BY GEORGE R. R. MARTIN

A SONG OF ICE AND FIRE
Book One: *A Game of Thrones*
Book Two: *A Clash of Kings*
Book Three: *A Storm of Swords*
Book Four: *A Feast for Crows*
Book Five: *A Dance with Dragons*

Dying of the Light
Windhaven (with Lisa Tuttle)
Fevre Dream
The Armageddon Rag
Dead Man's Hand (with John J. Miller)

SHORT STORY COLLECTIONS
Dreamsongs, Volume I
Dreamsongs, Volume II
A Song of Lya and Other Stories
Songs of Stars and Shadows
Sandkings
Songs the Dead Men Sing
Nightflyers
Tuf Voyaging
Portraits of His Children
Quartet

EDITED BY GEORGE R. R. MARTIN
New Voices in Science Fiction, Volumes 1–4
The Science Fiction Weight-Loss Book
(with Isaac Asimov and Martin Harry Greenberg)
The John W. Campbell Awards, Volume 5
Night Visions 3
Wild Card I–XXI

A GAME OF THRONES

BOOK ONE OF
A SONG OF ICE AND FIRE

GEORGE R. R. MARTIN

BANTAM BOOKS • NEW YORK

2011 Bantam Books Mass Market Edition

Published in the United States by Bantam Books, an imprint of The Random House Publishing Group, a division of Random House, Inc., New York.

BANTAM BOOKS and the rooster colophon are registered trademarks of Random House, Inc.

Originally published in hardcover in the United States by Bantam Spectra, a division of Random House, Inc., in 1996.

ISBN 978-0-553-57340-4
eBook ISBN 978-0-553-89784-5

Cover art copyright © 2011 by Larry Rostant
Cover design by David Stevenson

Maps by James Sinclair
Heraldic crests by Virginia Norey

Printed in the United States of America

www.bantamdell.com

65 64

this one is for Melinda

The South

- ♦ – Castle
- ◇ – Ruined Castle
- ● – City
- • – Town

N

Iron Islands

Pyke

Three Sisters

THE FINGERS

Seagard

Green Fork

The Kingsroad

VALE OF ARRYN

Blue Fork

The Eyrie

Red Fork

The Trident

Bloody Gate

Gulltown

Tumblestone

Riverrun

BAY OF CRABS

Golden Tooth

Harrenhal

Gods Eye

The Kingsroad

Casterly Rock

Dragonstone

Lannisport

The Goldroad

King's Landing

Blackwater Rush

THE REACH

Kingswood

The Sunroad

The Roseroad

Mander

Tarth

Storm's End

SHIPBREAKER BAY

Highgarden

The Dornish Marches

Rainwood

Cape Wrath

SEA OF DORNE

Oldtown

DORNE

Starfall

The Broken Arm

Sunspear

The Arbor

Map by
James Sinclair

PROLOGUE

"We should start back," Gared urged as the woods began to grow dark around them. "The wildlings are dead."

"Do the dead frighten you?" Ser Waymar Royce asked with just the hint of a smile.

Gared did not rise to the bait. He was an old man, past fifty, and he had seen the lordlings come and go. "Dead is dead," he said. "We have no business with the dead."

"Are they dead?" Royce asked softly. "What proof have we?"

"Will saw them," Gared said. "If he says they are dead, that's proof enough for me."

Will had known they would drag him into the quarrel sooner or later. He wished it had been later rather than sooner. "My mother told me that dead men sing no songs," he put in.

"My wet nurse said the same thing, Will," Royce replied. "Never believe anything you hear at a woman's tit. There are things to be learned even from the dead." His voice echoed, too loud in the twilit forest.

"We have a long ride before us," Gared pointed out. "Eight days, maybe nine. And night is falling."

Ser Waymar Royce glanced at the sky with disinterest. "It does that every day about this time. Are you unmanned by the dark, Gared?"

Will could see the tightness around Gared's mouth, the barely suppressed anger in his eyes under the thick black hood of his cloak. Gared had spent forty years in the Night's Watch, man and boy, and he was not accustomed to being made light of. Yet it was more than that. Under the wounded pride, Will could sense something else in the older man. You could taste it; a nervous tension that came perilous close to fear.

Will shared his unease. He had been four years on the Wall. The first time he had been sent beyond, all the old stories had come rushing back, and his bowels had turned to water. He had laughed about it afterward. He was a veteran of a hundred rangings by now, and the endless dark wilderness that the southron called the haunted forest had no more terrors for him.

Until tonight. Something was different tonight. There was an edge to this darkness that made his hackles rise. Nine days they had been riding, north and northwest and then north again, farther and farther from the Wall, hard on the track of a band of wildling raiders. Each day had been worse than the day that had come before it. Today was the worst of all. A cold wind was blowing out of the north, and it made the trees rustle like living things. All day, Will had felt as though something were watching him, something cold and implacable that loved him not. Gared had felt it too. Will wanted nothing so much as to ride hellbent for the safety of the Wall, but that was not a feeling to share with your commander.

Especially not a commander like this one.

Ser Waymar Royce was the youngest son of an ancient house with too many heirs. He was a handsome youth of eighteen, grey-eyed and graceful and slender as a knife. Mounted on his huge black destrier, the knight towered above Will and Gared on their smaller garrons. He wore black leather boots, black woolen pants, black moleskin gloves, and a fine supple coat of gleaming black ringmail over layers of black wool and boiled leather. Ser Waymar had been a Sworn Brother of the Night's Watch for less than half a year, but no one could say he had not prepared for his vocation. At least insofar as his wardrobe was concerned.

His cloak was his crowning glory; sable, thick and black and soft as sin. "Bet he killed them all himself, he did," Gared told the barracks over wine, "twisted their little heads off, our mighty warrior." They had all shared the laugh.

It is hard to take orders from a man you laughed at in your cups, Will reflected as he sat shivering atop his garron. Gared must have felt the same.

"Mormont said as we should track them, and we did," Gared said. "They're dead. They shan't trouble us no more. There's hard riding before us. I don't like this weather. If it snows, we could be a fortnight getting back, and snow's the best we can hope for. Ever seen an ice storm, my lord?"

The lordling seemed not to hear him. He studied the deepening twilight in that half-bored, half-distracted way he had. Will had ridden with the knight long enough to understand that it was best not to interrupt him when he looked like that. "Tell me again what you saw, Will. All the details. Leave nothing out."

Will had been a hunter before he joined the Night's Watch. Well, a poacher in truth. Mallister freeriders had caught him red-handed in the Mallisters' own woods, skinning one of the Mallisters' own bucks, and it had been a choice of putting on the black or losing a hand. No one could move through the woods as silent as Will, and it had not taken the black brothers long to discover his talent.

"The camp is two miles farther on, over that ridge, hard beside a stream," Will said. "I got close as I dared. There's eight of them, men and women both. No children I could see. They put up a lean-to against the rock. The snow's pretty well covered it now, but I could still make it out. No fire burning, but the firepit was still plain as day. No one moving. I watched a long time. No living man ever lay so still."

"Did you see any blood?"

"Well, no," Will admitted.

"Did you see any weapons?"

"Some swords, a few bows. One man had an axe.

Heavy-looking, double-bladed, a cruel piece of iron. It was on the ground beside him, right by his hand."

"Did you make note of the position of the bodies?"

Will shrugged. "A couple are sitting up against the rock. Most of them on the ground. Fallen, like."

"Or sleeping," Royce suggested.

"Fallen," Will insisted. "There's one woman up an ironwood, half-hid in the branches. A far-eyes." He smiled thinly. "I took care she never saw me. When I got closer, I saw that she wasn't moving neither." Despite himself, he shivered.

"You have a chill?" Royce asked.

"Some," Will muttered. "The wind, m'lord."

The young knight turned back to his grizzled man-at-arms. Frost-fallen leaves whispered past them, and Royce's destrier moved restlessly. "What do you think might have killed these men, Gared?" Ser Waymar asked casually. He adjusted the drape of his long sable cloak.

"It was the cold," Gared said with iron certainty. "I saw men freeze last winter, and the one before, when I was half a boy. Everyone talks about snows forty foot deep, and how the ice wind comes howling out of the north, but the real enemy is the cold. It steals up on you quieter than Will, and at first you shiver and your teeth chatter and you stamp your feet and dream of mulled wine and nice hot fires. It burns, it does. Nothing burns like the cold. But only for a while. Then it gets inside you and starts to fill you up, and after a while you don't have the strength to fight it. It's easier just to sit down or go to sleep. They say you don't feel any pain toward the end. First you go weak and drowsy, and everything starts to fade, and then it's like sinking into a sea of warm milk. Peaceful, like."

"Such eloquence, Gared," Ser Waymar observed. "I never suspected you had it in you."

"I've had the cold in me too, lordling." Gared pulled back his hood, giving Ser Waymar a good long look at the stumps where his ears had been. "Two ears, three toes, and the little finger off my left hand. I got off light. We found my brother frozen at his watch, with a smile on his face."

Ser Waymar shrugged. "You ought dress more warmly, Gared."

Gared glared at the lordling, the scars around his ear holes flushed red with anger where Maester Aemon had cut the ears away. "We'll see how warm you can dress when the winter comes." He pulled up his hood and hunched over his garron, silent and sullen.

"If Gared said it was the cold . . ." Will began.

"Have you drawn any watches this past week, Will?"

"Yes, m'lord." There never was a week when he did not draw a dozen bloody watches. What was the man driving at?

"And how did you find the Wall?"

"Weeping," Will said, frowning. He saw it clear enough, now that the lordling had pointed it out. "They couldn't have froze. Not if the Wall was weeping. It wasn't cold enough."

Royce nodded. "Bright lad. We've had a few light frosts this past week, and a quick flurry of snow now and then, but surely no cold fierce enough to kill eight grown men. Men clad in fur and leather, let me remind you, with shelter near at hand, and the means of making fire." The knight's smile was cocksure. "Will, lead us there. I would see these dead men for myself."

And then there was nothing to be done for it. The order had been given, and honor bound them to obey.

Will went in front, his shaggy little garron picking the way carefully through the undergrowth. A light snow had fallen the night before, and there were stones and roots and hidden sinks lying just under its crust, waiting for the careless and the unwary. Ser Waymar Royce came next, his great black destrier snorting impatiently. The warhorse was the wrong mount for ranging, but try and tell that to the lordling. Gared brought up the rear. The old man-at-arms muttered to himself as he rode.

Twilight deepened. The cloudless sky turned a deep purple, the color of an old bruise, then faded to black. The stars began to come out. A half-moon rose. Will was grateful for the light.

"We can make a better pace than this, surely," Royce said when the moon was full risen.

"Not with this horse," Will said. Fear had made him insolent. "Perhaps my lord would care to take the lead?"

Ser Waymar Royce did not deign to reply.

Somewhere off in the wood a wolf howled.

Will pulled his garron over beneath an ancient gnarled ironwood and dismounted.

"Why are you stopping?" Ser Waymar asked.

"Best go the rest of the way on foot, m'lord. It's just over that ridge."

Royce paused a moment, staring off into the distance, his face reflective. A cold wind whispered through the trees. His great sable cloak stirred behind like something half-alive.

"There's something wrong here," Gared muttered.

The young knight gave him a disdainful smile. "Is there?"

"Can't you feel it?" Gared asked. "Listen to the darkness."

Will could feel it. Four years in the Night's Watch, and he had never been so afraid. What was it?

"Wind. Trees rustling. A wolf. Which sound is it that unmans you so, Gared?" When Gared did not answer, Royce slid gracefully from his saddle. He tied the destrier securely to a low-hanging limb, well away from the other horses, and drew his longsword from its sheath. Jewels glittered in its hilt, and the moonlight ran down the shining steel. It was a splendid weapon, castle-forged, and new-made from the look of it. Will doubted it had ever been swung in anger.

"The trees press close here," Will warned. "That sword will tangle you up, m'lord. Better a knife."

"If I need instruction, I will ask for it," the young lord said. "Gared, stay here. Guard the horses."

Gared dismounted. "We need a fire. I'll see to it."

"How big a fool are you, old man? If there are enemies in this wood, a fire is the last thing we want."

"There's some enemies a fire will keep away," Gared said. "Bears and direwolves and . . . and other things . . ."

Ser Waymar's mouth became a hard line. "No fire."

Gared's hood shadowed his face, but Will could see the hard glitter in his eyes as he stared at the knight. For a moment he was afraid the older man would go for his sword. It was a short, ugly thing, its grip discolored by sweat, its edge nicked from hard use, but Will would not have given an iron bob for the lordling's life if Gared pulled it from its scabbard.

Finally Gared looked down. "No fire," he muttered, low under his breath.

Royce took it for acquiescence and turned away. "Lead on," he said to Will.

Will threaded their way through a thicket, then started up the slope to the low ridge where he had found his vantage point under a sentinel tree. Under the thin crust of snow, the ground was damp and muddy, slick footing, with rocks and hidden roots to trip you up. Will made no sound as he climbed. Behind him, he heard the soft metallic slither of the lordling's ringmail, the rustle of leaves, and muttered curses as reaching branches grabbed at his longsword and tugged on his splendid sable cloak.

The great sentinel was right there at the top of the ridge, where Will had known it would be, its lowest branches a bare foot off the ground. Will slid in underneath, flat on his belly in the snow and the mud, and looked down on the empty clearing below.

His heart stopped in his chest. For a moment he dared not breathe. Moonlight shone down on the clearing, the ashes of the firepit, the snow-covered lean-to, the great rock, the little half-frozen stream. Everything was just as it had been a few hours ago.

They were gone. All the bodies were gone.

"Gods!" he heard behind him. A sword slashed at a branch as Ser Waymar Royce gained the ridge. He stood there beside the sentinel, longsword in hand, his cloak billowing behind him as the wind came up, outlined nobly against the stars for all to see.

"Get *down!*" Will whispered urgently. "Something's wrong."

Royce did not move. He looked down at the empty clearing and laughed. "Your dead men seem to have moved camp, Will."

Will's voice abandoned him. He groped for words that did not come. It was not possible. His eyes swept back and forth over the abandoned campsite, stopped on the axe. A huge double-bladed battle-axe, still lying where he had seen it last, untouched. A valuable weapon . . .

"On your feet, Will," Ser Waymar commanded. "There's no one here. I won't have you hiding under a bush."

Reluctantly, Will obeyed.

Ser Waymar looked him over with open disapproval. "I am not going back to Castle Black a failure on my first ranging. We *will* find these men." He glanced around. "Up the tree. Be quick about it. Look for a fire."

Will turned away, wordless. There was no use to argue. The wind was moving. It cut right through him. He went to the tree, a vaulting grey-green sentinel, and began to climb. Soon his hands were sticky with sap, and he was lost among the needles. Fear filled his gut like a meal he could not digest. He whispered a prayer to the nameless gods of the wood, and slipped his dirk free of its sheath. He put it between his teeth to keep both hands free for climbing. The taste of cold iron in his mouth gave him comfort.

Down below, the lordling called out suddenly, "Who goes there?" Will heard uncertainty in the challenge. He stopped climbing; he listened; he watched.

The woods gave answer: the rustle of leaves, the icy rush of the stream, a distant hoot of a snow owl.

The Others made no sound.

Will saw movement from the corner of his eye. Pale shapes gliding through the wood. He turned his head, glimpsed a white shadow in the darkness. Then it was gone. Branches stirred gently in the wind, scratching at one another with wooden fingers. Will opened his mouth to call down a warning, and the words seemed to freeze in his throat. Perhaps he was wrong. Perhaps it had only been a bird, a reflection on the snow, some trick of the moonlight. What had he seen, after all?

"Will, where are you?" Ser Waymar called up. "Can you see anything?" He was turning in a slow circle, suddenly wary, his sword in hand. He must have felt them, as Will felt them. There was nothing to see. "Answer me! Why is it so cold?"

It *was* cold. Shivering, Will clung more tightly to his perch. His face pressed hard against the trunk of the sentinel. He could feel the sweet, sticky sap on his cheek.

A shadow emerged from the dark of the wood. It stood in front of Royce. Tall, it was, and gaunt and hard as old bones, with flesh pale as milk. Its armor seemed to change color as it moved; here it was white as new-fallen snow, there black as shadow, everywhere dappled with the deep grey-green of the trees. The patterns ran like moonlight on water with every step it took.

Will heard the breath go out of Ser Waymar Royce in a long hiss. "Come no farther," the lordling warned. His voice cracked like a boy's. He threw the long sable cloak back over his shoulders, to free his arms for battle, and took his sword in both hands. The wind had stopped. It was very cold.

The Other slid forward on silent feet. In its hand was a longsword like none that Will had ever seen. No human metal had gone into the forging of that blade. It was alive with moonlight, translucent, a shard of crystal so thin that it seemed almost to vanish when seen edge-on. There was a faint blue shimmer to the thing, a ghost-light that played around its edges, and somehow Will knew it was sharper than any razor.

Ser Waymar met him bravely. "Dance with me then." He lifted his sword high over his head, defiant. His hands trembled from the weight of it, or perhaps from the cold. Yet in that moment, Will thought, he was a boy no longer, but a man of the Night's Watch.

The Other halted. Will saw its eyes; blue, deeper and bluer than any human eyes, a blue that burned like ice. They fixed on the longsword trembling on high, watched the moonlight running cold along the metal. For a heartbeat he dared to hope.

They emerged silently from the shadows, twins to the first. Three of them . . . four . . . five . . . Ser Waymar may have felt the cold that came with them, but he never saw them, never heard them. Will had to call out. It was his duty. And his death, if he did. He shivered, and hugged the tree, and kept the silence.

The pale sword came shivering through the air.

Ser Waymar met it with steel. When the blades met, there was no ring of metal on metal; only a high, thin sound at the edge of hearing, like an animal screaming in pain. Royce checked a second blow, and a third, then fell back a step. Another flurry of blows, and he fell back again.

Behind him, to right, to left, all around him, the watchers stood patient, faceless, silent, the shifting patterns of their delicate armor making them all but invisible in the wood. Yet they made no move to interfere.

Again and again the swords met, until Will wanted to cover his ears against the strange anguished keening of their clash. Ser Waymar was panting from the effort now, his breath steaming in the moonlight. His blade was white with frost; the Other's danced with pale blue light.

Then Royce's parry came a beat too late. The pale sword bit through the ringmail beneath his arm. The young lord cried out in pain. Blood welled between the rings. It steamed in the cold, and the droplets seemed red as fire where they touched the snow. Ser Waymar's fingers brushed his side. His moleskin glove came away soaked with red.

The Other said something in a language that Will did not know; his voice was like the cracking of ice on a winter lake, and the words were mocking.

Ser Waymar Royce found his fury. "For Robert!" he shouted, and he came up snarling, lifting the frost-covered longsword with both hands and swinging it around in a flat sidearm slash with all his weight behind it. The Other's parry was almost lazy.

When the blades touched, the steel shattered.

A scream echoed through the forest night, and the longsword shivered into a hundred brittle pieces, the shards scattering like a rain of needles. Royce went to his knees, shrieking, and covered his eyes. Blood welled between his fingers.

The watchers moved forward together, as if some signal had been given. Swords rose and fell, all in a deathly silence. It was cold butchery. The pale blades sliced through ringmail as if it were silk. Will closed his eyes. Far beneath him, he heard their voices and laughter sharp as icicles.

When he found the courage to look again, a long time had passed, and the ridge below was empty.

He stayed in the tree, scarce daring to breathe, while the moon crept slowly across the black sky. Finally, his muscles cramping and his fingers numb with cold, he climbed down.

Royce's body lay facedown in the snow, one arm outflung. The thick sable cloak had been slashed in a dozen places. Lying dead like that, you saw how young he was. A boy.

He found what was left of the sword a few feet away,

the end splintered and twisted like a tree struck by lightning. Will knelt, looked around warily, and snatched it
up. The broken sword would be his proof. Gared would
know what to make of it, and if not him, then surely that
old bear Mormont or Maester Aemon. Would Gared still
be waiting with the horses? He had to hurry.

Will rose. Ser Waymar Royce stood over him.

His fine clothes were a tatter, his face a ruin. A shard
from his sword transfixed the blind white pupil of his left
eye.

The right eye was open. The pupil burned blue. It saw.

The broken sword fell from nerveless fingers. Will
closed his eyes to pray. Long, elegant hands brushed his
cheek, then tightened around his throat. They were
gloved in the finest moleskin and sticky with blood, yet
the touch was icy cold.

BRAN

T he morning had dawned clear and cold, with a
crispness that hinted at the end of summer. They
set forth at daybreak to see a man beheaded,
twenty in all, and Bran rode among them, nervous with
excitement. This was the first time he had been deemed
old enough to go with his lord father and his brothers to
see the king's justice done. It was the ninth year of summer, and the seventh of Bran's life.

The man had been taken outside a small holdfast in
the hills. Robb thought he was a wildling, his sword
sworn to Mance Rayder, the King-beyond-the-Wall. It
made Bran's skin prickle to think of it. He remembered
the hearth tales Old Nan told them. The wildlings were
cruel men, she said, slavers and slayers and thieves. They
consorted with giants and ghouls, stole girl children in
the dead of night, and drank blood from polished horns.
And their women lay with the Others in the Long Night
to sire terrible half-human children.

But the man they found bound hand and foot to the
holdfast wall awaiting the king's justice was old and
scrawny, not much taller than Robb. He had lost both
ears and a finger to frostbite, and he dressed all in black,

the same as a brother of the Night's Watch, except that his furs were ragged and greasy.

The breath of man and horse mingled, steaming, in the cold morning air as his lord father had the man cut down from the wall and dragged before them. Robb and Jon sat tall and still on their horses, with Bran between them on his pony, trying to seem older than seven, trying to pretend that he'd seen all this before. A faint wind blew through the holdfast gate. Over their heads flapped the banner of the Starks of Winterfell: a grey direwolf racing across an ice-white field.

Bran's father sat solemnly on his horse, long brown hair stirring in the wind. His closely trimmed beard was shot with white, making him look older than his thirty-five years. He had a grim cast to his grey eyes this day, and he seemed not at all the man who would sit before the fire in the evening and talk softly of the age of heroes and the children of the forest. He had taken off Father's face, Bran thought, and donned the face of Lord Stark of Winterfell.

There were questions asked and answers given there in the chill of morning, but afterward Bran could not recall much of what had been said. Finally his lord father gave a command, and two of his guardsmen dragged the ragged man to the ironwood stump in the center of the square. They forced his head down onto the hard black wood. Lord Eddard Stark dismounted and his ward Theon Greyjoy brought forth the sword. "Ice," that sword was called. It was as wide across as a man's hand, and taller even than Robb. The blade was Valyrian steel, spell-forged and dark as smoke. Nothing held an edge like Valyrian steel.

His father peeled off his gloves and handed them to Jory Cassel, the captain of his household guard. He took hold of Ice with both hands and said, "In the name of Robert of the House Baratheon, the First of his Name, King of the Andals and the Rhoynar and the First Men, Lord of the Seven Kingdoms and Protector of the Realm, by the word of Eddard of the House Stark, Lord of Winterfell and Warden of the North, I do sentence you to die." He lifted the greatsword high above his head.

Bran's bastard brother Jon Snow moved closer. "Keep

the pony well in hand," he whispered. "And don't look away. Father will know if you do."

Bran kept his pony well in hand, and did not look away.

His father took off the man's head with a single sure stroke. Blood sprayed out across the snow, as red as summerwine. One of the horses reared and had to be restrained to keep from bolting. Bran could not take his eyes off the blood. The snows around the stump drank it eagerly, reddening as he watched.

The head bounced off a thick root and rolled. It came up near Greyjoy's feet. Theon was a lean, dark youth of nineteen who found everything amusing. He laughed, put his boot on the head, and kicked it away.

"Ass," Jon muttered, low enough so Greyjoy did not hear. He put a hand on Bran's shoulder, and Bran looked over at his bastard brother. "You did well," Jon told him solemnly. Jon was fourteen, an old hand at justice.

It seemed colder on the long ride back to Winterfell, though the wind had died by then and the sun was higher in the sky. Bran rode with his brothers, well ahead of the main party, his pony struggling hard to keep up with their horses.

"The deserter died bravely," Robb said. He was big and broad and growing every day, with his mother's coloring, the fair skin, red-brown hair, and blue eyes of the Tullys of Riverrun. "He had courage, at the least."

"No," Jon Snow said quietly. "It was not courage. This one was dead of fear. You could see it in his eyes, Stark." Jon's eyes were a grey so dark they seemed almost black, but there was little they did not see. He was of an age with Robb, but they did not look alike. Jon was slender where Robb was muscular, dark where Robb was fair, graceful and quick where his half brother was strong and fast.

Robb was not impressed. "The Others take his eyes," he swore. "He died well. Race you to the bridge?"

"Done," Jon said, kicking his horse forward. Robb cursed and followed, and they galloped off down the trail, Robb laughing and hooting, Jon silent and intent. The hooves of their horses kicked up showers of snow as they went.

Bran did not try to follow. His pony could not keep up.

He had seen the ragged man's eyes, and he was thinking of them now. After a while, the sound of Robb's laughter receded, and the woods grew silent again.

So deep in thought was he that he never heard the rest of the party until his father moved up to ride beside him. "Are you well, Bran?" he asked, not unkindly.

"Yes, Father," Bran told him. He looked up. Wrapped in his furs and leathers, mounted on his great warhorse, his lord father loomed over him like a giant. "Robb says the man died bravely, but Jon says he was afraid."

"What do you think?" his father asked.

Bran thought about it. "Can a man still be brave if he's afraid?"

"That is the only time a man can be brave," his father told him. "Do you understand why I did it?"

"He was a wildling," Bran said. "They carry off women and sell them to the Others."

His lord father smiled. "Old Nan has been telling you stories again. In truth, the man was an oathbreaker, a deserter from the Night's Watch. No man is more dangerous. The deserter knows his life is forfeit if he is taken, so he will not flinch from any crime, no matter how vile. But you mistake me. The question was not why the man had to die, but why I must do it."

Bran had no answer for that. "King Robert has a headsman," he said, uncertainly.

"He does," his father admitted. "As did the Targaryen kings before him. Yet our way is the older way. The blood of the First Men still flows in the veins of the Starks, and we hold to the belief that the man who passes the sentence should swing the sword. If you would take a man's life, you owe it to him to look into his eyes and hear his final words. And if you cannot bear to do that, then perhaps the man does not deserve to die.

"One day, Bran, you will be Robb's bannerman, holding a keep of your own for your brother and your king, and justice will fall to you. When that day comes, you must take no pleasure in the task, but neither must you look away. A ruler who hides behind paid executioners soon forgets what death is."

That was when Jon reappeared on the crest of the hill before them. He waved and shouted down at them. *"Fa-*

ther, Bran, come quickly, see what Robb has found!"
Then he was gone again.

Jory rode up beside them. "Trouble, my lord?"

"Beyond a doubt," his lord father said. "Come, let us
see what mischief my sons have rooted out now." He sent
his horse into a trot. Jory and Bran and the rest came after.

They found Robb on the riverbank north of the bridge,
with Jon still mounted beside him. The late summer
snows had been heavy this moonturn. Robb stood knee-
deep in white, his hood pulled back so the sun shone in
his hair. He was cradling something in his arm, while the
boys talked in hushed, excited voices.

The riders picked their way carefully through the
drifts, groping for solid footing on the hidden, uneven
ground. Jory Cassel and Theon Greyjoy were the first to
reach the boys. Greyjoy was laughing and joking as
he rode. Bran heard the breath go out of him. *"Gods!"* he
exclaimed, struggling to keep control of his horse as he
reached for his sword.

Jory's sword was already out. "Robb, get away from
it!" he called as his horse reared under him.

Robb grinned and looked up from the bundle in his
arms. "She can't hurt you," he said. "She's dead, Jory."

Bran was afire with curiosity by then. He would have
spurred the pony faster, but his father made them dismount beside the bridge and approach on foot. Bran
jumped off and ran.

By then Jon, Jory, and Theon Greyjoy had all dismounted as well. "What in the seven hells is it?" Greyjoy
was saying.

"A wolf," Robb told him.

"A freak," Greyjoy said. "Look at the *size* of it."

Bran's heart was thumping in his chest as he pushed
through a waist-high drift to his brothers' side.

Half-buried in bloodstained snow, a huge dark shape
slumped in death. Ice had formed in its shaggy grey fur,
and the faint smell of corruption clung to it like a
woman's perfume. Bran glimpsed blind eyes crawling
with maggots, a wide mouth full of yellowed teeth. But it
was the size of it that made him gasp. It was bigger than
his pony, twice the size of the largest hound in his father's kennel.

"It's no freak," Jon said calmly. "That's a direwolf. They grow larger than the other kind."

Theon Greyjoy said, "There's not been a direwolf sighted south of the Wall in two hundred years."

"I see one now," Jon replied.

Bran tore his eyes away from the monster. That was when he noticed the bundle in Robb's arms. He gave a cry of delight and moved closer. The pup was a tiny ball of grey-black fur, its eyes still closed. It nuzzled blindly against Robb's chest as he cradled it, searching for milk among his leathers, making a sad little whimpery sound. Bran reached out hesitantly. "Go on," Robb told him. "You can touch him."

Bran gave the pup a quick nervous stroke, then turned as Jon said, "Here you go." His half brother put a second pup into his arms. "There are five of them." Bran sat down in the snow and hugged the wolf pup to his face. Its fur was soft and warm against his cheek.

"Direwolves loose in the realm, after so many years," muttered Hullen, the master of horse. "I like it not."

"It is a sign," Jory said.

Father frowned. "This is only a dead animal, Jory," he said. Yet he seemed troubled. Snow crunched under his boots as he moved around the body. "Do we know what killed her?"

"There's something in the throat," Robb told him, proud to have found the answer before his father even asked. "There, just under the jaw."

His father knelt and groped under the beast's head with his hand. He gave a yank and held it up for all to see. A foot of shattered antler, tines snapped off, all wet with blood.

A sudden silence descended over the party. The men looked at the antler uneasily, and no one dared to speak. Even Bran could sense their fear, though he did not understand.

His father tossed the antler to the side and cleansed his hands in the snow. "I'm surprised she lived long enough to whelp," he said. His voice broke the spell.

"Maybe she didn't," Jory said. "I've heard tales . . . maybe the bitch was already dead when the pups came."

"Born with the dead," another man put in. "Worse luck."

"No matter," said Hullen. "They be dead soon enough too."

Bran gave a wordless cry of dismay.

"The sooner the better," Theon Greyjoy agreed. He drew his sword. "Give the beast here, Bran."

The little thing squirmed against him, as if it heard and understood. *"No!"* Bran cried out fiercely. "It's mine."

"Put away your sword, Greyjoy," Robb said. For a moment he sounded as commanding as their father, like the lord he would someday be. "We will keep these pups."

"You cannot do that, boy," said Harwin, who was Hullen's son.

"It be a mercy to kill them," Hullen said.

Bran looked to his lord father for rescue, but got only a frown, a furrowed brow. "Hullen speaks truly, son. Better a swift death than a hard one from cold and starvation."

"No!" He could feel tears welling in his eyes, and he looked away. He did not want to cry in front of his father.

Robb resisted stubbornly. "Ser Rodrik's red bitch whelped again last week," he said. "It was a small litter, only two live pups. She'll have milk enough."

"She'll rip them apart when they try to nurse."

"Lord Stark," Jon said. It was strange to hear him call Father that, so formal. Bran looked at him with desperate hope. "There are five pups," he told Father. "Three male, two female."

"What of it, Jon?"

"You have five trueborn children," Jon said. "Three sons, two daughters. The direwolf is the sigil of your House. Your children were meant to have these pups, my lord."

Bran saw his father's face change, saw the other men exchange glances. He loved Jon with all his heart at that moment. Even at seven, Bran understood what his brother had done. The count had come right only because Jon had omitted himself. He had included the girls, included even Rickon, the baby, but not the bastard who bore the surname Snow, the name that custom decreed be given to all those in the north unlucky enough to be born with no name of their own.

Their father understood as well. "You want no pup for yourself, Jon?" he asked softly.

"The direwolf graces the banners of House Stark," Jon pointed out. "I am no Stark, Father."

Their lord father regarded Jon thoughtfully. Robb rushed into the silence he left. "I will nurse him myself, Father," he promised. "I will soak a towel with warm milk, and give him suck from that."

"Me too!" Bran echoed.

The lord weighed his sons long and carefully with his eyes. "Easy to say, and harder to do. I will not have you wasting the servants' time with this. If you want these pups, you will feed them yourselves. Is that understood?"

Bran nodded eagerly. The pup squirmed in his grasp, licked at his face with a warm tongue.

"You must train them as well," their father said. "*You* must train them. The kennelmaster will have nothing to do with these monsters, I promise you that. And the gods help you if you neglect them, or brutalize them, or train them badly. These are not dogs to beg for treats and slink off at a kick. A direwolf will rip a man's arm off his shoulder as easily as a dog will kill a rat. Are you sure you want this?"

"Yes, Father," Bran said.

"Yes," Robb agreed.

"The pups may die anyway, despite all you do."

"They won't die," Robb said. "We won't *let* them die."

"Keep them, then. Jory, Desmond, gather up the other pups. It's time we were back to Winterfell."

It was not until they were mounted and on their way that Bran allowed himself to taste the sweet air of victory. By then, his pup was snuggled inside his leathers, warm against him, safe for the long ride home. Bran was wondering what to name him.

Halfway across the bridge, Jon pulled up suddenly.

"What is it, Jon?" their lord father asked.

"Can't you hear it?"

Bran could hear the wind in the trees, the clatter of their hooves on the ironwood planks, the whimpering of his hungry pup, but Jon was listening to something else.

"There," Jon said. He swung his horse around and galloped back across the bridge. They watched him dismount where the direwolf lay dead in the snow, watched him kneel. A moment later he was riding back to them, smiling.

"He must have crawled away from the others," Jon said.

"Or been driven away," their father said, looking at the sixth pup. His fur was white, where the rest of the litter was grey. His eyes were as red as the blood of the ragged man who had died that morning. Bran thought it curious that this pup alone would have opened his eyes while the others were still blind.

"An albino," Theon Greyjoy said with wry amusement. "This one will die even faster than the others."

Jon Snow gave his father's ward a long, chilling look. "I think not, Greyjoy," he said. "This one belongs to me."

CATELYN

Catelyn had never liked this godswood.

She had been born a Tully, at Riverrun far to the south, on the Red Fork of the Trident. The godswood there was a garden, bright and airy, where tall redwoods spread dappled shadows across tinkling streams, birds sang from hidden nests, and the air was spicy with the scent of flowers.

The gods of Winterfell kept a different sort of wood. It was a dark, primal place, three acres of old forest untouched for ten thousand years as the gloomy castle rose around it. It smelled of moist earth and decay. No redwoods grew here. This was a wood of stubborn sentinel trees armored in grey-green needles, of mighty oaks, of ironwoods as old as the realm itself. Here thick black trunks crowded close together while twisted branches wove a dense canopy overhead and misshapen roots wrestled beneath the soil. This was a place of deep silence and brooding shadows, and the gods who lived here had no names.

But she knew she would find her husband here tonight. Whenever he took a man's life, afterward he would seek the quiet of the godswood.

Catelyn had been anointed with the seven oils and named in the rainbow of light that filled the sept of Riverrun. She was of the Faith, like her father and grandfather and his father before him. Her gods had names, and their faces were as familiar as the faces of her parents. Worship was a septon with a censer, the smell of incense, a seven-sided crystal alive with light, voices raised in song. The Tullys kept a godswood, as all the great houses did, but it was only a place to walk or read or lie in the sun. Worship was for the sept.

For her sake, Ned had built a small sept where she might sing to the seven faces of god, but the blood of the First Men still flowed in the veins of the Starks, and his own gods were the old ones, the nameless, faceless gods of the greenwood they shared with the vanished children of the forest.

At the center of the grove an ancient weirwood brooded over a small pool where the waters were black and cold. "The heart tree," Ned called it. The weirwood's bark was white as bone, its leaves dark red, like a thousand bloodstained hands. A face had been carved in the trunk of the great tree, its features long and melancholy, the deep-cut eyes red with dried sap and strangely watchful. They were old, those eyes; older than Winterfell itself. They had seen Brandon the Builder set the first stone, if the tales were true; they had watched the castle's granite walls rise around them. It was said that the children of the forest had carved the faces in the trees during the dawn centuries before the coming of the First Men across the narrow sea.

In the south the last weirwoods had been cut down or burned out a thousand years ago, except on the Isle of Faces where the green men kept their silent watch. Up here it was different. Here every castle had its godswood, and every godswood had its heart tree, and every heart tree its face.

Catelyn found her husband beneath the weirwood, seated on a moss-covered stone. The greatsword Ice was across his lap, and he was cleaning the blade in those waters black as night. A thousand years of humus lay thick upon the godswood floor, swallowing the sound of her feet, but the red eyes of the weirwood seemed to follow her as she came. "Ned," she called softly.

He lifted his head to look at her. "Catelyn," he said. His voice was distant and formal. "Where are the children?"

He would always ask her that. "In the kitchen, arguing about names for the wolf pups." She spread her cloak on the forest floor and sat beside the pool, her back to the weirwood. She could feel the eyes watching her, but she did her best to ignore them. "Arya is already in love, and Sansa is charmed and gracious, but Rickon is not quite sure."

"Is he afraid?" Ned asked.

"A little," she admitted. "He is only three."

Ned frowned. "He must learn to face his fears. He will not be three forever. And winter is coming."

"Yes," Catelyn agreed. The words gave her a chill, as they always did. The Stark words. Every noble house had its words. Family mottoes, touchstones, prayers of sorts, they boasted of honor and glory, promised loyalty and truth, swore faith and courage. All but the Starks. *Winter is coming,* said the Stark words. Not for the first time, she reflected on what a strange people these northerners were.

"The man died well, I'll give him that," Ned said. He had a swatch of oiled leather in one hand. He ran it lightly up the greatsword as he spoke, polishing the metal to a dark glow. "I was glad for Bran's sake. You would have been proud of Bran."

"I am always proud of Bran," Catelyn replied, watching the sword as he stroked it. She could see the rippling deep within the steel, where the metal had been folded back on itself a hundred times in the forging. Catelyn had no love for swords, but she could not deny that Ice had its own beauty. It had been forged in Valyria, before the Doom had come to the old Freehold, when the ironsmiths had worked their metal with spells as well as hammers. Four hundred years old it was, and as sharp as the day it was forged. The name it bore was older still, a legacy from the age of heroes, when the Starks were Kings in the North.

"He was the fourth this year," Ned said grimly. "The poor man was half-mad. Something had put a fear in him so deep that my words could not reach him." He sighed. "Ben writes that the strength of the Night's Watch is down below a thousand. It's not only desertions. They are losing men on rangings as well."

"Is it the wildlings?" she asked.

"Who else?" Ned lifted Ice, looked down the cool steel length of it. "And it will only grow worse. The day may come when I will have no choice but to call the banners and ride north to deal with this King-beyond-the-Wall for good and all."

"Beyond the Wall?" The thought made Catelyn shudder.

Ned saw the dread on her face. "Mance Rayder is nothing for us to fear."

"There are darker things beyond the Wall." She glanced behind her at the heart tree, the pale bark and red eyes, watching, listening, thinking its long slow thoughts.

His smile was gentle. "You listen to too many of Old Nan's stories. The Others are as dead as the children of the forest, gone eight thousand years. Maester Luwin will tell you they never lived at all. No living man has ever seen one."

"Until this morning, no living man had ever seen a direwolf either," Catelyn reminded him.

"I ought to know better than to argue with a Tully," he said with a rueful smile. He slid Ice back into its sheath. "You did not come here to tell me crib tales. I know how little you like this place. What is it, my lady?"

Catelyn took her husband's hand. "There was grievous news today, my lord. I did not wish to trouble you until you had cleansed yourself." There was no way to soften the blow, so she told him straight. "I am so sorry, my love. Jon Arryn is dead."

His eyes found hers, and she could see how hard it took him, as she had known it would. In his youth, Ned had fostered at the Eyrie, and the childless Lord Arryn had become a second father to him and his fellow ward, Robert Baratheon. When the Mad King Aerys II Targaryen had demanded their heads, the Lord of the Eyrie had raised his moon-and-falcon banners in revolt rather than give up those he had pledged to protect.

And one day fifteen years ago, this second father had become a brother as well, as he and Ned stood together in the sept at Riverrun to wed two sisters, the daughters of Lord Hoster Tully.

"Jon . . ." he said. "Is this news certain?"

"It was the king's seal, and the letter is in Robert's own hand. I saved it for you. He said Lord Arryn was taken quickly. Even Maester Pycelle was helpless, but he brought the milk of the poppy, so Jon did not linger long in pain."

"That is some small mercy, I suppose," he said. She could see the grief on his face, but even then he thought first of her. "Your sister," he said. "And Jon's boy. What word of them?"

"The message said only that they were well, and had returned to the Eyrie," Catelyn said. "I wish they had gone to Riverrun instead. The Eyrie is high and lonely, and it was ever her husband's place, not hers. Lord Jon's memory will haunt each stone. I know my sister. She needs the comfort of family and friends around her."

"Your uncle waits in the Vale, does he not? Jon named him Knight of the Gate, I'd heard."

Catelyn nodded. "Brynden will do what he can for her, and for the boy. That is some comfort, but still . . ."

"Go to her," Ned urged. "Take the children. Fill her halls with noise and shouts and laughter. That boy of hers needs other children about him, and Lysa should not be alone in her grief."

"Would that I could," Catelyn said. "The letter had other tidings. The king is riding to Winterfell to seek you out."

It took Ned a moment to comprehend her words, but when the understanding came, the darkness left his eyes. "Robert is coming here?" When she nodded, a smile broke across his face.

Catelyn wished she could share his joy. But she had heard the talk in the yards; a direwolf dead in the snow, a broken antler in its throat. Dread coiled within her like a snake, but she forced herself to smile at this man she loved, this man who put no faith in signs. "I knew that would please you," she said. "We should send word to your brother on the Wall."

"Yes, of course," he agreed. "Ben will want to be here. I shall tell Maester Luwin to send his swiftest bird." Ned rose and pulled her to her feet. "Damnation, how many years has it been? And he gives us no more notice than this? How many in his party, did the message say?"

"I should think a hundred knights, at the least, with all their retainers, and half again as many freeriders. Cersei and the children travel with them."

"Robert will keep an easy pace for their sakes," he said. "It is just as well. That will give us more time to prepare."

"The queen's brothers are also in the party," she told him.

Ned grimaced at that. There was small love between him and the queen's family, Catelyn knew. The Lannisters of Casterly Rock had come late to Robert's cause, when victory was all but certain, and he had never forgiven them. "Well, if the price for Robert's company is an infestation of Lannisters, so be it. It sounds as though Robert is bringing half his court."

"Where the king goes, the realm follows," she said.

"It will be good to see the children. The youngest was still sucking at the Lannister woman's teat the last time I saw him. He must be, what, five by now?"

"Prince Tommen is seven," she told him. "The same age as Bran. Please, Ned, guard your tongue. The Lannister woman is our queen, and her pride is said to grow with every passing year."

Ned squeezed her hand. "There must be a feast, of course, with singers, and Robert will want to hunt. I shall send Jory south with an honor guard to meet them on the kingsroad and escort them back. Gods, how are we going to feed them all? On his way already, you said? Damn the man. Damn his royal hide."

DAENERYS

Her brother held the gown up for her inspection. "This is beauty. Touch it. Go on. Caress the fabric."

Dany touched it. The cloth was so smooth that it seemed to run through her fingers like water. She could not remember ever wearing anything so soft. It frightened her. She pulled her hand away. "Is it really mine?"

"A gift from the Magister Illyrio," Viserys said, smiling. Her brother was in a high mood tonight. "The color will bring out the violet in your eyes. And you shall have gold as well, and jewels of all sorts. Illyrio has promised. Tonight you must look like a princess."

A princess, Dany thought. She had forgotten what that was like. Perhaps she had never really known. "Why does he give us so much?" she asked. "What does he want from us?" For nigh on half a year, they had lived in the magister's house, eating his food, pampered by his servants. Dany was thirteen, old enough to know that such gifts seldom come without their price, here in the free city of Pentos.

"Illyrio is no fool," Viserys said. He was a gaunt young man with nervous hands and a feverish look in his pale lilac eyes. "The magister knows that I will not forget my friends when I come into my throne."

Dany said nothing. Magister Illyrio was a dealer in spices, gemstones, dragonbone, and other, less savory things. He had friends in all of the Nine Free Cities, it was said, and even beyond, in Vaes Dothrak and the fabled lands beside the Jade Sea. It was also said that he'd never had a friend he wouldn't cheerfully sell for the right price. Dany listened to the talk in the streets, and she heard these things, but she knew better than to question her brother when he wove his webs of dream. His anger was a terrible thing when roused. Viserys called it "waking the dragon."

Her brother hung the gown beside the door. "Illyrio will send the slaves to bathe you. Be sure you wash off the stink of the stables. Khal Drogo has a thousand horses, tonight he looks for a different sort of mount." He studied her critically. "You still slouch. Straighten yourself." He pushed back her shoulders with his hands. "Let them see that you have a woman's shape now." His fingers brushed lightly over her budding breasts and tightened on a nipple. "You will not fail me tonight. If you do, it will go hard for you. You don't want to wake the dragon, do you?" His fingers twisted her, the pinch cruelly hard through the rough fabric of her tunic. *"Do you?"* he repeated.

"No," Dany said meekly.

Her brother smiled. "Good." He touched her hair, almost with affection. "When they write the history of my reign, sweet sister, they will say that it began tonight."

When he was gone, Dany went to her window and looked out wistfully on the waters of the bay. The square brick towers of Pentos were black silhouettes outlined against the setting sun. Dany could hear the singing of the red priests as they lit their night fires and the shouts of ragged children playing games beyond the walls of the estate. For a moment she wished she could be out there with them, barefoot and breathless and dressed in tatters, with no past and no future and no feast to attend at Khal Drogo's manse.

Somewhere beyond the sunset, across the narrow sea, lay a land of green hills and flowered plains and great rushing rivers, where towers of dark stone rose amidst magnificent blue-grey mountains, and armored knights rode to battle beneath the banners of their lords. The Dothraki called that land *Rhaesh Andahli*, the land of the Andals. In the Free Cities, they talked of Westeros and the Sunset Kingdoms. Her brother had a simpler name. "Our land," he called it. The words were like a prayer with him. If he said them enough, the gods were sure to hear. "Ours by blood right, taken from us by treachery, but ours still, ours forever. You do not steal from the dragon, oh, no. The dragon remembers."

And perhaps the dragon did remember, but Dany could not. She had never seen this land her brother said was theirs, this realm beyond the narrow sea. These places he talked of, Casterly Rock and the Eyrie, Highgarden and the Vale of Arryn, Dorne and the Isle of Faces, they were just words to her. Viserys had been a boy of eight when they fled King's Landing to escape the advancing armies of the Usurper, but Daenerys had been only a quickening in their mother's womb.

Yet sometimes Dany would picture the way it had been, so often had her brother told her the stories. The midnight flight to Dragonstone, moonlight shimmering on the ship's black sails. Her brother Rhaegar battling the Usurper in the bloody waters of the Trident and dying for the woman he loved. The sack of King's Landing by the ones Viserys called the Usurper's dogs, the lords Lannister and Stark. Princess Elia of Dorne pleading for mercy as Rhaegar's heir was ripped from her breast and murdered before her eyes. The polished skulls of the last dragons staring down sightlessly from the walls of the throne room while the Kingslayer opened Father's throat with a golden sword.

She had been born on Dragonstone nine moons after their flight, while a raging summer storm threatened to rip the island fastness apart. They said that storm was terrible. The Targaryen fleet was smashed while it lay at anchor, and huge stone blocks were ripped from the parapets and sent hurtling into the wild waters of the narrow sea. Her mother had died birthing her, and for that her brother Viserys had never forgiven her.

She did not remember Dragonstone either. They had run again, just before the Usurper's brother set sail with his new-built fleet. By then only Dragonstone itself, the ancient seat of their House, had remained of the Seven

Kingdoms that had once been theirs. It would not remain for long. The garrison had been prepared to sell them to the Usurper, but one night Ser Willem Darry and four loyal men had broken into the nursery and stolen them both, along with her wet nurse, and set sail under cover of darkness for the safety of the Braavosian coast.

She remembered Ser Willem dimly, a great grey bear of a man, half-blind, roaring and bellowing orders from his sickbed. The servants had lived in terror of him, but he had always been kind to Dany. He called her "Little Princess" and sometimes "My Lady," and his hands were soft as old leather. He never left his bed, though, and the smell of sickness clung to him day and night, a hot, moist, sickly sweet odor. That was when they lived in Braavos, in the big house with the red door. Dany had her own room there, with a lemon tree outside her window. After Ser Willem had died, the servants had stolen what little money they had left, and soon after they had been put out of the big house. Dany had cried when the red door closed behind them forever.

They had wandered since then, from Braavos to Myr, from Myr to Tyrosh, and on to Qohor and Volantis and Lys, never staying long in any one place. Her brother would not allow it. The Usurper's hired knives were close behind them, he insisted, though Dany had never seen one.

At first the magisters and archons and merchant princes were pleased to welcome the last Targaryens to their homes and tables, but as the years passed and the Usurper continued to sit upon the Iron Throne, doors closed and their lives grew meaner. Years past they had been forced to sell their last few treasures, and now even the coin they had gotten from Mother's crown had gone. In the alleys and wine sinks of Pentos, they called her brother "the beggar king." Dany did not want to know what they called her.

"We will have it all back someday, sweet sister," he would promise her. Sometimes his hands shook when he talked about it. "The jewels and the silks, Dragonstone and King's Landing, the Iron Throne and the Seven Kingdoms, all they have taken from us, we will have it back." Viserys lived for that day. All that Daenerys wanted back was the big house with the red door, the lemon tree outside her window, the childhood she had never known.

There came a soft knock on her door. "Come," Dany said, turning away from the window. Illyrio's servants entered, bowed, and set about their business. They were slaves, a gift from one of the magister's many Dothraki friends. There was no slavery in the free city of Pentos. Nonetheless, they were slaves. The old woman, small and grey as a mouse, never said a word, but the girl made up for it. She was Illyrio's favorite, a fair-haired, blue-eyed wench of sixteen who chattered constantly as she worked.

They filled her bath with hot water brought up from the kitchen and scented it with fragrant oils. The girl pulled the rough cotton tunic over Dany's head and helped her into the tub. The water was scalding hot, but Daenerys did not flinch or cry out. She liked the heat. It made her feel clean. Besides, her brother had often told her that it was never too hot for a Targaryen. "Ours is the house of the dragon," he would say. "The fire is in our blood."

The old woman washed her long, silver-pale hair and gently combed out the snags, all in silence. The girl scrubbed her back and her feet and told her how lucky she was. "Drogo is so rich that even his slaves wear golden collars. A hundred thousand men ride in his *khalasar*, and his palace in Vaes Dothrak has two hundred rooms and doors of solid silver." There was more like that, so much more, what a handsome man the *khal* was, so tall and fierce, fearless in battle, the best rider ever to mount a horse, a demon archer. Daenerys said nothing. She had always assumed that she would wed Viserys when she came of age. For centuries the Targaryens had married brother to sister, since Aegon the Conqueror had taken his sisters to bride. The line must be kept pure, Viserys had told her a thousand times; theirs was the kingsblood, the golden blood of old Valyria, the blood of the dragon. Dragons did not mate with the beasts of the field, and Targaryens did not mingle their blood with that of lesser men. Yet now Viserys schemed to sell her to a stranger, a barbarian.

When she was clean, the slaves helped her from the water and toweled her dry. The girl brushed her hair until it shone like molten silver, while the old woman anointed her with the spiceflower perfume of the Dothraki plains, a dab on each wrist, behind her ears, on the tips of her breasts, and one last one, cool on her lips, down there between her legs. They dressed her in the wisps that Magister Illyrio had sent up, and then the gown, a deep plum silk to bring out the violet in her eyes. The girl slid the gilded sandals onto her feet, while the old woman fixed the tiara in her hair, and slid golden bracelets crusted with amethysts around her wrists. Last of all came the collar, a heavy golden torc emblazoned with ancient Valyrian glyphs.

"Now you look all a princess," the girl said breathlessly when they were done. Dany glanced at her image in the silvered looking glass that Illyrio had so thoughtfully provided. *A princess*, she thought, but she remembered what the girl had said, how Khal Drogo was so rich even his slaves wore golden collars. She felt a sudden chill, and gooseflesh pimpled her bare arms.

Her brother was waiting in the cool of the entry hall, seated on the edge of the pool, his hand trailing in the water. He rose when she appeared and looked her over critically. "Stand there," he told her. "Turn around. Yes. Good. You look . . ."

"Regal," Magister Illyrio said, stepping through an archway. He moved with surprising delicacy for such a massive man. Beneath loose garments of flame-colored silk, rolls of fat jiggled as he walked. Gemstones glittered on every finger, and his man had oiled his forked yellow beard until it shone like real gold. "May the Lord of Light shower you with blessings on this most fortunate day, Princess Daenerys," the magister said as he took her hand. He bowed his head, showing a thin glimpse of crooked yellow teeth through the gold of his beard. "She is a vision, Your Grace, a vision," he told her brother. "Drogo will be enraptured."

"She's too skinny," Viserys said. His hair, the same silver-blond as hers, had been pulled back tightly behind his head and fastened with a dragonbone brooch. It was a severe look that emphasized the hard, gaunt lines of his face. He rested his hand on the hilt of the sword that Illyrio had lent him, and said, "Are you sure that Khal Drogo likes his women this young?"

"She has had her blood. She is old enough for the *khal*," Illyrio told him, not for the first time. "Look at her. That silver-gold hair, those purple eyes . . . she is the blood of old Valyria, no doubt, no doubt . . . and highborn, daughter of the old king, sister to the new, she cannot fail to entrance our Drogo." When he released her hand, Daenerys found herself trembling.

"I suppose," her brother said doubtfully. "The savages have queer tastes. Boys, horses, sheep . . ."

"Best not suggest this to Khal Drogo," Illyrio said.

Anger flashed in her brother's lilac eyes. "Do you take me for a fool?"

The magister bowed slightly. "I take you for a king. Kings lack the caution of common men. My apologies if I have given offense." He turned away and clapped his hands for his bearers.

The streets of Pentos were pitch-dark when they set out in Illyrio's elaborately carved palanquin. Two servants went ahead to light their way, carrying ornate oil lanterns with panes of pale blue glass, while a dozen strong men hoisted the poles to their shoulders. It was warm and close inside behind the curtains. Dany could smell the stench of Illyrio's pallid flesh through his heavy perfumes.

Her brother, sprawled out on his pillows beside her, never noticed. His mind was away across the narrow sea. "We won't need his whole *khalasar*," Viserys said. His fingers toyed with the hilt of his borrowed blade, though Dany knew he had never used a sword in earnest. "Ten thousand, that would be enough, I could sweep the Seven Kingdoms with ten thousand Dothraki screamers. The realm will rise for its rightful king. Tyrell, Redwyne, Darry, Greyjoy, they have no more love for the Usurper than I do. The Dornishmen burn to avenge Elia and her children. And the smallfolk will be with us. They cry out for their king." He looked at Illyrio anxiously. "They do, don't they?"

"They are your people, and they love you well," Magister Illyrio said amiably. "In holdfasts all across the realm, men lift secret toasts to your health while women sew dragon banners and hide them against the day of your return from across the water." He gave a massive shrug. "Or so my agents tell me."

Dany had no agents, no way of knowing what anyone was doing or thinking across the narrow sea, but she mistrusted Illyrio's sweet words as she mistrusted everything about Illyrio. Her brother was nodding eagerly, however. "I shall kill the Usurper myself," he promised, who had never killed anyone, "as he killed my brother Rhaegar. And Lannister too, the Kingslayer, for what he did to my father."

"That would be most fitting," Magister Illyrio said. Dany saw the smallest hint of a smile playing around his full lips, but her brother did not notice. Nodding, he pushed back a curtain and stared off into the night, and Dany knew he was fighting the Battle of the Trident once again.

The nine-towered manse of Khal Drogo sat beside the waters of the bay, its high brick walls overgrown with pale ivy. It had been given to the *khal* by the magisters of Pentos, Illyrio told them. The Free Cities were always generous with the horselords. "It is not that we fear these barbarians," Illyrio would explain with a smile. "The Lord of Light would hold our city walls against a million Dothraki, or so the red priests promise . . . yet why take chances, when their friendship comes so cheap?"

Their palanquin was stopped at the gate, the curtains pulled roughly back by one of the house guards. He had the copper skin and dark almond eyes of a Dothraki, but his face was hairless and he wore the spiked bronze cap of the Unsullied. He looked them over coldly. Magister Illyrio growled something to him in the rough Dothraki tongue; the guardsman replied in the same voice and waved them through the gates.

Dany noticed that her brother's hand was clenched tightly around the hilt of his borrowed sword. He looked almost as frightened as she felt. "Insolent eunuch," Viserys muttered as the palanquin lurched up toward the manse.

Magister Illyrio's words were honey. "Many important men will be at the feast tonight. Such men have enemies. The *khal* must protect his guests, yourself chief among them, Your Grace. No doubt the Usurper would pay well for your head."

"Oh, yes," Viserys said darkly. "He has tried, Illyrio, I promise you that. His hired knives follow us everywhere.

I am the last dragon, and he will not sleep easy while I live."

The palanquin slowed and stopped. The curtains were thrown back, and a slave offered a hand to help Daenerys out. His collar, she noted, was ordinary bronze. Her brother followed, one hand still clenched hard around his sword hilt. It took two strong men to get Magister Illyrio back on his feet.

Inside the manse, the air was heavy with the scent of spices, pinchfire and sweet lemon and cinnamon. They were escorted across the entry hall, where a mosaic of colored glass depicted the Doom of Valyria. Oil burned in black iron lanterns all along the walls. Beneath an arch of twining stone leaves, a eunuch sang their coming. "Viserys of the House Targaryen, the Third of his Name," he called in a high, sweet voice, "King of the Andals and the Rhoynar and the First Men, Lord of the Seven Kingdoms and Protector of the Realm. His sister, Daenerys Stormborn, Princess of Dragonstone. His honorable host, Illyrio Mopatis, Magister of the Free City of Pentos."

They stepped past the eunuch into a pillared courtyard overgrown in pale ivy. Moonlight painted the leaves in shades of bone and silver as the guests drifted among them. Many were Dothraki horselords, big men with red-brown skin, their drooping mustachios bound in metal rings, their black hair oiled and braided and hung with bells. Yet among them moved bravos and sellswords from Pentos and Myr and Tyrosh, a red priest even fatter than Illyrio, hairy men from the Port of Ibben, and lords from the Summer Isles with skin as black as ebony. Daenerys looked at them all in wonder . . . and realized, with a sudden start of fear, that she was the only woman there.

Illyrio whispered to them. "Those three are Drogo's bloodriders, there," he said. "By the pillar is Khal Moro, with his son Rhogoro. The man with the green beard is brother to the Archon of Tyrosh, and the man behind him is Ser Jorah Mormont."

The last name caught Daenerys. "A knight?"

"No less." Illyrio smiled through his beard. "Anointed with the seven oils by the High Septon himself."

"What is he doing here?" she blurted.

"The Usurper wanted his head," Illyrio told them. "Some trifling affront. He sold some poachers to a Tyroshi slaver instead of giving them to the Night's Watch. Absurd law. A man should be able to do as he likes with his own chattel."

"I shall wish to speak with Ser Jorah before the night is done," her brother said. Dany found herself looking at the knight curiously. He was an older man, past forty and balding, but still strong and fit. Instead of silks and cottons, he wore wool and leather. His tunic was a dark green, embroidered with the likeness of a black bear standing on two legs.

She was still looking at this strange man from the homeland she had never known when Magister Illyrio placed a moist hand on her bare shoulder. "Over there, sweet princess," he whispered, "there is the *khal* himself."

Dany wanted to run and hide, but her brother was looking at her, and if she displeased him she knew she would wake the dragon. Anxiously, she turned and looked at the man Viserys hoped would ask to wed her before the night was done.

The slave girl had not been far wrong, she thought. Khal Drogo was a head taller than the tallest man in the room, yet somehow light on his feet, as graceful as the panther in Illyrio's menagerie. He was younger than she'd thought, no more than thirty. His skin was the color of polished copper, his thick mustachios bound with gold and bronze rings.

"I must go and make my submissions," Magister Illyrio said. "Wait here. I shall bring him to you."

Her brother took her by the arm as Illyrio waddled over to the *khal*, his fingers squeezing so hard that they hurt. "Do you see his braid, sweet sister?"

Drogo's braid was black as midnight and heavy with scented oil, hung with tiny bells that rang softly as he moved. It swung well past his belt, below even his buttocks, the end of it brushing against the back of his thighs.

"You see how long it is?" Viserys said. "When Dothraki are defeated in combat, they cut off their braids in disgrace, so the world will know their shame. Khal Drogo has never lost a fight. He is Aegon the Dragonlord come again, and you will be his queen."

Dany looked at Khal Drogo. His face was hard and

cruel, his eyes as cold and dark as onyx. Her brother hurt
her sometimes, when she woke the dragon, but he did not
frighten her the way this man frightened her. "I don't
want to be his queen," she heard herself say in a small,
thin voice. "Please, *please*, Viserys, I don't want to, I want
to go home."

"Home?" He kept his voice low, but she could hear the
fury in his tone. "How are we to go home, sweet sister?
They took our home from us!" He drew her into the shadows, out of sight, his fingers digging into her skin. *"How
are we to go home?"* he repeated, meaning King's Landing, and Dragonstone, and all the realm they had lost.

Dany had only meant their rooms in Illyrio's estate, no
true home surely, though all they had, but her brother did
not want to hear that. There was no home there for him.
Even the big house with the red door had not been home
for him. His fingers dug hard into her arm, demanding an
answer. "I don't know . . ." she said at last, her voice
breaking. Tears welled in her eyes.

"I do," he said sharply. "We go home with an army,
sweet sister. With Khal Drogo's army, that is how we go
home. And if you must wed him and bed him for that,
you will." He smiled at her. "I'd let his whole *khalasar*
fuck you if need be, sweet sister, all forty thousand men,
and their horses too if that was what it took to get my
army. Be grateful it is only Drogo. In time you may even
learn to like him. Now dry your eyes. Illyrio is bringing
him over, and he will *not* see you crying."

Dany turned and saw that it was true. Magister Illyrio,
all smiles and bows, was escorting Khal Drogo over to
where they stood. She brushed away unfallen tears with
the back of her hand.

"Smile," Viserys whispered nervously, his hand falling
to the hilt of his sword. "And stand up straight. Let him
see that you have breasts. Gods know, you have little
enough as is."

Daenerys smiled, and stood up straight.

EDDARD

The visitors poured through the castle gates in a river of gold and silver and polished steel, three hundred strong, a pride of bannermen and knights, of sworn swords and freeriders. Over their heads a dozen golden banners whipped back and forth in the northern wind, emblazoned with the crowned stag of Baratheon.

Ned knew many of the riders. There came Ser Jaime Lannister with hair as bright as beaten gold, and there Sandor Clegane with his terrible burned face. The tall boy beside him could only be the crown prince, and that stunted little man behind them was surely the Imp, Tyrion Lannister.

Yet the huge man at the head of the column, flanked by two knights in the snow-white cloaks of the Kingsguard, seemed almost a stranger to Ned . . . until he vaulted off the back of his warhorse with a familiar roar, and crushed him in a bone-crunching hug. "*Ned!* Ah, but it is good to see that frozen face of yours." The king looked him over top to bottom, and laughed. "You have not changed at all."

Would that Ned had been able to say the same. Fifteen years past, when they had ridden forth to win a throne, the Lord of Storm's End had been clean-shaven, clear-eyed, and muscled like a maiden's fantasy. Six and a half feet tall, he towered over lesser men, and when he donned his armor and the great antlered helmet of his House, he became a veritable giant. He'd had a giant's strength too, his weapon of choice a spiked iron warhammer that Ned could scarcely lift. In those days, the smell of leather and blood had clung to him like perfume.

Now it was perfume that clung to him like perfume, and he had a girth to match his height. Ned had last seen the king nine years before during Balon Greyjoy's rebellion, when the stag and the direwolf had joined to end the pretensions of the self-proclaimed King of the Iron Islands. Since the night they had stood side by side in Greyjoy's fallen stronghold, where Robert had accepted the rebel lord's surrender and Ned had taken his son Theon as hostage and ward, the king had gained at least eight stone. A beard as coarse and black as iron wire covered his jaw to hide his double chin and the sag of the royal jowls, but nothing could hide his stomach or the dark circles under his eyes.

Yet Robert was Ned's king now, and not just a friend, so he said only, "Your Grace. Winterfell is yours."

By then the others were dismounting as well, and grooms were coming forward for their mounts. Robert's queen, Cersei Lannister, entered on foot with her younger children. The wheelhouse in which they had ridden, a huge double-decked carriage of oiled oak and gilded metal pulled by forty heavy draft horses, was too wide to pass through the castle gate. Ned knelt in the snow to kiss the queen's ring, while Robert embraced Catelyn like a long-lost sister. Then the children had been brought forward, introduced, and approved of by both sides.

No sooner had those formalities of greeting been completed than the king had said to his host, "Take me down to your crypt, Eddard. I would pay my respects."

Ned loved him for that, for remembering her still after all these years. He called for a lantern. No other words were needed. The queen had begun to protest. They had been riding since dawn, everyone was tired and cold, surely they should refresh themselves first. The dead would wait. She had said no more than that; Robert had looked at her, and her twin brother Jaime had taken her quietly by the arm, and she had said no more.

They went down to the crypt together, Ned and this king he scarcely recognized. The winding stone steps were narrow. Ned went first with the lantern. "I was starting to think we would never reach Winterfell," Robert complained as they descended. "In the south, the way they talk about my Seven Kingdoms, a man forgets that your part is as big as the other six combined."

"I trust you enjoyed the journey, Your Grace?"

Robert snorted. "Bogs and forests and fields, and scarcely a decent inn north of the Neck. I've never seen such a vast emptiness. Where are all your *people*?"

"Likely they were too shy to come out," Ned jested. He could feel the chill coming up the stairs, a cold breath from deep within the earth. "Kings are a rare sight in the north."

Robert snorted. "More likely they were hiding under the snow. *Snow,* Ned!" The king put one hand on the wall to steady himself as they descended.

"Late summer snows are common enough," Ned said. "I hope they did not trouble you. They are usually mild."

"The Others take your mild snows," Robert swore. "What will this place be like in winter? I shudder to think."

"The winters are hard," Ned admitted. "But the Starks will endure. We always have."

"You need to come south," Robert told him. "You need a taste of summer before it flees. In Highgarden there are fields of golden roses that stretch away as far as the eye can see. The fruits are so ripe they explode in your mouth—melons, peaches, fireplums, you've never tasted such sweetness. You'll see, I brought you some. Even at Storm's End, with that good wind off the bay, the days are so hot you can barely move. And you ought to see the towns, Ned! Flowers everywhere, the markets bursting with food, the summerwines so cheap and so good that you can get drunk just breathing the air. Everyone is fat and drunk and rich." He laughed and slapped his own ample stomach a thump. "And the *girls,* Ned!" he exclaimed, his eyes sparkling. "I swear, women lose all modesty in the heat. They swim naked in the river, right beneath the castle. Even in the streets, it's too damn hot for wool or fur, so they go around in these short gowns, silk if they have the silver and cotton if not, but it's all the same when they start sweating and the cloth sticks to their skin, they might as well be naked." The king laughed happily.

Robert Baratheon had always been a man of huge appetites, a man who knew how to take his pleasures. That was not a charge anyone could lay at the door of Eddard Stark. Yet Ned could not help but notice that those pleasures were taking a toll on the king. Robert was breathing heavily by the time they reached the bottom of the stairs, his face red in the lantern light as they stepped out into the darkness of the crypt.

"Your Grace," Ned said respectfully. He swept the lantern in a wide semicircle. Shadows moved and lurched. Flickering light touched the stones underfoot and brushed against a long procession of granite pillars that marched ahead, two by two, into the dark. Between the pillars, the dead sat on their stone thrones against the walls, backs against the sepulchres that contained their mortal remains. "She is down at the end, with Father and Brandon."

He led the way between the pillars and Robert followed wordlessly, shivering in the subterranean chill. It was always cold down here. Their footsteps rang off the stones and echoed in the vault overhead as they walked among the dead of House Stark. The Lords of Winterfell watched them pass. Their likenesses were carved into the stones that sealed the tombs. In long rows they sat, blind eyes staring out into eternal darkness, while great stone direwolves curled round their feet. The shifting shadows made the stone figures seem to stir as the living passed by.

By ancient custom an iron longsword had been laid across the lap of each who had been Lord of Winterfell, to keep the vengeful spirits in their crypts. The oldest had long ago rusted away to nothing, leaving only a few red stains where the metal had rested on stone. Ned wondered if that meant those ghosts were free to roam the castle now. He hoped not. The first Lords of Winterfell had been men hard as the land they ruled. In the centuries before the Dragonlords came over the sea, they had sworn allegiance to no man, styling themselves the Kings in the North.

Ned stopped at last and lifted the oil lantern. The crypt continued on into darkness ahead of them, but beyond this point the tombs were empty and unsealed; black holes waiting for their dead, waiting for him and his children. Ned did not like to think on that. "Here," he told his king.

Robert nodded silently, knelt, and bowed his head.

There were three tombs, side by side. Lord Rickard Stark, Ned's father, had a long, stern face. The stonemason had known him well. He sat with quiet dignity, stone fingers holding tight to the sword across his lap, but in life all swords had failed him. In two smaller sepulchres on either side were his children.

Brandon had been twenty when he died, strangled by order of the Mad King Aerys Targaryen only a few short days before he was to wed Catelyn Tully of Riverrun. His father had been forced to watch him die. He was the true heir, the eldest, born to rule.

Lyanna had only been sixteen, a child-woman of surpassing loveliness. Ned had loved her with all his heart. Robert had loved her even more. She was to have been his bride.

"She was more beautiful than that," the king said after a silence. His eyes lingered on Lyanna's face, as if he could will her back to life. Finally he rose, made awkward by his weight. "Ah, damn it, Ned, did you have to bury her in a place like *this*?" His voice was hoarse with remembered grief. "She deserved more than darkness . . ."

"She was a Stark of Winterfell," Ned said quietly. "This is her place."

"She should be on a hill somewhere, under a fruit tree, with the sun and clouds above her and the rain to wash her clean."

"I was with her when she died," Ned reminded the king. "She wanted to come home, to rest beside Brandon and Father." He could hear her still at times. *Promise me*, she had cried, in a room that smelled of blood and roses. *Promise me, Ned.* The fever had taken her strength and her voice had been faint as a whisper, but when he gave her his word, the fear had gone out of his sister's eyes. Ned remembered the way she had smiled then, how tightly her fingers had clutched his as she gave up her hold on life, the rose petals spilling from her palm, dead and black. After that he remembered nothing. They had found him still holding her body, silent with grief. The little crannogman, Howland Reed, had taken her hand from his. Ned could recall none of it. "I bring her flowers when I can," he said. "Lyanna was . . . fond of flowers."

The king touched her cheek, his fingers brushing across the rough stone as gently as if it were living flesh. "I vowed to kill Rhaegar for what he did to her."

"You did," Ned reminded him.

"Only once," Robert said bitterly.

They had come together at the ford of the Trident while the battle crashed around them, Robert with his warhammer and his great antlered helm, the Targaryen prince armored all in black. On his breastplate was the three-headed dragon of his House, wrought all in rubies that flashed like fire in the sunlight. The waters of the Trident ran red around the hooves of their destriers as they circled and clashed, again and again, until at last a crushing blow from Robert's hammer stove in the dragon and the chest beneath it. When Ned had finally come on the scene, Rhaegar lay dead in the stream, while men of both armies scrabbled in the swirling waters for rubies knocked free of his armor.

"In my dreams, I kill him every night," Robert admitted. "A thousand deaths will still be less than he deserves."

There was nothing Ned could say to that. After a quiet, he said, "We should return, Your Grace. Your wife will be waiting." .

"The Others take my wife," Robert muttered sourly, but he started back the way they had come, his footsteps falling heavily. "And if I hear 'Your Grace' once more, I'll have your head on a spike. We are more to each other than that."

"I had not forgotten," Ned replied quietly. When the king did not answer, he said, "Tell me about Jon."

Robert shook his head. "I have never seen a man sicken so quickly. We gave a tourney on my son's name day. If you had seen Jon then, you would have sworn he would live forever. A fortnight later he was dead. The sickness was like a fire in his gut. It burned right through him." He paused beside a pillar, before the tomb of a long-dead Stark. "I loved that old man."

"We both did." Ned paused a moment. "Catelyn fears for her sister. How does Lysa bear her grief?"

Robert's mouth gave a bitter twist. "Not well, in truth," he admitted. "I think losing Jon has driven the woman mad, Ned. She has taken the boy back to the Eyrie. Against my wishes. I had hoped to foster him with Tywin Lannister at Casterly Rock. Jon had no brothers, no other sons. Was I supposed to leave him to be raised by women?"

Ned would sooner entrust a child to a pit viper than to Lord Tywin, but he left his doubts unspoken. Some old wounds never truly heal, and bleed again at the slightest word. "The wife has lost the husband," he said carefully. "Perhaps the mother feared to lose the son. The boy is very young."

"Six, and sickly, and Lord of the Eyrie, gods have mercy," the king swore. "Lord Tywin had never taken a ward before. Lysa ought to have been honored. The Lannisters are a great and noble House. She refused to even hear of it. Then she left in the dead of night, without so much as a by-your-leave. Cersei was furious." He sighed deeply. "The boy is my namesake, did you know that? Robert Arryn. I am sworn to protect him. How can I do that if his mother steals him away?"

"I will take him as ward, if you wish," Ned said. "Lysa should consent to that. She and Catelyn were close as girls, and she would be welcome here as well."

"A generous offer, my friend," the king said, "but too late. Lord Tywin has already given his consent. Fostering the boy elsewhere would be a grievous affront to him."

"I have more concern for my nephew's welfare than I do for Lannister pride," Ned declared.

"That is because you do not sleep with a Lannister." Robert laughed, the sound rattling among the tombs and bouncing from the vaulted ceiling. His smile was a flash of white teeth in the thicket of the huge black beard. "Ah, Ned," he said, "you are still too serious." He put a massive arm around Ned's shoulders. "I had planned to wait a few days to speak to you, but I see now there's no need for it. Come, walk with me."

They started back down between the pillars. Blind

stone eyes seemed to follow them as they passed. The king kept his arm around Ned's shoulder. "You must have wondered why I finally came north to Winterfell, after so long."

Ned had his suspicions, but he did not give them voice. "For the joy of my company, surely," he said lightly. "And there is the Wall. You need to see it, Your Grace, to walk along its battlements and talk to those who man it. The Night's Watch is a shadow of what it once was. Benjen says—"

"No doubt I will hear what your brother says soon enough," Robert said. "The Wall has stood for what, eight thousand years? It can keep a few days more. I have more pressing concerns. These are difficult times. I need good men about me. Men like Jon Arryn. He served as Lord of the Eyrie, as Warden of the East, as the Hand of the King. He will not be easy to replace."

"His son . . ." Ned began.

"His son will succeed to the Eyrie and all its incomes," Robert said brusquely. "No more."

That took Ned by surprise. He stopped, startled, and turned to look at his king. The words came unbidden. "The Arryns have always been Wardens of the East. The title goes with the domain."

"Perhaps when he comes of age, the honor can be restored to him," Robert said. "I have this year to think of, and next. A six-year-old boy is no war leader, Ned."

"In peace, the title is only an honor. Let the boy keep it. For his father's sake if not his own. Surely you owe Jon that much for his service."

The king was not pleased. He took his arm from around Ned's shoulders. "Jon's service was the duty he owed his liege lord. I am not ungrateful, Ned. You of all men ought to know that. But the son is not the father. A mere boy cannot hold the east." Then his tone softened. "Enough of this. There is a more important office to discuss, and I would not argue with you." Robert grasped Ned by the elbow. "I have need of you, Ned."

"I am yours to command, Your Grace. Always." They were words he had to say, and so he said them, apprehensive about what might come next.

Robert scarcely seemed to hear him. "Those years we spent in the Eyrie . . . *gods*, those were good years. I want you at my side again, Ned. I want you down in King's Landing, not up here at the end of the world where you are no damned use to anybody." Robert looked off into the darkness, for a moment as melancholy as a Stark. "I swear to you, sitting a throne is a thousand times harder than winning one. Laws are a tedious business and counting coppers is worse. And the people . . . there is no end of them. I sit on that damnable iron chair and listen to them complain until my mind is numb and my ass is raw. They all want something, money or land or justice. The lies they tell . . . and my lords and ladies are no better. I am surrounded by flatterers and fools. It can drive a man to madness, Ned. Half of them don't dare tell me the truth, and the other half can't find it. There are nights I wish we had lost at the Trident. Ah, no, not truly, but . . ."

"I understand," Ned said softly.

Robert looked at him. "I think you do. If so, you are the only one, my old friend." He smiled. "Lord Eddard Stark, I would name you the Hand of the King."

Ned dropped to one knee. The offer did not surprise him; what other reason could Robert have had for coming so far? The Hand of the King was the second-most powerful man in the Seven Kingdoms. He spoke with the king's voice, commanded the king's armies, drafted the king's laws. At times he even sat upon the Iron Throne to dispense king's justice, when the king was absent, or sick, or otherwise indisposed. Robert was offering him a responsibility as large as the realm itself.

It was the last thing in the world he wanted.

"Your Grace," he said. "I am not worthy of the honor."

Robert groaned with good-humored impatience. "If I wanted to honor you, I'd let you retire. I am planning to make you run the kingdom and fight the wars while I eat and drink and wench myself into an early grave." He slapped his gut and grinned. "You know the saying, about the king and his Hand?"

Ned knew the saying. "What the king dreams," he said, "the Hand builds."

"I bedded a fishmaid once who told me the lowborn have a choicer way to put it. The king eats, they say, and the Hand takes the shit." He threw back his head and roared his laughter. The echoes rang through the darkness, and all around them the dead of Winterfell seemed to watch with cold and disapproving eyes.

Finally the laughter dwindled and stopped. Ned was still on one knee, his eyes upraised. "Damn it, Ned," the king complained. "You might at least humor me with a smile."

"They say it grows so cold up here in winter that a man's laughter freezes in his throat and chokes him to death," Ned said evenly. "Perhaps that is why the Starks have so little humor."

"Come south with me, and I'll teach you how to laugh again," the king promised. "You helped me win this damnable throne, now help me hold it. We were meant to rule together. If Lyanna had lived, we should have been brothers, bound by blood as well as affection. Well, it is not too late. I have a son. You have a daughter. My Joff and your Sansa shall join our houses, as Lyanna and I might once have done."

This offer *did* surprise him. "Sansa is only eleven."

Robert waved an impatient hand. "Old enough for betrothal. The marriage can wait a few years." The king smiled. "Now stand up and say yes, curse you."

"Nothing would give me greater pleasure, Your Grace," Ned answered. He hesitated. "These honors are all so unexpected. May I have some time to consider? I need to tell my wife . . ."

"Yes, yes, of course, tell Catelyn, sleep on it if you must." The king reached down, clasped Ned by the hand, and pulled him roughly to his feet. "Just don't keep me waiting too long. I am not the most patient of men."

For a moment Eddard Stark was filled with a terrible sense of foreboding. *This* was his place, here in the north. He looked at the stone figures all around them, breathed deep in the chill silence of the crypt. He could feel the eyes of the dead. They were all listening, he knew. And winter was coming.

JON

There were times—not many, but a few—when Jon Snow was glad he was a bastard. As he filled his wine cup once more from a passing flagon, it struck him that this might be one of them.

He settled back in his place on the bench among the younger squires and drank. The sweet, fruity taste of summerwine filled his mouth and brought a smile to his lips.

The Great Hall of Winterfell was hazy with smoke and heavy with the smell of roasted meat and fresh-baked bread. Its grey stone walls were draped with banners. White, gold, crimson: the direwolf of Stark, Baratheon's crowned stag, the lion of Lannister. A singer was playing the high harp and reciting a ballad, but down at this end of the hall his voice could scarcely be heard above the roar of the fire, the clangor of pewter plates and cups, and the low mutter of a hundred drunken conversations.

It was the fourth hour of the welcoming feast laid for the king. Jon's brothers and sisters had been seated with the royal children, beneath the raised platform where Lord and Lady Stark hosted the king and queen. In honor of the occasion, his lord father would doubtless permit each child a glass of wine, but no more than that. Down here on the benches, there was no one to stop Jon drinking as much as he had a thirst for.

And he was finding that he had a man's thirst, to the raucous delight of the youths around him, who urged him on every time he drained a glass. They were fine company, and Jon relished the stories they were telling, tales of battle and bedding and the hunt. He was certain that his companions were more entertaining than the king's offspring. He had sated his curiosity about the visitors when they made their entrance. The procession had passed not a foot from the place he had been given on the bench, and Jon had gotten a good long look at them all.

His lord father had come first, escorting the queen. She was as beautiful as men said. A jeweled tiara gleamed amidst her long golden hair, its emeralds a perfect match for the green of her eyes. His father helped her up the steps to the dais and led her to her seat, but the queen never so much as looked at him. Even at fourteen, Jon could see through her smile.

Next had come King Robert himself, with Lady Stark on his arm. The king was a great disappointment to Jon. His father had talked of him often: the peerless Robert Baratheon, demon of the Trident, the fiercest warrior of the realm, a giant among princes. Jon saw only a fat man, red-faced under his beard, sweating through his silks. He walked like a man half in his cups.

After them came the children. Little Rickon first, managing the long walk with all the dignity a three-year-old could muster. Jon had to urge him on when he stopped to visit. Close behind came Robb, in grey wool trimmed with white, the Stark colors. He had the Princess Myrcella on his arm. She was a wisp of a girl, not quite eight, her hair a cascade of golden curls under a jeweled net. Jon noticed the shy looks she gave Robb as they passed between the tables and the timid way she smiled at him. He decided she was insipid. Robb didn't even have the sense to realize how stupid she was; he was grinning like a fool.

His half sisters escorted the royal princes. Arya was paired with plump young Tommen, whose white-blond hair was longer than hers. Sansa, two years older, drew the crown prince, Joffrey Baratheon. He was twelve, younger than Jon or Robb, but taller than either, to Jon's vast dismay. Prince Joffrey had his sister's hair and his mother's deep green eyes. A thick tangle of blond curls dripped down past his golden choker and high velvet collar. Sansa looked radiant as she walked beside him, but Jon did not like Joffrey's pouty lips or the bored, disdainful way he looked at Winterfell's Great Hall.

He was more interested in the pair that came behind him: the queen's brothers, the Lannisters of Casterly Rock. The Lion and the Imp; there was no mistaking which was which. Ser Jaime Lannister was twin to Queen Cersei; tall and golden, with flashing green eyes and a smile that cut like a knife. He wore crimson silk, high black boots, a black satin cloak. On the breast of his tunic, the lion of his House was embroidered in gold thread, roaring its defiance. They called him the Lion of Lannister to his face and whispered "Kingslayer" behind his back.

Jon found it hard to look away from him. *This is what a king should look like,* he thought to himself as the man passed.

Then he saw the other one, waddling along half-hidden by his brother's side. Tyrion Lannister, the youngest of Lord Tywin's brood and by far the ugliest. All that the gods had given to Cersei and Jaime, they had denied Tyrion. He was a dwarf, half his brother's height, struggling to keep pace on stunted legs. His head was too large for his body, with a brute's squashed-in face beneath a swollen shelf of brow. One green eye and one black one peered out from under a lank fall of hair so blond it seemed white. Jon watched him with fascination.

The last of the high lords to enter were his uncle, Benjen Stark of the Night's Watch, and his father's ward, young Theon Greyjoy. Benjen gave Jon a warm smile as he went by. Theon ignored him utterly, but there was nothing new in that. After all had been seated, toasts were made, thanks were given and returned, and then the feasting began.

Jon had started drinking then, and he had not stopped.

Something rubbed against his leg beneath the table. Jon saw red eyes staring up at him. "Hungry again?" he asked. There was still half a honeyed chicken in the center of the table. Jon reached out to tear off a leg, then had a better idea. He knifed the bird whole and let the carcass slide to the floor between his legs. Ghost ripped into it in savage silence. His brothers and sisters had not been permitted to bring their wolves to the banquet, but there were more curs than Jon could count at this end of the hall, and no one had said a word about his pup. He told himself he was fortunate in that too.

His eyes stung. Jon rubbed at them savagely, cursing the smoke. He swallowed another gulp of wine and watched his direwolf devour the chicken.

Dogs moved between the tables, trailing after the serving girls. One of them, a black mongrel bitch with long yellow eyes, caught a scent of the chicken. She stopped and edged under the bench to get a share. Jon watched the confrontation. The bitch growled low in her throat and moved closer. Ghost looked up, silent, and fixed the dog with those hot red eyes. The bitch snapped an angry challenge. She was three times the size of the direwolf pup. Ghost did not move. He stood over his prize and opened his mouth, baring his fangs. The bitch tensed, barked again, then thought better of this fight. She turned and slunk away, with one last defiant snap to save her pride. Ghost went back to his meal.

Jon grinned and reached under the table to ruffle the shaggy white fur. The direwolf looked up at him, nipped gently at his hand, then went back to eating.

"Is this one of the direwolves I've heard so much of?" a familiar voice asked close at hand.

Jon looked up happily as his uncle Ben put a hand on his head and ruffled his hair much as Jon had ruffled the wolf's. "Yes," he said. "His name is Ghost."

One of the squires interrupted the bawdy story he'd been telling to make room at the table for their lord's brother. Benjen Stark straddled the bench with long legs and took the wine cup out of Jon's hand. "Summerwine," he said after a taste. "Nothing so sweet. How many cups have you had, Jon?"

Jon smiled.

Ben Stark laughed. "As I feared. Ah, well. I believe I was younger than you the first time I got truly and sincerely drunk." He snagged a roasted onion, dripping brown with gravy, from a nearby trencher and bit into it. It crunched.

His uncle was sharp-featured and gaunt as a mountain crag, but there was always a hint of laughter in his blue-grey eyes. He dressed in black, as befitted a man of the Night's Watch. Tonight it was rich black velvet, with high leather boots and a wide belt with a silver buckle. A heavy silver chain was looped round his neck. Benjen watched Ghost with amusement as he ate his onion. "A very quiet wolf," he observed.

"He's not like the others," Jon said. "He never makes a sound. That's why I named him Ghost. That, and because he's white. The others are all dark, grey or black."

"There are still direwolves beyond the Wall. We hear them on our rangings." Benjen Stark gave Jon a long look. "Don't you usually eat at table with your brothers?"

"Most times," Jon answered in a flat voice. "But tonight Lady Stark thought it might give insult to the royal family to seat a bastard among them."

"I see." His uncle glanced over his shoulder at the raised table at the far end of the hall. "My brother does not seem very festive tonight."

Jon had noticed that too. A bastard had to learn to notice things, to read the truth that people hid behind their eyes. His father was observing all the courtesies, but there was tightness in him that Jon had seldom seen before. He said little, looking out over the hall with hooded eyes, seeing nothing. Two seats away, the king had been drinking heavily all night. His broad face was flushed behind his great black beard. He made many a toast, laughed loudly at every jest, and attacked each dish like a starving man, but beside him the queen seemed as cold as an ice sculpture. "The queen is angry too," Jon told his uncle in a low, quiet voice. "Father took the king down to the crypts this afternoon. The queen didn't want him to go."

Benjen gave Jon a careful, measuring look. "You don't miss much, do you, Jon? We could use a man like you on the Wall."

Jon swelled with pride. "Robb is a stronger lance than I am, but I'm the better sword, and Hullen says I sit a horse as well as anyone in the castle."

"Notable achievements."

"Take me with you when you go back to the Wall," Jon said in a sudden rush. "Father will give me leave to go if you ask him, I know he will."

Uncle Benjen studied his face carefully. "The Wall is a hard place for a boy, Jon."

"I am almost a man grown," Jon protested. "I will turn fifteen on my next name day, and Maester Luwin says bastards grow up faster than other children."

"That's true enough," Benjen said with a downward twist of his mouth. He took Jon's cup from the table, filled it fresh from a nearby pitcher, and drank down a long swallow.

"Daeren Targaryen was only fourteen when he conquered Dorne," Jon said. The Young Dragon was one of his heroes.

"A conquest that lasted a summer," his uncle pointed out. "Your Boy King lost ten thousand men taking the place, and another fifty thousand trying to hold it. Someone should have told him that war isn't a game." He took another sip of wine. "Also," he said, wiping his mouth, "Daeren Targaryen was only eighteen when he died. Or have you forgotten that part?"

"I forget nothing," Jon boasted. The wine was making him bold. He tried to sit very straight, to make himself seem taller. "I want to serve in the Night's Watch, Uncle."

He had thought on it long and hard, lying abed at night while his brothers slept around him. Robb would someday inherit Winterfell, would command great armies as the Warden of the North. Bran and Rickon would be Robb's bannermen and rule holdfasts in his name. His sisters Arya and Sansa would marry the heirs of other great houses and go south as mistress of castles of their own. But what place could a bastard hope to earn?

"You don't know what you're asking, Jon. The Night's Watch is a sworn brotherhood. We have no families. None of us will ever father sons. Our wife is duty. Our mistress is honor."

"A bastard can have honor too," Jon said. "I am ready to swear your oath."

"You are a boy of fourteen," Benjen said. "Not a man, not yet. Until you have known a woman, you cannot understand what you would be giving up."

"I don't care about that!" Jon said hotly.

"You might, if you knew what it meant," Benjen said.

"If you knew what the oath would cost you, you might be less eager to pay the price, son."

Jon felt anger rise inside him. "I'm not your son!"

Benjen Stark stood up. "More's the pity." He put a hand on Jon's shoulder. "Come back to me after you've fathered a few bastards of your own, and we'll see how you feel."

Jon trembled. "I will never father a bastard," he said carefully. *"Never!"* He spat it out like venom.

Suddenly he realized that the table had fallen silent, and they were all looking at him. He felt the tears begin to well behind his eyes. He pushed himself to his feet.

"I must be excused," he said with the last of his dignity. He whirled and bolted before they could see him cry. He must have drunk more wine than he had realized. His feet got tangled under him as he tried to leave, and he lurched sideways into a serving girl and sent a flagon of spiced wine crashing to the floor. Laughter boomed all around him, and Jon felt hot tears on his cheeks. Someone tried to steady him. He wrenched free of their grip and ran, half-blind, for the door. Ghost followed close at his heels, out into the night.

The yard was quiet and empty. A lone sentry stood high on the battlements of the inner wall, his cloak pulled tight around him against the cold. He looked bored and miserable as he huddled there alone, but Jon would have traded places with him in an instant. Otherwise the castle was dark and deserted. Jon had seen an abandoned holdfast once, a drear place where nothing moved but the wind and the stones kept silent about whatever people had lived there. Winterfell reminded him of that tonight.

The sounds of music and song spilled through the open windows behind him. They were the last things Jon wanted to hear. He wiped away his tears on the sleeve of his shirt, furious that he had let them fall, and turned to go.

"Boy," a voice called out to him. Jon turned.

Tyrion Lannister was sitting on the ledge above the door to the Great Hall, looking for all the world like a gargoyle. The dwarf grinned down at him. "Is that animal a wolf?"

"A direwolf," Jon said. "His name is Ghost." He stared up at the little man, his disappointment suddenly forgotten. "What are you doing up there? Why aren't you at the feast?"

"Too hot, too noisy, and I'd drunk too much wine," the dwarf told him. "I learned long ago that it is considered rude to vomit on your brother. Might I have a closer look at your wolf?"

Jon hesitated, then nodded slowly. "Can you climb down, or shall I bring a ladder?"

"Oh, bleed that," the little man said. He pushed himself off the ledge into empty air. Jon gasped, then watched with awe as Tyrion Lannister spun around in a tight ball, landed lightly on his hands, then vaulted backward onto his legs.

Ghost backed away from him uncertainly.

The dwarf dusted himself off and laughed. "I believe I've frightened your wolf. My apologies."

"He's not scared," Jon said. He knelt and called out. "Ghost, come here. Come on. That's it."

The wolf pup padded closer and nuzzled at Jon's face, but he kept a wary eye on Tyrion Lannister, and when the dwarf reached out to pet him, he drew back and bared his fangs in a silent snarl. "Shy, isn't he?" Lannister observed.

"Sit, Ghost," Jon commanded. "That's it. Keep still." He looked up at the dwarf. "You can touch him now. He won't move until I tell him to. I've been training him."

"I see," Lannister said. He ruffled the snow-white fur between Ghost's ears and said, "Nice wolf."

"If I wasn't here, he'd tear out your throat," Jon said. It wasn't actually true yet, but it would be.

"In that case, you had best stay close," the dwarf said. He cocked his oversized head to one side and looked Jon over with his mismatched eyes. "I am Tyrion Lannister."

"I know," Jon said. He rose. Standing, he was taller than the dwarf. It made him feel strange.

"You're Ned Stark's bastard, aren't you?"

Jon felt a coldness pass right through him. He pressed his lips together and said nothing.

"Did I offend you?" Lannister said. "Sorry. Dwarfs don't have to be tactful. Generations of capering fools in motley have won me the right to dress badly and say any damn thing that comes into my head." He grinned. "You *are* the bastard, though."

"Lord Eddard Stark is my father," Jon admitted stiffly.

Lannister studied his face. "Yes," he said. "I can see it. You have more of the north in you than your brothers."

"Half brothers," Jon corrected. He was pleased by the dwarf's comment, but he tried not to let it show.

"Let me give you some counsel, bastard," Lannister said. "Never forget what you are, for surely the world will not. Make it your strength. Then it can never be your weakness. Armor yourself in it, and it will never be used to hurt you."

Jon was in no mood for anyone's counsel. "What do you know about being a bastard?"

"All dwarfs are bastards in their father's eyes."

"You are your mother's trueborn son of Lannister."

"Am I?" the dwarf replied, sardonic. "Do tell my lord father. My mother died birthing me, and he's never been sure."

"I don't even know who my mother was," Jon said.

"Some woman, no doubt. Most of them are." He favored Jon with a rueful grin. "Remember this, boy. All dwarfs may be bastards, yet not all bastards need be dwarfs." And with that he turned and sauntered back into the feast, whistling a tune. When he opened the door, the light from within threw his shadow clear across the yard, and for just a moment Tyrion Lannister stood tall as a king.

CATELYN

O f all the rooms in Winterfell's Great Keep, Catelyn's bedchambers were the hottest. She seldom had to light a fire. The castle had been built over natural hot springs, and the scalding waters rushed through its walls and chambers like blood through a man's body, driving the chill from the stone halls, filling the glass gardens with a moist warmth, keeping the earth from freezing. Open pools smoked day and night in a dozen small courtyards. That was a little thing, in summer; in winter, it was the difference between life and death.

Catelyn's bath was always hot and steaming, and her walls warm to the touch. The warmth reminded her of Riverrun, of days in the sun with Lysa and Edmure, but Ned could never abide the heat. The Starks were made for the cold, he would tell her, and she would laugh and tell him in that case they had certainly built their castle in the wrong place.

So when they had finished, Ned rolled off and climbed from her bed, as he had a thousand times before. He crossed the room, pulled back the heavy tapestries, and threw open the high narrow windows one by one, letting the night air into the chamber.

The wind swirled around him as he stood facing the dark, naked and empty-handed. Catelyn pulled the furs to her chin and watched him. He looked somehow smaller and more vulnerable, like the youth she had wed in the sept at Riverrun, fifteen long years gone. Her loins still ached from the urgency of his lovemaking. It was a good ache. She could feel his seed within her. She prayed that it might quicken there. It had been three years since Rickon. She was not too old. She could give him another son.

"I will refuse him," Ned said as he turned back to her. His eyes were haunted, his voice thick with doubt.

Catelyn sat up in the bed. "You cannot. You *must* not."

"My duties are here in the north. I have no wish to be Robert's Hand."

"He will not understand that. He is a king now, and kings are not like other men. If you refuse to serve him, he will wonder why, and sooner or later he will begin to suspect that you oppose him. Can't you see the danger that would put us in?"

Ned shook his head, refusing to believe. "Robert would never harm me or any of mine. We were closer than brothers. He loves me. If I refuse him, he will roar and curse and bluster, and in a week we will laugh about it together. I know the man!"

"You knew the man," she said. "The king is a stranger to you." Catelyn remembered the direwolf dead in the snow, the broken antler lodged deep in her throat. She had to make him see. "Pride is everything to a king, my lord. Robert came all this way to see you, to bring you these great honors, you cannot throw them back in his face."

"Honors?" Ned laughed bitterly.

"In his eyes, yes," she said.

"And in yours?"

"*And* in mine," she blazed, angry now. Why couldn't he see? "He offers his own son in marriage to our daughter, what else would you call that? Sansa might someday be queen. Her sons could rule from the Wall to the mountains of Dorne. What is so wrong with that?"

"Gods, Catelyn, Sansa is only *eleven*," Ned said. "And Joffrey . . . Joffrey is . . ."

She finished for him. ". . . crown prince, and heir to the Iron Throne. And I was only twelve when my father promised me to your brother Brandon."

That brought a bitter twist to Ned's mouth. "Brandon. Yes. Brandon would know what to do. He always did. It was all meant for Brandon. You, Winterfell, everything. He was born to be a King's Hand and a father to queens. I never asked for this cup to pass to me."

"Perhaps not," Catelyn said, "but Brandon is dead, and the cup has passed, and you must drink from it, like it or not."

Ned turned away from her, back to the night. He stood staring out in the darkness, watching the moon and the stars perhaps, or perhaps the sentries on the wall.

Catelyn softened then, to see his pain. Eddard Stark had married her in Brandon's place, as custom decreed, but the shadow of his dead brother still lay between them, as did the other, the shadow of the woman he would not name, the woman who had borne him his bastard son.

She was about to go to him when the knock came at the door, loud and unexpected. Ned turned, frowning. "What is it?"

Desmond's voice came through the door. "My lord, Maester Luwin is without and begs urgent audience."

"You told him I had left orders not to be disturbed?"

"Yes, my lord. He insists."

"Very well. Send him in."

Ned crossed to the wardrobe and slipped on a heavy robe. Catelyn realized suddenly how cold it had become. She sat up in bed and pulled the furs to her chin. "Perhaps we should close the windows," she suggested.

Ned nodded absently. Maester Luwin was shown in.

The maester was a small grey man. His eyes were grey, and quick, and saw much. His hair was grey, what little the years had left him. His robe was grey wool, trimmed with white fur, the Stark colors. Its great floppy sleeves had pockets hidden inside. Luwin was always tucking things into those sleeves and producing other things from them: books, messages, strange artifacts, toys for the children. With all he kept hidden in his sleeves, Catelyn was surprised that Maester Luwin could lift his arms at all.

The maester waited until the door had closed behind him before he spoke. "My lord," he said to Ned, "pardon for disturbing your rest. I have been left a message."

Ned looked irritated. "Been *left*? By whom? Has there been a rider? I was not told."

"There was no rider, my lord. Only a carved wooden box, left on a table in my observatory while I napped. My servants saw no one, but it must have been brought by someone in the king's party. We have had no other visitors from the south."

"A wooden box, you say?" Catelyn said.

"Inside was a fine new lens for the observatory, from Myr by the look of it. The lenscrafters of Myr are without equal."

Ned frowned. He had little patience for this sort of thing, Catelyn knew. "A lens," he said. "What has that to do with me?"

"I asked the same question," Maester Luwin said. "Clearly there was more to this than the seeming."

Under the heavy weight of her furs, Catelyn shivered. "A lens is an instrument to help us see."

"Indeed it is." He fingered the collar of his order; a heavy chain worn tight around the neck beneath his robe, each link forged from a different metal.

Catelyn could feel dread stirring inside her once again. "What is it that they would have us see more clearly?"

"The very thing I asked myself." Maester Luwin drew a tightly rolled paper out of his sleeve. "I found the true message concealed within a false bottom when I dismantled the box the lens had come in, but it is not for my eyes."

Ned held out his hand. "Let me have it, then."

Luwin did not stir. "Pardons, my lord. The message is not for you either. It is marked for the eyes of the Lady Catelyn, and her alone. May I approach?"

Catelyn nodded, not trusting to speak. The maester placed the paper on the table beside the bed. It was sealed with a small blob of blue wax. Luwin bowed and began to retreat.

"Stay," Ned commanded him. His voice was grave. He looked at Catelyn. "What is it? My lady, you're shaking."

"I'm afraid," she admitted. She reached out and took the letter in trembling hands. The furs dropped away from her nakedness, forgotten. In the blue wax was the moon-and-falcon seal of House Arryn. "It's from Lysa." Catelyn looked at her husband. "It will not make us glad," she told him. "There is grief in this message, Ned. I can feel it."

Ned frowned, his face darkening. "Open it."

Catelyn broke the seal.

Her eyes moved over the words. At first they made no sense to her. Then she remembered. "Lysa took no chances. When we were girls together, we had a private language, she and I."

"Can you read it?"

"Yes," Catelyn admitted.

"Then tell us."

"Perhaps I should withdraw," Maester Luwin said.

"No," Catelyn said. "We will need your counsel." She threw back the furs and climbed from the bed. The night air was as cold as the grave on her bare skin as she padded across the room.

Maester Luwin averted his eyes. Even Ned looked shocked. "What are you doing?" he asked.

"Lighting a fire," Catelyn told him. She found a dressing gown and shrugged into it, then knelt over the cold hearth.

"Maester Luwin—" Ned began.

"Maester Luwin has delivered all my children," Catelyn said. "This is no time for false modesty." She slid the paper in among the kindling and placed the heavier logs on top of it.

Ned crossed the room, took her by the arm, and pulled her to her feet. He held her there, his face inches from her. "My lady, tell me! What was this message?"

Catelyn stiffened in his grasp. "A warning," she said softly. "If we have the wits to hear."

His eyes searched her face. "Go on."

"Lysa says Jon Arryn was murdered."

His fingers tightened on her arm. "By whom?"

"The Lannisters," she told him. "The queen."

Ned released his hold on her arm. There were deep red marks on her skin. "Gods," he whispered. His voice was hoarse. "Your sister is sick with grief. She cannot know what she is saying."

"She knows," Catelyn said. "Lysa is impulsive, yes,

but this message was carefully planned, cleverly hidden. She knew it meant death if her letter fell into the wrong hands. To risk so much, she must have had more than mere suspicion." Catelyn looked to her husband. "Now we truly have no choice. You *must* be Robert's Hand. You must go south with him and learn the truth."

She saw at once that Ned had reached a very different conclusion. "The only truths I know are here. The south is a nest of adders I would do better to avoid."

Luwin plucked at his chain collar where it had chafed the soft skin of his throat. "The Hand of the King has great power, my lord. Power to find the truth of Lord Arryn's death, to bring his killers to the king's justice. Power to protect Lady Arryn and her son, if the worst be true."

Ned glanced helplessly around the bedchamber. Catelyn's heart went out to him, but she knew she could not take him in her arms just then. First the victory must be won, for her children's sake. "You say you love Robert like a brother. Would you leave your brother surrounded by Lannisters?"

"The Others take both of you," Ned muttered darkly. He turned away from them and went to the window. She did not speak, nor did the maester. They waited, quiet, while Eddard Stark said a silent farewell to the home he loved. When he turned away from the window at last, his voice was tired and full of melancholy, and moisture glittered faintly in the corners of his eyes. "My father went south once, to answer the summons of a king. He never came home again."

"A different time," Maester Luwin said. "A different king."

"Yes," Ned said dully. He seated himself in a chair by the hearth. "Catelyn, you shall stay here in Winterfell."

His words were like an icy draft through her heart. "No," she said, suddenly afraid. Was this to be her punishment? Never to see his face again, nor to feel his arms around her?

"Yes," Ned said, in words that would brook no argument. "You must govern the north in my stead, while I run Robert's errands. There must always be a Stark in Winterfell. Robb is fourteen. Soon enough, he will be a man grown. He must learn to rule, and I will not be here for him. Make him part of your councils. He must be ready when his time comes."

"Gods will, not for many years," Maester Luwin murmured.

"Maester Luwin, I trust you as I would my own blood. Give my wife your voice in all things great and small. Teach my son the things he needs to know. Winter is coming."

Maester Luwin nodded gravely. Then silence fell, until Catelyn found her courage and asked the question whose answer she most dreaded. "What of the other children?"

Ned stood, and took her in his arms, and held her face close to his. "Rickon is very young," he said gently. "He should stay here with you and Robb. The others I would take with me."

"I could not bear it," Catelyn said, trembling.

"You must," he said. "Sansa must wed Joffrey, that is clear now, we must give them no grounds to suspect our devotion. And it is past time that Arya learned the ways of a southron court. In a few years she will be of an age to marry too."

Sansa would shine in the south, Catelyn thought to herself, and the gods knew that Arya needed refinement. Reluctantly, she let go of them in her heart. But not Bran. Never Bran. "Yes," she said, "but please, Ned, for the love you bear me, let Bran remain here at Winterfell. He is only seven."

"I was eight when my father sent me to foster at the Eyrie," Ned said. "Ser Rodrik tells me there is bad feeling between Robb and Prince Joffrey. That is not healthy. Bran can bridge that distance. He is a sweet boy, quick to laugh, easy to love. Let him grow up with the young princes, let him become their friend as Robert became mine. Our House will be the safer for it."

He was right; Catelyn knew it. It did not make the pain any easier to bear. She would lose all four of them, then: Ned, and both girls, and her sweet, loving Bran. Only Robb and little Rickon would be left to her. She felt lonely already. Winterfell was such a vast place. "Keep him off the walls, then," she said bravely. "You know how Bran loves to climb."

Ned kissed the tears from her eyes before they could

fall. "Thank you, my lady," he whispered. "This is hard, I know."

"What of Jon Snow, my lord?" Maester Luwin asked.

Catelyn tensed at the mention of the name. Ned felt the anger in her, and pulled away.

Many men fathered bastards. Catelyn had grown up with that knowledge. It came as no surprise to her, in the first year of her marriage, to learn that Ned had fathered a child on some girl chance met on campaign. He had a man's needs, after all, and they had spent that year apart, Ned off at war in the south while she remained safe in her father's castle at Riverrun. Her thoughts were more of Robb, the infant at her breast, than of the husband she scarcely knew. He was welcome to whatever solace he might find between battles. And if his seed quickened, she expected he would see to the child's needs.

He did more than that. The Starks were not like other men. Ned brought his bastard home with him, and called him "son" for all the north to see. When the wars were over at last, and Catelyn rode to Winterfell, Jon and his wet nurse had already taken up residence.

That cut deep. Ned would not speak of the mother, not so much as a word, but a castle has no secrets, and Catelyn heard her maids repeating tales they heard from the lips of her husband's soldiers. They whispered of Ser Arthur Dayne, the Sword of the Morning, deadliest of the seven knights of Aerys's Kingsguard, and of how their young lord had slain him in single combat. And they told how afterward Ned had carried Ser Arthur's sword back to the beautiful young sister who awaited him in a castle called Starfall on the shores of the Summer Sea. The Lady Ashara Dayne, tall and fair, with haunting violet eyes. It had taken her a fortnight to marshal her courage, but finally, in bed one night, Catelyn had asked her husband the truth of it, asked him to his face.

That was the only time in all their years that Ned had ever frightened her. "Never ask me about Jon," he said, cold as ice. "He is my blood, and that is all you need to know. And now I will learn where you heard that name, my lady." She had pledged to obey; she told him; and from that day on, the whispering had stopped, and Ashara Dayne's name was never heard in Winterfell again.

Whoever Jon's mother had been, Ned must have loved

her fiercely, for nothing Catelyn said would persuade him to send the boy away. It was the one thing she could never forgive him. She had come to love her husband with all her heart, but she had never found it in her to love Jon. She might have overlooked a dozen bastards for Ned's sake, so long as they were out of sight. Jon was never out of sight, and as he grew, he looked more like Ned than any of the trueborn sons she bore him. Somehow that made it worse. "Jon must go," she said now.

"He and Robb are close," Ned said. "I had hoped . . ."

"He cannot stay here," Catelyn said, cutting him off. "He is your son, not mine. I will not have him." It was hard, she knew, but no less the truth. Ned would do the boy no kindness by leaving him here at Winterfell.

The look Ned gave her was anguished. "You know I cannot take him south. There will be no place for him at court. A boy with a bastard's name . . . you know what they will say of him. He will be shunned."

Catelyn armored her heart against the mute appeal in her husband's eyes. "They say your friend Robert has fathered a dozen bastards himself."

"And none of them has ever been seen at court!" Ned blazed. "The Lannister woman has seen to that. How can you be so damnably cruel, Catelyn? He is only a boy. He—"

His fury was on him. He might have said more, and worse, but Maester Luwin cut in. "Another solution presents itself," he said, his voice quiet. "Your brother Benjen came to me about Jon a few days ago. It seems the boy aspires to take the black."

Ned looked shocked. "He asked to join the Night's Watch?"

Catelyn said nothing. Let Ned work it out in his own mind; her voice would not be welcome now. Yet gladly would she have kissed the maester just then. His was the perfect solution. Benjen Stark was a Sworn Brother. Jon would be a son to him, the child he would never have. And in time the boy would take the oath as well. He would father no sons who might someday contest with Catelyn's own grandchildren for Winterfell.

Maester Luwin said, "There is great honor in service on the Wall, my lord."

"And even a bastard may rise high in the Night's

Watch," Ned reflected. Still, his voice was troubled. "Jon is so young. If he asked this when he was a man grown, that would be one thing, but a boy of fourteen . . ."

"A hard sacrifice," Maester Luwin agreed. "Yet these are hard times, my lord. His road is no crueler than yours or your lady's."

Catelyn thought of the three children she must lose. It was not easy keeping silent then.

Ned turned away from them to gaze out the window, his long face silent and thoughtful. Finally he sighed, and turned back. "Very well," he said to Maester Luwin. "I suppose it is for the best. I will speak to Ben."

"When shall we tell Jon?" the maester asked.

"When I must. Preparations must be made. It will be a fortnight before we are ready to depart. I would sooner let Jon enjoy these last few days. Summer will end soon enough, and childhood as well. When the time comes, I will tell him myself."

ARYA

Arya's stitches were crooked again.

She frowned down at them with dismay and glanced over to where her sister Sansa sat among the other girls. Sansa's needlework was exquisite. Everyone said so. "Sansa's work is as pretty as she is," Septa Mordane told their lady mother once. "She has such fine, delicate hands." When Lady Catelyn had asked about Arya, the septa had sniffed. "Arya has the hands of a blacksmith."

Arya glanced furtively across the room, worried that Septa Mordane might have read her thoughts, but the septa was paying her no attention today. She was sitting with the Princess Myrcella, all smiles and admiration. It was not often that the septa was privileged to instruct a royal princess in the womanly arts, as she had said when the queen brought Myrcella to join them. Arya thought that Myrcella's stitches looked a little crooked too, but you would never know it from the way Septa Mordane was cooing.

She studied her own work again, looking for some way to salvage it, then sighed and put down the needle. She looked glumly at her sister. Sansa was chatting away happily as she worked. Beth Cassel, Ser Rodrik's little girl, was sitting by her feet, listening to every word she said, and Jeyne Poole was leaning over to whisper something in her ear.

"What are you talking about?" Arya asked suddenly.

Jeyne gave her a startled look, then giggled. Sansa looked abashed. Beth blushed. No one answered.

"Tell me," Arya said.

Jeyne glanced over to make certain that Septa Mordane was not listening. Myrcella said something then, and the septa laughed along with the rest of the ladies.

"We were talking about the prince," Sansa said, her voice soft as a kiss.

Arya knew which prince she meant: Joffrey, of course. The tall, handsome one. Sansa got to sit with him at the feast. Arya had to sit with the little fat one. Naturally.

"Joffrey likes your sister," Jeyne whispered, proud as if she had something to do with it. She was the daughter of Winterfell's steward and Sansa's dearest friend. "He told her she was very beautiful."

"He's going to marry her," little Beth said dreamily, hugging herself. "Then Sansa will be queen of all the realm."

Sansa had the grace to blush. She blushed prettily. She did everything prettily, Arya thought with dull resentment. "Beth, you shouldn't make up stories," Sansa corrected the younger girl, gently stroking her hair to take the harshness out of her words. She looked at Arya. "What did you think of Prince Joff, sister? He's very gallant, don't you think?"

"Jon says he looks like a girl," Arya said.

Sansa sighed as she stitched. "Poor Jon," she said. "He gets jealous because he's a bastard."

"He's our brother," Arya said, much too loudly. Her voice cut through the afternoon quiet of the tower room.

Septa Mordane raised her eyes. She had a bony face, sharp eyes, and a thin lipless mouth made for frowning. It was frowning now. "What are you talking about, children?"

"Our half brother," Sansa corrected, soft and precise. She smiled for the septa. "Arya and I were remarking on how pleased we were to have the princess with us today," she said.

Septa Mordane nodded. "Indeed. A great honor for us all." Princess Myrcella smiled uncertainly at the compliment. "Arya, why aren't you at work?" the septa asked. She rose to her feet, starched skirts rustling as she started across the room. "Let me see your stitches."

Arya wanted to scream. It was just like Sansa to go and attract the septa's attention. "Here," she said, surrendering up her work.

The septa examined the fabric. "Arya, Arya, Arya," she said. "This will not do. This will not do at all."

Everyone was looking at her. It was too much. Sansa was too well bred to smile at her sister's disgrace, but Jeyne was smirking on her behalf. Even Princess Myrcella looked sorry for her. Arya felt tears filling her eyes. She pushed herself out of her chair and bolted for the door.

Septa Mordane called after her. "Arya, come back here! Don't you take another step! Your lady mother will hear of this. In front of our royal princess too! You'll shame us all!"

Arya stopped at the door and turned back, biting her lip. The tears were running down her cheeks now. She managed a stiff little bow to Myrcella. "By your leave, my lady."

Myrcella blinked at her and looked to her ladies for guidance. But if she was uncertain, Septa Mordane was not. "Just where do you think you are going, Arya?" the septa demanded.

Arya glared at her. "I have to go shoe a horse," she said sweetly, taking a brief satisfaction in the shock on the septa's face. Then she whirled and made her exit, running down the steps as fast as her feet would take her.

It wasn't fair. Sansa had everything. Sansa was two years older; maybe by the time Arya had been born, there had been nothing left. Often it felt that way. Sansa could sew and dance and sing. She wrote poetry. She knew how to dress. She played the high harp *and* the bells. Worse, she was beautiful. Sansa had gotten their mother's fine high cheekbones and the thick auburn hair of the Tullys. Arya took after their lord father. Her hair was a lusterless brown, and her face was long and solemn. Jeyne used to call her Arya Horseface, and neigh whenever she came near. It hurt that the one thing Arya could do better than her sister was ride a horse. Well, that and manage a household. Sansa had never had much of a head for figures. If she did marry Prince Joff, Arya hoped for his sake that he had a good steward.

Nymeria was waiting for her in the guardroom at the base of the stairs. She bounded to her feet as soon as she caught sight of Arya. Arya grinned. The wolf pup loved her, even if no one else did. They went everywhere together, and Nymeria slept in her room, at the foot of her bed. If Mother had not forbidden it, Arya would gladly have taken the wolf with her to needlework. Let Septa Mordane complain about her stitches *then*.

Nymeria nipped eagerly at her hand as Arya untied her. She had yellow eyes. When they caught the sunlight, they gleamed like two golden coins. Arya had named her after the warrior queen of the Rhoyne, who had led her people across the narrow sea. That had been a great scandal too. Sansa, of course, had named her pup "Lady." Arya made a face and hugged the wolfling tight. Nymeria licked her ear, and she giggled.

By now Septa Mordane would certainly have sent word to her lady mother. If she went to her room, they would find her. Arya did not care to be found. She had a better notion. The boys were at practice in the yard. She wanted to see Robb put gallant Prince Joffrey flat on his back. "Come," she whispered to Nymeria. She got up and ran, the wolf coming hard at her heels.

There was a window in the covered bridge between the armory and the Great Keep where you had a view of the whole yard. That was where they headed.

They arrived, flushed and breathless, to find Jon seated on the sill, one leg drawn up languidly to his chin. He was watching the action, so absorbed that he seemed unaware of her approach until his white wolf moved to meet them. Nymeria stalked closer on wary feet. Ghost, already larger than his litter mates, smelled her, gave her ear a careful nip, and settled back down.

Jon gave her a curious look. "Shouldn't you be working on your stitches, little sister?"

Arya made a face at him. "I wanted to see them fight."

He smiled. "Come here, then."

Arya climbed up on the window and sat beside him, to a chorus of thuds and grunts from the yard below.

To her disappointment, it was the younger boys drilling. Bran was so heavily padded he looked as though he had belted on a featherbed, and Prince Tommen, who was plump to begin with, seemed positively round. They were huffing and puffing and hitting at each other with padded wooden swords under the watchful eye of old Ser Rodrik Cassel, the master-at-arms, a great stout keg of a man with magnificent white cheek whiskers. A dozen spectators, man and boy, were calling out encouragement, Robb's voice the loudest among them. She spotted Theon Greyjoy beside him, his black doublet emblazoned with the golden kraken of his House, a look of wry contempt on his face. Both of the combatants were staggering. Arya judged that they had been at it awhile.

"A shade more exhausting than needlework," Jon observed.

"A shade more fun than needlework," Arya gave back at him. Jon grinned, reached over, and messed up her hair. Arya flushed. They had always been close. Jon had their father's face, as she did. They were the only ones. Robb and Sansa and Bran and even little Rickon all took after the Tullys, with easy smiles and fire in their hair. When Arya had been little, she had been afraid that meant that she was a bastard too. It had been Jon she had gone to in her fear, and Jon who had reassured her.

"Why aren't you down in the yard?" Arya asked him.

He gave her a half smile. "Bastards are not allowed to damage young princes," he said. "Any bruises they take in the practice yard must come from trueborn swords."

"Oh." Arya felt abashed. She should have realized. For the second time today, Arya reflected that life was not fair.

She watched her little brother whack at Tommen. "I could do just as good as Bran," she said. "He's only seven. I'm nine."

Jon looked her over with all his fourteen-year-old wisdom. "You're too skinny," he said. He took her arm to feel her muscle. Then he sighed and shook his head. "I doubt you could even lift a longsword, little sister, never mind swing one."

Arya snatched back her arm and glared at him. Jon messed up her hair again. They watched Bran and Tommen circle each other.

"You see Prince Joffrey?" Jon asked.

She hadn't, not at first glance, but when she looked again she found him to the back, under the shade of the high stone wall. He was surrounded by men she did not recognize, young squires in the livery of Lannister and Baratheon, strangers all. There were a few older men among them; knights, she surmised.

"Look at the arms on his surcoat," Jon suggested.

Arya looked. An ornate shield had been embroidered on the prince's padded surcoat. No doubt the needlework was exquisite. The arms were divided down the middle; on one side was the crowned stag of the royal House, on the other the lion of Lannister.

"The Lannisters are proud," Jon observed. "You'd think the royal sigil would be sufficient, but no. He makes his mother's House equal in honor to the king's."

"The woman is important too!" Arya protested.

Jon chuckled. "Perhaps you should do the same thing, little sister. Wed Tully to Stark in your arms."

"A wolf with a fish in its mouth?" It made her laugh. "That would look silly. Besides, if a girl can't fight, why should she have a coat of arms?"

Jon shrugged. "Girls get the arms but not the swords. Bastards get the swords but not the arms. I did not make the rules, little sister."

There was a shout from the courtyard below. Prince Tommen was rolling in the dust, trying to get up and failing. All the padding made him look like a turtle on its back. Bran was standing over him with upraised wooden sword, ready to whack him again once he regained his feet. The men began to laugh.

"Enough!" Ser Rodrik called out. He gave the prince a hand and yanked him back to his feet. "Well fought. Lew, Donnis, help them out of their armor." He looked around. "Prince Joffrey, Robb, will you go another round?"

Robb, already sweaty from a previous bout, moved forward eagerly. "Gladly."

Joffrey moved into the sunlight in response to Rodrik's summons. His hair shone like spun gold. He looked bored. "This is a game for children, Ser Rodrik."

Theon Greyjoy gave a sudden bark of laughter. "You are children," he said derisively.

"Robb may be a child," Joffrey said. "I am a prince. And I grow tired of swatting at Starks with a play sword."

"You got more swats than you gave, Joff," Robb said. "Are you afraid?"

Prince Joffrey looked at him. "Oh, terrified," he said. "You're so much older." Some of the Lannister men laughed.

Jon looked down on the scene with a frown. "Joffrey is truly a little shit," he told Arya.

Ser Rodrik tugged thoughtfully at his white whiskers. "What are you suggesting?" he asked the prince.

"Live steel."

"Done," Robb shot back. "You'll be sorry!"

The master-at-arms put a hand on Robb's shoulder to quiet him. "Live steel is too dangerous. I will permit you tourney swords, with blunted edges."

Joffrey said nothing, but a man strange to Arya, a tall knight with black hair and burn scars on his face, pushed forward in front of the prince. "This is your prince. Who are you to tell him he may not have an edge on his sword, *ser*?"

"Master-at-arms of Winterfell, Clegane, and you would do well not to forget it."

"Are you training women here?" the burned man wanted to know. He was muscled like a bull.

"I am training *knights*," Ser Rodrik said pointedly. "They will have steel when they are ready. When they are of an age."

The burned man looked at Robb. "How old are you, boy?"

"Fourteen," Robb said.

"I killed a man at twelve. You can be sure it was not with a blunt sword."

Arya could see Robb bristle. His pride was wounded. He turned on Ser Rodrik. "Let me do it. I can beat him."

"Beat him with a tourney blade, then," Ser Rodrik said.

Joffrey shrugged. "Come and see me when you're older, Stark. If you're not *too* old." There was laughter from the Lannister men.

Robb's curses rang through the yard. Arya covered her mouth in shock. Theon Greyjoy seized Robb's arm to keep him away from the prince. Ser Rodrik tugged at his whiskers in dismay.

Joffrey feigned a yawn and turned to his younger

brother. "Come, Tommen," he said. "The hour of play is done. Leave the children to their frolics."

That brought more laughter from the Lannisters, more curses from Robb. Ser Rodrik's face was beet-red with fury under the white of his whiskers. Theon kept Robb locked in an iron grip until the princes and their party were safely away.

Jon watched them leave, and Arya watched Jon. His face had grown as still as the pool at the heart of the godswood. Finally he climbed down off the window. "The show is done," he said. He bent to scratch Ghost behind the ears. The white wolf rose and rubbed against him. "You had best run back to your room, little sister. Septa Mordane will surely be lurking. The longer you hide, the sterner the penance. You'll be sewing all through winter. When the spring thaw comes, they will find your body with a needle still locked tight between your frozen fingers."

Arya didn't think it was funny. "I hate needlework!" she said with passion. "It's not fair!"

"Nothing is fair," Jon said. He messed up her hair again and walked away from her, Ghost moving silently beside him. Nymeria started to follow too, then stopped and came back when she saw that Arya was not coming.

Reluctantly she turned in the other direction.

It was worse than Jon had thought. It wasn't Septa Mordane waiting in her room. It was Septa Mordane *and* her mother.

BRAN

The hunt left at dawn. The king wanted wild boar at the feast tonight. Prince Joffrey rode with his father, so Robb had been allowed to join the hunters as well. Uncle Benjen, Jory, Theon Greyjoy, Ser Rodrik, and even the queen's funny little brother had all ridden out with them. It was the last hunt, after all. On the morrow they left for the south.

Bran had been left behind with Jon and the girls and Rickon. But Rickon was only a baby and the girls were only girls and Jon and his wolf were nowhere to be found. Bran did not look for him very hard. He thought Jon was angry at him. Jon seemed to be angry at everyone these days. Bran did not know why. He was going with Uncle Ben to the Wall, to join the Night's Watch. That was almost as good as going south with the king. Robb was the one they were leaving behind, not Jon.

For days, Bran could scarcely wait to be off. He was going to ride the kingsroad on a horse of his own, not a pony but a real horse. His father would be the Hand of the King, and they were going to live in the red castle at King's Landing, the castle the Dragonlords had built. Old Nan said there were ghosts there, and dungeons where terrible things had been done, and dragon heads on the walls. It gave Bran a shiver just to think of it, but he was not afraid. How could he be afraid? His father would be with him, and the king with all his knights and sworn swords.

Bran was going to be a knight himself someday, one of the Kingsguard. Old Nan said they were the finest swords in all the realm. There were only seven of them, and they wore white armor and had no wives or children, but lived only to serve the king. Bran knew all the stories. Their names were like music to him. Serwyn of the Mirror Shield. Ser Ryam Redwyne. Prince Aemon the Dragonknight. The twins Ser Erryk and Ser Arryk, who had died on one another's swords hundreds of years ago, when brother fought sister in the war the singers called the Dance of the Dragons. The White Bull, Gerold High-tower. Ser Arthur Dayne, the Sword of the Morning. Barristan the Bold.

Two of the Kingsguard had come north with King Robert. Bran had watched them with fascination, never quite daring to speak to them. Ser Boros was a bald man with a jowly face, and Ser Meryn had droopy eyes and a beard the color of rust. Ser Jaime Lannister looked more like the knights in the stories, and he was of the Kingsguard too, but Robb said he had killed the old mad king and shouldn't count anymore. The greatest living knight was Ser Barristan Selmy, Barristan the Bold, the Lord Commander of the Kingsguard. Father had promised that they would meet Ser Barristan when they reached King's Landing, and Bran had been marking the days on his wall, eager to depart, to see a world he had only dreamed of and begin a life he could scarcely imagine.

Yet now that the last day was at hand, suddenly Bran felt lost. Winterfell had been the only home he had ever known. His father had told him that he ought to say his farewells today, and he had tried. After the hunt had ridden out, he wandered through the castle with his wolf at his side, intending to visit the ones who would be left behind, Old Nan and Gage the cook, Mikken in his smithy, Hodor the stableboy who smiled so much and took care of his pony and never said anything but "Hodor," the man in the glass gardens who gave him a blackberry when he came to visit . . .

But it was no good. He had gone to the stable first, and seen his pony there in its stall, except it wasn't *his* pony anymore, he was getting a real horse and leaving the pony behind, and all of a sudden Bran just wanted to sit down and cry. He turned and ran off before Hodor and the other stableboys could see the tears in his eyes. That was the end of his farewells. Instead Bran spent the morning alone in the godswood, trying to teach his wolf to fetch a stick, and failing. The wolfling was smarter than any of the hounds in his father's kennel and Bran would have sworn he understood every word that was said to him, but he showed very little interest in chasing sticks.

He was still trying to decide on a name. Robb was calling his Grey Wind, because he ran so fast. Sansa had named hers Lady, and Arya named hers after some old witch queen in the songs, and little Rickon called his Shaggydog, which Bran thought was a pretty stupid name for a direwolf. Jon's wolf, the white one, was Ghost. Bran wished he had thought of that first, even though his wolf wasn't white. He had tried a hundred names in the last fortnight, but none of them sounded right.

Finally he got tired of the stick game and decided to go climbing. He hadn't been up to the broken tower for weeks with everything that had happened, and this might be his last chance.

He raced across the godswood, taking the long way around to avoid the pool where the heart tree grew. The heart tree had always frightened him; trees ought not have eyes, Bran thought, or leaves that looked like hands. His wolf came sprinting at his heels. "You stay here," he told him at the base of the sentinel tree near the armory wall. "Lie down. That's right. Now *stay*."

The wolf did as he was told. Bran scratched him behind the ears, then turned away, jumped, grabbed a low branch, and pulled himself up. He was halfway up the tree, moving easily from limb to limb, when the wolf got to his feet and began to howl.

Bran looked back down. His wolf fell silent, staring up at him through slitted yellow eyes. A strange chill went through him. He began to climb again. Once more the wolf howled. "Quiet," he yelled. "Sit down. Stay. You're worse than Mother." The howling chased him all the way up the tree, until finally he jumped off onto the armory roof and out of sight.

The rooftops of Winterfell were Bran's second home. His mother often said that Bran could climb before he could walk. Bran could not remember when he first learned to walk, but he could not remember when he started to climb either, so he supposed it must be true.

To a boy, Winterfell was a grey stone labyrinth of walls and towers and courtyards and tunnels spreading out in all directions. In the older parts of the castle, the halls slanted up and down so that you couldn't even be sure what floor you were on. The place had grown over the centuries like some monstrous stone tree, Maester Luwin told him once, and its branches were gnarled and thick and twisted, its roots sunk deep into the earth.

When he got out from under it and scrambled up near the sky, Bran could see all of Winterfell in a glance. He liked the way it looked, spread out beneath him, only birds wheeling over his head while all the life of the castle went on below. Bran could perch for hours among the shapeless, rain-worn gargoyles that brooded over the First Keep, watching it all: the men drilling with wood and steel in the yard, the cooks tending their vegetables in the glass garden, restless dogs running back and forth in the kennels, the silence of the godswood, the girls gossiping beside the washing well. It made him feel like he was lord of the castle, in a way even Robb would never know.

It taught him Winterfell's secrets too. The builders had not even leveled the earth; there were hills and valleys behind the walls of Winterfell. There was a covered bridge that went from the fourth floor of the bell tower across to the second floor of the rookery. Bran knew about that. And he knew you could get inside the inner wall by the south gate, climb three floors and run all the way around Winterfell through a narrow tunnel in the stone, and then come out *on ground level* at the north gate, with a hundred feet of wall looming over you. Even Maester Luwin didn't know *that,* Bran was convinced.

His mother was terrified that one day Bran would slip off a wall and kill himself. He told her that he wouldn't, but she never believed him. Once she made him promise that he would stay on the ground. He had managed to keep that promise for almost a fortnight, miserable every day, until one night he had gone out the window of his bedroom when his brothers were fast asleep.

He confessed his crime the next day in a fit of guilt. Lord Eddard ordered him to the godswood to cleanse himself. Guards were posted to see that Bran remained there alone all night to reflect on his disobedience. The next morning Bran was nowhere to be seen. They finally found him fast asleep in the upper branches of the tallest sentinel in the grove.

As angry as he was, his father could not help but laugh. "You're not my son," he told Bran when they fetched him down, "you're a squirrel. So be it. If you must climb, then climb, but try not to let your mother see you."

Bran did his best, although he did not think he ever really fooled her. Since his father would not forbid it, she turned to others. Old Nan told him a story about a bad little boy who climbed too high and was struck down by lightning, and how afterward the crows came to peck out his eyes. Bran was not impressed. There were crows' nests atop the broken tower, where no one ever went but him, and sometimes he filled his pockets with corn before he climbed up there and the crows ate it right out of his hand. None of them had ever shown the slightest bit of interest in pecking out his eyes.

Later, Maester Luwin built a little pottery boy and dressed him in Bran's clothes and flung him off the wall into the yard below, to demonstrate what would happen to Bran if he fell. That had been fun, but afterward Bran just looked at the maester and said, "I'm not made of clay. And anyhow, I never fall."

Then for a while the guards would chase him whenever they saw him on the roofs, and try to haul him down. That was the best time of all. It was like playing a game with his brothers, except that Bran always won. None of the guards could climb half so well as Bran, not even Jory. Most of the time they never saw him anyway. People never looked up. That was another thing he liked about climbing; it was almost like being invisible.

He liked how it felt too, pulling himself up a wall stone by stone, fingers and toes digging hard into the small crevices between. He always took off his boots and went barefoot when he climbed; it made him feel as if he had four hands instead of two. He liked the deep, sweet ache it left in the muscles afterward. He liked the way the air tasted way up high, sweet and cold as a winter peach. He liked the birds: the crows in the broken tower, the tiny little sparrows that nested in cracks between the stones, the ancient owl that slept in the dusty loft above the old armory. Bran knew them all.

Most of all, he liked going places that no one else could go, and seeing the grey sprawl of Winterfell in a way that no one else ever saw it. It made the whole castle Bran's secret place.

His favorite haunt was the broken tower. Once it had been a watchtower, the tallest in Winterfell. A long time ago, a hundred years before even his father had been born, a lightning strike had set it afire. The top third of the structure had collapsed inward, and the tower had never been rebuilt. Sometimes his father sent ratters into the base of the tower, to clean out the nests they always found among the jumble of fallen stones and charred and rotten beams. But no one ever got up to the jagged top of the structure now except for Bran and the crows.

He knew two ways to get there. You could climb straight up the side of the tower itself, but the stones were loose, the mortar that held them together long gone to ash, and Bran never liked to put his full weight on them.

The *best* way was to start from the godswood, shinny up the tall sentinel, and cross over the armory and the guards hall, leaping roof to roof, barefoot so the guards wouldn't hear you overhead. That brought you up to the blind side of the First Keep, the oldest part of the castle, a squat round fortress that was taller than it looked. Only rats and spiders lived there now but the old stones still made for good climbing. You could go straight up to where the gargoyles leaned out blindly over empty space, and swing from gargoyle to gargoyle, hand over hand, around to the north side. From there, if you really stretched, you could reach out and pull yourself over to the broken tower where it leaned close. The last part was the scramble up the blackened stones to the eyrie, no more than ten feet, and then the crows would come round to see if you'd brought any corn.

Bran was moving from gargoyle to gargoyle with the ease of long practice when he heard the voices. He was so startled he almost lost his grip. The First Keep had been empty all his life.

"I do not like it," a woman was saying. There was a row of windows beneath him, and the voice was drifting out of the last window on this side. "*You* should be the Hand."

"Gods forbid," a man's voice replied lazily. "It's not an honor I'd want. There's far too much work involved."

Bran hung, listening, suddenly afraid to go on. They might glimpse his feet if he tried to swing by.

"Don't you see the danger this puts us in?" the woman said. "Robert loves the man like a brother."

"Robert can barely stomach his brothers. Not that I blame him. Stannis would be enough to give anyone indigestion."

"Don't play the fool. Stannis and Renly are one thing, and Eddard Stark is quite another. Robert will *listen* to Stark. Damn them both. I should have *insisted* that he name you, but I was certain Stark would refuse him."

"We ought to count ourselves fortunate," the man said. "The king might as easily have named one of his brothers, or even Littlefinger, gods help us. Give me honorable enemies rather than ambitious ones, and I'll sleep more easily by night."

They were talking about Father, Bran realized. He wanted to hear more. A few more feet . . . but they would see him if he swung out in front of the window.

"We will have to watch him carefully," the woman said.

"I would sooner watch you," the man said. He sounded bored. "Come back here."

"Lord Eddard has never taken any interest in anything that happened south of the Neck," the woman said. "Never. I tell you, he means to move against us. Why else would he leave the seat of his power?"

"A hundred reasons. Duty. Honor. He yearns to write his name large across the book of history, to get away from his wife, or both. Perhaps he just wants to be warm for once in his life."

"His wife is Lady Arryn's sister. It's a wonder Lysa was not here to greet us with her accusations."

Bran looked down. There was a narrow ledge beneath

the window, only a few inches wide. He tried to lower himself toward it. Too far. He would never reach.

"You fret too much. Lysa Arryn is a frightened cow."

"That frightened cow shared Jon Arryn's bed."

"If she knew anything, she would have gone to Robert before she fled King's Landing."

"When he had already agreed to foster that weakling son of hers at Casterly Rock? I think not. She knew the boy's life would be hostage to her silence. She may grow bolder now that he's safe atop the Eyrie."

"Mothers." The man made the word sound like a curse. "I think birthing does something to your minds. You are all mad." He laughed. It was a bitter sound. "Let Lady Arryn grow as bold as she likes. Whatever she knows, whatever she thinks she knows, she has no proof." He paused a moment. "Or does she?"

"Do you think the king will require proof?" the woman said. "I tell you, he loves me not."

"And whose fault is that, sweet sister?"

Bran studied the ledge. He could drop down. It was too narrow to land on, but if he could catch hold as he fell past, pull himself up . . . except that might make a noise, draw them to the window. He was not sure what he was hearing, but he knew it was not meant for his ears.

"You are as blind as Robert," the woman was saying.

"If you mean I see the same thing, yes," the man said. "I see a man who would sooner die than betray his king."

"He betrayed one already, or have you forgotten?" the woman said. "Oh, I don't deny he's loyal to Robert, that's obvious. What happens when Robert dies and Joff takes the throne? And the sooner *that* comes to pass, the safer we'll all be. My husband grows more restless every day. Having Stark beside him will only make him worse. He's still in love with the sister, the insipid little dead sixteen-year-old. How long till he decides to put me aside for some new Lyanna?"

Bran was suddenly very frightened. He wanted nothing so much as to go back the way he had come, to find his brothers. Only what would he tell them? He had to get closer, Bran realized. He had to see who was talking.

The man sighed. "You should think less about the future and more about the pleasures at hand."

"Stop that!" the woman said. Bran heard the sudden slap of flesh on flesh, then the man's laughter.

Bran pulled himself up, climbed over the gargoyle, crawled out onto the roof. This was the easy way. He moved across the roof to the next gargoyle, right above the window of the room where they were talking.

"All this talk is getting very tiresome, sister," the man said. "Come here and be quiet."

Bran sat astride the gargoyle, tightened his legs around it, and swung himself around, upside down. He hung by his legs and slowly stretched his head down toward the window. The world looked strange upside down. A courtyard swam dizzily below him, its stones still wet with melted snow.

Bran looked in the window.

Inside the room, a man and a woman were wrestling. They were both naked. Bran could not tell who they were. The man's back was to him, and his body screened the woman from view as he pushed her up against a wall.

There were soft, wet sounds. Bran realized they were kissing. He watched, wide-eyed and frightened, his breath tight in his throat. The man had a hand down between her legs, and he must have been hurting her there, because the woman started to moan, low in her throat. "Stop it," she said, "stop it, stop it. Oh, *please* . . ." But her voice was low and weak, and she did not push him away. Her hands buried themselves in his hair, his tangled golden hair, and pulled his face down to her breast.

Bran saw her face. Her eyes were closed and her mouth was open, moaning. Her golden hair swung from side to side as her head moved back and forth, but still he recognized the queen.

He must have made a noise. Suddenly her eyes opened, and she was staring right at him. She screamed.

Everything happened at once then. The woman pushed the man away wildly, shouting and pointing. Bran tried to pull himself up, bending double as he reached for the gargoyle. He was in too much of a hurry. His hand scraped uselessly across smooth stone, and in his panic his legs slipped, and suddenly he was falling. There was an instant of vertigo, a sickening lurch as the window flashed past. He shot out a hand, grabbed for the ledge, lost it, caught it again with his other hand. He swung against the building, hard. The impact took the breath out of him. Bran dangled, one-handed, panting.

Faces appeared in the window above him.

The queen. And now Bran recognized the man beside her. They looked as much alike as reflections in a mirror.

"He *saw* us," the woman said shrilly.

"So he did," the man said.

Bran's fingers started to slip. He grabbed the ledge with his other hand. Fingernails dug into unyielding stone. The man reached down. "Take my hand," he said. "Before you fall."

Bran seized his arm and held on tight with all his strength. The man yanked him up to the ledge. "What are you doing?" the woman demanded.

The man ignored her. He was very strong. He stood Bran up on the sill. "How old are you, boy?"

"Seven," Bran said, shaking with relief. His fingers had dug deep gouges in the man's forearm. He let go sheepishly.

The man looked over at the woman. "The things I do for love," he said with loathing. He gave Bran a shove.

Screaming, Bran went backward out the window into empty air. There was nothing to grab on to. The courtyard rushed up to meet him.

Somewhere off in the distance, a wolf was howling. Crows circled the broken tower, waiting for corn.

TYRION

Somewhere in the great stone maze of Winterfell, a wolf howled. The sound hung over the castle like a flag of mourning.

Tyrion Lannister looked up from his books and shivered, though the library was snug and warm. Something about the howling of a wolf took a man right out of his here and now and left him in a dark forest of the mind, running naked before the pack.

When the direwolf howled again, Tyrion shut the heavy leather-bound cover on the book he was reading, a hundred-year-old discourse on the changing of the seasons by a long-dead maester. He covered a yawn with the back of his hand. His reading lamp was flickering, its oil all but gone, as dawn light leaked through the high windows. He had been at it all night, but that was nothing new. Tyrion Lannister was not much a one for sleeping.

His legs were stiff and sore as he eased down off the bench. He massaged some life back into them and limped heavily to the table where the septon was snoring softly, his head pillowed on an open book in front of him. Tyrion glanced at the title. A life of the Grand Maester Aethelmure, no wonder. "Chayle," he said softly. The young man jerked up, blinking, confused, the crystal of his order swinging wildly on its silver chain. "I'm off to break my fast. See that you return the books to the shelves. Be gentle with the Valyrian scrolls, the parchment is very dry. Ayrmidon's *Engines of War* is quite rare, and yours is the only complete copy I've ever seen." Chayle gaped at him, still half-asleep. Patiently, Tyrion repeated his instructions, then clapped the septon on the shoulder and left him to his tasks.

Outside, Tyrion swallowed a lungful of the cold morning air and began his laborious descent of the steep stone steps that corkscrewed around the exterior of the library tower. It was slow going; the steps were cut high and narrow, while his legs were short and twisted. The rising sun had not yet cleared the walls of Winterfell, but the men were already hard at it in the yard below. Sandor Clegane's rasping voice drifted up to him. "The boy is a long time dying. I wish he would be quicker about it."

Tyrion glanced down and saw the Hound standing with young Joffrey as squires swarmed around them. "At least he dies quietly," the prince replied. "It's the wolf that makes the noise. I could scarce sleep last night."

Clegane cast a long shadow across the hard-packed earth as his squire lowered the black helm over his head. "I could silence the creature, if it please you," he said through his open visor. His boy placed a longsword in his hand. He tested the weight of it, slicing at the cold morning air. Behind him, the yard rang to the clangor of steel on steel.

The notion seemed to delight the prince. "Send a dog to kill a dog!" he exclaimed. "Winterfell is so infested with wolves, the Starks would never miss one."

Tyrion hopped off the last step onto the yard. "I beg to differ, nephew," he said. "The Starks can count past six. Unlike some princes I might name."

Joffrey had the grace at least to blush.

"A voice from nowhere," Sandor said. He peered through his helm, looking this way and that. "Spirits of the air!"

The prince laughed, as he always laughed when his bodyguard did this mummer's farce. Tyrion was used to it. "Down here."

The tall man peered down at the ground, and pretended to notice him. "The little lord Tyrion," he said. "My pardons. I did not see you standing there."

"I am in no mood for your insolence today." Tyrion turned to his nephew. "Joffrey, it is past time you called on Lord Eddard and his lady, to offer them your comfort."

Joffrey looked as petulant as only a boy prince can look. "What good will my comfort do them?"

"None," Tyrion said. "Yet it is expected of you. Your absence has been noted."

"The Stark boy is nothing to me," Joffrey said. "I cannot abide the wailing of women."

Tyrion Lannister reached up and slapped his nephew hard across the face. The boy's cheek began to redden.

"One word," Tyrion said, "and I will hit you again."

"I'm going to tell Mother!" Joffrey exclaimed.

Tyrion hit him again. Now both cheeks flamed.

"You tell your mother," Tyrion told him. "But first you get yourself to Lord and Lady Stark, and you fall to your knees in front of them, and you tell them how very sorry you are, and that you are at their service if there is the slightest thing you can do for them or theirs in this desperate hour, and that all your prayers go with them. Do you understand? *Do you?*"

The boy looked as though he was going to cry. Instead, he managed a weak nod. Then he turned and fled headlong from the yard, holding his cheek. Tyrion watched him run.

A shadow fell across his face. He turned to find Clegane looming overhead like a cliff. His soot-dark armor seemed to blot out the sun. He had lowered the visor on his helm. It was fashioned in the likeness of a snarling black hound, fearsome to behold, but Tyrion had always thought it a great improvement over Clegane's hideously burned face.

"The prince will remember that, little lord," the Hound warned him. The helm turned his laugh into a hollow rumble.

"I pray he does," Tyrion Lannister replied. "If he forgets, be a good dog and remind him." He glanced around the courtyard. "Do you know where I might find my brother?"

"Breaking fast with the queen."

"Ah," Tyrion said. He gave Sandor Clegane a perfunctory nod and walked away as briskly as his stunted legs would carry him, whistling. He pitied the first knight to try the Hound today. The man did have a temper.

A cold, cheerless meal had been laid out in the morning room of the Guest House. Jaime sat at table with Cersei and the children, talking in low, hushed voices.

"Is Robert still abed?" Tyrion asked as he seated himself, uninvited, at the table.

His sister peered at him with the same expression of faint distaste she had worn since the day he was born. "The king has not slept at all," she told him. "He is with Lord Eddard. He has taken their sorrow deeply to heart."

"He has a large heart, our Robert," Jaime said with a lazy smile. There was very little that Jaime took seriously. Tyrion knew that about his brother, and forgave it. During all the terrible long years of his childhood, only Jaime had ever shown him the smallest measure of affection or respect, and for that Tyrion was willing to forgive him most anything.

A servant approached. "Bread," Tyrion told him, "and two of those little fish, and a mug of that good dark beer to wash them down. Oh, and some bacon. Burn it until it turns black." The man bowed and moved off. Tyrion turned back to his siblings. Twins, male and female. They looked very much the part this morning. Both had chosen a deep green that matched their eyes. Their blond curls were all a fashionable tumble, and gold ornaments shone at wrists and fingers and throats.

Tyrion wondered what it would be like to have a twin, and decided that he would rather not know. Bad enough to face himself in a looking glass every day. Another him was a thought too dreadful to contemplate.

Prince Tommen spoke up. "Do you have news of Bran, Uncle?"

"I stopped by the sickroom last night," Tyrion announced. "There was no change. The maester thought that a hopeful sign."

"I don't want Brandon to die," Tommen said timorously. He was a sweet boy. Not like his brother, but then Jaime and Tyrion were somewhat less than peas in a pod themselves.

"Lord Eddard had a brother named Brandon as well,"

Jaime mused. "One of the hostages murdered by Targaryen. It seems to be an unlucky name."

"Oh, not so unlucky as all that, surely," Tyrion said. The servant brought his plate. He ripped off a chunk of black bread.

Cersei was studying him warily. "What do you mean?"

Tyrion gave her a crooked smile. "Why, only that Tommen may get his wish. The maester thinks the boy may yet live." He took a sip of beer.

Myrcella gave a happy gasp, and Tommen smiled nervously, but it was not the children Tyrion was watching. The glance that passed between Jaime and Cersei lasted no more than a second, but he did not miss it. Then his sister dropped her gaze to the table. "That is no mercy. These northern gods are cruel to let the child linger in such pain."

"What were the maester's words?" Jaime asked.

The bacon crunched when he bit into it. Tyrion chewed thoughtfully for a moment and said, "He thinks that if the boy were going to die, he would have done so already. It has been four days with no change."

"Will Bran get better, Uncle?" little Myrcella asked. She had all of her mother's beauty, and none of her nature.

"His back is broken, little one," Tyrion told her. "The fall shattered his legs as well. They keep him alive with honey and water, or he would starve to death. Perhaps, if he wakes, he will be able to eat real food, but he will never walk again."

"If he wakes," Cersei repeated. "Is that likely?"

"The gods alone know," Tyrion told her. "The maester only hopes." He chewed some more bread. "I would swear that wolf of his is keeping the boy alive. The creature is outside his window day and night, howling. Every time they chase it away, it returns. The maester said they closed the window once, to shut out the noise, and Bran seemed to weaken. When they opened it again, his heart beat stronger."

The queen shuddered. "There is something unnatural about those animals," she said. "They are dangerous. I will *not* have any of them coming south with us."

Jaime said, "You'll have a hard time stopping them, sister. They follow those girls everywhere."

Tyrion started on his fish. "Are you leaving soon, then?"

"Not near soon enough," Cersei said. Then she frowned. "Are *we* leaving?" she echoed. "What about you? Gods, don't tell me you are staying *here*?"

Tyrion shrugged. "Benjen Stark is returning to the Night's Watch with his brother's bastard. I have a mind to go with them and see this Wall we have all heard so much of."

Jaime smiled. "I hope you're not thinking of taking the black on us, sweet brother."

Tyrion laughed. "What, me, celibate? The whores would go begging from Dorne to Casterly Rock. No, I just want to stand on top of the Wall and piss off the edge of the world."

Cersei stood abruptly. "The children don't need to hear this filth. Tommen, Myrcella, come." She strode briskly from the morning room, her train and her pups trailing behind her.

Jaime Lannister regarded his brother thoughtfully with those cool green eyes. "Stark will never consent to leave Winterfell with his son lingering in the shadow of death."

"He will if Robert commands it," Tyrion said. "And Robert *will* command it. There is nothing Lord Eddard can do for the boy in any case."

"He could end his torment," Jaime said. "I would, if it were my son. It would be a mercy."

"I advise against putting that suggestion to Lord Eddard, sweet brother," Tyrion said. "He would not take it kindly."

"Even if the boy does live, he will be a cripple. Worse than a cripple. A grotesque. Give me a good clean death."

Tyrion replied with a shrug that accentuated the twist of his shoulders. "Speaking for the grotesques," he said, "I beg to differ. Death is so terribly final, while life is full of possibilities."

Jaime smiled. "You are a perverse little imp, aren't you?"

"Oh, yes," Tyrion admitted. "I hope the boy does wake. I would be most interested to hear what he might have to say."

His brother's smile curdled like sour milk. "Tyrion,

my sweet brother," he said darkly, "there are times when you give me cause to wonder whose side you are on."

Tyrion's mouth was full of bread and fish. He took a swallow of strong black beer to wash it all down, and grinned up wolfishly at Jaime. "Why, Jaime, my sweet brother," he said, "you wound me. You know how much I love my family."

JON

Jon climbed the steps slowly, trying not to think that this might be the last time ever. Ghost padded silently beside him. Outside, snow swirled through the castle gates, and the yard was all noise and chaos, but inside the thick stone walls it was still warm and quiet. Too quiet for Jon's liking.

He reached the landing and stood for a long moment, afraid. Ghost nuzzled at his hand. He took courage from that. He straightened, and entered the room.

Lady Stark was there beside his bed. She had been there, day and night, for close on a fortnight. Not for a moment had she left Bran's side. She had her meals brought to her there, and chamber pots as well, and a small hard bed to sleep on, though it was said she had scarcely slept at all. She fed him herself, the honey and water and herb mixture that sustained life. Not once did she leave the room. So Jon had stayed away.

But now there was no more time.

He stood in the door for a moment, afraid to speak, afraid to come closer. The window was open. Below, a wolf howled. Ghost heard and lifted his head.

Lady Stark looked over. For a moment she did not

seem to recognize him. Finally she blinked. "What are *you* doing here?" she asked in a voice strangely flat and emotionless.

"I came to see Bran," Jon said. "To say good-bye."

Her face did not change. Her long auburn hair was dull and tangled. She looked as though she had aged twenty years. "You've said it. Now go away."

Part of him wanted only to flee, but he knew that if he did he might never see Bran again. He took a nervous step into the room. "Please," he said.

Something cold moved in her eyes. "I told you to leave," she said. "We don't want you here."

Once that would have sent him running. Once that might even have made him cry. Now it only made him angry. He would be a Sworn Brother of the Night's Watch soon, and face worse dangers than Catelyn Tully Stark. "He's my brother," he said.

"Shall I call the guards?"

"Call them," Jon said, defiant. "You can't stop me from seeing him." He crossed the room, keeping the bed between them, and looked down on Bran where he lay.

She was holding one of his hands. It looked like a claw. This was not the Bran he remembered. The flesh had all gone from him. His skin stretched tight over bones like sticks. Under the blanket, his legs bent in ways that made Jon sick. His eyes were sunken deep into black pits; open, but they saw nothing. The fall had shrunken him somehow. He looked half a leaf, as if the first strong wind would carry him off to his grave.

Yet under the frail cage of those shattered ribs, his chest rose and fell with each shallow breath.

"Bran," he said, "I'm sorry I didn't come before. I was afraid." He could feel the tears rolling down his cheeks. Jon no longer cared. "Don't die, Bran. Please. We're all waiting for you to wake up. Me and Robb and the girls, everyone . . ."

Lady Stark was watching. She had not raised a cry. Jon took that for acceptance. Outside the window, the direwolf howled again. The wolf that Bran had not had time to name.

"I have to go now," Jon said. "Uncle Benjen is waiting. I'm to go north to the Wall. We have to leave today, before the snows come." He remembered how excited Bran had been at the prospect of the journey. It was more than he could bear, the thought of leaving him behind like this. Jon brushed away his tears, leaned over, and kissed his brother lightly on the lips.

"I wanted him to stay here with me," Lady Stark said softly.

Jon watched her, wary. She was not even looking at him. She was talking to him, but for a part of her, it was as though he were not even in the room.

"I prayed for it," she said dully. "He was my special boy. I went to the sept and prayed seven times to the seven faces of god that Ned would change his mind and leave him here with me. Sometimes prayers are answered."

Jon did not know what to say. "It wasn't your fault," he managed after an awkward silence.

Her eyes found him. They were full of poison. "I need none of your absolution, bastard."

Jon lowered his eyes. She was cradling one of Bran's hands. He took the other, squeezed it. Fingers like the bones of birds. "Good-bye," he said.

He was at the door when she called out to him. "Jon," she said. He should have kept going, but she had never called him by his name before. He turned to find her looking at his face, as if she were seeing it for the first time.

"Yes?" he said.

"It should have been you," she told him. Then she turned back to Bran and began to weep, her whole body shaking with the sobs. Jon had never seen her cry before.

It was a long walk down to the yard.

Outside, everything was noise and confusion. Wagons were being loaded, men were shouting, horses were being harnessed and saddled and led from the stables. A light snow had begun to fall, and everyone was in an uproar to be off.

Robb was in the middle of it, shouting commands with the best of them. He seemed to have grown of late, as if Bran's fall and his mother's collapse had somehow made him stronger. Grey Wind was at his side.

"Uncle Benjen is looking for you," he told Jon. "He wanted to be gone an hour ago."

"I know," Jon said. "Soon." He looked around at all

the noise and confusion. "Leaving is harder than I thought."

"For me too," Robb said. He had snow in his hair, melting from the heat of his body. "Did you see him?"

Jon nodded, not trusting himself to speak.

"He's not going to die," Robb said. "I know it."

"You Starks are hard to kill," Jon agreed. His voice was flat and tired. The visit had taken all the strength from him.

Robb knew something was wrong. "My mother . . ."

"She was . . . very kind," Jon told him.

Robb looked relieved. "Good." He smiled. "The next time I see you, you'll be all in black."

Jon forced himself to smile back. "It was always my color. How long do you think it will be?"

"Soon enough," Robb promised. He pulled Jon to him and embraced him fiercely. "Farewell, Snow."

Jon hugged him back. "And you, Stark. Take care of Bran."

"I will." They broke apart and looked at each other awkwardly. "Uncle Benjen said to send you to the stables if I saw you," Robb finally said.

"I have one more farewell to make," Jon told him.

"Then I haven't seen you," Robb replied. Jon left him standing there in the snow, surrounded by wagons and wolves and horses. It was a short walk to the armory. He picked up his package and took the covered bridge across to the Keep.

Arya was in her room, packing a polished ironwood chest that was bigger than she was. Nymeria was helping. Arya would only have to point, and the wolf would bound across the room, snatch up some wisp of silk in her jaws, and fetch it back. But when she smelled Ghost, she sat down on her haunches and yelped at them.

Arya glanced behind her, saw Jon, and jumped to her feet. She threw her skinny arms tight around his neck. "I was afraid you were gone," she said, her breath catching in her throat. "They wouldn't let me out to say good-bye."

"What did you do now?" Jon was amused.

Arya disentangled herself from him and made a face. "Nothing. I was all packed and everything." She gestured at the huge chest, no more than a third full, and at the clothes that were scattered all over the room. "Septa Mordane says I have to do it all over. My things weren't properly folded, she says. A proper southron lady doesn't just throw her clothes inside her chest like old rags, she says."

"Is that what you did, little sister?"

"Well, they're going to get all messed up anyway," she said. "Who cares how they're folded?"

"Septa Mordane," Jon told her. "I don't think she'd like Nymeria helping, either." The she-wolf regarded him silently with her dark golden eyes. "It's just as well. I have something for you to take with you, and it has to be packed very carefully."

Her face lit up. "A present?"

"You could call it that. Close the door."

Wary but excited, Arya checked the hall. "Nymeria, here. Guard." She left the wolf out there to warn of intruders and closed the door. By then Jon had pulled off the rags he'd wrapped it in. He held it out to her.

Arya's eyes went wide. Dark eyes, like his. "A sword," she said in a small, hushed breath.

The scabbard was soft grey leather, supple as sin. Jon drew out the blade slowly, so she could see the deep blue sheen of the steel. "This is no toy," he told her. "Be careful you don't cut yourself. The edges are sharp enough to shave with."

"Girls don't shave," Arya said.

"Maybe they should. Have you ever seen the septa's legs?"

She giggled at him. "It's so skinny."

"So are you," Jon told her. "I had Mikken make this special. The bravos use swords like this in Pentos and Myr and the other Free Cities. It won't hack a man's head off, but it can poke him full of holes if you're fast enough."

"I can be fast," Arya said.

"You'll have to work at it every day." He put the sword in her hands, showed her how to hold it, and stepped back. "How does it feel? Do you like the balance?"

"I think so," Arya said.

"First lesson," Jon said. "Stick them with the pointy end."

Arya gave him a *whap* on the arm with the flat of her

blade. The blow stung, but Jon found himself grinning
like an idiot. "I know which end to use," Arya said. A
doubtful look crossed her face. "Septa Mordane will take
it away from me."

"Not if she doesn't know you have it," Jon said.

"Who will I practice with?"

"You'll find someone," Jon promised her. "King's
Landing is a true city, a thousand times the size of
Winterfell. Until you find a partner, watch how they fight
in the yard. Run, and ride, make yourself strong. And
whatever you do . . ."

Arya knew what was coming next. They said it together.

". . . don't . . . tell . . . Sansa!"

Jon messed up her hair. "I will miss you, little sister."
Suddenly she looked like she was going to cry. "I wish
you were coming with us."

"Different roads sometimes lead to the same castle.
Who knows?" He was feeling better now. He was not going to let himself be sad. "I better go. I'll spend my first
year on the Wall emptying chamber pots if I keep Uncle
Ben waiting any longer."

Arya ran to him for a last hug. "Put down the sword
first," Jon warned her, laughing. She set it aside almost
shyly and showered him with kisses.

When he turned back at the door, she was holding it
again, trying it for balance. "I almost forgot," he told her.
"All the best swords have names."

"Like Ice," she said. She looked at the blade in her
hand. "Does this have a name? Oh, tell me."

"Can't you guess?" Jon teased. "Your very favorite
thing."

Arya seemed puzzled at first. Then it came to her. She
was that quick. They said it together:

"Needle!"

The memory of her laughter warmed him on the long
ride north.

DAENERYS

Daenerys Targaryen wed Khal Drogo with fear and barbaric splendor in a field beyond the walls of Pentos, for the Dothraki believed that all things of importance in a man's life must be done beneath the open sky.

Drogo had called his *khalasar* to attend him and they had come, forty thousand Dothraki warriors and uncounted numbers of women, children, and slaves. Outside the city walls they camped with their vast herds, raising palaces of woven grass, eating everything in sight, and making the good folk of Pentos more anxious with every passing day.

"My fellow magisters have doubled the size of the city guard," Illyrio told them over platters of honey duck and orange snap peppers one night at the manse that had been Drogo's. The *khal* had joined his *khalasar*, his estate given over to Daenerys and her brother until the wedding.

"Best we get Princess Daenerys wedded quickly before they hand half the wealth of Pentos away to sellswords and bravos," Ser Jorah Mormont jested. The exile had offered her brother his sword the night Dany had been sold to Khal Drogo; Viserys had accepted eagerly. Mormont had been their constant companion ever since.

Magister Illyrio laughed lightly through his forked beard, but Viserys did not so much as smile. "He can have her tomorrow, if he likes," her brother said. He glanced over at Dany, and she lowered her eyes. "So long as he pays the price."

Illyrio waved a languid hand in the air, rings glittering on his fat fingers. "I have told you, all is settled. Trust me. The *khal* has promised you a crown, and you shall have it."

"Yes, but when?"

"When the *khal* chooses," Illyrio said. "He will have the girl first, and after they are wed he must make his procession across the plains and present her to the *dosh khaleen* at Vaes Dothrak. After that, perhaps. If the omens favor war."

Viserys seethed with impatience. "I piss on Dothraki omens. The Usurper sits on my father's throne. How long must I wait?"

Illyrio gave a massive shrug. "You have waited most of your life, great king. What is another few months, another few years?"

Ser Jorah, who had traveled as far east as Vaes Dothrak, nodded in agreement. "I counsel you to be patient, Your Grace. The Dothraki are true to their word, but they do things in their own time. A lesser man may beg a favor from the *khal*, but must never presume to berate him."

Viserys bristled. "Guard your tongue, Mormont, or I'll have it out. I am no lesser man, I am the rightful Lord of the Seven Kingdoms. The dragon does not beg."

Ser Jorah lowered his eyes respectfully. Illyrio smiled enigmatically and tore a wing from the duck. Honey and grease ran over his fingers and dripped down into his beard as he nibbled at the tender meat. *There are no more dragons,* Dany thought, staring at her brother, though she did not dare say it aloud.

Yet that night she dreamt of one. Viserys was hitting her, hurting her. She was naked, clumsy with fear. She ran from him, but her body seemed thick and ungainly. He struck her again. She stumbled and fell. "You woke the dragon," he screamed as he kicked her. "You woke the dragon, you woke the dragon." Her thighs were slick with blood. She closed her eyes and whimpered. As if in answer, there was a hideous *ripping* sound and the crackling of some great fire. When she looked again, Viserys was gone, great columns of flame rose all around, and in the midst of them was the dragon. It turned its great head slowly. When its molten eyes found hers, she woke, shaking and covered with a fine sheen of sweat. She had never been so afraid . . .

. . . until the day of her wedding came at last.

The ceremony began at dawn and continued until dusk, an endless day of drinking and feasting and fighting. A mighty earthen ramp had been raised amid the grass palaces, and there Dany was seated beside Khal Drogo, above the seething sea of Dothraki. She had never seen so many people in one place, nor people so strange and frightening. The horselords might put on rich fabrics and sweet perfumes when they visited the Free Cities, but out under the open sky they kept the old ways. Men and women alike wore painted leather vests over bare chests and horsehair leggings cinched by bronze medallion belts, and the warriors greased their long braids with fat from the rendering pits. They gorged themselves on horseflesh roasted with honey and peppers, drank themselves blind on fermented mare's milk and Illyrio's fine wines, and spat jests at each other across the fires, their voices harsh and alien in Dany's ears.

Viserys was seated just below her, splendid in a new black wool tunic with a scarlet dragon on the chest. Illyrio and Ser Jorah sat beside him. Theirs was a place of high honor, just below the *khal*'s own bloodriders, but Dany could see the anger in her brother's lilac eyes. He did not like sitting beneath her, and he fumed when the slaves offered each dish first to the *khal* and his bride, and served him from the portions they refused. He could do nothing but nurse his resentment, so nurse it he did, his mood growing blacker by the hour at each insult to his person.

Dany had never felt so alone as she did seated in the midst of that vast horde. Her brother had told her to smile, and so she smiled until her face ached and the tears came unbidden to her eyes. She did her best to hide them, knowing how angry Viserys would be if he saw her crying, terrified of how Khal Drogo might react. Food was brought to her, steaming joints of meat and thick black sausages and Dothraki blood pies, and later fruits and sweetgrass stews and delicate pastries from the kitchens of Pentos, but she waved it all away. Her stomach was a roil, and she knew she could keep none of it down.

There was no one to talk to. Khal Drogo shouted commands and jests down to his bloodriders, and laughed at their replies, but he scarcely glanced at Dany beside him. They had no common language. Dothraki was incomprehensible to her, and the *khal* knew only a few words of the bastard Valyrian of the Free Cities, and none at all of the Common Tongue of the Seven Kingdoms. She would even have welcomed the conversation of Illyrio and her brother, but they were too far below to hear her.

So she sat in her wedding silks, nursing a cup of honeyed wine, afraid to eat, talking silently to herself. *I am blood of the dragon*, she told herself. *I am Daenerys Stormborn, Princess of Dragonstone, of the blood and seed of Aegon the Conqueror.*

The sun was only a quarter of the way up the sky when she saw her first man die. Drums were beating as some of the women danced for the *khal*. Drogo watched without expression, but his eyes followed their movements, and from time to time he would toss down a bronze medallion for the women to fight over.

The warriors were watching too. One of them finally stepped into the circle, grabbed a dancer by the arm, pushed her down to the ground, and mounted her right there, as a stallion mounts a mare. Illyrio had told her that might happen. "The Dothraki mate like the animals in their herds. There is no privacy in a *khalasar*, and they do not understand sin or shame as we do."

Dany looked away from the coupling, frightened when she realized what was happening, but a second warrior stepped forward, and a third, and soon there was no way to avert her eyes. Then two men seized the same woman. She heard a shout, saw a shove, and in the blink of an eye the *arakhs* were out, long razor-sharp blades, half sword and half scythe. A dance of death began as the warriors circled and slashed, leaping toward each other, whirling the blades around their heads, shrieking insults at each clash. No one made a move to interfere.

It ended as quickly as it began. The *arakhs* shivered

together faster than Dany could follow, one man missed a
step, the other swung his blade in a flat arc. Steel bit into
flesh just above the Dothraki's waist, and opened him
from backbone to belly button, spilling his entrails into
the dust. As the loser died, the winner took hold of the
nearest woman—not even the one they had been quarreling over—and had her there and then. Slaves carried off
the body, and the dancing resumed.

Magister Illyrio had warned Dany about this too. "A
Dothraki wedding without at least three deaths is deemed
a dull affair," he had said. Her wedding must have been
especially blessed; before the day was over, a dozen men
had died.

As the hours passed, the terror grew in Dany, until it
was all she could do not to scream. She was afraid of the
Dothraki, whose ways seemed alien and monstrous, as if
they were beasts in human skins and not true men at all.
She was afraid of her brother, of what he might do if she
failed him. Most of all, she was afraid of what would happen tonight under the stars, when her brother gave her up
to the hulking giant who sat drinking beside her with a
face as still and cruel as a bronze mask.

I am the blood of the dragon, she told herself again.

When at last the sun was low in the sky, Khal Drogo
clapped his hands together, and the drums and the shouting and feasting came to a sudden halt. Drogo stood and
pulled Dany to her feet beside him. It was time for her
bride gifts.

And after the gifts, she knew, after the sun had gone
down, it would be time for the first ride and the consummation of her marriage. Dany tried to put the thought
aside, but it would not leave her. She hugged herself to try
to keep from shaking.

Her brother Viserys gifted her with three handmaids.
Dany knew they had cost him nothing; Illyrio no doubt
had provided the girls. Irri and Jhiqui were copper-skinned
Dothraki with black hair and almond-shaped eyes,
Doreah a fair-haired, blue-eyed Lysene girl. "These are no
common servants, sweet sister," her brother told her as
they were brought forward one by one. "Illyrio and I selected them personally for you. Irri will teach you riding,
Jhiqui the Dothraki tongue, and Doreah will instruct you

in the womanly arts of love." He smiled thinly. "She's very good, Illyrio and I can both swear to that."

Ser Jorah Mormont apologized for his gift. "It is a small thing, my princess, but all a poor exile could afford," he said as he laid a small stack of old books before her. They were histories and songs of the Seven Kingdoms, she saw, written in the Common Tongue. She thanked him with all her heart.

Magister Illyrio murmured a command, and four burly slaves hurried forward, bearing between them a great cedar chest bound in bronze. When she opened it, she found piles of the finest velvets and damasks the Free Cities could produce . . . and resting on top, nestled in the soft cloth, three huge eggs. Dany gasped. They were the most beautiful things she had ever seen, each different than the others, patterned in such rich colors that at first she thought they were crusted with jewels, and so large it took both of her hands to hold one. She lifted it delicately, expecting that it would be made of some fine porcelain or delicate enamel, or even blown glass, but it was much heavier than that, as if it were all of solid stone. The surface of the shell was covered with tiny scales, and as she turned the egg between her fingers, they shimmered like polished metal in the light of the setting sun. One egg was a deep green, with burnished bronze flecks that came and went depending on how Dany turned it. Another was pale cream streaked with gold. The last was black, as black as a midnight sea, yet alive with scarlet ripples and swirls. "What are they?" she asked, her voice hushed and full of wonder.

"Dragon's eggs, from the Shadow Lands beyond Asshai," said Magister Illyrio. "The eons have turned them to stone, yet still they burn bright with beauty."

"I shall treasure them always." Dany had heard tales of such eggs, but she had never seen one, nor thought to see one. It was a truly magnificent gift, though she knew that Illyrio could afford to be lavish. He had collected a fortune in horses and slaves for his part in selling her to Khal Drogo.

The *khal*'s bloodriders offered her the traditional three weapons, and splendid weapons they were. Haggo gave her a great leather whip with a silver handle, Cohollo a magnificent *arakh* chased in gold, and Qotho a double-curved dragonbone bow taller than she was. Magister Illyrio and Ser Jorah had taught her the traditional refusals for these offerings. "This is a gift worthy of a great warrior, O blood of my blood, and I am but a woman. Let my lord husband bear these in my stead." And so Khal Drogo too received his "bride gifts."

Other gifts she was given in plenty by other Dothraki: slippers and jewels and silver rings for her hair, medallion belts and painted vests and soft furs, sandsilks and jars of scent, needles and feathers and tiny bottles of purple glass, and a gown made from the skin of a thousand mice. "A handsome gift, *Khaleesi*," Magister Illyrio said of the last, after he had told her what it was. "Most lucky." The gifts mounted up around her in great piles, more gifts than she could possibly imagine, more gifts than she could want or use.

And last of all, Khal Drogo brought forth his own bride gift to her. An expectant hush rippled out from the center of the camp as he left her side, growing until it had swallowed the whole *khalasar*. When he returned, the dense press of Dothraki gift-givers parted before him, and he led the horse to her.

She was a young filly, spirited and splendid. Dany knew just enough about horses to know that this was no ordinary animal. There was something about her that took the breath away. She was grey as the winter sea, with a mane like silver smoke.

Hesitantly she reached out and stroked the horse's neck, ran her fingers through the silver of her mane. Khal Drogo said something in Dothraki and Magister Illyrio translated. "Silver for the silver of your hair, the *khal* says."

"She's beautiful," Dany murmured.

"She is the pride of the *khalasar*," Illyrio said. "Custom decrees that the *khaleesi* must ride a mount worthy of her place by the side of the *khal*."

Drogo stepped forward and put his hands on her waist. He lifted her up as easily as if she were a child and set her on the thin Dothraki saddle, so much smaller than the ones she was used to. Dany sat there uncertain for a moment. No one had told her about this part. "What should I do?" she asked Illyrio.

It was Ser Jorah Mormont who answered. "Take the reins and ride. You need not go far."

Nervously Dany gathered the reins in her hands and slid her feet into the short stirrups. She was only a fair rider; she had spent far more time traveling by ship and wagon and palanquin than by horseback. Praying that she would not fall off and disgrace herself, she gave the filly the lightest and most timid touch with her knees.

And for the first time in hours, she forgot to be afraid. Or perhaps it was for the first time ever.

The silver-grey filly moved with a smooth and silken gait, and the crowd parted for her, every eye upon them. Dany found herself moving faster than she had intended, yet somehow it was exciting rather than terrifying. The horse broke into a trot, and she smiled. Dothraki scrambled to clear a path. The slightest pressure with her legs, the lightest touch on the reins, and the filly responded. She sent it into a gallop, and now the Dothraki were hooting and laughing and shouting at her as they jumped out of her way. As she turned to ride back, a firepit loomed ahead, directly in her path. They were hemmed in on either side, with no room to stop. A daring she had never known filled Daenerys then, and she gave the filly her head.

The silver horse leapt the flames as if she had wings.

When she pulled up before Magister Illyrio, she said, "Tell Khal Drogo that he has given me the wind." The fat Pentoshi stroked his yellow beard as he repeated her words in Dothraki, and Dany saw her new husband smile for the first time.

The last sliver of sun vanished behind the high walls of Pentos to the west just then. Dany had lost all track of time. Khal Drogo commanded his bloodriders to bring forth his own horse, a lean red stallion. As the *khal* was saddling the horse, Viserys slid close to Dany on her silver, dug his fingers into her leg, and said, "Please him, sweet sister, or I swear, you will see the dragon wake as it has never woken before."

The fear came back to her then, with her brother's words. She felt like a child once more, only thirteen and all alone, not ready for what was about to happen to her.

They rode out together as the stars came out, leaving the *khalasar* and the grass palaces behind. Khal Drogo spoke no word to her, but drove his stallion at a hard trot through the gathering dusk. The tiny silver bells in his long braid rang softly as he rode. "I am the blood of the dragon," she whispered aloud as she followed, trying to keep her courage up. "I am the blood of the dragon. I am the blood of the dragon." The dragon was never afraid.

Afterward she could not say how far or how long they had ridden, but it was full dark when they stopped at a grassy place beside a small stream. Drogo swung off his horse and lifted her down from hers. She felt as fragile as glass in his hands, her limbs as weak as water. She stood there helpless and trembling in her wedding silks while he secured the horses, and when he turned to look at her, she began to cry.

Khal Drogo stared at her tears, his face strangely empty of expression. "No," he said. He lifted his hand and rubbed away the tears roughly with a callused thumb.

"You speak the Common Tongue," Dany said in wonder.

"No," he said again.

Perhaps he had only that word, she thought, but it was one word more than she had known he had, and somehow it made her feel a little better. Drogo touched her hair lightly, sliding the silver-blond strands between his fingers and murmuring softly in Dothraki. Dany did not understand the words, yet there was warmth in the tone, a tenderness she had never expected from this man.

He put his finger under her chin and lifted her head, so she was looking up into his eyes. Drogo towered over her as he towered over everyone. Taking her lightly under the arms, he lifted her and seated her on a rounded rock beside the stream. Then he sat on the ground facing her, legs crossed beneath him, their faces finally at a height. "No," he said.

"Is that the only word you know?" she asked him.

Drogo did not reply. His long heavy braid was coiled in the dirt beside him. He pulled it over his right shoulder and began to remove the bells from his hair, one by one. After a moment Dany leaned forward to help. When they were done, Drogo gestured. She understood. Slowly, carefully, she began to undo his braid.

It took a long time. All the while he sat there silently, watching her. When she was done, he shook his head, and his hair spread out behind him like a river of darkness, oiled and gleaming. She had never seen hair so long, so black, so thick.

Then it was his turn. He began to undress her.

His fingers were deft and strangely tender. He removed her silks one by one, carefully, while Dany sat unmoving, silent, looking at his eyes. When he bared her small breasts, she could not help herself. She averted her eyes and covered herself with her hands. "No," Drogo said. He pulled her hands away from her breasts, gently but firmly, then lifted her face again to make her look at him. "No," he repeated.

"No," she echoed back at him.

He stood her up then and pulled her close to remove the last of her silks. The night air was chilly on her bare skin. She shivered, and gooseflesh covered her arms and legs. She was afraid of what would come next, but for a while nothing happened. Khal Drogo sat with his legs crossed, looking at her, drinking in her body with his eyes.

After a while he began to touch her. Lightly at first, then harder. She could sense the fierce strength in his hands, but he never hurt her. He held her hand in his own and brushed her fingers, one by one. He ran a hand gently down her leg. He stroked her face, tracing the curve of her ears, running a finger gently around her mouth. He put both hands in her hair and combed it with his fingers. He turned her around, massaged her shoulders, slid a knuckle down the path of her spine.

It seemed as if hours passed before his hands finally went to her breasts. He stroked the soft skin underneath until it tingled. He circled her nipples with his thumbs, pinched them between thumb and forefinger, then began to pull at her, very lightly at first, then more insistently, until her nipples stiffened and began to ache.

He stopped then, and drew her down onto his lap. Dany was flushed and breathless, her heart fluttering in her chest. He cupped her face in his huge hands and she looked into his eyes. "No?" he said, and she knew it was a question.

She took his hand and moved it down to the wetness between her thighs. "Yes," she whispered as she put his finger inside her.

EDDARD

The summons came in the hour before the dawn, when the world was still and grey.

Alyn shook him roughly from his dreams and Ned stumbled into the predawn chill, groggy from sleep, to find his horse saddled and the king already mounted. Robert wore thick brown gloves and a heavy fur cloak with a hood that covered his ears, and looked for all the world like a bear sitting a horse. "Up, Stark!" he roared. "Up, up! We have matters of state to discuss."

"By all means," Ned said. "Come inside, Your Grace." Alyn lifted the flap of the tent.

"No, no, *no*," Robert said. His breath steamed with every word. "The camp is full of ears. Besides, I want to ride out and taste this country of yours." Ser Boros and Ser Meryn waited behind him with a dozen guardsmen, Ned saw. There was nothing to do but rub the sleep from his eyes, dress, and mount up.

Robert set the pace, driving his huge black destrier hard as Ned galloped along beside him, trying to keep up. He called out a question as they rode, but the wind blew his words away, and the king did not hear him. After that Ned rode in silence. They soon left the kingsroad and

took off across rolling plains dark with mist. By then the
guard had fallen back a small distance, safely out of earshot, but still Robert would not slow.

Dawn broke as they crested a low ridge, and finally the
king pulled up. By then they were miles south of the main
party. Robert was flushed and exhilarated as Ned reined
up beside him. "Gods," he swore, laughing, "it feels good
to get out and *ride* the way a man was meant to ride! I
swear, Ned, this creeping along is enough to drive a man
mad." He had never been a patient man, Robert
Baratheon. "That damnable wheelhouse, the way it
creaks and groans, climbing every bump in the road as if
it were a mountain . . . I promise you, if that wretched
thing breaks another axle, I'm going to burn it, and Cersei
can walk!"

Ned laughed. "I will gladly light the torch for you."

"Good man!" The king clapped him on the shoulder.
"I've half a mind to leave them all behind and just keep
going."

A smile touched Ned's lips. "I do believe you mean it."

"I do, I do," the king said. "What do you say, Ned? Just
you and me, two vagabond knights on the kingsroad, our
swords at our sides and the gods know what in front of us,
and maybe a farmer's daughter or a tavern wench to
warm our beds tonight."

"Would that we could," Ned said, "but we have duties
now, my liege . . . to the realm, to our children, I to my
lady wife and you to your queen. We are not the boys we
were."

"You were never the boy you were," Robert grumbled.
"More's the pity. And yet there was that one time . . .
what was her name, that common girl of yours? Becca?
No, she was one of mine, gods love her, black hair and
these sweet big eyes, you could drown in them. Yours
was . . . Aleena? No. You told me once. Was it Merryl?
You know the one I mean, your bastard's mother?"

"Her name was Wylla," Ned replied with cool courtesy, "and I would sooner not speak of her."

"Wylla. Yes." The king grinned. "She must have been a
rare wench if she could make Lord Eddard Stark forget his
honor, even for an hour. You never told me what she
looked like . . ."

Ned's mouth tightened in anger. "Nor will I. Leave it

be, Robert, for the love you say you bear me. I dishonored myself and I dishonored Catelyn, in the sight of gods and men."

"Gods have mercy, you scarcely *knew* Catelyn."

"I had taken her to wife. She was carrying my child."

"You are too hard on yourself, Ned. You always were. Damn it, no woman wants Baelor the Blessed in her bed." He slapped a hand on his knee. "Well, I'll not press you if you feel so strong about it, though I swear, at times you're so prickly you ought to take the hedgehog as your sigil."

The rising sun sent fingers of light through the pale white mists of dawn. A wide plain spread out beneath them, bare and brown, its flatness here and there relieved by long, low hummocks. Ned pointed them out to his king. "The barrows of the First Men."

Robert frowned. "Have we ridden onto a graveyard?"

"There are barrows everywhere in the north, Your Grace," Ned told him. "This land is old."

"And cold," Robert grumbled, pulling his cloak more tightly around himself. The guard had reined up well behind them, at the bottom of the ridge. "Well, I did not bring you out here to talk of graves or bicker about your bastard. There was a rider in the night, from Lord Varys in King's Landing. Here." The king pulled a paper from his belt and handed it to Ned.

Varys the eunuch was the king's master of whisperers. He served Robert now as he had once served Aerys Targaryen. Ned unrolled the paper with trepidation, thinking of Lysa and her terrible accusation, but the message did not concern Lady Arryn. "What is the source for this information?"

"Do you remember Ser Jorah Mormont?"

"Would that I might forget him," Ned said bluntly. The Mormonts of Bear Island were an old house, proud and honorable, but their lands were cold and distant and poor. Ser Jorah had tried to swell the family coffers by selling some poachers to a Tyroshi slaver. As the Mormonts were bannermen to the Starks, his crime had dishonored the north. Ned had made the long journey west to Bear Island, only to find when he arrived that Jorah had taken ship beyond the reach of Ice and the king's justice. Five years had passed since then.

"Ser Jorah is now in Pentos, anxious to earn a royal

pardon that would allow him to return from exile," Robert explained. "Lord Varys makes good use of him."

"So the slaver has become a spy," Ned said with distaste. He handed the letter back. "I would rather he become a corpse."

"Varys tells me that spies are more useful than corpses," Robert said. "Jorah aside, what do you make of his report?"

"Daenerys Targaryen has wed some Dothraki horselord. What of it? Shall we send her a wedding gift?"

The king frowned. "A knife, perhaps. A good sharp one, and a bold man to wield it."

Ned did not feign surprise; Robert's hatred of the Targaryens was a madness in him. He remembered the angry words they had exchanged when Tywin Lannister had presented Robert with the corpses of Rhaegar's wife and children as a token of fealty. Ned had named that murder; Robert called it war. When he had protested that the young prince and princess were no more than babes, his new-made king had replied, "I see no babes. Only dragonspawn." Not even Jon Arryn had been able to calm that storm. Eddard Stark had ridden out that very day in a cold rage, to fight the last battles of the war alone in the south. It had taken another death to reconcile them; Lyanna's death, and the grief they had shared over her passing.

This time, Ned resolved to keep his temper. "Your Grace, the girl is scarcely more than a child. You are no Tywin Lannister, to slaughter innocents." It was said that Rhaegar's little girl had cried as they dragged her from beneath her bed to face the swords. The boy had been no more than a babe in arms, yet Lord Tywin's soldiers had torn him from his mother's breast and dashed his head against a wall.

"And how long will this one remain an innocent?" Robert's mouth grew hard. "This *child* will soon enough spread her legs and start breeding more dragonspawn to plague me."

"Nonetheless," Ned said, "the murder of children . . . it would be vile . . . unspeakable . . ."

"*Unspeakable!*" the king roared. "What Aerys did to your brother Brandon was unspeakable. The way your lord father died, that was unspeakable. And Rhaegar . . . how many times do you think he raped your sister? How many *hundreds* of times?" His voice had grown so loud that his horse whinnied nervously beneath him. The king jerked the reins hard, quieting the animal, and pointed an angry finger at Ned. "I will kill every Targaryen I can get my hands on, until they are as dead as their dragons, and then I will piss on their graves."

Ned knew better than to defy him when the wrath was on him. If the years had not quenched Robert's thirst for revenge, no words of his would help. "You can't get your hands on this one, can you?" he said quietly.

The king's mouth twisted in a bitter grimace. "No, gods be cursed. Some pox-ridden Pentoshi cheesemonger had her brother and her walled up on his estate with pointy-hatted eunuchs all around them, and now he's handed them over to the Dothraki. I should have had them both killed years ago, when it was easy to get at them, but Jon was as bad as you. More fool I, I listened to him."

"Jon Arryn was a wise man and a good Hand."

Robert snorted. The anger was leaving him as suddenly as it had come. "This Khal Drogo is said to have a hundred thousand men in his horde. What would Jon say to *that*?"

"He would say that even a million Dothraki are no threat to the realm, so long as they remain on the other side of the narrow sea," Ned replied calmly. "The barbarians have no *ships*. They hate and fear the open sea."

The king shifted uncomfortably in his saddle. "Perhaps. There are ships to be had in the Free Cities, though. I tell you, Ned, I do not like this marriage. There are still those in the Seven Kingdoms who call me Usurper. Do you forget how many houses fought for Targaryen in the war? They bide their time for now, but give them half a chance, they will murder me in my bed, and my sons with me. If the beggar king crosses with a Dothraki horde at his back, the traitors will join him."

"He will not cross," Ned promised. "And if by some mischance he does, we will throw him back into the sea. Once you choose a new Warden of the East—"

The king groaned. "For the last time, I will not name the Arryn boy Warden. I know the boy is your nephew, but with Targaryens climbing in bed with Dothraki, I would be mad to rest one quarter of the realm on the shoulders of a sickly child."

Ned was ready for that. "Yet we still must have a Warden of the East. If Robert Arryn will not do, name one of your brothers. Stannis proved himself at the siege of Storm's End, surely."

He let the name hang there for a moment. The king frowned and said nothing. He looked uncomfortable.

"That is," Ned finished quietly, watching, "unless you have already promised the honor to another."

For a moment Robert had the grace to look startled. Just as quickly, the look became annoyance. "What if I have?"

"It's Jaime Lannister, is it not?"

Robert kicked his horse back into motion and started down the ridge toward the barrows. Ned kept pace with him. The king rode on, eyes straight ahead. "Yes," he said at last. A single hard word to end the matter.

"Kingslayer," Ned said. The rumors were true, then. He rode on dangerous ground now, he knew. "An able and courageous man, no doubt," he said carefully, "but his father is Warden of the West, Robert. In time Ser Jaime will succeed to that honor. No one man should hold both East and West." He left unsaid his real concern; that the appointment would put half the armies of the realm into the hands of Lannisters.

"I will fight that battle when the enemy appears on the field," the king said stubbornly. "At the moment, Lord Tywin looms eternal as Casterly Rock, so I doubt that Jaime will be succeeding anytime soon. Don't vex me about this, Ned, the stone has been set."

"Your Grace, may I speak frankly?"

"I seem unable to stop you," Robert grumbled. They rode through tall brown grasses.

"Can you trust Jaime Lannister?"

"He is my wife's twin, a Sworn Brother of the Kingsguard, his life and fortune and honor all bound to mine."

"As they were bound to Aerys Targaryen's," Ned pointed out.

"Why should I mistrust him? He has done everything I have ever asked of him. His sword helped win the throne I sit on."

His sword helped taint the throne you sit on, Ned

thought, but he did not permit the words to pass his lips. "He swore a vow to protect his king's life with his own. Then he opened that king's throat with a sword."

"Seven hells, *someone* had to kill Aerys!" Robert said, reining his mount to a sudden halt beside an ancient barrow. "If Jaime hadn't done it, it would have been left for you or me."

"We were not Sworn Brothers of the Kingsguard," Ned said. The time had come for Robert to hear the whole truth, he decided then and there. "Do you remember the Trident, Your Grace?"

"I won my crown there. How should I forget it?"

"You took a wound from Rhaegar," Ned reminded him. "So when the Targaryen host broke and ran, you gave the pursuit into my hands. The remnants of Rhaegar's army fled back to King's Landing. We followed. Aerys was in the Red Keep with several thousand loyalists. I expected to find the gates closed to us."

Robert gave an impatient shake of his head. "Instead you found that our men had already taken the city. What of it?"

"Not our men," Ned said patiently. "Lannister men. The lion of Lannister flew over the ramparts, not the crowned stag. And they had taken the city by treachery."

The war had raged for close to a year. Lords great and small had flocked to Robert's banners; others had remained loyal to Targaryen. The mighty Lannisters of Casterly Rock, the Wardens of the West, had remained aloof from the struggle, ignoring calls to arms from both rebels and royalists. Aerys Targaryen must have thought that his gods had answered his prayers when Lord Tywin Lannister appeared before the gates of King's Landing with an army twelve thousand strong, professing loyalty. So the mad king had ordered his last mad act. He had opened his city to the lions at the gate.

"Treachery was a coin the Targaryens knew well," Robert said. The anger was building in him again. "Lannister paid them back in kind. It was no less than they deserved. I shall not trouble my sleep over it."

"You were not there," Ned said, bitterness in his voice. Troubled sleep was no stranger to him. He had lived his lies for fourteen years, yet they still haunted him at night. "There was no honor in that conquest."

"The Others take your honor!" Robert swore. "What did any Targaryen ever know of honor? Go down into your crypt and ask Lyanna about the dragon's honor!"

"You avenged Lyanna at the Trident," Ned said, halting beside the king. *Promise me, Ned*, she had whispered.

"That did not bring her back." Robert looked away, off into the grey distance. "The gods be damned. It was a hollow victory they gave me. A crown . . . it was the *girl* I prayed them for. Your sister, safe . . . and mine again, as she was meant to be. I ask you, Ned, what good is it to wear a crown? The gods mock the prayers of kings and cowherds alike."

"I cannot answer for the gods, Your Grace . . . only for what I found when I rode into the throne room that day," Ned said. "Aerys was dead on the floor, drowned in his own blood. His dragon skulls stared down from the walls. Lannister's men were everywhere. Jaime wore the white cloak of the Kingsguard over his golden armor. I can see him still. Even his sword was gilded. He was seated on the Iron Throne, high above his knights, wearing a helm fashioned in the shape of a lion's head. How he glittered!"

"This is well known," the king complained.

"I was still mounted. I rode the length of the hall in silence, between the long rows of dragon skulls. It felt as though they were watching me, somehow. I stopped in front of the throne, looking up at him. His golden sword was across his legs, its edge red with a king's blood. My men were filling the room behind me. Lannister's men drew back. I never said a word. I looked at him seated there on the throne, and I waited. At last Jaime laughed and got up. He took off his helm, and he said to me, 'Have no fear, Stark. I was only keeping it warm for our friend Robert. It's not a very comfortable seat, I'm afraid.'"

The king threw back his head and roared. His laughter startled a flight of crows from the tall brown grass. They took to the air in a wild beating of wings. "You think I should mistrust Lannister because he sat on my throne for a few moments?" He shook with laughter again. "Jaime was all of seventeen, Ned. Scarce more than a boy."

"Boy or man, he had no right to that throne."

"Perhaps he was tired," Robert suggested. "Killing

kings is weary work. Gods know, there's no place else to rest your ass in that damnable room. And he spoke truly, it *is* a monstrous uncomfortable chair. In more ways than one." The king shook his head. "Well, now I know Jaime's dark sin, and the matter can be forgotten. I am heartily sick of secrets and squabbles and matters of state, Ned. It's all as tedious as counting coppers. Come, let's ride, you used to know how. I want to feel the wind in my hair again." He kicked his horse back into motion and galloped up over the barrow, raining earth down behind him.

For a moment Ned did not follow. He had run out of words, and he was filled with a vast sense of helplessness. Not for the first time, he wondered what he was doing here and why he had come. He was no Jon Arryn, to curb the wildness of his king and teach him wisdom. Robert would do what he pleased, as he always had, and nothing Ned could say or do would change that. He belonged in Winterfell. He belonged with Catelyn in her grief, and with Bran.

A man could not always be where he belonged, though. Resigned, Eddard Stark put his boots into his horse and set off after the king.

TYRION

The north went on forever.

Tyrion Lannister knew the maps as well as anyone, but a fortnight on the wild track that passed
for the kingsroad up here had brought home the lesson
that the map was one thing and the land quite another.

They had left Winterfell on the same day as the king,
amidst all the commotion of the royal departure, riding
out to the sound of men shouting and horses snorting, to
the rattle of wagons and the groaning of the queen's huge
wheelhouse, as a light snow flurried about them. The
kingsroad was just beyond the sprawl of castle and town.
There the banners and the wagons and the columns of
knights and freeriders turned south, taking the tumult
with them, while Tyrion turned north with Benjen Stark
and his nephew.

It had grown colder after that, and far more quiet.

West of the road were flint hills, grey and rugged, with
tall watchtowers on their stony summits. To the east the
land was lower, the ground flattening to a rolling plain
that stretched away as far as the eye could see. Stone
bridges spanned swift, narrow rivers, while small farms
spread in rings around holdfasts walled in wood and

stone. The road was well trafficked, and at night for their comfort there were rude inns to be found.

Three days ride from Winterfell, however, the farmland gave way to dense wood, and the kingsroad grew lonely. The flint hills rose higher and wilder with each passing mile, until by the fifth day they had turned into mountains, cold blue-grey giants with jagged promontories and snow on their shoulders. When the wind blew from the north, long plumes of ice crystals flew from the high peaks like banners.

With the mountains a wall to the west, the road veered north by northeast through the wood, a forest of oak and evergreen and black brier that seemed older and darker than any Tyrion had ever seen. "The wolfswood," Benjen Stark called it, and indeed their nights came alive with the howls of distant packs, and some not so distant. Jon Snow's albino direwolf pricked up his ears at the nightly howling, but never raised his own voice in reply. There was something very unsettling about that animal, Tyrion thought.

There were eight in the party by then, not counting the wolf. Tyrion traveled with two of his own men, as befit a Lannister. Benjen Stark had only his bastard nephew and some fresh mounts for the Night's Watch, but at the edge of the wolfswood they stayed a night behind the wooden walls of a forest holdfast, and there joined up with another of the black brothers, one Yoren. Yoren was stooped and sinister, his features hidden behind a beard as black as his clothing, but he seemed as tough as an old root and as hard as stone. With him were a pair of ragged peasant boys from the Fingers. "Rapers," Yoren said with a cold look at his charges. Tyrion understood. Life on the Wall was said to be hard, but no doubt it was preferable to castration.

Five men, three boys, a direwolf, twenty horses, and a cage of ravens given over to Benjen Stark by Maester Luwin. No doubt they made a curious fellowship for the kingsroad, or any road.

Tyrion noticed Jon Snow watching Yoren and his sullen companions, with an odd cast to his face that looked uncomfortably like dismay. Yoren had a twisted shoulder and a sour smell, his hair and beard were matted and greasy and full of lice, his clothing old, patched, and seldom washed. His two young recruits smelled even worse, and seemed as stupid as they were cruel.

No doubt the boy had made the mistake of thinking that the Night's Watch was made up of men like his uncle. If so, Yoren and his companions were a rude awakening. Tyrion felt sorry for the boy. He had chosen a hard life . . . or perhaps he should say that a hard life had been chosen for him.

He had rather less sympathy for the uncle. Benjen Stark seemed to share his brother's distaste for Lannisters, and he had not been pleased when Tyrion had told him of his intentions. "I warn you, Lannister, you'll find no inns at the Wall," he had said, looking down on him.

"No doubt you'll find some place to put me," Tyrion had replied. "As you might have noticed, I'm small."

One did not say no to the queen's brother, of course, so that had settled the matter, but Stark had not been happy. "You will not like the ride, I promise you that," he'd said curtly, and since the moment they set out, he had done all he could to live up to that promise.

By the end of the first week, Tyrion's thighs were raw from hard riding, his legs were cramping badly, and he was chilled to the bone. He did not complain. He was damned if he would give Benjen Stark that satisfaction.

He took a small revenge in the matter of his riding fur, a tattered bearskin, old and musty-smelling. Stark had offered it to him in an excess of Night's Watch gallantry, no doubt expecting him to graciously decline. Tyrion had accepted with a smile. He had brought his warmest clothing with him when they rode out of Winterfell, and soon discovered that it was nowhere near warm enough. It was *cold* up here, and growing colder. The nights were well below freezing now, and when the wind blew it was like a knife cutting right through his warmest woolens. By now Stark was no doubt regretting his chivalrous impulse. Perhaps he had learned a lesson. The Lannisters never declined, graciously or otherwise. The Lannisters took what was offered.

Farms and holdfasts grew scarcer and smaller as they pressed northward, ever deeper into the darkness of the wolfswood, until finally there were no more roofs to shelter under, and they were thrown back on their own resources.

Tyrion was never much use in making a camp or breaking one. Too small, too hobbled, too in-the-way. So while Stark and Yoren and the other men erected rude shelters, tended the horses, and built a fire, it became his custom to take his fur and a wineskin and go off by himself to read.

On the eighteenth night of their journey, the wine was a rare sweet amber from the Summer Isles that he had brought all the way north from Casterly Rock, and the book a rumination on the history and properties of dragons. With Lord Eddard Stark's permission, Tyrion had borrowed a few rare volumes from the Winterfell library and packed them for the ride north.

He found a comfortable spot just beyond the noise of the camp, beside a swift-running stream with waters clear and cold as ice. A grotesquely ancient oak provided shelter from the biting wind. Tyrion curled up in his fur with his back against the trunk, took a sip of the wine, and began to read about the properties of dragonbone. *Dragonbone is black because of its high iron content,* the book told him. *It is strong as steel, yet lighter and far more flexible, and of course utterly impervious to fire. Dragonbone bows are greatly prized by the Dothraki, and small wonder. An archer so armed can outrange any wooden bow.*

Tyrion had a morbid fascination with dragons. When he had first come to King's Landing for his sister's wedding to Robert Baratheon, he had made it a point to seek out the dragon skulls that had hung on the walls of Targaryen's throne room. King Robert had replaced them with banners and tapestries, but Tyrion had persisted until he found the skulls in the dank cellar where they had been stored.

He had expected to find them impressive, perhaps even frightening. He had not thought to find them beautiful. Yet they were. As black as onyx, polished smooth, so the bone seemed to shimmer in the light of his torch. They liked the fire, he sensed. He'd thrust the torch into the mouth of one of the larger skulls and made the shadows leap and dance on the wall behind him. The teeth were long, curving knives of black diamond. The flame of the torch was nothing to them; they had bathed in the heat of far greater fires. When he had moved away, Tyrion could have sworn that the beast's empty eye sockets had watched him go.

There were nineteen skulls. The oldest was more than three thousand years old; the youngest a mere century and a half. The most recent were also the smallest; a matched pair no bigger than mastiff's skulls, and oddly misshapen, all that remained of the last two hatchlings born on Dragonstone. They were the last of the Targaryen dragons, perhaps the last dragons anywhere, and they had not lived very long.

From there the skulls ranged upward in size to the three great monsters of song and story, the dragons that Aegon Targaryen and his sisters had unleashed on the Seven Kingdoms of old. The singers had given them the names of gods: Balerion, Meraxes, Vhaghar. Tyrion had stood between their gaping jaws, wordless and awed. You could have ridden a horse down Vhaghar's gullet, although you would not have ridden it out again. Meraxes was even bigger. And the greatest of them, Balerion, the Black Dread, could have swallowed an aurochs whole, or even one of the hairy mammoths said to roam the cold wastes beyond the Port of Ibben.

Tyrion stood in that dank cellar for a long time, staring at Balerion's huge, empty-eyed skull until his torch burned low, trying to grasp the size of the living animal, to imagine how it must have looked when it spread its great black wings and swept across the skies, breathing fire.

His own remote ancestor, King Loren of the Rock, had tried to stand against the fire when he joined with King Mern of the Reach to oppose the Targaryen conquest. That was close on three hundred years ago, when the Seven Kingdoms *were* kingdoms, and not mere provinces of a greater realm. Between them, the Two Kings had six hundred banners flying, five thousand mounted knights, and ten times as many freeriders and men-at-arms. Aegon Dragonlord had perhaps a fifth that number, the chroniclers said, and most of those were conscripts from the ranks of the last king he had slain, their loyalties uncertain.

The hosts met on the broad plains of the Reach, amidst golden fields of wheat ripe for harvest. When the Two Kings charged, the Targaryen army shivered and shattered and began to run. For a few moments, the chroniclers wrote, the conquest was at an end . . . but only for those few moments, before Aegon Targaryen and his sisters joined the battle.

It was the only time that Vhaghar, Meraxes, and Balerion were all unleashed at once. The singers called it the Field of Fire.

Near four thousand men had burned that day, among them King Mern of the Reach. King Loren had escaped, and lived long enough to surrender, pledge his fealty to the Targaryens, and beget a son, for which Tyrion was duly grateful.

"Why do you read so much?"

Tyrion looked up at the sound of the voice. Jon Snow was standing a few feet away, regarding him curiously. He closed the book on a finger and said, "Look at me and tell me what you see."

The boy looked at him suspiciously. "Is this some kind of trick? I see you. Tyrion Lannister."

Tyrion sighed. "You are remarkably polite for a bastard, Snow. What you see is a dwarf. You are what, twelve?"

"Fourteen," the boy said.

"Fourteen, and you're taller than I will ever be. My legs are short and twisted, and I walk with difficulty. I require a special saddle to keep from falling off my horse. A saddle of my own design, you may be interested to know. It was either that or ride a pony. My arms are strong enough, but again, too short. I will never make a swordsman. Had I been born a peasant, they might have left me out to die, or sold me to some slaver's grotesquerie. Alas, I was born a Lannister of Casterly Rock, and the grotesqueries are all the poorer. Things are expected of me. My father was the Hand of the King for twenty years. My brother later killed that very same king, as it turns out, but life is full of these little ironies. My sister married the new king and my repulsive nephew will be king after him. I must do my part for the honor of my House, wouldn't you agree? Yet how? Well, my legs may be too small for my body, but my head is too large, although I prefer to think it is just large enough for my mind. I have a realistic grasp of my own strengths and weaknesses. My mind is my weapon. My brother has his sword, King Robert has his warhammer, and I have my mind . . . and a mind needs books as a sword needs a whetstone, if it is to keep its edge." Tyrion tapped the leather cover of the book. "That's why I read so much, Jon Snow."

The boy absorbed that all in silence. He had the Stark face if not the name: long, solemn, guarded, a face that gave nothing away. Whoever his mother had been, she had left little of herself in her son. "What are you reading about?" he asked.

"Dragons," Tyrion told him.

"What good is that? There are no more dragons," the boy said with the easy certainty of youth.

"So they say," Tyrion replied. "Sad, isn't it? When I was your age, I used to dream of having a dragon of my own."

"You did?" the boy said suspiciously. Perhaps he thought Tyrion was making fun of him.

"Oh, yes. Even a stunted, twisted, ugly little boy can look down over the world when he's seated on a dragon's back." Tyrion pushed the bearskin aside and climbed to his feet. "I used to start fires in the bowels of Casterly Rock and stare at the flames for hours, pretending they were dragonfire. Sometimes I'd imagine my father burning. At other times, my sister." Jon Snow was staring at him, a look equal parts horror and fascination. Tyrion guffawed. "Don't look at me that way, bastard. I know your secret. You've dreamt the same kind of dreams."

"No," Jon Snow said, horrified. "I wouldn't . . ."

"No? Never?" Tyrion raised an eyebrow. "Well, no doubt the Starks have been terribly good to you. I'm certain Lady Stark treats you as if you were one of her own. And your brother Robb, he's always been kind, and why not? He gets Winterfell and you get the Wall. And your father . . . he must have good reasons for packing you off to the Night's Watch . . ."

"Stop it," Jon Snow said, his face dark with anger. "The Night's Watch is a noble calling!"

Tyrion laughed. "You're too smart to believe that. The Night's Watch is a midden heap for all the misfits of the realm. I've seen you looking at Yoren and his boys. Those are your new brothers, Jon Snow, how do you like them? Sullen peasants, debtors, poachers, rapers, thieves, and bastards like you all wind up on the Wall, watching for grumkins and snarks and all the other monsters your wet nurse warned you about. The good part is there are no grumkins or snarks, so it's scarcely dangerous work. The bad part is you freeze your balls off, but since you're not allowed to breed anyway, I don't suppose that matters."

"*Stop it!*" the boy screamed. He took a step forward, his hands coiling into fists, close to tears.

Suddenly, absurdly, Tyrion felt guilty. He took a step forward, intending to give the boy a reassuring pat on the shoulder or mutter some word of apology.

He never saw the wolf, where it was or how it came at him. One moment he was walking toward Snow and the next he was flat on his back on the hard rocky ground, the book spinning away from him as he fell, the breath going out of him at the sudden impact, his mouth full of dirt and blood and rotting leaves. As he tried to get up, his back spasmed painfully. He must have wrenched it in the fall. He ground his teeth in frustration, grabbed a root, and pulled himself back to a sitting position. "Help me," he said to the boy, reaching up a hand.

And suddenly the wolf was between them. He did not growl. The damned thing never made a sound. He only looked at him with those bright red eyes, and showed him his teeth, and that was more than enough. Tyrion sagged back to the ground with a grunt. "Don't help me, then. I'll sit right here until you leave."

Jon Snow stroked Ghost's thick white fur, smiling now. "Ask me nicely."

Tyrion Lannister felt the anger coiling inside him, and crushed it out with a will. It was not the first time in his life he had been humiliated, and it would not be the last. Perhaps he even deserved this. "I should be very grateful for your kind assistance, Jon," he said mildly.

"Down, Ghost," the boy said. The direwolf sat on his haunches. Those red eyes never left Tyrion. Jon came around behind him, slid his hands under his arms, and lifted him easily to his feet. Then he picked up the book and handed it back.

"Why did he attack me?" Tyrion asked with a sidelong glance at the direwolf. He wiped blood and dirt from his mouth with the back of his hand.

"Maybe he thought you were a grumkin."

Tyrion glanced at him sharply. Then he laughed, a raw

snort of amusement that came bursting out through his nose entirely without his permission. "Oh, gods," he said, choking on his laughter and shaking his head, "I suppose I do rather look like a grumkin. What does he do to snarks?"

"You don't want to know." Jon picked up the wineskin and handed it to Tyrion.

Tyrion pulled out the stopper, tilted his head, and squeezed a long stream into his mouth. The wine was cool fire as it trickled down his throat and warmed his belly. He held out the skin to Jon Snow. "Want some?"

The boy took the skin and tried a cautious swallow. "It's true, isn't it?" he said when he was done. "What you said about the Night's Watch."

Tyrion nodded.

Jon Snow set his mouth in a grim line. "If that's what it is, that's what it is."

Tyrion grinned at him. "That's good, bastard. Most men would rather deny a hard truth than face it."

"Most men," the boy said. "But not you."

"No," Tyrion admitted, "not me. I seldom even dream of dragons anymore. There are no dragons." He scooped up the fallen bearskin. "Come, we had better return to camp before your uncle calls the banners."

The walk was short, but the ground was rough underfoot and his legs were cramping badly by the time they got back. Jon Snow offered a hand to help him over a thick tangle of roots, but Tyrion shook him off. He would make his own way, as he had all his life. Still, the camp was a welcome sight. The shelters had been thrown up against the tumbledown wall of a long-abandoned hold-fast, a shield against the wind. The horses had been fed and a fire had been laid. Yoren sat on a stone, skinning a squirrel. The savory smell of stew filled Tyrion's nostrils. He dragged himself over to where his man Morrec was tending the stewpot. Wordlessly, Morrec handed him the ladle. Tyrion tasted and handed it back. "More pepper," he said.

Benjen Stark emerged from the shelter he shared with his nephew. "There you are. Jon, damn it, don't go off like that by yourself. I thought the Others had gotten you."

"It was the grumkins," Tyrion told him, laughing. Jon Snow smiled. Stark shot a baffled look at Yoren. The old man grunted, shrugged, and went back to his bloody work.

The squirrel gave some body to the stew, and they ate it with black bread and hard cheese that night around their fire. Tyrion shared around his skin of wine until even Yoren grew mellow. One by one the company drifted off to their shelters and to sleep, all but Jon Snow, who had drawn the night's first watch.

Tyrion was the last to retire, as always. As he stepped into the shelter his men had built for him, he paused and looked back at Jon Snow. The boy stood near the fire, his face still and hard, looking deep into the flames.

Tyrion Lannister smiled sadly and went to bed.

CATELYN

Ned and the girls were eight days gone when Maester Luwin came to her one night in Bran's sickroom, carrying a reading lamp and the books of account. "It is past time that we reviewed the figures, my lady," he said. "You'll want to know how much this royal visit cost us."

Catelyn looked at Bran in his sickbed and brushed his hair back off his forehead. It had grown very long, she realized. She would have to cut it soon. "I have no need to look at figures, Maester Luwin," she told him, never taking her eyes from Bran. "I know what the visit cost us. Take the books away."

"My lady, the king's party had healthy appetites. We must replenish our stores before—"

She cut him off. "I said, take the books away. The steward will attend to our needs."

"We have no steward," Maester Luwin reminded her. Like a little grey rat, she thought, he would not let go. "Poole went south to establish Lord Eddard's household at King's Landing."

Catelyn nodded absently. "Oh, yes. I remember." Bran looked so pale. She wondered whether they might move his bed under the window, so he could get the morning sun.

Maester Luwin set the lamp in a niche by the door and fiddled with its wick. "There are several appointments that require your immediate attention, my lady. Besides the steward, we need a captain of the guards to fill Jory's place, a new master of horse—"

Her eyes snapped around and found him. "A master of *horse*?" Her voice was a whip.

The maester was shaken. "Yes, my lady. Hullen rode south with Lord Eddard, so—"

"My son lies here broken and dying, Luwin, and you wish to discuss a new master of *horse*? Do you think I care what happens in the stables? Do you think it matters to me one whit? I would gladly butcher every horse in Winterfell with my own hands if it would open Bran's eyes, do you understand that? *Do you!*"

He bowed his head. "Yes, my lady, but the appointments—"

"I'll make the appointments," Robb said.

Catelyn had not heard him enter, but there he stood in the doorway, looking at her. She had been shouting, she realized with a sudden flush of shame. What was happening to her? She was so tired, and her head hurt all the time.

Maester Luwin looked from Catelyn to her son. "I have prepared a list of those we might wish to consider for the vacant offices," he said, offering Robb a paper plucked from his sleeve.

Her son glanced at the names. He had come from outside, Catelyn saw; his cheeks were red from the cold, his hair shaggy and windblown. "Good men," he said. "We'll talk about them tomorrow." He handed back the list of names.

"Very good, my lord." The paper vanished into his sleeve.

"Leave us now," Robb said. Maester Luwin bowed and departed. Robb closed the door behind him and turned to her. He was wearing a sword, she saw. "Mother, what are you doing?"

Catelyn had always thought Robb looked like her; like Bran and Rickon and Sansa, he had the Tully coloring, the auburn hair, the blue eyes. Yet now for the first time she saw something of Eddard Stark in his face, something as stern and hard as the north. "What am I doing?" she echoed, puzzled. "How can you ask that? What do you imagine I'm doing? I am taking care of your brother. I am taking care of Bran."

"Is that what you call it? You haven't left this room since Bran was hurt. You didn't even come to the gate when Father and the girls went south."

"I said my farewells to them here, and watched them ride out from that window." She had begged Ned not to go, not now, not after what had happened; everything had changed now, couldn't he see that? It was no use. He had no choice, he had told her, and then he left, choosing. "I can't leave him, even for a moment, not when any moment could be his last. I have to be with him, if . . . if . . ." She took her son's limp hand, sliding his fingers through her own. He was so frail and thin, with no strength left in his hand, but she could still feel the warmth of life through his skin.

Robb's voice softened. "He's not going to die, Mother. Maester Luwin says the time of greatest danger has passed."

"And what if Maester Luwin is wrong? What if Bran needs me and I'm not here?"

"*Rickon* needs you," Robb said sharply. "He's only three, he doesn't understand what's happening. He thinks everyone has deserted him, so he follows me around all day, clutching my leg and crying. I don't know what to do with him." He paused a moment, chewing on his lower lip the way he'd done when he was little. "Mother, *I* need you too. I'm trying but I can't . . . I can't do it all by myself." His voice broke with sudden emotion, and Catelyn remembered that he was only fourteen. She wanted to get up and go to him, but Bran was still holding her hand and she could not move.

Outside the tower, a wolf began to howl. Catelyn trembled, just for a second.

"Bran's." Robb opened the window and let the night air into the stuffy tower room. The howling grew louder. It was a cold and lonely sound, full of melancholy and despair.

"Don't," she told him. "Bran needs to stay warm."

"He needs to hear them sing," Robb said. Somewhere

out in Winterfell, a second wolf began to howl in chorus with the first. Then a third, closer. "Shaggydog and Grey Wind," Robb said as their voices rose and fell together. "You can tell them apart if you listen close."

Catelyn was shaking. It was the grief, the cold, the howling of the direwolves. Night after night, the howling and the cold wind and the grey empty castle, on and on they went, never changing, and her boy lying there broken, the sweetest of her children, the gentlest, Bran who loved to laugh and climb and dreamt of knighthood, all gone now, she would never hear him laugh again. Sobbing, she pulled her hand free of his and covered her ears against those terrible howls. "Make them stop!" she cried. "I can't stand it, make them stop, make them stop, kill them all if you must, just make them *stop!*"

She didn't remember falling to the floor, but there she was, and Robb was lifting her, holding her in strong arms. "Don't be afraid, Mother. They would never hurt him." He helped her to her narrow bed in the corner of the sickroom. "Close your eyes," he said gently. "Rest. Maester Luwin tells me you've hardly slept since Bran's fall."

"I *can't,*" she wept. "Gods forgive me, Robb, I can't, what if he dies while I'm asleep, what if he dies, what if he dies . . ." The wolves were still howling. She screamed and held her ears again. "Oh, gods, close the window!"

"If you swear to me you'll sleep." Robb went to the window, but as he reached for the shutters another sound was added to the mournful howling of the direwolves. "Dogs," he said, listening. "All the dogs are barking. They've never done that before . . ." Catelyn heard his breath catch in his throat. When she looked up, his face was pale in the lamplight. *"Fire,"* he whispered.

Fire, she thought, and then, *Bran!* "Help me," she said urgently, sitting up. "Help me with Bran."

Robb did not seem to hear her. "The library tower's on fire," he said.

Catelyn could see the flickering reddish light through the open window now. She sagged with relief. Bran was safe. The library was across the bailey, there was no way the fire would reach them here. "Thank the gods," she whispered.

Robb looked at her as if she'd gone mad. "Mother, stay here. I'll come back as soon as the fire's out." He ran then. She heard him shout to the guards outside the room, heard them descending together in a wild rush, taking the stairs two and three at a time.

Outside, there were shouts of "Fire!" in the yard, screams, running footsteps, the whinny of frightened horses, and the frantic barking of the castle dogs. The howling was gone, she realized as she listened to the cacophony. The direwolves had fallen silent.

Catelyn said a silent prayer of thanks to the seven faces of god as she went to the window. Across the bailey, long tongues of flame shot from the windows of the library. She watched the smoke rise into the sky and thought sadly of all the books the Starks had gathered over the centuries. Then she closed the shutters.

When she turned away from the window, the man was in the room with her.

"You weren't s'posed to be here," he muttered sourly. "No one was s'posed to be here."

He was a small, dirty man in filthy brown clothing, and he stank of horses. Catelyn knew all the men who worked in their stables, and he was none of them. He was gaunt, with limp blond hair and pale eyes deep-sunk in a bony face, and there was a dagger in his hand.

Catelyn looked at the knife, then at Bran. "No," she said. The word stuck in her throat, the merest whisper.

He must have heard her. "It's a mercy," he said. "He's dead already."

"No," Catelyn said, louder now as she found her voice again. "No, you *can't*." She spun back toward the window to scream for help, but the man moved faster than she would have believed. One hand clamped down over her mouth and yanked back her head, the other brought the dagger up to her windpipe. The stench of him was overwhelming.

She reached up with both hands and grabbed the blade with all her strength, pulling it away from her throat. She heard him cursing into her ear. Her fingers were slippery with blood, but she would not let go of the dagger. The hand over her mouth clenched more tightly, shutting off her air. Catelyn twisted her head to the side and managed to get a piece of his flesh between her teeth. She bit down hard into his palm. The man grunted in pain. She ground her teeth together and tore at him, and all of a sudden he let go. The taste of his blood filled her mouth. She sucked in air and screamed, and he grabbed her hair and pulled her away from him, and she stumbled and went down, and then he was standing over her, breathing hard, shaking. The dagger was still clutched tightly in his right hand, slick with blood. "You weren't s'posed to be here," he repeated stupidly.

Catelyn saw the shadow slip through the open door behind him. There was a low rumble, less than a snarl, the merest whisper of a threat, but he must have heard something, because he started to turn just as the wolf made its leap. They went down together, half sprawled over Catelyn where she'd fallen. The wolf had him under the jaw. The man's shriek lasted less than a second before the beast wrenched back its head, taking out half his throat.

His blood felt like warm rain as it sprayed across her face.

The wolf was looking at her. Its jaws were red and wet and its eyes glowed golden in the dark room. It was Bran's wolf, she realized. Of course it was. "Thank you," Catelyn whispered, her voice faint and tiny. She lifted her hand, trembling. The wolf padded closer, sniffed at her fingers, then licked at the blood with a wet rough tongue. When it had cleaned all the blood off her hand, it turned away silently and jumped up on Bran's bed and lay down beside him. Catelyn began to laugh hysterically.

That was the way they found them, when Robb and Maester Luwin and Ser Rodrik burst in with half the guards in Winterfell. When the laughter finally died in her throat, they wrapped her in warm blankets and led her back to the Great Keep, to her own chambers. Old Nan undressed her and helped her into a scalding hot bath and washed the blood off her with a soft cloth.

Afterward Maester Luwin arrived to dress her wounds. The cuts in her fingers went deep, almost to the bone, and her scalp was raw and bleeding where he'd pulled out a handful of hair. The maester told her the pain was just starting now, and gave her milk of the poppy to help her sleep.

Finally she closed her eyes.

When she opened them again, they told her that she had slept four days. Catelyn nodded and sat up in bed. It all seemed like a nightmare to her now, everything since Bran's fall, a terrible dream of blood and grief, but she had the pain in her hands to remind her that it was real. She felt weak and light-headed, yet strangely resolute, as if a great weight had lifted from her.

"Bring me some bread and honey," she told her servants, "and take word to Maester Luwin that my bandages want changing." They looked at her in surprise and ran to do her bidding.

Catelyn remembered the way she had been before, and she was ashamed. She had let them all down, her children, her husband, her House. It would not happen again. She would show these northerners how strong a Tully of Riverrun could be.

Robb arrived before her food. Rodrik Cassel came with him, and her husband's ward Theon Greyjoy, and lastly Hallis Mollen, a muscular guardsman with a square brown beard. He was the new captain of the guard, Robb said. Her son was dressed in boiled leather and ringmail, she saw, and a sword hung at his waist.

"Who was he?" Catelyn asked them.

"No one knows his name," Hallis Mollen told her. "He was no man of Winterfell, m'lady, but some says they seen him here and about the castle these past few weeks."

"One of the king's men, then," she said, "or one of the Lannisters'. He could have waited behind when the others left."

"Maybe," Hal said. "With all these strangers filling up Winterfell of late, there's no way of saying who he belonged to."

"He'd been hiding in your stables," Greyjoy said. "You could smell it on him."

"And how could he go unnoticed?" she said sharply.

Hallis Mollen looked abashed. "Between the horses Lord Eddard took south and them we sent north to the Night's Watch, the stalls were half-empty. It were no great trick to hide from the stableboys. Could be Hodor saw him, the talk is that boy's been acting queer, but simple as he is . . ." Hal shook his head.

"We found where he'd been sleeping," Robb put in.

"He had ninety silver stags in a leather bag buried beneath the straw."

"It's good to know my son's life was not sold cheaply," Catelyn said bitterly.

Hallis Mollen looked at her, confused. "Begging your grace, m'lady, you saying he was out to kill your *boy*?"

Greyjoy was doubtful. "That's madness."

"He came for Bran," Catelyn said. "He kept muttering how I wasn't supposed to be there. He set the library fire thinking I would rush to put it out, taking any guards with me. If I hadn't been half-mad with grief, it would have worked."

"Why would anyone want to kill Bran?" Robb said. "Gods, he's only a little boy, helpless, sleeping . . ."

Catelyn gave her firstborn a challenging look. "If you are to rule in the north, you must think these things through, Robb. Answer your own question. Why would anyone want to kill a sleeping child?"

Before he could answer, the servants returned with a plate of food fresh from the kitchen. There was much more than she'd asked for: hot bread, butter and honey and blackberry preserves, a rasher of bacon and a soft-boiled egg, a wedge of cheese, a pot of mint tea. And with it came Maester Luwin.

"How is my son, Maester?" Catelyn looked at all the food and found she had no appetite.

Maester Luwin lowered his eyes. "Unchanged, my lady."

It was the reply she had expected, no more and no less. Her hands throbbed with pain, as if the blade were still in her, cutting deep. She sent the servants away and looked back to Robb. "Do you have the answer yet?"

"Someone is afraid Bran might wake up," Robb said, "afraid of what he might say or do, afraid of something he knows."

Catelyn was proud of him. "Very good." She turned to the new captain of the guard. "We must keep Bran safe. If there was one killer, there could be others."

"How many guards do you want, m'lady?" Hal asked.

"So long as Lord Eddard is away, my son is the master of Winterfell," she told him.

Robb stood a little taller. "Put one man in the sickroom, night and day, one outside the door, two at the bottom of the stairs. No one sees Bran without my warrant or my mother's."

"As you say, m'lord."

"Do it now," Catelyn suggested.

"And let his wolf stay in the room with him," Robb added.

"Yes," Catelyn said. And then again: "Yes."

Hallis Mollen bowed and left the room.

"Lady Stark," Ser Rodrik said when the guardsman had gone, "did you chance to notice the dagger the killer used?"

"The circumstances did not allow me to examine it closely, but I can vouch for its edge," Catelyn replied with a dry smile. "Why do you ask?"

"We found the knife still in the villain's grasp. It seemed to me that it was altogether too fine a weapon for such a man, so I looked at it long and hard. The blade is Valyrian steel, the hilt dragonbone. A weapon like that has no business being in the hands of such as him. Someone gave it to him."

Catelyn nodded, thoughtful. "Robb, close the door."

He looked at her strangely, but did as she told him.

"What I am about to tell you must not leave this room," she told them. "I want your oaths on that. If even part of what I suspect is true, Ned and my girls have ridden into deadly danger, and a word in the wrong ears could mean their lives."

"Lord Eddard is a second father to me," said Theon Greyjoy. "I do so swear."

"You have my oath," Maester Luwin said.

"And mine, my lady," echoed Ser Rodrik.

She looked at her son. "And you, Robb?"

He nodded his consent.

"My sister Lysa believes the Lannisters murdered her husband, Lord Arryn, the Hand of the King," Catelyn told them. "It comes to me that Jaime Lannister did not join the hunt the day Bran fell. He remained here in the castle." The room was deathly quiet. "I do not think Bran fell from that tower," she said into the stillness. "I think he was thrown."

The shock was plain on their faces. "My lady, that is a monstrous suggestion," said Rodrik Cassel. "Even the

Kingslayer would flinch at the murder of an innocent child."

"Oh, would he?" Theon Greyjoy asked. "I wonder."

"There is no limit to Lannister pride or Lannister ambition," Catelyn said.

"The boy had always been surehanded in the past," Maester Luwin said thoughtfully. "He knew every stone in Winterfell."

"*Gods*," Robb swore, his young face dark with anger. "If this is true, he will pay for it." He drew his sword and waved it in the air. "I'll kill him myself!"

Ser Rodrik bristled at him. "Put that away! The Lannisters are a hundred leagues away. *Never* draw your sword unless you mean to use it. How many times must I tell you, foolish boy?"

Abashed, Robb sheathed his sword, suddenly a child again. Catelyn said to Ser Rodrik, "I see my son is wearing steel now."

The old master-at-arms said, "I thought it was time."

Robb was looking at her anxiously. "Past time," she said. "Winterfell may have need of all its swords soon, and they had best not be made of wood."

Theon Greyjoy put a hand on the hilt of his blade and said, "My lady, if it comes to that, my House owes yours a great debt."

Maester Luwin pulled at his chain collar where it chafed against his neck. "All we have is conjecture. This is the queen's beloved brother we mean to accuse. She will not take it kindly. We must have proof, or forever keep silent."

"Your proof is in the dagger," Ser Rodrik said. "A fine blade like that will not have gone unnoticed."

There was only one place to find the truth of it, Catelyn realized. "Someone must go to King's Landing."

"I'll go," Robb said.

"No," she told him. "Your place is here. There must always be a Stark in Winterfell." She looked at Ser Rodrik with his great white whiskers, at Maester Luwin in his grey robes, at young Greyjoy, lean and dark and impetuous. Who to send? Who would be believed? Then she knew. Catelyn struggled to push back the blankets, her bandaged fingers as stiff and unyielding as stone. She climbed out of bed. "I must go myself."

"My lady," said Maester Luwin, "is that wise? Surely the Lannisters would greet your arrival with suspicion."

"What about Bran?" Robb asked. The poor boy looked utterly confused now. "You can't mean to leave him."

"I have done everything I can for Bran," she said, laying a wounded hand on his arm. "His life is in the hands of the gods and Maester Luwin. As you reminded me yourself, Robb, I have other children to think of now."

"You will need a strong escort, my lady," Theon said.

"I'll send Hal with a squad of guardsmen," Robb said.

"No," Catelyn said. "A large party attracts unwelcome attention. I would not have the Lannisters know I am coming."

Ser Rodrik protested. "My lady, let me accompany you at least. The kingsroad can be perilous for a woman alone."

"I will not be taking the kingsroad," Catelyn replied. She thought for a moment, then nodded her consent. "Two riders can move as fast as one, and a good deal faster than a long column burdened by wagons and wheelhouses. I will welcome your company, Ser Rodrik. We will follow the White Knife down to the sea, and hire a ship at White Harbor. Strong horses and brisk winds should bring us to King's Landing well ahead of Ned and the Lannisters." *And then,* she thought, *we shall see what we shall see.*

SANSA

Eddard Stark had left before dawn, Septa Mordane informed Sansa as they broke their fast. "The king sent for him. Another hunt, I do believe. There are still wild aurochs in these lands, I am told."

"I've never seen an aurochs," Sansa said, feeding a piece of bacon to Lady under the table. The direwolf took it from her hand, as delicate as a queen.

Septa Mordane sniffed in disapproval. "A noble lady does not feed dogs at her table," she said, breaking off another piece of comb and letting the honey drip down onto her bread.

"She's not a dog, she's a direwolf," Sansa pointed out as Lady licked her fingers with a rough tongue. "Anyway, Father said we could keep them with us if we want."

The septa was not appeased. "You're a good girl, Sansa, but I do vow, when it comes to that creature you're as willful as your sister Arya." She scowled. "And where is Arya this morning?"

"She wasn't hungry," Sansa said, knowing full well that her sister had probably stolen down to the kitchen hours ago and wheedled a breakfast out of some cook's boy.

"Do remind her to dress nicely today. The grey velvet, perhaps. We are all invited to ride with the queen and Princess Myrcella in the royal wheelhouse, and we must look our best."

Sansa already looked her best. She had brushed out her long auburn hair until it shone, and picked her nicest blue silks. She had been looking forward to today for more than a week. It was a great honor to ride with the queen, and besides, Prince Joffrey might be there. Her betrothed. Just thinking it made her feel a strange fluttering inside, even though they were not to marry for years and years. Sansa did not really *know* Joffrey yet, but she was already in love with him. He was all she ever dreamt her prince should be, tall and handsome and strong, with hair like gold. She treasured every chance to spend time with him, few as they were. The only thing that scared her about today was Arya. Arya had a way of ruining everything. You never knew what she would do. "I'll tell her," Sansa said uncertainly, "but she'll dress the way she always does." She hoped it wouldn't be too embarrassing. "May I be excused?"

"You may." Septa Mordane helped herself to more bread and honey, and Sansa slid from the bench. Lady followed at her heels as she ran from the inn's common room.

Outside, she stood for a moment amidst the shouts and curses and the creak of wooden wheels as the men broke down the tents and pavilions and loaded the wagons for another day's march. The inn was a sprawling three-story structure of pale stone, the biggest that Sansa had ever seen, but even so, it had accommodations for less than a third of the king's party, which had swollen to more than four hundred with the addition of her father's household and the freeriders who had joined them on the road.

She found Arya on the banks of the Trident, trying to hold Nymeria still while she brushed dried mud from her fur. The direwolf was not enjoying the process. Arya was wearing the same riding leathers she had worn yesterday and the day before.

"You better put on something pretty," Sansa told her. "Septa Mordane said so. We're traveling in the queen's wheelhouse with Princess Myrcella today."

"I'm not," Arya said, trying to brush a tangle out of Nymeria's matted grey fur. "Mycah and I are going to ride upstream and look for rubies at the ford."

"Rubies," Sansa said, lost. "What rubies?"

Arya gave her a look like she was so stupid. "*Rhaegar's* rubies. This is where King Robert killed him and won the crown."

Sansa regarded her scrawny little sister in disbelief. "You can't look for rubies, the princess is expecting us. The queen invited us both."

"I don't care," Arya said. "The wheelhouse doesn't even have *windows*, you can't see a thing."

"What could you want to see?" Sansa said, annoyed. She had been thrilled by the invitation, and her stupid sister was going to ruin everything, just as she'd feared. "It's all just fields and farms and holdfasts."

"It is *not*," Arya said stubbornly. "If you came with us sometimes, you'd see."

"I *hate* riding," Sansa said fervently. "All it does is get you soiled and dusty and sore."

Arya shrugged. "Hold *still*," she snapped at Nymeria, "I'm not hurting you." Then to Sansa she said, "When we were crossing the Neck, I counted thirty-six flowers I never saw before, and Mycah showed me a lizard-lion."

Sansa shuddered. They had been twelve days crossing the Neck, rumbling down a crooked causeway through an endless black bog, and she had hated every moment of it. The air had been damp and clammy, the causeway so narrow they could not even make proper camp at night, they had to stop right on the kingsroad. Dense thickets of half-drowned trees pressed close around them, branches dripping with curtains of pale fungus. Huge flowers bloomed in the mud and floated on pools of stagnant water, but if you were stupid enough to leave the causeway to pluck them, there were quicksands waiting to suck you down, and snakes watching from the trees, and lizard-lions floating half-submerged in the water, like black logs with eyes and teeth.

None of which stopped Arya, of course. One day she came back grinning her horsey grin, her hair all tangled and her clothes covered in mud, clutching a raggedy bunch of purple and green flowers for Father. Sansa kept hoping he would tell Arya to behave herself and act like the highborn lady she was supposed to be, but he never did, he only hugged her and thanked her for the flowers. That just made her worse.

Then it turned out the purple flowers were called *poison kisses*, and Arya got a rash on her arms. Sansa would have thought that might have taught her a lesson, but Arya laughed about it, and the next day she rubbed *mud* all over her arms like some ignorant bog woman just because her friend Mycah told her it would stop the itching. She had bruises on her arms and shoulders too, dark purple welts and faded green-and-yellow splotches; Sansa had seen them when her sister undressed for sleep. How she had gotten *those* only the seven gods knew.

Arya was still going on, brushing out Nymeria's tangles and chattering about things she'd seen on the trek south. "Last week we found this haunted watchtower, and the day before we chased a herd of wild horses. You should have seen them run when they caught a scent of Nymeria." The wolf wriggled in her grasp and Arya scolded her. "Stop that, I have to do the other side, you're all muddy."

"You're not supposed to leave the column," Sansa reminded her. "Father said so."

Arya shrugged. "I didn't go far. Anyway, Nymeria was with me the whole time. I don't always go off, either. Sometimes it's fun just to ride along with the wagons and talk to people."

Sansa knew all about the sorts of people Arya liked to talk to: squires and grooms and serving girls, old men and naked children, rough-spoken freeriders of uncertain birth. Arya would make friends with *anybody*. This Mycah was the worst; a butcher's boy, thirteen and wild, he slept in the meat wagon and smelled of the slaughtering block. Just the sight of him was enough to make Sansa feel sick, but Arya seemed to prefer his company to hers.

Sansa was running out of patience now. "You have to come with me," she told her sister firmly. "You can't refuse the queen. Septa Mordane will expect you."

Arya ignored her. She gave a hard yank with the brush. Nymeria growled and spun away, affronted. "Come *back* here!"

"There's going to be lemon cakes and tea," Sansa went on, all adult and reasonable. Lady brushed against her leg.

Sansa scratched her ears the way she liked, and Lady sat beside her on her haunches, watching Arya chase Nymeria. "Why would you want to ride a smelly old horse and get all sore and sweaty when you could recline on feather pillows and eat cakes with the queen?"

"I don't like the queen," Arya said casually. Sansa sucked in her breath, shocked that even *Arya* would say such a thing, but her sister prattled on, heedless. "She won't even let me bring Nymeria." She thrust the brush under her belt and stalked her wolf. Nymeria watched her approach warily.

"A royal wheelhouse is no place for a *wolf*," Sansa said. "And Princess Myrcella is afraid of them, you know that."

"Myrcella is a little baby." Arya grabbed Nymeria around her neck, but the moment she pulled out the brush again the direwolf wriggled free and bounded off. Frustrated, Arya threw down the brush. "*Bad* wolf!" she shouted.

Sansa couldn't help but smile a little. The kennelmaster once told her that an animal takes after its master. She gave Lady a quick little hug. Lady licked her cheek. Sansa giggled. Arya heard and whirled around, glaring. "I don't care what you say, I'm going out riding." Her long horsey face got the stubborn look that meant she was going to do something willful.

"Gods be true, Arya, sometimes you act like such a *child*," Sansa said. "I'll go by myself then. It will be ever so much nicer that way. Lady and I will eat all the lemon cakes and just have the best time without you."

She turned to walk off, but Arya shouted after her, "They won't let you bring Lady either." She was gone before Sansa could think of a reply, chasing Nymeria along the river.

Alone and humiliated, Sansa took the long way back to the inn, where she knew Septa Mordane would be waiting. Lady padded quietly by her side. She was almost in tears. All she wanted was for things to be nice and pretty, the way they were in the songs. Why couldn't Arya be sweet and delicate and kind, like Princess Myrcella? She would have liked a sister like that.

Sansa could never understand how two sisters, born only two years apart, could be so different. It would have been easier if Arya had been a bastard, like their half brother Jon. She even *looked* like Jon, with the long face and brown hair of the Starks, and nothing of their lady mother in her face or her coloring. And Jon's mother had been *common*, or so people whispered. Once, when she was littler, Sansa had even asked Mother if perhaps there hadn't been some mistake. Perhaps the grumkins had stolen her *real* sister. But Mother had only laughed and said no, Arya was her daughter and Sansa's trueborn sister, blood of their blood. Sansa could not think why Mother would want to lie about it, so she supposed it had to be true.

As she neared the center of camp, her distress was quickly forgotten. A crowd had gathered around the queen's wheelhouse. Sansa heard excited voices buzzing like a hive of bees. The doors had been thrown open, she saw, and the queen stood at the top of the wooden steps, smiling down at someone. She heard her saying, "The council does us great honor, my good lords."

"What's happening?" she asked a squire she knew.

"The council sent riders from King's Landing to escort us the rest of the way," he told her. "An honor guard for the king."

Anxious to see, Sansa let Lady clear a path through the crowd. People moved aside hastily for the direwolf. When she got closer, she saw two knights kneeling before the queen, in armor so fine and gorgeous that it made her blink.

One knight wore an intricate suit of white enameled scales, brilliant as a field of new-fallen snow, with silver chasings and clasps that glittered in the sun. When he removed his helm, Sansa saw that he was an old man with hair as pale as his armor, yet he seemed strong and graceful for all that. From his shoulders hung the pure white cloak of the Kingsguard.

His companion was a man near twenty whose armor was steel plate of a deep forest-green. He was the handsomest man Sansa had ever set eyes upon; tall and powerfully made, with jet-black hair that fell to his shoulders and framed a clean-shaven face, and laughing green eyes to match his armor. Cradled under one arm was an antlered helm, its magnificent rack shimmering in gold.

At first Sansa did not notice the third stranger. He did

not kneel with the others. He stood to one side, beside their horses, a gaunt grim man who watched the proceedings in silence. His face was pockmarked and beardless, with deepset eyes and hollow cheeks. Though he was not an old man, only a few wisps of hair remained to him, sprouting above his ears, but those he had grown long as a woman's. His armor was iron-grey chainmail over layers of boiled leather, plain and unadorned, and it spoke of age and hard use. Above his right shoulder the stained leather hilt of the blade strapped to his back was visible; a two-handed greatsword, too long to be worn at his side.

"The king is gone hunting, but I know he will be pleased to see you when he returns," the queen was saying to the two knights who knelt before her, but Sansa could not take her eyes off the third man. He seemed to feel the weight of her gaze. Slowly he turned his head. Lady growled. A terror as overwhelming as anything Sansa Stark had ever felt filled her suddenly. She stepped backward and bumped into someone.

Strong hands grasped her by the shoulders, and for a moment Sansa thought it was her father, but when she turned, it was the burned face of Sandor Clegane looking down at her, his mouth twisted in a terrible mockery of a smile. "You are shaking, girl," he said, his voice rasping. "Do I frighten you so much?"

He did, and had since she had first laid eyes on the ruin that fire had made of his face, though it seemed to her now that he was not half so terrifying as the other. Still, Sansa wrenched away from him, and the Hound laughed, and Lady moved between them, rumbling a warning. Sansa dropped to her knees to wrap her arms around the wolf. They were all gathered around gaping, she could feel their eyes on her, and here and there she heard muttered comments and titters of laughter.

"A wolf," a man said, and someone else said, "Seven hells, that's a direwolf," and the first man said, "What's it doing in camp?" and the Hound's rasping voice replied, "The Starks use them for wet nurses," and Sansa realized that the two stranger knights were looking down on her and Lady, swords in their hands, and then she was frightened again, and ashamed. Tears filled her eyes.

She heard the queen say, "Joffrey, go to her."

And her prince was there.

"Leave her alone," Joffrey said. He stood over her, beautiful in blue wool and black leather, his golden curls shining in the sun like a crown. He gave her his hand, drew her to her feet. "What is it, sweet lady? Why are you afraid? No one will hurt you. Put away your swords, all of you. The wolf is her little pet, that's all." He looked at Sandor Clegane. "And you, dog, away with you, you're scaring my betrothed."

The Hound, ever faithful, bowed and slid away quietly through the press. Sansa struggled to steady herself. She felt like such a fool. She was a Stark of Winterfell, a noble lady, and someday she would be a queen. "It was not him, my sweet prince," she tried to explain. "It was the other one."

The two stranger knights exchanged a look. "Payne?" chuckled the young man in the green armor.

The older man in white spoke to Sansa gently. "Oft-times Ser Ilyn frightens me as well, sweet lady. He has a fearsome aspect."

"As well he should." The queen had descended from the wheelhouse. The spectators parted to make way for her. "If the wicked do not fear the King's Justice, you have put the wrong man in the office."

Sansa finally found her words. "Then surely you have chosen the right one, Your Grace," she said, and a gale of laughter erupted all around her.

"Well spoken, child," said the old man in white. "As befits the daughter of Eddard Stark. I am honored to know you, however irregular the manner of our meeting. I am Ser Barristan Selmy, of the Kingsguard." He bowed.

Sansa knew the name, and now the courtesies that Septa Mordane had taught her over the years came back to her. "The Lord Commander of the Kingsguard," she said, "and councillor to Robert our king and to Aerys Targaryen before him. The honor is mine, good knight. Even in the far north, the singers praise the deeds of Barristan the Bold."

The green knight laughed again. "Barristan the Old, you mean. Don't flatter him too sweetly, child, he thinks overmuch of himself already." He smiled at her. "Now, wolf girl, if you can put a name to me as well, then I must concede that you are truly our Hand's daughter."

Joffrey stiffened beside her. "Have a care how you address my betrothed."

"I can answer," Sansa said quickly, to quell her prince's anger. She smiled at the green knight. "Your helmet bears golden antlers, my lord. The stag is the sigil of the royal House. King Robert has two brothers. By your extreme youth, you can only be Renly Baratheon, Lord of Storm's End and councillor to the king, and so I name you."

Ser Barristan chuckled. "By his extreme youth, he can only be a prancing jackanapes, and so *I* name him."

There was general laughter, led by Lord Renly himself. The tension of a few moments ago was gone, and Sansa was beginning to feel comfortable . . . until Ser Ilyn Payne shouldered two men aside, and stood before her, unsmiling. He did not say a word. Lady bared her teeth and began to growl, a low rumble full of menace, but this time Sansa silenced the wolf with a gentle hand to the head. "I am sorry if I offended you, Ser Ilyn," she said.

She waited for an answer, but none came. As the headsman looked at her, his pale colorless eyes seemed to strip the clothes away from her, and then the skin, leaving her soul naked before him. Still silent, he turned and walked away.

Sansa did not understand. She looked at her prince. "Did I say something wrong, Your Grace? Why will he not speak to me?"

"Ser Ilyn has not been feeling talkative these past fourteen years," Lord Renly commented with a sly smile.

Joffrey gave his uncle a look of pure loathing, then took Sansa's hands in his own. "Aerys Targaryen had his tongue ripped out with hot pincers."

"He speaks most eloquently with his sword, however," the queen said, "and his devotion to our realm is unquestioned." Then she smiled graciously and said, "Sansa, the good councillors and I must speak together until the king returns with your father. I fear we shall have to postpone your day with Myrcella. Please give your sweet sister my apologies. Joffrey, perhaps you would be so kind as to entertain our guest today."

"It would be my pleasure, Mother," Joffrey said very formally. He took her by the arm and led her away from the wheelhouse, and Sansa's spirits took flight. A whole day with her prince! She gazed at Joffrey worshipfully. He was so gallant, she thought. The way he had rescued her from Ser Ilyn and the Hound, why, it was almost like the songs, like the time Serwyn of the Mirror Shield saved the Princess Daeryssa from the giants, or Prince Aemon the Dragonknight championing Queen Naerys's honor against evil Ser Morgil's slanders.

The touch of Joffrey's hand on her sleeve made her heart beat faster. "What would you like to do?"

Be with you, Sansa thought, but she said, "Whatever you'd like to do, my prince."

Joffrey reflected a moment. "We could go riding."

"Oh, I *love* riding," Sansa said.

Joffrey glanced back at Lady, who was following at their heels. "Your wolf is liable to frighten the horses, and my dog seems to frighten you. Let us leave them both behind and set off on our own, what do you say?"

Sansa hesitated. "If you like," she said uncertainly. "I suppose I could tie Lady up." She did not quite understand, though. "I didn't know you had a dog . . ."

Joffrey laughed. "He's my mother's dog, in truth. She has set him to guard me, and so he does."

"You mean the Hound," she said. She wanted to hit herself for being so slow. Her prince would never love her if she seemed stupid. "Is it safe to leave him behind?"

Prince Joffrey looked annoyed that she would even ask. "Have no fear, lady. I am almost a man grown, and I don't fight with wood like your brothers. All I need is this." He drew his sword and showed it to her; a longsword adroitly shrunken to suit a boy of twelve, gleaming blue steel, castle-forged and double-edged, with a leather grip and a lion's-head pommel in gold. Sansa exclaimed over it admiringly, and Joffrey looked pleased. "I call it Lion's Tooth," he said.

And so they left her direwolf and his bodyguard behind them, while they ranged east along the north bank of the Trident with no company save Lion's Tooth.

It was a glorious day, a magical day. The air was warm and heavy with the scent of flowers, and the woods here had a gentle beauty that Sansa had never seen in the north. Prince Joffrey's mount was a blood bay courser, swift as the wind, and he rode it with reckless abandon, so fast that Sansa was hard-pressed to keep up on her mare. It was a day for adventures. They explored the caves by the riverbank, and tracked a shadowcat to its lair, and when they grew hungry, Joffrey found a holdfast by its smoke and told them to fetch food and wine for their prince and his lady. They dined on trout fresh from the river, and Sansa drank more wine than she had ever drunk before. "My father only lets us have one cup, and only at feasts," she confessed to her prince.

"My betrothed can drink as much as she wants," Joffrey said, refilling her cup.

They went more slowly after they had eaten. Joffrey sang for her as they rode, his voice high and sweet and pure. Sansa was a little dizzy from the wine. "Shouldn't we be starting back?" she asked.

"Soon," Joffrey said. "The battleground is right up ahead, where the river bends. That was where my father killed Rhaegar Targaryen, you know. He smashed in his chest, *crunch*, right through the armor." Joffrey swung an imaginary warhammer to show her how it was done. "Then my uncle Jaime killed old Aerys, and my father was king. What's that sound?"

Sansa heard it too, floating through the woods, a kind of wooden clattering, *snack snack snack*. "I don't know," she said. It made her nervous, though. "Joffrey, let's go back."

"I want to see what it is." Joffrey turned his horse in the direction of the sounds, and Sansa had no choice but to follow. The noises grew louder and more distinct, the *clack* of wood on wood, and as they grew closer they heard heavy breathing as well, and now and then a grunt.

"Someone's there," Sansa said anxiously. She found herself thinking of Lady, wishing the direwolf was with her.

"You're safe with me." Joffrey drew his Lion's Tooth from its sheath. The sound of steel on leather made her tremble. "This way," he said, riding through a stand of trees.

Beyond, in a clearing overlooking the river, they came upon a boy and a girl playing at knights. Their swords were wooden sticks, broom handles from the look of them, and they were rushing across the grass, swinging at each other lustily. The boy was years older, a head taller, and much stronger, and he was pressing the attack. The girl, a scrawny thing in soiled leathers, was dodging and managing to get her stick in the way of most of the boy's blows, but not all. When she tried to lunge at him, he caught her stick with his own, swept it aside, and slid his wood down hard on her fingers. She cried out and lost her weapon.

Prince Joffrey laughed. The boy looked around, wide-eyed and startled, and dropped his stick in the grass. The girl glared at them, sucking on her knuckles to take the sting out, and Sansa was horrified. "*Arya!*" she called out incredulously.

"Go away," Arya shouted back at them, angry tears in her eyes. "What are you doing here? Leave us alone."

Joffrey glanced from Arya to Sansa and back again. "Your sister?" She nodded, blushing. Joffrey examined the boy, an ungainly lad with a coarse, freckled face and thick red hair. "And who are you, boy?" he asked in a commanding tone that took no notice of the fact that the other was a year his senior.

"Mycah," the boy muttered. He recognized the prince and averted his eyes. "M'lord."

"He's the butcher's boy," Sansa said.

"He's my friend," Arya said sharply. "You leave him alone."

"A butcher's boy who wants to be a knight, is it?" Joffrey swung down from his mount, sword in hand. "Pick up your sword, butcher's boy," he said, his eyes bright with amusement. "Let us see how good you are."

Mycah stood there, frozen with fear.

Joffrey walked toward him. "Go on, pick it up. Or do you only fight little girls?"

"She ast me to, m'lord," Mycah said. "She *ast* me to."

Sansa had only to glance at Arya and see the flush on her sister's face to know the boy was telling the truth, but Joffrey was in no mood to listen. The wine had made him wild. "Are you going to pick up your sword?"

Mycah shook his head. "It's only a stick, m'lord. It's not no sword, it's only a stick."

"And you're only a butcher's boy, and no knight." Joffrey lifted Lion's Tooth and laid its point on Mycah's cheek below the eye, as the butcher's boy stood trembling. "That was my lady's sister you were hitting, do you know that?" A bright bud of blood blossomed where his sword pressed into Mycah's flesh, and a slow red line trickled down the boy's cheek.

"*Stop it!*" Arya screamed. She grabbed up her fallen stick.

Sansa was afraid. "Arya, you stay out of this."

"I won't hurt him . . . much," Prince Joffrey told Arya, never taking his eyes off the butcher's boy.

Arya went for him.

Sansa slid off her mare, but she was too slow. Arya swung with both hands. There was a loud *crack* as the wood split against the back of the prince's head, and then everything happened at once before Sansa's horrified eyes. Joffrey staggered and whirled around, roaring curses. Mycah ran for the trees as fast as his legs would take him. Arya swung at the prince again, but this time Joffrey caught the blow on Lion's Tooth and sent her broken stick flying from her hands. The back of his head was all bloody and his eyes were on fire. Sansa was shrieking, "No, no, stop it, stop it, both of you, you're spoiling it," but no one was listening. Arya scooped up a rock and hurled it at Joffrey's head. She hit his horse instead, and the blood bay reared and went galloping off after Mycah. "*Stop it, don't, stop it!*" Sansa screamed. Joffrey slashed at Arya with his sword, screaming obscenities, terrible words, filthy words. Arya darted back, frightened now, but Joffrey followed, hounding her toward the woods, backing her up against a tree. Sansa didn't know what to do. She watched helplessly, almost blind from her tears.

Then a grey blur flashed past her, and suddenly Nymeria was there, leaping, jaws closing around Joffrey's sword arm. The steel fell from his fingers as the wolf knocked him off his feet, and they rolled in the grass, the wolf snarling and ripping at him, the prince shrieking in pain. "Get it *off*," he screamed. "Get it *off*!"

Arya's voice cracked like a whip. "*Nymeria!*"

The direwolf let go of Joffrey and moved to Arya's side. The prince lay in the grass, whimpering, cradling his mangled arm. His shirt was soaked in blood. Arya said, "She didn't hurt you . . . much." She picked up Lion's Tooth where it had fallen, and stood over him, holding the sword with both hands.

Joffrey made a scared whimpery sound as he looked up

at her. "No," he said, "don't hurt me. I'll tell my mother."

"You leave him alone!" Sansa screamed at her sister.

Arya whirled and heaved the sword into the air, putting her whole body into the throw. The blue steel flashed in the sun as the sword spun out over the river. It hit the water and vanished with a splash. Joffrey moaned. Arya ran off to her horse, Nymeria loping at her heels.

After they had gone, Sansa went to Prince Joffrey. His eyes were closed in pain, his breath ragged. Sansa knelt beside him. "Joffrey," she sobbed. "Oh, look what they did, look what they did. My poor prince. Don't be afraid. I'll ride to the holdfast and bring help for you." Tenderly she reached out and brushed back his soft blond hair.

His eyes snapped open and looked at her, and there was nothing but loathing there, nothing but the vilest contempt. "Then go," he spit at her. "And *don't touch me.*"

EDDARD

"**T**hey've found her, my lord."

Ned rose quickly. "Our men or Lannister's?"

"It was Jory," his steward Vayon Poole replied. "She's not been harmed."

"Thank the gods," Ned said. His men had been searching for Arya for four days now, but the queen's men had been out hunting as well. "Where is she? Tell Jory to bring her here at once."

"I am sorry, my lord," Poole told him. "The guards on the gate were Lannister men, and they informed the queen when Jory brought her in. She's being taken directly before the king . . ."

"*Damn* that woman!" Ned said, striding to the door. "Find Sansa and bring her to the audience chamber. Her voice may be needed." He descended the tower steps in a red rage. He had led searches himself for the first three days, and had scarcely slept an hour since Arya had disappeared. This morning he had been so heartsick and weary he could scarcely stand, but now his fury was on him, filling him with strength.

Men called out to him as he crossed the castle yard, but Ned ignored them in his haste. He would have run, but he was still the King's Hand, and a Hand must keep his dignity. He was aware of the eyes that followed him, of the muttered voices wondering what he would do.

The castle was a modest holding a half day's ride south of the Trident. The royal party had made themselves the uninvited guests of its lord, Ser Raymun Darry, while the hunt for Arya and the butcher's boy was conducted on both sides of the river. They were not welcome visitors. Ser Raymun lived under the king's peace, but his family had fought beneath Rhaegar's dragon banners at the Trident, and his three older brothers had died there, a truth neither Robert nor Ser Raymun had forgotten. With king's men, Darry men, Lannister men, and Stark men all crammed into a castle far too small for them, tensions burned hot and heavy.

The king had appropriated Ser Raymun's audience chamber, and that was where Ned found them. The room was crowded when he burst in. Too crowded, he thought; left alone, he and Robert might have been able to settle the matter amicably.

Robert was slumped in Darry's high seat at the far end of the room, his face closed and sullen. Cersei Lannister and her son stood beside him. The queen had her hand on Joffrey's shoulder. Thick silken bandages still covered the boy's arm.

Arya stood in the center of the room, alone but for Jory Cassel, every eye upon her. "Arya," Ned called loudly. He went to her, his boots ringing on the stone floor. When she saw him, she cried out and began to sob.

Ned went to one knee and took her in his arms. She was shaking. "I'm sorry," she sobbed, "I'm sorry, I'm sorry."

"I know," he said. She felt so tiny in his arms, nothing but a scrawny little girl. It was hard to see how she had caused so much trouble. "Are you hurt?"

"No." Her face was dirty, and her tears left pink tracks down her cheeks. "Hungry some. I ate some berries, but there was nothing else."

"We'll feed you soon enough," Ned promised. He rose to face the king. "What is the meaning of this?" His eyes swept the room, searching for friendly faces. But for his own men, they were few enough. Ser Raymun Darry guarded his look well. Lord Renly wore a half smile that might mean anything, and old Ser Barristan was grave; the rest were Lannister men, and hostile. Their only good fortune was that both Jaime Lannister and Sandor Clegane were missing, leading searches north of the Trident. "Why was I not told that my daughter had been found?" Ned demanded, his voice ringing. "Why was she not brought to me at once?"

He spoke to Robert, but it was Cersei Lannister who answered. "How *dare* you speak to your king in that manner!"

At that, the king stirred. "Quiet, woman," he snapped. He straightened in his seat. "I am sorry, Ned. I never meant to frighten the girl. It seemed best to bring her here and get the business done with quickly."

"And what business is that?" Ned put ice in his voice.

The queen stepped forward. "You know full well, Stark. This girl of yours attacked my son. Her and her butcher's boy. That animal of hers tried to tear his arm off."

"That's not true," Arya said loudly. "She just bit him a little. He was hurting Mycah."

"Joff told us what happened," the queen said. "You and the butcher boy beat him with clubs while you set your wolf on him."

"That's not how it was," Arya said, close to tears again. Ned put a hand on her shoulder.

"Yes it is!" Prince Joffrey insisted. "They all attacked me, and she threw Lion's Tooth in the river!" Ned noticed that he did not so much as glance at Arya as he spoke.

"Liar!" Arya yelled.

"Shut up!" the prince yelled back.

"Enough!" the king roared, rising from his seat, his voice thick with irritation. Silence fell. He glowered at Arya through his thick beard. "Now, child, you will tell me what happened. Tell it all, and tell it true. It is a great crime to lie to a king." Then he looked over at his son. "When she is done, you will have your turn. Until then, hold your tongue."

As Arya began her story, Ned heard the door open behind him. He glanced back and saw Vayon Poole enter with Sansa. They stood quietly at the back of the hall as Arya spoke. When she got to the part where she threw Joffrey's sword into the middle of the Trident, Renly

Baratheon began to laugh. The king bristled. "Ser Barristan, escort my brother from the hall before he chokes."

Lord Renly stifled his laughter. "My brother is too kind. I can find the door myself." He bowed to Joffrey. "Perchance later you'll tell me how a nine-year-old girl the size of a wet rat managed to disarm you with a broom handle and throw your sword in the river." As the door swung shut behind him, Ned heard him say, "Lion's Tooth," and guffaw once more.

Prince Joffrey was pale as he began his very different version of events. When his son was done talking, the king rose heavily from his seat, looking like a man who wanted to be anywhere but here. "What in all the seven hells am I supposed to make of this? He says one thing, she says another."

"They were not the only ones present," Ned said. "Sansa, come here." Ned had heard her version of the story the night Arya had vanished. He knew the truth. "Tell us what happened."

His eldest daughter stepped forward hesitantly. She was dressed in blue velvets trimmed with white, a silver chain around her neck. Her thick auburn hair had been brushed until it shone. She blinked at her sister, then at the young prince. "I don't know," she said tearfully, looking as though she wanted to bolt. "I don't remember. Everything happened so fast, I didn't see . . ."

"You rotten!" Arya shrieked. She flew at her sister like an arrow, knocking Sansa down to the ground, pummeling her. "Liar, liar, liar, liar."

"Arya, *stop it!*" Ned shouted. Jory pulled her off her sister, kicking. Sansa was pale and shaking as Ned lifted her back to her feet. "Are you hurt?" he asked, but she was staring at Arya, and she did not seem to hear.

"The girl is as wild as that filthy animal of hers," Cersei Lannister said. "Robert, I want her punished."

"Seven hells," Robert swore. "Cersei, look at her. She's a child. What would you have me do, whip her through the streets? Damn it, children fight. It's over. No lasting harm was done."

The queen was furious. "Joff will carry those scars for the rest of his life."

Robert Baratheon looked at his eldest son. "So he will.

Perhaps they will teach him a lesson. Ned, see that your daughter is disciplined. I will do the same with my son."

"Gladly, Your Grace," Ned said with vast relief.

Robert started to walk away, but the queen was not done. "And what of the direwolf?" she called after him. "What of the beast that savaged your son?"

The king stopped, turned back, frowned. "I'd forgotten about the damned wolf."

Ned could see Arya tense in Jory's arms. Jory spoke up quickly. "We found no trace of the direwolf, Your Grace."

Robert did not look unhappy. "No? So be it."

The queen raised her voice. "A hundred golden dragons to the man who brings me its skin!"

"A costly pelt," Robert grumbled. "I want no part of this, woman. You can damn well buy your furs with Lannister gold."

The queen regarded him coolly. "I had not thought you so niggardly. The king I'd thought to wed would have laid a wolfskin across my bed before the sun went down."

Robert's face darkened with anger. "That would be a fine trick, without a wolf."

"We have a wolf," Cersei Lannister said. Her voice was very quiet, but her green eyes shone with triumph.

It took them all a moment to comprehend her words, but when they did, the king shrugged irritably. "As you will. Have Ser Ilyn see to it."

"Robert, you cannot mean this," Ned protested.

The king was in no mood for more argument. "Enough, Ned, I will hear no more. A direwolf is a savage beast. Sooner or later it would have turned on your girl the same way the other did on my son. Get her a dog, she'll be happier for it."

That was when Sansa finally seemed to comprehend. Her eyes were frightened as they went to her father. "He doesn't mean Lady, does he?" She saw the truth on his face. "No," she said. "No, not Lady, Lady didn't bite anybody, she's good . . ."

"Lady wasn't there," Arya shouted angrily. "You leave her alone!"

"Stop them," Sansa pleaded, "don't let them do it, please, please, it wasn't Lady, it was Nymeria, Arya did it, you can't, it wasn't Lady, don't let them hurt Lady, I'll make her be good, I promise, I promise . . ." She started to cry.

All Ned could do was take her in his arms and hold her while she wept. He looked across the room at Robert. His old friend, closer than any brother. "Please, Robert. For the love you bear me. For the love you bore my sister. Please."

The king looked at them for a long moment, then turned his eyes on his wife. "Damn you, Cersei," he said with loathing.

Ned stood, gently disengaging himself from Sansa's grasp. All the weariness of the past four days had returned to him. "Do it yourself then, Robert," he said in a voice cold and sharp as steel. "At least have the courage to do it yourself."

Robert looked at Ned with flat, dead eyes and left without a word, his footsteps heavy as lead. Silence filled the hall.

"Where is the direwolf?" Cersei Lannister asked when her husband was gone. Beside her, Prince Joffrey was smiling.

"The beast is chained up outside the gatehouse, Your Grace," Ser Barristan Selmy answered reluctantly.

"Send for Ilyn Payne."

"No," Ned said. "Jory, take the girls back to their rooms and bring me Ice." The words tasted of bile in his throat, but he forced them out. "If it must be done, I will do it."

Cersei Lannister regarded him suspiciously. "You, Stark? Is this some trick? Why would you do such a thing?"

They were all staring at him, but it was Sansa's look that cut. "She is of the north. She deserves better than a butcher."

He left the room with his eyes burning and his daughter's wails echoing in his ears, and found the direwolf pup where they chained her. Ned sat beside her for a while. "Lady," he said, tasting the name. He had never paid much attention to the names the children had picked, but looking at her now, he knew that Sansa had chosen well. She was the smallest of the litter, the prettiest, the most gentle and trusting. She looked at him with bright golden eyes, and he ruffled her thick grey fur.

Shortly, Jory brought him Ice.

When it was over, he said, "Choose four men and have them take the body north. Bury her at Winterfell."

"All that way?" Jory said, astonished.

"All that way," Ned affirmed. "The Lannister woman shall never have *this* skin."

He was walking back to the tower to give himself up to sleep at last when Sandor Clegane and his riders came pounding through the castle gate, back from their hunt.

There was something slung over the back of his destrier, a heavy shape wrapped in a bloody cloak. "No sign of your daughter, Hand," the Hound rasped down, "but the day was not wholly wasted. We got her little pet." He reached back and shoved the burden off, and it fell with a thump in front of Ned.

Bending, Ned pulled back the cloak, dreading the words he would have to find for Arya, but it was not Nymeria after all. It was the butcher's boy, Mycah, his body covered in dried blood. He had been cut almost in half from shoulder to waist by some terrible blow struck from above.

"You rode him down," Ned said.

The Hound's eyes seemed to glitter through the steel of that hideous dog's-head helm. "He ran." He looked at Ned's face and laughed. "But not very fast."

BRAN

It seemed as though he had been falling for years.

Fly, a voice whispered in the darkness, but Bran did not know how to fly, so all he could do was fall.

Maester Luwin made a little boy of clay, baked him till he was hard and brittle, dressed him in Bran's clothes, and flung him off a roof. Bran remembered the way he shattered. "But I never fall," he said, falling.

The ground was so far below him he could barely make it out through the grey mists that whirled around him, but he could feel how fast he was falling, and he knew what was waiting for him down there. Even in dreams, you could not fall forever. He would wake up in the instant before he hit the ground, he knew. You always woke up in the instant before you hit the ground.

And if you don't? the voice asked.

The ground was closer now, still far far away, a thousand miles away, but closer than it had been. It was cold here in the darkness. There was no sun, no stars, only the ground below coming up to smash him, and the grey mists, and the whispering voice. He wanted to cry.

Not cry. Fly.

"I can't fly," Bran said. "I can't, I can't . . ."

How do you know? Have you ever tried?

The voice was high and thin. Bran looked around to see where it was coming from. A crow was spiraling down with him, just out of reach, following him as he fell. "Help me," he said.

I'm trying, the crow replied. *Say, got any corn?*

Bran reached into his pocket as the darkness spun dizzily around him. When he pulled his hand out, golden kernels slid from between his fingers into the air. They fell with him.

The crow landed on his hand and began to eat.

"Are you really a crow?" Bran asked.

Are you really falling? the crow asked back.

"It's just a dream," Bran said.

Is it? asked the crow.

"I'll wake up when I hit the ground," Bran told the bird.

You'll die when you hit the ground, the crow said. It went back to eating corn.

Bran looked down. He could see mountains now, their peaks white with snow, and the silver thread of rivers in dark woods. He closed his eyes and began to cry.

That won't do any good, the crow said. *I told you, the answer is flying, not crying. How hard can it be? I'm doing it.* The crow took to the air and flapped around Bran's hand.

"You have wings," Bran pointed out.

Maybe you do too.

Bran felt along his shoulders, groping for feathers.

There are different kinds of wings, the crow said.

Bran was staring at his arms, his legs. He was so skinny, just skin stretched taut over bones. Had he always been so thin? He tried to remember. A face swam up at him out of the grey mist, shining with light, golden. "The things I do for love," it said.

Bran screamed.

The crow took to the air, cawing. *Not that,* it shrieked at him. *Forget that, you do not need it now, put it aside, put it away.* It landed on Bran's shoulder, and pecked at him, and the shining golden face was gone.

Bran was falling faster than ever. The grey mists howled around him as he plunged toward the earth below. "What are you doing to me?" he asked the crow, tearful.

Teaching you how to fly.
"I can't fly!"
You're flying right now.
"I'm *falling!*"
Every flight begins with a fall, the crow said. *Look down.*
"I'm afraid . . ."
LOOK DOWN!
Bran looked down, and felt his insides turn to water. The ground was rushing up at him now. The whole world was spread out below him, a tapestry of white and brown and green. He could see everything so clearly that for a moment he forgot to be afraid. He could see the whole realm, and everyone in it.

He saw Winterfell as the eagles see it, the tall towers looking squat and stubby from above, the castle walls just lines in the dirt. He saw Maester Luwin on his balcony, studying the sky through a polished bronze tube and frowning as he made notes in a book. He saw his brother Robb, taller and stronger than he remembered him, practicing swordplay in the yard with real steel in his hand. He saw Hodor, the simple giant from the stables, carrying an anvil to Mikken's forge, hefting it onto his shoulder as easily as another man might heft a bale of hay. At the heart of the godswood, the great white weirwood brooded over its reflection in the black pool, its leaves rustling in a chill wind. When it felt Bran watching, it lifted its eyes from the still waters and stared back at him knowingly.

He looked east, and saw a galley racing across the waters of the Bite. He saw his mother sitting alone in a cabin, looking at a bloodstained knife on a table in front of her, as the rowers pulled at their oars and Ser Rodrik leaned across a rail, shaking and heaving. A storm was gathering ahead of them, a vast dark roaring lashed by lightning, but somehow they could not see it.

He looked south, and saw the great blue-green rush of the Trident. He saw his father pleading with the king, his face etched with grief. He saw Sansa crying herself to sleep at night, and he saw Arya watching in silence and holding her secrets hard in her heart. There were shadows all around them. One shadow was dark as ash, with the terrible face of a hound. Another was armored like the sun, golden and beautiful. Over them both loomed a giant in armor made of stone, but when he opened his visor, there was nothing inside but darkness and thick black blood.

He lifted his eyes and saw clear across the narrow sea, to the Free Cities and the green Dothraki sea and beyond, to Vaes Dothrak under its mountain, to the fabled lands of the Jade Sea, to Asshai by the Shadow, where dragons stirred beneath the sunrise.

Finally he looked north. He saw the Wall shining like blue crystal, and his bastard brother Jon sleeping alone in a cold bed, his skin growing pale and hard as the memory of all warmth fled from him. And he looked past the Wall, past endless forests cloaked in snow, past the frozen shore and the great blue-white rivers of ice and the dead plains where nothing grew or lived. North and north and north he looked, to the curtain of light at the end of the world, and then beyond that curtain. He looked deep into the heart of winter, and then he cried out, afraid, and the heat of his tears burned on his cheeks.

Now you know, the crow whispered as it sat on his shoulder. *Now you know why you must live.*

"Why?" Bran said, not understanding, falling, falling.

Because winter is coming.

Bran looked at the crow on his shoulder, and the crow looked back. It had three eyes, and the third eye was full of a terrible knowledge. Bran looked down. There was nothing below him now but snow and cold and death, a frozen wasteland where jagged blue-white spires of ice waited to embrace him. They flew up at him like spears. He saw the bones of a thousand other dreamers impaled upon their points. He was desperately afraid.

"Can a man still be brave if he's afraid?" he heard his own voice saying, small and far away.

And his father's voice replied to him. "That is the only time a man can be brave."

Now, Bran, the crow urged. *Choose. Fly or die.*

Death reached for him, screaming.

Bran spread his arms and flew.

Wings unseen drank the wind and filled and pulled him upward. The terrible needles of ice receded below him. The sky opened up above. Bran soared. It was better than climbing. It was better than anything. The world grew small beneath him.

"I'm flying!" he cried out in delight.

I've noticed, said the three-eyed crow. It took to the air, flapping its wings in his face, slowing him, blinding him. He faltered in the air as its pinions beat against his cheeks. Its beak stabbed at him fiercely, and Bran felt a sudden blinding pain in the middle of his forehead, between his eyes.

"What are you doing?" he shrieked.

The crow opened its beak and cawed at him, a shrill scream of fear, and the grey mists shuddered and swirled around him and ripped away like a veil, and he saw that the crow was really a woman, a serving woman with long black hair, and he knew her from somewhere, from Winterfell, yes, that was it, he remembered her now, and then he realized that he was in Winterfell, in a bed high in some chilly tower room, and the black-haired woman dropped a basin of water to shatter on the floor and ran down the steps, shouting, "He's awake, he's awake, he's awake."

Bran touched his forehead, between his eyes. The place where the crow had pecked him was still burning, but there was nothing there, no blood, no wound. He felt weak and dizzy. He tried to get out of bed, but nothing happened.

And then there was movement beside the bed, and something landed lightly on his legs. He felt nothing. A pair of yellow eyes looked into his own, shining like the sun. The window was open and it was cold in the room, but the warmth that came off the wolf enfolded him like a hot bath. His pup, Bran realized . . . or was it? He was so *big* now. He reached out to pet him, his hand trembling like a leaf.

When his brother Robb burst into the room, breathless from his dash up the tower steps, the direwolf was licking Bran's face. Bran looked up calmly. "His name is Summer," he said.

CATELYN

"**W**e will make King's Landing within the hour."

Catelyn turned away from the rail and forced herself to smile. "Your oarmen have done well by us, Captain. Each one of them shall have a silver stag, as a token of my gratitude."

Captain Moreo Tumitis favored her with a half bow. "You are far too generous, Lady Stark. The honor of carrying a great lady like yourself is all the reward they need."

"But they'll take the silver anyway."

Moreo smiled. "As you say." He spoke the Common Tongue fluently, with only the slightest hint of a Tyroshi accent. He'd been plying the narrow sea for thirty years, he'd told her, as oarman, quartermaster, and finally captain of his own trading galleys. The *Storm Dancer* was his fourth ship, and his fastest, a two-masted galley of sixty oars.

She had certainly been the fastest of the ships available in White Harbor when Catelyn and Ser Rodrik Cassel had arrived after their headlong gallop downriver. The Tyroshi were notorious for their avarice, and Ser Rodrik had argued for hiring a fishing sloop out of the Three Sisters, but

Catelyn had insisted on the galley. It was good that she had. The winds had been against them much of the voyage, and without the galley's oars they'd still be beating their way past the Fingers, instead of skimming toward King's Landing and journey's end.

So close, she thought. Beneath the linen bandages, her fingers still throbbed where the dagger had bitten. The pain was her scourge, Catelyn felt, lest she forget. She could not bend the last two fingers on her left hand, and the others would never again be dexterous. Yet that was a small enough price to pay for Bran's life.

Ser Rodrik chose that moment to appear on deck. "My good friend," said Moreo through his forked green beard. The Tyroshi loved bright colors, even in their facial hair. "It is so fine to see you looking better."

"Yes," Ser Rodrik agreed. "I haven't wanted to die for almost two days now." He bowed to Catelyn. "My lady."

He *was* looking better. A shade thinner than he had been when they set out from White Harbor, but almost himself again. The strong winds in the Bite and the roughness of the narrow sea had not agreed with him, and he'd almost gone over the side when the storm seized them unexpectedly off Dragonstone, yet somehow he had clung to a rope until three of Moreo's men could rescue him and carry him safely below decks.

"The captain was just telling me that our voyage is almost at an end," she said.

Ser Rodrik managed a wry smile. "So soon?" He looked odd without his great white side whiskers; smaller somehow, less fierce, and ten years older. Yet back on the Bite it had seemed prudent to submit to a crewman's razor, after his whiskers had become hopelessly befouled for the third time while he leaned over the rail and retched into the swirling winds.

"I will leave you to discuss your business," Captain Moreo said. He bowed and took his leave of them.

The galley skimmed the water like a dragonfly, her oars rising and falling in perfect time. Ser Rodrik held the rail and looked out over the passing shore. "I have not been the most valiant of protectors."

Catelyn touched his arm. "We are here, Ser Rodrik, and safely. That is all that truly matters." Her hand groped beneath her cloak, her fingers stiff and fumbling.

The dagger was still at her side. She found she had to touch it now and then, to reassure herself. "Now we must reach the king's master-at-arms, and pray that he can be trusted."

"Ser Aron Santagar is a vain man, but an honest one." Ser Rodrik's hand went to his face to stroke his whiskers and discovered once again that they were gone. He looked nonplussed. "He may know the blade, yes . . . but, my lady, the moment we go ashore we are at risk. And there are those at court who will know you on sight."

Catelyn's mouth grew tight. "Littlefinger," she murmured. His face swam up before her; a boy's face, though he was a boy no longer. His father had died several years before, so he was Lord Baelish now, yet still they called him Littlefinger. Her brother Edmure had given him that name, long ago at Riverrun. His family's modest holdings were on the smallest of the Fingers, and Petyr had been slight and short for his age.

Ser Rodrik cleared his throat. "Lord Baelish once, ah . . ." His thought trailed off uncertainly in search of the polite word.

Catelyn was past delicacy. "He was my father's ward. We grew up together in Riverrun. I thought of him as a brother, but his feelings for me were . . . more than brotherly. When it was announced that I was to wed Brandon Stark, Petyr challenged for the right to my hand. It was madness. Brandon was twenty, Petyr scarcely fifteen. I had to beg Brandon to spare Petyr's life. He let him off with a scar. Afterward my father sent him away. I have not seen him since." She lifted her face to the spray, as if the brisk wind could blow the memories away. "He wrote to me at Riverrun after Brandon was killed, but I burned the letter unread. By then I knew that Ned would marry me in his brother's place."

Ser Rodrik's fingers fumbled once again for nonexistent whiskers. "Littlefinger sits on the small council now."

"I knew he would rise high," Catelyn said. "He was always clever, even as a boy, but it is one thing to be clever and another to be wise. I wonder what the years have done to him."

High overhead, the far-eyes sang out from the rigging. Captain Moreo came scrambling across the deck, giving orders, and all around them the *Storm Dancer* burst into frenetic activity as King's Landing slid into view atop its three high hills.

Three hundred years ago, Catelyn knew, those heights had been covered with forest, and only a handful of fisherfolk had lived on the north shore of the Blackwater Rush where that deep, swift river flowed into the sea. Then Aegon the Conqueror had sailed from Dragonstone. It was here that his army had put ashore, and there on the highest hill that he built his first crude redoubt of wood and earth.

Now the city covered the shore as far as Catelyn could see; manses and arbors and granaries, brick storehouses and timbered inns and merchant's stalls, taverns and graveyards and brothels, all piled one on another. She could hear the clamor of the fish market even at this distance. Between the buildings were broad roads lined with trees, wandering crookback streets, and alleys so narrow that two men could not walk abreast. Visenya's hill was crowned by the Great Sept of Baelor with its seven crystal towers. Across the city on the hill of Rhaenys stood the blackened walls of the Dragonpit, its huge dome collapsing into ruin, its bronze doors closed now for a century. The Street of the Sisters ran between them, straight as an arrow. The city walls rose in the distance, high and strong.

A hundred quays lined the waterfront, and the harbor was crowded with ships. Deepwater fishing boats and river runners came and went, ferrymen poled back and forth across the Blackwater Rush, trading galleys unloaded goods from Braavos and Pentos and Lys. Catelyn spied the queen's ornate barge, tied up beside a fat-bellied whaler from the Port of Ibben, its hull black with tar, while upriver a dozen lean golden warships rested in their cribs, sails furled and cruel iron rams lapping at the water.

And above it all, frowning down from Aegon's high hill, was the Red Keep; seven huge drum-towers crowned with iron ramparts, an immense grim barbican, vaulted halls and covered bridges, barracks and dungeons and granaries, massive curtain walls studded with archers' nests, all fashioned of pale red stone. Aegon the Conqueror had commanded it built. His son Maegor the Cruel had seen it completed. Afterward he had taken the heads of every stonemason, woodworker, and builder who had labored on it. Only the blood of the dragon would ever know the secrets of the fortress the Dragonlords had built, he vowed.

Yet now the banners that flew from its battlements were golden, not black, and where the three-headed dragon had once breathed fire, now pranced the crowned stag of House Baratheon.

A high-masted swan ship from the Summer Isles was beating out from port, its white sails huge with wind. The *Storm Dancer* moved past it, pulling steadily for shore.

"My lady," Ser Rodrik said, "I have thought on how best to proceed while I lay abed. You must not enter the castle. I will go in your stead and bring Ser Aron to you in some safe place."

She studied the old knight as the galley drew near to a pier. Moreo was shouting in the vulgar Valyrian of the Free Cities. "You would be as much at risk as I would."

Ser Rodrik smiled. "I think not. I looked at my reflection in the water earlier and scarcely recognized myself. My mother was the last person to see me without whiskers, and she is forty years dead. I believe I am safe enough, my lady."

Moreo bellowed a command. As one, sixty oars lifted from the river, then reversed and backed water. The galley slowed. Another shout. The oars slid back inside the hull. As they thumped against the dock, Tyroshi seamen leapt down to tie up. Moreo came bustling up, all smiles. "King's Landing, my lady, as you did command, and never has a ship made a swifter or surer passage. Will you be needing assistance to carry your things to the castle?"

"We shall not be going to the castle. Perhaps you can suggest an inn, someplace clean and comfortable and not too far from the river."

The Tyroshi fingered his forked green beard. "Just so. I know of several establishments that might suit your needs. Yet first, if I may be so bold, there is the matter of the second half of the payment we agreed upon. And of course the extra silver you were so kind as to promise. Sixty stags, I believe it was."

"For the oarmen," Catelyn reminded him.

"Oh, of a certainty," said Moreo. "Though perhaps I should hold it for them until we return to Tyrosh. For the sake of their wives and children. If you give them the silver here, my lady, they will dice it away or spend it all for a night's pleasure."

"There are worse things to spend money on," Ser Rodrik put in. "Winter is coming."

"A man must make his own choices," Catelyn said. "They earned the silver. How they spend it is no concern of mine."

"As you say, my lady," Moreo replied, bowing and smiling.

Just to be sure, Catelyn paid the oarmen herself, a stag to each man, and a copper to the two men who carried their chests halfway up Visenya's hill to the inn that Moreo had suggested. It was a rambling old place on Eel Alley. The woman who owned it was a sour crone with a wandering eye who looked them over suspiciously and bit the coin that Catelyn offered her to make sure it was real. Her rooms were large and airy, though, and Moreo swore that her fish stew was the most savory in all the Seven Kingdoms. Best of all, she had no interest in their names.

"I think it best if you stay away from the common room," Ser Rodrik said, after they had settled in. "Even in a place like this, one never knows who may be watching." He wore ringmail, dagger, and longsword under a dark cloak with a hood he could pull up over his head. "I will be back before nightfall, with Ser Aron," he promised. "Rest now, my lady."

Catelyn *was* tired. The voyage had been long and fatiguing, and she was no longer as young as she had been. Her windows opened on the alley and rooftops, with a view of the Blackwater beyond. She watched Ser Rodrik set off, striding briskly through the busy streets until he was lost in the crowds, then decided to take his advice. The bedding was stuffed with straw instead of feathers, but she had no trouble falling asleep.

She woke to a pounding on her door.

Catelyn sat up sharply. Outside the window, the rooftops of King's Landing were red in the light of the setting sun. She had slept longer than she intended. A fist hammered at her door again, and a voice called out, "Open, in the name of the king."

"A moment," she called out. She wrapped herself in her cloak. The dagger was on the bedside table. She snatched it up before she unlatched the heavy wooden door.

The men who pushed into the room wore the black ringmail and golden cloaks of the City Watch. Their leader smiled at the dagger in her hand and said, "No need for that, m'lady. We're to escort you to the castle."

"By whose authority?" she said.

He showed her a ribbon. Catelyn felt her breath catch in her throat. The seal was a mockingbird, in grey wax. "Petyr," she said. So soon. Something must have happened to Ser Rodrik. She looked at the head guardsman. "Do you know who I am?"

"No, m'lady," he said. "M'lord Littlefinger said only to bring you to him, and see that you were not mistreated."

Catelyn nodded. "You may wait outside while I dress."

She bathed her hands in the basin and wrapped them in clean linen. Her fingers were thick and awkward as she struggled to lace up her bodice and knot a drab brown cloak about her neck. How could Littlefinger have known she was here? Ser Rodrik would never have told him. Old he might be, but he was stubborn, and loyal to a fault. Were they too late, had the Lannisters reached King's Landing before her? No, if that were true, Ned would be here too, and surely he would have come to her. How . . . ?

Then she thought, *Moreo.* The Tyroshi knew who they were and where they were, damn him. She hoped he'd gotten a good price for the information.

They had brought a horse for her. The lamps were being lit along the streets as they set out, and Catelyn felt the eyes of the city on her as she rode, surrounded by the guard in their golden cloaks. When they reached the Red Keep, the portcullis was down and the great gates sealed for the night, but the castle windows were alive with flickering lights. The guardsmen left their mounts outside the walls and escorted her through a narrow postern door, then up endless steps to a tower.

He was alone in the room, seated at a heavy wooden table, an oil lamp beside him as he wrote. When they ushered her inside, he set down his pen and looked at her. "Cat," he said quietly.

"Why have I been brought here in this fashion?"

He rose and gestured brusquely to the guards. "Leave

us." The men departed. "You were not mistreated, I trust," he said after they had gone. "I gave firm instructions." He noticed her bandages. "Your hands . . ."

Catelyn ignored the implied question. "I am not accustomed to being summoned like a serving wench," she said icily. "As a boy, you still knew the meaning of courtesy."

"I've angered you, my lady. That was never my intent." He looked contrite. The look brought back vivid memories for Catelyn. He had been a sly child, but after his mischiefs he always looked contrite; it was a gift he had. The years had not changed him much. Petyr had been a small boy, and he had grown into a small man, an inch or two shorter than Catelyn, slender and quick, with the sharp features she remembered and the same laughing grey-green eyes. He had a little pointed chin beard now, and threads of silver in his dark hair, though he was still shy of thirty. They went well with the silver mockingbird that fastened his cloak. Even as a child, he had always loved his silver.

"How did you know I was in the city?" she asked him.

"Lord Varys knows all," Petyr said with a sly smile. "He will be joining us shortly, but I wanted to see you alone first. It has been too long, Cat. How many years?"

Catelyn ignored his familiarity. There were more important questions. "So it was the King's Spider who found me."

Littlefinger winced. "You don't want to call him that. He's very sensitive. Comes of being an eunuch, I imagine. Nothing happens in this city without Varys knowing. Ofttimes he knows about it *before* it happens. He has informants everywhere. His little birds, he calls them. One of his little birds heard about your visit. Thankfully, Varys came to me first."

"Why you?"

He shrugged. "Why not me? I am master of coin, the king's own councillor. Selmy and Lord Renly rode north to meet Robert, and Lord Stannis is gone to Dragonstone, leaving only Maester Pycelle and me. I was the obvious choice. I was ever a friend to your sister Lysa, Varys knows that."

"Does Varys know about . . ."

"Lord Varys knows everything . . . except why you are here." He lifted an eyebrow. "Why *are* you here?"

"A wife is allowed to yearn for her husband, and if a mother needs her daughters close, who can tell her no?"

Littlefinger laughed. "Oh, very good, my lady, but please don't expect me to believe that. I know you too well. What were the Tully words again?"

Her throat was dry. *"Family, Duty, Honor,"* she recited stiffly. He did know her too well.

"Family, Duty, Honor," he echoed. "All of which required you to remain in Winterfell, where our Hand left you. No, my lady, something has happened. This sudden trip of yours bespeaks a certain urgency. I beg of you, let me help. Old sweet friends should never hesitate to rely upon each other." There was a soft knock on the door. "Enter," Littlefinger called out.

The man who stepped through the door was plump, perfumed, powdered, and as hairless as an egg. He wore a vest of woven gold thread over a loose gown of purple silk, and on his feet were pointed slippers of soft velvet. "Lady Stark," he said, taking her hand in both of his, "to see you again after so many years is such a joy." His flesh was soft and moist, and his breath smelled of lilacs. "Oh, your poor hands. Have you burned yourself, sweet lady? The fingers are so delicate . . . Our good Maester Pycelle makes a marvelous salve, shall I send for a jar?"

Catelyn slid her fingers from his grasp. "I thank you, my lord, but my own Maester Luwin has already seen to my hurts."

Varys bobbed his head. "I was grievous sad to hear about your son. And him so young. The gods are cruel."

"On that we agree, Lord Varys," she said. The title was but a courtesy due him as a council member; Varys was lord of nothing but the spiderweb, the master of none but his whisperers.

The eunuch spread his soft hands. "On more than that, I hope, sweet lady. I have great esteem for your husband, our new Hand, and I know we do both love King Robert."

"Yes," she was forced to say. "For a certainty."

"Never has a king been so beloved as our Robert," quipped Little finger. He smiled slyly. "At least in Lord Varys's hearing."

"Good lady," Varys said with great solicitude. "There

are men in the Free Cities with wondrous healing powers. Say only the word, and I will send for one for your dear Bran."

"Maester Luwin is doing all that can be done for Bran," she told him. She would not speak of Bran, not here, not with these men. She trusted Littlefinger only a little, and Varys not at all. She would not let them see her grief. "Lord Baelish tells me that I have you to thank for bringing me here."

Varys giggled like a little girl. "Oh, yes. I suppose I am guilty. I hope you forgive me, kind lady." He eased himself down into a seat and put his hands together. "I wonder if we might trouble you to show us the dagger?"

Catelyn Stark stared at the eunuch in stunned disbelief. He *was* a spider, she thought wildly, an enchanter or worse. He knew things no one could possibly know, unless . . . "What have you done to Ser Rodrik?" she demanded.

Littlefinger was lost. "I feel rather like the knight who arrives at the battle without his lance. What dagger are we talking about? Who is Ser Rodrik?"

"Ser Rodrik Cassel is master-at-arms at Winterfell," Varys informed him. "I assure you, Lady Stark, nothing at all has been done to the good knight. He did call here early this afternoon. He visited with Ser Aron Santagar in the armory, and they talked of a certain dagger. About sunset, they left the castle together and walked to that dreadful hovel where you were staying. They are still there, drinking in the common room, waiting for your return. Ser Rodrik was very distressed to find you gone."

"How could you know all that?"

"The whisperings of little birds," Varys said, smiling. "I know things, sweet lady. That is the nature of my service." He shrugged. "You *do* have the dagger with you, yes?"

Catelyn pulled it out from beneath her cloak and threw it down on the table in front of him. "Here. Perhaps your little birds will whisper the name of the man it belongs to."

Varys lifted the knife with exaggerated delicacy and ran a thumb along its edge. Blood welled, and he let out a squeal and dropped the dagger back on the table.

"Careful," Catelyn told him, "it's sharp."

"Nothing holds an edge like Valyrian steel," Littlefinger said as Varys sucked at his bleeding thumb and looked at Catelyn with sullen admonition. Littlefinger hefted the knife lightly in his hand, testing the grip. He flipped it in the air, caught it again with his other hand. "Such sweet balance. You want to find the owner, is that the reason for this visit? You have no need of Ser Aron for that, my lady. You should have come to me."

"And if I had," she said, "what would you have told me?"

"I would have told you that there was only one knife like this at King's Landing." He grasped the blade between thumb and forefinger, drew it back over his shoulder, and threw it across the room with a practiced flick of his wrist. It struck the door and buried itself deep in the oak, quivering. "It's mine."

"*Yours?*" It made no sense. Petyr had not been at Winterfell.

"Until the tourney on Prince Joffrey's name day," he said, crossing the room to wrench the dagger from the wood. "I backed Ser Jaime in the jousting, along with half the court." Petyr's sheepish grin made him look half a boy again. "When Loras Tyrell unhorsed him, many of us became a trifle poorer. Ser Jaime lost a hundred golden dragons, the queen lost an emerald pendant, and I lost my knife. Her Grace got the emerald back, but the winner kept the rest."

"*Who?*" Catelyn demanded, her mouth dry with fear. Her fingers ached with remembered pain.

"The Imp," said Littlefinger as Lord Varys watched her face. "Tyrion Lannister."

JON

The courtyard rang to the song of swords.

Under black wool, boiled leather, and mail, sweat trickled icily down Jon's chest as he pressed the attack. Grenn stumbled backward, defending himself clumsily. When he raised his sword, Jon went underneath it with a sweeping blow that crunched against the back of the other boy's leg and sent him staggering. Grenn's downcut was answered by an overhand that dented his helm. When he tried a sideswing, Jon swept aside his blade and slammed a mailed forearm into his chest. Grenn lost his footing and sat down hard in the snow. Jon knocked his sword from his fingers with a slash to his wrist that brought a cry of pain.

"Enough!" Ser Alliser Thorne had a voice with an edge like Valyrian steel.

Grenn cradled his hand. "The bastard broke my wrist."

"The bastard hamstrung you, opened your empty skull, and cut off your hand. Or would have, if these blades had an edge. It's fortunate for you that the Watch needs stableboys as well as rangers." Ser Alliser gestured at Jeren and Toad. "Get the Aurochs on his feet, he has funeral arrangements to make."

Jon took off his helm as the other boys were pulling Grenn to his feet. The frosty morning air felt good on his face. He leaned on his sword, drew a deep breath, and allowed himself a moment to savor the victory.

"That is a longsword, not an old man's cane," Ser Alliser said sharply. "Are your legs hurting, Lord Snow?"

Jon hated that name, a mockery that Ser Alliser had hung on him the first day he came to practice. The boys had picked it up, and now he heard it everywhere. He slid the longsword back into its scabbard. "No," he replied.

Thorne strode toward him, crisp black leathers whispering faintly as he moved. He was a compact man of fifty years, spare and hard, with grey in his black hair and eyes like chips of onyx. "The truth now," he commanded.

"I'm tired," Jon admitted. His arm burned from the weight of the longsword, and he was starting to feel his bruises now that the fight was done.

"What you are is weak."

"I won."

"No. The Aurochs lost."

One of the other boys sniggered. Jon knew better than to reply. He had beaten everyone that Ser Alliser had sent against him, yet it gained him nothing. The master-at-arms served up only derision. Thorne hated him, Jon had decided, of course, he hated the other boys even worse.

"That will be all," Thorne told them. "I can only stomach so much ineptitude in any one day. If the Others ever come for us, I pray they have archers, because you lot are fit for nothing more than arrow fodder."

Jon followed the rest back to the armory, walking alone. He often walked alone here. There were almost twenty in the group he trained with, yet not one he could call a friend. Most were two or three years his senior, yet not one was half the fighter Robb had been at fourteen. Dareon was quick but afraid of being hit. Pyp used his sword like a dagger, Jeren was weak as a girl, Grenn slow and clumsy. Halder's blows were brutally hard but he ran right into your attacks. The more time he spent with them, the more Jon despised them.

Inside, Jon hung sword and scabbard from a hook in the stone wall, ignoring the others around him. Methodically, he began to strip off his mail, leather, and sweat-soaked woolens. Chunks of coal burned in iron braziers at either end of the long room, but Jon found himself shivering. The chill was always with him here. In a few years he would forget what it felt like to be warm.

The weariness came on him suddenly, as he donned the roughspun blacks that were their everyday wear. He sat on a bench, his fingers fumbling with the fastenings on his cloak. *So cold,* he thought, remembering the warm halls of Winterfell, where the hot waters ran through the walls like blood through a man's body. There was scant warmth to be found in Castle Black; the walls were cold here, and the people colder.

No one had told him the Night's Watch would be like this; no one except Tyrion Lannister. The dwarf had given him the truth on the road north, but by then it had been too late. Jon wondered if his father had known what the Wall would be like. He must have, he thought; that only made it hurt the worse.

Even his uncle had abandoned him in this cold place at the end of the world. Up here, the genial Benjen Stark he had known became a different person. He was First Ranger, and he spent his days and nights with Lord Commander Mormont and Maester Aemon and the other high officers, while Jon was given over to the less than tender charge of Ser Alliser Thorne.

Three days after their arrival, Jon had heard that Benjen Stark was to lead a half-dozen men on a ranging into the haunted forest. That night he sought out his uncle in the great timbered common hall and pleaded to go with him. Benjen refused him curtly. "This is not Winterfell," he told him as he cut his meat with fork and dagger. "On the Wall, a man gets only what he earns. You're no ranger, Jon, only a green boy with the smell of summer still on you."

Stupidly, Jon argued. "I'll be fifteen on my name day," he said. "Almost a man grown."

Benjen Stark frowned. "A boy you are, and a boy you'll remain until Ser Alliser says you are fit to be a man of the Night's Watch. If you thought your Stark blood would win you easy favors, you were wrong. We put aside our old families when we swear our vows. Your father will always have a place in my heart, but *these* are my brothers now." He gestured with his dagger at the men around them, all the hard cold men in black.

Jon rose at dawn the next day to watch his uncle leave. One of his rangers, a big ugly man, sang a bawdy song as he saddled his garron, his breath steaming in the cold morning air. Ben Stark smiled at that, but he had no smile for his nephew. "How often must I tell you no, Jon? We'll speak when I return."

As he watched his uncle lead his horse into the tunnel, Jon had remembered the things that Tyrion Lannister told him on the kingsroad, and in his mind's eye he saw Ben Stark lying dead, his blood red on the snow. The thought made him sick. What was he becoming? Afterward he sought out Ghost in the loneliness of his cell, and buried his face in his thick white fur.

If he must be alone, he would make solitude his armor. Castle Black had no godswood, only a small sept and a drunken septon, but Jon could not find it in him to pray to any gods, old or new. If they were real, he thought, they were as cruel and implacable as winter.

He missed his true brothers: little Rickon, bright eyes shining as he begged for a sweet; Robb, his rival and best friend and constant companion; Bran, stubborn and curious, always wanting to follow and join in whatever Jon and Robb were doing. He missed the girls too, even Sansa, who never called him anything but "my half brother" since she was old enough to understand what *bastard* meant. And Arya . . . he missed her even more than Robb, skinny little thing that she was, all scraped knees and tangled hair and torn clothes, so fierce and willful. Arya never seemed to fit, no more than he had . . . yet she could always make Jon smile. He would give anything to be with her now, to muss up her hair once more and watch her make a face, to hear her finish a sentence with him.

"You broke my wrist, bastard boy."

Jon lifted his eyes at the sullen voice. Grenn loomed over him, thick of neck and red of face, with three of his friends behind him. He knew Todder, a short ugly boy with an unpleasant voice. The recruits all called him Toad. The other two were the ones Yoren had brought north with them, Jon remembered, rapers taken down in the Fingers. He'd forgotten their names. He hardly ever spoke to them, if he could help it. They were brutes and bullies, without a thimble of honor between them.

Jon stood up. "I'll break the other one for you if you ask nicely." Grenn was sixteen and a head taller than Jon. All four of them were bigger than he was, but they did not scare him. He'd beaten every one of them in the yard.

"Maybe we'll break you," one of the rapers said.

"Try." Jon reached back for his sword, but one of them grabbed his arm and twisted it behind his back.

"You make us look bad," complained Toad.

"You looked bad before I ever met you," Jon told him. The boy who had his arm jerked upward on him, hard. Pain lanced through him, but Jon would not cry out.

Toad stepped close. "The little lordling has a mouth on him," he said. He had pig eyes, small and shiny. "Is that your mommy's mouth, bastard? What was she, some whore? Tell us her name. Maybe I had her a time or two." He laughed.

Jon twisted like an eel and slammed a heel down across the instep of the boy holding him. There was a sudden cry of pain, and he was free. He flew at Toad, knocked him backward over a bench, and landed on his chest with both hands on his throat, slamming his head against the packed earth.

The two from the Fingers pulled him off, throwing him roughly to the ground. Grenn began to kick at him. Jon was rolling away from the blows when a booming voice cut through the gloom of the armory. "STOP THIS! *NOW!*"

Jon pulled himself to his feet. Donal Noye stood glowering at them. "The yard is for fighting," the armorer said. "Keep your quarrels out of my armory, or I'll make them *my* quarrels. You won't like that."

Toad sat on the floor, gingerly feeling the back of his head. His fingers came away bloody. "He tried to kill me."

" 'S true. I saw it," one of the rapers put in.

"He broke my wrist," Grenn said again, holding it out to Noye for inspection.

The armorer gave the offered wrist the briefest of glances. "A bruise. Perhaps a sprain. Maestor Aemon will give you a salve. Go with him, Todder, that head wants looking after. The rest of you, return to your cells. Not you, Snow. You stay."

Jon sat heavily on the long wooden bench as the others

left, oblivious to the looks they gave him, the silent promises of future retribution. His arm was throbbing.

"The Watch has need of every man it can get," Donal Noye said when they were alone. "Even men like Toad. You won't win any honors killing him."

Jon's anger flared. "He said my mother was—"

"—a whore. I heard him. What of it?"

"Lord Eddard Stark was not a man to sleep with whores," Jon said icily. "His honor—"

"—did not prevent him from fathering a bastard. Did it?"

Jon was cold with rage. "Can I go?"

"You go when I tell you to go."

Jon stared sullenly at the smoke rising from the brazier, until Noye took him under the chin, thick fingers twisting his head around. "Look at me when I'm talking to you, boy."

Jon looked. The armorer had a chest like a keg of ale and a gut to match. His nose was flat and broad, and he always seemed in need of a shave. The left sleeve of his black wool tunic was fastened at the shoulder with a silver pin in the shape of a longsword. "Words won't make your mother a whore. She was what she was, and nothing Toad says can change that. You know, we have men on the Wall whose mothers *were* whores."

Not my mother, Jon thought stubbornly. He knew nothing of his mother; Eddard Stark would not talk of her. Yet he dreamed of her at times, so often that he could almost see her face. In his dreams, she was beautiful, and highborn, and her eyes were kind.

"You think you had it hard, being a high lord's bastard?" the armorer went on. "That boy Jeren is a septon's get, and Cotter Pyke is the baseborn son of a tavern wench. Now he commands Eastwatch by the Sea."

"I don't care," Jon said. "I don't care about them and I don't care about you or Thorne or Benjen Stark or any of it. I hate it here. It's too . . . it's cold."

"Yes. Cold and hard and mean, that's the Wall, and the men who walk it. Not like the stories your wet nurse told you. Well, piss on the stories and piss on your wet nurse. This is the way it is, and you're here for life, same as the rest of us."

"Life," Jon repeated bitterly. The armorer could talk

about life. He'd had one. He'd only taken the black after he'd lost an arm at the siege of Storm's End. Before that he'd smithed for Stannis Baratheon, the king's brother. He'd seen the Seven Kingdoms from one end to the other; he'd feasted and wenched and fought in a hundred battles. They said it was Donal Noye who'd forged King Robert's warhammer, the one that crushed the life from Rhaegar Targaryen on the Trident. He'd done all the things that Jon would never do, and then when he was old, well past thirty, he'd taken a glancing blow from an axe and the wound had festered until the whole arm had to come off. Only then, crippled, had Donal Noye come to the Wall, when his life was all but over.

"Yes, life," Noye said. "A long life or a short one, it's up to you, Snow. The road you're walking, one of your brothers will slit your throat for you one night."

"They're not my brothers," Jon snapped. "They hate me because I'm better than they are."

"No. They hate you because you act like you're better than they are. They look at you and see a castle-bred bastard who thinks he's a lordling." The armorer leaned close. "You're no lordling. Remember that. You're a Snow, not a Stark. You're a bastard and a bully."

"A *bully*?" Jon almost choked on the word. The accusation was so unjust it took his breath away. "They were the ones who came after me. Four of them."

"Four that you've humiliated in the yard. Four who are probably afraid of you. I've watched you fight. It's not training with you. Put a good edge on your sword, and they'd be dead meat; you know it, I know it, they know it. You leave them nothing. You shame them. Does that make you proud?"

Jon hesitated. He did feel proud when he won. Why shouldn't he? But the armorer was taking that away too, making it sound as if he were doing something wrong. "They're all older than me," he said defensively.

"Older and bigger and stronger, that's the truth. I'll wager your master-at-arms taught you how to fight bigger men at Winterfell, though. Who was he, some old knight?"

"Ser Rodrik Cassel," Jon said warily. There was a trap here. He felt it closing around him.

Donal Noye leaned forward, into Jon's face. "Now

think on this, boy. None of these others have ever had a master-at-arms until Ser Alliser. Their fathers were farmers and wagonmen and poachers, smiths and miners and oars on a trading galley. What they know of fighting they learned between decks, in the alleys of Oldtown and Lannisport, in wayside brothels and taverns on the kingsroad. They may have clacked a few sticks together before they came here, but I promise you, not one in twenty was ever rich enough to own a real sword." His look was grim. "So how do you like the taste of your victories now, Lord Snow?"

"Don't call me that!" Jon said sharply, but the force had gone out of his anger. Suddenly he felt ashamed and guilty. "I never . . . I didn't think . . ."

"Best you start thinking," Noye warned him. "That, or sleep with a dagger by your bed. Now go."

By the time Jon left the armory, it was almost midday. The sun had broken through the clouds. He turned his back on it and lifted his eyes to the Wall, blazing blue and crystalline in the sunlight. Even after all these weeks, the sight of it still gave him the shivers. Centuries of wind-blown dirt had pocked and scoured it, covering it like a film, and it often seemed a pale grey, the color of an overcast sky . . . but when the sun caught it fair on a bright day, it *shone*, alive with light, a colossal blue-white cliff that filled up half the sky.

The largest structure ever built by the hands of man, Benjen Stark had told Jon on the kingsroad when they had first caught sight of the Wall in the distance. "And beyond a doubt the most useless," Tyrion Lannister had added with a grin, but even the Imp grew silent as they rode closer. You could see it from miles off, a pale blue line across the northern horizon, stretching away to the east and west and vanishing in the far distance, immense and unbroken. *This is the end of the world,* it seemed to say.

When they finally spied Castle Black, its timbered keeps and stone towers looked like nothing more than a handful of toy blocks scattered on the snow, beneath the vast wall of ice. The ancient stronghold of the black brothers was no Winterfell, no true castle at all. Lacking walls, it could not be defended, not from the south, or east, or west; but it was only the north that concerned the

Night's Watch, and to the north loomed the Wall. Almost seven hundred feet high it stood, three times the height of the tallest tower in the stronghold it sheltered. His uncle said the top was wide enough for a dozen armored knights to ride abreast. The gaunt outlines of huge catapults and monstrous wooden cranes stood sentry up there, like the skeletons of great birds, and among them walked men in black as small as ants.

As he stood outside the armory looking up, Jon felt almost as overwhelmed as he had that day on the kingsroad, when he'd seen it for the first time. The Wall was like that. Sometimes he could almost forget that it was there, the way you forgot about the sky or the earth underfoot, but there were other times when it seemed as if there was nothing else in the world. It was older than the Seven Kingdoms, and when he stood beneath it and looked up, it made Jon dizzy. He could feel the great weight of all that ice pressing down on him, as if it were about to topple, and somehow Jon knew that if it fell, the world fell with it.

"Makes you wonder what lies beyond," a familiar voice said.

Jon looked around. "Lannister. I didn't see—I mean, I thought I was alone."

Tyrion Lannister was bundled in furs so thickly he looked like a very small bear. "There's much to be said for taking people unawares. You never know what you might learn."

"You won't learn anything from me," Jon told him. He had seen little of the dwarf since their journey ended. As the queen's own brother, Tyrion Lannister had been an honored guest of the Night's Watch. The Lord Commander had given him rooms in the King's Tower—so-called, though no king had visited it for a hundred years—and Lannister dined at Mormont's own table and spent his days riding the Wall and his nights dicing and drinking with Ser Alliser and Bowen Marsh and the other high officers.

"Oh, I learn things everywhere I go." The little man gestured up at the Wall with a gnarled black walking stick. "As I was saying . . . why is it that when one man builds a wall, the next man immediately needs to know what's on the other side?" He cocked his head and looked at Jon with his curious mismatched eyes. "You *do* want to know what's on the other side, don't you?"

"It's nothing special," Jon said. He wanted to ride with Benjen Stark on his rangings, deep into the mysteries of the haunted forest, wanted to fight Mance Rayder's wildlings and ward the realm against the Others, but it was better not to speak of the things you wanted. "The rangers say it's just woods and mountains and frozen lakes, with lots of snow and ice."

"And the grumkins and the snarks," Tyrion said. "Let us not forget them, Lord Snow, or else what's that big thing for?"

"Don't call me Lord Snow."

The dwarf lifted an eyebrow. "Would you rather be called the Imp? Let them see that their words can cut you, and you'll never be free of the mockery. If they want to give you a name, take it, make it your own. Then they can't hurt you with it anymore." He gestured with his stick. "Come, walk with me. They'll be serving some vile stew in the common hall by now, and I could do with a bowl of something hot."

Jon was hungry too, so he fell in beside Lannister and slowed his pace to match the dwarf's awkward, waddling steps. The wind was rising, and they could hear the old wooden buildings creaking around them, and in the distance a heavy shutter banging, over and over, forgotten. Once there was a muffled *thump* as a blanket of snow slid from a roof and landed near them.

"I don't see your wolf," Lannister said as they walked.

"I chain him up in the old stables when we're training. They board all the horses in the east stables now, so no one bothers him. The rest of the time he stays with me. My sleeping cell is in Hardin's Tower."

"That's the one with the broken battlement, no? Shattered stone in the yard below, and a lean to it like our noble king Robert after a long night's drinking? I thought all those buildings had been abandoned."

Jon shrugged. "No one cares where you sleep. Most of the old keeps are empty, you can pick any cell you want." Once Castle Black had housed five thousand fighting men with all their horses and servants and weapons. Now it was home to a tenth that number, and parts of it were falling into ruin.

Tyrion Lannister's laughter steamed in the cold air. "I'll be sure to tell your father to arrest more stonemasons, before your tower collapses."

Jon could taste the mockery there, but there was no denying the truth. The Watch had built nineteen great strongholds along the Wall, but only three were still occupied: Eastwatch on its grey windswept shore, the Shadow Tower hard by the mountains where the Wall ended, and Castle Black between them, at the end of the kingsroad. The other keeps, long deserted, were lonely, haunted places, where cold winds whistled through black windows and the spirits of the dead manned the parapets.

"It's better that I'm by myself," Jon said stubbornly. "The rest of them are scared of Ghost."

"Wise boys," Lannister said. Then he changed the subject. "The talk is, your uncle is too long away."

Jon remembered the wish he'd wished in his anger, the vision of Benjen Stark dead in the snow, and he looked away quickly. The dwarf had a way of sensing things, and Jon did not want him to see the guilt in his eyes. "He said he'd be back by my name day," he admitted. His name day had come and gone, unremarked, a fortnight past. "They were looking for Ser Waymar Royce, his father is bannerman to Lord Arryn. Uncle Benjen said they might search as far as the Shadow Tower. That's all the way up in the mountains."

"I hear that a good many rangers have vanished of late," Lannister said as they mounted the steps to the common hall. He grinned and pulled open the door. "Perhaps the grumkins are hungry this year."

Inside, the hall was immense and drafty, even with a fire roaring in its great hearth. Crows nested in the timbers of its lofty ceiling. Jon heard their cries overhead as he accepted a bowl of stew and a heel of black bread from the day's cooks. Grenn and Toad and some of the others were seated at the bench nearest the warmth, laughing and cursing each other in rough voices. Jon eyed them thoughtfully for a moment. Then he chose a spot at the far end of the hall, well away from the other diners.

Tyrion Lannister sat across from him, sniffing at the stew suspiciously. "Barley, onion, carrot," he muttered. "Someone should tell the cooks that turnip isn't a meat."

"It's mutton stew." Jon pulled off his gloves and

warmed his hands in the steam rising from the bowl. The smell made his mouth water.

"Snow."

Jon knew Alliser Thorne's voice, but there was a curious note in it that he had not heard before. He turned.

"The Lord Commander wants to see you. Now."

For a moment Jon was too frightened to move. Why would the Lord Commander want to see him? They had heard something about Benjen, he thought wildly, he was dead, the vision had come true. "Is it my uncle?" he blurted. "Is he returned safe?"

"The Lord Commander is not accustomed to waiting," was Ser Alliser's reply. "And I am not accustomed to having my commands questioned by bastards."

Tyrion Lannister swung off the bench and rose. "Stop it, Thorne. You're frightening the boy."

"Keep out of matters that don't concern you, Lannister. You have no place here."

"I have a place at court, though," the dwarf said, smiling. "A word in the right ear, and you'll die a sour old man before you get another boy to train. Now tell Snow why the Old Bear needs to see him. Is there news of his uncle?"

"No," Ser Alliser said. "This is another matter entirely. A bird arrived this morning from Winterfell, with a message that concerns his brother." He corrected himself. "His half brother."

"Bran," Jon breathed, scrambling to his feet. "Something's happened to Bran."

Tyrion Lannister laid a hand on his arm. "Jon," he said. "I am truly sorry."

Jon scarcely heard him. He brushed off Tyrion's hand and strode across the hall. He was running by the time he hit the doors. He raced to the Commander's Keep, dashing through drifts of old snow. When the guards passed him, he took the tower steps two at a time. By the time he burst into the presence of the Lord Commander, his boots were soaked and Jon was wild-eyed and panting. "Bran," he said. "What does it say about Bran?"

Jeor Mormont, Lord Commander of the Night's Watch, was a gruff old man with an immense bald head and a shaggy grey beard. He had a raven on his arm, and he was feeding it kernels of corn. "I am told you can read." He shook the raven off, and it flapped its wings and flew to the window, where it sat watching as Mormont drew a roll of paper from his belt and handed it to Jon. *"Corn,"* it muttered in a raucous voice. *"Corn, corn."*

Jon's finger traced the outline of the direwolf in the white wax of the broken seal. He recognized Robb's hand, but the letters seemed to blur and run as he tried to read them. He realized he was crying. And then, through the tears, he found the sense in the words, and raised his head. "He woke up," he said. "The gods gave him back."

"Crippled," Mormont said. "I'm sorry, boy. Read the rest of the letter."

He looked at the words, but they didn't matter. Nothing mattered. Bran was going to live. "My brother is going to live," he told Mormont. The Lord Commander shook his head, gathered up a fistful of corn, and whistled. The raven flew to his shoulder, crying, *"Live! Live!"*

Jon ran down the stairs, a smile on his face and Robb's letter in his hand. "My brother is going to live," he told the guards. They exchanged a look. He ran back to the common hall, where he found Tyrion Lannister just finishing his meal. He grabbed the little man under the arms, hoisted him up in the air, and spun him around in a circle. *"Bran is going to live!"* he whooped. Lannister looked startled. Jon put him down and thrust the paper into his hands. "Here, read it," he said.

Others were gathering around and looking at him curiously. Jon noticed Grenn a few feet away. A thick woolen bandage was wrapped around one hand. He looked anxious and uncomfortable, not menacing at all. Jon went to him. Grenn edged backward and put up his hands. "Stay away from me now, you bastard."

Jon smiled at him. "I'm sorry about your wrist. Robb used the same move on me once, only with a wooden blade. It hurt like seven hells, but yours must be worse. Look, if you want, I can show you how to defend that."

Alliser Thorne overheard him. "Lord Snow wants to take my place now." He sneered. "I'd have an easier time teaching a wolf to juggle than you will training this aurochs."

"I'll take that wager, Ser Alliser," Jon said. "I'd love to see Ghost juggle."

Jon heard Grenn suck in his breath, shocked. Silence fell.

Then Tyrion Lannister guffawed. Three of the black brothers joined in from a nearby table. The laughter spread up and down the benches, until even the cooks joined in. The birds stirred in the rafters, and finally even Grenn began to chuckle.

Ser Alliser never took his eyes from Jon. As the laughter rolled around him, his face darkened, and his sword hand curled into a fist. "That was a grievous error, Lord Snow," he said at last in the acid tones of an enemy.

EDDARD

Eddard Stark rode through the towering bronze doors of the Red Keep sore, tired, hungry, and irritable. He was still ahorse, dreaming of a long hot soak, a roast fowl, and a featherbed, when the king's steward told him that Grand Maester Pycelle had convened an urgent meeting of the small council. The honor of the Hand's presence was requested as soon as it was convenient. "It will be convenient on the morrow," Ned snapped as he dismounted.

The steward bowed very low. "I shall give the councillors your regrets, my lord."

"No, damn it," Ned said. It would not do to offend the council before he had even begun. "I will see them. Pray give me a few moments to change into something more presentable."

"Yes, my lord," the steward said. "We have given you Lord Arryn's former chambers in the Tower of the Hand, if it please you. I shall have your things taken there."

"My thanks," Ned said as he ripped off his riding gloves and tucked them into his belt. The rest of his household was coming through the gate behind him. Ned saw Vayon Poole, his own steward, and called out. "It seems the council has urgent need of me. See that my daughters find their bedchambers, and tell Jory to keep them there. Arya is not to go exploring." Poole bowed. Ned turned back to the royal steward. "My wagons are still straggling through the city. I shall need appropriate garments."

"It will be my great pleasure," the steward said.

And so Ned had come striding into the council chambers, bone-tired and dressed in borrowed clothing, to find four members of the small council waiting for him.

The chamber was richly furnished. Myrish carpets covered the floor instead of rushes, and in one corner a hundred fabulous beasts cavorted in bright paints on a carved screen from the Summer Isles. The walls were hung with tapestries from Norvos and Qohor and Lys, and a pair of Valyrian sphinxes flanked the door, eyes of polished garnet smoldering in black marble faces.

The councillor Ned liked least, the eunuch Varys, accosted him the moment he entered. "Lord Stark, I was grievous sad to hear about your troubles on the kingsroad. We have all been visiting the sept to light candles for Prince Joffrey. I pray for his recovery." His hand left powder stains on Ned's sleeve, and he smelled as foul and sweet as flowers on a grave.

"Your gods have heard you," Ned replied, cool yet polite. "The prince grows stronger every day." He disentangled himself from the eunuch's grip and crossed the room to where Lord Renly stood by the screen, talking quietly with a short man who could only be Littlefinger. Renly had been a boy of eight when Robert won the throne, but he had grown into a man so like his brother that Ned found it disconcerting. Whenever he saw him, it was as if the years had slipped away and Robert stood before him, fresh from his victory on the Trident.

"I see you have arrived safely, Lord Stark," Renly said.

"And you as well," Ned replied. "You must forgive me, but sometimes you look the very image of your brother Robert."

"A poor copy," Renly said with a shrug.

"Though much better dressed," Littlefinger quipped. "Lord Renly spends more on clothing than half the ladies of the court."

It was true enough. Lord Renly was in dark green velvet, with a dozen golden stags embroidered on his doublet. A cloth-of-gold half cape was draped casually across one shoulder, fastened with an emerald brooch. "There are worse crimes," Renly said with a laugh. "The way *you* dress, for one."

Littlefinger ignored the jibe. He eyed Ned with a smile on his lips that bordered on insolence. "I have hoped to meet you for some years, Lord Stark. No doubt Lady Catelyn has mentioned me to you."

"She has," Ned replied with a chill in his voice. The sly arrogance of the comment rankled him. "I understand you knew my brother Brandon as well."

Renly Baratheon laughed. Varys shuffled over to listen.

"Rather too well," Littlefinger said. "I still carry a token of his esteem. Did Brandon speak of me too?"

"Often, and with some heat," Ned said, hoping that would end it. He had no patience with this game they played, this dueling with words.

"I should have thought that heat ill suits you Starks," Littlefinger said. "Here in the south, they say you are all made of ice, and melt when you ride below the Neck."

"I do not plan on melting soon, Lord Baelish. You may count on it." Ned moved to the council table and said, "Maester Pycelle, I trust you are well."

The Grand Maester smiled gently from his tall chair at the foot of the table. "Well enough for a man of my years, my lord," he replied, "yet I do tire easily, I fear." Wispy strands of white hair fringed the broad bald dome of his forehead above a kindly face. His maester's collar was no simple metal choker such as Luwin wore, but two dozen heavy chains wound together into a ponderous metal necklace that covered him from throat to breast. The links were forged of every metal known to man: black iron and red gold, bright copper and dull lead, steel and tin and pale silver, brass and bronze and platinum. Garnets and amethysts and black pearls adorned the metalwork, and here and there an emerald or ruby. "Perhaps we might begin soon," the Grand Maester said, hands knitting together atop his broad stomach. "I fear I shall fall asleep if we wait much longer."

"As you will." The king's seat sat empty at the head of the table, the crowned stag of Baratheon embroidered in gold thread on its pillows. Ned took the chair beside it, as the right hand of his king. "My lords," he said formally, "I am sorry to have kept you waiting."

"You are the King's Hand," Varys said. "We serve at your pleasure, Lord Stark."

As the others took their accustomed seats, it struck Eddard Stark forcefully that he did not belong here, in this room, with these men. He remembered what Robert had told him in the crypts below Winterfell. *I am surrounded by flatterers and fools,* the king had insisted. Ned looked down the council table and wondered which were the flatterers and which the fools. He thought he knew already. "We are but five," he pointed out.

"Lord Stannis took himself to Dragonstone not long after the king went north," Varys said, "and our gallant Ser Barristan no doubt rides beside the king as he makes his way through the city, as befits the Lord Commander of the Kingsguard."

"Perhaps we had best wait for Ser Barristan and the king to join us," Ned suggested.

Renly Baratheon laughed aloud. "If we wait for my brother to grace us with his royal presence, it could be a long sit."

"Our good King Robert has many cares," Varys said. "He entrusts some small matters to us, to lighten his load."

"What Lord Varys means is that all this business of coin and crops and justice bores my royal brother to tears," Lord Renly said, "so it falls to us to govern the realm. He does send us a command from time to time." He drew a tightly rolled paper from his sleeve and laid it on the table. "This morning he commanded me to ride ahead with all haste and ask Grand Maester Pycelle to convene this council at once. He has an urgent task for us."

Littlefinger smiled and handed the paper to Ned. It bore the royal seal. Ned broke the wax with his thumb and flattened the letter to consider the king's urgent command, reading the words with mounting disbelief. Was there no end to Robert's folly? And to do this in *his* name, that was salt in the wound. "Gods be good," he swore.

"What Lord Eddard means to say," Lord Renly announced, "is that His Grace instructs us to stage a great

tournament in honor of his appointment as the Hand of
the King."

"How much?" asked Littlefinger, mildly.

Ned read the answer off the letter. "Forty thousand
golden dragons to the champion. Twenty thousand to the
man who comes second, another twenty to the winner of
the melee, and ten thousand to the victor of the archery
competition."

"Ninety thousand gold pieces," Littlefinger sighed.
"And we must not neglect the other costs. Robert will
want a prodigious feast. That means cooks, carpenters,
serving girls, singers, jugglers, fools . . ."

"Fools we have in plenty," Lord Renly said.

Grand Maester Pycelle looked to Littlefinger and
asked, "Will the treasury bear the expense?"

"What treasury is that?" Littlefinger replied with a
twist of his mouth. "Spare me the foolishness, Maester.
You know as well as I that the treasury has been empty
for years. I shall have to borrow the money. No doubt the
Lannisters will be accommodating. We owe Lord Tywin
some three million dragons at present, what matter another hundred thousand?"

Ned was stunned. "Are you claiming that the Crown is
three million gold pieces in debt?"

"The Crown is more than *six* million gold pieces in
debt, Lord Stark. The Lannisters are the biggest part of it,
but we have also borrowed from Lord Tyrell, the Iron
Bank of Braavos, and several Tyroshi trading cartels. Of
late I've had to turn to the Faith. The High Septon haggles
worse than a Dornish fishmonger."

Ned was aghast. "Aerys Targaryen left a treasury flowing with gold. How could you let this happen?"

Littlefinger gave a shrug. "The master of coin finds the
money. The king and the Hand spend it."

"I will not believe that Jon Arryn allowed Robert to
beggar the realm," Ned said hotly.

Grand Maester Pycelle shook his great bald head, his
chains clinking softly. "Lord Arryn was a prudent man,
but I fear that His Grace does not always listen to wise
counsel."

"My royal brother loves tournaments and feasts,"
Renly Baratheon said, "and he loathes what he calls
'counting coppers.' "

"I will speak with His Grace," Ned said. "This tourney is an extravagance the realm cannot afford."

"Speak to him as you will," Lord Renly said, "we had still best make our plans."

"Another day," Ned said. Perhaps too sharply, from the looks they gave him. He would have to remember that he was no longer in Winterfell, where only the king stood higher; here, he was but first among equals. "Forgive me, my lords," he said in a softer tone. "I am tired. Let us call a halt for today and resume when we are fresher." He did not ask for their consent, but stood abruptly, nodded at them all, and made for the door.

Outside, wagons and riders were still pouring through the castle gates, and the yard was a chaos of mud and horseflesh and shouting men. The king had not yet arrived, he was told. Since the ugliness on the Trident, the Starks and their household had ridden well ahead of the main column, the better to separate themselves from the Lannisters and the growing tension. Robert had hardly been seen; the talk was he was traveling in the huge wheelhouse, drunk as often as not. If so, he might be hours behind, but he would still be here too soon for Ned's liking. He had only to look at Sansa's face to feel the rage twisting inside him once again. The last fortnight of their journey had been a misery. Sansa blamed Arya and told her that it should have been Nymeria who died. And Arya was lost after she heard what had happened to her butcher's boy. Sansa cried herself to sleep, Arya brooded silently all day long, and Eddard Stark dreamed of a frozen hell reserved for the Starks of Winterfell.

He crossed the outer yard, passed under a portcullis into the inner bailey, and was walking toward what he thought was the Tower of the Hand when Littlefinger appeared in front of him. "You're going the wrong way, Stark. Come with me."

Hesitantly, Ned followed. Littlefinger led him into a tower, down a stair, across a small sunken courtyard, and along a deserted corridor where empty suits of armor stood sentinel along the walls. They were relics of the Targaryens, black steel with dragon scales cresting their helms, now dusty and forgotten. "This is not the way to my chambers," Ned said.

"Did I say it was? I'm leading you to the dungeons to

slit your throat and seal your corpse up behind a wall," Littlefinger replied, his voice dripping with sarcasm. "We have no time for this, Stark. Your wife awaits."

"What game are you playing, Littlefinger? Catelyn is at Winterfell, hundreds of leagues from here."

"Oh?" Littlefinger's grey-green eyes glittered with amusement. "Then it appears someone has managed an astonishing impersonation. For the last time, come. Or don't come, and I'll keep her for myself." He hurried down the steps.

Ned followed him warily, wondering if this day would ever end. He had no taste for these intrigues, but he was beginning to realize that they were meat and mead to a man like Littlefinger.

At the foot of the steps was a heavy door of oak and iron. Petyr Baelish lifted the crossbar and gestured Ned through. They stepped out into the ruddy glow of dusk, on a rocky bluff high above the river. "We're outside the castle," Ned said.

"You are a hard man to fool, Stark," Littlefinger said with a smirk. "Was it the sun that gave it away, or the sky? Follow me. There are niches cut in the rock. Try not to fall to your death, Catelyn would never understand." With that, he was over the side of the cliff, descending as quick as a monkey.

Ned studied the rocky face of the bluff for a moment, then followed more slowly. The niches were there, as Littlefinger had promised, shallow cuts that would be invisible from below, unless you knew just where to look for them. The river was a long, dizzying distance below. Ned kept his face pressed to the rock and tried not to look down any more often than he had to.

When at last he reached the bottom, a narrow, muddy trail along the water's edge, Littlefinger was lazing against a rock and eating an apple. He was almost down to the core. "You are growing old and slow, Stark," he said, flipping the apple casually into the rushing water. "No matter, we ride the rest of the way." He had two horses waiting. Ned mounted up and trotted behind him, down the trail and into the city.

Finally Baelish drew rein in front of a ramshackle building, three stories, timbered, its windows bright with lamplight in the gathering dusk. The sounds of music and raucous laughter drifted out and floated over the water. Beside the door swung an ornate oil lamp on a heavy chain, with a globe of leaded red glass.

Ned Stark dismounted in a fury. "A brothel," he said as he seized Littlefinger by the shoulder and spun him around. "You've brought me all this way to take me to a brothel."

"Your wife is inside," Littlefinger said.

It was the final insult. "Brandon was too kind to you," Ned said as he slammed the small man back against a wall and shoved his dagger up under the little pointed chin beard.

"My lord, *no*," an urgent voice called out. "He speaks the truth." There were footsteps behind him.

Ned spun, knife in hand, as an old white-haired man hurried toward them. He was dressed in brown rough-spun, and the soft flesh under his chin wobbled as he ran. "This is no business of yours," Ned began; then, suddenly, the recognition came. He lowered the dagger, astonished. *"Ser Rodrik?"*

Rodrik Cassel nodded. "Your lady awaits you upstairs."

Ned was lost. "Catelyn is truly here? This is not some strange jape of Littlefinger's?" He sheathed his blade.

"Would that it were, Stark," Littlefinger said. "Follow me, and try to look a shade more lecherous and a shade less like the King's Hand. It would not do to have you recognized. Perhaps you could fondle a breast or two, just in passing."

They went inside, through a crowded common room where a fat woman was singing bawdy songs while pretty young girls in linen shifts and wisps of colored silk pressed themselves against their lovers and dandled on their laps. No one paid Ned the least bit of attention. Ser Rodrik waited below while Littlefinger led him up to the third floor, along a corridor, and through a door.

Inside, Catelyn was waiting. She cried out when she saw him, ran to him, and embraced him fiercely.

"My lady," Ned whispered in wonderment.

"Oh, very good," said Littlefinger, closing the door. "You recognized her."

"I feared you'd never come, my lord," she whispered against his chest. "Petyr has been bringing me reports. He told me of your troubles with Arya and the young prince. How are my girls?"

"Both in mourning, and full of anger," he told her. "Cat, I do not understand. What are you doing in King's Landing? What's happened?" Ned asked his wife. "Is it Bran? Is he . . ." *Dead* was the word that came to his lips, but he could not say it.

"It is Bran, but not as you think," Catelyn said.

Ned was lost. "Then how? Why are you here, my love? What is this place?"

"Just what it appears," Littlefinger said, easing himself onto a window seat. "A brothel. Can you think of a less likely place to find a Catelyn Tully?" He smiled. "As it chances, I own this particular establishment, so arrangements were easily made. I am most anxious to keep the Lannisters from learning that Cat is here in King's Landing."

"Why?" Ned asked. He saw her hands then, the awkward way she held them, the raw red scars, the stiffness of the last two fingers on her left. "You've been hurt." He took her hands in his own, turned them over. "Gods. Those are deep cuts . . . a gash from a sword or . . . how did this happen, my lady?"

Catelyn slid a dagger out from under her cloak and placed it in his hand. "This blade was sent to open Bran's throat and spill his life's blood."

Ned's head jerked up. "But . . . who . . . why would . . ."

She put a finger to his lips. "Let me tell it all, my love. It will go faster that way. Listen."

So he listened, and she told it all, from the fire in the library tower to Varys and the guardsmen and Littlefinger. And when she was done, Eddard Stark sat dazed beside the table, the dagger in his hand. Bran's wolf had saved the boy's life, he thought dully. What was it that Jon had said when they found the pups in the snow? *Your children were meant to have these pups, my lord.* And he had killed Sansa's, and for what? Was it guilt he was feeling? Or fear? If the gods had sent these wolves, what folly had he done?

Painfully, Ned forced his thoughts back to the dagger and what it meant. "The Imp's dagger," he repeated. It made no sense. His hand curled around the smooth dragonbone hilt, and he slammed the blade into the table, felt it bite into the wood. It stood mocking him. "Why should Tyrion Lannister want Bran dead? The boy has never done him harm."

"Do you Starks have nought but snow between your ears?" Littlefinger asked. "The Imp would never have acted alone."

Ned rose and paced the length of the room. "If the queen had a role in this or, gods forbid, the king himself . . . no, I will not believe that." Yet even as he said the words, he remembered that chill morning on the barrowlands, and Robert's talk of sending hired knives after the Targaryen princess. He remembered Rhaegar's infant son, the red ruin of his skull, and the way the king had turned away, as he had turned away in Darry's audience hall not so long ago. He could still hear Sansa pleading, as Lyanna had pleaded once.

"Most likely the king did *not* know," Littlefinger said. "It would not be the first time. Our good Robert is practiced at closing his eyes to things he would rather not see."

Ned had no reply for that. The face of the butcher's boy swam up before his eyes, cloven almost in two, and afterward the king had said not a word. His head was pounding.

Littlefinger sauntered over to the table, wrenched the knife from the wood. "The accusation is treason either way. Accuse the king and you will dance with Ilyn Payne before the words are out of your mouth. The queen . . . *if* you can find proof, and *if* you can make Robert listen, then perhaps . . ."

"We have proof," Ned said. "We have the dagger."

"This?" Littlefinger flipped the knife casually end over end. "A sweet piece of steel, but it cuts two ways, my lord. The Imp will no doubt swear the blade was lost or stolen while he was at Winterfell, and with his hireling dead, who is there to give him the lie?" He tossed the knife lightly to Ned. "My counsel is to drop that in the river and forget that it was ever forged."

Ned regarded him coldly. "Lord Baelish, I am a Stark of Winterfell. My son lies crippled, perhaps dying. He would be dead, and Catelyn with him, but for a wolf pup we found in the snow. If you truly believe I could forget that, you are as big a fool now as when you took up sword against my brother."

"A fool I may be, Stark . . . yet I'm still here, while your brother has been moldering in his frozen grave for some fourteen years now. If you are so eager to molder beside him, far be it from me to dissuade you, but I would rather not be included in the party, thank you very much."

"You would be the last man I would willingly include in any party, Lord Baelish."

"You wound me deeply." Littlefinger placed a hand over his heart. "For my part, I always found you Starks a tiresome lot, but Cat seems to have become attached to you, for reasons I cannot comprehend. I shall try to keep you alive for her sake. A fool's task, admittedly, but I could never refuse your wife anything."

"I told Petyr our suspicions about Jon Arryn's death," Catelyn said. "He has promised to help you find the truth."

That was not news that Eddard Stark welcomed, but it was true enough that they needed help, and Littlefinger had been almost a brother to Cat once. It would not be the first time that Ned had been forced to make common cause with a man he despised. "Very well," he said, thrusting the dagger into his belt. "You spoke of Varys. Does the eunuch know all of it?"

"Not from my lips," Catelyn said. "You did not wed a fool, Eddard Stark. But Varys has ways of learning things that no man could know. He has some dark art, Ned, I swear it."

"He has spies, that is well known," Ned said, dismissive.

"It is more than that," Catelyn insisted. "Ser Rodrik spoke to Ser Aron Santagar in all secrecy, yet somehow the Spider knew of their conversation. I fear that man."

Littlefinger smiled. "Leave Lord Varys to me, sweet lady. If you will permit me a small obscenity—and where better for it than here—I hold the man's balls in the palm of my hand." He cupped his fingers, smiling. "Or would, if he were a man, or had any balls. You see, if the pie is opened, the birds begin to sing, and Varys would not like that. Were I you, I would worry more about the Lannisters and less about the eunuch."

Ned did not need Littlefinger to tell him that. He was thinking back to the day Arya had been found, to the look on the queen's face when she said, *We have a wolf,* so soft and quiet. He was thinking of the boy Mycah, of Jon Arryn's sudden death, of Bran's fall, of old mad Aerys Targaryen dying on the floor of his throne room while his life's blood dried on a gilded blade. "My lady," he said, turning to Catelyn, "there is nothing more you can do here. I want you to return to Winterfell at once. If there was one assassin, there could be others. Whoever ordered Bran's death will learn soon enough that the boy still lives."

"I had hoped to see the girls . . ." Catelyn said.

"That would be most unwise," Littlefinger put in. "The Red Keep is full of curious eyes, and children talk."

"He speaks truly, my love," Ned told her. He embraced her. "Take Ser Rodrik and ride for Winterfell. I will watch over the girls. Go home to our sons and keep them safe."

"As you say, my lord." Catelyn lifted her face, and Ned kissed her. Her maimed fingers clutched against his back with a desperate strength, as if to hold him safe forever in the shelter of her arms.

"Would the lord and lady like the use of a bedchamber?" asked Littlefinger. "I should warn you, Stark, we usually charge for that sort of thing around here."

"A moment alone, that's all I ask," Catelyn said.

"Very well." Littlefinger strolled to the door. "Don't be too long. It is past time the Hand and I returned to the castle, before our absence is noted."

Catelyn went to him and took his hands in her own. "I will not forget the help you gave me, Petyr. When your men came for me, I did not know whether they were taking me to a friend or an enemy. I have found you more than a friend. I have found a brother I'd thought lost."

Petyr Baelish smiled. "I am desperately sentimental, sweet lady. Best not tell anyone. I have spent years convincing the court that I am wicked and cruel, and I should hate to see all that hard work go for naught."

Ned believed not a word of that, but he kept his voice polite as he said, "You have my thanks as well, Lord Baelish."

"Oh, now *there's* a treasure," Littlefinger said, exiting.

When the door had closed behind him, Ned turned back to his wife. "Once you are home, send word to Helman Tallhart and Galbart Glover under my seal. They are to raise a hundred bowmen each and fortify Moat Cailin. Two hundred determined archers can hold the Neck against an army. Instruct Lord Manderly that he is to strengthen and repair all his defenses at White Harbor, and see that they are well manned. And from this day on, I want a careful watch kept over Theon Greyjoy. If there is war, we shall have sore need of his father's fleet."

"War?" The fear was plain on Catelyn's face.

"It will not come to that," Ned promised her, praying it was true. He took her in his arms again. "The Lannisters are merciless in the face of weakness, as Aerys Targaryen learned to his sorrow, but they would not dare attack the north without all the power of the realm behind them, and that they shall not have. I must play out this fool's masquerade as if nothing is amiss. Remember why I came here, my love. If I find proof that the Lannisters murdered Jon Arryn . . ."

He felt Catelyn tremble in his arms. Her scarred hands clung to him. "If," she said, "what then, my love?"

That was the most dangerous part, Ned knew. "All justice flows from the king," he told her. "When I know the truth, I must go to Robert." *And pray that he is the man I think he is,* he finished silently, *and not the man I fear he has become.*

TYRION

"**A**re you certain that you must leave us so soon?" the Lord Commander asked him.

"Past certain, Lord Mormont," Tyrion replied. "My brother Jaime will be wondering what has become of me. He may decide that you have convinced me to take the black."

"Would that I could." Mormont picked up a crab claw and cracked it in his fist. Old as he was, the Lord Commander still had the strength of a bear. "You're a cunning man, Tyrion. We have need of men of your sort on the Wall."

Tyrion grinned. "Then I shall scour the Seven Kingdoms for dwarfs and ship them all to you, Lord Mormont." As they laughed, he sucked the meat from a crab leg and reached for another. The crabs had arrived from Eastwatch only this morning, packed in a barrel of snow, and they were succulent.

Ser Alliser Thorne was the only man at table who did not so much as crack a smile. "Lannister mocks us."

"Only you, Ser Alliser," Tyrion said. This time the laughter round the table had a nervous, uncertain quality to it.

Thorne's black eyes fixed on Tyrion with loathing. "You have a bold tongue for someone who is less than half a man. Perhaps you and I should visit the yard together."

"Why?" asked Tyrion. "The crabs are here."

The remark brought more guffaws from the others. Ser Alliser stood up, his mouth a tight line. "Come and make your japes with steel in your hand."

Tyrion looked pointedly at his right hand. "Why, I *have* steel in my hand, Ser Alliser, although it appears to be a crab fork. Shall we duel?" He hopped up on his chair and began poking at Thorne's chest with the tiny fork. Roars of laughter filled the tower room. Bits of crab flew from the Lord Commander's mouth as he began to gasp and choke. Even his raven joined in, cawing loudly from above the window. *"Duel! Duel! Duel!"*

Ser Alliser Thorne walked from the room so stiffly it looked as though he had a dagger up his butt.

Mormont was still gasping for breath. Tyrion pounded him on the back. "To the victor goes the spoils," he called out. "I claim Thorne's share of the crabs."

Finally the Lord Commander recovered himself. "You are a wicked man, to provoke our Ser Alliser so," he scolded.

Tyrion seated himself and took a sip of wine. "If a man paints a target on his chest, he should expect that sooner or later someone will loose an arrow at him. I have seen dead men with more humor than your Ser Alliser."

"Not so," objected the Lord Steward, Bowen Marsh, a man as round and red as a pomegranate. "You ought to hear the droll names he gives the lads he trains."

Tyrion had heard a few of those droll names. "I'll wager the lads have a few names for him as well," he said. "Chip the ice off your eyes, my good lords. Ser Alliser Thorne should be mucking out your stables, not drilling your young warriors."

"The Watch has no shortage of stableboys," Lord Mormont grumbled. "That seems to be all they send us these days. Stableboys and sneak thieves and rapers. Ser Alliser is an anointed knight, one of the few to take the black since I have been Lord Commander. He fought bravely at King's Landing."

"On the wrong side," Ser Jeremy Rykker commented

dryly. "I ought to know, I was there on the battlements beside him. Tywin Lannister gave us a splendid choice. Take the black, or see our heads on spikes before evenfall. No offense intended, Tyrion."

"None taken, Ser Jaremy. My father is very fond of spiked heads, especially those of people who have annoyed him in some fashion. And a face as noble as yours, well, no doubt he saw you decorating the city wall above the King's Gate. I think you would have looked very striking up there."

"Thank you," Ser Jaremy replied with a sardonic smile.

Lord Commander Mormont cleared his throat. "Sometimes I fear Ser Alliser saw you true, Tyrion. You *do* mock us and our noble purpose here."

Tyrion shrugged. "We all need to be mocked from time to time, Lord Mormont, lest we start to take ourselves too seriously. More wine, please." He held out his cup.

As Rykker filled it for him, Bowen Marsh said, "You have a great thirst for a small man."

"Oh, I think that Lord Tyrion is quite a large man," Maester Aemon said from the far end of the table. He spoke softly, yet the high officers of the Night's Watch all fell quiet, the better to hear what the ancient had to say. "I think he is a giant come among us, here at the end of the world."

Tyrion answered gently, "I've been called many things, my lord, but *giant* is seldom one of them."

"Nonetheless," Maester Aemon said as his clouded, milk-white eyes moved to Tyrion's face, "I think it is true."

For once, Tyrion Lannister found himself at a loss for words. He could only bow his head politely and say, "You are too kind, Maester Aemon."

The blind man smiled. He was a tiny thing, wrinkled and hairless, shrunken beneath the weight of a hundred years so his maester's collar with its links of many metals hung loose about his throat. "I have been called many things, my lord," he said, "but *kind* is seldom one of them." This time Tyrion himself led the laughter.

Much later, when the serious business of eating was done and the others had left, Mormont offered Tyrion a chair beside the fire and a cup of mulled spirits so strong they brought tears to his eyes. "The kingsroad can be perilous this far north," the Lord Commander told him as they drank.

"I have Jyck and Morrec," Tyrion said, "and Yoren is riding south again."

"Yoren is only one man. The Watch shall escort you as far as Winterfell," Mormont announced in a tone that brooked no argument. "Three men should be sufficient."

"If you insist, my lord," Tyrion said. "You might send young Snow. He would be glad for a chance to see his brothers."

Mormont frowned through his thick grey beard. "Snow? Oh, the Stark bastard. I think not. The young ones need to forget the lives they left behind them, the brothers and mothers and all that. A visit home would only stir up feelings best left alone. I know these things. My own blood kin . . . my sister Maege rules Bear Island now, since my son's dishonor. I have nieces I have never seen." He took a swallow. "Besides, Jon Snow is only a boy. You shall have three strong swords, to keep you safe."

"I am touched by your concern, Lord Mormont." The strong drink was making Tyrion light-headed, but not so drunk that he did not realize that the Old Bear wanted something from him. "I hope I can repay your kindness."

"You can," Mormont said bluntly. "Your sister sits beside the king. Your brother is a great knight, and your father the most powerful lord in the Seven Kingdoms. Speak to them for us. Tell them of our need here. You have seen for yourself, my lord. The Night's Watch is dying. Our strength is less than a thousand now. Six hundred here, two hundred in the Shadow Tower, even fewer at Eastwatch, and a scant third of those fighting men. The Wall is a hundred leagues long. Think on that. Should an attack come, I have three men to defend each mile of wall."

"Three and a third," Tyrion said with a yawn.

Mormont scarcely seemed to hear him. The old man warmed his hands before the fire. "I sent Benjen Stark to search after Yohn Royce's son, lost on his first ranging. The Royce boy was green as summer grass, yet he insisted on the honor of his own command, saying it was his due as a knight. I did not wish to offend his lord father, so I yielded. I sent him out with two men I deemed as good as any in the Watch. More fool I."

"*Fool*," the raven agreed. Tyrion glanced up. The bird peered down at him with those beady black eyes, ruffling its wings. "*Fool*," it called again. Doubtless old Mormont would take it amiss if he throttled the creature. A pity.

The Lord Commander took no notice of the irritating bird. "Gared was near as old as I am and longer on the Wall," he went on, "yet it would seem he forswore himself and fled. I should never have believed it, not of him, but Lord Eddard sent me his head from Winterfell. Of Royce, there is no word. One deserter and two men lost, and now Ben Stark too has gone missing." He sighed deeply. "Who am I to send searching after *him*? In two years I will be seventy. Too old and too weary for the burden I bear, yet if I set it down, who will pick it up? Alliser Thorne? Bowen Marsh? I would have to be as blind as Maester Aemon not to see what *they* are. The Night's Watch has become an army of sullen boys and tired old men. Apart from the men at my table tonight, I have perhaps twenty who can read, and even fewer who can think, or plan, or *lead*. Once the Watch spent its summers building, and each Lord Commander raised the Wall higher than he found it. Now it is all we can do to stay alive."

He was in deadly earnest, Tyrion realized. He felt faintly embarrassed for the old man. Lord Mormont had spent a good part of his life on the Wall, and he needed to believe if those years were to have any meaning. "I promise, the king will hear of your need," Tyrion said gravely, "and I will speak to my father and my brother Jaime as well." And he would. Tyrion Lannister was as good as his word. He left the rest unsaid; that King Robert would ignore him, Lord Tywin would ask if he had taken leave of his senses, and Jaime would only laugh.

"You are a young man, Tyrion," Mormont said. "How many winters have you seen?"

He shrugged. "Eight, nine. I misremember."

"And all of them short."

"As you say, my lord." He had been born in the dead of winter, a terrible cruel one that the maesters said had lasted near three years, but Tyrion's earliest memories were of spring.

"When I was a boy, it was said that a long summer always meant a long winter to come. This summer has lasted *nine years*, Tyrion, and a tenth will soon be upon us. Think on that."

"When *I* was a boy," Tyrion replied, "my wet nurse told me that one day, if men were good, the gods would give the world a summer without ending. Perhaps we've been better than we thought, and the Great Summer is finally at hand." He grinned.

The Lord Commander did not seem amused. "You are not fool enough to believe that, my lord. Already the days grow shorter. There can be no mistake, Aemon has had letters from the Citadel, findings in accord with his own. The end of summer stares us in the face." Mormont reached out and clutched Tyrion tightly by the hand. "You must *make* them understand. I tell you, my lord, the darkness is coming. There are wild things in the woods, direwolves and mammoths and snow bears the size of aurochs, and I have seen darker shapes in my dreams."

"In your dreams," Tyrion echoed, thinking how badly he needed another strong drink.

Mormont was deaf to the edge in his voice. "The fisherfolk near Eastwatch have glimpsed white walkers on the shore."

This time Tyrion could not hold his tongue. "The fisherfolk of Lannisport often glimpse merlings."

"Denys Mallister writes that the mountain people are moving south, slipping past the Shadow Tower in numbers greater than ever before. They are running, my lord . . . but running from *what*?" Lord Mormont moved to the window and stared out into the night. "These are old bones, Lannister, but they have never felt a chill like this. Tell the king what I say, I pray you. Winter *is* coming, and when the Long Night falls, only the Night's Watch will stand between the realm and the darkness that sweeps from the north. The gods help us all if we are not ready."

"The gods help *me* if I do not get some sleep tonight. Yoren is determined to ride at first light." Tyrion got to his feet, sleepy from wine and tired of doom. "I thank you for all the courtesies you have done me, Lord Mormont."

"Tell them, Tyrion. Tell them and make them believe. That is all the thanks I need." He whistled, and his raven flew to him and perched on his shoulder. Mormont smiled and gave the bird some corn from his pocket, and that was how Tyrion left him.

It was bitter cold outside. Bundled thickly in his furs, Tyrion Lannister pulled on his gloves and nodded to the poor frozen wretches standing sentry outside the Commander's Keep. He set off across the yard for his own chambers in the King's Tower, walking as briskly as his legs could manage. Patches of snow crunched beneath his feet as his boots broke the night's crust, and his breath steamed before him like a banner. He shoved his hands into his armpits and walked faster, praying that Morrec had remembered to warm his bed with hot bricks from the fire.

Behind the King's Tower, the Wall glimmered in the light of the moon, immense and mysterious. Tyrion stopped for a moment to look up at it. His legs ached of cold and haste.

Suddenly a strange madness took hold of him, a yearning to look once more off the end of the world. It would be his last chance, he thought; tomorrow he would ride south, and he could not imagine why he would ever want to return to this frozen desolation. The King's Tower was before him, with its promise of warmth and a soft bed, yet Tyrion found himself walking past it, toward the vast pale palisade of the Wall.

A wooden stair ascended the south face, anchored on huge rough-hewn beams sunk deep into the ice and frozen in place. Back and forth it switched, clawing its way upward as crooked as a bolt of lightning. The black brothers assured him that it was much stronger than it looked, but Tyrion's legs were cramping too badly for him to even contemplate the ascent. He went instead to the iron cage beside the well, clambered inside, and yanked hard on the bell rope, three quick pulls.

He had to wait what seemed an eternity, standing there inside the bars with the Wall to his back. Long enough for Tyrion to begin to wonder why he was doing this. He had just about decided to forget his sudden whim and go to bed when the cage gave a jerk and began to ascend.

He moved upward slowly, by fits and starts at first, then more smoothly. The ground fell away beneath him, the cage swung, and Tyrion wrapped his hands around the iron bars. He could feel the cold of the metal even through his gloves. Morrec had a fire burning in his room, he noted with approval, but the Lord Commander's tower was dark. The Old Bear had more sense than he did, it seemed.

Then he was above the towers, still inching his way upward. Castle Black lay below him, etched in moonlight. You could see how stark and empty it was from up here; windowless keeps, crumbling walls, courtyards choked with broken stone. Farther off, he could see the lights of Mole's Town, the little village half a league south along the kingsroad, and here and there the bright glitter of moonlight on water where icy streams descended from the mountain heights to cut across the plains. The rest of the world was a bleak emptiness of windswept hills and rocky fields spotted with snow.

Finally a thick voice behind him said, "Seven hells, it's the dwarf," and the cage jerked to a sudden stop and hung there, swinging slowly back and forth, the ropes creaking.

"Bring him in, damn it." There was a grunt and a loud groaning of wood as the cage slid sideways and then the Wall was beneath him. Tyrion waited until the swinging had stopped before he pushed open the cage door and hopped down onto the ice. A heavy figure in black was leaning on the winch, while a second held the cage with a gloved hand. Their faces were muffled in woolen scarves so only their eyes showed, and they were plump with layers of wool and leather, black on black. "And what will you be wanting, this time of night?" the one by the winch asked.

"A last look."

The men exchanged sour glances. "Look all you want," the other one said. "Just have a care you don't fall off, little man. The Old Bear would have our hides." A small wooden shack stood under the great crane, and Tyrion saw the dull glow of a brazier and felt a brief gust of warmth when the winch men opened the door and went back inside. And then he was alone.

It was bitingly cold up here, and the wind pulled at his clothes like an insistent lover. The top of the Wall was wider than the kingsroad often was, so Tyrion had no fear of falling, although the footing was slicker than he would have liked. The brothers spread crushed stone across the walkways, but the weight of countless footsteps would melt the Wall beneath, so the ice would seem to grow around the gravel, swallowing it, until the path was bare again and it was time to crush more stone.

Still, it was nothing that Tyrion could not manage. He looked off to the east and west, at the Wall stretching before him, a vast white road with no beginning and no end and a dark abyss on either side. West, he decided, for no special reason, and he began to walk that way, following the pathway nearest the north edge, where the gravel looked freshest.

His bare cheeks were ruddy with the cold, and his legs complained more loudly with every step, but Tyrion ignored them. The wind swirled around him, gravel crunched beneath his boots, while ahead the white ribbon followed the lines of the hills, rising higher and higher, until it was lost beyond the western horizon. He passed a massive catapult, as tall as a city wall, its base sunk deep into the Wall. The throwing arm had been taken off for repairs and then forgotten; it lay there like a broken toy, half-embedded in the ice.

On the far side of the catapult, a muffled voice called out a challenge. "Who goes there? Halt!"

Tyrion stopped. "If I halt too long I'll freeze in place, Jon," he said as a shaggy pale shape slid toward him silently and sniffed at his furs. "Hello, Ghost."

Jon Snow moved closer. He looked bigger and heavier in his layers of fur and leather, the hood of his cloak pulled down over his face. "Lannister," he said, yanking loose the scarf to uncover his mouth. "This is the last place I would have expected to see you." He carried a heavy spear tipped in iron, taller than he was, and a sword hung at his side in a leather sheath. Across his chest was a gleaming black warhorn, banded with silver.

"This is the last place I would have expected to be seen," Tyrion admitted. "I was captured by a whim. If I touch Ghost, will he chew my hand off?"

"Not with me here," Jon promised.

Tyrion scratched the white wolf behind the ears. The red eyes watched him impassively. The beast came up as high as his chest now. Another year, and Tyrion had the gloomy feeling he'd be looking *up* at him. "What are *you* doing up here tonight?" he asked. "Besides freezing your manhood off . . ."

"I have drawn night guard," Jon said. "Again. Ser Alliser has kindly arranged for the watch commander to take a special interest in me. He seems to think that if they keep me awake half the night, I'll fall asleep during morning drill. So far I have disappointed him."

Tyrion grinned. "And has Ghost learned to juggle yet?"

"No," said Jon, smiling, "but Grenn held his own against Halder this morning, and Pyp is no longer dropping his sword quite so often as he did."

"Pyp?"

"Pypar is his real name. The small boy with the large ears. He saw me working with Grenn and asked for help. Thorne had never even shown him the proper way to grip a sword." He turned to look north. "I have a mile of Wall to guard. Will you walk with me?"

"If you walk slowly," Tyrion said.

"The watch commander tells me I must walk, to keep my blood from freezing, but he never said how fast."

They walked, with Ghost pacing along beside Jon like a white shadow. "I leave on the morrow," Tyrion said.

"I know." Jon sounded strangely sad.

"I plan to stop at Winterfell on the way south. If there is any message that you would like me to deliver . . ."

"Tell Robb that I'm going to command the Night's Watch and keep him safe, so he might as well take up needlework with the girls and have Mikken melt down his sword for horseshoes."

"Your brother is bigger than me," Tyrion said with a laugh. "I decline to deliver any message that might get me killed."

"Rickon will ask when I'm coming home. Try to explain where I've gone, if you can. Tell him he can have all my things while I'm away, he'll like that."

People seemed to be asking a great deal of him today, Tyrion Lannister thought. "You could put all this in a letter, you know."

"Rickon can't read yet. Bran . . ." He stopped suddenly. "I don't know what message to send to Bran. Help him, Tyrion."

"What help could I give him? I am no maester, to ease his pain. I have no spells to give him back his legs."

"You gave me help when I needed it," Jon Snow said.

"I gave you nothing," Tyrion said. "Words."

"Then give your words to Bran too."

"You're asking a lame man to teach a cripple how to dance," Tyrion said. "However sincere the lesson, the result is likely to be grotesque. Still, I know what it is to love a brother, Lord Snow. I will give Bran whatever small help is in my power."

"Thank you, my lord of Lannister." He pulled off his glove and offered his bare hand. "Friend."

Tyrion found himself oddly touched. "Most of my kin are bastards," he said with a wry smile, "but you're the first I've had to friend." He pulled a glove off with his teeth and clasped Snow by the hand, flesh against flesh. The boy's grip was firm and strong.

When he had donned his glove again, Jon Snow turned abruptly and walked to the low, icy northern parapet. Beyond him the Wall fell away sharply; beyond him there was only the darkness and the wild. Tyrion followed him, and side by side they stood upon the edge of the world.

The Night's Watch permitted the forest to come no closer than half a mile of the north face of the Wall. The thickets of ironwood and sentinel and oak that had once grown there had been harvested centuries ago, to create a broad swath of open ground through which no enemy could hope to pass unseen. Tyrion had heard that elsewhere along the Wall, between the three fortresses, the wildwood had come creeping back over the decades, that there were places where grey-green sentinels and pale white weirwoods had taken root in the shadow of the Wall itself, but Castle Black had a prodigious appetite for firewood, and here the forest was still kept at bay by the axes of the black brothers.

It was never far, though. From up here Tyrion could see it, the dark trees looming beyond the stretch of open ground, like a second wall built parallel to the first, a wall of night. Few axes had ever swung in *that* black wood, where even the moonlight could not penetrate the ancient tangle of root and thorn and grasping limb. Out there the trees grew huge, and the rangers said they seemed to brood and knew not men. It was small wonder the Night's Watch named it the haunted forest.

As he stood there and looked at all that darkness with

no fires burning anywhere, with the wind blowing and the cold like a spear in his guts, Tyrion Lannister felt as though he could almost believe the talk of the Others, the enemy in the night. His jokes of grumkins and snarks no longer seemed quite so droll.

"My uncle is out there," Jon Snow said softly, leaning on his spear as he stared off into the darkness. "The first night they sent me up here, I thought, Uncle Benjen will ride back tonight, and I'll see him first and blow the horn. He never came, though. Not that night and not any night."

"Give him time," Tyrion said.

Far off to the north, a wolf began to howl. Another voice picked up the call, then another. Ghost cocked his head and listened. "If he doesn't come back," Jon Snow promised, "Ghost and I will go find him." He put his hand on the direwolf's head.

"I believe you," Tyrion said, but what he thought was, *And who will go find you?* He shivered.

ARYA

Her father had been fighting with the council again. Arya could see it on his face when he came to table, late again, as he had been so often. The first course, a thick sweet soup made with pumpkins, had already been taken away when Ned Stark strode into the Small Hall. They called it that to set it apart from the Great Hall, where the king could feast a thousand, but it was a long room with a high vaulted ceiling and bench space for two hundred at its trestle tables.

"My lord," Jory said when Father entered. He rose to his feet, and the rest of the guard rose with him. Each man wore a new cloak, heavy grey wool with a white satin border. A hand of beaten silver clutched the woolen folds of each cloak and marked their wearers as men of the Hand's household guard. There were only fifty of them, so most of the benches were empty.

"Be seated," Eddard Stark said. "I see you have started without me. I am pleased to know there are still some men of sense in this city." He signaled for the meal to resume. The servants began bringing out platters of ribs, roasted in a crust of garlic and herbs.

"The talk in the yard is we shall have a tourney, my

lord," Jory said as he resumed his seat. "They say that knights will come from all over the realm to joust and feast in honor of your appointment as Hand of the King."

Arya could see that her father was not very happy about that. "Do they also say this is the last thing in the world I would have wished?"

Sansa's eyes had grown wide as the plates. "A *tourney*," she breathed. She was seated between Septa Mordane and Jeyne Poole, as far from Arya as she could get without drawing a reproach from Father. "Will we be permitted to go, Father?"

"You know my feelings, Sansa. It seems I must arrange Robert's games and pretend to be honored for his sake. That does not mean I must subject my daughters to this folly."

"Oh, *please*," Sansa said. "I want to see."

Septa Mordane spoke up. "Princess Myrcella will be there, my lord, and her younger than Lady Sansa. All the ladies of the court will be expected at a grand event like this, and as the tourney is in your honor, it would look queer if your family did not attend."

Father looked pained. "I suppose so. Very well, I shall arrange a place for you, Sansa." He saw Arya. "For both of you."

"I don't care about their stupid tourney," Arya said. She knew Prince Joffrey would be there, and she hated Prince Joffrey.

Sansa lifted her head. "It will be a *splendid* event. You shan't be wanted."

Anger flashed across Father's face. "*Enough*, Sansa. More of that and you will change my mind. I am weary unto death of this endless war you two are fighting. You are sisters. I expect you to behave like sisters, is that understood?"

Sansa bit her lip and nodded. Arya lowered her face to stare sullenly at her plate. She could feel tears stinging her eyes. She rubbed them away angrily, determined not to cry.

The only sound was the clatter of knives and forks. "Pray excuse me," her father announced to the table. "I find I have small appetite tonight." He walked from the hall.

After he was gone, Sansa exchanged excited whispers

with Jeyne Poole. Down the table Jory laughed at a joke, and Hullen started in about horseflesh. "Your warhorse, now, he may not be the best one for the joust. Not the same thing, oh, no, not the same at all." The men had heard it all before; Desmond, Jacks, and Hullen's son Harwin shouted him down together, and Porther called for more wine.

No one talked to Arya. She didn't care. She liked it that way. She would have eaten her meals alone in her bedchamber if they let her. Sometimes they did, when Father had to dine with the king or some lord or the envoys from this place or that place. The rest of the time, they ate in his solar, just him and her and Sansa. That was when Arya missed her brothers most. She wanted to tease Bran and play with baby Rickon and have Robb smile at her. She wanted Jon to muss up her hair and call her "little sister" and finish her sentences with her. But all of them were gone. She had no one left but Sansa, and Sansa wouldn't even talk to her unless Father made her.

Back at Winterfell, they had eaten in the Great Hall almost half the time. Her father used to say that a lord needed to eat with his men, if he hoped to keep them. "Know the men who follow you," she heard him tell Robb once, "and let them know you. Don't ask your men to die for a stranger." At Winterfell, he always had an extra seat set at his own table, and every day a different man would be asked to join him. One night it would be Vayon Poole, and the talk would be coppers and bread stores and servants. The next time it would be Mikken, and her father would listen to him go on about armor and swords and how hot a forge should be and the best way to temper steel. Another day it might be Hullen with his endless horse talk, or Septon Chayle from the library, or Jory, or Ser Rodrik, or even Old Nan with her stories.

Arya had loved nothing better than to sit at her father's table and listen to them talk. She had loved listening to the men on the benches too; to freeriders tough as leather, courtly knights and bold young squires, grizzled old men-at-arms. She used to throw snowballs at them and help them steal pies from the kitchen. Their wives gave her scones and she invented names for their babies and played monsters-and-maidens and hide-the-treasure and come-into-my-castle with their children. Fat Tom used to call her "Arya Underfoot," because he said that was where she always was. She'd liked that a lot better than "Arya Horseface."

Only that was Winterfell, a world away, and now everything was changed. This was the first time they had supped with the men since arriving in King's Landing. Arya hated it. She hated the sounds of their voices now, the way they laughed, the stories they told. They'd been her friends, she'd felt safe around them, but now she knew that was a lie. They'd let the queen kill Lady, that was horrible enough, but then the Hound found Mycah. Jeyne Poole had told Arya that he'd cut him up in so many pieces that they'd given him back to the butcher in a bag, and at first the poor man had thought it was a pig they'd slaughtered. And no one had raised a voice or drawn a blade or *anything*, not Harwin who always talked so bold, or Alyn who was going to be a knight, or Jory who was captain of the guard. Not even her father.

"He was my *friend*," Arya whispered into her plate, so low that no one could hear. Her ribs sat there untouched, grown cold now, a thin film of grease congealing beneath them on the plate. Arya looked at them and felt ill. She pushed away from the table.

"Pray, where do you think you are going, young lady?" Septa Mordane asked.

"I'm not hungry." Arya found it an effort to remember her courtesies. "May I be excused, please?" she recited stiffly.

"You may not," the septa said. "You have scarcely touched your food. You will sit down and clean your plate."

"You clean it!" Before anyone could stop her, Arya bolted for the door as the men laughed and Septa Mordane called loudly after her, her voice rising higher and higher.

Fat Tom was at his post, guarding the door to the Tower of the Hand. He blinked when he saw Arya rushing toward him and heard the septa's shouts. "Here now, little one, hold on," he started to say, reaching, but Arya slid between his legs and then she was running up the winding tower steps, her feet hammering on the stone while Fat Tom huffed and puffed behind her.

Her bedchamber was the only place that Arya liked in all of King's Landing, and the thing she liked best about it was the door, a massive slab of dark oak with black iron bands. When she slammed that door and dropped the heavy crossbar, nobody could get into her room, not Septa Mordane or Fat Tom or Sansa or Jory or the Hound, *nobody!* She slammed it now.

When the bar was down, Arya finally felt safe enough to cry.

She went to the window seat and sat there, sniffling, hating them all, and herself most of all. It was all her fault, everything bad that had happened. Sansa said so, and Jeyne too.

Fat Tom was knocking on her door. "Arya girl, what's wrong?" he called out. "You in there?"

"No!" she shouted. The knocking stopped. A moment later she heard him going away. Fat Tom was always easy to fool.

Arya went to the chest at the foot of her bed. She knelt, opened the lid, and began pulling her clothes out with both hands, grabbing handfuls of silk and satin and velvet and wool and tossing them on the floor. It was there at the bottom of the chest, where she'd hidden it. Arya lifted it out almost tenderly and drew the slender blade from its sheath.

Needle.

She thought of Mycah again and her eyes filled with tears. Her fault, her fault, her fault. If she had never asked him to play at swords with her . . .

There was a pounding at her door, louder than before. *"Arya Stark, you open this door at once, do you hear me!"*

Arya spun around, with Needle in her hand. "You better not come in here!" she warned. She slashed at the air savagely.

"The Hand will hear of this!" Septa Mordane raged.

"I don't care," Arya screamed. "Go away."

"You will rue this insolent behavior, young lady, I promise you that." Arya listened at the door until she heard the sound of the septa's receding footsteps.

She went back to the window, Needle in hand, and looked down into the courtyard below. If only she could climb like Bran, she thought; she would go out the window and down the tower, run away from this horrible place, away from Sansa and Septa Mordane and Prince

Joffrey, from all of them. Steal some food from the kitchens, take Needle and her good boots and a warm cloak. She could find Nymeria in the wild woods below the Trident, and together they'd return to Winterfell, or run to Jon on the Wall. She found herself wishing that Jon was here with her now. Then maybe she wouldn't feel so alone.

A soft knock at the door behind her turned Arya away from the window and her dreams of escape. "Arya," her father's voice called out. "Open the door. We need to talk."

Arya crossed the room and lifted the crossbar. Father was alone. He seemed more sad than angry. That made Arya feel even worse. "May I come in?" Arya nodded, then dropped her eyes, ashamed. Father closed the door. "Whose sword is that?"

"Mine." Arya had almost forgotten Needle, in her hand.

"Give it to me."

Reluctantly Arya surrendered her sword, wondering if she would ever hold it again. Her father turned it in the light, examining both sides of the blade. He tested the point with his thumb. "A bravo's blade," he said. "Yet it seems to me that I know this maker's mark. This is Mikken's work."

Arya could not lie to him. She lowered her eyes.

Lord Eddard Stark sighed. "My nine-year-old daughter is being armed from my own forge, and I know nothing of it. The Hand of the King is expected to rule the Seven Kingdoms, yet it seems I cannot even rule my own household. How is it that you come to own a sword, Arya? Where did you get this?"

Arya chewed her lip and said nothing. She would not betray Jon, not even to their father.

After a while, Father said, "I don't suppose it matters, truly." He looked down gravely at the sword in his hands. "This is no toy for children, least of all for a girl. What would Septa Mordane say if she knew you were playing with swords?"

"I wasn't *playing*," Arya insisted. "I hate Septa Mordane."

"That's enough." Her father's voice was curt and hard. "The septa is doing no more than is her duty, though gods know you have made it a struggle for the poor woman. Your mother and I have charged her with the impossible task of making you a lady."

"I don't *want* to be a lady!" Arya flared.

"I ought to snap this toy across my knee here and now, and put an end to this nonsense."

"Needle wouldn't break," Arya said defiantly, but her voice betrayed her words.

"It has a name, does it?" Her father sighed. "Ah, Arya. You have a wildness in you, child. 'The wolf blood,' my father used to call it. Lyanna had a touch of it, and my brother Brandon more than a touch. It brought them both to an early grave." Arya heard sadness in his voice; he did not often speak of his father, or of the brother and sister who had died before she was born. "Lyanna might have carried a sword, if my lord father had allowed it. You remind me of her sometimes. You even look like her."

"Lyanna was beautiful," Arya said, startled. Everybody said so. It was not a thing that was ever said of Arya.

"She was," Eddard Stark agreed, "beautiful, and willful, and dead before her time." He lifted the sword, held it out between them. "Arya, what did you think to do with this . . . Needle? Who did you hope to skewer? Your sister? Septa Mordane? Do you know the first thing about sword fighting?"

All she could think of was the lesson Jon had given her. "Stick them with the pointy end," she blurted out.

Her father snorted back laughter. "That *is* the essence of it, I suppose."

Arya desperately wanted to explain, to make him see. "I was trying to learn, but . . ." Her eyes filled with tears. "I asked Mycah to practice with me." The grief came on her all at once. She turned away, shaking. "I *asked* him," she cried. "It was my fault, it was me . . ."

Suddenly her father's arms were around her. He held her gently as she turned to him and sobbed against his chest. "No, sweet one," he murmured. "Grieve for your friend, but never blame yourself. You did not kill the butcher's boy. That murder lies at the Hound's door, him and the cruel woman he serves."

"I hate them," Arya confided, red-faced, sniffling. "The Hound and the queen and the king and Prince Joffrey. I hate all of them. Joffrey *lied*, it wasn't the way he said. I hate Sansa too. She *did* remember, she just lied so Joffrey would like her."

"We all lie," her father said. "Or did you truly think I'd believe that Nymeria ran off?"

Arya blushed guiltily. "Jory promised not to tell."

"Jory kept his word," her father said with a smile. "There are some things I do not need to be told. Even a blind man could see that wolf would never have left you willingly."

"We had to throw rocks," she said miserably. "I *told* her to run, to go be free, that I didn't want her anymore. There were other wolves for her to play with, we heard them howling, and Jory said the woods were full of game, so she'd have deer to hunt. Only she kept following, and finally we had to throw rocks. I hit her twice. She whined and looked at me and I felt so 'shamed, but it was right, wasn't it? The queen would have killed her."

"It was right," her father said. "And even the lie was . . . not without honor." He'd put Needle aside when he went to Arya to embrace her. Now he took the blade up again and walked to the window, where he stood for a moment, looking out across the courtyard. When he turned back, his eyes were thoughtful. He seated himself on the window seat, Needle across his lap. "Arya, sit down. I need to try and explain some things to you."

She perched anxiously on the edge of her bed. "You are too young to be burdened with all my cares," he told her, "but you are also a Stark of Winterfell. You know our words."

"Winter is coming," Arya whispered.

"The hard cruel times," her father said. "We tasted them on the Trident, child, and when Bran fell. You were born in the long summer, sweet one, you've never known anything else, but now the winter is truly coming. Remember the sigil of our House, Arya."

"The direwolf," she said, thinking of Nymeria. She hugged her knees against her chest, suddenly afraid.

"Let me tell you something about wolves, child. When the snows fall and the white winds blow, the lone wolf dies, but the pack survives. Summer is the time for squabbles. In winter, we must protect one another, keep each other warm, share our strengths. So if you must hate, Arya, hate those who would truly do us harm. Septa

Mordane is a good woman, and Sansa . . . Sansa is your sister. You may be as different as the sun and the moon, but the same blood flows through both your hearts. You need her, as she needs you . . . and I need both of you, gods help me."

He sounded so tired that it made Arya sad. "I don't hate Sansa," she told him. "Not truly." It was only half a lie.

"I do not mean to frighten you, but neither will I lie to you. We have come to a dark dangerous place, child. This is not Winterfell. We have enemies who mean us ill. We cannot fight a war among ourselves. This willfulness of yours, the running off, the angry words, the disobedience . . . at home, these were only the summer games of a child. Here and now, with winter soon upon us, that is a different matter. It is time to begin growing up."

"I will," Arya vowed. She had never loved him so much as she did in that instant. "I can be strong too. I can be as strong as Robb."

He held Needle out to her, hilt first. "Here."

She looked at the sword with wonder in her eyes. For a moment she was afraid to touch it, afraid that if she reached for it it would be snatched away again, but then her father said, "Go on, it's yours," and she took it in her hand.

"I can keep it?" she said. "For true?"

"For true." He smiled. "If I took it away, no doubt I'd find a morningstar hidden under your pillow within the fortnight. Try not to stab your sister, whatever the provocation."

"I won't. I promise." Arya clutched Needle tightly to her chest as her father took his leave.

The next morning, as they broke their fast, she apologized to Septa Mordane and asked for her pardon. The septa peered at her suspiciously, but Father nodded.

Three days later, at midday, her father's steward Vayon Poole sent Arya to the Small Hall. The trestle tables had been dismantled and the benches shoved against the walls. The hall seemed empty, until an unfamiliar voice said, "You are late, boy." A slight man with a bald head and a great beak of a nose stepped out of the shadows, holding a pair of slender wooden swords. "Tomorrow you will be here at midday." He had an accent, the lilt of the Free Cities, Braavos perhaps, or Myr.

"Who are you?" Arya asked.

"I am your dancing master." He tossed her one of the wooden blades. She grabbed for it, missed, and heard it clatter to the floor. "Tomorrow you will catch it. Now pick it up."

It was not just a stick, but a true wooden sword complete with grip and guard and pommel. Arya picked it up and clutched it nervously with both hands, holding it out in front of her. It was heavier than it looked, much heavier than Needle.

The bald man clicked his teeth together. "That is not the way, boy. This is not a greatsword that is needing two hands to swing it. You will take the blade in one hand."

"It's too heavy," Arya said.

"It is heavy as it needs to be to make you strong, and for the balancing. A hollow inside is filled with lead, just so. One hand now is all that is needing."

Arya took her right hand off the grip and wiped her sweaty palm on her pants. She held the sword in her left hand. He seemed to approve. "The left is good. All is reversed, it will make your enemies more awkward. Now you are standing wrong. Turn your body sideface, yes, so. You are skinny as the shaft of a spear, do you know. That is good too, the target is smaller. Now the grip. Let me see." He moved closer and peered at her hand, prying her fingers apart, rearranging them. "Just so, yes. Do not squeeze it so tight, no, the grip must be deft, delicate."

"What if I drop it?" Arya said.

"The steel must be part of your arm," the bald man told her. "Can you drop part of your arm? No. Nine years Syrio Forel was first sword to the Sealord of Braavos, he knows these things. Listen to him, boy."

It was the third time he had called her "boy." "I'm a girl," Arya objected.

"Boy, girl," Syrio Forel said. "You are a sword, that is all." He clicked his teeth together. "Just so, that is the grip. You are not holding a battle-axe, you are holding a—"

"—*needle*," Arya finished for him, fiercely.

"Just so. Now we will begin the dance. Remember, child, this is not the iron dance of Westeros we are learning, the knight's dance, hacking and hammering, no. This is the bravo's dance, the water dance, swift and sudden. All men are made of water, do you know this? When you pierce them, the water leaks out and they die." He took a step backward, raised his own wooden blade. "Now you will try to strike me."

Arya tried to strike him. She tried for four hours, until every muscle in her body was sore and aching, while Syrio Forel clicked his teeth together and told her what to do.

The next day their real work began.

DAENERYS

"The Dothraki sea," Ser Jorah Mormont said as he reined to a halt beside her on the top of the ridge. Beneath them, the plain stretched out immense and empty, a vast flat expanse that reached to the distant horizon and beyond. It *was* a sea, Dany thought. Past here, there were no hills, no mountains, no trees nor cities nor roads, only the endless grasses, the tall blades rippling like waves when the winds blew. "It's so green," she said.

"Here and now," Ser Jorah agreed. "You ought to see it when it blooms, all dark red flowers from horizon to horizon, like a sea of blood. Come the dry season, and the world turns the color of old bronze. And this is only *hranna*, child. There are a hundred kinds of grass out there, grasses as yellow as lemon and as dark as indigo, blue grasses and orange grasses and grasses like rainbows. Down in the Shadow Lands beyond Asshai, they say there are oceans of ghost grass, taller than a man on horseback with stalks as pale as milkglass. It murders all other grass and glows in the dark with the spirits of the damned. The Dothraki claim that someday ghost grass will cover the entire world, and then all life will end."

That thought gave Dany the shivers. "I don't want to talk about that now," she said. "It's so beautiful here, I don't want to think about everything dying."

"As you will, *Khaleesi*," Ser Jorah said respectfully.

She heard the sound of voices and turned to look behind her. She and Mormont had outdistanced the rest of their party, and now the others were climbing the ridge below them. Her handmaid Irri and the young archers of her *khas* were fluid as centaurs, but Viserys still struggled with the short stirrups and the flat saddle. Her brother was miserable out here. He ought never have come. Magister Illyrio had urged him to wait in Pentos, had offered him the hospitality of his manse, but Viserys would have none of it. He would stay with Drogo until the debt had been paid, until he had the crown he had been promised. "And if he tries to cheat me, he will learn to his sorrow what it means to wake the dragon," Viserys had vowed, laying a hand on his borrowed sword. Illyrio had blinked at that and wished him good fortune.

Dany realized that she did not want to listen to any of her brother's complaints right now. The day was too perfect. The sky was a deep blue, and high above them a hunting hawk circled. The grass sea swayed and sighed with each breath of wind, the air was warm on her face, and Dany felt at peace. She would not let Viserys spoil it.

"Wait here," Dany told Ser Jorah. "Tell them all to stay. Tell them I command it."

The knight smiled. Ser Jorah was not a handsome man. He had a neck and shoulders like a bull, and coarse black hair covered his arms and chest so thickly that there was none left for his head. Yet his smiles gave Dany comfort. "You are learning to talk like a queen, Daenerys."

"Not a queen," said Dany. "A *khaleesi*." She wheeled her horse about and galloped down the ridge alone.

The descent was steep and rocky, but Dany rode fearlessly, and the joy and the danger of it were a song in her heart. All her life Viserys had told her she was a princess, but not until she rode her silver had Daenerys Targaryen ever felt like one.

At first it had not come easy. The *khalasar* had broken camp the morning after her wedding, moving east toward Vaes Dothrak, and by the third day Dany thought she was going to die. Saddle sores opened on her bottom, hideous and bloody. Her thighs were chafed raw, her hands blistered from the reins, the muscles of her legs and back so wracked with pain that she could scarcely sit. By the time dusk fell, her handmaids would need to help her down from her mount.

Even the nights brought no relief. Khal Drogo ignored her when they rode, even as he had ignored her during their wedding, and spent his evenings drinking with his warriors and bloodriders, racing his prize horses, watching women dance and men die. Dany had no place in these parts of his life. She was left to sup alone, or with Ser Jorah and her brother, and afterward to cry herself to sleep. Yet every night, some time before the dawn, Drogo would come to her tent and wake her in the dark, to ride her as relentlessly as he rode his stallion. He always took her from behind, Dothraki fashion, for which Dany was grateful; that way her lord husband could not see the tears that wet her face, and she could use her pillow to muffle her cries of pain. When he was done, he would close his eyes and begin to snore softly and Dany would lie beside him, her body bruised and sore, hurting too much for sleep.

Day followed day, and night followed night, until Dany knew she could not endure a moment longer. She would kill herself rather than go on, she decided one night . . .

Yet when she slept that night, she dreamt the dragon dream again. Viserys was not in it this time. There was only her and the dragon. Its scales were black as night, wet and slick with blood. *Her* blood, Dany sensed. Its eyes were pools of molten magma, and when it opened its mouth, the flame came roaring out in a hot jet. She could hear it singing to her. She opened her arms to the fire, embraced it, let it swallow her whole, let it cleanse her and temper her and scour her clean. She could feel her flesh sear and blacken and slough away, could feel her blood boil and turn to steam, and yet there was no pain. She felt strong and new and fierce.

And the next day, strangely, she did not seem to hurt quite so much. It was as if the gods had heard her and taken pity. Even her handmaids noticed the change. "*Khaleesi,*" Jhiqui said, "what is wrong? Are you sick?"

"I was," she answered, standing over the dragon's eggs

that Illyrio had given her when she wed. She touched one, the largest of the three, running her hand lightly over the shell. *Black-and-scarlet*, she thought, *like the dragon in my dream.* The stone felt strangely warm beneath her fingers . . . or was she still dreaming? She pulled her hand back nervously.

From that hour onward, each day was easier than the one before it. Her legs grew stronger; her blisters burst and her hands grew callused; her soft thighs toughened, supple as leather.

The *khal* had commanded the handmaid Irri to teach Dany to ride in the Dothraki fashion, but it was the filly who was her real teacher. The horse seemed to know her moods, as if they shared a single mind. With every passing day, Dany felt surer in her seat. The Dothraki were a hard and unsentimental people, and it was not their custom to name their animals, so Dany thought of her only as the silver. She had never loved anything so much.

As the riding became less an ordeal, Dany began to notice the beauties of the land around her. She rode at the head of the *khalasar* with Drogo and his bloodriders, so she came to each country fresh and unspoiled. Behind them the great horde might tear the earth and muddy the rivers and send up clouds of choking dust, but the fields ahead of them were always green and verdant.

They crossed the rolling hills of Norvos, past terraced farms and small villages where the townsfolk watched anxiously from atop white stucco walls. They forded three wide placid rivers and a fourth that was swift and narrow and treacherous, camped beside a high blue waterfall, skirted the tumbled ruins of a vast dead city where ghosts were said to moan among blackened marble columns. They raced down Valyrian roads a thousand years old and straight as a Dothraki arrow. For half a moon, they rode through the Forest of Qohor, where the leaves made a golden canopy high above them, and the trunks of the trees were as wide as city gates. There were great elk in that wood, and spotted tigers, and lemurs with silver fur and huge purple eyes, but all fled before the approach of the *khalasar* and Dany got no glimpse of them.

By then her agony was a fading memory. She still ached after a long day's riding, yet somehow the pain had a sweetness to it now, and each morning she came willingly to her saddle, eager to know what wonders waited for her in the lands ahead. She began to find pleasure even in her nights, and if she still cried out when Drogo took her, it was not always in pain.

At the bottom of the ridge, the grasses rose around her, tall and supple. Dany slowed to a trot and rode out onto the plain, losing herself in the green, blessedly alone. In the *khalasar* she was never alone. Khal Drogo came to her only after the sun went down, but her handmaids fed her and bathed her and slept by the door of her tent, Drogo's bloodriders and the men of her *khas* were never far, and her brother was an unwelcome shadow, day and night. Dany could hear him on the top of the ridge, his voice shrill with anger as he shouted at Ser Jorah. She rode on, submerging herself deeper in the Dothraki sea.

The green swallowed her up. The air was rich with the scents of earth and grass, mixed with the smell of horse-flesh and Dany's sweat and the oil in her hair. Dothraki smells. They seemed to belong here. Dany breathed it all in, laughing. She had a sudden urge to feel the ground beneath her, to curl her toes in that thick black soil. Swinging down from her saddle, she let the silver graze while she pulled off her high boots.

Viserys came upon her as sudden as a summer storm, his horse rearing beneath him as he reined up too hard. "You *dare!*" he screamed at her. "You give commands to *me*? To *me*!" He vaulted off the horse, stumbling as he landed. His face was flushed as he struggled back to his feet. He grabbed her, shook her. "Have you forgotten who you are? Look at you. *Look at you!*"

Dany did not need to look. She was barefoot, with oiled hair, wearing Dothraki riding leathers and a painted vest given her as a bride gift. She looked as though she belonged here. Viserys was soiled and stained in city silks and ringmail.

He was still screaming. "You do *not* command the dragon. Do you understand? I am the Lord of the Seven Kingdoms, I will not hear orders from some horselord's slut, do you hear me?" His hand went under her vest, his fingers digging painfully into her breast. "*Do you hear me?*"

Dany shoved him away, hard.

Viserys stared at her, his lilac eyes incredulous. She

had never defied him. Never fought back. Rage twisted his features. He would hurt her now, and badly, she knew that.

Crack.

The whip made a sound like thunder. The coil took Viserys around the throat and yanked him backward. He went sprawling in the grass, stunned and choking. The Dothraki riders hooted at him as he struggled to free himself. The one with the whip, young Jhogo, rasped a question. Dany did not understand his words, but by then Irri was there, and Ser Jorah, and the rest of her *khas*. "Jhogo asks if you would have him dead, *Khaleesi*," Irri said.

"No," Dany replied. "No."

Jhogo understood that. One of the others barked out a comment, and the Dothraki laughed. Irri told her, "Quaro thinks you should take an ear to teach him respect."

Her brother was on his knees, his fingers digging under the leather coils, crying incoherently, struggling for breath. The whip was tight around his windpipe.

"Tell them I do not wish him harmed," Dany said.

Irri repeated her words in Dothraki. Jhogo gave a pull on the whip, yanking Viserys around like a puppet on a string. He went sprawling again, freed from the leather embrace, a thin line of blood under his chin where the whip had cut deep.

"I warned him what would happen, my lady," Ser Jorah Mormont said. "I told him to stay on the ridge, as you commanded."

"I know you did," Dany replied, watching Viserys. He lay on the ground, sucking in air noisily, red-faced and sobbing. He was a pitiful thing. He had always been a pitiful thing. Why had she never seen that before? There was a hollow place inside her where her fear had been.

"Take his horse," Dany commanded Ser Jorah. Viserys gaped at her. He could not believe what he was hearing; nor could Dany quite believe what she was saying. Yet the words came. "Let my brother walk behind us back to the *khalasar*." Among the Dothraki, the man who does not ride was no man at all, the lowest of the low, without honor or pride. "Let everyone see him as he is."

"*No!*" Viserys screamed. He turned to Ser Jorah, pleading in the Common Tongue with words the horsemen would not understand. "Hit her, Mormont. Hurt her.

Your king commands it. Kill this Dothraki dogs and teach her."

The exile knight looked from Dany to her brother; she barefoot, with dirt between her toes and oil in her hair, he with his silks and steel. Dany could see the decision on his face. "He shall walk, *Khaleesi*," he said. He took her brother's horse in hand while Dany remounted her silver.

Viserys gaped at him, and sat down in the dirt. He kept his silence, but he would not move, and his eyes were full of poison as they rode away. Soon he was lost in the tall grass. When they could not see him anymore, Dany grew afraid. "Will he find his way back?" she asked Ser Jorah as they rode.

"Even a man as blind as your brother should be able to follow our trail," he replied.

"He is proud. He may be too shamed to come back."

Jorah laughed. "Where else should he go? If he cannot find the *khalasar*, the *khalasar* will most surely find him. It is hard to drown in the Dothraki sea, child."

Dany saw the truth of that. The *khalasar* was like a city on the march, but it did not march blindly. Always scouts ranged far ahead of the main column, alert for any sign of game or prey or enemies, while outriders guarded their flanks. They missed nothing, not here, in this land, the place where they had come from. These plains were a part of them . . . and of her, now.

"I hit him," she said, wonder in her voice. Now that it was over, it seemed like some strange dream that she had dreamed. "Ser Jorah, do you think . . . he'll be so angry when he gets back . . ." She shivered. "I woke the dragon, didn't I?"

Ser Jorah snorted. "Can you wake the dead, girl? Your brother Rhaegar was the last dragon, and he died on the Trident. Viserys is less than the shadow of a snake."

His blunt words startled her. It seemed as though all the things she had always believed were suddenly called into question. "You . . . you swore him your sword . . ."

"That I did, girl," Ser Jorah said. "And if your brother is the shadow of a snake, what does that make his servants?" His voice was bitter.

"He is still the true king. He is . . ."

Jorah pulled up his horse and looked at her. "Truth now. Would you want to see Viserys sit a throne?"

Dany thought about that. "He would not be a very good king, would he?"

"There have been worse . . . but not many." The knight gave his heels to his mount and started off again.

Dany rode close beside him. "Still," she said, "the common people are waiting for him. Magister Illyrio says they are sewing dragon banners and praying for Viserys to return from across the narrow sea to free them."

"The common people pray for rain, healthy children, and a summer that never ends," Ser Jorah told her. "It is no matter to them if the high lords play their game of thrones, so long as they are left in peace." He gave a shrug. "They never are."

Dany rode along quietly for a time, working his words like a puzzle box. It went against everything that Viserys had ever told her to think that the people could care so little whether a true king or a usurper reigned over them. Yet the more she thought on Jorah's words, the more they rang of truth.

"What do *you* pray for, Ser Jorah?" she asked him.

"Home," he said. His voice was thick with longing.

"I pray for home too," she told him, believing it.

Ser Jorah laughed. "Look around you then, *Khaleesi.*"

But it was not the plains Dany saw then. It was King's Landing and the great Red Keep that Aegon the Conqueror had built. It was Dragonstone where she had been born. In her mind's eye they burned with a thousand lights, a fire blazing in every window. In her mind's eye, all the doors were red.

"My brother will never take back the Seven Kingdoms," Dany said. She had known that for a long time, she realized. She had known it all her life. Only she had never let herself say the words, even in a whisper, but now she said them for Jorah Mormont and all the world to hear.

Ser Jorah gave her a measuring look. "You think not."

"He could not lead an army even if my lord husband gave him one," Dany said. "He has no coin and the only knight who follows him reviles him as less than a snake. The Dothraki make mock of his weakness. He will never take us home."

"Wise child." The knight smiled.

"I am no child," she told him fiercely. Her heels pressed into the sides of her mount, rousing the silver to a gallop. Faster and faster she raced, leaving Jorah and Irri and the others far behind, the warm wind in her hair and the setting sun red on her face. By the time she reached the *khalasar*, it was dusk.

The slaves had erected her tent by the shore of a spring-fed pool. She could hear rough voices from the woven grass palace on the hill. Soon there would be laughter, when the men of her *khas* told the story of what had happened in the grasses today. By the time Viserys came limping back among them, every man, woman, and child in the camp would know him for a walker. There were no secrets in the *khalasar*.

Dany gave the silver over to the slaves for grooming and entered her tent. It was cool and dim beneath the silk. As she let the door flap close behind her, Dany saw a finger of dusty red light reach out to touch her dragon's eggs across the tent. For an instant a thousand droplets of scarlet flame swam before her eyes. She blinked, and they were gone.

Stone, she told herself. *They are only stone, even Illyrio said so, the dragons are all dead.* She put her palm against the black egg, fingers spread gently across the curve of the shell. The stone was warm. Almost hot. "The sun," Dany whispered. "The sun warmed them as they rode."

She commanded her handmaids to prepare her a bath. Doreah built a fire outside the tent, while Irri and Jhiqui fetched the big copper tub—another bride gift—from the packhorses and carried water from the pool. When the bath was steaming, Irri helped her into it and climbed in after her.

"Have you ever seen a dragon?" she asked as Irri scrubbed her back and Jhiqui sluiced sand from her hair. She had heard that the first dragons had come from the east, from the Shadow Lands beyond Asshai and the islands of the Jade Sea. Perhaps some were still living there, in realms strange and wild.

"Dragons are gone, *Khaleesi*," Irri said.

"Dead," agreed Jhiqui. "Long and long ago."

Viserys had told her that the last Targaryen dragons

had died no more than a century and a half ago, during the reign of Aegon III, who was called the Dragonbane. That did not seem so long ago to Dany. "Everywhere?" she said, disappointed. "Even in the east?" Magic had died in the west when the Doom fell on Valyria and the Lands of the Long Summer, and neither spell-forged steel nor stormsingers nor dragons could hold it back, but Dany had always heard that the east was different. It was said that manticores prowled the islands of the Jade Sea, that basilisks infested the jungles of Yi Ti, that spellsingers, warlocks, and aeromancers practiced their arts openly in Asshai, while shadowbinders and bloodmages worked terrible sorceries in the black of night. Why shouldn't there be dragons too?

"No dragon," Irri said. "Brave men kill them, for dragon terrible evil beasts. It is known."

"It is known," agreed Jhiqui.

"A trader from Qarth once told me that dragons came from the moon," blond Doreah said as she warmed a towel over the fire. Jhiqui and Irri were of an age with Dany, Dothraki girls taken as slaves when Drogo destroyed their father's *khalasar*. Doreah was older, almost twenty. Magister Illyrio had found her in a pleasure house in Lys.

Silvery-wet hair tumbled across her eyes as Dany turned her head, curious. "The moon?"

"He told me the moon was an egg, *Khaleesi*," the Lysene girl said. "Once there were two moons in the sky, but one wandered too close to the sun and cracked from the heat. A thousand thousand dragons poured forth, and drank the fire of the sun. That is why dragons breathe flame. One day the other moon will kiss the sun too, and then it will crack and the dragons will return."

The two Dothraki girls giggled and laughed. "You are foolish strawhead slave," Irri said. "Moon is no egg. Moon is god, woman wife of sun. It is known."

"It is known," Jhiqui agreed.

Dany's skin was flushed and pink when she climbed from the tub. Jhiqui laid her down to oil her body and scrape the dirt from her pores. Afterward Irri sprinkled her with spiceflower and cinnamon. While Doreah brushed her hair until it shone like spun silver, she thought about the moon, and eggs, and dragons.

Her supper was a simple meal of fruit and cheese and fry bread, with a jug of honeyed wine to wash it down. "Doreah, stay and eat with me," Dany commanded when she sent her other handmaids away. The Lysene girl had hair the color of honey, and eyes like the summer sky.

She lowered those eyes when they were alone. "You honor me, *Khaleesi*," she said, but it was no honor, only service. Long after the moon had risen, they sat together, talking.

That night, when Khal Drogo came, Dany was waiting for him. He stood in the door of her tent and looked at her with surprise. She rose slowly and opened her sleeping silks and let them fall to the ground. "This night we must go outside, my lord," she told him, for the Dothraki believed that all things of importance in a man's life must be done beneath the open sky.

Khal Drogo followed her out into the moonlight, the bells in his hair tinkling softly. A few yards from her tent was a bed of soft grass, and it was there that Dany drew him down. When he tried to turn her over, she put a hand on his chest. "No," she said. "This night I would look on your face."

There is no privacy in the heart of the *khalasar*. Dany felt the eyes on her as she undressed him, heard the soft voices as she did the things that Doreah had told her to do. It was nothing to her. Was she not *khaleesi*? His were the only eyes that mattered, and when she mounted him she saw something there that she had never seen before. She rode him as fiercely as ever she had ridden her silver, and when the moment of his pleasure came, Khal Drogo called out her name.

They were on the far side of the Dothraki sea when Jhiqui brushed the soft swell of Dany's stomach with her fingers and said, "*Khaleesi*, you are with child."

"I know," Dany told her.

It was her fourteenth name day.

BRAN

In the yard below, Rickon ran with the wolves.

Bran watched from his window seat. Wherever the boy went, Grey Wind was there first, loping ahead to cut him off, until Rickon saw him, screamed in delight, and went pelting off in another direction. Shaggydog ran at his heels, spinning and snapping if the other wolves came too close. His fur had darkened until he was all black, and his eyes were green fire. Bran's Summer came last. He was silver and smoke, with eyes of yellow gold that saw all there was to see. Smaller than Grey Wind, and more wary. Bran thought he was the smartest of the litter. He could hear his brother's breathless laughter as Rickon dashed across the hard-packed earth on little baby legs.

His eyes stung. He wanted to be down there, laughing and running. Angry at the thought, Bran knuckled away the tears before they could fall. His eighth name day had come and gone. He was almost a man grown now, too old to cry.

"It was just a lie," he said bitterly, remembering the crow from his dream. "I can't fly. I can't even run."

"Crows are all liars," Old Nan agreed, from the chair

where she sat doing her needlework. "I know a story about a crow."

"I don't want any more stories," Bran snapped, his voice petulant. He had liked Old Nan and her stories once. Before. But it was different now. They left her with him all day now, to watch over him and clean him and keep him from being lonely, but she just made it worse. "I hate your stupid stories."

The old woman smiled at him toothlessly. "My stories? No, my little lord, not mine. The stories *are*, before me and after me, before you too."

She was a very ugly old woman, Bran thought spitefully; shrunken and wrinkled, almost blind, too weak to climb stairs, with only a few wisps of white hair left to cover a mottled pink scalp. No one really knew how old she was, but his father said she'd been called Old Nan even when he was a boy. She was the oldest person in Winterfell for certain, maybe the oldest person in the Seven Kingdoms. Nan had come to the castle as a wet nurse for a Brandon Stark whose mother had died birthing him. He had been an older brother of Lord Rickard, Bran's grandfather, or perhaps a younger brother, or a brother to *Lord Rickard's* father. Sometimes Old Nan told it one way and sometimes another. In all the stories the little boy died at three of a summer chill, but Old Nan stayed on at Winterfell with her own children. She had lost both her sons to the war when King Robert won the throne, and her grandson was killed on the walls of Pyke during Balon Greyjoy's rebellion. Her daughters had long ago married and moved away and died. All that was left of her own blood was Hodor, the simpleminded giant who worked in the stables, but Old Nan just lived on and on, doing her needlework and telling her stories.

"I don't care whose stories they are," Bran told her, "I hate them." He didn't want stories and he didn't want Old Nan. He wanted his mother and father. He wanted to go running with Summer loping beside him. He wanted to climb the broken tower and feed corn to the crows. He wanted to ride his pony again with his brothers. He wanted it to be the way it had been before.

"I know a story about a boy who hated stories," Old Nan said with her stupid little smile, her needles moving all the while, *click click click*, until Bran was ready to scream at her.

It would never be the way it had been, he knew. The crow had tricked him into flying, but when he woke up he was broken and the world was changed. They had all left him, his father and his mother and his sisters and even his bastard brother Jon. His father had promised he would ride a real horse to King's Landing, but they'd gone without him. Maester Luwin had sent a bird after Lord Eddard with a message, and another to Mother and a third to Jon on the Wall, but there had been no answers. "Ofttimes the birds are lost, child," the maester had told him. "There's many a mile and many a hawk between here and King's Landing, the message may not have reached them." Yet to Bran it felt as if they had all died while he had slept . . . or perhaps Bran had died, and they had forgotten him. Jory and Ser Rodrik and Vayon Poole had gone too, and Hullen and Harwin and Fat Tom and a quarter of the guard.

Only Robb and baby Rickon were still here, and Robb was changed. He was Robb the Lord now, or trying to be. He wore a real sword and never smiled. His days were spent drilling the guard and practicing his swordplay, making the yard ring with the sound of steel as Bran watched forlornly from his window. At night he closeted himself with Maester Luwin, talking or going over account books. Sometimes he would ride out with Hallis Mollen and be gone for days at a time, visiting distant holdfasts. Whenever he was away more than a day, Rickon would cry and ask Bran if Robb was ever coming back. Even when he was home at Winterfell, Robb the Lord seemed to have more time for Hallis Mollen and Theon Greyjoy than he ever did for his brothers.

"I could tell you the story about Brandon the Builder," Old Nan said. "That was always your favorite."

Thousands and thousands of years ago, Brandon the Builder had raised Winterfell, and some said the Wall. Bran knew the story, but it had never been his favorite. Maybe one of the other Brandons had liked that story. Sometimes Nan would talk to him as if he were *her* Brandon, the baby she had nursed all those years ago, and sometimes she confused him with his uncle Brandon, who was killed by the Mad King before Bran was even born. She had lived so long, Mother had told him once, that all the Brandon Starks had become one person in her head.

"That's not my favorite," he said. "My favorites were the scary ones." He heard some sort of commotion outside and turned back to the window. Rickon was running across the yard toward the gatehouse, the wolves following him, but the tower faced the wrong way for Bran to see what was happening. He smashed a fist on his thigh in frustration and felt nothing.

"Oh, my sweet summer child," Old Nan said quietly, "what do *you* know of fear? Fear is for the winter, my little lord, when the snows fall a hundred feet deep and the ice wind comes howling out of the north. Fear is for the long night, when the sun hides its face for years at a time, and little children are born and live and die all in darkness while the direwolves grow gaunt and hungry, and the white walkers move through the woods."

"You mean the Others," Bran said querulously.

"The Others," Old Nan agreed. "Thousands and thousands of years ago, a winter fell that was cold and hard and endless beyond all memory of man. There came a night that lasted a generation, and kings shivered and died in their castles even as the swineherds in their hovels. Women smothered their children rather than see them starve, and cried, and felt their tears freeze on their cheeks." Her voice and her needles fell silent, and she glanced up at Bran with pale, filmy eyes and asked, "So, child. This is the sort of story you like?"

"Well," Bran said reluctantly, "yes, only . . ."

Old Nan nodded. "In that darkness, the Others came for the first time," she said as her needles went *click click click*. "They were cold things, dead things, that hated iron and fire and the touch of the sun, and every creature with hot blood in its veins. They swept over holdfasts and cities and kingdoms, felled heroes and armies by the score, riding their pale dead horses and leading hosts of the slain. All the swords of men could not stay their advance, and even maidens and suckling babes found no pity in them. They hunted the maids through frozen forests, and fed their dead servants on the flesh of human children."

Her voice had dropped very low, almost to a whisper, and Bran found himself leaning forward to listen.

"Now these were the days before the Andals came, and long before the women fled across the narrow sea from the cities of the Rhoyne, and the hundred kingdoms of those times were the kingdoms of the First Men, who had taken these lands from the children of the forest. Yet here and there in the fastness of the woods the children still lived in their wooden cities and hollow hills, and the faces in the trees kept watch. So as cold and death filled the earth, the last hero determined to seek out the children, in the hopes that their ancient magics could win back what the armies of men had lost. He set out into the dead lands with a sword, a horse, a dog, and a dozen companions. For years he searched, until he despaired of ever finding the children of the forest in their secret cities. One by one his friends died, and his horse, and finally even his dog, and his sword froze so hard the blade snapped when he tried to use it. And the Others smelled the hot blood in him, and came silent on his trail, stalking him with packs of pale white spiders big as hounds—"

The door opened with a *bang*, and Bran's heart leapt up into his mouth in sudden fear, but it was only Maester Luwin, with Hodor looming in the stairway behind him. "Hodor!" the stableboy announced, as was his custom, smiling hugely at them all.

Maester Luwin was not smiling. "We have visitors," he announced, "and your presence is required, Bran."

"I'm listening to a story now," Bran complained.

"Stories wait, my little lord, and when you come back to them, why, there they are," Old Nan said. "Visitors are not so patient, and ofttimes they bring stories of their own."

"Who is it?" Bran asked Maester Luwin.

"Tyrion Lannister, and some men of the Night's Watch, with word from your brother Jon. Robb is meeting with them now. Hodor, will you help Bran down to the hall?"

"Hodor!" Hodor agreed happily. He ducked to get his great shaggy head under the door. Hodor was nearly seven feet tall. It was hard to believe that he was the same blood as Old Nan. Bran wondered if he would shrivel up as small as his great-grandmother when he was old. It did not seem likely, even if Hodor lived to be a thousand.

Hodor lifted Bran as easy as if he were a bale of hay, and cradled him against his massive chest. He always smelled faintly of horses, but it was not a bad smell. His arms were thick with muscle and matted with brown hair. "Hodor," he said again. Theon Greyjoy had once commented that Hodor did not know much, but no one could doubt that he knew his name. Old Nan had cackled like a hen when Bran told her that, and confessed that Hodor's real name was Walder. No one knew where "Hodor" had come from, she said, but when he started saying it, they started calling him by it. It was the only word he had.

They left Old Nan in the tower room with her needles and her memories. Hodor hummed tunelessly as he carried Bran down the steps and through the gallery, with Maester Luwin following behind, hurrying to keep up with the stableboy's long strides.

Robb was seated in Father's high seat, wearing ringmail and boiled leather and the stern face of Robb the Lord. Theon Greyjoy and Hallis Mollen stood behind him. A dozen guardsmen lined the grey stone walls beneath tall narrow windows. In the center of the room the dwarf stood with his servants, and four strangers in the black of the Night's Watch. Bran could sense the anger in the hall the moment that Hodor carried him through the doors.

"Any man of the Night's Watch is welcome here at Winterfell for as long as he wishes to stay," Robb was saying with the voice of Robb the Lord. His sword was across his knees, the steel bare for all the world to see. Even Bran knew what it meant to greet a guest with an unsheathed sword.

"Any man of the Night's Watch," the dwarf repeated, "but not me, do I take your meaning, boy?"

Robb stood and pointed at the little man with his sword. "I am the lord here while my mother and father are away, Lannister. I am not your boy."

"If you are a lord, you might learn a lord's courtesy," the little man replied, ignoring the sword point in his face. "Your bastard brother has all your father's graces, it would seem."

"*Jon,*" Bran gasped out from Hodor's arms.

The dwarf turned to look at him. "So it is true, the boy lives. I could scarce believe it. You Starks are hard to kill."

"You Lannisters had best remember that," Robb said, lowering his sword. "Hodor, bring my brother here."

"Hodor," Hodor said, and he trotted forward smiling and set Bran in the high seat of the Starks, where the Lords of Winterfell had sat since the days when they called themselves the Kings in the North. The seat was cold stone, polished smooth by countless bottoms; the carved heads of direwolves snarled on the ends of its massive arms. Bran clasped them as he sat, his useless legs dangling. The great seat made him feel half a baby.

Robb put a hand on his shoulder. "You said you had business with Bran. Well, here he is, Lannister."

Bran was uncomfortably aware of Tyrion Lannister's eyes. One was black and one was green, and both were looking at him, studying him, weighing him. "I am told you were quite the climber, Bran," the little man said at last. "Tell me, how is it you happened to fall that day?"

"I *never*," Bran insisted. He never fell, never never *never*.

"The child does not remember anything of the fall, or the climb that came before it," said Maester Luwin gently.

"Curious," said Tyrion Lannister.

"My brother is not here to answer questions, Lannister," Robb said curtly. "Do your business and be on your way."

"I have a gift for you," the dwarf said to Bran. "Do you like to ride, boy?"

Maester Luwin came forward. "My lord, the child has lost the use of his legs. He cannot sit a horse."

"Nonsense," said Lannister. "With the right horse and the right saddle, even a cripple can ride."

The word was a knife through Bran's heart. He felt tears come unbidden to his eyes. "I'm *not* a cripple!"

"Then I am not a dwarf," the dwarf said with a twist of his mouth. "My father will rejoice to hear it." Greyjoy laughed.

"What sort of horse and saddle are you suggesting?" Maester Luwin asked.

"A smart horse," Lannister replied. "The boy cannot

use his legs to command the animal, so you must shape the horse to the rider, teach it to respond to the reins, to the voice. I would begin with an unbroken yearling, with no old training to be unlearned." He drew a rolled paper from his belt. "Give this to your saddler. He will provide the rest."

Maester Luwin took the paper from the dwarf's hand, curious as a small grey squirrel. He unrolled it, studied it. "I see. You draw nicely, my lord. Yes, this ought to work. I should have thought of this myself."

"It came easier to me, Maester. It is not terribly unlike my own saddles."

"Will I truly be able to ride?" Bran asked. He wanted to believe them, but he was afraid. Perhaps it was just another lie. The crow had promised him that he could fly.

"You will," the dwarf told him. "And I swear to you, boy, on horseback you will be as tall as any of them."

Robb Stark seemed puzzled. "Is this some trap, Lannister? What's Bran to you? Why should you want to help him?"

"Your brother Jon asked it of me. And I have a tender spot in my heart for cripples and bastards and broken things." Tyrion Lannister placed a hand over his heart and grinned.

The door to the yard flew open. Sunlight came streaming across the hall as Rickon burst in, breathless. The direwolves were with him. The boy stopped by the door, wide-eyed, but the wolves came on. Their eyes found Lannister, or perhaps they caught his scent. Summer began to growl first. Grey Wind picked it up. They padded toward the little man, one from the right and one from the left.

"The wolves do not like your smell, Lannister," Theon Greyjoy commented.

"Perhaps it's time I took my leave," Tyrion said. He took a step backward . . . and Shaggydog came out of the shadows behind him, snarling. Lannister recoiled, and Summer lunged at him from the other side. He reeled away, unsteady on his feet, and Grey Wind snapped at his arm, teeth ripping at his sleeve and tearing loose a scrap of cloth.

"No!" Bran shouted from the high seat as Lannister's men reached for their steel. "Summer, *here.* Summer, to me!"

The direwolf heard the voice, glanced at Bran, and again at Lannister. He crept backward, away from the little man, and settled down below Bran's dangling feet.

Robb had been holding his breath. He let it out with a sigh and called, "Grey Wind." His direwolf moved to him, swift and silent. Now there was only Shaggydog, rumbling at the small man, his eyes burning like green fire.

"Rickon, call him," Bran shouted to his baby brother, and Rickon remembered himself and screamed, "Home, Shaggy, home now." The black wolf gave Lannister one final snarl and bounded off to Rickon, who hugged him tightly around the neck.

Tyrion Lannister undid his scarf, mopped at his brow, and said in a flat voice, "How interesting."

"Are you well, my lord?" asked one of his men, his sword in hand. He glanced nervously at the direwolves as he spoke.

"My sleeve is torn and my breeches are unaccountably damp, but nothing was harmed save my dignity."

Even Robb looked shaken. "The wolves . . . I don't know why they did that . . ."

"No doubt they mistook me for dinner." Lannister bowed stiffly to Bran. "I thank you for calling them off, young ser. I promise you, they would have found me quite indigestible. And now I *will* be leaving, truly."

"A moment, my lord," Maester Luwin said. He moved to Robb and they huddled close together, whispering. Bran tried to hear what they were saying, but their voices were too low.

Robb Stark finally sheathed his sword. "I . . . I may have been hasty with you," he said. "You've done Bran a kindness, and, well . . ." Robb composed himself with an effort. "The hospitality of Winterfell is yours if you wish it, Lannister."

"Spare me your false courtesies, boy. You do not love me and you do not want me here. I saw an inn outside your walls, in the winter town. I'll find a bed there, and both of us will sleep easier. For a few coppers I may even find a comely wench to warm the sheets for me." He spoke to one of the black brothers, an old man with a twisted back and a tangled beard. "Yoren, we go south at daybreak. You will find me on the road, no doubt." With that he made his exit, struggling across the hall on his short legs, past Rickon and out the door. His men followed.

The four of the Night's Watch remained. Robb turned to them uncertainly. "I have had rooms prepared, and you'll find no lack of hot water to wash off the dust of the road. I hope you will honor us at table tonight." He spoke the words so awkwardly that even Bran took note; it was a speech he had learned, not words from the heart, but the black brothers thanked him all the same.

Summer followed them up the tower steps as Hodor carried Bran back to his bed. Old Nan was asleep in her chair. Hodor said "Hodor," gathered up his great-grandmother, and carried her off, snoring softly, while Bran lay thinking. Robb had promised that he could feast with the Night's Watch in the Great Hall. "Summer," he called. The wolf bounded up on the bed. Bran hugged him so hard he could feel the hot breath on his cheek. "I can ride now," he whispered to his friend. "We can go hunting in the woods soon, wait and see." After a time he slept.

In his dream he was climbing again, pulling himself up an ancient windowless tower, his fingers forcing themselves between blackened stones, his feet scrabbling for purchase. Higher and higher he climbed, through the clouds and into the night sky, and still the tower rose before him. When he paused to look down, his head swam dizzily and he felt his fingers slipping. Bran cried out and clung for dear life. The earth was a thousand miles beneath him and he could not fly. *He could not fly.* He waited until his heart had stopped pounding, until he could breathe, and he began to climb again. There was no way to go but up. Far above him, outlined against a vast pale moon, he thought he could see the shapes of gargoyles. His arms were sore and aching, but he dared not rest. He forced himself to climb faster. The gargoyles watched him ascend. Their eyes glowed red as hot coals in a brazier. Perhaps once they had been lions, but now they were twisted and grotesque. Bran could hear them whispering to each other in soft stone voices terrible to hear. He must not listen, he told himself, he must not hear, so long as he did not hear them he was safe. But when the gargoyles pulled themselves loose from the stone and padded down the side of the tower to where Bran clung, he knew he was not safe after all. "I didn't hear," he wept as they came closer and closer, "I didn't, I didn't."

He woke gasping, lost in darkness, and saw a vast shadow looming over him. "I didn't hear," he whispered, trembling in fear, but then the shadow said "Hodor," and lit the candle by the bedside, and Bran sighed with relief.

Hodor washed the sweat from him with a warm, damp cloth and dressed him with deft and gentle hands. When it was time, he carried him down to the Great Hall, where a long trestle table had been set up near the fire. The lord's seat at the head of the table had been left empty, but Robb sat to the right of it, with Bran across from him. They ate suckling pig that night, and pigeon pie, and turnips soaking in butter, and afterward the cook had promised honeycombs. Summer snatched table scraps from Bran's hand, while Grey Wind and Shaggydog fought over a bone in the corner. Winterfell's dogs would not come near the hall now. Bran had found that strange at first, but he was growing used to it.

Yoren was senior among the black brothers, so the steward had seated him between Robb and Maester Luwin. The old man had a sour smell, as if he had not washed in a long time. He ripped at the meat with his teeth, cracked the ribs to suck out the marrow from the bones, and shrugged at the mention of Jon Snow. "Ser Alliser's bane," he grunted, and two of his companions shared a laugh that Bran did not understand. But when Robb asked for news of their uncle Benjen, the black brothers grew ominously quiet.

"What is it?" Bran asked.

Yoren wiped his fingers on his vest. "There's hard news, m'lords, and a cruel way to pay you for your meat and mead, but the man as asks the question must bear the answer. Stark's gone."

One of the other men said, "The Old Bear sent him out to look for Waymar Royce, and he's late returning, my lord."

"Too long," Yoren said. "Most like he's dead."

"My uncle is not dead," Robb Stark said loudly, anger in his tones. He rose from the bench and laid his hand on the hilt of his sword. "Do you hear me? *My uncle is not dead!*" His voice rang against the stone walls, and Bran was suddenly afraid.

Old sour-smelling Yoren looked up at Robb, unimpressed. "Whatever you say, m'lord," he said. He sucked at a piece of meat between his teeth.

The youngest of the black brothers shifted uncomfortably in his seat. "There's not a man on the Wall knows the haunted forest better than Benjen Stark. He'll find his way back."

"Well," said Yoren, "maybe he will and maybe he won't. Good men have gone into those woods before, and never come out."

All Bran could think of was Old Nan's story of the Others and the last hero, hounded through the white woods by dead men and spiders big as hounds. He was afraid for a moment, until he remembered how that story ended. "The children will help him," he blurted, "the children of the forest!"

Theon Greyjoy sniggered, and Maester Luwin said, "Bran, the children of the forest have been dead and gone for thousands of years. All that is left of them are the faces in the trees."

"Down here, might be that's true, Maester," Yoren said, "but up past the Wall, who's to say? Up there, a man can't always tell what's alive and what's dead."

That night, after the plates had been cleared, Robb carried Bran up to bed himself. Grey Wind led the way, and Summer came close behind. His brother was strong for his age, and Bran was as light as a bundle of rags, but the stairs were steep and dark, and Robb was breathing hard by the time they reached the top.

He put Bran into bed, covered him with blankets, and blew out the candle. For a time Robb sat beside him in the dark. Bran wanted to talk to him, but he did not know what to say. "We'll find a horse for you, I promise," Robb whispered at last.

"Are they ever coming back?" Bran asked him.

"Yes," Robb said with such hope in his voice that Bran knew he was hearing his brother and not just Robb the Lord. "Mother will be home soon. Maybe we can ride out to meet her when she comes. Wouldn't that surprise her, to see you ahorse?" Even in the dark room, Bran could feel his brother's smile. "And afterward, we'll ride north to see the Wall. We won't even tell Jon we're coming, we'll just be there one day, you and me. It will be an adventure."

"An adventure," Bran repeated wistfully. He heard his brother sob. The room was so dark he could not see the tears on Robb's face, so he reached out and found his hand. Their fingers twined together.

EDDARD

"Lord Arryn's death was a great sadness for all of us, my lord," Grand Maester Pycelle said. "I would be more than happy to tell you what I can of the manner of his passing. Do be seated. Would you care for refreshments? Some dates, perhaps? I have some very fine persimmons as well. Wine no longer agrees with my digestion, I fear, but I can offer you a cup of iced milk, sweetened with honey. I find it most refreshing in this heat."

There was no denying the heat; Ned could feel the silk tunic clinging to his chest. Thick, moist air covered the city like a damp woolen blanket, and the riverside had grown unruly as the poor fled their hot, airless warrens to jostle for sleeping places near the water, where the only breath of wind was to be found. "That would be most kind," Ned said, seating himself.

Pycelle lifted a tiny silver bell with thumb and forefinger and tinkled it gently. A slender young serving girl hurried into the solar. "Iced milk for the King's Hand and myself, if you would be so kind, child. Well sweetened."

As the girl went to fetch their drinks, the Grand Maester knotted his fingers together and rested his hands on his stomach. "The smallfolk say that the last year of summer is always the hottest. It is not so, yet ofttimes it feels that way, does it not? On days like this, I envy you northerners your summer snows." The heavy jeweled chain around the old man's neck chinked softly as he shifted in his seat. "To be sure, King Maekar's summer was hotter than this one, and near as long. There were fools, even in the Citadel, who took that to mean that the Great Summer had come at last, the summer that never ends, but in the seventh year it broke suddenly, and we had a short autumn and a terrible long winter. Still, the heat was fierce while it lasted. Oldtown steamed and sweltered by day and came alive only by night. We would walk in the gardens by the river and argue about the gods. I remember the *smells* of those nights, my lord—perfume and sweat, melons ripe to bursting, peaches and pomegranates, nightshade and moonbloom. I was a young man then, still forging my chain. The heat did not exhaust me as it does now." Pycelle's eyes were so heavily lidded he looked half-asleep. "My pardons, Lord Eddard. You did not come to hear foolish meanderings of a summer forgotten before your father was born. Forgive an old man his wanderings, if you would. Minds are like swords, I do fear. The old ones go to rust. Ah, and here is our milk." The serving girl placed the tray between them, and Pycelle gave her a smile. "Sweet child." He lifted a cup, tasted, nodded. "Thank you. You may go."

When the girl had taken her leave, Pycelle peered at Ned through pale, rheumy eyes. "Now where were we? Oh, yes. You asked about Lord Arryn . . ."

"I did." Ned sipped politely at the iced milk. It was pleasantly cold, but oversweet to his taste.

"If truth be told, the Hand had not seemed quite himself for some time," Pycelle said. "We had sat together on council many a year, he and I, and the signs were there to read, but I put them down to the great burdens he had borne so faithfully for so long. Those broad shoulders were weighed down by all the cares of the realm, and more besides. His son was ever sickly, and his lady wife so anxious that she would scarcely let the boy out of her sight. It was enough to weary even a strong man, and the Lord Jon was not young. Small wonder if he seemed melancholy and tired. Or so I thought at the time. Yet now I am less certain." He gave a ponderous shake of his head.

"What can you tell me of his final illness?"

The Grand Maester spread his hands in a gesture of helpless sorrow. "He came to me one day asking after a certain book, as hale and healthy as ever, though it did seem to me that something was troubling him deeply. The next morning he was twisted over in pain, too sick to rise from bed. Maester Colemon thought it was a chill on the stomach. The weather had been hot, and the Hand often iced his wine, which can upset the digestion. When Lord Jon continued to weaken, I went to him myself, but the gods did not grant me the power to save him."

"I have heard that you sent Maester Colemon away."

The Grand Maester's nod was as slow and deliberate as a glacier. "I did, and I fear the Lady Lysa will never forgive me that. Maybe I was wrong, but at the time I thought it best. Maester Colemon is like a son to me, and I yield to none in my esteem for his abilities, but he is young, and the young ofttimes do not comprehend the frailty of an older body. He was purging Lord Arryn with wasting potions and pepper juice, and I feared he might kill him."

"Did Lord Arryn say anything to you during his final hours?"

Pycelle wrinkled his brow. "In the last stage of his fever, the Hand called out the name *Robert* several times, but whether he was asking for his son or for the king I could not say. Lady Lysa would not permit the boy to enter the sickroom, for fear that he too might be taken ill. The king did come, and he sat beside the bed for hours, talking and joking of times long past in hopes of raising Lord Jon's spirits. His love was fierce to see."

"Was there nothing else? No final words?"

"When I saw that all hope had fled, I gave the Hand the milk of the poppy, so he should not suffer. Just before he closed his eyes for the last time, he whispered something to the king and his lady wife, a blessing for his son. *The seed is strong*, he said. At the end, his speech was too slurred to comprehend. Death did not come until the next morning, but Lord Jon was at peace after that. He never spoke again."

Ned took another swallow of milk, trying not to gag on

the sweetness of it. "Did it seem to you that there was anything unnatural about Lord Arryn's death?"

"Unnatural?" The aged maester's voice was thin as a whisper. "No, I could not say so. Sad, for a certainty. Yet in its own way, death is the most natural thing of all, Lord Eddard. Jon Arryn rests easy now, his burdens lifted at last."

"This illness that took him," said Ned. "Had you ever seen its like before, in other men?"

"Near forty years I have been Grand Maester of the Seven Kingdoms," Pycelle replied. "Under our good King Robert, and Aerys Targaryen before him, and his father Jaehaerys the Second before him, and even for a few short months under Jaehaerys's father, Aegon the Fortunate, the Fifth of His Name. I have seen more of illness than I care to remember, my lord. I will tell you this: Every case is different, and every case is alike. Lord Jon's death was no stranger than any other."

"His wife thought otherwise."

The Grand Maester nodded. "I recall now, the widow is sister to your own noble wife. If an old man may be forgiven his blunt speech, let me say that grief can derange even the strongest and most disciplined of minds, and the Lady Lysa was never that. Since her last stillbirth, she has seen enemies in every shadow, and the death of her lord husband left her shattered and lost."

"So you are quite certain that Jon Arryn died of a sudden illness?"

"I am," Pycelle replied gravely. "If not illness, my good lord, what else could it be?"

"Poison," Ned suggested quietly.

Pycelle's sleepy eyes flicked open. The aged maester shifted uncomfortably in his seat. "A disturbing thought. We are not the Free Cities, where such things are common. Grand Maester Aethelmure wrote that all men carry murder in their hearts, yet even so, the poisoner is beneath contempt." He fell silent for a moment, his eyes lost in thought. "What you suggest is possible, my lord, yet I do not think it likely. Every hedge maester knows the common poisons, and Lord Arryn displayed none of the signs. And the Hand was loved by all. What sort of monster in man's flesh would dare to murder such a noble lord?"

"I have heard it said that poison is a woman's weapon."

Pycelle stroked his beard thoughtfully. "It is said. Women, cravens . . . and eunuchs." He cleared his throat and spat a thick glob of phlegm onto the rushes. Above them, a raven cawed loudly in the rookery. "The Lord Varys was born a slave in Lys, did you know? Put not your trust in spiders, my lord."

That was scarcely anything Ned needed to be told; there was something about Varys that made his flesh crawl. "I will remember that, Maester. And I thank you for your help. I have taken enough of your time." He stood.

Grand Maester Pycelle pushed himself up from his chair slowly and escorted Ned to the door. "I hope I have helped in some small way to put your mind at ease. If there is any other service I might perform, you need only ask."

"One thing," Ned told him. "I should be curious to examine the book that you lent Jon the day before he fell ill."

"I fear you would find it of little interest," Pycelle said. "It was a ponderous tome by Grand Maester Malleon on the lineages of the great houses."

"Still, I should like to see it."

The old man opened the door. "As you wish. I have it here somewhere. When I find it, I shall have it sent to your chambers straightaway."

"You have been most courteous," Ned told him. Then, almost as an afterthought, he said, "One last question, if you would be so kind. You mentioned that the king was at Lord Arryn's bedside when he died. I wonder, was the queen with him?"

"Why, no," Pycelle said. "She and the children were making the journey to Casterly Rock, in company with her father. Lord Tywin had brought a retinue to the city for the tourney on Prince Joffrey's name day, no doubt hoping to see his son Jaime win the champion's crown. In that he was sadly disappointed. It fell to me to send the queen word of Lord Arryn's sudden death. Never have I sent off a bird with a heavier heart."

"Dark wings, dark words," Ned murmured. It was a proverb Old Nan had taught him as a boy.

"So the fishwives say," Grand Maester Pycelle agreed, "but we know it is not always so. When Maester Luwin's bird brought the word about your Bran, the message lifted every true heart in the castle, did it not?"

"As you say, Maester."

"The gods are merciful." Pycelle bowed his head. "Come to me as often as you like, Lord Eddard. I am here to serve."

Yes, Ned thought as the door swung shut, *but whom?*

On the way back to his chambers, he came upon his daughter Arya on the winding steps of the Tower of the Hand, windmilling her arms as she struggled to balance on one leg. The rough stone had scuffed her bare feet. Ned stopped and looked at her. "Arya, what are you doing?"

"Syrio says a water dancer can stand on one toe for hours." Her hands flailed at the air to steady herself.

Ned had to smile. "Which toe?" he teased.

"*Any* toe," Arya said, exasperated with the question. She hopped from her right leg to her left, swaying dangerously before she regained her balance.

"Must you do your standing here?" he asked. "It's a long hard fall down these steps."

"Syrio says a water dancer *never* falls." She lowered her leg to stand on two feet. "Father, will Bran come and live with us now?"

"Not for a long time, sweet one," he told her. "He needs to win his strength back."

Arya bit her lip. "What will Bran do when he's of age?"

Ned knelt beside her. "He has years to find that answer, Arya. For now, it is enough to know that he will live." The night the bird had come from Winterfell, Eddard Stark had taken the girls to the castle godswood, an acre of elm and alder and black cottonwood overlooking the river. The heart tree there was a great oak, its ancient limbs overgrown with smokeberry vines; they knelt before it to offer their thanksgiving, as if it had been a weirwood. Sansa drifted to sleep as the moon rose, Arya several hours later, curling up in the grass under Ned's cloak. All through the dark hours he kept his vigil alone. When dawn broke over the city, the dark red blooms of dragon's breath surrounded the girls where they lay. "I dreamed of Bran," Sansa had whispered to him. "I saw him smiling."

"He was going to be a knight," Arya was saying now. "A knight of the Kingsguard. Can he still be a knight?"

"No," Ned said. He saw no use in lying to her. "Yet someday he may be the lord of a great holdfast and sit on the king's council. He might raise castles like Brandon the Builder, or sail a ship across the Sunset Sea, or enter your mother's Faith and become the High Septon." *But he will never run beside his wolf again,* he thought with a sadness too deep for words, *or lie with a woman, or hold his own son in his arms.*

Arya cocked her head to one side. "Can I be a king's councillor and build castles and become the High Septon?"

"You," Ned said, kissing her lightly on the brow, "will marry a king and rule his castle, and your sons will be knights and princes and lords and, yes, perhaps even a High Septon."

Arya screwed up her face. "No," she said, "that's *Sansa.*" She folded up her right leg and resumed her balancing. Ned sighed and left her there.

Inside his chambers, he stripped off his sweat-stained silks and sluiced cold water over his head from the basin beside the bed. Alyn entered as he was drying his face. "My lord," he said, "Lord Baelish is without and begs audience."

"Escort him to my solar," Ned said, reaching for a fresh tunic, the lightest linen he could find. "I'll see him at once."

Littlefinger was perched on the window seat when Ned entered, watching the knights of the Kingsguard practice at swords in the yard below. "If only old Selmy's mind were as nimble as his blade," he said wistfully, "our council meetings would be a good deal livelier."

"Ser Barristan is as valiant and honorable as any man in King's Landing." Ned had come to have a deep respect for the aged, white-haired Lord Commander of the Kingsguard.

"And as tiresome," Littlefinger added, "though I daresay he should do well in the tourney. Last year he unhorsed the Hound, and it was only four years ago that he was champion."

The question of who might win the tourney interested Eddard Stark not in the least. "Is there a reason for this visit, Lord Petyr, or are you here simply to enjoy the view from my window?"

Littlefinger smiled. "I promised Cat I would help you in your inquiries, and so I have."

That took Ned aback. Promise or no promise, he could not find it in him to trust Lord Petyr Baelish, who struck him as too clever by half. "You have something for me?"

"Some*one*," Littlefinger corrected. "Four someones, if truth be told. Had you thought to question the Hand's servants?"

Ned frowned. "Would that I could. Lady Arryn took her household back to the Eyrie." Lysa had done him no favor in that regard. All those who had stood closest to her husband had gone with her when she fled: Jon's maester, his steward, the captain of his guard, his knights and retainers.

"*Most* of her household," Littlefinger said, "not all. A few remain. A pregnant kitchen girl hastily wed to one of Lord Renly's grooms, a stablehand who joined the City Watch, a potboy discharged from service for theft, and Lord Arryn's squire."

"His squire?" Ned was pleasantly surprised. A man's squire often knew a great deal of his comings and goings.

"Ser Hugh of the Vale," Littlefinger named him. "The king knighted the boy after Lord Arryn's death."

"I shall send for him," Ned said. "And the others."

Littlefinger winced. "My lord, step over here to the window, if you would be so kind."

"Why?"

"Come, and I'll show you, my lord."

Frowning, Ned crossed to the window. Petyr Baelish made a casual gesture. "There, across the yard, at the door of the armory, do you see the boy squatting by the steps honing a sword with an oilstone?"

"What of him?"

"He reports to Varys. The Spider has taken a great interest in you and all your doings." He shifted in the window seat. "Now glance at the wall. Farther west, above the stables. The guardsman leaning on the ramparts?"

Ned saw the man. "Another of the eunuch's whisperers?"

"No, this one belongs to the queen. Notice that he enjoys a fine view of the door to this tower, the better to note who calls on you. There are others, many unknown even to me. The Red Keep is full of eyes. Why do you think I hid Cat in a brothel?"

Eddard Stark had no taste for these intrigues. "Seven hells," he swore. It *did* seem as though the man on the walls was watching him. Suddenly uncomfortable, Ned moved away from the window. "Is everyone someone's informer in this cursed city?"

"Scarcely," said Littlefinger. He counted on the fingers on his hand. "Why, there's me, you, the king . . . although, come to think on it, the king tells the queen much too much, and I'm less than certain about you." He stood up. "Is there a man in your service that you trust utterly and completely?"

"Yes," said Ned.

"In that case, I have a delightful palace in Valyria that I would dearly love to sell you," Littlefinger said with a mocking smile. "The wiser answer was *no*, my lord, but be that as it may. Send this paragon of yours to Ser Hugh and the others. Your own comings and goings will be noted, but even Varys the Spider cannot watch every man in your service every hour of the day." He started for the door.

"Lord Petyr," Ned called after him. "I . . . am grateful for your help. Perhaps I was wrong to distrust you."

Littlefinger fingered his small pointed beard. "You are slow to learn, Lord Eddard. Distrusting me was the wisest thing you've done since you climbed down off your horse."

JON

Jon was showing Dareon how best to deliver a side-stroke when the new recruit entered the practice yard. "Your feet should be farther apart," he urged. "You don't want to lose your balance. That's good. Now pivot as you deliver the stroke, get all your weight behind the blade."

Dareon broke off and lifted his visor. "Seven gods," he murmured. "Would you look at this, Jon."

Jon turned. Through the eye slit of his helm, he beheld the fattest boy he had ever seen standing in the door of the armory. By the look of him, he must have weighed twenty stone. The fur collar of his embroidered surcoat was lost beneath his chins. Pale eyes moved nervously in a great round moon of a face, and plump sweaty fingers wiped themselves on the velvet of his doublet. "They . . . they told me I was to come here for . . . for training," he said to no one in particular.

"A lordling," Pyp observed to Jon. "Southron, most like near Highgarden." Pyp had traveled the Seven Kingdoms with a mummers' troupe, and bragged that he could tell what you were and where you'd been born just from the sound of your voice.

A striding huntsman had been worked in scarlet thread upon the breast of the fat boy's fur-trimmed surcoat. Jon did not recognize the sigil. Ser Alliser Thorne looked over his new charge and said, "It would seem they have run short of poachers and thieves down south. Now they send us pigs to man the Wall. Is fur and velvet your notion of armor, my Lord of Ham?"

It was soon revealed that the new recruit had brought his own armor with him; padded doublet, boiled leather, mail and plate and helm, even a great wood-and-leather shield blazoned with the same striding huntsman he wore on his surcoat. As none of it was black, however, Ser Alliser insisted that he reequip himself from the armory. That took half the morning. His girth required Donal Noye to take apart a mail hauberk and refit it with leather panels at the sides. To get a helm over his head the armorer had to detach the visor. His leathers bound so tightly around his legs and under his arms that he could scarcely move. Dressed for battle, the new boy looked like an overcooked sausage about to burst its skin. "Let us hope you are not as inept as you look," Ser Alliser said. "Halder, see what Ser Piggy can do."

Jon Snow winced. Halder had been born in a quarry and apprenticed as a stonemason. He was sixteen, tall and muscular, and his blows were as hard as any Jon had ever felt. "This will be uglier than a whore's ass," Pyp muttered, and it was.

The fight lasted less than a minute before the fat boy was on the ground, his whole body shaking as blood leaked through his shattered helm and between his pudgy fingers. "I yield," he shrilled. "No more, I yield, don't hit me." Rast and some of the other boys were laughing.

Even then, Ser Alliser would not call an end. "On your feet, Ser Piggy," he called. "Pick up your sword." When the boy continued to cling to the ground, Thorne gestured to Halder. "Hit him with the flat of your blade until he finds his feet." Halder delivered a tentative smack to his foe's upraised cheeks. "You can hit harder than that," Thorne taunted. Halder took hold of his longsword with both hands and brought it down so hard the blow split leather, even on the flat. The new boy screeched in pain.

Jon Snow took a step forward. Pyp laid a mailed hand

on his arm. "Jon, *no*," the small boy whispered with an anxious glance at Ser Alliser Thorne.

"On your feet," Thorne repeated. The fat boy struggled to rise, slipped, and fell heavily again. "Ser Piggy is starting to grasp the notion," Ser Alliser observed. "Again."

Halder lifted the sword for another blow. "Cut us off a ham!" Rast urged, laughing.

Jon shook off Pyp's hand. "Halder, *enough*."

Halder looked to Ser Alliser.

"The Bastard speaks and the peasants tremble," the master-at-arms said in that sharp, cold voice of his. "I remind you that I am the master-at-arms here, Lord Snow."

"Look at him, Halder," Jon urged, ignoring Thorne as best he could. "There's no honor in beating a fallen foe. He yielded." He knelt beside the fat boy.

Halder lowered his sword. "He yielded," he echoed.

Ser Alliser's onyx eyes were fixed on Jon Snow. "It would seem our Bastard is in love," he said as Jon helped the fat boy to his feet. "Show me your steel, Lord Snow."

Jon drew his longsword. He dared defy Ser Alliser only to a point, and he feared he was well beyond it now.

Thorne smiled. "The Bastard wishes to defend his lady love, so we shall make an exercise of it. Rat, Pimple, help our Stone Head here." Rast and Albett moved to join Halder. "Three of you ought to be sufficient to make Lady Piggy squeal. All you need do is get past the Bastard."

"Stay behind me," Jon said to the fat boy. Ser Alliser had often sent two foes against him, but never three. He knew he would likely go to sleep bruised and bloody tonight. He braced himself for the assault.

Suddenly Pyp was beside him. "Three to two will make for better sport," the small boy said cheerfully. He dropped his visor and slid out his sword. Before Jon could even think to protest, Grenn had stepped up to make a third.

The yard had grown deathly quiet. Jon could feel Ser Alliser's eyes. "Why are you waiting?" he asked Rast and the others in a voice gone deceptively soft, but it was Jon who moved first. Halder barely got his sword up in time.

Jon drove him backward, attacking with every blow, keeping the older boy on the heels. *Know your foe,* Ser Rodrik had taught him once; Jon knew Halder, brutally strong but short of patience, with no taste for defense. Frustrate him, and he would leave himself open, as certain as sunset.

The clang of steel echoed through the yard as the others joined battle around him. Jon blocked a savage cut at his head, the shock of impact running up his arm as the swords crashed together. He slammed a sidestroke into Halder's ribs, and was rewarded with a muffled grunt of pain. The counterstroke caught Jon on the shoulder. Chainmail crunched, and pain flared up his neck, but for an instant Halder was unbalanced. Jon cut his left leg from under him, and he fell with a curse and a crash.

Grenn was standing his ground as Jon had taught him, giving Albett more than he cared for, but Pyp was hard-pressed. Rast had two years and forty pounds on him. Jon stepped up behind him and rang the raper's helm like a bell. As Rast went reeling, Pyp slid in under his guard, knocked him down, and leveled a blade at his throat. By then Jon had moved on. Facing two swords, Albett backed away. "I yield," he shouted.

Ser Alliser Thorne surveyed the scene with disgust. "The mummer's farce has gone on long enough for today." He walked away. The session was at an end.

Dareon helped Halder to his feet. The quarryman's son wrenched off his helm and threw it across the yard. "For an instant, I thought I finally had you, Snow."

"For an instant, you did," Jon replied. Under his mail and leather, his shoulder was throbbing. He sheathed his sword and tried to remove his helm, but when he raised his arm, the pain made him grit his teeth.

"Let me," a voice said. Thick-fingered hands unfastened helm from gorget and lifted it off gently. "Did he hurt you?"

"I've been bruised before." He touched his shoulder and winced. The yard was emptying around them.

Blood matted the fat boy's hair where Halder had split his helm asunder. "My name is Samwell Tarly, of Horn . . ." He stopped and licked his lips. "I mean, I *was* of Horn Hill, until I . . . left. I've come to take the black. My father is Lord Randyll, a bannerman to the Tyrells of Highgarden. I used to be his heir, only . . ." His voice trailed off.

"I'm Jon Snow, Ned Stark's bastard, of Winterfell."

Samwell Tarly nodded. "I . . . if you want, you can call me Sam. My mother calls me Sam."

"You can call *him* Lord Snow," Pyp said as he came up to join them. "You don't want to know what his mother calls him."

"These two are Grenn and Pypar," Jon said.

"Grenn's the ugly one," Pyp said.

Grenn scowled. "You're uglier than me. At least I don't have ears like a bat."

"My thanks to all of you," the fat boy said gravely.

"Why didn't you get up and fight?" Grenn demanded.

"I wanted to, truly. I just . . . I couldn't. I didn't want him to hit me anymore." He looked at the ground. "I . . . I fear I'm a coward. My lord father always said so."

Grenn looked thunderstruck. Even Pyp had no words to say to that, and Pyp had words for everything. What sort of man would proclaim himself a coward?

Samwell Tarly must have read their thoughts on their faces. His eyes met Jon's and darted away, quick as frightened animals. "I . . . I'm sorry," he said. "I don't mean to . . . to be like I am." He walked heavily toward the armory.

Jon called after him. "You were hurt," he said. "Tomorrow you'll do better."

Sam looked mournfully back over one shoulder. "No I won't," he said, blinking back tears. "I never do better."

When he was gone, Grenn frowned. "Nobody likes cravens," he said uncomfortably. "I wish we hadn't helped him. What if they think we're craven too?"

"You're too stupid to be craven," Pyp told him.

"I am not," Grenn said.

"Yes you are. If a bear attacked you in the woods, you'd be too stupid to run away."

"I would not," Grenn insisted. "I'd run away faster than you." He stopped suddenly, scowling when he saw Pyp's grin and realized what he'd just said. His thick neck flushed a dark red. Jon left them there arguing as he returned to the armory, hung up his sword, and stripped off his battered armor.

Life at Castle Black followed certain patterns; the mornings were for swordplay, the afternoons for work. The black brothers set new recruits to many different tasks, to learn where their skills lay. Jon cherished the rare afternoons when he was sent out with Ghost ranging at his side to bring back game for the Lord Commander's table, but for every day spent hunting, he gave a dozen to Donal Noye in the armory, spinning the whetstone while the one-armed smith sharpened axes grown dull from use, or pumping the bellows as Noye hammered out a new sword. Other times he ran messages, stood at guard, mucked out stables, fletched arrows, assisted Maester Aemon with his birds or Bowen Marsh with his counts and inventories.

That afternoon, the watch commander sent him to the winch cage with four barrels of fresh-crushed stone, to scatter gravel over the icy footpaths atop the Wall. It was lonely and boring work, even with Ghost along for company, but Jon found he did not mind. On a clear day you could see half the world from the top of the Wall, and the air was always cold and bracing. He could think here, and he found himself thinking of Samwell Tarly . . . and, oddly, of Tyrion Lannister. He wondered what Tyrion would have made of the fat boy. *Most men would rather deny a hard truth than face it,* the dwarf had told him, grinning. The world was full of cravens who pretended to be heroes; it took a queer sort of courage to admit to cowardice as Samwell Tarly had.

His sore shoulder made the work go slowly. It was late afternoon before Jon finished graveling the paths. He lingered on high to watch the sun go down, turning the western sky the color of blood. Finally, as dusk was settling over the north, Jon rolled the empty barrels back into the cage and signaled the winch men to lower him.

The evening meal was almost done by the time he and Ghost reached the common hall. A group of the black brothers were dicing over mulled wine near the fire. His friends were at the bench nearest the west wall, laughing. Pyp was in the middle of a story. The mummer's boy with the big ears was a born liar with a hundred different voices, and he did not tell his tales so much as live them, playing all the parts as needed, a king one moment and a swineherd the next. When he turned into an alehouse girl or a virgin princess, he used a high falsetto voice that reduced them all to tears of helpless laughter, and his eunuchs were always eerily accurate caricatures of Ser Alliser. Jon took as much pleasure from Pyp's antics as anyone . . . yet that night he turned away and went instead to the end of the bench, where Samwell Tarly sat alone, as far from the others as he could get.

He was finishing the last of the pork pie the cooks had served up for supper when Jon sat down across from him. The fat boy's eyes widened at the sight of Ghost. "Is that a wolf?"

"A direwolf," Jon said. "His name is Ghost. The direwolf is the sigil of my father's House."

"Ours is a striding huntsman," Samwell Tarly said.

"Do you like to hunt?"

The fat boy shuddered. "I hate it." He looked as though he was going to cry again.

"What's wrong now?" Jon asked him. "Why are you always so frightened?"

Sam stared at the last of his pork pie and gave a feeble shake of his head, too scared even to talk. A burst of laughter filled the hall. Jon heard Pyp squeaking in a high voice. He stood. "Let's go outside."

The round fat face looked up at him, suspicious. "Why? What will we do outside?"

"Talk," Jon said. "Have you seen the Wall?"

"I'm fat, not blind," Samwell Tarly said. "Of course I saw it, it's seven hundred feet high." Yet he stood up all the same, wrapped a fur-lined cloak over his shoulders, and followed Jon from the common hall, still wary, as if he suspected some cruel trick was waiting for him in the night. Ghost padded along beside them. "I never thought it would be like this," Sam said as they walked, his words steaming in the cold air. Already he was huffing and puffing as he tried to keep up. "All the buildings are falling down, and it's so . . . so . . ."

"Cold?" A hard frost was settling over the castle, and Jon could hear the soft crunch of grey weeds beneath his boots.

Sam nodded miserably. "I hate the cold," he said. "Last night I woke up in the dark and the fire had gone out and I was certain I was going to freeze to death by morning."

"It must have been warmer where you come from."

"I never saw snow until last month. We were crossing the barrowlands, me and the men my father sent to see me north, and this white stuff began to fall, like a soft rain. At first I thought it was so beautiful, like feathers drifting from the sky, but it kept on and on, until I was frozen to the bone. The men had crusts of snow in their beards and more on their shoulders, and still it kept coming. I was afraid it would never end."

Jon smiled.

The Wall loomed before them, glimmering palely in the light of the half moon. In the sky above, the stars burned clear and sharp. "Are they going to make me go up there?" Sam asked. His face curdled like old milk as he looked at the great wooden stairs. "I'll die if I have to climb that."

"There's a winch," Jon said, pointing. "They can draw you up in a cage."

Samwell Tarly sniffled. "I don't like high places."

It was too much. Jon frowned, incredulous. "Are you afraid of *everything*?" he asked. "I don't understand. If you are truly so craven, why are you here? Why would a coward want to join the Night's Watch?"

Samwell Tarly looked at him for a long moment, and his round face seemed to cave in on itself. He sat down on the frost-covered ground and began to cry, huge choking sobs that made his whole body shake. Jon Snow could only stand and watch. Like the snowfall on the barrowlands, it seemed the tears would never end.

It was Ghost who knew what to do. Silent as shadow, the pale direwolf moved closer and began to lick the warm tears off Samwell Tarly's face. The fat boy cried out, startled . . . and somehow, in a heartbeat, his sobs turned to laughter.

Jon Snow laughed with him. Afterward they sat on the frozen ground, huddled in their cloaks with Ghost between them. Jon told the story of how he and Robb had found the pups newborn in the late summer snows. It seemed a thousand years ago now. Before long he found himself talking of Winterfell.

"Sometimes I dream about it," he said. "I'm walking down this long empty hall. My voice echoes all around, but no one answers, so I walk faster, opening doors, shouting names. I don't even know who I'm looking for. Most nights it's my father, but sometimes it's Robb instead, or my little sister Arya, or my uncle." The thought of Benjen Stark saddened him; his uncle was still missing. The Old Bear had sent out rangers in search of him. Ser

Jaremy Rykker had led two sweeps, and Quorin Halfhand had gone forth from the Shadow Tower, but they'd found nothing aside from a few blazes in the trees that his uncle had left to mark his way. In the stony highlands to the northwest, the marks stopped abruptly and all trace of Ben Stark vanished.

"Do you ever find anyone in your dream?" Sam asked.

Jon shook his head. "No one. The castle is always empty." He had never told anyone of the dream, and he did not understand why he was telling Sam now, yet somehow it felt good to talk of it. "Even the ravens are gone from the rookery, and the stables are full of bones. That always scares me. I start to run then, throwing open doors, climbing the tower three steps at a time, screaming for someone, for anyone. And then I find myself in front of the door to the crypts. It's black inside, and I can see the steps spiraling down. Somehow I know I have to go down there, but I don't want to. I'm afraid of what might be waiting for me. The old Kings of Winter are down there, sitting on their thrones with stone wolves at their feet and iron swords across their laps, but it's not them I'm afraid of. I scream that I'm not a Stark, that this isn't my place, but it's no good, I have to go anyway, so I start down, feeling the walls as I descend, with no torch to light the way. It gets darker and darker, until I want to scream." He stopped, frowning, embarrassed. "That's when I always wake." His skin cold and clammy, shivering in the darkness of his cell. Ghost would leap up beside him, his warmth as comforting as daybreak. He would go back to sleep with his face pressed into the direwolf's shaggy white fur. "Do you dream of Horn Hill?" Jon asked.

"No." Sam's mouth grew tight and hard. "I hated it there." He scratched Ghost behind the ear, brooding, and Jon let the silence breathe. After a long while Samwell Tarly began to talk, and Jon Snow listened quietly, and learned how it was that a self-confessed coward found himself on the Wall.

The Tarlys were a family old in honor, bannermen to Mace Tyrell, Lord of Highgarden and Warden of the South. The eldest son of Lord Randyll Tarly, Samwell was born heir to rich lands, a strong keep, and a storied two-handed greatsword named Heartsbane, forged of Valyrian steel and passed down from father to son near five hundred years.

Whatever pride his lord father might have felt at Samwell's birth vanished as the boy grew up plump, soft, and awkward. Sam loved to listen to music and make his own songs, to wear soft velvets, to play in the castle kitchen beside the cooks, drinking in the rich smells as he snitched lemon cakes and blueberry tarts. His passions were books and kittens and dancing, clumsy as he was. But he grew ill at the sight of blood, and wept to see even a chicken slaughtered. A dozen masters-at-arms came and went at Horn Hill, trying to turn Samwell into the knight his father wanted. The boy was cursed and caned, slapped and starved. One man had him sleep in his chainmail to make him more martial. Another dressed him in his mother's clothing and paraded him through the bailey to shame him into valor. He only grew fatter and more frightened, until Lord Randyll's disappointment turned to anger and then to loathing. "One time," Sam confided, his voice dropping from a whisper, "two men came to the castle, warlocks from Qarth with white skin and blue lips. They slaughtered a bull aurochs and made me bathe in the hot blood, but it didn't make me brave as they'd promised. I got sick and retched. Father had them scourged."

Finally, after three girls in as many years, Lady Tarly gave her lord husband a second son. From that day, Lord Randyll ignored Sam, devoting all his time to the younger boy, a fierce, robust child more to his liking. Samwell had known several years of sweet peace with his music and his books.

Until the dawn of his fifteenth name day, when he had been awakened to find his horse saddled and ready. Three men-at-arms had escorted him into a wood near Horn Hill, where his father was skinning a deer. "You are almost a man grown now, and my heir," Lord Randyll Tarly had told his eldest son, his long knife laying bare the carcass as he spoke. "You have given me no cause to disown you, but neither will I allow you to inherit the land and title that should be Dickon's. Heartsbane must go to a man strong enough to wield her, and you are not worthy to touch her hilt. So I have decided that you shall this day announce that you wish to take the black. You will forsake all claim to your brother's inheritance and start north before evenfall.

"If you do not, then on the morrow we shall have a hunt, and somewhere in these woods your horse will stumble, and you will be thrown from the saddle to die . . . or so I will tell your mother. She has a woman's heart and finds it in her to cherish even you, and I have no wish to cause her pain. Please do not imagine that it will truly be that easy, should you think to defy me. Nothing would please me more than to hunt you down like the pig you are." His arms were red to the elbow as he laid the skinning knife aside. "So. There is your choice. The Night's Watch"—he reached inside the deer, ripped out its heart, and held it in his fist, red and dripping—"or this."

Sam told the tale in a calm, dead voice, as if it were something that had happened to someone else, not to him. And strangely, Jon thought, he did not weep, not even once. When he was done, they sat together and listened to the wind for a time. There was no other sound in all the world.

Finally Jon said, "We should go back to the common hall."

"Why?" Sam asked.

Jon shrugged. "There's hot cider to drink, or mulled wine if you prefer. Some nights Dareon sings for us, if the mood is on him. He was a singer, before . . . well, not truly, but almost, an apprentice singer."

"How did he come here?" Sam asked.

"Lord Rowan of Goldengrove found him in bed with his daughter. The girl was two years older, and Dareon swears she helped him through her window, but under her father's eye she named it rape, so here he is. When Maester Aemon heard him sing, he said his voice was honey poured over thunder." Jon smiled. "Toad sometimes sings too, if you call it singing. Drinking songs he learned in his father's winesink. Pyp says his voice is piss poured over a fart." They laughed at that together.

"I should like to hear them both," Sam admitted, "but they would not want me there." His face was troubled. "He's going to make me fight again on the morrow, isn't he?"

"He is," Jon was forced to say.

Sam got awkwardly to his feet. "I had better try to sleep." He huddled down in his cloak and plodded off.

The others were still in the common room when Jon returned, alone but for Ghost. "Where have *you* been?" Pyp asked.

"Talking with Sam," he said.

"He truly is craven," said Grenn. "At supper, there were still places on the bench when he got his pie, but he was too scared to come sit with us."

"The Lord of Ham thinks he's too good to eat with the likes of us," suggested Jeren.

"I saw him eat a pork pie," Toad said, smirking. "Do you think it was a brother?" He began to make *oink*ing noises.

"Stop it!" Jon snapped angrily.

The other boys fell silent, taken aback by his sudden fury. "Listen to me," Jon said into the quiet, and he told them how it was going to be. Pyp backed him, as he'd known he would, but when Halder spoke up, it was a pleasant surprise. Grenn was anxious at the first, but Jon knew the words to move him. One by one the rest fell in line. Jon persuaded some, cajoled some, shamed the others, made threats where threats were required. At the end they had all agreed . . . all but Rast.

"You girls do as you please," Rast said, "but if Thorne sends me against Lady Piggy, I'm going to slice me off a rasher of bacon." He laughed in Jon's face and left them there.

Hours later, as the castle slept, three of them paid a call on his cell. Grenn held his arms while Pyp sat on his legs. Jon could hear Rast's rapid breathing as Ghost leapt onto his chest. The direwolf's eyes burned red as embers as his teeth nipped lightly at the soft skin of the boy's throat, just enough to draw blood. "Remember, we know where you sleep," Jon said softly.

The next morning Jon heard Rast tell Albett and Toad how his razor had slipped while he shaved.

From that day forth, neither Rast nor any of the others would hurt Samwell Tarly. When Ser Alliser matched them against him, they would stand their ground and swat aside his slow, clumsy strokes. If the master-at-arms screamed for an attack, they would dance in and tap Sam lightly on breastplate or helm or leg. Ser Alliser raged and threatened and called them all cravens and women and worse, yet Sam remained unhurt. A few nights later, at Jon's urging, he joined them for the evening meal, taking a place on the bench beside Halder. It was another fortnight before he found the nerve to join their talk, but in time he was laughing at Pyp's faces and teasing Grenn with the best of them.

Fat and awkward and frightened he might be, but Samwell Tarly was no fool. One night he visited Jon in his cell. "I don't know what you did," he said, "but I know you did it." He looked away shyly. "I've never had a friend before."

"We're not friends," Jon said. He put a hand on Sam's broad shoulder. "We're brothers."

And so they were, he thought to himself after Sam had taken his leave. Robb and Bran and Rickon were his father's sons, and he loved them still, yet Jon knew that he had never truly been one of them. Catelyn Stark had seen to that. The grey walls of Winterfell might still haunt his dreams, but Castle Black was his life now, and his brothers were Sam and Grenn and Halder and Pyp and the other cast-outs who wore the black of the Night's Watch.

"My uncle spoke truly," he whispered to Ghost. He wondered if he would ever see Benjen Stark again, to tell him.

EDDARD

"It's the Hand's tourney that's the cause of all the trouble, my lords," the Commander of the City Watch complained to the king's council.

"The king's tourney," Ned corrected, wincing. "I assure you, the Hand wants no part of it."

"Call it what you will, my lord. Knights have been arriving from all over the realm, and for every knight we get two freeriders, three craftsmen, six men-at-arms, a dozen merchants, two dozen whores, and more thieves than I dare guess. This cursed heat had half the city in a fever to start, and now with all these visitors . . . last night we had a drowning, a tavern riot, three knife fights, a rape, two fires, robberies beyond count, and a drunken horse race down the Street of the Sisters. The night before a woman's head was found in the Great Sept, floating in the rainbow pool. No one seems to know how it got there or who it belongs to."

"How dreadful," Varys said with a shudder.

Lord Renly Baratheon was less sympathetic. "If you cannot keep the king's peace, Janos, perhaps the City Watch should be commanded by someone who can."

Stout, jowly Janos Slynt puffed himself up like an angry frog, his bald pate reddening. "Aegon the Dragon himself could not keep the peace, Lord Renly. I need more men."

"How many?" Ned asked, leaning forward. As ever, Robert had not troubled himself to attend the council session, so it fell to his Hand to speak for him.

"As many as can be gotten, Lord Hand."

"Hire fifty new men," Ned told him. "Lord Baelish will see that you get the coin."

"I will?" Littlefinger said.

"You will. You found forty thousand golden dragons for a champion's purse, surely you can scrape together a few coppers to keep the king's peace." Ned turned back to Janos Slynt. "I will also give you twenty good swords from my own household guard, to serve with the Watch until the crowds have left."

"All thanks, Lord Hand," Slynt said, bowing. "I promise you, they shall be put to good use."

When the Commander had taken his leave, Eddard Stark turned to the rest of the council. "The sooner this folly is done with, the better I shall like it." As if the expense and trouble were not irksome enough, all and sundry insisted on salting Ned's wound by calling it "the Hand's tourney," as if he were the cause of it. And Robert honestly seemed to think he should feel honored!

"The realm prospers from such events, my lord," Grand Maester Pycelle said. "They bring the great the chance of glory, and the lowly a respite from their woes."

"And put coins in many a pocket," Littlefinger added. "Every inn in the city is full, and the whores are walking bowlegged and jingling with each step."

Lord Renly laughed. "We're fortunate my brother Stannis is not with us. Remember the time he proposed to outlaw brothels? The king asked him if perhaps he'd like to outlaw eating, shitting, and breathing while he was at it. If truth be told, I ofttimes wonder how Stannis ever got that ugly daughter of his. He goes to his marriage bed like a man marching to a battlefield, with a grim look in his eyes and a determination to do his duty."

Ned had not joined the laughter. "I wonder about your brother Stannis as well. I wonder when he intends to end his visit to Dragonstone and resume his seat on this council."

"No doubt as soon as we've scourged all those whores into the sea," Littlefinger replied, provoking more laughter.

"I have heard quite enough about whores for one day," Ned said, rising. "Until the morrow."

Harwin had the door when Ned returned to the Tower of the Hand. "Summon Jory to my chambers and tell your father to saddle my horse," Ned told him, too brusquely.

"As you say, my lord."

The Red Keep and the "Hand's tourney" were chafing him raw, Ned reflected as he climbed. He yearned for the comfort of Catelyn's arms, for the sounds of Robb and Jon crossing swords in the practice yard, for the cool days and cold nights of the north.

In his chambers he stripped off his council silks and sat for a moment with the book while he waited for Jory to arrive. *The Lineages and Histories of the Great Houses of the Seven Kingdoms, With Descriptions of Many High Lords and Noble Ladies and Their Children*, by Grand Maester Malleon. Pycelle had spoken truly; it made for ponderous reading. Yet Jon Arryn had asked for it, and Ned felt certain he had reasons. There was something here, some truth buried in these brittle yellow pages, if only he could see it. But *what?* The tome was over a century old. Scarcely a man now alive had yet been born when Malleon had compiled his dusty lists of weddings, births, and deaths.

He opened to the section on House Lannister once more, and turned the pages slowly, hoping against hope that something would leap out at him. The Lannisters were an old family, tracing their descent back to Lann the Clever, a trickster from the Age of Heroes who was no doubt as legendary as Bran the Builder, though far more beloved of singers and taletellers. In the songs, Lann was the fellow who winkled the Casterlys out of Casterly Rock with no weapon but his wits, and stole gold from the sun to brighten his curly hair. Ned wished he were here now, to winkle the truth out of this damnable book.

A sharp rap on the door heralded Jory Cassel. Ned closed Malleon's tome and bid him enter. "I've promised the City Watch twenty of my guard until the tourney is done," he told him. "I rely on you to make the choice. Give Alyn the command, and make certain the men understand that they are needed to stop fights, not start them." Rising, Ned opened a cedar chest and removed a light linen undertunic. "Did you find the stableboy?"

"The watchman, my lord," Jory said. "He vows he'll never touch another horse."

"What did he have to say?"

"He claims he knew Lord Arryn well. Fast friends, they were." Jory snorted. "The Hand always gave the lads a copper on their name days, he says. Had a way with horses. Never rode his mounts too hard, and brought them carrots and apples, so they were always pleased to see him."

"Carrots and apples," Ned repeated. It sounded as if this boy would be even less use than the others. And he was the last of the four Littlefinger had turned up. Jory had spoken to each of them in turn. Ser Hugh had been brusque and uninformative, and arrogant as only a new-made knight can be. If the Hand wished to talk to him, he should be pleased to receive him, but he would not be questioned by a mere captain of guards . . . even if said captain was ten years older and a hundred times the swordsman. The serving girl had at least been pleasant. She said Lord Jon had been reading more than was good for him, that he was troubled and melancholy over his young son's frailty, and gruff with his lady wife. The pot-boy, now cordwainer, had never exchanged so much as a word with Lord Jon, but he was full of oddments of kitchen gossip: the lord had been quarreling with the king, the lord only picked at his food, the lord was sending his boy to be fostered on Dragonstone, the lord had taken a great interest in the breeding of hunting hounds, the lord had visited a master armorer to commission a new suit of plate, wrought all in pale silver with a blue jasper falcon and a mother-of-pearl moon on the breast. The king's own brother had gone with him to help choose the design, the potboy said. No, not Lord Renly, the other one, Lord Stannis.

"Did our watchman recall anything else of note?"

"The lad swears Lord Jon was as strong as a man half his age. Often went riding with Lord Stannis, he says."

Stannis again, Ned thought. He found that curious. Jon Arryn and he had been cordial, but never friendly. And while Robert had been riding north to Winterfell, Stannis had removed himself to Dragonstone, the Targaryen island fastness he had conquered in his brother's name. He had given no word as to when he might return. "Where did they go on these rides?" Ned asked.

"The boy says that they visited a brothel."

"A brothel?" Ned said. "The Lord of the Eyrie and Hand of the King visited a brothel with *Stannis Baratheon*?" He shook his head, incredulous, wondering what Lord Renly would make of this tidbit. Robert's lusts were the subject of ribald drinking songs throughout the realm, but Stannis was a different sort of man; a bare year younger than the king, yet utterly unlike him, stern, humorless, unforgiving, grim in his sense of duty.

"The boy insists it's true. The Hand took three guardsmen with him, and the boy says they were joking of it when he took their horses afterward."

"Which brothel?" Ned asked.

"The boy did not know. The guards would."

"A pity Lysa carried them off to the Vale," Ned said dryly. "The gods are doing their best to vex us. Lady Lysa, Maester Colemon, Lord Stannis . . . everyone who might actually know the truth of what happened to Jon Arryn is a thousand leagues away."

"Will you summon Lord Stannis back from Dragonstone?"

"Not yet," Ned said. "Not until I have a better notion of what this is all about and where he stands." The matter nagged at him. Why did Stannis leave? Had he played some part in Jon Arryn's murder? Or was he afraid? Ned found it hard to imagine what could frighten Stannis Baratheon, who had once held Storm's End through a year of siege, surviving on rats and boot leather while the Lords Tyrell and Redwyne sat outside with their hosts, banqueting in sight of his walls.

"Bring me my doublet, if you would. The grey, with the direwolf sigil. I want this armorer to know who I am. It might make him more forthcoming."

Jory went to the wardrobe. "Lord Renly is brother to Lord Stannis as well as the king."

"Yet it seems that he was not invited on these rides." Ned was not sure what to make of Renly, with all his friendly ways and easy smiles. A few days past, he had taken Ned aside to show him an exquisite rose gold locklet. Inside was a miniature painted in the vivid Myrish style, of a lovely young girl with doe's eyes and a cascade of soft brown hair. Renly had seemed anxious to know if the girl reminded him of anyone, and when Ned had no answer but a shrug, he had seemed disappointed. The maid was Loras Tyrell's sister Margaery, he'd confessed, but there were those who said she looked like Lyanna. "No," Ned had told him, bemused. Could it be that Lord Renly, who looked so like a young Robert, had conceived a passion for a girl he fancied to be a young Lyanna? That struck him as more than passing queer.

Jory held out the doublet, and Ned slid his hands through the armholes. "Perhaps Lord Stannis will return for Robert's tourney," he said as Jory laced the garment up the back.

"That would be a stroke of fortune, my lord," Jory said.

Ned buckled on a longsword. "In other words, not bloody likely." His smile was grim.

Jory draped Ned's cloak across his shoulders and clasped it at the throat with the Hand's badge of office. "The armorer lives above his shop, in a large house at the top of the Street of Steel. Alyn knows the way, my lord."

Ned nodded. "The gods help this potboy if he's sent me off haring after shadows." It was a slim enough staff to lean on, but the Jon Arryn that Ned Stark had known was not one to wear jeweled and silvered plate. Steel was steel; it was meant for protection, not ornament. He might have changed his views, to be sure. He would scarcely have been the first man who came to look on things differently after a few years at court . . . but the change was marked enough to make Ned wonder.

"Is there any other service I might perform?"

"I suppose you'd best begin visiting whorehouses."

"Hard duty, my lord." Jory grinned. "The men will be glad to help. Porther has made a fair start already."

Ned's favorite horse was saddled and waiting in the yard. Varly and Jacks fell in beside him as he rode through the yard. Their steel caps and shirts of mail must have been sweltering, yet they said no word of complaint. As Lord Eddard passed beneath the King's Gate into the stink of the city, his grey and white cloak streaming from his shoulders, he saw eyes everywhere and kicked his mount into a trot. His guard followed.

He looked behind him frequently as they made their way through the crowded city streets. Tomard and Desmond had left the castle early this morning to take up positions on the route they must take, and watch for anyone following them, but even so, Ned was uncertain. The shadow of the King's Spider and his little birds had him fretting like a maiden on her wedding night.

The Street of Steel began at the market square beside the River Gate, as it was named on maps, or the Mud Gate, as it was commonly called. A mummer on stilts was striding through the throngs like some great insect, with a horde of barefoot children trailing behind him, hooting. Elsewhere, two ragged boys no older than Bran were dueling with sticks, to the loud encouragement of some and the furious curses of others. An old woman ended the contest by leaning out of her window and emptying a bucket of slops on the heads of the combatants. In the shadow of the wall, farmers stood beside their wagons, bellowing out, "Apples, the best apples, cheap at twice the price," and "Blood melons, sweet as honey," and "Turnips, onions, roots, here you go here, here you go, turnips, onions, roots, here you go here."

The Mud Gate was open, and a squad of City Watchmen stood under the portcullis in their golden cloaks, leaning on spears. When a column of riders appeared from the west, the guardsmen sprang into action, shouting commands and moving the carts and foot traffic aside to let the knight enter with his escort. The first rider through the gate carried a long black banner. The silk rippled in the wind like a living thing; across the fabric was blazoned a night sky slashed with purple lightning. *"Make way for Lord Beric!"* the rider shouted. *"Make way for Lord Beric!"* And close behind came the young lord himself, a dashing figure on a black courser, with red-gold hair and a black satin cloak dusted with stars. "Here to fight in the Hand's tourney, my lord?" a guardsman called out to him. "Here to *win* the Hand's tourney," Lord Beric shouted back as the crowd cheered.

Ned turned off the square where the Street of Steel began and followed its winding path up a long hill, past blacksmiths working at open forges, freeriders haggling over mail shirts, and grizzled ironmongers selling old blades and razors from their wagons. The farther they climbed, the larger the buildings grew. The man they wanted was all the way at the top of the hill, in a huge house of timber and plaster whose upper stories loomed over the narrow street. The double doors showed a hunting scene carved in ebony and weirwood. A pair of stone knights stood sentry at the entrance, armored in fanciful suits of polished red steel that transformed them into griffin and unicorn. Ned left his horse with Jacks and shouldered his way inside.

The slim young serving girl took quick note of Ned's badge and the sigil on his doublet, and the master came hurrying out, all smiles and bows. "Wine for the King's Hand," he told the girl, gesturing Ned to a couch. "I am Tobho Mott, my lord, please, please, put yourself at ease." He wore a black velvet coat with hammers embroidered on the sleeves in silver thread. Around his neck was a heavy silver chain and a sapphire as large as a pigeon's egg. "If you are in need of new arms for the Hand's tourney, you have come to the right shop." Ned did not bother to correct him. "My work is costly, and I make no apologies for that, my lord," he said as he filled two matching silver goblets. "You will not find craftsmanship equal to mine anywhere in the Seven Kingdoms, I promise you. Visit every forge in King's Landing if you like, and compare for yourself. Any village smith can hammer out a shirt of mail; my work is art."

Ned sipped his wine and let the man go on. The Knight of Flowers bought all his armor here, Tobho boasted, and many high lords, the ones who knew fine steel, and even Lord Renly, the king's own brother. Perhaps the Hand had seen Lord Renly's new armor, the green plate with the golden antlers? No other armorer in the city could get that deep a green; he knew the secret of putting color in the steel itself, paint and enamel were the crutches of a journeyman. Or mayhaps the Hand wanted a blade? Tobho had learned to work Valyrian steel at the forges of Qohor as a boy. Only a man who knew the spells could take old weapons and forge them anew. "The direwolf is the sigil of House Stark, is it not? I could fashion a direwolf helm so real that children will run from you in the street," he vowed.

Ned smiled. "Did you make a falcon helm for Lord Arryn?"

Tobho Mott paused a long moment and set aside his wine. "The Hand did call upon me, with Lord Stannis, the king's brother. I regret to say, they did not honor me with their patronage."

Ned looked at the man evenly, saying nothing, waiting. He had found over the years that silence sometimes yielded more than questions. And so it was this time.

"They asked to see the boy," the armorer said, "so I took them back to the forge."

"The boy," Ned echoed. He had no notion who the boy might be. "I should like to see the boy as well."

Tobho Mott gave him a cool, careful look. "As you wish, my lord," he said with no trace of his former friendliness. He led Ned out a rear door and across a narrow yard, back to the cavernous stone barn where the work was done. When the armorer opened the door, the blast of hot air that came through made Ned feel as though he were walking into a dragon's mouth. Inside, a forge blazed in each corner, and the air stank of smoke and sulfur. Journeymen armorers glanced up from their hammers and tongs just long enough to wipe the sweat from their brows, while bare-chested apprentice boys worked the bellows.

The master called over a tall lad about Robb's age, his arms and chest corded with muscle. "This is Lord Stark, the new Hand of the King," he told him as the boy looked at Ned through sullen blue eyes and pushed back sweat-soaked hair with his fingers. Thick hair, shaggy and unkempt and black as ink. The shadow of a new beard darkened his jaw. "This is Gendry. Strong for his age, and he works hard. Show the Hand that helmet you made, lad." Almost shyly, the boy led them to his bench, and a steel helm shaped like a bull's head, with two great curving horns.

Ned turned the helm over in his hands. It was raw steel, unpolished but expertly shaped. "This is fine work. I would be pleased if you would let me buy it."

The boy snatched it out of his hands. "It's not for sale."

Tobho Mott looked horror-struck. "Boy, this is the King's Hand. If his lordship wants this helm, make him a gift of it. He honors you by asking."

"I made it for me," the boy said stubbornly.

"A hundred pardons, my lord," his master said hurriedly to Ned. "The boy is crude as new steel, and like new steel would profit from some beating. That helm is journeyman's work at best. Forgive him and I promise I will craft you a helm like none you have ever seen."

"He's done nothing that requires my forgiveness. Gendry, when Lord Arryn came to see you, what did you talk about?"

"He asked me questions is all, m'lord."

"What sort of questions?"

The boy shrugged. "How was I, and was I well treated, and if I liked the work, and stuff about my mother. Who she was and what she looked like and all."

"What did you tell him?" Ned asked.

The boy shoved a fresh fall of black hair off his forehead. "She died when I was little. She had yellow hair, and sometimes she used to sing to me, I remember. She worked in an alehouse."

"Did Lord Stannis question you as well?"

"The bald one? No, not him. He never said no word, just glared at me, like I was some raper who done for his daughter."

"Mind your filthy tongue," the master said. "This is the King's own Hand." The boy lowered his eyes. "A smart boy, but stubborn. That helm . . . the others call him bullheaded, so he threw it in their teeth."

Ned touched the boy's head, fingering the thick black hair. "Look at me, Gendry." The apprentice lifted his face. Ned studied the shape of his jaw, the eyes like blue ice. *Yes,* he thought, *I see it.* "Go back to your work, lad. I'm sorry to have bothered you." He walked back to the house with the master. "Who paid the boy's apprentice fee?" he asked lightly.

Mott looked fretful. "You saw the boy. Such a strong boy. Those hands of his, those hands were made for hammers. He had such promise, I took him on without a fee."

"The truth now," Ned urged. "The streets are full of strong boys. The day you take on an apprentice without a fee will be the day the Wall comes down. Who paid for him?"

"A lord," the master said reluctantly. "He gave no name, and wore no sigil on his coat. He paid in gold, twice the customary sum, and said he was paying once for the boy, and once for my silence."

"Describe him."

"He was stout, round of shoulder, not so tall as you. Brown beard, but there was a bit of red in it, I'll swear. He wore a rich cloak, that I do remember, heavy purple velvet worked with silver threads, but the hood shadowed his face and I never did see him clear." He hesitated a moment. "My lord, I want no trouble."

"None of us wants trouble, but I fear these are troubled times, Master Mott," Ned said. "You know who the boy is."

"I am only an armorer, my lord. I know what I'm told."

"You know who the boy is," Ned repeated patiently. "That is not a question."

"The boy is my apprentice," the master said. He looked Ned in the eye, stubborn as old iron. "Who he was before he came to me, that's none of my concern."

Ned nodded. He decided that he liked Tobho Mott, master armorer. "If the day ever comes when Gendry would rather wield a sword than forge one, send him to me. He has the look of a warrior. Until then, you have my thanks, Master Mott, and my promise. Should I ever want a helm to frighten children, this will be the first place I visit."

His guard was waiting outside with the horses. "Did you find anything, my lord?" Jacks asked as Ned mounted up.

"I did," Ned told him, wondering. What had Jon Arryn wanted with a king's bastard, and why was it worth his life?

CATELYN

"**M**y lady, you ought cover your head," Ser Rodrik told her as their horses plodded north. "You will take a chill."

"It is only water, Ser Rodrik," Catelyn replied. Her hair hung wet and heavy, a loose strand stuck to her forehead, and she could imagine how ragged and wild she must look, but for once she did not care. The southern rain was soft and warm. Catelyn liked the feel of it on her face, gentle as a mother's kisses. It took her back to her childhood, to long grey days at Riverrun. She remembered the godswood, drooping branches heavy with moisture, and the sound of her brother's laughter as he chased her through piles of damp leaves. She remembered making mud pies with Lysa, the weight of them, the mud slick and brown between her fingers. They had served them to Littlefinger, giggling, and he'd eaten so much mud he was sick for a week. How young they all had been.

Catelyn had almost forgotten. In the north, the rain fell cold and hard, and sometimes at night it turned to ice. It was as likely to kill a crop as nurture it, and it sent grown men running for the nearest shelter. That was no rain for little girls to play in.

"I am soaked through," Ser Rodrik complained. "Even my bones are wet." The woods pressed close around them, and the steady pattering of rain on leaves was accompanied by the small sucking sounds their horses made as their hooves pulled free of the mud. "We will want a fire tonight, my lady, and a hot meal would serve us both."

"There is an inn at the crossroads up ahead," Catelyn told him. She had slept many a night there in her youth, traveling with her father. Lord Hoster Tully had been a restless man in his prime, always riding somewhere. She still remembered the innkeep, a fat woman named Masha Heddle who chewed sourleaf night and day and seemed to have an endless supply of smiles and sweet cakes for the children. The sweet cakes had been soaked with honey, rich and heavy on the tongue, but how Catelyn had dreaded those smiles. The sourleaf had stained Masha's teeth a dark red, and made her smile a bloody horror.

"An inn," Ser Rodrik repeated wistfully. "If only . . . but we dare not risk it. If we wish to remain unknown, I think it best we seek out some small holdfast . . ." He broke off as they heard sounds up the road; splashing water, the clink of mail, a horse's whinny. "Riders," he warned, his hand dropping to the hilt of his sword. Even on the kingsroad, it never hurt to be wary.

They followed the sounds around a lazy bend of the road and saw them; a column of armed men noisily fording a swollen stream. Catelyn reined up to let them pass. The banner in the hand of the foremost rider hung sodden and limp, but the guardsmen wore indigo cloaks and on their shoulders flew the silver eagle of Seagard. "Mallisters," Ser Rodrik whispered to her, as if she had not known. "My lady, best pull up your hood."

Catelyn made no move. Lord Jason Mallister himself rode with them, surrounded by his knights, his son Patrek by his side and their squires close behind. They were riding for King's Landing and the Hand's tourney, she knew. For the past week, the travelers had been thick as flies upon the kingsroad; knights and freeriders, singers with their harps and drums, heavy wagons laden with hops or corn or casks of honey, traders and craftsmen and whores, and all of them moving south.

She studied Lord Jason boldly. The last time she had

seen him he had been jesting with her uncle at her wedding feast; the Mallisters stood bannermen to the Tullys, and his gifts had been lavish. His brown hair was salted with white now, his face chiseled gaunt by time, yet the years had not touched his pride. He rode like a man who feared nothing. Catelyn envied him that; she had come to fear so much. As the riders passed, Lord Jason nodded a curt greeting, but it was only a high lord's courtesy to strangers chance met on the road. There was no recognition in those fierce eyes, and his son did not even waste a look.

"He did not know you," Ser Rodrik said after, wondering.

"He saw a pair of mud-spattered travelers by the side of the road, wet and tired. It would never occur to him to suspect that one of them was the daughter of his liege lord. I think we shall be safe enough at the inn, Ser Rodrik."

It was near dark when they reached it, at the crossroads north of the great confluence of the Trident. Masha Heddle was fatter and greyer than Catelyn remembered, still chewing her sourleaf, but she gave them only the most cursory of looks, with nary a hint of her ghastly red smile. "Two rooms at the top of the stair, that's all there is," she said, chewing all the while. "They're under the bell tower, you won't be missing meals, though there's some thinks it too noisy. Can't be helped. We're full up, or near as makes no matter. It's those rooms or the road."

It was those rooms, low, dusty garrets at the top of a cramped narrow staircase. "Leave your boots down here," Masha told them after she'd taken their coin. "The boy will clean them. I won't have you tracking mud up my stairs. Mind the bell. Those who come late to meals don't eat." There were no smiles, and no mention of sweet cakes.

When the supper bell rang, the sound was deafening. Catelyn had changed into dry clothes. She sat by the window, watching rain run down the pane. The glass was milky and full of bubbles, and a wet dusk was falling outside. Catelyn could just make out the muddy crossing where the two great roads met.

The crossroads gave her pause. If they turned west from here, it was an easy ride down to Riverrun. Her father had always given her wise counsel when she needed it most, and she yearned to talk to him, to warn him of the gathering storm. If Winterfell needed to brace for war, how much more so Riverrun, so much closer to King's Landing, with the power of Casterly Rock looming to the west like a shadow. If only her father had been stronger, she might have chanced it, but Hoster Tully had been bedridden these past two years, and Catelyn was loath to tax him now.

The eastern road was wilder and more dangerous, climbing through rocky foothills and thick forests into the Mountains of the Moon, past high passes and deep chasms to the Vale of Arryn and the stony Fingers beyond. Above the Vale, the Eyrie stood high and impregnable, its towers reaching for the sky. There she would find her sister . . . and, perhaps, some of the answers Ned sought. Surely Lysa knew more than she had dared to put in her letter. She might have the very proof that Ned needed to bring the Lannisters to ruin, and if it came to war, they would need the Arryns and the eastern lords who owed them service.

Yet the mountain road was perilous. Shadowcats prowled those passes, rock slides were common, and the mountain clans were lawless brigands, descending from the heights to rob and kill and melting away like snow whenever the knights rode out from the Vale in search of them. Even Jon Arryn, as great a lord as any the Eyrie had ever known, had always traveled in strength when he crossed the mountains. Catelyn's only strength was one elderly knight, armored in loyalty.

No, she thought, Riverrun and the Eyrie would have to wait. Her path ran north to Winterfell, where her sons and her duty were waiting for her. As soon as they were safely past the Neck, she could declare herself to one of Ned's bannermen, and send riders racing ahead with orders to mount a watch on the kingsroad.

The rain obscured the fields beyond the crossroads, but Catelyn saw the land clear enough in her memory. The marketplace was just across the way, and the village a mile farther on, half a hundred white cottages surrounding a small stone sept. There would be more now; the summer had been long and peaceful. North of here the kingsroad ran along the Green Fork of the Trident, through fertile valleys and green woodlands, past thriving towns and stout holdfasts and the castles of the river lords.

Catelyn knew them all: the Blackwoods and the Brackens, ever enemies, whose quarrels her father was obliged to settle; Lady Whent, last of her line, who dwelt with her ghosts in the cavernous vaults of Harrenhal; irascible Lord Frey, who had outlived seven wives and filled his twin castles with children, grandchildren, and great-grandchildren, and bastards and grandbastards as well. All of them were bannermen to the Tullys, their swords sworn to the service of Riverrun. Catelyn wondered if that would be enough, if it came to war. Her father was the staunchest man who'd ever lived, and she had no doubt that he would call his banners . . . but would the banners come? The Darrys and Rygers and Mootons had sworn oaths to Riverrun as well, yet they had fought with Rhaegar Targaryen on the Trident, while Lord Frey had arrived with his levies well after the battle was over, leaving some doubt as to which army he had planned to join (theirs, he had assured the victors solemnly in the aftermath, but ever after her father had called him the Late Lord Frey). It must *not* come to war, Catelyn thought fervently. They must not let it.

Ser Rodrik came for her just as the bell ceased its clangor. "We had best make haste if we hope to eat tonight, my lady."

"It might be safer if we were not knight and lady until we pass the Neck," she told him. "Common travelers attract less notice. A father and daughter taken to the road on some family business, say."

"As you say, my lady," Ser Rodrik agreed. It was only when she laughed that he realized what he'd done. "The old courtesies die hard, my—my daughter." He tried to tug on his missing whiskers, and sighed with exasperation.

Catelyn took his arm. "Come, Father," she said. "You'll find that Masha Heddle sets a good table, I think, but try not to praise her. You truly don't want to see her smile."

The common room was long and drafty, with a row of huge wooden kegs at one end and a fireplace at the other. A serving boy ran back and forth with skewers of meat while Masha drew beer from the kegs, chewing her sourleaf all the while.

The benches were crowded, townsfolk and farmers mingling freely with all manner of travelers. The crossroads made for odd companions; dyers with black and purple hands shared a bench with rivermen reeking of fish, an ironsmith thick with muscle squeezed in beside a wizened old septon, hard-bitten sellswords and soft plump merchants swapped news like boon companions.

The company included more swords than Catelyn would have liked. Three by the fire wore the red stallion badge of the Brackens, and there was a large party in blue steel ringmail and capes of a silvery grey. On their shoulder was another familiar sigil, the twin towers of House Frey. She studied their faces, but they were all too young to have known her. The senior among them would have been no older than Bran when she went north.

Ser Rodrik found them an empty place on the bench near the kitchen. Across the table a handsome youth was fingering a woodharp. "Seven blessings to you, goodfolk," he said as they sat. An empty wine cup stood on the table before him.

"And to you, singer," Catelyn returned. Ser Rodrik called for bread and meat and beer in a tone that meant *now*. The singer, a youth of some eighteen years, eyed them boldly and asked where they were going, and from whence they had come, and what news they had, letting the questions fly as quick as arrows and never pausing for an answer. "We left King's Landing a fortnight ago," Catelyn replied, answering the safest of his questions.

"That's where I'm bound," the youth said. As she had suspected, he was more interested in telling his own story than in hearing theirs. Singers loved nothing half so well as the sound of their own voices. "The Hand's tourney means rich lords with fat purses. The last time I came away with more silver than I could carry . . . or would have, if I hadn't lost it all betting on the Kingslayer to win the day."

"The gods frown on the gambler," Ser Rodrik said sternly. He was of the north, and shared the Stark views on tournaments.

"They frowned on me, for certain," the singer said.

"Your cruel gods and the Knight of Flowers altogether did me in."

"No doubt that was a lesson for you," Ser Rodrik said.

"It was. This time my coin will champion Ser Loras."

Ser Rodrik tried to tug at whiskers that were not there, but before he could frame a rebuke the serving boy came scurrying up. He laid trenchers of bread before them and filled them with chunks of browned meat off a skewer, dripping with hot juice. Another skewer held tiny onions, fire peppers, and fat mushrooms. Ser Rodrik set to lustily as the lad ran back to fetch them beer.

"My name is Marillion," the singer said, plucking a string on his woodharp. "Doubtless you've heard me play somewhere?"

His manner made Catelyn smile. Few wandering singers ever ventured as far north as Winterfell, but she knew his like from her girlhood in Riverrun. "I fear not," she told him.

He drew a plaintive chord from the woodharp. "That is your loss," he said. "Who was the finest singer you've ever heard?"

"Alia of Braavos," Ser Rodrik answered at once.

"Oh, I'm *much* better than that old stick," Marillion said. "If you have the silver for a song, I'll gladly show you."

"I might have a copper or two, but I'd sooner toss it down a well than pay for your howling," Ser Rodrik groused. His opinion of singers was well known; music was a lovely thing for girls, but he could not comprehend why any healthy boy would fill his hand with a harp when he might have had a sword.

"Your grandfather has a sour nature," Marillion said to Catelyn. "I meant to do you honor. An homage to your beauty. In truth, I was made to sing for kings and high lords."

"Oh, I can see that," Catelyn said. "Lord Tully is fond of song, I hear. No doubt you've been to Riverrun."

"A hundred times," the singer said airily. "They keep a chamber for me, and the young lord is like a brother."

Catelyn smiled, wondering what Edmure would think of that. Another singer had once bedded a girl her brother fancied; he had hated the breed ever since. "And Winterfell?" she asked him. "Have you traveled north?"

"Why would I?" Marillion asked. "It's all blizzards and bearskins up there, and the Starks know no music but the howling of wolves." Distantly, she was aware of the door banging open at the far end of the room.

"Innkeep," a servant's voice called out behind her, "we have horses that want stabling, and my lord of Lannister requires a room and a hot bath."

"Oh, gods," Ser Rodrik said before Catelyn reached out to silence him, her fingers tightening hard around his forearm.

Masha Heddle was bowing and smiling her hideous red smile. "I'm sorry, m'lord, truly, we're full up, every room."

There were four of them, Catelyn saw. An old man in the black of the Night's Watch, two servants . . . and him, standing there small and bold as life. "My men will sleep in your stable, and as for myself, well, I do not require a *large* room, as you can plainly see." He flashed a mocking grin. "So long as the fire's warm and the straw reasonably free of fleas, I am a happy man."

Masha Heddle was beside herself. "M'lord, there's nothing, it's the tourney, there's no help for it, oh . . ."

Tyrion Lannister pulled a coin from his purse and flicked it up over his head, caught it, tossed it again. Even across the room, where Catelyn sat, the wink of gold was unmistakable.

A freerider in a faded blue cloak lurched to his feet. "You're welcome to my room, m'lord."

"Now there's a clever man," Lannister said as he sent the coin spinning across the room. The freerider snatched it from the air. "And a nimble one to boot." The dwarf turned back to Masha Heddle. "You will be able to manage food, I trust?"

"Anything you like, m'lord, anything at all," the innkeep promised. *And may he choke on it,* Catelyn thought, but it was Bran she saw choking, drowning on his own blood.

Lannister glanced at the nearest tables. "My men will have whatever you're serving these people. Double portions, we've had a long hard ride. I'll take a roast fowl— chicken, duck, pigeon, it makes no matter. And send up a flagon of your best wine. Yoren, will you sup with me?"

"Aye, m'lord, I will," the black brother replied.

The dwarf had not so much as glanced toward the far end of the room, and Catelyn was thinking how grateful she was for the crowded benches between them when suddenly Marillion bounded to his feet. *"My lord of Lannister!"* he called out. "I would be pleased to entertain you while you eat. Let me sing you the lay of your father's great victory at King's Landing!"

"Nothing would be more likely to ruin my supper," the dwarf said dryly. His mismatched eyes considered the singer briefly, started to move away . . . and found Catelyn. He looked at her for a moment, puzzled. She turned her face away, but too late. The dwarf was smiling. "Lady Stark, what an unexpected pleasure," he said. "I was sorry to miss you at Winterfell."

Marillion gaped at her, confusion giving way to chagrin as Catelyn rose slowly to her feet. She heard Ser Rodrik curse. If only the man had lingered at the Wall, she thought, if only . . .

"Lady . . . Stark?" Masha Heddle said thickly.

"I was still Catelyn Tully the last time I bedded here," she told the innkeep. She could hear the muttering, feel the eyes upon her. Catelyn glanced around the room, at the faces of the knights and sworn swords, and took a deep breath to slow the frantic beating of her heart. Did she dare take the risk? There was no time to think it through, only the moment and the sound of her own voice ringing in her ears. "You in the corner," she said to an older man she had not noticed until now. "Is that the black bat of Harrenhal I see embroidered on your surcoat, ser?"

The man got to his feet. "It is, my lady."

"And is Lady Whent a true and honest friend to my father, Lord Hoster Tully of Riverrun?"

"She is," the man replied stoutly.

Ser Rodrik rose quietly and loosened his sword in its scabbard. The dwarf was blinking at them, blank-faced, with puzzlement in his mismatched eyes.

"The red stallion was ever a welcome sight in Riverrun," she said to the trio by the fire. "My father counts Jonos Bracken among his oldest and most loyal bannermen."

The three men-at-arms exchanged uncertain looks.

"Our lord is honored by his trust," one of them said hesitantly.

"I envy your father all these fine friends," Lannister quipped, "but I do not quite see the purpose of this, Lady Stark."

She ignored him, turning to the large party in blue and grey. They were the heart of the matter; there were more than twenty of them. "I know your sigil as well: the twin towers of Frey. How fares your good lord, sers?"

Their captain rose. "Lord Walder is well, my lady. He plans to take a new wife on his ninetieth name day, and has asked your lord father to honor the wedding with his presence."

Tyrion Lannister sniggered. That was when Catelyn knew he was hers. "This man came a guest into my house, and there conspired to murder my son, a boy of seven," she proclaimed to the room at large, pointing. Ser Rodrik moved to her side, his sword in hand. "In the name of King Robert and the good lords you serve, I call upon you to seize him and help me return him to Winterfell to await the king's justice."

She did not know what was more satisfying: the sound of a dozen swords drawn as one or the look on Tyrion Lannister's face.

SANSA

Sansa rode to the Hand's tourney with Septa Mordane and Jeyne Poole, in a litter with curtains of yellow silk so fine she could see right through them. They turned the whole world gold. Beyond the city walls, a hundred pavilions had been raised beside the river, and the common folk came out in the thousands to watch the games. The splendor of it all took Sansa's breath away; the shining armor, the great chargers caparisoned in silver and gold, the shouts of the crowd, the banners snapping in the wind . . . and the knights themselves, the knights most of all.

"It is better than the songs," she whispered when they found the places that her father had promised her, among the high lords and ladies. Sansa was dressed beautifully that day, in a green gown that brought out the auburn of her hair, and she knew they were looking at her and smiling.

They watched the heroes of a hundred songs ride forth, each more fabulous than the last. The seven knights of the Kingsguard took the field, all but Jaime Lannister in scaled armor the color of milk, their cloaks as white as fresh-fallen snow. Ser Jaime wore the white cloak as well, but beneath it he was shining gold from head to foot, with a lion's-head helm and a golden sword. Ser Gregor Clegane, the Mountain That Rides, thundered past them like an avalanche. Sansa remembered Lord Yohn Royce, who had guested at Winterfell two years before. "His armor is bronze, thousands and thousands of years old, engraved with magic runes that ward him against harm," she whispered to Jeyne. Septa Mordane pointed out Lord Jason Mallister, in indigo chased with silver, the wings of an eagle on his helm. He had cut down three of Rhaegar's bannermen on the Trident. The girls giggled over the warrior priest Thoros of Myr, with his flapping red robes and shaven head, until the septa told them that he had once scaled the walls of Pyke with a flaming sword in hand.

Other riders Sansa did not know; hedge knights from the Fingers and Highgarden and the mountains of Dorne, unsung freeriders and new-made squires, the younger sons of high lords and the heirs of lesser houses. Younger men, most had done no great deeds as yet, but Sansa and Jeyne agreed that one day the Seven Kingdoms would resound to the sound of their names. Ser Balon Swann. Lord Bryce Caron of the Marches. Bronze Yohn's heir, Ser Andar Royce, and his younger brother Ser Robar, their silvered steel plate filigreed in bronze with the same ancient runes that warded their father. The twins Ser Horas and Ser Hobber, whose shields displayed the grape cluster sigil of the Redwynes, burgundy on blue. Patrek Mallister, Lord Jason's son. Six Freys of the Crossing: Ser Jared, Ser Hosteen, Ser Danwell, Ser Emmon, Ser Theo, Ser Perwyn, sons and grandsons of old Lord Walder Frey, and his bastard son Martyn Rivers as well.

Jeyne Poole confessed herself frightened by the look of Jalabhar Xho, an exile prince from the Summer Isles who wore a cape of green and scarlet feathers over skin as dark as night, but when she saw young Lord Beric Dondarrion, with his hair like red gold and his black shield slashed by lightning, she pronounced herself willing to marry him on the instant.

The Hound entered the lists as well, and so too the king's brother, handsome Lord Renly of Storm's End. Jory, Alyn, and Harwin rode for Winterfell and the north. "Jory looks a beggar among these others," Septa Mordane sniffed when he appeared. Sansa could only agree. Jory's armor was blue-grey plate without device or ornament, and a thin grey cloak hung from his shoulders like a soiled rag. Yet he acquitted himself well, unhorsing Horas Redwyne in his first joust and one of the Freys in his second. In his third match, he rode three passes at a free-rider named Lothor Brune whose armor was as drab as his own. Neither man lost his seat, but Brune's lance was steadier and his blows better placed, and the king gave him the victory. Alyn and Harwin fared less well; Harwin was unhorsed in his first tilt by Ser Meryn of the Kingsguard, while Alyn fell to Ser Balon Swann.

The jousting went all day and into the dusk, the hooves of the great warhorses pounding down the lists until the field was a ragged wasteland of torn earth. A dozen times Jeyne and Sansa cried out in unison as riders crashed together, lances exploding into splinters while the commons screamed for their favorites. Jeyne covered her eyes whenever a man fell, like a frightened little girl, but Sansa was made of sterner stuff. A great lady knew how to behave at tournaments. Even Septa Mordane noted her composure and nodded in approval.

The Kingslayer rode brilliantly. He overthrew Ser Andar Royce and the Marcher Lord Bryce Caron as easily as if he were riding at rings, and then took a hard-fought match from white-haired Barristan Selmy, who had won his first two tilts against men thirty and forty years his junior.

Sandor Clegane and his immense brother, Ser Gregor the Mountain, seemed unstoppable as well, riding down one foe after the next in ferocious style. The most terrifying moment of the day came during Ser Gregor's second joust, when his lance rode up and struck a young knight from the Vale under the gorget with such force that it drove through his throat, killing him instantly. The youth fell not ten feet from where Sansa was seated. The point of Ser Gregor's lance had snapped off in his neck, and his life's blood flowed out in slow pulses, each weaker than the one before. His armor was shiny new; a bright streak of fire ran down his outstretched arm, as the steel caught the light. Then the sun went behind a cloud, and it was gone. His cloak was blue, the color of the sky on a clear summer's day, trimmed with a border of crescent moons, but as his blood seeped into it, the cloth darkened and the moons turned red, one by one.

Jeyne Poole wept so hysterically that Septa Mordane finally took her off to regain her composure, but Sansa sat with her hands folded in her lap, watching with a strange fascination. She had never seen a man die before. She ought to be crying too, she thought, but the tears would not come. Perhaps she had used up all her tears for Lady and Bran. It would be different if it had been Jory or Ser Rodrik or Father, she told herself. The young knight in the blue cloak was nothing to her, some stranger from the Vale of Arryn whose name she had forgotten as soon as she heard it. And now the world would forget his name too, Sansa realized; there would be no songs sung for him. That was sad.

After they carried off the body, a boy with a spade ran onto the field and shoveled dirt over the spot where he had fallen, to cover up the blood. Then the jousts resumed.

Ser Balon Swann also fell to Gregor, and Lord Renly to the Hound. Renly was unhorsed so violently that he seemed to fly backward off his charger, legs in the air. His head hit the ground with an audible *crack* that made the crowd gasp, but it was just the golden antler on his helm. One of the tines had snapped off beneath him. When Lord Renly climbed to his feet, the commons cheered wildly, for King Robert's handsome young brother was a great favorite. He handed the broken tine to his conqueror with a gracious bow. The Hound snorted and tossed the broken antler into the crowd, where the commons began to punch and claw over the little bit of gold, until Lord Renly walked out among them and restored the peace. By then Septa Mordane had returned, alone. Jeyne had been feeling ill, she explained; she had helped her back to the castle. Sansa had almost forgotten about Jeyne.

Later a hedge knight in a checkered cloak disgraced himself by killing Beric Dondarrion's horse, and was declared forfeit. Lord Beric shifted his saddle to a new mount, only to be knocked right off it by Thoros of Myr. Ser Aron Santagar and Lothor Brune tilted thrice without result; Ser Aron fell afterward to Lord Jason Mallister, and Brune to Yohn Royce's younger son, Robar.

In the end it came down to four; the Hound and his

monstrous brother Gregor, Jaime Lannister the King-slayer, and Ser Loras Tyrell, the youth they called the Knight of Flowers.

Ser Loras was the youngest son of Mace Tyrell, the Lord of Highgarden and Warden of the South. At sixteen, he was the youngest rider on the field, yet he had un-horsed three knights of the Kingsguard that morning in his first three jousts. Sansa had never seen anyone so beautiful. His plate was intricately fashioned and enam-eled as a bouquet of a thousand different flowers, and his snow-white stallion was draped in a blanket of red and white roses. After each victory, Ser Loras would remove his helm and ride slowly round the fence, and finally pluck a single white rose from the blanket and toss it to some fair maiden in the crowd.

His last match of the day was against the younger Royce. Ser Robar's ancestral runes proved small protec-tion as Ser Loras split his shield and drove him from his saddle to crash with an awful clangor in the dirt. Robar lay moaning as the victor made his circuit of the field. Finally they called for a litter and carried him off to his tent, dazed and unmoving. Sansa never saw it. Her eyes were only for Ser Loras. When the white horse stopped in front of her, she thought her heart would burst.

To the other maidens he had given white roses, but the one he plucked for her was red. "Sweet lady," he said, "no victory is half so beautiful as you." Sansa took the flower timidly, struck dumb by his gallantry. His hair was a mass of lazy brown curls, his eyes like liquid gold. She inhaled the sweet fragrance of the rose and sat clutching it long after Ser Loras had ridden off.

When Sansa finally looked up, a man was standing over her, staring. He was short, with a pointed beard and a silver streak in his hair, almost as old as her father. "You must be one of her daughters," he said to her. He had grey-green eyes that did not smile when his mouth did. "You have the Tully look."

"I'm Sansa Stark," she said, ill at ease. The man wore a heavy cloak with a fur collar, fastened with a silver mock-ingbird, and he had the effortless manner of a high lord, but she did not know him. "I have not had the honor, my lord."

Septa Mordane quickly took a hand. "Sweet child, this is Lord Petyr Baelish, of the king's small council."

"Your mother was *my* queen of beauty once," the man said quietly. His breath smelled of mint. "You have her hair." His fingers brushed against her cheek as he stroked one auburn lock. Quite abruptly he turned and walked away.

By then, the moon was well up and the crowd was tired, so the king decreed that the last three matches would be fought the next morning, before the melee. While the commons began their walk home, talking of the day's jousts and the matches to come on the morrow, the court moved to the riverside to begin the feast. Six monstrous huge aurochs had been roasting for hours, turning slowly on wooden spits while kitchen boys basted them with butter and herbs until the meat crackled and spit. Tables and benches had been raised outside the pavilions, piled high with sweetgrass and strawberries and fresh-baked bread.

Sansa and Septa Mordane were given places of high honor, to the left of the raised dais where the king himself sat beside his queen. When Prince Joffrey seated himself to her right, she felt her throat tighten. He had not spoken a word to her since the awful thing had happened, and she had not dared to speak to him. At first she thought she hated him for what they'd done to Lady, but after Sansa had wept her eyes dry, she told herself that it had not been Joffrey's doing, not truly. The queen had done it; she was the one to hate, her and Arya. Nothing bad would have happened except for Arya.

She could not hate Joffrey tonight. He was too beautiful to hate. He wore a deep blue doublet studded with a double row of golden lion's heads, and around his brow a slim coronet made of gold and sapphires. His hair was as bright as the metal. Sansa looked at him and trembled, afraid that he might ignore her or, worse, turn hateful again and send her weeping from the table.

Instead Joffrey smiled and kissed her hand, handsome and gallant as any prince in the songs, and said, "Ser Loras has a keen eye for beauty, sweet lady."

"He was too kind," she demurred, trying to remain modest and calm, though her heart was singing. "Ser

Loras is a true knight. Do you think he will win tomorrow, my lord?"

"No," Joffrey said. "My dog will do for him, or perhaps my uncle Jaime. And in a few years, when I am old enough to enter the lists, I shall do for them all." He raised his hand to summon a servant with a flagon of iced summerwine, and poured her a cup. She looked anxiously at Septa Mordane, until Joffrey leaned over and filled the septa's cup as well, so she nodded and thanked him graciously and said not another word.

The servants kept the cups filled all night, yet afterward Sansa could not recall ever tasting the wine. She needed no wine. She was drunk on the magic of the night, giddy with glamour, swept away by beauties she had dreamt of all her life and never dared hope to know. Singers sat before the king's pavilion, filling the dusk with music. A juggler kept a cascade of burning clubs spinning through the air. The king's own fool, the pie-faced simpleton called Moon Boy, danced about on stilts, all in motley, making mock of everyone with such deft cruelty that Sansa wondered if he was simple after all. Even Septa Mordane was helpless before him; when he sang his little song about the High Septon, she laughed so hard she spilled wine on herself.

And Joffrey was the soul of courtesy. He talked to Sansa all night, showering her with compliments, making her laugh, sharing little bits of court gossip, explaining Moon Boy's japes. Sansa was so captivated that she quite forgot all her courtesies and ignored Septa Mordane, seated to her left.

All the while the courses came and went. A thick soup of barley and venison. Salads of sweetgrass and spinach and plums, sprinkled with crushed nuts. Snails in honey and garlic. Sansa had never eaten snails before; Joffrey showed her how to get the snail out of the shell, and fed her the first sweet morsel himself. Then came trout fresh from the river, baked in clay; her prince helped her crack open the hard casing to expose the flaky white flesh within. And when the meat course was brought out, he served her himself, slicing a queen's portion from the joint, smiling as he laid it on her plate. She could see from the way he moved that his right arm was still troubling him, yet he uttered not a word of complaint.

Later came sweetbreads and pigeon pie and baked apples fragrant with cinnamon and lemon cakes frosted in sugar, but by then Sansa was so stuffed that she could not manage more than two little lemon cakes, as much as she loved them. She was wondering whether she might attempt a third when the king began to shout.

King Robert had grown louder with each course. From time to time Sansa could hear him laughing or roaring a command over the music and the clangor of plates and cutlery, but they were too far away for her to make out his words.

Now everybody heard him. *"No,"* he thundered in a voice that drowned out all other speech. Sansa was shocked to see the king on his feet, red of face, reeling. He had a goblet of wine in one hand, and he was drunk as a man could be. "You do not tell me what to do, woman," he screamed at Queen Cersei. "I am king here, do you understand? I rule here, and if I say that I will fight tomorrow, *I will fight!"*

Everyone was staring. Sansa saw Ser Barristan, and the king's brother Renly, and the short man who had talked to her so oddly and touched her hair, but no one made a move to interfere. The queen's face was a mask, so bloodless that it might have been sculpted from snow. She rose from the table, gathered her skirts around her, and stormed off in silence, servants trailing behind.

Jaime Lannister put a hand on the king's shoulder, but the king shoved him away hard. Lannister stumbled and fell. The king guffawed. "The great knight. I can still knock you in the dirt. Remember that, Kingslayer." He slapped his chest with the jeweled goblet, splashing wine all over his satin tunic. "Give me my hammer and not a man in the realm can stand before me!"

Jaime Lannister rose and brushed himself off. "As you say, Your Grace." His voice was stiff.

Lord Renly came forward, smiling. "You've spilled your wine, Robert. Let me bring you a fresh goblet."

Sansa started as Joffrey laid his hand on her arm. "It grows late," the prince said. He had a queer look on his face, as if he were not seeing her at all. "Do you need an escort back to the castle?"

"No," Sansa began. She looked for Septa Mordane, and was startled to find her with her head on the table, snoring soft and ladylike snores. "I mean to say . . . yes, thank you, that would be most kind. I *am* tired, and the way is so dark. I should be glad for some protection."

Joffrey called out, *"Dog!"*

Sandor Clegane seemed to take form out of the night, so quickly did he appear. He had exchanged his armor for a red woolen tunic with a leather dog's head sewn on the front. The light of the torches made his burned face shine a dull red. "Yes, Your Grace?" he said.

"Take my betrothed back to the castle, and see that no harm befalls her," the prince told him brusquely. And without even a word of farewell, Joffrey strode off, leaving her there.

Sansa could *feel* the Hound watching her. "Did you think Joff was going to take you himself?" He laughed. He had a laugh like the snarling of dogs in a pit. "Small chance of that." He pulled her unresisting to her feet. "Come, you're not the only one needs sleep. I've drunk too much, and I may need to kill my brother tomorrow." He laughed again.

Suddenly terrified, Sansa pushed at Septa Mordane's shoulder, hoping to wake her, but she only snored the louder. King Robert had stumbled off and half the benches were suddenly empty. The feast was over, and the beautiful dream had ended with it.

The Hound snatched up a torch to light their way. Sansa followed close beside him. The ground was rocky and uneven; the flickering light made it seem to shift and move beneath her. She kept her eyes lowered, watching where she placed her feet. They walked among the pavilions, each with its banner and its armor hung outside, the silence weighing heavier with every step. Sansa could not bear the sight of him, he frightened her so, yet she had been raised in all the ways of courtesy. A true lady would not notice his face, she told herself. "You rode gallantly today, Ser Sandor," she made herself say.

Sandor Clegane snarled at her. "Spare me your empty little compliments, girl . . . and your *ser*'s. I am no knight. I spit on them and their vows. My brother is a knight. Did you see him ride today?"

"Yes," Sansa whispered, trembling. "He was . . ."

"Gallant?" the Hound finished.

He was mocking her, she realized. "No one could

withstand him," she managed at last, proud of herself. It was no lie.

Sandor Clegane stopped suddenly in the middle of a dark and empty field. She had no choice but to stop beside him. "Some septa trained you well. You're like one of those birds from the Summer Isles, aren't you? A pretty little talking bird, repeating all the pretty little words they taught you to recite."

"That's unkind." Sansa could feel her heart fluttering in her chest. "You're frightening me. I want to go now."

"No one could withstand him," the Hound rasped. "That's truth enough. No one could ever withstand Gregor. That boy today, his second joust, oh, that was a pretty bit of business. You saw that, did you? Fool boy, he had no business riding in this company. No money, no squire, no one to help him with that armor. That gorget wasn't fastened proper. You think Gregor didn't notice that? You think *Ser* Gregor's lance rode up by chance, do you? Pretty little talking girl, you believe that, you're empty-headed as a bird for true. Gregor's lance goes where Gregor wants it to go. Look at me. *Look at me!*" Sandor Clegane put a huge hand under her chin and forced her face up. He squatted in front of her, and moved the torch close. "There's a pretty for you. Take a good long stare. You know you want to. I've watched you turning away all the way down the kingsroad. Piss on that. Take your look."

His fingers held her jaw as hard as an iron trap. His eyes watched hers. Drunken eyes, sullen with anger. She had to look.

The right side of his face was gaunt, with sharp cheekbones and a grey eye beneath a heavy brow. His nose was large and hooked, his hair thin, dark. He wore it long and brushed it sideways, because no hair grew on the *other* side of that face.

The left side of his face was a ruin. His ear had been burned away; there was nothing left but a hole. His eye was still good, but all around it was a twisted mass of scar, slick black flesh hard as leather, pocked with craters and fissured by deep cracks that gleamed red and wet when he moved. Down by his jaw, you could see a hint of bone where the flesh had been seared away.

Sansa began to cry. He let go of her then, and snuffed

out the torch in the dirt. "No pretty words for that, girl? No little compliment the septa taught you?" When there was no answer, he continued. "Most of them, they think it was some battle. A siege, a burning tower, an enemy with a torch. One fool asked if it was dragonsbreath." His laugh was softer this time, but just as bitter. "I'll tell you what it was, girl," he said, a voice from the night, a shadow leaning so close now that she could smell the sour stench of wine on his breath. "I was younger than you, six, maybe seven. A woodcarver set up shop in the village under my father's keep, and to buy favor he sent us gifts. The old man made marvelous toys. I don't remember what I got, but it was Gregor's gift I wanted. A wooden knight, all painted up, every joint pegged separate and fixed with strings, so you could make him fight. Gregor is five years older than me, the toy was nothing to him, he was already a squire, near six foot tall and muscled like an ox. So I took his knight, but there was no joy to it, I tell you. I was scared all the while, and true enough, he found me. There was a brazier in the room. Gregor never said a word, just picked me up under his arm and shoved the side of my face down in the burning coals and held me there while I screamed and screamed. You saw how strong he is. Even then, it took three grown men to drag him off me. The septons preach about the seven hells. What do they know? Only a man who's been burned knows what hell is truly like.

"My father told everyone my bedding had caught fire, and our maester gave me ointments. *Ointments!* Gregor got his ointments too. Four years later, they anointed him with the seven oils and he recited his knightly vows and Rhaegar Targaryen tapped him on the shoulder and said, 'Arise, Ser Gregor.'"

The rasping voice trailed off. He squatted silently before her, a hulking black shape shrouded in the night, hidden from her eyes. Sansa could hear his ragged breathing. She was sad for him, she realized. Somehow, the fear had gone away.

The silence went on and on, so long that she began to grow afraid once more, but she was afraid for him now, not for herself. She found his massive shoulder with her hand. "He was no true knight," she whispered to him.

The Hound threw back his head and roared. Sansa

stumbled back, away from him, but he caught her arm. "No," he growled at her, "no, little bird, he was no true knight."

The rest of the way into the city, Sandor Clegane said not a word. He led her to where the carts were waiting, told a driver to take them back to the Red Keep, and climbed in after her. They rode in silence through the King's Gate and up torchlit city streets. He opened the postern door and led her into the castle, his burned face twitching and his eyes brooding, and he was one step behind her as they climbed the tower stairs. He took her safe all the way to the corridor outside her bedchamber.

"Thank you, my lord," Sansa said meekly.

The Hound caught her by the arm and leaned close. "The things I told you tonight," he said, his voice sounding even rougher than usual. "If you ever tell Joffrey . . . your sister, your father . . . any of them . . ."

"I won't," Sansa whispered. "I promise."

It was not enough. "If you ever tell *anyone*," he finished, "I'll kill you."

EDDARD

"**I** stood last vigil for him myself," Ser Barristan Selmy said as they looked down at the body in the back of the cart. "He had no one else. A mother in the Vale, I am told."

In the pale dawn light, the young knight looked as though he were sleeping. He had not been handsome, but death had smoothed his rough-hewn features and the silent sisters had dressed him in his best velvet tunic, with a high collar to cover the ruin the lance had made of his throat. Eddard Stark looked at his face, and wondered if it had been for his sake that the boy had died. Slain by a Lannister bannerman before Ned could speak to him; could that be mere happenstance? He supposed he would never know.

"Hugh was Jon Arryn's squire for four years," Selmy went on. "The king knighted him before he rode north, in Jon's memory. The lad wanted it desperately, yet I fear he was not ready."

Ned had slept badly last night and he felt tired beyond his years. "None of us is ever ready," he said.

"For knighthood?"

"For death." Gently Ned covered the boy with his

cloak, a bloodstained bit of blue bordered in crescent moons. When his mother asked why her son was dead, he reflected bitterly, they would tell her he had fought to honor the King's Hand, Eddard Stark. "This was needless. War should not be a game." Ned turned to the woman beside the cart, shrouded in grey, face hidden but for her eyes. The silent sisters prepared men for the grave, and it was ill fortune to look on the face of death. "Send his armor home to the Vale. The mother will want to have it."

"It is worth a fair piece of silver," Ser Barristan said. "The boy had it forged special for the tourney. Plain work, but good. I do not know if he had finished paying the smith."

"He paid yesterday, my lord, and he paid dearly," Ned replied. And to the silent sister he said, "Send the mother the armor. I will deal with this smith." She bowed her head.

Afterward Ser Barristan walked with Ned to the king's pavilion. The camp was beginning to stir. Fat sausages sizzled and spit over firepits, spicing the air with the scents of garlic and pepper. Young squires hurried about on errands as their masters woke, yawning and stretching, to meet the day. A serving man with a goose under his arm bent his knee when he caught sight of them. "M'lords," he muttered as the goose honked and pecked at his fingers. The shields displayed outside each tent heralded its occupant: the silver eagle of Seagard, Bryce Caron's field of nightingales, a cluster of grapes for the Redwynes, brindled boar, red ox, burning tree, white ram, triple spiral, purple unicorn, dancing maiden, blackadder, twin towers, horned owl, and last the pure white blazons of the Kingsguard, shining like the dawn.

"The king means to fight in the melee today," Ser Barristan said as they were passing Ser Meryn's shield, its paint sullied by a deep gash where Loras Tyrell's lance had scarred the wood as he drove him from his saddle.

"Yes," Ned said grimly. Jory had woken him last night to bring him that news. Small wonder he had slept so badly.

Ser Barristan's look was troubled. "They say night's beauties fade at dawn, and the children of wine are oft disowned in the morning light."

"They say so," Ned agreed, "but not of Robert." Other men might reconsider words spoken in drunken bravado, but Robert Baratheon would remember and, remembering, would never back down.

The king's pavilion was close by the water, and the morning mists off the river had wreathed it in wisps of grey. It was all of golden silk, the largest and grandest structure in the camp. Outside the entrance, Robert's warhammer was displayed beside an immense iron shield blazoned with the crowned stag of House Baratheon.

Ned had hoped to discover the king still abed in a wine-soaked sleep, but luck was not with him. They found Robert drinking beer from a polished horn and roaring his displeasure at two young squires who were trying to buckle him into his armor. "Your Grace," one was saying, almost in tears, "it's made too small, it won't go." He fumbled, and the gorget he was trying to fit around Robert's thick neck tumbled to the ground.

"Seven hells!" Robert swore. "Do I have to do it myself? Piss on the both of you. Pick it up. Don't just stand there gaping, Lancel, *pick it up!"* The lad jumped, and the king noticed his company. "Look at these oafs, Ned. My wife insisted I take these two to squire for me, and they're worse than useless. Can't even put a man's armor on him properly. Squires, they say. *I* say they're swineherds dressed up in silk."

Ned only needed a glance to understand the difficulty. "The boys are not at fault," he told the king. "You're too fat for your armor, Robert."

Robert Baratheon took a long swallow of beer, tossed the empty horn onto his sleeping furs, wiped his mouth with the back of his hand, and said darkly, "Fat? *Fat,* is it? Is that how you speak to your king?" He let go his laughter, sudden as a storm. "Ah, damn you, Ned, why are you always right?"

The squires smiled nervously until the king turned on them. "You. Yes, both of you. You heard the Hand. The king is too fat for his armor. Go find Ser Aron Santagar. Tell him I need the breastplate stretcher. *Now! What are you waiting for?"*

The boys tripped over each other in their haste to be quit of the tent. Robert managed to keep a stern face until they were gone. Then he dropped back into a chair, shaking with laughter.

Ser Barristan Selmy chuckled with him. Even Eddard Stark managed a smile. Always, though, the graver thoughts crept in. He could not help taking note of the two squires: handsome boys, fair and well made. One was Sansa's age, with long golden curls; the other perhaps fifteen, sandy-haired, with a wisp of a mustache and the emerald-green eyes of the queen.

"Ah, I wish I could be there to see Santagar's face," Robert said. "I hope he'll have the wit to send them to someone else. We ought to keep them running all day!"

"Those boys," Ned asked him. "Lannisters?"

Robert nodded, wiping tears from his eyes. "Cousins. Sons of Lord Tywin's brother. One of the dead ones. Or perhaps the live one, now that I come to think on it. I don't recall. My wife comes from a very large family, Ned."

A very ambitious family, Ned thought. He had nothing against the squires, but it troubled him to see Robert surrounded by the queen's kin, waking and sleeping. The Lannister appetite for offices and honors seemed to know no bounds. "The talk is you and the queen had angry words last night."

The mirth curdled on Robert's face. "The woman tried to forbid me to fight in the melee. She's sulking in the castle now, damn her. Your sister would never have shamed me like that."

"You never knew Lyanna as I did, Robert," Ned told him. "You saw her beauty, but not the iron underneath. She would have told you that you have no business in the melee."

"You too?" The king frowned. "You are a sour man, Stark. Too long in the north, all the juices have frozen inside you. Well, *mine* are still running." He slapped his chest to prove it.

"You are the king," Ned reminded him.

"I sit on the damn iron seat when I must. Does that mean I don't have the same hungers as other men? A bit of wine now and again, a girl squealing in bed, the feel of a horse between my legs? Seven hells, Ned, I want to *hit* someone."

Ser Barristan Selmy spoke up. "Your Grace," he said,

"it is not seemly that the king should ride into the melee. It would not be a fair contest. Who would dare strike you?"

Robert seemed honestly taken aback. "Why, all of them, damn it. If they can. And the last man left standing . . ."

". . . will be you," Ned finished. He saw at once that Selmy had hit the mark. The dangers of the melee were only a savor to Robert, but this touched on his pride. "Ser Barristan is right. There's not a man in the Seven Kingdoms who would dare risk your displeasure by hurting you."

The king rose to his feet, his face flushed. "Are you telling me those prancing cravens will *let me win*?"

"For a certainty," Ned said, and Ser Barristan Selmy bowed his head in silent accord.

For a moment Robert was so angry he could not speak. He strode across the tent, whirled, strode back, his face dark and angry. He snatched up his breastplate from the ground and threw it at Barristan Selmy in a wordless fury. Selmy dodged. "Get out," the king said then, coldly. "Get out before I kill you."

Ser Barristan left quickly. Ned was about to follow when the king called out again. "Not you, Ned."

Ned turned back. Robert took up his horn again, filled it with beer from a barrel in the corner, and thrust it at Ned. "Drink," he said brusquely.

"I've no thirst—"

"*Drink*. Your king commands it."

Ned took the horn and drank. The beer was black and thick, so strong it stung the eyes.

Robert sat down again. "Damn you, Ned Stark. You and Jon Arryn, I loved you both. What have you done to me? You were the one should have been king, you or Jon."

"You had the better claim, Your Grace."

"I told you to drink, not to argue. You made me king, you could at least have the courtesy to listen when I talk, damn you. Look at me, Ned. Look at what kinging has done to me. Gods, too fat for my armor, how did it ever come to this?"

"Robert . . ."

"Drink and stay quiet, the king is talking. I swear to you, I was never so alive as when I was winning this throne, or so dead as now that I've won it. And Cersei . . . I have Jon Arryn to thank for her. I had no wish to marry after Lyanna was taken from me, but Jon said the realm needed an heir. Cersei Lannister would be a good match, he told me, she would bind Lord Tywin to me should Viserys Targaryen ever try to win back his father's throne." The king shook his head. "I loved that old man, I swear it, but now I think he was a bigger fool than Moon Boy. Oh, Cersei is lovely to look at, truly, but *cold* . . . the way she guards her cunt, you'd think she had all the gold of Casterly Rock between her legs. Here, give me that beer if you won't drink it." He took the horn, upended it, belched, wiped his mouth. "I am sorry for your girl, Ned. Truly. About the wolf, I mean. My son was lying, I'd stake my soul on it. My son . . . you love your children, don't you?"

"With all my heart," Ned said.

"Let me tell you a secret, Ned. More than once, I have dreamed of giving up the crown. Take ship for the Free Cities with my horse and my hammer, spend my time warring and whoring, that's what I was made for. The sellsword king, how the singers would love me. You know what stops me? The thought of Joffrey on the throne, with Cersei standing behind him whispering in his ear. My son. How could I have made a son like that, Ned?"

"He's only a boy," Ned said awkwardly. He had small liking for Prince Joffrey, but he could hear the pain in Robert's voice. "Have you forgotten how wild you were at his age?"

"It would not trouble me if the boy was wild, Ned. You don't know him as I do." He sighed and shook his head. "Ah, perhaps you are right. Jon despaired of me often enough, yet I grew into a good king." Robert looked at Ned and scowled at his silence. "You might speak up and agree now, you know."

"Your Grace . . ." Ned began, carefully.

Robert slapped Ned on the back. "Ah, say that I'm a better king than Aerys and be done with it. You never could lie for love nor honor, Ned Stark. I'm still young, and now that you're here with me, things will be different. We'll make this a reign to sing of, and damn the Lannisters to seven hells. I smell bacon. Who do you think our champion will be today? Have you seen Mace Tyrell's boy? The Knight of Flowers, they call him. Now there's a son any man would be proud to own to. Last tourney, he dumped the Kingslayer on his golden rump, you ought to have seen the look on Cersei's face. I laughed till my sides hurt. Renly says he has this sister, a maid of fourteen, lovely as a dawn . . ."

They broke their fast on black bread and boiled goose eggs and fish fried up with onions and bacon, at a trestle table by the river's edge. The king's melancholy melted away with the morning mist, and before long Robert was eating an orange and waxing fond about a morning at the Eyrie when they had been boys. ". . . had given Jon a barrel of oranges, remember? Only the things had gone rotten, so I flung mine across the table and hit Dacks right in the nose. You remember, Redfort's pock-faced squire? He tossed one back at me, and before Jon could so much as fart, there were oranges flying across the High Hall in every direction." He laughed uproariously, and even Ned smiled, remembering.

This was the boy he had grown up with, he thought; this was the Robert Baratheon he'd known and loved. If he could prove that the Lannisters were behind the attack on Bran, prove that they had murdered Jon Arryn, this man would listen. Then Cersei would fall, and the Kingslayer with her, and if Lord Tywin dared to rouse the west, Robert would smash him as he had smashed Rhaegar Targaryen on the Trident. He could see it all so clearly.

That breakfast tasted better than anything Eddard Stark had eaten in a long time, and afterward his smiles came easier and more often, until it was time for the tournament to resume.

Ned walked with the king to the jousting field. He had promised to watch the final tilts with Sansa; Septa Mordane was ill today, and his daughter was determined not to miss the end of the jousting. As he saw Robert to his place, he noted that Cersei Lannister had chosen not to appear; the place beside the king was empty. That too gave Ned cause to hope.

He shouldered his way to where his daughter was seated and found her as the horns blew for the day's first joust. Sansa was so engrossed she scarcely seemed to notice his arrival.

Sandor Clegane was the first rider to appear. He wore an olive-green cloak over his soot-grey armor. That, and his hound's-head helm, were his only concession to ornament.

"A hundred golden dragons on the Kingslayer," Littlefinger announced loudly as Jaime Lannister entered the lists, riding an elegant blood bay destrier. The horse wore a blanket of gilded ringmail, and Jaime glittered from head to heel. Even his lance was fashioned from the golden wood of the Summer Isles.

"Done," Lord Renly shouted back. "The Hound has a hungry look about him this morning."

"Even hungry dogs know better than to bite the hand that feeds them," Littlefinger called dryly.

Sandor Clegane dropped his visor with an audible *clang* and took up his position. Ser Jaime tossed a kiss to some woman in the commons, gently lowered his visor, and rode to the end of the lists. Both men couched their lances.

Ned Stark would have loved nothing so well as to see them both lose, but Sansa was watching it all moist-eyed and eager. The hastily erected gallery trembled as the horses broke into a gallop. The Hound leaned forward as he rode, his lance rock steady, but Jaime shifted his seat deftly in the instant before impact. Clegane's point was turned harmlessly against the golden shield with the lion blazon, while his own hit square. Wood shattered, and the Hound reeled, fighting to keep his seat. Sansa gasped. A ragged cheer went up from the commons.

"I wonder how I ought spend your money," Littlefinger called down to Lord Renly.

The Hound just managed to stay in his saddle. He jerked his mount around hard and rode back to the lists for the second pass. Jaime Lannister tossed down his broken lance and snatched up a fresh one, jesting with his squire. The Hound spurred forward at a hard gallop. Lannister rode to meet him. This time, when Jaime shifted his seat, Sandor Clegane shifted with him. Both lances exploded, and by the time the splinters had settled, a riderless blood bay was trotting off in search of grass while Ser Jaime Lannister rolled in the dirt, golden and dented.

Sansa said, "I knew the Hound would win."

Littlefinger overheard. "If you know who's going to win the second match, speak up now before Lord Renly plucks me clean," he called to her. Ned smiled.

"A pity the Imp is not here with us," Lord Renly said. "I should have won twice as much."

Jaime Lannister was back on his feet, but his ornate lion helmet had been twisted around and dented in his fall, and now he could not get it off. The commons were hooting and pointing, the lords and ladies were trying to stifle their chuckles, and failing, and over it all Ned could hear King Robert laughing, louder than anyone. Finally they had to lead the Lion of Lannister off to a blacksmith, blind and stumbling.

By then Ser Gregor Clegane was in position at the head of the lists. He was huge, the biggest man that Eddard Stark had ever seen. Robert Baratheon and his brothers were all big men, as was the Hound, and back at Winterfell there was a simpleminded stableboy named Hodor who dwarfed them all, but the knight they called the Mountain That Rides would have towered over Hodor. He was well over seven feet tall, closer to eight, with massive shoulders and arms thick as the trunks of small trees. His destrier seemed a pony in between his armored legs, and the lance he carried looked as small as a broom handle.

Unlike his brother, Ser Gregor did not live at court. He was a solitary man who seldom left his own lands, but for wars and tourneys. He had been with Lord Tywin when King's Landing fell, a new-made knight of seventeen years, even then distinguished by his size and his implacable ferocity. Some said it had been Gregor who'd dashed the skull of the infant prince Aegon Targaryen against a wall, and whispered that afterward he had raped the mother, the Dornish princess Elia, before putting her to the sword. These things were not said in Gregor's hearing.

Ned Stark could not recall ever speaking to the man, though Gregor had ridden with them during Balon Greyjoy's rebellion, one knight among thousands. He watched him with disquiet. Ned seldom put much stock in gossip, but the things said of Ser Gregor were more than ominous. He was soon to be married for the third time, and one heard dark whisperings about the deaths of his first two wives. It was said that his keep was a grim place where servants disappeared unaccountably and even the dogs were afraid to enter the hall. And there had been a sister who had died young under queer circumstances, and the fire that had disfigured his brother, and the hunting accident that had killed their father. Gregor had inherited the keep, the gold, and the family estates. His younger brother Sandor had left the same day to take service with the Lannisters as a sworn sword, and it was said that he had never returned, not even to visit.

When the Knight of Flowers made his entrance, a murmur ran through the crowd, and he heard Sansa's fervent whisper, "Oh, he's so *beautiful*." Ser Loras Tyrell was slender as a reed, dressed in a suit of fabulous silver armor polished to a blinding sheen and filigreed with twining black vines and tiny blue forget-me-nots. The commons realized in the same instant as Ned that the blue of the flowers came from sapphires; a gasp went up from a thousand throats. Across the boy's shoulders his cloak hung heavy. It was woven of forget-me-nots, real ones, hundreds of fresh blooms sewn to a heavy woolen cape.

His courser was as slim as her rider, a beautiful grey mare, built for speed. Ser Gregor's huge stallion trumpeted as he caught her scent. The boy from Highgarden did something with his legs, and his horse pranced sideways, nimble as a dancer. Sansa clutched at his arm. "Father, don't let Ser Gregor hurt him," she said. Ned saw she was wearing the rose that Ser Loras had given her yesterday. Jory had told him about that as well.

"These are tourney lances," he told his daughter. "They make them to splinter on impact, so no one is hurt." Yet he remembered the dead boy in the cart with his cloak of crescent moons, and the words were raw in his throat.

Ser Gregor was having trouble controlling his horse. The stallion was screaming and pawing the ground, shaking his head. The Mountain kicked at the animal savagely with an armored boot. The horse reared and almost threw him.

The Knight of Flowers saluted the king, rode to the far end of the list, and couched his lance, ready. Ser Gregor brought his animal to the line, fighting with the reins. And suddenly it began. The Mountain's stallion broke in

a hard gallop, plunging forward wildly, while the mare
charged as smooth as a flow of silk. Ser Gregor wrenched
his shield into position, juggled with his lance, and all the
while fought to hold his unruly mount on a straight line,
and suddenly Loras Tyrell was on him, placing the point
of his lance just *there*, and in an eye blink the Mountain
was falling. He was so huge that he took his horse down
with him in a tangle of steel and flesh.

Ned heard applause, cheers, whistles, shocked gasps,
excited muttering, and over it all the rasping, raucous
laughter of the Hound. The Knight of Flowers reined up at
the end of the lists. His lance was not even broken. His
sapphires winked in the sun as he raised his visor, smiling. The commons went mad for him.

In the middle of the field, Ser Gregor Clegane disentangled himself and came boiling to his feet. He wrenched off
his helm and slammed it down onto the ground. His face
was dark with fury and his hair fell down into his eyes.
"My sword," he shouted to his squire, and the boy ran it
out to him. By then his stallion was back on its feet as
well.

Gregor Clegane killed the horse with a single blow of
such ferocity that it half severed the animal's neck.
Cheers turned to shrieks in a heartbeat. The stallion went
to its knees, screaming as it died. By then Gregor was
striding down the lists toward Ser Loras Tyrell, his bloody
sword clutched in his fist. "*Stop him!*" Ned shouted, but
his words were lost in the roar. Everyone else was yelling
as well, and Sansa was crying.

It all happened so fast. The Knight of Flowers was
shouting for his own sword as Ser Gregor knocked his
squire aside and made a grab for the reins of his horse.
The mare scented blood and reared. Loras Tyrell kept his
seat, but barely. Ser Gregor swung his sword, a savage
two-handed blow that took the boy in the chest and
knocked him from the saddle. The courser dashed away
in panic as Ser Loras lay stunned in the dirt. But as Gregor
lifted his sword for the killing blow, a rasping voice
warned, "*Leave him be,*" and a steel-clad hand wrenched
him away from the boy.

The Mountain pivoted in wordless fury, swinging his
longsword in a killing arc with all his massive strength
behind it, but the Hound caught the blow and turned it,

and for what seemed an eternity the two brothers stood hammering at each other as a dazed Loras Tyrell was helped to safety. Thrice Ned saw Ser Gregor aim savage blows at the hound's-head helmet, yet not once did Sandor send a cut at his brother's unprotected face.

It was the king's voice that put an end to it . . . the king's voice and twenty swords. Jon Arryn had told them that a commander needs a good battlefield voice, and Robert had proved the truth of that on the Trident. He used that voice now. *"STOP THIS MADNESS,"* he boomed, *"IN THE NAME OF YOUR KING!"*

The Hound went to one knee. Ser Gregor's blow cut air, and at last he came to his senses. He dropped his sword and glared at Robert, surrounded by his Kingsguard and a dozen other knights and guardsmen. Wordlessly, he turned and strode off, shoving past Barristan Selmy. "Let him go," Robert said, and as quickly as that, it was over.

"Is the Hound the champion now?" Sansa asked Ned.

"No," he told her. "There will be one final joust, between the Hound and the Knight of Flowers."

But Sansa had the right of it after all. A few moments later Ser Loras Tyrell walked back onto the field in a simple linen doublet and said to Sandor Clegane, "I owe you my life. The day is yours, ser."

"I am no *ser*," the Hound replied, but he took the victory, and the champion's purse, and, for perhaps the first time in his life, the love of the commons. They cheered him as he left the lists to return to his pavilion.

As Ned walked with Sansa to the archery field, Littlefinger and Lord Renly and some of the others fell in with them. "Tyrell had to know the mare was in heat," Littlefinger was saying. "I swear the boy planned the whole thing. Gregor has always favored huge, ill-tempered stallions with more spirit than sense." The notion seemed to amuse him.

It did not amuse Ser Barristan Selmy. "There is small honor in tricks," the old man said stiffly.

"Small honor and twenty thousand golds." Lord Renly smiled.

That afternoon a boy named Anguy, an unheralded commoner from the Dornish Marches, won the archery competition, outshooting Ser Balon Swann and Jalabhar Xho at a hundred paces after all the other bowmen had been eliminated at the shorter distances. Ned sent Alyn to seek him out and offer him a position with the Hand's guard, but the boy was flush with wine and victory and riches undreamed of, and he refused.

The melee went on for three hours. Near forty men took part, freeriders and hedge knights and new-made squires in search of a reputation. They fought with blunted weapons in a chaos of mud and blood, small troops fighting together and then turning on each other as alliances formed and fractured, until only one man was left standing. The victor was the red priest, Thoros of Myr, a madman who shaved his head and fought with a flaming sword. He had won melees before; the fire sword frightened the mounts of the other riders, and nothing frightened Thoros. The final tally was three broken limbs, a shattered collarbone, a dozen smashed fingers, two horses that had to be put down, and more cuts, sprains, and bruises than anyone cared to count. Ned was desperately pleased that Robert had not taken part.

That night at the feast, Eddard Stark was more hopeful than he had been in a great while. Robert was in high good humor, the Lannisters were nowhere to be seen, and even his daughters were behaving. Jory brought Arya down to join them, and Sansa spoke to her sister pleasantly. "The tournament was *magnificent*," she sighed. "You should have come. How was your dancing?"

"I'm sore all over," Arya reported happily, proudly displaying a huge purple bruise on her leg.

"You must be a terrible dancer," Sansa said doubtfully.

Later, while Sansa was off listening to a troupe of singers perform the complex round of interwoven ballads called the "Dance of the Dragons," Ned inspected the bruise himself. "I hope Forel is not being too hard on you," he said.

Arya stood on one leg. She was getting much better at that of late. "Syrio says that every hurt is a lesson, and every lesson makes you better."

Ned frowned. The man Syrio Forel had come with an excellent reputation, and his flamboyant Braavosi style was well suited to Arya's slender blade, yet still . . . a few days ago, she had been wandering around with a swatch of black silk tied over her eyes. Syrio was teaching her to see with her ears and her nose and her skin, she told him. Before that, he had her doing spins and back flips. "Arya, are you certain you want to persist in this?"

She nodded. "Tomorrow we're going to catch cats."

"Cats." Ned sighed. "Perhaps it was a mistake to hire this Braavosi. If you like, I will ask Jory to take over your lessons. Or I might have a quiet word with Ser Barristan. He was the finest sword in the Seven Kingdoms in his youth."

"I don't want them," Arya said. "I want Syrio."

Ned ran his fingers through his hair. Any decent master-at-arms could give Arya the rudiments of slash-and-parry without this nonsense of blindfolds, cartwheels, and hopping about on one leg, but he knew his youngest daughter well enough to know there was no arguing with that stubborn jut of jaw. "As you wish," he said. Surely she would grow tired of this soon. "Try to be careful."

"I will," she promised solemnly as she hopped smoothly from her right leg to her left.

Much later, after he had taken the girls back through the city and seen them both safe in bed, Sansa with her dreams and Arya with her bruises, Ned ascended to his own chambers atop the Tower of the Hand. The day had been warm and the room was close and stuffy. Ned went to the window and unfastened the heavy shutters to let in the cool night air. Across the Great Yard, he noticed the flickering glow of candlelight from Littlefinger's windows. The hour was well past midnight. Down by the river, the revels were only now beginning to dwindle and die.

He took out the dagger and studied it. Littlefinger's blade, won by Tyrion Lannister in a tourney wager, sent to slay Bran in his sleep. *Why?* Why would the dwarf want Bran dead? Why would *anyone* want Bran dead?

The dagger, Bran's fall, all of it was linked somehow to the murder of Jon Arryn, he could feel it in his gut, but the truth of Jon's death remained as clouded to him as when he had started. Lord Stannis had not returned to King's Landing for the tourney. Lysa Arryn held her silence behind the high walls of the Eyrie. The squire was dead, and Jory was still searching the whorehouses. What did he have but Robert's bastard?

That the armorer's sullen apprentice was the king's son, Ned had no doubt. The Baratheon look was stamped on his face, in his jaw, his eyes, that black hair. Renly was too young to have fathered a boy of that age, Stannis too cold and proud in his honor. Gendry had to be Robert's.

Yet knowing all that, what had he learned? The king had other baseborn children scattered throughout the Seven Kingdoms. He had openly acknowledged one of his bastards, a boy of Bran's age whose mother was highborn. The lad was being fostered by Lord Renly's castellan at Storm's End.

Ned remembered Robert's first child as well, a daughter born in the Vale when Robert was scarcely more than a boy himself. A sweet little girl; the young lord of Storm's End had doted on her. He used to make daily visits to play with the babe, long after he had lost interest in the mother. Ned was often dragged along for company, whether he willed it or not. The girl would be seventeen or eighteen now, he realized; older than Robert had been when he fathered her. A strange thought.

Cersei could not have been pleased by her lord husband's by-blows, yet in the end it mattered little whether the king had one bastard or a hundred. Law and custom gave the baseborn few rights. Gendry, the girl in the Vale, the boy at Storm's End, none of them could threaten Robert's trueborn children . . .

His musings were ended by a soft rap on his door. "A man to see you, my lord," Harwin called. "He will not give his name."

"Send him in," Ned said, wondering.

The visitor was a stout man in cracked, mud-caked boots and a heavy brown robe of the coarsest roughspun, his features hidden by a cowl, his hands drawn up into voluminous sleeves.

"Who are you?" Ned asked.

"A friend," the cowled man said in a strange, low voice. "We must speak alone, Lord Stark."

Curiosity was stronger than caution. "Harwin, leave us," he commanded. Not until they were alone behind closed doors did his visitor draw back his cowl.

"*Lord Varys!*" Ned said in astonishment.

"Lord Stark," Varys said politely, seating himself. "I wonder if I might trouble you for a drink?"

Ned filled two cups with summerwine and handed one to Varys. "I might have passed within a foot of you and never recognized you," he said, incredulous. He had never seen the eunuch dress in anything but silk and velvet and the richest damasks, and this man smelled of sweat instead of lilacs.

"That was my dearest hope," Varys said. "It would not do if certain people learned that we had spoken in private. The queen watches you closely. This wine is very choice. Thank you."

"How did you get past my other guards?" Ned asked. Porther and Cayn had been posted outside the tower, and Alyn on the stairs.

"The Red Keep has ways known only to ghosts and spiders." Varys smiled apologetically. "I will not keep you long, my lord. There are things you must know. You are the King's Hand, and the king is a fool." The eunuch's cloying tones were gone; now his voice was thin and sharp as a whip. "Your friend, I know, yet a fool nonetheless . . . and doomed, unless you save him. Today was a near thing. They had hoped to kill him during the melee."

For a moment Ned was speechless with shock. *"Who?"*

Varys sipped his wine. "If I truly need to tell you that, you are a bigger fool than Robert and I am on the wrong side."

"The Lannisters," Ned said. "The queen . . . no, I will not believe that, not even of Cersei. She asked him not to fight!"

"She *forbade* him to fight, in front of his brother, his knights, and half the court. Tell me truly, do you know any surer way to force King Robert into the melee? I ask you."

Ned had a sick feeling in his gut. The eunuch had hit upon a truth; tell Robert Baratheon he could not, should not, or must not do a thing, and it was as good as done. "Even if he'd fought, who would have dared to strike the king?"

Varys shrugged. "There were forty riders in the melee. The Lannisters have many friends. Amidst all that chaos, with horses screaming and bones breaking and Thoros of Myr waving that absurd firesword of his, who could name it murder if some chance blow felled His Grace?" He went to the flagon and refilled his cup. "After the deed was done, the slayer would be beside himself with grief. I can almost hear him weeping. So sad. Yet no doubt the gracious and compassionate widow would take pity, lift the poor unfortunate to his feet, and bless him with a gentle kiss of forgiveness. Good King Joffrey would have no choice but to pardon him." The eunuch stroked his cheek. "Or perhaps Cersei would let Ser Ilyn strike off his head. Less risk for the Lannisters that way, though quite an unpleasant surprise for their little friend."

Ned felt his anger rise. "You knew of this plot, and yet you did nothing."

"I command whisperers, not warriors."

"You might have come to me earlier."

"Oh, yes, I confess it. And you would have rushed straight to the king, yes? And when Robert heard of his peril, what would he have done? I wonder."

Ned considered that. "He would have damned them all, and fought anyway, to show he did not fear them."

Varys spread his hands. "I will make another confession, Lord Eddard. I was curious to see what you would do. *Why not come to me?* you ask, and I must answer, *Why, because I did not trust you, my lord.*"

"*You* did not trust *me?*" Ned was frankly astonished.

"The Red Keep shelters two sorts of people, Lord Eddard," Varys said. "Those who are loyal to the realm, and those who are loyal only to themselves. Until this morning, I could not say which you might be . . . so I waited to see . . . and now I know, for a certainty." He smiled a plump tight little smile, and for a moment his private face and public mask were one. "I begin to comprehend why the queen fears you so much. Oh, yes I do."

"You are the one she ought to fear," Ned said.

"No. I am what I am. The king makes use of me, but it shames him. A most puissant warrior is our Robert, and such a manly man has little love for sneaks and spies and eunuchs. If a day should come when Cersei whispers, 'Kill that man,' Ilyn Payne will snick my head off in a twinkling, and who will mourn poor Varys then? North or south, they sing no songs for spiders." He reached out and touched Ned with a soft hand. "But you, Lord Stark . . . I think . . . no, I *know* . . . he would not kill you, not even for his queen, and there may lie our salvation."

It was all too much. For a moment Eddard Stark wanted nothing so much as to return to Winterfell, to the clean simplicity of the north, where the enemies were winter and the wildlings beyond the Wall. "Surely Robert has other loyal friends," he protested. "His brothers, his—"

"—wife?" Varys finished, with a smile that cut. "His brothers hate the Lannisters, true enough, but hating the queen and loving the king are not quite the same thing, are they? Ser Barristan loves his honor, Grand Maester Pycelle loves his office, and Littlefinger loves Little-finger."

"The Kingsguard—"

"A paper shield," the eunuch said. "*Try* not to look so shocked, Lord Stark. Jaime Lannister is himself a Sworn Brother of the White Swords, and we all know what *his* oath is worth. The days when men like Ryam Redwyne and Prince Aemon the Dragonknight wore the white cloak are gone to dust and song. Of these seven, only Ser Barristan Selmy is made of the true steel, and Selmy is *old*. Ser Boros and Ser Meryn are the queen's creatures to the bone, and I have deep suspicions of the others. No, my lord, when the swords come out in earnest, you will be the only true friend Robert Baratheon will have."

"Robert must be told," Ned said. "If what you say is true, if even a part of it is true, the king must hear it for himself."

"And what proof shall we lay before him? My words against theirs? My little birds against the queen and the Kingslayer, against his brothers and his council, against the Wardens of East and West, against all the might of Casterly Rock? Pray, send for Ser Ilyn directly, it will save us all some time. I know where that road ends."

"Yet if what you say is true, they will only bide their time and make another attempt."

"Indeed they will," said Varys, "and sooner rather than later, I do fear. You are making them most anxious, Lord Eddard. But my little birds will be listening, and together we may be able to forestall them, you and I." He rose and pulled up his cowl so his face was hidden once more. "Thank you for the wine. We will speak again. When you see me next at council, be certain to treat me with your accustomed contempt. You should not find it difficult."

He was at the door when Ned called, *"Varys."* The eunuch turned back. "How did Jon Arryn die?"

"I wondered when you would get around to that."

"Tell me."

"The tears of Lys, they call it. A rare and costly thing, clear and sweet as water, and it leaves no trace. I begged Lord Arryn to use a taster, in this very room I begged him, but he would not hear of it. Only one who was less than a man would even think of such a thing, he told me."

Ned had to know the rest. "Who gave him the poison?"

"Some dear sweet friend who often shared meat and mead with him, no doubt. Oh, but which one? There were many such. Lord Arryn was a kindly, trusting man." The eunuch sighed. "There *was* one boy. All he was, he owed Jon Arryn, but when the widow fled to the Eyrie with her household, he stayed in King's Landing and prospered. It always gladdens my heart to see the young rise in the world." The whip was in his voice again, every word a stroke. "He must have cut a gallant figure in the tourney, him in his bright new armor, with those crescent moons on his cloak. A pity he died so untimely, before you could talk to him . . ."

Ned felt half-poisoned himself. "The squire," he said. "Ser Hugh." Wheels within wheels within wheels. Ned's head was pounding. "*Why?* Why now? Jon Arryn had been Hand for fourteen years. What was he doing that they had to kill him?"

"Asking questions," Varys said, slipping out the door.

TYRION

As he stood in the predawn chill watching Chiggen butcher his horse, Tyrion Lannister chalked up one more debt owed the Starks. Steam rose from inside the carcass when the squat sellsword opened the belly with his skinning knife. His hands moved deftly, with never a wasted cut; the work had to be done quickly, before the stink of blood brought shadowcats down from the heights.

"None of us will go hungry tonight," Bronn said. He was near a shadow himself; bone thin and bone hard, with black eyes and black hair and a stubble of beard.

"Some of us may," Tyrion told him. "I am not fond of eating horse. Particularly *my* horse."

"Meat is meat," Bronn said with a shrug. "The Dothraki like horse more than beef or pork."

"Do you take me for a Dothraki?" Tyrion asked sourly. The Dothraki ate horse, in truth; they also left deformed children out for the feral dogs who ran behind their *khalasars*. Dothraki customs had scant appeal for him.

Chiggen sliced a thin strip of bloody meat off the carcass and held it up for inspection. "Want a taste, dwarf?"

"My brother Jaime gave me that mare for my twenty-third name day," Tyrion said in a flat voice.

"Thank him for us, then. If you ever see him again." Chiggen grinned, showing yellow teeth, and swallowed the raw meat in two bites. "Tastes well bred."

"Better if you fry it up with onions," Bronn put in.

Wordlessly, Tyrion limped away. The cold had settled deep in his bones, and his legs were so sore he could scarcely walk. Perhaps his dead mare was the lucky one. *He* had hours more riding ahead of him, followed by a few mouthfuls of food and a short, cold sleep on hard ground, and then another night of the same, and another, and another, and the gods only knew how it would end. "Damn her," he muttered as he struggled up the road to rejoin his captors, remembering, "damn her and all the Starks."

The memory was still bitter. One moment he'd been ordering supper, and an eye blink later he was facing a room of armed men, with Jyck reaching for a sword and the fat innkeep shrieking, "No swords, not *here*, please, m'lords."

Tyrion wrenched down Jyck's arm hurriedly, before he got them both hacked to pieces. "Where are your courtesies, Jyck? Our good hostess said no swords. Do as she asks." He forced a smile that must have looked as queasy as it felt. "You're making a sad mistake, Lady Stark. I had no part in any attack on your son. On my honor—"

"Lannister honor," was all she said. She held up her hands for all the room to see. "His dagger left these scars. The blade he sent to open my son's throat."

Tyrion felt the anger all around him, thick and smoky, fed by the deep cuts in the Stark woman's hands. "Kill him," hissed some drunken slattern from the back, and other voices took up the call, faster than he would have believed. Strangers all, friendly enough only a moment ago, and yet now they cried for his blood like hounds on a trail.

Tyrion spoke up loudly, trying to keep the quaver from his voice. "If Lady Stark believes I have some crime to answer for, I will go with her and answer for it."

It was the only possible course. Trying to cut their way out of this was a sure invitation to an early grave. A good dozen swords had responded to the Stark woman's plea for help: the Harrenhal man, the three Brackens, a pair of unsavory sellswords who looked as though they'd kill him as soon as spit, and some fool field hands who doubtless had no idea what they were doing. Against that, what did Tyrion have? A dagger at his belt, and two men. Jyck swung a fair enough sword, but Morrec scarcely counted; he was part groom, part cook, part body servant, and no soldier. As for Yoren, whatever his feelings might have been, the black brothers were sworn to take no part in the quarrels of the realm. Yoren would do nothing.

And indeed, the black brother stepped aside silently when the old knight by Catelyn Stark's side said, "Take their weapons," and the sellsword Bronn stepped forward to pull the sword from Jyck's fingers and relieve them all of their daggers. "Good," the old man said as the tension in the common room ebbed palpably, "excellent." Tyrion recognized the gruff voice; Winterfell's master-at-arms, shorn of his whiskers.

Scarlet-tinged spittle flew from the fat innkeep's mouth as she begged of Catelyn Stark, "Don't kill him here!"

"Don't kill him anywhere," Tyrion urged.

"Take him somewheres else, no blood here, m'lady, I wants no high lordlin's quarrels."

"We are taking him back to Winterfell," she said, and Tyrion thought, *Well, perhaps* . . . By then he'd had a moment to glance over the room and get a better idea of the situation. He was not altogether displeased by what he saw. Oh, the Stark woman had been clever, no doubt of it. Force them to make a public affirmation of the oaths sworn her father by the lords they served, and then call on them for succor, and her a woman, yes, that was sweet. Yet her success was not as complete as she might have liked. There were close to fifty in the common room by his rough count. Catelyn Stark's plea had roused a bare dozen; the others looked confused, or frightened, or sullen. Only two of the Freys had stirred, Tyrion noted, and they'd sat back down quick enough when their captain failed to move. He might have smiled if he'd dared.

"Winterfell it is, then," he said instead. That was a long ride, as he could well attest, having just ridden it the other way. So many things could happen along the way. "My father will wonder what has become of me," he added, catching the eye of the swordsman who'd offered to yield up his room. "He'll pay a handsome reward to any man who brings him word of what happened here today." Lord Tywin would do no such thing, of course, but Tyrion would make up for it if he won free.

Ser Rodrik glanced at his lady, his look worried, as well it might be. "His men come with him," the old knight announced. "And we'll thank the rest of you to stay quiet about what you've seen here."

It was all Tyrion could do not to laugh. *Quiet?* The old fool. Unless he took the whole inn, the word would begin to spread the instant they were gone. The freerider with the gold coin in his pocket would fly to Casterly Rock like an arrow. If not him, then someone else. Yoren would carry the story south. That fool singer might make a lay of it. The Freys would report back to their lord, and the gods only knew what he might do. Lord Walder Frey might be sworn to Riverrun, but he was a cautious man who had lived a long time by making certain he was always on the winning side. At the very least he would send his birds winging south to King's Landing, and he might well dare more than that.

Catelyn Stark wasted no time. "We must ride at once. We'll want fresh mounts, and provisions for the road. You men, know that you have the eternal gratitude of House Stark. If any of you choose to help us guard our captives and get them safe to Winterfell, I promise you shall be well rewarded." That was all it took; the fools came rushing forward. Tyrion studied their faces; they would indeed be well rewarded, he vowed to himself, but perhaps not quite as they imagined.

Yet even as they were bundling him outside, saddling the horses in the rain, and tying his hands with a length of coarse rope, Tyrion Lannister was not truly afraid. They would never get him to Winterfell, he would have given odds on that. Riders would be after them within the day, birds would take wing, and surely one of the river lords would want to curry favor with his father enough to take a hand. Tyrion was congratulating himself on his subtlety when someone pulled a hood down over his eyes and lifted him up onto a saddle.

They set out through the rain at a hard gallop, and before long Tyrion's thighs were cramped and aching and his butt throbbed with pain. Even when they were safely away from the inn, and Catelyn Stark slowed them to a trot, it was a miserable pounding journey over rough ground, made worse by his blindness. Every twist and turn put him in danger of falling off his horse. The hood muffled sound, so he could not make out what was being said around him, and the rain soaked through the cloth and made it cling to his face, until even breathing was a struggle. The rope chafed his wrists raw and seemed to grow tighter as the night wore on. *I was about to settle down to a warm fire and a roast fowl, and that wretched singer had to open his mouth,* he thought mournfully. The wretched singer had come along with them. "There is a great song to be made from this, and I'm the one to make it," he told Catelyn Stark when he announced his intention of riding with them to see how the "splendid adventure" turned out. Tyrion wondered whether the boy would think the adventure quite so splendid once the Lannister riders caught up with them.

The rain had finally stopped and dawn light was seeping through the wet cloth over his eyes when Catelyn Stark gave the command to dismount. Rough hands pulled him down from his horse, untied his wrists, and yanked the hood off his head. When he saw the narrow stony road, the foothills rising high and wild all around them, and the jagged snowcapped peaks on the distant horizon, all the hope went out of him in a rush. "This is the high road," he gasped, looking at Lady Stark with accusation. "The *eastern* road. You said we were riding for Winterfell!"

Catelyn Stark favored him with the faintest of smiles. "Often and loudly," she agreed. "No doubt your friends will ride that way when they come after us. I wish them good speed."

Even now, long days later, the memory filled him with a bitter rage. All his life Tyrion had prided himself on his cunning, the only gift the gods had seen fit to give him, and yet this seven-times-damned she-wolf Catelyn Stark had outwitted him at every turn. The knowledge was more galling than the bare fact of his abduction.

They stopped only as long as it took to feed and water the horses, and then they were off again. This time Tyrion was spared the hood. After the second night they no longer bound his hands, and once they had gained the heights they scarcely bothered to guard him at all. It seemed they did not fear his escape. And why should they? Up here the land was harsh and wild, and the high road little more than a stony track. If he did run, how far could he hope to go, alone and without provisions? The shadowcats would make a morsel of him, and the clans that dwelt in the mountain fastnesses were brigands and murderers who bowed to no law but the sword.

Yet still the Stark woman drove them forward relentlessly. He knew where they were bound. He had known it since the moment they pulled off his hood. These mountains were the domain of House Arryn, and the late Hand's widow was a Tully, Catelyn Stark's sister . . . and no friend to the Lannisters. Tyrion had known the Lady Lysa slightly during her years at King's Landing, and did not look forward to renewing the acquaintance.

His captors were clustered around a stream a short ways down the high road. The horses had drunk their fill of the icy cold water, and were grazing on clumps of brown grass that grew from clefts in the rock. Jyck and Morrec huddled close, sullen and miserable. Mohor stood over them, leaning on his spear and wearing a rounded iron cap that made him look as if he had a bowl on his head. Nearby, Marillion the singer sat oiling his woodharp, complaining of what the damp was doing to his strings.

"We must have some rest, my lady," the hedge knight Ser Willis Wode was saying to Catelyn Stark as Tyrion approached. He was Lady Whent's man, stiff-necked and stolid, and the first to rise to aid Catelyn Stark back at the inn.

"Ser Willis speaks truly, my lady," Ser Rodrik said. "This is the third horse we have lost—"

"We will lose more than horses if we're overtaken by the Lannisters," she reminded them. Her face was windburnt and gaunt, but it had lost none of its determination.

"Small chance of that here," Tyrion put in.

"The lady did not ask your views, dwarf," snapped Kurleket, a great fat oaf with short-cropped hair and a pig's face. He was one of the Brackens, a man-at-arms in the service of Lord Jonos. Tyrion had made a special effort to learn all their names, so he might thank them later for

their tender treatment of him. A Lannister always paid
his debts. Kurleket would learn that someday, as would
his friends Lharys and Mohor, and the good Ser Willis,
and the sellswords Bronn and Chiggen. He planned an especially sharp lesson for Marillion, him of the woodharp
and the sweet tenor voice, who was struggling so manfully to rhyme *imp* with *gimp* and *limp* so he could make
a song of this outrage.

"Let him speak," Lady Stark commanded.

Tyrion Lannister seated himself on a rock. "By now
our pursuit is likely racing across the Neck, chasing your
lie up the kingsroad . . . assuming there *is* a pursuit,
which is by no means certain. Oh, no doubt the word has
reached my father . . . but my father does not love me
overmuch, and I am not at all sure that he will bother to
bestir himself." It was only half a lie; Lord Tywin Lannister cared not a fig for his deformed son, but he tolerated no slights on the honor of his House. "This is a cruel
land, Lady Stark. You'll find no succor until you reach the
Vale, and each mount you lose burdens the others all the
more. Worse, you risk losing *me*. I am small, and not
strong, and if I die, then what's the point?" That was no
lie at all; Tyrion did not know how much longer he could
endure this pace.

"It might be said that your death *is* the point, Lannister," Catelyn Stark replied.

"I think not," Tyrion said. "If you wanted me dead,
you had only to say the word, and one of these staunch
friends of yours would gladly have given me a red smile."
He looked at Kurleket, but the man was too dim to taste
the mockery.

"The Starks do not murder men in their beds."

"Nor do I," he said. "I tell you again, I had no part in
the attempt to kill your son."

"The assassin was armed with your dagger."

Tyrion felt the heat rise in him. "It was not my dagger," he insisted. "How many times must I swear to that?
Lady Stark, whatever you may believe of me, I am not a
stupid man. Only a fool would arm a common footpad
with his own blade."

Just for a moment, he thought he saw a flicker of doubt
in her eyes, but what she said was, "Why would Petyr lie
to me?"

"Why does a bear shit in the woods?" he demanded. "Because it is his nature. Lying comes as easily as breathing to a man like Littlefinger. *You* ought to know that, you of all people."

She took a step toward him, her face tight. "And what does that mean, Lannister?"

Tyrion cocked his head. "Why, every man at court has heard him tell how he took your maidenhead, my lady."

"That is a lie!" Catelyn Stark said.

"Oh, wicked little imp," Marillion said, shocked.

Kurleket drew his dirk, a vicious piece of black iron. "At your word, m'lady, I'll toss his lying tongue at your feet." His pig eyes were wet with excitement at the prospect.

Catelyn Stark stared at Tyrion with a coldness on her face such as he had never seen. "Petyr Baelish loved me once. He was only a boy. His passion was a tragedy for all of us, but it was real, and pure, and nothing to be made mock of. He wanted my hand. That is the truth of the matter. You are truly an evil man, Lannister."

"And you are truly a fool, Lady Stark. Littlefinger has never loved anyone but Littlefinger, and I promise you that it is not your *hand* that he boasts of, it's those ripe breasts of yours, and that sweet mouth, and the heat between your legs."

Kurleket grabbed a handful of hair and yanked his head back in a hard jerk, baring his throat. Tyrion felt the cold kiss of steel beneath his chin. "Shall I bleed him, my lady?"

"Kill me and the truth dies with me," Tyrion gasped.

"Let him talk," Catelyn Stark commanded.

Kurleket let go of Tyrion's hair, reluctantly.

Tyrion took a deep breath. "How did Littlefinger tell you I came by this dagger of his? Answer me that."

"You won it from him in a wager, during the tourney on Prince Joffrey's name day."

"When my brother Jaime was unhorsed by the Knight of Flowers, that was his story, no?"

"It was," she admitted. A line creased her brow.

"Riders!"

The shriek came from the wind-carved ridge above them. Ser Rodrik had sent Lharys scrambling up the rock face to watch the road while they took their rest.

For a long second, no one moved. Catelyn Stark was the first to react. "Ser Rodrik, Ser Willis, to horse," she shouted. "Get the other mounts behind us. Mohor, guard the prisoners—"

"Arm us!" Tyrion sprang to his feet and seized her by the arm. "You will need every sword."

She knew he was right, Tyrion could see it. The mountain clans cared nothing for the enmities of the great houses; they would slaughter Stark and Lannister with equal fervor, as they slaughtered each other. They might spare Catelyn herself; she was still young enough to bear sons. Still, she hesitated.

"I hear them!" Ser Rodrik called out. Tyrion turned his head to listen, and there it was: hoofbeats, a dozen horses or more, coming nearer. Suddenly everyone was moving, reaching for weapons, running to their mounts.

Pebbles rained down around them as Lharys came springing and sliding down the ridge. He landed breathless in front of Catelyn Stark, an ungainly-looking man with wild tufts of rust-colored hair sticking out from under a conical steel cap. "Twenty men, maybe twenty-five," he said, breathless. "Milk Snakes or Moon Brothers, by my guess. They must have eyes out, m'lady . . . hidden watchers . . . they know we're here."

Ser Rodrik Cassel was already ahorse, a longsword in hand. Mohor crouched behind a boulder, both hands on his iron-tipped spear, a dagger between his teeth. "You, singer," Ser Willis Wode called out. "Help me with this breastplate." Marillion sat frozen, clutching his wood-harp, his face as pale as milk, but Tyrion's man Morrec bounded quickly to his feet and moved to help the knight with his armor.

Tyrion kept his grip on Catelyn Stark. "You have no choice," he told her. "Three of us, and a fourth man wasted guarding us . . . four men can be the difference between life and death up here."

"Give me your word that you will put down your swords again after the fight is done."

"My word?" The hoofbeats were louder now. Tyrion grinned crookedly. "Oh, that you have, my lady . . . on my honor as a Lannister."

For a moment he thought she would spit at him, but instead she snapped, "Arm them," and as quick as that she was pulling away. Ser Rodrik tossed Jyck his sword and scabbard, and wheeled to meet the foe. Morrec helped himself to a bow and quiver, and went to one knee beside the road. He was a better archer than swordsman. And Bronn rode up to offer Tyrion a double-bladed axe.

"I have never fought with an axe." The weapon felt awkward and unfamiliar in his hands. It had a short haft, a heavy head, a nasty spike on top.

"Pretend you're splitting logs," Bronn said, drawing his longsword from the scabbard across his back. He spat, and trotted off to form up beside Chiggen and Ser Rodrik. Ser Willis mounted up to join them, fumbling with his helmet, a metal pot with a thin slit for his eyes and a long black silk plume.

"Logs don't bleed," Tyrion said to no one in particular. He felt naked without armor. He looked around for a rock and ran over to where Marillion was hiding. "Move over."

"Go away!" the boy screamed back at him. "I'm a singer, I want no part of this fight!"

"What, lost your taste for adventure?" Tyrion kicked at the youth until he slid over, and not a moment too soon. A heartbeat later, the riders were on them.

There were no heralds, no banners, no horns nor drums, only the twang of bowstrings as Morrec and Lharys let fly, and suddenly the clansmen came thundering out of the dawn, lean dark men in boiled leather and mismatched armor, faces hidden behind barred halfhelms. In gloved hands were clutched all manner of weapons: longswords and lances and sharpened scythes, spiked clubs and daggers and heavy iron mauls. At their head rode a big man in a striped shadowskin cloak, armed with a two-handed greatsword.

Ser Rodrik shouted *"Winterfell!"* and rode to meet him, with Bronn and Chiggen beside him, screaming some wordless battle cry. Ser Willis Wode followed, swinging a spiked morningstar around his head. "Harrenhal! Harrenhal!" he sang. Tyrion felt a sudden urge to leap up, brandish his axe, and boom out, "Casterly Rock!" but the insanity passed quickly and he crouched down lower.

He heard the screams of frightened horses and the crash of metal on metal. Chiggen's sword raked across the naked face of a mailed rider, and Bronn plunged through the clansmen like a whirlwind, cutting down foes right and left. Ser Rodrik hammered at the big man in the shadowskin cloak, their horses dancing round each other as they traded blow for blow. Jyck vaulted onto a horse and galloped bareback into the fray. Tyrion saw an arrow sprout from the throat of the man in the shadowskin cloak. When he opened his mouth to scream, only blood came out. By the time he fell, Ser Rodrik was fighting someone else.

Suddenly Marillion shrieked, covering his head with his woodharp as a horse leapt over their rock. Tyrion scrambled to his feet as the rider turned to come back at them, hefting a spiked maul. Tyrion swung his axe with both hands. The blade caught the charging horse in the throat with a meaty *thunk*, angling upward, and Tyrion almost lost his grip as the animal screamed and collapsed. He managed to wrench the axe free and lurch clumsily out of the way. Marillion was less fortunate. Horse and rider crashed to the ground in a tangle on top of the singer. Tyrion danced back in while the brigand's leg was still pinned beneath his fallen mount, and buried the axe in the man's neck, just above the shoulder blades.

As he struggled to yank the blade loose, he heard Marillion moaning under the bodies. "Someone help me," the singer gasped. "Gods have mercy, I'm *bleeding*."

"I believe that's horse blood," Tyrion said. The singer's hand came crawling out from beneath the dead animal, scrabbling in the dirt like a spider with five legs. Tyrion put his heel on the grasping fingers and felt a satisfying crunch. "Close your eyes and pretend you're dead," he advised the singer before he hefted the axe and turned away.

After that, things ran together. The dawn was full of shouts and screams and heavy with the scent of blood, and the world had turned to chaos. Arrows hissed past his ear and clattered off the rocks. He saw Bronn unhorsed, fighting with a sword in each hand. Tyrion kept on the fringes of the fight, sliding from rock to rock and darting out of the shadows to hew at the legs of passing horses. He found a wounded clansman and left him dead, helping himself to the man's halfhelm. It fit too snugly, but Tyrion was glad of any protection at all. Jyck was cut down from behind while he sliced at a man in front of him, and later Tyrion stumbled over Kurleket's body. The pig face had been smashed in with a mace, but Tyrion recognized the dirk as he plucked it from the man's dead fingers. He was sliding it through his belt when he heard a woman's scream.

Catelyn Stark was trapped against the stone face of the mountain with three men around her, one still mounted and the other two on foot. She had a dagger clutched awkwardly in her maimed hands, but her back was to the rock now and they had penned her on three sides. *Let them have the bitch*, Tyrion thought, *and welcome to her*, yet somehow he was moving. He caught the first man in the back of the knee before they even knew he was there, and the heavy axehead split flesh and bone like rotten wood. *Logs that bleed*, Tyrion thought inanely as the second man came for him. Tyrion ducked under his sword, lashed out with the axe, the man reeled backward . . . and Catelyn Stark stepped up behind him and opened his throat. The horseman remembered an urgent engagement elsewhere and galloped off suddenly.

Tyrion looked around. The enemy were all vanquished or vanished. Somehow the fighting had ended when he wasn't looking. Dying horses and wounded men lay all around, screaming or moaning. To his vast astonishment, he was not one of them. He opened his fingers and let the axe *thunk* to the ground. His hands were sticky with blood. He could have sworn they had been fighting for half a day, but the sun seemed scarcely to have moved at all.

"Your first battle?" Bronn asked later as he bent over Jyck's body, pulling off his boots. They were good boots, as befit one of Lord Tywin's men; heavy leather, oiled and supple, much finer than what Bronn was wearing.

Tyrion nodded. "My father will be *so* proud," he said. His legs were cramping so badly he could scarcely stand. Odd, he had never once noticed the pain during the battle.

"You need a woman now," Bronn said with a glint in his black eyes. He shoved the boots into his saddlebag. "Nothing like a woman after a man's been blooded, take my word."

Chiggen stopped looting the corpses of the brigands long enough to snort and lick his lips.

Tyrion glanced over to where Lady Stark was dressing Ser Rodrik's wounds. "I'm willing if she is," he said. The freeriders broke into laughter, and Tyrion grinned and thought, *There's a start.*

Afterward he knelt by the stream and washed the blood off his face in water cold as ice. As he limped back to the others, he glanced again at the slain. The dead clansmen were thin, ragged men, their horses scrawny and undersized, with every rib showing. What weapons Bronn and Chiggen had left them were none too impressive. Mauls, clubs, a *scythe* . . . He remembered the big man in the shadowskin cloak who had dueled Ser Rodrik with a two-handed greatsword, but when he found his corpse sprawled on the stony ground, the man was not so big after all, the cloak was gone, and Tyrion saw that the blade was badly notched, its cheap steel spotted with rust. Small wonder the clansmen had left nine bodies on the ground.

They had only three dead; two of Lord Bracken's men-at-arms, Kurleket and Mohor, and his own man Jyck, who had made such a bold show with his bareback charge. *A fool to the end*, Tyrion thought.

"Lady Stark, I urge you to press on, with all haste," Ser Willis Wode said, his eyes scanning the ridgetops warily through the slit in his helm. "We drove them off for the moment, but they will not have gone far."

"We must bury our dead, Ser Willis," she said. "These were brave men. I will not leave them to the crows and shadowcats."

"This soil is too stony for digging," Ser Willis said.

"Then we shall gather stones for cairns."

"Gather all the stones you want," Bronn told her, "but do it without me or Chiggen. I've better things to do than pile rocks on dead men . . . breathing, for one." He looked over the rest of the survivors. "Any of you who hope to be alive come nightfall, ride with us."

"My lady, I fear he speaks the truth," Ser Rodrik said wearily. The old knight had been wounded in the fight, a deep gash in his left arm and a spear thrust that grazed his neck, and he sounded his age. "If we linger here, they will be on us again for a certainty, and we may not live through a second attack."

Tyrion could see the anger in Catelyn's face, but she

had no choice. "May the gods forgive us, then. We will ride at once."

There was no shortage of horses now. Tyrion moved his saddle to Jyck's spotted gelding, who looked strong enough to last another three or four days at least. He was about to mount when Lharys stepped up and said, "I'll take that dirk now, dwarf."

"Let him keep it." Catelyn Stark looked down from her horse. "And see that he has his axe back as well. We may have need of it if we are attacked again."

"You have my thanks, lady," Tyrion said, mounting up.

"Save them," she said curtly. "I trust you no more than I did before." She was gone before he could frame a reply.

Tyrion adjusted his stolen helm and took the axe from Bronn. He remembered how he had begun the journey, with his wrists bound and a hood pulled down over his head, and decided that this was a definite improvement. Lady Stark could keep her trust; so long as he could keep the axe, he would count himself ahead in the game.

Ser Willis Wode led them out. Bronn took the rear, with Lady Stark safely in the middle, Ser Rodrik a shadow beside her. Marillion kept throwing sullen looks back at Tyrion as they rode. The singer had broken several ribs, his woodharp, and all four fingers on his playing hand, yet the day had not been an utter loss to him; somewhere he had acquired a magnificent shadowskin cloak, thick black fur slashed by stripes of white. He huddled beneath its folds silently, and for once had nothing to say.

They heard the deep growls of shadowcats behind them before they had gone half a mile, and later the wild snarling of the beasts fighting over the corpses they had left behind. Marillion grew visibly pale. Tyrion trotted up beside him. *"Craven,"* he said, "rhymes nicely with *raven."* He kicked his horse and moved past the singer, up to Ser Rodrik and Catelyn Stark.

She looked at him, lips pressed tightly together.

"As I was saying before we were so rudely interrupted," Tyrion began, "there is a serious flaw in Littlefinger's fable. Whatever you may believe of me, Lady Stark, I promise you this—I *never* bet against my family."

ARYA

The one-eared black tom arched his back and hissed at her.

Arya padded down the alley, balanced lightly on the balls of her bare feet, listening to the flutter of her heart, breathing slow deep breaths. *Quiet as a shadow,* she told herself, *light as a feather.* The tomcat watched her come, his eyes wary.

Catching cats was hard. Her hands were covered with half-healed scratches, and both knees were scabbed over where she had scraped them raw in tumbles. At first even the cook's huge fat kitchen cat had been able to elude her, but Syrio had kept her at it day and night. When she'd run to him with her hands bleeding, he had said, "So slow? Be quicker, girl. Your enemies will give you more than scratches." He had dabbed her wounds with Myrish fire, which burned so bad she had had to bite her lip to keep from screaming. Then he sent her out after more cats.

The Red Keep was *full* of cats: lazy old cats dozing in the sun, cold-eyed mousers twitching their tails, quick little kittens with claws like needles, ladies' cats all combed and trusting, ragged shadows prowling the midden heaps. One by one Arya had chased them down and snatched them up and brought them proudly to Syrio Forel . . . all but this one, this one-eared black devil of a tomcat. "That's the real king of this castle right there," one of the gold cloaks had told her. "Older than sin and twice as mean. One time, the king was feasting the queen's father, and that black bastard hopped up on the table and snatched a roast quail right out of Lord Tywin's fingers. Robert laughed so hard he like to burst. You stay away from that one, child."

He had run her halfway across the castle; twice around the Tower of the Hand, across the inner bailey, through the stables, down the serpentine steps, past the small kitchen and the pig yard and the barracks of the gold cloaks, along the base of the river wall and up more steps and back and forth over Traitor's Walk, and then down again and through a gate and around a well and in and out of strange buildings until Arya didn't know where she was.

Now at last she had him. High walls pressed close on either side, and ahead was a blank windowless mass of stone. *Quiet as a shadow,* she repeated, sliding forward, *light as a feather.*

When she was three steps away from him, the tomcat bolted. Left, then right, he went; and right, then left, went Arya, cutting off his escape. He hissed again and tried to dart between her legs. *Quick as a snake,* she thought. Her hands closed around him. She hugged him to her chest, whirling and laughing aloud as his claws raked at the front of her leather jerkin. Ever so fast, she kissed him right between the eyes, and jerked her head back an instant before his claws would have found her face. The tomcat yowled and spit.

"What's he doing to that cat?"

Startled, Arya dropped the cat and whirled toward the voice. The tom bounded off in the blink of an eye. At the end of the alley stood a girl with a mass of golden curls, dressed as pretty as a doll in blue satin. Beside her was a plump little blond boy with a prancing stag sewn in pearls across the front of his doublet and a miniature sword at his belt. *Princess Myrcella and Prince Tommen,* Arya thought. A septa as large as a draft horse hovered over them, and behind her two big men in crimson cloaks, Lannister house guards.

"What were you doing to that cat, boy?" Myrcella
asked again, sternly. To her brother she said, "He's a ragged boy, isn't he? Look at him." She giggled.

"A ragged dirty smelly boy," Tommen agreed.

They don't know me, Arya realized. *They don't even
know I'm a girl.* Small wonder; she was barefoot and
dirty, her hair tangled from the long run through the castle, clad in a jerkin ripped by cat claws and brown roughspun pants hacked off above her scabby knees. You don't
wear skirts and silks when you're catching cats. Quickly
she lowered her head and dropped to one knee. Maybe
they *wouldn't* recognize her. If they did, she would never
hear the end of it. Septa Mordane would be mortified, and
Sansa would never speak to her again from the shame.

The old fat septa moved forward. "Boy, how did you
come here? You have no business in this part of the castle."

"You can't keep this sort out," one of the red cloaks
said. "Like trying to keep out rats."

"Who do you belong to, boy?" the septa demanded.
"Answer me. What's wrong with you, are you mute?"

Arya's voice caught in her throat. If she answered,
Tommen and Myrcella would know her for certain.

"Godwyn, bring him here," the septa said. The taller of
the guardsmen started down the alley.

Panic gripped her throat like a giant's hand. Arya could
not have spoken if her life had hung on it. *Calm as still
water,* she mouthed silently.

As Godwyn reached for her, Arya moved. *Quick as a
snake.* She leaned to her left, letting his fingers brush her
arm, spinning around him. *Smooth as summer silk.* By
the time he got himself turned, she was sprinting down
the alley. *Swift as a deer.* The septa was screeching at her.
Arya slid between legs as thick and white as marble columns, bounded to her feet, bowled into Prince Tommen
and hopped over him when he sat down hard and said
"Oof," spun away from the second guard, and then she
was past them all, running full out.

She heard shouts, then pounding footsteps, closing behind her. She dropped and rolled. The red cloak went ca-
reening past her, stumbling. Arya sprang back to her feet.
She saw a window above her, high and narrow, scarcely
more than an arrow slit. Arya leapt, caught the sill, pulled

herself up. She held her breath as she wriggled through. *Slippery as an eel.* Dropping to the floor in front of a startled scrubwoman, she hopped up, brushed the rushes off her clothes, and was off again, out the door and along a long hall, down a stair, across a hidden courtyard, around a corner and over a wall and through a low narrow window into a pitch-dark cellar. The sounds grew more and more distant behind her.

Arya was out of breath and quite thoroughly lost. She was in for it now if they had recognized her, but she didn't think they had. She'd moved too fast. *Swift as a deer.*

She hunkered down in the dark against a damp stone wall and listened for the pursuit, but the only sound was the beating of her own heart and a distant drip of water. *Quiet as a shadow,* she told herself. She wondered where she was. When they had first come to King's Landing, she used to have bad dreams about getting lost in the castle. Father said the Red Keep was smaller than Winterfell, but in her dreams it had been immense, an endless stone maze with walls that seemed to shift and change behind her. She would find herself wandering down gloomy halls past faded tapestries, descending endless circular stairs, darting through courtyards or over bridges, her shouts echoing unanswered. In some of the rooms the red stone walls would seem to drip blood, and nowhere could she find a window. Sometimes she would hear her father's voice, but always from a long way off, and no matter how hard she ran after it, it would grow fainter and fainter, until it faded to nothing and Arya was alone in the dark.

It was very dark right now, she realized. She hugged her bare knees tight against her chest and shivered. She would wait quietly and count to ten thousand. By then it would be safe for her to come creeping back out and find her way home.

By the time she had reached eighty-seven, the room had begun to lighten as her eyes adjusted to the blackness. Slowly the shapes around her took on form. Huge empty eyes stared at her hungrily through the gloom, and dimly she saw the jagged shadows of long teeth. She had lost the count. She closed her eyes and bit her lip and sent the fear away. When she looked again, the monsters would be gone. Would never have been. She pretended that Syrio was beside her in the dark, whispering in her ear. *Calm as still water,* she told herself. *Strong as a bear. Fierce as a wolverine.* She opened her eyes again.

The monsters were still there, but the fear was gone.

Arya got to her feet, moving warily. The heads were all around her. She touched one, curious, wondering if it was real. Her fingertips brushed a massive jaw. It *felt* real enough. The bone was smooth beneath her hand, cold and hard to the touch. She ran her fingers down a tooth, black and sharp, a dagger made of darkness. It made her shiver.

"It's dead," she said aloud. "It's just a skull, it can't hurt me." Yet somehow the monster seemed to know she was there. She could feel its empty eyes watching her through the gloom, and there was something in that dim, cavernous room that did not love her. She edged away from the skull and backed into a second, larger than the first. For an instant she could feel its teeth digging into her shoulder, as if it wanted a bite of her flesh. Arya whirled, felt leather catch and tear as a huge fang nipped at her jerkin, and then she was running. Another skull loomed ahead, the biggest monster of all, but Arya did not even slow. She leapt over a ridge of black teeth as tall as swords, dashed through hungry jaws, and threw herself against the door.

Her hands found a heavy iron ring set in the wood, and she yanked at it. The door resisted a moment, before it slowly began to swing inward, with a *creak* so loud Arya was certain it could be heard all through the city. She opened the door just far enough to slip through, into the hallway beyond.

If the room with the monsters had been dark, the hall was the blackest pit in the seven hells. *Calm as still water,* Arya told herself, but even when she gave her eyes a moment to adjust, there was nothing to see but the vague grey outline of the door she had come through. She wiggled her fingers in front of her face, felt the air move, saw nothing. She was blind. *A water dancer sees with all her senses,* she reminded herself. She closed her eyes and steadied her breathing one two three, drank in the quiet, reached out with her hands.

Her fingers brushed against rough unfinished stone to her left. She followed the wall, her hand skimming along the surface, taking small gliding steps through the darkness. *All halls lead somewhere. Where there is a way in, there is a way out. Fear cuts deeper than swords.* Arya would not be afraid. It seemed as if she had been walking a long ways when the wall ended abruptly and a draft of cold air blew past her cheek. Loose hairs stirred faintly against her skin.

From somewhere far below her, she heard noises. The scrape of boots, the distant sound of voices. A flickering light brushed the wall ever so faintly, and she saw that she stood at the top of a great black well, a shaft twenty feet across plunging deep into the earth. Huge stones had been set into the curving walls as steps, circling down and down, dark as the steps to hell that Old Nan used to tell them of. And *something* was coming up out of the darkness, out of the bowels of the earth . . .

Arya peered over the edge and felt the cold black breath on her face. Far below, she saw the light of a single torch, small as the flame of a candle. Two men, she made out. Their shadows writhed against the sides of the well, tall as giants. She could hear their voices, echoing up the shaft.

". . . found one bastard," one said. "The rest will come soon. A day, two days, a fortnight . . ."

"And when he learns the truth, what will he do?" a second voice asked in the liquid accents of the Free Cities.

"The gods alone know," the first voice said. Arya could see a wisp of grey smoke drifting up off the torch, writhing like a snake as it rose. "The fools tried to kill his son, and what's worse, they made a mummer's farce of it. He's not a man to put that aside. I warn you, the wolf and lion will soon be at each other's throats, whether we will it or no."

"Too soon, too soon," the voice with the accent complained. "What good is war *now*? We are not ready. Delay."

"As well bid me stop time. Do you take me for a wizard?"

The other chuckled. "No less." Flames licked at the cold air. The tall shadows were almost on top of her. An instant later the man holding the torch climbed into her sight, his companion beside him. Arya crept back away from the well, dropped to her stomach, and flattened herself against the wall. She held her breath as the men reached the top of the steps.

"What would you have me do?" asked the torchbearer, a stout man in a leather half cape. Even in heavy boots, his feet seemed to glide soundlessly over the ground. A round scarred face and a stubble of dark beard showed under his steel cap, and he wore mail over boiled leather, and a dirk and shortsword at his belt. It seemed to Arya there was something oddly familiar about him.

"If one Hand can die, why not a second?" replied the man with the accent and the forked yellow beard. "You have danced the dance before, my friend." He was no one Arya had ever seen before, she was certain of it. Grossly fat, yet he seemed to walk lightly, carrying his weight on the balls of his feet as a water dancer might. His rings glimmered in the torchlight, red-gold and pale silver, crusted with rubies, sapphires, slitted yellow tiger eyes. Every finger wore a ring; some had two.

"Before is not now, and this Hand is not the other," the scarred man said as they stepped out into the hall. *Still as stone,* Arya told herself, *quiet as a shadow.* Blinded by the blaze of their own torch, they did not see her pressed flat against the stone, only a few feet away.

"Perhaps so," the forked beard replied, pausing to catch his breath after the long climb. "Nonetheless, we must have time. The princess is with child. The *khal* will not bestir himself until his son is born. You know how they are, these savages."

The man with the torch pushed at something. Arya heard a deep rumbling. A huge slab of rock, red in the torchlight, slid down out of the ceiling with a resounding crash that almost made her cry out. Where the entry to the well had been was nothing but stone, solid and unbroken.

"If he does not bestir himself soon, it may be too late," the stout man in the steel cap said. "This is no longer a game for two players, if ever it was. Stannis Baratheon and Lysa Arryn have fled beyond my reach, and the whispers say they are gathering swords around them. The Knight of Flowers writes Highgarden, urging his lord father to send his sister to court. The girl is a maid of fourteen, sweet and beautiful and tractable, and Lord Renly and Ser Loras intend that Robert should bed her, wed her, and make a new queen. Littlefinger . . . the gods only know what game Littlefinger is playing. Yet Lord Stark's the one who troubles my sleep. He has the bastard, he has the book, and soon enough he'll have the truth. And now his wife has abducted Tyrion Lannister, thanks to Littlefinger's meddling. Lord Tywin will take that for an outrage, and Jaime has a queer affection for the Imp. If the Lannisters move north, that will bring the Tullys in as well. *Delay,* you say. *Make haste,* I reply. Even the finest of jugglers cannot keep a hundred balls in the air forever."

"You are more than a juggler, old friend. You are a true sorcerer. All I ask is that you work your magic awhile longer." They started down the hall in the direction Arya had come, past the room with the monsters.

"What I can do, I will," the one with the torch said softly. "I must have gold, and another fifty birds."

She let them get a long way ahead, then went creeping after them. *Quiet as a shadow.*

"So many?" The voices were fainter as the light dwindled ahead of her. "The ones you need are hard to find . . . so young, to know their letters . . . perhaps older . . . not die so easy . . ."

"No. The younger are safer . . . treat them gently . . ."

". . . if they kept their tongues . . ."

". . . the risk . . ."

Long after their voices had faded away, Arya could still see the light of the torch, a smoking star that bid her follow. Twice it seemed to disappear, but she kept on straight, and both times she found herself at the top of steep, narrow stairs, the torch glimmering far below her. She hurried after it, down and down. Once she stumbled over a rock and fell against the wall, and her hand found raw earth supported by timbers, whereas before the tunnel had been dressed stone.

She must have crept after them for miles. Finally they were gone, but there was no place to go but forward. She found the wall again and followed, blind and lost, pretending that Nymeria was padding along beside her in the darkness. At the end she was knee-deep in foul-smelling water, wishing she could dance upon it as Syrio might have, and wondering if she'd ever see light again. It was full dark when finally Arya emerged into the night air.

She found herself standing at the mouth of a sewer where it emptied into the river. She stank so badly that she stripped right there, dropping her soiled clothing on the riverbank as she dove into the deep black waters. She swam until she felt clean, and crawled out shivering. Some riders went past along the river road as Arya was washing her clothes, but if they saw the scrawny naked girl scrubbing her rags in the moonlight, they took no notice.

She was miles from the castle, but from anywhere in King's Landing you needed only to look up to see the Red Keep high on Aegon's Hill, so there was no danger of losing her way. Her clothes were almost dry by the time she reached the gatehouse. The portcullis was down and the gates barred, so she turned aside to a postern door. The gold cloaks who had the watch sneered when she told them to let her in. "Off with you," one said. "The kitchen scraps are gone, and we'll have no begging after dark."

"I'm not a beggar," she said. "I live here."

"I said, *off with you.* Do you need a clout on the ear to help your hearing?"

"I want to see my father."

The guards exchanged a glance. "I want to fuck the queen myself, for all the good it does me," the younger one said.

The older scowled. "Who's this father of yours, boy, the city ratcatcher?"

"The Hand of the King," Arya told him.

Both men laughed, but then the older one swung his fist at her, casually, as a man would swat a dog. Arya saw the blow coming even before it began. She danced back out of the way, untouched. "I'm not a boy," she spat at them. "I'm Arya Stark of Winterfell, and if you lay a hand on me my lord father will have both your heads on spikes. If you don't believe me, fetch Jory Cassel or Vayon Poole from the Tower of the Hand." She put her hands on her hips. "Now are you going to open the gate, or do you need a clout on the ear to help your hearing?"

Her father was alone in the solar when Harwin and Fat Tom marched her in, an oil lamp glowing softly at his elbow. He was bent over the biggest book Arya had ever seen, a great thick tome with cracked yellow pages of crabbed script, bound between faded leather covers, but he closed it to listen to Harwin's report. His face was stern as he sent the men away with thanks.

"You realize I had half my guard out searching for you?" Eddard Stark said when they were alone. "Septa Mordane is beside herself with fear. She's in the sept praying for your safe return. Arya, you *know* you are never to go beyond the castle gates without my leave."

"I didn't go out the gates," she blurted. "Well, I didn't mean to. I was down in the dungeons, only they turned into this tunnel. It was all dark, and I didn't have a torch or a candle to see by, so I had to follow. I couldn't go back the way I came on account of the monsters. Father, they were talking about *killing* you! Not the monsters, the two men. They didn't see me, I was being still as stone and quiet as a shadow, but I heard them. They said you had a book and a bastard and if one Hand could die, why not a second? Is that the book? Jon's the bastard, I bet."

"Jon? Arya, what are you talking about? Who said this?"

"*They* did," she told him. "There was a fat one with rings and a forked yellow beard, and another in mail and a steel cap, and the fat one said they had to delay but the other one told him he couldn't keep juggling and the wolf and the lion were going to eat each other and it was a mummer's farce." She tried to remember the rest. She hadn't quite understood everything she'd heard, and now it was all mixed up in her head. "The fat one said the princess was with child. The one in the steel cap, he had the torch, he said that they had to hurry. I think he was a wizard."

"A wizard," said Ned, unsmiling. "Did he have a long white beard and tall pointed hat speckled with stars?"

"No! It wasn't like Old Nan's stories. He didn't *look* like a wizard, but the fat one said he was."

"I warn you, Arya, if you're spinning this thread of air—"

"No, I *told* you, it was in the dungeons, by the place with the secret wall. I was chasing cats, and well . . ." She screwed up her face. If she admitted knocking over Prince Tommen, he would be *really* angry with her. ". . . well, I went in this window. That's where I found the monsters."

"Monsters *and* wizards," her father said. "It would

seem you've had quite an adventure. These men you heard, you say they spoke of juggling and mummery?"

"Yes," Arya admitted, "only—"

"Arya, they were mummers," her father told her. "There must be a dozen troupes in King's Landing right now, come to make some coin off the tourney crowds. I'm not certain what these two were doing in the castle, but perhaps the king has asked for a show."

"No." She shook her head stubbornly. "They weren't—"

"You shouldn't be following people about and spying on them in any case. Nor do I cherish the notion of my daughter climbing in strange windows after stray cats. Look at you, sweetling. Your arms are covered with scratches. This has gone on long enough. Tell Syrio Forel that I want a word with him—"

He was interrupted by a short, sudden knock. "Lord Eddard, pardons," Desmond called out, opening the door a crack, "but there's a black brother here begging audience. He says the matter is urgent. I thought you would want to know."

"My door is always open to the Night's Watch," Father said.

Desmond ushered the man inside. He was stooped and ugly, with an unkempt beard and unwashed clothes, yet Father greeted him pleasantly and asked his name.

"Yoren, as it please m'lord. My pardons for the hour." He bowed to Arya. "And this must be your son. He has your look."

"I'm a *girl*," Arya said, exasperated. If the old man was down from the Wall, he must have come by way of Winterfell. "Do you know my brothers?" she asked excitedly. "Robb and Bran are at Winterfell, and Jon's on the Wall. Jon Snow, he's in the Night's Watch too, you must know him, he has a direwolf, a white one with red eyes. Is Jon a ranger yet? I'm Arya Stark." The old man in his smelly black clothes was looking at her oddly, but Arya could not seem to stop talking. "When you ride back to the Wall, would you bring Jon a letter if I wrote one?" She wished Jon were here right now. *He'd* believe her about the dungeons and the fat man with the forked beard and the wizard in the steel cap.

"My daughter often forgets her courtesies," Eddard

Stark said with a faint smile that softened his words. "I beg your forgiveness, Yoren. Did my brother Benjen send you?"

"No one *sent* me, m'lord, saving old Mormont. I'm here to find men for the Wall, and when Robert next holds court, I'll bend the knee and cry our need, see if the king and his Hand have some scum in the dungeons they'd be well rid of. You might say as Benjen Stark is why we're talking, though. His blood ran black. Made him my brother as much as yours. It's for his sake I'm come. Rode hard, I did, near killed my horse the way I drove her, but I left the others well behind."

"The others?"

Yoren spat. "Sellswords and freeriders and like trash. That inn was full o' them, and I saw them take the scent. The scent of blood or the scent of gold, they smell the same in the end. Not all o' them made for King's Landing, either. Some went galloping for Casterly Rock, and the Rock lies closer. Lord Tywin will have gotten the word by now, you can count on it."

Father frowned. "What word is this?"

Yoren eyed Arya. "One best spoken in private, m'lord, begging your pardons."

"As you say. Desmond, see my daughter to her chambers." He kissed her on the brow. "We'll finish our talk on the morrow."

Arya stood rooted to the spot. "Nothing bad's happened to Jon, has it?" she asked Yoren. "Or Uncle Benjen?"

"Well, as to Stark, I can't say. The Snow boy was well enough when I left the Wall. It's not them as concerns me."

Desmond took her hand. "Come along, milady. You heard your lord father."

Arya had no choice but to go with him, wishing it had been Fat Tom. With Tom, she might have been able to linger at the door on some excuse and hear what Yoren was saying, but Desmond was too single-minded to trick. "How many guards does my father have?" she asked him as they descended to her bedchamber.

"Here at King's Landing? Fifty."

"You wouldn't let anyone kill him, would you?" she asked.

Desmond laughed. "No fear on that count, little lady. Lord Eddard's guarded night and day. He'll come to no harm."

"The Lannisters have more than fifty men," Arya pointed out.

"So they do, but every northerner is worth ten of these southron swords, so you can sleep easy."

"What if a wizard was sent to kill him?"

"Well, as to that," Desmond replied, drawing his longsword, "wizards die the same as other men, once you cut their heads off."

EDDARD

"**R**obert, I beg of you," Ned pleaded, "hear what you are saying. You are talking of murdering a child."

"*The whore is pregnant!*" The king's fist slammed down on the council table loud as a thunderclap. "I warned you this would happen, Ned. Back in the barrowlands, I warned you, but you did not care to hear it. Well, you'll hear it now. I want them dead, mother and child both, and that fool Viserys as well. Is that plain enough for you? *I want them dead.*"

The other councillors were all doing their best to pretend that they were somewhere else. No doubt they were wiser than he was. Eddard Stark had seldom felt quite so alone. "You will dishonor yourself forever if you do this."

"Then let it be on my head, so long as it is done. I am not so blind that I cannot see the shadow of the axe when it is hanging over my own neck."

"There is no axe," Ned told his king. "Only the shadow of a shadow, twenty years removed . . . if it exists at all."

"*If?*" Varys asked softly, wringing powdered hands together. "My lord, you wrong me. Would I bring lies to king and council?"

Ned looked at the eunuch coldly. "You would bring us the whisperings of a traitor half a world away, my lord. Perhaps Mormont is wrong. Perhaps he is lying."

"Ser Jorah would not dare deceive me," Varys said with a sly smile. "Rely on it, my lord. The princess is with child."

"So you say. If you are wrong, we need not fear. If the girl miscarries, we need not fear. If she births a daughter in place of a son, we need not fear. If the babe dies in infancy, we need not fear."

"But if it *is* a boy?" Robert insisted. "If he lives?"

"The narrow sea would still lie between us. I shall fear the Dothraki the day they teach their horses to run on water."

The king took a swallow of wine and glowered at Ned across the council table. "So you would counsel me to do nothing until the dragonspawn has landed his army on my shores, is that it?"

"This 'dragonspawn' is in his mother's belly," Ned said. "Even Aegon did no conquering until after he was weaned."

"*Gods!* You are stubborn as an aurochs, Stark." The king looked around the council table. "Have the rest of you mislaid your tongues? Will no one talk sense to this frozen-faced fool?"

Varys gave the king an unctuous smile and laid a soft hand on Ned's sleeve. "I understand your qualms, Lord Eddard, truly I do. It gave me no joy to bring this grievous news to council. It is a terrible thing we contemplate, a *vile* thing. Yet we who presume to rule must do vile things for the good of the realm, howevermuch it pains us."

Lord Renly shrugged. "The matter seems simple enough to me. We ought to have had Viserys and his sister killed years ago, but His Grace my brother made the mistake of listening to Jon Arryn."

"Mercy is never a mistake, Lord Renly," Ned replied. "On the Trident, Ser Barristan here cut down a dozen good men, Robert's friends and mine. When they brought him to us, grievously wounded and near death, Roose Bolton urged us to cut his throat, but your brother said, 'I will not kill a man for loyalty, nor for fighting well,' and sent his own maester to tend Ser Barristan's wounds." He gave the king a long cool look. "Would that man were here today."

Robert had shame enough to blush. "It was not the same," he complained. "Ser Barristan was a knight of the Kingsguard."

"Whereas Daenerys is a fourteen-year-old girl." Ned knew he was pushing this well past the point of wisdom, yet he could not keep silent. "Robert, I ask you, what did we rise against Aerys Targaryen for, if not to put an end to the murder of children?"

"To put an end to *Targaryens*!" the king growled.

"Your Grace, I never knew you to fear Rhaegar." Ned fought to keep the scorn out of his voice, and failed. "Have the years so unmanned you that you tremble at the shadow of an unborn child?"

Robert purpled. "No more, Ned," he warned, pointing. "Not another word. Have you forgotten who is king here?"

"No, Your Grace," Ned replied. "Have you?"

"Enough!" the king bellowed. "I am sick of talk. I'll be done with this, or be damned. What say you all?"

"She must be killed," Lord Renly declared.

"We have no choice," murmured Varys. "Sadly, sadly . . ."

Ser Barristan Selmy raised his pale blue eyes from the table and said, "Your Grace, there is honor in facing an enemy on the battlefield, but none in killing him in his mother's womb. Forgive me, but I must stand with Lord Eddard."

Grand Maester Pycelle cleared his throat, a process that seemed to take some minutes. "My order serves the realm, not the ruler. Once I counseled King Aerys as loyally as I counsel King Robert now, so I bear this girl child of his no ill will. Yet I ask you this—should war come again, how many soldiers will die? How many towns will burn? How many children will be ripped from their mothers to perish on the end of a spear?" He stroked his luxuriant white beard, infinitely sad, infinitely weary. "Is it not wiser, even *kinder*, that Daenerys Targaryen should die now so that tens of thousands might live?"

"Kinder," Varys said. "Oh, well and truly spoken, Grand Maester. It is so true. Should the gods in their caprice grant Daenerys Targaryen a son, the realm must bleed."

Littlefinger was the last. As Ned looked to him, Lord Petyr stifled a yawn. "When you find yourself in bed with an ugly woman, the best thing to do is close your eyes and get on with it," he declared. "Waiting won't make the maid any prettier. Kiss her and be done with it."

"Kiss her?" Ser Barristan repeated, aghast.

"A steel kiss," said Littlefinger.

Robert turned to face his Hand. "Well, there it is, Ned. You and Selmy stand alone on this matter. The only question that remains is, who can we find to kill her?"

"Mormont craves a royal pardon," Lord Renly reminded them.

"Desperately," Varys said, "yet he craves life even more. By now, the princess nears Vaes Dothrak, where it is death to draw a blade. If I told you what the Dothraki would do to the poor man who used one on a *khaleesi*, none of you would sleep tonight." He stroked a powdered cheek. "Now, poison . . . the tears of Lys, let us say. Khal Drogo need never know it was not a natural death."

Grand Maester Pycelle's sleepy eyes flicked open. He squinted suspiciously at the eunuch.

"Poison is a coward's weapon," the king complained.

Ned had heard enough. "You send hired knives to kill a fourteen-year-old girl and still quibble about honor?" He pushed back his chair and stood. "Do it yourself, Robert. The man who passes the sentence should swing the sword. Look her in the eyes before you kill her. See her tears, hear her last words. You owe her that much at least."

"Gods," the king swore, the word exploding out of him as if he could barely contain his fury. "You mean it, damn you." He reached for the flagon of wine at his elbow, found it empty, and flung it away to shatter against the wall. "I am out of wine and out of patience. Enough of this. Just have it done."

"I will not be part of murder, Robert. Do as you will, but do not ask me to fix my seal to it."

For a moment Robert did not seem to understand what Ned was saying. Defiance was not a dish he tasted often. Slowly his face changed as comprehension came. His eyes narrowed and a flush crept up his neck past the velvet collar. He pointed an angry finger at Ned. "You are the King's Hand, Lord Stark. You will do as I command you, or I'll find me a Hand who will."

"I wish him every success." Ned unfastened the heavy clasp that clutched at the folds of his cloak, the ornate silver hand that was his badge of office. He laid it on the table in front of the king, saddened by the memory of the man who had pinned it on him, the friend he had loved. "I thought you a better man than this, Robert. I thought we had made a nobler king."

Robert's face was purple. "*Out*," he croaked, choking on his rage. "Out, damn you, I'm done with you. What are you waiting for? Go, run back to Winterfell. And make certain I never look on your face again, or I swear, I'll have your head on a spike!"

Ned bowed, and turned on his heel without another word. He could feel Robert's eyes on his back. As he strode from the council chambers, the discussion resumed with scarcely a pause. "On Braavos there is a society called the Faceless Men," Grand Maester Pycelle offered.

"Do you have any idea how *costly* they are?" Littlefinger complained. "You could hire an army of common sellswords for half the price, and that's for a merchant. I don't dare think what they might ask for a princess."

The closing of the door behind him silenced the voices. Ser Boros Blount was stationed outside the chamber, wearing the long white cloak and armor of the Kingsguard. He gave Ned a quick, curious glance from the corner of his eye, but asked no questions.

The day felt heavy and oppressive as he crossed the bailey back to the Tower of the Hand. He could feel the threat of rain in the air. Ned would have welcomed it. It might have made him feel a trifle less unclean. When he reached his solar, he summoned Vayon Poole. The steward came at once. "You sent for me, my lord Hand?"

"Hand no longer," Ned told him. "The king and I have quarreled. We shall be returning to Winterfell."

"I shall begin making arrangements at once, my lord. We will need a fortnight to ready everything for the journey."

"We may not have a fortnight. We may not have a day. The king mentioned something about seeing my head on a spike." Ned frowned. He did not truly believe the king would harm him, not Robert. He was angry now, but once Ned was safely out of sight, his rage would cool as it always did.

Always? Suddenly, uncomfortably, he found himself recalling Rhaegar Targaryen. *Fifteen years dead, yet Robert hates him as much as ever.* It was a disturbing notion . . . and there was the other matter, the business with Catelyn and the dwarf that Yoren had warned him of last night. That would come to light soon, as sure as sunrise, and with the king in such a black fury . . . Robert might not care a fig for Tyrion Lannister, but it would touch on his pride, and there was no telling what the queen might do.

"It might be safest if I went on ahead," he told Poole. "I will take my daughters and a few guardsmen. The rest of you can follow when you are ready. Inform Jory, but tell no one else, and do nothing until the girls and I have gone. The castle is full of eyes and ears, and I would rather my plans were not known."

"As you command, my lord."

When he had gone, Eddard Stark went to the window and sat brooding. Robert had left him no choice that he could see. He ought to thank him. It would be good to return to Winterfell. He ought never have left. His sons were waiting there. Perhaps he and Catelyn would make a new son together when he returned, they were not so old yet. And of late he had often found himself dreaming of snow, of the deep quiet of the wolfswood at night.

And yet, the thought of leaving angered him as well. So much was still undone. Robert and his council of cravens and flatterers would beggar the realm if left unchecked . . . or, worse, sell it to the Lannisters in payment of their loans. And the truth of Jon Arryn's death still eluded him. Oh, he had found a few pieces, enough to convince him that Jon had indeed been murdered, but that was no more than the spoor of an animal on the forest floor. He had not sighted the beast itself yet, though he sensed it was there, lurking, hidden, treacherous.

It struck him suddenly that he might return to Winterfell by sea. Ned was no sailor, and ordinarily would have preferred the kingsroad, but if he took ship he could stop at Dragonstone and speak with Stannis Baratheon.

Pycelle had sent a raven off across the water, with a polite letter from Ned requesting Lord Stannis to return to his seat on the small council. As yet, there had been no reply, but the silence only deepened his suspicions. Lord Stannis shared the secret Jon Arryn had died for, he was certain of it. The truth he sought might very well be waiting for him on the ancient island fortress of House Targaryen.

And when you have it, what then? Some secrets are safer kept hidden. Some secrets are too dangerous to share, even with those you love and trust. Ned slid the dagger that Catelyn had brought him out of the sheath on his belt. The Imp's knife. Why would the dwarf want Bran dead? To silence him, surely. Another secret, or only a different strand of the same web?

Could *Robert* be part of it? He would not have thought so, but once he would not have thought Robert could command the murder of women and children either. Catelyn had tried to warn him. *You knew the man,* she had said. *The king is a stranger to you.* The sooner he was quit of King's Landing, the better. If there was a ship sailing north on the morrow, it would be well to be on it.

He summoned Vayon Poole again and sent him to the docks to make inquiries, quietly but quickly. "Find me a fast ship with a skilled captain," he told the steward. "I care nothing for the size of its cabins or the quality of its appointments, so long as it is swift and safe. I wish to leave at once."

Poole had no sooner taken his leave than Tomard announced a visitor. "Lord Baelish to see you, m'lord."

Ned was half-tempted to turn him away, but thought better of it. He was not free yet; until he was, he must play their games. "Show him in, Tom."

Lord Petyr sauntered into the solar as if nothing had gone amiss that morning. He wore a slashed velvet doublet in cream-and-silver, a grey silk cloak trimmed with black fox, and his customary mocking smile.

Ned greeted him coldly. "Might I ask the reason for this visit, Lord Baelish?"

"I won't detain you long, I'm on my way to dine with Lady Tanda. Lamprey pie and roast suckling pig. She has some thought to wed me to her younger daughter, so her table is always astonishing. If truth be told, I'd sooner marry the pig, but don't tell her. I do love lamprey pie."

"Don't let me keep you from your eels, my lord," Ned said with icy disdain. "At the moment, I cannot think of anyone whose company I desire less than yours."

"Oh, I'm certain if you put your mind to it, you could come up with a few names. Varys, say. Cersei. Or Robert. His Grace is most wroth with you. He went on about you at some length after you took your leave of us this morning. The words *insolence* and *ingratitude* came into it frequently, I seem to recall."

Ned did not honor that with a reply. Nor did he offer his guest a seat, but Littlefinger took one anyway. "After you stormed out, it was left to me to convince them not to hire the Faceless Men," he continued blithely. "Instead Varys will quietly let it be known that we'll make a lord of whoever does in the Targaryen girl."

Ned was disgusted. "So now we grant titles to assassins."

Littlefinger shrugged. "Titles are cheap. The Faceless Men are expensive. If truth be told, I did the Targaryen girl more good than you with all your talk of honor. *Let* some sellsword drunk on visions of lordship try to kill her. Likely he'll make a botch of it, and afterward the Dothraki will be on their guard. If we'd sent a Faceless Man after her, she'd be as good as buried."

Ned frowned. "You sit in council and talk of ugly women and steel kisses, and now you expect me to believe that you tried to protect the girl? How big a fool do you take me for?"

"Well, quite an enormous one, actually," said Littlefinger, laughing.

"Do you always find murder so amusing, Lord Baelish?"

"It's not murder I find amusing, Lord Stark, it's you. You rule like a man dancing on rotten ice. I daresay you will make a noble splash. I believe I heard the first crack this morning."

"The first and last," said Ned. "I've had my fill."

"When do you mean to return to Winterfell, my lord?"

"As soon as I can. What concern is that of yours?"

"None . . . but if perchance you're still here come evenfall, I'd be pleased to take you to this brothel your man Jory has been searching for so ineffectually." Littlefinger smiled. "And I won't even tell the Lady Catelyn."

CATELYN

"**M**y lady, you should have sent word of your coming," Ser Donnel Waynwood told her as their horses climbed the pass. "We would have sent an escort. The high road is not as safe as it once was, for a party as small as yours."

"We learned that to our sorrow, Ser Donnel," Catelyn said. Sometimes she felt as though her heart had turned to stone; six brave men had died to bring her this far, and she could not even find it in her to weep for them. Even their names were fading. "The clansmen harried us day and night. We lost three men in the first attack, and two more in the second, and Lannister's serving man died of a fever when his wounds festered. When we heard your men approaching, I thought us doomed for certain." They had drawn up for a last desperate fight, blades in hand and backs to the rock. The dwarf had been whetting the edge of his axe and making some mordant jest when Bronn spotted the banner the riders carried before them, the moon-and-falcon of House Arryn, sky-blue and white. Catelyn had never seen a more welcome sight.

"The clans have grown bolder since Lord Jon died," Ser Donnel said. He was a stocky youth of twenty years, earnest and homely, with a wide nose and a shock of thick brown hair. "If it were up to me, I would take a hundred men into the mountains, root them out of their fast-nesses, and teach them some sharp lessons, but your sis-ter has forbidden it. She would not even permit her knights to fight in the Hand's tourney. She wants all our swords kept close to home, to defend the Vale . . . against what, no one is certain. Shadows, some say." He looked at her anxiously, as if he had suddenly remem-bered who she was. "I hope I have not spoken out of turn, my lady. I meant no offense."

"Frank talk does not offend me, Ser Donnel." Catelyn knew what her sister feared. *Not shadows, Lannisters,* she thought to herself, glancing back to where the dwarf rode beside Bronn. The two of them had grown thick as thieves since Chiggen had died. The little man was more cunning than she liked. When they had entered the mountains, he had been her captive, bound and helpless. What was he now? Her captive still, yet he rode along with a dirk through his belt and an axe strapped to his saddle, wearing the shadowskin cloak he'd won dicing with the singer and the chainmail hauberk he'd taken off Chiggen's corpse. Two score men flanked the dwarf and the rest of her ragged band, knights and men-at-arms in service to her sister Lysa and Jon Arryn's young son, and yet Tyrion betrayed no hint of fear. *Could I be wrong?* Catelyn wondered, not for the first time. Could he be in-nocent after all, of Bran and Jon Arryn and all the rest? And if he was, what did that make her? Six men had died to bring him here.

Resolute, she pushed her doubts away. "When we reach your keep, I would take it kindly if you could send for Maester Colemon at once. Ser Rodrik is feverish from his wounds." More than once she had feared the gallant old knight would not survive the journey. Toward the end he could scarcely sit his horse, and Bronn had urged her to leave him to his fate, but Catelyn would not hear of it. They had tied him in the saddle instead, and she had com-manded Marillion the singer to watch over him.

Ser Donnel hesitated before he answered. "The Lady Lysa has commanded the maester to remain at the Eyrie at all times, to care for Lord Robert," he said. "We have a septon at the gate who tends to our wounded. He can see to your man's hurts."

Catelyn had more faith in a maester's learning than a septon's prayers. She was about to say as much when she saw the battlements ahead, long parapets built into the very stone of the mountains on either side of them. Where the pass shrank to a narrow defile scarce wide enough for four men to ride abreast, twin watchtowers clung to the rocky slopes, joined by a covered bridge of weathered grey stone that arched above the road. Silent faces watched from arrow slits in tower, battlements, and bridge. When they had climbed almost to the top, a knight rode out to meet them. His horse and his armor were grey, but his cloak was the rippling blue-and-red of Riverrun, and a shiny black fish, wrought in gold and obsidian, pinned its folds against his shoulder. "Who would pass the Bloody Gate?" he called.

"Ser Donnel Waynwood, with the Lady Catelyn Stark and her companions," the young knight answered.

The Knight of the Gate lifted his visor. "I thought the lady looked familiar. You are far from home, little Cat."

"And you, Uncle," she said, smiling despite all she had been through. Hearing that hoarse, smoky voice again took her back twenty years, to the days of her childhood.

"My home is at my back," he said gruffly.

"Your home is in my heart," Catelyn told him. "Take off your helm. I would look on your face again."

"The years have not improved it, I fear," Brynden Tully said, but when he lifted off the helm, Catelyn saw that he lied. His features were lined and weathered, and time had stolen the auburn from his hair and left him only grey, but the smile was the same, and the bushy eyebrows fat as caterpillars, and the laughter in his deep blue eyes. "Did Lysa know you were coming?"

"There was no time to send word ahead," Catelyn told him. The others were coming up behind her. "I fear we ride before the storm, Uncle."

"May we enter the Vale?" Ser Donnel asked. The Waynwoods were ever ones for ceremony.

"In the name of Robert Arryn, Lord of the Eyrie, Defender of the Vale, True Warden of the East, I bid you enter freely, and charge you to keep his peace," Ser Brynden replied. "Come."

And so she rode behind him, beneath the shadow of the Bloody Gate where a dozen armies had dashed themselves to pieces in the Age of Heroes. On the far side of the stoneworks, the mountains opened up suddenly upon a vista of green fields, blue sky, and snowcapped mountains that took her breath away. The Vale of Arryn bathed in the morning light.

It stretched before them to the misty east, a tranquil land of rich black soil, wide slow-moving rivers, and hundreds of small lakes that shone like mirrors in the sun, protected on all sides by its sheltering peaks. Wheat and corn and barley grew high in its fields, and even in Highgarden the pumpkins were no larger nor the fruit any sweeter than here. They stood at the western end of the valley, where the high road crested the last pass and began its winding descent to the bottomlands two miles below. The Vale was narrow here, no more than a half day's ride across, and the northern mountains seemed so close that Catelyn could almost reach out and touch them. Looming over them all was the jagged peak called the Giant's Lance, a mountain that even mountains looked up to, its head lost in icy mists three and a half miles above the valley floor. Over its massive western shoulder flowed the ghost torrent of Alyssa's Tears. Even from this distance, Catelyn could make out the shining silver thread, bright against the dark stone.

When her uncle saw that she had stopped, he moved his horse closer and pointed. "It's there, beside Alyssa's Tears. All you can see from here is a flash of white every now and then, if you look hard and the sun hits the walls just right."

Seven towers, Ned had told her, *like white daggers thrust into the belly of the sky, so high you can stand on the parapets and look down on the clouds.* "How long a ride?" she asked.

"We can be at the mountain by evenfall," Uncle Brynden said, "but the climb will take another day."

Ser Rodrik Cassel spoke up from behind. "My lady," he said, "I fear I can go no farther today." His face sagged beneath his ragged, new-grown whiskers, and he looked so weary Catelyn feared he might fall off his horse.

"Nor should you," she said. "You have done all I could have asked of you, and a hundred times more. My uncle will see me the rest of the way to the Eyrie. Lannister must come with me, but there is no reason that you and the others should not rest here and recover your strength."

"We should be honored to have them to guest," Ser Donnel said with the grave courtesy of the young. Beside Ser Rodrik, only Bronn, Ser Willis Wode, and Marillion the singer remained of the party that had ridden with her from the inn by the crossroads.

"My lady," Marillion said, riding forward. "I beg you allow me to accompany you to the Eyrie, to see the end of the tale as I saw its beginnings." The boy sounded haggard, yet strangely determined; he had a fevered shine to his eyes.

Catelyn had never asked the singer to ride with them; that choice he had made himself, and how he had come to survive the journey when so many braver men lay dead and unburied behind them, she could never say. Yet here he was, with a scruff of beard that made him look almost a man. Perhaps she owed him something for having come this far. "Very well," she told him.

"I'll come as well," Bronn announced.

She liked that less well. Without Bronn she would never have reached the Vale, she knew; the sellsword was as fierce a fighter as she had ever seen, and his sword had helped cut them through to safety. Yet for all that, Catelyn misliked the man. Courage he had, and strength, but there was no kindness in him, and little loyalty. And she had seen him riding beside Lannister far too often, talking in low voices and laughing at some private joke. She would have preferred to separate him from the dwarf here and now, but having agreed that Marillion might continue to the Eyrie, she could see no gracious way to deny that same right to Bronn. "As you wish," she said, although she noted that he had not actually asked her permission.

Ser Willis Wode remained with Ser Rodrik, a soft-spoken septon fussing over their wounds. Their horses were left behind as well, poor ragged things. Ser Donnel promised to send birds ahead to the Eyrie and the Gates of the Moon with the word of their coming. Fresh mounts were brought forth from the stables, surefooted mountain stock with shaggy coats, and within the hour they set forth once again. Catelyn rode beside her uncle as they began the descent to the valley floor. Behind came Bronn, Tyrion Lannister, Marillion, and six of Brynden's men.

Not until they were a third of the way down the mountain path, well out of earshot of the others, did Brynden Tully turn to her and say, "So, child. Tell me about this storm of yours."

"I have not been a child in many years, Uncle," Catelyn said, but she told him nonetheless. It took longer than she would have believed to tell it all, Lysa's letter and Bran's fall, the assassin's dagger and Littlefinger and her chance meeting with Tyrion Lannister in the crossroads inn.

Her uncle listened silently, heavy brows shadowing his eyes as his frown grew deeper. Brynden Tully had always known how to listen . . . to anyone but her father. He was Lord Hoster's brother, younger by five years, but the two of them had been at war as far back as Catelyn could remember. During one of their louder quarrels, when Catelyn was eight, Lord Hoster had called Brynden "the black goat of the Tully flock." Laughing, Brynden had pointed out that the sigil of their house was a leaping trout, so he ought to be a black *fish* rather than a black goat, and from that day forward he had taken it as his personal emblem.

The war had not ended until the day she and Lysa had been wed. It was at their wedding feast that Brynden told his brother he was leaving Riverrun to serve Lysa and her new husband, the Lord of the Eyrie. Lord Hoster had not spoken his brother's name since, from what Edmure told her in his infrequent letters.

Nonetheless, during all those years of Catelyn's girlhood, it had been Brynden the Blackfish to whom Lord Hoster's children had run with their tears and their tales, when Father was too busy and Mother too ill. Catelyn, Lysa, Edmure . . . and yes, even Petyr Baelish, their father's ward . . . he had listened to them all patiently, as he listened now, laughing at their triumphs and sympathizing with their childish misfortunes.

When she was done, her uncle remained silent for a long time, as his horse negotiated the steep, rocky trail. "Your father must be told," he said at last. "If the Lannisters should march, Winterfell is remote and the Vale walled up behind its mountains, but Riverrun lies right in their path."

"I'd had the same fear," Catelyn admitted. "I shall ask Maester Colemon to send a bird when we reach the Eyrie." She had other messages to send as well; the commands that Ned had given her for his bannermen, to ready the defenses of the north. "What is the mood in the Vale?" she asked.

"Angry," Brynden Tully admitted. "Lord Jon was much loved, and the insult was keenly felt when the king named Jaime Lannister to an office the Arryns had held for near three hundred years. Lysa has commanded us to call her son the *True* Warden of the East, but no one is fooled. Nor is your sister alone in wondering at the manner of the Hand's death. None dare say Jon was murdered, not openly, but suspicion casts a long shadow." He gave Catelyn a look, his mouth tight. "And there is the boy."

"The boy? What of him?" She ducked her head as they passed under a low overhang of rock, and around a sharp turn.

Her uncle's voice was troubled. "Lord Robert," he sighed. "Six years old, sickly, and prone to weep if you take his dolls away. Jon Arryn's trueborn heir, by all the gods, yet there are some who say he is too weak to sit his father's seat. Nestor Royce has been high steward these past fourteen years, while Lord Jon served in King's Landing, and many whisper that he should rule until the boy comes of age. Others believe that Lysa must marry again, and soon. Already the suitors gather like crows on a battlefield. The Eyrie is full of them."

"I might have expected that," Catelyn said. Small wonder there; Lysa was still young, and the kingdom of Mountain and Vale made a handsome wedding gift. "Will Lysa take another husband?"

"She says yes, provided she finds a man who suits her," Brynden Tully said, "but she has already rejected Lord Nestor and a dozen other suitable men. She swears that this time *she* will choose her lord husband."

"You of all people can scarce fault her for that."

Ser Brynden snorted. "Nor do I, but . . . it seems to me Lysa is only playing at courtship. She enjoys the sport, but I believe your sister intends to rule herself until her boy is old enough to be Lord of the Eyrie in truth as well as name."

"A woman can rule as wisely as a man," Catelyn said.

"The *right* woman can," her uncle said with a sideways glance. "Make no mistake, Cat. Lysa is not you." He hesitated a moment. "If truth be told, I fear you may not find your sister as . . . helpful as you would like."

She was puzzled. "What do you mean?"

"The Lysa who came back from King's Landing is not the same girl who went south when her husband was named Hand. Those years were hard for her. You must know. Lord Arryn was a dutiful husband, but their marriage was made from politics, not passion."

"As was my own."

"They began the same, but your ending has been happier than your sister's. Two babes stillborn, twice as many miscarriages, Lord Arryn's death . . . Catelyn, the gods gave Lysa only the one child, and he is all your sister lives for now, poor boy. Small wonder she fled rather than see him handed over to the Lannisters. Your sister is *afraid*, child, and the Lannisters are what she fears most. She ran to the Vale, stealing away from the Red Keep like a thief in the night, and all to snatch her son out of the lion's mouth . . . and now you have brought the lion to her door."

"In chains," Catelyn said. A crevasse yawned on her right, falling away into darkness. She reined up her horse and picked her way along step by careful step.

"Oh?" Her uncle glanced back, to where Tyrion Lannister was making his slow descent behind them. "I see an axe on his saddle, a dirk at his belt, and a sellsword that trails after him like a hungry shadow. Where are the chains, sweet one?"

Catelyn shifted uneasily in her seat. "The dwarf is here, and not by choice. Chains or no, he is my prisoner. Lysa will want him to answer for his crimes no less than I. It was her own lord husband the Lannisters murdered, and her own letter that first warned us against them."

Brynden Blackfish gave her a weary smile. "I hope you are right, child," he sighed, in tones that said she was wrong.

The sun was well to the west by the time the slope began to flatten beneath the hooves of their horses. The road widened and grew straight, and for the first time Catelyn noticed wildflowers and grasses growing. Once they reached the valley floor, the going was faster and they made good time, cantering through verdant greenwoods and sleepy little hamlets, past orchards and golden wheat fields, splashing across a dozen sunlit streams. Her uncle sent a standard-bearer ahead of them, a double banner flying from his staff; the moon-and-falcon of House Arryn on high, and below it his own black fish. Farm wagons and merchants' carts and riders from lesser houses moved aside to let them pass.

Even so, it was full dark before they reached the stout castle that stood at the foot of the Giant's Lance. Torches flickered atop its ramparts, and the horned moon danced upon the dark waters of its moat. The drawbridge was up and the portcullis down, but Catelyn saw lights burning in the gatehouse and spilling from the windows of the square towers beyond.

"The Gates of the Moon," her uncle said as the party drew rein. His standard-bearer rode to the edge of the moat to hail the men in the gatehouse. "Lord Nestor's seat. He should be expecting us. Look up."

Catelyn raised her eyes, up and up and up. At first all she saw was stone and trees, the looming mass of the great mountain shrouded in night, as black as a starless sky. Then she noticed the glow of distant fires well above them; a tower keep, built upon the steep side of the mountain, its lights like orange eyes staring down from above. Above that was another, higher and more distant, and still higher a third, no more than a flickering spark in the sky. And finally, up where the falcons soared, a flash of white in the moonlight. Vertigo washed over her as she stared upward at the pale towers, so far above.

"The Eyrie," she heard Marillion murmur, awed.

The sharp voice of Tyrion Lannister broke in. "The Arryns must not be overfond of company. If you're planning to make us climb that mountain in the dark, I'd rather you kill me here."

"We'll spend the night here and make the ascent on the morrow," Brynden told him.

"I can scarcely wait," the dwarf replied. "How do we get up there? I've no experience at riding goats."

"Mules," Brynden said, smiling.

"There are steps carved into the mountain," Catelyn said. Ned had told her about them when he talked of his youth here with Robert Baratheon and Jon Arryn.

Her uncle nodded. "It is too dark to see them, but the steps are there. Too steep and narrow for horses, but mules can manage them most of the way. The path is guarded by three waycastles, Stone and Snow and Sky. The mules will take us as far up as Sky."

Tyrion Lannister glanced up doubtfully. "And beyond that?"

Brynden smiled. "Beyond that, the path is too steep even for mules. We ascend on foot the rest of the way. Or perchance you'd prefer to ride a basket. The Eyrie clings to the mountain directly above Sky, and in its cellars are six great winches with long iron chains to draw supplies up from below. If you prefer, my lord of Lannister, I can arrange for you to ride up with the bread and beer and apples."

The dwarf gave a bark of laughter. "Would that I were a pumpkin," he said. "Alas, my lord father would no doubt be most chagrined if his son of Lannister went to his fate like a load of turnips. If you ascend on foot, I fear I must do the same. We Lannisters do have a certain pride."

"Pride?" Catelyn snapped. His mocking tone and easy manner made her angry. "Arrogance, some might call it. Arrogance and avarice and lust for power."

"My brother is undoubtedly arrogant," Tyrion Lannister replied. "My father is the soul of avarice, and my sweet sister Cersei lusts for power with every waking breath. I, however, am innocent as a little lamb. Shall I bleat for you?" He grinned.

The drawbridge came creaking down before she could reply, and they heard the sound of oiled chains as the portcullis was drawn up. Men-at-arms carried burning brands out to light their way, and her uncle led them across the moat. Lord Nestor Royce, High Steward of the Vale and Keeper of the Gates of the Moon, was waiting in the yard to greet them, surrounded by his knights. "Lady Stark," he said, bowing. He was a massive, barrel-chested man, and his bow was clumsy.

Catelyn dismounted to stand before him. "Lord Nestor," she said. She knew the man only by reputation; Bronze Yohn's cousin, from a lesser branch of House

Royce, yet still a formidable lord in his own right. "We have had a long and tiring journey. I would beg the hospitality of your roof tonight, if I might."

"My roof is yours, my lady," Lord Nestor returned gruffly, "but your sister the Lady Lysa has sent down word from the Eyrie. She wishes to see you at once. The rest of your party will be housed here and sent up at first light."

Her uncle swung off his horse. "What madness is this?" he said bluntly. Brynden Tully had never been a man to blunt the edge of his words. "A night ascent, with the moon not even full? Even Lysa should know that's an invitation to a broken neck."

"The mules know the way, Ser Brynden." A wiry girl of seventeen or eighteen years stepped up beside Lord Nestor. Her dark hair was cropped short and straight around her head, and she wore riding leathers and a light shirt of silvered ringmail. She bowed to Catelyn, more gracefully than her lord. "I promise you, my lady, no harm will come to you. It would be my honor to take you up. I've made the dark climb a hundred times. Mychel says my father must have been a goat."

She sounded so cocky that Catelyn had to smile. "Do you have a name, child?"

"Mya Stone, if it please you, my lady," the girl said.

It did not please her; it was an effort for Catelyn to keep the smile on her face. *Stone* was a bastard's name in the Vale, as *Snow* was in the north, and *Flowers* in Highgarden; in each of the Seven Kingdoms, custom had fashioned a surname for children born with no names of their own. Catelyn had nothing against this girl, but suddenly she could not help but think of Ned's bastard on the Wall, and the thought made her angry and guilty, both at once. She struggled to find words for a reply.

Lord Nestor filled the silence. "Mya's a clever girl, and if she vows she will bring you safely to the Lady Lysa, I believe her. She has not failed me yet."

"Then I put myself in your hands, Mya Stone," Catelyn said. "Lord Nestor, I charge you to keep a close guard on my prisoner."

"And I charge you to bring the prisoner a cup of wine and a nicely crisped capon, before he dies of hunger," Lannister said. "A girl would be pleasant as well, but I suppose that's too much to ask of you." The sellsword Bronn laughed aloud.

Lord Nestor ignored the banter. "As you say, my lady, so it will be done." Only then did he look at the dwarf. "See our lord of Lannister to a tower cell, and bring him meat and mead."

Catelyn took her leave of her uncle and the others as Tyrion Lannister was led off, then followed the bastard girl through the castle. Two mules were waiting in the upper bailey, saddled and ready. Mya helped her mount one while a guardsman in a sky-blue cloak opened the narrow postern gate. Beyond was dense forest of pine and spruce, and the mountain like a black wall, but the steps were there, chiseled deep into the rock, ascending into the sky. "Some people find it easier if they close their eyes," Mya said as she led the mules through the gate into the dark wood. "When they get frightened or dizzy, sometimes they hold on to the mule too tight. They don't like that."

"I was born a Tully and wed to a Stark," Catelyn said. "I do not frighten easily. Do you plan to light a torch?" The steps were black as pitch.

The girl made a face. "Torches just blind you. On a clear night like this, the moon and the stars are enough. Mychel says I have the eyes of the owl." She mounted and urged her mule up the first step. Catelyn's animal followed of its own accord.

"You mentioned Mychel before," Catelyn said. The mules set the pace, slow but steady. She was perfectly content with that.

"Mychel's my love," Mya explained. "Mychel Redfort. He's squire to Ser Lyn Corbray. We're to wed as soon as he becomes a knight, next year or the year after."

She sounded so like Sansa, so happy and innocent with her dreams. Catelyn smiled, but the smile was tinged with sadness. The Redforts were an old name in the Vale, she knew, with the blood of the First Men in their veins. His love she might be, but no Redfort would ever wed a bastard. His family would arrange a more suitable match for him, to a Corbray or a Waynwood or a Royce, or perhaps a daughter of some greater house outside the Vale. If Mychel Redfort laid with this girl at all, it would be on the wrong side of the sheet.

The ascent was easier than Catelyn had dared hope. The trees pressed close, leaning over the path to make a rustling green roof that shut out even the moon, so it seemed as though they were moving up a long black tunnel. But the mules were surefooted and tireless, and Mya Stone did indeed seem blessed with night-eyes. They plodded upward, winding their way back and forth across the face of the mountain as the steps twisted and turned. A thick layer of fallen needles carpeted the path, so the shoes of their mules made only the softest sound on the rock. The quiet soothed her, and the gentle rocking motion set Catelyn to swaying in her saddle. Before long she was fighting sleep.

Perhaps she did doze for a moment, for suddenly a massive ironbound gate was looming before them. "Stone," Mya announced cheerily, dismounting. Iron spikes were set along the tops of formidable stone walls, and two fat round towers overtopped the keep. The gate swung open at Mya's shout. Inside, the portly knight who commanded the waycastle greeted Mya by name and offered them skewers of charred meat and onions still hot from the spit. Catelyn had not realized how hungry she was. She ate standing in the yard, as stablehands moved their saddles to fresh mules. The hot juices ran down her chin and dripped onto her cloak, but she was too famished to care.

Then it was up onto a new mule and out again into the starlight. The second part of the ascent seemed more treacherous to Catelyn. The trail was steeper, the steps more worn, and here and there littered with pebbles and broken stone. Mya had to dismount a half-dozen times to move fallen rocks from their path. "You don't want your mule to break a leg up here," she said. Catelyn was forced to agree. She could feel the altitude more now. The trees were sparser up here, and the wind blew more vigorously, sharp gusts that tugged at her clothing and pushed her hair into her eyes. From time to time the steps doubled back on themselves, and she could see Stone below them, and the Gates of the Moon farther down, its torches no brighter than candles.

Snow was smaller than Stone, a single fortified tower and a timber keep and stable hidden behind a low wall of unmortared rock. Yet it nestled against the Giant's Lance in such a way as to command the entire stone stair above the lower waycastle. An enemy intent on the Eyrie would have to fight his way from Stone step by step, while rocks and arrows rained down from Snow above. The commander, an anxious young knight with a pockmarked face, offered bread and cheese and the chance to warm themselves before his fire, but Mya declined. "We ought to keep going, my lady," she said. "If it please you." Catelyn nodded.

Again they were given fresh mules. Hers was white. Mya smiled when she saw him. "Whitey's a good one, my lady. Sure of foot, even on ice, but you need to be careful. He'll kick if he doesn't like you."

The white mule seemed to like Catelyn; there was no kicking, thank the gods. There was no ice either, and she was grateful for that as well. "My mother says that hundreds of years ago, this was where the snow began," Mya told her. "It was always white above here, and the ice never melted." She shrugged. "I can't remember ever seeing snow this far down the mountain, but maybe it was that way once, in the olden times."

So young, Catelyn thought, trying to remember if she had ever been like that. The girl had lived half her life in summer, and that was all she knew. *Winter is coming, child,* she wanted to tell her. The words were on her lips; she almost said them. Perhaps she was becoming a Stark at last.

Above Snow, the wind was a living thing, howling around them like a wolf in the waste, then falling off to nothing as if to lure them into complacency. The stars seemed brighter up here, so close that she could almost touch them, and the horned moon was huge in the clear black sky. As they climbed, Catelyn found it was better to look up than down. The steps were cracked and broken from centuries of freeze and thaw and the tread of countless mules, and even in the dark the heights put her heart in her throat. When they came to a high saddle between two spires of rock, Mya dismounted. "It's best to lead the mules over," she said. "The wind can be a little scary here, my lady."

Catelyn climbed stiffly from the shadows and looked at the path ahead; twenty feet long and close to three feet wide, but with a precipitous drop to either side. She could hear the wind shrieking. Mya stepped lightly out, her mule following as calmly as if they were crossing a bailey. It was her turn. Yet no sooner had she taken her first step than fear caught Catelyn in its jaws. She could *feel* the emptiness, the vast black gulfs of air that yawned around her. She stopped, trembling, afraid to move. The wind screamed at her and wrenched at her cloak, trying to pull her over the edge. Catelyn edged her foot backward, the most timid of steps, but the mule was behind her, and she could not retreat. *I am going to die here,* she thought. She could feel cold sweat trickling down her back.

"Lady Stark," Mya called across the gulf. The girl sounded a thousand leagues away. "Are you well?"

Catelyn Tully Stark swallowed what remained of her pride. "I . . . I cannot do this, child," she called out.

"Yes you can," the bastard girl said. "I know you can. Look how wide the path is."

"I don't want to look." The world seemed to be spinning around her, mountain and sky and mules, whirling like a child's top. Catelyn closed her eyes to steady her ragged breathing.

"I'll come back for you," Mya said. "Don't move, my lady."

Moving was about the last thing Catelyn was about to do. She listened to the skirling of the wind and the scuffling sound of leather on stone. Then Mya was there, taking her gently by the arm. "Keep your eyes closed if you like. Let go of the rope now, Whitey will take care of himself. Very good, my lady. I'll lead you over, it's easy, you'll see. Give me a step now. That's it, move your foot, just slide it forward. See. Now another. Easy. You could run across. Another one, go on. Yes." And so, foot by foot, step by step, the bastard girl led Catelyn across, blind and trembling, while the white mule followed placidly behind them.

The waycastle called Sky was no more than a high, crescent-shaped wall of unmortared stone raised against the side of the mountain, but even the topless towers of Valyria could not have looked more beautiful to Catelyn Stark. Here at last the snow crown began; Sky's weathered stones were rimed with frost, and long spears of ice hung from the slopes above.

Dawn was breaking in the east as Mya Stone *hallooed*

for the guards, and the gates opened before them. Inside the walls there was only a series of ramps and a great tumble of boulders and stones of all sizes. No doubt it would be the easiest thing in the world to begin an avalanche from here. A mouth yawned in the rock face in front of them. "The stables and barracks are in there," Mya said. "The last part is inside the mountain. It can be a little dark, but at least you're out of the wind. This is as far as the mules can go. Past here, well, it's a sort of chimney, more like a stone ladder than proper steps, but it's not too bad. Another hour and we'll be there."

Catelyn looked up. Directly overhead, pale in the dawn light, she could see the foundations of the Eyrie. It could not be more than six hundred feet above them. From below it looked like a small white honeycomb. She remembered what her uncle had said of baskets and winches. "The Lannisters may have their pride," she told Mya, "but the Tullys are born with better sense. I have ridden all day and the best part of a night. Tell them to lower a basket. I shall ride with the turnips."

The sun was well above the mountains by the time Catelyn Stark finally reached the Eyrie. A stocky, silver-haired man in a sky-blue cloak and hammered moon-and-falcon breastplate helped her from the basket; Ser Vardis Egen, captain of Jon Arryn's household guard. Beside him stood Maester Colemon, thin and nervous, with too little hair and too much neck. "Lady Stark," Ser Vardis said, "the pleasure is as great as it is unanticipated." Maester Colemon bobbed his head in agreement. "Indeed it is, my lady, indeed it is. I have sent word to your sister. She left orders to be awakened the instant you arrived."

"I hope she had a good night's rest," Catelyn said with a certain bite in her tone that seemed to go unnoticed.

The men escorted her from the winch room up a spiral stair. The Eyrie was a small castle by the standards of the great houses; seven slender white towers bunched as tightly as arrows in a quiver on a shoulder of the great mountain. It had no need of stables nor smithys nor kennels, but Ned said its granary was as large as Winterfell's, and its towers could house five hundred men. Yet it seemed strangely deserted to Catelyn as she passed through it, its pale stone halls echoing and empty.

Lysa was waiting alone in her solar, still clad in her bed

robes. Her long auburn hair tumbled unbound across bare white shoulders and down her back. A maid stood behind her, brushing out the night's tangles, but when Catelyn entered, her sister rose to her feet, smiling. "Cat," she said. "Oh, Cat, how good it is to see you. My sweet sister." She ran across the chamber and wrapped her sister in her arms. "How long it has been," Lysa murmured against her. "Oh, how very very long."

It had been five years, in truth; five cruel years, for Lysa. They had taken their toll. Her sister was two years the younger, yet she looked older now. Shorter than Catelyn, Lysa had grown thick of body, pale and puffy of face. She had the blue eyes of the Tullys, but hers were pale and watery, never still. Her small mouth had turned petulant. As Catelyn held her, she remembered the slender, high-breasted girl who'd waited beside her that day in the sept at Riverrun. How lovely and full of hope she had been. All that remained of her sister's beauty was the great fall of thick auburn hair that cascaded to her waist.

"You look well," Catelyn lied, "but . . . tired."

Her sister broke the embrace. "Tired. Yes. Oh, yes." She seemed to notice the others then; her maid, Maester Colemon, Ser Vardis. "Leave us," she told them. "I wish to speak to my sister alone." She held Catelyn's hand as they withdrew . . .

. . . and dropped it the instant the door closed. Catelyn saw her face change. It was as if the sun had gone behind a cloud. "Have you taken leave of your *senses*?" Lysa snapped at her. "To bring him *here*, without a word of permission, without so much as a warning, to drag us into your quarrels with the Lannisters . . ."

"*My* quarrels?" Catelyn could scarce believe what she was hearing. A great fire burned in the hearth, but there was no trace of warmth in Lysa's voice. "They were your quarrels first, sister. It was you who sent me that cursed letter, you who wrote that the Lannisters had murdered your husband."

"To warn you, so you could stay away from them! I never meant to *fight* them! Gods, Cat, do you know what you've *done*?"

"Mother?" a small voice said. Lysa whirled, her heavy robe swirling around her. Robert Arryn, Lord of the Eyrie, stood in the doorway, clutching a ragged cloth doll and looking at them with large eyes. He was a painfully thin child, small for his age and sickly all his days, and from time to time he trembled. The shaking sickness, the maesters called it. "I heard voices."

Small wonder, Catelyn thought; Lysa had almost been shouting. Still, her sister looked daggers at her. "This is your aunt Catelyn, baby. My sister, Lady Stark. Do you remember?"

The boy glanced at her blankly. "I think so," he said, blinking, though he had been less than a year old the last time Catelyn had seen him.

Lysa seated herself near the fire and said, "Come to Mother, my sweet one." She straightened his bedclothes and fussed with his fine brown hair. "Isn't he beautiful? And strong too, don't you believe the things you hear. Jon knew. *The seed is strong,* he told me. His last words. He kept saying Robert's name, and he grabbed my arm so hard he left marks. *Tell them, the seed is strong.* His seed. He wanted everyone to know what a good strong boy my baby was going to be."

"Lysa," Catelyn said, "if you're right about the Lannisters, all the more reason we must act quickly. We—"

"Not in front of the *baby*," Lysa said. "He has a delicate temper, don't you, sweet one?"

"The boy is Lord of the Eyrie and Defender of the Vale," Catelyn reminded her, "and these are not times for delicacy. Ned thinks it may come to war."

"*Quiet!*" Lysa snapped at her. "You're scaring the boy." Little Robert took a quick peek over his shoulder at Catelyn and began to tremble. His doll fell to the rushes, and he pressed himself against his mother. "Don't be afraid, my sweet baby," Lysa whispered. "Mother's here, nothing will hurt you." She opened her robe and drew out a pale, heavy breast, tipped with red. The boy grabbed for it eagerly, buried his face against her chest, and began to suck. Lysa stroked his hair.

Catelyn was at a loss for words. *Jon Arryn's son,* she thought incredulously. She remembered her own baby, three-year-old Rickon, half the age of this boy and five times as fierce. Small wonder the lords of the Vale were restive. For the first time she understood why the king had tried to take the child away from his mother to foster with the Lannisters . . .

"We're safe here," Lysa was saying. Whether to her or to the boy, Catelyn was not sure.

"Don't be a fool," Catelyn said, the anger rising in her. "No one is safe. If you think hiding here will make the Lannisters forget you, you are sadly mistaken."

Lysa covered her boy's ear with her hand. "Even if they could bring an army through the mountains and past the Bloody Gate, the Eyrie is impregnable. You saw for yourself. No enemy could ever reach us up here."

Catelyn wanted to slap her. Uncle Brynden had tried to warn her, she realized. "No castle is impregnable."

"This one is," Lysa insisted. "Everyone says so. The only thing is, what am I to do with this Imp you have brought me?"

"Is he a bad man?" the Lord of the Eyrie asked, his mother's breast popping from his mouth, the nipple wet and red.

"A very bad man," Lysa told him as she covered herself, "but Mother won't let him harm my little baby."

"Make him fly," Robert said eagerly.

Lysa stroked her son's hair. "Perhaps we will," she murmured. "Perhaps that is just what we will do."

EDDARD

He found Littlefinger in the brothel's common room, chatting amiably with a tall, elegant woman who wore a feathered gown over skin as black as ink. By the hearth, Heward and a buxom wench were playing at forfeits. From the look of it, he'd lost his belt, his cloak, his mail shirt, and his right boot so far, while the girl had been forced to unbutton her shift to the waist. Jory Cassel stood beside a rain-streaked window with a wry smile on his face, watching Heward turn over tiles and enjoying the view.

Ned paused at the foot of the stair and pulled on his gloves. "It's time we took our leave. My business here is done."

Heward lurched to his feet, hurriedly gathering up his things. "As you will, my lord," Jory said. "I'll help Wyl bring round the horses." He strode to the door.

Littlefinger took his time saying his farewells. He kissed the black woman's hand, whispered some joke that made her laugh aloud, and sauntered over to Ned. "Your business," he said lightly, "or Robert's? They say the Hand dreams the king's dreams, speaks with the king's voice, and rules with the king's sword. Does that also mean you fuck with the king's—"

"Lord Baelish," Ned interrupted, "you presume too much. I am not ungrateful for your help. It might have taken us years to find this brothel without you. That does not mean I intend to endure your mockery. And I am no longer the King's Hand."

"The direwolf must be a prickly beast," said Littlefinger with a sharp twist of his mouth.

A warm rain was pelting down from a starless black sky as they walked to the stables. Ned drew up the hood of his cloak. Jory brought out his horse. Young Wyl came right behind him, leading Littlefinger's mare with one hand while the other fumbled with his belt and the lacings of his trousers. A barefoot whore leaned out of the stable door, giggling at him.

"Will we be going back to the castle now, my lord?" Jory asked. Ned nodded and swung into the saddle. Littlefinger mounted up beside him. Jory and the others followed.

"Chataya runs a choice establishment," Littlefinger said as they rode. "I've half a mind to buy it. Brothels are a much sounder investment than ships, I've found. Whores seldom sink, and when they are boarded by pirates, why, the pirates pay good coin like everyone else." Lord Petyr chuckled at his own wit.

Ned let him prattle on. After a time, he quieted and they rode in silence. The streets of King's Landing were dark and deserted. The rain had driven everyone under their roofs. It beat down on Ned's head, warm as blood and relentless as old guilts. Fat drops of water ran down his face.

"Robert will never keep to one bed," Lyanna had told him at Winterfell, on the night long ago when their father had promised her hand to the young Lord of Storm's End. "I hear he has gotten a child on some girl in the Vale." Ned had held the babe in his arms; he could scarcely deny her, nor would he lie to his sister, but he had assured her that what Robert did before their betrothal was of no matter, that he was a good man and true who would love her with all his heart. Lyanna had only smiled. "Love is sweet, dearest Ned, but it cannot change a man's nature."

The girl had been so young Ned had not dared to ask

her age. No doubt she'd been a virgin; the better brothels could always find a virgin, if the purse was fat enough. She had light red hair and a powdering of freckles across the bridge of her nose, and when she slipped free a breast to give her nipple to the babe, he saw that her bosom was freckled as well. "I named her Barra," she said as the child nursed. "She looks so like him, does she not, milord? She has his nose, and his hair . . ."

"She does." Eddard Stark had touched the baby's fine, dark hair. It flowed through his fingers like black silk. Robert's firstborn had had the same fine hair, he seemed to recall.

"Tell him that when you see him, milord, as it . . . as it please you. Tell him how beautiful she is."

"I will," Ned had promised her. That was his curse. Robert would swear undying love and forget them before evenfall, but Ned Stark kept his vows. He thought of the promises he'd made Lyanna as she lay dying, and the price he'd paid to keep them.

"And tell him I've not been with no one else. I swear it, milord, by the old gods and new. Chataya said I could have half a year, for the baby, and for hoping he'd come back. So you'll tell him I'm waiting, won't you? I don't want no jewels or nothing, just him. He was always good to me, truly."

Good to you, Ned thought hollowly. "I will tell him, child, and I promise you, Barra shall not go wanting."

She had smiled then, a smile so tremulous and sweet that it cut the heart out of him. Riding through the rainy night, Ned saw Jon Snow's face in front of him, so like a younger version of his own. If the gods frowned so on bastards, he thought dully, why did they fill men with such lusts? "Lord Baelish, what do you know of Robert's bastards?"

"Well, he has more than you, for a start."

"How many?"

Littlefinger shrugged. Rivulets of moisture twisted down the back of his cloak. "Does it matter? If you bed enough women, some will give you presents, and His Grace has never been shy on that count. I know he's acknowledged that boy at Storm's End, the one he fathered the night Lord Stannis wed. He could hardly do otherwise. The mother was a Florent, niece to the Lady Selyse, one of her bedmaids. Renly says that Robert carried the girl upstairs during the feast, and broke in the wedding bed while Stannis and his bride were still dancing. Lord Stannis seemed to think that was a blot on the honor of his wife's House, so when the boy was born, he shipped him off to Renly." He gave Ned a sideways glance. "I've also heard whispers that Robert got a pair of twins on a serving wench at Casterly Rock, three years ago when he went west for Lord Tywin's tourney. Cersei had the babes killed, and sold the mother to a passing slaver. Too much an affront to Lannister pride, that close to home."

Ned Stark grimaced. Ugly tales like that were told of every great lord in the realm. He could believe it of Cersei Lannister readily enough . . . but would the king stand by and let it happen? The Robert he had known would not have, but the Robert he had known had never been so practiced at shutting his eyes to things he did not wish to see. "Why would Jon Arryn take a sudden interest in the king's baseborn children?"

The short man gave a sodden shrug. "He was the King's Hand. Doubtless Robert asked him to see that they were provided for."

Ned was soaked through to the bone, and his soul had grown cold. "It had to be more than that, or why kill him?"

Littlefinger shook the rain from his hair and laughed. "Now I see. Lord Arryn learned that His Grace had filled the bellies of some whores and fishwives, and for that he had to be silenced. Small wonder. Allow a man like that to live, and next he's like to blurt out that the sun rises in the east."

There was no answer Ned Stark could give to that but a frown. For the first time in years, he found himself remembering Rhaegar Targaryen. He wondered if Rhaegar had frequented brothels; somehow he thought not.

The rain was falling harder now, stinging the eyes and drumming against the ground. Rivers of black water were running down the hill when Jory called out, *"My lord,"* his voice hoarse with alarm. And in an instant, the street was full of soldiers.

Ned glimpsed ringmail over leather, gauntlets and greaves, steel helms with golden lions on the crests. Their cloaks clung to their backs, sodden with rain. He had no time to count, but there were ten at least, a line of them, on foot, blocking the street, with longswords and iron-tipped spears. *"Behind!"* he heard Wyl cry, and when he turned his horse, there were more in back of them, cutting off their retreat. Jory's sword came singing from its scabbard. "Make way or die!"

"The wolves are howling," their leader said. Ned could see rain running down his face. "Such a small pack, though."

Littlefinger walked his horse forward, step by careful step. "What is the meaning of this? This is the Hand of the King."

"He *was* the Hand of the King." The mud muffled the hooves of the blood bay stallion. The line parted before him. On a golden breastplate, the lion of Lannister roared its defiance. "Now, if truth be told, I'm not sure what he is."

"Lannister, this is madness," Littlefinger said. "Let us pass. We are expected back at the castle. What do you think you're doing?"

"He knows what he's doing," Ned said calmly.

Jaime Lannister smiled. "Quite true. I'm looking for my brother. You remember my brother, don't you, Lord Stark? He was with us at Winterfell. Fair-haired, mismatched eyes, sharp of tongue. A short man."

"I remember him well," Ned replied.

"It would seem he has met some trouble on the road. My lord father is quite vexed. You would not perchance have any notion of who might have wished my brother ill, would you?"

"Your brother has been taken at my command, to answer for his crimes," Ned Stark said.

Littlefinger groaned in dismay. "My lords—"

Ser Jaime ripped his longsword from its sheath and urged his stallion forward. "Show me your steel, Lord Eddard. I'll butcher you like Aerys if I must, but I'd sooner you died with a blade in your hand." He gave Littlefinger a cool, contemptuous glance. "Lord Baelish, I'd leave here in some haste if I did not care to get bloodstains on my costly clothing."

Littlefinger did not need to be urged. "I will bring the City Watch," he promised Ned. The Lannister line parted to let him through, and closed behind him. Littlefinger put his heels to his mare and vanished around a corner.

Ned's men had drawn their swords, but they were three against twenty. Eyes watched from nearby windows and doors, but no one was about to intervene. His party was mounted, the Lannisters on foot save for Jaime himself. A charge might win them free, but it seemed to Eddard Stark that they had a surer, safer tactic. "Kill me," he warned the Kingslayer, "and Catelyn will most certainly slay Tyrion."

Jaime Lannister poked at Ned's chest with the gilded sword that had sipped the blood of the last of the Dragonkings. "Would she? The noble Catelyn Tully of Riverrun murder a hostage? I think . . . not." He sighed. "But I am not willing to chance my brother's life on a woman's honor." Jaime slid the golden sword into its sheath. "So I suppose I'll let you run back to Robert to tell him how I frightened you. I wonder if he'll care." Jaime pushed his wet hair back with his fingers and wheeled his horse around. When he was beyond the line of swordsmen, he glanced back at his captain. "Tregar, see that no harm comes to Lord Stark."

"As you say, m'lord."

"Still . . . we wouldn't want him to leave here *entirely* unchastened, so"—through the night and the rain, he glimpsed the white of Jaime's smile—"kill his men."

"No!" Ned Stark screamed, clawing for his sword. Jaime was already cantering off down the street as he heard Wyl shout. Men closed from both sides. Ned rode one down, cutting at phantoms in red cloaks who gave way before him. Jory Cassel put his heels into his mount and charged. A steel-shod hoof caught a Lannister guardsman in the face with a sickening *crunch*. A second man reeled away and for an instant Jory was free. Wyl cursed as they pulled him off his dying horse, swords slashing in the rain. Ned galloped to him, bringing his longsword down on Tregar's helm. The jolt of impact made him grit his teeth. Tregar stumbled to his knees, his lion crest sheared in half, blood running down his face. Heward was hacking at the hands that had seized his bridle when a spear caught him in the belly. Suddenly Jory was back among them, a red rain flying from his sword. *"No!"* Ned shouted. "Jory, *away!"* Ned's horse slipped under him

and came crashing down in the mud. There was a moment of blinding pain and the taste of blood in his mouth.

He saw them cut the legs from Jory's mount and drag him to the earth, swords rising and falling as they closed in around him. When Ned's horse lurched back to its feet, he tried to rise, only to fall again, choking on his scream. He could see the splintered bone poking through his calf. It was the last thing he saw for a time. The rain came down and down and down.

When he opened his eyes again, Lord Eddard Stark was alone with his dead. His horse moved closer, caught the rank scent of blood, and galloped away. Ned began to drag himself through the mud, gritting his teeth at the agony in his leg. It seemed to take years. Faces watched from candlelit windows, and people began to emerge from alleys and doors, but no one moved to help.

Littlefinger and the City Watch found him there in the street, cradling Jory Cassel's body in his arms.

Somewhere the gold cloaks found a litter, but the trip back to the castle was a blur of agony, and Ned lost consciousness more than once. He remembered seeing the Red Keep looming ahead of him in the first grey light of dawn. The rain had darkened the pale pink stone of the massive walls to the color of blood.

Then Grand Maester Pycelle was looming over him, holding a cup, whispering, "Drink, my lord. Here. The milk of the poppy, for your pain." He remembered swallowing, and Pycelle was telling someone to heat the wine to boiling and fetch him clean silk, and that was the last he knew.

DAENERYS

The Horse Gate of Vaes Dothrak was made of two gigantic bronze stallions, rearing, their hooves meeting a hundred feet above the roadway to form a pointed arch.

Dany could not have said why the city needed a gate when it had no walls . . . and no *buildings* that she could see. Yet there it stood, immense and beautiful, the great horses framing the distant purple mountain beyond. The bronze stallions threw long shadows across the waving grasses as Khal Drogo led the *khalasar* under their hooves and down the godsway, his bloodriders beside him.

Dany followed on her silver, escorted by Ser Jorah Mormont and her brother Viserys, mounted once more. After the day in the grass when she had left him to walk back to the *khalasar*, the Dothraki had laughingly called him *Khal Rhae Mhar*, the Sorefoot King. Khal Drogo had offered him a place in a cart the next day, and Viserys had accepted. In his stubborn ignorance, he had not even known he was being mocked; the carts were for eunuchs, cripples, women giving birth, the very young and the very old. That won him yet another name: *Khal Rhaggat*, the

Cart King. Her brother had thought it was the *khal*'s way of apologizing for the wrong Dany had done him. She had begged Ser Jorah not to tell him the truth, lest he be shamed. The knight had replied that the king could well do with a bit of shame . . . yet he had done as she bid. It had taken much pleading, and all the pillow tricks Doreah had taught her, before Dany had been able to make Drogo relent and allow Viserys to rejoin them at the head of the column.

"Where is the *city*?" she asked as they passed beneath the bronze arch. There were no buildings to be seen, no people, only the grass and the road, lined with ancient monuments from all the lands the Dothraki had sacked over the centuries.

"Ahead," Ser Jorah answered. "Under the mountain."

Beyond the horse gate, plundered gods and stolen heroes loomed to either side of them. The forgotten deities of dead cities brandished their broken thunderbolts at the sky as Dany rode her silver past their feet. Stone kings looked down on her from their thrones, their faces chipped and stained, even their names lost in the mists of time. Lithe young maidens danced on marble plinths, draped only in flowers, or poured air from shattered jars. Monsters stood in the grass beside the road; black iron dragons with jewels for eyes, roaring griffins, manticores with their barbed tails poised to strike, and other beasts she could not name. Some of the statues were so lovely they took her breath away, others so misshapen and terrible that Dany could scarcely bear to look at them. Those, Ser Jorah said, had likely come from the Shadow Lands beyond Asshai.

"So many," she said as her silver stepped slowly onward, "and from so many lands."

Viserys was less impressed. "The trash of dead cities," he sneered. He was careful to speak in the Common Tongue, which few Dothraki could understand, yet even so Dany found herself glancing back at the men of her *khas*, to make certain he had not been overheard. He went on blithely. "All these savages know how to do is steal the things better men have built . . . and kill." He laughed. "They *do* know how to kill. Otherwise I'd have no use for them at all."

"They are my people now," Dany said. "You should not call them savages, brother."

"The dragon speaks as he likes," Viserys said . . . in the Common Tongue. He glanced over his shoulder at Aggo and Rakharo, riding behind them, and favored them with a mocking smile. "See, the savages lack the wit to understand the speech of civilized men." A moss-eaten stone monolith loomed over the road, fifty feet tall. Viserys gazed at it with boredom in his eyes. "How long must we linger amidst these ruins before Drogo gives me my army? I grow tired of waiting."

"The princess must be presented to the *dosh khaleen* . . ."

"The crones, yes," her brother interrupted, "and there's to be some mummer's show of a prophecy for the whelp in her belly, you told me. What is that to me? I'm tired of eating horsemeat and I'm sick of the stink of these savages." He sniffed at the wide, floppy sleeve of his tunic, where it was his custom to keep a sachet. It could not have helped much. The tunic was filthy. All the silk and heavy wools that Viserys had worn out of Pentos were stained by hard travel and rotted from sweat.

Ser Jorah Mormont said, "The Western Market will have food more to your taste, Your Grace. The traders from the Free Cities come there to sell their wares. The *khal* will honor his promise in his own time."

"He had better," Viserys said grimly. "I was promised a crown, and I mean to have it. The dragon is not mocked." Spying an obscene likeness of a woman with six breasts and a ferret's head, he rode off to inspect it more closely.

Dany was relieved, yet no less anxious. "I pray that my sun-and-stars will not keep him waiting too long," she told Ser Jorah when her brother was out of earshot.

The knight looked after Viserys doubtfully. "Your brother should have bided his time in Pentos. There is no place for him in a *khalasar*. Illyrio tried to warn him."

"He will go as soon as he has his ten thousand. My lord husband promised a golden crown."

Ser Jorah grunted. "Yes, *Khaleesi*, but . . . the Dothraki look on these things differently than we do in the west. I have told him as much, as Illyrio told him, but your brother does not listen. The horselords are no traders. Viserys thinks he sold you, and now he wants his price. Yet Khal Drogo would say he had you as a gift. He will give Viserys a gift in return, yes . . . in his own time. You do not *demand* a gift, not of a *khal*. You do not demand anything of a *khal*."

"It is not right to make him wait." Dany did not know why she was defending her brother, yet she was. "Viserys says he could sweep the Seven Kingdoms with ten thousand Dothraki screamers."

Ser Jorah snorted. "Viserys could not sweep a stable with ten thousand brooms."

Dany could not pretend to surprise at the disdain in his tone. "What . . . what if it were not Viserys?" she asked. "If it were someone else who led them? Someone stronger? Could the Dothraki truly conquer the Seven Kingdoms?"

Ser Jorah's face grew thoughtful as their horses trod together down the godsway. "When I first went into exile, I looked at the Dothraki and saw half-naked barbarians, as wild as their horses. If you had asked me then, Princess, I should have told you that a thousand good knights would have no trouble putting to flight a hundred times as many Dothraki."

"But if I asked you now?"

"Now," the knight said, "I am less certain. They are better riders than any knight, utterly fearless, and their bows outrange ours. In the Seven Kingdoms, most archers fight on foot, from behind a shieldwall or a barricade of sharpened stakes. The Dothraki fire from horseback, charging or retreating, it makes no matter, they are full as deadly . . . and there are so *many* of them, my lady. Your lord husband alone counts forty thousand mounted warriors in his *khalasar*."

"Is that truly so many?"

"Your brother Rhaegar brought as many men to the Trident," Ser Jorah admitted, "but of that number, no more than a tenth were knights. The rest were archers, freeriders, and foot soldiers armed with spears and pikes. When Rhaegar fell, many threw down their weapons and fled the field. How long do you imagine such a rabble would stand against the charge of forty thousand screamers howling for blood? How well would boiled leather jerkins and mailed shirts protect them when the arrows fall like rain?"

"Not long," she said, "not well."

He nodded. "Mind you, Princess, if the lords of the Seven Kingdoms have the wit the gods gave a goose, it will never come to that. The riders have no taste for siegecraft. I doubt they could take even the weakest castle in the Seven Kingdoms, but if Robert Baratheon were fool enough to give them battle . . ."

"Is he?" Dany asked. "A fool, I mean?"

Ser Jorah considered that for a moment. "Robert should have been born Dothraki," he said at last. "Your *khal* would tell you that only a coward hides behind stone walls instead of facing his enemy with a blade in hand. The Usurper would agree. He is a strong man, brave . . . and rash enough to meet a Dothraki horde in the open field. But the men around him, well, their pipers play a different tune. His brother Stannis, Lord Tywin Lannister, Eddard Stark . . ." He spat.

"You hate this Lord Stark," Dany said.

"He took from me all I loved, for the sake of a few lice-ridden poachers and his precious honor," Ser Jorah said bitterly. From his tone, she could tell the loss still pained him. He changed the subject quickly. "There," he announced, pointing. "Vaes Dothrak. The city of the horselords."

Khal Drogo and his bloodriders led them through the great bazaar of the Western Market, down the broad ways beyond. Dany followed close on her silver, staring at the strangeness about her. Vaes Dothrak was at once the largest city and the smallest that she had ever known. She thought it must be ten times as large as Pentos, a vastness without walls or limits, its broad windswept streets paved in grass and mud and carpeted with wildflowers. In the Free Cities of the west, towers and manses and hovels and bridges and shops and halls all crowded in on one another, but Vaes Dothrak sprawled languorously, baking in the warm sun, ancient, arrogant, and empty.

Even the buildings were so queer to her eyes. She saw carved stone pavilions, manses of woven grass as large as castles, rickety wooden towers, stepped pyramids faced with marble, log halls open to the sky. In place of walls, some palaces were surrounded by thorny hedges. "None of them are alike," she said.

"Your brother had part of the truth," Ser Jorah admitted. "The Dothraki do not build. A thousand years ago, to make a house, they would dig a hole in the earth and cover it with a woven grass roof. The buildings you see were made by slaves brought here from lands they've plundered, and they built each after the fashion of their own peoples."

Most of the halls, even the largest, seemed deserted. "Where are the people who live here?" Dany asked. The bazaar had been full of running children and men shouting, but elsewhere she had seen only a few eunuchs going about their business.

"Only the crones of the *dosh khaleen* dwell permanently in the sacred city, them and their slaves and servants," Ser Jorah replied, "yet Vaes Dothrak is large enough to house every man of every *khalasar*, should all the *khals* return to the Mother at once. The crones have prophesied that one day that will come to pass, and so Vaes Dothrak must be ready to embrace all its children."

Khal Drogo finally called a halt near the Eastern Market where the caravans from Yi Ti and Asshai and the Shadow Lands came to trade, with the Mother of Mountains looming overhead. Dany smiled as she recalled Magister Illyrio's slave girl and her talk of a palace with two hundred rooms and doors of solid silver. The "palace" was a cavernous wooden feasting hall, its rough-hewn timbered walls rising forty feet, its roof sewn silk, a vast billowing tent that could be raised to keep out the rare rains, or lowered to admit the endless sky. Around the hall were broad grassy horse yards fenced with high hedges, firepits, and hundreds of round earthen houses that bulged from the ground like miniature hills, covered with grass.

A small army of slaves had gone ahead to prepare for Khal Drogo's arrival. As each rider swung down from his saddle, he unbelted his *arakh* and handed it to a waiting slave, and any other weapons he carried as well. Even Khal Drogo himself was not exempt. Ser Jorah had explained that it was forbidden to carry a blade in Vaes Dothrak, or to shed a free man's blood. Even warring *khalasars* put aside their feuds and shared meat and mead together when they were in sight of the Mother of Mountains. In this place, the crones of the *dosh khaleen* had decreed, all Dothraki were one blood, one *khalasar*, one herd.

Cohollo came to Dany as Irri and Jhiqui were helping her down off her silver. He was the oldest of Drogo's three bloodriders, a squat bald man with a crooked nose and a mouth full of broken teeth, shattered by a mace twenty years before when he saved the young *khalakka* from sellswords who hoped to sell him to his father's enemies. His life had been bound to Drogo's the day her lord husband was born.

Every *khal* had his bloodriders. At first Dany had thought of them as a kind of Dothraki Kingsguard, sworn to protect their lord, but it went further than that. Jhiqui had taught her that a bloodrider was more than a guard; they were the *khal's* brothers, his shadows, his fiercest friends. "Blood of my blood," Drogo called them, and so it was; they shared a single life. The ancient traditions of the horselords demanded that when the *khal* died, his bloodriders died with him, to ride at his side in the night lands. If the *khal* died at the hands of some enemy, they lived only long enough to avenge him, and then followed him joyfully into the grave. In some *khalasars*, Jhiqui said, the bloodriders shared the *khal's* wine, his tent, and even his wives, though never his horses. A man's mount was his own.

Daenerys was glad that Khal Drogo did not hold to those ancient ways. She should not have liked being shared. And while old Cohollo treated her kindly enough, the others frightened her; Haggo, huge and silent, often glowered as if he had forgotten who she was, and Qotho had cruel eyes and quick hands that liked to hurt. He left bruises on Doreah's soft white skin whenever he touched her, and sometimes made Irri sob in the night. Even his horses seemed to fear him.

Yet they were bound to Drogo for life and death, so Daenerys had no choice but to accept them. And sometimes she found herself wishing her father had been protected by such men. In the songs, the white knights of the Kingsguard were ever noble, valiant, and true, and yet King Aerys had been murdered by one of them, the handsome boy they now called the Kingslayer, and a second, Ser Barristan the Bold, had gone over to the Usurper. She wondered if all men were as false in the Seven Kingdoms.

When her son sat the Iron Throne, she would see that he had bloodriders of his own to protect him against treachery in his Kingsguard.

"*Khaleesi,*" Cohollo said to her, in Dothraki. "Drogo, who is blood of my blood, commands me to tell you that he must ascend the Mother of Mountains this night, to sacrifice to the gods for his safe return."

Only men were allowed to set foot on the Mother, Dany knew. The *khal's* bloodriders would go with him, and return at dawn. "Tell my sun-and-stars that I dream of him, and wait anxious for his return," she replied, thankful. Dany tired more easily as the child grew within her; in truth, a night of rest would be most welcome. Her pregnancy only seemed to have inflamed Drogo's desire for her, and of late his embraces left her exhausted.

Doreah led her to the hollow hill that had been prepared for her and her *khal.* It was cool and dim within, like a tent made of earth. "Jhiqui, a bath, please," she commanded, to wash the dust of travel from her skin and soak her weary bones. It was pleasant to know that they would linger here for a while, that she would not need to climb back on her silver on the morrow.

The water was scalding hot, as she liked it. "I will give my brother his gifts tonight," she decided as Jhiqui was washing her hair. "He should look a king in the sacred city. Doreah, run and find him and invite him to sup with me." Viserys was nicer to the Lysene girl than to her Dothraki handmaids, perhaps because Magister Illyrio had let him bed her back in Pentos. "Irri, go to the bazaar and buy fruit and meat. Anything but horseflesh."

"Horse is best," Irri said. "Horse makes a man strong."

"Viserys hates horsemeat."

"As you say, *Khaleesi.*"

She brought back a haunch of goat and a basket of fruits and vegetables. Jhiqui roasted the meat with sweetgrass and firepods, basting it with honey as it cooked, and there were melons and pomegranates and plums and some queer eastern fruit Dany did not know. While her handmaids prepared the meal, Dany laid out the clothing she'd had made to her brother's measure: a tunic and leggings of crisp white linen, leather sandals that laced up to the knee, a bronze medallion belt, a leather vest painted with fire-breathing dragons. The Dothraki would respect him more if he looked less a beggar, she hoped, and perhaps he would forgive her for shaming him that day in the grass. He was still her king, after all, and her brother. They were both blood of the dragon.

She was arranging the last of his gifts—a sandsilk cloak, green as grass, with a pale grey border that would bring out the silver in his hair—when Viserys arrived, dragging Doreah by the arm. Her eye was red where he'd hit her. "How *dare* you send this whore to give me commands," he said. He shoved the handmaid roughly to the carpet.

The anger took Dany utterly by surprise. "I only wanted . . . Doreah, what did you say?"

"*Khaleesi*, pardons, forgive me. I went to him, as you bid, and told him you commanded him to join you for supper."

"No one commands the dragon," Viserys snarled. "*I am your king!* I should have sent you back her head!"

The Lysene girl quailed, but Dany calmed her with a touch. "Don't be afraid, he won't hurt you. Sweet brother, please, forgive her, the girl misspoke herself, I told her to *ask* you to sup with me, if it pleases Your Grace." She took him by the hand and drew him across the room. "Look. These are for you."

Viserys frowned suspiciously. "What is all this?"

"New raiment. I had it made for you." Dany smiled shyly.

He looked at her and sneered. "Dothraki rags. Do you presume to dress me now?"

"Please . . . you'll be cooler and more comfortable, and I thought . . . maybe if you dressed like them, the Dothraki . . ." Dany did not know how to say it without waking his dragon.

"Next you'll want to braid my hair."

"I'd never . . ." Why was he always so cruel? She had only wanted to help. "You have no right to a braid, you have won no victories yet."

It was the wrong thing to say. Fury shone from his lilac eyes, yet he dared not strike her, not with her handmaids watching and the warriors of her *khas* outside. Viserys picked up the cloak and sniffed at it. "This stinks of manure. Perhaps I shall use it as a horse blanket."

"I had Doreah sew it specially for you," she told him, wounded. "These are garments fit for a *khal.*"

"I am the Lord of the Seven Kingdoms, not some grass-stained savage with bells in his hair," Viserys spat back at her. He grabbed her arm. "You forget yourself, slut. Do you think that big belly will protect you if you wake the dragon?"

His fingers dug into her arm painfully and for an instant Dany felt like a child again, quailing in the face of his rage. She reached out with her other hand and grabbed the first thing she touched, the belt she'd hoped to give him, a heavy chain of ornate bronze medallions. She swung it with all her strength.

It caught him full in the face. Viserys let go of her. Blood ran down his cheek where the edge of one of the medallions had sliced it open. "You are the one who forgets himself," Dany said to him. "Didn't you learn *anything* that day in the grass? Leave me now, before I summon my *khas* to drag you out. And pray that Khal Drogo does not hear of this, or he will cut open your belly and feed you your own entrails."

Viserys scrambled back to his feet. "When I come into my kingdom, you will rue this day, slut." He walked off, holding his torn face, leaving her gifts behind him.

Drops of his blood had spattered the beautiful sandsilk cloak. Dany clutched the soft cloth to her cheek and sat cross-legged on her sleeping mats.

"Your supper is ready, *Khaleesi,*" Jhiqui announced.

"I'm not hungry," Dany said sadly. She was suddenly very tired. "Share the food among yourselves, and send some to Ser Jorah, if you would." After a moment she added, "Please, bring me one of the dragon's eggs."

Irri fetched the egg with the deep green shell, bronze flecks shining amid its scales as she turned it in her small hands. Dany curled up on her side, pulling the sandsilk cloak across her and cradling the egg in the hollow between her swollen belly and small, tender breasts. She liked to hold them. They were so beautiful, and sometimes just being close to them made her feel stronger, braver, as if somehow she were drawing strength from the stone dragons locked inside.

She was lying there, holding the egg, when she felt the

child move within her . . . as if he were reaching out, brother to brother, blood to blood. *"You* are the dragon," Dany whispered to him, "the *true* dragon. I know it. I know it." And she smiled, and went to sleep dreaming of home.

BRAN

A light snow was falling. Bran could feel the flakes on his face, melting as they touched his skin like the gentlest of rains. He sat straight atop his horse, watching as the iron portcullis was winched upward. Try as he might to keep calm, his heart was fluttering in his chest.

"Are you ready?" Robb asked.

Bran nodded, trying not to let his fear show. He had not been outside Winterfell since his fall, but he was determined to ride out as proud as any knight.

"Let's ride, then." Robb put his heels into his big grey-and-white gelding, and the horse walked under the portcullis.

"Go," Bran whispered to his own horse. He touched her neck lightly, and the small chestnut filly started forward. Bran had named her Dancer. She was two years old, and Joseth said she was smarter than any horse had a right to be. They had trained her special, to respond to rein and voice and touch. Up to now, Bran had only ridden her around the yard. At first Joseth or Hodor would lead her, while Bran sat strapped to her back in the oversize saddle the Imp had drawn up for him, but for the past fortnight he had been riding her on his own, trotting her round and round, and growing bolder with every circuit.

They passed beneath the gatehouse, over the drawbridge, through the outer walls. Summer and Grey Wind came loping beside them, sniffing at the wind. Close behind came Theon Greyjoy, with his longbow and a quiver of broadheads; he had a mind to take a deer, he had told them. He was followed by four guardsmen in mailed shirts and coifs, and Joseth, a stick-thin stableman whom Robb had named master of horse while Hullen was away. Maester Luwin brought up the rear, riding on a donkey. Bran would have liked it better if he and Robb had gone off alone, just the two of them, but Hal Mollen would not hear of it, and Maester Luwin backed him. If Bran fell off his horse or injured himself, the maester was determined to be with him.

Beyond the castle lay the market square, its wooden stalls deserted now. They rode down the muddy streets of the village, past rows of small neat houses of log and undressed stone. Less than one in five were occupied, thin tendrils of woodsmoke curling up from their chimneys. The rest would fill up one by one as it grew colder. When the snow fell and the ice winds howled down out of the north, Old Nan said, farmers left their frozen fields and distant holdfasts, loaded up their wagons, and then the winter town came alive. Bran had never seen it happen, but Maester Luwin said the day was looming closer. The end of the long summer was near at hand. *Winter is coming.*

A few villagers eyed the direwolves anxiously as the riders went past, and one man dropped the wood he was carrying as he shrank away in fear, but most of the townfolk had grown used to the sight. They bent the knee when they saw the boys, and Robb greeted each of them with a lordly nod.

With his legs unable to grip, the swaying motion of the horse made Bran feel unsteady at first, but the huge saddle with its thick horn and high back cradled him comfortingly, and the straps around his chest and thighs would not allow him to fall. After a time the rhythm began to feel almost natural. His anxiety faded, and a tremulous smile crept across his face.

Two serving wenches stood beneath the sign of the

Smoking Log, the local alehouse. When Theon Greyjoy called out to them, the younger girl turned red and covered her face. Theon spurred his mount to move up beside Robb. "Sweet Kyra," he said with a laugh. "She squirms like a weasel in bed, but say a word to her on the street, and she blushes pink as a maid. Did I ever tell you about the night that she and Bessa—"

"Not where my brother can hear, Theon," Robb warned him with a glance at Bran.

Bran looked away and pretended not to have heard, but he could feel Greyjoy's eyes on him. No doubt he was smiling. He smiled a lot, as if the world were a secret joke that only he was clever enough to understand. Robb seemed to admire Theon and enjoy his company, but Bran had never warmed to his father's ward.

Robb rode closer. "You are doing well, Bran."

"I want to go faster," Bran replied.

Robb smiled. "As you will." He sent his gelding into a trot. The wolves raced after him. Bran snapped the reins sharply, and Dancer picked up her pace. He heard a shout from Theon Greyjoy, and the hoofbeats of the other horses behind him.

Bran's cloak billowed out, rippling in the wind, and the snow seemed to rush at his face. Robb was well ahead, glancing back over his shoulder from time to time to make sure Bran and the others were following. He snapped the reins again. Smooth as silk, Dancer slid into a gallop. The distance closed. By the time he caught Robb on the edge of the wolfswood, two miles beyond the winter town, they had left the others well behind. "I can *ride!*" Bran shouted, grinning. It felt almost as good as flying.

"I'd race you, but I fear you'd win." Robb's tone was light and joking, yet Bran could tell that something was troubling his brother underneath the smile.

"I don't want to race." Bran looked around for the direwolves. Both had vanished into the wood. "Did you hear Summer howling last night?"

"Grey Wind was restless too," Robb said. His auburn hair had grown shaggy and unkempt, and a reddish stubble covered his jaw, making him look older than his fifteen years. "Sometimes I think they know things . . .

sense things . . ." Robb sighed. "I never know how much to tell you, Bran. I wish you were older."

"I'm eight now!" Bran said. "Eight isn't so much younger than fifteen, and I'm the heir to Winterfell, after you."

"So you are." Robb sounded sad, and even a little scared. "Bran, I need to tell you something. There was a bird last night. From King's Landing. Maester Luwin woke me."

Bran felt a sudden dread. *Dark wings, dark words,* Old Nan always said, and of late the messenger ravens had been proving the truth of the proverb. When Robb wrote to the Lord Commander of the Night's Watch, the bird that came back brought word that Uncle Benjen was still missing. Then a message had arrived from the Eyrie, from Mother, but that had not been good news either. She did not say when she meant to return, only that she had taken the Imp as prisoner. Bran had sort of liked the little man, yet the name *Lannister* sent cold fingers creeping up his spine. There was something about the Lannisters, something he ought to remember, but when he tried to think what, he felt dizzy and his stomach clenched hard as a stone. Robb spent most of that day locked behind closed doors with Maester Luwin, Theon Greyjoy, and Hallis Mollen. Afterward, riders were sent out on fast horses, carrying Robb's commands throughout the north. Bran heard talk of Moat Cailin, the ancient stronghold the First Men had built at the top of the Neck. No one ever told him what was happening, yet he knew it was not good.

And now another raven, another message. Bran clung to hope. "Was the bird from Mother? Is she coming home?"

"The message was from Alyn in King's Landing. Jory Cassel is dead. And Wyl and Heward as well. Murdered by the Kingslayer." Robb lifted his face to the snow, and the flakes melted on his cheeks. "May the gods give them rest."

Bran did not know what to say. He felt as if he'd been punched. Jory had been captain of the household guard at Winterfell since before Bran was born. "They killed Jory?" He remembered all the times Jory had chased him over the roofs. He could picture him striding across the yard in mail and plate, or sitting at his accustomed place on the bench in the Great Hall, joking as he ate. "Why would anyone kill Jory?"

Robb shook his head numbly, the pain plain in his eyes. "I don't know, and . . . Bran, that's not the worst of it. Father was caught beneath a falling horse in the fight. Alyn says his leg was shattered, and . . . Maester Pycelle has given him the milk of the poppy, but they aren't sure when . . . when he . . ." The sound of hoof-beats made him glance down the road, to where Theon and the others were coming up. "When he will wake," Robb finished. He laid his hand on the pommel of his sword then, and went on in the solemn voice of Robb the Lord. "Bran, I promise you, whatever might happen, I will not let this be forgotten."

Something in his tone made Bran even more fearful. "What will you do?" he asked as Theon Greyjoy reined in beside them.

"Theon thinks I should call the banners," Robb said.

"Blood for blood." For once Greyjoy did not smile. His lean, dark face had a hungry look to it, and black hair fell down across his eyes.

"Only the lord can call the banners," Bran said as the snow drifted down around them.

"If your father dies," Theon said, "Robb will be Lord of Winterfell."

"He *won't* die!" Bran screamed at him.

Robb took his hand. "He won't die, not Father," he said calmly. "Still . . . the honor of the north is in my hands now. When our lord father took his leave of us, he told me to be strong for you and for Rickon. I'm almost a man grown, Bran."

Bran shivered. "I wish Mother was back," he said miserably. He looked around for Maester Luwin; his donkey was visible in the far distance, trotting over a rise. "Does Maester Luwin say to call the banners too?"

"The maester is timid as an old woman," said Theon.

"Father always listened to his counsel," Bran reminded his brother. "Mother too."

"I listen to him," Robb insisted. "I listen to everyone."

The joy Bran had felt at the ride was gone, melted away like the snowflakes on his face. Not so long ago, the thought of Robb calling the banners and riding off to war would have filled him with excitement, but now he felt only dread. "Can we go back now?" he asked. "I'm cold."

Robb glanced around. "We need to find the wolves. Can you stand to go a bit longer?"

"I can go as long as you can." Maester Luwin had warned him to keep the ride short, for fear of saddle sores, but Bran would not admit to weakness in front of his brother. He was sick of the way everyone was always fussing over him and asking how he was.

"Let's hunt down the hunters, then," Robb said. Side by side, they urged their mounts off the kingsroad and struck out into the wolfswood. Theon dropped back and followed well behind them, talking and joking with the guardsmen.

It was nice under the trees. Bran kept Dancer to a walk, holding the reins lightly and looking all around him as they went. He knew this wood, but he had been so long confined to Winterfell that he felt as though he were seeing it for the first time. The smells filled his nostrils; the sharp fresh tang of pine needles, the earthy odor of wet rotting leaves, the hints of animal musk and distant cooking fires. He caught a glimpse of a black squirrel moving through the snow-covered branches of an oak, and paused to study the silvery web of an empress spider.

Theon and the others fell farther and farther behind, until Bran could no longer hear their voices. From ahead came the faint sound of rushing waters. It grew louder until they reached the stream. Tears stung his eyes.

"Bran?" Robb asked. "What's wrong?"

Bran shook his head. "I was just remembering," he said. "Jory brought us here once, to fish for trout. You and me and Jon. Do you remember?"

"I remember," Robb said, his voice quiet and sad.

"I didn't catch anything," Bran said, "but Jon gave me his fish on the way back to Winterfell. Will we ever see Jon again?"

"We saw Uncle Benjen when the king came to visit," Robb pointed out. "Jon will visit too, you'll see."

The stream was running high and fast. Robb dismounted and led his gelding across the ford. In the deepest part of the crossing, the water came up to midthigh. He tied his horse to a tree on the far side, and waded back across for Bran and Dancer. The current foamed around rock and root, and Bran could feel the spray on his face as Robb led him over. It made him smile. For a moment he felt strong again, and whole. He looked up at the trees and dreamed of climbing them, right up to the very top, with the whole forest spread out beneath him.

They were on the far side when they heard the howl, a long rising wail that moved through the trees like a cold wind. Bran raised his head to listen. "Summer," he said. No sooner had he spoken than a second voice joined the first.

"They've made a kill," Robb said as he remounted. "I'd best go and bring them back. Wait here, Theon and the others should be along shortly."

"I want to go with you," Bran said.

"I'll find them faster by myself." Robb spurred his gelding and vanished into the trees.

Once he was gone, the woods seemed to close in around Bran. The snow was falling more heavily now. Where it touched the ground it melted, but all about him rock and root and branch wore a thin blanket of white. As he waited, he was conscious of how uncomfortable he felt. He could not feel his legs, hanging useless in the stirrups, but the strap around his chest was tight and chafing, and the melting snow had soaked through his gloves to chill his hands. He wondered what was keeping Theon and Maester Luwin and Joseth and the rest.

When he heard the rustle of leaves, Bran used the reins to make Dancer turn, expecting to see his friends, but the ragged men who stepped out onto the bank of the stream were strangers.

"Good day to you," he said nervously. One look, and Bran knew they were neither foresters nor farmers. He was suddenly conscious of how richly he was dressed. His surcoat was new, dark grey wool with silver buttons, and a heavy silver pin fastened his fur-trimmed cloak at the shoulders. His boots and gloves were lined with fur as well.

"All alone, are you?" said the biggest of them, a bald man with a raw windburnt face. "Lost in the wolfswood, poor lad."

"I'm not lost." Bran did not like the way the strangers were looking at him. He counted four, but when he turned his head, he saw two others behind him. "My brother rode off just a moment ago, and my guard will be here shortly."

"Your guard, is it?" a second man said. Grey stubble covered his gaunt face. "And what would they be guarding, my little lord? Is that a silver pin I see there on your cloak?"

"Pretty," said a woman's voice. She scarcely looked like a woman, tall and lean, with the same hard face as the others, her hair hidden beneath a bowl-shaped halfhelm. The spear she held was eight feet of black oak, tipped in rusted steel.

"Let's have a look," said the big bald man.

Bran watched him anxiously. The man's clothes were filthy, fallen almost to pieces, patched here with brown and here with blue and there with a dark green, and faded everywhere to grey, but once that cloak might have been black. The grey stubbly man wore black rags too, he saw with a sudden start. Suddenly Bran remembered the oathbreaker his father had beheaded, the day they had found the wolf pups; that man had worn black as well, and Father said he had been a deserter from the Night's Watch. *No man is more dangerous,* he remembered Lord Eddard saying. *The deserter knows his life is forfeit if he is taken, so he will not flinch from any crime, no matter how vile or cruel.*

"The pin, lad," the big man said. He held out his hand.

"We'll take the horse too," said another of them, a woman shorter than Robb, with a broad flat face and lank yellow hair. "Get down, and be quick about it." A knife slid from her sleeve into her hand, its edge jagged as a saw.

"No," Bran blurted. "I can't . . ."

The big man grabbed his reins before Bran could think to wheel Dancer around and gallop off. "You can, lordling . . . and will, if you know what's good for you."

"Stiv, look how he's strapped on." The tall woman pointed with her spear. "Might be it's the truth he's telling."

"Straps, is it?" Stiv said. He drew a dagger from a sheath at his belt. "There's ways to deal with straps."

"You some kind of cripple?" asked the short woman.

Bran flared. "I'm Brandon Stark of Winterfell, and you better let go of my horse, or I'll see you all dead."

The gaunt man with the grey stubbled face laughed. "The boy's a Stark, true enough. Only a Stark would be fool enough to threaten where smarter men would beg."

"Cut his little cock off and stuff it in his mouth," suggested the short woman. "That should shut him up."

"You're as stupid as you are ugly, Hali," said the tall woman. "The boy's worth nothing dead, but alive . . . gods be damned, think what Mance would give to have Benjen Stark's own blood to hostage!"

"Mance be damned," the big man cursed. "You want to go back there, Osha? More fool you. Think the white walkers will care if you have a hostage?" He turned back to Bran and slashed at the strap around his thigh. The leather parted with a sigh.

The stroke had been quick and careless, biting deep. Looking down, Bran glimpsed pale flesh where the wool of his leggings had parted. Then the blood began to flow. He watched the red stain spread, feeling light-headed, curiously apart; there had been no pain, not even a hint of feeling. The big man grunted in surprise.

"Put down your steel now, and I promise you shall have a quick and painless death," Robb called out.

Bran looked up in desperate hope, and there he was. The strength of the words were undercut by the way his voice cracked with strain. He was mounted, the bloody carcass of an elk slung across the back of his horse, his sword in a gloved hand.

"The brother," said the man with the grey stubbly face.

"He's a fierce one, he is," mocked the short woman. Hali, they called her. "You mean to fight us, boy?"

"Don't be a fool, lad. You're one against six." The tall woman, Osha, leveled her spear. "Off the horse, and throw down the sword. We'll thank you kindly for the mount and for the venison, and you and your brother can be on your way."

Robb whistled. They heard the faint sound of soft feet on wet leaves. The undergrowth parted, low-hanging branches giving up their accumulation of snow, and Grey Wind and Summer emerged from the green. Summer sniffed the air and growled.

"Wolves," gasped Hali.

"Direwolves," Bran said. Still half-grown, they were as

large as any wolf he had ever seen, but the differences were easy to spot, if you knew what to look for. Maester Luwin and Farlen the kennelmaster had taught him. A direwolf had a bigger head and longer legs in proportion to its body, and its snout and jaw were markedly leaner and more pronounced. There was something gaunt and terrible about them as they stood there amid the gently falling snow. Fresh blood spotted Grey Wind's muzzle.

"Dogs," the big bald man said contemptuously. "Yet I'm told there's nothing like a wolfskin cloak to warm a man by night." He made a sharp gesture. "Take them."

Robb shouted, *"Winterfell!"* and kicked his horse. The gelding plunged down the bank as the ragged men closed. A man with an axe rushed in, shouting and heedless. Robb's sword caught him full in the face with a sickening *crunch* and a spray of bright blood. The man with the gaunt stubbly face made a grab for the reins, and for half a second he had them . . . and then Grey Wind was on him, bearing him down. He fell back into the stream with a splash and a shout, flailing wildly with his knife as his head went under. The direwolf plunged in after him, and the white water turned red where they had vanished.

Robb and Osha matched blows in midstream. Her long spear was a steel-headed serpent, flashing out at his chest, once, twice, three times, but Robb parried every thrust with his longsword, turning the point aside. On the fourth or fifth thrust, the tall woman overextended herself and lost her balance, just for a second. Robb charged, riding her down.

A few feet away, Summer darted in and snapped at Hali. The knife bit at his flank. Summer slid away, snarling, and came rushing in again. This time his jaws closed around her calf. Holding the knife with both hands, the small woman stabbed down, but the direwolf seemed to sense the blade coming. He pulled free for an instant, his mouth full of leather and cloth and bloody flesh. When Hali stumbled and fell, he came at her again, slamming her backward, teeth tearing at her belly.

The sixth man ran from the carnage . . . but not far. As he went scrambling up the far side of the bank, Grey Wind emerged from the stream, dripping wet. He shook the water off and bounded after the running man, hamstringing him with a single snap of his teeth, and going for the throat as the screaming man slid back down toward the water.

And then there was no one left but the big man, Stiv. He slashed at Bran's chest strap, grabbed his arm, and yanked. Suddenly Bran was falling. He sprawled on the ground, his legs tangled under him, one foot in the stream. He could not feel the cold of the water, but he felt the steel when Stiv pressed his dagger to his throat. "Back away," the man warned, "or I'll open the boy's windpipe, I swear it."

Robb reined his horse in, breathing hard. The fury went out of his eyes, and his sword arm dropped.

In that moment Bran saw everything. Summer was savaging Hali, pulling glistening blue snakes from her belly. Her eyes were wide and staring. Bran could not tell whether she was alive or dead. The grey stubbly man and the one with the axe lay unmoving, but Osha was on her knees, crawling toward her fallen spear. Grey Wind padded toward her, dripping wet. "Call him off!" the big man shouted. "Call them both off, or the cripple boy dies now!"

"Grey Wind, Summer, to me," Robb said.

The direwolves stopped, turned their heads. Grey Wind loped back to Robb. Summer stayed where he was, his eyes on Bran and the man beside him. He growled. His muzzle was wet and red, but his eyes burned.

Osha used the butt end of her spear to lever herself back to her feet. Blood leaked from a wound on the upper arm where Robb had cut her. Bran could see sweat trickling down the big man's face. Stiv was as scared as he was, he realized. "Starks," the man muttered, "bloody Starks." He raised his voice. "Osha, kill the wolves and get his sword."

"Kill them yourself," she replied. "I'll not be getting near those monsters."

For a moment Stiv was at a loss. His hand trembled; Bran felt a trickle of blood where the knife pressed against his neck. The stench of the man filled his nose; he smelled of fear. "You," he called out to Robb. "You have a name?"

"I am Robb Stark, the heir to Winterfell."

"This is your brother?"

"Yes."

"You want him alive, you do what I say. Off the horse."

Robb hesitated a moment. Then, slowly and deliberately, he dismounted and stood with his sword in hand.

"Now kill the wolves."

Robb did not move.

"You do it. The wolves or the boy."

"*No!*" Bran screamed. If Robb did as they asked, Stiv would kill them both anyway, once the direwolves were dead.

The bald man took hold of his hair with his free hand and twisted it cruelly, till Bran sobbed in pain. "You shut your mouth, cripple, you hear me?" He twisted harder. "*You hear me?*"

A low *thrum* came from the woods behind them. Stiv gave a choked gasp as a half foot of razor-tipped broadhead suddenly exploded out of his chest. The arrow was bright red, as if it had been painted in blood.

The dagger fell away from Bran's throat. The big man swayed and collapsed, facedown in the stream. The arrow broke beneath him. Bran watched his life go swirling off in the water.

Osha glanced around as Father's guardsmen appeared from beneath the trees, steel in hand. She threw down her spear. "Mercy, m'lord," she called to Robb.

The guardsmen had a strange, pale look to their faces as they took in the scene of slaughter. They eyed the wolves uncertainly, and when Summer returned to Hali's corpse to feed, Joseth dropped his knife and scrambled for the bush, heaving. Even Maester Luwin seemed shocked as he stepped from behind a tree, but only for an instant. Then he shook his head and waded across the stream to Bran's side. "Are you hurt?"

"He cut my leg," Bran said, "but I couldn't feel it."

As the maester knelt to examine the wound, Bran turned his head. Theon Greyjoy stood beside a sentinel tree, his bow in hand. He was smiling. Ever smiling. A half-dozen arrows were thrust into the soft ground at his feet, but it had taken only one. "A dead enemy is a thing of beauty," he announced.

"Jon always said you were an ass, Greyjoy," Robb said loudly. "I ought to chain you up in the yard and let Bran take a few practice shots at *you.*"

"You should be thanking me for saving your brother's life."

"What if you had missed the shot?" Robb said. "What if you'd only wounded him? What if you had made his hand jump, or hit Bran instead? For all you knew, the man might have been wearing a breastplate, all you could see was the back of his cloak. What would have happened to my brother then? Did you ever think of *that*, Greyjoy?"

Theon's smile was gone. He gave a sullen shrug and began to pull his arrows from the ground, one by one.

Robb glared at his guardsmen. "Where were you?" he demanded of them. "I was sure you were close behind us."

The men traded unhappy glances. "We were following, m'lord," said Quent, the youngest of them, his beard a soft brown fuzz. "Only first we waited for Maester Luwin and his ass, begging your pardons, and then, well, as it were . . ." He glanced over at Theon and quickly looked away, abashed.

"I spied a turkey," Theon said, annoyed by the question. "How was I to know that you'd leave the boy alone?"

Robb turned his head to look at Theon once more. Bran had never seen him so angry, yet he said nothing. Finally he knelt beside Maester Luwin. "How badly is my brother wounded?"

"No more than a scratch," the maester said. He wet a cloth in the stream to clean the cut. "Two of them wear the black," he told Robb as he worked.

Robb glanced over at where Stiv lay sprawled in the stream, his ragged black cloak moving fitfully as the rushing waters tugged at it. "Deserters from the Night's Watch," he said grimly. "They must have been fools, to come so close to Winterfell."

"Folly and desperation are ofttimes hard to tell apart," said Maester Luwin.

"Shall we bury them, m'lord?" asked Quent.

"They would not have buried us," Robb said. "Hack off their heads, we'll send them back to the Wall. Leave the rest for the carrion crows."

"And this one?" Quent jerked a thumb toward Osha.

Robb walked over to her. She was a head taller than he

was, but she dropped to her knees at his approach. "Give me my life, m'lord of Stark, and I am yours."

"Mine? What would I do with an oathbreaker?"

"I broke no oaths. Stiv and Wallen flew down off the Wall, not me. The black crows got no place for women."

Theon Greyjoy sauntered closer. "Give her to the wolves," he urged Robb. The woman's eyes went to what was left of Hali, and just as quickly away. She shuddered. Even the guardsmen looked queasy.

"She's a woman," Robb said.

"A wildling," Bran told him. "She said they should keep me alive so they could take me to Mance Rayder."

"Do you have a name?" Robb asked her.

"Osha, as it please the lord," she muttered sourly.

Maester Luwin stood. "We might do well to question her."

Bran could see the relief on his brother's face. "As you say, Maester. Wayn, bind her hands. She'll come back to Winterfell with us . . . and live or die by the truths she gives us."

TYRION

"You want eat?" Mord asked, glowering. He had a plate of boiled beans in one thick, stub-fingered hand.

Tyrion Lannister was starved, but he refused to let this brute see him cringe. "A leg of lamb would be pleasant," he said, from the heap of soiled straw in the corner of his cell. "Perhaps a dish of peas and onions, some fresh baked bread with butter, and a flagon of mulled wine to wash it down. Or beer, if that's easier. I try not to be overly particular."

"Is beans," Mord said. "Here." He held out the plate.

Tyrion sighed. The turnkey was twenty stone of gross stupidity, with brown rotting teeth and small dark eyes. The left side of his face was slick with scar where an axe had cut off his ear and part of his cheek. He was as predictable as he was ugly, but Tyrion *was* hungry. He reached up for the plate.

Mord jerked it away, grinning. "Is here," he said, holding it out beyond Tyrion's reach.

The dwarf climbed stiffly to his feet, every joint aching. "Must we play the same fool's game with every meal?" He made another grab for the beans.

Mord shambled backward, grinning through his rotten teeth. "Is here, dwarf man." He held the plate out at arm's length, over the edge where the cell ended and the sky began. "You not want eat? Here. Come take."

Tyrion's arms were too short to reach the plate, and he was not about to step that close to the edge. All it would take would be a quick shove of Mord's heavy white belly, and he would end up a sickening red splotch on the stones of Sky, like so many other prisoners of the Eyrie over the centuries. "Come to think on it, I'm not hungry after all," he declared, retreating to the corner of his cell.

Mord grunted and opened his thick fingers. The wind took the plate, flipping it over as it fell. A handful of beans sprayed back at them as the food tumbled out of sight. The turnkey laughed, his gut shaking like a bowl of pudding.

Tyrion felt a pang of rage. "You fucking son of a pox-ridden ass," he spat. "I hope you die of a bloody flux."

For that, Mord gave him a kick, driving a steel-toed boot hard into Tyrion's ribs on the way out. "I take it back!" he gasped as he doubled over on the straw. "I'll kill you myself, I swear it!" The heavy iron-bound door slammed shut. Tyrion heard the rattle of keys.

For a small man, he had been cursed with a danger-ously big mouth, he reflected as he crawled back to his corner of what the Arryns laughably called their dungeon. He huddled beneath the thin blanket that was his only bedding, staring out at a blaze of empty blue sky and dis-tant mountains that seemed to go on forever, wishing he still had the shadowskin cloak he'd won from Marillion at dice, after the singer had stolen it off the body of that brigand chief. The skin had smelled of blood and mold, but it was warm and thick. Mord had taken it the mo-ment he laid eyes on it.

The wind tugged at his blanket with gusts sharp as talons. His cell was miserably small, even for a dwarf. Not five feet away, where a wall ought to have been, where a wall *would* be in a proper dungeon, the floor ended and the sky began. He had plenty of fresh air and sunshine, and the moon and stars by night, but Tyrion would have traded it all in an instant for the dankest, gloomiest pit in the bowels of the Casterly Rock.

"You fly," Mord had promised him, when he'd shoved

him into the cell. "Twenty day, thirty, fifty maybe. Then you fly."

The Arryns kept the only dungeon in the realm where the prisoners were welcome to escape at will. That first day, after girding up his courage for hours, Tyrion had lain flat on his stomach and squirmed to the edge, to poke out his head and look down. Sky was six hundred feet below, with nothing between but empty air. If he craned his neck out as far as it could go, he could see other cells to his right and left and above him. He was a bee in a stone honeycomb, and someone had torn off his wings.

It was cold in the cell, the wind screamed night and day, and worst of all, the floor *sloped*. Ever so slightly, yet it was enough. He was afraid to close his eyes, afraid that he might roll over in his sleep and wake in sudden terror as he went sliding off the edge. Small wonder the sky cells drove men mad.

Gods save me, some previous tenant had written on the wall in something that looked suspiciously like blood, *the blue is calling.* At first Tyrion wondered who he'd been, and what had become of him; later, he decided that he would rather not know.

If only he had shut his mouth . . .

The wretched boy had started it, looking down on him from a throne of carved weirwood beneath the moon-and-falcon banners of House Arryn. Tyrion Lannister had been looked down on all his life, but seldom by rheumy-eyed six-year-olds who needed to stuff fat cushions under their cheeks to lift them to the height of a man. "Is he the bad man?" the boy had asked, clutching his doll.

"He is," the Lady Lysa had said from the lesser throne beside him. She was all in blue, powdered and perfumed for the suitors who filled her court.

"He's so *small,*" the Lord of the Eyrie said, giggling.

"This is Tyrion the Imp, of House Lannister, who murdered your father." She raised her voice so it carried down the length of High Hall of the Eyrie, ringing off the milk-white walls and the slender pillars, so every man could hear it. *"He slew the Hand of the King!"*

"Oh, did I kill him too?" Tyrion had said, like a fool.

That would have been a very good time to have kept his mouth closed and his head bowed. He could see that now; seven hells, he had seen it then. The High Hall of the Arryns was long and austere, with a forbidding coldness to its walls of blue-veined white marble, but the faces around him had been colder by far. The power of Casterly Rock was far away, and there were no friends of the Lannisters in the Vale of Arryn. Submission and silence would have been his best defenses.

But Tyrion's mood had been too foul for sense. To his shame, he had faltered during the last leg of their day-long climb up to the Eyrie, his stunted legs unable to take him any higher. Bronn had carried him the rest of the way, and the humiliation poured oil on the flames of his anger. "It would seem I've been a busy little fellow," he said with bitter sarcasm. "I wonder when I found the time to do all this slaying and murdering."

He ought to have remembered who he was dealing with. Lysa Arryn and her half-sane weakling son had not been known at court for their love of wit, especially when it was directed at them.

"Imp," Lysa said coldly, "you will guard that mocking tongue of yours and speak to my son politely, or I promise you will have cause to regret it. Remember where you are. This is the Eyrie, and these are knights of the Vale you see around you, true men who loved Jon Arryn well. Every one of them would die for me."

"Lady Arryn, should any harm come to me, my brother Jaime will be pleased to see that they do." Even as he spat out the words, Tyrion knew they were folly.

"Can you fly, my lord of Lannister?" Lady Lysa asked. "Does a dwarf have wings? If not, you would be wiser to swallow the next threat that comes to mind."

"I made no threats," Tyrion said. "That was a promise."

Little Lord Robert hopped to his feet at that, so upset he dropped his doll. "You can't hurt us," he screamed. "No one can hurt us here. Tell him, Mother, tell him he can't hurt us here." The boy began to twitch.

"The Eyrie is impregnable," Lysa Arryn declared calmly. She drew her son close, holding him safe in the circle of her plump white arms. "The Imp is trying to frighten us, sweet baby. The Lannisters are all liars. No one will hurt my sweet boy."

The hell of it was, she was no doubt right. Having seen what it took to get here, Tyrion could well imagine how it would be for a knight trying to fight his way up in armor, while stones and arrows poured down from above and enemies contested with him for every step. *Nightmare* did not begin to describe it. Small wonder the Eyrie had never been taken.

Still, Tyrion had been unable to silence himself. "Not impregnable," he said, "merely inconvenient."

Young Robert pointed down, his hand trembling. "You're a *liar*. Mother, I want to see him fly." Two guardsmen in sky-blue cloaks seized Tyrion by the arms, lifting him off his floor.

The gods only know what might have happened then were it not for Catelyn Stark. "Sister," she called out from where she stood below the thrones, "I beg you to remember, this man is *my* prisoner. I will not have him harmed."

Lysa Arryn glanced at her sister coolly for a moment, then rose and swept down on Tyrion, her long skirts trailing after her. For an instant he feared she would strike him, but instead she commanded them to release him. Her men shoved him to the floor, his legs went out from under him, and Tyrion fell.

He must have made quite a sight as he struggled to his knees, only to feel his right leg spasm, sending him sprawling once more. Laughter boomed up and down the High Hall of the Arryns.

"My sister's little guest is too weary to stand," Lady Lysa announced. "Ser Vardis, take him down to the dungeon. A rest in one of our sky cells will do him much good."

The guardsmen jerked him upright. Tyrion Lannister dangled between them, kicking feebly, his face red with shame. "I will remember this," he told them all as they carried him off.

And so he did, for all the good it did him.

At first he had consoled himself that this imprisonment could not last long. Lysa Arryn wanted to humble him, that was all. She would send for him again, and soon. If not her, then Catelyn Stark would want to question him. This time he would guard his tongue more closely. They dare not kill him out of hand; he was still a Lannister of Casterly Rock, and if they shed his blood, it would mean war. Or so he had told himself.

Now he was not so certain.

Perhaps his captors only meant to let him rot here, but he feared he did not have the strength to rot for long. He was growing weaker every day, and it was only a matter of time until Mord's kicks and blows did him serious harm, provided the gaoler did not starve him to death first. A few more nights of cold and hunger, and the blue would start calling to him too.

He wondered what was happening beyond the walls (such as they were) of his cell. Lord Tywin would surely have sent out riders when the word reached him. Jaime might be leading a host through the Mountains of the Moon even now . . . unless he was riding north against Winterfell instead. Did anyone outside the Vale even suspect where Catelyn Stark had taken him? He wondered what Cersei would do when she heard. The king could order him freed, but would Robert listen to his queen or his Hand? Tyrion had no illusions about the king's love for his sister.

If Cersei kept her wits about her, she would insist the king sit in judgment of Tyrion himself. Even Ned Stark could scarcely object to that, not without impugning the honor of the king. And Tyrion would be only too glad to take his chances in a trial. Whatever murders they might lay at his door, the Starks had no proof of anything so far as he could see. Let them make their case before the Iron Throne and the lords of the land. It would be the end of them. If only Cersei were clever enough to see that . . .

Tyrion Lannister sighed. His sister was not without a certain low cunning, but her pride blinded her. She would see the insult in this, not the opportunity. And Jaime was even worse, rash and headstrong and quick to anger. His brother never untied a knot when he could slash it in two with his sword.

He wondered which of them had sent the footpad to silence the Stark boy, and whether they had truly conspired at the death of Lord Arryn. If the old Hand had been murdered, it was deftly and subtly done. Men of his age died of sudden illness all the time. In contrast, sending some oaf with a stolen knife after Brandon Stark struck him as unbelievably clumsy. And wasn't *that* peculiar, come to think on it . . .

Tyrion shivered. Now *there* was a nasty suspicion. Perhaps the direwolf and the lion were not the only beasts in the woods, and if that was true, someone was using him as a catspaw. Tyrion Lannister hated being used.

He would have to get out of here, and soon. His chances of overpowering Mord were small to none, and no one was about to smuggle him a six-hundred-foot-long rope, so he would have to talk himself free. His mouth had gotten him into this cell; it could damn well get him out.

Tyrion pushed himself to his feet, doing his best to ignore the slope of the floor beneath him, with its ever-so-subtle tug toward the edge. He hammered on the door with a fist. *"Mord!"* he shouted. *"Turnkey! Mord, I want you!"* He had to keep it up a good ten minutes before he heard footsteps. Tyrion stepped back an instant before the door opened with a crash.

"Making noise," Mord growled, with blood in his eyes. Dangling from one meaty hand was a leather strap, wide and thick, doubled over in his fist.

Never show them you're afraid, Tyrion reminded himself. "How would you like to be rich?" he asked.

Mord hit him. He swung the strap backhand, lazily, but the leather caught Tyrion high on the arm. The force of it staggered him, and the pain made him grit his teeth. "No mouth, dwarf man," Mord warned him.

"Gold," Tyrion said, miming a smile. "Casterly Rock is full of gold . . . *ahhhh* . . ." This time the blow was a forehand, and Mord put more of his arm into the swing, making the leather *crack* and jump. It caught Tyrion in the ribs and dropped him to his knees, whimpering. He forced himself to look up at the gaoler. "As rich as the Lannisters," he wheezed. "That's what they say, Mord—"

Mord grunted. The strap whistled through the air and smashed Tyrion full in the face. The pain was so bad he did not remember falling, but when he opened his eyes again he was on the floor of his cell. His ear was ringing, and his mouth was full of blood. He groped for purchase, to push himself up, and his fingers brushed against . . . nothing. Tyrion snatched his hand back as fast as if it had been scalded, and tried his best to stop breathing. He had fallen right on the edge, inches from the blue.

"More to say?" Mord held the strap between his fists

and gave it a sharp pull. The *snap* made Tyrion jump. The turnkey laughed.

He won't push me over, Tyrion told himself desperately as he crawled away from the edge. *Catelyn Stark wants me alive, he doesn't dare kill me.* He wiped the blood off his lips with the back of his hand, grinned, and said, "That was a stiff one, Mord." The gaoler squinted at him, trying to decide if he was being mocked. "I could make good use of a strong man like you." The strap flew at him, but this time Tyrion was able to cringe away from it. He took a glancing blow to the shoulder, nothing more. "Gold," he repeated, scrambling backward like a crab, "more gold than you'll see here in a lifetime. Enough to buy land, women, horses . . . you could be a lord. Lord Mord." Tyrion hawked up a glob of blood and phlegm and spat it out into the sky.

"Is no gold," Mord said.

He's listening! Tyrion thought. "They relieved me of my purse when they captured me, but the gold is still mine. Catelyn Stark might take a man prisoner, but she'd never stoop to rob him. That wouldn't be honorable. Help me, and all the gold is yours." Mord's strap licked out, but it was a halfhearted, desultory swing, slow and contemptuous. Tyrion caught the leather in his hand and held it prisoned. "There will be no risk to you. All you need do is deliver a message."

The gaoler yanked his leather strap free of Tyrion's grasp. "Message," he said, as if he had never heard the word before. His frown made deep creases in his brow.

"You heard me, my lord. Only carry my word to your lady. Tell her . . ." *What? What would possibly make Lysa Arryn relent?* The inspiration came to Tyrion Lannister suddenly. ". . . tell her that I wish to confess my crimes."

Mord raised his arm and Tyrion braced himself for another blow, but the turnkey hesitated. Suspicion and greed warred in his eyes. He wanted that gold, yet he feared a trick; he had the look of a man who had often been tricked. "Is lie," he muttered darkly. "Dwarf man cheat me."

"I will put my promise in writing," Tyrion vowed.

Some illiterates held writing in disdain; others seemed to have a superstitious reverence for the written word, as if it were some sort of magic. Fortunately, Mord was one of the latter. The turnkey lowered the strap. "Writing down gold. Much gold."

"Oh, *much* gold," Tyrion assured him. "The purse is just a taste, my friend. My brother wears armor of solid gold plate." In truth, Jaime's armor was gilded steel, but this oaf would never know the difference.

Mord fingered his strap thoughtfully, but in the end, he relented and went to fetch paper and ink. When the letter was written, the gaoler frowned at it suspiciously. "Now deliver my message," Tyrion urged.

He was shivering in his sleep when they came for him, late that night. Mord opened the door but kept his silence. Ser Vardis Egen woke Tyrion with the point of his boot. "On your feet, Imp. My lady wants to see you."

Tyrion rubbed the sleep from his eyes and put on a grimace he scarcely felt. "No doubt she does, but what makes you think I wish to see her?"

Ser Vardis frowned. Tyrion remembered him well from the years he had spent at King's Landing as the captain of the Hand's household guard. A square, plain face, silver hair, a heavy build, and no humor whatsoever. "Your wishes are not my concern. On your feet, or I'll have you carried."

Tyrion clambered awkwardly to his feet. "A cold night," he said casually, "and the High Hall is so drafty. I don't wish to catch a chill. Mord, if you would be so good, fetch my cloak."

The gaoler squinted at him, face dull with suspicion.

"My *cloak*," Tyrion repeated. "The shadowskin you took from me for safekeeping. You recall."

"Get him the damnable cloak," Ser Vardis said.

Mord did not dare grumble. He gave Tyrion a glare that promised future retribution, yet he went for the cloak. When he draped it around his prisoner's neck, Tyrion smiled. "My thanks. I shall think of you whenever I wear it." He flung the trailing end of the long fur over his right shoulder, and felt warm for the first time in days. "Lead on, Ser Vardis."

The High Hall of the Arryns was aglow with the light of fifty torches, burning in the sconces along the walls. The Lady Lysa wore black silk, with the moon-and-falcon sewn on her breast in pearls. Since she did not look the sort to join the Night's Watch, Tyrion could only imagine that she had decided mourning clothes were appropriate garb for a confession. Her long auburn hair, woven into an elaborate braid, fell across her left shoulder. The taller throne beside her was empty; no doubt the little Lord of the Eyrie was off shaking in his sleep. Tyrion was thankful for that much, at least.

He bowed deeply and took a moment to glance around the hall. Lady Arryn had summoned her knights and retainers to hear his confession, as he had hoped. He saw Ser Brynden Tully's craggy face and Lord Nestor Royce's bluff one. Beside Nestor stood a younger man with fierce black side-whiskers who could only be his heir, Ser Albar. Most of the principal houses of the Vale were represented. Tyrion noted Ser Lyn Corbray, slender as a sword, Lord Hunter with his gouty legs, the widowed Lady Waynwood surrounded by her sons. Others sported sigils he did not know; broken lance, green viper, burning tower, winged chalice.

Among the lords of the Vale were several of his companions from the high road; Ser Rodrik Cassel, pale from half-healed wounds, stood with Ser Willis Wode beside him. Marillion the singer had found a new woodharp. Tyrion smiled; whatever happened here tonight, he did not wish it to happen in secret, and there was no one like a singer for spreading a story near and far.

In the rear of the hall, Bronn lounged beneath a pillar. The freerider's black eyes were fixed on Tyrion, and his hand lay lightly on the pommel of his sword. Tyrion gave him a long look, wondering . . .

Catelyn Stark spoke first. "You wish to confess your crimes, we are told."

"I do, my lady," Tyrion answered.

Lysa Arryn smiled at her sister. "The sky cells always break them. The gods can see them there, and there is no darkness to hide in."

"He does not look broken to me," Lady Catelyn said.

Lady Lysa paid her no mind. "Say what you will," she commanded Tyrion.

And now to roll the dice, he thought with another quick glance back at Bronn. "Where to begin? I am a vile little man, I confess it. My crimes and sins are beyond counting, my lords and ladies. I have lain with whores,

not once but hundreds of times. I have wished my own
lord father dead, and my sister, our gracious queen, as
well." Behind him, someone chuckled. "I have not always
treated my servants with kindness. I have gambled. I have
even cheated, I blush to admit. I have said many cruel and
malicious things about the noble lords and ladies of the
court." That drew outright laughter. "Once I—"

"Silence!" Lysa Arryn's pale round face had turned a
burning pink. "What do you imagine you are doing,
dwarf?"

Tyrion cocked his head to one side. "Why, confessing
my crimes, my lady."

Catelyn Stark took a step forward. "You are accused of
sending a hired knife to slay my son Bran in his bed, and
of conspiring to murder Lord Jon Arryn, the Hand of the
King."

Tyrion gave a helpless shrug. *"Those* crimes I cannot
confess, I fear. I know nothing of any murders."

Lady Lysa rose from her weirwood throne. "I will *not*
be made mock of. You have had your little jape, Imp. I
trust you enjoyed it. Ser Vardis, take him back to the dungeon . . . but this time find him a smaller cell, with a
floor more sharply sloped."

"Is *this* how justice is done in the Vale?" Tyrion
roared, so loudly that Ser Vardis froze for an instant.
"Does honor stop at the Bloody Gate? You accuse me of
crimes, I deny them, so you throw me into an open cell to
freeze and starve." He lifted his head, to give them all a
good look at the bruises Mord had left on his face. "Where
is the king's justice? Is the Eyrie not part of the Seven
Kingdoms? I stand accused, you say. Very well. *I demand
a trial!* Let me speak, and let my truth or falsehood be
judged openly, in the sight of gods and men."

A low murmuring filled the High Hall. He had her,
Tyrion knew. He was highborn, the son of the most powerful lord in the realm, the brother of the queen. He could
not be denied a trial. Guardsmen in sky-blue cloaks had
started toward Tyrion, but Ser Vardis bid them halt and
looked to Lady Lysa.

Her small mouth twitched in a petulant smile. "If you
are tried and found to be guilty of the crimes for which
you stand accused, then by the king's own laws, you must

pay with your life's blood. We keep no headsman in the Eyrie, my lord of Lannister. Open the Moon Door."

The press of spectators parted. A narrow weirwood door stood between two slender marble pillars, a crescent moon carved in the white wood. Those standing closest edged backward as a pair of guardsmen marched through. One man removed the heavy bronze bars; the second pulled the door inward. Their blue cloaks rose snapping from their shoulders, caught in the sudden gust of wind that came howling through the open door. Beyond was the emptiness of the night sky, speckled with cold uncaring stars.

"Behold the king's justice," Lysa Arryn said. Torch flames fluttered like pennons along the walls, and here and there the odd torch guttered out.

"Lysa, I think this unwise," Catelyn Stark said as the black wind swirled around the hall.

Her sister ignored her. "You want a trial, my lord of Lannister. Very well, a trial you shall have. My son will listen to whatever you care to say, and you shall hear his judgment. Then you may leave . . . by one door or the other."

She looked so pleased with herself, Tyrion thought, and small wonder. How could a trial threaten her, when her weakling son was the lord judge? Tyrion glanced at her Moon Door. *Mother, I want to see him fly!* the boy had said. How many men had the snot-nosed little wretch sent through that door already?

"I thank you, my good lady, but I see no need to trouble Lord Robert," Tyrion said politely. "The gods know the truth of my innocence. I will have their verdict, not the judgment of men. I demand trial by combat."

A storm of sudden laughter filled the High Hall of the Arryns. Lord Nestor Royce snorted, Ser Willis chuckled, Ser Lyn Corbray guffawed, and others threw back their heads and howled until tears ran down their faces. Marillion clumsily plucked a gay note on his new woodharp with the fingers of his broken hand. Even the wind seemed to whistle with derision as it came skirling through the Moon Door.

Lysa Arryn's watery blue eyes looked uncertain. He had caught her off balance. "You have that right, to be sure."

The young knight with the green viper embroidered on his surcoat stepped forward and went to one knee. "My lady, I beg the boon of championing your cause."

"The honor should be mine," old Lord Hunter said. "For the love I bore your lord husband, let me avenge his death."

"My father served Lord Jon faithfully as High Steward of the Vale," Ser Albar Royce boomed. "Let me serve his son in this."

"The gods favor the man with the just cause," said Ser Lyn Corbray, "yet often that turns out to be the man with the surest sword. We all know who that is." He smiled modestly.

A dozen other men all spoke at once, clamoring to be heard. Tyrion found it disheartening to realize so many strangers were eager to kill him. Perhaps this had not been such a clever plan after all.

Lady Lysa raised a hand for silence. "I thank you, my lords, as I know my son would thank you if he were among us. No men in the Seven Kingdoms are as bold and true as the knights of the Vale. Would that I could grant you all this honor. Yet I can choose only one." She gestured. "Ser Vardis Egen, you were ever my lord husband's good right hand. You shall be our champion."

Ser Vardis had been singularly silent. "My lady," he said gravely, sinking to one knee, "pray give this burden to another, I have no taste for it. The man is no warrior. Look at him. A dwarf, half my size and lame in the legs. It would be shameful to slaughter such a man and call it justice."

Oh, *excellent*, Tyrion thought. "I agree."

Lysa glared at him. "You demanded a trial by combat."

"And now I demand a champion, such as you have chosen for yourself. My brother Jaime will gladly take my part, I know."

"Your precious Kingslayer is hundreds of leagues from here," snapped Lysa Arryn.

"Send a bird for him. I will gladly await his arrival."

"You will face Ser Vardis on the morrow."

"Singer," Tyrion said, turning to Marillion, "when you make a ballad of this, be certain you tell them how Lady Arryn denied the dwarf the right to a champion, and sent him forth lame and bruised and hobbling to face her finest knight."

"I deny you *nothing*!" Lysa Arryn said, her voice peeved and shrill with irritation. "Name your champion, Imp . . . if you think you can find a man to die for you."

"If it is all the same to you, I'd sooner find one to kill for me." Tyrion looked over the long hall. No one moved. For a long moment he wondered if it had all been a colossal blunder.

Then there was a stirring in the rear of the chamber. "I'll stand for the dwarf," Bronn called out.

EDDARD

He dreamt an old dream, of three knights in white cloaks, and a tower long fallen, and Lyanna in her bed of blood.

In the dream his friends rode with him, as they had in life. Proud Martyn Cassel, Jory's father; faithful Theo Wull; Ethan Glover, who had been Brandon's squire; Ser Mark Ryswell, soft of speech and gentle of heart; the crannogman, Howland Reed; Lord Dustin on his great red stallion. Ned had known their faces as well as he knew his own once, but the years leech at a man's memories, even those he has vowed never to forget. In the dream they were only shadows, grey wraiths on horses made of mist.

They were seven, facing three. In the dream as it had been in life. Yet these were no ordinary three. They waited before the round tower, the red mountains of Dorne at their backs, their white cloaks blowing in the wind. And these were no shadows; their faces burned clear, even now. Ser Arthur Dayne, the Sword of the Morning, had a sad smile on his lips. The hilt of the greatsword Dawn poked up over his right shoulder. Ser Oswell Whent was on one knee, sharpening his blade with a whetstone. Across his white-enameled helm, the black bat of his House spread its wings. Between them stood fierce old Ser Gerold Hightower, the White Bull, Lord Commander of the Kingsguard.

"I looked for you on the Trident," Ned said to them.

"We were not there," Ser Gerold answered.

"Woe to the Usurper if we had been," said Ser Oswell.

"When King's Landing fell, Ser Jaime slew your king with a golden sword, and I wondered where you were."

"Far away," Ser Gerold said, "or Aerys would yet sit the Iron Throne, and our false brother would burn in seven hells."

"I came down on Storm's End to lift the siege," Ned told them, "and the Lords Tyrell and Redwyne dipped their banners, and all their knights bent the knee to pledge us fealty. I was certain you would be among them."

"Our knees do not bend easily," said Ser Arthur Dayne.

"Ser Willem Darry is fled to Dragonstone, with your queen and Prince Viserys. I thought you might have sailed with him."

"Ser Willem is a good man and true," said Ser Oswell.

"But not of the Kingsguard," Ser Gerold pointed out. "The Kingsguard does not flee."

"Then or now," said Ser Arthur. He donned his helm.

"We swore a vow," explained old Ser Gerold.

Ned's wraiths moved up beside him, with shadow swords in hand. They were seven against three.

"And now it begins," said Ser Arthur Dayne, the Sword of the Morning. He unsheathed Dawn and held it with both hands. The blade was pale as milkglass, alive with light.

"No," Ned said with sadness in his voice. "Now it ends." As they came together in a rush of steel and shadow, he could hear Lyanna screaming. *"Eddard!"* she called. A storm of rose petals blew across a blood-streaked sky, as blue as the eyes of death.

"Lord Eddard," Lyanna called again.

"I promise," he whispered. "Lya, I promise . . ."

"Lord Eddard," a man echoed from the dark.

Groaning, Eddard Stark opened his eyes. Moonlight streamed through the tall windows of the Tower of the Hand.

"Lord Eddard?" A shadow stood over the bed.

"How . . . how long?" The sheets were tangled, his leg splinted and plastered. A dull throb of pain shot up his side.

"Six days and seven nights." The voice was Vayon Poole's. The steward held a cup to Ned's lips. "Drink, my lord."

"What . . . ?"

"Only water. Maester Pycelle said you would be thirsty."

Ned drank. His lips were parched and cracked. The water tasted sweet as honey.

"The king left orders," Vayon Poole told him when the cup was empty. "He would speak with you, my lord."

"On the morrow," Ned said. "When I am stronger." He could not face Robert now. The dream had left him weak as a kitten.

"My lord," Poole said, "he commanded us to send you to him the moment you opened your eyes." The steward busied himself lighting a bedside candle.

Ned cursed softly. Robert was never known for his patience. "Tell him I'm too weak to come to him. If he wishes to speak with me, I should be pleased to receive him here. I hope you wake him from a sound sleep. And summon . . ." He was about to say *Jory* when he remembered. "Summon the captain of my guard."

Alyn stepped into the bedchamber a few moments after the steward had taken his leave. "My lord."

"Poole tells me it has been six days," Ned said. "I must know how things stand."

"The Kingslayer is fled the city," Alyn told him. "The talk is he's ridden back to Casterly Rock to join his father. The story of how Lady Catelyn took the Imp is on every lip. I have put on extra guards, if it please you."

"It does," Ned assured him. "My daughters?"

"They have been with you every day, my lord. Sansa prays quietly, but Arya . . ." He hesitated. "She has not said a word since they brought you back. She is a fierce little thing, my lord. I have never seen such anger in a girl."

"Whatever happens," Ned said, "I want my daughters kept safe. I fear this is only the beginning."

"No harm will come to them, Lord Eddard," Alyn said. "I stake my life on that."

"Jory and the others . . ."

"I gave them over to the silent sisters, to be sent north to Winterfell. Jory would want to lie beside his grandfather."

It would have to be his grandfather, for Jory's father was buried far to the south. Martyn Cassel had perished with the rest. Ned had pulled the tower down afterward, and used its bloody stones to build eight cairns upon the ridge. It was said that Rhaegar had named that place the tower of joy, but for Ned it was a bitter memory. They had been seven against three, yet only two had lived to ride away; Eddard Stark himself and the little crannogman, Howland Reed. He did not think it omened well that he should dream that dream again after so many years.

"You've done well, Alyn," Ned was saying when Vayon Poole returned. The steward bowed low. "His Grace is without, my lord, and the queen with him."

Ned pushed himself up higher, wincing as his leg trembled with pain. He had not expected Cersei to come. It did not bode well that she had. "Send them in, and leave us. What we have to say should not go beyond these walls." Poole withdrew quietly.

Robert had taken time to dress. He wore a black velvet doublet with the crowned stag of Baratheon worked upon the breast in golden thread, and a golden mantle with a cloak of black and gold squares. A flagon of wine was in his hand, his face already flushed from drink. Cersei Lannister entered behind him, a jeweled tiara in her hair.

"Your Grace," Ned said. "Your pardons. I cannot rise."

"No matter," the king said gruffly. "Some wine? From the Arbor. A good vintage."

"A small cup," Ned said. "My head is still heavy from the milk of the poppy."

"A man in your place should count himself fortunate that his head is still on his shoulders," the queen declared.

"Quiet, woman," Robert snapped. He brought Ned a cup of wine. "Does the leg still pain you?"

"Some," Ned said. His head was swimming, but it would not do to admit to weakness in front of the queen.

"Pycelle swears it will heal clean." Robert frowned. "I take it you know what Catelyn has done?"

"I do." Ned took a small swallow of wine. "My lady wife is blameless, Your Grace. All she did she did at my command."

"I am *not* pleased, Ned," Robert grumbled.

"By what right do you dare lay hands on my blood?" Cersei demanded. "Who do you think you are?"

"The Hand of the King," Ned told her with icy courtesy. "Charged by your own lord husband to keep the king's peace and enforce the king's justice."

"You *were* the Hand," Cersei began, "but now—"

"Silence!" the king roared. "You asked him a question and he answered it." Cersei subsided, cold with anger, and Robert turned back to Ned. "Keep the king's peace, you say. Is this how you keep my peace, Ned? Seven men are dead . . ."

"Eight," the queen corrected. "Tregar died this morning, of the blow Lord Stark gave him."

"Abductions on the kingsroad and drunken slaughter in my streets," the king said. "I will not have it, Ned."

"Catelyn had good reason for taking the Imp—"

"I said, I will *not* have it! To hell with her reasons. You will command her to release the dwarf at once, *and* you will make your peace with Jaime."

"Three of my men were butchered before my eyes, because Jaime Lannister wished to *chasten* me. Am I to forget that?"

"My brother was not the cause of this quarrel," Cersei told the king. "Lord Stark was returning drunk from a brothel. His men attacked Jaime and his guards, even as his wife attacked Tyrion on the kingsroad."

"You know me better than that, Robert," Ned said. "Ask Lord Baelish if you doubt me. He was there."

"I've talked to Littlefinger," Robert said. "He claims he rode off to bring the gold cloaks before the fighting began, but he admits you were returning from some whorehouse."

"*Some* whorehouse? Damn your eyes, Robert, I went there to have a look at your daughter! Her mother has named her Barra. She looks like that first girl you fathered, when we were boys together in the Vale." He watched the queen as he spoke; her face was a mask, still and pale, betraying nothing.

Robert flushed. "Barra," he grumbled. "Is that supposed to please me? Damn the girl. I thought she had more sense."

"She cannot be more than fifteen, and a whore, and you thought she had *sense*?" Ned said, incredulous. His leg was beginning to pain him sorely. It was hard to keep his temper. "The fool child is in love with you, Robert."

The king glanced at Cersei. "This is no fit subject for the queen's ears."

"Her Grace will have no liking for anything I have to say," Ned replied. "I am told the Kingslayer has fled the city. Give me leave to bring him back to justice."

The king swirled the wine in his cup, brooding. He took a swallow. "No," he said. "I want no more of this. Jaime slew three of your men, and you five of his. Now it ends."

"Is that your notion of justice?" Ned flared. "If so, I am pleased that I am no longer your Hand."

The queen looked to her husband. "If any man had dared speak to a Targaryen as he has spoken to you—"

"Do you take me for Aerys?" Robert interrupted.

"I took you for a *king*. Jaime and Tyrion are your own brothers, by all the laws of marriage and the bonds we share. The Starks have driven off the one and seized the other. This man dishonors you with every breath he takes, and yet you stand there meekly, asking if his leg pains him and would he like some wine."

Robert's face was dark with anger. "How many times must I tell you to hold your tongue, woman?"

Cersei's face was a study in contempt. "What a jape the gods have made of us two," she said. "By all rights, you ought to be in skirts and me in mail."

Purple with rage, the king lashed out, a vicious backhand blow to the side of the head. She stumbled against the table and fell hard, yet Cersei Lannister did not cry out. Her slender fingers brushed her cheek, where the pale smooth skin was already reddening. On the morrow the bruise would cover half her face. "I shall wear this as a badge of honor," she announced.

"Wear it in silence, or I'll honor you again," Robert vowed. He shouted for a guard. Ser Meryn Trant stepped into the room, tall and somber in his white armor. "The queen is tired. See her to her bedchamber." The knight helped Cersei to her feet and led her out without a word.

Robert reached for the flagon and refilled his cup. "You see what she does to me, Ned." The king seated himself, cradling his wine cup. "My loving wife. The mother of my children." The rage was gone from him now; in his eyes Ned saw something sad and scared. "I should not have hit her. That was not . . . that was not *kingly*." He stared down at his hands, as if he did not quite know what they were. "I was always strong . . . no one could stand before me, no one. How do you fight someone if you can't hit them?" Confused, the king shook his head. "Rhaegar . . . Rhaegar *won*, damn him. I killed him, Ned, I drove the spike right through that black armor into his black heart, and he died at my feet. They made up songs about it. Yet somehow he still won. He has Lyanna now, and I have *her*." The king drained his cup.

"Your Grace," Ned Stark said, "we must talk . . ."

Robert pressed his fingertips against his temples. "I am sick unto death of talk. On the morrow I'm going to the kingswood to hunt. Whatever you have to say can wait until I return."

"If the gods are good, I shall not be here on your return. You commanded me to return to Winterfell, remember?"

Robert stood up, grasping one of the bedposts to steady himself. "The gods are seldom good, Ned. Here, this is yours." He pulled the heavy silver hand clasp from a pocket in the lining of his cloak and tossed it on the bed. "Like it or not, you are my Hand, damn you. I forbid you to leave."

Ned picked up the silver clasp. He was being given no choice, it seemed. His leg throbbed, and he felt as helpless as a child. "The Targaryen girl—"

The king groaned. "Seven hells, don't start with her again. That's done, I'll hear no more of it."

"Why would you want me as your Hand, if you refuse to listen to my counsel?"

"Why?" Robert laughed. "Why not? Someone has to rule this damnable kingdom. Put on the badge, Ned. It suits you. And if you ever throw it in my face again, I swear to you, I'll pin the damned thing on Jaime Lannister."

CATELYN

The eastern sky was rose and gold as the sun broke over the Vale of Arryn. Catelyn Stark watched the light spread, her hands resting on the delicate carved stone of the balustrade outside her window. Below her the world turned from black to indigo to green as dawn crept across fields and forests. Pale white mists rose off Alyssa's Tears, where the ghost waters plunged over the shoulder of the mountain to begin their long tumble down the face of the Giant's Lance. Catelyn could feel the faint touch of spray on her face.

Alyssa Arryn had seen her husband, her brothers, and all her children slain, and yet in life she had never shed a tear. So in death, the gods had decreed that she would know no rest until her weeping watered the black earth of the Vale, where the men she had loved were buried. Alyssa had been dead six thousand years now, and still no drop of the torrent had ever reached the valley floor far below. Catelyn wondered how large a waterfall her own tears would make when she died. "Tell me the rest of it," she said.

"The Kingslayer is massing a host at Casterly Rock," Ser Rodrik Cassel answered from the room behind her.

"Your brother writes that he has sent riders to the Rock, demanding that Lord Tywin proclaim his intent, but he has had no answer. Edmure has commanded Lord Vance and Lord Piper to guard the pass below the Golden Tooth. He vows to you that he will yield no foot of Tully land without first watering it with Lannister blood."

Catelyn turned away from the sunrise. Its beauty did little to lighten her mood; it seemed cruel for a day to dawn so fair and end so foul as this one promised to. "Edmure has sent riders and made vows," she said, "but Edmure is not the Lord of Riverrun. What of my lord father?"

"The message made no mention of Lord Hoster, my lady." Ser Rodrik tugged at his whiskers. They had grown in white as snow and bristly as a thornbush while he was recovering from his wounds; he looked almost himself again.

"My father would not have given the defense of Riverrun over to Edmure unless he was very sick," she said, worried. "I should have been woken as soon as this bird arrived."

"Your lady sister thought it better to let you sleep, Maester Colemon told me."

"I should have been woken," she insisted.

"The maester tells me your sister planned to speak with you after the combat," Ser Rodrik said.

"Then she still plans to go through with this mummer's farce?" Catelyn grimaced. "The dwarf has played her like a set of pipes, and she is too deaf to hear the tune. Whatever happens this morning, Ser Rodrik, it is past time we took our leave. My place is at Winterfell with my sons. If you are strong enough to travel, I shall ask Lysa for an escort to see us to Gulltown. We can take ship from there."

"Another ship?" Ser Rodrik looked a shade green, yet he managed not to shudder. "As you say, my lady."

The old knight waited outside her door as Catelyn summoned the servants Lysa had given her. If she spoke to her sister before the duel, perhaps she could change her mind, she thought as they dressed her. Lysa's policies varied with her moods, and her moods changed hourly. The shy girl she had known at Riverrun had grown into a woman who was by turns proud, fearful, cruel, dreamy, reckless, timid, stubborn, vain, and, above all, *inconstant*.

When that vile turnkey of hers had come crawling to tell them that Tyrion Lannister wished to confess, Catelyn had urged Lysa to have the dwarf brought to them privately, but no, nothing would do but that her sister must make a show of him before half the Vale. And now this . . .

"Lannister is *my* prisoner," she told Ser Rodrik as they descended the tower stairs and made their way through the Eyrie's cold white halls. Catelyn wore plain grey wool with a silvered belt. "My sister must be reminded of that."

At the doors to Lysa's apartments, they met her uncle storming out. "Going to join the fool's festival?" Ser Brynden snapped. "I'd tell you to slap some sense into your sister, if I thought it would do any good, but you'd only bruise your hand."

"There was a bird from Riverrun," Catelyn began, "a letter from Edmure . . ."

"I know, child." The black fish that fastened his cloak was Brynden's only concession to ornament. "I had to hear it from Maester Colemon. I asked your sister for leave to take a thousand seasoned men and ride for Riverrun with all haste. Do you know what she told me? *The Vale cannot spare a thousand swords, nor even one, Uncle*, she said. *You are the Knight of the Gate. Your place is here*." A gust of childish laughter drifted through the open doors behind him, and her uncle glanced darkly over his shoulder. "Well, I told her she could bloody well find herself a new Knight of the Gate. Black fish or no, I am still a Tully. I shall leave for Riverrun by evenfall."

Catelyn could not pretend to surprise. "Alone? You know as well as I that you will never survive the high road. Ser Rodrik and I are returning to Winterfell. Come with us, Uncle. I will give you your thousand men. Riverrun will not fight alone."

Brynden thought a moment, then nodded a brusque agreement. "As you say. It's the long way home, but I'm more like to get there. I'll wait for you below." He went striding off, his cloak swirling behind him.

Catelyn exchanged a look with Ser Rodrik. They went

through the doors to the high, nervous sound of a child's giggles.

Lysa's apartments opened over a small garden, a circle of dirt and grass planted with blue flowers and ringed on all sides by tall white towers. The builders had intended it as a godswood, but the Eyrie rested on the hard stone of the mountain, and no matter how much soil was hauled up from the Vale, they could not get a weirwood to take root here. So the Lords of the Eyrie planted grass and scattered statuary amidst low, flowering shrubs. It was there the two champions would meet to place their lives, and that of Tyrion Lannister, into the hands of the gods.

Lysa, freshly scrubbed and garbed in cream velvet with a rope of sapphires and moonstones around her milk-white neck, was holding court on the terrace overlooking the scene of the combat, surrounded by her knights, retainers, and lords high and low. Most of them still hoped to wed her, bed her, and rule the Vale of Arryn by her side. From what Catelyn had seen during her stay at the Eyrie, it was a vain hope.

A wooden platform had been built to elevate Robert's chair; there the Lord of the Eyrie sat, giggling and clapping his hands as a humpbacked puppeteer in blue-and-white motley made two wooden knights hack and slash at each other. Pitchers of thick cream and baskets of blackberries had been set out, and the guests were sipping a sweet orange-scented wine from engraved silver cups. *A fool's festival,* Brynden had called it, and small wonder.

Across the terrace, Lysa laughed gaily at some jest of Lord Hunter's, and nibbled a blackberry from the point of Ser Lyn Corbray's dagger. They were the suitors who stood highest in Lysa's favor . . . today, at least. Catelyn would have been hard-pressed to say which man was more unsuitable. Eon Hunter was even older than Jon Arryn had been, half-crippled by gout, and cursed with three quarrelsome sons, each more grasping than the last. Ser Lyn was a different sort of folly; lean and handsome, heir to an ancient but impoverished house, but vain, reckless, hot-tempered . . . and, it was whispered, notoriously uninterested in the intimate charms of women.

When Lysa espied Catelyn, she welcomed her with a sisterly embrace and a moist kiss on the cheek. "Isn't it a lovely morning? The gods are smiling on us. Do try a cup of the wine, sweet sister. Lord Hunter was kind enough to send for it, from his own cellars."

"Thank you, no. Lysa, we must talk."

"After," her sister promised, already beginning to turn away from her.

"Now." Catelyn spoke more loudly than she'd intended. Men were turning to look. "Lysa, you cannot mean to go ahead with this folly. Alive, the Imp has value. Dead, he is only food for crows. And if his champion should prevail here—"

"Small chance of that, my lady," Lord Hunter assured her, patting her shoulder with a liver-spotted hand. "Ser Vardis is a doughty fighter. He will make short work of the sellsword."

"Will he, my lord?" Catelyn said coolly. "I wonder." She had seen Bronn fight on the high road; it was no accident that he had survived the journey while other men had died. He moved like a panther, and that ugly sword of his seemed a part of his arm.

Lysa's suitors were gathering around them like bees round a blossom. "Women understand little of these things," Ser Morton Waynwood said. "Ser Vardis is a knight, sweet lady. This other fellow, well, his sort are all cowards at heart. Useful enough in a battle, with thousands of their fellows around them, but stand them up alone and the manhood leaks right out of them."

"Say you have the truth of it, then," Catelyn said with a courtesy that made her mouth ache. "What will we gain by the dwarf's death? Do you imagine that Jaime will care a fig that we gave his brother a *trial* before we flung him off a mountain?"

"Behead the man," Ser Lyn Corbray suggested. "When the Kingslayer receives the Imp's head, it will be a warning to him."

Lysa gave an impatient shake of her waist-long auburn hair. "Lord Robert wants to see him fly," she said, as if that settled the matter. "And the Imp has only himself to blame. It was he who demanded a trial by combat."

"Lady Lysa had no honorable way to deny him, even if she'd wished to," Lord Hunter intoned ponderously.

Ignoring them all, Catelyn turned all her force on her sister. "I remind you, Tyrion Lannister is *my* prisoner."

"And I remind *you*, the dwarf murdered my lord husband!" Her voice rose. "He poisoned the Hand of the King and left my sweet baby fatherless, and now I mean to see him pay!" Whirling, her skirts swinging around her, Lysa stalked across the terrace. Ser Lyn and Ser Morton and the other suitors excused themselves with cool nods and trailed after her.

"Do you think he did?" Ser Rodrik asked her quietly when they were alone again. "Murder Lord Jon, that is? The Imp still denies it, and most fiercely . . ."

"I believe the Lannisters murdered Lord Arryn," Catelyn replied, "but whether it was Tyrion, or Ser Jaime, or the queen, or all of them together, I could not begin to say." Lysa had named Cersei in the letter she had sent to Winterfell, but now she seemed certain that Tyrion was the killer . . . perhaps because the dwarf was here, while the queen was safe behind the walls of the Red Keep, hundreds of leagues to the south. Catelyn almost wished she had burned her sister's letter *before* reading it.

Ser Rodrik tugged at his whiskers. "Poison, well . . . that could be the dwarf's work, true enough. Or Cersei's. It's said poison is a woman's weapon, begging your pardons, my lady. The Kingslayer, now . . . I have no great liking for the man, but he's not the sort. Too fond of the sight of blood on that golden sword of his. *Was* it poison, my lady?"

Catelyn frowned, vaguely uneasy. "How else could they make it look a natural death?" Behind her, Lord Robert shrieked with delight as one of the puppet knights sliced the other in half, spilling a flood of red sawdust onto the terrace. She glanced at her nephew and sighed. "The boy is utterly without discipline. He will never be strong enough to rule unless he is taken away from his mother for a time."

"His lord father agreed with you," said a voice at her elbow. She turned to behold Maester Colemon, a cup of wine in his hand. "He was planning to send the boy to Dragonstone for fostering, you know . . . oh, but I'm speaking out of turn." The apple of his throat bobbed anxiously beneath the loose maester's chain. "I fear I've had too much of Lord Hunter's excellent wine. The prospect of bloodshed has my nerves all a-fray . . ."

"You are mistaken, Maester," Catelyn said. "It was Casterly Rock, not Dragonstone, and those arrangements were made after the Hand's death, without my sister's consent."

The maester's head jerked so vigorously at the end of his absurdly long neck that he looked half a puppet himself. "No, begging your forgiveness, my lady, but it was Lord Jon who—"

A bell tolled loudly below them. High lords and serving girls alike broke off what they were doing and moved to the balustrade. Below, two guardsmen in sky-blue cloaks led forth Tyrion Lannister. The Eyrie's plump septon escorted him to the statue in the center of the garden, a weeping woman carved in veined white marble, no doubt meant to be Alyssa.

"The bad little man," Lord Robert said, giggling. "Mother, can I make him fly? I want to see him fly."

"Later, my sweet baby," Lysa promised him.

"Trial first," drawled Ser Lyn Corbray, "*then* execution."

A moment later the two champions appeared from opposite sides of the garden. The knight was attended by two young squires, the sellsword by the Eyrie's master-at-arms.

Ser Vardis Egen was steel from head to heel, encased in heavy plate armor over mail and padded surcoat. Large circular rondels, enameled cream-and-blue in the moon-and-falcon sigil of House Arryn, protected the vulnerable juncture of arm and breast. A skirt of lobstered metal covered him from waist to midthigh, while a solid gorget encircled his throat. Falcon's wings sprouted from the temples of his helm, and his visor was a pointed metal beak with a narrow slit for vision.

Bronn was so lightly armored he looked almost naked beside the knight. He wore only a shirt of black oiled ringmail over boiled leather, a round steel halfhelm with a noseguard, and a mail coif. High leather boots with steel shinguards gave some protection to his legs, and discs of black iron were sewn into the fingers of his gloves. Yet Catelyn noted that the sellsword stood half a hand taller than his foe, with a longer reach . . . and Bronn was fifteen years younger, if she was any judge.

They knelt in the grass beneath the weeping woman, facing each other, with Lannister between them. The septon removed a faceted crystal sphere from the soft cloth bag at his waist. He lifted it high above his head, and the light shattered. Rainbows danced across the Imp's face. In a high, solemn, singsong voice, the septon asked the gods to look down and bear witness, to find the truth in this man's soul, to grant him life and freedom if he was innocent, death if he was guilty. His voice echoed off the surrounding towers.

When the last echo had died away, the septon lowered his crystal and made a hasty departure. Tyrion leaned over and whispered something in Bronn's ear before the guardsmen led him away. The sellsword rose laughing and brushed a blade of grass from his knee.

Robert Arryn, Lord of the Eyrie and Defender of the Vale, was fidgeting impatiently in his elevated chair. "When are they going to fight?" he asked plaintively.

Ser Vardis was helped back to his feet by one of his squires. The other brought him a triangular shield almost four feet tall, heavy oak dotted with iron studs. They strapped it to his left forearm. When Lysa's master-at-arms offered Bronn a similar shield, the sellsword spat and waved it away. Three days growth of coarse black beard covered his jaw and cheeks, but if he did not shave it was not for want of a razor; the edge of his sword had the dangerous glimmer of steel that had been honed every day for hours, until it was too sharp to touch.

Ser Vardis held out a gauntleted hand, and his squire placed a handsome double-edged longsword in his grasp. The blade was engraved with a delicate silver tracery of a mountain sky; its pommel was a falcon's head, its cross-guard fashioned into the shape of wings. "I had that sword crafted for Jon in King's Landing," Lysa told her guests proudly as they watched Ser Vardis try a practice cut. "He wore it whenever he sat the Iron Throne in King Robert's place. Isn't it a lovely thing? I thought it only fitting that our champion avenge Jon with his own blade."

The engraved silver blade was beautiful beyond a doubt, but it seemed to Catelyn that Ser Vardis might have been more comfortable with his own sword. Yet she said nothing; she was weary of futile arguments with her sister.

"Make them fight!" Lord Robert called out.

Ser Vardis faced the Lord of the Eyrie and lifted his sword in salute. "For the Eyrie and the Vale!"

Tyrion Lannister had been seated on a balcony across the garden, flanked by his guards. It was to him that Bronn turned with a cursory salute.

"They await your command," Lady Lysa said to her lord son.

"*Fight!*" the boy screamed, his arms trembling as they clutched at his chair.

Ser Vardis swiveled, bringing up his heavy shield. Bronn turned to face him. Their swords rang together, once, twice, a testing. The sellsword backed off a step. The knight came after, holding his shield before him. He tried a slash, but Bronn jerked back, just out of reach, and the silver blade cut only air. Bronn circled to his right. Ser Vardis turned to follow, keeping his shield between them. The knight pressed forward, placing each foot carefully on the uneven ground. The sellsword gave way, a faint smile playing over his lips. Ser Vardis attacked, slashing, but Bronn leapt away from him, hopping lightly over a low, moss-covered stone. Now the sellsword circled left, away from the shield, toward the knight's unprotected side. Ser Vardis tried a hack at his legs, but he did not have the reach. Bronn danced farther to his left. Ser Vardis turned in place.

"The man is craven," Lord Hunter declared. "Stand and fight, coward!" Other voices echoed the sentiment.

Catelyn looked to Ser Rodrik. Her master-at-arms gave a curt shake of his head. "He wants to make Ser Vardis chase him. The weight of armor and shield will tire even the strongest man."

She had seen men practice at their swordplay near every day of her life, had viewed half a hundred tourneys in her time, but this was something different and deadlier: a dance where the smallest misstep meant death. And as she watched, the memory of another duel in another time came back to Catelyn Stark, as vivid as if it had been yesterday.

They met in the lower bailey of Riverrun. When Brandon saw that Petyr wore only helm and breastplate and mail, he took off most of his armor. Petyr had begged her for a favor he might wear, but she had turned him away. Her lord father promised her to Brandon Stark, and so it was to him that she gave her token, a pale blue handscarf she had embroidered with the leaping trout of Riverrun.

As she pressed it into his hand, she pleaded with him. "He is only a foolish boy, but I have loved him like a brother. It would grieve me to see him die." And her betrothed looked at her with the cool grey eyes of a Stark and promised to spare the boy who loved her.

That fight was over almost as soon as it began. Brandon was a man grown, and he drove Littlefinger all the way across the bailey and down the water stair, raining steel on him with every step, until the boy was staggering and bleeding from a dozen wounds. "Yield!" he called, more than once, but Petyr would only shake his head and fight on, grimly. When the river was lapping at their ankles, Brandon finally ended it, with a brutal backhand cut that bit through Petyr's rings and leather into the soft flesh below the ribs, so deep that Catelyn was certain that the wound was mortal. He looked at her as he fell and murmured "Cat" as the bright blood came flowing out between his mailed fingers. She thought she had forgotten that.

That was the last time she had seen his face . . . until the day she was brought before him in King's Landing.

A fortnight passed before Littlefinger was strong enough to leave Riverrun, but her lord father forbade her to visit him in the tower where he lay abed. Lysa helped their maester nurse him; she had been softer and shyer in those days. Edmure had called on him as well, but Petyr had sent him away. Her brother had acted as Brandon's squire at the duel, and Littlefinger would not forgive that. As soon as he was strong enough to be moved, Lord Hoster Tully sent Petyr Baelish away in a closed litter, to finish his healing on the Fingers, upon the windswept jut of rock where he'd been born.

The ringing clash of steel on steel jarred Catelyn back to the present. Ser Vardis was coming hard at Bronn, driving into him with shield and sword. The sellsword scrambled backward, checking each blow, stepping lithely over rock and root, his eyes never leaving his foe. He was quicker, Catelyn saw; the knight's silvered sword never came near to touching him, but his own ugly grey blade hacked a notch from Ser Vardis's shoulder plate.

The brief flurry of fighting ended as swiftly as it had begun when Bronn sidestepped and slid behind the statue of the weeping woman. Ser Vardis lunged at where he had been, striking a spark off the pale marble of Alyssa's thigh.

"They're not fighting good, Mother," the Lord of the Eyrie complained. "I want them to *fight*."

"They will, sweet baby," his mother soothed him. "The sellsword can't run all day."

Some of the lords on Lysa's terrace were making wry jests as they refilled their wine cups, but across the garden, Tyrion Lannister's mismatched eyes watched the champions dance as if there were nothing else in the world.

Bronn came out from behind the statue hard and fast, still moving left, aiming a two-handed cut at the knight's unshielded right side. Ser Vardis blocked, but clumsily, and the sellsword's blade flashed upward at his head. Metal rang, and a falcon's wing collapsed with a crunch. Ser Vardis took a half step back to brace himself, raised his shield. Oak chips flew as Bronn's sword hacked at the wooden wall. The sellsword stepped left again, away from the shield, and caught Ser Vardis across the stomach, the razor edge of his blade leaving a bright gash when it bit into the knight's plate.

Ser Vardis drove forward off his back foot, his own silver blade descending in a savage arc. Bronn slammed it aside and danced away. The knight crashed into the weeping woman, rocking her on her plinth. Staggered, he stepped backward, his head turning this way and that as he searched for his foe. The slit visor of his helm narrowed his vision.

"Behind you, ser!" Lord Hunter shouted, too late. Bronn brought his sword down with both hands, catching Ser Vardis in the elbow of his sword arm. The thin lobstered metal that protected the joint *crunched*. The knight grunted, turning, wrenching his weapon up. This time Bronn stood his ground. The swords flew at each other, and their steel song filled the garden and rang off the white towers of the Eyrie.

"Ser Vardis is hurt," Ser Rodrik said, his voice grave.

Catelyn did not need to be told; she had eyes, she could see the bright finger of blood running along the knight's forearm, the wetness inside the elbow joint. Every parry was a little slower and a little lower than the one before. Ser Vardis turned his side to his foe, trying to use his shield to block instead, but Bronn slid around him, quick as a cat. The sellsword seemed to be getting stronger. His cuts were leaving their marks now. Deep shiny gashes gleamed all over the knight's armor, on his right thigh, his beaked visor, crossing on his breastplate, a long one along the front of his gorget. The moon-and-falcon rondel over Ser Vardis's right arm was sheared clean in half, hanging by its strap. They could hear his labored breath, rattling through the air holes in his visor.

Blind with arrogance as they were, even the knights and lords of the Vale could see what was happening below them, yet her sister could not. "Enough, Ser Vardis!" Lady Lysa called down. "Finish him now, my baby is growing tired."

And it must be said of Ser Vardis Egen that he was true to his lady's command, even to the last. One moment he was reeling backward, half-crouched behind his scarred shield; the next he charged. The sudden bull rush caught Bronn off balance. Ser Vardis crashed into him and slammed the lip of his shield into the sellsword's face. Almost, *almost*, Bronn lost his feet . . . he staggered back, tripped over a rock, and caught hold of the weeping woman to keep his balance. Throwing aside his shield, Ser Vardis lurched after him, using both hands to raise his sword. His right arm was blood from elbow to fingers now, yet his last desperate blow would have opened Bronn from neck to navel . . . if the sellsword had stood to receive it.

But Bronn jerked back. Jon Arryn's beautiful engraved silver sword glanced off the marble elbow of the weeping woman and snapped clean a third of the way up the blade. Bronn put his shoulder into the statue's back. The weathered likeness of Alyssa Arryn tottered and fell with a great crash, and Ser Vardis Egen went down beneath her.

Bronn was on him in a heartbeat, kicking what was left of his shattered rondel aside to expose the weak spot between arm and breastplate. Ser Vardis was lying on his side, pinned beneath the broken torso of the weeping woman. Catelyn heard the knight groan as the sellsword lifted his blade with both hands and drove it down and in with all his weight behind it, under the arm and through the ribs. Ser Vardis Egen shuddered and lay still.

Silence hung over the Eyrie. Bronn yanked off his

halfhelm and let it fall to the grass. His lip was smashed and bloody where the shield had caught him, and his coal-black hair was soaked with sweat. He spit out a broken tooth.

"Is it over, Mother?" the Lord of the Eyrie asked.

No, Catelyn wanted to tell him, *it's only now beginning.*

"Yes," Lysa said glumly, her voice as cold and dead as the captain of her guard.

"Can I make the little man fly now?"

Across the garden, Tyrion Lannister got to his feet. "Not *this* little man," he said. "This little man is going down in the turnip hoist, thank you very much."

"You presume—" Lysa began.

"I presume that House Arryn remembers its own words," the Imp said. *"As High as Honor."*

"You promised I could make him fly," the Lord of the Eyrie screamed at his mother. He began to shake.

Lady Lysa's face was flushed with fury. "The gods have seen fit to proclaim him innocent, child. We have no choice but to free him." She lifted her voice. "Guards. Take my lord of Lannister and his . . . *creature* here out of my sight. Escort them to the Bloody Gate and set them free. See that they have horses and supplies sufficient to reach the Trident, and make certain all their goods and weapons are returned to them. They shall need them on the high road."

"The high road," Tyrion Lannister said. Lysa allowed herself a faint, satisfied smile. It was another sort of death sentence, Catelyn realized. Tyrion Lannister must know that as well. Yet the dwarf favored Lady Arryn with a mocking bow. "As you command, my lady," he said. "I believe we know the way."

JON

"**Y**ou are as hopeless as any boys I have ever trained," Ser Alliser Thorne announced when they had all assembled in the yard. "Your hands were made for manure shovels, not for swords, and if it were up to me, the lot of you would be set to herding swine. But last night I was told that Gueren is marching five new boys up the kingsroad. One or two may even be worth the price of piss. To make room for them, I have decided to pass eight of you on to the Lord Commander to do with as he will." He called out the names one by one. "Toad. Stone Head. Aurochs. Lover. Pimple. Monkey. Ser Loon." Last, he looked at Jon. "And the Bastard."

Pyp let fly a *whoop* and thrust his sword into the air. Ser Alliser fixed him with a reptile stare. "They will call you men of Night's Watch now, but you are bigger fools than the Mummer's Monkey here if you believe that. You are boys still, green and stinking of summer, and when the winter comes you will die like flies." And with that, Ser Alliser Thorne took his leave of them.

The other boys gathered round the eight who had been named, laughing and cursing and offering congratulations. Halder smacked Toad on the butt with the flat of his sword and shouted, "Toad, of the Night's Watch!" Yelling that a black brother needed a horse, Pyp leapt onto Grenn's shoulders, and they tumbled to the ground, rolling and punching and hooting. Dareon dashed inside the armory and returned with a skin of sour red. As they passed the wine from hand to hand, grinning like fools, Jon noticed Samwell Tarly standing by himself beneath a bare dead tree in the corner of the yard. Jon offered him the skin. "A swallow of wine?"

Sam shook his head. "No thank you, Jon."

"Are you well?"

"Very well, truly," the fat boy lied. "I am so happy for you all." His round face quivered as he forced a smile. "You will be First Ranger someday, just as your uncle was."

"*Is*," Jon corrected. He would not accept that Benjen Stark was dead. Before he could say more, Halder cried, "Here, you planning to drink that all yourself?" Pyp snatched the skin from his hand and danced away, laughing. While Grenn seized his arm, Pyp gave the skin a squeeze, and a thin stream of red squirted Jon in the face. Halder howled in protest at the waste of good wine. Jon sputtered and struggled. Matthar and Jeren climbed the wall and began pelting them all with snowballs.

By the time he wrenched free, with snow in his hair and wine stains on his surcoat, Samwell Tarly had gone.

That night, Three-Finger Hobb cooked the boys a special meal to mark the occasion. When Jon arrived at the common hall, the Lord Steward himself led him to the bench near the fire. The older men clapped him on the arm in passing. The eight soon-to-be brothers feasted on rack of lamb baked in a crust of garlic and herbs, garnished with sprigs of mint, and surrounded by mashed yellow turnips swimming in butter. "From the Lord Commander's own table," Bowen Marsh told them. There were salads of spinach and chickpeas and turnip greens, and afterward bowls of iced blueberries and sweet cream.

"Do you think they'll keep us together?" Pyp wondered as they gorged themselves happily.

Toad made a face. "I hope not. I'm sick of looking at those ears of yours."

"Ho," said Pyp. "Listen to the crow call the raven

black. You're certain to be a ranger, Toad. They'll want you as far from the castle as they can. If Mance Rayder attacks, lift your visor and show your face, and he'll run off screaming."

Everyone laughed but Grenn. "I hope *I'm* a ranger."

"You and everyone else," said Matthar. Every man who wore the black walked the Wall, and every man was expected to take up steel in its defense, but the rangers were the true fighting heart of the Night's Watch. It was they who dared ride beyond the Wall, sweeping through the haunted forest and the icy mountain heights west of the Shadow Tower, fighting wildlings and giants and monstrous snow bears.

"Not everyone," said Halder. "It's the builders for me. What use would rangers be if the Wall fell down?"

The order of builders provided the masons and carpenters to repair keeps and towers, the miners to dig tunnels and crush stone for roads and footpaths, the woodsmen to clear away new growth wherever the forest pressed too close to the Wall. Once, it was said, they had quarried immense blocks of ice from frozen lakes deep in the haunted forest, dragging them south on sledges so the Wall might be raised ever higher. Those days were centuries gone, however; now, it was all they could do to ride the Wall from Eastwatch to the Shadow Tower, watching for cracks or signs of melt and making what repairs they could.

"The Old Bear's no fool," Dareon observed. "You're certain to be a builder, and Jon's certain to be a ranger. He's the best sword and the best rider among us, and his uncle was the First before he . . ." His voice trailed off awkwardly as he realized what he had almost said.

"Benjen Stark is still First Ranger," Jon Snow told him, toying with his bowl of blueberries. The rest might have given up all hope of his uncle's safe return, but not him. He pushed away the berries, scarcely touched, and rose from the bench.

"Aren't you going to eat those?" Toad asked.

"They're yours." Jon had hardly tasted Hobb's great feast. "I could not eat another bite." He took his cloak from its hook near the door and shouldered his way out.

Pyp followed him. "Jon, what is it?"

"Sam," he admitted. "He was not at table tonight."

"It's not like him to miss a meal," Pyp said thoughtfully. "Do you suppose he's taken ill?"

"He's frightened. We're leaving him." He remembered the day he had left Winterfell, all the bittersweet farewells; Bran lying broken, Robb with snow in his hair, Arya raining kisses on him after he'd given her Needle. "Once we say our words, we'll all have duties to attend to. Some of us may be sent away, to Eastwatch or the Shadow Tower. Sam will remain in training, with the likes of Rast and Cuger and these new boys who are coming up the kingsroad. Gods only know what they'll be like, but you can bet Ser Alliser will send them against him, first chance he gets."

Pyp made a grimace. "You did all you could."

"All we could wasn't enough," Jon said.

A deep restlessness was on him as he went back to Hardin's Tower for Ghost. The direwolf walked beside him to the stables. Some of the more skittish horses kicked at their stalls and laid back their ears as they entered. Jon saddled his mare, mounted, and rode out from Castle Black, south across the moonlit night. Ghost raced ahead of him, flying over the ground, gone in the blink of an eye. Jon let him go. A wolf needed to hunt.

He had no destination in mind. He wanted only to ride. He followed the creek for a time, listening to the icy trickle of water over rock, then cut across the fields to the kingsroad. It stretched out before him, narrow and stony and pocked with weeds, a road of no particular promise, yet the sight of it filled Jon Snow with a vast longing. Winterfell was down that road, and beyond it Riverrun and King's Landing and the Eyrie and so many other places; Casterly Rock, the Isles of Faces, the red mountains of Dorne, the hundred islands of Braavos in the sea, the smoking ruins of old Valyria. All the places that Jon would never see. The world was down that road . . . and he was here.

Once he swore his vow, the Wall would be his home until he was old as Maester Aemon. "I have not sworn yet," he muttered. He was no outlaw, bound to take the black or pay the penalty for his crimes. He had come here freely, and he might leave freely . . . until he said the words. He need only ride on, and he could leave it all behind. By the time the moon was full again, he would be back in Winterfell with his brothers.

Your *half* brothers, a voice inside reminded him. *And Lady Stark, who will not welcome you.* There was no place for him in Winterfell, no place in King's Landing either. Even his own mother had not had a place for him. The thought of her made him sad. He wondered who she had been, what she had looked like, why his father had left her. *Because she was a whore or an adulteress, fool. Something dark and dishonorable, or else why was Lord Eddard too ashamed to speak of her?*

Jon Snow turned away from the kingsroad to look behind him. The fires of Castle Black were hidden behind a hill, but the Wall was there, pale beneath the moon, vast and cold, running from horizon to horizon.

He wheeled his horse around and started for home.

Ghost returned as he crested a rise and saw the distant glow of lamplight from the Lord Commander's Tower. The direwolf's muzzle was red with blood as he trotted beside the horse. Jon found himself thinking of Samwell Tarly again on the ride back. By the time he reached the stables, he knew what he must do.

Maester Aemon's apartments were in a stout wooden keep below the rookery. Aged and frail, the maester shared his chambers with two of the younger stewards, who tended to his needs and helped him in his duties. The brothers joked that he had been given the two ugliest men in the Night's Watch; being blind, he was spared having to look at them. Clydas was short, bald, and chinless, with small pink eyes like a mole. Chett had a wen on his neck the size of a pigeon's egg, and a face red with boils and pimples. Perhaps that was why he always seemed so angry.

It was Chett who answered Jon's knock. "I need to speak to Maester Aemon," Jon told him.

"The maester is abed, as you should be. Come back on the morrow and maybe he'll see you." He began to shut the door.

Jon jammed it open with his boot. "I need to speak to him now. The morning will be too late."

Chett scowled. "The maester is not accustomed to being woken in the night. Do you know how old he is?"

"Old enough to treat visitors with more courtesy than

you," Jon said. "Give him my pardons. I would not disturb his rest if it were not important."

"And if I refuse?"

Jon had his boot wedged solidly in the door. "I can stand here all night if I must."

The black brother made a disgusted noise and opened the door to admit him. "Wait in the library. There's wood. Start a fire. I won't have the maester catching a chill on account of you."

Jon had the logs crackling merrily by the time Chett led in Maester Aemon. The old man was clad in his bed robe, but around his throat was the chain collar of his order. A maester did not remove it even to sleep. "The chair beside the fire would be pleasant," he said when he felt the warmth on his face. When he was settled comfortably, Chett covered his legs with a fur and went to stand by the door.

"I am sorry to have woken you, Maester," Jon Snow said.

"You did not wake me," Maester Aemon replied. "I find I need less sleep as I grow older, and I am grown very old. I often spend half the night with ghosts, remembering times fifty years past as if they were yesterday. The mystery of a midnight visitor is a welcome diversion. So tell me, Jon Snow, why have you come calling at this strange hour?"

"To ask that Samwell Tarly be taken from training and accepted as a brother of the Night's Watch."

"This is no concern of Maester Aemon," Chett complained.

"Our Lord Commander has given the training of recruits into the hands of Ser Alliser Thorne," the maester said gently. "Only he may say when a boy is ready to swear his vow, as you surely know. Why then come to me?"

"The Lord Commander listens to you," Jon told him. "And the wounded and the sick of the Night's Watch are in your charge."

"And is your friend Samwell wounded or sick?"

"He will be," Jon promised, "unless you help."

He told them all of it, even the part where he'd set Ghost at Rast's throat. Maester Aemon listened silently, blind eyes fixed on the fire, but Chett's face darkened with each word. "Without us to keep him safe, Sam will have no chance," Jon finished. "He's *hopeless* with a sword. My sister Arya could tear him apart, and she's not yet ten. If Ser Alliser makes him fight, it's only a matter of time before he's hurt or killed."

Chett could stand no more. "I've seen this fat boy in the common hall," he said. "He *is* a pig, and a hopeless craven as well, if what you say is true."

"Maybe it is so," Maester Aemon said. "Tell me, Chett, what would you have us do with such a boy?"

"Leave him where he is," Chett said. "The Wall is no place for the weak. Let him train until he is ready, no matter how many years that takes. Ser Alliser shall make a man of him or kill him, as the gods will."

"That's *stupid*," Jon said. He took a deep breath to gather his thoughts. "I remember once I asked Maester Luwin why he wore a chain around his throat."

Maester Aemon touched his own collar lightly, his bony, wrinkled finger stroking the heavy metal links. "Go on."

"He told me that a maester's collar is made of chain to remind him that he is sworn to serve," Jon said, remembering. "I asked why each link was a different metal. A silver chain would look much finer with his grey robes, I said. Maester Luwin laughed. A maester forges his chain with study, he told me. The different metals are each a different kind of learning, gold for the study of money and accounts, silver for healing, iron for warcraft. And he said there were other meanings as well. The collar is supposed to remind a maester of the realm he serves, isn't that so? Lords are gold and knights steel, but two links can't make a chain. You also need silver and iron and lead, tin and copper and bronze and all the rest, and those are farmers and smiths and merchants and the like. A chain needs all sorts of metals, and a land needs all sorts of people."

Maester Aemon smiled. "And so?"

"The Night's Watch needs all sorts too. Why else have rangers and stewards and builders? Lord Randyll couldn't make Sam a warrior, and Ser Alliser won't either. You can't hammer tin into iron, no matter how hard you beat it, but that doesn't mean tin is useless. Why shouldn't Sam be a steward?"

Chett gave an angry scowl. "*I'm* a steward. You think

it's easy work, fit for cowards? The order of stewards keeps the Watch alive. We hunt and farm, tend the horses, milk the cows, gather firewood, cook the meals. Who do you think makes your clothing? Who brings up supplies from the south? The stewards."

Maester Aemon was gentler. "Is your friend a hunter?"

"He hates hunting," Jon had to admit.

"Can he plow a field?" the maester asked. "Can he drive a wagon or sail a ship? Could he butcher a cow?"

"No."

Chett gave a nasty laugh. "I've seen what happens to soft lordlings when they're put to work. Set them to churning butter and their hands blister and bleed. Give them an axe to split logs, and they cut off their own foot."

"I know one thing Sam could do better than anyone."

"Yes?" Maester Aemon prompted.

Jon glanced warily at Chett, standing beside the door, his boils red and angry. "He could help you," he said quickly. "He can do sums, and he knows how to read and write. I know Chett can't read, and Clydas has weak eyes. Sam read every book in his father's library. He'd be good with the ravens too. Animals seem to like him. Ghost took to him straight off. There's a lot he could do, besides fighting. The Night's Watch needs every man. Why kill one, to no end? Make use of him instead."

Maester Aemon closed his eyes, and for a brief moment Jon was afraid that he had gone to sleep. Finally he said, "Maester Luwin taught you well, Jon Snow. Your mind is as deft as your blade, it would seem."

"Does that mean . . . ?"

"It means I shall think on what you have said," the maester told him firmly. "And now, I believe I am ready to sleep. Chett, show our young brother to the door."

TYRION

They had taken shelter beneath a copse of aspens just off the high road. Tyrion was gathering deadwood while their horses took water from a mountain stream. He stooped to pick up a splintered branch and examined it critically. "Will this do? I am not practiced at starting fires. Morrec did that for me."

"A *fire*?" Bronn said, spitting. "Are you so hungry to die, dwarf? Or have you taken leave of your senses? A fire will bring the clansmen down on us from miles around. I mean to survive this journey, Lannister."

"And how do you hope to do that?" Tyrion asked. He tucked the branch under his arm and poked around through the sparse undergrowth, looking for more. His back ached from the effort of bending; they had been riding since daybreak, when a stone-faced Ser Lyn Corbray had ushered them through the Bloody Gate and commanded them never to return.

"We have no chance of fighting our way back," Bronn said, "but two can cover more ground than ten, and attract less notice. The fewer days we spend in these mountains, the more like we are to reach the riverlands. Ride hard and fast, I say. Travel by night and hole up by day, avoid the road where we can, make no noise and light no fires."

Tyrion Lannister sighed. "A splendid plan, Bronn. Try it, as you like . . . and forgive me if I do not linger to bury you."

"You think to outlive *me*, dwarf?" The sellsword grinned. He had a dark gap in his smile where the edge of Ser Vardis Egen's shield had cracked a tooth in half.

Tyrion shrugged. "Riding hard and fast by night is a sure way to tumble down a mountain and crack your skull. I prefer to make my crossing slow and easy. I know you love the taste of horse, Bronn, but if our mounts die under us this time, we'll be trying to saddle shadowcats . . . and if truth be told, I think the clans will find us no matter what we do. Their eyes are all around us." He swept a gloved hand over the high, wind-carved crags that surrounded them.

Bronn grimaced. "Then we're dead men, Lannister."

"If so, I prefer to die comfortable," Tyrion replied. "We need a fire. The nights are cold up here, and hot food will warm our bellies and lift our spirits. Do you suppose there's any game to be had? Lady Lysa has kindly provided us with a veritable feast of salt beef, hard cheese, and stale bread, but I would hate to break a tooth so far from the nearest maester."

"I can find meat." Beneath a fall of black hair, Bronn's dark eyes regarded Tyrion suspiciously. "I should leave you here with your fool's fire. If I took your horse, I'd have twice the chance to make it through. What would you do then, dwarf?"

"Die, most like." Tyrion stooped to get another stick.

"You don't think I'd do it?"

"You'd do it in an instant, if it meant your life. You were quick enough to silence your friend Chiggen when he caught that arrow in his belly." Bronn had yanked back the man's head by the hair and driven the point of his dirk in under the ear, and afterward told Catelyn Stark that the other sellsword had died of his wound.

"He was good as dead," Bronn said, "and his moaning was bringing them down on us. Chiggen would have done the same for me . . . and he was no friend, only a man I rode with. Make no mistake, dwarf. I fought for you, but I do not love you."

"It was your blade I needed," Tyrion said, "not your love." He dumped his armful of wood on the ground.

Bronn grinned. "You're bold as any sellsword, I'll give you that. How did you know I'd take your part?"

"Know?" Tyrion squatted awkwardly on his stunted legs to build the fire. "I tossed the dice. Back at the inn, you and Chiggen helped take me captive. Why? The others saw it as their duty, for the honor of the lords they served, but not you two. You had no lord, no duty, and precious little honor, so why trouble to involve yourselves?" He took out his knife and whittled some thin strips of bark off one of the sticks he'd gathered, to serve as kindling. "Well, why do sellswords do anything? For gold. You were thinking Lady Catelyn would reward you for your help, perhaps even take you into her service. Here, that should do, I hope. Do you have a flint?"

Bronn slid two fingers into the pouch at his belt and tossed down a flint. Tyrion caught it in the air.

"My thanks," he said. "The thing is, you did not know the Starks. Lord Eddard is a proud, honorable, and honest man, and his lady wife is worse. Oh, no doubt she would have found a coin or two for you when this was all over, and pressed it in your hand with a polite word and a look of distaste, but that's the most you could have hoped for. The Starks look for courage and loyalty and honor in the men they choose to serve them, and if truth be told, you and Chiggen were lowborn scum." Tyrion struck the flint against his dagger, trying for a spark. Nothing.

Bronn snorted. "You have a bold tongue, little man. One day someone is like to cut it out and make you eat it."

"Everyone tells me that." Tyrion glanced up at the sellsword. "Did I offend you? My pardons . . . but you *are* scum, Bronn, make no mistake. Duty, honor, friendship, what's that to you? No, don't trouble yourself, we both know the answer. Still, you're not stupid. Once we reached the Vale, Lady Stark had no more need of you . . . but I did, and the one thing the Lannisters have never lacked for is gold. When the moment came to toss the dice, I was counting on your being smart enough to know where your best interest lay. Happily for me, you did." He slammed stone and steel together again, fruitlessly.

"Here," said Bronn, squatting, "I'll do it." He took the knife and flint from Tyrion's hands and struck sparks on his first try. A curl of bark began to smolder.

"Well done," Tyrion said. "Scum you may be, but you're undeniably useful, and with a sword in your hand you're almost as good as my brother Jaime. What do you want, Bronn? Gold? Land? Women? Keep me alive, and you'll have it."

Bronn blew gently on the fire, and the flames leapt up higher. "And if you die?"

"Why then, I'll have one mourner whose grief is sincere," Tyrion said, grinning. "The gold ends when I do."

The fire was blazing up nicely. Bronn stood, tucked the flint back into his pouch, and tossed Tyrion his dagger. "Fair enough," he said. "My sword's yours, then . . . but don't go looking for me to bend the knee and m'lord you every time you take a shit. I'm no man's toady."

"Nor any man's friend," Tyrion said. "I've no doubt you'd betray me as quick as you did Lady Stark, if you saw a profit in it. If the day ever comes when you're tempted to sell me out, remember this, Bronn—I'll match their price, whatever it is. I like living. And now, do you think you could do something about finding us some supper?"

"Take care of the horses," Bronn said, unsheathing the long dirk he wore at his hip. He strode into the trees.

An hour later the horses had been rubbed down and fed, the fire was crackling away merrily, and a haunch of a young goat was turning above the flames, spitting and hissing. "All we lack now is some good wine to wash down our kid," Tyrion said.

"That, a woman, and another dozen swords," Bronn said. He sat cross-legged beside the fire, honing the edge of his longsword with an oilstone. There was something strangely reassuring about the rasping sound it made when he drew it down the steel. "It will be full dark soon," the sellsword pointed out. "I'll take first watch . . . for all the good it will do us. It might be kinder to let them kill us in our sleep."

"Oh, I imagine they'll be here long before it comes to sleep." The smell of the roasting meat made Tyrion's mouth water.

Bronn watched him across the fire. "You have a plan," he said flatly, with a scrape of steel on stone.

"A hope, call it," Tyrion said. "Another toss of the dice."

"With our lives as the stake?"

Tyrion shrugged. "What choice do we have?" He leaned over the fire and sawed a thin slice of meat from the kid. "Ahhhh," he sighed happily as he chewed. Grease ran down his chin. "A bit tougher than I'd like, and in want of spicing, but I'll not complain too loudly. If I were back at the Eyrie, I'd be dancing on a precipice in hopes of a boiled bean."

"And yet you gave the turnkey a purse of gold," Bronn said.

"A Lannister always pays his debts."

Even Mord had scarcely believed it when Tyrion tossed him the leather purse. The gaoler's eyes had gone big as boiled eggs as he yanked open the drawstring and beheld the glint of gold. "I kept the silver," Tyrion had told him with a crooked smile, "but you were promised the gold, and there it is." It was more than a man like Mord could hope to earn in a lifetime of abusing prisoners. "And remember what I said, this is only a taste. If you ever grow tired of Lady Arryn's service, present yourself at Casterly Rock, and I'll pay you the rest of what I owe you." With golden dragons spilling out of both hands, Mord had fallen to his knees and promised that he would do just that.

Bronn yanked out his dirk and pulled the meat from the fire. He began to carve thick chunks of charred meat off the bone as Tyrion hollowed out two heels of stale bread to serve as trenchers. "If we do reach the river, what will you do then?" the sellsword asked as he cut.

"Oh, a whore and a featherbed and a flagon of wine, for a start." Tyrion held out his trencher, and Bronn filled it with meat. "And then to Casterly Rock or King's Landing, I think. I have some questions that want answering, concerning a certain dagger."

The sellsword chewed and swallowed. "So you were telling it true? It was not your knife?"

Tyrion smiled thinly. "Do I look a liar to you?"

By the time their bellies were full, the stars had come out and a half-moon was rising over the mountains. Tyrion spread his shadowskin cloak on the ground and stretched out with his saddle for a pillow. "Our friends are taking their sweet time."

"If I were them, I'd fear a trap," Bronn said. "Why else would we be so open, if not to lure them in?"

Tyrion chuckled. "Then we ought to sing and send them fleeing in terror." He began to whistle a tune.

"You're mad, dwarf," Bronn said as he cleaned the grease out from under his nails with his dirk.

"Where's your love of music, Bronn?"

"If it was music you wanted, you should have gotten the singer to champion you."

Tyrion grinned. "That would have been amusing. I can just see him fending off Ser Vardis with his woodharp." He resumed his whistling. "Do you know this song?" he asked.

"You hear it here and there, in inns and whorehouses."

"Myrish. 'The Seasons of My Love.' Sweet and sad, if you understand the words. The first girl I ever bedded used to sing it, and I've never been able to put it out of my head." Tyrion gazed up at the sky. It was a clear cold night and the stars shone down upon the mountains as bright and merciless as truth. "I met her on a night like this," he heard himself saying. "Jaime and I were riding back from Lannisport when we heard a scream, and she came running out into the road with two men dogging her heels, shouting threats. My brother unsheathed his sword and went after them, while I dismounted to protect the girl. She was scarcely a year older than I was, dark-haired, slender, with a face that would break your heart. It certainly broke mine. Lowborn, half-starved, unwashed . . . yet lovely. They'd torn the rags she was wearing half off her back, so I wrapped her in my cloak while Jaime chased the men into the woods. By the time he came trotting back, I'd gotten a name out of her, and a story. She was a crofter's child, orphaned when her father died of fever, on her way to . . . well, nowhere, really.

"Jaime was all in a lather to hunt down the men. It was not often outlaws dared prey on travelers so near to Casterly Rock, and he took it as an insult. The girl was too frightened to send off by herself, though, so I offered to take her to the closest inn and feed her while my brother rode back to the Rock for help.

"She was hungrier than I would have believed. We finished two whole chickens and part of a third, and drank a flagon of wine, talking. I was only thirteen, and the wine went to my head, I fear. The next thing I knew, I was sharing her bed. If she was shy, I was shyer. I'll never know where I found the courage. When I broke her maidenhead, she wept, but afterward she kissed me and sang her little song, and by morning I was in love."

"You?" Bronn's voice was amused.

"Absurd, isn't it?" Tyrion began to whistle the song again. "I married her," he finally admitted.

"A Lannister of Casterly Rock wed to a crofter's daughter," Bronn said. "How did you manage that?"

"Oh, you'd be astonished at what a boy can make of a few lies, fifty pieces of silver, and a drunken septon. I dared not bring my bride home to Casterly Rock, so I set her up in a cottage of her own, and for a fortnight we played at being man and wife. And then the septon sobered and confessed all to my lord father." Tyrion was surprised at how desolate it made him feel to say it, even after all these years. Perhaps he was just tired. "That was the end of my marriage." He sat up and stared at the dying fire, blinking at the light.

"He sent the girl away?"

"He did better than that," Tyrion said. "First he made my brother tell me the truth. The girl was a whore, you see. Jaime arranged the whole affair, the road, the outlaws, all of it. He thought it was time I had a woman. He paid double for a maiden, knowing it would be my first time.

"After Jaime had made his confession, to drive home the lesson, Lord Tywin brought my wife in and gave her to his guards. They paid her fair enough. A silver for each man, how many whores command that high a price? He sat me down in the corner of the barracks and bade me watch, and at the end she had so many silvers the coins were slipping through her fingers and rolling on the floor, she . . ." The smoke was stinging his eyes. Tyrion cleared his throat and turned away from the fire, to gaze out into darkness. "Lord Tywin had me go last," he said in a quiet voice. "And he gave me a gold coin to pay her, because I was a Lannister, and worth more."

After a time he heard the noise again, the rasp of steel on stone as Bronn sharpened his sword. "Thirteen or thirty or three, I would have killed the man who did that to me."

Tyrion swung around to face him. "You may get that chance one day. Remember what I told you. A Lannister always pays his debts." He yawned. "I think I will try and sleep. Wake me if we're about to die."

He rolled himself up in the shadowskin and shut his eyes. The ground was stony and cold, but after a time Tyrion Lannister did sleep. He dreamt of the sky cell. This time he was the gaoler, not the prisoner, *big,* with a strap in his hand, and he was hitting his father, driving him back, toward the abyss . . .

"Tyrion." Bronn's warning was low and urgent.

Tyrion was awake in the blink of an eye. The fire had burned down to embers, and the shadows were creeping in all around them. Bronn had raised himself to one knee, his sword in one hand and his dirk in the other. Tyrion held up a hand: *stay still,* it said. "Come share our fire, the night is cold," he called out to the creeping shadows. "I fear we've no wine to offer you, but you're welcome to some of our goat."

All movement stopped. Tyrion saw the glint of moonlight on metal. "Our mountain," a voice called out from the trees, deep and hard and unfriendly. "Our goat."

"Your goat," Tyrion agreed. "Who are you?"

"When you meet your gods," a different voice replied, "say it was Gunthor son of Gurn of the Stone Crows who sent you to them." A branch cracked underfoot as he stepped into the light; a thin man in a horned helmet, armed with a long knife.

"And Shagga son of Dolf." That was the first voice, deep and deadly. A boulder shifted to their left, and stood, and became a man. Massive and slow and strong he seemed, dressed all in skins, with a club in his right hand and an axe in his left. He smashed them together as he lumbered closer.

Other voices called other names, Conn and Torrek and Jaggot and more that Tyrion forgot the instant he heard them; ten at least. A few had swords and knives; others brandished pitchforks and scythes and wooden spears. He waited until they were done shouting out their names before he gave them answer. "I am Tyrion son of Tywin, of the Clan Lannister, the Lions of the Rock. We will gladly pay you for the goat we ate."

"What do you have to give us, Tyrion son of Tywin?" asked the one who named himself Gunthor, who seemed to be their chief.

"There is silver in my purse," Tyrion told them. "This hauberk I wear is large for me, but it should fit Conn nicely, and the battle-axe I carry would suit Shagga's mighty hand far better than that wood-axe he holds."

"The halfman would pay us with our own coin," said Conn.

"Conn speaks truly," Gunthor said. "Your silver is ours. Your horses are ours. Your hauberk and your battle-axe and the knife at your belt, those are ours too. You have nothing to give us but your lives. How would you like to die, Tyrion son of Tywin?"

"In my own bed, with a belly full of wine and a maiden's mouth around my cock, at the age of eighty," he replied.

The huge one, Shagga, laughed first and loudest. The others seemed less amused. "Conn, take their horses," Gunthor commanded. "Kill the other and seize the halfman. He can milk the goats and make the mothers laugh."

Bronn sprang to his feet. "Who dies first?"

"*No!*" Tyrion said sharply. "Gunthor son of Gurn, hear me. My House is rich and powerful. If the Stone Crows will see us safely through these mountains, my lord father will shower you with gold."

"The gold of a lowland lord is as worthless as a halfman's promises," Gunthor said.

"Half a man I may be," Tyrion said, "yet I have the courage to face my enemies. What do the Stone Crows do, but hide behind rocks and shiver with fear as the knights of the Vale ride by?"

Shagga gave a roar of anger and clashed club against axe. Jaggot poked at Tyrion's face with the fire-hardened point of a long wooden spear. He did his best not to flinch. "Are these the best weapons you could steal?" he said. "Good enough for killing sheep, perhaps . . . if the sheep do not fight back. My father's smiths shit better steel."

"Little boyman," Shagga roared, "will you mock my

axe after I chop off your manhood and feed it to the goats?"

But Gunthor raised a hand. "No. I would hear his words. The mothers go hungry, and steel fills more mouths than gold. What would you give us for your lives, Tyrion son of Tywin? Swords? Lances? Mail?"

"All that, and more, Gunthor son of Gurn," Tyrion Lannister replied, smiling. "I will give you the Vale of Arryn."

EDDARD

Through the high narrow windows of the Red Keep's cavernous throne room, the light of sunset spilled across the floor, laying dark red stripes upon the walls where the heads of dragons had once hung. Now the stone was covered with hunting tapestries, vivid with greens and browns and blues, and yet still it seemed to Ned Stark that the only color in the hall was the red of blood.

He sat high upon the immense ancient seat of Aegon the Conqueror, an ironwork monstrosity of spikes and jagged edges and grotesquely twisted metal. It was, as Robert had warned him, a hellishly uncomfortable chair, and never more so than now, with his shattered leg throbbing more sharply every minute. The metal beneath him had grown harder by the hour, and the fanged steel behind made it impossible to lean back. *A king should never sit easy*, Aegon the Conqueror had said, when he commanded his armorers to forge a great seat from the swords laid down by his enemies. *Damn Aegon for his arrogance*, Ned thought sullenly, *and damn Robert and his hunting as well.*

"You are quite certain these were more than brigands?" Varys asked softly from the council table beneath the throne. Grand Maester Pycelle stirred uneasily beside him, while Littlefinger toyed with a pen. They were the only councillors in attendance. A white hart had been sighted in the kingswood, and Lord Renly and Ser Barristan had joined the king to hunt it, along with Prince Joffrey, Sandor Clegane, Balon Swann, and half the court. So Ned must needs sit the Iron Throne in his absence.

At least he *could* sit. Save the council, the rest must stand respectfully, or kneel. The petitioners clustered near the tall doors, the knights and high lords and ladies beneath the tapestries, the smallfolk in the gallery, the mailed guards in their cloaks, gold or grey: all stood.

The villagers were kneeling: men, women, and children, alike tattered and bloody, their faces drawn by fear. The three knights who had brought them here to bear witness stood behind them.

"*Brigands*, Lord Varys?" Ser Raymun Darry's voice dripped scorn. "Oh, they were brigands, beyond a doubt. Lannister brigands."

Ned could feel the unease in the hall, as high lords and servants alike strained to listen. He could not pretend to surprise. The west had been a tinderbox since Catelyn had seized Tyrion Lannister. Both Riverrun and Casterly Rock had called their banners, and armies were massing in the pass below the Golden Tooth. It had only been a matter of time until the blood began to flow. The sole question that remained was how best to stanch the wound.

Sad-eyed Ser Karyl Vance, who would have been handsome but for the winestain birthmark that discolored his face, gestured at the kneeling villagers. "This is all the remains of the holdfast of Sherrer, Lord Eddard. The rest are dead, along with the people of Wendish Town and the Mummer's Ford."

"Rise," Ned commanded the villagers. He never trusted what a man told him from his knees. "All of you, up."

In ones and twos, the holdfast of Sherrer struggled to its feet. One ancient needed to be helped, and a young girl in a bloody dress stayed on her knees, staring blankly at Ser Arys Oakheart, who stood by the foot of the throne in the white armor of the Kingsguard, ready to protect and defend the king . . . or, Ned supposed, the King's Hand.

"Joss," Ser Raymun Darry said to a plump balding man in a brewer's apron. "Tell the Hand what happened at Sherrer."

Joss nodded. "If it please His Grace—"

"His Grace is hunting across the Blackwater," Ned said, wondering how a man could live his whole life a few days ride from the Red Keep and still have no notion what his king looked like. Ned was clad in a white linen doublet with the direwolf of Stark on the breast; his black wool cloak was fastened at the collar by his silver hand of office. Black and white and grey, all the shades of truth. "I am Lord Eddard Stark, the King's Hand. Tell me who you are and what you know of these raiders."

"I keep . . . I *kept* . . . I kept an alehouse, m'lord, in Sherrer, by the stone bridge. The finest ale south of the Neck, everyone said so, begging your pardons, m'lord. It's gone now like all the rest, m'lord. They come and drank their fill and spilled the rest before they fired my roof, and they would of spilled my blood too, if they'd caught me. M'lord."

"They burnt us out," a farmer beside him said. "Come riding in the dark, up from the south, and fired the fields and the houses alike, killing them as tried to stop them. They weren't no raiders, though, m'lord. They had no mind to steal our stock, not these, they butchered my milk cow where she stood and left her for the flies and the crows."

"They rode down my 'prentice boy," said a squat man with a smith's muscles and a bandage around his head. He had put on his finest clothes to come to court, but his breeches were patched, his cloak travel-stained and dusty. "Chased him back and forth across the fields on their horses, poking at him with their lances like it was a game, them laughing and the boy stumbling and screaming till the big one pierced him clean through."

The girl on her knees craned her head up at Ned, high above her on the throne. "They killed my mother too, Your Grace. And they . . . they . . ." Her voice trailed off, as if she had forgotten what she was about to say. She began to sob.

Ser Raymun Darry took up the tale. "At Wendish

Town, the people sought shelter in their holdfast, but the walls were timbered. The raiders piled straw against the wood and burnt them all alive. When the Wendish folk opened their gates to flee the fire, they shot them down with arrows as they came running out, even women with suckling babes."

"Oh, dreadful," murmured Varys. "How cruel can men be?"

"They would of done the same for us, but the Sherrer holdfast's made of stone," Joss said. "Some wanted to smoke us out, but the big one said there was riper fruit upriver, and they made for the Mummer's Ford."

Ned could feel cold steel against his fingers as he leaned forward. Between each finger was a blade, the points of twisted swords fanning out like talons from arms of the throne. Even after three centuries, some were still sharp enough to cut. The Iron Throne was full of traps for the unwary. The songs said it had taken a thousand blades to make it, heated white-hot in the furnace breath of Balerion the Black Dread. The hammering had taken fifty-nine days. The end of it was this hunched black beast made of razor edges and barbs and ribbons of sharp metal; a chair that could kill a man, and had, if the stories could be believed.

What Eddard Stark was doing sitting there he would never comprehend, yet there he sat, and these people looked to him for justice. "What proof do you have that these were Lannisters?" he asked, trying to keep his fury under control. "Did they wear crimson cloaks or fly a lion banner?"

"Even Lannisters are not so blind stupid as that," Ser Marq Piper snapped. He was a swaggering bantam rooster of a youth, too young and too hot-blooded for Ned's taste, though a fast friend of Catelyn's brother, Edmure Tully.

"Every man among them was mounted and mailed, my lord," Ser Karyl answered calmly. "They were armed with steel-tipped lances and longswords, with battle-axes for the butchering." He gestured toward one of the ragged survivors. "You. Yes, you, no one's going to hurt you. Tell the Hand what you told me."

The old man bobbed his head. "Concerning their horses," he said, "it were warhorses they rode. Many a year I worked in old Ser Willum's stables, so I knows the difference. Not a one of these ever pulled a plow, gods bear witness if I'm wrong."

"Well-mounted brigands," observed Littlefinger. "Perhaps they stole the horses from the last place they raided."

"How many men were there in this raiding party?" Ned asked.

"A hundred, at the least," Joss answered, in the same instant as the bandaged smith said, "Fifty," and the grandmother behind him, "Hunnerds and hunnerds, m'lord, an army they was."

"You are more right than you know, goodwoman," Lord Eddard told her. "You say they flew no banners. What of the armor they wore? Did any of you note ornaments or decorations, devices on shield or helm?"

The brewer, Joss, shook his head. "It grieves me, m'lord, but no, the armor they showed us was plain, only . . . the one who led them, he was armored like the rest, but there was no mistaking him all the same. It was the size of him, m'lord. Those as say the giants are all dead never saw this one, I swear. Big as an ox he was, and a voice like stone breaking."

"*The Mountain!*" Ser Marq said loudly. "Can any man doubt it? This was Gregor Clegane's work."

Ned heard muttering from beneath the windows and the far end of the hall. Even in the galley, nervous whispers were exchanged. High lords and smallfolk alike knew what it could mean if Ser Marq was proved right. Ser Gregor Clegane stood bannerman to Lord Tywin Lannister.

He studied the frightened faces of the villagers. Small wonder they had been so fearful; they had thought they were being dragged here to name Lord Tywin a red-handed butcher before a king who was his son by marriage. He wondered if the knights had given them a choice.

Grand Maester Pycelle rose ponderously from the council table, his chain of office clinking. "Ser Marq, with respect, you cannot know that this outlaw was Ser Gregor. There are many large men in the realm."

"As large as the Mountain That Rides?" Ser Karyl said. "I have never met one."

"Nor has any man here," Ser Raymun added hotly. "Even his brother is a pup beside him. My lords, open your eyes. Do you need to see his seal on the corpses? It was Gregor."

"Why should Ser Gregor turn brigand?" Pycelle asked. "By the grace of his liege lord, he holds a stout keep and lands of his own. The man is an anointed knight."

"A false knight!" Ser Marq said. "Lord Tywin's mad dog."

"My lord Hand," Pycelle declared in a stiff voice, "I urge you to remind this *good* knight that Lord Tywin Lannister is the father of our own gracious queen."

"Thank you, Grand Maester Pycelle," Ned said. "I fear we might have forgotten that if you had not pointed it out."

From his vantage point atop the throne, he could see men slipping out the door at the far end of the hall. Hares going to ground, he supposed . . . or rats off to nibble the queen's cheese. He caught a glimpse of Septa Mordane in the gallery, with his daughter Sansa beside her. Ned felt a flash of anger; this was no place for a girl. But the septa could not have known that today's court would be anything but the usual tedious business of hearing petitions, settling disputes between rival holdfasts, and adjudicating the placement of boundary stones.

At the council table below, Petyr Baelish lost interest in his quill and leaned forward. "Ser Marq, Ser Karyl, Ser Raymun—perhaps I might ask you a question? These holdfasts were under your protection. Where were you when all this slaughtering and burning was going on?"

Ser Karyl Vance answered. "I was attending my lord father in the pass below the Golden Tooth, as was Ser Marq. When the word of these outrages reached Ser Edmure Tully, he sent word that we should take a small force of men to find what survivors we could and bring them to the king."

Ser Raymun Darry spoke up. "Ser Edmure had summoned me to Riverrun with all my strength. I was camped across the river from his walls, awaiting his commands, when the word reached me. By the time I could return to my own lands, Clegane and his vermin were back across the Red Fork, riding for Lannister's hills."

Littlefinger stroked the point of his beard thoughtfully. "And if they come again, ser?"

"If they come again, we'll use their blood to water the fields they burnt," Ser Marq Piper declared hotly.

"Ser Edmure has sent men to every village and holdfast within a day's ride of the border," Ser Karyl explained. "The next raider will not have such an easy time of it."

And that may be precisely what Lord Tywin wants, Ned thought to himself, *to bleed off strength from Riverrun, goad the boy into scattering his swords.* His wife's brother was young, and more gallant than wise. He would try to hold every inch of his soil, to defend every man, woman, and child who named him lord, and Tywin Lannister was shrewd enough to know that.

"If your fields and holdfasts are safe from harm," Lord Petyr was saying, "what then do you ask of the throne?"

"The lords of the Trident keep the king's peace," Ser Raymun Darry said. "The Lannisters have broken it. We ask leave to answer them, steel for steel. We ask justice for the smallfolk of Sherrer and Wendish Town and the Mummer's Ford."

"Edmure agrees, we must pay Gregor Clegane back his bloody coin," Ser Marq declared, "but old Lord Hoster commanded us to come here and beg the king's leave before we strike."

Thank the gods for old Lord Hoster, then. Tywin Lannister was as much fox as lion. If indeed he'd sent Ser Gregor to burn and pillage—and Ned did not doubt that he had—he'd taken care to see that he rode under cover of night, without banners, in the guise of a common brigand. Should Riverrun strike back, Cersei and her father would insist that it had been the Tullys who broke the king's peace, not the Lannisters. The gods only knew what Robert would believe.

Grand Maester Pycelle was on his feet again. "My lord Hand, if these good folk believe that Ser Gregor has forsaken his holy vows for plunder and rape, let them go to his liege lord and make their complaint. These crimes are no concern of the throne. Let them seek Lord Tywin's justice."

"It is all the king's justice," Ned told him. "North, south, east, or west, all we do we do in Robert's name."

"The *king's* justice," Grand Maester Pycelle said. "So it is, and so we should defer this matter until the king—"

"The king is hunting across the river and may not return for days," Lord Eddard said. "Robert bid me to sit here in his place, to listen with his ears, and to speak with his voice. I mean to do just that . . . though I agree that he must be told." He saw a familiar face beneath the tapestries. "Ser Robar."

Ser Robar Royce stepped forward and bowed. "My lord."

"Your father is hunting with the king," Ned said. "Will you bring them word of what was said and done here today?"

"At once, my lord."

"Do we have your leave to take our vengeance against Ser Gregor, then?" Marq Piper asked the throne.

"Vengeance?" Ned said. "I thought we were speaking of justice. Burning Clegane's fields and slaughtering his people will not restore the king's peace, only your injured pride." He glanced away before the young knight could voice his outraged protest, and addressed the villagers. "People of Sherrer, I cannot give you back your homes or your crops, nor can I restore your dead to life. But perhaps I can give you some small measure of justice, in the name of our king, Robert."

Every eye in the hall was fixed on him, waiting. Slowly Ned struggled to his feet, pushing himself up from the throne with the strength of his arms, his shattered leg screaming inside its cast. He did his best to ignore the pain; it was no moment to let them see his weakness. "The First Men believed that the judge who called for death should wield the sword, and in the north we hold to that still. I mislike sending another to do my killing . . . yet it seems I have no choice." He gestured at his broken leg.

"Lord Eddard!" The shout came from the west side of the hall as a handsome stripling of a boy strode forth boldly. Out of his armor, Ser Loras Tyrell looked even younger than his sixteen years. He wore pale blue silk, his belt a linked chain of golden roses, the sigil of his House. "I beg you the honor of acting in your place. Give this task to me, my lord, and I swear I shall not fail you."

Littlefinger chuckled. "Ser Loras, if we send you off alone, Ser Gregor will send us back your head with a plum stuffed in that pretty mouth of yours. The Mountain is not the sort to bend his neck to any man's justice."

"I do not fear Gregor Clegane," Ser Loras said haughtily.

Ned eased himself slowly back onto the hard iron seat of Aegon's misshapen throne. His eyes searched the faces along the wall. "Lord Beric," he called out. "Thoros of Myr. Ser Gladden. Lord Lothar." The men named stepped forward one by one. "Each of you is to assemble twenty men, to bring my word to Gregor's keep. Twenty of my own guards shall go with you. Lord Beric Dondarrion, you shall have the command, as befits your rank."

The young lord with the red-gold hair bowed. "As you command, Lord Eddard."

Ned raised his voice, so it carried to the far end of the throne room. "In the name of Robert of the House Baratheon, the First of his Name, King of the Andals and the Rhoynar and the First Men, Lord of the Seven Kingdoms and Protector of the Realm, by the word of Eddard of the House Stark, his Hand, I charge you to ride to the westlands with all haste, to cross the Red Fork of the Trident under the king's flag, and there bring the king's justice to the false knight Gregor Clegane, and to all those who shared in his crimes. I denounce him, and attaint him, and strip him of all rank and titles, of all lands and incomes and holdings, and do sentence him to death. May the gods take pity on his soul."

When the echo of his words had died away, the Knight of Flowers seemed perplexed. "Lord Eddard, what of me?"

Ned looked down on him. From on high, Loras Tyrell seemed almost as young as Robb. "No one doubts your valor, Ser Loras, but we are about justice here, and what you seek is vengeance." He looked back to Lord Beric. "Ride at first light. These things are best done quickly." He held up a hand. "The throne will hear no more petitions today."

Alyn and Porther climbed the steep iron steps to help him back down. As they made their descent, he could feel Loras Tyrell's sullen stare, but the boy had stalked away before Ned reached the floor of the throne room.

At the base of the Iron Throne, Varys was gathering papers from the council table. Littlefinger and Grand Maester Pycelle had already taken their leave. "You are a bolder man than I, my lord," the eunuch said softly.

"How so, Lord Varys?" Ned asked brusquely. His leg was throbbing, and he was in no mood for word games.

"Had it been me up there, I should have sent Ser Loras. He *so* wanted to go . . . and a man who has the Lannisters for his enemies would do well to make the Tyrells his friends."

"Ser Loras is young," said Ned. "I daresay he will outgrow the disappointment."

"And Ser Ilyn?" The eunuch stroked a plump, powdered cheek. "He *is* the King's Justice, after all. Sending other men to do his office . . . some might construe that as a grave insult."

"No slight was intended." In truth, Ned did not trust the mute knight, though perhaps that was only because he misliked executioners. "I remind you, the Paynes are bannermen to House Lannister. I thought it best to choose men who owed Lord Tywin no fealty."

"Very prudent, no doubt," Varys said. "Still, I chanced to see Ser Ilyn in the back of the hall, staring at us with those pale eyes of his, and I must say, he did not look pleased, though to be sure it is hard to tell with our silent knight. I hope he outgrows his disappointment as well. He does so *love* his work . . ."

SANSA

"**H**e wouldn't send Ser Loras," Sansa told Jeyne Poole that night as they shared a cold supper by lamplight. "I think it was because of his leg."

Lord Eddard had taken his supper in his bedchamber with Alyn, Harwin, and Vayon Poole, the better to rest his broken leg, and Septa Mordane had complained of sore feet after standing in the gallery all day. Arya was supposed to join them, but she was late coming back from her dancing lesson.

"His leg?" Jeyne said uncertainly. She was a pretty, dark-haired girl of Sansa's own age. "Did Ser Loras hurt his leg?"

"Not *his* leg," Sansa said, nibbling delicately at a chicken leg. "*Father's* leg, silly. It hurts him ever so much, it makes him cross. Otherwise I'm certain he would have sent Ser Loras."

Her father's decision still bewildered her. When the Knight of Flowers had spoken up, she'd been sure she was about to see one of Old Nan's stories come to life. Ser Gregor was the monster and Ser Loras the true hero who would slay him. He even *looked* a true hero, so slim and beautiful, with golden roses around his slender waist and his rich brown hair tumbling down into his eyes. And then Father had *refused* him! It had upset her more than she could tell. She had said as much to Septa Mordane as they descended the stairs from the gallery, but the septa had only told her it was not her place to question her lord father's decisions.

That was when Lord Baelish had said, "Oh, I don't know, Septa. Some of her lord father's decisions could do with a bit of questioning. The young lady is as wise as she is lovely." He made a sweeping bow to Sansa, so deep she was not quite sure if she was being complimented or mocked.

Septa Mordane had been *very* upset to realize that Lord Baelish had overheard them. "The girl was just talking, my lord," she'd said. "Foolish chatter. She meant nothing by the comment."

Lord Baelish stroked his little pointed beard and said, "Nothing? Tell me, child, why would you have sent Ser Loras?"

Sansa had no choice but to explain about heroes and monsters. The king's councillor smiled. "Well, those are not the reasons I'd have given, but . . ." He had touched her cheek, his thumb lightly tracing the line of a cheekbone. "Life is not a song, sweetling. You may learn that one day to your sorrow."

Sansa did not feel like telling all that to Jeyne, however; it made her uneasy just to think back on it.

"Ser Ilyn's the King's Justice, not Ser Loras," Jeyne said. "Lord Eddard should have sent him."

Sansa shuddered. Every time she looked at Ser Ilyn Payne, she shivered. He made her feel as though something dead were slithering over her naked skin. "Ser Ilyn's almost like a *second* monster. I'm glad Father didn't pick him."

"Lord Beric is as much a hero as Ser Loras. He's ever so brave and gallant."

"I suppose," Sansa said doubtfully. Beric Dondarrion was handsome enough, but he was awfully *old*, almost twenty-two; the Knight of Flowers would have been much better. Of course, Jeyne had been in love with Lord Beric ever since she had first glimpsed him in the lists. Sansa thought she was being silly; Jeyne was only a steward's daughter, after all, and no matter how much she

mooned after him, Lord Beric would never look at someone so far beneath him, even if she hadn't been half his
age.

It would have been unkind to say so, however, so Sansa
took a sip of milk and changed the subject. "I had a dream
that Joffrey would be the one to take the white hart," she
said. It had been more of a wish, actually, but it sounded
better to call it a dream. Everyone knew that dreams were
prophetic. White harts were supposed to be very rare and
magical, and in her heart she knew her gallant prince was
worthier than his drunken father.

"A dream? Truly? Did Prince Joffrey just go up to it
and touch it with his bare hand and do it no harm?"

"No," Sansa said. "He shot it with a golden arrow and
brought it back for me." In the songs, the knights never
killed magical beasts, they just went up to them and
touched them and did them no harm, but she knew Joffrey liked hunting, especially the killing part. Only animals, though. Sansa was certain her prince had no part in
murdering Jory and those other poor men; that had been
his wicked uncle, the Kingslayer. She knew her father
was still angry about that, but it wasn't fair to blame Joff.
That would be like blaming her for something that Arya
had done.

"I saw your sister this afternoon," Jeyne blurted out, as
if she'd been reading Sansa's thoughts. "She was walking
through the stables on her hands. Why would she do a
thing like that?"

"I'm sure I don't know why Arya does anything."
Sansa hated stables, smelly places full of manure and
flies. Even when she went riding, she liked the boy to
saddle the horse and bring it to her in the yard. "Do you
want to hear about the court or not?"

"I do," Jeyne said.

"There was a black brother," Sansa said, "begging men
for the Wall, only he was kind of old and smelly." She
hadn't liked that at all. She had always imagined the
Night's Watch to be men like Uncle Benjen. In the songs,
they were called the black knights of the Wall. But this
man had been crookbacked and hideous, and he looked as
though he might have lice. If this was what the Night's
Watch was truly like, she felt sorry for her bastard half
brother, Jon. "Father asked if there were any knights in

the hall who would do honor to their houses by taking the
black, but no one came forward, so he gave this Yoren his
pick of the king's dungeons and sent him on his way. And
later these two brothers came before him, freeriders from
the Dornish Marches, and pledged their swords to the service of the king. Father accepted their oaths . . ."

Jeyne yawned. "Are there any lemon cakes?"

Sansa did not like being interrupted, but she had to
admit, lemon cakes sounded more interesting than most
of what had gone on in the throne room. "Let's see," she
said.

The kitchen yielded no lemon cakes, but they did find
half of a cold strawberry pie, and that was almost as good.
They ate it on the tower steps, giggling and gossiping and
sharing secrets, and Sansa went to bed that night feeling
almost as wicked as Arya.

The next morning she woke before first light and crept
sleepily to her window to watch Lord Beric form up his
men. They rode out as dawn was breaking over the city,
with three banners going before them; the crowned stag of
the king flew from the high staff, the direwolf of Stark
and Lord Beric's own forked lightning standard from
shorter poles. It was all so exciting, a song come to life;
the clatter of swords, the flicker of torchlight, banners
dancing in the wind, horses snorting and whinnying, the
golden glow of sunrise slanting through the bars of the
portcullis as it jerked upward. The Winterfell men looked
especially fine in their silvery mail and long grey cloaks.

Alyn carried the Stark banner. When she saw him rein
in beside Lord Beric to exchange words, it made Sansa feel
ever so proud. Alyn was handsomer than Jory had been;
he was going to be a knight one day.

The Tower of the Hand seemed so empty after they left
that Sansa was even pleased to see Arya when she went
down to break her fast. "Where is everyone?" her sister
wanted to know as she ripped the skin from a blood orange. "Did Father send them to hunt down Jaime Lannister?"

Sansa sighed. "They rode with Lord Beric, to behead
Ser Gregor Clegane." She turned to Septa Mordane, who
was eating porridge with a wooden spoon. "Septa, will
Lord Beric spike Ser Gregor's head on his own gate or

bring it back here for the king?" She and Jeyne Poole had been arguing over that last night.

The septa was horror-struck. "A lady does not discuss such things over her porridge. Where are your courtesies, Sansa? I swear, of late you've been near as bad as your sister."

"What did Gregor do?" Arya asked.

"He burned down a holdfast and murdered a lot of people, women and children too."

Arya screwed up her face in a scowl. "Jaime Lannister murdered Jory and Heward and Wyl, and the Hound murdered Mycah. Somebody should have beheaded *them*."

"It's not the same," Sansa said. "The Hound is Joffrey's sworn shield. Your butcher's boy attacked the prince."

"Liar," Arya said. Her hand clenched the blood orange so hard that red juice oozed between her fingers.

"Go ahead, call me all the names you want," Sansa said airily. "You won't dare when I'm married to Joffrey. You'll have to bow to me and call me Your Grace." She shrieked as Arya flung the orange across the table. It caught her in the middle of the forehead with a wet squish and plopped down into her lap.

"You have juice on your face, Your Grace," Arya said.

It was running down her nose and stinging her eyes. Sansa wiped it away with a napkin. When she saw what the fruit in her lap had done to her beautiful ivory silk dress, she shrieked again. "You're *horrible*," she screamed at her sister. "They should have killed *you* instead of Lady!"

Septa Mordane came lurching to her feet. "Your lord father will hear of this! Go to your chambers, at once. *At once!*"

"Me too?" Tears welled in Sansa's eyes. "That's not fair."

"The matter is not subject to discussion. Go!"

Sansa stalked away with her head up. She was to be a queen, and queens did not cry. At least not where people could see. When she reached her bedchamber, she barred the door and took off her dress. The blood orange had left a blotchy red stain on the silk. "I *hate* her!" she screamed. She balled up the dress and flung it into the cold hearth, on top of the ashes of last night's fire. When she saw that the stain had bled through onto her underskirt, she began to sob despite herself. She ripped off the rest of her clothes wildly, threw herself into bed, and cried herself back to sleep.

It was midday when Septa Mordane knocked upon her door. "Sansa. Your lord father will see you now."

Sansa sat up. "Lady," she whispered. For a moment it was as if the direwolf was there in the room, looking at her with those golden eyes, sad and knowing. She had been dreaming, she realized. Lady was with her, and they were running together, and . . . and . . . trying to remember was like trying to catch the rain with her fingers. The dream faded, and Lady was dead again.

"Sansa." The rap came again, sharply. "Do you hear me?"

"Yes, Septa," she called out. "Might I have a moment to dress, please?" Her eyes were red from crying, but she did her best to make herself beautiful.

Lord Eddard was bent over a huge leather-bound book when Septa Mordane marched her into the solar, his plaster-wrapped leg stiff beneath the table. "Come here, Sansa," he said, not unkindly, when the septa had gone for her sister. "Sit beside me." He closed the book.

Septa Mordane returned with Arya squirming in her grasp. Sansa had put on a lovely pale green damask gown and a look of remorse, but her sister was still wearing the ratty leathers and roughspun she'd worn at breakfast. "Here is the other one," the septa announced.

"My thanks, Septa Mordane. I would talk to my daughters alone, if you would be so kind." The septa bowed and left.

"Arya started it," Sansa said quickly, anxious to have the first word. "She called me a liar and threw an orange at me and spoiled my dress, the ivory silk, the one Queen Cersei gave me when I was betrothed to Prince Joffrey. She hates that I'm going to marry the prince. She tries to spoil *everything*, Father, she can't stand for anything to be beautiful or nice or splendid."

"*Enough*, Sansa." Lord Eddard's voice was sharp with impatience.

Arya raised her eyes. "I'm sorry, Father. I was wrong and I beg my sweet sister's forgiveness."

Sansa was so startled that for a moment she was

speechless. Finally she found her voice. "What about my dress?"

"Maybe . . . I could wash it," Arya said doubtfully.

"Washing won't do any good," Sansa said. "Not if you scrubbed all day and all night. The silk is *ruined.*"

"Then I'll . . . make you a new one," Arya said.

Sansa threw back her head in disdain. "*You?* You couldn't sew a dress fit to clean the pigsties."

Their father sighed. "I did not call you here to talk of dresses. I'm sending you both back to Winterfell."

For the second time Sansa found herself too stunned for words. She felt her eyes grow moist again.

"You *can't,*" Arya said.

"Please, Father," Sansa managed at last. "Please don't."

Eddard Stark favored his daughters with a tired smile. "At last we've found something you agree on."

"I didn't do anything wrong," Sansa pleaded with him. "I don't want to go back." She loved King's Landing; the pagaentry of the court, the high lords and ladies in their velvets and silks and gemstones, the great city with all its people. The tournament had been the most magical time of her whole life, and there was so much she had not seen yet, harvest feasts and masked balls and mummer shows. She could not bear the thought of losing it all. "Send Arya away, she started it, Father, I swear it. I'll be good, you'll see, just let me stay and I promise to be as fine and noble and courteous as the queen."

Father's mouth twitched strangely. "Sansa, I'm not sending you away for fighting, though the gods know I'm sick of you two squabbling. I want you back in Winterfell for your own safety. Three of my men were cut down like dogs not a league from where we sit, and what does Robert do? He goes *hunting.*"

Arya was chewing at her lip in that disgusting way she had. "Can we take Syrio back with us?"

"Who cares about your stupid *dancing master?*" Sansa flared. "Father, I only just now remembered, I *can't* go away, I'm to marry Prince Joffrey." She tried to smile bravely for him. "I love him, Father, I truly truly do, I love him as much as Queen Naerys loved Prince Aemon the Dragonknight, as much as Jonquil loved Ser Florian. I want to be his queen and have his babies."

"Sweet one," her father said gently, "listen to me. When you're old enough, I will make you a match with a high lord who's worthy of you, someone brave and gentle and strong. This match with Joffrey was a terrible mistake. That boy is no Prince Aemon, you must believe me."

"He *is!*" Sansa insisted. "I don't want someone brave and gentle, I want *him.* We'll be ever so happy, just like in the songs, you'll see. I'll give him a son with golden hair, and one day he'll be the king of all the realm, the greatest king that ever was, as brave as the wolf and as proud as the lion."

Arya made a face. "Not if Joffrey's his father," she said. "He's a liar and a craven and anyhow he's a stag, not a lion."

Sansa felt tears in her eyes. "He is *not!* He's not the least bit like that old drunken king," she screamed at her sister, forgetting herself in her grief.

Father looked at her strangely. *"Gods,"* he swore softly, "out of the mouth of babes . . ." He shouted for Septa Mordane. To the girls he said, "I am looking for a fast trading galley to take you home. These days, the sea is safer than the kingsroad. You will sail as soon as I can find a proper ship, with Septa Mordane and a complement of guards . . . and yes, with Syrio Forel, if he agrees to enter my service. But say nothing of this. It's better if no one knows of our plans. We'll talk again tomorrow."

Sansa cried as Septa Mordane marched them down the steps. They were going to take it all away; the tournaments and the court and her prince, everything, they were going to send her back to the bleak grey walls of Winterfell and lock her up forever. Her life was over before it had begun.

"Stop that weeping, child," Septa Mordane said sternly. "I am certain your lord father knows what is best for you."

"It won't be so bad, Sansa," Arya said. "We're going to sail on a galley. It will be an adventure, and then we'll be with Bran and Robb again, and Old Nan and Hodor and the rest." She touched her on the arm.

"Hodor!" Sansa yelled. "You ought to marry Hodor, you're just like him, stupid and hairy and ugly!" She wrenched away from her sister's hand, stormed into her bedchamber, and barred the door behind her.

EDDARD

"**P**ain is a gift from the gods, Lord Eddard," Grand Maester Pycelle told him. "It means the bone is knitting, the flesh healing itself. Be thankful."

"I will be thankful when my leg stops throbbing."

Pycelle set a stoppered flask on the table by the bed. "The milk of the poppy, for when the pain grows too onerous."

"I sleep too much already."

"Sleep is the great healer."

"I had hoped that was you."

Pycelle smiled wanly. "It is good to see you in such a fierce humor, my lord." He leaned close and lowered his voice. "There was a raven this morning, a letter for the queen from her lord father. I thought you had best know."

"Dark wings, dark words," Ned said grimly. "What of it?"

"Lord Tywin is greatly wroth about the men you sent after Ser Gregor Clegane," the maester confided. "I feared he would be. You will recall, I said as much in council."

"Let him be wroth," Ned said. Every time his leg throbbed, he remembered Jaime Lannister's smile, and Jory dead in his arms. "Let him write all the letters to the queen he likes. Lord Beric rides beneath the king's own banner. If Lord Tywin attempts to interfere with the king's justice, he will have Robert to answer to. The only thing His Grace enjoys more than hunting is making war on lords who defy him."

Pycelle pulled back, his maester's chain jangling. "As you say. I shall visit again on the morrow." The old man hurriedly gathered up his things and took his leave. Ned had little doubt that he was bound straight for the royal apartments, to whisper at the queen. *I thought you had best know,* indeed . . . as if Cersei had not instructed him to pass along her father's threats. He hoped his response rattled those perfect teeth of hers. Ned was not near as confident of Robert as he pretended, but there was no reason Cersei need know that.

When Pycelle was gone, Ned called for a cup of honeyed wine. That clouded the mind as well, yet not as badly. He needed to be able to think. A thousand times, he asked himself what Jon Arryn might have done, had he lived long enough to act on what he'd learned. Or perhaps he *had* acted, and died for it.

It was queer how sometimes a child's innocent eyes can see things that grown men are blind to. Someday, when Sansa was grown, he would have to tell her how she had made it all come clear for him. *He's not the least bit like that old drunken king,* she had declared, angry and unknowing, and the simple truth of it had twisted inside him, cold as death. *This was the sword that killed Jon Arryn,* Ned thought then, *and it will kill Robert as well, a slower death but full as certain.* Shattered legs may heal in time, but some betrayals fester and poison the soul.

Littlefinger came calling an hour after the Grand Maester had left, clad in a plum-colored doublet with a mockingbird embroidered on the breast in black thread, and a striped cloak of black and white. "I cannot visit long, my lord," he announced. "Lady Tanda expects me to lunch with her. No doubt she will roast me a fatted calf. If it's near as fatted as her daughter, I'm like to rupture and die. And how is your leg?"

"Inflamed and painful, with an itch that is driving me mad."

Littlefinger lifted an eyebrow. "In future, try not to let

any horses fall on it. I would urge you to heal quickly. The realm grows restive. Varys has heard ominous whispers from the west. Freeriders and sellswords have been flocking to Casterly Rock, and not for the thin pleasure of Lord Tywin's conversation."

"Is there word of the king?" Ned demanded. "Just how long does Robert intend to hunt?"

"Given his preferences, I believe he'd stay in the forest until you and the queen both die of old age," Lord Petyr replied with a faint smile. "Lacking that, I imagine he'll return as soon as he's killed something. They found the white hart, it seems . . . or rather, what remained of it. Some wolves found it first, and left His Grace scarcely more than a hoof and a horn. Robert was in a fury, until he heard talk of some monstrous boar deeper in the forest. Then nothing would do but he must have it. Prince Joffrey returned this morning, with the Royces, Ser Balon Swann, and some twenty others of the party. The rest are still with the king."

"The Hound?" Ned asked, frowning. Of all the Lannister party, Sandor Clegane was the one who concerned him the most, now that Ser Jaime had fled the city to join his father.

"Oh, returned with Joffrey, and went straight to the queen." Littlefinger smiled. "I would have given a hundred silver stags to have been a roach in the rushes when he learned that Lord Beric was off to behead his brother."

"Even a blind man could see the Hound loathed his brother."

"Ah, but Gregor was *his* to loathe, not yours to kill. Once Dondarrion lops the summit off our Mountain, the Clegane lands and incomes will pass to Sandor, but I wouldn't hold my water waiting for his thanks, not that one. And now you must forgive me. Lady Tanda awaits with her fatted calves."

On the way to the door, Lord Petyr spied Grand Maester Malleon's massive tome on the table and paused to idly flip open the cover. *"The Lineages and Histories of the Great Houses of the Seven Kingdoms, With Descriptions of Many High Lords and Noble Ladies and Their Children,"* he read. "Now there is tedious reading if ever I saw it. A sleeping potion, my lord?"

For a brief moment Ned considered telling him all of

it, but there was something in Littlefinger's japes that irked him. The man was too clever by half, a mocking smile never far from his lips. "Jon Arryn was studying this volume when he was taken sick," Ned said in a careful tone, to see how he might respond.

And he responded as he always did: with a quip. "In that case," he said, "death must have come as a blessed relief." Lord Petyr Baelish bowed and took his leave.

Eddard Stark allowed himself a curse. Aside from his own retainers, there was scarcely a man in this city he trusted. Littlefinger had concealed Catelyn and helped Ned in his inquiries, yet his haste to save his own skin when Jaime and his swords had come out of the rain still rankled. Varys was worse. For all his protestations of loyalty, the eunuch knew too much and did too little. Grand Maester Pycelle seemed more Cersei's creature with every passing day, and Ser Barristan was an old man, and rigid. He would tell Ned to do his duty.

Time was perilously short. The king would return from his hunt soon, and honor would require Ned to go to him with all he had learned. Vayon Poole had arranged for Sansa and Arya to sail on the *Wind Witch* out of Braavos, three days hence. They would be back at Winterfell before the harvest. Ned could no longer use his concern for their safety to excuse his delay.

Yet last night he had dreamt of Rhaegar's children. Lord Tywin had laid the bodies beneath the Iron Throne, wrapped in the crimson cloaks of his house guard. That was clever of him; the blood did not show so badly against the red cloth. The little princess had been barefoot, still dressed in her bed gown, and the boy . . . the boy . . .

Ned could not let that happen again. The realm could not withstand a second mad king, another dance of blood and vengeance. He must find some way to save the children.

Robert could be merciful. Ser Barristan was scarcely the only man he had pardoned. Grand Maester Pycelle, Varys the Spider, Lord Balon Greyjoy; each had been counted an enemy to Robert once, and each had been welcomed into friendship and allowed to retain honors and office for a pledge of fealty. So long as a man was brave and honest, Robert would treat him with all the honor and respect due a valiant enemy.

This was something else: poison in the dark, a knife thrust to the soul. This he could never forgive, no more than he had forgiven Rhaegar. *He will kill them all*, Ned realized.

And yet, he knew he could not keep silent. He had a duty to Robert, to the realm, to the shade of Jon Arryn . . . and to Bran, who surely must have stumbled on some part of the truth. Why else would they have tried to slay him?

Late that afternoon he summoned Tomard, the portly guardsman with the ginger-colored whiskers his children called Fat Tom. With Jory dead and Alyn gone, Fat Tom had command of his household guard. The thought filled Ned with vague disquiet. Tomard was a solid man; affable, loyal, tireless, capable in a limited way, but he was near fifty, and even in his youth he had never been energetic. Perhaps Ned should not have been so quick to send off half his guard, and all his best swords among them.

"I shall require your help," Ned said when Tomard appeared, looking faintly apprehensive, as he always did when called before his lord. "Take me to the godswood."

"Is that wise, Lord Eddard? With your leg and all?"

"Perhaps not. But necessary."

Tomard summoned Varly. With one arm around each man's shoulders, Ned managed to descend the steep tower steps and hobble across the bailey. "I want the guard doubled," he told Fat Tom. "No one enters or leaves the Tower of the Hand without my leave."

Tom blinked. "M'lord, with Alyn and the others away, we are hard-pressed already—"

"It will only be a short while. Lengthen the watches."

"As you say, m'lord," Tom answered. "Might I ask why—"

"Best not," Ned answered crisply.

The godswood was empty, as it always was here in this citadel of the southron gods. Ned's leg was screaming as they lowered him to the grass beside the heart tree. "Thank you." He drew a paper from his sleeve, sealed with the sigil of his House. "Kindly deliver this at once."

Tomard looked at the name Ned had written on the paper and licked his lips anxiously. "My lord . . ."

"Do as I bid you, Tom," Ned said.

How long he waited in the quiet of the godswood, he

could not say. It was peaceful here. The thick walls shut out the clamor of the castle, and he could hear birds singing, the murmur of crickets, leaves rustling in a gentle wind. The heart tree was an oak, brown and faceless, yet Ned Stark still felt the presence of his gods. His leg did not seem to hurt so much.

She came to him at sunset, as the clouds reddened above the walls and towers. She came alone, as he had bid her. For once she was dressed simply, in leather boots and hunting greens. When she drew back the hood of her brown cloak, he saw the bruise where the king had struck her. The angry plum color had faded to yellow, and the swelling was down, but there was no mistaking it for anything but what it was.

"Why here?" Cersei Lannister asked as she stood over him.

"So the gods can see."

She sat beside him on the grass. Her every move was graceful. Her curling blond hair moved in the wind, and her eyes were green as the leaves of summer. It had been a long time since Ned Stark had seen her beauty, but he saw it now. "I know the truth Jon Arryn died for," he told her.

"Do you?" The queen watched his face, wary as a cat. "Is that why you called me here, Lord Stark? To pose me riddles? Or is it your intent to seize me, as your wife seized my brother?"

"If you truly believed that, you would never have come." Ned touched her cheek gently. "Has he done this before?"

"Once or twice." She shied away from his hand. "Never on the face before. Jaime would have killed him, even if it meant his own life." Cersei looked at him defiantly. "My brother is worth a hundred of your friend."

"Your brother?" Ned said. "Or your lover?"

"Both." She did not flinch from the truth. "Since we were children together. And why not? The Targaryens wed brother to sister for three hundred years, to keep the bloodlines pure. And Jaime and I are more than brother and sister. We are one person in two bodies. We shared a womb together. He came into this world holding my foot, our old maester said. When he is in me, I feel . . . whole." The ghost of a smile flitted over her lips.

"My son Bran . . ."

To her credit, Cersei did not look away. "He saw us. You love your children, do you not?"

Robert had asked him the very same question, the morning of the melee. He gave her the same answer. "With all my heart."

"No less do I love mine."

Ned thought, *If it came to that, the life of some child I did not know, against Robb and Sansa and Arya and Bran and Rickon, what would I do? Even more so, what would* Catelyn *do, if it were Jon's life, against the children of her body?* He did not know. He prayed he never would.

"All three are Jaime's," he said. It was not a question.

"Thank the gods."

The seed is strong, Jon Arryn had cried on his deathbed, and so it was. All those bastards, all with hair as black as night. Grand Maester Malleon recorded the last mating between stag and lion, some ninety years ago, when Tya Lannister wed Gowen Baratheon, third son of the reigning lord. Their only issue, an unnamed boy described in Malleon's tome as a *large and lusty lad born with a full head of black hair,* died in infancy. Thirty years before that a male Lannister had taken a Baratheon maid to wife. She had given him three daughters and a son, each black-haired. No matter how far back Ned searched in the brittle yellowed pages, always he found the gold yielding before the coal.

"A dozen years," Ned said. "How is it that you have had no children by the king?"

She lifted her head, defiant. "Your Robert got me with child once," she said, her voice thick with contempt. "My brother found a woman to cleanse me. He never knew. If truth be told, I can scarcely bear for him to touch me, and I have not let him inside me for years. I know other ways to pleasure him, when he leaves his whores long enough to stagger up to my bedchamber. Whatever we do, the king is usually so drunk that he's forgotten it all by the next morning."

How could they have all been so blind? The truth was there in front of them all the time, written on the children's faces. Ned felt sick. "I remember Robert as he was the day he took the throne, every inch a king," he said quietly. "A thousand other women might have loved him with all their hearts. What did he do to make you hate him so?"

Her eyes burned, green fire in the dusk, like the lioness that was her sigil. "The night of our wedding feast, the first time we shared a bed, he called me by your sister's name. He was on top of me, *in* me, stinking of wine, and he whispered *Lyanna*."

Ned Stark thought of pale blue roses, and for a moment he wanted to weep. "I do not know which of you I pity most."

The queen seemed amused by that. "Save your pity for yourself, Lord Stark. I want none of it."

"You know what I must do."

"*Must?*" She put her hand on his good leg, just above the knee. "A true man does what he will, not what he must." Her fingers brushed lightly against his thigh, the gentlest of promises. "The realm needs a strong Hand. Joff will not come of age for years. No one wants war again, least of all me." Her hand touched his face, his hair. "If friends can turn to enemies, enemies can become friends. Your wife is a thousand leagues away, and my brother has fled. Be kind to me, Ned. I swear to you, you shall never regret it."

"Did you make the same offer to Jon Arryn?"

She slapped him.

"I shall wear that as a badge of honor," Ned said dryly.

"*Honor*," she spat. "How dare you play the noble lord with me! What do you take me for? You've a bastard of your own, I've seen him. Who was the mother, I wonder? Some Dornish peasant you raped while her holdfast burned? A whore? Or was it the grieving sister, the Lady Ashara? She threw herself into the sea, I'm told. Why was that? For the brother you slew, or the child you stole? Tell me, my *honorable* Lord Eddard, how are you any different from Robert, or me, or Jaime?"

"For a start," said Ned, "I do not kill children. You would do well to listen, my lady. I shall say this only once. When the king returns from his hunt, I intend to lay the truth before him. You must be gone by then. You and your children, all three, and not to Casterly Rock. If I were you, I should take ship for the Free Cities, or even farther, to the Summer Isles or the Port of Ibben. As far as the winds blow."

"Exile," she said. "A bitter cup to drink from."

"A sweeter cup than your father served Rhaegar's children," Ned said, "and kinder than you deserve. Your father and your brothers would do well to go with you. Lord Tywin's gold will buy you comfort and hire swords to keep you safe. You shall need them. I promise you, no matter where you flee, Robert's wrath will follow you, to the back of beyond if need be."

The queen stood. "And what of my wrath, Lord Stark?" she asked softly. Her eyes searched his face. "You should have taken the realm for yourself. It was there for the taking. Jaime told me how you found him on the Iron Throne the day King's Landing fell, and made him yield it up. That was your moment. All you needed to do was climb those steps, and sit. Such a sad mistake."

"I have made more mistakes than you can possibly imagine," Ned said, "but that was not one of them."

"Oh, but it was, my lord," Cersei insisted. "When you play the game of thrones, you win or you die. There is no middle ground."

She turned up her hood to hide her swollen face and left him there in the dark beneath the oak, amidst the quiet of the godswood, under a blue-black sky. The stars were coming out.

DAENERYS

The heart was steaming in the cool evening air when Khal Drogo set it before her, raw and bloody. His arms were red to the elbow. Behind him, his bloodriders knelt on the sand beside the corpse of the wild stallion, stone knives in their hands. The stallion's blood looked black in the flickering orange glare of the torches that ringed the high chalk walls of the pit.

Dany touched the soft swell of her belly. Sweat beaded her skin and trickled down her brow. She could feel the old women watching her, the ancient crones of Vaes Dothrak, with eyes that shone dark as polished flint in their wrinkled faces. She must not flinch or look afraid. *I am the blood of the dragon*, she told herself as she took the stallion's heart in both hands, lifted it to her mouth, and plunged her teeth into the tough, stringy flesh.

Warm blood filled her mouth and ran down over her chin. The taste threatened to gag her, but she made herself chew and swallow. The heart of a stallion would make her son strong and swift and fearless, or so the Dothraki believed, but only if the mother could eat it all. If she choked on the blood or retched up the flesh, the omens were less favorable; the child might be stillborn, or come forth weak, deformed, or female.

Her handmaids had helped her ready herself for the ceremony. Despite the tender mother's stomach that had afflicted her these past two moons, Dany had dined on bowls of half-clotted blood to accustom herself to the taste, and Irri made her chew strips of dried horseflesh until her jaws were aching. She had starved herself for a day and a night before the ceremony in the hopes that hunger would help her keep down the raw meat.

The wild stallion's heart was all muscle, and Dany had to worry it with her teeth and chew each mouthful a long time. No steel was permitted within the sacred confines of Vaes Dothrak, beneath the shadow of the Mother of Mountains; she had to rip the heart apart with teeth and nails. Her stomach roiled and heaved, yet she kept on, her face smeared with the heartsblood that sometimes seemed to explode against her lips.

Khal Drogo stood over her as she ate, his face as hard as a bronze shield. His long black braid was shiny with oil. He wore gold rings in his mustache, gold bells in his braid, and a heavy belt of solid gold medallions around his waist, but his chest was bare. She looked at him whenever she felt her strength failing; looked at him, and chewed and swallowed, chewed and swallowed, chewed and swallowed. Toward the end, Dany thought she glimpsed a fierce pride in his dark, almond-shaped eyes, but she could not be sure. The *khal's* face did not often betray the thoughts within.

And finally it was done. Her cheeks and fingers were sticky as she forced down the last of it. Only then did she turn her eyes back to the old women, the crones of the *dosh khaleen.*

"Khalakka dothrae mr'anha!" she proclaimed in her best Dothraki. *A prince rides inside me!* She had practiced the phrase for days with her handmaid Jhiqui.

The oldest of the crones, a bent and shriveled stick of a woman with a single black eye, raised her arms on high. *"Khalakka dothrae!"* she shrieked. *The prince is riding!*

"He is riding!" the other women answered. *"Rakh! Rakh! Rakh haj!"* they proclaimed. *A boy, a boy, a strong boy.*

Bells rang, a sudden clangor of bronze birds. A deep-throated warhorn sounded its long low note. The old women began to chant. Underneath their painted leather vests, their withered dugs swayed back and forth, shiny with oil and sweat. The eunuchs who served them threw bundles of dried grasses into a great bronze brazier, and clouds of fragrant smoke rose up toward the moon and the stars. The Dothraki believed the stars were horses made of fire, a great herd that galloped across the sky by night.

As the smoke ascended, the chanting died away and the ancient crone closed her single eye, the better to peer into the future. The silence that fell was complete. Dany could hear the distant call of night birds, the hiss and crackle of the torches, the gentle lapping of water from the lake. The Dothraki stared at her with eyes of night, waiting.

Khal Drogo laid his hand on Dany's arm. She could feel the tension in his fingers. Even a *khal* as mighty as Drogo could know fear when the *dosh khaleen* peered into smoke of the future. At her back, her handmaids fluttered anxiously.

Finally the crone opened her eye and lifted her arms. "I have seen his face, and heard the thunder of his hooves," she proclaimed in a thin, wavery voice.

"The thunder of his hooves!" the others chorused.

"As swift as the wind he rides, and behind him his *khalasar* covers the earth, men without number, with *arakhs* shining in their hands like blades of razor grass. Fierce as a storm this prince will be. His enemies will tremble before him, and their wives will weep tears of blood and rend their flesh in grief. The bells in his hair will sing his coming, and the milk men in the stone tents will fear his name." The old woman trembled and looked at Dany almost as if she were afraid. "The prince is riding, and he shall be the stallion who mounts the world."

"The stallion who mounts the world!" the onlookers cried in echo, until the night rang to the sound of their voices.

The one-eyed crone peered at Dany. "What shall he be called, the stallion who mounts the world?"

She stood to answer. "He shall be called Rhaego," she said, using the words that Jhiqui had taught her. Her hands touched the swell beneath her breasts protectively as a roar went up from the Dothraki. *"Rhaego,"* they screamed. *"Rhaego, Rhaego, Rhaego!"*

The name was still ringing in her ears as Khal Drogo led her from the pit. His bloodriders fell in behind them. A procession followed them out onto the godsway, the broad grassy road that ran through the heart of Vaes Dothrak, from the horse gate to the Mother of Mountains. The crones of the *dosh khaleen* came first, with their eunuchs and slaves. Some supported themselves with tall carved staffs as they struggled along on ancient, shaking legs, while others walked as proud as any horselord. Each of the old women had been a *khaleesi* once. When their lord husbands died and a new *khal* took his place at the front of his riders, with a new *khaleesi* mounted beside him, they were sent here, to reign over the vast Dothraki nation. Even the mightiest of *khals* bowed to the wisdom and authority of the *dosh khaleen*. Still, it gave Dany the shivers to think that one day she might be sent to join them, whether she willed it or no.

Behind the wise women came the others; Khal Ogo and his son, the *khalakka* Fogo, Khal Jommo and his wives, the chief men of Drogo's *khalasar*, Dany's handmaids, the *khal*'s servants and slaves, and more. Bells rang and drums beat a stately cadence as they marched along the godsway. Stolen heroes and the gods of dead peoples brooded in the darkness beyond the road. Alongside the procession, slaves ran lightly through the grass with torches in their hands, and the flickering flames made the great monuments seem almost alive.

"What is meaning, name Rhaego?" Khal Drogo asked as they walked, using the Common Tongue of the Seven Kingdoms. She had been teaching him a few words when she could. Drogo was quick to learn when he put his mind to it, though his accent was so thick and barbarous that neither Ser Jorah nor Viserys could understand a word he said.

"My brother Rhaegar was a fierce warrior, my sun-and-stars," she told him. "He died before I was born. Ser Jorah says that he was the last of the dragons."

Khal Drogo looked down at her. His face was a copper mask, yet under the long black mustache, drooping beneath the weight of its gold rings, she thought she glimpsed the shadow of a smile. "Is good name, Dan Ares wife, moon of my life," he said.

They rode to the lake the Dothraki called the Womb of the World, surrounded by a fringe of reeds, its water still and calm. A thousand thousand years ago, Jhiqui told her, the first man had emerged from its depths, riding upon the back of the first horse.

The procession waited on the grassy shore as Dany stripped and let her soiled clothing fall to the ground. Naked, she stepped gingerly into the water. Irri said the lake had no bottom, but Dany felt soft mud squishing between her toes as she pushed through the tall reeds. The moon floated on the still black waters, shattering and re-forming as her ripples washed over it. Goose pimples rose on her pale skin as the coldness crept up her thighs and kissed her lower lips. The stallion's blood had dried on her hands and around her mouth. Dany cupped her fingers and lifted the sacred waters over her head, cleansing herself and the child inside her while the *khal* and the others looked on. She heard the old women of the *dosh khaleen* muttering to each other as they watched, and wondered what they were saying.

When she emerged from the lake, shivering and dripping, her handmaid Doreah hurried to her with a robe of painted sandsilk, but Khal Drogo waved her away. He was looking on her swollen breasts and the curve of her belly with approval, and Dany could see the shape of his manhood pressing through his horsehide trousers, below the heavy gold medallions of his belt. She went to him and helped him unlace. Then her huge *khal* took her by the hips and lifted her into the air, as he might lift a child. The bells in his hair rang softly.

Dany wrapped her arms around his shoulders and pressed her face against his neck as he thrust himself inside her. Three quick strokes and it was done. *"The stallion who mounts the world,"* Drogo whispered hoarsely. His hands still smelled of horse blood. He bit at her throat, hard, in the moment of his pleasure, and when he lifted her off, his seed filled her and trickled down the inside of her thighs. Only then was Doreah permitted to drape her in the scented sandsilk, and Irri to fit soft slippers to her feet.

Khal Drogo laced himself up and spoke a command,

and horses were brought to the lakeshore. Cohollo had the honor of helping the *khaleesi* onto her silver. Drogo spurred his stallion, and set off down the godsway beneath the moon and stars. On her silver, Dany easily kept pace.

The silk tenting that roofed Khal Drogo's hall had been rolled up tonight, and the moon followed them inside. Flames leapt ten feet in the air from three huge stone-lined firepits. The air was thick with the smells of roasting meat and curdled, fermented mare's milk. The hall was crowded and noisy when they entered, the cushions packed with those whose rank and name were not sufficient to allow them at the ceremony. As Dany rode beneath the arched entry and up the center aisle, every eye was on her. The Dothraki screamed out comments on her belly and her breasts, hailing the life within her. She could not understand all they shouted, but one phrase came clear. *"The stallion that mounts the world,"* she heard, bellowed in a thousand voices.

The sounds of drums and horns swirled up into the night. Half-clothed women spun and danced on the low tables, amid joints of meat and platters piled high with plums and dates and pomegranates. Many of the men were drunk on clotted mare's milk, yet Dany knew no *arakh* would clash tonight, not here in the sacred city, where blades and bloodshed were forbidden.

Khal Drogo dismounted and took his place on the high bench. Khal Jommo and Khal Ogo, who had been in Vaes Dothrak with their *khalasars* when they arrived, were given seats of high honor to Drogo's right and left. The bloodriders of the three *khals* sat below them, and farther down Khal Jommo's four wives.

Dany climbed off her silver and gave the reins to one of the slaves. As Doreah and Irri arranged her cushions, she searched for her brother. Even across the length of the crowded hall, Viserys should have been conspicuous with his pale skin, silvery hair, and beggar's rags, but she did not see him anywhere.

Her glance roamed the crowded tables near the walls, where men whose braids were even shorter than their manhoods sat on frayed rugs and flat cushions around the low tables, but all the faces she saw had black eyes and copper skin. She spied Ser Jorah Mormont near the center of the hall, close to the middle firepit. It was a place of respect, if not high honor; the Dothraki esteemed the knight's prowess with a sword. Dany sent Jhiqui to bring him to her table. Mormont came at once, and went to one knee before her. *"Khaleesi,"* he said, "I am yours to command."

She patted the stuffed horsehide cushion beside her. "Sit and talk with me."

"You honor me." The knight seated himself cross-legged on the cushion. A slave knelt before him, offering a wooden platter full of ripe figs. Ser Jorah took one and bit it in half.

"Where is my brother?" Dany asked. "He ought to have come by now, for the feast."

"I saw His Grace this morning," he told her. "He told me he was going to the Western Market, in search of wine."

"Wine?" Dany said doubtfully. Viserys could not abide the taste of the fermented mare's milk the Dothraki drank, she knew that, and he was oft at the bazaars these days, drinking with the traders who came in the great caravans from east and west. He seemed to find their company more congenial than hers.

"Wine," Ser Jorah confirmed, "and he has some thought to recruit men for his army from the sellswords who guard the caravans." A serving girl laid a blood pie in front of him, and he attacked it with both hands.

"Is that wise?" she asked. "He has no gold to pay soldiers. What if he's betrayed?" Caravan guards were seldom troubled much by thoughts of honor, and the Usurper in King's Landing would pay well for her brother's head. "You ought to have gone with him, to keep him safe. You are his sworn sword."

"We are in Vaes Dothrak," he reminded her. "No one may carry a blade here or shed a man's blood."

"Yet men die," she said. "Jhogo told me. Some of the traders have eunuchs with them, huge men who strangle thieves with wisps of silk. That way no blood is shed and the gods are not angered."

"Then let us hope your brother will be wise enough not to steal anything." Ser Jorah wiped the grease off his mouth with the back of his hand and leaned close over the table. "He had planned to take your dragon's eggs, until I warned him that I'd cut off his hand if he so much as touched them."

For a moment Dany was so shocked she had no words. "My eggs . . . but they're *mine*, Magister Illyrio gave them to me, a bride gift, why would Viserys want . . . they're only stones . . ."

"The same could be said of rubies and diamonds and fire opals, Princess . . . and dragon's eggs are rarer by far. Those traders he's been drinking with would sell their own manhoods for even one of those *stones*, and with all three Viserys could buy as many sellswords as he might need."

Dany had not known, had not even suspected. "Then . . . he should have them. He does not need to steal them. He had only to ask. He is my brother . . . and my true king."

"He is your brother," Ser Jorah acknowledged.

"You do not understand, ser," she said. "My mother died giving me birth, and my father and my brother Rhaegar even before that. I would never have known so much as their names if Viserys had not been there to tell me. He was the only one left. The only one. He is all I have."

"Once," said Ser Jorah. "No longer, *Khaleesi*. You belong to the Dothraki now. In your womb rides the stallion who mounts the world." He held out his cup, and a slave filled it with fermented mare's milk, sour-smelling and thick with clots.

Dany waved her away. Even the smell of it made her feel ill, and she would take no chances of bringing up the horse heart she had forced herself to eat. "What does it mean?" she asked. "What is this stallion? Everyone was shouting it at me, but I don't understand."

"The stallion is the *khal* of *khals* promised in ancient prophecy, child. He will unite the Dothraki into a single *khalasar* and ride to the ends of the earth, or so it was promised. All the people of the world will be his herd."

"Oh," Dany said in a small voice. Her hand smoothed her robe down over the swell of her stomach. "I named him Rhaego."

"A name to make the Usurper's blood run cold."

Suddenly Doreah was tugging at her elbow. *"My lady,"* the handmaid whispered urgently, "your brother . . ."

Dany looked down the length of the long, roofless hall

and there he was, striding toward her. From the lurch in his step, she could tell at once that Viserys had found his wine . . . and something that passed for courage.

He was wearing his scarlet silks, soiled and travel-stained. His cloak and gloves were black velvet, faded from the sun. His boots were dry and cracked, his silver-blond hair matted and tangled. A longsword swung from his belt in a leather scabbard. The Dothraki eyed the sword as he passed; Dany heard curses and threats and angry muttering rising all around her, like a tide. The music died away in a nervous stammering of drums.

A sense of dread closed around her heart. "Go to him," she commanded Ser Jorah. "Stop him. Bring him here. Tell him he can have the dragon's eggs if that is what he wants." The knight rose swiftly to his feet.

"Where is my sister?" Viserys shouted, his voice thick with wine. "I've come for her feast. How dare you presume to eat without me? No one eats before the king. Where is she? The whore can't hide from the dragon."

He stopped beside the largest of the three firepits, peering around at the faces of the Dothraki. There were five thousand men in the hall, but only a handful who knew the Common Tongue. Yet even if his words were incomprehensible, you had only to look at him to know that he was drunk.

Ser Jorah went to him swiftly, whispered something in his ear, and took him by the arm, but Viserys wrenched free. "Keep your hands off me! No one touches the dragon without leave."

Dany glanced anxiously up at the high bench. Khal Drogo was saying something to the other *khals* beside him. Khal Jommo grinned, and Khal Ogo began to guffaw loudly.

The sound of laughter made Viserys lift his eyes. "Khal Drogo," he said thickly, his voice almost polite. "I'm here for the feast." He staggered away from Ser Jorah, making to join the three *khals* on the high bench.

Khal Drogo rose, spat out a dozen words in Dothraki, faster than Dany could understand, and pointed. "Khal Drogo says your place is not on the high bench," Ser Jorah translated for her brother. "Khal Drogo says your place is there."

Viserys glanced where the *khal* was pointing. At the

back of the long hall, in a corner by the wall, deep in shadow so better men would not need to look on them, sat the lowest of the low; raw unblooded boys, old men with clouded eyes and stiff joints, the dim-witted and the maimed. Far from the meat, and farther from honor. "That is no place for a king," her brother declared.

"Is place," Khal Drogo answered, in the Common Tongue that Dany had taught him, "for Sorefoot King." He clapped his hands together. "A cart! Bring cart for *Khal Rhaggat!*"

Five thousand Dothraki began to laugh and shout. Ser Jorah was standing beside Viserys, screaming in his ear, but the roar in the hall was so thunderous that Dany could not hear what he was saying. Her brother shouted back and the two men grappled, until Mormont knocked Viserys bodily to the floor.

Her brother drew his sword.

The bared steel shone a fearful red in the glare from the firepits. *"Keep away from me!"* Viserys hissed. Ser Jorah backed off a step, and her brother climbed unsteadily to his feet. He waved the sword over his head, the borrowed blade that Magister Illyrio had given him to make him seem more kingly. Dothraki were shrieking at him from all sides, screaming vile curses.

Dany gave a wordless cry of terror. She knew what a drawn sword meant here, even if her brother did not.

Her voice made Viserys turn his head, and he saw her for the first time. "There she is," he said, smiling. He stalked toward her, slashing at the air as if to cut a path through a wall of enemies, though no one tried to bar his way.

"The blade . . . you must not," she begged him. "Please, Viserys. It is forbidden. Put down the sword and come share my cushions. There's drink, food . . . is it the dragon's eggs you want? You can have them, only throw away the sword."

"Do as she tells you, fool," Ser Jorah shouted, "before you get us all killed."

Viserys laughed. "They can't kill us. They can't shed blood here in the sacred city . . . but *I* can." He laid the point of his sword between Daenerys's breasts and slid it downward, over the curve of her belly. "I want what I came for," he told her. "I want the crown he promised me. He bought you, but he never paid for you. Tell him I want what I bargained for, or I'm taking you back. You and the eggs both. He can keep his bloody foal. I'll cut the bastard out and leave it for him." The sword point pushed through her silks and pricked at her navel. Viserys was weeping, she saw; weeping and laughing, both at the same time, this man who had once been her brother.

Distantly, as from far away, Dany heard her handmaid Jhiqui sobbing in fear, pleading that she dared not translate, that the *khal* would bind her and drag her behind his horse all the way up the Mother of Mountains. She put her arm around the girl. "Don't be afraid," she said. "I shall tell him."

She did not know if she had enough words, yet when she was done Khal Drogo spoke a few brusque sentences in Dothraki, and she knew he understood. The sun of her life stepped down from the high bench. "What did he say?" the man who had been her brother asked her, flinching.

It had grown so silent in the hall that she could hear the bells in Khal Drogo's hair, chiming softly with each step he took. His bloodriders followed him, like three copper shadows. Daenerys had gone cold all over. "He says you shall have a splendid golden crown that men shall tremble to behold."

Viserys smiled and lowered his sword. That was the saddest thing, the thing that tore at her afterward . . . the way he smiled. "That was all I wanted," he said. "What was promised."

When the sun of her life reached her, Dany slid an arm around his waist. The *khal* said a word, and his bloodriders leapt forward. Qotho seized the man who had been her brother by the arms. Haggo shattered his wrist with a single, sharp twist of his huge hands. Cohollo pulled the sword from his limp fingers. Even now Viserys did not understand. "No," he shouted, "you cannot touch me, I am the dragon, the *dragon*, and I will be *crowned!*"

Khal Drogo unfastened his belt. The medallions were pure gold, massive and ornate, each one as large as a man's hand. He shouted a command. Cook slaves pulled a heavy iron stew pot from the firepit, dumped the stew onto the ground, and returned the pot to the flames. Drogo tossed in the belt and watched without expression as the medallions turned red and began to lose their shape. She could see fires dancing in the onyx of his eyes. A slave handed him a pair of thick horsehair mittens, and he pulled them on, never so much as looking at the man.

Viserys began to scream the high, wordless scream of the coward facing death. He kicked and twisted, whimpered like a dog and wept like a child, but the Dothraki held him tight between them. Ser Jorah had made his way to Dany's side. He put a hand on her shoulder. "Turn away, my princess, I beg you."

"No." She folded her arms across the swell of her belly, protectively.

At the last, Viserys looked at her. "Sister, please . . . Dany, tell them . . . make them . . . sweet sister . . ."

When the gold was half-melted and starting to run, Drogo reached into the flames, snatched out the pot. "Crown!" he roared. "Here. A crown for Cart King!" And upended the pot over the head of the man who had been her brother.

The sound Viserys Targaryen made when that hideous iron helmet covered his face was like nothing human. His feet hammered a frantic beat against the dirt floor, slowed, stopped. Thick globs of molten gold dripped down onto his chest, setting the scarlet silk to smoldering . . . yet no drop of blood was spilled.

He was no dragon, Dany thought, curiously calm. *Fire cannot kill a dragon.*

EDDARD

He was walking through the crypts beneath Winterfell, as he had walked a thousand times before. The Kings of Winter watched him pass with eyes of ice, and the direwolves at their feet turned their great stone heads and snarled. Last of all, he came to the tomb where his father slept, with Brandon and Lyanna beside him. *"Promise me, Ned,"* Lyanna's statue whispered. She wore a garland of pale blue roses, and her eyes wept blood.

Eddard Stark jerked upright, his heart racing, the blankets tangled around him. The room was black as pitch, and someone was hammering on the door. "Lord Eddard," a voice called loudly.

"A moment." Groggy and naked, he stumbled his way across the darkened chamber. When he opened the door, he found Tomard with an upraised fist, and Cayn with a taper in hand. Between them stood the king's own steward.

The man's face might have been carved of stone, so little did it show. "My lord Hand," he intoned. "His Grace the King commands your presence. At once."

So Robert had returned from his hunt. It was long past

time. "I shall need a few moments to dress." Ned left the man waiting without. Cayn helped him with his clothes; white linen tunic and grey cloak, trousers cut open down his plaster-sheathed leg, his badge of office, and last of all a belt of heavy silver links. He sheathed the Valyrian dagger at his waist.

The Red Keep was dark and still as Cayn and Tomard escorted him across the inner bailey. The moon hung low over the walls, ripening toward full. On the ramparts, a guardsman in a gold cloak walked his rounds.

The royal apartments were in Maegor's Holdfast, a massive square fortress that nestled in the heart of the Red Keep behind walls twelve feet thick and a dry moat lined with iron spikes, a castle-within-a-castle. Ser Boros Blount guarded the far end of the bridge, white steel armor ghostly in the moonlight. Within, Ned passed two other knights of the Kingsguard; Ser Preston Greenfield stood at the bottom of the steps, and Ser Barristan Selmy waited at the door of the king's bedchamber. *Three men in white cloaks,* he thought, remembering, and a strange chill went through him. Ser Barristan's face was as pale as his armor. Ned had only to look at him to know that something was dreadfully wrong. The royal steward opened the door. "Lord Eddard Stark, the Hand of the King," he announced.

"Bring him here," Robert's voice called, strangely thick.

Fires blazed in the twin hearths at either end of the bedchamber, filling the room with a sullen red glare. The heat within was suffocating. Robert lay across the canopied bed. At the bedside hovered Grand Maester Pycelle, while Lord Renly paced restlessly before the shuttered windows. Servants moved back and forth, feeding logs to the fire and boiling wine. Cersei Lannister sat on the edge of the bed beside her husband. Her hair was tousled, as if from sleep, but there was nothing sleepy in her eyes. They followed Ned as Tomard and Cayn helped him cross the room. He seemed to move very slowly, as if he were still dreaming.

The king still wore his boots. Ned could see dried mud and blades of grass clinging to the leather where Robert's feet stuck out beneath the blanket that covered him. A green doublet lay on the floor, slashed open and discarded, the cloth crusted with red-brown stains. The room smelled of smoke and blood and death.

"Ned," the king whispered when he saw him. His face was pale as milk. "Come . . . closer."

His men brought him close. Ned steadied himself with a hand on the bedpost. He had only to look down at Robert to know how bad it was. "What . . . ?" he began, his throat clenched.

"A boar." Lord Renly was still in his hunting greens, his cloak spattered with blood.

"A devil," the king husked. "My own fault. Too much wine, damn me to hell. Missed my thrust."

"And where were the rest of you?" Ned demanded of Lord Renly. "Where was Ser Barristan and the Kingsguard?"

Renly's mouth twitched. "My brother commanded us to stand aside and let him take the boar alone."

Eddard Stark lifted the blanket.

They had done what they could to close him up, but it was nowhere near enough. The boar must have been a fearsome thing. It had ripped the king from groin to nipple with its tusks. The wine-soaked bandages that Grand Maester Pycelle had applied were already black with blood, and the smell off the wound was hideous. Ned's stomach turned. He let the blanket fall.

"Stinks," Robert said. "The stink of death, don't think I can't smell it. Bastard did me good, eh? But I . . . I paid him back in kind, Ned." The king's smile was as terrible as his wound, his teeth red. "Drove a knife right through his eye. Ask them if I didn't. Ask them."

"Truly," Lord Renly murmured. "We brought the carcass back with us, at my brother's command."

"For the feast," Robert whispered. "Now leave us. The lot of you. I need to speak with Ned."

"Robert, my sweet lord . . ." Cersei began.

"I said *leave*," Robert insisted with a hint of his old fierceness. "What part of that don't you understand, woman?"

Cersei gathered up her skirts and her dignity and led the way to the door. Lord Renly and the others followed. Grand Maester Pycelle lingered, his hands shaking as he offered the king a cup of thick white liquid. "The milk of the poppy, Your Grace," he said. "Drink. For your pain."

Robert knocked the cup away with the back of his hand. "Away with you. I'll sleep soon enough, old fool. Get out."

Grand Maester Pycelle gave Ned a stricken look as he shuffled from the room.

"Damn you, Robert," Ned said when they were alone. His leg was throbbing so badly he was almost blind with pain. Or perhaps it was grief that fogged his eyes. He lowered himself to the bed, beside his friend. "Why do you always have to be so headstrong?"

"Ah, fuck you, Ned," the king said hoarsely. "I killed the bastard, didn't I?" A lock of matted black hair fell across his eyes as he glared up at Ned. "Ought to do the same for you. Can't leave a man to hunt in peace. Ser Robar found me. Gregor's head. Ugly thought. Never told the Hound. Let Cersei surprise him." His laugh turned into a grunt as a spasm of pain hit him. "Gods have mercy," he muttered, swallowing his agony. "The girl. Daenerys. Only a child, you were right . . . that's why, the girl . . . the gods sent the boar . . . sent to punish me . . ." The king coughed, bringing up blood. "Wrong, it was wrong, I . . . only a girl . . . Varys, Littlefinger, even my brother . . . worthless . . . no one to tell me *no* but you, Ned . . . only you . . ." He lifted his hand, the gesture pained and feeble. "Paper and ink. There, on the table. Write what I tell you."

Ned smoothed the paper out across his knee and took up the quill. "At your command, Your Grace."

"This is the will and word of Robert of House Baratheon, the First of his Name, King of the Andals and all the rest—put in the damn titles, you know how it goes. I do hereby command Eddard of House Stark, Lord of Winterfell and Hand of the King, to serve as Lord Regent and Protector of the Realm upon my . . . upon my death . . . to rule in my . . . in my stead, until my son Joffrey does come of age . . ."

"Robert . . ." *Joffrey is not your son,* he wanted to say, but the words would not come. The agony was written too plainly across Robert's face; he could not hurt him more. So Ned bent his head and wrote, but where the king had said "my son Joffrey," he scrawled "my heir" instead. The deceit made him feel soiled. *The lies we tell for love,* he thought. *May the gods forgive me.* "What else would you have me say?"

"Say . . . whatever you need to. Protect and defend, gods old and new, you have the words. Write. I'll sign it. You give it to the council when I'm dead."

"Robert," Ned said in a voice thick with grief, "you must not do this. Don't die on me. The realm needs you."

Robert took his hand, fingers squeezing hard. "You are . . . such a bad liar, Ned Stark," he said through his pain. "The realm . . . the realm knows . . . what a wretched king I've been. Bad as Aerys, the gods spare me."

"No," Ned told his dying friend, "not so bad as Aerys, Your Grace. Not near so bad as Aerys."

Robert managed a weak red smile. "At the least, they will say . . . this last thing . . . this I did right. You won't fail me. You'll rule now. You'll hate it, worse than I did . . . but you'll do well. Are you done with the scribbling?"

"Yes, Your Grace." Ned offered Robert the paper. The king scrawled his signature blindly, leaving a smear of blood across the letter. "The seal should be witnessed."

"Serve the boar at my funeral feast," Robert rasped. "Apple in its mouth, skin seared crisp. Eat the bastard. Don't care if you choke on him. Promise me, Ned."

"I promise." *Promise me, Ned,* Lyanna's voice echoed.

"The girl," the king said. "Daenerys. Let her live. If you can, if it . . . not too late . . . talk to them . . . Varys, Littlefinger . . . don't let them kill her. And help my son, Ned. Make him be . . . better than me." He winced. "Gods have mercy."

"They will, my friend," Ned said. "They will."

The king closed his eyes and seemed to relax. "Killed by a pig," he muttered. "Ought to laugh, but it hurts too much."

Ned was not laughing. "Shall I call them back?"

Robert gave a weak nod. "As you will. Gods, why is it so *cold* in here?"

The servants rushed back in and hurried to feed the fires. The queen had gone; that was some small relief, at least. If she had any sense, Cersei would take her children and fly before the break of day, Ned thought. She had lingered too long already.

King Robert did not seem to miss her. He bid his

brother Renly and Grand Maester Pycelle to stand in witness as he pressed his seal into the hot yellow wax that Ned had dripped upon his letter. "Now give me something for the pain and let me die."

Hurriedly Grand Maester Pycelle mixed him another draught of the milk of the poppy. This time the king drank deeply. His black beard was beaded with thick white droplets when he threw the empty cup aside. "Will I dream?"

Ned gave him his answer. "You will, my lord."

"Good," he said, smiling. "I will give Lyanna your love, Ned. Take care of my children for me."

The words twisted in Ned's belly like a knife. For a moment he was at a loss. He could not bring himself to lie. Then he remembered the bastards: little Barra at her mother's breast, Mya in the Vale, Gendry at his forge, and all the others. "I shall . . . guard your children as if they were my own," he said slowly.

Robert nodded and closed his eyes. Ned watched his old friend sag softly into the pillows as the milk of the poppy washed the pain from his face. Sleep took him.

Heavy chains jangled softly as Grand Maester Pycelle came up to Ned. "I will do all in my power, my lord, but the wound has mortified. It took them two days to get him back. By the time I saw him, it was too late. I can lessen His Grace's suffering, but only the gods can heal him now."

"How long?" Ned asked.

"By rights, he should be dead already. I have never seen a man cling to life so fiercely."

"My brother was always strong," Lord Renly said. "Not wise, perhaps, but strong." In the sweltering heat of the bedchamber, his brow was slick with sweat. He might have been Robert's ghost as he stood there, young and dark and handsome. "He slew the boar. His entrails were sliding from his belly, yet somehow he slew the boar." His voice was full of wonder.

"Robert was never a man to leave the battleground so long as a foe remained standing," Ned told him.

Outside the door, Ser Barristan Selmy still guarded the tower stairs. "Maester Pycelle has given Robert the milk of the poppy," Ned told him. "See that no one disturbs his rest without leave from me."

"It shall be as you command, my lord." Ser Barristan seemed old beyond his years. "I have failed my sacred trust."

"Even the truest knight cannot protect a king against himself," Ned said. "Robert loved to hunt boar. I have seen him take a thousand of them." He would stand his ground without flinching, his legs braced, the great spear in his hands, and as often as not he would curse the boar as it charged, and wait until the last possible second, until it was almost on him, before he killed it with a single sure and savage thrust. "No one could know this one would be his death."

"You are kind to say so, Lord Eddard."

"The king himself said as much. He blamed the wine."

The white-haired knight gave a weary nod. "His Grace was reeling in his saddle by the time we flushed the boar from his lair, yet he commanded us all to stand aside."

"I wonder, Ser Barristan," asked Varys, so quietly, "who gave the king this wine?"

Ned had not heard the eunuch approach, but when he looked around, there he stood. He wore a black velvet robe that brushed the floor, and his face was freshly powdered.

"The wine was from the king's own skin," Ser Barristan said.

"Only one skin? Hunting is such thirsty work."

"I did not keep count. More than one, for a certainty. His squire would fetch him a fresh skin whenever he required it."

"Such a dutiful boy," said Varys, "to make certain His Grace did not lack for refreshment."

Ned had a bitter taste in his mouth. He recalled the two fair-haired boys Robert had sent chasing after a breastplate stretcher. The king had told everyone the tale that night at the feast, laughing until he shook. "Which squire?"

"The elder," said Ser Barristan. "Lancel."

"I know the lad well," said Varys. "A stalwart boy, Ser Kevan Lannister's son, nephew to Lord Tywin and cousin to the queen. I hope the dear sweet lad does not blame himself. Children are so vulnerable in the innocence of their youth, how well do I remember."

Certainly Varys had once been young. Ned doubted

that he had ever been innocent. "You mention children. Robert had a change of heart concerning Daenerys Targaryen. Whatever arrangements you made, I want unmade. At once."

"Alas," said Varys. "At once may be too late. I fear those birds have flown. But I shall do what I can, my lord. With your leave." He bowed and vanished down the steps, his soft-soled slippers whispering against the stone as he made his descent.

Cayn and Tomard were helping Ned across the bridge when Lord Renly emerged from Maegor's Holdfast. "Lord Eddard," he called after Ned, "a moment, if you would be so kind."

Ned stopped. "As you wish."

Renly walked to his side. "Send your men away." They met in the center of the bridge, the dry moat beneath them. Moonlight silvered the cruel edges of the spikes that lined its bed.

Ned gestured. Tomard and Cayn bowed their heads and backed away respectfully. Lord Renly glanced warily at Ser Boros on the far end of the span, at Ser Preston in the doorway behind them. "That letter." He leaned close. "Was it the regency? Has my brother named you Protector?" He did not wait for a reply. "My lord, I have thirty men in my personal guard, and other friends beside, knights and lords. Give me an hour, and I can put a hundred swords in your hand."

"And what should I do with a hundred swords, my lord?"

"*Strike!* Now, while the castle sleeps." Renly looked back at Ser Boros again and dropped his voice to an urgent whisper. "We must get Joffrey away from his mother and take him in hand. Protector or no, the man who holds the king holds the kingdom. We should seize Myrcella and Tommen as well. Once we have her children, Cersei will not dare oppose us. The council will confirm you as Lord Protector and make Joffrey your ward."

Ned regarded him coldly. "Robert is not dead yet. The gods may spare him. If not, I shall convene the council to hear his final words and consider the matter of the succession, but I will not dishonor his last hours on earth by shedding blood in his halls and dragging frightened children from their beds."

Lord Renly took a step back, taut as a bowstring. "Every moment you delay gives Cersei another moment to prepare. By the time Robert dies, it may be too late . . . for both of us."

"Then we should pray that Robert does not die."

"Small chance of that," said Renly.

"Sometimes the gods are merciful."

"The Lannisters are not." Lord Renly turned away and went back across the moat, to the tower where his brother lay dying.

By the time Ned returned to his chambers, he felt weary and heartsick, yet there was no question of his going back to sleep, not now. *When you play the game of thrones, you win or you die,* Cersei Lannister had told him in the godswood. He found himself wondering if he had done the right thing by refusing Lord Renly's offer. He had no taste for these intrigues, and there was no honor in threatening children, and yet . . . if Cersei elected to fight rather than flee, he might well have need of Renly's hundred swords, and more besides.

"I want Littlefinger," he told Cayn. "If he's not in his chambers, take as many men as you need and search every winesink and whorehouse in King's Landing until you find him. Bring him to me before break of day." Cayn bowed and took his leave, and Ned turned to Tomard. "The *Wind Witch* sails on the evening tide. Have you chosen the escort?"

"Ten men, with Porther in command."

"Twenty, and you will command," Ned said. Porther was a brave man, but headstrong. He wanted someone more solid and sensible to keep watch over his daughters.

"As you wish, m'lord," Tom said. "Can't say I'll be sad to see the back of this place. I miss the wife."

"You will pass near Dragonstone when you turn north. I need you to deliver a letter for me."

Tom looked apprehensive. "To Dragonstone, m'lord?" The island fortress of House Targaryen had a sinister repute.

"Tell Captain Qos to hoist my banner as soon as he comes in sight of the island. They may be wary of unexpected visitors. If he is reluctant, offer him whatever it takes. I will give you a letter to place into the hand of Lord Stannis Baratheon. No one else. Not his steward, nor the captain of his guard, nor his lady wife, but only Lord Stannis himself."

"As you command, m'lord."

When Tomard had left him, Lord Eddard Stark sat staring at the flame of the candle that burned beside him on the table. For a moment his grief overwhelmed him. He wanted nothing so much as to seek out the godswood, to kneel before the heart tree and pray for the life of Robert Baratheon, who had been more than a brother to him. Men would whisper afterward that Eddard Stark had betrayed his king's friendship and disinherited his sons; he could only hope that the gods would know better, and that Robert would learn the truth of it in the land beyond the grave.

Ned took out the king's last letter. A roll of crisp white parchment sealed with golden wax, a few short words and a smear of blood. How small the difference between victory and defeat, between life and death.

He drew out a fresh sheet of paper and dipped his quill in the inkpot. *To His Grace, Stannis of the House Baratheon,* he wrote. *By the time you receive this letter, your brother Robert, our King these past fifteen years, will be dead. He was savaged by a boar whilst hunting in the kingswood . . .*

The letters seemed to writhe and twist on the paper as his hand trailed to a stop. Lord Tywin and Ser Jaime were not men to suffer disgrace meekly; they would fight rather than flee. No doubt Lord Stannis was wary, after the murder of Jon Arryn, but it was imperative that he sail for King's Landing at once with all his power, before the Lannisters could march.

Ned chose each word with care. When he was done, he signed the letter *Eddard Stark, Lord of Winterfell, Hand of the King, and Protector of the Realm,* blotted the paper, folded it twice, and melted the sealing wax over the candle flame.

His regency would be a short one, he reflected as the wax softened. The new king would choose his own Hand. Ned would be free to go home. The thought of Winterfell brought a wan smile to his face. He wanted to hear Bran's laughter once more, to go hawking with Robb; to watch Rickon at play. He wanted to drift off to a dreamless sleep in his own bed with his arms wrapped tight around his lady, Catelyn.

Cayn returned as he was pressing the direwolf seal down into the soft white wax. Desmond was with him, and between them Littlefinger. Ned thanked his guards and sent them away.

Lord Petyr was clad in a blue velvet tunic with puffed sleeves, his silvery cape patterned with mockingbirds. "I suppose congratulations are in order," he said as he seated himself.

Ned scowled. "The king lies wounded and near to death."

"I know," Littlefinger said. "I also know that Robert has named you Protector of the Realm."

Ned's eyes flicked to the king's letter on the table beside him, its seal unbroken. "And how is it you know that, my lord?"

"Varys hinted as much," Littlefinger said, "and you have just confirmed it."

Ned's mouth twisted in anger. "Damn Varys and his little birds. Catelyn spoke truly, the man has some black art. I do not trust him."

"Excellent. You're learning." Littlefinger leaned forward. "Yet I'll wager you did not drag me here in the black of night to discuss the eunuch."

"No," Ned admitted. "I know the secret Jon Arryn was murdered to protect. Robert will leave no trueborn son behind him. Joffrey and Tommen are Jaime Lannister's bastards, born of his incestuous union with the queen."

Littlefinger lifted an eyebrow. "Shocking," he said in a tone that suggested he was not shocked at all. "The girl as well? No doubt. So when the king dies . . ."

"The throne by rights passes to Lord Stannis, the elder of Robert's two brothers."

Lord Petyr stroked his pointed beard as he considered the matter. "So it would seem. Unless . . ."

"*Unless,* my lord? There is no *seeming* to this. Stannis is the heir. Nothing can change that."

"Stannis cannot take the throne without your help. If you're wise, you'll make certain Joffrey succeeds."

Ned gave him a stony stare. "Have you no shred of honor?"

"Oh, a *shred,* surely," Littlefinger replied negligently.

"Hear me out. Stannis is no friend of yours, nor of mine. Even his brothers can scarcely stomach him. The man is iron, hard and unyielding. He'll give us a new Hand and a new council, for a certainty. No doubt he'll thank you for handing him the crown, but he won't love you for it. And his ascent will mean war. Stannis cannot rest easy on the throne until Cersei and her bastards are dead. Do you think Lord Tywin will sit idly while his daughter's head is measured for a spike? Casterly Rock will rise, and not alone. Robert found it in him to pardon men who served King Aerys, so long as they did him fealty. Stannis is less forgiving. He will not have forgotten the siege of Storm's End, and the Lords Tyrell and Redwyne dare not. Every man who fought beneath the dragon banner or rose with Balon Greyjoy will have good cause to fear. Seat Stannis on the Iron Throne and I promise you, the realm will bleed.

"Now look at the other side of the coin. Joffrey is but twelve, and Robert gave *you* the regency, my lord. You are the Hand of the King and Protector of the Realm. The power is yours, Lord Stark. All you need do is reach out and take it. Make your peace with the Lannisters. Release the Imp. Wed Joffrey to your Sansa. Wed your younger girl to Prince Tommen, and your heir to Myrcella. It will be four years before Joffrey comes of age. By then he will look to you as a second father, and if not, well . . . four years is a good long while, my lord. Long enough to dispose of Lord Stannis. Then, should Joffrey prove troublesome, we can reveal his little secret and put Lord Renly on the throne."

"We?" Ned repeated.

Littlefinger gave a shrug. "You'll need someone to share your burdens. I assure you, my price would be modest."

"Your price." Ned's voice was ice. "Lord Baelish, what you suggest is treason."

"Only if we lose."

"You forget," Ned told him. "You forget Jon Arryn. You forget Jory Cassel. And you forget this." He drew the dagger and laid it on the table between them; a length of dragonbone and Valyrian steel, as sharp as the difference between right and wrong, between true and false, between life and death. "They sent a man to *cut my son's throat*, Lord Baelish."

Littlefinger sighed. "I fear I did forget, my lord. Pray forgive me. For a moment I did not remember that I was talking to a Stark." His mouth quirked. "So it will be Stannis, and war?"

"It is not a choice. Stannis is the heir."

"Far be it from me to dispute the Lord Protector. What would you have of me, then? Not my wisdom, for a certainty."

"I shall do my best to forget your . . . wisdom," Ned said with distaste. "I called you here to ask for the help you promised Catelyn. This is a perilous hour for all of us. Robert has named me Protector, true enough, but in the eyes of the world, Joffrey is still his son and heir. The queen has a dozen knights and a hundred men-at-arms who will do whatever she commands . . . enough to overwhelm what remains of my own household guard. And for all I know, her brother Jaime may be riding for King's Landing even as we speak, with a Lannister host at his back."

"And you without an army." Littlefinger toyed with the dagger on the table, turning it slowly with a finger. "There is small love lost between Lord Renly and the Lannisters. Bronze Yohn Royce, Ser Balon Swann, Ser Loras, Lady Tanda, the Redwyne twins . . . each of them has a retinue of knights and sworn swords here at court."

"Renly has thirty men in his personal guard, the rest even fewer. It is not enough, even if I could be certain that all of them will choose to give me their allegiance. I must have the gold cloaks. The City Watch is two thousand strong, sworn to defend the castle, the city, and the king's peace."

"Ah, but when the queen proclaims one king and the Hand another, whose peace do they protect?" Lord Petyr flicked at the dagger with his finger, setting it spinning in place. Round and round it went, wobbling as it turned. When at last it slowed to a stop, the blade pointed at Littlefinger. "Why, there's your answer," he said, smiling. "They follow the man who pays them." He leaned back and looked Ned full in the face, his grey-green eyes bright with mockery. "You wear your honor like a suit of armor, Stark. You think it keeps you safe, but all it does is weigh you down and make it hard for you to move. Look at you now. You know why you summoned me here. You know what you want to ask me to do. You know it has to be done . . . but it's not *honorable*, so the words stick in your throat.''

Ned's neck was rigid with tension. For a moment he was so angry that he did not trust himself to speak.

Littlefinger laughed. "I ought to make you say it, but that would be cruel . . . so have no fear, my good lord. For the sake of the love I bear for Catelyn, I will go to Janos Slynt this very hour and make certain that the City Watch is yours. Six thousand gold pieces should do it. A third for the Commander, a third for the officers, a third for the men. We might be able to buy them for half that much, but I prefer not to take chances." Smiling, he plucked up the dagger and offered it to Ned, hilt first.

JON

Jon was breaking his fast on applecakes and blood sausage when Samwell Tarly plopped himself down on the bench. "I've been summoned to the sept," Sam said in an excited whisper. "They're passing me out of training. I'm to be made a brother with the rest of you. Can you believe it?"

"No, truly?"

"Truly. I'm to assist Maester Aemon with the library and the birds. He needs someone who can read and write letters."

"You'll do well at that," Jon said, smiling.

Sam glanced about anxiously. "Is it time to go? I shouldn't be late, they might change their minds." He was fairly bouncing as they crossed the weed-strewn courtyard. The day was warm and sunny. Rivulets of water trickled down the sides of the Wall, so the ice seemed to sparkle and shine.

Inside the sept, the great crystal caught the morning light as it streamed through the south-facing window and spread it in a rainbow on the altar. Pyp's mouth dropped open when he caught sight of Sam, and Toad poked Grenn in the ribs, but no one dared say a word. Septon Celladar was swinging a censer, filling the air with fragrant incense that reminded Jon of Lady Stark's little sept in Winterfell. For once the septon seemed sober.

The high officers arrived in a body; Maester Aemon leaning on Clydas, Ser Alliser cold-eyed and grim, Lord Commander Mormont resplendent in a black wool doublet with silvered bearclaw fastenings. Behind them came the senior members of the three orders: red-faced Bowen Marsh the Lord Steward, First Builder Othell Yarwyck, and Ser Jaremy Rykker, who commanded the rangers in the absence of Benjen Stark.

Mormont stood before the altar, the rainbow shining on his broad bald head. "You came to us outlaws," he began, "poachers, rapers, debtors, killers, and thieves. You came to us children. You came to us alone, in chains, with neither friends nor honor. You came to us rich, and you came to us poor. Some of you bear the names of proud houses. Others have only bastards' names, or no names at all. It makes no matter. All that is past now. On the Wall, we are all one house.

"At evenfall, as the sun sets and we face the gathering night, you shall take your vows. From that moment, you will be a Sworn Brother of the Night's Watch. Your crimes will be washed away, your debts forgiven. So too you must wash away your former loyalties, put aside your grudges, forget old wrongs and old loves alike. Here you begin anew.

"A man of the Night's Watch lives his life for the realm. Not for a king, nor a lord, nor the honor of this house or that house, neither for gold nor glory nor a woman's love, but for the *realm*, and all the people in it. A man of the Night's Watch takes no wife and fathers no sons. Our wife is duty. Our mistress is honor. And you are the only sons we shall ever know.

"You have learned the words of the vow. Think carefully before you say them, for once you have taken the black, there is no turning back. The penalty for desertion is death." The Old Bear paused for a moment before he said, "Are there any among you who wish to leave our company? If so, go now, and no one shall think the less of you."

No one moved.

"Well and good," said Mormont. "You may take your

vows here at evenfall, before Septon Celladar and the first of your order. Do any of you keep to the old gods?"

Jon stood. "I do, my lord."

"I expect you will want to say your words before a heart tree, as your uncle did," Mormont said.

"Yes, my lord," Jon said. The gods of the sept had nothing to do with him; the blood of the First Men flowed in the veins of the Starks.

He heard Grenn whispering behind him. "There's no godswood here. Is there? I never saw a godswood."

"You wouldn't see a herd of aurochs until they trampled you into the snow," Pyp whispered back.

"I would so," Grenn insisted. "I'd see them a long way off."

Mormont himself confirmed Grenn's doubts. "Castle Black has no need of a godswood. Beyond the Wall the haunted forest stands as it stood in the Dawn Age, long before the Andals brought the Seven across the narrow sea. You will find a grove of weirwoods half a league from this spot, and mayhap your gods as well."

"My lord." The voice made Jon glance back in surprise. Samwell Tarly was on his feet. The fat boy wiped his sweaty palms against his tunic. "Might I . . . might I go as well? To say my words at this heart tree?"

"Does House Tarly keep the old gods too?" Mormont asked.

"No, my lord," Sam replied in a thin, nervous voice. The high officers frightened him, Jon knew, the Old Bear most of all. "I was named in the light of the Seven at the sept on Horn Hill, as my father was, and his father, and all the Tarlys for a thousand years."

"Why would you forsake the gods of your father and your House?" wondered Ser Jaremy Rykker.

"The Night's Watch is my House now," Sam said. "The Seven have never answered my prayers. Perhaps the old gods will."

"As you wish, boy," Mormont said. Sam took his seat again, as did Jon. "We have placed each of you in an order, as befits our need and your own strengths and skills." Bowen Marsh stepped forward and handed him a paper. The Lord Commander unrolled it and began to read. "Halder, to the builders," he began. Halder gave a stiff nod of approval. "Grenn, to the rangers. Albett, to the builders.

Pypar, to the rangers." Pyp looked over at Jon and wiggled his ears. "Samwell, to the stewards." Sam sagged with relief, mopping at his brow with a scrap of silk. "Matthar, to the rangers. Dareon, to the stewards. Todder, to the rangers. Jon, to the stewards."

The *stewards?* For a moment Jon could not believe what he had heard. Mormont must have read it wrong. He started to rise, to open his mouth, to tell them there had been a mistake . . . and then he saw Ser Alliser studying him, eyes shiny as two flakes of obsidian, and he knew.

The Old Bear rolled up the paper. "Your firsts will instruct you in your duties. May all the gods preserve you, brothers." The Lord Commander favored them with a half bow, and took his leave. Ser Alliser went with him, a thin smile on his face. Jon had never seen the master-at-arms look quite so happy.

"Rangers with me," Ser Jaremy Rykker called when they were gone. Pyp was staring at Jon as he got slowly to his feet. His ears were red. Grenn, grinning broadly, did not seem to realize that anything was amiss. Matt and Toad fell in beside them, and they followed Ser Jaremy from the sept.

"Builders," announced lantern-jawed Othell Yarwyck. Halder and Albett trailed out after him.

Jon looked around him in sick disbelief. Maester Aemon's blind eyes were raised toward the light he could not see. The septon was arranging crystals on the altar. Only Sam and Dareon remained on the benches; a fat boy, a singer . . . and him.

Lord Steward Bowen Marsh rubbed his plump hands together. "Samwell, you will assist Maester Aemon in the rookery and library. Chett is going to the kennels, to help with the hounds. You shall have his cell, so as to be close to the maester night and day. I trust you will take good care of him. He is very old and very precious to us.

"Dareon, I am told that you sang at many a high lord's table and shared their meat and mead. We are sending you to Eastwatch. It may be your palate will be some help to Cotter Pyke when merchant galleys come trading. We are paying too dear for salt beef and pickled fish, and the quality of the olive oil we're getting has been frightful. Present yourself to Borcas when you arrive, he will keep you busy between ships."

Marsh turned his smile on Jon. "Lord Commander Mormont has requested you for his personal steward, Jon. You'll sleep in a cell beneath his chambers, in the Lord Commander's tower."

"And what will my duties be?" Jon asked sharply. "Will I serve the Lord Commander's meals, help him fasten his clothes, fetch hot water for his bath?"

"Certainly." Marsh frowned at Jon's tone. "And you will run his messages, keep a fire burning in his chambers, change his sheets and blankets daily, and do all else that the Lord Commander might require of you."

"Do you take me for a servant?"

"No," Maester Aemon said, from the back of the sept. Clydas helped him stand. "We took you for a man of Night's Watch . . . but perhaps we were wrong in that."

It was all Jon could do to stop himself from walking out. Was he supposed to churn butter and sew doublets like a girl for the rest of his days? "May I go?" he asked stiffly.

"As you wish," Bowen Marsh responded.

Dareon and Sam left with him. They descended to the yard in silence. Outside, Jon looked up at the Wall shining in the sun, the melting ice creeping down its side in a hundred thin fingers. Jon's rage was such that he would have smashed it all in an instant, and the world be damned.

"Jon," Samwell Tarly said excitedly. "Wait. Don't you see what they're doing?"

Jon turned on him in a fury. "I see Ser Alliser's bloody hand, that's all I see. He wanted to shame me, and he has."

Dareon gave him a look. "The stewards are fine for the likes of you and me, Sam, but not for Lord Snow."

"I'm a better swordsman and a better rider than any of you," Jon blazed back. "It's not *fair!*"

"Fair?" Dareon sneered. "The girl was waiting for me, naked as the day she was born. She pulled me through the window, and you talk to me of *fair?*" He walked off.

"There is no shame in being a steward," Sam said.

"Do you think I want to spend the rest of my life washing an old man's smallclothes?"

"The old man is Lord Commander of the Night's Watch," Sam reminded him. "You'll be with him day and night. Yes, you'll pour his wine and see that his bed linen is fresh, but you'll also take his letters, attend him at meetings, squire for him in battle. You'll be as close to him as his shadow. You'll know everything, be a part of everything . . . and the Lord Steward said Mormont asked for you *himself*!

"When I was little, my father used to insist that I attend him in the audience chamber whenever he held court. When he rode to Highgarden to bend his knee to Lord Tyrell, he made me come. Later, though, he started to take Dickon and leave me at home, and he no longer cared whether I sat through his audiences, so long as Dickon was there. He wanted his *heir* at his side, don't you see? To watch and listen and learn from all he did. I'll wager that's why Lord Mormont requested you, Jon. What else could it be? He wants to groom you for *command*!"

Jon was taken aback. It was true, Lord Eddard had often made Robb part of his councils back at Winterfell. Could Sam be right? Even a bastard could rise high in the Night's Watch, they said. "I never asked for this," he said stubbornly.

"None of us are here for *asking*," Sam reminded him.

And suddenly Jon Snow was ashamed.

Craven or not, Samwell Tarly had found the courage to accept his fate like a man. *On the Wall, a man gets only what he earns*, Benjen Stark had said the last night Jon had seen him alive. *You're no ranger, Jon, only a green boy with the smell of summer still on you*. He'd heard it said that bastards grow up faster than other children; on the Wall, you grew up or you died.

Jon let out a deep sigh. "You have the right of it. I was acting the boy."

"Then you'll stay and say your words with me?"

"The old gods will be expecting us." He made himself smile.

They set out late that afternoon. The Wall had no gates as such, neither here at Castle Black nor anywhere along its three hundred miles. They led their horses down a narrow tunnel cut through the ice, cold dark walls pressing in around them as the passage twisted and turned. Three times their way was blocked by iron bars, and they had to stop while Bowen Marsh drew out his keys and unlocked the massive chains that secured them. Jon could sense the vast weight pressing down on him as he waited behind the Lord Steward. The air was colder than a tomb, and more still. He felt a strange relief when they reemerged into the afternoon light on the north side of the Wall.

Sam blinked at the sudden glare and looked around apprehensively. "The wildlings . . . they wouldn't . . . they'd never dare come this close to the Wall. Would they?"

"They never have." Jon climbed into his saddle. When Bowen Marsh and their ranger escort had mounted, Jon put two fingers in his mouth and whistled. Ghost came loping out of the tunnel.

The Lord Steward's garron whickered and backed away from the direwolf. "Do you mean to take that beast?"

"Yes, my lord," Jon said. Ghost's head lifted. He seemed to taste the air. In the blink of an eye he was off, racing across the broad, weed-choked field to vanish in the trees.

Once they had entered the forest, they were in a different world. Jon had often hunted with his father and Jory and his brother Robb. He knew the wolfswood around Winterfell as well as any man. The haunted forest was much the same, and yet the feel of it was very different.

Perhaps it was all in the knowing. They had ridden past the end of the world; somehow that changed everything. Every shadow seemed darker, every sound more ominous. The trees pressed close and shut out the light of the setting sun. A thin crust of snow cracked beneath the hooves of their horses, with a sound like breaking bones. When the wind set the leaves to rustling, it was like a chilly finger tracing a path up Jon's spine. The Wall was at their backs, and only the gods knew what lay ahead.

The sun was sinking below the trees when they reached their destination, a small clearing in the deep of the wood where nine weirwoods grew in a rough circle. Jon drew in a breath, and he saw Sam Tarly staring. Even in the wolfswood, you never found more than two or three of the white trees growing together; a grove of nine was unheard of. The forest floor was carpeted with fallen leaves, bloodred on top, black rot beneath. The wide smooth trunks were bone pale, and nine faces stared inward. The dried sap that crusted in the eyes was red and hard as ruby. Bowen Marsh commanded them to leave their horses outside the circle. "This is a sacred place, we will not defile it."

When they entered the grove, Samwell Tarly turned slowly looking at each face in turn. No two were quite alike. "They're watching us," he whispered. "The old gods."

"Yes." Jon knelt, and Sam knelt beside him.

They said the words together, as the last light faded in the west and grey day became black night.

"Hear my words, and bear witness to my vow," they recited, their voices filling the twilit grove. "Night gathers, and now my watch begins. It shall not end until my death. I shall take no wife, hold no lands, father no children. I shall wear no crowns and win no glory. I shall live and die at my post. I am the sword in the darkness. I am the watcher on the walls. I am the fire that burns against the cold, the light that brings the dawn, the horn that wakes the sleepers, the shield that guards the realms of men. I pledge my life and honor to the Night's Watch, for this night and all the nights to come."

The woods fell silent. "You knelt as boys," Bowen Marsh intoned solemnly. "Rise now as men of the Night's Watch."

Jon held out a hand to pull Sam back to his feet. The rangers gathered round to offer smiles and congratulations, all but the gnarled old forester Dywen. "Best we be starting back, m'lord," he said to Bowen Marsh. "Dark's falling, and there's something in the smell o' the night that I mislike."

And suddenly Ghost was back, stalking softly between two weirwoods. *White fur and red eyes,* Jon realized, disquieted. *Like the trees . . .*

The wolf had something in his jaws. Something black. "What's he got there?" asked Bowen Marsh, frowning.

"To me, Ghost." Jon knelt. "Bring it here."

The direwolf trotted to him. Jon heard Samwell Tarly's sharp intake of breath.

"Gods be good," Dywen muttered. "That's a hand."

EDDARD

The grey light of dawn was streaming through his window when the thunder of hoofbeats awoke Eddard Stark from his brief, exhausted sleep. He lifted his head from the table to look down into the yard. Below, men in mail and leather and crimson cloaks were making the morning ring to the sound of swords, and riding down mock warriors stuffed with straw. Ned watched Sandor Clegane gallop across the hard-packed ground to drive an iron-tipped lance through a dummy's head. Canvas ripped and straw exploded as Lannister guardsmen joked and cursed.

Is this brave show for my benefit? he wondered. If so, Cersei was a greater fool than he'd imagined. *Damn her,* he thought, *why is the woman not fled? I have given her chance after chance . . .*

The morning was overcast and grim. Ned broke his fast with his daughters and Septa Mordane. Sansa, still disconsolate, stared sullenly at her food and refused to eat, but Arya wolfed down everything that was set in front of her. "Syrio says we have time for one last lesson before we take ship this evening," she said. "Can I, Father? All my things are packed."

"A short lesson, and make certain you leave yourself time to bathe and change. I want you ready to leave by midday, is that understood?"

"By midday," Arya said.

Sansa looked up from her food. "If she can have a dancing lesson, why won't you let me say farewell to Prince Joffrey?"

"I would gladly go with her, Lord Eddard," Septa Mordane offered. "There would be no question of her missing the ship."

"It would not be wise for you to go to Joffrey right now, Sansa. I'm sorry."

Sansa's eyes filled with tears. "But *why?*"

"Sansa, your lord father knows best," Septa Mordane said. "You are not to question his decisions."

"It's not *fair!*" Sansa pushed back from her table, knocked over her chair, and ran weeping from the solar.

Septa Mordane rose, but Ned gestured her back to her seat. "Let her go, Septa. I will try to make her understand when we are all safely back in Winterfell." The septa bowed her head and sat down to finish her breakfast.

It was an hour later when Grand Maester Pycelle came to Eddard Stark in his solar. His shoulders slumped, as if the weight of the great maester's chain around his neck had become too great to bear. "My lord," he said, "King Robert is gone. The gods give him rest."

"No," Ned answered. "He hated rest. The gods give him love and laughter, and the joy of righteous battle." It was strange how empty he felt. He had been expecting the visit, and yet with those words, something died within him. He would have given all his titles for the freedom to weep . . . but he was Robert's Hand, and the hour he dreaded had come. "Be so good as to summon the members of the council here to my solar," he told Pycelle. The Tower of the Hand was as secure as he and Tomard could make it; he could not say the same for the council chambers.

"My lord?" Pycelle blinked. "Surely the affairs of the kingdom will keep till the morrow, when our grief is not so fresh."

Ned was quiet but firm. "I fear we must convene at once."

Pycelle bowed. "As the Hand commands." He called

his servants and sent them running, then gratefully accepted Ned's offer of a chair and a cup of sweet beer.

Ser Barristan Selmy was the first to answer the summons, immaculate in white cloak and enameled scales. "My lords," he said, "my place is beside the young king now. Pray give me leave to attend him."

"Your place is here, Ser Barristan," Ned told him.

Littlefinger came next, still garbed in the blue velvets and silver mockingbird cape he had worn the night previous, his boots dusty from riding. "My lords," he said, smiling at nothing in particular before he turned to Ned. "That little task you set me is accomplished, Lord Eddard."

Varys entered in a wash of lavender, pink from his bath, his plump face scrubbed and freshly powdered, his soft slippers all but soundless. "The little birds sing a grievous song today," he said as he seated himself. "The realm weeps. Shall we begin?"

"When Lord Renly arrives," Ned said.

Varys gave him a sorrowful look. "I fear Lord Renly has left the city."

"Left the *city*?" Ned had counted on Renly's support.

"He took his leave through a postern gate an hour before dawn, accompanied by Ser Loras Tyrell and some fifty retainers," Varys told them. "When last seen, they were galloping south in some haste, no doubt bound for Storm's End or Highgarden."

So much for Renly and his hundred swords. Ned did not like the smell of that, but there was nothing to be done for it. He drew out Robert's last letter. "The king called me to his side last night and commanded me to record his final words. Lord Renly and Grand Maester Pycelle stood witness as Robert sealed the letter, to be opened by the council after his death. Ser Barristan, if you would be so kind?"

The Lord Commander of the Kingsguard examined the paper. "King Robert's seal, and unbroken." He opened the letter and read. "Lord Eddard Stark is herein named Protector of the Realm, to rule as regent until the heir comes of age."

And as it happens, he is of age, Ned reflected, but he did not give voice to the thought. He trusted neither Pycelle nor Varys, and Ser Barristan was honor-bound to protect and defend the boy he thought his new king. The old knight would not abandon Joffrey easily. The need for deceit was a bitter taste in his mouth, but Ned knew he must tread softly here, must keep his counsel and play the game until he was firmly established as regent. There would be time enough to deal with the succession when Arya and Sansa were safely back in Winterfell, and Lord Stannis had returned to King's Landing with all his power.

"I would ask this council to confirm me as Lord Protector, as Robert wished," Ned said, watching their faces, wondering what thoughts hid behind Pycelle's half-closed eyes, Littlefinger's lazy half-smile, and the nervous flutter of Varys's fingers.

The door opened. Fat Tom stepped into the solar. "Pardon, my lords, the king's steward insists . . ."

The royal steward entered and bowed. "Esteemed lords, the king demands the immediate presence of his small council in the throne room."

Ned had expected Cersei to strike quickly; the summons came as no surprise. "The king is dead," he said, "but we shall go with you nonetheless. Tom, assemble an escort, if you would."

Littlefinger gave Ned his arm to help him down the steps. Varys, Pycelle, and Ser Barristan followed close behind. A double column of men-at-arms in chainmail and steel helms was waiting outside the tower, eight strong. Grey cloaks snapped in the wind as the guardsmen marched them across the yard. There was no Lannister crimson to be seen, but Ned was reassured by the number of gold cloaks visible on the ramparts and at the gates.

Janos Slynt met them at the door to the throne room, armored in ornate black-and-gold plate, with a high-crested helm under one arm. The Commander bowed stiffly. His men pushed open the great oaken doors, twenty feet tall and banded with bronze.

The royal steward led them in. "All hail His Grace, Joffrey of the Houses Baratheon and Lannister, the First of his Name, King of the Andals and the Rhoynar and the First Men, Lord of the Seven Kingdoms and Protector of the Realm," he sang out.

It was a long walk to the far end of the hall, where Joffrey waited atop the Iron Throne. Supported by Littlefinger, Ned Stark slowly limped and hopped toward the boy who called himself king. The others followed. The first time he had come this way, he had been on horseback, sword in hand, and the Targaryen dragons had watched from the walls as he forced Jaime Lannister down from the throne. He wondered if Joffrey would step down quite so easily.

Five knights of the Kingsguard—all but Ser Jaime and Ser Barristan—were arrayed in a crescent around the base of the throne. They were in full armor, enameled steel from helm to heel, long pale cloaks over their shoulders, shining white shields strapped to their left arms. Cersei Lannister and her two younger children stood behind Ser Boros and Ser Meryn. The queen wore a gown of sea-green silk, trimmed with Myrish lace as pale as foam. On her finger was a golden ring with an emerald the size of a pigeon's egg, on her head a matching tiara.

Above them, Prince Joffrey sat amidst the barbs and spikes in a cloth-of-gold doublet and a red satin cape. Sandor Clegane was stationed at the foot of the throne's steep narrow stair. He wore mail and soot-grey plate and his snarling dog's-head helm.

Behind the throne, twenty Lannister guardsmen waited with longswords hanging from their belts. Crimson cloaks draped their shoulders and steel lions crested their helms. But Littlefinger had kept his promise; all along the walls, in front of Robert's tapestries with their scenes of hunt and battle, the gold-cloaked ranks of the City Watch stood stiffly to attention, each man's hand clasped around the haft of an eight-foot-long spear tipped in black iron. They outnumbered the Lannisters five to one.

Ned's leg was a blaze of pain by the time he stopped. He kept a hand on Littlefinger's shoulder to help support his weight.

Joffrey stood. His red satin cape was patterned in gold thread; fifty roaring lions to one side, fifty prancing stags to the other. "I command the council to make all the necessary arrangements for my coronation," the boy proclaimed. "I wish to be crowned within the fortnight. Today I shall accept oaths of fealty from my loyal councillors."

Ned produced Robert's letter. "Lord Varys, be so kind as to show this to my lady of Lannister."

The eunuch carried the letter to Cersei. The queen glanced at the words. "Protector of the Realm," she read. "Is this meant to be your shield, my lord? A piece of paper?" She ripped the letter in half, ripped the halves in quarters, and let the pieces flutter to the floor.

"Those were the king's words," Ser Barristan said, shocked.

"We have a new king now," Cersei Lannister replied. "Lord Eddard, when last we spoke, you gave me some counsel. Allow me to return the courtesy. Bend the knee, my lord. Bend the knee and swear fealty to my son, and we shall allow you to step down as Hand and live out your days in the grey waste you call home."

"Would that I could," Ned said grimly. If she was so determined to force the issue here and now, she left him no choice. "Your son has no claim to the throne he sits. Lord Stannis is Robert's true heir."

"Liar!" Joffrey screamed, his face reddening.

"Mother, what does he mean?" Princess Myrcella asked the queen plaintively. "Isn't Joff the king now?"

"You condemn yourself with your own mouth, Lord Stark," said Cersei Lannister. "Ser Barristan, seize this traitor."

The Lord Commander of the Kingsguard hesitated. In the blink of an eye he was surrounded by Stark guardsmen, bare steel in their mailed fists.

"And now the treason moves from words to deeds," Cersei said. "Do you think Ser Barristan stands alone, my lord?" With an ominous rasp of metal on metal, the Hound drew his longsword. The knights of the Kingsguard and twenty Lannister guardsmen in crimson cloaks moved to support him.

"Kill him!" the boy king screamed down from the Iron Throne. *"Kill all of them, I command it!"*

"You leave me no choice," Ned told Cersei Lannister. He called out to Janos Slynt. "Commander, take the queen and her children into custody. Do them no harm, but escort them back to the royal apartments and keep them there, under guard."

"Men of the Watch!" Janos Slynt shouted, donning his

helm. A hundred gold cloaks leveled their spears and closed.

"I want no bloodshed," Ned told the queen. "Tell your men to lay down their swords, and no one need—"

With a single sharp thrust, the nearest gold cloak drove his spear into Tomard's back. Fat Tom's blade dropped from nerveless fingers as the wet red point burst out through his ribs, piercing leather and mail. He was dead before his sword hit the floor.

Ned's shout came far too late. Janos Slynt himself slashed open Varly's throat. Cayn whirled, steel flashing, drove back the nearest spearman with a flurry of blows; for an instant it looked as though he might cut his way free. Then the Hound was on him. Sandor Clegane's first cut took off Cayn's sword hand at the wrist; his second drove him to his knees and opened him from shoulder to breastbone.

As his men died around him, Littlefinger slid Ned's dagger from its sheath and shoved it up under his chin. His smile was apologetic. "I *did* warn you not to trust me, you know."

ARYA

"High," Syrio Forel called out, slashing at her head. The stick swords *clack*ed as Arya parried. "Left," he shouted, and his blade came whistling. Hers darted to meet it. The *clack* made him click his teeth together.

"Right," he said, and "Low," and "Left," and "Left" again, faster and faster, moving forward. Arya retreated before him, checking each blow.

"Lunge," he warned, and when he thrust she side-stepped, swept his blade away, and slashed at his shoulder. She almost touched him, *almost*, so close it made her grin. A strand of hair dangled in her eyes, limp with sweat. She pushed it away with the back of her hand.

"Left," Syrio sang out. "Low." His sword was a blur, and the Small Hall echoed to the *clack clack .clack*. "Left. Left. High. Left. Right. Left. Low. *Left!*"

The wooden blade caught her high in the breast, a sudden stinging blow that hurt all the more because it came from the wrong side. "*Ow*," she cried out. She would have a fresh bruise there by the time she went to sleep, somewhere out at sea. *A bruise is a lesson*, she told herself, *and each lesson makes us better*.

Syrio stepped back. "You are dead now."

Arya made a face. "You cheated," she said hotly. "You said left and you went right."

"Just so. And now you are a dead girl."

"But you *lied!*"

"My words lied. My eyes and my arm shouted out the truth, but you were not seeing."

"I was so," Arya said. "I watched you every second!"

"Watching is not seeing, dead girl. The water dancer sees. Come, put down the sword, it is time for listening now."

She followed him over to the wall, where he settled onto a bench. "Syrio Forel was first sword to the Sealord of Braavos, and are you knowing how that came to pass?"

"You were the finest swordsman in the city."

"Just so, but why? Other men were stronger, faster, younger, why was Syrio Forel the best? I will tell you now." He touched the tip of his little finger lightly to his eyelid. "The seeing, the true seeing, that is the heart of it.

"Hear me. The ships of Braavos sail as far as the winds blow, to lands strange and wonderful, and when they return their captains fetch queer animals to the Sealord's menagerie. Such animals as you have never seen, striped horses, great spotted things with necks as long as stilts, hairy mouse-pigs as big as cows, stinging manticores, tigers that carry their cubs in a pouch, terrible walking lizards with scythes for claws. Syrio Forel has seen these things.

"On the day I am speaking of, the first sword was newly dead, and the Sealord sent for me. Many bravos had come to him, and as many had been sent away, none could say why. When I came into his presence, he was seated, and in his lap was a fat yellow cat. He told me that one of his captains had brought the beast to him, from an island beyond the sunrise. 'Have you ever seen her like?' he asked of me.

"And to him I said, 'Each night in the alleys of Braavos I see a thousand like him,' and the Sealord laughed, and that day I was named the first sword."

Arya screwed up her face. "I don't understand."

Syrio clicked his teeth together. "The cat was an ordinary cat, no more. The others expected a fabulous beast, so that is what they saw. How large it was, they said. It was no larger than any other cat, only fat from indolence, for the Sealord fed it from his own table. What curious small ears, they said. Its ears had been chewed away in kitten fights. And it was plainly a tomcat, yet the Sealord said 'her,' and that is what the others saw. Are you hearing?"

Arya thought about it. "You saw what was there."

"Just so. Opening your eyes is all that is needing. The heart lies and the head plays tricks with us, but the eyes see true. Look with your eyes. Hear with your ears. Taste with your mouth. Smell with your nose. Feel with your skin. *Then* comes the thinking, afterward, and in that way knowing the truth."

"Just so," said Arya, grinning.

Syrio Forel allowed himself a smile. "I am thinking that when we are reaching this Winterfell of yours, it will be time to put this needle in your hand."

"Yes!" Arya said eagerly. "Wait till I show Jon—"

Behind her the great wooden doors of the Small Hall flew open with a resounding crash. Arya whirled.

A knight of the Kingsguard stood beneath the arch of the door with five Lannister guardsmen arrayed behind him. He was in full armor, but his visor was up. Arya remembered his droopy eyes and rust-colored whiskers from when he had come to Winterfell with the king: Ser Meryn Trant. The red cloaks wore mail shirts over boiled leather and steel caps with lion crests. "Arya Stark," the knight said, "come with us, child."

Arya chewed her lip uncertainly. "What do you want?"

"Your father wants to see you."

Arya took a step forward, but Syrio Forel held her by the arm. "And why is it that Lord Eddard is sending Lannister men in the place of his own? I am wondering."

"Mind your place, dancing master," Ser Meryn said. "This is no concern of yours."

"My father wouldn't send *you*," Arya said. She snatched up her stick sword. The Lannisters laughed.

"Put down the stick, girl," Ser Meryn told her. "I am a Sworn Brother of the Kingsguard, the White Swords."

"So was the Kingslayer when he killed the old king," Arya said. "I don't have to go with you if I don't want."

Ser Meryn Trant ran out of patience. "Take her," he said to his men. He lowered the visor of his helm.

Three of them started forward, chainmail clinking softly with each step. Arya was suddenly afraid. *Fear cuts deeper than swords,* she told herself, to slow the racing of her heart.

Syrio Forel stepped between them, tapping his wooden sword lightly against his boot. "You will be stopping there. Are you men or dogs that you would threaten a child?"

"Out of the way, old man," one of the red cloaks said.

Syrio's stick came whistling up and rang against his helm. "I am Syrio Forel, and you will now be speaking to me with more respect."

"Bald bastard." The man yanked free his longsword. The stick moved again, blindingly fast. Arya heard a loud *crack* as the sword went clattering to the stone floor. "My *hand*," the guardsman yelped, cradling his broken fingers.

"You are quick, for a dancing master," said Ser Meryn.

"You are slow, for a knight," Syrio replied.

"Kill the Braavosi and bring me the girl," the knight in the white armor commanded.

Four Lannister guardsmen unsheathed their swords. The fifth, with the broken fingers, spat and pulled free a dagger with his left hand.

Syrio Forel clicked his teeth together, sliding into his water dancer's stance, presenting only his side to the foe. "Arya child," he called out, never looking, never taking his eyes off the Lannisters, "we are done with dancing for the day. Best you are going now. Run to your father."

Arya did not want to leave him, but he had taught her to do as he said. *"Swift as a deer,"* she whispered.

"Just so," said Syrio Forel as the Lannisters closed.

Arya retreated, her own sword stick clutched tightly in her hand. Watching him now, she realized that Syrio had only been toying with her when they dueled. The red cloaks came at him from three sides with steel in their hands. They had chainmail over their chest and arms, and steel codpieces sewn into their pants, but only leather on their legs. Their hands were bare, and the caps they wore had noseguards, but no visor over the eyes.

Syrio did not wait for them to reach him, but spun to his left. Arya had never seen a man move as fast. He checked one sword with his stick and whirled away from a second. Off balance, the second man lurched into the first. Syrio put a boot to his back and the red cloaks went down together. The third guard came leaping over them, slashing at the water dancer's head. Syrio ducked under his blade and thrust upward. The guardsman fell screaming as blood welled from the wet red hole where his left eye had been.

The fallen men were getting up. Syrio kicked one in the face and snatched the steel cap off the other's head. The dagger man stabbed at him. Syrio caught the thrust in the helmet and shattered the man's kneecap with his stick. The last red cloak shouted a curse and charged, hacking down with both hands on his sword. Syrio rolled right, and the butcher's cut caught the helmetless man between neck and shoulder as he struggled to his knees. The longsword crunched through mail and leather and flesh. The man on his knees shrieked. Before his killer could wrench free his blade, Syrio jabbed him in the apple of his throat. The guardsman gave a choked cry and staggered back, clutching at his neck, his face blackening.

Five men were down, dead, or dying by the time Arya reached the back door that opened on the kitchen. She heard Ser Meryn Trant curse. "Bloody oafs," he swore, drawing his longsword from its scabbard.

Syrio Forel resumed his stance and clicked his teeth together. "Arya child," he called out, never looking at her, "be gone now."

Look with your eyes, he had said. She saw: the knight in his pale armor head to foot, legs, throat, and hands sheathed in metal, eyes hidden behind his high white helm, and in his hand cruel steel. Against that: Syrio, in a leather vest, with a wooden sword in his hand. "Syrio, *run,*" she screamed.

"The first sword of Braavos does not run," he sang as Ser Meryn slashed at him. Syrio danced away from his cut, his stick a blur. In a heartbeat, he had bounced blows off the knight's temple, elbow, and throat, the wood ringing against the metal of helm, gauntlet, and gorget. Arya stood frozen. Ser Meryn advanced; Syrio backed away. He checked the next blow, spun away from the second, deflected the third.

The fourth sliced his stick in two, splintering the wood and shearing through the lead core.

Sobbing, Arya spun and ran.

She plunged through the kitchens and buttery, blind with panic, weaving between cooks and potboys. A baker's helper stepped in front of her, holding a wooden tray. Arya bowled her over, scattering fragrant loaves of fresh-baked bread on the floor. She heard shouting behind her as she spun around a portly butcher who stood gaping at her with a cleaver in his hands. His arms were red to the elbow.

All that Syrio Forel had taught her went racing through her head. *Swift as a deer. Quiet as a shadow. Fear cuts deeper than swords. Quick as a snake. Calm as still water. Fear cuts deeper than swords. Strong as a bear. Fierce as a wolverine. Fear cuts deeper than swords. The man who fears losing has already lost. Fear cuts deeper than swords. Fear cuts deeper than swords. Fear cuts deeper than swords.* The grip of her wooden sword was slick with sweat, and Arya was breathing hard when she reached the turret stair. For an instant she froze. Up or down? Up would take her to the covered bridge that spanned the small court to the Tower of the Hand, but that would be the way they'd expect her to go, for certain. *Never do what they expect,* Syrio once said. Arya went down, around and around, leaping over the narrow stone steps two and three at a time. She emerged in a cavernous vaulted cellar, surrounded by casks of ale stacked twenty feet tall. The only light came through narrow slanting windows high in the wall.

The cellar was a dead end. There was no way out but the way she had come in. She dare not go back up those steps, but she couldn't stay here, either. She had to find her father and tell him what had happened. Her father would protect her.

Arya thrust her wooden sword through her belt and began to climb, leaping from cask to cask until she could reach the window. Grasping the stone with both hands, she pulled herself up. The wall was three feet thick, the window a tunnel slanting up and out. Arya wriggled toward daylight. When her head reached ground level, she peered across the bailey to the Tower of the Hand.

The stout wooden door hung splintered and broken, as if by axes. A dead man sprawled facedown on the steps, his cloak tangled beneath him, the back of his mailed shirt soaked red. The corpse's cloak was grey wool trimmed with white satin, she saw with sudden terror. She could not tell who he was.

"*No,*" she whispered. What was happening? Where was her father? Why had the red cloaks come for her? She remembered what the man with the yellow beard had said, the day she had found the monsters. *If one Hand can die, why not a second?* Arya felt tears in her eyes. She held her breath to listen. She heard the sounds of fighting, shouts, screams, the clang of steel on steel, coming through the windows of the Tower of the Hand.

She could not go back. Her father . . .

Arya closed her eyes. For a moment she was too frightened to move. They had killed Jory and Wyl and Heward, and that guardsman on the step, whoever he had been. They could kill her father too, and her if they caught her. "*Fear cuts deeper than swords,*" she said aloud, but it was no good pretending to be a water dancer, Syrio had been a water dancer and the white knight had probably killed him, and anyhow she was only a little girl with a wooden stick, alone and afraid.

She squirmed out into the yard, glancing around warily as she climbed to her feet. The castle seemed deserted. The Red Keep was *never* deserted. All the people must be hiding inside, their doors barred. Arya glanced up longingly at her bedchamber, then moved away from the Tower of the Hand, keeping close to the wall as she slid from shadow to shadow. She pretended she was chasing cats . . . except she was the cat now, and if they caught her, they would kill her.

Moving between buildings and over walls, keeping stone to her back wherever possible so no one could surprise her, Arya reached the stables almost without incident. A dozen gold cloaks in mail and plate ran past as she was edging across the inner bailey, but without knowing whose side they were on, she hunched down low in the shadows and let them pass.

Hullen, who had been master of horse at Winterfell as long as Arya could remember, was slumped on the ground by the stable door. He had been stabbed so many times it looked as if his tunic was patterned with scarlet flowers. Arya was certain he was dead, but when she crept closer, his eyes opened. "Arya Underfoot," he whispered. "You must . . . warn your . . . your lord father . . ." Frothy red spittle bubbled from his mouth. The master of horse closed his eyes again and said no more.

Inside were more bodies; a groom she had played with, and three of her father's household guard. A wagon, laden with crates and chests, stood abandoned near the door of the stable. The dead men must have been loading it for the trip to the docks when they were attacked. Arya snuck closer. One of the corpses was Desmond, who'd shown her his longsword and promised to protect her father. He lay on his back, staring blindly at the ceiling as flies crawled across his eyes. Close to him was a dead man in the red cloak and lion-crest helm of the Lannisters. Only one, though. *Every northerner is worth ten of these southron swords,* Desmond had told her. "You *liar!*" she said, kicking his body in a sudden fury.

The animals were restless in their stalls, whickering and snorting at the scent of blood. Arya's only plan was to saddle a horse and flee, away from the castle and the city. All she had to do was stay on the kingsroad and it would take her back to Winterfell. She took a bridle and harness off the wall.

As she crossed in back of the wagon, a fallen chest caught her eye. It must have been knocked down in the fight or dropped as it was being loaded. The wood had split, the lid opening to spill the chest's contents across the ground. Arya recognized silks and satins and velvets she never wore. She might need warm clothes on the kingsroad, though . . . and besides . . .

Arya knelt in the dirt among the scattered clothes. She found a heavy woolen cloak, a velvet skirt and a silk tunic and some smallclothes, a dress her mother had embroidered for her, a silver baby bracelet she might sell. Shoving the broken lid out of the way, she groped inside the chest for Needle. She had hidden it way down at the bottom, under everything, but her stuff had all been jumbled around when the chest was dropped. For a moment Arya was afraid someone had found the sword and stolen it. Then her fingers felt the hardness of metal under a satin gown.

"*There* she is," a voice hissed close behind her.

Startled, Arya whirled. A stableboy stood behind her, a smirk on his face, his filthy white undertunic peeking out from beneath a soiled jerkin. His boots were covered with manure, and he had a pitchfork in one hand. "Who are you?" she asked.

"She don't know me," he said, "but I knows her, oh, yes. The wolf girl."

"Help me saddle a horse," Arya pleaded, reaching back into the chest, groping for Needle. "My father's the Hand of the King, he'll reward you."

"Father's *dead*," the boy said. He shuffled toward her. "It's the queen who'll be rewarding me. Come here, girl."

"Stay away!" Her fingers closed around Needle's hilt.

"I says, *come*." He grabbed her arm, hard.

Everything Syrio Forel had ever taught her vanished in a heartbeat. In that instant of sudden terror, the only lesson Arya could remember was the one Jon Snow had given her, the very first.

She stuck him with the pointy end, driving the blade upward with a wild, hysterical strength.

Needle went through his leather jerkin and the white flesh of his belly and came out between his shoulder blades. The boy dropped the pitchfork and made a soft noise, something between a gasp and a sigh. His hands closed around the blade. "Oh, gods," he moaned, as his undertunic began to redden. "Take it out."

When she took it out, he died.

The horses were screaming. Arya stood over the body, still and frightened in the face of death. Blood had gushed from the boy's mouth as he collapsed, and more was seeping from the slit in his belly, pooling beneath his body. His palms were cut where he'd grabbed at the blade. She backed away slowly, Needle red in her hand. She had to get away, someplace far from here, someplace safe away from the stableboy's accusing eyes.

She snatched up the bridle and harness again and ran to her mare, but as she lifted the saddle to the horse's back, Arya realized with a sudden sick dread that the castle gates would be closed. Even the postern doors would likely be guarded. Maybe the guards wouldn't recognize her. If they thought she was a boy, perhaps they'd let her . . . no, they'd have orders not to let *anyone* out, it wouldn't matter whether they knew her or not.

But there was another way out of the castle . . .

The saddle slipped from Arya's fingers and fell to the dirt with a thump and a puff of dust. Could she find the room with the monsters again? She wasn't certain, yet she knew she had to try.

She found the clothing she'd gathered and slipped into the cloak, concealing Needle beneath its folds. The rest of her things she tied in a roll. With the bundle under her arm, she crept to the far end of the stable. Unlatching the back door, she peeked out anxiously. She could hear the distant sound of swordplay, and the shivery wail of a man screaming in pain across the bailey. She would need to go down the serpentine steps, past the small kitchen and the pig yard, that was how she'd gone last time, chasing the black tomcat . . . only that would take her right past the barracks of the gold cloaks. She couldn't go that way. Arya tried to think of another way. If she crossed to the other side of the castle, she could creep along the river wall and through the little godswood . . . but first she'd have to cross the yard, in the plain view of the guards on the walls.

She had never seen so many men on the walls. Gold cloaks, most of them, armed with spears. Some of them knew her by sight. What would they do if they saw her running across the yard? She'd look so small from up there, would they be able to tell who she was? Would they care?

She had to leave *now*, she told herself, but when the moment came, she was too frightened to move.

Calm as still water, a small voice whispered in her ear. Arya was so startled she almost dropped her bundle. She looked around wildly, but there was no one in the stable but her, and the horses, and the dead men.

Quiet as a shadow, she heard. Was it her own voice, or Syrio's? She could not tell, yet somehow it calmed her fears.

She stepped out of the stable.

It was the scariest thing she'd ever done. She wanted to run and hide, but she made herself *walk* across the yard, slowly, putting one foot in front of the other as if she had all the time in the world and no reason to be afraid of anyone. She thought she could feel their eyes, like bugs crawling on her skin under her clothes. Arya never looked up. If she saw them watching, all her courage would desert her, she knew, and she would drop the bundle of clothes and run and cry like a baby, and then they would have her. She kept her gaze on the ground. By the time she reached the shadow of the royal sept on the far side of the yard, Arya was cold with sweat, but no one had raised the hue and cry.

The sept was open and empty. Inside, half a hundred prayer candles burned in a fragrant silence. Arya figured the gods would never miss two. She stuffed them up her sleeves, and left by a back window. Sneaking back to the alley where she had cornered the one-eared tom was easy, but after that she got lost. She crawled in and out of windows, hopped over walls, and felt her way through dark cellars, quiet as a shadow. Once she heard a woman weeping. It took her more than an hour to find the low narrow window that slanted down to the dungeon where the monsters waited.

She tossed her bundle through and doubled back to light her candle. That was chancy; the fire she'd remembered seeing had burnt down to embers, and she heard voices as she was blowing on the coals. Cupping her fingers around the flickering candle, she went out the window as they were coming in the door, without ever getting a glimpse of who it was.

This time the monsters did not frighten her. They seemed almost old friends. Arya held the candle over her head. With each step she took, the shadows moved against the walls, as if they were turning to watch her pass. "*Dragons*," she whispered. She slid Needle out from under her cloak. The slender blade seemed very small and the dragons very big, yet somehow Arya felt better with steel in her hand.

The long windowless hall beyond the door was as black as she remembered. She held Needle in her left hand, her sword hand, the candle in her right fist. Hot wax ran down across her knuckles. The entrance to the well had been to the left, so Arya went right. Part of her wanted to run, but she was afraid of snuffing out her candle. She heard the faint squeaking of rats and glimpsed a pair of tiny glowing eyes on the edge of the light, but rats did not scare her. Other things did. It would be so easy to hide here, as she had hidden from the wizard and the man with the forked beard. She could almost see the stableboy standing against the wall, his hands curled into claws with the blood still dripping from the deep gashes in his palms where Needle had cut him. He might be waiting to grab her as she passed. He would see her candle coming a long way off. Maybe she would be better off without the light . . .

Fear cuts deeper than swords, the quiet voice inside her whispered. Suddenly Arya remembered the crypts at Winterfell. They were a lot scarier than this place, she told herself. She'd been just a little girl the first time she saw them. Her brother Robb had taken them down, her and Sansa and baby Bran, who'd been no bigger than Rickon was now. They'd only had one candle between them, and Bran's eyes had gotten as big as saucers as he stared at the stone faces of the Kings of Winter, with their wolves at their feet and their iron swords across their laps.

Robb took them all the way down to the end, past Grandfather and Brandon and Lyanna, to show them their own tombs. Sansa kept looking at the stubby little candle, anxious that it might go out. Old Nan had told her there were spiders down here, and rats as big as dogs. Robb smiled when she said that. "There are worse things than spiders and rats," he whispered. "This is where the dead walk." That was when they heard the sound, low and deep and shivery. Baby Bran had clutched at Arya's hand.

When the spirit stepped out of the open tomb, pale white and moaning for blood, Sansa ran shrieking for the stairs, and Bran wrapped himself around Robb's leg, sobbing. Arya stood her ground and gave the spirit a punch. It was only Jon, covered with flour. "You *stupid,*" she told him, "you scared the baby," but Jon and Robb just laughed and laughed, and pretty soon Bran and Arya were laughing too.

The memory made Arya smile, and after that the darkness held no more terrors for her. The stableboy was dead, she'd killed him, and if he jumped out at her she'd kill him again. She was going home. Everything would be better once she was home again, safe behind Winterfell's grey granite walls.

Her footsteps sent soft echoes hurrying ahead of her as Arya plunged deeper into the darkness.

SANSA

They came for Sansa on the third day.

She chose a simple dress of dark grey wool, plainly cut but richly embroidered around the collar and sleeves. Her fingers felt thick and clumsy as she struggled with the silver fastenings without the benefit of servants. Jeyne Poole had been confined with her, but Jeyne was useless. Her face was puffy from all her crying, and she could not seem to stop sobbing about her father.

"I'm certain your father is well," Sansa told her when she had finally gotten the dress buttoned right. "I'll ask the queen to let you see him." She thought that kindness might lift Jeyne's spirits, but the other girl just looked at her with red, swollen eyes and began to cry all the harder. She was such a *child*.

Sansa had wept too, the first day. Even within the stout walls of Maegor's Holdfast, with her door closed and barred, it was hard not to be terrified when the killing began. She had grown up to the sound of steel in the yard, and scarcely a day of her life had passed without hearing the clash of sword on sword, yet somehow knowing that the fighting was real made all the difference in the world. She heard it as she had never heard it before, and there were other sounds as well, grunts of pain, angry curses, shouts for help, and the moans of wounded and dying men. In the songs, the knights never screamed nor begged for mercy.

So she wept, pleading through her door for them to tell her what was happening, calling for her father, for Septa Mordane, for the king, for her gallant prince. If the men guarding her heard her pleas, they gave no answer. The only time the door opened was late that night, when they thrust Jeyne Poole inside, bruised and shaking. *"They're killing everyone,"* the steward's daughter had shrieked at her. She went on and on. The Hound had broken down her door with a warhammer, she said. There were bodies on the stair of the Tower of the Hand, and the steps were slick with blood. Sansa dried her own tears as she struggled to comfort her friend. They went to sleep in the same bed, cradled in each other's arms like sisters.

The second day was even worse. The room where Sansa had been confined was at the top of the highest tower of Maegor's Holdfast. From its window, she could see that the heavy iron portcullis in the gatehouse was down, and the drawbridge drawn up over the deep dry moat that separated the keep-within-a-keep from the larger castle that surrounded it. Lannister guardsmen prowled the walls with spears and crossbows to hand. The fighting was over, and the silence of the grave had settled over the Red Keep. The only sounds were Jeyne Poole's endless whimpers and sobs.

They were fed—hard cheese and fresh-baked bread and milk to break their fast, roast chicken and greens at midday, and a late supper of beef and barley stew—but the servants who brought the meals would not answer Sansa's questions. That evening, some women brought her clothes from the Tower of the Hand, and some of Jeyne's things as well, but they seemed nearly as frightened as Jeyne, and when she tried to talk to them, they fled from her as if she had the grey plague. The guards outside the door still refused to let them leave the room.

"Please, I need to speak to the queen again," Sansa told them, as she told everyone she saw that day. "She'll want to talk to me, I know she will. Tell her I want to see her, please. If not the queen, then Prince Joffrey, if you'd be so kind. We're to marry when we're older."

At sunset on the second day, a great bell began to ring. Its voice was deep and sonorous, and the long slow clanging filled Sansa with a sense of dread. The ringing went on and on, and after a while they heard other bells answering from the Great Sept of Baelor on Visenya's Hill. The sound rumbled across the city like thunder, warning of the storm to come.

"What is it?" Jeyne asked, covering her ears. "Why are they ringing the bells?"

"The king is dead." Sansa could not say how she knew it, yet she did. The slow, endless clanging filled their room, as mournful as a dirge. Had some enemy stormed the castle and murdered King Robert? Was that the meaning of the fighting they had heard?

She went to sleep wondering, restless, and fearful. Was her beautiful Joffrey the king now? Or had they killed him too? She was afraid for him, and for her father. If only they would tell her what was happening . . .

That night Sansa dreamt of Joffrey on the throne, with herself seated beside him in a gown of woven gold. She had a crown on her head, and everyone she had ever known came before her, to bend the knee and say their courtesies.

The next morning, the morning of the third day, Ser Boros Blount of the Kingsguard came to escort her to the queen.

Ser Boros was an ugly man with a broad chest and short, bandy legs. His nose was flat, his cheeks baggy with jowls, his hair grey and brittle. Today he wore white velvet, and his snowy cloak was fastened with a lion brooch. The beast had the soft sheen of gold, and his eyes were tiny rubies. "You look very handsome and splendid this morning, Ser Boros," Sansa told him. A lady remembered her courtesies, and she was resolved to be a lady no matter what.

"And you, my lady," Ser Boros said in a flat voice. "Her Grace awaits. Come with me."

There were guards outside her door, Lannister men-at-arms in crimson cloaks and lion-crested helms. Sansa made herself smile at them pleasantly and bid them a good morning as she passed. It was the first time she had been allowed outside the chamber since Ser Arys Oakheart had led her there two mornings past. "To keep you safe, my sweet one," Queen Cersei had told her. "Joffrey would never forgive me if anything happened to his precious."

Sansa had expected that Ser Boros would escort her to the royal apartments, but instead he led her out of Maegor's Holdfast. The bridge was down again. Some workmen were lowering a man on ropes into the depths of the dry moat. When Sansa peered down, she saw a body impaled on the huge iron spikes below. She averted her eyes quickly, afraid to ask, afraid to look too long, afraid he might be someone she knew.

They found Queen Cersei in the council chambers, seated at the head of a long table littered with papers, candles, and blocks of sealing wax. The room was as splendid as any that Sansa had ever seen. She stared in awe at the carved wooden screen and the twin sphinxes that sat beside the door.

"Your Grace," Ser Boros said when they were ushered inside by another of the Kingsguard, Ser Mandon of the curiously dead face, "I've brought the girl."

Sansa had hoped Joffrey might be with her. Her prince was not there, but three of the king's councillors were. Lord Petyr Baelish sat on the queen's left hand, Grand Maester Pycelle at the end of the table, while Lord Varys hovered over them, smelling flowery. All of them were clad in black, she realized with a feeling of dread. Mourning clothes . . .

The queen wore a high-collared black silk gown, with a hundred dark red rubies sewn into her bodice, covering her from neck to bosom. They were cut in the shape of teardrops, as if the queen were weeping blood. Cersei smiled to see her, and Sansa thought it was the sweetest and saddest smile she had ever seen. "Sansa, my sweet child," she said, "I know you've been asking for me. I'm sorry that I could not send for you sooner. Matters have been very unsettled, and I have not had a moment. I trust my people have been taking good care of you?"

"Everyone has been very sweet and pleasant, Your Grace, thank you ever so much for asking," Sansa said politely. "Only, well, no one will talk to us or tell us what's happened . . ."

"Us?" Cersei seemed puzzled.

"We put the steward's girl in with her," Ser Boros said. "We did not know what else to do with her."

The queen frowned. "Next time, you will ask," she said, her voice sharp. "The gods only know what sort of tales she's been filling Sansa's head with."

"Jeyne's scared," Sansa said. "She won't stop crying. I promised her I'd ask if she could see her father."

Old Grand Maester Pycelle lowered his eyes.

"Her father is well, isn't he?" Sansa said anxiously. She knew there had been fighting, but surely no one would harm a steward. Vayon Poole did not even wear a sword.

Queen Cersei looked at each of the councillors in turn. "I won't have Sansa fretting needlessly. What shall we do with this little friend of hers, my lords?"

Lord Petyr leaned forward. "I'll find a place for her."

"Not in the city," said the queen.

"Do you take me for a fool?"

The queen ignored that. "Ser Boros, escort this girl to Lord Petyr's apartments and instruct his people to keep her there until he comes for her. Tell her that Littlefinger will be taking her to see her father, that ought to calm her down. I want her gone before Sansa returns to her chamber."

"As you command, Your Grace," Ser Boros said. He bowed deeply, spun on his heel, and took his leave, his long white cloak stirring the air behind him.

Sansa was confused. "I don't understand," she said. "Where is Jeyne's father? Why can't Ser Boros take her to him instead of Lord Petyr having to do it?" She had promised herself she would be a lady, gentle as the queen and as strong as her mother, the Lady Catelyn, but all of a sudden she was scared again. For a second she thought she might cry. "Where are you sending her? She hasn't done anything wrong, she's a good girl."

"She's upset you," the queen said gently. "We can't be having that. Not another word, now. Lord Baelish will see that Jeyne's well taken care of, I promise you." She patted the chair beside her. "Sit down, Sansa. I want to talk to you."

Sansa seated herself beside the queen. Cersei smiled again, but that did not make her feel any less anxious. Varys was wringing his soft hands together, Grand

Maester Pycelle kept his sleepy eyes on the papers in front of him, but she could feel Littlefinger staring. Something about the way the small man looked at her made Sansa feel as though she had no clothes on. Goose bumps pimpled her skin.

"Sweet Sansa," Queen Cersei said, laying a soft hand on her wrist. "Such a beautiful child. I do hope you know how much Joffrey and I love you."

"You *do?*" Sansa said, breathless. Littlefinger was forgotten. Her prince loved her. Nothing else mattered.

The queen smiled. "I think of you almost as my own daughter. And I know the love you bear for Joffrey." She gave a weary shake of her head. "I am afraid we have some grave news about your lord father. You must be brave, child."

Her quiet words gave Sansa a chill. "What is it?"

"Your father is a traitor, dear," Lord Varys said.

Grand Maester Pycelle lifted his ancient head. "With my own ears, I heard Lord Eddard swear to our beloved King Robert that he would protect the young princes as if they were his own sons. And yet the moment the king was dead, he called the small council together to steal Prince Joffrey's rightful throne."

"No," Sansa blurted. "He wouldn't do that. He *wouldn't!*"

The queen picked up a letter. The paper was torn and stiff with dried blood, but the broken seal was her father's, the direwolf stamped in pale wax. "We found this on the captain of your household guard, Sansa. It is a letter to my late husband's brother Stannis, inviting him to take the crown."

"Please, Your Grace, there's been a mistake." Sudden panic made her dizzy and faint. "Please, send for my father, he'll tell you, he would never write such a letter, the king was his friend."

"Robert thought so," said the queen. "This betrayal would have broken his heart. The gods are kind, that he did not live to see it." She sighed. "Sansa, sweetling, you must see what a dreadful position this has left us in. You are innocent of any wrong, we all know that, and yet you are the daughter of a traitor. How can I allow you to marry my son?"

"But I *love* him," Sansa wailed, confused and frightened. What did they mean to do to her? What had they done to her father? It was not supposed to happen this way. She had to wed Joffrey, they were betrothed, he was promised to her, she had even dreamed about it. It wasn't fair to take him away from her on account of whatever her father might have done.

"How well I know that, child," Cersei said, her voice so kind and sweet. "Why else should you have come to me and told me of your father's plan to send you away from us, if not for love?"

"It *was* for love," Sansa said in a rush. "Father wouldn't even give me leave to say farewell." She was the good girl, the obedient girl, but she had felt as wicked as Arya that morning, sneaking away from Septa Mordane, defying her lord father. She had never done anything so willful before, and she would never have done it then if she hadn't loved Joffrey as much as she did. "He was going to take me back to Winterfell and marry me to some hedge knight, even though it was Joff I wanted. I told him, but he wouldn't listen." The king had been her last hope. The king could *command* Father to let her stay in King's Landing and marry Prince Joffrey, Sansa knew he could, but the king had always frightened her. He was loud and rough-voiced and drunk as often as not, and he would probably have just sent her back to Lord Eddard, if they even let her see him. So she went to the queen instead, and poured out her heart, and Cersei had listened and thanked her sweetly . . . only then Ser Arys had escorted her to the high room in Maegor's Holdfast and posted guards, and a few hours later, the fighting had begun outside. "Please," she finished, "you *have* to let me marry Joffrey, I'll be ever so good a wife to him, you'll see. I'll be a queen just like you, I promise."

Queen Cersei looked to the others. "My lords of the council, what do you say to her plea?"

"The poor child," murmured Varys. "A love so true and innocent, Your Grace, it would be cruel to deny it . . . and yet, what can we do? Her father stands condemned." His soft hands washed each other in a gesture of helpless distress.

"A child born of traitor's seed will find that betrayal comes naturally to her," said Grand Maester Pycelle.

"She is a sweet thing now, but in ten years, who can say what treasons she may hatch?"

"No," Sansa said, horrified. "I'm not, I'd never . . . I wouldn't betray Joffrey, I love him, I swear it, I do."

"Oh, so poignant," said Varys. "And yet, it is truly said that blood runs truer than oaths."

"She reminds me of the mother, not the father," Lord Petyr Baelish said quietly. "Look at her. The hair, the eyes. She is the very image of Cat at the same age."

The queen looked at her, troubled, and yet Sansa could see kindness in her clear green eyes. "Child," she said, "if I could truly believe that you were not like your father, why nothing should please me more than to see you wed to my Joffrey. I know he loves you with all his heart." She sighed. "And yet, I fear that Lord Varys and the Grand Maester have the right of it. The blood will tell. I have only to remember how your sister set her wolf on my son."

"I'm not like Arya," Sansa blurted. "She has the traitor's blood, not me. I'm *good*, ask Septa Mordane, she'll tell you, I only want to be Joffrey's loyal and loving wife."

She felt the weight of Cersei's eyes as the queen studied her face. "I believe you mean it, child." She turned to face the others. "My lords, it seems to me that if the rest of her kin were to remain loyal in this terrible time, that would go a long way toward laying our fears to rest."

Grand Maester Pycelle stroked his huge soft beard, his wide brow furrowed in thought. "Lord Eddard has three sons."

"Mere boys," Lord Petyr said with a shrug. "I should be more concerned with Lady Catelyn and the Tullys."

The queen took Sansa's hand in both of hers. "Child, do you know your letters?"

Sansa nodded nervously. She could read and write better than any of her brothers, although she was hopeless at sums.

"I am pleased to hear that. Perhaps there is hope for you and Joffrey still . . ."

"What do you want me to do?"

"You must write your lady mother, and your brother, the eldest . . . what is his name?"

"Robb," Sansa said.

"The word of your lord father's treason will no doubt

reach them soon. Better that it should come from you. You must tell them how Lord Eddard betrayed his king."

Sansa wanted Joffrey desperately, but she did not think she had the courage to do as the queen was asking. "But he never . . . I don't . . . Your Grace, I wouldn't know what to say . . ."

The queen patted her hand. "We will tell you what to write, child. The important thing is that you urge Lady Catelyn and your brother to keep the king's peace."

"It will go hard for them if they don't," said Grand Maester Pycelle. "By the love you bear them, you must urge them to walk the path of wisdom."

"Your lady mother will no doubt fear for you dreadfully," the queen said. "You must tell her that you are well and in our care, that we are treating you gently and seeing to your every want. Bid them to come to King's Landing and pledge their fealty to Joffrey when he takes his throne. If they do that . . . why, then we shall know that there is no taint in your blood, and when you come into the flower of your womanhood, you shall wed the king in the Great Sept of Baelor, before the eyes of gods and men."

. . . *wed the king* . . . The words made her breath come faster, yet still Sansa hesitated. "Perhaps . . . if I might see my father, talk to him about . . ."

"Treason?" Lord Varys hinted.

"You disappoint me, Sansa," the queen said, with eyes gone hard as stones. "We've told you of your father's crimes. If you are truly as loyal as you say, why should you want to see him?"

"I . . . I only meant . . ." Sansa felt her eyes grow wet. "He's not . . . please, he hasn't been . . . hurt, or . . . or . . ."

"Lord Eddard has not been harmed," the queen said.

"But . . . what's to become of him?"

"That is a matter for the king to decide," Grand Maester Pycelle announced ponderously.

The *king!* Sansa blinked back her tears. Joffrey was the king now, she thought. Her gallant prince would never hurt her father, no matter what he might have done. If she went to him and pleaded for mercy, she was certain he'd listen. He *had* to listen, he loved her, even the queen said so. Joff would need to punish Father, the lords would expect it, but perhaps he could send him back to Winterfell, or exile him to one of the Free Cities across the narrow sea. It would only have to be for a few years. By then she and Joffrey would be married. Once she was queen, she could persuade Joff to bring Father back and grant him a pardon.

Only . . . if Mother or Robb did anything treasonous, called the banners or refused to swear fealty or *anything*, it would all go wrong. Her Joffrey was good and kind, she knew it in her heart, but a king had to be stern with rebels. She had to make them understand, she *had* to!

"I'll . . . I'll write the letters," Sansa told them.

With a smile as warm as the sunrise, Cersei Lannister leaned close and kissed her gently on the cheek. "I knew you would. Joffrey will be so proud when I tell him what courage and good sense you've shown here today."

In the end, she wrote four letters. To her mother, the Lady Catelyn Stark, and to her brothers at Winterfell, and to her aunt and her grandfather as well, Lady Lysa Arryn of the Eyrie, and Lord Hoster Tully of Riverrun. By the time she had done, her fingers were cramped and stiff and stained with ink. Varys had her father's seal. She warmed the pale white beeswax over a candle, poured it carefully, and watched as the eunuch stamped each letter with the direwolf of House Stark.

Jeyne Poole and all her things were gone when Ser Mandon Moore returned Sansa to the high tower of Maegor's Holdfast. No more weeping, she thought gratefully. Yet somehow it seemed colder with Jeyne gone, even after she'd built a fire. She pulled a chair close to the hearth, took down one of her favorite books, and lost herself in the stories of Florian and Jonquil, of Lady Shella and the Rainbow Knight, of valiant Prince Aemon and his doomed love for his brother's queen.

It was not until later that night, as she was drifting off to sleep, that Sansa realized she had forgotten to ask about her sister.

JON

"Othor," announced Ser Jaremy Rykker, "beyond a doubt. And this one was Jafer Flowers." He turned the corpse over with his foot, and the dead white face stared up at the overcast sky with blue, blue eyes. "They were Ben Stark's men, both of them."

My uncle's men, Jon thought numbly. He remembered how he'd pleaded to ride with them. *Gods, I was such a green boy. If he had taken me, it might be me lying here . . .*

Jafer's right wrist ended in the ruin of torn flesh and splintered bone left by Ghost's jaws. His right hand was floating in a jar of vinegar back in Maester Aemon's tower. His left hand, still at the end of his arm, was as black as his cloak.

"Gods have mercy," the Old Bear muttered. He swung down from his garron, handing his reins to Jon. The morning was unnaturally warm; beads of sweat dotted the Lord Commander's broad forehead like dew on a melon. His horse was nervous, rolling her eyes, backing away from the dead men as far as her lead would allow. Jon led her off a few paces, fighting to keep her from bolt-

ing. The horses did not like the feel of this place. For that
matter, neither did Jon.

The dogs liked it least of all. Ghost had led the party
here; the pack of hounds had been useless. When Bass the
kennelmaster had tried to get them to take the scent from
the severed hand, they had gone wild, yowling and barking, fighting to get away. Even now they were snarling
and whimpering by turns, pulling at their leashes while
Chett cursed them for curs.

It is only a wood, Jon told himself, *and they're only
dead men.* He had seen dead men before . . .

Last night he had dreamt the Winterfell dream again.
He was wandering the empty castle, searching for his father, descending into the crypts. Only this time the
dream had gone further than before. In the dark he'd
heard the scrape of stone on stone. When he turned he
saw that the vaults were opening, one after the other. As
the dead kings came stumbling from their cold black
graves, Jon had woken in pitch-dark, his heart hammering. Even when Ghost leapt up on the bed to nuzzle at his
face, he could not shake his deep sense of terror. He dared
not go back to sleep. Instead he had climbed the Wall and
walked, restless, until he saw the light of the dawn off to
the east. *It was only a dream. I am a brother of the
Night's Watch now, not a frightened boy.*

Samwell Tarly huddled beneath the trees, half-hidden
behind the horses. His round fat face was the color of
curdled milk. So far he had not lurched off to the woods
to retch, but he had not so much as glanced at the dead
men either. "I can't look," he whispered miserably.

"You have to look," Jon told him, keeping his voice
low so the others would not hear. "Maester Aemon sent
you to be his eyes, didn't he? What good are eyes if they're
shut?"

"Yes, but . . . I'm such a coward, Jon."

Jon put a hand on Sam's shoulder. "We have a dozen
rangers with us, and the dogs, even Ghost. No one will
hurt you, Sam. Go ahead and look. The first look is the
hardest."

Sam gave a tremulous nod, working up his courage
with a visible effort. Slowly he swiveled his head. His
eyes widened, but Jon held his arm so he could not turn
away.

"Ser Jaremy," the Old Bear asked gruffly, "Ben Stark had six men with him when he rode from the Wall. Where are the others?"

Ser Jaremy shook his head. "Would that I knew."

Plainly Mormont was not pleased with that answer. "Two of our brothers butchered almost within sight of the Wall, yet your rangers heard nothing, saw nothing. Is this what the Night's Watch has fallen to? Do we still sweep these woods?"

"Yes, my lord, but—"

"Do we still mount watches?"

"We do, but—"

"This man wears a hunting horn." Mormont pointed at Othor. "Must I suppose that he died without sounding it? Or have your rangers all gone deaf as well as blind?"

Ser Jaremy bristled, his face taut with anger. "No horn was blown, my lord, or my rangers would have heard it. I do not have sufficient men to mount as many patrols as I should like . . . and since Benjen was lost, we have stayed closer to the Wall than we were wont to do before, by your own command."

The Old Bear grunted. "Yes. Well. Be that as it may." He made an impatient gesture. "Tell me how they died."

Squatting beside the dead man he had named Jafer Flowers, Ser Jaremy grasped his head by the scalp. The hair came out between his fingers, brittle as straw. The knight cursed and shoved at the face with the heel of his hand. A great gash in the side of the corpse's neck opened like a mouth, crusted with dried blood. Only a few ropes of pale tendon still attached the head to the neck. "This was done with an axe."

"Aye," muttered Dywen, the old forester. "Belike the axe that Othor carried, m'lord."

Jon could feel his breakfast churning in his belly, but he pressed his lips together and made himself look at the second body. Othor had been a big ugly man, and he made a big ugly corpse. No axe was in evidence. Jon remembered Othor; he had been the one bellowing the bawdy song as the rangers rode out. His singing days were done. His flesh was blanched white as milk, everywhere but his hands. His hands were black like Jafer's. Blossoms of hard cracked blood decorated the mortal wounds that covered him like a rash, breast and groin and throat. Yet his eyes were still open. They stared up at the sky, blue as sapphires.

Ser Jaremy stood. "The wildlings have axes too."

Mormont rounded on him. "So you believe this is Mance Rayder's work? This close to the Wall?"

"Who else, my lord?"

Jon could have told him. He knew, they all knew, yet no man of them would say the words. *The Others are only a story, a tale to make children shiver. If they ever lived at all, they are gone eight thousand years.* Even the thought made him feel foolish; he was a man grown now, a black brother of the Night's Watch, not the boy who'd once sat at Old Nan's feet with Bran and Robb and Arya.

Yet Lord Commander Mormont gave a snort. "If Ben Stark had come under wildling attack a half day's ride from Castle Black, he would have returned for more men, chased the killers through all seven hells and brought me back their heads."

"Unless he was slain as well," Ser Jaremy insisted.

The words hurt, even now. It had been so long, it seemed folly to cling to the hope that Ben Stark was still alive, but Jon Snow was nothing if not stubborn.

"It has been close on half a year since Benjen left us, my lord," Ser Jaremy went on. "The forest is vast. The wildlings might have fallen on him anywhere. I'd wager these two were the last survivors of his party, on their way back to us . . . but the enemy caught them before they could reach the safety of the Wall. The corpses are still fresh, these men cannot have been dead more than a day . . ."

"*No,*" Samwell Tarly squeaked.

Jon was startled. Sam's nervous, high-pitched voice was the last he would have expected to hear. The fat boy was frightened of the officers, and Ser Jaremy was not known for his patience.

"I did not ask for your views, boy," Rykker said coldly.

"Let him speak, ser," Jon blurted.

Mormont's eyes flicked from Sam to Jon and back again. "If the lad has something to say, I'll hear him out. Come closer, boy. We can't see you behind those horses."

Sam edged past Jon and the garrons, sweating profusely. "My lord, it . . . it can't be a day or . . . look . . . the blood . . ."

"Yes?" Mormont growled impatiently. "Blood, what of it?"

"He soils his smallclothes at the sight of it," Chett shouted out, and the rangers laughed.

Sam mopped at the sweat on his brow. "You . . . you can see where Ghost . . . Jon's direwolf . . . you can see where he tore off that man's hand, and yet . . . the stump hasn't bled, look . . ." He waved a hand. "My father . . . L-lord Randyll, he, he made me watch him dress animals sometimes, when . . . after . . ." Sam shook his head from side to side, his chins quivering. Now that he had looked at the bodies, he could not seem to look away. "A fresh kill . . . the blood would still flow, my lords. Later . . . later it would be clotted, like a . . . a jelly, thick and . . . and . . ." He looked as though he was going to be sick. "This man . . . look at the wrist, it's all . . . *crusty* . . . dry . . . like . . ."

Jon saw at once what Sam meant. He could see the torn veins in the dead man's wrist, iron worms in the pale flesh. His blood was a black dust. Yet Jaremy Rykker was unconvinced. "If they'd been dead much longer than a day, they'd be ripe by now, boy. They don't even smell."

Dywen, the gnarled old forester who liked to boast that he could smell snow coming on, sidled closer to the corpses and took a whiff. "Well, they're no pansy flowers, but . . . m'lord has the truth of it. There's no corpse stink."

"They . . . they aren't rotting." Sam pointed, his fat finger shaking only a little. "Look, there's . . . there's no maggots or . . . or . . . worms or anything . . . they've been lying here in the woods, but they . . . they haven't been chewed or eaten by animals . . . only Ghost . . . otherwise they're . . . they're . . ."

"Untouched," Jon said softly. "And Ghost is different. The dogs and the horses won't go near them."

The rangers exchanged glances; they could see it was true, every man of them. Mormont frowned, glancing from the corpses to the dogs. "Chett, bring the hounds closer."

Chett tried, cursing, yanking on the leashes, giving one animal a lick of his boot. Most of the dogs just whimpered and planted their feet. He tried dragging one. The bitch resisted, growling and squirming as if to escape her collar.

Finally she lunged at him. Chett dropped the leash and stumbled backward. The dog leapt over him and bounded off into the trees.

"This . . . this is all wrong," Sam Tarly said earnestly. "The blood . . . there's bloodstains on their clothes, and . . . and their flesh, dry and hard, but . . . there's none on the ground, or . . . anywhere. With those . . . those . . . those . . ." Sam made himself swallow, took a deep breath. "With those *wounds* . . . terrible wounds . . . there should be blood all over. Shouldn't there?"

Dywen sucked at his wooden teeth. "Might be they didn't die here. Might be someone brought 'em and left 'em for us. A warning, as like." The old forester peered down suspiciously. "And might be I'm a fool, but I don't know that Othor never had no blue eyes afore."

Ser Jaremy looked startled. "Neither did Flowers," he blurted, turning to stare at the dead man.

A silence fell over the wood. For a moment all they heard was Sam's heavy breathing and the wet sound of Dywen sucking on his teeth. Jon squatted beside Ghost.

"Burn them," someone whispered. One of the rangers; Jon could not have said who. "Yes, burn them," a second voice urged.

The Old Bear gave a stubborn shake of his head. "Not yet. I want Maester Aemon to have a look at them. We'll bring them back to the Wall."

Some commands are more easily given than obeyed. They wrapped the dead men in cloaks, but when Hake and Dywen tried to tie one onto a horse, the animal went mad, screaming and rearing, lashing out with its hooves, even biting at Ketter when he ran to help. The rangers had no better luck with the other garrons; not even the most placid wanted any part of these burdens. In the end they were forced to hack off branches and fashion crude slings to carry the corpses back on foot. It was well past midday by the time they started back.

"I will have these woods searched," Mormont commanded Ser Jaremy as they set out. "Every tree, every rock, every bush, and every foot of muddy ground within ten leagues of here. Use all the men you have, and if you do not have enough, borrow hunters and foresters from the stewards. If Ben and the others are out here, dead or alive, I will have them found. And if there is anyone *else* in these woods, I will know of it. You are to track them and take them, alive if possible. Is that understood?"

"It is, my lord," Ser Jaremy said. "It will be done."

After that, Mormont rode in silence, brooding. Jon followed close behind him; as the Lord Commander's steward, that was his place. The day was grey, damp, overcast, the sort of day that made you wish for rain. No wind stirred the wood; the air hung humid and heavy, and Jon's clothes clung to his skin. It was warm. Too warm. The Wall was weeping copiously, had been weeping for days, and sometimes Jon even imagined it was shrinking.

The old men called this weather *spirit summer*, and said it meant the season was giving up its ghosts at last. After this the cold would come, they warned, and a long summer always meant a long winter. This summer had lasted ten years. Jon had been a babe in arms when it began.

Ghost ran with them for a time and then vanished among the trees. Without the direwolf, Jon felt almost naked. He found himself glancing at every shadow with unease. Unbidden, he thought back on the tales that Old Nan used to tell them, when he was a boy at Winterfell. He could almost hear her voice again, and the *click-click-click* of her needles. *In that darkness, the Others came riding*, she used to say, dropping her voice lower and lower. *Cold and dead they were, and they hated iron and fire and the touch of the sun, and every living creature with hot blood in its veins. Holdfasts and cities and kingdoms of men all fell before them, as they moved south on pale dead horses, leading hosts of the slain. They fed their dead servants on the flesh of human children . . .*

When he caught his first glimpse of the Wall looming above the tops of an ancient gnarled oak, Jon was vastly relieved. Mormont reined up suddenly and turned in his saddle. "Tarly," he barked, "come here."

Jon saw the start of fright on Sam's face as he lumbered up on his mare; doubtless he thought he was in trouble. "You're fat but you're not stupid, boy," the Old Bear said gruffly. "You did well back there. And you, Snow."

Sam blushed a vivid crimson and tripped over his own tongue as he tried to stammer out a courtesy. Jon had to smile.

When they emerged from under the trees, Mormont spurred his tough little garron to a trot. Ghost came streaking out from the woods to meet them, licking his chops, his muzzle red from prey. High above, the men on the Wall saw the column approaching. Jon heard the deep, throaty call of the watchman's great horn, calling out across the miles; a single long blast that shuddered through the trees and echoed off the ice.

UUUUUUUooooooooooooooooooooooooooooooooooooo.

The sound faded slowly to silence. One blast meant rangers returning, and Jon thought, *I was a ranger for one day, at least. Whatever may come, they cannot take that away from me.*

Bowen Marsh was waiting at the first gate as they led their garrons through the icy tunnel. The Lord Steward was red-faced and agitated. "My lord," he blurted at Mormont as he swung open the iron bars, "there's been a bird, you must come at once."

"What is it, man?" Mormont said gruffly.

Curiously, Marsh glanced at Jon before he answered. "Maester Aemon has the letter. He's waiting in your solar."

"Very well. Jon, see to my horse, and tell Ser Jaremy to put the dead men in a storeroom until the maester is ready for them." Mormont strode away grumbling.

As they led their horses back to the stable, Jon was uncomfortably aware that people were watching him. Ser Alliser Thorne was drilling his boys in the yard, but he broke off to stare at Jon, a faint half smile on his lips. One-armed Donal Noye stood in the door of the armory. "The gods be with you, Snow," he called out.

Something's wrong, Jon thought. *Something's very wrong.*

The dead men were carried to one of the storerooms along the base of the Wall, a dark cold cell chiseled from the ice and used to keep meat and grain and sometimes even beer. Jon saw that Mormont's horse was fed and watered and groomed before he took care of his own. Afterward he sought out his friends. Grenn and Toad were on watch, but he found Pyp in the common hall. "What's happened?" he asked.

Pyp lowered his voice. "The king's dead."

Jon was stunned. Robert Baratheon had looked old and

fat when he visited Winterfell, yet he'd seemed hale enough, and there'd been no talk of illness. "How can you know?"

"One of the guards overheard Clydas reading the letter to Maester Aemon." Pyp leaned close. "Jon, I'm sorry. He was your father's friend, wasn't he?"

"They were as close as brothers, once." Jon wondered if Joffrey would keep his father as the King's Hand. It did not seem likely. That might mean Lord Eddard would return to Winterfell, and his sisters as well. He might even be allowed to visit them, with Lord Mormont's permission. It would be good to see Arya's grin again and to talk with his father. *I will ask him about my mother*, he resolved. *I am a man now, it is past time he told me. Even if she was a whore, I don't care, I want to know.*

"I heard Hake say the dead men were your uncle's," Pyp said.

"Yes," Jon replied. "Two of the six he took with him. They'd been dead a long time, only . . . the bodies are queer."

"Queer?" Pyp was all curiosity. "How queer?"

"Sam will tell you." Jon did not want to talk of it. "I should see if the Old Bear has need of me."

He walked to the Lord Commander's Tower alone, with a curious sense of apprehension. The brothers on guard eyed him solemnly as he approached. "The Old Bear's in his solar," one of them announced. "He was asking for you."

Jon nodded. He should have come straight from the stable. He climbed the tower steps briskly. *He wants wine or a fire in his hearth, that's all,* he told himself.

When he entered the solar, Mormont's raven screamed at him. *"Corn!"* the bird shrieked. *"Corn! Corn! Corn!"*

"Don't you believe it, I just fed him," the Old Bear growled. He was seated by the window, reading a letter. "Bring me a cup of wine, and pour one for yourself."

"For myself, my lord?"

Mormont lifted his eyes from the letter to stare at Jon. There was pity in that look; he could taste it. "You heard me."

Jon poured with exaggerated care, vaguely aware that he was drawing out the act. When the cups were filled, he would have no choice but to face whatever was in that letter. Yet all too soon, they were filled. "Sit, boy," Mormont commanded him. "Drink."

Jon remained standing. "It's my father, isn't it?"

The Old Bear tapped the letter with a finger. "Your father and the king," he rumbled. "I won't lie to you, it's grievous news. I never thought to see another king, not at my age, with Robert half my years and strong as a bull." He took a gulp of wine. "They say the king loved to hunt. The things we love destroy us every time, lad. Remember that. My son loved that young wife of his. Vain woman. If not for her, he would never have thought to sell those poachers."

Jon could scarcely follow what he was saying. "My lord, I don't understand. What's happened to my father?"

"I told you to sit," Mormont grumbled. *"Sit,"* the raven screamed. "And have a drink, damn you. That's a command, Snow."

Jon sat, and took a sip of wine.

"Lord Eddard has been imprisoned. He is charged with treason. It is said he plotted with Robert's brothers to deny the throne to Prince Joffrey."

"No," Jon said at once. "That couldn't be. My father would never betray the king!"

"Be that as it may," said Mormont. "It is not for me to say. Nor for you."

"But it's a *lie,*" Jon insisted. How could they think his father was a traitor, had they all gone mad? Lord Eddard Stark would never dishonor himself . . . would he?

He fathered a bastard, a small voice whispered inside him. *Where was the honor in that? And your mother, what of her? He will not even speak her name.*

"My lord, what will happen to him? Will they kill him?"

"As to that, I cannot say, lad. I mean to send a letter. I knew some of the king's councillors in my youth. Old Pycelle, Lord Stannis, Ser Barristan . . . Whatever your father has done, or hasn't done, he is a great lord. He must be allowed to take the black and join us here. Gods knows, we need men of Lord Eddard's ability."

Jon knew that other men accused of treason had been allowed to redeem their honor on the Wall in days past. Why not Lord Eddard? His father *here.* That was a strange thought, and strangely uncomfortable. It would be a mon-

strous injustice to strip him of Winterfell and force him to
take the black, and yet if it meant his life . . .

And would Joffrey allow it? He remembered the prince
at Winterfell, the way he'd mocked Robb and Ser Rodrik
in the yard. Jon himself he had scarcely even noticed; bastards were beneath even his contempt. "My lord, will the
king listen to you?"

The Old Bear shrugged. "A boy king . . . I imagine
he'll listen to his mother. A pity the dwarf isn't with
them. He's the lad's uncle, and he saw our need when he
visited us. It was a bad thing, your lady mother taking
him captive—"

"Lady Stark is not my mother," Jon reminded him
sharply. Tyrion Lannister had been a friend to him. If Lord
Eddard was killed, she would be as much to blame as the
queen. "My lord, what of my sisters? Arya and Sansa,
they were with my father, do you know—"

"Pycelle makes no mention of them, but doubtless
they'll be treated gently. I will ask about them when I
write." Mormont shook his head. "This could not have
happened at a worse time. If ever the realm needed a
strong king . . . there are dark days and cold nights
ahead, I feel it in my bones . . ." He gave Jon a long
shrewd look. "I hope you are not thinking of doing anything stupid, boy."

He's my father, Jon wanted to say, but he knew that
Mormont would not want to hear it. His throat was dry.
He made himself take another sip of wine.

"Your duty is here now," the Lord Commander reminded him. "Your old life ended when you took the
black." His bird made a raucous echo. *"Black."* Mormont
took no notice. "Whatever they do in King's Landing is
none of our concern." When Jon did not answer, the old
man finished his wine and said, "You're free to go. I'll
have no further need of you today. On the morrow you
can help me write that letter."

Jon did not remember standing or leaving the solar.
The next he knew, he was descending the tower steps,
thinking, *This is my father, my sisters, how can it be
none of my concern?*

Outside, one of the guards looked at him and said, "Be
strong, boy. The gods are cruel."

They know, Jon realized. "My father is no traitor," he

said hoarsely. Even the words stuck in his throat, as if to choke him. The wind was rising, and it seemed colder in the yard than it had when he'd gone in. Spirit summer was drawing to an end.

The rest of the afternoon passed as if in a dream. Jon could not have said where he walked, what he did, who he spoke with. Ghost was with him, he knew that much. The silent presence of the direwolf gave him comfort. *The girls do not even have that much*, he thought. *Their wolves might have kept them safe, but Lady is dead and Nymeria's lost, they're all alone.*

A north wind had begun to blow by the time the sun went down. Jon could hear it skirling against the Wall and over the icy battlements as he went to the common hall for the evening meal. Hobb had cooked up a venison stew, thick with barley, onions, and carrots. When he spooned an extra portion onto Jon's plate and gave him the crusty heel of the bread, he knew what it meant. *He knows.* He looked around the hall, saw heads turn quickly, eyes politely averted. *They all know.*

His friends rallied to him. "We asked the septon to light a candle for your father," Matthar told him. "It's a lie, we all know it's a lie, even *Grenn* knows it's a lie," Pyp chimed in. Grenn nodded, and Sam clasped Jon's hand, "You're my brother now, so he's my father too," the fat boy said. "If you want to go out to the weirwoods and pray to the old gods, I'll go with you."

The weirwoods were beyond the Wall, yet he knew Sam meant what he said. *They* are *my brothers*, he thought. *As much as Robb and Bran and Rickon . . .*

And then he heard the laughter, sharp and cruel as a whip, and the voice of Ser Alliser Thorne. "Not only a bastard, but a *traitor's* bastard," he was telling the men around him.

In the blink of an eye, Jon had vaulted onto the table, dagger in his hand. Pyp made a grab for him, but he wrenched his leg away, and then he was sprinting down the table and kicking the bowl from Ser Alliser's hand. Stew went flying everywhere, spattering the brothers. Thorne recoiled. People were shouting, but Jon Snow did not hear them. He lunged at Ser Alliser's face with the dagger, slashing at those cold onyx eyes, but Sam threw himself between them and before Jon could get around him, Pyp was on his back clinging like a monkey, and Grenn was grabbing his arm while Toad wrenched the knife from his fingers.

Later, much later, after they had marched him back to his sleeping cell, Mormont came down to see him, raven on his shoulder. "I told you not to do anything stupid, boy," the Old Bear said. *"Boy,"* the bird chorused. Mormont shook his head, disgusted. "And to think I had high hopes for you."

They took his knife and his sword and told him he was not to leave his cell until the high officers met to decide what was to be done with him. And then they placed a guard outside his door to make certain he obeyed. His friends were not allowed to see him, but the Old Bear did relent and permit him Ghost, so he was not utterly alone.

"My father is no traitor," he told the direwolf when the rest had gone. Ghost looked at him in silence. Jon slumped against the wall, hands around his knees, and stared at the candle on the table beside his narrow bed. The flame flickered and swayed, the shadows moved around him, the room seemed to grow darker and colder. *I will not sleep tonight,* Jon thought.

Yet he must have dozed. When he woke, his legs were stiff and cramped and the candle had long since burned out. Ghost stood on his hind legs, scrabbling at the door. Jon was startled to see how tall he'd grown. "Ghost, what is it?" he called softly. The direwolf turned his head and looked down at him, baring his fangs in a silent snarl. *Has he gone mad?* Jon wondered. "It's me, Ghost," he murmured, trying not to sound afraid. Yet he was trembling, violently. When had it gotten so cold?

Ghost backed away from the door. There were deep gouges where he'd raked the wood. Jon watched him with mounting disquiet. "There's someone out there, isn't there?" he whispered. Crouching, the direwolf crept backward, white fur rising on the back of his neck. *The guard,* he thought, *they left a man to guard my door, Ghost smells him through the door, that's all it is.*

Slowly, Jon pushed himself to his feet. He was shivering uncontrollably, wishing he still had a sword. Three quick steps brought him to the door. He grabbed the handle and pulled it inward. The *creak* of the hinges almost made him jump.

His guard was sprawled bonelessly across the narrow steps, looking up at him. Looking *up* at him, even though he was lying on his stomach. His head had been twisted completely around.

It can't be, Jon told himself. *This is the Lord Commander's Tower, it's guarded day and night, this couldn't happen, it's a dream, I'm having a nightmare.*

Ghost slid past him, out the door. The wolf started up the steps, stopped, looked back at Jon. That was when he heard it, the soft scrape of a boot on stone, the sound of a latch turning. The sounds came from above. From the Lord Commander's chambers.

A nightmare this might be, yet it was no dream.

The guard's sword was in its sheath. Jon knelt and worked it free. The heft of steel in his fist made him bolder. He moved up the steps, Ghost padding silently before him. Shadows lurked in every turn of the stair. Jon crept up warily, probing any suspicious darkness with the point of his sword.

Suddenly he heard the shriek of Mormont's raven. *"Corn,"* the bird was screaming. *"Corn, corn, corn, corn, corn, corn."* Ghost bounded ahead, and Jon came scrambling after. The door to Mormont's solar was wide open. The direwolf plunged through. Jon stopped in the doorway, blade in hand, giving his eyes a moment to adjust. Heavy drapes had been pulled across the windows, and the darkness was black as ink. *"Who's there?"* he called out.

Then he saw it, a shadow in the shadows, sliding toward the inner door that led to Mormont's sleeping cell, a man-shape all in black, cloaked and hooded . . . but beneath the hood, its eyes shone with an icy blue radiance . . .

Ghost leapt. Man and wolf went down together with neither scream nor snarl, rolling, smashing into a chair, knocking over a table laden with papers. Mormont's raven was flapping overhead, screaming, *"Corn, corn, corn, corn."* Jon felt as blind as Maester Aemon. Keeping the wall to his back, he slid toward the window and ripped down the curtain. Moonlight flooded the solar. He glimpsed black hands buried in white fur, swollen dark fingers tightening around his direwolf's throat. Ghost was twisting and snapping, legs flailing in the air, but he could not break free.

Jon had no time to be afraid. He threw himself forward, shouting, bringing down the longsword with all his weight behind it. Steel sheared through sleeve and skin and bone, yet the sound was *wrong* somehow. The smell that engulfed him was so queer and cold he almost gagged. He saw arm and hand on the floor, black fingers wriggling in a pool of moonlight. Ghost wrenched free of the other hand and crept away, red tongue lolling from his mouth.

The hooded man lifted his pale moon face, and Jon slashed at it without hesitation. The sword laid the intruder open to the bone, taking off half his nose and opening a gash cheek to cheek under those eyes, eyes, eyes like blue stars burning. Jon knew that face. *Othor*, he thought, reeling back. *Gods, he's dead, he's dead, I saw him dead.*

He felt something scrabble at his ankle. Black fingers clawed at his calf. The arm was crawling up his leg, ripping at wool and flesh. Shouting with revulsion, Jon pried the fingers off his leg with the point of his sword and flipped the thing away. It lay writhing, fingers opening and closing.

The corpse lurched forward. There was no blood. One-armed, face cut near in half, it seemed to feel nothing. Jon held the longsword before him. "Stay away!" he commanded, his voice gone shrill. *"Corn,"* screamed the raven, *"corn, corn."* The severed arm was wriggling out of its torn sleeve, a pale snake with a black five-fingered head. Ghost pounced and got it between his teeth. Finger bones crunched. Jon hacked at the corpse's neck, felt the steel bite deep and hard.

Dead Othor slammed into him, knocking him off his feet.

Jon's breath went out of him as the fallen table caught him between his shoulder blades. The sword, where was the sword? He'd lost the damned *sword*! When he opened his mouth to scream, the wight jammed its black corpse fingers into Jon's mouth. Gagging, he tried to shove it off, but the dead man was too heavy. Its hand forced itself farther down his throat, icy cold, choking him. Its face was against his own, filling the world. Frost covered its eyes, sparkling blue. Jon raked cold flesh with his nails and kicked at the thing's legs. He tried to bite, tried to punch, tried to breathe . . .

And suddenly the corpse's weight was gone, its fingers ripped from his throat. It was all Jon could do to roll over, retching and shaking. Ghost had it again. He watched as the direwolf buried his teeth in the wight's gut and began to rip and tear. He watched, only half conscious, for a long moment before he finally remembered to look for his sword . . .

. . . and saw Lord Mormont, naked and groggy from sleep, standing in the doorway with an oil lamp in hand. Gnawed and fingerless, the arm thrashed on the floor, wriggling toward him.

Jon tried to shout, but his voice was gone. Staggering to his feet, he kicked the arm away and snatched the lamp from the Old Bear's fingers. The flame flickered and almost died. *"Burn!"* the raven cawed. *"Burn, burn, burn!"*

Spinning, Jon saw the drapes he'd ripped from the window. He flung the lamp into the puddled cloth with both hands. Metal crunched, glass shattered, oil spewed, and the hangings went up in a great *whoosh* of flame. The heat of it on his face was sweeter than any kiss Jon had ever known. "Ghost!" he shouted.

The direwolf wrenched free and came to him as the wight struggled to rise, dark snakes spilling from the great wound in its belly. Jon plunged his hand into the flames, grabbed a fistful of the burning drapes, and whipped them at the dead man. *Let it burn*, he prayed as the cloth smothered the corpse, *gods, please, please, let it burn.*

BRAN

The Karstarks came in on a cold windy morning, bringing three hundred horsemen and near two thousand foot from their castle at Karhold. The steel points of their pikes winked in the pale sunlight as the column approached. A man went before them, pounding out a slow, deep-throated marching rhythm on a drum that was bigger than he was, *boom, boom, boom*.

Bran watched them come from a guard turret atop the outer wall, peering through Maester Luwin's bronze far-eye while perched on Hodor's shoulders. Lord Rickard himself led them, his sons Harrion and Eddard and Torrhen riding beside him beneath night-black banners emblazoned with the white sunburst of their House. Old Nan said they had Stark blood in them, going back hundreds of years, but they did not look like Starks to Bran. They were big men, and fierce, faces covered with thick beards, hair worn loose past the shoulders. Their cloaks were made of skins, the pelts of bear and seal and wolf.

They were the last, he knew. The other lords were already here, with their hosts. Bran yearned to ride out among them, to see the winter houses full to bursting, the jostling crowds in the market square every morning, the streets rutted and torn by wheel and hoof. But Robb had forbidden him to leave the castle. "We have no men to spare to guard you," his brother had explained.

"I'll take Summer," Bran argued.

"Don't act the boy with me, Bran," Robb said. "You know better than that. Only two days ago one of Lord Bolton's men knifed one of Lord Cerwyn's at the Smoking Log. Our lady mother would skin me for a pelt if I let you put yourself at risk." He was using the voice of Robb the Lord when he said it; Bran knew that meant there was no appeal.

It was because of what had happened in the wolfs-wood, he knew. The memory still gave him bad dreams. He had been as helpless as a baby, no more able to defend himself than Rickon would have been. Less, even . . . Rickon would have kicked them, at the least. It shamed him. He was only a few years younger than Robb; if his brother was almost a man grown, so was he. He should have been able to protect himself.

A year ago, *before,* he would have visited the town even if it meant climbing over the walls by himself. In those days he could run down stairs, get on and off his pony by himself, and wield a wooden sword good enough to knock Prince Tommen in the dirt. Now he could only watch, peering out through Maester Luwin's lens tube. The maester had taught him all the banners: the mailed fist of the Glovers, silver on scarlet; Lady Mormont's black bear; the hideous flayed man that went before Roose Bolton of the Dreadfort; a bull moose for the Hornwoods; a battle-axe for the Cerwyns; three sentinel trees for the Tallharts; and the fearsome sigil of House Umber, a roaring giant in shattered chains.

And soon enough he learned the faces too, when the lords and their sons and knights retainer came to Winterfell to feast. Even the Great Hall was not large enough to seat all of them at once, so Robb hosted each of the principal bannermen in turn. Bran was always given the place of honor at his brother's right hand. Some of the lords bannermen gave him queer hard stares as he sat there, as if they wondered by what right a green boy should be placed above them, and him a cripple too.

"How many is it now?" Bran asked Maester Luwin as

Lord Karstark and his sons rode through the gates in the outer wall.

"Twelve thousand men, or near enough as makes no matter."

"How many knights?"

"Few enough," the maester said with a touch of impatience. "To be a knight, you must stand your vigil in a sept, and be anointed with the seven oils to consecrate your vows. In the north, only a few of the great houses worship the Seven. The rest honor the old gods, and name no knights . . . but those lords and their sons and sworn swords are no less fierce or loyal or honorable. A man's worth is not marked by a *ser* before his name. As I have told you a hundred times before."

"Still," said Bran, "how many knights?"

Maester Luwin sighed. "Three hundred, perhaps four . . . among three thousand armored lances who are not knights."

"Lord Karstark is the last," Bran said thoughtfully. "Robb will feast him tonight."

"No doubt he will."

"How long before . . . before they go?"

"He must march soon, or not at all," Maester Luwin said. "The winter town is full to bursting, and this army of his will eat the countryside clean if it camps here much longer. Others are waiting to join him all along the kingsroad, barrow knights and crannogmen and the Lords Manderly and Flint. The fighting has begun in the riverlands, and your brother has many leagues to go."

"I know." Bran felt as miserable as he sounded. He handed the bronze tube back to the maester, and noticed how thin Luwin's hair had grown on top. He could see the pink of scalp showing through. It felt queer to look down on him this way, when he'd spent his whole life looking up at him, but when you sat on Hodor's back you looked down on everyone. "I don't want to watch anymore. Hodor, take me back to the keep."

"Hodor," said Hodor.

Maester Luwin tucked the tube up his sleeve. "Bran, your lord brother will not have time to see you now. He must greet Lord Karstark and his sons and make them welcome."

"I won't trouble Robb. I want to visit the godswood."
He put his hand on Hodor's shoulder. "Hodor."

A series of chisel-cut handholds made a ladder in the
granite of the tower's inner wall. Hodor hummed tunelessly as he went down hand under hand, Bran bouncing
against his back in the wicker seat that Maester Luwin
had fashioned for him. Luwin had gotten the idea from
the baskets the women used to carry firewood on their
backs; after that it had been a simple matter of cutting
legholes and attaching some new straps to spread Bran's
weight more evenly. It was not as good as riding Dancer,
but there were places Dancer could not go, and this did
not shame Bran the way it did when Hodor carried him in
his arms like a baby. Hodor seemed to like it too, though
with Hodor it was hard to tell. The only tricky part was
doors. Sometimes Hodor *forgot* that he had Bran on his
back, and that could be painful when he went through a
door.

For near a fortnight there had been so many comings
and goings that Robb ordered both portcullises kept up
and the drawbridge down between them, even in the dead
of night. A long column of armored lancers was crossing
the moat between the walls when Bran emerged from the
tower; Karstark men, following their lords into the castle.
They wore black iron halfhelms and black woolen cloaks
patterned with the white sunburst. Hodor trotted along
beside them, smiling to himself, his boots thudding
against the wood of the drawbridge. The riders gave them
queer looks as they went by, and once Bran heard someone guffaw. He refused to let it trouble him. "Men will
look at you," Maester Luwin had warned him the first
time they had strapped the wicker basket around Hodor's
chest. "They will look, and they will talk, and some will
mock you." *Let them mock*, Bran thought. No one
mocked him in his bedchamber, but he would not live his
life in bed.

As they passed beneath the gatehouse portcullis, Bran
put two fingers into his mouth and whistled. Summer
came loping across the yard. Suddenly the Karstark lancers were fighting for control, as their horses rolled their
eyes and whickered in dismay. One stallion reared,
screaming, his rider cursing and hanging on desperately.
The scent of the direwolves sent horses into a frenzy of

fear if they were not accustomed to it, but they'd quiet soon enough once Summer was gone. "The godswood," Bran reminded Hodor.

Even Winterfell itself was crowded. The yard rang to the sound of sword and axe, the rumble of wagons, and the barking of dogs. The armory doors were open, and Bran glimpsed Mikken at his forge, his hammer ringing as sweat dripped off his bare chest. Bran had never seen as many strangers in all his years, not even when King Robert had come to visit Father.

He tried not to flinch as Hodor ducked through a low door. They walked down a long dim hallway, Summer padding easily beside them. The wolf glanced up from time to time, eyes smoldering like liquid gold. Bran would have liked to touch him, but he was riding too high for his hand to reach.

The godswood was an island of peace in the sea of chaos that Winterfell had become. Hodor made his way through the dense stands of oak and ironwood and sentinels, to the still pool beside the heart tree. He stopped under the gnarled limbs of the weirwood, humming. Bran reached up over his head and pulled himself out of his seat, drawing the dead weight of his legs up through the holes in the wicker basket. He hung for a moment, dangling, the dark red leaves brushing against his face, until Hodor lifted him and lowered him to the smooth stone beside the water. "I want to be by myself for a while," he said. "You go soak. Go to the pools."

"Hodor." Hodor stomped through the trees and vanished. Across the godswood, beneath the windows of the Guest House, an underground hot spring fed three small ponds. Steam rose from the water day and night, and the wall that loomed above was thick with moss. Hodor hated cold water, and would fight like a treed wildcat when threatened with soap, but he would happily immerse himself in the hottest pool and sit for hours, giving a loud burp to echo the spring whenever a bubble rose from the murky green depths to break upon the surface.

Summer lapped at the water and settled down at Bran's side. He rubbed the wolf under the jaw, and for a moment boy and beast both felt at peace. Bran had always liked the godswood, even *before*, but of late he found himself drawn to it more and more. Even the heart tree no longer

scared him the way it used to. The deep red eyes carved
into the pale trunk still watched him, yet somehow he
took comfort from that now. The gods were looking over
him, he told himself; the old gods, gods of the Starks and
the First Men and the children of the forest, his *father's*
gods. He felt safe in their sight, and the deep silence of the
trees helped him think. Bran had been thinking a lot since
his fall; thinking, and dreaming, and talking with the
gods.

"Please make it so Robb won't go away," he prayed
softly. He moved his hand through the cold water, sending ripples across the pool. "Please make him stay. Or if
he has to go, bring him home safe, with Mother and Father and the girls. And make it . . . make it so Rickon
understands."

His baby brother had been wild as a winter storm since
he learned Robb was riding off to war, weeping and angry
by turns. He'd refused to eat, cried and screamed for most
of a night, even punched Old Nan when she tried to sing
him to sleep, and the next day he'd vanished. Robb had
set half the castle searching for him, and when at last
they'd found him down in the crypts, Rickon had slashed
at them with a rusted iron sword he'd snatched from a
dead king's hand, and Shaggydog had come slavering out
of the darkness like a green-eyed demon. The wolf was
near as wild as Rickon; he'd bitten Gage on the arm and
torn a chunk of flesh from Mikken's thigh. It had taken
Robb himself and Grey Wind to bring him to bay. Farlen
had the black wolf chained up in the kennels now, and
Rickon cried all the more for being without him.

Maester Luwin counseled Robb to remain at
Winterfell, and Bran pleaded with him too, for his own
sake as much as Rickon's, but his brother only shook his
head stubbornly and said, "I don't want to go. I *have* to."

It was only half a lie. Someone had to go, to hold the
Neck and help the Tullys against the Lannisters, Bran
could understand that, but it did not *have* to be Robb. His
brother might have given the command to Hal Mollen or
Theon Greyjoy, or to one of his lords bannermen. Maester
Luwin urged him to do just that, but Robb would not hear
of it. "My lord father would never have sent men off to
die while he huddled like a craven behind the walls of
Winterfell," he said, all Robb the Lord.

Robb seemed half a stranger to Bran now, transformed, a lord in truth, though he had not yet seen his sixteenth name day. Even their father's bannermen seemed to sense it. Many tried to test him, each in his own way. Roose Bolton and Robett Glover both demanded the honor of battle command, the first brusquely, the second with a smile and a jest. Stout, grey-haired Maege Mormont, dressed in mail like a man, told Robb bluntly that he was young enough to be her grandson, and had no business giving her commands . . . but as it happened, she had a granddaughter she would be willing to have him marry. Soft-spoken Lord Cerwyn had actually brought his daughter with him, a plump, homely maid of thirty years who sat at her father's left hand and never lifted her eyes from her plate. Jovial Lord Hornwood had no daughters, but he did bring gifts, a horse one day, a haunch of venison the next, a silver-chased hunting horn the day after, and he asked nothing in return . . . nothing but a certain hold-fast taken from his grandfather, and hunting rights north of a certain ridge, and leave to dam the White Knife, if it please the lord.

Robb answered each of them with cool courtesy, much as Father might have, and somehow he bent them to his will.

And when Lord Umber, who was called the Greatjon by his men and stood as tall as Hodor and twice as wide, threatened to take his forces home if he was placed behind the Hornwoods or the Cerwyns in the order of march, Robb told him he was welcome to do so. "And when we are done with the Lannisters," he promised, scratching Grey Wind behind the ear, "we will march back north, root you out of your keep, and hang you for an oathbreaker." Cursing, the Greatjon flung a flagon of ale into the fire and bellowed that Robb was so green he must piss grass. When Hallis Mollen moved to restrain him, he knocked him to the floor, kicked over a table, and unsheathed the biggest, ugliest greatsword that Bran had ever seen. All along the benches, his sons and brothers and sworn swords leapt to their feet, grabbing for their steel.

Yet Robb only said a quiet word, and in a snarl and the blink of an eye Lord Umber was on his back, his sword spinning on the floor three feet away and his hand drip-

ping blood where Grey Wind had bitten off two fingers.
"My lord father taught me that it was death to bare steel
against your liege lord," Robb said, "but doubtless you
only meant to cut my meat." Bran's bowels went to water
as the Greatjon struggled to rise, sucking at the red
stumps of fingers . . . but then, astonishingly, the huge
man *laughed*. "Your meat," he roared, "is bloody *tough*."

And somehow after that the Greatjon became Robb's
right hand, his staunchest champion, loudly telling all
and sundry that the boy lord was a Stark after all, and
they'd damn well better bend their knees if they didn't
fancy having them chewed off.

Yet that very night, his brother came to Bran's bedchamber pale and shaken, after the fires had burned low
in the Great Hall. "I thought he was going to kill me,"
Robb confessed. "Did you see the way he threw down
Hal, like he was no bigger than Rickon? Gods, I was so
scared. And the Greatjon's not the worst of them, only
the loudest. Lord Roose never says a word, he only looks
at me, and all I can think of is that room they have in the
Dreadfort, where the Boltons hang the skins of their enemies."

"That's just one of Old Nan's stories," Bran said. A
note of doubt crept into his voice. "Isn't it?"

"I don't know." He gave a weary shake of his head.
"Lord Cerwyn means to take his daughter south with us.
To cook for him, he says. Theon is certain I'll find the girl
in my bedroll one night. I wish . . . I wish Father was
here . . ."

That was the one thing they could agree on, Bran and
Rickon and Robb the Lord; they all wished Father was
here. But Lord Eddard was a thousand leagues away, a
captive in some dungeon, a hunted fugitive running for
his life, or even dead. No one seemed to know for certain;
every traveler told a different tale, each more terrifying
than the last. The heads of Father's guardsmen were rotting on the walls of the Red Keep, impaled on spikes. King
Robert was dead at Father's hands. The Baratheons had
laid siege to King's Landing. Lord Eddard had fled south
with the king's wicked brother Renly. Arya and Sansa had
been murdered by the Hound. Mother had killed Tyrion
the Imp and hung his body from the walls of Riverrun.
Lord Tywin Lannister was marching on the Eyrie, burning

and slaughtering as he went. One wine-sodden taleteller even claimed that Rhaegar Targaryen had returned from the dead and was marshaling a vast host of ancient heroes on Dragonstone to reclaim his father's throne.

When the raven came, bearing a letter marked with Father's own seal and written in Sansa's hand, the cruel truth seemed no less incredible. Bran would never forget the look on Robb's face as he stared at their sister's words. "She says Father conspired at treason with the king's brothers," he read. "King Robert is dead, and Mother and I are summoned to the Red Keep to swear fealty to Joffrey. She says we must be loyal, and when she marries Joffrey she will plead with him to spare our lord father's life." His fingers closed into a fist, crushing Sansa's letter between them. "And she says nothing of Arya, *nothing*, not so much as a word. Damn her! What's wrong with the girl?"

Bran felt all cold inside. "She lost her wolf," he said, weakly, remembering the day when four of his father's guardsmen had returned from the south with Lady's bones. Summer and Grey Wind and Shaggydog had begun to howl before they crossed the drawbridge, in voices drawn and desolate. Beneath the shadow of the First Keep was an ancient lichyard, its headstones spotted with pale lichen, where the old Kings of Winter had laid their faithful servants. It was there they buried Lady, while her brothers stalked between the graves like restless shadows. She had gone south, and only her bones had returned.

Their grandfather, old Lord Rickard, had gone as well, with his son Brandon who was Father's brother, and two hundred of his best men. None had ever returned. And Father had gone south, with Arya and Sansa, and Jory and Hullen and Fat Tom and the rest, and later Mother and Ser Rodrik had gone, and *they* hadn't come back either. And now Robb meant to go. Not to King's Landing and not to swear fealty, but to Riverrun, with a sword in his hand. And if their lord father were truly a prisoner, that could mean his death for a certainty. It frightened Bran more than he could say.

"If Robb has to go, watch over him," Bran entreated the old gods, as they watched him with the heart tree's red eyes, "and watch over his men, Hal and Quent and the rest, and Lord Umber and Lady Mormont and the other lords. And Theon too, I suppose. Watch them and keep them safe, if it please you, gods. Help them defeat the Lannisters and save Father and bring them home."

A faint wind sighed through the godswood and the red leaves stirred and whispered. Summer bared his teeth. "You hear them, boy?" a voice asked.

Bran lifted his head. Osha stood across the pool, beneath an ancient oak, her face shadowed by leaves. Even in irons, the wildling moved quiet as a cat. Summer circled the pool, sniffed at her. The tall woman flinched.

"Summer, to me," Bran called. The direwolf took one final sniff, spun, and bounded back. Bran wrapped his arms around him. "What are *you* doing here?" He had not seen Osha since they'd taken her captive in the wolfswood, though he knew she'd been set to working in the kitchens.

"They are my gods too," Osha said. "Beyond the Wall, they are the only gods." Her hair was growing out, brown and shaggy. It made her look more womanly, that and the simple dress of brown roughspun they'd given her when they took her mail and leather. "Gage lets me have my prayers from time to time, when I feel the need, and I let him do as he likes under my skirt, when he feels the need. It's nothing to me. I like the smell of flour on his hands, and he's gentler than Stiv." She gave an awkward bow. "I'll leave you. There's pots that want scouring."

"No, stay," Bran commanded her. "Tell me what you meant, about hearing the gods."

Osha studied him. "You asked them and they're answering. Open your ears, listen, you'll hear."

Bran listened. "It's only the wind," he said after a moment, uncertain. "The leaves are rustling."

"Who do you think sends the wind, if not the gods?" She seated herself across the pool from him, clinking faintly as she moved. Mikken had fixed iron manacles to her ankles, with a heavy chain between them; she could walk, so long as she kept her strides small, but there was no way for her to run, or climb, or mount a horse. "They see you, boy. They hear you talking. That rustling, that's them talking back."

"What are they saying?"

"They're sad. Your lord brother will get no help from them, not where he's going. The old gods have no power in the south. The weirwoods there were all cut down, thousands of years ago. How can they watch your brother when they have no eyes?"

Bran had not thought of that. It frightened him. If even the gods could not help his brother, what hope was there? Maybe Osha wasn't hearing them right. He cocked his head and tried to listen again. He thought he could hear the sadness now, but nothing more than that.

The rustling grew louder. Bran heard muffled footfalls and a low humming, and Hodor came blundering out of the trees, naked and smiling. "Hodor!"

"He must have heard our voices," Bran said. "Hodor, you forgot your clothes."

"Hodor," Hodor agreed. He was dripping wet from the neck down, steaming in the chill air. His body was covered with brown hair, thick as a pelt. Between his legs, his manhood swung long and heavy.

Osha eyed him with a sour smile. "Now there's a big man," she said. "He has giant's blood in him, or I'm the queen."

"Maester Luwin says there are no more giants. He says they're all dead, like the children of the forest. All that's left of them are old bones in the earth that men turn up with plows from time to time."

"Let Maester Luwin ride beyond the Wall," Osha said. "He'll find giants then, or they'll find him. My brother killed one. Ten foot tall she was, and stunted at that. They've been known to grow big as twelve and thirteen feet. Fierce things they are too, all hair and teeth, and the wives have beards like their husbands, so there's no telling them apart. The women take human men for lovers, and it's from them the half bloods come. It goes harder on the women they catch. The men are so big they'll rip a maid apart before they get her with child." She grinned at him. "But you don't know what I mean, do you, boy?"

"Yes I do," Bran insisted. He understood about mating; he had seen dogs in the yard, and watched a stallion mount a mare. But talking about it made him uncomfortable. He looked at Hodor. "Go back and bring your clothes, Hodor," he said. "Go dress."

"Hodor." He walked back the way he had come, ducking under a low-hanging tree limb.

He *was* awfully big, Bran thought as he watched him

go. "Are there truly giants beyond the Wall?" he asked Osha, uncertainly.

"Giants and worse than giants, Lordling. I tried to tell your brother when he asked his questions, him and your maester and that smiley boy Greyjoy. The cold winds are rising, and men go out from their fires and never come back . . . or if they do, they're not *men* no more, but only wights, with blue eyes and cold black hands. Why do you think I run south with Stiv and Hali and the rest of them fools? Mance thinks he'll fight, the brave sweet stubborn man, like the white walkers were no more than rangers, but what does he know? He can call himself King-beyond-the-Wall all he likes, but he's still just another old black crow who flew down from the Shadow Tower. He's never tasted winter. I was *born* up there, child, like my mother and her mother before her and *her* mother before her, born of the Free Folk. We remember." Osha stood, her chains rattling together. "I tried to tell your lordling brother. Only yesterday, when I saw him in the yard. 'M'lord Stark,' I called to him, respectful as you please, but he looked through me, and that sweaty oaf Greatjon Umber shoves me out of the path. So be it. I'll wear my irons and hold my tongue. A man who won't listen can't hear."

"Tell *me*. Robb will listen to me, I know he will."

"Will he now? We'll see. You tell him this, m'lord. You tell him he's bound on marching the wrong way. It's north he should be taking his swords. *North*, not south. You hear me?"

Bran nodded. "I'll tell him."

But that night, when they feasted in the Great Hall, Robb was not with them. He took his meal in the solar instead, with Lord Rickard and the Greatjon and the other lords bannermen, to make the final plans for the long march to come. It was left to Bran to fill his place at the head of the table, and act the host to Lord Karstark's sons and honored friends. They were already at their places when Hodor carried Bran into the hall on his back, and knelt beside the high seat. Two of the serving men helped lift him from his basket. Bran could feel the eyes of every stranger in the hall. It had grown quiet. "My lords," Hallis Mollen announced, "Brandon Stark, of Winterfell."

"I welcome you to our fires," Bran said stiffly, "and offer you meat and mead in honor of our friendship."

Harrion Karstark, the oldest of Lord Rickard's sons, bowed, and his brothers after him, yet as they settled back in their places he heard the younger two talking in low voices, over the clatter of wine cups. ". . . sooner die than live like that," muttered one, his father's namesake Eddard, and his brother Torrhen said likely the boy was broken inside as well as out, too craven to take his own life.

Broken, Bran thought bitterly as he clutched his knife. Is that what he was now? Bran the Broken? "I don't want to be broken," he whispered fiercely to Maester Luwin, who'd been seated to his right. "I want to be a knight."

"There are some who call my order the knights of the mind," Luwin replied. "You are a surpassing clever boy when you work at it, Bran. Have you ever thought that you might wear a maester's chain? There is no limit to what you might learn."

"I want to learn *magic,*" Bran told him. "The crow promised that I would fly."

Maester Luwin sighed. "I can teach you history, healing, herblore. I can teach you the speech of ravens, and how to build a castle, and the way a sailor steers his ship by the stars. I can teach you to measure the days and mark the seasons, and at the Citadel in Oldtown they can teach you a thousand things more. But, Bran, no man can teach you magic."

"The children could," Bran said. "The children of the forest." That reminded him of the promise he had made to Osha in the godswood, so he told Luwin what she had said.

The maester listened politely. "The wildling woman could give Old Nan lessons in telling tales, I think," he said when Bran was done. "I will talk with her again if you like, but it would be best if you did not trouble your brother with this folly. He has more than enough to concern him without fretting over giants and dead men in the woods. It's the Lannisters who hold your lord father, Bran, not the children of the forest." He put a gentle hand on Bran's arm. "Think on what I said, child."

And two days later, as a red dawn broke across a windswept sky, Bran found himself in the yard beneath the gatehouse, strapped atop Dancer as he said his farewells to his brother.

"You are the lord in Winterfell now," Robb told him. He was mounted on a shaggy grey stallion, his shield hung from the horse's side; wood banded with iron, white and grey, and on it the snarling face of a direwolf. His brother wore grey chainmail over bleached leathers, sword and dagger at his waist, a fur-trimmed cloak across his shoulders. "You must take my place, as I took Father's, until we come home."

"I know," Bran replied miserably. He had never felt so little or alone or scared. He did not know how to be a lord.

"Listen to Maester Luwin's counsel, and take care of Rickon. Tell him that I'll be back as soon as the fighting is done."

Rickon had refused to come down. He was up in his chamber, red-eyed and defiant. *"No!"* he'd screamed when Bran had asked if he didn't want to say farewell to Robb. *"NO farewell!"*

"I told him," Bran said. "He says no one ever comes back."

"He can't be a baby forever. He's a Stark, and near four." Robb sighed. "Well, Mother will be home soon. And I'll bring back Father, I promise."

He wheeled his courser around and trotted away. Grey Wind followed, loping beside the warhorse, lean and swift. Hallis Mollen went before them through the gate, carrying the rippling white banner of House Stark atop a high standard of grey ash. Theon Greyjoy and the Greatjon fell in on either side of Robb, and their knights formed up in a double column behind them, steel-tipped lances glinting in the sun.

Uncomfortably, he remembered Osha's words. *He's marching the wrong way,* he thought. For an instant he wanted to gallop after him and shout a warning, but when Robb vanished beneath the portcullis, the moment was gone.

Beyond the castle walls, a roar of sound went up. The foot soldiers and townsfolk were cheering Robb as he rode past, Bran knew; cheering for Lord Stark, for the Lord of Winterfell on his great stallion, with his cloak streaming and Grey Wind racing beside him. They would never cheer for him that way, he realized with a dull ache. He might be the lord in Winterfell while his brother and father were gone, but he was still Bran the Broken. He could not even get off his own horse, except to fall.

When the distant cheers had faded to silence and the yard was empty at last, Winterfell seemed deserted and dead. Bran looked around at the faces of those who remained, women and children and old men . . . and Hodor. The huge stableboy had a lost and frightened look to his face. "Hodor?" he said sadly.

"Hodor," Bran agreed, wondering what it meant.

DAENERYS

When he had taken his pleasure, Khal Drogo rose from their sleeping mats to tower above her. His skin shone dark as bronze in the ruddy light from the brazier, the faint lines of old scars visible on his broad chest. Ink-black hair, loose and unbound, cascaded over his shoulders and down his back, well past his waist. His manhood glistened wetly. The *khal*'s mouth twisted in a frown beneath the droop of his long mustachio. "The stallion who mounts the world has no need of iron chairs."

Dany propped herself on an elbow to look up at him, so tall and magnificent. She loved his hair especially. It had never been cut; he had never known defeat. "It was prophesied that the stallion will ride to the ends of the earth," she said.

"The earth ends at the black salt sea," Drogo answered at once. He wet a cloth in a basin of warm water to wipe the sweat and oil from his skin. "No horse can cross the poison water."

"In the Free Cities, there are ships by the thousand," Dany told him, as she had told him before. "Wooden horses with a hundred legs, that fly across the sea on wings full of wind."

Khal Drogo did not want to hear it. "We will speak no more of wooden horses and iron chairs." He dropped the cloth and began to dress. "This day I will go to the grass and hunt, woman wife," he announced as he shrugged into a painted vest and buckled on a wide belt with heavy medallions of silver, gold, and bronze.

"Yes, my sun-and-stars," Dany said. Drogo would take his bloodriders and ride in search of *hrakkar*, the great white lion of the plains. If they returned triumphant, her lord husband's joy would be fierce, and he might be willing to hear her out.

Savage beasts he did not fear, nor any man who had ever drawn breath, but the sea was a different matter. To the Dothraki, water that a horse could not drink was something foul; the heaving grey-green plains of the ocean filled them with superstitious loathing. Drogo was a bolder man than the other horselords in half a hundred ways, she had found . . . but not in this. If only she could get him onto a ship . . .

After the *khal* and his bloodriders had ridden off with their bows, Dany summoned her handmaids. Her body felt so fat and ungainly now that she welcomed the help of their strong arms and deft hands, whereas before she had often been uncomfortable with the way they fussed and fluttered about her. They scrubbed her clean and dressed her in sandsilk, loose and flowing. As Doreah combed out her hair, she sent Jhiqui to find Ser Jorah Mormont.

The knight came at once. He wore horsehair leggings and painted vest, like a rider. Coarse black hair covered his thick chest and muscular arms. "My princess. How may I serve you?"

"You must talk to my lord husband," Dany said. "Drogo says the stallion who mounts the world will have all the lands of the earth to rule, and no need to cross the poison water. He talks of leading his *khalasar* east after Rhaego is born, to plunder the lands around the Jade Sea."

The knight looked thoughtful. "The *khal* has never seen the Seven Kingdoms," he said. "They are nothing to him. If he thinks of them at all, no doubt he thinks of islands, a few small cities clinging to rocks in the manner of Lorath or Lys, surrounded by stormy seas. The riches of the east must seem a more tempting prospect."

"But he must ride *west*," Dany said, despairing. "Please, help me make him understand." She had never seen the Seven Kingdoms either, no more than Drogo, yet she felt as though she knew them from all the tales her brother had told her. Viserys had promised her a thousand times that he would take her back one day, but he was dead now and his promises had died with him.

"The Dothraki do things in their own time, for their own reasons," the knight answered. "Have patience, Princess. Do not make your brother's mistake. We will go home, I promise you."

Home? The word made her feel sad. Ser Jorah had his Bear Island, but what was home to her? A few tales, names recited as solemnly as the words of a prayer, the fading memory of a red door . . . was Vaes Dothrak to be her home forever? When she looked at the crones of the *dosh khaleen*, was she looking at her future?

Ser Jorah must have seen the sadness on her face. "A great caravan arrived during the night, *Khaleesi*. Four hundred horses, from Pentos by way of Norvos and Qohor, under the command of Merchant Captain Byan Votyris. Illyrio may have sent a letter. Would you care to visit the Western Market?"

Dany stirred. "Yes," she said. "I would like that." The markets came alive when a caravan had come in. You could never tell what treasures the traders might bring this time, and it would be good to hear men speaking Valyrian again, as they did in the Free Cities. "Irri, have them prepare a litter."

"I shall tell your *khas*," Ser Jorah said, withdrawing.

If Khal Drogo had been with her, Dany would have ridden her silver. Among the Dothraki, mothers stayed on horseback almost up to the moment of birth, and she did not want to seem weak in her husband's eyes. But with the *khal* off hunting, it was pleasant to lie back on soft cushions and be carried across Vaes Dothrak, with red silk curtains to shield her from the sun. Ser Jorah saddled up and rode beside her, with the four young men of her *khas* and her handmaids.

The day was warm and cloudless, the sky a deep blue. When the wind blew, she could smell the rich scents of grass and earth. As her litter passed beneath the stolen monuments, she went from sunlight to shadow and back again. Dany swayed along, studying the faces of dead heroes and forgotten kings. She wondered if the gods of burned cities could still answer prayers.

If I were not the blood of the dragon, she thought wistfully, *this could be my home.* She was *khaleesi,* she had a strong man and a swift horse, handmaids to serve her, warriors to keep her safe, an honored place in the *dosh khaleen* awaiting her when she grew old . . . and in her womb grew a son who would one day bestride the world. That should be enough for any woman . . . but not for the dragon. With Viserys gone, Daenerys was the last, the very last. She was the seed of kings and conquerors, and so too the child inside her. She must not forget.

The Western Market was a great square of beaten earth surrounded by warrens of mud-baked brick, animal pens, whitewashed drinking halls. Hummocks rose from the ground like the backs of great subterranean beasts breaking the surface, yawning black mouths leading down to cool and cavernous storerooms below. The interior of the square was a maze of stalls and crookback aisles, shaded by awnings of woven grass.

A hundred merchants and traders were unloading their goods and setting up in stalls when they arrived, yet even so the great market seemed hushed and deserted compared to the teeming bazaars that Dany remembered from Pentos and the other Free Cities. The caravans made their way to Vaes Dothrak from east and west not so much to sell to the Dothraki as to trade with each other, Ser Jorah had explained. The riders let them come and go unmolested, so long as they observed the peace of the sacred city, did not profane the Mother of Mountains or the Womb of the World, and honored the crones of the *dosh khaleen* with the traditional gifts of salt, silver, and seed. The Dothraki did not truly comprehend this business of buying and selling.

Dany liked the strangeness of the Eastern Market too, with all its queer sights and sounds and smells. She often spent her mornings there, nibbling tree eggs, locust pie, and green noodles, listening to the high ululating voices of the spellsingers, gaping at manticores in silver cages and immense grey elephants and the striped black-and-white horses of the Jogos Nhai. She enjoyed watching all the people too: dark solemn Asshai'i and tall pale Qartheen, the bright-eyed men of Yi Ti in monkey-tail hats, warrior maids from Bayasabhad, Shamyriana, and Kayakayanaya with iron rings in their nipples and rubies in their cheeks, even the dour and frightening Shadow Men, who covered their arms and legs and chests with tattoos and hid their faces behind masks. The Eastern Market was a place of wonder and magic for Dany.

But the Western Market smelled of home.

As Irri and Jhiqui helped her from her litter, she sniffed, and recognized the sharp odors of garlic and pepper, scents that reminded Dany of days long gone in the alleys of Tyrosh and Myr and brought a fond smile to her face. Under that she smelled the heady sweet perfumes of Lys. She saw slaves carrying bolts of intricate Myrish lace and fine wools in a dozen rich colors. Caravan guards wandered among the aisles in copper helmets and knee-length tunics of quilted yellow cotton, empty scabbards swinging from their woven leather belts. Behind one stall an armorer displayed steel breastplates worked with gold and silver in ornate patterns, and helms hammered in the shapes of fanciful beasts. Next to him was a pretty young woman selling Lannisport goldwork, rings and brooches and torcs and exquisitely wrought medallions suitable for belting. A huge eunuch guarded her stall, mute and hairless, dressed in sweat-stained velvets and scowling at anyone who came close. Across the aisle, a fat cloth trader from Yi Ti was haggling with a Pentoshi over the price of some green dye, the monkey tail on his hat swaying back and forth as he shook his head.

"When I was a little girl, I loved to play in the bazaar," Dany told Ser Jorah as they wandered down the shady aisle between the stalls. "It was so *alive* there, all the people shouting and laughing, so many wonderful things to look at . . . though we seldom had enough coin to buy anything . . . well, except for a sausage now and again, or honeyfingers . . . do they have honeyfingers in the Seven Kingdoms, the kind they bake in Tyrosh?"

"Cakes, are they? I could not say, Princess." The knight bowed. "If you would pardon me for a time, I will seek out the captain and see if he has letters for us."

"Very well. I'll help you find him."

"There is no need for you to trouble yourself." Ser Jorah glanced away impatiently. "Enjoy the market. I will rejoin you when my business is concluded."

Curious, Dany thought as she watched him stride off through the throngs. She didn't see why she should not go with him. Perhaps Ser Jorah meant to find a woman after he met with the merchant captain. Whores frequently traveled with the caravans, she knew, and some men were queerly shy about their couplings. She gave a shrug. "Come," she told the others.

Her handmaids trailed along as Dany resumed her stroll through the market. "Oh, look," she exclaimed to Doreah, "those are the kind of sausages I meant." She pointed to a stall where a wizened little woman was grilling meat and onions on a hot firestone. "They make them with lots of garlic and hot peppers." Delighted with her discovery, Dany insisted the others join her for a sausage. Her handmaids wolfed theirs down giggling and grinning, though the men of her *khas* sniffed at the grilled meat suspiciously. "They taste different than I remember," Dany said after her first few bites.

"In Pentos, I make them with pork," the old woman said, "but all my pigs died on the Dothraki sea. These are made of horsemeat, *Khaleesi,* but I spice them the same."

"Oh." Dany felt disappointed, but Quaro liked his sausage so well he decided to have another one, and Rakharo had to outdo him and eat three more, belching loudly. Dany giggled.

"You have not laughed since your brother the *Khal Rhaggat* was crowned by Drogo," said Irri. "It is good to see, *Khaleesi.*"

Dany smiled shyly. It *was* sweet to laugh. She felt half a girl again.

They wandered for half the morning. She saw a beautiful feathered cloak from the Summer Isles, and took it for a gift. In return, she gave the merchant a silver medallion from her belt. That was how it was done among the Dothraki. A birdseller taught a green-and-red parrot to say her name, and Dany laughed again, yet still refused to take him. What would she do with a green-and-red parrot in a *khalasar*? She did take a dozen flasks of scented oils, the perfumes of her childhood; she had only to close her eyes and sniff them and she could see the big house with the red door once more. When Doreah looked longingly at a fertility charm at a magician's booth, Dany took that too and gave it to the handmaid, thinking that now she should find something for Irri and Jhiqui as well.

Turning a corner, they came upon a wine merchant offering thimble-sized cups of his wares to the passersby. "Sweet reds," he cried in fluent Dothraki, "I have sweet reds, from Lys and Volantis and the Arbor. Whites from Lys, Tyroshi pear brandy, firewine, pepperwine, the pale green nectars of Myr. Smokeberry browns and Andalish sours, I have them, I have them." He was a small man, slender and handsome, his flaxen hair curled and perfumed after the fashion of Lys. When Dany paused before his stall, he bowed low. "A taste for the *khaleesi*? I have a sweet red from Dorne, my lady, it sings of plums and cherries and rich dark oak. A cask, a cup, a swallow? One taste, and you will name your child after me."

Dany smiled. "My son has his name, but I will try your summerwine," she said in Valyrian, Valyrian as they spoke it in the Free Cities. The words felt strange on her tongue, after so long. "Just a taste, if you would be so kind."

The merchant must have taken her for Dothraki, with her clothes and her oiled hair and sun-browned skin. When she spoke, he gaped at her in astonishment. "My lady, you are . . . Tyroshi? Can it be so?"

"My speech may be Tyroshi, and my garb Dothraki, but I am of Westeros, of the Sunset Kingdoms," Dany told him.

Doreah stepped up beside her. "You have the honor to address Daenerys of the House Targaryen, Daenerys Stormborn, *khaleesi* of the riding men and princess of the Seven Kingdoms."

The wine merchant dropped to his knees. "Princess," he said, bowing his head.

"Rise," Dany commanded him. "I would still like to taste that summerwine you spoke of."

The man bounded to his feet. "That? Dornish swill. It is not worthy of a princess. I have a dry red from the Arbor, crisp and delectable. Please, let me give you a cask."

Khal Drogo's visits to the Free Cities had given him a taste for good wine, and Dany knew that such a noble

vintage would please him. "You honor me, ser," she murmured sweetly.

"The honor is mine." The merchant rummaged about
in the back of his stall and produced a small oaken cask.
Burned into the wood was a cluster of grapes. "The
Redwyne sigil," he said, pointing, "for the Arbor. There is
no finer drink."

"Khal Drogo and I will share it together. Aggo, take
this back to my litter, if you'd be so kind." The wineseller
beamed as the Dothraki hefted the cask.

She did not realize that Ser Jorah had returned until
she heard the knight say, *"No."* His voice was strange,
brusque. "Aggo, put down that cask."

Aggo looked at Dany. She gave a hesitant nod. "Ser
Jorah, is something wrong?"

"I have a thirst. Open it, wineseller."

The merchant frowned. "The wine is for the *khaleesi,*
not for the likes of you, ser."

Ser Jorah moved closer to the stall. "If you don't open
it, I'll crack it open with your head." He carried no weapons here in the sacred city, save his hands—yet his hands
were enough, big, hard, dangerous, his knuckles covered
with coarse dark hairs. The wineseller hesitated a moment, then took up his hammer and knocked the plug
from the cask.

"Pour," Ser Jorah commanded. The four young warriors of Dany's *khas* arrayed themselves behind him,
frowning, watching with their dark, almond-shaped eyes.

"It would be a crime to drink this rich a wine without
letting it breathe." The wineseller had not put his hammer down.

Jhogo reached for the whip coiled at his belt, but Dany
stopped him with a light touch on the arm. "Do as Ser
Jorah says," she said. People were stopping to watch.

The man gave her a quick, sullen glance. "As the princess commands." He had to set aside his hammer to lift
the cask. He filled two thimble-sized tasting cups, pouring so deftly he did not spill a drop.

Ser Jorah lifted a cup and sniffed at the wine, frowning.

"Sweet, isn't it?" the wineseller said, smiling. "Can
you smell the fruit, ser? The perfume of the Arbor. Taste
it, my lord, and tell me it isn't the finest, richest wine
that's ever touched your tongue."

Ser Jorah offered him the cup. "You taste it first."

"Me?" The man laughed. "I am not worthy of this vintage, my lord. And it's a poor wine merchant who drinks up his own wares." His smile was amiable, yet she could see the sheen of sweat on his brow.

"You *will* drink," Dany said, cold as ice. "Empty the cup, or I will tell them to hold you down while Ser Jorah pours the whole cask down your throat."

The wineseller shrugged, reached for the cup . . . and grabbed the cask instead, flinging it at her with both hands. Ser Jorah bulled into her, knocking her out of the way. The cask bounced off his shoulder and smashed open on the ground. Dany stumbled and lost her feet. *"No,"* she screamed, thrusting her hands out to break her fall . . . and Doreah caught her by the arm and wrenched her backward, so she landed on her legs and not her belly.

The trader vaulted over the stall, darting between Aggo and Rakharo. Quaro reached for an *arakh* that was not there as the blond man slammed him aside. He raced down the aisle. Dany heard the snap of Jhogo's whip, saw the leather lick out and coil around the wineseller's leg. The man sprawled face first in the dirt.

A dozen caravan guards had come running. With them was the master himself, Merchant Captain Byan Votyris, a diminutive Norvoshi with skin like old leather and a bristling blue mustachio that swept up to his ears. He seemed to know what had happened without a word being spoken. "Take this one away to await the pleasure of the *khal*," he commanded, gesturing at the man on the ground. Two guards hauled the wineseller to his feet. "His goods I gift to you as well, Princess," the merchant captain went on. "Small token of regret, that one of mine would do this thing."

Doreah and Jhiqui helped Dany back to her feet. The poisoned wine was leaking from the broken cask into the dirt. "How did you know?" she asked Ser Jorah, trembling. *"How?"*

"I did not know, *Khaleesi,* not until the man refused to drink, but once I read Magister Illyrio's letter, I feared." His dark eyes swept over the faces of the strangers in the market. "Come. Best not to talk of it here."

Dany was near tears as they carried her back. The taste in her mouth was one she had known before: fear. For years she had lived in terror of Viserys, afraid of waking the dragon. This was even worse. It was not just for herself that she feared now, but for her baby. He must have sensed her fright, for he moved restlessly inside her. Dany stroked the swell of her belly gently, wishing she could reach him, touch him, soothe him. "You are the blood of the dragon, little one," she whispered as her litter swayed along, curtains drawn tight. "You are the blood of the dragon, and the dragon does not fear."

Under the hollow hummock of earth that was her home in Vaes Dothrak, Dany ordered them to leave her—all but Ser Jorah. "Tell me," she commanded as she lowered herself onto her cushions. "Was it the Usurper?"

"Yes." The knight drew out a folded parchment. "A letter to Viserys, from Magister Illyrio. Robert Baratheon offers lands and lordships for your death, or your brother's."

"My brother?" Her sob was half a laugh. "He does not know yet, does he? The Usurper owes Drogo a lordship." This time her laugh was half a sob. She hugged herself protectively. "And me, you said. Only me?"

"You and the child," Ser Jorah said, grim.

"No. He cannot have my son." She would not weep, she decided. She would not shiver with fear. *The Usurper has woken the dragon now,* she told herself . . . and her eyes went to the dragon's eggs resting in their nest of dark velvet. The shifting lamplight limned their stony scales, and shimmering motes of jade and scarlet and gold swam in the air around them, like courtiers around a king.

Was it madness that seized her then, born of fear? Or some strange wisdom buried in her blood? Dany could not have said. She heard her own voice saying, "Ser Jorah, light the brazier."

"Khaleesi?" The knight looked at her strangely. "It is so hot. Are you certain?"

She had never been so certain. "Yes. I . . . I have a chill. Light the brazier."

He bowed. "As you command."

When the coals were afire, Dany sent Ser Jorah from her. She had to be alone to do what she must do. *This is madness,* she told herself as she lifted the black-and-scarlet egg from the velvet. *It will only crack and burn, and it's so beautiful, Ser Jorah will call me a fool if I ruin it,* and yet, and yet . . .

Cradling the egg with both hands, she carried it to the fire and pushed it down amongst the burning coals. The black scales seemed to glow as they drank the heat. Flames licked against the stone with small red tongues. Dany placed the other two eggs beside the black one in the fire. As she stepped back from the brazier, the breath trembled in her throat.

She watched until the coals had turned to ashes. Drifting sparks floated up and out of the smokehole. Heat shimmered in waves around the dragon's eggs. And that was all.

Your brother Rhaegar was the last dragon, Ser Jorah had said. Dany gazed at her eggs sadly. What had she expected? A thousand thousand years ago they had been alive, but now they were only pretty rocks. They could not make a dragon. A dragon was air and fire. Living flesh, not dead stone.

The brazier was cold again by the time Khal Drogo returned. Cohollo was leading a packhorse behind him, with the carcass of a great white lion slung across its back. Above, the stars were coming out. The *khal* laughed as he swung down off his stallion and showed her the scars on his leg where the *hrakkar* had raked him through his leggings. "I shall make you a cloak of its skin, moon of my life," he swore.

When Dany told him what had happened at the market, all laughter stopped, and Khal Drogo grew very quiet.

"This poisoner was the first," Ser Jorah Mormont warned him, "but he will not be the last. Men will risk much for a lordship."

Drogo was silent for a time. Finally he said, "This seller of poisons ran from the moon of my life. Better he should run after her. So he will. Jhogo, Jorah the Andal, to each of you I say, choose any horse you wish from my herds, and it is yours. Any horse save my red and the silver that was my bride gift to the moon of my life. I make this gift to you for what you did.

"And to Rhaego son of Drogo, the stallion who will mount the world, to him I also pledge a gift. To him I will give this iron chair his mother's father sat in. I will give him Seven Kingdoms. I, Drogo, *khal*, will do this thing."

His voice rose, and he lifted his fist to the sky. "I will take my *khalasar* west to where the world ends, and ride the wooden horses across the black salt water as no *khal* has done before. I will kill the men in the iron suits and tear down their stone houses. I will rape their women, take their children as slaves, and bring their broken gods back to Vaes Dothrak to bow down beneath the Mother of Mountains. This I vow, I, Drogo son of Bharbo. This I swear before the Mother of Mountains, as the stars look down in witness."

His *khalasar* left Vaes Dothrak two days later, striking south and west across the plains. Khal Drogo led them on his great red stallion, with Daenerys beside him on her silver. The wineseller hurried behind them, naked, on foot, chained at throat and wrists. His chains were fastened to the halter of Dany's silver. As she rode, he ran after her, barefoot and stumbling. No harm would come to him . . . so long as he kept up.

CATELYN

It was too far to make out the banners clearly, but even through the drifting fog she could see that they were white, with a dark smudge in their center that could only be the direwolf of Stark, grey upon its icy field. When she saw it with her own eyes, Catelyn reined up her horse and bowed her head in thanks. The gods were good. She was not too late.

"They await our coming, my lady," Ser Wylis Manderly said, "as my lord father swore they would."

"Let us not keep them waiting any longer, ser." Ser Brynden Tully put the spurs to his horse and trotted briskly toward the banners. Catelyn rode beside him.

Ser Wylis and his brother Ser Wendel followed, leading their levies, near fifteen hundred men: some twenty-odd knights and as many squires, two hundred mounted lances, swordsmen, and freeriders, and the rest foot, armed with spears, pikes and tridents. Lord Wyman had remained behind to see to the defenses of White Harbor. A man of near sixty years, he had grown too stout to sit a horse. "If I had thought to see war again in my lifetime, I should have eaten a few less eels," he'd told Catelyn when he met her ship, slapping his massive belly with both hands. His fingers were fat as sausages. "My boys will see you safe to your son, though, have no fear."

His "boys" were both older than Catelyn, and she might have wished that they did not take after their father quite so closely. Ser Wylis was only a few eels short of not being able to mount his own horse; she pitied the poor animal. Ser Wendel, the younger boy, would have been the fattest man she'd ever known, had she only neglected to meet his father and brother. Wylis was quiet and formal, Wendel loud and boisterous; both had ostentatious walrus mustaches and heads as bare as a baby's bottom; neither seemed to own a single garment that was not spotted with food stains. Yet she liked them well enough; they had gotten her to Robb, as their father had vowed, and nothing else mattered.

She was pleased to see that her son had sent eyes out, even to the east. The Lannisters would come from the south when they came, but it was good that Robb was being careful. *My son is leading a host to war,* she thought, still only half believing it. She was desperately afraid for him, and for Winterfell, yet she could not deny feeling a certain pride as well. A year ago he had been a boy. What was he now? she wondered.

Outriders spied the Manderly banners—the white merman with trident in hand, rising from a blue-green sea—and hailed them warmly. They were led to a spot of high ground dry enough for a camp. Ser Wylis called a halt there, and remained behind with his men to see the fires laid and the horses tended, while his brother Wendel rode on with Catelyn and her uncle to present their father's respects to their liege lord.

The ground under their horses' hooves was soft and wet. It fell away slowly beneath them as they rode past smoky peat fires, lines of horses, and wagons heavy-laden with hardbread and salt beef. On a stony outcrop of land higher than the surrounding country, they passed a lord's pavilion with walls of heavy sailcloth. Catelyn recognized the banner, the bull moose of the Hornwoods, brown on its dark orange field.

Just beyond, through the mists, she glimpsed the walls and towers of Moat Cailin . . . or what remained of them. Immense blocks of black basalt, each as large as a crofter's cottage, lay scattered and tumbled like a child's wooden blocks, half-sunk in the soft boggy soil. Nothing else remained of a curtain wall that had once stood as high as Winterfell's. The wooden keep was gone entirely, rotted away a thousand years past, with not so much as a timber to mark where it had stood. All that was left of the great stronghold of the First Men were three towers . . . three where there had once been twenty, if the taletellers could be believed.

The Gatehouse Tower looked sound enough, and even boasted a few feet of standing wall to either side of it. The Drunkard's Tower, off in the bog where the south and west walls had once met, leaned like a man about to spew a bellyful of wine into the gutter. And the tall, slender Children's Tower, where legend said the children of the forest had once called upon their nameless gods to send the hammer of the waters, had lost half its crown. It looked as if some great beast had taken a bite out of the crenellations along the tower top, and spit the rubble across the bog. All three towers were green with moss. A tree was growing out between the stones on the north side of the Gatehouse Tower, its gnarled limbs festooned with ropy white blankets of ghostskin.

"Gods have mercy," Ser Brynden exclaimed when he saw what lay before them. "*This* is Moat Cailin? It's no more than a—"

"—death trap," Catelyn finished. "I know how it looks, Uncle. I thought the same the first time I saw it, but Ned assured me that this *ruin* is more formidable than it seems. The three surviving towers command the causeway from all sides, and any enemy must pass between them. The bogs here are impenetrable, full of quicksands and suckholes and teeming with snakes. To assault any of the towers, an army would need to wade through waist-deep black muck, cross a moat full of lizard-lions, and scale walls slimy with moss, all the while exposing themselves to fire from archers in the other towers." She gave her uncle a grim smile. "And when night falls, there are said to be ghosts, cold vengeful spirits of the north who hunger for southron blood."

Ser Brynden chuckled. "Remind me not to linger here. Last I looked, I was southron myself."

Standards had been raised atop all three towers. The Karstark sunburst hung from the Drunkard's Tower, beneath the direwolf; on the Children's Tower it was the Greatjon's giant in shattered chains. But on the Gatehouse Tower, the Stark banner flew alone. That was where Robb had made his seat. Catelyn made for it, with Ser Brynden and Ser Wendel behind her, their horses stepping slowly down the log-and-plank road that had been laid across the green-and-black fields of mud.

She found her son surrounded by his father's lords bannermen, in a drafty hall with a peat fire smoking in a black hearth. He was seated at a massive stone table, a pile of maps and papers in front of him, talking intently with Roose Bolton and the Greatjon. At first he did not notice her . . . but his wolf did. The great grey beast was lying near the fire, but when Catelyn entered he lifted his head, and his golden eyes met hers. The lords fell silent one by one, and Robb looked up at the sudden quiet and saw her. *"Mother!"* he said, his voice thick with emotion.

Catelyn wanted to run to him, to kiss his sweet brow, to wrap him in her arms and hold him so tightly that he would never come to harm . . . but here in front of his lords, she dared not. He was playing a man's part now, and she would not take that away from him. So she held herself at the far end of the basalt slab they were using for a table. The direwolf got to his feet and padded across the room to where she stood. It seemed bigger than a wolf ought to be. "You've grown a beard," she said to Robb, while Grey Wind sniffed her hand.

He rubbed his stubbled jaw, suddenly awkward. "Yes." His chin hairs were redder than the ones on his head.

"I like it." Catelyn stroked the wolf's head, gently. "It makes you look like my brother Edmure." Grey Wind nipped at her fingers, playful, and trotted back to his place by the fire.

Ser Helman Tallhart was the first to follow the direwolf across the room to pay his respects, kneeling before her and pressing his brow to her hand. "Lady Catelyn," he said, "you are fair as ever, a welcome sight in troubled times." The Glovers followed, Galbart and Robett, and Greatjon Umber, and the rest, one by one. Theon Greyjoy was the last. "I had not looked to see you here, my lady," he said as he knelt.

"I had not thought to be here," Catelyn said, "until I came ashore at White Harbor, and Lord Wyman told me that Robb had called the banners. You know his son, Ser Wendel." Wendel Manderly stepped forward and bowed as low as his girth would allow. "And my uncle, Ser Brynden Tully, who has left my sister's service for mine."

"The Blackfish," Robb said. "Thank you for joining us, ser. We need men of your courage. And you, Ser Wendel, I am glad to have you here. Is Ser Rodrik with you as well, Mother? I've missed him."

"Ser Rodrik is on his way north from White Harbor. I have named him castellan and commanded him to hold Winterfell till our return. Maester Luwin is a wise counsellor, but unskilled in the arts of war."

"Have no fear on that count, Lady Stark," the Greatjon told her in his bass rumble. "Winterfell is safe. We'll shove our swords up Tywin Lannister's bunghole soon enough, begging your pardons, and then it's on to the Red Keep to free Ned."

"My lady, a question, as it please you." Roose Bolton, Lord of the Dreadfort, had a small voice, yet when he spoke larger men quieted to listen. His eyes were curiously pale, almost without color, and his look disturbing. "It is said that you hold Lord Tywin's dwarf son as captive. Have you brought him to us? I vow, we should make good use of such a hostage."

"I did hold Tyrion Lannister, but no longer," Catelyn was forced to admit. A chorus of consternation greeted the news. "I was no more pleased than you, my lords. The gods saw fit to free him, with some help from my fool of a sister." She ought not to be so open in her contempt, she knew, but her parting from the Eyrie had not been pleasant. She had offered to take Lord Robert with her, to foster him at Winterfell for a few years. The company of other boys would do him good, she had dared to suggest. Lysa's rage had been frightening to behold. "Sister or no," she had replied, "if you try to steal my son, you will leave by the Moon Door." After that there was no more to be said.

The lords were anxious to question her further, but Catelyn raised a hand. "No doubt we will have time for all this later, but my journey has fatigued me. I would speak with my son alone. I know you will forgive me, my lords." She gave them no choice; led by the ever-obliging Lord Hornwood, the bannermen bowed and took their leave. "And you, Theon," she added when Greyjoy lingered. He smiled and left them.

There was ale and cheese on the table. Catelyn filled a horn, sat, sipped, and studied her son. He seemed taller than when she'd left, and the wisps of beard did make him look older. "Edmure was sixteen when he grew his first whiskers."

"I will be sixteen soon enough," Robb said.

"And you are fifteen now. Fifteen, and leading a host to battle. Can you understand why I might fear, Robb?"

His look grew stubborn. "There was no one else."

"No one?" she said. "Pray, who were those men I saw here a moment ago? Roose Bolton, Rickard Karstark, Galbart and Robett Glover, the Greatjon, Helman Tallhart . . . you might have given the command to *any* of them. Gods be good, you might even have sent Theon, though he would not be my choice."

"They are not Starks," he said.

"They are *men*, Robb, seasoned in battle. You were fighting with wooden swords less than a year past."

She saw anger in his eyes at that, but it was gone as quick as it came, and suddenly he was a boy again. "I know," he said, abashed. "Are you . . . are you sending me back to Winterfell?"

Catelyn sighed. "I should. You ought never have left. Yet I dare not, not now. You have come too far. Someday these lords will look to you as their liege. If I pack you off now, like a child being sent to bed without his supper, they will remember, and laugh about it in their cups. The day will come when you need them to respect you, even fear you a little. Laughter is poison to fear. I will not do that to you, much as I might wish to keep you safe."

"You have my thanks, Mother," he said, his relief obvious beneath the formality.

She reached across his table and touched his hair. "You are my firstborn, Robb. I have only to look at you to remember the day you came into the world, red-faced and squalling."

He rose, clearly uncomfortable with her touch, and walked to the hearth. Grey Wind rubbed his head against his leg. "You know . . . about Father?"

"Yes." The reports of Robert's sudden death and Ned's fall had frightened Catelyn more than she could say, but she would not let her son see her fear. "Lord Manderly told me when I landed at White Harbor. Have you had any word of your sisters?"

"There was a letter," Robb said, scratching his direwolf under the jaw. "One for you as well, but it came to Winterfell with mine." He went to the table, rummaged among some maps and papers, and returned with a crumpled parchment. "This is the one she wrote me, I never thought to bring yours."

Something in Robb's tone troubled her. She smoothed out the paper and read. Concern gave way to disbelief, then to anger, and lastly to fear. "This is Cersei's letter, not your sister's," she said when she was done. "The real message is in what Sansa does not say. All this about how kindly and gently the Lannisters are treating her . . . I know the sound of a threat, even whispered. They have Sansa hostage, and they mean to keep her."

"There's no mention of Arya," Robb pointed out, miserable.

"No." Catelyn did not want to think what that might mean, not now, not here.

"I had hoped . . . if you still held the Imp, a trade of hostages . . ." He took Sansa's letter and crumpled it in his fist, and she could tell from the way he did it that it was not the first time. "Is there word from the Eyrie? I wrote to Aunt Lysa, asking help. Has she called Lord Arryn's banners, do you know? Will the knights of the Vale come join us?"

"Only one," she said, "the best of them, my uncle . . . but Brynden Blackfish was a Tully first. My sister is not about to stir beyond her Bloody Gate."

Robb took it hard. "Mother, what are we going to *do*? I brought this whole army together, eighteen thousand men, but I don't . . . I'm not certain . . ." He looked to her, his eyes shining, the proud young lord melted away in an instant, and quick as that he was a child again, a fifteen-year-old boy looking to his mother for answers.

It would not do.

"What are you so afraid of, Robb?" she asked gently.

"I . . ." He turned his head away, to hide the first tear. "If we march . . . even if we win . . . the Lannisters hold Sansa, and Father. They'll kill them, won't they?"

"They want us to think so."

"You mean they're lying?"

"I do not know, Robb. What I do know is that you have no choice. If you go to King's Landing and swear fealty, you will never be allowed to leave. If you turn your tail and retreat to Winterfell, your lords will lose all respect for you. Some may even go over to the Lannisters. Then the queen, with that much less to fear, can do as she likes with her prisoners. Our best hope, our *only* true hope, is that you can defeat the foe in the field. If you should chance to take Lord Tywin or the Kingslayer captive, why then a trade might very well be possible, but that is not the heart of it. So long as you have power enough that they must fear you, Ned and your sister should be safe. Cersei is wise enough to know that she may need them to make her peace, should the fighting go against her."

"What if the fighting *doesn't* go against her?" Robb asked. "What if it goes against us?"

Catelyn took his hand. "Robb, I will not soften the truth for you. If you lose, there is no hope for any of us. They say there is naught but stone at the heart of Casterly Rock. Remember the fate of Rhaegar's children."

She saw the fear in his young eyes then, but there was a strength as well. "Then I will not lose," he vowed.

"Tell me what you know of the fighting in the riverlands," she said. She had to learn if he was truly ready.

"Less than a fortnight past, they fought a battle in the hills below the Golden Tooth," Robb said. "Uncle Edmure had sent Lord Vance and Lord Piper to hold the pass, but the Kingslayer descended on them and put them to flight. Lord Vance was slain. The last word we had was that Lord Piper was falling back to join your brother and his other bannermen at Riverrun, with Jaime Lannister on his heels. That's not the worst of it, though. All the time they were battling in the pass, Lord Tywin was bringing a second Lannister army around from the south. It's said to be even larger than Jaime's host.

"Father must have known that, because he sent out some men to oppose them, under the king's own banner. He gave the command to some southron lordling, Lord Erik or Derik or something like that, but Ser Raymun Darry rode with him, and the letter said there were other knights as well, and a force of Father's own guardsmen. Only it was a trap. Lord Derik had no sooner crossed the

Red Fork than the Lannisters fell upon him, the king's banner be damned, and Gregor Clegane took them in the rear as they tried to pull back across the Mummer's Ford. This Lord Derik and a few others may have escaped, no one is certain, but Ser Raymun was killed, and most of our men from Winterfell. Lord Tywin has closed off the kingsroad, it's said, and now he's marching north toward Harrenhal, burning as he goes."

Grim and grimmer, thought Catelyn. It was worse than she'd imagined. "You mean to meet him here?" she asked.

"If he comes so far, but no one thinks he will," Robb said. "I've sent word to Howland Reed, Father's old friend at Greywater Watch. If the Lannisters come up the Neck, the crannogmen will bleed them every step of the way, but Galbart Glover says Lord Tywin is too smart for that, and Roose Bolton agrees. He'll stay close to the Trident, they believe, taking the castles of the river lords one by one, until Riverrun stands alone. We need to march south to meet him."

The very idea of it chilled Catelyn to the bone. What chance would a fifteen-year-old boy have against seasoned battle commanders like Jaime and Tywin Lannister? "Is that wise? You are strongly placed here. It's said that the old Kings in the North could stand at Moat Cailin and throw back hosts ten times the size of their own."

"Yes, but our food and supplies are running low, and this is not land we can live off easily. We've been waiting for Lord Manderly, but now that his sons have joined us, we need to march."

She was hearing the lords bannermen speaking with her son's voice, she realized. Over the years, she had hosted many of them at Winterfell, and been welcomed with Ned to their own hearths and tables. She knew what sorts of men they were, each one. She wondered if Robb did.

And yet there was sense in what they said. This host her son had assembled was not a standing army such as the Free Cities were accustomed to maintain, nor a force of guardsmen paid in coin. Most of them were smallfolk: crofters, fieldhands, fishermen, sheepherders, the sons of innkeeps and traders and tanners, leavened with a smattering of sellswords and freeriders hungry for plunder.

When their lords called, they came . . . but not forever. "Marching is all very well," she said to her son, "but *where*, and to what purpose? What do you mean to do?"

Robb hesitated. "The Greatjon thinks we should take the battle to Lord Tywin and surprise him," he said, "but the Glovers and the Karstarks feel we'd be wiser to go around his army and join up with Uncle Ser Edmure against the Kingslayer." He ran his fingers through his shaggy mane of auburn hair, looking unhappy. "Though by the time we reach Riverrun . . . I'm not certain . . ."

"*Be* certain," Catelyn told her son, "or go home and take up that wooden sword again. You cannot afford to seem indecisive in front of men like Roose Bolton and Rickard Karstark. Make no mistake, Robb—these are your bannermen, not your friends. You named yourself battle commander. *Command.*"

Her son looked at her, startled, as if he could not credit what he was hearing. "As you say, Mother."

"I'll ask you again. What do *you* mean to do?"

Robb drew a map across the table, a ragged piece of old leather covered with lines of faded paint. One end curled up from being rolled; he weighed it down with his dagger. "Both plans have virtues, but . . . look, if we try to swing around Lord Tywin's host, we take the risk of being caught between him and the Kingslayer, and if we attack him . . . by all reports, he has more men than I do, and a lot more armored horse. The Greatjon says that won't matter if we catch him with his breeches down, but it seems to me that a man who has fought as many battles as Tywin Lannister won't be so easily surprised."

"Good," she said. She could hear echoes of Ned in his voice, as he sat there, puzzling over the map. "Tell me more."

"I'd leave a small force here to hold Moat Cailin, archers mostly, and march the rest down the causeway," he said, "but once we're below the Neck, I'd split our host in two. The foot can continue down the kingsroad, while our horsemen cross the Green Fork at the Twins." He pointed. "When Lord Tywin gets word that we've come south, he'll march north to engage our main host, leaving our riders free to hurry down the west bank to Riverrun." Robb sat back, not quite daring to smile, but pleased with himself and hungry for her praise.

Catelyn frowned down at the map. "You'd put a river between the two parts of your army."

"*And* between Jaime and Lord Tywin," he said eagerly. The smile came at last. "There's no crossing on the Green Fork above the ruby ford, where Robert won his crown. Not until the Twins, all the way up here, and Lord Frey controls that bridge. He's your father's bannerman, isn't that so?"

The Late Lord Frey, Catelyn thought. "He is," she admitted, "but my father has never trusted him. Nor should you."

"I won't," Robb promised. "What do you think?"

She was impressed despite herself. *He looks like a Tully*, she thought, *yet he's still his father's son, and Ned taught him well.* "Which force would you command?"

"The horse," he answered at once. Again like his father; Ned would always take the more dangerous task himself.

"And the other?"

"The Greatjon is always saying that we should smash Lord Tywin. I thought I'd give him the honor."

It was his first misstep, but how to make him see it without wounding his fledgling confidence? "Your father once told me that the Greatjon was as fearless as any man he had ever known."

Robb grinned. "Grey Wind ate two of his fingers, and he *laughed* about it. So you agree, then?"

"Your father is not fearless," Catelyn pointed out. "He is brave, but that is very different."

Her son considered that for a moment. "The eastern host will be all that stands between Lord Tywin and Winterfell," he said thoughtfully. "Well, them and whatever few bowmen I leave here at the Moat. So I don't want someone fearless, do I?"

"No. You want cold cunning, I should think, not courage."

"Roose Bolton," Robb said at once. "That man scares me."

"Then let us pray he will scare Tywin Lannister as well."

Robb nodded and rolled up the map. "I'll give the commands, and assemble an escort to take you home to Winterfell."

Catelyn had fought to keep herself strong, for Ned's sake and for this stubborn brave son of theirs. She had put despair and fear aside, as if they were garments she did not choose to wear . . . but now she saw that she had donned them after all.

"I am not going to Winterfell," she heard herself say, surprised at the sudden rush of tears that blurred her vision. "My father may be dying behind the walls of Riverrun. My brother is surrounded by foes. I must go to them."

TYRION

Chella daughter of Cheyk of the Black Ears had gone ahead to scout, and it was she who brought back word of the army at the crossroads. "By their fires I call them twenty thousand strong," she said. "Their banners are red, with a golden lion."

"Your father?" Bronn asked.

"Or my brother Jaime," Tyrion said. "We shall know soon enough." He surveyed his ragged band of brigands: near three hundred Stone Crows, Moon Brothers, Black Ears, and Burned Men, and those just the seed of the army he hoped to grow. Gunthor son of Gurn was raising the other clans even now. He wondered what his lord father would make of them in their skins and bits of stolen steel. If truth be told, he did not know what to make of them himself. Was he their commander or their captive? Most of the time, it seemed to be a little of both. "It might be best if I rode down alone," he suggested.

"Best for Tyrion son of Tywin," said Ulf, who spoke for the Moon Brothers.

Shagga glowered, a fearsome sight to see. "Shagga son of Dolf likes this not. Shagga will go with the boyman, and if the boyman lies, Shagga will chop off his man-hood—"

"—and feed it to the goats, yes," Tyrion said wearily. "Shagga, I give you my word as a Lannister, I will return."

"Why should we trust your word?" Chella was a small hard woman, flat as a boy, and no fool. "Lowland lords have lied to the clans before."

"You wound me, Chella," Tyrion said. "Here I thought we had become such friends. But as you will. You shall ride with me, and Shagga and Conn for the Stone Crows, Ulf for the Moon Brothers, and Timett son of Timett for the Burned Men." The clansmen exchanged wary looks as he named them. "The rest shall wait here until I send for you. *Try* not to kill and maim each other while I'm gone."

He put his heels to his horse and trotted off, giving them no choice but to follow or be left behind. Either was fine with him, so long as they did not sit down to *talk* for a day and a night. That was the trouble with the clans; they had an absurd notion that every man's voice should be heard in council, so they argued about *everything*, endlessly. Even their women were allowed to speak. Small wonder that it had been hundreds of years since they last threatened the Vale with anything beyond an occasional raid. Tyrion meant to change that.

Bronn rode with him. Behind them—after a quick bit of grumbling—the five clansmen followed on their under-size garrons, scrawny things that looked like ponies and scrambled up rock walls like goats.

The Stone Crows rode together, and Chella and Ulf stayed close as well, as the Moon Brothers and Black Ears had strong bonds between them. Timett son of Timett rode alone. Every clan in the Mountains of the Moon feared the Burned Men, who mortified their flesh with fire to prove their courage and (the others said) roasted babies at their feasts. And even the other Burned Men feared Timett, who had put out his own left eye with a white-hot knife when he reached the age of manhood. Tyrion gathered that it was more customary for a boy to burn off a nipple, a finger, or (if he was truly brave, or truly mad) an ear. Timett's fellow Burned Men were so awed by his choice of an eye that they promptly named him a red hand, which seemed to be some sort of a war chief.

"I wonder what their king burned off," Tyrion said to Bronn when he heard the tale. Grinning, the sellsword had tugged at his crotch . . . but even Bronn kept a respectful tongue around Timett. If a man was mad enough to put out his own eye, he was unlikely to be gentle to his enemies.

Distant watchers peered down from towers of unmortared stone as the party descended through the foothills, and once Tyrion saw a raven take wing. Where the high road twisted between two rocky outcrops, they came to the first strong point. A low earthen wall four feet high closed off the road, and a dozen crossbowmen manned the heights. Tyrion halted his followers out of range and rode to the wall alone. "Who commands here?" he shouted up.

The captain was quick to appear, and even quicker to give them an escort when he recognized his lord's son. They trotted past blackened fields and burned holdfasts, down to the riverlands and the Green Fork of the Trident. Tyrion saw no bodies, but the air was full of ravens and carrion crows; there had been fighting here, and recently.

Half a league from the crossroads, a barricade of sharpened stakes had been erected, manned by pikemen and archers. Behind the line, the camp spread out to the far distance. Thin fingers of smoke rose from hundreds of cookfires, mailed men sat under trees and honed their blades, and familiar banners fluttered from staffs thrust into the muddy ground.

A party of mounted horsemen rode forward to challenge them as they approached the stakes. The knight who led them wore silver armor inlaid with amethysts and a striped purple-and-silver cloak. His shield bore a unicorn sigil, and a spiral horn two feet long jutted up from the brow of his horsehead helm. Tyrion reined up to greet him. "Ser Flement."

Ser Flement Brax lifted his visor. "Tyrion," he said in astonishment. "My lord, we all feared you dead, or . . ." He looked at the clansmen uncertainly. "These . . . companions of yours . . ."

"Bosom friends and loyal retainers," Tyrion said. "Where will I find my lord father?"

"He has taken the inn at the crossroads for his quarters."

Tyrion laughed. The inn at the crossroads! Perhaps the gods were just after all. "I will see him at once."

"As you say, my lord." Ser Flement wheeled his horse about and shouted commands. Three rows of stakes were pulled from the ground to make a hole in the line. Tyrion led his party through.

Lord Tywin's camp spread over leagues. Chella's estimate of twenty thousand men could not be far wrong. The common men camped out in the open, but the knights had thrown up tents, and some of the high lords had erected pavilions as large as houses. Tyrion spied the red ox of the Presters, Lord Crakehall's brindled boar, the burning tree of Marbrand, the badger of Lydden. Knights called out to him as he cantered past, and men-at-arms gaped at the clansmen in open astonishment.

Shagga was gaping back; beyond a certainty, he had never seen so many men, horses, and weapons in all his days. The rest of the mountain brigands did a better job of guarding their faces, but Tyrion had no doubts that they were full as much in awe. Better and better. The more impressed they were with the power of the Lannisters, the easier they would be to command.

The inn and its stables were much as he remembered, though little more than tumbled stones and blackened foundations remained where the rest of the village had stood. A gibbet had been erected in the yard, and the body that swung there was covered with ravens. At Tyrion's approach they took to the air, squawking and flapping their black wings. He dismounted and glanced up at what remained of the corpse. The birds had eaten her lips and eyes and most of her cheeks, baring her stained red teeth in a hideous smile. "A room, a meal, and a flagon of wine, that was all I asked," he reminded her with a sigh of reproach.

Boys emerged hesitantly from the stables to see to their horses. Shagga did not want to give his up. "The lad won't steal your mare," Tyrion assured him. "He only wants to give her some oats and water and brush out her coat." Shagga's coat could have used a good brushing too, but it would have been less than tactful to mention it. "You have my word, the horse will not be harmed."

Glaring, Shagga let go his grip on the reins. "This is the horse of Shagga son of Dolf," he roared at the stableboy.

"If he doesn't give her back, chop off his manhood and feed it to the goats," Tyrion promised. "Provided you can find some."

A pair of house guards in crimson cloaks and lion-crested helms stood under the inn's sign, on either side of the door. Tyrion recognized their captain. "My father?"

"In the common room, m'lord."

"My men will want meat and mead," Tyrion told him. "See that they get it." He entered the inn, and there was Father.

Tywin Lannister, Lord of Casterly Rock and Warden of the West, was in his middle fifties, yet hard as a man of twenty. Even seated, he was tall, with long legs, broad shoulders, a flat stomach. His thin arms were corded with muscle. When his once-thick golden hair had begun to recede, he had commanded his barber to shave his head; Lord Tywin did not believe in half measures. He razored his lip and chin as well, but kept his side-whiskers, two great thickets of wiry golden hair that covered most of his cheeks from ear to jaw. His eyes were a pale green, flecked with gold. A fool more foolish than most had once jested that even Lord Tywin's shit was flecked with gold. Some said the man was still alive, deep in the bowels of Casterly Rock.

Ser Kevan Lannister, his father's only surviving brother, was sharing a flagon of ale with Lord Tywin when Tyrion entered the common room. His uncle was portly and balding, with a close-cropped yellow beard that followed the line of his massive jaw. Ser Kevan saw him first. "Tyrion," he said in surprise.

"Uncle," Tyrion said, bowing. "And my lord father. What a pleasure to find you here."

Lord Tywin did not stir from his chair, but he did give his dwarf son a long, searching look. "I see that the rumors of your demise were unfounded."

"Sorry to disappoint you, Father," Tyrion said. "No need to leap up and embrace me, I wouldn't want you to strain yourself." He crossed the room to their table, acutely conscious of the way his stunted legs made him waddle with every step. Whenever his father's eyes were on him, he became uncomfortably aware of all his deformities and shortcomings. "Kind of you to go to war for me," he said as he climbed into a chair and helped himself to a cup of his father's ale.

"By my lights, it was you who started this," Lord Tywin replied. "Your brother Jaime would never have meekly submitted to capture at the hands of a woman."

"That's one way we differ, Jaime and I. He's taller as well, you may have noticed."

His father ignored the sally. "The honor of our House was at stake. I had no choice but to ride. No man sheds Lannister blood with impunity."

"Hear Me Roar," Tyrion said, grinning. The Lannister words. "Truth be told, none of my blood was actually shed, although it was a close thing once or twice. Morrec and Jyck were killed."

"I suppose you will be wanting some new men."

"Don't trouble yourself, Father, I've acquired a few of my own." He tried a swallow of the ale. It was brown and yeasty, so thick you could almost chew it. Very fine, in truth. A pity his father had hanged the innkeep. "How is your war going?"

His uncle answered. "Well enough, for the nonce. Ser Edmure had scattered small troops of men along his borders to stop our raiding, and your lord father and I were able to destroy most of them piecemeal before they could regroup."

"Your brother has been covering himself with glory," his father said. "He smashed the Lords Vance and Piper at the Golden Tooth, and met the massed power of the Tullys under the walls of Riverrun. The lords of the Trident have been put to rout. Ser Edmure Tully was taken captive, with many of his knights and bannermen. Lord Blackwood led a few survivors back to Riverrun, where Jaime has them under siege. The rest fled to their own strongholds."

"Your father and I have been marching on each in turn," Ser Kevan said. "With Lord Blackwood gone, Raventree fell at once, and Lady Whent yielded Harrenhal for want of men to defend it. Ser Gregor burnt out the Pipers and the Brackens . . ."

"Leaving you unopposed?" Tyrion said.

"Not wholly," Ser Kevan said. "The Mallisters still hold Seagard and Walder Frey is marshaling his levies at the Twins."

"No matter," Lord Tywin said. "Frey only takes the field when the scent of victory is in the air, and all he smells now is ruin. And Jason Mallister lacks the strength to fight alone. Once Jaime takes Riverrun, they will both be quick enough to bend the knee. Unless the Starks and the Arryns come forth to oppose us, this war is good as won."

"I would not fret overmuch about the Arryns if I were you," Tyrion said. "The Starks are another matter. Lord Eddard—"

"—is our hostage," his father said. "He will lead no armies while he rots in a dungeon under the Red Keep."

"No," Ser Kevan agreed, "but his son has called the banners and sits at Moat Cailin with a strong host around him."

"No sword is strong until it's been tempered," Lord Tywin declared. "The Stark boy is a child. No doubt he likes the sound of warhorns well enough, and the sight of his banners fluttering in the wind, but in the end it comes down to butcher's work. I doubt he has the stomach for it."

Things *had* gotten interesting while he'd been away, Tyrion reflected. "And what is our fearless monarch doing whilst all this 'butcher's work' is being done?" he wondered. "How has my lovely and persuasive sister gotten Robert to agree to the imprisonment of his dear friend Ned?"

"Robert Baratheon is dead," his father told him. "Your nephew reigns in King's Landing."

That *did* take Tyrion aback. "My sister, you mean." He took another gulp of ale. The realm would be a much different place with Cersei ruling in place of her husband.

"If you have a mind to make yourself of use, I will give you a command," his father said. "Marq Piper and Karyl Vance are loose in our rear, raiding our lands across the Red Fork."

Tyrion made a *tsk*ing sound. "The gall of them, fighting back. Ordinarily I'd be glad to punish such rudeness, Father, but the truth is, I have pressing business elsewhere."

"Do you?" Lord Tywin did not seem awed. "We also

have a pair of Ned Stark's afterthoughts making a nuisance of themselves by harassing my foraging parties. Beric Dondarrion, some young lordling with delusions of valor. He has that fat jape of a priest with him, the one who likes to set his sword on fire. Do you think you might be able to deal with them as you scamper off? Without making too much a botch of it?"

Tyrion wiped his mouth with the back of his hand and smiled. "Father, it warms my heart to think that you might entrust me with . . . what, twenty men? Fifty? Are you sure you can spare so many? Well, no matter. If I should come across Thoros and Lord Beric, I shall spank them both." He climbed down from his chair and waddled to the sideboard, where a wheel of veined white cheese sat surrounded by fruit. "First, though, I have some promises of my own to keep," he said as he sliced off a wedge. "I shall require three thousand helms and as many hauberks, plus swords, pikes, steel spearheads, maces, battle-axes, gauntlets, gorgets, greaves, breastplates, wagons to carry all this—"

The door behind him opened with a crash, so violently that Tyrion almost dropped his cheese. Ser Kevan leapt up swearing as the captain of the guard went flying across the room to smash against the hearth. As he tumbled down into the cold ashes, his lion helm askew, Shagga snapped the man's sword in two over a knee thick as a tree trunk, threw down the pieces, and lumbered into the common room. He was preceded by his stench, riper than the cheese and overpowering in the closed space. "Little redcape," he snarled, "when next you bare steel on Shagga son of Dolf, I will chop off your manhood and roast it in the fire."

"What, no goats?" Tyrion said, taking a bite of cheese.

The other clansmen followed Shagga into the common room, Bronn with them. The sellsword gave Tyrion a rueful shrug.

"Who might you be?" Lord Tywin asked, cool as snow.

"They followed me home, Father," Tyrion explained. "May I keep them? They don't eat much."

No one was smiling. "By what right do you savages intrude on our councils?" demanded Ser Kevan.

"Savages, lowlander?" Conn might have been handsome if you washed him. "We are free men, and free men by rights sit on all war councils."

"Which one is the lion lord?" Chella asked.

"They are both old men," announced Timett son of Timett, who had yet to see his twentieth year.

Ser Kevan's hand went to his sword hilt, but his brother placed two fingers on his wrist and held him fast. Lord Tywin seemed unperturbed. "Tyrion, have you forgotten your courtesies? Kindly acquaint us with our . . . honored guests."

Tyrion licked his fingers. "With pleasure," he said. "The fair maid is Chella daughter of Cheyk of the Black Ears."

"I'm no maid," Chella protested. "My sons have taken fifty ears among them."

"May they take fifty more." Tyrion waddled away from her. "This is Conn son of Coratt. Shagga son of Dolf is the one who looks like Casterly Rock with hair. They are Stone Crows. Here is Ulf son of Umar of the Moon Brothers, and here Timett son of Timett, a red hand of the Burned Men. And this is Bronn, a sellsword of no particular allegiance. He has already changed sides twice in the short time I've known him, you and he ought to get on famously, Father." To Bronn and the clansmen he said, "May I present my lord father, Tywin son of Tytos of House Lannister, Lord of Casterly Rock, Warden of the West, Shield of Lannisport, and once and future Hand of the King."

Lord Tywin rose, dignified and correct. "Even in the west, we know the prowess of the warrior clans of the Mountains of the Moon. What brings you down from your strongholds, my lords?"

"Horses," said Shagga.

"A promise of silk and steel," said Timett son of Timett.

Tyrion was about to tell his lord father how he proposed to reduce the Vale of Arryn to a smoking wasteland, but he was never given the chance. The door banged open again. The messenger gave Tyrion's clansmen a quick, queer look as he dropped to one knee before Lord Tywin. "My lord," he said, "Ser Addam bid me tell you that the Stark host is moving down the causeway."

Lord Tywin Lannister did not smile. Lord Tywin *never*

smiled, but Tyrion had learned to read his father's pleasure all the same, and it was there on his face. "So the wolfling is leaving his den to play among the lions," he said in a voice of quiet satisfaction. "Splendid. Return to Ser Addam and tell him to fall back. He is not to engage the northerners until we arrive, but I want him to harass their flanks and draw them farther south."

"It will be as you command." The rider took his leave.

"We are well situated here," Ser Kevan pointed out. "Close to the ford and ringed by pits and spikes. If they are coming south, I say let them come, and break themselves against us."

"The boy may hang back or lose his courage when he sees our numbers," Lord Tywin replied. "The sooner the Starks are broken, the sooner I shall be free to deal with Stannis Baratheon. Tell the drummers to beat assembly, and send word to Jaime that I am marching against Robb Stark."

"As you will," Ser Kevan said.

Tyrion watched with a grim fascination as his lord father turned next to the half-wild clansmen. "It is said that the men of the mountain clans are warriors without fear."

"It is said truly," Conn of the Stone Crows answered.

"And the women," Chella added.

"Ride with me against my enemies, and you shall have all my son promised you, and more," Lord Tywin told them.

"Would you pay us with our own coin?" Ulf son of Umar said. "Why should we need the father's promise, when we have the son's?"

"I said nothing of *need*," Lord Tywin replied. "My words were courtesy, nothing more. You need not join us. The men of the winterlands are made of iron and ice, and even my boldest knights fear to face them."

Oh, deftly done, Tyrion thought, smiling crookedly.

"The Burned Men fear nothing. Timett son of Timett will ride with the lions."

"Wherever the Burned Men go, the Stone Crows have been there first," Conn declared hotly. "We ride as well."

"Shagga son of Dolf will chop off their manhoods and feed them to the crows."

"We will ride with you, lion lord," Chella daughter of

Cheyk agreed, "but only if your halfman son goes with us. He has bought his breath with promises. Until we hold the steel he has pledged us, his life is ours."

Lord Tywin turned his gold-flecked eyes on his son.

"Joy," Tyrion said with a resigned smile.

SANSA

The walls of the throne room had been stripped bare, the hunting tapestries that King Robert loved taken down and stacked in the corner in an untidy heap.

Ser Mandon Moore went to take his place under the throne beside two of his fellows of the Kingsguard. Sansa hovered by the door, for once unguarded. The queen had given her freedom of the castle as a reward for being good, yet even so, she was escorted everywhere she went. "Honor guards for my daughter-to-be," the queen called them, but they did not make Sansa feel honored.

"Freedom of the castle" meant that she could go wherever she chose within the Red Keep so long as she promised not to go beyond the walls, a promise Sansa had been more than willing to give. She couldn't have gone beyond the walls anyway. The gates were watched day and night by Janos Slynt's gold cloaks, and Lannister house guards were always about as well. Besides, even if she could leave the castle, where would she go? It was enough that she could walk in the yard, pick flowers in Myrcella's garden, and visit the sept to pray for her father. Sometimes she prayed in the godswood as well, since the Starks kept the old gods.

This was the first court session of Joffrey's reign, so Sansa looked about nervously. A line of Lannister house guards stood beneath the western windows, a line of gold-cloaked City Watchmen beneath the east. Of smallfolk and commoners, she saw no sign, but under the gallery a cluster of lords great and small milled restlessly. There were no more than twenty, where a hundred had been accustomed to wait upon King Robert.

Sansa slipped in among them, murmuring greetings as she worked her way toward the front. She recognized black-skinned Jalabhar Xho, gloomy Ser Aron Santagar, the Redwyne twins Horror and Slobber . . . only none of them seemed to recognize *her*. Or if they did, they shied away as if she had the grey plague. Sickly Lord Gyles covered his face at her approach and feigned a fit of coughing, and when funny drunken Ser Dontos started to hail her, Ser Balon Swann whispered in his ear and he turned away.

And so many others were missing. Where had the rest of them gone? Sansa wondered. Vainly, she searched for friendly faces. Not one of them would meet her eyes. It was as if she had become a ghost, dead before her time.

Grand Maester Pycelle was seated alone at the council table, seemingly asleep, his hands clasped together atop his beard. She saw Lord Varys hurry into the hall, his feet making no sound. A moment later Lord Baelish entered through the tall doors in the rear, smiling. He chatted amiably with Ser Balon and Ser Dontos as he made his way to the front. Butterflies fluttered nervously in Sansa's stomach. *I shouldn't be afraid,* she told herself. *I have nothing to be afraid of, it will all come out well, Joff loves me and the queen does too, she said so.*

A herald's voice rang out. "All hail His Grace, Joffrey of the Houses Baratheon and Lannister, the First of his Name, King of the Andals, the Rhoynar, and the First Men, and Lord of the Seven Kingdoms. All hail his lady mother, Cersei of House Lannister, Queen Regent, Light of the West, and Protector of the Realm."

Ser Barristan Selmy, resplendent in white plate, led them in. Ser Arys Oakheart escorted the queen, while Ser Boros Blount walked beside Joffrey, so six of the Kingsguard were now in the hall, all the White Swords save

Jaime Lannister alone. Her prince—no, her *king* now!—
took the steps of the Iron Throne two at a time, while his
mother was seated with the council. Joff wore plush black
velvets slashed with crimson, a shimmering cloth-of-gold
cape with a high collar, and on his head a golden crown
crusted with rubies and black diamonds.

When Joffrey turned to look out over the hall, his eye
caught Sansa's. He smiled, seated himself, and spoke. "It
is a king's duty to punish the disloyal and reward those
who are true. Grand Maester Pycelle, I command you to
read my decrees."

Pycelle pushed himself to his feet. He was clad in a
magnificent robe of thick red velvet, with an ermine collar and shiny gold fastenings. From a drooping sleeve,
heavy with gilded scrollwork, he drew a parchment, unrolled it, and began to read a long list of names, commanding each in the name of king and council to present
themselves and swear their fealty to Joffrey. Failing that,
they would be adjudged traitors, their lands and titles forfeit to the throne.

The names he read made Sansa hold her breath. Lord
Stannis Baratheon, his lady wife, his daughter. Lord Renly
Baratheon. Both Lord Royces and their sons. Ser Loras
Tyrell. Lord Mace Tyrell, his brothers, uncles, sons. The
red priest, Thoros of Myr. Lord Beric Dondarrion. Lady
Lysa Arryn and her son, the little Lord Robert. Lord
Hoster Tully, his brother Ser Brynden, his son Ser
Edmure. Lord Jason Mallister. Lord Bryce Caron of the
Marches. Lord Tytos Blackwood. Lord Walder Frey and his
heir Ser Stevron. Lord Karyl Vance. Lord Jonos Bracken.
Lady Shella Whent. Doran Martell, Prince of Dorne, and
all his sons. *So many,* she thought as Pycelle read on and
on, *it will take a whole flock of ravens to send out these
commands.*

And at the end, near last, came the names Sansa had
been dreading. Lady Catelyn Stark. Robb Stark. Brandon
Stark, Rickon Stark, Arya Stark. Sansa stifled a gasp.
Arya. They wanted Arya to present herself and swear an
oath . . . it must mean her sister had fled on the galley,
she must be safe at Winterfell by now . . .

Grand Maester Pycelle rolled up the list, tucked it up
his left sleeve, and pulled another parchment from his
right. He cleared his throat and resumed. "In the place of

the traitor Eddard Stark, it is the wish of His Grace that Tywin Lannister, Lord of Casterly Rock and Warden of the West, take up the office of Hand of the King, to speak with his voice, lead his armies against his enemies, and carry out his royal will. So the king has decreed. The small council consents.

"In the place of the traitor Stannis Baratheon, it is the wish of His Grace that his lady mother, the Queen Regent Cersei Lannister, who has ever been his staunchest support, be seated upon his small council, that she may help him rule wisely and with justice. So the king has decreed. The small council consents."

Sansa heard a soft murmuring from the lords around her, but it was quickly stilled. Pycelle continued.

"It is also the wish of His Grace that his loyal servant, Janos Slynt, Commander of the City Watch of King's Landing, be at once raised to the rank of lord and granted the ancient seat of Harrenhal with all its attendant lands and incomes, and that his sons and grandsons shall hold these honors after him until the end of time. It is moreover his command that *Lord* Slynt be seated immediately upon his small council, to assist in the governance of the realm. So the king has decreed. The small council consents."

Sansa glimpsed motion from the corner of her eye as Janos Slynt made his entrance. This time the muttering was louder and angrier. Proud lords whose houses went back thousands of years made way reluctantly for the balding, frog-faced commoner as he marched past. Golden scales had been sewn onto the black velvet of his doublet and rang together softly with each step. His cloak was checked black-and-gold satin. Two ugly boys who must have been his sons went before him, struggling with the weight of a heavy metal shield as tall as they were. For his sigil he had taken a bloody spear, gold on a night-black field. The sight of it raised goose prickles up and down Sansa's arms.

As Lord Slynt took his place, Grand Maester Pycelle resumed. "Lastly, in these times of treason and turmoil, with our beloved Robert so lately dead, it is the view of the council that the life and safety of King Joffrey is of paramount importance . . ." He looked to the queen.

Cersei stood. "Ser Barristan Selmy, stand forth."

Ser Barristan had been standing at the foot of the Iron Throne, as still as any statue, but now he went to one knee and bowed his head. "Your Grace, I am yours to command."

"Rise, Ser Barristan," Cersei Lannister said. "You may remove your helm."

"My lady?" Standing, the old knight took off his high white helm, though he did not seem to understand why.

"You have served the realm long and faithfully, good ser, and every man and woman in the Seven Kingdoms owes you thanks. Yet now I fear your service is at an end. It is the wish of king and council that you lay down your heavy burden."

"My . . . burden? I fear I . . . I do not . . ."

The new-made lord, Janos Slynt, spoke up, his voice heavy and blunt. "Her Grace is trying to tell you that you are relieved as Lord Commander of the Kingsguard."

The tall, white-haired knight seemed to shrink as he stood there, scarcely breathing. "Your Grace," he said at last. "The Kingsguard is a Sworn Brotherhood. Our vows are taken for life. Only death may relieve the Lord Commander of his sacred trust."

"Whose death, Ser Barristan?" The queen's voice was soft as silk, but her words carried the whole length of the hall. "Yours, or your king's?"

"You let my father die," Joffrey said accusingly from atop the Iron Throne. "You're too old to protect anybody."

Sansa watched as the knight peered up at his new king. She had never seen him look his years before, yet now he did. "Your Grace," he said. "I was chosen for the White Swords in my twenty-third year. It was all I had ever dreamed, from the moment I first took sword in hand. I gave up all claim to my ancestral keep. The girl I was to wed married my cousin in my place, I had no need of land or sons, my life would be lived for the realm. Ser Gerold Hightower himself heard my vows . . . to ward the king with all my strength . . . to give my blood for his . . . I fought beside the White Bull and Prince Lewyn of Dorne . . . beside Ser Arthur Dayne, the Sword of the Morning. Before I served your father, I helped shield King Aerys, and his father Jaehaerys before him . . . three kings . . ."

"And all of them dead," Littlefinger pointed out.

"Your time is done," Cersei Lannister announced. "Joffrey requires men around him who are young and strong. The council has determined that Ser Jaime Lannister will take your place as the Lord Commander of Sworn Brothers of the White Swords."

"The Kingslayer," Ser Barristan said, his voice hard with contempt. "The false knight who profaned his blade with the blood of the king he had sworn to defend."

"Have a care for your words, ser," the queen warned. "You are speaking of our beloved brother, your king's own blood."

Lord Varys spoke, gentler than the others. "We are not unmindful of your service, good ser. Lord Tywin Lannister has generously agreed to grant you a handsome tract of land north of Lannisport, beside the sea, with gold and men sufficient to build you a stout keep, and servants to see to your every need."

Ser Barristan looked up sharply. "A hall to die in, and men to bury me. I thank you, my lords . . . but I spit upon your pity." He reached up and undid the clasps that held his cloak in place, and the heavy white garment slithered from his shoulders to fall in a heap on the floor. His helmet dropped with a *clang*. "I am a knight," he told them. He opened the silver fastenings of his breastplate and let that fall as well. "I shall die a knight."

"A naked knight, it would seem," quipped Littlefinger.

They all laughed then, Joffrey on his throne, and the lords standing attendance, Janos Slynt and Queen Cersei and Sandor Clegane and even the other men of the Kingsguard, the five who had been his brothers until a moment ago. *Surely that must have hurt the most,* Sansa thought. Her heart went out to the gallant old man as he stood shamed and red-faced, too angry to speak. Finally he drew his sword.

Sansa heard someone gasp. Ser Boros and Ser Meryn moved forward to confront him, but Ser Barristan froze them in place with a look that dripped contempt. "Have no fear, sers, your king is safe . . . no thanks to you. Even now, I could cut through the five of you as easy as a dagger cuts cheese. If you would serve under the King-slayer, not a one of you is fit to wear the white." He flung his sword at the foot of the Iron Throne. "Here, boy. Melt it down and add it to the others, if you like. It will do you more good than the swords in the hands of these five. Perhaps Lord Stannis will chance to sit on it when he takes your throne."

He took the long way out, his steps ringing loud against the floor and echoing off the bare stone walls. Lords and ladies parted to let him pass. Not until the pages had closed the great oak-and-bronze doors behind him did Sansa hear sounds again: soft voices, uneasy stirrings, the shuffle of papers from the council table. "He called me *boy*," Joffrey said peevishly, sounding younger than his years. "He talked about my uncle Stannis too."

"Idle talk," said Varys the eunuch. "Without meaning . . ."

"He could be making plots with my uncles. I want him seized and questioned." No one moved. Joffrey raised his voice. "I said, *I want him seized!*"

Janos Slynt rose from the council table. "My gold cloaks will see to it, Your Grace."

"Good," said King Joffrey. Lord Janos strode from the hall, his ugly sons double-stepping to keep up as they lugged the great metal shield with the arms of House Slynt.

"Your Grace," Littlefinger reminded the king. "If we might resume, the seven are now six. We find ourselves in need of a new sword for your Kingsguard."

Joffrey smiled. "Tell them, Mother."

"The king and council have determined that no man in the Seven Kingdoms is more fit to guard and protect His Grace than his sworn shield, Sandor Clegane."

"How do you like that, dog?" King Joffrey asked.

The Hound's scarred face was hard to read. He took a long moment to consider. "Why not? I have no lands nor wife to forsake, and who'd care if I did?" The burned side of his mouth twisted. "But I warn you, I'll say no knight's vows."

"The Sworn Brothers of the Kingsguard have always been knights," Ser Boros said firmly.

"Until now," the Hound said in his deep rasp, and Ser Boros fell silent.

When the king's herald moved forward, Sansa realized the moment was almost at hand. She smoothed down the cloth of her skirt nervously. She was dressed in mourning, as a sign of respect for the dead king, but she had taken special care to make herself beautiful. Her gown was the ivory silk that the queen had given her, the one Arya had ruined, but she'd had them dye it black and you couldn't see the stain at all. She had fretted over her jewelry for hours and finally decided upon the elegant simplicity of a plain silver chain.

The herald's voice boomed out. "If any man in this hall has other matters to set before His Grace, let him speak now or go forth and hold his silence."

Sansa quailed. *Now,* she told herself, *I must do it now. Gods give me courage.* She took one step, then another. Lords and knights stepped aside silently to let her pass, and she felt the weight of their eyes on her. *I must be as strong as my lady mother.* "Your Grace," she called out in a soft, tremulous voice.

The height of the Iron Throne gave Joffrey a better vantage point than anyone else in the hall. He was the first to see her. "Come forward, my lady," he called out, smiling.

His smile emboldened her, made her feel beautiful and strong. *He does love me, he does.* Sansa lifted her head and walked toward him, not too slow and not too fast. She must not let them see how nervous she was.

"The Lady Sansa, of House Stark," the herald cried.

She stopped under the throne, at the spot where Ser Barristan's white cloak lay puddled on the floor beside his helm and breastplate. "Do you have some business for king and council, Sansa?" the queen asked from the council table.

"I do." She knelt on the cloak, so as not to spoil her gown, and looked up at her prince on his fearsome black throne. "As it please Your Grace, I ask mercy for my father, Lord Eddard Stark, who was the Hand of the King." She had practiced the words a hundred times.

The queen sighed. "Sansa, you disappoint me. What did I tell you about traitor's blood?"

"Your father has committed grave and terrible crimes, my lady," Grand Maester Pycelle intoned.

"Ah, poor sad thing," sighed Varys. "She is only a babe, my lords, she does not know what she asks."

Sansa had eyes only for Joffrey. *He must listen to me, he must,* she thought. The king shifted on his seat. "Let her speak," he commanded. "I want to hear what she says."

"Thank you, Your Grace." Sansa smiled, a shy secret smile, just for him. He was listening. She knew he would.

"Treason is a noxious weed," Pycelle declared solemnly. "It must be torn up, root and stem and seed, lest new traitors sprout from every roadside."

"Do you deny your father's crime?" Lord Baelish asked.

"No, my lords." Sansa knew better than that. "I know he must be punished. All I ask is mercy. I know my lord father must regret what he did. He was King Robert's friend and he loved him, you all know he loved him. He never wanted to be Hand until the king asked him. They must have lied to him. Lord Renly or Lord Stannis or . . . or *somebody*, they must have lied, otherwise . . ."

King Joffrey leaned forward, hands grasping the arms of the throne. Broken sword points fanned out between his fingers. "He said I wasn't the king. Why did he say that?"

"His leg was broken," Sansa replied eagerly. "It hurt ever so much, Maester Pycelle was giving him milk of the poppy, and they say that milk of the poppy fills your head with clouds. Otherwise he would never have said it."

Varys said, "A child's faith . . . such sweet innocence . . . and yet, they say wisdom oft comes from the mouths of babes."

"Treason is treason," Pycelle replied at once.

Joffrey rocked restlessly on the throne. "Mother?"

Cersei Lannister considered Sansa thoughtfully. "If Lord Eddard were to confess his crime," she said at last, "we would know he had repented his folly."

Joffrey pushed himself to his feet. *Please,* Sansa thought, *please, please, be the king I know you are, good and kind and noble, please.* "Do you have any more to say?" he asked her.

"Only . . . that as you love me, you do me this kindness, my prince," Sansa said.

King Joffrey looked her up and down. "Your sweet words have moved me," he said gallantly, nodding, as if to say all would be well. "I shall do as you ask . . . but first your father has to confess. He has to confess and say that I'm the king, or there will be no mercy for him."

"He will," Sansa said, heart soaring. "Oh, I know he will."

EDDARD

The straw on the floor stank of urine. There was no window, no bed, not even a slop bucket. He remembered walls of pale red stone festooned with patches of nitre, a grey door of splintered wood, four inches thick and studded with iron. He had seen them, briefly, a quick glimpse as they shoved him inside. Once the door had slammed shut, he had seen no more. The dark was absolute. He had as well been blind.

Or dead. Buried with his king. "Ah, Robert," he murmured as his groping hand touched a cold stone wall, his leg throbbing with every motion. He remembered the jest the king had shared in the crypts of Winterfell, as the Kings of Winter looked on with cold stone eyes. *The king eats*, Robert had said, *and the Hand takes the shit*. How he had laughed. Yet he had gotten it wrong. *The king dies*, Ned Stark thought, *and the Hand is buried*.

The dungeon was under the Red Keep, deeper than he dared imagine. He remembered the old stories about Maegor the Cruel, who murdered all the masons who labored on his castle, so they might never reveal its secrets.

He damned them all: Littlefinger, Janos Slynt and his gold cloaks, the queen, the Kingslayer, Pycelle and Varys and Ser Barristan, even Lord Renly, Robert's own blood, who had run when he was needed most. Yet in the end he blamed himself. *"Fool,"* he cried to the darkness, "thrice-damned blind fool."

Cersei Lannister's face seemed to float before him in the darkness. Her hair was full of sunlight, but there was mockery in her smile. "When you play the game of thrones, you win or you die," she whispered. Ned had played and lost, and his men had paid the price of his folly with their life's blood.

When he thought of his daughters, he would have wept gladly, but the tears would not come. Even now, he was a Stark of Winterfell, and his grief and his rage froze hard inside him.

When he kept very still, his leg did not hurt so much, so he did his best to lie unmoving. For how long he could not say. There was no sun and no moon. He could not see to mark the walls. Ned closed his eyes and opened them; it made no difference. He slept and woke and slept again. He did not know which was more painful, the waking or the sleeping. When he slept, he dreamed: dark disturbing dreams of blood and broken promises. When he woke, there was nothing to do but think, and his waking thoughts were worse than nightmares. The thought of Cat was as painful as a bed of nettles. He wondered where she was, what she was doing. He wondered whether he would ever see her again.

Hours turned to days, or so it seemed. He could feel a dull ache in his shattered leg, an itch beneath the plaster. When he touched his thigh, the flesh was hot to his fingers. The only sound was his breathing. After a time, he began to talk aloud, just to hear a voice. He made plans to keep himself sane, built castles of hope in the dark. Robert's brothers were out in the world, raising armies at Dragonstone and Storm's End. Alyn and Harwin would return to King's Landing with the rest of his household guard once they had dealt with Ser Gregor. Catelyn would raise the north when the word reached her, and the lords of river and mountain and Vale would join her.

He found himself thinking of Robert more and more. He saw the king as he had been in the flower of his youth, tall and handsome, his great antlered helm on his head, his warhammer in hand, sitting his horse like a horned

god. He heard his laughter in the dark, saw his eyes, blue
and clear as mountain lakes. "Look at us, Ned," Robert
said. "Gods, how did we come to this? You here, and me
killed by a pig. We won a throne together . . ."

I failed you, Robert, Ned thought. He could not say
the words. *I lied to you, hid the truth. I let them kill you.*

The king heard him. "You stiff-necked fool," he muttered, "too proud to listen. Can you eat pride, Stark? Will
honor shield your children?" Cracks ran down his face,
fissures opening in the flesh, and he reached up and ripped
the mask away. It was not Robert at all; it was Littlefinger, grinning, mocking him. When he opened his
mouth to speak, his lies turned to pale grey moths and
took wing.

Ned was half-asleep when the footsteps came down
the hall. At first he thought he dreamt them; it had been
so long since he had heard anything but the sound of his
own voice. Ned was feverish by then, his leg a dull agony,
his lips parched and cracked. When the heavy wooden
door creaked open, the sudden light was painful to his
eyes.

A gaoler thrust a jug at him. The clay was cool and
beaded with moisture. Ned grasped it with both hands
and gulped eagerly. Water ran from his mouth and dripped
down through his beard. He drank until he thought he
would be sick. "How long . . . ?" he asked weakly when
he could drink no more.

The gaoler was a scarecrow of a man with a rat's face
and frayed beard, clad in a mail shirt and a leather half
cape. "No talking," he said as he wrenched the jug from
Ned's hands.

"Please," Ned said, "my daughters . . ." The door
crashed shut. He blinked as the light vanished, lowered
his head to his chest, and curled up on the straw. It no
longer stank of urine and shit. It no longer smelled at all.

He could no longer tell the difference between waking
and sleeping. The memory came creeping upon him in
the darkness, as vivid as a dream. It was the year of false
spring, and he was eighteen again, down from the Eyrie to
the tourney at Harrenhal. He could see the deep green of
the grass, and smell the pollen on the wind. Warm days
and cool nights and the sweet taste of wine. He remembered Brandon's laughter, and Robert's berserk valor in

the melee, the way he laughed as he unhorsed men left and right. He remembered Jaime Lannister, a golden youth in scaled white armor, kneeling on the grass in front of the king's pavilion and making his vows to protect and defend King Aerys. Afterward, Ser Oswell Whent helped Jaime to his feet, and the White Bull himself, Lord Commander Ser Gerold Hightower, fastened the snowy cloak of the Kingsguard about his shoulders. All six White Swords were there to welcome their newest brother.

Yet when the jousting began, the day belonged to Rhaegar Targaryen. The crown prince wore the armor he would die in: gleaming black plate with the three-headed dragon of his House wrought in rubies on the breast. A plume of scarlet silk streamed behind him when he rode, and it seemed no lance could touch him. Brandon fell to him, and Bronze Yohn Royce, and even the splendid Ser Arthur Dayne, the Sword of the Morning.

Robert had been jesting with Jon and old Lord Hunter as the prince circled the field after unhorsing Ser Barristan in the final tilt to claim the champion's crown. Ned remembered the moment when all the smiles died, when Prince Rhaegar Targaryen urged his horse past his own wife, the Dornish princess Elia Martell, to lay the queen of beauty's laurel in Lyanna's lap. He could see it still: a crown of winter roses, blue as frost.

Ned Stark reached out his hand to grasp the flowery crown, but beneath the pale blue petals the thorns lay hidden. He felt them clawing at his skin, sharp and cruel, saw the slow trickle of blood run down his fingers, and woke, trembling, in the dark.

Promise me, Ned, his sister had whispered from her bed of blood. She had loved the scent of winter roses.

"Gods save me," Ned wept. "I am going mad."

The gods did not deign to answer.

Each time the turnkey brought him water, he told himself another day had passed. At first he would beg the man for some word of his daughters and the world beyond his cell. Grunts and kicks were his only replies. Later, when the stomach cramps began, he begged for food instead. It made no matter; he was not fed. Perhaps the Lannisters meant for him to starve to death. "No," he told himself. If Cersei had wanted him dead, he would have been cut down in the throne room with his men. She wanted him alive. Weak, desperate, yet alive. Catelyn held her brother; she dare not kill him or the Imp's life would be forfeit as well.

From outside his cell came the rattle of iron chains. As the door creaked open, Ned put a hand to the damp wall and pushed himself toward the light. The glare of a torch made him squint. "Food," he croaked.

"Wine," a voice answered. It was not the rat-faced man; this gaoler was stouter, shorter, though he wore the same leather half cape and spiked steel cap. "Drink, Lord Eddard." He thrust a wineskin into Ned's hands.

The voice was strangely familiar, yet it took Ned Stark a moment to place it. *"Varys?"* he said groggily when it came. He touched the man's face. "I'm not . . . not dreaming this. You're here." The eunuch's plump cheeks were covered with a dark stubble of beard. Ned felt the coarse hair with his fingers. Varys had transformed himself into a grizzled turnkey, reeking of sweat and sour wine. "How did you . . . what sort of magician are you?"

"A thirsty one," Varys said. "Drink, my lord."

Ned's hands fumbled at the skin. "Is this the same poison they gave Robert?"

"You wrong me," Varys said sadly. "Truly, no one loves a eunuch. Give me the skin." He drank, a trickle of red leaking from the corner of his plump mouth. "Not the equal of the vintage you offered me the night of the tourney, but no more poisonous than most," he concluded, wiping his lips. "Here."

Ned tried a swallow. "Dregs." He felt as though he were about to bring the wine back up.

"All men must swallow the sour with the sweet. High lords and eunuchs alike. Your hour has come, my lord."

"My daughters . . ."

"The younger girl escaped Ser Meryn and fled," Varys told him. "I have not been able to find her. Nor have the Lannisters. A kindness, there. Our new king loves her not. Your older girl is still betrothed to Joffrey. Cersei keeps her close. She came to court a few days ago to plead that you be spared. A pity you couldn't have been there, you would have been touched." He leaned forward intently. "I trust you realize that you are a dead man, Lord Eddard?"

"The queen will not kill me," Ned said. His head swam; the wine was strong, and it had been too long since he'd eaten. "Cat . . . Cat holds her brother . . ."

"The *wrong* brother," Varys sighed. "And lost to her, in any case. She let the Imp slip through her fingers. I expect he is dead by now, somewhere in the Mountains of the Moon."

"If that is true, slit my throat and have done with it." He was dizzy from the wine, tired and heartsick.

"Your blood is the last thing I desire."

Ned frowned. "When they slaughtered my guard, you stood beside the queen and watched, and said not a word."

"And would again. I seem to recall that I was unarmed, unarmored, and surrounded by Lannister swords." The eunuch looked at him curiously, tilting his head. "When I was a young boy, before I was cut, I traveled with a troupe of mummers through the Free Cities. They taught me that each man has a role to play, in life as well as mummery. So it is at court. The King's Justice must be fearsome, the master of coin must be frugal, the Lord Commander of the Kingsguard must be valiant . . . and the master of whisperers must be sly and obsequious and without scruple. A courageous informer would be as useless as a cowardly knight." He took the wineskin back and drank.

Ned studied the eunuch's face, searching for truth beneath the mummer's scars and false stubble. He tried some more wine. This time it went down easier. "Can you free me from this pit?"

"I could . . . but *will* I? No. Questions would be asked, and the answers would lead back to me."

Ned had expected no more. "You are blunt."

"A eunuch has no honor, and a spider does not enjoy the luxury of scruples, my lord."

"Would you at least consent to carry a message out for me?"

"That would depend on the message. I will gladly provide you with paper and ink, if you like. And when you have written what you will, I will take the letter and read it, and deliver it or not, as best serves my own ends."

"Your own ends. What ends are those, Lord Varys?"

"Peace," Varys replied without hesitation. "If there

was one soul in King's Landing who was truly desperate to keep Robert Baratheon alive, it was me." He sighed. "For fifteen years I protected him from his enemies, but I could not protect him from his friends. What strange fit of madness led you to tell the queen that you had learned the truth of Joffrey's birth?"

"The madness of mercy," Ned admitted.

"Ah," said Varys. "To be sure. You are an honest and honorable man, Lord Eddard. Ofttimes I forget that. I have met so few of them in my life." He glanced around the cell. "When I see what honesty and honor have won you, I understand why."

Ned Stark laid his head back against the damp stone wall and closed his eyes. His leg was throbbing. "The king's wine . . . did you question Lancel?"

"Oh, indeed. Cersei gave him the wineskins, and told him it was Robert's favorite vintage." The eunuch shrugged. "A hunter lives a perilous life. If the boar had not done for Robert, it would have been a fall from a horse, the bite of a wood adder, an arrow gone astray . . . the forest is the abbatoir of the gods. It was not wine that killed the king. It was your *mercy*."

Ned had feared as much. "Gods forgive me."

"If there are gods," Varys said, "I expect they will. The queen would not have waited long in any case. Robert was becoming unruly, and she needed to be rid of him to free her hands to deal with his brothers. They are quite a pair, Stannis and Renly. The iron gauntlet and the silk glove." He wiped his mouth with the back of his hand. "You have been foolish, my lord. You ought to have heeded Littlefinger when he urged you to support Joffrey's succession."

"How . . . how could you know of that?"

Varys smiled. "I know, that's all that need concern you. I also know that on the morrow the queen will pay you a visit."

Slowly Ned raised his eyes. "Why?"

"Cersei is frightened of you, my lord . . . but she has other enemies she fears even more. Her beloved Jaime is fighting the river lords even now. Lysa Arryn sits in the Eyrie, ringed in stone and steel, and there is no love lost between her and the queen. In Dorne, the Martells still brood on the murder of Princess Elia and her babes. And now your son marches down the Neck with a northern host at his back."

"Robb is only a boy," Ned said, aghast.

"A boy with an army," Varys said. "Yet only a boy, as you say. The king's brothers are the ones giving Cersei sleepless nights . . . Lord Stannis in particular. His claim is the true one, he is known for his prowess as a battle commander, and he is utterly without mercy. There is no creature on earth half so terrifying as a truly just man. No one knows what Stannis has been doing on Dragonstone, but I will wager you that he's gathered more swords than seashells. So here is Cersei's nightmare: while her father and brother spend their power battling Starks and Tullys, Lord Stannis will land, proclaim himself king, and lop off her son's curly blond head . . . and her own in the bargain, though I truly believe she cares more about the boy."

"Stannis Baratheon is Robert's true heir," Ned said. "The throne is his by rights. I would welcome his ascent."

Varys *tsk*ed. "Cersei will not want to hear that, I promise you. Stannis may win the throne, but only your rotting head will remain to cheer unless you guard that tongue of yours. Sansa begged so sweetly, it would be a shame if you threw it all away. You are being given your life back, if you'll take it. Cersei is no fool. She knows a tame wolf is of more use than a dead one."

"You want me to *serve* the woman who murdered my king, butchered my men, and crippled my son?" Ned's voice was thick with disbelief.

"I want you to serve the realm," Varys said. "Tell the queen that you will confess your vile treason, command your son to lay down his sword, and proclaim Joffrey as the true heir. Offer to denounce Stannis and Renly as faithless usurpers. Our green-eyed lioness knows you are a man of honor. If you will give her the peace she needs and the time to deal with Stannis, and pledge to carry her secret to your grave, I believe she will allow you to take the black and live out the rest of your days on the Wall, with your brother and that baseborn son of yours."

The thought of Jon filled Ned with a sense of shame, and a sorrow too deep for words. If only he could see the boy again, sit and talk with him . . . pain shot through his broken leg, beneath the filthy grey plaster of his cast. He winced, his fingers opening and closing helplessly. "Is this your own scheme," he gasped out at Varys, "or are you in league with Littlefinger?"

That seemed to amuse the eunuch. "I would sooner wed the Black Goat of Qohor. Littlefinger is the second most devious man in the Seven Kingdoms. Oh, I feed him choice whispers, sufficient so that he *thinks* I am his . . . just as I allow Cersei to believe I am hers."

"And just as you let me believe that you were mine. Tell me, Lord Varys, who do you truly serve?"

Varys smiled thinly. "Why, the realm, my good lord, how ever could you doubt that? I swear it by my lost manhood. I serve the realm, and the realm needs peace." He finished the last swallow of wine, and tossed the empty skin aside. "So what is your answer, Lord Eddard? Give me your word that you'll tell the queen what she wants to hear when she comes calling."

"If I did, my word would be as hollow as an empty suit of armor. My life is not so precious to me as that."

"Pity." The eunuch stood. "And your daughter's life, my lord? How precious is that?"

A chill pierced Ned's heart. "My daughter . . ."

"Surely you did not think I'd forgotten about your sweet innocent, my lord? The queen most certainly has not."

"*No*," Ned pleaded, his voice cracking. "Varys, gods have mercy, do as you like with me, but leave my daughter out of your schemes. Sansa's no more than a child."

"Rhaenys was a child too. Prince Rhaegar's daughter. A precious little thing, younger than your girls. She had a small black kitten she called Balerion, did you know? I always wondered what happened to him. Rhaenys liked to pretend he was the true Balerion, the Black Dread of old, but I imagine the Lannisters taught her the difference between a kitten and a dragon quick enough, the day they broke down her door." Varys gave a long weary sigh, the sigh of a man who carried all the sadness of the world in a sack upon his shoulders. "The High Septon once told me that as we sin, so do we suffer. If that's true, Lord Eddard, tell me . . . why is it always the innocents who suffer most, when you high lords play your game of thrones? Ponder it, if you would, while you wait upon the queen.

And spare a thought for this as well: The next visitor who calls on you could bring you bread and cheese and the milk of the poppy for your pain . . . or he could bring you Sansa's head.

"The choice, my dear lord Hand, is *entirely* yours."

CATELYN

As the host trooped down the causeway through the black bogs of the Neck and spilled out into the riverlands beyond, Catelyn's apprehensions grew. She masked her fears behind a face kept still and stern, yet they were there all the same, growing with every league they crossed. Her days were anxious, her nights restless, and every raven that flew overhead made her clench her teeth.

She feared for her lord father, and wondered at his ominous silence. She feared for her brother Edmure, and prayed that the gods would watch over him if he must face the Kingslayer in battle. She feared for Ned and her girls, and for the sweet sons she had left behind at Winterfell. And yet there was nothing she could do for any of them, and so she made herself put all thought of them aside. *You must save your strength for Robb,* she told herself. *He is the only one you can help. You must be as fierce and hard as the north, Catelyn Tully. You must be a Stark for true now, like your son.*

Robb rode at the front of the column, beneath the flapping white banner of Winterfell. Each day he would ask one of his lords to join him, so they might confer as they marched; he honored every man in turn, showing no favorites, listening as his lord father had listened, weighing the words of one against the other. *He has learned so much from Ned,* she thought as she watched him, *but has he learned enough?*

The Blackfish had taken a hundred picked men and a hundred swift horses and raced ahead to screen their movements and scout the way. The reports Ser Brynden's riders brought back did little to reassure her. Lord Tywin's host was still many days to the south . . . but Walder Frey, Lord of the Crossing, had assembled a force of near four thousand men at his castles on the Green Fork.

"Late again," Catelyn murmured when she heard. It was the Trident all over, damn the man. Her brother Edmure had called the banners; by rights, Lord Frey should have gone to join the Tully host at Riverrun, yet here he sat.

"Four thousand men," Robb repeated, more perplexed than angry. "Lord Frey cannot hope to fight the Lannisters by himself. Surely he means to join his power to ours."

"Does he?" Catelyn asked. She had ridden forward to join Robb and Robert Glover, his companion of the day. The vanguard spread out behind them, a slow-moving forest of lances and banners and spears. "I wonder. Expect nothing of Walder Frey, and you will never be surprised."

"He's your father's bannerman."

"Some men take their oaths more seriously than others, Robb. And Lord Walder was always friendlier with Casterly Rock than my father would have liked. One of his sons is wed to Tywin Lannister's sister. That means little of itself, to be sure. Lord Walder has sired a great many children over the years, and they must needs marry someone. Still . . ."

"Do you think he means to betray us to the Lannisters, my lady?" Robert Glover asked gravely.

Catelyn sighed. "If truth be told, I doubt even Lord Frey knows what Lord Frey intends to do. He has an old man's caution and a young man's ambition, and has never lacked for cunning."

"We must have the Twins, Mother," Robb said heatedly. "There is no other way across the river. You know that."

"Yes. And so does Walder Frey, you can be sure of that."

That night they made camp on the southern edge of the bogs, halfway between the kingsroad and the river. It was there Theon Greyjoy brought them further word from her uncle. "Ser Brynden says to tell you he's crossed swords with the Lannisters. There are a dozen scouts who won't be reporting back to Lord Tywin anytime soon. Or ever." He grinned. "Ser Addam Marbrand commands their outriders, and he's pulling back south, burning as he goes. He knows where we are, more or less, but the Blackfish vows he will not know when we split."

"Unless Lord Frey tells him," Catelyn said sharply. "Theon, when you return to my uncle, tell him he is to place his best bowmen around the Twins, day and night, with orders to bring down any raven they see leaving the battlements. I want no birds bringing word of my son's movements to Lord Tywin."

"Ser Brynden has seen to it already, my lady," Theon replied with a cocky smile. "A few more blackbirds, and we should have enough to bake a pie. I'll save you their feathers for a hat."

She ought to have known that Brynden Blackfish would be well ahead of her. "What have the Freys been doing while the Lannisters burn their fields and plunder their holdfasts?"

"There's been some fighting between Ser Addam's men and Lord Walder's," Theon answered. "Not a day's ride from here, we found two Lannister scouts feeding the crows where the Freys had strung them up. Most of Lord Walder's strength remains massed at the Twins, though."

That bore Walder Frey's seal beyond a doubt, Catelyn thought bitterly; hold back, wait, watch, take no risk unless forced to it.

"If he's been fighting the Lannisters, perhaps he does mean to hold to his vows," Robb said.

Catelyn was less encouraged. "Defending his own lands is one thing, open battle against Lord Tywin quite another."

Robb turned back to Theon Greyjoy. "Has the Blackfish found any other way across the Green Fork?"

Theon shook his head. "The river's running high and

fast. Ser Brynden says it can't be forded, not this far north."

"I *must* have that crossing!" Robb declared, fuming. "Oh, our horses might be able to swim the river, I suppose, but not with armored men on their backs. We'd need to build rafts to pole our steel across, helms and mail and lances, and we don't have the trees for that. *Or* the time. Lord Tywin is marching north . . ." He balled his hand into a fist.

"Lord Frey would be a fool to try and bar our way," Theon Greyjoy said with his customary easy confidence. "We have five times his numbers. You can take the Twins if you need to, Robb."

"Not easily," Catelyn warned them, "and not in time. While you were mounting your siege, Tywin Lannister would bring up his host and assault you from the rear."

Robb glanced from her to Greyjoy, searching for an answer and finding none. For a moment he looked even younger than his fifteen years, despite his mail and sword and the stubble on his cheeks. "What would my lord father do?" he asked her.

"Find a way across," she told him. "Whatever it took."

The next morning it was Ser Brynden Tully himself who rode back to them. He had put aside the heavy plate and helm he'd worn as the Knight of the Gate for the lighter leather-and-mail of an outrider, but his obsidian fish still fastened his cloak.

Her uncle's face was grave as he swung down off his horse. "There has been a battle under the walls of Riverrun," he said, his mouth grim. "We had it from a Lannister outrider we took captive. The Kingslayer has destroyed Edmure's host and sent the lords of the Trident reeling in flight."

A cold hand clutched at Catelyn's heart. "And my brother?"

"Wounded and taken prisoner," Ser Brynden said. "Lord Blackwood and the other survivors are under siege inside Riverrun, surrounded by Jaime's host."

Robb looked fretful. "We must get across this accursed river if we're to have any hope of relieving them in time."

"That will not be easily done," her uncle cautioned. "Lord Frey has pulled his whole strength back inside his castles, and his gates are closed and barred."

"Damn the man," Robb swore. "If the old fool does not relent and let me cross, he'll leave me no choice but to storm his walls. I'll pull the Twins down around his ears if I have to, we'll see how well he likes that!"

"You sound like a sulky boy, Robb," Catelyn said sharply. "A child sees an obstacle, and his first thought is to run around it or knock it down. A lord must learn that sometimes words can accomplish what swords cannot."

Robb's neck reddened at the rebuke. "Tell me what you mean, Mother," he said meekly.

"The Freys have held the crossing for six hundred years, and for six hundred years they have never failed to exact their toll."

"What toll? What does he *want*?"

She smiled. "That is what we must discover."

"And what if I do not choose to pay this toll?"

"Then you had best retreat back to Moat Cailin, deploy to meet Lord Tywin in battle . . . or grow wings. I see no other choices." Catelyn put her heels to her horse and rode off, leaving her son to ponder her words. It would not do to make him feel as if his mother were usurping his place. *Did you teach him wisdom as well as valor, Ned?* she wondered. *Did you teach him how to kneel?* The graveyards of the Seven Kingdoms were full of brave men who had never learned that lesson.

It was near midday when their vanguard came in sight of the Twins, where the Lords of the Crossing had their seat.

The Green Fork ran swift and deep here, but the Freys had spanned it many centuries past and grown rich off the coin men paid them to cross. Their bridge was a massive arch of smooth grey rock, wide enough for two wagons to pass abreast; the Water Tower rose from the center of the span, commanding both road and river with its arrow slits, murder holes, and portcullises. It had taken the Freys three generations to complete their bridge; when they were done they'd thrown up stout timber keeps on either bank, so no one might cross without their leave.

The timber had long since given way to stone. The Twins—two squat, ugly, formidable castles, identical in every respect, with the bridge arching between—had guarded the crossing for centuries. High curtain walls, deep moats, and heavy oak-and-iron gates protected the approaches, the bridge footings rose from within stout inner keeps, there was a barbican and portcullis on either bank, and the Water Tower defended the span itself.

One glance was sufficient to tell Catelyn that the castle would not be taken by storm. The battlements bristled with spears and swords and scorpions, there was an archer at every crenel and arrow slit, the drawbridge was up, the portcullis down, the gates closed and barred.

The Greatjon began to curse and swear as soon as he saw what awaited them. Lord Rickard Karstark glowered in silence. "That cannot be assaulted, my lords," Roose Bolton announced.

"Nor can we take it by siege, without an army on the far bank to invest the other castle," Helman Tallhart said gloomily. Across the deep-running green waters, the western twin stood like a reflection of its eastern brother. "Even if we had the time. Which, to be sure, we do not."

As the northern lords studied the castle, a sally port opened, a plank bridge slid across the moat, and a dozen knights rode forth to confront them, led by four of Lord Walder's many sons. Their banner bore twin towers, dark blue on a field of pale silver-grey. Ser Stevron Frey, Lord Walder's heir, spoke for them. The Freys all looked like weasels; Ser Stevron, past sixty with grandchildren of his own, looked like an especially old and tired weasel, yet he was polite enough. "My lord father has sent me to greet you, and inquire as to who leads this mighty host."

"I do." Robb spurred his horse forward. He was in his armor, with the direwolf shield of Winterfell strapped to his saddle and Grey Wind padding by his side.

The old knight looked at her son with a faint flicker of amusement in his watery grey eyes, though his gelding whickered uneasily and sidled away from the direwolf. "My lord father would be most honored if you would share meat and mead with him in the castle and explain your purpose here."

His words crashed among the lords bannermen like a great stone from a catapult. Not one of them approved. They cursed, argued, shouted down each other.

"You must not do this, my lord," Galbart Glover pleaded with Robb. "Lord Walder is not to be trusted."

Roose Bolton nodded. "Go in there alone and you're

his. He can sell you to the Lannisters, throw you in a dungeon, or slit your throat, as he likes."

"If he wants to talk to us, let him open his gates, and we will *all* share his meat and mead," declared Ser Wendel Manderly.

"Or let him come out and treat with Robb here, in plain sight of his men and ours," suggested his brother, Ser Wylis.

Catelyn Stark shared all their doubts, but she had only to glance at Ser Stevron to see that he was not pleased by what he was hearing. A few more words and the chance would be lost. She had to act, and quickly. *"I will go,"* she said loudly.

"You, my lady?" The Greatjon furrowed his brow.

"Mother, are you certain?" Clearly, Robb was not.

"Never more," Catelyn lied glibly. "Lord Walder is my father's bannerman. I have known him since I was a girl. He would never offer me any harm." *Unless he saw some profit in it,* she added silently, but some truths did not bear saying, and some lies were necessary.

"I am certain my lord father would be pleased to speak to the Lady Catelyn," Ser Stevron said. "To vouchsafe for our good intentions, my brother Ser Perwyn will remain here until she is safely returned to you."

"He shall be our honored guest," said Robb. Ser Perwyn, the youngest of the four Freys in the party, dismounted and handed the reins of his horse to a brother. "I require my lady mother's return by evenfall, Ser Stevron," Robb went on. "It is not my intent to linger here long."

Ser Stevron Frey gave a polite nod. "As you say, my lord." Catelyn spurred her horse forward and did not look back. Lord Walder's sons and envoys fell in around her.

Her father had once said of Walder Frey that he was the only lord in the Seven Kingdoms who could field an army out of his breeches. When the Lord of the Crossing welcomed Catelyn in the great hall of the east castle, surrounded by twenty living sons (minus Ser Perwyn, who would have made twenty-one), thirty-six grandsons, nineteen great-grandsons, and numerous daughters, granddaughters, bastards, and grandbastards, she understood just what he had meant.

Lord Walder was ninety, a wizened pink weasel with a bald spotted head, too gouty to stand unassisted. His newest wife, a pale frail girl of sixteen years, walked beside his litter when they carried him in. She was the eighth Lady Frey.

"It is a great pleasure to see you again after so many years, my lord," Catelyn said.

The old man squinted at her suspiciously. "Is it? I doubt that. Spare me your sweet words, Lady Catelyn, I am too old. Why are you here? Is your boy too proud to come before me himself? What am I to do with *you?*"

Catelyn had been a girl the last time she had visited the Twins, but even then Lord Walder had been irascible, sharp of tongue, and blunt of manner. Age had made him worse than ever, it would seem. She would need to choose her words with care, and do her best to take no offense from his.

"Father," Ser Stevron said reproachfully, "you forget yourself. Lady Stark is here at your invitation."

"Did I ask *you?* You are not Lord Frey yet, not until I die. Do I look dead? I'll hear no instructions from you."

"This is no way to speak in front of our noble guest, Father," one of his younger sons said.

"Now my bastards presume to teach me courtesy," Lord Walder complained. "I'll speak any way I like, damn you. I've had three kings to guest in my life, and queens as well, do you think I require lessons from the likes of you, Ryger? Your mother was milking goats the first time I gave her my seed." He dismissed the red-faced youth with a flick of his fingers and gestured to two of his other sons. "Danwell, Whalen, help me to my chair."

They shifted Lord Walder from his litter and carried him to the high seat of the Freys, a tall chair of black oak whose back was carved in the shape of two towers linked by a bridge. His young wife crept up timidly and covered his legs with a blanket. When he was settled, the old man beckoned Catelyn forward and planted a papery dry kiss on her hand. "There," he announced. "Now that I have observed the courtesies, my lady, perhaps my sons will do me the honor of shutting their mouths. Why are you here?"

"To ask you to open your gates, my lord," Catelyn replied politely. "My son and his lords bannermen are most anxious to cross the river and be on their way."

"To Riverrun?" He sniggered. "Oh, no need to tell me,

no need. I'm not blind yet. The old man can still read a map."

"To Riverrun," Catelyn confirmed. She saw no reason to deny it. "Where I might have expected to find you, my lord. You are still my father's bannerman, are you not?"

"Heh," said Lord Walder, a noise halfway between a laugh and a grunt. "I called my swords, yes I did, here they are, you saw them on the walls. It was my intent to march as soon as all my strength was assembled. Well, to send my sons. I am well past marching myself, Lady Catelyn." He looked around for likely confirmation and pointed to a tall, stooped man of fifty years. "Tell her, Jared. Tell her that was my intent."

"It was, my lady," said Ser Jared Frey, one of his sons by his second wife. "On my honor."

"Is it my fault that your fool brother lost his battle before we could march?" He leaned back against his cushions and scowled at her, as if challenging her to dispute his version of events. "I am told the Kingslayer went through him like an axe through ripe cheese. Why should my boys hurry south to die? All those who did go south are running north again."

Catelyn would gladly have spitted the querulous old man and roasted him over a fire, but she had only till evenfall to open the bridge. Calmly, she said, "All the more reason that we must reach Riverrun, and soon. Where can we go to talk, my lord?"

"We're talking now," Lord Frey complained. The spotted pink head snapped around. "What are you all looking at?" he shouted at his kin. "Get out of here. Lady Stark wants to speak to me in private. Might be she has designs on my fidelity, *heh.* Go, all of you, find something useful to do. Yes, you too, woman. Out, out, *out.*" As his sons and grandsons and daughters and bastards and nieces and nephews streamed from the hall, he leaned close to Catelyn and confessed, "They're all waiting for me to die. Stevron's been waiting for forty years, but I keep disappointing him. *Heh.* Why should I die just so he can be a lord? I ask you. I won't do it."

"I have every hope that you will live to be a hundred."

"That" would boil them, to be sure. Oh, to be sure. Now, what do you want to say?"

"We want to cross," Catelyn told him.

"Oh, *do* you? That's blunt. Why should I let you?"

For a moment her anger flared. "If you were strong enough to climb your own battlements, Lord Frey, you would see that my son has twenty thousand men outside your walls."

"They'll be twenty thousand fresh corpses when Lord Tywin gets here," the old man shot back. "Don't you try and frighten me, my lady. Your husband's in some traitor's cell under the Red Keep, your father's sick, might be dying, and Jaime Lannister's got your brother in chains. What do you have that I should fear? That son of yours? I'll match you son for son, and I'll still have eighteen when yours are all dead."

"You swore an oath to my father," Catelyn reminded him.

He bobbed his head side to side, smiling. "Oh, yes, I said some words, but I swore oaths to the crown too, it seems to me. Joffrey's the king now, and that makes you and your boy and all those fools out there no better than rebels. If I had the sense the gods gave a fish, I'd help the Lannisters boil you all."

"Why don't you?" she challenged him.

Lord Walder snorted with disdain. "Lord Tywin the proud and splendid, Warden of the West, Hand of the King, oh, what a great man *that* one is, him and his gold this and gold that and lions here and lions there. I'll wager you, he eats too many beans, he breaks wind just like me, but you'll never hear *him* admit it, oh, no. What's *he* got to be so puffed up about anyway? Only two sons, and one of them's a twisted little monster. I'll match *him* son for son, and I'll still have nineteen and a *half* left when all of his are dead!" He cackled. "If Lord Tywin wants my help, he can bloody well *ask* for it."

That was all Catelyn needed to hear. "I am asking for your help, my lord," she said humbly. "And my father and my brother and my lord husband and my sons are asking with my voice."

Lord Walder jabbed a bony finger at her face. "Save your sweet words, my lady. Sweet words I get from my wife. Did you see her? Sixteen she is, a little flower, and her honey's only for me. I wager she gives me a son by this time next year. Perhaps I'll make *him* heir, wouldn't that boil the rest of them?"

"I'm certain she will give you many sons."

His head bobbed up and down. "Your lord father did not come to the wedding. An insult, as I see it. Even if he is dying. He never came to my last wedding either. He calls me the Late Lord Frey, you know. Does he think I'm dead? I'm not dead, and I promise you, I'll outlive him as I outlived his father. Your family has always pissed on me, don't deny it, don't lie, you know it's true. Years ago, I went to your father and suggested a match between his son and my daughter. Why not? I had a daughter in mind, sweet girl, only a few years older than Edmure, but if your brother didn't warm to her, I had others he might have had, young ones, old ones, virgins, widows, whatever he wanted. No, Lord Hoster would not hear of it. Sweet words he gave me, excuses, but what I *wanted* was to get rid of a daughter.

"And your sister, that one, she's full as bad. It was, oh, a year ago, no more, Jon Arryn was still the King's Hand, and I went to the city to see my sons ride in the tourney. Stevron and Jared are too old for the lists now, but Danwell and Hosteen rode, Perwyn as well, and a couple of my bastards tried the melee. If I'd known how they'd shame me, I would never have troubled myself to make the journey. Why did I need to ride all that way to see Hosteen knocked off his horse by that Tyrell whelp? I ask you. The boy's half his age, Ser Daisy they call him, something like that. And Danwell was unhorsed by a hedge knight! Some days I wonder if those two are truly mine. My third wife was a Crakehall, all of the Crakehall women are sluts. Well, never mind about that, she died before you were born, what do you care?

"I was speaking of your sister. I proposed that Lord and Lady Arryn foster two of my grandsons at court, and offered to take their own son to ward here at the Twins. Are my grandsons unworthy to be seen at the king's court? They are sweet boys, quiet and mannerly. Walder is Merrett's son, named after me, and the other one . . . *heh*, I don't recall . . . he might have been another Walder, they're always naming them Walder so I'll favor them, but his father . . . which one was his father now?" His face wrinkled up. "Well, whoever he was, Lord Arryn wouldn't have him, or the other one, and I blame your lady sister for that. She frosted up as if I'd suggested sell-

ing her boy to a mummer's show or making a eunuch out
of him, and when Lord Arryn said the child was going to
Dragonstone to foster with Stannis Baratheon, she
stormed off without a word of regrets and all the Hand
could give me was apologies. What good are apologies? I
ask you."

Catelyn frowned, disquieted. "I had understood that
Lysa's boy was to be fostered with Lord Tywin at Casterly
Rock."

"No, it was Lord Stannis," Walder Frey said irritably.
"Do you think I can't tell Lord Stannis from Lord Tywin?
They're both bungholes who think they're too noble to
shit, but never mind about that, I know the difference. Or
do you think I'm so old I can't remember? I'm ninety and
I remember very well. I remember what to do with a
woman too. That wife of mine will give me a son before
this time next year, I'll wager. Or a daughter, that can't be
helped. Boy or girl, it will be red, wrinkled, and squalling,
and like as not she'll want to name it Walder or Walda."

Catelyn was not concerned with what Lady Frey might
choose to name her child. "Jon Arryn was going to foster
his son with Lord Stannis, you are quite certain of that?"

"Yes, yes, yes," the old man said. "Only he died, so
what does it matter? You say you want to cross the
river?"

"We do."

"Well, you can't!" Lord Walder announced crisply.
"Not unless I allow it, and why should I? The Tullys and
the Starks have never been friends of mine." He pushed
himself back in his chair and crossed his arms, smirking,
waiting for her answer.

The rest was only haggling.

A swollen red sun hung low against the western hills
when the gates of the castle opened. The drawbridge
creaked down, the portcullis winched up, and Lady Catelyn Stark rode forth to rejoin her son and his lords bannermen. Behind her came Ser Jared Frey, Ser Hosteen
Frey, Ser Danwell Frey, and Lord Walder's bastard son
Ronel Rivers, leading a long column of pikemen, rank on
rank of shuffling men in blue steel ringmail and silvery
grey cloaks.

Robb galloped out to meet her, with Grey Wind racing
beside his stallion. "It's done," she told him. "Lord

Walder will grant you your crossing. His swords are yours as well, less four hundred he means to keep back to hold the Twins. I suggest that you leave four hundred of your own, a mixed force of archers and swordsmen. He can scarcely object to an offer to augment his garrison . . . but make certain you give the command to a man you can trust. Lord Walder may need help keeping faith."

"As you say, Mother," Robb answered, gazing at the ranks of pikemen. "Perhaps . . . Ser Helman Tallhart, do you think?"

"A fine choice."

"What . . . what did he want of us?"

"If you can spare a few of your swords, I need some men to escort two of Lord Frey's grandsons north to Winterfell," she told him. "I have agreed to take them as wards. They are young boys, aged eight years and seven. It would seem they are both named Walder. Your brother Bran will welcome the companionship of lads near his own age, I should think."

"Is that all? Two fosterlings? That's a small enough price to—"

"Lord Frey's son Olyvar will be coming with us," she went on. "He is to serve as your personal squire. His father would like to see him knighted, in good time."

"A squire." He shrugged. "Fine, that's fine, if he's—"

"Also, if your sister Arya is returned to us safely, it is agreed that she will marry Lord Walder's youngest son, Elmar, when the two of them come of age."

Robb looked nonplussed. "Arya won't like that one bit."

"And you are to wed one of his daughters, once the fighting is done," she finished. "His lordship has graciously consented to allow you to choose whichever girl you prefer. He has a number he thinks might be suitable."

To his credit, Robb did not flinch. "I see."

"Do you consent?"

"Can I refuse?"

"Not if you wish to cross."

"I consent," Robb said solemnly. He had never seemed more manly to her than he did in that moment. Boys might play with swords, but it took a lord to make a marriage pact, knowing what it meant.

They crossed at evenfall as a horned moon floated

upon the river. The double column wound its way through the gate of the eastern twin like a great steel snake, slithering across the courtyard, into the keep and over the bridge, to issue forth once more from the second castle on the west bank.

Catelyn rode at the head of the serpent, with her son and her uncle Ser Brynden and Ser Stevron Frey. Behind followed nine tenths of their horse; knights, lancers, freeriders, and mounted bowmen. It took hours for them all to cross. Afterward, Catelyn would remember the clatter of countless hooves on the drawbridge, the sight of Lord Walder Frey in his litter watching them pass, the glitter of eyes peering down through the slats of the murder holes in the ceiling as they rode through the Water Tower.

The larger part of the northern host, pikes and archers and great masses of men-at-arms on foot, remained upon the east bank under the command of Roose Bolton. Robb had commanded him to continue the march south, to confront the huge Lannister army coming north under Lord Tywin.

For good or ill, her son had thrown the dice.

JON

"**A**re you well, Snow?" Lord Mormont asked, scowling.

"*Well*," his raven squawked. "*Well*."

"I am, my lord," Jon lied . . . loudly, as if that could make it true. "And you?"

Mormont frowned. "A dead man tried to kill me. How well could I be?" He scratched under his chin. His shaggy grey beard had been singed in the fire, and he'd hacked it off. The pale stubble of his new whiskers made him look old, disreputable, and grumpy. "You do not look well. How is your hand?"

"Healing." Jon flexed his bandaged fingers to show him. He had burned himself more badly than he knew throwing the flaming drapes, and his right hand was swathed in silk halfway to the elbow. At the time he'd felt nothing; the agony had come after. His cracked red skin oozed fluid, and fearsome blood blisters rose between his fingers, big as roaches. "The maester says I'll have scars, but otherwise the hand should be as good as it was before."

"A scarred hand is nothing. On the Wall, you'll be wearing gloves often as not."

"As you say, my lord." It was not the thought of scars that troubled Jon; it was the rest of it. Maester Aemon had given him milk of the poppy, yet even so, the pain had been hideous. At first it had felt as if his hand were still aflame, burning day and night. Only plunging it into basins of snow and shaved ice gave any relief at all. Jon thanked the gods that no one but Ghost saw him writhing on his bed, whimpering from the pain. And when at last he *did* sleep, he dreamt, and that was even worse. In the dream, the corpse he fought had blue eyes, black hands, and his father's face, but he dared not tell Mormont *that*.

"Dywen and Hake returned last night," the Old Bear said. "They found no sign of your uncle, no more than the others did."

"I know." Jon had dragged himself to the common hall to sup with his friends, and the failure of the rangers' search had been all the men had been talking of.

"You know," Mormont grumbled. "How is it that everyone knows everything around here?" He did not seem to expect an answer. "It would seem there were only the two of . . . of those *creatures*, whatever they were, I will not call them men. And thank the gods for that. Any more and . . . well, that doesn't bear thinking of. There will be more, though. I can feel it in these old bones of mine, and Maester Aemon agrees. The cold winds are rising. Summer is at an end, and a winter is coming such as this world has never seen."

Winter is coming. The Stark words had never sounded so grim or ominous to Jon as they did now. "My lord," he asked hesitantly, "it's said there was a bird last night . . ."

"There was. What of it?"

"I had hoped for some word of my father."

"Father," taunted the old raven, bobbing its head as it walked across Mormont's shoulders. *"Father."*

The Lord Commander reached up to pinch its beak shut, but the raven hopped up on his head, fluttered its wings, and flew across the chamber to light above a window. "Grief and noise," Mormont grumbled. "That's all they're good for, ravens. Why I put up with that pestilential bird . . . if there was news of Lord Eddard, don't you think I would have sent for you? Bastard or no, you're still his blood. The message concerned Ser Barristan Selmy. It seems he's been removed from the Kingsguard. They gave his place to that black dog Clegane, and now Selmy's wanted for treason. The fools sent some watchmen to seize him, but he slew two of them and escaped." Mormont snorted, leaving no doubt of his view of men who'd send gold cloaks against a knight as renowed as Barristan the Bold. "We have white shadows in the woods and unquiet dead stalking our halls, and a *boy* sits the Iron Throne," he said in disgust.

The raven laughed shrilly. *"Boy, boy, boy, boy."*

Ser Barristan had been the Old Bear's best hope, Jon remembered; if he had fallen, what chance was there that Mormont's letter would be heeded? He curled his hand into a fist. Pain shot through his burned fingers. "What of my sisters?"

"The message made no mention of Lord Eddard or the girls." He gave an irritated shrug. "Perhaps they never got my letter. Aemon sent two copies, with his best birds, but who can say? More like, Pycelle did not deign to reply. It would not be the first time, nor the last. I fear we count for less than nothing in King's Landing. They tell us what they want us to know, and that's little enough."

And you tell me *what you want* me *to know, and that's less,* Jon thought resentfully. His brother Robb had called the banners and ridden south to war, yet no word of that had been breathed to him . . . save by Samwell Tarly, who'd read the letter to Maester Aemon and whispered its contents to Jon that night in secret, all the time saying how he shouldn't. Doubtless they thought his brother's war was none of his concern. It troubled him more than he could say. Robb was marching and he was not. No matter how often Jon told himself that his place was here now, with his new brothers on the Wall, he still felt craven.

"Corn," the raven was crying. *"Corn, corn."*

"Oh, be quiet," the Old Bear told it. "Snow, how soon does Maester Aemon say you'll have use of that hand back?"

"Soon," Jon replied.

"Good." On the table between them, Lord Mormont laid a large sword in a black metal scabbard banded with silver. "Here. You'll be ready for this, then."

The raven flapped down and landed on the table, strutting toward the sword, head cocked curiously. Jon hesitated. He had no inkling what this meant. "My lord?"

"The fire melted the silver off the pommel and burnt the crossguard and grip. Well, dry leather and old wood, what could you expect? The blade, now . . . you'd need a fire a hundred times as hot to harm the blade." Mormont shoved the scabbard across the rough oak planks. "I had the rest made anew. Take it."

"Take it," echoed his raven, preening. *"Take it, take it."*

Awkwardly, Jon took the sword in hand. His *left* hand; his bandaged right was still too raw and clumsy. Carefully he pulled it from its scabbard and raised it level with his eyes.

The pommel was a hunk of pale stone weighted with lead to balance the long blade. It had been carved into the likeness of a snarling wolf's head, with chips of garnet set into the eyes. The grip was virgin leather, soft and black, as yet unstained by sweat or blood. The blade itself was a good half foot longer than those Jon was used to, tapered to thrust as well as slash, with three fullers deeply incised in the metal. Where Ice was a true two-handed greatsword, this was a hand-and-a-halfer, sometimes named a "bastard sword." Yet the wolf sword actually seemed lighter than the blades he had wielded before. When Jon turned it sideways, he could see the ripples in the dark steel where the metal had been folded back on itself again and again. "This is Valyrian steel, my lord," he said wonderingly. His father had let him handle Ice often enough; he knew the look, the feel.

"It is," the Old Bear told him. "It was my father's sword, and his father's before him. The Mormonts have carried it for five centuries. I wielded it in my day and passed it on to my son when I took the black."

He is giving me his son's sword. Jon could scarcely believe it. The blade was exquisitely balanced. The edges glimmered faintly as they kissed the light. "Your son—"

"My son brought dishonor to House Mormont, but at least he had the grace to leave the sword behind when he fled. My sister returned it to my keeping, but the very sight of it reminded me of Jorah's shame, so I put it aside and thought no more of it until we found it in the ashes of my bedchamber. The original pommel was a bear's head, silver, yet so worn its features were all but indistinguishable. For you, I thought a white wolf more apt. One of our builders is a fair stonecarver."

When Jon had been Bran's age, he had dreamed of doing great deeds, as boys always did. The details of his feats changed with every dreaming, but quite often he imagined saving his father's life. Afterward Lord Eddard would declare that Jon had proved himself a true Stark, and place Ice in his hand. Even then he had known it was only a child's folly; no bastard could ever hope to wield a father's sword. Even the memory shamed him. What kind of man stole his own brother's birthright? *I have no right to this,* he thought, *no more than to Ice.* He twitched his burned fingers, feeling a throb of pain deep under the skin. "My lord, you honor me, but—"

"Spare me your *but*'s, boy," Lord Mormont interrupted. "I would not be sitting here were it not for you and that beast of yours. You fought bravely . . . and more to the point, you thought quickly. *Fire!* Yes, damn it. We ought to have known. We ought to have *remembered.* The Long Night has come before. Oh, eight thousand years is a good while, to be sure . . . yet if the Night's Watch does not remember, who will?"

"Who will," chimed the talkative raven. *"Who will."*

Truly, the gods had heard Jon's prayer that night; the fire had caught in the dead man's clothing and consumed him as if his flesh were candle wax and his bones old dry wood. Jon had only to close his eyes to see the thing staggering across the solar, crashing against the furniture and flailing at the flames. It was the face that haunted him most; surrounded by a nimbus of fire, hair blazing like straw, the dead flesh melting away and sloughing off its skull to reveal the gleam of bone beneath.

Whatever demonic force moved Othor had been driven out by the flames; the twisted thing they had found in the ashes had been no more than cooked meat and charred bone. Yet in his nightmare he faced it again . . . and this time the burning corpse wore Lord Eddard's features. It was his father's skin that burst and blackened, his father's eyes that ran liquid down his cheeks like jellied tears. Jon did not understand why that should be or what it might mean, but it frightened him more than he could say.

"A sword's small payment for a life," Mormont concluded. "Take it, I'll hear no more of it, is that understood?"

"Yes, my lord." The soft leather gave beneath Jon's fingers, as if the sword were molding itself to his grip already. He knew he should be honored, and he was, and yet . . .

He is not my father. The thought leapt unbidden to Jon's mind. *Lord Eddard Stark is my father. I will not forget him, no matter how many swords they give me.* Yet he could scarcely tell Lord Mormont that it was another man's sword he dreamt of . . .

"I want no courtesies either," Mormont said, "so thank me no thanks. Honor the steel with deeds, not words."

Jon nodded. "Does it have a name, my lord?"

"It did, once. Longclaw, it was called."

"Claw," the raven cried. *"Claw."*

"Longclaw is an apt name." Jon tried a practice cut. He was clumsy and uncomfortable with his left hand, yet even so the steel seemed to flow through the air, as if it had a will of its own. "Wolves have claws, as much as bears."

The Old Bear seemed pleased by that. "I suppose they do. You'll want to wear that over the shoulder, I imagine. It's too long for the hip, at least until you've put on a few inches. And you'll need to work at your two-handed strikes as well. Ser Endrew can show you some moves, when your burns have healed."

"Ser Endrew?" Jon did not know the name.

"Ser Endrew Tarth, a good man. He's on his way from the Shadow Tower to assume the duties of master-at-arms. Ser Alliser Thorne left yestermorn for Eastwatch-by-the-Sea."

Jon lowered the sword. "Why?" he said, stupidly.

Mormont snorted. "Because I *sent* him, why do you think? He's bringing the hand your Ghost tore off the end of Jafer Flowers's wrist. I have commanded him to take ship to King's Landing and lay it before this boy king. *That* should get young Joffrey's attention, I'd think . . . and Ser Alliser's a knight, highborn, anointed, with old friends at court, altogether harder to ignore than a glorified crow."

"Crow." Jon thought the raven sounded faintly indignant.

"As well," the Lord Commander continued, ignoring the bird's protest, "it puts a thousand leagues twixt him and you without it seeming a rebuke." He jabbed a finger up at Jon's face. "And don't think this means I approve of that nonsense in the common hall. Valor makes up for a fair amount of folly, but you're not a boy anymore, however many years you've seen. That's a man's sword you have there, and it will take a man to wield her. I'll expect you to act the part, henceforth."

"Yes, my lord." Jon slid the sword back into the silver-banded scabbard. If not the blade he would have chosen, it was nonetheless a noble gift, and freeing him from Alliser Thorne's malignance was nobler still.

The Old Bear scratched at his chin. "I had forgotten how much a new beard itches," he said. "Well, no help for that. Is that hand of yours healed enough to resume your duties?"

"Yes, my lord."

"Good. The night will be cold, I'll want hot spice wine. Find me a flagon of red, not too sour, and don't skimp on the spices. And tell Hobb that if he sends me boiled mutton again I'm like to boil *him.* That last haunch was grey. Even the bird wouldn't touch it." He stroked the raven's head with his thumb, and the bird made a contented *quork*ing sound. "Away with you. I've work to do."

The guards smiled at him from their niches as he wound his way down the turret stair, carrying the sword in his good hand. "Sweet steel," one man said. "You earned that, Snow," another told him. Jon made himself smile back at them, but his heart was not in it. He knew he should be pleased, yet he did not feel it. His hand ached, and the taste of anger was in his mouth, though he could not have said who he was angry with or why.

A half dozen of his friends were lurking outside when he left the King's Tower, where Lord Commander Mormont now made his residence. They'd hung a target on the granary doors, so they could seem to be honing their skills as archers, but he knew lurkers when he saw them. No sooner did he emerge than Pyp called out, "Well, come about, let's have a look."

"At what?" Jon said.

Toad sidled close. "Your rosy butt cheeks, what else?"

"The sword," Grenn stated. "We want to see the sword."

Jon raked them with an accusing look. "You knew."

Pyp grinned. "We're not all as dumb as Grenn."

"You are so," insisted Grenn. "You're dumber."

Halder gave an apologetic shrug. "I helped Pate carve the stone for the pommel," the builder said, "and your friend Sam bought the garnets in Mole's Town."

"We knew even before that, though," Grenn said. "Rudge has been helping Donal Noye in the forge. He was there when the Old Bear brought him the burnt blade."

"The *sword*!" Matt insisted. The others took up the chant. "The *sword*, the *sword*, the *sword*."

Jon unsheathed Longclaw and showed it to them, turning it this way and that so they could admire it. The bastard blade glittered in the pale sunlight, dark and deadly. "Valyrian steel," he declared solemnly, trying to sound as pleased and proud as he ought to have felt.

"I heard of a man who had a razor made of Valyrian steel," declared Toad. "He cut his head off trying to shave."

Pyp grinned. "The Night's Watch is thousands of years old," he said, "but I'll wager Lord Snow's the first brother ever honored for burning down the Lord Commander's Tower."

The others laughed, and even Jon had to smile. The fire he'd started had not, in truth, burned down that formidable stone tower, but it had done a fair job of gutting the interior of the top two floors, where the Old Bear had his chambers. No one seemed to mind that very much, since it had also destroyed Othor's murderous corpse.

The other wight, the one-handed thing that had once been a ranger named Jafer Flowers, had also been destroyed, cut near to pieces by a dozen swords . . . but not before it had slain Ser Jaremy Rykker and four other men. Ser Jaremy had finished the job of hacking its head off, yet had died all the same when the headless corpse pulled his own dagger from its sheath and buried it in his bowels. Strength and courage did not avail much against foemen who would not fall because they were already dead; even arms and armor offered small protection.

That grim thought soured Jon's fragile mood. "I need

to see Hobb about the Old Bear's supper," he announced brusquely, sliding Longclaw back into its scabbard. His friends meant well, but they did not understand. It was not their fault, truly; they had not had to face Othor, they had not seen the pale glow of those dead blue eyes, had not felt the cold of those dead black fingers. Nor did they know of the fighting in the riverlands. How could they hope to comprehend? He turned away from them abruptly and strode off, sullen. Pyp called after him, but Jon paid him no mind.

They had moved him back to his old cell in tumble-down Hardin's Tower after the fire, and it was there he returned. Ghost was curled up asleep beside the door, but he lifted his head at the sound of Jon's boots. The direwolf's red eyes were darker than garnets and wiser than men. Jon knelt, scratched his ear, and showed him the pommel of the sword. "Look. It's you."

Ghost sniffed at his carved stone likeness and tried a lick. Jon smiled. "You're the one deserves an honor," he told the wolf . . . and suddenly he found himself remembering how he'd found him, that day in the late summer snow. They had been riding off with the other pups, but Jon had heard a noise and turned back, and there he was, white fur almost invisible against the drifts. *He was all alone,* he thought, *apart from the others in the litter. He was different, so they drove him out.*

"Jon?" He looked up. Samwell Tarly stood rocking nervously on his heels. His cheeks were red, and he was wrapped in a heavy fur cloak that made him look ready for hibernation.

"Sam." Jon stood. "What is it? Do you want to see the sword?" If the others had known, no doubt Sam did too.

The fat boy shook his head. "I was heir to my father's blade once," he said mournfully. "Heartsbane. Lord Randyll let me hold it a few times, but it always scared me. It was Valyrian steel, beautiful but so sharp I was afraid I'd hurt one of my sisters. Dickon will have it now." He wiped sweaty hands on his cloak. "I . . . ah . . . Maester Aemon wants to see you."

It was not time for his bandages to be changed. Jon frowned suspiciously. "Why?" he demanded. Sam looked miserable. That was answer enough. "You told him, didn't you?" Jon said angrily. "You told him that you told me."

"I . . . he . . . Jon, I didn't want to . . . he asked . . . I mean . . . I think he *knew*, he sees things no one else sees . . ."

"He's *blind*," Jon pointed out forcefully, disgusted. "I can find the way myself." He left Sam standing there, openmouthed and quivering.

He found Maester Aemon up in the rookery, feeding the ravens. Clydas was with him, carrying a bucket of chopped meat as they shuffled from cage to cage. "Sam said you wanted me?"

The maester nodded. "I did indeed. Clydas, give Jon the bucket. Perhaps he will be kind enough to assist me." The hunched, pink-eyed brother handed Jon the bucket and scurried down the ladder. "Toss the meat into the cages," Aemon instructed him. "The birds will do the rest."

Jon shifted the bucket to his right hand and thrust his left down into the bloody bits. The ravens began to scream noisily and fly at the bars, beating at the metal with night-black wings. The meat had been chopped into pieces no larger than a finger joint. He filled his fist and tossed the raw red morsels into the cage, and the squawking and squabbling grew hotter. Feathers flew as two of the larger birds fought over a choice piece. Quickly Jon grabbed a second handful and threw it in after the first. "Lord Mormont's raven likes fruit and corn."

"He is a rare bird," the maester said. "Most ravens will eat grain, but they prefer flesh. It makes them strong, and I fear they relish the taste of blood. In that they are like men . . . and like men, not all ravens are alike."

Jon had nothing to say to that. He threw meat, wondering why he'd been summoned. No doubt the old man would tell him, in his own good time. Maester Aemon was not a man to be hurried.

"Doves and pigeons can also be trained to carry messages," the maester went on, "though the raven is a stronger flyer, larger, bolder, far more clever, better able to defend itself against hawks . . . yet ravens are black, and they eat the dead, so some godly men abhor them. Baelor the Blessed tried to replace all the ravens with doves, did you know?" The maester turned his white eyes on Jon, smiling. "The Night's Watch prefers ravens."

Jon's fingers were in the bucket, blood up to the wrist. "Dywen says the wildlings call us crows," he said uncertainly.

"The crow is the raven's poor cousin. They are both beggars in black, hated and misunderstood."

Jon wished he understood what they were talking about, and why. What did he care about ravens and doves? If the old man had something to say to him, why couldn't he just say it?

"Jon, did you ever wonder *why* the men of the Night's Watch take no wives and father no children?" Maester Aemon asked.

Jon shrugged. "No." He scattered more meat. The fingers of his left hand were slimy with blood, and his right throbbed from the weight of the bucket.

"So they will not love," the old man answered, "for love is the bane of honor, the death of duty."

That did not sound right to Jon, yet he said nothing. The maester was a hundred years old, and a high officer of the Night's Watch; it was not his place to contradict him.

The old man seemed to sense his doubts. "Tell me, Jon, if the day should ever come when your lord father must needs choose between honor on the one hand and those he loves on the other, what would he do?"

Jon hesitated. He wanted to say that Lord Eddard would never dishonor himself, not even for love, yet inside a small sly voice whispered, *He fathered a bastard, where was the honor in that? And your mother, what of his duty to her, he will not even say her name.* "He would do whatever was right," he said . . . ringingly, to make up for his hesitation. "No matter what."

"Then Lord Eddard is a man in ten thousand. Most of us are not so strong. What is honor compared to a woman's love? What is duty against the feel of a newborn son in your arms . . . or the memory of a brother's smile? Wind and words. Wind and words. We are only human, and the gods have fashioned us for love. That is our great glory, and our great tragedy.

"The men who formed the Night's Watch knew that only their courage shielded the realm from the darkness to the north. They knew they must have no divided loyalties to weaken their resolve. So they vowed they would have no wives nor children.

"Yet brothers they had, and sisters. Mothers who gave them birth, fathers who gave them names. They came from a hundred quarrelsome kingdoms, and they knew times may change, but men do not. So they pledged as well that the Night's Watch would take no part in the battles of the realms it guarded.

"They kept their pledge. When Aegon slew Black Harren and claimed his kingdom, Harren's brother was Lord Commander on the Wall, with ten thousand swords to hand. He did not march. In the days when the Seven Kingdoms *were* seven kingdoms, not a generation passed that three or four of them were not at war. The Watch took no part. When the Andals crossed the narrow sea and swept away the kingdoms of the First Men, the sons of the fallen kings held true to their vows and remained at their posts. So it has always been, for years beyond counting. Such is the price of honor.

"A craven can be as brave as any man, when there is nothing to fear. And we all do our duty, when there is no cost to it. How easy it seems then, to walk the path of honor. Yet soon or late in every man's life comes a day when it is *not* easy, a day when he must choose."

Some of the ravens were still eating, long stringy bits of meat dangling from their beaks. The rest seemed to be watching him. Jon could feel the weight of all those tiny black eyes. "And this is my day . . . is that what you're saying?"

Maester Aemon turned his head and *looked* at him with those dead white eyes. It was as if he were seeing right into his heart. Jon felt naked and exposed. He took the bucket in both hands and flung the rest of the slops through the bars. Strings of meat and blood flew everywhere, scattering the ravens. They took to the air, shrieking wildly. The quicker birds snatched morsels on the wing and gulped them down greedily. Jon let the empty bucket clang to the floor.

The old man laid a withered, spotted hand on his shoulder. "It hurts, boy," he said softly. "Oh, yes. Choosing . . . it has always hurt. And always will. I know."

"You *don't* know," Jon said bitterly. "No one knows. Even if I am his bastard, he's still my *father* . . ."

Maester Aemon sighed. "Have you heard nothing I've told you, Jon? Do you think you are the first?" He shook his ancient head, a gesture weary beyond words. "Three times the gods saw fit to test my vows. Once when I was a boy, once in the fullness of my manhood, and once when I had grown old. By then my strength was fled, my eyes grown dim, yet that last choice was as cruel as the first. My ravens would bring the news from the south, words darker than their wings, the ruin of my House, the death of my kin, disgrace and desolation. What could I have done, old, blind, frail? I was helpless as a suckling babe, yet still it grieved me to sit forgotten as they cut down my brother's poor grandson, and *his* son, and even the little children . . ."

Jon was shocked to see the shine of tears in the old man's eyes. "Who are you?" he asked quietly, almost in dread.

A toothless smile quivered on the ancient lips. "Only a maester of the Citadel, bound in service to Castle Black and the Night's Watch. In my order, we put aside our house names when we take our vows and don the collar." The old man touched the maester's chain that hung loosely around his thin, fleshless neck. "My father was Maekar, the First of his Name, and my brother Aegon reigned after him in my stead. My grandfather named me for Prince Aemon the Dragonknight, who was his uncle, or his father, depending on which tale you believe. Aemon, he called me . . ."

"Aemon . . . *Targaryen?*" Jon could scarcely believe it.

"Once," the old man said. "Once. So you see, Jon, I *do* know . . . and knowing, I will not tell you *stay* or *go*. You must make that choice yourself, and live with it all the rest of your days. As I have." His voice fell to a whisper. "As I have . . ."

DAENERYS

When the battle was done, Dany rode her silver through the fields of the dead. Her handmaids and the men of her *khas* came after, smiling and jesting among themselves.

Dothraki hooves had torn the earth and trampled the rye and lentils into the ground, while *arakhs* and arrows had sown a terrible new crop and watered it with blood. Dying horses lifted their heads and screamed at her as she rode past. Wounded men moaned and prayed. *Jaqqa rhan* moved among them, the mercy men with their heavy axes, taking a harvest of heads from the dead and dying alike. After them would scurry a flock of small girls, pulling arrows from the corpses to fill their baskets. Last of all the dogs would come sniffing, lean and hungry, the feral pack that was never far behind the *khalasar*.

The sheep had been dead longest. There seemed to be thousands of them, black with flies, arrow shafts bristling from each carcass. Khal Ogo's riders had done that, Dany knew; no man of Drogo's *khalasar* would be such a fool as to waste his arrows on sheep when there were shepherds yet to kill.

The town was afire, black plumes of smoke roiling and

tumbling as they rose into a hard blue sky. Beneath broken walls of dried mud, riders galloped back and forth, swinging their long whips as they herded the survivors from the smoking rubble. The women and children of Ogo's *khalasar* walked with a sullen pride, even in defeat and bondage; they were slaves now, but they seemed not to fear it. It was different with the townsfolk. Dany pitied them; she remembered what terror felt like. Mothers stumbled along with blank, dead faces, pulling sobbing children by the hand. There were only a few men among them, cripples and cowards and grandfathers.

Ser Jorah said the people of this country named themselves the Lhazareen, but the Dothraki called them *haesh rakhi*, the Lamb Men. Once Dany might have taken them for Dothraki, for they had the same copper skin and almond-shaped eyes. Now they looked alien to her, squat and flat-faced, their black hair cropped unnaturally short. They were herders of sheep and eaters of vegetables, and Khal Drogo said they belonged south of the river bend. The grass of the Dothraki sea was not meant for sheep.

Dany saw one boy bolt and run for the river. A rider cut him off and turned him, and the others boxed him in, cracking their whips in his face, running him this way and that. One galloped behind him, lashing him across the buttocks until his thighs ran red with blood. Another snared his ankle with a lash and sent him sprawling. Finally, when the boy could only crawl, they grew bored of the sport and put an arrow through his back.

Ser Jorah met her outside the shattered gate. He wore a dark green surcoat over his mail. His gauntlets, greaves, and greathelm were dark grey steel. The Dothraki had mocked him for a coward when he donned his armor, but the knight had spit insults right back in their teeth, tempers had flared, longsword had clashed with *arakh*, and the rider whose taunts had been loudest had been left behind to bleed to death.

Ser Jorah lifted the visor of his flat-topped greathelm as he rode up. "Your lord husband awaits you within the town."

"Drogo took no harm?"

"A few cuts," Ser Jorah answered, "nothing of consequence. He slew two *khals* this day. Khal Ogo first, and then the son, Fogo, who became *khal* when Ogo fell. His bloodriders cut the bells from their hair, and now Khal Drogo's every step rings louder than before."

Ogo and his son had shared the high bench with her lord husband at the naming feast where Viserys had been crowned, but that was in Vaes Dothrak, beneath the Mother of Mountains, where every rider was a brother and all quarrels were put aside. It was different out in the grass. Ogo's *khalasar* had been attacking the town when Khal Drogo caught him. She wondered what the Lamb Men had thought, when they first saw the dust of their horses from atop those cracked-mud walls. Perhaps a few, the younger and more foolish who still believed that the gods heard the prayers of desperate men, took it for deliverance.

Across the road, a girl no older than Dany was sobbing in a high thin voice as a rider shoved her over a pile of corpses, facedown, and thrust himself inside her. Other riders dismounted to take their turns. That was the sort of deliverance the Dothraki brought the Lamb Men.

I am the blood of the dragon, Daenerys Targaryen reminded herself as she turned her face away. She pressed her lips together and hardened her heart and rode on toward the gate.

"Most of Ogo's riders fled," Ser Jorah was saying. "Still, there may be as many as ten thousand captives."

Slaves, Dany thought. Khal Drogo would drive them downriver to one of the towns on Slaver's Bay. She wanted to cry, but she told herself that she must be strong. *This is war, this is what it looks like, this is the price of the Iron Throne.*

"I've told the *khal* he ought to make for Meereen," Ser Jorah said. "They'll pay a better price than he'd get from a slaving caravan. Illyrio writes that they had a plague last year, so the brothels are paying double for healthy young girls, and triple for boys under ten. If enough children survive the journey, the gold will buy us all the ships we need, and hire men to sail them."

Behind them, the girl being raped made a heartrending sound, a long sobbing wail that went on and on and on. Dany's hand clenched hard around the reins, and she turned the silver's head. "Make them stop," she commanded Ser Jorah.

"*Khaleesi?*" The knight sounded perplexed.

"You heard my words," she said. "Stop them." She spoke to her *khas* in the harsh accents of Dothraki. "Jhogo, Quaro, you will aid Ser Jorah. I want no rape."

The warriors exchanged a baffled look.

Jorah Mormont spurred his horse closer. "Princess," he said, "you have a gentle heart, but you do not understand. This is how it has always been. Those men have shed blood for the *khal*. Now they claim their reward."

Across the road, the girl was still crying, her high sing-song tongue strange to Dany's ears. The first man was done with her now, and a second had taken his place.

"She is a lamb girl," Quaro said in Dothraki. "She is nothing, *Khaleesi*. The riders do her honor. The Lamb Men lay with sheep, it is known."

"It is known," her handmaid Irri echoed.

"It is known," agreed Jhogo, astride the tall grey stallion that Drogo had given him. "If her wailing offends your ears, *Khaleesi*, Jhogo will bring you her tongue." He drew his *arakh*.

"I will not have her harmed," Dany said. "I claim her. Do as I command you, or Khal Drogo will know the reason why."

"*Ai, Khaleesi,*" Jhogo replied, kicking his horse. Quaro and the others followed his lead, the bells in their hair chiming.

"Go with them," she commanded Ser Jorah.

"As you command." The knight gave her a curious look. "You are your brother's sister, in truth."

"Viserys?" She did not understand.

"No," he answered. "Rhaegar." He galloped off.

Dany heard Jhogo shout. The rapers laughed at him. One man shouted back. Jhogo's *arakh* flashed, and the man's head went tumbling from his shoulders. Laughter turned to curses as the horsemen reached for weapons, but by then Quaro and Aggo and Rakharo were there. She saw Aggo point across the road to where she sat upon her silver. The riders looked at her with cold black eyes. One spat. The others scattered to their mounts, muttering.

All the while the man atop the lamb girl continued to plunge in and out of her, so intent on his pleasure that he seemed unaware of what was going on around him. Ser Jorah dismounted and wrenched him off with a mailed hand. The Dothraki went sprawling in the mud, bounced up with a knife in hand, and died with Aggo's arrow through his throat. Mormont pulled the girl off the pile of corpses and wrapped her in his blood-spattered cloak. He led her across the road to Dany. "What do you want done with her?"

The girl was trembling, her eyes wide and vague. Her hair was matted with blood. "Doreah, see to her hurts. You do not have a rider's look, perhaps she will not fear you. The rest, with me." She urged the silver through the broken wooden gate.

It was worse inside the town. Many of the houses were afire, and the *jaqqa rhan* had been about their grisly work. Headless corpses filled the narrow, twisty lanes. They passed other women being raped. Each time Dany reined up, sent her *khas* to make an end to it, and claimed the victim as slave. One of them, a thick-bodied, flat-nosed woman of forty years, blessed Dany haltingly in the Common Tongue, but from the others she got only flat black stares. They were suspicious of her, she realized with sadness; afraid that she had saved them for some worse fate.

"You cannot claim them all, child," Ser Jorah said, the fourth time they stopped, while the warriors of her *khas* herded her new slaves behind her.

"I am *khaleesi*, heir to the Seven Kingdoms, the blood of the dragon," Dany reminded him. "It is not for you to tell me what I cannot do." Across the city, a building collapsed in a great gout of fire and smoke, and she heard distant screams and the wailing of frightened children.

They found Khal Drogo seated before a square windowless temple with thick mud walls and a bulbous dome like some immense brown onion. Beside him was a pile of heads taller than he was. One of the short arrows of the Lamb Men stuck through the meat of his upper arm, and blood covered the left side of his bare chest like a splash of paint. His three bloodriders were with him.

Jhiqui helped Dany dismount; she had grown clumsy as her belly grew larger and heavier. She knelt before the *khal.* "My sun-and-stars is wounded." The *arakh* cut was wide but shallow; his left nipple was gone, and a flap of bloody flesh and skin dangled from his chest like a wet rag.

"Is scratch, moon of life, from *arakh* of one bloodrider

to Khal Ogo," Khal Drogo said in the Common Tongue. "I kill him for it, and Ogo too." He turned his head, the bells in his braid ringing softly. "Is Ogo you hear, and Fogo his *khalakka*, who was *khal* when I slew him."

"No man can stand before the sun of my life," Dany said, "the father of the stallion who mounts the world."

A mounted warrior rode up and vaulted from his saddle. He spoke to Haggo, a stream of angry Dothraki too fast for Dany to understand. The huge bloodrider gave her a heavy look before he turned to his *khal*. "This one is Mago, who rides in the *khas* of Ko Jhaqo. He says the *khaleesi* has taken his spoils, a daughter of the lambs who was his to mount."

Khal Drogo's face was still and hard, but his black eyes were curious as they went to Dany. "Tell me the truth of this, moon of my life," he commanded in Dothraki.

Dany told him what she had done, in his own tongue so the *khal* would understand her better, her words simple and direct.

When she was done, Drogo was frowning. "This is the way of war. These women are our slaves now, to do with as we please."

"It pleases me to hold them safe," Dany said, wondering if she had dared too much. "If your warriors would mount these women, let them take them gently and keep them for wives. Give them places in the *khalasar* and let them bear you sons."

Qotho was ever the cruelest of the bloodriders. It was he who laughed. "Does the horse breed with the sheep?"

Something in his tone reminded her of Viserys. Dany turned on him angrily. "The dragon feeds on horse and sheep alike."

Khal Drogo smiled. "See how fierce she grows!" he said. "It is my son inside her, the stallion who mounts the world, filling her with his fire. Ride slowly, Qotho . . . if the mother does not burn you where you sit, the son will trample you into the mud. And you, Mago, hold your tongue and find another lamb to mount. These belong to my *khaleesi*." He started to reach out a hand to Daenerys, but as he lifted his arm Drogo grimaced in sudden pain and turned his head.

Dany could almost feel his agony. The wounds were worse than Ser Jorah had led her to believe. "Where are the healers?" she demanded. The *khalasar* had two sorts: barren women and eunuch slaves. The herbwomen dealt in potions and spells, the eunuchs in knife, needle, and fire. "Why do they not attend the *khal*?"

"The *khal* sent the hairless men away, *Khaleesi*," old Cohollo assured her. Dany saw the bloodrider had taken a wound himself; a deep gash in his left shoulder.

"Many riders are hurt," Khal Drogo said stubbornly. "Let them be healed first. This arrow is no more than the bite of a fly, this little cut only a new scar to boast of to my son."

Dany could see the muscles in his chest where the skin had been cut away. A trickle of blood ran from the arrow that pierced his arm. "It is not for Khal Drogo to wait," she proclaimed. "Jhogo, seek out these eunuchs and bring them here at once."

"Silver Lady," a woman's voice said behind her, "I can help the Great Rider with his hurts."

Dany turned her head. The speaker was one of the slaves she had claimed, the heavy, flat-nosed woman who had blessed her.

"The *khal* needs no help from women who lie with sheep," barked Qotho. "Aggo, cut out her tongue."

Aggo grabbed her hair and pressed a knife to her throat. Dany lifted a hand. "No. She is mine. Let her speak."

Aggo looked from her to Qotho. He lowered his knife.

"I meant no wrong, fierce riders." The woman spoke Dothraki well. The robes she wore had once been the lightest and finest of woolens, rich with embroidery, but now they were mud-caked and bloody and ripped. She clutched the torn cloth of her bodice to her heavy breasts. "I have some small skill in the healing arts."

"Who are you?" Dany asked her.

"I am named Mirri Maz Duur. I am godswife of this temple."

"*Maegi*," grunted Haggo, fingering his *arakh*. His look was dark. Dany remembered the word from a terrifying story that Jhiqui had told her one night by the cookfire. A *maegi* was a woman who lay with demons and practiced the blackest of sorceries, a vile thing, evil and soulless, who came to men in the dark of night and sucked life and strength from their bodies.

"I am a healer," Mirri Maz Duur said.

"A healer of sheeps," sneered Qotho. "Blood of my blood, I say kill this *maegi* and wait for the hairless men."

Dany ignored the bloodrider's outburst. This old, homely, thick-bodied woman did not look like a *maegi* to her. "Where did you learn your healing, Mirri Maz Duur?"

"My mother was godswife before me, and taught me all the songs and spells most pleasing to the Great Shepherd, and how to make the sacred smokes and ointments from leaf and root and berry. When I was younger and more fair, I went in caravan to Asshai by the Shadow, to learn from their mages. Ships from many lands come to Asshai, so I lingered long to study the healing ways of distant peoples. A moonsinger of the Jogos Nhai gifted me with her birthing songs, a woman of your own riding people taught me the magics of grass and corn and horse, and a maester from the Sunset Lands opened a body for me and showed me all the secrets that hide beneath the skin."

Ser Jorah Mormont spoke up. "A maester?"

"Marwyn, he named himself," the woman replied in the Common Tongue. "From the sea. Beyond the sea. The Seven Lands, he said. Sunset Lands. Where men are iron and dragons rule. He taught me this speech."

"A maester in Asshai," Ser Jorah mused. "Tell me, Godswife, what did this Marwyn wear about his neck?"

"A chain so tight it was like to choke him, Iron Lord, with links of many metals."

The knight looked at Dany. "Only a man trained in the Citadel of Oldtown wears such a chain," he said, "and such men do know much of healing."

"Why should you want to help my *khal*?"

"All men are one flock, or so we are taught," replied Mirri Maz Duur. "The Great Shepherd sent me to earth to heal his lambs, wherever I might find them."

Qotho gave her a stinging slap. "We are no sheep, *maegi*."

"Stop it," Dany said angrily. "She is mine. I will not have her harmed."

Khal Drogo grunted. "The arrow must come out, Qotho."

"Yes, Great Rider," Mirri Maz Duur answered, touching her bruised face. "And your breast must be washed and sewn, lest the wound fester."

"Do it, then," Khal Drogo commanded.

"Great Rider," the woman said, "my tools and potions are inside the god's house, where the healing powers are strongest."

"I will carry you, blood of my blood," Haggo offered.

Khal Drogo waved him away. "I need no man's help," he said, in a voice proud and hard. He stood, unaided, towering over them all. A fresh wave of blood ran down his breast, from where Ogo's *arakh* had cut off his nipple. Dany moved quickly to his side. "I am no man," she whispered, "so you may lean on me." Drogo put a huge hand on her shoulder. She took some of his weight as they walked toward the great mud temple. The three blood-riders followed. Dany commanded Ser Jorah and the warriors of her *khas* to guard the entrance and make certain no one set the building afire while they were still inside.

They passed through a series of anterooms, into the high central chamber under the onion. Faint light shone down through hidden windows above. A few torches burnt smokily from sconces on the walls. Sheepskins were scattered across the mud floor. "There," Mirri Maz Duur said, pointing to the altar, a massive blue-veined stone carved with images of shepherds and their flocks. Khal Drogo lay upon it. The old woman threw a handful of dried leaves onto a brazier, filling the chamber with fragrant smoke. "Best if you wait outside," she told the rest of them.

"We are blood of his blood," Cohollo said. "Here we wait."

Qotho stepped close to Mirri Maz Duur. "Know this, wife of the Lamb God. Harm the *khal* and you suffer the same." He drew his skinning knife and showed her the blade.

"She will do no harm." Dany felt she could trust this old, plain-faced woman with her flat nose; she had saved her from the hard hands of her rapers, after all.

"If you must stay, then help," Mirri told the blood-riders. "The Great Rider is too strong for me. Hold him still while I draw the arrow from his flesh." She let the rags of her gown fall to her waist as she opened a carved chest, and busied herself with bottles and boxes, knives and needles. When she was ready, she broke off the barbed arrowhead and pulled out the shaft, chanting in the sing-song tongue of the Lhazareen. She heated a flagon of wine to boiling on the brazier, and poured it over his wounds. Khal Drogo cursed her, but he did not move. She bound the arrow wound with a plaster of wet leaves and turned to the gash on his breast, smearing it with a pale green paste before she pulled the flap of skin back in place. The *khal* ground his teeth together and swallowed a scream. The godswife took out a silver needle and a bobbin of silk thread and began to close the flesh. When she was done she painted the skin with red ointment, covered it with more leaves, and bound the breast in a ragged piece of lambskin. "You must say the prayers I give you and keep the lambskin in place for ten days and ten nights," she said. "There will be fever, and itching, and a great scar when the healing is done."

Khal Drogo sat, bells ringing. "I sing of my scars, sheep woman." He flexed his arm and scowled.

"Drink neither wine nor the milk of the poppy," she cautioned him. "Pain you will have, but you must keep your body strong to fight the poison spirits."

"I am *khal*," Drogo said. "I spit on pain and drink what I like. Cohollo, bring my vest." The older man hastened off.

"Before," Dany said to the ugly Lhazareen woman, "I heard you speak of birthing songs . . ."

"I know every secret of the bloody bed, Silver Lady, nor have I ever lost a babe," Mirri Maz Duur replied.

"My time is near," Dany said. "I would have you attend me when he comes, if you would."

Khal Drogo laughed. "Moon of my life, you do not ask a slave, you tell her. She will do as you command." He jumped down from the altar. "Come, my blood. The stallions call, this place is ashes. It is time to ride."

Haggo followed the *khal* from the temple, but Qotho lingered long enough to favor Mirri Maz Duur with a stare. "Remember, *maegi*, as the *khal* fares, so shall you."

"As you say, rider," the woman answered him, gathering up her jars and bottles. "The Great Shepherd guards the flock."

TYRION

On a hill overlooking the kingsroad, a long trestle table of rough-hewn pine had been erected beneath an elm tree and covered with a golden cloth. There, beside his pavilion, Lord Tywin took his evening meal with his chief knights and lords bannermen, his great crimson-and-gold standard waving overhead from a lofty pike.

Tyrion arrived late, saddlesore, and sour, all too vividly aware of how amusing he must look as he waddled up the slope to his father. The day's march had been long and tiring. He thought he might get quite drunk tonight. It was twilight, and the air was alive with drifting fireflies.

The cooks were serving the meat course: five suckling pigs, skin seared and crackling, a different fruit in every mouth. The smell made his mouth water. "My pardons," he began, taking his place on the bench beside his uncle.

"Perhaps I'd best charge you with burying our dead, Tyrion," Lord Tywin said. "If you are as late to battle as you are to table, the fighting will all be done by the time you arrive."

"Oh, surely you can save me a peasant or two, Father," Tyrion replied. "Not too many, I wouldn't want to be greedy." He filled his wine cup and watched a serving man carve into the pig. The crisp skin crackled under his knife, and hot juice ran from the meat. It was the loveliest sight Tyrion had seen in ages.

"Ser Addam's outriders say the Stark host has moved south from the Twins," his father reported as his trencher was filled with slices of pork. "Lord Frey's levies have joined them. They are likely no more than a day's march north of us."

"Please, Father," Tyrion said. "I'm about to eat."

"Does the thought of facing the Stark boy unman you, Tyrion? Your brother Jaime would be eager to come to grips with him."

"I'd sooner come to grips with that pig. Robb Stark is not half so tender, and he never smelled as good."

Lord Lefford, the sour bird who had charge of their stores and supplies, leaned forward. "I hope your savages do not share your reluctance, else we've wasted our good steel on them."

"My savages will put your steel to excellent use, my lord," Tyrion replied. When he had told Lefford he needed arms and armor to equip the three hundred men Ulf had fetched down out of the foothills, you would have thought he'd asked the man to turn his virgin daughters over to their pleasure.

Lord Lefford frowned. "I saw that great hairy one today, the one who insisted that he must have *two* battle-axes, the heavy black steel ones with twin crescent blades."

"Shagga likes to kill with either hand," Tyrion said as a trencher of steaming pork was laid in front of him.

"He still had that wood-axe of his strapped to his back."

"Shagga is of the opinion that three axes are even better than two." Tyrion reached a thumb and forefinger into the salt dish, and sprinkled a healthy pinch over his meat.

Ser Kevan leaned forward. "We had a thought to put you and your wildlings in the vanguard when we come to battle."

Ser Kevan seldom "had a thought" that Lord Tywin had not had first. Tyrion had skewered a chunk of meat on the point of his dagger and brought it to his mouth. Now he lowered it. "The vanguard?" he repeated dubiously. Either his lord father had a new respect for Tyrion's abilities, or he'd decided to rid himself of his embarrassing get for good. Tyrion had the gloomy feeling he knew which.

"They seem ferocious enough," Ser Kevan said.

"Ferocious?" Tyrion realized he was echoing his uncle like a trained bird. His father watched, judging him, weighing every word. "Let me tell you how ferocious they are. Last night, a Moon Brother stabbed a Stone Crow over a sausage. So today as we made camp three Stone Crows seized the man and opened his throat for him. Perhaps they were hoping to get the sausage back, I couldn't say. Bronn managed to keep Shagga from chopping off the dead man's cock, which was fortunate, but even so Ulf is demanding blood money, which Conn and Shagga refuse to pay."

"When soldiers lack discipline, the fault lies with their lord commander," his father said.

His brother Jaime had always been able to make men follow him eagerly, and die for him if need be. Tyrion lacked that gift. He bought loyalty with gold, and compelled obedience with his name. "A *bigger* man would be able to put the fear in them, is that what you're saying, my lord?"

Lord Tywin Lannister turned to his brother. "If my son's men will not obey his commands, perhaps the vanguard is not the place for him. No doubt he would be more comfortable in the rear, guarding our baggage train."

"Do me no kindnesses, Father," he said angrily. "If you have no other command to offer me, I'll lead your van."

Lord Tywin studied his dwarf son. "I said nothing about command. You will serve under Ser Gregor."

Tyrion took one bite of pork, chewed a moment, and spit it out angrily. "I find I am not hungry after all," he said, climbing awkwardly off the bench. "Pray excuse me, my lords."

Lord Tywin inclined his head, dismissing him. Tyrion turned and walked away. He was conscious of their eyes on his back as he waddled down the hill. A great gust of laughter went up from behind him, but he did not look back. He hoped they all choked on their suckling pigs.

Dusk had settled, turning all the banners black. The Lannister camp sprawled for miles between the river and the kingsroad. In amongst the men and the horses and the trees, it was easy to get lost, and Tyrion did. He passed a dozen great pavilions and a hundred cookfires. Fireflies drifted amongst the tents like wandering stars. He caught the scent of garlic sausage, spiced and savory, so tempting it made his empty stomach growl. Away in the distance, he heard voices raised in some bawdy song. A giggling woman raced past him, naked beneath a dark cloak, her drunken pursuer stumbling over tree roots. Farther on, two spearmen faced each other across a little trickle of a stream, practicing their thrust-and-parry in the fading light, their chests bare and slick with sweat.

No one looked at him. No one spoke to him. No one paid him any mind. He was surrounded by men sworn to House Lannister, a vast host twenty thousand strong, and yet he was alone.

When he heard the deep rumble of Shagga's laughter booming through the dark, he followed it to the Stone Crows in their small corner of the night. Conn son of Coratt waved a tankard of ale. "Tyrion Halfman! Come, sit by our fire, share meat with the Stone Crows. We have an ox."

"I can see that, Conn son of Coratt." The huge red carcass was suspended over a roaring fire, skewered on a spit the size of a small tree. No doubt it *was* a small tree. Blood and grease dripped down into the flames as two Stone Crows turned the meat. "I thank you. Send for me when the ox is cooked." From the look of it, that might even be before the battle. He walked on.

Each clan had its own cookfire; Black Ears did not eat with Stone Crows, Stone Crows did not eat with Moon Brothers, and no one ate with Burned Men. The modest tent he had coaxed out of Lord Lefford's stores had been erected in the center of the four fires. Tyrion found Bronn sharing a skin of wine with the new servants. Lord Tywin had sent him a groom and a body servant to see to his needs, and even insisted he take a squire. They were seated around the embers of a small cookfire. A girl was with them; slim, dark-haired, no more than eighteen by the look of her. Tyrion studied her face for a moment, before he spied fishbones in the ashes. "What did you eat?"

"Trout, m'lord," said his groom. "Bronn caught them."

Trout, he thought. *Suckling pig. Damn my father.* He stared mournfully at the bones, his belly rumbling.

His squire, a boy with the unfortunate name of Podrick Payne, swallowed whatever he had been about to say. The lad was a distant cousin to Ser Ilyn Payne, the king's headsman . . . and almost as quiet, although not for want of a tongue. Tyrion had made him stick it out once, just to be certain. "Definitely a tongue," he had said. "Someday you must learn to use it."

At the moment, he did not have the patience to try and coax a thought out of the lad, whom he suspected had been inflicted on him as a cruel jape. Tyrion turned his attention back to the girl. "Is this her?" he asked Bronn.

She rose gracefully and looked down at him from the lofty height of five feet or more. "It is, m'lord, and she can speak for herself, if it please you."

He cocked his head to one side. "I am Tyrion, of House Lannister. Men call me the Imp."

"My mother named me Shae. Men call me . . . often."

Bronn laughed, and Tyrion had to smile. "Into the tent, Shae, if you would be so kind." He lifted the flap and held it for her. Inside, he knelt to light a candle.

The life of a soldier was not without certain compensations. Wherever you have a camp, you are certain to have camp followers. At the end of the day's march, Tyrion had sent Bronn back to find him a likely whore. "I would prefer one who is reasonably young, with as pretty a face as you can find," he had said. "If she has washed sometime this year, I shall be glad. If she hasn't, wash her. Be certain that you tell her who I am, and warn her of *what* I am." Jyck had not always troubled to do that. There was a look the girls got in their eyes sometimes when they first beheld the lordling they'd been hired to pleasure . . . a look that Tyrion Lannister did not ever care to see again.

He lifted the candle and looked her over. Bronn had done well enough; she was doe-eyed and slim, with small firm breasts and a smile that was by turns shy, insolent, and wicked. He liked that. "Shall I take my gown off, m'lord?" she asked.

"In good time. Are you a maiden, Shae?"

"If it please you, m'lord," she said demurely.

"What would please me would be the truth of you, girl."

"Aye, but that will cost you double."

Tyrion decided they would get along splendidly. "I am a Lannister. Gold I have in plenty, and you'll find me generous . . . but I'll want more from you than what you've got between your legs, though I'll want that too. You'll share my tent, pour my wine, laugh at my jests, rub the ache from my legs after each day's ride . . . and whether I keep you a day or a year, for so long as we are together you will take no other men into your bed."

"Fair enough." She reached down to the hem of her thin roughspun gown and pulled it up over her head in one smooth motion, tossing it aside. There was nothing underneath but Shae. "If he don't put down that candle, m'lord will burn his fingers."

Tyrion put down the candle, took her hand in his, and pulled her gently to him. She bent to kiss him. Her mouth tasted of honey and cloves, and her fingers were deft and practiced as they found the fastenings of his clothes.

When he entered her, she welcomed him with whispered endearments and small, shuddering gasps of pleasure. Tyrion suspected her delight was feigned, but she did it so well that it did not matter. *That* much truth he did not crave.

He had needed her, Tyrion realized afterward, as she lay quietly in his arms. Her or someone like her. It had been nigh on a year since he'd lain with a woman, since before he had set out for Winterfell in company with his brother and King Robert. He could well die on the morrow or the day after, and if he did, he would sooner go to his grave thinking of Shae than of his lord father, Lysa Arryn, or the Lady Catelyn Stark.

He could feel the softness of her breasts pressed against his arm as she lay beside him. That was a good feeling. A song filled his head. Softly, quietly, he began to whistle.

"What's that, m'lord?" Shae murmured against him.

"Nothing," he told her. "A song I learned as a boy, that's all. Go to sleep, sweetling."

When her eyes were closed and her breathing deep and steady, Tyrion slid out from beneath her, gently, so as not to disturb her sleep. Naked, he crawled outside, stepped over his squire, and walked around behind his tent to make water.

Bronn was seated cross-legged under a chestnut tree, near where they'd tied the horses. He was honing the edge of his sword, wide awake; the sellsword did not seem to sleep like other men. "Where did you find her?" Tyrion asked him as he pissed.

"I took her from a knight. The man was loath to give her up, but your name changed his thinking somewhat . . . that, and my dirk at his throat."

"Splendid," Tyrion said dryly, shaking off the last drops. "I seem to recall saying *find me a whore*, not *make me an enemy*."

"The pretty ones were all claimed," Bronn said. "I'll be pleased to take her back if you'd prefer a toothless drab."

Tyrion limped closer to where he sat. "My lord father would call that insolence, and send you to the mines for impertinence."

"Good for me you're not your father," Bronn replied. "I saw one with boils all over her nose. Would you like her?"

"What, and break your heart?" Tyrion shot back. "I shall keep Shae. Did you perchance note the *name* of this knight you took her from? I'd rather not have him beside me in the battle."

Bronn rose, cat-quick and cat-graceful, turning his sword in his hand. "You'll have me beside you in the battle, dwarf."

Tyrion nodded. The night air was warm on his bare skin. "See that I survive this battle, and you can name your reward."

Bronn tossed the longsword from his right hand to his left, and tried a cut. "Who'd want to kill the likes of you?"

"My lord father, for one. He's put me in the van."

"I'd do the same. A small man with a big shield. You'll give the archers fits."

"I find you oddly cheering," Tyrion said. "I must be mad."

Bronn sheathed his sword. "Beyond a doubt."

When Tyrion returned to his tent, Shae rolled onto her elbow and murmured sleepily, "I woke and m'lord was gone."

"M'lord is back now." He slid in beside her.

Her hand went between his stunted legs, and found him hard. "Yes he is," she whispered, stroking him.

He asked her about the man Bronn had taken her from, and she named the minor retainer of an insignificant lordling. "You need not fear his like, m'lord," the girl said, her fingers busy at his cock. "He is a small man."

"And what am I, pray?" Tyrion asked her. "A giant?"

"Oh, yes," she purred, "my giant of Lannister." She mounted him then, and for a time, she almost made him believe it. Tyrion went to sleep smiling . . .

. . . and woke in darkness to the blare of trumpets. Shae was shaking him by the shoulder. "M'lord," she whispered. "Wake up, m'lord. I'm frightened."

Groggy, he sat up and threw back the blanket. The horns called through the night, wild and urgent, a cry that said *hurry hurry hurry*. He heard shouts, the clatter of spears, the whicker of horses, though nothing yet that spoke to him of fighting. "My lord father's trumpets," he said. "Battle assembly. I thought Stark was yet a day's march away."

Shae shook her head, lost. Her eyes were wide and white.

Groaning, Tyrion lurched to his feet and pushed his way outside, shouting for his squire. Wisps of pale fog drifted through the night, long white fingers off the river. Men and horses blundered through the predawn chill; saddles were being cinched, wagons loaded, fires extinguished. The trumpets blew again: *hurry hurry hurry*. Knights vaulted onto snorting coursers while men-at-arms buckled their sword belts as they ran. When he found Pod, the boy was snoring softly. Tyrion gave him a sharp poke in the ribs with his toe. "My armor," he said, "and be quick about it." Bronn came trotting out of the mists, already armored and ahorse, wearing his battered halfhelm. "Do you know what's happened?" Tyrion asked him.

"The Stark boy stole a march on us," Bronn said. "He crept down the kingsroad in the night, and now his host is less than a mile north of here, forming up in battle array."

Hurry, the trumpets called, *hurry hurry hurry*.

"See that the clansmen are ready to ride." Tyrion ducked back inside his tent. "Where are my clothes?" he barked at Shae. "There. No, the leather, damn it. Yes. Bring me my boots."

By the time he was dressed, his squire had laid out his armor, such that it was. Tyrion owned a fine suit of heavy plate, expertly crafted to fit his misshapen body. Alas, it was safe at Casterly Rock, and he was not. He had to make do with oddments assembled from Lord Lefford's wagons: mail hauberk and coif, a dead knight's gorget, lobstered greaves and gauntlets and pointed steel boots. Some of it was ornate, some plain; not a bit of it matched, or fit as it should. His breastplate was meant for a bigger man; for his oversize head, they found a huge bucket-shaped greathelm topped with a foot-long triangular spike.

Shae helped Pod with the buckles and clasps. "If I die, weep for me," Tyrion told the whore.

"How will you know? You'll be dead."

"I'll know."

"I believe you would." Shae lowered the greathelm down over his head, and Pod fastened it to his gorget. Tyrion buckled on his belt, heavy with the weight of shortsword and dirk. By then his groom had brought up his mount, a formidable brown courser armored as heavily as he was. He needed help to mount; he felt as though he weighed a thousand stone. Pod handed him up his shield, a massive slab of heavy ironwood banded with steel. Lastly they gave him his battle-axe. Shae stepped back and looked him over. "M'lord looks fearsome."

"M'lord looks a dwarf in mismatched armor," Tyrion answered sourly, "but I thank you for the kindness. Podrick, should the battle go against us, see the lady safely home." He saluted her with his axe, wheeled his horse about, and trotted off. His stomach was a hard knot, so tight it pained him. Behind, his servants hurriedly began to strike his tent. Pale crimson fingers fanned out to the east as the first rays of the sun broke over the horizon. The western sky was a deep purple, speckled with stars. Tyrion wondered whether this was the last sunrise he would ever see . . . and whether wondering was a mark of cowardice. Did his brother Jaime ever contemplate death before a battle?

A warhorn sounded in the far distance, a deep mournful note that chilled the soul. The clansmen climbed onto their scrawny mountain horses, shouting curses and rude jokes. Several appeared to be drunk. The rising sun was burning off the drifting tendrils of fog as Tyrion led them off. What grass the horses had left was heavy with dew, as if some passing god had scattered a bag of diamonds over the earth. The mountain men fell in behind him, each clan arrayed behind its own leaders.

In the dawn light, the army of Lord Tywin Lannister unfolded like an iron rose, thorns gleaming.

His uncle would lead the center. Ser Kevan had raised his standards above the kingsroad. Quivers hanging from their belts, the foot archers arrayed themselves into three long lines, to east and west of the road, and stood calmly stringing their bows. Between them, pikemen formed squares; behind were rank on rank of men-at-arms with spear and sword and axe. Three hundred heavy horse surrounded Ser Kevan and the lords bannermen Lefford, Lydden, and Serrett with all their sworn retainers.

The right wing was all cavalry, some four thousand men, heavy with the weight of their armor. More than three quarters of the knights were there, massed together like a great steel fist. Ser Addam Marbrand had the command. Tyrion saw his banner unfurl as his standard-bearer shook it out; a burning tree, orange and smoke. Behind him flew Ser Flement's purple unicorn, the brindled boar of Crakehall, the bantam rooster of Swyft, and more.

His lord father took his place on the hill where he had slept. Around him, the reserve assembled; a huge force, half mounted and half foot, five thousand strong. Lord Tywin almost always chose to command the reserve; he would take the high ground and watch the battle unfold below him, committing his forces when and where they were needed most.

Even from afar, his lord father was resplendent. Tywin Lannister's battle armor put his son Jaime's gilded suit to shame. His greatcloak was sewn from countless layers of cloth-of-gold, so heavy that it barely stirred even when he charged, so large that its drape covered most of his stallion's hindquarters when he took the saddle. No ordinary clasp would suffice for such a weight, so the greatcloak was held in place by a matched pair of miniature lionesses crouching on his shoulders, as if poised to spring. Their mate, a male with a magnificent mane, reclined atop Lord

Tywin's greathelm, one paw raking the air as he roared. All three lions were wrought in gold, with ruby eyes. His armor was heavy steel plate, enameled in a dark crimson, greaves and gauntlets inlaid with ornate gold scrollwork. His rondels were golden sunbursts, all his fastenings were gilded, and the red steel was burnished to such a high sheen that it shone like fire in the light of the rising sun.

Tyrion could hear the rumble of the foemen's drums now. He remembered Robb Stark as he had last seen him, in his father's high seat in the Great Hall of Winterfell, a sword naked and shining in his hands. He remembered how the direwolves had come at him out of the shadows, and suddenly he could see them again, snarling and snapping, teeth bared in his face. Would the boy bring his wolves to war with him? The thought made him uneasy.

The northerners would be exhausted after their long sleepless march. Tyrion wondered what the boy had been thinking. Did he think to take them unawares while they slept? Small chance of that; whatever else might be said of him, Tywin Lannister was no man's fool.

The van was massing on the left. He saw the standard first, three black dogs on a yellow field. Ser Gregor sat beneath it, mounted on the biggest horse Tyrion had ever seen. Bronn took one look at him and grinned. "Always follow a big man into battle."

Tyrion threw him a hard look. "And why is that?"

"They make such splendid targets. That one, he'll draw the eyes of every bowman on the field."

Laughing, Tyrion regarded the Mountain with fresh eyes. "I confess, I had not considered it in that light."

Clegane had no splendor about him; his armor was steel plate, dull grey, scarred by hard use and showing neither sigil nor ornament. He was pointing men into position with his blade, a two-handed greatsword that Ser Gregor waved about with one hand as a lesser man might wave a dagger. "Any man runs, I'll cut him down myself," he was roaring when he caught sight of Tyrion. "Imp! Take the left. Hold the river. If you can."

The left of the left. To turn their flank, the Starks would need horses that could run on water. Tyrion led his men toward the riverbank. "Look," he shouted, pointing with his axe. "The river." A blanket of pale mist still clung to the surface of the water, the murky green current swirling past underneath. The shallows were muddy and choked with reeds. "That river is ours. Whatever happens, keep close to the water. Never lose sight of it. Let no enemy come between us and our river. If they dirty our waters, hack off their cocks and feed them to the fishes."

Shagga had an axe in either hand. He smashed them together and made them ring. *"Halfman!"* he shouted. Other Stone Crows picked up the cry, and the Black Ears and Moon Brothers as well. The Burned Men did not shout, but they rattled their swords and spears. *"Halfman! Halfman! Halfman!"*

Tyrion turned his courser in a circle to look over the field. The ground was rolling and uneven here; soft and muddy near the river, rising in a gentle slope toward the kingsroad, stony and broken beyond it, to the east. A few trees spotted the hillsides, but most of the land had been cleared and planted. His heart pounded in his chest in time to the drums, and under his layers of leather and steel his brow was cold with sweat. He watched Ser Gregor as the Mountain rode up and down the line, shouting and gesticulating. This wing too was all cavalry, but where the right was a mailed fist of knights and heavy lancers, the vanguard was made up of the sweepings of the west: mounted archers in leather jerkins, a swarming mass of undisciplined freeriders and sellswords, field-hands on plow horses armed with scythes and their fathers' rusted swords, half-trained boys from the stews of Lannisport . . . and Tyrion and his mountain clansmen.

"Crow food," Bronn muttered beside him, giving voice to what Tyrion had left unsaid. He could only nod. Had his lord father taken leave of his senses? No pikes, too few bowmen, a bare handful of knights, the ill-armed and unarmored, commanded by an unthinking brute who led with his rage . . . how could his father expect this travesty of a battle to hold his left?

He had no time to think about it. The drums were so near that the beat crept under his skin and set his hands to twitching. Bronn drew his longsword, and suddenly the enemy was there before them, boiling over the tops of the hills, advancing with measured tread behind a wall of shields and pikes.

Gods be damned, look at them all, Tyrion thought, though he knew his father had more men on the field.

Their captains led them on armored warhorses, standard-bearers riding alongside with their banners. He glimpsed the bull moose of the Hornwoods, the Karstark sunburst, Lord Cerwyn's battle-axe, and the mailed fist of the Glovers . . . *and* the twin towers of Frey, blue on grey. So much for his father's certainty that Lord Walder would not bestir himself. The white of House Stark was seen everywhere, the grey direwolves seeming to run and leap as the banners swirled and streamed from the high staffs. *Where is the boy?* Tyrion wondered.

A warhorn blew. *Haroooooooooooooooooooooooooo,* it cried, its voice as long and low and chilling as a cold wind from the north. The Lannister trumpets answered, *da-DA da-DA da-DAAAAAAAAA,* brazen and defiant, yet it seemed to Tyrion that they sounded somehow smaller, more anxious. He could feel a fluttering in his bowels, a queasy liquid feeling; he hoped he was not going to die sick.

As the horns died away, a hissing filled the air; a vast flight of arrows arched up from his right, where the archers stood flanking the road. The northerners broke into a run, shouting as they came, but the Lannister arrows fell on them like hail, hundreds of arrows, thousands, and shouts turned to screams as men stumbled and went down. By then a second flight was in the air, and the archers were fitting a third arrow to their bowstrings.

The trumpets blared again, *da-DAAA da-DAAA da-DA da-DA da-DAAAAAAA.* Ser Gregor waved his huge sword and bellowed a command, and a thousand other voices screamed back at him. Tyrion put his spurs to his horse and added one more voice to the cacophony, and the van surged forward. "The river!" he shouted at his clansmen as they rode. "Remember, hew to the river." He was still leading when they broke a canter, until Chella gave a bloodcurdling shriek and galloped past him, and Shagga howled and followed. The clansmen charged after them, leaving Tyrion in their dust.

A crescent of enemy spearmen had formed ahead, a double hedgehog bristling with steel, waiting behind tall oaken shields marked with the sunburst of Karstark. Gregor Clegane was the first to reach them, leading a wedge of armored veterans. Half the horses shied at the last second, breaking their charge before the row of spears. The others died, sharp steel points ripping through their chests. Tyrion saw a dozen men go down. The Mountain's stallion reared, lashing out with iron-shod hooves as a barbed spearhead raked across his neck. Maddened, the beast lunged into the ranks. Spears thrust at him from every side, but the shield wall broke beneath his weight. The northerners stumbled away from the animal's death throes. As his horse fell, snorting blood and biting with his last red breath, the Mountain rose untouched, laying about him with his two-handed greatsword.

Shagga went bursting through the gap before the shields could close, other Stone Crows hard behind him. Tyrion shouted, "Burned Men! Moon Brothers! After me!" but most of them were *ahead* of him. He glimpsed Timett son of Timett vault free as his mount died under him in full stride, saw a Moon Brother impaled on a Karstark spear, watched Conn's horse shatter a man's ribs with a kick. A flight of arrows descended on them; where they came from he could not say, but they fell on Stark and Lannister alike, rattling off armor or finding flesh. Tyrion lifted his shield and hid beneath it.

The hedgehog was crumbling, the northerners reeling back under the impact of the mounted assault. Tyrion saw Shagga catch a spearman full in the chest as the fool came on at a run, saw his axe shear through mail and leather and muscle and lungs. The man was dead on his feet, the axehead lodged in his breast, yet Shagga rode on, cleaving a shield in two with his left-hand battle-axe while the corpse was bouncing and stumbling bonelessly along on his right. Finally the dead man slid off. Shagga smashed the two axes together and roared.

By then the enemy was on him, and Tyrion's battle shrunk to the few feet of ground around his horse. A man-at-arms thrust at his chest and his axe lashed out, knocking the spear aside. The man danced back for another try, but Tyrion spurred his horse and rode right over him. Bronn was surrounded by three foes, but he lopped the head off the first spear that came at him, and raked his blade across a second man's face on his backslash.

A thrown spear came hurtling at Tyrion from the left and lodged in his shield with a woody *chunk*. He wheeled and raced after the thrower, but the man raised his own shield over his head. Tyrion circled around him, raining axe blows down on the wood. Chips of oak went flying, until the northerner lost his feet and slipped, falling flat on his back with his shield on top of him. He was below the reach of Tyrion's axe and it was too much bother to dismount, so he left him there and rode after another man, taking him from behind with a sweeping downcut that sent a jolt of impact up his arm. That won him a moment's respite. Reining up, he looked for the river. There it was, off to the right. Somehow he had gotten turned around.

A Burned Man rode past, slumped against his horse. A spear had entered his belly and come out through his back. He was past any help, but when Tyrion saw one of the northerners run up and make a grab for his reins, he charged.

His quarry met him sword in hand. He was tall and spare, wearing a long chainmail hauberk and gauntlets of lobstered steel, but he'd lost his helm and blood ran down into his eyes from a gash across his forehead. Tyrion aimed a swipe at his face, but the tall man slammed it aside. "Dwarf," he screamed. "Die." He turned in a circle as Tyrion rode around him, hacking at his head and shoulders. Steel rang on steel, and Tyrion soon realized that the tall man was quicker and stronger than he was. Where in the seven hells was Bronn? "Die," the man grunted, chopping at him savagely. Tyrion barely got his shield up in time, and the wood seemed to explode inward under the force of the blow. The shattered pieces fell away from his arm. *"Die!"* the swordsman bellowed, shoving in close and whanging Tyrion across the temple so hard his head rang. The blade made a hideous scraping sound as he drew it back over the steel. The tall man grinned . . . until Tyrion's destrier bit, quick as a snake, laying his cheek bare to the bone. Then he screamed. Tyrion buried his axe in his head. *"You* die," he told him, and he did.

As he wrenched the blade free, he heard a shout. *"Ed-dard!"* a voice rang out. *"For Eddard and Winterfell!"* The knight came thundering down on him, swinging the spiked ball of a morningstar around his head. Their war-horses slammed together before Tyrion could so much as open his mouth to shout for Bronn. His right elbow exploded with pain as the spikes punched through the thin metal around the joint. His axe was gone, as fast as that. He clawed for his sword, but the morningstar was circling again, coming at his face. A sickening *crunch*, and he was falling. He did not recall hitting the ground, but when he looked up there was only sky above him. He rolled onto his side and tried to find his feet, but pain shuddered through him and the world throbbed. The knight who had felled him drew up above him. "Tyrion the Imp," he boomed down. "You are mine. Do you yield, Lannister?"

Yes, Tyrion thought, but the word caught in his throat. He made a croaking sound and fought his way to his knees, fumbling for a weapon. His sword, his dirk, anything . . .

"Do you yield?" The knight loomed overhead on his armored warhorse. Man and horse both seemed immense. The spiked ball swung in a lazy circle. Tyrion's hands were numb, his vision blurred, his scabbard empty. "Yield or die," the knight declared, his flail whirling faster and faster.

Tyrion lurched to his feet, driving his head into the horse's belly. The animal gave a hideous scream and reared. It tried to twist away from the agony, a shower of blood and viscera poured down over Tyrion's face, and the horse fell like an avalanche. The next he knew, his visor was packed with mud and something was crushing his foot. He wriggled free, his throat so tight he could scarce talk. ". . . yield . . ." he managed to croak faintly.

"Yes," a voice moaned, thick with pain.

Tyrion scraped the mud off his helm so he could see again. The horse had fallen away from him, onto its rider. The knight's leg was trapped, the arm he'd used to break his fall twisted at a grotesque angle. "Yield," he repeated. Fumbling at his belt with his good hand, he drew a sword and flung it at Tyrion's feet. "I yield, my lord."

Dazed, the dwarf knelt and lifted the blade. Pain hammered through his elbow when he moved his arm. The battle seemed to have moved beyond him. No one remained on his part of the field save a large number of corpses. Ravens were already circling and landing to feed. He saw that Ser Kevan had brought up his center in support of the van; his huge mass of pikemen had pushed the northerners back against the hills. They were struggling on the slopes, pikes thrusting against another wall of shields, these oval and reinforced with iron studs. As he watched, the air filled with arrows again, and the men behind the oak wall crumbled beneath the murderous fire. "I believe you are losing, ser," he told the knight under the horse. The man made no reply.

The sound of hooves coming up behind him made him whirl, though he could scarcely lift the sword he held for the agony in his elbow. Bronn reined up and looked down on him.

"Small use you turned out to be," Tyrion told him.

"It would seem you did well enough on your own," Bronn answered. "You've lost the spike off your helm, though."

Tyrion groped at the top of the greathelm. The spike had snapped off clean. "I haven't lost it. I know just where it is. Do you see my horse?"

By the time they found it, the trumpets had sounded again and Lord Tywin's reserve came sweeping up along the river. Tyrion watched his father fly past, the crimson-and-gold banner of Lannister rippling over his head as he thundered across the field. Five hundred knights surrounded him, sunlight flashing off the points of their lances. The remnants of the Stark lines shattered like glass beneath the hammer of their charge.

With his elbow swollen and throbbing inside his armor, Tyrion made no attempt to join the slaughter. He and Bronn went looking for his men. Many he found among the dead. Ulf son of Umar lay in a pool of congealing blood, his arm gone at the elbow, a dozen of his Moon Brothers sprawled around him. Shagga was slumped beneath a tree, riddled with arrows, Conn's head in his lap. Tyrion thought they were both dead, but as he dismounted, Shagga opened his eyes and said, "They have killed Conn son of Coratt." Handsome Conn had no mark but for the red stain over his breast, where the spear thrust had killed him. When Bronn pulled Shagga to his feet, the big man seemed to notice the arrows for the first time. He plucked them out one by one, cursing the holes they had made in his layers of mail and leather, and yowling like a babe at the few that had buried themselves in his flesh. Chella daughter of Cheyk rode up as they were yanking arrows out of Shagga, and showed them four ears she had taken. Timett they discovered looting the bodies of the slain with his Burned Men. Of the three hundred clansmen who had ridden to battle behind Tyrion Lannister, perhaps half had survived.

He left the living to look after the dead, sent Bronn to take charge of his captive knight, and went alone in search of his father. Lord Tywin was seated by the river, sipping wine from a jeweled cup as his squire undid the fastenings on his breastplate. "A fine victory," Ser Kevan said when he saw Tyrion. "Your wild men fought well."

His father's eyes were on him, pale green flecked with gold, so cool they gave Tyrion a chill. "Did that surprise you, Father?" he asked. "Did it upset your plans? We were supposed to be butchered, were we not?"

Lord Tywin drained his cup, his face expressionless. "I put the least disciplined men on the left, yes. I anticipated that they would break. Robb Stark is a green boy, more like to be brave than wise. I'd hoped that if he saw our left collapse, he might plunge into the gap, eager for a rout. Once he was fully committed, Ser Kevan's pikes would wheel and take him in the flank, driving him into the river while I brought up the reserve."

"And you thought it best to place me in the midst of this carnage, yet keep me ignorant of your plans."

"A feigned rout is less convincing," his father said, "and I am not inclined to trust my plans to a man who consorts with sellswords and savages."

"A pity my savages ruined your dance." Tyrion pulled off his steel gauntlet and let it fall to the ground, wincing at the pain that stabbed up his arm.

"The Stark boy proved more cautious than I expected for one of his years," Lord Tywin admitted, "but a victory is a victory. You appear to be wounded."

Tyrion's right arm was soaked with blood. "Good of you to notice, Father," he said through clenched teeth. "Might I trouble you to send for your maesters? Unless you relish the notion of having a *one-armed* dwarf for a son . . ."

An urgent shout of *"Lord Tywin!"* turned his father's head before he could reply. Tywin Lannister rose to his feet as Ser Addam Marbrand leapt down off his courser. The horse was lathered and bleeding from the mouth. Ser Addam dropped to one knee, a rangy man with dark copper hair that fell to his shoulders, armored in burnished bronzed steel with the fiery tree of his House etched black on his breastplate. "My liege, we have taken some of their commanders. Lord Cerwyn, Ser Wylis Manderly, Harrion Karstark, four Freys. Lord Hornwood is dead, and I fear Roose Bolton has escaped us."

"And the boy?" Lord Tywin asked.

Ser Addam hesitated. "The Stark boy was not with them, my lord. They say he crossed at the Twins with the great part of his horse, riding hard for Riverrun."

A green boy, Tyrion remembered, *more like to be brave than wise*. He would have laughed, if he hadn't hurt so much.

CATELYN

The woods were full of whispers.

Moonlight winked on the tumbling waters of the stream below as it wound its rocky way along the floor of the valley. Beneath the trees, warhorses whickered softly and pawed at the moist, leafy ground, while men made nervous jests in hushed voices. Now and again, she heard the chink of spears, the faint metallic slither of chain mail, but even those sounds were muffled.

"It should not be long now, my lady," Hallis Mollen said. He had asked for the honor of protecting her in the battle to come; it was his right, as Winterfell's captain of guards, and Robb had not refused it to him. She had thirty men around her, charged to keep her unharmed and see her safely home to Winterfell if the fighting went against them. Robb had wanted fifty; Catelyn had insisted that ten would be enough, that he would need every sword for the fight. They made their peace at thirty, neither happy with it.

"It will come when it comes," Catelyn told him. When it came, she knew it would mean death. Hal's death perhaps . . . or hers, or Robb's. No one was safe. No life was certain. Catelyn was content to wait, to listen to the whispers in the woods and the faint music of the brook, to feel the warm wind in her hair.

She was no stranger to waiting, after all. Her men had always made her wait. "Watch for me, little cat," her father would always tell her, when he rode off to court or fair or battle. And she would, standing patiently on the battlements of Riverrun as the waters of the Red Fork and the Tumblestone flowed by. He did not always come when he said he would, and days would ofttimes pass as Catelyn stood her vigil, peering out between crenels and through arrow loops until she caught a glimpse of Lord Hoster on his old brown gelding, trotting along the rivershore toward the landing. "Did you watch for me?" he'd ask when he bent to hug her. "Did you, little cat?"

Brandon Stark had bid her wait as well. "I shall not be long, my lady," he had vowed. "We will be wed on my return." Yet when the day came at last, it was his brother Eddard who stood beside her in the sept.

Ned had lingered scarcely a fortnight with his new bride before he too had ridden off to war with promises on his lips. At least he had left her with more than words; he had given her a son. Nine moons had waxed and waned, and Robb had been born in Riverrun while his father still warred in the south. She had brought him forth in blood and pain, not knowing whether Ned would ever see him. Her son. He had been so small . . .

And now it was for Robb that she waited . . . for Robb, and for Jaime Lannister, the gilded knight who men said had never learned to wait at all. "The Kingslayer is restless, and quick to anger," her uncle Brynden had told Robb. And he had wagered their lives and their best hope of victory on the truth of what he said.

If Robb was frightened, he gave no sign of it. Catelyn watched her son as he moved among the men, touching one on the shoulder, sharing a jest with another, helping a third to gentle an anxious horse. His armor clinked softly when he moved. Only his head was bare. Catelyn watched a breeze stir his auburn hair, so like her own, and wondered when her son had grown so big. Fifteen, and near as tall as she was.

Let him grow taller, she asked the gods. *Let him know sixteen, and twenty, and fifty. Let him grow as tall as his father, and hold his own son in his arms. Please, please,*

please. As she watched him, this tall young man with the new beard and the direwolf prowling at his heels, all she could see was the babe they had laid at her breast at Riverrun, so long ago.

The night was warm, but the thought of Riverrun was enough to make her shiver. *Where are they?* she wondered. Could her uncle have been wrong? So much rested on the truth of what he had told them. Robb had given the Blackfish three hundred picked men, and sent them ahead to screen his march. "Jaime does not know," Ser Brynden said when he rode back. "I'll stake my life on that. No bird has reached him, my archers have seen to that. We've seen a few of his outriders, but those that saw us did not live to tell of it. He ought to have sent out more. He does not know."

"How large is his host?" her son asked.

"Twelve thousand foot, scattered around the castle in three separate camps, with the rivers between," her uncle said, with the craggy smile she remembered so well. "There is no other way to besiege Riverrun, yet still, that will be their undoing. Two or three thousand horse."

"The Kingslayer has us three to one," said Galbart Glover.

"True enough," Ser Brynden said, "yet there is one thing Ser Jaime lacks."

"Yes?" Robb asked.

"Patience."

Their host was greater than it had been when they left the Twins. Lord Jason Mallister had brought his power out from Seagard to join them as they swept around the headwaters of the Blue Fork and galloped south, and others had crept forth as well, hedge knights and small lords and masterless men-at-arms who had fled north when her brother Edmure's army was shattered beneath the walls of Riverrun. They had driven their horses as hard as they dared to reach this place before Jaime Lannister had word of their coming, and now the hour was at hand.

Catelyn watched her son mount up. Olyvar Frey held his horse for him, Lord Walder's son, two years older than Robb, and ten years younger and more anxious. He strapped Robb's shield in place and handed up his helm. When he lowered it over the face she loved so well, a tall young knight sat on his grey stallion where her son had been. It was dark among the trees, where the moon did not reach. When Robb turned his head to look at her, she could see only black inside his visor. "I must ride down the line, Mother," he told her. "Father says you should let the men see you before a battle."

"Go, then," she said. "Let them see you."

"It will give them courage," Robb said.

And who will give me courage? she wondered, yet she kept her silence and made herself smile for him. Robb turned the big grey stallion and walked him slowly away from her, Grey Wind shadowing his steps. Behind him his battle guard formed up. When he'd forced Catelyn to accept her protectors, she had insisted that he be guarded as well, and the lords bannermen had agreed. Many of their sons had clamored for the honor of riding with the Young Wolf, as they had taken to calling him. Torrhen Karstark and his brother Eddard were among his thirty, and Patrek Mallister, Smalljon Umber, Daryn Hornwood, Theon Greyjoy, no less than five of Walder Frey's vast brood, along with older men like Ser Wendel Manderly and Robin Flint. One of his companions was even a woman: Dacey Mormont, Lady Maege's eldest daughter and heir to Bear Island, a lanky six-footer who had been given a morningstar at an age when most girls were given dolls. Some of the other lords muttered about that, but Catelyn would not listen to their complaints. "This is not about the honor of your houses," she told them. "This is about keeping my son alive and whole."

And if it comes to that, she wondered, *will thirty be enough? Will six thousand be enough?*

A bird called faintly in the distance, a high sharp trill that felt like an icy hand on Catelyn's neck. Another bird answered; a third, a fourth. She knew their call well enough, from her years at Winterfell. Snow shrikes. Sometimes you saw them in the deep of winter, when the godswood was white and still. They were northern birds.

They are coming, Catelyn thought.

"They're coming, my lady," Hal Mollen whispered. He was always a man for stating the obvious. "Gods be with us."

She nodded as the woods grew still around them. In the quiet she could hear them, far off yet moving closer; the tread of many horses, the rattle of swords and spears and armor, the murmur of human voices, with here a laugh, and there a curse.

Eons seemed to come and go. The sounds grew louder. She heard more laughter, a shouted command, splashing as they crossed and recrossed the little stream. A horse snorted. A man swore. And then at last she saw him . . . only for an instant, framed between the branches of the trees as she looked down at the valley floor, yet she knew it was him. Even at a distance, Ser Jaime Lannister was unmistakable. The moonlight had silvered his armor and the gold of his hair, and turned his crimson cloak to black. He was not wearing a helm.

He was there and he was gone again, his silvery armor obscured by the trees once more. Others came behind him, long columns of them, knights and sworn swords and freeriders, three quarters of the Lannister horse.

"He is no man for sitting in a tent while his carpenters build siege towers," Ser Brynden had promised. "He has ridden out with his knights thrice already, to chase down raiders or storm a stubborn holdfast."

Nodding, Robb had studied the map her uncle had drawn him. Ned had taught him to read maps. "Raid him *here*," he said, pointing. "A few hundred men, no more. Tully banners. When he comes after you, we will be waiting"—his finger moved an inch to the left—"*here.*"

Here was a hush in the night, moonlight and shadows, a thick carpet of dead leaves underfoot, densely wooded ridges sloping gently down to the streambed, the underbrush thinning as the ground fell away.

Here was her son on his stallion, glancing back at her one last time and lifting his sword in salute.

Here was the call of Maege Mormont's warhorn, a long low blast that rolled down the valley from the east, to tell them that the last of Jaime's riders had entered the trap.

And Grey Wind threw back his head and howled.

The sound seemed to go right through Catelyn Stark, and she found herself shivering. It was a terrible sound, a frightening sound, yet there was music in it too. For a second she felt something like pity for the Lannisters below. *So this is what death sounds like,* she thought.

HAArooooooooooooooooooooooooooo came the answer from the far ridge as the Greatjon winded his own horn. To east and west, the trumpets of the Mallisters and Freys blew vengeance. North, where the valley narrowed and bent like a cocked elbow, Lord Karstark's warhorns added their own deep, mournful voices to the dark chorus. Men were shouting and horses rearing in the stream below.

The whispering wood let out its breath all at once, as the bowmen Robb had hidden in the branches of the trees let fly their arrows and the night erupted with the screams of men and horses. All around her, the riders raised their lances, and the dirt and leaves that had buried the cruel bright points fell away to reveal the gleam of sharpened steel. *"Winterfell!"* she heard Robb shout as the arrows sighed again. He moved away from her at a trot, leading his men downhill.

Catelyn sat on her horse, unmoving, with Hal Mollen and her guard around her, and she waited as she had waited before, for Brandon and Ned and her father. She was high on the ridge, and the trees hid most of what was going on beneath her. A heartbeat, two, four, and suddenly it was as if she and her protectors were alone in the wood. The rest were melted away into the green.

Yet when she looked across the valley to the far ridge, she saw the Greatjon's riders emerge from the darkness beneath the trees. They were in a long line, an endless line, and as they burst from the wood there was an instant, the smallest part of a heartbeat, when all Catelyn saw was the moonlight on the points of their lances, as if a thousand willowisps were coming down the ridge, wreathed in silver flame.

Then she blinked, and they were only men, rushing down to kill or die.

Afterward, she could not claim she had seen the battle. Yet she could hear, and the valley rang with echoes. The *crack* of a broken lance, the clash of swords, the cries of "Lannister" and "Winterfell" and "Tully! Riverrun and Tully!" When she realized there was no more to see, she closed her eyes and listened. The battle came alive around her. She heard hoofbeats, iron boots splashing in shallow water, the woody sound of swords on oaken shields and the scrape of steel against steel, the hiss of arrows, the thunder of drums, the terrified screaming of a thousand horses. Men shouted curses and begged for mercy, and got it (or not), and lived (or died). The ridges seemed to play queer tricks with sound. Once she heard Robb's voice, as clear as if he'd been standing at her side, calling, "To me! To me!" And she heard his direwolf, snarling and growling, heard the snap of those long teeth, the tearing of flesh, shrieks of fear and pain from man and horse alike. Was there only one wolf? It was hard to be certain.

Little by little, the sounds dwindled and died, until at last there was only the wolf. As a red dawn broke in the east, Grey Wind began to howl again.

Robb came back to her on a different horse, riding a piebald gelding in the place of the grey stallion he had taken down into the valley. The wolf's head on his shield was slashed half to pieces, raw wood showing where deep gouges had been hacked in the oak, but Robb himself seemed unhurt. Yet when he came closer, Catelyn saw that his mailed glove and the sleeve of his surcoat were black with blood. "You're hurt," she said.

Robb lifted his hand, opened and closed his fingers. "No," he said. "This is . . . Torrhen's blood, perhaps, or . . ." He shook his head. "I do not know."

A mob of men followed him up the slope, dirty and dented and grinning, with Theon and the Greatjon at their head. Between them they dragged Ser Jaime Lannister. They threw him down in front of her horse. "The Kingslayer," Hal announced, unnecessarily.

Lannister raised his head. "Lady Stark," he said from his knees. Blood ran down one cheek from a gash across his scalp, but the pale light of dawn had put the glint of gold back in his hair. "I would offer you my sword, but I seem to have mislaid it."

"It is not your sword I want, ser," she told him. "Give me my father and my brother Edmure. Give me my daughters. Give me my lord husband."

"I have mislaid them as well, I fear."

"A pity," Catelyn said coldly.

"Kill him, Robb," Theon Greyjoy urged. "Take his head off."

"No," her son answered, peeling off his bloody glove. "He's more use alive than dead. And my lord father never condoned the murder of prisoners after a battle."

"A wise man," Jaime Lannister said, "and honorable."

"Take him away and put him in irons," Catelyn said.

"Do as my lady mother says," Robb commanded, "and

make certain there's a strong guard around him. Lord Karstark will want his head on a pike."

"That he will," the Greatjon agreed, gesturing. Lannister was led away to be bandaged and chained.

"Why should Lord Karstark want him dead?" Catelyn asked.

Robb looked away into the woods, with the same brooding look that Ned often got. "He . . . he killed them . . ."

"Lord Karstark's sons," Galbart Glover explained.

"Both of them," said Robb. "Torrhen and Eddard. And Daryn Hornwood as well."

"No one can fault Lannister on his courage," Glover said. "When he saw that he was lost, he rallied his retainers and fought his way up the valley, hoping to reach Lord Robb and cut him down. And almost did."

"He *mislaid* his sword in Eddard Karstark's neck, after he took Torrhen's hand off and split Daryn Hornwood's skull open," Robb said. "All the time he was shouting for me. If they hadn't tried to stop him—"

"—I should then be mourning in place of Lord Karstark," Catelyn said. "Your men did what they were sworn to do, Robb. They died protecting their liege lord. Grieve for them. Honor them for their valor. But not now. You have no time for grief. You may have lopped the head off the snake, but three quarters of the body is still coiled around my father's castle. We have won a battle, not a war."

"But *such* a battle!" said Theon Greyjoy eagerly. "My lady, the realm has not seen such a victory since the Field of Fire. I vow, the Lannisters lost ten men for every one of ours that fell. We've taken close to a hundred knights captive, and a dozen lords bannermen. Lord Westerling, Lord Banefort, Ser Garth Greenfield, Lord Estren, Ser Tytos Brax, Mallor the Dornishman . . . *and* three Lannisters besides Jaime, Lord Tywin's own nephews, two of his sister's sons and one of his dead brother's . . ."

"And Lord Tywin?" Catelyn interrupted. "Have you perchance taken Lord Tywin, Theon?"

"No," Greyjoy answered, brought up short.

"Until you do, this war is far from done."

Robb raised his head and pushed his hair back out of his eyes. "My mother is right. We still have Riverrun."

DAENERYS

The flies circled Khal Drogo slowly, their wings buzzing, a low thrum at the edge of hearing that filled Dany with dread.

The sun was high and pitiless. Heat shimmered in waves off the stony outcrops of low hills. A thin finger of sweat trickled slowly between Dany's swollen breasts. The only sounds were the steady clop of their horses' hooves, the rhythmic tingle of the bells in Drogo's hair, and the distant voices behind them.

Dany watched the flies.

They were as large as bees, gross, purplish, glistening. The Dothraki called them *bloodflies*. They lived in marshes and stagnant pools, sucked blood from man and horse alike, and laid their eggs in the dead and dying. Drogo hated them. Whenever one came near him, his hand would shoot out quick as a striking snake to close around it. She had never seen him miss. He would hold the fly inside his huge fist long enough to hear its frantic buzzing. Then his fingers would tighten, and when he opened his hand again, the fly would be only a red smear on his palm.

Now one crept across the rump of his stallion, and the

horse gave an angry flick of its tail to brush it away. The others flitted about Drogo, closer and closer. The *khal* did not react. His eyes were fixed on distant brown hills, the reins loose in his hands. Beneath his painted vest, a plaster of fig leaves and caked blue mud covered the wound on his breast. The herbwomen had made it for him. Mirri Maz Duur's poultice had itched and burned, and he had torn it off six days ago, cursing her for a *maegi.* The mud plaster was more soothing, and the herbwomen made him poppy wine as well. He'd been drinking it heavily these past three days; when it was not poppy wine, it was fermented mare's milk or pepper beer.

Yet he scarcely touched his food, and he thrashed and groaned in the night. Dany could see how drawn his face had become. Rhaego was restless in her belly, kicking like a stallion, yet even that did not stir Drogo's interest as it had. Every morning her eyes found fresh lines of pain on his face when he woke from his troubled sleep. And now this silence. It was making her afraid. Since they had mounted up at dawn, he had said not a word. When she spoke, she got no answer but a grunt, and not even that much since midday.

One of the bloodflies landed on the bare skin of the *khal*'s shoulder. Another, circling, touched down on his neck and crept up toward his mouth. Khal Drogo swayed in the saddle, bells ringing, as his stallion kept onward at a steady walking pace.

Dany pressed her heels into her silver and rode closer. "My lord," she said softly. "Drogo. My sun-and-stars."

He did not seem to hear. The bloodfly crawled up under his drooping mustache and settled on his cheek, in the crease beside his nose. Dany gasped, *"Drogo."* Clumsily she reached over and touched his arm.

Khal Drogo reeled in the saddle, tilted slowly, and fell heavily from his horse. The flies scattered for a heartbeat, and then circled back to settle on him where he lay.

"No," Dany said, reining up. Heedless of her belly for once, she scrambled off her silver and ran to him.

The grass beneath him was brown and dry. Drogo cried out in pain as Dany knelt beside him. His breath rattled harshly in his throat, and he looked at her without recognition. "My horse," he gasped. Dany brushed the flies off his chest, smashing one as he would have. His skin burned beneath her fingers.

The *khal*'s bloodriders had been following just behind them. She heard Haggo shout as they galloped up. Cohollo vaulted from his horse. "Blood of my blood," he said as he dropped to his knees. The other two kept to their mounts.

"No," Khal Drogo groaned, struggling in Dany's arms. "Must ride. Ride. No."

"He fell from his horse," Haggo said, staring down. His broad face was impassive, but his voice was leaden.

"You must not say that," Dany told him. "We have ridden far enough today. We will camp here."

"Here?" Haggo looked around them. The land was brown and sere, inhospitable. "This is no camping ground."

"It is not for a woman to bid us halt," said Qotho, "not even a *khaleesi*."

"We camp here," Dany repeated. "Haggo, tell them Khal Drogo commanded the halt. If any ask why, say to them that my time is near and I could not continue. Cohollo, bring up the slaves, they must put up the *khal*'s tent at once. Qotho—"

"You do not command me, *Khaleesi*," Qotho said.

"Find Mirri Maz Duur," she told him. The godswife would be walking among the other Lamb Men, in the long column of slaves. "Bring her to me, with her chest."

Qotho glared down at her, his eyes hard as flint. "The *maegi*." He spat. "This I will not do."

"You will," Dany said, "or when Drogo wakes, he will hear why you defied me."

Furious, Qotho wheeled his stallion around and galloped off in anger . . . but Dany knew he would return with Mirri Maz Duur, however little he might like it. The slaves erected Khal Drogo's tent beneath a jagged outcrop of black rock whose shadow gave some relief from the heat of the afternoon sun. Even so, it was stifling under the sandsilk as Irri and Doreah helped Dany walk Drogo inside. Thick patterned carpets had been laid down over the ground, and pillows scattered in the corners. Eroeh, the timid girl Dany had rescued outside the mud walls of the Lamb Men, set up a brazier. They stretched Drogo out on a woven mat. "No," he muttered in the Common

Tongue. "No, no." It was all he said, all he seemed capable of saying.

Doreah unhooked his medallion belt and stripped off his vest and leggings, while Jhiqui knelt by his feet to undo the laces of his riding sandals. Irri wanted to leave the tent flaps open to let in the breeze, but Dany forbade it. She would not have any see Drogo this way, in delirium and weakness. When her *khas* came up, she posted them outside at guard. "Admit no one without my leave," she told Jhogo. "No one."

Eroeh stared fearfully at Drogo where he lay. "He dies," she whispered.

Dany slapped her. "The *khal* cannot die. He is the father of the stallion who mounts the world. His hair has never been cut. He still wears the bells his father gave him."

"*Khaleesi*," Jhiqui said, "he fell from his horse."

Trembling, her eyes full of sudden tears, Dany turned away from them. *He fell from his horse!* It was so, she had seen it, and the bloodriders, and no doubt her handmaids and the men of her *khas* as well. And how many more? They could not keep it secret, and Dany knew what that meant. A *khal* who could not ride could not rule, and Drogo had fallen from his horse.

"We must bathe him," she said stubbornly. She must not allow herself to despair. "Irri, have the tub brought at once. Doreah, Eroeh, find water, cool water, he's so hot." He was a fire in human skin.

The slaves set up the heavy copper tub in the corner of the tent. When Doreah brought the first jar of water, Dany wet a length of silk to lay across Drogo's brow, over the burning skin. His eyes looked at her, but he did not see. When his lips opened, no words escaped them, only a moan. "Where is Mirri Maz Duur?" she demanded, her patience rubbed raw with fear.

"Qotho will find her," Irri said.

Her handmaids filled the tub with tepid water that stank of sulfur, sweetening it with jars of bitter oil and handfuls of crushed mint leaves. While the bath was being prepared, Dany knelt awkwardly beside her lord husband, her belly great with their child within. She undid his braid with anxious fingers, as she had on the night he'd taken her for the first time, beneath the stars. His bells she laid aside carefully, one by one. He would want them again when he was well, she told herself.

A breath of air entered the tent as Aggo poked his head through the silk. *"Khaleesi,"* he said, "the Andal is come, and begs leave to enter."

"The Andal" was what the Dothraki called Ser Jorah. "Yes," she said, rising clumsily, "send him in." She trusted the knight. He would know what to do if anyone did.

Ser Jorah Mormont ducked through the door flap and waited a moment for his eyes to adjust to the dimness. In the fierce heat of the south, he wore loose trousers of mottled sandsilk and open-toed riding sandals that laced up to his knee. His scabbard hung from a twisted horse-hair belt. Under a bleached white vest, he was bare-chested, skin reddened by the sun. "Talk goes from mouth to ear, all over the *khalasar*," he said. "It is said Khal Drogo fell from his horse."

"Help him," Dany pleaded. "For the love you say you bear me, help him now."

The knight knelt beside her. He looked at Drogo long and hard, and then at Dany. "Send your maids away."

Wordlessly, her throat tight with fear, Dany made a gesture. Irri herded the other girls from the tent.

When they were alone, Ser Jorah drew his dagger. Deftly, with a delicacy surprising in such a big man, he began to scrape away the black leaves and dried blue mud from Drogo's chest. The plaster had caked hard as the mud walls of the Lamb Men, and like those walls it cracked easily. Ser Jorah broke the dry mud with his knife, pried the chunks from the flesh, peeled off the leaves one by one. A foul, sweet smell rose from the wound, so thick it almost choked her. The leaves were crusted with blood and pus, Drogo's breast black and glistening with corruption.

"No," Dany whispered as tears ran down her cheeks. "No, please, gods hear me, *no*."

Khal Drogo thrashed, fighting some unseen enemy. Black blood ran slow and thick from his open wound.

"Your *khal* is good as dead, Princess."

"No, he can't die, he *mustn't*, it was only a cut." Dany took his large callused hand in her own small ones, and held it tight between them. "I will not let him die . . ."

Ser Jorah gave a bitter laugh. "*Khaleesi* or queen, that command is beyond your power. Save your tears, child. Weep for him tomorrow, or a year from now. We do not have time for grief. We must go, and quickly, before he dies."

Dany was lost. "Go? Where should we go?"

"Asshai, I would say. It lies far to the south, at the end of the known world, yet men say it is a great port. We will find a ship to take us back to Pentos. It will be a hard journey, make no mistake. Do you trust your *khas*? Will they come with us?"

"Khal Drogo commanded them to keep me safe," Dany replied uncertainly, "but if he dies . . ." She touched the swell of her belly. "I don't understand. Why should we flee? I am *khaleesi*. I carry Drogo's heir. He will be *khal* after Drogo . . ."

Ser Jorah frowned. "Princess, hear me. The Dothraki will not follow a suckling babe. Drogo's strength was what they bowed to, and only that. When he is gone, Jhaqo and Pono and the other *kos* will fight for his place, and this *khalasar* will devour itself. The winner will want no more rivals. The boy will be taken from your breast the moment he is born. They will give him to the dogs . . ."

Dany hugged herself. "But *why*?" she cried plaintively. "Why should they kill a little baby?"

"He is Drogo's son, and the crones say he will be the stallion who mounts the world. It was prophesied. Better to kill the child than to risk his fury when he grows to manhood."

The child kicked inside her, as if he had heard. Dany remembered the story Viserys had told her, of what the Usurper's dogs had done to Rhaegar's children. His son had been a babe as well, yet they had ripped him from his mother's breast and dashed his head against a wall. That was the way of men. "They must not hurt my son!" she cried. "I will order my *khas* to keep him safe, and Drogo's bloodriders will—"

Ser Jorah held her by the shoulders. "A bloodrider dies with his *khal*. You know that, child. They will take you to Vaes Dothrak, to the crones, that is the last duty they owe him in life . . . when it is done, they will join Drogo in the night lands."

Dany did not want to go back to Vaes Dothrak and live the rest of her life among those terrible old women, yet she knew that the knight spoke the truth. Drogo had been more than her sun-and-stars; he had been the shield that kept her safe. "I will not leave him," she said stubbornly, miserably. She took his hand again. "I will not."

A stirring at the tent flap made Dany turn her head. Mirri Maz Duur entered, bowing low. Days on the march, trailing behind the *khalasar*, had left her limping and haggard, with blistered and bleeding feet and hollows under her eyes. Behind her came Qotho and Haggo, carrying the godswife's chest between them. When the bloodriders caught sight of Drogo's wound, the chest slipped from Haggo's fingers and crashed to the floor of the tent, and Qotho swore an oath so foul it seared the air.

Mirri Maz Duur studied Drogo, her face still and dead. "The wound has festered."

"This is your work, *maegi*," Qotho said. Haggo laid his fist across Mirri's cheek with a meaty *smack* that drove her to the ground. Then he kicked her where she lay.

"*Stop it!*" Dany screamed.

Qotho pulled Haggo away, saying, "Kicks are too merciful for a *maegi*. Take her outside. We will stake her to the earth, to be the mount of every passing man. And when they are done with her, the dogs will use her as well. Weasels will tear out her entrails and carrion crows feast upon her eyes. The flies off the river shall lay their eggs in her womb and drink pus from the ruins of her breasts . . ." He dug iron-hard fingers into the soft, wobbly flesh under the godswife's arm and hauled her to her feet.

"No," Dany said. "I will not have her harmed."

Qotho's lips skinned back from his crooked brown teeth in a terrible mockery of a smile. "No? You say me *no*? Better you should pray that we do not stake you out beside your *maegi*. You did this, as much as the other."

Ser Jorah stepped between them, loosening his long-sword in its scabbard. "Rein in your tongue, bloodrider. The princess is still your *khaleesi*."

"Only while the blood-of-my-blood still lives," Qotho told the knight. "When he dies, she is nothing."

Dany felt a tightness inside her. "Before I was *khaleesi*,

I was the blood of the dragon. Ser Jorah, summon my *khas*."

"No," said Qotho. "We will go. For now . . . *Khaleesi*." Haggo followed him from the tent, scowling.

"That one means you no good, Princess," Mormont said. "The Dothraki say a man and his bloodriders share one life, and Qotho sees it ending. A dead man is beyond fear."

"No one has died," Dany said. "Ser Jorah, I may have need of your blade. Best go don your armor." She was more frightened than she dared admit, even to herself.

The knight bowed. "As you say." He strode from the tent.

Dany turned back to Mirri Maz Duur. The woman's eyes were wary. "So you have saved me once more."

"And now you must save him," Dany said. "Please . . ."

"You do not ask a slave," Mirri replied sharply, "you tell her." She went to Drogo burning on his mat, and gazed long at his wound. "Ask or tell, it makes no matter. He is beyond a healer's skills." The *khal*'s eyes were closed. She opened one with her fingers. "He has been dulling the hurt with milk of the poppy."

"Yes," Dany admitted.

"I made him a poultice of firepod and sting-me-not and bound it in a lambskin."

"It burned, he said. He tore it off. The herbwomen made him a new one, wet and soothing."

"It burned, yes. There is great healing magic in fire, even your hairless men know that."

"Make him another poultice," Dany begged. "This time I will make certain he wears it."

"The time for that is past, my lady," Mirri said. "All I can do now is ease the dark road before him, so he might ride painless to the night lands. He will be gone by morning."

Her words were a knife through Dany's breast. What had she ever done to make the gods so cruel? She had finally found a safe place, had finally tasted love and hope. She was finally going home. And now to lose it all . . . "No," she pleaded. "Save him, and I will free you, I swear it. You must know a way . . . some magic, some . . ."

Mirri Maz Duur sat back on her heels and studied Daenerys through eyes as black as night. "There is a spell." Her voice was quiet, scarcely more than a whisper. "But it is hard, lady, and dark. Some would say that death is cleaner. I learned the way in Asshai, and paid dear for the lesson. My teacher was a bloodmage from the Shadow Lands."

Dany went cold all over. "Then you truly are a *maegi* . . ."

"Am I?" Mirri Maz Duur smiled. "Only a *maegi* can save your rider now, Silver Lady."

"Is there no other way?"

"No other."

Khal Drogo gave a shuddering gasp.

"Do it," Dany blurted. She must not be afraid; she was the blood of the dragon. "Save him."

"There is a price," the godswife warned her.

"You'll have gold, horses, whatever you like."

"It is not a matter of gold or horses. This is blood-magic, lady. Only death may pay for life."

"Death?" Dany wrapped her arms around herself protectively, rocked back and forth on her heels. "My death?" She told herself she would die for him, if she must. She was the blood of the dragon, she would not be afraid. Her brother Rhaegar had died for the woman he loved.

"No," Mirri Maz Duur promised. "Not your death, *Khaleesi*."

Dany trembled with relief. "Do it."

The *maegi* nodded solemnly. "As you speak, so it shall be done. Call your servants."

Khal Drogo writhed feebly as Rakharo and Quaro lowered him into the bath. "No," he muttered, "no. Must ride." Once in the water, all the strength seemed to leak out of him.

"Bring his horse," Mirri Maz Duur commanded, and so it was done. Jhogo led the great red stallion into the tent. When the animal caught the scent of death, he screamed and reared, rolling his eyes. It took three men to subdue him.

"What do you mean to do?" Dany asked her.

"We need the blood," Mirri answered. "That is the way."

Jhogo edged back, his hand on his *arakh*. He was a youth of sixteen years, whip-thin, fearless, quick to laugh, with the faint shadow of his first mustachio on his upper lip. He fell to his knees before her. "*Khaleesi*," he pleaded, "you must not do this thing. Let me kill this *maegi*."

"Kill her and you kill your *khal*," Dany said.

"This is bloodmagic," he said. "It is forbidden."

"I am *khaleesi*, and I say it is not forbidden. In Vaes Dothrak, Khal Drogo slew a stallion and I ate his heart, to give our son strength and courage. This is the same. The *same*."

The stallion kicked and reared as Rakharo, Quaro, and Aggo pulled him close to the tub where the *khal* floated like one already dead, pus and blood seeping from his wound to stain the bathwaters. Mirri Maz Duur chanted words in a tongue that Dany did not know, and a knife appeared in her hand. Dany never saw where it came from. It looked old; hammered red bronze, leaf-shaped, its blade covered with ancient glyphs. The *maegi* drew it across the stallion's throat, under the noble head, and the horse screamed and shuddered as the blood poured out of him in a red rush. He would have collapsed, but the men of her *khas* held him up. "Strength of the mount, go into the rider," Mirri sang as horse blood swirled into the waters of Drogo's bath. "Strength of the beast, go into the man."

Jhogo looked terrified as he struggled with the stallion's weight, afraid to touch the dead flesh, yet afraid to let go as well. *Only a horse,* Dany thought. If she could buy Drogo's life with the death of a horse, she would pay a thousand times over.

When they let the stallion fall, the bath was a dark red, and nothing showed of Drogo but his face. Mirri Maz Duur had no use for the carcass. "Burn it," Dany told them. It was what they did, she knew. When a man died, his mount was killed and placed beneath him on the funeral pyre, to carry him to the night lands. The men of her *khas* dragged the carcass from the tent. The blood had gone everywhere. Even the sandsilk walls were spotted with red, and the rugs underfoot were black and wet.

Braziers were lit. Mirri Maz Duur tossed a red powder onto the coals. It gave the smoke a spicy scent, a pleasant

enough smell, yet Eroeh fled sobbing, and Dany was filled
with fear. But she had gone too far to turn back now. She
sent her handmaids away. "Go with them, Silver Lady,"
Mirri Maz Duur told her.

"I will stay," Dany said. "The man took me under the
stars and gave life to the child inside me. I will not leave
him."

"You must. Once I begin to sing, no one must enter
this tent. My song will wake powers old and dark. The
dead will dance here this night. No living man must look
on them."

Dany bowed her head, helpless. "No one will enter."
She bent over the tub, over Drogo in his bath of blood,
and kissed him lightly on the brow. *"Bring him back to
me,"* she whispered to Mirri Maz Duur before she fled.

Outside, the sun was low on the horizon, the sky a
bruised red. The *khalasar* had made camp. Tents and
sleeping mats were scattered as far as the eye could see. A
hot wind blew. Jhogo and Aggo were digging a firepit to
burn the dead stallion. A crowd had gathered to stare at
Dany with hard black eyes, their faces like masks of
beaten copper. She saw Ser Jorah Mormont, wearing mail
and leather now, sweat beading on his broad, balding forehead. He pushed his way through the Dothraki to Dany's
side. When he saw the scarlet footprints her boots had left
on the ground, the color seemed to drain from his face.
"What have you done, you little fool?" he asked hoarsely.

"I had to save him."

"We could have fled," he said. "I would have seen you
safe to Asshai, Princess. There was no need . . ."

"Am I truly your princess?" she asked him.

"You know you are, gods save us both."

"Then help me now."

Ser Jorah grimaced. "Would that I knew how."

Mirri Maz Duur's voice rose to a high, ululating wail
that sent a shiver down Dany's back. Some of the
Dothraki began to mutter and back away. The tent was
aglow with the light of braziers within. Through the
blood-spattered sandsilk, she glimpsed shadows moving.

Mirri Maz Duur was dancing, and not alone.

Dany saw naked fear on the faces of the Dothraki.
"This *must not be*," Qotho thundered.

She had not seen the bloodrider return. Haggo and

Cohollo were with him. They had brought the hairless men, the eunuchs who healed with knife and needle and fire.

"This *will* be," Dany replied.

"*Maegi*," Haggo growled. And old Cohollo—Cohollo who had bound his life to Drogo's on the day of his birth, Cohollo who had always been kind to her—Cohollo spat full in her face.

"You will die, *maegi*," Qotho promised, "but the other must die first." He drew his *arakh* and made for the tent.

"No," she shouted, "you *mustn't*." She caught him by the shoulder, but Qotho shoved her aside. Dany fell to her knees, crossing her arms over her belly to protect the child within. "Stop him," she commanded her *khas*, "kill him."

Rakharo and Quaro stood beside the tent flap. Quaro took a step forward, reaching for the handle of his whip, but Qotho spun graceful as a dancer, the curved *arakh* rising. It caught Quaro low under the arm, the bright sharp steel biting up through leather and skin, through muscle and rib bone. Blood fountained as the young rider reeled backward, gasping.

Qotho wrenched the blade free. "*Horselord*," Ser Jorah Mormont called. "Try me." His longsword slid from its scabbard.

Qotho whirled, cursing. The *arakh* moved so fast that Quaro's blood flew from it in a fine spray, like rain in a hot wind. The longsword caught it a foot from Ser Jorah's face, and held it quivering for an instant as Qotho howled in fury. The knight was clad in chainmail, with gauntlets and greaves of lobstered steel and a heavy gorget around his throat, but he had not thought to don his helm.

Qotho danced backward, *arakh* whirling around his head in a shining blur, flickering out like lightning as the knight came on in a rush. Ser Jorah parried as best he could, but the slashes came so fast that it seemed to Dany that Qotho had four *arakhs* and as many arms. She heard the crunch of sword on mail, saw sparks fly as the long curved blade glanced off a gauntlet. Suddenly it was Mormont stumbling backward, and Qotho leaping to the attack. The left side of the knight's face ran red with blood, and a cut to the hip opened a gash in his mail and left him limping. Qotho screamed taunts at him, calling him a craven, a milk man, a eunuch in an iron suit. "You die now!" he promised, *arakh* shivering through the red twilight. Inside Dany's womb, her son kicked wildly. The curved blade slipped past the straight one and bit deep into the knight's hip where the mail gaped open.

Mormont grunted, stumbled. Dany felt a sharp pain in her belly, a wetness on her thighs. Qotho shrieked triumph, but his *arakh* had found bone, and for half a heartbeat it caught.

It was enough. Ser Jorah brought his longsword down with all the strength left him, through flesh and muscle and bone, and Qotho's forearm dangled loose, flopping on a thin cord of skin and sinew. The knight's next cut was at the Dothraki's ear, so savage that Qotho's face seemed almost to explode.

The Dothraki were shouting, Mirri Maz Duur wailing inside the tent like nothing human, Quaro pleading for water as he died. Dany cried out for help, but no one heard. Rakharo was fighting Haggo, *arakh* dancing with *arakh* until Jhogo's whip cracked, loud as thunder, the lash coiling around Haggo's throat. A yank, and the blood-rider stumbled backward, losing his feet and his sword. Rakharo sprang forward, howling, swinging his *arakh* down with both hands through the top of Haggo's head. The point caught between his eyes, red and quivering. Someone threw a stone, and when Dany looked, her shoulder was torn and bloody. "No," she wept, "no, please, stop it, it's too high, the price is too high." More stones came flying. She tried to crawl toward the tent, but Cohollo caught her. Fingers in her hair, he pulled her head back and she felt the cold touch of his knife at her throat. "My baby," she screamed, and perhaps the gods heard, for as quick as that, Cohollo was dead. Aggo's arrow took him under the arm, to pierce his lungs and heart.

When at last Daenerys found the strength to raise her head, she saw the crowd dispersing, the Dothraki stealing silently back to their tents and sleeping mats. Some were saddling horses and riding off. The sun had set. Fires burned throughout the *khalasar*, great orange blazes that crackled with fury and spit embers at the sky. She tried to rise, and agony seized her and squeezed her like a giant's fist. The breath went out of her; it was all she could do to gasp. The sound of Mirri Maz Duur's voice was like a funeral dirge. Inside the tent, the shadows whirled.

An arm went under her waist, and then Ser Jorah was lifting her off her feet. His face was sticky with blood, and Dany saw that half his ear was gone. She convulsed in his arms as the pain took her again, and heard the knight shouting for her handmaids to help him. *Are they all so afraid?* She knew the answer. Another pain grasped her, and Dany bit back a scream. It felt as if her son had a knife in each hand, as if he were hacking at her to cut his way out. "Doreah, curse you," Ser Jorah roared. "Come here. Fetch the birthing women."

"They will not come. They say she is accursed."

"They'll come or I'll have their heads."

Doreah wept. "They are gone, my lord."

"The *maegi*," someone else said. Was that Aggo? "Take her to the *maegi*."

No, Dany wanted to say, *no, not that, you mustn't,* but when she opened her mouth, a long wail of pain escaped, and the sweat broke over her skin. *What was wrong with them, couldn't they see?* Inside the tent the shapes were dancing, circling the brazier and the bloody bath, dark against the sandsilk, and some did not look human. She glimpsed the shadow of a great wolf, and another like a man wreathed in flames.

"The Lamb Woman knows the secrets of the birthing bed," Irri said. "She said so, I heard her."

"Yes," Doreah agreed, "I heard her too."

No, she shouted, or perhaps she only thought it, for no whisper of sound escaped her lips. She was being carried. Her eyes opened to gaze up at a flat dead sky, black and bleak and starless. *Please, no.* The sound of Mirri Maz Duur's voice grew louder, until it filled the world. *The shapes!* she screamed. *The dancers!*

Ser Jorah carried her inside the tent.

ARYA

The scent of hot bread drifting from the shops along the Street of Flour was sweeter than any perfume Arya had ever smelled. She took a deep breath and stepped closer to the pigeon. It was a plump one, speckled brown, busily pecking at a crust that had fallen between two cobblestones, but when Arya's shadow touched it, it took to the air.

Her stick sword whistled out and caught it two feet off the ground, and it went down in a flurry of brown feathers. She was on it in the blink of an eye, grabbing a wing as the pigeon flapped and fluttered. It pecked at her hand. She grabbed its neck and twisted until she felt the bone snap.

Compared with catching cats, pigeons were *easy*.

A passing septon was looking at her askance. "Here's the best place to find pigeon," Arya told him as she brushed herself off and picked up her fallen stick sword. "They come for the crumbs." He hurried away.

She tied the pigeon to her belt and started down the street. A man was pushing a load of tarts by on a two-wheeled cart; the smells sang of blueberries and lemons and apricots. Her stomach made a hollow rumbly noise.

"Could I have one?" she heard herself say. "A lemon, or . . . or any kind."

The pushcart man looked her up and down. Plainly he did not like what he saw. "Three coppers."

Arya tapped her wooden sword against the side of her boot. "I'll trade you a fat pigeon," she said.

"The Others take your pigeon," the pushcart man said.

The tarts were still warm from the oven. The smells were making her mouth water, but she did not have three coppers . . . or one. She gave the pushcart man a look, remembering what Syrio had told her about *seeing*. He was short, with a little round belly, and when he moved he seemed to favor his left leg a little. She was just thinking that if she snatched a tart and ran he would never be able to catch her when he said, "You be keepin' your filthy hands off. The gold cloaks know how to deal with thieving little gutter rats, that they do."

Arya glanced warily behind her. Two of the City Watch were standing at the mouth of an alley. Their cloaks hung almost to the ground, the heavy wool dyed a rich gold; their mail and boots and gloves were black. One wore a longsword at his hip, the other an iron cudgel. With a last wistful glance at the tarts, Arya edged back from the cart and hurried off. The gold cloaks had not been paying her any special attention, but the sight of them tied her stomach in knots. Arya had been staying as far from the castle as she could get, yet even from a distance she could see the heads rotting atop the high red walls. Flocks of crows squabbled noisily over each head, thick as flies. The talk in Flea Bottom was that the gold cloaks had thrown in with the Lannisters, their commander raised to a lord, with lands on the Trident and a seat on the king's council.

She had also heard other things, scary things, things that made no sense to her. Some said her father had murdered King Robert and been slain in turn by Lord Renly. Others insisted that *Renly* had killed the king in a drunken quarrel between brothers. Why else should he have fled in the night like a common thief? One story said the king had been killed by a boar while hunting, another that he'd died *eating* a boar, stuffing himself so full that he'd ruptured at the table. No, the king had died at table, others said, but only because Varys the Spider poisoned him. No, it had been *the queen* who poisoned him. No, he had died of a pox. No, he had choked on a fish bone.

One thing all the stories agreed on: King Robert was dead. The bells in the seven towers of the Great Sept of Baelor had tolled for a day and a night, the thunder of their grief rolling across the city in a bronze tide. They only rang the bells like that for the death of a king, a tanner's boy told Arya.

All she wanted was to go home, but leaving King's Landing was not so easy as she had hoped. Talk of war was on every lip, and gold cloaks were as thick on the city walls as fleas on . . . well, her, for one. She had been sleeping in Flea Bottom, on rooftops and in stables, wherever she could find a place to lie down, and it hadn't taken her long to learn that the district was well named.

Every day since her escape from the Red Keep, Arya had visited each of the seven city gates in turn. The Dragon Gate, the Lion Gate, and the Old Gate were closed and barred. The Mud Gate and the Gate of the Gods were open, but only to those who wanted to enter the city; the guards let no one out. Those who were allowed to leave left by the King's Gate or the Iron Gate, but Lannister men-at-arms in crimson cloaks and lion-crested helms manned the guard posts there. Spying down from the roof of an inn by the King's Gate, Arya saw them searching wagons and carriages, forcing riders to open their saddlebags, and questioning everyone who tried to pass on foot.

Sometimes she thought about swimming the river, but the Blackwater Rush was wide and deep, and everyone agreed that its currents were wicked and treacherous. She had no coin to pay a ferryman or take passage on a ship.

Her lord father had taught her never to steal, but it was growing harder to remember why. If she did not get out soon, she would have to take her chances with the gold cloaks. She hadn't gone hungry much since she learned to knock down birds with her stick sword, but she feared so much pigeon was making her sick. A couple she'd eaten raw, before she found Flea Bottom.

In the Bottom there were pot-shops along the alleys where huge tubs of stew had been simmering for years, and you could trade half your bird for a heel of yesterday's bread and a "bowl o' brown," and they'd even stick the other half in the fire and crisp it up for you, so long as you plucked the feathers yourself. Arya would have given anything for a cup of milk and a lemon cake, but the brown wasn't so bad. It usually had barley in it, and chunks of carrot and onion and turnip, and sometimes even apple, with a film of grease swimming on top. Mostly she tried not to think about the meat. Once she had gotten a piece of fish.

The only thing was, the pot-shops were never empty, and even as she bolted down her food, Arya could feel them watching. Some of them stared at her boots or her cloak, and she knew what they were thinking. With others, she could almost feel their eyes crawling under her leathers; she *didn't* know what they were thinking, and that scared her even more. A couple times, she was followed out into the alleys and chased, but so far no one had been able to catch her.

The silver bracelet she'd hoped to sell had been stolen her first night out of the castle, along with her bundle of good clothes, snatched while she slept in a burnt-out house off Pig Alley. All they left her was the cloak she had been huddled in, the leathers on her back, her wooden practice sword . . . and Needle. She'd been lying on top of Needle, or else it would have been gone too; it was worth more than all the rest together. Since then Arya had taken to walking around with her cloak draped over her right arm, to conceal the blade at her hip. The wooden sword she carried in her left hand, out where everybody could see it, to scare off robbers, but there were men in the pot-shops who wouldn't have been scared off if she'd had a battle-axe. It was enough to make her lose her taste for pigeon and stale bread. Often as not, she went to bed hungry rather than risk the stares.

Once she was outside the city, she would find berries to pick, or orchards she might raid for apples and cherries. Arya remembered seeing some from the kingsroad on the journey south. And she could dig for roots in the forest, even run down some rabbits. In the city, the only things to run down were rats and cats and scrawny dogs. The pot-shops would give you a fistful of coppers for a litter of pups, she'd heard, but she didn't like to think about that.

Down below the Street of Flour was a maze of twisting alleys and cross streets. Arya scrambled through the crowds, trying to put distance between her and the gold cloaks. She had learned to keep to the center of the street. Sometimes she had to dodge wagons and horses, but at least you could see them coming. If you walked near the buildings, people grabbed you. In some alleys you couldn't help but brush against the walls; the buildings leaned in so close they almost met.

A whooping gang of small children went running past, chasing a rolling hoop. Arya stared at them with resentment, remembering the times she'd played at hoops with Bran and Jon and their baby brother Rickon. She wondered how big Rickon had grown, and whether Bran was sad. She would have given anything if Jon had been here to call her "little sister" and muss her hair. Not that it needed mussing. She'd seen her reflection in puddles, and she didn't think hair got any more mussed than hers.

She had tried talking to the children she saw in the street, hoping to make a friend who would give her a place to sleep, but she must have talked wrong or something. The little ones only looked at her with quick, wary eyes and ran away if she came too close. Their big brothers and sisters asked questions Arya couldn't answer, called her names, and tried to steal from her. Only yesterday, a scrawny barefoot girl twice her age had knocked her down and tried to pull the boots off her feet, but Arya gave her a *crack* on her ear with her stick sword that sent her off sobbing and bleeding.

A gull wheeled overhead as she made her way down the hill toward Flea Bottom. Arya glanced at it thoughtfully, but it was well beyond the reach of her stick. It made her think of the sea. Maybe *that* was the way out. Old Nan used to tell stories of boys who stowed away on trading galleys and sailed off into all kinds of adventures. Maybe Arya could do that too. She decided to visit the riverfront. It was on the way to the Mud Gate anyway, and she hadn't checked that one today.

The wharfs were oddly quiet when Arya got there. She spied another pair of gold cloaks, walking side by side through the fish market, but they never so much as looked at her. Half the stalls were empty, and it seemed to her that there were fewer ships at dock than she remembered. Out on the Blackwater, three of the king's war galleys moved in formation, gold-painted hulls splitting the water as their oars rose and fell. Arya watched them for a bit, then began to make her way along the river.

When she saw the guardsmen on the third pier, in grey woolen cloaks trimmed with white satin, her heart almost stopped in her chest. The sight of Winterfell's colors brought tears to her eyes. Behind them, a sleek three-banked trading galley rocked at her moorings. Arya could not read the name painted on the hull; the words were strange, Myrish, Braavosi, perhaps even High Valyrian. She grabbed a passing longshoreman by the sleeve. "Please," she said, "what ship is this?"

"She's the *Wind Witch,* out of Myr," the man said.

"She's *still here,*" Arya blurted. The longshoreman gave her a queer look, shrugged, and walked away. Arya ran toward the pier. The *Wind Witch* was the ship Father had hired to take her home . . . still waiting! She'd imagined it had sailed ages ago.

Two of the guardsmen were dicing together while the third walked rounds, his hand on the pommel of his sword. Ashamed to let them see her crying like a baby, she stopped to rub at her eyes. Her eyes her eyes her eyes, why did . . .

Look with your eyes, she heard Syrio whisper.

Arya looked. She knew all of her father's men. The three in the grey cloaks were strangers. "You," the one walking rounds called out. "What do you want here, boy?" The other two looked up from their dice.

It was all Arya could do not to bolt and run, but she knew that if she did, they would be after her at once. She made herself walk closer. They were looking for a girl, but he thought she was a boy. She'd *be* a boy, then. "Want to buy a pigeon?" She showed him the dead bird.

"Get out of here," the guardsman said.

Arya did as he told her. She did not have to pretend to be frightened. Behind her, the men went back to their dice.

She could not have said how she got back to Flea Bottom, but she was breathing hard by the time she reached the narrow crooked unpaved streets between the hills. The Bottom had a stench to it, a stink of pigsties and stables and tanner's sheds, mixed in with the sour smell of winesinks and cheap whorehouses. Arya wound her way through the maze dully. It was not until she caught a whiff of bubbling brown coming through a pot-shop door that she realized her pigeon was gone. It must have slipped from her belt as she ran, or someone had stolen it and she'd never noticed. For a moment she wanted to cry again. She'd have to walk all the way back to the Street of Flour to find another one that plump.

Far across the city, bells began to ring.

Arya glanced up, listening, wondering what the ringing meant this time.

"What's this now?" a fat man called from the pot-shop.

"The bells again, gods ha'mercy," wailed an old woman.

A red-haired whore in a wisp of painted silk pushed open a second-story window. "Is it the boy king that's died now?" she shouted down, leaning out over the street. "Ah, that's a boy for you, they never last long." As she laughed, a naked man slid his arms around her from behind, biting her neck and rubbing the heavy white breasts that hung loose beneath her shift.

"Stupid slut," the fat man shouted up. "The king's not dead, that's only summoning bells. One tower tolling. When the king dies, they ring every bell in the city."

"Here, quit your biting, or I'll ring *your* bells," the woman in the window said to the man behind her, pushing him off with an elbow. "So who is it died, if not the king?"

"It's a summoning," the fat man repeated.

Two boys close to Arya's age scampered past, splashing through a puddle. The old woman cursed them, but they kept right on going. Other people were moving too, heading up the hill to see what the noise was about. Arya ran after the slower boy. "Where you going?" she shouted when she was right behind him. "What's happening?"

He glanced back without slowing. "The gold cloaks is carryin' him to the sept."

"Who?" she yelled, running hard.

"The *Hand*! They'll be taking his head off, Buu says."

A passing wagon had left a deep rut in the street. The boy leapt over, but Arya never saw it. She tripped and fell, face first, scraping her knee open on a stone and smashing her fingers when her hands hit the hard-packed earth. Needle tangled between her legs. She sobbed as she struggled to her knees. The thumb of her left hand was covered with blood. When she sucked on it, she saw that half the thumbnail was gone, ripped off in her fall. Her hands throbbed, and her knee was all bloody too.

"Make way!" someone shouted from the cross street. *"Make way for my lords of Redwyne!"* It was all Arya could do to get out of the road before they ran her down, four guardsmen on huge horses, pounding past at a gallop. They wore checked cloaks, blue-and-burgundy. Behind them, two young lordlings rode side by side on a pair of chestnut mares alike as peas in a pod. Arya had seen them in the bailey a hundred times; the Redwyne twins, Ser Horas and Ser Hobber, homely youths with orange hair and square, freckled faces. Sansa and Jeyne Poole used to call them Ser Horror and Ser Slobber, and giggle whenever they caught sight of them. They did not look funny now.

Everyone was moving in the same direction, all in a hurry to see what the ringing was all about. The bells seemed louder now, clanging, calling. Arya joined the stream of people. Her thumb hurt so bad where the nail had broken that it was all she could do not to cry. She bit her lip as she limped along, listening to the excited voices around her.

"—the King's Hand, Lord Stark. They're carrying him up to Baelor's Sept."

"I heard he was dead."

"Soon enough, soon enough. Here, I got me a silver stag says they lop his head off."

"Past time, the traitor." The man spat.

Arya struggled to find a voice. "He *never*—" she started, but she was only a child and they talked right over her.

"Fool! They ain't neither going to lop him. Since when do they knick traitors on the steps of the Great Sept?"

"Well, they don't mean to anoint him no knight. I heard it was Stark killed old King Robert. Slit his throat in the woods, and when they found him, he stood there cool as you please and said it was some old boar did for His Grace."

"Ah, that's not true, it was his own brother did him, that Renly, him with his gold antlers."

"You shut your lying mouth, woman. You don't know what you're saying, his lordship's a fine true man."

By the time they reached the Street of the Sisters, they

were packed in shoulder to shoulder. Arya let the human current carry her along, up to the top of Visenya's Hill. The white marble plaza was a solid mass of people, all yammering excitedly at each other and straining to get closer to the Great Sept of Baelor. The bells were very loud here.

Arya squirmed through the press, ducking between the legs of horses and clutching tight to her sword stick. From the middle of the crowd, all she could see were arms and legs and stomachs, and the seven slender towers of the sept looming overhead. She spotted a wood wagon and thought to climb up on the back where she might be able to see, but others had the same idea. The teamster cursed at them and drove them off with a crack of his whip.

Arya grew frantic. Forcing her way to the front of the crowd, she was shoved up against the stone of a plinth. She looked up at Baelor the Blessed, the septon king. Sliding her stick sword through her belt, Arya began to climb. Her broken thumbnail left smears of blood on the painted marble, but she made it up, and wedged herself in between the king's feet.

That was when she saw her father.

Lord Eddard stood on the High Septon's pulpit outside the doors of the sept, supported between two of the gold cloaks. He was dressed in a rich grey velvet doublet with a white wolf sewn on the front in beads, and a grey wool cloak trimmed with fur, but he was thinner than Arya had ever seen him, his long face drawn with pain. He was not standing so much as being held up; the cast over his broken leg was grey and rotten.

The High Septon himself stood behind him, a squat man, grey with age and ponderously fat, wearing long white robes and an immense crown of spun gold and crystal that wreathed his head with rainbows whenever he moved.

Clustered around the doors of the sept, in front of the raised marble pulpit, were a knot of knights and high lords. Joffrey was prominent among them, his raiment all crimson, silk and satin patterned with prancing stags and roaring lions, a gold crown on his head. His queen mother stood beside him in a black mourning gown slashed with crimson, a veil of black diamonds in her hair. Arya recognized the Hound, wearing a snowy white cloak over his dark grey armor, with four of the Kingsguard around him. She saw Varys the eunuch gliding among the lords in soft slippers and a patterned damask robe, and she thought the short man with the silvery cape and pointed beard might be the one who had once fought a duel for Mother.

And there in their midst was Sansa, dressed in sky-blue silk, with her long auburn hair washed and curled and silver bracelets on her wrists. Arya scowled, wondering what her sister was doing here, why she looked so happy.

A long line of gold-cloaked spearmen held back the crowd, commanded by a stout man in elaborate armor, all black lacquer and gold filigree. His cloak had the metallic shimmer of true cloth-of-gold.

When the bell ceased to toll, a quiet slowly settled across the great plaza, and her father lifted his head and began to speak, his voice so thin and weak she could scarcely make him out. People behind her began to shout out, *"What?"* and *"Louder!"* The man in the black-and-gold armor stepped up behind Father and prodded him sharply. *You leave him alone!* Arya wanted to shout, but she knew no one would listen. She chewed her lip.

Her father raised his voice and began again. "I am Eddard Stark, Lord of Winterfell and Hand of the King," he said more loudly, his voice carrying across the plaza, "and I come before you to confess my treason in the sight of gods and men."

"No," Arya whimpered. Below her, the crowd began to scream and shout. Taunts and obscenities filled the air. Sansa had hidden her face in her hands.

Her father raised his voice still higher, straining to be heard. "I betrayed the faith of my king and the trust of my friend, Robert," he shouted. "I swore to defend and protect his children, yet before his blood was cold, I plotted to depose and murder his son and seize the throne for myself. Let the High Septon and Baelor the Beloved and the Seven bear witness to the truth of what I say: Joffrey Baratheon is the one true heir to the Iron Throne, and by the grace of all the gods, Lord of the Seven Kingdoms and Protector of the Realm."

A stone came sailing out of the crowd. Arya cried out as she saw her father hit. The gold cloaks kept him from falling. Blood ran down his face from a deep gash across his forehead. More stones followed. One struck the guard to Father's left. Another went clanging off the breastplate of the knight in the black-and-gold armor. Two of the Kingsguard stepped in front of Joffrey and the queen, protecting them with their shields.

Her hand slid beneath her cloak and found Needle in its sheath. She tightened her fingers around the grip, squeezing as hard as she had ever squeezed anything. *Please, gods, keep him safe,* she prayed. *Don't let them hurt my father.*

The High Septon knelt before Joffrey and his mother. "As we sin, so do we suffer," he intoned, in a deep swelling voice much louder than Father's. "This man has confessed his crimes in the sight of gods and men, here in this holy place." Rainbows danced around his head as he lifted his hands in entreaty. "The gods are just, yet Blessed Baelor taught us that they are also merciful. What shall be done with this traitor, Your Grace?"

A thousand voices were screaming, but Arya never heard them. Prince Joffrey . . . no, *King* Joffrey . . . stepped out from behind the shields of his Kingsguard. "My mother bids me let Lord Eddard take the black, and Lady Sansa has begged mercy for her father." He looked straight at Sansa then, and *smiled*, and for a moment Arya thought that the gods had heard her prayer, until Joffrey turned back to the crowd and said, "But they have the soft hearts of women. So long as I am your king, treason shall never go unpunished. Ser Ilyn, bring me his head!"

The crowd roared, and Arya felt the statue of Baelor rock as they surged against it. The High Septon clutched at the king's cape, and Varys came rushing over waving his arms, and even the queen was saying something to him, but Joffrey shook his head. Lords and knights moved aside as *he* stepped through, tall and fleshless, a skeleton in iron mail, the King's Justice. Dimly, as if from far off, Arya heard her sister scream. Sansa had fallen to her knees, sobbing hysterically. Ser Ilyn Payne climbed the steps of the pulpit.

Arya wriggled between Baelor's feet and threw herself into the crowd, drawing Needle. She landed on a man in a butcher's apron, knocking him to the ground. Immediately someone slammed into her back and she almost went down herself. Bodies closed in around her, stumbling and pushing, trampling on the poor butcher. Arya slashed at them with Needle.

High atop the pulpit, Ser Ilyn Payne gestured and the knight in black-and-gold gave a command. The gold cloaks flung Lord Eddard to the marble, with his head and chest out over the edge.

"Here, you!" an angry voice shouted at Arya, but she bowled past, shoving people aside, squirming between them, slamming into anyone in her way. A hand fumbled at her leg and she hacked at it, kicked at shins. A woman stumbled and Arya ran up her back, cutting to both sides, but it was no good, *no good*, there were too many people, no sooner did she make a hole than it closed again. Someone buffeted her aside. She could still hear Sansa screaming.

Ser Ilyn drew a two-handed greatsword from the scabbard on his back. As he lifted the blade above his head, sunlight seemed to ripple and dance down the dark metal, glinting off an edge sharper than any razor. *Ice*, she thought, *he has Ice!* Her tears streamed down her face, blinding her.

And then a hand shot out of the press and closed round her arm like a wolf trap, so hard that Needle went flying from her hand. Arya was wrenched off her feet. She would have fallen if he hadn't held her up, as easy as if she were a doll. A face pressed close to hers, long black hair and tangled beard and rotten teeth. *"Don't look!"* a thick voice snarled at her.

"I . . . I . . . I . . ." Arya sobbed.

The old man shook her so hard her teeth rattled. "Shut your mouth and close your eyes, *boy*." Dimly, as if from far away, she heard a . . . a *noise* . . . a soft sighing sound, as if a million people had let out their breath at once. The old man's fingers dug into her arm, stiff as iron. "Look at me. Yes, that's the way of it, at *me*." Sour wine perfumed his breath. "Remember, *boy*?"

It was the smell that did it. Arya saw the matted greasy hair, the patched, dusty black cloak that covered his twisted shoulders, the hard black eyes squinting at her. And she remembered the black brother who had come to visit her father.

"Know me now, do you? There's a bright boy." He

spat. "They're done here. You'll be coming with me, and you'll be keeping your mouth shut." When she started to reply, he shook her again, even harder. "*Shut,* I said."

The plaza was beginning to empty. The press dissolved around them as people drifted back to their lives. But Arya's life was gone. Numb, she trailed along beside . . . *Yoren, yes, his name is Yoren.* She did not recall him finding Needle, until he handed the sword back to her. "Hope you can use that, boy."

"I'm not—" she started.

He shoved her into a doorway, thrust dirty fingers through her hair, and gave it a twist, yanking her head back. "—not a smart *boy,* that what you mean to say?"

He had a knife in his other hand.

As the blade flashed toward her face, Arya threw herself backward, kicking wildly, wrenching her head from side to side, but he had her by the hair, so *strong,* she could feel her scalp tearing, and on her lips the salt taste of tears.

BRAN

The oldest were men grown, seventeen and eighteen years from the day of their naming. One was past twenty. Most were younger, sixteen or less.

Bran watched them from the balcony of Maester Luwin's turret, listening to them grunt and strain and curse as they swung their staves and wooden swords. The yard was alive to the *clack* of wood on wood, punctuated all too often by *thwacks* and yowls of pain when a blow struck leather or flesh. Ser Rodrik strode among the boys, face reddening beneath his white whiskers, muttering at them one and all. Bran had never seen the old knight look so fierce. "No," he kept saying. "No. No. No."

"They don't fight very well," Bran said dubiously. He scratched Summer idly behind the ears as the direwolf tore at a haunch of meat. Bones crunched between his teeth.

"For a certainty," Maester Luwin agreed with a deep sigh. The maester was peering through his big Myrish lens tube, measuring shadows and noting the position of the comet that hung low in the morning sky. "Yet given time . . . Ser Rodrik has the truth of it, we need men to walk the walls. Your lord father took the cream of his guard to King's Landing, and your brother took the rest, along with all the likely lads for leagues around. Many will not come back to us, and we must needs find the men to take their places."

Bran stared resentfully at the sweating boys below. "If I still had my legs, I could beat them all." He remembered the last time he'd held a sword in his hand, when the king had come to Winterfell. It was only a wooden sword, yet he'd knocked Prince Tommen down half a hundred times. "Ser Rodrik should teach me to use a poleaxe. If I had a poleaxe with a big long haft, Hodor could be my legs. We could be a knight together."

"I think that . . . unlikely," Maester Luwin said. "Bran, when a man fights, his arms and legs and thoughts must be as one."

Below in the yard, Ser Rodrik was yelling. "You fight like a goose. He pecks you and you peck him harder. *Parry!* Block the blow. Goose fighting will not suffice. If those were real swords, the first peck would take your arm off!" One of the other boys laughed, and the old knight rounded on him. "You laugh. You. Now that is gall. *You* fight like a hedgehog . . ."

"There was a knight once who couldn't see," Bran said stubbornly, as Ser Rodrik went on below. "Old Nan told me about him. He had a long staff with blades at both ends and he could spin it in his hands and chop two men at once."

"Symeon Star-Eyes," Luwin said as he marked numbers in a book. "When he lost his eyes, he put star sapphires in the empty sockets, or so the singers claim. Bran, that is only a story, like the tales of Florian the Fool. A fable from the Age of Heroes." The maester *tsk*ed. "You must put these dreams aside, they will only break your heart."

The mention of dreams reminded him. "I dreamed about the crow again last night. The one with three eyes. He flew into my bedchamber and told me to come with him, so I did. We went down to the crypts. Father was there, and we talked. He was sad."

"And why was that?" Luwin peered through his tube.

"It was something to do about Jon, I think." The dream had been deeply disturbing, more so than any of the other crow dreams. "Hodor won't go down into the crypts."

The maester had only been half listening, Bran could tell. He lifted his eye from the tube, blinking. "Hodor won't . . . ?"

"Go down into the crypts. When I woke, I told him to take me down, to see if Father was truly there. At first he didn't know what I was saying, but I got him to the steps by telling him to go here and go there, only then he wouldn't go down. He just stood on the top step and said 'Hodor,' like he was scared of the dark, but I *had* a torch. It made me so mad I almost gave him a swat in the head, like Old Nan is always doing." He saw the way the maester was frowning and hurriedly added, "I didn't, though."

"Good. Hodor is a man, not a mule to be beaten."

"In the dream I flew down with the crow, but I can't do that when I'm awake," Bran explained.

"Why would you want to go down to the crypts?"

"I told you. To look for Father."

The maester tugged at the chain around his neck, as he often did when he was uncomfortable. "Bran, sweet child, one day Lord Eddard will sit below in stone, beside his father and his father's father and all the Starks back to the old Kings in the North . . . but that will not be for many years, gods be good. Your father is a prisoner of the queen in King's Landing. You will not find him in the crypts."

"He was there last night. I talked to him."

"Stubborn boy," the maester sighed, setting his book aside. "Would you like to go see?"

"I can't. Hodor won't go, and the steps are too narrow and twisty for Dancer."

"I believe I can solve that difficulty."

In place of Hodor, the wildling woman Osha was summoned. She was tall and tough and uncomplaining, willing to go wherever she was commanded. "I lived my life beyond the Wall, a hole in the ground won't fret me none, m'lords," she said.

"Summer, come," Bran called as she lifted him in wiry-strong arms. The direwolf left his bone and followed as Osha carried Bran across the yard and down the spiral steps to the cold vault under the earth. Maester Luwin went ahead with a torch. Bran did not even mind—*too* badly—that she carried him in her arms and not on her back. Ser Rodrik had ordered Osha's chain struck off, since she had served faithfully and well since she had been at Winterfell. She still wore the heavy iron shackles around her ankles—a sign that she was not yet wholly trusted—but they did not hinder her sure strides down the steps.

Bran could not recall the last time he had been in the crypts. It had been *before*, for certain. When he was little, he used to play down here with Robb and Jon and his sisters.

He wished they were here now; the vault might not have seemed so dark and scary. Summer stalked out in the echoing gloom, then stopped, lifted his head, and sniffed the chill dead air. He bared his teeth and crept backward, eyes glowing golden in the light of the maester's torch. Even Osha, hard as old iron, seemed uncomfortable. "Grim folk, by the look of them," she said as she eyed the long row of granite Starks on their stone thrones.

"They were the Kings of Winter," Bran whispered. Somehow it felt wrong to talk too loudly in this place.

Osha smiled. "Winter's got no king. If you'd seen it, you'd know that, summer boy."

"They were the Kings in the North for thousands of years," Maester Luwin said, lifting the torch high so the light shone on the stone faces. Some were hairy and bearded, shaggy men fierce as the wolves that crouched by their feet. Others were shaved clean, their features gaunt and sharp-edged as the iron longswords across their laps. "Hard men for a hard time. Come." He strode briskly down the vault, past the procession of stone pillars and the endless carved figures. A tongue of flame trailed back from the upraised torch as he went.

The vault was cavernous, longer than Winterfell itself, and Jon had told him once that there were other levels underneath, vaults even deeper and darker where the older kings were buried. It would not do to lose the light. Summer refused to move from the steps, even when Osha followed the torch, Bran in her arms.

"Do you recall your history, Bran?" the maester said as they walked. "Tell Osha who they were and what they did, if you can."

He looked at the passing faces and the tales came back to him. The maester had told him the stories, and Old

Nan had made them come alive. "That one is Jon Stark. When the sea raiders landed in the east, he drove them out and built the castle at White Harbor. His son was Rickard Stark, not my father's father but another Rickard, he took the Neck away from the Marsh King and married his daughter. Theon Stark's the real thin one with the long hair and the skinny beard. They called him the 'Hungry Wolf,' because he was always at war. That's a Brandon, the tall one with the dreamy face, he was Brandon the Shipwright, because he loved the sea. His tomb is empty. He tried to sail west across the Sunset Sea and was never seen again. His son was Brandon the Burner, because he put the torch to all his father's ships in grief. There's Rodrik Stark, who won Bear Island in a wrestling match and gave it to the Mormonts. And that's Torrhen Stark, the King Who Knelt. He was the last King in the North and the first Lord of Winterfell, after he yielded to Aegon the Conqueror. Oh, there, he's Cregan Stark. He fought with Prince Aemon once, and the Dragonknight said he'd never faced a finer swordsman." They were almost at the end now, and Bran felt a sadness creeping over him. "And there's my grandfather, Lord Rickard, who was beheaded by Mad King Aerys. His daughter Lyanna and his son Brandon are in the tombs beside him. Not me, another Brandon, my father's brother. They're not supposed to have statues, that's only for the lords and the kings, but my father loved them so much he had them done."

"The maid's a fair one," Osha said.

"Robert was betrothed to marry her, but Prince Rhaegar carried her off and raped her," Bran explained. "Robert fought a war to win her back. He killed Rhaegar on the Trident with his hammer, but Lyanna died and he never got her back at all."

"A sad tale," said Osha, "but those empty holes are sadder."

"Lord Eddard's tomb, for when his time comes," Maester Luwin said. "Is this where you saw your father in your dream, Bran?"

"Yes." The memory made him shiver. He looked around the vault uneasily, the hairs on the back of his neck bristling. Had he heard a noise? Was there someone here?

Maester Luwin stepped toward the open sepulchre, torch in hand. "As you see, he's not here. Nor will he be, for many a year. Dreams are only dreams, child." He thrust his arm into the blackness inside the tomb, as into the mouth of some great beast. "Do you see? It's quite empt—"

The darkness sprang at him, snarling.

Bran saw eyes like green fire, a flash of teeth, fur as black as the pit around them. Maester Luwin yelled and threw up his hands. The torch went flying from his fingers, caromed off the stone face of Brandon Stark, and tumbled to the statue's feet, the flames licking up his legs. In the drunken shifting torchlight, they saw Luwin struggling with the direwolf, beating at his muzzle with one hand while the jaws closed on the other.

"Summer!" Bran screamed.

And Summer came, shooting from the dimness behind them, a leaping shadow. He slammed into Shaggydog and knocked him back, and the two direwolves rolled over and over in a tangle of grey and black fur, snapping and biting at each other, while Maester Luwin struggled to his knees, his arm torn and bloody. Osha propped Bran up against Lord Rickard's stone wolf as she hurried to assist the maester. In the light of the guttering torch, shadow wolves twenty feet tall fought on the wall and roof.

"Shaggy," a small voice called. When Bran looked up, his little brother was standing in the mouth of Father's tomb. With one final snap at Summer's face, Shaggydog broke off and bounded to Rickon's side. "You let my father be," Rickon warned Luwin. "You let him be."

"Rickon," Bran said softly. "Father's not here."

"Yes he is. I saw him." Tears glistened on Rickon's face. "I saw him last night."

"In your dream . . . ?"

Rickon nodded. "You leave him. You leave him be. He's coming home now, like he promised. He's coming home."

Bran had never seen Maester Luwin look so uncertain before. Blood dripped down his arm where Shaggydog had shredded the wool of his sleeve and the flesh beneath. "Osha, the torch," he said, biting through his pain, and she snatched it up before it went out. Soot stains blackened both legs of his uncle's likeness. "That . . . that *beast,*" Luwin went on, "is supposed to be chained up in the kennels."

Rickon patted Shaggydog's muzzle, damp with blood. "I let him loose. He doesn't like chains." He licked at his fingers.

"Rickon," Bran said, "would you like to come with me?"

"No. I like it here."

"It's dark here. And cold."

"I'm not afraid. I have to wait for Father."

"You can wait with me," Bran said. "We'll wait together, you and me and our wolves." Both of the direwolves were licking wounds now, and would bear close watching.

"Bran," the maester said firmly, "I know you mean well, but Shaggydog is too wild to run loose. I'm the third man he's savaged. Give him the freedom of the castle and it's only a question of time before he kills someone. The truth is hard, but the wolf has to be chained, or . . ." He hesitated.

. . . *or killed,* Bran thought, but what he said was, "He was not made for chains. We will wait in your tower, all of us."

"That is quite impossible," Maester Luwin said.

Osha grinned. "The boy's the lordling here, as I recall." She handed Luwin back his torch and scooped Bran up into her arms again. "The maester's tower it is."

"Will you come, Rickon?"

His brother nodded. "If Shaggy comes too," he said, running after Osha and Bran, and there was nothing Maester Luwin could do but follow, keeping a wary eye on the wolves.

Maester Luwin's turret was so cluttered that it seemed to Bran a wonder that he ever found anything. Tottering piles of books covered tables and chairs, rows of stoppered jars lined the shelves, candle stubs and puddles of dried wax dotted the furniture, the bronze Myrish lens tube sat on a tripod by the terrace door, star charts hung from the walls, shadow maps lay scattered among the rushes, papers, quills, and pots of inks were everywhere, and all of it was spotted with droppings from the ravens in the rafters. Their strident *quorks* drifted down from above as Osha washed and cleaned and bandaged the maester's wounds, under Luwin's terse instruction. "This is folly," the small grey man said while she dabbed at the wolf bites with a stinging ointment. "I agree that it is odd that both you boys dreamed the same dream, yet when you stop to consider it, it's only natural. You miss your lord father, and you know that he is a captive. Fear can fever a man's mind and give him queer thoughts. Rickon is too young to comprehend—"

"I'm four now," Rickon said. He was peeking through the lens tube at the gargoyles on the First Keep. The direwolves sat on opposite sides of the large round room, licking their wounds and gnawing on bones.

"—too young, and—*ooh*, seven hells, that burns, no, don't stop, more. Too young, as I say, but you, Bran, you're old enough to know that dreams are only dreams."

"Some are, some aren't." Osha poured pale red firemilk into a long gash. Luwin gasped. "The children of the forest could tell you a thing or two about dreaming."

Tears were streaming down the maester's face, yet he shook his head doggedly. "The children . . . live only in dreams. Now. Dead and gone. Enough, that's enough. Now the bandages. Pads and then wrap, and make it tight, I'll be bleeding."

"Old Nan says the children knew the songs of the trees, that they could fly like birds and swim like fish and talk to the animals," Bran said. "She says that they made music so beautiful that it made you cry like a little baby just to hear it."

"And all this they did with magic," Maester Luwin said, distracted. "I wish they were here now. A spell would heal my arm less painfully, and they could talk to Shaggydog and tell him not to bite." He gave the big black wolf an angry glance out of the corner of his eye. "Take a lesson, Bran. The man who trusts in spells is dueling with a glass sword. As the children did. Here, let me show you something." He stood abruptly, crossed the room, and returned with a green jar in his good hand. "Have a look at these," he said as he pulled the stopper and shook out a handful of shiny black arrowheads.

Bran picked one up. "It's made of glass." Curious, Rickon drifted closer to peer over the table.

"Dragonglass," Osha named it as she sat down beside Luwin, bandagings in hand.

"Obsidian," Maester Luwin insisted, holding out his wounded arm. "Forged in the fires of the gods, far below the earth. The children of the forest hunted with that, thousands of years ago. The children worked no metal. In place of mail, they wore long shirts of woven leaves and bound their legs in bark, so they seemed to melt into the wood. In place of swords, they carried blades of obsidian."

"And still do." Osha placed soft pads over the bites on the maester's forearm and bound them tight with long strips of linen.

Bran held the arrowhead up close. The black glass was slick and shiny. He thought it beautiful. "Can I keep one?"

"As you wish," the maester said.

"I want one too," Rickon said. "I want four. *I'm* four."

Luwin made him count them out. "Careful, they're still sharp. Don't cut yourself."

"Tell me about the children," Bran said. It was important.

"What do you wish to know?"

"Everything."

Maester Luwin tugged at his chain collar where it chafed against his neck. "They were people of the Dawn Age, the very first, before kings and kingdoms," he said. "In those days, there were no castles or holdfasts, no cities, not so much as a market town to be found between here and the sea of Dorne. There were no men at all. Only the children of the forest dwelt in the lands we now call the Seven Kingdoms.

"They were a people dark and beautiful, small of stature, no taller than children even when grown to manhood. They lived in the depths of the wood, in caves and crannogs and secret tree towns. Slight as they were, the children were quick and graceful. Male and female hunted together, with weirwood bows and flying snares. Their gods were the gods of the forest, stream, and stone, the old gods whose names are secret. Their wise men were called *greenseers*, and carved strange faces in the weirwoods to keep watch on the woods. How long the children reigned here or where they came from, no man can know.

"But some twelve thousand years ago, the First Men appeared from the east, crossing the Broken Arm of Dorne before it was broken. They came with bronze swords and great leathern shields, riding horses. No horse had ever been seen on this side of the narrow sea. No doubt the children were as frightened by the horses as the First Men were by the faces in the trees. As the First Men carved out holdfasts and farms, they cut down the faces and gave them to the fire. Horror-struck, the children went to war. The old songs say that the greenseers used dark magics to make the seas rise and sweep away the land, shattering the Arm, but it was too late to close the door. The wars went on until the earth ran red with blood of men and children both, but more children than men, for men were bigger and stronger, and wood and stone and obsidian make a poor match for bronze. Finally the wise of both races prevailed, and the chiefs and heroes of the First Men met the greenseers and wood dancers amidst the weirwood groves of a small island in the great lake called Gods Eye.

"There they forged the Pact. The First Men were given the coastlands, the high plains and bright meadows, the mountains and bogs, but the deep woods were to remain forever the children's, and no more weirwoods were to be put to the axe anywhere in the realm. So the gods might bear witness to the signing, every tree on the island was given a face, and afterward, the sacred order of green men was formed to keep watch over the Isle of Faces.

"The Pact began four thousand years of friendship between men and children. In time, the First Men even put aside the gods they had brought with them, and took up the worship of the secret gods of the wood. The signing of the Pact ended the Dawn Age, and began the Age of Heroes."

Bran's fist curled around the shiny black arrowhead. "But the children of the forest are all gone now, you said."

"Here, they are," said Osha, as she bit off the end of the last bandage with her teeth. "North of the Wall, things are different. That's where the children went, and the giants, and the other old races."

Maester Luwin sighed. "Woman, by rights you ought to be dead or in chains. The Starks have treated you more gently than you deserve. It is unkind to repay them for their kindness by filling the boys' heads with folly."

"Tell me where they went," Bran said. "I want to know."

"Me too," Rickon echoed.

"Oh, very well," Luwin muttered. "So long as the kingdoms of the First Men held sway, the Pact endured, all through the Age of Heroes and the Long Night and the birth of the Seven Kingdoms, yet finally there came a time, many centuries later, when other peoples crossed the narrow sea.

"The Andals were the first, a race of tall, fair-haired warriors who came with steel and fire and the seven-pointed star of the new gods painted on their chests. The wars lasted hundreds of years, but in the end the six southron kingdoms all fell before them. Only here, where the King in the North threw back every army that tried to cross the Neck, did the rule of the First Men endure. The Andals burnt out the weirwood groves, hacked down the faces, slaughtered the children where they found them, and everywhere proclaimed the triumph of the Seven over the old gods. So the children fled north—"

Summer began to howl.

Maester Luwin broke off, startled. When Shaggydog bounded to his feet and added his voice to his brother's, dread clutched at Bran's heart. *"It's coming,"* he whispered, with the certainty of despair. He had known it since last night, he realized, since the crow had led him down into the crypts to say farewell. He had known it, but he had not believed. He had wanted Maester Luwin to be right. *The crow,* he thought, *the three-eyed crow . . .*

The howling stopped as suddenly as it had begun. Summer padded across the tower floor to Shaggydog, and began to lick at a mat of bloody fur on the back of his brother's neck. From the window came a flutter of wings.

A raven landed on the grey stone sill, opened its beak, and gave a harsh, raucous rattle of distress.

Rickon began to cry. His arrowheads fell from his hand one by one and clattered on the floor. Bran pulled him close and hugged him.

Maester Luwin stared at the black bird as if it were a scorpion with feathers. He rose, slow as a sleepwalker, and moved to the window. When he whistled, the raven hopped onto his bandaged forearm. There was dried blood on its wings. "A hawk," Luwin murmured, "perhaps an owl. Poor thing, a wonder it got through." He took the letter from its leg.

Bran found himself shivering as the maester unrolled the paper. "What is it?" he said, holding his brother all the harder.

"You know what it is, boy," Osha said, not unkindly. She put her hand on his head.

Maester Luwin looked up at them numbly, a small grey man with blood on the sleeve of his grey wool robe and tears in his bright grey eyes. "My lords," he said to the sons, in a voice gone hoarse and shrunken, "we . . . we shall need to find a stonecarver who knew his likeness well . . ."

SANSA

In the tower room at the heart of Maegor's Holdfast, Sansa gave herself to the darkness.

She drew the curtains around her bed, slept, woke weeping, and slept again. When she could not sleep she lay under her blankets shivering with grief. Servants came and went, bringing meals, but the sight of food was more than she could bear. The dishes piled up on the table beneath her window, untouched and spoiling, until the servants took them away again.

Sometimes her sleep was leaden and dreamless, and she woke from it more tired than when she had closed her eyes. Yet those were the best times, for when she dreamed, she dreamed of Father. Waking or sleeping, she saw him, saw the gold cloaks fling him down, saw Ser Ilyn striding forward, unsheathing Ice from the scabbard on his back, saw the moment . . . the moment when . . . she had wanted to look away, she had *wanted* to, her legs had gone out from under her and she had fallen to her knees, yet somehow she could not turn her head, and all the people were screaming and shouting, and her prince had smiled at her, he'd *smiled* and she'd felt safe, but only for a heartbeat, until he said those words, and her father's legs . . . that was what she remembered, his legs, the way they'd *jerked* when Ser Ilyn . . . when the sword . . .

Perhaps I will die too, she told herself, and the thought did not seem so terrible to her. If she flung herself from the window, she could put an end to her suffering, and in the years to come the singers would write songs of her grief. Her body would lie on the stones below, broken and innocent, shaming all those who had betrayed her. Sansa went so far as to cross the bedchamber and throw open the shutters . . . but then her courage left her, and she ran back to her bed, sobbing.

The serving girls tried to talk to her when they brought her meals, but she never answered them. Once Grand Maester Pycelle came with a box of flasks and bottles, to ask if she was ill. He felt her brow, made her undress, and touched her all over while her bedmaid held her down. When he left he gave her a potion of honeywater and herbs and told her to drink a swallow every night. She drank it all right then and went back to sleep.

She dreamt of footsteps on the tower stair, an ominous scraping of leather on stone as a man climbed slowly toward her bedchamber, step by step. All she could do was huddle behind her door and listen, trembling, as he came closer and closer. It was Ser Ilyn Payne, she knew, coming for her with Ice in his hand, coming to take her head. There was no place to run, no place to hide, no way to bar the door. Finally the footsteps stopped and she knew he was just outside, standing there silent with his dead eyes and his long pocked face. That was when she realized she was naked. She crouched down, trying to cover herself with her hands, as her door began to swing open, creaking, the point of the greatsword poking through . . .

She woke murmuring, "Please, please, I'll be good, I'll be *good*, please don't," but there was no one to hear.

When they finally came for her in truth, Sansa never heard their footsteps. It was Joffrey who opened her door, not Ser Ilyn but the boy who had been her prince. She was in bed, curled up tight, her curtains drawn, and she could not have said if it was noon or midnight. The first thing she heard was the slam of the door. Then her bed hangings were yanked back, and she threw up a hand against the sudden light and saw them standing over her.

"You will attend me in court this afternoon," Joffrey said. "See that you bathe and dress as befits my betrothed." Sandor Clegane stood at his shoulder in a plain brown doublet and green mantle, his burned face hideous in the morning light. Behind them were two knights of the Kingsguard in long white satin cloaks.

Sansa drew her blanket up to her chin to cover herself. "No," she whimpered, "please . . . leave me be."

"If you won't rise and dress yourself, my Hound will do it for you," Joffrey said.

"I beg of you, my prince . . ."

"I'm king now. Dog, get her out of bed."

Sandor Clegane scooped her up around the waist and lifted her off the featherbed as she struggled feebly. Her blanket fell to the floor. Underneath she had only a thin bedgown to cover her nakedness. "Do as you're bid, child," Clegane said. "Dress." He pushed her toward her wardrobe, almost gently.

Sansa backed away from them. "I did as the queen asked, I wrote the letters, I wrote what she told me. You promised you'd be merciful. Please, let me go home. I won't do any treason, I'll be good, I swear it, I don't have traitor's blood, I *don't*. I only want to go home." Remembering her courtesies, she lowered her head. "As it please you," she finished weakly.

"It does *not* please me," Joffrey said. "Mother says I'm still to marry you, so you'll stay here, and you'll obey."

"I don't *want* to marry you," Sansa wailed. "You chopped off my father's *head*!"

"He was a traitor. I never promised to spare him, only that I'd be merciful, and I was. If he hadn't been your father, I would have had him torn or flayed, but I gave him a clean death."

Sansa stared at him, seeing him for the first time. He was wearing a padded crimson doublet patterned with lions and a cloth-of-gold cape with a high collar that framed his face. She wondered how she could ever have thought him handsome. His lips were as soft and red as the worms you found after a rain, and his eyes were vain and cruel. "I hate you," she whispered.

King Joffrey's face hardened. "My mother tells me that

it isn't fitting that a king should strike his wife. Ser Meryn."

The knight was on her before she could think, yanking back her hand as she tried to shield her face and backhanding her across the ear with a gloved fist. Sansa did not remember falling, yet the next she knew she was sprawled on one knee amongst the rushes. Her head was ringing. Ser Meryn Trant stood over her, with blood on the knuckles of his white silk glove.

"Will you obey now, or shall I have him chastise you again?"

Sansa's ear felt numb. She touched it, and her fingertips came away wet and red. "I . . . as . . . as you command, my lord."

"*Your Grace*," Joffrey corrected her. "I shall look for you in court." He turned and left.

Ser Meryn and Ser Arys followed him out, but Sandor Clegane lingered long enough to yank her roughly to her feet. "Save yourself some pain, girl, and give him what he wants."

"What . . . what does he want? Please, tell me."

"He wants you to smile and smell sweet and be his lady love," the Hound rasped. "He wants to hear you recite all your pretty little words the way the septa taught you. He wants you to love him . . . and fear him."

After he was gone, Sansa sank back onto the rushes, staring at the wall until two of her bedmaids crept timidly into the chamber. "I will need hot water for my bath, please," she told them, "and perfume, and some powder to hide this bruise." The right side of her face was swollen and beginning to ache, but she knew Joffrey would want her to be beautiful.

The hot water made her think of Winterfell, and she took strength from that. She had not washed since the day her father died, and she was startled at how filthy the water became. Her maids sluiced the blood off her face, scrubbed the dirt from her back, washed her hair and brushed it out until it sprang back in thick auburn curls. Sansa did not speak to them, except to give them commands; they were Lannister servants, not her own, and she did not trust them. When the time came to dress, she chose the green silk gown that she had worn to the tourney. She recalled how gallant Joff had been to her that night at the feast. Perhaps it would make him remember as well, and treat her more gently.

She drank a glass of buttermilk and nibbled at some sweet biscuits as she waited, to settle her stomach. It was midday when Ser Meryn returned. He had donned his white armor; a shirt of enameled scales chased with gold, a tall helm with a golden sunburst crest, greaves and gorget and gauntlet and boots of gleaming plate, a heavy wool cloak clasped with a golden lion. His visor had been removed from his helm, to better show his dour face; pouchy bags under his eyes, a wide sour mouth, rusty hair spotted with grey. "My lady," he said, bowing, as if he had not beaten her bloody only three hours past. "His Grace has instructed me to escort you to the throne room."

"Did he instruct you to hit me if I refused to come?"

"Are you refusing to come, my lady?" The look he gave her was without expression. He did not so much as glance at the bruise he had left her.

He did not hate her, Sansa realized; neither did he love her. He felt nothing for her at all. She was only a . . . a *thing* to him. "No," she said, rising. She wanted to rage, to hurt him as he'd hurt her, to warn him that when she was queen she would have him exiled if he ever dared strike her again . . . but she remembered what the Hound had told her, so all she said was, "I shall do whatever His Grace commands."

"As I do," he replied.

"Yes . . . but you are no true knight, Ser Meryn."

Sandor Clegane would have laughed at that, Sansa knew. Other men might have cursed her, warned her to keep silent, even begged for her forgiveness. Ser Meryn Trant did none of these. Ser Meryn Trant simply did not care.

The balcony was deserted save for Sansa. She stood with her head bowed, fighting to hold back her tears, while below Joffrey sat on his Iron Throne and dispensed what it pleased him to call justice. Nine cases out of ten seemed to bore him; those he allowed his council to handle, squirming restlessly while Lord Baelish, Grand Maester Pycelle, or Queen Cersei resolved the matter. When he did choose to make a ruling, though, not even his queen mother could sway him.

A thief was brought before him and he had Ser Ilyn chop his hand off, right there in court. Two knights came to him with a dispute about some land, and he decreed that they should duel for it on the morrow. "To the *death*," he added. A woman fell to her knees to plead for the head of a man executed as a traitor. She had loved him, she said, and she wanted to see him decently buried. "If you loved a traitor, you must be a traitor too," Joffrey said. Two gold cloaks dragged her off to the dungeons.

Frog-faced Lord Slynt sat at the end of the council table wearing a black velvet doublet and a shiny cloth-of-gold cape, nodding with approval every time the king pronounced a sentence. Sansa stared hard at his ugly face, remembering how he had thrown down her father for Ser Ilyn to behead, wishing she could hurt him, wishing that some hero would throw *him* down and cut off his head. But a voice inside her whispered, *There are no heroes,* and she remembered what Lord Petyr had said to her, here in this very hall. "Life is not a song, sweetling," he'd told her. "You may learn that one day to your sorrow." *In life, the monsters win,* she told herself, and now it was the Hound's voice she heard, a cold rasp, metal on stone. "Save yourself some pain, girl, and give him what he wants."

The last case was a plump tavern singer, accused of making a song that ridiculed the late King Robert. Joff commanded them to fetch his woodharp and ordered him to perform the song for the court. The singer wept and swore he would never sing that song again, but the king insisted. It was sort of a funny song, all about Robert fighting with a pig. The pig was the boar who'd killed him, Sansa knew, but in some verses it almost sounded as if he were singing about the queen. When the song was done, Joffrey announced that he'd decided to be merciful. The singer could keep either his fingers or his tongue. He would have a day to make his choice. Janos Slynt nodded.

That was the final business of the afternoon, Sansa saw with relief, but her ordeal was not yet done. When the herald's voice dismissed the court, she fled the balcony, only to find Joffrey waiting for her at the base of the curving stairs. The Hound was with him, and Ser Meryn as well. The young king examined her critically, top to bottom. "You look much better than you did."

"Thank you, Your Grace," Sansa said. Hollow words, but they made him nod and smile.

"Walk with me," Joffrey commanded, offering her his arm. She had no choice but to take it. The touch of his hand would have thrilled her once; now it made her flesh crawl. "My name day will be here soon," Joffrey said as they slipped out the rear of the throne room. "There will be a great feast, and gifts. What are you going to give me?"

"I . . . I had not thought, my lord."

"*Your Grace,*" he said sharply. "You truly are a stupid girl, aren't you? My mother says so."

"She does?" After all that had happened, his words should have lost their power to hurt her, yet somehow they had not. The queen had always been so kind to her.

"Oh, yes. She worries about our children, whether they'll be stupid like you, but I told her not to trouble herself." The king gestured, and Ser Meryn opened a door for them.

"Thank you, Your Grace," she murmured. *The Hound was right,* she thought, *I am only a little bird, repeating the words they taught me.* The sun had fallen below the western wall, and the stones of the Red Keep glowed dark as blood.

"I'll get you with child as soon as you're able," Joffrey said as he escorted her across the practice yard. "If the first one is stupid, I'll chop off your head and find a smarter wife. When do you think you'll be able to have children?"

Sansa could not look at him, he shamed her so. "Septa Mordane says most . . . most highborn girls have their flowering at twelve or thirteen."

Joffrey nodded. "This way." He led her into the gatehouse, to the base of the steps that led up to the battlements.

Sansa jerked back away from him, trembling. Suddenly she knew where they were going. "*No,*" she said, her voice a frightened gasp. "Please, no, don't make me, I beg you . . ."

Joffrey pressed his lips together. "I want to show you what happens to traitors."

Sansa shook her head wildly. "I won't. I *won't.*"

"I can have Ser Meryn drag you up," he said. "You won't like that. You had better do what I say." Joffrey reached for her, and Sansa cringed away from him, backing into the Hound.

"Do it, girl," Sandor Clegane told her, pushing her back toward the king. His mouth twitched on the burned side of his face and Sansa could almost hear the rest of it. *He'll have you up there no matter what, so give him what he wants.*

She forced herself to take King Joffrey's hand. The climb was something out of a nightmare; every step was a struggle, as if she were pulling her feet out of ankle-deep mud, and there were more steps than she would have believed, a thousand thousand steps, and horror waiting on the ramparts.

From the high battlements of the gatehouse, the whole world spread out below them. Sansa could see the Great Sept of Baelor on Visenya's hill, where her father had died. At the other end of the Street of the Sisters stood the fire-blackened ruins of the Dragonpit. To the west, the swollen red sun was half-hidden behind the Gate of the Gods. The salt sea was at her back, and to the south was the fish market and the docks and the swirling torrent of the Blackwater Rush. And to the north . . .

She turned that way, and saw only the city, streets and alleys and hills and bottoms and more streets and more alleys and the stone of distant walls. Yet she knew that beyond them was open country, farms and fields and forests, and beyond that, north and north and north again, stood Winterfell.

"What are you looking at?" Joffrey said. "This is what I wanted you to see, right here."

A thick stone parapet protected the outer edge of the rampart, reaching as high as Sansa's chin, with crenellations cut into it every five feet for archers. The heads were mounted between the crenels, along the top of the wall, impaled on iron spikes so they faced out over the city. Sansa had noted them the moment she'd stepped out onto the wallwalk, but the river and the bustling streets and the setting sun were ever so much prettier. *He can make me look at the heads,* she told herself, *but he can't make me see them.*

"This one is your father," he said. "This one here. Dog, turn it around so she can see him."

Sandor Clegane took the head by the hair and turned

it. The severed head had been dipped in tar to preserve it
longer. Sansa looked at it calmly, not seeing it at all. It did
not really look like Lord Eddard, she thought; it did not
even look *real*. "How long do I have to look?"

Joffrey seemed disappointed. "Do you want to see the
rest?" There was a long row of them.

"If it please Your Grace."

Joffrey marched her down the wallwalk, past a dozen
more heads and two empty spikes. "I'm saving those for
my uncle Stannis and my uncle Renly," he explained.
The other heads had been dead and mounted much longer
than her father. Despite the tar, most were long past being
recognizable. The king pointed to one and said, "That's
your septa there," but Sansa could not even have told that
it was a woman. The jaw had rotted off her face, and birds
had eaten one ear and most of a cheek.

Sansa had wondered what had happened to Septa
Mordane, although she supposed she had known all along.
"Why did you kill *her*?" she asked. "She was god-
sworn . . ."

"She was a traitor." Joffrey looked pouty; somehow
she was upsetting him. "You haven't said what you mean
to give me for my name day. Maybe I should give you
something instead, would you like that?"

"If it please you, my lord," Sansa said.

When he smiled, she knew he was mocking her. "Your
brother is a traitor too, you know." He turned Septa
Mordane's head back around. "I remember your brother
from Winterfell. My dog called him the lord of the
wooden sword. Didn't you, dog?"

"Did I?" the Hound replied. "I don't recall."

Joffrey gave a petulant shrug. "Your brother defeated
my uncle Jaime. My mother says it was treachery and
deceit. She wept when she heard. Women are all weak,
even her, though she pretends she isn't. She says we need
to stay in King's Landing in case my other uncles attack,
but I don't care. After my name day feast, I'm going to
raise a host and kill your brother myself. That's what I'll
give you, Lady Sansa. Your brother's head."

A kind of madness took over her then, and she heard
herself say, "Maybe my brother will give me *your* head."

Joffrey scowled. "You must never mock me like that.

A true wife does not mock her lord. Ser Meryn, teach her."

This time the knight grasped her beneath the jaw and held her head still as he struck her. He hit her twice, left to right, and harder, right to left. Her lip split and blood ran down her chin, to mingle with the salt of her tears.

"You shouldn't be crying all the time," Joffrey told her. "You're more pretty when you smile and laugh."

Sansa made herself smile, afraid that he would have Ser Meryn hit her again if she did not, but it was no good, the king still shook his head. "Wipe off the blood, you're all messy."

The outer parapet came up to her chin, but along the inner edge of the walk was nothing, nothing but a long plunge to the bailey seventy or eighty feet below. All it would take was a shove, she told herself. He was standing right there, right *there*, smirking at her with those fat wormlips. *You could do it,* she told herself. *You could. Do it right now.* It wouldn't even matter if she went over with him. It wouldn't matter at all.

"Here, girl." Sandor Clegane knelt before her, *between* her and Joffrey. With a delicacy surprising in such a big man, he dabbed at the blood welling from her broken lip.

The moment was gone. Sansa lowered her eyes. "Thank you," she said when he was done. She was a good girl, and always remembered her courtesies.

DAENERYS

Wings shadowed her fever dreams.

"You don't want to wake the dragon, do you?"

She was walking down a long hall beneath high stone arches. She could not look behind her, *must* not look behind her. There was a door ahead of her, tiny with distance, but even from afar, she saw that it was painted red. She walked faster, and her bare feet left bloody footprints on the stone.

"You don't want to wake the dragon, do you?"

She saw sunlight on the Dothraki sea, the living plain, rich with the smells of earth and death. Wind stirred the grasses, and they rippled like water. Drogo held her in strong arms, and his hand stroked her sex and opened her and woke that sweet wetness that was his alone, and the stars smiled down on them, stars in a daylight sky. "Home," she whispered as he entered her and filled her with his seed, but suddenly the stars were gone, and across the blue sky swept the great wings, and the world took flame.

". . . don't want to wake the dragon, do you?"

Ser Jorah's face was drawn and sorrowful. "Rhaegar

was the last dragon," he told her. He warmed translucent hands over a glowing brazier where stone eggs smouldered red as coals. One moment he was there and the next he was fading, his flesh colorless, less substantial than the wind. "The last dragon," he whispered, thin as a wisp, and was gone. She felt the dark behind her, and the red door seemed farther away than ever.

". . . don't want to wake the dragon, do you?"

Viserys stood before her, screaming. "The dragon does not beg, slut. You do not command the dragon. I am the dragon, and I will be crowned." The molten gold trickled down his face like wax, burning deep channels in his flesh. *"I am the dragon and I will be crowned!"* he shrieked, and his fingers snapped like snakes, biting at her nipples, pinching, twisting, even as his eyes burst and ran like jelly down seared and blackened cheeks.

". . . don't want to wake the dragon . . ."

The red door was so far ahead of her, and she could feel the icy breath behind, sweeping up on her. If it caught her she would die a death that was more than death, howling forever alone in the darkness. She began to run.

". . . don't want to wake the dragon . . ."

She could feel the heat inside her, a terrible burning in her womb. Her son was tall and proud, with Drogo's copper skin and her own silver-gold hair, violet eyes shaped like almonds. And he smiled for her and began to lift his hand toward hers, but when he opened his mouth the fire poured out. She saw his heart burning through his chest, and in an instant he was gone, consumed like a moth by a candle, turned to ash. She wept for her child, the promise of a sweet mouth on her breast, but her tears turned to steam as they touched her skin.

". . . want to wake the dragon . . ."

Ghosts lined the hallway, dressed in the faded raiment of kings. In their hands were swords of pale fire. They had hair of silver and hair of gold and hair of platinum white, and their eyes were opal and amethyst, tourmaline and jade. "Faster," they cried, "faster, faster." She raced, her feet melting the stone wherever they touched. *"Faster!"* the ghosts cried as one, and she screamed and threw herself forward. A great knife of pain ripped down her back, and she felt her skin tear open and smelled the stench of burning blood and saw the shadow of wings. And Daenerys Targaryen flew.

"... *wake the dragon* ..."

The door loomed before her, the red door, so close, so close, the hall was a blur around her, the cold receding behind. And now the stone was gone and she flew across the Dothraki sea, high and higher, the green rippling beneath, and all that lived and breathed fled in terror from the shadow of her wings. She could smell home, she could see it, there, just beyond that door, green fields and great stone houses and arms to keep her warm, *there*. She threw open the door.

"... *the dragon* ..."

And saw her brother Rhaegar, mounted on a stallion as black as his armor. Fire glimmered red through the narrow eye slit of his helm. "The last dragon," Ser Jorah's voice whispered faintly. "The last, the last." Dany lifted his polished black visor. The face within was her own.

After that, for a long time, there was only the pain, the fire within her, and the whisperings of stars.

She woke to the taste of ashes.

"No," she moaned, "no, please."

"*Khaleesi?*" Jhiqui hovered over her, a frightened doe.

The tent was drenched in shadow, still and close. Flakes of ash drifted upward from a brazier, and Dany followed them with her eyes through the smoke hole above. *Flying*, she thought. *I had wings, I was flying.* But it was only a dream. "Help me," she whispered, struggling to rise. "Bring me ..." Her voice was raw as a wound, and she could not think what she wanted. Why did she hurt so much? It was as if her body had been torn to pieces and remade from the scraps. "I want ..."

"Yes, *Khaleesi.*" Quick as that Jhiqui was gone, bolting from the tent, shouting. Dany needed ... something ... someone ... what? It was important, she knew. It was the only thing in the world that mattered. She rolled onto her side and got an elbow under her, fighting the blanket tangled about her legs. It was so hard to move. The world swam dizzily. *I have to ...*

They found her on the carpet, crawling toward her dragon eggs. Ser Jorah Mormont lifted her in his arms and carried her back to her sleeping silks, while she struggled feebly against him. Over his shoulder she saw her three handmaids, Jhogo with his little wisp of mustache, and the flat broad face of Mirri Maz Duur. "I must," she tried to tell them, "I have to . . ."

". . . sleep, Princess," Ser Jorah said.

"No," Dany said. "Please. Please."

"Yes." He covered her with silk, though she was burning. "Sleep and grow strong again, *Khaleesi*. Come back to us." And then Mirri Maz Duur was there, the *maegi*, tipping a cup against her lips. She tasted sour milk, and something else, something thick and bitter. Warm liquid ran down her chin. Somehow she swallowed. The tent grew dimmer, and sleep took her again. This time she did not dream. She floated, serene and at peace, on a black sea that knew no shore.

After a time—a night, a day, a year, she could not say—she woke again. The tent was dark, its silken walls flapping like wings when the wind gusted outside. This time Dany did not attempt to rise. "Irri," she called, "Jhiqui. Doreah." They were there at once. "My throat is dry," she said, "so dry," and they brought her water. It was warm and flat, yet Dany drank it eagerly, and sent Jhiqui for more. Irri dampened a soft cloth and stroked her brow. "I have been sick," Dany said. The Dothraki girl nodded. "How long?" The cloth was soothing, but Irri seemed so sad, it frightened her. "*Long*," she whispered. When Jhiqui returned with more water, Mirri Maz Duur came with her, eyes heavy from sleep. "Drink," she said, lifting Dany's head to the cup once more, but this time it was only wine. Sweet, sweet wine. Dany drank, and lay back, listening to the soft sound of her own breathing. She could feel the heaviness in her limbs, as sleep crept in to fill her up once more. "Bring me . . ." she murmured, her voice slurred and drowsy. "Bring . . . I want to hold . . ."

"Yes?" the *maegi* asked. "What is it you wish, *Khaleesi*?"

"Bring me . . . egg . . . dragon's egg . . . please . . ." Her lashes turned to lead, and she was too weary to hold them up.

When she woke the third time, a shaft of golden sunlight was pouring through the smoke hole of the tent, and her arms were wrapped around a dragon's egg. It was the pale one, its scales the color of butter cream, veined with whorls of gold and bronze, and Dany could feel the heat of it. Beneath her bedsilks, a fine sheen of perspiration covered her bare skin. *Dragondew,* she thought. Her fingers trailed lightly across the surface of the shell, tracing the wisps of gold, and deep in the stone she felt something twist and stretch in response. It did not frighten her. All her fear was gone, burned away.

Dany touched her brow. Under the film of sweat, her skin was cool to the touch, her fever gone. She made herself sit. There was a moment of dizziness, and the deep ache between her thighs. Yet she felt strong. Her maids came running at the sound of her voice. "Water," she told them, "a flagon of water, cold as you can find it. And fruit, I think. Dates."

"As you say, *Khaleesi.*"

"I want Ser Jorah," she said, standing. Jhiqui brought a sandsilk robe and draped it over her shoulders. "And a warm bath, and Mirri Maz Duur, and . . ." Memory came back to her all at once, and she faltered. "Khal Drogo," she forced herself to say, watching their faces with dread. "Is he—?"

"The *khal* lives," Irri answered quietly . . . yet Dany saw a darkness in her eyes when she said the words, and no sooner had she spoken than she rushed away to fetch water.

She turned to Doreah. "Tell me."

"I . . . I shall bring Ser Jorah," the Lysene girl said, bowing her head and fleeing the tent.

Jhiqui would have run as well, but Dany caught her by the wrist and held her captive. "What is it? I must know. Drogo . . . and my child." Why had she not remembered the child until now? "My son . . . Rhaego . . . where is he? I want him."

Her handmaid lowered her eyes. "The boy . . . he did not live, *Khaleesi.*" Her voice was a frightened whisper.

Dany released her wrist. *My son is dead,* she thought as Jhiqui left the tent. She had known somehow. She had known since she woke the first time to Jhiqui's tears. No, she had known *before* she woke. Her dream came back to her, sudden and vivid, and she remembered the tall man with the copper skin and long silver-gold braid, bursting into flame.

She should weep, she knew, yet her eyes were dry as

ash. She had wept in her dream, and the tears had turned to steam on her cheeks. *All the grief has been burned out of me,* she told herself. She felt sad, and yet . . . she could feel Rhaego receding from her, as if he had never been.

Ser Jorah and Mirri Maz Duur entered a few moments later, and found Dany standing over the other dragon's eggs, the two still in their chest. It seemed to her that they felt as hot as the one she had slept with, which was passing strange. "Ser Jorah, come here," she said. She took his hand and placed it on the black egg with the scarlet swirls. "What do you feel?"

"Shell, hard as rock." The knight was wary. "Scales."

"Heat?"

"No. Cold stone." He took his hand away. "Princess, are you well? Should you be up, weak as you are?"

"Weak? I am strong, Jorah." To please him, she reclined on a pile of cushions. "Tell me how my child died."

"He never lived, my princess. The women say . . ." He faltered, and Dany saw how the flesh hung loose on him, and the way he limped when he moved.

"Tell me. Tell me what the women say."

He turned his face away. His eyes were haunted. "They say the child was . . ."

She waited, but Ser Jorah could not say it. His face grew dark with shame. He looked half a corpse himself.

"Monstrous," Mirri Maz Duur finished for him. The knight was a powerful man, yet Dany understood in that moment that the *maegi* was stronger, and crueler, and infinitely more dangerous. "Twisted. I drew him forth myself. He was scaled like a lizard, blind, with the stub of a tail and small leather wings like the wings of a bat. When I touched him, the flesh sloughed off the bone, and inside he was full of graveworms and the stink of corruption. He had been dead for years."

Darkness, Dany thought. The terrible darkness sweeping up behind to devour her. If she looked back she was lost. "My son was alive and strong when Ser Jorah carried me into this tent," she said. "I could feel him kicking, fighting to be born."

"That may be as it may be," answered Mirri Maz

Duur, "yet the creature that came forth from your womb was as I said. Death was in that tent, *Khaleesi*."

"Only shadows," Ser Jorah husked, but Dany could hear the doubt in his voice. "I saw, *maegi*. I saw you, alone, dancing with the shadows."

"The grave casts long shadows, Iron Lord," Mirri said. "Long and dark, and in the end no light can hold them back."

Ser Jorah had killed her son, Dany knew. He had done what he did for love and loyalty, yet he had carried her into a place no living man should go and fed her baby to the darkness. He knew it too; the grey face, the hollow eyes, the limp. "The shadows have touched you too, Ser Jorah," she told him. The knight made no reply. Dany turned to the godswife. "You warned me that only death could pay for life. I thought you meant the horse."

"No," Mirri Maz Duur said. "That was a lie you told yourself. You knew the price."

Had she? Had she? *If I look back I am lost.* "The price was paid," Dany said. "The horse, my child, Quaro and Qotho, Haggo and Cohollo. The price was paid and paid and paid." She rose from her cushions. "Where is Khal Drogo? Show him to me, godswife, *maegi*, bloodmage, whatever you are. Show me Khal Drogo. Show me what I bought with my son's life."

"As you command, *Khaleesi*," the old woman said. "Come, I will take you to him."

Dany was weaker than she knew. Ser Jorah slipped an arm around her and helped her stand. "Time enough for this later, my princess," he said quietly.

"I would see him now, Ser Jorah."

After the dimness of the tent, the world outside was blinding bright. The sun burned like molten gold, and the land was seared and empty. Her handmaids waited with fruit and wine and water, and Jhogo moved close to help Ser Jorah support her. Aggo and Rakharo stood behind. The glare of sun on sand made it hard to see more, until Dany raised her hand to shade her eyes. She saw the ashes of a fire, a few score horses milling listlessly and searching for a bite of grass, a scattering of tents and bedrolls. A small crowd of children had gathered to watch her, and beyond she glimpsed women going about their work, and withered old men staring at the flat blue sky with tired eyes, swatting feebly at bloodflies. A count might show a hundred people, no more. Where the other forty thousand had made their camp, only the wind and dust lived now.

"Drogo's *khalasar* is gone," she said.

"A *khal* who cannot ride is no *khal*," said Jhogo.

"The Dothraki follow only the strong," Ser Jorah said. "I am sorry, my princess. There was no way to hold them. Ko Pono left first, naming himself Khal Pono, and many followed him. Jhaqo was not long to do the same. The rest slipped away night by night, in large bands and small. There are a dozen new *khalasars* on the Dothraki sea, where once there was only Drogo's."

"The old remain," said Aggo. "The frightened, the weak, and the sick. And we who swore. We remain."

"They took Khal Drogo's herds, *Khaleesi*," Rakharo said. "We were too few to stop them. It is the right of the strong to take from the weak. They took many slaves as well, the *khal*'s and yours, yet they left some few."

"Eroeh?" asked Dany, remembering the frightened child she had saved outside the city of the Lamb Men.

"Mago seized her, who is Khal Jhaqo's bloodrider now," said Jhogo. "He mounted her high and low and gave her to his *khal*, and Jhaqo gave her to his other bloodriders. They were six. When they were done with her, they cut her throat."

"It was her fate, *Khaleesi*," said Aggo.

If I look back I am lost. "It was a cruel fate," Dany said, "yet not so cruel as Mago's will be. I promise you that, by the old gods and the new, by the lamb god and the horse god and every god that lives. I swear it by the Mother of Mountains and the Womb of the World. Before I am done with them, Mago and Ko Jhaqo will plead for the mercy they showed Eroeh."

The Dothraki exchanged uncertain glances. "*Khaleesi*," the handmaid Irri explained, as if to a child, "Jhaqo is a *khal* now, with twenty thousand riders at his back."

She lifted her head. "And I am Daenerys Stormborn, Daenerys of House Targaryen, of the blood of Aegon the Conqueror and Maegor the Cruel and old Valyria before them. I am the dragon's daughter, and I swear to you, these men will die screaming. Now bring me to Khal Drogo."

He was lying on the bare red earth, staring up at the sun.

A dozen bloodflies had settled on his body, though he did not seem to feel them. Dany brushed them away and knelt beside him. His eyes were wide open but did not see, and she knew at once that he was blind. When she whispered his name, he did not seem to hear. The wound on his breast was as healed as it would ever be, the scar that covered it grey and red and hideous.

"Why is he out here alone, in the sun?" she asked them.

"He seems to like the warmth, Princess," Ser Jorah said. "His eyes follow the sun, though he does not see it. He can walk after a fashion. He will go where you lead him, but no farther. He will eat if you put food in his mouth, drink if you dribble water on his lips."

Dany kissed her sun-and-stars gently on the brow, and stood to face Mirri Maz Duur. "Your spells are costly, *maegi*."

"He lives," said Mirri Maz Duur. "You asked for life. You paid for life."

"This is not life, for one who was as Drogo was. His life was laughter, and meat roasting over a firepit, and a horse between his legs. His life was an *arakh* in his hand and his bells ringing in his hair as he rode to meet an enemy. His life was his bloodriders, and me, and the son I was to give him."

Mirri Maz Duur made no reply.

"When will he be as he was?" Dany demanded.

"When the sun rises in the west and sets in the east," said Mirri Maz Duur. "When the seas go dry and mountains blow in the wind like leaves. When your womb quickens again, and you bear a living child. Then he will return, and not before."

Dany gestured at Ser Jorah and the others. "Leave us. I would speak with this *maegi* alone." Mormont and the Dothraki withdrew. "You *knew*," Dany said when they were gone. She ached, inside and out, but her fury gave her strength. "You knew what I was buying, and you knew the price, and yet you let me pay it."

"It was wrong of them to burn my temple," the heavy, flat-nosed woman said placidly. "That angered the Great Shepherd."

"This was no god's work," Dany said coldly. *If I look back I am lost.* "You cheated me. You murdered my child within me."

"The stallion who mounts the world will burn no cities now. His *khalasar* shall trample no nations into dust."

"I spoke for you," she said, anguished. "I saved you."

"*Saved* me?" The Lhazareen woman spat. "Three riders had taken me, not as a man takes a woman but from behind, as a dog takes a bitch. The fourth was in me when you rode past. How then did you save me? I saw my god's house burn, where I had healed good men beyond counting. My home they burned as well, and in the street I saw piles of heads. I saw the head of a baker who made my bread. I saw the head of a boy I had saved from deadeye fever, only three moons past. I heard children crying as the riders drove them off with their whips. Tell me again what you saved."

"Your life."

Mirri Maz Duur laughed cruelly. "Look to your *khal* and see what life is worth, when all the rest is gone."

Dany called out for the men of her *khas* and bid them take Mirri Maz Duur and bind her hand and foot, but the *maegi* smiled at her as they carried her off, as if they shared a secret. A word, and Dany could have her head off . . . yet then what would she have? A head? If life was worthless, what was death?

They led Khal Drogo back to her tent, and Dany commanded them to fill a tub, and this time there was no blood in the water. She bathed him herself, washing the dirt and the dust from his arms and chest, cleaning his face with a soft cloth, soaping his long black hair and combing the knots and tangles from it till it shone again as she remembered. It was well past dark before she was done, and Dany was exhausted. She stopped for drink and food, but it was all she could do to nibble at a fig and keep down a mouthful of water. Sleep would have been a release, but she had slept enough . . . too long, in truth. She owed this night to Drogo, for all the nights that had been, and yet might be.

The memory of their first ride was with her when she led him out into the darkness, for the Dothraki believed that all things of importance in a man's life must be done beneath the open sky. She told herself that there were powers stronger than hatred, and spells older and truer than any the *maegi* had learned in Asshai. The night was black and moonless, but overhead a million stars burned bright. She took that for an omen.

No soft blanket of grass welcomed them here, only the hard dusty ground, bare and strewn with stones. No trees stirred in the wind, and there was no stream to soothe her fears with the gentle music of water. Dany told herself that the stars would be enough. "Remember, Drogo," she whispered. "Remember our first ride together, the day we wed. Remember the night we made Rhaego, with the *khalasar* all around us and your eyes on my face. Remember how cool and clean the water was in the Womb of the World. Remember, my sun-and-stars. Remember, and come back to me."

The birth had left her too raw and torn to take him inside of her, as she would have wanted, but Doreah had taught her other ways. Dany used her hands, her mouth, her breasts. She raked him with her nails and covered him with kisses and whispered and prayed and told him stories, and by the end she had bathed him with her tears. Yet Drogo did not feel, or speak, or rise.

And when the bleak dawn broke over an empty horizon, Dany knew that he was truly lost to her. "When the sun rises in the west and sets in the east," she said sadly. "When the seas go dry and mountains blow in the wind like leaves. When my womb quickens again, and I bear a living child. Then you will return, my sun-and-stars, and not before."

Never, the darkness cried, *never never never.*

Inside the tent Dany found a cushion, soft silk stuffed with feathers. She clutched it to her breasts as she walked back out to Drogo, to her sun-and-stars. *If I look back I am lost.* It hurt even to walk, and she wanted to sleep, to sleep and not to dream.

She knelt, kissed Drogo on the lips, and pressed the cushion down across his face.

TYRION

"They have my son," Tywin Lannister said.

"They do, my lord." The messenger's voice was dulled by exhaustion. On the breast of his torn surcoat, the brindled boar of Crakehall was half-obscured by dried blood.

One of your sons, Tyrion thought. He took a sip of wine and said not a word, thinking of Jaime. When he lifted his arm, pain shot through his elbow, reminding him of his own brief taste of battle. He loved his brother, but he would not have wanted to be with him in the Whispering Wood for all the gold in Casterly Rock.

His lord father's assembled captains and bannermen had fallen very quiet as the courier told his tale. The only sound was the crackle and hiss of the log burning in the hearth at the end of the long, drafty common room.

After the hardships of the long relentless drive south, the prospect of even a single night in an inn had cheered Tyrion mightily . . . though he rather wished it had not been *this* inn again, with all its memories. His father had set a grueling pace, and it had taken its toll. Men wounded in the battle kept up as best they could or were abandoned to fend for themselves. Every morning they left a few more by the roadside, men who went to sleep never to wake. Every afternoon a few more collapsed along the way. And every evening a few more deserted, stealing off into the dusk. Tyrion had been half-tempted to go with them.

He had been upstairs, enjoying the comfort of a feather-bed and the warmth of Shae's body beside him, when his squire had woken him to say that a rider had arrived with dire news of Riverrun. So it had all been for nothing. The rush south, the endless forced marches, the bodies left beside the road . . . all for naught. Robb Stark had reached Riverrun days and days ago.

"How could this happen?" Ser Harys Swyft moaned. "*How?* Even after the Whispering Wood, you had Riverrun ringed in iron, surrounded by a great host . . . what madness made Ser Jaime decide to split his men into three separate camps? Surely he knew how vulnerable that would leave them?"

Better than you, you chinless craven, Tyrion thought. Jaime might have lost Riverrun, but it angered him to hear his brother slandered by the likes of Swyft, a shameless lickspittle whose greatest accomplishment was marrying his equally chinless daughter to Ser Kevan, and thereby attaching himself to the Lannisters.

"I would have done the same," his uncle responded, a good deal more calmly than Tyrion might have. "You have never seen Riverrun, Ser Harys, or you would know that Jaime had little choice in the matter. The castle is situated at the end of the point of land where the Tumblestone flows into the Red Fork of the Trident. The rivers form two sides of a triangle, and when danger threatens, the Tullys open their sluice gates upstream to create a wide moat on the third side, turning Riverrun into an island. The walls rise sheer from the water, and from their towers the defenders have a commanding view of the opposite shores for many leagues around. To cut off all the approaches, a besieger must needs place one camp north of the Tumblestone, one south of the Red Fork, and a third between the rivers, west of the moat. There is no other way, none."

"Ser Kevan speaks truly, my lords," the courier said. "We'd built palisades of sharpened stakes around the camps, yet it was not enough, not with no warning and the rivers cutting us off from each other. They came down on the north camp first. No one was expecting an attack. Marq Piper had been raiding our supply trains, but he had no more than fifty men. Ser Jaime had gone out to deal with them the night before . . . well, with what we *thought* was them. We were told the Stark host was east of the Green Fork, marching south . . ."

"And your outriders?" Ser Gregor Clegane's face might have been hewn from rock. The fire in the hearth gave a somber orange cast to his skin and put deep shadows in the hollows of his eyes. "They saw nothing? They gave you no warning?"

The bloodstained messenger shook his head. "Our outriders had been vanishing. Marq Piper's work, we thought. The ones who did come back had seen nothing."

"A man who sees nothing has no use for his eyes," the Mountain declared. "Cut them out and give them to your next outrider. Tell him you hope that four eyes might see better than two . . . and if not, the man after him will have six."

Lord Tywin Lannister turned his face to study Ser Gregor. Tyrion saw a glimmer of gold as the light shone off his father's pupils, but he could not have said whether the look was one of approval or disgust. Lord Tywin was oft quiet in council, preferring to listen before he spoke, a habit Tyrion himself tried to emulate. Yet this silence was uncharacteristic even for him, and his wine was untouched.

"You said they came at night," Ser Kevan prompted.

The man gave a weary nod. "The Blackfish led the van, cutting down our sentries and clearing away the palisades for the main assault. By the time our men knew what was happening, riders were pouring over the ditch banks and galloping through the camp with swords and torches in hand. I was sleeping in the west camp, between the rivers. When we heard the fighting and saw the tents being fired, Lord Brax led us to the rafts and we tried to pole across, but the current pushed us downstream and the Tullys started flinging rocks at us with the catapults on their walls. I saw one raft smashed to kindling and three others overturned, men swept into the river and drowned . . . and those who did make it across found the Starks waiting for them on the riverbanks."

Ser Flement Brax wore a silver-and-purple tabard and the look of a man who cannot comprehend what he has just heard. "My lord father—"

"Sorry, my lord," the messenger said. "Lord Brax was clad in plate-and-mail when his raft overturned. He was very gallant."

He was a fool, Tyrion thought, swirling his cup and staring down into the winy depths. Crossing a river at night on a crude raft, wearing armor, with an enemy waiting on the other side—if that was gallantry, he would take cowardice every time. He wondered if Lord Brax had felt especially gallant as the weight of his steel pulled him under the black water.

"The camp between the rivers was overrun as well," the messenger was saying. "While we were trying to cross, more Starks swept in from the west, two columns of armored horse. I saw Lord Umber's giant-in-chains and the Mallister eagle, but it was the boy who led them, with a monstrous wolf running at his side. I wasn't there to see, but it's said the beast killed four men and ripped apart a dozen horses. Our spearmen formed up a shieldwall and held against their first charge, but when the Tullys saw them engaged, they opened the gates of Riverrun and Tytos Blackwood led a sortie across the drawbridge and took them in the rear."

"Gods save us," Lord Lefford swore.

"Greatjon Umber fired the siege towers we were building, and Lord Blackwood found Ser Edmure Tully in chains among the other captives, and made off with them all. Our south camp was under the command of Ser Forley Prester. He retreated in good order when he saw that the other camps were lost, with two thousand spears and as many bowmen, but the Tyroshi sellsword who led his freeriders struck his banners and went over to the foe."

"Curse the man." His uncle Kevan sounded more angry than surprised. "I warned Jaime not to trust that one. A man who fights for coin is loyal only to his purse."

Lord Tywin wove his fingers together under his chin. Only his eyes moved as he listened. His bristling golden side-whiskers framed a face so still it might have been a mask, but Tyrion could see tiny beads of sweat dappling his father's shaven head.

"How could it *happen*?" Ser Harys Swyft wailed again.

"Ser Jaime taken, the siege broken . . . this is a *catastrophe*!"

Ser Addam Marbrand said, "I am sure we are all grateful to you for pointing out the obvious, Ser Harys. The question is, what shall we do about it?"

"What *can* we do? Jaime's host is all slaughtered or taken or put to flight, and the Starks and the Tullys sit squarely across our line of supply. We are cut off from the west! They can march on Casterly Rock if they so choose, and what's to stop them? My lords, we are beaten. We must sue for peace."

"Peace?" Tyrion swirled his wine thoughtfully, took a deep draft, and hurled his empty cup to the floor, where it shattered into a thousand pieces. "There's your peace, Ser Harys. My sweet nephew broke it for good and all when he decided to ornament the Red Keep with Lord Eddard's head. You'll have an easier time drinking wine from that cup than you will convincing Robb Stark to make peace *now*. He's *winning* . . . or hadn't you noticed?"

"Two battles do not make a war," Ser Addam insisted. "We are far from lost. I should welcome the chance to try my own steel against this Stark boy."

"Perhaps they would consent to a truce, and allow us to trade our prisoners for theirs," offered Lord Lefford.

"Unless they trade three-for-one, we still come out light on those scales," Tyrion said acidly. "And what are we to offer for my brother? Lord Eddard's rotting head?"

"I had heard that Queen Cersei has the Hand's daughters," Lefford said hopefully. "If we give the lad his sisters back . . ."

Ser Addam snorted disdainfully. "He would have to be an utter ass to trade Jaime Lannister's life for two girls."

"Then we must ransom Ser Jaime, whatever it costs," Lord Lefford said.

Tyrion rolled his eyes. "If the Starks feel the need for gold, they can melt down Jaime's armor."

"If we ask for a truce, they will think us weak," Ser Addam argued. "We should march on them at once."

"Surely our friends at court could be prevailed upon to join us with fresh troops," said Ser Harys. "And someone might return to Casterly Rock to raise a new host."

Lord Tywin Lannister rose to his feet. *"They have my*

son," he said once more, in a voice that cut through the babble like a sword through suet. "Leave me. All of you."

Ever the soul of obedience, Tyrion rose to depart with the rest, but his father gave him a look. "Not you, Tyrion. Remain. And you as well, Kevan. The rest of you, out."

Tyrion eased himself back onto the bench, startled into speechlessness. Ser Kevan crossed the room to the wine casks. "Uncle," Tyrion called, "if you would be so kind—".

"Here." His father offered him his cup, the wine untouched.

Now Tyrion truly *was* nonplussed. He drank.

Lord Tywin seated himself. "You have the right of it about Stark. Alive, we might have used Lord Eddard to forge a peace with Winterfell and Riverrun, a peace that would have given us the time we need to deal with Robert's brothers. Dead . . ." His hand curled into a fist. "Madness. Rank madness."

"Joff's only a boy," Tyrion pointed out. "At his age, I committed a few follies of my own."

His father gave him a sharp look. "I suppose we ought to be grateful that he has not yet married a whore."

Tyrion sipped at his wine, wondering how Lord Tywin would look if he flung the cup in his face.

"Our position is worse than you know," his father went on. "It would seem we have a new king."

Ser Kevan looked poleaxed. "A new—*who?* What have they done to Joffrey?"

The faintest flicker of distaste played across Lord Tywin's thin lips. "Nothing . . . yet. My grandson still sits the Iron Throne, but the eunuch has heard whispers from the south. Renly Baratheon wed Margaery Tyrell at Highgarden this fortnight past, and now he has claimed the crown. The bride's father and brothers have bent the knee and sworn him their swords."

"Those are grave tidings." When Ser Kevan frowned, the furrows in his brow grew deep as canyons.

"My daughter commands us to ride for King's Landing at once, to defend the Red Keep against King Renly and the Knight of Flowers." His mouth tightened. "*Commands* us, mind you. In the name of the king and council."

"How is King Joffrey taking the news?" Tyrion asked with a certain black amusement.

"Cersei has not seen fit to tell him yet," Lord Tywin said. "She fears he might insist on marching against Renly himself."

"With what army?" Tyrion asked. "You don't plan to give him *this* one, I hope?"

"He talks of leading the City Watch," Lord Tywin said.

"If he takes the Watch, he'll leave the city undefended," Ser Kevan said. "And with Lord Stannis on Dragonstone . . ."

"Yes." Lord Tywin looked down at his son. "I had thought you were the one made for motley, Tyrion, but it would appear that I was wrong."

"Why, Father," said Tyrion, "that almost sounds like praise." He leaned forward intently. "What of Stannis? He's the elder, not Renly. How does he feel about his brother's claim?"

His father frowned. "I have felt from the beginning that Stannis was a greater danger than all the others combined. Yet he does nothing. Oh, Varys hears his whispers. Stannis is building ships, Stannis is hiring sellswords, Stannis is bringing a shadowbinder from Asshai. What does it mean? Is any of it true?" He gave an irritated shrug. "Kevan, bring us the map."

Ser Kevan did as he was bid. Lord Tywin unrolled the leather, smoothing it flat. "Jaime has left us in a bad way. Roose Bolton and the remnants of his host are north of us. Our enemies hold the Twins and Moat Cailin. Robb Stark sits to the west, so we cannot retreat to Lannisport and the Rock unless we choose to give battle. Jaime is taken, and his army for all purposes has ceased to exist. Thoros of Myr and Beric Dondarrion continue to plague our foraging parties. To our east we have the Arryns, Stannis Baratheon sits on Dragonstone, and in the south Highgarden and Storm's End are calling their banners."

Tyrion smiled crookedly. "Take heart, Father. At least Rhaegar Targaryen is still dead."

"I had hoped you might have more to offer us than japes, Tyrion," Lord Tywin Lannister said.

Ser Kevan frowned over the map, forehead creasing. "Robb Stark will have Edmure Tully and the lords of the Trident with him now. Their combined power may ex-

ceed our own. And with Roose Bolton behind us . . .
Tywin, if we remain here, I fear we might be caught between three armies."

"I have no intention of remaining here. We must finish
our business with young Lord Stark before Renly
Baratheon can march from Highgarden. Bolton does not
concern me. He is a wary man, and we made him warier
on the Green Fork. He will be slow to give pursuit. So
. . . on the morrow, we make for Harrenhal. Kevan, I
want Ser Addam's outriders to screen our movements.
Give him as many men as he requires, and send them out
in groups of four. I will have no vanishings."

"As you say, my lord, but . . . why Harrenhal? That
is a grim, unlucky place. Some call it cursed."

"Let them," Lord Tywin said. "Unleash Ser Gregor and
send him before us with his reavers. Send forth Vargo
Hoat and his freeriders as well, and Ser Amory Lorch.
Each is to have three hundred horse. Tell them I want to
see the riverlands afire from the Gods Eye to the Red
Fork."

"They will burn, my lord," Ser Kevan said, rising. "I
shall give the commands." He bowed and made for the
door.

When they were alone, Lord Tywin glanced at Tyrion.
"Your savages might relish a bit of rapine. Tell them they
may ride with Vargo Hoat and plunder as they like—
goods, stock, women, they may take what they want and
burn the rest."

"Telling Shagga and Timett how to pillage is like telling a rooster how to crow," Tyrion commented, "but I
should prefer to keep them with me." Uncouth and unruly they might be, yet the wildlings were *his*, and he
trusted them more than any of his father's men. He was
not about to hand them over.

"Then you had best learn to control them. I will not
have the city plundered."

"The city?" Tyrion was lost. "What city would that
be?"

"King's Landing. I am sending you to court."

It was the last thing Tyrion Lannister would ever have
anticipated. He reached for his wine, and considered for a
moment as he sipped. "And what am I to do there?"

"Rule," his father said curtly.

Tyrion hooted with laughter. "My sweet sister might have a word or two to say about that!"

"Let her say what she likes. Her son needs to be taken in hand before he ruins us all. I blame those jackanapes on the council—our friend Petyr, the venerable Grand Maester, and that cockless wonder Lord Varys. What sort of counsel are they giving Joffrey when he lurches from one folly to the next? Whose notion was it to make this Janos Slynt a lord? The man's father was a *butcher*, and they grant him Harrenhal. *Harrenhal*, that was the seat of kings! Not that he will ever set foot inside it, if I have a say. I am told he took a bloody spear for his sigil. A bloody cleaver would have been my choice." His father had not raised his voice, yet Tyrion could see the anger in the gold of his eyes. "And dismissing Selmy, where was the sense in that? Yes, the man was old, but the name of Barristan the Bold still has meaning in the realm. He lent honor to any man he served. Can anyone say the same of the Hound? You feed your dog bones under the table, you do not seat him beside you on the high bench." He pointed a finger at Tyrion's face. "If Cersei cannot curb the boy, you must. And if these councillors are playing us false . . ."

Tyrion knew. "Spikes," he sighed. "Heads. Walls."

"I see you have taken a few lessons from me."

"More than you know, Father," Tyrion answered quietly. He finished his wine and set the cup aside, thoughtful. A part of him was more pleased than he cared to admit. Another part was remembering the battle upriver, and wondering if he was being sent to hold the left again. "Why me?" he asked, cocking his head to one side. "Why not my uncle? Why not Ser Addam or Ser Flement or Lord Serrett? Why not a . . . *bigger* man?"

Lord Tywin rose abruptly. "You are my son."

That was when he knew. *You have given him up for lost,* he thought. *You bloody bastard, you think Jaime's good as dead, so I'm all you have left.* Tyrion wanted to slap him, to spit in his face, to draw his dagger and cut the heart out of him and see if it was made of old hard gold, the way the smallfolks said. Yet he sat there, silent and still.

The shards of the broken cup crunched beneath his father's heels as Lord Tywin crossed the room. "One last thing," he said at the door. "You will not take the whore to court."

Tyrion sat alone in the common room for a long while after his father was gone. Finally he climbed the steps to his cozy garret beneath the bell tower. The ceiling was low, but that was scarcely a drawback for a dwarf. From the window, he could see the gibbet his father had erected in the yard. The innkeep's body turned slowly on its rope whenever the night wind gusted. Her flesh had grown as thin and ragged as Lannister hopes.

Shae murmured sleepily and rolled toward him when he sat on the edge of the featherbed. He slid his hand under the blanket and cupped a soft breast, and her eyes opened. "M'lord," she said with a drowsy smile.

When he felt her nipple stiffen, Tyrion kissed her. "I have a mind to take you to King's Landing, sweetling," he whispered.

JON

The mare whickered softly as Jon Snow tightened the cinch. "Easy, sweet lady," he said in a soft voice, quieting her with a touch. Wind whispered through the stable, a cold dead breath on his face, but Jon paid it no mind. He strapped his roll to the saddle, his scarred fingers stiff and clumsy. "Ghost," he called softly, "to me." And the wolf was there, eyes like embers.

"Jon, please. You must not do this."

He mounted, the reins in his hand, and wheeled the horse around to face the night. Samwell Tarly stood in the stable door, a full moon peering over his shoulder. He threw a giant's shadow, immense and black. "Get out of my way, Sam."

"Jon, you *can't*," Sam said. "I won't let you."

"I would sooner not hurt you," Jon told him. "Move aside, Sam, or I'll ride you down."

"You won't. You have to listen to me. Please . . ."

Jon put his spurs to horseflesh, and the mare bolted for the door. For an instant Sam stood his ground, his face as round and pale as the moon behind him, his mouth a widening O of surprise. At the last moment, when they were almost on him, he jumped aside as Jon had known he would, stumbled, and fell. The mare leapt over him, out into the night.

Jon raised the hood of his heavy cloak and gave the horse her head. Castle Black was silent and still as he rode out, with Ghost racing at his side. Men watched from the Wall behind him, he knew, but their eyes were turned north, not south. No one would see him go, no one but Sam Tarly, struggling back to his feet in the dust of the old stables. He hoped Sam hadn't hurt himself, falling like that. He was so heavy and so ungainly, it would be just like him to break a wrist or twist his ankle getting out of the way. "I warned him," Jon said aloud. "It was nothing to do with him, anyway." He flexed his burned hand as he rode, opening and closing the scarred fingers. They still pained him, but it felt good to have the wrappings off.

Moonlight silvered the hills as he followed the twisting ribbon of the kingsroad. He needed to get as far from the Wall as he could before they realized he was gone. On the morrow he would leave the road and strike out overland through field and bush and stream to throw off pursuit, but for the moment speed was more important than deception. It was not as though they would not guess where he was going.

The Old Bear was accustomed to rise at first light, so Jon had until dawn to put as many leagues as he could between him and the Wall . . . *if* Sam Tarly did not betray him. The fat boy was dutiful and easily frightened, but he loved Jon like a brother. If questioned, Sam would doubtless tell them the truth, but Jon could not imagine him braving the guards in front of the King's Tower to wake Mormont from sleep.

When Jon did not appear to fetch the Old Bear's breakfast from the kitchen, they'd look in his cell and find Longclaw on the bed. It had been hard to abandon it, but Jon was not so lost to honor as to take it with him. Even Jorah Mormont had not done that, when he fled in disgrace. Doubtless Lord Mormont would find someone more worthy of the blade. Jon felt bad when he thought of the old man. He knew his desertion would be salt in the still-raw wound of his son's disgrace. That seemed a poor way to repay him for his trust, but it couldn't be helped.

No matter what he did, Jon felt as though he were betraying someone.

Even now, he did not know if he was doing the honorable thing. The southron had it easier. They had their septons to talk to, someone to tell them the gods' will and help sort out right from wrong. But the Starks worshiped the old gods, the nameless gods, and if the heart trees heard, they did not speak.

When the last lights of Castle Black vanished behind him, Jon slowed his mare to a walk. He had a long journey ahead and only the one horse to see him through. There were holdfasts and farming villages along the road south where he might be able to trade the mare for a fresh mount when he needed one, but not if she were injured or blown.

He would need to find new clothes soon; most like, he'd need to steal them. He was clad in black from head to heel; high leather riding boots, roughspun breeches and tunic, sleeveless leather jerkin, and heavy wool cloak. His longsword and dagger were sheathed in black moleskin, and the hauberk and coif in his saddlebag were black ringmail. Any bit of it could mean his death if he were taken. A stranger wearing black was viewed with cold suspicion in every village and holdfast north of the Neck, and men would soon be watching for him. Once Maester Aemon's ravens took flight, Jon knew he would find no safe haven. Not even at Winterfell. Bran might want to let him in, but Maester Luwin had better sense. He would bar the gates and send Jon away, as he should. Better not to call there at all.

Yet he saw the castle clear in his mind's eye, as if he had left it only yesterday; the towering granite walls, the Great Hall with its smells of smoke and dog and roasting meat, his father's solar, the turret room where he had slept. Part of him wanted nothing so much as to hear Bran laugh again, to sup on one of Gage's beef-and-bacon pies, to listen to Old Nan tell her tales of the children of the forest and Florian the Fool.

But he had not left the Wall for that; he had left because he was after all his father's son, and Robb's brother. The gift of a sword, even a sword as fine as Longclaw, did not make him a Mormont. Nor was he Aemon Targaryen. Three times the old man had chosen, and three times he had chosen honor, but that was him. Even now, Jon could not decide whether the maester had stayed because he was weak and craven, or because he was strong and true. Yet he understood what the old man had meant, about the pain of choosing; he understood that all too well.

Tyrion Lannister had claimed that most men would rather deny a hard truth than face it, but Jon was done with denials. He was who he was; Jon Snow, bastard and oathbreaker, motherless, friendless, and damned. For the rest of his life—however long that might be—he would be condemned to be an outsider, the silent man standing in the shadows who dares not speak his true name. Wherever he might go throughout the Seven Kingdoms, he would need to live a lie, lest every man's hand be raised against him. But it made no matter, so long as he lived long enough to take his place by his brother's side and help avenge his father.

He remembered Robb as he had last seen him, standing in the yard with snow melting in his auburn hair. Jon would have to come to him in secret, disguised. He tried to imagine the look on Robb's face when he revealed himself. His brother would shake his head and smile, and he'd say . . . he'd say . . .

He could not see the smile. Hard as he tried, he could not see it. He found himself thinking of the deserter his father had beheaded the day they'd found the direwolves. "You said the words," Lord Eddard had told him. "You took a vow, before your brothers, before the old gods and the new." Desmond and Fat Tom had dragged the man to the stump. Bran's eyes had been wide as saucers, and Jon had to remind him to keep his pony in hand. He remembered the look on Father's face when Theon Greyjoy brought forth Ice, the spray of blood on the snow, the way Theon had kicked the head when it came rolling at his feet.

He wondered what Lord Eddard might have done if the deserter had been his brother Benjen instead of that ragged stranger. Would it have been any different? It must, surely, *surely* . . . and Robb would welcome him, for a certainty. He *had* to, or else . . .

It did not bear thinking about. Pain throbbed, deep in his fingers, as he clutched the reins. Jon put his heels into his horse and broke into a gallop, racing down the kings-

road, as if to outrun his doubts. Jon was not afraid of
death, but he did not want to die like that, trussed and
bound and beheaded like a common brigand. If he must
perish, let it be with a sword in his hand, fighting his
father's killers. He was no true Stark, had never been one
. . . but he could die like one. Let them say that Eddard
Stark had fathered four sons, not three.

Ghost kept pace with them for almost half a mile, red
tongue lolling from his mouth. Man and horse alike lowered their heads as he asked the mare for more speed. The
wolf slowed, stopped, watching, his eyes glowing red in
the moonlight. He vanished behind, but Jon knew he
would follow, at his own pace.

Scattered lights flickered through the trees ahead of
him, on both sides of the road: Mole's Town. A dog
barked as he rode through, and he heard a mule's raucous
haw from the stable, but otherwise the village was still.
Here and there the glow of hearth fires shone through
shuttered windows, leaking between wooden slats, but
only a few.

Mole's Town was bigger than it seemed, but three
quarters of it was under the ground, in deep warm cellars
connected by a maze of tunnels. Even the whorehouse
was down there, nothing on the surface but a wooden
shack no bigger than a privy, with a red lantern hung over
the door. On the Wall, he'd heard men call the whores
"buried treasures." He wondered whether any of his
brothers in black were down there tonight, mining. That
was oathbreaking too, yet no one seemed to care.

Not until he was well beyond the village did Jon slow
again. By then both he and the mare were damp with
sweat. He dismounted, shivering, his burned hand aching.
A bank of melting snow lay under the trees, bright in the
moonlight, water trickling off to form small shallow
pools. Jon squatted and brought his hands together, cupping the runoff between his fingers. The snowmelt was
icy cold. He drank, and splashed some on his face, until
his cheeks tingled. His fingers were throbbing worse than
they had in days, and his head was pounding too. *I am
doing the right thing,* he told himself, *so why do I feel so
bad?*

The horse was well lathered, so Jon took the lead and
walked her for a while. The road was scarcely wide

enough for two riders to pass abreast, its surface cut by tiny streams and littered with stone. That run had been truly stupid, an invitation to a broken neck. Jon wondered what had gotten into him. Was he in such a great rush to die?

Off in the trees, the distant scream of some frightened animal made him look up. His mare whinnied nervously. Had his wolf found some prey? He cupped his hands around his mouth. *"Ghost!"* he shouted. "Ghost, to me." The only answer was a rush of wings behind him as an owl took flight.

Frowning, Jon continued on his way. He led the mare for half an hour, until she was dry. Ghost did not appear. Jon wanted to mount up and ride again, but he was concerned about his missing wolf. *"Ghost,"* he called again. "Where are you? To me! *Ghost!"* Nothing in these woods could trouble a direwolf, even a half-grown direwolf, unless . . . no, Ghost was too smart to attack a bear, and if there was a wolf pack anywhere close Jon would have surely heard them howling.

He should eat, he decided. Food would settle his stomach and give Ghost the chance to catch up. There was no danger yet; Castle Black still slept. In his saddlebag, he found a biscuit, a piece of cheese, and a small withered brown apple. He'd brought salt beef as well, and a rasher of bacon he'd filched from the kitchens, but he would save the meat for the morrow. After it was gone he'd need to hunt, and that would slow him.

Jon sat under the trees and ate his biscuit and cheese while his mare grazed along the kingsroad. He kept the apple for last. It had gone a little soft, but the flesh was still tart and juicy. He was down to the core when he heard the sounds: horses, and from the north. Quickly Jon leapt up and strode to his mare. Could he outrun them? No, they were too close, they'd hear him for a certainty, and if they were from Castle Black . . .

He led the mare off the road, behind a thick stand of grey-green sentinels. "Quiet now," he said in a hushed voice, crouching down to peer through the branches. If the gods were kind, the riders would pass by. Likely as not, they were only smallfolk from Mole's Town, farmers on their way to their fields, although what they were doing out in the middle of the night . . .

He listened to the sound of hooves growing steadily louder as they trotted briskly down the kingsroad. From the sound, there were five or six of them at the least. Their voices drifted through the trees.

". . . certain he came this way?"

"We *can't* be certain."

"He could have ridden east, for all you know. Or left the road to cut through the woods. That's what I'd do."

"In the dark? Stupid. If you didn't fall off your horse and break your neck, you'd get lost and wind up back at the Wall when the sun came up."

"I would not." Grenn sounded peeved. "I'd just ride south, you can tell south by the stars."

"What if the sky was cloudy?" Pyp asked.

"Then I wouldn't go."

Another voice broke in. "You know where *I'd* be if it was me? I'd be in Mole's Town, digging for buried treasure." Toad's shrill laughter boomed through the trees. Jon's mare snorted.

"Keep quiet, all of you," Halder said. "I thought I heard something."

"Where? I didn't hear anything." The horses stopped.

"*You* can't hear yourself fart."

"I can too," Grenn insisted.

"*Quiet!*"

They all fell silent, listening. Jon found himself holding his breath. *Sam,* he thought. He hadn't gone to the Old Bear, but he hadn't gone to bed either, he'd woken the other boys. Damn them all. Come dawn, if they were not in their beds, they'd be named deserters too. What did they think they were doing?

The hushed silence seemed to stretch on and on. From where Jon crouched, he could see the legs of their horses through the branches. Finally Pyp spoke up. "What did you hear?"

"I don't know," Halder admitted. "A sound, I thought it might have been a horse but . . ."

"There's nothing here."

Out of the corner of his eye, Jon glimpsed a pale shape moving through the trees. Leaves rustled, and Ghost came bounding out of the shadows, so suddenly that Jon's mare started and gave a whinny. "*There!*" Halder shouted.

"I heard it too!"

"Traitor," Jon told the direwolf as he swung up into the saddle. He turned the mare's head to slide off through the trees, but they were on him before he had gone ten feet.

"Jon!" Pyp shouted after him.

"Pull up," Grenn said. "You can't outrun us all."

Jon wheeled around to face them, drawing his sword. "Get back. I don't wish to hurt you, but I will if I have to."

"One against seven?" Halder gave a signal. The boys spread out, surrounding him.

"What do you want with me?" Jon demanded.

"We want to take you back where you belong," Pyp said.

"I belong with my brother."

"We're your brothers now," Grenn said.

"They'll cut off your head if they catch you, you know," Toad put in with a nervous laugh. "This is so stupid, it's like something the Aurochs would do."

"I would not," Grenn said. "I'm no oathbreaker. I said the words and I meant them."

"So did I," Jon told them. "Don't you understand? They murdered my *father.* It's war, my brother Robb is fighting in the riverlands—"

"We know," said Pyp solemnly. "Sam told us everything."

"We're sorry about your father," Grenn said, "but it doesn't matter. Once you say the words, you can't leave, no matter what."

"I *have* to," Jon said fervently.

"You said the words," Pyp reminded him. *"Now my watch begins,* you said it. *It shall not end until my death."*

"I shall live and die at my post," Grenn added, nodding.

"You don't have to tell me the words, I know them as well as you do." He was angry now. Why couldn't they let him go in peace? They were only making it harder.

"I am the sword in the darkness," Halder intoned.

"The watcher on the walls," piped Toad.

Jon cursed them all to their faces. They took no notice. Pyp spurred his horse closer, reciting, *"I am the fire that burns against the cold, the light that brings the dawn, the horn that wakes the sleepers, the shield that guards the realms of men."*

"Stay back," Jon warned him, brandishing his sword. "I mean it, Pyp." They weren't even wearing armor, he could cut them to pieces if he had to.

Matthar had circled behind him. He joined the chorus. *"I pledge my life and honor to the Night's Watch."*

Jon kicked his mare, spinning her in a circle. The boys were all around him now, closing from every side.

"For this night . . ." Halder trotted in from the left.

". . . and all the nights to come," finished Pyp. He reached over for Jon's reins. "So here are your choices. Kill me, or come back with me."

Jon lifted his sword . . . and lowered it, helpless. "Damn you," he said. "Damn you all."

"Do we have to bind your hands, or will you give us your word you'll ride back peaceful?" asked Halder.

"I won't run, if that's what you mean." Ghost moved out from under the trees and Jon glared at him. "Small help you were," he said. The deep red eyes looked at him knowingly.

"We had best hurry," Pyp said. "If we're not back before first light, the Old Bear will have *all* our heads."

Of the ride back, Jon Snow remembered little. It seemed shorter than the journey south, perhaps because his mind was elsewhere. Pyp set the pace, galloping, walking, trotting, and then breaking into another gallop. Mole's Town came and went, the red lantern over the brothel long extinguished. They made good time. Dawn was still an hour off when Jon glimpsed the towers of Castle Black ahead of them, dark against the pale immensity of the Wall. It did not seem like home this time.

They could take him back, Jon told himself, but they could not make him stay. The war would not end on the morrow, or the day after, and his friends could not watch him day and night. He would bide his time, make them think he was content to remain here . . . and then, when they had grown lax, he would be off again. Next time he would avoid the kingsroad. He could follow the Wall east, perhaps all the way to the sea, a longer route but a safer one. Or even west, to the mountains, and then south over the high passes. That was the wildling's way, hard and perilous, but at least no one would follow him. He wouldn't stray within a hundred leagues of Winterfell or the kingsroad.

Samwell Tarly awaited them in the old stables, slumped on the ground against a bale of hay, too anxious to sleep. He rose and brushed himself off. "I . . . I'm glad they found you, Jon."

"I'm not," Jon said, dismounting.

Pyp hopped off his horse and looked at the lightening sky with disgust. "Give us a hand bedding down the horses, Sam," the small boy said. "We have a long day before us, and no sleep to face it on, thanks to Lord Snow."

When day broke, Jon walked to the kitchens as he did every dawn. Three-Finger Hobb said nothing as he gave him the Old Bear's breakfast. Today it was three brown eggs boiled hard, with fried bread and ham steak and a bowl of wrinkled plums. Jon carried the food back to the King's Tower. He found Mormont at the window seat, writing. His raven was walking back and forth across his shoulders, muttering, *"Corn, corn, corn."* The bird shrieked when Jon entered. "Put the food on the table," the Old Bear said, glancing up. "I'll have some beer."

Jon opened a shuttered window, took the flagon of beer off the outside ledge, and filled a horn. Hobb had given him a lemon, still cold from the Wall. Jon crushed it in his fist. The juice trickled through his fingers. Mormont drank lemon in his beer every day, and claimed that was why he still had his own teeth.

"Doubtless you loved your father," Mormont said when Jon brought him his horn. "The things we love destroy us every time, lad. Remember when I told you that?"

"I remember," Jon said sullenly. He did not care to talk of his father's death, not even to Mormont.

"See that you never forget it. The hard truths are the ones to hold tight. Fetch me my plate. Is it ham again? So be it. You look weary. Was your moonlight ride so tiring?"

Jon's throat was dry. "You know?"

"Know," the raven echoed from Mormont's shoulder. *"Know."*

The Old Bear snorted. "Do you think they chose me

Lord Commander of the Night's Watch because I'm dumb as a stump, Snow? Aemon told me you'd go. I told him you'd be back. I know my men . . . and my *boys* too. Honor set you on the kingsroad . . . and honor brought you back."

"My friends brought me back," Jon said.

"Did I say it was *your* honor?" Mormont inspected his plate.

"They killed my father. Did you expect me to do nothing?"

"If truth be told, we expected you to do just as you did." Mormont tried a plum, spit out the pit. "I ordered a watch kept over you. You were seen leaving. If your brothers had not fetched you back, you would have been taken along the way, and not by friends. Unless you have a horse with wings like a raven. Do you?"

"No." Jon felt like a fool.

"Pity, we could use a horse like that."

Jon stood tall. He told himself that he would die well; that much he could do, at the least. "I know the penalty for desertion, my lord. I'm not afraid to die."

"Die!" the raven cried.

"Nor live, I hope," Mormont said, cutting his ham with a dagger and feeding a bite to the bird. "You have not deserted—yet. Here you stand. If we beheaded every boy who rode to Mole's Town in the night, only ghosts would guard the Wall. Yet maybe you mean to flee again on the morrow, or a fortnight from now. Is that it? Is that your hope, boy?"

Jon kept silent.

"I thought so." Mormont peeled the shell off a boiled egg. "Your father is dead, lad. Do you think you can bring him back?"

"No," he answered, sullen.

"Good," Mormont said. "We've seen the dead come back, you and me, and it's not something I care to see again." He ate the egg in two bites and flicked a bit of shell out from between his teeth. "Your brother is in the field with all the power of the north behind him. Any one of his lords bannermen commands more swords than you'll find in all the Night's Watch. Why do you imagine that they need *your* help? Are you such a mighty warrior, or do you carry a grumkin in your pocket to magic up your sword?"

Jon had no answer for him. The raven was pecking at an egg, breaking the shell. Pushing his beak through the hole, he pulled out morsels of white and yoke.

The Old Bear sighed. "You are not the only one touched by this war. Like as not, my sister is marching in your brother's host, her and those daughters of hers, dressed in men's mail. Maege is a hoary old snark, stubborn, short-tempered, and willful. Truth be told, I can hardly stand to be around the wretched woman, but that does not mean my love for her is any less than the love you bear your half sisters." Frowning, Mormont took his last egg and squeezed it in his fist until the shell crunched. "Or perhaps it does. Be that as it may, I'd still grieve if she were slain, yet you don't see me running off. I said the words, just as you did. My place is here . . . where is yours, boy?"

I have no place, Jon wanted to say, *I'm a bastard, I have no rights, no name, no mother, and now not even a father.* The words would not come. "I don't know."

"I do," said Lord Commander Mormont. "The cold winds are rising, Snow. Beyond the Wall, the shadows lengthen. Cotter Pyke writes of vast herds of elk, streaming south and east toward the sea, and mammoths as well. He says one of his men discovered huge, misshapen footprints not three leagues from Eastwatch. Rangers from the Shadow Tower have found whole villages abandoned, and at night Ser Denys says they see fires in the mountains, huge blazes that burn from dusk till dawn. Quorin Halfhand took a captive in the depths of the Gorge, and the man swears that Mance Rayder is massing all his people in some new, secret stronghold he's found, to what end the gods only know. Do you think your uncle Benjen was the only ranger we've lost this past year?"

"*Ben Jen,*" the raven squawked, bobbing its head, bits of egg dribbling from its beak. "*Ben Jen. Ben Jen.*"

"No," Jon said. There had been others. Too many.

"Do you think your brother's war is more important than ours?" the old man barked.

Jon chewed his lip. The raven flapped its wings at him. "*War, war, war, war,*" it sang.

"It's not," Mormont told him. "Gods save us, boy,

you're not blind and you're not stupid. When dead men come hunting in the night, do you think it matters who sits the Iron Throne?"

"No." Jon had not thought of it that way.

"Your lord father sent you to us, Jon. Why, who can say?"

"Why? Why? Why?" the raven called.

"All I know is that the blood of the First Men flows in the veins of the Starks. The First Men built the Wall, and it's said they remember things otherwise forgotten. And that beast of yours . . . he led us to the wights, warned you of the dead man on the steps. Ser Jaremy would doubtless call that happenstance, yet Ser Jaremy is dead and I'm not." Lord Mormont stabbed a chunk of ham with the point of his dagger. "I think you were meant to be here, and I want you and that wolf of yours with us when we go beyond the Wall."

His words sent a chill of excitement down Jon's back. "Beyond the Wall?"

"You heard me. I mean to find Ben Stark, alive or dead." He chewed and swallowed. "I will not sit here meekly and wait for the snows and the ice winds. We must know what is happening. This time the Night's Watch will ride in force, against the King-beyond-the-Wall, the Others, and anything else that may be out there. I mean to command them myself." He pointed his dagger at Jon's chest. "By custom, the Lord Commander's steward is his squire as well . . . but I do not care to wake every dawn wondering if you've run off again. So I will have an answer from you, Lord Snow, and I will have it now. Are you a brother of the Night's Watch . . . or only a bastard boy who wants to play at war?"

Jon Snow straightened himself and took a long deep breath. *Forgive me, Father. Robb, Arya, Bran . . . forgive me, I cannot help you. He has the truth of it. This is my place.* "I am . . . yours, my lord. Your man. I swear it. I will not run again."

The Old Bear snorted. "Good. Now go put on your sword."

CATELYN

I t seemed a thousand years ago that Catelyn Stark had carried her infant son out of Riverrun, crossing the Tumblestone in a small boat to begin their journey north to Winterfell. And it was across the Tumblestone that they came home now, though the boy wore plate and mail in place of swaddling clothes.

Robb sat in the bow with Grey Wind, his hand resting on his direwolf's head as the rowers pulled at their oars. Theon Greyjoy was with him. Her uncle Brynden would come behind in the second boat, with the Greatjon and Lord Karstark.

Catelyn took a place toward the stern. They shot down the Tumblestone, letting the strong current push them past the looming Wheel Tower. The splash and rumble of the great waterwheel within was a sound from her girlhood that brought a sad smile to Catelyn's face. From the sandstone walls of the castle, soldiers and servants shouted down her name, and Robb's, and "Winterfell!" From every rampart waved the banner of House Tully: a leaping trout, silver, against a rippling blue-and-red field. It was a stirring sight, yet it did not lift her heart. She wondered if indeed her heart would ever lift again. *Oh, Ned . . .*

Below the Wheel Tower, they made a wide turn and knifed through the churning water. The men put their backs into it. The wide arch of the Water Gate came into view, and she heard the creak of heavy chains as the great iron portcullis was winched upward. It rose slowly as they approached, and Catelyn saw that the lower half of it was red with rust. The bottom foot dripped brown mud on them as they passed underneath, the barbed spikes mere inches above their heads. Catelyn gazed up at the bars and wondered how deep the rust went and how well the portcullis would stand up to a ram and whether it ought to be replaced. Thoughts like that were seldom far from her mind these days.

They passed beneath the arch and under the walls, moving from sunlight to shadow and back into sunlight. Boats large and small were tied up all around them, secured to iron rings set in the stone. Her father's guards waited on the water stair with her brother. Ser Edmure Tully was a stocky young man with a shaggy head of auburn hair and a fiery beard. His breastplate was scratched and dented from battle, his blue-and-red cloak stained by blood and smoke. At his side stood the Lord Tytos Blackwood, a hard pike of a man with close-cropped salt-and-pepper whiskers and a hook nose. His bright yellow armor was inlaid with jet in elaborate vine-and-leaf patterns, and a cloak sewn from raven feathers draped his thin shoulders. It had been Lord Tytos who led the sortie that plucked her brother from the Lannister camp.

"Bring them in," Ser Edmure commanded. Three men scrambled down the stairs knee-deep in the water and pulled the boat close with long hooks. When Grey Wind bounded out, one of them dropped his pole and lurched back, stumbling and sitting down abruptly in the river. The others laughed, and the man got a sheepish look on his face. Theon Greyjoy vaulted over the side of the boat and lifted Catelyn by the waist, setting her on a dry step above him as water lapped around his boots.

Edmure came down the steps to embrace her. "Sweet sister," he murmured hoarsely. He had deep blue eyes and a mouth made for smiles, but he was not smiling now. He looked worn and tired, battered by battle and haggard from strain. His neck was bandaged where he had taken a wound. Catelyn hugged him fiercely.

"Your grief is mine, Cat," he said when they broke apart. "When we heard about Lord Eddard . . . the Lannisters will pay, I swear it, you will have your vengeance."

"Will that bring Ned back to me?" she said sharply. The wound was still too fresh for softer words. She could not think about Ned now. She would not. It would not do. She had to be strong. "All that will keep. I must see Father."

"He awaits you in his solar," Edmure said.

"Lord Hoster is bedridden, my lady," her father's steward explained. When had that good man grown so old and grey? "He instructed me to bring you to him at once."

"I'll take her." Edmure escorted her up the water stair and across the lower bailey, where Petyr Baelish and Brandon Stark had once crossed swords for her favor. The massive sandstone walls of the keep loomed above them. As they pushed through a door between two guardsmen in fish-crest helms, she asked, "How bad is he?" dreading the answer even as she said the words.

Edmure's look was somber. "He will not be with us long, the maesters say. The pain is . . . constant, and grievous."

A blind rage filled her, a rage at all the world; at her brother Edmure and her sister Lysa, at the Lannisters, at the maesters, at Ned and her father and the monstrous gods who would take them both away from her. "You should have told me," she said. "You should have sent word as soon as you knew."

"He forbade it. He did not want his enemies to know that he was dying. With the realm so troubled, he feared that if the Lannisters suspected how frail he was . . ."

". . . they might attack?" Catelyn finished, hard. *It was your doing, yours,* a voice whispered inside her. *If you had not taken it upon yourself to seize the dwarf . . .*

They climbed the spiral stair in silence.

The keep was three-sided, like Riverrun itself, and Lord Hoster's solar was triangular as well, with a stone balcony that jutted out to the east like the prow of some great sandstone ship. From there the lord of the castle could look down on his walls and battlements, and beyond, to where the waters met. They had moved her father's bed out onto the balcony. "He likes to sit in the sun and watch the rivers," Edmure explained. "Father, see who I've brought. Cat has come to see you . . ."

Hoster Tully had always been a big man; tall and broad in his youth, portly as he grew older. Now he seemed shrunken, the muscle and meat melted off his bones. Even his face sagged. The last time Catelyn had seen him, his hair and beard had been brown, well streaked with grey. Now they had gone white as snow.

His eyes opened to the sound of Edmure's voice. "Little cat," he murmured in a voice thin and wispy and wracked by pain. "My little cat." A tremulous smile touched his face as his hand groped for hers. "I watched for you . . ."

"I shall leave you to talk," her brother said, kissing their lord father gently on the brow before he withdrew.

Catelyn knelt and took her father's hand in hers. It was a big hand, but fleshless now, the bones moving loosely under the skin, all the strength gone from it. "You should have told me," she said. "A rider, a raven . . ."

"Riders are taken, questioned," he answered. "Ravens are brought down . . ." A spasm of pain took him, and his fingers clutched hers hard. "The crabs are in my belly . . . pinching, always pinching. Day and night. They have fierce claws, the crabs. Maester Vyman makes me dreamwine, milk of the poppy . . . I sleep a lot . . . but I wanted to be awake to see you, when you came. I was afraid . . . when the Lannisters took your brother, the camps all around us . . . I was afraid I would go, before I could see you again . . . I was afraid . . ."

"I'm here, Father," she said. "With Robb, my son. He'll want to see you too."

"Your boy," he whispered. "He had my eyes, I remember . . ."

"He did, and does. And we've brought you Jaime Lannister, in irons. Riverrun is free again, Father."

Lord Hoster smiled. "I saw. Last night, when it began, I told them . . . had to see. They carried me to the gatehouse . . . watched from the battlements. Ah, that was beautiful . . . the torches came in a wave, I could hear the cries floating across the river . . . sweet cries . . .

when that siege tower went up, gods . . . would have died then, and glad, if only I could have seen you children first. Was it your boy who did it? Was it your Robb?"

"Yes," Catelyn said, fiercely proud. "It was Robb . . . and Brynden. Your brother is here as well, my lord."

"Him." Her father's voice was a faint whisper. "The Blackfish . . . came back? From the Vale?"

"Yes."

"And Lysa?" A cool wind moved through his thin white hair. "Gods be good, your sister . . . did she come as well?"

He sounded so full of hope and yearning that it was hard to tell the truth. "No. I'm sorry . . ."

"Oh." His face fell, and some light went out of his eyes. "I'd hoped . . . I would have liked to see her, before . . ."

"She's with her son, in the Eyrie."

Lord Hoster gave a weary nod. "Lord Robert now, poor Arryn's gone . . . I remember . . . why did she not come with you?"

"She is frightened, my lord. In the Eyrie she feels safe." She kissed his wrinkled brow. "Robb will be waiting. Will you see him? And Brynden?"

"Your son," he whispered. "Yes. Cat's child . . . he had my eyes, I remember. When he was born. Bring him . . . yes."

"And your brother?"

Her father glanced out over the rivers. "Blackfish," he said. "Has he wed yet? Taken some . . . girl to wife?"

Even on his deathbed, Catelyn thought sadly. "He has not wed. You know that, Father. Nor will he ever."

"I told him . . . *commanded* him. Marry! I was his lord. He knows. My right, to make his match. A good match. A Redwyne. Old House. Sweet girl, pretty . . . freckles . . . Bethany, yes. Poor child. Still waiting. Yes. Still . . ."

"Bethany Redwyne wed Lord Rowan years ago," Catelyn reminded him. "She has three children by him."

"Even so," Lord Hoster muttered. "Even so. Spit on the girl. The Redwynes. Spit on *me.* His lord, his brother . . . that Blackfish. I had other offers. Lord Bracken's girl. Walder Frey . . . any of three, he said . . . Has he wed? Anyone? Anyone?"

"No one," Catelyn said, "yet he has come many leagues to see you, fighting his way back to Riverrun. I would not be here now, if Ser Brynden had not helped us."

"He was ever a warrior," her father husked. "That he could do. Knight of the Gate, yes." He leaned back and closed his eyes, inutterably weary. "Send him. Later. I'll sleep now. Too sick to fight. Send him up later, the Blackfish . . ."

Catelyn kissed him gently, smoothed his hair, and left him there in the shade of his keep, with his rivers flowing beneath. He was asleep before she left the solar.

When she returned to the lower bailey, Ser Brynden Tully stood on the water stairs with wet boots, talking with the captain of Riverrun's guards. He came to her at once. "Is he—?"

"Dying," she said. "As we feared."

Her uncle's craggy face showed his pain plain. He ran his fingers through his thick grey hair. "Will he see me?"

She nodded. "He says he is too sick to fight."

Brynden Blackfish chuckled. "I am too old a soldier to believe that. Hoster will be chiding me about the Redwyne girl even as we light his funeral pyre, damn his bones."

Catelyn smiled, knowing it was true. "I do not see Robb."

"He went with Greyjoy to the hall, I believe."

Theon Greyjoy was seated on a bench in Riverrun's Great Hall, enjoying a horn of ale and regaling her father's garrison with an account of the slaughter in the Whispering Wood. "Some tried to flee, but we'd pinched the valley shut at both ends, and we rode out of the darkness with sword and lance. The Lannisters must have thought the Others themselves were on them when that wolf of Robb's got in among them. I saw him tear one man's arm from his shoulder, and their horses went mad at the scent of him. I couldn't tell you how many men were thrown—"

"Theon," she interrupted, "where might I find my son?"

"Lord Robb went to visit the godswood, my lady."

It was what Ned would have done. *He is his father's son as much as mine, I must remember. Oh, gods, Ned . . .*

She found Robb beneath the green canopy of leaves, surrounded by tall redwoods and great old elms, kneeling before the heart tree, a slender weirwood with a face more sad than fierce. His longsword was before him, the point thrust in the earth, his gloved hands clasped around the hilt. Around him others knelt: Greatjon Umber, Rickard Karstark, Maege Mormont, Galbart Glover, and more. Even Tytos Blackwood was among them, the great raven cloak fanned out behind him. *These are the ones who keep the old gods*, she realized. She asked herself what gods she kept these days, and could not find an answer.

It would not do to disturb them at their prayers. The gods must have their due . . . even cruel gods who would take Ned from her, and her lord father as well. So Catelyn waited. The river wind moved through the high branches, and she could see the Wheel Tower to her right, ivy crawling up its side. As she stood there, all the memories came flooding back to her. Her father had taught her to ride amongst these trees, and that was the elm that Edmure had fallen from when he broke his arm, and over there, beneath that bower, she and Lysa had played at kissing with Petyr.

She had not thought of that in years. How young they all had been—she no older than Sansa, Lysa younger than Arya, and Petyr younger still, yet eager. The girls had traded him between them, serious and giggling by turns. It came back to her so vividly she could almost feel his sweaty fingers on her shoulders and taste the mint on his breath. There was always mint growing in the godswood, and Petyr had liked to chew it. He had been such a bold little boy, always in trouble. "He tried to put his tongue in my mouth," Catelyn had confessed to her sister afterward, when they were alone. "He did with me too," Lysa had whispered, shy and breathless. "I liked it."

Robb got to his feet slowly and sheathed his sword, and Catelyn found herself wondering whether her son had ever kissed a girl in the godswood. Surely he must have. She had seen Jeyne Poole giving him moist-eyed glances, and some of the serving girls, even ones as old as eighteen . . . he had ridden in battle and killed men with a sword, surely he had been kissed. There were tears in her eyes. She wiped them away angrily.

"Mother," Robb said when he saw her standing there. "We must call a council. There are things to be decided."

"Your grandfather would like to see you," she said. "Robb, he's very sick."

"Ser Edmure told me. I am sorry, Mother . . . for Lord Hoster and for you. Yet first we must meet. We've had word from the south. Renly Baratheon has claimed his brother's crown."

"Renly?" she said, shocked. "I had thought, surely it would be Lord Stannis . . ."

"So did we all, my lady," Galbart Glover said.

The war council convened in the Great Hall, at four long trestle tables arranged in a broken square. Lord Hoster was too weak to attend, asleep on his balcony, dreaming of the sun on the rivers of his youth. Edmure sat in the high seat of the Tullys, with Brynden Blackfish at his side, and his father's bannermen arrayed to right and left and along the side tables. Word of the victory at River-run had spread to the fugitive lords of the Trident, draw-ing them back. Karyl Vance came in, a lord now, his father dead beneath the Golden Tooth. Ser Marq Piper was with him, and they brought a Darry, Ser Raymun's son, a lad no older than Bran. Lord Jonos Bracken arrived from the ruins of Stone Hedge, glowering and blustering, and took a seat as far from Tytos Blackwood as the tables would permit.

The northern lords sat opposite, with Catelyn and Robb facing her brother across the tables. They were fewer. The Greatjon sat at Robb's left hand, and then Theon Greyjoy; Galbart Glover and Lady Mormont were to the right of Catelyn. Lord Rickard Karstark, gaunt and hollow-eyed in his grief, took his seat like a man in a nightmare, his long beard uncombed and unwashed. He had left two sons dead in the Whispering Wood, and there was no word of the third, his eldest, who had led the Karstark spears against Tywin Lannister on the Green Fork.

The arguing raged on late into the night. Each lord had a right to speak, and speak they did . . . and shout, and curse, and reason, and cajole, and jest, and bargain, and slam tankards on the table, and threaten, and walk out, and return sullen or smiling. Catelyn sat and listened to it all.

Roose Bolton had re-formed the battered remnants of their other host at the mouth of the causeway. Ser Helman Tallhart and Walder Frey still held the Twins. Lord Tywin's army had crossed the Trident, and was making for Harrenhal. And there were two kings in the realm. Two kings, and no agreement.

Many of the lords bannermen wanted to march on Harrenhal at once, to meet Lord Tywin and end Lannister power for all time. Young, hot-tempered Marq Piper urged a strike west at Casterly Rock instead. Still others counseled patience. Riverrun sat athwart the Lannister supply lines, Jason Mallister pointed out; let them bide their time, denying Lord Tywin fresh levies and provisions while they strengthened their defenses and rested their weary troops. Lord Blackwood would have none of it. They should finish the work they began in the Whispering Wood. March to Harrenhal and bring Roose Bolton's army down as well. What Blackwood urged, Bracken opposed, as ever; Lord Jonos Bracken rose to insist they ought pledge their fealty to King Renly, and move south to join their might to his.

"Renly is not the king," Robb said. It was the first time her son had spoken. Like his father, he knew how to listen.

"You cannot mean to hold to Joffrey, my lord," Galbart Glover said. "He put your father to death."

"That makes him evil," Robb replied. "I do not know that it makes Renly king. Joffrey is still Robert's eldest trueborn son, so the throne is rightfully his by all the laws of the realm. Were he to die, and I mean to see that he does, he has a younger brother. Tommen is next in line after Joffrey."

"Tommen is no less a Lannister," Ser Marq Piper snapped.

"As you say," said Robb, troubled. "Yet if neither one is king, still, how could it be Lord Renly? He's Robert's *younger* brother. Bran can't be Lord of Winterfell before me, and Renly can't be king before Lord Stannis."

Lady Mormont agreed. "Lord Stannis has the better claim."

"Renly is *crowned*," said Marq Piper. "Highgarden and Storm's End support his claim, and the Dornishmen will not be laggardly. If Winterfell and Riverrun add their strength to his, he will have five of the seven great houses behind him. *Six*, if the Arryns bestir themselves! Six against the Rock! My lords, within the year, we will have all their heads on pikes, the queen and the boy king, Lord Tywin, the Imp, the Kingslayer, Ser Kevan, *all* of them! That is what we shall win if we join with King Renly. What does Lord Stannis have against that, that we should cast it all aside?"

"The right," said Robb stubbornly. Catelyn thought he sounded eerily like his father as he said it.

"So you mean us to declare for Stannis?" asked Edmure.

"I don't know," said Robb. "I prayed to know what to do, but the gods did not answer. The Lannisters killed my father for a traitor, and we know that was a lie, but if Joffrey is the lawful king and we fight against him, we *will* be traitors."

"My lord father would urge caution," aged Ser Stevron said, with the weaselly smile of a Frey. "Wait, let these two kings play their game of thrones. When they are done fighting, we can bend our knees to the victor, or oppose him, as we choose. With Renly arming, likely Lord Tywin would welcome a truce . . . and the safe return of his son. Noble lords, allow me to go to him at Harrenhal and arrange good terms and ransoms . . ."

A roar of outrage drowned out his voice. *"Craven!"* the Greatjon thundered. "Begging for a truce will make us seem weak," declared Lady Mormont. "Ransoms be damned, we must *not* give up the Kingslayer," shouted Rickard Karstark.

"Why not a peace?" Catelyn asked.

The lords looked at her, but it was Robb's eyes she felt, his and his alone. "My lady, they murdered my lord father, your husband," he said grimly. He unsheathed his longsword and laid it on the table before him, the bright steel on the rough wood. "This is the only peace I have for Lannisters."

The Greatjon bellowed his approval, and other men added their voices, shouting and drawing swords and pounding their fists on the table. Catelyn waited until they had quieted. "My lords," she said then, "Lord Eddard was your liege, but I shared his bed and bore his children. Do you think I love him any less than you?" Her voice almost broke with her grief, but Catelyn took a long breath and steadied herself. "Robb, if that sword could bring him back, I should never let you sheathe it until Ned stood at my side once more . . . but he is gone, and a hundred Whispering Woods will not change that. Ned is gone, and Daryn Hornwood, and Lord Karstark's valiant sons, and many other good men besides, and none of them will return to us. Must we have more deaths still?"

"You are a woman, my lady," the Greatjon rumbled in his deep voice. "Women do not understand these things."

"You are the gentle sex," said Lord Karstark, with the lines of grief fresh on his face. "A man has a need for vengeance."

"Give me Cersei Lannister, Lord Karstark, and you would see how *gentle* a woman can be," Catelyn replied. "Perhaps I do not understand tactics and strategy . . . but I understand futility. We went to war when Lannister armies were ravaging the riverlands, and Ned was a prisoner, falsely accused of treason. We fought to defend ourselves, and to win my lord's freedom.

"Well, the one is done, and the other forever beyond our reach. I will mourn for Ned until the end of my days, but I must think of the living. I want my daughters back, and the queen holds them still. If I must trade our four Lannisters for their two Starks, I will call that a bargain and thank the gods. I want you safe, Robb, ruling at Winterfell from your father's seat. I want you to live your life, to kiss a girl and wed a woman and father a son. I want to write an end to this. I want to go home, my lords, and weep for my husband."

The hall was very quiet when Catelyn finished speaking.

"Peace," said her uncle Brynden. "Peace is sweet, my lady . . . but on what terms? It is no good hammering your sword into a plowshare if you must forge it again on the morrow."

"What did Torrhen and my Eddard die for, if I am to return to Karhold with nothing but their bones?" asked Rickard Karstark.

"Aye," said Lord Bracken. "Gregor Clegane laid waste to my fields, slaughtered my smallfolk, and left Stone Hedge a smoking ruin. Am I now to bend the knee to the ones who sent him? What have we fought for, if we are to put all back as it was before?"

Lord Blackwood agreed, to Catelyn's surprise and dismay. "And if we do make peace with King Joffrey, are we not then traitors to King Renly? What if the stag should prevail against the lion, where would that leave us?"

"Whatever you may decide for yourselves, I shall never call a Lannister my king," declared Marq Piper.

"Nor I!" yelled the little Darry boy. "I never will!"

Again the shouting began. Catelyn sat despairing. She had come so close, she thought. They had almost listened, *almost* . . . but the moment was gone. There would be no peace, no chance to heal, no safety. She looked at her son, watched him as he listened to the lords debate, frowning, troubled, yet wedded to his war. He had pledged himself to marry a daughter of Walder Frey, but she saw his true bride plain before her now: the sword he had laid on the table.

Catelyn was thinking of her girls, wondering if she would ever see them again, when the Greatjon lurched to his feet.

"MY LORDS!" he shouted, his voice booming off the rafters. "Here is what I say to these two kings!" He spat. "Renly Baratheon is nothing to me, nor Stannis neither. Why should they rule over me and mine, from some flowery seat in Highgarden or Dorne? What do they know of the Wall or the wolfswood or the barrows of the First Men? Even their *gods* are wrong. The Others take the Lannisters too, I've had a bellyful of them." He reached back over his shoulder and drew his immense two-handed greatsword. "Why shouldn't we rule ourselves again? It was the dragons we married, and the dragons are all dead!" He pointed at Robb with the blade. *"There* sits the only king I mean to bow *my* knee to, m'lords," he thundered. "The King in the North!"

And he knelt, and laid his sword at her son's feet.

"I'll have peace on *those* terms," Lord Karstark said. "They can keep their red castle and their iron chair as well." He eased his longsword from its scabbard. "The King in the North!" he said, kneeling beside the Greatjon.

Maege Mormont stood. "The King of Winter!" she declared, and laid her spiked mace beside the swords. And the river lords were rising too, Blackwood and Bracken and Mallister, houses who had never been ruled from Winterfell, yet Catelyn watched them rise and draw their blades, bending their knees and shouting the old words that had not been heard in the realm for more than three hundred years, since Aegon the Dragon had come to make the Seven Kingdoms one . . . yet now were heard again, ringing from the timbers of her father's hall:

"The King in the North!"

"The King in the North!"

"THE KING IN THE NORTH!"

DAENERYS

The land was red and dead and parched, and good wood was hard to come by. Her foragers returned with gnarled cottonwoods, purple brush, sheaves of brown grass. They took the two straightest trees, hacked the limbs and branches from them, skinned off their bark, and split them, laying the logs in a square. Its center they filled with straw, brush, bark shavings, and bundles of dry grass. Rakharo chose a stallion from the small herd that remained to them; he was not the equal of Khal Drogo's red, but few horses were. In the center of the square, Aggo fed him a withered apple and dropped him in an instant with an axe blow between the eyes.

Bound hand and foot, Mirri Maz Duur watched from the dust with disquiet in her black eyes. "It is not enough to kill a horse," she told Dany. "By itself, the blood is nothing. You do not have the words to make a spell, nor the wisdom to find them. Do you think bloodmagic is a game for children? You call me *maegi* as if it were a curse, but all it means is *wise*. You are a child, with a child's ignorance. Whatever you mean to do, it will not work. Loose me from these bonds and I will help you."

"I am tired of the *maegi*'s braying," Dany told Jhogo.

He took his whip to her, and after that the godswife kept silent.

Over the carcass of the horse, they built a platform of hewn logs; trunks of smaller trees and limbs from the greater, and the thickest straightest branches they could find. They laid the wood east to west, from sunrise to sunset. On the platform they piled Khal Drogo's treasures: his great tent, his painted vests, his saddles and harness, the whip his father had given him when he came to manhood, the *arakh* he had used to slay Khal Ogo and his son, a mighty dragonbone bow. Aggo would have added the weapons Drogo's bloodriders had given Dany for bride gifts as well, but she forbade it. "Those are mine," she told him, "and I mean to keep them." Another layer of brush was piled about the *khal*'s treasures, and bundles of dried grass scattered over them.

Ser Jorah Mormont drew her aside as the sun was creeping toward its zenith. "Princess . . ." he began.

"Why do you call me that?" Dany challenged him. "My brother Viserys was your king, was he not?"

"He was, my lady."

"Viserys is dead. I am his heir, the last blood of House Targaryen. Whatever was his is mine now."

"My . . . queen," Ser Jorah said, going to one knee. "My sword that was his is yours, Daenerys. And my heart as well, that never belonged to your brother. I am only a knight, and I have nothing to offer you but exile, but I beg you, hear me. Let Khal Drogo go. You shall not be alone. I promise you, no man shall take you to Vaes Dothrak unless you wish to go. You need not join the *dosh khaleen*. Come east with me. Yi Ti, Qarth, the Jade Sea, Asshai by the Shadow. We will see all the wonders yet unseen, and drink what wines the gods see fit to serve us. Please, *Khaleesi*. I know what you intend. Do not. *Do not*."

"I must," Dany told him. She touched his face, fondly, sadly. "You do not understand."

"I understand that you loved him," Ser Jorah said in a voice thick with despair. "I loved my lady wife once, yet I did not die with her. You are my queen, my sword is yours, but do not ask me to stand aside as you climb on Drogo's pyre. I will not watch you burn."

"Is that what you fear?" Dany kissed him lightly on

his broad forehead. "I am not such a child as that, sweet ser."

"You do not mean to die with him? You swear it, my queen?"

"I swear it," she said in the Common Tongue of the Seven Kingdoms that by rights were hers.

The third level of the platform was woven of branches no thicker than a finger, and covered with dry leaves and twigs. They laid them north to south, from ice to fire, and piled them high with soft cushions and sleeping silks. The sun had begun to lower toward the west by the time they were done. Dany called the Dothraki around her. Fewer than a hundred were left. How many had Aegon started with? she wondered. It did not matter.

"You will be my *khalasar*," she told them. "I see the faces of slaves. I free you. Take off your collars. Go if you wish, no one shall harm you. If you stay, it will be as brothers and sisters, husbands and wives." The black eyes watched her, wary, expressionless. "I see the children, women, the wrinkled faces of the aged. I was a child yesterday. Today I am a woman. Tomorrow I will be old. To each of you I say, give me your hands and your hearts, and there will always be a place for you." She turned to the three young warriors of her *khas*. "Jhogo, to you I give the silver-handled whip that was my bride gift, and name you *ko*, and ask your oath, that you will live and die as blood of my blood, riding at my side to keep me safe from harm."

Jhogo took the whip from her hands, but his face was confused. *"Khaleesi,"* he said hesitantly, "this is not done. It would shame me, to be bloodrider to a woman."

"Aggo," Dany called, paying no heed to Jhogo's words. *If I look back I am lost.* "To you I give the dragonbone bow that was my bride gift." It was double-curved, shiny black and exquisite, taller than she was. "I name you *ko*, and ask your oath, that you should live and die as blood of my blood, riding at my side to keep me safe from harm."

Aggo accepted the bow with lowered eyes. "I cannot say these words. Only a man can lead a *khalasar* or name a *ko*."

"Rakharo," Dany said, turning away from the refusal, "you shall have the great *arakh* that was my bride gift, with hilt and blade chased in gold. And you too I name my *ko*, and ask that you live and die as blood of my blood, riding at my side to keep me safe from harm."

"You are *khaleesi*," Rakharo said, taking the *arakh*. "I shall ride at your side to Vaes Dothrak beneath the Mother of Mountains, and keep you safe from harm until you take your place with the crones of the *dosh khaleen*. No more can I promise."

She nodded, as calmly as if she had not heard his answer, and turned to the last of her champions. "Ser Jorah Mormont," she said, "first and greatest of my knights, I have no bride gift to give you, but I swear to you, one day you shall have from my hands a longsword like none the world has ever seen, dragon-forged and made of Valyrian steel. And I would ask for your oath as well."

"You have it, my queen," Ser Jorah said, kneeling to lay his sword at her feet. "I vow to serve you, to obey you, to die for you if need be."

"Whatever may come?"

"Whatever may come."

"I shall hold you to that oath. I pray you never regret the giving of it." Dany lifted him to his feet. Stretching on her toes to reach his lips, she kissed the knight gently and said, "You are the first of my Queensguard."

She could feel the eyes of the *khalasar* on her as she entered her tent. The Dothraki were muttering and giving her strange sideways looks from the corners of their dark almond eyes. They thought her mad, Dany realized. Perhaps she was. She would know soon enough. *If I look back I am lost.*

Her bath was scalding hot when Irri helped her into the tub, but Dany did not flinch or cry aloud. She liked the heat. It made her feel clean. Jhiqui had scented the water with the oils she had found in the market in Vaes Dothrak; the steam rose moist and fragrant. Doreah washed her hair and combed it out, working loose the mats and tangles. Irri scrubbed her back. Dany closed her eyes and let the smell and the warmth enfold her. She could feel the heat soaking through the soreness between her thighs. She shuddered when it entered her, and her pain and stiffness seemed to dissolve. She floated.

When she was clean, her handmaids helped her from

the water. Irri and Jhiqui fanned her dry, while Doreah brushed her hair until it fell like a river of liquid silver down her back. They scented her with spiceflower and cinnamon; a touch on each wrist, behind her ears, on the tips of her milk-heavy breasts. The last dab was for her sex. Irri's finger felt as light and cool as a lover's kiss as it slid softly up between her lips.

Afterward, Dany sent them all away, so she might prepare Khal Drogo for his final ride into the night lands. She washed his body clean and brushed and oiled his hair, running her fingers through it for the last time, feeling the weight of it, remembering the first time she had touched it, the night of their wedding ride. His hair had never been cut. How many men could die with their hair uncut? She buried her face in it and inhaled the dark fragrance of the oils. He smelled like grass and warm earth, like smoke and semen and horses. He smelled like Drogo. *Forgive me, sun of my life,* she thought. *Forgive me for all I have done and all I must do. I paid the price, my star, but it was too high, too high . . .*

Dany braided his hair and slid the silver rings onto his mustache and hung his bells one by one. So many bells, gold and silver and bronze. Bells so his enemies would hear him coming and grow weak with fear. She dressed him in horsehair leggings and high boots, buckling a belt heavy with gold and silver medallions about his waist. Over his scarred chest she slipped a painted vest, old and faded, the one Drogo had loved best. For herself she chose loose sandsilk trousers, sandals that laced halfway up her legs, and a vest like Drogo's.

The sun was going down when she called them back to carry his body to the pyre. The Dothraki watched in silence as Jhogo and Aggo bore him from the tent. Dany walked behind them. They laid him down on his cushions and silks, his head toward the Mother of Mountains far to the northeast.

"Oil," she commanded, and they brought forth the jars and poured them over the pyre, soaking the silks and the brush and the bundles of dry grass, until the oil trickled from beneath the logs and the air was rich with fragrance. "Bring my eggs," Dany commanded her handmaids. Something in her voice made them run.

Ser Jorah took her arm. "My queen, Drogo will have no use for dragon's eggs in the night lands. Better to sell them in Asshai. Sell one and we can buy a ship to take us back to the Free Cities. Sell all three and you will be a wealthy woman all your days."

"They were not given to me to sell," Dany told him.

She climbed the pyre herself to place the eggs around her sun-and-stars. The black beside his heart, under his arm. The green beside his head, his braid coiled around it. The cream-and-gold down between his legs. When she kissed him for the last time, Dany could taste the sweetness of the oil on his lips.

As she climbed down off the pyre, she noticed Mirri Maz Duur watching her. "You are mad," the godswife said hoarsely.

"Is it so far from madness to wisdom?" Dany asked. "Ser Jorah, take this *maegi* and bind her to the pyre."

"To the . . . my queen, no, hear me . . ."

"Do as I say." Still he hesitated, until her anger flared. "You swore to obey me, whatever might come. Rakharo, help him."

The godswife did not cry out as they dragged her to Khal Drogo's pyre and staked her down amidst his treasures. Dany poured the oil over the woman's head herself. "I thank you, Mirri Maz Duur," she said, "for the lessons you have taught me."

"You will not hear me scream," Mirri responded as the oil dripped from her hair and soaked her clothing.

"I will," Dany said, "but it is not your screams I want, only your life. I remember what you told me. Only death can pay for life." Mirri Maz Duur opened her mouth, but made no reply. As she stepped away, Dany saw that the contempt was gone from the *maegi*'s flat black eyes; in its place was something that might have been fear. Then there was nothing to be done but watch the sun and look for the first star.

When a horselord dies, his horse is slain with him, so he might ride proud into the night lands. The bodies are burned beneath the open sky, and the *khal* rises on his fiery steed to take his place among the stars. The more fiercely the man burned in life, the brighter his star will shine in the darkness.

Jhogo spied it first. *"There,"* he said in a hushed voice. Dany looked and saw it, low in the east. The first star was a comet, burning red. Bloodred; fire red; the dragon's tail. She could not have asked for a stronger sign.

Dany took the torch from Aggo's hand and thrust it between the logs. The oil took the fire at once, the brush and dried grass a heartbeat later. Tiny flames went darting up the wood like swift red mice, skating over the oil and leaping from bark to branch to leaf. A rising heat puffed at her face, soft and sudden as a lover's breath, but in seconds it had grown too hot to bear. Dany stepped backward. The wood crackled, louder and louder. Mirri Maz Duur began to sing in a shrill, ululating voice. The flames whirled and writhed, racing each other up the platform. The dusk shimmered as the air itself seemed to liquefy from the heat. Dany heard logs spit and crack. The fires swept over Mirri Maz Duur. Her song grew louder, shriller . . . then she gasped, again and again, and her song became a shuddering wail, thin and high and full of agony.

And now the flames reached her Drogo, and now they were all around him. His clothing took fire, and for an instant the *khal* was clad in wisps of floating orange silk and tendrils of curling smoke, grey and greasy. Dany's lips parted and she found herself holding her breath. Part of her wanted to go to him as Ser Jorah had feared, to rush into the flames to beg for his forgiveness and take him inside her one last time, the fire melting the flesh from their bones until they were as one, forever.

She could smell the odor of burning flesh, no different than horseflesh roasting in a firepit. The pyre roared in the deepening dusk like some great beast, drowning out the fainter sound of Mirri Maz Duur's screaming and sending up long tongues of flame to lick at the belly of the night. As the smoke grew thicker, the Dothraki backed away, coughing. Huge orange gouts of fire unfurled their banners in that hellish wind, the logs hissing and cracking, glowing cinders rising on the smoke to float away into the dark like so many newborn fireflies. The heat beat at the air with great red wings, driving the Dothraki back, driving off even Mormont, but Dany stood her ground. She was the blood of the dragon, and the fire was in her.

She had sensed the truth of it long ago, Dany thought as she took a step closer to the conflagration, but the brazier had not been hot enough. The flames writhed before her like the women who had danced at her wedding, whirling and singing and spinning their yellow and orange and crimson veils, fearsome to behold, yet lovely, so lovely, alive with heat. Dany opened her arms to them, her skin flushed and glowing. *This is a wedding, too,* she thought. Mirri Maz Duur had fallen silent. The godswife thought her a child, but children grow, and children learn.

Another step, and Dany could feel the heat of the sand on the soles of her feet, even through her sandals. Sweat ran down her thighs and between her breasts and in rivulets over her cheeks, where tears had once run. Ser Jorah was shouting behind her, but he did not matter anymore, only the fire mattered. The flames were so beautiful, the loveliest things she had ever seen, each one a sorcerer robed in yellow and orange and scarlet, swirling long smoky cloaks. She saw crimson firelions and great yellow serpents and unicorns made of pale blue flame; she saw fish and foxes and monsters, wolves and bright birds and flowering trees, each more beautiful than the last. She saw a horse, a great grey stallion limned in smoke, its flowing mane a nimbus of blue flame. *Yes, my love, my sun-and-stars, yes, mount now, ride now.*

Her vest had begun to smolder, so Dany shrugged it off and let it fall to the ground. The painted leather burst into sudden flame as she skipped closer to the fire, her breasts bare to the blaze, streams of milk flowing from her red and swollen nipples. *Now,* she thought, *now,* and for an instant she glimpsed Khal Drogo before her, mounted on his smoky stallion, a flaming lash in his hand. He smiled, and the whip snaked down at the pyre, hissing.

She heard a *crack*, the sound of shattering stone. The platform of wood and brush and grass began to shift and collapse in upon itself. Bits of burning wood slid down at her, and Dany was showered with ash and cinders. And something else came crashing down, bouncing and rolling, to land at her feet; a chunk of curved rock, pale and veined with gold, broken and smoking. The roaring filled the world, yet dimly through the firefall Dany heard women shriek and children cry out in wonder.

Only death can pay for life.

And there came a second *crack*, loud and sharp as thunder, and the smoke stirred and whirled around her and the pyre shifted, the logs exploding as the fire touched their secret hearts. She heard the screams of frightened horses, and the voices of the Dothraki raised in shouts of fear and terror, and Ser Jorah calling her name and cursing. *No,* she wanted to shout to him, *no, my good knight, do not fear for me. The fire is mine. I am Daenerys Stormborn, daughter of dragons, bride of dragons, mother of dragons, don't you see? Don't you SEE?* With a belch of flame and smoke that reached thirty feet into the sky, the pyre collapsed and came down around her. Unafraid, Dany stepped forward into the firestorm, calling to her children.

The third *crack* was as loud and sharp as the breaking of the world.

When the fire died at last and the ground became cool enough to walk upon, Ser Jorah Mormont found her amidst the ashes, surrounded by blackened logs and bits of glowing ember and the burnt bones of man and woman and stallion. She was naked, covered with soot, her clothes turned to ash, her beautiful hair all crisped away . . . yet she was unhurt.

The cream-and-gold dragon was suckling at her left breast, the green-and-bronze at the right. Her arms cradled them close. The black-and-scarlet beast was draped across her shoulders, its long sinuous neck coiled under her chin. When it saw Jorah, it raised its head and looked at him with eyes as red as coals.

Wordless, the knight fell to his knees. The men of her *khas* came up behind him. Jhogo was the first to lay his *arakh* at her feet. "Blood of my blood," he murmured, pushing his face to the smoking earth. "Blood of my blood," she heard Aggo echo. "Blood of my blood," Rakharo shouted.

And after them came her handmaids, and then the others, all the Dothraki, men and women and children, and Dany had only to look at their eyes to know that they were hers now, today and tomorrow and forever, hers as they had never been Drogo's.

As Daenerys Targaryen rose to her feet, her black

hissed, pale smoke venting from its mouth and nostrils. The other two pulled away from her breasts and added their voices to the call, translucent wings unfolding and stirring the air, and for the first time in hundreds of years, the night came alive with the music of dragons.

APPENDIX

HOUSE BARATHEON

The youngest of the Great Houses, born during the Wars of Conquest. Its founder, Orys Baratheon, was rumored to be Aegon the Dragon's bastard brother. Orys rose through the ranks to become one of Aegon's fiercest commanders. When he defeated and slew Argilac the Arrogant, the last Storm King, Aegon rewarded him with Argilac's castle, lands, and daughter. Orys took the girl to bride, and adopted the banner, honors, and words of her line. The Baratheon sigil is a crowned stag, black, on a golden field. Their words are *Ours is the Fury*.

KING ROBERT BARATHEON, the First of His Name,
— his wife, QUEEN CERSEI, of House Lannister,
— their children:
— PRINCE JOFFREY, heir to the Iron Throne, twelve,
— PRINCESS MYRCELLA, a girl of eight,
— PRINCE TOMMEN, a boy of seven,

— his brothers:
  — STANNIS BARATHEON, Lord of
    Dragonstone,
    — his wife, LADY SELYSE of House
      Florent,
    — their daughter, SHIREEN, a girl of
      nine,
  — RENLY BARATHEON, Lord of Storm's
    End,
— his small council:
  — GRAND MAESTER PYCELLE,
  — LORD PETYR BAELISH, called
    LITTLEFINGER, master of coin,
  — LORD STANNIS BARATHEON, master
    of ships,
  — LORD RENLY BARATHEON, master of
    laws,
  — SER BARRISTAN SELMY, Lord
    Commander of the Kingsguard,
  — VARYS, a eunuch, called the Spider,
    master of whisperers,
— his court and retainers:
  — SER ILYN PAYNE, the King's Justice, a
    headsman,
  — SANDOR CLEGANE, called the Hound,
    sworn shield to Prince Joffrey,
  — JANOS SLYNT, a commoner,
commander of the City Watch of King's
Landing,
  — JALABHAR XHO, an exile prince from
    the Summer Isles,
  — MOON BOY, a jester and fool,

— LANCEL and TYREK LANNISTER,
  squires to the king, the queen's cousins,
— SER ARON SANTAGAR, master-at-
  arms,
— his Kingsguard:
— SER BARRISTAN SELMY, Lord
  Commander,
— SER JAIME LANNISTER, called the
  Kingslayer,
— SER BOROS BLOUNT,
— SER MERYN TRANT,
— SER ARYS OAKHEART,
— SER PRESTON GREENFIELD,
— SER MANDON MOORE,

The principal houses sworn to Storm's End are
Selmy, Wylde, Trant, Penrose, Errol, Estermont,
Tarth, Swann, Dondarrion, Caron.

The principal houses sworn to Dragonstone are Celtigar, Velaryon, Seaworth, Bar Emmon, and Sunglass.

HOUSE STARK

The Starks trace their descent from Brandon the Builder and the ancient Kings of Winter. For thousands of years, they ruled from Winterfell as Kings in the North, until Torrhen Stark, the King Who Knelt, chose to swear fealty to Aegon the Dragon rather than give battle. Their blazon is a grey direwolf on an ice-white field. The Stark words are *Winter Is Coming.*

EDDARD STARK, Lord of Winterfell, Warden of the North,
— his wife, LADY CATELYN, of House Tully,
— their children:
  — ROBB, the heir to Winterfell, fourteen years of age,
  — SANSA, the eldest daughter, eleven,
  — ARYA, the younger daughter, a girl of nine,
  — BRANDON, called Bran, seven,
  — RICKON, a boy of three,

— his bastard son, JON SNOW, a boy of fourteen,

— his ward, THEON GREYJOY, heir to the Iron Islands,

— his siblings:

  — {BRANDON}, his elder brother, murdered by the command of Aerys II Targaryen,

  — {LYANNA}, his younger sister, died in the mountains of Dorne,

  — BENJEN, his younger brother, a man of the Night's Watch,

— his household:

  — MAESTER LUWIN, counselor, healer, and tutor,

  — VAYON POOLE, steward of Winterfell,

    — JEYNE, his daughter, Sansa's closest friend,

  — JORY CASSEL, captain of the guard,

    — HALLIS MOLLEN, DESMOND, JACKS, PORTHER, QUENT, ALYN, TOMARD, VARLY, HEWARD, CAYN, WYL, guardsmen,

  — SER RODRIK CASSEL, master-at-arms, Jory's uncle,

    — BETH, his young daughter,

  — SEPTA MORDANE, tutor to Lord Eddard's daughters,

  — SEPTON CHAYLE, keeper of the castle sept and library,

  — HULLEN, master of horse,

    — his son, HARWIN, a guardsman,

— JOSETH, a stableman and horse trainer,
— FARLEN, kennelmaster,
— OLD NAN, storyteller, once a wet nurse,
  — HODOR, her great-grandson, a simpleminded stableboy,
— GAGE, the cook,
— MIKKEN, smith and armorer,
— his principal lords bannermen:
— SER HELMAN TALLHART,
— RICKARD KARSTARK, Lord of Karhold,
— ROOSE BOLTON, Lord of the Dreadfort,
— JON UMBER, called the Greatjon,
— GALBART and ROBETT GLOVER,
— WYMAN MANDERLY, Lord of White Harbor,
— MAEGE MORMONT, the Lady of Bear Island,

The principal houses sworn to Winterfell are Karstark, Umber, Flint, Mormont, Hornwood, Cerwyn, Reed, Manderly, Glover, Tallhart, Bolton.

HOUSE LANNISTER

Fair-haired, tall, and handsome, the Lannisters are the blood of Andal adventurers who carved out a mighty kingdom in the western hills and valleys. Through the female line they boast of descent from Lann the Clever, the legendary trickster of the Age of Heroes. The gold of Casterly Rock and the Golden Tooth has made them the wealthiest of the Great Houses. Their sigil is a golden lion upon a crimson field. The Lannister words are *Hear Me Roar!*

TYWIN LANNISTER, Lord of Casterly Rock, Warden of the West, Shield of Lannisport,
— his wife, {LADY JOANNA}, a cousin, died in childbed,
— their children:
— SER JAIME, called the Kingslayer, heir to Casterly Rock, a twin to Cersei,
— QUEEN CERSEI, wife of King Robert I Baratheon, a twin to Jaime,
— TYRION, called the Imp, a dwarf,

— his siblings:
- — SER KEVAN, his eldest brother,
  - — his wife, DORNA, of House Swyft,
  - — their eldest son, LANCEL, squire to the king,
  - — their twin sons, WILLEM and MARTYN,
  - — their infant daughter, JANEI,
- — GENNA, his sister, wed to Ser Emmon Frey,
  - — their son, SER CLEOS FREY,
  - — their son, TION FREY, a squire,
- — {SER TYGETT}, his second brother, died of a pox,
  - — his widow, DARLESSA, of House Marbrand,
  - — their son, TYREK, squire to the king,
- — {GERION}, his youngest brother, lost at sea,
  - — his bastard daughter, JOY, a girl of ten,
— their cousin, SER STAFFORD LANNISTER, brother to the late Lady Joanna,
- — his daughters, CERENNA and MYRIELLE,
- — his son, SER DAVEN LANNISTER,
— his counselor, MAESTER CREYLEN,
— his chief knights and lords bannermen:
- — LORD LEO LEFFORD,
- — SER ADDAM MARBRAND,
- — SER GREGOR CLEGANE, the Mountain That Rides,

— SER HARYS SWYFT, father by marriage to Ser Kevan,
— LORD ANDROS BRAX,
— SER FORLEY PRESTER,
— SER AMORY LORCH,
— VARGO HOAT, of the Free City of Qohor, a sellsword,

Principal houses sworn to Casterly Rock are Payne, Swyft, Marbrand, Lydden, Banefort, Lefford, Crakehall, Serrett, Broom, Clegane, Prester, and Westerling.

HOUSE ARRYN

The Arryns are descended from the Kings of Mountain and Vale, one of the oldest and purest lines of Andal nobility. Their sigil is the moon-and-falcon, white, upon a sky blue field. The Arryn words are *As High As Honor.*

{JON ARRYN}, Lord of the Eyrie, Defender of the Vale, Warden of the East, Hand of the King, recently deceased,
— his first wife, {LADY JEYNE, of House Royce}, died in childbed, her daughter stillborn,
— his second wife, {LADY ROWENA, of House Arryn}, his cousin, died of a winter chill, childless,
— his third wife and widow, LADY LYSA, of House Tully,
— their son:
— ROBERT ARRYN, a sickly boy of six years, now Lord of the Eyrie and Defender of the Vale,

— their retainers and household:
- MAESTER COLEMON, counselor, healer, and tutor,
- SER VARDIS EGEN, captain of the guard,
- SER BRYNDEN TULLY, called the Blackfish, Knight of the Gate and uncle to the Lady Lysa,
- LORD NESTOR ROYCE, High Steward of the Vale,
  - SER ALBAR ROYCE, his son,
  - MYA STONE, a bastard girl in his service,
- LORD EON HUNTER, suitor to Lady Lysa,
- SER LYN CORBRAY, suitor to Lady Lysa,
  - MYCHEL REDFORT, his squire,
- LADY ANYA WAYNWOOD, a widow,
  - SER MORTON WAYNWOOD, her son, suitor to Lady Lysa,
  - SER DONNEL WAYNWOOD, her son,
- MORD, a brutal gaoler,

The principal houses sworn to the Eyrie are Royce, Baelish, Egen, Waynwood, Hunter, Redfort, Corbray, Belmore, Melcolm, and Hersy.

HOUSE TULLY

The Tullys never reigned as kings, though they held rich lands and the great castle at Riverrun for a thousand years. During the Wars of Conquest, the riverlands belonged to Harren the Black, King of the Isles. Harren's grandfather, King Harwyn Hardhand, had taken the Trident from Arrec the Storm King, whose ancestors had conquered all the way to the Neck three hundred years earlier, slaying the last of the old River Kings. A vain and bloody tyrant, Harren the Black was little loved by those he ruled, and many of the river lords deserted him to join Aegon's host. First among them was Edmyn Tully of Riverrun. When Harren and his line perished in the burning of Harrenhal, Aegon rewarded House Tully by raising Lord Edmyn to dominion over the lands of the Trident and requiring the other river lords to swear him fealty. The Tully sigil is a leaping trout, silver, on a field of rippling blue and red. The Tully words are *Family, Duty, Honor.*

HOSTER TULLY, Lord of Riverrun,

— his wife, {LADY MINISA, of House Whent}, died in childbed,
— their children:
  — CATELYN, the eldest daughter, wed to Lord Eddard Stark,
  — LYSA, the younger daughter, wed to Lord Jon Arryn,
  — SER EDMURE, heir to Riverrun,
— his brother, SER BRYNDEN, called the Blackfish,
— his household:
  — MAESTER VYMAN, counselor, healer, and tutor,
  — SER DESMOND GRELL, master-at-arms,
  — SER ROBIN RYGER, captain of the guard,
  — UTHERYDES WAYN, steward of Riverrun,
— his knights and lords bannermen:
  — JASON MALLISTER, Lord of Seagard,
    — PATREK MALLISTER, his son and heir,
  — WALDER FREY, Lord of the Crossing,
    — his numerous sons, grandsons, and bastards,
  — JONOS BRACKEN, Lord of the Stone Hedge,
  — TYTOS BLACKWOOD, Lord of Raventree,
  — SER RAYMUN DARRY,
  — SER KARYL VANCE,
  — SER MARQ PIPER,

— SHELLA WHENT, Lady of Harrenhal,
  — SER WILLIS WODE, a knight in her
    service,

Lesser houses sworn to Riverrun include Darry,
Frey, Mallister, Bracken, Blackwood, Whent, Ryger,
Piper, Vance.

HOUSE TYRELL

The Tyrells rose to power as stewards to the Kings of the Reach, whose domain included the fertile plains of the southwest from the Dornish marches and Blackwater Rush to the shores of the Sunset Sea. Through the female line, they claim descent from Garth Greenhand, gardener king of the First Men, who wore a crown of vines and flowers and made the land bloom. When King Mern, last of the old line, perished on the Field of Fire, his steward Harlen Tyrell surrendered Highgarden to Aegon Targaryen, pledging fealty. Aegon granted him the castle and dominion over the Reach. The Tyrell sigil is a golden rose on a grass-green field. Their words are *Growing Strong.*

> MACE TYRELL, Lord of Highgarden, Warden of the South, Defender of the Marches, High Marshal of the Reach,
> — his wife, LADY ALERIE, of House Hightower of Oldtown,
> — their children:

- WILLAS, their eldest son, heir to
  Highgarden,
- SER GARLAN, called the Gallant, their
  second son,
- SER LORAS, the Knight of Flowers,
  their youngest son,
- MARGAERY, their daughter, a maid of
  fourteen years,
- his widowed mother, LADY OLENNA of
House Redwyne, called the Queen of
Thorns,
- his sisters:
  - MINA, wed to Lord Paxter Redwyne,
  - JANNA, wed to Ser Jon Fossoway,
- his uncles:
  - GARTH, called the Gross, Lord
    Seneschal of Highgarden,
    - his bastard sons, GARSE and
      GARRETT FLOWERS,
  - SER MORYN, Lord Commander of the
    City Watch of Oldtown,
  - MAESTER GORMON, a scholar of the
    Citadel,
- his household:
  - MAESTER LOMYS, counselor, healer,
    and tutor,
  - IGON VYRWEL, captain of the guard,
  - SER VORTIMER CRANE, master-at-
    arms,
- his knights and lord bannermen:
  - PAXTER REDWYNE, Lord of the Arbor,
    - his wife, LADY MINA, of House
      Tyrell,

— their children:
— SER HORAS, mocked as Horror,
twin to Hobber,
— SER HOBBER, mocked as Slobber,
twin to Horas,
— DESMERA, a maid of fifteen,
— RANDYLL TARLY, Lord of Horn Hill,
— SAMWELL, his elder son, of the
Night's Watch,
— DICKON, his younger son, heir to
Horn Hill,
— ARWYN OAKHEART, Lady of Old Oak,
— MATHIS ROWAN, Lord of Goldengrove,
— LEYTON HIGHTOWER, Voice of
Oldtown, Lord of the Port,
— SER JON FOSSOWAY,

Principal houses sworn to Highgarden are Vyrwel, Florent, Oakheart, Hightower, Crane, Tarly, Redwyne, Rowan, Fossoway, and Mullendore.

HOUSE GREYJOY

The Greyjoys of Pyke claim descent from the Grey King of the Age of Heroes. Legend says the Grey King ruled not only the western isles but the sea itself, and took a mermaid to wife.

For thousands of years, raiders from the Iron Islands —called "ironmen" by those they plundered—were the terrors of the seas, sailing as far as the Port of Ibben and the Summer Isles. They prided themselves on their fierceness in battle and their sacred freedoms. Each island had its own "salt king" and "rock king." The High King of the Isles was chosen from among their number, until King Urron made the throne hereditary by murdering the other kings when they assembled for a choosing. Urron's own line was extinguished a thousand years later when the Andals swept over the islands. The Greyjoys, like other island lords, intermarried with the conquerers.

The Iron Kings extended their rule far beyond the isles themselves, carving kingdoms out of the mainland with fire and sword. King Qhored could truth-fully boast that his writ ran "wherever men can smell salt water or hear the crash of waves." In later centuries, Qhored's descendents lost the Arbor, Oldtown, Bear Island, and much of the western shore. Still, come the Wars of Conquest, King Harren the Black ruled all the lands between the mountains, from the Neck to the Blackwater Rush. When Harren and his sons perished in the fall of Harrenhal, Aegon Targaryen granted the riverlands to House Tully, and allowed the surviving lords of the Iron Islands to revive their ancient custom and chose who should have the primacy among them. They chose Lord Vickon Greyjoy of Pyke.

The Greyjoy sigil is a golden kraken upon a black field. Their words are *We Do Not Sow*.

BALON GREYJOY, Lord of the Iron Islands,
    King of Salt and Rock, Son of the Sea Wind,
    Lord Reaper of Pyke,
    — his wife, LADY ALANNYS, of House
      Harlaw,
    — their children:
      — {RODRIK}, their eldest son, slain at
        Seagard during Greyjoy's Rebellion,
      — {MARON}, their second son, slain on
        the walls of Pyke during Greyjoy's
        Rebellion,
      — ASHA, their daughter, captain of the
        Black Wind,
      — THEON, their sole surviving son, heir
        to Pyke, a ward of Lord Eddard Stark,

— his brothers:
- — EURON, called Crow's Eye, captain of the *Silence*, an outlaw, pirate, and raider,
- — VICTARION, Lord Captain of the Iron Fleet,
- — AERON, called Damphair, a priest of the Drowned God,

Lesser houses sworn to Pyke include Harlaw, Stonehouse, Merlyn, Sunderly, Botley, Tawney, Wynch, Goodbrother.

HOUSE MARTELL

Nymeria, the warrior queen of the Rhoyne, brought her ten thousand ships to land in Dorne, the southernmost of the Seven Kingdoms, and took Lord Mors Martell to husband. With her help, he vanquished his rivals to rule all Dorne. The Rhoynar influence remains strong. Thus Dornish rulers style themselves "Prince" rather than "King." Under Dornish law, lands and titles pass to the eldest child, not the eldest male. Dorne, alone of the Seven Kingdoms, was never conquered by Aegon the Dragon. It was not permanently joined to the realm until two hundred years later, and then by marriage and treaty, not the sword. Peaceable King Daeron II succeeded where the warriors had failed by wedding the Dornish princess Myriah and giving his own sister in marriage to the reigning Prince of Dorne. The Martell banner is a red sun pierced by a golden spear. Their words are *Unbowed, Unbent, Unbroken*.

DORAN NYMEROS MARTELL, Lord of
   Sunspear, Prince of Dorne,

— his wife, MELLARIO, of the Free City of Norvos,
— their children:
  — PRINCESS ARIANNE, their eldest daughter, heir to Sunspear,
  — PRINCE QUENTYN, their elder son,
  — PRINCE TRYSTANE, their younger son,
— his siblings:
  — his sister, {PRINCESS ELIA}, wed to Prince Rhaegar Targaryen, slain during the Sack of King's Landing,
    — their children:
      — {PRINCESS RHAENYS}, a young girl, slain during the Sack of King's Landing,
      — {PRINCE AEGON}, a babe, slain during the Sack of King's Landing,
  — his brother, PRINCE OBERYN, the Red Viper,
— his household:
  — AREO HOTAH, a Norvoshi sellsword, captain of guards,
  — MAESTER CALEOTTE, counselor, healer, and tutor,
— his knights and lord bannermen:
  — EDRIC DAYNE, Lord of Starfall,

The principal houses sworn to Sunspear include Jordayne, Santagar, Allyrion, Toland, Yronwood, Wyl, Fowler, and Dayne.

The Old Dynasty
HOUSE TARGARYEN

The Targaryens are the blood of the dragon, descended from the high lords of the ancient Freehold of Valyria, their heritage proclaimed in a striking (some say inhuman) beauty, with lilac or indigo or violet eyes and hair of silver-gold or platinum white.

Aegon the Dragon's ancestors escaped the Doom of Valyria and the chaos and slaughter that followed to settle on Dragonstone, a rocky island in the narrow sea. It was from there that Aegon and his sisters Visenya and Rhaenys sailed to conquer the Seven Kingdoms. To preserve the blood royal and keep it pure, House Targaryen has often followed the Valyrian custom of wedding brother to sister. Aegon himself took both his sisters to wife, and fathered sons on each. The Targaryen banner is a three-headed dragon, red on black, the three heads representing Aegon and his sisters. The Targaryen words are *Fire and Blood*.

THE TARGARYEN SUCCESSION
dated by years after Aegon's Landing

1–37	Aegon I	Aegon the Conquerer, Aegon the Dragon,
37–42	Aenys I	son of Aegon and Rhaenys,
42–48	Maegor I	Maegor the Cruel, son of Aegon and Visenya,
48–103	Jaehaerys I	the Old King, the Conciliator, Aenys' son,
103–129	Viserys I	grandson to Jaehaerys,
129–131	Aegon II	eldest son of Viserys, [Aegon II's ascent was disputed by his sister Rhaenyra, a year his elder. Both perished in the war between them, called by singers the Dance of the Dragons.]
131–157	Aegon III	the Dragonbane, Rhaenyra's son, [The last of the Targaryen dragons died during the reign of Aegon III.]
157–161	Daeron I	the Young Dragon, the Boy King, eldest son of Aegon III, [Daeron conquered Dorne, but was unable to hold it, and died young.]
161–171	Baelor I	the Beloved, the Blessed, septon and king, second son of Aegon III,
171–172	Viserys II	younger brother of Aegon III,
172–184	Aegon IV	the Unworthy, eldest son of Viserys, [His younger brother, Prince Aemon the Dragonknight, was champion and some say lover to Queen Naerys.]

184–209	Daeron II	Queen Naerys' son, by Aegon or Aemon, [Daeron brought Dorne into the realm by wedding the Dornish princess Myriah.]
209–221	Aerys I	second son to Daeron II (left no issue),
221–233	Maekar I	fourth son of Daeron II,
233–259	Aegon V	the Unlikely, Maekar's fourth son,
259–262	Jaehaerys II	second son of Aegon the Unlikely,
262–283	Aerys II	the Mad King, only son to Jaehaerys,

Therein the line of the dragon kings ended, when Aerys II was dethroned and killed, along with his heir, the crown prince Rhaegar Targaryen, slain by Robert Baratheon on the Trident.

THE LAST TARGARYENS

{KING AERYS TARGARYEN}, the Second of His Name, slain by Jaime Lannister during the Sack of King's Landing,
— his sister and wife, {QUEEN RHAELLA} of House Targaryen, died in childbed on Dragonstone,
— their children:
— {PRINCE RHAEGAR}, heir to the Iron Throne, slain by Robert Baratheon on the Trident,
— his wife, {PRINCESS ELIA} of House Martell, slain during the Sack of King's Landing,
— their children:
— {PRINCESS RHAENYS}, a young girl, slain during the Sack of King's Landing,

— {PRINCE AEGON}, a babe, slain during the Sack of King's Landing,
— PRINCE VISERYS, styling himself Viserys, the Third of His Name, Lord of the Seven Kingdoms, called the Beggar King,
— PRINCESS DAENERYS, called Daenerys Stormborn, a maid of thirteen years.

ACKNOWLEDGMENTS

The devil is in the details, they say.

A book this size has a *lot* of devils, any one of which will bite you if you don't watch out. Fortunately, I know a lot of angels.

Thanks and appreciation, therefore, to all those good folks who so kindly lent me their ears and their expertise (and in some cases their books) so I could get all those little details right—to Sage Walker, Martin Wright, Melinda Snodgrass, Carl Keim, Bruce Baugh, Tim O'Brien, Roger Zelazny, Jane Lindskold, and Laura J. Mixon, and of course to Parris.

And a special thanks to Jennifer Hershey, for labors above and beyond the call . . .

ABOUT THE AUTHOR

GEORGE R. R. MARTIN sold his first story in 1971 and hasn't stopped. As a writer/producer, he worked on *The Twilight Zone, Beauty and the Beast,* and various feature films and pilots that were never made. In the mid '90s he returned to prose and began work on A Song of Ice and Fire. He has been in the Seven Kingdoms ever since. He lives in Santa Fe, New Mexico, with the lovely Parris.

George R. R. Martin's
epic fantasy saga
A Song of Ice and Fire

begins with
A GAME OF THRONES

and continues in
A CLASH OF KINGS

A STORM OF SWORDS

A FEAST FOR CROWS

Don't miss any volume in the series!

Now, here's a special preview of
the next book in

George R. R. Martin's

landmark series

A CLASH OF KINGS

the riveting sequel to
A GAME OF THRONES

On sale now

THEON

There was no safe anchorage at Pyke, but Theon Greyjoy wished to look on his father's castle from the sea, to see it as he had seen it last, ten years before, when Robert Baratheon's war galley had borne him from the island to be a ward of Eddard Stark. On that day he had stood beside the rail, listening to the stroke of the oars and the pounding of the master's drum while he watched Pyke grow smaller and smaller in the distance, until it vanished beneath a green horizon. Now he wanted to see it grow larger, to rise from the sea before him.

Obedient to his wishes, the *Myraham* beat her way past the point with her sails snapping and her captain cursing the wind and his crew and the follies of highborn lordlings. Theon drew the hood of his cloak up against the spray, and looked for home.

The shore was all sharp rocks and glowering cliffs, and the castle seemed one with the rest, its towers and walls and bridges quarried from the same grey-black stone, wet by the same salt waves, festooned with the same spreading patches of dark green moss, speckled by the droppings of the same sea birds. The point of land on which the Greyjoys had raised their fortress had once thrust like a sword into the bowels of the ocean, but the great waves had hammered at it day and night until the land broke and shattered, thousands of years past. All that remained were three bare and barren islands and a dozen towering stacks of rock that rose from the water like the pillars of some sea god's temple, while the angry waves foamed and crashed around them.

Drear, dark, forbidding, Pyke stood atop those islands and pillars, almost a part of them, its curtain walls closing off the headland to guard the foot of the great stone bridge that leapt from the clifftop to the largest islet, dominated by massive bulk of the Great Keep, whose walls still bore the scars of Robert Baratheon's assault. Further out were the Kitchen Keep and the Bloody Keep, each on its own stony island at the end of a high, vaulting bridge. Towers and outbuildings clung to the stacks beyond, linked to each other by covered archways when the pillars stood close, by long swaying walks of wood and rope when they did not. The Sea Tower rose from the outmost island at the point of the broken sword, the oldest part of the castle, round and tall, the sheer-sided pillar on which it stood half eaten through by the endless battering of the waves. The base of the tower was white from centuries of salt spray, the upper stories green from the moss that crawled over it like a thick blanket, the jagged crown black with soot from its nightly watchfire.

Above the Sea Tower snapped his father's sigil on a long banner with three tails. The *Myraham* was too far off for Theon to see more than the cloth itself, but he knew the device it bore: the golden kraken of House Greyjoy, arms writhing and reaching against the black field. The banner streamed from an iron mast, shivering and twisting as the wind gusted, like a bird struggling to take flight. Best of all, the direwolf of Stark did not fly above, casting its shadow down upon the Greyjoy kraken.

Theon had never seen a more stirring sight. In the sky behind the castle, the fine red tail of the comet was visible through thin, scuttling clouds. All the way from Riverrun to Seagard, the Mallisters had argued about its meaning. *It is my comet*, Theon told himself, sliding a hand into his fur-lined cloak to touch the oilskin pouch snug in its pocket. Inside was the letter Robb Stark had given him, paper as good as a crown.

"Does the castle look as you remember it, milord?" the captain's daughter asked as she pressed herself against his arm.

"It looks smaller," Theon confessed, "though perhaps that is only the distance." The *Myraham* was a fat-bellied southron merchanter up from Oldtown, carrying wine and spice and seed to trade for iron ore. Her captain was a fat-bellied southron merchanter as well, and the stony sea that foamed at the feet of the castle made his plump lips quiver, so he stayed well out, further than Theon would have liked. An ironborn captain in a longship would have taken them along the cliffs and under the high bridge that spanned the gap between the gatehouse and the Great Keep, but this plump Oldtowner had neither the craft, the crew, nor the courage to attempt such a thing. So they sailed past at a safe distance, and Theon must content himself with seeing Pyke from afar. Even so, the *Myraham* had to struggle mightily to keep itself off those rocks.

"It must be windy there," the captain's daughter observed.

He laughed. "Windy and cold and damp. A miserable hard place, in truth . . . but my lord father once told me that hard places breed hard men, and hard men rule the world."

The captain's face was as green as the sea when he came bowing up to Theon and asked, "May we make for port now, milord?"

"You may," Theon said, a faint smile playing about his lips. The promise of gold had turned the Oldtowner into a shameless lickspittle. It would have been a much different voyage if a longship from the islands had been waiting at Seagard, as he'd hoped. Ironborn captains were proud and wilful, and did not go in awe of a man's blood. The islands were too small for awe, and a longship smaller still. If every captain was a king aboard his own ship, as was often said, it was small wonder they named the islands the land of ten thousand kings. And when you have seen your kings shit over the rail and turn green in a storm, it was hard to bend the knee and pretend they were a god. "The Drowned God makes men," old King Urron Redhand had once said, thousands of years ago, "but it's men who make crowns."

The *Myraham* was rounding a wooded point. Below the pine-clad bluffs, a dozen fishing boats were pulling in their nets. The big merchanter stayed well out from them, tacking. Theon moved to the bow for a better view. He saw the castle first, the stronghold of the Botleys, a lesser house sworn to his father. When he was a boy it had been timber and wattle, but Robert Baratheon had razed that structure to the ground. Lord Sawane had rebuilt in stone, for now a small square keep crowned the hill. Pale green flags drooped from the squat corner towers; the Botley banner, he knew, emblazoned with a shoal of silvery fish.

Beneath the dubious protection of the fish-ridden little castle lay the village of Lordsport, its harbor aswarm with ships. When last he'd seen Lordsport, it had been a smoking wasteland, the skeletons of burnt galleys lying black on the stony shore like the bones of dead leviathans, the houses no more than broken walls and cold ashes. After ten years, few traces of the war remained. The smallfolk had built new hovels with the stones of the old, and cut fresh sod for their roofs. A new inn had risen beside the landing, twice the size of the old one, with a lower story of cut stone and two upper stories of timber. The sept beyond had never been rebuilt, though; only a seven-sided foundation remained to show where it had stood. Robert Baratheon's fury had soured the ironmen's taste for the new gods, it would seem.

Theon was more interested in ships than gods. Among the masts of countless fishing boats, he spied a Tyroshi trading galley offloading beside a lumbering Ibbenese cog with her black-tarred hull. A great number of longships, fifty or sixty at the least, stood out to sea or lay beached on the pebbled shore to the north. *So many*, he thought, uneasy. Theon could not recall ever seeing this many longships in Lordsport before, save on the eve of his father's ill-fated rebellion. And some of the sails bore devices from the other islands; the blood moon of Wynch, Lord Goodbrother's banded black warhorn, Harlaw's silver scythe. He searched for a glimpse of his uncle Euron's *Silence*. Of that lean and terrible red ship he saw no sign, but his father's *Great Kraken* was there, looming over the lesser craft, her bow ornamented with a grey iron ram in the shape of its namesake.

Had Lord Balon anticipated him and called the Greyjoy banners when he received Robb's message from Riverrun? His hand went inside his cloak again, to the oilskin pouch. No one knew of his letter but Robb Stark; they were no fools, and only a fool entrusted his secrets to a bird. Still, Lord Balon was no fool either. He might well have guessed why his son was coming home at long last, and acted accordingly.

The thought did not please him. His father's war was long done, and lost. This was Theon's hour—his plan, his glory, and in time, his crown. *Yet if the longships are hosting . . .*

It might be only a caution, now that he thought on it. A defensive move, lest the war spill out across the sea. Old men were cautious by nature. His father was old now, and so too his uncle Victarion, who commanded the Iron Fleet. His uncle Euron was a different song, to be sure, but the *Silence* did not seem to be in port. *It is for the good*, Theon told himself. *This way, I shall be able to strike all the more quickly.*

As the *Myraham* made her way landward, Theon paced the deck restlessly, scanning the shore. He had not thought to find Lord Balon himself waiting at quayside, but surely his father would have sent someone to meet him. Old Sylas Sourmouth the steward, or perhaps Lord Botley or Dagmer Cleftjaw. They knew he was coming. Robb had sent word before Theon left Riverrun, and when they'd found no longship waiting at Seagard, Lord Jason Mallister had sent his own birds to Pyke, supposing that Robb's were lost.

Yet he saw no familiar faces on the landing, no honor guard of riders to escort him from Lordsport to Pyke, only smallfolk going about their small business. Shorehands rolled casks of wine off the Tyroshi trader, fisherfolk cried the day's catch, children ran and played. A priest in the sea-water robes of the Drowned God was leading a pair of horses along the pebbled shore, while above him a slattern leaned out a window in the inn, calling out to some passing Ibbanese sailors.

A handful of Lordsport merchants had gathered to meet the ship. They shouted up questions as the *Myraham* was tying up. "We're out of Oldtown," the captain called down in reply, "bearing apples and oranges, wines from the Arbor, feathers from the Summer Isles. I have pepper, woven leathers, a bolt of Myrish lace, mirrors for milady, a pair of Oldtown woodharps sweet as any you ever heard." The gangplank descended with a creak and a thud. "And I've brought your heir back to you."

The Lordsport men gazed on Theon with blank, bovine eyes, and he realized that they did not know who he was. It made him angry. He pressed a golden dragon into the captain's palm. "Have your men bring my things." Without waiting for a reply, he strode down the gangplank. "Innkeep," he barked, "I require a horse."

"As you say, m'lord," the man responded, without so much as a bow. He had forgotten how bold the ironborn could be. "Happens as I have one might do. Where would you be riding, m'lord?"

"Pyke," Theon snapped curtly. The fool *still* did not know him. He should have worn his good doublet, with the kraken embroidered on the breast, that would have left no question.

"You'll want to be off soon, to reach Pyke afore dark," the innkeep said. "My boy will go with you and show you the way."

"Your boy will not be needed," a deep voice called, "nor your horse. I shall see my nephew back to his father's house."

The speaker was the priest he had seen leading the horses along the shoreline. As the man approached, the smallfolk bent the knee, and Theon heard the innkeep murmur, "Damphair."

Tall and thin, with fierce black eyes and a beak of a nose, the priest was garbed in mottled robes of green and grey and blue, the swirling colors of the Drowned God. A waterskin hung under his arm on a leather strap, and ropes of dried seaweed were braided through his waist-long black hair and untrimmed beard.

Theon frowned at the prod of memory. In one of his few curt letters, Lord Balon had written of his youngest brother going down in a storm, and turning holy when he washed up safe on shore. "Uncle Aeron?" he said, doubtfully.

"Nephew Theon," the priest replied. "Your lord father bid me fetch you. Come."

"In a moment, uncle." He turned back to the *Myraham*. "My things," he commanded the captain.

A sailor fetched him down his tall yew bow and quiver of arrows, but it was the captain's daughter who brought the pack with his good clothing. "Milord." Her eyes were red. When he took the pack, she made as if to embrace him, there in front of her own father and his priestly uncle and half the island.

Theon turned deftly aside. "You have my thanks."

"Please," she said, "I do love you well, milord."

"I must go." He hurried after his uncle, who was already well down the pier. Theon caught him with a dozen long strides. "I had not looked for you, uncle. After ten years, I thought perhaps my lord father and lady mother might come themselves, or send Dagmer with an honor guard."

"It is not for you to question the commands of the Lord Reaper of Pyke." The priest's manner was chilly, most unlike the man Theon remembered. Aeron Greyjoy had been the most amiable of his uncles, feckless and quick to laugh, fond of songs, ale, and women. "As to Dagmer, the Cleftjaw is gone to Old Wyk at your father's behest, to roust the Stonehouses and the Drumms."

"To what purpose?" Theon asked sharply. "Why are the longships hosting?"

"Why have longships ever hosted?" His uncle had left the horses tied up in front of the waterside inn. When they reached them, he turned to Theon. "Tell me true, nephew. Do you pray to the wolf gods now?"

Theon seldom prayed at all, but that was not something you confessed to a priest, even your father's own brother. "Ned Stark prayed to a tree. No, I care nothing for Stark's gods."

"Good. Kneel."

The ground was all stones and mud. "Uncle, I—"

"*Kneel*. Or are you too proud now, a lordling of the green lands come among us?"

Scowling, Theon knelt. He had a purpose here, and might need Aeron's help to achieve it. A crown was worth a little mud and horseshit on his breeches, he supposed.

"Bow your head." Lifting the skin, his uncle pulled the cork and directed a thin stream of seawater down upon Theon's head. It drenched his hair and ran over his forehead into his eyes. Sheets washed down his cheeks, and a finger crept under his cloak and doublet and down his back, a cold rivulet along his spine. The salt made his eyes burn, until it was all he could do not to cry out. He could taste the ocean on his lips. "Let Theon your servant be born again from the sea, as you were," Aeron Greyjoy intoned. "Bless him with salt, bless him with stone, bless him with steel. Nephew, do you still know the words?"

"What is dead may never die," Theon said, remembering.

"What is dead may never die," his uncle echoed, "but rises again, harder and stronger. Stand."

Theon stood, blinking back tears from the salt in his eyes. Wordless, his uncle corked the waterskin, untied his horse, and mounted. Theon did the same. They set off together, leaving the inn and the harbor behind them, up past the castle of Lord Botley into the stony hills. The priest ventured no further word.

"I have been half my life away from home," Theon ventured at last. "Will I find the islands changed?"

"Men fish the sea, dig in the earth, and die. Women birth children in blood and pain, and die. Night follows day. The winds and tides remain. The islands are as our god made them."

Gods, he has grown grim, Theon thought. "Will I find my sister and my lady mother at Pyke?"

"You will not. Your mother dwells on Harlaw, with her own sister. It is less raw there, and her cough troubles her. Your sister has taken *Black Wind* to Great Wyk, with messages from your lord father. She will return e'er long, you may be sure."

Theon did not need to be told that *Black Wind* was Asha's longship. He had not seen his sister in ten years, but that much he knew of her. Odd that she would call it that, when Robb Stark had a wolf named Grey Wind. "Stark is grey and Greyjoy's black," he murmured, smiling, "but it seems we're both windy."

The priest had nothing to say to that.

"And what of you, uncle?" Theon asked. "You were no priest when I was taken from Pyke. I remember how you would sing the old reaving songs standing on the table with a horn of ale in hand."

"Young I was, and vain," Aeron Greyjoy said, "but the sea washed my follies and my vanities away. That man drowned, nephew. His lungs filled with seawater, and the fish ate the scales off his eyes. When I rose again, I saw clearly."

He is mad as he is sour, Theon thought, saddened. He had liked what he remembered of the old Aeron Greyjoy. "Uncle, why has my father called his swords and sails?"

"Doubtless he will tell you at Pyke."

"I would know his plans now," Theon said.

"From me, you shall not. We are commanded not to speak of this to any man."

"Even to *me?*" Theon's anger flared. He'd led men in war, hunted with a king, won honor in tourney melees, ridden with Brynden Blackfish and Greatjon Umber, fought in the Whispering Wood, bedded more girls than he could name, and yet this uncle was treating him as though he were still a child of ten. "If my father makes plans for war, I must know of them. I am not '*any man*,' I am heir to Pyke and the Iron Islands."

"As to that," his uncle said, "we shall see."

The words were a slap in the face. "What does that mean, *we shall see?*" Theon said scornfully. "My brothers are both dead. I am my lord father's only living son."

"Your sister lives." Aeron gave Theon not so much as the courtesy of a glance.

Asha, he thought, confounded. She was three years older than Theon, yet still . . . "A woman may inherit only if there is no male heir in the direct line," he insisted loudly. "I will not be cheated of my rights, I warn you."

His uncle grunted. "You *warn* a servant of the Drowned God, boy? You have forgotten more than you know. And you are a great fool if you believe your lord father will ever hand these holy islands over to a Stark. Now be silent. The ride is long enough without your magpie chatterings."

Theon held his tongue, though not without struggle. *So that is the way of it*, he thought. He almost laughed. As if ten years in Winterfell could make a Stark. Lord Eddard may have raised him among his own children, but Theon had never truly felt one of them. The whole castle, from Ned Stark himself to the lowliest kitchen scullion, knew he was there as hostage to his father's good behavior, and treated him accordingly. Even the bastard Jon Snow had been accorded more honor than he had.

Lord Eddard had tried to play the father to him from time to time, but to Theon he had always remained the man who'd brought blood and fire to Pyke and taken him from his home. As a boy, he had lived in fear of Stark's stern face and great dark sword. His lady wife was, if anything, even more distant and suspicious.

As for their children, the younger ones had been mewling babes for most of his years at Winterfell. Only Robb and his baseborn half-brother Jon Snow had been old enough to be worth his notice. The bastard was a sullen boy, quick to sense a slight, jealous of Theon's high birth and Robb's regard for him. For Robb himself, Theon did have a certain affection, as for a younger brother . . . but it would be best not to mention that. In Pyke, it would seem, the old wars were still being fought. That ought not surprise him. The Iron Islands lived in the past; the present was too hard and bitter to be borne. Besides, his father and uncles were old, and the old lords were like that; they took their dusty feuds to the grave, forgetting nothing and forgiving less.

The path they rode wound up and up, into bare and stony hills. Soon they were out of sight of the sea, though the smell of salt still hung sharp in the damp air. They kept a steady plodding pace, past a shepherd's croft and the abandoned workings of a mine. This new, holy Aeron Greyjoy was not much for talk. They rode in a gloom of silence. Finally Theon could suffer it no longer. "Robb Stark is Lord of Winterfell now," he said.

Aeron rode on. "One wolf is much like the other."

"Robb has broken fealty with the Iron Throne and crowned himself King in the North. There's war."

"The maester's ravens fly over salt as soon as rock. This news is old and cold."

"It means a new day, uncle," Theon promised.

"Every morning brings a new day, much like the old."

"In Riverrun, they would tell you different," he said. "I've heard it said that the red comet is a herald of a new age. A messenger from the gods, they say."

"A sign it is," the priest agreed, "but from our god, not theirs. A burning brand it is, such as our people carried of old. It is the flame the Drowned God brought from the sea, and it proclaims a rising tide. It is time to hoist our sails and go forth into the world with fire and sword, as he did."

Theon smiled. "I could not agree more."

"A man agrees with god as a raindrop with the storm."

This raindrop will one day be a king, old man. Theon had suffered quite enough of his uncle's gloom. He put his spurs into his horse and trotted on ahead, smiling.

It was nigh on sunset when they reached the walls of Pyke, a crescent of dark stone that ran from cliff to cliff, with the gatehouse in the center and three square towers to either side. Theon could still make out the scars left by the stones of Robert Baratheon's catapults. A new south tower had risen from the ruins of the old, its stone a paler shade of grey, and as yet unmarred by patches of lichen. That was where Robert had made his breach, swarming in over the rubble and corpses with his warhammer in hand and Ned Stark at his side. Theon had watched from the safety of the Sea Tower, and sometimes he still saw the torches in his dreams, and heard the dull thunder of the collapse.

The gates stood open to him, the rusted iron portcullis drawn up. The guards atop the battlements watched with strangers' eyes as Theon Greyjoy came home at last.

Beyond the curtain wall were half a hundred acres of headland hard against the sky and the sea. The stables were here, and the kennels, and a scatter of other outbuildings. Sheep and swine huddled in their pens, and the castle dogs ran free. To the south were the cliffs, and the wide stone bridge to the Great Keep. Theon could hear the crashing of waves as he swung down from his saddle. A stableman came to take his horse. A pair of gaunt children and some serving men stared at him with dull eyes, but there was no sign of his lord father, nor anyone else he recalled from boyhood. *A bleak and bitter homecoming*, he thought.

The priest had not dismounted. "Will you not stay the night and share our meat and mead, uncle?"

"Bring you, I was told. You are brought. Now I return to our god's business." Aeron Greyjoy turned his horse and rode slowly out beneath the muddy spikes of the portcullis.

A bentback old crone in a shapeless grey dress approached him warily. "M'lord," she said, "I am sent to make you welcome and show you to chambers."

"By whose bidding?"

"Your lord father, m'lord."

Theon pulled off his gloves. "So you *do* know who I am. Why is my father not here to greet me?"

"He awaits you in the Sea Tower, m'lord. When you are rested from your trip."

And I thought Ned Stark cold. "And who are you?"

"Helya, who keeps this castle for your lord father."

"Sylas was steward here. They called him Sourmouth." Even now, Theon could recall the winey stench of the old man's breath.

"Dead these five years, m'lord."

"And what of Maester Qalen, where is he?"

"He sleeps in the sea. Wendamyr keeps the ravens now, but he is gone south to Oldtown on some maester's business."

It is as if I were a stranger here, Theon thought. *Nothing has changed, and yet everything has changed.* "Show me to my chambers, woman," he commanded. Bowing stiffly, she led him across the headland to the bridge. That at least was as he remembered; the ancient stones slick with spray and spotted by lichen and moss, the sea foaming under their feet like some great wild beast, the salt wind clutching at their clothes.

When he had imagined his homecoming, he had always pictured himself returning to the snug bedchamber in the Sea Tower where he'd slept as a child. Instead the old woman led him to the Bloody Keep. The halls were larger and better furnished, if no less cold nor damp. Theon was given a suite of chilly rooms with ceilings so high that they were lost in gloom. He might have been more impressed if he had not known that these were the very chambers that had given the Bloody Keep its name. A thousand years before, the sons of the River King had been slaughtered here, hacked to bits in their beds so the pieces of their bodies might be sent back to their father on the mainland.

But Theon was a Greyjoy, and Greyjoys were not murdered in Pyke, except once in a great while by their brothers, and his brothers were both mercifully dead. It was not the memories of ancient murders that made him glance about with distaste. The wall hangings were green with mildew, the mattress musty-smelling and sagging, and rushes old and brittle. It had been years since these chambers had last been opened. The damp went bone deep.

"I'll have a basin of hot water, and a fire in this hearth," he told the crone. "See that they light braziers in the other rooms to drive out some of the chill. And gods be good, get someone in here at once to change these rushes."

"Yes, m'lord. As you command." She fled.

After some time, they brought the hot water he had asked for. It was only tepid, and soon cold, and seawater in the bargain, but it served to wash the dust of the long ride from his face and hair and hands. As bondservants scurried about lighting braziers, Theon stripped off his travel-stained clothing and dressed to meet his father. He chose boots of supple black leather, soft lambswool breeches of silvery-grey, a black velvet doublet with the golden kraken of the Greyjoys embroidered on the breast. Around his throat he fastened a slender gold chain, around his waist a belt of bleached white leather. He hung a dirk at one hip and a longsword at the other, in scabbards striped black-and-gold. Drawing the dirk, he tested its edge with his thumb, pulled a whetstone from his belt pouch, and gave it a few licks. He prided himself on keeping his weapons sharp. "When I return, I shall expect a warm room and clean rushes," he warned the bondservants as he drew on a pair of black gloves, the silk decorated with a delicate scrollwork tracery in golden thread.

Theon returned to the Great Keep through a covered stone walkway, the echoes of his footsteps mingling with the ceaseless rumble of the sea below. To get to the Sea Tower on its crooked pillar, he must needs cross three further bridges, each narrower than the one before. The last was made of rope and wood, and the wet salt wind made it sway underfoot like a living thing. Theon's heart was in his mouth by the time he was halfway across. A long way below, the waves threw up tall plumes of spray as they crashed against the rock. As a boy, he used to run across this bridge, even in the black of night. *Boys believe nothing can hurt them*, his doubt whispered. *Grown men know better.*

The door was narrow, made of grey wood studded with iron, and Theon found it barred from the inside. He hammered on it with a fist, and cursed when a splinter snagged the fine silk of his glove. The wood was damp and moldy, the iron studs rusted.

After a moment the door was opened from within by a guard in a black iron breastplate and pothelm. "You are the son?"

"Out of my way, or you'll learn who I am, to your sorrow." The man stood aside. Theon climbed the twisting steps to the solar. He found his father seated beside a brazier, beneath a robe of musty sealskins that covered him foot to chin. At the sound of boots on stone, the Lord of the Iron Islands lifted his eyes to behold his last living son. He was smaller than Theon remembered him. And so gaunt. Balon

Greyjoy had always been thin, but now he looked as though the gods had put him in a cauldron and boiled every spare ounce of flesh from his bones, until nothing remained but hair and skin. Bone thin and bone hard he was, with a face that might have been chipped from flint. His eyes were flinty too, black and sharp, but the years and the salt winds had turned his hair the grey of a winter sea, flecked with white-caps. Unbound, it hung past the small of the back.

"Nine years, is it?" Lord Balon said at last.

"Ten," Theon answered, pulling off his torn gloves.

"A boy they took," his father said. "What are you now?"

"A man," Theon answered. "Your blood and your heir."

Lord Balon grunted. "We shall see."

"You shall," Theon promised.

"Ten years, you say. Stark had you as long as I. And now you come as his envoy."

"Not his," Theon said. "Lord Eddard is dead, beheaded by the Lannister queen."

"They are both dead," Lord Balon said. "Stark, and that Robert who took broke my walls with his stones. Once I vowed I'd live to see them both in their graves, and now I have." He grimaced. "Yet the cold and the damp still make my joints ache, as when they were alive. So what does it serve?"

"It serves." Theon moved closer. "I bring a letter—"

"Did Ned Stark dress you like that?" his father interrupted, squinting up from beneath his robe. "Was it his pleasure to garb you in velvets and silks and make you his own sweet daughter?"

Theon felt the blood rising to his face. "I am no man's daughter. If you mislike my garb, I will change it."

"You will," Lord Balon agreed brusquely. Throwing off the fur robe, he pushed himself to his feet. He was not so tall as Theon remembered. "That bauble around your neck—did you buy it with gold or iron?"

Theon touched the gold chain, at a loss for words. He had forgotten. *It has been so long . . .* In the Old Way, only women decorated themselves with ornaments bought with coin. A warrior wore only the jewelry he took off the corpses of enemies slain by his own hand. *Paying the iron price*, it was called.

"You blush red as a maid, Theon," his father said. "A question was asked. Is it the gold price you paid, or the iron?"

"The gold," Theon admitted.

His father slid his fingers under the necklace and gave it a yank so hard it was like to take Theon's head off, had the chain not snapped first. "My daughter has taken an axe for a lover," Lord Balon said. "I will not have my son bedeck himself like a whore." He dropped the broken chain onto the brazier, where it slid down among the coals. "It is as I feared. The green lands have made you soft, and the Starks have made you theirs."

"You're wrong," Theon said. "Ned Stark was my gaoler, but my blood is still salt and iron."

Lord Balon turned away and warmed his boney hands over the brazier. "Yet the Stark pup sends you to me like a well-trained raven, clutching his little message."

"There is nothing small about the letter I bear," Theon said, "and the offer he makes is one *I* suggested to him."

"This wolf king heeds your counsel, does he?" The notion seemed to amuse Lord Balon.

"He heeds me, yes. I've hunted with him, trained with him, shared meat and mead with him, warred at his side. I have earned his trust. He looks on me as an older brother, he—"

"*No.*" His father jabbed a finger at his face. "Not here, not in Pyke, not in my hearing, you will not name him *brother*, this son of the man who put your true brothers to the sword. Or have you forgotten Rodrik and Maron, who were your own blood?"

"I forget nothing." Theon might have reminded his father that Ned Stark had killed neither of his sons, in truth. Rodrik had been slain by Lord Jason Mallister at Seagard, Maron crushed in the collapse of the old south tower . . . but Stark *would* have done for them just as quick had the tide of battle chanced to sweep them together. "I remember my brothers very well," he said instead. Chiefly he remembered Rodrik's drunken cuffs and Maron's cruel japes and endless lies. "I remember when my father was a king, too." He took out the letter Robb had given him, and thrust it forward. "Here. Read it . . . Your Grace."

Lord Balon broke the seal and unfolded the parchment. His black eyes flicked back and forth. "So the boy would give me a crown again," he said, "and all I need do is destroy his enemies." His thin lips twisted in a smile.

"By now Robb is likely besieging the Golden Tooth," Theon said. "Once it falls, he'll be through the hills in a day. Lord Tywin and his host are at Harrenhal, cut off from the west. The Kingslayer is a captive at Riverrun. Only Ser Stafford Lannister and the raw green levies he's been gathering remain to oppose Robb in the west. Ser Stafford will have no choice but to put himself between Robb's army and Lannisport . . . which means the city will be undefended when we descend on it by sea. If the gods are with us, even Casterly Rock itself may fall before the Lannisters so much as realize that we are upon them."

Lord Balon grunted. "Casterly Rock has never fallen."

"Until now." Theon smiled. *And how sweet that will be.*

His father did not return the smile. "So this is why Robb Stark sends you back to me, after so long? So you might win my consent to this plan of his?"

"It is my plan, not Robb's," Theon said proudly. *Mine, as the victory will be mine, and in time the crown.* "I will lead the attack myself, if it please you. As my reward I would ask that you grant me Casterly Rock for my own seat, once we have taken it from the Lannisters." With the Rock, he could hold Lannisport and the green lands of the west, and the gold-rich hills that surrounded them. It would mean wealth and power such as House Greyjoy had never known.

"You reward yourself handsomely for a notion and a few lines of scribbling." His father read the letter again. "The pup says nothing about a reward. Only that you speak for him, and I am to listen, and give him my sails and swords, and in return he will give me a crown." His flinty eyes lifted to meet his son's. "He will *give* me a crown," he repeated, his voice growing sharp.

"A poor choice of words, what is meant is—"

"What is meant is what is said. The boy will *give* me a crown. And what is given can be taken away." Lord Balon tossed the letter onto the brazier, atop the necklace. The parchment curled, blackened, and took flame.

Theon was aghast. "Have you gone mad?"

His father laid a stinging backhand across his cheek. "Mind your tongue. You are not in Winterfell now, and I am not Robb the Boy, that you should speak to me so. I am the Greyjoy, Lord Reaper of Pyke, King of Salt and Rock, Son of the Sea Wind, and no man gives me a crown. I pay the iron price. I will *take* my crown, as Urron Redhand did five thousand years ago."

Also by
GEORGE R. R. MARTIN

── Novels ──

The
Armageddon Rag

Fevre Dream

Windhaven

Dying of the Light

── Short Stories ──

Dreamsongs:
Volume I

Dreamsongs:
Volume II

Also available in Audio and eBook
THE RANDOM HOUSE PUBLISHING GROUP
www.GeorgeRRMartin.com

GAME OF THRONES

THE COMPLETE FIRST SEASON

Includes hours of bonus content including interactive guides, seven audio commentaries, and never-before-seen footage from the set.

NOW AVAILABLE
ON BLU-RAY™, DVD
and DIGITAL DOWNLOAD

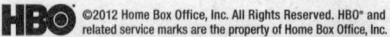

Praise for George R. R. Martin's

A GAME OF THRONES

"Grabs hold and won't let go. It's brilliant."
—Robert Jordan

"Reminiscent of T. H. White's *The Once and Future King*, this novel is an absorbing combination of the mythic, the sweepingly historical, and the intensely personal."—*Chicago Sun-Times*

"Perhaps the best of the epic fantasies—readable and realistic."—Marion Zimmer Bradley

"The major fantasy of the decade."—*The Denver Post*

"I would be very surprised if this is not the major fantasy publishing event of 1996, and I'm already impatient for the next installment."
—*Science Fiction Chronicle*

"Such a splendid tale and such a fantistorical! I read my eyes out."—Ann McCaffrey

"Martin makes a triumphant return to high fantasy with this extraordinary rich new novel. . . . Martin's trophy case is already stuffed with major prizes, including Hugos, Nebulas, Locus awards and a Bram Stoker. He's probably going to have to add another shelf, at least."
—*Publishers Weekly*

"George R. R. Martin is one of our very best science fiction writers, and this is one of his very best books."
—Raymond E. Feist

"A colorful, majestic tapestry of characters, action and plot that deserves a spot on any reader's wall . . . the pages seem to pass in a blur as you read."
—*Albuquerque Journal*

"George Martin is assuredly a new master craftsman in the guild of heroic fantasy."—Katharine Kerr

By George R. R. Martin

A Song of Ice and Fire
Book One: *A Game of Thrones*
Book Two: *A Clash of Kings*
Book Three: *A Storm of Swords*
Book Four: *A Feast for Crows*
Book Five: *A Dance with Dragons*

Dying of the Light
Windhaven (with Lisa Tuttle)
Fevre Dream
The Armageddon Rag
Dead Man's Hand (with John J. Miller)

Short Story Collections
Dreamsongs, Volume I
Dreamsongs, Volume II
A Song of Lya and Other Stories
Songs of Stars and Shadows
Sandkings
Songs the Dead Men Sing
Nightflyers
Tuf Voyaging
Portraits of His Children
Quartet

Edited by George R. R. Martin
New Voices in Science Fiction, Volumes 1–4
The Science Fiction Weight-Loss Book
(with Isaac Asimov and Martin Harry Greenberg)
The John W. Campbell Awards, Volume 5
Night Visions 3
Wild Card I–XXI

A CLASH OF KINGS

BOOK TWO OF
A SONG OF ICE AND FIRE

GEORGE R. R. MARTIN

BANTAM BOOKS • NEW YORK

2011 Bantam Books Mass Market Edition

Copyright © 1999 by George R. R. Martin
Excerpt from *A Storm of Swords* copyright © 2000 by George R. R. Martin
All rights reserved.

Published in the United States by Bantam Books, an imprint of The Random House Publishing Group, a division of Random House, Inc., New York.

BANTAM BOOKS and the rooster colophon are registered trademarks of Random House, Inc.

Originally published in hardcover in the United States by Bantam Spectra, a division of Random House, Inc., in 1999.

ISBN 978-0-553-57990-1
eBook ISBN 978-0-553-89785-2

Cover art copyright © 2011 by Larry Rostant
Cover design by David Stevenson

Maps by James Sinclair
Heraldic crests by Virginia Norey

Printed in the United States of America

www.bantamdell.com

58 57 56 55 54 53 52 51 50 49

to John and Gail
for all the meat and mead we've shared

PROLOGUE

The comet's tail spread across the dawn, a red slash that bled above the crags of Dragonstone like a wound in the pink and purple sky.

The maester stood on the windswept balcony outside his chambers. It was here the ravens came, after long flight. Their droppings speckled the gargoyles that rose twelve feet tall on either side of him, a hellhound and a wyvern, two of the thousand that brooded over the walls of the ancient fortress. When first he came to Dragonstone, the army of stone grotesques had made him uneasy, but as the years passed he had grown used to them. Now he thought of them as old friends. The three of them watched the sky together with foreboding.

The maester did not believe in omens. And yet . . . old as he was, Cressen had never seen a comet half so bright, nor yet that color, that terrible color, the color of blood and flame and sunsets. He wondered if his gargoyles had ever seen its like. They had been here so much longer than he had, and would still be here long after he was gone. If stone tongues could speak . . .

Such folly. He leaned against the battlement, the sea crashing beneath him, the black stone rough beneath his fingers. *Talking gargoyles and prophecies in the sky. I am an old done man, grown giddy as a child again.* Had a lifetime's hard-won wisdom fled him along with his health and strength? He was a maester, trained and chained in the great Citadel of Oldtown. What had he come to, when superstition filled his head as if he were an ignorant fieldhand?

And yet . . . and yet . . . the comet burned even by day now, while pale grey steam rose from the hot vents of Dragonmont behind the castle, and yestermorn a white raven had brought word from the Citadel itself, word long-expected but no less fearful for all that, word of summer's end. Omens, all. Too many to deny. *What does it all mean?* he wanted to cry.

"Maester Cressen, we have visitors." Pylos spoke softly, as if loath to disturb Cressen's solemn meditations. Had he known what drivel filled his head, he would have shouted. "The princess would see the white raven." Ever correct, Pylos called her *princess* now, as her lord father was a king. King of a smoking rock in the great salt sea, yet a king nonetheless. "Her fool is with her."

The old man turned away from the dawn, keeping a hand on his wyvern to steady himself. "Help me to my chair and show them in."

Taking his arm, Pylos led him inside. In his youth, Cressen had walked briskly, but he was not far from his eightieth name day now, and his legs were frail and unsteady. Two years past, he had fallen and shattered a hip, and it had never mended properly. Last year when he took ill, the Citadel had sent Pylos out from Oldtown, mere days before Lord Stannis had closed the isle . . . to help him in his labors, it was said, but Cressen knew the truth. Pylos had come to replace him when he died. He did not mind. Someone must take his place, and sooner than he would like . . .

He let the younger man settle him behind his books and papers. "Go bring her. It is ill to keep a lady waiting." He waved a hand, a feeble gesture of haste from a man no longer capable of hastening. His flesh was wrinkled and spotted, the skin so papery thin that he could see the web of veins and the shape of bones beneath. And how they trembled, these hands of his that had once been so sure and deft . . .

When Pylos returned the girl came with him, shy as ever. Behind her, shuffling and hopping in that queer sideways walk of his, came her fool. On his head was a mock helm fashioned from an old tin bucket, with a rack of deer antlers strapped to the crown and hung with cowbells. With his every lurching step, the bells rang, each with a different voice, *clang-a-dang bong-dong ring-a-ling clong clong clong.*

"Who comes to see us so early, Pylos?" Cressen said.

"It's me and Patches, Maester." Guileless blue eyes blinked at him. Hers was not a pretty face, alas. The child had her lord father's square jut of jaw and her mother's unfortunate ears, along with a disfigurement all her own, the legacy of the bout of greyscale that had almost claimed her in the crib. Across half one cheek and well down her neck, her flesh was stiff and dead, the skin cracked and flaking, mottled black and grey and stony to the touch. "Pylos said we might see the white raven."

"Indeed you may," Cressen answered. As if he would ever deny her. She had been denied too often in her time. Her name was Shireen. She would be ten on her next name day, and she was the saddest child that Maester Cressen had ever known. *Her sadness is my shame,* the old man thought, *another mark of my failure.* "Maester Pylos, do me a kindness and bring the bird down from the rookery for the Lady Shireen."

"It would be my pleasure." Pylos was a polite youth, no more than five-and-twenty, yet solemn as a man of sixty. If only he had more humor, more *life* in him; that was what was needed here. Grim places needed lightening, not solemnity, and Dragonstone was grim beyond a doubt, a lonely citadel in the wet waste surrounded by storm and salt, with the smoking shadow of the mountain at its back. A maester must go where he is sent, so Cressen had come here with his lord some twelve years past, and he had served, and served well. Yet he had never loved Dragonstone, nor ever felt truly at home here. Of late, when he woke from restless dreams in which the red woman figured disturbingly, he often did not know where he was.

The fool turned his patched and piebald head to watch Pylos climb the steep iron steps to the rookery. His bells rang with the motion. "Under the sea, the birds have scales for feathers," he said, *clang-a-langing.* "I know, I know, oh, oh, oh."

Even for a fool, Patchface was a sorry thing. Perhaps once he could evoke gales of laughter with a quip, but the sea had taken that power from him, along with half his wits and all his memory. He was soft and obese, subject to twitches and trembles, incoherent as often as not. The girl was the only one who laughed at him now, the only one who cared if he lived or died.

An ugly little girl and a sad fool, and maester makes three . . . now there is a tale to make men weep. "Sit with me, child." Cressen beckoned her closer. "This is early to come calling, scarce past dawn. You should be snug in your bed."

"I had bad dreams," Shireen told him. "About the dragons. They were coming to eat me."

The child had been plagued by nightmares as far back as Maester Cressen could recall. "We have talked of this before," he said gently. "The dragons cannot come to life. They are carved of stone, child. In olden days, our island was the westernmost outpost of the great Freehold of Valyria. It was the Valyrians who raised this citadel, and they had ways of shaping stone since lost to us. A castle must have towers wherever two walls meet at an angle, for defense. The Valyrians fashioned these towers in the shape of dragons to make their fortress seem more fearsome, just as they crowned their walls with a thousand gargoyles instead of simple crenellations." He took her small pink hand in his own frail spotted one and gave it a gentle squeeze. "So you see, there is nothing to fear."

Shireen was unconvinced. "What about the thing in the sky? Dalla and Matrice were talking by the well, and Dalla said she heard the red woman tell Mother that it was dragonsbreath. If the dragons are breathing, doesn't that mean they are coming to life?"

The red woman, Maester Cressen thought sourly. *Ill enough that she's filled the head of the mother with her madness, must she poison the daughter's dreams as well?* He would have a stern word with Dalla, warn her not to spread such tales. "The thing in the sky is a comet, sweet child. A star with a tail, lost in the heavens. It will be gone soon enough, never to be seen again in our lifetimes. Watch and see."

Shireen gave a brave little nod. "Mother said the white raven means it's not summer anymore."

"That is so, my lady. The white ravens fly only from the Citadel." Cressen's fingers went to the chain about his neck, each link forged from a different metal, each symbolizing his mastery of another branch of learning; the maester's collar, mark of his order. In the pride of his youth, he had worn it easily, but now it seemed heavy to him, the metal cold against his skin. "They are larger than other ravens, and more clever, bred to carry only the most important messages. This one came to tell us that the Conclave has met, considered the reports and measurements made by maesters all over the realm, and declared this great summer done at last. Ten years, two turns, and sixteen days it lasted, the longest summer in living memory."

"Will it get cold now?" Shireen was a summer child, and had never known true cold.

"In time," Cressen replied. "If the gods are good, they will grant us a warm autumn and bountiful harvests, so we might prepare for the winter to come." The smallfolk said that a long summer meant an even longer winter, but the maester saw no reason to frighten the child with such tales.

Patchface rang his bells. "It is *always* summer under

the sea," he intoned. "The merwives wear nennymoans in their hair and weave gowns of silver seaweed. I know, I know, oh, oh, oh."

Shireen giggled. "I should like a gown of silver seaweed."

"Under the sea, it snows up," said the fool, "and the rain is dry as bone. I know, I know, oh, oh, oh."

"Will it truly snow?" the child asked.

"It will," Cressen said. *But not for years yet, I pray, and then not for long.* "Ah, here is Pylos with the bird."

Shireen gave a cry of delight. Even Cressen had to admit the bird made an impressive sight, white as snow and larger than any hawk, with the bright black eyes that meant it was no mere albino, but a truebred white raven of the Citadel. "Here," he called. The raven spread its wings, leapt into the air, and flapped noisily across the room to land on the table beside him.

"I'll see to your breakfast now," Pylos announced. Cressen nodded. "This is the Lady Shireen," he told the raven. The bird bobbed its pale head up and down, as if it were bowing. *"Lady,"* it croaked. *"Lady."*

The child's mouth gaped open. "It *talks!*"

"A few words. As I said, they are clever, these birds."

"Clever bird, clever man, clever clever fool," said Patchface, jangling. "Oh, clever clever clever fool." He began to sing. *"The shadows come to dance, my lord, dance my lord, dance my lord,"* he sang, hopping from one foot to the other and back again. *"The shadows come to stay, my lord, stay my lord, stay my lord."* He jerked his head with each word, the bells in his antlers sending up a clangor.

The white raven screamed and went flapping away to perch on the iron railing of the rookery stairs. Shireen seemed to grow smaller. "He sings that all the time. I told him to stop but he won't. It makes me scared. Make him stop."

And how do I do that? the old man wondered. *Once I might have silenced him forever, but now . . .*

Patchface had come to them as a boy. Lord Steffon of cherished memory had found him in Volantis, across the narrow sea. The king—the old king, Aerys II Targaryen, who had not been quite so mad in those days—had sent his lordship to seek a bride for Prince Rhaegar, who had no sisters to wed. "We have found the most splendid fool," he wrote Cressen, a fortnight before he was to return home from his fruitless mission. "Only a boy, yet nimble as a monkey and witty as a dozen courtiers. He juggles and riddles and does magic, and he can sing prettily in four tongues. We have bought his freedom and hope to bring him home with us. Robert will be delighted with him, and perhaps in time he will even teach Stannis how to laugh."

It saddened Cressen to remember that letter. No one had ever taught Stannis how to laugh, least of all the boy Patchface. The storm came up suddenly, howling, and Shipbreaker Bay proved the truth of its name. The lord's two-masted galley *Windproud* broke up within sight of his castle. From its parapets his two eldest sons had watched as their father's ship was smashed against the rocks and swallowed by the waters. A hundred oarsmen and sailors went down with Lord Steffon Baratheon and his lady wife, and for days thereafter every tide left a fresh crop of swollen corpses on the strand below Storm's End.

The boy washed up on the third day. Maester Cressen had come down with the rest, to help put names to the dead. When they found the fool he was naked, his skin white and wrinkled and powdered with wet sand. Cressen had thought him another corpse, but when Jommy grabbed his ankles to drag him off to the burial wagon, the boy coughed water and sat up. To his dying day, Jommy had sworn that Patchface's flesh was clammy cold.

No one ever explained those two days the fool had been lost in the sea. The fisherfolk liked to say a mermaid had taught him to breathe water in return for his seed. Patchface himself had said nothing. The witty, clever lad that Lord Steffon had written of never reached Storm's End; the boy they found was someone else, broken in body and mind, hardly capable of speech, much less of wit. Yet his fool's face left no doubt of who he was. It was the fashion in the Free City of Volantis to tattoo the faces of slaves and servants; from neck to scalp the boy's skin had been patterned in squares of red and green motley.

"The wretch is mad, and in pain, and no use to anyone, least of all himself," declared old Ser Harbert, the castellan of Storm's End in those years. "The kindest thing you could do for that one is fill his cup with the milk of the poppy. A painless sleep, and there's an end to it. He'd bless you if he had the wit for it." But Cressen had refused, and in the end he had won. Whether Patchface had gotten any joy of that victory he could not say, not even today, so many years later.

"The shadows come to dance, my lord, dance my lord, dance my lord," the fool sang on, swinging his head and making his bells clang and clatter. *Bong dong, ring-a-ling, bong dong.*

"Lord," the white raven shrieked. *"Lord, lord, lord."*

"A fool sings what he will," the maester told his anxious princess. "You must not take his words to heart. On the morrow he may remember another song, and this one will never be heard again." *He can sing prettily in four tongues,* Lord Steffon had written . . .

Pylos strode through the door. "Maester, pardons."

"You have forgotten the porridge," Cressen said, amused. That was most unlike Pylos.

"Maester, Ser Davos returned last night. They were talking of it in the kitchen. I thought you would want to know at once."

"Davos . . . last night, you say? Where is he?"

"With the king. They have been together most of the night."

There was a time when Lord Stannis would have woken him, no matter the hour, to have him there to give his counsel. "I should have been told," Cressen complained. "I should have been woken." He disentangled his fingers from Shireen's. "Pardons, my lady, but I must speak with your lord father. Pylos, give me your arm. There are too many steps in this castle, and it seems to me they add a few every night, just to vex me."

Shireen and Patchface followed them out, but the child soon grew restless with the old man's creeping pace and dashed ahead, the fool lurching after her with his cowbells clanging madly.

Castles are not friendly places for the frail, Cressen was reminded as he descended the turnpike stairs of Sea Dragon Tower. Lord Stannis would be found in the Chamber of the Painted Table, atop the Stone Drum, Dragonstone's central keep, so named for the way its ancient walls boomed and rumbled during storms. To reach him they must cross the gallery, pass through the middle and inner walls with their guardian gargoyles and black iron gates, and ascend more steps than Cressen cared to contemplate. Young men climbed steps two at a time; for old men with bad hips, every one was a torment. But Lord Stannis would not think to come to him, so the maester resigned himself to the ordeal. He had Pylos to help him, at the least, and for that he was grateful.

Shuffling along the gallery, they passed before a row of tall arched windows with commanding views of the outer bailey, the curtain wall, and the fishing village beyond. In the yard, archers were firing at practice butts to the call of "Notch, draw, loose." Their arrows made a sound like a flock of birds taking wing. Guardsmen strode the wallwalks, peering between the gargoyles on the host camped without. The morning air was hazy with the smoke of cookfires, as three thousand men sat down to break their fasts beneath the banners of their lords. Past the sprawl of the camp, the anchorage was crowded with ships. No craft that had come within sight of Dragonstone this past half year had been allowed to leave again. Lord Stannis's *Fury*, a triple-decked war galley of three hundred oars, looked almost small beside some of the big-bellied carracks and cogs that surrounded her.

The guardsmen outside the Stone Drum knew the maesters by sight, and passed them through. "Wait here," Cressen told Pylos, within. "It's best I see him alone."

"It is a long climb, Maester."

Cressen smiled. "You think I have forgotten? I have climbed these steps so often I know each one by name."

Halfway up, he regretted his decision. He had stopped to catch his breath and ease the pain in his hip when he heard the scuff of boots on stone, and came face-to-face with Ser Davos Seaworth, descending.

Davos was a slight man, his low birth written plain upon a common face. A well-worn green cloak, stained by salt and spray and faded from the sun, draped his thin shoulders, over brown doublet and breeches that matched brown eyes and hair. About his neck a pouch of worn leather hung from a thong. His small beard was well peppered with grey, and he wore a leather glove on his maimed left hand. When he saw Cressen, he checked his descent.

"Ser Davos," the maester said. "When did you return?"

"In the black of morning. My favorite time." It was said that no one had ever handled a ship by night half so well as Davos Shorthand. Before Lord Stannis had knighted him, he had been the most notorious and elusive smuggler in all the Seven Kingdoms.

"And?"

The man shook his head. "It is as you warned him. They will not rise, Maester. Not for him. They do not love him."

No, Cressen thought. *Nor will they ever. He is strong, able, just . . . aye, just past the point of wisdom . . . yet it is not enough. It has never been enough.* "You spoke to them all?"

"All? No. Only those that would see me. They do not love me either, these highborns. To them I'll always be the Onion Knight." His left hand closed, stubby fingers locking into a fist; Stannis had hacked the ends off at the last joint, all but the thumb. "I broke bread with Gulian Swann and old Penrose, and the Tarths consented to a midnight meeting in a grove. The others—

well, Beric Dondarrion is gone missing, some say dead, and Lord Caron is with Renly. Bryce the Orange, of the Rainbow Guard."

"The Rainbow Guard?"

"Renly's made his own Kingsguard," the onetime smuggler explained, "but these seven don't wear white. Each one has his own color. Loras Tyrell's their Lord Commander."

It was just the sort of notion that would appeal to Renly Baratheon; a splendid new order of knighthood, with gorgeous new raiment to proclaim it. Even as a boy, Renly had loved bright colors and rich fabrics, and he had loved his games as well. "Look at me!" he would shout as he ran laughing through the halls of Storm's End. "Look at me, I'm a dragon," or "Look at me, I'm a wizard," or "Look at me, look at me, I'm the rain god."

The bold little boy with wild black hair and laughing eyes was a man grown now, one-and-twenty, and still he played his games. *Look at me, I'm a king*, Cressen thought sadly. *Oh, Renly, Renly, dear sweet child, do you know what you are doing? And would you care if you did? Is there anyone who cares for him but me?* "What reasons did the lords give for their refusals?" he asked Ser Davos.

"Well, as to that, some gave me soft words and some blunt, some made excuses, some promises, some only lied." He shrugged. "In the end words are just wind."

"You could bring him no hope?"

"Only the false sort, and I'd not do that," Davos said. "He had the truth from me."

Maester Cressen remembered the day Davos had been knighted, after the siege of Storm's End. Lord Stannis and a small garrison had held the castle for close to a year, against the great host of the Lords Tyrell and Redwyne. Even the sea was closed against them, watched day and night by Redwyne galleys flying the burgundy banners of the Arbor. Within Storm's End, the horses had long since been eaten, the dogs and cats were gone, and the garrison was down to roots and rats. Then came a night when the moon was new and black clouds hid the stars. Cloaked in that darkness, Davos the smuggler had dared the Redwyne cordon and the rocks of Shipbreaker Bay alike. His little ship had a black hull, black sails, black oars, and a hold crammed with onions and salt fish. Little enough, yet it had kept the garrison alive long enough for Eddard Stark to reach Storm's End and break the siege.

Lord Stannis had rewarded Davos with choice lands on Cape Wrath, a small keep, and a knight's honors . . . but he had also decreed that he lose a joint of each finger on his left hand, to pay for all his years of smuggling. Davos had submitted, on the condition that Stannis wield the knife himself; he would accept no punishment from lesser hands. The lord had used a butcher's cleaver, the better to cut clean and true. Afterward, Davos had chosen the name Seaworth for his new-made house, and he took for his banner a black ship on a pale grey field—with an onion on its sails. The onetime smuggler was fond of saying that Lord Stannis had done him a boon, by giving him four less fingernails to clean and trim.

No, Cressen thought, a man like that would give no false hope, nor soften a hard truth. "Ser Davos, truth can be a bitter draught, even for a man like Lord Stannis. He thinks only of returning to King's Landing in the fullness of his power, to tear down his enemies and claim what is rightfully his. Yet now . . ."

"If he takes this meager host to King's Landing, it will be only to die. He does not have the numbers. I told him as much, but you know his pride." Davos held up his gloved hand. "My fingers will grow back before that man bends to sense."

The old man sighed. "You have done all you could. Now I must add my voice to yours." Wearily, he resumed his climb.

Lord Stannis Baratheon's refuge was a great round room with walls of bare black stone and four tall narrow windows that looked out to the four points of the compass. In the center of the chamber was the great table from which it took its name, a massive slab of carved wood fashioned at the command of Aegon Targaryen in the days before the Conquest. The Painted Table was more than fifty feet long, perhaps half that wide at its widest point, but less than four feet across at its narrowest. Aegon's carpenters had shaped it after the land of Westeros, sawing out each bay and peninsula until the table nowhere ran straight. On its surface, darkened by near three hundred years of varnish, were painted the Seven Kingdoms as they had been in Aegon's day; rivers and mountains, castles and cities, lakes and forests.

There was a single chair in the room, carefully positioned in the precise place that Dragonstone occupied off the coast of Westeros, and raised up to give a good view of the tabletop. Seated in the chair was a man in a tight-laced leather jerkin and breeches of roughspun brown wool. When Maester Cressen entered, he glanced up. "I knew *you* would come, old man, whether I summoned you or no." There was no hint of warmth in his voice; there seldom was.

Stannis Baratheon, Lord of Dragonstone and by the grace of the gods rightful heir to the Iron Throne of the Seven Kingdoms of Westeros, was broad of shoulder and sinewy of limb, with a tightness to his face and flesh that spoke of leather cured in the sun until it was as tough as steel. *Hard* was the word men used when they spoke of Stannis, and hard he was. Though he was not yet five-and-thirty, only a fringe of thin black hair remained on his head, circling behind his ears like the shadow of a crown. His brother, the late King Robert, had grown a beard in his final years. Maester Cressen had never seen it, but they said it was a wild thing, thick and fierce. As if in answer, Stannis kept his own whiskers cropped tight and short. They lay like a blue-black shadow across his square jaw and the bony hollows of his cheeks. His eyes were open wounds beneath his heavy brows, a blue as dark as the sea by night. His mouth would have given despair to even the drollest of fools; it was a mouth made for frowns and scowls and sharply worded commands, all thin pale lips and clenched muscles, a mouth that had forgotten how to smile and had never known how to laugh. Sometimes when the world grew very still and silent of a night, Maester Cressen fancied he could hear Lord Stannis grinding his teeth half a castle away.

"Once you would have woken me," the old man said.

"Once you were young. Now you are old and sick, and need your sleep." Stannis had never learned to soften his speech, to dissemble or flatter; he said what he thought, and those that did not like it could be damned. "I knew you'd learn what Davos had to say soon enough. You always do, don't you?"

"I would be of no help to you if I did not," Cressen said. "I met Davos on the stair."

"And he told all, I suppose? I should have had the man's tongue shortened along with his fingers."

"He would have made you a poor envoy then."

"He made me a poor envoy in any case. The storm lords will not rise for me. It seems they do not like me, and the justice of my cause means nothing to them. The cravenly ones will sit behind their walls waiting to see how the wind rises and who is likely to triumph. The bold ones have already declared for Renly. For *Renly*!" He spat out the name like poison on his tongue.

"Your brother has been the Lord of Storm's End these past thirteen years. These lords are his sworn bannermen—"

"*His*," Stannis broke in, "when by rights they should be mine. I never asked for Dragonstone. I never wanted it. I took it because Robert's enemies were here and he commanded me to root them out. I built his fleet and did his work, dutiful as a younger brother should be to an elder, as Renly should be to me. And what was Robert's thanks? He names me Lord of Dragonstone, and gives Storm's End and its incomes to *Renly*. Storm's End belonged to House Baratheon for three hundred years; by rights it should have passed to me when Robert took the Iron Throne."

It was an old grievance, deeply felt, and never more so than now. Here was the heart of his lord's weakness; for Dragonstone, old and strong though it was, commanded the allegiance of only a handful of lesser lords, whose stony island holdings were too thinly peopled to yield up the men that Stannis needed. Even with the sellswords he had brought across the narrow sea from the Free Cities of Myr and Lys, the host camped outside his walls was far too small to bring down the power of House Lannister.

"Robert did you an injustice," Maester Cressen replied carefully, "yet he had sound reasons. Dragonstone had long been the seat of House Targaryen. He needed a man's strength to rule here, and Renly was but a child."

"He is a child still," Stannis declared, his anger ringing loud in the empty hall, "a thieving child who thinks to snatch the crown off my brow. What has Renly ever done to earn a throne? He sits in council and jests with Littlefinger, and at tourneys he dons his splendid suit of armor and allows himself to be knocked off his horse by a better man. That is the sum of my brother Renly, who thinks he ought to be a king. I ask you, why did the gods inflict me with *brothers*?"

"I cannot answer for the gods."

"You seldom answer at all these days, it seems to me. Who maesters for Renly? Perchance I should send for him, I might like his counsel better. What do you think this maester said when my brother decided to steal my crown? What counsel did your colleague offer to this traitor blood of mine?"

"It would surprise me if Lord Renly sought counsel, Your Grace." The youngest of Lord Steffon's three sons had grown into a man bold but heedless, who acted from impulse rather than calculation. In that, as in so much else, Renly was like his brother Robert, and utterly unlike Stannis.

"*Your Grace*," Stannis repeated bitterly. "You mock me with a king's style, yet what am I king of? Dragonstone and a few rocks in the narrow sea, there is my kingdom." He descended the steps of his chair to stand before the table, his shadow falling across the mouth of the Blackwater Rush and the painted forest where King's Landing now stood. There he stood, brooding over the realm he sought to claim, so near at hand and yet so far away. "Tonight I am to sup with my lords bannermen, such as they are. Celtigar, Velaryon, Bar Emmon, the whole paltry lot of them. A poor crop, if truth be told, but they are what my brothers have left me. That Lysene pirate Salladhor Saan will be there with the latest tally of what I owe him, and Morosh the Myrman will caution me with talk of tides and autumn gales, while Lord Sunglass mutters piously of the will of the Seven. Celtigar will want to know which storm lords are joining us. Velaryon will threaten to take his levies home unless we strike at once. What am I to tell them? What must I do now?"

"Your true enemies are the Lannisters, my lord," Maester Cressen answered. "If you and your brother were to make common cause against them—"

"I will not treat with Renly," Stannis answered in a tone that brooked no argument. "Not while he calls himself a king."

"Not Renly, then," the maester yielded. His lord was stubborn and proud; when he had set his mind, there was no changing it. "Others might serve your needs as well. Eddard Stark's son has been proclaimed King in the North, with all the power of Winterfell and River-run behind him."

"A green boy," said Stannis, "and another false king. Am I to accept a broken realm?"

"Surely half a kingdom is better than none," Cressen said, "and if you help the boy avenge his father's murder—"

"Why should I avenge Eddard Stark? The man was nothing to me. Oh, *Robert* loved him, to be sure. Loved him as a brother, how often did I hear that? *I* was his brother, not Ned Stark, but you would never have known it by the way he treated me. I held Storm's End for him, watching good men starve while Mace Tyrell and Paxter Redwyne feasted within sight of my walls. Did Robert thank me? No. He thanked *Stark,* for lifting the siege when we were down to rats and radishes. I built a fleet at Robert's command, took Dragonstone in his name. Did he take my hand and say, *Well done, brother, whatever should I do without you?* No, he blamed me for letting Willem Darry steal away Viserys and the babe, as if I could have stopped it. I sat on his council for fifteen years, helping Jon Arryn rule his realm while Robert drank and whored, but when Jon died, did my brother name me his Hand? No, he went galloping off to his dear friend Ned Stark, and offered him the honor. And small good it did either of them."

"Be that as it may, my lord," Maester Cressen said gently. "Great wrongs have been done you, but the past is dust. The future may yet be won if you join with the Starks. There are others you might sound out as well. What of Lady Arryn? If the queen murdered her husband, surely she will want justice for him. She has a young son, Jon Arryn's heir. If you were to betroth Shireen to him—"

"The boy is weak and sickly," Lord Stannis objected. "Even his father saw how it was, when he asked me to foster him on Dragonstone. Service as a page might have done him good, but that damnable Lannister woman had Lord Arryn poisoned before it could be done, and now Lysa hides him in the Eyrie. She'll never part with the boy, I promise you that."

"Then you must send Shireen to the Eyrie," the maester urged. "Dragonstone is a grim home for a child. Let her fool go with her, so she will have a familiar face about her."

"Familiar and hideous." Stannis furrowed his brow in thought. "Still . . . perhaps it is worth the trying . . ."

"Must the rightful Lord of the Seven Kingdoms beg for help from widow women and usurpers?" a woman's voice asked sharply.

Maester Cressen turned, and bowed his head. "My lady," he said, chagrined that he had not heard her enter.

Lord Stannis scowled. "I do not beg. Of anyone. Mind you remember that, woman."

"I am pleased to hear it, my lord." Lady Selyse was as tall as her husband, thin of body and thin of face, with

prominent ears, a sharp nose, and the faintest hint of a
mustache on her upper lip. She plucked it daily and
cursed it regularly, yet it never failed to return. Her eyes
were pale, her mouth stern, her voice a whip. She
cracked it now. "Lady Arryn owes you her allegiance, as
do the Starks, your brother Renly, and all the rest. You
are their one true king. It would not be fitting to plead
and bargain with them for what is rightfully yours by
the grace of god."

God, she said, not *gods.* The red woman had won her,
heart and soul, turning her from the gods of the Seven
Kingdoms, both old and new, to worship the one they
called the Lord of Light.

"Your god can keep his grace," said Lord Stannis, who
did not share his wife's fervent new faith. "It's swords I
need, not blessings. Do you have an army hidden somewhere that you've not told me of?" There was no affection in his tone. Stannis had always been uncomfortable
around women, even his own wife. When he had gone
to King's Landing to sit on Robert's council, he had left
Selyse on Dragonstone with their daughter. His letters
had been few, his visits fewer; he did his duty in the
marriage bed once or twice a year, but took no joy in it,
and the sons he had once hoped for had never come.

"My brothers and uncles and cousins have armies,"
she told him. "House Florent will rally to your banner."

"House Florent can field two thousand swords at
best." It was said that Stannis knew the strength of every house in the Seven Kingdoms. "And you have a deal
more faith in your brothers and uncles than I do, my
lady. The Florent lands lie too close to Highgarden for
your lord uncle to risk Mace Tyrell's wrath."

"There is another way." Lady Selyse moved closer.
"Look out your windows, my lord. There is the sign you
have waited for, blazoned on the sky. Red, it is, the red
of flame, red for the fiery heart of the true god. It is *his*
banner—and yours! See how it unfurls across the heavens like a dragon's hot breath, and you the Lord of
Dragonstone. It means your time has come, Your Grace.
Nothing is more certain. You are meant to sail from this

desolate rock as Aegon the Conqueror once sailed, to sweep all before you as he did. Only say the word, and embrace the power of the Lord of Light."

"How many swords will the Lord of Light put into my hand?" Stannis demanded again.

"All you need," his wife promised. "The swords of Storm's End and Highgarden for a start, and all their lords bannermen."

"Davos would tell you different," Stannis said. "Those swords are sworn to Renly. They love my charming young brother, as they once loved Robert . . . and as they have never loved me."

"Yes," she answered, "but if Renly should die . . ."

Stannis looked at his lady with narrowed eyes, until Cressen could not hold his tongue. "It is not to be thought. Your Grace, whatever follies Renly has committed—"

"*Follies?* I call them treasons." Stannis turned back to his wife. "My brother is young and strong, and he has a vast host around him, and these rainbow knights of his."

"Melisandre has gazed into the flames, and seen him dead."

Cressen was horrorstruck. "Fratricide . . . my lord, this is *evil*, unthinkable . . . please, listen to me."

Lady Selyse gave him a measured look. "And what will you tell him, Maester? How he might win half a kingdom if he goes to the Starks on his knees and sells our daughter to Lysa Arryn?"

"I have heard your counsel, Cressen," Lord Stannis said. "Now I will hear hers. You are dismissed."

Maester Cressen bent a stiff knee. He could feel Lady Selyse's eyes on his back as he shuffled slowly across the room. By the time he reached the bottom of the steps it was all he could do to stand erect. "Help me," he said to Pylos.

When he was safe back in his own rooms, Cressen sent the younger man away and limped to his balcony once more, to stand between his gargoyles and stare out to sea. One of Salladhor Saan's warships was sweeping past the castle, her gaily striped hull slicing through the grey-green waters as her oars rose and fell. He watched until she vanished behind a headland. *Would that my fears could vanish so easily.* Had he lived so long for this?

When a maester donned his collar, he put aside the hope of children, yet Cressen had oft felt a father nonetheless. Robert, Stannis, Renly . . . three sons he had raised after the angry sea claimed Lord Steffon. Had he done so ill that now he must watch one kill the other? He could not allow it, *would* not allow it.

The woman was the heart of it. Not the Lady Selyse, the *other* one. The red woman, the servants had named her, afraid to speak her name. "I will speak her name," Cressen told his stone hellhound. "Melisandre. *Her.*" Melisandre of Asshai, sorceress, shadowbinder, and priestess to R'hllor, the Lord of Light, the Heart of Fire, the God of Flame and Shadow. Melisandre, whose madness must not be allowed to spread beyond Dragonstone.

His chambers seemed dim and gloomy after the brightness of the morning. With fumbling hands, the old man lit a candle and carried it to the workroom beneath the rookery stair, where his ointments, potions, and medicines stood neatly on their shelves. On the bottom shelf behind a row of salves in squat clay jars he found a vial of indigo glass, no larger than his little finger. It rattled when he shook it. Cressen blew away a layer of dust and carried it back to his table. Collapsing into his chair, he pulled the stopper and spilled out the vial's contents. A dozen crystals, no larger than seeds, rattled across the parchment he'd been reading. They shone like jewels in the candlelight, so purple that the maester found himself thinking that he had never truly seen the color before.

The chain around his throat felt very heavy. He touched one of the crystals lightly with the tip of his little finger. *Such a small thing to hold the power of life and death.* It was made from a certain plant that grew only on the islands of the Jade Sea, half a world away.

The leaves had to be aged, and soaked in a wash of limes and sugar water and certain rare spices from the Summer Isles. Afterward they could be discarded, but the potion must be thickened with ash and allowed to crystallize. The process was slow and difficult, the necessaries costly and hard to acquire. The alchemists of Lys knew the way of it, though, and the Faceless Men of Braavos . . . and the maesters of his order as well, though it was not something talked about beyond the walls of the Citadel. All the world knew that a maester forged his silver link when he learned the art of healing—but the world preferred to forget that men who knew how to heal also knew how to kill.

Cressen no longer recalled the name the Asshai'i gave the leaf, or the Lysene poisoners the crystal. In the Citadel, it was simply called the strangler. Dissolved in wine, it would make the muscles of a man's throat clench tighter than any fist, shutting off his windpipe. They said a victim's face turned as purple as the little crystal seed from which his death was grown, but so too did a man choking on a morsel of food.

And this very night Lord Stannis would feast his bannermen, his lady wife . . . and the red woman, Melisandre of Asshai.

I must rest, Maester Cressen told himself. *I must have all my strength come dark. My hands must not shake, nor my courage flag. It is a dreadful thing I do, yet it must be done. If there are gods, surely they will forgive me.* He had slept so poorly of late. A nap would refresh him for the ordeal ahead. Wearily, he tottered off to his bed. Yet when he closed his eyes, he could still see the light of the comet, red and fiery and vividly alive amidst the darkness of his dreams. *Perhaps it is my comet*, he thought drowsily at the last, just before sleep took him. *An omen of blood, foretelling murder . . . yes . . .*

When he woke it was full dark, his bedchamber was black, and every joint in his body ached. Cressen pushed himself up, his head throbbing. Clutching for his cane, he rose unsteady to his feet. *So late*, he thought. *They did not summon me.* He was always summoned for feasts, seated near the salt, close to Lord Stannis. His lord's face swam up before him, not the man he was but the boy he had been, standing cold in the shadows while the sun shone on his elder brother. Whatever he did, Robert had done first, and better. Poor boy . . . he must hurry, for *his* sake.

The maester found the crystals where he had left them, and scooped them off the parchment. Cressen owned no hollow rings, such as the poisoners of Lys were said to favor, but a myriad of pockets great-and small were sewn inside the loose sleeves of his robe. He secreted the strangler seeds in one of them, threw open his door, and called, "Pylos? Where are you?" When he heard no reply, he called again, louder. "Pylos, I need help." Still there came no answer. That was queer; the young maester had his cell only a half turn down the stair, within easy earshot.

In the end, Cressen had to shout for the servants. "Make haste," he told them. "I have slept too long. They will be feasting by now . . . drinking . . . I should have been woken." What had happened to Maester Pylos? Truly, he did not understand.

Again he had to cross the long gallery. A night wind whispered through the great windows, sharp with the smell of the sea. Torches flickered along the walls of Dragonstone, and in the camp beyond, he could see hundreds of cookfires burning, as if a field of stars had fallen to the earth. Above, the comet blazed red and malevolent. *I am too old and wise to fear such things,* the maester told himself.

The doors to the Great Hall were set in the mouth of a stone dragon. He told the servants to leave him outside. It would be better to enter alone; he must not appear feeble. Leaning heavily on his cane, Cressen climbed the last few steps and hobbled beneath the gateway teeth. A pair of guardsmen opened the heavy red doors before him, unleashing a sudden blast of noise and light. Cressen stepped down into the dragon's maw.

Over the clatter of knife and plate and the low mutter

of table talk, he heard Patchface singing, ". . . *dance, my lord, dance my lord,*" to the accompaniment of jangling cowbells. The same dreadful song he'd sung this morning. *"The shadows come to stay, my lord, stay my lord, stay my lord."* The lower tables were crowded with knights, archers, and sellsword captains, tearing apart loaves of black bread to soak in their fish stew. Here there was no loud laughter, no raucous shouting such as marred the dignity of other men's feasts; Lord Stannis did not permit such.

Cressen made his way toward the raised platform where the lords sat with the king. He had to step wide around Patchface. Dancing, his bells ringing, the fool neither saw nor heard his approach. As he hopped from one leg to the other, Patchface lurched into Cressen, knocking his cane out from under him. They went crashing down together amidst the rushes in a tangle of arms and legs, while a sudden gale of laughter went up around them. No doubt it was a comical sight.

Patchface sprawled half on top of him, motley fool's face pressed close to his own. He had lost his tin helm with its antlers and bells. "Under the sea, you fall *up,*" he declared. "I know, I know, oh, oh, oh." Giggling, the fool rolled off, bounded to his feet, and did a little dance.

Trying to make the best of it, the maester smiled feebly and struggled to rise, but his hip was in such pain that for a moment he was half afraid that he had broken it all over again. He felt strong hands grasp him under the arms and lift him back to his feet. "Thank you, ser," he murmured, turning to see which knight had come to his aid . . .

"Maester," said Lady Melisandre, her deep voice flavored with the music of the Jade Sea. "You ought take more care." As ever, she wore red head to heel, a long loose gown of flowing silk as bright as fire, with dagged sleeves and deep slashes in the bodice that showed glimpses of a darker bloodred fabric beneath. Around her throat was a red gold choker tighter than any maester's chain, ornamented with a single great ruby. Her hair was not the orange or strawberry color of common red-haired men, but a deep burnished copper that shone in the light of the torches. Even her eyes were red . . . but her skin was smooth and white, unblemished, pale as cream. Slender she was, graceful, taller than most knights, with full breasts and narrow waist and a heart-shaped face. Men's eyes that once found her did not quickly look away, not even a maester's eyes. Many called her beautiful. She was not beautiful. She was red, and terrible, and red.

"I . . . thank you, my lady."

"A man your age must look to where he steps," Melisandre said courteously. "The night is dark and full of terrors."

He knew the phrase, some prayer of her faith. *It makes no matter, I have a faith of my own.* "Only children fear the dark," he told her. Yet even as he said the words, he heard Patchface take up his song again. *"The shadows come to dance, my lord, dance my lord, dance my lord."*

"Now here is a riddle," Melisandre said. "A clever fool and a foolish wise man." Bending, she picked up Patchface's helm from where it had fallen and set it on Cressen's head. The cowbells rang softly as the tin bucket slid down over his ears. "A crown to match your chain, Lord Maester," she announced. All around them, men were laughing.

Cressen pressed his lips together and fought to still his rage. She thought he was feeble and helpless, but she would learn otherwise before the night was done. Old he might be, yet he was still a maester of the Citadel. "I need no crown but truth," he told her, removing the fool's helm from his head.

"There are truths in this world that are not taught at Oldtown." Melisandre turned from him in a swirl of red silk and made her way back to the high table, where King Stannis and his queen were seated. Cressen handed the antlered tin bucket back to Patchface, and made to follow.

Maester Pylos sat in his place.

The old man could only stop and stare. "Maester Pylos," he said at last. "You . . . you did not wake me."

"His Grace commanded me to let you rest." Pylos had at least the grace to blush. "He told me you were not needed here."

Cressen looked over the knights and captains and lords sitting silent. Lord Celtigar, aged and sour, wore a mantle patterned with red crabs picked out in garnets. Handsome Lord Velaryon chose sea-green silk, the white gold seahorse at his throat matching his long fair hair. Lord Bar Emmon, that plump boy of fourteen, was swathed in purple velvet trimmed with white seal, Ser Axell Florent remained homely even in russet and fox fur, pious Lord Sunglass wore moonstones at throat and wrist and finger, and the Lysene captain Salladhor Saan was a sunburst of scarlet satin, gold, and jewels. Only Ser Davos dressed simply, in brown doublet and green wool mantle, and only Ser Davos met his gaze, with pity in his eyes.

"You are too ill and too confused to be of use to me, old man." It sounded so like Lord Stannis's voice, but it could not be, it could not. "Pylos will counsel me henceforth. Already he works with the ravens, since you can no longer climb to the rookery. I will not have you kill yourself in my service."

Maester Cressen blinked. *Stannis, my lord, my sad sullen boy, son I never had, you must not do this, don't you know how I have cared for you, lived for you, loved you despite all? Yes, loved you, better than Robert even, or Renly, for you were the one unloved, the one who needed me most.* Yet all he said was, "As you command, my lord, but . . . but I am hungry. Might not I have a place at your table?" *At your side, I belong at your side . . .*

Ser Davos rose from the bench. "I should be honored if the maester would sit here beside me, Your Grace."

"As you will." Lord Stannis turned away to say something to Melisandre, who had seated herself at his right hand, in the place of high honor. Lady Selyse was on his left, flashing a smile as bright and brittle as her jewels.

Too far, Cressen thought dully, looking at where Ser Davos was seated. Half of the lords bannermen were between the smuggler and the high table. *I must be closer to her if I am to get the strangler into her cup, yet how?*

Patchface was capering about as the maester made his slow way around the table to Davos Seaworth. "Here we eat fish," the fool declared happily, waving a cod about like a scepter. "Under the sea, the fish eat us. I know, I know, oh, oh, oh."

Ser Davos moved aside to make room on the bench. "We all should be in motley tonight," he said gloomily as Cressen seated himself, "for this is fool's business we're about. The red woman has seen victory in her flames, so Stannis means to press his claim, no matter what the numbers. Before she's done we're all like to see what Patchface saw, I fear—the bottom of the sea."

Cressen slid his hands up into his sleeves as if for warmth. His fingers found the hard lumps the crystals made in the wool. "Lord Stannis."

Stannis turned from the red woman, but it was Lady Selyse who replied. "*King* Stannis. You forget yourself, Maester."

"He is old, his mind wanders," the king told her gruffly. "What is it, Cressen? Speak your mind."

"As you intend to sail, it is vital that you make common cause with Lord Stark and Lady Arryn . . ."

"I make common cause with no one," Stannis Baratheon said.

"No more than light makes common cause with darkness." Lady Selyse took his hand.

Stannis nodded. "The Starks seek to steal half my kingdom, even as the Lannisters have stolen my throne and my own sweet brother the swords and service and strongholds that are mine by rights. They are all usurpers, and they are all my enemies."

I have lost him, Cressen thought, despairing. If only

he could somehow approach Melisandre unseen . . .
he needed but an instant's access to her cup. "You are
the rightful heir to your brother Robert, the true Lord of
the Seven Kingdoms, and King of the Andals, the
Rhoynar, and the First Men," he said desperately, "but
even so, you cannot hope to triumph without allies."

"He has an ally," Lady Selyse said. "R'hllor, the Lord
of Light, the Heart of Fire, the God of Flame and
Shadow."

"Gods make uncertain allies at best," the old man
insisted, "and *that* one has no power here."

"You think not?" The ruby at Melisandre's throat
caught the light as she turned her head, and for an instant it seemed to glow bright as the comet. "If you will
speak such folly, Maester, you ought to wear your
crown again."

"Yes," Lady Selyse agreed. "Patches's helm. It suits
you well, old man. Put it on again, I command you."

"Under the sea, no one wears hats," Patchface said. "I
know, I know, oh, oh, oh."

Lord Stannis's eyes were shadowed beneath his heavy
brow, his mouth tight as his jaw worked silently. He
always ground his teeth when he was angry. "Fool," he
growled at last, "my lady wife commands. Give Cressen
your helm."

No, the old maester thought, *this is not you, not your
way, you were always just, always hard yet never cruel,
never, you did not understand mockery, no more than
you understood laughter.*

Patchface danced closer, his cowbells ringing,
clang-a-lang, ding-ding, clink-clank-clink-clank. The
maester sat silent while the fool set the antlered bucket
on his brow. Cressen bowed his head beneath the
weight. His bells clanged. "Perhaps he ought sing his
counsel henceforth," Lady Selyse said.

"You go too far, woman," Lord Stannis said. "He is an
old man, and he's served me well."

*And I will serve you to the last, my sweet lord, my
poor lonely son,* Cressen thought, for suddenly he saw
the way. Ser Davos's cup was before him, still half-full

of sour red. He found a hard flake of crystal in his sleeve, held it tight between thumb and forefinger as he reached for the cup. *Smooth motions, deft, I must not fumble now,* he prayed, and the gods were kind. In the blink of an eye, his fingers were empty. His hands had not been so steady for years, nor half so fluid. Davos saw, but no one else, he was certain. Cup in hand, he rose to his feet. "Mayhaps I have been a fool. Lady Melisandre, will you share a cup of wine with me? A cup in honor of your god, your Lord of Light? A cup to toast his power?"

The red woman studied him. "If you wish."

He could feel them all watching him. Davos clutched at him as he left the bench, catching his sleeve with the fingers that Lord Stannis had shortened. "What are you doing?" he whispered.

"A thing that must be done," Maester Cressen answered, "for the sake of the realm, and the soul of my lord." He shook off Davos's hand, spilling a drop of wine on the rushes.

She met him beneath the high table with every man's eyes upon them. But Cressen saw only her. Red silk, red eyes, the ruby red at her throat, red lips curled in a faint smile as she put her hand atop his own, around the cup. Her skin felt hot, feverish. "It is not too late to spill the wine, Maester."

"No," he whispered hoarsely. "No."

"As you will." Melisandre of Asshai took the cup from his hands and drank long and deep. There was only half a swallow of wine remaining when she offered it back to him. "And now you."

His hands were shaking, but he made himself be strong. A maester of the Citadel must not be afraid. The wine was sour on his tongue. He let the empty cup drop from his fingers to shatter on the floor. "He *does* have power here, my lord," the woman said. "And fire cleanses." At her throat, the ruby shimmered redly.

Cressen tried to reply, but his words caught in his throat. His cough became a terrible thin whistle as he strained to suck in air. Iron fingers tightened round his neck. As he sank to his knees, still he shook his head, denying her, denying her power, denying her magic, denying her god. And the cowbells peeled in his antlers, singing *fool, fool, fool* while the red woman looked down on him in pity, the candle flames dancing in her red red eyes.

ARYA

At Winterfell they had called her "Arya Horseface" and she'd thought nothing could be
worse, but that was before the orphan boy
Lommy Greenhands had named her "Lumpyhead."

Her head *felt* lumpy when she touched it. When
Yoren had dragged her into that alley she'd thought he
meant to kill her, but the sour old man had only held
her tight, sawing through her mats and tangles with his
dagger. She remembered how the breeze sent the fistfuls
of dirty brown hair skittering across the paving stones,
toward the sept where her father had died. "I'm taking
men and boys from the city," Yoren growled as the
sharp steel scraped at her head. "Now you hold still,
boy." By the time he had finished, her scalp was nothing but tufts and stubble.

Afterward he told her that from there to Winterfell
she'd be Arry the orphan boy. "Gate shouldn't be hard,
but the road's another matter. You got a long way to go
in bad company. I got thirty this time, men and boys all
bound for the Wall, and don't be thinking they're like

that bastard brother o' yours." He shook her. "Lord Eddard gave me pick o' the dungeons, and I didn't find no little lordlings down there. This lot, half o' them would turn you over to the queen quick as spit for a pardon and maybe a few silvers. The other half'd do the same, only they'd rape you first. So you keep to yourself and make your water in the woods, alone. That'll be the hardest part, the pissing, so don't drink no more'n you need."

Leaving King's Landing was easy, just like he'd said. The Lannister guardsmen on the gate were stopping everyone, but Yoren called one by name and their wagons were waved through. No one spared Arya a glance. They were looking for a highborn girl, daughter of the King's Hand, not for a skinny boy with his hair chopped off. Arya never looked back. She wished the Rush would rise and wash the whole city away, Flea Bottom and the Red Keep and the Great Sept and *everything*, and everyone too, especially Prince Joffrey and his mother. But she knew it wouldn't, and anyhow Sansa was still in the city and would wash away too. When she remembered that, Arya decided to wish for Winterfell instead.

Yoren was wrong about the pissing, though. That wasn't the hardest part at all; Lommy Greenhands and Hot Pie were the hardest part. Orphan boys. Yoren had plucked some from the streets with promises of food for their bellies and shoes for their feet. The rest he'd found in chains. "The Watch needs good men," he told them as they set out, "but you lot will have to do."

Yoren had taken grown men from the dungeons as well, thieves and poachers and rapers and the like. The worst were the three he'd found in the black cells who must have scared even him, because he kept them fettered hand and foot in the back of a wagon, and vowed they'd stay in irons all the way to the Wall. One had no nose, only the hole in his face where it had been cut off, and the gross fat bald one with the pointed teeth and the weeping sores on his cheeks had eyes like nothing human.

They took five wagons out of King's Landing, laden

with supplies for the Wall: hides and bolts of cloth, bars of pig iron, a cage of ravens, books and paper and ink, a bale of sourleaf, jars of oil, and chests of medicine and spices. Teams of plow horses pulled the wagons, and Yoren had bought two coursers and a half-dozen donkeys for the boys. Arya would have preferred a real horse, but the donkey was better than riding on a wagon.

The men paid her no mind, but she was not so lucky with the boys. She was two years younger than the youngest orphan, not to mention smaller and skinnier, and Lommy and Hot Pie took her silence to mean she was scared, or stupid, or deaf. "Look at that sword Lumpyhead's got there," Lommy said one morning as they made their plodding way past orchards and wheat fields. He'd been a dyer's apprentice before he was caught stealing, and his arms were mottled green to the elbow. When he laughed he brayed like the donkeys they were riding. "Where's a gutter rat like Lumpyhead get him a sword?"

Arya chewed her lip sullenly. She could see the back of Yoren's faded black cloak up ahead of the wagons, but she was determined not to go crying to him for help.

"Maybe he's a little squire," Hot Pie put in. His mother had been a baker before she died, and he'd pushed her cart through the streets all day, shouting *"Hot pies! Hot pies!"* "Some lordy lord's little squire boy, that's it."

"He ain't no squire, look at him. I bet that's not even a real sword. I bet it's just some play sword made of tin."

Arya hated them making fun of Needle. "It's castle-forged steel, you stupid," she snapped, turning in the saddle to glare at them, "and you better shut your mouth."

The orphan boys hooted. "Where'd you get a blade like that, Lumpyface?" Hot Pie wanted to know.

"Lumpy*head*," corrected Lommy. "He prob'ly stole it."

"I did *not*!" she shouted. Jon Snow had given her Needle. Maybe she had to let them call her Lumpyhead, but she wasn't going to let them call Jon a thief.

"If he stole it, we could take it off him," said Hot Pie. "It's not his anyhow. I could use me a sword like that."

Lommy egged him on. "Go on, take it off him, I dare you."

Hot Pie kicked his donkey, riding closer. "Hey, Lumpyface, you gimme that sword." His hair was the color of straw, his fat face all sunburnt and peeling. "You don't know how to use it."

Yes I do, Arya could have said. *I killed a boy, a fat boy like you, I stabbed him in the belly and he died, and I'll kill you too if you don't let me alone.* Only she did not dare. Yoren didn't know about the stableboy, but she was afraid of what he might do if he found out. Arya was pretty sure that some of the other men were killers too, the three in the manacles for sure, but the queen wasn't looking for *them*, so it wasn't the same.

"Look at him," brayed Lommy Greenhands. "I bet he's going to cry now. You want to cry, Lumpyhead?"

She had cried in her sleep the night before, dreaming of her father. Come morning, she'd woken red-eyed and dry, and could not have shed another tear if her life had hung on it.

"He's going to wet his pants," Hot Pie suggested.

"Leave him be," said the boy with the shaggy black hair who rode behind them. Lommy had named *him* the Bull, on account of this horned helm he had that he polished all the time but never wore. Lommy didn't dare mock the Bull. He was older, and big for his age, with a broad chest and strong-looking arms.

"You better give Hot Pie the sword, Arry," Lommy said. "Hot Pie wants it bad. He kicked a boy to death. He'll do the same to you, I bet."

"I knocked him down and I kicked him in the balls, and I kept kicking him there until he was dead," Hot Pie boasted. "I kicked him all to pieces. His balls were broke open and bloody and his cock turned black. You better gimme the sword."

Arya slid her practice sword from her belt. "You can have this one," she told Hot Pie, not wanting to fight.

"That's just some stick." He rode nearer and tried to reach over for Needle's hilt.

Arya made the stick whistle as she laid the wood across his donkey's hindquarters. The animal *hawed* and bucked, dumping Hot Pie on the ground. She vaulted off her own donkey and poked him in the gut as he tried to get up and he sat back down with a grunt. Then she whacked him across the face and his nose made a *crack* like a branch breaking. Blood dribbled from his nostrils. When Hot Pie began to wail, Arya whirled toward Lommy Greenhands, who was sitting on his donkey openmouthed. "You want some sword too?" she yelled, but he didn't. He raised dyed green hands in front of his face and squealed at her to get away.

The Bull shouted, "Behind you," and Arya spun. Hot Pie was on his knees, his fist closing around a big jagged rock. She let him throw it, ducking her head as it sailed past. Then she flew at him. He raised a hand and she hit it, and then his cheek, and then his knee. He grabbed for her, and she danced aside and bounced the wood off the back of his head. He fell down and got up and stumbled after her, his red face all smeared with dirt and blood. Arya slid into a water dancer's stance and waited. When he came close enough, she lunged, right between his legs, so hard that if her wooden sword had had a point it would have come out between his butt cheeks.

By the time Yoren pulled her off him, Hot Pie was sprawled out on the ground with his breeches brown and smelly, crying as Arya whapped him over and over and over. "*Enough*," the black brother roared, prying the stick sword from her fingers, "you want to kill the fool?" When Lommy and some others started to squeal, the old man turned on them too. "Shut your mouths, or I'll be shutting them for you. Any more o' this, I'll tie you lot behind the wagons and *drag* you to the Wall." He spat. "And that goes twice for you, Arry. You come with me, boy. *Now.*"

They were all looking at her, even the three chained and manacled in the back of the wagon. The fat one snapped his pointy teeth together and *hissed*, but Arya ignored him.

The old man dragged her well off the road into a tangle of trees, cursing and muttering all the while. "If I had a thimble o' sense, I would've left you in King's Landing. You hear me, *boy*?" He always snarled that word, putting a bite in it so she would be certain to hear. "Unlace your breeches and pull 'em down. Go on, there's no one here to see. Do it." Sullenly, Arya did as he said. "Over there, against the oak. Yes, like that." She wrapped her arms around the trunk and pressed her face to the rough wood. "You scream now. You scream loud."

I won't, Arya thought stubbornly, but when Yoren laid the wood against the back of her bare thighs, the shriek burst out of her anyway. "Think that hurt?" he said. "Try this one." The stick came whistling. Arya shrieked again, clutching the tree to keep from falling. "One more." She held on tight, chewing her lip, flinching when she heard it coming. The stroke made her jump and howl. *I won't cry*, she thought, *I won't do that. I'm a Stark of Winterfell, our sigil is the direwolf, direwolves don't cry.* She could feel a thin trickle of blood running down her left leg. Her thighs and cheeks were ablaze with pain. "Might be I got your attention now," Yoren said. "Next time you take that stick to one of your brothers, you'll get twice what you give, you hear me? Now cover yourself."

They're not my brothers, Arya thought as she bent to yank up her breeches, but she knew better than to say so. Her hands fumbled with her belt and laces.

Yoren was looking at her. "You hurt?"

Calm as still water, she told herself, the way Syrio Forel had taught her. "Some."

He spat. "That pie boy's hurting worse. It wasn't him as killed your father, girl, nor that thieving Lommy neither. Hitting them won't bring him back."

"I know," Arya muttered sullenly.

"Here's something you don't know. It wasn't supposed to happen like it did. I was set to leave, wagons bought and loaded, and a man comes with a boy for me, and a purse of coin, and a message, never mind who it's from. Lord Eddard's to take the black, he says to me, wait, he'll be going with you. Why d'you think I was there? Only something went queer."

"Joffrey," Arya breathed. "Someone should kill *him!*"

"Someone will, but it won't be me, nor you neither." Yoren tossed back her stick sword. "Got sourleaf back at the wagons," he said as they made their way back to the road. "You'll chew some, it'll help with the sting."

It did help, some, though the taste of it was foul and it made her spit look like blood. Even so, she walked for the rest of that day, and the day after, and the day after *that*, too raw to sit a donkey. Hot Pie was worse off; Yoren had to shift some barrels around so he could lie in the back of a wagon on some sacks of barley, and he whimpered every time the wheels hit a rock. Lommy Greenhands wasn't even hurt, yet he stayed as far away from Arya as he could get. "Every time you look at him, he twitches," the Bull told her as she walked beside his donkey. She did not answer. It seemed safer not to talk to anyone.

That night she lay upon her thin blanket on the hard ground, staring up at the great red comet. The comet was splendid and scary all at once. "The Red Sword," the Bull named it; he claimed it looked like a sword, the blade still red-hot from the forge. When Arya squinted the right way she could see the sword too, only it wasn't a new sword, it was Ice, her father's greatsword, all ripply Valyrian steel, and the red was Lord Eddard's blood on the blade after Ser Ilyn the King's Justice had cut off his head. Yoren had made her look away when it happened, yet it seemed to her that the comet looked like Ice must have, after.

When at last she slept, she dreamed of home. The kingsroad wound its way past Winterfell on its way to the Wall, and Yoren had promised he'd leave her there with no one any wiser about who she'd been. She yearned to see her mother again, and Robb and Bran and Rickon . . . but it was Jon Snow she thought of most. She wished somehow they could come to the Wall *before* Winterfell, so Jon might muss up her hair and call her "little sister." She'd tell him, "I missed you," and he'd say it too at the very same moment, the way they always used to say things together. She would have liked that. She would have liked that better than anything.

SANSA

The morning of King Joffrey's name day dawned bright and windy, with the long tail of the great comet visible through the high scuttling clouds. Sansa was watching it from her tower window when Ser Arys Oakheart arrived to escort her down to the tourney grounds. "What do you think it means?" she asked him.

"Glory to your betrothed," Ser Arys answered at once. "See how it flames across the sky today on His Grace's name day, as if the gods themselves had raised a banner in his honor. The smallfolk have named it King Joffrey's Comet."

Doubtless that was what they told Joffrey; Sansa was not so sure. "I've heard servants calling it the Dragon's Tail."

"King Joffrey sits where Aegon the Dragon once sat, in the castle built by his son," Ser Arys said. "He is the dragon's heir—and crimson is the color of House Lannister, another sign. This comet is sent to herald

Joffrey's ascent to the throne, I have no doubt. It means that he will triumph over his enemies."

Is it true? she wondered. *Would the gods be so cruel?* Her mother was one of Joffrey's enemies now, her brother Robb another. Her father had died by the king's command. Must Robb and her lady mother die next? The comet *was* red, but Joffrey was Baratheon as much as Lannister, and their sigil was a black stag on a golden field. Shouldn't the gods have sent Joff a golden comet?

Sansa closed the shutters and turned sharply away from the window. "You look very lovely today, my lady," Ser Arys said.

"Thank you, ser." Knowing that Joffrey would require her to attend the tourney in his honor, Sansa had taken special care with her face and clothes. She wore a gown of pale purple silk and a moonstone hair net that had been a gift from Joffrey. The gown had long sleeves to hide the bruises on her arms. Those were Joffrey's gifts as well. When they told him that Robb had been proclaimed King in the North, his rage had been a fearsome thing, and he had sent Ser Boros to beat her.

"Shall we go?" Ser Arys offered his arm and she let him lead her from her chamber. If she must have one of the Kingsguard dogging her steps, Sansa preferred that it be him. Ser Boros was short-tempered, Ser Meryn cold, and Ser Mandon's strange dead eyes made her uneasy, while Ser Preston treated her like a lackwit child. Arys Oakheart was courteous, and would talk to her cordially. Once he even objected when Joffrey commanded him to hit her. He *did* hit her in the end, but not hard as Ser Meryn or Ser Boros might have, and at least he had argued. The others obeyed without question . . . except for the Hound, but Joff never asked the Hound to punish her. He used the other five for that.

Ser Arys had light brown hair and a face that was not unpleasant to look upon. Today he made quite the dashing figure, with his white silk cloak fastened at the shoulder by a golden leaf, and a spreading oak tree worked upon the breast of his tunic in shining gold thread. "Who do you think will win the day's honors?" Sansa asked as they descended the steps arm in arm.

"I will," Ser Arys answered, smiling. "Yet I fear the triumph will have no savor. This will be a small field, and poor. No more than two score will enter the lists, including squires and freeriders. There is small honor in unhorsing green boys."

The last tourney had been different, Sansa reflected. King Robert had staged it in her father's honor. High lords and fabled champions had come from all over the realm to compete, and the whole city had turned out to watch. She remembered the splendor of it: the field of pavilions along the river with a knight's shield hung before each door, the long rows of silken pennants waving in the wind, the gleam of sunlight on bright steel and gilded spurs. The days had rung to the sounds of trumpets and pounding hooves, and the nights had been full of feasts and song. Those had been the most magical days of her life, but they seemed a memory from another age now. Robert Baratheon was dead, and her father as well, beheaded for a traitor on the steps of the Great Sept of Baelor. Now there were three kings in the land, and war raged beyond the Trident while the city filled with desperate men. Small wonder that they had to hold Joff's tournament behind the thick stone walls of the Red Keep.

"Will the queen attend, do you think?" Sansa always felt safer when Cersei was there to restrain her son.

"I fear not, my lady. The council is meeting, some urgent business." Ser Arys dropped his voice. "Lord Tywin has gone to ground at Harrenhal instead of bringing his army to the city as the queen commanded. Her Grace is furious." He fell silent as a column of Lannister guardsmen marched past, in crimson cloaks and lion-crested helms. Ser Arys was fond of gossip, but only when he was certain that no one was listening.

The carpenters had erected a gallery and lists in the outer bailey. It was a poor thing indeed, and the meager throng that had gathered to watch filled but half the seats. Most of the spectators were guardsmen in the gold cloaks of the City Watch or the crimson of House Lannister; of lords and ladies there were but a paltry few, the handful that remained at court. Grey-faced Lord Gyles Rosby was coughing into a square of pink silk. Lady Tanda was bracketed by her daughters, placid dull Lollys and acid-tongued Falyse. Ebon-skinned Jalabhar Xho was an exile who had no other refuge, Lady Ermesande a babe seated on her wet nurse's lap. The talk was she would soon be wed to one of the queen's cousins, so the Lannisters might claim her lands.

The king was shaded beneath a crimson canopy, one leg thrown negligently over the carved wooden arm of his chair. Princess Myrcella and Prince Tommen sat behind him. In the back of the royal box, Sandor Clegane stood at guard, his hands resting on his swordbelt. The white cloak of the Kingsguard was draped over his broad shoulders and fastened with a jeweled brooch, the snowy cloth looking somehow unnatural against his brown roughspun tunic and studded leather jerkin. "Lady Sansa," the Hound announced curtly when he saw her. His voice was as rough as the sound of a saw on wood. The burn scars on his face and throat made one side of his mouth twitch when he spoke.

Princess Myrcella nodded a shy greeting at the sound of Sansa's name, but plump little Prince Tommen jumped up eagerly. "Sansa, did you hear? I'm to ride in the tourney today. Mother said I could." Tommen was all of eight. He reminded her of her own little brother, Bran. They were of an age. Bran was back at Winterfell, a cripple, yet safe.

Sansa would have given anything to be with him. "I fear for the life of your foeman," she told Tommen solemnly.

"His foeman will be stuffed with straw," Joff said as he rose. The king was clad in a gilded breastplate with a roaring lion engraved upon its chest, as if he expected the war to engulf them at any moment. He was thirteen today, and tall for his age, with the green eyes and golden hair of the Lannisters.

"Your Grace," she said, dipping in a curtsy.

Ser Arys bowed. "Pray pardon me, Your Grace. I must equip myself for the lists."

Joffrey waved a curt dismissal while he studied Sansa from head to heels. "I'm pleased you wore my stones."

So the king had decided to play the gallant today. Sansa was relieved. "I thank you for them . . . and for your tender words. I pray you a lucky name day, Your Grace."

"Sit," Joff commanded, gesturing her to the empty seat beside his own. "Have you heard? The Beggar King is dead."

"Who?" For a moment Sansa was afraid he meant Robb.

"Viserys. The last son of Mad King Aerys. He's been going about the Free Cities since before I was born, calling himself a king. Well, Mother says the Dothraki finally crowned him. With molten gold." He laughed. "That's funny, don't you think? The dragon was their sigil. It's almost as good as if some wolf killed your traitor brother. Maybe I'll feed him to wolves after I've caught him. Did I tell you, I intend to challenge him to single combat?"

"I should like to see that, Your Grace." *More than you know.* Sansa kept her tone cool and polite, yet even so Joffrey's eyes narrowed as he tried to decide whether she was mocking him. "Will you enter the lists today?" she asked quickly.

The king frowned. "My lady mother said it was not fitting, since the tourney is in my honor. Otherwise I would have been champion. Isn't that so, dog?"

The Hound's mouth twitched. "Against this lot? Why not?"

He had been the champion in her father's tourney, Sansa remembered. "Will you joust today, my lord?" she asked him.

Clegane's voice was thick with contempt. "Wouldn't be worth the bother of arming myself. This is a tournament of gnats."

The king laughed. "My dog has a fierce bark. Perhaps

I should command him to fight the day's champion. To the death." Joffrey was fond of making men fight to the death.

"You'd be one knight the poorer." The Hound had never taken a knight's vows. His brother was a knight, and he hated his brother.

A blare of trumpets sounded. The king settled back in his seat and took Sansa's hand. Once that would have set her heart to pounding, but that was before he had answered her plea for mercy by presenting her with her father's head. His touch filled her with revulsion now, but she knew better than to show it. She made herself sit very still.

"Ser Meryn Trant of the Kingsguard," a herald called.

Ser Meryn entered from the west side of the yard, clad in gleaming white plate chased with gold and mounted on a milk-white charger with a flowing grey mane. His cloak streamed behind him like a field of snow. He carried a twelve-foot lance.

"Ser Hobber of House Redwyne, of the Arbor," the herald sang. Ser Hobber trotted in from the east, riding a black stallion caparisoned in burgundy and blue. His lance was striped in the same colors, and his shield bore the grape cluster sigil of his House. The Redwyne twins were the queen's unwilling guests, even as Sansa was. She wondered whose notion it had been for them to ride in Joffrey's tourney. Not their own, she thought.

At a signal from the master of revels, the combatants couched their lances and put their spurs to their mounts. There were shouts from the watching guardsmen and the lords and ladies in the gallery. The knights came together in the center of the yard with a great shock of wood and steel. The white lance and the striped one exploded in splinters within a second of each other. Hobber Redwyne reeled at the impact, yet somehow managed to keep his seat. Wheeling their horses about at the far end of the lists, the knights tossed down their broken lances and accepted replacements from the squires. Ser Horas Redwyne, Ser Hobber's twin, shouted encouragement to his brother.

But on their second pass Ser Meryn swung the point of his lance to strike Ser Hobber in the chest, driving him from the saddle to crash resoundingly to the earth. Ser Horas cursed and ran out to help his battered brother from the field.

"Poorly ridden," declared King Joffrey.

"Ser Balon Swann, of Stonehelm in the Red Watch," came the herald's cry. Wide white wings ornamented Ser Balon's greathelm, and black and white swans fought on his shield. *"Morros of House Slynt, heir to Lord Janos of Harrenhal."*

"Look at that upjumped oaf," Joff hooted, loud enough for half the yard to hear. Morros, a mere squire and a new-made squire at that, was having difficulty managing lance and shield. The lance was a knight's weapon, Sansa knew, the Slynts lowborn. Lord Janos had been no more than commander of the City Watch before Joffrey had raised him to Harrenhal and the council.

I hope he falls and shames himself, she thought bitterly. *I hope Ser Balon kills him.* When Joffrey proclaimed her father's death, it had been Janos Slynt who seized Lord Eddard's severed head by the hair and raised it on high for king and crowd to behold, while Sansa wept and screamed.

Morros wore a checkered black-and-gold cloak over black armor inlaid with golden scrollwork. On his shield was the bloody spear his father had chosen as the sigil of their new-made house. But he did not seem to know what to do with the shield as he urged his horse forward, and Ser Balon's point struck the blazon square. Morros dropped his lance, fought for balance, and lost. One foot caught in a stirrup as he fell, and the runaway charger dragged the youth to the end of the lists, head bouncing against the ground. Joff hooted derision. Sansa was appalled, wondering if the gods had heard her vengeful prayer. But when they disentangled Morros Slynt from his horse, they found him bloodied but alive. "Tommen, we picked the wrong foe for you," the king told his brother. "The straw knight jousts better than that one."

Next came Ser Horas Redwyne's turn. He fared better than his twin, vanquishing an elderly knight whose mount was bedecked with silver griffins against a striped blue-and-white field. Splendid as he looked, the old man made a poor contest of it. Joffrey curled his lip. "This is a feeble show."

"I warned you," said the Hound. "Gnats."

The king was growing bored. It made Sansa anxious. She lowered her eyes and resolved to keep quiet, no matter what. When Joffrey Baratheon's mood darkened, any chance word might set off one of his rages.

"Lothor Brune, freerider in the service of Lord Baelish," cried the herald. *"Ser Dontos the Red, of House Hollard."*

The freerider, a small man in dented plate without device, duly appeared at the west end of the yard, but of his opponent there was no sign. Finally a chestnut stallion trotted into view in a swirl of crimson and scarlet silks, but Ser Dontos was not on it. The knight appeared a moment later, cursing and staggering, clad in breastplate and plumed helm and nothing else. His legs were pale and skinny, and his manhood flopped about obscenely as he chased after his horse. The watchers roared and shouted insults. Catching his horse by the bridle, Ser Dontos tried to mount, but the animal would not stand still and the knight was so drunk that his bare foot kept missing the stirrup.

By then the crowd was howling with laughter . . . all but the king. Joffrey had a look in his eyes that Sansa remembered well, the same look he'd had at the Great Sept of Baelor the day he pronounced death on Lord Eddard Stark. Finally Ser Dontos the Red gave it up for a bad job, sat down in the dirt, and removed his plumed helm. "I lose," he shouted. "Fetch me some wine."

The king stood. "A cask from the cellars! I'll see him drowned in it."

Sansa heard herself gasp. *"No, you can't."*

Joffrey turned his head. "What did you say?"

Sansa could not believe she had spoken. Was she mad? To tell him *no* in front of half the court? She hadn't meant to say anything, only . . . Ser Dontos was drunk and silly and useless, but he meant no harm.

"Did you say I *can't*? Did you?"

"Please," Sansa said, "I only meant . . . it would be ill luck, Your Grace . . . to, to kill a man on your name day."

"You're lying," Joffrey said. "I ought to drown you with him, if you care for him so much."

"I don't care for him, Your Grace." The words tumbled out desperately. "Drown him or have his head off, only . . . kill him on the morrow, if you like, but please . . . not today, not on your name day. I couldn't bear for you to have ill luck . . . terrible luck, even for kings, the singers all say so . . ."

Joffrey scowled. He knew she was lying, she could see it. He would make her bleed for this.

"The girl speaks truly," the Hound rasped. "What a man sows on his name day, he reaps throughout the year." His voice was flat, as if he did not care a whit whether the king believed him or no. Could it be *true*? Sansa had not known. It was just something she'd said, desperate to avoid punishment.

Unhappy, Joffrey shifted in his seat and flicked his fingers at Ser Dontos. "Take him away. I'll have him killed on the morrow, the fool."

"He is," Sansa said. "A fool. You're so clever, to see it. He's better fitted to be a fool than a knight, isn't he? You ought to dress him in motley and make him clown for you. He doesn't deserve the mercy of a quick death."

The king studied her a moment. "Perhaps you're not so stupid as Mother says." He raised his voice. "Did you hear my lady, Dontos? From this day on, you're my new fool. You can sleep with Moon Boy and dress in motley."

Ser Dontos, sobered by his near brush with death, crawled to his knees. "Thank you, Your Grace. And you, my lady. Thank you."

As a brace of Lannister guardsmen led him off, the

master of revels approached the box. "Your Grace," he said, "shall I summon a new challenger for Brune, or proceed with the next tilt?"

"Neither. These are gnats, not knights. I'd have them all put to death, only it's my name day. The tourney is done. Get them all out of my sight."

The master of revels bowed, but Prince Tommen was not so obedient. "I'm supposed to ride against the straw man."

"Not today."

"But I want to ride!"

"I don't care what you want."

"Mother *said* I could ride."

"She said," Princess Myrcella agreed.

"Mother *said*," mocked the king. "Don't be childish."

"We're children," Myrcella declared haughtily. "We're *supposed* to be childish."

The Hound laughed. "She has you there."

Joffrey was beaten. "Very well. Even my brother couldn't tilt any worse than these others. Master, bring out the quintain, Tommen wants to be a gnat."

Tommen gave a shout of joy and ran off to be readied, his chubby little legs pumping hard. "Luck," Sansa called to him.

They set up the quintain at the far end of the lists while the prince's pony was being saddled. Tommen's opponent was a child-sized leather warrior stuffed with straw and mounted on a pivot, with a shield in one hand and a padded mace in the other. Someone had fastened a pair of antlers to the knight's head. Joffrey's father King Robert had worn antlers on his helm, Sansa remembered . . . but so did his uncle Lord Renly, Robert's brother, who had turned traitor and crowned himself king.

A pair of squires buckled the prince into his ornate silver-and-crimson armor. A tall plume of red feathers sprouted from the crest of his helm, and the lion of Lannister and crowned stag of Baratheon frolicked together on his shield. The squires helped him mount, and Ser Aron Santagar, the Red Keep's master-at-arms, stepped forward and handed Tommen a blunted silver longsword with a leaf-shaped blade, crafted to fit an eight-year-old hand.

Tommen raised the blade high. "Casterly Rock!" he shouted in a high boyish voice as he put his heels into his pony and started across the hard-packed dirt at the quintain. Lady Tanda and Lord Gyles started a ragged cheer, and Sansa added her voice to theirs. The king brooded in silence.

Tommen got his pony up to a brisk trot, waved his sword vigorously, and struck the knight's shield a solid blow as he went by. The quintain spun, the padded mace flying around to give the prince a mighty whack in the back of his head. Tommen spilled from the saddle, his new armor rattling like a bag of old pots as he hit the ground. His sword went flying, his pony cantered away across the bailey, and a great gale of derision went up. King Joffrey laughed longest and loudest of all.

"Oh," Princess Myrcella cried. She scrambled out of the box and ran to her little brother.

Sansa found herself possessed of a queer giddy courage. "You should go with her," she told the king. "Your brother might be hurt."

Joffrey shrugged. "What if he is?"

"You should help him up and tell him how well he rode." Sansa could not seem to stop herself.

"He got knocked off his horse and fell in the dirt," the king pointed out. "That's not riding well."

"Look," the Hound interrupted. "The boy has courage. He's going to try again."

They were helping Prince Tommen mount his pony. *If only Tommen were the elder instead of Joffrey,* Sansa thought. *I wouldn't mind marrying Tommen.*

The sounds from the gatehouse took them by surprise. Chains rattled as the portcullis was drawn upward, and the great gates opened to the creak of iron hinges. "Who told them to open the gate?" Joff demanded. With the troubles in the city, the gates of the Red Keep had been closed for days.

A column of riders emerged from beneath the portcullis with a clink of steel and a clatter of hooves. Clegane stepped close to the king, one hand on the hilt of his longsword. The visitors were dinted and haggard and dusty, yet the standard they carried was the lion of Lannister, golden on its crimson field. A few wore the red cloaks and mail of Lannister men-at-arms, but more were freeriders and sellswords, armored in oddments and bristling with sharp steel . . . and there were others, monstrous savages out of one of Old Nan's tales, the scary ones Bran used to love. They were clad in shabby skins and boiled leather, with long hair and fierce beards. Some wore bloodstained bandages over their brows or wrapped around their hands, and others were missing eyes, ears, and fingers.

In their midst, riding on a tall red horse in a strange high saddle that cradled him back and front, was the queen's dwarf brother Tyrion Lannister, the one they called the Imp. He had let his beard grow to cover his pushed-in face, until it was a bristly tangle of yellow and black hair, coarse as wire. Down his back flowed a shadowskin cloak, black fur striped with white. He held the reins in his left hand and carried his right arm in a white silk sling, but otherwise looked as grotesque as Sansa remembered from when he had visited Winterfell. With his bulging brow and mismatched eyes, he was still the ugliest man she had ever chanced to look upon.

Yet Tommen put his spurs into his pony and galloped headlong across the yard, shouting with glee. One of the savages, a huge shambling man so hairy that his face was all but lost beneath his whiskers, scooped the boy out of his saddle, armor and all, and deposited him on the ground beside his uncle. Tommen's breathless laughter echoed off the walls as Tyrion clapped him on the backplate, and Sansa was startled to see that the two were of a height. Myrcella came running after her brother, and the dwarf picked her up by the waist and spun her in a circle, squealing.

When he lowered her back to the ground, the little man kissed her lightly on the brow and came waddling across the yard toward Joffrey. Two of his men followed close behind him; a black-haired black-eyed sellsword who moved like a stalking cat, and a gaunt youth with an empty socket where one eye should have been. Tommen and Myrcella trailed after them.

The dwarf went to one knee before the king. "Your Grace."

"You," Joffrey said.

"Me," the Imp agreed, "although a more courteous greeting might be in order, for an uncle and an elder."

"They said you were dead," the Hound said.

The little man gave the big one a look. One of his eyes was green, one was black, and both were cool. "I was speaking to the king, not to his cur."

"*I'm* glad you're not dead," said Princess Myrcella.

"We share that view, sweet child." Tyrion turned to Sansa. "My lady, I am sorry for your losses. Truly, the gods are cruel."

Sansa could not think of a word to say to him. How could he be sorry for her losses? Was he mocking her? It wasn't the gods who'd been cruel, it was Joffrey.

"I am sorry for your loss as well, Joffrey," the dwarf said.

"What loss?"

"Your royal father? A large fierce man with a black beard; you'll recall him if you try. He was king before you."

"Oh, *him*. Yes, it was very sad, a boar killed him."

"Is that what 'they' say, Your Grace?"

Joffrey frowned. Sansa felt that she ought to say something. What was it that Septa Mordane used to tell her? *A lady's armor is courtesy*, that was it. She donned her armor and said, "I'm sorry my lady mother took you captive, my lord."

"A great many people are sorry for that," Tyrion replied, "and before I am done, some may be a deal sorrier . . . yet I thank you for the sentiment. Joffrey, where might I find your mother?"

"She's with my council," the king answered. "Your brother Jaime keeps losing battles." He gave Sansa an angry look, as if it were *her* fault. "He's been taken by the Starks and we've lost Riverrun and now her stupid brother is calling himself a king."

The dwarf smiled crookedly. "All sorts of people are calling themselves kings these days."

Joff did not know what to make of that, though he looked suspicious and out of sorts. "Yes. Well. I am pleased you're not dead, Uncle. Did you bring me a gift for my name day?"

"I did. My wits."

"I'd sooner have Robb Stark's head," Joff said with a sly glance at Sansa. "Tommen, Myrcella, come."

Sandor Clegane lingered behind a moment. "I'd guard that tongue of yours, little man," he warned, before he strode off after his liege.

Sansa was left with the dwarf and his monsters. She tried to think of what else she might say. "You hurt your arm," she managed at last.

"One of your northmen hit me with a morningstar during the battle on the Green Fork. I escaped him by falling off my horse." His grin turned into something softer as he studied her face. "Is it grief for your lord father that makes you so sad?"

"My father was a traitor," Sansa said at once. "And my brother and lady mother are traitors as well." That reflex she had learned quickly. "I am loyal to my beloved Joffrey."

"No doubt. As loyal as a deer surrounded by wolves."

"Lions," she whispered, without thinking. She glanced about nervously, but there was no one close enough to hear.

Lannister reached out and took her hand, and gave it a squeeze. "I am only a little lion, child, and I vow, I shall not savage you." Bowing, he said, "But now you must excuse me. I have urgent business with queen and council."

Sansa watched him walk off, his body swaying heavily from side to side with every step, like something from a grotesquerie. *He speaks more gently than Joffrey,* she thought, *but the queen spoke to me gently too. He's still a Lannister, her brother and Joff's uncle, and no friend.* Once she had loved Prince Joffrey with all her heart, and admired and trusted his mother, the queen. They had repaid that love and trust with her father's head. Sansa would never make that mistake again.

TYRION

In the chilly white raiment of the Kingsguard, Ser Mandon Moore looked like a corpse in a shroud. "Her Grace left orders, the council in session is not to be disturbed."

"I would be only a small disturbance, ser." Tyrion slid the parchment from his sleeve. "I bear a letter from my father, Lord Tywin Lannister, the Hand of the King. There is his seal."

"Her Grace does not wish to be disturbed," Ser Mandon repeated slowly, as if Tyrion were a dullard who had not heard him the first time.

Jaime had once told him that Moore was the most dangerous of the Kingsguard—excepting himself, always—because his face gave no hint as what he might do next. Tyrion would have welcomed a hint. Bronn and Timett could likely kill the knight if it came to swords, but it would scarcely bode well if he began by slaying one of Joffrey's protectors. Yet if he let the man turn him away, where was his authority? He made himself smile. "Ser Mandon, you have not met my companions.

This is Timett son of Timett, a red hand of the Burned Men. And this is Bronn. Perchance you recall Ser Vardis Egen, who was captain of Lord Arryn's household guard?"

"I know the man." Ser Mandon's eyes were pale grey, oddly flat and lifeless.

"Knew," Bronn corrected with a thin smile.

Ser Mandon did not deign to show that he had heard that.

"Be that as it may," Tyrion said lightly, "I truly must see my sister and present my letter, ser. If you would be so kind as to open the door for us?"

The white knight did not respond. Tyrion was almost at the point of trying to force his way past when Ser Mandon abruptly stood aside. "You may enter. They may not."

A small victory, he thought, *but sweet.* He had passed his first test. Tyrion Lannister shouldered through the door, feeling almost tall. Five members of the king's small council broke off their discussion suddenly. "You," his sister Cersei said in a tone that was equal parts disbelief and distaste.

"I can see where Joffrey learned his courtesies." Tyrion paused to admire the pair of Valyrian sphinxes that guarded the door, affecting an air of casual confidence. Cersei could smell weakness the way a dog smells fear.

"What are you doing here?" His sister's lovely green eyes studied him without the least hint of affection.

"Delivering a letter from our lord father." He sauntered to the table and placed the tightly rolled parchment between them.

The eunuch Varys took the letter and turned it in his delicate powdered hands. "How kind of Lord Tywin. And his sealing wax is such a lovely shade of gold." Varys gave the seal a close inspection. "It gives every appearance of being genuine."

"Of course it's genuine." Cersei snatched it out of his hands. She broke the wax and unrolled the parchment.

Tyrion watched her read. His sister had taken the

king's seat for herself—he gathered Joffrey did not often trouble to attend council meetings, no more than Robert had—so Tyrion climbed up into the Hand's chair. It seemed only appropriate.

"This is absurd," the queen said at last. "My lord father has sent my brother to sit in his place in this council. He bids us accept Tyrion as the Hand of the King, until such time as he himself can join us."

Grand Maester Pycelle stroked his flowing white beard and nodded ponderously. "It would seem that a welcome is in order."

"Indeed." Jowly, balding Janos Slynt looked rather like a frog, a smug frog who had gotten rather above himself. "We have sore need of you, my lord. Rebellion everywhere, this grim omen in the sky, rioting in the city streets . . ."

"And whose fault is that, Lord Janos?" Cersei lashed out. "Your gold cloaks are charged with keeping order. As to you, Tyrion, you could better serve us on the field of battle."

He laughed. "No, I'm done with fields of battle, thank you. I sit a chair better than a horse, and I'd sooner hold a wine goblet than a battle-axe. All that about the thunder of the drums, sunlight flashing on armor, magnificent destriers snorting and prancing? Well, the drums gave me headaches, the sunlight flashing on my armor cooked me up like a harvest day goose, and those magnificent destriers shit *everywhere*. Not that I am complaining. Compared to the hospitality I enjoyed in the Vale of Arryn, drums, horseshit, and fly bites are my favorite things."

Littlefinger laughed. "Well said, Lannister. A man after my own heart."

Tyrion smiled at him, remembering a certain dagger with a dragonbone hilt and a Valyrian steel blade. *We must have a talk about that, and soon.* He wondered if Lord Petyr would find that subject amusing as well. "Please," he told them, "do let me be of service, in whatever *small* way I can."

Cersei read the letter again. "How many men have you brought with you?"

"A few hundred. My own men, chiefly. Father was loath to part with any of his. He *is* fighting a war, after all."

"What use will your few hundred men be if Renly marches on the city, or Stannis sails from Dragonstone? I ask for an army and my father sends me a dwarf. The *king* names the Hand, with the consent of council. Joffrey named our lord father."

"And our lord father named me."

"He cannot do that. Not without Joff's consent."

"Lord Tywin is at Harrenhal with his host, if you'd care to take it up with him," Tyrion said politely. "My lords, perchance you would permit me a private word with my sister?"

Varys slithered to his feet, smiling in that unctuous way he had. "How you must have yearned for the sound of your sweet sister's voice. My lords, please, let us give them a few moments together. The woes of our troubled realm shall keep."

Janos Slynt rose hesitantly and Grand Maester Pycelle ponderously, yet they rose. Littlefinger was the last. "Shall I tell the steward to prepare chambers in Maegor's Holdfast?"

"My thanks, Lord Petyr, but I will be taking Lord Stark's former quarters in the Tower of the Hand."

Littlefinger laughed. "You're a braver man than me, Lannister. You *do* know the fate of our last two Hands?"

"Two? If you mean to frighten me, why not say four?"

"Four?" Littlefinger raised an eyebrow. "Did the Hands before Lord Arryn meet some dire end in the Tower? I'm afraid I was too young to pay them much mind."

"Aerys Targaryen's last Hand was killed during the Sack of King's Landing, though I doubt he'd had time to settle into the Tower. He was only Hand for a fortnight. The one before him was burned to death. And before them came two others who died landless and penniless in exile, and counted themselves lucky. I believe my lord father was the last Hand to depart King's Landing with his name, properties, and parts all intact."

"Fascinating," said Littlefinger. "And all the more reason I'd sooner bed down in the dungeon."

Perhaps you'll get that wish, Tyrion thought, but he said, "Courage and folly are cousins, or so I've heard. Whatever curse may linger over the Tower of the Hand, I pray I'm small enough to escape its notice."

Janos Slynt laughed, Littlefinger smiled, and Grand Maester Pycelle followed them both out, bowing gravely.

"I hope Father did not send you all this way to plague us with history lessons," his sister said when they were alone.

"How I have yearned for the sound of your sweet voice," Tyrion sighed to her.

"How I have yearned to have that eunuch's tongue pulled out with hot pincers," Cersei replied. "Has father lost his senses? Or did you forge this letter?" She read it once more, with mounting annoyance. "Why would he inflict *you* on me? I wanted him to come himself." She crushed Lord Tywin's letter in her fingers. "I am Joffrey's regent, and I sent him a royal *command!*"

"And he ignored you," Tyrion pointed out. "He has quite a large army, he can do that. Nor is he the first. Is he?"

Cersei's mouth tightened. He could see her color rising. "If I name this letter a forgery and tell them to throw you in a dungeon, no one will ignore *that*, I promise you."

He was walking on rotten ice now, Tyrion knew. One false step and he would plunge through. "No one," he agreed amiably, "least of all our father. The one with the army. But why should you want to throw me into a dungeon, sweet sister, when I've come all this long way to help you?"

"I do not require *your* help. It was our father's presence that I commanded."

"Yes," he said quietly, "but it's Jaime you want."

His sister fancied herself subtle, but he had grown up with her. He could read her face like one of his favorite books, and what he read now was rage, and fear, and despair. "Jaime—"

"—is my brother no less than yours," Tyrion interrupted. "Give me your support and I promise you, we will have Jaime freed and returned to us unharmed."

"How?" Cersei demanded. "The Stark boy and his mother are not like to forget that we beheaded Lord Eddard."

"True," Tyrion agreed, "yet you still hold his daughters, don't you? I saw the older girl out in the yard with Joffrey."

"Sansa," the queen said. "I've given it out that I have the younger brat as well, but it's a lie. I sent Meryn Trant to take her in hand when Robert died, but her wretched dancing master interfered and the girl fled. No one has seen her since. Likely she's dead. A great many people died that day."

Tyrion had hoped for both Stark girls, but he supposed one would have to do. "Tell me about our friends on the council."

His sister glanced at the door. "What of them?"

"Father seems to have taken a dislike to them. When I left him, he was wondering how their heads might look on the wall beside Lord Stark's." He leaned forward across the table. "Are you certain of their loyalty? Do you trust them?"

"I trust no one," Cersei snapped. "I need them. Does Father believe they are playing us false?"

"Suspects, rather."

"Why? What does he know?"

Tyrion shrugged. "He knows that your son's short reign has been a long parade of follies and disasters. That suggests that someone is giving Joffrey some very bad counsel."

Cersei gave him a searching look. "Joff has had no lack of good counsel. He's always been strong-willed. Now that he's king, he believes he should do as he pleases, not as he's bid."

"Crowns do queer things to the heads beneath them," Tyrion agreed. "This business with Eddard Stark . . . Joffrey's work?"

The queen grimaced. "He was instructed to pardon Stark, to allow him to take the black. The man would have been out of our way forever, and we might have made peace with that son of his, but Joff took it upon himself to give the mob a better show. What was I to do? He called for Lord Eddard's head in front of half the city. And Janos Slynt and Ser Ilyn went ahead blithely and shortened the man without a word from me!" Her hand tightened into a fist. "The High Septon claims we profaned Baelor's Sept with blood, after lying to him about our intent."

"It would seem he has a point," said Tyrion. "So this *Lord* Slynt, he was part of it, was he? Tell me, whose fine notion was it to grant him Harrenhal and name him to the council?"

"Littlefinger made the arrangements. We needed Slynt's gold cloaks. Eddard Stark was plotting with Renly and he'd written to Lord Stannis, offering him the throne. We might have lost all. Even so, it was a close thing. If Sansa hadn't come to me and told me all her father's plans . . ."

Tyrion was surprised. "Truly? His own daughter?" Sansa had always seemed such a sweet child, tender and courteous.

"The girl was wet with love. She would have done *anything* for Joffrey, until he cut off her father's head and called it mercy. That put an end to that."

"His Grace has a unique way of winning the hearts of his subjects," Tyrion said with a crooked smile. "Was it Joffrey's wish to dismiss Ser Barristan Selmy from his Kingsguard too?"

Cersei sighed. "Joff wanted someone to blame for Robert's death. Varys suggested Ser Barristan. Why not? It gave Jaime command of the Kingsguard and a seat on the small council, and allowed Joff to throw a bone to his dog. He is very fond of Sandor Clegane. We were prepared to offer Selmy some land and a towerhouse, more than the useless old fool deserved."

"I hear that useless old fool slew two of Slynt's gold cloaks when they tried to seize him at the Mud Gate."

His sister looked very unhappy. "Janos should have sent more men. He is not as competent as might be wished."

"Ser Barristan was the Lord Commander of Robert Baratheon's Kingsguard," Tyrion reminded her pointedly. "He and Jaime are the only survivors of Aerys Targaryen's seven. The smallfolk talk of him in the same way they talk of Serwyn of the Mirror Shield and Prince Aemon the Dragonknight. What do you imagine they'll think when they see Barristan the Bold riding beside Robb Stark or Stannis Baratheon?"

Cersei glanced away. "I had not considered that."

"Father did," said Tyrion. "*That* is why he sent me. To put an end to these follies and bring your son to heel."

"Joff will be no more tractable for you than for me."

"He might."

"Why should he?"

"He knows *you* would never hurt him."

Cersei's eyes narrowed. "If you believe I'd ever allow you to harm my son, you're sick with fever."

Tyrion sighed. She'd missed the point, as she did so often. "Joffrey is as safe with me as he is with you," he assured her, "but so long as the boy *feels* threatened, he'll be more inclined to listen." He took her hand. "I *am* your brother, you know. You need me, whether you care to admit it or no. Your son needs me, if he's to have a hope of retaining that ugly iron chair."

His sister seemed shocked that he would touch her. "You have always been cunning."

"In my own small way." He grinned.

"It may be worth the trying . . . but make no mistake, Tyrion. If I accept you, you shall be the King's Hand in name, but *my* Hand in truth. You will share all your plans and intentions with me before you act, and you will do *nothing* without my consent. Do you understand?"

"Oh, yes."

"Do you agree?"

"Certainly," he lied. "I am yours, sister." *For as long as I need to be.* "So, now that we are of one purpose, we ought have no more secrets between us. You say Joffrey had Lord Eddard killed, Varys dismissed Ser Barristan, and Littlefinger gifted us with Lord Slynt. Who murdered Jon Arryn?"

Cersei yanked her hand back. "How should I know?"

"The grieving widow in the Eyrie seems to think it was me. Where did she come by that notion, I wonder?"

"I'm sure I don't know. That fool Eddard Stark accused me of the same thing. He hinted that Lord Arryn suspected or . . . well, believed . . ."

"That you were fucking our sweet Jaime?"

She slapped him.

"Did you think I was as blind as Father?" Tyrion rubbed his cheek. "Who you lie with is no matter to me . . . although it doesn't seem quite just that you should open your legs for one brother and not the other."

She slapped him.

"Be gentle, Cersei, I'm only jesting with you. If truth be told, I'd sooner have a nice whore. I never understood what Jaime saw in you, apart from his own reflection."

She slapped him.

His cheeks were red and burning, yet he smiled. "If you keep doing that, I may get angry."

That stayed her hand. "Why should I care if you do?"

"I have some new friends," Tyrion confessed. "You won't like them at all. How did you kill Robert?"

"He did that himself. All we did was help. When Lancel saw that Robert was going after boar, he gave him strongwine. His favorite sour red, but fortified, three times as potent as he was used to. The great stinking fool loved it. He could have stopped swilling it down anytime he cared to, but no, he drained one skin and told Lancel to fetch another. The boar did the rest.

You should have been at the feast, Tyrion. There has never been a boar so delicious. They cooked it with mushrooms and apples, and it tasted like triumph."

"Truly, sister, you were born to be a widow." Tyrion had rather liked Robert Baratheon, great blustering oaf that he was . . . doubtless in part because his sister loathed him so. "Now, if you are done slapping me, I will be off." He twisted his legs around and clambered down awkwardly from the chair.

Cersei frowned. "I haven't given you leave to depart. I want to know how you intend to free Jaime."

"I'll tell you when I know. Schemes are like fruit, they require a certain ripening. Right now, I have a mind to ride through the streets and take the measure of this city." Tyrion rested his hand on the head of the sphinx beside the door. "One parting request. Kindly make certain no harm comes to Sansa Stark. It would not do to lose *both* the daughters."

Outside the council chamber, Tyrion nodded to Ser Mandon and made his way down the long vaulted hall. Bronn fell in beside him. Of Timett son of Timett there was no sign. "Where's our red hand?" Tyrion asked.

"He felt an urge to explore. His kind was not made for waiting about in halls."

"I hope he doesn't kill anyone important." The clansmen Tyrion had brought down from their fastnesses in the Mountains of the Moon were loyal in their own fierce way, but they were proud and quarrelsome as well, prone to answer insults real or imagined with steel. "Try to find him. And while you are at it, see that the rest have been quartered and fed. I want them in the barracks beneath the Tower of the Hand, but don't let the steward put the Stone Crows near the Moon Brothers, and tell him the Burned Men must have a hall all to themselves."

"Where will you be?"

"I'm riding back to the Broken Anvil."

Bronn grinned insolently. "Need an escort? The talk is, the streets are dangerous."

"I'll call upon the captain of my sister's household

guard, and remind him that I am no less a Lannister than she is. He needs to recall that his oath is to Casterly Rock, not to Cersei or Joffrey."

An hour later, Tyrion rode from the Red Keep accompanied by a dozen Lannister guardsmen in crimson cloaks and lion-crested halfhelms. As they passed beneath the portcullis, he noted the heads mounted atop the walls. Black with rot and old tar, they had long since become unrecognizable. "Captain Vylarr," he called, "I want those taken down on the morrow. Give them to the silent sisters for cleaning." It would be hell to match them with the bodies, he supposed, yet it must be done. Even in the midst of war, certain decencies needed to be observed.

Vylarr grew hesitant. "His Grace has told us he wishes the traitors' heads to remain on the walls until he fills those last three empty spikes there on the end."

"Let me hazard a wild stab. One is for Robb Stark, the others for Lords Stannis and Renly. Would that be right?"

"Yes, my lord."

"My nephew is thirteen years old today, Vylarr. Try and recall that. I'll have the heads down on the morrow, or one of those empty spikes may have a different lodger. Do you take my meaning, Captain?"

"I'll see that they're taken down myself, my lord."

"Good." Tyrion put his heels into his horse and trotted away, leaving the red cloaks to follow as best they could.

He had told Cersei he intended to take the measure of the city. That was not entirely a lie. Tyrion Lannister was not pleased by much of what he saw. The streets of King's Landing had always been teeming and raucous and noisy, but now they reeked of danger in a way that he did not recall from past visits. A naked corpse sprawled in the gutter near the Street of Looms, being torn at by a pack of feral dogs, yet no one seemed to care. Watchmen were much in evidence, moving in pairs through the alleys in their gold cloaks and shirts of black ringmail, iron cudgels never far from their hands.

The markets were crowded with ragged men selling their household goods for any price they could get . . . and conspicuously empty of farmers selling food. What little produce he did see was three times as costly as it had been a year ago. One peddler was hawking rats roasted on a skewer. *"Fresh rats,"* he cried loudly, *"fresh rats."* Doubtless fresh rats were to be preferred to old stale rotten rats. The frightening thing was, the rats looked more appetizing than most of what the butchers were selling. On the Street of Flour, Tyrion saw guards at every other shop door. When times grew lean, even bakers found sellswords cheaper than bread, he reflected.

"There is no food coming in, is there?" he said to Vylarr.

"Little enough," the captain admitted. "With the war in the riverlands and Lord Renly raising rebels in Highgarden, the roads are closed to south and west."

"And what has my good sister done about this?"

"She is taking steps to restore the king's peace," Vylarr assured him. "Lord Slynt has tripled the size of the City Watch, and the queen has put a thousand craftsmen to work on our defenses. The stonemasons are strengthening the walls, carpenters are building scorpions and catapults by the hundred, fletchers are making arrows, the smiths are forging blades, and the Alchemists' Guild has pledged ten thousand jars of wildfire."

Tyrion shifted uncomfortably in his saddle. He was pleased that Cersei had not been idle, but wildfire was treacherous stuff, and ten thousand jars were enough to turn all of King's Landing into cinders. "Where has my sister found the coin to pay for all of this?" It was no secret that King Robert had left the crown vastly in debt, and alchemists were seldom mistaken for altruists.

"Lord Littlefinger always finds a way, my lord. He has imposed a tax on those wishing to enter the city."

"Yes, that would work," Tyrion said, thinking, *Clever. Clever and cruel.* Tens of thousands had fled the fighting for the supposed safety of King's Landing. He had seen them on the kingsroad, troupes of mothers and children and anxious fathers who had gazed on his horses and wagons with covetous eyes. Once they reached the city they would doubtless pay over all they had to put those high comforting walls between them and the war . . . though they might think twice if they knew about the wildfire.

The inn beneath the sign of the broken anvil stood within sight of those walls, near the Gate of the Gods where they had entered that morning. As they rode into its courtyard, a boy ran out to help Tyrion down from his horse. "Take your men back to the castle," he told Vylarr. "I'll be spending the night here."

The captain looked dubious. "Will you be safe, my lord?"

"Well, as to that, Captain, when I left the inn this morning it was full of Black Ears. One is never quite safe when Chella daughter of Cheyk is about." Tyrion waddled toward the door, leaving Vylarr to puzzle at his meaning.

A gust of merriment greeted him as he shoved into the inn's common room. He recognized Chella's throaty chuckle and the lighter music of Shae's laughter. The girl was seated by the hearth, sipping wine at a round wooden table with three of the Black Ears he'd left to guard her and a plump man whose back was to him. The innkeeper, he assumed . . . until Shae called Tyrion by name and the intruder rose. "My good lord, I am *so* pleased to see you," he gushed, a soft eunuch's smile on his powdered face.

Tyrion stumbled. "Lord Varys. I had not thought to see you here." *The Others take him, how did he find them so quickly?*

"Forgive me if I intrude," Varys said. "I was taken by a sudden urge to meet your young lady."

"Young lady," Shae repeated, savoring the words. "You're half right, m'lord. I'm young."

Eighteen, Tyrion thought. *Eighteen, and a whore, but quick of wit, nimble as a cat between the sheets, with large dark eyes and fine black hair and a sweet, soft, hungry little mouth . . . and mine! Damn you, eunuch.* "I fear I'm the intruder, Lord Varys," he said with forced courtesy. "When I came in, you were in the midst of some merriment."

"M'lord Varys complimented Chella on her ears and said she must have killed many men to have such a fine necklace," Shae explained. It grated on him to hear her call Varys *m'lord* in that tone; that was what she called him in their pillow play. "And Chella told him only cowards kill the vanquished."

"Braver to leave the man alive, with a chance to cleanse his shame by winning back his ear," explained Chella, a small dark woman whose grisly neckware was hung with no less than forty-six dried, wrinkled ears. Tyrion had counted them once. "Only so can you prove you do not fear your enemies."

Shae hooted. "And then m'lord says if he was a Black Ear he'd never sleep, for dreams of one-eared men."

"A problem I will never need face," Tyrion said. "I'm terrified of my enemies, so I kill them all."

Varys giggled. "Will you take some wine with us, my lord?"

"I'll take some wine." Tyrion seated himself beside Shae. He understood what was happening here, if Chella and the girl did not. Varys was delivering a message. When he said, *I was taken by a sudden urge to meet your young lady,* what he meant was, *You tried to hide her, but I knew where she was, and who she was, and here I am.* He wondered who had betrayed him. The innkeeper, that boy in the stable, a guard on the gate . . . or one of his own?

"I always like to return to the city through the Gate of the Gods," Varys told Shae as he filled the wine cups. "The carvings on the gatehouse are exquisite, they make me weep each time I see them. The eyes . . . so expressive, don't you think? They almost seem to follow you as you ride beneath the portcullis."

"I never noticed, m'lord," Shae replied. "I'll look again on the morrow, if it please you."

Don't bother, sweetling, Tyrion thought, swirling the wine in the cup. *He cares not a whit about carvings. The eyes he boasts of are his own. What he means is that he was watching, that he knew we were here the moment we passed through the gates.*

"Do be careful, child," Varys urged. "King's Landing is not wholly safe these days. I know these streets well, and yet I almost feared to come today, alone and unarmed as I was. Lawless men are everywhere in this dark time, oh, yes. Men with cold steel and colder hearts." *Where I can come alone and unarmed, others can come with swords in their fists,* he was saying.

Shae only laughed. "If they try and bother me, they'll be one ear short when Chella runs them off."

Varys hooted as if that was the funniest thing he had ever heard, but there was no laughter in his eyes when he turned them on Tyrion. "Your young lady has an amiable way to her. I should take very good care of her if I were you."

"I intend to. Any man who tries to harm her—well, I'm too small to be a Black Ear, and I make no claims to courage." *See? I speak the same tongue you do, eunuch. Hurt her, and I'll have your head.*

"I will leave you." Varys rose. "I know how weary you must be. I only wished to welcome you, my lord, and tell you how very pleased I am by your arrival. We have dire need of you on the council. Have you seen the comet?"

"I'm short, not blind," Tyrion said. Out on the kingsroad, it had seemed to cover half the sky, outshining the crescent moon.

"In the streets, they call it the Red Messenger," Varys said. "They say it comes as a herald before a king, to warn of fire and blood to follow." The eunuch rubbed his powdered hands together. "May I leave you with a bit of a riddle, Lord Tyrion?" He did not wait for an answer. "In a room sit three great men, a king, a priest, and a rich man with his gold. Between them stands a sellsword, a little man of common birth and no great mind. Each of the great ones bids him slay the other two. 'Do it,' says the king, 'for I am your lawful ruler.' 'Do it,' says the priest, 'for I command you in the names of the gods.' 'Do it,' says the rich man, 'and all this gold shall be yours.' So tell me—who lives and who dies?'' Bowing deeply, the eunuch hurried from the common room on soft slippered feet.

When he was gone, Chella gave a snort and Shae wrinkled up her pretty face. "The rich man lives. Doesn't he?"

Tyrion sipped at his wine, thoughtful. "Perhaps. Or not. That would depend on the sellsword, it seems." He set down his cup. "Come, let's go upstairs."

She had to wait for him at the top of the steps, for her legs were slim and supple while his were short and stunted and full of aches. But she was smiling when he reached her. "Did you miss me?" she teased as she took his hand.

"Desperately," Tyrion admitted. Shae only stood a shade over five feet, yet still he must look up to her . . . but in her case he found he did not mind. She was sweet to look up at.

"You'll miss me all the time in your Red Keep," she said as she led him to her room. "All alone in your cold bed in your Tower of the Hand."

"Too true." Tyrion would gladly have kept her with him, but his lord father had forbidden it. *You will not take the whore to court,* Lord Tywin had commanded. Bringing her to the city was as much defiance as he dared. All his authority derived from his father, the girl had to understand that. "You won't be far," he promised. "You'll have a house, with guards and servants, and I'll visit as often as I'm able."

Shae kicked shut the door. Through the cloudy panes of the narrow window, he could make out the Great Sept of Baelor crowning Visenya's Hill, but Tyrion was distracted by a different sight. Bending, Shae took her gown by the hem, drew it over her head, and tossed it aside. She did not believe in smallclothes. "You'll never be able to rest," she said as she stood before him, pink and nude and lovely, one hand braced on her hip.

"You'll think of me every time you go to bed. Then you'll get hard and you'll have no one to help you and you'll never be able to sleep unless you"—she grinned that wicked grin Tyrion liked so well—"is *that* why they call it the Tower of the Hand, m'lord?"

"Be quiet and kiss me," he commanded.

He could taste the wine on her lips, and feel her small firm breasts pressed against him as her fingers moved to the lacings of his breeches. "My lion," she whispered when he broke off the kiss to undress. "My sweet lord, my giant of Lannister." Tyrion pushed her toward the bed. When he entered her, she screamed loud enough to wake Baelor the Blessed in his tomb, and her nails left gouges in his back. He'd never had a pain he liked half so well.

Fool, he thought to himself afterward, as they lay in the center of the sagging mattress amidst the rumpled sheets. *Will you never learn, dwarf? She's a whore, damn you, it's your coin she loves, not your cock. Remember Tysha?* Yet when his fingers trailed lightly over one nipple, it stiffened at the touch, and he could see the mark on her breast where he'd bitten her in his passion.

"So what will you do, m'lord, now that you're the Hand of the King?" Shae asked him as he cupped that warm sweet flesh.

"Something Cersei will never expect," Tyrion murmured softly against her slender neck. "I'll do . . . justice."

BRAN

Bran preferred the hard stone of the window seat to the comforts of his featherbed and blankets. Abed, the walls pressed close and the ceiling hung heavy above him; abed, the room was his cell, and Winterfell his prison. Yet outside his window, the wide world still called.

He could not walk, nor climb nor hunt nor fight with a wooden sword as once he had, but he could still *look*. He liked to watch the windows begin to glow all over Winterfell as candles and hearth fires were lit behind the diamond-shaped panes of tower and hall, and he loved to listen to the direwolves sing to the stars.

Of late, he often dreamed of wolves. *They are talking to me, brother to brother,* he told himself when the direwolves howled. He could almost understand them . . . not quite, not truly, but *almost* . . . as if they were singing in a language he had once known and somehow forgotten. The Walders might be scared of them, but the Starks had wolf blood. Old Nan told him so. "Though it is stronger in some than in others," she warned.

Summer's howls were long and sad, full of grief and longing. Shaggydog's were more savage. Their voices echoed through the yards and halls until the castle rang and it seemed as though some great pack of direwolves haunted Winterfell, instead of only two . . . two where there had once been six. *Do they miss their brothers and sisters too?* Bran wondered. *Are they calling to Grey Wind and Ghost, to Nymeria and Lady's Shade? Do they want them to come home and be a pack together?*

"Who can know the mind of a wolf?" Ser Rodrik Cassel said when Bran asked him why they howled. Bran's lady mother had named him castellan of Winterfell in her absence, and his duties left him little time for idle questions.

"It's freedom they're calling for," declared Farlen, who was kennelmaster and had no more love for the direwolves than his hounds did. "They don't like being walled up, and who's to blame them? Wild things belong in the wild, not in a castle."

"They want to hunt," agreed Gage the cook as he tossed cubes of suet in a great kettle of stew. "A wolf smells better'n any man. Like as not, they've caught the scent o' prey."

Maester Luwin did not think so. "Wolves often howl at the moon. These are howling at the comet. See how bright it is, Bran? Perchance they think it *is* the moon."

When Bran repeated that to Osha, she laughed aloud. "Your wolves have more wit than your maester," the wildling woman said. "They know truths the grey man has forgotten." The way she said it made him shiver, and when he asked what the comet meant, she answered, "Blood and fire, boy, and nothing sweet."

Bran asked Septon Chayle about the comet while they were sorting through some scrolls snatched from the library fire. "It is the sword that slays the season," he replied, and soon after the white raven came from

Oldtown bringing word of autumn, so doubtless he was right.

Though Old Nan did not think so, and she'd lived longer than any of them. "Dragons," she said, lifting her head and sniffing. She was near blind and could not see the comet, yet she claimed she could *smell* it. "It be dragons, boy," she insisted. Bran got no *princes* from Nan, no more than he ever had.

Hodor said only, "Hodor." That was all he ever said.

And still the direwolves howled. The guards on the walls muttered curses, hounds in the kennels barked furiously, horses kicked at their stalls, the Walders shivered by their fire, and even Maester Luwin complained of sleepless nights. Only Bran did not mind. Ser Rodrik had confined the wolves to the godswood after Shaggydog bit Little Walder, but the stones of Winterfell played queer tricks with sound, and sometimes it sounded as if they were in the yard right below Bran's window. Other times he would have sworn they were up on the curtain walls, loping round like sentries. He wished that he could see them.

He *could* see the comet hanging above the Guards Hall and the Bell Tower, and farther back the First Keep, squat and round, its gargoyles black shapes against the bruised purple dusk. Once Bran had known every stone of those buildings, inside and out; he had climbed them all, scampering up walls as easily as other boys ran down stairs. Their rooftops had been his secret places, and the crows atop the broken tower his special friends.

And then he had fallen.

Bran did not remember falling, yet they said he had, so he supposed it must be true. He had almost died. When he saw the weatherworn gargoyles atop the First Keep where it had happened, he got a queer tight feeling in his belly. And now he could not climb, nor walk nor run nor swordfight, and the dreams he'd dreamed of knighthood had soured in his head.

Summer had howled the day Bran had fallen, and for long after as he lay broken in his bed; Robb had told him so before he went away to war. Summer had mourned for him, and Shaggydog and Grey Wind had joined in his grief. And the night the bloody raven had brought word of their father's death, the wolves had known that too. Bran had been in the maester's turret with Rickon talking of the children of the forest when Summer and Shaggydog had drowned out Luwin with their howls.

Who are they mourning now? Had some enemy slain the King in the North, who used to be his brother Robb? Had his bastard brother Jon Snow fallen from the Wall? Had his mother died, or one of his sisters? Or was this something else, as maester and septon and Old Nan seemed to think?

If I were truly a direwolf, I would understand the song, he thought wistfully. In his wolf dreams, he could race up the sides of mountains, jagged icy mountains taller than any tower, and stand at the summit beneath the full moon with all the world below him, the way it used to be.

"Oooo," Bran cried tentatively. He cupped his hands around his mouth and lifted his head to the comet. "*Oooooooooooooooooooo, ahoooooooooooooooo,*" he howled. It sounded stupid, high and hollow and quavering, a little boy's howl, not a wolf's. Yet Summer gave answer, his deep voice drowning out Bran's thin one, and Shaggydog made it a chorus. Bran *haroooed* again. They howled together, last of their pack.

The noise brought a guard to his door, Hayhead with the wen on his nose. He peered in, saw Bran howling out the window, and said, "What's this, my prince?"

It made Bran feel queer when they called him prince, though he *was* Robb's heir, and Robb was King in the North now. He turned his head to howl at the guard. "*Oooooooo. Oo-oo-ooooooooooooo.*"

Hayhead screwed up his face. "Now you stop that there."

"*Ooo-ooo-oooooo. Ooo-ooo-oooooooooooooooooo.*"

The guardsman retreated. When he came back, Maester Luwin was with him, all in grey, his chain tight about his neck. "Bran, those beasts make sufficient noise without your help." He crossed the room and put his hand on the boy's brow. "The hour grows late, you ought to be fast asleep."

"I'm talking to the wolves." Bran brushed the hand away.

"Shall I have Hayhead carry you to your bed?"

"I can get to bed myself." Mikken had hammered a row of iron bars into the wall, so Bran could pull himself about the room with his arms. It was slow and hard and it made his shoulders ache, but he hated being carried. "Anyway, I don't have to sleep if I don't want to."

"All men must sleep, Bran. Even princes."

"When I sleep I turn into a wolf." Bran turned his face away and looked back out into the night. "Do wolves dream?"

"All creatures dream, I think, yet not as men do."

"Do dead men dream?" Bran asked, thinking of his father. In the dark crypts below Winterfell, a stonemason was chiseling out his father's likeness in granite.

"Some say yes, some no," the maester answered. "The dead themselves are silent on the matter."

"Do trees dream?"

"Trees? No . . ."

"They do," Bran said with sudden certainty. "They dream tree dreams. I dream of a tree sometimes. A weirwood, like the one in the godswood. It calls to me. The wolf dreams are better. I smell things, and sometimes I can taste the blood."

Maester Luwin tugged at his chain where it chafed his neck. "If you would only spend more time with the other children—"

"I hate the other children," Bran said, meaning the Walders. "I commanded you to send them away."

Luwin grew stern. "The Freys are your lady mother's wards, sent here to be fostered at her express command. It is not for you to expel them, nor is it kind. If we turned them out, where would they go?"

"Home. It's their fault you won't let me have Summer."

"The Frey boy did not ask to be attacked," the maester said, "no more than I did."

"That was Shaggydog." Rickon's big black wolf was so wild he even frightened Bran at times. "Summer never bit anyone."

"Summer ripped out a man's throat in this very chamber, or have you forgotten? The truth is, those sweet pups you and your brothers found in the snow have grown into dangerous beasts. The Frey boys are wise to be wary of them."

"We should put the Walders in the godswood. They could play lord of the crossing all they want, and Summer could sleep with me again. If I'm the prince, why won't you heed me? I wanted to ride Dancer, but Alebelly wouldn't let me past the gate."

"And rightly so. The wolfswood is full of danger; your last ride should have taught you that. Would you want some outlaw to take you captive and sell you to the Lannisters?"

"Summer would save me," Bran insisted stubbornly. "Princes should be allowed to sail the sea and hunt boar in the wolfswood and joust with lances."

"Bran, child, why do you torment yourself so? One day you may do some of these things, but now you are only a boy of eight."

"I'd sooner be a wolf. Then I could live in the wood and sleep when I wanted, and I could find Arya and Sansa. I'd *smell* where they were and go save them, and when Robb went to battle I'd fight beside him like Grey Wind. I'd tear out the Kingslayer's throat with my teeth, *rip*, and then the war would be over and everyone would come back to Winterfell. If I was a wolf . . ." He howled. *"Ooo-ooo-oooooooooooooo."*

Luwin raised his voice. "A true prince would welcome—"

"AAHOOOOOOOO," Bran howled, louder. *"OOOO-OOOO-OOOO."*

The maester surrendered. "As you will, child." With a look that was part grief and part disgust, he left the bedchamber.

Howling lost its savor once Bran was alone. After a time he quieted. *I did welcome them,* he told himself, resentful. *I was the lord in Winterfell, a true lord, he can't say I wasn't.* When the Walders had arrived from the Twins, it had been Rickon who wanted them gone. A baby of four, he had screamed that he wanted Mother and Father and Robb, not these strangers. It had been up to Bran to soothe him and bid the Freys welcome. He had offered them meat and mead and a seat by the fire, and even Maester Luwin had said afterward that he'd done well.

Only that was before the game.

The game was played with a log, a staff, a body of water, and a great deal of shouting. The water was the most important, Walder and Walder assured Bran. You could use a plank or even a series of stones, and a branch could be your staff. You didn't *have* to shout. But without water, there was no game. As Maester Luwin and Ser Rodrik were not about to let the children go wandering off into the wolfswood in search of a stream, they made do with one of the murky pools in the godswood. Walder and Walder had never seen hot water bubbling from the ground before, but they both allowed how it would make the game even better.

Both of them were called Walder Frey. Big Walder said there were bunches of Walders at the Twins, all named after the boys' grandfather, Lord Walder Frey. "We have our *own* names at Winterfell," Rickon told them haughtily when he heard that.

The way their game was played, you laid the log across the water, and one player stood in the middle with the stick. He was the lord of the crossing, and when one of the other players came up, he had to say, "I am the lord of the crossing, who goes there?" And the other player had to make up a speech about who they were and why they should be allowed to cross. The lord could make them swear oaths and answer questions. They didn't have to tell the truth, but the oaths were binding unless they said "Mayhaps," so the trick was to say "Mayhaps" so the lord of the crossing didn't notice. Then you could try and knock the lord into the water and *you* got to be lord of the crossing, but only if you'd

said "Mayhaps." Otherwise you were out of the game.
The lord got to knock anyone in the water anytime he
pleased, and he was the only one who got to use a stick.

In practice, the game seemed to come down to mostly
shoving, hitting, and falling into the water, along with a
lot of loud arguments about whether or not someone
had said "Mayhaps." Little Walder was lord of the crossing more often than not.

He was Little Walder even though he was tall and
stout, with a red face and a big round belly. Big Walder
was sharp-faced and skinny and half a foot shorter.
"He's fifty-two days older than me," Little Walder explained, "so he was bigger at first, but I grew faster."

"We're cousins, not brothers," added Big Walder, the
little one. "I'm Walder son of Jammos. My father was
Lord Walder's son by his fourth wife. He's Walder son of
Merrett. His grandmother was Lord Walder's third wife,
the Crakehall. He's ahead of me in the line of succession even though I'm older."

"Only by fifty-two days," Little Walder objected.
"And neither of us will ever hold the Twins, stupid."

"I will," Big Walder declared. "We're not the only
Walders either. Ser Stevron has a grandson, Black
Walder, he's fourth in line of succession, and there's
Red Walder, Ser Emmon's son, and Bastard Walder, who
isn't in the line at all. He's called Walder Rivers not
Walder Frey. Plus there's girls named Walda."

"And Tyr. You always forget Tyr."

"He's Wal*tyr*, not Walder," Big Walder said airily.
"And he's after us, so he doesn't matter. Anyhow, I
never liked him."

Ser Rodrik decreed that they would share Jon Snow's
old bedchamber, since Jon was in the Night's Watch and
never coming back. Bran hated that; it made him feel as
if the Freys were trying to steal Jon's place.

He had watched wistfully while the Walders contested with Turnip the cook's boy and Joseth's girls
Bandy and Shyra. The Walders had decreed that Bran
should be the judge and decide whether or not people

had said "Mayhaps," but as soon as they started playing they forgot all about him.

The shouts and splashes soon drew others: Palla the kennel girl, Cayn's boy Calon, TomToo whose father Fat Tom had died with Bran's father at King's Landing. Before very long, every one of them was soaked and muddy. Palla was brown from head to heel, with moss in her hair, breathless from laughter. Bran had not heard so much laughing since the night the bloody raven came. *If I had my legs, I'd knock all of them into the water,* he thought bitterly. *No one would ever be lord of the crossing but me.*

Finally Rickon came running into the godswood, Shaggydog at his heels. He watched Turnip and Little Walder struggle for the stick until Turnip lost his footing and went in with a huge splash, arms waving. Rickon yelled, "Me! Me now! I want to play!" Little Walder beckoned him on, and Shaggydog started to follow. "No, Shaggy," his brother commanded. "Wolves can't play. You stay with Bran." And he did . . .

. . . until Little Walder had smacked Rickon with the stick, square across his belly. Before Bran could blink, the black wolf was flying over the plank, there was blood in the water, the Walders were shrieking red murder, Rickon sat in the mud laughing, and Hodor came lumbering in shouting "Hodor! Hodor! Hodor!"

After that, oddly, Rickon decided he *liked* the Walders. They never played lord of the crossing again, but they played other games—monsters and maidens, rats and cats, come-into-my-castle, all sorts of things. With Rickon by their side, the Walders plundered the kitchens for pies and honeycombs, raced round the walls, tossed bones to the pups in the kennels, and trained with wooden swords under Ser Rodrik's sharp eye. Rickon even showed them the deep vaults under the earth where the stonemason was carving father's tomb. "You had no right!" Bran screamed at his brother when he heard. "That was our place, a *Stark* place!" But Rickon never cared.

The door to his bedchamber opened. Maester Luwin

was carrying a green jar, and this time Osha and Hayhead came with him. "I've made you a sleeping draught, Bran."

Osha scooped him up in her bony arms. She was very tall for a woman, and wiry strong. She bore him effortlessly to his bed.

"This will give you dreamless sleep," Maester Luwin said as he pulled the stopper from the jar. "Sweet, dreamless sleep."

"It will?" Bran said, wanting to believe.

"Yes. Drink."

Bran drank. The potion was thick and chalky, but there was honey in it, so it went down easy.

"Come the morn, you'll feel better." Luwin gave Bran a smile and a pat as he took his leave.

Osha lingered behind. "Is it the wolf dreams again?"

Bran nodded.

"You should not fight so hard, boy. I see you talking to the heart tree. Might be the gods are trying to talk back."

"The gods?" he murmured, drowsy already. Osha's face grew blurry and grey. *Sweet, dreamless sleep,* Bran thought.

Yet when the darkness closed over him, he found himself in the godswood, moving silently beneath green-grey sentinels and gnarled oaks as old as time. *I am walking,* he thought, exulting. Part of him knew that it was only a dream, but even the dream of walking was better than the truth of his bedchamber, walls and ceiling and door.

It was dark amongst the trees, but the comet lit his way, and his feet were sure. He was moving on four *good* legs, strong and swift, and he could feel the ground underfoot, the soft crackling of fallen leaves, thick roots and hard stones, the deep layers of humus. It was a good feeling.

The smells filled his head, alive and intoxicating; the green muddy stink of the hot pools, the perfume of rich rotting earth beneath his paws, the squirrels in the oaks. The scent of squirrel made him remember the taste of hot blood and the way the bones would crack between his teeth. Slaver filled his mouth. He had eaten no more than half a day past, but there was no joy in dead meat, even deer. He could hear the squirrels chittering and rustling above him, safe among their leaves, but they knew better than to come down to where his brother and he were prowling.

He could smell his brother too, a familiar scent, strong and earthy, his scent as black as his coat. His brother was loping around the walls, full of fury. Round and round he went, night after day after night, tireless, searching . . . for prey, for a way out, for his mother, his littermates, his pack . . . searching, searching, and never finding.

Behind the trees the walls rose, piles of dead manrock that loomed all about this speck of living wood. Speckled grey they rose, and moss-spotted, yet thick and strong and higher than any wolf could hope to leap. Cold iron and splintery wood closed off the only holes through the piled stones that hemmed them in. His brother would stop at every hole and bare his fangs in rage, but the ways stayed closed.

He had done the same the first night, and learned that it was no good. Snarls would open no paths here. Circling the walls would not push them back. Lifting a leg and marking the trees would keep no men away. The world had tightened around them, but beyond the walled wood still stood the great grey caves of manrock. *Winterfell*, he remembered, the sound coming to him suddenly. Beyond its sky-tall man-cliffs the true world was calling, and he knew he must answer or die.

ARYA

They traveled dawn to dusk, past woods and
orchards and neatly tended fields, through small
villages, crowded market towns, and stout holdfasts. Come dark, they would make camp and eat by the
light of the Red Sword. The men took turns standing
watch. Arya would glimpse firelight flickering through
the trees from the camps of other travelers. There
seemed to be more camps every night, and more traffic
on the kingsroad by day.

Morn, noon, and night they came, old folks and little
children, big men and small ones, barefoot girls and
women with babes at their breasts. Some drove farm
wagons or bumped along in the back of ox carts. More
rode: draft horses, ponies, mules, donkeys, anything
that would walk or run or roll. One woman led a milk
cow with a little girl on its back. Arya saw a smith
pushing a wheelbarrow with his tools inside, hammers
and tongs and even an anvil, and a little while later a
different man with a different wheelbarrow, only inside
this one were two babies in a blanket. Most came on

foot, with their goods on their shoulders and weary, wary looks upon their faces. They walked south, toward the city, toward King's Landing, and only one in a hundred spared so much as a word for Yoren and his charges, traveling north. She wondered why no one else was going the same way as them.

Many of the travelers were armed; Arya saw daggers and dirks, scythes and axes, and here and there a sword. Some had made clubs from tree limbs, or carved knobby staffs. They fingered their weapons and gave lingering looks at the wagons as they rolled by, yet in the end they let the column pass. Thirty was too many, no matter what they had in those wagons.

Look with your eyes, Syrio had said, *listen with your ears.*

One day a madwoman began to scream at them from the side of the road. "Fools! They'll kill you, fools!" She was scarecrow thin, with hollow eyes and bloody feet.

The next morning, a sleek merchant on a grey mare reined up by Yoren and offered to buy his wagons and everything in them for a quarter of their worth. "It's war, they'll take what they want, you'll do better selling to me, my friend." Yoren turned away with a twist of his crooked shoulders, and spat.

Arya noticed the first grave that same day; a small mound beside the road, dug for a child. A crystal had been set in the soft earth, and Lommy wanted to take it until the Bull told him he'd better leave the dead alone. A few leagues farther on, Praed pointed out more graves, a whole row freshly dug. After that, a day hardly passed without one.

One time Arya woke in the dark, frightened for no reason she could name. Above, the Red Sword shared the sky with half a thousand stars. The night seemed oddly quiet to her, though she could hear Yoren's muttered snores, the crackle of the fire, even the muffled stirrings of the donkeys. Yet somehow it felt as though the world were holding its breath, and the silence made her shiver. She went back to sleep clutching Needle.

Come morning, when Praed did not awaken, Arya realized that it had been his coughing she had missed. They dug a grave of their own then, burying the sellsword where he'd slept. Yoren stripped him of his valuables before they threw the dirt on him. One man claimed his boots, another his dagger. His mail shirt and helm were parceled out. His longsword Yoren handed to the Bull. "Arms like yours, might be you can learn to use this," he told him. A boy called Tarber tossed a handful of acorns on top of Praed's body, so an oak might grow to mark his place.

That evening they stopped in a village at an ivy-covered inn. Yoren counted the coins in his purse and decided they had enough for a hot meal. "We'll sleep outside, same as ever, but they got a bathhouse here, if any of you feels the need o' hot water and a lick o' soap."

Arya did not dare, even though she smelled as bad as Yoren by now, all sour and stinky. Some of the creatures living in her clothes had come all the way from Flea Bottom with her; it didn't seem right to drown them. Tarber and Hot Pie and the Bull joined the line of men headed for the tubs. Others settled down in front of the bathhouse. The rest crowded into the common room. Yoren even sent Lommy out with tankards for the three in fetters, who'd been left chained up in the back of their wagon.

Washed and unwashed alike supped on hot pork pies and baked apples. The innkeeper gave them a round of beer on the house. "I had a brother took the black, years ago. Serving boy, clever, but one day he got seen filching pepper from m'lord's table. He liked the taste of it, is all. Just a pinch o' pepper, but Ser Malcolm was a hard man. You get pepper on the Wall?" When Yoren shook his head, the man sighed. "Shame. Lync loved that pepper."

Arya sipped at her tankard cautiously, between spoonfuls of pie still warm from the oven. Her father sometimes let them have a cup of beer, she remembered. Sansa used to make a face at the taste and say that wine was ever so much finer, but Arya had liked it well enough. It made her sad to think of Sansa and her father.

The inn was full of people moving south, and the common room erupted in scorn when Yoren said they were traveling the other way. "You'll be back soon enough," the innkeeper vowed. "There's no going north. Half the fields are burnt, and what folks are left are walled up inside their holdfasts. One bunch rides off at dawn and another one shows up by dusk."

"That's nothing to us," Yoren insisted stubbornly. "Tully or Lannister, makes no matter. The Watch takes no part."

Lord Tully is my grandfather, Arya thought. It mattered to *her,* but she chewed her lip and kept quiet, listening.

"It's more than Lannister and Tully," the innkeeper said. "There's wild men down from the Mountains of the Moon, try telling *them* you take no part. And the Starks are in it too, the young lord's come down, the dead Hand's son . . ."

Arya sat up straight, straining to hear. Did he mean *Robb*?

"I heard the boy rides to battle on a wolf," said a yellow-haired man with a tankard in his hand.

"Fool's talk." Yoren spat.

"The man I heard it from, he saw it himself. A wolf big as a horse, he swore."

"Swearing don't make it true, Hod," the innkeeper said. "You keep swearing you'll pay what you owe me, and I've yet to see a copper." The common room erupted in laughter, and the man with the yellow hair turned red.

"It's been a bad year for wolves," volunteered a sallow man in a travel-stained green cloak. "Around the Gods Eye, the packs have grown bolder'n anyone can remember. Sheep, cows, dogs, makes no matter, they kill as they like, and they got no fear of men. It's worth your life to go into those woods by night."

"Ah, that's more tales, and no more true than the other."

"I heard the same thing from my cousin, and she's not the sort to lie," an old woman said. "She says there's this great pack, hundreds of them, mankillers. The one that leads them is a she-wolf, a bitch from the seventh hell."

A she-wolf. Arya sloshed her beer, wondering. Was the Gods Eye near the Trident? She wished she had a map. It had been near the Trident that she'd left Nymeria. She hadn't wanted to, but Jory said they had no choice, that if the wolf came back with them she'd be killed for biting Joffrey, even though he'd deserved it. They'd had to shout and scream and throw stones, and it wasn't until a few of Arya's stones struck home that the direwolf had finally stopped following them. *She probably wouldn't even know me now*, Arya thought. *Or if she did, she'd hate me.*

The man in the green cloak said, "I heard how this hellbitch walked into a village one day . . . a market day, people everywhere, and she walks in bold as you please and tears a baby from his mother's arms. When the tale reached Lord Mooton, him and his sons swore they'd put an end to her. They tracked her to her lair with a pack of wolfhounds, and barely escaped with their skins. Not one of those dogs came back, not one."

"That's just a story," Arya blurted out before she could stop herself. "Wolves don't eat babies."

"And what would you know about it, lad?" asked the man in the green cloak.

Before she could think of an answer, Yoren had her by the arm. "The boy's greensick on beer, that's all it is."

"No I'm not. They *don't* eat babies . . ."

"Outside, *boy* . . . and see that you stay there until you learn to shut your mouth when men are talking." He gave her a stiff shove, toward the side door that led back to the stables. "Go on now. See that the stableboy has watered our horses."

Arya went outside, stiff with fury. "They *don't*," she muttered, kicking at a rock as she stalked off. It went rolling and fetched up under the wagons.

"Boy," a friendly voice called out. "Lovely boy."

One of the men in irons was talking to her. Warily, Arya approached the wagon, one hand on Needle's hilt.

The prisoner lifted an empty tankard, his chains rattling. "A man could use another taste of beer. A man has a thirst, wearing these heavy bracelets." He was the youngest of the three, slender, fine-featured, always smiling. His hair was red on one side and white on the other, all matted and filthy from cage and travel. "A man could use a bath too," he said, when he saw the way Arya was looking at him. "A boy could make a friend."

"I have friends," Arya said.

"None I can see," said the one without a nose. He was squat and thick, with huge hands. Black hair covered his arms and legs and chest, even his back. He reminded Arya of a drawing she had once seen in a book, of an ape from the Summer Isles. The hole in his face made it hard to look at him for long.

The bald one opened his mouth and *hissed* like some immense white lizard. When Arya flinched back, startled, he opened his mouth wide and waggled his tongue at her, only it was more a stump than a tongue. "Stop that," she blurted.

"A man does not choose his companions in the black cells," the handsome one with the red-and-white hair said. Something about the way he talked reminded her of Syrio; it was the same, yet different too. "These two, they have no courtesy. A man must ask forgiveness. You are called Arry, is that not so?"

"Lumpyhead," said the noseless one. "Lumpyhead Lumpyface Stickboy. Have a care, Lorath, he'll hit you with his stick."

"A man must be ashamed of the company he keeps, Arry," the handsome one said. "This man has the honor to be Jaqen H'ghar, once of the Free City of Lorath. Would that he were home. This man's ill-bred companions in captivity are named Rorge"—he waved his tankard at the noseless man—"and Biter." Biter *hissed* at her again, displaying a mouthful of yellowed teeth filed into points. "A man must have some name, is that not so? Biter cannot speak and Biter cannot write, yet his teeth are very sharp, so a man calls him Biter and he smiles. Are you charmed?"

Arya backed away from the wagon. "No." *They can't hurt me,* she told herself, *they're all chained up.*

He turned his tankard upside down. "A man must weep."

Rorge, the noseless one, flung his drinking cup at her with a curse. His manacles made him clumsy, yet even so he would have sent the heavy pewter tankard crashing into her head if Arya hadn't leapt aside. "You get us some beer, pimple. *Now!*"

"You shut your mouth!" Arya tried to think what Syrio would have done. She drew her wooden practice sword.

"Come closer," Rorge said, "and I'll shove that stick up your bunghole and fuck you bloody."

Fear cuts deeper than swords. Arya made herself approach the wagon. Every step was harder than the one before. *Fierce as a wolverine, calm as still water.* The words sang in her head. Syrio would not have been afraid. She was almost close enough to touch the wheel when Biter lurched to his feet and grabbed for her, his irons clanking and rattling. The manacles brought his hands up short, half a foot from her face. He *hissed.*

She hit him. Hard, right between his little eyes.

Screaming, Biter reeled back, and then threw all his weight against his chains. The links slithered and turned and grew taut, and Arya heard the creak of old dry wood as the great iron rings strained against the floorboards of the wagon. Huge pale hands groped for her while veins bulged along Biter's arms, but the bonds held, and finally the man collapsed backward. Blood ran from the weeping sores on his cheeks.

"A boy has more courage than sense," the one who had named himself Jaqen H'ghar observed.

Arya edged backward away from the wagon. When she felt the hand on her shoulder, she whirled, bringing up her stick sword again, but it was only the Bull. "What are you doing?"

He raised his hands defensively. "Yoren said none of us should go near those three."

"They don't scare me," Arya said.

"Then you're stupid. They scare *me*." The Bull's hand fell to the hilt of his sword, and Rorge began to laugh. "Let's get away from them."

Arya scuffed at the ground with her foot, but she let the Bull lead her around to the front of the inn. Rorge's laughter and Biter's hissing followed them. "Want to fight?" she asked the Bull. She wanted to hit something.

. He blinked at her, startled. Strands of thick black hair, still wet from the bathhouse, fell across his deep blue eyes. "I'd hurt you."

"You would not."

"You don't know how strong I am."

"You don't know how quick I am."

"You're asking for it, Arry." He drew Praed's long-sword. "This is cheap steel, but it's a real sword."

Arya unsheathed Needle. "This is good steel, so it's realer than yours."

The Bull shook his head. "Promise not to cry if I cut you?"

"I'll promise if you will." She turned sideways, into her water dancer's stance, but the Bull did not move. He was looking at something behind her. "What's wrong?"

"Gold cloaks." His face closed up tight.

It couldn't be, Arya thought, but when she glanced back, they were riding up the kingsroad, six in the black ringmail and golden cloaks of the City Watch. One was an officer; he wore a black enamel breastplate ornamented with four golden disks. They drew up in front of the inn. *Look with your eyes*, Syrio's voice seemed to whisper. Her eyes saw white lather under their saddles; the horses had been ridden long and hard. Calm as still water, she took the Bull by the arm and drew him back behind a tall flowering hedge.

"What is it?" he asked. "What are you doing? Let go."

"Quiet as a shadow," she whispered, pulling him down.

Some of Yoren's other charges were sitting in front of

the bathhouse, waiting their turn at a tub. "You men," one of the gold cloaks shouted. "You the ones left to take the black?"

"We might be," came the cautious answer.

"We'd rather join you boys," old Reysen said. "We hear it's *cold* on that Wall."

The gold cloak officer dismounted. "I have a warrant for a certain boy—"

Yoren stepped out of the inn, fingering his tangled black beard. "Who is it wants this boy?"

The other gold cloaks were dismounting to stand beside their horses. "Why are we hiding?" the Bull whispered.

"It's me they want," Arya whispered back. His ear smelled of soap. "You be quiet."

"The queen wants him, old man, not that it's your concern," the officer said, drawing a ribbon from his belt. "Here, Her Grace's seal and warrant."

Behind the hedge, the Bull shook his head doubtfully. "Why would the queen want *you*, Arry?"

She punched his shoulder. "Be *quiet*!"

Yoren fingered the warrant ribbon with its blob of golden wax. "Pretty." He spit. "Thing is, the boy's in the Night's Watch now. What he done back in the city don't mean piss-all."

"The queen's not interested in your views, old man, and neither am I," the officer said. "I'll have the boy."

Arya thought about running, but she knew she wouldn't get far on her donkey when the gold cloaks had horses. And she was so tired of running. She'd run when Ser Meryn came for her, and again when they killed her father. If she was a real water dancer, she would go out there with Needle and kill all of them, and never run from anyone ever again.

"You'll have no one," Yoren said stubbornly. "There's laws on such things."

The gold cloak drew a shortsword. "Here's your law."

Yoren looked at the blade. "That's no law, just a sword. Happens I got one too."

The officer smiled. "Old fool. I have five men with me."

Yoren spat. "Happens I got thirty."

The gold cloak laughed. "This lot?" said a big lout with a broken nose. "Who's first?" he shouted, showing his steel.

Tarber plucked a pitchfork out of a bale of hay. "I am."

"No, I am," called Cutjack, the plump stonemason, pulling his hammer off the leather apron he always wore.

"Me." Kurz came up off the ground with his skinning knife in hand.

"Me and him." Koss strung his longbow.

"All of us," said Reysen, snatching up the tall hardwood walking staff he carried.

Dobber stepped naked out of the bathhouse with his clothes in a bundle, saw what was happening, and dropped everything but his dagger. "Is it a fight?" he asked.

"I guess," said Hot Pie, scrambling on all fours for a big rock to throw. Arya could not believe what she was seeing. She *hated* Hot Pie! Why would he risk himself for her?

The one with the broken nose still thought it was funny. "You girls put away them rocks and sticks before you get spanked. None of you knows what end of a sword to hold."

"*I do!*" Arya wouldn't let them die for her like Syrio. She wouldn't! Shoving through the hedge with Needle in hand, she slid into a water dancer's stance.

Broken Nose guffawed. The officer looked her up and down. "Put the blade away, little girl, no one wants to hurt you."

"I'm *not* a girl!" she yelled, furious. What was wrong with them? They rode all this way for her and here she was and they were just smiling at her. "I'm the one you want."

"*He's* the one we want." The officer jabbed his shortsword toward the Bull, who'd come forward to stand beside her, Praed's cheap steel in his hand.

But it was a mistake to take his eyes off Yoren, even for an instant. Quick as that, the black brother's sword was pressed to the apple of the officer's throat. "Neither's the one you get, less you want me to see if your apple's ripe yet. I got me ten, fifteen more brothers in that inn, if you still need convincing. I was you, I'd let loose of that gutcutter, spread my cheeks over that fat little horse, and gallop on back to the city." He spat, and poked harder with the point of his sword. "Now."

The officer's fingers uncurled. His sword fell in the dust.

"We'll just keep that," Yoren said. "Good steel's always needed on the Wall."

"As you say. For now. Men." The gold cloaks sheathed and mounted up. "You'd best scamper up to that Wall of yours in a hurry, old man. The next time I catch you, I believe I'll have your head to go with the bastard boy's."

"Better men than you have tried." Yoren slapped the rump of the officer's horse with the flat of his sword and sent him reeling off down the kingsroad. His men followed.

When they were out of sight, Hot Pie began to whoop, but Yoren looked angrier than ever. "Fool! You think he's done with us? Next time he won't prance up and hand me no damn ribbon. Get the rest out o' them baths, we need to be moving. Ride all night, maybe we can stay ahead o' them for a bit." He scooped up the shortsword the officer had dropped. "Who wants this?"

"Me!" Hot Pie yelled.

"Don't be using it on Arry." He handed the boy the sword, hilt first, and walked over to Arya, but it was the Bull he spoke to. "Queen wants you bad, boy."

Arya was lost. "Why should she want *him*?"

The Bull scowled at her. "Why should she want *you*? You're nothing but a little gutter rat!"

"Well, you're nothing but a bastard boy!" Or maybe

he was only *pretending* to be a bastard boy. "What's your true name?"

"Gendry," he said, like he wasn't quite sure.

"Don't see why no one wants neither o' you," Yoren said, "but they can't have you regardless. You ride them two coursers. First sight of a gold cloak, make for the Wall like a dragon's on your tail. The rest o' us don't mean spit to them."

"Except for you," Arya pointed out. "That man said he'd take your head too."

"Well, as to that," Yoren said, "if he can get it off my shoulders, he's welcome to it."

JON

"S am?" Jon called softly.

The air smelled of paper and dust and years. Before him, tall wooden shelves rose up into dimness, crammed with leatherbound books and bins of ancient scrolls. A faint yellow glow filtered through the stacks from some hidden lamp. Jon blew out the taper he carried, preferring not to risk an open flame amidst so much old dry paper. Instead he followed the light, wending his way down the narrow aisles beneath barrel-vaulted ceilings. All in black, he was a shadow among shadows, dark of hair, long of face, grey of eye. Black moleskin gloves covered his hands; the right because it was burned, the left because a man felt half a fool wearing only one glove.

Samwell Tarly sat hunched over a table in a niche carved into the stone of the wall. The glow came from the lamp hung over his head. He looked up at the sound of Jon's steps.

"Have you been here all night?"

"Have I?" Sam looked startled.

"You didn't break your fast with us, and your bed hadn't been slept in." Rast suggested that maybe Sam had deserted, but Jon never believed it. Desertion required its own sort of courage, and Sam had little enough of that.

"Is it morning? Down here there's no way to know."

"Sam, you're a sweet fool," Jon said. "You'll miss that bed when we're sleeping on the cold hard ground, I promise you."

Sam yawned. "Maester Aemon sent me to find maps for the Lord Commander. I never thought . . . Jon, the *books*, have you ever seen their like? There are *thousands*!"

He gazed about him. "The library at Winterfell has more than a hundred. Did you find the maps?"

"Oh, yes." Sam's hand swept over the table, fingers plump as sausages indicating the clutter of books and scrolls before him. "A dozen, at the least." He unfolded a square of parchment. "The paint has faded, but you can see where the mapmaker marked the sites of wildling villages, and there's another book . . . where is it now? I was reading it a moment ago." He shoved some scrolls aside to reveal a dusty volume bound in rotted leather. *"This,"* he said reverently, "is the account of a journey from the Shadow Tower all the way to Lorn Point on the Frozen Shore, written by a ranger named Redwyn. It's not dated, but he mentions a Dorren Stark as King in the North, so it must be from before the Conquest. Jon, they fought *giants*! Redwyn even traded with the children of the forest, it's all here." Ever so delicately, he turned pages with a finger. "He drew maps as well, see . . ."

"Maybe you could write an account of our ranging, Sam."

He'd meant to sound encouraging, but it was the wrong thing to say. The last thing Sam needed was to be reminded of what faced them on the morrow. He shuffled the scrolls about aimlessly. "There's more maps. If I had time to search . . . everything's a jumble. *I* could set it all to order, though; I know I could, but it would take time . . . well, *years*, in truth."

"Mormont wanted those maps a little sooner than that." Jon plucked a scroll from a bin, blew off the worst of the dust. A corner flaked off between his fingers as he unrolled it. "Look, this one is crumbling," he said, frowning over the faded script.

"Be gentle." Sam came around the table and took the scroll from his hand, holding it as if it were a wounded animal. "The important books used to be copied over when they needed them. Some of the oldest have been copied half a hundred times, probably."

"Well, don't bother copying that one. Twenty-three barrels of pickled cod, eighteen jars of fish oil, a cask of salt . . ."

"An inventory," Sam said, "or perhaps a bill of sale."

"Who cares how much pickled cod they ate six hundred years ago?" Jon wondered.

"I would." Sam carefully replaced the scroll in the bin from which Jon had plucked it. "You can learn so much from ledgers like that, truly you can. It can tell you how many men were in the Night's Watch then, how they lived, what they ate . . ."

"They ate food," said Jon, "and they lived as we live."

"You'd be surprised. This vault is a treasure, Jon."

"If you say so." Jon was doubtful. Treasure meant gold, silver, and jewels, not dust, spiders, and rotting leather.

"I do," the fat boy blurted. He was older than Jon, a man grown by law, but it was hard to think of him as anything but a boy. "I found drawings of the faces in the trees, and a book about the tongue of the children of the forest . . . works that even the Citadel doesn't have, scrolls from old Valyria, counts of the seasons written by maesters dead a thousand years . . ."

"The books will still be here when we return."

"*If* we return . . ."

"The Old Bear is taking two hundred seasoned men, three-quarters of them rangers. Qhorin Halfhand will be bringing another hundred brothers from the Shadow

Tower. You'll be as safe as if you were back in your lord father's castle at Horn Hill."

Samwell Tarly managed a sad little smile. "I was never very safe in my father's castle either."

The gods play cruel jests, Jon thought. Pyp and Toad, all a lather to be a part of the great ranging, were to remain at Castle Black. It was Samwell Tarly, the self-proclaimed coward, grossly fat, timid, and near as bad a rider as he was with a sword, who must face the haunted forest. The Old Bear was taking two cages of ravens, so they might send back word as they went. Maester Aemon was blind and far too frail to ride with them, so his steward must go in his place. "We need you for the ravens, Sam. And someone has to help me keep Grenn humble."

Sam's chins quivered. "You could care for the ravens, or Grenn could, or *anyone,*" he said with a thin edge of desperation in his voice. "I could show you how. You know your letters too, you could write down Lord Mormont's messages as well as I."

"I'm the Old Bear's steward. I'll need to squire for him, tend his horse, set up his tent; I won't have time to watch over birds as well. Sam, you said the words. You're a brother of the Night's Watch now."

"A brother of the Night's Watch shouldn't be so scared."

"We're all scared. We'd be fools if we weren't." Too many rangers had been lost the past two years, even Benjen Stark, Jon's uncle. They had found two of his uncle's men in the wood, slain, but the corpses had risen in the chill of night. Jon's burnt fingers twitched as he remembered. He still saw the wight in his dreams, dead Othor with the burning blue eyes and the cold black hands, but that was the last thing Sam needed to be reminded of. "There's no shame in fear, my father told me, what matters is how we face it. Come, I'll help you gather up the maps."

Sam nodded unhappily. The shelves were so closely spaced that they had to walk single file as they left. The vault opened onto one of the tunnels the brothers called the wormwalks, winding subterranean passages that linked the keeps and towers of Castle Black under the earth. In summer the wormwalks were seldom used, save by rats and other vermin, but winter was a different matter. When the snows drifted forty and fifty feet high and the ice winds came howling out of the north, the tunnels were all that held Castle Black together.

Soon, Jon thought as they climbed. He'd seen the harbinger that had come to Maester Aemon with word of summer's end, the great raven of the Citadel, white and silent as Ghost. He had seen a winter once, when he was very young, but everyone agreed that it had been a short one, and mild. This one would be different. He could feel it in his bones.

The steep stone steps had Sam puffing like a blacksmith's bellows by the time they reached the surface. They emerged into a brisk wind that made Jon's cloak swirl and snap. Ghost was stretched out asleep beneath the wattle-and-daub wall of the granary, but he woke when Jon appeared, bushy white tail held stiffly upright as he trotted to them.

Sam squinted up at the Wall. It loomed above them, an icy cliff seven hundred feet high. Sometimes it seemed to Jon almost a living thing, with moods of its own. The color of the ice was wont to change with every shift of the light. Now it was the deep blue of frozen rivers, now the dirty white of old snow, and when a cloud passed before the sun it darkened to the pale grey of pitted stone. The Wall stretched east and west as far as the eye could see, so huge that it shrunk the timbered keeps and stone towers of the castle to insignificance. It was the end of the world.

And we are going beyond it.

The morning sky was streaked by thin grey clouds, but the pale red line was there behind them. The black brothers had dubbed the wanderer Mormont's Torch, saying (only half in jest) that the gods must have sent it to light the old man's way through the haunted forest.

"The comet's so bright you can see it by day now," Sam said, shading his eyes with a fistful of books.

"Never mind about comets, it's maps the Old Bear wants."

Ghost loped ahead of them. The grounds seemed deserted this morning, with so many rangers off at the brothel in Mole's Town, digging for buried treasure and drinking themselves blind. Grenn had gone with them. Pyp and Halder and Toad had offered to buy him his first woman to celebrate his first ranging. They'd wanted Jon and Sam to come as well, but Sam was almost as frightened of whores as he was of the haunted forest, and Jon had wanted no part of it. "Do what you want," he told Toad, "I took a vow."

As they passed the sept, he heard voices raised in song. *Some men want whores on the eve of battle, and some want gods.* Jon wondered who felt better afterward. The sept tempted him no more than the brothel; his own gods kept their temples in the wild places, where the weirwoods spread their bone-white branches. *The Seven have no power beyond the Wall,* he thought, *but my gods will be waiting.*

Outside the armory, Ser Endrew Tarth was working with some raw recruits. They'd come in last night with Conwy, one of the wandering crows who roamed the Seven Kingdoms collecting men for the Wall. This new crop consisted of a greybeard leaning on a staff, two blond boys with the look of brothers, a foppish youth in soiled satin, a raggy man with a clubfoot, and some grinning loon who must have fancied himself a warrior. Ser Endrew was showing him the error of that presumption. He was a gentler master-at-arms than Ser Alliser Thorne had been, but his lessons would still raise bruises. Sam winced at every blow, but Jon Snow watched the swordplay closely.

"What do you make of them, Snow?" Donal Noye stood in the door of his armory, bare-chested under a leather apron, the stump of his left arm uncovered for once. With his big gut and barrel chest, his flat nose and bristly black jaw, Noye did not make a pretty sight, but he was a welcome one nonetheless. The armorer had proved himself a good friend.

"They smell of summer," Jon said as Ser Endrew bull-rushed his foe and knocked him sprawling. "Where did Conwy find them?"

"A lord's dungeon near Gulltown," the smith replied. "A brigand, a barber, a beggar, two orphans, and a boy whore. With such do we defend the realms of men."

"They'll do." Jon gave Sam a private smile. "We did."

Noye drew him closer. "You've heard these tidings of your brother?"

"Last night." Conwy and his charges had brought the news north with them, and the talk in the common room had been of little else. Jon was still not certain how he felt about it. Robb a king? The brother he'd played with, fought with, shared his first cup of wine with? *But not mother's milk, no. So now Robb will sip summerwine from jeweled goblets, while I'm kneeling beside some stream sucking snowmelt from cupped hands.* "Robb will make a good king," he said loyally.

"Will he now?" The smith eyed him frankly. "I hope that's so, boy, but once I might have said the same of Robert."

"They say you forged his warhammer," Jon remembered.

"Aye. I was his man, a Baratheon man, smith and armorer at Storm's End until I lost the arm. I'm old enough to remember Lord Steffon before the sea took him, and I knew those three sons of his since they got their names. I tell you this—Robert was never the same after he put on that crown. Some men are like swords, made for fighting. Hang them up and they go to rust."

"And his brothers?" Jon asked.

The armorer considered that a moment. "Robert was the true steel. Stannis is pure iron, black and hard and strong, yes, but brittle, the way iron gets. He'll break before he bends. And Renly, that one, he's copper, bright and shiny, pretty to look at but not worth all that much at the end of the day."

And what metal is Robb? Jon did not ask. Noye was a Baratheon man; likely he thought Joffrey the lawful king and Robb a traitor. Among the brotherhood of the

Night's Watch, there was an unspoken pact never to probe too deeply into such matters. Men came to the Wall from all of the Seven Kingdoms, and old loves and loyalties were not easily forgotten, no matter how many oaths a man swore . . . as Jon himself had good reason to know. Even Sam—his father's House was sworn to Highgarden, whose Lord Tyrell supported King Renly. Best not to talk of such things. The Night's Watch took no sides. "Lord Mormont awaits us," Jon said.

"I won't keep you from the Old Bear." Noye clapped him on the shoulder and smiled. "May the gods go with you on the morrow, Snow. You bring back that uncle of yours, you hear?"

"We will," Jon promised him.

Lord Commander Mormont had taken up residence in the King's Tower after the fire had gutted his own. Jon left Ghost with the guards outside the door. "More stairs," said Sam miserably as they started up. "I hate stairs."

"Well, that's one thing we won't face in the wood."

When they entered the solar, the raven spied them at once. *"Snow!"* the bird shrieked. Mormont broke off his conversation. "Took you long enough with those maps." He pushed the remains of breakfast out of the way to make room on the table. "Put them here. I'll have a look at them later."

Thoren Smallwood, a sinewy ranger with a weak chin and a weaker mouth hidden under a thin scraggle of beard, gave Jon and Sam a cool look. He had been one of Alliser Thorne's henchmen, and had no love for either of them. "The Lord Commander's place is at Castle Black, lording and commanding," he told Mormont, ignoring the newcomers, "it seems to me."

The raven flapped big black wings. *"Me, me, me."*

"If you are ever Lord Commander, you may do as you please," Mormont told the ranger, "but it seems to *me* that I have not died yet, nor have the brothers put you in my place."

"I'm First Ranger now, with Ben Stark lost and Ser

Jaremy killed," Smallwood said stubbornly. "The command should be mine."

Mormont would have none of it. "I sent out Ben Stark, and Ser Waymar before him. I do not mean to send you after them and sit wondering how long I must wait before I give you up for lost as well." He pointed. "And Stark remains First Ranger until we know for a certainty that he is dead. Should that day come, it will be me who names his successor, not you. Now stop wasting my time. We ride at first light, or have you forgotten?"

Smallwood pushed to his feet. "As my lord commands." On the way out, he frowned at Jon, as if it were somehow his fault.

"First Ranger!" The Old Bear's eyes lighted on Sam. "I'd sooner name *you* First Ranger. He has the effrontery to tell me to my face that I'm too old to ride with him. Do I look old to you, boy?" The hair that had retreated from Mormont's spotted scalp had regrouped beneath his chin in a shaggy grey beard that covered much of his chest. He thumped it hard. "Do I look *frail*?"

Sam opened his mouth, gave a little squeak. The Old Bear terrified him. "No, my lord," Jon offered quickly. "You look strong as a . . . a . . ."

"Don't cozen me, Snow, you know I won't have it. Let me have a look at these maps." Mormont pawed through them brusquely, giving each no more than a glance and a grunt. "Was this all you could find?"

"I . . . m-m-my lord," Sam stammered, "there . . . there were more, b-b-but . . . the dis-disorder . . ."

"These are old," Mormont complained, and his raven echoed him with a sharp cry of *"Old, old."*

"The villages may come and go, but the hills and rivers will be in the same places," Jon pointed out.

"True enough. Have you chosen your ravens yet, Tarly?"

"M-m-maester Aemon m-means to p-pick them come evenfall, after the f-f-feeding."

"I'll have his best. Smart birds, and strong."

"*Strong,*" his own bird said, preening. "*Strong, strong.*"

"If it happens that we're all butchered out there, I mean for my successor to know where and how we died."

Talk of butchery reduced Samwell Tarly to speechlessness. Mormont leaned forward. "Tarly, when I was a lad half your age, my lady mother told me that if I stood about with my mouth open, a weasel was like to mistake it for his lair and run down my throat. If you have something to say, say it. Otherwise, beware of weasels." He waved a brusque dismissal. "Off with you, I'm too busy for folly. No doubt the maester has some work you can do."

Sam swallowed, stepped back, and scurried out so quickly he almost tripped over the rushes.

"Is that boy as big a fool as he seems?" the Lord Commander asked when he'd gone. "*Fool,*" the raven complained. Mormont did not wait for Jon to answer. "His lord father stands high in King Renly's councils, and I had half a notion to dispatch him . . . no, best not. Renly is not like to heed a quaking fat boy. I'll send Ser Arnell. He's a deal steadier, and his mother was one of the green-apple Fossoways."

"If it please my lord, what would you have of King Renly?"

"The same things I'd have of all of them, lad. Men, horses, swords, armor, grain, cheese, wine, wool, nails . . . the Night's Watch is not proud, we take what is offered." His fingers drummed against the rough-hewn planks of the table. "If the winds have been kind, Ser Alliser should reach King's Landing by the turn of the moon, but whether this boy Joffrey will pay him any heed, I do not know. House Lannister has never been a friend to the Watch."

"Thorne has the wight's hand to show them." A grisly pale thing with black fingers, it was, that twitched and stirred in its jar as if it were still alive.

"Would that we had another hand to send to Renly."

"Dywen says you can find anything beyond the Wall."

"Aye, Dywen says. And the last time he went ranging, he says he saw a bear fifteen feet tall." Mormont snorted. "My sister is said to have taken a bear for her lover. I'd believe *that* before I'd believe one fifteen feet tall. Though in a world where dead come walking . . . ah, even so, a man must believe his eyes. I have seen the dead walk. I've not seen any giant bears." He gave Jon a long, searching look. "But we were speaking of hands. How is yours?"

"Better." Jon peeled off his moleskin glove and showed him. Scars covered his arm halfway to the elbow, and the mottled pink flesh still felt tight and tender, but it was healing. "It itches, though. Maester Aemon says that's good. He gave me a salve to take with me when we ride."

"You can wield Longclaw despite the pain?"

"Well enough." Jon flexed his fingers, opening and closing his fist the way the maester had shown him. "I'm to work the fingers every day to keep them nimble, as Maester Aemon said."

"Blind he may be, but Aemon knows what he's about. I pray the gods let us keep him another twenty years. Do you know that he might have been king?"

Jon was taken by surprise. "He told me his father was king, but not . . . I thought him perhaps a younger son."

"So he was. His father's father was Daeron Targaryen, the Second of His Name, who brought Dorne into the realm. Part of the pact was that he wed a Dornish princess. She gave him four sons. Aemon's father Maekar was the youngest of those, and Aemon was *his* third son. Mind you, all this happened long before I was born, ancient as Smallwood would make me."

"Maester Aemon was named for the Dragonknight."

"So he was. Some say Prince Aemon was King Daeron's true father, not Aegon the Unworthy. Be that as it may, our Aemon lacked the Dragonknight's martial nature. He likes to say he had a slow sword but quick wits. Small wonder his grandfather packed him off to the Citadel. He was nine or ten, I believe . . . and ninth or tenth in the line of succession as well."

Maester Aemon had counted more than a hundred name days, Jon knew. Frail, shrunken, wizened, and blind, it was hard to imagine him as a little boy no older than Arya.

Mormont continued. "Aemon was at his books when the eldest of his uncles, the heir apparent, was slain in a tourney mishap. He left two sons, but they followed him to the grave not long after, during the Great Spring Sickness. King Daeron was also taken, so the crown passed to Daeron's second son, Aerys."

"The Mad King?" Jon was confused. Aerys had been king before Robert, that wasn't so long ago.

"No, this was Aerys the First. The one Robert deposed was the second of that name."

"How long ago was this?"

"Eighty years or close enough," the Old Bear said, "and no, I *still* hadn't been born, though Aemon had forged half a dozen links of his maester's chain by then. Aerys wed his own sister, as the Targaryens were wont to do, and reigned for ten or twelve years. Aemon took his vows and left the Citadel to serve at some lordling's court . . . until his royal uncle died without issue. The Iron Throne passed to the last of King Daeron's four sons. That was Maekar, Aemon's father. The new king summoned all his sons to court and would have made Aemon part of his councils, but he refused, saying that would usurp the place rightly belonging to the Grand Maester. Instead he served at the keep of his eldest brother, another Daeron. Well, that one died too, leaving only a feeble-witted daughter as heir. Some pox he caught from a whore, I believe. The next brother was Aerion."

"Aerion the Monstrous?" Jon knew that name. "The Prince Who Thought He Was a Dragon" was one of Old Nan's more gruesome tales. His little brother Bran had loved it.

"The very one, though he named himself Aerion

Brightflame. One night, in his cups, he drank a jar of wildfire, after telling his friends it would transform him into a dragon, but the gods were kind and it transformed him into a corpse. Not quite a year after, King Maekar died in battle against an outlaw lord."

Jon was not entirely innocent of the history of the realm; his own maester had seen to that. "That was the year of the Great Council," he said. "The lords passed over Prince Aerion's infant son and Prince Daeron's daughter and gave the crown to Aegon."

"Yes and no. First they offered it, quietly, to Aemon. And quietly he refused. The gods meant for him to serve, not to rule, he told them. He had sworn a vow and would not break it, though the High Septon himself offered to absolve him. Well, no sane man wanted any blood of Aerion's on the throne, and Daeron's girl was a lackwit besides being female, so they had no choice but to turn to Aemon's younger brother—Aegon, the Fifth of His Name. Aegon the Unlikely, they called him, born the fourth son of a fourth son. Aemon knew, and rightly, that if he remained at court those who disliked his brother's rule would seek to use him, so he came to the Wall. And here he has remained, while his brother and his brother's son and *his* son each reigned and died in turn, until Jaime Lannister put an end to the line of the Dragonkings."

"King," croaked the raven. The bird flapped across the solar to land on Mormont's shoulder. *"King,"* it said again, strutting back and forth.

"He likes that word," Jon said, smiling.

"An easy word to say. An easy word to like."

"King," the bird said again.

"I think he means for you to have a crown, my lord."

"The realm has three kings already, and that's two too many for my liking." Mormont stroked the raven under the beak with a finger, but all the while his eyes never left Jon Snow.

It made him feel odd. "My lord, why have you told me this, about Maester Aemon?"

"Must I have a reason?" Mormont shifted in his seat,

frowning. "Your brother Robb has been crowned King in the North. You and Aemon have that in common. A king for a brother."

"And this too," said Jon. "A vow."

The Old Bear gave a loud snort, and the raven took flight, flapping in a circle about the room. "Give me a man for every vow I've seen broken and the Wall will never lack for defenders."

"I've always known that Robb would be Lord of Winterfell."

Mormont gave a whistle, and the bird flew to him again and settled on his arm. "A lord's one thing, a king's another." He offered the raven a handful of corn from his pocket. "They will garb your brother Robb in silks, satins, and velvets of a hundred different colors, while you live and die in black ringmail. He will wed some beautiful princess and father sons on her. You'll have no wife, nor will you ever hold a child of your own blood in your arms. Robb will rule, you will serve. Men will call you a crow. Him they'll call *Your Grace*. Singers will praise every little thing he does, while your greatest deeds all go unsung. Tell me that none of this troubles you, Jon . . . and I'll name you a liar, and know I have the truth of it."

Jon drew himself up, taut as a bowstring. "And if it *did* trouble me, what might I do, bastard as I am?"

"What *will* you do?" Mormont asked. "Bastard as you are?"

"Be troubled," said Jon, "and keep my vows."

CATELYN

Her son's crown was fresh from the forge, and it seemed to Catelyn Stark that the weight of it pressed heavy on Robb's head.

The ancient crown of the Kings of Winter had been lost three centuries ago, yielded up to Aegon the Conqueror when Torrhen Stark knelt in submission. What Aegon had done with it no man could say. Lord Hoster's smith had done his work well, and Robb's crown looked much as the other was said to have looked in the tales told of the Stark kings of old; an open circlet of hammered bronze incised with the runes of the First Men, surmounted by nine black iron spikes wrought in the shape of longswords. Of gold and silver and gemstones, it had none; bronze and iron were the metals of winter, dark and strong to fight against the cold.

As they waited in Riverrun's Great Hall for the prisoner to be brought before them, she saw Robb push back the crown so it rested upon the thick auburn mop of his hair; moments later, he moved it forward again; later he gave it a quarter turn, as if that might make it sit more easily on his brow. *It is no easy thing to wear a crown*, Catelyn thought, watching, *especially for a boy of fifteen years.*

When the guards brought in the captive, Robb called for his sword. Olyvar Frey offered it up hilt first, and her son drew the blade and laid it bare across his knees, a threat plain for all to see. "Your Grace, here is the man you asked for," announced Ser Robin Ryger, captain of the Tully household guard.

"Kneel before the king, Lannister!" Theon Greyjoy shouted. Ser Robin forced the prisoner to his knees.

He did not look a lion, Catelyn reflected. This Ser Cleos Frey was a son of the Lady Genna who was sister to Lord Tywin Lannister, but he had none of the fabled Lannister beauty, the fair hair and green eyes. Instead he had inherited the stringy brown locks, weak chin, and thin face of his sire, Ser Emmon Frey, old Lord Walder's second son. His eyes were pale and watery and he could not seem to stop blinking, but perhaps that was only the light. The cells below Riverrun were dark and damp . . . and these days crowded as well.

"Rise, Ser Cleos." Her son's voice was not as icy as his father's would have been, but he did not sound a boy of fifteen either. War had made a man of him before his time. Morning light glimmered faintly against the edge of the steel across his knees.

Yet it was not the sword that made Ser Cleos Frey anxious; it was the beast. Grey Wind, her son had named him. A direwolf large as any elkhound, lean and smoke-dark, with eyes like molten gold. When the beast padded forward and sniffed at the captive knight, every man in that hall could smell the scent of fear. Ser Cleos had been taken during the battle in the Whispering Wood, where Grey Wind had ripped out the throats of half a dozen men.

The knight scrambled up, edging away with such alacrity that some of the watchers laughed aloud. "Thank you, my lord."

"Your Grace," barked Lord Umber, the Greatjon, ever the loudest of Robb's northern bannermen . . . and the

truest and fiercest as well, or so he insisted. He had been the first to proclaim her son King in the North, and he would brook no slight to the honor of his new-made sovereign.

"Your Grace," Ser Cleos corrected hastily. "Pardons."

He is not a bold man, this one, Catelyn thought. More of a Frey than a Lannister, in truth. His cousin the Kingslayer would have been a much different matter. They would never have gotten that honorific through Ser Jaime Lannister's perfect teeth.

"I brought you from your cell to carry my message to your cousin Cersei Lannister in King's Landing. You'll travel under a peace banner, with thirty of my best men to escort you."

Ser Cleos was visibly relieved. "Then I should be most glad to bring His Grace's message to the queen."

"Understand," Robb said, "I am not giving you your freedom. Your grandfather Lord Walder pledged me his support and that of House Frey. Many of your cousins and uncles rode with us in the Whispering Wood, but *you* chose to fight beneath the lion banner. That makes you a Lannister, not a Frey. I want your pledge, on your honor as a knight, that after you deliver my message you'll return with the queen's reply, and resume your captivity."

Ser Cleos answered at once. "I do so vow."

"Every man in this hall has heard you," warned Catelyn's brother Ser Edmure Tully, who spoke for Riverrun and the lords of the Trident in the place of their dying father. "If you do not return, the whole realm will know you forsworn."

"I will do as I pledged," Ser Cleos replied stiffly. "What is this message?"

"An offer of peace." Robb stood, longsword in hand. Grey Wind moved to his side. The hall grew hushed. "Tell the Queen Regent that if she meets my terms, I will sheath this sword, and make an end to the war between us."

In the back of the hall, Catelyn glimpsed the tall, gaunt figure of Lord Rickard Karstark shove through a rank of guards and out the door. No one else moved. Robb paid the disruption no mind. "Olyvar, the paper," he commanded. The squire took his longsword and handed up a rolled parchment.

Robb unrolled it. "First, the queen must release my sisters and provide them with transport by sea from King's Landing to White Harbor. It is to be understood that Sansa's betrothal to Joffrey Baratheon is at an end. When I receive word from my castellan that my sisters have returned unharmed to Winterfell, I will release the queen's cousins, the squire Willem Lannister and your brother Tion Frey, and give them safe escort to Casterly Rock or wheresoever she desires them delivered."

Catelyn Stark wished she could read the thoughts that hid behind each face, each furrowed brow and pair of tightened lips.

"Secondly, my lord father's bones will be returned to us, so he may rest beside his brother and sister in the crypts beneath Winterfell, as he would have wished. The remains of the men of his household guard who died in his service at King's Landing must also be returned."

Living men had gone south, and cold bones would return. *Ned had the truth of it*, she thought. *His place was at Winterfell, he said as much, but would I hear him? No. Go, I told him, you must be Robert's Hand, for the good of our House, for the sake of our children . . . my doing, mine, no other . . .*

"Third, my father's greatsword Ice will be delivered to my hand, here at Riverrun."

She watched her brother Ser Edmure Tully as he stood with his thumbs hooked over his swordbelt, his face as still as stone.

"Fourth, the queen will command her father Lord Tywin to release those knights and lords bannermen of mine that he took captive in the battle on the Green Fork of the Trident. Once he does so, I shall release my own captives taken in the Whispering Wood and the Battle of the Camps, save Jaime Lannister alone, who will remain my hostage for his father's good behavior."

She studied Theon Greyjoy's sly smile, wondering what it meant. That young man had a way of looking as though he knew some secret jest that only he was privy to; Catelyn had never liked it.

"Lastly, King Joffrey and the Queen Regent must renounce all claims to dominion over the north. Henceforth we are no part of their realm, but a free and independent kingdom, as of old. Our domain shall include all the Stark lands north of the Neck, and in addition the lands watered by the River Trident and its vassal streams, bounded by the Golden Tooth to the west and the Mountains of the Moon in the east."

"THE KING IN THE NORTH!" boomed Greatjon Umber, a ham-sized fist hammering at the air as he shouted. *"Stark! Stark! The King in the North!"*

Robb rolled up the parchment again. "Maester Vyman has drawn a map, showing the borders we claim. You shall have a copy for the queen. Lord Tywin must withdraw beyond these borders, and cease his raiding, burning, and pillage. The Queen Regent and her son shall make no claims to taxes, incomes, nor service from my people, and shall free my lords and knights from all oaths of fealty, vows, pledges, debts, and obligations owed to the Iron Throne and the Houses Baratheon and Lannister. Additionally, the Lannisters shall deliver ten highborn hostages, to be mutually agreed upon, as a pledge of peace. These I will treat as honored guests, according to their station. So long as the terms of this pact are abided with faithfully, I shall release two hostages every year, and return them safely to their families." Robb tossed the rolled parchment at the knight's feet. "There are the terms. If she meets them, I'll give her peace. If not"—he whistled, and Grey Wind moved forward snarling—"I'll give her another Whispering Wood."

"Stark!" the Greatjon roared again, and now other voices took up the cry. *"Stark, Stark, King in the North!"* The direwolf threw back his head and howled.

Ser Cleos had gone the color of curdled milk. "The queen shall hear your message, my—Your Grace."

"Good," Robb said. "Ser Robin, see that he has a good meal and clean clothing. He's to ride at first light."

"As you command, Your Grace," Ser Robin Ryger replied.

"Then we are done." The assembled knights and lords bannermen bent their knees as Robb turned to leave, Grey Wind at his heels. Olyvar Frey scrambled ahead to open the door. Catelyn followed them out, her brother at her side.

"You did well," she told her son in the gallery that led from the rear of the hall, "though that business with the wolf was japery more befitting a boy than a king."

Robb scratched Grey Wind behind the ear. "Did you see the look on his face, Mother?" he asked, smiling.

"What I saw was Lord Karstark, walking out."

"As did I." Robb lifted off his crown with both hands and gave it to Olyvar. "Take this thing back to my bedchamber."

"At once, Your Grace." The squire hurried off.

"I'll wager there were others who felt the same as Lord Karstark," her brother Edmure declared. "How can we talk of peace while the Lannisters spread like a pestilence over my father's domains, stealing his crops and slaughtering his people? I say again, we ought to be marching on Harrenhal."

"We lack the strength," Robb said, though unhappily.

Edmure persisted. "Do we grow stronger sitting here? Our host dwindles every day."

"And whose doing is that?" Catelyn snapped at her brother. It had been at Edmure's insistence that Robb had given the river lords leave to depart after his crowning, each to defend his own lands. Ser Marq Piper and Lord Karyl Vance had been the first to go. Lord Jonos Bracken had followed, vowing to reclaim the burnt shell of his castle and bury his dead, and now Lord Jason Mallister had announced his intent to return to his seat at Seagard, still mercifully untouched by the fighting.

"You cannot ask my river lords to remain idle while their fields are being pillaged and their people put to the sword," Ser Edmure said, "but Lord Karstark is a north-man. It would be an ill thing if he were to leave us."

"I'll speak with him," said Robb. "He lost two sons in the Whispering Wood. Who can blame him if he does not want to make peace with their killers . . . with my father's killers . . ."

"More bloodshed will not bring your father back to us, or Lord Rickard's sons," Catelyn said. "An offer had to be made—though a wiser man might have offered sweeter terms."

"Any sweeter and I would have gagged." Her son's beard had grown in redder than his auburn hair. Robb seemed to think it made him look fierce, royal . . . older. But bearded or no, he was still a youth of fifteen, and wanted vengeance no less than Rickard Karstark. It had been no easy thing to convince him to make even this offer, poor as it was.

"Cersei Lannister will *never* consent to trade your sisters for a pair of cousins. It's her brother she'll want, as you know full well." She had told him as much before, but Catelyn was finding that kings do not listen half so attentively as sons.

"I can't release the Kingslayer, not even if I wanted to. My lords would never abide it."

"Your lords made you their king."

"And can *unmake* me just as easy."

"If your crown is the price we must pay to have Arya and Sansa returned safe, we should pay it willingly. Half your lords would like to murder Lannister in his cell. If he should die while he's your prisoner, men will say—"

"—that he well deserved it," Robb finished.

"And your sisters?" Catelyn asked sharply. "Will they deserve their deaths as well? I promise you, if any harm comes to her brother, Cersei will pay us back blood for blood—"

"Lannister won't die," Robb said. "No one so much as speaks to him without my warrant. He has food, wa-ter, clean straw, more comfort than he has any right to. But I won't free him, not even for Arya and Sansa."

Her son was looking *down* at her, Catelyn realized.

Was it war that made him grow so fast, she wondered, *or the crown they had put on his head?* "Are you afraid to have Jaime Lannister in the field again, is that the truth of it?"

Grey Wind growled, as if he sensed Robb's anger, and Edmure Tully put a brotherly hand on Catelyn's shoulder. "Cat, don't. The boy has the right of this."

"Don't call me *the boy,*" Robb said, rounding on his uncle, his anger spilling out all at once on poor Edmure, who had only meant to support him. "I'm almost a man grown, and a king—*your* king, ser. And I don't fear Jaime Lannister. I defeated him once, I'll defeat him again if I must, only . . .'" He pushed a fall of hair out of his eyes and gave a shake of the head. "I might have been able to trade the Kingslayer for Father, but . . .'"

". . . but not for the girls?" Her voice was icy quiet. "Girls are not important enough, are they?"

Robb made no answer, but there was hurt in his eyes. Blue eyes, Tully eyes, eyes she had given him. She had wounded him, but he was too much his father's son to admit it.

That was unworthy of me, she told herself. *Gods be good, what is to become of me? He is doing his best, trying so hard, I know it, I see it, and yet . . . I have lost my Ned, the rock my life was built on, I could not bear to lose the girls as well . . .*

"I'll do all I can for my sisters," Robb said. "If the queen has any sense, she'll accept my terms. If not, I'll make her rue the day she refused me." Plainly, he'd had enough of the subject. "Mother, are you certain you will not consent to go to the Twins? You would be farther from the fighting, and you could acquaint yourself with Lord Frey's daughters to help me choose my bride when the war is done."

He wants me gone, Catelyn thought wearily. *Kings are not supposed to have mothers, it would seem, and I tell him things he does not want to hear.* "You're old enough to decide which of Lord Walder's girls you prefer without your mother's help, Robb."

"Then go with Theon. He leaves on the morrow.

He'll help the Mallisters escort that lot of captives to Seagard and then take ship for the Iron Islands. You could find a ship as well, and be back at Winterfell with a moon's turn, if the winds are kind. Bran and Rickon need you."

And you do not, is that what you mean to say? "My lord father has little enough time remaining him. So long as your grandfather lives, my place is at Riverrun with him."

"I could command you to go. As king. I could."

Catelyn ignored that. "I'll say again, I would sooner you sent someone else to Pyke, and kept Theon close to you."

"Who better to treat with Balon Greyjoy than his son?"

"Jason Mallister," offered Catelyn. "Tytos Blackwood. Stevron Frey. Anyone . . . but not Theon."

Her son squatted beside Grey Wind, ruffling the wolf's fur and incidentally avoiding her eyes. "Theon's fought bravely for us. I told you how he saved Bran from those wildlings in the wolfswood. If the Lannisters won't make peace, I'll have need of Lord Greyjoy's longships."

"You'll have them sooner if you keep his son as hostage."

"He's been a hostage half his life."

"For good reason," Catelyn said. "Balon Greyjoy is not a man to be trusted. He wore a crown himself, remember, if only for a season. He may aspire to wear one again."

Robb stood. "I will not grudge him that. If I'm King in the North, let him be King of the Iron Islands, if that's his desire. I'll give him a crown gladly, so long as he helps us bring down the Lannisters."

"Robb—"

"I'm sending Theon. Good day, Mother. Grey Wind, come." Robb walked off briskly, the direwolf padding beside him.

Catelyn could only watch him go. Her son and now her king. How queer that felt. *Command*, she had told him back in Moat Cailin. And so he did. "I am going to visit Father," she announced abruptly. "Come with me, Edmure."

"I need to have a word with those new bowmen Ser Desmond is training. I'll visit him later."

If he still lives, Catelyn thought, but she said nothing. Her brother would sooner face battle than that sickroom.

The shortest way to the central keep where her father lay dying was through the godswood, with its grass and wildflowers and thick stands of elm and redwood. A wealth of rustling leaves still clung to the branches of the trees, all ignorant of the word the white raven had brought to Riverrun a fortnight past. Autumn had come, the Conclave had declared, but the gods had not seen fit to tell the winds and woods as yet. For that Catelyn was duly grateful. Autumn was always a fearful time, with the specter of winter looming ahead. Even the wisest man never knew whether his next harvest would be the last.

Hoster Tully, Lord of Riverrun, lay abed in his solar, with its commanding view to the east where the rivers Tumblestone and Red Fork met beyond the walls of his castle. He was sleeping when Catelyn entered, his hair and beard as white as his featherbed, his once portly frame turned small and frail by the death that grew within him.

Beside the bed, still dressed in mail hauberk and travel-stained cloak, sat her father's brother, the Blackfish. His boots were dusty and spattered with dried mud. "Does Robb know you are returned, Uncle?" Ser Brynden Tully was Robb's eyes and ears, the commander of his scouts and outriders.

"No. I came here straight from the stables, when they told me the king was holding court. His Grace will want to hear my tidings in private first, I'd think." The Blackfish was a tall, lean man, grey of hair and precise in his movements, his clean-shaven face lined and windburnt. "How is he?" he asked, and she knew he did not mean Robb.

"Much the same. The maester gives him dreamwine and milk of the poppy for his pain, so he sleeps most of the time, and eats too little. He seems weaker with each day that passes."

"Does he speak?"

"Yes . . . but there is less and less sense to the things he says. He talks of his regrets, of unfinished tasks, of people long dead and times long past. Sometimes he does not know what season it is, or who I am. Once he called me by Mother's name."

"He misses her still," Ser Brynden answered. "You have her face. I can see it in your cheekbones, and your jaw . . ."

"You remember more of her than I do. It has been a long time." She seated herself on the bed and brushed away a strand of fine white hair that had fallen across her father's face.

"Each time I ride out, I wonder if I shall find him alive or dead on my return." Despite their quarrels, there was a deep bond between her father and the brother he had once disowned.

"At least you made your peace with him."

They sat for a time in silence, until Catelyn raised her head. "You spoke of tidings that Robb needed to hear?" Lord Hoster moaned and rolled onto his side, almost as if he had heard.

Brynden stood. "Come outside. Best if we do not wake him."

She followed him out onto the stone balcony that jutted three-sided from the solar like the prow of a ship. Her uncle glanced up, frowning. "You can see it by day now. My men call it the Red Messenger . . . but what is the message?"

Catelyn raised her eyes, to where the faint red line of the comet traced a path across the deep blue sky like a long scratch across the face of god. "The Greatjon told Robb that the old gods have unfurled a red flag of vengeance for Ned. Edmure thinks it's an omen of victory for Riverrun—he sees a fish with a long tail, in the Tully colors, red against blue." She sighed. "I wish I had their faith. Crimson is a Lannister color."

"That thing's not crimson," Ser Brynden said. "Nor Tully red, the mud red of the river. That's blood up there, child, smeared across the sky."

"Our blood or theirs?"

"Was there ever a war where only one side bled?" Her uncle gave a shake of the head. "The riverlands are awash in blood and flame all around the Gods Eye. The fighting has spread south to the Blackwater and north across the Trident, almost to the Twins. Marq Piper and Karyl Vance have won some small victories, and this southron lordling Beric Dondarrion has been raiding the raiders, falling upon Lord Tywin's foraging parties and vanishing back into the woods. It's said that Ser Burton Crakehall was boasting that he'd slain Dondarrion, until he led his column into one of Lord Beric's traps and got every man of them killed."

"Some of Ned's guard from King's Landing are with this Lord Beric," Catelyn recalled. "May the gods preserve them."

"Dondarrion and this red priest who rides with him are clever enough to preserve themselves, if the tales be true," her uncle said, "but your father's bannermen make a sadder tale. Robb should never have let them go. They've scattered like quail, each man trying to protect his own, and it's folly, Cat, folly. Jonos Bracken was wounded in the fighting amidst the ruins of his castle, and his nephew Hendry slain. Tytos Blackwood's swept the Lannisters off his lands, but they took every cow and pig and speck of grain and left him nothing to defend but Raventree Hall and a scorched desert. Darry men recaptured their lord's keep but held it less than a fortnight before Gregor Clegane descended on them and put the whole garrison to the sword, even their lord."

Catelyn was horrorstruck. "Darry was only a child."

"Aye, and the last of his line as well. The boy would have brought a fine ransom, but what does gold mean to a frothing dog like Gregor Clegane? That beast's head would make a noble gift for all the people of the realm, I vow."

Catelyn knew Ser Gregor's evil reputation, yet still . . . "Don't speak to me of heads, Uncle. Cersei has mounted Ned's on a spike above the walls of the Red Keep, and left it for the crows and flies." Even now, it was hard for her to believe that he was truly gone. Some nights she would wake in darkness, half-asleep, and for an instant expect to find him there beside her. "Clegane is no more than Lord Tywin's catspaw." For Tywin Lannister—Lord of Casterly Rock, Warden of the West, father to Queen Cersei, Ser Jaime the Kingslayer, and Tyrion the Imp, and grandfather to Joffrey Baratheon, the new-crowned boy king—was the true danger, Catelyn believed.

"True enough," Ser Brynden admitted. "And Tywin Lannister is no man's fool. He sits safe behind the walls of Harrenhal, feeding his host on our harvest and burning what he does not take. Gregor is not the only dog he's loosed. Ser Amory Lorch is in the field as well, and some sellsword out of Qohor who'd sooner maim a man than kill him. I've seen what they leave behind them. Whole villages put to the torch, women raped and mutilated, butchered children left unburied to draw wolves and wild dogs . . . it would sicken even the dead."

"When Edmure hears this, he will rage."

"And that will be just as Lord Tywin desires. Even terror has its purpose, Cat. Lannister wants to provoke us to battle."

"Robb is like to give him that wish," Catelyn said, fretful. "He is restless as a cat sitting here, and Edmure and the Greatjon and the others will urge him on." Her son had won two great victories, smashing Jaime Lannister in the Whispering Wood and routing his leaderless host outside the walls of Riverrun in the Battle of the Camps, but from the way some of his bannermen spoke of him, he might have been Aegon the Conqueror reborn.

Brynden Blackfish arched a bushy grey eyebrow. "More fool they. My first rule of war, Cat—*never give* the enemy his wish. Lord Tywin would like to fight on a field of his own choosing. He wants us to march on Harrenhal."

"Harrenhal." Every child of the Trident knew the tales told of Harrenhal, the vast fortress that King Harren the Black had raised beside the waters of Gods Eye three hundred years past, when the Seven Kingdoms had *been* seven kingdoms, and the riverlands were ruled by the ironmen from the islands. In his pride, Harren had desired the highest hall and tallest towers in all Westeros. Forty years it had taken, rising like a great shadow on the shore of the lake while Harren's armies plundered his neighbors for stone, lumber, gold, and workers. Thousands of captives died in his quarries, chained to his sledges, or laboring on his five colossal towers. Men froze by winter and sweltered in summer. Weirwoods that had stood three thousand years were cut down for beams and rafters. Harren had beggared the riverlands and the Iron Islands alike to ornament his dream. And when at last Harrenhal stood complete, on the very day King Harren took up residence, Aegon the Conqueror had come ashore at King's Landing.

Catelyn could remember hearing Old Nan tell the story to her own children, back at Winterfell. "And King Harren learned that thick walls and high towers are small use against dragons," the tale always ended. "For dragons *fly*." Harren and all his line had perished in the fires that engulfed his monstrous fortress, and every house that held Harrenhal since had come to misfortune. Strong it might be, but it was a dark place, and cursed.

"I would not have Robb fight a battle in the shadow of that keep," Catelyn admitted. "Yet we must do *something*, Uncle."

"And soon," her uncle agreed. "I have not told you the worst of it, child. The men I sent west have brought back word that a new host is gathering at Casterly Rock."

Another Lannister army. The thought made her ill. "Robb must be told at once. Who will command?"

"Ser Stafford Lannister, it's said." He turned to gaze out over the rivers, his red-and-blue cloak stirring in the breeze.

"Another nephew?" The Lannisters of Casterly Rock were a damnably large and fertile house.

"Cousin," Ser Brynden corrected. "Brother to Lord Tywin's late wife, so twice related. An old man and a bit of a dullard, but he has a son, Ser Daven, who is more formidable."

"Then let us hope it is the father and not the son who takes this army into the field."

"We have some time yet before we must face them. This lot will be sellswords, freeriders, and green boys from the stews of Lannisport. Ser Stafford must see that they are armed and drilled before he dare risk battle . . . and make no mistake, Lord Tywin is not the Kingslayer. He will not rush in heedless. He will wait patiently for Ser Stafford to march before he stirs from behind the walls of Harrenhal."

"Unless . . ." said Catelyn.

"Yes?" Ser Brynden prompted.

"Unless he *must* leave Harrenhal," she said, "to face some other threat."

Her uncle looked at her thoughtfully. "Lord Renly."

"*King* Renly." If she would ask help from the man, she would need to grant him the style he had claimed for himself.

"Perhaps." The Blackfish smiled a dangerous smile. "He'll want something, though."

"He'll want what kings always want," she said. "Homage."

TYRION

Janos Slynt was a butcher's son, and he laughed like a man chopping meat. "More wine?" Tyrion asked him.

"I should not object," Lord Janos said, holding out his cup. He was built like a keg, and had a similar capacity. "I should not object at all. That's a fine red. From the Arbor?"

"Dornish." Tyrion gestured, and his serving man poured. But for the servants, he and Lord Janos were alone in the Small Hall, at a small candlelit table surrounded by darkness. "Quite the find. Dornish wines are not often so rich."

"Rich," said the big frog-faced man, taking a healthy gulp. He was not a man for sipping, Janos Slynt. Tyrion had made note of that at once. "Yes, rich, that's the very word I was searching for, the *very* word. You have a gift for words, Lord Tyrion, if I might say so. And you tell a droll tale. Droll, yes."

"I'm pleased you think so . . . but I'm not a lord, as

you are. A simple *Tyrion* will suffice for me, Lord Janos."

"As you wish." He took another swallow, dribbling wine on the front of his black satin doublet. He was wearing a cloth-of-gold half cape fastened with a miniature spear, its point enameled in dark red. And he was well and truly drunk.

Tyrion covered his mouth and belched politely. Unlike Lord Janos he had gone easy on the wine, but he was very full. The first thing he had done after taking up residence in the Tower of the Hand was inquire after the finest cook in the city and take her into his service. This evening they had supped on oxtail soup, summer greens tossed with pecans, grapes, red fennel, and crumbled cheese, hot crab pie, spiced squash, and quails drowned in butter. Each dish had come with its own wine. Lord Janos allowed that he had never eaten half so well. "No doubt that will change when you take your seat in Harrenhal," Tyrion said.

"For a certainty. Perhaps I should ask this cook of yours to enter my service, what do you say?"

"Wars have been fought over less," he said, and they both had a good long laugh. "You're a bold man to take Harrenhal for your seat. Such a grim place, and *huge* . . . costly to maintain. And some say cursed as well."

"Should I fear a pile of stone?" He hooted at the notion. "A bold man, you said. You must be bold, to rise. As I have. To Harrenhal, yes! And why not? You know. You are a bold man too, I sense. Small, mayhap, but *bold*."

"You are too kind. More wine?"

"No. No, truly, I . . . oh, gods be damned, *yes*. Why not? A bold man drinks his fill!"

"Truly." Tyrion filled Lord Slynt's cup to the brim. "I have been glancing over the names you put forward to take your place as Commander of the City Watch."

"Good men. Fine men. Any of the six will do, but I'd choose Allar Deem. My right arm. Good good man.

Loyal. Pick him and you won't be sorry. If he pleases the king."

"To be sure." Tyrion took a small sip of his own wine. "I had been considering Ser Jacelyn Bywater. He's been captain on the Mud Gate for three years, and he served with valor during Balon Greyjoy's Rebellion. King Robert knighted him at Pyke. And yet his name does not appear on your list."

Lord Janos Slynt took a gulp of wine and sloshed it around in his mouth for a moment before swallowing. "Bywater. Well. Brave man, to be sure, yet . . . he's *rigid*, that one. A queer dog. The men don't like him. A cripple too, lost his hand at Pyke, that's what got him knighted. A poor trade, if you ask me, a hand for a *ser*." He laughed. "Ser Jacelyn thinks overmuch of himself and his honor, as I see it. You'll do better leaving that one where he is, my lor—Tyrion. Allar Deem's the man for you."

"Deem is little loved in the streets, I am told."

"He's feared. That's better."

"What was it I heard of him? Some trouble in a brothel?"

"That. Not his fault, my lo—Tyrion. No. He never meant to kill the woman, that was her own doing. He warned her to stand aside and let him do his duty."

"Still . . . mothers and children, he might have expected she'd try to save the babe." Tyrion smiled. "Have some of this cheese, it goes splendidly with the wine. Tell me, why did you choose Deem for that unhappy task?"

"A good commander knows his men, Tyrion. Some are good for one job, some for another. Doing for a babe, and her still on the tit, that takes a certain sort. Not every man'd do it. Even if it was only some whore and her whelp."

"I suppose that's so," said Tyrion, hearing *only some whore* and thinking of Shae, and Tysha long ago, and all the other women who had taken his coin and his seed over the years.

Slynt went on, oblivious. "A hard man for a hard job,

is Deem. Does as he's told, and never a word after-
ward." He cut a slice off the cheese. "This *is* fine. Sharp.
Give me a good sharp knife and a good sharp cheese and
I'm a happy man."

Tyrion shrugged. "Enjoy it while you can. With the
riverlands in flame and Renly king in Highgarden, good
cheese will soon be hard to come by. So who sent you
after the whore's bastard?"

Lord Janos gave Tyrion a wary look, then laughed and
wagged a wedge of cheese at him. "You're a sly one,
Tyrion. Thought you could trick me, did you? It takes
more than wine and cheese to make Janos Slynt tell
more than he should. I pride myself. Never a question,
and never a word afterward, not with me."

"As with Deem."

"Just the same. You make him your Commander
when I'm off to Harrenhal, and you won't regret it."

Tyrion broke off a nibble of the cheese. It was sharp
indeed, and veined with wine; very choice. "Whoever
the king names will not have an easy time stepping into
your armor, I can tell. Lord Mormont faces the same
problem."

Lord Janos looked puzzled. "I thought she was a lady.
Mormont. Beds down with bears, that's the one?"

"It was her brother I was speaking of. Jeor Mormont,
the Lord Commander of the Night's Watch. When I was
visiting with him on the Wall, he mentioned how concerned he was about finding a good man to take his
place. The Watch gets so few good men these days."
Tyrion grinned. "He'd sleep easier if he had a man like
you, I imagine. Or the valiant Allar Deem."

Lord Janos roared. "Small chance of that!"

"One would think," Tyrion said, "but life does take
queer turns. Consider Eddard Stark, my lord. I don't
suppose he ever imagined his life would end on the
steps of Baelor's Sept."

"There were damn few as did," Lord Janos allowed,
chuckling.

Tyrion chuckled too. "A pity I wasn't here to see it.
They say even Varys was surprised."

Lord Janos laughed so hard his gut shook. "The Spider," he said. "Knows everything, they say. Well, he didn't know *that*."

"How could he?" Tyrion put the first hint of a chill in his tone. "He had helped persuade my sister that Stark should be pardoned, on the condition that he take the black."

"Eh?" Janos Slynt blinked vaguely at Tyrion.

"My sister Cersei," Tyrion repeated, a shade more strongly, in case the fool had some doubt who he meant. "The Queen Regent."

"Yes." Slynt took a swallow. "As to that, well . . . the king commanded it, m'lord. The king himself."

"The king is thirteen," Tyrion reminded him.

"Still. He *is* the king." Slynt's jowls quivered when he frowned. "The Lord of the Seven Kingdoms."

"Well, one or two of them, at least," Tyrion said with a sour smile. "Might I have a look at your spear?"

"My spear?" Lord Janos blinked in confusion.

Tyrion pointed. "The clasp that fastens your cape."

Hesitantly, Lord Janos drew out the ornament and handed it to Tyrion.

"We have goldsmiths in Lannisport who do better work," he opined. "The red enamel blood is a shade much, if you don't mind my saying. Tell me, my lord, did you drive the spear into the man's back yourself, or did you only give the command?"

"I gave the command, and I'd give it again. Lord Stark was a traitor." The bald spot in the middle of Slynt's head was beet-red, and his cloth-of-gold cape had slithered off his shoulders onto the floor. "The man tried to buy me."

"Little dreaming that you had already been sold."

Slynt slammed down his wine cup. "Are you drunk? If you think I will sit here and have my honor questioned . . ."

"What honor is that? I do admit, you made a better bargain than Ser Jacelyn. A lordship and a castle for a spear thrust in the back, and you didn't even need to thrust the spear." He tossed the golden ornament back to Janos Slynt. It bounced off his chest and clattered to the floor as the man rose.

"I mislike the tone of your voice, my lo—*Imp.* I am the Lord of Harrenhal and a member of the king's council, who are you to chastise me like this?"

Tyrion cocked his head sideways. "I think you know quite well who I am. How many sons do you have?"

"What are my sons to you, dwarf?"

"Dwarf?" His anger flashed. "You should have stopped at Imp. I am Tyrion of House Lannister, and someday, if you have the sense the gods gave a sea slug, you will drop to your knees in thanks that it was me you had to deal with, and not my lord father. Now, *how many sons do you have?"*

Tyrion could see the sudden fear in Janos Slynt's eyes. "Th-three, m'lord. And a daughter. Please, m'lord—"

"You need not beg." He slid off his chair. "You have my word, no harm will come to them. The younger boys will be fostered out as squires. If they serve well and loyally, they may be knights in time. Let it never be said that House Lannister does not reward those who serve it. Your eldest son will inherit the title Lord Slynt, and this appalling sigil of yours." He kicked at the little golden spear and sent it skittering across the floor. "Lands will be found for him, and he can build a seat for himself. It will not be Harrenhal, but it will be sufficient. It will be up to him to make a marriage for the girl."

Janos Slynt's face had gone from red to white. "Wh-what . . . what do you . . . ?" His jowls were quivering like mounds of suet.

"What do I mean to do with *you?"* Tyrion let the oaf tremble for a moment before he answered. "The carrack *Summer's Dream* sails on the morning tide. Her master tells me she will call at Gulltown, the Three Sisters, the isle of Skagos, and Eastwatch-by-the-Sea. When you see Lord Commander Mormont, give him my fond regards, and tell him that I have not forgotten the needs of the Night's Watch. I wish you long life and good service, my lord."

Once Janos Slynt realized he was not to be summarily executed, color returned to his face. He thrust his jaw out. "We will see about this, Imp. *Dwarf.* Perhaps it will be you on that ship, what do you think of that? Perhaps it will be you on the Wall." He gave a bark of anxious laughter. "You and your threats, well, we will see. I am the king's friend, you know. We shall hear what Joffrey has to say about this. And Littlefinger and the queen, oh, yes. Janos Slynt has a good many friends. We will see who goes sailing, I promise you. Indeed we will."

Slynt spun on his heel like the watchman he'd once been, and strode the length of the Small Hall, boots ringing on the stone. He clattered up the steps, threw open the door . . . and came face-to-face with a tall, lantern-jawed man in black breastplate and gold cloak. Strapped to the stump of his right wrist was an iron hand. "Janos," he said, deep-set eyes glinting under a prominent brow ridge and a shock of salt-and-pepper hair. Six gold cloaks moved quietly into the Small Hall behind him as Janos Slynt backed away.

"Lord Slynt," Tyrion called out, "I believe you know Ser Jacelyn Bywater, our new Commander of the City Watch."

"We have a litter waiting for you, my lord," Ser Jacelyn told Slynt. "The docks are dark and distant, and the streets are not safe by night. Men."

As the gold cloaks ushered out their onetime commander, Tyrion called Ser Jacelyn to his side and handed him a roll of parchment. "It's a long voyage, and Lord Slynt will want for company. See that these six join him on the *Summer's Dream.*"

Bywater glanced over the names and smiled. "As you will."

"There's one," Tyrion said quietly. "Deem. Tell the captain it would not be taken amiss if that one should happen to be swept overboard before they reach Eastwatch."

"I'm told those northern waters are very stormy, my lord." Ser Jacelyn bowed and took his leave, his cloak rippling behind him. He trod on Slynt's cloth-of-gold cape on his way.

Tyrion sat alone, sipping at what remained of the fine sweet Dornish wine. Servants came and went, clearing the dishes from the table. He told them to leave the wine. When they were done, Varys came gliding into the hall, wearing flowing lavender robes that matched his smell. "Oh, sweetly done, my good lord."

"Then why do I have this bitter taste in my mouth?" He pressed his fingers into his temples. "I told them to throw Allar Deem into the sea. I am sorely tempted to do the same with you."

"You might be disappointed by the result," Varys replied. "The storms come and go, the waves crash overhead, the big fish eat the little fish, and I keep on paddling. Might I trouble you for a taste of the wine that Lord Slynt enjoyed so much?"

Tyrion waved at the flagon, frowning.

Varys filled a cup. "Ah. Sweet as summer." He took another sip. "I hear the grapes singing on my tongue."

"I wondered what that noise was. Tell the grapes to keep still, my head is about to split. It was my sister. That was what the oh-so-loyal Lord Janos refused to say. *Cersei* sent the gold cloaks to that brothel."

Varys tittered nervously. So he had known all along.

"You left that part out," Tyrion said accusingly.

"Your own sweet sister," Varys said, so grief-stricken he looked close to tears. "It is a hard thing to tell a man, my lord. I was fearful how you might take it. Can you forgive me?"

"No," Tyrion snapped. "Damn you. Damn *her*." He could not touch Cersei, he knew. Not yet, not even if he'd wanted to, and he was far from certain that he did. Yet it rankled, to sit here and make a mummer's show of justice by punishing the sorry likes of Janos Slynt and Allar Deem, while his sister continued on her savage course. "In future, you will tell me what you know, Lord Varys. *All* of what you know."

The eunuch's smile was sly. "That might take rather a long time, my good lord. I know quite a lot."

"Not enough to save this child, it would seem."

"Alas, no. There was another bastard, a boy, older. I took steps to see him removed from harm's way . . . but I confess, I never dreamed the babe would be at risk. A baseborn girl, less than a year old, with a whore for a mother. What threat could she pose?"

"She was Robert's," Tyrion said bitterly. "That was enough for Cersei, it would seem."

"Yes. It is grievous sad. I must blame myself for the poor sweet babe and her mother, who was so young and loved the king."

"Did she?" Tyrion had never seen the dead girl's face, but in his mind she was Shae and Tysha both. "Can a whore truly love anyone, I wonder? No, don't answer. Some things I would rather not know." He had settled Shae in a sprawling stone-and-timber manse, with its own well and stable and garden; he had given her servants to see to her wants, a white bird from the Summer Isles to keep her company, silks and silver and gemstones to adorn her, guards to protect her. And yet she seemed restive. She wanted to be with him more, she told him; she wanted to serve him and help him. "You help me most here, between the sheets," he told her one night after their loving as he lay beside her, his head pillowed against her breast, his groin aching with a sweet soreness. She made no reply, save with her eyes. He could see there that it was not what she'd wanted to hear.

Sighing, Tyrion started to reach for the wine again, then remembered Lord Janos and pushed the flagon away. "It does seem my sister was telling the truth about Stark's death. We have my nephew to thank for that madness."

"King Joffrey gave the command. Janos Slynt and Ser Ilyn Payne carried it out, swiftly, without hesitation . . ."

". . . almost as if they had expected it. Yes, we have been over this ground before, without profit. A folly."

"With the City Watch in hand, my lord, you are well placed to see to it that His Grace commits no further . . . follies? To be sure, there is still the queen's household guard to consider . . ."

"The red cloaks?" Tyrion shrugged. "Vylarr's loyalty is to Casterly Rock. He knows I am here with my father's authority. Cersei would find it hard to use his men against me . . . besides, they are only a hundred. I have half again as many men of my own. *And* six thousand gold cloaks, if Bywater is the man you claim."

"You will find Ser Jacelyn to be courageous, honorable, obedient . . . and most grateful."

"To whom, I wonder?" Tyrion did not trust Varys, though there was no denying his value. He knew things, beyond a doubt. "Why *are* you so helpful, my lord Varys?" he asked, studying the man's soft hands, the bald powdered face, the slimy little smile.

"You are the Hand. I serve the realm, the king, and you."

"As you served Jon Arryn and Eddard Stark?"

"I served Lord Arryn and Lord Stark as best I could. I was saddened and horrified by their most untimely deaths."

"Think how *I* feel. I'm like to be next."

"Oh, I think not," Varys said, swirling the wine in his cup. "Power is a curious thing, my lord. Perchance you have considered the riddle I posed you that day in the inn?"

"It has crossed my mind a time or two," Tyrion admitted. "The king, the priest, the rich man—who lives and who dies? Who will the swordsman obey? It's a riddle without an answer, or rather, too many answers. All depends on the man with the sword."

"And yet he is no one," Varys said. "He has neither crown nor gold nor favor of the gods, only a piece of pointed steel."

"That piece of steel is the power of life and death."

"Just so . . . yet if it is the swordsmen who rule us in truth, why do we pretend our kings hold the power? Why should a strong man with a sword *ever* obey a child king like Joffrey, or a wine-sodden oaf like his father?"

"Because these child kings and drunken oafs can call other strong men, with other swords."

"Then these other swordsmen have the true power. Or do they? Whence came their swords? Why do *they* obey?" Varys smiled. "Some say knowledge is power. Some tell us that all power comes from the gods. Others say it derives from law. Yet that day on the steps of Baelor's Sept, our godly High Septon and the lawful Queen Regent and your ever-so-knowledgeable servant were as powerless as any cobbler or cooper in the crowd. Who truly killed Eddard Stark, do you think? Joffrey, who gave the command? Ser Ilyn Payne, who swung the sword? Or . . . another?"

Tyrion cocked his head sideways. "Did you mean to answer your damned riddle, or only to make my head ache worse?"

Varys smiled. "Here, then. Power resides where men *believe* it resides. No more and no less."

"So power is a mummer's trick?"

"A shadow on the wall," Varys murmured, "yet shadows can kill. And ofttimes a very small man can cast a very large shadow."

Tyrion smiled. "Lord Varys, I am growing strangely fond of you. I may kill you yet, but I think I'd feel sad about it."

"I will take that as high praise."

"What are you, Varys?" Tyrion found he truly wanted to know. "A spider, they say."

"Spies and informers are seldom loved, my lord. I am but a loyal servant of the realm."

"And a eunuch. Let us not forget that."

"I seldom do."

"People have called me a halfman too, yet I think the gods have been kinder to me. I am small, my legs are twisted, and women do not look upon me with any great yearning . . . yet I'm still a man. Shae is not the first to grace my bed, and one day I may take a wife and sire a son. If the gods are good, he'll look like his uncle and think like his father. You have no such hope to sustain you. Dwarfs are a jape of the gods . . . but men make eunuchs. Who cut you, Varys? When and why? Who *are* you, truly?"

The eunuch's smile never flickered, but his eyes glittered with something that was not laughter. "You are kind to ask, my lord, but my tale is long and sad, and we have treasons to discuss." He drew a parchment from the sleeve of his robe. "The master of the King's Galley *White Hart* plots to slip anchor three days hence to offer his sword and ship to Lord Stannis."

Tyrion sighed. "I suppose we must make some sort of bloody lesson out of the man?"

"Ser Jacelyn could arrange for him to vanish, but a trial before the king would help assure the continued loyalty of the other captains."

And keep my royal nephew occupied as well. "As you say. Put him down for a dose of Joffrey's justice."

Varys made a mark on the parchment. "Ser Horas and Ser Hobber Redwyne have bribed a guard to let them out a postern gate, the night after next. Arrangements have been made for them to sail on the Pentoshi galley *Moonrunner*, disguised as oarsmen."

"Can we *keep* them on those oars for a few years, see how they fancy it?" He smiled. "No, my sister would be distraught to lose such treasured guests. Inform Ser Jacelyn. Seize the man they bribed and explain what an honor it is to serve as a brother of the Night's Watch. And have men posted around the *Moonrunner*, in case the Redwynes find a second guard short of coin."

"As you will." Another mark on the parchment. "Your man Timett slew a wineseller's son this evening, at a gambling den on the Street of Silver. He accused him of cheating at tiles."

"Was it true?"

"Oh, beyond a doubt."

"Then the honest men of the city owe Timett a debt of gratitude. I shall see that he has the king's thanks."

The eunuch gave a nervous giggle and made another mark. "We also have a sudden plague of holy men. The comet has brought forth all manner of queer priests, preachers, and prophets, it would seem. They beg in the winesinks and pot-shops and foretell doom and destruction to anyone who stops to listen."

Tyrion shrugged. "We are close on the three hundredth year since Aegon's Landing, I suppose it is only to be expected. Let them rant."

"They are spreading fear, my lord."

"I thought that was your job."

Varys covered his mouth with his hand. "You are very cruel to say so. One last matter. Lady Tanda gave a small supper last night. I have the menu and the guest list for your inspection. When the wine was poured, Lord Gyles rose to lift a cup to the king, and Ser Balon Swann was heard to remark, *'We'll need three cups for that.'* Many laughed . . ."

Tyrion raised a hand. "Enough. Ser Balon made a jest. I am not interested in treasonous table talk, Lord Varys."

"You are as wise as you are gentle, my lord." The parchment vanished up the eunuch's sleeve. "We both have much to do. I shall leave you."

When the eunuch had departed, Tyrion sat for a long time watching the candle and wondering how his sister would take the news of Janos Slynt's dismissal. Not happily, if he was any judge, but beyond sending an angry protest to Lord Tywin in Harrenhal, he did not see what Cersei could hope to do about it. Tyrion had the City Watch now, plus a hundred-and-a-half fierce clansmen and a growing force of sellswords recruited by Bronn. He would seem well protected.

Doubtless Eddard Stark thought the same.

The Red Keep was dark and still when Tyrion left the Small Hall. Bronn was waiting in his solar. "Slynt?" he asked.

"Lord Janos will be sailing for the Wall on the morning tide. Varys would have me believe that I have replaced one of Joffrey's men with one of my own. More likely, I have replaced Littlefinger's man with one belonging to Varys, but so be it."

"You'd best know, Timett killed a man—"

"Varys told me."

The sellsword seemed unsurprised. "The fool figured a one-eyed man would be easier to cheat. Timett pinned his wrist to the table with a dagger and ripped out his throat barehanded. He has this trick where he stiffens his fingers—"

"Spare me the grisly details, my supper is sitting badly in my belly," Tyrion said. "How goes your recruiting?"

"Well enough. Three new men tonight."

"How do you know which ones to hire?"

"I look them over. I question them, to learn where they've fought and how well they lie." Bronn smiled. "And then I give them a chance to kill me, while I do the same for them."

"Have you killed any?"

"No one we could have used."

"And if one of them kills you?"

"He'll be one you'll want to hire."

Tyrion was a little drunk, and very tired. "Tell me, Bronn. If I told you to kill a babe . . . an infant girl, say, still at her mother's breast . . . would you do it? Without question?"

"Without question? No." The sellsword rubbed thumb and forefinger together. "I'd ask how much."

And why would I ever need your Allar Deem, Lord Slynt? Tyrion thought. *I have a hundred of my own.* He wanted to laugh; he wanted to weep; most of all, he wanted Shae.

ARYA

The road was little more than two ruts through the weeds.

The good part was, with so little traffic there'd be no one to point the finger and say which way they'd gone. The human flood that had flowed down the kingsroad was only a trickle here.

The bad part was, the road wound back and forth like a snake, tangling with even smaller trails and sometimes seeming to vanish entirely only to reappear half a league farther on when they had all but given up hope. Arya hated it. The land was gentle enough, rolling hills and terraced fields interspersed with meadows and woodlands and little valleys where willows crowded close to slow shallow streams. Even so, the path was so narrow and crooked that their pace had dropped to a crawl.

It was the wagons that slowed them, lumbering along, axles creaking under the weight of their heavy loads. A dozen times a day they had to stop to free a wheel that had stuck in a rut, or double up the teams to climb a muddy slope. Once, in the middle of a dense stand of oak, they came face-to-face with three men pulling a load of firewood in an ox cart, with no way for either to get around. There had been nothing for it but to wait while the foresters unhitched their ox, led him through the trees, spun the cart, hitched the ox up again, and started back the way they'd come. The ox was even *slower* than the wagons, so that day they hardly got anywhere at all.

Arya could not help looking over her shoulder, wondering when the gold cloaks would catch them. At night, she woke at every noise to grab for Needle's hilt. They never made camp without putting out sentries now, but Arya did not trust them, especially the orphan boys. They might have done well enough in the alleys of King's Landing, but out here they were lost. When she was being quiet as a shadow, she could sneak past all of them, flitting out by starlight to make her water in the woods where no one would see. Once, when Lommy Greenhands had the watch, she shimmied up an oak and moved from tree to tree until she was right above his head, and he never saw a thing. She would have jumped down on top of him, but she knew his scream would wake the whole camp, and Yoren might take a stick to her again.

Lommy and the other orphans all treated the Bull like someone special now because the queen wanted his head, though he would have none of it. "I never did nothing to no queen," he said angrily. "I did my work, is all. Bellows and tongs and fetch and carry. I was s'posed to be an armorer, and one day Master Mott says I got to join the Night's Watch, that's all I know." Then he'd go off to polish his helm. It was a beautiful helm, rounded and curved, with a slit visor and two great metal bull's horns. Arya would watch him polish the metal with an oilcloth, shining it so bright you could see the flames of the cookfire reflected in the steel. Yet he never actually put it on his head.

"I bet he's that traitor's bastard," Lommy said one

night, in a hushed voice so Gendry would not hear. "The wolf lord, the one they nicked on Baelor's steps."

"He is not," Arya declared. *My father only had one bastard, and that's Jon.* She stalked off into the trees, wishing she could just saddle her horse and ride home. She was a good horse, a chestnut mare with a white blaze on her forehead. And Arya had always been a good rider. She could gallop off and never see any of them, unless she wanted to. Only then she'd have no one to scout ahead of her, or watch behind, or stand guard while she napped, and when the gold cloaks caught her, she'd be all alone. It was safer to stay with Yoren and the others.

"We're not far from Gods Eye," the black brother said one morning. "The kingsroad won't be safe till we're across the Trident. So we'll come up around the lake along the western shore, they're not like to look for us there." At the next spot where two ruts cut cross each other, he turned the wagons west.

Here farmland gave way to forest, the villages and holdfasts were smaller and farther apart, the hills higher and the valleys deeper. Food grew harder to come by. In the city, Yoren had loaded up the wagons with salt fish, hard bread, lard, turnips, sacks of beans and barley, and wheels of yellow cheese, but every bite of it had been eaten. Forced to live off the land, Yoren turned to Koss and Kurz, who'd been taken as poachers. He would send them ahead of the column, into the woods, and come dusk they would be back with a deer slung between them on a pole or a brace of quail swinging from their belts. The younger boys would be set to picking blackberries along the road, or climbing fences to fill a sack with apples if they happened upon an orchard.

Arya was a skilled climber and a fast picker, and she liked to go off by herself. One day she came across a rabbit, purely by happenstance. It was brown and fat, with long ears and a twitchy nose. Rabbits ran faster than cats, but they couldn't climb trees half so well. She whacked it with her stick and grabbed it by its ears, and Yoren stewed it with some mushrooms and wild onions. Arya was given a whole leg, since it was her rabbit. She shared it with Gendry. The rest of them each got a spoonful, even the three in manacles. Jaqen H'ghar thanked her politely for the treat, and Biter licked the grease off his dirty fingers with a blissful look, but Rorge, the noseless one, only laughed and said, "There's a hunter now. Lumpyface Lumpyhead Rabbitkiller."

Outside a holdfast called Briarwhite, some fieldhands surrounded them in a cornfield, demanding coin for the ears they'd taken. Yoren eyed their scythes and tossed them a few coppers. "Time was, a man in black was feasted from Dorne to Winterfell, and even high lords called it an honor to shelter him under their roofs," he said bitterly. "Now cravens like you want hard coin for a bite of wormy apple." He spat.

"It's sweetcorn, better'n a stinking old black bird like you deserves," one of them answered roughly. "You get out of our field now, and take these sneaks and stabbers with you, or we'll stake you up in the corn to scare the other crows away."

They roasted the sweetcorn in the husk that night, turning the ears with long forked sticks, and ate it hot right off the cob. Arya thought it tasted wonderful, but Yoren was too angry to eat. A cloud seemed to hang over him, ragged and black as his cloak. He paced about the camp restlessly, muttering to himself.

The next day Koss came racing back to warn Yoren of a camp ahead. "Twenty or thirty men, in mail and halfhelms," he said. "Some of them are cut up bad, and one's dying, from the sound of him. With all the noise he was making, I got right up close. They got spears and shields, but only one horse, and that's lame. I think they been there awhile, from the stink of the place."

"See a banner?"

"Spotted treecat, yellow and black, on a mud-brown field."

Yoren folded a sourleaf into his mouth and chewed. "Can't say," he admitted. "Might be one side, might be t'other. If they're hurt that bad, likely they'd take our mounts no matter who they are. Might be they'd take more than that. I believe we'll go wide around them." It took them miles out of their way, and cost them two days at the least, but the old man said it was cheap at the price. "You'll have time enough on the Wall. The rest o' your lives, most like. Seems to me there's no rush to get there."

Arya saw men guarding the fields more and more when they turned north again. Often they stood silently beside the road, giving a cold eye to anyone who passed. Elsewhere they patrolled on horses, riding their fence lines with axes strapped to their saddles. At one place, she spotted a man perched up in a dead tree, with a bow in his hand and a quiver hanging from the branch beside him. The moment he spied them, he notched an arrow to his bowstring, and never looked away until the last wagon was out of sight. All the while, Yoren cursed. "Him in his tree, let's see how well he likes it up there when the Others come to take him. He'll scream for the Watch then, that he will."

A day later Dobber spied a red glow against the evening sky. "Either this road went and turned again, or that sun's setting in the north."

Yoren climbed a rise to get a better look. "Fire," he announced. He licked a thumb and held it up. "Wind should blow it away from us. Still bears watching."

And watch it they did. As the world darkened, the fire seemed to grow brighter and brighter, until it looked as though the whole north was ablaze. From time to time, they could even smell the smoke, though the wind held steady and the flames never got any closer. By dawn the fire had burned itself out, but none of them slept very well that night.

It was midday when they arrived at the place where the village had been. The fields were a charred desolation for miles around, the houses blackened shells. The carcasses of burnt and butchered animals dotted the ground, under living blankets of carrion crows that rose, cawing furiously, when disturbed. Smoke still drifted from inside the holdfast. Its timber palisade looked strong from afar, but had not proved strong enough.

Riding out in front of the wagons on her horse, Arya saw burnt bodies impaled on sharpened stakes atop the walls, their hands drawn up tight in front of their faces as if to fight off the flames that had consumed them. Yoren called a halt when they were still some distance off, and told Arya and the other boys to guard the wagons while he and Murch and Cutjack went in on foot. A flock of ravens rose from inside the walls when they climbed through the broken gate, and the caged ravens in their wagons called out to them with *quorks* and raucous shrieks.

"Should we go in after them?" Arya asked Gendry after Yoren and the others had been gone a long time.

"Yoren said wait." Gendry's voice sounded hollow. When Arya turned to look, she saw that he was wearing his helm, all shiny steel and great curving horns.

When they finally returned, Yoren had a little girl in his arms, and Murch and Cutjack were carrying a woman in a sling made of an old torn quilt. The girl was no older than two and she cried all the time, a whimpery sound, like something was caught in her throat. Either she couldn't talk yet or she had forgotten how. The woman's right arm ended in a bloody stump at her elbow, and her eyes didn't seem to see anything, even when she was looking right at it. She talked, but she only said one thing. "Please," she cried, over and over. "Please. Please." Rorge thought that was funny. He laughed through the hole in his face where his nose had been, and Biter started laughing too, until Murch cursed them and told them to shut up.

Yoren had them fix the woman a place in the back of a wagon. "And be quick about it," he said. "Come dark, there'll be wolves here, and worse."

"I'm scared," Hot Pie murmured when he saw the one-armed woman thrashing in the wagon.

"Me too," Arya confessed.

He squeezed her shoulder. "I never truly kicked no boy to death, Arry. I just sold my mommy's pies, is all."

Arya rode as far ahead of the wagons as she dared, so she wouldn't have to hear the little girl crying or listen

to the woman whisper, "Please." She remembered a
story Old Nan had told once, about a man imprisoned
in a dark castle by evil giants. He was very brave and
smart and he tricked the giants and escaped . . . but no
sooner was he outside the castle than the Others took
him, and drank his hot red blood. Now she knew how
he must have felt.

The one-armed woman died at evenfall. Gendry and
Cutjack dug her grave on a hillside beneath a weeping
willow. When the wind blew, Arya thought she could
hear the long trailing branches whispering, "Please.
Please. Please." The little hairs on the back of her neck
rose, and she almost ran from the graveside.

"No fire tonight," Yoren told them. Supper was a
handful of wild radishes Koss found, a cup of dry beans,
water from a nearby brook. The water had a funny taste
to it, and Lommy told them it was the taste of bodies,
rotting someplace upstream. Hot Pie would have hit
him if old Reysen hadn't pulled them apart.

Arya drank too much water, just to fill her belly with
something. She never thought she'd be able to sleep, yet
somehow she did. When she woke, it was pitch-black
and her bladder was full to bursting. Sleepers huddled
all around her, wrapped in blankets and cloaks. Arya
found Needle, stood, listened. She heard the soft footfalls of a sentry, men turning in restless sleep, Rorge's
rattling snores, and the queer hissing sound that Biter
made when he slept. From a different wagon came the
steady rhythmic scrape of steel on stone as Yoren sat,
chewing sourleaf and sharpening the edge of his dirk.

Hot Pie was one of the boys on watch. "Where you
going?" he asked when he saw Arya heading for the
trees.

Arya waved vaguely at the woods.

"No you're not," Hot Pie said. He had gotten bolder
again now that he had a sword on his belt, even though
it was just a shortsword and he handled it like a cleaver.
"The old man said for everyone to stay close tonight."

"I need to make water," Arya explained.

"Well, use that tree right there." He pointed. "You

don't know what's out there, Arry. I heard wolves before."

Yoren wouldn't like it if she fought with him. She
tried to look afraid. "Wolves? For true?"

"I heard," he assured her.

"I don't think I need to go after all." She went back to
her blanket and pretended to sleep until she heard Hot
Pie's footsteps going away. Then she rolled over and
slipped off into the woods on the other side of the camp,
quiet as a shadow. There were sentries out this way too,
but Arya had no trouble avoiding them. Just to make
sure, she went out twice as far as usual. When she was
sure there was no one near, she skinned down her
breeches and squatted to do her business.

She was making water, her clothing tangled about her
ankles, when she heard rustling from under the trees.
Hot Pie, she thought in panic, *he followed me*. Then
she saw the eyes shining out from the wood, bright with
reflected moonlight. Her belly clenched tight as she
grabbed for Needle, not caring if she pissed herself,
counting eyes, two four eight twelve, a whole pack . . .

One of them came padding out from under the trees.
He stared at her, and bared his teeth, and all she could
think was how stupid she'd been and how Hot Pie
would gloat when they found her half-eaten body the
next morning. But the wolf turned and raced back into
the darkness, and quick as that the eyes were gone.
Trembling, she cleaned herself and laced up and followed a distant scraping sound back to camp, and to
Yoren. Arya climbed up into the wagon beside him,
shaken. "Wolves," she whispered hoarsely. "In the
woods."

"Aye. They would be." He never looked at her.

"They scared me."

"Did they?" He spat. "Seems to me your kind was
fond o' wolves."

"Nymeria was a direwolf." Arya hugged herself.
"That's different. Anyhow, she's gone. Jory and I threw
rocks at her until she ran off, or else the queen would
have killed her." It made her sad to talk about it. "I bet

if she'd been in the city, she wouldn't have let them cut off Father's head."

"Orphan boys got no fathers," Yoren said, "or did you forget that?" The sourleaf had turned his spit red, so it looked like his mouth was bleeding. "The only wolves we got to fear are the ones wear manskin, like those who done for that village."

"I wish I was home," she said miserably. She tried so hard to be brave, to be fierce as a wolverine and all, but sometimes she felt like she was just a little girl after all.

The black brother peeled a fresh sourleaf from the bale in the wagon and stuffed it into his mouth. "Might be I should of left you where I found you, boy. All of you. Safer in the city, seems to me."

"I don't care. I want to go home."

"Been bringing men to the Wall for close on thirty years." Froth shone on Yoren's lips, like bubbles of blood. "All that time, I only lost three. Old man died of a fever, city boy got snakebit taking a shit, and one fool tried to kill me in my sleep and got a red smile for his trouble." He drew the dirk across his throat, to show her. "Three in thirty years." He spat out the old sourleaf. "A ship now, might have been wiser. No chance o' finding more men on the way, but still . . . clever man, he'd go by ship, but me . . . thirty years I been taking this kingsroad." He sheathed his dirk. "Go to sleep, boy. Hear me?"

She did try. Yet as she lay under her thin blanket, she could hear the wolves howling . . . and another sound, fainter, no more than a whisper on the wind, that might have been screams.

DAVOS

The morning air was dark with the smoke of burning gods.

They were all afire now, Maid and Mother, Warrior and Smith, the Crone with her pearl eyes and the Father with his gilded beard; even the Stranger, carved to look more animal than human. The old dry wood and countless layers of paint and varnish blazed with a fierce hungry light. Heat rose shimmering through the chill air; behind, the gargoyles and stone dragons on the castle walls seemed blurred, as if Davos were seeing them through a veil of tears. *Or as if the beasts were trembling, stirring . . .*

"An ill thing," Allard declared, though at least he had the sense to keep his voice low. Dale muttered agreement.

"Silence," said Davos. "Remember where you are." His sons were good men, but young, and Allard especially was rash. *Had I stayed a smuggler, Allard would have ended on the Wall. Stannis spared him from that end, something else I owe him . . .*

Hundreds had come to the castle gates to bear witness to the burning of the Seven. The smell in the air was ugly. Even for soldiers, it was hard not to feel uneasy at such an affront to the gods most had worshiped all their lives.

The red woman walked round the fire three times, praying once in the speech of Asshai, once in High Valyrian, and once in the Common Tongue. Davos understood only the last. "R'hllor, come to us in our darkness," she called. "Lord of Light, we offer you these false gods, these seven who are one, and him the enemy. Take them and cast your light upon us, for the night is dark and full of terrors." Queen Selyse echoed the words. Beside her, Stannis watched impassively, his jaw hard as stone under the blue-black shadow of his tight-cropped beard. He had dressed more richly than was his wont, as if for the sept.

Dragonstone's sept had been where Aegon the Conqueror knelt to pray the night before he sailed. That had not saved it from the queen's men. They had overturned the altars, pulled down the statues, and smashed the stained glass with warhammers. Septon Barre could only curse them, but Ser Hubard Rambton led his three sons to the sept to defend their gods. The Rambtons had slain four of the queen's men before the others overwhelmed them. Afterward Guncer Sunglass, mildest and most pious of lords, told Stannis he could no longer support his claim. Now he shared a sweltering cell with the septon and Ser Hubard's two surviving sons. The other lords had not been slow to take the lesson.

The gods had never meant much to Davos the smuggler, though like most men he had been known to make offerings to the Warrior before battle, to the Smith when he launched a ship, and to the Mother whenever his wife grew great with child. He felt ill as he watched them burn, and not only from the smoke.

Maester Cressen would have stopped this. The old man had challenged the Lord of Light and been struck down for his impiety, or so the gossips told each other. Davos knew the truth. He had seen the maester slip something into the wine cup. *Poison. What else could it be? He drank a cup of death to free Stannis from Melisandre, but somehow her god shielded her.* He would gladly have killed the red woman for that, yet what chance would he have where a maester of the Citadel had failed? He was only a smuggler raised high, Davos of Flea Bottom, the Onion Knight.

The burning gods cast a pretty light, wreathed in their robes of shifting flame, red and orange and yellow. Septon Barre had once told Davos how they'd been carved from the masts of the ships that had carried the first Targaryens from Valyria. Over the centuries, they had been painted and repainted, gilded, silvered, jeweled. "Their beauty will make them more pleasing to R'hllor," Melisandre said when she told Stannis to pull them down and drag them out the castle gates.

The Maiden lay athwart the Warrior, her arms widespread as if to embrace him. The Mother seemed almost to shudder as the flames came licking up her face. A longsword had been thrust through her heart, and its leather grip was alive with flame. The Father was on the bottom, the first to fall. Davos watched the hand of the Stranger writhe and curl as the fingers blackened and fell away one by one, reduced to so much glowing charcoal. Nearby, Lord Celtigar coughed fitfully and covered his wrinkled face with a square of linen embroidered in red crabs. The Myrmen swapped jokes as they enjoyed the warmth of the fire, but young Lord Bar Emmon had turned a splotchy grey, and Lord Velaryon was watching the king rather than the conflagration.

Davos would have given much to know what he was thinking, but one such as Velaryon would never confide in him. The Lord of the Tides was of the blood of ancient Valyria, and his House had thrice provided brides for Targaryen princes; Davos Seaworth stank of fish and onions. It was the same with the other lordlings. He could trust none of them, nor would they ever include him in their private councils. They scorned his sons as well. *My grandsons will joust with theirs, though, and one day their blood may wed with mine. In time my*

*little black ship will fly as high as Velaryon's seahorse
or Celtigar's red crabs.*

That is, if Stannis won his throne. If he lost . . .

Everything I am, I owe to him. Stannis had raised
him to knighthood. He had given him a place of honor
at his table, a war galley to sail in place of a smuggler's
skiff. Dale and Allard captained galleys as well, Maric
was oarmaster on the *Fury*, Matthos served his father
on *Black Betha*, and the king had taken Devan as a
royal squire. One day he would be knighted, and the
two little lads as well. Marya was mistress of a small
keep on Cape Wrath, with servants who called her
m'lady, and Davos could hunt red deer in his own
woods. All this he had of Stannis Baratheon, for the
price of a few finger joints. *It was just, what he did to
me. I had flouted the king's laws all my life. He has
earned my loyalty.* Davos touched the little pouch that
hung from the leather thong about his neck. His fingers
were his luck, and he needed luck now. *As do we all.
Lord Stannis most of all.*

Pale flames licked at the grey sky. Dark smoke rose,
twisting and curling. When the wind pushed it toward
them, men blinked and wept and rubbed their eyes.
Allard turned his head away, coughing and cursing. *A
taste of things to come,* thought Davos. Many and more
would burn before this war was done.

Melisandre was robed all in scarlet satin and blood
velvet, her eyes as red as the great ruby that glistened at
her throat as if it too were afire. "In ancient books of
Asshai it is written that there will come a day after a
long summer when the stars bleed and the cold breath
of darkness falls heavy on the world. In this dread hour
a warrior shall draw from the fire a burning sword. And
that sword shall be Lightbringer, the Red Sword of Heroes, and he who clasps it shall be Azor Ahai come
again, and the darkness shall flee before him." She lifted
her voice, so it carried out over the gathered host. *"Azor
Ahai, beloved of R'hllor! The Warrior of Light, the Son
of Fire! Come forth, your sword awaits you! Come forth
and take it into your hand!"*

Stannis Baratheon strode forward like a soldier marching into battle. His squires stepped up to attend him. Davos watched as his son Devan pulled a long padded glove over the king's right hand. The boy wore a cream-colored doublet with a fiery heart sewn on the breast. Bryen Farring was similarly garbed as he tied a stiff leather cape around His Grace's neck. Behind, Davos heard a faint clank and clatter of bells. "Under the sea, smoke rises in bubbles, and flames burn green and blue and black," Patchface sang somewhere. "I know, I know, oh, oh, oh."

The king plunged into the fire with his teeth clenched, holding the leather cloak before him to keep off the flames. He went straight to the Mother, grasped the sword with his gloved hand, and wrenched it free of the burning wood with a single hard jerk. Then he was retreating, the sword held high, jade-green flames swirling around cherry-red steel. Guards rushed to beat out the cinders that clung to the king's clothing.

"A sword of fire!" shouted Queen Selyse. Ser Axell Florent and the other queen's men took up the cry. *"A sword of fire! It burns! It burns! A sword of fire!"*

Melisandre lifted her hands above her head. *"Behold! A sign was promised, and now a sign is seen! Behold Lightbringer! Azor Ahai has come again! All hail the Warrior of Light! All hail the Son of Fire!"*

A ragged wave of shouts gave answer, just as Stannis's glove began to smolder. Cursing, the king thrust the point of the sword into the damp earth and beat out the flames against his leg.

"Lord, cast your light upon us!" Melisandre called out.

"For the night is dark and full of terrors," Selyse and her queen's men replied. *Should I speak the words as well?* Davos wondered. *Do I owe Stannis that much? Is this fiery god truly his own?* His shortened fingers twitched.

Stannis peeled off the glove and let it fall to the ground. The gods in the pyre were scarcely recognizable anymore. The head fell off the Smith with a puff of ash and embers. Melisandre sang in the tongue of Asshai, her voice rising and falling like the tides of the sea. Stannis untied his singed leather cape and listened in silence. Thrust in the ground, Lightbringer still glowed ruddy hot, but the flames that clung to the sword were dwindling and dying.

By the time the song was done, only charwood remained of the gods, and the king's patience had run its course. He took the queen by the elbow and escorted her back into Dragonstone, leaving Lightbringer where it stood. The red woman remained a moment to watch as Devan knelt with Byren Farring and rolled up the burnt and blackened sword in the king's leather cloak. *The Red Sword of Heroes looks a proper mess*, thought Davos.

A few of the lords lingered to speak in quiet voices upwind of the fire. They fell silent when they saw Davos looking at them. *Should Stannis fall, they will pull me down in an instant.* Neither was he counted one of the queen's men, that group of ambitious knights and minor lordlings who had given themselves to this Lord of Light and so won the favor and patronage of Lady—*no, Queen, remember?*—Selyse.

The fire had started to dwindle by the time Melisandre and the squires departed with the precious sword. Davos and his sons joined the crowd making its way down to the shore and the waiting ships. "Devan acquitted himself well," he said as they went.

"He fetched the glove without dropping it, yes," said Dale.

Allard nodded. "That badge on Devan's doublet, the fiery heart, what was that? The Baratheon sigil is a crowned stag."

"A lord can choose more than one badge," Davos said.

Dale smiled. "A black ship *and* an onion, Father?"

Allard kicked at a stone. "The Others take our onion . . . *and* that flaming heart. It was an ill thing to burn the Seven."

"When did you grow so devout?" Davos said. "What does a smuggler's son know of the doings of gods?"

"I'm a knight's son, Father. If you won't remember, why should they?"

"A knight's son, but not a knight," said Davos. "Nor will you ever be, if you meddle in affairs that do not concern you. Stannis is our rightful king, it is not for us to question him. We sail his ships and do his bidding. That is all."

"As to that, Father," Dale said, "I mislike these water casks they've given me for *Wraith*. Green pine. The water will spoil on a voyage of any length."

"I got the same for *Lady Marya*," said Allard. "The queen's men have laid claim to all the seasoned wood."

"I will speak to the king about it," Davos promised. Better it come from him than from Allard. His sons were good fighters and better sailors, but they did not know how to talk to lords. *They were lowborn, even as I was, but they do not like to recall that. When they look at our banner, all they see is a tall black ship flying on the wind. They close their eyes to the onion.*

The port was as crowded as Davos had ever known it. Every dock teemed with sailors loading provisions, and every inn was packed with soldiers dicing or drinking or looking for a whore . . . a vain search, since Stannis permitted none on his island. Ships lined the strand; war galleys and fishing vessels, stout carracks and fat-bottomed cogs. The best berths had been taken by the largest vessels: Stannis's flagship *Fury* rocking between *Lord Steffon* and *Stag of the Sea*, Lord Velaryon's silver-hulled *Pride of Driftmark* and her three sisters, Lord Celtigar's ornate *Red Claw*, the ponderous *Swordfish* with her long iron prow. Out to sea at anchor rode Salladhor Saan's great *Valyrian* amongst the striped hulls of two dozen smaller Lysene galleys.

A weathered little inn sat on the end of the stone pier where *Black Betha*, *Wraith*, and *Lady Marya* shared mooring space with a half-dozen other galleys of one hundred oars or less. Davos had a thirst. He took his leave of his sons and turned his steps toward the inn. Out front squatted a waist-high gargoyle, so eroded by rain and salt that his features were all but obliterated.

He and Davos were old friends, though. He gave a pat to the stone head as he went in. "Luck," he murmured.

Across the noisy common room, Salladhor Saan sat eating grapes from a wooden bowl. When he spied Davos, he beckoned him closer. "Ser knight, come sit with me. Eat a grape. Eat two. They are marvelously sweet." The Lyseni was a sleek, smiling man whose flamboyance was a byword on both sides of the narrow sea. Today he wore flashing cloth-of-silver, with dagged sleeves so long the ends of them pooled on the floor. His buttons were carved jade monkeys, and atop his wispy white curls perched a jaunty green cap decorated with a fan of peacock feathers.

Davos threaded his way through the tables to a chair. In the days before his knighthood, he had often bought cargoes from Salladhor Saan. The Lyseni was a smuggler himself, as well as a trader, a banker, a notorious pirate, and the self-styled Prince of the Narrow Sea. *When a pirate grows rich enough, they make him a prince.* It had been Davos who had made the journey to Lys to recruit the old rogue to Lord Stannis's cause.

"You did not see the gods burn, my lord?" he asked.

"The red priests have a great temple on Lys. Always they are burning this and burning that, crying out to their R'hllor. They bore me with their fires. Soon they will bore King Stannis too, it is to be hoped." He seemed utterly unconcerned that someone might over-hear him, eating his grapes and dribbling the seeds out onto his lip, flicking them off with a finger. "My *Bird of Thousand Colors* came in yesterday, good ser. She is not a warship, no, but a trader, and she paid a call on King's Landing. Are you sure you will not have a grape? Chil-dren go hungry in the city, it is said." He dangled the grapes before Davos and smiled.

"It's ale I need, and news."

"The men of Westeros are ever rushing," complained Salladhor Saan. "What good is this, I ask you? He who hurries through life hurries to his grave." He belched. "The Lord of Casterly Rock has sent his dwarf to see to King's Landing. Perhaps he hopes that his ugly face will frighten off attackers, eh? Or that we will laugh ourselves dead when the Imp capers on the battlements, who can say? The dwarf has chased off the lout who ruled the gold cloaks and put in his place a knight with an iron hand." He plucked a grape, and squeezed it between thumb and forefinger until the skin burst. Juice ran down between his fingers.

A serving girl pushed her way through, swatting at the hands that groped her as she passed. Davos ordered a tankard of ale, turned back to Saan, and said, "How well is the city defended?"

The other shrugged. "The walls are high and strong, but who will man them? They are building scorpions and spitfires, oh, yes, but the men in the golden cloaks are too few and too green, and there are no others. A swift strike, like a hawk plummeting at a hare, and the great city will be ours. Grant us wind to fill our sails, and your king could sit upon his Iron Throne by evenfall on the morrow. We could dress the dwarf in motley and prick his little cheeks with the points of our spears to make him dance for us, and mayhaps your goodly king would make me a gift of the beautiful Queen Cersei to warm my bed for a night. I have been too long away from my wives, and all in his service."

"Pirate," said Davos. "You have no wives, only concubines, and you have been well paid for every day and every ship."

"Only in promises," said Salladhor Saan mournfully. "Good ser, it is gold I crave, not words on papers." He popped a grape into his mouth.

"You'll have your gold when we take the treasury in King's Landing. No man in the Seven Kingdoms is more honorable than Stannis Baratheon. He will keep his word." Even as Davos spoke, he thought, *This world is twisted beyond hope, when lowborn smugglers must vouch for the honor of kings.*

"So he has said and said. And so I say, let us do this thing. Even these grapes could be no more ripe than that city, my old friend."

The serving girl returned with his ale. Davos gave her

a copper. "Might be we could take King's Landing, as you say," he said as he lifted the tankard, "but how long would we hold it? Tywin Lannister is known to be at Harrenhal with a great host, and Lord Renly . . ."

"Ah, yes, the young brother," said Salladhor Saan. "That part is not so good, my friend. King Renly bestirs himself. No, here he is *Lord* Renly, my pardons. So many kings, my tongue grows weary of the word. The brother Renly has left Highgarden with his fair young queen, his flowered lords and shining knights, and a mighty host of foot. He marches up your road of roses toward the very same great city we were speaking of."

"He takes his *bride*?"

The other shrugged. "He did not tell me why. Perhaps he is loath to part with the warm burrow between her thighs, even for a night. Or perhaps he is that certain of his victory."

"The king must be told."

"I have attended to it, good ser. Though His Grace frowns so whenever he does see me that I tremble to come before him. Do you think he would like me better if I wore a hair shirt and never smiled? Well, I will not do it. I am an honest man, he must suffer me in silk and samite. Or else I shall take my ships where I am better loved. That sword was not Lightbringer, my friend."

The sudden shift in subject left Davos uneasy. "Sword?"

"A sword plucked from fire, yes. Men tell me things, it is my pleasant smile. How shall a burnt sword serve Stannis?"

"A *burning* sword," corrected Davos.

"Burnt," said Salladhor Saan, "and be glad of that, my friend. Do you know the tale of the forging of Lightbringer? I shall tell it to you. It was a time when darkness lay heavy on the world. To oppose it, the hero must have a hero's blade, oh, like none that had ever been. And so for thirty days and thirty nights Azor Ahai labored sleepless in the temple, forging a blade in the sacred fires. Heat and hammer and fold, heat and hammer and fold, oh, yes, until the sword was done. Yet when he plunged it into water to temper the steel it burst asunder.

"Being a hero, it was not for him to shrug and go in search of excellent grapes such as these, so again he began. The second time it took him fifty days and fifty nights, and this sword seemed even finer than the first. Azor Ahai captured a lion, to temper the blade by plunging it through the beast's red heart, but once more the steel shattered and split. Great was his woe and great was his sorrow then, for he knew what he must do.

"A hundred days and a hundred nights he labored on the third blade, and as it glowed white-hot in the sacred fires, he summoned his wife. 'Nissa Nissa,' he said to her, for that was her name, 'bare your breast, and know that I love you best of all that is in this world.' She did this thing, why I cannot say, and Azor Ahai thrust the smoking sword through her living heart. It is said that her cry of anguish and ecstasy left a crack across the face of the moon, but her blood and her soul and her strength and her courage all went into the steel. Such is the tale of the forging of Lightbringer, the Red Sword of Heroes.

"Now do you see my meaning? Be glad that it is just a burnt sword that His Grace pulled from that fire. Too much light can hurt the eyes, my friend, and fire *burns*." Salladhor Saan finished the last grape and smacked his lips. "When do you think the king will bid us sail, good ser?"

"Soon, I think," said Davos, "if his god wills it."

"*His* god, ser friend? Not yours? Where is the god of Ser Davos Seaworth, knight of the onion ship?"

Davos sipped his ale to give himself a moment. *The inn is crowded, and you are not Salladhor Saan,* he reminded himself. *Be careful how you answer.* "King Stannis is my god. He made me and blessed me with his trust."

"I will remember." Salladhor Saan got to his feet. "My pardons. These grapes have given me a hunger, and dinner awaits on my *Valyrian*. Minced lamb with pepper and roasted gull stuffed with mushrooms and fennel and onion. Soon we shall eat together in King's Landing, yes? In the Red Keep we shall feast, while the dwarf sings us a jolly tune. When you speak to King Stannis, mention if you would that he will owe me another thirty thousand dragons come the black of the moon. He ought to have given those gods to me. They were too beautiful to burn, and might have brought a noble price in Pentos or Myr. Well, if he grants me Queen Cersei for a night I shall forgive him." The Lyseni clapped Davos on the back, and swaggered from the inn as if he owned it.

Ser Davos Seaworth lingered over his tankard for a good while, thinking. A year ago, he had been with Stannis in King's Landing when King Robert staged a tourney for Prince Joffrey's name day. He remembered the red priest Thoros of Myr, and the flaming sword he had wielded in the melee. The man had made for a colorful spectacle, his red robes flapping while his blade writhed with pale green flames, but everyone knew there was no true magic to it, and in the end his fire had guttered out and Bronze Yohn Royce had brained him with a common mace.

A true sword of fire, now, that would be a wonder to behold. Yet at such a cost . . . When he thought of Nissa Nissa, it was his own Marya he pictured, a good-natured plump woman with sagging breasts and a kindly smile, the best woman in the world. He tried to picture himself driving a sword through her, and shuddered. *I am not made of the stuff of heroes,* he decided. If that was the price of a magic sword, it was more than he cared to pay.

Davos finished his ale, pushed away the tankard, and left the inn. On the way out he patted the gargoyle on the head and muttered, "Luck." They would all need it.

It was well after dark when Devan came down to *Black Betha,* leading a snow-white palfrey. "My lord father," he announced, "His Grace commands you to attend him in the Chamber of the Painted Table. You are to ride the horse and come at once."

It was good to see Devan looking so splendid in his squire's raiment, but the summons made Davos uneasy. *Will he bid us sail?* he wondered. Salladhor Saan was not the only captain who felt that King's Landing was ripe for an attack, but a smuggler must learn patience. *We have no hope of victory. I said as much to Maester Cressen, the day I returned to Dragonstone, and nothing has changed. We are too few, the foes too many. If we dip our oars, we die.* Nonetheless, he climbed onto the horse.

When Davos arrived at the Stone Drum, a dozen highborn knights and great bannermen were just leaving. Lords Celtigar and Velaryon each gave him a curt nod and walked on while the others ignored him utterly, but Ser Axell Florent stopped for a word.

Queen Selyse's uncle was a keg of a man with thick arms and bandy legs. He had the prominent ears of a Florent, even larger than his niece's. The coarse hair that sprouted from his did not stop him hearing most of what went on in the castle. For ten years Ser Axell had served as castellan of Dragonstone while Stannis sat on Robert's council in King's Landing, but of late he had emerged as the foremost of the queen's men. "Ser Davos, it is good to see you, as ever," he said.

"And you, my lord."

"I made note of you this morning as well. The false gods burned with a merry light, did they not?"

"They burned brightly." Davos did not trust this man, for all his courtesy. House Florent had declared for Renly.

"The Lady Melisandre tells us that sometimes R'hllor permits his faithful servants to glimpse the future in flames. It seemed to me as I watched the fire this morning that I was looking at a dozen beautiful dancers, maidens garbed in yellow silk spinning and swirling before a great king. I think it was a true vision, ser. A glimpse of the glory that awaits His Grace after we take King's Landing and the throne that is his by rights."

Stannis has no taste for such dancing, Davos

thought, but he dared not offend the queen's uncle. "I saw only fire," he said, "but the smoke was making my eyes water. You must pardon me, ser, the king awaits." He pushed past, wondering why Ser Axell had troubled himself. *He is a queen's man and I am the king's.*

Stannis sat at his Painted Table with Maester Pylos at his shoulder, an untidy pile of papers before them. "Ser," the king said when Davos entered, "come have a look at this letter."

Obediently, he selected a paper at random. "It looks handsome enough, Your Grace, but I fear I cannot read the words." Davos could decipher maps and charts as well as any, but letters and other writings were beyond his powers. *But my Devan has learned his letters, and young Steffon and Stannis as well.*

"I'd forgotten." A furrow of irritation showed between the king's brows. "Pylos, read it to him."

"Your Grace." The maester took up one of the parchments and cleared his throat. *"All men know me for the trueborn son of Steffon Baratheon, Lord of Storm's End, by his lady wife Cassana of House Estermont. I declare upon the honor of my House that my beloved brother Robert, our late king, left no trueborn issue of his body, the boy Joffrey, the boy Tommen, and the girl Myrcella being abominations born of incest between Cersei Lannister and her brother Jaime the Kingslayer. By right of birth and blood, I do this day lay claim to the Iron Throne of the Seven Kingdoms of Westeros. Let all true men declare their loyalty. Done in the Light of the Lord, under the sign and seal of Stannis of House Baratheon, the First of His Name, King of the Andals, the Rhoynar, and the First Men, and Lord of the Seven Kingdoms."* The parchment rustled softly as Pylos laid it down.

"Make it *Ser* Jaime the Kingslayer henceforth," Stannis said, frowning. "Whatever else the man may be, he remains a knight. I don't know that we ought to call Robert my *beloved* brother either. He loved me no more than he had to, nor I him."

"A harmless courtesy, Your Grace," Pylos said.

"A lie. Take it out." Stannis turned to Davos. "The maester tells me that we have one hundred seventeen ravens on hand. I mean to use them all. One hundred seventeen ravens will carry one hundred seventeen copies of my letter to every corner of the realm, from the Arbor to the Wall. Perhaps a hundred will win through against storm and hawk and arrow. If so, a hundred maesters will read my words to as many lords in as many solars and bedchambers . . . and then the letters will like as not be consigned to the fire, and lips pledged to silence. These great lords love Joffrey, or Renly, or Robb Stark. I am their rightful king, but they will deny me if they can. So I have need of you."

"I am yours to command, my king. As ever."

Stannis nodded. "I mean for you to sail *Black Betha* north, to Gulltown, the Fingers, the Three Sisters, even White Harbor. Your son Dale will go south in *Wraith*, past Cape Wrath and the Broken Arm, all along the coast of Dorne as far as the Arbor. Each of you will carry a chest of letters, and you will deliver one to every port and holdfast and fishing village. Nail them to the doors of septs and inns for every man to read who can."

Davos said, "That will be few enough."

"Ser Davos speaks truly, Your Grace," said Maester Pylos. "It would be better to have the letters read aloud."

"Better, but more dangerous," said Stannis. "These words will not be kindly received."

"Give me knights to do the reading," Davos said. "That will carry more weight than anything I might say."

Stannis seemed well satisfied with that. "I can give you such men, yes. I have a hundred knights who would sooner read than fight. Be open where you can and stealthy where you must. Use every smuggler's trick you know, the black sails, the hidden coves, whatever it requires. If you run short of letters, capture a few septons and set them to copying out more. I mean to use your second son as well. He will take *Lady Marya* across the narrow sea, to Braavos and the other Free Cities, to deliver other letters to the men who rule there. The world will know of my claim, and of Cersei's infamy."

You can tell them, Davos thought, *but will they believe?* He glanced thoughtfully at Maester Pylos. The king caught the look. "Maester, perhaps you ought get to your writing. We will need a great many letters, and soon."

"As you will." Pylos bowed, and took his leave.

The king waited until he was gone before he said, "What is it you would not say in the presence of my maester, Davos?"

"My liege, Pylos is pleasant enough, but I cannot see the chain about his neck without mourning for Maester Cressen."

"Is it his fault the old man died?" Stannis glanced into the fire. "I never wanted Cressen at that feast. He'd angered me, yes, he'd given me bad counsel, but I did not want him dead. I'd hoped he might be granted a few years of ease and comfort. He had earned that much, at least, but"—he ground his teeth together—"but he died. And Pylos serves me ably."

"Pylos is the least of it. The letter . . . What did your lords make of it, I wonder?"

Stannis snorted. "Celtigar pronounced it admirable. If I showed him the contents of my privy, he would declare that admirable as well. The others bobbed their heads up and down like a flock of .geese, all but Velaryon, who said that steel would decide the matter, not words on parchment. As if I had never suspected. The Others take my lords, I'll hear your views."

"Your words were blunt and strong."

"And true."

"And true. Yet you have no proof. Of this incest. No more than you did a year ago."

"There's proof of a sort at Storm's End. Robert's bastard. The one he fathered on my wedding night, in the very bed they'd made up for me and my bride. Delena was a Florent, and a maiden when he took her, so Robert acknowledged the babe. Edric Storm, they call him. He is said to be the very image of my brother. If men were to see him, and then look again at Joffrey and Tommen, they could not help but wonder, I would think."

"Yet how are men to see him, if he is at Storm's End?"

Stannis drummed his fingers on the Painted Table. "It is a difficulty. One of many." He raised his eyes. "You have more to say about the letter. Well, get on with it. I did not make you a knight so you could learn to mouth empty courtesies. I have my lords for that. Say what you would say, Davos."

Davos bowed his head. "There was a phrase at the end. How did it go? *Done in the Light of the Lord . . .*"

"Yes." The king's jaw was clenched.

"Your people will mislike those words."

"As you did?" said Stannis sharply.

"If you were to say instead, *Done in the sight of gods and men,* or *By the grace of the gods old and new . . .*"

"Have you gone devout on me, smuggler?"

"That was to be my question for you, my liege."

"Was it now? It sounds as though you love my new god no more than you love my new maester."

"I do not know this Lord of Light," Davos admitted, "but I knew the gods we burned this morning. The Smith has kept my ships safe, while the Mother has given me seven strong sons."

"Your wife has given you seven strong sons. Do you pray to her? It was wood we burned this morning."

"That may be so," Davos said, "but when I was a boy in Flea Bottom begging for a copper, sometimes the septons would feed me."

"*I* feed you now."

"You have given me an honored place at your table. And in return I give you truth. Your people will not love you if you take from them the gods they have always worshiped, and give them one whose very name sounds queer on their tongues."

Stannis stood abruptly. *"R'hllor.* Why is that so hard? They will not love me, you say? When have they ever loved me? How can I lose something I have never owned?" He moved to the south window to gaze out at the moonlit sea. "I stopped believing in gods the day I saw the *Windproud* break up across the bay. Any gods so monstrous as to drown my mother and father would never have *my* worship, I vowed. In King's Landing, the High Septon would prattle at me of how all justice and goodness flowed from the Seven, but all I ever saw of either was made by men."

"If you do not believe in gods—"

"—why trouble with this new one?" Stannis broke in. "I have asked myself as well. I know little and care less of gods, but the red priestess has power."

Yes, but what sort of power? "Cressen had wisdom."

"I trusted in his wisdom and your wiles, and what did they avail me, smuggler? The storm lords sent you packing. I went to them a beggar and they laughed at me. Well, there will be no more begging, and no more laughing either. The Iron Throne is mine by rights, but how am I to take it? There are four kings in the realm, and three of them have more men and more gold than I do. I have ships . . . and I have *her.* The red woman. Half my knights are afraid even to say her name, did you know? If she can do nothing else, a sorceress who can inspire such dread in grown men is not to be despised. A frightened man is a beaten man. And perhaps she *can* do more. I mean to find out.

"When I was a lad I found an injured goshawk and nursed her back to health. *Proudwing,* I named her. She would perch on my shoulder and flutter from room to room after me and take food from my hand, but she would not soar. Time and again I would take her hawking, but she never flew higher than the treetops. Robert called her *Weakwing.* He owned a gyrfalcon named Thunderclap who never missed her strike. One day our great-uncle Ser Harbert told me to try a different bird. I was making a fool of myself with Proudwing, he said,

and he was right." Stannis Baratheon turned away from
the window, and the ghosts who moved upon the southern sea. "The Seven have never brought me so much as
a sparrow. It is time I tried another hawk, Davos. A *red*
hawk."

THEON

There was no safe anchorage at Pyke, but Theon
Greyjoy wished to look on his father's castle
from the sea, to see it as he had seen it last, ten
years before, when Robert Baratheon's war galley had
borne him away to be a ward of Eddard Stark. On that
day he had stood beside the rail, listening to the stroke
of the oars and the pounding of the master's drum while
he watched Pyke dwindle in the distance. Now he
wanted to see it grow larger, to rise from the sea before
him.

Obedient to his wishes, the *Myraham* beat her way
past the point with her sails snapping and her captain
cursing the wind and his crew and the follies of highborn lordlings. Theon drew the hood of his cloak up
against the spray, and looked for home.

The shore was all sharp rocks and glowering cliffs,
and the castle seemed one with the rest, its towers and
walls and bridges quarried from the same grey-black
stone, wet by the same salt waves, festooned with the
same spreading patches of dark green lichen, speckled

by the droppings of the same seabirds. The point of land on which the Greyjoys had raised their fortress had once thrust like a sword into the bowels of the ocean, but the waves had hammered at it day and night until the land broke and shattered, thousands of years past. All that remained were three bare and barren islands and a dozen towering stacks of rock that rose from the water like the pillars of some sea god's temple, while the angry waves foamed and crashed among them.

Drear, dark, forbidding, Pyke stood atop those islands and pillars, almost a part of them, its curtain wall closing off the headland around the foot of the great stone bridge that leapt from the clifftop to the largest islet, dominated by the massive bulk of the Great Keep. Farther out were the Kitchen Keep and the Bloody Keep, each on its own island. Towers and outbuildings clung to the stacks beyond, linked to each other by covered archways when the pillars stood close, by long swaying walks of wood and rope when they did not.

The Sea Tower rose from the outmost island at the point of the broken sword, the oldest part of the castle, round and tall, the sheer-sided pillar on which it stood half-eaten through by the endless battering of the waves. The base of the tower was white from centuries of salt spray, the upper stories green from the lichen that crawled over it like a thick blanket, the jagged crown black with soot from its nightly watchfire.

Above the Sea Tower snapped his father's banner. The *Myraham* was too far off for Theon to see more than the cloth itself, but he knew the device it bore: the golden kraken of House Greyjoy, arms writhing and reaching against a black field. The banner streamed from an iron mast, shivering and twisting as the wind gusted, like a bird struggling to take flight. And here at least the direwolf of Stark did not fly above, casting its shadow down upon the Greyjoy kraken.

Theon had never seen a more stirring sight. In the sky behind the castle, the fine red tail of the comet was visible through thin, scuttling clouds. All the way from Riverrun to Seagard, the Mallisters had argued about its meaning. *It is my comet,* Theon told himself, sliding a hand into his fur-lined cloak to touch the oilskin pouch snug in its pocket. Inside was the letter Robb Stark had given him, paper as good as a crown.

"Does the castle look as you remember it, milord?" the captain's daughter asked as she pressed herself against his arm.

"It looks smaller," Theon confessed, "though perhaps that is only the distance." The *Myraham* was a fat-bellied southron merchanter up from Oldtown, carrying wine and cloth and seed to trade for iron ore. Her captain was a fat-bellied southron merchanter as well, and the stony sea that foamed at the feet of the castle made his plump lips quiver, so he stayed well out, farther than Theon would have liked. An ironborn captain in a longship would have taken them along the cliffs and under the high bridge that spanned the gap between the gatehouse and the Great Keep, but this plump Oldtowner had neither the craft, the crew, nor the courage to attempt such a thing. So they sailed past at a safe distance, and Theon must content himself with seeing Pyke from afar. Even so, the *Myraham* had to struggle mightily to keep itself off those rocks.

"It must be windy there," the captain's daughter observed.

He laughed. "Windy and cold and damp. A miserable hard place, in truth . . . but my lord father once told me that hard places breed hard men, and hard men rule the world."

The captain's face was as green as the sea when he came bowing up to Theon and asked, "May we make for port now, milord?"

"You may," Theon said, a faint smile playing about his lips. The promise of gold had turned the Oldtowner into a shameless lickspittle. It would have been a much different voyage if a longship from the islands had been waiting at Seagard as he'd hoped. Ironborn captains were proud and willful, and did not go in awe of a man's blood. The islands were too small for awe, and a longship smaller still. If every captain was a king aboard his own ship, as was often said, it was small wonder they named the islands the land of ten thousand kings. And when you have seen your kings shit over the rail and turn green in a storm, it was hard to bend the knee and pretend they were gods. "The Drowned God makes men," old King Urron Redhand had once said, thousands of years ago, "but it's men who make crowns."

A longship would have made the crossing in half the time as well. The *Myraham* was a wallowing tub, if truth be told, and he would not care to be aboard her in a storm. Still, Theon could not be too unhappy. He was here, undrowned, and the voyage had offered certain other amusements. He put an arm around the captain's daughter. "Summon me when we make Lordsport," he told her father. "We'll be below, in my cabin." He led the girl away aft, while her father watched them go in sullen silence.

The cabin was the captain's, in truth, but it had been turned over to Theon's use when they sailed from Seagard. The captain's daughter had not been turned over to his use, but she had come to his bed willingly enough all the same. A cup of wine, a few whispers, and there she was. The girl was a shade plump for his taste, with skin as splotchy as oatmeal, but her breasts filled his hands nicely and she had been a maiden the first time he took her. That was surprising at her age, but Theon found it diverting. He did not think the captain approved, and that was amusing as well, watching the man struggle to swallow his outrage while performing his courtesies to the high lord, the rich purse of gold he'd been promised never far from his thoughts.

As Theon shrugged out of his wet cloak, the girl said, "You must be so happy to see your home again, milord. How many years have you been away?"

"Ten, or close as makes no matter," he told her. "I was a boy of ten when I was taken to Winterfell as a ward of Eddard Stark." A ward in name, a hostage in truth. Half his days a hostage . . . but no longer. His life was his own again, and nowhere a Stark to be seen.

He drew the captain's daughter close and kissed her on her ear. "Take off your cloak."

She dropped her eyes, suddenly shy, but did as he bid her. When the heavy garment, sodden with spray, fell from her shoulders to the deck, she gave him a little bow and smiled anxiously. She looked rather stupid when she smiled, but he had never required a woman to be clever. "Come here," he told her.

She did. "I have never seen the Iron Islands."

"Count yourself fortunate." Theon stroked her hair. It was fine and dark, though the wind had made a tangle of it. "The islands are stern and stony places, scant of comfort and bleak of prospect. Death is never far here, and life is mean and meager. Men spend their nights drinking ale and arguing over whose lot is worse, the fisherfolk who fight the sea or the farmers who try and scratch a crop from the poor thin soil. If truth be told, the miners have it worse than either, breaking their backs down in the dark, and for what? Iron, lead, tin, those are our treasures. Small wonder the ironmen of old turned to raiding."

The stupid girl did not seem to be listening. "I could go ashore with you," she said. "I would, if it please you . . ."

"You could go ashore," Theon agreed, squeezing her breast, "but not with me, I fear."

"I'd work in your castle, milord. I can clean fish and bake bread and churn butter. Father says my peppercrab stew is the best he's ever tasted. You could find me a place in your kitchens and I could make you peppercrab stew."

"And warm my bed by night?" He reached for the laces of her bodice and began to undo them, his fingers deft and practiced. "Once I might have carried you home as a prize, and kept you to wife whether you willed it or no. The ironmen of old did such things. A man had his rock wife, his true bride, ironborn like himself, but he had his salt wives too, women captured on raids."

The girl's eyes grew wide, and not because he had bared her breasts. "I would be your salt wife, milord."

"I fear those days are gone." Theon's finger circled one heavy teat, spiraling in toward the fat brown nipple. "No longer may we ride the wind with fire and sword, taking what we want. Now we scratch in the ground and toss lines in the sea like other men, and count ourselves lucky if we have salt cod and porridge enough to get us through a winter." He took her nipple in his mouth, and bit it until she gasped.

"You can put it in me again, if it please you," she whispered in his ear as he sucked.

When he raised his head from her breast, the skin was dark red where his mouth had marked her. "It would please me to teach you something new. Unlace me and pleasure me with your mouth."

"With my mouth?"

His thumb brushed lightly over her full lips. "It's what those lips were made for, sweetling. If you were my salt wife, you'd do as I command."

She was timid at first, but learned quickly for such a stupid girl, which pleased him. Her mouth was as wet and sweet as her cunt, and this way he did not have to listen to her mindless prattle. *Once I would have kept her as a salt wife in truth,* he thought to himself as he slid his fingers through her tangled hair. *Once. When we still kept the Old Way, lived by the axe instead of the pick, taking what we would, be it wealth, women, or glory.* In those days, the ironborn did not work mines; that was labor for the captives brought back from the hostings, and so too the sorry business of farming and tending goats and sheep. War was an ironman's proper trade. The Drowned God had made them to reave and rape, to carve out kingdoms and write their names in fire and blood and song.

Aegon the Dragon had destroyed the Old Way when he burned Black Harren, gave Harren's kingdom back to the weakling rivermen, and reduced the Iron Islands to an insignificant backwater of a much greater realm. Yet the old red tales were still told around driftwood fires and smoky hearths all across the islands, even behind the high stone halls of Pyke. Theon's father numbered among his titles the style of Lord Reaper, and the Greyjoy words boasted that *We Do Not Sow.*

It had been to bring back the Old Way more than for the empty vanity of a crown that Lord Balon had staged his great rebellion. Robert Baratheon had written a bloody end to that hope, with the help of his friend Eddard Stark, but both men were dead now. Mere boys ruled in their stead, and the realm that Aegon the Conqueror had forged was smashed and sundered. *This is the season*, Theon thought as the captain's daughter slid her lips up and down the length of him, *the season, the year, the day, and I am the man.* He smiled crookedly, wondering what his father would say when Theon told him that he, the last-born, babe and hostage, *he* had succeeded where Lord Balon himself had failed.

His climax came on him sudden as a storm, and he filled the girl's mouth with his seed. Startled, she tried to pull away, but Theon held her tight by the hair. Afterward, she crawled up beside him. "Did I please milord?"

"Well enough," he told her.

"It tasted salty," she murmured.

"Like the sea?"

She nodded. "I have always loved the sea, milord."

"As I have," he said, rolling her nipple idly between his fingers. It was true. The sea meant freedom to the men of the Iron Islands. He had forgotten that until the *Myraham* had raised sail at Seagard. The sounds brought old feelings back; the creak of wood and rope, the captain's shouted commands, the snap of the sails as the wind filled them, each as familiar as the beating of his own heart, and as comforting. *I must remember this*, Theon vowed to himself. *I must never go far from the sea again.*

"Take me with you, milord," the captain's daughter begged. "I don't need to go to your castle. I can stay in some town, and be your salt wife." She reached out to stroke his cheek.

Theon Greyjoy pushed her hand aside and climbed off the bunk. "My place is Pyke, and yours is on this ship."

"I can't stay here now."

He laced up his breeches. "Why not?"

"My father," she told him. "Once you're gone, he'll punish me, milord. He'll call me names and hit me."

Theon swept his cloak off its peg and over his shoulders. "Fathers are like that," he admitted as he pinned the folds with a silver clasp. "Tell him he should be pleased. As many times as I've fucked you, you're likely with child. It's not every man who has the honor of raising a king's bastard." She looked at him stupidly, so he left her there.

The *Myraham* was rounding a wooded point. Below the pine-clad bluffs, a dozen fishing boats were pulling in their nets. The big cog stayed well out from them, tacking. Theon moved to the bow for a better view. He saw the castle first, the stronghold of the Botleys. When he was a boy it had been timber and wattle, but Robert Baratheon had razed that structure to the ground. Lord Sawane had rebuilt in stone, for now a small square keep crowned the hill. Pale green flags drooped from the squat corner towers, each emblazoned with a shoal of silvery fish.

Beneath the dubious protection of the fish-ridden little castle lay the village of Lordsport, its harbor aswarm with ships. When last he'd seen Lordsport, it had been a smoking wasteland, the skeletons of burnt longships and smashed galleys littering the stony shore like the bones of dead leviathans, the houses no more than broken walls and cold ashes. After ten years, few traces of the war remained. The smallfolk had built new hovels with the stones of the old, and cut fresh sod for their roofs. A new inn had risen beside the landing, twice the size of the old one, with a lower story of cut stone and two upper stories of timber. The sept beyond had never been rebuilt, though; only a seven-sided foundation remained where it had stood. Robert Baratheon's fury had soured the ironmen's taste for the new gods, it would seem.

Theon was more interested in ships than gods. Among the masts of countless fishing boats, he spied a Tyroshi trading galley off-loading beside a lumbering Ibbenese cog with her black-tarred hull. A great number of longships, fifty or sixty at the least, stood out to sea or lay beached on the pebbled shore to the north. Some of the sails bore devices from the other islands; the blood moon of Wynch, Lord Goodbrother's banded black warhorn, Harlaw's silver scythe. Theon searched for his uncle Euron's *Silence*. Of that lean and terrible red ship he saw no sign, but his father's *Great Kraken* was there, her bow ornamented with a grey iron ram in the shape of its namesake.

Had Lord Balon anticipated him and called the Greyjoy banners? His hand went inside his cloak again, to the oilskin pouch. No one knew of his letter but Robb Stark; they were no fools, to entrust their secrets to a bird. Still, Lord Balon was no fool either. He might well have guessed why his son was coming home at long last, and acted accordingly.

The thought did not please him. His father's war was long done, and lost. This was Theon's hour—his plan, his glory, and in time his crown. *Yet if the longships are hosting . . .*

It might be only a caution, now that he thought on it. A defensive move, lest the war spill out across the sea. Old men were cautious by nature. His father was old now, and so too his uncle Victarion, who commanded the Iron Fleet. His uncle Euron was a different song, to be sure, but the *Silence* did not seem to be in port. *It's all for the good,* Theon told himself. *This way, I shall be able to strike all the more quickly.*

As the *Myraham* made her way landward, Theon paced the deck restlessly, scanning the shore. He had not thought to find Lord Balon himself at quayside, but surely his father would have sent someone to meet him. Sylas Sourmouth the steward, Lord Botley, perhaps even Dagmer Cleftjaw. It would be good to look on Dagmer's hideous old face again. It was not as though they had no word of his arrival. Robb had sent ravens from Riverrun, and when they'd found no longship at Seagard, Jason Mallister had sent his own birds to Pyke, supposing that Robb's were lost.

Yet he saw no familiar faces, no honor guard waiting to escort him from Lordsport to Pyke, only smallfolk going about their small business. Shorehands rolled casks of wine off the Tyroshi trader, fisherfolk cried the day's catch, children ran and played. A priest in the sea-water robes of the Drowned God was leading a pair of horses along the pebbled shore, while above him a slat-tern leaned out a window in the inn, calling out to some passing Ibbenese sailors.

A handful of Lordsport merchants had gathered to meet the ship. They shouted questions as the *Myraham* was tying up. "We're out of Oldtown," the captain called down, "bearing apples and oranges, wines from the Arbor, feathers from the Summer Isles. I have pep-per, woven leathers, a bolt of Myrish lace, mirrors for milady, a pair of Oldtown woodharps sweet as any you ever heard." The gangplank descended with a creak and a thud. "And I've brought your heir back to you."

The Lordsport men gazed on Theon with blank, bo-vine eyes, and he realized that they did not know who he was. It made him angry. He pressed a golden dragon into the captain's palm. "Have your men bring my things." Without waiting for a reply, he strode down the gangplank. "Innkeeper," he barked, "I require a horse."

"As you say, m'lord," the man responded, without so much as a bow. He had forgotten how bold the ironborn could be. "Happens as I have one might do. Where would you be riding, m'lord?"

"Pyke." The fool *still* did not know him. He should have worn his good doublet, with the kraken embroi-dered on the breast.

"You'll want to be off soon, to reach Pyke afore dark," the innkeeper said. "My boy will go with you and show you the way."

"Your boy will not be needed," a deep voice called, "nor your horse. I shall see my nephew back to his fa-ther's house."

The speaker was the priest he had seen leading the horses along the shoreline. As the man approached, the smallfolk bent the knee, and Theon heard the innkeeper murmur, "Damphair."

Tall and thin, with fierce black eyes and a beak of a nose, the priest was garbed in mottled robes of green and grey and blue, the swirling colors of the Drowned God. A waterskin hung under his arm on a leather strap, and ropes of dried seaweed were braided through his waist-long black hair and untrimmed beard.

A memory prodded at Theon. In one of his rare curt letters, Lord Balon had written of his youngest brother going down in a storm, and turning holy when he washed up safe on shore. "Uncle Aeron?" he said doubtfully.

"Nephew Theon," the priest replied. "Your lord father bid me fetch you. Come."

"In a moment, Uncle." He turned back to the *Myraham*. "My things," he commanded the captain.

A sailor fetched him down his tall yew bow and quiver of arrows, but it was the captain's daughter who brought the pack with his good clothing. "Milord." Her eyes were red. When he took the pack, she made as if to embrace him, there in front of her own father and his priestly uncle and half the island.

Theon turned deftly aside. "You have my thanks."

"Please," she said, "I do love you well, milord."

"I must go." He hurried after his uncle, who was already well down the pier. Theon caught him with a dozen long strides. "I had not looked for you, Uncle. After ten years, I thought perhaps my lord father and lady mother might come themselves, or send Dagmer with an honor guard."

"It is not for you to question the commands of the Lord Reaper of Pyke." The priest's manner was chilly, most unlike the man Theon remembered. Aeron Greyjoy had been the most amiable of his uncles, feckless and quick to laugh, fond of songs, ale, and women. "As to Dagmer, the Cleftjaw is gone to Old Wyk at your father's behest, to roust the Stonehouses and the Drumms."

"To what purpose? Why are the longships hosting?"

"Why have longships ever hosted?" His uncle had left the horses tied up in front of the waterside inn. When they reached them, he turned to Theon. "Tell me true, nephew. Do you pray to the wolf gods now?"

Theon seldom prayed at all, but that was not something you confessed to a priest, even your father's own brother. "Ned Stark prayed to a tree. No, I care nothing for Stark's gods."

"Good. Kneel."

The ground was all stones and mud. "Uncle, I—"

"*Kneel.* Or are you too proud now, a lordling of the green lands come among us?"

Theon knelt. He had a purpose here, and might need Aeron's help to achieve it. A crown was worth a little mud and horseshit on his breeches, he supposed.

"Bow your head." Lifting the skin, his uncle pulled the cork and directed a thin stream of seawater down upon Theon's head. It drenched his hair and ran over his forehead into his eyes. Sheets washed down his cheeks, and a finger crept under his cloak and doublet and down his back, a cold rivulet along his spine. The salt made his eyes burn, until it was all he could do not to cry out. He could taste the ocean on his lips. "Let Theon your servant be born again from the sea, as you were," Aeron Greyjoy intoned. "Bless him with salt, bless him with stone, bless him with steel. Nephew, do you still know the words?"

"What is dead may never die," Theon said, remembering.

"What is dead may never die," his uncle echoed, "but rises again, harder and stronger. Stand."

Theon stood, blinking back tears from the salt in his eyes. Wordless, his uncle corked the waterskin, untied his horse, and mounted. Theon did the same. They set off together, leaving the inn and the harbor behind them, up past the castle of Lord Botley into the stony hills. The priest ventured no further word.

"I have been half my life away from home," Theon ventured at last. "Will I find the islands changed?"

"Men fish the sea, dig in the earth, and die. Women birth children in blood and pain, and die. Night follows day. The winds and tides remain. The islands are as our god made them."

Gods, he has grown grim, Theon thought. "Will I find my sister and my lady mother at Pyke?"

"You will not. Your mother dwells on Harlaw, with her own sister. It is less raw there, and her cough troubles her. Your sister has taken *Black Wind* to Great Wyk, with messages from your lord father. She will return e'er long, you may be sure."

Theon did not need to be told that *Black Wind* was Asha's longship. He had not seen his sister in ten years, but that much he knew of her. Odd that she would call it that, when Robb Stark had a wolf named Grey Wind. "Stark is grey and Greyjoy's black," he murmured, smiling, "but it seems we're both windy."

The priest had nothing to say to that.

"And what of you, Uncle?" Theon asked. "You were no priest when I was taken from Pyke. I remember how you would sing the old reaving songs standing on the table with a horn of ale in hand."

"Young I was, and vain," Aeron Greyjoy said, "but the sea washed my follies and my vanities away. That man drowned, nephew. His lungs filled with seawater, and the fish ate the scales off his eyes. When I rose again, I saw clearly."

He is as mad as he is sour. Theon had liked what he remembered of the old Aeron Greyjoy. "Uncle, why has my father called his swords and sails?"

"Doubtless he will tell you at Pyke."

"I would know his plans now."

"From me, you shall not. We are commanded not to speak of this to any man."

"Even to *me*?" Theon's anger flared. He'd led men in war, hunted with a king, won honor in tourney melees, ridden with Brynden Blackfish and Greatjon Umber, fought in the Whispering Wood, bedded more girls than he could name, and yet this uncle was treating him as though he were still a child of ten. "If my father makes plans for war, I must know of them. I am not *'any man,'* I am heir to Pyke and the Iron Islands."

"As to that," his uncle said, "we shall see."

The words were a slap in the face. "*We shall see?* My brothers are both dead. I am my lord father's only living son."

"Your sister lives."

Asha, he thought, confounded. She was three years older than Theon, yet still . . . "A woman may inherit only if there is no male heir in the direct line," he insisted loudly. "I will not be cheated of my rights, I warn you."

His uncle grunted. "You *warn* a servant of the Drowned God, boy? You have forgotten more than you know. And you are a great fool if you believe your lord father will ever hand these holy islands over to a Stark. Now be silent. The ride is long enough without your magpie chatterings."

Theon held his tongue, though not without struggle. *So that is the way of it,* he thought. As if ten years in Winterfell could make a Stark. Lord Eddard had raised him among his own children, but Theon had never been one of them. The whole castle, from Lady Stark to the lowliest kitchen scullion, knew he was hostage to his father's good behavior, and treated him accordingly. Even the bastard Jon Snow had been accorded more honor than he had.

Lord Eddard had tried to play the father from time to time, but to Theon he had always remained the man who'd brought blood and fire to Pyke and taken him from his home. As a boy, he had lived in fear of Stark's stern face and great dark sword. His wife was, if anything, even more distant and suspicious.

As for their children, the younger ones had been mewling babes for most of his years at Winterfell. Only Robb and his baseborn half brother Jon Snow had been old enough to be worth his notice. The bastard was a sullen boy, quick to sense a slight, jealous of Theon's

high birth and Robb's regard for him. For Robb himself,
Theon did have a certain affection, as for a younger
brother . . . but it would be best not to mention that.
In Pyke, it would seem, the old wars were still being
fought. That ought not surprise him. The Iron Islands
lived in the past; the present was too hard and bitter to
be borne. Besides, his father and uncles were old, and
the old lords were like that; they took their dusty feuds
to the grave, forgetting nothing and forgiving less.

It had been the same with the Mallisters, his companions on the ride from Riverrun to Seagard. Patrek Mallister was not too ill a fellow; they shared a taste for
wenches, wine, and hawking. But when old Lord Jason
saw his heir growing overly fond of Theon's company,
he had taken Patrek aside to remind him that Seagard
had been built to defend the coast against reavers from
the Iron Islands, the Greyjoys of Pyke chief among
them. Their Booming Tower was named for its immense bronze bell, rung of old to call the townsfolk and
farmhands into the castle when longships were sighted
on the western horizon.

"Never mind that the bell has been rung just once in
three hundred years," Patrek had told Theon the day
after, as he shared his father's cautions and a jug of
green-apple wine.

"When my brother stormed Seagard," Theon said.
Lord Jason had slain Rodrik Greyjoy under the walls of
the castle, and thrown the ironmen back into the bay.
"If your father supposes I bear him some enmity for
that, it's only because he never knew Rodrik."

They had a laugh over that as they raced ahead to an
amorous young miller's wife that Patrek knew. *Would
that Patrek were with me now.* Mallister or no, he was
a more amiable riding companion than this sour old
priest that his uncle Aeron had turned into.

The path they rode wound up and up, into bare and
stony hills. Soon they were out of sight of the sea,
though the smell of salt still hung sharp in the damp air.
They kept a steady plodding pace, past a shepherd's
croft and the abandoned workings of a mine. This new,

holy Aeron Greyjoy was not much for talk. They rode in a gloom of silence. Finally Theon could suffer it no longer. "Robb Stark is Lord of Winterfell now," he said.

Aeron rode on. "One wolf is much like the other."

"Robb has broken fealty with the Iron Throne and crowned himself King in the North. There's war."

"The maester's ravens fly over salt as soon as rock. This news is old and cold."

"It means a new day, Uncle."

"Every morning brings a new day, much like the old."

"In Riverrun, they would tell you different. They say the red comet is a herald of a new age. A messenger from the gods."

"A sign it is," the priest agreed, "but from our god, not theirs. A burning brand it is, such as our people carried of old. It is the flame the Drowned God brought from the sea, and it proclaims a rising tide. It is time to hoist our sails and go forth into the world with fire and sword, as he did."

Theon smiled. "I could not agree more."

"A man agrees with god as a raindrop with the storm."

This raindrop will one day be a king, old man. Theon had suffered quite enough of his uncle's gloom. He put his spurs into his horse and trotted on ahead, smiling.

It was nigh on sunset when they reached the walls of Pyke, a crescent of dark stone that ran from cliff to cliff, with the gatehouse in the center and three square towers to either side. Theon could still make out the scars left by the stones of Robert Baratheon's catapults. A new south tower had risen from the ruins of the old, its stone a paler shade of grey, and as yet unmarred by patches of lichen. That was where Robert had made his breach, swarming in over the rubble and corpses with his warhammer in hand and Ned Stark at his side. Theon had watched from the safety of the Sea Tower, and sometimes he still saw the torches in his dreams, and heard the dull thunder of the collapse.

The gates stood open to him, the rusted iron portcullis drawn up. The guards atop the battlements watched with strangers' eyes as Theon Greyjoy came home at last.

Beyond the curtain wall were half a hundred acres of headland hard against the sky and the sea. The stables were here, and the kennels, and a scatter of other out-buildings. Sheep and swine huddled in their pens while the castle dogs ran free. To the south were the cliffs, and the wide stone bridge to the Great Keep. Theon could hear the crashing of waves as he swung down from his saddle. A stableman came to take his horse. A pair of gaunt children and some thralls stared at him with dull eyes, but there was no sign of his lord father, nor anyone else he recalled from boyhood. *A bleak and bitter homecoming*, he thought.

The priest had not dismounted. "Will you not stay the night and share our meat and mead, Uncle?"

"Bring you, I was told. You are brought. Now I return to our god's business." Aeron Greyjoy turned his horse and rode slowly out beneath the muddy spikes of the portcullis.

A bentback old crone in a shapeless grey dress approached him warily. "M'lord, I am sent to show you to chambers."

"By whose bidding?"

"Your lord father, m'lord."

Theon pulled off his gloves. "So you *do* know who I am. Why is my father not here to greet me?"

"He awaits you in the Sea Tower, m'lord. When you are rested from your trip."

And I thought Ned Stark cold. "And who are you?"

"Helya, who keeps this castle for your lord father."

"Sylas was steward here. They called him Sourmouth." Even now, Theon could recall the winey stench of the old man's breath.

"Dead these five years, m'lord."

"And what of Maester Qalen, where is he?"

"He sleeps in the sea. Wendamyr keeps the ravens now."

It is as if I were a stranger here, Theon thought. *Nothing has changed, and yet everything has changed.*

"Show me to my chambers, woman," he commanded. Bowing stiffly, she led him across the headland to the bridge. That at least was as he remembered; the ancient stones slick with spray and spotted by lichen, the sea foaming under their feet like some great wild beast, the salt wind clutching at their clothes.

Whenever he'd imagined his homecoming, he had always pictured himself returning to the snug bedchamber in the Sea Tower, where he'd slept as a child. Instead the old woman led him to the Bloody Keep. The halls here were larger and better furnished, if no less cold nor damp. Theon was given a suite of chilly rooms with ceilings so high that they were lost in gloom. He might have been more impressed if he had not known that these were the very chambers that had given the Bloody Keep its name. A thousand years before, the sons of the River King had been slaughtered here, hacked to bits in their beds so that pieces of their bodies might be sent back to their father on the mainland.

But Greyjoys were not murdered in Pyke except once in a great while by their brothers, and his brothers were both dead. It was not fear of ghosts that made him glance about with distaste. The wall hangings were green with mildew, the mattress musty-smelling and sagging, the rushes old and brittle. Years had come and gone since these chambers had last been opened. The damp went bone deep. "I'll have a basin of hot water and a fire in this hearth," he told the crone. "See that they light braziers in the other rooms to drive out some of the chill. And gods be good, get someone in here at once to change these rushes."

"Yes, m'lord. As you command." She fled.

After some time, they brought the hot water he had asked for. It was only tepid, and soon cold, and seawater in the bargain, but it served to wash the dust of the long ride from his face and hair and hands. While two thralls lit his braziers, Theon stripped off his travel-stained clothing and dressed to meet his father. He chose boots of supple black leather, soft lambswool breeches of silvery-grey, a black velvet doublet with the golden kraken of the Greyjoys embroidered on the breast. Around his throat he fastened a slender gold chain, around his waist a belt of bleached white leather. He hung a dirk at one hip and a longsword at the other, in scabbards striped black-and-gold. Drawing the dirk, he tested its edge with his thumb, pulled a whetstone from his belt pouch, and gave it a few licks. He prided himself on keeping his weapons sharp. "When I return, I shall expect a warm room and clean rushes," he warned the thralls as he drew on a pair of black gloves, the silk decorated with a delicate scrollwork tracery in golden thread.

Theon returned to the Great Keep through a covered stone walkway, the echoes of his footsteps mingling with the ceaseless rumble of the sea below. To get to the Sea Tower on its crooked pillar, he had to cross three further bridges, each narrower than the one before. The last was made of rope and wood, and the wet salt wind made it sway underfoot like a living thing. Theon's heart was in his mouth by the time he was halfway across. A long way below, the waves threw up tall plumes of spray as they crashed against the rock. As a boy, he used to *run* across this bridge, even in the black of night. *Boys believe nothing can hurt them*, his doubt whispered. *Grown men know better.*

The door was grey wood studded with iron, and Theon found it barred from the inside. He hammered on it with a fist, and cursed when a splinter snagged the fabric of his glove. The wood was damp and moldy, the iron studs rusted.

After a moment the door was opened from within by a guard in a black iron breastplate and pothelm. "You are the son?"

"Out of my way, or you'll learn who I am." The man stood aside. Theon climbed the twisting steps to the solar. He found his father seated beside a brazier, beneath a robe of musty sealskins that covered him foot to chin. At the sound of boots on stone, the Lord of the Iron Islands lifted his eyes to behold his last living son. He was smaller than Theon remembered him. And so gaunt. Balon Greyjoy had always been thin, but now he looked as though the gods had put him in a cauldron and boiled every spare ounce of flesh from his bones, until nothing remained but hair and skin. Bone thin and bone hard he was, with a face that might have been chipped from flint. His eyes were flinty too, black and sharp, but the years and the salt winds had turned his hair the grey of a winter sea, flecked with whitecaps. Unbound, it hung past the small of the back.

"Nine years, is it?" Lord Balon said at last.

"Ten," Theon answered, pulling off his torn gloves.

"A boy they took," his father said. "What are you now?"

"A man," Theon answered. "Your blood and your heir."

Lord Balon grunted. "We shall see."

"You shall," Theon promised.

"Ten years, you say. Stark had you as long as I. And now you come as his envoy."

"Not his," Theon said. "Lord Eddard is dead, beheaded by the Lannister queen."

"They are both dead, Stark and that Robert who broke my walls with his stones. I vowed I'd live to see them both in their graves, and I have." He grimaced. "Yet the cold and the damp still make my joints ache, as when they were alive. So what does it serve?"

"It serves." Theon moved closer. "I bring a letter—"

"Did Ned Stark dress you like that?" his father interrupted, squinting up from beneath his robe. "Was it his pleasure to garb you in velvets and silks and make you his own sweet daughter?"

Theon felt the blood rising to his face. "I am no man's daughter. If you mislike my garb, I will change it."

"You will." Throwing off the furs, Lord Balon pushed himself to his feet. He was not so tall as Theon remembered. "That bauble around your neck—was it bought with gold or iron?"

Theon touched the gold chain. He had forgotten. *It has been so long* . . . In the Old Way, women might decorate themselves with ornaments bought with coin, but a warrior wore only the jewelry he took off the corpses of enemies slain by his own hand. *Paying the iron price*, it was called.

"You blush red as a maid, Theon. A question was asked. Is it the gold price you paid, or the iron?"

"The gold," Theon admitted.

His father slid his fingers under the necklace and gave it a yank so hard it was like to take Theon's head off, had the chain not snapped first. "My daughter has taken an axe for a lover," Lord Balon said. "I will not have my son bedeck himself like a whore." He dropped the broken chain onto the brazier, where it slid down among the coals. "It is as I feared. The green lands have made you soft, and the Starks have made you theirs."

"You're wrong. Ned Stark was my gaoler, but my blood is still salt and iron."

Lord Balon turned away to warm his bony hands over the brazier. "Yet the Stark pup sends you to me like a well-trained raven, clutching his little message."

"There is nothing small about the letter I bear," Theon said, "and the offer he makes is one *I* suggested to him."

"This wolf king heeds your counsel, does he?" The notion seemed to amuse Lord Balon.

"He heeds me, yes. I've hunted with him, trained with him, shared meat and mead with him, warred at his side. I have earned his trust. He looks on me as an older brother, he—"

"*No.*" His father jabbed a finger at his face. "Not here, not in Pyke, not in my hearing, you will not name him *brother*, this son of the man who put your true brothers to the sword. Or have you forgotten Rodrik and Maron, who were your own blood?"

"I forget nothing." Ned Stark had killed neither of his brothers, in truth. Rodrik had been slain by Lord Jason Mallister at Seagard, Maron crushed in the collapse of the old south tower . . . but Stark *would* have done for them just as quick had the tide of battle chanced to sweep them together. "I remember my brothers very well," Theon insisted. Chiefly he remembered Rodrik's drunken cuffs and Maron's cruel japes and endless lies. "I remember when my father was a king too." He took out Robb's letter and thrust it forward. "Here. Read it . . . Your Grace."

Lord Balon broke the seal and unfolded the parchment. His black eyes flicked back and forth. "So the boy would give me a crown again," he said, "and all I need do is destroy his enemies." His thin lips twisted in a smile.

"By now Robb is at the Golden Tooth," Theon said. "Once it falls, he'll be through the hills in a day. Lord Tywin's host is at Harrenhal, cut off from the west. The Kingslayer is a captive at Riverrun. Only Ser Stafford Lannister and the raw green levies he's been gathering remain to oppose Robb in the west. Ser Stafford will put himself between Robb's army and Lannisport, which means the city will be undefended when we descend on it by sea. If the gods are with us, even Casterly Rock itself may fall before the Lannisters so much as realize that we are upon them."

Lord Balon grunted. "Casterly Rock has never fallen."

"Until now." Theon smiled. *And how sweet that will be.*

His father did not return the smile. "So this is why Robb Stark sends you back to me, after so long? So you might win my consent to this plan of his?"

"It is my plan, not Robb's," Theon said proudly. *Mine, as the victory will be mine, and in time the crown.* "I will lead the attack myself, if it please you. As my reward I would ask that you grant me Casterly Rock for my own seat, once we have taken it from the Lannisters." With the Rock, he could hold Lannisport and the golden lands of the west. It would mean wealth and power such as House Greyjoy had never known.

"You reward yourself handsomely for a notion and a few lines of scribbling." His father read the letter again. "The pup says nothing about a reward. Only that you speak for him, and I am to listen, and give him my sails and swords, and in return he will give me a crown." His flinty eyes lifted to meet his son's. "He will *give* me a crown," he repeated, his voice growing sharp.

"A poor choice of words, what is meant is—"

"What is meant is what is said. The boy will *give* me a crown. And what is given can be taken away." Lord Balon tossed the letter onto the brazier, atop the necklace. The parchment curled, blackened, and took flame.

Theon was aghast. "Have you gone mad?"

His father laid a stinging backhand across his cheek. "Mind your tongue. You are not in Winterfell now, and I am not Robb the Boy, that you should speak to me so. I am the Greyjoy, Lord Reaper of Pyke, King of Salt and Rock, Son of the Sea Wind, and no man gives me a crown. I pay the iron price. I will *take* my crown, as Urron Redhand did five thousand years ago."

Theon edged backward, away from the sudden fury in his father's tone. "Take it, then," he spat, his cheek still tingling. "Call yourself King of the Iron Islands, no one will care . . . until the wars are over, and the victor looks about and spies the old fool perched off his shore with an iron crown on his head."

Lord Balon laughed. "Well, at the least you are no craven. No more than I'm a fool. Do you think I gather my ships to watch them rock at anchor? I mean to carve out a kingdom with fire and sword . . . but not from the west, and not at the bidding of King Robb the Boy. Casterly Rock is too strong, and Lord Tywin too cunning by half. Aye, we might take Lannisport, but we should never keep it. No. I hunger for a different plum . . . not so juicy sweet, to be sure, yet it hangs there ripe and undefended."

Where? Theon might have asked, but by then he knew.

DAENERYS

The Dothraki named the comet *shierak qiya*, the Bleeding Star. The old men muttered that it omened ill, but Daenerys Targaryen had seen it first on the night she had burned Khal Drogo, the night her dragons had awakened. *It is the herald of my coming,* she told herself as she gazed up into the night sky with wonder in her heart. *The gods have sent it to show me the way.*

Yet when she put the thought into words, her handmaid Doreah quailed. "That way lies the red lands, *Khaleesi.* A grim place and terrible, the riders say."

"The way the comet points is the way we must go," Dany insisted . . . though in truth, it was the only way open to her.

She dare not turn north onto the vast ocean of grass they called the Dothraki sea. The first *khalasar* they met would swallow up her ragged band, slaying the warriors and slaving the rest. The lands of the Lamb Men south of the river were likewise closed to them. They were too few to defend themselves even against that unwarlike folk, and the Lhazareen had small reason to love them. She might have struck downriver for the ports at Meereen and Yunkai and Astapor, but Rakharo warned her that Pono's *khalasar* had ridden that way, driving thousands of captives before them to sell in the flesh marts that festered like open sores on the shores of Slaver's Bay. "Why should I fear Pono?" Dany objected. "He was Drogo's *ko*, and always spoke me gently."

"Ko Pono spoke you gently," Ser Jorah Mormont said. "Khal Pono will kill you. He was the first to abandon Drogo. Ten thousand warriors went with him. You have a hundred."

No, Dany thought. *I have four. The rest are women, old sick men, and boys whose hair has never been braided.* "I have the dragons," she pointed out.

"Hatchlings," Ser Jorah said. "One swipe from an *arakh* would put an end to them, though Pono is more like to seize them for himself. Your dragon eggs were more precious than rubies. A living dragon is beyond price. In all the world, there are only three. Every man who sees them will want them, my queen."

"They are *mine*," she said fiercely. They had been born from her faith and her need, given life by the deaths of her husband and unborn son and the *maegi* Mirri Maz Duur. Dany had walked into the flames as they came forth, and they had drunk milk from her swollen breasts. "No man will take them from me while I live."

"You will not live long should you meet Khal Pono. Nor Khal Jhaqo, nor any of the others. You must go where they do not."

Dany had named him the first of her Queensguard . . . and when Mormont's gruff counsel and the omens agreed, her course was clear. She called her people together and mounted her silver mare. Her hair had burned away in Drogo's pyre, so her handmaids garbed her in the skin of the *hrakkar* Drogo had slain, the white lion of the Dothraki sea. Its fearsome head made a hood to cover her naked scalp, its pelt a cloak that flowed across her shoulders and down her back. The cream-colored dragon sunk sharp black claws into the lion's mane and coiled its tail around her arm, while Ser Jorah took his accustomed place by her side.

"We follow the comet," Dany told her *khalasar*. Once it was said, no word was raised against it. They had been Drogo's people, but they were hers now. *The Unburnt*, they called her, and *Mother of Dragons*. Her word was their law.

They rode by night, and by day took refuge from the sun beneath their tents. Soon enough Dany learned the truth of Doreah's words. This was no kindly country. They left a trail of dead and dying horses behind them as they went, for Pono, Jhaqo, and the others had seized the best of Drogo's herds, leaving to Dany the old and the scrawny, the sickly and the lame, the broken animals and the ill-tempered. It was the same with the people. *They are not strong*, she told herself, *so I must be their strength. I must show no fear, no weakness, no doubt. However frightened my heart, when they look upon my face they must see only Drogo's queen.* She felt older than her fourteen years. If ever she had truly been a girl, that time was done.

Three days into the march, the first man died. A toothless oldster with cloudy blue eyes, he fell exhausted from his saddle and could not rise again. An hour later he was done. Blood flies swarmed about his corpse and carried his ill luck to the living. "His time was past," her handmaid Irri declared. "No man should live longer than his teeth." The others agreed. Dany bid them kill the weakest of their dying horses, so the dead man might go mounted into the night lands.

Two nights later, it was an infant girl who perished. Her mother's anguished wailing lasted all day, but there was nothing to be done. The child had been too young to ride, poor thing. Not for her the endless black grasses of the night lands; she must be born again.

There was little forage in the red waste, and less water. It was a sere and desolate land of low hills and barren windswept plains. The rivers they crossed were dry as dead men's bones. Their mounts subsisted on the tough brown devilgrass that grew in clumps at the base of rocks and dead trees. Dany sent outriders ranging ahead of the column, but they found neither wells nor springs, only bitter pools, shallow and stagnant, shrinking in the hot sun. The deeper they rode into the waste, the smaller the pools became, while the distance between them grew. If there were gods in this trackless wilderness of stone and sand and red clay, they were hard dry gods, deaf to prayers for rain.

Wine gave out first, and soon thereafter the clotted mare's milk the horselords loved better than mead. Then their stores of flatbread and dried meat were exhausted as well. Their hunters found no game, and only the flesh of their dead horses filled their bellies. Death followed death. Weak children, wrinkled old women, the sick and the stupid and the heedless, the cruel land claimed them all. Doreah grew gaunt and hollow-eyed, and her soft golden hair turned brittle as straw.

Dany hungered and thirsted with the rest of them. The milk in her breasts dried up, her nipples cracked and bled, and the flesh fell away from her day by day until she was lean and hard as a stick, yet it was her dragons she feared for. Her father had been slain before she was born, and her splendid brother Rhaegar as well. Her mother had died bringing her into the world while the storm screamed outside. Gentle Ser Willem Darry, who must have loved her after a fashion, had been taken by a wasting sickness when she was very young. Her brother Viserys, Khal Drogo who was her sun-and-stars, even her unborn son, the gods had claimed them all. *They will not have my dragons,* Dany vowed. *They will not.*

The dragons were no larger than the scrawny cats she had once seen skulking along the walls of Magister Illyrio's estate in Pentos . . . until they unfolded their wings. Their span was three times their length, each wing a delicate fan of translucent skin, gorgeously colored, stretched taut between long thin bones. When you looked hard, you could see that most of their body was neck, tail, and wing. *Such little things,* she thought as she fed them by hand. Or rather, tried to feed them, for the dragons would not eat. They would hiss and spit at each bloody morsel of horsemeat, steam rising from their nostrils, yet they would not take the food . . . until Dany recalled something Viserys had told her when they were children.

Only dragons and men eat cooked meat, he had said.

When she had her handmaids char the horsemeat black, the dragons ripped at it eagerly, their heads striking like snakes. So long as the meat was seared, they gulped down several times their own weight every day, and at last began to grow larger and stronger. Dany marveled at the smoothness of their scales, and the *heat* that poured off them, so palpable that on cold nights their whole bodies seemed to steam.

Each evenfall as the *khalasar* set out, she would choose a dragon to ride upon her shoulder. Irri and Jhiqui carried the others in a cage of woven wood slung between their mounts, and rode close behind her, so Dany was never out of their sight. It was the only way to keep them quiescent.

"Aegon's dragons were named for the gods of Old Valyria," she told her bloodriders one morning after a long night's journey. "Visenya's dragon was Vhagar, Rhaenys had Meraxes, and Aegon rode Balerion, the Black Dread. It was said that Vhagar's breath was so hot that it could melt a knight's armor and cook the man inside, that Meraxes swallowed horses whole, and Balerion . . . his fire was as black as his scales, his wings so vast that whole towns were swallowed up in their shadow when he passed overhead."

The Dothraki looked at her hatchlings uneasily. The largest of her three was shiny black, his scales slashed with streaks of vivid scarlet to match his wings and horns. *"Khaleesi,"* Aggo murmured, "there sits Balerion, come again."

"It may be as you say, blood of my blood," Dany replied gravely, "but he shall have a new name for this new life. I would name them all for those the gods have taken. The green one shall be Rhaegal, for my valiant brother who died on the green banks of the Trident. The cream-and-gold I call Viserion. Viserys was cruel and weak and frightened, yet he was my brother still. His dragon will do what he could not."

"And the black beast?" asked Ser Jorah Mormont.

"The black," she said, "is Drogon."

Yet even as her dragons prospered, her *khalasar* withered and died. Around them the land turned ever more desolate. Even devilgrass grew scant; horses dropped in their tracks, leaving so few that some of her people must trudge along on foot. Doreah took a fever and grew worse with every league they crossed. Her lips and hands broke with blood blisters, her hair came out in clumps, and one evenfall she lacked the strength to mount her horse. Jhogo said they must leave her or bind her to her saddle, but Dany remembered a night on the Dothraki sea, when the Lysene girl had taught her secrets so that Drogo might love her more. She gave Doreah water from her own skin, cooled her brow with a damp cloth, and held her hand until she died, shivering. Only then would she permit the *khalasar* to press on.

They saw no sign of other travelers. The Dothraki began to mutter fearfully that the comet had led them to some hell. Dany went to Ser Jorah one morning as they made camp amidst a jumble of black wind-scoured stones. "Are we lost?" she asked him. "Does this waste have no end to it?"

"It has an end," he answered wearily. "I have seen the maps the traders draw, my queen. Few caravans come this way, that is so, yet there are great kingdoms to the east, and cities full of wonders. Yi Ti, Qarth, Asshai by the Shadow . . ."

"Will we live to see them?"

"I will not lie to you. The way is harder than I dared think." The knight's face was grey and exhausted. The wound he had taken to his hip the night he fought Khal Drogo's bloodriders had never fully healed; she could see how he grimaced when he mounted his horse, and he seemed to slump in his saddle as they rode. "Perhaps we are doomed if we press on . . . but I know for a certainty that we are doomed if we turn back."

Dany kissed him lightly on the cheek. It heartened her to see him smile. *I must be strong for him as well,* she thought grimly. *A knight he may be, but I am the blood of the dragon.*

The next pool they found was scalding hot and stinking of brimstone, but their skins were almost empty. The Dothraki cooled the water in jars and pots and drank it tepid. The taste was no less foul, but water was water, and all of them thirsted. Dany looked at the horizon with despair. They had lost a third of their number, and still the waste stretched before them, bleak and red and endless. *The comet mocks my hopes,* she thought, lifting her eyes to where it scored the sky. *Have I crossed half the world and seen the birth of dragons only to die with them in this hard hot desert!* She would not believe it.

The next day, dawn broke as they were crossing a cracked and fissured plain of hard red earth. Dany was about to command them to make camp when her outriders came racing back at a gallop. "A city, *Khaleesi,*" they cried. "A city pale as the moon and lovely as a maid. An hour's ride, no more."

"Show me," she said.

When the city appeared before her, its walls and towers shimmering white behind a veil of heat, it looked so beautiful that Dany was certain it must be a mirage. "Do you know what place this might be?" she asked Ser Jorah.

The exile knight gave a weary shake of the head. "No, my queen. I have never traveled this far east."

The distant white walls promised rest and safety, a chance to heal and grow strong, and Dany wanted nothing so much as to rush toward them. Instead she turned to her bloodriders. "Blood of my blood, go ahead of us and learn the name of this city, and what manner of welcome we should expect."

"*Ai, Khaleesi,*" said Aggo.

Her riders were not long in returning. Rakharo swung

down from his saddle. From his medallion belt hung the great curving *arakh* that Dany had bestowed on him when she named him bloodrider. "This city is dead, *Khaleesi*. Nameless and godless we found it, the gates broken, only wind and flies moving through the streets."

Jhiqui shuddered. "When the gods are gone, the evil ghosts feast by night. Such places are best shunned. It is known."

"It is known," Irri agreed.

"Not to me." Dany put her heels into her horse and showed them the way, trotting beneath the shattered arch of an ancient gate and down a silent street. Ser Jorah and her bloodriders followed, and then, more slowly, the rest of the Dothraki.

How long the city had been deserted she could not know, but the white walls, so beautiful from afar, were cracked and crumbling when seen up close. Inside was a maze of narrow crooked alleys. The buildings pressed close, their facades blank, chalky, windowless. Everything was white, as if the people who lived here had known nothing of color. They rode past heaps of sun-washed rubble where houses had fallen in, and elsewhere saw the faded scars of fire. At a place where six alleys came together, Dany passed an empty marble plinth. Dothraki had visited this place before, it would seem. Perhaps even now the missing statue stood among the other stolen gods in Vaes Dothrak. She might have ridden past it a hundred times, never knowing. On her shoulder, Viserion *hissed*.

They made camp before the remnants of a gutted palace, on a windswept plaza where devilgrass grew between the paving stones. Dany sent out men to search the ruins. Some went reluctantly, yet they went . . . and one scarred old man returned a brief time later, hopping and grinning, his hands overflowing with figs. They were small, withered things, yet her people grabbed for them greedily, jostling and pushing at each other, stuffing the fruit into their cheeks and chewing blissfully.

Other searchers returned with tales of other fruit trees, hidden behind closed doors in secret gardens. Aggo showed her a courtyard overgrown with twisting vines and tiny green grapes, and Jhogo discovered a well where the water was pure and cold. Yet they found bones too, the skulls of the unburied dead, bleached and broken. "Ghosts," Irri muttered. "Terrible ghosts. We must not stay here, *Khaleesi*, this is their place."

"I fear no ghosts. Dragons are more powerful than ghosts." *And figs are more important.* "Go with Jhiqui and find me some clean sand for a bath, and trouble me no more with silly talk."

In the coolness of her tent, Dany blackened horse-meat over a brazier and reflected on her choices. There was food and water here to sustain them, and enough grass for the horses to regain their strength. How pleasant it would be to wake every day in the same place, to linger among shady gardens, eat figs, and drink cool water, as much as she might desire.

When Irri and Jhiqui returned with pots of white sand, Dany stripped and let them scrub her clean. "Your hair is coming back, *Khaleesi*," Jhiqui said as she scraped sand off her back. Dany ran a hand over the top of her head, feeling the new growth. Dothraki men wore their hair in long oiled braids, and cut them only when defeated. *Perhaps I should do the same,* she thought, *to remind them that Drogo's strength lives within me now.* Khal Drogo had died with his hair uncut, a boast few men could make.

Across the tent, Rhaegal unfolded green wings to flap and flutter a half foot before thumping to the carpet. When he landed, his tail lashed back and forth in fury, and he raised his head and screamed. *If I had wings, I would want to fly too,* Dany thought. The Targaryens of old had ridden upon dragonback when they went to war. She tried to imagine what it would feel like, to straddle a dragon's neck and soar high into the air. *It would be like standing on a mountaintop, only better. The whole world would be spread out below. If I flew high enough,*

I could even see the Seven Kingdoms, and reach up and touch the comet.

Irri broke her reverie to tell her that Ser Jorah Mormont was outside, awaiting her pleasure. "Send him in," Dany commanded, sand-scrubbed skin tingling. She wrapped herself in the lionskin. The *hrakkar* had been much bigger than Dany, so the pelt covered everything that wanted covering.

"I've brought you a peach," Ser Jorah said, kneeling. It was so small she could almost hide it in her palm, and overripe too, but when she took the first bite, the flesh was so sweet she almost cried. She ate it slowly, savoring every mouthful, while Ser Jorah told her of the tree it had been plucked from, in a garden near the western wall.

"Fruit and water and shade," Dany said, her cheeks sticky with peach juice. "The gods were good to bring us to this place."

"We should rest here until we are stronger," the knight urged. "The red lands are not kind to the weak."

"My handmaids say there are ghosts here."

"There are ghosts everywhere," Ser Jorah said softly. "We carry them with us wherever we go."

Yes, she thought. *Viserys, Khal Drogo, my son Rhaego, they are with me always.* "Tell me the name of your ghost, Jorah. You know all of mine."

His face grew very still. "Her name was Lynesse."

"Your wife?"

"My second wife."

It pains him to speak of her, Dany saw, but she wanted to know the truth. "Is that all you would say of her?" The lion pelt slid off one shoulder and she tugged it back into place. "Was she beautiful?"

"Very beautiful." Ser Jorah lifted his eyes from her shoulder to her face. "The first time I beheld her, I thought she was a goddess come to earth, the Maid herself made flesh. Her birth was far above my own. She was the youngest daughter of Lord Leyton Hightower of Oldtown. The White Bull who commanded your fa-

ther's Kingsguard was her great-uncle. The Hightowers
are an ancient family, very rich and very proud."

"And loyal," Dany said. "I remember, Viserys said the
Hightowers were among those who stayed true to my
father."

"That's so," he admitted.

"Did your fathers make the match?"

"No," he said. "Our marriage . . . that makes a long
tale and a dull one, Your Grace. I would not trouble you
with it."

"I have nowhere to go," she said. "Please."

"As my queen commands." Ser Jorah frowned. "My
home . . . you must understand that to understand the
rest. Bear Island is beautiful, but remote. Imagine old
gnarled oaks and tall pines, flowering thornbushes, grey
stones bearded with moss, little creeks running icy
down steep hillsides. The hall of the Mormonts is built
of huge logs and surrounded by an earthen palisade.
Aside from a few crofters, my people live along the
coasts and fish the seas. The island lies far to the north,
and our winters are more terrible than you can imagine,
Khaleesi.

"Still, the island suited me well enough, and I never
lacked for women. I had my share of fishwives and
crofter's daughters, before and after I was wed. I married
young, to a bride of my father's choosing, a Glover of
Deepwood Motte. Ten years we were wed, or near
enough as makes no matter. She was a plain-faced
woman, but not unkind. I suppose I came to love her
after a fashion, though our relations were dutiful rather
than passionate. Three times she miscarried while trying to give me an heir. The last time she never recovered. She died not long after."

Dany put her hand on his and gave his fingers a
squeeze. "I am sorry for you, truly."

Ser Jorah nodded. "By then my father had taken the
black, so I was Lord of Bear Island in my own right. I
had no lack of marriage offers, but before I could reach a
decision Lord Balon Greyjoy rose in rebellion against
the Usurper, and Ned Stark called his banners to help

his friend Robert. The final battle was on Pyke. When Robert's stonethrowers opened a breach in King Balon's wall, a priest from Myr was the first man through, but I was not far behind. For that I won my knighthood.

"To celebrate his victory, Robert ordained that a tourney should be held outside Lannisport. It was there I saw Lynesse, a maid half my age. She had come up from Oldtown with her father to see her brothers joust. I could not take my eyes off her. In a fit of madness, I begged her favor to wear in the tourney, never dreaming she would grant my request, yet she did.

"I fight as well as any man, *Khaleesi*, but I have never been a tourney knight. Yet with Lynesse's favor knotted round my arm, I was a different man. I won joust after joust. Lord Jason Mallister fell before me, and Bronze Yohn Royce. Ser Ryman Frey, his brother Ser Hosteen, Lord Whent, Strongboar, even Ser Boros Blount of the Kingsguard, I unhorsed them all. In the last match, I broke nine lances against Jaime Lannister to no result, and King Robert gave me the champion's laurel. I crowned Lynesse queen of love and beauty, and that very night went to her father and asked for her hand. I was drunk, as much on glory as on wine. By rights I should have gotten a contemptuous refusal, but Lord Leyton accepted my offer. We were married there in Lannisport, and for a fortnight I was the happiest man in the wide world."

"Only a fortnight?" asked Dany. *Even I was given more happiness than that, with Drogo who was my sun-and-stars.*

"A fortnight was how long it took us to sail from Lannisport back to Bear Island. My home was a great disappointment to Lynesse. It was too cold, too damp, too far away, my castle no more than a wooden longhall. We had no masques, no mummer shows, no balls or fairs. Seasons might pass without a singer ever coming to play for us, and there's not a goldsmith on the island. Even meals became a trial. My cook knew little beyond his roasts and stews, and Lynesse soon lost her taste for fish and venison.

"I lived for her smiles, so I sent all the way to Oldtown for a new cook, and brought a harper from Lannisport. Goldsmiths, jewelers, dressmakers, whatever she wanted I found for her, but it was never enough. Bear Island is rich in bears and trees, and poor in aught else. I built a fine ship for her and we sailed to Lannisport and Oldtown for festivals and fairs, and once even to Braavos, where I borrowed heavily from the moneylenders. It was as a tourney champion that I had won her hand and heart, so I entered other tourneys for her sake, but the magic was gone. I never distinguished myself again, and each defeat meant the loss of another charger and another suit of jousting armor, which must needs be ransomed or replaced. The cost could not be borne. Finally I insisted we return home, but there matters soon grew even worse than before. I could no longer pay the cook and the harper, and Lynesse grew wild when I spoke of pawning her jewels.

"The rest . . . I did things it shames me to speak of. For gold. So Lynesse might keep her jewels, her harper, and her cook. In the end it cost me all. When I heard that Eddard Stark was coming to Bear Island, I was so lost to honor that rather than stay and face his judgment, I took her with me into exile. Nothing mattered but our love, I told myself. We fled to Lys, where I sold my ship for gold to keep us."

His voice was thick with grief, and Dany was reluctant to press him any further, yet she had to know how it ended. "Did she die there?" she asked him gently.

"Only to me," he said. "In half a year my gold was gone, and I was obliged to take service as a sellsword. While I was fighting Braavosi on the Rhoyne, Lynesse moved into the manse of a merchant prince named Tregar Ormollen. They say she is his chief concubine now, and even his wife goes in fear of her."

Dany was horrified. "Do you hate her?"

"Almost as much as I love her," Ser Jorah answered. "Pray excuse me, my queen. I find I am very tired."

She gave him leave to go, but as he was lifting the flap of her tent, she could not stop herself calling after him with one last question. "What did she look like, your Lady Lynesse?"

Ser Jorah smiled sadly. "Why, she looked a bit like you, Daenerys." He bowed low. "Sleep well, my queen."

Dany shivered, and pulled the lionskin tight about her. *She looked like me.* It explained much that she had not truly understood. *He wants me,* she realized. *He loves me as he loved her, not as a knight loves his queen but as a man loves a woman.* She tried to imagine herself in Ser Jorah's arms, kissing him, pleasuring him, letting him enter her. It was no good. When she closed her eyes, his face kept changing into Drogo's.

Khal Drogo had been her sun-and-stars, her first, and perhaps he must be her last. The *maegi* Mirri Maz Duur had sworn she should never bear a living child, and what man would want a barren wife? And what man could hope to rival Drogo, who had died with his hair uncut and rode now through the night lands, the stars his *khalasar*?

She had heard the longing in Ser Jorah's voice when he spoke of his Bear Island. *He can never have me, but one day I can give him back his home and honor. That much I can do for him.*

No ghosts troubled her sleep that night. She dreamed of Drogo and the first ride they had taken together on the night they were wed. In the dream it was not horses they rode, but dragons.

The next morn, she summoned her bloodriders. "Blood of my blood," she told the three of them, "I have need of you. Each of you is to choose three horses, the hardiest and healthiest that remain to us. Load as much water and food as your mounts can bear, and ride forth for me. Aggo shall strike southwest, Rakharo due south. Jhogo, you are to follow *shierak qiya* on southeast."

"What shall we seek, *Khaleesi*?" asked Jhogo.

"Whatever there is," Dany answered. "Seek for other cities, living and dead. Seek for caravans and people. Seek for rivers and lakes and the great salt sea. Find how far this waste extends before us, and what lies on the other side. When I leave this place, I do not mean to strike out blind again. I will know where I am bound, and how best to get there.''

And so they went, the bells in their hair ringing softly, while Dany settled down with her small band of survivors in the place they named *Vaes Tolorro*, the city of bones. Day followed night followed day. Women harvested fruit from the gardens of the dead. Men groomed their mounts and mended saddles, stirrups, and shoes. Children wandered the twisty alleys and found old bronze coins and bits of purple glass and stone flagons with handles carved like snakes. One woman was stung by a red scorpion, but hers was the only death. The horses began to put on some flesh. Dany tended Ser Jorah's wound herself, and it began to heal.

Rakharo was the first to return. Due south the red waste stretched on and on, he reported, until it ended on a bleak shore beside the poison water. Between here and there lay only swirling sand, wind-scoured rocks, and plants bristly with sharp thorns. He had passed the bones of a dragon, he swore, so immense that he had ridden his horse through its great black jaws. Other than that, he had seen nothing.

Dany gave him charge of a dozen of her strongest men, and set them to pulling up the plaza to get to the earth beneath. If devilgrass could grow between the paving stones, other grasses would grow when the stones were gone. They had wells enough, no lack of water. Given seed, they could make the plaza bloom.

Aggo was back next. The southwest was barren and burnt, he swore. He had found the ruins of two more cities, smaller than Vaes Tolorro but otherwise the same. One was warded by a ring of skulls mounted on rusted iron spears, so he dared not enter, but he had explored the second for as long as he could. He showed Dany an iron bracelet he had found, set with a uncut fire opal the size of her thumb. There were scrolls as well, but they were dry and crumbling and Aggo had left them where they lay.

Dany thanked him and told him to see to the repair of

the gates. If enemies had crossed the waste to destroy these cities in ancient days, they might well come again. "If so, we must be ready," she declared.

Jhogo was gone so long that Dany feared him lost, but finally when they had all but ceased to look for him, he came riding up from the southeast. One of the guards that Aggo had posted saw him first and gave a shout, and Dany rushed to the walls to see for herself. It was true. Jhogo came, yet not alone. Behind him rode three queerly garbed strangers atop ugly humped creatures that dwarfed any horse.

They drew rein before the city gates, and looked up to see Dany on the wall above them. "Blood of my blood," Jhogo called, "I have been to the great city Qarth, and returned with three who would look on you with their own eyes."

Dany stared down at the strangers. "Here I stand. Look, if that is your pleasure . . . but first tell me your names."

The pale man with the blue lips replied in guttural Dothraki, "I am Pyat Pree, the great warlock."

The bald man with the jewels in his nose answered in the Valyrian of the Free Cities, "I am Xaro Xhoan Daxos of the Thirteen, a merchant prince of Qarth."

The woman in the lacquered wooden mask said in the Common Tongue of the Seven Kingdoms, "I am Quaithe of the Shadow. We come seeking dragons."

"Seek no more," Daenerys Targaryen told them. "You have found them."

JON

Whitetree, the village was named on Sam's old maps. Jon did not think it much of a village. Four tumbledown one-room houses of un-mortared stone surrounded an empty sheepfold and a well. The houses were roofed with sod, the windows shuttered with ragged pieces of hide. And above them loomed the pale limbs and dark red leaves of a monstrous great weirwood.

It was the biggest tree Jon Snow had ever seen, the trunk near eight feet wide, the branches spreading so far that the entire village was shaded beneath their canopy. The size did not disturb him so much as the face . . . the mouth especially, no simple carved slash, but a jagged hollow large enough to swallow a sheep.

Those are not sheep bones, though. Nor is that a sheep's skull in the ashes.

"An old tree." Mormont sat his horse, frowning. "Old," his raven agreed from his shoulder. "Old, old, old."

"And powerful." Jon could feel the power.

Thoren Smallwood dismounted beside the trunk, dark in his plate and mail. "Look at that face. Small wonder men feared them, when they first came to Westeros. I'd like to take an axe to the bloody thing myself."

Jon said, "My lord father believed no man could tell a lie in front of a heart tree. The old gods know when men are lying."

"My father believed the same," said the Old Bear. "Let me have a look at that skull."

Jon dismounted. Slung across his back in a black leather shoulder sheath was Longclaw, the hand-and-a-half bastard blade the Old Bear had given him for saving his life. *A bastard sword for a bastard,* the men joked. The hilt had been fashioned new for him, adorned with a wolf's-head pommel in pale stone, but the blade itself was Valyrian steel, old and light and deadly sharp.

He knelt and reached a gloved hand down into the maw. The inside of the hollow was red with dried sap and blackened by fire. Beneath the skull he saw another, smaller, the jaw broken off. It was half-buried in ash and bits of bone.

When he brought the skull to Mormont, the Old Bear lifted it in both hands and stared into the empty sockets. "The wildlings burn their dead. We've always known that. Now I wished I'd asked them why, when there were still a few around to ask."

Jon Snow remembered the wight rising, its eyes shining blue in the pale dead face. He knew why, he was certain.

"Would that bones could talk," the Old Bear grumbled. "This fellow could tell us much. How he died. Who burned him, and why. Where the wildlings have gone." He sighed. "The children of the forest could speak to the dead, it's said. But I can't." He tossed the skull back into the mouth of the tree, where it landed with a puff of fine ash. "Go through all these houses. Giant, get to the top of this tree, have a look. I'll have the hounds brought up too. Perchance this time the trail will be fresher." His tone did not suggest that he held out much hope of the last.

Two men went through each house, to make certain nothing was missed. Jon was paired with dour Eddison Tollett, a squire grey of hair and thin as a pike, whom the other brothers called Dolorous Edd. "Bad enough when the dead come walking," he said to Jon as they crossed the village, "now the Old Bear wants them talking as well? No good will come of *that*, I'll warrant. And who's to say the bones wouldn't lie? Why should death make a man truthful, or even clever? The dead are likely dull fellows, full of tedious complaints—the ground's too cold, my gravestone should be larger, why does *he* get more worms than I do . . ."

Jon had to stoop to pass through the low door. Within he found a packed dirt floor. There were no furnishings, no sign that people had lived here but for some ashes beneath the smoke hole in the roof. "What a dismal place to live," he said.

"I was born in a house much like this," declared Dolorous Edd. "Those were my enchanted years. Later I fell on hard times." A nest of dry straw bedding filled one corner of the room. Edd looked at it with longing. "I'd give all the gold in Casterly Rock to sleep in a bed again."

"You call that a bed?"

"If it's softer than the ground and has a roof over it, I call it a bed." Dolorous Edd sniffed the air. "I smell dung."

The smell was very faint. "Old dung," said Jon. The house felt as though it had been empty for some time. Kneeling, he searched through the straw with his hands to see if anything had been concealed beneath, then made a round of the walls. It did not take very long. "There's nothing here."

Nothing was what he had expected; Whitetree was the fourth village they had passed, and it had been the same in all of them. The people were gone, vanished with their scant possessions and whatever animals they may have had. None of the villages showed any signs of

having been attacked. They were simply . . . empty.
"What do you think happened to them all?" Jon asked.

"Something worse than we can imagine," suggested
Dolorous Edd. "Well, *I* might be able to imagine it, but
I'd sooner not. Bad enough to know you're going to
come to some awful end without thinking about it
aforetime."

Two of the hounds were sniffing around the door as
they reemerged. Other dogs ranged through the village.
Chett was cursing them loudly, his voice thick with the
anger he never seemed to put aside. The light filtering
through the red leaves of the weirwood made the boils
on his face look even more inflamed than usual. When
he saw Jon his eyes narrowed; there was no love lost
between them.

The other houses had yielded no wisdom. *"Gone,"*
cried Mormont's raven, flapping up into the weirwood
to perch above them. *"Gone, gone, gone."*

"There were wildlings at Whitetree only a year ago."
Thoren Smallwood looked more a lord than Mormont
did, clad in Ser Jaremy Rykker's gleaming black mail
and embossed breastplate. His heavy cloak was richly
trimmed with sable, and clasped with the crossed hammers of the Rykkers, wrought in silver. Ser Jaremy's
cloak, once . . . but the wight had claimed Ser Jaremy,
and the Night's Watch wasted nothing.

"A year ago Robert was king, and the realm was at
peace," declared Jarman Buckwell, the square stolid
man who commanded the scouts. "Much can change in
a year's time."

"One thing hasn't changed," Ser Mallador Locke insisted. "Fewer wildlings means fewer worries. I won't
mourn, whatever's become of them. Raiders and murderers, the lot of them."

Jon heard a rustling from the red leaves above. Two
branches parted, and he glimpsed a little man moving
from limb to limb as easily as a squirrel. Bedwyck stood
no more than five feet tall, but the grey streaks in his
hair showed his age. The other rangers called him
Giant. He sat in a fork of the tree over their heads and

said, "There's water to the north. A lake, might be. A few flint hills rising to the west, not very high. Nothing else to see, my lords."

"We might camp here tonight," Smallwood suggested.

The Old Bear glanced up, searching for a glimpse of sky through the pale limbs and red leaves of the weirwood. "No," he declared. "Giant, how much daylight remains to us?"

"Three hours, my lord."

"We'll press on north," Mormont decided. "If we reach this lake, we can make camp by the shore, perchance catch a few fish. Jon, fetch me paper, it's past time I wrote Maester Aemon."

Jon found parchment, quill, and ink in his saddlebag and brought them to the Lord Commander. *At Whitetree,* Mormont scrawled. *The fourth village. All empty. The wildlings are gone.* "Find Tarly and see that he gets this on its way," he said as he handed Jon the message. When he whistled, his raven came flapping down to land on his horse's head. *"Corn,"* the raven suggested, bobbing. The horse whickered.

Jon mounted his garron, wheeled him about, and trotted off. Beyond the shade of the great weirwood the men of the Night's Watch stood beneath lesser trees, tending their horses, chewing strips of salt beef, pissing, scratching, and talking. When the command was given to move out again, the talk died, and they climbed back into their saddles. Jarman Buckwell's scouts rode out first, with the vanguard under Thoren Smallwood heading the column proper. Then came the Old Bear with the main force, Ser Mallador Locke with the baggage train and packhorses, and finally Ser Ottyn Wythers and the rear guard. Two hundred men all told, with half again as many mounts.

By day they followed game trails and streambeds, the "ranger's roads" that led them ever deeper into the wilderness of leaf and root. At night they camped beneath a starry sky and gazed up at the comet. The black brothers had left Castle Black in good spirits, joking and trading tales, but of late the brooding silence of the wood seemed to have sombered them all. Jests had grown fewer and tempers shorter. No one would admit to being afraid—they were men of the Night's Watch, after all—but Jon could feel the unease. Four empty villages, no wildlings anywhere, even the game seemingly fled. The haunted forest had never seemed more haunted, even veteran rangers agreed.

As he rode, Jon peeled off his glove to air his burned fingers. *Ugly things.* He remembered suddenly how he used to muss Arya's hair. His little stick of a sister. He wondered how she was faring. It made him a little sad to think that he might never muss her hair again. He began to flex his hand, opening and closing the fingers. If he let his sword hand stiffen and grow clumsy, it well might be the end of him, he knew. A man needed his sword beyond the Wall.

Jon found Samwell Tarly with the other stewards, watering his horses. He had three to tend: his own mount, and two packhorses, each bearing a large wire-and-wicker cage full of ravens. The birds flapped their wings at Jon's approach and screamed at him through the bars. A few shrieks sounded suspiciously like words. "Have you been teaching them to talk?" he asked Sam.

"A few words. Three of them can say *snow.*"

"One bird croaking my name was bad enough," said Jon, "and snow's nothing a black brother wants to hear about." Snow often meant death in the north.

"Was there anything in Whitetree?"

"Bones, ashes, and empty houses." Jon handed Sam the roll of parchment. "The Old Bear wants word sent back to Aemon."

Sam took a bird from one of the cages, stroked its feathers, attached the message, and said, "Fly home now, brave one. Home." The raven *quorked* something unintelligible back at him, and Sam tossed it into the air. Flapping, it beat its way skyward through the trees. "I wish he could carry me with him."

"Still?"

"Well," said Sam, "yes, but . . . I'm not as frightened as I was, truly. The first night, every time I heard someone getting up to make water, I thought it was wildlings creeping in to slit my throat. I was afraid that if I closed my eyes, I might never open them again, only . . . well . . . dawn came after all." He managed a wan smile. "I may be craven, but I'm not *stupid.* I'm sore and my back aches from riding and from sleeping on the ground, but I'm hardly scared at all. Look." He held out a hand for Jon to see how steady it was. "I've been working on my maps."

The world is strange, Jon thought. Two hundred brave men had left the Wall, and the only one who was not growing more fearful was Sam, the self-confessed coward. "We'll make a ranger of you yet," he joked. "Next thing, you'll want to be an outrider like Grenn. Shall I speak to the Old Bear?"

"Don't you dare!" Sam pulled up the hood of his enormous black cloak and clambered awkwardly back onto his horse. It was a plow horse, big and slow and clumsy, but better able to bear his weight than the little garrons the rangers rode. "I had hoped we might stay the night in the village," he said wistfully. "It would be nice to sleep under a roof again."

"Too few roofs for all of us." Jon mounted again, gave Sam a parting smile, and rode off. The column was well under way, so he swung wide around the village to avoid the worst of the congestion. He had seen enough of Whitetree.

Ghost emerged from the undergrowth so suddenly that the garron shied and reared. The white wolf hunted well away from the line of march, but he was not having much better fortune than the foragers Smallwood sent out after game. The woods were as empty as the villages, Dywen had told him one night around the fire. "We're a large party," Jon had said. "The game's probably been frightened away by all the noise we make on the march."

"Frightened away by *something,* no doubt," Dywen said.

Once the horse had settled, Ghost loped along easily

beside him. Jon caught up to Mormont as he was wending his way around a hawthorn thicket. "Is the bird
away?" the Old Bear asked.

"Yes, my lord. Sam is teaching them to talk."

The Old Bear snorted. "He'll regret that. Damned
things make a lot of noise, but they never say a thing
worth hearing."

They rode in silence, until Jon said, "If my uncle
found all these villages empty as well—"

"—he would have made it his purpose to learn why,"
Lord Mormont finished for him, "and it may well be
someone or something did not want that known. Well,
we'll be three hundred when Qhorin joins us. Whatever
enemy waits out here will not find us so easy to deal
with. We will find them, Jon, I promise you."

Or they will find us, thought Jon.

ARYA

The river was a blue-green ribbon shining in the morning sun. Reeds grew thick in the shallows along the banks, and Arya saw a water snake skimming across the surface, ripples spreading out behind it as it went. Overhead a hawk flew in lazy circles.

It seemed a peaceful place . . . until Koss spotted the dead man. "There, in the reeds." He pointed, and Arya saw it. The body of a soldier, shapeless and swollen. His sodden green cloak had hung up on a rotted log, and a school of tiny silver fishes were nibbling at his face. "I told you there was bodies," Lommy announced. "I could taste them in that water."

When Yoren saw the corpse, he spat. "Dobber, see if he's got anything worth the taking. Mail, knife, a bit o' coin, what have you." He spurred his gelding and rode out into the river, but the horse struggled in the soft mud and beyond the reeds the water deepened. Yoren rode back angry, his horse covered in brown slime up to the knees. "We won't be crossing here. Koss, you'll come with me upriver, look for a ford. Woth, Gerren, you go downstream. The rest o' you wait here. Put a guard out."

Dobber found a leather purse in the dead man's belt. Inside were four coppers and a little hank of blond hair tied up with a red ribbon. Lommy and Tarber stripped naked and went wading, and Lommy scooped up handfuls of slimy mud and threw them at Hot Pie, shouting, "Mud Pie! Mud Pie!" In the back of their wagon, Rorge cursed and threatened and told them to unchain him while Yoren was gone, but no one paid him any mind. Kurz caught a fish with his bare hands. Arya saw how he did it, standing over a shallow pool, calm as still water, his hand darting out quick as a snake when the fish swam near. It didn't look as hard as catching cats. Fish didn't have claws.

It was midday when the others returned. Woth reported a wooden bridge half a mile downstream, but someone had burned it up. Yoren peeled a sourleaf off the bale. "Might be we could swim the horses over, maybe the donkeys, but there's no way we'll get those wagons across. And there's smoke to the north and west, more fires, could be this side o' the river's the place we want to be." He picked up a long stick and drew a circle in the mud, a line trailing down from it. "That's Gods Eye, with the river flowing south. We're here." He poked a hole beside the line of the river, under the circle. "We can't go round west of the lake, like I thought. East takes us back to the kingsroad." He moved the stick up to where the line and circle met. "Near as I recall, there's a town here. The holdfast's stone, and there's a lordling got his seat there too, just a towerhouse, but he'll have a guard, might be a knight or two. We follow the river north, should be there before dark. They'll have boats, so I mean to sell all we got and hire us one." He drew the stick up through the circle of the lake, from bottom to top. "Gods be good, we'll find a wind and sail across the Gods Eye to Harrentown." He thrust the point down at the top of the circle. "We can buy new mounts there, or else take shelter at

Harrenhal. That's Lady Whent's seat, and she's always been a friend o' the Watch."

Hot Pie's eyes got wide. "There's ghosts in Harrenhal . . ."

Yoren spat. "There's for your ghosts." He tossed the stick down in the mud. "Mount up."

Arya was remembering the stories Old Nan used to tell of Harrenhal. Evil King Harren had walled himself up inside, so Aegon unleashed his dragons and turned the castle into a pyre. Nan said that fiery spirits still haunted the blackened towers. Sometimes men went to sleep safe in their beds and were found dead in the morning, all burnt up. Arya didn't really believe that, and anyhow it had all happened a long time ago. Hot Pie was being silly; it wouldn't be ghosts at Harrenhal, it would be *knights*. Arya could reveal herself to Lady Whent, and the knights would escort her home and keep her safe. That was what knights did; they kept you safe, especially women. Maybe Lady Whent would even help the crying girl.

The river track was no kingsroad, yet it was not half bad for what it was, and for once the wagons rolled along smartly. They saw the first house an hour shy of evenfall, a snug little thatch-roofed cottage surrounded by fields of wheat. Yoren rode out ahead, hallooing, but got no answer. "Dead, might be. Or hiding. Dobber, Rey, with me." The three men went into the cottage. "Pots is gone, no sign o' any coin laid by," Yoren muttered when they returned. "No animals. Run, most like. Might be we met 'em on the kingsroad." At least the house and field had not been burned, and there were no corpses about. Tarber found a garden out back, and they pulled some onions and radishes and filled a sack with cabbages before they went on their way.

A little farther up the road, they glimpsed a forester's cabin surrounded by old trees and neatly stacked logs ready for the splitting, and later a ramshackle stilt-house leaning over the river on poles ten feet tall, both deserted. They passed more fields, wheat and corn and barley ripening in the sun, but here there were no men sitting in trees, nor walking the rows with scythes. Finally the town came into view; a cluster of white houses spread out around the walls of the holdfast, a big sept with a shingled wooden roof, the lord's towerhouse sitting on a small rise to the west . . . and no sign of any people, anywhere.

Yoren sat on his horse, frowning through his tangle of beard. "Don't like it," he said, "but there it is. We'll go have us a look. A *careful* look. See maybe there's some folk hiding. Might be they left a boat behind, or some weapons we can use."

The black brother left ten to guard the wagons and the whimpery little girl, and split the rest of them into four groups of five to search the town. "Keep your eyes and ears open," he warned them, before he rode off to the towerhouse to see if there was any sign of the lordling or his guards.

Arya found herself with Gendry, Hot Pie, and Lommy. Squat, kettle-bellied Woth had pulled an oar on a galley once, which made him the next best thing they had to a sailor, so Yoren told him to take them down to the lakefront and see if they could find a boat. As they rode between the silent white houses, gooseprickles crawled up Arya's arms. This empty town frightened her almost as much as the burnt holdfast where they'd found the crying girl and the one-armed woman. Why would people run off and leave their homes and everything? What could scare them so much?

The sun was low to the west, and the houses cast long dark shadows. A sudden clap of sound made Arya reach for Needle, but it was only a shutter banging in the wind. After the open river shore, the closeness of the town unnerved her.

When she glimpsed the lake ahead between houses and trees, Arya put her knees into her horse, galloping past Woth and Gendry. She burst out onto the grassy sward beside the pebbled shore. The setting sun made the tranquil surface of the water shimmer like a sheet of beaten copper. It was the biggest lake she had ever seen, with no hint of a far shore. She saw a rambling inn to her left, built out over the water on heavy wooden pilings. To her right, a long pier jutted into the lake, and there were other docks farther east, wooden fingers reaching out from the town. But the only boat in view was an upside-down rowboat abandoned on the rocks beneath the inn, its bottom thoroughly rotted out. "They're gone," Arya said, dejected. What would they do now?

"There's an inn," Lommy said, when the others rode up. "Do you think they left any food? Or ale?"

"Let's go see," Hot Pie suggested.

"Never you mind about no inn," snapped Woth. "Yoren said we're to find a boat."

"They took the boats." Somehow Arya knew it was true; they could search the whole town, and they'd find no more than the upside-down rowboat. Despondent, she climbed off her horse and knelt by the lake. The water lapped softly around her legs. A few lantern bugs were coming out, their little lights blinking on and off. The green water was warm as tears, but there was no salt in it. It tasted of summer and mud and growing things. Arya plunged her face down into it to wash off the dust and dirt and sweat of the day. When she leaned back the trickles ran down the back of her neck and under her collar. They felt good. She wished she could take off her clothes and swim, gliding through the warm water like an skinny pink otter. Maybe she could swim all the way to Winterfell.

Woth was shouting at her to help search, so she did, peering into boathouses and sheds while her horse grazed along the shore. They found some sails, some nails, buckets of tar gone hard, and a mother cat with a litter of new-born kittens. But no boats.

The town was as dark as any forest when Yoren and the others reappeared. "Tower's empty," he said. "Lord's gone off to fight maybe, or to get his smallfolk to safety, no telling. Not a horse or pig left in town, but we'll eat. Saw a goose running loose, and some chickens, and there's good fish in the Gods Eye."

"The boats are gone," Arya reported.

"We could patch the bottom of that rowboat," said Koss.

"Might do for four o' us," Yoren said.

"There's nails," Lommy pointed out. "And there's trees all around. We could build us all boats."

Yoren spat. "You know anything 'bout boat-building, dyer's boy?" Lommy looked blank.

"A raft," suggested Gendry. "Anyone can build a raft, and long poles for pushing."

Yoren looked thoughtful. "Lake's too deep to pole across, but if we stayed to the shallows near shore . . . it'd mean leaving the wagons. Might be that's best. I'll sleep on it."

"Can we stay at the inn?" Lommy asked.

"We'll stay in the holdfast, with the gates barred," the old man said. "I like the feel o' stone walls about me when I sleep."

Arya could not keep quiet. "We shouldn't stay here," she blurted. "The people didn't. They all ran off, even their lord."

"Arry's scared," Lommy announced, braying laughter.

"I'm *not*," she snapped back, "but *they* were."

"Smart boy," said Yoren. "Thing is, the folks who lived here were at war, like it or no. We're not. Night's Watch takes no part, so no man's our enemy."

And no man's our friend, she thought, but this time she held her tongue. Lommy and the rest were looking at her, and she did not want to seem craven in front of them.

The holdfast gates were studded with iron nails. Within, they found a pair of iron bars the size of saplings, with post holes in the ground and metal brackets on the gate. When they slotted the bars through the brackets, they made a huge X brace. It was no Red Keep, Yoren announced when they'd explored the holdfast top to bottom, but it was better than most, and should do for a night well enough. The walls were rough unmortared stone ten feet high, with a wooden catwalk inside the battlements. There was a postern gate to the north, and Gerren discovered a trap under the straw in the old wooden barn, leading to a narrow, winding tunnel. He followed it a long way under the earth and came out by the lake. Yoren had them roll a wagon on top of the trap, to make certain no one came in that way. He divided them into three watches, and sent Tarber, Kurz, and Cutjack off to the abandoned towerhouse to keep an eye out from on high. Kurz had a hunting horn to sound if danger threatened.

They drove their wagons and animals inside and barred the gates behind them. The barn was a ramshackle thing, large enough to hold half the animals in the town. The haven, where the townfolk would shelter in times of trouble, was even larger, low and long and built of stone, with a thatched roof. Koss went out the postern gate and brought the goose back, and two chickens as well, and Yoren allowed a cookfire. There was a big kitchen inside the holdfast, though all the pots and kettles had been taken. Gendry, Dobber, and Arya drew cook duty. Dobber told Arya to pluck the fowl while Gendry split wood. "Why can't I split the wood?" she asked, but no one listened. Sullenly, she set to plucking a chicken while Yoren sat on the end of the bench sharpening the edge of his dirk with a whetstone.

When the food was ready, Arya ate a chicken leg and a bit of onion. No one talked much, not even Lommy. Gendry went off by himself afterward, polishing his helm with a look on his face like he wasn't even there. The crying girl whimpered and wept, but when Hot Pie offered her a bit of goose she gobbled it down and looked for more.

Arya drew second watch, so she found a straw pallet in the haven. Sleep did not come easy, so she borrowed Yoren's stone and set to honing Needle. Syrio Forel had said that a dull blade was like a lame horse. Hot Pie squatted on the pallet beside her, watching her work.

"Where'd you get a good sword like that?" he asked. When he saw the look she gave him, he raised his hands defensively. "I never said you stole it, I just wanted to know where you got it, is all."

"My brother gave it to me," she muttered.

"I never knew you had no brother."

Arya paused to scratch under her shirt. There were fleas in the straw, though she couldn't see why a few more would bother her. "I have lots of brothers."

"You do? Are they bigger than you, or littler?"

I shouldn't be talking like this. Yoren said I should keep my mouth shut. "Bigger," she lied. "They have swords too, big longswords, and they showed me how to kill people who bother me."

"I was talking, not bothering." Hot Pie went off and let her alone and Arya curled up on her pallet. She could hear the crying girl from the far side of the haven. *I wish she'd just be quiet. Why does she have to cry all the time?*

She must have slept, though she never remembered closing her eyes. She dreamed a wolf was howling, and the sound was so terrible that it woke her at once. Arya sat up on her pallet with her heart thumping. "Hot Pie, wake up." She scrambled to her feet. "Woth, Gendry, didn't you hear?" She pulled on a boot.

All around her, men and boys stirred and crawled from their pallets. "What's wrong?" Hot Pie asked. "Hear what?" Gendry wanted to know. "Arry had a bad dream," someone else said.

"No, I heard it," she insisted. "A wolf."

"Arry has wolves in his head," sneered Lommy. "Let them howl," Gerren said, "they're out there, we're in here." Woth agreed. "Never saw no wolf could storm a holdfast." Hot Pie was saying, "I never heard nothing."

"It was a *wolf*," she shouted at them as she yanked on her second boot. "Something's wrong, someone's coming, get *up!*"

Before they could hoot her down again, the sound came shuddering through the night—only it was no wolf this time, it was Kurz blowing his hunting horn, sounding danger. In a heartbeat, all of them were pulling on clothes and snatching for whatever weapons they owned. Arya ran for the gate as the horn sounded again. As she dashed past the barn, Biter threw himself furiously against his chains, and Jaqen H'ghar called out from the back of their wagon. "Boy! Sweet boy! Is it war, red war? Boy, free us. A man can fight. *Boy!"* She ignored him and plunged on. By then she could hear horses and shouts beyond the wall.

She scrambled up onto the catwalk. The parapets were a bit too high and Arya a bit too short; she had to wedge her toes into the holes between the stones to see over. For a moment she thought the town was full of lantern bugs. Then she realized they were men with torches, galloping between the houses. She saw a roof go up, flames licking at the belly of the night with hot orange tongues as the thatch caught. Another followed, and then another, and soon there were fires blazing everywhere.

Gendry climbed up beside her, wearing his helm. "How many?"

Arya tried to count, but they were riding too fast, torches spinning through the air as they flung them. "A hundred," she said. "Two hundred, I don't know." Over the roar of the flames, she could hear shouts. "They'll come for us soon."

"There," Gendry said, pointing.

A column of riders moved between the burning buildings toward the holdfast. Firelight glittered off metal helms and spattered their mail and plate with orange and yellow highlights. One carried a banner on a tall lance. She thought it was red, but it was hard to tell in the night, with the fires roaring all around. Everything seemed red or black or orange.

The fire leapt from one house to another. Arya saw a tree consumed, the flames creeping across its branches until it stood against the night in robes of living orange. Everyone was awake now, manning the catwalks or struggling with the frightened animals below. She could hear Yoren shouting commands. Something bumped against her leg, and she glanced down to discover the crying girl clutching her. "Get away!" She wrenched her leg free. "What are you doing up here? Run and hide someplace, you stupid." She shoved the girl away.

The riders reined up before the gates. *"You in the holdfast!"* shouted a knight in a tall helm with a spiked crest. *"Open, in the name of the king!"*

"Aye, and which king is that?" old Reysen yelled back down, before Woth cuffed him into silence.

Yoren climbed the battlement beside the gate, his faded black cloak tied to a wooden staff. *"You men hold down here!"* he shouted. *"The townfolk's gone."*

"And who are you, old man? One of Lord Beric's cravens?" called the knight in the spiked helm. "If that fat fool Thoros is in there, ask him how he likes *these* fires."

"Got no such man here," Yoren shouted back. "Only some lads for the Watch. Got no part o' your war." He hoisted up the staff, so they could all see the color of his cloak. "Have a look. That's black, for the Night's Watch."

"Or black for House Dondarrion," called the man who bore the enemy banner. Arya could see its colors more clearly now in the light of the burning town: a golden lion on red. "Lord Beric's sigil is a purple lightning bolt on a black field."

Suddenly Arya remembered the morning she had thrown the orange in Sansa's face and gotten juice all over her stupid ivory silk gown. There had been some southron lordling at the tourney, her sister's stupid friend Jeyne was in love with him. He had a lightning bolt on his shield and her father had sent him out to behead the Hound's brother. It seemed a thousand years ago now, something that had happened to a different person in a different life . . . to Arya Stark the Hand's daughter, not Arry the orphan boy. How would Arry know lords and such?

"Are you blind, man?" Yoren waved his staff back and

forth, making the cloak ripple. "You see a bloody light-ning bolt?"

"By night all banners look black," the knight in the spiked helm observed. "Open, or we'll know you for outlaws in league with the king's enemies."

Yoren spat. "Who's got your command?"

"I do." The reflections of burning houses glimmered dully on the armor of his warhorse as the others parted to let him pass. He was a stout man with a manticore on his shield, and ornate scrollwork crawling across his steel breastplate. Through the open visor of his helm, a face pale and piggy peered up. "Ser Amory Lorch, bannerman to Lord Tywin Lannister of Casterly Rock, the Hand of the King. The *true* king, Joffrey." He had a high, thin voice. "In his name, I command you to open these gates."

All around them, the town burned. The night air was full of smoke, and the drifting red embers outnumbered the stars. Yoren scowled. "Don't see the need. Do what you want to the town, it's naught to me, but leave us be. We're no foes to you."

Look with your eyes, Arya wanted to shout at the men below. "Can't they *see* we're no lords or knights?" she whispered.

"I don't think they care, Arry," Gendry whispered back.

And she looked at Ser Amory's face, the way Syrio had taught her to look, and she saw that he was right.

"If you are no traitors, open your gates," Ser Amory called. "We'll make certain you're telling it true and be on our way."

Yoren was chewing sourleaf. "Told you, no one here but us. You got my word on that."

The knight in the spiked helm laughed. "The crow gives us his *word*."

"You lost, old man?" mocked one of the spearmen. "The Wall's a long way north o' here."

"I command you once more, in King Joffrey's name, to prove the loyalty you profess and open these gates," said Ser Amory.

For a long moment Yoren considered, chewing. Then he spat. "Don't think I will."

"So be it. You defy the king's command, and so proclaim yourselves rebels, black cloaks or no."

"Got me young boys in here," Yoren shouted down.

"Young boys and old men die the same." Ser Amory raised a lanquid fist, and a spear came hurtling from the fire-bright shadows behind. Yoren must have been the target, but it was Woth beside him who was hit. The spearhead went in his throat and exploded out the back of his neck, dark and wet. Woth grabbed at the shaft, and fell boneless from the walk.

"Storm the walls and kill them all," Ser Amory said in a bored voice. More spears flew. Arya yanked down Hot Pie by the back of his tunic. From outside came the rattle of armor, the scrape of swords on scabbards, the banging of spears on shields, mingled with curses and the hoofbeats of racing horses. A torch sailed spinning above their heads, trailing fingers of fire as it thumped down in the dirt of the yard.

"Blades!" Yoren shouted. "Spread apart, defend the wall wherever they hit. Koss, Urreg, hold the postern. Lommy, pull that spear out of Woth and get up where he was."

Hot Pie dropped his shortsword when he tried to unsheath it. Arya shoved the blade back into his hand. "I don't know how to swordfight," he said, white-eyed.

"It's easy," Arya said, but the lie died in her throat as a *hand* grasped the top of the parapet. She saw it by the light of the burning town, so clear that it was as if time had stopped. The fingers were blunt, callused, wiry black hairs grew between the knuckles, there was dirt under the nail of the thumb. *Fear cuts deeper than swords*, she remembered as the top of a pothelm loomed up behind the hand.

She slashed down hard, and Needle's castle-forged steel bit into the grasping fingers between the knuckles. *"Winterfell!"* she screamed. Blood spurted, fingers flew, and the helmed face vanished as suddenly as it had appeared. "Behind!" Hot Pie yelled. Arya whirled. The second man was bearded and helmetless, his dirk between his teeth to leave both hands free for climbing. As he swung his leg over the parapet, she drove her point at his eyes. Needle never touched him; he reeled backward and fell. *I hope he falls on his face and cuts off his tongue.* "Watch *them*, not me!" she screamed at Hot Pie. The next time someone tried to climb their part of the wall, the boy hacked at his hands with his swordshort until the man dropped away.

Ser Amory had no ladders, but the holdfast walls were rough-cut and unmortared, easy to climb, and there seemed to be no end to the foes. For each one Arya cut or stabbed or shoved back, another was coming over the wall. The knight in the spiked helm reached the rampart, but Yoren tangled his black banner around his spike, and forced the point of his dirk through his armor while the man was fighting the cloth. Every time Arya looked up, more torches were flying, trailing long tongues of flame that lingered behind her eyes. She saw a gold lion on a red banner and thought of Joffrey, wishing he was here so she could drive Needle through his sneery face. When four men assaulted the gate with axes, Koss shot them down with arrows, one by one. Dobber wrestled a man off the walk, and Lommy smashed his head with a rock before he could rise, and hooted until he saw the knife in Dobber's belly and realized he wouldn't be getting up either. Arya jumped over a dead boy no older than Jon, lying with his arm cut off. She didn't think she'd done it, but she wasn't sure. She heard Qyle beg for mercy before a knight with a wasp on his shield smashed his face in with a spiked mace. Everything smelled of blood and smoke and iron and piss, but after a time it seemed like that was only one smell. She never saw how the skinny man got over the wall, but when he did she fell on him with Gendry and Hot Pie. Gendry's sword shattered on the man's helm, tearing it off his head. Underneath he was bald and scared-looking, with missing teeth and a speckly grey beard, but even as she was feeling sorry for him she was killing him, shouting, *"Winterfell! Winterfell!"* while Hot Pie screamed *"Hot Pie!"* beside her as he hacked at the man's scrawny neck.

When the skinny man was dead, Gendry stole his sword and leapt down into the yard to fight some more. Arya looked past him, and saw steel shadows running through the holdfast, firelight shining off mail and blades, and she knew that they'd gotten over the wall somewhere, or broken through at the postern. She jumped down beside Gendry, landing the way Syrio had taught her. The night rang to the clash of steel and the cries of the wounded and dying. For a moment Arya stood uncertain, not knowing which way to go. Death was all around her.

And then Yoren was there, shaking her, screaming in her face. *"Boy!"* he yelled, the way he always yelled it. "Get *out*, it's done, we've lost. Herd up all you can, you and him and the others, the boys, you get them out. *Now!"*

"How?" Arya said.

"That trap," he screamed. "Under the barn."

Quick as that he was gone, off to fight, sword in hand. Arya grabbed Gendry by the arm. "He said *go*," she shouted, "the barn, the way out." Through the slits of his helm, the Bull's eyes shone with reflected fire. He nodded. They called Hot Pie down from the wall and found Lommy Greenhands where he lay bleeding from a spear thrust through his calf. They found Gerren too, but he was hurt too bad to move. As they were running toward the barn, Arya spied the crying girl sitting in the middle of the chaos, surrounded by smoke and slaughter. She grabbed her by the hand and pulled her to her feet as the others raced ahead. The girl wouldn't walk, even when slapped. Arya dragged her with her right hand while she held Needle in the left. Ahead, the night was a sullen red. *The barn's on fire*, she thought. Flames were licking up its sides from where a torch had fallen on straw, and she could hear the screaming of the animals trapped within. Hot Pie stepped out of the barn. "Arry, *come on!* Lommy's *gone*, leave her if she won't come!"

Stubbornly, Arya dragged all the harder, pulling the crying girl along. Hot Pie scuttled back inside, abandoning them . . . but Gendry came back, the fire shining so bright on his polished helm that the horns seemed to glow orange. He ran to them, and hoisted the crying girl up over his shoulder. *"Run!"*

Rushing through the barn doors was like running into a furnace. The air was swirling with smoke, the back wall a sheet of fire ground to roof. Their horses and donkeys were kicking and rearing and screaming. *The poor animals*, Arya thought. Then she saw the wagon, and the three men manacled to its bed. Biter was flinging himself against the chains, blood running down his arms from where the irons clasped his wrists. Rorge screamed curses, kicking at the wood. "Boy!" called Jaqen H'ghar. "Sweet boy!"

The open trap was only a few feet ahead, but the fire was spreading fast, consuming the old wood and dry straw faster than she would have believed. Arya remembered the Hound's horrible burned face. "Tunnel's narrow," Gendry shouted. "How do we get her through?"

"Pull her," Arya said. "Push her."

"Good boys, kind boys," called Jaqen H'ghar, coughing.

"Get these fucking chains off!" Rorge screamed.

Gendry ignored them. "You go first, then her, then me. Hurry, it's a long way."

"When you split the firewood," Arya remembered, "where did you leave the axe?"

"Out by the haven." He spared a glance for the chained men. "I'd save the donkeys first. There's no time."

"You take her!" she yelled. "You get her out! You do it!" The fire beat at her back with hot red wings as she fled the burning barn. It felt blessedly cool outside, but men were dying all around her. She saw Koss throw down his blade to yield, and she saw them kill him where he stood. Smoke was everywhere. There was no sign of Yoren, but the axe was where Gendry had left it, by the woodpile outside the haven. As she wrenched it free, a mailed hand grabbed her arm. Spinning, Arya drove the head of the axe hard between his legs. She never saw his face, only the dark blood seeping between the links of his hauberk. Going back into that barn was the hardest thing she ever did. Smoke was pouring out the open door like a writhing black snake, and she could hear the screams of the poor animals inside, donkeys and horses and men. She chewed her lip, and darted through the doors, crouched low where the smoke wasn't quite so thick.

A donkey was caught in a ring of fire, shrieking in terror and pain. She could smell the stench of burning hair. The roof was gone up too, and things were falling down, pieces of flaming wood and bits of straw and hay. Arya put a hand over her mouth and nose. She couldn't see the wagon for the smoke, but she could still hear Biter screaming. She crawled toward the sound.

And then a wheel was looming over her. The wagon *jumped* and moved a half foot when Biter threw himself against his chains again. Jaqen saw her, but it was too hard to breathe, let alone talk. She threw the axe into the wagon. Rorge caught it and lifted it over his head, rivers of sooty sweat pouring down his noseless face. Arya was running, coughing. She heard the steel crash through the old wood, and again, again. An instant later came a *crack* as loud as thunder, and the bottom of the wagon came ripping loose in an explosion of splinters.

Arya rolled headfirst into the tunnel and dropped five feet. She got dirt in her mouth but she didn't care, the taste was fine, the taste was mud and water and worms and life. Under the earth the air was cool and dark. Above was nothing but blood and roaring red and choking smoke and the screams of dying horses. She moved her belt around so Needle would not be in her way, and began to crawl. A dozen feet down the tunnel she heard the sound, like the roar of some monstrous beast, and a cloud of hot smoke and black dust came billowing up behind her, smelling of hell. Arya held her breath and kissed the mud on the floor of the tunnel and cried. For whom, she could not say.

TYRION

The queen was not disposed to wait on Varys. "Treason is vile enough," she declared furiously, "but this is barefaced naked villainy, and I do not need that mincing eunuch to tell me what must be done with villains."

Tyrion took the letters from his sister's hand and compared them side by side. There were two copies, the words exactly alike, though they had been written by different hands.

"Maester Frenken received the first missive at Castle Stokeworth," Grand Maester Pycelle explained. "The second copy came through Lord Gyles."

Littlefinger fingered his beard. "If Stannis bothered with *them*, it's past certain every other lord in the Seven Kingdoms saw a copy as well."

"I want these letters burned, every one," Cersei declared. "No hint of this must reach my son's ears, or my father's."

"I imagine Father's heard rather more than a hint by now," Tyrion said dryly. "Doubtless Stannis sent a bird to Casterly Rock, and another to Harrenhal. As for burning the letters, to what point? The song is sung, the wine is spilled, the wench is pregnant. And this is not as dire as it seems, in truth."

Cersei turned on him in green-eyed fury. "Are you utterly witless? Did you read what he says? *The boy Joffrey*, he calls him. And he dares to accuse *me* of incest, adultery, and treason!"

Only because you're guilty. It was astonishing to see how angry Cersei could wax over accusations she knew perfectly well to be true. *If we lose the war, she ought to take up mummery, she has a gift for it.* Tyrion waited until she was done and said, "Stannis must have some pretext to justify his rebellion. What did you expect him to write? 'Joffrey is my brother's trueborn son and heir, but I mean to take his throne for all that'?"

"I will not suffer to be called a whore!"

Why, sister, he never claims Jaime paid you. Tyrion made a show of glancing over the writing again. There had been some niggling phrase . . . "Done in the Light of the Lord," he read. "A queer choice of words, that."

Pycelle cleared his throat. "These words often appear in letters and documents from the Free Cities. They mean no more than, let us say, *written in the sight of god.* The god of the red priests. It is their usage, I do believe."

"Varys told us some years past that Lady Selyse had taken up with a red priest," Littlefinger reminded them.

Tyrion tapped the paper. "And now it would seem her lord husband has done the same. We can use that against him. Urge the High Septon to reveal how Stannis has turned against the gods as well as his rightful king . . ."

"Yes, yes," the queen said impatiently, "but first we must stop this filth from spreading further. The council must issue an edict. Any man heard speaking of incest or calling Joff a bastard should lose his tongue for it."

"A prudent measure," said Grand Maester Pycelle, his chain of office clinking as he nodded.

"A folly," sighed Tyrion. "When you tear out a man's

tongue, you are not proving him a liar, you're only telling the world that you fear what he might say."

"So what would *you* have us do?" his sister demanded.

"Very little. Let them whisper, they'll grow bored with the tale soon enough. Any man with a thimble of sense will see it for a clumsy attempt to justify usurping the crown. Does Stannis offer proof? How could he, when it never happened?" Tyrion gave his sister his sweetest smile.

"That's so," she had to say. "Still . . ."

"Your Grace, your brother has the right of this." Petyr Baelish steepled his fingers. "If we attempt to silence this talk, we only lend it credence. Better to treat it with contempt, like the pathetic lie it is. And meantime, fight fire with fire."

Cersei gave him a measuring look. "What sort of fire?"

"A tale of somewhat the same nature, perhaps. But more easily believed. Lord Stannis has spent most of his marriage apart from his wife. Not that I fault him, I'd do the same were I married to Lady Selyse. Nonetheless, if we put it about that her daughter is baseborn and Stannis a cuckold, well . . . the smallfolk are always eager to believe the worst of their lords, particularly those as stern, sour, and prickly proud as Stannis Baratheon."

"He has never been much loved, that's true." Cersei considered a moment. "So we pay him back in his own coin. Yes, I like this. Who can we name as Lady Selyse's lover? She has two brothers, I believe. And one of her uncles has been with her on Dragonstone all this time . . ."

"Ser Axell Florent is her castellan." Loath as Tyrion was to admit it, Littlefinger's scheme had promise. Stannis had never been enamored of his wife, but he was bristly as a hedgehog where his honor was concerned and mistrustful by nature. If they could sow discord between him and his followers, it could only help their cause. "The child has the Florent ears, I'm told."

Littlefinger gestured languidly. "A trade envoy from Lys once observed to me that Lord Stannis must love his daughter very well, since he'd erected hundreds of statues of her all along the walls of Dragonstone. 'My lord,' I had to tell him, 'those are gargoyles.'" He chuckled. "Ser Axell might serve for Shireen's father, but in my experience, the more bizarre and shocking a tale the more apt it is to be repeated. Stannis keeps an especially grotesque fool, a lackwit with a tattooed face."

Grand Maester Pycelle gaped at him, aghast. "Surely you do not mean to suggest that Lady Selyse would bring a *fool* into her bed?"

"You'd have to be a fool to want to bed Selyse Florent," said Littlefinger. "Doubtless Patchface reminded her of Stannis. And the best lies contain within them nuggets of truth, enough to give a listener pause. As it happens, this fool is utterly devoted to the girl and follows her everywhere. They even look somewhat alike. Shireen has a mottled, half-frozen face as well."

Pycelle was lost. "But that is from the greyscale that near killed her as a babe, poor thing."

"I like my tale better," said Littlefinger, "and so will the smallfolk. Most of them believe that if a woman eats rabbit while pregnant, her child will be born with long floppy ears."

Cersei smiled the sort of smile she customarily reserved for Jaime. "Lord Petyr, you are a wicked creature."

"Thank you, Your Grace."

"And a most accomplished liar," Tyrion added, less warmly. *This one is more dangerous than I knew,* he reflected.

Littlefinger's grey-green eyes met the dwarf's mismatched stare with no hint of unease. "We all have our gifts, my lord."

The queen was too caught up in her revenge to take note of the exchange. "Cuckolded by a halfwit fool! Stannis will be laughed at in every winesink this side of the narrow sea."

"The story should not come from us," Tyrion said, "or it will be seen for a self-serving lie." *Which it is, to be sure.*

Once more Littlefinger supplied the answer. "Whores love to gossip, and as it happens I own a brothel or three. And no doubt Varys can plant seeds in the alehouses and pot-shops."

"Varys," Cersei said, frowning. "Where *is* Varys?"

"I have been wondering about that myself, Your Grace."

"The Spider spins his secret webs day and night," Grand Maester Pycelle said ominously. "I mistrust that one, my lords."

"And he speaks so kindly of you." Tyrion pushed himself off his chair. As it happened, he knew what the eunuch was about, but it was nothing the other councillors needed to hear. "Pray excuse me, my lords. Other business calls."

Cersei was instantly suspicious. "King's business?"

"Nothing you need trouble yourself about."

"I'll be the judge of that."

"Would you spoil my surprise?" Tyrion said. "I'm having a gift made for Joffrey. A little chain."

"What does he need with another chain? He has gold chains and silver, more than he can wear. If you think for a moment you can buy Joff's love with gifts—"

"Why, surely I *have* the king's love, as he has mine. And *this* chain I believe he may one day treasure above all others." The little man bowed and waddled to the door.

Bronn was waiting outside the council chambers to escort him back to the Tower of the Hand. "The smiths are in your audience chamber, waiting your pleasure," he said as they crossed the ward.

"Waiting my pleasure. I like the ring of that, Bronn. You almost sound a proper courtier. Next you'll be kneeling."

"Fuck you, dwarf."

"That's Shae's task." Tyrion heard Lady Tanda calling to him merrily from the top of the serpentine steps.

Pretending not to notice her, he waddled a bit faster. "See that my litter is readied, I'll be leaving the castle as soon as I'm done here." Two of the Moon Brothers had the door guard. Tyrion greeted them pleasantly, and grimaced before starting up the stairs. The climb to his bedchamber made his legs ache.

Within he found a boy of twelve laying out clothing on the bed; his squire, such that he was. Podrick Payne was so shy he was furtive. Tyrion had never quite gotten over the suspicion that his father had inflicted the boy on him as a joke.

"Your garb, my lord," the boy mumbled when Tyrion entered, staring down at his boots. Even when he worked up the courage to speak, Pod could never quite manage to look at you. "For the audience. And your chain. The Hand's chain."

"Very good. Help me dress." The doublet was black velvet covered with golden studs in the shape of lions' heads, the chain a loop of solid gold hands, the fingers of each clasping the wrist of the next. Pod brought him a cloak of crimson silk fringed in gold, cut to his height. On a normal man, it would be no more than a half cape.

The Hand's private audience chamber was not so large as the king's, nor a patch on the vastness of the throne room, but Tyrion liked its Myrish rugs, wall hangings, and sense of intimacy. As he entered, his steward cried out, "Tyrion Lannister, Hand of the King." He liked that too. The gaggle of smiths, armorers, and ironmongers that Bronn had collected fell to their knees.

He hoisted himself up into the high seat under the round golden window and bid them rise. "Goodmen, I know you are all busy, so I will be succinct. Pod, if you please." The boy handed him a canvas sack. Tyrion yanked the drawstring and upended the bag. Its contents spilled onto the rug with a muffled *thunk* of metal on wool. "I had these made at the castle forge. I want a thousand more just like them."

One of the smiths knelt to inspect the object: three

immense steel links, twisted together. "A mighty chain."

"Mighty, but short," the dwarf replied. "Somewhat like me. I fancy one a good deal longer. Do you have a name?"

",They call me Ironbelly, m'lord." The smith was squat and broad, plainly dressed in wool and leather, but his arms were as thick as a bull's neck.

"I want every forge in King's Landing turned to making these links and joining them. All other work is to be put aside. I want every man who knows the art of working metal set to this task, be he master, journeyman, or apprentice. When I ride up the Street of Steel, I want to hear hammers ringing, night or day. And I want a man, a strong man, to see that all this is done. Are you that man, Goodman Ironbelly?"

"Might be I am, m'lord. But what of the mail and swords the queen was wanting?"

Another smith spoke up. "Her Grace commanded us to make chainmail and armor, swords and daggers and axes, all in great numbers. For arming her new gold cloaks, m'lord."

"That work can wait," Tyrion said. "The chain first."

"M'lord, begging your pardon, Her Grace said those as didn't meet their numbers would have their hands crushed," the anxious smith persisted. "Smashed on their own anvils, she said."

Sweet Cersei, always striving to make the smallfolk love us. "No one will have their hands smashed. You have my word on it."

"Iron is grown dear," Ironbelly declared, "and this chain will be needing much of it, and coke beside, for the fires."

"Lord Baelish will see that you have coin as you need it," Tyrion promised. He could count on Littlefinger for that much, he hoped. "I will command the City Watch to help you find iron. Melt down every horseshoe in this city if you must."

An older man moved forward, richly dressed in a damask tunic with silver fastenings and a cloak lined with foxfur. He knelt to examine the great steel links Tyrion had dumped on the floor. "My lord," he announced gravely, "this is crude work at best. There is no art to it. Suitable labor for common smiths, no doubt, for men who bend horseshoes and hammer out kettles, but I am a master armorer, as it please my lord. This is no work for me, nor my fellow masters. We make swords as sharp as song, armor such as a god might wear. Not *this*."

Tyrion tilted his head to the side and gave the man a dose of his mismatched eyes. "What is your name, master armorer?"

"Salloreon, as it please my lord. If the King's Hand will permit, I should be *most* honored to forge him a suit of armor suitable to his House and high office." Two of the others sniggered, but Salloreon plunged ahead, heedless. "Plate and scale, I think. The scales gilded bright as the sun, the plate enameled a deep Lannister crimson. I would suggest a demon's head for a helm, crowned with tall golden horns. When you ride into battle, men will shrink away in fear."

A demon's head, Tyrion thought ruefully, *now what does that say of me?* "Master Salloreon, I plan to fight the rest of my battles from this chair. It's links I need, not demon horns. So let me put it to you this way. You will make chains, or you will wear them. The choice is yours." He rose, and took his leave with nary a backward glance.

Bronn was waiting by the gate with his litter and an escort of mounted Black Ears. "You know where we're bound," Tyrion told him. He accepted a hand up into the litter. He had done all he could to feed the hungry city—he'd set several hundred carpenters to building fishing boats in place of catapults, opened the kingswood to any hunter who dared to cross the river, even sent gold cloaks foraging to the west and south—yet he still saw accusing eyes everywhere he rode. The litter's curtains shielded him from that, and besides gave him leisure to think.

As they wound their slow way down twisty Shadowblack Lane to the foot of Aegon's High Hill, Tyrion reflected on the events of the morning. His sister's ire had led her to overlook the true significance of Stannis Baratheon's letter. Without proof, his accusations were nothing; what mattered was that he had named himself a king. *And what will Renly make of that?* They could not *both* sit the Iron Throne.

Idly, he pushed the curtain back a few inches to peer out at the streets. Black Ears rode on both sides of him, their grisly necklaces looped about their throats, while Bronn went in front to clear the way. He watched the passersby watching him, and played a little game with himself, trying to sort the informers from the rest. *The ones who look the most suspicious are likely innocent,* he decided. *It's the ones who look innocent I need to beware.*

His destination was behind the hill of Rhaenys, and the streets were crowded. Almost an hour had passed before the litter swayed to a stop. Tyrion was dozing, but he woke abruptly when the motion ceased, rubbed the sand from his eyes, and accepted Bronn's hand to climb down.

The house was two stories tall, stone below and timber above. A round turret rose from one corner of the structure. Many of the windows were leaded. Over the door swung an ornate lamp, a globe of gilded metal and scarlet glass.

"A brothel," Bronn said. "What do you mean to do here?"

"What does one usually do in a brothel?"

The sellsword laughed. "Shae's not enough?"

"She was pretty enough for a camp follower, but I'm no longer in camp. Little men have big appetites, and I'm told the girls here are fit for a king."

"Is the boy old enough?"

"Not Joffrey. Robert. This house was a great favorite of his." *Although Joffrey may indeed be old enough. An interesting notion, that.* "If you and the Black Ears care to amuse yourselves, feel free, but Chataya's girls are costly. You'll find cheaper houses all along the street.

Leave one man here who'll know where to find the others when I wish to return."

Bronn nodded. "As you say." The Black Ears were all grins.

Inside the door, a tall woman in flowing silks was waiting for him. She had ebon skin and sandalwood eyes. "I am Chataya," she announced, bowing deeply. "And you are—"

"Let us not get into the habit of names. Names are dangerous." The air smelled of some exotic spice, and the floor beneath his feet displayed a mosaic of two women entwined in love. "You have a pleasant establishment."

"I have labored long to make it so. I am glad the Hand is pleased." Her voice was flowing amber, liquid with the accents of the distant Summer Isles.

"Titles can be as dangerous as names," Tyrion warned. "Show me a few of your girls."

"It will be my great delight. You will find that they are all as sweet as they are beautiful, and skilled in every art of love." She swept off gracefully, leaving Tyrion to waddle after as best he could on legs half the length of hers.

From behind an ornate Myrish screen carved with flowers and fancies and dreaming maidens, they peered unseen into a common room where an old man was playing a cheerful air on the pipes. In a cushioned alcove, a drunken Tyroshi with a purple beard dandled a buxom young wench on his knee. He'd unlaced her bodice and was tilting his cup to pour a thin trickle of wine over her breasts so he might lap it off. Two other girls sat playing at tiles before a leaded glass window. The freckled one wore a chain of blue flowers in her honeyed hair. The other had skin as smooth and black as polished jet, wide dark eyes, small pointed breasts. They dressed in flowing silks cinched at the waist with beaded belts. The sunlight pouring through the colored glass outlined their sweet young bodies through the thin cloth, and Tyrion felt a stirring in his groin. "I would respectfully suggest the dark-skinned girl," said Chataya.

"She's young."

"She has sixteen years, my lord."

A good age for Joffrey, he thought, remembering what Bronn had said. His first had been even younger. Tyrion remembered how shy she'd seemed as he drew her dress up over her head the first time. Long dark hair and blue eyes you could drown in, and he had. So long ago . . . *What a wretched fool you are, dwarf.* "Does she come from your home lands, this girl?"

"Her blood is the blood of summer, my lord, but my daughter was born here in King's Landing." His surprise must have shown on his face, for Chataya continued, "My people hold that there is no shame to be found in the pillow house. In the Summer Isles, those who are skilled at giving pleasure are greatly esteemed. Many highborn youths and maidens serve for a few years after their flowerings, to honor the gods."

"What do the gods have to do with it?"

"The gods made our bodies as well as our souls, is it not so? They give us voices, so we might worship them with song. They give us hands, so we might build them temples. And they give us desire, so we might mate and worship them in that way."

"Remind me to tell the High Septon," said Tyrion. "If I could pray with my cock, I'd be much more religious." He waved a hand. "I will gladly accept your suggestion."

"I shall summon my daughter. Come."

The girl met him at the foot of the stairs. Taller than Shae, though not so tall as her mother, she had to kneel before Tyrion could kiss her. "My name is Alayaya," she said, with only the slightest hint of her mother's accent. "Come, my lord." She took him by the hand and drew him up two flights of stairs, then down a long hall. Gasps and shrieks of pleasure were coming from behind one of the closed doors, giggles and whispers from another. Tyrion's cock pressed against the lacings of his breeches. *This could be humiliating*, he thought as he followed Alayaya up another stair to the turret room. There was only one door. She led him through and closed it. Within the room was a great canopied bed, a tall wardrobe decorated with erotic carvings, and a narrow window of leaded glass in a pattern of red and yellow diamonds.

"You are very beautiful, Alayaya," Tyrion told her when they were alone. "From head to heels, every part of you is lovely. Yet just now the part that interests me most is your tongue."

"My lord will find my tongue well schooled. When I was a girl I learned when to use it, and when not."

"That pleases me." Tyrion smiled. "So what shall we do now? Perchance you have some suggestion?"

"Yes," she said. "If my lord will open the wardrobe, he will find what he seeks."

Tyrion kissed her hand, and climbed inside the empty wardrobe. Alayaya closed it after him. He groped for the back panel, felt it slide under his fingers, and pushed it all the way aside. The hollow space behind the walls was pitch-black, but he fumbled until he felt metal. His hand closed around the rung of a ladder. He found a lower rung with his foot, and started down. Well below street level, the shaft opened onto a slanting earthen tunnel, where he found Varys waiting with candle in hand.

Varys did not look at all like himself. A scarred face and a stubble of dark beard showed under his spiked steel cap, and he wore mail over boiled leather, dirk and shortsword at his belt. "Was Chataya's to your satisfaction, my lord?"

"Almost too much so," admitted Tyrion. "You're certain this woman can be relied on?"

"I am certain of nothing in this fickle and treacherous world, my lord. Chataya has no cause to love the queen, though, and she knows that she has you to thank for ridding her of Allar Deem. Shall we go?" He started down the tunnel.

Even his walk is different, Tyrion observed. The scent of sour wine and garlic clung to Varys instead of lavender. "I like this new garb of yours," he offered as they went.

"The work I do does not permit me to travel the streets amid a column of knights. So when I leave the castle, I adopt more suitable guises, and thus live to serve you longer."

"Leather becomes you. You ought to come like this to our next council session."

"Your sister would not approve, my lord."

"My sister would soil her smallclothes." He smiled in the dark. "I saw no signs of any of her spies skulking after me."

"I am pleased to hear it, my lord. Some of your sister's hirelings are mine as well, unbeknownst to her. I should hate to think they had grown so sloppy as to be seen."

"Well, *I'd* hate to think I was climbing through wardrobes and suffering the pangs of frustrated lust all for naught."

"Scarcely for naught," Varys assured him. "They know you are here. Whether any will be bold enough to enter Chataya's in the guise of patrons I cannot say, but I find it best to err on the side of caution."

"How is it a brothel happens to have a secret entrance?"

"The tunnel was dug for another King's Hand, whose honor would not allow him to enter such a house openly. Chataya has closely guarded the knowledge of its existence."

"And yet *you* knew of it."

"Little birds fly through many a dark tunnel. Careful, the steps are steep."

They emerged through a trap at the back of a stable, having come perhaps a distance of three blocks under Rhaenys's Hill. A horse whickered in his stall when Tyrion let the door slam shut. Varys blew out the candle and set it on a beam and Tyrion gazed about. A mule and three horses occupied the stalls. He waddled over to the piebald gelding and took a look at his teeth. "Old," he said, "and I have my doubts about his wind."

"He is not a mount to carry you into battle, true,"

Varys replied, "but he will serve, and attract no notice. As will the others. And the stableboys see and hear only the animals." The eunuch took a cloak from a peg. It was roughspun, sun-faded, and threadbare, but very ample in its cut. "If you will permit me." When he swept it over Tyrion's shoulders it enveloped him head to heel, with a cowl that could be pulled forward to drown his face in shadows. "Men see what they expect to see," Varys said as he fussed and pulled. "Dwarfs are not so common a sight as children, so a child is what they will see. A boy in an old cloak on his father's horse, going about his father's business. Though it would be best if you came most often by night."

"I plan to . . . after today. At the moment, though, Shae awaits me." He had put her up in a walled manse at the far northeast corner of King's Landing, not far from the sea, but he had not dared visit her there for fear of being followed.

"Which horse will you have?"

Tyrion shrugged. "This one will do well enough."

"I shall saddle him for you." Varys took tack and saddle down from a peg.

Tyrion adjusted the heavy cloak and paced restlessly. "You missed a lively council. Stannis has crowned himself, it seems."

"I know."

"He accuses my brother and sister of incest. I wonder how he came by that suspicion."

"Perhaps he read a book and looked at the color of a bastard's hair, as Ned Stark did, and Jon Arryn before him. Or perhaps someone whispered it in his ear." The eunuch's laugh was not his usual giggle, but deeper and more throaty.

"Someone like you, perchance?"

"Am I suspected? It was not me."

"If it had been, would you admit it?"

"No. But why should I betray a secret I have kept so long? It is one thing to deceive a king, and quite another to hide from the cricket in the rushes and the little bird in the chimney. Besides, the bastards were there for all to see."

"Robert's bastards? What of them?"

"He fathered eight, to the best of my knowing," Varys said as he wrestled with the saddle. "Their mothers were copper and honey, chestnut and butter, yet the babes were all black as ravens . . . and as ill-omened, it would seem. So when Joffrey, Myrcella, and Tommen slid out between your sister's thighs, each as golden as the sun, the truth was not hard to glimpse."

Tyrion shook his head. *If she had borne only one child for her husband, it would have been enough to disarm suspicion . . . but then she would not have been Cersei.* "If you were not this whisperer, who was?"

"Some traitor, doubtless." Varys tightened the cinch.

"Littlefinger?"

"I named no name."

Tyrion let the eunuch help him mount. "Lord Varys," he said from the saddle, "sometimes I feel as though you are the best friend I have in King's Landing, and sometimes I feel you are my worst enemy."

"How odd. I think quite the same of you."

BRAN

Long before the first pale fingers of light pried apart Bran's shutters, his eyes were open.

There were guests in Winterfell, visitors come for the harvest feast. This morning they would be tilting at quintains in the yard. Once that prospect would have filled him with excitement, but that was *before*.

Not now. The Walders would break lances with the squires of Lord Manderly's escort, but Bran would have no part of it. He must play the prince in his father's solar. "Listen, and it may be that you will learn something of what lordship is all about," Maester Luwin had said.

Bran had never asked to be a prince. It was knighthood he had always dreamed of; bright armor and streaming banners, lance and sword, a warhorse between his legs. Why must he waste his days listening to old men speak of things he only half understood? *Because you're broken*, a voice inside reminded him. A lord on his cushioned chair might be crippled—the Walders said their grandfather was so feeble he had to be carried everywhere in a litter—but not a knight on his destrier. Besides, it was his duty. "You are your brother's heir and the Stark in Winterfell," Ser Rodrik said, reminding him of how Robb used to sit with their lord father when his bannermen came to see him.

Lord Wyman Manderly had arrived from White Harbor two days past, traveling by barge and litter, as he was too fat to sit a horse. With him had come a long tail of retainers: knights, squires, lesser lords and ladies, heralds, musicians, even a juggler, all aglitter with banners and surcoats in what seemed half a hundred colors. Bran had welcomed them to Winterfell from his father's high stone seat with the direwolves carved into the arms, and afterward Ser Rodrik had said he'd done well. If that had been the end of it, he would not have minded. But it was only the beginning.

"The feast makes a pleasant pretext," Ser Rodrik explained, "but a man does not cross a hundred leagues for a sliver of duck and a sip of wine. Only those who have matters of import to set before us are like to make the journey."

Bran gazed up at the rough stone ceiling above his head. Robb would tell him not to play the boy, he knew. He could almost hear him, and their lord father as well. *Winter is coming, and you are almost a man grown, Bran. You have a duty.*

When Hodor came bustling in, smiling and humming tunelessly, he found the boy resigned to his fate. Together they got him washed and brushed. "The white wool doublet today," Bran commanded. "And the silver brooch. Ser Rodrik will want me to look lordly." As much as he could, Bran preferred to dress himself, but there were some tasks—pulling on breeches, lacing his boots—that vexed him. They went quicker with Hodor's help. Once he had been taught to do something, he did it deftly. His hands were always gentle, though his strength was astonishing. "You could have been a knight too, I bet," Bran told him. "If the gods hadn't taken your wits, you would have been a great knight."

"Hodor?" Hodor blinked at him with guileless brown eyes, eyes innocent of understanding.

"Yes," said Bran. "Hodor." He pointed.

On the wall beside the door hung a basket, stoutly made of wicker and leather, with holes cut for Bran's legs. Hodor slid his arms through the straps and cinched the wide belt tight around his chest, then knelt beside the bed. Bran used the bars sunk into the wall to support himself as he swung the dead weight of his legs into the basket and through the holes.

"Hodor," Hodor said again, rising. The stableboy stood near seven feet tall all by himself; on his back Bran's head almost brushed the ceiling. He ducked low as they passed through the door. One time Hodor smelled bread baking and *ran* to the kitchens, and Bran got such a crack that Maester Luwin had to sew up his scalp. Mikken had given him a rusty old visorless helm from the armory, but Bran seldom troubled to wear it. The Walders laughed whenever they saw it on his head.

He rested his hands on Hodor's shoulders as they descended the winding stair. Outside, the sounds of sword and shield and horse already rang through the yard. It made a sweet music. *I'll just have a look*, Bran thought, *a quick look, that's all.*

The White Harbor lordlings would emerge later in the morning, with their knights and men-at-arms. Until then, the yard belonged to their squires, who ranged in age from ten to forty. Bran wished he were one of them so badly that his stomach hurt with the wanting.

Two quintains had been erected in the courtyard, each a stout post supporting a spinning crossbeam with a shield at one end and a padded butt at the other. The shields had been painted red-and-gold, though the Lannister lions were lumpy and misshapen, and already well scarred by the first boys to take a tilt at them.

The sight of Bran in his basket drew stares from those who had not seen it before, but he had learned to ignore stares. At least he had a good view; on Hodor's back, he towered over everyone. The Walders were mounting up, he saw. They'd brought fine armor up from the Twins, shining silver plate with enameled blue chasings. Big Walder's crest was shaped like a castle, while Little Walder favored streamers of blue and grey silk. Their shields and surcoats also set them apart from each other. Little Walder quartered the twin towers of Frey with the brindled boar of his grandmother's House and the plowman of his mother's: Crakehall and Darry, respectively. Big Walder's quarterings were the tree-and-ravens of House Blackwood and the twining snakes of the Paeges. *They must be hungry for honor*, Bran thought as he watched them take up their lances. *A Stark needs only the direwolf.*

Their dappled grey coursers were swift, strong, and beautifully trained. Side by side they charged the quintains. Both hit the shields cleanly and were well past before the padded butts came spinning around. Little Walder struck the harder blow, but Bran thought Big Walder sat his horse better. He would have given both his useless legs for the chance to ride against either.

Little Walder cast his splintered lance aside, spied Bran, and reined up. "Now there's an ugly horse," he said of Hodor.

"Hodor's no horse," Bran said.

"Hodor," said Hodor.

Big Walder trotted up to join his cousin. "Well, he's not as *smart* as a horse, that's for certain." A few of the White Harbor lads poked each other and laughed.

"Hodor." Beaming genially, Hodor looked from one Frey to the other, oblivious to their taunting. "Hodor hodor?"

Little Walder's mount whickered. "See, they're talking to each other. Maybe *hodor* means 'I love you' in horse."

"You shut up, Frey." Bran could feel his color rising.

Little Walder spurred his horse closer, giving Hodor a bump that pushed him backward. "What will you do if I don't?"

"He'll set his wolf on you, cousin," warned Big Walder.

"Let him. I always wanted a wolfskin cloak."

"Summer would tear your fat head off," Bran said.

Little Walder banged a mailed fist against his breast-plate. "Does your wolf have steel teeth, to bite through plate and mail?"

"Enough!" Maester Luwin's voice cracked through the clangor of the yard as loud as a thunderclap. How much he had overheard, Bran could not say . . . but it was enough to anger him, clearly. "These threats are unseemly, and I'll hear no more of them. Is this how you behave at the Twins, Walder Frey?"

"If I want to." Atop his courser, Little Walder gave Luwin a sullen glare, as if to say, *You are only a maester, who are you to reproach a Frey of the Crossing?*

"Well, it is not how Lady Stark's wards ought behave at Winterfell. What's at the root of this?" The maester looked at each boy in turn. "One of you will tell me, I swear, or—"

"We were having a jape with Hodor," confessed Big Walder. "I am sorry if we offended Prince Bran. We only meant to be amusing." He at least had the grace to look abashed.

Little Walder only looked peevish. "And me," he said. "I was only being amusing too."

The bald spot atop the maester's head had turned red, Bran could see; if anything, Luwin was more angry than before. "A good lord comforts and protects the weak and helpless," he told the Freys. "I will not have you making Hodor the butt of cruel jests, do you hear me? He's a good-hearted lad, dutiful and obedient, which is more than I can say for either of you." The maester wagged a finger at Little Walder. "And you will stay *out* of the godswood and away from those wolves, or answer for it." Sleeves flapping, he turned on his heels, stalked off a few paces, and glanced back. "Bran. Come. Lord Wyman awaits."

"Hodor, go with the maester," Bran commanded.

"Hodor," said Hodor. His long strides caught up with the maester's furiously pumping legs on the steps of the Great Keep. Maester Luwin held the door open, and

Bran hugged Hodor's neck and ducked as they went through.

"The Walders—" he began.

"I'll hear no more of that, it's done." Maester Luwin looked worn-out and frayed. "You were right to defend Hodor, but you should never have been there. Ser Rodrik and Lord Wyman have broken their fast already while they waited for you. Must I come myself to fetch you, as if you were a little child?"

"No," Bran said, ashamed. "I'm sorry. I only wanted . . ."

"I know what you wanted," Maester Luwin said, more gently. "Would that it could be, Bran. Do you have any questions before we begin this audience?"

"Will we talk of the war?"

"*You* will talk of naught." The sharpness was back in Luwin's voice. "You are still a child of eight . . ."

"Almost nine!"

"Eight," the maester repeated firmly. "Speak nothing but courtesies unless Ser Rodrik or Lord Wyman puts you a question."

Bran nodded. "I'll remember."

"I will say nothing to Ser Rodrik of what passed between you and the Frey boys."

"Thank you."

They put Bran in his father's oak chair with the grey velvet cushions, behind a long plank-and-trestle table. Ser Rodrik sat on his right hand and Maester Luwin to his left, armed with quills and inkpots and a sheaf of blank parchment to write down all that transpired. Bran ran a hand across the rough wood of the table and begged Lord Wyman's pardons for being late.

"Why, no prince is ever late," the Lord of White Harbor responded amiably. "Those who arrive before him have come early, that's all." Wyman Manderly had a great booming laugh. It was small wonder he could not sit a saddle; he looked as if he outweighed most horses. As windy as he was vast, he began by asking Winterfell to confirm the new customs officers he had appointed for White Harbor. The old ones had been holding back silver for King's Landing rather than paying it over to the new King in the North. "King Robb needs his own coinage as well," he declared, "and White Harbor is the very place to mint it." He offered to take charge of the matter, as it please the king, and went from that to speak of how he had strengthened the port's defenses, detailing the cost of every improvement.

In addition to a mint, Lord Manderly also proposed to build Robb a warfleet. "We have had no strength at sea for hundreds of years, since Brandon the Burner put the torch to his father's ships. Grant me the gold and within the year I will float you sufficient galleys to take Dragonstone and King's Landing both."

Bran's interest pricked up at talk of warships. No one asked him, but he thought Lord Wyman's notion a splendid one. In his mind's eye he could see them already. He wondered if a cripple had ever commanded a warship. But Ser Rodrik promised only to send the proposal on to Robb for his consideration, while Maester Luwin scratched at the parchment.

Midday came and went. Maester Luwin sent Poxy Tym down to the kitchens, and they dined in the solar on cheese, capons, and brown oatbread. While tearing apart a bird with fat fingers, Lord Wyman made polite inquiry after Lady Hornwood, who was a cousin of his. "She was born a Manderly, you know. Perhaps, when her grief has run its course, she would like to be a Manderly again, eh?" He took a bite from a wing, and smiled broadly. "As it happens, I am a widower these past eight years. Past time I took another wife, don't you agree, my lords? A man does get lonely." Tossing the bones aside, he reached for a leg. "Or if the lady fancies a younger lad, well, my son Wendel is unwed as well. He is off south guarding Lady Catelyn, but no doubt he will wish to take a bride on his return. A valiant boy, and jolly. Just the man to teach her to laugh again, eh?" He wiped a bit of grease off his chin with the sleeve of his tunic.

Bran could hear the distant clash of arms through the

windows. He cared nothing about marriages. *I wish I was down in the yard.*

His lordship waited until the table had been cleared before he raised the matter of a letter he had received from Lord Tywin Lannister, who held his elder son, Ser Wylis, taken captive on the Green Fork. "He offers him back to me without ransom, provided I withdraw my levies from His Grace and vow to fight no more."

"You will refuse him, of course," said Ser Rodrik.

"Have no fear on that count," the lord assured them. "King Robb has no more loyal servant than Wyman Manderly. I would be loath to see my son languish at Harrenhal any longer than he must, however. That is an ill place. Cursed, they say. Not that I am the sort to swallow such tales, but still, there it is. Look at what's befallen this Janos Slynt. Raised up to Lord of Harrenhal by the queen, and cast down by her brother. Shipped off to the Wall, they say. I pray some equitable exchange of captives can be arranged before too very long. I know Wylis would not want to sit out the rest of the war. Gallant, that son of mine, and fierce as a mastiff."

Bran's shoulders were stiff from sitting in the same chair by the time the audience drew to a close. And that night, as he sat to supper, a horn sounded to herald the arrival of another guest. Lady Donella Hornwood brought no tail of knights and retainers; only herself, and six tired men-at-arms with a moosehead badge on their dusty orange livery. "We are very sorry for all you have suffered, my lady," Bran said when she came before him to speak her words of greetings. Lord Hornwood had been killed in the battle on the Green Fork, their only son cut down in the Whispering Wood. "Winterfell will remember."

"That is good to know." She was a pale husk of a woman, every line of her face etched with grief. "I am very weary, my lord. If I might have leave to rest, I should be thankful."

"To be sure," Ser Rodrik said. "There is time enough for talk on the morrow."

When the morrow came, most of the morning was

given over to talk of grains and greens and salting meat. Once the maesters in their Citadel had proclaimed the first of autumn, wise men put away a portion of each harvest . . . though how large a portion was a matter that seemed to require much talk. Lady Hornwood was storing a fifth of her harvest. At Maester Luwin's suggestion, she vowed to increase that to a quarter.

"Bolton's bastard is massing men at the Dreadfort," she warned them. "I hope he means to take them south to join his father at the Twins, but when I sent to ask his intent, he told me that no Bolton would be questioned by a woman. As if he were trueborn and had a right to that name."

"Lord Bolton has never acknowledged the boy, so far as I know," Ser Rodrik said. "I confess, I do not know him."

"Few do," she replied. "He lived with his mother until two years past, when young Domeric died and left Bolton without an heir. That was when he brought his bastard to the Dreadfort. The boy is a sly creature by all accounts, and he has a servant who is almost as cruel as he is. Reek, they call the man. It's said he never bathes. They hunt together, the Bastard and this Reek, and not for deer. I've heard tales, things I can scarce believe, even of a Bolton. And now that my lord husband and my sweet son have gone to the gods, the Bastard looks at my lands hungrily."

Bran wanted to give the lady a hundred men to defend her rights, but Ser Rodrik only said, "He may look, but should he do more I promise you there will be dire retribution. You will be safe enough, my lady . . . though perhaps in time, when your grief is passed, you may find it prudent to wed again."

"I am past my childbearing years, what beauty I had long fled," she replied with a tired half smile, "yet men come sniffing after me as they never did when I was a maid."

"You do not look favorably on these suitors?" asked Luwin.

"I shall wed again if His Grace commands it," Lady

Hornwood replied, "but Mors Crowfood is a drunken brute, and older than my father. As for my noble cousin of Manderly, my lord's bed is not large enough to hold one of his majesty, and I am surely too small and frail to lie beneath him."

Bran knew that men slept on top of women when they shared a bed. Sleeping under Lord Manderly would be like sleeping under a fallen horse, he imagined. Ser Rodrik gave the widow a sympathetic nod. "You will have other suitors, my lady. We shall try and find you a prospect more to your taste."

"Perhaps you need not look very far, ser."

After she had taken her leave, Maester Luwin smiled. "Ser Rodrik, I do believe my lady fancies you."

Ser Rodrik cleared his throat and looked uncomfortable.

"She was very sad," said Bran.

Ser Rodrik nodded. "Sad and gentle, and not at all uncomely for a woman of her years, for all her modesty. Yet a danger to the peace of your brother's realm nonetheless."

"Her?" Bran said, astonished.

Maester Luwin answered. "With no direct heir, there are sure to be many claimants contending for the Hornwood lands. The Tallharts, Flints, and Karstarks all have ties to House Hornwood through the female line, and the Glovers are fostering Lord Harys's bastard at Deepwood Motte. The Dreadfort has no claim that I know, but the lands adjoin, and Roose Bolton is not one to overlook such a chance."

Ser Rodrik tugged at his whiskers. "In such cases, her liege lord must find her a suitable match."

"Why *can't* you marry her?" Bran asked. "You said she was comely, and Beth would have a mother."

The old knight put a hand on Bran's arm. "A kindly thought, my prince, but I am only a knight, and besides too old. I might hold her lands for a few years, but as soon as I died Lady Hornwood would find herself back in the same mire, and Beth's prospects might be perilous as well."

"Then let Lord Hornwood's bastard be the heir," Bran said, thinking of his half brother Jon.

Ser Rodrik said, "That would please the Glovers, and perhaps Lord Hornwood's shade as well, but I do not think Lady Hornwood would love us. The boy is not of her blood."

"Still," said Maester Luwin, "it must be considered. Lady Donella is past her fertile years, as she said herself. If not the bastard, who?"

"May I be excused?" Bran could hear the squires at their swordplay in the yard below, the ring of steel on steel.

"As you will, my prince," said Ser Rodrik. "You did well." Bran flushed with pleasure. Being a lord was not so tedious as he had feared, and since Lady Hornwood had been so much briefer than Lord Manderly, he even had a few hours of daylight left to visit with Summer. He liked to spend time with his wolf every day, when Ser Rodrik and the maester allowed it.

No sooner had Hodor entered the godswood than Summer emerged from under an oak, almost as if he had known they were coming. Bran glimpsed a lean black shape watching from the undergrowth as well. "Shaggy," he called. "Here, Shaggydog. To me." But Rickon's wolf vanished as swiftly as he'd appeared.

Hodor knew Bran's favorite place, so he took him to the edge of the pool beneath the great spread of the heart tree, where Lord Eddard used to kneel to pray. Ripples were running across the surface of the water when they arrived, making the reflection of the weirwood shimmer and dance. There was no wind, though. For an instant Bran was baffled.

And then Osha exploded up out of the pool with a great splash, so sudden that even Summer leapt back, snarling. Hodor jumped away, wailing "Hodor, *Hodor*" in dismay until Bran patted his shoulder to soothe his fears. "How can you swim in there?" he asked Osha. "Isn't it cold?"

"As a babe I suckled on icicles, boy. I like the cold." Osha swam to the rocks and rose dripping. She was naked, her skin bumpy with gooseprickles. Summer crept close and sniffed at her. "I wanted to touch the bottom."

"I never knew there was a bottom."

"Might be there isn't." She grinned. "What are you staring at, boy? Never seen a woman before?"

"I have so." Bran had bathed with his sisters hundreds of times and he'd seen serving women in the hot pools too. Osha looked different, though, hard and sharp instead of soft and curvy. Her legs were all sinew, her breasts flat as two empty purses. "You've got a lot of scars."

"Every one hard earned." She picked up her brown shift, shook some leaves off of it, and pulled it down over her head.

"Fighting giants?" Osha claimed there were still giants beyond the Wall. *One day maybe I'll even see one . . .*

"Fighting men." She belted herself with a length of rope. "Black crows, oft as not. Killed me one too," she said, shaking out her hair. It had grown since she'd come to Winterfell, well down past her ears. She looked softer than the woman who had once tried to rob and kill him in the wolfswood. "Heard some yattering in the kitchen today about you and them Freys."

"Who? What did they say?"

She gave him a sour grin. "That it's a fool boy who mocks a giant, and a mad world when a cripple has to defend him."

"Hodor never knew they were mocking him," Bran said. "Anyhow he never fights." He remembered once when he was little, going to the market square with his mother and Septa Mordane. They brought Hodor to carry for them, but he had wandered away, and when they found him some boys had him backed into an alley, poking him with sticks. *"Hodor!"* he kept shouting, cringing and covering himself, but he had never raised a hand against his tormentors. "Septon Chayle says he has a gentle spirit."

"Aye," she said, "and hands strong enough to twist a

man's head off his shoulders, if he takes a mind to. All the same, he better watch his back around that Walder. Him and you both. The big one they call little, it comes to me he's well named. Big outside, little inside, and mean down to the bones."

"He'd never dare hurt me. He's scared of Summer, no matter what he says."

"Then might be he's not so stupid as he seems." Osha was always wary around the direwolves. The day she was taken, Summer and Grey Wind between them had torn three wildlings to bloody pieces. "Or might be he is. And that tastes of trouble too." She tied up her hair. "You have more of them wolf dreams?"

"No." He did not like to talk about the dreams.

"A prince should lie better than that." Osha laughed. "Well, your dreams are your business. Mine's in the kitchens, and I'd best be getting back before Gage starts to shouting and waving that big wooden spoon of his. By your leave, my prince."

She should never have talked about the wolf dreams, Bran thought as Hodor carried him up the steps to his bedchamber. He fought against sleep as long as he could, but in the end it took him as it always did. On this night he dreamed of the weirwood. It was looking at him with its deep red eyes, calling to him with its twisted wooden mouth, and from its pale branches the three-eyed crow came flapping, pecking at his face and crying his name in a voice as sharp as swords.

The blast of horns woke him. Bran pushed himself onto his side, grateful for the reprieve. He heard horses and boisterous shouting. *More guests have come, and half-drunk by the noise of them.* Grasping his bars he pulled himself from the bed and over to the window seat. On their banner was a giant in shattered chains that told him that these were Umber men, down from the northlands beyond the Last River.

The next day two of them came together to audience; the Greatjon's uncles, blustery men in the winter of their days with beards as white as the bearskin cloaks they wore. A crow had once taken Mors for dead and pecked out his eye, so he wore a chunk of dragonglass in its stead. As Old Nan told the tale, he'd grabbed the crow in his fist and bitten its head off, so they named him Crowfood. She would never tell Bran why his gaunt brother Hother was called Whoresbane.

No sooner had they been seated than Mors asked for leave to wed Lady Hornwood. "The Greatjon's the Young Wolf's strong right hand, all know that to be true. Who better to protect the widow's lands than an Umber, and what Umber better than me?"

"Lady Donella is still grieving," Maester Luwin said.

"I have a cure for grief under my furs." Mors laughed.

Ser Rodrik thanked him courteously and promised to bring the matter before the lady and the king.

Hother wanted ships. "There's wildlings stealing down from the north, more than I've ever seen before. They cross the Bay of Seals in little boats and wash up on our shores. The crows in Eastwatch are too few to stop them, and they go to ground quick as weasels. It's longships we need, aye, and strong men to sail them. The Greatjon took too many. Half our harvest is gone to seed for want of arms to swing the scythes."

Ser Rodrik pulled at his whiskers. "You have forests of tall pine and old oak. Lord Manderly has shipwrights and sailors in plenty. Together you ought to be able to float enough longships to guard both your coasts."

"Manderly?" Mors Umber snorted. "That great waddling sack of suet? His own people mock him as Lord Lamprey, I've heard. The man can scarce walk. If you stuck a sword in his belly, ten thousand eels would wriggle out."

"He is fat," Ser Rodrik admitted, "but he is not stupid. You will work with him, or the king will know the reason why." And to Bran's astonishment, the truculent Umbers agreed to do as he commanded, though not without grumbling.

While they were sitting at audience, the Glover men arrived from Deepwood Motte, and a large party of Tallharts from Torrhen's Square. Galbart and Robett Glover had left Deepwood in the hands of Robett's wife, but it was their steward who came to Winterfell. "My lady begs that you excuse her absence. Her babes are still too young for such a journey, and she was loath to leave them." Bran soon realized that it was the steward, not Lady Glover, who truly ruled at Deepwood Motte. The man allowed that he was at present setting aside only a tenth of his harvest. A hedge wizard had told him there would be a bountiful spirit summer before the cold set in, he claimed. Maester Luwin had a number of choice things to say about hedge wizards. Ser Rodrik commanded the man to set aside a fifth, and questioned the steward closely about Lord Hornwood's bastard, the boy Larence Snow. In the north, all highborn bastards took the surname *Snow*. This lad was near twelve, and the steward praised his wits and courage.

"Your notion about the bastard may have merit, Bran," Maester Luwin said after. "One day you will be a good lord for Winterfell, I think."

"No I won't." Bran knew he would never be a lord, no more than he could be a knight. "Robb's to marry some Frey girl, you told me so yourself, and the Walders say the same. He'll have sons, and they'll be the lords of Winterfell after him, not me."

"It may be so, Bran," Ser Rodrik said, "but I was wed three times and my wives gave me daughters. Now only Beth remains to me. My brother Martyn fathered four strong sons, yet only Jory lived to be a man. When he was slain, Martyn's line died with him. When we speak of the morrow nothing is ever certain."

Leobald Tallhart had his turn the following day. He spoke of weather portents and the slack wits of smallfolk, and told how his nephew itched for battle. "Benfred has raised his own company of lances. Boys, none older than nineteen years, but every one thinks he's another young wolf. When I told them they were only young rabbits, they laughed at me. Now they call themselves the Wild Hares and gallop about the country with rabbitskins tied to the ends of their lances, singing songs of chivalry."

Bran thought that sounded grand. He remembered

Benfred Tallhart, a big bluff loud boy who had often visited Winterfell with his father, Ser Helman, and had been friendly with Robb and with Theon Greyjoy. But Ser Rodrik was clearly displeased by what he heard. "If the king were in need of more men, he would send for them," he said. "Instruct your nephew that he is to remain at Torrhen's Square, as his lord father commanded."

"I will, ser," said Leobald, and only then raised the matter of Lady Hornwood. Poor thing, with no husband to defend her lands nor son to inherit. His own lady wife was a Hornwood, sister to the late Lord Halys, doubtless they recalled. "An empty hall is a sad one. I had a thought to send my younger son to Lady Donella to foster as her own. Beren is near ten, a likely lad, and her own nephew. He would cheer her, I am certain, and perhaps he would even take the name Hornwood . . ."

"If he were named heir?" suggested Maester Luwin.

". . . so the House might continue," finished Leobald.

Bran knew what to say. "Thank you for the notion, my lord," he blurted out before Ser Rodrik could speak. "We will bring the matter to my brother Robb. Oh, and Lady Hornwood."

Leobald seemed surprised that he had spoken. "I'm grateful, my prince," he said, but Bran saw pity in his pale blue eyes, mingled perhaps with a little gladness that the cripple was, after all, not *his* son. For a moment he hated the man.

Maester Luwin liked him better, though. "Beren Tallhart may well be our best answer," he told them when Leobald had gone. "By blood he is half Hornwood. If he takes his uncle's name . . ."

". . . he will still be a boy," said Ser Rodrik, "and hard-pressed to hold his lands against the likes of Mors Umber or this bastard of Roose Bolton's. We must think on this carefully. Robb should have our best counsel before he makes his decision."

"It may come down to practicalities," said Maester Luwin. "Which lord he most needs to court. The riverlands are part of his realm, he may wish to cement the alliance by wedding Lady Hornwood to one of the lords of the Trident. A Blackwood, perhaps, or a Frey—"

· "Lady Hornwood can have one of our Freys," said Bran. "She can have both of them if she likes."

"You are not kind, my prince," Ser Rodrik chided gently.

Neither are the Walders. Scowling, Bran stared down at the table and said nothing.

In the days that followed, ravens arrived from other lordly houses, bearing regrets. The bastard of the Dreadfort would not be joining them, the Mormonts and Karstarks had all gone south with Robb, Lord Locke was too old to dare the journey, Lady Flint was heavy with child, there was sickness at Widow's Watch. Finally all of the principal vassals of House Stark had been heard from save for Howland Reed the crannogman, who had not set foot outside his swamps for many a year, and the Cerwyns whose castle lay a half day's ride from Winterfell. Lord Cerwyn was a captive of the Lannisters, but his son, a lad of fourteen, arrived one bright, blustery morning at the head of two dozen lances. Bran was riding Dancer around the yard when they came through the gate. He trotted over to greet them. Cley Cerwyn had always been a friend to Bran and his brothers.

"Good morrow, Bran," Cley called out cheerfully. "Or must I call you Prince Bran now?"

"Only if you want."

Cley laughed. "Why not? Everyone else is a king or prince these days. Did Stannis write Winterfell as well?"

· "Stannis? I don't know."

"He's a king now too," Cley confided. "He says Queen Cersei bedded her brother, so Joffrey is a bastard."

"Joffrey the Illborn," one of the Cerwyn knights growled. "Small wonder he's faithless, with the Kingslayer for a father."

"Aye," said another, "the gods hate incest. Look how they brought down the Targaryens."

For a moment Bran felt as though he could not breathe. A giant hand was crushing his chest. He felt as though he was falling, and clutched desperately at Dancer's reins.

His terror must have shown on his face. "Bran?" Cley Cerwyn said. "Are you unwell? It's only another king."

"Robb will beat him too." He turned Dancer's head toward the stables, oblivious to the puzzled stares the Cerwyns gave him. His blood was roaring in his ears, and had he not been strapped onto his saddle he might well have fallen.

That night Bran prayed to his father's gods for dreamless sleep. If the gods heard, they mocked his hopes, for the nightmare they sent was worse than any wolf dream.

"Fly or die!" cried the three-eyed crow as it pecked at him. He wept and pleaded but the crow had no pity. It put out his left eye and then his right, and when he was blind in the dark it pecked at his brow, driving its terrible sharp beak deep into his skull. He screamed until he was certain his lungs must burst. The pain was an axe splitting his head apart, but when the crow wrenched out its beak all slimy with bits of bone and brain, Bran could see again. What he saw made him gasp in fear. He was clinging to a tower miles high, and his fingers were slipping, nails scrabbling at the stone, his legs dragging him down, stupid useless dead legs. *"Help me!"* he cried. A golden man appeared in the sky above him and pulled him up. "The things I do for love," he murmured softly as he tossed him out kicking into empty air.

TYRION

"I do not sleep as I did when I was younger," Grand
Maester Pycelle told him, by way of apology for
the dawn meeting. "I would sooner be up, though
the world be dark, than lie restless abed, fretting on
tasks undone," he said—though his heavy-lidded eyes
made him look half-asleep as he said it.

In the airy chambers beneath the rookery, his girl
served them boiled eggs, stewed plums, and porridge,
while Pycelle served the pontifications. "In these sad
times, when so many hunger, I think it only fitting to
keep my table spare."

"Commendable," Tyrion admitted, breaking a large
brown egg that reminded him unduly of the Grand
Maester's bald spotted head. "I take a different view. If
there is food I eat it, in case there is none on the morrow." He smiled. "Tell me, are your ravens early risers
as well?"

Pycelle stroked the snowy beard that flowed down his
chest. "To be sure. Shall I send for quill and ink after we
have eaten?"

"No need." Tyrion laid the letters on the table beside his porridge, twin parchments tightly rolled and sealed with wax at both ends. "Send your girl away, so we can talk."

"Leave us, child," Pycelle commanded. The serving girl hurried from the room. "These letters, now . . ."

"For the eyes of Doran Martell, Prince of Dorne." Tyrion peeled the cracked shell away from his egg and took a bite. It wanted salt. "One letter, in two copies. Send your swiftest birds. The matter is of great import."

"I shall dispatch them as soon as we have broken our fast."

"Dispatch them now. Stewed plums will keep. The realm may not. Lord Renly is leading his host up the roseroad, and no one can say when Lord Stannis will sail from Dragonstone."

Pycelle blinked. "If my lord prefers—"

"He does."

"I am here to serve." The maester pushed himself ponderously to his feet, his chain of office clinking softly. It was a heavy thing, a dozen maester's collars threaded around and through each other and ornamented with gemstones. And it seemed to Tyrion that the gold and silver and platinum links far outnumbered those of baser metals.

Pycelle moved so slowly that Tyrion had time to finish his egg and taste the plums—overcooked and watery, to his taste—before the sound of wings prompted him to rise. He spied the raven, dark in the dawn sky, and turned briskly toward the maze of shelves at the far end of the room.

The maester's medicines made an impressive display; dozens of pots sealed with wax, hundreds of stoppered vials, as many milkglass bottles, countless jars of dried herbs, each container neatly labeled in Pycelle's precise hand. *An orderly mind*, Tyrion reflected, and indeed, once you puzzled out the arrangement, it was easy to see that every potion had its place. *And such interesting things.* He noted sweetsleep and nightshade, milk of the poppy, the tears of Lys, powdered greycap, wolfsbane and demon's dance, basilisk venom, blindeye, widow's blood . . .

Standing on his toes and straining upward, he managed to pull a small dusty bottle off the high shelf. When he read the label, he smiled and slipped it up his sleeve.

He was back at the table peeling another egg when Grand Maester Pycelle came creeping down the stairs. "It is done, my lord." The old man seated himself. "A matter like this . . . best done promptly, indeed, indeed . . . of great import, you say?"

"Oh, yes." The porridge was too thick, Tyrion felt, and wanted butter and honey. To be sure, butter and honey were seldom seen in King's Landing of late, though Lord Gyles kept them well supplied in the castle. Half of the food they ate these days came from his lands or Lady Tanda's. Rosby and Stokeworth lay near the city to the north, and were yet untouched by war.

"The Prince of Dorne, himself. Might I ask . . ."

"Best not."

"As you say." Pycelle's curiosity was so ripe that Tyrion could almost taste it. "Mayhaps . . . the king's council . . ."

Tyrion tapped his wooden spoon against the edge of the bowl. "The council exists to *advise* the king, Maester."

"Just so," said Pycelle, "and the king—"

"—is a boy of thirteen. I speak with his voice."

"So you do. Indeed. The King's Own Hand. Yet . . . your most gracious sister, our Queen Regent, she . . ."

". . . bears a great weight upon those lovely white shoulders of hers. I have no wish to add to her burdens. Do you?" Tyrion cocked his head and gave the Grand Maester an inquiring stare.

Pycelle dropped his gaze back to his food. Something about Tyrion's mismatched green-and-black eyes made men squirm; knowing that, he made good use of them. "Ah," the old man muttered into his plums. "Doubtless you have the right of it, my lord. It is most considerate of you to . . . spare her this . . . burden."

"That's just the sort of fellow I am." Tyrion returned to the unsatisfactory porridge. "Considerate. Cersei is my own sweet sister, after all."

"And a woman, to be sure," Grand Maester Pycelle said. "A most uncommon woman, and yet . . . it is no small thing, to tend to all the cares of the realm, despite the frailty of her sex . . ."

Oh, yes, she's a frail dove, just ask Eddard Stark. "I'm pleased you share my concern. And I thank you for the hospitality of your table. But a long day awaits." He swung his legs out and clambered down from his chair. "Be so good as to inform me at once should we receive a reply from Dorne?"

"As you say, my lord."

"And *only* me?"

"Ah . . . to be sure." Pycelle's spotted hand was clutching at his beard the way a drowning man clutches for a rope. It made Tyrion's heart glad. *One,* he thought.

He waddled out into the lower bailey; his stunted legs complained of the steps. The sun was well up now, and the castle was stirring. Guardsmen walked the walls, and knights and men-at-arms were training with blunted weapons. Nearby, Bronn sat on the lip of a well. A pair of comely serving girls sauntered past carrying a wicker basket of rushes between them, but the sellsword never looked. "Bronn, I despair of you." Tyrion gestured at the wenches. "With sweet sights like that before you, all you see is a gaggle of louts raising a clangor."

"There are a hundred whorehouses in this city where a clipped copper will buy me all the cunt I want," Bronn answered, "but one day my life may hang on how close I've watched your louts." He stood. "Who's the boy in the checkered blue surcoat with the three eyes on his shield?"

"Some hedge knight. Tallad, he names himself. Why?"

Bronn pushed a fall of hair from his eyes. "He's the best of them. But watch him, he falls into a rhythm, delivering the same strokes in the same order each time he attacks." He grinned. "That will be the death of him, the day he faces me."

"He's pledged to Joffrey; he's not like to face you." They set off across the bailey, Bronn matching his long stride to Tyrion's short one. These days the sellsword was looking almost respectable. His dark hair was washed and brushed, he was freshly shaved, and he wore the black breastplate of an officer of the City Watch. From his shoulders trailed a cloak of Lannister crimson patterned with golden hands. Tyrion had made him a gift of it when he named him captain of his personal guard. "How many supplicants do we have today?" he inquired.

"Thirty odd," answered Bronn. "Most with complaints, or wanting something, as ever. Your pet was back."

He groaned. "Lady Tanda?"

"Her page. She invites you to sup with her again. There's to be a haunch of venison, she says, a brace of stuffed geese sauced with mulberries, and—"

"—her daughter," Tyrion finished sourly. Since the hour he had arrived in the Red Keep, Lady Tanda had been stalking him, armed with a never-ending arsenal of lamprey pies, wild boars, and savory cream stews. Somehow she had gotten the notion that a dwarf lordling would be the perfect consort for her daughter Lollys, a large, soft, dim-witted girl who rumor said was still a maid at thirty-and-three. "Send her my regrets."

"No taste for stuffed goose?" Bronn grinned evilly.

"Perhaps you should eat the goose and marry the maid. Or better still, send Shagga."

"Shagga's more like to eat the maid and marry the goose," observed Bronn. "Anyway, Lollys outweighs him."

"There is that," Tyrion admitted as they passed under the shadow of a covered walkway between two towers. "Who else wants me?"

The sellsword grew more serious. "There's a moneylender from Braavos, holding fancy papers and the like, requests to see the king about payment on some loan."

"As if Joff could count past twenty. Send the man to Littlefinger, he'll find a way to put him off. Next?"

"A lordling down from the Trident, says your father's men burned his keep, raped his wife, and killed all his peasants."

"I believe they call that *war*." Tyrion smelled Gregor Clegane's work, or that of Ser Amory Lorch or his father's other pet hellhound, the Qohorik. "What does he want of Joffrey?"

"New peasants," Bronn said. "He walked all this way to sing how loyal he is and beg for recompense."

"I'll make time for him on the morrow." Whether truly loyal or merely desperate, a compliant river lord might have his uses. "See that he's given a comfortable chamber and a hot meal. Send him a new pair of boots as well, good ones, courtesy of King Joffrey." A show of generosity never hurt.

Bronn gave a curt nod. "There's also a great gaggle of bakers, butchers, and greengrocers clamoring to be heard."

"I told them last time, I have nothing to give them." Only a thin trickle of food was coming into King's Landing, most of it earmarked for castle and garrison. Prices had risen sickeningly high on greens, roots, flour, and fruit, and Tyrion did not want to think about what sorts of flesh might be going into the kettles of the potshops down in Flea Bottom. Fish, he hoped. They still had the river and the sea . . . at least until Lord Stannis sailed.

"They want protection. Last night a baker was roasted in his own oven. The mob claimed he charged too much for bread."

"Did he?"

"He's not apt to deny it."

"They didn't eat him, did they?"

"Not that I've heard."

"Next time they will," Tyrion said grimly. "I give them what protection I can. The gold cloaks—"

"They claim there were gold cloaks in the mob," Bronn said. "They're demanding to speak to the king himself."

"Fools." Tyrion had sent them off with regrets; his nephew would send them off with whips and spears. He was half-tempted to allow it . . . but no, he dare not. Soon or late, some enemy would march on King's Landing, and the last thing he wanted was willing traitors within the city walls. "Tell them King Joffrey shares their fears and will do all he can for them."

"They want bread, not promises."

"If I give them bread today, on the morrow I'll have twice as many at the gates. Who else?"

"A black brother down from the Wall. The steward says he brought some rotted hand in a jar."

Tyrion smiled wanly. "I'm surprised no one ate it. I suppose I ought to see him. It's not Yoren, perchance?"

"No. Some knight. Thorne."

"Ser *Alliser* Thorne?" Of all the black brothers he'd met on the Wall, Tyrion Lannister had liked Ser Alliser Thorne the least. A bitter, mean-spirited man with too great a sense of his own worth. "Come to think on it, I don't believe I care to see Ser Alliser just now. Find him a snug cell where no one has changed the rushes in a year, and let his hand rot a little more."

Bronn snorted laughter and went his way, while Tyrion struggled up the serpentine steps. As he limped across the outer yard, he heard the portcullis rattling up. His sister and a large party were waiting by the main gate.

Mounted on her white palfrey, Cersei towered high above him, a goddess in green. "Brother," she called out, not warmly. The queen had not been pleased by the way he'd dealt with Janos Slynt.

"Your Grace." Tyrion bowed politely. "You look lovely this morning." Her crown was gold, her cloak ermine. Her retinue sat their mounts behind her: Ser Boros Blount of the Kingsguard, wearing white scale and his favorite scowl; Ser Balon Swann, bow slung from his silver-inlay saddle; Lord Gyles Rosby, his wheezing cough worse than ever; Hallyne the Pyromancer of the Alchemists' Guild; and the queen's newest favorite, their cousin Ser Lancel Lannister, her late husband's squire upjumped to knight at his widow's insistence. Vylarr and twenty guardsmen rode escort. "Where are you bound this day, sister?" Tyrion asked.

"I'm making a round of the gates to inspect the new scorpions and spitfires. I would not have it thought that all of us are as indifferent to the city's defense as you seem to be." Cersei fixed him with those clear green eyes of hers, beautiful even in their contempt. "I am informed that Renly Baratheon has marched from Highgarden. He is making his way up the roseroad, with all his strength behind him."

"Varys gave me the same report."

"He could be here by the full moon."

"Not at his present leisurely pace," Tyrion assured her. "He feasts every night in a different castle, and holds court at every crossroads he passes."

"And every day, more men rally to his banners. His host is now said to be a hundred thousand strong."

"That seems rather high."

"He has the power of Storm's End and Highgarden behind him, you little fool," Cersei snapped down at him. "All the Tyrell bannermen but for the Redwynes, and you have me to thank for that. So long as I hold those poxy twins of his, Lord Paxter will squat on the Arbor and count himself fortunate to be out of it."

"A pity you let the Knight of Flowers slip through your pretty fingers. Still, Renly has other concerns besides us. Our father at Harrenhal, Robb Stark at Riverrun . . . were I he, I would do much as he is doing. Make my progress, flaunt my power for the realm to see, watch, wait. Let my rivals contend while I bide my own sweet time. If Stark defeats us, the south will fall into Renly's hands like a windfall from the gods, and he'll not have lost a man. And if it goes the other way, he can descend on us while we are weakened."

Cersei was not appeased. "I want you to make Father bring his army to King's Landing."

Where it will serve no purpose but to make you feel safe. "When have I ever been able to *make* Father do anything?"

She ignored the question. "And when do you plan to free Jaime? He's worth a hundred of you."

Tyrion grinned crookedly. "Don't tell Lady Stark, I beg you. We don't have a hundred of me to trade."

"Father must have been mad to send you. You're worse than useless." The queen jerked on her reins and wheeled her palfrey around. She rode out the gate at a brisk trot, ermine cloak streaming behind her. Her retinue hastened after.

In truth, Renly Baratheon did not frighten Tyrion half so much as his brother Stannis did. Renly was beloved of the commons, but he had never before led men in war. Stannis was otherwise: hard, cold, inexorable. If only they had some way of knowing what was happening on Dragonstone . . . but not one of the fisherfolk he had paid to spy out the island had ever returned, and even the informers the eunuch claimed to have placed in Stannis's household had been ominously silent. The striped hulls of Lysene war galleys had been seen offshore, though, and Varys had reports from Myr of sellsail captains taking service with Dragonstone. *If Stannis attacks by sea while his brother Renly storms the gates, they'll soon be mounting Joffrey's head on a spike. Worse, mine will be beside him.* A depressing thought. He ought to make plans to get Shae safely out of the city, should the worst seem likely.

Podrick Payne stood at the door of his solar, studying the floor. "He's inside," he announced to Tyrion's belt buckle. "Your solar. My lord. Sorry."

Tyrion sighed. "*Look* at me, Pod. It unnerves me when you talk to my codpiece, especially when I'm not wearing one. Who is inside my solar?"

"Lord Littlefinger." Podrick managed a quick look at his face, then hastily dropped his eyes. "I meant, Lord Petyr. Lord Baelish. The master of coin."

"You make him sound a crowd." The boy hunched down as if struck, making Tyrion feel absurdly guilty.

Lord Petyr was seated on his window seat, languid and elegant in a plush plum-colored doublet and a yellow satin cape, one gloved hand resting on his knee. "The king is fighting hares with a crossbow," he said. "The hares are winning. Come see."

Tyrion had to stand on his toes to get a look. A dead hare lay on the ground below; another, long ears twitching, was about to expire from the bolt in his side. Spent quarrels lay strewn across the hard-packed earth like straws scattered by a storm. "Now!" Joff shouted. The gamesman released the hare he was holding, and he went bounding off. Joffrey jerked the trigger on the crossbow. The bolt missed by two feet. The hare stood on his hind legs and twitched his nose at the king. Cursing, Joff spun the wheel to winch back his string, but the animal was gone before he was loaded. "Another!" The gamesman reached into the hutch. This one made a brown streak against the stones, while Joffrey's hurried shot almost took Ser Preston in the groin.

Littlefinger turned away. "Boy, are you fond of potted hare?" he asked Podrick Payne.

Pod stared at the visitor's boots, lovely things of red-dyed leather ornamented with black scrollwork. "To eat, my lord?"

"Invest in pots," Littlefinger advised. "Hares will soon overrun the castle. We'll be eating hare thrice a day."

"Better than rats on a skewer," said Tyrion. "Pod, leave us. Unless Lord Petyr would care for some refreshment?"

"Thank you, but no." Littlefinger flashed his mocking smile. "Drink with the dwarf, it's said, and you wake up walking the Wall. Black brings out my unhealthy pallor."

Have no fear, my lord, Tyrion thought, *it's not the Wall I have in mind for you.* He seated himself in a high chair piled with cushions and said, "You look very elegant today, my lord."

"I'm wounded. I strive to look elegant *every* day."

"Is the doublet new?"

"It is. You're most observant."

"Plum and yellow. Are those the colors of your House?"

"No. But a man gets bored wearing the same colors day in and day out, or so I've found."

"That's a handsome knife as well."

"Is it?" There was mischief in Littlefinger's eyes. He drew the knife and glanced at it casually, as if he had never seen it before. "Valyrian steel, and a dragonbone hilt. A trifle plain, though. It's yours, if you would like it."

"Mine?" Tyrion gave him a long look. "No. I think not. Never mine." *He knows, the insolent wretch. He knows and he knows that I know, and he thinks that I cannot touch him.*

If ever truly a man had armored himself in gold, it was Petyr Baelish, not Jaime Lannister. Jaime's famous armor was but gilded steel, but Littlefinger, ah . . . Tyrion had learned a few things about sweet Petyr, to his growing disquiet.

Ten years ago, Jon Arryn had given him a minor sinecure in customs, where Lord Petyr had soon distinguished himself by bringing in three times as much as any of the king's other collectors. King Robert had been a prodigious spender. A man like Petyr Baelish, who had a gift for rubbing two golden dragons together to breed a third, was invaluable to his Hand. Littlefinger's rise had been arrow-swift. Within three years of his coming to court, he was master of coin and a member of the small council, and today the crown's revenues were ten times what they had been under his beleaguered predecessor . . . though the crown's debts had grown vast as well. A master juggler was Petyr Baelish.

Oh, he was clever. He did not simply collect the gold and lock it in a treasure vault, no. He paid the king's debts in promises, and put the king's gold to work. He bought wagons, shops, ships, houses. He bought grain when it was plentiful and sold bread when it was scarce. He bought wool from the north and linen from the south and lace from Lys, stored it, moved it, dyed it, sold it. The golden dragons bred and multiplied, and Littlefinger lent them out and brought them home with hatchlings.

And in the process, he moved his own men into place. The Keepers of the Keys were his, all four. The King's Counter and the King's Scales were men he'd named. The officers in charge of all three mints. Harbormasters, tax farmers, customs sergeants, wool factors, toll collectors, pursers, wine factors; nine of every ten belonged to Littlefinger. They were men of middling birth, by and large; merchants' sons, lesser lordlings, sometimes even foreigners, but judging from their results, far more able than their highborn predecessors.

No one had ever thought to question the appointments, and why should they? Littlefinger was no threat to anyone. A clever, smiling, genial man, everyone's friend, always able to find whatever gold the king or his Hand required, and yet of such undistinguished birth, one step up from a hedge knight, he was not a man to fear. He had no banners to call, no army of retainers, no great stronghold, no holdings to speak of, no prospects of a great marriage.

But do I dare touch him? Tyrion wondered. *Even if he is a traitor?* He was not at all certain he could, least of all now, while the war raged. Given time, he could replace Littlefinger's men with his own in key positions, but . . .

A shout rang up from the yard. "Ah, His Grace has killed a hare," Lord Baelish observed.

"No doubt a slow one," Tyrion said. "My lord, you were fostered at Riverrun. I've heard it said that you grew close to the Tullys."

"You might say so. The girls especially."

"How close?"

"I had their maidenhoods. Is that close enough?"

The lie—Tyrion was fairly certain it was a lie—was delivered with such an air of nonchalance that one could almost believe it. Could it have been Catelyn Stark who lied? About her defloration, and the dagger as well? The longer he lived, the more Tyrion realized that nothing was simple and little was true. "Lord Hoster's daughters do not love me," he confessed. "I doubt they would listen to any proposal I might make. Yet coming from you, the same words might fall more sweetly on their ears."

"That would depend on the words. If you mean to offer Sansa in return for your brother, waste someone else's time. Joffrey will never surrender his plaything, and Lady Catelyn is not so great a fool as to barter the Kingslayer for a slip of a girl."

"I mean to have Arya as well. I have men searching."

"Searching is not finding."

"I'll keep that in mind, my lord. In any case, it was Lady Lysa I hoped you might sway. For her, I have a sweeter offer."

"Lysa is more tractable than Catelyn, true . . . but also more fearful, and I understand she hates you."

"She believes she has good reason. When I was her guest in the Eyrie, she insisted that I'd murdered her husband, and was not inclined to listen to denials." He leaned forward. "If I gave her Jon Arryn's true killer, she might think more kindly of me."

That made Littlefinger sit up. "True killer? I confess, you make me curious. Who do you propose?"

It was Tyrion's turn to smile. "Gifts I give my friends, freely. Lysa Arryn would need to understand that."

"Is it her friendship you require, or her swords?"

"Both."

Littlefinger stroked the neat spike of his beard. "Lysa has woes of her own. Clansmen raiding out of the Mountains of the Moon, in greater numbers than ever before . . . and better armed."

"Distressing," said Tyrion Lannister, who had armed them. "I could help her with that. A word from me . . ."

"And what would this word cost her?"

"I want Lady Lysa and her son to acclaim Joffrey as king, to swear fealty, and to—"

"—make war on the Starks and Tullys?" Littlefinger shook his head. "There's the roach in your pudding,

Lannister. Lysa will never send her knights against Riverrun."

"Nor would I ask it. We have no lack of enemies. I'll use her power to oppose Lord Renly, or Lord Stannis, should he stir from Dragonstone. In return, I will give her justice for Jon Arryn and peace in the Vale. I will even name that appalling child of hers Warden of the East, as his father was before him." *I want to see him fly,* a boy's voice whispered faintly in memory. "And to seal the bargain, I will give her my niece."

He had the pleasure of seeing a look of genuine surprise in Petyr Baelish's grey-green eyes. "Myrcella?"

"When she comes of age, she can wed little Lord Robert. Until such time, she'll be Lady Lysa's ward at the Eyrie."

"And what does Her Grace the queen think of this ploy?" When Tyrion shrugged, Littlefinger burst into laughter. "I thought not. You're a dangerous little man, Lannister. Yes, I could sing this song to Lysa." Again the sly smile, the mischief in his glance. "If I cared to."

Tyrion nodded, waiting, knowing Littlefinger could never abide a long silence.

"So," Lord Petyr continued after a pause, utterly unabashed, "what's in your pot for me?"

"Harrenhal."

It was interesting to watch his face. Lord Petyr's father had been the smallest of small lords, his grandfather a landless hedge knight; by birth, he held no more than a few stony acres on the windswept shore of the Fingers. Harrenhal was one of the richest plums in the Seven Kingdoms, its lands broad and rich and fertile, its great castle as formidable as any in the realm . . . and so large as to dwarf Riverrun, where Petyr Baelish had been fostered by House Tully, only to be brusquely expelled when he dared raise his sights to Lord Hoster's daughter.

Littlefinger took a moment to adjust the drape of his cape, but Tyrion had seen the flash of hunger in those sly cat's eyes. *I have him,* he knew. "Harrenhal is cursed," Lord Petyr said after a moment, trying to sound bored.

"Then raze it to the ground and build anew to suit yourself. You'll have no lack of coin. I mean to make you liege lord of the Trident. These river lords have proven they cannot be trusted. Let them do you fealty for their lands."

"Even the Tullys?"

"If there are any Tullys left when we are done."

Littlefinger looked like a boy who had just taken a furtive bite from a honeycomb. He was *trying* to watch for bees, but the honey was so sweet. "Harrenhal and all its lands and incomes," he mused. "With a stroke, you'd make me one of the greatest lords in the realm. Not that I'm ungrateful, my lord, but—why?"

"You served my sister well in the matter of the succession."

"As did Janos Slynt. On whom this same castle of Harrenhal was quite recently bestowed—only to be snatched away when he was no longer of use."

Tyrion laughed. "You have me, my lord. What can I say? I need you to deliver the Lady Lysa. I did not need Janos Slynt." He gave a crooked shrug. "I'd sooner have you seated in Harrenhal than Renly seated on the Iron Throne. What could be plainer?"

"What indeed. You realize that I may need to bed Lysa Arryn again to get her consent to this marriage?"

"I have little doubt you'll be equal to the task."

"I once told Ned Stark that when you find yourself naked with an ugly woman, the only thing to do is close your eyes and get on with it." Littlefinger steepled his fingers and gazed into Tyrion's mismatched eyes. "Give me a fortnight to conclude my affairs and arrange for a ship to carry me to Gulltown."

"That will do nicely."

His guest rose. "This has been quite the pleasant morning, Lannister. And profitable . . . for both of us, I trust." He bowed, his cape a swirl of yellow as he strode out the door.

Two, thought Tyrion.

He went up to his bedchamber to await Varys, who would soon be making an appearance. Evenfall, he guessed. Perhaps as late as moonrise, though he hoped not. He hoped to visit Shae tonight. He was pleasantly surprised when Galt of the Stone Crows informed him not an hour later that the powdered man was at his door. "You are a cruel man, to make the Grand Maester squirm so," the eunuch scolded. "The man cannot abide a secret."

"Is that a crow I hear, calling the raven black? Or would you sooner not hear what I've proposed to Doran Martell?"

Varys giggled. "Perhaps my little birds have told me."

"Have they, indeed?" He wanted to hear this. "Go on."

"The Dornishmen thus far have held aloof from these wars. Doran Martell has called his banners, but no more. His hatred for House Lannister is well known, and it is commonly thought he will join Lord Renly. You wish to dissuade him."

"All this is obvious," said Tyrion.

"The only puzzle is what you might have offered for his allegiance. The prince is a sentimental man, and he still mourns his sister Elia and her sweet babe."

"My father once told me that a lord never lets sentiment get in the way of ambition . . . and it happens we have an empty seat on the small council, now that Lord Janos has taken the black."

"A council seat is not to be despised," Varys admitted, "yet will it be enough to make a proud man forget his sister's murder?"

"Why forget?" Tyrion smiled. "I've promised to deliver his sister's killers, alive or dead, as he prefers. *After* the war is done, to be sure."

Varys gave him a shrewd look. "My little birds tell me that Princess Elia cried a . . . certain name . . . when they came for her."

"Is a secret still a secret if everyone knows it?" In Casterly Rock, it was common knowledge that Gregor Clegane had killed Elia and her babe. They said he had raped the princess with her son's blood and brains still on his hands.

"*This* secret is your lord father's sworn man."

"My father would be the first to tell you that fifty thousand Dornishmen are worth one rabid dog."

Varys stroked a powdered cheek. "And if Prince Doran demands the blood of the lord who gave the command as well as the knight who did the deed . . ."

"Robert Baratheon led the rebellion. All commands came from him, in the end."

"Robert was not at King's Landing."

"Neither was Doran Martell."

"So. Blood for his pride, a chair for his ambition. Gold and land, that goes without saying. A sweet offer . . . yet sweets can be poisoned. If I were the prince, something more would I require before I should reach for this honeycomb. Some token of good faith, some sure safeguard against betrayal." Varys smiled his slimiest smile. "Which one will you give him, I wonder?"

Tyrion sighed. "You know, don't you?"

"Since you put it that way—yes. Tommen. You could scarcely offer Myrcella to Doran Martell and Lysa Arryn both."

"Remind me never to play these guessing games with you again. You cheat."

"Prince Tommen is a good boy."

"If I pry him away from Cersei and Joffrey while he's still young, he may even grow to be a good man."

"And a good king?"

"Joffrey is king."

"And Tommen is heir, should anything ill befall His Grace. Tommen, whose nature is so sweet, and notably . . . tractable."

"You have a suspicious mind, Varys."

"I shall take that as a tribute, my lord. In any case, Prince Doran will hardly be insensible of the great honor you do him. Very deftly done, I would say . . . but for one small flaw."

The dwarf laughed. "Named Cersei?"

"What avails statecraft against the love of a mother

for the sweet fruit of her womb? Perhaps, for the glory of her House and the safety of the realm, the queen might be persuaded to send away Tommen or Myrcella. But both of them? Surely not."

"What Cersei does not know will never hurt me."

"And if Her Grace were to discover your intentions before your plans are ripe?"

"Why," he said, "then I would know the man who told her to be my certain enemy." And when Varys giggled, he thought, *Three*.

SANSA

Come to the godswood tonight, if you want to go home.

The words were the same on the hundredth reading as they'd been on the first, when Sansa had discovered the folded sheet of parchment beneath her pillow. She did not know how it had gotten there or who had sent it. The note was unsigned, unsealed, and the hand unfamiliar. She crushed the parchment to her chest and whispered the words to herself. "Come to the godswood tonight, if you want to go home," she breathed, ever so faintly.

What could it mean? Should she take it to the queen to prove that she was being good? Nervously, she rubbed her stomach. The angry purple bruise Ser Meryn had given her had faded to an ugly yellow, but still hurt. His fist had been mailed when he hit her. It was her own fault. She must learn to hide her feelings better, so as not to anger Joffrey. When she heard that the Imp had sent Lord Slynt to the Wall, she had forgotten herself and said, "I hope the Others get him." The king had not been pleased.

Come to the godswood tonight, if you want to go home.

Sansa had prayed so hard. Could this be her answer at last, a true knight sent to save her? Perhaps it was one of the Redwyne twins, or bold Ser Balon Swann . . . or even Beric Dondarrion, the young lord her friend Jeyne Poole had loved, with his red-gold hair and the spray of stars on his black cloak.

Come to the godswood tonight, if you want to go home.

What if it was some cruel jape of Joffrey's, like the day he had taken her up to the battlements to show her Father's head? Or perhaps it was some subtle snare to prove she was not loyal. If she went to the godswood, would she find Ser Ilyn Payne waiting for her, sitting silent under the heart tree with Ice in his hand, his pale eyes watching to see if she'd come?

Come to the godswood tonight, if you want to go home.

When the door opened, she hurriedly stuffed the note under her sheet and sat on it. It was her bedmaid, the mousy one with the limp brown hair. "What do you want?" Sansa demanded.

"Will milady be wanting a bath tonight?"

"A fire, I think . . . I feel a chill." She *was* shivering, though the day had been hot.

"As you wish."

Sansa watched the girl suspiciously. Had she seen the note? Had she put it under the pillow? It did not seem likely; she seemed a stupid girl, not one you'd want delivering secret notes, but Sansa did not know her. The queen had her servants changed every fortnight, to make certain none of them befriended her.

When a fire was blazing in the hearth, Sansa thanked the maid curtly and ordered her out. The girl was quick to obey, as ever, but Sansa decided there was something sly about her eyes. Doubtless, she was scurrying off to report to the queen, or maybe Varys. All her maids spied on her, she was certain.

Once alone, she thrust the note in the flames, watching the parchment curl and blacken. *Come to the godswood tonight, if you want to go home.* She drifted to her window. Below, she could see a short knight in moon-pale armor and a heavy white cloak pacing the drawbridge. From his height, it could only be Ser Preston Greenfield. The queen had given her freedom of the castle, but even so, he would want to know where she was going if she tried to leave Maegor's Holdfast at this time of night. What was she to tell him? Suddenly she was glad she had burned the note.

She unlaced her gown and crawled into her bed, but she did not sleep. *Was he still there?* she wondered. *How long will he wait?* It was so cruel, to send her a note and tell her nothing. The thoughts went round and round in her head.

If only she had someone to tell her what to do. She missed Septa Mordane, and even more Jeyne Poole, her truest friend. The septa had lost her head with the rest, for the crime of serving House Stark. Sansa did not know what had happened to Jeyne, who had disappeared from her rooms afterward, never to be mentioned again. She tried not to think of them too often, yet sometimes the memories came unbidden, and then it was hard to hold back the tears. Once in a while, Sansa even missed her sister. By now Arya was safe back in Winterfell, dancing and sewing, playing with Bran and baby Rickon, even riding through the winter town if she liked. Sansa was allowed to go riding too, but only in the bailey, and it got boring going round in a circle all day.

She was wide awake when she heard the shouting. Distant at first, then growing louder. Many voices yelling together. She could not make out the words. And there were horses as well, and pounding feet, shouts of command. She crept to her window and saw men running on the walls, carrying spears and torches. *Go back to your bed,* Sansa told herself, *this is nothing that*

concerns you, just some new trouble out in the city.
The talk at the wells had all been of troubles in the city
of late. People were crowding in, running from the war,
and many had no way to live save by robbing and killing
each other. *Go to bed.*

But when she looked, the white knight was gone, the
bridge across the dry moat down but undefended.

Sansa turned away without thinking and ran to her
wardrobe. *Oh, what am I doing?* she asked herself as
she dressed. *This is madness.* She could see the lights of
many torches on the curtain walls. Had Stannis and
Renly come at last to kill Joffrey and claim their
brother's throne? If so, the guards would raise the drawbridge, cutting off Maegor's Holdfast from the outer castle. Sansa threw a plain grey cloak over her shoulders
and picked up the knife she used to cut her meat. *If it is
some trap, better that I die than let them hurt me
more,* she told herself. She hid the blade under her
cloak.

A column of red-cloaked swordsmen ran past as she
slipped out into the night. She waited until they were
well past before she darted across the undefended drawbridge. In the yard, men were buckling on swordbelts
and cinching the saddles of their horses. She glimpsed
Ser Preston near the stables with three others of the
Kingsguard, white cloaks bright as the moon as they
helped Joffrey into his armor. Her breath caught in her
throat when she saw the king. Thankfully, he did not
see her. He was shouting for his sword and crossbow.

The noise receded as she moved deeper into the castle, never daring to look back for fear that Joffrey might
be watching . . . or worse, following. The serpentine
steps twisted ahead, striped by bars of flickering light
from the narrow windows above. Sansa was panting by
the time she reached the top. She ran down a shadowy
colonnade and pressed herself against a wall to catch
her breath. When something brushed against her leg,
she almost jumped out of her skin, but it was only a cat,
a ragged black tom with a chewed-off ear. The creature
spit at her and leapt away.

By the time she reached the godswood, the noises had faded to a faint rattle of steel and a distant shouting. Sansa pulled her cloak tighter. The air was rich with the smells of earth and leaf. *Lady would have liked this place*, she thought. There was something wild about a godswood; even here, in the heart of the castle at the heart of the city, you could feel the old gods watching with a thousand unseen eyes.

Sansa had favored her mother's gods over her father's. She loved the statues, the pictures in leaded glass, the fragrance of burning incense, the septons with their robes and crystals, the magical play of the rainbows over altars inlaid with mother-of-pearl and onyx and lapis lazuli. Yet she could not deny that the godswood had a certain power too. Especially by night. *Help me*, she prayed, *send me a friend, a true knight to champion me . . .*

She moved from tree to tree, feeling the roughness of the bark beneath her fingers. Leaves brushed at her cheeks. Had she come too late? He would not have left so soon, would he? Or had he even been here? Dare she risk calling out? It seemed so hushed and still here . . .

"I feared you would not come, child."

Sansa whirled. A man stepped out of the shadows, heavyset, thick of neck, shambling. He wore a dark grey robe with the cowl pulled forward, but when a thin sliver of moonlight touched his cheek, she knew him at once by the blotchy skin and web of broken veins beneath. "Ser Dontos," she breathed, heartbroken. "Was it you?"

"Yes, my lady." When he moved closer, she could smell the sour stench of wine on his breath. "Me." He reached out a hand.

Sansa shrank back. *"Don't!"* She slid her hand under her cloak, to her hidden knife. "What . . . what do you want with me?"

"Only to help you," Dontos said, "as you helped me."

"You're drunk, aren't you?"

"Only one cup of wine, to help my courage. If they catch me now, they'll strip the skin off my back."

And what will they do to me? Sansa found herself thinking of Lady again. She could smell out falsehood, she *could*, but she was dead, Father had killed her, on account of Arya. She drew the knife and held it before her with both hands.

"Are you going to stab me?" Dontos asked.

"I will," she said. "Tell me who sent you."

"No one, sweet lady. I swear it on my honor as a knight."

"A knight?" Joffrey had decreed that he was to be a knight no longer, only a fool, lower even than Moon Boy. "I prayed to the gods for a knight to come save me," she said. "I prayed and prayed. Why would they send me a drunken old fool?"

"I deserve that, though . . . I know it's queer, but . . . all those years I was a knight, I was truly a fool, and now that I am a fool I think . . . I think I may find it in me to be a knight again, sweet lady. And all because of you . . . your grace, your courage. You saved me, not only from Joffrey, but from myself." His voice dropped. "The singers say there was another fool once who was the greatest knight of all . . ."

"Florian," Sansa whispered. A shiver went through her.

"Sweet lady, I would be your Florian," Dontos said humbly, falling to his knees before her.

Slowly, Sansa lowered the knife. Her head seemed terribly light, as if she were floating. *This is madness, to trust myself to this drunkard, but if I turn away will the chance ever come again?* "How . . . how would you do it? Get me away?"

Ser Dontos raised his face to her. "Taking you from the castle, that will be the hardest. Once you're out, there are ships that would take you home. I'd need to find the coin and make the arrangements, that's all."

"Could we go now?" she asked, hardly daring to hope.

"This very night? No, my lady, I fear not. First I must find a sure way to get you from the castle when the hour is ripe. It will not be easy, nor quick. They watch me as well." He licked his lips nervously. "Will you put away your blade?"

Sansa slipped the knife beneath her cloak. "Rise, ser."

"Thank you, sweet lady." Ser Dontos lurched clumsily to his feet, and brushed earth and leaves from his knees. "Your lord father was as true a man as the realm has ever known, but I stood by and let them slay him. I said nothing, did nothing . . . and yet, when Joffrey would have slain me, you spoke up. Lady, I have never been a hero, no Ryam Redwyne or Barristan the Bold. I've won no tourneys, no renown in war . . . but I *was* a knight once, and you have helped me remember what that meant. My life is a poor thing, but it is yours." Ser Dontos placed a hand on the gnarled bole of the heart tree. He was shaking, she saw. "I vow, with your father's gods as witness, that I shall send you home."

He swore. A solemn oath, before the gods. "Then . . . I will put myself in your hands, ser. But how will I know, when it is time to go? Will you send me another note?"

Ser Dontos glanced about anxiously. "The risk is too great. You must come here, to the godswood. As often as you can. This is the safest place. The *only* safe place. Nowhere else. Not in your chambers nor mine nor on the steps nor in the yard, even if it seems we are alone. The stones have ears in the Red Keep, and only here may we talk freely."

"Only here," Sansa said. "I'll remember."

"And if I should seem cruel or mocking or indifferent when men are watching, forgive me, child. I have a role to play, and you must do the same. One misstep and our heads will adorn the walls as did your father's."

She nodded. "I understand."

"You will need to be brave and strong . . . and patient, patient above all."

"I will be," she promised, "but . . . please . . . make it as soon as you can. I'm afraid . . ."

"So am I," Ser Dontos said, smiling wanly. "And now you must go, before you are missed."

"You will not come with me?"

"Better if we are never seen together."

Nodding, Sansa took a step . . . then spun back, nervous, and softly laid a kiss on his cheek, her eyes closed. "My Florian," she whispered. "The gods heard my prayer."

She flew along the river walk, past the small kitchen, and through the pig yard, her hurried footsteps lost beneath the squealing of the hogs in their pens. *Home,* she thought, *home, he is going to take me home, he'll keep me safe, my Florian.* The songs about Florian and Jonquil were her very favorites. *Florian was homely too, though not so old.*

She was racing headlong down the serpentine steps when a man lurched out of a hidden doorway. Sansa caromed into him and lost her balance. Iron fingers caught her by the wrist before she could fall, and a deep voice rasped at her. "It's a long roll down the serpentine, little bird. Want to kill us both?" His laughter was rough as a saw on stone. "Maybe you do."

The Hound. "No, my lord, pardons, I'd never." Sansa averted her eyes but it was too late, he'd seen her face. "Please, you're hurting me." She tried to wriggle free.

"And what's Joff's little bird doing flying down the serpentine in the black of night?" When she did not answer, he shook her. *"Where were you?"*

"The g-g-godswood, my lord," she said, not daring to lie. "Praying . . . praying for my father, and . . . for the king, praying that he'd not be hurt."

"Think I'm so drunk that I'd believe *that?*" He let go his grip on her arm, swaying slightly as he stood, stripes of light and darkness falling across his terrible burnt face. "You look almost a woman . . . face, teats, and you're taller too, almost . . . ah, you're still a stupid little bird, aren't you? Singing all the songs they taught you . . . sing me a song, why don't you? Go on. Sing to me. Some song about knights and fair maids. You like knights, don't you?"

He was scaring her. "T-true knights, my lord."

"*True* knights," he mocked. "And I'm no lord, no more than I'm a knight. Do I need to beat that into you?" Clegane reeled and almost fell. "*Gods,*" he swore, "too much wine. Do you like wine, little bird? *True* wine? A flagon of sour red, dark as blood, all a man needs. Or a woman." He laughed, shook his head. "Drunk as a dog, damn me. You come now. Back to your cage, little bird. I'll take you there. Keep you safe for the king." The Hound gave her a push, oddly gentle, and followed her down the steps. By the time they reached the bottom, he had lapsed back into a brooding silence, as if he had forgotten she was there.

When they reached Maegor's Holdfast, she was alarmed to see that it was Ser Boros Blount who now held the bridge. His high white helm turned stiffly at the sound of their footsteps. Sansa flinched away from his gaze. Ser Boros was the worst of the Kingsguard, an ugly man with a foul temper, all scowls and jowls.

"That one is nothing to fear, girl." The Hound laid a heavy hand on her shoulder. "Paint stripes on a toad, he does not become a tiger."

Ser Boros lifted his visor. "Ser, where—"

"Fuck your *ser*, Boros. You're the knight, not me. I'm the king's dog, remember?"

"The king was looking for his dog earlier."

"The dog was drinking. It was your night to shield him, *ser*. You and my other *brothers.*"

Ser Boros turned to Sansa. "How is it you are not in your chambers at this hour, lady?"

"I went to the godswood to pray for the safety of the king." The lie sounded better this time, almost true.

"You expect her to sleep with all the noise?" Clegane said. "What was the trouble?"

"Fools at the gate," Ser Boros admitted. "Some loose tongues spread tales of the preparations for Tyrek's wedding feast, and these wretches got it in their heads they should be feasted too. His Grace led a sortie and sent them scurrying."

"A brave boy," Clegane said, mouth twitching.

Let us see how brave he is when he faces my brother, Sansa thought. The Hound escorted her across the drawbridge. As they were winding their way up the steps, she said, "Why do you let people call you a dog? You won't let *anyone* call you a knight."

"I like dogs better than knights. My father's father was kennelmaster at the Rock. One autumn year, Lord Tytos came between a lioness and her prey. The lioness didn't give a shit that she was Lannister's own sigil. Bitch tore into my lord's horse and would have done for my lord too, but my grandfather came up with the hounds. Three of his dogs died running her off. My grandfather lost a leg, so Lannister paid him for it with lands and a towerhouse, and took his son to squire. The three dogs on our banner are the three that died, in the yellow of autumn grass. A hound will die for you, but never lie to you. And he'll look you straight in the face." He cupped her under the jaw, raising her chin, his fingers pinching her painfully. "And that's more than little birds can do, isn't it? I never got my song."

"I . . . I know a song about Florian and Jonquil."

"Florian and Jonquil? A fool and his cunt. Spare me. But one day I'll have a song from you, whether you will it or no."

"I will sing it for you gladly."

Sandor Clegane snorted. "Pretty thing, and such a bad liar. A dog can smell a lie, you know. Look around you, and take a good whiff. They're all liars here . . . and every one better than you."

ARYA

When she climbed all the way up to the highest branch, Arya could see chimneys poking through the trees. Thatched roofs clustered along the shore of the lake and the small stream that emptied into it, and a wooden pier jutted out into the water beside a low long building with a slate roof.

She skinnied farther out, until the branch began to sag under her weight. No boats were tied to the pier, but she could see thin tendrils of smoke rising from some of the chimneys, and part of a wagon jutting out behind a stable.

Someone's there. Arya chewed her lip. All the other places they'd come upon had been empty and desolate. Farms, villages, castles, septs, barns, it made no matter. If it could burn, the Lannisters had burned it; if it could die, they'd killed it. They had even set the woods ablaze where they could, though the leaves were still green and wet from recent rains, and the fires had not spread. "They would have burned the lake if they could have,"

Gendry had said, and Arya knew he was right. On the night of their escape, the flames of the burning town had shimmered so brightly on the water that it had seemed that the lake *was* afire.

When they finally summoned the nerve to steal back into the ruins the next night, nothing remained but blackened stones, the hollow shells of houses, and corpses. In some places wisps of pale smoke still rose from the ashes. Hot Pie had pleaded with them not to go back, and Lommy called them fools and swore that Ser Amory would catch them and kill them too, but Lorch and his men had long gone by the time they reached the holdfast. They found the gates broken down, the walls partly demolished, and the inside strewn with the unburied dead. One look was enough for Gendry. "They're killed, every one," he said. "And dogs have been at them too, look."

"Or wolves."

"Dogs, wolves, it makes no matter. It's done here."

But Arya would not leave until they found Yoren. They couldn't have killed *him*, she told herself, he was too hard and tough, and a brother of the Night's Watch besides. She said as much to Gendry as they searched among the corpses.

The axe blow that had killed him had split his skull apart, but the great tangled beard could be no one else's, or the garb, patched and unwashed and so faded it was more grey than black. Ser Amory Lorch had given no more thought to burying his own dead than to those he had murdered, and the corpses of four Lannister men-at-arms were heaped near Yoren's. Arya wondered how many it had taken to bring him down.

He was going to take me home, she thought as they dug the old man's hole. There were too many dead to bury them all, but Yoren at least must have a grave, Arya had insisted. *He was going to bring me safe to Winterfell, he promised.* Part of her wanted to cry. The other part wanted to kick him.

It was Gendry who thought of the lord's towerhouse and the three that Yoren had sent to hold it. They had come under attack as well, but the round tower had only one entry, a second-story door reached by a ladder. Once that had been pulled inside, Ser Amory's men could not get at them. The Lannisters had piled brush around the tower's base and set it afire, but the stone would not burn, and Lorch did not have the patience to starve them out. Cutjack opened the door at Gendry's shout, and when Kurz said they'd be better pressing on north than going back, Arya had clung to the hope that she still might reach Winterfell.

Well, this village was no Winterfell, but those thatched roofs promised warmth and shelter and maybe even food, if they were bold enough to risk them. *Unless it's Lorch there. He had horses; he would have traveled faster than us.*

She watched from the tree for a long time, hoping she might see something; a man, a horse, a banner, anything that would help her know. A few times she glimpsed motion, but the buildings were so far off it was hard to be certain. Once, very clearly, she heard the whinny of a horse.

The air was full of birds, crows mostly. From afar, they were no larger than flies as they wheeled and flapped above the thatched roofs. To the east, Gods Eye was a sheet of sun-hammered blue that filled half the world. Some days, as they made their slow way up the muddy shore (Gendry wanted no part of any roads, and even Hot Pie and Lommy saw the sense in that), Arya felt as though the lake were calling her. She wanted to leap into those placid blue waters, to feel clean again, to swim and splash and bask in the sun. But she dare not take off her clothes where the others could see, not even to wash them. At the end of the day she would often sit on a rock and dangle her feet in the cool water. She had finally thrown away her cracked and rotted shoes. Walking barefoot was hard at first, but the blisters had finally broken, the cuts had healed, and her soles had turned to leather. The mud was nice between her toes, and she liked to feel the earth underfoot when she walked.

From up here, she could see a small wooded island off to the northeast. Thirty yards from shore, three black swans were gliding over the water, so serene . . . no one had told them that war had come, and they cared nothing for burning towns and butchered men. She stared at them with yearning. Part of her wanted to be a swan. The other part wanted to eat one. She had broken her fast on some acorn paste and a handful of bugs. Bugs weren't so bad when you got used to them. Worms were worse, but still not as bad as the pain in your belly after days without food. Finding bugs was easy, all you had to do was kick over a rock. Arya had eaten a bug once when she was little, just to make Sansa screech, so she hadn't been afraid to eat another. Weasel wasn't either, but Hot Pie retched up the beetle he tried to swallow, and Lommy and Gendry wouldn't even try. Yesterday Gendry had caught a frog and shared it with Lommy, and, a few days before, Hot Pie had found blackberries and stripped the bush bare, but mostly they had been living on water and acorns. Kurz had told them how to use rocks and make a kind of acorn paste. It tasted awful.

She wished the poacher hadn't died. He'd known more about the woods than all the rest of them together, but he'd taken an arrow through the shoulder pulling in the ladder at the towerhouse. Tarber had packed it with mud and moss from the lake, and for a day or two Kurz swore the wound was nothing, even though the flesh of his throat was turning dark while angry red welts crept up his jaw and down his chest. Then one morning he couldn't find the strength to get up, and by the next he was dead.

They buried him under a mound of stones, and Cutjack had claimed his sword and hunting horn, while Tarber helped himself to bow and boots and knife. They'd taken it all when they left. At first they thought the two had just gone hunting, that they'd soon return with game and feed them all. But they waited and waited, until finally Gendry made them move on. Maybe Tarber and Cutjack figured they would stand a better chance without a gaggle of orphan boys to herd along. They probably would too, but that didn't stop her hating them for leaving.

Beneath her tree, Hot Pie barked like a dog. Kurz had told them to use animal sounds to signal to each other. An old poacher's trick, he'd said, but he'd died before he could teach them how to make the sounds right. Hot Pie's bird calls were awful. His dog was better, but not much.

Arya hopped from the high branch to one beneath it, her hands out for balance. *A water dancer never falls.* Lightfoot, her toes curled tight around the branch, she walked a few feet, hopped down to a larger limb, then swung hand over hand through the tangle of leaves until she reached the trunk. The bark was rough beneath her fingers, against her toes. She descended quickly, jumping down the final six feet, rolling when she landed.

Gendry gave her a hand to pull her up. "You were up there a long time. What could you see?"

"A fishing village, just a little place, north along the shore. Twenty-six thatch roofs and one slate, I counted. I saw part of a wagon. Someone's there."

At the sound of her voice, Weasel came creeping out from the bushes. Lommy had named her that. He said she looked like a weasel, which wasn't true, but they couldn't keep on calling her the crying girl after she finally stopped crying. Her mouth was filthy. Arya hoped she hadn't been eating mud again.

"Did you see people?" asked Gendry.

"Mostly just roofs," Arya admitted, "but some chimneys were smoking, and I heard a horse." The Weasel put her arms around her leg, clutching tight. Sometimes she did that now.

"If there's people, there's food," Hot Pie said, too loudly. Gendry was always telling him to be more quiet, but it never did any good. "Might be they'd give us some."

"Might be they'd kill us too," Gendry said.

"Not if we yielded," Hot Pie said hopefully.

"Now you sound like Lommy."

Lommy Greenhands sat propped up between two thick roots at the foot of an oak. A spear had taken him through his left calf during the fight at the holdfast. By the end of the next day, he had to limp along one-legged with an arm around Gendry, and now he couldn't even do *that*. They'd hacked branches off trees to make a litter for him, but it was slow, hard work carrying him along, and he whimpered every time they jounced him.

"We have to yield," he said. "That's what Yoren should have done. He should have opened the gates like they said."

Arya was sick of Lommy going on about how Yoren should have yielded. It was all he talked about when they carried him, that and his leg and his empty belly.

Hot Pie agreed. "They *told* Yoren to open the gates, they told him in the king's name. You have to do what they tell you in the king's name. It was that stinky old man's fault. If he'd of yielded, they would have left us be."

Gendry frowned. "Knights and lordlings, they take each other captive and pay ransoms, but they don't care if the likes of you yield or not." He turned to Arya. "What else did you see?"

"If it's a fishing village, they'd sell us fish, I bet," said Hot Pie. The lake teemed with fresh fish, but they had nothing to catch them with. Arya had tried to use her hands, the way she'd seen Koss do, but fish were quicker than pigeons and the water played tricks on her eyes.

"I don't know about fish." Arya tugged at the Weasel's matted hair, thinking it might be best to hack it off. "There's crows down by the water. Something's dead there."

"Fish, washed up on shore," Hot Pie said. "If the crows eat it, I bet we could."

"We should catch some crows, we could eat *them*," said Lommy. "We could make a fire and roast them like chickens."

Gendry looked fierce when he scowled. His beard had grown in thick and black as briar. "I said, no fires."

"Lommy's *hungry,*" Hot Pie whined, "and I am too."

"We're all hungry," said Arya.

"*You're* not," Lommy spat from the ground. "Worm breath."

Arya could have kicked him in his wound. "I *said* I'd dig worms for you too, if you wanted."

Lommy made a disgusted face. "If it wasn't for my leg, I'd hunt us some boars."

"Some boars," she mocked. "You need a boarspear to hunt boars, and horses and dogs, and men to flush the boar from its lair." Her father had hunted boar in the wolfswood with Robb and Jon. Once he even took Bran, but never Arya, even though she was older. Septa Mordane said boar hunting was not for ladies, and Mother only promised that when she was older she might have her own hawk. She was older now, but if she had a hawk she'd *eat* it.

"What do *you* know about hunting boars?" said Hot Pie.

"More than you."

Gendry was in no mood to hear it. "Quiet, both of you, I need to think what to do." He always looked pained when he tried to think, like it hurt him something fierce.

"Yield," Lommy said.

"I told you to shut up about the yielding. We don't even know who's in there. Maybe we can steal some food."

"Lommy could steal, if it wasn't for his leg," said Hot Pie. "He was a thief in the city."

"A bad thief," Arya said, "or he wouldn't have got caught."

Gendry squinted up at the sun. "Evenfall will be the best time to sneak in. I'll go scout come dark."

"No, I'll go," Arya said. "You're too noisy."

Gendry got that look on his face. "We'll both go."

"Arry should go," said Lommy. "He's sneakier than you are."

"We'll *both* go, I said."

"But what if you don't come back? Hot Pie can't carry me by himself, you know he can't . . ."

"And there's wolves," Hot Pie said. "I heard them last night, when I had the watch. They sounded close."

Arya had heard them too. She'd been asleep in the branches of an elm, but the howling had woken her. She'd sat awake for a good hour, listening to them, prickles creeping up her spine.

"And you won't even let us have a fire to keep them off," Hot Pie said. "It's not right, leaving us for the wolves."

"No one is leaving you," Gendry said in disgust. "Lommy has his spear if the wolves come, and you'll be with him. We're just going to go see, that's all; we're coming back."

"Whoever it is, you should yield to them," Lommy whined. "I need some potion for my leg, it hurts bad."

"If we see any leg potion, we'll bring it," Gendry said. "Arry, let's go, I want to get near before the sun is down. Hot Pie, you keep Weasel here, I don't want her following."

"Last time she kicked me."

"*I'll* kick you if you don't keep her here." Without waiting for an answer, Gendry donned his steel helm and walked off.

Arya had to scamper to keep up. Gendry was five years older and a foot taller than she was, and long of leg as well. For a while he said nothing, just plowed on through the trees with an angry look on his face, making too much noise. But finally he stopped and said, "I think Lommy's going to die."

She was not surprised. Kurz had died of his wound, and he'd been a lot stronger than Lommy. Whenever it was Arya's turn to help carry him, she could feel how warm his skin was, and smell the stink off his leg. "Maybe we could find a maester . . ."

"You only find maesters in castles, and even if we found one, he wouldn't dirty his hands on the likes of Lommy." Gendry ducked under a low-hanging limb.

"That's not true." Maester Luwin would have helped anyone who came to him, she was certain.

"He's going to die, and the sooner he does it, the better for the rest of us. We should just leave him, like he says. If it was you or me hurt, you know he'd leave us." They scrambled down a steep cut and up the other side, using roots for handholds. "I'm sick of carrying him, and I'm sick of all his talk about yielding too. If he could stand up, I'd knock his teeth in. Lommy's no use to anyone. That crying girl's no use either."

"You leave Weasel alone, she's just scared and hungry is all." Arya glanced back, but the girl was not following for once. Hot Pie must have grabbed her, like Gendry had told him.

"She's no use," Gendry repeated stubbornly. "Her and Hot Pie and Lommy, they're slowing us down, and they're going to get us killed. You're the only one of the bunch who's good for anything. Even if you are a girl."

Arya froze in her steps. *"I'm not a girl!"*

"Yes you are. Do you think I'm as stupid as they are?"

"No, you're stupider. The Night's Watch doesn't take girls, everyone knows that."

"That's true. I don't know why Yoren brought you, but he must have had some reason. You're still a girl."

"I am not!"

"Then pull out your cock and take a piss. Go on."

"I don't need to take a piss. If I wanted to I could."

"Liar. You can't take out your cock because you don't have one. I never noticed before when there were thirty of us, but you always go off in the woods to make your water. You don't see Hot Pie doing that, nor me neither. If you're not a girl, you must be some eunuch."

"You're the eunuch."

"You know I'm not." Gendry smiled. "You want me to take out my cock and prove it? I don't have anything to hide."

"Yes you do," Arya blurted, desperate to escape the subject of the cock she didn't have. "Those gold cloaks were after you at the inn, and you won't tell us why."

"I wish I knew. I think Yoren knew, but he never told me. Why did you think they were after you, though?"

Arya bit her lip. She remembered what Yoren had said, the day he had hacked off her hair. *This lot, half o' them would turn you over to the queen quick as spit for a pardon and maybe a few silvers. The other half'd do the same, only they'd rape you first.* Only Gendry was different, the queen wanted him too. "I'll tell you if you'll tell me," she said warily.

"I would if I knew, Arry . . . is that really what you're called, or do you have some girl's name?"

Arya glared at the gnarled root by her feet. She realized that the pretense was done. Gendry knew, and she had nothing in her pants to convince him otherwise. She could draw Needle and kill him where he stood, or else trust him. She wasn't certain she'd be able to kill him, even if she tried; he had his own sword, and he was a *lot* stronger. All that was left was the truth. "Lommy and Hot Pie can't know," she said.

"They won't," he swore. "Not from me."

"Arya." She raised her eyes to his. "My name is Arya. Of House Stark."

"Of House . . ." It took him a moment before he said, "The King's Hand was named Stark. The one they killed for a traitor."

"He was never a traitor. He was my father."

Gendry's eyes widened. "So *that*'s why you thought . . ."

She nodded. "Yoren was taking me home to Winterfell."

"I . . . you're highborn then, a . . . you'll be a lady . . ."

Arya looked down at her ragged clothes and bare feet, all cracked and calloused. She saw the dirt under her nails, the scabs on her elbows, the scratches on her hands. *Septa Mordane wouldn't even know me, I bet. Sansa might, but she'd pretend not to.* "My mother's a lady, and my sister, but I never was."

"Yes you were. You were a lord's daughter and you lived in a castle, didn't you? And you . . . gods be

good, I never . . ." All of a sudden Gendry seemed uncertain, almost afraid. "All that about cocks, I never
should have said that. And I been pissing in front of you
and everything, I . . . I beg your pardon, m'lady."

"*Stop that!*" Arya hissed. Was he mocking her?

"I know my courtesies, m'lady," Gendry said, stubborn as ever. "Whenever highborn girls came into the
shop with their fathers, my master told me I was to
bend the knee, and speak only when they spoke to me,
and call them *m'lady.*"

"If you start calling me m'lady, even *Hot Pie* is going
to notice. And you better keep on pissing the same way
too."

"As m'lady commands."

Arya slammed his chest with both hands. He tripped
over a stone and sat down with a thump. "What kind of
lord's daughter are you?" he said, laughing.

"*This* kind." She kicked him in the side, but it only
made him laugh harder. "You laugh all you like. *I'm*
going to see who's in the village." The sun had already
fallen below the trees; dusk would be on them in no
time at all. For once it was Gendry who had to hurry
after. "You smell that?" she asked.

He sniffed the air. "Rotten fish?"

"You know it's not."

"We better be careful. I'll go around west, see if
there's some road. There must be if you saw a wagon.
You take the shore. If you need help, bark like a dog."

"That's stupid. If I need help, I'll shout *help.*" She
darted away, bare feet silent in the grass. When she
glanced back over her shoulder, he was watching her
with that pained look on his face that meant he was
thinking. *He's probably thinking that he shouldn't be
letting m'lady go stealing food.* Arya just knew he was
going to be stupid now.

The smell grew stronger as she got closer to the village. It did not smell like rotten fish to her. This stench
was ranker, fouler. She wrinkled her nose.

Where the trees began to thin, she used the undergrowth, slipping from bush to bush quiet as a shadow.

Every few yards she stopped to listen. The third time, she heard horses, and a man's voice as well. And the smell got worse. *Dead man's stink, that's what it is.* She had smelled it before, with Yoren and the others.

A dense thicket of brambles grew south of the village. By the time she reached it, the long shadows of sunset had begun to fade, and the lantern bugs were coming out. She could see thatched roofs just beyond the hedge. She crept along until she found a gap and squirmed through on her belly, keeping well hidden until she saw what made the smell.

Beside the gently lapping waters of Gods Eye, a long gibbet of raw green wood had been thrown up, and things that had once been men dangled there, their feet in chains, while crows pecked at their flesh and flapped from corpse to corpse. For every crow there were a hundred flies. When the wind blew off the lake, the nearest corpse twisted on its chain, ever so slightly. The crows had eaten most of its face, and something else had been at it as well, something much larger. Throat and chest had been torn apart, and glistening green entrails and ribbons of ragged flesh dangled from where the belly had been opened. One arm had been ripped right off the shoulder; Arya saw the bones a few feet away, gnawed and cracked, picked clean of meat.

She made herself look at the next man and the one beyond him and the one beyond *him*, telling herself she was hard as a stone. Corpses all, so savaged and decayed that it took her a moment to realize they had been stripped before they were hanged. They did not look like naked people; they hardly looked like people at all. The crows had eaten their eyes, and sometimes their faces. Of the sixth in the long row, nothing remained but a single leg, still tangled in its chains, swaying with each breeze.

Fear cuts deeper than swords. Dead men could not hurt her, but whoever had killed them could. Well beyond the gibbet, two men in mail hauberks stood leaning on their spears in front of the long low building by the water, the one with the slate roof. A pair of tall poles had been driven into the muddy ground in front of it, banners drooping from each staff. One looked red and one paler, white or yellow maybe, but both were limp and with the dusk settling, she could not even be certain that red one was Lannister crimson. *I don't need to see the lion, I can see all the dead people, who else would it be but Lannisters?*

Then there was a shout.

The two spearmen turned at the cry, and a third man came into view, shoving a captive before him. It was growing too dark to make out faces, but the prisoner was wearing a shiny steel helm, and when Arya saw the horns she knew it was Gendry. *You stupid stupid stupid STUPID!* she thought. If he'd been here she would have kicked him again.

The guards were talking loudly, but she was too far away to make out the words, especially with the crows gabbling and flapping closer to hand. One of the spearmen snatched the helm off Gendry's head and asked him a question, but he must not have liked the answer, because he smashed him across the face with the butt of his spear and knocked him down. The one who'd captured him gave him a kick, while the second spearman was trying on the bull's-head helm. Finally they pulled him to his feet and marched him off toward the storehouse. When they opened the heavy wooden doors, a small boy darted out, but one of the guards grabbed his arm and flung him back inside. Arya heard sobbing from inside the building, and then a shriek so loud and full of pain that it made her bite her lip.

The guards shoved Gendry inside with the boy and barred the doors behind them. Just then, a breath of wind came sighing off the lake, and the banners stirred and lifted. The one on the tall staff bore the golden lion, as she'd feared. On the other, three sleek black shapes ran across a field as yellow as butter. Dogs, she thought. Arya had seen those dogs before, but where?

It didn't matter. The only thing that mattered was that they had Gendry. Even if he *was* stubborn and stupid, she had to get him out. She wondered if they knew that the queen wanted him.

One of the guards took off his helm and donned Gendry's instead. It made her angry to see him wearing it, but she knew there was nothing she could do to stop him. She thought she heard more screams from inside the windowless storehouse, muffled by the masonry, but it was hard to be certain.

She stayed long enough to see the guard changed, and much more besides. Men came and went. They led their horses down to the stream to drink. A hunting party returned from the wood, carrying a deer's carcass slung from a pole. She watched them clean and gut it and build a cookfire on the far side of the stream, and the smell of cooking meat mingled queerly with the stench of corruption. Her empty belly roiled and she thought she might retch. The prospect of food brought other men out of the houses, near all of them wearing bits of mail or boiled leather. When the deer was cooked, the choicest portions were carried to one of the houses.

She thought that the dark might let her crawl close and free Gendry, but the guards kindled torches off the cookfire. A squire brought meat and bread to the two guarding the storehouse, and later two more men joined them and they all passed a skin of wine from hand to hand. When it was empty the others left, but the two guards remained, leaning on their spears.

Arya's arms and legs were stiff when she finally wriggled out from under the briar into the dark of the wood. It was a black night, with a thin sliver of moon appearing and disappearing as the clouds blew past. *Silent as a shadow*, she told herself as she moved through the trees. In this darkness she dared not run, for fear of tripping on some unseen root or losing her way. On her left Gods Eye lapped calmly against its shores. On her right a wind sighed through the branches, and leaves rustled and stirred. Far off, she heard the howling of wolves.

Lommy and Hot Pie almost shit themselves when she stepped out of the trees behind them. "Quiet," she told them, putting an arm around Weasel when the little girl came running up.

Hot Pie stared at her with big eyes. "We thought you left us." He had his shortsword in hand, the one Yoren had taken off the gold cloak. "I was scared you was a wolf."

"Where's the Bull?" asked Lommy.

"They caught him," Arya whispered. "We have to get him out. Hot Pie, you got to help. We'll sneak up and kill the guards, and then I'll open the door."

Hot Pie and Lommy exchanged a look. "How many?"

"I couldn't count," Arya admitted. "Twenty at least, but only two on the door."

Hot Pie looked as if he were going to cry. "We can't fight *twenty*."

"You only need to fight *one*. I'll do the other and we'll get Gendry out and run."

"We should yield," Lommy said. "Just go in and yield."

Arya shook her head stubbornly.

"Then just leave him, Arry," Lommy pleaded. "They don't know about the rest of us. If we hide, they'll go away, you know they will. It's not our fault Gendry's captured."

"You're stupid, Lommy," Arya said angrily. "You'll *die* if we don't get Gendry out. Who's going to carry you?"

"You and Hot Pie."

"All the time, with no one else to help? We'll never do it. Gendry was the strong one. Anyhow, I don't care what you say, I'm going back for him." She looked at Hot Pie. "Are you coming?"

Hot Pie glanced at Lommy, at Arya, at Lommy again. "I'll come," he said reluctantly.

"Lommy, you keep Weasel here."

He grabbed the little girl by the hand and pulled her close. "What if the wolves come?"

"Yield," Arya suggested.

Finding their way back to the village seemed to take hours. Hot Pie kept stumbling in the dark and losing his

way, and Arya had to wait for him and double back.
Finally she took him by the hand and led him along
through the trees. "Just be quiet and follow." When
they could make out the first faint glow of the village
fires against the sky, she said, "There's dead men hanging on the other side of the hedge, but they're nothing to
be scared of, just remember fear cuts deeper than
swords. We have to go real quiet and slow." Hot Pie
nodded.

She wriggled under the briar first and waited for him
on the far side, crouched low. Hot Pie emerged pale and
panting, face and arms bloody with long scratches. He
started to say something, but Arya put a finger to his
lips. On hands and knees, they crawled along the gibbet,
beneath the swaying dead. Hot Pie never once looked
up, nor made a sound.

Until the crow landed on his back, and he gave a muffled gasp. *"Who's there?"* a voice boomed suddenly from
the dark.

Hot Pie leapt to his feet. *"I yield!"* He threw away his
sword as dozens of crows rose shrieking and complaining to flap about the corpses. Arya grabbed his leg
and tried to drag him back down, but he wrenched loose
and ran forward, waving his arms. "I yield, I yield."

She bounced up and drew Needle, but by then men
were all around her. Arya slashed at the nearest, but he
blocked her with a steel-clad arm, and someone else
slammed into her and dragged her to the ground, and a
third man wrenched the sword from her grasp. When
she tried to bite, her teeth snapped shut on cold dirty
chainmail. "Oho, a fierce one," the man said, laughing.
The blow from his iron-clad fist near knocked her head
off.

They talked over her as she lay hurting, but Arya
could not seem to understand the words. Her ears rang.
When she tried to crawl off, the earth moved beneath
her. *They took Needle.* The shame of that hurt worse
than the pain, and the pain hurt a lot. Jon had given her
that sword. Syrio had taught her to use it.

Finally someone grabbed the front of her jerkin,

yanked her to her knees. Hot Pie was kneeling too, before the tallest man Arya had ever seen, a monster from one of Old Nan's stories. She never saw where the giant had come from. Three black dogs raced across his faded yellow surcoat, and his face looked as hard as if it had been cut from stone. Suddenly Arya knew where she had seen those dogs before. The night of the tourney at King's Landing, all the knights had hung their shields outside their pavilions. "That one belongs to the Hound's brother," Sansa had confided when they passed the black dogs on the yellow field. "He's even bigger than Hodor, you'll see. They call him *the Mountain That Rides.*"

Arya let her head droop, only half aware of what was going on around her. Hot Pie was yielding some more. The Mountain said, "You'll lead us to these others," and walked off. Next she was stumbling past the dead men on their gibbet, while Hot Pie told their captors he'd bake them pies and tarts if they didn't hurt him. Four men went with them. One carried a torch, one a longsword; two had spears.

They found Lommy where they'd left him, under the oak. "I yield," he called out at once when he saw them. He'd flung away his own spear and raised his hands, splotchy green with old dye. "I yield. Please."

The man with the torch searched around under the trees. "Are you the last? Baker boy said there was a girl."

"She ran off when she heard you coming," Lommy said. "You made a lot of noise." And Arya thought, *Run, Weasel, run as far as you can, run and hide and never come back.*

"Tell us where we can find that whoreson Dondarrion, and there'll be a hot meal in it for you."

"Who?" said Lommy blankly.

"I told you, this lot don't know no more than those cunts in the village. Waste o' bloody time."

One of the spearmen drifted over to Lommy. "Something wrong with your leg, boy?"

"It got hurt."

"Can you walk?" He sounded concerned.

"No," said Lommy. "You got to carry me."

"Think so?" The man lifted his spear casually and drove the point through the boy's soft throat. Lommy never even had time to yield again. He jerked once, and that was all. When the man pulled his spear loose, blood sprayed out in a dark fountain. "Carry him, he says," he muttered, chuckling.

TYRION

They had warned him to dress warmly. Tyrion
Lannister took them at their word. He was
garbed in heavy quilted breeches and a woolen
doublet, and over it all he had thrown the shadowskin
cloak he had acquired in the Mountains of the Moon.
The cloak was absurdly long, made for a man twice his
height. When he was not ahorse, the only way to wear
the thing was to wrap it around him several times,
which made him look like a ball of striped fur.

Even so, he was glad he had listened. The chill in the
long dank vault went bone deep. Timett had chosen to
retreat back up to the cellar after a brief taste of the cold
below. They were somewhere under the hill of
Rhaenys, behind the Guildhall of the Alchemists. The
damp stone walls were splotchy with nitre, and the only
light came from the sealed iron-and-glass oil lamp that
Hallyne the Pyromancer carried so gingerly.

*Gingerly indeed . . . and these would be the ginger
jars.* Tyrion lifted one for inspection. It was round and
ruddy, a fat clay grapefruit. A little big for his hand, but

it would fit comfortably in the grip of a normal man, he knew. The pottery was thin, so fragile that even he had been warned not to squeeze too tightly, lest he crush it in his fist. The clay felt roughened, pebbled. Hallyne told him that was intentional. "A smooth pot is more apt to slip from a man's grasp."

The wildfire oozed slowly toward the lip of the jar when Tyrion tilted it to peer inside. The color would be a murky green, he knew, but the poor light made that impossible to confirm. "Thick," he observed.

"That is from the cold, my lord," said Hallyne, a pallid man with soft damp hands and an obsequious manner. He was dressed in striped black-and-scarlet robes trimmed with sable, but the fur looked more than a little patchy and moth-eaten. "As it warms, the substance will flow more easily, like lamp oil."

The substance was the pyromancers' own term for wildfire. They called each other *wisdom* as well, which Tyrion found almost as annoying as their custom of hinting at the vast secret stores of knowledge that they wanted him to think they possessed. Once theirs had been a powerful guild, but in recent centuries the maesters of the Citadel had supplanted the alchemists almost everywhere. Now only a few of the older order remained, and they no longer even pretended to transmute metals . . .

. . . but they *could* make wildfire. "Water will not quench it, I am told."

"That is so. Once it takes fire, the substance will burn fiercely until it is no more. More, it will seep into cloth, wood, leather, even steel, so they take fire as well."

Tyrion remembered the red priest Thoros of Myr and his flaming sword. Even a thin coating of wildfire could burn for an hour. Thoros always needed a new sword after a melee, but Robert had been fond of the man and ever glad to provide one. "Why doesn't it seep into the clay as well?"

"Oh, but it does," said Hallyne. "There is a vault below this one where we store the older pots. Those from

King Aerys's day. It was his fancy to have the jars made in the shapes of fruits. Very perilous fruits indeed, my lord Hand, and, hmmm, *riper* now than ever, if you take my meaning. We have sealed them with wax and pumped the lower vault full of water, but even so . . . by rights they ought to have been destroyed, but so many of our masters were murdered during the Sack of King's Landing, the few acolytes who remained were unequal to the task. And much of the stock we made for Aerys was lost. Only last year, two hundred jars were discovered in a storeroom beneath the Great Sept of Baelor. No one could recall how they came there, but I'm sure I do not need to tell you that the High Septon was beside himself with terror. I myself saw that they were safely moved. I had a cart filled with sand, and sent our most able acolytes. We worked only by night, we—"

"—did a splendid job, I have no doubt." Tyrion placed the jar he'd been holding back among its fellows. They covered the table, standing in orderly rows of four and marching away into the subterranean dimness. And there were other tables beyond, many other tables. "These, ah, *fruits* of the late King Aerys, can they still be used?"

"Oh, yes, most certainly . . . but *carefully*, my lord, ever so carefully. As it ages, the substance grows ever more, hmmmm, *fickle*, let us say. Any flame will set it afire. Any spark. Too much heat and jars will blaze up of their own accord. It is not wise to let them sit in sunlight, even for a short time. Once the fire begins within, the heat causes the substance to expand violently, and the jars shortly fly to pieces. If other jars should happen to be stored in the same vicinity, those go up as well, and so—"

"How many jars do you have at present?"

"This morning the Wisdom Munciter told me that we had seven thousand eight hundred and forty. That count includes four thousand jars from King Aerys's day, to be sure."

"Our overripe fruits?"

Hallyne bobbed his head. "Wisdom Malliard believes we shall be able to provide a full ten thousand jars, as was promised the queen. I concur." The pyromancer looked indecently pleased with that prospect.

Assuming our enemies give you the time. The pyromancers kept their recipe for wildfire a closely guarded secret, but Tyrion knew that it was a lengthy, dangerous, and time-consuming process. He had assumed the promise of ten thousand jars was a wild boast, like that of the bannerman who vows to marshal ten thousand swords for his lord and shows up on the day of battle with a hundred and two. *If they can truly give us ten thousand . . .*

He did not know whether he ought to be delighted or terrified. *Perhaps a smidge of both.* "I trust that your guild brothers are not engaging in any unseemly haste, Wisdom. We do not want ten thousand jars of defective wildfire, nor even one . . . and we most certainly do not want any mishaps."

"There will be no mishaps, my lord Hand. The substance is prepared by trained acolytes in a series of bare stone cells, and each jar is removed by an apprentice and carried down here the instant it is ready. Above each work cell is a room filled entirely with sand. A protective spell has been laid on the floors, hmmm, most powerful. Any fire in the cell below causes the floors to fall away, and the sand smothers the blaze at once."

"Not to mention the careless acolyte." By *spell* Tyrion imagined Hallyne meant *clever trick.* He thought he would like to inspect one of these false-ceilinged cells to see how it worked, but this was not the time. Perhaps when the war was won.

"My brethren are never careless," Hallyne insisted. "If I may be, hmmmm, *frank . . .*"

"Oh, do."

"The substance flows through my veins, and lives in the heart of every pyromancer. We respect its power. But the common soldier, hmmmm, the crew of one of the queen's spitfires, say, in the unthinking frenzy of battle . . . any little mistake can bring catastrophe. That cannot be said too often. My father often told King Aerys as much, as *his* father told old King Jaehaerys."

"They must have listened," Tyrion said. "If they had burned the city down, someone would have told me. So your counsel is that we had best be careful?"

"Be *very* careful," said Hallyne. "Be *very very* careful."

"These clay jars . . . do you have an ample supply?"

"We do, my lord, and thank you for asking."

"You won't mind if I take some, then. A few thousand."

"A few *thousand*?"

"Or however many your guild can spare, without interfering with production. It's *empty* pots I'm asking for, understand. Have them sent round to the captains on each of the city gates."

"I will, my lord, but why . . . ?"

Tyrion smiled up at him. "When you tell me to dress warmly, I dress warmly. When you tell me to be careful, well . . ." He gave a shrug. "I've seen enough. Perhaps you would be so good as to escort me back up to my litter?"

"It would be my great, hmmm, pleasure, my lord." Hallyne lifted the lamp and led the way back to the stairs. "It was good of you to visit us. A great honor, hmmm. It has been too long since the King's Hand graced us with his presence. Not since Lord Rossart, and he was of our order. That was back in King Aerys's day. King Aerys took a great interest in our work."

King Aerys used you to roast the flesh off his enemies. His brother Jaime had told him a few stories of the Mad King and his pet pyromancers. "Joffrey will be interested as well, I have no doubt." *Which is why I'd best keep him well away from you.*

"It is our great hope to have the king visit our Guildhall in his own royal person. I have spoken of it to your royal sister. A great feast . . ."

It was growing warmer as they climbed. "His Grace has prohibited all feasting until such time as the war is won." *At my insistence.* "The king does not think it fitting to banquet on choice food while his people go without bread."

"A most, hmmm, *loving* gesture, my lord. Perhaps instead some few of us might call upon the king at the Red Keep. A small demonstration of our powers, as it were, to distract His Grace from his many cares for an evening. Wildfire is but one of the dread secrets of our ancient order. Many and wondrous are the things we might show you."

"I will take it up with my sister." Tyrion had no objection to a few magic tricks, but Joff's fondness for making men fight to the death was trial enough; he had no intention of allowing the boy to taste the possibilities of burning them alive.

When at last they reached the top of the steps, Tyrion shrugged out of his shadowskin fur and folded it over his arm. The Guildhall of the Alchemists was an imposing warren of black stone, but Hallyne led him through the twists and turns until they reached the Gallery of the Iron Torches, a long echoing chamber where columns of green fire danced around black metal columns twenty feet tall. Ghostly flames shimmered off the polished black marble of the walls and floor and bathed the hall in an emerald radiance. Tyrion would have been more impressed if he hadn't known that the great iron torches had only been lit this morning in honor of his visit, and would be extinguished the instant the doors closed behind him. Wildfire was too costly to squander.

They emerged atop the broad curving steps that fronted on the Street of the Sisters, near the foot of Visenya's Hill. He bid Hallyne farewell and waddled down to where Timett son of Timett waited with an escort of Burned Men. Given his purpose today, it had seemed a singularly appropriate choice for his guard. Besides, their scars struck terror in the hearts of the city rabble. That was all to the good these days. Only three nights past, another mob had gathered at the gates of the Red Keep, chanting for food. Joff had unleashed a storm of arrows against them, slaying four, and then shouted down that they had his leave to eat their dead. *Winning us still more friends.*

Tyrion was surprised to see Bronn standing beside the litter as well. "What are you doing here?"

"Delivering your messages," Bronn said. "Ironhand wants you urgently at the Gate of the Gods. He won't say why. And you've been summoned to Maegor's too."

"Summoned?" Tyrion knew of only one person who would presume to use that word. "And what does Cersei want of me?"

Bronn shrugged. "The queen commands you to return to the castle at once and attend her in her chambers. That stripling cousin of yours delivered the message. Four hairs on his lip and he thinks he's a man."

"Four hairs and a knighthood. He's *Ser* Lancel now, never forget." Tyrion knew that Ser Jacelyn would not send for him unless the matter was of import. "I'd best see what Bywater wants. Inform my sister that I will attend her on my return."

"She won't like that," Bronn warned.

"Good. The longer Cersei waits, the angrier she'll become, and anger makes her stupid. I much prefer angry and stupid to composed and cunning." Tyrion tossed his folded cloak into his litter, and Timett helped him up after it.

The market square inside the Gate of the Gods, which in normal times would have been thronged with farmers selling vegetables, was near deserted when Tyrion crossed it. Ser Jacelyn met him at the gate, and raised his iron hand in brusque salute. "My lord. Your cousin Cleos Frey is here, come from Riverrun under a peace banner with a letter from Robb Stark."

"Peace terms?"

"So he says."

"Sweet cousin. Show me to him."

The gold cloaks had confined Ser Cleos to a windowless guardroom in the gatehouse. He rose when they entered. "Tyrion, you are a most welcome sight."

"That's not something I hear often, cousin."

"Has Cersei come with you?"

"My sister is otherwise occupied. Is this Stark's letter?" He plucked it off the table. "Ser Jacelyn, you may leave us."

Bywater bowed and departed. "I was asked to bring the offer to the Queen Regent," Ser Cleos said as the door shut.

"I shall." Tyrion glanced over the map that Robb Stark had sent with his letter. "All in good time, cousin. Sit. Rest. You look gaunt and haggard." He looked worse than that, in truth.

"Yes." Ser Cleos lowered himself onto a bench. "It is bad in the riverlands, Tyrion. Around the Gods Eye and along the kingsroad especially. The river lords are burning their own crops to try and starve us, and your father's foragers are torching every village they take and putting the smallfolk to the sword."

That was the way of war. The smallfolk were slaughtered, while the highborn were held for ransom. *Remind me to thank the gods that I was born a Lannister.*

Ser Cleos ran a hand through his thin brown hair. "Even with a peace banner, we were attacked twice. Wolves in mail, hungry to savage anyone weaker than themselves. The gods alone know what side they started on, but they're on their own side now. Lost three men, and twice as many wounded."

"What news of our foe?" Tyrion turned his attention back to Stark's terms. *The boy does not want too much. Only half the realm, the release of our captives, hostages, his father's sword . . . oh, yes, and his sisters.*

"The boy sits idle at Riverrun," Ser Cleos said. "I think he fears to face your father in the field. His strength grows less each day. The river lords have departed, each to defend his own lands."

Is this what Father intended? Tyrion rolled up Stark's map. "These terms will never do."

"Will you at least consent to trade the Stark girls for Tion and Willem?" Ser Cleos asked plaintively.

Tion Frey was his younger brother, Tyrion recalled. "No," he said gently, "but we'll propose our own exchange of captives. Let me consult with Cersei and the council. We shall send you back to Riverrun with *our* terms."

Clearly, the prospect did not cheer him. "My lord, I do not believe Robb Stark will yield easily. It is Lady Catelyn who wants this peace, not the boy."

"Lady Catelyn wants her daughters." Tyrion pushed himself down from the bench, letter and map in hand. "Ser Jacelyn will see that you have food and fire. You look in dire need of sleep, cousin. I will send for you when we know more."

He found Ser Jacelyn on the ramparts, watching several hundred new recruits drilling in the field below. With so many seeking refuge in King's Landing, there was no lack of men willing to join the City Watch for a full belly and a bed of straw in the barracks, but Tyrion had no illusions about how well these ragged defenders of theirs would fight if it came to battle.

"You did well to send for me," Tyrion said. "I shall leave Ser Cleos in your hands. He is to have every hospitality."

"And his escort?" the commander wanted to know.

"Give them food and clean garb, and find a maester to see to their hurts. They are not to set foot inside the city, is that understood?" It would never do to have the truth of conditions in King's Landing reach Robb Stark in Riverrun.

"Well understood, my lord."

"Oh, and one more thing. The alchemists will be sending a large supply of clay pots to each of the city gates. You're to use them to train the men who will work your spitfires. Fill the pots with green paint and have them drill at loading and firing. Any man who spatters should be replaced. When they have mastered the paint pots, substitute lamp oil and have them work at lighting the jars and firing them while aflame. Once they learn to do that without burning themselves, they may be ready for wildfire."

Ser Jacelyn scratched at his cheek with his iron hand.

"Wise measures. Though I have no love for that alchemist's piss."

"Nor I, but I use what I'm given."

Once back inside his litter, Tyrion Lannister drew the curtains and plumped a cushion under his elbow. Cersei would be displeased to learn that he had intercepted Stark's letter, but his father had sent him here to rule, not to please Cersei.

It seemed to him that Robb Stark had given them a golden chance. Let the boy wait at Riverrun dreaming of an easy peace. Tyrion would reply with terms of his own, giving the King in the North just enough of what he wanted to keep him hopeful. Let Ser Cleos wear out his bony Frey rump riding to and fro with offers and counters. All the while, their cousin Ser Stafford would be training and arming the new host he'd raised at Casterly Rock. Once he was ready, he and Lord Tywin could smash the Tullys and Starks between them.

Now if only Robert's brothers would be so accommodating. Glacial as his progress was, still Renly Baratheon crept north and east with his huge southron host, and scarcely a night passed that Tyrion did not dread being awakened with the news that Lord Stannis was sailing his fleet up the Blackwater Rush. *Well, it would seem I have a goodly stock of wildfire, but still . . .*

The sound of some hubbub in the street intruded on his worries. Tyrion peered out cautiously between the curtains. They were passing through Cobbler's Square, where a sizable crowd had gathered beneath the leather awnings to listen to the rantings of a prophet. A robe of undyed wool belted with a hempen rope marked him for one of the begging brothers.

"Corruption!" the man cried shrilly. "There is the warning! Behold the Father's scourge!" He pointed at the fuzzy red wound in the sky. From this vantage, the distant castle on Aegon's High Hill was directly behind him, with the comet hanging forebodingly over its towers. *A clever choice of stage,* Tyrion reflected. "We have become swollen, bloated, foul. Brother couples with sis-

ter in the bed of kings, and the fruit of their incest capers in his palace to the piping of a twisted little
monkey demon. Highborn ladies fornicate with fools
and give birth to monsters! Even the High Septon has
forgotten the gods! He bathes in scented waters and
grows fat on lark and lamprey while his people starve!
Pride comes before prayer, maggots rule our castles, and
gold is all . . . but *no more!* The Rotten Summer is at
an end, and the Whoremonger King is brought low!
When the boar did open him, a great stench rose to
heaven and a thousand snakes slid forth from his belly,
hissing and biting!" He jabbed his bony finger back at
comet and castle. "There comes the Harbinger! Cleanse
yourselves, the gods cry out, lest ye be cleansed! Bathe
in the wine of righteousness, or you shall be bathed in
fire! *Fire!*"

"*Fire!*" other voices echoed, but the hoots of derision
almost drowned them out. Tyrion took solace from
that. He gave the command to continue, and the litter
rocked like a ship on a rough sea as the Burned Men
cleared a path. *Twisted little monkey demon indeed.*
The wretch did have a point about the High Septon, to
be sure. What was it that Moon Boy had said of him the
other day? *A pious man who worships the Seven so fervently that he eats a meal for each of them whenever
he sits to table.* The memory of the fool's jape made
Tyrion smile.

He was pleased to reach the Red Keep without further
incident. As he climbed the steps to his chambers,
Tyrion felt a deal more hopeful than he had at dawn.
*Time, that's all I truly need, time to piece it all to-
gether. Once the chain is done . . .* He opened the
door to his solar.

Cersei turned away from the window, her skirts
swirling around her slender hips. "How *dare* you ignore
my summons!"

"Who admitted you to my tower?"

"*Your* tower? This is my son's royal castle."

"So they tell me." Tyrion was not amused. Crawn

would be even less so; his Moon Brothers had the guard today. "I was about to come to you, as it happens."

"Were you?"

He swung the door shut behind him. "You doubt me?"

"Always, and with good reason."

"I'm hurt." Tyrion waddled to the sideboard for a cup of wine. He knew no surer way to work up a thirst than talking with Cersei. "If I've given you offense, I would know how."

"What a disgusting little worm you are. Myrcella is my only daughter. Did you truly imagine that I would allow you to sell her like a bag of oats?"

Myrcella, he thought. *Well, that egg has hatched. Let's see what color the chick is.* "Hardly a bag of oats. Myrcella is a princess. Some would say this is what she was born for. Or did you plan to marry her to Tommen?"

Her hand lashed out, knocking the wine cup from his hand to spill on the floor. "Brother or no, I should have your tongue out for that. *I* am Joffrey's regent, not you, and I say that Myrcella will not be shipped off to this Dornishman the way I was shipped to Robert Baratheon."

Tyrion shook wine off his fingers and sighed. "Why not? She'd be a deal safer in Dorne than she is here."

"Are you utterly ignorant or simply perverse? You know as well as I that the Martells have no cause to love us."

"The Martells have every cause to hate us. Nonetheless, I expect them to agree. Prince Doran's grievance against House Lannister goes back only a generation, but the Dornishmen have warred against Storm's End and Highgarden for a thousand years, and Renly has taken Dorne's allegiance for granted. Myrcella is nine, Trystane Martell eleven. I have proposed they wed when she reaches her fourteenth year. Until such time, she would be an honored guest at Sunspear, under Prince Doran's protection."

"A hostage," Cersei said, mouth tightening.

"An honored guest," Tyrion insisted, "and I suspect Martell will treat Myrcella more kindly than Joffrey has treated Sansa Stark. I had in mind to send Ser Arys Oakheart with her. With a knight of the Kingsguard as her sworn shield, no one is like to forget who or what she is."

"Small good Ser Arys will do her if Doran Martell decides that my daughter's death would wash out his sister's."

"Martell is too honorable to murder a nine-year-old girl, particularly one as sweet and innocent as Myrcella. So long as he holds her he can be reasonably certain that we'll keep faith on our side, and the terms are too rich to refuse. Myrcella is the least part of it. I've also offered him his sister's killer, a council seat, some castles on the Marches . . ."

"Too much." Cersei paced away from him, restless as a lioness, skirts swirling. "You've offered too much, and without my authority or consent."

"This is the Prince of Dorne we are speaking of. If I'd offered less, he'd likely spit in my face."

"*Too much!*" Cersei insisted, whirling back.

"What would *you* have offered him, that hole between your legs?" Tyrion said, his own anger flaring.

This time he saw the slap coming. His head snapped around with a *crack*. "Sweet sweet sister," he said, "I promise you, that was the last time you will ever strike me."

His sister laughed. "Don't threaten me, little man. Do you think Father's letter keeps you safe? A piece of paper. Eddard Stark had a piece of paper too, for all the good it did him."

Eddard Stark did not have the City Watch, Tyrion thought, *nor my clansmen, nor the sellswords that Bronn has hired. I do.* Or so he hoped. Trusting in Varys, in Ser Jacelyn Bywater, in Bronn. Lord Stark had probably had his delusions as well.

Yet he said nothing. A wise man did not pour wildfire on a brazier. Instead he poured a fresh cup of wine. "How safe do you think Myrcella will be if King's Landing falls? Renly and Stannis will mount her head beside yours."

And Cersei began to cry.

Tyrion Lannister could not have been more astonished if Aegon the Conqueror himself had burst into the room, riding on a dragon and juggling lemon pies. He had not seen his sister weep since they were children together at Casterly Rock. Awkwardly, he took a step toward her. When your sister cries, you were supposed to comfort her . . . but this was *Cersei!* He reached a tentative hand for her shoulder.

"Don't *touch* me," she said, wrenching away. It should not have hurt, yet it did, more than any slap. Red-faced, as angry as she was grief-stricken, Cersei struggled for breath. "Don't look at me, not . . . not like this . . . not *you.*"

Politely, Tyrion turned his back. "I did not mean to frighten you. I promise you, nothing will happen to Myrcella."

"Liar," she said behind him. "I'm not a child, to be soothed with empty promises. You told me you would free Jaime too. Well, where is he?"

"In Riverrun, I should imagine. Safe and under guard, until I find a way to free him."

Cersei sniffed. "I should have been born a man. I would have no need of any of you then. None of this would have been allowed to happen. How could Jaime let himself be captured by that *boy?* And Father, I trusted in him, fool that I am, but where is he now that he's wanted? What is he *doing?*"

"Making war."

"From behind the walls of Harrenhal?" she said scornfully. "A curious way of fighting. It looks suspiciously like hiding."

"Look again."

"What else would you call it? Father sits in one castle, and Robb Stark sits in another, and no one *does* anything."

"There is sitting and there is sitting," Tyrion suggested. "Each one waits for the other to move, but the lion is still, poised, his tail twitching, while the fawn is frozen by fear, bowels turned to jelly. No matter which way he bounds, the lion will have him, and he knows it."

"And you're *quite* certain that Father is the lion?"

Tyrion grinned. "It's on all our banners."

She ignored the jest. "If it was Father who'd been taken captive, Jaime would not be sitting by idly, I promise you."

Jaime would be battering his host to bloody bits against the walls of Riverrun, and the Others take their chances. He never did have any patience, no more than you, sweet sister. "Not all of us can be as bold as Jaime, but there are other ways to win wars. Harrenhal is strong and well situated."

"And King's Landing is *not*, as we both know perfectly well. While Father plays lion and fawn with the Stark boy, Renly marches up the roseroad. He could be at our gates any day now!"

"The city will not fall in a day. From Harrenhal it is a straight, swift march down the kingsroad. Renly will scarce have unlimbered his siege engines before Father takes him in the rear. His host will be the hammer, the city walls the anvil. It makes a lovely picture."

Cersei's green eyes bored into him, wary, yet hungry for the reassurance he was feeding her. "And if Robb Stark marches?"

"Harrenhal is close enough to the fords of the Trident so that Roose Bolton cannot bring the northern foot across to join with the Young Wolf's horse. Stark cannot march on King's Landing without taking Harrenhal first, and even with Bolton he is not strong enough to do that." Tyrion tried his most winning smile. "Meanwhile Father lives off the fat of the riverlands, while our uncle Stafford gathers fresh levies at the Rock."

Cersei regarded him suspiciously. "How could you know all this? Did Father tell you his intentions when he sent you here?"

"No. I glanced at a map."

Her look turned to disdain. "You've conjured up every

word of this in that grotesque head of yours, haven't you, Imp?"

Tyrion *tsk*ed. "Sweet sister, I ask you, if we weren't winning, would the Starks have sued for peace?" He drew out the letter that Ser Cleos Frey had brought. "The Young Wolf has sent us terms, you see. Unacceptable terms, to be sure, but still, a beginning. Would you care to see them?"

"Yes." That fast, she was all queen again. "How do *you* come to have them? They should have come to me."

"What else is a Hand for, if not to hand you things?" Tyrion handed her the letter. His cheek still throbbed where Cersei's hand had left its mark. *Let her flay half my face, it will be a small price to pay for her consent to the Dornish marriage.* He would have that now, he could sense it.

And certain knowledge of an informer too . . . well, that was the plum in his pudding.

BRAN

Dancer was draped in bardings of snowy white wool emblazoned with the grey direwolf of House Stark, while Bran wore grey breeches and white doublet, his sleeves and collar trimmed with vair. Over his heart was his wolf's-head brooch of silver and polished jet. He would sooner have had Summer than a silver wolf on his breast, but Ser Rodrik had been unyielding.

The low stone steps balked Dancer only for a moment. When Bran urged her on, she took them easily. Beyond the wide oak-and-iron doors, eight long rows of trestle tables filled Winterfell's Great Hall, four on each side of the center aisle. Men crowded shoulder to shoulder on the benches. "Stark!" they called as Bran trotted past, rising to their feet. "Winterfell! *Winterfell!*"

He was old enough to know that it was not truly *him* they shouted for—it was the harvest they cheered, it was Robb and his victories, it was his lord father and his grandfather and all the Starks going back eight thousand years. Still, it made him swell with pride. For so long as it took him to ride the length of that hall he forgot that he was broken. Yet when he reached the dais, with every eye upon him, Osha and Hodor undid his straps and buckles, lifted him off Dancer's back, and carried him to the high seat of his fathers.

Ser Rodrik was seated to Bran's left, his daughter Beth beside him. Rickon was to his right, his mop of shaggy auburn hair grown so long that it brushed his ermine mantle. He had refused to let anyone cut it since their mother had gone. The last girl to try had been bitten for her efforts. "I wanted to ride too," he said as Hodor led Dancer away. "I ride better than you."

"You don't, so hush up," he told his brother. Ser Rodrik bellowed for quiet. Bran raised his voice. He bid them welcome in the name of his brother, the King in the North, and asked them to thank the gods old and new for Robb's victories and the bounty of the harvest. "May there be a hundred more," he finished, raising his father's silver goblet.

"*A hundred more!*" Pewter tankards, clay cups, and iron-banded drinking horns clashed together. Bran's wine was sweetened with honey and fragrant with cinnamon and cloves, but stronger than he was used to. He could feel its hot snaky fingers wriggling through his chest as he swallowed. By the time he set down the goblet, his head was swimming.

"You did well, Bran," Ser Rodrik told him. "Lord Eddard would have been most proud." Down the table, Maester Luwin nodded his agreement as the servers began to carry in the food.

Such food Bran had never seen; course after course after course, so much that he could not manage more than a bite or two of each dish. There were great joints of aurochs roasted with leeks, venison pies chunky with carrots, bacon, and mushrooms, mutton chops sauced in honey and cloves, savory duck, peppered boar, goose, skewers of pigeon and capon, beef-and-barley stew, cold fruit soup. Lord Wyman had brought twenty casks of fish from White Harbor packed in salt and seaweed; whitefish and winkles, crabs and mussels, clams, herring, cod, salmon, lobster and lampreys. There was black bread and honeycakes and oaten biscuits; there were turnips and pease and beets, beans and squash and huge red onions; there were baked apples and berry tarts and pears poached in strongwine. Wheels of white cheese were set at every table, above and below the salt, and flagons of hot spice wine and chilled autumn ale were passed up and down the tables.

Lord Wyman's musicians played bravely and well, but harp and fiddle and horn were soon drowned beneath a tide of talk and laughter, the clash of cup and plate, and the snarling of hounds fighting for table scraps. The singer sang good songs, "Iron Lances" and "The Burning of the Ships" and "The Bear and the Maiden Fair," but only Hodor seemed to be listening. He stood beside the piper, hopping from one foot to the other.

The noise swelled to a steady rumbling roar, a great heady stew of sound. Ser Rodrik talked with Maester Luwin above Beth's curly head, while Rickon screamed happily at the Walders. Bran had not wanted the Freys at the high table, but the maester reminded him that they would soon be kin. Robb was to marry one of their aunts, and Arya one of their uncles. "She never will," Bran said, "not Arya," but Maester Luwin was unyielding, so there they were beside Rickon.

The serving men brought every dish to Bran first, that he might take the lord's portion if he chose. By the time they reached the ducks, he could eat no more. After that he nodded approval at each course in turn, and waved it away. If the dish smelled especially choice, he would send it to one of the lords on the dais, a gesture of friendship and favor that Maester Luwin told him he must make. He sent some salmon down to poor sad Lady Hornwood, the boar to the boisterous Umbers, a dish of goose-in-berries to Cley Cerwyn, and a huge lobster to Joseth the master of horse, who was neither lord nor guest, but had seen to Dancer's training and made it possible for Bran to ride. He sent sweets to Hodor and Old Nan as well, for no reason but he loved them. Ser Rodrik reminded him to send something to his foster brothers, so he sent Little Walder some boiled beets and Big Walder the buttered turnips.

On the benches below, Winterfell men mixed with smallfolk from the winter town, friends from the nearer holdfasts, and the escorts of their lordly guests. Some faces Bran had never seen before, others he knew as well as his own, yet they all seemed equally foreign to him. He watched them as from a distance, as if he still sat in the window of his bedchamber, looking down on the yard below, seeing everything yet a part of nothing.

Osha moved among the tables, pouring ale. One of Leobald Tallhart's men slid a hand up under her skirts and she broke the flagon over his head, to roars of laughter. Yet Mikken had his hand down some woman's bodice, and she seemed not to mind. Bran watched Farlen make his red bitch beg for bones and smiled at Old Nan plucking at the crust of a hot pie with wrinkled fingers. On the dais, Lord Wyman attacked a steaming plate of lampreys as if they were an enemy host. He was so fat that Ser Rodrik had commanded that a special wide chair be built for him to sit in, but he laughed loud and often, and Bran thought he liked him. Poor wan Lady Hornwood sat beside him, her face a stony mask as she picked listlessly at her food. At the opposite end of the high table, Hothen and Mors were playing a drinking game, slamming their horns together as hard as knights meeting in joust.

It is too hot here, and too noisy, and they are all getting drunk. Bran itched under his grey and white woolens, and suddenly he wished he were anywhere but here. *It is cool in the godswood now. Steam is rising off the hot pools, and the red leaves of the weirwood are rustling. The smells are richer than here, and before long the moon will rise and my brother will sing to it.*

"Bran?" Ser Rodrik said. "You do not eat."

The waking dream had been so vivid, for a moment Bran had not known where he was. "I'll have more later," he said. "My belly's full to bursting."

The old knight's white mustache was pink with wine. "You have done well, Bran. Here, and at the audiences. You will be an especial fine lord one day, I think."

I want to be a knight. Bran took another sip of the spiced honey wine from his father's goblet, grateful for something to clutch. The lifelike head of a snarling direwolf was raised on the side of the cup. He felt the silver muzzle pressing against his palm, and remembered the last time he had seen his lord father drink from this goblet.

It had been the night of the welcoming feast, when King Robert had brought his court to Winterfell. Summer still reigned then. His parents had shared the dais with Robert and his queen, with her brothers beside her. Uncle Benjen had been there too, all in black. Bran and his brothers and sisters sat with the king's children, Joffrey and Tommen and Princess Myrcella, who'd spent the whole meal gazing at Robb with adoring eyes. Arya made faces across the table when no one was looking; Sansa listened raptly while the king's high harper sang songs of chivalry, and Rickon kept asking why Jon wasn't with them. "Because he's a bastard," Bran finally had to whisper to him.

And now they are all gone. It was as if some cruel god had reached down with a great hand and swept them all away, the girls to captivity, Jon to the Wall, Robb and Mother to war, King Robert and Father to their graves, and perhaps Uncle Benjen as well . . .

Even down on the benches, there were new men at the tables. Jory was dead, and Fat Tom, and Porther, Alyn, Desmond, Hullen who had been master of horse, Harwin his son . . . all those who had gone south with his father, even Septa Mordane and Vayon Poole. The rest had ridden to war with Robb, and might soon be dead as well for all Bran knew. He liked Hayhead and Poxy Tym and Skittrick and the other new men well enough, but he missed his old friends.

He looked up and down the benches at all the faces happy and sad, and wondered who would be missing next year and the year after. He might have cried then, but he couldn't. He was the Stark in Winterfell, his father's son and his brother's heir, and almost a man grown.

At the foot of the hall, the doors opened and a gust of cold air made the torches flame brighter for an instant. Alebelly led two new guests into the feast. "The Lady Meera of House Reed," the rotund guardsman bellowed over the clamor. "With her brother, Jojen, of Greywater Watch."

Men looked up from their cups and trenchers to eye the newcomers. Bran heard Little Walder mutter, "Frogeaters," to Big Walder beside him. Ser Rodrik climbed to his feet. "Be welcome, friends, and share this harvest with us." Serving men hurried to lengthen the table on the dais, fetching trestles and chairs.

"Who are *they*?" Rickon asked.

"Mudmen," answered Little Walder disdainfully. "They're thieves and cravens, and they have green teeth from eating frogs."

Maester Luwin crouched beside Bran's seat to whisper counsel in his ear. "You must greet these ones warmly. I had not thought to see them here, but . . . you know who they are?"

Bran nodded. "Crannogmen. From the Neck."

"Howland Reed was a great friend to your father," Ser Rodrik told him. "These two are his, it would seem."

As the newcomers walked the length of the hall, Bran saw that one was indeed a girl, though he would never have known it by her dress. She wore lambskin breeches soft with long use, and a sleeveless jerkin armored in bronze scales. Though near Robb's age, she was slim as a boy, with long brown hair knotted behind her head and only the barest suggestion of breasts. A woven net hung from one slim hip, a long bronze knife from the other; under her arm she carried an old iron greathelm spotted with rust; a frog spear and round leathern shield were strapped to her back.

Her brother was several years younger and bore no weapons. All his garb was green, even to the leather of his boots, and when he came closer Bran saw that his eyes were the color of moss, though his teeth looked as white as anyone else's. Both Reeds were slight of build, slender as swords and scarcely taller than Bran himself. They went to one knee before the dais.

"My lords of Stark," the girl said. "The years have passed in their hundreds and their thousands since my folk first swore their fealty to the King in the North. My lord father has sent us here to say the words again, for all our people."

She is looking at me, Bran realized. He had to make some answer. "My brother Robb is fighting in the south," he said, "but you can say your words to me, if you like."

"To Winterfell we pledge the faith of Greywater," they said together. "Hearth and heart and harvest we yield up to you, my lord. Our swords and spears and arrows are yours to command. Grant mercy to our weak, help to our helpless, and justice to all, and we shall never fail you."

"I swear it by earth and water," said the boy in green.

"I swear it by bronze and iron," his sister said.

"We swear it by ice and fire," they finished together.

Bran groped for words. Was he supposed to swear something back to them? Their oath was not one he had been taught. "May your winters be short and your summers bountiful," he said. That was usually a good thing to say. "Rise. I'm Brandon Stark."

The girl, Meera, got to her feet and helped her brother up. The boy stared at Bran all the while. "We bring you gifts of fish and frog and fowl," he said.

"I thank you." Bran wondered if he would have to eat a frog to be polite. "I offer you the meat and mead of Winterfell." He tried to recall all he had been taught of the crannogmen, who dwelt amongst the bogs of the Neck and seldom left their wetlands. They were a poor folk, fishers and frog-hunters who lived in houses of thatch and woven reeds on floating islands hidden in the deeps of the swamp. It was said that they were a cowardly people who fought with poisoned weapons and preferred to hide from foes rather than face them in open battle. And yet Howland Reed had been one of

Father's staunchest companions during the war for King Robert's crown, before Bran was born.

The boy, Jojen, looked about the hall curiously as he took his seat. "Where are the direwolves?"

"In the godswood," Rickon answered. "Shaggy was bad."

"My brother would like to see them," the girl said.

Little Walder spoke up loudly. "He'd best watch they don't see him, or they'll take a bite out of him."

"They won't bite if I'm there." Bran was pleased that they wanted to see the wolves. "Summer won't anyway, and he'll keep Shaggydog away." He was curious about these mudmen. He could not recall ever seeing one before. His father had sent letters to the Lord of Greywater over the years, but none of the crannogmen had ever called at Winterfell. He would have liked to talk to them more, but the Great Hall was so noisy that it was hard to hear anyone who wasn't right beside you.

Ser Rodrik was right beside Bran. "Do they truly eat frogs?" he asked the old knight.

"Aye," Ser Rodrik said. "Frogs and fish and lizard-lions, and all manner of birds."

Maybe they don't have sheep and cattle, Bran thought. He commanded the serving men to bring them mutton chops and a slice off the aurochs and fill their trenchers with beef-and-barley stew. They seemed to like that well enough. The girl caught him staring at her and smiled. Bran blushed and looked away.

Much later, after all the sweets had been served and washed down with gallons of summerwine, the food was cleared and the tables shoved back against the walls to make room for the dancing. The music grew wilder, the drummers joined in, and Hother Umber brought forth a huge curved warhorn banded in silver. When the singer reached the part in "The Night That Ended" where the Night's Watch rode forth to meet the Others in the Battle for the Dawn, he blew a blast that set all the dogs to barking.

Two Glover men began a spinning skirl on bladder and woodharp. Mors Umber was the first on his feet. He seized a passing serving girl by the arm, knocking the flagon of wine out of her hands to shatter on the floor. Amidst the rushes and bones and bits of bread that littered the stone, he whirled her and spun her and tossed her in the air. The girl squealed with laughter and turned red as her skirts swirled and lifted.

Others soon joined in. Hodor began to dance all by himself, while Lord Wyman asked little Beth Cassel to partner him. For all his size, he moved gracefully. When he tired, Cley Cerwyn danced with the child in his stead. Ser Rodrik approached Lady Hornwood, but she made her excuses and took her leave. Bran watched long enough to be polite, and then had Hodor summoned. He was hot and tired, flushed from the wine, and the dancing made him sad. It was something else he could never do. "I want to go."

"Hodor," Hodor shouted back, kneeling. Maester Luwin and Hayhead lifted him into his basket. The folk of Winterfell had seen this sight half a hundred times, but doubtless it looked queer to the guests, some of whom were more curious than polite. Bran felt the stares.

They went out the rear rather than walk the length of the hall, Bran ducking his head as they passed through the lord's door. In the dim-lit gallery outside the Great Hall, they came upon Joseth the master of horse engaged in a different sort of riding. He had some woman Bran did not know shoved up against the wall, her skirts around her waist. She was giggling until Hodor stopped to watch. Then she screamed. "Leave them be, Hodor," Bran had to tell him. "Take me to my bedchamber."

Hodor carried him up the winding steps to his tower and knelt beside one of the iron bars that Mikken had driven into the wall. Bran used the bars to move himself to the bed, and Hodor pulled off his boots and breeches. "You can go back to the feast now, but don't go bothering Joseth and that woman," Bran said.

"Hodor," Hodor replied, bobbing his head.

When he blew out his bedside candle, darkness covered him like a soft, familiar blanket. The faint sound of music drifted through his shuttered window.

Something his father had told him once when he was little came back to him suddenly. He had asked Lord Eddard if the Kingsguard were truly the finest knights in the Seven Kingdoms. "No longer," he answered, "but once they were a marvel, a shining lesson to the world."

"Was there one who was best of all?"

"The finest knight I ever saw was Ser Arthur Dayne, who fought with a blade called Dawn, forged from the heart of a fallen star. They called him the Sword of the Morning, and he would have killed me but for Howland Reed." Father had gotten sad then, and he would say no more. Bran wished he had asked him what he meant.

He went to sleep with his head full of knights in gleaming armor, fighting with swords that shone like starfire, but when the dream came he was in the godswood again. The smells from the kitchen and the Great Hall were so strong that it was almost as if he had never left the feast. He prowled beneath the trees, his brother close behind him. This night was wildly alive, full of the howling of the man-pack at their play. The sounds made him restless. He wanted to run, to hunt, he wanted to—

The rattle of iron made his ears prick up. His brother heard it too. They raced through the undergrowth toward the sound. Bounding across the still water at the foot of the old white one, he caught the scent of a stranger, the man-smell well mixed with leather and earth and iron.

The intruders had pushed a few yards into the wood when he came upon them; a female and a young male, with no taint of fear to them, even when he showed them the white of his teeth. His brother growled low in his throat, yet still they did not run.

"Here they come," the female said. *Meera*, some part of him whispered, some wisp of the sleeping boy lost in the wolf dream. "Did you know they would be so big?"

"They will be bigger still before they are grown," the young male said, watching them with eyes large, green, and unafraid. "The black one is full of fear and rage, but the grey is strong . . . stronger than he knows . . . can you feel him, sister?"

"No," she said, moving a hand to the hilt of the long brown knife she wore. "Go careful, Jojen."

"He won't hurt me. This is not the day I die." The male walked toward them, unafraid, and reached out for his muzzle, a touch as light as a summer breeze. Yet at the brush of those fingers the wood dissolved and the very ground turned to smoke beneath his feet and swirled away laughing, and then he was spinning and falling, falling, *falling* . . .

CATELYN

A s she slept amidst the rolling grasslands, Catelyn dreamt that Bran was whole again, that Arya and Sansa held hands, that Rickon was still a babe at her breast. Robb, crownless, played with a wooden sword, and when all were safe asleep, she found Ned in her bed, smiling.

Sweet it was, sweet and gone too soon. Dawn came cruel, a dagger of light. She woke aching and alone and weary; weary of riding, weary of hurting, weary of duty. *I want to weep,* she thought. *I want to be comforted. I'm so tired of being strong. I want to be foolish and frightened for once. Just for a small while, that's all . . . a day . . . an hour . . .*

Outside her tent, men were stirring. She heard the whicker of horses, Shadd complaining of stiffness in his back, Ser Wendel calling for his bow. Catelyn wished they would all go away. They were good men, loyal, yet she was tired of them all. It was her children she yearned after. One day, she promised herself as she lay abed, one day she would allow herself to be less than strong.

But not today. It could not be today.

Her fingers seemed more clumsy than usual as she fumbled on her clothes. She supposed she ought to be grateful that she had any use of her hands at all. The dagger had been Valyrian steel, and Valyrian steel bites deep and sharp. She had only to look at the scars to remember.

Outside, Shadd was stirring oats into a kettle, while Ser Wendel Manderly sat stringing his bow. "My lady," he said when Catelyn emerged. "There are birds in this grass. Would you fancy a roast quail to break your fast this morning?"

"Oats and bread are sufficient . . . for all of us, I think. We have many leagues yet to ride, Ser Wendel."

"As you will, my lady." The knight's moon face looked crestfallen, the tips of his great walrus mustache twitching with disappointment. "Oats and bread, and what could be better?" He was one of the fattest men Catelyn had ever known, but howevermuch he loved his food, he loved his honor more.

"Found some nettles and brewed a tea," Shadd announced. "Will m'lady take a cup?"

"Yes, with thanks."

She cradled the tea in her scarred hands and blew on it to cool it. Shadd was one of the Winterfell men. Robb had sent twenty of his best to see her safely to Renly. He had sent five lordlings as well, whose names and high birth would add weight and honor to her mission. As they made their way south, staying well clear of towns and holdfasts, they had seen bands of mailed men more than once, and glimpsed smoke on the eastern horizon, but none had dared molest them. They were too weak to be a threat, too many to be easy prey. Once across the Blackwater, the worst was behind. For the past four days, they had seen no signs of war.

Catelyn had never wanted this. She had told Robb as much, back in Riverrun. "When last I saw Renly, he was a boy no older than Bran. I do not know him. Send someone else. My place is here with my father, for whatever time he has left."

Her son had looked at her unhappily. "There is no one else. I cannot go myself. Your father's too ill. The Blackfish is my eyes and ears, I dare not lose him. Your brother I need to hold Riverrun when we march—"

"March?" No one had said a word to her of marching.

"I cannot sit at Riverrun waiting for peace. It makes me look as if I were afraid to take the field again. When there are no battles to fight, men start to think of hearth and harvest, Father told me that. Even my northmen grow restless."

My northmen, she thought. *He is even starting to talk like a king.* "No one has ever died of restlessness, but rashness is another matter. We've planted seeds, let them grow."

Robb shook his head stubbornly. "We've tossed some seeds in the wind, that's all. If your sister Lysa was coming to aid us, we would have heard by now. How many birds have we sent to the Eyrie, four? I want peace too, but why should the Lannisters give me *anything* if all I do is sit here while my army melts away around me swift as summer snow?"

"So rather than look craven, you will dance to Lord Tywin's pipes?" she threw back. "He *wants* you to march on Harrenhal, ask your uncle Brynden if—"

"I said nothing of Harrenhal," Robb said. "Now, will you go to Renly for me, or must I send the Greatjon?"

The memory brought a wan smile to her face. Such an obvious ploy, that, yet deft for a boy of fifteen. Robb knew how ill-suited a man like Greatjon Umber would be to treat with a man like Renly Baratheon, and he knew that she knew it as well. What could she do but accede, praying that her father would live until her return? Had Lord Hoster been well, he would have gone himself, she knew. Still, that leavetaking was hard, hard. He did not even know her when she came to say farewell. "Minisa," he called her, "where are the children? My little Cat, my sweet Lysa . . ." Catelyn had kissed him on the brow and told him his babes were well. "Wait for me, my lord," she said as his eyes closed. "I waited for you, oh, so many times. Now you must wait for me."

Fate drives me south and south again, Catelyn thought as she sipped the astringent tea, *when it is north I should be going, north to home.* She had written to Bran and Rickon, that last night at Riverrun. *I do not forget you, my sweet ones, you must believe that. It is only that your brother needs me more.*

"We ought to reach the upper Mander today, my lady," Ser Wendel announced while Shadd spooned out the porridge. "Lord Renly will not be far, if the talk be true."

And what do I tell him when I find him? That my son holds him no true king? She did not relish this meeting. They needed friends, not more enemies, yet Robb would never bend the knee in homage to a man he felt had no claim to the throne.

Her bowl was empty, though she could scarce remember tasting the porridge. She laid it aside. "It is time we were away." The sooner she spoke to Renly, the sooner she could turn for home. She was the first one mounted, and she set the pace for the column. Hal Mollen rode beside her, bearing the banner of House Stark, the grey direwolf on an ice-white field.

They were still a half day's ride from Renly's camp when they were taken. Robin Flint had ranged ahead to scout, and he came galloping back with word of a far-eyes watching from the roof of a distant windmill. By the time Catelyn's party reached the mill, the man was long gone. They pressed on, covering not quite a mile before Renly's outriders came swooping down on them, twenty men mailed and mounted, led by a grizzled greybeard of a knight with bluejays on his surcoat.

When he saw her banners, he trotted up to her alone. "My lady," he called, "I am Ser Colen of Greenpools, as it please you. These are dangerous lands you cross."

"Our business is urgent," she answered him. "I come as envoy from my son, Robb Stark, the King in the

North, to treat with Renly Baratheon, the King in the South."

"King Renly is the crowned and anointed lord of *all* the Seven Kingdoms, my lady," Ser Colen answered, though courteously enough. "His Grace is encamped with his host near Bitterbridge, where the roseroad crosses the Mander. It shall be my great honor to escort you to him." The knight raised a mailed hand, and his men formed a double column flanking Catelyn and her guard. *Escort or captor?* she wondered. There was nothing to be done but trust in Ser Colen's honor, and Lord Renly's.

They saw the smoke of the camp's fires when they were still an hour from the river. Then the sound came drifting across farm and field and rolling plain, indistinct as the murmur of some distant sea, but swelling as they rode closer. By the time they caught sight of the Mander's muddy waters glinting in the sun, they could make out the voices of men, the clatter of steel, the whinny of horses. Yet neither sound nor smoke prepared them for the host itself.

Thousands of cookfires filled the air with a pale smoky haze. The horse lines alone stretched out over leagues. A forest had surely been felled to make the tall staffs that held the banners. Great siege engines lined the grassy verge of the roseroad, mangonels and trebuchets and rolling rams mounted on wheels taller than a man on horseback. The steel points of pikes flamed red with sunlight, as if already blooded, while the pavilions of the knights and high lords sprouted from the grass like silken mushrooms. She saw men with spears and men with swords, men in steel caps and mail shirts, camp followers strutting their charms, archers fletching arrows, teamsters driving wagons, swineherds driving pigs, pages running messages, squires honing swords, knights riding palfreys, grooms leading ill-tempered destriers. "This is a fearsome lot of men," Ser Wendel Manderly observed as they crossed the ancient stone span from which Bitterbridge took its name.

"That it is," Catelyn agreed.

Near all the chivalry of the south had come to Renly's call, it seemed. The golden rose of Highgarden was seen everywhere: sewn on the right breast of armsmen and servants, flapping and fluttering from the green silk banners that adorned lance and pike, painted upon the shields hung outside the pavilions of the sons and brothers and cousins and uncles of House Tyrell. As well Catelyn spied the fox-and-flowers of House Florent, Fossoway apples red and green, Lord Tarly's striding huntsman, oak leaves for Oakheart, cranes for Crane, a cloud of black-and-orange butterflies for the Mullendores.

Across the Mander, the storm lords had raised their standards—Renly's own bannermen, sworn to House Baratheon and Storm's End. Catelyn recognized Bryce Caron's nightingales, the Penrose quills, and Lord Estermont's sea turtle, green on green. Yet for every shield she knew, there were a dozen strange to her, borne by the small lords sworn to the bannermen, and by hedge knights and freeriders who had come swarming to make Renly Baratheon a king in fact as well as name.

Renly's own standard flew high over all. From the top of his tallest siege tower, a wheeled oaken immensity covered with rawhides, streamed the largest war banner that Catelyn had ever seen—a cloth big enough to carpet many a hall, shimmering gold, with the crowned stag of Baratheon black upon it, prancing proud and tall.

"My lady, do you hear that noise?" asked Hallis Mollen, trotting close. "What is that?"

She listened. Shouts, and horses screaming, and the clash of steel, and . . . "Cheering," she said. They had been riding up a gentle slope toward a line of brightly colored pavilions on the height. As they passed between them, the press of men grew thicker, the sounds louder. And then she saw.

Below, beneath the stone-and-timber battlements of a small castle, a melee was in progress.

A field had been cleared off, fences and galleries and tilting barriers thrown up. Hundreds were gathered to watch, perhaps thousands. From the looks of the grounds, torn and muddy and littered with bits of dinted armor and broken lances, they had been at it for a day or more, but now the end was near. Fewer than a score of knights remained ahorse, charging and slashing at each other as watchers and fallen combatants cheered them on. She saw two destriers collide in full armor, going down in a tangle of steel and horseflesh. "A tourney," Hal Mollen declared. He had a penchant for loudly announcing the obvious.

"Oh, splendid," Ser Wendel Manderly said as a knight in a rainbow-striped cloak wheeled to deliver a backhand blow with a long-handled axe that shattered the shield of the man pursuing him and sent him reeling in his stirrups.

The press in front of them made further progress difficult. "Lady Stark," Ser Colen said, "if your men would be so good as to wait here, I'll present you to the king."

"As you say." She gave the command, though she had to raise her voice to be heard above the tourney din. Ser Colen walked his horse slowly through the throngs, with Catelyn riding in his wake. A roar went up from the crowd as a helmetless red-bearded man with a griffin on his shield went down before a big knight in blue armor. His steel was a deep cobalt, even the blunt morningstar he wielded with such deadly effect, his mount barded in the quartered sun-and-moon heraldry of House Tarth.

"Red Ronnet's down, gods be damned," a man cursed.

"Loras'll do for that blue—" a companion answered before a roar drowned out the rest of his words.

Another man was fallen, trapped beneath his injured horse, both of them screaming in pain. Squires rushed out to aid them.

This is madness, Catelyn thought. *Real enemies on every side and half the realm in flames, and Renly sits here playing at war like a boy with his first wooden sword.*

The lords and ladies in the gallery were as engrossed in the melee as the men on the ground. Catelyn marked them well. Her father had oft treated with the southron lords, and not a few had been guests at Riverrun. She recognized Lord Mathis Rowan, stouter and more florid than ever, the golden tree of his House spread across his white doublet. Below him sat Lady Oakheart, tiny and delicate, and to her left Lord Randyll Tarly of Horn Hill, his greatsword Heartsbane propped up against the back of his seat. Others she knew only by their sigils, and some not at all.

In their midst, watching and laughing with his young queen by his side, sat a ghost in a golden crown.

Small wonder the lords gather around him with such fervor, she thought, *he is Robert come again.* Renly was handsome as Robert had been handsome; long of limb and broad of shoulder, with the same coal-black hair, fine and straight, the same deep blue eyes, the same easy smile. The slender circlet around his brows seemed to suit him well. It was soft gold, a ring of roses exquisitely wrought; at the front lifted a stag's head of dark green jade, adorned with golden eyes and golden antlers.

The crowned stag decorated the king's green velvet tunic as well, worked in gold thread upon his chest; the Baratheon sigil in the colors of Highgarden. The girl who shared the high seat with him was also of Highgarden: his young queen, Margaery, daughter to Lord Mace Tyrell. Their marriage was the mortar that held the great southron alliance together, Catelyn knew. Renly was one-and-twenty, the girl no older than Robb, very pretty, with a doe's soft eyes and a mane of curling brown hair that fell about her shoulders in lazy ringlets. Her smile was shy and sweet.

Out in the field, another man lost his seat to the knight in the rainbow-striped cloak, and the king shouted approval with the rest. "*Loras!*" she heard him call. "*Loras! Highgarden!*" The queen clapped her hands together in excitement.

Catelyn turned to see the end of it. Only four men were left in the fight now, and there was small doubt whom king and commons favored. She had never met Ser Loras Tyrell, but even in the distant north one heard

tales of the prowess of the young Knight of Flowers. Ser
Loras rode a tall white stallion in silver mail, and fought
with a long-handled axe. A crest of golden roses ran
down the center of his helm.

Two of the other survivors had made common cause.
They spurred their mounts toward the knight in the
cobalt armor. As they closed to either side, the blue
knight reined hard, smashing one man full in the face
with his splintered shield while his black destrier
lashed out with a steel-shod hoof at the other. In a
blink, one combatant was unhorsed, the other reeling.
The blue knight let his broken shield drop to the ground
to free his left arm, and then the Knight of Flowers was
on him. The weight of his steel seemed to hardly diminish the grace and quickness with which Ser Loras
moved, his rainbow cloak swirling about him.

The white horse and the black one wheeled like lovers at a harvest dance, the riders throwing steel in place
of kisses. Longaxe flashed and morningstar whirled.
Both weapons were blunted, yet still they raised an awful clangor. Shieldless, the blue knight was getting
much the worse of it. Ser Loras rained down blows on
his head and shoulders, to shouts of *"Highgarden!"*
from the throng. The other gave answer with his
morningstar, but whenever the ball came crashing in,
Ser Loras interposed his battered green shield, emblazoned with three golden roses. When the longaxe
caught the blue knight's hand on the backswing and
sent the morningstar flying from his grasp, the crowd
screamed like a rutting beast. The Knight of Flowers
raised his axe for the final blow.

The blue knight charged into it. The stallions
slammed together, the blunted axehead smashed
against the scarred blue breastplate . . . but somehow
the blue knight had the haft locked between steel-
gauntleted fingers. He wrenched it from Ser Loras's
hand, and suddenly the two were grappling mount-to-
mount, and an instant later they were falling. As their
horses pulled apart, they crashed to the ground with
bone-jarring force. Loras Tyrell, on the bottom, took the

brunt of the impact. The blue knight pulled a long dirk free and flicked open Tyrell's visor. The roar of the crowd was too loud for Catelyn to hear what Ser Loras said, but she saw the word form on his split, bloody lips. *Yield.*

The blue knight climbed unsteady to his feet, and raised his dirk in the direction of Renly Baratheon, the salute of a champion to his king. Squires dashed onto the field to help the vanquished knight to his feet. When they got his helm off, Catelyn was startled to see how young he was. He could not have had more than two years on Robb. The boy might have been as comely as his sister, but the broken lip, unfocused eyes, and blood trickling through his matted hair made it hard to be certain.

"Approach," King Renly called to the champion.

He limped toward the gallery. At close hand, the brilliant blue armor looked rather less splendid; everywhere it showed scars, the dents of mace and warhammer, the long gouges left by swords, chips in the enameled breastplate and helm. His cloak hung in rags. From the way he moved, the man within was no less battered. A few voices hailed him with cries of *"Tarth!"* and, oddly, *"A Beauty! A Beauty!"* but most were silent. The blue knight knelt before the king. "Grace," he said, his voice muffled by his dented greathelm.

"You are all your lord father claimed you were." Renly's voice carried over the field. "I've seen Ser Loras unhorsed once or twice . . . but never quite in *that* fashion."

"That were no proper unhorsing," complained a drunken archer nearby, a Tyrell rose sewn on his jerkin. "A vile trick, pulling the lad down."

The press had begun to open up. "Ser Colen," Catelyn said to her escort, "who is this man, and why do they mislike him so?"

Ser Colen frowned. "Because he is no man, my lady. That's Brienne of Tarth, daughter to Lord Selwyn the Evenstar."

"Daughter!" Catelyn was horrified.

"Brienne the Beauty, they name her . . . though not to her face, lest they be called upon to defend those words with their bodies."

She heard King Renly declare the Lady Brienne of Tarth the victor of the great melee at Bitterbridge, last mounted of one hundred sixteen knights. "As champion, you may ask of me any boon that you desire. If it lies in my power, it is yours."

"Your Grace," Brienne answered, "I ask the honor of a place among your Rainbow Guard. I would be one of your seven, and pledge my life to yours, to go where you go, ride at your side, and keep you safe from all hurt and harm."

"Done," he said. "Rise, and remove your helm."

She did as he bid her. And when the greathelm was lifted, Catelyn understood Ser Colen's words.

Beauty, they called her . . . mocking. The hair beneath the visor was a squirrel's nest of dirty straw, and her face . . . Brienne's eyes were large and very blue, a young girl's eyes, trusting and guileless, but the rest . . . her features were broad and coarse, her teeth prominent and crooked, her mouth too wide, her lips so plump they seemed swollen. A thousand freckles speckled her cheeks and brow, and her nose had been broken more than once. Pity filled Catelyn's heart. *Is there any creature on earth as unfortunate as an ugly woman?*

And yet, when Renly cut away her torn cloak and fastened a rainbow in its place, Brienne of Tarth did not look unfortunate. Her smile lit up her face, and her voice was strong and proud as she said, "My life for yours, Your Grace. From this day on, I am your shield, I swear it by the old gods and the new." The way she looked at the king—looked *down* at him, she was a good hand higher, though Renly was near as tall as his brother had been—was painful to see.

"Your Grace!" Ser Colen of Greenpools swung down off his horse to approach the gallery. "I beg your leave." He went to one knee. "I have the honor to bring you the

Lady Catelyn Stark, sent as envoy by her son Robb, Lord of Winterfell."

"Lord of Winterfell and King in the North, ser," Catelyn corrected him. She dismounted and moved to Ser Colen's side.

King Renly looked surprised. "Lady Catelyn? We are most pleased." He turned to his young queen. "Margaery my sweet, this is the Lady Catelyn Stark of Winterfell."

"You are most welcome here, Lady Stark," the girl said, all soft courtesy. "I am sorry for your loss."

"You are kind," said Catelyn.

"My lady, I swear to you, I will see that the Lannisters answer for your husband's murder," the king declared. "When I take King's Landing, I'll send you Cersei's head."

And will that bring my Ned back to me? she thought. "It will be enough to know that justice has been done, my lord."

"Your Grace," Brienne the Blue corrected sharply. "And you should kneel when you approach the king."

"The distance between a *lord* and a *grace* is a small one, my lady," Catelyn said. "Lord Renly wears a crown, as does my son. If you wish, we may stand here in the mud and debate what honors and titles are rightly due to each, but it strikes me that we have more pressing matters to consider."

Some of Renly's lords bristled at that, but the king only laughed. "Well said, my lady. There will be time enough for *grace*s when these wars are done. Tell me, when does your son mean to march against Harrenhal?"

Until she knew whether this king was friend or foe, Catelyn was not about to reveal the least part of Robb's dispositions. "I do not sit on my son's war councils, my lord."

"So long as he leaves a few Lannisters for me, I'll not complain. What has he done with the Kingslayer?"

"Jaime Lannister is held prisoner at Riverrun."

"Still alive?" Lord Mathis Rowan seemed dismayed.

Bemused, Renly said, "It would seem the direwolf is gentler than the lion."

"Gentler than the Lannisters," murmured Lady Oakheart with a bitter smile, "is drier than the sea."

"I call it weak." Lord Randyll Tarly had a short, bristly grey beard and a reputation for blunt speech. "No disrespect to you, Lady Stark, but it would have been more seemly had Lord Robb come to pay homage to the king himself, rather than hiding behind his mother's skirts."

"*King* Robb is warring, my lord," Catelyn replied with icy courtesy, "not playing at tourney."

Renly grinned. "Go softly, Lord Randyll, I fear you're overmatched." He summoned a steward in the livery of Storm's End. "Find a place for the lady's companions, and see that they have every comfort. Lady Catelyn shall have my own pavilion. Since Lord Caswell has been so kind as to give me use of his castle, I have no need of it. My lady, when you are rested, I would be honored if you would share our meat and mead at the feast Lord Caswell is giving us tonight. A farewell feast. I fear his lordship is eager to see the heels of my hungry horde."

"Not true, Your Grace," protested a wispy young man who must have been Caswell. "What is mine is yours."

"Whenever someone said that to my brother Robert, he took them at their word," Renly said. "Do you have daughters?"

"Yes, Your Grace. Two."

"Then thank the gods that I am not Robert. My sweet queen is all the woman I desire." Renly held out his hand to help Margaery to her feet. "We'll talk again when you've had a chance to refresh yourself, Lady Catelyn."

Renly led his bride back toward the castle while his steward conducted Catelyn to the king's green silk pavilion. "If you have need of anything, you have only to ask, my lady."

Catelyn could scarcely imagine what she might need that had not already been provided. The pavilion was larger than the common rooms of many an inn and furnished with every comfort: feather mattress and sleeping furs, a wood-and-copper tub large enough for two, braziers to keep off the night's chill, slung leather camp chairs, a writing table with quills and inkpot, bowls of peaches, plums, and pears, a flagon of wine with a set of matched silver cups, cedar chests packed full of Renly's clothing, books, maps, game boards, a high harp, a tall bow and a quiver of arrows, a pair of red-tailed hunting hawks, a vertible armory of fine weapons. *He does not stint himself, this Renly,* she thought as she looked about. *Small wonder this host moves so slowly.*

Beside the entrance, the king's armor stood sentry; a suit of forest-green plate, its fittings chased with gold, the helm crowned by a great rack of golden antlers. The steel was polished to such a high sheen that she could see her reflection in the breastplate, gazing back at her as if from the bottom of a deep green pond. *The face of a drowned woman,* Catelyn thought. *Can you drown in grief?* She turned away sharply, angry with her own frailty. She had no time for the luxury of self-pity. She must wash the dust from her hair and change into a gown more fitting for a king's feast.

Ser Wendel Manderly, Lucas Blackwood, Ser Perwyn Frey, and the rest of her highborn companions accompanied her to the castle. The great hall of Lord Caswell's keep was great only by courtesy, yet room was found on the crowded benches for Catelyn's men, amidst Renly's own knights. Catelyn was assigned a place on the dais between red-faced Lord Mathis Rowan and genial Ser Jon Fossoway of the green-apple Fossoways. Ser Jon made jests, while Lord Mathis inquired politely after the health of her father, brother, and children.

Brienne of Tarth had been seated at the far end of the high table. She did not gown herself as a lady, but chose a knight's finery instead, a velvet doublet quartered rose-and-azure, breeches and boots and a fine-tooled swordbelt, her new rainbow cloak flowing down her back. No garb could disguise her plainness, though; the huge freckled hands, the wide flat face, the thrust of her teeth. Out of armor, her body seemed ungainly, broad of hip and thick of limb, with hunched muscular shoulders but no bosom to speak of. And it was clear from her every action that Brienne knew it, and suffered for it. She spoke only in answer, and seldom lifted her gaze from her food.

Of food there was plenty. The war had not touched the fabled bounty of Highgarden. While singers sang and tumblers tumbled, they began with pears poached in wine, and went on to tiny savory fish rolled in salt and cooked crisp, and capons stuffed with onions and mushrooms. There were great loaves of brown bread, mounds of turnips and sweetcorn and pease, immense hams and roast geese and trenchers dripping full of venison stewed with beer and barley. For the sweet, Lord Caswell's servants brought down trays of pastries from his castle kitchens, cream swans and spun-sugar unicorns, lemon cakes in the shape of roses, spiced honey biscuits and blackberry tarts, apple crisps and wheels of buttery cheese.

The rich foods made Catelyn queasy, but it would never do to show frailty when so much depended on her strength. She ate sparingly, while she watched this man who would be king. Renly sat with his young bride on his left hand and her brother on the right. Apart from the white linen bandage around his brow, Ser Loras seemed none the worse for the day's misadventures. He was indeed as comely as Catelyn had suspected he might be. When not glazed, his eyes were lively and intelligent, his hair an artless tumble of brown locks that many a maid might have envied. He had replaced his tattered tourney cloak with a new one; the same brilliantly striped silk of Renly's Rainbow Guard, clasped with the golden rose of Highgarden.

From time to time, King Renly would feed Margaery some choice morsel off the point of his dagger, or lean over to plant the lightest of kisses on her cheek, but it was Ser Loras who shared most of his jests and confidences. The king enjoyed his food and drink, that was plain to see, yet he seemed neither glutton nor drunkard. He laughed often, and well, and spoke amiably to highborn lords and lowly serving wenches alike.

Some of his guests were less moderate. They drank too much and boasted too loudly, to her mind. Lord Willum's sons Josua and Elyas disputed heatedly about who would be first over the walls of King's Landing. Lord Varner dandled a serving girl on his lap, nuzzling at her neck while one hand went exploring down her bodice. Guyard the Green, who fancied himself a singer, diddled a harp and gave them a verse about tying lions' tails in knots, parts of which rhymed. Ser Mark Mullendore brought a black-and-white monkey and fed him morsels from his own plate, while Ser Tanton of the red-apple Fossoways climbed on the table and swore to slay Sandor Clegane in single combat. The vow might have been taken more solemnly if Ser Tanton had not had one foot in a gravy boat when he made it.

The height of folly was reached when a plump fool came capering out in gold-painted tin with a cloth lion's head, and chased a dwarf around the tables, whacking him over the head with a bladder. Finally King Renly demanded to know why he was beating his brother. "Why, Your Grace, I'm the Kinslayer," the fool said.

"It's *King*slayer, fool of a fool," Renly said, and the hall rang with laughter.

Lord Rowan beside her did not join the merriment. "They are all so young," he said.

It was true. The Knight of Flowers could not have reached his second name day when Robert slew Prince Rhaegar on the Trident. Few of the others were very much older. They had been babes during the Sack of King's Landing, and no more than boys when Balon Greyjoy raised the Iron Islands in rebellion. *They are still unblooded*, Catelyn thought as she watched Lord Bryce goad Ser Robar into juggling a brace of daggers. *It is all a game to them still, a tourney writ large, and all they see is the chance for glory and honor and spoils. They are boys drunk on song and story, and like all boys, they think themselves immortal.*

"War will make them old," Catelyn said, "as it did

us." She had been a girl when Robert and Ned and Jon
Arryn raised their banners against Aerys Targaryen, a
woman by the time the fighting was done. "I pity
them."

"Why?" Lord Rowan asked her. "Look at them.
They're young and strong, full of life and laughter. And
lust, aye, more lust than they know what to do with.
There will be many a bastard bred this night, I promise
you. Why pity?"

"Because it will not last," Catelyn answered, sadly.
"Because they are the knights of summer, and winter is
coming."

"Lady Catelyn, you are wrong." Brienne regarded her
with eyes as blue as her armor. "Winter will never come
for the likes of us. Should we die in battle, they will
surely sing of us, and it's always summer in the songs.
In the songs all knights are gallant, all maids are beautiful, and the sun is always shining."

Winter comes for all of us, Catelyn thought. *For me,
it came when Ned died. It will come for you too, child,
and sooner than you like.* She did not have the heart to
say it.

The king saved her. "Lady Catelyn," Renly called
down. "I feel the need of some air. Will you walk with
me?"

Catelyn stood at once. "I should be honored."

Brienne was on her feet as well. "Your Grace, give me
but a moment to don my mail. You should not be without protection."

King Renly smiled. "If I am not safe in the heart of
Lord Caswell's castle, with my own host around me,
one sword will make no matter . . . not even *your*
sword, Brienne. Sit and eat. If I have need of you, I'll
send for you."

His words seemed to strike the girl harder than any
blow she had taken that afternoon. "As you will, Your
Grace." Brienne sat, eyes downcast. Renly took
Catelyn's arm and led her from the hall, past a slouching guardsman who straightened so hurriedly that he

near dropped his spear. Renly clapped the man on the shoulder and made a jest of it.

"This way, my lady." The king took her through a low door into a stair tower. As they started up, he said, "Perchance, is Ser Barristan Selmy with your son at Riverrun?"

"No," she answered, puzzled. "Is he no longer with Joffrey? He was the Lord Commander of the Kingsguard."

Renly shook his head. "The Lannisters told him he was too old and gave his cloak to the Hound. I'm told he left King's Landing vowing to take up service with the true king. That cloak Brienne claimed today was the one I was keeping for Selmy, in hopes that he might offer me his sword. When he did not turn up at Highgarden, I thought perhaps he had gone to Riverrun instead."

"We have not seen him."

"He was old, yes, but a good man still. I hope he has not come to harm. The Lannisters are great fools." They climbed a few more steps. "On the night of Robert's death, I offered your husband a hundred swords and urged him to take Joffrey into his power. Had he listened, he would be regent today, and there would have been no need for me to claim the throne."

"Ned refused you." She did not have to be told.

"He had sworn to protect Robert's children," Renly said. "I lacked the strength to act alone, so when Lord Eddard turned me away, I had no choice but to flee. Had I stayed, I knew the queen would see to it that I did not long outlive my brother."

Had you stayed, and lent your support to Ned, he might still be alive, Catelyn thought bitterly.

"I liked your husband well enough, my lady. He was a loyal friend to Robert, I know . . . but he would not listen and he would not bend. Here, I wish to show you something." They had reached the top of the stairwell. Renly pushed open a wooden door, and they stepped out onto the roof.

Lord Caswell's keep was scarcely tall enough to call a

tower, but the country was low and flat and Catelyn could see for leagues in all directions. Wherever she looked, she saw fires. They covered the earth like fallen stars, and like the stars there was no end to them. "Count them if you like, my lady," Renly said quietly. "You will still be counting when dawn breaks in the east. How many fires burn around Riverrun tonight, I wonder?"

Catelyn could hear faint music drifting from the Great Hall, seeping out into the night. She dare not count the stars.

"I'm told your son crossed the Neck with twenty thousand swords at his back," Renly went on. "Now that the lords of the Trident are with him, perhaps he commands forty thousand."

No, she thought, *not near so many, we have lost men in battle, and others to the harvest.*

"I have twice that number here," Renly said, "and this is only part of my strength. Mace Tyrell remains at Highgarden with another ten thousand, I have a strong garrison holding Storm's End, and soon enough the Dornishmen will join me with all their power. And never forget my brother Stannis, who holds Dragonstone and commands the lords of the narrow sea."

"It would seem that you are the one who has forgotten Stannis," Catelyn said, more sharply than she'd intended.

"His claim, you mean?" Renly laughed. "Let us be blunt, my lady. Stannis would make an appalling king. Nor is he like to become one. Men respect Stannis, even fear him, but precious few have ever loved him."

"He is still your elder brother. If either of you can be said to have a right to the Iron Throne, it must be Lord Stannis."

Renly shrugged. "Tell me, what right did my brother Robert ever have to the Iron Throne?" He did not wait for an answer. "Oh, there was talk of the blood ties between Baratheon and Targaryen, of weddings a hundred years past, of second sons and elder daughters. No one but the maesters care about any of it. Robert won the throne with his warhammer." He swept a hand across the campfires that burned from horizon to horizon. "Well, there is my claim, as good as Robert's ever was. If your son supports me as his father supported Robert, he'll not find me ungenerous. I will gladly confirm him in all his lands, titles, and honors. He can rule in Winterfell as he pleases. He can even go on calling himself King in the North if he likes, so long as he bends the knee and does me homage as his overlord. *King* is only a word, but fealty, loyalty, service . . . those I must have."

"And if he will not give them to you, my lord?"

"I mean to be king, my lady, and not of a broken kingdom. I cannot say it plainer than that. Three hundred years ago, a Stark king knelt to Aegon the Dragon, when he saw he could not hope to prevail. That was wisdom. Your son must be wise as well. Once he joins me, this war is good as done. We—" Renly broke off suddenly, distracted. "What's this now?"

The rattle of chains heralded the raising of the portcullis. Down in the yard below, a rider in a winged helm urged his well-lathered horse under the spikes. "Summon the king!" he called.

Renly vaulted up into a crenel. "I'm here, ser."

"Your Grace." The rider spurred his mount closer. "I came swift as I could. From Storm's End. We are besieged, Your Grace, Ser Cortnay defies them, but . . ."

"But . . . that's not possible. I would have been told if Lord Tywin left Harrenhal."

"These are no Lannisters, my liege. It's Lord Stannis at your gates. *King* Stannis, he calls himself now."

JON

A blowing rain lashed at Jon's face as he spurred his horse across the swollen stream. Beside him, Lord Commander Mormont gave the hood of his cloak a tug, muttering curses on the weather. His raven sat on his shoulder, feathers ruffled, as soaked and grumpy as the Old Bear himself. A gust of wind sent wet leaves flapping round them like a flock of dead birds. *The haunted forest*, Jon thought ruefully. *The drowned forest, more like it.*

He hoped Sam was holding up, back down the column. He was not a good rider even in fair weather, and six days of rain had made the ground treacherous, all soft mud and hidden rocks. When the wind blew, it drove the water right into their eyes. The Wall would be flowing off to the south, the melting ice mingling with warm rain to wash down in sheets and rivers. Pyp and Toad would be sitting near the fire in the common room, drinking cups of mulled wine before their supper. Jon envied them. His wet wool clung to him sodden and itching, his neck and shoulders ached fiercely from the weight of mail and sword, and he was sick of salt cod, salt beef, and hard cheese.

Up ahead a hunting horn sounded a quavering note, half drowned beneath the constant patter of the rain. "Buckwell's horn," the Old Bear announced. "The gods are good; Craster's still there." His raven gave a single flap of his big wings, croaked *"Corn,"* and ruffled his feathers up again.

Jon had often heard the black brothers tell tales of Craster and his keep. Now he would see it with his own eyes. After seven empty villages, they had all come to dread finding Craster's as dead and desolate as the rest, but it seemed they would be spared that. *Perhaps the Old Bear will finally get some answers,* he thought. *Anyway, we'll be out of the rain.*

Thoren Smallwood swore that Craster was a friend to the Watch, despite his unsavory reputation. "The man's half-mad, I won't deny it," he'd told the Old Bear, "but you'd be the same if you'd spent your life in this cursed wood. Even so, he's never turned a ranger away from his fire, nor does he love Mance Rayder. He'll give us good counsel."

So long as he gives us a hot meal and a chance to dry our clothes, I'll be happy. Dywen said Craster was a kinslayer, liar, raper, and craven, and hinted that he trafficked with slavers and demons. "And worse," the old forester would add, clacking his wooden teeth. "There's a *cold* smell to that one, there is."

"Jon," Lord Mormont commanded, "ride back along the column and spread the word. And remind the officers that I want no trouble about Craster's wives. The men are to mind their hands and speak to these women as little as need be."

"Aye, my lord." Jon turned his horse back the way they'd come. It was pleasant to have the rain out of his face, if only for a little while. Everyone he passed seemed to be weeping. The march was strung out through half a mile of woods.

In the midst of the baggage train, Jon passed Samwell Tarly, slumped in his saddle under a wide floppy hat. He was riding one dray horse and leading the others. The drumming of the rain against the hoods of their cages had the ravens squawking and fluttering. "You put a fox in with them?" Jon called out.

Water ran off the brim of Sam's hat as he lifted his head. "Oh, hullo, Jon. No, they just hate the rain, the same as us."

"How are you faring, Sam?"

"Wetly." The fat boy managed a smile. "Nothing has killed me yet, though."

"Good. Craster's Keep is just ahead. If the gods are good, he'll let us sleep by his fire."

Sam looked dubious. "Dolorous Edd says Craster's a terrible savage. He marries his daughters and obeys no laws but those he makes himself. And Dywen told Grenn he's got black blood in his veins. His mother was a wildling woman who lay with a ranger, so he's a bas . . ." Suddenly he realized what he was about to say.

"A bastard," Jon said with a laugh. "You can say it, Sam. I've heard the word before." He put the spurs to his surefooted little garron. "I need to hunt down Ser Ottyn. Be careful around Craster's women." As if Samwell Tarly needed warning on that score. "We'll talk later, after we've made camp."

Jon carried the word back to Ser Ottyn Wythers, plodding along with the rear guard. A small prune-faced man of an age with Mormont, Ser Ottyn always looked tired, even at Castle Black, and the rain had beaten him down unmercifully. "Welcome tidings," he said. "This wet has soaked my bones, and even my saddle sores complain of saddle sores."

On his way back, Jon swung wide of the column's line of march and took a shorter path through the thick of the wood. The sounds of man and horse diminished, swallowed up by the wet green wild, and soon enough he could hear only the steady wash of rain against leaf and tree and rock. It was midafternoon, yet the forest seemed as dark as dusk. Jon wove a path between rocks and puddles, past great oaks, grey-green sentinels, and black-barked ironwoods. In places the branches wove a canopy overhead and he was given a moment's respite from the drumming of the rain against his head. As he rode past a lightning-blasted chestnut tree overgrown with wild white roses, he heard something rustling in the underbrush. *"Ghost,"* he called out. "Ghost, to me."

But it was Dywen who emerged from the greenery, forking a shaggy grey garron with Grenn ahorse beside him. The Old Bear had deployed outriders to either side of the main column, to screen their march and warn of the approach of any enemies, and even there he took no chances, sending the men out in pairs.

"Ah, it's you, Lord Snow." Dywen smiled an oaken smile; his teeth were carved of wood, and fit badly. "Thought me and the boy had us one o' them Others to deal with. Lose your wolf?"

"He's off hunting." Ghost did not like to travel with the column, but he would not be far. When they made camp for the night, he'd find his way to Jon at the Lord Commander's tent.

"Fishing, I'd call it, in this wet," Dywen said.

"My mother always said rain was good for growing crops," Grenn put in hopefully.

"Aye, a good crop of mildew," Dywen said. "The best thing about a rain like this, it saves a man from taking baths." He made a clacking sound on his wooden teeth.

"Buckwell's found Craster," Jon told them.

"Had he lost him?" Dywen chuckled. "See that you young bucks don't go nosing about Craster's wives, you hear?"

Jon smiled. "Want them all for yourself, Dywen?"

Dywen clacked his teeth some more. "Might be I do. Craster's got ten fingers and one cock, so he don't count but to eleven. He'd never miss a couple."

"How many wives does he have, truly?" Grenn asked.

"More'n you ever will, brother. Well, it's not so hard when you breed your own. There's your beast, Snow."

Ghost was trotting along beside Jon's horse with tail held high, his white fur ruffed up thick against the rain.

He moved so silently Jon could not have said just when he appeared. Grenn's mount shied at the scent of him; even now, after more than a year, the horses were uneasy in the presence of the direwolf. "With me, Ghost." Jon spurred off to Craster's Keep.

He had never thought to find a stone castle on the far side of the Wall, but he *had* pictured some sort of motte-and-bailey with a wooden palisade and a timber tower keep. What they found instead was a midden heap, a pigsty, an empty sheepfold, and a windowless daub-and-wattle hall scarce worthy of the name. It was long and low, chinked together from logs and roofed with sod. The compound stood atop a rise too modest to name a hill, surrounded by an earthen dike. Brown rivulets flowed down the slope where the rain had eaten gaping holes in the defenses, to join a rushing brook that curved around to the north, its thick waters turned into a murky torrent by the rains.

On the southwest, he found an open gate flanked by a pair of animal skulls on high poles: a bear to one side, a ram to the other. Bits of flesh still clung to the bear skull, Jon noted as he joined the line riding past. Within, Jarmen Buckwell's scouts and men from Thoren Smallwood's van were setting up horse lines and struggling to raise tents. A host of piglets rooted about three huge sows in the sty. Nearby, a small girl pulled carrots from a garden, naked in the rain, while two women tied a pig for slaughter. The animal's squeals were high and horrible, almost human in their distress. Chett's hounds barked wildly in answer, snarling and snapping despite his curses, with a pair of Craster's dogs barking back. When they saw Ghost, some of the dogs broke off and ran, while others began to bay and growl. The direwolf ignored them, as did Jon.

Well, thirty of us will be warm and dry, Jon thought once he'd gotten a good look at the hall. *Perhaps as many as fifty.* The place was much too small to sleep two hundred men, so most would need to remain outside. And where to put them? The rain had turned half the compound yard to ankle-deep puddles and the rest to sucking mud. Another dismal night was in prospect.

The Lord Commander had entrusted his mount to Dolorous Edd. He was cleaning mud out of the horse's hooves as Jon dismounted. "Lord Mormont's in the hall," he announced. "He said for you to join him. Best leave the wolf outside, he looks hungry enough to eat one of Craster's children. Well, truth be told, *I'm* hungry enough to eat one of Craster's children, so long as he was served hot. Go on, I'll see to your horse. If it's warm and dry inside, don't tell me, I wasn't asked in." He flicked a glob of wet mud out from under a horseshoe. "Does this mud look like shit to you? Could it be that this whole hill is made of Craster's shit?"

Jon smiled. "Well, I hear he's been here a long time."

"You cheer me not. Go see the Old Bear."

"Ghost, stay," he commanded. The door to Craster's Keep was made of two flaps of deerhide. Jon shoved between them, stooping to pass under the low lintel. Two dozen of the chief rangers had preceded him, and were standing around the firepit in the center of the dirt floor while puddles collected about their boots. The hall stank of soot, dung, and wet dog. The air was heavy with smoke, yet somehow still damp. Rain leaked through the smoke hole in the roof. It was all a single room, with a sleeping loft above reached by a pair of splintery ladders.

Jon remembered how he'd felt the day they had left the Wall: nervous as a maiden, but eager to glimpse the mysteries and wonders beyond each new horizon. *Well, here's one of the wonders*, he told himself, gazing about the squalid, foul-smelling hall. The acrid smoke was making his eyes water. *A pity that Pyp and Toad can't see all they're missing.*

Craster sat above the fire, the only man to enjoy his own chair. Even Lord Commander Mormont must seat himself on the common bench, with his raven muttering on his shoulder. Jarman Buckwell stood behind, dripping from patched mail and shiny wet leather, beside Thoren Smallwood in the late Ser Jaremy's heavy breastplate and sable-trimmed cloak.

Craster's sheepskin jerkin and cloak of sewn skins made a shabby contrast, but around one thick wrist was a heavy ring that had the glint of gold. He looked to be a powerful man, though well into the winter of his days now, his mane of hair grey going to white. A flat nose and a drooping mouth gave him a cruel look, and one of his ears was missing. *So this is a wildling.* Jon remembered Old Nan's tales of the savage folk who drank blood from human skulls. Craster seemed to be drinking a thin yellow beer from a chipped stone cup. Perhaps he had not heard the stories.

"I've not seen Benjen Stark for three years," he was telling Mormont. "And if truth be told, I never once missed him." A half-dozen black puppies and the odd pig or two skulked among the benches, while women in ragged deerskins passed horns of beer, stirred the fire, and chopped carrots and onions into a kettle.

"He ought to have passed here last year," said Thoren Smallwood. A dog came sniffing round his leg. He kicked it and sent it off yipping.

Lord Mormont said, "Ben was searching for Ser Waymar Royce, who'd vanished with Gared and young Will."

"Aye, those three I recall. The lordling no older than one of these pups. Too proud to sleep under my roof, him in his sable cloak and black steel. My wives give him big cow eyes all the same." He turned his squint on the nearest of the women. "Gared says they were chasing raiders. I told him, with a commander that green, best not catch 'em. Gared wasn't half-bad, for a crow. Had less ears than me, that one. The 'bite took 'em, same as mine." Craster laughed. "Now I hear he got no head neither. The 'bite do that too?"

Jon remembered a spray of red blood on white snow, and the way Theon Greyjoy had kicked the dead man's head. *The man was a deserter.* On the way back to Winterfell, Jon and Robb had raced, and found six direwolf pups in the snow. A thousand years ago.

"When Ser Waymar left you, where was he bound?"

Craster gave a shrug. "Happens I have better things to do than tend to the comings and goings of crows." He drank a pull of beer and set the cup aside. "Had no good southron wine up here for a bear's night. I could use me some wine, and a new axe. Mine's lost its bite, can't have that, I got me women to protect." He gazed around at his scurrying wives.

"You are few here, and isolated," Mormont said. "If you like, I'll detail some men to escort you south to the Wall."

The raven seemed to like the notion. *"Wall,"* it screamed, spreading black wings like a high collar behind Mormont's head.

Their host gave a nasty smile, showing a mouthful of broken brown teeth. "And what would we do there, serve you at supper? We're free folk here. Craster serves no man."

"These are bad times to dwell alone in the wild. The cold winds are rising."

"Let them rise. My roots are sunk deep." Craster grabbed a passing woman by the wrist. "Tell him, wife. Tell the Lord Crow how well content we are."

The woman licked at thin lips. "This is our place. Craster keeps us safe. Better to die free than live a slave."

"Slave," muttered the raven.

Mormont leaned forward. "Every village we have passed has been abandoned. Yours are the first living faces we've seen since we left the Wall. The people are gone . . . whether dead, fled, or taken, I could not say. The animals as well. Nothing is left. And earlier, we found the bodies of two of Ben Stark's rangers only a few leagues from the Wall. They were pale and cold, with black hands and black feet and wounds that did not bleed. Yet when we took them back to Castle Black they rose in the night and killed. One slew Ser Jaremy Rykker and the other came for me, which tells me that they remember some of what they knew when they lived, but there was no human mercy left in them."

The woman's mouth hung open, a wet pink cave, but Craster only gave a snort. "We've had no such troubles here . . . and I'll thank you not to tell such evil tales under my roof. I'm a godly man, and the gods keep me safe. If wights come walking, I'll know how to send them back to their graves. Though I could use me a sharp new axe." He sent his wife scurrying with a slap on her leg and a shout of "More beer, and be quick about it."

"No trouble from the dead," Jarmen Buckwell said, "but what of the living, my lord? What of your king?"

"*King!*" cried Mormont's raven. "*King, king, king.*"

"That Mance Rayder?" Craster spit into the fire. "King-beyond-the-Wall. What do free folk want with kings?" He turned his squint on Mormont. "There's much I could tell you o' Rayder and his doings, if I had a mind. This o' the empty villages, that's his work. You would have found this hall abandoned as well, if I were a man to scrape to such. He sends a rider, tells me I must leave my own keep to come grovel at his feet. I sent the man back, but kept his tongue. It's nailed to that wall there." He pointed. "Might be that I could tell you where to seek Mance Rayder. If I had a mind." The brown smile again. "But we'll have time enough for that. You'll be wanting to sleep beneath my roof, belike, and eat me out of pigs."

"A roof would be most welcome, my lord," Mormont said. "We've had hard riding, and too much wet."

"Then you'll guest here for a night. No longer, I'm not that fond o' crows. The loft's for me and mine, but you'll have all the floor you like. I've meat and beer for twenty, no more. The rest o' your black crows can peck after their own corn."

"We've packed in our own supplies, my lord," said the Old Bear. "We should be pleased to share our food and wine."

Craster wiped his drooping mouth with the back of a hairy hand. "I'll taste your wine, Lord Crow, that I will. One more thing. Any man lays a hand on my wives, he loses the hand."

"Your roof, your rule," said Thoren Smallwood, and Lord Mormont nodded stiffly, though he looked none too pleased.

"That's settled, then." Craster grudged them a grunt. "D'ya have a man can draw a map?"

"Sam Tarly can." Jon pushed forward. "Sam loves maps."

Mormont beckoned him closer. "Send him here after he's eaten. Have him bring quill and parchment. And find Tollett as well. Tell him to bring my axe. A guest gift for our host."

"Who's this one now?" Craster said before Jon could go. "He has the look of a Stark."

"My steward and squire, Jon Snow."

"A bastard, is it?" Craster looked Jon up and down. "Man wants to bed a woman, seems like he ought to take her to wife. That's what I do." He shooed Jon off with a wave. "Well, run and do your service, bastard, and see that axe is good and sharp now, I've no use for dull steel."

Jon Snow bowed stiffly and took his leave. Ser Ottyn Wythers was coming in as he was leaving, and they almost collided at the deerhide door. Outside, the rain seemed to have slackened. Tents had gone up all over the compound. Jon could see the tops of others under the trees.

Dolorous Edd was feeding the horses. "Give the wildling an axe, why not?" He pointed out Mormont's weapon, a short-hafted battle-axe with gold scrollwork inlaid on the black steel blade. "He'll give it back, I vow. Buried in the Old Bear's skull, like as not. Why not give him *all* our axes, and our swords as well? I mislike the way they clank and rattle as we ride. We'd travel faster without them, straight to hell's door. Does it rain in hell, I wonder? Perhaps Craster would like a nice hat instead."

Jon smiled. "He wants an axe. And wine as well."

"See, the Old Bear's clever. If we get the wildling well and truly drunk, perhaps he'll only cut off an ear when he tries to slay us with that axe. I have two ears but only one head."

"Smallwood says Craster is a friend to the Watch."

"Do you know the difference between a wildling who's a friend to the Watch and one who's not?" asked the dour squire. "Our enemies leave our bodies for the crows and the wolves. Our friends bury us in secret graves. I wonder how long that bear's been nailed up on that gate, and what Craster had there before we came hallooing?" Edd looked at the axe doubtfully, the rain running down his long face. "Is it dry in there?"

"Drier than out here."

"If I lurk about after, not too close to the fire, belike they'll take no note of me till morn. The ones under his roof will be the first he murders, but at least we'll die dry."

Jon had to laugh. "Craster's one man. We're two hundred. I doubt he'll murder anyone."

"You cheer me," said Edd, sounding utterly morose. "And besides, there's much to be said for a good sharp axe. I'd hate to be murdered with a maul. I saw a man hit in the brow with a maul once. Scarce split the skin at all, but his head turned mushy and swelled up big as a gourd, only purply-red. A comely man, but he died ugly. It's good that we're not giving them mauls." Edd walked away shaking his head, his sodden black cloak shedding rain behind him.

Jon got the horses fed before he stopped to think of his own supper. He was wondering where to find Sam when he heard a shout of fear. *"Wolf!"* He sprinted around the hall toward the cry, the earth sucking at his boots. One of Craster's women was backed up against the mud-spattered wall of the keep. "Keep away," she was shouting at Ghost. "You keep away!" The direwolf had a rabbit in his mouth and another dead and bloody on the ground before him. "Get it away, m'lord," she pleaded when she saw him.

"He won't hurt you." He knew at once what had happened; a wooden hutch, its slats shattered, lay on its side in the wet grass. "He must have been hungry. We haven't seen much game." Jon whistled. The direwolf bolted down the rabbit, crunching the small bones between his teeth, and padded over to him.

The woman regarded them with nervous eyes. She was younger than he'd thought at first. A girl of fifteen or sixteen years, he judged, dark hair plastered across a gaunt face by the falling rain, her bare feet muddy to the ankles. The body under the sewn skins was showing in the early turns of pregnancy. "Are you one of Craster's daughters?" he asked.

She put a hand over her belly. "Wife now." Edging away from the wolf, she knelt mournfully beside the broken hutch. "I was going to breed them rabbits. There's no sheep left."

"The Watch will make good for them." Jon had no coin of his own, or he would have offered it to her . . . though he was not sure what good a few coppers or even a silver piece would do her beyond the Wall. "I'll speak to Lord Mormont on the morrow."

She wiped her hands on her skirt. "M'lord—"

"I'm no lord."

But others had come crowding round, drawn by the woman's scream and the crash of the rabbit hutch. "Don't you believe him, girl," called out Lark the Sisterman, a ranger mean as a cur. "That's Lord Snow himself."

"Bastard of Winterfell and brother to kings," mocked Chett, who'd left his hounds to see what the commotion was about.

"That wolf's looking at you hungry, girl," Lark said. "Might be it fancies that tender bit in your belly."

Jon was not amused. "You're scaring her."

"Warning her, more like." Chett's grin was as ugly as the boils that covered most of his face.

"We're not to talk to you," the girl remembered suddenly.

"Wait," Jon said, too late. She bolted, ran.

Lark made a grab for the second rabbit, but Ghost was quicker. When he bared his teeth, the Sisterman slipped in the mud and went down on his bony butt. The others laughed. The direwolf took the rabbit in his mouth and brought it to Jon.

"There was no call to scare the girl," he told them.

"We'll hear no scolds from you, bastard." Chett blamed Jon for the loss of his comfortable position with Maester Aemon, and not without justice. If he had not gone to Aemon about Sam Tarly, Chett would still be tending an old blind man instead of a pack of ill-tempered hunting hounds. "You may be the Lord Commander's pet, but you're not the Lord Commander . . . and you wouldn't talk so bloody bold without that monster of yours always about."

"I'll not fight a brother while we're beyond the Wall," Jon answered, his voice cooler than he felt.

Lark got to one knee. "He's afraid of you, Chett. On the Sisters, we have a name for them like him."

"I know all the names. Save your breath." He walked away, Ghost at his side. The rain had dwindled to a thin drizzle by the time he reached the gate. Dusk would be on them soon, followed by another wet dark dismal night. The clouds would hide moon and stars and Mormont's Torch, turning the woods black as pitch. Every piss would be an adventure, if not quite of the sort Jon Snow had once envisioned.

Out under the trees, some rangers had found enough duff and dry wood to start a fire beneath a slanting ridge of slate. Others had raised tents or made rude shelters by stretching their cloaks over low branches. Giant had crammed himself inside the hollow of a dead oak. "How d'ye like my castle, Lord Snow?"

"It looks snug. You know where Sam is?"

"Keep on the way you were. If you come on Ser Ottyn's pavilion, you've gone too far." Giant smiled. "Unless Sam's found him a tree too. What a tree *that* would be."

It was Ghost who found Sam in the end. The direwolf shot ahead like a quarrel from a crossbow. Under an outcrop of rock that gave some small degree of shelter from the rain, Sam was feeding the ravens. His boots squished when he moved. "My feet are soaked through," he admitted miserably. "When I climbed off my horse, I stepped in a hole and went in up to my knees."

"Take off your boots and dry your stockings. I'll find some dry wood. If the ground's not wet under the rock, we might be able to get a fire burning." Jon showed Sam the rabbit. "And we'll feast."

"Won't you be attending Lord Mormont in the hall?"

"No, but you will. The Old Bear wants you to map for him. Craster says he'll find Mance Rayder for us."

"Oh." Sam did not look anxious to meet Craster, even if it meant a warm fire.

"He said eat first, though. Dry your feet." Jon went to gather fuel, digging down under deadfalls for the drier wood beneath and peeling back layers of sodden pine needles until he found likely kindling. Even then, it seemed to take forever for a spark to catch. He hung his cloak from the rock to keep the rain off his smoky little fire, making them a small snug alcove.

As he knelt to skin the rabbit, Sam pulled off his boots. "I think there's moss growing between my toes," he declared mournfully, wriggling the toes in question. "The rabbit will taste good. I don't even mind about the blood and all." He looked away. "Well, only a little . . ."

Jon spitted the carcass, banked the fire with a pair of rocks, and balanced their meal atop them. The rabbit had been a scrawny thing, but as it cooked it smelled like a king's feast. Other rangers gave them envious looks. Even Ghost looked up hungrily, flames shining in his red eyes as he sniffed. "You had yours before," Jon reminded him.

"Is Craster as savage as the rangers say?" Sam asked. The rabbit was a shade underdone, but tasted wonderful. "What's his castle like?"

"A midden heap with a roof and a firepit." Jon told Sam what he had seen and heard in Craster's Keep.

By the time the telling was done, it was dark outside and Sam was licking his fingers. "That was good, but now I'd like a leg of lamb. A whole leg, just for me, sauced with mint and honey and cloves. Did you see any lambs?"

"There was a sheepfold, but no sheep."

"How does he feed all his men?"

"I didn't see any men. Just Craster and his women and a few small girls. I wonder he's able to hold the place. His defenses were nothing to speak of, only a muddy dike. You had better go up to the hall and draw that map. Can you find the way?"

"If I don't fall in the mud." Sam struggled back into his boots, collected quill and parchment, and shouldered out into the night, the rain pattering down on his cloak and floppy hat.

Ghost laid his head on his paws and went to sleep by the fire. Jon stretched out beside him, grateful for the warmth. He was cold and wet, but not so cold and wet as he'd been a short time before. *Perhaps tonight the Old Bear will learn something that will lead us to Uncle Benjen.*

He woke to the sight of his own breath misting in the cold morning air. When he moved, his bones ached. Ghost was gone, the fire burnt out. Jon reached to pull aside the cloak he'd hung over the rock, and found it stiff and frozen. He crept beneath it and stood up in a forest turned to crystal.

The pale pink light of dawn sparkled on branch and leaf and stone. Every blade of grass was carved from emerald, every drip of water turned to diamond. Flowers and mushrooms alike wore coats of glass. Even the mud puddles had a bright brown sheen. Through the shimmering greenery, the black tents of his brothers were encased in a fine glaze of ice.

So there is magic beyond the Wall after all. He found himself thinking of his sisters, perhaps because he'd dreamed of them last night. Sansa would call this an enchantment, and tears would fill her eyes at the wonder of it, but Arya would run out laughing and shouting, wanting to touch it all.

"Lord Snow?" he heard. Soft and meek. He turned. Crouched atop the rock that had sheltered him during

the night was the rabbit keeper, wrapped in a black cloak so large it drowned her. *Sam's cloak,* Jon realized at once. *Why is she wearing Sam's cloak?* "The fat one told me I'd find you here, m'lord," she said.

"We ate the rabbit, if that's what you came for." The admission made him feel absurdly guilty.

"Old Lord Crow, him with the talking bird, he gave Craster a crossbow worth a hundred rabbits." Her arms closed over the swell of her belly. "Is it true, m'lord? Are you brother to a king?"

"A half brother," he admitted. "I'm Ned Stark's bastard. My brother Robb is the King in the North. Why are you here?"

"The fat one, that Sam, he said to see you. He give me his cloak, so no one would say I didn't belong."

"Won't Craster be angry with you?"

"My father drank overmuch of the Lord Crow's wine last night. He'll sleep most of the day." Her breath frosted the air in small nervous puffs. "They say the king gives justice and protects the weak." She started to climb off the rock, awkwardly, but the ice had made it slippery and her foot went out from under her. Jon caught her before she could fall, and helped her safely down. The woman knelt on the icy ground. "M'lord, I beg you—"

"Don't beg me anything. Go back to your hall, you shouldn't be here. We were commanded not to speak to Craster's women."

"You don't have to speak with me, m'lord. Just take me with you, when you go, that's all I ask."

All she asks, he thought. *As if that were nothing.*

"I'll . . . I'll be your wife, if you like. My father, he's got nineteen now, one less won't hurt him none."

"Black brothers are sworn never to take wives, don't you know that? And we're guests in your father's hall besides."

"Not *you,*" she said. "I watched. You never ate at his board, nor slept by his fire. He never gave you guest-right, so you're not bound to him. It's for the baby I have to go."

"I don't even know your name."

"Gilly, he called me. For the gillyflower."

"That's pretty." He remembered Sansa telling him once that he should say that whenever a lady told him her name. He could not help the girl, but perhaps the courtesy would please her. "Is it Craster who frightens you, Gilly?"

"For the baby, not for me. If it's a girl, that's not so bad, she'll grow a few years and he'll marry her. But Nella says it's to be a boy, and she's had six and knows these things. He gives the boys to the gods. Come the white cold, he does, and of late it comes more often. That's why he started giving them sheep, even though he has a taste for mutton. Only now the sheep's gone too. Next it will be dogs, till . . ." She lowered her eyes and stroked her belly.

"What gods?" Jon was remembering that they'd seen no boys in Craster's Keep, nor men either, save Craster himself.

"The cold gods," she said. "The ones in the night. The white shadows."

And suddenly Jon was back in the Lord Commander's Tower again. A severed hand was climbing his calf and when he pried it off with the point of his longsword, it lay writhing, fingers opening and closing. The dead man rose to his feet, blue eyes shining in that gashed and swollen face. Ropes of torn flesh hung from the great wound in his belly, yet there was no blood.

"What color are their eyes?" he asked her.

"Blue. As bright as blue stars, and as cold."

She has seen them, he thought. *Craster lied.*

"Will you take me? Just so far as the Wall—"

"We do not ride for the Wall. We ride north, after Mance Rayder and these Others, these white shadows and their wights. We *seek* them, Gilly. Your babe would not be safe with us."

Her fear was plain on her face. "You will come back, though. When your warring's done, you'll pass this way again."

"We may." *If any of us still live.* "That's for the Old

Bear to say, the one you call the Lord Crow. I'm only his squire. I do not choose the road I ride."

"No." He could hear the defeat in her voice. "Sorry to be of trouble, m'lord. I only . . . they said the king keeps people safe, and I thought . . ." Despairing, she ran, Sam's cloak flapping behind her like great black wings.

Jon watched her go, his joy in the morning's brittle beauty gone. *Damn her*, he thought resentfully, *and damn Sam twice for sending her to me. What did he think I could do for her? We're here to fight wildlings, not save them.*

Other men were crawling from their shelters, yawning and stretching. The magic was already faded, icy brightness turning back to common dew in the light of the rising sun. Someone had gotten a fire started; he could smell woodsmoke drifting through the trees, and the smoky scent of bacon. Jon took down his cloak and snapped it against the rock, shattering the thin crust of ice that had formed in the night, then gathered up Longclaw and shrugged an arm through a shoulder strap. A few yards away he made water into a frozen bush, his piss steaming in the cold air and melting the ice wherever it fell. Afterward he laced up his black wool breeches and followed the smells.

Grenn and Dywen were among the brothers who had gathered round the fire. Hake handed Jon a hollow heel of bread filled with burnt bacon and chunks of salt fish warmed in bacon grease. He wolfed it down while listening to Dywen boast of having three of Craster's women during the night.

"You did not," Grenn said, scowling. "I would have seen."

Dywen whapped him up alongside his ear with the back of his hand. "You? Seen? You're blind as Maester Aemon. You never even saw that bear."

"What bear? Was there a bear?"

"There's always a bear," declared Dolorous Edd in his usual tone of gloomy resignation. "One killed my brother when I was young. Afterward it wore his teeth around its neck on a leather thong. And they were good teeth too, better than mine. I've had nothing but trouble with my teeth."

"Did Sam sleep in the hall last night?" Jon asked him.

"I'd not call it sleeping. The ground was hard, the rushes ill-smelling, and my brothers snore frightfully. Speak of bears if you will, none ever growled so fierce as Brown Bernarr. I was warm, though. Some dogs crawled atop me during the night. My cloak was almost dry when one of them pissed in it. Or perhaps it was Brown Bernarr. Have you noticed that the rain stopped the instant I had a roof above me? It will start again now that I'm back out. Gods and dogs alike delight to piss on me."

"I'd best go see to Lord Mormont," said Jon.

The rain might have stopped, but the compound was still a morass of shallow lakes and slippery mud. Black brothers were folding their tents, feeding their horses, and chewing on strips of salt beef. Jarman Buckwell's scouts were tightening the girths on their saddles before setting out. "Jon," Buckwell greeted him from horseback. "Keep a good edge on that bastard sword of yours. We'll be needing it soon enough."

Craster's hall was dim after daylight. Inside, the night's torches had burned low, and it was hard to know that the sun had risen. Lord Mormont's raven was the first to spy him enter. Three lazy flaps of its great black wings, and it perched atop Longclaw's hilt. *"Corn?"* It nipped at a strand of Jon's hair.

"Ignore that wretched beggar bird, Jon, it's just had half my bacon." The Old Bear sat at Craster's board, breaking his fast with the other officers on fried bread, bacon, and sheepgut sausage. Craster's new axe was on the table, its gold inlay gleaming faintly in the torchlight. Its owner was sprawled unconscious in the sleeping loft above, but the women were all up, moving about and serving. "What sort of day do we have?"

"Cold, but the rain has stopped."

"Very good. See that my horse is saddled and ready. I

mean for us to ride within the hour. Have you eaten?
Craster serves plain fare, but filling."

I will not eat Craster's food, he decided suddenly. "I
broke my fast with the men, my lord." Jon shooed the
raven off Longclaw. The bird hopped back to Mormont's
shoulder, where it promptly shat. "You might have
done that on Snow instead of saving it for me," the Old
Bear grumbled. The raven *quorked*.

He found Sam behind the hall, standing with Gilly at
the broken rabbit hutch. She was helping him back into
his cloak, but when she saw Jon she stole away. Sam
gave him a look of wounded reproach. "I thought you
would help her."

"And how was I to do that?" Jon said sharply. "Take
her with us, wrapped up in your cloak? We were commanded not to—"

"I know," said Sam guiltily, "but she was afraid. I
know what it is to be afraid. I told her . . ." He swallowed.

"*What?* That we'd take her with us?"

Sam's fat face blushed a deep red. "On the way
home." He could not meet Jon's eyes. "She's going to
have a baby."

"Sam, have you taken leave of all your sense? We may
not even return this way. And if we do, do you think the
Old Bear is going to let you pack off one of Craster's
wives?"

"I thought . . . maybe by then I could think of a
way . . ."

"I have no time for this, I have horses to groom and
saddle." Jon walked away as confused as he was angry.
Sam's heart was a big as the rest of him, but for all his
reading he could be as thick as Grenn at times. It was
impossible, and dishonorable besides. *So why do I feel
so ashamed?*

Jon took his accustomed position at Mormont's side
as the Night's Watch streamed out past the skulls on
Craster's gate. They struck off north and west along a
crooked game trail. Melting ice dripped down all about
them, a slower sort of rain with its own soft music.

North of the compound, the brook was in full spate, choked with leaves and bits of wood, but the scouts had found where the ford lay and the column was able to splash across. The water ran as high as a horse's belly. Ghost swam, emerging on the bank with his white fur dripping brown. When he shook, spraying mud and water in all directions, Mormont said nothing, but on his shoulder the raven screeched.

"My lord," Jon said quietly as the wood closed in around them once more. "Craster has no sheep. Nor any sons."

Mormont made no answer.

"At Winterfell one of the serving women told us stories," Jon went on. "She used to say that there were wildlings who would lay with the Others to birth half-human children."

"Hearth tales. Does Craster seem less than human to you?"

In half a hundred ways. "He gives his sons to the wood."

A long silence. Then: "Yes." And *"Yes,"* the raven muttered, strutting. *"Yes, yes, yes."*

"You knew?"

"Smallwood told me. Long ago. All the rangers know, though few will talk of it."

"Did my uncle know?"

"All the rangers," Mormont repeated. "You think I ought to stop him. Kill him if need be." The Old Bear sighed. "Were it only that he wished to rid himself of some mouths, I'd gladly send Yoren or Conwys to collect the boys. We could raise them to the black and the Watch would be that much the stronger. But the wildlings serve crueler gods than you or I. These boys are Craster's offerings. His prayers, if you will."

His wives must offer different prayers, Jon thought.

"How is it you came to know this?" the Old Bear asked him. "From one of Craster's wives?"

"Yes, my lord," Jon confessed. "I would sooner not tell you which. She was frightened and wanted help."

"The wide world is full of people wanting help, Jon.

Would that some could find the courage to help themselves. Craster sprawls in his loft even now, stinking of wine and lost to sense. On his board below lies a sharp new axe. Were it me, I'd name it 'Answered Prayer' and make an end."

Yes. Jon thought of Gilly. She and her sisters. They were nineteen, and Craster was one, but . . .

"Yet it would be an ill day for us if Craster died. Your uncle could tell you of the times Craster's Keep made the difference between life and death for our rangers."

"My father . . ." He hesitated.

"Go on, Jon. Say what you would say."

"My father once told me that some men are not worth having," Jon finished. "A bannerman who is brutal or unjust dishonors his liege lord as well as himself."

"Craster is his own man. He has sworn us no vows. Nor is he subject to our laws. Your heart is noble, Jon, but learn a lesson here. We cannot set the world to rights. That is not our purpose. The Night's Watch has other wars to fight."

Other wars. Yes. I must remember. "Jarman Buckwell said I might have need of my sword soon."

"Did he?" Mormont did not seem pleased. "Craster said much and more last night, and confirmed enough of my fears to condemn me to a sleepless night on his floor. Mance Rayder is gathering his people together in the Frostfangs. That's why the villages are empty. It is the same tale that Ser Denys Mallister had from the wildling his men captured in the Gorge, but Craster has added the *where*, and that makes all the difference."

"Is he making a city, or an army?"

"Now, that is the question. How many wildlings are there? How many men of fighting age? No one knows with certainty. The Frostfangs are cruel, inhospitable, a wilderness of stone and ice. They will not long sustain any great number of people. I can see only one purpose in this gathering. Mance Rayder means to strike south, into the Seven Kingdoms."

"Wildlings have invaded the realm before." Jon had heard the tales from Old Nan and Maester Luwin both, back at Winterfell. "Raymun Redbeard led them south in the time of my grandfather's grandfather, and before him there was a king named Bael the Bard."

"Aye, and long before them came the Horned Lord and the brother kings Gendel and Gorne, and in ancient days Joramun, who blew the Horn of Winter and woke giants from the earth. Each man of them broke his strength on the Wall, or was broken by the power of Winterfell on the far side . . . but the Night's Watch is only a shadow of what we were, and who remains to oppose the wildlings besides us? The Lord of Winterfell is dead, and his heir has marched his strength south to fight the Lannisters. The wildlings may never again have such a chance as this. I knew Mance Rayder, Jon. He is an oathbreaker, yes . . . but he has eyes to see, and no man has ever dared to name him faintheart."

"What will we do?" asked Jon.

"Find him," said Mormont. "Fight him. Stop him."

Three hundred, thought Jon, *against the fury of the wild.* His fingers opened and closed.

THEON

She was undeniably a beauty. *But your first is always beautiful,* Theon Greyjoy thought.

"Now there's a pretty grin," a woman's voice said behind him. "The lordling likes the look of her, does he?"

Theon turned to give her an appraising glance. He liked what he saw. Ironborn, he knew at a glance; lean and long-legged, with black hair cut short, wind-chafed skin, strong sure hands, a dirk at her belt. Her nose was too big and too sharp for her thin face, but her smile made up for it. He judged her a few years older than he was, but no more than five-and-twenty. She moved as if she were used to a deck beneath her feet.

"Yes, she's a sweet sight," he told her, "though not half so sweet as you."

"Oho." She grinned. "I'd best be careful. This lordling has a honeyed tongue."

"Taste it and see."

"Is it that way, then?" she said, eyeing him boldly. There were women on the Iron Islands—not many, but a few—who crewed the longships along with their men, and it was said that salt and sea changed them, gave them a man's appetites. "Have you been that long at sea, lordling? Or were there no women where you came from?"

"Women enough, but none like you."

"And how would you know what I'm like?"

"My eyes can see your face. My ears can hear your laughter. And my cock's gone hard as a mast for you."

The woman stepped close and pressed a hand to the front of his breeches. "Well, you're no liar," she said, giving him a squeeze through the cloth. "How bad does it hurt?"

"Fiercely."

"Poor lordling." She released him and stepped back. "As it happens, I'm a woman wed, and new with child."

"The gods are good," Theon said. "No chance I'd give you a bastard that way."

"Even so, my man wouldn't thank you."

"No, but you might."

"And why would that be? I've had lords before. They're made the same as other men."

"Have you ever had a prince?" he asked her. "When you're wrinkled and grey and your teats hang past your belly, you can tell your children's children that once you loved a king."

"Oh, is it love we're talking now? And here I thought it was just cocks and cunts."

"Is it love you fancy?" He'd decided that he liked this wench, whoever she was; her sharp wit was a welcome respite from the damp gloom of Pyke. "Shall I name my longship after you, and play you the high harp, and keep you in a tower room in my castle with only jewels to wear, like a princess in a song?"

"You *ought* to name your ship after me," she said, ignoring all the rest. "It was me who built her."

"Sigrin built her. My lord father's shipwright."

"I'm Esgred. Ambrode's daughter, and wife to Sigrin."

He had not known that Ambrode had a daughter, or Sigrin a wife . . . but he'd met the younger shipwright only once, and the older one he scarce remembered. "You're wasted on Sigrin."

"Oho. Sigrin told me this sweet ship is wasted on you."

Theon bristled. "Do you know who I am?"

"Prince Theon of House Greyjoy. Who else? Tell me true, my lord, how well do you love her, this new maid of yours? Sigrin will want to know."

The longship was so new that she still smelled of pitch and resin. His uncle Aeron would bless her on the morrow, but Theon had ridden over from Pyke to get a look at her before she was launched. She was not so large as Lord Balon's own *Great Kraken* or his uncle Victarion's *Iron Victory*, but she looked swift and sweet, even sitting in her wooden cradle on the strand; lean black hull a hundred feet long, a single tall mast, fifty long oars, deck enough for a hundred men . . . and at the prow, the great iron ram in the shape of an arrowhead. "Sigrin did me good service," he admitted. "Is she as fast as she looks?"

"Faster—for a master that knows how to handle her."

"It has been a few years since I sailed a ship." *And I've never captained one, if truth be told.* "Still, I'm a Greyjoy, and an ironman. The sea is in my blood."

"And your blood will be in the sea, if you sail the way you talk," she told him.

"I would never mistreat such a fair maiden."

"Fair maiden?" She laughed. "She's a sea bitch, this one."

"There, and now you've named her. *Sea Bitch.*"

That amused her; he could see the sparkle in her dark eyes. "And you said you'd name her after me," she said in a voice of wounded reproach.

"I did." He caught her hand. "Help me, my lady. In the green lands, they believe a woman with child means good fortune for any man who beds her."

"And what would they know about ships in the green lands? Or women, for that matter? Besides, I think you made that up."

"If I confess, will you still love me?"

"Still? When have I ever loved you?"

"Never," he admitted, "but I am trying to repair that lack, my sweet Esgred. The wind is cold. Come aboard my ship and let me warm you. On the morrow my uncle Aeron will pour seawater over her prow and mumble a prayer to the Drowned God, but I'd sooner bless her with the milk of my loins, and yours."

"The Drowned God might not take that kindly."

"Bugger the Drowned God. If he troubles us, I'll drown him again. We're off to war within a fortnight. Would you send me into battle all sleepless with longing?"

"Gladly."

"A cruel maid. My ship is well named. If I steer her onto the rocks in my distraction, you'll have yourself to blame."

"Do you plan to steer with this?" Esgred brushed the front of his breeches once more, and smiled as a finger traced the iron outline of his manhood.

"Come back to Pyke with me," he said suddenly, thinking, *What will Lord Balon say? And why should I care? I am a man grown, if I want to bring a wench to bed it is no one's business but my own.*

"And what would I do in Pyke?" Her hand stayed where it was.

"My father will feast his captains tonight." He had them to feast every night, while he waited for the last stragglers to arrive, but Theon saw no need to tell all that.

"Would you make me your captain for the night, my lord prince?" She had the wickedest smile he'd ever seen on a woman.

"I might. If I knew you'd steer me safe into port."

"Well, I know which end of the oar goes in the sea, and there's no one better with ropes and knots." One-handed, she undid the lacing of his breeches, then grinned and stepped lightly away from him. "A pity I'm a woman wed, and new with child."

Flustered, Theon laced himself back up. "I need to start back to the castle. If you do not come with me, I may lose my way for grief, and all the islands would be poorer."

"We couldn't have that . . . but I have no horse, my lord."

"You could take my squire's mount."

"And leave your poor squire to walk all the way to Pyke?"

"Share mine, then."

"You'd like that well enough." The smile again. "Now, would I be behind you, or in front?"

"You would be wherever you liked."

"I like to be on top."

Where has this wench been all my life? "My father's hall is dim and dank. It needs Esgred to make the fires blaze."

"The lordling has a honeyed tongue."

"Isn't that where we began?"

She threw up her hands. "And where we end. Esgred is yours, sweet prince. Take me to your castle. Let me see your proud towers rising from the sea."

"I left my horse at the inn. Come." They walked down the strand together, and when Theon took her arm, she did not pull away. He liked the way she walked; there was a boldness to it, part saunter and part sway, that suggested she would be just as bold beneath the blankets.

Lordsport was as crowded as he'd ever seen it, swarming with the crews of the longships that lined the pebbled shore and rode at anchor well out past the breakwater. Ironmen did not bend their knees often nor easily, but Theon noted that oarsmen and townfolk alike grew quiet as they passed, and acknowledged him with respectful bows of the head. *They have finally learned who I am,* he thought. *And past time too.*

Lord Goodbrother of Great Wyk had come in the night before with his main strength, near forty longships. His men were everywhere, conspicuous in their striped goat's hair sashes. It was said about the inn that Otter Gimpknee's whores were being fucked bowlegged by beardless boys in sashes. The boys were welcome to them so far as Theon was concerned. A poxier den of slatterns he hoped he'd never see. His present companion was more to his taste. That she was wed to his father's shipwright and pregnant to boot only made her more intriguing.

"Has my lord prince begun choosing his crew?" Esgred asked as they made their way toward the stable. "Ho, Bluetooth," she shouted to a passing seafarer, a tall man in bearskin vest and raven-winged helm. "How fares your bride?"

"Fat with child, and talking of twins."

"So soon?" Esgred smiled that wicked smile. "You got your oar in the water quickly."

"Aye, and stroked and stroked and *stroked*," roared the man.

"A big man," Theon observed. "Bluetooth, was it? Should I choose him for my *Sea Bitch*?"

"Only if you mean to insult him. Bluetooth has a sweet ship of his own."

"I have been too long away to know one man from another," Theon admitted. He'd looked for a few of the friends he'd played with as a boy, but they were gone, dead, or grown into strangers. "My uncle Victarion has loaned me his own steersman."

"Rymolf Stormdrunk? A good man, so long as he's sober." She saw more faces she knew, and called out to a passing trio, "Uller, Qarl. Where's your brother, Skyte?"

"The Drowned God needed a strong oarsman, I fear," replied the stocky man with the white streak in his beard.

"What he means is, Eldiss drank too much wine and his fat belly burst," said the pink-cheeked youth beside him.

"What's dead may never die," Esgred said.

"What's dead may never die."

Theon muttered the words with them. "You seem well known," he said to the woman when the men had passed on.

"Every man loves the shipwright's wife. He had better, lest he wants his ship to sink. If you need men to pull your oars, you could do worse than those three."

"Lordsport has no lack of strong arms." Theon had given the matter no little thought. It was fighters he wanted, and men who would be loyal to *him*, not to his lord father or his uncles. He was playing the part of a dutiful young prince for the moment, while he waited for Lord Balon to reveal the fullness of his plans. If it turned out that he did not like those plans or his part in them, however, well . . .

"Strength is not enough. A longship's oars must move as one if you would have her best speed. Choose men who have rowed together before, if you're wise."

"Sage counsel. Perhaps you'd help me choose them." *Let her believe I want her wisdom, women fancy that.*

"I may. If you treat me kindly."

"How else?"

Theon quickened his stride as they neared the *Myraham*, rocking high and empty by the quay. Her captain had tried to sail a fortnight past, but Lord Balon would not permit it. None of the merchantmen that called at Lordsport had been allowed to depart again; his father wanted no word of the hosting to reach the mainland before he was ready to strike.

"Milord," a plaintive voice called down from the forecastle of the merchanter. The captain's daughter leaned over the rail, gazing after him. Her father had forbidden her to come ashore, but whenever Theon came to Lordsport he spied her wandering forlornly about the deck. "Milord, a moment," she called after him. "As it please milord . . ."

"Did she?" Esgred asked as Theon hurried her past the cog. "Please milord?"

He saw no sense in being coy with this one. "For a time. Now she wants to be my salt wife."

"Oho. Well, she'd profit from some salting, no doubt. Too soft and bland, that one. Or am I wrong?"

"You're not wrong." *Soft and bland. Precisely. How had she known?*

He had told Wex to wait at the inn. The common

room was so crowded that Theon had to push his way through the door. Not a seat was to be had at bench nor table. Nor did he see his squire. *"Wex,"* he shouted over the din and clatter. *If he's up with one of those poxy whores, I'll strip the hide off him*, he was thinking when he finally spied the boy, dicing near the hearth . . . and winning too, by the look of the pile of coins before him.

"Time to go," Theon announced. When the boy paid him no mind, he seized him by the ear and pulled him from the game. Wex grabbed up a fistful of coppers and came along without a word. That was one of the things Theon liked best about him. Most squires have loose tongues, but Wex had been born dumb . . . which didn't seem to keep him from being clever as any twelve-year-old had a right to be. He was a baseborn son of one of Lord Botley's half brothers. Taking him as squire had been part of the price Theon had paid for his horse.

When Wex saw Esgred, his eyes went round. *You'd think he'd never seen a woman before*, Theon thought. "Esgred will be riding with me back to Pyke. Saddle the horses, and be quick about it."

The boy had ridden in on a scrawny little garron from Lord Balon's stable, but Theon's mount was quite another sort of beast. "Where did you find that hellhorse?" Esgred asked when she saw him, but from the way she laughed he knew she was impressed.

"Lord Botley bought him in Lannisport a year past, but he proved to be too much horse for him, so Botley was pleased to sell." The Iron Islands were too sparse and rocky for breeding good horses. Most of the islanders were indifferent riders at best, more comfortable on the deck of a longship than in the saddle. Even the lords rode garrons or shaggy Harlaw ponies, and ox carts were more common than drays. The smallfolk too poor to own either one pulled their own plows through the thin, stony soil.

But Theon had spent ten years in Winterfell, and did not intend to go to war without a good mount beneath him. Lord Botley's misjudgment was his good fortune: a stallion with a temper as black as his hide, larger than a courser if not quite so big as most destriers. As Theon was not quite so big as most knights, that suited him admirably. The animal had fire in his eyes. When he'd met his new owner, he'd pulled back his lips and tried to bite off his face.

"Does he have a name?" Esgred asked Theon as he mounted.

"Smiler." He gave her a hand, and pulled her up in front of him, where he could put his arms around her as they rode. "I knew a man once who told me that I smiled at the wrong things."

"Do you?"

"Only by the lights of those who smile at nothing." He thought of his father and his uncle Aeron.

"Are you smiling now, my lord prince?"

"Oh, yes." Theon reached around her to take the reins. She was almost of a height with him. Her hair could have used a wash and she had a faded pink scar on her pretty neck, but he liked the smell of her, salt and sweat and woman.

The ride back to Pyke promised to be a good deal more interesting than the ride down had been.

When they were well beyond Lordsport, Theon put a hand on her breast. Esgred reached up and plucked it away. "I'd keep both hands on the reins, or this black beast of yours is like to fling us both off and kick us to death."

"I broke him of that." Amused, Theon behaved himself for a while, chatting amiably of the weather (grey and overcast, as it had been since he arrived, with frequent rains) and telling her of the men he'd killed in the Whispering Wood. When he reached the part about coming *that* close to the Kingslayer himself, he slid his hand back up to where it had been. Her breasts were small, but he liked the firmness of them.

"You don't want to do that, my lord prince."

"Oh, but I do." Theon gave her a squeeze.

"Your squire is watching you."

"Let him. He'll never speak of it, I swear."

Esgred pried his fingers off her breast. This time she kept him firmly prisoned. She had strong hands.

"I like a woman with a good tight grip."

She snorted. "I'd not have thought it, by that wench on the waterfront."

"You must not judge me by her. She was the only woman on the ship."

"Tell me of your father. Will he welcome me kindly to his castle?"

"Why should he? He scarcely welcomed *me*, his own blood, the heir to Pyke and the Iron Islands."

"Are you?" she asked mildly. "It's said that you have uncles, brothers, a sister."

"My brothers are long dead, and my sister . . . well, they say Asha's favorite gown is a chainmail hauberk that hangs down past her knees, with boiled leather smallclothes beneath. Men's garb won't make her a man, though. I'll make a good marriage alliance with her once we've won the war, if I can find a man to take her. As I recall, she had a nose like a vulture's beak, a ripe crop of pimples, and no more chest than a boy."

"You can marry off your sister," Esgred observed, "but not your uncles."

"My uncles . . ." Theon's claim took precedence over those of his father's three brothers, but the woman had touched on a sore point nonetheless. In the islands it was scarce unheard of for a strong, ambitious uncle to dispossess a weak nephew of his rights, and usually murder him in the bargain. *But I am not weak*, Theon told himself, *and I mean to be stronger yet by the time my father dies.* "My uncles pose no threat to me," he declared. "Aeron is drunk on seawater and sanctity. He lives only for his god—"

"*His* god? Not yours?"

"Mine as well. What is dead can never die." He smiled thinly. "If I make pious noises as required, Damphair will give me no trouble. And my uncle Victarion—"

"Lord Captain of the Iron Fleet, and a fearsome warrior. I have heard them sing of him in the alehouses."

"During my lord father's rebellion, he sailed into Lannisport with my uncle Euron and burned the Lannister fleet where it lay at anchor," Theon recalled. "The plan was Euron's, though. Victarion is like some great grey bullock, strong and tireless and dutiful, but not like to win any races. No doubt, he'll serve me as loyally as he has served my lord father. He has neither the wits nor the ambition to plot betrayal."

"Euron Crow's eye has no lack of cunning, though. I've heard men say terrible things of that one."

Theon shifted his seat. "My uncle Euron has not been seen in the islands for close on two years. He may be dead." If so, it might be for the best. Lord Balon's eldest brother had never given up the Old Way, even for a day. His *Silence*, with its black sails and dark red hull, was infamous in every port from Ibben to Asshai, it was said.

"He may be dead," Esgred agreed, "and if he lives, why, he has spent so long at sea, he'd be half a stranger here. The ironborn would never seat a stranger in the Seastone Chair."

"I suppose not," Theon replied, before it occurred to him that some would call *him* a stranger as well. The thought made him frown. *Ten years is a long while, but I am back now, and my father is far from dead. I have time to prove myself.*

He considered fondling Esgred's breast again, but she would probably only take his hand away, and all this talk of his uncles had dampened his ardor somewhat. Time enough for such play at the castle, in the privacy of his chambers. "I will speak to Helya when we reach Pyke, and see that you have an honored place at the feast," he said. "I must sit on the dais, at my father's right hand, but I will come down and join you when he leaves the hall. He seldom lingers long. He has no belly for drink these days."

"A grievous thing when a great man grows old."

"Lord Balon is but the *father* of a great man."

"A modest lordling."

"Only a fool humbles himself when the world is so full of men eager to do that job for him." He kissed her lightly on the nape of her neck.

"What shall I wear to this great feast?" She reached back and pushed his face away.

"I'll ask Helya to garb you. One of my lady mother's gowns might do. She is off on Harlaw, and not expected to return."

"The cold winds have worn her away, I hear. Will you not go see her? Harlaw is only a day's sail, and surely Lady Greyjoy yearns for a last sight of her son."

"Would that I could. I am kept too busy here. My father relies on me, now that I am returned. Come peace, perhaps . . ."

"Your coming might bring *her* peace."

"Now you sound a woman," Theon complained.

"I confess, I am . . . and new with child."

Somehow that thought excited him. "So you say, but your body shows no signs of it. How shall it be proven? Before I believe you, I shall need to see your breasts grow ripe, and taste your mother's milk."

"And what will my husband say to this? Your father's own sworn man and servant?"

"We'll give him so many ships to build, he'll never know you've left him."

She laughed. "It's a cruel lordling who's seized me. If I promise you that one day you may watch my babe get suck, will you tell me more of your war, Theon of House Greyjoy? There are miles and mountains still ahead of us, and I would hear of this wolf king you served, and the golden lions he fights."

Ever anxious to please her, Theon obliged. The rest of the long ride passed swiftly as he filled her pretty head with tales of Winterfell and war. Some of the things he said astonished him. *She is easy to talk to, gods praise her*, he reflected. *I feel as though I've known her for years. If the wench's pillow play is half the equal of her wit, I'll need to keep her* . . . He thought of Sigrin the Shipwright, a thick-bodied, thick-witted man, flaxen hair already receding from a pimpled brow, and shook his head. *A waste. A most tragic waste.*

It seemed scarcely any time at all before the great curtain wall of Pyke loomed up before them.

The gates were open. Theon put his heels into Smiler and rode through at a brisk trot. The hounds were barking wildly as he helped Esgred dismount. Several came bounding up, tails wagging. They shot straight past him and almost bowled the woman over, leaping all around her, yapping and licking. *"Off,"* Theon shouted, aiming an ineffectual kick at one big brown bitch, but Esgred was laughing and wrestling with them.

A stableman came pounding up after the dogs. "Take the horse," Theon commanded him, "and get these damn dogs away—"

The lout paid him no mind. His face broke into a huge gap-toothed smile and he said, "Lady Asha. You're back."

"Last night," she said. "I sailed from Great Wyk with Lord Goodbrother, and spent the night at the inn. My little brother was kind enough to let me ride with him from Lordsport." She kissed one of the dogs on the nose and grinned at Theon.

All he could do was stand and gape at her. *Asha. No. She cannot be Asha.* He realized suddenly that there were two Ashas in his head. One was the little girl he had known. The other, more vaguely imagined, looked something like her mother. Neither looked a bit like this . . . this . . . this . . .

"The pimples went when the breasts came," she explained while she tussled with a dog, "but I kept the vulture's beak."

Theon found his voice. *"Why didn't you tell me?"*

Asha let go of the hound and straightened. "I wanted to see who you were first. And I did." She gave him a mocking half bow. "And now, little brother, pray excuse me. I need to bathe and dress for the feast. I wonder if I still have that chainmail gown I like to wear over my boiled leather smallclothes?" She gave him that evil grin, and crossed the bridge with that walk he'd liked so well, half saunter and half sway.

When Theon turned away, Wex was smirking at him. He gave the boy a clout on the ear. "That's for enjoying this so much." And another, harder. "And that's for not warning me. Next time, grow a tongue."

His own chambers in the Guest Keep had never seemed so chilly, though the thralls had left a brazier burning. Theon kicked his boots off, let his cloak fall to the floor, and poured himself a cup of wine, remembering a gawky girl with knob knees and pimples. *She unlaced my breeches,* he thought, outraged, *and she said . . . oh, gods, and I said . . .* He groaned. He could not possibly have made a more appalling fool of himself.

No, he thought then. *She was the one who made me a fool. The evil bitch must have enjoyed every moment of it. And the way she kept reaching for my cock . . .*

He took his cup and went to the window seat, where he sat drinking and watching the sea while the sun darkened over Pyke. *I have no place here,* he thought, *and Asha is the reason, may the Others take her!* The water below turned from green to grey to black. By then he could hear distant music, and he knew it was time to change for the feast.

Theon chose plain boots and plainer clothes, somber shades of black and grey to fit his mood. No ornament; he had nothing bought with iron. *I might have taken something off that wildling I killed to save Bran Stark, but he had nothing worth the taking. That's my cursed luck, I kill the poor.*

The long smoky hall was crowded with his father's lords and captains when Theon entered, near four hundred of them. Dagmer Cleftjaw had not yet returned from Old Wyk with the Stonehouses and Drumms, but all the rest were there—Harlaws from Harlaw, Blacktydes from Blacktyde, Sparrs, Merlyns, and Goodbrothers from Great Wyk, Saltcliffes and Sunderlies from Saltcliffe, and Botleys and Wynches from the other side of Pyke. The thralls were pouring ale, and there was music, fiddles and skins and drums. Three burly men were doing the finger dance, spinning short-hafted axes at each other. The trick was to catch the axe or leap over it without missing a step. It was called the finger dance because it usually ended when one of the dancers lost one . . . or two, or five.

Neither the dancers nor the drinkers took much note of Theon Greyjoy as he strode to the dais. Lord Balon occupied the Seastone Chair, carved in the shape of a great kraken from an immense block of oily black stone. Legend said that the First Men had found it standing on the shore of Old Wyk when they came to the Iron Islands. To the left of the high seat were Theon's uncles. Asha was ensconced at his right hand, in the place of honor. "You come late, Theon," Lord Balon observed.

"I ask your pardon." Theon took the empty seat beside Asha. Leaning close, he hissed in her ear, "You're in my place."

She turned to him with innocent eyes. "Brother, surely you are mistaken. Your place is at Winterfell." Her smile cut. "And where are all your pretty clothes? I heard you fancied silk and velvet against your skin." She was in soft green wool herself, simply cut, the fabric clinging to the slender lines of her body.

"Your hauberk must have rusted away, sister," he threw back. "A great pity. I'd like to see you all in iron."

Asha only laughed. "You may yet, little brother . . . if you think your *Sea Bitch* can keep up with my *Black Wind*." One of their father's thralls came near, bearing a flagon of wine. "Are you drinking ale or wine tonight, Theon?" She leaned over close. "Or is it still a taste of my mother's milk you thirst for?"

He flushed. "Wine," he told the thrall. Asha turned away and banged on the table, shouting for ale.

Theon hacked a loaf of bread in half, hollowed out a trencher, and summoned a cook to fill it with fish stew. The smell of the thick cream made him a little ill, but he forced himself to eat some. He'd drunk enough wine to float him through two meals. *If I retch, it will be on her.* "Does Father know that you've married his ship-wright?" he asked his sister.

"No more than Sigrin does." She gave a shrug. *"Esgred* was the first ship he built. He named her after his mother. I would be hard-pressed to say which he loves best."

"Every word you spoke to me was a lie."

"Not *every* word. Remember when I told you I like to be on top?" Asha grinned.

That only made him angrier. "All that about being a woman wed, and new with child . . ."

"Oh, that part was true enough." Asha leapt to her feet. *"Rolfe, here,"* she shouted down at one of the finger dancers, holding up a hand. He saw her, spun, and suddenly an axe came flying from his hand, the blade gleaming as it tumbled end over end through the torchlight. Theon had time for a choked gasp before Asha snatched the axe from the air and slammed it down into the table, splitting his trencher in two and splattering his mantle with drippings. "There's my lord husband." His sister reached down inside her gown and drew a dirk from between her breasts. "And here's my sweet suckling babe."

He could not imagine how he looked at that moment, but suddenly Theon Greyjoy realized that the Great Hall was ringing with laughter, all of it at him. Even his father was smiling, gods be damned, and his uncle Victarion chuckled aloud. The best response he could summon was a queasy grin. *We shall see who is laughing when all this is done, bitch.*

Asha wrenched the axe out of the table and flung it back down at the dancers, to whistles and loud cheers. "You'd do well to heed what I told you about choosing a crew." A thrall offered them a platter, and she stabbed a salted fish and ate it off the end of her dirk. "If you had troubled to learn the first thing of Sigrin, I could never have fooled you. Ten years a wolf, and you land here and think to prince about the islands, but you know nothing and no one. Why should men fight and die for you?"

"I am their lawful prince," Theon said stiffly.

"By the laws of the green lands, you might be. But we make our own laws here, or have you forgotten?"

Scowling, Theon turned to contemplate the leaking trencher before him. He would have stew in his lap before long. He shouted for a thrall to clean it up. *Half my life I have waited to come home, and for what? Mockery and disregard!* This was not the Pyke he remembered. Or *did* he remember? He had been so young when they took him away to hold hostage.

The feast was a meager enough thing, a succession of fish stews, black bread, and spiceless goat. The tastiest thing Theon found to eat was an onion pie. Ale and wine continued to flow well after the last of the courses had been cleared away.

Lord Balon Greyjoy rose from the Seastone Chair. "Have done with your drink and come to my solar," he commanded his companions on the dais. "We have plans to lay." He left them with no other word, flanked by two of his guards. His brothers followed in short order. Theon rose to go after them.

"My little brother is in a rush to be off." Asha raised her drinking horn and beckoned for more ale.

"Our lord father is waiting."

"And has, for many a year. It will do him no harm to wait a little longer . . . but if you fear his wrath, scurry after him by all means. You ought to have no trouble catching our uncles." She smiled. "One is drunk on seawater, after all, and the other is a great grey bullock so dim he'll probably get lost."

Theon sat back down, annoyed. "I run after no man."

"No man, but every woman?"

"It was not me who grabbed your cock."

"I don't have one, remember? You grabbed every other bit of me quick enough."

He could feel the flush creeping up his cheeks. "I'm a man with a man's hungers. What sort of unnatural creature are you?"

"Only a shy maid." Asha's hand darted out under the table to give his cock a squeeze. Theon nearly jumped from his chair. "What, don't you want me to steer you into port, brother?"

"Marriage is not for you," Theon decided. "When I rule, I believe I will pack you off to the silent sisters." He lurched to his feet and strode off unsteadily to find his father.

Rain was falling by the time he reached the swaying bridge out to the Sea Tower. His stomach was crashing and churning like the waves below, and wine had unsteadied his feet. Theon gritted his teeth and gripped the rope tightly as he made his way across, pretending that it was Asha's neck he was clutching.

The solar was as damp and drafty as ever. Buried under his sealskin robes, his father sat before the brazier with his brothers on either side of him. Victarion was talking of tides and winds when Theon entered, but Lord Balon waved him silent. "I have made my plans. It is time you heard them."

"I have some suggestions—"

"When I require your counsel I shall ask for it," his father said. "We have had a bird from Old Wyk. Dagmer is bringing the Drumms and Stonehouses. If the god grants us good winds, we will sail when they arrive . . . or *you* will. I mean for you to strike the first blow, Theon. You shall take eight longships north—"

"*Eight?*" His face reddened. "What can I hope to accomplish with only eight longships?"

"You are to harry the Stony Shore, raiding the fishing villages and sinking any ships you chance to meet. It may be that you will draw some of the northern lords out from behind their stone walls. Aeron will accompany you, and Dagmer Cleftjaw."

"May the Drowned God bless our swords," the priest said.

Theon felt as if he'd been slapped. He was being sent to do reaver's work, burning fishermen out of their hovels and raping their ugly daughters, and yet it seemed Lord Balon did not trust him sufficiently to do even that much. Bad enough to have to suffer the Damphair's scowls and chidings. With Dagmer Cleftjaw along as well, his command would be purely nominal.

"Asha my daughter," Lord Balon went on, and Theon turned to see that his sister had slipped in silently, "you shall take thirty longships of picked men round Sea Dragon Point. Land upon the tidal flats north of Deepwood Motte. March quickly, and the castle may fall before they even know you are upon them."

Asha smiled like a cat in cream. "I've always wanted a castle," she said sweetly.

"Then take one."

Theon had to bite his tongue. Deepwood Motte was the stronghold of the Glovers. With both Robett and Galbart warring in the south, it would be lightly held, and once the castle fell the ironmen would have a secure base in the heart of the north. *I should be the one sent to take Deepwood.* He *knew* Deepwood Motte, he had visited the Glovers several times with Eddard Stark.

"Victarion," Lord Balon said to his brother, "the main thrust shall fall to you. When my sons have struck their blows, Winterfell must respond. You should meet small opposition as you sail up Saltspear and the Fever River. At the headwaters, you will be less than twenty miles from Moat Cailin. The Neck is the key to the kingdom. Already we command the western seas. Once we hold Moat Cailin, the pup will not be able to win back to the north . . . and if he is fool enough to try, his enemies will seal the south end of the causeway behind him, and Robb the boy will find himself caught like a rat in a bottle."

Theon could keep silent no longer. "A bold plan, Father, but the lords in their castles—"

Lord Balon rode over him. "The lords are gone south with the pup. Those who remained behind are the cravens, old men, and green boys. They will yield or fall, one by one. Winterfell may defy us for a year, but what of it? The rest shall be ours, forest and field and hall, and we shall make the folk our thralls and salt wives."

Aeron Damphair raised his arms. "And the waters of

wrath will rise high, and the Drowned God will spread his dominion across the green lands!"

"What is dead can never die," Victarion intoned. Lord Balon and Asha echoed his words, and Theon had no choice but to mumble along with them. And then it was done.

Outside the rain was falling harder than ever. The rope bridge twisted and writhed under his feet. Theon Greyjoy stopped in the center of the span and contemplated the rocks below. The sound of the waves was a crashing roar, and he could taste the salt spray on his lips. A sudden gust of wind made him lose his footing, and he stumbled to his knees.

Asha helped him rise. "You can't hold your wine either, brother."

Theon leaned on her shoulder and let her guide him across the rain-slick boards. "I liked you better when you were Esgred," he told her accusingly.

She laughed. "That's fair. I liked *you* better when you were nine."

TYRION

Through the door came the soft sound of the high harp, mingled with a trilling of pipes. The singer's voice was muffled by the thick walls, yet Tyrion knew the verse. *I loved a maid as fair as summer*, he remembered, *with sunlight in her hair . . .*

Ser Meryn Trant guarded the queen's door this night. His muttered "My lord" struck Tyrion as a tad grudging, but he opened the door nonetheless. The song broke off abruptly as he strode into his sister's bedchamber.

Cersei was reclining on a pile of cushions. Her feet were bare, her golden hair artfully tousled, her robe a green-and-gold samite that caught the light of the candles and shimmered as she looked up. "Sweet sister," Tyrion said, "how beautiful you look tonight." He turned to the singer. "And you as well, cousin. I had no notion you had such a lovely voice."

The compliment made Ser Lancel sulky; perhaps he thought he was being mocked. It seemed to Tyrion that the lad had grown three inches since being knighted. Lancel had thick sandy hair, green Lannister eyes, and a line of soft blond fuzz on his upper lip. At sixteen, he was cursed with all the certainty of youth, unleavened by any trace of humor or self-doubt, and wed to the arrogance that came so naturally to those born blond and strong and handsome. His recent elevation had only made him worse. "Did Her Grace send for you?" the boy demanded.

"Not that I recall," Tyrion admitted. "It grieves me to disturb your revels, Lancel, but as it happens, I have matters of import to discuss with my sister."

Cersei regarded him suspiciously. "If you are here about those begging brothers, Tyrion, spare me your reproaches. I won't have them spreading their filthy treasons in the streets. They can preach to each other in the dungeons."

"And count themselves lucky that they have such a gentle queen," added Lancel. "I would have had their tongues out."

"One even dared to say that the gods were punishing us because Jaime murdered the rightful king," Cersei declared. "It will not be borne, Tyrion. I gave you ample opportunity to deal with these lice, but you and your Ser Jacelyn did nothing, so I commanded Vylarr to attend to the matter."

"And so he did." Tyrion *had* been annoyed when the red cloaks had dragged a half dozen of the scabrous prophets down to the dungeons without consulting him, but they were not important enough to battle over. "No doubt we will all be better off for a little quiet in the streets. That is not why I came. I have tidings I know you will be anxious to hear, sweet sister, but they are best spoken of privily."

"Very well." The harpist and the piper bowed and hurried out, while Cersei kissed her cousin chastely on the cheek. "Leave us, Lancel. My brother's harmless when he's alone. If he'd brought his pets, we'd smell them."

The young knight gave his cousin a baleful glance and pulled the door shut forcefully behind him. "I'll have you know I make Shagga bathe once a fortnight," Tyrion said when he was gone.

"You're very pleased with yourself, aren't you? Why?"

"Why not?" Tyrion said. Every day, every night, hammers rang along the Street of Steel, and the great chain grew longer. He hopped up onto the great canopied bed. "Is this the bed where Robert died? I'm surprised you kept it."

"It gives me sweet dreams," she said. "Now spit out your business and waddle away, Imp."

Tyrion smiled. "Lord Stannis has sailed from Dragonstone."

Cersei bolted to her feet. "And yet you sit there grinning like a harvest-day pumpkin? Has Bywater called out the City Watch? We must send a bird to Harrenhal at once." He was laughing by then. She seized him by the shoulders and shook him. "Stop it. Are you mad, or drunk? *Stop it!*"

It was all he could do to get out the words. "I can't," he gasped. "It's too . . . gods, too funny . . . Stannis . . ."

"What?"

"He hasn't sailed against us," Tyrion managed. "He's laid siege to Storm's End. Renly is riding to meet him."

His sister's nails dug painfully into his arms. For a moment she stared incredulous, as if he had begun to gibber in an unknown tongue. "Stannis and Renly are fighting *each other?*" When he nodded, Cersei began to chuckle. "Gods be good," she gasped, "I'm starting to believe that Robert was the *clever* one."

Tyrion threw back his head and roared. They laughed together. Cersei pulled him off the bed and whirled him around and even hugged him, for a moment as giddy as a girl. By the time she let go of him, Tyrion was breathless and dizzy. He staggered to her sideboard and put out a hand to steady himself.

"Do you think it will truly come to battle between them? If they should come to some accord—"

"They won't," Tyrion said. "They are too different

and yet too much alike, and neither could ever stomach the other."

"And Stannis has always felt he was cheated of Storm's End," Cersei said thoughtfully. "The ancestral seat of House Baratheon, his by rights . . . if you knew how many times he came to Robert singing that same dull song in that gloomy aggrieved tone he has. When Robert gave the place to Renly, Stannis clenched his jaw so tight I thought his teeth would shatter."

"He took it as a slight."

"It was meant as a slight," Cersei said.

"Shall we raise a cup to brotherly love?"

"Yes," she answered, breathless. "Oh, gods, yes."

His back was to her as he filled two cups with sweet Arbor red. It was the easiest thing in the world to sprinkle a pinch of fine powder into hers. "To Stannis!" he said as he handed her the wine. *Harmless when I'm alone, am I?*

"To Renly!" she replied, laughing. "May they battle long and hard, and the Others take them both!"

Is this the Cersei that Jaime sees? When she smiled, you saw how beautiful she was, truly. *I loved a maid as fair as summer, with sunlight in her hair.* He almost felt sorry for poisoning her.

It was the next morning as he broke his fast that her messenger arrived. The queen was indisposed and would not be able to leave her chambers. *Not able to leave her privy, more like.* Tyrion made the proper sympathetic noises and sent word to Cersei to rest easy, he would treat with Ser Cleos as they'd planned.

The Iron Throne of Aegon the Conqueror was a tangle of nasty barbs and jagged metal teeth waiting for any fool who tried to sit too comfortably, and the steps made his stunted legs cramp as he climbed up to it, all too aware of what an absurd spectacle he must be. Yet there was one thing to be said for it. It was *high.*

Lannister guardsmen stood silent in their crimson cloaks and lion-crested halfhelms. Ser Jacelyn's gold cloaks faced them across the hall. The steps to the throne were flanked by Bronn and Ser Preston of the

Kingsguard. Courtiers filled the gallery while supplicants clustered near the towering oak-and-bronze doors.
Sansa Stark looked especially lovely this morning,
though her face was as pale as milk. Lord Gyles stood
coughing, while poor cousin Tyrek wore his bridegroom's mantle of miniver and velvet. Since his marriage to little Lady Ermesande three days past, the other
squires had taken to calling him "Wet Nurse" and asking him what sort of swaddling clothes his bride wore
on their wedding night.

Tyrion looked down on them all, and found he liked
it. "Call forth Ser Cleos Frey." His voice rang off the
stone walls and down the length of the hall. He liked
that too. *A pity Shae could not be here to see this,* he
reflected. She'd asked to come, but it was impossible.

Ser Cleos made the long walk between the gold
cloaks and the crimson, looking neither right nor left.
As he knelt, Tyrion observed that his cousin was losing
his hair.

"Ser Cleos," Littlefinger said from the council table,
"you have our thanks for bringing us this peace offer
from Lord Stark."

Grand Maester Pycelle cleared his throat. "The
Queen Regent, the King's Hand, and the small council
have considered the terms offered by this self-styled
King in the North. Sad to say, they will not do, and you
must tell these northmen so, ser."

"Here are *our* terms," said Tyrion. "Robb Stark must
lay down his sword, swear fealty, and return to
Winterfell. He must free my brother unharmed, and
place his host under Jaime's command, to march
against the rebels Renly and Stannis Baratheon. Each of
Stark's bannermen must send us a son as hostage. A
daughter will suffice where there is no son. They shall
be treated gently and given high places here at court, so
long as their fathers commit no new treasons."

Cleos Frey looked ill. "My lord Hand," he said, "Lord
Stark will never consent to these terms."

We never expected he would, Cleos. "Tell him that
we have raised another great host at Casterly Rock, that

soon it will march on him from the west while my lord father advances from the east. Tell him that he stands alone, without hope of allies. Stannis and Renly Baratheon war against each other, and the Prince of Dorne has consented to wed his son Trystane to the Princess Myrcella." Murmurs of delight and consternation alike arose from the gallery and the back of the hall.

"As to this of my cousins," Tyrion went on, "we offer Harrion Karstark and Ser Wylis Manderly for Willem Lannister, and Lord Cerwyn and Ser Donnel Locke for your brother Tion. Tell Stark that two Lannisters are worth four northmen in any season." He waited for the laughter to die. "His father's bones he shall have, as a gesture of Joffrey's good faith."

"Lord Stark asked for his sisters and his father's sword as well," Ser Cleos reminded him.

Ser Ilyn Payne stood mute, the hilt of Eddard Stark's greatsword rising over one shoulder. "Ice," said Tyrion. "He'll have that when he makes his peace with us, not before."

"As you say. And his sisters?"

Tyrion glanced toward Sansa, and felt a stab of pity as he said, "Until such time as he frees my brother Jaime, unharmed, they shall remain here as hostages. How well they are treated depends on him." *And if the gods are good, Bywater will find Arya alive, before Robb learns she's gone missing.*

"I shall bring him your message, my lord."

Tyrion plucked at one of the twisted blades that sprang from the arm of the throne. *And now the thrust.* "Vylarr," he called.

"My lord."

"The men Stark sent are sufficient to protect Lord Eddard's bones, but a Lannister should have a Lannister escort," Tyrion declared. "Ser Cleos is the queen's cousin, and mine. We shall sleep more easily if you would see him safely back to Riverrun."

"As you command. How many men should I take?"

"Why, all of them."

Vylarr stood like a man made of stone. It was Grand Maester Pycelle who rose, gasping, "My lord Hand, that cannot . . . your father, Lord Tywin himself, he sent these good men to our city to protect Queen Cersei and her children . . ."

"The Kingsguard and the City Watch protect them well enough. The gods speed you on your way, Vylarr."

At the council table Varys smiled knowingly, Littlefinger sat feigning boredom, and Pycelle gaped like a fish, pale and confused. A herald stepped forward. "If any man has other matters to set before the King's Hand, let him speak now or go forth and hold his silence."

"*I* will be heard." A slender man all in black pushed his way between the Redwyne twins.

"Ser *Alliser!*" Tyrion exclaimed. "Why, I had no notion that you'd come to court. You should have sent me word."

"I have, as well you know." Thorne was as prickly as his name, a spare, sharp-featured man of fifty, hard-eyed and hard-handed, his black hair streaked with grey. "I have been shunned, ignored, and left to wait like some baseborn servant."

"Truly? Bronn, this was not well done. Ser Alliser and I are old friends. We walked the Wall together."

"Sweet Ser Alliser," murmured Varys, "you must not think too harshly of us. So many seek our Joffrey's grace, in these troubled and tumultuous times."

"More troubled than you know, eunuch."

"To his face we call him *Lord* Eunuch," quipped Littlefinger.

"How may we be of help to you, good brother?" Grand Maester Pycelle asked in soothing tones.

"The Lord Commander sent me to His Grace the king," Thorne answered. "The matter is too grave to be left to servants."

"The king is playing with his new crossbow," Tyrion said. Ridding himself of Joffrey had required only an ungainly Myrish crossbow that threw three quarrels at a time, and nothing would do but that he try it at once. "You can speak to servants or hold your silence."

"As you will," Ser Alliser said, displeasure in every word. "I am sent to tell you that we found two rangers, long missing. They were dead, yet when we brought the corpses back to the Wall they rose again in the night. One slew Ser Jaremy Rykker, while the second tried to murder the Lord Commander."

Distantly, Tyrion heard someone snigger. *Does he mean to mock me with this folly?* He shifted uneasily and glanced down at Varys, Littlefinger, and Pycelle, wondering if one of them had a role in this. A dwarf enjoyed at best a tenuous hold on dignity. Once the court and kingdom started to laugh at him, he was doomed. And yet . . . and yet . . .

Tyrion remembered a cold night under the stars when he'd stood beside the boy Jon Snow and a great white wolf atop the Wall at the end of the world, gazing out at the trackless dark beyond. He had felt—what?—*something,* to be sure, a dread that had cut like that frigid northern wind. A wolf had howled off in the night, and the sound had sent a shiver through him.

Don't be a fool, he told himself. *A wolf, a wind, a dark forest, it meant nothing. And yet . . .* He had come to have a liking for old Jeor Mormont during his time at Castle Black. "I trust that the Old Bear survived this attack?"

"He did."

"And that your brothers killed these, ah, dead men?"

"We did."

"You're certain that they are dead this time?" Tyrion asked mildly. When Bronn choked on a snort of laughter, he knew how he must proceed. "Truly truly dead?"

"They were dead the first time," Ser Alliser snapped. "Pale and cold, with black hands and feet. I brought Jared's hand, torn from his corpse by the bastard's wolf."

Littlefinger stirred. "And where is this charming token?"

Ser Alliser frowned uncomfortably. "It . . . rotted to

pieces while I waited, unheard. There's naught left to show but bones."

Titters echoed through the hall. "Lord Baelish," Tyrion called down to Littlefinger, "buy our brave Ser Alliser a hundred spades to take back to the Wall with him."

"Spades?" Ser Alliser narrowed his eyes suspiciously.

"If you *bury* your dead, they won't come walking," Tyrion told him, and the court laughed openly. "Spades will end your troubles, with some strong backs to wield them. Ser Jacelyn, see that the good brother has his pick of the city dungeons."

Ser Jacelyn Bywater said, "As you will, my lord, but the cells are near empty. Yoren took all the likely men."

"Arrest some more, then," Tyrion told him. "Or spread the word that there's bread and turnips on the Wall, and they'll go of their own accord." The city had too many mouths to feed, and the Night's Watch a perpetual need of men. At Tyrion's signal, the herald cried an end, and the hall began to empty.

Ser Alliser Thorne was not so easily dismissed. He was waiting at the foot of the Iron Throne when Tyrion descended. "Do you think I sailed all the way from Eastwatch-by-the-Sea to be mocked by the likes of you?" he fumed, blocking the way. "This is no jape. I saw it with my own eyes. I tell you, the dead walk."

"You should try to kill them more thoroughly." Tyrion pushed past. Ser Alliser made to grab his sleeve, but Preston Greenfield thrust him back. "No closer, ser."

Thorne knew better than to challenge a knight of the Kingsguard. "You are a fool, Imp," he shouted at Tyrion's back.

The dwarf turned to face him. "Me? Truly? Then why were they laughing at you, I wonder?" He smiled wanly. "You came for men, did you not?"

"The cold winds are rising. The Wall must be held."

"And to hold it you need men, which I've given you . . . as you might have noted, if your ears heard anything but insults. Take them, thank me, and begone before I'm forced to take a crab fork to you again. Give my warm regards to Lord Mormont . . . and to Jon Snow as well." Bronn seized Ser Alliser by the elbow and marched him forcefully from the hall.

Grand Maester Pycelle had already scuttled off, but Varys and Littlefinger had watched it all, start to finish. "I grow ever more admiring of you, my lord," confessed the eunuch. "You appease the Stark boy with his father's bones and strip your sister of her protectors in one swift stroke. You give that black brother the men he seeks, rid the city of some hungry mouths, yet make it all seem mockery so none may say that the dwarf fears snarks and grumkins. Oh, deftly done."

Littlefinger stroked his beard. "Do you truly mean to send away all your guards, Lannister?"

"No, I mean to send away all my *sister's* guards."

"The queen will never allow that."

"Oh, I think she may. I *am* her brother, and when you've known me longer, you'll learn that I mean everything I say."

"Even the lies?"

"*Especially* the lies. Lord Petyr, I sense that you are unhappy with me."

"I love you as much as I ever have, my lord. Though I do not relish being played for a fool. If Myrcella weds Trystane Martell, she can scarcely wed Robert Arryn, can she?"

"Not without causing a great scandal," he admitted. "I regret my little ruse, Lord Petyr, but when we spoke, I could not know the Dornishmen would accept my offer."

Littlefinger was not appeased. "I do not like being lied to, my lord. Leave me out of your next deception."

Only if you'll do the same for me, Tyrion thought, glancing at the dagger sheathed at Littlefinger's hip. "If I have given offense, I am deeply sorry. All men know how much we love you, my lord. And how much we need you."

"Try and remember that." With that Littlefinger left them.

"Walk with me, Varys," said Tyrion. They left through the king's door behind the throne, the eunuch's slippers whisking lightly over the stone.

"Lord Baelish has the truth of it, you know. The queen will never permit you to send away her guard."

"She will. You'll see to that."

A smile flickered across Varys's plump lips. "Will I?"

"Oh, for a certainty. You'll tell her it is part of my scheme to free Jaime."

Varys stroked a powdered cheek. "This would doubtless involve the four men your man Bronn searched for so diligently in all the low places of King's Landing. A thief, a poisoner, a mummer, and a murderer."

"Put them in crimson cloaks and lion helms, they'll look no different from any other guardsmen. I searched for some time for a ruse that might get them into Riverrun before I thought to hide them in plain sight. They'll ride in by the main gate, flying Lannister banners and escorting Lord Eddard's bones." He smiled crookedly. "Four men alone would be watched vigilantly. Four among a hundred can lose themselves. So I must send the true guardsmen as well as the false . . . as you'll tell my sister."

"And for the sake of her beloved brother, she will consent, despite her misgivings." They made their way down a deserted colonnade. "Still, the loss of her red cloaks will surely make her uneasy."

"I like her uneasy," said Tyrion.

Ser Cleos Frey left that very afternoon, escorted by Vylarr and a hundred red-cloaked Lannister guardsmen. The men Robb Stark had sent joined them at the King's Gate for the long ride west.

Tyrion found Timett dicing with his Burned Men in the barracks. "Come to my solar at midnight." Timett gave him a hard one-eyed stare, a curt nod. He was not one for long speeches.

That night he feasted with the Stone Crows and Moon Brothers in the Small Hall, though he shunned the wine for once. He wanted all his wits about him. "Shagga, what moon is this?"

Shagga's frown was a fierce thing. "Black, I think."

"In the west, they call that a traitor's moon. Try not to get too drunk tonight, and see that your axe is sharp."

"A Stone Crow's axe is always sharp, and Shagga's axes are sharpest of all. Once I cut off a man's head, but he did not know it until he tried to brush his hair. Then it fell off."

"Is that why you never brush yours?" The Stone Crows roared and stamped their feet, Shagga hooting loudest of all.

By midnight, the castle was silent and dark. Doubtless a few gold cloaks on the walls spied them leaving the Tower of the Hand, but no one raised a voice. He was the Hand of the King, and where he went was his own affair.

The thin wooden door split with a thunderous *crack* beneath the heel of Shagga's boot. Pieces went flying inward, and Tyrion heard a woman's gasp of fear. Shagga hacked the door apart with three great blows of his axe and kicked his way through the ruins. Timett followed, and then Tyrion, stepping gingerly over the splinters. The fire had burned down to a few glowing embers, and shadows lay thick across the bedchamber. When Timett ripped the heavy curtains off the bed, the naked serving girl stared up with wide white eyes. "Please, my lords," she pleaded, "don't hurt me." She cringed away from Shagga, flushed and fearful, trying to cover her charms with her hands and coming up a hand short.

"Go," Tyrion told her. "It's not you we want."

"Shagga wants this woman."

"Shagga wants every whore in this city of whores," complained Timett son of Timett.

"Yes," Shagga said, unabashed. "Shagga would give her a strong child."

"If she wants a strong child, she'll know whom to seek," Tyrion said. "Timett, see her out . . . gently, if you would."

The Burned Man pulled the girl from the bed and half marched, half dragged her across the chamber. Shagga

watched them go, mournful as a puppy. The girl stumbled over the shattered door and out into the hall,
helped along by a firm shove from Timett. Above their
heads, the ravens were screeching.

Tyrion dragged the soft blanket off the bed, uncover-
ing Grand Maester Pycelle beneath. "Tell me, does the
Citadel approve of you bedding the serving wenches,
Maester?"

The old man was as naked as the girl, though he made
a markedly less attractive sight. For once, his heavy-
lidded eyes were open wide. "W-what is the meaning of
this? I am an old man, your loyal servant . . ."

Tyrion hoisted himself onto the bed. "So loyal that
you sent only one of my letters to Doran Martell. The
other you gave to my sister."

"N-no," squealed Pycelle. "No, a falsehood, I swear
it, it was not me. Varys, it was Varys, the Spider, I
warned you—"

"Do all maesters lie so poorly? I told Varys that I was
giving Prince Doran my nephew Tommen to foster. I
told Littlefinger that I planned to wed Myrcella to Lord
Robert of the Eyrie. I told no one that I had offered
Myrcella to the Dornish . . . that truth was only in the
letter I entrusted to *you*."

Pycelle clutched for a corner of the blanket. "Birds are
lost, messages stolen or sold . . . it was Varys, there
are things I might tell you of that eunuch that would
chill your blood . . ."

"My lady prefers my blood hot."

"Make no mistake, for every secret the eunuch whispers in your ear, he holds seven back. And Littlefinger,
that one . . ."

"I know all about Lord Petyr. He's almost as untrustworthy as you. Shagga, cut off his manhood and feed it
to the goats."

Shagga hefted the huge double-bladed axe. "There are
no goats, Halfman."

"Make do."

Roaring, Shagga leapt forward. Pycelle shrieked and
wet the bed, urine spraying in all directions as he tried

to scramble back out of reach. The wildling caught him by the end of his billowy white beard and hacked off three-quarters of it with a single slash of the axe.

"Timett, do you suppose our friend will be more forthcoming without those whiskers to hide behind?" Tyrion used a bit of the sheet to wipe the piss off his boots.

"He will tell the truth soon." Darkness pooled in the empty pit of Timett's burned eye. "I can smell the stink of his fear."

Shagga tossed a handful of hair down to the rushes, and seized what beard was left. "Hold still, Maester," urged Tyrion. "When Shagga gets angry, his hands shake."

"Shagga's hands never shake," the huge man said indignantly, pressing the great crescent blade under Pycelle's quivering chin and sawing through another tangle of beard.

"How long have you been spying for my sister?" Tyrion asked.

Pycelle's breathing was rapid and shallow. "All I did, I did for House Lannister." A sheen of sweat covered the broad dome of the old man's brow, and wisps of white hair clung to his wrinkled skin. "Always . . . for years . . . your lord father, ask him, I was ever his true servant . . . 'twas I who bid Aerys open his gates . . ."

That took Tyrion by surprise. He had been no more than an ugly boy at Casterly Rock when the city fell. "So the Sack of King's Landing was your work as well?"

"For the realm! Once Rhaegar died, the war was done. Aerys was mad, Viserys too young, Prince Aegon a babe at the breast, but the realm needed a king . . . I prayed it should be your good father, but Robert was too strong, and Lord Stark moved too swiftly . . ."

"How many have you betrayed, I wonder? Aerys, Eddard Stark, me . . . King Robert as well? Lord Arryn, Prince Rhaegar? Where does it begin, Pycelle?" He *knew* where it ended.

The axe scratched at the apple of Pycelle's throat and stroked the soft wobbly skin under his jaw, scraping away the last hairs. "You . . . were not here," he gasped when the blade moved upward to his cheeks. "Robert . . . his wounds . . . if you had seen them, smelled them, you would have no doubt . . ."

"Oh, I know the boar did your work for you . . . but if he'd left the job half done, doubtless you would have finished it."

"He was a wretched king . . . vain, drunken, lecherous . . . he would have set your sister aside, his own queen . . . please . . . Renly was plotting to bring the Highgarden maid to court, to entice his brother . . . it is the gods' own truth . . ."

"And what was Lord Arryn plotting?"

"He *knew*," Pycelle said. "About . . . about . . ."

"I know what he knew about," snapped Tyrion, who was not anxious for Shagga and Timett to know as well.

"He was sending his wife back to the Eyrie, and his son to be fostered on Dragonstone . . . he meant to act . . ."

"So you poisoned him first."

"No." Pycelle struggled feebly. Shagga growled and grabbed his head. The clansman's hand was so big he could have crushed the maester's skull like an eggshell had he squeezed.

Tyrion *tsked* at him. "I saw the tears of Lys among your potions. And you sent away Lord Arryn's own maester and tended him yourself, so you could make certain that he died."

"A falsehood!"

"Shave him closer," Tyrion suggested. "The throat again."

The axe swept back down, rasping over the skin. A thin film of spit bubbled on Pycelle's lips as his mouth trembled. "I tried to save Lord Arryn. I vow—"

"Careful now, Shagga, you've cut him."

Shagga growled. "Dolf fathered warriors, not barbers."

When he felt the blood trickling down his neck and onto his chest, the old man shuddered, and the last strength went out of him. He looked shrunken, both smaller and frailer than he had been when they burst in on him. "Yes," he whimpered, "*yes,* Colemon was purging, so I sent him away. The queen needed Lord Arryn dead, she did not say so, could not, Varys was listening, always listening, but when I looked at her I knew. It was not me who gave him the poison, though, I swear it." The old man wept. "Varys will tell you, it was the boy, his squire, Hugh he was called, he must surely have done it, ask your sister, ask her."

Tyrion was disgusted. "Bind him and take him away," he commanded. "Throw him down in one of the black cells."

They dragged him out the splintered door. "Lannister," he moaned, "all I've done has been for Lannister . . ."

When he was gone, Tyrion made a leisurely search of the quarters and collected a few more small jars from his shelves. The ravens muttered above his head as he worked, a strangely peaceful noise. He would need to find someone to tend the birds until the Citadel sent a man to replace Pycelle.

He was the one I'd hoped to trust. Varys and Littlefinger were no more loyal, he suspected . . . only more subtle, and thus more dangerous. Perhaps his father's way would have been best: summon Ilyn Payne, mount three heads above the gates, and have done. *And wouldn't that be a pretty sight,* he thought.

ARYA

Fear cuts deeper than swords, Arya would tell herself, but that did not make the fear go away. It was as much a part of her days as stale bread and the blisters on her toes after a long day of walking the hard, rutted road.

She had thought she had known what it meant to be afraid, but she learned better in that storehouse beside the Gods Eye. Eight days she had lingered there before the Mountain gave the command to march, and every day she had seen someone die.

The Mountain would come into the storehouse after he had broken his fast and pick one of the prisoners for questioning. The village folk would never look at him. Maybe they thought that if they did not notice him, he would not notice them . . . but he saw them anyway and picked whom he liked. There was no place to hide, no tricks to play, no way to be safe.

One girl shared a soldier's bed three nights running; the Mountain picked her on the fourth day, and the soldier said nothing.

A smiley old man mended their clothing and babbled about his son, off serving in the gold cloaks at King's Landing. "A king's man, he is," he would say, "a good king's man like me, all for Joffrey." He said it so often the other captives began to call him All-for-Joffrey whenever the guards weren't listening. All-for-Joffrey was picked on the fifth day.

A young mother with a pox-scarred face offered to freely tell them all she knew if they'd promise not to hurt her daughter. The Mountain heard her out; the next morning he picked her daughter, to be certain she'd held nothing back.

The ones chosen were questioned in full view of the other captives, so they could see the fate of rebels and traitors. A man the others called the Tickler asked the questions. His face was so ordinary and his garb so plain that Arya might have thought him one of the villagers before she had seen him at his work. "Tickler makes them howl so hard they piss themselves," old stoop-shoulder Chiswyck told them. He was the man she'd tried to bite, who'd called her a fierce little thing and smashed her head with a mailed fist. Sometimes he helped the Tickler. Sometimes others did that. Ser Gregor Clegane himself would stand motionless, watching and listening, until the victim died.

The questions were always the same. Was there gold hidden in the village? Silver, gems? Was there more food? Where was Lord Beric Dondarrion? Which of the village folk had aided him? When he rode off, where did he go? How many men were with them? How many knights, how many bowmen, how many men-at-arms? How were they armed? How many were horsed? How many were wounded? What other enemy had they seen? How many? When? What banners did they fly? Where did they go? Was there gold hidden in the village? Silver, gems? Where was Lord Beric Dondarrion? How many men were with him? By the third day, Arya could have asked the questions herself.

They found a little gold, a little silver, a great sack of copper pennies, and a dented goblet set with garnets that two soldiers almost came to blows over. They learned that Lord Beric had ten starvelings with him, or else a hundred mounted knights; that he had ridden west, or north, or south; that he had crossed the lake in a boat; that he was strong as an aurochs or weak from the bloody flux. No one ever survived the Tickler's questioning; no man, no woman, no child. The strongest lasted past evenfall. Their bodies were hung beyond the fires for the wolves.

By the time they marched, Arya knew she was no water dancer. Syrio Forel would never have let them knock him down and take his sword away, nor stood by when they killed Lommy Greenhands. Syrio would never have sat silent in that storehouse nor shuffled along meekly among the other captives. The direwolf was the sigil of the Starks, but Arya felt more a lamb, surrounded by a herd of other sheep. She hated the villagers for their sheepishness, almost as much as she hated herself.

The Lannisters had taken everything: father, friends, home, hope, courage. One had taken Needle, while another had broken her wooden stick sword over his knee. They had even taken her stupid secret. The storehouse had been big enough for her to creep off and make her water in some corner when no one was looking, but it was different on the road. She held it as long as she could, but finally she had to squat by a bush and skin down her breeches in front of all of them. It was that or wet herself. Hot Pie gaped at her with big moon eyes, but no one else even troubled to look. Girl sheep or boy sheep, Ser Gregor and his men did not seem to care.

Their captors permitted no chatter. A broken lip taught Arya to hold her tongue. Others never learned at all. One boy of three would not stop calling for his father, so they smashed his face in with a spiked mace. Then the boy's mother started screaming and Raff the Sweetling killed her as well.

Arya watched them die and did nothing. What good did it do you to be brave? One of the women picked for questioning had tried to be brave, but she had died screaming like all the rest. There were no brave people on that march, only scared and hungry ones. Most were women and children. The few men were very old or very young; the rest had been chained to that gibbet and left for the wolves and the crows. Gendry was only spared because he'd admitted to forging the horned helm himself; smiths, even apprentice smiths, were too valuable to kill.

They were being taken to serve Lord Tywin Lannister at Harrenhal, the Mountain told them. "You're traitors and rebels, so thank your gods that Lord Tywin's giving you this chance. It's more than you'd get from the outlaws. Obey, serve, and live."

"It's not just, it's not," she heard one wizened old woman complain to another when they had bedded down for the night. "We never did no treason, the others come in and took what they wanted, same as this bunch."

"Lord Beric did us no hurt, though," her friend whispered. "And that red priest with him, he paid for all they took."

"Paid? He took two of my chickens and gave me a bit of paper with a mark on it. Can I eat a bit of raggy old paper, I ask you? Will it give me eggs?" She looked about to see that no guards were near, and spat three times. "There's for the Tullys and there's for the Lannisters and there's for the Starks."

"It's a sin and a shame," an old man hissed. "When the old king was still alive, he'd not have stood for this."

"King Robert?" Arya asked, forgetting herself.

"King *Aerys*, gods grace him," the old man said, too loudly. A guard came sauntering over to shut them up. The old man lost both his teeth, and there was no more talk that night.

Besides his captives, Ser Gregor was bringing back a dozen pigs, a cage of chickens, a scrawny milk cow, and nine wagons of salt fish. The Mountain and his men had horses, but the captives were all afoot, and those too weak to keep up were killed out of hand, along with anyone foolish enough to flee. The guards took women off into the bushes at night, and most seemed to expect it and went along meekly enough. One girl, prettier than the others, was made to go with four or five different men every night, until finally she hit one with a rock. Ser Gregor made everyone watch while he took off her head with a sweep of his massive two-handed greatsword. "Leave the body for the wolves," he commanded when the deed was done, handing the sword to his squire to be cleaned.

Arya glanced sidelong at Needle, sheathed at the hip of a black-bearded, balding man-at-arms called Polliver. *It's good that they took it away,* she thought. Otherwise she would have tried to stab Ser Gregor, and he would have cut her right in half, and the wolves would eat her too.

Polliver was not so bad as some of the others, even though he'd stolen Needle. The night she was caught, the Lannister men had been nameless strangers with faces as alike as their nasal helms, but she'd come to know them all. You had to know who was lazy and who was cruel, who was smart and who was stupid. You had to learn that even though the one they called Shitmouth had the foulest tongue she'd ever heard, he'd give you an extra piece of bread if you asked, while jolly old Chiswyck and soft-spoken Raff would just give you the back of their hand.

Arya watched and listened and polished her hates the way Gendry had once polished his horned helm. Dunsen wore those bull's horns now, and she hated him for it. She hated Polliver for Needle, and she hated old Chiswyck who thought he was funny. And Raff the Sweetling, who'd driven his spear through Lommy's throat, she hated even more. She hated Ser Amory Lorch for Yoren, and she hated Ser Meryn Trant for Syrio, the Hound for killing the butcher's boy Mycah, and Ser Ilyn and Prince Joffrey and the queen for the sake of her father and Fat Tom and Desmond and the rest, and even for Lady, Sansa's wolf. The Tickler was almost too scary to hate. At times she could almost forget he was still with them; when he was not asking questions, he was just another soldier, quieter than most, with a face like a thousand other men.

Every night Arya would say their names. "Ser Gregor," she'd whisper to her stone pillow. "Dunsen, Polliver, Chiswyck, Raff the Sweetling. The Tickler and the Hound. Ser Amory, Ser Ilyn, Ser Meryn, King Joffrey, Queen Cersei." Back in Winterfell, Arya had prayed with her mother in the sept and with her father in the godswood, but there were no gods on the road to Harrenhal, and her names were the only prayer she cared to remember.

Every day they marched, and every night she said her names, until finally the trees thinned and gave way to a patchwork landscape of rolling hills, meandering streams, and sunlit fields, where the husks of burnt holdfasts thrust up black as rotten teeth. It was another long day's march before they glimpsed the towers of Harrenhal in the distance, hard beside the blue waters of the lake.

It would be better once they got to Harrenhal, the captives told each other, but Arya was not so certain. She remembered Old Nan's stories of the castle built on fear. Harren the Black had mixed human blood in the mortar, Nan used to say, dropping her voice so the children would need to lean close to hear, but Aegon's dragons had roasted Harren and all his sons within their great walls of stone. Arya chewed her lip as she walked along on feet grown hard with callus. It would not be much longer, she told herself; those towers could not be more than a few miles off.

Yet they walked all that day and most of the next before at last they reached the fringes of Lord Tywin's army, encamped west of the castle amidst the scorched remains of a town. Harrenhal was deceptive from afar, because it was so *huge.* Its colossal curtain walls rose beside the lake, sheer and sudden as mountain cliffs, while atop their battlements the rows of wood-and-iron scorpions looked as small as the bugs for which they were named.

The stink of the Lannister host reached Arya well before she could make out the devices on the banners that sprouted along the lakeshore, atop the pavilions of the westermen. From the smell, Arya could tell that Lord Tywin had been here some time. The latrines that ringed the encampment were overflowing and swarming with flies, and she saw faint greenish fuzz on many of the sharpened stakes that protected the perimeters.

Harrenhal's gatehouse, itself as large as Winterfell's Great Keep, was as scarred as it was massive, its stones fissured and discolored. From outside, only the tops of five immense towers could be seen beyond the walls. The shortest of them was half again as tall as the highest tower in Winterfell, but they did not soar the way a proper tower did. Arya thought they looked like some old man's gnarled, knuckly fingers groping after a passing cloud. She remembered Nan telling how the stone had melted and flowed like candlewax down the steps and in the windows, glowing a sullen searing red as it sought out Harren where he hid. Arya could believe every word; each tower was more grotesque and misshapen than the last, lumpy and runneled and cracked.

"I don't want to go there," Hot Pie squeaked as Harrenhal opened its gates to them. "There's ghosts in there."

Chiswyck heard him, but for once he only smiled. "Baker boy, here's your choice. Come join the ghosts, or be one."

Hot Pie went in with the rest of them.

In the echoing stone-and-timber bathhouse, the captives were stripped and made to scrub and scrape themselves raw in tubs of scalding hot water. Two fierce old women supervised the process, discussing them as bluntly as if they were newly acquired donkeys. When Arya's turn came round, Goodwife Amabel clucked in dismay at the sight of her feet, while Goodwife Harra felt the callus on her fingers that long hours of practice with Needle had earned her. "Got those churning butter, I'll wager," she said. "Some farmer's whelp, are you? Well, never you mind, girl, you have a chance to win a higher place in this world if you work hard. If you won't work hard, you'll be beaten. And what do they call you?"

Arya dared not say her true name, but Arry was no good either, it was a boy's name and they could see she was no boy. "Weasel," she said, naming the first girl she could think of. "Lommy called me Weasel."

"I can see why," sniffed Goodwife Amabel. "That hair is a fright and a nest for lice as well. We'll have it off, and then you're for the kitchens."

"I'd sooner tend the horses." Arya liked horses, and maybe if she was in the stables she'd be able to steal one and escape.

Goodwife Harra slapped her so hard that her swollen lip broke open all over again. "And keep that tongue to yourself or you'll get worse. No one asked your views."

The blood in her mouth had a salty metal tang to it. Arya dropped her gaze and said nothing. *If I still had Needle, she wouldn't dare hit me*, she thought sullenly.

"Lord Tywin and his knights have grooms and squires to tend their horses, they don't need the likes of you," Goodwife Amabel said. "The kitchens are snug and clean, and there's always a warm fire to sleep by and plenty to eat. You might have done well there, but I can see you're not a clever girl. Harra, I believe we should give this one to Weese."

"If you think so, Amabel." They gave her a shift of grey roughspun wool and a pair of ill-fitting shoes, and sent her off.

Weese was understeward for the Wailing Tower, a squat man with a fleshy carbuncle of a nose and a nest of angry red boils near one corner of his plump lips. Arya was one of six sent to him. He looked them all over with a gimlet eye. "The Lannisters are generous to those as serve them well, an honor none of your sort deserve, but in war a man makes do with what's to hand. Work hard and mind your place and might be one day you'll rise as high as me. If you think to presume on his lordship's kindness, though, you'll find *me* waiting after m'lord has gone, y'see." He strutted up and down before them, telling them how they must never look the highborn in the eye, nor speak until spoken to, nor get in his lordship's way. "My nose never lies," he boasted. "I can smell defiance, I can smell pride, I can smell disobedience. I catch a whiff of any such stinks, you'll answer for it. When I sniff you, all I want to smell is fear."

DAENERYS

On the walls of Qarth, men beat gongs to herald her coming, while others blew curious horns that encircled their bodies like great bronze snakes. A column of camelry emerged from the city as her honor guards. The riders wore scaled copper armor and snouted helms with copper tusks and long black silk plumes, and sat high on saddles inlaid with rubies and garnets. Their camels were dressed in blankets of a hundred different hues.

"Qarth is the greatest city that ever was or ever will be," Pyat Pree had told her, back amongst the bones of Vaes Tolorro. "It is the center of the world, the gate between north and south, the bridge between east and west, ancient beyond memory of man and so magnificent that Saathos the Wise put out his eyes after gazing upon Qarth for the first time, because he knew that all he saw thereafter should look squalid and ugly by comparison."

Dany took the warlock's words well salted, but the magnificence of the great city was not to be denied.

Three thick walls encircled Qarth, elaborately carved. The outer was red sandstone, thirty feet high and decorated with animals: snakes slithering, kites flying, fish swimming, intermingled with wolves of the red waste and striped zorses and monstrous elephants. The middle wall, forty feet high, was grey granite alive with scenes of war: the clash of sword and shield and spear, arrows in flight, heroes at battle and babes being butchered, pyres of the dead. The innermost wall was fifty feet of black marble, with carvings that made Dany blush until she told herself that she was being a fool. She was no maid; if she could look on the grey wall's scenes of slaughter, why should she avert her eyes from the sight of men and women giving pleasure to one another?

The outer gates were banded with copper, the middle with iron; the innermost were studded with golden eyes. All opened at Dany's approach. As she rode her silver into the city, small children rushed out to scatter flowers in her path. They wore golden sandals and bright paint, no more.

All the colors that had been missing from Vaes Tolorro had found their way to Qarth; buildings crowded about her fantastical as a fever dream in shades of rose, violet, and umber. She passed under a bronze arch fashioned in the likeness of two snakes mating, their scales delicate flakes of jade, obsidian, and lapis lazuli. Slim towers stood taller than any Dany had ever seen, and elaborate fountains filled every square, wrought in the shapes of griffins and dragons and manticores.

The Qartheen lined the streets and watched from delicate balconies that looked too frail to support their weight. They were tall pale folk in linen and samite and tiger fur, every one a lord or lady to her eyes. The women wore gowns that left one breast bare, while the men favored beaded silk skirts. Dany felt shabby and barbaric as she rode past them in her lionskin robe with black Drogon on one shoulder. Her Dothraki called the Qartheen "Milk Men" for their paleness, and Khal Drogo had dreamed of the day when he might sack the great cities of the east. She glanced at her bloodriders, their dark almond-shaped eyes giving no hint of their thoughts. *Is it only the plunder they see?* she wondered. *How savage we must seem to these Qartheen.*

Pyrat Pree conducted her little *khalasar* down the center of a great arcade where the city's ancient heroes stood thrice life-size on columns of white and green marble. They passed through a bazaar in a cavernous building whose latticework ceiling was home to a thousand gaily colored birds. Trees and flowers bloomed on the terraced walls above the stalls, while below it seemed as if everything the gods had put into the world was for sale.

Her silver shied as the merchant prince Xaro Xhoan Daxos rode up to her; the horses could not abide the close presence of camels, she had found. "If you see here anything that you would desire, O most beautiful of women, you have only to speak and it is yours," Xaro called down from his ornate horned saddle.

"Qarth itself is hers, she has no need of baubles," blue-lipped Pyat Pree sang out from her other side. "It shall be as I promised, *Khaleesi.* Come with me to the House of the Undying, and you shall drink of truth and wisdom."

"Why should she need your Palace of Dust, when I can give her sunlight and sweet water and silks to sleep in?" Xaro said to the warlock. "The Thirteen shall set a crown of black jade and fire opals upon her lovely head."

"The only palace I desire is the red castle at King's Landing, my lord Pyat." Dany was wary of the warlock; the *maegi* Mirri Maz Duur had soured her on those who played at sorcery. "And if the great of Qarth would give me gifts, Xaro, let them give me ships and swords to win back what is rightfully mine."

Pyat's blue lips curled upward in a gracious smile. "It shall be as you command, *Khaleesi.*" He moved away, swaying with his camel's motion, his long beaded robes trailing behind.

"The young queen is wise beyond her years," Xaro

Xhoan Daxos murmured down at her from his high saddle. "There is a saying in Qarth. A warlock's house is built of bones and lies."

"Then why do men lower their voices when they speak of the warlocks of Qarth? All across the east, their power and wisdom are revered."

"Once they were mighty," Xaro agreed, "but now they are as ludicrous as those feeble old soldiers who boast of their prowess long after strength and skill have left them. They read their crumbling scrolls, drink shade-of-the-evening until their lips turn blue, and hint of dread powers, but they are hollow husks compared to those who went before. Pyat Pree's gifts will turn to dust in your hands, I warn you." He gave his camel a lick of his whip and sped away.

"The crow calls the raven black," muttered Ser Jorah in the Common Tongue of Westeros. The exile knight rode at her right hand, as ever. For their entrance into Qarth, he had put away his Dothraki garb and donned again the plate and mail and wool of the Seven Kingdoms half a world away. "You would do well to avoid both those men, Your Grace."

"Those men will help me to my crown," she said. "Xaro has vast wealth, and Pyat Pree—"

"—pretends to power," the knight said brusquely. On his dark green surcoat, the bear of House Mormont stood on its hind legs, black and fierce. Jorah looked no less ferocious as he scowled at the crowd that filled the bazaar. "I would not linger here long, my queen. I mislike the very smell of this place."

Dany smiled. "Perhaps it's the camels you're smelling. The Qartheen themselves seem sweet enough to my nose."

"Sweet smells are sometimes used to cover foul ones."

My great bear, Dany thought. *I am his queen, but I will always be his cub as well, and he will always guard me.* It made her feel safe, but sad as well. She wished she could love him better than she did.

Xaro Xhoan Daxos had offered Dany the hospitality of

his home while she was in the city. She had expected something grand. She had not expected a palace larger than many a market town. *It makes Magister Illyrio's manse in Pentos look like a swineherd's hovel,* she thought. Xaro swore that his home could comfortably house all of her people and their horses besides; indeed, it swallowed them. An entire wing was given over to her. She would have her own gardens, a marble bathing pool, a scrying tower and warlock's maze. Slaves would tend her every need. In her private chambers, the floors were green marble, the walls draped with colorful silk hangings that shimmered with every breath of air. "You are too generous," she told Xaro Xhoan Daxos.

"For the Mother of Dragons, no gift is too great." Xaro was a languid, elegant man with a bald head and a great beak of a nose crusted with rubies, opals, and flakes of jade. "On the morrow, you shall feast upon peacock and lark's tongue, and hear music worthy of the most beautiful of women. The Thirteen will come to do you homage, and all the great of Qarth."

All the great of Qarth will come to see my dragons, Dany thought, yet she thanked Xaro for his kindness before she sent him on his way. Pyat Pree took his leave as well, vowing to petition the Undying Ones for an audience. "A honor rare as summer snows." Before he left he kissed her bare feet with his pale blue lips and pressed on her a gift, a jar of ointment that he swore would let her see the spirits of the air. Last of the three seekers to depart was Quaithe the shadowbinder. From her Dany received only a warning. "Beware," the woman in the red lacquer mask said.

"Of whom?"

"Of all. They shall come day and night to see the wonder that has been born again into the world, and when they see they shall lust. For dragons are fire made flesh, and fire is power."

When Quaithe too was gone, Ser Jorah said, "She speaks truly, my queen . . . though I like her no more than the others."

"I do not understand her." Pyat and Xaro had showered Dany with promises from the moment they first glimpsed her dragons, declaring themselves her loyal servants in all things, but from Quaithe she had gotten only the rare cryptic word. And it disturbed her that she had never seen the woman's face. *Remember Mirri Maz Duur*, she told herself. *Remember treachery.* She turned to her bloodriders. "We will keep our own watch so long as we are here. See that no one enters this wing of the palace without my leave, and take care that the dragons are always well guarded."

"It shall be done, *Khaleesi*," Aggo said.

"We have seen only the parts of Qarth that Pyat Pree wished us to see," she went on. "Rakharo, go forth and look on the rest, and tell me what you find. Take good men with you—and women, to go places where men are forbidden."

"As you say, I do, blood of my blood," said Rakharo.

"Ser Jorah, find the docks and see what manner of ships lie at anchor. It has been half a year since I last heard tidings from the Seven Kingdoms. Perhaps the gods will have blown some good captain here from Westeros with a ship to carry us home."

The knight frowned. "That would be no kindness. The Usurper will kill you, sure as sunrise." Mormont hooked his thumbs through his swordbelt. "My place is here at your side."

"Jhogo can guard me as well. You have more languages than my bloodriders, and the Dothraki mistrust the sea and those who sail her. Only you can serve me in this. Go among the ships and speak to the crews, learn where they are from and where they are bound and what manner of men command them."

Reluctantly, the exile nodded. "As you say, my queen."

When all the men had gone, her handmaids stripped off the travel-stained silks she wore, and Dany padded out to where the marble pool sat in the shade of a portico. The water was deliciously cool, and the pool was stocked with tiny golden fish that nibbled curiously at her skin and made her giggle. It felt good to close her eyes and float, knowing she could rest as long as she liked. She wondered whether Aegon's Red Keep had a pool like this, and fragrant gardens full of lavender and mint. *It must, surely. Viserys always said the Seven Kingdoms were more beautiful than any other place in the world.*

The thought of home disquieted her. If her sun-and-stars had lived, he would have led his *khalasar* across the poison water and swept away her enemies, but his strength had left the world. Her bloodriders remained, sworn to her for life and skilled in slaughter, but only in the ways of the horselords. The Dothraki sacked cities and plundered kingdoms, they did not rule them. Dany had no wish to reduce King's Landing to a blackened ruin full of unquiet ghosts. She had supped enough on tears. *I want to make my kingdom beautiful, to fill it with fat men and pretty maids and laughing children. I want my people to smile when they see me ride by, the way Viserys said they smiled for my father.*

But before she could do that she must conquer.

The Usurper will kill you, sure as sunrise, Mormont had said. Robert had slain her gallant brother Rhaegar, and one of his creatures had crossed the Dothraki sea to poison her and her unborn son. They said Robert Baratheon was strong as a bull and fearless in battle, a man who loved nothing better than war. And with him stood the great lords her brother had named the Usurper's dogs, cold-eyed Eddard Stark with his frozen heart, and the golden Lannisters, father and son, so rich, so powerful, so treacherous.

How could she hope to overthrow such men? When Khal Drogo had lived, men trembled and made him gifts to stay his wrath. If they did not, he took their cities, wealth and wives and all. But his *khalasar* had been vast, while hers was meager. Her people had followed her across the red waste as she chased her comet, and would follow her across the poison water too, but they would not be enough. Even her dragons might not be enough. Viserys had believed that the realm would rise for its rightful king . . . but Viserys had been a fool, and fools believe in foolish things.

Her doubts made her shiver. Suddenly the water felt cold to her, and the little fish prickling at her skin annoying. Dany stood and climbed from the pool. "Irri," she called, "Jhiqui."

As the handmaids toweled her dry and wrapped her in a sandsilk robe, Dany's thoughts went to the three who had sought her out in the City of Bones. *The Bleeding Star led me to Qarth for a purpose. Here I will find what I need, if I have the strength to take what is offered, and the wisdom to avoid the traps and snares. If the gods mean for me to conquer, they will provide, they will send me a sign, and if not . . . if not . . .*

It was near evenfall and Dany was feeding her dragons when Irri stepped through the silken curtains to tell her that Ser Jorah had returned from the docks . . . and not alone. "Send him in, with whomever he has brought," she said, curious.

When they entered, she was seated on a mound of cushions, her dragons all about her. The man he brought with him wore a cloak of green and yellow feathers and had skin as black as polished jet. "Your Grace," the knight said, "I bring you Quhuru Mo, captain of the *Cinnamon Wind* out of Tall Trees Town."

The black man knelt. "I am greatly honored, my queen," he said, not in the tongue of the Summer Isles, which Dany did not know, but in the liquid Valyrian of the Nine Free Cities.

"The honor is mine, Quhuru Mo," said Dany in the same language. "Have you come from the Summer Isles?"

"This is so, Your Grace, but before, not half a year past, we called at Oldtown. From there I bring you a wondrous gift."

"A gift?"

"A gift of news. Dragonmother, Stormborn, I tell you true, Robert Baratheon is dead."

Outside her walls, dusk was settling over Qarth, but a sun had risen in Dany's heart. "Dead?" she repeated. In her lap, black Drogon *hissed*, and pale smoke rose before her face like a veil. "You are certain? The Usurper is dead?"

"So it is said in Oldtown, and Dorne, and Lys, and all the other ports where we have called."

He sent me poisoned wine, yet I live and he is gone. "What was the manner of his death?" On her shoulder, pale Viserion flapped wings the color of cream, stirring the air.

"Torn by a monstrous boar whilst hunting in his kingswood, or so I heard in Oldtown. Others say his queen betrayed him, or his brother, or Lord Stark who was his Hand. Yet all the tales agree in this: King Robert is dead and in his grave."

Dany had never looked upon the Usurper's face, yet seldom a day had passed when she had not thought of him. His great shadow had lain across her since the hour of her birth, when she came forth amidst blood and storm into a world where she no longer had a place. And now this ebony stranger had lifted that shadow.

"The boy sits the Iron Throne now," Ser Jorah said.

"King Joffrey reigns," Quhuru Mo agreed, "but the Lannisters rule. Robert's brothers have fled King's Landing. The talk is, they mean to claim the crown. And the Hand has fallen, Lord Stark who was King Robert's friend. He has been seized for treason."

"Ned Stark a traitor?" Ser Jorah snorted. "Not bloody likely. The Long Summer will come again before that one would besmirch his precious honor."

"What honor could he have?" Dany said. "He was a traitor to his true king, as were these Lannisters." It pleased her to hear that the Usurper's dogs were fighting amongst themselves, though she was unsurprised. The same thing happened when her Drogo died, and his great *khalasar* tore itself to pieces. "My brother is dead as well, Viserys who was the true king," she told the Summer Islander. "Khal Drogo my lord husband killed him with a crown of molten gold." Would her brother have been any wiser, had he known that the vengeance he had prayed for was so close at hand?

"Then I grieve for you, Dragonmother, and for bleeding Westeros, bereft of its rightful king."

Beneath Dany's gentle fingers, green Rhaegal stared at the stranger with eyes of molten gold. When his mouth opened, his teeth gleamed like black needles. "When does your ship return to Westeros, Captain?"

"Not for a year or more, I fear. From here the *Cinnamon Wind* sails east, to make the trader's circle round the Jade Sea."

"I see," said Dany, disappointed. "I wish you fair winds and good trading, then. You have brought me a precious gift."

"I have been amply repaid, great queen."

She puzzled at that. "How so?"

His eyes gleamed. "I have seen dragons."

Dany laughed. "And will see more of them one day, I hope. Come to me in King's Landing when I am on my father's throne, and you shall have a great reward."

The Summer Islander promised he would do so, and kissed her lightly on the fingers as he took his leave. Jhiqui showed him out, while Ser Jorah Mormont remained.

"Khaleesi," the knight said when they were alone, "I should not speak so freely of your plans, if I were you. This man will spread the tale wherever he goes now."

"Let him," she said. "Let the whole world know my purpose. The Usurper is dead, what does it matter?"

"Not every sailor's tale is true," Ser Jorah cautioned, "and even if Robert be truly dead, his son rules in his place. This changes nothing, truly."

"This changes *everything.*" Dany rose abruptly. Screeching, her dragons uncoiled and spread their wings. Drogon flapped and clawed up to the lintel over the archway. The others skittered across the floor, wingtips scrabbling on the marble. "Before, the Seven Kingdoms were like my Drogo's *khalasar*, a hundred thousand made as one by his strength. Now they fly to pieces, even as the *khalasar* did after my *khal* lay dead."

"The high lords have always fought. Tell me who's won and I'll tell you what it means. *Khaleesi*, the Seven

Kingdoms are not going to fall into your hands like so many ripe peaches. You will need a fleet, gold, armies, alliances—"

"All this I know." She took his hands in hers and looked up into his dark suspicious eyes. *Sometimes he thinks of me as a child he must protect, and sometimes as a woman he would like to bed, but does he ever truly see me as his queen?* "I am not the frightened girl you met in Pentos. I have counted only fifteen name days, true . . . but I am as old as the crones in the *dosh khaleen* and as young as my dragons, Jorah. I have borne a child, burned a *khal,* and crossed the red waste and the Dothraki sea. Mine is the blood of the dragon."

"As was your brother's," he said stubbornly.

"I am not Viserys."

"No," he admitted. "There is more of Rhaegar in you, I think, but even Rhaegar could be slain. Robert proved that on the Trident, with no more than a warhammer. Even dragons can die."

"Dragons die." She stood on her toes to kiss him lightly on an unshaven cheek. "But so do dragon-slayers."

BRAN

Meera moved in a wary circle, her net dangling loose in her left hand, the slender three-pronged frog spear poised in her right. Summer followed her with his golden eyes, turning, his tail held stiff and tall. Watching, watching . . .

"Yai!" the girl shouted, the spear darting out. The wolf slid to the left and leapt before she could draw back the spear. Meera cast her net, the tangles unfolding in the air before her. Summer's leap carried him into it. He dragged it with him as he slammed into her chest and knocked her over backward. Her spear went spinning away. The damp grass cushioned her fall but the breath went out of her in an "Oof." The wolf crouched atop her.

Bran hooted. "You lose."

"She wins," her brother Jojen said. "Summer's snared."

He was right, Bran saw. Thrashing and growling at the net, trying to rip free, Summer was only ensnaring himself worse. Nor could he bite through. "Let him out."

Laughing, the Reed girl threw her arms around the tangled wolf and rolled them both. Summer gave a piteous whine, his legs kicking against the cords that bound them. Meera knelt, undid a twist, pulled at a corner, tugged deftly here and there, and suddenly the direwolf was bounding free.

"Summer, to me." Bran spread his arms. "Watch," he said, an instant before the wolf bowled into him. He clung with all his strength as the wolf dragged him bumping through the grass. They wrestled and rolled and clung to each other, one snarling and yapping, the other laughing. In the end it was Bran sprawled on top, the mud-spattered direwolf under him. "Good wolf," he panted. Summer licked him across the ear.

Meera shook her head. "Does he never grow angry?"

"Not with me." Bran grabbed the wolf by his ears and Summer snapped at him fiercely, but it was all in play. "Sometimes he tears my garb but he's never drawn blood."

"*Your* blood, you mean. If he'd gotten past my net . . ."

"He wouldn't hurt you. He knows I like you." All of the other lords and knights had departed within a day or two of the harvest feast, but the Reeds had stayed to become Bran's constant companions. Jojen was so solemn that Old Nan called him "little grandfather," but Meera reminded Bran of his sister Arya. She wasn't scared to get dirty, and she could run and fight and throw as good as a boy. She was older than Arya, though, almost sixteen, a woman grown. They were both older than Bran, even though his ninth name day had finally come and gone, but they never treated him like a child.

"I wish you were our wards instead of the Walders." He began to struggle toward the nearest tree. His dragging and wriggling was unseemly to watch, but when Meera moved to lift him he said, "No, don't help me." He rolled clumsily and pushed and squirmed backward, using the strength of his arms, until he was sitting with his back to the trunk of a tall ash. "See, I told you." Summer lay down with his head in Bran's lap. "I never knew anyone who fought with a net before," he told Meera while he scratched the direwolf between the ears. "Did your master-at-arms teach you net-fighting?"

"My father taught me. We have no knights at Greywater. No master-at-arms, and no maester."

"Who keeps your ravens?"

She smiled. "Ravens can't find Greywater Watch, no more than our enemies can."

"Why not?"

"Because it moves," she told him.

Bran had never heard of a moving castle before. He looked at her uncertainly, but he couldn't tell whether she was teasing him or not. "I wish I could see it. Do you think your lord father would let me come visit when the war is over?"

"You would be most welcome, my prince. Then or now."

"Now?" Bran had spent his whole life at Winterfell. He yearned to see far places. "I could ask Ser Rodrik when he returns." The old knight was off east, trying to set to rights the trouble there. Roose Bolton's bastard had started it by seizing Lady Hornwood as she returned from the harvest feast, marrying her that very night even though he was young enough to be her son. Then Lord Manderly had taken her castle. To protect the Hornwood holdings from the Boltons, he had written, but Ser Rodrik had been almost as angry with him as with the bastard. "Ser Rodrik might let me go. Maester Luwin never would."

Sitting cross-legged under the weirwood, Jojen Reed regarded him solemnly. "It would be good if you left Winterfell, Bran."

"It would?"

"Yes. And sooner rather than later."

"My brother has the greensight," said Meera. "He dreams things that haven't happened, but sometimes they do."

"There is no *sometimes*, Meera." A look passed between them; him sad, her defiant.

"Tell me what's going to happen," Bran said.

"I will," said Jojen, "if you'll tell me about your dreams."

The godswood grew quiet. Bran could hear leaves rustling, and Hodor's distant splashing from the hot pools. He thought of the golden man and the three-eyed crow, remembered the crunch of bones between his jaws and the coppery taste of blood. "I don't have dreams. Maester Luwin gives me sleeping draughts."

"Do they help?"

"Sometimes."

Meera said, "All of Winterfell knows you wake at night shouting and sweating, Bran. The women talk of it at the well, and the guards in their hall."

"Tell us what frightens you so much," said Jojen.

"I don't want to. Anyway, it's only dreams. Maester Luwin says dreams might mean anything or nothing."

"My brother dreams as other boys do, and those dreams might mean anything," Meera said, "but the green dreams are different."

Jojen's eyes were the color of moss, and sometimes when he looked at you he seemed to be seeing something else. Like now. "I dreamed of a winged wolf bound to earth with grey stone chains," he said. "It was a green dream, so I knew it was true. A crow was trying to peck through the chains, but the stone was too hard and his beak could only chip at them."

"Did the crow have three eyes?"

Jojen nodded.

Summer raised his head from Bran's lap, and gazed at the mudman with his dark golden eyes.

"When I was little I almost died of greywater fever. That was when the crow came to me."

"He came to me after I fell," Bran blurted. "I was asleep for a long time. He said I had to fly or die, and I woke up, only I was broken and I couldn't fly after all."

"You can if you want to." Picking up her net, Meera

shook out the last tangles and began arranging it in loose folds.

"*You* are the winged wolf, Bran," said Jojen. "I wasn't sure when we first came, but now I am. The crow sent us here to break your chains."

"Is the crow at Greywater?"

"No. The crow is in the north."

"At the Wall?" Bran had always wanted to see the Wall. His bastard brother Jon was there now, a man of the Night's Watch.

"Beyond the Wall." Meera Reed hung the net from her belt. "When Jojen told our lord father what he'd dreamed, he sent us to Winterfell."

"How would I break the chains, Jojen?" Bran asked.

"Open your eye."

"They *are* open Can't you *see*?"

"Two are open." Jojen pointed. "One, two."

"I only *have* two."

"You have three. The crow gave you the third, but you will not open it." He had a slow soft way of speaking. "With two eyes you see my face. With three you could see my heart. With two you can see that oak tree there. With three you could see the acorn the oak grew from and the stump that it will one day become. With two you see no farther than your walls. With three you would gaze south to the Summer Sea and north beyond the Wall."

Summer got to his feet. "I don't need to see so far." Bran made a nervous smile. "I'm tired of talking about crows. Let's talk about wolves. Or lizard-lions. Have you ever hunted one, Meera? We don't have them here."

Meera plucked her frog spear out of the bushes. "They live in the water. In slow streams and deep swamps—"

Her brother interrupted. "Did you dream of a lizard-lion?"

"No," said Bran. "I told you, I don't want—"

"Did you dream of a wolf?"

He was making Bran angry. "I don't have to tell you my dreams. I'm the prince. I'm the Stark in Winterfell."

"Was it Summer?"

"You be quiet."

"The night of the harvest feast, you dreamed you were Summer in the godswood, didn't you?"

"Stop it!" Bran shouted. Summer slid toward the weirwood, his white teeth bared.

Jojen Reed took no mind. "When I touched Summer, I felt you in him. Just as you are in him now."

"You couldn't have. I was in bed. I was sleeping."

"You were in the godswood, all in grey."

"It was only a bad dream . . ."

Jojen stood. "I felt you. I felt you fall. Is that what scares you, the falling?"

The falling, Bran thought, *and the golden man, the queen's brother, he scares me too, but mostly the falling.* He did not say it, though. How could he? He had not been able to tell Ser Rodrik or Maester Luwin, and he could not tell the Reeds either. If he didn't talk about it, maybe he would forget. He had never wanted to remember. It might not even be a true remembering.

"Do you fall every night, Bran?" Jojen asked quietly.

A low rumbling growl rose from Summer's throat, and there was no play in it. He stalked forward, all teeth and hot eyes. Meera stepped between the wolf and her brother, spear in hand. "Keep him back, Bran."

"Jojen is making him angry."

Meera shook out her net.

"It's your anger, Bran," her brother said. "Your fear."

"It isn't. I'm not a wolf." Yet he'd howled with them in the night, and tasted blood in his wolf dreams.

"Part of you is Summer, and part of Summer is you. You know that, Bran."

Summer rushed forward, but Meera blocked him, jabbing with the three-pronged spear. The wolf twisted aside, circling, stalking. Meera turned to face him. "Call him back, Bran."

"Summer!" Bran shouted. "To me, Summer!" He slapped an open palm down on the meat of his thigh. His hand tingled, though his dead leg felt nothing.

The direwolf lunged again, and again Meera's spear darted out. Summer dodged, circled back. The bushes rustled, and a lean black shape came padding from behind the weirwood, teeth bared. The scent was strong; his brother had smelled his rage. Bran felt hairs rise on the back of his neck. Meera stood beside her brother, with wolves to either side. "Bran, call them off."

"I *can't*!"

"Jojen, up the tree."

"There's no need. Today is not the day I die."

"*Do it!*" she screamed, and her brother scrambled up the trunk of the weirwood, using the face for his handholds. The direwolves closed. Meera abandoned spear and net, jumped up, and grabbed the branch above her head. Shaggy's jaws snapped shut beneath her ankle as she swung up and over the limb. Summer sat back on his haunches and howled, while Shaggydog worried the net, shaking it in his teeth.

Only then did Bran remember that they were not alone. He cupped hands around his mouth. "Hodor!" he shouted. "*Hodor! Hodor!*" He was badly frightened and somehow ashamed. "They won't hurt Hodor," he assured his treed friends.

A few moments passed before they heard a tuneless humming. Hodor arrived half-dressed and mud-spattered from his visit to the hot pools, but Bran had never been so glad to see him. "Hodor, help me. Chase off the wolves. Chase them off."

Hodor went to it gleefully, waving his arms and stamping his huge feet, shouting "Hodor, Hodor," running first at one wolf and then the other. Shaggydog was the first to flee, slinking back into the foliage with a final snarl. When Summer had enough, he came back to Bran and lay down beside him.

No sooner did Meera touch ground than she snatched up her spear and net again. Jojen never took his eyes off Summer. "We will talk again," he promised Bran.

It was the wolves, it wasn't me. He did not understand why they'd gotten so wild. *Maybe Maester Luwin was right to lock them in the godswood.* "Hodor," he said, "bring me to Maester Luwin."

The maester's turret below the rookery was one of

Bran's favorite places. Luwin was hopelessly untidy, but his clutter of books and scrolls and bottles was as familiar and comforting to Bran as his bald spot and the flapping sleeves of his loose grey robes. He liked the ravens too.

He found Luwin perched on a high stool, writing. With Ser Rodrik gone, all of the governance of the castle had fallen on his shoulders. "My prince," he said when Hodor entered, "you're early for lessons today." The maester spent several hours every afternoon tutoring Bran, Rickon, and the Walder Freys.

"Hodor, stand still." Bran grasped a wall sconce with both hands and used it to pull himself up and out of the basket. He hung for a moment by his arms until Hodor carried him to a chair. "Meera says her brother has the greensight."

Maester Luwin scratched at the side of his nose with his writing quill. "Does she now?"

He nodded. "You told me that the children of the forest had the greensight. I remember."

"Some claimed to have that power. Their wise men were called *greenseers.*"

"Was it magic?"

"Call it that for want of a better word, if you must. At heart it was only a different sort of knowledge."

"What was it?"

Luwin set down his quill. "No one truly knows, Bran. The children are gone from the world, and their wisdom with them. It had to do with the faces in the trees, we think. The First Men believed that the greenseers could see through the eyes of the weirwoods. That was why they cut down the trees whenever they warred upon the children. Supposedly the greenseers also had power over the beasts of the wood and the birds in the trees. Even fish. Does the Reed boy claim such powers?"

"No. I don't think. But he has dreams that come true sometimes, Meera says."

"All of us have dreams that come true sometimes. You dreamed of your lord father in the crypts before we knew he was dead, remember?"

"Rickon did too. We dreamed the same dream."

"Call it greensight, if you wish . . . but remember as well all those tens of thousands of dreams that you and Rickon have dreamed that did *not* come true. Do you perchance recall what I taught you about the chain collar that every maester wears?"

Bran thought for a moment, trying to remember. "A maester forges his chain in the Citadel of Oldtown. It's a chain because you swear to serve, and it's made of different metals because you serve the realm and the realm has different sorts of people. Every time you learn something you get another link. Black iron is for ravenry, silver for healing, gold for sums and numbers. I don't remember them all."

Luwin slid a finger up under his collar and began to turn it, inch by inch. He had a thick neck for a small man, and the chain was tight, but a few pulls had it all the way around. "This is Valyrian steel," he said when the link of dark grey metal lay against the apple of his throat. "Only one maester in a hundred wears such a link. This signifies that I have studied what the Citadel calls *the higher mysteries*—magic, for want of a better word. A fascinating pursuit, but of small use, which is why so few maesters trouble themselves with it.

"All those who study the higher mysteries try their own hand at spells, soon or late. I yielded to the temptation too, I must confess it. Well, I was a boy, and what boy does not secretly wish to find hidden powers in himself? I got no more for my efforts than a thousand boys before me, and a thousand since. Sad to say, magic does not work."

"Sometimes it does," Bran protested. "I had that dream, and Rickon did too. And there are mages and warlocks in the east . . ."

"There are men who *call* themselves mages and warlocks," Maester Luwin said. "I had a friend at the Citadel who could pull a rose out of your ear, but he was no more magical than I was. Oh, to be sure, there is much we do not understand. The years pass in their hundreds and their thousands, and what does any man see of life but a few summers, a few winters? We look at mountains and call them eternal, and so they seem . . . but in the course of time, mountains rise and fall, rivers change their courses, stars fall from the sky, and great cities sink beneath the sea. Even gods die, we think. Everything changes.

"Perhaps magic was once a mighty force in the world, but no longer. What little remains is no more than the wisp of smoke that lingers in the air after a great fire has burned out, and even that is fading. Valyria was the last ember, and Valyria is gone. The dragons are no more, the giants are dead, the children of the forest forgotten with all their lore.

"No, my prince. Jojen Reed may have had a dream or two that he believes came true, but he does not have the greensight. No living man has that power."

Bran said as much to Meera Reed when she came to him at dusk as he sat in his window seat watching the lights flicker to life. "I'm sorry for what happened with the wolves. Summer shouldn't have tried to hurt Jojen, but Jojen shouldn't have said all that about my dreams. The crow lied when he said I could fly, and your brother lied too."

"Or perhaps your maester is wrong."

"He isn't. Even my father relied on his counsel."

"Your father listened, I have no doubt. But in the end, he decided for himself. Bran, will you let me tell you about a dream Jojen dreamed of you and your fosterling brothers?"

"The Walders aren't my brothers."

She paid that no heed. "You were sitting at supper, but instead of a servant, Maester Luwin brought you your food. He served you the king's cut off the roast, the meat rare and bloody, but with a savory smell that made everyone's mouth water. The meat he served the Freys was old and grey and dead. Yet they liked their supper better than you liked yours."

"I don't understand."

"You will, my brother says. When you do, we'll talk again."

Bran was almost afraid to sit to supper that night, but when he did, it was pigeon pie they set before him. Everyone else was served the same, and he couldn't see that anything was wrong with the food they served the Walders. *Maester Luwin has the truth of it,* he told himself. Nothing bad was coming to Winterfell, no matter what Jojen said. Bran was relieved . . . but disappointed too. So long as there was magic, anything could happen. Ghosts could walk, trees could talk, and broken boys could grow up to be knights. "But there isn't," he said aloud in the darkness of his bed. "There's no magic, and the stories are just stories."

And he would never walk, nor fly, nor be a knight.

TYRION

The rushes were scratchy under the soles of his bare feet. "My cousin chooses a queer hour to come visiting," Tyrion told a sleep-befuddled Podrick Payne, who'd doubtless expected to be well roasted for waking him. "See him to my solar and tell him I'll be down shortly."

It was well past midnight, he judged from the black outside the window. *Does Lancel think to find me drowsy and slow of wit at this hour?* he wondered. *No, Lancel scarce thinks at all, this is Cersei's doing.* His sister would be disappointed. Even abed, he worked well into the morning—reading by the flickering light of a candle, scrutinizing the reports of Varys's whisperers, and poring over Littlefinger's books of accounts until the columns blurred and his eyes ached.

He splashed some tepid water on his face from the basin beside his bed and took his time squatting in the garderobe, the night air cold on his bare skin. Ser Lancel was sixteen, and not known for his patience. Let him wait, and grow more anxious in the waiting. When his bowels were empty, Tyrion slipped on a bedrobe and roughed his thin flaxen hair with his fingers, all the more to look as if he had wakened from sleep.

Lancel was pacing before the ashes of the hearth, garbed in slashed red velvet with black silk undersleeves, a jeweled dagger and a gilded scabbard hanging from his swordbelt. "Cousin," Tyrion greeted him. "Your visits are too few. To what do I owe this undeserved pleasure?"

"Her Grace the Queen Regent has sent me to command you to release Grand Maester Pycelle." Ser Lancel showed Tyrion a crimson ribbon, bearing Cersei's lion seal impressed in golden wax. "Here is her warrant."

"So it is." Tyrion waved it away. "I hope my sister is not overtaxing her strength, so soon after her illness. It would be a great pity if she were to suffer a relapse."

"Her Grace is quite recovered," Ser Lancel said curtly.

"Music to my ears." *Though not a tune I'm fond of. I should have given her a larger dose.* Tyrion had hoped for a few more days without Cersei's interference, but he was not too terribly surprised by her return to health. She was Jaime's twin, after all. He made himself smile pleasantly. "Pod, build us a fire, the air is too chilly for my taste. Will you take a cup with me, Lancel? I find that mulled wine helps me sleep."

"I need no help sleeping," Ser Lancel said. "I am come at Her Grace's behest, not to drink with you, Imp."

Knighthood had made the boy bolder, Tyrion reflected—that, and the sorry part he had played in murdering King Robert. "Wine does have its dangers." He smiled as he poured. "As to Grand Maester Pycelle . . . if my sweet sister is so concerned for him, I would have thought she'd come herself. Instead she sends you. What am I to make of that?"

"Make of it what you will, so long as you release your prisoner. The Grand Maester is a staunch friend to the Queen Regent, and under her personal protection." A hint of a sneer played about the lad's lips; he was enjoying this. *He takes his lessons from Cersei.* "Her

Grace will never consent to this outrage. She reminds you that *she* is Joffrey's regent."

"As I am Joffrey's Hand."

"The Hand serves," the young knight informed him airily. "The regent *rules* until the king is of age."

"Perhaps you ought write that down so I'll remember it better." The fire was crackling merrily. "You may leave us, Pod," Tyrion told his squire. Only when the boy was gone did he turn back to Lancel. "There is more?"

"Yes. Her Grace bids me inform you that Ser Jacelyn Bywater defied a command issued in the king's own name."

Which means that Cersei has already ordered Bywater to release Pycelle, and been rebuffed. "I see."

"She insists that the man be removed from his office and placed under arrest for treason. I warn you—"

He set aside his wine cup. "I'll hear no warnings from you, boy."

"*Ser*," Lancel said stiffly. He touched his sword, perhaps to remind Tyrion that he wore one. "Have a care how you speak to me, Imp." Doubtless he meant to sound threatening, but that absurd wisp of a mustache ruined the effect.

"Oh, unhand your sword. One cry from me and Shagga will burst in and kill you. With an axe, not a wineskin."

Lancel reddened; was he such a fool as to believe his part in Robert's death had gone unnoted? "I am a knight—"

"So I've noted. Tell me—did Cersei have you knighted before or after she took you into her bed?"

The flicker in Lancel's green eyes was all the admission Tyrion needed. So Varys told it true. *Well, no one can ever claim that my sister does not love her family.* "What, nothing to say? No more warnings for me, *ser*?"

"You will withdraw these filthy accusations or—"

"Please. Have you given any thought to what Joffrey will do when I tell him you murdered his father to bed his mother?"

"It was not like that!" Lancel protested, horrified.

"No? What *was* it like, pray?"

"The queen gave me the strongwine! Your own father Lord Tywin, when I was named the king's squire, he told me to obey her in everything."

"Did he tell you to fuck her too?" *Look at him. Not quite so tall, his features not so fine, and his hair is sand instead of spun gold, yet still . . . even a poor copy of Jaime is sweeter than an empty bed, I suppose.* "No, I thought not."

"I never meant . . . I only did as I was bid, I . . ."

". . . hated every instant of it, is that what you would have me believe? A high place at court, knighthood, my sister's legs opening for you at night, oh, yes, it must have been terrible for you." Tyrion pushed himself to his feet. "Wait here. His Grace will want to hear this."

The defiance went from Lancel all at once. The young knight fell to his knees a frightened boy. "Mercy, my lord, I beg you."

"Save it for Joffrey. He likes a good beg."

"My lord, it was your sister's bidding, the queen, as you said, but His Grace . . . he'd never understand . . ."

"Would you have me keep the truth from the king?"

"For my father's sake! I'll leave the city, it will be as if it never happened! I swear, I will end it . . ."

It was hard not to laugh. "I think not."

Now the lad looked lost. "My lord?"

"You heard me. My father told you to obey my sister? Very well, obey her. Stay close to her side, keep her trust, pleasure her as often as she requires it. No one need ever know . . . so long as you keep faith with me. I want to know what Cersei is doing. Where she goes, who she sees, what they talk of, what plans she is hatching. All. And you will be the one to tell me, won't you?"

"Yes, my lord." Lancel spoke without a moment's hesitation. Tyrion liked that. "I will. I swear it. As you command."

"Rise." Tyrion filled the second cup and pressed it on him. "Drink to our understanding. I promise, there are no boars in the castle that I know of." Lancel lifted the cup and drank, albeit stiffly. "Smile, cousin. My sister is a beautiful woman, and it's all for the good of the realm. You could do well out of this. Knighthood is nothing. If you're clever, you'll have a lordship from me before you're done." Tyrion swirled the wine in his cup. "We want Cersei to have every faith in you. Go back and tell her I beg her forgiveness. Tell her that you frightened me, that I want no conflict between us, that henceforth I shall do nothing without her consent."

"But . . . her demands . . ."

"Oh, I'll give her Pycelle."

"You will?" Lancel seemed astonished.

Tyrion smiled. "I'll release him on the morrow. I could swear that I hadn't harmed a hair on his head, but it wouldn't be strictly true. In any case, he's well enough, though I won't vouch for his vigor. The black cells are not a healthy place for a man his age. Cersei can keep him as a pet or send him to the Wall, I don't care which, but I won't have him on the council."

"And Ser Jacelyn?"

"Tell my sister you believe you can win him away from me, given time. That ought to content her for a while."

"As you say." Lancel finished his wine.

"One last thing. With King Robert dead, it would be most embarrassing should his grieving widow suddenly grow great with child."

"My lord, I . . . we . . . the queen has commanded me not to . . ." His ears had turned Lannister crimson. "I spill my seed on her belly, my lord."

"A lovely belly, I have no doubt. Moisten it as often as you wish . . . but see that your dew falls nowhere else. I want no more nephews, is that clear?"

Ser Lancel made a stiff bow and took his leave.

Tyrion allowed himself a moment to feel sorry for the boy. *Another fool, and a weakling as well, but he does not deserve what Cersei and I are doing to him.* It was a kindness that his uncle Kevan had two other sons; this one was unlikely to live out the year. Cersei would have him killed out of hand if she learned he was betraying her, and if by some grace of the gods she did not, Lancel would never survive the day Jaime Lannister returned to King's Landing. The only question would be whether Jaime cut him down in a jealous rage, or Cersei murdered him first to keep Jaime from finding out. Tyrion's silver was on Cersei.

A restlessness was on him, and Tyrion knew full well he would not get back to sleep tonight. *Not here, in any case.* He found Podrick Payne asleep in a chair outside the door of the solar, and shook him by the shoulder. "Summon Bronn, and then run down to the stables and have two horses saddled."

The squire's eyes were cloudy with sleep. "Horses."

"Those big brown animals that love apples, I'm sure you've seen them. Four legs and a tail. But Bronn first."

The sellsword was not long in appearing. "Who pissed in your soup?" he demanded.

"Cersei, as ever. You'd think I'd be used to the taste by now, but never mind. My gentle sister seems to have mistaken me for Ned Stark."

"I hear he was taller."

"Not after Joff took off his head. You ought to have dressed more warmly, the night is chill."

"Are we going somewhere?"

"Are all sellswords as clever as you?"

The city streets were dangerous, but with Bronn beside him Tyrion felt safe enough. The guards let him out a postern gate in the north wall, and they rode down Shadowblack Lane to the foot of Aegon's High Hill, and thence onto Pigrun Alley, past rows of shuttered windows and tall timber-and-stone buildings whose upper stories leaned out so far over the street they almost kissed. The moon seemed to follow them as they went, playing peek-and-sneak among the chimneys. They encountered no one but a lone old crone, carrying a dead cat by the tail. She gave them a fearful look, as if she were afraid they might try to steal her dinner, and slunk off into the shadows without a word.

Tyrion reflected on the men who had been Hand before him, who had proved no match for his sister's wiles. *How could they be? Men like that . . . too honest to live, too noble to shit, Cersei devours such fools every morning when she breaks her fast. The only way to defeat my sister is to play her own game, and that was something the Lords Stark and Arryn would never do.* Small wonder that both of them were dead, while Tyrion Lannister had never felt more alive. His stunted legs might make him a comic grotesque at a harvest ball, but *this* dance he knew.

Despite the hour, the brothel was crowded. Chataya greeted them pleasantly and escorted them to the common room. Bronn went upstairs with a dark-eyed girl from Dorne, but Alayaya was busy entertaining. "She will be so pleased to know you've come," said Chataya. "I will see that the turret room is made ready for you. Will my lord take a cup of wine while he waits?"

"I will," he said.

The wine was poor stuff compared to the vintages from the Arbor the house normally served. "You must forgive us, my lord," Chataya said. "I cannot find good wine at any price of late."

"You are not alone in that, I fear."

Chataya commiserated with him a moment, then excused herself and glided off. *A handsome woman,* Tyrion reflected as he watched her go. He had seldom seen such elegance and dignity in a whore. Though to be sure, she saw herself more as a kind of priestess. *Perhaps that is the secret. It is not what we do, so much as why we do it.* Somehow that thought comforted him.

A few of the other patrons were giving him sideways looks. The last time he ventured out, a man had spit on him . . . well, had tried to. Instead he'd spit on Bronn, and in future would do his spitting without teeth.

"Is milord feeling unloved?" Dancy slid into his lap and nibbled at his ear. "I have a cure for that."

Smiling, Tyrion shook his head. "You are too beautiful for words, sweetling, but I've grown fond of Alayaya's remedy."

"You've never *tried* mine. Milord never chooses anyone but 'Yaya. She's good but I'm better, don't you want to see?"

"Next time, perhaps." Tyrion had no doubt that Dancy would be a lively handful. She was pug-nosed and bouncy, with freckles and a mane of thick red hair that tumbled down past her waist. But he had Shae waiting for him at the manse.

Giggling, she put her hand between his thighs and squeezed him through his breeches. "I don't think *he* wants to wait till next time," she announced. "He wants to come out and count all my freckles, I think."

"Dancy." Alayaya stood in the doorway, dark and cool in gauzy green silk. "His lordship is come to visit me."

Tyrion gently disentangled himself from the other girl and stood. Dancy did not seem to mind. "Next time," she reminded him. She put a finger in her mouth and sucked it.

As the black-skinned girl led him up the stairs, she said, "Poor Dancy. She has a fortnight to get my lord to choose her. Elsewise she loses her black pearls to Marei."

Marei was a cool, pale, delicate girl Tyrion had noticed once or twice. Green eyes and porcelain skin, long straight silvery hair, very lovely, but too solemn by half. "I'd hate to have the poor child lose her pearls on account of me."

"Then take her upstairs next time."

"Maybe I will."

She smiled. "I think not, my lord."

She's right, Tyrion thought, *I won't. Shae may be only a whore, but I am faithful to her after my fashion.*

In the turret room, as he opened the door of the wardrobe, he looked at Alayaya curiously. "What do you do while I'm gone?"

She raised her arms and stretched like some sleek

black cat. "Sleep. I am much better rested since you began to visit us, my lord. And Marei is teaching us to read, perhaps soon I will be able to pass the time with a book."

"Sleep is good," he said. "And books are better." He gave her a quick kiss on the cheek. Then it was down the shaft and through the tunnel.

As he left the stable on his piebald gelding, Tyrion heard the sound of music drifting over the rooftops. It was pleasant to think that men still sang, even in the midst of butchery and famine. Remembered notes filled his head, and for a moment he could almost hear Tysha as she'd sung to him half a lifetime ago. He reined up to listen. The tune was wrong, the words too faint to hear. A different song then, and why not? His sweet innocent Tysha had been a lie start to finish, only a whore his brother Jaime had hired to make him a man.

I'm free of Tysha now, he thought. *She's haunted me half my life, but I don't need her anymore, no more than I need Alayaya or Dancy or Marei, or the hundreds like them I've bedded with over the years. I have Shae now. Shae.*

The gates of the manse were closed and barred. Tyrion pounded until the ornate bronze eye clacked open. "It's me." The man who admitted him was one of Varys's prettier finds, a Braavosi daggerman with a harelip and a lazy eye. Tyrion had wanted no handsome young guardsmen loitering about Shae day after day. "Find me old, ugly, scarred men, preferably impotent," he had told the eunuch. "Men who prefer boys. Or men who prefer sheep, for that matter." Varys had not managed to come up with any sheeplovers, but he did find a eunuch strangler and a pair of foul-smelling Ibbenese who were as fond of axes as they were of each other. The others were as choice a lot of mercenaries as ever graced a dungeon, each uglier than the last. When Varys had paraded them before him, Tyrion had been afraid he'd gone too far, but Shae had never uttered a word of complaint. *And why would she? She has never com-*

plained of me, and I'm more hideous than all her guards together. Perhaps she does not even see ugliness.

Even so, Tyrion would sooner have used some of his mountain clansmen to guard the manse; Chella's Black Ears perhaps, or the Moon Brothers. He had more faith in their iron loyalties and sense of honor than in the greed of sellswords. The risk was too great, however. All King's Landing knew the wildlings were his. If he sent the Black Ears here, it would only be a matter of time until the whole city knew the King's Hand was keeping a concubine.

One of the Ibbenese took his horse. "Have you woken her?" Tyrion asked him.

"No, m'lord."

"Good."

The fire in the bedchamber had burned down to embers, but the room was still warm. Shae had kicked off her blankets and sheets as she slept. She lay nude atop the featherbed, the soft curves of her young body limned in the faint glow from the hearth. Tyrion stood in the door and drank in the sight of her. *Younger than Marei, sweeter than Dancy, more beautiful than Alayaya, she's all I need and more.* How could a whore look so clean and sweet and innocent, he wondered?

He had not intended to disturb her, but the sight of her was enough to make him hard. He let his garments fall to the floor, then crawled onto the bed and gently pushed her legs apart and kissed her between the thighs. Shae murmured in her sleep. He kissed her again, and licked at her secret sweetness, on and on until his beard and her cunt were both soaked. When she gave a soft moan and shuddered, he climbed up and thrust himself inside her and exploded almost at once.

Her eyes were open. She smiled and stroked his head and whispered, "I just had the sweetest dream, m'lord."

Tyrion nipped at her small hard nipple and nestled his head on her shoulder. He did not pull out of her; would that he never had to pull out of her. "This is no dream," he promised her. *It is real, all of it,* he thought, *the wars, the intrigues, the great bloody game, and me in* the center of it . . . me, the dwarf, the monster, the one they scorned and laughed at, but now I hold it all, the power, the city, the girl. This was what I was made for, and gods forgive me, but I do love it . . .

And her. And her.

ARYA

Whatever names Harren the Black had meant to give his towers were long forgotten. They were called the Tower of Dread, the Widow's Tower, the Wailing Tower, the Tower of Ghosts, and Kingspyre Tower. Arya slept in a shallow niche in the cavernous vaults beneath the Wailing Tower, on a bed of straw. She had water to wash in whenever she liked, a chunk of soap. The work was hard, but no harder than walking miles every day. Weasel did not need to find worms and bugs to eat, as Arry had; there was bread every day, and barley stews with bits of carrot and turnip, and once a fortnight even a bite of meat.

Hot Pie ate even better; he was where he belonged, in the kitchens, a round stone building with a domed roof that was a world unto itself. Arya took her meals at a trestle table in the undercroft with Weese and his other charges, but sometimes she would be chosen to help fetch their food, and she and Hot Pie could steal a moment to talk. He could never remember that she was now Weasel and kept calling her Arry, even though he knew she was a girl. Once he tried to slip her a hot apple tart, but he made such a clumsy job of it that two of the cooks saw. They took the tart away and beat him with a big wooden spoon.

Gendry had been sent to the forge; Arya seldom saw him. As for those she served with, she did not even want to know their names. That only made it hurt worse when they died. Most of them were older than she was and content to let her alone.

Harrenhal was vast, much of it far gone in decay. Lady Whent had held the castle as bannerman to House Tully, but she'd used only the lower thirds of two of the five towers, and let the rest go to ruin. Now she was fled, and the small household she'd left could not begin to tend the needs of all the knights, lords, and highborn prisoners Lord Tywin had brought, so the Lannisters must forage for servants as well as for plunder and provender. The talk was that Lord Tywin planned to restore Harrenhal to glory, and make it his new seat once the war was done.

Weese used Arya to run messages, draw water, and fetch food, and sometimes to serve at table in the Barracks Hall above the armory, where the men-at-arms took their meals. But most of her work was cleaning. The ground floor of the Wailing Tower was given over to storerooms and granaries, and two floors above housed part of the garrison, but the upper stories had not been occupied for eighty years. Now Lord Tywin had commanded that they be made fit for habitation again. There were floors to be scrubbed, grime to be washed off windows, broken chairs and rotted beds to be carried off. The topmost story was infested with nests of the huge black bats that House Whent had used for its sigil, and there were rats in the cellars as well . . . and ghosts, some said, the spirits of Harren the Black and his sons.

Arya thought that was stupid. Harren and his sons had died in Kingspyre Tower, that was why it had that name, so why should they cross the yard to haunt her? The Wailing Tower only wailed when the wind blew from the north, and that was just the sound the air made blowing through the cracks in the stones where they had fissured from the heat. If there *were* ghosts in Harrenhal, they never troubled her. It was the living men she feared, Weese and Ser Gregor Clegane and Lord Tywin Lannister himself, who kept his apartments in Kingspyre Tower, still the tallest and mightiest of all, though lopsided beneath the weight of the slagged stone that made it look like some giant half-melted black candle.

She wondered what Lord Tywin would do if she marched up to him and confessed to being Arya Stark, but she knew she'd never get near enough to talk to him, and anyhow he'd never believe her if she did, and afterward Weese would beat her bloody.

In his own small strutting way, Weese was nearly as scary as Ser Gregor. The Mountain swatted men like flies, but most of the time he did not even seem to know the fly was there. Weese *always* knew you were there, and what you were doing, and sometimes what you were thinking. He would hit at the slightest provocation, and he had a dog who was near as bad as he was, an ugly spotted bitch that smelled worse than any dog Arya had ever known. Once she saw him set the dog on a latrine boy who'd annoyed him. She tore a big chunk out of the boy's calf while Weese laughed.

It took him only three days to earn the place of honor in her nightly prayers. "Weese," she would whisper, first of all. "Dunsen, Chiswyck, Polliver, Raff the Sweetling. The Tickler and the Hound. Ser Gregor, Ser Amory, Ser Ilyn, Ser Meryn, King Joffrey, Queen Cersei." If she let herself forget even one of them, how would she ever find him again to kill him?

On the road Arya had felt like a sheep, but Harrenhal turned her into a mouse. She was grey as a mouse in her scratchy wool shift, and like a mouse she kept to the crannies and crevices and dark holes of the castle, scurrying out of the way of the mighty.

Sometimes she thought they were *all* mice within those thick walls, even the knights and the great lords. The size of the castle made even Gregor Clegane seem small. Harrenhal covered thrice as much ground as Winterfell, and its buildings were so much larger they could scarcely be compared. Its stables housed a thousand horses, its godswood covered twenty acres, its kitchens were as large as Winterfell's Great Hall, and its own great hall, grandly named the Hall of a Hundred Hearths even though it only had thirty and some (Arya had tried to count them, twice, but she came up with thirty-three once and thirty-five the other time) was so cavernous that Lord Tywin could have feasted his entire host, though he never did. Walls, doors, halls, steps, everything was built to an inhuman scale that made Arya remember the stories Old Nan used to tell of the giants who lived beyond the Wall.

And as lords and ladies never notice the little grey mice under their feet, Arya heard all sorts of secrets just by keeping her ears open as she went about her duties. Pretty Pia from the buttery was a slut who was working her way through every knight in the castle. The wife of the gaoler was with child, but the real father was either Ser Alyn Stackspear or a singer called Whitesmile Wat. Lord Lefford made mock of ghosts at table, but always kept a candle burning by his bed. Ser Dunaver's squire Jodge could not hold his water when he slept. The cooks despised Ser Harys Swyft and spit in all his food. Once she even overheard Maester Tothmure's serving girl confiding to her brother about some message that said Joffrey was a bastard and not the rightful king at all. "Lord Tywin told him to burn the letter and never speak such filth again," the girl whispered.

King Robert's brothers Stannis and Renly had joined the fighting, she heard. "And both of them kings now," Weese said. "Realm's got more kings than a castle's got rats." Even Lannister men questioned how long Joffrey would hold the Iron Throne. "The lad's got no army but them gold cloaks, and he's ruled by a eunuch, a dwarf, and a woman," she heard a lordling mutter in his cups. "What good will the likes of them be if it comes to battle?" There was always talk of Beric Dondarrion. A fat archer once said the Bloody Mummers had slain him, but the others only laughed. "Lorch killed the man at Rushing Falls, and the Mountain's slain him twice. Got me a silver stag says he don't stay dead this time neither."

Arya did not know who Bloody Mummers were until a fortnight later, when the queerest company of men she'd ever seen arrived at Harrenhal. Beneath the standard of a black goat with bloody horns rode copper men with bells in their braids; lancers astride striped black-and-white horses; bowmen with powdered cheeks; squat hairy men with shaggy shields; brown-skinned men in feathered cloaks; a wispy fool in green-and-pink motley; swordsmen with fantastic forked beards dyed green and purple and silver; spearmen with colored scars that covered their cheeks; a slender man in septon's robes, a fatherly one in maester's grey, and a sickly one whose leather cloak was fringed with long blond hair.

At their head was a man stick-thin and very tall, with a drawn emaciated face made even longer by the ropy black beard that grew from his pointed chin nearly to his waist. The helm that hung from his saddle horn was black steel, fashioned in the shape of a goat's head. About his neck he wore a chain made of linked coins of many different sizes, shapes, and metals, and his horse was one of the strange black-and-white ones.

"You don't want to know that lot, Weasel," Weese said when he saw her looking at the goat-helmed man. Two of his drinking friends were with him, men-at-arms in service to Lord Lefford.

"Who are they?" she asked.

One of the soldiers laughed. "The Footmen, girl. Toes of the Goat. Lord Tywin's Bloody Mummers."

"Pease for wits. You get her flayed, *you* can scrub the

bloody steps," said Weese. "They're sellswords, Weasel
girl. Call themselves the Brave Companions. Don't use
them other names where they can hear, or they'll hurt
you bad. The goat-helm's their captain, Lord Vargo
Hoat."

"He's no fucking lord," said the second soldier. "I
heard Ser Amory say so. He's just some sellsword with a
mouth full of slobber and a high opinion of hisself."

"Aye," said Weese, "but she better *call* him lord if she
wants to keep all her parts."

Arya looked at Vargo Hoat again. *How many monsters does Lord Tywin have?*

The Brave Companions were housed in the Widow's
Tower, so Arya need not serve them. She was glad of
that; on the very night they arrived, fighting broke out
between the sellswords and some Lannister men. Ser
Harys Swyft's squire was stabbed to death and two of
the Bloody Mummers were wounded. The next morning Lord Tywin hanged them both from the gatehouse
walls, along with one of Lord Lydden's archers. Weese
said the archer had started all the trouble by taunting
the sellswords over Beric Dondarrion. After the hanged
men had stopped kicking, Vargo Hoat and Ser Harys
embraced and kissed and swore to love each other always as Lord Tywin looked on. Arya thought it was
funny the way Vargo Hoat lisped and slobbered, but she
knew better than to laugh.

The Bloody Mummers did not linger long at
Harrenhal, but before they rode out again, Arya heard
one of them saying how a northern army under Roose
Bolton had occupied the ruby ford of the Trident. "If he
crosses, Lord Tywin will smash him again like he did on
the Green Fork," a Lannister bowmen said, but his fellows jeered him down. "Bolton'll never cross, not till
the Young Wolf marches from Riverrun with his wild
northmen and all them wolves."

Arya had not known her brother was so near. Riverrun was much closer than Winterfell, though she was
not certain where it lay in relation to Harrenhal. *I could*

find out somehow, I know I could, if only I could get away. When she thought of seeing Robb's face again Arya had to bite her lip. *And I want to see Jon too, and Bran and Rickon, and Mother. Even Sansa . . . I'll kiss her and beg her pardons like a proper lady, she'll like that.*

From the courtyard talk she'd learned that the upper chambers of the Tower of Dread housed three dozen captives taken during some battle on the Green Fork of the Trident. Most had been given freedom of the castle in return for their pledge not to attempt escape. *They vowed not to escape,* Arya told herself, *but they never swore not to help* me *escape.*

The captives ate at their own table in the Hall of a Hundred Hearths, and could often be seen about the grounds. Four brothers took their exercise together every day, fighting with staves and wooden shields in the Flowstone Yard. Three of them were Freys of the Crossing, the fourth their bastard brother. They were only there a short time, though; one morning two other brothers arrived under a peace banner with a chest of gold, and ransomed them from the knights who'd captured them. The six Freys all left together.

No one ransomed the northmen, though. One fat lordling haunted the kitchens, Hot Pie told her, always looking for a morsel. His mustache was so bushy that it covered his mouth, and the clasp that held his cloak was a silver-and-sapphire trident. He belonged to Lord Tywin, but the fierce, bearded young man who liked to walk the battlements alone in a black cloak patterned with white suns had been taken by some hedge knight who meant to get rich off him. Sansa would have known who he was, and the fat one too, but Arya had never taken much interest in titles and sigils. Whenever Septa Mordane had gone on about the history of this house and that house, she was inclined to drift and dream and wonder when the lesson would be done.

She *did* remember Lord Cerwyn, though. His lands had been close to Winterfell, so he and his son Cley had often visited. Yet as fate would have it, he was the only captive who was never seen; he was abed in a tower cell, recovering from a wound. For days and days Arya tried to work out how she might steal past the door guards to see him. If he knew her, he would be honor bound to help her. A lord would have gold for a certainty, they all did; perhaps he would pay some of Lord Tywin's own sellswords to take her to Riverrun. Father had always said that most sellswords would betray anyone for enough gold.

Then one morning she spied three women in the cowled grey robes of the silent sisters loading a corpse into their wagon. The body was sewn into a cloak of the finest silk, decorated with a battle-axe sigil. When Arya asked who it was, one of the guards told her that Lord Cerwyn had died. The words felt like a kick in the belly. *He could never have helped you anyway,* she thought as the sisters drove the wagon through the gate. *He couldn't even help himself, you stupid mouse.*

After that it was back to scrubbing and scurrying and listening at doors. Lord Tywin would soon march on Riverrun, she heard. Or he would drive south to Highgarden, no one would ever expect that. No, he must defend King's Landing, Stannis was the greatest threat. He'd sent Gregor Clegane and Vargo Hoat to destroy Roose Bolton and remove the dagger from his back. He'd sent ravens to the Eyrie, he meant to wed the Lady Lysa Arryn and win the Vale. He'd bought a ton of silver to forge magic swords that would slay the Stark wargs. He was writing Lady Stark to make a peace, the Kingslayer would soon be freed.

Though ravens came and went every day, Lord Tywin himself spent most of his days behind closed doors with his war council. Arya caught glimpses of him, but always from afar—once walking the walls in the company of three maesters and the fat captive with the bushy mustache, once riding out with his lords bannermen to visit the encampments, but most often standing in an arch of the covered gallery watching men at practice in the yard below. He stood with his hands locked together on the gold pommel of his longsword. They said Lord Tywin loved gold most of all; he even *shit* gold, she heard one squire jest. The Lannister lord was strong-looking for an old man, with stiff golden whiskers and a bald head. There was something in his face that reminded Arya of her own father, even though they looked nothing alike. *He has a lord's face, that's all*, she told herself. She remembered hearing her lady mother tell Father to put on his lord's face and go deal with some matter. Father had laughed at that. She could not imagine Lord Tywin ever laughing at anything.

One afternoon, while she was waiting her turn to draw a pail of water from the well, she heard the hinges of the east gate groaning. A party of men rode under the portcullis at a walk. When she spied the manticore crawling across the shield of their leader, a stab of hate shot through her.

In the light of day, Ser Amory Lorch looked less frightening than he had by torchlight, but he still had the pig's eyes she recalled. One of the women said that his men had ridden all the way around the lake chasing Beric Dondarrion and slaying rebels. *We weren't rebels*, Arya thought. *We were the Night's Watch; the Night's Watch takes no side.* Ser Amory had fewer men than she remembered, though, and many wounded. *I hope their wounds fester. I hope they all die.*

Then she saw the three near the end of the column.

Rorge had donned a black halfhelm with a broad iron nasal that made it hard to see that he did not have a nose. Biter rode ponderously beside him on a destrier that looked ready to collapse under his weight. Half-healed burns covered his body, making him even more hideous than before.

But Jaqen H'ghar still smiled. His garb was still ragged and filthy, but he had found time to wash and brush his hair. It streamed down across his shoulders, red and white and shiny, and Arya heard the girls giggling to each other in admiration.

I should have let the fire have them. Gendry said to, I

should have listened. If she hadn't thrown them that axe they'd all be dead. For a moment she was afraid, but they rode past her without a flicker of interest. Only Jaqen H'ghar so much as glanced in her direction, and his eyes passed right over her. *He does not know me,* she thought. *Arry was a fierce little boy with a sword, and I'm just a grey mouse girl with a pail.*

She spent the rest of that day scrubbing steps inside the Wailing Tower. By evenfall her hands were raw and bleeding and her arms so sore they trembled when she lugged the pail back to the cellar. Too tired even for food, Arya begged Weese's pardons and crawled into her straw to sleep. "Weese," she yawned. "Dunsen, Chiswyck, Polliver, Raff the Sweetling. The Tickler and the Hound. Ser Gregor, Ser Amory, Ser Ilyn, Ser Meryn, King Joffrey, Queen Cersei." She thought she might add three more names to her prayer, but she was too tired to decide tonight.

Arya was dreaming of wolves running wild through the wood when a strong hand clamped down over her mouth like smooth warm stone, solid and unyielding. She woke at once, squirming and struggling. "A girl says nothing," a voice whispered close behind her ear. "A girl keeps her lips closed, no one hears, and friends may talk in secret. Yes?"

Heart pounding, Arya managed the tiniest of nods.

Jaqen H'ghar took his hand away. The cellar was black as pitch and she could not see his face, even inches away. She could *smell* him, though; his skin smelled clean and soapy, and he had scented his hair. "A boy becomes a girl," he murmured.

"I was *always* a girl. I didn't think you saw me."

"A man sees. A man knows."

She remembered that she hated him. "You scared me. You're one of *them* now, I should have let you burn. What are you doing here? Go away or I'll yell for Weese."

"A man pays his debts. A man owes three."

"Three?"

"The Red God has his due, sweet girl, and only death may pay for life. This girl took three that were his. This girl must give three in their places. Speak the names, and a man will do the rest."

He wants to help me, Arya realized with a rush of hope that made her dizzy. "Take me to Riverrun, it's not far, if we stole some horses we could—"

He laid a finger on her lips. "Three lives you shall have of me. No more, no less. Three and we are done. So a girl must ponder." He kissed her hair softly. "But not too long."

By the time Arya lit her stub of a candle, only a faint smell remained of him, a whiff of ginger and cloves lingering in the air. The woman in the next niche rolled over on her straw and complained of the light, so Arya blew it out. When she closed her eyes, she saw faces swimming before her. Joffrey and his mother, Ilyn Payne and Meryn Trant and Sandor Clegane . . . but they were in King's Landing hundreds of miles away, and Ser Gregor had lingered only a few nights before departing again for more foraging, taking Raff and Chiswyck and the Tickler with him. Ser Amory Lorch was here, though, and she hated him almost as much. Didn't she? She wasn't certain. And there was always Weese.

She thought of him again the next morning, when lack of sleep made her yawn. "Weasel," Weese purred, "next time I see that mouth droop open, I'll pull out your tongue and feed it to my bitch." He twisted her ear between his fingers to make certain she'd heard, and told her to get back to those steps, he wanted them clean down to the third landing by nightfall.

As she worked, Arya thought about the people she wanted dead. She pretended she could see their faces on the steps, and scrubbed harder to wipe them away. The Starks were at war with the Lannisters and she was a Stark, so she should kill as many Lannisters as she could, that was what you did in wars. But she didn't think she should trust Jaqen. *I should kill them myself.* Whenever her father had condemned a man to death, he did the deed himself with Ice, his greatsword. "If you would take a man's life, you owe it to him to look him in the face and hear his last words," she'd heard him tell Robb and Jon once.

The next day she avoided Jaqen H'ghar, and the day after that. It was not hard. She was very small and Harrenhal was very large, full of places where a mouse could hide.

And then Ser Gregor returned, earlier than expected, driving a herd of goats this time in place of a herd of prisoners. She heard he'd lost four men in one of Lord Beric's night raids, but those Arya hated returned unscathed and took up residence on the second floor of the Wailing Tower. Weese saw that they were well supplied with drink. "They always have a good thirst, that lot," he grumbled. "Weasel, go up and ask if they've got any clothes that need mending, I'll have the women see to it."

Arya ran up her well-scrubbed steps. No one paid her any mind when she entered. Chiswyck was seated by the fire with a horn of ale to hand, telling one of his funny stories. She dared not interrupt, unless she wanted a bloody lip.

"After the Hand's tourney, it were, before the war come," Chiswyck was saying. "We were on our ways back west, seven of us with Ser Gregor. Raff was with me, and young Joss Stilwood, he'd squired for Ser in the lists. Well, we come on this pisswater river, running high on account there'd been rains. No way to ford, but there's an alehouse near, so there we repair. Ser rousts the brewer and tells him to keep our horns full till the waters fall, and you should see the man's pig eyes shine at the sight o' silver. So he's fetching us ale, him and his daughter, and poor thin stuff it is, no more'n brown piss, which don't make me any happier, nor Ser neither. And all the time this brewer's saying how glad he is to have us, custom being slow on account o' them rains. The fool won't shut his yap, not him, though Ser is saying not a word, just brooding on the Knight o' Pansies and that bugger's trick he played. You can see how tight his mouth sits, so me and the other lads we know better'n to say a squeak to him, but this brewer he's got to talk, he even asks how m'lord fared in the jousting. Ser just gave him this look." Chiswyck cackled, quaffed his ale, and wiped the foam away with the back of his hand. "Meanwhile, this daughter of his has been fetching and pouring, a fat little thing, eighteen or so—"

"Thirteen, more like," Raff the Sweetling drawled.

"Well, be that as it may, she's not much to look at, but Eggon's been drinking and gets to touching her, and might be I did a little touching meself, and Raff's telling young Stilwood that he ought t' drag the girl upstairs and make hisself a man, giving the lad courage as it were. Finally Joss reaches up under her skirt, and she shrieks and drops her flagon and goes running off to the kitchen. Well, it would have ended right there, only what does the old fool do but he goes to *Ser* and asks him to make us leave the girl alone, him being an anointed knight and all such.

"Ser Gregor, he wasn't paying no mind to none of our fun, but now he *looks*, you know how he does, and he commands that the girl be brought before him. Now the old man has to drag her out of the kitchen, and no one to blame but hisself. Ser looks her over and says, 'So this is the whore you're so concerned for,' and this besotted old fool says, 'My Layna's no whore, ser,' right to Gregor's face. Ser, he never blinks, just says, 'She is now,' tosses the old man another silver, rips the dress off the wench, and takes her right there on the table in front of her da, her flopping and wiggling like a rabbit and making these noises. The look on the old man's face, I laughed so hard ale was coming out me nose. Then this boy hears the noise, the son I figure, and comes rushing up from the cellar, so Raff has to stick a dirk in his belly. By then Ser's done, so he goes back to his drinking and we all have a turn. Tobbot, you know how he is, he flops her over and goes in the back way. The girl was done fighting by the time I had her, maybe she'd decided she liked it after all, though to tell the truth I wouldn't have minded a little wiggling. And now here's the best bit . . . when it's all done, Ser tells the old man that he wants his change. The girl wasn't worth a silver, he says . . . and damned if that old man didn't fetch a fistful of coppers, beg m'lord's pardon, and *thank him for the custom*!"

The men all roared, none louder than Chiswyck himself, who laughed so hard at his own story that snot dribbled from his nose down into his scraggy grey beard. Arya stood in the shadows of the stairwell and watched him. She crept back down to the cellars without saying a word. When Weese found that she hadn't asked about the clothes, he yanked down her breeches and caned her until blood ran down her thighs, but Arya closed her eyes and thought of all the sayings Syrio had taught her, so she scarcely felt it.

Two nights later, he sent her to the Barracks Hall to serve at table. She was carrying a flagon of wine and pouring when she glimpsed Jaqen H'ghar at his trencher across the aisle. Chewing her lip, Arya glanced around warily to make certain Weese was not in sight. *Fear cuts deeper than swords*, she told herself.

She took a step, and another, and with each she felt less a mouse. She worked her way down the bench, filling wine cups. Rorge sat to Jaqen's right, deep drunk, but he took no note of her. Arya leaned close and whispered, "Chiswyck," right in Jaqen's ear. The Lorathi gave no sign that he had heard.

When her flagon was empty, Arya hurried down to the cellars to refill it from the cask, and quickly returned to her pouring. No one had died of thirst while she was gone, nor even noted her brief absence.

Nothing happened the next day, nor the day after, but on the third day Arya went to the kitchens with Weese to fetch their dinner. "One of the Mountain's men fell off a wallwalk last night and broke his fool neck," she heard Weese tell a cook.

"Drunk?" the woman asked.

"No more'n usual. Some are saying it was Harren's

ghost flung him down." He snorted to show what *he* thought of such notions.

It wasn't Harren, Arya wanted to say, *it was me*. She had killed Chiswyck with a whisper, and she would kill two more before she was through. *I'm the ghost in Harrenhal*, she thought. And that night, there was one less name to hate.

CATELYN

The meeting place was a grassy sward dotted with pale grey mushrooms and the raw stumps of felled trees.

"We are the first, my lady," Hallis Mollen said as they reined up amidst the stumps, alone between the armies. The direwolf banner of House Stark flapped and fluttered atop the lance he bore. Catelyn could not see the sea from here, but she could feel how close it was. The smell of salt was heavy on the wind gusting from the east.

Stannis Baratheon's foragers had cut the trees down for his siege towers and catapults. Catelyn wondered how long the grove had stood, and whether Ned had rested here when he led his host south to lift the last siege of Storm's End. He had won a great victory that day, all the greater for being bloodless.

Gods grant that I shall do the same, Catelyn prayed. Her own liege men thought she was mad even to come. "This is no fight of ours, my lady," Ser Wendel

Manderly had said. "I know the king would not wish his mother to put herself at risk."

"We are all at risk," she told him, perhaps too sharply. "Do you think I wish to be here, ser?" *I belong at Riverrun with my dying father, at Winterfell with my sons.* "Robb sent me south to speak for him, and speak for him I shall." It would be no easy thing to forge a peace between these brothers, Catelyn knew, yet for the good of the realm, it must be tried.

Across rain-sodden fields and stony ridges, she could see the great castle of Storm's End rearing up against the sky, its back to the unseen sea. Beneath that mass of pale grey stone, the encircling army of Lord Stannis Baratheon looked as small and insignificant as mice with banners.

The songs said that Storm's End had been raised in ancient days by Durran, the first Storm King, who had won the love of the fair Elenei, daughter of the sea god and the goddess of the wind. On the night of their wedding, Elenei had yielded her maidenhood to a mortal's love and thus doomed herself to a mortal's death, and her grieving parents had unleashed their wrath and sent the winds and waters to batter down Durran's hold. His friends and brothers and wedding guests were crushed beneath collapsing walls or blown out to sea, but Elenei sheltered Durran within her arms so he took no harm, and when the dawn came at last he declared war upon the gods and vowed to rebuild.

Five more castles he built, each larger and stronger than the last, only to see them smashed asunder when the gale winds came howling up Shipbreaker Bay, driving great walls of water before them. His lords pleaded with him to build inland; his priests told him he must placate the gods by giving Elenei back to the sea; even his smallfolk begged him to relent. Durran would have none of it. A seventh castle he raised, most massive of all. Some said the children of the forest helped him build it, shaping the stones with magic; others claimed that a small boy told him what he must do, a boy who would grow to be Bran the Builder. No matter how the tale was told, the end was the same. Though the angry gods threw storm after storm against it, the seventh castle stood defiant, and Durran Godsgrief and fair Elenei dwelt there together until the end of their days.

Gods do not forget, and still the gales came raging up the narrow sea. Yet Storm's End endured, through centuries and tens of centuries, a castle like no other. Its great curtain wall was a hundred feet high, unbroken by arrow slit or postern, everywhere rounded, curving, smooth, its stones fit so cunningly together that nowhere was crevice nor angle nor gap by which the wind might enter. That wall was said to be forty feet thick at its narrowest, and near eighty on the seaward face, a double course of stones with an inner core of sand and rubble. Within that mighty bulwark, the kitchens and stables and yards sheltered safe from wind and wave. Of towers, there was but one, a colossal drum tower, windowless where it faced the sea, so large that it was granary and barracks and feast hall and lord's dwelling all in one, crowned by massive battlements that made it look from afar like a spiked fist atop an upthrust arm.

"My lady," Hal Mollen called. Two riders had emerged from the tidy little camp beneath the castle, and were coming toward them at a slow walk. "That will be King Stannis."

"No doubt." Catelyn watched them come. *Stannis it must be, yet that is not the Baratheon banner.* It was a bright yellow, not the rich gold of Renly's standards, and the device it bore was red, though she could not make out its shape.

Renly would be last to arrive. He had told her as much when she set out. He did not propose to mount his horse until he saw his brother well on his way. The first to arrive must wait on the other, and Renly would do no waiting. *It is a sort of game kings play,* she told herself. Well, she was no king, so she need not play it. Catelyn was practiced at waiting.

As he neared, she saw that Stannis wore a crown of red gold with points fashioned in the shape of flames. His belt was studded with garnets and yellow topaz, and a great square-cut ruby was set in the hilt of the sword he wore. Otherwise his dress was plain: studded leather jerkin over quilted doublet, worn boots, breeches of brown roughspun. The device on his sun-yellow banner showed a red heart surrounded by a blaze of orange fire. The crowned stag was there, yes . . . shrunken and enclosed within the heart. Even more curious was his standard bearer—a woman, garbed all in reds, face shadowed within the deep hood of her scarlet cloak. *A red priestess*, Catelyn thought, wondering. The sect was numerous and powerful in the Free Cities and the distant east, but there were few in the Seven Kingdoms.

"Lady Stark," Stannis Baratheon said with chill courtesy as he reined up. He inclined his head, balder than she remembered.

"Lord Stannis," she returned.

Beneath the tight-trimmed beard his heavy jaw clenched hard, yet he did not hector her about titles. For that she was duly grateful. "I had not thought to find you at Storm's End."

"I had not thought to be here."

His deepset eyes regarded her uncomfortably. This was not a man made for easy courtesies. "I am sorry for your lord's death," he said, "though Eddard Stark was no friend to me."

"He was never your enemy, my lord. When the Lords Tyrell and Redwyne held you prisoned in that castle, starving, it was Eddard Stark who broke the siege."

"At my brother's command, not for love of me," Stannis answered. "Lord Eddard did his duty, I will not deny it. Did I ever do less? *I* should have been Robert's Hand."

"That was your brother's will. Ned never wanted it."

"Yet he took it. That which should have been mine. Still, I give you my word, you shall have justice for his murder."

How they loved to promise heads, these men who would be king. "Your brother promised me the same. But if truth be told, I would sooner have my daughters back, and leave justice to the gods. Cersei still holds my

Sansa, and of Arya there has been no word since the day of Robert's death."

"If your children are found when I take the city, they shall be sent to you." *Alive or dead*, his tone implied.

"And when shall that be, Lord Stannis? King's Landing is close to your Dragonstone, but I find you here instead."

"You are frank, Lady Stark. Very well, I'll answer you frankly. To take the city, I need the power of these southron lords I see across the field. My brother has them. I must needs take them from him."

"Men give their allegiance where they will, my lord. These lords swore fealty to Robert and House Baratheon. If you and your brother were to put aside your quarrel—"

"I have no quarrel with Renly, should he prove dutiful. I am his elder, and his king. I want only what is mine by rights. Renly owes me loyalty and obedience. I mean to have it. From him, and from these other lords." Stannis studied her face. "And what cause brings you to this field, my lady? Has House Stark cast its lot with my brother, is that the way of it?"

This one will never bend, she thought, yet she must try nonetheless. Too much was at stake. "My son reigns as King in the North, by the will of our lords and people. He bends the knee to no man, but holds out the hand of friendship to all."

"Kings have no friends," Stannis said bluntly, "only subjects and enemies."

"And brothers," a cheerful voice called out behind her. Catelyn glanced over her shoulder as Lord Renly's palfrey picked her way through the stumps. The younger Baratheon was splendid in his green velvet doublet and satin cloak trimmed in vair. The crown of golden roses girded his temples, jade stag's head rising over his forehead, long black hair spilling out beneath. Jagged chunks of black diamond studded his swordbelt, and a chain of gold and emeralds looped around his neck.

Renly had chosen a woman to carry his banner as

well, though Brienne hid face and form behind plate armor that gave no hint of her sex. Atop her twelve-foot lance, the crowned stag pranced black-on-gold as the wind off the sea rippled the cloth.

His brother's greeting was curt. "Lord Renly."

"*King* Renly. Can that truly be you, Stannis?"

Stannis frowned. "Who else should it be?"

Renly gave an easy shrug. "When I saw that standard, I could not be certain. Whose banner do you bear?"

"Mine own."

The red-clad priestess spoke up. "The king has taken for his sigil the fiery heart of the Lord of Light."

Renly seemed amused by that. "All for the good. If we both use the same banner, the battle will be terribly confused."

Catelyn said, "Let us hope there will be no battle. We three share a common foe who would destroy us all."

Stannis studied her, unsmiling. "The Iron Throne is mine by rights. All those who deny that are my foes."

"The whole of the realm denies it, brother," said Renly. "Old men deny it with their death rattle, and unborn children deny it in their mothers' wombs. They deny it in Dorne and they deny it on the Wall. No one wants you for their king. Sorry."

Stannis clenched his jaw, his face taut. "I swore I would never treat with you while you wore your traitor's crown. Would that I had kept to that vow."

"This is folly," Catelyn said sharply. "Lord Tywin sits at Harrenhal with twenty thousand swords. The remnants of the Kingslayer's army have regrouped at the Golden Tooth, another Lannister host gathers beneath the shadow of Casterly Rock, and Cersei and her son hold King's Landing and your precious Iron Throne. You each name yourself *king*, yet the kingdom bleeds, and no one lifts a sword to defend it but my son."

Renly shrugged. "Your son has won a few battles. I shall win the war. The Lannisters can wait my pleasure."

"If you have proposals to make, make them," Stannis said brusquely, "or I will be gone."

"Very well," said Renly. "I propose that you dismount, bend your knee, and swear me your allegiance."

Stannis choked back rage. "That you shall never have."

"You served Robert, why not me?"

"Robert was my elder brother. You are the younger."

"Younger, bolder, and *far* more comely . . ."

". . . and a thief and a usurper besides."

Renly shrugged. "The Targaryens called Robert usurper. He seemed to be able to bear the shame. So shall I."

This will not do. "Listen to yourselves! If you were sons of mine, I would bang your heads together and lock you in a bedchamber until you remembered that you were brothers."

Stannis frowned at her. "You presume too much, Lady Stark. I am the rightful king, and your son no less a traitor than my brother here. His day will come as well."

The naked threat fanned her fury. "You are very free to name others traitor and usurper, my lord, yet how are you any different? You say you alone are the rightful king, yet it seems to me that Robert had two sons. By all the laws of the Seven Kingdoms, Prince Joffrey is his rightful heir, and Tommen after him . . . and we are *all* traitors, however good our reasons."

Renly laughed. "You must forgive Lady Catelyn, Stannis. She's come all the way down from Riverrun, a long way ahorse. I fear she never saw your little letter."

"Joffrey is not my brother's seed," Stannis said bluntly. "Nor is Tommen. They are bastards. The girl as well. All three of them abominations born of incest."

Would even Cersei be so mad? Catelyn was speechless.

"Isn't that a sweet story, my lady?" Renly asked. "I was camped at Horn Hill when Lord Tarly received his letter, and I must say, it took my breath away." He smiled at his brother. "I had never suspected you were so clever, Stannis. Were it only true, you would indeed be Robert's heir."

"*Were* it true? Do you name me a liar?"

"Can you prove any word of this fable?"

Stannis ground his teeth.

Robert could never have known, Catelyn thought, *or Cersei would have lost her head in an instant.* "Lord Stannis," she asked, "if you knew the queen to be guilty of such monstrous crimes, why did you keep silent?"

"I did not keep silent," Stannis declared. "I brought my suspicions to Jon Arryn."

"Rather than your own brother?"

"My brother's regard for me was never more than dutiful," said Stannis. "From me, such accusations would have seemed peevish and self-serving, a means of placing myself first in the line of succession. I believed Robert would be more disposed to listen if the charges came from Lord Arryn, whom he loved."

"Ah," said Renly. "So we have the word of a dead man."

"Do you think he died by happenstance, you purblind fool? Cersei had him poisoned, for fear he would reveal her. Lord Jon had been gathering certain proofs—"

"—which doubtless died with him. How inconvenient."

Catelyn was remembering, fitting pieces together. "My sister Lysa accused the queen of killing her husband in a letter she sent me at Winterfell," she admitted. "Later, in the Eyrie, she laid the murder at the feet of the queen's brother Tyrion."

Stannis snorted. "If you step in a nest of snakes, does it matter which one bites you first?"

"All this of snakes and incest is droll, but it changes nothing. You may well have the better claim, Stannis, but I still have the larger army." Renly's hand slid inside his cloak. Stannis saw, and reached at once for the hilt of his sword, but before he could draw steel his brother produced . . . a peach. "Would you like one, brother?" Renly asked, smiling. "From Highgarden. You've never tasted anything so sweet, I promise you." He took a bite. Juice ran from the corner of his mouth.

"I did not come here to eat fruit." Stannis was fuming.

"My lords!" Catelyn said. "We ought to be hammering out the terms of an alliance, not trading taunts."

"A man should never refuse to taste a peach," Renly said as he tossed the stone away. "He may never get the chance again. Life is short, Stannis. Remember what the Starks say. Winter is coming." He wiped his mouth with the back of his hand.

"I did not come here to be threatened, either."

"Nor were you," Renly snapped back. "When I make threats, you'll know it. If truth be told, I've never liked you, Stannis, but you *are* my own blood, and I have no wish to slay you. So if it is Storm's End you want, take it . . . as a brother's gift. As Robert once gave it to me, I give it to you."

"It is not yours to give. It is mine by rights."

Sighing, Renly half turned in the saddle. "What am I to do with this brother of mine, Brienne? He refuses my peach, he refuses my castle, he even shunned my wedding . . ."

"We both know your wedding was a mummer's farce. A year ago you were scheming to make the girl one of Robert's whores."

"A year ago I was scheming to make the girl Robert's queen," Renly said, "but what does it matter? The boar got Robert and I got Margaery. You'll be pleased to know she came to me a maid."

"In your bed she's like to die that way."

"Oh, I expect I'll get a son on her within the year. Pray, how many sons do you have, Stannis? Oh, yes— none." Renly smiled innocently. "As to your daughter, I understand. If my wife looked like yours, I'd send my fool to service her as well."

"Enough!" Stannis roared. "I will not be mocked to my face, do you hear me? *I will not!"* He yanked his longsword from its scabbard. The steel gleamed strangely bright in the wan sunlight, now red, now yellow, now blazing white. The air around it seemed to shimmer, as if from heat.

Catelyn's horse whinnied and backed away a step, but Brienne moved between the brothers, her own blade in hand. "Put up your steel!" she shouted at Stannis.

Cersei Lannister is laughing herself breathless, Catelyn thought wearily.

Stannis pointed his shining sword at his brother. "I am not without mercy," thundered he who was notoriously without mercy. "Nor do I wish to sully Lightbringer with a brother's blood. For the sake of the mother who bore us both, I will give you this night to rethink your folly, Renly. Strike your banners and come to me before dawn, and I will grant you Storm's End and your old seat on the council and even name you my heir until a son is born to me. Otherwise, I shall destroy you."

Renly laughed. "Stannis, that's a very pretty sword, I'll grant you, but I think the glow off it has ruined your eyes. Look across the fields, brother. Can you see all those banners?"

"Do you think a few bolts of cloth will make you king?"

"Tyrell swords will make me king. Rowan and Tarly and Caron will make me king, with axe and mace and warhammer. Tarth arrows and Penrose lances, Fossoway, Cuy, Mullendore, Estermont, Selmy, Hightower, Oakheart, Crane, Caswell, Blackbar, Morrigen, Beesbury, Shermer, Dunn, Footly . . . even House Florent, your own wife's brothers and uncles, they will make me king. All the chivalry of the south rides with me, and that is the least part of my power. My foot is coming behind, a hundred thousand swords and spears and pikes. And you will *destroy* me? With what, pray? That paltry rabble I see there huddled under the castle walls? I'll call them five thousand and be generous, codfish lords and onion knights and sellswords. Half of them are like to come over to me before the battle starts. You have fewer than four hundred horse, my scouts tell me—freeriders in boiled leather who will not stand an instant against armored lances. I do not care how seasoned a warrior you think you are, Stannis, that host of yours won't survive the first charge of my vanguard."

"We shall see, brother." Some of the light seemed to go out of the world when Stannis slid his sword back into its scabbard. "Come the dawn, we shall see."

"I hope your new god's a merciful one, brother."

Stannis snorted and galloped away, disdainful. The red priestess lingered a moment behind. "Look to your own sins, Lord Renly," she said as she wheeled her horse around.

Catelyn and Lord Renly returned together to the camp where his thousands and her few waited their return. "That was amusing, if not terribly profitable," he commented. "I wonder where I can get a sword like that? Well, doubtless Loras will make me a gift of it after the battle. It grieves me that it must come to this."

"You have a cheerful way of grieving," said Catelyn, whose distress was not feigned.

"Do I?" Renly shrugged. "So be it. Stannis was never the most cherished of brothers, I confess. Do you suppose this tale of his is true? If Joffrey is the Kingslayer's get—"

"—your brother is the lawful heir."

"While he lives," Renly admitted. "Though it's a fool's law, wouldn't you agree? Why the oldest son, and not the best-fitted? The crown will suit me, as it never suited Robert and would not suit Stannis. I have it in me to be a great king, strong yet generous, clever, just, diligent, loyal to my friends and terrible to my enemies, yet capable of forgiveness, patient—"

"—humble?" Catelyn supplied.

Renly laughed. "You must allow a king *some* flaws, my lady."

Catelyn felt very tired. It had all been for nothing. The Baratheon brothers would drown each other in blood while her son faced the Lannisters alone, and nothing she could say or do would stop it. *It is past time I went back to Riverrun to close my father's eyes,* she thought. *That much at least I can do. I may be a poor envoy, but I am a good mourner, gods save me.*

Their camp was well sited atop a low stony ridge that ran from north to south. It was far more orderly than the sprawling encampment on the Mander, though only a quarter as large. When he'd learned of his brother's assault on Storm's End, Renly had split his forces, much as Robb had done at the Twins. His great mass of foot he had left behind at Bitterbridge with his young queen, his wagons, carts, draft animals, and all his cumbersome siege machinery, while Renly himself led his knights and freeriders in a swift dash east.

How like his brother Robert he was, even in that . . . only Robert had always had Eddard Stark to temper his boldness with caution. Ned would surely have prevailed upon Robert to bring up his *whole* force, to encircle Stannis and besiege the besiegers. That choice Renly had denied himself in his headlong rush to come to grips with his brother. He had outdistanced his supply lines, left food and forage days behind with all his wagons and mules and oxen. He *must* come to battle soon, or starve.

Catelyn sent Hal Mollen to tend to their horses while she accompanied Renly back to the royal pavilion at the heart of the encampment. Inside the walls of green silk, his captains and lords bannermen were waiting to hear word of the parley. "My brother has not changed," their young king told them as Brienne unfastened his cloak and lifted the gold-and-jade crown from his brow. "Castles and courtesies will not appease him, he must have blood. Well, I am of a mind to grant his wish."

"Your Grace, I see no need for battle here," Lord Mathis Rowan put in. "The castle is strongly garrisoned and well provisioned, Ser Cortnay Penrose is a seasoned commander, and the trebuchet has not been built that could breach the walls of Storm's End. Let Lord Stannis have his siege. He will find no joy in it, and whilst he sits cold and hungry and profitless, we will take King's Landing."

"And have men say I feared to face Stannis?"

"Only fools will say that," Lord Mathis argued.

Renly looked to the others. "What say you all?"

"I say that Stannis is a danger to you," Lord Randyll Tarly declared. "Leave him unblooded and he will only grow stronger, while your own power is diminished by battle. The Lannisters will not be beaten in a day. By the time you are done with them, Lord Stannis may be as strong as you . . . or stronger."

Others chorused their agreement. The king looked pleased. "We shall fight, then."

I have failed Robb as I failed Ned, Catelyn thought. "My lord," she announced. "If you are set on battle, my purpose here is done. I ask your leave to return to Riverrun."

"You do not have it." Renly seated himself on a camp chair.

She stiffened. "I had hoped to help you make a peace, my lord. I will not help you make a war."

Renly gave a shrug. "I daresay we'll prevail without your five-and-twenty, my lady. I do not mean for you to take part in the battle, only to watch it."

"I was at the Whispering Wood, my lord. I have seen enough butchery. I came here an envoy—"

"And an envoy you shall leave," Renly said, "but wiser than you came. You shall see what befalls rebels with your own eyes, so your son can hear it from your own lips. We'll keep you safe, never fear." He turned away to make his dispositions. "Lord Mathis, you shall lead the center of my main battle. Bryce, you'll have the left. The right is mine. Lord Estermont, you shall command the reserve."

"I shall not fail you, Your Grace," Lord Estermont replied.

Lord Mathis Rowan spoke up. "Who shall have the van?"

"Your Grace," said Ser Jon Fossoway, "I beg the honor."

"Beg all you like," said Ser Guyard the Green, "by rights it should be one of the seven who strikes the first blow."

"It takes more than a pretty cloak to charge a shield wall," Randyll Tarly announced. "I was leading Mace

Tyrell's van when you were still sucking on your mother's teat, Guyard.''

A clamor filled the pavilion, as other men loudly set forth their claims. *The knights of summer,* Catelyn thought. Renly raised a hand. "Enough, my lords. If I had a dozen vans, all of you should have one, but the greatest glory by rights belongs to the greatest knight. Ser Loras shall strike the first blow."

"With a glad heart, Your Grace." The Knight of Flowers knelt before the king. "Grant me your blessing, and a knight to ride beside me with your banner. Let the stag and rose go to battle side by side."

Renly glanced about him. "Brienne."

"Your Grace?" She was still armored in her blue steel, though she had taken off her helm. The crowded tent was hot, and sweat plastered limp yellow hair to her broad, homely face. "My place is at your side. I am your sworn shield . . ."

"One of seven," the king reminded her. "Never fear, four of your fellows will be with me in the fight."

Brienne dropped to her knees. "If I must part from Your Grace, grant me the honor of arming you for battle."

Catelyn heard someone snigger behind her. *She loves him, poor thing,* she thought sadly. *She'd play his squire just to touch him, and never care how great a fool they think her.*

"Granted," Renly said. "Now leave me, all of you. Even kings must rest before a battle."

"My lord," Catelyn said, "there was a small sept in the last village we passed. If you will not permit me to depart for Riverrun, grant me leave to go there and pray."

"As you will. Ser Robar, give Lady Stark safe escort to this sept . . . but see that she returns to us by dawn."

"You might do well to pray yourself," Catelyn added.

"For victory?"

"For wisdom."

Renly laughed. "Loras, stay and help me pray. It's been so long I've quite forgotten how. As to the rest of you, I want every man in place by first light, armed, armored, and horsed. We shall give Stannis a dawn he will not soon forget."

Dusk was falling when Catelyn left the pavilion. Ser Robar Royce fell in beside her. She knew him slightly—one of Bronze Yohn's sons, comely in a rough-hewn way, a tourney warrior of some renown. Renly had gifted him with a rainbow cloak and a suit of blood red armor, and named him one of his seven. "You are a long way from the Vale, ser," she told him.

"And you far from Winterfell, my lady."

"I know what brought me here, but why have you come? This is not your battle, no more than it is mine."

"I made it my battle when I made Renly my king."

"The Royces are bannermen to House Arryn."

"My lord father owes Lady Lysa fealty, as does his heir. A second son must find glory where he can." Ser Robar shrugged. "A man grows weary of tourneys."

He could not be older than one-and-twenty, Catelyn thought, of an age with his king . . . but *her* king, her Robb, had more wisdom at fifteen than this youth had ever learned. Or so she prayed.

In Catelyn's small corner of the camp, Shadd was slicing carrots into a kettle, Hal Mollen was dicing with three of his Winterfell men, and Lucas Blackwood sat sharpening his dagger. "Lady Stark," Lucas said when he saw her, "Mollen says it is to be battle at dawn."

"Hal has the truth of it," she answered. *And a loose tongue as well, it would seem.*

"Do we fight or flee?"

"We pray, Lucas," she answered him. "We pray."

SANSA

"The longer you keep him waiting, the worse it will go for you," Sandor Clegane warned her.

Sansa tried to hurry, but her fingers fumbled at buttons and knots. The Hound was always rough-tongued, but something in the way he had looked at her filled her with dread. Had Joffrey found out about her meetings with Ser Dontos? *Please no*, she thought as she brushed out her hair. Ser Dontos was her only hope. *I have to look pretty, Joff likes me to look pretty, he's always liked me in this gown, this color.* She smoothed the cloth down. The fabric was tight across her chest.

When she emerged, Sansa walked on the Hound's left, away from the burned side of his face. "Tell me what I've done."

"Not you. Your kingly brother."

"Robb's a traitor." Sansa knew the words by rote. "I had no part in whatever he did." *Gods be good, don't let it be the Kingslayer.* If Robb had harmed Jaime Lannister, it would mean her life. She thought of Ser

Ilyn, and how those terrible pale eyes staring pitilessly out of that gaunt pockmarked face.

The Hound snorted. "They trained you well, little bird." He conducted her to the lower bailey, where a crowd had gathered around the archery butts. Men moved aside to let them through. She could hear Lord Gyles coughing. Loitering stablehands eyed her insolently, but Ser Horas Redwyne averted his gaze as she passed, and his brother Hobber pretended not to see her. A yellow cat was dying on the ground, mewling piteously, a crossbow quarrel through its ribs. Sansa stepped around it, feeling ill.

Ser Dontos approached on his broomstick horse; since he'd been too drunk to mount his destrier at the tourney, the king had decreed that henceforth he must always go horsed. "Be brave," he whispered, squeezing her arm.

Joffrey stood in the center of the throng, winding an ornate crossbow. Ser Boros and Ser Meryn were with him. The sight of them was enough to tie her insides in knots.

"Your Grace." She fell to her knees.

"Kneeling won't save you now," the king said. "Stand up. You're here to answer for your brother's latest treasons."

"Your Grace, whatever my traitor brother has done, I had no part. You know that, I beg you, please—"

"*Get her up!*"

The Hound pulled her to her feet, not ungently.

"Ser Lancel," Joff said, "tell her of this outrage."

Sansa had always thought Lancel Lannister comely and well spoken, but there was neither pity nor kindness in the look he gave her. "Using some vile sorcery, your brother fell upon Ser Stafford Lannister with an army of wargs, not three days ride from Lannisport. Thousands of good men were butchered as they slept, without the chance to lift sword. After the slaughter, the northmen feasted on the flesh of the slain."

Horror coiled cold hands around Sansa's throat.

"You have nothing to say?" asked Joffrey.

"Your Grace, the poor child is shocked witless," murmured Ser Dontos.

"Silence, fool." Joffrey lifted his crossbow and pointed it at her face. "You Starks are as unnatural as those wolves of yours. I've not forgotten how your monster savaged me."

"That was Arya's wolf," she said. "Lady never hurt you, but you killed her anyway."

"No, your father did," Joff said, "but I killed your father. I wish I'd done it myself. I killed a man last night who was bigger than your father. They came to the gate shouting my name and calling for bread like I was some *baker*, but I taught them better. I shot the loudest one right through the throat."

"And he died?" With the ugly iron head of the quarrel staring her in the face, it was hard to think what else to say.

"Of course he died, he had my quarrel in his throat. There was a woman throwing rocks, I got her as well, but only in the arm." Frowning, he lowered the crossbow. "I'd shoot you too, but if I do Mother says they'd kill my uncle Jaime. Instead you'll just be punished and we'll send word to your brother about what will happen to you if he doesn't yield. Dog, hit her."

"Let me beat her!" Ser Dontos shoved forward, tin armor clattering. He was armed with a "morningstar" whose head was a melon. *My Florian.* She could have kissed him, blotchy skin and broken veins and all. He trotted his broomstick around her, shouting "Traitor, traitor" and whacking her over the head with the melon. Sansa covered herself with her hands, staggering every time the fruit pounded her, her hair sticky by the second blow. People were laughing. The melon flew to pieces. *Laugh, Joffrey,* she prayed as the juice ran down her face and the front of her blue silk gown. *Laugh and be satisfied.*

Joffrey did not so much as snigger. "Boros. Meryn."

Ser Meryn Trant seized Dontos by the arm and flung him brusquely away. The red-faced fool went sprawling, broomstick, melon, and all. Ser Boros seized Sansa.

"Leave her face," Joffrey commanded. "I like her pretty."

Boros slammed a fist into Sansa's belly, driving the air out of her. When she doubled over, the knight grabbed her hair and drew his sword, and for one hideous instant she was certain he meant to open her throat. As he laid the flat of the blade across her thighs, she thought her legs might break from the force of the blow. Sansa screamed. Tears welled in her eyes. *It will be over soon.* She soon lost count of the blows.

"Enough," she heard the Hound rasp.

"No it isn't," the king replied. "Boros, make her naked."

Boros shoved a meaty hand down the front of Sansa's bodice and gave a hard yank. The silk came tearing away, baring her to the waist. Sansa covered her breasts with her hands. She could hear sniggers, far off and cruel. "Beat her bloody," Joffrey said, "we'll see how her brother fancies—"

"What is the meaning of this?"

The Imp's voice cracked like a whip, and suddenly Sansa was free. She stumbled to her knees, arms crossed over her chest, her breath ragged. "Is this your notion of chivalry, Ser Boros?" Tyrion Lannister demanded angrily. His pet sellsword stood with him, and one of his wildlings, the one with the burned eye. "What sort of knight beats helpless maids?"

"The sort who serves his king, Imp." Ser Boros raised his sword, and Ser Meryn stepped up beside him, his blade scraping clear of its scabbard.

"Careful with those," warned the dwarf's sellsword. "You don't want to get blood all over those pretty white cloaks."

"Someone give the girl something to cover herself with," the Imp said. Sandor Clegane unfastened his cloak and tossed it at her. Sansa clutched it against her chest, fists bunched hard in the white wool. The coarse weave was scratchy against her skin, but no velvet had ever felt so fine.

"This girl's to be your queen," the Imp told Joffrey. "Have you no regard for her honor?"

"I'm punishing her."

"For what crime? She did not fight her brother's battle."

"She has the blood of a wolf."

"And you have the wits of a goose."

"You can't talk to me that way. The king can do as he likes."

"Aerys Targaryen did as he liked. Has your mother ever told you what happened to him?"

Ser Boros Blount *harrumphed*. "No man threatens His Grace in the presence of the Kingsguard."

Tyrion Lannister raised an eyebrow. "I am not threatening the king, ser, I am educating my nephew. Bronn, Timett, the next time Ser Boros opens his mouth, kill him." The dwarf smiled. "Now *that* was a threat, ser. See the difference?"

Ser Boros turned a dark shade of red. "The queen will hear of this!"

"No doubt she will. And why wait? Joffrey, shall we send for your mother?"

The king flushed.

"Nothing to say, Your Grace?" his uncle went on. "Good. Learn to use your ears more and your mouth less, or your reign will be shorter than I am. Wanton brutality is no way to win your people's love . . . or your queen's."

"Fear is better than love, Mother says." Joffrey pointed at Sansa. "*She* fears me."

The Imp sighed. "Yes, I see. A pity Stannis and Renly aren't twelve-year-old girls as well. Bronn, Timett, bring her."

Sansa moved as if in a dream. She thought the Imp's men would take her back to her bedchamber in Maegor's Holdfast, but instead they conducted her to the Tower of the Hand. She had not set foot inside that place since the day her father fell from grace, and it made her feel faint to climb those steps again.

Some serving girls took charge of her, mouthing

meaningless comforts to stop her shaking. One stripped
off the ruins of her gown and smallclothes, and another
bathed her and washed the sticky juice from her face
and her hair. As they scrubbed her down with soap and
sluiced warm water over her head, all she could see
were the faces from the bailey. *Knights are sworn to
defend the weak, protect women, and fight for the
right, but none of them did a thing.* Only Ser Dontos
had tried to help, and he was no longer a knight, no
more than the Imp was, nor the Hound . . . the Hound
hated knights . . . *I hate them too,* Sansa thought.
They are no true knights, not one of them.

After she was clean, plump ginger-headed Maester
Frenken came to see her. He bid her lie facedown on the
mattress while he spread a salve across the angry red
welts that covered the backs of her legs. Afterward he
mixed her a draught of dreamwine, with some honey so
it might go down easier. "Sleep a bit, child. When you
wake, all this will seem a bad dream."

No it won't, you stupid man, Sansa thought, but she
drank the dreamwine anyway, and slept.

It was dark when she woke again, not quite knowing
where she was, the room both strange and strangely familiar. As she rose, a stab of pain went through her legs
and brought it all back. Tears filled her eyes. Someone
had laid out a robe for her beside the bed. Sansa slipped
it on and opened the door. Outside stood a hard-faced
woman with leathery brown skin, three necklaces
looped about her scrawny neck. One was gold and one
was silver and one was made of human ears. "Where
does she think she's going?" the woman asked, leaning
on a tall spear.

"The godswood." She had to find Ser Dontos, beg him
to take her home *now* before it was too late.

"The halfman said you're not to leave," the woman
said. "Pray here, the gods will hear."

Meekly, Sansa dropped her eyes and retreated back
inside. She realized suddenly why this place seemed so
familiar. *They've put me in Arya's old bedchamber,
from when Father was the Hand of the King. All her*

things are gone and the furnishings have been moved around, but it's the same . . .

A short time later, a serving girl brought a platter of cheese and bread and olives, with a flagon of cold water. "Take it away," Sansa commanded, but the girl left the food on a table. She *was* thirsty, she realized. Every step sent knives through her thighs, but she made herself cross the room. She drank two cups of water, and was nibbling on an olive when the knock came.

Anxiously, she turned toward the door, smoothed down the folds of her robe. "Yes?"

The door opened, and Tyrion Lannister stepped inside. "My lady. I trust I am not disturbing you?"

"Am I your prisoner?"

"My guest." He was wearing his chain of office, a necklace of linked golden hands. "I thought we might talk."

"As my lord commands." Sansa found it hard not to stare; his face was so ugly it held a queer fascination for her.

"The food and garments are to your satisfaction?" he asked. "If there is anything else you need, you have only to ask."

"You are most kind. And this morning . . . it was very good of you to help me."

"You have a right to know why Joffrey was so wroth. Six nights gone, your brother fell upon my uncle Stafford, encamped with his host at a village called Oxcross not three days ride from Casterly Rock. Your northerners won a crushing victory. We received word only this morning."

Robb will kill you all, she thought, exulting. "It's . . . terrible, my lord. My brother is a vile traitor."

The dwarf smiled wanly. "Well, he's no fawn, he's made that clear enough."

"Ser Lancel said Robb led an army of wargs . . ."

The Imp gave a disdainful bark of laughter. "Ser Lancel's a wineskin warrior who wouldn't know a warg from a wart. Your brother had his direwolf with him, but I suspect that's as far as it went. The northmen crept into my uncle's camp and cut his horse lines, and Lord Stark sent his wolf among them. Even war-trained destriers went mad. Knights were trampled to death in their pavilions, and the rabble woke in terror and fled, casting aside their weapons to run the faster. Ser Stafford was slain as he chased after a horse. Lord Rickard Karstark drove a lance through his chest. Ser Rubert Brax is also dead, along with Ser Lymond Vikary, Lord Crakehall, and Lord Jast. Half a hundred more have been taken captive, including Jast's sons and my nephew Martyn Lannister. Those who survived are spreading wild tales and swearing that the old gods of the north march with your brother."

"Then . . . there was no sorcery?"

Lannister snorted. "Sorcery is the sauce fools spoon over failure to hide the flavor of their own incompetence. My mutton-headed uncle had not even troubled to post sentries, it would seem. His host was raw—apprentice boys, miners, fieldhands, fisherfolk, the sweepings of Lannisport. The only mystery is how your brother reached him. Our forces still hold the stronghold at the Golden Tooth, and they swear he did not pass." The dwarf gave an irritated shrug. "Well, Robb Stark is my father's bane. Joffrey is mine. Tell me, what do you feel for my kingly nephew?"

"I love him with all my heart," Sansa said at once.

"Truly?" He did not sound convinced. "Even now?"

"My love for His Grace is greater than it has ever been."

The Imp laughed aloud. "Well, someone has taught you to lie well. You may be grateful for that one day, child. You *are* a child still, are you not? Or have you flowered?"

Sansa blushed. It was a rude question, but the shame of being stripped before half the castle made it seem like nothing. "No, my lord."

"That's all to the good. If it gives you any solace, I do not intend that you ever wed Joffrey. No marriage will reconcile Stark and Lannister after all that has happened, I fear. More's the pity. The match was one of King Robert's better notions, if Joffrey hadn't mucked it up."

She knew she ought to say something, but the words caught in her throat.

"You grow very quiet," Tyrion Lannister observed. "Is this what you want? An end to your betrothal?"

"I . . ." Sansa did not know what to say. *Is it a trick? Will he punish me if I tell the truth?* She stared at the dwarf's brutal bulging brow, the hard black eye and the shrewd green one, the crooked teeth and wiry beard. "I only want to be loyal."

"Loyal," the dwarf mused, "and far from any Lannisters. I can scarce blame you for that. When I was your age, I wanted the same thing." He smiled. "They tell me you visit the godswood every day. What do you pray for, Sansa?"

I pray for Robb's victory and Joffrey's death . . . and for home. For Winterfell. "I pray for an end to the fighting."

"We'll have that soon enough. There will be another battle, between your brother Robb and my lord father, and that will settle the issue."

Robb will beat him, Sansa thought. *He beat your uncle and your brother Jaime, he'll beat your father too.*

It was as if her face were an open book, so easily did the dwarf read her hopes. "Do not take Oxcross too much to heart, my lady," he told her, not unkindly. "A battle is not a war, and my lord father is assuredly not my uncle Stafford. The next time you visit the godswood, pray that your brother has the wisdom to bend the knee. Once the north returns to the king's peace, I mean to send you home." He hopped down off the window seat and said, "You may sleep here tonight. I'll give you some of my own men as a guard, some Stone Crows perhaps—"

"No," Sansa blurted out, aghast. If she was locked in the Tower of the Hand, guarded by the dwarf's men, how would Ser Dontos ever spirit her away to freedom?

"Would you prefer Black Ears? I'll give you Chella if a woman would make you more at ease."

"Please, no, my lord, the wildlings frighten me."

He grinned. "Me as well. But more to the point, they frighten Joffrey and that nest of sly vipers and lickspittle dogs he calls a Kingsguard. With Chella or Timett by your side, no one would dare offer you harm."

"I would sooner return to my own bed." A lie came to her suddenly, but it seemed so *right* that she blurted it out at once. "This tower was where my father's men were slain. Their ghosts would give me terrible dreams, and I would see their blood wherever I looked."

Tyrion Lannister studied her face. "I am no stranger to nightmares, Sansa. Perhaps you are wiser than I knew. Permit me at least to escort you safely back to your own chambers."

CATELYN

It was full dark before they found the village. Catelyn found herself wondering if the place had a name. If so, its people had taken that knowledge with them when they fled, along with all they owned, down to the candles in the sept. Ser Wendel lit a torch and led her through the low door.

Within, the seven walls were cracked and crooked. *God is one*, Septon Osmynd had taught her when she was a girl, *with seven aspects, as the sept is a single building, with seven walls.* The wealthy septs of the cities had statues of the Seven and an altar to each. In Winterfell, Septon Chayle hung carved masks from each wall. Here Catelyn found only rough charcoal drawings. Ser Wendel set the torch in a sconce near the door, and left to wait outside with Robar Royce.

Catelyn studied the faces. The Father was bearded, as ever. The Mother smiled, loving and protective. The Warrior had his sword sketched in beneath his face, the Smith his hammer. The Maid was beautiful, the Crone wizened and wise.

And the seventh face . . . the Stranger was neither male nor female, yet both, ever the outcast, the wanderer from far places, less and more than human, unknown and unknowable. Here the face was a black oval, a shadow with stars for eyes. It made Catelyn uneasy. She would get scant comfort there.

She knelt before the Mother. "My lady, look down on this battle with a mother's eyes. They are all sons, every one. Spare them if you can, and spare my own sons as well. Watch over Robb and Bran and Rickon. Would that I were with them."

A crack ran down through the Mother's left eye. It made her look as if she were crying. Catelyn could hear Ser Wendel's booming voice, and now and again Ser Robar's quiet answers, as they talked of the coming battle. Otherwise the night was still. Not even a cricket could be heard, and the gods kept their silence. *Did your old gods ever answer you, Ned?* she wondered. *When you knelt before your heart tree, did they hear you?*

Flickering torchlight danced across the walls, making the faces seem half-alive, twisting them, changing them. The statues in the great septs of the cities wore the faces the stonemasons had given them, but these charcoal scratchings were so crude they might be anyone. The Father's face made her think of her own father, dying in his bed at Riverrun. The Warrior was Renly and Stannis, Robb and Robert, Jaime Lannister and Jon Snow. She even glimpsed Arya in those lines, just for an instant. Then a gust of wind through the door made the torch sputter, and the semblance was gone, washed away in orange glare.

The smoke was making her eyes burn. She rubbed at them with the heels of her scarred hands. When she looked up at the Mother again, it was her own mother she saw. Lady Minisa Tully had died in childbed, trying to give Lord Hoster a second son. The baby had perished with her, and afterward some of the life had gone out of Father. *She was always so calm,* Catelyn thought, remembering her mother's soft hands, her warm smile. *If*

she had lived, how different our lives might have been.
She wondered what Lady Minisa would make of her eldest daughter, kneeling here before her. *I have come so many thousands of leagues, and for what? Who have I served? I have lost my daughters, Robb does not want me, and Bran and Rickon must surely think me a cold and unnatural mother. I was not even with Ned when he died . . .*

Her head swam, and the sept seemed to move around her. The shadows swayed and shifted, furtive animals racing across the cracked white walls. Catelyn had not eaten today. Perhaps that had been unwise. She told herself that there had been no time, but the truth was that food had lost its savor in a world without Ned. *When they took his head off, they killed me too.*

Behind her the torch spit, and suddenly it seemed to her that it was her sister's face on the wall, though the eyes were harder than she recalled, not Lysa's eyes but Cersei's. *Cersei is a mother too. No matter who fathered those children, she felt them kick inside her, brought them forth with her pain and blood, nursed them at her breast. If they are truly Jaime's . . .*

"Does Cersei pray to you too, my lady?" Catelyn asked the Mother. She could see the proud, cold, lovely features of the Lannister queen etched upon the wall. The crack was still there; even Cersei could weep for her children. "Each of the Seven embodies all of the Seven," Septon Osmynd had told her once. There was as much beauty in the Crone as in the Maiden, and the Mother could be fiercer than the Warrior when her children were in danger. *Yes . . .*

She had seen enough of Robert Baratheon at Winterfell to know that the king did not regard Joffrey with any great warmth. If the boy was truly Jaime's seed, Robert would have put him to death along with his mother, and few would have condemned him. Bastards were common enough, but incest was a monstrous sin to both old gods and new, and the children of such wickedness were named abominations in sept and godswood alike. The dragon kings had wed brother to sister, but they were the blood of old Valyria where such practices had been common, and like their dragons the Targaryens answered to neither gods nor men.

Ned must have known, and Lord Arryn before him. Small wonder that the queen had killed them both. *Would I do any less for my own?* Catelyn clenched her hands, feeling the tightness in her scarred fingers where the assassin's steel had cut to the bone as she fought to save her son. "Bran knows too," she whispered, lowering her head. *Gods be good, he must have seen something, heard something, that was why they tried to kill him in his bed.*

Lost and weary, Catelyn Stark gave herself over to her gods. She knelt before the Smith, who fixed things that were broken, and asked that he give her sweet Bran his protection. She went to the Maid and beseeched her to lend her courage to Arya and Sansa, to guard them in their innocence. To the Father, she prayed for justice, the strength to seek it and the wisdom to know it, and she asked the Warrior to keep Robb strong and shield him in his battles. Lastly she turned to the Crone, whose statues often showed her with a lamp in one hand. "Guide me, wise lady," she prayed. "Show me the path I must walk, and do not let me stumble in the dark places that lie ahead."

Finally there were footsteps behind her, and a noise at the door. "My lady," Ser Robar said gently, "pardon, but our time is at an end. We must be back before the dawn breaks."

Catelyn rose stiffly. Her knees ached, and she would have given much for a featherbed and a pillow just then. "Thank you, ser. I am ready."

They rode in silence through sparse woodland where the trees leaned drunkenly away from the sea. The nervous whinny of horses and the clank of steel guided them back to Renly's camp. The long ranks of man and horse were armored in darkness, as black as if the Smith had hammered night itself into steel. There were banners to her right, banners to her left, and rank on rank of banners before her, but in the predawn gloom, neither colors nor sigils could be discerned. *A grey army,* Catelyn thought. *Grey men on grey horses beneath grey banners.* As they sat their horses waiting, Renly's shadow knights pointed their lances upward, so she rode through a forest of tall naked trees, bereft of leaves and life. Where Storm's End stood was only a deeper darkness, a wall of black through which no stars could shine, but she could see torches moving across the fields where Lord Stannis had made his camp.

The candles within Renly's pavilion made the shimmering silken walls seem to glow, transforming the great tent into a magical castle alive with emerald light. Two of the Rainbow Guard stood sentry at the door to the royal pavilion. The green light shone strangely against the purple plums of Ser Parmen's surcoat, and gave a sickly hue to the sunflowers that covered every inch of Ser Emmon's enameled yellow plate. Long silken plumes flew from their helms, and rainbow cloaks draped their shoulders.

Within, Catelyn found Brienne armoring the king for battle while the Lords Tarly and Rowan spoke of dispositions and tactics. It was pleasantly warm inside, the heat shimmering off the coals in a dozen small iron braziers. "I must speak with you, Your Grace," she said, granting him a king's style for once, anything to make him heed her.

"In a moment, Lady Catelyn," Renly replied. Brienne fit backplate to breastplate over his quilted tunic. The king's armor was a deep green, the green of leaves in a summer wood, so dark it drank the candlelight. Gold highlights gleamed from inlay and fastenings like distant fires in that wood, winking every time he moved. "Pray continue, Lord Mathis."

"Your Grace," Mathis Rowan said with a sideways glance at Catelyn. "As I was saying, our battles are well drawn up. Why wait for daybreak? Sound the advance."

"And have it said that I won by treachery, with an unchivalrous attack? Dawn was the chosen hour."

"Chosen by Stannis," Randyll Tarly pointed out.

"He'd have us charge into the teeth of the rising sun. We'll be half-blind."

"Only until first shock," Renly said confidently. "Ser Loras will break them, and after that it will be chaos." Brienne tightened green leather straps and buckled golden buckles. "When my brother falls, see that no insult is done to his corpse. He is my own blood, I will not have his head paraded about on a spear."

"And if he yields?" Lord Tarly asked.

"Yields?" Lord Rowan laughed. "When Mace Tyrell laid siege to Storm's End, Stannis ate rats rather than open his gates."

"Well I remember." Renly lifted his chin to allow Brienne to fasten his gorget in place. "Near the end, Ser Gawen Wylde and three of his knights tried to steal out a postern gate to surrender. Stannis caught them and ordered them flung from the walls with catapults. I can still see Gawen's face as they strapped him down. He had been our master-at-arms."

Lord Rowan appeared puzzled. "No men were hurled from the walls. I would surely remember that."

"Maester Cressen told Stannis that we might be forced to eat our dead, and there was no gain in flinging away good meat." Renly pushed back his hair. Brienne bound it with a velvet tie and pulled a padded cap down over his ears, to cushion the weight of his helm. "Thanks to the Onion Knight we were never reduced to dining on corpses, but it was a close thing. Too close for Ser Gawen, who died in his cell."

"Your Grace." Catelyn had waited patiently, but time grew short. "You promised me a word."

Renly nodded. "See to your battles, my lords . . . oh, and if Barristan Selmy is at my brother's side, I want him spared."

"There's been no word of Ser Barristan since Joffrey cast him out," Lord Rowan objected.

"I know that old man. He needs a king to guard, or who is he? Yet he never came to me, and Lady Catelyn says he is not with Robb Stark at Riverrun. Where else but with Stannis?"

"As you say, Your Grace. No harm will come to him." The lords bowed deeply and departed.

"Say your say, Lady Stark," Renly said. Brienne swept his cloak over his broad shoulders. It was cloth-of-gold, heavy, with the crowned stag of Baratheon picked out in flakes of jet.

"The Lannisters tried to kill my son Bran. A thousand times I have asked myself why. Your brother gave me my answer. There was a hunt the day he fell. Robert and Ned and most of the other men rode out after boar, but Jaime Lannister remained at Winterfell, as did the queen."

Renly was not slow to take the implication. "So you believe the boy caught them at their incest . . ."

"I beg you, my lord, grant me leave to go to your brother Stannis and tell him what I suspect."

"To what end?"

"Robb will set aside his crown if you and your brother will do the same," she said, hoping it was true. She would *make* it true if she must; Robb would listen to her, even if his lords would not. "Let the three of you call for a Great Council, such as the realm has not seen for a hundred years. We will send to Winterfell, so Bran may tell his tale and all men may know the Lannisters for the true usurpers. Let the assembled lords of the Seven Kingdoms choose who shall rule them."

Renly laughed. "Tell me, my lady, do direwolves vote on who should lead the pack?" Brienne brought the king's gauntlets and greathelm, crowned with golden antlers that would add a foot and a half to his height. "The time for talk is done. Now we see who is stronger." Renly pulled a lobstered green-and-gold gauntlet over his left hand, while Brienne knelt to buckle on his belt, heavy with the weight of longsword and dagger.

"I beg you in the name of the Mother," Catelyn began when a sudden gust of wind flung open the door of the tent. She thought she glimpsed movement, but when she turned her head, it was only the king's shadow shifting against the silken walls. She heard Renly begin a jest, his shadow moving, lifting its sword, black on green, candles guttering, shivering, something was queer, wrong, and then she saw Renly's sword still in its scabbard, sheathed still, but the shadowsword . . .

"Cold," said Renly in a small puzzled voice, a heartbeat before the steel of his gorget parted like cheesecloth beneath the shadow of a blade that was not there. He had time to make a small thick gasp before the blood came gushing out of his throat.

"Your Gr—*no!*" cried Brienne the Blue when she saw that evil flow, sounding as scared as any little girl. The king stumbled into her arms, a sheet of blood creeping down the front of his armor, a dark red tide that drowned his green and gold. More candles guttered out. Renly tried to speak, but he was choking on his own blood. His legs collapsed, and only Brienne's strength held him up. She threw back her head and screamed, wordless in her anguish.

The shadow. Something dark and evil had happened here, she knew, something that she could not begin to understand. *Renly never cast that shadow. Death came in that door and blew the life out of him as swift as the wind snuffed out his candles.*

Only a few instants passed before Robar Royce and Emmon Cuy came bursting in, though it felt like half the night. A pair of men-at-arms crowded in behind with torches. When they saw Renly in Brienne's arms, and her drenched with the king's blood, Ser Robar gave a cry of horror. "Wicked woman!" screamed Ser Emmon, he of the sunflowered steel. "Away from him, you vile creature!"

"Gods be good, Brienne, *why?*" asked Ser Robar.

Brienne looked up from her king's body. The rainbow cloak that hung from her shoulders had turned red where the king's blood had soaked into the cloth. "I . . . I . . ."

"You'll die for this." Ser Emmon snatched up a long-handled battle-axe from the weapons piled near the door. "You'll pay for the king's life with your own!"

"*NO!*" Catelyn Stark screamed, finding her voice at

last, but it was too late, the blood madness was on them, and they rushed forward with shouts that drowned her softer words.

Brienne moved faster than Catelyn would have believed. Her own sword was not to hand, so she snatched Renly's from its scabbard and raised it to catch Emmon's axe on the downswing. A spark flashed blue-white as steel met steel with a rending crash, and Brienne sprang to her feet, the body of the dead king thrust rudely aside. Ser Emmon stumbled over it as he tried to close, and Brienne's blade sheared through the wooden haft to send his axehead spinning. Another man thrust a flaming torch at her back, but the rainbow cloak was too sodden with blood to burn. Brienne spun and cut, and torch and hand went flying. Flames crept across the carpet. The maimed man began to scream. Ser Emmon dropped the axe and fumbled for his sword. The second man-at-arms lunged, Brienne parried, and their swords danced and clanged against each other. When Emmon Cuy came wading back in, Brienne was forced to retreat, yet somehow she held them both at bay. On the ground, Renly's head rolled sickeningly to one side, and a second mouth yawned wide, the blood coming from him now in slow pulses.

Ser Robar had hung back, uncertain, but now he was reaching for his hilt. "Robar, no, listen." Catelyn seized his arm. "You do her wrong, it was not her. *Help her!* Hear me, it was Stannis." The name was on her lips before she could think how it got there, but as she said it, she knew that it was true. "I swear it, you know me, it was *Stannis* killed him."

The young rainbow knight stared at this madwoman with pale and frightened eyes. "Stannis? How?"

"I do not know. Sorcery, some dark magic, there was a shadow, a *shadow*." Her own voice sounded wild and crazed to her, but the words poured out in a rush as the blades continued to clash behind her. "A shadow with a sword, I swear it, I saw. Are you blind, the girl *loved* him! *Help her!*" She glanced back, saw the second guardsman fall, his blade dropping from limp fingers.

Outside there was shouting. More angry men would be bursting in on them any instant, she knew. "She is innocent, Robar. You have my word, on my husband's grave and my honor as a Stark!"

That resolved him. "I will hold them," Ser Robar said. "Get her away." He turned and went out.

The fire had reached the wall and was creeping up the side of the tent. Ser Emmon was pressing Brienne hard, him in his enameled yellow steel and her in wool. He had forgotten Catelyn, until the iron brazier came crashing into the back of his head. Helmed as he was, the blow did no lasting harm, but it sent him to his knees. "Brienne, with me," Catelyn commanded. The girl was not slow to see the chance. A slash, and the green silk parted. They stepped out into darkness and the chill of dawn. Loud voices came from the other side of the pavilion. "This way," Catelyn urged, "and slowly. We must not run, or they will ask why. Walk easy, as if nothing were amiss."

Brienne thrust her sword blade through her belt and fell in beside Catelyn. The night air smelled of rain. Behind them, the king's pavilion was well ablaze, flames rising high against the dark. No one made any move to stop them. Men rushed past them, shouting of fire and murder and sorcery. Others stood in small groups and spoke in low voices. A few were praying, and one young squire was on his knees, sobbing openly.

Renly's battles were already coming apart as the rumors spread from mouth to mouth. The nightfires had burned low, and as the east began to lighten the immense mass of Storm's End emerged like a dream of stone while wisps of pale mist raced across the field, flying from the sun on wings of wind. *Morning ghosts,* she had heard Old Nan call them once, spirits returning to their graves. And Renly one of them now, gone like his brother Robert, like her own dear Ned.

"I never held him but as he died," Brienne said quietly as they walked through the spreading chaos. Her voice sounded as if she might break at any instant. "He was laughing one moment, and suddenly the blood was everywhere . . . my lady, I do not understand. Did you see, did you . . . ?"

"I saw a shadow. I thought it was Renly's shadow at the first, but it was his brother's."

"Lord Stannis?"

"I *felt* him. It makes no sense, I know . . ."

It made sense enough for Brienne. "I will kill him," the tall homely girl declared. "With my lord's own sword, I will kill him. I swear it. I swear it. I swear it."

Hal Mollen and the rest of her escort were waiting with the horses. Ser Wendel Manderly was all in a lather to know what was happening. "My lady, the camp has gone mad," he blurted when he saw them. "Lord Renly, is he—" He stopped suddenly, staring at Brienne and the blood that drenched her.

"Dead, but not by our hands."

"The battle—" Hal Mollen began.

"There will be no battle." Catelyn mounted, and her escort formed up about her, with Ser Wendel to her left and Ser Perwyn Frey on her right. "Brienne, we brought mounts enough for twice our number. Choose one, and come with us."

"I have my own horse, my lady. And my armor—"

"Leave them. We must be well away before they think to look for us. We were both with the king when he was killed. That will not be forgotten." Wordless, Brienne turned and did as she was bid. "Ride," Catelyn commanded her escort when they were all ahorse. "If any man tries to stop us, cut him down."

As the long fingers of dawn fanned across the fields, color was returning to the world. Where grey men had sat grey horses armed with shadow spears, the points of ten thousand lances now glinted silvery cold, and on the myriad flapping banners Catelyn saw the blush of red and pink and orange, the richness of blues and browns, the blaze of gold and yellow. All the power of Storm's End and Highgarden, the power that had been Renly's an hour ago. *They belong to Stannis now,* she realized, *even if they do not know it themselves yet. Where else are they to turn, if not to the last*

Baratheon? Stannis has won all with a single evil stroke.

I am the rightful king, he had declared, his jaw clenched hard as iron, *and your son no less a traitor than my brother here. His day will come as well.*

A chill went through her.

JON

The hill jutted above the dense tangle of forest, rising solitary and sudden, its windswept heights visible from miles off. The wildlings called it the Fist of the First Men, rangers said. It *did* look like a fist, Jon Snow thought, punching up through earth and wood, its bare brown slopes knuckled with stone.

He rode to the top with Lord Mormont and the officers, leaving Ghost below under the trees. The direwolf had run off three times as they climbed, twice returning reluctantly to Jon's whistle. The third time, the Lord Commander lost patience and snapped, "Let him go, boy. I want to reach the crest before dusk. Find the wolf later."

The way up was steep and stony, the summit crowned by a chest-high wall of tumbled rocks. They had to circle some distance west before they found a gap large enough to admit the horses. "This is good ground, Thoren," the Old Bear proclaimed when at last they attained the top. "We could scarce hope for better. We'll make our camp here to await Halfhand." The Lord Commander swung down off his saddle, dislodging the raven from his shoulder. Complaining loudly, the bird took to the air.

The views atop the hill were bracing, yet it was the ringwall that drew Jon's eye, the weathered grey stones with their white patches of lichen, their beards of green moss. It was said that the Fist had been a ringfort of the First Men in the Dawn Age. "An old place, and strong," Thoren Smallwood said.

"Old," Mormont's raven screamed as it flapped in noisy circles about their heads. *"Old, old, old."*

"Quiet," Mormont growled up at the bird. The Old Bear was too proud to admit to weakness, but Jon was not deceived. The strain of keeping up with younger men was taking its toll.

"These heights will be easy to defend, if need be," Thoren pointed out as he walked his horse along the ring of stones; his sable-trimmed cloak stirring in the wind.

"Yes, this place will do." The Old Bear lifted a hand to the wind, and raven landed on his forearm, claws scrabbling against his black ringmail.

"What about water, my lord?" Jon wondered.

"We crossed a brook at the foot of the hill."

"A long climb for a drink," Jon pointed out, "and outside the ring of stones."

Thoren said, "Are you too lazy to climb a hill, boy?"

When Lord Mormont said, "We're not like to find another place as strong. We'll carry water, and make certain we are well supplied," Jon knew better than to argue. So the command was given, and the brothers of the Night's Watch raised their camp behind the stone ring the First Men had made. Black tents sprouted like mushrooms after a rain, and blankets and bedrolls covered the bare ground. Stewards tethered the garrons in long lines, and saw them fed and watered. Foresters took their axes to the trees in the waning afternoon light to harvest enough wood to see them through the night. A score of builders set to clearing brush, digging latrines, and untying their bundles of fire-hardened stakes. "I will have every opening in the ringwall ditched and staked before dark," the Old Bear had commanded.

Once he'd put up the Lord Commander's tent and seen to their horses, Jon Snow descended the hill in search of Ghost. The direwolf came at once, all in silence. One moment Jon was striding beneath the trees, whistling and shouting, alone in the green, pinecones and fallen leaves under his feet; the next, the great white direwolf was walking beside him, pale as morning mist.

But when they reached the ringfort, Ghost balked again. He padded forward warily to sniff at the gap in the stones, and then retreated, as if he did not like what he'd smelled. Jon tried to grab him by the scruff of his neck and haul him bodily inside the ring, no easy task; the wolf weighed as much as he did, and was stronger by far. "Ghost, what's *wrong* with you?" It was not like him to be so unsettled. In the end Jon had to give it up. "As you will," he told the wolf. "Go, hunt." The red eyes watched him as he made his way back through the mossy stones.

They ought to be safe here. The hill offered commanding views, and the slopes were precipitous to the north and west and only slightly more gentle to the east. Yet as the dusk deepened and darkness seeped into the hollows between the trees, Jon's sense of foreboding grew. *This is the haunted forest,* he told himself. *Maybe there are ghosts here, the spirits of the First Men. This was their place, once.*

"Stop acting the boy," he told himself. Clambering atop the piled rocks, Jon gazed off toward the setting sun. He could see the light shimmering like hammered gold off the surface of the Milkwater as it curved away to the south. Upriver the land was more rugged, the dense forest giving way to a series of bare stony hills that rose high and wild to the north and west. On the horizon stood the mountains like a great shadow, range on range of them receding into the blue-grey distance, their jagged peaks sheathed eternally in snow. Even from afar they looked vast and cold and inhospitable.

Closer at hand, it was the trees that ruled. To south and east the wood went on as far as Jon could see, a vast tangle of root and limb painted in a thousand shades of green, with here and there a patch of red where a weirwood shouldered through the pines and sentinels, or a blush of yellow where some broadleafs had begun to turn. When the wind blew, he could hear the creak and groan of branches older than he was. A thousand leaves fluttered, and for a moment the forest seemed a deep green sea, storm-tossed and heaving, eternal and unknowable.

Ghost was not like to be alone down there, he thought. Anything could be moving under that sea, creeping toward the ringfort through the dark of the wood, concealed beneath those trees. *Anything.* How would they ever know? He stood there for a long time, until the sun vanished behind the saw-toothed mountains and darkness began to creep through the forest.

"Jon?" Samwell Tarly called up. "I thought it looked like you. Are you well?"

"Well enough." Jon hopped down. "How did you fare today?"

"Well. I fared well. Truly."

Jon was not about to share his disquiet with his friend, not when Samwell Tarly was at last beginning to find his courage. "The Old Bear means to wait here for Qhorin Halfhand and the men from the Shadow Tower."

"It seems a strong place," said Sam. "A ringfort of the First Men. Do you think there were battles fought here?"

"No doubt. You'd best get a bird ready. Mormont will want to send back word."

"I wish I could send them all. They hate being caged."

"You would too, if you could fly."

"If I could fly, I'd be back at Castle Black eating a pork pie," said Sam.

Jon clapped him on the shoulder with his burned

hand. They walked back through the camp together. Cookfires were being lit all around them. Overhead, the stars were coming out. The long red tail of Mormont's Torch burned as bright as the moon. Jon heard the ravens before he saw them. Some were calling his name. The birds were not shy when it came to making noise.

They feel it too. "I'd best see to the Old Bear," he said. "He gets noisy when he isn't fed as well."

He found Mormont talking with Thoren Smallwood and half a dozen other officers. "There you are," the old man said gruffly. "Bring us some hot wine, if you would. The night is chilly."

"Yes, my lord." Jon built a cookfire, claimed a small cask of Mormont's favorite robust red from stores, and poured it into a kettle. He hung the kettle above the flames while he gathered the rest of his ingredients. The Old Bear was particular about his hot spiced wine. So much cinnamon and so much nutmeg and so much honey, not a drop more. Raisins and nuts and dried berries, but no lemon, that was the rankest sort of southron heresy—which was queer, since he always took lemon in his morning beer. The drink must be hot to warm a man properly, the Lord Commander insisted, but the wine must never be allowed to come to a boil. Jon kept a careful eye on the kettle.

As he worked, he could hear the voices from inside the tent. Jarman Buckwell said, "The easiest road up into the Frostfangs is to follow the Milkwater back to its source. Yet if we go that path, Rayder will know of our approach, certain as sunrise."

"The Giant's Stair might serve," said Ser Mallador Locke, "or the Skirling Pass, if it's clear."

The wine was steaming. Jon lifted the kettle off the fire, filled eight cups, and carried them into the tent. The Old Bear was peering at the crude map Sam had drawn him that night back in Craster's Keep. He took a cup from Jon's tray, tried a swallow of wine, and gave a brusque nod of approval. His raven hopped down his arm. *"Corn,"* it said. *"Corn. Corn."*

Ser Ottyn Wythers waved the wine away. "I would

not go into the mountains at all," he said in a thin, tired voice. "The Frostfangs have a cruel bite even in summer, and now . . . if we should be caught by a storm . . ."

"I do not mean to risk the Frostfangs unless I must," said Mormont. "Wildlings can no more live on snow and stone than we can. They will emerge from the heights soon, and for a host of any size, the only route is along the Milkwater. If so, we are strongly placed here. They cannot hope to slip by us."

"They may not wish to. They are thousands, and we will be three hundred when the Halfhand reaches us." Ser Mallador accepted a cup from Jon.

"If it comes to battle, we could not hope for better ground than here," declared Mormont. "We'll strengthen the defenses. Pits and spikes, caltrops scattered on the slopes, every breach mended. Jarman, I'll want your sharpest eyes as watchers. A ring of them, all around us and along the river, to warn of any approach. Hide them up in trees. And we had best start bringing up water too, more than we need. We'll dig cisterns. It will keep the men occupied, and may prove needful later."

"My rangers—" started Thoren Smallwood.

"Your rangers will limit their ranging to this side of the river until the Halfhand reaches us. After that, we'll see. I will not lose more of my men."

"Mance Rayder might be massing his host a day's ride from here, and we'd never know," Smallwood complained.

"We know where the wildlings are massing," Mormont came back. "We had it from Craster. I mislike the man, but I do not think he lied to us in this."

"As you say." Smallwood took a sullen leave. The others finished their wine and followed, more courteously.

"Shall I bring you supper, my lord?" Jon asked.

"*Corn*," the raven cried. Mormont did not answer at once. When he did he said only, "Did your wolf find game today?"

"He's not back yet."

"We could do with fresh meat." Mormont dug into a sack and offered his raven a handful of corn. "You think I'm wrong to keep the rangers close?"

"That's not for me to say, my lord."

"It is if you're asked."

"If the rangers must stay in sight of the Fist, I don't see how they can hope to find my uncle," Jon admitted.

"They can't." The raven pecked at the kernels in the Old Bear's palm. "Two hundred men or ten thousand, the country is too vast." The corn gone, Mormont turned his hand over.

"You would not give up the search?"

"Maester Aemon thinks you clever." Mormont moved the raven to his shoulder. The bird tilted its head to one side, little eyes a-glitter.

The answer was there. "Is it . . . it seems to me that it might be easier for one man to find two hundred than for two hundred to find one."

The raven gave a cackling scream, but the Old Bear smiled through the grey of his beard. "This many men and horses leave a trail even Aemon could follow. On this hill, our fires ought to be visible as far off as the foothills of the Frostfangs. If Ben Stark is alive and free, he will come to us, I have no doubt."

"Yes," said Jon, "but . . . what if . . ."

". . . he's dead?" Mormont asked, not unkindly.

Jon nodded, reluctantly.

"*Dead*," the raven said. "*Dead. Dead.*"

"He may come to us anyway," the Old Bear said. "As Othor did, and Jafer Flowers. I dread that as much as you, Jon, but we must admit the possibility."

"*Dead*," his raven cawed, ruffling its wings. Its voice grew louder and more shrill. "*Dead.*"

Mormont stroked the bird's black feathers, and stifled a sudden yawn with the back of his hand. "I will forsake supper, I believe. Rest will serve me better. Wake me at first light."

"Sleep well, my lord." Jon gathered up the empty cups and stepped outside. He heard distant laughter, the plaintive sound of pipes. A great blaze was crackling in the center of the camp, and he could smell stew cooking. The Old Bear might not be hungry, but Jon was. He drifted over toward the fire.

Dywen was holding forth, spoon in hand. "I know this wood as well as any man alive, and I tell you, I wouldn't care to ride through it alone tonight. Can't you smell it?"

Grenn was staring at him with wide eyes, but Dolorous Edd said, "All I smell is the shit of two hundred horses. And this stew. Which has a similar aroma, now that I come to sniff it."

"I've got your *similar aroma* right here." Hake patted his dirk. Grumbling, he filled Jon's bowl from the kettle.

The stew was thick with barley, carrot, and onion, with here and there a ragged shred of salt beef, softened in the cooking.

"What is it you smell, Dywen?" asked Grenn.

The forester sucked on his spoon a moment. He had taken out his teeth. His face was leathery and wrinkled, his hands gnarled as old roots. "Seems to me like it smells . . . well . . . *cold.*"

"Your head's as wooden as your teeth," Hake told him. "There's no smell to cold."

There is, thought Jon, remembering the night in the Lord Commander's chambers. *It smells like death.* Suddenly he was not hungry anymore. He gave his stew to Grenn, who looked in need of an extra supper to warm him against the night.

The wind was blowing briskly when he left. By morning, frost would cover the ground, and the tent ropes would be stiff and frozen. A few fingers of spiced wine sloshed in the bottom of the kettle. Jon fed fresh wood to the fire and put the kettle over the flames to reheat. He flexed his fingers as he waited, squeezing and spreading until the hand tingled. The first watch had taken up their stations around the perimeter of the camp. Torches flickered all along the ringwall. The night was moonless, but a thousand stars shone overhead.

A sound rose out of the darkness, faint and distant, but unmistakable: the howling of wolves. Their voices rose and fell, a chilly song, and lonely. It made the hairs rise along the back of his neck. Across the fire, a pair of red eyes regarded him from the shadows. The light of the flames made them glow.

"Ghost," Jon breathed, surprised. "So you came inside after all, eh?" The white wolf often hunted all night; he had not expected to see him again till daybreak. "Was the hunting so bad?" he asked. "Here. To me, Ghost."

The direwolf circled the fire, sniffing Jon, sniffing the wind, never still. It did not seem as if he were after meat right now. *When the dead came walking, Ghost knew. He woke me, warned me.* Alarmed, he got to his feet. "Is something out there? Ghost, do you have a scent?" *Dywen said he smelled cold.*

The direwolf loped off, stopped, looked back. *He wants me to follow.* Pulling up the hood of his cloak, Jon walked away from the tents, away from the warmth of his fire, past the lines of shaggy little garrons. One of the horses whickered nervously when Ghost padded by. Jon soothed him with a word and paused to stroke his muzzle. He could hear the wind whistling through cracks in the rocks as they neared the ringwall. A voice called out a challenge. Jon stepped into the torchlight. "I need to fetch water for the Lord Commander."

"Go on, then," the guard said. "Be quick about it." Huddled beneath his black cloak, with his hood drawn up against the wind, the man never even looked to see if he had a bucket.

Jon slipped sideways between two sharpened stakes while Ghost slid beneath them. A torch had been thrust down into a crevice, its flames flying pale orange banners when the gusts came. He snatched it up as he squeezed through the gap between the stones. Ghost went racing down the hill. Jon followed more slowly, the torch thrust out before him as he made his descent. The camp sounds faded behind him. The night was black, the slope steep, stony, and uneven. A moment's inattention would be a sure way to break an ankle . . . or his neck. *What am I doing?* he asked himself as he picked his way down.

The trees stood beneath him, warriors armored in bark and leaf, deployed in their silent ranks awaiting the command to storm the hill. Black, they seemed . . . it was only when his torchlight brushed against them that Jon glimpsed a flash of green. Faintly, he heard the sound of water flowing over rocks. Ghost vanished in the underbrush. Jon struggled after him, listening to the call of the brook, to the leaves sighing in the wind. Branches clutched at his cloak, while overhead thick limbs twined together and shut out the stars.

He found Ghost lapping from the stream. *"Ghost,"* he called, "to me. *Now.*" When the direwolf raised his head, his eyes glowed red and baleful, and water streamed down from his jaws like slaver. There was something fierce and terrible about him in that instant. And then he was off, bounding past Jon, racing through the trees. "Ghost, *no*, stay," he shouted, but the wolf paid no heed. The lean white shape was swallowed by the dark, and Jon had only two choices—to climb the hill again, alone, or to follow.

He followed, angry, holding the torch out low so he could see the rocks that threatened to trip him with every step, the thick roots that seemed to grab as his feet, the holes where a man could twist an ankle. Every few feet he called again for Ghost, but the night wind was swirling amongst the trees and it drank the words. *This is madness*, he thought as he plunged deeper into the trees. He was about to turn back when he glimpsed a flash of white off ahead and to the right, back toward the hill. He jogged after it, cursing under his breath.

A quarter way around the Fist he chased the wolf before he lost him again. Finally he stopped to catch his breath amidst the scrub, thorns, and tumbled rocks at the base of the hill. Beyond the torchlight, the dark pressed close.

A soft scrabbling noise made him turn. Jon moved toward the sound, stepping carefully among boulders and thornbushes. Behind a fallen tree, he came on Ghost again. The direwolf was digging furiously, kicking up dirt.

"What have you found?" Jon lowered the torch, revealing a rounded mound of soft earth. *A grave,* he thought. *But whose?*

He knelt, jammed the torch into the ground beside him. The soil was loose, sandy. Jon pulled it out by the fistful. There were no stones, no roots. Whatever was here had been put here recently. Two feet down, his fingers touched cloth. He had been expecting a corpse, fearing a corpse, but this was something else. He pushed against the fabric and felt small, hard shapes beneath, unyielding. There was no smell, no sign of graveworms. Ghost backed off and sat on his haunches, watching.

Jon brushed the loose soil away to reveal a rounded bundle perhaps two feet across. He jammed his fingers down around the edges and worked it loose. When he pulled it free, whatever was inside shifted and clinked. *Treasure,* he thought, but the shapes were wrong to be coins, and the *sound* was wrong for metal.

A length of frayed rope bound the bundle together. Jon unsheathed his dagger and cut it, groped for the edges of the cloth, and pulled. The bundle turned, and its contents spilled out onto the ground, glittering dark and bright. He saw a dozen knives, leaf-shaped spearheads, numerous arrowheads. Jon picked up a dagger blade, featherlight and shiny black, hiltless. Torchlight ran along its edge, a thin orange line that spoke of razor sharpness. *Dragonglass. What the maesters call obsidian.* Had Ghost uncovered some ancient cache of the children of the forest, buried here for thousands of years? The Fist of the First Men was an old place, only . . .

Beneath the dragonglass was an old warhorn, made from an auroch's horn and banded in bronze. Jon shook the dirt from inside it, and a stream of arrowheads fell out. He let them fall, and pulled up a corner of the cloth the weapons had been wrapped in, rubbing it between his fingers. *Good wool, thick, a double weave, damp but not rotted.* It could not have been long in the ground. And it was *dark.* He seized a handful and pulled it close to the torch. *Not dark. Black.*

Even before Jon stood and shook it out, he knew what he had: the black cloak of a Sworn Brother of the Night's Watch.

BRAN

Alebelly found him in the forge, working the bellows for Mikken. "Maester wants you in the turret, m'lord prince. There's been a bird from the king."

"From Robb?" Excited, Bran did not wait for Hodor, but let Alebelly carry him up the steps. He was a big man, though not so big as Hodor and nowhere near as strong. By the time they reached the maester's turret he was red-faced and puffing. Rickon was there before them, and both Walder Freys as well.

Maester Luwin sent Alebelly away and closed his door. "My lords," he said gravely, "we have had a message from His Grace, with both good news and ill. He has won a great victory in the west, shattering a Lannister army at a place named Oxcross, and has taken several castles as well. He writes us from Ashemark, formerly the stronghold of House Marbrand."

Rickon tugged at the maester's robe. "Is Robb coming home?"

"Not just yet, I fear. There are battles yet to fight."

"Was it Lord Tywin he defeated?" asked Bran.

"No," said the maester. "Ser Stafford Lannister commanded the enemy host. He was slain in the battle."

Bran had never even heard of Ser Stafford Lannister. He found himself agreeing with Big Walder when he said, "Lord Tywin is the only one who matters."

"Tell Robb I want him to come home," said Rickon. "He can bring his wolf home too, and Mother and Father." Though he knew Lord Eddard was dead, sometimes Rickon forgot . . . willfully, Bran suspected. His little brother was stubborn as only a boy of four can be.

Bran was glad for Robb's victory, but disquieted as well. He remembered what Osha had said the day that his brother had led his army out of Winterfell. *He's marching the wrong way,* the wildling woman had insisted.

"Sadly, no victory is without cost." Maester Luwin turned to the Walders. "My lords, your uncle Ser Stevron Frey was among those who lost their lives at Oxcross. He took a wound in the battle, Robb writes. It was not thought to be serious, but three days later he died in his tent, asleep."

Big Walder shrugged. "He was very old. Five-and-sixty, I think. Too old for battles. He was always saying he was tired."

Little Walder hooted. "Tired of waiting for our grandfather to die, you mean. Does this mean Ser Emmon's the heir now?"

"Don't be stupid," his cousin said. "The sons of the first son come before the second son. Ser Ryman is next in line, and then Edwyn and Black Walder and Petyr Pimple. And then Aegon and all *his* sons."

"Ryman is old too," said Little Walder. "Past forty, I bet. And he has a bad belly. Do you think he'll be lord?"

"*I'll* be lord. I don't care if he is."

Maester Luwin cut in sharply. "You ought to be ashamed of such talk, my lords. Where is your grief? Your uncle is dead."

"Yes," said Little Walder. "We're very sad."

They weren't, though. Bran got a sick feeling in his

belly. *They like the taste of this dish better than I do.*
He asked Maester Luwin to be excused.

"Very well." The maester rang for help. Hodor must
have been busy in the stables. It was Osha who came.
She was stronger than Alebelly, though, and had no
trouble lifting Bran in her arms and carrying him down
the steps.

"Osha," Bran asked as they crossed the yard. "Do you
know the way north? To the Wall and . . . and even
past?"

"The way's easy. Look for the Ice Dragon, and chase
the blue star in the rider's eye." She backed through a
door and started up the winding steps.

"And there are still giants there, and . . . the
rest . . . the Others, and the children of the forest
too?"

"The giants I've seen, the children I've heard tell of,
and the white walkers . . . why do you want to
know?"

"Did you ever see a three-eyed crow?"

"No." She laughed. "And I can't say I'd want to."
Osha kicked open the door to his bedchamber and set
him in his window seat, where he could watch the yard
below.

It seemed only a few heartbeats after she took her
leave that the door opened again, and Jojen Reed entered
unbidden, with his sister Meera behind him. "You
heard about the bird?" Bran asked. The other boy nodded. "It wasn't a supper like you said. It was a letter
from Robb, and we didn't eat it, but—"

"The green dreams take strange shapes sometimes,"
Jojen admitted. "The truth of them is not always easy to
understand."

"Tell me the bad thing you dreamed," Bran said. "The
bad thing that is coming to Winterfell."

"Does my lord prince believe me now? Will he trust
my words, no matter how queer they sound in his
ears?"

Bran nodded.

"It is the sea that comes."

"The *sea?*"

"I dreamed that the sea was lapping all around Winterfell. I saw black waves crashing against the gates and towers, and then the salt water came flowing over the walls and filled the castle. Drowned men were floating in the yard. When I first dreamed the dream, back at Greywater, I didn't know their faces, but now I do. That Alebelly is one, the guard who called our names at the feast. Your septon's another. Your smith as well."

"Mikken?" Bran was as confused as he was dismayed. "But the sea is hundreds and hundreds of leagues away, and Winterfell's walls are so high the water couldn't get in even if it did come."

"In the dark of night the salt sea will flow over these walls," said Jojen. "I saw the dead, bloated and drowned."

"We have to tell them," Bran said. "Alebelly and Mikken, and Septon Chayle. Tell them not to drown."

"It will not save them," replied the boy in green.

Meera came to the window seat and put a hand on his shoulder. "They will not believe, Bran. No more than you did."

Jojen sat on Bran's bed. "Tell me what *you* dream."

He was scared, even then, but he had sworn to trust them, and a Stark of Winterfell keeps his sworn word. "There's different kinds," he said slowly. "There's the wolf dreams, those aren't so bad as the others. I run and hunt and kill squirrels. And there's dreams where the crow comes and tells me to fly. Sometimes the tree is in those dreams too, calling my name. That frightens me. But the worst dreams are when I fall." He looked down into the yard, feeling miserable. "I never used to fall before. When I climbed. I went everyplace, up on the roofs and along the walls, I used to feed the crows in the Burned Tower. Mother was afraid that I would fall but I knew I never would. Only I did, and now when I sleep I fall all the time."

Meera gave his shoulder a squeeze. "Is that all?"

"I guess."

"*Warg,*" said Jojen Reed.

Bran looked at him, his eyes wide. "What?"

"Warg. Shapechanger. Beastling. That is what they will call you, if they should ever hear of your wolf dreams."

The names made him afraid again. "*Who* will call me?"

"Your own folk. In fear. Some will hate you if they know what you are. Some will even try to kill you."

Old Nan told scary stories of beastlings and shapechangers sometimes. In the stories they were always evil. "I'm not like that," Bran said. "I'm *not*. It's only dreams."

"The wolf dreams are no true dreams. You have your eye closed tight whenever you're awake, but as you drift off it flutters open and your soul seeks out its other half. The power is strong in you."

"I don't want it. I want to be a *knight*."

"A knight is what you want. A warg is what you are. You can't change that, Bran, you can't deny it or push it away. You are the winged wolf, but you will never fly." Jojen got up and walked to the window. "Unless you *open your eye*." He put two fingers together and poked Bran in the forehead, hard.

When he raised his hand to the spot, Bran felt only the smooth unbroken skin. There was no eye, not even a closed one. "How can I open it if it's not there?"

"You will never find the eye with your fingers, Bran. You must search with your heart." Jojen studied Bran's face with those strange green eyes. "Or are you afraid?"

"Maester Luwin says there's nothing in dreams that a man need fear."

"There is," said Jojen.

"What?"

"The past. The future. The truth."

They left him more muddled than ever. When he was alone, Bran tried to open his third eye, but he didn't know how. No matter how he wrinkled his forehead and poked at it, he couldn't see any different than he'd done before. In the days that followed, he tried to warn others about what Jojen had seen, but it didn't go as he wanted. Mikken thought it was funny. "The sea, is it? Happens I always wanted to see the sea. Never got where I could go to it, though. So now it's coming to me, is it? The gods are good, to take such trouble for a poor smith."

"The gods will take me when they see fit," Septon Chayle said quietly, "though I scarcely think it likely that I'll drown, Bran. I grew up on the banks of the White Knife, you know. I'm quite the strong swimmer."

Alebelly was the only one who paid the warning any heed. He went to talk to Jojen himself, and afterward stopped bathing and refused to go near the well. Finally he stank so bad that six of the other guards threw him into a tub of scalding water and scrubbed him raw while he screamed that they were going to drown him like the frogboy had said. Thereafter he scowled whenever he saw Bran or Jojen about the castle, and muttered under his breath.

It was a few days after Alebelly's bath that Ser Rodrik returned to Winterfell with his prisoner, a fleshy young man with fat moist lips and long hair who smelled like a privy, even worse than Alebelly had. "Reek, he's called," Hayhead said when Bran asked who it was. "I never heard his true name. He served the Bastard of Bolton and helped him murder Lady Hornwood, they say."

The Bastard himself was dead, Bran learned that evening over supper. Ser Rodrik's men had caught him on Hornwood land doing something horrible (Bran wasn't quite sure what, but it seemed to be something you did without your clothes) and shot him down with arrows as he tried to ride away. They came too late for poor Lady Hornwood, though. After their wedding, the Bastard had locked her in a tower and neglected to feed her. Bran had heard men saying that when Ser Rodrik had smashed down the door he found her with her mouth all bloody and her fingers chewed off.

"The monster has tied us a thorny knot," the old knight told Maester Luwin. "Like it or no, Lady Hornwood was his wife. He made her say the vows before both septon and heart tree, and bedded her that very night before witnesses. She signed a will naming him as heir and fixed her seal to it."

"Vows made at sword point are not valid," the maester argued.

"Roose Bolton may not agree. Not with land at issue." Ser Rodrik looked unhappy. "Would that I could take this serving man's head off as well, he's as bad as his master. But I fear I must keep him alive until Robb returns from his wars. He is the only witness to the worst of the Bastard's crimes. Perhaps when Lord Bolton hears his tale, he will abandon his claim, but meantime we have Manderly knights and Dreadfort men killing one another in Hornwood forests, and I lack the strength to stop them." The old knight turned in his seat and gave Bran a stern look. "And what have you been about while I've been away, my lord prince? Commanding our guardsmen not to wash? Do you want them smelling like this Reek, is that it?"

"The sea is coming here," Bran said. "Jojen saw it in a green dream. Alebelly is going to drown."

Maester Luwin tugged at his chain collar. "The Reed boy believes he sees the future in his dreams, Ser Rodrik. I've spoken to Bran about the uncertainty of such prophecies, but if truth be told, there *is* trouble along the Stony Shore. Raiders in longships, plundering fishing villages. Raping and burning. Leobald Tallhart has sent his nephew Benfred to deal with them, but I expect they'll take to their ships and flee at the first sight of armed men."

"Aye, and strike somewhere else. The Others take all such cowards. They would never dare, no more than the Bastard of Bolton, if our main strength were not a thousand leagues south." Ser Rodrik looked at Bran. "What else did the lad tell you?"

"He said the water would flow over our walls. He saw Alebelly drowned, and Mikken and Septon Chayle too."

Ser Rodrik frowned. "Well, should it happen that I need to ride against these raiders myself, I shan't take

Alebelly, then. He didn't see *me* drowned, did he? No? Good."

It heartened Bran to hear that. *Maybe they won't drown, then,* he thought. *If they stay away from the sea.*

Meera thought so too, later that night when she and Jojen met Bran in his room to play a three-sided game of tiles, but her brother shook his head. "The things I see in green dreams can't be changed."

That made his sister angry. "Why would the gods send a warning if we can't heed it and change what's to come?"

"I don't know," Jojen said sadly.

"If you were Alebelly, you'd probably jump into the well to have done with it! He should *fight,* and Bran should too."

"Me?" Bran felt suddenly afraid. "What should I fight? Am I going to drown too?"

Meera looked at him guiltily. "I shouldn't have said . . ."

He could tell that she was hiding something. "Did you see me in a green dream?" he asked Jojen nervously. "Was I drowned?"

"Not drowned." Jojen spoke as if every word pained him. "I dreamed of the man who came today, the one they call Reek. You and your brother lay dead at his feet, and he was skinning off your faces with a long red blade."

Meera rose to her feet. "If I went to the dungeon, I could drive a spear right through his heart. How could he murder Bran if he was dead?"

"The gaolers will stop you," Jojen said. "The guards. And if you tell them why you want him dead, they'll never believe."

"I have guards too," Bran reminded them. "Alebelly and Poxy Tym and Hayhead and the rest."

Jojen's mossy eyes were full of pity. "They won't be able to stop him, Bran. I couldn't see why, but I saw the end of it. I saw you and Rickon in your crypts, down in the dark with all the dead kings and their stone wolves."

No, Bran thought. *No.* "If I went away . . . to Greywater, or to the crow, someplace far where they couldn't find me . . ."

"It will not matter. The dream was green, Bran, and the green dreams do not lie."

TYRION

Varys stood over the brazier, warming his soft hands. "It would appear Renly was murdered most fearfully in the very midst of his army. His throat was opened from ear to ear by a blade that passed through steel and bone as if they were soft cheese."

"Murdered by whose hand?" Cersei demanded.

"Have you ever considered that too many answers are the same as no answer at all? My informers are not always as highly placed as we might like. When a king dies, fancies sprout like mushrooms in the dark. A groom says that Renly was slain by a knight of his own Rainbow Guard. A washerwoman claims Stannis stole through the heart of his brother's army with his magic sword. Several men-at-arms believe a woman did the fell deed, but cannot agree on *which* woman. A maid that Renly had spurned, claims one. A camp follower brought in to serve his pleasure on the eve of battle, says a second. The third ventures that it might have been the Lady Catelyn Stark."

The queen was not pleased. "Must you waste our time with every rumor the fools care to tell?"

"You pay me well for these rumors, my gracious queen."

"We pay you for the truth, Lord Varys. Remember that, or this small council may grow smaller still."

Varys tittered nervously. "You and your noble brother will leave His Grace with no council at all if you continue."

"I daresay, the realm could survive a few less councillors," said Littlefinger with a smile.

"Dear dear Petyr," said Varys, "are you not concerned that yours might be the next name on the Hand's little list?"

"Before you, Varys? I should never dream of it."

"Mayhaps we will be brothers on the Wall together, you and I." Varys giggled again.

"Sooner than you'd like, if the next words out of your mouth are not something useful, eunuch." From the look of her eyes, Cersei was prepared to castrate Varys all over again.

"Might this be some ruse?" asked Littlefinger.

"If so, it is a ruse of surpassing cleverness," said Varys. "It has certainly hoodwinked me."

Tyrion had heard enough. "Joff will be so disappointed," he said. "He was saving such a nice spike for Renly's head. But whoever did the deed, we must assume Stannis was behind it. The gain is clearly his." He did not like this news; he had counted on the brothers Baratheon decimating each other in bloody battle. He could feel his elbow throbbing where the morningstar had laid it open. It did that sometimes in the damp. He squeezed it uselessly in his hand and asked, "What of Renly's host?"

"The greater part of his foot remains at Bitterbridge." Varys abandoned the brazier to take his seat at the table. "Most of the lords who rode with Lord Renly to Storm's End have gone over banner-and-blade to Stannis, with all their chivalry."

"Led by the Florents, I'd wager," said Littlefinger.

Varys gave him a simpering smile. "You would win, my lord. Lord Alester was indeed the first to bend the knee. Many others followed."

"Many," Tyrion said pointedly, "but not all?"

"Not all," agreed the eunuch. "Not Loras Tyrell, nor Randyll Tarly, nor Mathis Rowan. And Storm's End itself has not yielded. Ser Cortnay Penrose holds the castle in Renly's name, and will not believe his liege is dead. He demands to see the mortal remains before he opens his gates, but it seems that Renly's corpse has unaccountably vanished. Carried away, most likely. A fifth of Renly's knights departed with Ser Loras rather than bend the knee to Stannis. It's said the Knight of Flowers went mad when he saw his king's body, and slew three of Renly's guards in his wrath, among them Emmon Cuy and Robar Royce."

A pity he stopped at three, thought Tyrion.

"Ser Loras is likely making for Bitterbridge," Varys went on. "His sister is there, Renly's queen, as well as a great many soldiers who suddenly find themselves kingless. Which side will they take now? A ticklish question. Many serve the lords who remained at Storm's End, and those lords now belong to Stannis."

Tyrion leaned forward. "There is a chance here, it seems to me. Win Loras Tyrell to our cause and Lord Mace Tyrell and his bannermen might join us as well. They may have sworn their swords to Stannis for the moment, yet they cannot love the man, or they would have been his from the start."

"Is their love for us any greater?" asked Cersei.

"Scarcely," said Tyrion. "They loved Renly, clearly, but Renly is slain. Perhaps we can give them good and sufficient reasons to prefer Joffrey to Stannis . . . *if* we move quickly."

"What sort of reasons do you mean to give them?"

"Gold reasons," Littlefinger suggested at once.

Varys made a *tsk*ing sound. "Sweet Petyr, surely you do not mean to suggest that these puissant lords and noble knights could be *bought* like so many chickens in the market."

"Have you been to our markets of late, Lord Varys?" asked Littlefinger. "You'd find it easier to buy a lord than a chicken, I daresay. Of course, lords cluck prouder than chickens, and take it ill if you offer them coin like a tradesman, but they are seldom adverse to taking gifts . . . honors, lands, castles . . ."

"Bribes might sway some of the lesser lords," Tyrion said, "but never Highgarden."

"True," Littlefinger admitted. "The Knight of Flowers is the key there. Mace Tyrell has two older sons, but Loras has always been his favorite. Win him, and Highgarden will be yours."

Yes, Tyrion thought. "It seems to me we should take a lesson from the late Lord Renly. We can win the Tyrell alliance as he did. With a marriage."

Varys understood the quickest. "You think to wed King Joffrey to Margaery Tyrell."

"I do." Renly's young queen was no more than fifteen, sixteen, he seemed to recall . . . older than Joffrey, but a few years were nothing, it was so neat and sweet he could taste it.

"Joffrey is betrothed to Sansa Stark," Cersei objected.

"Marriage contracts can be broken. What advantage is there in wedding the king to the daughter of a dead traitor?"

Littlefinger spoke up. "You might point out to His Grace that the Tyrells are much wealthier than the Starks, and that Margaery is said to be lovely . . . and beddable besides."

"Yes," said Tyrion, "Joff ought to like that well enough."

"My son is too young to care about such things."

"You think so?" asked Tyrion. "He's thirteen, Cersei. The same age at which I married."

"You shamed us all with that sorry episode. Joffrey is made of finer stuff."

"So fine that he had Ser Boros rip off Sansa's gown."

"He was angry with the girl."

"He was angry with that cook's boy who spilled the soup last night as well, but he didn't strip him naked."

"This was not a matter of some spilled soup—"

No, it was a matter of some pretty teats. After that business in the yard, Tyrion had spoken with Varys about how they might arrange for Joffrey to visit Chataya's. A taste of honey might sweeten the boy, he hoped. He might even be *grateful*, gods forbid, and Tyrion could do with a shade more gratitude from his sovereign. It would need to be done secretly, of course. The tricky bit would be parting him from the Hound. "The dog is never far from his master's heels," he'd observed to Varys, "but all men sleep. And some gamble and whore and visit winesinks as well."

"The Hound does all these things, if that is your question."

"No," said Tyrion. "My question is *when*."

Varys had laid a finger on his cheek, smiling enigmatically. "My lord, a suspicious man might think you wished to find a time when Sandor Clegane was not protecting King Joffrey, the better to do the boy some harm."

"Surely you know me better than that, Lord Varys," Tyrion said. "Why, all I want is for Joffrey to love me."

The eunuch had promised to look into the matter. The war made its own demands, though; Joffrey's initiation into manhood would need to wait. "Doubtless you know your son better than I do," he made himself tell Cersei, "but regardless, there's still much to be said for a Tyrell marriage. It may be the only way that Joffrey lives long enough to reach his wedding night."

Littlefinger agreed. "The Stark girl brings Joffrey nothing but her body, sweet as that may be. Margaery Tyrell brings fifty thousand swords and all the strength of Highgarden."

"Indeed." Varys laid a soft hand on the queen's sleeve. "You have a mother's heart, and I know His Grace loves his little sweetling. Yet kings must learn to put the needs of the realm before their own desires. I say this offer must be made."

The queen pulled free of the eunuch's touch. "You would not speak so if you were women. Say what you will, my lords, but Joffrey is too proud to settle for Renly's leavings. He will never consent."

Tyrion shrugged. "When the king comes of age in three years, he may give or withhold his consent as he pleases. Until then, you are his regent and I am his Hand, and he will marry whomever we tell him to marry. Leavings or no."

Cersei's quiver was empty. "Make your offer then, but gods save you all if Joff does not like this girl."

"I'm so pleased we can agree," Tyrion said. "Now, which of us shall go to Bitterbridge? We must reach Ser Loras with our offer before his blood can cool."

"You mean to send one of the council?"

"I can scarcely expect the Knight of Flowers to treat with Bronn or Shagga, can I? The Tyrells are proud."

His sister wasted no time trying to twist the situation to her advantage. "Ser Jacelyn Bywater is nobly born. Send him."

Tyrion shook his head. "We need someone who can do more than repeat our words and fetch back a reply. Our envoy must speak for king and council and settle the matter quickly."

"The Hand speaks with the king's voice." Candlelight gleamed green as wildfire in Cersei's eyes. "If we send you, Tyrion, it will be as if Joffrey went himself. And who better? You wield words as skillfully as Jaime wields a sword."

Are you that eager to get me out of the city, Cersei? "You are too kind, sister, but it seems to me that a boy's mother is better fitted to arrange his marriage than any uncle. And you have a gift for winning friends that I could never hope to match."

Her eyes narrowed. "Joff needs me at his side."

"Your Grace, my lord Hand," said Littlefinger, "the king needs both of you here. Let me go in your stead."

"You?" *What gain does he see in this?* Tyrion wondered.

"I am of the king's council, yet not the king's blood,

so I would make a poor hostage. I knew Ser Loras passing well when he was here at court, and gave him no cause to mislike me. Mace Tyrell bears me no enmity that I know of, and I flatter myself that I am not unskilled in negotiation."

He has us. Tyrion did not trust Petyr Baelish, nor did he want the man out of his sight, yet what other choice was left him? It must be Littlefinger or Tyrion himself, and he knew full well that if he left King's Landing for any length of time, all that he had managed to accomplish would be undone. "There is fighting between here and Bitterbridge," he said cautiously. "And you can be past certain that Lord Stannis will be dispatching his own shepherds to gather in his brother's wayward lambs."

"I've never been frightened of shepherds. It's the sheep who trouble me. Still, I suppose an escort might be in order."

"I can spare a hundred gold cloaks," Tyrion said.

"Five hundred."

"Three hundred."

"And forty more—twenty knights with as many squires. If I arrive without a knightly tail, the Tyrells will think me of small account."

That was true enough. "Agreed."

"I'll include Horror and Slobber in my party, and send them on to their lord father afterward. A gesture of goodwill. We need Paxter Redwyne, he's Mace Tyrell's oldest friend, and a great power in his own right."

"And a traitor," the queen said, balking. "The Arbor would have declared for Renly with all the rest, except that Redwyne knew full well his whelps would suffer for it."

"Renly is dead, Your Grace," Littlefinger pointed out, "and neither Stannis nor Lord Paxter will have forgotten how Redwyne galleys closed the sea during the siege of Storm's End. Restore the twins and perchance we may win Redwyne's love."

Cersei remained unconvinced. "The Others can keep his love, I want his swords and sails. Holding tight to those twins is the best way to make certain that we'll have them."

Tyrion had the answer. "Then let us send Ser Hobber back to the Arbor and keep Ser Horas here. Lord Paxter ought to be clever enough to riddle out the meaning of that, I should think."

The suggestion was carried without protest, but Littlefinger was not done. "We'll want horses. Swift and strong. The fighting will make remounts hard to come by. A goodly supply of gold will also be needed, for those gifts we spoke of earlier."

"Take as much as you require. If the city falls, Stannis will steal it all anyway."

"I'll want my commission in writing. A document that will leave Mace Tyrell in no doubt as to my authority, granting me full power to treat with him concerning this match and any other arrangements that might be required, and to make binding pledges in the king's name. It should be signed by Joffrey and every member of this council, and bear all our seals."

Tyrion shifted uncomfortably. "Done. Will that be all? I remind you, there's a long road between here and Bitterbridge."

"I'll be riding it before dawn breaks." Littlefinger rose. "I trust that on my return, the king will see that I am suitably rewarded for my valiant efforts in his cause?"

Varys giggled. "Joffrey is such a grateful sovereign, I'm certain you will have no cause to complain, my good brave lord."

The queen was more direct. "What do you want, Petyr?"

Littlefinger glanced at Tyrion with a sly smile. "I shall need to give that some consideration. No doubt I'll think of something." He sketched an airy bow and took his leave, as casual as if he were off to one of his brothels.

Tyrion glanced out the window. The fog was so thick that he could not even see the curtain wall across the yard. A few dim lights shone indistinct through that greyness. *A foul day for travel,* he thought. He did not envy Petyr Baelish. "We had best see to drawing up those documents. Lord Varys, send for parchment and quill. And someone will need to wake Joffrey."

It was still grey and dark when the meeting finally ended. Varys scurried off alone, his soft slippers whisking along the floor. The Lannisters lingered a moment by the door. "How comes your chain, brother?" the queen asked as Ser Preston fastened a vair-lined cloth-of-silver cloak about her shoulders.

"Link by link, it grows longer. We should thank the gods that Ser Cortnay Penrose is as stubborn as he is. Stannis will never march north with Storm's End untaken in his rear."

"Tyrion, I know we do not always agree on policy, but it seems to me that I was wrong about you. You are not so big a fool as I imagined. In truth, I realize now that you have been a great help. For that I thank you. You must forgive me if I have spoken to you harshly in the past."

"Must I?" He gave her a shrug, a smile. "Sweet sister, you have said nothing that requires forgiveness."

"Today, you mean?" They both laughed . . . and Cersei leaned over and planted a quick, soft kiss on his brow.

Too astonished for words, Tyrion could only watch her stride off down the hall, Ser Preston at her side. "Have I lost my wits, or did my sister just kiss me?" he asked Bronn when she was gone.

"Was it so sweet?"

"It was . . . unanticipated." Cersei had been behaving queerly of late. Tyrion found it very unsettling. "I am trying to recall the last time she kissed me. I could not have been more than six or seven. Jaime had dared her to do it."

"The woman's finally taken note of your charms."

"No," Tyrion said. "No, the woman is hatching something. Best find out what, Bronn. You know I hate surprises."

THEON

Theon wiped the spittle off his cheek with the back of his hand. "Robb will gut you, Greyjoy," Benfred Tallheart screamed. "He'll feed your turncloak's heart to his wolf, you piece of sheep dung."

Aeron Damphair's voice cut through the insults like a sword through cheese. "Now you must kill him."

"I have questions for him first," said Theon.

"*Fuck* your questions." Benfred hung bleeding and helpless between Stygg and Werlag. "You'll choke on them before you get any answers from me, craven. Turncloak."

Uncle Aeron was relentless. "When he spits on you, he spits on all of us. He spits on the Drowned God. He must die."

"My father gave *me* the command here, Uncle."

"And sent me to counsel you."

And to watch me. Theon dare not push matters too far with his uncle. The command was his, yes, but his men had a faith in the Drowned God that they did not have in him, and they were terrified of Aeron Damphair. *I cannot fault them for that.*

"You'll lose your head for this, Greyjoy. The crows will eat the jelly of your eyes." Benfred tried to spit again, but only managed a little blood. "The Others bugger your wet god."

Tallhart, you've spit away your life, Theon thought. "Stygg, silence him," he said.

They forced Benfred to his knees. Werlag tore the rabbitskin off his belt and jammed it between his teeth to stop his shouting. Stygg unlimbered his axe.

"No," Aeron Damphair declared. "He must be given to the god. The old way."

What does it matter? Dead is dead. "Take him, then."

"You will come as well. You command here. The offering should come from you."

That was more than Theon could stomach. "You are the priest, Uncle, I leave the god to you. Do me the same kindness and leave the battles to me." He waved his hand, and Werlag and Stygg began to drag their captive off toward the shore. Aeron Damphair gave his nephew a reproachful look, then followed. Down to the pebbled beach they would go, to drown Benfred Tallhart in salt water. The old way.

Perhaps it's a kindness, Theon told himself as he stalked off in the other direction. Stygg was hardly the most expert of headsmen, and Benfred had a neck thick as a boar's, heavy with muscle and fat. *I used to mock him for it, just to see how angry I could make him,* he remembered. That had been, what, three years past? When Ned Stark had ridden to Torrhen's Square to see Ser Helman, Theon had accompanied him and spent a fortnight in Benfred's company.

He could hear the rough noises of victory from the crook in the road where the battle had been fought . . . if you'd go so far as to call it a battle. *More like slaughtering sheep, if truth be told. Sheep fleeced in steel, but sheep nonetheless.*

Climbing a jumble of stone, Theon looked down on

the dead men and dying horses. The horses had deserved better. Tymor and his brothers had gathered up
what mounts had come through the fight unhurt, while
Urzen and Black Lorren silenced the animals too badly
wounded to be saved. The rest of his men were looting
the corpses. Gevin Harlaw knelt on a dead man's chest,
sawing off his finger to get at a ring. *Paying the iron
price. My lord father would approve.* Theon thought of
seeking out the bodies of the two men he'd slain himself to see if they had any jewelry worth the taking, but
the notion left a bitter taste in his mouth. He could
imagine what Eddard Stark would have said. Yet that
thought made him angry too. *Stark is dead and rotting,
and naught to me,* he reminded himself.

Old Botley, who was called Fishwhiskers, sat scowling by his pile of plunder while his three sons added to
it. One of them was in a shoving match with a fat man
named Todric, who was reeling among the slain with a
horn of ale in one hand and an axe in the other, clad in a
cloak of white foxfur only slightly stained by the blood
of its previous owner. *Drunk,* Theon decided, watching
him bellow. It was said that the ironmen of old had oft
been blood-drunk in battle, so berserk that they felt no
pain and feared no foe, but this was a common ale-
drunk.

"Wex, my bow and quiver." The boy ran and fetched
them. Theon bent the bow and slipped the string into
its notches as Todric knocked down the Botley boy and
flung ale into his eyes. Fishwhiskers leapt up cursing,
but Theon was quicker. He drew on the hand that
clutched the drinking horn, figuring to give them a shot
to talk about, but Todric spoiled it by lurching to one
side just as he loosed. The arrow took him through the
belly.

The looters stopped to gape. Theon lowered his bow.
"No drunkards, I said, and no squabbles over plunder."
On his knees, Todric was dying noisily. "Botley, silence
him." Fishwhiskers and his sons were quick to obey.
They slit Todric's throat as he kicked feebly, and were

stripping him of cloak and rings and weapons before he was even dead.

Now they know I mean what I say. Lord Balon might have given him the command, but Theon knew that some of his men saw only a soft boy from the green lands when they looked at him. "Anyone else have a thirst?" No one replied. "Good." He kicked at Benfred's fallen banner, clutched in the dead hand of the squire who'd borne it. A rabbitskin had been tied below the flag. *Why rabbitskins?* he had meant to ask, but being spat on had made him forget his questions. He tossed his bow back to Wex and strode off, remembering how elated he'd felt after the Whispering Wood, and wondering why this did not taste as sweet. *Tallhart, you bloody overproud fool, you never even sent out a scout.*

They'd been joking and even *singing* as they'd come on, the three trees of Tallhart streaming above them while rabbitskins flapped stupidly from the points of their lances. The archers concealed behind the gorse had spoiled the song with a rain of arrows, and Theon himself had led his men-at-arms out to finish the butcher's work with dagger, axe, and warhammer. He had ordered their leader spared for questioning.

Only he had not expected it to be Benfred Tallhart.

His limp body was being dragged from the surf when Theon returned to his *Sea Bitch.* The masts of his longships stood outlined against the sky along the pebbled beach. Of the fishing village, nothing remained but cold ashes that stank when it rained. The men had been put to the sword, all but a handful that Theon had allowed to flee to bring the word to Torrhen's Square. Their wives and daughters had been claimed for salt wives, those who were young enough and fair. The crones and the ugly ones had simply been raped and killed, or taken for thralls if they had useful skills and did not seem likely to cause trouble.

Theon had planned that attack as well, bringing his ships up to the shore in the chill darkness before the dawn and leaping from the prow with a longaxe in his hand to lead his men into the sleeping village. He did not like the taste of any of this, but what choice did he have?

His thrice-damned sister was sailing her *Black Wind* north even now, sure to win a castle of her own. Lord Balon had let no word of the hosting escape the Iron Islands, and Theon's bloody work along the Stony Shore would be put down to sea raiders out for plunder. The northmen would not realize their true peril, not until the hammers fell on Deepwood Motte and Moat Cailin. *And after all is done and won, they will make songs for that bitch Asha, and forget that I was even here.* That is, if he allowed it.

Dagmer Cleftjaw stood by the high carved prow of his longship, *Foamdrinker*. Theon had assigned him the task of guarding the ships; otherwise men would have called it Dagmer's victory, not his. A more prickly man might have taken that for a slight, but the Cleftjaw had only laughed.

"The day is won," Dagmer called down. "And yet you do not smile, boy. The living should smile, for the dead cannot." He smiled himself to show how it was done. It made for a hideous sight. Under a snowy white mane of hair, Dagmer Cleftjaw had the most gut-churning scar Theon had ever seen, the legacy of the longaxe that had near killed him as a boy. The blow had splintered his jaw, shattered his front teeth, and left him four lips where other men had but two. A shaggy beard covered his cheeks and neck, but the hair would not grow over the scar, so a shiny seam of puckered, twisted flesh divided his face like a crevasse through a snowfield. "We could hear them singing," the old warrior said. "It was a good song, and they sang it bravely."

"They sang better than they fought. Harps would have done them as much good as their lances did."

"How many men are lost?"

"Of ours?" Theon shrugged. "Todric. I killed him for getting drunk and fighting over loot."

"Some men are born to be killed." A lesser man might have been afraid to show a smile as frightening as his, yet Dagmer grinned more often and more broadly than Lord Balon ever had.

Ugly as it was, that smile brought back a hundred memories. Theon had seen it often as a boy, when he'd jumped a horse over a mossy wall, or flung an axe and split a target square. He'd seen it when he blocked a blow from Dagmer's sword, when he put an arrow through a seagull on the wing, when he took the tiller in hand and guided a longship safely through a snarl of foaming rocks. *He gave me more smiles than my father and Eddard Stark together.* Even Robb . . . he ought to have won a smile the day he'd saved Bran from that wildling, but instead he'd gotten a scolding, as if he were some cook who'd burned the stew.

"You and I must talk, Uncle," Theon said. Dagmer was no true uncle, only a sworn man with perhaps a pinch of Greyjoy blood four or five lives back, and that from the wrong side of the blanket. Yet Theon had always called him uncle nonetheless.

"Come onto my deck, then." There were no *m'lords* from Dagmer, not when he stood on his own deck. On the Iron Islands, every captain was a king aboard his own ship.

He climbed the plank to the deck of the *Foamdrinker* in four long strides, and Dagmer led him back to the cramped aft cabin, where the old man poured a horn of sour ale and offered Theon the same. He declined. "We did not capture enough horses. A few, but . . . well, I'll make do with what I have, I suppose. Fewer men means more glory."

"What need do we have of horses?" Like most ironmen, Dagmer preferred to fight on foot or from the deck of a ship. "Horses will only shit on our decks and get in our way."

"If we sailed, yes," Theon admitted. "I have another plan." He watched the other carefully to see how he would take that. Without the Cleftjaw he could not hope to succeed. Command or no, the men would never follow him if both Aeron and Dagmer opposed him, and he had no hope of winning over the sour-faced priest.

"Your lord father commanded us to harry the coast, no more." Eyes pale as sea foam watched Theon from under those shaggy white eyebrows. Was it disapproval he saw there, or a spark of interest? The latter, he thought . . . hoped . . .

"You are my father's man."

"His *best* man, and always have been."

Pride, Theon thought. *He is proud, I must use that, his pride will be the key.* "There is no man in the Iron Islands half so skilled with spear or sword."

"You have been too long away, boy. When you left, it was as you say, but I am grown old in Lord Greyjoy's service. The singers call Andrik best now. Andrik the Unsmiling, they name him. A giant of a man. He serves Lord Drumm of Old Wyk. And Black Lorren and Qarl the Maid are near as dread."

"This Andrik may be a great fighter, but men do not fear him as they fear you."

"Aye, that's so," Dagmer said. The fingers curled around the drinking horn were heavy with rings, gold and silver and bronze, set with chunks of sapphire and garnet and dragonglass. He had paid the iron price for every one, Theon knew.

"If I had a man like you in my service, I should not waste him on this child's business of harrying and burning. This is no work for Lord Balon's best man . . ."

Dagmer's grin twisted his lips apart and showed the brown splinters of his teeth. "Nor for his trueborn son?" He hooted. "I know you too well, Theon. I saw you take your first step, helped you bend your first bow. 'Tis not me who feels wasted."

"By rights I should have my sister's command," he admitted, uncomfortably aware of how peevish that sounded.

"You take this business too hard, boy. It is only that your lord father does not know you. With your brothers dead and you taken by the wolves, your sister was his solace. He learned to rely on her, and she has never failed him."

"Nor have I. The Starks knew my worth. I was one of

Brynden Blackfish's picked scouts, and I charged with the first wave in the Whispering Wood. I was *that* close to crossing swords with the Kingslayer himself." Theon held his hands two feet apart. "Daryn Hornwood came between us, and died for it."

"Why do you tell me this?" Dagmer asked. "It was me who put your first sword in your hand. I know you are no craven."

"Does my father?"

The hoary old warrior looked as if he had bitten into something he did not like the taste of. "It is only . . . Theon, the Boy Wolf is your friend, and these Starks had you for ten years."

"I am no Stark." *Lord Eddard saw to that.* "I am a Greyjoy, and I mean to be my father's heir. How can I do that unless I prove myself with some great deed?"

"You are young. Other wars will come, and you shall do your great deeds. For now, we are commanded to harry the Stony Shore."

"Let my uncle Aeron see to it. I'll give him six ships, all but *Foamdrinker* and *Sea Bitch*, and he can burn and drown to his god's surfeit."

"The command was given you, not Aeron Damphair."

"So long as the harrying is done, what does it matter? No priest could do what I mean to, nor what I ask of you. I have a task that only Dagmer Cleftjaw can accomplish."

Dagmer took a long draught from his horn. "Tell me."

He is tempted, Theon thought. *He likes this reaver's work no better than I do.* "If my sister can take a castle, so can I."

"Asha has four or five times the men we do."

Theon allowed himself a sly smile. "But we have four times the wits, and five times the courage."

"Your father—"

"—will thank me, when I hand him his kingdom. I mean to do a deed that the harpers will sing of for a thousand years."

He knew that would give Dagmer pause. A singer had made a song about the axe that cracked his jaw in half, and the old man loved to hear it. Whenever he was in his cups he would call for a reaving song, something loud and stormy that told of dead heroes and deeds of wild valor. *His hair is white and his teeth are rotten, but he still has a taste for glory.*

"What would my part be in this scheme of yours, boy?" Dagmer Cleftjaw asked after a long silence, and Theon knew he had won.

"To strike terror into the heart of the foe, as only one of your name could do. You'll take the great part of our force and march on Torrhen's Square. Helman Tallhart took his best men south, and Benfred died here with their sons. His uncle Leobald will remain, with some small garrison." *If I had been able to question Benfred, I would know just how small.* "Make no secret of your approach. Sing all the brave songs you like. I want them to close their gates."

"Is this Torrhen's Square a strong keep?"

"Strong enough. The walls are stone, thirty feet high, with square towers at each corner and a square keep within."

"Stone walls cannot be fired. How are we to take them? We do not have the numbers to storm even a small castle."

"You will make camp outside their walls and set to building catapults and siege engines."

"That is not the Old Way. Have you forgotten? Ironmen fight with swords and axes, not by flinging rocks. There is no glory in starving out a foeman."

"Leobald will not know that. When he sees you raising siege towers, his old woman's blood will run cold, and he will bleat for help. Stay your archers, Uncle, and let the raven fly. The castellan at Winterfell is a brave man, but age has stiffened his wits as well as his limbs. When he learns that one of his king's bannermen is under attack by the fearsome Dagmer Cleftjaw, he will summon his strength and ride to Tallhart's aid. It is his duty. Ser Rodrik is nothing if not dutiful."

"Any force he summons will be larger than mine," Dagmer said, "and these old knights are more cunning than you think, or they would never have lived to see their first grey hair. You set us a battle we cannot hope to win, Theon. This Torrhen's Square will never fall."

Theon smiled. "It's not Torrhen's Square I mean to take."

ARYA

Confusion and clangor ruled the castle. Men stood on the beds of wagons loading casks of wine, sacks of flour, and bundles of new-fletched arrows. Smiths straightened swords, knocked dents from breastplates, and shoed destriers and pack mules alike. Mail shirts were tossed in barrels of sand and rolled across the lumpy surface of the Flowstone Yard to scour them clean. Weese's women had twenty cloaks to mend, a hundred more to wash. The high and humble crowded into the sept together to pray. Outside the walls, tents and pavilions were coming down. Squires tossed pails of water over cookfires, while soldiers took out their oilstones to give their blades one last good lick. The noise was a swelling tide: horses blowing and whickering, lords shouting commands, men-at-arms trading curses, camp followers squabbling.

Lord Tywin Lannister was marching at last.

Ser Addam Marbrand was the first of the captains to depart, a day before the rest. He made a gallant show of it, riding a spirited red courser whose mane was the

same copper color as the long hair that streamed past
Ser Addam's shoulders. The horse was barded in bronze-
colored trappings dyed to match the rider's cloak and
emblazoned with the burning tree. Some of the castle
women sobbed to see him go. Weese said he was a great
horseman and sword fighter, Lord Tywin's most daring
commander.

I hope he dies, Arya thought as she watched him ride
out the gate, his men streaming after him in a double
column. *I hope they all die.* They were going to fight
Robb, she knew. Listening to the talk as she went about
her work, Arya had learned that Robb had won some
great victory in the west. He'd burned Lannisport, some
said, or else he meant to burn it. He'd captured Casterly
Rock and put everyone to the sword, or he was besieging the Golden Tooth . . . but *something* had happened, that much was certain.

Weese had her running messages from dawn to dusk.
Some of them even took her beyond the castle walls,
out into the mud and madness of the camp. *I could flee,*
she thought as a wagon rumbled past her. *I could hop
on the back of a wagon and hide, or fall in with the
camp followers, no one would stop me.* She might have
done it if not for Weese. He'd told them more than once
what he'd do to anyone who tried to run off on him. "It
won't be no beating, oh, no. I won't lay a finger on you.
I'll just save you for the Qohorik, yes I will, I'll save you
for the Crippler. Vargo Hoat his name is, and when he
gets back he'll cut off your feet." *Maybe if Weese were
dead,* Arya thought . . . but not when she was with
him. He could look at you and smell what you were
thinking, he always said so.

Weese never imagined she could read, though, so he
never bothered to seal the messages he gave her. Arya
peeked at them all, but they were never anything good,
just stupid stuff sending this cart to the granary and that
one to the armory. One was a demand for payment on a
gambling debt, but the knight she gave it to couldn't
read. When she told him what it said he tried to hit her,
but Arya ducked under the blow, snatched a silver-

banded drinking horn off his saddle, and darted away. The knight roared and came after her, but she slid between two wayns, wove through a crowd of archers, and jumped a latrine trench. In his mail he couldn't keep up. When she gave the horn to Weese, he told her that a smart little Weasel like her deserved a reward. "I've got my eye on a plump crisp capon to sup on tonight. We'll share it, me and you. You'll like that."

Everywhere she went, Arya searched for Jaqen H'ghar, wanting to whisper another name to him before those she hated were all gone out of her reach, but amidst the chaos and confusion the Lorathi sellsword was not to be found. He still owed her two deaths, and she was worried she would never get them if he rode off to battle with the rest. Finally she worked up the courage to ask one of the gate guards if he'd gone. "One of Lorch's men, is he?" the man said. "He won't be going, then. His lordship's named Ser Amory castellan of Harrenhal. That whole lot's staying right here, to hold the castle. The Bloody Mummers will be left as well, to do the foraging. That goat Vargo Hoat is like to spit, him and Lorch have always hated each other."

The Mountain would be leaving with Lord Tywin, though. He would command the van in battle, which meant that Dunsen, Polliver, and Raff would all slip between her fingers unless she could find Jaqen and have him kill one of them before they left.

"Weasel," Weese said that afternoon. "Get to the armory and tell Lucan that Ser Lyonel notched his sword in practice and needs a new one. Here's his mark." He handed her a square of paper. "Be quick about it now, he's to ride with Ser Kevan Lannister."

Arya took the paper and ran. The armory adjoined the castle smithy, a long high-roofed tunnel of a building with twenty forges built into its walls and long stone water troughs for tempering the steel. Half of the forges were at work when she entered. The walls rang with the sound of hammers, and burly men in leather aprons stood sweating in the sullen heat as they bent over bellows and anvils. When she spied Gendry, his bare chest was slick with sweat, but the blue eyes under the heavy black hair had the stubborn look she remembered. Arya didn't know that she even wanted to talk to him. It was his fault they'd all been caught. "Which one is Lucan?" She thrust out the paper. "I'm to get a new sword for Ser Lyonel."

"Never mind about Ser Lyonel." He drew her aside by the arm. "Last night Hot Pie asked me if I heard you yell *Winterfell* back at the holdfast, when we were all fighting on the wall."

"I never did!"

"Yes you did. I heard you too."

"Everyone was yelling stuff," Arya said defensively. "Hot Pie yelled *hot pie.* He must have yelled it a hundred times."

"It's what *you* yelled that matters. I told Hot Pie he should clean the wax out of his ears, that all you yelled was *Go to hell!* If he asks you, you better say the same."

"I will," she said, even though she thought *go to hell* was a stupid thing to yell. She didn't dare tell Hot Pie who she really was. *Maybe I should say Hot Pie's name to Jaqen.*

"I'll get Lucan," Gendry said.

Lucan grunted at the writing (though Arya did not think he could read it), and pulled down a heavy longsword. "This is too good for that oaf, and you tell him I said so," he said as he gave her the blade.

"I will," she lied. If she did any such thing, Weese would beat her bloody. Lucan could deliver his own insults.

The longsword was a lot heavier than Needle had been, but Arya liked the feel of it. The weight of steel in her hands made her feel stronger. *Maybe I'm not a water dancer yet, but I'm not a mouse either. A mouse couldn't use a sword but I can.* The gates were open, soldiers coming and going, drays rolling in empty and going out creaking and swaying under their loads. She thought about going to the stables and telling them that Ser Lyonel wanted a new horse. She had the paper, the stableboys wouldn't be able to read it any better than

Lucan had. *I could take the horse and the sword and just ride out. If the guards tried to stop me I'd show them the paper and say I was bringing everything to Ser Lyonel.* She had no notion what Ser Lyonel looked like or where to find him, though. If they questioned her, they'd know, and then Weese . . . Weese . . .

As she chewed her lip, trying not to think about how it would feel to have her feet cut off, a group of archers in leather jerkins and iron helms went past, their bows slung across their shoulders. Arya heard snatches of their talk.

". . . giants I tell you, he's got *giants* twenty foot tall come down from beyond the Wall, follow him like dogs . . ."

". . . not natural, coming on them so fast, in the night and all. He's more wolf than man, all them Starks are . . ."

". . . shit on your wolves and giants, the boy'd piss his pants if he knew we was coming. He wasn't man enough to march on Harrenhal, was he? Ran t'other way, didn't he? He'd run now if he knew what was best for him."

"So you say, but might be the boy knows something we don't, maybe it's *us* ought to be run . . ."

Yes, Arya thought. *Yes, it's you who ought to run, you and Lord Tywin and the Mountain and Ser Addam and Ser Amory and stupid Ser Lyonel whoever he is, all of you better run or my brother will kill you, he's a Stark, he's more wolf than man, and so am I.*

"Weasel." Weese's voice cracked like a whip. She never saw where he came from, but suddenly he was right in front of her. "Give me that. Took you long enough." He snatched the sword from her fingers, and dealt her a stinging slap with the back of his hand. "Next time be quicker about it."

For a moment she had been a wolf again, but Weese's slap took it all away and left her with nothing but the taste of her own blood in her mouth. She'd bitten her tongue when he hit her. She hated him for that.

"You want another?" Weese demanded. "You'll get it

too. I'll have none of your insolent looks. Get down to the brewhouse and tell Tuffleberry that I have two dozen barrels for him, but he better send his lads to fetch them or I'll find someone wants 'em worse." Arya started off, but not quick enough for Weese. "You *run* if you want to eat tonight," he shouted, his promises of a plump crisp capon already forgotten. "And don't be getting lost again, or I swear I'll beat you bloody."

You won't, Arya thought. *You won't ever again.* But she ran. The old gods of the north must have been guiding her steps. Halfway to the brewhouse, as she passing under the stone bridge that arched between Widow's Tower and Kingspyre, she heard harsh, growling laughter. Rorge came around a corner with three other men, the manticore badge of Ser Amory sewn over their hearts. When he saw her, he stopped and grinned, showing a mouthful of crooked brown teeth under the leather flap he wore sometimes to cover the hole in his face. "Yoren's little cunt," he called her. "Guess we know why that black bastard wanted *you* on the Wall, don't we?" He laughed again, and the others laughed with him. "Where's your stick now?" Rorge demanded suddenly, the smile gone as quick as it had come. "Seems to me I promised to fuck you with it." He took a step toward her. Arya edged backward. "Not so brave now that I'm not in chains, are you?"

"I *saved* you." She kept a good yard between them, ready to run quick as a snake if he made a grab for her.

"Owe you another fucking for that, seems like. Did Yoren pump your cunny, or did he like that tight little ass better?"

"I'm looking for Jaqen," she said. "There's a message."

Rorge halted. Something in his eyes . . . could it be that he was *scared* of Jaqen H'ghar? "The bathhouse. Get out of my way."

Arya whirled and ran, swift as a deer, her feet flying over the cobbles all the way to the bathhouse. She found Jaqen soaking in a tub, steam rising around him as a serving girl sluiced hot water over his head. His long hair, red on one side and white on the other, fell down across his shoulders, wet and heavy.

She crept up quiet as a shadow, but he opened his eyes all the same. "She steals in on little mice feet, but a man hears," he said. *How could he hear me?* she wondered, and it seemed as if he heard that as well. "The scuff of leather on stone sings loud as warhorns to a man with open ears. Clever girls go barefoot."

"I have a message." Arya eyed the serving girl uncertainly. When she did not seem likely to go away, she leaned in until her mouth was almost touching his ear. "Weese," she whispered.

Jaqen H'ghar closed his eyes again, floating languid, half-asleep. "Tell his lordship a man shall attend him at his leisure." His hand moved suddenly, splashing hot water at her, and Arya had to leap back to keep from getting drenched.

When she told Tuffleberry what Weese had said, the brewer cursed loudly. "You tell Weese my lads got duties to attend to, and you tell him he's a pox-ridden bastard too, and the seven hells will freeze over before he gets another horn of my ale. I'll have them barrels within the hour or Lord Tywin will hear of it, see if he don't."

Weese cursed too when Arya brought back that message, even though she left out the pox-ridden bastard part. He fumed and threatened, but in the end he rounded up six men and sent them off grumbling to fetch the barrels down to the brewhouse.

Supper that evening was a thin stew of barley, onion, and carrots, with a wedge of stale brown bread. One of the women had taken to sleeping in Weese's bed, and she got a piece of ripe blue cheese as well, and a wing off the capon that Weese had spoken of that morning. He ate the rest himself, the grease running down in a shiny line through the boils that festered at the corner of his mouth. The bird was almost gone when he glanced up from his trencher and saw Arya staring. "Weasel, come here."

A few mouthfuls of dark meat still clung to one thigh.

He forgot, but now he's remembered, Arya thought. It made her feel bad for telling Jaqen to kill him. She got off the bench and went to the head of the table.

"I saw you looking at me." Weese wiped his fingers on the front of her shift. Then he grabbed her throat with one hand and slapped her with the other. "What did I tell you?" He slapped her again, backhand. "Keep those eyes to yourself, or next time I'll spoon one out and feed it to my bitch." A shove sent her stumbling to the floor. Her hem caught on a loose nail in the splintered wooden bench and ripped as she fell. "You'll mend that before you sleep," Weese announced as he pulled the last bit of meat off the capon. When he was finished he sucked his fingers noisily, and threw the bones to his ugly spotted dog.

"Weese," Arya whispered that night as she bent over the tear in her shift. "Dunsen, Polliver, Raff the Sweetling," she said, calling a name every time she pushed the bone needle through the undyed wool. "The Tickler and the Hound. Ser Gregor, Ser Amory, Ser Ilyn, Ser Meryn, King Joffrey, Queen Cersei." She wondered how much longer she would have to include Weese in her prayer, and drifted off to sleep dreaming that on the morrow, when she woke, he'd be dead.

But it was the sharp toe of Weese's boot that woke her, as ever. The main strength of Lord Tywin's host would ride this day, he told them as they broke their fast on oatcakes. "Don't none of you be thinking how easy it'll be here once m'lord of Lannister is gone," he warned. "The castle won't grow no smaller, I promise you that, only now there'll be fewer hands to tend to it. You lot of slugabeds are going to learn what work is now, yes you are."

Not from you. Arya picked at her oaten cake. Weese frowned at her, as if he smelled her secret. Quickly she dropped her gaze to her food, and dared not raise her eyes again.

Pale light filled the yard when Lord Tywin Lannister took his leave of Harrenhal. Arya watched from an arched window halfway up the Wailing Tower. His charger wore a blanket of enameled crimson scales and gilded crinet and chamfron, while Lord Tywin himself sported a thick ermine cloak. His brother Ser Kevan looked near as splendid. No less than four standard-bearers went before them, carrying huge crimson banners emblazoned with the golden lion. Behind the Lannisters came their great lords and captains. Their banners flared and flapped, a pageant of color: red ox and golden mountain, purple unicorn and bantam rooster, brindled boar and badger, a silver ferret and a juggler in motley, stars and sunbursts, peacock and panther, chevron and dagger, black hood and blue beetle and green arrow.

Last of all came Ser Gregor Clegane in his grey plate steel, astride a stallion as bad-tempered as his rider. Polliver rode beside him, with the black dog standard in his hand and Gendry's horned helm on his head. He was a tall man, but he looked no more than a half-grown boy when he rode in his master's shadow.

A shiver crept up Arya's spine as she watched them pass under the great iron portcullis of Harrenhal. Suddenly she knew that she had made a terrible mistake. *I'm so stupid,* she thought. Weese did not matter, no more than Chiswyck had. *These* were the men who mattered, the ones she ought to have killed. Last night she could have whispered any of them dead, if only she hadn't been so mad at Weese for hitting her and lying about the capon. *Lord Tywin, why didn't I say Lord Tywin?*

Perhaps it was not too late to change her mind. Weese was not killed yet. If she could find Jaqen, tell him . . .

Hurriedly, Arya ran down the twisting steps, her chores forgotten. She heard the rattle of chains as the portcullis was slowly lowered, its spikes sinking deep into the ground . . . and then another sound, a shriek of pain and fear.

A dozen people got there before her, though none was coming any too close. Arya squirmed between them. Weese was sprawled across the cobbles, his throat a red ruin, eyes gaping sightlessly up at a bank of grey cloud.

His ugly spotted dog stood on his chest, lapping at the blood pulsing from his neck, and every so often ripping a mouthful of flesh out of the dead man's face.

Finally someone brought a crossbow and shot the spotted dog dead while she was worrying at one of Weese's ears.

"Damnedest thing," she heard a man say. "He had that bitch dog since she was a pup."

"This place is cursed," the man with the crossbow said.

"It's Harren's ghost, that's what it is," said Goodwife Amabel. "I'll not sleep here another night, I swear it."

Arya lifted her gaze from the dead man and his dead dog. Jaqen H'ghar was leaning up against the side of the Wailing Tower. When he saw her looking, he lifted a hand to his face and laid two fingers casually against his cheek.

CATELYN

Two days ride from Riverrun, a scout spied them watering their horses beside a muddy steam. Catelyn had never been so glad to see the twin tower badge of House Frey.

When she asked him to lead them to her uncle, he said, "The Blackfish is gone west with the king, my lady. Martyn Rivers commands the outriders in his stead."

"I see." She had met Rivers at the Twins; a baseborn son of Lord Walder Frey, half brother to Ser Perwyn. It did not surprise her to learn that Robb had struck at the heart of Lannister power; clearly he had been contemplating just that when he sent her away to treat with Renly. "Where is Rivers now?"

"His camp is two hours ride, my lady."

"Take us to him," she commanded. Brienne helped her back into her saddle, and they set out at once.

"Have you come from Bitterbridge, my lady?" the scout asked.

"No." She had not dared. With Renly dead, Catelyn

had been uncertain of the reception she might receive from his young widow and her protectors. Instead she had ridden through the heart of the war, through fertile riverlands turned to blackened desert by the fury of the Lannisters, and each night her scouts brought back tales that made her ill. "Lord Renly is slain," she added.

"We'd hoped that tale was some Lannister lie, or—"

"Would that it were. My brother commands in Riverrun?"

"Yes, my lady. His Grace left Ser Edmure to hold Riverrun and guard his rear."

Gods grant him the strength to do so, Catelyn thought. *And the wisdom as well.* "Is there word from Robb in the west?"

"You have not heard?" The man seemed surprised. "His Grace won a great victory at Oxcross. Ser Stafford Lannister is dead, his host scattered."

Ser Wendel Manderly gave a *whoop* of pleasure, but Catelyn only nodded. Tomorrow's trials concerned her more than yesterday's triumphs.

Martyn Rivers had made his camp in the shell of a shattered holdfast, beside a roofless stable and a hundred fresh graves. He went to one knee when Catelyn dismounted. "Well met, my lady. Your brother charged us to keep an eye out for your party, and escort you back to Riverrun in all haste should we come upon you."

Catelyn scarce liked the sound of that. "Is it my father?"

"No, my lady. Lord Hoster is unchanged." Rivers was a ruddy man with scant resemblance to his half brothers. "It is only that we feared you might chance upon Lannister scouts. Lord Tywin has left Harrenhal and marches west with all his power."

"Rise," she told Rivers, frowning. Stannis Baratheon would soon be on the march as well, gods help them all. "How long until Lord Tywin is upon us?"

"Three days, perhaps four, it is hard to know. We have eyes out along all the roads, but it would be best not to linger."

Nor did they. Rivers broke his camp quickly and saddled up beside her, and they set off again, near fifty strong now, flying beneath the direwolf, the leaping trout, the twin towers.

Her men wanted to hear more of Robb's victory at Oxcross, and Rivers obliged. "There's a singer come to Riverrun, calls himself Rymund the Rhymer, he's made a song of the fight. Doubtless you'll hear it sung tonight, my lady. 'Wolf in the Night,' this Rymund calls it." He went on to tell how the remnants of Ser Stafford's host had fallen back on Lannisport. Without siege engines there was no way to storm Casterly Rock, so the Young Wolf was paying the Lannisters back in kind for the devastation they'd inflicted on the riverlands. Lords Karstark and Glover were raiding along the coast, Lady Mormont had captured thousands of cattle and was driving them back toward Riverrun, while the Greatjon had seized the gold mines at Castamere, Nunn's Deep, and the Pendric Hills. Ser Wendel laughed. "Nothing's more like to bring a Lannister running than a threat to his gold."

"How did the king ever take the Tooth?" Ser Perwyn Frey asked his bastard brother. "That's a hard strong keep, and it commands the hill road."

"He never took it. He slipped around it in the night. It's said the direwolf showed him the way, that Grey Wind of his. The beast sniffed out a goat track that wound down a defile and up along beneath a ridge, a crooked and stony way, yet wide enough for men riding single file. The Lannisters in their watchtowers got not so much a glimpse of them." Rivers lowered his voice. "There's some say that after the battle, the king cut out Stafford Lannister's heart and fed it to the wolf."

"I would not believe such tales," Catelyn said sharply. "My son is no savage."

"As you say, my lady. Still, it's no more than the beast deserved. That is no common wolf, that one. The Greatjon's been heard to say that the old gods of the north sent those direwolves to your children."

Catelyn remembered the day when her boys had found the pups in the late summer snows. There had been five, three male and two female for the five true-born children of House Stark . . . and a sixth, white of fur and red of eye, for Ned's bastard son Jon Snow. *No common wolves,* she thought. *No indeed.*

That night as they made their camp, Brienne sought out her tent. "My lady, you are safely back among your own now, a day's ride from your brother's castle. Give me leave to go."

Catelyn should not have been surprised. The homely young woman had kept to herself all through their journey, spending most of her time with the horses, brushing out their coats and pulling stones from their shoes. She had helped Shadd cook and clean game as well, and soon proved that she could hunt as well as any. Any task Catelyn asked her to turn her hand to, Brienne had performed deftly and without complaint, and when she was spoken to she answered politely, but she never chattered, nor wept, nor laughed. She had ridden with them every day and slept among them every night without ever truly becoming one of them.

It was the same when she was with Renly, Catelyn thought. *At the feast, in the melee, even in Renly's pavilion with her brothers of the Rainbow Guard. There are walls around this one higher than Winterfell's.*

"If you left us, where would you go?" Catelyn asked her.

"Back," Brienne said. "To Storm's End."

"Alone." It was not a question.

The broad face was a pool of still water, giving no hint of what might live in the depths below. "Yes."

"You mean to kill Stannis."

Brienne closed her thick callused fingers around the hilt of her sword. The sword that had been his. "I swore a vow. Three times I swore. You heard me."

"I did," Catelyn admitted. The girl had kept the rainbow cloak when she discarded the rest of her blood-stained clothing, she knew. Brienne's own things had been left behind during their flight, and she had been forced to clothe herself in odd bits of Ser Wendel's spare garb, since no one else in their party had garments large enough to fit her. "Vows should be kept, I agree, but Stannis has a great host around him, and his own guards sworn to keep him safe."

"I am not afraid of his guards. I am as good as any of them. I should never have fled."

"Is that what troubles you, that some fool might call you craven?" She sighed. "Renly's death was no fault of yours. You served him valiantly, but when you seek to follow him into the earth, you serve no one." She stretched out a hand, to give what comfort a touch could give. "I know how hard it is—"

Brienne shook off her hand. "No one knows."

"You're wrong," Catelyn said sharply. "Every morning, when I wake, I remember that Ned is gone. I have no skill with swords, but that does not mean that I do not dream of riding to King's Landing and wrapping my hands around Cersei Lannister's white throat and squeezing until her face turns black."

The Beauty raised her eyes, the only part of her that was truly beautiful. "If you dream that, why would you seek to hold me back? Is it because of what Stannis said at the parley?"

Was it! Catelyn glanced across the camp. Two men were walking sentry, spears in hand. "I was taught that good men must fight evil in this world, and Renly's death was evil beyond all doubt. Yet I was also taught that the gods make kings, not the swords of men. If Stannis is our rightful king—"

"He's not. Robert was never the rightful king either, even Renly said as much. Jaime Lannister *murdered* the rightful king, after Robert killed his lawful heir on the Trident. Where were the gods then? The gods don't care about men, no more than kings care about peasants."

"A good king does care."

"Lord Renly . . . His Grace, he . . . he would have been the *best* king, my lady, he was so good, he . . ."

"He is gone, Brienne," she said, as gently as she could. "Stannis and Joffrey remain . . . and so does my son."

"He wouldn't . . . you'd never make a *peace* with Stannis, would you? Bend the knee? You wouldn't . . ."

"I will tell you true, Brienne. I do not know. My son may be a king, but I am no queen . . . only a mother who would keep her children safe, however she could."

"I am not made to be a mother. I need to fight."

"Then fight . . . but for the living, not the dead. Renly's enemies are Robb's enemies as well."

Brienne stared at the ground and shuffled her feet. "I do not know your son, my lady." She looked up. "I could serve you. If you would have me."

Catelyn was startled. "Why me?"

The question seemed to trouble Brienne. "You helped me. In the pavilion . . . when they thought that I had . . . that I had . . ."

"You were innocent."

"Even so, you did not have to do that. You could have let them kill me. I was nothing to you."

Perhaps I did not want to be the only one who knew the dark truth of what had happened there, Catelyn thought. "Brienne, I have taken many wellborn ladies into my service over the years, but never one like you. I am no battle commander."

"No, but you have courage. Not battle courage perhaps but . . . I don't know . . . a kind of *woman's* courage. And I think, when the time comes, you will not try and hold me back. Promise me that. That you will not hold me back from Stannis."

Catelyn could still hear Stannis saying that Robb's turn too would come in time. It was like a cold breath on the back of her neck. "When the time comes, I will not hold you back."

The tall girl knelt awkwardly, unsheathed Renly's longsword, and laid it at her feet. "Then I am yours, my lady. Your liege man, or . . . whatever you would have me be. I will shield your back and keep your counsel and give my life for yours, if need be. I swear it by the old gods and the new."

"And I vow that you shall always have a place by my hearth and meat and mead at my table, and pledge to ask no service of you that might bring you into dishonor. I swear it by the old gods and the new. Arise." As she clasped the other woman's hands between her own, Catelyn could not help but smile. *How many times did I watch Ned accept a man's oath of service?* She wondered what he would think if he could see her now.

They forded the Red Fork late the next day, upstream of Riverrun where the river made a wide loop and the waters grew muddy and shallow. The crossing was guarded by a mixed force of archers and pikemen wearing the eagle badge of the Mallisters. When they saw Catelyn's banners, they emerged from behind their sharpened stakes and sent a man over from the far bank to lead her party across. "Slow and careful like, milady," he warned as he took the bridle of her horse. "We've planted iron spikes under the water, y'see, and there's caltrops scattered among them rocks there. It's the same on all the fords, by your brother's command."

Edmure thinks to fight here. The realization gave her a queasy feeling in the bowels, but she held her tongue.

Between the Red Fork and the Tumblestone, they joined a stream of smallfolk making for the safety of Riverrun. Some were driving animals before them, others pulling wayns, but they made way as Catelyn rode past, and cheered her with cries of "Tully!" or "Stark!" Half a mile from the castle, she passed through a large encampment where the scarlet banner of the Blackwoods waved above the lord's tent. Lucas took his leave of her there, to seek out his father, Lord Tytos. The rest rode on.

Catelyn spied a second camp strung out along the bank north of the Tumblestone, familiar standards flapping in the wind—Marq Piper's dancing maiden, Darry's plowman, the twining red-and-white snakes of the Paeges. They were all her father's bannermen, lords of the Trident. Most had left Riverrun before she had, to defend their own lands. If they were here again, it could only mean that Edmure had called them back. *Gods save us, it's true, he means to offer battle to Lord Tywin.*

Something dark was dangling against the walls of Riverrun, Catelyn saw from a distance. When she rode close, she saw dead men hanging from the battlements, slumped at the ends of long ropes with hempen nooses tight around their necks, their faces swollen and black. The crows had been at them, but their crimson cloaks still showed bright against the sandstone walls.

"They have hanged some Lannisters," Hal Mollen observed.

"A pretty sight," Ser Wendel Manderly said cheerfully.

"Our friends have begun without us," Perwyn Frey jested. The others laughed, all but Brienne, who gazed up at the row of bodies unblinking, and neither spoke nor smiled.

If they have slain the Kingslayer, then my daughters are dead as well. Catelyn spurred her horse to a canter. Hal Mollen and Robin Flint raced past at a gallop, halooing to the gatehouse. The guards on the walls had doubtless spied her banners some time ago, for the portcullis was up as they approached.

Edmure rode out from the castle to meet her, surrounded by three of her father's sworn men—great-bellied Ser Desmond Grell the master-at-arms, Utherydes Wayn the steward, and Ser Robin Ryger, Riverrun's big bald captain of guards. They were all three of an age with Lord Hoster, men who had spent their lives in her father's service. *Old men,* Catelyn realized.

Edmure wore a blue-and-red cloak over a tunic embroidered with silver fish. From the look of him, he had not shaved since she rode south; his beard was a fiery bush. "Cat, it is good to have you safely back. When we heard of Renly's death, we feared for your life. And Lord Tywin is on the march as well."

"So I am told. How fares our father?"

"One day he seems stronger, the next . . ." He shook

his head. "He's asked for you. I did not know what to tell him."

"I will go to him soon," she vowed. "Has there been word from Storm's End since Renly died? Or from Bitterbridge?" No ravens came to men on the road, and Catelyn was anxious to know what had happened behind her.

"Nothing from Bitterbridge. From Storm's End, three birds from the castellan, Ser Cortnay Penrose, all carrying the same plea. Stannis has him surrounded by land and sea. He offers his allegiance to whatsoever king will break the siege. He fears for the boy, he says. What boy would that be, do you know?"

"Edric Storm," Brienne told them. "Robert's bastard son."

Edmure looked at her curiously. "Stannis has sworn that the garrison might go free, unharmed, provided they yield the castle within the fortnight and deliver the boy into his hands, but Ser Cortnay will not consent."

He risks all for a baseborn boy whose blood is not even his own, Catelyn thought. "Did you send him an answer?"

Edmure shook his head. "Why, when we have neither help nor hope to offer? And Stannis is no enemy of ours."

Ser Robin Ryger spoke. "My lady, can you tell us the manner of Lord Renly's death? The tales we've heard have been queer."

"Cat," her brother said, "some say *you* killed Renly. Others claim it was some southron woman." His glance lingered on Brienne.

"My king was murdered," the girl said quietly, "and not by Lady Catelyn. I swear it on my sword, by the gods old and new."

"This is Brienne of Tarth, the daughter of Lord Selwyn the Evenstar, who served in Renly's Rainbow Guard," Catelyn told them. "Brienne, I am honored to acquaint you with my brother Ser Edmure Tully, heir to

Riverrun. His steward Utherydes Wayn. Ser Robin Ryger and Ser Desmond Grell."

"Honored," said Ser Desmond. The others echoed him. The girl flushed, embarrassed even at this commonplace courtesy. If Edmure thought her a curious sort of lady, at least he had the grace not to say so.

"Brienne was with Renly when he was killed, as was I," said Catelyn, "but we had no part in his death." She did not care to speak of the shadow, here in the open with men all around, so she waved a hand at the bodies. "Who are these men you've hanged?"

Edmure glanced up uncomfortably. "They came with Ser Cleos when he brought the queen's answer to our peace offer."

Catelyn was shocked. "You've killed *envoys!*"

"False envoys," Edmure declared. "They pledged me their peace and surrendered their weapons, so I allowed them freedom of the castle, and for three nights they ate my meat and drank my mead whilst I talked with Ser Cleos. On the fourth night, they tried to free the King-slayer." He pointed up. "That big brute killed two guards with naught but those ham hands of his, caught them by the throats and smashed their skulls together while that skinny lad beside him was opening Lannister's cell with a bit of wire, gods curse him. The one on the end was some sort of damned mummer. He used my own voice to command that the River Gate be opened. The guardsmen swear to it, Enger and Delp and Long Lew, all three. If you ask me, the man sounded nothing like me, and yet the oafs were raising the portcullis all the same."

This was the Imp's work, Catelyn suspected; it stank of the same sort of cunning he had displayed at the Eyrie. Once, she would have named Tyrion the least dangerous of the Lannisters. Now she was not so certain. "How is it you caught them?"

"Ah, as it happened, I was not in the castle. I'd crossed the Tumblestone to, ah . . . ."

"You were whoring or wenching. Get on with the tale."

Edmure's cheeks flamed as red as his beard. "It was the hour before dawn, and I was only then returning. When Long Lew saw my boat and recognized me, he finally thought to wonder who was standing below barking commands, and raised a cry."

"Tell me the Kingslayer was retaken."

"Yes, though not easily. Jaime got hold of a sword, slew Poul Pemford and Ser Desmond's squire Myles, and wounded Delp so badly that Maester Vyman fears he'll soon die as well. It was a bloody mess. At the sound of steel, some of the other red cloaks rushed to join him, barehand or no. I hanged those beside the four who freed him, and threw the rest in the dungeons. Jaime too. We'll have no more escapes from that one. He's down in the dark this time, chained hand and foot and bolted to the wall."

"And Cleos Frey?"

"He swears he knew naught of the plot. Who can say? The man is half Lannister, half Frey, and all liar. I put him in Jaime's old tower cell."

"You say he brought terms?"

"If you can call them that. You'll like them no more than I did, I promise."

"Can we hope for no help from the south, Lady Stark?" asked Utherydes Wayn, her father's steward. "This charge of incest . . . Lord Tywin does not suffer such slights lightly. He will seek to wash the stain from his daughter's name with the blood of her accuser, Lord Stannis must see that. He has no choice but to make common cause with us."

Stannis has made common cause with a power greater and darker. "Let us speak of these matters later." Catelyn trotted over the drawbridge, putting the grisly row of dead Lannisters behind her. Her brother kept pace. As they rode out into the bustle of Riverrun's upper bailey, a naked toddler ran in front of the horses. Catelyn jerked her reins hard to avoid him, glancing about in dismay. Hundreds of smallfolk had been admitted to the castle, and allowed to erect crude shelters against the walls. Their children were everywhere underfoot, and the yard teemed with their cows, sheep, and chickens. "Who are all these folk?"

"My people," Edmure answered. "They were afraid."

Only my sweet brother would crowd all these useless mouths into a castle that might soon be under siege. Catelyn knew that Edmure had a soft heart; sometimes she thought his head was even softer. She loved him for it, yet still . . .

"Can Robb be reached by raven?"

"He's in the field, my lady," Ser Desmond replied. "The bird would have no way to find him."

Utherydes Wayn coughed. "Before he left us, the young king instructed us to send you on to the Twins upon your return, Lady Stark. He asks that you learn more of Lord Walder's daughters, to help him select his bride when the time comes."

"We'll provide you with fresh mounts and provisions," her brother promised. "You'll want to refresh yourself before—"

"I'll want to stay," Catelyn said, dismounting. She had no intention of leaving Riverrun and her dying father to pick Robb's wife for him. *Robb wants me safe, I cannot fault him for that, but his pretext is growing threadbare.* "Boy," she called, and an urchin from the stables ran out to take the reins of her horse.

Edmure swung down from his saddle. He was a head taller than she was, but he would always be her little brother. "Cat," he said unhappily, "Lord Tywin is coming—"

"He is making for the west, to defend his own lands. If we close our gates and shelter behind the walls, we can watch him pass with safety."

"This is Tully land," Edmure declared. "If Tywin Lannister thinks to cross it unbloodied, I mean to teach him a hard lesson."

The same lesson you taught his son? Her brother could be stubborn as river rock when his pride was touched, but neither of them was likely to forget how Ser Jaime had cut Edmure's host to bloody pieces the last time he had offered battle. "We have nothing to gain and everything to lose by meeting Lord Tywin in the field," Catelyn said tactfully.

"The yard is not the place to discuss my battle plans."

"As you will. Where shall we go?"

Her brother's face darkened. For a moment she thought he was about to lose his temper with her, but finally he snapped, "The godswood. If you will insist."

She followed him along a gallery to the godswood gate. Edmure's anger had always been a sulky, sullen thing. Catelyn was sorry she had wounded him, but the matter was too important for her to concern herself with his pride. When they were alone beneath the trees, Edmure turned to face her.

"You do not have the strength to meet the Lannisters in the field," she said bluntly.

"When all my strength is marshaled, I should have eight thousand foot and three thousand horse," Edmure said.

"Which means Lord Tywin will have near twice your numbers."

"Robb's won his battles against worse odds," Edmure replied, "and I have a plan. You've forgotten Roose Bolton. Lord Tywin defeated him on the Green Fork, but failed to pursue. When Lord Tywin went to Harrenhal, Bolton took the ruby ford and the crossroads. He has ten thousand men. I've sent word to Helman Tallhart to join him with the garrison Robb left at the Twins—"

"Edmure, Robb left those men to *hold* the Twins and make certain Lord Walder keeps faith with us."

"He has," Edmure said stubbornly. "The Freys fought bravely in the Whispering Wood, and old Ser Stevron died at Oxcross, we hear. Ser Ryman and Black Walder and the rest are with Robb in the west, Martyn has been of great service scouting, and Ser Perwyn helped see you safe to Renly. Gods be good, how much more can we ask of them? Robb's betrothed to one of Lord Walder's daughters, and Roose Bolton wed another, I hear. And haven't you taken two of his grandsons to be fostered at Winterfell?"

"A ward can easily become a hostage, if need be." She had not known that Ser Stevron was dead, nor of Bolton's marriage.

"If we're two hostages to the good, all the more reason Lord Walder dare not play us false. Bolton needs Frey's men, and Ser Helman's as well. I've commanded him to retake Harrenhal."

"That's like to be a bloody business."

"Yes, but once the castle falls, Lord Tywin will have no safe retreat. My own levies will defend the fords of Red Fork against his crossing. If he attacks across the river, he'll end as Rhaegar did when he tried to cross the Trident. If he holds back, he'll be caught between Riverrun and Harrenhal, and when Robb returns from the west we can finish him for good and all."

Her brother's voice was full of brusque confidence, but Catelyn found herself wishing that Robb had not taken her uncle Brynden west with him. The Blackfish was the veteran of half a hundred battles; Edmure was the veteran of one, and that one lost.

"The plan's a good one," he concluded. "Lord Tytos says so, and Lord Jonos as well. When did Blackwood and Bracken agree about *anything* that was not certain, I ask you?"

"Be that as it may." She was suddenly weary. Perhaps she was wrong to oppose him. Perhaps it was a splendid plan, and her misgivings only a woman's fears. She wished Ned were here, or her uncle Brynden, or . . . "Have you asked Father about this?"

"Father is in no state to weigh strategies. Two days ago he was making plans for your marriage to Brandon Stark! Go see him yourself if you do not believe me. This plan will work, Cat, you'll see."

"I hope so, Edmure. I truly do." She kissed him on the cheek, to let him know she meant it, and went to find her father.

Lord Hoster Tully was much as she had left him—

abed, haggard, flesh pale and clammy. The room smelled of sickness, a cloying odor made up in equal parts of stale sweat and medicine. When she pulled back the drapes, her father gave a low moan, and his eyes fluttered open. He stared at her as if he could not comprehend who she was or what she wanted.

"Father." She kissed him. "I am returned."

He seemed to know her then. "You've come," he whispered faintly, lips barely moving.

"Yes," she said. "Robb sent me south, but I hurried back."

"South . . . where . . . is the Eyrie south, sweetling? I don't recall . . . oh, dear heart, I was afraid . . . have you forgiven me, child?" Tears ran down his cheeks.

"You've done nothing that needs forgiveness, Father." She stroked his limp white hair and felt his brow. The fever still burned him from within, despite all the maester's potions.

"It was best," her father whispered. "Jon's a good man, good . . . strong, kind . . . take care of you . . . he will . . . and well born, listen to me, you must, I'm your father . . . your father . . . you'll wed when Cat does, yes you *will* . . ."

He thinks I'm Lysa, Catelyn realized. *Gods be good, he talks as if we were not married yet.*

Her father's hands clutched at hers, fluttering like two frightened white birds. "That stripling . . . wretched boy . . . not speak that name to me, your duty . . . your mother, she would . . ." Lord Hoster cried as a spasm of pain washed over him. "Oh, gods forgive me, forgive me, *forgive* me. My medicine . . ."

And then Maester Vyman was there, holding a cup to his lips. Lord Hoster sucked at the thick white potion as eager as a babe at the breast, and Catelyn could see peace settle over him once more. "He'll sleep now, my lady," the maester said when the cup was empty. The milk of the poppy had left a thick white film around her father's mouth. Maester Vyman wiped it away with a sleeve.

Catelyn could watch no more. Hoster Tully had been a strong man, and proud. It hurt her to see him reduced to this. She went out to the terrace. The yard below was crowded with refugees and chaotic with their noises, but beyond the walls the rivers flowed clean and pure and endless. *Those are his rivers, and soon he will return to them for his last voyage.*

Maester Vyman had followed her out. "My lady," he said softly, "I cannot keep the end at bay much longer. We ought send a rider after his brother. Ser Brynden would wish to be here."

"Yes," Catelyn said, her voice thick with her grief.

"And the Lady Lysa as well, perhaps?"

"Lysa will not come."

"If you wrote her yourself, perhaps . . ."

"I will put some words to paper, if that please you." She wondered who Lysa's "wretched stripling" had been. Some young squire or hedge knight, like as not . . . though by the vehemence with which Lord Hoster had opposed him, he might have been a tradesman's son or baseborn apprentice, even a singer. Lysa had always been too fond of singers. *I must not blame her. Jon Arryn was twenty years older than our father, however noble.*

The tower her brother had set aside for her use was the very same that she and Lysa had shared as maids. It would feel good to sleep on a featherbed again, with a warm fire in the hearth; when she was rested the world would seem less bleak.

But outside her chambers she found Utherydes Wayn waiting with two women clad in grey, their faces cowled save for their eyes. Catelyn knew at once why they were here. *"Ned?"*

The sisters lowered their gaze. Utherydes said, "Ser Cleos brought him from King's Landing, my lady."

"Take me to him," she commanded.

They had laid him out on a trestle table and covered him with a banner, the white banner of House Stark with its grey direwolf sigil. "I would look on him," Catelyn said.

"Only the bones remain, my lady."

"I would look on him," she repeated.

One of the silent sisters turned down the banner.

Bones, Catelyn thought. *This is not Ned, this is not the man I loved, the father of my children.* His hands were clasped together over his chest, skeletal fingers curled about the hilt of some longsword, but they were not Ned's hands, so strong and full of life. They had dressed the bones in Ned's surcoat, the fine white velvet with the direwolf badge over the heart, but nothing remained of the warm flesh that had pillowed her head so many nights, the arms that had held her. The head had been rejoined to the body with fine silver wire, but one skull looks much like another, and in those empty hollows she found no trace of her lord's dark grey eyes, eyes that could be soft as a fog or hard as stone. *They gave his eyes to crows,* she remembered.

Catelyn turned away. "That is not his sword."

"Ice was not returned to us, my lady," Utherydes said. "Only Lord Eddard's bones."

"I suppose I must thank the queen for even that much."

"Thank the Imp, my lady. It was his doing."

One day I will thank them all. "I am grateful for your service, sisters," Catelyn said, "but I must lay another task upon you. Lord Eddard was a Stark, and his bones must be laid to rest beneath Winterfell." *They will make a statue of him, a stone likeness that will sit in the dark with a direwolf at his feet and a sword across his knees.* "Make certain the sisters have fresh horses, and aught else they need for the journey," she told Utherydes Wayn. "Hal Mollen will escort them back to Winterfell, it is his place as captain of guards." She gazed down at the bones that were all that remained of her lord and love. "Now leave me, all of you. I would be alone with Ned tonight."

The women in grey bowed their heads. *The silent sisters do not speak to the living,* Catelyn remembered dully, *but some say they can talk to the dead.* And how she envied that . . .

DAENERYS

The drapes kept out the dust and heat of the streets, but they could not keep out disappointment. Dany climbed inside wearily, glad for the refuge from the sea of Qartheen eyes. "Make way," Jhogo shouted at the crowd from horseback, snapping his whip, "make way, make way for the Mother of Dragons."

Reclining on cool satin cushions, Xaro Xhoan Daxos poured ruby-red wine into matched goblets of jade and gold, his hands sure and steady despite the sway of the palanquin. "I see a deep sadness written upon your face, my light of love." He offered her a goblet. "Could it be the sadness of a lost dream?"

"A dream delayed, no more." Dany's tight silver collar was chafing against her throat. She unfastened it and flung it aside. The collar was set with an enchanted amethyst that Xaro swore would ward her against all poisons. The Pureborn were notorious for offering poisoned wine to those they thought dangerous, but they had not given Dany so much as a cup of water.

They never saw me for a queen, she thought bitterly. *I was only an afternoon's amusement, a horse girl with a curious pet.*

Rhaegal hissed and dug sharp black claws into her bare shoulder as Dany stretched out a hand for the wine. Wincing, she shifted him to her other shoulder, where he could claw her gown instead of her skin. She was garbed after the Qartheen fashion. Xaro had warned her that the Enthroned would never listen to a Dothraki, so she had taken care to go before them in flowing green samite with one breast bared, silvered sandals on her feet, with a belt of black-and-white pearls about her waist. *For all the help they offered, I could have gone naked. Perhaps I should have.* She drank deep.

Descendants of the ancient kings and queens of Qarth, the Pureborn commanded the Civic Guard and the fleet of ornate galleys that ruled the straits between the seas. Daenerys Targaryen had wanted that fleet, or part of it, and some of their soldiers as well. She made the traditional sacrifice in the Temple of Memory, offered the traditional bribe to the Keeper of the Long List, sent the traditional persimmon to the Opener of the Door, and finally received the traditional blue silk slippers summoning her to the Hall of a Thousand Thrones.

The Pureborn heard her pleas from the great wooden seats of their ancestors, rising in curved tiers from a marble floor to a high-domed ceiling painted with scenes of Qarth's vanished glory. The chairs were immense, fantastically carved, bright with goldwork and studded with amber, onyx, lapis, and jade, each one different from all the others, and each striving to be the most fabulous. Yet the men who sat in them seemed so listless and world-weary that they might have been asleep. *They listened, but they did not hear, or care,* she thought. *They are Milk Men indeed. They never meant to help me. They came because they were curious. They came because they were bored, and the dragon on my shoulder interested them more than I did.*

"Tell me the words of the Pureborn," prompted Xaro Xhoan Daxos. "Tell me what they said to sadden the queen of my heart."

"They said no." The wine tasted of pomegranates and hot summer days. "They said it with great courtesy, to be sure, but under all the lovely words, it was still no."

"Did you flatter them?"

"Shamelessly."

"Did you weep?"

"The blood of the dragon does not weep," she said testily.

Xaro sighed. "You ought to have wept." The Qartheen wept often and easily; it was considered a mark of the civilized man. "The men we bought, what did they say?"

"Mathos said nothing. Wendello praised the way I spoke. The Exquisite refused me with the rest, but he wept afterward."

"Alas, that Qartheen should be so faithless." Xaro was not himself of the Pureborn, but he had told her whom to bribe and how much to offer. "Weep, weep, for the treachery of men."

Dany would sooner have wept for her gold. The bribes she'd tendered to Mathos Mallarawan, Wendello Qar Deeth, and Egon Emeros the Exquisite might have bought her a ship, or hired a score of sellswords. "Suppose I sent Ser Jorah to demand the return of my gifts?" she asked.

"Suppose a Sorrowful Man came to my palace one night and killed you as you slept," said Xaro. The Sorrowful Men were an ancient sacred guild of assassins, so named because they always whispered, "I am so sorry," to their victims before they killed them. The Qartheen were nothing if not polite. "It is wisely said that it is easier to milk the Stone Cow of Faros than to wring gold from the Pureborn."

Dany did not know where Faros was, but it seemed to her that Qarth was full of stone cows. The merchant princes, grown vastly rich off the trade between the seas, were divided into three jealous factions: the Ancient Guild of Spicers, the Tourmaline Brotherhood, and the Thirteen, to which Xaro belonged. Each vied with the others for dominance, and all three contended endlessly with the Pureborn. And brooding over all were the warlocks, with their blue lips and dread powers, seldom seen but much feared.

She would have been lost without Xaro. The gold that she had squandered to open the doors of the Hall of a Thousand Thrones was largely a product of the merchant's generosity and quick wits. As the rumor of living dragons had spread through the east, ever more seekers had come to learn if the tale was true—and Xaro Xhoan Daxos saw to it that the great and the humble alike offered some token to the Mother of Dragons.

The trickle he started soon swelled to a flood. Trader captains brought lace from Myr, chests of saffron from Yi Ti, amber and dragonglass out of Asshai. Merchants offered bags of coin, silversmiths rings and chains. Pipers piped for her, tumblers tumbled, and jugglers juggled, while dyers draped her in colors she had never known existed. A pair of Jogos Nhai presented her with one of their striped zorses, black and white and fierce. A widow brought the dried corpse of her husband, covered with a crust of silvered leaves; such remnants were believed to have great power, especially if the deceased had been a sorcerer, as this one had. And the Tourmaline Brotherhood pressed on her a crown wrought in the shape of a three-headed dragon; the coils were yellow gold, the wings silver, the heads carved from jade, ivory, and onyx.

The crown was the only offering she'd kept. The rest she sold, to gather the wealth she had wasted on the Pureborn. Xaro would have sold the crown too—the Thirteen would see that she had a much finer one, he swore—but Dany forbade it. "Viserys sold my mother's crown, and men called him a beggar. I shall keep this one, so men will call me a queen." And so she did, though the weight of it made her neck ache.

Yet even crowned, I am a beggar still, Dany thought. *I have become the most splendid beggar in the world, but a beggar all the same.* She hated it, as her brother must have. *All those years of running from city to city one step ahead of the Usurper's knives, pleading for help from archons and princes and magisters, buying our food with flattery. He must have known how they mocked him. Small wonder he turned so angry and bitter.* In the end it had driven him mad. *It will do the same to me if I let it.* Part of her would have liked nothing more than to lead her people back to Vaes Tolorro, and make the dead city bloom. *No, that is defeat. I have something Viserys never had. I have the dragons. The dragons are all the difference.*

She stroked Rhaegal. The green dragon closed his teeth around the meat of her hand and nipped hard. Outside, the great city murmured and thrummed and seethed, all its myriad voices blending into one low sound like the surge of the sea. "Make way, you Milk Men, make way for the Mother of Dragons," Jhogo cried, and the Qartheen moved aside, though perhaps the oxen had more to do with that than his voice. Through the swaying draperies, Dany caught glimpses of him astride his grey stallion. From time to time he gave one of the oxen a flick with the silver-handled whip she had given him. Aggo guarded on her other side, while Rakharo rode behind the procession, watching the faces in the crowd for any sign of danger. Ser Jorah she had left behind today, to guard her other dragons; the exile knight had been opposed to this folly from the start. *He distrusts everyone,* she reflected, *and perhaps for good reason.*

As Dany lifted her goblet to drink, Rhaegal sniffed at the wine and drew his head back, hissing. "Your dragon has a good nose." Xaro wiped his lips. "The wine is ordinary. It is said that across the Jade Sea they make a golden vintage so fine that one sip makes all other wines taste like vinegar. Let us take my pleasure barge and go in search of it, you and I."

"The Arbor makes the best wine in the world," Dany declared. Lord Redwyne had fought for her father against the Usurper, she remembered, one of the few to remain true to the last. *Will he fight for me as well?* There was no way to be certain after so many years. "Come with me to the Arbor, Xaro, and you'll have the finest vintages you ever tasted. But we'll need to go in a warship, not a pleasure barge."

"I have no warships. War is bad for trade. Many times I have told you, Xaro Xhoan Daxos is a man of peace."

Xaro Xhoan Daxos is a man of gold, she thought, *and gold will buy me all the ships and swords I need.* "I have not asked you to take up a sword, only to lend me your ships."

He smiled modestly. "Of trading ships I have a few, that is so. Who can say how many? One may be sinking even now, in some stormy corner of the Summer Sea. On the morrow, another will fall afoul of corsairs. The next day, one of my captains may look at the wealth in his hold and think, *All this should belong to me.* Such are the perils of trade. Why, the longer we talk, the fewer ships I am likely to have. I grow poorer by the instant."

"Give me ships, and I will make you rich again."

"Marry me, bright light, and sail the ship of my heart. I cannot sleep at night for thinking of your beauty."

Dany smiled. Xaro's flowery protestations of passion amused her, but his manner was at odds with his words. While Ser Jorah had scarcely been able to keep his eyes from her bare breast when he'd helped her into the palanquin, Xaro hardly deigned to notice it, even in these close confines. And she had seen the beautiful boys who surrounded the merchant prince, flitting through his palace halls in wisps of silk. "You speak sweetly, Xaro, but under your words I hear another *no.*"

"This Iron Throne you speak of sounds monstrous cold and hard. I cannot bear the thought of jagged barbs cutting your sweet skin." The jewels in Xaro's nose gave him the aspect of some strange glittery bird. His long, elegant fingers waved dismissal. "Let this be your kingdom, most exquisite of queens, and let me be your king. I will give you a throne of gold, if you like. When Qarth begins to pall, we can journey round Yi Ti and search for the dreaming city of the poets, to sip the wine of wisdom from a dead man's skull."

"I mean to sail to Westeros, and drink the wine of vengeance from the skull of the Usurper." She scratched Rhaegal under one eye, and his jade-green wings unfolded for a moment, stirring the still air in the palanquin.

A single perfect tear ran down the cheek of Xaro Xhoan Daxos. "Will nothing turn you from this madness?"

"Nothing," she said, wishing she was as certain as she sounded. "If each of the Thirteen would lend me ten ships—"

"You would have one hundred thirty ships, and no crew to sail them. The justice of your cause means naught to the common men of Qarth. Why should my sailors care who sits upon the throne of some kingdom at the edge of the world?"

"I will pay them to care."

"With what coin, sweet star of my heaven?"

"With the gold the seekers bring."

"That you may do," Xaro acknowledged, "but so much caring will cost dear. You will need to pay them far more than I do, and all of Qarth laughs at my ruinous generosity."

"If the Thirteen will not aid me, perhaps I should ask the Guild of Spicers or the Tourmaline Brotherhood?"

Xaro gave a languid shrug. "They will give you nothing but flattery and lies. The Spicers are dissemblers and braggarts and the Brotherhood is full of pirates."

"Then I must heed Pyat Pree, and go to the warlocks."

The merchant prince sat up sharply. "Pyat Pree has blue lips, and it is truly said that blue lips speak only lies. Heed the wisdom of one who loves you. Warlocks are bitter creatures who eat dust and drink of shadows. They will give you naught. They have naught to give."

"I would not need to seek sorcerous help if my friend Xaro Xhoan Daxos would give me what I ask."

"I have given you my home and heart, do they mean

nothing to you? I have given you perfume and pomegranates, tumbling monkeys and spitting snakes, scrolls
from lost Valyria, an idol's head and a serpent's foot. I
have given you this palanquin of ebony and gold, and a
matched set of bullocks to bear it, one white as ivory
and one black as jet, with horns inlaid with jewels."

"Yes," Dany said. "But it was ships and soldiers I
wanted."

"Did I not give you an army, sweetest of women? A
thousand knights, each in shining armor."

The armor had been made of silver and gold, the
knights of jade and beryl and onyx and tourmaline, of
amber and opal and amethyst, each as tall as her little
finger. "A thousand lovely knights," she said, "but not
the sort my enemies need fear. And my bullocks cannot
carry me across the water, I—why are we stopping?"
The oxen had slowed notably.

"*Khaleesi*," Aggo called through the drapes as the palanquin jerked to a sudden halt. Dany rolled onto an elbow to lean out. They were on the fringes of the bazaar,
the way ahead blocked by a solid wall of people. "What
are they looking at?"

Jhogo rode back to her. "A firemage, *Khaleesi*."

"I want to see."

"Then you must." The Dothraki offered a hand down.
When she took it, he pulled her up onto his horse and
sat her in front of him, where she could see over the
heads of the crowd. The firemage had conjured a ladder
in the air, a crackling orange ladder of swirling flame
that rose unsupported from the floor of the bazaar,
reaching toward the high latticed roof.

Most of the spectators, she noticed, were not of the
city: she saw sailors off trading ships, merchants come
by caravan, dusty men out of the red waste, wandering
soldiers, craftsmen, slavers. Jhogo slid one hand about
her waist and leaned close. "The Milk Men shun him.
Khaleesi, do you see the girl in the felt hat? There, behind the fat priest. She is a—"

"—cutpurse," finished Dany. She was no pampered
lady, blind to such things. She had seen cutpurses

aplenty in the streets of the Free Cities, during the years she'd spent with her brother, running from the Usurper's hired knives.

The mage was gesturing, urging the flames higher and higher with broad sweeps of his arms. As the watchers craned their necks upward, the cutpurses squirmed through the press, small blades hidden in their palms. They relieved the prosperous of their coin with one hand while pointing upward with the other.

When the fiery ladder stood forty feet high, the mage leapt forward and began to climb it, scrambling up hand over hand as quick as a monkey. Each rung he touched dissolved behind him, leaving no more than a wisp of silver smoke. When he reached the top, the ladder was gone and so was he.

"A fine trick," announced Jhogo with admiration.

"No trick," a woman said in the Common Tongue.

Dany had not noticed Quaithe in the crowd, yet there she stood, eyes wet and shiny behind the implacable red lacquer mask. "What mean you, my lady?"

"Half a year gone, that man could scarcely wake fire from dragonglass. He had some small skill with powders and wildfire, sufficient to entrance a crowd while his cutpurses did their work. He could walk across hot coals and make burning roses bloom in the air, but he could no more aspire to climb the fiery ladder than a common fisherman could hope to catch a kraken in his nets."

Dany looked uneasily at where the ladder had stood. Even the smoke was gone now, and the crowd was breaking up, each man going about his business. In a moment more than a few would find their purses flat and empty. "And now?"

"And now his powers grow, *Khaleesi*. And you are the cause of it."

"Me?" She laughed. "How could that be?"

The woman stepped closer and lay two fingers on Dany's wrist. "You are the Mother of Dragons, are you not?"

"She is, and no spawn of shadows may touch her."

Jhogo brushed Quaithe's fingers away with the handle of his whip.

The woman took a step backward. "You must leave this city soon, Daenerys Targaryen, or you will never be permitted to leave it at all."

Dany's wrist still tingled where Quaithe had touched her. "Where would you have me go?" she asked.

"To go north, you must journey south. To reach the west, you must go east. To go forward you must go back, and to touch the light you must pass beneath the shadow."

Asshai, Dany thought. *She would have me go to Asshai.* "Will the Asshai'i give me an army?" she demanded. "Will there be gold for me in Asshai? Will there be ships? What is there in Asshai that I will not find in Qarth?"

"Truth," said the woman in the mask. And bowing, she faded back into the crowd.

Rakharo snorted contempt through his drooping black mustachios. "*Khaleesi*, better a man should swallow scorpions than trust in the spawn of shadows, who dare not show their face beneath the sun. It is known."

"It is known," Aggo agreed.

Xaro Xhoan Daxos had watched the whole exchange from his cushions. When Dany climbed back into the palanquin beside him, he said, "Your savages are wiser than they know. Such truths as the Asshai'i hoard are not like to make you smile." Then he pressed another cup of wine on her, and spoke of love and lust and other trifles all the way back to his manse.

In the quiet of her chambers, Dany stripped off her finery and donned a loose robe of purple silk. Her dragons were hungry, so she chopped up a snake and charred the pieces over a brazier. *They are growing*, she realized as she watched them snap and squabble over the blackened flesh. *They must weigh twice what they had in Vaes Tolorro.* Even so, it would be years before they were large enough to take to war. *And they must be trained as well, or they will lay my kingdom waste.* For all her Targaryen blood, Dany had not the least idea of how to train a dragon.

Ser Jorah Mormont came to her as the sun was going down. "The Pureborn refused you?"

"As you said they would. Come, sit, give me your counsel." Dany drew him down to the cushions beside her, and Jhiqui brought them a bowl of purple olives and onions drowned in wine.

"You will get no help in this city, *Khaleesi*." Ser Jorah took an onion between thumb and forefinger. "Each day I am more convinced of that than the day before. The Pureborn see no farther than the walls of Qarth, and Xaro . . ."

"He asked me to marry him again."

"Yes, and I know why." When the knight frowned, his heavy black brows joined together above his deep-set eyes.

"He dreams of me, day and night." She laughed.

"Forgive me, my queen, but it is your dragons he dreams of."

"Xaro assures me that in Qarth, man and woman each retain their own property after they are wed. The dragons are mine." She smiled as Drogon came hopping and flapping across the marble floor to crawl up on the cushion beside her.

"He tells it true as far as it goes, but there's one thing he failed to mention. The Qartheen have a curious wedding custom, my queen. On the day of their union, a wife may ask a token of love from her husband. Whatsoever she desires of his worldly goods, he must grant. And he may ask the same of her. One thing only may be asked, but whatever is named may not be denied."

"One thing," she repeated. "And it may not be denied?"

"With one dragon, Xaro Xhoan Daxos would rule this city, but one ship will further our cause but little."

Dany nibbled at an onion and reflected ruefully on the faithlessness of men. "We passed through the bazaar on our way back from the Hall of a Thousand Thrones," she told Ser Jorah. "Quaithe was there." She told him of the firemage and the fiery ladder, and what the woman in the red mask had told her.

"I would be glad to leave this city, if truth be told," the knight said when she was done. "But not for Asshai."

"Where, then?"

"East," he said.

"I am half a world away from my kingdom even here. If I go any farther east I may never find my way home to Westeros."

"If you go west, you risk your life."

"House Targaryen has friends in the Free Cities," she reminded him. "Truer friends than Xaro or the Pureborn."

"If you mean Illyrio Mopatis, I wonder. For sufficient gold, Illyrio would sell you as quickly as he would a slave."

"My brother and I were guests in Illyrio's manse for half a year. If he meant to sell us, he could have done it then."

"He did sell you," Ser Jorah said. "To Khal Drogo."

Dany flushed. He had the truth of it, but she did not like the sharpness with which he put it. "Illyrio protected us from the Usurper's knives, and he believed in my brother's cause."

"Illyrio believes in no cause but Illyrio. Gluttons are greedy men as a rule, and magisters are devious. Illyrio Mopatis is both. What do you truly know of him?"

"I know that he gave me my dragon eggs."

He snorted. "If he'd known they were like to hatch, he'd would have sat on them himself."

That made her smile despite herself. "Oh, I have no doubt of that, ser. I know Illyrio better than you think. I was a child when I left his manse in Pentos to wed my sun-and-stars, but I was neither deaf nor blind. And I am no child now."

"Even if Illyrio is the friend you think him," the knight said stubbornly, "he is not powerful enough to enthrone you by himself, no more than he could your brother."

"He is rich," she said. "Not so rich as Xaro, perhaps, but rich enough to hire ships for me, and men as well."

"Sellswords have their uses," Ser Jorah admitted, "but you will not win your father's throne with sweepings from the Free Cities. Nothing knits a broken realm together so quick as an invading army on its soil."

"I am their rightful queen," Dany protested.

"You are a stranger who means to land on their shores with an army of outlanders who cannot even speak the Common Tongue. The lords of Westeros do not know you, and have every reason to fear and mistrust you. You must win them over before you sail. A few at least."

"And how am I to do that, if I go east as you counsel?"

He ate an olive and spit out the pit into his palm. "I do not know, Your Grace," he admitted, "but I do know that the longer you remain in one place, the easier it will be for your enemies to find you. The name *Targaryen* still frightens them, so much so that they sent a man to murder you when they heard you were with child. What will they do when they learn of your dragons?"

Drogon was curled up beneath her arm, as hot as a stone that has soaked all day in the blazing sun. Rhaegal and Viserion were fighting over a scrap of meat, buffeting each other with their wings as smoke hissed from their nostrils. *My furious children,* she thought. *They must not come to harm.* "The comet led me to Qarth for a reason. I had hoped to find my army here, but it seems that will not be. What else remains, I ask myself?" *I am afraid,* she realized, *but I must be brave.* "Come the morrow, you must go to Pyat Pree."

TYRION

The girl never wept. Young as she was, Myrcella Baratheon was a princess born. *And a Lannister, despite her name*, Tyrion reminded himself, *as much Jaime's blood as Cersei's.*

To be sure, her smile was a shade tremulous when her brothers took their leave of her on the deck of the *Seaswift*, but the girl knew the proper words to say, and she said them with courage and dignity. When the time came to part, it was Prince Tommen who cried, and Myrcella who gave him comfort.

Tyrion looked down upon the farewells from the high deck of *King Robert's Hammer*, a great war galley of four hundred oars. *Rob's Hammer*, as her oarsmen called her, would form the main strength of Myrcella's escort. *Lionstar*, *Bold Wind*, and *Lady Lyanna* would sail with her as well.

It made Tyrion more than a little uneasy to detach so great a part of their already inadequate fleet, depleted as it was by the loss of all those ships that had sailed with Lord Stannis to Dragonstone and never returned, but

Cersei would hear of nothing less. Perhaps she was wise. If the girl was captured before she reached Sunspear, the Dornish alliance would fall to pieces. So far Doran Martell had done no more than call his banners. Once Myrcella was safe in Braavos, he had pledged to move his strength to the high passes, where the threat might make some of the Marcher lords rethink their loyalties and give Stannis pause about marching north. It was purely a feint, however. The Martells would not commit to actual battle unless Dorne itself was attacked, and Stannis was not so great a fool. *Though some of his bannermen may be*, Tyrion reflected. *I should think on that.*

He cleared his throat. "You know your orders, Captain."

"I do, my lord. We are to follow the coast, staying always in sight of land, until we reach Cracklaw Point. From there we are to strike out across the narrow sea for Braavos. On no account are we to sail within sight of Dragonstone."

"And if our foes should chance upon you nonetheless?"

"If a single ship, we are to run them off or destroy them. If there are more, the *Bold Wind* will cleave to the *Seaswift* to protect her while the rest of the fleet does battle."

Tyrion nodded. If the worst happened, the little *Seaswift* ought to be able to outrun pursuit. A small ship with big sails, she was faster than any warship afloat, or so her captain had claimed. Once Myrcella reached Braavos, she ought to be safe. He was sending Ser Arys Oakheart as her sworn shield, and had engaged the Braavosi to bring her the rest of the way to Sunspear. Even Lord Stannis would hesitate to wake the anger of the greatest and most powerful of the Free Cities. Traveling from King's Landing to Dorne by way of Braavos was scarcely the most direct of routes, but it was the safest . . . or so he hoped.

If Lord Stannis knew of this sailing, he could not choose a better time to send his fleet against us. Tyrion glanced back to where the Rush emptied out into Black-water Bay and was relieved to see no signs of sails on the wide green horizon. At last report, the Baratheon fleet still lay off Storm's End, where Ser Cortnay Penrose continued to defy the besiegers in dead Renly's name. Meanwhile, Tyrion's winch towers stood three-quarters complete. Even now men were hoisting heavy blocks of stone into place, no doubt cursing him for making them work through the festivities. Let them curse. *Another fortnight, Stannis, that's all I require. Another fortnight and it will be done.*

Tyrion watched his niece kneel before the High Septon to receive his blessing on her voyage. Sunlight caught in his crystal crown and spilled rainbows across Myrcella's upturned face. The noise from the riverside made it impossible to hear the prayers. He hoped the gods had sharper ears. The High Septon was as fat as a house, and more pompous and long of wind than even Pycelle. *Enough, old man, make an end to it,* Tyrion thought irritably. *The gods have better things to do than listen to you, and so do I.*

When at last the droning and mumbling was done, Tyrion took his farewell of the captain of *Rob's Hammer.* "Deliver my niece safely to Braavos, and there will be a knighthood waiting for you on your return," he promised.

As he made his way down the steep plank to the quay, Tyrion could feel unkind eyes upon him. The galley rocked gently and the movement underfoot made his waddle worse than ever. *I'll wager they'd love to snigger.* No one dared, not openly, though he heard mutterings mingled with the creak of wood and rope and the rush of the river around the pilings. *They do not love me,* he thought. *Well, small wonder. I'm well fed and ugly, and they are starving.*

Bronn escorted him through the crowd to join his sister and her sons. Cersei ignored him, preferring to lavish her smiles on their cousin. He watched her charming Lancel with eyes as green as the rope of emeralds around her slim white throat, and smiled a small sly smile to himself. *I know your secret, Cersei,* he thought. His sister had oft called upon the High Septon of late, to seek the blessings of the gods in their coming struggle with Lord Stannis . . . or so she would have him believe. In truth, after a brief call at the Great Sept of Baelor, Cersei would don a plain brown traveler's cloak and steal off to meet a certain hedge knight with the unlikely name of Ser Osmund Kettleblack, and his equally unsavory brothers Osney and Osfryd. Lancel had told him all about them. Cersei meant to use the Kettleblacks to buy her own force of sellswords.

Well, let her enjoy her plots. She was much sweeter when she thought she was outwitting him. The Kettleblacks would charm her, take her coin, and promise her anything she asked, and why not, when Bronn was matching every copper penny, coin for coin? Amiable rogues all three, the brothers were in truth much more skilled at deceit than they'd ever been at bloodletting. Cersei had managed to buy herself three hollow drums; they would make all the fierce booming sounds she required, but there was nothing inside. It amused Tyrion no end.

Horns blew fanfares as *Lionstar* and *Lady Lyanna* pushed out from shore, moving downriver to clear the way for *Seaswift*. A few cheers went up from the crush along the banks, as thin and ragged as the clouds scuttling overhead. Myrcella smiled and waved from the deck. Behind her stood Arys Oakheart, his white cloak streaming. The captain ordered lines cast off, and oars pushed the *Seaswift* out into the lusty current of the Blackwater Rush, where her sails blossomed in the wind—common white sails, as Tyrion had insisted, not sheets of Lannister crimson. Prince Tommen sobbed. "You mew like a suckling babe," his brother hissed at him. "Princes aren't supposed to cry."

"Prince Aemon the Dragonknight cried the day Princess Naerys wed his brother Aegon," Sansa Stark said, "and the twins Ser Arryk and Ser Erryk died with tears on their cheeks after each had given the other a mortal wound."

"Be quiet, or I'll have Ser Meryn give *you* a mortal wound," Joffrey told his betrothed. Tyrion glanced at his sister, but Cersei was engrossed in something Ser Balon Swann was telling her. *Can she truly be so blind as to what he is?* he wondered.

Out on the river, *Bold Wind* unshipped her oars and glided downstream in the wake of *Seaswift.* Last came *King Robert's Hammer,* the might of the royal fleet . . . or at least that portion that had not fled to Dragonstone last year with Stannis. Tyrion had chosen the ships with care, avoiding any whose captains might be of doubtful loyalty, according to Varys . . . but as Varys himself was of doubtful loyalty, a certain amount of apprehension remained. *I rely too much on Varys,* he reflected. *I need my own informers. Not that I'd trust them either.* Trust would get you killed.

He wondered again about Littlefinger. There had been no word from Petyr Baelish since he had ridden off for Bitterbridge. That might mean nothing—or everything. Even Varys could not say. The eunuch had suggested that perhaps Littlefinger had met some misfortune on the roads. He might even be slain. Tyrion had snorted in derision. "If Littlefinger is dead, then I'm a giant." More likely, the Tyrells were balking at the proposed marriage. Tyrion could scarcely blame them. *If I were Mace Tyrell, I would sooner have Joffrey's head on a pike than his cock in my daughter.*

The little fleet was well out into the bay when Cersei indicated that it was time to go. Bronn brought Tyrion's horse and helped him mount. That was Podrick Payne's task, but they had left Pod back at the Red Keep. The gaunt sellsword made for a much more reassuring presence than the boy would have.

The narrow streets were lined by men of the City Watch, holding back the crowd with the shafts of their spears. Ser Jacelyn Bywater went in front, heading a wedge of mounted lancers in black ringmail and golden cloaks. Behind him came Ser Aron Santagar and Ser Balon Swann, bearing the king's banners, the lion of Lannister and crowned stag of Baratheon.

King Joffrey followed on a tall grey palfrey, a golden crown set upon his golden curls. Sansa Stark rode a chestnut mare at his side, looking neither right nor left, her thick auburn hair flowing to her shoulders beneath a net of moonstones. Two of the Kingsguard flanked the couple, the Hound on the king's right hand and Ser Mandon Moore to the left of the Stark girl.

Next came Tommen, snuffling, with Ser Preston Greenfield in his white armor and cloak, and then Cersei, accompanied by Ser Lancel and protected by Meryn Trant and Boros Blount. Tyrion fell in with his sister. After them followed the High Septon in his litter, and a long tail of other courtiers—Ser Horas Redwyne, Lady Tanda and her daughter, Jalabhar Xho, Lord Gyles Rosby, and the rest. A double column of guardsmen brought up the rear.

The unshaven and the unwashed stared at the riders with dull resentment from behind the line of spears. *I like this not one speck*, Tyrion thought. Bronn had a score of sellswords scattered through the crowd with orders to stop any trouble before it started. Perhaps Cersei had similarly disposed her Kettleblacks. Somehow Tyrion did not think it would help much. If the fire was too hot, you could hardly keep the pudding from scorching by tossing a handful of raisins in the pot.

They crossed Fishmonger's Square and rode along Muddy Way before turning onto the narrow, curving Hook to begin their climb up Aegon's High Hill. A few voices raised a cry of *"Joffrey! All hail, all hail!"* as the young king rode by, but for every man who picked up the shout, a hundred kept their silence. The Lannisters moved through a sea of ragged men and hungry women, breasting a tide of sullen eyes. Just ahead of him, Cersei was laughing at something Lancel had said, though he suspected her merriment was feigned. She could not be oblivious to the unrest around them, but his sister always believed in putting on the brave show.

Halfway along the route, a wailing woman forced her way between two watchmen and ran out into the street in front of the king and his companions, holding the corpse of her dead baby above her head. It was blue and swollen, grotesque, but the real horror was the mother's eyes. Joffrey looked for a moment as if he meant to ride her down, but Sansa Stark leaned over and said something to him. The king fumbled in his purse, and flung the woman a silver stag. The coin bounced off the child and rolled away, under the legs of the gold cloaks and into the crowd, where a dozen men began to fight for it. The mother never once blinked. Her skinny arms were trembling from the dead weight of her son.

"Leave her, Your Grace," Cersei called out to the king, "she's beyond our help, poor thing."

The mother heard her. Somehow the queen's voice cut through the woman's ravaged wits. Her slack face twisted in loathing. *Whore!* she shrieked. *"Kingslayer's whore! Brotherfucker!"* Her dead child dropped from her arms like a sack of flour as she pointed at Cersei. *"Brotherfucker brotherfucker brotherfucker."*

Tyrion never saw who threw the dung. He only heard Sansa's gasp and Joffrey's bellowed curse, and when he turned his head, the king was wiping brown filth from his cheek. There was more caked in his golden hair and spattered over Sansa's legs.

"Who threw that?" Joffrey screamed. He pushed his fingers into his hair, made a furious face, and flung away another handful of dung. "I want the man who threw that!" he shouted. "A hundred golden dragons to the man who gives him up."

"He was up there!" someone shouted from the crowd. The king wheeled his horse in a circle to survey the rooftops and open balconies above them. In the crowd people were pointing, shoving, cursing one another and the king.

"Please, Your Grace, let him go," Sansa pleaded.

The king paid her no heed. "Bring me the man who flung that filth!" Joffrey commanded. "He'll lick it off me or I'll have his head. Dog, you bring him here!"

Obedient, Sandor Clegane swung down from his saddle, but there was no way through that wall of flesh, let alone to the roof. Those closest to him began to squirm and shove to get away, while others pushed forward to see. Tyrion smelled disaster. "Clegane, leave off, the man is long fled."

"I *want* him!" Joffrey pointed at the roof. "He was up there! Dog, cut through them and bring—"

A tumult of sound drowned his last words, a rolling thunder of rage and fear and hatred that engulfed them from all sides. *"Bastard!"* someone screamed at Joffrey, *"bastard monster."* Other voices flung calls of *"Whore"* and *"Brotherfucker"* at the queen, while Tyrion was pelted with shouts of *"Freak"* and *"Halfman."* Mixed in with the abuse, he heard a few cries of *"Justice"* and *"Robb, King Robb, the Young Wolf,"* of *"Stannis!"* and even *"Renly!"* From both sides of the street, the crowd surged against the spear shafts while the gold cloaks struggled to hold the line. Stones and dung and fouler things whistled overhead. "Feed us!" a woman shrieked. "Bread!" boomed a man behind her. *"We want bread,* bastard!" In a heartbeat, a thousand voices took up the chant. King Joffrey and King Robb and King Stannis were forgotten, and King Bread ruled alone. *"Bread,"* they clamored. *"Bread, bread!"*

Tyrion spurred to his sister's side, yelling, "Back to the castle. *Now."* Cersei gave a curt nod, and Ser Lancel unsheathed his sword. Ahead of the column, Jacelyn Bywater was roaring commands. His riders lowered their lances and drove forward in a wedge. The king was wheeling his palfrey around in anxious circles while hands reached past the line of gold cloaks, grasping for him. One managed to get hold of his leg, but only for an instant. Ser Mandon's sword slashed down, parting hand from wrist. *"Ride!"* Tyrion shouted at his nephew, giving the horse a sharp *smack* on the rump. The animal reared, trumpeting, and plunged ahead, the press shattering before him.

Tyrion drove into the gap hard on the king's hooves. Bronn kept pace, sword in hand. A jagged rock flew past his head as he rode, and a rotten cabbage exploded against Ser Mandon's shield. To their left, three gold cloaks went down under the surge, and then the crowd was rushing forward, trampling the fallen men. The Hound had vanished behind, though his riderless horse galloped beside them. Tyrion saw Aron Santagar pulled from the saddle, the gold-and-black Baratheon stag torn from his grasp. Ser Balon Swann dropped the Lannister lion to draw his longsword. He slashed right and left as the fallen banner was ripped apart, the thousand ragged pieces swirling away like crimson leaves in a storm-wind. In an instant they were gone. Someone staggered in front of Joffrey's horse and shrieked as the king rode him down. Whether it had been man, woman, or child Tyrion could not have said. Joffrey was galloping at his side, whey-faced, with Ser Mandon Moore a white shadow on his left.

And suddenly the madness was behind and they were clattering across the cobbled square that fronted on the castle barbican. A line of spearmen held the gates. Ser Jacelyn was wheeling his lances around for another charge. The spears parted to let the king's party pass under the portcullis. Pale red walls loomed up about them, reassuringly high and aswarm with cross-bowmen.

Tyrion did not recall dismounting. Ser Mandon was helping the shaken king off his horse when Cersei, Tommen, and Lancel rode through the gates with Ser Meryn and Ser Boros close behind. Boros had blood smeared along his blade, while Meryn's white cloak had been torn from his back. Ser Balon Swann rode in helmetless, his mount lathered and bleeding at the mouth. Horas Redwyne brought in Lady Tanda, half-crazed with fear for her daughter Lollys, who had been knocked from the saddle and left behind. Lord Gyles, more grey of face than ever, stammered out a tale of seeing the High Septon spilled from his litter, screeching prayers as the crowd swept over him. Jalabhar Xho said he thought he'd seen Ser Preston Greenfield of the Kingsguard riding back toward the High Septon's overturned litter, but he was not certain.

Tyrion was dimly aware of a maester asking if he was injured. He pushed his way across the yard to where his nephew stood, his dung-encrusted crown askew. "Traitors," Joffrey was babbling excitedly, "I'll have all their heads, I'll—"

The dwarf slapped his flushed face so hard the crown flew from Joffrey's head. Then he shoved him with both hands and knocked him sprawling. "You blind bloody *fool*."

"They were traitors," Joffrey squealed from the ground. "They called me names and attacked me!"

"You set your dog on them! What did you imagine they would do, bend the knee meekly while the Hound lopped off some limbs? You spoiled witless little *boy*, you've killed Clegane and gods know how many more, and yet *you* come through unscratched. *Damn you!"* And he kicked him. It felt so good he might have done more, but Ser Mandon Moore pulled him off as Joffrey howled, and then Bronn was there to take him in hand. Cersei knelt over her son, while Ser Balon Swann restrained Ser Lancel. Tyrion wrenched free of Bronn's grip. "How many are still out there?" he shouted to no one and everyone.

"My daughter," cried Lady Tanda. "Please, someone must go back for Lollys . . ."

"Ser Preston is not returned," Ser Boros Blount reported, "nor Aron Santagar."

"Nor Wet Nurse," said Ser Horas Redwyne. That was the mocking name the other squires had hung on young Tyrek Lannister.

Tyrion glanced round the yard. "Where's the Stark girl?"

For a moment no one answered. Finally Joffrey said, "She was riding by me. I don't know where she went."

Tyrion pressed blunt fingers into his throbbing temples. If Sansa Stark had come to harm, Jaime was as good as dead. "Ser Mandon, you were her shield."

Ser Mandon Moore remained untroubled. "When they mobbed the Hound, I thought first of the king."

"And rightly so," Cersei put in. "Boros, Meryn, go back and find the girl."

"And my daughter," Lady Tanda sobbed. "Please, sers . . ."

Ser Boros did not look pleased at the prospect of leaving the safety of the castle. "Your Grace," he told the queen, "the sight of our white cloaks might enrage the mob."

Tyrion had stomached all he cared to. "The Others take your fucking cloaks! *Take them off* if you're afraid to wear them, you bloody oaf . . . but *find me Sansa Stark* or I swear, I'll have Shagga split that ugly head of yours in two to see if there's anything inside but black pudding."

Ser Boros went purple with rage. "You would call *me* ugly, *you?*" He started to raise the bloody sword still clutched in his mailed fist. Bronn shoved Tyrion unceremoniously behind him.

"Stop it!" Cersei snapped. "Boros, you'll do as you're bid, or we'll find someone else to wear that cloak. Your oath—"

"There she is!" Joffrey shouted, pointing.

Sandor Clegane cantered briskly through the gates astride Sansa's chestnut courser. The girl was seated behind, both arms tight around the Hound's chest.

Tyrion called to her. "Are you hurt, Lady Sansa?"

Blood was trickling down Sansa's brow from a deep gash on her scalp. "They . . . they were throwing things . . . rocks and filth, eggs . . . I tried to tell them, I had no bread to give them. A man tried to pull me from the saddle. The Hound killed him, I think . . . his arm . . ." Her eyes widened and she put a hand over her mouth. "He *cut off his arm.*"

Clegane lifted her to the ground. His white cloak was torn and stained, and blood seeped through a jagged tear in his left sleeve. "The little bird's bleeding. Someone take her back to her cage and see to that cut." Maester Frenken scurried forward to obey. "They did for Santagar," the Hound continued. "Four men held him down and took turns bashing at his head with a cobblestone. I gutted one, not that it did Ser Aron much good."

Lady Tanda approached him. "My daughter—"

"Never saw her." The Hound glanced around the yard, scowling. "Where's my horse? If anything's happened to that horse, someone's going to pay."

"He was running with us for a time," Tyrion said, "but I don't know what became of him after that."

"*Fire!*" a voice screamed down from atop the barbican. "My lords, there's smoke in the city. Flea Bottom's afire."

Tyrion was inutterably weary, but there was no *time* for despair. "Bronn, take as many men as you need and see that the water wagons are not molested." *Gods be good, the wildfire, if any blaze should reach that . . .* "We can lose all of Flea Bottom if we must, but on no account must the fire reach the Guildhall of the Alchemists, is that understood? Clegane, you'll go with him."

For half a heartbeat, Tyrion thought he glimpsed fear in the Hound's dark eyes. *Fire,* he realized. *The Others take me, of course he hates fire, he's tasted it too well.* The look was gone in an instant, replaced by Clegane's familiar scowl. "I'll go," he said, "though not by *your* command. I need to find that horse."

Tyrion turned to the three remaining knights of the Kingsguard. "Each of you will ride escort to a herald. Command the people to return to their homes. Any man found on the streets after the last peal of the evenfall bell will be killed."

"Our place is beside the king," Ser Meryn said, complacent.

Cersei reared up like a viper. "Your place is where my brother says it is," she spit. "The Hand speaks with the king's own voice, and disobedience is treason."

Boros and Meryn exchanged a look. "Should we wear our cloaks, Your Grace?" Ser Boros asked.

"Go naked for all I care. It might remind the mob that you're men. They're like to have forgotten after seeing the way you behaved out there in the street."

Tyrion let his sister rage. His head was throbbing. He thought he could smell smoke, though perhaps it was just the scent of his nerves fraying. Two of the Stone

Crows guarded the door of the Tower of the Hand. "Find me Timett son of Timett."

"Stone Crows do not run squeaking after Burned Men," one of the wildlings informed him haughtily.

For a moment Tyrion had forgotten who he was dealing with. "Then find me Shagga."

"Shagga sleeps."

It was an effort not to scream. "Wake. Him."

"It is no easy thing to wake Shagga son of Dolf," the man complained. "His wrath is fearsome." He went off grumbling.

The clansman wandered in yawning and scratching. "Half the city is rioting, the other half is burning, and Shagga lies snoring," Tyrion said.

"Shagga mislikes your muddy water here, so he must drink your weak ale and sour wine, and after his head hurts."

"I have Shae in a manse near the Iron Gate. I want you to go to her and keep her safe, whatever may come."

The huge man smiled, his teeth a yellow crevasse in the hairy wilderness of his beard. "Shagga will fetch her here."

"Just see that no harm comes to her. Tell her I will come to her as soon as I may. This very night, perhaps, or on the morrow for a certainty."

Yet by evenfall the city was still in turmoil, though Bronn reported that the fires were quenched and most of the roving mobs dispersed. Much as Tyrion yearned for the comfort of Shae's arms, he realized he would go nowhere that night.

Ser Jacelyn Bywater delivered the butcher's bill as he was supping on a cold capon and brown bread in the gloom of his solar. Dusk had faded to darkness by then, but when his servants came to light his candles and start a fire in the hearth, Tyrion had roared at them and sent them running. His mood was as black as the chamber, and Bywater said nothing to lighten it.

The list of the slain was topped by the High Septon, ripped apart as he squealed to his gods for mercy. *Starv-*

ing men take a hard view of priests too fat to walk,
Tyrion reflected.

Ser Preston's corpse had been overlooked at first; the
gold cloaks had been searching for a knight in white
armor, and he had been stabbed and hacked so cruelly
that he was red-brown from head to heel.

Ser Aron Santagar had been found in a gutter, his head
a red pulp inside a crushed helm.

Lady Tanda's daughter had surrendered her maidenhood to half a hundred shouting men behind a tanner's
shop. The gold cloaks found her wandering naked on
Sowbelly Row.

Tyrek was still missing, as was the High Septon's
crystal crown. Nine gold cloaks had been slain, two
score wounded. No one had troubled to count how
many of the mob had died.

"I want Tyrek found, alive or dead," Tyrion said
curtly when Bywater was done. "He's no more than a
boy. Son to my late uncle Tygett. His father was always
kind to me."

"We'll find him. The septon's crown as well."

"The Others can bugger each other with the septon's
crown, for all I care."

"When you named me to command the Watch, you
told me you wanted plain truth, always."

"Somehow I have a feeling I am not going to like
whatever you're about to say," Tyrion said gloomily.

"We held the city today, my lord, but I make no
promises for the morrow. The kettle is close to boiling.
So many thieves and murderers are abroad that no
man's house is safe, the bloody flux is spreading in the
stews along Pisswater Bend, there's no food to be had
for copper nor silver. Where before you heard only mutterings from the gutter, now there's open talk of treason
in guildhalls and markets."

"Do you need more men?"

"I do not trust half the men I have now. Slynt tripled
the size of the Watch, but it takes more than a gold
cloak to make a watchman. There are good men and
loyal among the new recruits, but also more brutes,

sots, cravens, and traitors than you'd care to know. They're half-trained and undisciplined, and what loyalty they have is to their own skins. If it comes to battle, they'll not hold, I fear."

"I never expected them to," said Tyrion. "Once our walls are breached, we are lost, I've known that from the start."

"My men are largely drawn from the smallfolk. They walk the same streets, drink in the same winesinks, spoon down their bowls of brown in the same potshops. Your eunuch must have told you, there is small love for the Lannisters in King's Landing. Many still remember how your lord father sacked the city, when Aerys opened the gates to him. They whisper that the gods are punishing us for the sins of your House—for your brother's murder of King Aerys, for the butchery of Rhaegar's children, for the execution of Eddard Stark and the savagery of Joffrey's justice. Some talk openly of how much better things were when Robert was king, and hint that times would be better again with Stannis on the throne. In pot-shops and winesinks and brothels, you hear these things—and in the barracks and guardhalls as well, I fear."

"They hate my family, is that what you are telling me?"

"Aye . . . and will turn on them, if the chance comes."

"Me as well?"

"Ask your eunuch."

"I'm asking you."

Bywater's deep-set eyes met the dwarf's mismatched ones, and did not blink. "You most of all, my lord."

"Most of all?" The injustice was like to choke him. "It was Joffrey who told them to eat their dead, Joffrey who set his dog on them. How could they blame me?"

"His Grace is but a boy. In the streets, it is said that he has evil councillors. The queen has never been known as a friend to the commons, nor is Lord Varys called the Spider out of love . . . but it is you they blame most. Your sister and the eunuch were here when times were better under King Robert, but you were not. They say that you've filled the city with swaggering sellswords and unwashed savages, brutes who take what they want and follow no laws but their own. They say you exiled Janos Slynt because you found him too bluff and honest for your liking. They say you threw wise and gentle Pycelle into the dungeons when he dared raise his voice against you. Some even claim that you mean to seize the Iron Throne for your own."

"Yes, and I am a monster besides, hideous and misshapen, never forget that." His hand coiled into a fist. "I've heard enough. We both have work to attend to. Leave me."

Perhaps my lord father was right to despise me all these years, if this is the best I can achieve, Tyrion thought when he was alone. He stared down at the remains of his supper, his belly roiling at the sight of the cold greasy capon. Disgusted, he pushed it away, shouted for Pod, and sent the boy running to summon Varys and Bronn. *My most trusted advisers are a eunuch and a sellsword, and my lady's a whore. What does that say of me?*

Bronn complained of the gloom when he arrived, and insisted on a fire in the hearth. It was blazing by the time Varys made his appearance. "Where have you been?" Tyrion demanded.

"About the king's business, my sweet lord."

"Ah, yes, the *king*," Tyrion muttered. "My nephew is not fit to sit a privy, let alone the Iron Throne."

Varys shrugged. "An apprentice must be taught his trade."

"Half the 'prentices on Reeking Lane could rule better than this king of yours." Bronn seated himself across the table and pulled a wing off the capon.

Tyrion had made a practice of ignoring the sellsword's frequent insolences, but tonight he found it galling. "I don't recall giving you leave to finish my supper."

"You didn't look to be eating it," Bronn said through a mouthful of meat. "City's starving, it's a crime to waste food. You have any wine?"

Next he'll want me to pour it for him, Tyrion thought darkly. "You go too far," he warned.

"And you never go far enough." Bronn tossed the wingbone to the rushes. "Ever think how easy life would be if the other one had been born first?" He thrust his fingers inside the capon and tore off a handful of breast. "The weepy one, Tommen. Seems like he'd do whatever he was told, as a good king should."

A chill crept down Tyrion's spine as he realized what the sellsword was hinting at. *If Tommen was king . . .*

There was only one way Tommen would become king. No, he could not even think it. Joffrey was his own blood, and Jaime's son as much as Cersei's. "I could have your head off for saying that," he told Bronn, but the sellsword only laughed.

"Friends," said Varys, "quarreling will not serve us. I beg you both, take heart."

"Whose?" asked Tyrion sourly. He could think of several tempting choices.

DAVOS

Ser Cortnay Penrose wore no armor. He sat a sorrel stallion, his standard-bearer a dapple grey. Above them flapped Baratheon's crowned stag and the crossed quills of Penrose, white on a russet field. Ser Cortnay's spade-shaped beard was russet as well, though he'd gone wholly bald on top. If the size and splendor of the king's party impressed him, it did not show on that weathered face.

They trotted up with much clinking of chain and rattle of plate. Even Davos wore mail, though he could not have said why; his shoulders and lower back ached from the unaccustomed weight. It made him feel cumbered and foolish, and he wondered once more why he was here. *It is not for me to question the king's commands, and yet . . .*

Every man of the party was of better birth and higher station than Davos Seaworth, and the great lords glittered in the morning sun. Silvered steel and gold inlay brightened their armor, and their warhelms were crested in a riot of silken plumes, feathers, and cunningly wrought heraldic beasts with gemstone eyes. Stannis himself looked out of place in this rich and royal company. Like Davos, the king was plainly garbed in wool and boiled leather, though the circlet of red gold about his temples lent him a certain grandeur. Sunlight flashed off its flame-shaped points whenever he moved his head.

This was the closest Davos had come to His Grace in the eight days since *Black Betha* had joined the rest of the fleet off Storm's End. He'd sought an audience within an hour of his arrival, only to be told that the king was occupied. The king was often occupied, Davos learned from his son Devan, one of the royal squires. Now that Stannis Baratheon had come into his power, the lordlings buzzed around him like flies round a corpse. *He looks half a corpse too, years older than when I left Dragonstone.* Devan said the king scarcely slept of late. "Since Lord Renly died, he has been troubled by terrible nightmares," the boy had confided to his father. "Maester's potions do not touch them. Only the Lady Melisandre can soothe him to sleep."

Is that why she shares his pavilion now? Davos wondered. *To pray with him? Or does she have another way to soothe him to sleep?* It was an unworthy question, and one he dared not ask, even of his own son. Devan was a good boy, but he wore the flaming heart proudly on his doublet, and his father had seen him at the nightfires as dusk fell, beseeching the Lord of Light to bring the dawn. *He is the king's squire,* he told himself, *it is only to be expected that he would take the king's god.*

Davos had almost forgotten how high and thick the walls of Storm's End loomed up close. King Stannis halted beneath them, a few feet from Ser Cortnay and his standard-bearer. "Ser," he said with stiff courtesy. He made no move to dismount.

"My lord." That was less courteous, but not unexpected.

"It is customary to grant a king the style *Your Grace*," announced Lord Florent. A red gold fox poked its shining snout out from his breastplate through a circle of lapis lazuli flowers. Very tall, very courtly, and very rich, the Lord of Brightwater Keep had been the first of Renly's bannermen to declare for Stannis, and the first to renounce his old gods and take up the Lord of Light. Stannis had left his queen on Dragonstone along with her uncle Axell, but the queen's men were more numerous and powerful than ever, and Alester Florent was the foremost.

Ser Cortnay Penrose ignored him, preferring to address Stannis. "This is a notable company. The great lords Estermont, Errol, and Varner. Ser Jon of the green-apple Fossoways and Ser Bryan of the red. Lord Caron and Ser Guyard of King Renly's Rainbow Guard . . . *and* the puissant Lord Alester Florent of Brightwater, to be sure. Is that your Onion Knight I spy to the rear? Well met, Ser Davos. I fear I do not know the lady."

"I am named Melisandre, ser." She alone came unarmored, but for her flowing red robes. At her throat the great ruby drank the daylight. "I serve your king, and the Lord of Light."

"I wish you well of them, my lady," Ser Cortnay answered, "but I bow to other gods, and a different king."

"There is but one true king, and one true god," announced Lord Florent.

"Are we here to dispute theology, my lord? Had I known, I would have brought a septon."

"You know full well why we are here," said Stannis. "You have had a fortnight to consider my offer. You sent your ravens. No help has come. Nor will it. Storm's End stands alone, and I am out of patience. One last time, ser, I command you to open your gates, and deliver me that which is mine by rights."

"And the terms?" asked Ser Cortnay.

"Remain as before," said Stannis. "I will pardon you for your treason, as I have pardoned these lords you see behind me. The men of your garrison will be free to enter my service or to return unmolested to their homes. You may keep your weapons and as much property as a man can carry. I will require your horses and pack animals, however."

"And what of Edric Storm?"

"My brother's bastard must be surrendered to me."

"Then my answer is still no, my lord."

The king clenched his jaw. He said nothing.

Melisandre spoke instead. "May the Lord of Light protect you in your darkness, Ser Cortnay."

"May the Others bugger your Lord of Light," Penrose spat back, "and wipe his arse with that rag you bear."

Lord Alester Florent cleared his throat. "Ser Cortnay, mind your tongue. His Grace means the boy no harm. The child is his own blood, and mine as well. My niece Delena was the mother, as all men know. If you will not trust to the king, trust to me. You know me for a man of honor—"

"I know you for a man of ambition," Ser Cortnay broke in. "A man who changes kings and gods the way I change my boots. As do these other turncloaks I see before me."

An angry clamor went up from the king's men. *He is not far wrong,* Davos thought. Only a short time before, the Fossoways, Guyard Morrigen, and the Lords Caron, Varner, Errol, and Estermont had all belonged to Renly. They had sat in his pavilion, helped him make his battle plans, plotted how Stannis might be brought low. And Lord Florent had been with them—he might be Queen Selyse's own uncle, but that had not kept the Lord of Brightwater from bending his knee to Renly when Renly's star was rising.

Bryce Caron walked his horse forward a few paces, his long rainbow-striped cloak twisting in the wind off the bay. "No man here is a turncloak, ser. My fealty belongs to Storm's End, and King Stannis is its rightful lord . . . *and* our true king. He is the last of House Baratheon, Robert's heir and Renly's."

"If that is so, why is the Knight of Flowers not among you? And where is Mathis Rowan? Randyll Tarly? Lady Oakheart? Why are they not here in your company, they who loved Renly best? *Where is Brienne of Tarth, I ask you?*"

"That one?" Ser Guyard Morrigen laughed harshly. "She ran. As well she might. Hers was the hand that slew the king."

"A lie," Ser Cortnay said. "I knew Brienne when she was no more than a girl playing at her father's feet in Evenfall Hall, and I knew her still better when the Evenstar sent her here to Storm's End. She loved Renly Baratheon from the first moment she laid eyes on him, a blind man could see it."

"To be sure," declared Lord Florent airily, "and she would scarcely be the first maid maddened to murder by a man who spurned her. Though for my own part, I believe it was Lady Stark who slew the king. She had journeyed all the way from Riverrun to plead for an alliance, and Renly had refused her. No doubt she saw him as a danger to her son, and so removed him."

"It was Brienne," insisted Lord Caron. "Ser Emmon Cuy swore as much before he died. You have my oath on that, Ser Cortnay."

Contempt thickened Ser Cortnay's voice. "And what is that worth? You wear your cloak of many colors, I see. The one Renly gave you when you swore your *oath* to protect him. If he is dead, how is it you are not?" He turned his scorn on Guyard Morrigen. "I might ask the same of you, ser. Guyard the Green, yes? Of the Rainbow Guard? Sworn to give his own life for his king's? If I had such a cloak, I would be ashamed to wear it."

Morrigen bristled. "Be glad this is a parley, Penrose, or I would have your tongue for those words."

"And cast it in the same fire where you left your manhood?"

"*Enough!*" Stannis said. "The Lord of Light willed that my brother die for his treason. Who did the deed matters not."

"Not to *you*, perhaps," said Ser Cortnay. "I have heard your proposal, Lord Stannis. Now here is mine." He pulled off his glove and flung it full in the king's face. "Single combat. Sword, lance, or any weapon you care to name. Or if you fear to hazard your magic sword and royal skin against an old man, name you a champion, and I shall do the same." He gave Guyard Morrigen and Bryce Caron a scathing look. "Either of these pups would do nicely, I should think."

Ser Guyard Morrigen grew dark with fury. "I will take up the gage, if it please the king."

"As would I." Bryce Caron looked to Stannis.

The king ground his teeth. "No."

Ser Cortnay did not seem surprised. "Is it the justice of your cause you doubt, my lord, or the strength of your arm? Are you afraid I'll piss on your burning sword and put it out?"

"Do you take me for an utter fool, ser?" asked Stannis. "I have twenty thousand men. You are besieged by land and sea. Why would I choose single combat when my eventual victory is certain?" The king pointed a finger at him. "I give you fair warning. If you force me to take my castle by storm, you may expect no mercy. I will hang you for traitors, every one of you."

"As the gods will it. Bring on your storm, my lord—and recall, if you do, the *name* of this castle." Ser Cortnay gave a pull on his reins and rode back toward the gate.

Stannis said no word, but turned his horse around and started back toward his camp. The others followed. "If we storm these walls thousands will die," fretted ancient Lord Estermont, who was the king's grandfather on his mother's side. "Better to hazard but a single life, surely? Our cause is righteous, so the gods must surely bless our champion's arms with victory."

God, old man, thought Davos. *You forget, we have only one now, Melisandre's Lord of Light.*

Ser Jon Fossoway said, "I would gladly take this challenge myself, though I'm not half the swordsman Lord Caron is, or Ser Guyard. Renly left no notable knights at Storm's End. Garrison duty is for old men and green boys."

Lord Caron agreed. "An easy victory, to be sure. And what glory, to win Storm's End with a single stroke!"

Stannis raked them all with a look. "You chatter like magpies, and with less sense. I will have quiet." The king's eyes fell on Davos. "Ser. Ride with me." He spurred his horse away from his followers. Only Melisandre kept pace, bearing the great standard of the fiery heart with the crowned stag within. *As if it had been swallowed whole.*

Davos saw the looks that passed between the lordlings as he rode past them to join the king. These were no onion knights, but proud men from houses whose names were old in honor. Somehow he knew that Renly had never chided them in such a fashion. The youngest of the Baratheons had been born with a gift for easy courtesy that his brother sadly lacked.

He eased back to a slow trot when his horse came up beside the king's. "Your Grace." Seen at close hand, Stannis looked worse than Davos had realized from afar. His face had grown haggard, and he had dark circles under his eyes.

"A smuggler must be a fair judge of men," the king said. "What do you make of this Ser Cortnay Penrose?"

"A stubborn man," said Davos carefully.

"Hungry for death, I call it. He throws my pardon in my face. Aye, and throws his life away in the bargain, and the lives of every man inside those walls. *Single combat!*" The king snorted in derision. "No doubt he mistook me for Robert."

"More like he was desperate. What other hope does he have?"

"None. The castle will fall. But how to do it quickly?" Stannis brooded on that for a moment. Under the steady *clop-clop* of hooves, Davos could hear the faint sound of the king grinding his teeth. "Lord Alester urges me to bring old Lord Penrose here. Ser Cortnay's father. You know the man, I believe?"

"When I came as your envoy, Lord Penrose received me more courteously than most," Davos said. "He is an old done man, sire. Sickly and failing."

"Florent would have him fail more visibly. In his son's sight, with a noose about his neck."

It was dangerous to oppose the queen's men, but Davos had vowed always to tell his king the truth. "I think that would be ill done, my liege. Ser Cortnay will watch his father die before he would ever betray his trust. It would gain us nothing, and bring dishonor to our cause."

"What dishonor?" Stannis bristled. "Would you have me spare the lives of traitors?"

"You have spared the lives of those behind us."

"Do you scold me for that, smuggler?"

"It is not my place." Davos feared he had said too much.

The king was relentless. "You esteem this Penrose more than you do my lords bannermen. Why?"

"He keeps faith."

"A misplaced faith in a dead usurper."

"Yes," Davos admitted, "but still, he keeps faith."

"As those behind us do not?"

Davos had come too far with Stannis to play coy now. "Last year they were Robert's men. A moon ago they were Renly's. This morning they are yours. Whose will they be on the morrow?"

And Stannis laughed. A sudden gust, rough and full of scorn. "I told you, Melisandre," he said to the red woman, "my Onion Knight tells me the truth."

"I see you know him well, Your Grace," the red woman said.

"Davos, I have missed you sorely," the king said. "Aye, I have a tail of traitors, your nose does not deceive you. My lords bannermen are inconstant even in their treasons. I need them, but you should know how it sickens me to pardon such as these when I have punished better men for lesser crimes. You have every right to reproach me, Ser Davos."

"You reproach yourself more than I ever could, Your Grace. You must have these great lords to win your throne—"

"Fingers and all, it seems." Stannis smiled grimly.

Unthinking, Davos raised his maimed hand to the

pouch at his throat, and felt the fingerbones within. *Luck.*

The king saw the motion. "Are they still there, Onion Knight? You have not lost them?"

"No."

"Why do you keep them? I have often wondered."

"They remind me of what I was. Where I came from. They remind me of your justice, my liege."

"It *was* justice," Stannis said. "A good act does not wash out the bad, nor a bad act the good. Each should have its own reward. You were a hero *and* a smuggler." He glanced behind at Lord Florent and the others, rainbow knights and turncloaks, who were following at a distance. "These pardoned lords would do well to reflect on that. Good men and true will fight for Joffrey, wrongly believing him the true king. A northman might even say the same of Robb Stark. But these lords who flocked to my brother's banners *knew* him for a usurper. They turned their backs on their rightful king for no better reason than dreams of power and glory, and I have marked them for what they are. Pardoned them, yes. Forgiven. But not forgotten." He fell silent for a moment, brooding on his plans for justice. And then, abruptly, he said, "What do the smallfolk say of Renly's death?"

"They grieve. Your brother was well loved."

"Fools love a fool," grumbled Stannis, "but I grieve for him as well. For the boy he was, not the man he grew to be." He was silent for a time, and then he said, "How did the commons take the news of Cersei's incest?"

"While we were among them they shouted for King Stannis. I cannot speak for what they said once we had sailed."

"So you do not think they believed?"

"When I was smuggling, I learned that some men believe everything and some nothing. We met both sorts. And there is another tale being spread as well—"

"Yes." Stannis bit off the word. "Selyse has given me horns, and tied a fool's bells to the end of each. My daughter fathered by a halfwit jester! A tale as vile as it is absurd. Renly threw it in my teeth when we met to parley. You would need to be as mad as Patchface to believe such a thing."

"That may be so, my liege . . . but whether they believe the story or no, they delight to tell it." In many places it had come before them, poisoning the well for their own true tale.

"Robert could piss in a cup and men would call it wine, but I offer them pure cold water and they squint in suspicion and mutter to each other about how queer it tastes." Stannis ground his teeth. "If someone said I had magicked myself into a boar to kill Robert, likely they would believe that as well."

"You cannot stop them talking, my liege," Davos said, "but when you take your vengeance on your brothers' true killers, the realm will know such tales for lies."

Stannis only seemed to half hear him. "I have no doubt that Cersei had a hand in Robert's death. I will have justice for him. Aye, and for Ned Stark and Jon Arryn as well."

"And for Renly?" The words were out before Davos could stop to consider them.

For a long time the king did not speak. Then, very softly, he said, "I dream of it sometimes. Of Renly's dying. A green tent, candles, a woman screaming. And blood." Stannis looked down at his hands. "I was still abed when he died. Your Devan will tell you. He tried to wake me. Dawn was nigh and my lords were waiting, fretting. I should have been ahorse, armored. I knew Renly would attack at break of day. Devan says I thrashed and cried out, but what does it matter? It was a dream. I was in my tent when Renly died, and when I woke my hands were clean."

Ser Davos Seaworth could feel his phantom fingertips start to itch. *Something is wrong here,* the onetime smuggler thought. Yet he nodded and said, "I see."

"Renly offered me a peach. At our parley. Mocked me, defied me, threatened me, and offered me a peach. I thought he was drawing a blade and went for mine own. Was that his purpose, to make me show fear? Or was it one of his pointless jests? When he spoke of how sweet the peach was, did his words have some hidden meaning?" The king gave a shake of his head, like a dog shaking a rabbit to snap its neck. "Only Renly could vex me so with a piece of fruit. He brought his doom on himself with his treason, but I did love him, Davos. I know that now. I swear, I will go to my grave thinking of my brother's peach."

By then they were in amongst the camp, riding past the ordered rows of tents, the blowing banners, and the stacks of shields and spears. The stink of horse dung was heavy in the air, mingled with the woodsmoke and the smell of cooking meat. Stannis reined up long enough to bark a brusque dismissal to Lord Florent and the others, commanding them to attend him in his pavilion one hour hence for a council of war. They bowed their heads and dispersed, while Davos and Melisandre rode to the king's pavilion.

The tent had to be large, since it was there his lords bannermen came to council. Yet there was nothing grand about it. It was a soldier's tent of heavy canvas, dyed the dark yellow that sometimes passed for gold. Only the royal banner that streamed atop the center pole marked it as a king's. That, and the guards without; queen's men leaning on tall spears, with the badge of the fiery heart sewn over their own.

Grooms came up to help them dismount. One of the guards relieved Melisandre of her cumbersome standard, driving the staff deep into the soft ground. Devan stood to one side of the door, waiting to lift the flap for the king. An older squire waited beside him. Stannis took off his crown and handed it to Devan. "Cold water, cups for two. Davos, attend me. My lady, I shall send for you when I require you."

"As the king commands." Melisandre bowed.

After the brightness of the morning, the interior of the pavilion seemed cool and dim. Stannis seated himself on a plain wooden camp stool and waved Davos to another. "One day I may make you a lord, smuggler. If only to irk Celtigar and Florent. You will not thank me, though. It will mean you must suffer through these councils, and feign interest in the braying of mules."

"Why do you have them, if they serve no purpose?"

"The mules love the sound of their own braying, why else? And I need them to haul my cart. Oh, to be sure, once in a great while some useful notion is put forth. But not today, I think—ah, here's your son with our water."

Devan set the tray on the table and filled two clay cups. The king sprinkled a pinch of salt in his cup before he drank; Davos took his water straight, wishing it were wine. "You were speaking of your council?"

"Let me tell you how it will go. Lord Velaryon will urge me to storm the castle walls at first light, grapnels and scaling ladders against arrows and boiling oil. The young mules will think this a splendid notion. Estermont will favor settling down to starve them out, as Tyrell and Redwyne once tried with me. That might take a year, but old mules are patient. And Lord Caron and the others who like to kick will want to take up Ser Cortnay's gauntlet and hazard all upon a single combat. Each one imagining *he* will be my champion and win undying fame." The king finished his water. "What would *you* have me do, smuggler?"

Davos considered a moment before he answered. "Strike for King's Landing at once."

The king snorted. "And leave Storm's End untaken?"

"Ser Cortnay does not have the power to harm you. The Lannisters do. A siege would take too long, single combat is too chancy, and an assault would cost thousands of lives with no certainty of success. And there is no need. Once you dethrone Joffrey this castle must come to you with all the rest. It is said about the camp that Lord Tywin Lannister rushes west to rescue Lannisport from the vengeance of the northmen . . ."

"You have a passing clever father, Devan," the king told the boy standing by his elbow. "He makes me wish I had more smugglers in my service. And fewer lords.

Though you are wrong in one respect, Davos. There *is* a need. If I leave Storm's End untaken in my rear, it will be said I was defeated here. And that I cannot permit. Men do not love me as they loved my brothers. They follow me because they fear me . . . and defeat is death to fear. The castle must fall." His jaw ground side to side. "Aye, and *quickly.* Doran Martell has called his banners and fortified the mountain passes. His Dornishmen are poised to sweep down onto the Marches. And Highgarden is far from spent. My brother left the greater part of his power at Bitterbridge, near sixty thousand foot. I sent my wife's brother Ser Errol with Ser Parmen Crane to take them under my command, but they have not returned. I fear that Ser Loras Tyrell reached Bitterbridge before my envoys, and took that host for his own."

"All the more reason to take King's Landing as soon as we may. Salladhor Saan told me—"

"Salladhor Saan thinks only of gold!" Stannis exploded. "His head is full of dreams of the treasure he fancies lies under the Red Keep, so let us hear no more of Salladhor Saan. The day I need military counsel from a Lysene brigand is the day I put off my crown and take the black." The king made a fist. "Are you here to serve me, smuggler? Or to vex me with arguments?"

"I am yours," Davos said.

"Then hear me. Ser Cortnay's lieutenant is cousin to the Fossoways. Lord Meadows, a green boy of twenty. Should some ill chance strike down Penrose, command of Storm's End would pass to this stripling, and his cousins believe he would accept my terms and yield up the castle."

"I remember another stripling who was given command of Storm's End. He could not have been much more than twenty."

"Lord Meadows is not as stonehead stubborn as I was."

"Stubborn or craven, what does it matter? Ser Cortnay Penrose seemed hale and hearty to me."

"So did my brother, the day before his death. The night is dark and full of terrors, Davos."

Davos Seaworth felt the small hairs rising on the back of his neck. "My lord, I do not understand you."

"I do not require your understanding. Only your service. Ser Cortnay will be dead within the day. Melisandre has seen it in the flames of the future. His death and the manner of it. He will not die in knightly combat, needless to say." Stannis held out his cup, and Devan filled it again from the flagon. "Her flames do not lie. She saw Renly's doom as well. On Dragonstone she saw it, and told Selyse. Lord Velaryon and your friend Salladhor Saan would have had me sail against Joffrey, but Melisandre told me that if I went to Storm's End, I would win the best part of my brother's power, and she was right."

"B-but," Davos stammered, "Lord Renly only came here because you had laid siege to the castle. He was marching toward King's Landing before, against the Lannisters, he would have—"

Stannis shifted in his seat, frowning. "Was, would have, what is that? He did what he did. He came here with his banners and his peaches, to his doom . . . and it was well for me he did. Melisandre saw another day in her flames as well. A morrow where Renly rode out of the south in his green armor to smash my host beneath the walls of King's Landing. Had I met my brother there, it might have been me who died in place of him."

"Or you might have joined your strength to his to bring down the Lannisters," Davos protested. "Why not that? If she saw two futures, well . . . *both* cannot be true."

King Stannis pointed a finger. "There you err, Onion Knight. Some lights cast more than one shadow. Stand before the nightfire and you'll see for yourself. The flames shift and dance, never still. The shadows grow tall and short, and every man casts a dozen. Some are fainter than others, that's all. Well, men cast their shadows across the future as well. One shadow or many. Melisandre sees them all.

"You do not love the woman. I know that, Davos, I am not blind. My lords mislike her too. Estermont thinks the flaming heart ill-chosen and begs to fight beneath the crowned stag as of old. Ser Guyard says a woman should not be my standard-bearer. Others whisper that she has no place in my war councils, that I ought to send her back to Asshai, that it is sinful to keep her in my tent of a night. Aye, they whisper . . . while she serves."

"Serves how?" Davos asked, dreading the answer.

"As needed." The king looked at him. "And you?"

"I . . ." Davos licked his lips. "I am yours to command. What would you have me do?"

"Nothing you have not done before. Only land a boat beneath the castle, unseen, in the black of night. Can you do that?"

"Yes. Tonight?"

The king gave a curt nod. "You will need a small boat. Not *Black Betha*. No one must know what you do."

Davos wanted to protest. He was a knight now, no longer a smuggler, and he had never been an assassin. Yet when he opened his mouth, the words would not come. This was *Stannis*, his just lord, to whom he owed all he was. And he had his sons to consider as well. *Gods be good, what has she done to him?*

"You are quiet," Stannis observed.

And should remain so, Davos told himself, yet instead he said, "My liege, you must have the castle, I see that now, but surely there are other ways. *Cleaner* ways. Let Ser Cortnay keep the bastard boy and he may well yield."

"I must have the boy, Davos. *Must*. Melisandre has seen that in the flames as well."

Davos groped for some other answer. "Storm's End holds no knight who can match Ser Guyard or Lord Caron, or any of a hundred others sworn to your service. This single combat . . . could it be that Ser Cortnay seeks for a way to yield with honor? Even if it means his own life?"

A troubled look crossed the king's face like a passing

cloud. "More like he plans some treachery. There will be no combat of champions. Ser Cortnay was dead before he ever threw that glove. The flames do not lie, Davos."

Yet they require me to make them true, he thought. It had been a long time since Davos Seaworth felt so sad.

And so it was that he found himself once more crossing Shipbreaker Bay in the dark of night, steering a tiny boat with a black sail. The sky was the same, and the sea. The same salt smell was in the air, and the water chuckling against the hull was just as he remembered it. A thousand flickering campfires burned around the castle, as the fires of the Tyrells and Redwynes had sixteen years before. But all the rest was different.

The last time it was life I brought to Storm's End, shaped to look like onions. This time it is death, in the shape of Melisandre of Asshai. Sixteen years ago, the sails had cracked and snapped with every shift of wind, until he'd pulled them down and gone on with muffled oars. Even so, his heart had been in his gullet. The men on the Redwyne galleys had grown lax after so long, however, and they had slipped through the cordon smooth as black satin. This time, the only ships in sight belonged to Stannis, and the only danger would come from watchers on the castle walls. Even so, Davos was taut as a bowstring.

Melisandre huddled upon a thwart, lost in the folds of a dark red cloak that covered her from head to heels, her face a paleness beneath the cowl. Davos loved the water. He slept best when he had a deck rocking beneath him, and the sighing of the wind in his rigging was a sweeter sound to him than any a singer could make with his harp strings. Even the sea brought him no comfort tonight, though. "I can smell the fear on you, ser knight," the red woman said softly.

"Someone once told me the night is dark and full of terrors. And tonight I am no knight. Tonight I am Davos the smuggler again. Would that you were an onion."

She laughed. "Is it me you fear? Or what we do?"

"What *you* do. I'll have no part of it."

"Your hand raised the sail. Your hand holds the tiller."

Silent, Davos tended to his course. The shore was a snarl of rocks, so he was taking them well out across the bay. He would wait for the tide to turn before coming about. Storm's End dwindled behind them, but the red woman seemed unconcerned. "Are you a good man, Davos Seaworth?" she asked.

Would a good man be doing this? "I am a man," he said. "I am kind to my wife, but I have known other women. I have tried to be a father to my sons, to help make them a place in this world. Aye, I've broken laws, but I never felt evil until tonight. I would say my parts are mixed, m'lady. Good *and* bad."

"A grey man," she said. "Neither white nor black, but partaking of both. Is that what you are, Ser Davos?"

"What if I am? It seems to me that most men are grey."

"If half of an onion is black with rot, it is a rotten onion. A man is good, or he is evil."

The fires behind them had melted into one vague glow against the black sky, and the land was almost out of sight. It was time to come about. "Watch your head, my lady." He pushed on the tiller, and the small boat threw up a curl of black water as she turned. Melisandre leaned under the swinging yard, one hand on the gunwale, calm as ever. Wood creaked, canvas cracked, and water splashed, so loudly a man might swear the castle was sure to hear. Davos knew better. The endless crash of wave on rock was the only sound that ever penetrated the massive seaward walls of Storm's End, and that but faintly.

A rippling wake spread out behind as they swung back toward the shore. "You speak of men and onions," Davos said to Melisandre. "What of women? Is it not the same for them? Are you good or evil, my lady?"

That made her chuckle. "Oh, good. I am a knight of sorts myself, sweet ser. A champion of light and life."

"Yet you mean to kill a man tonight," he said. "As you killed Maester Cressen."

"Your maester poisoned himself. He meant to poison me, but I was protected by a greater power and he was not."

"And Renly Baratheon? Who was it who killed him?"

Her head turned. Beneath the shadow of the cowl, her eyes burned like pale red candle flames. "Not I."

"Liar." Davos was certain now.

Melisandre laughed again. "You are lost in darkness and confusion, Ser Davos."

"And a good thing." Davos gestured at the distant lights flickering along the walls of Storm's End. "Feel how cold the wind is? The guards will huddle close to those torches. A little warmth, a little light, they're a comfort on a night like this. Yet that will blind them, so they will not see us pass." *I hope.* "The god of darkness protects us now, my lady. Even you."

The flames of her eyes seemed to burn a little brighter at that. "Speak not that name, ser. Lest you draw his black eye upon us. He protects no man, I promise you. He is the enemy of all that lives. It is the torches that hide us, you have said so yourself. Fire. The bright gift of the Lord of Light."

"Have it your way."

"His way, rather."

The wind was shifting, Davos could feel it, see it in the way the black canvas rippled. He reached for the halyards. "Help me bring in the sail. I'll row us the rest of the way."

Together they tied off the sail as the boat rocked beneath them. As Davos unshipped the oars and slid them into the choppy black water, he said, "Who rowed you to Renly?"

"There was no need," she said. "He was unprotected. But here . . . this Storm's End is an old place. There are spells woven into the stones. Dark walls that no shadow can pass—ancient, forgotten, yet still in place."

"Shadow?" Davos felt his flesh prickling. "A shadow is a thing of darkness."

"You are more ignorant than a child, ser knight. There are no shadows in the dark. Shadows are the servants of light, the children of fire. The brightest flame casts the darkest shadows."

Frowning, Davos hushed her then. They were coming close to shore once more, and voices carried across the water. He rowed, the faint sound of his oars lost in the rhythm of the waves. The seaward side of Storm's End perched upon a pale white cliff, the chalky stone sloping up steeply to half again the height of the massive curtain wall. A mouth yawned in the cliff, and it was that Davos steered for, as he had sixteen years before. The tunnel opened on a cavern under the castle, where the storm lords of old had built their landing.

The passage was navigable only during high tide, and was never less than treacherous, but his smuggler's skills had not deserted him. Davos threaded their way deftly between the jagged rocks until the cave mouth loomed up before them. He let the waves carry them inside. They crashed around him, slamming the boat this way and that and soaking them to the skin. A half-seen finger of rock came rushing up out of the gloom, snarling foam, and Davos barely kept them off it with an oar.

Then they were past, engulfed in darkness, and the waters smoothed. The little boat slowed and swirled. The sound of their breathing echoed until it seemed to surround them. Davos had not expected the blackness. The last time, torches had burned all along the tunnel, and the eyes of starving men had peered down through the murder holes in the ceiling. The portcullis was somewhere ahead, he knew. Davos used the oars to slow them, and they drifted against it almost gently.

"This is as far as we go, unless you have a man inside to lift the gate for us." His whispers scurried across the lapping water like a line of mice on soft pink feet.

"Have we passed within the walls?"

"Yes. Beneath. But we can go no farther. The portcullis goes all the way to the bottom. And the bars are too closely spaced for even a child to squeeze through."

There was no answer but a soft rustling. And then a light bloomed amidst the darkness.

Davos raised a hand to shield his eyes, and his breath caught in his throat. Melisandre had thrown back her cowl and shrugged out of the smothering robe. Beneath, she was naked, and huge with child. Swollen breasts hung heavy against her chest, and her belly bulged as if near to bursting. *"Gods preserve us,"* he whispered, and heard her answering laugh, deep and throaty. Her eyes were hot coals, and the sweat that dappled her skin seemed to glow with a light of its own. Melisandre *shone.*

Panting, she squatted and spread her legs. Blood ran down her thighs, black as ink. Her cry might have been agony or ecstasy or both. And Davos saw the crown of the child's head push its way out of her. Two arms wriggled free, grasping, black fingers coiling around Melisandre's straining thighs, pushing, until the whole of the shadow slid out into the world and rose taller than Davos, tall as the tunnel, towering above the boat. He had only an instant to look at it before it was gone, twisting between the bars of the portcullis and racing across the surface of the water, but that instant was long enough.

He knew that shadow. As he knew the man who'd cast it.

JON

The call came drifting through the black of night. Jon pushed himself onto an elbow, his hand reaching for Longclaw by force of habit as the camp began to stir. *The horn that wakes the sleepers*, he thought.

The long low note lingered at the edge of hearing. The sentries at the ringwall stood still in their footsteps, breath frosting and heads turned toward the west. As the sound of the horn faded, even the wind ceased to blow. Men rolled from their blankets and reached for spears and swordbelts, moving quietly, listening. A horse whickered and was hushed. For a heartbeat it seemed as if the whole forest were holding its breath. The brothers of the Night's Watch waited for a second blast, praying they should not hear it, fearing that they would.

When the silence had stretched unbearably long and the men knew at last that the horn would not wind again, they grinned at one another sheepishly, as if to deny that they had been anxious. Jon Snow fed a few sticks to the fire, buckled on his swordbelt, pulled on his boots, shook the dirt and dew from the cloak, and fastened it around his shoulders. The flames blazed up beside him, welcome heat beating against his face as he dressed. He could hear the Lord Commander moving inside the tent. After a moment Mormont lifted the flap. "One blast?" On his shoulder, his raven sat fluffed and silent, looking miserable.

"One, my lord," Jon agreed. "Brothers returning."

Mormont moved to the fire. "The Halfhand. And past time." He had grown more restive every day they waited; much longer and he would have been fit to whelp cubs. "See that there's hot food for the men and fodder for the horses. I'll see Qhorin at once."

"I'll bring him, my lord." The men from the Shadow Tower had been expected days ago. When they had not appeared, the brothers had begun to wonder. Jon had heard gloomy mutterings around the cookfire, and not just from Dolorous Edd. Ser Ottyn Wythers was for retreating to Castle Black as soon as possible. Ser Mallador Locke would strike for the Shadow Tower, hoping to pick up Qhorin's trail and learn what had befallen him. And Thoren Smallwood wanted to push on into the mountains. "Mance Rayder knows he must battle the Watch," Thoren had declared, "but he will never look for us so far north. If we ride up the Milkwater, we can take him unawares and cut his host to ribbons before he knows we are on him."

"The numbers would be greatly against us," Ser Ottyn had objected. "Craster said he was gathering a great host. Many thousands. Without Qhorin, we are only two hundred."

"Send two hundred wolves against ten thousand sheep, ser, and see what happens," said Smallwood confidently.

"There are goats among these sheep, Thoren," warned Jarman Buckwell. "Aye, and maybe a few lions. Rattleshirt, Harma the Dogshead, Alfyn Crowkiller . . ."

"I know them as well as you do, Buckwell," Thoren

Smallwood snapped back. "And I mean to have their heads, every one. These are *wildlings*. No soldiers. A few hundred heroes, drunk most like, amidst a great horde of women, children, and thralls. We will sweep over them and send them howling back to their hovels."

They had argued for many hours, and reached no agreement. The Old Bear was too stubborn to retreat, but neither would he rush headlong up the Milkwater, seeking battle. In the end, nothing had been decided but to wait a few more days for the men from the Shadow Tower, and talk again if they did not appear.

And now they had, which meant that the decision could be delayed no longer. Jon was glad of that much, at least. If they must battle Mance Rayder, let it be soon.

He found Dolorous Edd at the fire, complaining about how difficult it was for him to sleep when people insisted on blowing horns in the woods. Jon gave him something new to complain about. Together they woke Hake, who received the Lord Commander's orders with a stream of curses, but got up all the same and soon had a dozen brothers cutting roots for a soup.

Sam came puffing up as Jon crossed the camp. Under the black hood his face was as pale and round as the moon. "I heard the horn. Has your uncle come back?"

"It's only the men from the Shadow Tower." It was growing harder to cling to the hope of Benjen Stark's safe return. The cloak he had found beneath the Fist could well have belonged to his uncle or one of his men, even the Old Bear admitted as much, though why they would have buried it there, wrapped around the cache of dragonglass, no one could say. "Sam, I have to go."

At the ringwall, he found the guards sliding spikes from the half-frozen earth to make an opening. It was not long until the first of the brothers from the Shadow Tower began wending their way up the slope. All in leather and fur they were, with here and there a bit of steel or bronze; heavy beards covered hard lean faces, and made them look as shaggy as their garrons. Jon was surprised to see some of them were riding two to a horse. When he looked more closely, it was plain that many of them were wounded. *There has been trouble on the way.*

Jon knew Qhorin Halfhand the instant he saw him, though they had never met. The big ranger was half a legend in the Watch; a man of slow words and swift action, tall and straight as a spear, long-limbed and solemn. Unlike his men, he was clean-shaven. His hair fell from beneath his helm in a heavy braid touched with hoarfrost, and the blacks he wore were so faded they might have been greys. Only thumb and forefinger remained on the hand that held the reins; the other fingers had been sheared off catching a wildling's axe that would otherwise have split his skull. It was told that he had thrust his maimed fist into the face of the axeman so the blood spurted into his eyes, and slew him while he was blind. Since that day, the wildlings beyond the Wall had known no foe more implacable.

Jon hailed him. "Lord Commander Mormont would see you at once. I'll show you to his tent."

Qhorin swung down from his saddle. "My men are hungry, and our horses require tending."

"They'll all be seen to."

The ranger gave his horse into the care of one of his men and followed. "You are Jon Snow. You have your father's look."

"Did you know him, my lord?"

"I am no lordling. Only a brother of the Night's Watch. I knew Lord Eddard, yes. And his father before him."

Jon had to hurry his steps to keep up with Qhorin's long strides. "Lord Rickard died before I was born."

"He was a friend to the Watch." Qhorin glanced behind. "It is said that a direwolf runs with you."

"Ghost should be back by dawn. He hunts at night."

They found Dolorous Edd frying a rasher of bacon and boiling a dozen eggs in a kettle over the Old Bear's cookfire. Mormont sat in his wood-and-leather camp chair.

"I had begun to fear for you. Did you meet with trouble?"

"We met with Alfyn Crowkiller. Mance had sent him to scout along the Wall, and we chanced on him returning." Qhorin removed his helm. "Alfyn will trouble the realm no longer, but some of his company escaped us. We hunted down as many as we could, but it may be that a few will win back to the mountains."

"And the cost?"

"Four brothers dead. A dozen wounded. A third as many as the foe. And we took captives. One died quickly from his wounds, but the other lived long enough to be questioned."

"Best talk of this inside. Jon will fetch you a horn of ale. Or would you prefer hot spiced wine?"

"Boiled water will suffice. An egg and a bite of bacon."

"As you wish." Mormont lifted the flap of the tent and Qhorin Halfhand stooped and stepped through.

Edd stood over the kettle swishing the eggs about with a spoon. "I envy those eggs," he said. "I could do with a bit of boiling about now. If the kettle were larger, I might jump in. Though I would sooner it were wine than water. There are worse ways to die than warm and drunk. I knew a brother drowned himself in wine once. It was a poor vintage, though, and his corpse did not improve it."

"You *drank* the wine?"

"It's an awful thing to find a brother dead. You'd have need of a drink as well, Lord Snow." Edd stirred the kettle and added a pinch more nutmeg.

Restless, Jon squatted by the fire and poked at it with a stick. He could hear the Old Bear's voice inside the tent, punctuated by the raven's squawks and Qhorin Halfhand's quieter tones, but he could not make out the words. *Alfyn Crowkiller dead, that's good.* He was one of the bloodiest of the wildling raiders, taking his name from the black brothers he'd slain. *So why does Qhorin sound so grave, after such a victory?*

Jon had hoped that the arrival of men from the

Shadow Tower would lift the spirits in the camp. Only last night, he was coming back through the dark from a piss when he heard five or six men talking in low voices around the embers of a fire. When he heard Chett muttering that it was past time they turned back, Jon stopped to listen. "It's an old man's folly, this ranging," he heard. "We'll find nothing but our graves in them mountains."

"There's giants in the Frostfangs, and wargs, and worse things," said Lark the Sisterman.

"I'll not be going there, I promise you."

"The Old Bear's not like to give you a choice."

"Might be we won't give him one," said Chett.

Just then one of the dogs had raised his head and growled, and he had to move away quickly, before he was seen. *I was not meant to hear that,* he thought. He considered taking the tale to Mormont, but he could not bring himself to inform on his brothers, even brothers such as Chett and the Sisterman. *It was just empty talk,* he told himself. *They are cold and afraid; we all are.* It was hard waiting here, perched on the stony summit above the forest, wondering what the morrow might bring. *The unseen enemy is always the most fearsome.*

Jon slid his new dagger from its sheath and studied the flames as they played against the shiny black glass. He had fashioned the wooden hilt himself, and wound hempen twine around it to make a grip. Ugly, but it served. Dolorous Edd opined that glass knives were about as useful as nipples on a knight's breastplate, but Jon was not so certain. The dragonglass blade was sharper than steel, albeit far more brittle.

It must have been buried for a reason.

He had made a dagger for Grenn as well, and another for the Lord Commander. The warhorn he had given to Sam. On closer examination the horn had proved cracked, and even after he had cleaned all the dirt out, Jon had been unable to get any sound from it. The rim was chipped as well, but Sam liked old things, even worthless old things. "Make a drinking horn out of it,"

Jon told him, "and every time you take a drink you'll remember how you ranged beyond the Wall, all the way to the Fist of the First Men." He gave Sam a spearhead and a dozen arrowheads as well, and passed the rest out among his other friends for luck.

The Old Bear had seemed pleased by the dagger, but he preferred a steel knife at his belt, Jon had noticed. Mormont could offer no answers as to who might have buried the cloak or what it might mean. *Perhaps Qhorin will know.* The Halfhand had ventured deeper into the wild than any other living man.

"You want to serve, or shall I?"

Jon sheathed the dagger. "I'll do it." He wanted to hear what they were saying.

Edd cut three thick slices off a stale round of oat bread, stacked them on a wooden platter, covered them with bacon and bacon drippings, and filled a bowl with hard-cooked eggs. Jon took the bowl in one hand and the platter in the other and backed into the Lord Commander's tent.

Qhorin was seated cross-legged on the floor, his spine as straight as a spear. Candlelight flickered against the hard flat planes of his cheeks as he spoke. ". . . Rattleshirt, the Weeping Man, and every other chief great and small," he was saying. "They have wargs as well, and mammoths, and more strength than we would have dreamed. Or so he claimed. I will not swear as to the truth of it. Ebben believes the man was telling us tales to make his life last a little longer."

"True or false, the Wall must be warned," the Old Bear said as Jon placed the platter between them. "And the king."

"Which king?"

"All of them. The true and the false alike. If they would claim the realm, let them defend it."

The Halfhand helped himself to an egg and cracked it on the edge of the bowl. "These kings will do what they will," he said, peeling away the shell. "Likely it will be little enough. The best hope is Winterfell. The Starks must rally the north."

"Yes. To be sure." The Old Bear unrolled a map, frowned at it, tossed it aside, opened another. He was pondering where the hammer would fall, Jon could see it. The Watch had once manned seventeen castles along the hundred leagues of the Wall, but they had been abandoned one by one as the brotherhood dwindled. Only three were now garrisoned, a fact that Mance Rayder knew as well as they did. "Ser Alliser Thorne will bring back fresh levies from King's Landing, we can hope. If we man Greyguard from the Shadow Tower and the Long Barrow from Eastwatch . . ."

"Greyguard has largely collapsed. Stonedoor would serve better, if the men could be found. Icemark and Deep Lake as well, mayhaps. With daily patrols along the battlements between."

"Patrols, aye. Twice a day, if we can. The Wall itself is a formidable obstacle. Undefended, it cannot stop them, yet it will delay them. The larger the host, the longer they'll require. From the emptiness they've left behind, they must mean to bring their women with them. Their young as well, and beasts . . . have you ever seen a goat climb a ladder? A rope? They will need to build a stair, or a great ramp . . . it will take a moon's turn at the least, perhaps longer. Mance will know his best chance is to pass *beneath* the Wall. Through a gate, or . . ."

"A breach."

Mormont's head came up sharply. "What?"

"They do not plan to climb the Wall nor to burrow beneath it, my lord. They plan to break it."

"The Wall is seven hundred feet high, and so thick at the base that it would take a hundred men a year to cut through it with picks and axes."

"Even so."

Mormont plucked at his beard, frowning. "How?"

"How else? Sorcery." Qhorin bit the egg in half. "Why else would Mance choose to gather his strength in the Frostfangs? Bleak and hard they are, and a long weary march from the Wall."

"I'd hoped he chose the mountains to hide his muster from the eyes of my rangers."

"Perhaps," said Qhorin, finishing the egg, "but there is more, I think. He is seeking something in the high cold places. He is searching for something he needs."

"Something?" Mormont's raven lifted its head and screamed. The sound was sharp as a knife in the closeness of the tent.

"Some power. What it is, our captive could not say. He was questioned perhaps too sharply, and died with much unsaid. I doubt he knew in any case."

Jon could hear the wind outside. It made a high thin sound as it shivered through the stones of the ringwall and tugged at the tent ropes. Mormont rubbed his mouth thoughtfully. "Some power," he repeated. "I must know."

"Then you must send scouts into the mountains."

"I am loath to risk more men."

"We can only die. Why else do we don these black cloaks, but to die in defense of the realm? I would send fifteen men, in three parties of five. One to probe the Milkwater, one the Skirling Pass, one to climb the Giant's Stair. Jarman Buckwell, Thoren Smallwood, and myself to command. To learn what waits in those mountains."

"Waits," the raven cried. *"Waits."*

Lord Commander Mormont sighed deep in his chest. "I see no other choice," he conceded, "but if you do not return . . ."

"Someone will come down out of the Frostfangs, my lord," the ranger said. "If us, all well and good. If not, it will be Mance Rayder, and you sit square in his path. He cannot march south and leave you behind, to follow and harry his rear. He must attack. This is a strong place."

"Not that strong," said Mormont.

"Belike we shall all die, then. Our dying will buy time for our brothers on the Wall. Time to garrison the empty castles and freeze shut the gates, time to summon lords and kings to their aid, time to hone their axes and repair their catapults. Our lives will be coin well spent."

"*Die*," the raven muttered, pacing along Mormont's shoulders. "*Die, die, die, die.*" The Old Bear sat slumped and silent, as if the burden of speech had grown too heavy for him to bear. But at last he said, "May the gods forgive me. Choose your men."

Qhorin Halfhand turned his head. His eyes met Jon's, and held them for a long moment. "Very well. I choose Jon Snow."

Mormont blinked. "He is hardly more than a boy. And my steward besides. Not even a ranger."

"Tollett can care for you as well, my lord." Qhorin lifted his maimed, two-fingered hand. "The old gods are still strong beyond the Wall. The gods of the First Men . . . and the Starks."

Mormont looked at Jon. "What is your will in this?"

"To go," he said at once.

The old man smiled sadly. "I thought it might be."

Dawn had broken when Jon stepped from the tent beside Qhorin Halfhand. The wind swirled around them, stirring their black cloaks and sending a scatter of red cinders flying from the fire.

"We ride at noon," the ranger told him. "Best find that wolf of yours."

TYRION

"The queen intends to send Prince Tommen away." They knelt alone in the hushed dimness of the sept, surrounded by shadows and flickering candles, but even so Lancel kept his voice low. "Lord Gyles will take him to Rosby, and conceal him there in the guise of a page. They plan to darken his hair and tell everyone that he is the son of a hedge knight."

"Is it the mob she fears? Or me?"

"Both," said Lancel.

"Ah." Tyrion had known nothing of this ploy. Had Varys's little birds failed him for once? Even spiders must nod, he supposed . . . or was the eunuch playing a deeper and more subtle game than he knew? "You have my thanks, ser."

"Will you grant me the boon I asked of you?"

"Perhaps." Lancel wanted his own command in the next battle. A splendid way to die before he finished growing that mustache, but young knights always think themselves invincible.

Tyrion lingered after his cousin had slipped away. At

the Warrior's altar, he used one candle to light another. *Watch over my brother, you bloody bastard, he's one of yours.* He lit a second candle to the Stranger, for himself.

That night, when the Red Keep was dark, Bronn arrived to find him sealing a letter. "Take this to Ser Jacelyn Bywater." The dwarf dribbled hot golden wax down onto the parchment.

"What does it say?" Bronn could not read, so he asked impudent questions.

"That he's to take fifty of his best swords and scout the roseroad." Tyrion pressed his seal into the soft wax.

"Stannis is more like to come up the kingsroad."

"Oh, I know. Tell Bywater to disregard what's in the letter and take his men north. He's to lay a trap along the Rosby road. Lord Gyles will depart for his castle in a day or two, with a dozen men-at-arms, some servants, and my nephew. Prince Tommen may be dressed as a page."

"You want the boy brought back, is that it?"

"No. I want him taken on to the castle." Removing the boy from the city was one of his sister's better notions, Tyrion had decided. At Rosby, Tommen would be safe from the mob, and keeping him apart from his brother also made things more difficult for Stannis; even if he took King's Landing and executed Joffrey, he'd still have a Lannister claimant to contend with. "Lord Gyles is too sickly to run and too craven to fight. He'll command his castellan to open the gates. Once inside the walls, Bywater is to expel the garrison and hold Tommen there safe. Ask him how he likes the sound of *Lord* Bywater."

"Lord Bronn would sound better. I could grab the boy for you just as well. I'll dandle him on my knee and sing him nursery songs if there's a lordship in it."

"I need you here," said Tyrion. *And I don't trust you with my nephew.* Should any ill befall Joffrey, the Lannister claim to the Iron Throne would rest on Tommen's young shoulders. Ser Jacelyn's gold cloaks would defend the boy; Bronn's sellswords were more apt to sell him to his enemies.

"What should the new lord do with the old one?"

"Whatever he pleases, so long as he remembers to feed him. I don't want him dying." Tyrion pushed away from the table. "My sister will send one of the Kingsguard with the prince."

Bronn was not concerned. "The Hound is Joffrey's dog, he won't leave him. Ironhand's gold cloaks should be able to handle the others easy enough."

"If it comes to killing, tell Ser Jacelyn I won't have it done in front of Tommen." Tyrion donned a heavy cloak of dark brown wool. "My nephew is tender-hearted."

"Are you certain he's a Lannister?"

"I'm certain of nothing but winter and battle," he said. "Come. I'm riding with you part of the way."

"Chataya's?"

"You know me too well."

They left through a postern gate in the north wall. Tyrion put his heels into his horse and clattered down Shadowblack Lane. A few furtive shapes darted into alleys at the sound of hoofbeats on the cobbles, but no one dared accost them. The council had extended his curfew; it was death to be taken on the streets after the evenfall bells had sung. The measure had restored a degree of peace to King's Landing and quartered the number of corpses found in the alleys of a morning, yet Varys said the people cursed him for it. *They should be thankful they have the breath to curse.* A pair of gold cloaks confronted them as they were making their way along Coppersmith's Wynd, but when they realized whom they'd challenged they begged the Hand's pardons and waved them on. Bronn turned south for the Mud Gate and they parted company.

Tyrion rode on toward Chataya's, but suddenly his patience deserted him. He twisted in the saddle, scanning the street behind. There were no signs of followers. Every window was dark or tightly shuttered. He heard nothing but the wind swirling down the alleys. *If Cersei has someone stalking me tonight, he must be disguised as a rat.* "Bugger it all," he muttered. He was sick of caution. Wheeling his horse around, he dug in his spurs. *If anyone's after me, we'll see how well they ride.* He flew through the moonlight streets, clattering over cobbles, darting down narrow alleys and up twisty wynds, racing to his love.

As he hammered on the gate he heard music wafting faintly over the spiked stone walls. One of the Ibbenese ushered him inside. Tyrion gave the man his horse and said, "Who is that?" The diamond-shaped panes of the longhall windows shone with yellow light, and he could hear a man singing.

The Ibbenese shrugged. "Fatbelly singer."

The sound swelled as he walked from the stable to the house. Tyrion had never been fond of singers, and he liked this one even less than the run of the breed, sight unseen. When he pushed open the door, the man broke off. "My lord Hand." He knelt, balding and kettle-bellied, murmuring, "An honor, an honor."

"M'lord." Shae smiled at the sight of him. He liked that smile, the quick unthinking way it came to her pretty face. The girl wore her purple silk, belted with a cloth-of-silver sash. The colors favored her dark hair and the smooth cream of her skin.

"Sweetling," he called her. "And who is this?"

The singer raised his eyes. "I am called Symon Silver Tongue, my lord. A player, a singer, a taleteller—"

"And a great fool," Tyrion finished. "What did you call me, when I entered?"

"Call? I only . . ." The silver in Symon's tongue seemed to have turned to lead. "My lord Hand, I said, an honor . . ."

"A wiser man would have pretended not to recognize me. Not that I would have been fooled, but you ought to have tried. What am I to do with you now? You know of my sweet Shae, you know where she dwells, you know that I visit by night alone."

"I swear, I'll tell no one . . ."

"On that much we agree. Good night to you." Tyrion led Shae up the stairs.

"My singer may never sing again now," she teased. "You've scared the voice from him."

"A little fear will help him reach those high notes."

She closed the door to their bedchamber. "You won't hurt him, will you?" She lit a scented candle and knelt to pull off his boots. "His songs cheer me on the nights you don't come."

"Would that I could come every night," he said as she rubbed his bare feet. "How well does he sing?"

"Better than some. Not so good as others."

Tyrion opened her robe and buried his face between her breasts. She always smelled clean to him, even in this reeking sty of a city. "Keep him if you like, but keep him close. I won't have him wandering the city spreading tales in pot-shops."

"He won't—" she started.

Tyrion covered her mouth with his own. He'd had talk enough; he needed the sweet simplicity of the pleasure he found between Shae's thighs. Here, at least, he was welcome, wanted.

Afterward, he eased his arm out from under her head, slipped on his tunic, and went down to the garden. A half-moon silvered the leaves of the fruit trees and shone on the surface of the stone bathing pond. Tyrion seated himself beside the water. Somewhere off to his right a cricket was chirping, a curiously homey sound. *It is peaceful here,* he thought, *but for how long?*

A whiff of something rank made him turn his head. Shae stood in the door behind him, dressed in the silvery robe he'd given her. *I loved a maid as white as winter, with moonglow in her hair.* Behind her stood one of the begging brothers, a portly man in filthy patched robes, his bare feet crusty with dirt, a bowl hung about his neck on a leather thong where a septon would have worn a crystal. The smell of him would have gagged a rat.

"Lord Varys has come to see you," Shae announced. The begging brother blinked at her, astonished.

Tyrion laughed. "To be sure. How is it you knew him when I did not?"

She shrugged. "It's still him. Only dressed different."

"A different look, a different smell, a different way of walking," said Tyrion. "Most men would be deceived."

"And most women, maybe. But not whores. A whore learns to see the man, not his garb, or she turns up dead in an alley."

Varys looked pained, and not because of the false scabs on his feet. Tyrion chuckled. "Shae, would you bring us some wine?" He might need a drink. Whatever brought the eunuch here in the dead of night was not like to be good.

"I almost fear to tell you why I've come, my lord," Varys said when Shae had left them. "I bring dire tidings."

"You ought to dress in black feathers, Varys, you're as bad an omen as any raven." Awkwardly, Tyrion pushed to his feet, half afraid to ask the next question. "Is it Jaime?" *If they have harmed him, nothing will save them.*

"No, my lord. A different matter. Ser Cortnay Penrose is dead. Storm's End has opened its gates to Stannis Baratheon."

Dismay drove all other thoughts from Tyrion's mind. When Shae returned with the wine, he took one sip and flung the cup away to explode against the side of the house. She raised a hand to shield herself from the shards as the wine ran down the stones in long fingers, black in the moonlight. "*Damn* him!" Tyrion said.

Varys smiled, showing a mouth full of rotted teeth. "Who, my lord? Ser Cortnay or Lord Stannis?"

"Both of them." Storm's End was strong, it should have been able to hold out for half a year or more . . . time enough for his father to finish with Robb Stark. "How did this happen?"

Varys glanced at Shae. "My lord, must we trouble your sweet lady's sleep with such grim and bloody talk?"

"A lady might be afraid," said Shae, "but I'm not."

"You should be," Tyrion told her. "With Storm's End fallen, Stannis will soon turn his attention toward King's Landing." He regretted flinging away that wine now. "Lord Varys, give us a moment, and I'll ride back to the castle with you."

"I shall wait in the stables." He bowed and stomped off.

Tyrion drew Shae down beside him. "You are not safe here."

"I have my walls, and the guards you gave me."

"Sellswords," Tyrion said. "They like my gold well enough, but will they die for it? As for these walls, a man could stand on another's shoulders and be over in a heartbeat. A manse much like this one was burned during the riots. They killed the goldsmith who owned it for the crime of having a full larder, just as they tore the High Septon to pieces, raped Lollys half a hundred times, and smashed Ser Aron's skull in. What do you think they would do if they got their hands on the Hand's lady?"

"The Hand's whore, you mean?" She looked at him with those big bold eyes of hers. "Though I would be your lady, m'lord. I'd dress in all the beautiful things you gave me, in satin and samite and cloth-of-gold, and I'd wear your jewels and hold your hand and sit by you at feasts. I could give you sons, I know I could . . . and I vow I'd never shame you."

My love for you shames me enough. "A sweet dream, Shae. Now put it aside, I beg you. It can never be."

"Because of the queen? I'm not afraid of her either."

"I am."

"Then *kill* her and be done with it. It's not as if there was any love between you."

Tyrion sighed. "She's my sister. The man who kills his own blood is cursed forever in the sight of gods and men. Moreover, whatever you and I may think of Cersei, my father and brother hold her dear. I can scheme with any man in the Seven Kingdoms, but the gods have not equipped me to face Jaime with swords in hand."

"The Young Wolf and Lord Stannis have swords and they don't scare you."

How little you know, sweetling. "Against them I have all the power of House Lannister. Against Jaime or my father, I have no more than a twisted back and a pair of stunted legs."

"You have me." Shae kissed him, her arms sliding around his neck as she pressed her body to his.

The kiss aroused him, as her kisses always did, but this time Tyrion gently disentangled himself. "Not now. Sweetling, I have . . . well, call it the seed of a plan. I think I might be able to bring you into the castle kitchens."

Shae's face went still. "The kitchens?"

"Yes. If I act through Varys, no one will be the wiser."

She giggled. "M'lord, I'd poison you. Every man who's tasted my cooking has told me what a good whore I am."

"The Red Keep has sufficient cooks. Butchers and bakers too. You'd need to pose as a scullion."

"A pot girl," she said, "in scratchy brown roughspun. Is that how m'lord wants to see me?"

"M'lord wants to see you alive," Tyrion said. "You can scarcely scour pots in silk and velvet."

"Has m'lord grown tired of me?" She reached a hand under his tunic and found his cock. In two quick strokes she had it hard. "*He* still wants me." She laughed. "Would you like to fuck your kitchen wench, m'lord? You can dust me with flour and suck gravy off my titties if you . . ."

"Stop it." The way she was acting reminded him of Dancy, who had tried so hard to win her wager. He yanked her hand away to keep her from further mischief. "This is not the time for bed sport, Shae. Your life may be at stake."

Her grin was gone. "If I've displeased m'lord, I never meant it, only . . . couldn't you just give me more guards?"

Tyrion breathed a deep sigh. *Remember how young she is,* he told himself. He took her hand. "Your gems can be replaced, and new gowns can be sewn twice as lovely as the old. To me, you're the most precious thing within these walls. The Red Keep is not safe either, but it's a deal safer than here. I want you there."

"In the kitchens." Her voice was flat. "Scouring pots."

"For a short while."

"My father made me his kitchen wench," she said, her mouth twisting. "That was why I ran off."

"You told me you ran off because your father made you his whore," he reminded her.

"That too. I didn't like scouring his pots no more than I liked his cock in me." She tossed her head. "Why can't you keep me in your tower? Half the lords at court keep bedwarmers."

"I was expressly forbidden to take you to court."

"By your stupid father." Shae pouted. "You're old enough to keep all the whores you want. Does he take you for a beardless boy? What could he do, spank you?"

He slapped her. Not hard, but hard enough. "Damn you," he said. "*Damn* you. *Never* mock me. Not *you.*"

For a moment Shae did not speak. The only sound was the cricket, chirping, chirping. "Beg pardon, m'lord," she said at last, in a heavy wooden voice. "I never meant to be impudent."

And I never meant to strike you. Gods be good, am I turning into Cersei? "That was ill done," he said. "On both our parts. Shae, you do not understand." Words he had never meant to speak came tumbling out of him like mummers from a hollow horse. "When I was thirteen, I wed a crofter's daughter. Or so I thought her. I was blind with love for her, and thought she felt the same for me, but my father rubbed my face in the truth. My bride was a whore Jaime had hired to give me my first taste of manhood." *And I believed all of it, fool that I was.* "To drive the lesson home, Lord Tywin gave my wife to a barracks of his guardsmen to use as they pleased, and commanded me to watch." *And to take her one last time, after the rest were done. One last time, with no trace of love or tenderness remaining.* "So you *will remember her as she truly is,"* he said, *and I should have defied him, but my cock betrayed me, and I did as I was bid.* "After he was done with her, my father had the marriage undone. It was as if we had never been wed, the septons said." He squeezed her hand. "Please, let's have no more talk of the Tower of the Hand. You will be in the kitchens only a little while. Once we're done with Stannis, you'll have another manse, and silks as soft as your hands."

Shae's eyes had grown large but he could not read what lay behind them. "My hands won't be soft if I clean ovens and scrape plates all day. Will you still want them touching you when they're all red and raw and cracked from hot water and lye soap?"

"More than ever," he said. "When I look at them, they'll remind me how brave you were."

He could not say if she believed him. She lowered her eyes. "I am yours to command, m'lord."

It was as much acceptance as she could give tonight, he saw that plain enough. He kissed her cheek where he'd struck her, to take some sting from the blow. "I will send for you."

Varys was waiting in the stables, as promised. His horse looked spavined and half-dead. Tyrion mounted up; one of the sellswords opened the gates. They rode out in silence. *Why did I tell her about Tysha, gods help me?* he asked himself, suddenly afraid. There were some secrets that should never be spoken, some shames a man should take to his grave. What did he want from her, forgiveness? The way she had looked at him, what did that mean? Did she hate the thought of scouring pots that much, or was it his confession? *How could I tell her that and still think she would love me?* part of him said, and another part mocked, saying, *Fool of a dwarf, it is only the gold and jewels the whore loves.*

His scarred elbow was throbbing, jarred every time the horse set down a hoof. Sometimes he could almost fancy he heard the bones grinding together inside. Perhaps he should see a maester, get some potion for the pain . . . but since Pycelle had revealed himself for what he was, Tyrion Lannister mistrusted the maesters. The gods only knew who they were conspiring with, or what they had mixed in those potions they gave you. "Varys," he said. "I need to bring Shae into the castle without Cersei becoming aware." Briefly, he sketched out his kitchen scheme.

When he was done, the eunuch made a little clucking sound. "I will do as my lord commands, of course . . . but I must warn you, the kitchens are full of eyes and ears. Even if the girl falls under no particular suspicion, she will be subject to a thousand questions. Where was she born? Who were her parents? How did she come to King's Landing? The truth will never do, so she must lie . . . and lie, and lie." He glanced down at Tyrion. "And such a pretty young kitchen wench will incite lust as well as curiosity. She will be touched, pinched, patted, and fondled. Pot boys will crawl under her blankets of a night. Some lonely cook may seek to wed her. Bakers will knead her breasts with floured hands."

"I'd sooner have her fondled than stabbed," said Tyrion.

Varys rode on a few paces and said, "It might be that there is another way. As it happens, the maidservant who attends Lady Tanda's daughter has been filching her jewels. Were I to inform Lady Tanda, she would be forced to dismiss the girl at once. And the daughter would require a new maidservant."

"I see." This had possibilities, Tyrion saw at once. A lady's bedmaid wore finer garb than a scullion, and often even a jewel or two. Shae should be pleased by that. And Cersei thought Lady Tanda tedious and hysterical, and Lollys a bovine lackwit. She was not like to pay them any friendly calls.

"Lollys is timid and trusting," Varys said. "She will accept any tale she is told. Since the mob took her maidenhood she is afraid to leave her chambers, so Shae will be out of sight . . . but conveniently close, should you have need of comfort."

"The Tower of the Hand is watched, you know as

well as I. Cersei would be certain to grow curious if Lollys's bedmaid starting paying me calls."

"I might be able to slip the child into your bedchamber unseen. Chataya's is not the only house to boast a hidden door."

"A secret access? To *my* chambers?" Tyrion was more annoyed than surprised. Why else would Maegor the Cruel have ordered death for all the builders who had worked on his castle, except to preserve such secrets? "Yes, I suppose there would be. Where will I find the door? In my solar? My bedchamber?"

"My friend, you would not force me to reveal *all* my little secrets, would you?"

"Henceforth think of them as *our* little secrets, Varys." Tyrion glanced up at the eunuch in his smelly mummer's garb. "Assuming you *are* on my side . . ."

"Can you doubt it?"

"Why no, I trust you implicitly." A bitter laugh echoed off the shuttered windows. "I trust you like one of my own blood, in truth. Now tell me how Cortnay Penrose died."

"It is said that he threw himself from a tower."

"Threw *himself?* No, I will not believe that!"

"His guards saw no man enter his chambers, nor did they find any within afterward."

"Then the killer entered earlier and hid under the bed," Tyrion suggested, "or he climbed down from the roof on a rope. Perhaps the guards are lying. Who's to say they did not do the thing themselves?"

"Doubtless you are right, my lord."

His smug tone said otherwise. "But you do not think so? How was it done, then?"

For a long moment Varys said nothing. The only sound was the stately *clack* of horseshoes on cobbles. Finally the eunuch cleared his throat. "My lord, do you believe in the old powers?"

"Magic, you mean?" Tyrion said impatiently. "Bloodspells, curses, shapeshifting, those sorts of things?" He snorted. "Do you mean to suggest that Ser Cortnay was magicked to his death?"

"Ser Cortnay had challenged Lord Stannis to single combat on the morning he died. I ask you, is this the act of a man lost to despair? Then there is the matter of Lord Renly's mysterious and most fortuitous murder, even as his battle lines were forming up to sweep his brother from the field." The eunuch paused a moment. "My lord, you once asked me how it was that I was cut."

"I recall," said Tyrion. "You did not want to talk of it."

"Nor do I, but . . ." This pause was longer than the one before, and when Varys spoke again his voice was different somehow. "I was an orphan boy apprenticed to a traveling folly. Our master owned a fat little cog and we sailed up and down the narrow sea performing in all the Free Cities and from time to time in Oldtown and King's Landing.

"One day at Myr, a certain man came to our folly. After the performance, he made an offer for me that my master found too tempting to refuse. I was in terror. I feared the man meant to use me as I had heard men used small boys, but in truth the only part of me he had need of was my manhood. He gave me a potion that made me powerless to move or speak, yet did nothing to dull my senses. With a long hooked blade, he sliced me root and stem, chanting all the while. I watched him burn my manly parts on a brazier. The flames turned blue, and I heard a voice answer his call, though I did not understand the words they spoke.

"The mummers had sailed by the time he was done with me. Once I had served his purpose, the man had no further interest in me, so he put me out. When I asked him what I should do now, he answered that he supposed I should die. To spite him, I resolved to live. I begged, I stole, and I sold what parts of my body still remained to me. Soon I was as good a thief as any in Myr, and when I was older I learned that often the contents of a man's letters are more valuable than the contents of his purse.

"Yet I still dream of that night, my lord. Not of the

sorcerer, nor his blade, nor even the way my manhood shriveled as it burned. I dream of the voice. The voice from the flames. Was it a god, a demon, some conjurer's trick? I could not tell you, and I know all the tricks. All I can say for a certainty is that he called it, and it answered, and since that day I have hated magic and all those who practice it. If Lord Stannis is one such, I mean to see him dead."

When he was done, they rode in silence for a time. Finally Tyrion said, "A harrowing tale. I'm sorry."

The eunuch sighed. "You are sorry, but you do not believe me. No, my lord, no need to apologize. I was drugged and in pain and it was a very long time ago and far across the sea. No doubt I dreamed that voice. I've told myself as much a thousand times."

"I believe in steel swords, gold coins, and men's wits," said Tyrion. "And I believe there once were dragons. I've seen their skulls, after all."

"Let us hope that is the worst thing you ever see, my lord."

"On that we agree." Tyrion smiled. "And for Ser Cortnay's death, well, we know Stannis hired sellsails from the Free Cities. Perhaps he bought himself a skilled assassin as well."

"A *very* skilled assassin."

"There are such. I used to dream that one day I'd be rich enough to send a Faceless Man after my sweet sister."

"Regardless of how Ser Cortnay died," said Varys, "he is dead, the castle fallen. Stannis is free to march."

"Any chance we might convince the Dornishmen to descend on the Marches?" asked Tyrion.

"None."

"A pity. Well, the threat may serve to keep the Marcher lords close to their castles, at least. What news of my father?"

"If Lord Tywin has won across the Red Fork, no word has reached me yet. If he does not hasten, he may be trapped between his foes. The Oakheart leaf and the Rowan tree have been seen north of the Mander."

"No word from Littlefinger?"

"Perhaps he never reached Bitterbridge. Or perhaps he's died there. Lord Tarly has seized Renly's stores and put a great many to the sword; Florents, chiefly. Lord Caswell has shut himself up in his castle."

Tyrion threw back his head and laughed.

Varys reined up, nonplussed. "My lord?"

"Don't you see the jest, Lord Varys?" Tyrion waved a hand at the shuttered windows, at all the sleeping city. "Storm's End is fallen and Stannis is coming with fire and steel and the gods alone know what dark powers, and the good folk don't have Jaime to protect them, nor Robert nor Renly nor Rhaegar nor their precious Knight of Flowers. Only me, the one they hate." He laughed again. "The dwarf, the evil counselor, the twisted little monkey demon. I'm all that stands between them and chaos."

CATELYN

Tell Father I have gone to make him proud." Her brother swung up into his saddle, every inch the lord in his bright mail and flowing mud-and-water cloak. A silver trout ornamented the crest of his greathelm, twin to the one painted on his shield.

"He was always proud of you, Edmure. And he loves you fiercely. Believe that."

"I mean to give him better reason than mere birth." He wheeled his warhorse about and raised a hand. Trumpets sounded, a drum began to boom, the drawbridge descended in fits and starts, and Ser Edmure Tully led his men out from Riverrun with lances raised and banners streaming.

I have a greater host than yours, brother, Catelyn thought as she watched them go. *A host of doubts and fears.*

Beside her, Brienne's misery was almost palpable. Catelyn had ordered garments sewn to her measure, handsome gowns to suit her birth and sex, yet still she preferred to dress in oddments of mail and boiled leather, a swordbelt cinched around her waist. She would have been happier riding to war with Edmure, no doubt, but even walls as strong as Riverrun's required swords to hold them. Her brother had taken every able-bodied man for the fords, leaving Ser Desmond Grell to command a garrison made up of the wounded, the old, and the sick, along with a few squires and some untrained peasant boys still shy of manhood. This, to defend a castle crammed full of women and children.

When the last of Edmure's foot had shuffled under the portcullis, Brienne asked, "What shall we do now, my lady?"

"Our duty." Catelyn's face was drawn as she started across the yard. *I have always done my duty*, she thought. Perhaps that was why her lord father had always cherished her best of all his children. Her two older brothers had both died in infancy, so she had been son as well as daughter to Lord Hoster until Edmure was born. Then her mother had died and her father had told her that she must be the lady of Riverrun now, and she had done that too. And when Lord Hoster promised her to Brandon Stark, she had thanked him for making her such a splendid match.

I gave Brandon my favor to wear, and never comforted Petyr once after he was wounded, nor bid him farewell when Father sent him off. And when Brandon was murdered and Father told me I must wed his brother, I did so gladly, though I never saw Ned's face until our wedding day. I gave my maidenhood to this solemn stranger and sent him off to his war and his king and the woman who bore him his bastard, because I always did my duty.

Her steps took her to the sept, a seven-sided sandstone temple set amidst her mother's gardens and filled with rainbow light. It was crowded when they entered; Catelyn was not alone in her need for prayer. She knelt before the painted marble image of the Warrior and lit a scented candle for Edmure and another for Robb off beyond the hills. *Keep them safe and help them to vic-*

tory, she prayed, *and bring peace to the souls of the slain and comfort to those they leave behind.*

The septon entered with his censer and crystal while she was at her prayers, so Catelyn lingered for the celebration. She did not know this septon, an earnest young man close to Edmure's age. He performed his office well enough, and his voice was rich and pleasant when he sang the praises to the Seven, but Catelyn found herself yearning for the thin quavering tones of Septon Osmynd, long dead. Osmynd would have listened patiently to the tale of what she had seen and felt in Renly's pavilion, and he might have known what it meant as well, and what she must do to lay to rest the shadows that stalked her dreams. *Osmynd, my father, Uncle Brynden, old Maester Kym, they always seemed to know everything, but now there is only me, and it seems I know nothing, not even my duty. How can I do my duty if I do not know where it lies?*

Catelyn's knees were stiff by the time she rose, though she felt no wiser. Perhaps she would go to the godswood tonight, and pray to Ned's gods as well. They were older than the Seven.

Outside, she found song of a very different sort. Rymund the Rhymer sat by the brewhouse amidst a circle of listeners, his deep voice ringing as he sang of Lord Deremond at the Bloody Meadow.

And there he stood with sword in hand,
the last of Darry's ten . . .

Brienne paused to listen for a moment, broad shoulders hunched and thick arms crossed against her chest. A mob of ragged boys raced by, screeching and flailing at each other with sticks. *Why do boys so love to play at war?* Catelyn wondered if Rymund was the answer. The singer's voice swelled as he neared the end of his song.

And red the grass beneath his feet,
and red his banners bright,

and red the glow of setting sun
that bathed him in its light.
"Come on, come on," the great lord called,
"my sword is hungry still."
And with a cry of savage rage,
They swarmed across the rill . . .

"Fighting is better than this waiting," Brienne said. "You don't feel so helpless when you fight. You have a sword and a horse, sometimes an axe. When you're armored it's hard for anyone to hurt you."

"Knights die in battle," Catelyn reminded her.

Brienne looked at her with those blue and beautiful eyes. "As ladies die in childbed. No one sings songs about *them*."

"Children are a battle of a different sort." Catelyn started across the yard. "A battle without banners or warhorns, but no less fierce. Carrying a child, bringing it into the world . . . your mother will have told you of the pain . . ."

"I never knew my mother," Brienne said. "My father had ladies . . . a different lady every year, but . . ."

"Those were no ladies," Catelyn said. "As hard as birth can be, Brienne, what comes after is even harder. At times I feel as though I am being torn apart. Would that there were five of me, one for each child, so I might keep them all safe."

"And who would keep *you* safe, my lady?"

Her smile was wan and tired. "Why, the men of my House. Or so my lady mother taught me. My lord father, my brother, my uncle, my husband, they will keep me safe . . . but while they are away from me, I suppose you must fill their place, Brienne."

Brienne bowed her head. "I shall try, my lady."

Later that day, Maester Vyman brought a letter. She saw him at once, hoping for some word from Robb, or from Ser Rodrik in Winterfell, but the message proved to be from one Lord Meadows, who named himself castellan of Storm's End. It was addressed to her father, her brother, her son, "or whoever now holds Riverrun." Ser

Cortnay Penrose was dead, the man wrote, and Storm's End had opened its gate to Stannis Baratheon, the true-born and rightful heir. The castle garrison had sworn their swords to his cause, one and all, and no man of them had suffered harm.

"Save Cortnay Penrose," Catelyn murmured. She had never met the man, yet she grieved to hear of his passing. "Robb should know of this at once," she said. "Do we know where he is?"

"At last word he was marching toward the Crag, the seat of House Westerling," said Maester Vyman. "If I dispatched a raven to Ashemark, it may be that they could send a rider after him."

"Do so."

Catelyn read the letter again after the maester was gone. "Lord Meadows says nothing of Robert's bastard," she confided to Brienne. "I suppose he yielded the boy with the rest, though I confess, I do not understand why Stannis wanted him so badly."

"Perhaps he fears the boy's claim."

"A bastard's claim? No, it's something else . . . what does this child look like?"

"He is seven or eight, comely, with black hair and bright blue eyes. Visitors oft thought him Lord Renly's own son."

"And Renly favored Robert." Catelyn had a glimmer of understanding. "Stannis means to parade his brother's bastard before the realm, so men might see Robert in his face and wonder why there is no such likeness in Joffrey."

"Would that mean so much?"

"Those who favor Stannis will call it proof. Those who support Joffrey will say it means nothing." Her own children had more Tully about them than Stark. Arya was the only one to show much of Ned in her features. *And Jon Snow, but he was never mine.* She found herself thinking of Jon's mother, that shadowy secret love her husband would never speak of. *Does she grieve for Ned as I do? Or did she hate him for leaving*

*her bed for mine? Does she pray for her son as I have
prayed for mine?*

They were uncomfortable thoughts, and futile. If Jon
had been born of Ashara Dayne of Starfall, as some
whispered, the lady was long dead; if not, Catelyn had
no clue who or where his mother might be. And it made
no matter. Ned was gone now, and his loves and his
secrets had all died with him.

Still, she was struck again by how strangely men behaved when it came to their bastards. Ned had always
been fiercely protective of Jon, and Ser Cortnay Penrose
had given up his life for this Edric Storm, yet Roose
Bolton's bastard had meant less to him than one of his
dogs, to judge from the tone of the queer cold letter
Edmure had gotten from him not three days past. He
had crossed the Trident and was marching on Harrenhal
as commanded, he wrote. "A strong castle, and well garrisoned, but His Grace shall have it, if I must kill every
living soul within to make it so." He hoped His Grace
would weigh that against the crimes of his bastard son,
whom Ser Rodrik Cassel had put to death. "A fate he no
doubt earned," Bolton had written. "Tainted blood is
ever treacherous, and Ramsay's nature was sly, greedy,
and cruel. I count myself well rid of him. The trueborn
sons my young wife has promised me would never have
been safe while he lived."

The sound of hurrying footsteps drove the morbid
thoughts from her head. Ser Desmond's squire dashed
panting into the room and knelt. "My lady . . . Lannisters . . . across the river."

"Take a long breath, lad, and tell it slowly."

He did as she bid him. "A column of armored men,"
he reported. "Across the Red Fork. They are flying a
purple unicorn below the lion of Lannister."

Some son of Lord Brax. Brax had come to Riverrun
once when she was a girl, to propose wedding one of his
sons to her or Lysa. She wondered whether it was this
same son out there now, leading the attack.

The Lannisters had ridden out of the southeast beneath a blaze of banners, Ser Desmond told her when

she ascended to the battlements to join him. "A few outriders, no more," he assured her. "The main strength of Lord Tywin's host is well to the south. We are in no danger here."

South of the Red Fork the land stretched away open and flat. From the watchtower Catelyn could see for miles. Even so, only the nearest ford was visible. Edmure had entrusted Lord Jason Mallister with its defense, as well as that of three others farther upriver. The Lannister riders were milling about uncertainly near the water, crimson and silver banners flapping in the wind. "No more than fifty, my lady," Ser Desmond estimated.

Catelyn watched the riders spread out in a long line. Lord Jason's men waited to receive them behind rocks and grass and hillocks. A trumpet blast sent the horsemen forward at a ponderous walk, splashing down into the current. For a moment they made a brave show, all bright armor and streaming banners, the sun flashing off the points of their lances.

"Now," she heard Brienne mutter.

It was hard to make out what was happening, but the screams of the horses seemed loud even at this remove, and beneath them Catelyn heard the fainter clash of steel on steel. A banner vanished suddenly as its bearer was swept under, and soon after the first dead man drifted past their walls, borne along by the current. By then the Lannisters had pulled back in confusion. She watched as they re-formed, conferred briefly, and galloped back the way they had come. The men on the walls shouted taunts after them, though they were already too far off to hear.

Ser Desmond slapped his belly. "Would that Lord Hoster could have seen that. It would have made him dance."

"My father's dancing days are past, I fear," Catelyn said, "and this fight is just begun. The Lannisters will come again. Lord Tywin has twice my brother's numbers."

"He could have ten times and it would not matter,"

Ser Desmond said. "The west bank of the Red Fork is higher than the east, my lady, and well wooded. Our bowmen have good cover, and a clear field for their shafts . . . and should any breach occur, Edmure will have his best knights in reserve, ready to ride wherever they are most sorely needed. The river will hold them."

"I pray that you are right," Catelyn said gravely.

That night they came again. She had commanded them to wake her at once if the enemy returned, and well after midnight a serving girl touched her gently by the shoulder. Catelyn sat up at once. "What is it?"

"The ford again, my lady."

Wrapped in a bedrobe, Catelyn climbed to the roof of the keep. From there she could see over the walls and the moonlit river to where the battle raged. The defenders had built watchfires along the bank, and perhaps the Lannisters thought to find them night-blind or unwary. If so, it was folly. Darkness was a chancy ally at best. As they waded in to breast their way across, men stepped in hidden pools and went down splashing, while others stumbled over stones or gashed their feet on the hidden caltrops. The Mallister bowmen sent a storm of fire arrows hissing across the river, strangely beautiful from afar. One man, pierced through a dozen times, his clothes afire, danced and whirled in the knee-deep water until at last he fell and was swept downstream. By the time his body came bobbing past Riverrun, the fires and his life had both been extinguished.

A small victory, Catelyn thought when the fighting had ended and the surviving foemen had melted back into the night, *yet a victory nonetheless.* As they descended the winding turret steps, Catelyn asked Brienne for her thoughts. "That was the brush of Lord Tywin's fingertip, my lady," the girl said. "He is probing, feeling for a weak point, an undefended crossing. If he does not find one, he will curl all his fingers into a fist and try and make one." Brienne hunched her shoulders. "That's what I'd do. Were I him." Her hand went to the hilt of her sword and gave it a little pat, as if to make certain it was still there.

And may the gods help us then, Catelyn thought. Yet there was nothing she could do for it. That was Edmure's battle out there on the river; hers was here inside the castle.

The next morning as she broke her fast, she sent for her father's aged steward, Utherydes Wayn. "Have Ser Cleos Frey brought a flagon of wine. I mean to question him soon, and I want his tongue well loosened."

"As you command, my lady."

Not long after, a rider with the Mallister eagle sewn on his breast arrived with a message from Lord Jason, telling of another skirmish and another victory. Ser Flement Brax had tried to force a crossing at a different ford six leagues to the south. This time the Lannisters shortened their lances and advanced across the river behind on foot, but the Mallister bowmen had rained high arcing shots down over their shields, while the scorpions Edmure had mounted on the riverbank sent heavy stones crashing through to break up the formation. "They left a dozen dead in the water, only two reaching the shallows, where we dealt with them briskly," the rider reported. He also told of fighting farther upstream, where Lord Karyl Vance held the fords. "Those thrusts too were turned aside, at grievous cost to our foes."

Perhaps Edmure was wiser than I knew, Catelyn thought. *His lords all saw the sense in his battle plans, why was I so blind? My brother is not the little boy I remember, no more than Robb is.*

She waited until evening before going to pay her call upon Ser Cleos Frey, reasoning that the longer she delayed, the drunker he was likely to be. As she entered the tower cell, Ser Cleos stumbled to his knees. "My lady, I knew naught of any escape. The Imp said a Lannister must needs have a Lannister escort, on my oath as a knight—"

"Arise, ser." Catelyn seated herself. "I know no grandson of Walder Frey would be an oathbreaker." *Unless it served his purpose.* "You brought peace terms, my brother said."

"I did." Ser Cleos lurched to his feet. She was pleased to see how unsteady he was.

"Tell me," she commanded, and he did.

When he was done, Catelyn sat frowning. Edmure had been right, these were no terms at all, except . . . "Lannister will exchange Arya and Sansa for his brother?"

"Yes. He sat on the Iron Throne and swore it."

"Before witnesses?"

"Before all the court, my lady. And the gods as well. I said as much to Ser Edmure, but he told me it was not possible, that His Grace Robb would never consent."

"He told you true." She could not even say that Robb was wrong. Arya and Sansa were children. The Kingslayer, alive and free, was as dangerous as any man in the realm. That road led nowhere. "Did you see my girls? Are they treated well?"

Ser Cleos hesitated. "I . . . yes, they seemed . . ."

He is fumbling for a lie, Catelyn realized, *but the wine has fuddled his wits.* "Ser Cleos," she said coolly, "you forfeited the protection of your peace banner when your men played us false. Lie to me, and you'll hang from the walls beside them. Believe that. I shall ask you once more—*did you see my daughters?*"

His brow was damp with sweat. "I saw Sansa at the court, the day Tyrion told me his terms. She looked most beautiful, my lady. Perhaps a, a bit wan. Drawn, as it were."

Sansa, but not Arya. That might mean anything. Arya had always been harder to tame. Perhaps Cersei was reluctant to parade her in open court for fear of what she might say or do. They might have her locked safely out of sight. *Or they might have killed her.* Catelyn shoved the thought away. "*His* terms, you said . . . yet Cersei is Queen Regent."

"Tyrion spoke for both of them. The queen was not there. She was indisposed that day, I was told."

"Curious." Catelyn thought back to that terrible trek through the Mountains of the Moon, and the way Tyrion Lannister had somehow seduced that sellsword from her service to his own. *The dwarf is too clever by half.* She could not imagine how he had survived the high road after Lysa had sent him from the Vale, yet it did not surprise her. *He had no part in Ned's murder, at the least. And he came to my defense when the clansmen attacked us. If I could trust his word . . .*

She opened her hands to look down at the scars across her fingers. *His dagger's marks,* she reminded herself. *His dagger, in the hand of the killer he paid to open Bran's throat.* Though the dwarf denied it, to be sure. Even after Lysa locked him in one of her sky cells and threatened him with her moon door, he had still denied it. "He lied," she said, rising abruptly. "The Lannisters are liars every one, and the dwarf is the worst of them. The killer was armed with his own knife."

Ser Cleos stared. "I know nothing of any—"

"You know nothing," she agreed, sweeping from the cell. Brienne fell in beside her, silent. *It is simpler for her,* Catelyn thought with a pang of envy. She was like a man in that. For men the answer was always the same, and never farther away than the nearest sword. For a woman, a mother, the way was stonier and harder to know.

She took a late supper in the Great Hall with her garrison, to give them what encouragement she could. Rymund the Rhymer sang through all the courses, sparing her the need to talk. He closed with the song he had written about Robb's victory at Oxcross. *"And the stars in the night were the eyes of his wolves, and the wind itself was their song."* Between the verses, Rymund threw back his head and howled, and by the end, half of the hall was howling along with him, even Desmond Grell, who was well in his cups. Their voices rang off the rafters.

Let them have their songs, if it makes them brave, Catelyn thought, toying with her silver goblet.

"There was always a singer at Evenfall Hall when I was a girl," Brienne said quietly. "I learned all the songs by heart."

"Sansa did the same, though few singers ever cared to

make the long journey north to Winterfell." *I told her there would be singers at the king's court, though. I told her she would hear music of all sorts, that her father could find some master to help her learn the high harp. Oh, gods forgive me . . .*

Brienne said, "I remember a woman . . . she came from some place across the narrow sea. I could not even say what language she sang in, but her voice was as lovely as she was. She had eyes the color of plums and her waist was so tiny my father could put his hands around it. His hands were almost as big as mine." She closed her long, thick fingers, as if to hide them.

"Did you sing for your father?" Catelyn asked.

Brienne shook her head, staring down at her trencher as if to find some answer in the gravy.

"For Lord Renly?"

The girl reddened. "Never, I . . . his fool, he made cruel japes sometimes, and I . . ."

"Someday you must sing for me."

"I . . . please, I have no gift." Brienne pushed back from the table. "Forgive me, my lady. Do I have your leave to go?"

Catelyn nodded. The tall, ungainly girl left the hall with long strides, almost unnoticed amidst the revelry. *May the gods go with her,* she thought as she returned listlessly to her supper.

It was three days later when the hammer blow that Brienne had foretold fell, and five days before they heard of it. Catelyn was sitting with her father when Edmure's messenger arrived. The man's armor was dinted, his boots dusty, and he had a ragged hole in his surcoat, but the look on his face as he knelt was enough to tell her that the news was good. "Victory, my lady." He handed her Edmure's letter. Her hand trembled as she broke the seal.

Lord Tywin had tried to force a crossing at a dozen different fords, her brother wrote, but every thrust had been thrown back. Lord Lefford had been drowned, the Crakehall knight called Strongboar taken captive, Ser Addam Marbrand thrice forced to retreat . . . but the fiercest battle had been fought at Stone Mill, where Ser Gregor Clegane had led the assault. So many of his men had fallen that their dead horses threatened to dam the flow. In the end the Mountain and a handful of his best had gained the west bank, but Edmure had thrown his reserve at them, and they had shattered and reeled away bloody and beaten. Ser Gregor himself had lost his horse and staggered back across the Red Fork bleeding from a dozen wounds while a rain of arrows and stones fell all around him. "They shall not cross, Cat," Edmure scrawled, "Lord Tywin is marching to the southeast. A feint perhaps, or full retreat, it matters not. *They shall not cross.*"

Ser Desmond Grell had been elated. "Oh, if only I might have been with him," the old knight said when she read him the letter. "Where is that fool Rymund? There's a song in this, by the gods, and one that even Edmure will want to hear. The mill that ground the Mountain down, I could almost make the words myself, had I the singer's gift."

"I'll hear no songs until the fighting's done," Catelyn said, perhaps too sharply. Yet she allowed Ser Desmond to spread the word, and agreed when he suggested breaking open some casks in honor of Stone Mill. The mood within Riverrun had been strained and somber; they would all be better for a little drink and hope.

That night the castle rang to the sounds of celebration. *"Riverrun!"* the smallfolk shouted, and "Tully! Tully!" They'd come frightened and helpless, and her brother had taken them in when most lords would have closed their gates. Their voices floated in through the high windows, and seeped under the heavy redwood doors. Rymund played his harp, accompanied by a pair of drummers and a youth with a set of reed pipes. Catelyn listened to girlish laughter, and the excited chatter of the green boys her brother had left her for a garrison. Good sounds . . . and yet they did not touch her. She could not share their happiness.

In her father's solar she found a heavy leatherbound book of maps and opened it to the riverlands. Her eyes found the path of the Red Fork and traced it by flickering candlelight. *Marching to the southeast,* she thought. By now they had likely reached the headwaters of the Blackwater Rush, she decided.

She closed the book even more uneasy than before. The gods had granted them victory after victory. At Stone Mill, at Oxcross, in the Battle of the Camps, at the Whispering Wood . . .

But if we are winning, why am I so afraid!

BRAN

The sound was the faintest of *clinks*, a scraping of steel over stone. He lifted his head from his paws, listening, sniffing at the night.

The evening's rain had woken a hundred sleeping smells and made them ripe and strong again. Grass and thorns, blackberries broken on the ground, mud, worms, rotting leaves, a rat creeping through the bush. He caught the shaggy black scent of his brother's coat and the sharp coppery tang of blood from the squirrel he'd killed. Other squirrels moved through the branches above, smelling of wet fur and fear, their little claws scratching at the bark. The noise had sounded something like that.

And he heard it again, *clink* and scrape. It brought him to his feet. His ears pricked and his tail rose. He howled, a long deep shivery cry, a howl to wake the sleepers, but the piles of man-rock were dark and dead. A still wet night, a night to drive men into their holes. The rain had stopped, but the men still hid from the damp, huddled by the fires in their caves of piled stone.

His brother came sliding through the trees, moving almost as quiet as another brother he remembered dimly from long ago, the white one with the eyes of blood. *This* brother's eyes were pools of shadow, but the fur on the back of his neck was bristling. He had heard the sounds as well, and known they meant danger.

This time the *clink* and scrape were followed by a slithering and the soft swift patter of skinfeet on stone. The wind brought the faintest whiff of a man-smell he did not know. *Stranger. Danger. Death.*

He ran toward the sound, his brother racing beside him. The stone dens rose before them, walls slick and wet. He bared his teeth, but the man-rock took no notice. A gate loomed up, a black iron snake coiled tight about bar and post. When he crashed against it, the gate shuddered and the snake clanked and slithered and held. Through the bars he could look down the long stone burrow that ran between the walls to the stony field beyond, but there was no way through. He could force his muzzle between the bars, but no more. Many a time his brother had tried to crack the black bones of the gate between his teeth, but they would not break. They had tried to dig under, but there were great flat stones beneath, half-covered by earth and blown leaves.

Snarling, he paced back and forth in front of the gate, then threw himself at it once more. It moved a little and slammed him back. *Locked,* something whispered. *Chained.* The voice he did not hear, the scent without a smell. The other ways were closed as well. Where doors opened in the walls of man-rock, the wood was thick and strong. There was no way out.

There is, the whisper came, and it seemed as if he could see the shadow of a great tree covered in needles, slanting up out of the black earth to ten times the height of a man. Yet when he looked about, it was not there. *The other side of the godswood, the sentinel, hurry, hurry . . .*

Through the gloom of night came a muffled shout, cut short.

Swiftly, swiftly, he whirled and bounded back into

the trees, wet leaves rustling beneath his paws, branches whipping at him as he rushed past. He could hear his brother following close. They plunged under the heart tree and around the cold pool, through the blackberry bushes, under a tangle of oaks and ash and hawthorn scrub, to the far side of the wood . . . and there it was, the shadow he'd glimpsed without seeing, the slanting tree pointing at the rooftops. *Sentinel,* came the thought.

He remembered how it was to climb it then. The needles everywhere, scratching at his bare face and falling down the back of his neck, the sticky sap on his hands, the sharp piney smell of it. It was an easy tree for a boy to climb, leaning as it did, crooked, the branches so close together they almost made a ladder, slanting right up to the roof.

Growling, he sniffed around the base of the tree, lifted a leg and marked it with a stream of urine. A low branch brushed his face, and he snapped at it, twisting and pulling until the wood cracked and tore. His mouth was full of needles and the bitter taste of the sap. He shook his head and snarled.

His brother sat back on his haunches and lifted his voice in a ululating howl, his song black with mourning. The way was no way. They were not squirrels, nor the cubs of men, they could not wriggle up the trunks of trees, clinging with soft pink paws and clumsy feet. They were runners, hunters, prowlers.

Off across the night, beyond the stone that hemmed them close, the dogs woke and began to bark. One and then another and then all of them, a great clamor. They smelled it too; the scent of foes and fear.

A desperate fury filled him, hot as hunger. He sprang away from the wall, loped off beneath the trees, the shadows of branch and leaf dappling his grey fur . . . and then he turned and raced back in a rush. His feet flew, kicking up wet leaves and pine needles, and for a little time he was a hunter and an antlered stag was fleeing before him and he could see it, smell it, and he ran full out in pursuit. The smell of fear made his heart thunder and slaver ran from his jaws, and he reached the falling tree in stride and threw himself up the trunk, claws scrabbling at the bark for purchase. Upward he bounded, *up*, two bounds, three, hardly slowing, until he was among the lower limbs. Branches tangled his feet and whipped at his eyes, grey-green needles scattered as he shouldered through them, snapping. He had to slow. Something snagged at his foot and he wrenched it free, snarling. The trunk narrowed under him, the slope steeper, almost straight up, and wet. The bark tore like skin when he tried to claw at it. He was a third of the way up, halfway, more, the roof was almost within reach . . . and then he put down a foot and felt it slip off the curve of wet wood, and suddenly he was sliding, stumbling. He yowled in fear and fury, falling, *falling*, and twisted around while the ground rushed up to break him . . .

And then Bran was back abed in his lonely tower room, tangled in his blankets, his breath coming hard. "Summer," he cried aloud. "Summer." His shoulder seemed to ache, as if he had fallen on it, but he knew it was only the ghost of what the wolf was feeling. *Jojen told it true. I am a beastling.* Outside he could hear the faint barking of dogs. *The sea has come. It's flowing over the walls, just as Jojen saw.* Bran grabbed the bar overhead and pulled himself up, shouting for help. No one came, and after a moment he remembered that no one would. They had taken the guard off his door. Ser Rodrik had needed every man of fighting age he could lay his hands on, so Winterfell had been left with only a token garrison.

The rest had left eight days past, six hundred men from Winterfell and the nearest holdfasts. Cley Cerwyn was bringing three hundred more to join them on the march, and Maester Luwin had sent ravens before them, summoning levies from White Harbor and the barrowlands and even the deep places inside the wolfswood. Torrhen's Square was under attack by some monstrous war chief named Dagmer Cleftjaw. Old Nan said he couldn't be killed, that once a foe had cut his head in two with an axe, but Dagmer was so fierce he'd just pushed the two halves back together and held them until they healed up. *Could Dagmer have won?* Torrhen's Square was many days from Winterfell, yet still . . .

Bran pulled himself from the bed, moving bar to bar until he reached the windows. His fingers fumbled a little as he swung back the shutters. The yard was empty, and all the windows he could see were black. Winterfell slept. *"Hodor!"* he shouted down, as loud as he could. Hodor would be asleep above the stables, but maybe if he yelled loud enough he'd hear, or *somebody* would. *"Hodor, come fast! Osha! Meera, Jojen, anyone!"* Bran cupped his hands around his mouth. *"HOOOOODOOOOOR!"*

But when the door crashed open behind him, the man who stepped through was no one Bran knew. He wore a leather jerkin sewn with overlapping iron disks, and carried a dirk in one hand and an axe strapped to his back. "What do you want?" Bran demanded, afraid. "This is my room. You get out of here."

Theon Greyjoy followed him into the bedchamber. "We're not here to harm you, Bran."

"Theon?" Bran felt dizzy with relief. "Did Robb send you? Is he here too?"

"Robb's far away. He can't help you now."

"Help me?" He was confused. "Don't scare me, Theon."

"I'm *Prince* Theon now. We're both princes, Bran. Who would have dreamed it? But I've taken your castle, my prince."

"Winterfell?" Bran shook his head. "No, you *couldn't.*"

"Leave us, Werlag." The man with the dirk withdrew. Theon seated himself on the bed. "I sent four men over the walls with grappling claws and ropes, and they opened a postern gate for the rest of us. My men are dealing with yours even now. I promise you, Winterfell is mine."

Bran did not understand. "But you're Father's *ward.*"

"And now you and your brother are *my* wards. As

soon as the fighting's done, my men will be bringing the rest of your people together in the Great Hall. You and I are going to speak to them. You'll tell them how you've yielded Winterfell to me, and command them to serve and obey their new lord as they did the old."

"I *won't*," said Bran. "We'll fight you and throw you out. I never yielded, you can't make me say I did."

"This is no game, Bran, so don't play the boy with me, I won't stand for it. The castle is mine, but these people are still yours. If the prince would keep them safe, he'd best do as he's told." He rose and went to the door. "Someone will come dress you and carry you to the Great Hall. Think carefully on what you want to say."

The waiting made Bran feel even more helpless than before. He sat in the window seat, staring out at dark towers and walls black as shadow. Once he thought he heard shouting beyond the Guards Hall, and something that might have been the clash of swords, but he did not have Summer's ears to hear, nor his nose to smell. *Awake, I am still broken, but when I sleep, when I'm Summer, I can run and fight and hear and smell.*

He had expected that Hodor would come for him, or maybe one of the serving girls, but when the door next opened it was Maester Luwin, carrying a candle. "Bran," he said, "you . . . know what has happened? You have been told?" The skin was broken above his left eye, and blood ran down that side of his face.

"Theon came. He said Winterfell was his now."

The maester set down the candle and wiped the blood off his cheek. "They swam the moat. Climbed the walls with hook and rope. Came over wet and dripping, steel in hand." He sat on the chair by the door, as fresh blood flowed. "Alebelly was on the gate, they surprised him in the turret and killed him. Hayhead's wounded as well. I had time to send off two ravens before they burst in. The bird to White Harbor got away, but they brought down the other with an arrow." The maester stared at the rushes. "Ser Rodrik took too many of our men, but I am to blame as much as he is. I never saw this danger, I never . . ."

Jojen saw it, Bran thought. "You better help me dress."

"Yes, that's so." In the heavy ironbound chest at the foot of Bran's bed the maester found smallclothes, breeches, and tunic. "You are the Stark in Winterfell, and Robb's heir. You must look princely." Together they garbed him as befit a lord.

"Theon wants me to yield the castle," Bran said as the maester was fastening the cloak with his favorite wolf's-head clasp of silver and jet.

"There is no shame in that. A lord must protect his smallfolk. Cruel places breed cruel peoples, Bran, remember that as you deal with these ironmen. Your lord father did what he could to gentle Theon, but I fear it was too little and too late."

The ironman who came for them was a squat thick-bodied man with a coal-black beard that covered half his chest. He bore the boy easily enough, though he looked none too happy with the task. Rickon's bedchamber was a half turn down the steps. The four-year-old was cranky at being woken. "I want Mother," he said. "I *want* her. And Shaggydog too."

"Your mother is far away, my prince." Maester Luwin pulled a bedrobe over the child's head. "But I'm here, and Bran." He took Rickon by the hand and led him out.

Below, they came on Meera and Jojen being herded from their room by a bald man whose spear was three feet taller than he was. When Jojen looked at Bran, his eyes were green pools full of sorrow. Other ironmen had rousted the Freys. "Your brother's lost his kingdom," Little Walder told Bran. "You're no prince now, just a hostage."

"So are you," Jojen said, "and me, and all of us."

"No one was talking to you, frogeater."

One of the ironmen went before them carrying a torch, but the rain had started again and soon drowned it out. As they hurried across the yard they could hear the direwolves howling in the godswood. *I hope Summer wasn't hurt falling from the tree.*

Theon Greyjoy was seated in the high seat of the Starks. He had taken off his cloak. Over a shirt of fine mail he wore a black surcoat emblazoned with the golden kraken of his House. His hands rested on the wolves' heads carved at the ends of the wide stone arms. "Theon's sitting in Robb's chair," Rickon said.

"Hush, Rickon." Bran could feel the menace around them, but his brother was too young. A few torches had been lit, and a fire kindled in the great hearth, but most of the hall remained in darkness. There was no place to sit with the benches stacked against the walls, so the castle folk stood in small groups, not daring to speak. He saw Old Nan, her toothless mouth opening and closing. Hayhead was carried in between two of the other guards, a bloodstained bandage wrapped about his bare chest. Poxy Tym wept inconsolably, and Beth Cassel cried with fear.

"What have we here?" Theon asked of the Reeds and Freys.

"These are Lady Catelyn's wards, both named Walder Frey," Maester Luwin explained. "And this is Jojen Reed and his sister Meera, son and daughter to Howland Reed of Greywater Watch, who came to renew their oaths of fealty to Winterfell."

"Some might call that ill-timed," said Theon, "though not for me. Here you are and here you'll stay." He vacated the high seat. "Bring the prince here, Lorren." The black-bearded man dumped Bran onto the stone as if he were a sack of oats.

People were still being driven into the Great Hall, prodded along with shouts and the butts of the spears. Gage and Osha arrived from the kitchens, spotted with flour from making the morning bread. Mikken they dragged in cursing. Farlen entered limping, struggling to support Palla. Her dress had been ripped in two; she held it up with a clenched fist and walked as if every step were agony. Septon Chayle rushed to lend a hand, but one of the ironmen knocked him to the floor.

The last man marched through the doors was the prisoner Reek, whose stench preceded him, ripe and pungent. Bran felt his stomach twist at the smell of him. "We found this one locked in a tower cell," announced his escort, a beardless youth with ginger-colored hair and sodden clothing, doubtless one of those who'd swum the moat. "He says they call him Reek."

"Can't think why," Theon said, smiling. "Do you always smell so bad, or did you just finish fucking a pig?"

"Haven't fucked no one since they took me, m'lord. Heke's me true name. I was in service to the Bastard o' the Dreadfort till the Starks give him an arrow in the back for a wedding gift."

Theon found that amusing. "Who did he marry?"

"The widow o' Hornwood, m'lord."

"That crone? Was he blind? She has teats like empty wineskins, dry and withered."

"It wasn't her teats he wed her for, m'lord."

The ironmen slammed shut the tall doors at the foot of the hall. From the high seat, Bran could see about twenty of them. *He probably left some guards on the gates and the armory.* Even so, there couldn't be more than thirty.

Theon raised his hands for quiet. "You all know me—"

"Aye, we know you for a sack of steaming dung!" shouted Mikken, before the bald man drove the butt of his spear into his gut, then smashed him across the face with the shaft. The smith stumbled to his knees and spat out a tooth.

"Mikken, you be silent." Bran tried to sound stern and lordly, the way Robb did when he made a command, but his voice betrayed him and the words came out in a shrill squeak.

"Listen to your little lordling, Mikken," said Theon. "He has more sense than you do."

A good lord protects his people, he reminded himself. "I've yielded Winterfell to Theon."

"Louder, Bran. And call me prince."

He raised his voice. "I have yielded Winterfell to

Prince Theon. All of you should do as he commands you."

"Damned if I will!" bellowed Mikken.

Theon ignored the outburst. "My father has donned the ancient crown of salt and rock, and declared himself King of the Iron Islands. He claims the north as well, by right of conquest. You are all his subjects."

"Bugger that." Mikken wiped the blood from his mouth. "I serve the Starks, not some treasonous squid of—*aah.*" The butt of the spear smashed him face first into the stone floor.

"Smiths have strong arms and weak heads," observed Theon. "But if the rest of you serve me as loyally as you served Ned Stark, you'll find me as generous a lord as you could want."

On his hands and knees, Mikken spat blood. *Please don't,* Bran wished at him, but the blacksmith shouted, "If you think you can hold the north with this sorry lot o'—"

The bald man drove the point of his spear into the back of Mikken's neck. Steel slid through flesh and came out his throat in a welter of blood. A woman screamed, and Meera wrapped her arms around Rickon. *It's blood he drowned on,* Bran thought numbly. *His own blood.*

"Who else has something to say?" asked Theon Greyjoy.

"Hodor hodor hodor hodor," shouted Hodor, eyes wide.

"Someone kindly shut that halfwit up."

Two ironmen began to beat Hodor with the butts of their spears. The stableboy dropped to the floor, trying to shield himself with his hands.

"I will be as good a lord to you as Eddard Stark ever was." Theon raised his voice to be heard above the smack of wood on flesh. "Betray me, though, and you'll wish you hadn't. And don't think the men you see here are the whole of my power. Torrhen's Square and Deepwood Motte will soon be ours as well, and my uncle is sailing up the Saltspear to seize Moat Cailin. If Robb

Stark can stave off the Lannisters, he may reign as King of the Trident hereafter, but House Greyjoy holds the north now."

"Stark's lords will fight you," the man Reek called out. "That bloated pig at White Harbor for one, and them Umbers and Karstarks too. You'll need men. Free me and I'm yours."

Theon weighed him a moment. "You're cleverer than you smell, but I could not suffer that stench."

"Well," said Reek, "I could wash some. If I was free."

"A man of rare good sense." Theon smiled. "Bend the knee."

One of the ironmen handed Reek a sword, and he laid it at Theon's feet and swore obedience to House Greyjoy and King Balon. Bran could not look. The green dream was coming true.

"M'lord Greyjoy!" Osha stepped past Mikken's body. "I was brought here captive too. You were there the day I was taken."

I thought you were a friend, Bran thought, hurt.

"I need fighters," Theon declared, "not kitchen sluts."

"It was Robb Stark put me in the kitchens. For the best part of a year, I've been left to scour kettles, scrape grease, and warm the straw for this one." She threw a look at Gage. "I've had a bellyful of it. Put a spear in my hand again."

"I got a spear for you right here," said the bald man who'd killed Mikken. He grabbed his crotch, grinning.

Osha drove her bony knee up between his legs. "You keep that soft pink thing." She wrested the spear from him and used the butt to knock him off his feet. "I'll have me the wood and iron." The bald man writhed on the floor while the other reavers sent up gales of laughter.

Theon laughed with the rest. "You'll do," he said. "Keep the spear; Stygg can find another. Now bend the knee and swear."

When no one else rushed forward to pledge service, they were dismissed with a warning to do their work and make no trouble. Hodor was given the task of bearing Bran back to his bed. His face was all ugly from the beating, his nose swollen and one eye closed. "Hodor," he sobbed between cracked lips as he lifted Bran in huge strong arms and bloody hands and carried him back out into the rain.

ARYA

There's ghosts, I know there is." Hot Pie was kneading bread, his arms floured up to his elbows. "Pia saw something in the buttery last night."

Arya made a rude noise. Pia was always seeing things in the buttery. Usually they were men. "Can I have a tart?" she asked. "You baked a whole tray."

"I need a whole tray. Ser Amory is partial to them."

She hated Ser Amory. "Let's spit on them."

Hot Pie looked around nervously. The kitchens were full of shadows and echoes, but the other cooks and scullions were all asleep in the cavernous lofts above the ovens. "He'll know."

"He will not," Arya said. "You can't taste *spit*."

"If he does, it's me they'll whip." Hot Pie stopped his kneading. "You shouldn't even *be* here. It's the black of night."

It was, but Arya never minded. Even in the black of night, the kitchens were never still; there was always someone rolling dough for the morning bread, stirring a kettle with a long wooden spoon, or butchering a hog for Ser Amory's breakfast bacon. Tonight it was Hot Pie.

"If Pinkeye wakes and finds you gone—" Hot Pie said.

"Pinkeye never wakes." His true name was Mebble, but everyone called him Pinkeye for his runny eyes. "Not once he's passed out." Each morning he broke his fast with ale. Each evening he fell into a drunken sleep after supper, wine-colored spit running down his chin. Arya would wait until she heard him snoring, then creep barefoot up the servant's stair, making no more noise than the mouse she'd been. She carried neither candle nor taper. Syrio had told her once that darkness could be her friend, and he was right. If she had the moon and the stars to see by, that was enough. "I bet we could escape, and Pinkeye wouldn't even notice I was gone," she told Hot Pie.

"I don't want to escape. It's better here than it was in them woods. I don't want to eat no worms. Here, sprinkle some flour on the board."

Arya cocked her head. "What's that?"

"What? I don't—"

"Listen with your *ears*, not your mouth. That was a warhorn. Two blasts, didn't you hear? And there, that's the portcullis chains, someone's going out or coming in. Want to go see?" The gates of Harrenhal had not been opened since the morning Lord Tywin had marched with his host.

"I'm making the morning bread," Hot Pie complained. "Anyhow I don't like it when it's dark, I told you."

"I'm going. I'll tell you after. Can I have a tart?"

"No."

She filched one anyway, and ate it on her way out. It was stuffed with chopped nuts and fruit and cheese, the crust flaky and still warm from the oven. Eating Ser Amory's tart made Arya feel daring. *Barefoot surefoot lightfoot*, she sang under her breath. *I am the ghost in Harrenhal.*

The horn had stirred the castle from sleep; men were coming out into the ward to see what the commotion was about. Arya fell in with the others. A line of ox carts were rumbling under the portcullis. *Plunder*, she knew at once. The riders escorting the carts spoke in a babble of queer tongues. Their armor glinted pale in the moonlight, and she saw a pair of striped black-and-white zorses. *The Bloody Mummers.* Arya withdrew a little deeper into the shadows, and watched as a huge black bear rolled by, caged in the back of a wagon. Other carts were loaded down with silver plate, weapons and shields, bags of flour, pens of squealing hogs and scrawny dogs and chickens. Arya was thinking how long it had been since she'd had a slice off a pork roast when she saw the first of the prisoners.

By his bearing and the proud way he held his head, he must have been a lord. She could see mail glinting beneath his torn red surcoat. At first Arya took him for a Lannister, but when he passed near a torch she saw his device was a silver fist, not a lion. His wrists were bound tightly, and a rope around one ankle tied him to the man behind him, and him to the man behind him, so the whole column had to shuffle along in a lurching lockstep. Many of the captives were wounded. If any halted, one of the riders would trot up and give him a lick of the whip to get him moving again. She tried to judge how many prisoners there were, but lost count before she got to fifty. There were twice that many at least. Their clothing was stained with mud and blood, and in the torchlight it was hard to make out all their badges and sigils, but some of those Arya glimpsed she recognized. Twin towers. Sunburst. Bloody man. Battle-axe. *The battle-axe is for Cerwyn, and the white sun on black is Karstark. They're northmen. My father's men, and Robb's.* She didn't like to think what that might mean.

The Bloody Mummers began to dismount. Stableboys emerged sleepy from their straw to tend their lathered horses. One of the riders was shouting for ale. The noise brought Ser Amory Lorch out onto the covered gallery above the ward, flanked by two torchbearers. Goat-helmed Vargo Hoat reined up below him. "My lord cathellan," the sellsword said. He had a thick, slobbery voice, as if his tongue was too big for his mouth.

"What's all this, Hoat?" Ser Amory demanded, frowning.

"Captiths. Rooth Bolton thought to croth the river, but my Brafe Companions cut his van to pieceth. Killed many, and thent Bolton running. Thith ith their lord commander, Glover, and the one behind ith Ther Aenyth Frey."

Ser Amory Lorch stared down at the roped captives with his little pig eyes. Arya did not think he was pleased. Everyone in the castle knew that he and Vargo Hoat hated each other. "Very well," he said. "Ser Cadwyn, take these men to the dungeons."

The lord with the mailed fist on his surcoat raised his eyes. "We were promised honorable treatment—" he began.

"Silenth!" Vargo Hoat screamed at him, spraying spittle.

Ser Amory addressed the captives. "What Hoat promised you is nothing to me. Lord Tywin made *me* the castellan of Harrenhal, and I shall do with you as I please." He gestured to his guards. "The great cell under the Widow's Tower ought to hold them all. Any who do not care to go are free to die here."

As his men herded off the captives at spearpoint, Arya saw Pinkeye emerge from the stairwell, blinking at the torchlight. If he found her missing, he would shout and threaten to whip the bloody hide off her, but she was not afraid. He was no Weese. He was forever threatening to whip the bloody hide off this one or that one, but Arya never actually knew him to *hit*. Still, it would be better if he never saw her. She glanced around. The oxen were being unharnessed, the carts unloaded, while the Brave Companions clamored for drink and the curious gathered around the caged bear. In the commotion, it was not hard to slip off unseen. She went back the way she had come, wanting to be out of sight before someone noticed her and thought to put her to work.

Away from the gates and the stables, the great castle

was largely deserted. The noise dwindled behind her. A swirling wind gusted, drawing a high shivery scream from the cracks in the Wailing Tower. Leaves had begun to fall from the trees in the godswood, and she could hear them moving through the deserted courtyards and between the empty buildings, making a faint skittery sound as the wind drove them across the stones. Now that Harrenhal was near empty once again, sound did queer things here. Sometimes the stones seemed to drink up noise, shrouding the yards in a blanket of silence. Other times, the echoes had a life of their own, so every footfall became the tread of a ghostly army, and every distant voice a ghostly feast. The funny sounds were one of the things that bothered Hot Pie, but not Arya.

Quiet as a shadow, she flitted across the middle bailey, around the Tower of Dread, and through the empty mews, where people said the spirits of dead falcons stirred the air with ghostly wings. She could go where she would. The garrison numbered no more than a hundred men, so small a troop that they were lost in Harrenhal. The Hall of a Hundred Hearths was closed off, along with many of the lesser buildings, even the Wailing Tower. Ser Amory Lorch resided in the castellan's chambers in Kingspyre, themselves as spacious as a lord's, and Arya and the other servants had moved to the cellars beneath him so they would be close at hand. While Lord Tywin had been in residence, there was always a man-at-arms wanting to know your business. But now there were only a hundred men left to guard a thousand doors, and no one seemed to know who should be where, or care much.

As she passed the armory, Arya heard the ring of a hammer. A deep orange glow shone through the high windows. She climbed to the roof and peeked down. Gendry was beating out a breastplate. When he worked, nothing existed for him but metal, bellows, fire. The hammer was like part of his arm. She watched the play of muscles in his chest and listened to the steel music he made. *He's strong*, she thought. As he took up the

long-handled tongs to dip the breastplate into the
quenching trough, Arya slithered through the window
and leapt down to the floor beside him.

He did not seem surprised to see her. "You should be
abed, girl." The breastplate hissed like a cat as he
dipped it in the cold water. "What was all that noise?"

"Vargo Hoat's come back with prisoners. I saw their
badges. There's a Glover, from Deepwood Motte, he's
my father's man. The rest too, mostly." All of a sudden,
Arya knew why her feet had brought her here. "You
have to help me get them out."

Gendry laughed. "And how do we do that?"

"Ser Amory sent them down to the dungeon. The one
under the Widow's Tower, that's just one big cell. You
could smash the door open with your hammer—"

"While the guards watch and make bets on how many
swings it will take me, maybe?"

Arya chewed her lips. "We'd need to kill the guards."

"How are we supposed to do that?"

"Maybe there won't be a lot of them."

"If there's *two*, that's too many for you and me. You
never learned nothing in that village, did you? You try
this and Vargo Hoat will cut off your hands and feet, the
way he does." Gendry took up the tongs again.

"You're *afraid*."

"Leave me alone, girl."

"Gendry, there's a *hundred* northmen. Maybe more, I
couldn't count them all. That's as many as Ser Amory
has. Well, not counting the Bloody Mummers. We just
have to get them out and we can take over the castle
and escape."

"Well, you can't get them out, no more'n you could
save Lommy." Gendry turned the breastplate with the
tongs to look at it closely. "And if we did escape, where
would we go?"

"Winterfell," she said at once. "I'd tell Mother how
you helped me, and you could stay—"

"Would m'lady permit? Could I shoe your horses for
you, and make swords for your lordly brothers?"

Sometimes he made her so *angry*. "You stop that!"

"Why should I wager my feet for the chance to sweat in Winterfell in place of Harrenhal? You know old Ben Blackthumb? He came here as a boy. Smithed for Lady Whent and her father before her and his father before him, and even for Lord Lothston who held Harrenhal before the Whents. Now he smiths for Lord Tywin, and you know what he says? A sword's a sword, a helm's a helm, and if you reach in the fire you get burned, no matter who you're serving. Lucan's a fair enough master. I'll stay here."

"The queen will catch you, then. She didn't send gold cloaks after Ben *Blackthumb*!"

"Likely it wasn't even me they wanted."

"It was too, you know it. You're *somebody*."

"I'm a 'prentice smith, and one day might be I'll make a master armorer . . . *if* I don't run off and lose my feet or get myself killed." He turned away from her, picked up his hammer once more, and began to bang.

Arya's hands curled into helpless fists. "The next helm you make, put *mule's ears* on it in place of bull's horns!" She had to flee, or else she would have started hitting him. *He probably wouldn't even feel it if I did. When they find who he is and cut off his stupid mulehead, he'll be sorry he didn't help.* She was better off without him anyhow. He was the one who got her caught at the village.

But thinking of the village made her remember the march, and the storeroom, and the Tickler. She thought of the little boy who'd been hit in the face with the mace, of stupid old All-for-Joffrey, of Lommy Greenhands. *I was a sheep, and then I was a mouse, I couldn't do anything but hide.* Arya chewed her lip and tried to think when her courage had come back. *Jaqen made me brave again. He made me a ghost instead of a mouse.*

She had been avoiding the Lorathi since Weese's death. Chiswyck had been *easy*, anyone could push a man off the wallwalk, but Weese had raised that ugly spotted dog from a pup, and only some dark magic could have turned the animal against him. *Yoren found Jaqen*

in a black cell, the same as Rorge and Biter, she remembered. *Jaqen did something horrible and Yoren
knew, that's why he kept him in chains.* If the Lorathi
was a wizard, Rorge and Biter could be demons he called
up from some hell, not men at all.

Jaqen still owed her one death. In Old Nan's stories
about men who were given magic wishes by a grumkin,
you had to be especially careful with the third wish,
because it was the last. Chiswyck and Weese hadn't
been very important. *The last death has to count,* Arya
told herself every night when she whispered her names.
But now she wondered if that was truly the reason she
had hesitated. So long as she could kill with a whisper,
Arya need not be afraid of anyone . . . but once she
used up the last death, she would only be a mouse
again.

With Pinkeye awake, she dared not go back to her
bed. Not knowing where else to hide, she made for the
godswood. She liked the sharp smell of the pines and
sentinels, the feel of grass and dirt between her toes,
and the sound the wind made in the leaves. A slow little
stream meandered through the wood, and there was one
spot where it had eaten the ground away beneath a
deadfall.

There, beneath rotting wood and twisted splintered
branches, she found her hidden sword.

Gendry was too stubborn to make one for her, so she
had made her own by breaking the bristles off a broom.
Her blade was much too light and had no proper grip,
but she liked the sharp jagged splintery end. Whenever
she had a free hour she stole away to work at the drills
Syrio had taught her, moving barefoot over the fallen
leaves, slashing at branches and whacking down leaves.
Sometimes she even climbed the trees and danced
among the upper branches, her toes gripping the limbs
as she moved back and forth, teetering a little less every
day as her balance returned to her. Night was the best
time; no one ever bothered her at night.

Arya climbed. Up in the kingdom of the leaves, she
unsheathed and for a time forgot them all, Ser Amory

and the Mummers and her father's men alike, losing herself in the feel of rough wood beneath the soles of her feet and the *swish* of sword through air. A broken branch became Joffrey. She struck at it until it fell away. The queen and Ser Ilyn and Ser Meryn and the Hound were only leaves, but she killed them all as well, slashing them to wet green ribbons. When her arm grew weary, she sat with her legs over a high limb to catch her breath in the cool dark air, listening to the squeak of bats as they hunted. Through the leafy canopy she could see the bone-white branches of the heart tree. *It looks just like the one in Winterfell from here.* If only it had been . . . then when she climbed down she would have been home again, and maybe find her father sitting under the weirwood where he always sat.

Shoving her sword through her belt, she slipped down branch to branch until she was back on the ground. The light of the moon painted the limbs of the weirwood silvery white as she made her way toward it, but the five-pointed red leaves turned black by night. Arya stared at the face carved into its trunk. It was a terrible face, its mouth twisted, its eyes flaring and full of hate. Is that what a god looked like? Could gods be hurt, the same as people? *I should pray,* she thought suddenly.

Arya went to her knees. She wasn't sure how she should begin. She clasped her hands together. *Help me, you old gods,* she prayed silently. *Help me get those men out of the dungeon so we can kill Ser Amory, and bring me home to Winterfell. Make me a water dancer and a wolf and not afraid again, ever.*

Was that enough? Maybe she should pray aloud if she wanted the old gods to hear. Maybe she should pray longer. Sometimes her father had prayed a long time, she remembered. But the old gods had never helped him. Remembering that made her angry. "You should have saved him," she scolded the tree. "He prayed to you all the time. I don't care if you help me or not. I don't think you could even if you wanted to."

"Gods are not mocked, girl."

The voice startled her. She leapt to her feet and drew

her wooden sword. Jaqen H'ghar stood so still in the darkness that he seemed one of the trees. "A man comes to hear a name. One and two and then comes three. A man would have done."

Arya lowered the splintery point toward the ground. "How did you know I was here?"

"A man sees. A man hears. A man knows."

She regarded him suspiciously. Had the gods sent him? "How'd you make the dog kill Weese? Did you call Rorge and Biter up from hell? Is Jaqen H'ghar your true name?"

"Some men have many names. Weasel. Arry. *Arya.*"

She backed away from him, until she was pressed against the heart tree. "Did Gendry tell?"

"A man knows," he said again. "My lady of Stark."

Maybe the gods *had* sent him in answer to her prayers. "I need you to help me get those men out of the dungeons. That Glover and those others, all of them. We have to kill the guards and open the cell some-how—"

"A girl forgets," he said quietly. "Two she has had, three were owed. If a guard must die, she needs only speak his name."

"But *one* guard won't be enough, we need to kill them all to open the cell." Arya bit her lip hard to stop from crying. "I want you to save the northmen like I saved you."

He looked down at her pitilessly. "Three lives were snatched from a god. Three lives must be repaid. The gods are not mocked." His voice was silk and steel.

"I never mocked." She thought for a moment. "The name . . . can I name *anyone*? And you'll kill him?"

Jaqen H'ghar inclined his head. "A man has said."

"*Anyone?*" she repeated. "A man, a woman, a little baby, or Lord Tywin, or the High Septon, or your fa-ther?"

"A man's sire is long dead, but did he live, and did you know his name, he would die at your command."

"Swear it," Arya said. "Swear it by the gods."

"By all the gods of sea and air, and even him of fire, I

swear it." He placed a hand in the mouth of the weirwood. "By the seven new gods and the old gods beyond count, I swear it."

He has sworn. "Even if I named the king . . ."

"Speak the name, and death will come. On the morrow, at the turn of the moon, a year from this day, it will come. A man does not fly like a bird, but one foot moves and then another and one day a man is there, and a king dies." He knelt beside her, so they were face-to-face. "A girl whispers if she fears to speak aloud. Whisper it now. Is it *Joffrey?*"

Arya put her lips to his ear. "It's *Jaqen H'ghar.*"

Even in the burning barn, with walls of flame towering all around and him in chains, he had not seemed so distraught as he did now. "A girl . . . she makes a jest."

"You swore. The gods heard you swear."

"The gods did hear." There was a knife in his hand suddenly, its blade thin as her little finger. Whether it was meant for her or him, Arya could not say. "A girl will weep. A girl will lose her only friend."

"You're not my friend. A friend would *help* me." She stepped away from him, balanced on the balls of her feet in case he threw his knife. "I'd never kill a *friend.*"

Jaqen's smile came and went. "A girl might . . . name another name then, if a friend did help?"

"A girl might," she said. "If a friend did help."

The knife vanished. "Come."

"Now?" She had never thought he would act so quickly.

"A man hears the whisper of sand in a glass. A man will not sleep until a girl unsays a certain name. Now, evil child."

I'm not an evil child, she thought, *I am a direwolf, and the ghost in Harrenhal.* She put her broomstick back in its hiding place and followed him from the godswood.

Despite the hour, Harrenhal stirred with fitful life. Vargo Hoat's arrival had thrown off all the routines. Ox carts, oxen, and horses had all vanished from the yard,

but the bear cage was still there. It had been hung from
the arched span of the bridge that divided the outer and
middle wards, suspended on heavy chains, a few feet off
the ground. A ring of torches bathed the area in light.
Some of the boys from the stables were tossing stones
to make the bear roar and grumble. Across the ward,
light spilled through the door of the Barracks Hall, accompanied by the clatter of tankards and men calling
for more wine. A dozen voices took up a song in a guttural tongue strange to Arya's ears.

They're drinking and eating before they sleep, she realized. *Pinkeye would have sent to wake me, to help
with the serving. He'll know I'm not abed.* But likely he
was busy pouring for the Brave Companions and those
of Ser Amory's garrison who had joined them. The noise
they were making would be a good distraction.

"The hungry gods will feast on blood tonight, if a
man would do this thing," Jaqen said. "Sweet girl, kind
and gentle. Unsay one name and say another and cast
this mad dream aside."

"I won't."

"Just so." He seemed resigned. "The thing will be
done, but a girl must obey. A man has no time for talk."

"A girl will obey," Arya said. "What should I do?"

"A hundred men are hungry, they must be fed, the
lord commands hot broth. A girl must run to the kitchens and tell her pie boy."

"Broth," she repeated. "Where will you be?"

"A girl will help make broth, and wait in the kitchens
until a man comes for her. Go. Run."

Hot Pie was pulling his loaves from the ovens when
she burst into the kitchen, but he was no longer alone.
They'd woken the cooks to feed Vargo Hoat and his
Bloody Mummers. Serving men were carrying off baskets of Hot Pie's bread and tarts, the chief cook was
carving cold slices off a ham, spit boys were turning
rabbits while the pot girls basted them with honey,
women were chopping onions and carrots. "What do
you want, Weasel?" the chief cook asked when he saw
her.

"Broth," she announced. "My lord wants broth."

He jerked his carving knife at the black iron kettles hung over the flames. "What do you think that is? Though I'd soon as piss in it as serve it to that goat. Can't even let a man have a night's sleep." He spat. "Well, never you mind, run back and tell him a kettle can't be hurried."

"I'm to wait here until it's done."

"Then stay out of the way. Or better yet, make yourself of use. Run to the buttery; his goatship will be wanting butter and cheese. Wake up Pia and tell her she'd best be nimble for once, if she wants to keep both of her feet."

She ran as fast as she could. Pia was awake in the loft, moaning under one of the Mummers, but she slipped back into her clothes quick enough when she heard Arya shout. She filled six baskets with crocks of butter and big wedges of stinky cheese wrapped in cloth. "Here, help me with these," she told Arya.

"I can't. But you better hurry or Vargo Hoat will chop off your foot." She darted off before Pia could grab her. On the way back, she wondered why none of the captives had their hands or feet chopped off. Maybe Vargo Hoat was afraid to make Robb angry. Though he didn't seem the sort to be afraid of *anyone*.

Hot Pie was stirring the kettles with a long wooden spoon when Arya returned to the kitchens. She grabbed up a second spoon and started to help. For a moment she thought maybe she should tell him, but then she remembered the village and decided not to. *He'd only yield again.*

Then she heard the ugly sound of Rorge's voice. "*Cook,*" he shouted. "We'll take your bloody broth." Arya let go of the spoon in dismay. *I never told him to bring them.* Rorge wore his iron helmet, with the nasal that half hid his missing nose. Jaqen and Biter followed him into the kitchen.

"The bloody broth isn't bloody ready yet," the cook said. "It needs to simmer. We only now put in the onions and—"

"Shut your hole, or I'll shove a spit up your ass and we'll baste you for a turn or two. I said broth and I said now."

Hissing, Biter grabbed a handful of half-charred rabbit right off the spit, and tore into it with his pointed teeth while honey dripped between his fingers.

The cook was beaten. "Take your bloody broth, then, but if the goat asks why it tastes so thin, you tell him."

Biter licked the grease and honey off his fingers as Jaqen H'ghar donned a pair of heavy padded mitts. He gave a second pair to Arya. "A weasel will help." The broth was boiling hot, and the kettles were heavy. Arya and Jaqen wrestled one between them, Rorge carried one by himself, and Biter grabbed two more, hissing in pain when the handles burned his hands. Even so, he did not drop them. They lugged the kettles out of the kitchens and across the ward. Two guards had been posted at the door of the Widow's Tower. "What's this?" one said to Rorge.

"A pot of boiling piss, want some?"

Jaqen smiled disarmingly. "A prisoner must eat too."

"No one said nothing about—"

Arya cut him off. "It's for *them*, not you."

The second guard waved them past. "Bring it down, then."

Inside the door a winding stair led down to the dungeons. Rorge led the way, with Jaqen and Arya bringing up the rear. "A girl will stay out of the way," he told her.

The steps opened onto a dank stone vault, long, gloomy, and windowless. A few torches burned in sconces at the near end where a group of Ser Amory's guards sat around a scarred wooden table, talking and playing at tiles. Heavy iron bars separated them from where the captives were crowded together in the dark. The smell of the broth brought many up to the bars.

Arya counted eight guards. They smelled the broth as well. "There's the ugliest serving wench I ever saw," their captain said to Rorge. "What's in the kettle?"

"Your cock and balls. You want to eat or not?"

One of the guards had been pacing, one standing near the bars, a third sitting on the floor with his back to the wall, but the prospect of food drew all of them to the table.

"About bloody time they fed us."

"That onions I smell?"

"So where's the bread?"

"Fuck, we need bowls, cups, spoons—"

"No you don't." Rorge heaved the scalding hot broth across the table, full in their faces. Jaqen H'ghar did the same. Biter threw his kettles too, swinging them underarm so they spun across the dungeon, raining soup. One caught the captain in the temple as he tried to rise. He went down like a sack of sand and lay still. The rest were screaming in agony, praying, or trying to crawl off.

Arya pressed back against the wall as Rorge began to cut throats. Biter preferred to grab the men behind the head and under the chin and crack their necks with a single twist of his huge pale hands. Only one of the guards managed to get a blade out. Jaqen danced away from his slash, drew his own sword, drove the man back into a corner with a flurry of blows, and killed him with a thrust to the heart. The Lorathi brought the blade to Arya still red with heart's blood and wiped it clean on the front of her shift. "A girl should be bloody too. This is her work."

The key to the cell hung from a hook on the wall above the table. Rorge took it down and opened the door. The first man through was the lord with the mailed fist on his surcoat. "Well done," he said. "I am Robett Glover."

"My lord." Jaqen gave him a bow.

Once freed, the captives stripped the dead guards of their weapons and darted up the steps with steel in hand. Their fellows crowded after them, bare-handed. They went swiftly, and with scarcely a word. None of them seemed quite so badly wounded as they had when Vargo Hoat had marched them through the gates of Harrenhal. "This of the soup, that was clever," the man

Glover was saying. "I did not expect that. Was it Lord Hoat's idea?"

Rorge began to laugh. He laughed so hard that snot flew out the hole where his nose had been. Biter sat on top of one of the dead men, holding a limp hand as he gnawed at the fingers. Bones cracked between his teeth.

"Who are you men?" A crease appeared between Robett Glover's brows. "You were not with Hoat when he came to Lord Bolton's encampment. Are you of the Brave Companions?"

Rorge wiped the snot off his chin with the back of his hand. "We are now."

"This man has the honor to be Jaqen H'ghar, once of the Free City of Lorath. This man's discourteous companions are named Rorge and Biter. A lord will know which is Biter." He waved a hand toward Arya. "And here—"

"I'm Weasel," she blurted, before he could tell who she *really* was. She did not want her name said here, where Rorge might hear, and Biter, and all these others she did not know.

She saw Glover dismiss her. "Very well," he said. "Let's make an end to this bloody business."

When they climbed back up the winding stair, they found the door guards lying in pools of their own blood. Northmen were running across the ward. Arya heard shouts. The door of Barracks Hall burst open and a wounded man staggered out screaming. Three others ran after him and silenced him with spear and sword. There was fighting around the gatehouse as well. Rorge and Biter rushed off with Glover, but Jaqen H'ghar knelt beside Arya. "A girl does not understand?"

"Yes I do," she said, though she didn't, not truly.

The Lorathi must have seen it on her face. "A goat has no loyalty. Soon a wolf banner is raised here, I think. But first a man would hear a certain name unsaid."

"I take back the name." Arya chewed her lip. "Do I still have a third death?"

"A girl is greedy." Jaqen touched one of the dead

guards and showed her his bloody fingers. "Here is three and there is four and eight more lie dead below. The debt is paid."

"The debt is paid," Arya agreed reluctantly. She felt a little sad. Now she was just a mouse again.

"A god has his due. And now a man must die." A strange smile touched the lips of Jaqen H'ghar.

"Die?" she said, confused. What did he mean? "But I unsaid the name. You don't need to die now."

"I do. My time is done." Jaqen passed a hand down his face from forehead to chin, and where it went he *changed.* His cheeks grew fuller, his eyes closer; his nose hooked, a scar appeared on his right cheek where no scar had been before. And when he shook his head, his long straight hair, half red and half white, dissolved away to reveal a cap of tight black curls.

Arya's mouth hung open. "Who *are* you?" she whispered, too astonished to be afraid. "How did you *do* that? Was it hard?"

He grinned, revealing a shiny gold tooth. "No harder than taking a new name, if you know the way."

"Show me," she blurted. "I want to do it too."

"If you would learn, you must come with me."

Arya grew hesitant. "Where?"

"Far and away, across the narrow sea."

"I can't. I have to go home. To Winterfell."

"Then we must part," he said, "for I have duties too." He lifted her hand and pressed a small coin into her palm. "Here."

"What is it?"

"A coin of great value."

Arya bit it. It was so hard it could only be iron. "Is it worth enough to buy a horse?"

"It is not meant for the buying of horses."

"Then what good is it?"

"As well ask what good is life, what good is death? If the day comes when you would find me again, give that coin to any man from Braavos, and say these words to him—*valar morghulis.*"

"Valar morghulis," Arya repeated. It wasn't hard. Her

fingers closed tight over the coin. Across the yard, she could hear men dying. "Please don't go, Jaqen."

"Jaqen is as dead as Arry," he said sadly, "and I have promises to keep. *Valar morghulis*, Arya Stark. Say it again."

"*Valar morghulis*," she said once more, and the stranger in Jaqen's clothes bowed to her and stalked off through the darkness, cloak swirling. She was alone with the dead men. *They deserved to die*, Arya told herself, remembering all those Ser Amory Lorch had killed at the holdfast by the lake.

The cellars under Kingspyre were empty when she returned to her bed of straw. She whispered her names to her pillow, and when she was done she added, "*Valar morghulis*," in a small soft voice, wondering what it meant.

Come dawn, Pinkeye and the others were back, all but one boy who'd been killed in the fighting for no reason that anyone could say. Pinkeye went up alone to see how matters stood by light of day, complaining all the while that his old bones could not abide steps. When he returned, he told them that Harrenhal had been taken. "Them Bloody Mummers killed some of Ser Amory's lot in their beds, and the rest at table after they were good and drunk. The new lord will be here before the day's out, with his whole host. He's from the wild north up where that Wall is, and they say he's a hard one. This lord or that lord, there's still work to be done. Any foolery and I'll whip the skin off your back." He looked at Arya when he said that, but never said a word to her about where she had been the night before.

All morning she watched the Bloody Mummers strip the dead of their valuables and drag the corpses to the Flowstone Yard, where a pyre was laid to dispose of them. Shagwell the Fool hacked the heads off two dead knights and pranced about the castle swinging them by the hair and making them talk. "What did you die of?" one head asked. "Hot weasel soup," replied the second.

Arya was set to mopping up dried blood. No one said a word to her beyond the usual, but every so often she would notice people looking at her strangely. Robett Glover and the other men they'd freed must have talked about what had happened down in the dungeon, and then Shagwell and his stupid talking heads started in about the weasel soup. She would have told him to shut up, but she was scared to. The fool was half-mad, and she'd heard that he'd once killed a man for not laughing at one of his japes. *He better shut his mouth or I'll put him on my list with the rest*, she thought as she scrubbed at a reddish-brown stain.

It was almost evenfall when the new master of Harrenhal arrived. He had a plain face, beardless and ordinary, notable only for his queer pale eyes. Neither plump, thin, nor muscular, he wore black ringmail and a spotted pink cloak. The sigil on his banner looked like a man dipped in blood. "On your knees for the Lord of the Dreadfort!" shouted his squire, a boy no older than Arya, and Harrenhal knelt.

Vargo Hoat came forward. "My lord, Harrenhal ith yourth."

The lord gave answer, but too softly for Arya to hear. Robett Glover and Ser Aenys Frey, freshly bathed and clad in clean new doublets and cloaks, came up to join them. After some brief talk, Ser Aenys led them over to Rorge and Biter. Arya was surprised to see them still here; somehow she would have expected them to vanish when Jaqen did. Arya heard the harsh sound of Rorge's voice, but not what he was saying. Then Shagwell pounced on her, dragging her out across the yard. "My lord, my lord," he sang, tugging at her wrist, "here's the weasel who made the soup!"

"Let *go*," Arya said, wriggling out of his grasp.

The lord regarded her. Only his eyes moved; they were very pale, the color of ice. "How old are you, child?"

She had to think for a moment to remember. "Ten."

"Ten, *my lord*," he reminded her. "Are you fond of animals?"

"Some kinds. My lord."

A thin smile twitched across his lips. "But not lions, it would seem. Nor manticores."

She did not know what to say to that, so she said nothing.

"They tell me you are called Weasel. That will not serve. What name did your mother give you?"

She bit her lip, groping for another name. Lommy had called her Lumpyhead, Sansa used Horseface, and her father's men once dubbed her Arya Underfoot, but she did not think any of those were the sort of name he wanted.

"Nymeria," she said. "Only she called me Nan for short."

"You will call me *my lord* when you speak to me, Nan," the lord said mildly. "You are too young to be a Brave Companion, I think, and of the wrong sex. Are you afraid of leeches, child?"

"They're only leeches. My lord."

"My squire could take a lesson from you, it would seem. Frequent leechings are the secret of a long life. A man must purge himself of bad blood. You will do, I think. For so long as I remain at Harrenhal, Nan, you shall be my cupbearer, and serve me at table and in chambers."

This time she knew better than to say that she'd sooner work in the stables. "Yes, your lord. I mean, my lord."

The lord waved a hand. "Make her presentable," he said to no one in particular, "and make certain she knows how to pour wine without spilling it." Turning away, he lifted a hand and said, "Lord Hoat, see to those banners above the gatehouse."

Four Brave Companions climbed to the ramparts and hauled down the lion of Lannister and Ser Amory's own black manticore. In their place they raised the flayed man of the Dreadfort and the direwolf of Stark. And that evening, a page named Nan poured wine for Roose Bolton and Vargo Hoat as they stood on the gallery, watching the Brave Companions parade Ser Amory Lorch naked through the middle ward. Ser Amory pleaded and sobbed and clung to the legs of his captors, until Rorge pulled him loose, and Shagwell kicked him down into the bear pit.

The bear is all in black, Arya thought. *Like Yoren.* She filled Roose Bolton's cup, and did not spill a drop.

DAENERYS

In this city of splendors, Dany had expected the House of the Undying Ones to be the most splendid of all, but she emerged from her palanquin to behold a grey and ancient ruin.

Long and low, without towers or windows, it coiled like a stone serpent through a grove of black-barked trees whose inky blue leaves made the stuff of the sorcerous drink the Qartheen called *shade of the evening*. No other buildings stood near. Black tiles covered the palace roof, many fallen or broken; the mortar between the stones was dry and crumbling. She understood now why Xaro Xhoan Daxos called it the Palace of Dust. Even Drogon seemed disquieted by the sight of it. The black dragon *hissed*, smoke seeping out between his sharp teeth.

"Blood of my blood," Jhogo said in Dothraki, "this is an evil place, a haunt of ghosts and *maegi*. See how it drinks the morning sun? Let us go before it drinks us as well."

Ser Jorah Mormont came up beside them. "What power can they have if they live in *that*?"

"Heed the wisdom of those who love you best," said Xaro Xhoan Daxos, lounging inside the palanquin. "Warlocks are bitter creatures who eat dust and drink of shadows. They will give you naught. They have naught to give."

Aggo put a hand on his *arakh*. "*Khaleesi*, it is said that many go into the Palace of Dust, but few come out."

"It is said," Jhogo agreed.

"We are blood of your blood," said Aggo, "sworn to live and die as you do. Let us walk with you in this dark place, to keep you safe from harm."

"Some places even a *khal* must walk alone," Dany said.

"Take me, then," Ser Jorah urged. "The risk—"

"Queen Daenerys must enter alone, or not at all." The warlock Pyat Pree stepped out from under the trees. *Has he been there all along?* Dany wondered. "Should she turn away now, the doors of wisdom shall be closed to her forevermore."

"My pleasure barge awaits, even now," Xaro Xhoan Daxos called out. "Turn away from this folly, most stubborn of queens. I have flutists who will soothe your troubled soul with sweet music, and a small girl whose tongue will make you sigh and melt."

Ser Jorah Mormont gave the merchant prince a sour look. "Your Grace, remember Mirri Maz Duur."

"I do," Dany said, suddenly decided. "I remember that she had knowledge. And she was only a *maegi*."

Pyat Pree smiled thinly. "The child speaks as sagely as a crone. Take my arm, and let me lead you."

"I am no child." Dany took his arm nonetheless.

It was darker than she would have thought under the black trees, and the way was longer. Though the path seemed to run straight from the street to the door of the palace, Pyat Pree soon turned aside. When she questioned him, the warlock said only, "The front way leads in, but never out again. Heed my words, my queen. The House of the Undying Ones was not made for mortal men. If you value your soul, take care and do just as I tell you."

"I will do as you say," Dany promised.

"When you enter, you will find yourself in a room with four doors: the one you have come through and three others. Take the door to your right. Each time, the door to your right. If you should come upon a stairwell, climb. Never go down, and never take any door but the first door to your right."

"The door to my right," Dany repeated. "I understand. And when I leave, the opposite?"

"By no means," Pyat Pree said. "Leaving and coming, it is the same. Always up. Always the door to your right. Other doors may open to you. Within, you will see many things that disturb you. Visions of loveliness and visions of horror, wonders and terrors. Sights and sounds of days gone by and days to come and days that never were. Dwellers and servitors may speak to you as you go. Answer or ignore them as you choose, but *enter no room* until you reach the audience chamber."

"I understand."

"When you come to the chamber of the Undying, be patient. Our little lives are no more than a flicker of a moth's wing to them. Listen well, and write each word upon your heart."

When they reached the door—a tall oval mouth, set in a wall fashioned in the likeness of a human face—the smallest dwarf Dany had ever seen was waiting on the threshold. He stood no higher than her knee, his faced pinched and pointed, snoutish, but he was dressed in delicate livery of purple and blue, and his tiny pink hands held a silver tray. Upon it rested a slender crystal glass filled with a thick blue liquid: *shade of the evening*, the wine of warlocks. "Take and drink," urged Pyat Pree.

"Will it turn my lips blue?"

"One flute will serve only to unstop your ears and dissolve the caul from off your eyes, so that you may hear and see the truths that will be laid before you."

Dany raised the glass to her lips. The first sip tasted like ink and spoiled meat, foul, but when she swallowed it seemed to come to life within her. She could feel tendrils spreading through her chest, like fingers of fire coiling around her heart, and on her tongue was a taste like honey and anise and cream, like mother's milk and Drogo's seed, like red meat and hot blood and molten gold. It was all the tastes she had ever known, and none of them . . . and then the glass was empty.

"Now you may enter," said the warlock. Dany put the glass back on the servitor's tray, and went inside.

She found herself in a stone anteroom with four doors, one on each wall. With never a hesitation, she went to the door on her right and stepped through. The second room was a twin to the first. Again she turned to the right-hand door. When she pushed it open she faced yet another small antechamber with four doors. *I am in the presence of sorcery.*

The fourth room was oval rather than square and walled in worm-eaten wood in place of stone. Six passages led out from it in place of four. Dany chose the rightmost, and entered a long, dim, high-ceilinged hall. Along the right hand was a row of torches burning with a smoky orange light, but the only doors were to her left. Drogon unfolded wide black wings and beat the stale air. He flew twenty feet before thudding to an undignified crash. Dany strode after him.

The mold-eaten carpet under her feet had once been gorgeously colored, and whorls of gold could still be seen in the fabric, glinting broken amidst the faded grey and mottled green. What remained served to muffle her footfalls, but that was not all to the good. Dany could hear sounds within the walls, a faint scurrying and scrabbling that made her think of rats. Drogon heard them too. His head moved as he followed the sounds, and when they stopped he gave an angry scream. Other sounds, even more disturbing, came through some of the closed doors. One shook and thumped, as if someone were trying to break through. From another came a dissonant piping that made the dragon lash his tail wildly from side to side. Dany hurried quickly past.

Not all the doors were closed. *I will not look,* Dany told herself, but the temptation was too strong.

In one room, a beautiful woman sprawled naked on the floor while four little men crawled over her. They had rattish pointed faces and tiny pink hands, like the servitor who had brought her the glass of shade. One was pumping between her thighs. Another savaged her breasts, worrying at the nipples with his wet red mouth, tearing and chewing.

Farther on she came upon a feast of corpses. Savagely slaughtered, the feasters lay strewn across overturned chairs and hacked trestle tables, asprawl in pools of congealing blood. Some had lost limbs, even heads. Severed hands clutched bloody cups, wooden spoons, roast fowl, heels of bread. In a throne above them sat a dead man with the head of a wolf. He wore an iron crown and held a leg of lamb in one hand as a king might hold a scepter, and his eyes followed Dany with mute appeal.

She fled from him, but only as far as the next open door. *I know this room,* she thought. She remembered those great wooden beams and the carved animal faces that adorned them. And there outside the window, a lemon tree! The sight of it made her heart ache with longing. *It is the house with the red door, the house in Braavos.* No sooner had she thought it than old Ser Willem came into the room, leaning heavily on his stick. "Little princess, there you are," he said in his gruff kind voice. "Come," he said, "come to me, my lady, you're home now, you're safe now." His big wrinkled hand reached for her, soft as old leather, and Dany wanted to take it and hold it and kiss it, she wanted that as much as she had ever wanted anything. Her foot edged forward, and then she thought, *He's dead, he's dead, the sweet old bear, he died a long time ago.* She backed away and ran.

The long hall went on and on and on, with endless doors to her left and only torches to her right. She ran past more doors than she could count, closed doors and open ones, doors of wood and doors of iron, carved doors and plain ones, doors with pulls and doors with locks and doors with knockers. Drogon lashed against her back, urging her on, and Dany ran until she could run no more.

Finally a great pair of bronze doors appeared to her left, grander than the rest. They swung open as she neared, and she had to stop and look. Beyond loomed a cavernous stone hall, the largest she had ever seen. The skulls of dead dragons looked down from its walls. Upon a towering barbed throne sat an old man in rich robes, an old man with dark eyes and long silver-grey hair. "Let him be king over charred bones and cooked meat," he said to a man below him. "Let him be the king of ashes." Drogon shrieked, his claws digging through silk and skin, but the king on his throne never heard, and Dany moved on.

Viserys, was her first thought the next time she paused, but a second glance told her otherwise. The man had her brother's hair, but he was taller, and his eyes were a dark indigo rather than lilac. "Aegon," he said to a woman nursing a newborn babe in a great wooden bed. "What better name for a king?"

"Will you make a song for him?" the woman asked.

"He has a song," the man replied. "He is the prince that was promised, and his is the song of ice and fire." He looked up when he said it and his eyes met Dany's, and it seemed as if he saw her standing there beyond the door. "There must be one more," he said, though whether he was speaking to her or the woman in the bed she could not say. "The dragon has three heads." He went to the window seat, picked up a harp, and ran his fingers lightly over its silvery strings. Sweet sadness filled the room as man and wife and babe faded like the morning mist, only the music lingering behind to speed her on her way.

It seemed as though she walked for another hour before the long hall finally ended in a steep stone stair, descending into darkness. Every door, open or closed, had been to her left. Dany looked back behind her. The torches were going out, she realized with a start of fear. Perhaps twenty still burned. Thirty at most. One more guttered out even as she watched, and the darkness came a little farther down the hall, creeping toward her. And as she listened it seemed as if she heard something else coming, shuffling and dragging itself slowly along the faded carpet. Terror filled her. She could not go back and she was afraid to stay here, but how could she go on? There was no door on her right, and the steps went down, not up.

Yet another torch went out as she stood pondering, and the sounds grew faintly louder. Drogon's long neck snaked out and he opened his mouth to scream, steam rising from between his teeth. *He hears it too.* Dany turned to the blank wall once more, but there was nothing. *Could there be a secret door, a door I cannot see?* Another torch went out. Another. *The first door on the right, he said, always the first door on the right. The first door on the right . . .*

It came to her suddenly. *. . . is the last door on the left!*

She flung herself through. Beyond was another small room with four doors. To the right she went, and to the right, and to the right, and to the right, and to the right, and to the right, and to the right, until she was dizzy and out of breath once more.

When she stopped, she found herself in yet another dank stone chamber . . . but this time the door opposite was round, shaped like an open mouth, and Pyat Pree stood outside in the grass beneath the trees. "Can it be that the Undying are done with you so soon?" he asked in disbelief when he saw her.

"So soon?" she said, confused. "I've walked for hours, and still not found them."

"You have taken a wrong turning. Come, I will lead you." Pyat Pree held out his hand.

Dany hesitated. There was a door to her right, still closed . . .

"That's not the way," Pyat Pree said firmly, his blue

lips prim with disapproval. "The Undying Ones will not wait forever."

"Our little lives are no.more than a flicker of a moth's wing to them," Dany said, remembering.

"Stubborn child. You will be lost, and never found."

She walked away from him, to the door on the right.

"No," Pyat screeched. "No, to me, come to me, to *meeeeeee*." His face crumbled inward, changing to something pale and wormlike.

Dany left him behind, entering a stairwell. She began to climb. Before long her legs were aching. She recalled that the House of the Undying Ones had seemed to have no towers.

Finally the stair opened. To her right, a set of wide wooden doors had been thrown open. They were fashioned of ebony and weirwood, the black and white grains swirling and twisting in strange interwoven patterns. They were very beautiful, yet somehow frightening. *The blood of the dragon must not be afraid.* Dany said a quick prayer, begging the Warrior for courage and the Dothraki horse god for strength. She made herself walk forward.

Beyond the doors was a great hall and a splendor of wizards. Some wore sumptuous robes of ermine, ruby velvet, and cloth of gold. Others fancied elaborate armor studded with gemstones, or tall pointed hats speckled with stars. There were women among them, dressed in gowns of surpassing loveliness. Shafts of sunlight slanted through windows of stained glass, and the air was alive with the most beautiful music she had ever heard.

A kingly man in rich robes rose when he saw her, and smiled. "Daenerys of House Targaryen, be welcome. Come and share the food of forever. We are the Undying of Qarth."

"Long have we awaited you," said a woman beside him, clad in rose and silver. The breast she had left bare in the Qartheen fashion was as perfect as a breast could be.

"We knew you were to come to us," the wizard king

said. "A thousand years ago we knew, and have been waiting all this time. We sent the comet to show you the way."

"We have knowledge to share with you," said a warrior in shining emerald armor, "and magic weapons to arm you with. You have passed every trial. Now come and sit with us, and all your questions shall be answered."

She took a step forward. But then Drogon leapt from her shoulder. He flew to the top of the ebony-and-weirwood door, perched there, and began to bite at the carved wood.

"A willful beast," laughed a handsome young man. "Shall we teach you the secret speech of dragonkind? Come, come."

Doubt seized her. The great door was so heavy it took all of Dany's strength to budge it, but finally it began to move. Behind was another door, hidden. It was old grey wood, splintery and plain . . . but it stood to the right of the door through which she'd entered. The wizards were beckoning her with voices sweeter than song. She ran from them, Drogon flying back down to her. Through the narrow door she passed, into a chamber awash in gloom.

A long stone table filled this room. Above it floated a human heart, swollen and blue with corruption, yet still alive. It beat, a deep ponderous throb of sound, and each pulse sent out a wash of indigo light. The figures around the table were no more than blue shadows. As Dany walked to the empty chair at the foot of the table, they did not stir, nor speak, nor turn to face her. There was no sound but the slow, deep beat of the rotting heart.

. . . *mother of dragons* . . . came a voice, part whisper and part moan . . . *dragons* . . . *dragons* . . . *dragons* . . . other voices echoed in the gloom. Some were male and some female. One spoke with the timbre of a child. The floating heart pulsed from dimness to darkness. It was hard to summon the will to speak, to recall the words she had practiced so assiduously. "I am Daenerys Stormborn of House Targaryen, Queen of the Seven Kingdoms of Westeros." *Do they hear me? Why don't they move?* She sat, folding her hands in her lap. "Grant me your counsel, and speak to me with the wisdom of those who have conquered death."

Through the indigo murk, she could make out the wizened features of the Undying One to her right, an old old man, wrinkled and hairless. His flesh was a ripe violet-blue, his lips and nails bluer still, so dark they were almost black. Even the whites of his eyes were blue. They stared unseeing at the ancient woman on the opposite side of the table, whose gown of pale silk had rotted on her body. One withered breast was left bare in the Qartheen manner, to show a pointed blue nipple hard as leather.

She is not breathing. Dany listened to the silence. *None of them are breathing, and they do not move, and those eyes see nothing. Could it be that the Undying Ones were dead?*

Her answer was a whisper as thin as a mouse's whisker. . . . *we   live* . . . *live* . . . *live* . . . it sounded. Myriad other voices whispered echoes. . . . *and know* . . . *know* . . . *know* . . . *know* . . .

"I have come for the gift of truth," Dany said. "In the long hall, the things I saw . . . were they true visions, or lies? Past things, or things to come? What did they mean?"

. . . *the shape of shadows* . . . *morrows not yet made* . . . *drink from the cup of ice* . . . *drink from the cup of fire* . . .

. . . *mother of dragons* . . . *child of three* . . .

"Three?" She did not understand.

. . . *three heads has the dragon* . . . the ghost chorus yammered inside her skull with never a lip moving, never a breath stirring the still blue air. . . . *mother of dragons* . . . *child of storm* . . . The whispers became a swirling song. . . . *three fires must you light* . . . *one for life and one for death and one to love* . . . Her own heart was beating in unison to the one that floated before her, blue and corrupt . . . *three mounts must you ride . . . one to bed and one to dread and one to love* . . . The voices were growing louder, she realized, and it seemed her heart was slowing, and even her breath. . . . *three treasons will you know . . . once for blood and once for gold and once for love* . . .

"I don't . . ." Her voice was no more than a whisper, almost as faint as theirs. What was happening to her? "I don't understand," she said, more loudly. Why was it so hard to talk here? "Help me. Show me."

. . . *help her* . . . the whispers mocked. . . . *show her* . . .

Then phantoms shivered through the murk, images in indigo. Viserys screamed as the molten gold ran down his cheeks and filled his mouth. A tall lord with copper skin and silver-gold hair stood beneath the banner of a fiery stallion, a burning city behind him. Rubies flew like drops of blood from the chest of a dying prince, and he sank to his knees in the water and with his last breath murmured a woman's name. . . . *mother of dragons, daughter of death* . . . Glowing like sunset, a red sword was raised in the hand of a blue-eyed king who cast no shadow. A cloth dragon swayed on poles amidst a cheering crowd. From a smoking tower, a great stone beast took wing, breathing shadow fire. . . . *mother of dragons, slayer of lies* . . . Her silver was trotting through the grass, to a darkling stream beneath a sea of stars. A corpse stood at the prow of a ship, eyes bright in his dead face, grey lips smiling sadly. A blue flower grew from a chink in a wall of ice, and filled the air with sweetness. . . . *mother of dragons, bride of fire* . . .

Faster and faster the visions came, one after the other, until it seemed as if the very air had come alive. Shadows whirled and danced inside a tent, boneless and terrible. A little girl ran barefoot toward a big house with a red door. Mirri Maz Duur shrieked in the flames, a dragon bursting from her brow. Behind a silver horse the bloody corpse of a naked man bounced and dragged. A white lion ran through grass taller than a man. Beneath the Mother of Mountains, a line of naked crones crept from a great lake and knelt shivering before her, their grey heads bowed. Ten thousand slaves lifted blood-stained hands as she raced by on her silver, riding like the wind. *"Mother!"* they cried. *"Mother, mother!"* They were reaching for her, touching her, tugging at her cloak, the hem of her skirt, her foot, her leg, her breast. They wanted her, needed her, the fire, the life, and Dany gasped and opened her arms to give herself to them . . .

But then black wings buffeted her round the head, and a scream of fury cut the indigo air, and suddenly the visions were gone, ripped away, and Dany's gasp turned to horror. The Undying were all around her, blue and cold, whispering as they reached for her, pulling, strok-ing, tugging at her clothes, touching her with their dry cold hands, twining their fingers through her hair. All the strength had left her limbs. She could not move. Even her heart had ceased to beat. She felt a hand on her bare breast, twisting her nipple. Teeth found the soft skin of her throat. A mouth descended on one eye, lick-ing, sucking, *biting* . . .

Then indigo turned to orange, and whispers turned to screams. Her heart was pounding, racing, the hands and mouths were gone, heat washed over her skin, and Dany blinked at a sudden glare. Perched above her, the dragon spread his wings and tore at the terrible dark heart, ripping the rotten flesh to ribbons, and when his head snapped forward, fire flew from his open jaws, bright and hot. She could hear the shrieks of the Undy-ing as they burned, their high thin papery voices crying out in tongues long dead. Their flesh was crumbling parchment, their bones dry wood soaked in tallow. They danced as the flames consumed them; they stag-gered and writhed and spun and raised blazing hands on high, their fingers bright as torches.

Dany pushed herself to her feet and bulled through them. They were light as air, no more than husks, and they fell at a touch. The whole room was ablaze by the time she reached the door. *"Drogon,"* she called, and he flew to her through the fire.

Outside a long dim passageway stretched serpentine before her, lit by the flickering orange glare from behind. Dany ran, searching for a door, a door to her right, a door to her left, any door, but there was nothing, only twisty stone walls, and a floor that seemed to move slowly under her feet, writhing as if to trip her. She kept her feet and ran faster, and suddenly the door was there ahead of her, a door like an open mouth.

When she spilled out into the sun, the bright light made her stumble. Pyat Pree was gibbering in some unknown tongue and hopping from one foot to the other. When Dany looked behind her, she saw thin tendrils of smoke forcing their way through cracks in the ancient stone walls of the Palace of Dust, and rising from between the black tiles of the roof.

Howling curses, Pyat Pree drew a knife and danced toward her, but Drogon flew at his face. Then she heard the *crack* of Jhogo's whip, and never was a sound so sweet. The knife went flying, and an instant later Rakharo was slamming Pyat to the ground. Ser Jorah Mormont knelt beside Dany in the cool green grass and put his arm around her shoulder.

TYRION

I f you die stupidly, I'm going to feed your body to the goats," Tyrion threatened as the first load of Stone Crows pushed off from the quay.

Shagga laughed. "The Halfman has no goats."

"I'll get some just for you."

Dawn was breaking, and pale ripples of light shimmered on the surface of the river, shattering under the poles and re-forming when the ferry had passed. Timett had taken his Burned Men into the kingswood two days before. Yesterday the Black Ears and Moon Brothers followed, today the Stone Crows.

"Whatever you do, don't try and fight a battle," Tyrion said. "Strike at their camps and baggage train. Ambush their scouts and hang the bodies from trees ahead of their line of march, loop around and cut down stragglers. I want night attacks, so many and so sudden that they'll be afraid to sleep—"

Shagga laid a hand atop Tyrion's head. "All this I learned from Dolf son of Holger before my beard had grown. This is the way of war in the Mountains of the Moon.''

"The kingswood is not the Mountains of the Moon, and you won't be fighting Milk Snakes and Painted Dogs. And *listen* to the guides I'm sending, they know this wood as well as you know your mountains. Heed their counsel and they'll serve you well.''

"Shagga will listen to the Halfman's pets,'' the clansman promised solemnly. And then it was time for him to lead his garron onto the ferry. Tyrion watched them push off and pole out toward the center of the Blackwater. He felt a queer twinge in the pit of his stomach as Shagga faded in the morning mist. He was going to feel naked without his clansmen.

He still had Bronn's hirelings, near eight hundred of them now, but sellswords were notoriously fickle. Tyrion had done what he could to buy their continued loyalty, promising Bronn and a dozen of his best men lands and knighthoods when the battle was won. They'd drunk his wine, laughed at his jests, and called each other *ser* until they were all staggering . . . all but Bronn himself, who'd only smiled that insolent dark smile of his and afterward said, "They'll kill for that knighthood, but don't ever think they'll die for it.''

Tyrion had no such delusion.

The gold cloaks were almost as uncertain a weapon. Six thousand men in the City Watch, thanks to Cersei, but only a quarter of them could be relied upon. "There's few out-and-out traitors, though there's some, even your spider hasn't found them all,'' Bywater had warned him. "But there's hundreds greener than spring grass, men who joined for bread and ale and safety. No man likes to look craven in the sight of his fellows, so they'll fight brave enough at the start, when it's all warhorns and blowing banners. But if the battle looks to be going sour they'll break, and they'll break bad. The first man to throw down his spear and run will have a thousand more trodding on his heels.''

To be sure, there were seasoned men in the City Watch, the core of two thousand who'd gotten their gold cloaks from Robert, not Cersei. Yet even those . . . a watchman was not truly a soldier, Lord Tywin Lannister had been fond of saying. Of knights and squires and men-at-arms, Tyrion had no more than three hundred. Soon enough, he must test the truth of another of his father's sayings: One man on a wall was worth ten beneath it.

Bronn and the escort were waiting at the foot of the quay, amidst swarming beggars, strolling whores, and fishwives crying the catch. The fishwives did more business than all the rest combined. Buyers flocked around the barrels and stalls to haggle over winkles, clams, and river pike. With no other food coming into the city, the price of fish was ten times what it had been before the war, and still rising. Those who had coin came to the riverfront each morning and each evening, in hopes of bringing home an eel or a pot of red crabs; those who did not slipped between the stalls hoping to steal, or stood gaunt and forlorn beneath the walls.

The gold cloaks cleared a path through the press, shoving people aside with the shafts of their spears. Tyrion ignored the muttered curses as best he could. A fish came sailing out of the crowd, slimy and rotten. It landed at his feet and flew to pieces. He stepped over it gingerly and climbed into his saddle. Children with swollen bellies were already fighting over pieces of the stinking fish.

Mounted, he gazed along the riverfront. Hammers rang in the morning air as carpenters swarmed over the Mud Gate, extending wooden hoardings from the battlements. Those were coming well. He was a deal less pleased by the clutter of ramshackle structures that had been allowed to grow up behind the quays, attaching themselves to the city walls like barnacles on the hull of a ship; bait shacks and pot-shops, warehouses, merchants' stalls, alehouses, the cribs where the cheaper sort of whores spread their legs. *It has to go, every bit of it.* As it was, Stannis would hardly need scaling ladders to storm the walls.

He called Bronn to his side. "Assemble a hundred

men and burn everything you see here between the water's edge and the city walls." He waved his stubby fingers, taking in all the waterfront squalor. "I want nothing left standing, do you understand?"

The black-haired sellsword turned his head, considering the task. "Them as own all this won't like that much."

"I never imagined they would. So be it; they'll have something else to curse the evil monkey demon for."

"Some may fight."

"See that they lose."

"What do we do with those that live here?"

"Let them have a reasonable time to remove their property, and then move them out. Try not to kill any of them, they're not the enemy. And no more rapes! Keep your men in line, damn it."

"They're sellswords, not septons," said Bronn. "Next you'll be telling me you want them sober."

"It couldn't hurt."

Tyrion only wished he could as easily make city walls twice as tall and three times as thick. Though perhaps it did not matter. Massive walls and tall towers had not saved Storm's End, nor Harrenhal, nor even Winterfell.

He remembered Winterfell as he had last seen it. Not as grotesquely huge as Harrenhal, nor as solid and impregnable to look at as Storm's End, yet there had been a great strength in those stones, a sense that within those walls a man might feel safe. The news of the castle's fall had come as a wrenching shock. "The gods give with one hand and take with the other," he muttered under his breath when Varys told him. They had given the Starks Harrenhal and taken Winterfell, a dismal exchange.

No doubt he should be rejoicing. Robb Stark would have to turn north now. If he could not defend his own home and hearth, he was no sort of king at all. It meant reprieve for the west, for House Lannister, and yet . . .

Tyrion had only the vaguest memory of Theon Greyjoy from his time with the Starks. A callow youth, always smiling, skilled with a bow; it was hard to imagine him as Lord of Winterfell. The Lord of Winterfell would always be a Stark.

He remembered their godswood; the tall sentinels armored in their grey-green needles, the great oaks, the hawthorn and ash and soldier pines, and at the center the heart tree standing like some pale giant frozen in time. He could almost smell the place, earthy and brooding, the smell of centuries, and he remembered how dark the wood had been even by day. *That wood was Winterfell. It was the north. I never felt so out of place as I did when I walked there, so much an unwelcome intruder.* He wondered if the Greyjoys would feel it too. The castle might well be theirs, but never that godswood. Not in a year, or ten, or fifty.

Tyrion Lannister walked his horse slowly toward the Mud Gate. *Winterfell is nothing to you,* he reminded himself. *Be glad the place has fallen, and look to your own walls.* The gate was open. Inside, three great trebuchets stood side by side in the market square, peering over the battlements like three huge birds. Their throwing arms were made from the trunks of old oaks, and banded with iron to keep them from splitting. The gold cloaks had named them the Three Whores, because they'd be giving Lord Stannis such a lusty welcome. *Or so we hope.*

Tyrion put his heels into his horse and trotted through the Mud Gate, breasting the human tide. Once beyond the Whores, the press grew thinner and the street opened up around him.

The ride back to the Red Keep was uneventful, but at the Tower of the Hand he found a dozen angry trader captains waiting in his audience chamber to protest the seizure of their ships. He gave them a sincere apology and promised compensation once the war was done. That did little to appease them. "What if you should lose, my lord?" one Braavosi asked.

"Then apply to King Stannis for your compensation."

By the time he rid himself of them, bells were ringing and Tyrion knew he would be late for the installation. He waddled across the yard almost at a run and crowded into the back of the castle sept as Joffrey fastened white silk cloaks about the shoulders of the two newest members of his Kingsguard. The rite seemed to require that everyone stand, so Tyrion saw nothing but a wall of courtly arses. On the other hand, once the new High Septon was finished leading the two knights through their solemn vows and anointing them in the names of the Seven, he would be well positioned to be first out the doors.

He approved of his sister's choice of Ser Balon Swann to take the place of the slain Preston Greenfield. The Swanns were Marcher lords, proud, powerful, and cautious. Pleading illness, Lord Gulian Swann had remained in his castle, taking no part in the war, but his eldest son had ridden with Renly and now Stannis, while Balon, the younger, served at King's Landing. If he'd had a third son, Tyrion suspected he'd be off with Robb Stark. It was not perhaps the most honorable course, but it showed good sense; whoever won the Iron Throne, the Swanns intended to survive. In addition to being well born, young Ser Balon was valiant, courtly, and skilled at arms; good with a lance, better with a morningstar, superb with the bow. He would serve with honor and courage.

Alas, Tyrion could not say the same for Cersei's second choice. Ser Osmund Kettleblack *looked* formidable enough. He stood six feet and six inches, most of it sinew and muscle, and his hook nose, bushy eyebrows, and spade-shaped brown beard gave his face a fierce aspect, so long as he did not smile. Lowborn, no more than a hedge knight, Kettleblack was utterly dependent on Cersei for his advancement, which was doubtless why she'd picked him. "Ser Osmund is as loyal as he is brave," she'd told Joffrey when she put forward his name. It was true, unfortunately. The good Ser Osmund had been selling her secrets to Bronn since the day she'd hired him, but Tyrion could scarcely *tell* her that.

He supposed he ought not complain. The appointment gave him another ear close to the king, unbeknownst to his sister. And even if Ser Osmund proved an utter craven, he would be no worse than Ser Boros Blount, currently residing in a dungeon at Rosby. Ser Boros had been escorting Tommen and Lord Gyles when Ser Jacelyn Bywater and his gold cloaks had surprised them, and had yielded up his charge with an alacrity that would have enraged old Ser Barristan Selmy as much as it did Cersei; a knight of the Kingsguard was supposed to die in defense of the king and royal family. His sister had insisted that Joffrey strip Blount of his white cloak on the grounds of treason and cowardice. *And now she replaces him with another man just as hollow.*

The praying, vowing, and anointing seemed to take most of the morning. Tyrion's legs soon began to ache. He shifted his weight from one foot to the other, restless. Lady Tanda stood several rows up, he saw, but her daughter was not with her. He had been half hoping to catch a glimpse of Shae. Varys said she was doing well, but he would prefer to see for himself.

"Better a lady's maid than a pot girl," Shae had said when Tyrion told her the eunuch's scheme. "Can I take my belt of silver flowers and my gold collar with the black diamonds you said looked like my eyes? I won't wear them if you say I shouldn't."

Loath as he was to disappoint her, Tyrion had to point out that while Lady Tanda was by no means a clever woman, even she might wonder if her daughter's bedmaid seemed to own more jewelry than her daughter. "Choose two or three dresses, no more," he commanded her. "Good wool, no silk, no samite, and no fur. The rest I'll keep in my own chambers for when you visit me." It was not the answer Shae had wanted, but at least she was safe.

When the investiture was finally done Joffrey marched out between Ser Balon and Ser Osmund in their new white cloaks, while Tyrion lingered for a word with the new High Septon (who was *his* choice, and wise enough to know who put the honey on his bread). "I want the gods on our side," Tyrion told him bluntly. "Tell them that Stannis has vowed to burn the Great Sept of Baelor."

"Is it true, my lord?" asked the High Septon, a small, shrewd man with a wispy white beard and wizened face.

Tyrion shrugged. "It may be. Stannis burned the gods-wood at Storm's End as an offering to the Lord of Light. If he'd offend the old gods, why should he spare the new? Tell them that. Tell them that any man who thinks to give aid to the usurper betrays the gods as well as his rightful king."

"I shall, my lord. And I shall command them to pray for the health of the king and his Hand as well."

Hallyne the Pyromancer was waiting on him when Tyrion returned to his solar, and Maester Frenken had brought messages. He let the alchemist wait a little longer while he read what the ravens had brought him. There was an old letter from Doran Martell, warning him that Storm's End had fallen, and a much more in-triguing one from Balon Greyjoy on Pyke, who styled himself *King of the Isles and the North*. He invited King Joffrey to send an envoy to the Iron Islands to fix the borders between their realms and discuss a possible alli-ance.

Tyrion read the letter three times and set it aside. Lord Balon's longships would have been a great help against the fleet sailing up from Storm's End, but they were thousands of leagues away on the wrong side of Westeros, and Tyrion was far from certain that he wanted to give away half the realm. *Perhaps I should spill this one in Cersei's lap, or take it to the council.*

Only then did he admit Hallyne with the latest tallies from the alchemists. "This cannot be true," said Tyrion as he pored over the ledgers. "Almost thirteen thousand jars? Do you take me for a fool? I'm not about to pay the king's gold for empty jars and pots of sewage sealed with wax, I warn you."

"No, no," Hallyne squeaked, "the sums are accurate, I swear. We have been, hmmm, most fortunate, my lord Hand. Another cache of Lord Rossart's was found, more than three hundred jars. Under the Dragonpit! Some

whores have been using the ruins to entertain their patrons, and one of them fell through a patch of rotted
floor into a cellar. When he felt the jars, he mistook
them for wine. He was so drunk he broke the seal and
drank some."

"There was a prince who tried that once," said Tyrion
dryly. "I haven't seen any dragons rising over the city,
so it would seem it didn't work this time either." The
Dragonpit atop the hill of Rhaenys had been abandoned
for a century and a half. He supposed it was as good a
place as any to store wildfire, and better than most, but
it would have been nice if the late Lord Rossart had *told*
someone. "Three hundred jars, you say? That still does
not account for these totals. You are several *thousand*
jars ahead of the best estimate you gave me when last
we met."

"Yes, yes, that's so." Hallyne mopped at his pale brow
with the sleeve of his black-and-scarlet robe. "We have
been working very hard, my lord Hand, hmmm."

"That would doubtless explain why you are making
so much more of the substance than before." Smiling,
Tyrion fixed the pyromancer with his mismatched
stare. "Though it does raise the question of why you did
not begin working hard until now."

Hallyne had the complexion of a mushroom, so it was
hard to see how he could turn any paler, yet somehow
he managed. "We *were*, my lord Hand, my brothers and
I have been laboring day and night from the first, I assure you. It is only, hmmm, we have made so much of
the substance that we have become, hmmm, more *practiced* as it were, and also"—the alchemist shifted uncomfortably—"certain spells, hmmm, ancient secrets of
our order, very delicate, very troublesome, but necessary if the substance is to be, hmmm, all it should
be . . ."

Tyrion was growing impatient. Ser Jacelyn Bywater
was likely here by now, and Ironhand misliked waiting.
"Yes, you have secret spells; how splendid. What of
them?"

"They, hmmm, seem to be working better than they

were." Hallyne smiled weakly. "You don't suppose there are any dragons about, do you?"

"Not unless you found one under the Dragonpit. Why?"

"Oh, pardon, I was just remembering something old Wisdom Pollitor told me once, when I was an acolyte. I'd asked him why so many of our spells seemed, well, not as *effectual* as the scrolls would have us believe, and he said it was because magic had begun to go out of the world the day the last dragon died."

"Sorry to disappoint you, but I've seen no dragons. I have noticed the King's Justice lurking about, however. Should any of these fruits you're selling me turn out to be filled with anything but wildfire, you'll be seeing him as well."

Hallyne fled so quickly that he almost bowled over Ser Jacelyn—no, *Lord* Jacelyn, he must remember that. Ironhand was mercifully direct, as ever. He'd returned from Rosby to deliver a fresh levy of spearmen recruited from Lord Gyles's estates and resume his command of the City Watch. "How does my nephew fare?" Tyrion asked when they were done discussing the city's defenses.

"Prince Tommen is hale and happy, my lord. He has adopted a fawn some of my men brought home from a hunt. He had one once before, he says, but Joffrey skinned her for a jerkin. He asks about his mother sometimes, and often begins letters to the Princess Myrcella, though he never seems to finish any. His brother, however, he does not seem to miss at all."

"You have made suitable arrangements for him, should the battle be lost?"

"My men have their instructions."

"Which are?"

"You commanded me to tell no one, my lord."

That made him smile. "I'm pleased you remember." Should King's Landing fall, he might well be taken alive. Better if he did not know where Joffrey's heir might be found.

Varys appeared not long after Lord Jacelyn had left.

"Men are such faithless creatures," he said by way of greeting.

Tyrion sighed. "Who's the traitor today?"

The eunuch handed him a scroll. "So much villainy, it sings a sad song for our age. Did honor die with our fathers?"

"My father is not dead yet." Tyrion scanned the list. "I know some of these names. These are rich men. Traders, merchants, craftsmen. Why should they conspire against us?"

"It seems they believe that Lord Stannis must win, and wish to share his victory. They call themselves the Antler Men, after the crowned stag."

"Someone should tell them that Stannis changed his sigil. Then they can be the Hot Hearts." It was no matter for jests, though; it appeared that these Antler Men had armed several hundred followers, to seize the Old Gate once battle was joined, and admit the enemy to the city. Among the names on the list was the master armorer Salloreon. "I suppose this means I won't be getting that terrifying helm with the demon horns," Tyrion complained as he scrawled the order for the man's arrest.

THEON

One moment he was asleep; the next, awake.

Kyra nestled against him, one arm draped lightly over his, her breasts brushing his back. He could hear her breathing, soft and steady. The sheet was tangled about them. It was the black of night. The bedchamber was dark and still.

What is it? Did I hear something? Someone?

Wind sighed faintly against the shutters. Somewhere, far off, he heard the yowl of a cat in heat. Nothing else. *Sleep, Greyjoy,* he told himself. *The castle is quiet, and you have guards posted. At your door, at the gates, on the armory.*

He might have put it down to a bad dream, but he did not remember dreaming. Kyra had worn him out. Until Theon had sent for her, she had lived all of her eighteen years in the winter town without ever setting foot inside the walls of the castle. She came to him wet and eager and lithe as a weasel, and there had been a certain undeniable spice to fucking a common tavern wench in Lord Eddard Stark's own bed.

She murmured sleepily as Theon slid out from under her arm and got to his feet. A few embers still smoldered in the hearth. Wex slept on the floor at the foot of the bed, rolled up inside his cloak and dead to the world. Nothing moved. Theon crossed to the window and threw open the shutters. Night touched him with cold fingers, and gooseprickles rose on his bare skin. He leaned against the stone sill and looked out on dark towers, empty yards, black sky, and more stars than a man could ever count if he lived to be a hundred. A half-moon floated above the Bell Tower and cast its reflection on the roof of the glass gardens. He heard no alarums, no voices, not so much as a footfall.

All's well, Greyjoy. Hear the quiet? You ought to be drunk with joy. You took Winterfell with fewer than thirty men, a feat to sing of. Theon started back to bed. He'd roll Kyra on her back and fuck her again, that ought to banish these phantoms. Her gasps and giggles would make a welcome respite from this silence.

He stopped. He had grown so used to the howling of the direwolves that he scarcely heard it anymore . . . but some part of him, some hunter's instinct, heard its absence.

Urzen stood outside his door, a sinewy man with a round shield slung over his back. "The wolves are quiet," Theon told him. "Go see what they're doing, and come straight back." The thought of the direwolves running loose gave him a queasy feeling. He remembered the day in the wolfswood when the wildlings had attacked Bran. Summer and Grey Wind had torn them to pieces.

When he prodded Wex with the toe of his boot, the boy sat up and rubbed his eyes. "Make certain Bran Stark and his little brother are in their beds, and be quick about it."

"M'lord?" Kyra called sleepily.

"Go back to sleep, this does not concern you." Theon poured himself a cup of wine and drank it down. All the time he was listening, hoping to hear a howl. *Too few men*, he thought sourly. *I have too few men. If Asha does not come . . .*

Wex returned the quickest, shaking his head side to side. Cursing, Theon found his tunic and breeches on the floor where he had dropped them in his haste to get at Kyra. Over the tunic he donned a jerkin of iron-studded leather, and he belted a longsword and dagger at his waist. His hair was wild as the wood, but he had larger concerns.

By then Urzen was back. "The wolves be gone."

Theon told himself he must be as cold and deliberate as Lord Eddard. "Rouse the castle," he said. "Herd them out into the yard, everyone, we'll see who's missing. And have Lorren make a round of the gates. Wex, with me."

He wondered if Stygg had reached Deepwood Motte yet. The man was not as skilled a rider as he claimed—none of the ironmen were much good in the saddle—but there'd been time enough. Asha might well be on her way. *And if she learns that I have lost the Starks . . .* It did not bear thinking about.

Bran's bedchamber was empty, as was Rickon's half a turn below. Theon cursed himself. He should have kept a guard on them, but he'd deemed it more important to have men walking the walls and protecting the gates than to nursemaid a couple of children, one a cripple.

Outside he heard sobbing as the castle folk were pulled from their beds and driven into the yard. *I'll give them reason to sob. I've used them gently, and this is how they repay me.* He'd even had two of his own men whipped bloody for raping that kennel girl, to show them he meant to be just. *They still blame me for the rape, though. And the rest.* He deemed that unfair. Mikken had killed himself with his mouth, just as Benfred had. As for Chayle, he had to give *someone* to the Drowned God, his men expected it. "I bear you no ill will," he'd told the septon before they threw him down the well, "but you and your gods have no place here now." You'd think the others might be grateful he hadn't chosen one of them, but no. He wondered how many of them were part of this plot against him.

Urzen returned with Black Lorren. "The Hunter's Gate," Lorren said. "Best come see."

The Hunter's Gate was conveniently sited close to the kennels and kitchens. It opened directly on fields and forests, allowing riders to come and go without first passing through the winter town, and so was favored by hunting parties. "Who had the guard here?" Theon demanded.

"Drennan and Squint."

Drennan was one of the men who'd raped Palla. "If they've let the boys escape, I'll have more than a little skin off their back this time, I swear it."

"No need for that," Black Lorren said curtly.

Nor was there. They found Squint floating facedown in the moat, his entrails drifting behind him like a nest of pale snakes. Drennan lay half-naked in the gatehouse, in the snug room where the drawbridge was worked. His throat had been opened ear to ear. A ragged tunic concealed the half-healed scars on his back, but his boots were scattered amidst the rushes, and his breeches tangled about his feet. There was cheese on a small table near the door, beside an empty flagon. And two cups.

Theon picked one up and sniffed at the dregs of wine in the bottom. "Squint was up on the wallwalk, no?"

"Aye," said Lorren.

Theon flung the cup into the hearth. "I'd say Drennan was pulling down his breeches to stick it in the woman when she stuck it in him. His own cheese knife, by the look of it. Someone find a pike and fish the other fool out of the moat."

The other fool was in a deal worse shape than Drennan. When Black Lorren drew him out of the water, they saw that one of his arms had been wrenched off at the elbow, half of his neck was missing, and there was a ragged hole where his navel and groin once had been. The pike tore through his bowels as Lorren was pulling him in. The stench was awful.

"The direwolves," Theon said. "Both of them, at a guess." Disgusted, he walked back to the drawbridge. Winterfell was encircled by two massive granite walls, with a wide moat between them. The outer wall stood eighty feet high, the inner more than a hundred. Lacking men, Theon had been forced to abandon the outer defenses and post his guards along the higher inner walls. He dared not risk having them on the wrong side of the moat should the castle rise against him.

There had to be two or more, he decided. *While the woman was entertaining Drennan, the others freed the wolves.*

Theon called for a torch and led them up the steps to the wallwalk. He swept the flame low before him, looking for . . . *there.* On the inside of the rampart and in the wide crenel between two upthrust merlons. "Blood," he announced, "clumsily mopped up. At a guess, the woman killed Drennan and lowered the drawbridge. Squint heard the clank of chains, came to have a look, and got this far. They pushed the corpse through the crenel into the moat so he wouldn't be found by another sentry."

Urzen peered along the walls. "The other watch turrets are not far. I see torches burning—"

"Torches, but no guards," Theon said testily. "Winterfell has more turrets than I have men."

"Four guards at the main gate," said Black Lorren, "and five walking the walls beside Squint."

Urzen said, "If he had sounded his horn—"

I am served by fools. "Try and imagine it was you up here, Urzen. It's dark and cold. You have been walking sentry for hours, looking forward to the end of your watch. Then you hear a noise and move toward the gate, and suddenly you see *eyes* at the top of the stair, glowing green and gold in the torchlight. Two shadows come rushing toward you faster than you can believe. You catch a glimpse of teeth, start to level your spear, and they *slam* into you and open your belly, tearing through leather as if it were cheesecloth." He gave

Urzen a hard shove. "And now you're down on your back, your guts are spilling out, and one of them has his teeth around your neck." Theon grabbed the man's scrawny throat, tightened his fingers, and smiled. "Tell me, at what moment during all of this do you stop to *blow your fucking horn?*" He shoved Urzen away roughly, sending him stumbling back against a merlon. The man rubbed his throat. *I should have had those beasts put down the day we took the castle,* he thought angrily. *I'd seen them kill, I knew how dangerous they were.*

"We must go after them," Black Lorren said.

"Not in the dark." Theon did not relish the idea of chasing direwolves through the wood by night; the hunters could easily become the hunted. "We'll wait for daylight. Until then, I had best go speak with my loyal subjects."

Down in the yard, a uneasy crowd of men, women, and children had been pushed up against the wall. Many had not been given time to dress; they covered themselves with woolen blankets, or huddled naked under cloaks or bedrobes. A dozen ironmen hemmed them in, torches in one hand and weapons in the other. The wind was gusting, and the flickering orange light reflected dully off steel helms, thick beards, and unsmiling eyes.

Theon walked up and down before the prisoners, studying the faces. They *all* looked guilty to him. "How many are missing?"

"Six." Reek stepped up behind him, smelling of soap, his long hair moving in the wind. "Both Starks, that bog boy and his sister, the halfwit from the stables, and your wildling woman."

Osha. He had suspected her from the moment he saw that second cup. *I should have known better than to trust that one. She's as unnatural as Asha. Even their names sound alike.*

"Has anyone had a look at the stables?"

"Aggar says no horses are missing."

"Dancer is still in his stall?"

"Dancer?" Reek frowned. "Aggar says the horses are all there. Only the halfwit is missing."

They're afoot, then. That was the best news he'd heard since he woke. Bran would be riding in his basket on Hodor's back, no doubt. Osha would need to carry Rickon; his little legs wouldn't take him far on their own. Theon was confident that he'd soon have them back in his hands. "Bran and Rickon have fled," he told the castle folk, watching their eyes. "Who knows where they've gone?" No one answered. "They could not have escaped without help," Theon went on. "Without food, clothing, weapons." He had locked away every sword and axe in Winterfell, but no doubt some had been hidden from him. "I'll have the names of all those who aided them. All those who turned a blind eye." The only sound was the wind. "Come first light, I mean to bring them back." He hooked his thumbs through his swordbelt. "I need huntsmen. Who wants a nice warm wolfskin to see them through the winter? Gage?" The cook had always greeted him cheerfully when he returned from the hunt, to ask whether he'd brought anything choice for the table, but he had nothing to say now. Theon walked back the way he had come, searching their faces for the least sign of guilty knowledge. "The wild is no place for a cripple. And Rickon, young as he is, how long will he last out there? Nan, think how frightened he must be." The old woman had nattered at him for ten years, telling her endless stories, but now she gaped at him as if he were some stranger. "I might have killed every man of you and given your women to my soldiers for their pleasure, but instead I protected you. Is this the thanks you offer?" Joseth who'd groomed his horses, Farlen who'd taught him all he knew of hounds, Barth the brewer's wife who'd been his first—not one of them would meet his eyes. *They hate me,* he realized.

Reek stepped close. "Strip off their skins," he urged, his thick lips glistening. "Lord Bolton, he used to say a naked man has few secrets, but a flayed man's got none."

The flayed man was the sigil of House Bolton, Theon knew; ages past, certain of their lords had gone so far as to cloak themselves in the skins of dead enemies. A number of Starks had ended thus. Supposedly all that had stopped a thousand years ago, when the Boltons had bent their knees to Winterfell. *Or so they say, but old ways die hard, as well I know.*

"There will be no flaying in the north so long as I rule in Winterfell," Theon said loudly. *I am your only protection against the likes of him,* he wanted to scream. He could not be that blatant, but perhaps some were clever enough to take the lesson.

The sky was greying over the castle walls. Dawn could not be far off. "Joseth, saddle Smiler and a horse for yourself. Murch, Gariss, Poxy Tym, you'll come as well." Murch and Gariss were the best huntsmen in the castle, and Tym was a fine bowman. "Aggar, Rednose, Gelmarr, Reek, Wex." He needed his own to watch his back. "Farlen, I'll want hounds, and you to handle them."

The grizzled kennelmaster crossed his arms. "And why would I care to hunt down my own trueborn lords, and babes at that?"

Theon moved close. "I am your trueborn lord now, and the man who keeps Palla safe."

He saw the defiance die in Farlen's eyes. "Aye, m'lord."

Stepping back, Theon glanced about to see who else he might add. "Maester Luwin," he announced.

"I know nothing of hunting."

No, but I don't trust you in the castle in my absence. "Then it's past time you learned."

"Let me come too. I want that wolfskin cloak." A boy stepped forward, no older than Bran. It took Theon a moment to remember him. "I've hunted lots of times before," Walder Frey said. "Red deer and elk, and even boar."

His cousin laughed at him. "He rode on a boar hunt with his father, but they never let him near the boar."

Theon look at the boy doubtfully. "Come if you like,

but if you can't keep up, don't think that I'll nurse you
along." He turned back to Black Lorren. "Winterfell is
yours in my absence. If we do not return, do with it as
you will." *That bloody well ought to have them praying for my success.*

They assembled by the Hunter's Gate as the first pale
rays of the sun brushed the top of the Bell Tower, their
breath frosting in the cold morning air. Gelmarr had
equipped himself with a longaxe whose reach would allow him to strike before the wolves were on him. The
blade was heavy enough to kill with a single blow.
Aggar wore steel greaves. Reek arrived carrying a boar
spear and an overstuffed washerwoman's sack bulging
with god knows what. Theon had his bow; he needed
nothing else. Once he had saved Bran's life with an arrow. He hoped he would not need to take it with another, but if it came to that, he would.

Eleven men, two boys, and a dozen dogs crossed the
moat. Beyond the outer wall, the tracks were plain to
read in the soft ground; the pawprints of the wolves,
Hodor's heavy tread, the shallower marks left by the
feet of the two Reeds. Once under the trees, the stony
ground and fallen leaves made the trail harder to see,
but by then Farlen's red bitch had the scent. The rest of
the dogs were close behind, the hounds sniffing and
barking, a pair of monstrous mastiffs bringing up the
rear. Their size and ferocity might make the difference
against a cornered direwolf.

He'd have guessed that Osha might run south to Ser
Rodrik, but the trail led north by northwest, into the
very heart of the wolfswood. Theon did not like that
one bit. It would be a bitter irony if the Starks made for
Deepwood Motte and delivered themselves right into
Asha's hands. *I'd sooner have them dead,* he thought
bitterly. *It is better to be seen as cruel than foolish.*

Wisps of pale mist threaded between the trees. Sentinels and soldier pines grew thick about here, and there
was nothing as dark and gloomy as an evergreen forest.
The ground was uneven, and the fallen needles dis-

guised the softness of the turf and made the footing treacherous for the horses, so they had to go slowly. *Not as slowly as a man carrying a cripple, though, or a bony harridan with a four-year-old on her back.* He told himself to be patient. He'd have them before the day was out.

Maester Luwin trotted up to him as they were following a game trail along the lip of a ravine. "Thus far hunting seems indistinguishable from riding through the woods, my lord."

Theon smiled. "There are similarities. But with hunting, there's blood at the end."

"Must it be so? This flight was great folly, but will you not be merciful? These are your foster brothers we seek."

"No Stark but Robb was ever brotherly toward me, but Bran and Rickon have more value to me living than dead."

"The same is true of the Reeds. Moat Cailin sits on the edge of the bogs. Lord Howland can make your uncle's occupation a visit to hell if he chooses, but so long as you hold his heirs he must stay his hand."

Theon had not considered that. In truth, he had scarcely considered the mudmen at all, beyond eyeing Meera once or twice and wondering if she was still a maiden. "You may be right. We will spare them if we can."

"And Hodor too, I hope. The boy is simple, you know that. He does as he is told. How many times has he groomed your horse, soaped your saddle, scoured your mail?"

Hodor was nothing to him. "If he does not fight us, we will let him live." Theon pointed a finger. "But say one word about sparing the wildling, and you can die with her. She swore me an oath, and pissed on it."

The maester inclined his head. "I make no apologies for oathbreakers. Do what you must. I thank you for your mercy."

Mercy, thought Theon as Luwin dropped back. *There's a bloody trap. Too much and they call you weak, too little and you're monstrous.* Yet the maester had given him good counsel, he knew. His father thought only in terms of conquest, but what good was it to take a kingdom if you could not hold it? Force and fear could carry you only so far. A pity Ned Stark had taken his daughters south; elsewise Theon could have tightened his grip on Winterfell by marrying one of them. Sansa was a pretty little thing too, and by now likely even ripe for bedding. But she was a thousand leagues away, in the clutches of the Lannisters. A shame.

The wood grew ever wilder. The pines and sentinels gave way to huge dark oaks. Tangles of hawthorn concealed treacherous gullies and cuts. Stony hills rose and fell. They passed a crofter's cottage, deserted and overgown, and skirted a flooded quarry where the still water had a sheen as grey as steel. When the dogs began to bay, Theon figured the fugitives were near at hand. He spurred Smiler and followed at a trot, but what he found was only the carcass of a young elk . . . or what remained of it.

He dismounted for a closer look. The kill was still fresh, and plainly the work of wolves. The dogs sniffed round it eagerly, and one of the mastiffs buried his teeth in a haunch until Farlen shouted him off. *No part of this animal has been butchered,* Theon realized. *The wolves ate, but not the men.* Even if Osha did not want to risk a fire, she ought to have cut them a few steaks. It made no sense to leave so much good meat to rot. "Farlen, are you certain we're on the right trail?" he demanded. "Could your dogs be chasing the wrong wolves?"

"My bitch knows the smell of Summer and Shaggy well enough."

"I hope so. For your sake."

Less than an hour later, the trail led down a slope toward a muddy brook swollen by the recent rains. It was there the dogs lost the scent. Farlen and Wex waded across with the hounds and came back shaking their heads while the animals ranged up and down the far bank, sniffing. "They went in here, m'lord, but I can't see where they come out," the kennelmaster said.

Theon dismounted and knelt beside the stream. He dipped a hand in it. The water was cold. "They won't have stayed long in this," he said. "Take half the dogs downstream, I'll go up—"

Wex clapped his hands together loudly.

"What is it?" Theon said.

The mute boy pointed.

The ground near the water was sodden and muddy. The tracks the wolves had left were plain enough. "Pawprints, yes. So?"

Wex drove his heel into the mud, and pivoted his foot this way and that. It left a deep gouge.

Joseth understood. "A man the size of Hodor ought to have left a deep print in this mud," he said. "More so with the weight of a boy on his back. Yet the only boot prints here are our own. See for yourself."

Appalled, Theon saw it was true. The wolves had gone into the turgid brown water alone. "Osha must have turned aside back of us. Before the elk, most likely. She sent the wolves on by themselves, hoping we'd chase after them." He rounded on his huntsmen. "If you two have played me false—"

"There's been only the one trail, my lord, I swear it," said Gariss defensively. "And the direwolves would never have parted from them boys. Not for long."

That's so, Theon thought. Summer and Shaggydog might have gone off to hunt, but soon or late they would return to Bran and Rickon. "Gariss, Murch, take four dogs and double back, find where we lost them. Aggar, you watch them, I'll have no trickery. Farlen and I will follow the direwolves. Give a blast on the horn when you pick up the trail. Two blasts if you catch sight of the beasts themselves. Once we find where they went, they'll lead us back to their masters."

He took Wex, the Frey boy, and Gynir Rednose to search upstream. He and Wex rode on one side of the brook, Rednose and Walder Frey on the other, each with a pair of hounds. The wolves might have come out on either bank. Theon kept an eye out for tracks, spoor, broken branches, any hint as to where the direwolves might have left the water. He spied the prints of deer, elk, and badger easily enough. Wex surprised a vixen drinking at the stream, and Walder flushed three rabbits from the underbrush and managed to put an arrow in one. They saw the claw marks where a bear had shredded the bark of a tall birch. But of the direwolves there was no sign.

A little farther, Theon told himself. *Past that oak, over that rise, past the next bend of the stream, we'll find something there.* He pressed on long after he knew he should turn back, a growing sense of anxiety gnawing at his belly. It was midday when he wrenched Smiler's head round in disgust and gave up.

Somehow Osha and the wretched boys were eluding him. It should not have been possible, not on foot, burdened with a cripple and a young child. Every passing hour increased the likelihood that they would make good their escape. *If they reach a village . . .* The people of the north would never deny Ned Stark's sons, Robb's brothers. They'd have mounts to speed them on their way, food. Men would fight for the honor of protecting them. The whole bloody north would rally around them.

The wolves went downstream, that's all. He clung to that thought. *That red bitch will sniff where they came out of the water and we'll be after them again.*

But when they joined up with Farlen's party, one look at the kennelmaster's face smashed all of Theon's hopes to shards. "The only thing those dogs are fit for is a bear baiting," he said angrily. "Would that I had a bear."

"The dogs are not at fault." Farlen knelt between a mastiff and his precious red bitch, a hand on each. "Running water don't hold no scents, m'lord."

"The wolves had to come out of the stream *somewhere.*"

"No doubt they did. Upstream or down. We keep on, we'll find the place, but which way?"

"I never knew a wolf to run up a streambed for miles," said Reek. "A man might. If he knew he was being hunted, he might. But a wolf?"

Yet Theon wondered. These beasts were not as other wolves. *I should have skinned the cursed things.*

It was the same tale all over again when they rejoined Gariss, Murch, and Aggar. The huntsmen had retraced their steps halfway to Winterfell without finding any sign of where the Starks might have parted company with the direwolves. Farlen's hounds seemed as frustrated as their masters, sniffing forlornly at trees and rocks and snapping irritably at each other.

Theon dared not admit defeat. "We'll return to the brook. Search again. This time we'll go as far as we must."

"We won't find them," the Frey boy said suddenly. "Not so long as the frogeaters are with them. Mudmen are sneaks, they won't fight like decent folks, they skulk and use poison arrows. You never see them, but they see you. Those who go into the bogs after them get lost and never come out. Their houses *move*, even the castles like Greywater Watch." He glanced nervously at greenery that encircled them on all sides. "They might be out there right now, listening to everything we say."

Farlen laughed to show what he thought of that notion. "My dogs would smell anything in them bushes. Be all over them before you could break wind, boy."

"Frogeaters don't smell like men," Frey insisted. "They have a boggy stink, like frogs and trees and scummy water. Moss grows under their arms in place of hair, and they can live with nothing to eat but mud and breathe swamp water."

Theon was about to tell him what he ought to do with his wet nurse's fable when Maester Luwin spoke up. "The histories say the crannogmen grew close to the children of the forest in the days when the greenseers tried to bring the hammer of the waters down upon the Neck. It may be that they have secret knowledge."

Suddenly the wood seemed a deal darker than it had a

moment before, as if a cloud had passed before the sun. It was one thing to have some fool boy spouting folly, but maesters were supposed to be wise. "The only children that concern me are Bran and Rickon," Theon said. "Back to the stream. Now."

For a moment he did not think they were going to obey, but in the end old habit asserted itself. They followed sullenly, but they followed. The Frey boy was as jumpy as those rabbits he'd flushed earlier. Theon put men on either bank and followed the current. They rode for miles, going slow and careful, dismounting to lead the horses over treacherous ground, letting the good-for-bear-bait hounds sniff at every bush. Where a fallen tree dammed the flow, the hunters were forced to loop around a deep green pool, but if the direwolves had done the same they'd left neither print nor spoor. The beasts had taken to swimming, it seemed. *When I catch them, they'll have all the swimming they can stomach. I'll give them both to the Drowned God.*

When the woods began to darken, Theon Greyjoy knew he was beaten. Either the crannogmen *did* know the magic of the children of the forest, or else Osha had deceived them with some wildling trick. He made them press on through the dusk, but when the last light faded Joseth finally worked up the courage to say, "This is fruitless, my lord. We will lame a horse, break a leg."

"Joseth has the right of it," said Maester Luwin. "Groping through the woods by torchlight will avail us nothing."

Theon could taste bile at the back of his throat, and his stomach was a nest of snakes twining and snapping at each other. If he crept back to Winterfell empty-handed, he might as well dress in motley henceforth and wear a pointed hat; the whole north would know him for a fool. *And when my father hears, and Asha . . .*

"M'lord prince." Reek urged his horse near. "Might be them Starks never came this way. If I was them, I would have gone north and east, maybe. To the Umbers.

Good Stark men, they are. But their lands are a long way. The boys will shelter someplace nearer. Might be I know where."

Theon looked at him suspiciously. "Tell me."

"You know that old mill, sitting lonely on the Acorn Water? We stopped there when I was being dragged to Winterfell a captive. The miller's wife sold us hay for our horses while that old knight clucked over her brats. Might be the Starks are hiding there."

Theon knew the mill. He had even tumbled the miller's wife a time or two. There was nothing special about it, or her. "Why there? There are a dozen villages and holdfasts just as close."

Amusement shone in those pale eyes. "Why? Now that's past knowing. But they're there, I have a feeling."

He was growing sick of the man's sly answers. *His lips look like two worms fucking.* "What are you saying? If you've kept some knowledge from me—"

"M'lord prince?" Reek dismounted, and beckoned Theon to do the same. When they were both afoot, he pulled open the cloth sack he'd fetched from Winterfell. "Have a look here."

It was growing hard to see. Theon thrust his hand into the sack impatiently, groping amongst soft fur and rough scratchy wool. A sharp point pricked his skin, and his fingers closed around something cold and hard. He drew out a wolf's-head brooch, silver and jet. Understanding came suddenly. His hand closed into a fist. "Gelmarr," he said, wondering whom he could trust. *None of them.* "Aggar. Rednose. With us. The rest of you may return to Winterfell with the hounds. I'll have no further need of them. I know where Bran and Rickon are hiding now."

"Prince Theon," Maester Luwin entreated, "you will remember your promise? Mercy, you said."

"Mercy was for this morning," said Theon. *It is better to be feared than laughed at.* "Before they made me angry."

JON

They could see the fire in the night, glimmering against the side of the mountain like a fallen star. It burned redder than the other stars, and did not twinkle, though sometimes it flared up bright and sometimes dwindled down to no more than a distant spark, dull and faint.

Half a mile ahead and two thousand feet up, Jon judged, *and perfectly placed to see anything moving in the pass below.*

"Watchers in the Skirling Pass," wondered the oldest among them. In the spring of his youth, he had been squire to a king, so the black brothers still called him Squire Dalbridge. "What is it Mance Rayder fears, I wonder?"

"If he knew they'd lit a fire, he'd flay the poor bastards," said Ebben, a squat bald man muscled like a bag of rocks.

"Fire is life up here," said Qhorin Halfhand, "but it can be death as well." By his command, they'd risked no open flames since entering the mountains. They ate cold salt beef, hard bread, and harder cheese, and slept clothed and huddled beneath a pile of cloaks and furs, grateful for each other's warmth. It made Jon remember cold nights long ago at Winterfell, when he'd shared a bed with his brothers. These men were brothers too, though the bed they shared was stone and earth.

"They'll have a horn," said Stonesnake.

The Halfhand said, "A horn they must not blow."

"That's a long cruel climb by night," Ebben said as he eyed the distant spark through a cleft in the rocks that sheltered them. The sky was cloudless, the jagged mountains rising black on black until the very top, where their cold crowns of snow and ice shone palely in the moonlight.

"And a longer fall," said Qhorin Halfhand. "Two men, I think. There are like to be two up there, sharing the watch."

"Me." The ranger they called Stonesnake had already shown that he was the best climber among them. It would have to be him.

"And me," said Jon Snow.

Qhorin Halfhand looked at him. Jon could hear the wind keening as it shivered through the high pass above them. One of the garrons whickered and pawed at the thin stony soil of the hollow where they had taken shelter. "The wolf will remain with us," Qhorin said. "White fur is seen too easily by moonlight." He turned to Stonesnake. "When it's done, throw down a burning brand. We'll come when we see it fall."

"No better time to start than now," said Stonesnake.

They each took a long coil of rope. Stonesnake carried a bag of iron spikes as well, and a small hammer with its head wrapped in thick felt. Their garrons they left behind, along with their helms, mail, and Ghost. Jon knelt and let the direwolf nuzzle him before they set off. "Stay," he commanded. "I'll be back for you."

Stonesnake took the lead. He was a short wiry man, near fifty and grey of beard but stronger than he seemed, and he had the best night eyes of anyone Jon had ever known. He needed them tonight. By day the mountains were blue-grey, brushed with frost, but once the sun vanished behind the jagged peaks they turned black. Now the rising moon had limned them in white and silver.

The black brothers moved through black shadows amidst black rocks, working their way up a steep, twisting trail as their breath frosted in the black air. Jon felt almost naked without his mail, but he did not miss its weight. This was hard going, and slow. To hurry here was to risk a broken ankle or worse. Stonesnake seemed to know where to put his feet as if by instinct, but Jon needed to be more careful on the broken, uneven ground.

The Skirling Pass was really a series of passes, a long twisting course that went up around a succession of icy wind-carved peaks and down through hidden valleys that seldom saw the sun. Apart from his companions, Jon had glimpsed no living man since they'd left the wood behind and begun to make their way upward. The Frostfangs were as cruel as any place the gods had made, and as inimical to men. The wind cut like a knife up here, and shrilled in the night like a mother mourning her slain children. What few trees they saw were stunted, grotesque things growing sideways out of cracks and fissures. Tumbled shelves of rock often overhung the trail, fringed with hanging icicles that looked like long white teeth from a distance.

Yet even so, Jon Snow was not sorry he had come. There were wonders here as well. He had seen sunlight flashing on icy thin waterfalls as they plunged over the lips of sheer stone cliffs, and a mountain meadow full of autumn wildflowers, blue coldsnaps and bright scarlet frostfires and stands of piper's grass in russet and gold. He had peered down ravines so deep and black they seemed certain to end in some hell, and he had ridden his garron over a wind-eaten bridge of natural stone with nothing but sky to either side. Eagles nested in the heights and came down to hunt the valleys, circling effortlessly on great blue-grey wings that seemed almost part of the sky. Once he had watched a shadowcat stalk a ram, flowing down the mountainside like liquid smoke until it was ready to pounce.

Now it is our turn to pounce. He wished he could move as sure and silent as that shadowcat, and kill as quickly. Longclaw was sheathed across his back, but he might not have room to use it. He carried dirk and dagger for closer work. *They will have weapons as well, and I am not armored.* He wondered who would prove the shadowcat by night's end, and who the ram.

For a long way they stayed to the trail, following its twists and turns as it snaked along the side of the mountain, upward, ever upward. Sometimes the mountain folded back on itself and they lost sight of the fire, but soon or late it would always reappear. The path Stonesnake chose would never have served for the horses. In places Jon had to put his back to the cold stone and shuffle along sideways like a crab, inch by inch. Even where the track widened it was treacherous; there were cracks big enough to swallow a man's leg, rubble to stumble over, hollow places where the water pooled by day and froze hard by night. *One step and then another,* Jon told himself. *One step and then another, and I will not fall.*

He had not shaved since leaving the Fist of the First Men, and the hair on his lip was soon stiff with frost. Two hours into the climb, the wind kicked up so fiercely that it was all he could do to hunch down and cling to the rock, praying he would not be blown off the mountain. *One step and then another,* he resumed when the gale subsided. *One step and then another, and I will not fall.*

Soon they were high enough so that looking down was best not considered. There was nothing below but yawning blackness, nothing above but moon and stars. "The mountain is your mother," Stonesnake had told him during an easier climb a few days past. "Cling to her, press your face up against her teats, and she won't drop you." Jon had made a joke of it, saying how he'd always wondered who his mother was, but never thought to find her in the Frostfangs. It did not seem nearly so amusing now. *One step and then another*, he thought, clinging tight.

The narrow track ended abruptly where a massive shoulder of black granite thrust out from the side of the mountain. After the bright moonlight, its shadow was so black that it felt like stepping into a cave. "Straight up here," the ranger said in a quiet voice. "We want to get above them." He peeled off his gloves, tucked them through his belt, tied one end of his rope around his waist, the other end around Jon. "Follow me when the rope grows taut." The ranger did not wait for an answer but started at once, moving upward with fingers and feet, faster than Jon would have believed. The long rope unwound slowly. Jon watched him closely, making note of how he went, and where he found each handhold, and when the last loop of hemp uncoiled, he took off his own gloves and followed, much more slowly.

Stonesnake had passed the rope around the smooth spike of rock he was waiting on, but as soon as Jon reached him he shook it loose and was off again. This time there was no convenient cleft when he reached the end of their tether, so he took out his felt-headed hammer and drove a spike deep into a crack in the stone with a series of gentle taps. Soft as the sounds were, they echoed off the stone so loudly that Jon winced with every blow, certain that the wildlings must hear them too. When the spike was secure, Stonesnake secured the rope to it, and Jon started after him. *Suck on the mountain's teat*, he reminded himself. *Don't look down. Keep your weight above your feet. Don't look down. Look at the rock in front of you. There's a good handhold, yes. Don't look down. I can catch a breath on that ledge there, all I need to do is reach it. Never look down.*

Once his foot slipped as he put his weight on it and his heart stopped in his chest, but the gods were good and he did not fall. He could feel the cold seeping off the rock into his fingers, but he dared not don his gloves; gloves would slip, no matter how tight they seemed, cloth and fur moving between skin and stone, and up here that could kill him. His burned hand was stiffening up on him, and soon it began to ache. Then he ripped open his thumbnail somehow, and after that he left smears of blood wherever he put his hand. He hoped he still had all his fingers by the end of the climb.

Up they went, and up, and up, black shadows creeping across the moonlit wall of rock. Anyone down on the floor of the pass could have seen them easily, but the mountain hid them from the view of the wildlings by their fire. They were close now, though. Jon could sense it. Even so, he did not think of the foes who were waiting for him, all unknowing, but of his brother at Winterfell. *Bran used to love to climb. I wish I had a tenth part of his courage.*

The wall was broken two-thirds of the way up by a crooked fissure of icy stone. Stonesnake reached down a hand to help him up. He had donned his gloves again, so Jon did the same. The ranger moved his head to the left, and the two of them crawled along the shelf three hundred yards or more, until they could see the dull orange glow beyond the lip of the cliff.

The wildlings had built their watchfire in a shallow depression above the narrowest part of the pass, with a sheer drop below and rock behind to shelter them from the worst of the wind. That same windbreak allowed the black brothers to crawl within a few feet of them, creeping along on their bellies until they were looking down on the men they must kill.

One was asleep, curled up tight and buried beneath a great mound of skins. Jon could see nothing of him but his hair, bright red in the firelight. The second sat close to the flames, feeding them twigs and branches and complaining of the wind in a querulous tone. The third watched the pass, though there was little to see, only a vast bowl of darkness ringed by the snowy shoulders of the mountains. It was the watcher who wore the horn.

Three. For a moment Jon was uncertain. *There was only supposed to be two.* One was asleep, though. And whether there was two or three or twenty, he still must do what he had come to do. Stonesnake touched his arm, pointed at the wildling with the horn. Jon nodded toward the one by the fire. It felt queer, picking a man to kill. Half the days of his life had been spent with sword and shield, training for this moment. *Did Robb feel this way before his first battle?* he wondered, but there was no time to ponder the question. Stonesnake moved as fast as his namesake, leaping down on the wildlings in a rain of pebbles. Jon slid Longclaw from its sheath and followed.

It all seemed to happen in a heartbeat. Afterward Jon could admire the courage of the wildling who reached first for his horn instead of his blade. He got it to his lips, but before he could sound it Stonesnake knocked the horn aside with a swipe of his shortsword. Jon's man leapt to his feet, thrusting at his face with a burning brand. He could feel the heat of the flames as he flinched back. Out of the corner of his eye, he saw the sleeper stirring, and knew he must finish his man quick. When the brand swung again, he bulled into it, swinging the bastard sword with both hands. The Valyrian steel sheared through leather, fur, wool, and flesh, but when the wildling fell he twisted, ripping the sword from Jon's grasp. On the ground the sleeper sat up beneath his furs. Jon slid his dirk free, grabbing the man by the hair and jamming the point of the knife up under his chin as he reached for his—no, *her*—

His hand froze. "A girl."

"A watcher," said Stonesnake. "A wildling. Finish her."

Jon could see fear and fire in her eyes. Blood ran down her white throat from where the point of his dirk had pricked her. *One thrust and it's done,* he told himself. He was so close he could smell onion on her breath. *She is no older than I am.* Something about her made him think of Arya, though they looked nothing at all alike. "Will you yield?" he asked, giving the dirk a half turn. *And if she doesn't?*

"I yield." Her words steamed in the cold air.

"You're our captive, then." He pulled the dirk away from the soft skin of her throat.

"Qhorin said nothing of taking captives," said Stonesnake.

"He never said not to." Jon let go his grip on the girl's hair, and she scuttled backward, away from them.

"She's a spearwife." Stonesnake gestured at the long-hafted axe that lay beside her sleeping furs. "She was reaching for that when you grabbed her. Give her half a chance and she'll bury it between your eyes."

"I won't give her half a chance." Jon kicked the axe well out of the girl's reach. "Do you have a name?"

"Ygritte." Her hand rubbed at her throat and came away bloody. She stared at the wetness.

Sheathing his dirk, he wrenched Longclaw free from the body of the man he'd killed. "You are my captive, Ygritte."

"I gave you my name."

"I'm Jon Snow."

She flinched. "An evil name."

"A bastard name," he said. "My father was Lord Eddard Stark of Winterfell."

The girl watched him warily, but Stonesnake gave a mordant chuckle. "It's the captive supposed to tell things, remember?" The ranger thrust a long branch into the fire. "Not that she will. I've known wildlings to bite off their own tongues before they'd answer a question." When the end of the branch was blazing merrily, he took two steps and flung it out over the pass. It fell through the night spinning until it was lost to sight.

"You ought to burn them you killed," said Ygritte.

"Need a bigger fire for that, and big fires burn bright." Stonesnake turned, his eyes scanning the black distance for any spark of light. "Are there more wildlings close by, is that it?"

"Burn them," the girl repeated stubbornly, "or it might be you'll need them swords again."

Jon remembered dead Othor and his cold black hands. "Maybe we should do as she says."

"There are other ways." Stonesnake knelt beside the man he'd slain, stripped him of cloak and boots and belt and vest, then hoisted the body over one thin shoulder and carried it to the edge. He grunted as he tossed it over. A moment later they heard a wet, heavy smack well below them. By then the ranger had the second body down to the skin and was dragging it by the arms. Jon took the feet and together they flung the dead man out in the blackness of the night.

Ygritte watched and said nothing. She was older than he'd thought at first, Jon realized; maybe as old as twenty, but short for her age, bandy-legged, with a round face, small hands, and a pug nose. Her shaggy mop of red hair stuck out in all directions. She looked plump as she crouched there, but most of that was layers of fur and wool and leather. Underneath all that she could be as skinny as Arya.

"Were you sent to watch for us?" Jon asked her.

"You, and others."

Stonesnake warmed his hands over the fire. "What waits beyond the pass?"

"The free folk."

"How many?"

"Hundreds and thousands. More than you ever saw, crow." She smiled. Her teeth were crooked, but very white.

She doesn't know how many. "Why come here?"

Ygritte fell silent.

"What's in the Frostfangs that your king could want? You can't stay here, there's no food."

She turned her face away from him.

"Do you mean to march on the Wall? When?"

She stared at the flames as if she could not hear him.

"Do you know anything of my uncle, Benjen Stark?"

Ygritte ignored him. Stonesnake laughed. "If she spits out her tongue, don't say I didn't warn you."

A low rumbling growl echoed off the rock. *Shadowcat,* Jon knew at once. As he rose he heard another, closer at hand. He pulled his sword and turned, listening.

"They won't trouble us," Ygritte said. "It's the dead they've come for. Cats can smell blood six miles off. They'll stay near the bodies till they've eaten every last stringy shred o' meat, and cracked the bones for the marrow."

Jon could hear the sounds of their feeding echoing off the rocks. It gave him an uneasy feeling. The warmth of the fire made him realize how bone-tired he was, but he dared not sleep. He had taken a captive, and it was on him to guard her. "Were they your kin?" he asked her quietly. "The two we killed?"

"No more than you are."

"Me?" He frowned. "What do you mean?"

"You said you were the Bastard o' Winterfell."

"I am."

"Who was your mother?"

"Some woman. Most of them are." Someone had said that to him once. He did not remember who.

She smiled again, a flash of white teeth. "And she never sung you the song o' the winter rose?"

"I never knew my mother. Or any such song."

"Bael the Bard made it," said Ygritte. "He was King-beyond-the-Wall a long time back. All the free folk know his songs, but might be you don't sing them in the south."

"Winterfell's not in the south," Jon objected.

"Yes it is. Everything below the Wall's south to us."

He had never thought of it that way. "I suppose it's all in where you're standing."

"Aye," Ygritte agreed. "It always is."

"Tell me," Jon urged her. It would be hours before Qhorin came up, and a story would help keep him awake. "I want to hear this tale of yours."

"Might be you won't like it much."

"I'll hear it all the same."

"Brave black crow," she mocked. "Well, long before he was king over the free folk, Bael was a great raider."

Stonesnake gave a snort. "A murderer, robber, and raper, is what you mean."

"That's all in where you're standing too," Ygritte said. "The Stark in Winterfell wanted Bael's head, but never could take him, and the taste o' failure galled him. One day in his bitterness he called Bael a craven who preyed only on the weak. When word o' that got back, Bael vowed to teach the lord a lesson. So he scaled the Wall, skipped down the kingsroad, and walked into Winterfell one winter's night with harp in hand, naming himself Sygerrik of Skagos. *Sygerrik* means 'deceiver' in the Old Tongue, that the First Men spoke, and the giants still speak.

"North or south, singers always find a ready welcome, so Bael ate at Lord Stark's own table, and played for the lord in his high seat until half the night was gone. The old songs he played, and new ones he'd made himself, and he played and sang so well that when he was done, the lord offered to let him name his own reward. 'All I ask is a flower,' Bael answered, 'the fairest flower that blooms in the gardens o' Winterfell.'

"Now as it happened the winter roses had only then come into bloom, and no flower is so rare nor precious. So the Stark sent to his glass gardens and commanded that the most beautiful o' the winter roses be plucked for the singer's payment. And so it was done. But when morning come, the singer had vanished . . . and so had Lord Brandon's maiden daughter. Her bed they found empty, but for the pale blue rose that Bael had left on the pillow where her head had lain."

Jon had never heard this tale before. "Which Brandon was this supposed to be? Brandon the Builder lived in the Age of Heroes, thousands of years before Bael. There was Brandon the Burner and his father Brandon the Shipwright, but—"

"This was Brandon the Daughterless," Ygritte said sharply. "Would you hear the tale, or no?"

He scowled. "Go on."

"Lord Brandon had no other children. At his behest, the black crows flew forth from their castles in the hundreds, but nowhere could they find any sign o' Bael or this maid. For most a year they searched, till the lord lost heart and took to his bed, and it seemed as though the line o' Starks was at its end. But one night as he lay waiting to die, Lord Brandon heard a child's cry. He followed the sound and found his daughter back in her bedchamber, asleep with a babe at her breast."

"Bael had brought her back?"

"No. They had been in Winterfell all the time, hiding with the dead beneath the castle. The maid loved Bael so dearly she bore him a son, the song says . . . though if truth be told, all the maids love Bael in them songs he wrote. Be that as it may, what's certain is that Bael left the child in payment for the rose he'd plucked unasked, and that the boy grew to be the next Lord Stark. So there it is—you have Bael's blood in you, same as me."

"It never happened," Jon said.

She shrugged. "Might be it did, might be it didn't. It is a good song, though. My mother used to sing it to me. She was a woman too, Jon Snow. Like yours." She rubbed her throat where his dirk had cut her. "The song ends when they find the babe, but there is a darker end to the story. Thirty years later, when Bael was King-beyond-the-Wall and led the free folk south, it was young Lord Stark who met him at the Frozen Ford . . . and killed him, for Bael would not harm his own son when they met sword to sword."

"So the son slew the father instead," said Jon.

"Aye," she said, "but the gods hate kinslayers, even when they kill unknowing. When Lord Stark returned from the battle and his mother saw Bael's head upon his spear, she threw herself from a tower in her grief. Her son did not long outlive her. One o' his lords peeled the skin off him and wore him for a cloak."

"Your Bael was a liar," he told her, certain now.

"No," Ygritte said, "but a bard's truth is different than yours or mine. Anyway, you asked for the story, so I told it." She turned away from him, closed her eyes, and seemed to sleep.

Dawn and Qhorin Halfhand arrived together. The black stones had turned to grey and the eastern sky had gone indigo when Stonesnake spied the rangers below, wending their way upward. Jon woke his captive and held her by the arm as they descended to meet them. Thankfully, there was another way off the mountain to the north and west, along paths much gentler than the one that had brought them up here. They were waiting in a narrow defile when their brothers appeared, leading their garrons. Ghost raced ahead at first scent of them. Jon squatted to let the direwolf close his jaws around his wrist, tugging his hand back and forth. It was a game they played. But when he glanced up, he saw Ygritte watching with eyes as wide and white as hen's eggs.

Qhorin Halfhand made no comment when he saw the prisoner. "There were three," Stonesnake told him. No more than that.

"We passed two," Ebben said, "or what the cats had left of them." He eyed the girl sourly, suspicion plain on his face.

"She yielded," Jon felt compelled to say.

Qhorin's face was impassive. "Do you know who I am?"

"Qhorin Halfhand." The girl looked half a child beside him, but she faced him boldly.

"Tell me true. If I fell into the hands of your people and yielded myself, what would it win me?"

"A slower death than elsewise."

The big ranger looked to Jon. "We have no food to feed her, nor can we spare a man to watch her."

"The way before us is perilous enough, lad," said Squire Dalbridge. "One shout when we need silence, and every man of us is doomed."

Ebben drew his dagger. "A steel kiss will keep her quiet."

Jon's throat was raw. He looked at them all helplessly. "She yielded herself to me."

"Then you must do what needs be done," Qhorin Halfhand said. "You are the blood of Winterfell and a man of the Night's Watch." He looked at the others. "Come, brothers. Leave him to it. It will go easier for him if we do not watch." And he led them up the steep twisting trail toward the pale pink glow of the sun where it broke through a mountain cleft, and before very long only Jon and Ghost remained with the wildling girl.

He thought Ygritte might try to run, but she only stood there, waiting, looking at him. "You never killed a woman before, did you?" When he shook his head, she said, "We die the same as men. But you don't need to do it. Mance would take you, I know he would. There's secret ways. Them crows would never catch us."

"I'm as much a crow as they are," Jon said.

She nodded, resigned. "Will you burn me, after?"

"I can't. The smoke might be seen."

"That's so." She shrugged. "Well, there's worse places to end up than the belly of a shadowcat."

He pulled Longclaw over a shoulder. "Aren't you afraid?"

"Last night I was," she admitted. "But now the sun's up." She pushed her hair aside to bare her neck, and knelt before him. "Strike hard and true, crow, or I'll come back and haunt you."

Longclaw was not so long or heavy a sword as his father's Ice, but it was Valyrian steel all the same. He touched the edge of the blade to mark where the blow must fall, and Ygritte shivered. "That's cold," she said. "Go on, be quick about it."

He raised Longclaw over his head, both hands tight around the grip. *One cut, with all my weight behind it.* He could give her a quick clean death, at least. He was his father's son. Wasn't he? Wasn't he?

"Do it," she urged him after a moment. "Bastard. *Do it.* I can't stay brave forever." When the blow did not fall she turned her head to look at him.

Jon lowered his sword. "Go," he muttered.

Ygritte stared.

"Now," he said, "before my wits return. *Go."*

She went.

SANSA

The southern sky was black with smoke. It rose swirling off a hundred distant fires, its sooty fingers smudging out the stars. Across the Blackwater Rush, a line of flame burned nightly from horizon to horizon, while on this side the Imp had fired the whole riverfront: docks and warehouses, homes and brothels, everything outside the city walls.

Even in the Red Keep, the air tasted of ashes. When Sansa found Ser Dontos in the quiet of the godswood, he asked if she'd been crying. "It's only from the smoke," she lied. "It looks as though half the kingswood is burning."

"Lord Stannis wants to smoke out the Imp's savages." Dontos swayed as he spoke, one hand on the trunk of a chestnut tree. A wine stain discolored the red-and-yellow motley of his tunic. "They kill his scouts and raid his baggage train. And the wildlings have been lighting fires too. The Imp told the queen that Stannis had better train his horses to eat ash, since he would find no blade of grass. I heard him say so. I hear all sorts of things as a fool that I never heard when I was a knight. They talk as though I am not there, and"—he leaned close, breathing his winey breath right in her face—"the Spider pays in gold for any little trifle. I think Moon Boy has been his for years."

He is drunk again. My poor Florian he names himself, and so he is. But he is all I have. "Is it true Lord Stannis burned the godswood at Storm's End?"

Dontos nodded. "He made a great pyre of the trees as an offering to his new god. The red priestess made him do it. They say she rules him now, body and soul. He's vowed to burn the Great Sept of Baelor too, if he takes the city."

"Let him." When Sansa had first beheld the Great Sept with its marble walls and seven crystal towers, she'd thought it was the most beautiful building in the world, but that had been before Joffrey beheaded her father on its steps. "I want it burned."

"Hush, child, the gods will hear you."

"Why should they? They never hear my prayers."

"Yes they do. They sent me to you, didn't they?"

Sansa picked at the bark of a tree. She felt light-headed, almost feverish. "They sent you, but what good have you done? You promised you would take me home, but I'm still here."

Dontos patted her arm. "I've spoken to a certain man I know, a good friend to me . . . and you, my lady. He will hire a swift ship to take us to safety, when the time is right."

"The time is right now," Sansa insisted, "before the fighting starts. They've forgotten about me. I know we could slip away if we tried."

"Child, child." Dontos shook his head. "Out of the castle, yes, we could do that, but the city gates are more heavily guarded than ever, and the Imp has even closed off the river."

It was true. The Blackwater Rush was as empty as Sansa had ever seen it. All the ferries had been withdrawn to the north bank, and the trading galleys had fled or been seized by the Imp to be made over for battle. The only ships to be seen were the king's war galleys. They rowed endlessly up and down, staying to the deep water in the middle of the river and exchanging flights of arrows with Stannis's archers on the south shore.

Lord Stannis himself was still on the march, but his vanguard had appeared two nights ago during the black of the moon. King's Landing had woken to the sight of their tents and banners. They were five thousand, Sansa had heard, near as many as all the gold cloaks in the city. They flew the red or green apples of House Fossoway, the turtle of Estermont, and the fox-and-flowers of Florent, and their commander was Ser Guyard Morrigen, a famous southron knight who men now called Guyard the Green. His standard showed a crow in flight, its black wings spread wide against a storm-green sky. But it was the pale yellow banners that worried the city. Long ragged tails streamed behind them like flickering flames, and in place of a lord's sigil they bore the device of a god: the burning heart of the Lord of Light.

"When Stannis comes, he'll have ten times as many men as Joffrey does, everyone says so."

Dontos squeezed her shoulder. "The size of his host does not matter, sweetling, so long as they are on the wrong side of the river. Stannis cannot cross without ships."

"He *has* ships. More than Joffrey."

"It's a long sail from Storm's End, the fleet will need to come up Massey's Hook and through the Gullet and across Blackwater Bay. Perhaps the good gods will send a storm to sweep them from the seas." Dontos gave a hopeful smile. "It is not easy for you, I know. You must be patient, child. When my friend returns to the city, we shall have our ship. Have faith in your Florian, and try not to be afraid."

Sansa dug her nails into her hand. She could feel the fear in her tummy, twisting and pinching, worse every day. Nightmares of the day Princess Myrcella had sailed still troubled her sleep; dark suffocating dreams that woke her in the black of night, struggling for breath. She could hear the people screaming at her, screaming without words, like animals. They had hemmed her in and thrown filth at her and tried to pull her off her horse, and would have done worse if the Hound had not cut his way to her side. They had torn the High Septon to pieces and smashed in Ser Aron's head with a rock. *Try not to be afraid!* he said.

The whole city was afraid. Sansa could see it from the castle walls. The smallfolk were hiding themselves behind closed shutters and barred doors as if that would keep them safe. The last time King's Landing had fallen, the Lannisters looted and raped as they pleased and put hundreds to the sword, even though the city had opened its gates. This time the Imp meant to fight, and a city that fought could expect no mercy at all.

Dontos was prattling on. "If I were still a knight, I should have to put on armor and man the walls with the rest. I ought to kiss King Joffrey's feet and thank him sweetly."

"If you thanked him for making you a fool, he'd make you a knight again," Sansa said sharply.

Dontos chuckled. "My Jonquil's a clever girl, isn't she?"

"Joffrey and his mother say I'm stupid."

"Let them. You're safer that way, sweetling. Queen Cersei and the Imp and Lord Varys and their like, they all watch each other keen as hawks, and pay this one and that one to spy out what the others are doing, but no one ever troubles themselves about Lady Tanda's daughter, do they?" Dontos covered his mouth to stifle a burp. "Gods preserve you, my little Jonquil." He was growing weepy. The wine did that to him. "Give your Florian a little kiss now. A kiss for luck." He swayed toward her.

Sansa dodged the wet groping lips, kissed him lightly on an unshaven cheek, and bid him good night. It took all her strength not to weep. She had been weeping too much of late. It was unseemly, she knew, but she could not seem to help herself; the tears would come, sometimes over a trifle, and nothing she did could hold them back.

The drawbridge to Maegor's Holdfast was unguarded. The Imp had moved most of the gold cloaks to the city walls, and the white knights of the Kingsguard had duties more important than dogging her heels. Sansa could go where she would so long as she did not try to leave the castle, but there was nowhere she wanted to go.

She crossed over the dry moat with its cruel iron spikes and made her way up the narrow turnpike stair, but when she reached the door of her bedchamber she could not bear to enter. The very walls of the room made her feel trapped; even with the window opened wide it felt as though there were no air to breathe.

Turning back to the stair, Sansa climbed. The smoke blotted out the stars and the thin crescent of moon, so the roof was dark and thick with shadows. Yet from here she could see everything: the Red Keep's tall towers and great cornerforts, the maze of city streets beyond, to south and west the river running black, the bay to the east, the columns of smoke and cinders, and fires, fires everywhere. Soldiers crawled over the city walls like ants with torches, and crowded the hoardings that had sprouted from the ramparts. Down by the Mud Gate, outlined against the drifting smoke, she could make out the vague shape of the three huge catapults, the biggest anyone had ever seen, overtopping the walls by a good twenty feet. Yet none of it made her feel less fearful. A stab went through her, so sharp that Sansa sobbed and clutched at her belly. She might have fallen, but a shadow moved suddenly, and strong fingers grabbed her arm and steadied her.

She grabbed a merlon for support, her fingers scrabbling at the rough stone. "Let go of me," she cried. "Let go."

"The little bird thinks she has wings, does she? Or do you mean to end up crippled like that brother of yours?"

Sansa twisted in his grasp. "I wasn't going to fall. It was only . . . you startled me, that's all."

"You mean I scared you. And still do."

She took a deep breath to calm herself. "I thought I was alone, I . . ." She glanced away.

"The little bird still can't bear to look at me, can she?" The Hound released her. "You were glad enough to see my face when the mob had you, though. Remember?"

Sansa remembered all too well. She remembered the way they had howled, the feel of the blood running down her cheek from where the stone had struck her, and the garlic stink on the breath of the man who had tried to pull her from her horse. She could still feel the cruel pinch of fingers on her wrist as she lost her balance and began to fall.

She'd thought she was going to die then, but the fingers had twitched, all five at once, and the man had shrieked loud as a horse. When his hand fell away, another hand, stronger, shoved her back into her saddle. The man with the garlicky breath was on the ground, blood pumping out the stump of his arm, but there were others all around, some with clubs in hand. The Hound leapt at them, his sword a blur of steel that trailed a red mist as it swung. When they broke and ran before him he had laughed, his terrible burned face for a moment transformed.

She made herself look at that face now, really look. It was only courteous, and a lady must never forget her courtesies. *The scars are not the worst part, nor even the way his mouth twitches. It's his eyes.* She had never seen eyes so full of anger. "I . . . I should have come to you after," she said haltingly. "To thank you, for . . . for saving me . . . you were so brave."

"Brave?" His laugh was half a snarl. "A dog doesn't need courage to chase off rats. They had me thirty to one, and not a man of them dared face me."

She hated the way he talked, always so harsh and angry. "Does it give you joy to scare people?"

"No, it gives me joy to kill people." His mouth twitched. "Wrinkle up your face all you like, but spare me this false piety. You were a high lord's get. Don't tell me Lord Eddard Stark of Winterfell never killed a man."

"That was his duty. He never liked it."

"Is that what he told you?" Clegane laughed again. "Your father lied. Killing is the sweetest thing there is." He drew his longsword. "*Here's* your truth. Your precious father found that out on Baelor's steps. Lord of Winterfell, Hand of the King, Warden of the North, the mighty Eddard Stark, of a line eight thousand years old . . . but Ilyn Payne's blade went through his neck all the same, didn't it? Do you remember the dance he did when his head came off his shoulders?"

Sansa hugged herself, suddenly cold. "Why are you always so hateful? I was *thanking* you . . ."

"Just as if I was one of those true knights you love so well, yes. What do you think a knight is *for*, girl? You think it's all taking favors from ladies and looking fine in gold plate? Knights are for *killing*." He laid the edge of his longsword against her neck, just under her ear. Sansa could feel the sharpness of the steel. "I killed my first man at twelve. I've lost count of how many I've killed since then. High lords with old names, fat rich men dressed in velvet, knights puffed up like bladders with their honors, yes, and women and children too— they're all meat, and I'm the butcher. Let them have their lands and their gods and their gold. Let them have their *ser*s." Sandor Clegane spat at her feet to show what he thought of that. "So long as I have this," he said, lifting the sword from her throat, "there's no man on earth I need fear."

Except your brother, Sansa thought, but she had better sense than to say it aloud. *He is a dog, just as he says. A half-wild, mean-tempered dog that bites any hand that tries to pet him, and yet will savage any man who tries to hurt his masters.* "Not even the men across the river?"

Clegane's eyes turned toward the distant fires. "All this burning." He sheathed his sword. "Only cowards fight with fire."

"Lord Stannis is no coward."

"He's not the man his brother was either. Robert never let a little thing like a river stop him."

"What will you do when he crosses?"

"Fight. Kill. Die, maybe."

"Aren't you afraid? The gods might send you down to some terrible hell for all the evil you've done."

"What evil?" He laughed. "What gods?"

"The gods who made us all."

"All?" he mocked. "Tell me, little bird, what kind of god makes a monster like the Imp, or a halfwit like Lady Tanda's daughter? If there are gods, they made sheep so wolves could eat mutton, and they made the weak for the strong to play with."

"True knights protect the weak."

He snorted. "There are no true knights, no more than there are gods. If you can't protect yourself, die and get out of the way of those who can. Sharp steel and strong arms rule this world, don't ever believe any different."

Sansa backed away from him. "You're awful."

"I'm honest. It's the world that's awful. Now fly away, little bird, I'm sick of you peeping at me."

Wordless, she fled. She was afraid of Sandor Clegane . . . and yet, some part of her wished that Ser Dontos had a little of the Hound's ferocity. *There are gods*, she told herself, *and there are true knights too. All the stories can't be lies.*

That night Sansa dreamed of the riot again. The mob surged around her, shrieking, a maddened beast with a thousand faces. Everywhere she turned she saw faces twisted into monstrous inhuman masks. She wept and told them she had never done them hurt, yet they dragged her from her horse all the same. "No," she cried, "no, please, don't, *don't*," but no one paid her any heed. She shouted for Ser Dontos, for her brothers, for her dead father and her dead wolf, for gallant Ser Loras who had given her a red rose once, but none of them came. She called for the heroes from the songs, for Florian and Ser Ryam Redwyne and Prince Aemon the Dragonknight, but no one heard. Women swarmed over her like weasels, pinching her legs and kicking her in the belly, and someone hit her in the face and she felt her teeth shatter. Then she saw the bright glimmer of steel. The knife plunged into her belly and tore and tore and tore, until there was nothing left of her down there but shiny wet ribbons.

When she woke, the pale light of morning was slanting through her window, yet she felt as sick and achy as if she had not slept at all. There was something sticky on her thighs. When she threw back the blanket and saw the blood, all she could think was that her dream had somehow come true. She remembered the knives inside her, twisting and ripping. She squirmed away in horror, kicking at the sheets and falling to the floor, breathing raggedly, naked, bloodied, and afraid.

But as she crouched there, on her hands and knees, understanding came. "No, please," Sansa whimpered, "please, no." She didn't want this happening to her, not now, not here, not now, not now, not now, not now.

Madness took hold of her. Pulling herself up by the bedpost, she went to the basin and washed between her legs, scrubbing away all the stickiness. By the time she was done, the water was pink with blood. When her maidservants saw it they would *know*. Then she remembered the bedclothes. She rushed back to the bed and stared in horror at the dark red stain and the tale it told. All she could think was that she had to get rid of it, or else they'd see. She couldn't let them see, or they'd marry her to Joffrey and make her lay with him.

Snatching up her knife, Sansa hacked at the sheet, cutting out the stain. *If they ask me about the hole, what will I say?* Tears ran down her face. She pulled the torn sheet from the bed, and the stained blanket as well. *I'll have to burn them.* She balled up the evidence, stuffed it in the fireplace, drenched it in oil from her bedside lamp, and lit it afire. Then she realized that the blood had soaked through the sheet into the featherbed, so she bundled that up as well, but it was big and cumbersome, hard to move. Sansa could get only half of it into the fire. She was on her knees, struggling to shove the mattress into the flames as thick grey smoke eddied around her and filled the room, when the door burst open and she heard her maid gasp.

In the end it took three of them to pull her away. And it was all for nothing. The bedclothes were burnt, but by the time they carried her off her thighs were bloody again. It was as if her own body had betrayed her to Joffrey, unfurling a banner of Lannister crimson for all the world to see.

When the fire was out, they carried off the singed featherbed, fanned away the worst of the smoke, and brought up a tub. Women came and went, muttering and looking at her strangely. They filled the tub with scalding hot water, bathed her and washed her hair and gave her a cloth to wear between her legs. By then Sansa was calm again, and ashamed for her folly. The smoke had ruined most of her clothing. One of the women went away and came back with a green wool shift that was almost her size. "It's not as pretty as your own things, but it will serve," she announced when she'd pulled it down over Sansa's head. "Your shoes weren't burned, so at least you won't need to go barefoot to the queen."

Cersei Lannister was breaking her fast when Sansa was ushered into her solar. "You may sit," the queen said graciously. "Are you hungry?" She gestured at the table. There was porridge, honey, milk, boiled eggs, and crisp fried fish.

The sight of the food made Sansa feel ill. Her tummy was tied in a knot. "No, thank you, Your Grace."

"I don't blame you. Between Tyrion and Lord Stannis, everything I eat tastes of ash. And now you're setting fires as well. What did you hope to accomplish?"

Sansa lowered her head. "The blood frightened me."

"The blood is the seal of your womanhood. Lady Catelyn might have prepared you. You've had your first flowering, no more."

Sansa had never felt less flowery. "My lady mother told me, but I . . . I thought it would be different."

"Different how?"

"I don't know. Less . . . less messy, and more magical."

Queen Cersei laughed. "Wait until you birth a child,

Sansa. A woman's life is nine parts mess to one part magic, you'll learn that soon enough . . . and the parts that look like magic often turn out to be messiest of all." She took a sip of milk. "So now you are a woman. Do you have the least idea of what that means?"

"It means that I am now fit to be wedded and bedded," said Sansa, "and to bear children for the king."

The queen gave a wry smile. "A prospect that no longer entices you as it once did, I can see. I will not fault you for that. Joffrey has always been difficult. Even his birth . . . I labored a day and a half to bring him forth. You cannot imagine the pain, Sansa. I screamed so loudly that I fancied Robert might hear me in the kingswood."

"His Grace was not with you?"

"Robert? Robert was hunting. That was his custom. Whenever my time was near, my royal husband would flee to the trees with his huntsmen and hounds. When he returned he would present me with some pelts or a stag's head, and I would present him with a baby.

"Not that I *wanted* him to stay, mind you. I had Grand Maester Pycelle and an army of midwives, and I had my brother. When they told Jaime he was not allowed in the birthing room, he smiled and asked which of them proposed to keep him out.

"Joffrey will show you no such devotion, I fear. You could thank your sister for that, if she weren't dead. He's never been able to forget that day on the Trident when you saw her shame him, so he shames you in turn. You're stronger than you seem, though. I expect you'll survive a bit of humiliation. I did. You may never love the king, but you'll love his children."

"I love His Grace with all my heart," Sansa said.

The queen sighed. "You had best learn some new lies, and quickly. Lord Stannis will not like that one, I promise you."

"The new High Septon said that the gods will never permit Lord Stannis to win, since Joffrey is the rightful king."

A half smile flickered across the queen's face.

"Robert's trueborn son and heir. Though Joff would cry whenever Robert picked him up. His Grace did not like that. His bastards had always gurgled at him happily, and sucked his finger when he put it in their little base-born mouths. Robert wanted smiles and cheers, always, so he went where he found them, to his friends and his whores. Robert wanted to be loved. My brother Tyrion has the same disease. Do you want to be loved, Sansa?"

"Everyone wants to be loved."

"I see flowering hasn't made you any brighter," said Cersei. "Sansa, permit me to share a bit of womanly wisdom with you on this very special day. Love is poison. A sweet poison, yes, but it will kill you all the same."

JON

It was dark in the Skirling Pass. The great stone flanks of the mountains hid the sun for most of the day, so they rode in shadow, the breath of man and horse steaming in the cold air. Icy fingers of water trickled down from the snowpack above into small frozen pools that cracked and broke beneath the hooves of their garrons. Sometimes they would see a few weeds struggling from some crack in the rock or a splotch of pale lichen, but there was no grass, and they were above the trees now.

The track was as steep as it was narrow, wending its way ever upward. Where the pass was so constricted that rangers had to go single file, Squire Dalbridge would take the lead, scanning the heights as he went, his longbow ever close to hand. It was said he had the keenest eyes in the Night's Watch.

Ghost padded restlessly by Jon's side. From time to time he would stop and turn, his ears pricked, as if he heard something behind them. Jon did not think the shadowcats would attack living men, not unless they were starving, but he loosened Longclaw in its scabbard even so.

A wind-carved arch of grey stone marked the highest point of the pass. Here the way broadened as it began its long descent toward the valley of the Milkwater. Qhorin decreed that they would rest here until the shadows began to grow again. "Shadows are friends to men in black," he said.

Jon saw the sense of that. It would be pleasant to ride in the light for a time, to let the bright mountain sun soak through their cloaks and chase the chill from their bones, but they dared not. Where there were three watchers there might be others, waiting to sound the alarm.

Stonesnake curled up under his ragged fur cloak and was asleep almost at once. Jon shared his salt beef with Ghost while Ebben and Squire Dalbridge fed the horses. Qhorin Halfhand sat with his back to a rock, honing the edge of his longsword with long slow strokes. Jon watched the ranger for a few moments, then summoned his courage and went to him. "My lord," he said, "you never asked me how it went. With the girl."

"I am no lord, Jon Snow." Qhorin slid the stone smoothly along the steel with his two-fingered hand.

"She told me Mance would take me, if I ran with her."

"She told you true."

"She even claimed we were kin. She told me a story . . ."

". . . of Bael the Bard and the rose of Winterfell. So Stonesnake told me. It happens I know the song. Mance would sing it of old, when he came back from a ranging. He had a passion for wildling music. Aye, and for their women as well."

"You knew him?"

"We all knew him." His voice was sad. *They were friends as well as brothers,* Jon realized, *and now they are sworn foes.* "Why did he desert?"

"For a wench, some say. For a crown, others would have it." Qhorin tested the edge of his sword with the ball of his thumb. "He liked women, Mance did, and he was not a man whose knees bent easily, that's true. But it was more than that. He loved the wild better than the Wall. It was in his blood. He was wildling born, taken as a child when some raiders were put to the sword. When he left the Shadow Tower he was only going home again."

"Was he a good ranger?"

"He was the best of us," said the Halfhand, "and the worst as well. Only fools like Thoren Smallwood despise the wildlings. They are as brave as we are, Jon. As strong, as quick, as clever. But they have no discipline. They name themselves the free folk, and each one thinks himself as good as a king and wiser than a maester. Mance was the same. He never learned how to obey."

"No more than me," said Jon quietly.

Qhorin's shrewd grey eyes seemed to see right through him. "So you let her go?" He did not sound the least surprised.

"You know?"

"Now. Tell me why you spared her."

It was hard to put into words. "My father never used a headsman. He said he owed it to men he killed to look into their eyes and hear their last words. And when I looked into Ygritte's eyes, I . . ." Jon stared down at his hands helplessly. "I know she was an enemy, but there was no evil in her."

"No more than in the other two."

"It was their lives or ours," Jon said. "If they had seen us, if they had sounded that horn . . ."

"The wildlings would hunt us down and slay us, true enough."

"Stonesnake has the horn now, though, and we took Ygritte's knife and axe. She's behind us, afoot, unarmed . . ."

"And not like to be a threat," Qhorin agreed. "If I had needed her dead, I would have left her with Ebben, or done the thing myself."

"Then why did you command it of me?"

"I did not command it. I told you to do what needed to be done, and left you to decide what that would be." Qhorin stood and slid his longsword back into its scabbard. "When I want a mountain scaled, I call on Stonesnake. Should I need to put an arrow through the eye of some foe across a windy battlefield, I summon Squire Dalbridge. Ebben can make any man give up his secrets. To lead men you must know them, Jon Snow. I know more of you now than I did this morning."

"And if I had slain her?" asked Jon.

"She would be dead, and I would know you better than I had before. But enough talk. You ought be sleeping. We have leagues to go, and dangers to face. You will need your strength."

Jon did not think sleep would come easily, but he knew the Halfhand was right. He found a place out of the wind, beneath an overhang of rock, and took off his cloak to use it for a blanket. "Ghost," he called. "Here. To me." He always slept better with the great white wolf beside him; there was comfort in the smell of him, and welcome warmth in that shaggy pale fur. This time, though, Ghost did no more than look at him. Then he turned away and padded around the garrons, and quick as that he was gone. *He wants to hunt*, Jon thought. Perhaps there were goats in these mountains. The shadowcats must live on something. "Just don't try and bring down a 'cat," he muttered. Even for a direwolf, that would be dangerous. He tugged his cloak over him and stretched out beneath the rock.

When he closed his eyes, he dreamed of direwolves.

There were five of them when there should have been six, and they were scattered, each apart from the others. He felt a deep ache of emptiness, a sense of incompleteness. The forest was vast and cold, and they were so small, so lost. His brothers were out there somewhere, and his sister, but he had lost their scent. He sat on his haunches and lifted his head to the darkening sky, and his cry echoed through the forest, a long lonely mournful sound. As it died away, he pricked up his ears, listening for an answer, but the only sound was the sigh of blowing snow.

Jon?

The call came from behind him, softer than a whisper, but strong too. Can a shout be silent? He turned his head, searching for his brother, for a glimpse of a lean grey shape moving beneath the trees, but there was nothing, only . . .

A weirwood.

It seemed to sprout from solid rock, its pale roots twisting up from a myriad of fissures and hairline cracks. The tree was slender compared to other weirwoods he had seen, no more than a sapling, yet it was growing as he watched, its limbs thickening as they reached for the sky. Wary, he circled the smooth white trunk until he came to the face. Red eyes looked at him. Fierce eyes they were, yet glad to see him. The weirwood had his brother's face. Had his brother always had three eyes?

Not always, came the silent shout. *Not before the crow.*

He sniffed at the bark, smelled wolf and tree and boy, but behind that there were other scents, the rich brown smell of warm earth and the hard grey smell of stone and something else, something terrible. Death, he knew. He was smelling death. He cringed back, his hair bristling, and bared his fangs.

Don't be afraid, I like it in the dark. No one can see you, but you can see them. But first you have to open your eyes. See? Like this. And the tree reached down and touched him.

And suddenly he was back in the mountains, his paws sunk deep in a drift of snow as he stood upon the edge of a great precipice. Before him the Skirling Pass opened up into airy emptiness, and a long vee-shaped valley lay spread beneath him like a quilt, awash in all the colors of an autumn afternoon.

A vast blue-white wall plugged one end of the vale, squeezing between the mountains as if it had shoul- dered them aside, and for a moment he thought he had dreamed himself back to Castle Black. Then he realized he was looking at a river of ice several thousand feet high. Under that glittering cold cliff was a great lake, its deep cobalt waters reflecting the snowcapped peaks that ringed it. There were men down in the valley, he saw now; many men, thousands, a huge host. Some were tearing great holes in the half-frozen ground, while others trained for war. He watched as a swarming mass of riders charged a shield wall, astride horses no larger than ants. The sound of their mock battle was a rustling of steel leaves, drifting faintly on the wind. Their encampment had no plan to it; he saw no ditches, no sharpened stakes, no neat rows of horse lines. Everywhere crude earthen shelters and hide tents sprouted haphazardly, like a pox on the face of the earth. He spied untidy mounds of hay, smelled goats and sheep, horses and pigs, dogs in great profusion. Tendrils of dark smoke rose from a thousand cookfires.

This is no army, no more than it is a town. This is a whole people come together.

Across the long lake, one of the mounds moved. He watched it more closely and saw that it was not dirt at all, but alive, a shaggy lumbering beast with a snake for a nose and tusks larger than those of the greatest boar that had ever lived. And the thing riding it was huge as well, and his shape was wrong, too thick in the leg and hips to be a man.

Then a sudden gust of cold made his fur stand up, and the air thrilled to the sound of wings. As he lifted his eyes to the ice-white mountain heights above, a shadow plummeted out of the sky. A shrill scream split the air. He glimpsed blue-grey pinions spread wide, shutting out the sun . . .

"*Ghost!*" Jon shouted, sitting up. He could still feel the talons, the *pain.* "Ghost, to me!"

Ebben appeared, grabbed him, shook him. "Quiet! You mean to bring the wildlings down on us? What's wrong with you, boy?"

"A dream," said Jon feebly. "I was Ghost, I was on the edge of the mountain looking down on a frozen river, and something attacked me. A bird . . . an eagle, I think . . ."

Squire Dalbridge smiled. "It's always pretty women in my dreams. Would that I dreamed more often."

Qhorin came up beside him. "A frozen river, you say?"

"The Milkwater flows from a great lake at the foot of a glacier," Stonesnake put in.

"There was a tree with my brother's face. The wildlings . . . there were *thousands*, more than I ever knew existed. And giants riding mammoths." From the way the light had shifted, Jon judged that he had been asleep for four or five hours. His head ached, and the back of his neck where the talons had burned through him. *But that was in the dream.*

"Tell me all that you remember, from first to last," said Qhorin Halfhand.

Jon was confused. "It was only a dream."

"A wolf dream," the Halfhand said. "Craster told the Lord Commander that the wildlings were gathering at the source of the Milkwater. That may be why you dreamed it. Or it may be that you saw what waits for us, a few hours farther on. Tell me."

It made him feel half a fool to talk of such things to Qhorin and the other rangers, but he did as he was commanded. None of the black brothers laughed at him, however. By the time he was done, even Squire Dalbridge was no longer smiling.

"Skinchanger?" said Ebben grimly, looking at the Halfhand. *Does he mean the eagle?* Jon wondered. *Or me?* Skinchangers and wargs belonged in Old Nan's stories, not in the world he had lived in all his life. Yet here, in this strange bleak wilderness of rock and ice, it was not hard to believe.

"The cold winds are rising. Mormont feared as much. Benjen Stark felt it as well. Dead men walk and the trees have eyes again. Why should we balk at wargs and giants?"

"Does this mean my dreams are true as well?" asked

Squire Dalbridge. "Lord Snow can keep his mammoths, I want my women."

"Man and boy I've served the Watch, and ranged as far as any," said Ebben. "I've seen the bones of giants, and heard many a queer tale, but no more. I want to see them with my own eyes."

"Be careful they don't see you, Ebben," Stonesnake said.

Ghost did not reappear as they set out again. The shadows covered the floor of the pass by then, and the sun was sinking fast toward the jagged twin peaks of the huge mountain the rangers named Forktop. *If the dream was true . . .* Even the thought scared him. Could the eagle have hurt Ghost, or knocked him off the precipice? And what about the weirwood with his brother's face, that smelled of death and darkness?

The last ray of sun vanished behind the peaks of Forktop. Twilight filled the Skirling Pass. It seemed to grow colder almost at once. They were no longer climbing. In fact, the ground had begun to descend, though as yet not sharply. It was littered with cracks and broken boulders and tumbled heaps of rock. *It will be dark soon, and still no sight of Ghost.* It was tearing Jon apart, yet he dare not shout for the direwolf as he would have liked. Other things might be listening as well.

"Qhorin," Squire Dalbridge called softly. "There. Look."

The eagle was perched on a spine of rock far above them, outlined against the darkening sky. *We've seen other eagles,* Jon thought. *That need not be the one I dreamed of.*

Even so, Ebben would have loosed a shaft at it, but the squire stopped him. "The bird's well out of bowshot."

"I don't like it watching us."

The squire shrugged. "Nor me, but you won't stop it. Only waste a good arrow."

Qhorin sat in his saddle, studying the eagle for a long time. "We press on," he finally said. The rangers resumed their descent.

Ghost, Jon wanted to shout, *where are you!*

He was about to follow Qhorin and the others when he glimpsed a flash of white between two boulders. *A patch of old snow,* he thought, until he saw it stir. He was off his horse at once. As he went to his knees, Ghost lifted his head. His neck glistened wetly, but he made no sound when Jon peeled off a glove and touched him. The talons had torn a bloody path through fur and flesh, but the bird had not been able to snap his neck.

Qhorin Halfhand was standing over him. "How bad?"

As if in answer, Ghost struggled to his feet.

"The wolf is strong," the ranger said. "Ebben, water. Stonesnake, your skin of wine. Hold him still, Jon."

Together they washed the caked blood from the direwolf's fur. Ghost struggled and bared his teeth when Qhorin poured the wine into the ragged red gashes the eagle had left him, but Jon wrapped his arms around him and murmured soothing words, and soon enough the wolf quieted. By the time they'd ripped a strip from Jon's cloak to wrap the wounds, full dark had settled. Only a dusting of stars set the black of sky apart from the black of stone. "Do we press on?" Stonesnake wanted to know.

Qhorin went to his garron. "Back, not on."

"Back?" Jon was taken by surprise.

"Eagles have sharper eyes than men. We are seen. So now we run." The Halfhand wound a long black scarf around his face and swung up into the saddle.

The other rangers exchanged a look, but no man thought to argue. One by one they mounted and turned their mounts toward home. "Ghost, come," he called, and the direwolf followed, a pale shadow moving through the night.

All night they rode, feeling their way up the twisting pass and through the stretches of broken ground. The wind grew stronger. Sometimes it was so dark that they dismounted and went ahead on foot, each man leading his garron. Once Ebben suggested that some torches might serve them well, but Qhorin said, "No fire," and that was the end of that. They reached the stone bridge at the summit and began to descend again. Off in the darkness a shadowcat screamed in fury, its voice bouncing off the rocks so it seemed as though a dozen other 'cats were giving answer. Once Jon thought he saw a pair of glowing eyes on a ledge overhead, as big as harvest moons.

In the black hour before dawn, they stopped to let the horses drink and fed them each a handful of oats and a twist or two of hay. "We are not far from the place the wildlings died," said Qhorin. "From there, one man could hold a hundred. The right man." He looked at Squire Dalbridge.

The squire bowed his head. "Leave me as many arrows as you can spare, brothers." He stroked his longbow. "And see my garron has an apple when you're home. He's earned it, poor beastie."

He's staying to die, Jon realized.

Qhorin clasped the squire's forearm with a gloved hand. "If the eagle flies down for a look at you . . ."

". . . he'll sprout some new feathers."

The last Jon saw of Squire Dalbridge was his back as he clambered up the narrow path to the heights.

When dawn broke, Jon looked up into a cloudless sky and saw a speck moving through the blue. Ebben saw it too, and cursed, but Qhorin told him to be quiet. "Listen."

Jon held his breath, and heard it. Far away and behind them, the call of a hunting horn echoed against the mountains.

"And now they come," said Qhorin.

TYRION

Pod dressed him for his ordeal in a plush velvet
tunic of Lannister crimson and brought him his
chain of office. Tyrion left it on the bedside table. His sister misliked being reminded that he was the
King's Hand, and he did not wish to inflame the relations between them any further.

Varys caught up with him as he was crossing the yard.
"My lord," he said, a little out of breath. "You had best
read this at once." He held out a parchment in a soft
white hand. "A report from the north."

"Good news or bad?" Tyrion asked.

"That is not for me to judge."

Tyrion unrolled the parchment. He had to squint to
read the words in the torchlit yard. "Gods be good," he
said softly. "Both of them?"

"I fear so, my lord. It is so sad. So grievous sad. And
them so young and innocent."

Tyrion remembered how the wolves had howled
when the Stark boy had fallen. *Are they howling now, I
wonder!* "Have you told anyone else?" he asked.

"Not as yet, though of course I must."

He rolled up the letter. "I'll tell my sister." He wanted to see how she took the news. He wanted that very much.

The queen looked especially lovely that night. She wore a low-cut gown of deep green velvet that brought out the color of her eyes. Her golden hair tumbled across her bare shoulders, and around her waist was a woven belt studded with emeralds. Tyrion waited until he had been seated and served a cup of wine before thrusting the letter at her. He said not a word. Cersei blinked at him innocently and took the parchment from his hand.

"I trust you're pleased," he said as she read. "You wanted the Stark boy dead, I believe."

Cersei made a sour face. "It was Jaime who threw him from that window, not me. For love, he said, as if that would please me. It was a stupid thing to do, and dangerous besides, but when did our sweet brother ever stop to think?"

"The boy saw you," Tyrion pointed out.

"He was a child. I could have frightened him into silence." She looked at the letter thoughtfully. "Why must I suffer accusations every time some Stark stubs his toe? This was Greyjoy's work, I had nothing to do with it."

"Let us hope Lady Catelyn believes that."

Her eyes widened. "She wouldn't—"

"—kill Jaime? Why not? What would you do if Joffrey and Tommen were murdered?"

"I still hold Sansa!" the queen declared.

"We still hold Sansa," he corrected her, "and we had best take good care of her. Now where is this supper you've promised me, sweet sister?"

Cersei set a tasty table, that could not be denied. They started with a creamy chestnut soup, crusty hot bread, and greens dressed with apples and pine nuts. Then came lamprey pie, honeyed ham, buttered carrots, white beans and bacon, and roast swan stuffed with mushrooms and oysters. Tyrion was exceedingly courteous; he offered his sister the choice portions of every dish, and made certain he ate only what she did. Not that he truly thought she'd poison him, but it never hurt to be careful.

The news about the Starks had soured her, he could see. "We've had no word from Bitterbridge?" she asked anxiously as she speared a bit of apple on the point of her dagger and ate it with small, delicate bites.

"None."

"I've never trusted Littlefinger. For enough coin, he'd go over to Stannis in a heartbeat."

"Stannis Baratheon is too bloody righteous to buy men. Nor would he make a comfortable lord for the likes of Petyr. This war has made for some queer bedfellows, I agree, but those two? No."

As he carved some slices off the ham, she said, "We have Lady Tanda to thank for the pig."

"A token of her love?"

"A bribe. She begs leave to return to her castle. Your leave as well as mine. I suspect she fears you'll arrest her on the road, as you did Lord Gyles."

"Does she plan to make off with the heir to the throne?" Tyrion served his sister a cut of ham and took one for himself. "I'd sooner she remain. If she wants to feel safe, tell her to bring down her garrison from Stokeworth. As many men as she has."

"If we need men so badly, why did you send away your savages?" A certain testiness crept into Cersei's voice.

"It was the best use I could have made of them," he told her truthfully. "They're fierce warriors, but not soldiers. In formal battle, discipline is more important than courage. They've already done us more good in the kingswood than they would ever have done us on the city walls."

As the swan was being served, the queen questioned him about the conspiracy of the Antler Men. She seemed more annoyed than afraid. "Why are we plagued with so many treasons? What injury has House Lannister ever done these wretches?"

"None," said Tyrion, "but they think to be on the winning side . . . which makes them fools as well as traitors."

"Are you certain you've found them all?"

"Varys says so." The swan was too rich for his taste.

A line appeared on Cersei's pale white brow, between those lovely eyes. "You put too much trust in that eunuch."

"He serves me well."

"Or so he'd have you believe. You think you're the only one he whispers secrets to? He gives each of us just enough to convince us that we'd be helpless without him. He played the same game with me, when I first wed Robert. For years, I was convinced I had no truer friend at court, but now . . ." She studied his face for a moment. "He says you mean to take the Hound from Joffrey."

Damn Varys. "I need Clegane for more important duties."

"Nothing is more important than the life of the king."

"The life of the king is not at risk. Joff will have brave Ser Osmund guarding him, and Meryn Trant as well." *They're good for nothing better.* "I need Balon Swann and the Hound to lead sorties, to make certain Stannis gets no toehold on our side of the Blackwater."

"Jaime would lead the sorties himself."

"From Riverrun? That's quite a sortie."

"Joff's only a boy."

"A boy who wants to be part of this battle, and for once he's showing some sense. I don't intend to put him in the thick of the fighting, but he needs to be seen. Men fight more fiercely for a king who shares their peril than one who hides behind his mother's skirts."

"He's *thirteen*, Tyrion."

"Remember Jaime at thirteen? If you want the boy to be his father's son, let him play the part. Joff wears the finest armor gold can buy, and he'll have a dozen gold cloaks around him at all times. If the city looks to be in the least danger of falling, I'll have him escorted back to the Red Keep at once."

He had thought that might reassure her, but he saw no sign of pleasure in those green eyes. "*Will* the city fall?"

"No." *But if it does, pray that we can hold the Red Keep long enough for our lord father to march to our relief.*

"You've lied to me before, Tyrion."

"Always with good reason, sweet sister. I want amity between us as much as you do. I've decided to release Lord Gyles." He had kept Gyles safe for just this gesture. "You can have Ser Boros Blount back as well."

The queen's mouth tightened. "Ser Boros can rot at Rosby," she said, "but Tommen—"

"—stays where he is. He's safer under Lord Jacelyn's protection than he would ever have been with Lord Gyles."

Serving men cleared away the swan, hardly touched. Cersei beckoned for the sweet. "I hope you like blackberry tarts."

"I love all sorts of tarts."

"Oh, I've known that a long while. Do you know why Varys is so dangerous?"

"Are we playing at riddles now? No."

"He doesn't have a cock."

"Neither do you." *And don't you just hate that, Cersei?*

"Perhaps I'm dangerous too. You, on the other hand, are as big a fool as every other man. That worm between your legs does half your thinking."

Tyrion licked the crumbs off his fingers. He did not like his sister's smile. "Yes, and just now my worm is thinking that perhaps it is time I took my leave."

"Are you unwell, brother?" She leaned forward, giving him a good look at the top of her breasts. "Suddenly you appear somewhat flustered."

"Flustered?" Tyrion glanced at the door. He thought he'd heard something outside. He was beginning to regret coming here alone. "You've never shown much interest in my cock before."

"It's not your cock that interests me, so much as what you stick it in. I don't depend on the eunuch for everything, as you do. I have my own ways of finding out things . . . especially things that people don't want me to know."

"What are you trying to say?"

"Only this—*I have your little whore.*"

Tyrion reached for his wine cup, buying a moment to gather his thoughts. "I thought men were more to your taste."

"You're such a droll little fellow. Tell me, have you married this one yet?" When he gave her no answer she laughed and said, "Father will be ever so relieved."

His belly felt as if it were full of eels. How had she found Shae? Had Varys betrayed him? Or had all his precautions been undone by his impatience the night he rode directly to the manse? "Why should you care who I choose to warm my bed?"

"A Lannister always pays his debts," she said. "You've been scheming against me since the day you came to King's Landing. You sold Myrcella, stole Tommen, and now you plot to have Joff killed. You want him dead so you can rule through Tommen."

Well, I can't say the notion isn't tempting. "This is madness, Cersei. Stannis will be here in days. You need me."

"For what? Your great prowess in battle?"

"Bronn's sellswords will never fight without me," he lied.

"Oh, I think they will. It's your gold they love, not your impish wit. Have no fear, though, they won't be without you. I won't say I haven't thought of slitting your throat from time to time, but Jaime would never forgive me if I did."

"And the whore?" He would not call her by name. *If I can convince her Shae means nothing to me, perhaps . . .*

"She'll be treated gently enough, so long as no harm

comes to my sons. If Joff should be killed, however, or if
Tommen should fall into the hands of our enemies,
your little cunt will die more painfully than you can
possibly imagine."

She truly believes I mean to kill my own nephew.
"The boys are safe," he promised her wearily. "Gods be
good, Cersei, they're my own blood! What sort of man
do you take me for?"

"A small and twisted one."

Tyrion stared at the dregs on the bottom of his wine
cup. *What would Jaime do in my place?* Kill the bitch,
most likely, and worry about the consequences afterward. But Tyrion did not have a golden sword, nor the
skill to wield one. He loved his brother's reckless wrath,
but it was their lord father he must try and emulate.
*Stone, I must be stone, I must be Casterly Rock, hard
and unmovable. If I fail this test, I had as lief seek out
the nearest grotesquerie.* "For all I know, you've killed
her already," he said.

"Would you like to see her? I thought you might."
Cersei crossed the room and threw open the heavy
oaken door. "Bring in my brother's whore."

Ser Osmund's brothers Osney and Osfryd were peas
from the same pod, tall men with hooked noses, dark
hair, and cruel smiles. She hung between them, eyes
wide and white in her dark face. Blood trickled from her
broken lip, and he could see bruises through her torn
clothing. Her hands were bound with rope, and they'd
gagged her so she could not speak.

"You said she wouldn't be hurt."

"She fought." Unlike his brothers, Osney Kettleblack
was clean-shaven, so the scratches showed plainly on
his bare cheeks. "Got claws like a shadowcat, this one."

"Bruises heal," said Cersei in a bored tone. "The
whore will live. So long as Joff does."

Tyrion wanted to laugh at her. It would have been so
sweet, so very very sweet, but it would have given the
game away. *You've lost, Cersei, and the Kettleblacks
are even bigger fools than Bronn claimed.* All he needed
to do was say the words.

Instead he looked at the girl's face and said, "You swear you'll release her after the battle?"

"If you release Tommen, yes."

He pushed himself to his feet. "Keep her then, but keep her safe. If these animals think they can use her . . . well, sweet sister, let me point out that a scale tips two ways." His tone was calm, flat, uncaring; he'd reached for his father's voice, and found it. "Whatever happens to her happens to Tommen as well, and that includes the beatings and rapes." *If she thinks me such a monster, I'll play the part for her.*

Cersei had not expected that. "You would not dare."

Tyrion made himself smile, slow and cold. Green and black, his eyes laughed at her. "Dare? I'll do it myself."

His sister's hand flashed at his face, but he caught her wrist and bent it back until she cried out. Osfryd moved to her rescue. "One more step and I'll break her arm," the dwarf warned him. The man stopped. "You remember when I said you'd never hit me again, Cersei?" He shoved her to the floor and turned back to the Kettleblacks. "Untie her and remove that gag."

The rope had been so tight as to cut off the blood to her hands. She cried out in pain as the circulation returned. Tyrion massaged her fingers gently until feeling returned. "Sweetling," he said, "you must be brave. I am sorry they hurt you."

"I know you'll free me, my lord."

"I will," he promised, and Alayaya bent over and kissed him on the brow. Her broken lips left a smear of blood on his forehead. *A bloody kiss is more than I deserve,* Tyrion thought. *She would never have been hurt but for me.*

Her blood still marked him as he looked down at the queen. "I have never liked you, Cersei, but you were my own sister, so I never did you harm. You've ended that. I will hurt you for this. I don't know how yet, but give me time. A day will come when you think yourself safe and happy, and suddenly your joy will turn to ashes in your mouth, and you'll know the debt is paid."

In war, his father had told him once, the battle is over in the instant one army breaks and flees. No matter that they're as numerous as they were a moment before, still armed and armored; once they had run before you they would not turn to fight again. So it was with Cersei. "Get out!" was all the answer she could summon. "Get out of my sight!"

Tyrion bowed. "Good night, then. And pleasant dreams."

He made his way back to the Tower of the Hand with a thousand armored feet marching through his skull. *I ought to have seen this coming the first time I slipped through the back of Chataya's wardrobe.* Perhaps he had not *wanted* to see. His legs were aching badly by the time he had made the climb. He sent Pod for a flagon of wine and pushed his way into his bedchamber.

Shae sat cross-legged in the canopied bed, nude but for the heavy golden chain that looped across the swell of her breasts: a chain of linked golden hands, each clasping the next.

Tyrion had not expected her. "What are you doing here?"

Laughing, she stroked the chain. "I wanted some hands on my titties . . . but these little gold ones are cold."

For a moment he did know what to say. How could he tell her that another woman had taken the beating meant for her, and might well die in her place should some mischance of battle fell Joffrey? He wiped Alayaya's blood from his brow with the heel of his hand. "The Lady Lollys—"

"She's asleep. Sleep's all she ever wants to do, the great cow. She sleeps and she eats. Sometimes she falls asleep while she's eating. The food falls under the blankets and she *rolls* in it, and I have to clean her." She made a disgusted face. "All they did was *fuck* her."

"Her mother says she's sick."

"She has a baby in her belly, that's all."

Tyrion gazed around the room. Everything seemed

much as he left it. "How did you enter? Show me the hidden door."

She gave a shrug. "Lord Varys made me wear a hood. I couldn't see, except . . . there was one place, I got a peep at the floor out the bottom of the hood. It was all tiles, you know, the kind that make a picture?"

"A mosaic?"

Shae nodded. "They were colored red and black. I think the picture was a dragon. Otherwise, everything was dark. We went down a ladder and walked a long ways, until I was all twisted around. Once we stopped so he could unlock an iron gate. I brushed against it when we went through. The dragon was past the gate. Then we went up another ladder, with a tunnel at the top. I had to stoop, and I think Lord Varys was crawling."

Tyrion made a round of the bedchamber. One of the sconces looked loose. He stood on his toes and tried to turn it. It revolved slowly, scraping against the stone wall. When it was upside down, the stub of the candle fell out. The rushes scattered across the cold stone floor did not show any particular disturbance. "Doesn't m'lord want to bed me?" asked Shae.

"In a moment." Tyrion threw open his wardrobe, shoved the clothing aside, and pushed against the rear panel. What worked for a whorehouse might work for a castle as well . . . but no, the wood was solid, unyielding. A stone beside the window seat drew his eye, but all his tugging and prodding went for naught. He returned to the bed frustrated and annoyed.

Shae undid his laces and threw her arms around his neck. "Your shoulders feel as hard as rocks," she murmured. "Hurry, I want to feel you inside me." Yet as her legs locked around his waist, his manhood left him. When she felt him go soft, Shae slid down under the sheets and took him in her mouth, but even that could not rouse him.

After a few moments he stopped her. "What's wrong?" she asked. All the sweet innocence of the world was written there in the lines of her young face.

Innocence? Fool, she's a whore, Cersei was right, you think with your cock, fool, fool.

"Just go to sleep, sweetling," he urged, stroking her hair. Yet long after Shae had taken his advice, Tyrion himself still lay awake, his fingers cupped over one small breast as he listened to her breathing.

CATELYN

The Great Hall of Riverrun was a lonely place for two to sit to supper. Deep shadows draped the walls. One of the torches had guttered out, leaving only three. Catelyn sat staring into her wine goblet. The vintage tasted thin and sour on her tongue. Brienne was across from her. Between them, her father's high seat was as empty as the rest of the hall. Even the servants were gone. She had given them leave to join the celebration.

The walls of the keep were thick, yet even so, they could hear the muffled sounds of revelry from the yard outside. Ser Desmond had brought twenty casks up from the cellars, and the smallfolk were celebrating Edmure's imminent return and Robb's conquest of the Crag by hoisting horns of nut-brown ale.

I cannot blame them, Catelyn thought. *They do not know. And if they did, why should they care? They never knew my sons. Never watched Bran climb with their hearts in their throats, pride and terror so mingled they seemed as one, never heard him laugh, never smiled to see Rickon trying so fiercely to be like his older brothers.* She stared at the supper set before her: trout wrapped in bacon, salad of turnip greens and red fennel and sweetgrass, pease and onions and hot bread. Brienne was eating methodically, as if supper were another chore to be accomplished. *I am become a sour woman,* Catelyn thought. *I take no joy in mead nor meat, and song and laughter have become suspicious strangers to me. I am a creature of grief and dust and bitter longings. There is an empty place within me where my heart was once.*

The sound of the other woman's eating had become intolerable to her. "Brienne, I am no fit company. Go join the revels, if you would. Drink a horn of ale and dance to Rymund's harping."

"I am not made for revels, my lady." Her big hands tore apart a heel of black bread. Brienne stared at the chunks as if she had forgotten what they were. "If you command it, I . . ."

Catelyn could sense her discomfort. "I only thought you might enjoy happier company than mine."

"I'm well content." The girl used the bread to sop up some of the bacon grease the trout had been fried in.

"There was another bird this morning." Catelyn did not know why she said it. "The maester woke me at once. That was dutiful, but not kind. Not kind at all." She had not meant to tell Brienne. No one knew but her and Maester Vyman, and she had meant to keep it that way until . . . until . . .

Until what? Foolish woman, will holding it secret in your heart make it any less true? If you never tell, never speak of it, will it become only a dream, less than a dream, a nightmare half-remembered? Oh, if only the gods would be so good.

"Is it news of King's Landing?" asked Brienne.

"Would that it was. The bird came from Castle Cerwyn, from Ser Rodrik, my castellan." *Dark wings, dark words.* "He has gathered what power he could and is marching on Winterfell, to take the castle back."

How unimportant all that sounded now. "But he said ... he wrote ... he told me, he ...."

"My lady, what is it? Is it some news of your sons?"

Such a simple question that was; would that the answer could be as simple. When Catelyn tried to speak, the words caught in her throat. "I have no sons but Robb." She managed those terrible words without a sob, and for that much she was glad.

Brienne looked at her with horror. "My lady?"

"Bran and Rickon tried to escape, but were taken at a mill on the Acorn Water. Theon Greyjoy has mounted their heads on the walls of Winterfell. Theon Greyjoy, who ate at my table since he was a boy of ten." *I have said it, gods forgive me. I have said it and made it true.*

Brienne's face was a watery blur. She reached across the table, but her fingers stopped short of Catelyn's, as if the touch might be unwelcome. "I ... there are no words, my lady. My good lady. Your sons, they ... they're with the gods now."

"Are they?" Catelyn said sharply. "What god would let this happen? Rickon was only a baby. How could he deserve such a death? And Bran ... when I left the north, he had not opened his eyes since his fall. I had to go before he woke. Now I can never return to him, or hear him laugh again." She showed Brienne her palms, her fingers. "These scars ... they sent a man to cut Bran's throat as he lay sleeping. He would have died then, and me with him, but Bran's wolf tore out the man's throat." That gave her a moment's pause. "I suppose Theon killed the wolves too. He must have, elsewise ... I was certain the boys would be safe so long as the direwolves were with them. Like Robb with his Grey Wind. But my daughters have no wolves now."

The abrupt shift of topic left Brienne bewildered. "Your daughters ..."

"Sansa was a lady at three, always so courteous and eager to please. She loved nothing so well as tales of knightly valor. Men would say she had my look, but she will grow into a woman far more beautiful than I ever was, you can see that. I often sent away her maid so I could brush her hair myself. She had auburn hair, lighter than mine, and so thick and soft . . . the red in it would catch the light of the torches and shine like copper.

"And Arya, well ·. . . Ned's visitors would oft mistake her for a stableboy if they rode into the yard unannounced. Arya was a trial, it must be said. Half a boy and half a wolf pup. Forbid her anything and it became her heart's desire. She had Ned's long face, and brown hair that always looked as though a bird had been nesting in it. I despaired of ever making a lady of her. She collected scabs as other girls collect dolls, and would say anything that came into her head. I think she must be dead too." When she said that, it felt as though a giant hand were squeezing her chest. "I want them all dead, Brienne. Theon Greyjoy first, then Jaime Lannister and Cersei and the Imp, every one, every one. But my girls . . . my girls will . . ."

"The queen . . . she has a little girl of her own," Brienne said awkwardly. "And sons too, of an age with yours. When she hears, perhaps she . . . she may take pity, and . . ."

"Send my daughters back unharmed?" Catelyn smiled sadly. "There is a sweet innocence about you, child. I could wish . . . but no. Robb will avenge his brothers. Ice can kill as dead as fire. *Ice* was Ned's great-sword. Valyrian steel, marked with the ripples of a thousand foldings, so sharp I feared to touch it. Robb's blade is dull as a cudgel compared to Ice. It will not be easy for him to get Theon's head off, I fear. The Starks do not use headsmen. Ned always said that the man who passes the sentence should swing the blade, though he never took any joy in the duty. But *I* would, oh, yes." She stared at her scarred hands, opened and closed them, then slowly raised her eyes. "I've sent him wine."

"Wine?" Brienne was lost. "Robb? Or . . . Theon Greyjoy?"

"The Kingslayer." The ploy had served her well with Cleos Frey. *I hope you're thirsty, Jaime. I hope your throat is dry and tight.* "I would like you to come with me."

"I am yours to command, my lady."

"Good." Catelyn rose abruptly. "Stay, finish your meal in peace. I will send for you later. At midnight."

"So late, my lady?"

"The dungeons are windowless. One hour is much like another down there, and for me, all hours are midnight." Her footsteps rang hollowly when Catelyn left the hall. As she climbed to Lord Hoster's solar, she could hear them outside, shouting, "Tully!" and "A cup! A cup to the brave young lord!" *My father is not dead,* she wanted to shout down at them. *My sons are dead, but my father lives, damn you all, and he is your lord still.*

Lord Hoster was deep in sleep. "He had a cup of dreamwine not so long ago, my lady," Maester Vyman said. "For the pain. He will not know you are here."

"It makes no matter," Catelyn said. *He is more dead than alive, yet more alive than my poor sweet sons.*

"My lady, is there aught I might do for you? A sleeping draught, perhaps?"

"Thank you, Maester, but no. I will not sleep away my grief. Bran and Rickon deserve better from me. Go and join the celebration, I will sit with my father for a time."

"As you will, my lady." Vyman bowed and left her.

Lord Hoster lay on his back, mouth open, his breath a faint whistling sigh. One hand hung over the edge of the mattress, a pale frail fleshless thing, but warm when she touched it. She slid her fingers through his and closed them. *No matter how tightly I hold him, I cannot keep him here,* she thought sadly. *Let him go.* Yet her fingers would not seem to unbend.

"I have no one to talk with, Father," she told him. "I pray, but the gods do not answer." Lightly she kissed his hand. The skin was warm, blue veins branching like rivers beneath his pale translucent skin. Outside the greater rivers flowed, the Red Fork and the Tumblestone, and they would flow forever, but not so the rivers in her father's hand. Too soon that current would grow still. "Last night I dreamed of that time Lysa and I got lost while riding back from Seagard. Do you remember? That strange·fog came up and we fell behind the rest of the party. Everything was grey, and I could not see a foot past the nose of my horse. We lost the road. The branches of the trees were like long skinny arms reaching out to grab us as we passed. Lysa started to cry, and when I shouted the fog seemed to swallow the sound. But Petyr knew where we were, and he rode back and found us . . .

"But there's no one to find me now, is there? This time I have to find our own way, and it is hard, so hard.

"I keep remembering the Stark words. Winter has come, Father. For me. For me. Robb must fight the Greyjoys now as well as the Lannisters, and for what? For a gold hat and an iron chair? Surely the land has bled enough. I want my girls back, I want Robb to lay down his sword and pick some homely daughter of Walder Frey to make him happy and give him sons. I want Bran and Rickon back, I want . . ." Catelyn hung her head. "I want," she said once more, and then her words were gone.

After a time the candle guttered and went out. Moonlight slanted between the slats of the shutters, laying pale silvery bars across her father's face. She could hear the soft whisper of his labored breathing, the endless rush of waters, the faint chords of some love song drifting up from the yard, so sad and sweet. *"I loved a maid as red as autumn,"* Rymund sang, *"with sunset in her hair."*

Catelyn never noticed when the singing ended. Hours had passed, yet it seemed only a heartbeat before Brienne was at the door. "My lady," she announced softly. "Midnight has come."

Midnight has come, Father, she thought, *and I must do my duty.* She let go of his hand.

The gaoler was a furtive little man with broken veins in his nose. They found him bent over a tankard of ale and the remains of a pigeon pie, more than a little drunk. He squinted at them suspiciously. "Begging your forgiveness, m'lady, but Lord Edmure says no one is to see the Kingslayer without a writing from him, with his seal upon it."

"*Lord* Edmure? Has my father died, and no one told me?"

The gaoler licked his lips. "No, m'lady, not as I knows."

"You will open the cell, or you will come with me to Lord Hoster's solar and tell him why you saw fit to defy me."

His eyes fell. "As m'lady says." The keys were chained to the studded leather belt that girdled his waist. He muttered under his breath as he sorted through them, until he found the one that fit the door to the Kingslayer's cell.

"Go back to your ale and leave us," she commanded. An oil lamp hung from a hook on the low ceiling. Catelyn took it down and turned up the flame. "Brienne, see that I am not disturbed."

Nodding, Brienne took up a position just outside the cell, her hand resting on the pommel of her sword. "My lady will call if she has need of me."

Catelyn shouldered aside the heavy wood-and-iron door and stepped into foul darkness. This was the bowels of Riverrun, and smelled the part. Old straw crackled underfoot. The walls were discolored with patches of nitre. Through the stone, she could hear the faint rush of the Tumblestone. The lamplight revealed a pail overflowing with feces in one corner and a huddled shape in another. The flagon of wine stood beside the door, untouched. *So much for that ploy. I ought to be thankful that the gaoler did not drink it himself, I suppose.*

Jaime raised his hands to cover his face, the chains around his wrists clanking. "Lady Stark," he said, in a voice hoarse with disuse. "I fear I am in no condition to receive you."

"Look at me, ser."

"The light hurts my eyes. A moment, if you would."

Jaime Lannister had been allowed no razor since the night he was taken in the Whispering Wood, and a shaggy beard covered his face, once so like the queen's. Glinting gold in the lamplight, the whiskers made him look like some great yellow beast, magnificent even in chains. His unwashed hair fell to his shoulders in ropes and tangles, the clothes were rotting on his body, his face was pale and wasted . . . and even so, the power and the beauty of the man were still apparent.

"I see you had no taste for the wine I sent you."

"Such sudden generosity seemed somewhat suspect."

"I can have your head off anytime I want. Why would I need to poison you?"

"Death by poison can seem natural. Harder to claim that my head simply fell off." He squinted up from the floor, his cat-green eyes slowly becoming accustomed to the light. "I'd invite you to sit, but your brother has neglected to provide me a chair."

"I can stand well enough."

"Can you? You look terrible, I must say. Though perhaps it's just the light in here." He was fettered at wrist and ankle, each cuff chained to the others, so he could neither stand nor lie comfortably. The ankle chains were bolted to the wall. "Are my bracelets heavy enough for you, or did you come to add a few more? I'll rattle them prettily if you like."

"You brought this on yourself," she reminded him. "We granted you the comfort of a tower cell befitting your birth and station. You repaid us by trying to escape."

"A cell is a cell. Some under Casterly Rock make this one seem a sunlit garden. One day perhaps I'll show them to you."

If he is cowed, he hides it well, Catelyn thought. "A man chained hand and foot should keep a more courteous tongue in his mouth, ser. I did not come here to be threatened."

"No? Then surely it was to have your pleasure of me? It's said that widows grow weary of their empty beds. We of the Kingsguard vow never to wed, but I suppose I could still service you if that's what you need. Pour us some of that wine and slip out of that gown and we'll see if I'm up to it."

Catelyn stared down at him in revulsion. *Was there ever a man as beautiful or as vile as this one?* "If you said that in my son's hearing, he would kill you for it."

"Only so long as I was wearing these." Jaime Lannister rattled his chains at her. "We both know the boy is afraid to face me in single combat."

"My son may be young, but if you take him for a fool, you are sadly mistaken . . . and it seems to me that you were not so quick to make challenges when you had an army at your back."

"Did the old Kings of Winter hide behind their mothers' skirts as well?"

"I grow weary of this, ser. There are things I must know."

"Why should I tell you anything?"

"To save your life."

"You think I fear death?" That seemed to amuse him.

"You should. Your crimes will have earned you a place of torment in the deepest of the seven hells, if the gods are just."

"What gods are those, Lady Catelyn? The trees your husband prayed to? How well did they serve him when my sister took his head off?" Jaime gave a chuckle. "If there are gods, why is the world so full of pain and injustice?"

"Because of men like you."

"There are no men like me. There's only me."

There is nothing here but arrogance and pride, and the empty courage of a madman. I am wasting my breath with this one. If there was ever a spark of honor in him, it is long dead. "If you will not speak with me, so be it. Drink the wine or piss in it, ser, it makes no matter to me."

Her hand was at the door pull when he said, "Lady Stark." She turned, waited. "Things go to rust in this damp," Jaime went on. "Even a man's courtesies. Stay, and you shall have your answers . . . for a price."

He has no shame. "Captives do not set prices."

"Oh, you'll find mine modest enough. Your turnkey tells me nothing but vile lies, and he cannot even keep them straight. One day he says Cersei has been flayed, and the next it's my father. Answer my questions and I'll answer yours."

"Truthfully?"

"Oh, it's *truth* you want? Be careful, my lady. Tyrion says that people often claim to hunger for truth, but seldom like the taste when it's served up."

"I am strong enough to hear anything you care to say."

"As you will, then. But first, if you'd be so kind . . . the wine. My throat is raw."

Catelyn hung the lamp from the door and moved the cup and flagon closer. Jaime sloshed the wine around his mouth before he swallowed. "Sour and vile," he said, "but it will do." He put his back to the wall, drew his knees up to his chest, and stared at her. "Your first question, Lady Catelyn?"

Not knowing how long this game might continue, Catelyn wasted no time. "Are you Joffrey's father?"

"You would never ask unless you knew the answer."

"I want it from your own lips."

He shrugged. "Joffrey is mine. As are the rest of Cersei's brood, I suppose."

"You admit to being your sister's lover?"

"I've always loved my sister, and you owe me two answers. Do all my kin still live?"

"Ser Stafford Lannister was slain at Oxcross, I am told."

Jaime was unmoved. "Uncle Dolt, my sister called him. It's Cersei and Tyrion who concern me. As well as my lord father."

"They live, all three." *But not long, if the gods are good.*

Jaime drank some more wine. "Ask your next."

Catelyn wondered if he would dare answer her next question with anything but a lie. "How did my son Bran come to fall?"

"I flung him from a window."

The easy way he said it took her voice away for an instant. *If I had a knife, I would kill him now,* she thought, until she remembered the girls. Her throat constricted as she said, "You were a knight, sworn to defend the weak and innocent."

"He was weak enough, but perhaps not so innocent. He was spying on us."

"Bran would not spy."

"Then blame those precious gods of yours, who brought the boy to our window and gave him a glimpse of something he was never meant to see."

"Blame the *gods*?" she said, incredulous. "Yours was the hand that threw him. You meant for him to die."

His chains chinked softly. "I seldom fling children from towers to improve their health. Yes, I meant for him to die."

"And when he did not, you knew your danger was worse than ever, so you gave your catspaw a bag of silver to make certain Bran would never wake."

"Did I now?" Jaime lifted his cup and took a long swallow. "I won't deny we talked of it, but you were with the boy day and night, your maester and Lord Eddard attended him frequently, and there were guards, even those damned direwolves . . . it would have required cutting my way through half of Winterfell. And why bother, when the boy seemed like to die of his own accord?"

"If you lie to me, this session is at an end." Catelyn held out her hands, to show him her fingers and palms. "The man who came to slit Bran's throat gave me these scars. You swear you had no part in sending him?"

"On my honor as a Lannister."

"Your honor as a Lannister is worth less than *this*." She kicked over the waste pail. Foul-smelling brown ooze crept across the floor of the cell, soaking into the straw.

Jaime Lannister backed away from the spill as far as his chains would allow. "I may indeed have shit for honor, I won't deny it, but I have never yet hired anyone to do my killing. Believe what you will, Lady Stark, but if I had wanted your Bran dead I would have slain him myself."

Gods be merciful, he's telling the truth. "If you did not send the killer, your sister did."

"If so, I'd know. Cersei keeps no secrets from me."

"Then it was the Imp."

"Tyrion is as innocent as your Bran. *He* wasn't climbing around outside of anyone's window, spying."

"Then why did the assassin have his dagger?"

"What dagger was this?"

"It was so long," she said, holding her hands apart, "plain, but finely made, with a blade of Valyrian steel and a dragonbone hilt. Your brother won it from Lord Baelish at the tourney on Prince Joffrey's name day."

Lannister poured, drank, poured, and stared into his wine cup. "This wine seems to be improving as I drink it. Imagine that. I seem to remember that dagger, now that you describe it. Won it, you say? How?"

"Wagering on you when you tilted against the Knight of Flowers." Yet when she heard her own words Catelyn knew she had gotten it wrong. "No . . . was it the other way?"

"Tyrion always backed me in the lists," Jaime said, "but that day Ser Loras unhorsed me. A mischance, I took the boy too lightly, but no matter. Whatever my brother wagered, he lost . . . but that dagger *did* change hands, I recall it now. Robert showed it to me that night at the feast. His Grace loved to salt my wounds, especially when drunk. And when was he not drunk?"

Tyrion Lannister had said much the same thing as they rode through the Mountains of the Moon, Catelyn remembered. She had refused to believe him. Petyr had sworn otherwise, Petyr who had been almost a brother, Petyr who loved her so much he fought a duel for her hand . . . and yet if Jaime and Tyrion told the same tale, what did that mean? The brothers had not seen each other since departing Winterfell more than a year ago. "Are you trying to deceive me?" Somewhere there was a trap here.

"I've admitted to shoving your precious urchin out a window, what would it gain me to lie about this knife?" He tossed down another cup of wine. "Believe what you will, I'm past caring what people say of me. And it's my turn. Have Robert's brothers taken the field?"

"They have."

"Now there's a niggardly response. Give me more than that, or your next answer will be as poor."

"Stannis marches against King's Landing," she said grudgingly. "Renly is dead, murdered at Bitterbridge by his brother, through some black art I do not understand."

"A pity," Jaime said. "I rather liked Renly, though Stannis is quite another tale. What side have the Tyrells taken?"

"Renly, at first. Now, I could not say."

"Your boy must be feeling lonely."

"Robb was sixteen a few days past . . . a man grown, and a king. He's won every battle he's fought. The last word we had from him, he had taken the Crag from the Westerlings."

"He hasn't faced my father yet, has he?"

"When he does, he'll defeat him. As he did you."

"He took me unawares. A craven's trick."

"You dare talk of tricks? Your brother Tyrion sent us cutthroats in envoy's garb, under a peace banner."

"If it were one of your sons in this cell, wouldn't his brothers do as much for him?"

My son has no brothers, she thought, but she would not share her pain with a creature such as this.

Jaime drank some more wine. "What's a brother's life when honor is at stake, eh?" Another sip. "Tyrion is clever enough to realize that your son will never consent to ransom me."

Catelyn could not deny it. "Robb's bannermen would sooner see you dead. Rickard Karstark in particular. You slew two of his sons in the Whispering Wood."

"The two with the white sunburst, were they?" Jaime

gave a shrug. "If truth be told, it was *your* son that I was trying to slay. The others got in my way. I killed them in fair fight, in the heat of battle. Any other knight would have done the same."

"How can you still count yourself a knight, when you have forsaken every vow you ever swore?"

Jaime reached for the flagon to refill his cup. "So many vows . . . they make you swear and swear. Defend the king. Obey the king. Keep his secrets. Do his bidding. Your life for his. But obey your father. Love your sister. Protect the innocent. Defend the weak. Respect the gods. Obey the laws. It's too much. No matter what you do, you're forsaking one vow or the other." He took a healthy swallow of wine and closed his eyes for an instant, leaning his head back against the patch of nitre on the wall. "I was the youngest man ever to wear the white cloak."

"And the youngest to betray all it stood for, Kingslayer."

"Kingslayer," he pronounced carefully. "And such a king he was!" He lifted his cup. "To Aerys Targaryen, the Second of His Name, Lord of the Seven Kingdoms and *Protector* of the Realm. And to the sword that opened his throat. A *golden* sword, don't you know. Until his blood ran red down the blade. Those are the Lannister colors, red and gold."

As he laughed, she realized the wine had done its work; Jaime had drained most of the flagon, and he was drunk. "Only a man like you would be proud of such an act."

"I told you, there are no men like me. Answer me this, Lady Stark—did your Ned ever tell you the manner of his father's death? Or his brother's?"

"They strangled Brandon while his father watched, and then killed Lord Rickard as well." An ugly tale, and sixteen years old. Why was he asking about it now?

"Killed, yes, but *how*?"

"The cord or the axe, I suppose."

Jaime took a swallow, wiped his mouth. "No doubt Ned wished to spare you. His sweet young bride, if not quite a maiden. Well, you wanted truth. Ask me. We made a bargain, I can deny you nothing. Ask."

"Dead is dead." *I do not want to know this.*

"Brandon was different from his brother, wasn't he? He had blood in his veins instead of cold water. More like me."

"Brandon was nothing like you."

"If you say so. You and he were to wed."

"He was on his way to Riverrun when . . ." Strange, how telling it still made her throat grow tight, after all these years. ". . . when he heard about Lyanna, and went to King's Landing instead. It was a rash thing to do." She remembered how her own father had raged when the news had been brought to Riverrun. *The gallant fool,* was what he called Brandon.

Jaime poured the last half cup of wine. "He rode into the Red Keep with a few companions, shouting for Prince Rhaegar to come out and die. But Rhaegar wasn't there. Aerys sent his guards to arrest them all for plotting his son's murder. The others were lords' sons too, it seems to me."

"Ethan Glover was Brandon's squire," Catelyn said. "He was the only one to survive. The others were Jeffory Mallister, Kyle Royce, and Elbert Arryn, Jon Arryn's nephew and heir." It was queer how she still remembered the names, after so many years. "Aerys accused them of treason and summoned their fathers to court to answer the charge, with the sons as hostages. When they came, he had them murdered without trial. Fathers and sons both."

"There were trials. Of a sort. Lord Rickard demanded trial by combat, and the king granted the request. Stark armored himself as for battle, thinking to duel one of the Kingsguard. Me, perhaps. Instead they took him to the throne room and suspended him from the rafters while two of Aerys's pyromancers kindled a blaze beneath him. The king told him that *fire* was the champion of House Targaryen. So all Lord Rickard needed to do to prove himself innocent of treason was . . . well, not burn.

"When the fire was blazing, Brandon was brought in. His hands were chained behind his back, and around his neck was a wet leathern cord attached to a device the king had brought from Tyrosh. His legs were left free, though, and his longsword was set down just beyond his reach.

"The pyromancers roasted Lord Rickard slowly, banking and fanning that fire carefully to get a nice even heat. His cloak caught first, and then his surcoat, and soon he wore nothing but metal and ashes. Next he would start to cook, Aerys promised . . . unless his son could free him. Brandon tried, but the more he struggled, the tighter the cord constricted around his throat. In the end he strangled himself.

"As for Lord Rickard, the steel of his breastplate turned cherry-red before the end, and his gold melted off his spurs and dripped down into the fire. I stood at the foot of the Iron Throne in my white armor and white cloak, filling my head with thoughts of Cersei. After, Gerold Hightower himself took me aside and said to me, 'You swore a vow to guard the king, not to judge him.' That was the White Bull, loyal to the end and a better man than me, all agree."

"Aerys . . ." Catelyn could taste bile at the back of her throat. The story was so hideous she suspected it had to be true. "Aerys was mad, the whole realm knew it, but if you would have me believe you slew him to avenge Brandon Stark . . ."

"I made no such claim. The Starks were nothing to me. I will say, I think it passing odd that I am loved by one for a kindness I never did, and reviled by so many for my finest act. At Robert's coronation, I was made to kneel at the royal feet beside Grand Maester Pycelle and Varys the eunuch, so that he might *forgive* us our crimes before he took us into his service. As for your Ned, he should have kissed the hand that slew Aerys, but he preferred to scorn the arse he found sitting on Robert's throne. I think Ned Stark loved Robert better than he ever loved his brother or his father . . . or even you, my lady. He was never unfaithful to Robert, was he?" Jaime gave a drunken laugh. "Come, Lady Stark, don't you find this all terribly amusing?"

"I find nothing about you amusing, Kingslayer."

"That name again. I don't think I'll fuck you after all, Littlefinger had you first, didn't he? I never eat off another man's trencher. Besides, you're not half so lovely as my sister." His smile cut. "I've never lain with any woman but Cersei. In my own way, I have been truer than your Ned ever was. Poor old dead Ned. So who has shit for honor now, I ask you? What was the name of that bastard he fathered?"

Catelyn took a step backward. *"Brienne."*

"No, that wasn't it." Jaime Lannister upended the flagon. A trickle ran down onto his face, bright as blood. "Snow, that was the one. Such a *white* name . . . like the pretty cloaks they give us in the Kingsguard when we swear our pretty oaths."

Brienne pushed open the door and stepped inside the cell. "You called, my lady?"

"Give me your sword." Catelyn held out her hand.

THEON

The sky was a gloom of cloud, the woods dead and frozen. Roots grabbed at Theon's feet as he ran, and bare branches lashed his face, leaving thin stripes of blood across his cheeks. He crashed through heedless, breathless, icicles flying to pieces before him. *Mercy*, he sobbed. From behind came a shuddering howl that curdled his blood. *Mercy, mercy.* When he glanced back over his shoulder he saw them coming, great wolves the size of horses with the heads of small children. *Oh, mercy, mercy.* Blood dripped from their mouths black as pitch, burning holes in the snow where it fell. Every stride brought them closer. Theon tried to run faster, but his legs would not obey. The trees all had faces, and they were laughing at him, laughing, and the howl came again. He could smell the hot breath of the beasts behind him, a stink of brimstone and corruption. *They're dead, dead, I saw them killed,* he tried to shout, *I saw their heads dipped in tar,* but when he opened his mouth only a moan emerged, and then something *touched* him and he whirled, shouting . . .

. . . flailing for the dagger he kept by his bedside and managing only to knock it to the floor. Wex danced away from him. Reek stood behind the mute, his face lit from below by the candle he carried. "What?" Theon cried. *Mercy.* "What do you want? Why are you in my bedchamber? *Why?*"

"My lord prince," said Reek, "your sister has come to Winterfell. You asked to be informed at once if she arrived."

"Past time," Theon muttered, pushing his fingers through his hair. He had begun to fear that Asha meant to leave him to his fate. *Mercy.* He glanced outside the window, where the first vague light of dawn was just brushing the towers of Winterfell. "Where is she?"

"Lorren took her and her men to the Great Hall to break their fast. Will you see her now?"

"Yes." Theon pushed off the blankets. The fire had burned down to embers. "Wex, hot water." He could not let Asha see him disheveled and soaked with sweat. *Wolves with children's faces* . . . He shivered. "Close the shutters." The bedchamber felt as cold as the dream forest had been.

All his dreams had been cold of late, and each more hideous than the one before. Last night he had dreamed himself back in the mill again, on his knees dressing the dead. Their limbs were already stiffening, so they seemed to resist sullenly as he fumbled at them with half-frozen fingers, tugging up breeches and knotting laces, yanking fur-trimmed boots over hard unbending feet, buckling a studded leather belt around a waist no bigger than the span of his hands. "This was never what I wanted," he told them as he worked. "They gave me no choice." The corpses made no answer, but only grew colder and heavier.

The night before, it had been the miller's wife. Theon had forgotten her name, but he remembered her body, soft pillowy breasts and stretch marks on her belly, the way she clawed his back when he fucked her. Last night in his dream he had been in bed with her once again, but this time she had teeth above *and* below, and she tore out his throat even as she was gnawing off his manhood. It was madness. He'd seen her die too. Gelmarr had cut her down with one blow of his axe as she cried to Theon for mercy. *Leave me, woman. It was him who killed you, not me. And he's dead as well.* At least Gelmarr did not haunt Theon's sleep.

The dream had receded by the time Wex returned with the water. Theon washed the sweat and sleep from his body and took his own good time dressing. Asha had let him wait long enough; now it was her turn. He chose a satin tunic striped black and gold and a fine leather jerkin with silver studs . . . and only then remembered that his wretched sister put more stock in blades than beauty. Cursing, he tore off the clothes and dressed again, in felted black wool and ringmail. Around his waist he buckled sword and dagger, remembering the night she had humiliated him at his own father's table. *Her sweet suckling babe, yes. Well, I have a knife too, and know how to use it.*

Last of all, he donned his crown, a band of cold iron slim as a finger, set with heavy chunks of black diamond and nuggets of gold. It was misshapen and ugly, but there was no help for that. Mikken lay buried in the lichyard, and the new smith was capable of little more than nails and horseshoes. Theon consoled himself with the reminder that it was only a prince's crown. He would have something much finer when he was crowned king.

Outside his door, Reek waited with Urzen and Kromm. Theon fell in with them. These days, he took guards with him everywhere he went, even to the privy. Winterfell wanted him dead. The very night they had returned from Acorn Water, Gelmarr the Grim had tumbled down some steps and broken his back. The next day, Aggar turned up with his throat slit ear to ear. Gynir Rednose became so wary that he shunned wine, took to sleeping in byrnie, coif, and helm, and adopted the noisiest dog in the kennels to give him warning should anyone try to steal up on his sleeping place. All the same, one morning the castle woke to the sound of the little dog barking wildly. They found the pup racing around the well, and Rednose floating in it, drowned.

He could not let the killings go unpunished. Farlen was as likely a suspect as any, so Theon sat in judgment, called him guilty, and condemned him to death. Even that went sour. As he knelt to the block, the kennelmaster said, "M'lord Eddard always did his own killings." Theon had to take the axe himself or look a weakling. His hands were sweating, so the shaft twisted in his grip as he swung and the first blow landed between Farlen's shoulders. It took three more cuts to hack through all that bone and muscle and sever the head from the body, and afterward he was sick, remembering all the times they'd sat over a cup of mead talking of hounds and hunting. *I had no choice,* he wanted to scream at the corpse. *The ironborn can't keep secrets, they had to die, and someone had to take the blame for it.* He only wished he had killed him cleaner. Ned Stark had never needed more than a single blow to take a man's head.

The killings stopped after Farlen's death, but even so his men continued sullen and anxious. "They fear no foe in open battle," Black Lorren told him, "but it is another thing to dwell among enemies, never knowing if the washerwoman means to kiss you or kill you, or whether the serving boy is filling your cup with ale or bale. We would do well to leave this place."

"I am the Prince of Winterfell!" Theon had shouted. "This is my seat, no man will drive me from it. No, nor woman either!"

Asha. It was her doing. My own sweet sister, may the Others bugger her with a sword. She wanted him dead, so she could steal his place as their father's heir. That was why she had let him languish here, ignoring the urgent commands he had sent her.

He found her in the high seat of the Starks, ripping a capon apart with her fingers. The hall rang with the voices of her men, sharing stories with Theon's own as they drank together. They were so loud that his entrance went all but unnoticed. "Where are the rest?" he demanded of Reek. There were no more than fifty men at the trestle tables, most of them his. Winterfell's Great Hall could have seated ten times the number.

"This is the whole o' the company, m'lord prince."

"The *whole*—how many men did she bring?"

"Twenty, by my count."

Theon Greyjoy strode to where his sister was sprawled. Asha was laughing at something one of her men had said, but broke off at his approach. "Why, 'tis the Prince of Winterfell." She tossed a bone to one of the dogs sniffing about the hall. Under that hawk's beak of a nose, her wide mouth twisted in a mocking grin. "Or is it Prince of Fools?"

"Envy ill becomes a maid."

Asha sucked grease from her fingers. A lock of black hair fell across her eyes. Her men were shouting for bread and bacon. They made a deal of noise, as few as they were. "Envy, Theon?"

"What else would you call it? With thirty men, I captured Winterfell in a night. You needed a thousand and a moon's turn to take Deepwood Motte."

"Well, I'm no great warrior like you, brother." She quaffed half a horn of ale and wiped her mouth with the back of her hand. "I saw the heads above your gates. Tell me true, which one gave you the fiercest fight, the cripple or the babe?"

Theon could feel the blood rushing to his face. He took no joy from those heads, no more than he had in displaying the headless bodies of the children before the castle. Old Nan stood with her soft toothless mouth opening and closing soundlessly, and Farlen threw himself at Theon, snarling like one of his hounds. Urzen and Cadwyl had to beat him senseless with the butts of their spears. *How did I come to this?* he remembered thinking as he stood over the fly-speckled bodies.

Only Maester Luwin had the stomach to come near. Stone-faced, the small grey man had begged leave to sew the boys' heads back onto their shoulders, so they might be laid in the crypts below with the other Stark dead.

"No," Theon had told him. "Not the crypts."

"But why, my lord? Surely they cannot harm you now. It is where they belong. All the bones of the Starks—"

"I said *no*." He needed the heads for the wall, but he had burned the headless bodies that very day, in all their finery. Afterward he had knelt amongst the bones and ashes to retrieve a slag of melted silver and cracked jet, all that remained of the wolf's-head brooch that had once been Bran's. He had it still.

"I treated Bran and Rickon generously," he told his sister. "They brought their fate on themselves."

"As do we all, little brother."

His patience was at an end. "How do you expect me to hold Winterfell if you bring me only twenty men?"

"Ten," Asha corrected. "The others return with me. You wouldn't want your own sweet sister to brave the dangers of the wood without an escort, would you? There are direwolves prowling the dark." She uncoiled from the great stone seat and rose to her feet. "Come, let us go somewhere we can speak more privily."

She was right, he knew, though it galled him that she would make that decision. *I should never have come to the hall*, he realized belatedly. *I should have summoned her to me.*

It was too late for that now, however. Theon had no choice but to lead Asha to Ned Stark's solar. There, before the ashes of a dead fire, he blurted, "Dagmer's lost the fight at Torrhen's Square—"

"The old castellan broke his shield wall, yes," Asha said calmly. "What did you expect? This Ser Rodrik knows the land intimately, as the Cleftjaw does not, and many of the northmen were mounted. The ironborn lack the discipline to stand a charge of armored horse. Dagmer lives, be grateful for that much. He's leading the survivors back toward the Stony Shore."

She knows more than I do, Theon realized. That only made him angrier. "The victory has given Leobald Tallhart the courage to come out from behind his walls and join Ser Rodrik. And I've had reports that Lord

Manderly has sent a dozen barges upriver packed with knights, warhorses, and siege engines. The Umbers are gathering beyond the Last River as well. I'll have an *army* at my gates before the moon turns, and you bring me only *ten men?*"

"I need not have brought you any."

"I commanded you—"

"*Father* commanded me to take Deepwood Motte," she snapped. "He said nothing of me having to rescue my little brother."

"Bugger Deepwood," he said. "It's a wooden pisspot on a hill. Winterfell is the heart of the land, but how am I to hold it without a garrison?"

"You might have thought of that before you took it. Oh, it was cleverly done, I'll grant you. If only you'd had the good sense to raze the castle and carry the two little princelings back to Pyke as hostages, you might have won the war in a stroke."

"You'd like that, wouldn't you? To see my prize reduced to ruins and ashes."

"Your prize will be the doom of you. Krakens rise from the *sea*, Theon, or did you forget that during your years among the wolves? Our strength is in our long-ships. My wooden pisspot sits close enough to the sea for supplies and fresh men to reach me whenever they are needful. But Winterfell is hundreds of leagues inland, ringed by woods, hills, and hostile holdfasts and castles. And every man in a thousand leagues is your enemy now, make no mistake. You made certain of that when you mounted those heads on your gatehouse." Asha shook her head. "How could you be such a bloody fool? *Children . . .*"

"*They defied me!*" he shouted in her face. "And it was blood for blood besides, two sons of Eddard Stark to pay for Rodrik and Maron." The words tumbled out heedlessly, but Theon knew at once that his father would approve. "I've laid my brothers' ghosts to rest."

"*Our* brothers," Asha reminded him, with a half smile that suggested she took his talk of vengeance well salted. "Did you bring their ghosts from Pyke, brother? And here I thought they haunted only Father."

"When has a maid ever understood a man's need for revenge?" Even if his father did not appreciate the gift of Winterfell, he *must* approve of Theon avenging his brothers!

Asha snorted back a laugh. "This Ser Rodrik may well feel the same manly need, did you think of that? You are blood of my blood, Theon, whatever else you may be. For the sake of the mother who bore us both, return to Deepwood Motte with me. Put Winterfell to the torch and fall back while you still can."

"No." Theon adjusted his crown. "I took this castle and I mean to hold it."

His sister looked at him a long time. "Then hold it you shall," she said, "for the rest of your life." She sighed. "I say it tastes like folly, but what would a shy maid know of such things?" At the door she gave him one last mocking smile. "You ought to know, that's the ugliest crown I've ever laid eyes on. Did you make it yourself?"

She left him fuming, and lingered no longer than was needful to feed and water her horses. Half the men she'd brought returned with her as threatened, riding out the same Hunter's Gate that Bran and Rickon had used for their escape.

Theon watched them go from atop the wall. As his sister vanished into the mists of the wolfswood he found himself wondering why he had not listened and gone with her.

"Gone, has she?" Reek was at his elbow.

Theon had not heard him approach, nor smelled him either. He could not think of anyone he wanted to see less. It made him uneasy to see the man walking around breathing, with what he knew. *I should have had him killed after he did the others,* he reflected, but the notion made him nervous. Unlikely as it seemed, Reek could read and write, and he was possessed of enough base cunning to have hidden an account of what they'd done.

"M'lord prince, if you'll pardon me saying, it's not right for her to abandon you. And ten men, that won't be near enough."

"I am well aware of that," Theon said. *So was Asha.*

"Well, might be I could help you," said Reek. "Give me a horse and bag o' coin, and I could find you some good fellows."

Theon narrowed his eyes. "How many?"

"A hundred, might be. Two hundred. Maybe more." He smiled, his pale eyes glinting. "I was born up north here. I know many a man, and many a man knows Reek."

Two hundred men were not an army, but you didn't need thousands to hold a castle as strong as Winterfell. So long as they could learn which end of a spear did the killing, they might make all the difference. "Do as you say and you'll not find me ungrateful. You can name your own reward."

"Well, m'lord, I haven't had no woman since I was with Lord Ramsay," Reek said. "I've had my eye on that Palla, and I hear she's already been had, so . . ."

He had gone too far with Reek to turn back now. "Two hundred men and she's yours. But a man less and you can go back to fucking pigs."

Reek was gone before the sun went down, carrying a bag of Stark silver and the last of Theon's hopes. *Like as not, I'll never see the wretch again,* he thought bitterly, but even so the chance had to be taken.

That night he dreamed of the feast Ned Stark had thrown when King Robert came to Winterfell. The hall rang with music and laughter, though the cold winds were rising outside. At first it was all wine and roast meat, and Theon was making japes and eyeing the serving girls and having himself a fine time . . . until he noticed that the room was growing darker. The music did not seem so jolly then; he heard discords and strange silences, and notes that hung in the air bleeding. Suddenly the wine turned bitter in his mouth, and when he looked up from his cup he saw that he was dining with the dead.

King Robert sat with his guts spilling out on the table from the great gash in his belly, and Lord Eddard was headless beside him. Corpses lined the benches below, grey-brown flesh sloughing off their bones as they raised their cups to toast, worms crawling in and out of the holes that were their eyes. He knew them, every one; Jory Cassel and Fat Tom, Porther and Cayn and Hullen the master of horse, and all the others who had ridden south to King's Landing never to return. Mikken and Chayle sat together, one dripping blood and the other water. Benfred Tallhart and his Wild Hares filled most of a table. The miller's wife was there as well, and Farlen, even the wildling Theon had killed in the wolfs-wood the day he had saved Bran's life.

But there were others with faces he had never known in life, faces he had seen only in stone. The slim, sad girl who wore a crown of pale blue roses and a white gown spattered with gore could only be Lyanna. Her brother Brandon stood beside her, and their father Lord Rickard just behind. Along the walls figures half-seen moved through the shadows, pale shades with long grim faces. The sight of them sent fear shivering through Theon sharp as a knife. And then the tall doors opened with a crash, and a freezing gale blew down the hall, and Robb came walking out of the night. Grey Wind stalked beside, eyes burning, and man and wolf alike bled from half a hundred savage wounds.

Theon woke with a scream, startling Wex so badly that the boy ran naked from the room. When his guards burst in with drawn swords, he ordered them to bring him the maester. By the time Luwin arrived rumpled and sleepy, a cup of wine had steadied Theon's hands, and he was feeling ashamed of his panic. "A dream," he muttered, "that was all it was. It meant nothing."

"Nothing," Luwin agreed solemnly. He left a sleeping draught, but Theon poured it down the privy shaft the moment he was gone. Luwin was a man as well as a maester, and the man had no love for him. *He wants me to sleep, yes . . . to sleep and never wake. He'd like that as much as Asha would.*

He sent for Kyra, kicked shut the door, climbed on top of her, and fucked the wench with a fury he'd never known was in him. By the time he finished, she was sobbing, her neck and breasts covered with bruises and bite marks. Theon shoved her from the bed and threw her a blanket. "Get out."

Yet even then, he could not sleep.

Come dawn, he dressed and went outside, to walk along the outer walls. A brisk autumn wind was swirling through the battlements. It reddened his cheeks and stung his eyes. He watched the forest go from grey to green below him as light filtered through the silent trees. On his left he could see tower tops above the inner wall, their roofs gilded by the rising sun. The red leaves of the weirwood were a blaze of flame among the green. *Ned Stark's tree,* he thought, and *Stark's wood, Stark's castle, Stark's sword, Stark's gods. This is their place, not mine. I am a Greyjoy of Pyke, born to paint a kraken on my shield and sail the great salt sea. I should have gone with Asha.*

On their iron spikes atop the gatehouse, the heads waited.

Theon gazed at them silently while the wind tugged on his cloak with small ghostly hands. The miller's boys had been of an age with Bran and Rickon, alike in size and coloring, and once Reek had flayed the skin from their faces and dipped their heads in tar, it was easy to see familiar features in those misshapen lumps of rotting flesh. People were such fools. *If we'd said they were rams' heads, they would have seen horns.*

SANSA

They had been singing in the sept all morning, since the first report of enemy sails had reached the castle. The sound of their voices mingled with the whicker of horses, the clank of steel, and the groaning hinges of the great bronze gates to make a strange and fearful music. *In the sept they sing for the Mother's mercy but on the walls it's the Warrior they pray to, and all in silence.* She remembered how Septa Mordane used to tell them that the Warrior and the Mother were only two faces of the same great god. *But if there is only one, whose prayers will be heard?*

Ser Meryn Trant held the blood bay for Joffrey to mount. Boy and horse alike wore gilded mail and enameled crimson plate, with matching golden lions on their heads. The pale sunlight flashed off the golds and reds every time Joff moved. *Bright, shining, and empty,* Sansa thought.

The Imp was mounted on a red stallion, armored more plainly than the king in battle gear that made him look like a little boy dressed up in his father's clothes.

But there was nothing childish about the battle-axe slung below his shield. Ser Mandon Moore rode at his side, white steel icy bright. When Tyrion saw her he turned his horse her way. "Lady Sansa," he called from the saddle, "surely my sister has asked you to join the other highborn ladies in Maegor's?"

"She has, my lord, but King Joffrey sent for me to see him off. I mean to visit the sept as well, to pray."

"I won't ask for whom." His mouth twisted oddly; if that was a smile, it was the queerest she had ever seen. "This day may change all. For you as well as for House Lannister. I ought to have sent you off with Tommen, now that I think on it. Still, you should be safe enough in Maegor's, so long as—"

"Sansa!" The boyish shout rang across the yard; Joffrey had seen her. "Sansa, here!"

He calls me as if he were calling a dog, she thought.

"His Grace has need of you," Tyrion Lannister observed. "We'll talk again after the battle, if the gods permit."

Sansa threaded her way through a file of gold-cloaked spearmen as Joffrey beckoned her closer. "It will be battle soon, everyone says so."

"May the gods have mercy on us all."

"My uncle's the one who will need mercy, but I won't give him any." Joffrey drew his sword. The pommel was a ruby cut in the shape of a heart, set between a lion's jaws. Three fullers were deeply incised in the blade. "My new blade, Hearteater."

He'd owned a sword named Lion's Tooth once, Sansa remembered. Arya had taken it from him and thrown it in a river. *I hope Stannis does the same with this one.* "It is beautifully wrought, Your Grace."

"Bless my steel with a kiss." He extended the blade down to her. "Go on, kiss it."

He had never sounded more like a stupid little boy. Sansa touched her lips to the metal, thinking that she would kiss any number of swords sooner than Joffrey. The gesture seemed to please him, though. He sheathed the blade with a flourish. "You'll kiss it again when I return, and taste my uncle's blood."

Only if one of your Kingsguard kills him for you. Three of the White Swords would go with Joffrey and his uncle: Ser Meryn, Ser Mandon, and Ser Osmund Kettleblack. "Will you lead your knights into battle?" Sansa asked, hoping.

"I would, but my uncle the Imp says my uncle Stannis will never cross the river. I'll command the Three Whores, though. I'm going to see to the traitors myself." The prospect made Joff smile. His plump pink lips always made him look pouty. Sansa had liked that once, but now it made her sick.

"They say my brother Robb always goes where the fighting is thickest," she said recklessly. "Though he's older than Your Grace, to be sure. A man grown."

That made him frown. "I'll deal with your brother after I'm done with my traitor uncle. I'll gut him with Hearteater, you'll see." He wheeled his horse about and spurred toward the gate. Ser Meryn and Ser Osmund fell in to his right and left, the gold cloaks following four abreast. The Imp and Ser Mandon Moore brought up the rear. The guards saw them off with shouts and cheers. When the last was gone, a sudden stillness settled over the yard, like the hush before a storm.

Through the quiet, the singing pulled at her. Sansa turned toward the sept. Two stableboys followed, and one of the guards whose watch was ended. Others fell in behind them.

Sansa had never seen the sept so crowded, nor so brightly lit; great shafts of rainbow-colored sunlight slanted down through the crystals in the high windows, and candles burned on every side, their little flames twinkling like stars. The Mother's altar and the Warrior's swam in light, but Smith and Crone and Maid and Father had their worshipers as well, and there were even a few flames dancing below the Stranger's half-human face . . . for what was Stannis Baratheon, if not the Stranger come to judge them? Sansa visited each of the Seven in turn, lighting a candle at each altar, and then found herself a place on the benches between a wizened old washerwoman and a boy no older than Rickon, dressed in the fine linen tunic of a knight's son. The old woman's hand was bony and hard with callus, the boy's small and soft, but it was good to have someone to hold on to. The air was hot and heavy, smelling of incense and sweat, crystal-kissed and candle-bright; it made her dizzy to breathe it.

She knew the hymn; her mother had taught it to her once, a long time ago in Winterfell. She joined her voice to theirs.

> *Gentle Mother, font of mercy,*
> *save our sons from war, we pray,*
> *stay the swords and stay the arrows,*
> *let them know a better day.*
> *Gentle Mother, strength of women,*
> *help our daughters through this fray,*
> *soothe the wrath and tame the fury,*
> *teach us all a kinder way.*

Across the city, thousands had jammed into the Great Sept of Baelor on Visenya's Hill, and they would be singing too, their voices swelling out over the city, across the river, and up into the sky. *Surely the gods must hear us*, she thought.

Sansa knew most of the hymns, and followed along on those she did not know as best she could. She sang along with grizzled old serving men and anxious young wives, with serving girls and soldiers, cooks and falconers, knights and knaves, squires and spit boys and nursing mothers. She sang with those inside the castle walls and those without, sang with all the city. She sang for mercy, for the living and the dead alike, for Bran and Rickon and Robb, for her sister Arya and her bastard brother Jon Snow, away off on the Wall. She sang for her mother and her father, for her grandfather Lord Hoster and her uncle Edmure Tully, for her friend Jeyne Poole, for old drunken King Robert, for Septa Mordane and Ser Dontos and Jory Cassel and Maester Luwin, for all the brave knights and soldiers who would die today, and for the children and the wives who would mourn them, and finally, toward the end, she even sang for Tyrion the Imp and for the Hound. *He is no true knight but he saved me all the same*, she told the Mother. *Save him if you can, and gentle the rage inside him*.

But when the septon climbed on high and called upon the gods to protect and defend their true and noble king, Sansa got to her feet. The aisles were jammed with people. She had to shoulder through while the septon called upon the Smith to lend strength to Joffrey's sword and shield, the Warrior to give him courage, the Father to defend him in his need. *Let his sword break and his shield shatter*, Sansa thought coldly as she shoved out through the doors, *let his courage fail him and every man desert him*.

A few guards paced along on the gatehouse battlements, but otherwise the castle seemed empty. Sansa stopped and listened. Away off, she could hear the sounds of battle. The singing almost drowned them out, but the sounds were there if you had the ears to hear: the deep moan of warhorns, the creak and thud of catapults flinging stones, the splashes and splinterings, the crackle of burning pitch and *thrum* of scorpions loosing their yard-long iron-headed shafts . . . and beneath it all, the cries of dying men.

It was another sort of song, a terrible song. Sansa pulled the hood of her cloak up over her ears, and hurried toward Maegor's Holdfast, the castle-within-a-castle where the queen had promised they would all be safe. At the foot of the drawbridge, she came upon Lady Tanda and her two daughters. Falyse had arrived yesterday from Castle Stokeworth with a small troop of soldiers. She was trying to coax her sister onto the bridge, but Lollys clung to her maid, sobbing, "I don't want to, I don't want to, I don't want to."

"The battle is *begun*," Lady Tanda said in a brittle voice.

"I don't want to, I don't want to."

There was no way Sansa could avoid them. She greeted them courteously. "May I be of help?"

Lady Tanda flushed with shame. "No, my lady, but we thank you kindly. You must forgive my daughter, she has not been well."

"I don't want to." Lollys clutched at her maid, a slender, pretty girl with short dark hair who looked as though she wanted nothing so much as to shove her mistress into the dry moat, onto those iron spikes. "Please, please, I don't want to."

Sansa spoke to her gently. "We'll all be thrice protected inside, and there's to be food and drink and song as well."

Lollys gaped at her, mouth open. She had dull brown eyes that always seemed to be wet with tears. "I don't want to."

"You *have* to," her sister Falyse said sharply, "and that is the end of it. Shae, help me." They each took an elbow, and together half dragged and half carried Lollys across the bridge. Sansa followed with their mother. "She's been sick," Lady Tanda said. *If a babe can be termed a sickness*, Sansa thought. It was common gossip that Lollys was with child.

The two guards at the door wore the lion-crested helms and crimson cloaks of House Lannister, but Sansa knew they were only dressed-up sellswords. Another sat at the foot of the stair—a real guard would have been standing, not sitting on a step with his halberd across his knees—but he rose when he saw them and opened the door to usher them inside.

The Queen's Ballroom was not a tenth the size of the castle's Great Hall, only half as big as the Small Hall in the Tower of the Hand, but it could still seat a hundred, and it made up in grace what it lacked in space. Beaten silver mirrors backed every wall sconce, so the torches burned twice as bright; the walls were paneled in richly carved wood, and sweet-smelling rushes covered the floors. From the gallery above drifted down the merry strains of pipes and fiddle. A line of arched windows ran along the south wall, but they had been closed off with heavy draperies. Thick velvet hangings admitted no thread of light, and would muffle the sound of prayer and war alike. *It makes no matter,* Sansa thought. *The war is with us.*

Almost every highborn woman in the city sat at the long trestle tables, along with a handful of old men and young boys. The women were wives, daughters, mothers, and sisters. Their men had gone out to fight Lord Stannis. Many would not return. The air was heavy with the knowledge. As Joffrey's betrothed, Sansa had the seat of honor on the queen's right hand. She was climbing the dais when she saw the man standing in the shadows by the back wall. He wore a long hauberk of oiled black mail, and held his sword before him: her father's greatsword, Ice, near as tall as he was. Its point rested on the floor, and his hard bony fingers curled around the crossguard on either side of the grip. Sansa's breath caught in her throat. Ser Ilyn Payne seemed to sense her stare. He turned his gaunt, pox-ravaged face toward her.

"What is *he* doing here?" she asked Osfryd Kettleblack. He captained the queen's new red cloak guard.

Osfryd grinned. "Her Grace expects she'll have need of him before the night's done."

Ser Ilyn was the King's Justice. There was only one service he might be needed for. *Whose head does she want?*

"All rise for Her Grace, Cersei of House Lannister, Queen Regent and Protector of the Realm," the royal steward cried.

Cersei's gown was snowy linen, white as the cloaks of the Kingsguard. Her long dagged sleeves showed a lining of gold satin. Masses of bright yellow hair tumbled to her bare shoulders in thick curls. Around her slender neck hung a rope of diamonds and emeralds. The white made her look strangely innocent, almost maidenly, but there were points of color on her cheeks.

"Be seated," the queen said when she had taken her place on the dais, "and be welcome." Osfryd Kettleblack held her chair; a page performed the same service for Sansa. "You look pale, Sansa," Cersei observed. "Is your red flower still blooming?"

"Yes."

"How apt. The men will bleed out there, and you in here." The queen signaled for the first course to be served.

"Why is Ser Ilyn here?" Sansa blurted out.

The queen glanced at the mute headsman. "To deal with treason, and to defend us if need be. He was a knight before he was a headsman." She pointed her spoon toward the end of the hall, where the tall wooden doors had been closed and barred. "When the axes smash down those doors, you may be glad of him."

I would be gladder if it were the Hound, Sansa thought. Harsh as he was, she did not believe Sandor Clegane would let any harm come to her. "Won't your guards protect us?"

"And who will protect us from my guards?" The queen gave Osfryd a sideways look. "Loyal sellswords are rare as virgin whores. If the battle is lost, my guards will trip on those crimson cloaks in their haste to rip them off. They'll steal what they can and flee, along with the serving men, washerwomen, and stableboys, all out to save their own worthless hides. Do you have any notion what happens when a city is sacked, Sansa? No, you wouldn't, would you? All you know of life you learned from singers, and there's such a dearth of good sacking songs."

"True knights would never harm women and children." The words rang hollow in her ears even as she said them.

"True knights." The queen seemed to find that wonderfully amusing. "No doubt you're right. So why don't you just eat your broth like a good girl and wait for Symeon Star-Eyes and Prince Aemon the Dragonknight to come rescue you, sweetling. I'm sure it won't be very long now."

DAVOS

Blackwater Bay was rough and choppy, whitecaps everywhere. *Black Betha* rode the flood tide, her sail cracking and snapping at each shift of wind. *Wraith* and *Lady Marya* sailed beside her, no more than twenty yards between their hulls. His sons could keep a line. Davos took pride in that.

Across the sea warhorns boomed, deep throaty moans like the calls of monstrous serpents, repeated ship to ship. "Bring down the sail," Davos commanded. "Lower mast. Oarsmen to your oars." His son Matthos relayed the commands. The deck of *Black Betha* churned as crewmen ran to their tasks, pushing through the soldiers who always seemed to be in the way no matter where they stood. Ser Imry had decreed that they would enter the river on oars alone, so as not to expose their sails to the scorpions and spitfires on the walls of King's Landing.

Davos could make out *Fury* well to the southeast, her sails shimmering golden as they came down, the crowned stag of Baratheon blazoned on the canvas.

From her decks Stannis Baratheon had commanded the assault on Dragonstone sixteen years before, but this time he had chosen to ride with his army, trusting *Fury* and the command of his fleet to his wife's brother Ser Imry, who'd come over to his cause at Storm's End with Lord Alester and all the other Florents.

Davos knew *Fury* as well as he knew his own ships. Above her three hundred oars was a deck given over wholly to scorpions, and topside she mounted catapults fore and aft, large enough to fling barrels of burning pitch. A most formidable ship, and very swift as well, although Ser Imry had packed her bow to stern with armored knights and men-at-arms, at some cost to her speed.

The warhorns sounded again, commands drifting back from the *Fury*. Davos felt a tingle in his missing fingertips. "Out oars," he shouted. "Form line." A hundred blades dipped down into the water as the oarmaster's drum began to boom. The sound was like the beating of a great slow heart, and the oars moved at every stroke, a hundred men pulling as one.

Wooden wings had sprouted from the *Wraith* and *Lady Marya* as well. The three galleys kept pace, their blades churning the water. "Slow cruise," Davos called. Lord Velaryon's silver-hulled *Pride of Driftmark* had moved into her position to port of *Wraith*, and *Bold Laughter* was coming up fast, but *Harridan* was only now getting her oars into the water and *Seahorse* was still struggling to bring down her mast. Davos looked astern. Yes, there, far to the south, that could only be *Swordfish*, lagging as ever. She dipped two hundred oars and mounted the largest ram in the fleet, though Davos had grave doubts about her captain.

He could hear soldiers shouting encouragement to each other across the water. They'd been little more than ballast since Storm's End, and were eager to get at the foe, confident of victory. In that, they were of one mind with their admiral, Lord High Captain Ser Imry Florent.

Three days past, he had summoned all his captains to

a war council aboard the *Fury* while the fleet lay anchored at the mouth of the Wendwater, in order to acquaint them with his dispositions. Davos and his sons had been assigned a place in the second line of battle, well out on the dangerous starboard wing. "A place of honor," Allard had declared, well satisfied with the chance to prove his valor. "A place of peril," his father had pointed out. His sons had given him pitying looks, even young Maric. *The Onion Knight has become an old woman*, he could hear them thinking, *still a smuggler at heart*.

Well, the last was true enough, he would make no apologies for it. *Seaworth* had a lordly ring to it, but down deep he was still Davos of Flea Bottom, coming home to his city on its three high hills. He knew as much of ships and sails and shores as any man in the Seven Kingdoms, and had fought his share of desperate fights sword to sword on a wet deck. But to this sort of battle he came a maiden, nervous and afraid. Smugglers do not sound warhorns and raise banners. When they smell danger, they raise sail and run before the wind.

Had he been admiral, he might have done it all differently. For a start, he would have sent a few of his swiftest ships to probe upriver and see what awaited them, instead of smashing in headlong. When he had suggested as much to Ser Imry, the Lord High Captain had thanked him courteously, but his eyes were not as polite. *Who is this lowborn craven?* those eyes asked. *Is he the one who bought his knighthood with an onion?*

With four times as many ships as the boy king, Ser Imry saw no need for caution or deceptive tactics. He had organized the fleet into ten lines of battle, each of twenty ships. The first two lines would sweep up the river to engage and destroy Joffrey's little fleet, or "the boy's toys" as Ser Imry dubbed them, to the mirth of his lordly captains. Those that followed would land companies of archers and spearmen beneath the city walls, and only then join the fight on the river. The smaller, slower ships to the rear would ferry over the main part of Stannis's host from the south bank, protected by

Salladhor Saan and his Lyseni, who would stand out in
the bay in case the Lannisters had other ships hidden up
along the coast, poised to sweep down on their rear.

To be fair, there was reason for Ser Imry's haste. The
winds had not used them kindly on the voyage up from
Storm's End. They had lost two cogs to the rocks of
Shipbreaker Bay on the very day they set sail, a poor
way to begin. One of the Myrish galleys had foundered
in the Straits of Tarth, and a storm had overtaken them
as they were entering the Gullet, scattering the fleet
across half the narrow sea. All but twelve ships had finally regrouped behind the sheltering spine of Massey's
Hook, in the calmer waters of Blackwater Bay, but not
before they had lost considerable time.

Stannis would have reached the Rush days ago. The
kingsroad ran from Storm's End straight to King's Landing, a much shorter route than by sea, and his host was
largely mounted; near twenty thousand knights, light
horse, and freeriders, Renly's unwilling legacy to his
brother. They would have made good time, but armored
destriers and twelve-foot lances would avail them little
against the deep waters of the Blackwater Rush and the
high stone walls of the city. Stannis would be camped
with his lords on the south bank of the river, doubtless
seething with impatience and wondering what Ser Imry
had done with his fleet.

Off Merling Rock two days before, they had sighted a
half-dozen fishing skiffs. The fisherfolk had fled before
them, but one by one they had been overtaken and
boarded. "A small spoon of victory is just the thing to
settle the stomach before battle," Ser Imry had declared
happily. "It makes the men hungry for a larger helping."
But Davos had been more interested in what the captives had to say about the defenses at King's Landing.
The dwarf had been busy building some sort of boom to
close off the mouth of the river, though the fishermen
differed as to whether the work had been completed or
not. He found himself wishing it had. If the river was
closed to them, Ser Imry would have no choice but to
pause and take stock.

The sea was full of sound: shouts and calls, warhorns and drums and the trill of pipes, the slap of wood on water as thousands of oars rose and fell. *"Keep line,"* Davos shouted. A gust of wind tugged at his old green cloak. A jerkin of boiled leather and a pothelm at his feet were his only armor. At sea, heavy steel was as like to cost a man his life as to save it, he believed. Ser Imry and the other highborn captains did not share his view; they glittered as they paced their decks.

Harridan and *Seahorse* had slipped into their places now, and Lord Celtigar's *Red Claw* beyond them. To starboard of Allard's *Lady Marya* were the three galleys that Stannis had seized from the unfortunate Lord Sunglass, *Piety*, *Prayer*, and *Devotion*, their decks crawling with archers. Even *Swordfish* was closing, lumbering and rolling through a thickening sea under both oars and sail. *A ship of that many oars ought to be much faster*, Davos reflected with disapproval. *It's that ram she carries, it's too big, she has no balance.*

The wind was gusting from the south, but under oars it made no matter. They would be sweeping in on the flood tide, but the Lannisters would have the river current to their favor, and the Blackwater Rush flowed strong and swift where it met the sea. The first shock would inevitably favor the foe. *We are fools to meet them on the Blackwater*, Davos thought. In any encounter on the open sea, their battle lines would envelop the enemy fleet on both flanks, driving them inward to destruction. On the river, though, the numbers and weight of Ser Imry's ships would count for less. They could not dress more than twenty ships abreast, lest they risk tangling their oars and colliding with each other.

Beyond the line of warships, Davos could see the Red Keep up on Aegon's High Hill, dark against a lemon sky, with the mouth of the Rush opening out below. Across the river the south shore was black with men and horses, stirring like angry ants as they caught sight of the approaching ships. Stannis would have kept them busy building rafts and fletching arrows, yet even so the waiting would have been a hard thing to bear. Trumpets sounded from among them, tiny and brazen, soon swallowed by the roar of a thousand shouts. Davos closed his stubby hand around the pouch that held his fingerbones, and mouthed a silent prayer for luck.

Fury herself would center the first line of battle, flanked by the *Lord Steffon* and the *Stag of the Sea*, each of two hundred oars. On the port and starboard wings were the hundreds: *Lady Harra, Brightfish, Laughing Lord, Sea Demon, Horned Honor, Ragged Jenna, Trident Three, Swift Sword, Princess Rhaenys, Dog's Nose, Sceptre, Faithful, Red Raven, Queen Alysanne, Cat, Courageous,* and *Dragonsbane.* From every stern streamed the fiery heart of the Lord of Light, red and yellow and orange. Behind Davos and his sons came another line of hundreds commanded by knights and lordly captains, and then the smaller, slower Myrish contingent, none dipping more than eighty oars. Farther back would come the sailed ships, carracks and lumbering great cogs, and last of all Salladhor Saan in his proud *Valyrian,* a towering three-hundred, paced by the rest of his galleys with their distinctive striped hulls. The flamboyant Lyseni princeling had not been pleased to be assigned the rear guard, but it was clear that Ser Imry trusted him no more than Stannis did. *Too many complaints, and too much talk of the gold he was owed.* Davos was sorry nonetheless. Salladhor Saan was a resourceful old pirate, and his crews were born seamen, fearless in a fight. They were wasted in the rear.

Ahooooooooooooooooooooooooooo. The call rolled across whitecaps and churning oars from the forecastle of the *Fury:* Ser Imry was sounding the attack. *Ahooooooooooooooooooooooo, ahooooooooooooooooooooooooooo.*

Swordfish had joined the line at last, though she still had her sail raised. "Fast cruise," Davos barked. The drum began to beat more quickly, and the stroke picked up, the blades of the oars cutting water, *splash-swoosh, splash-swoosh, splash-swoosh.* On deck, soldiers banged sword against shield, while archers quietly strung their bows and pulled the first arrow from the

quivers at their belts. The galleys of the first line of
battle obscured his vision, so Davos paced the deck
searching for a better view. He saw no sign of any boom;
the mouth of the river was open, as if to swallow them
all. Except . . .

In his smuggling days, Davos had often jested that he
knew the waterfront at King's Landing a deal better
than the back of his hand, since he had not spent a good
part of his life sneaking in and out of the back of his
hand. The squat towers of raw new stone that stood
opposite one another at the mouth of the Blackwater
might mean nothing to Ser Imry Florent, but to him it
was as if two extra fingers had sprouted from his knuckles.

Shading his eyes against the westering sun, he peered
at those towers more closely. They were too small to
hold much of a garrison. The one on the north bank was
built against the bluff with the Red Keep frowning
above; its counterpart on the south shore had its footing
in the water. *They dug a cut through the bank,* he knew
at once. That would make the tower very difficult to
assault; attackers would need to wade through the water or bridge the little channel. Stannis had posted bowmen below, to fire up at the defenders whenever one
was rash enough to lift his head above the ramparts, but
otherwise had not troubled.

Something flashed down low where the dark water
swirled around the base of the tower. It was sunlight on
steel, and it told Davos Seaworth all he needed to know.
*A chain boom . . . and yet they have not closed the
river against us. Why?*

He could make a guess at that as well, but there was
no time to consider the question. A shout went up from
the ships ahead, and the warhorns blew again: the enemy was before them.

Between the flashing oars of *Sceptre* and *Faithful,*
Davos saw a thin line of galleys drawn across the river,
the sun glinting off the gold paint that marked their
hulls. He knew those ships as well as he knew his own.
When he had been a smuggler, he'd always felt safer

knowing whether the sail on the horizon marked a fast
ship or a slow one, and whether her captain was a young
man hungry for glory or an old one serving out his days.

Ahoooooooooooooooooooooooooooo, the warhorns
called. "Battle speed," Davos shouted. On port and starboard he heard Dale and Allard giving the same command. Drums began to beat furiously, oars rose and fell,
and *Black Betha* surged forward. When he glanced
toward *Wraith,* Dale gave him a salute. *Swordfish* was
lagging once more, wallowing in the wake of the
smaller ships to either side; elsewise the line was
straight as a shield wall.

The river that had seemed so narrow from a distance
now stretched wide as a sea, but the city had grown
gigantic as well. Glowering down from Aegon's High
Hill, the Red Keep commanded the approaches. Its
iron-crowned battlements, massive towers, and thick
red walls gave it the aspect of a ferocious beast
hunched above river and streets. The bluffs on which it
crouched were steep and rocky, spotted with lichen
and gnarled thorny trees. The fleet would have to pass
below the castle to reach the harbor and city beyond.

The first line was in the river now, but the enemy
galleys were backing water. *They mean to draw us in.
They want us jammed close, constricted, no way to
sweep around their flanks . . . and with that boom behind us.* He paced his deck, craning his neck for a better
look at Joffrey's fleet. The boy's toys included the ponderous *Godsgrace,* he saw, the old slow *Prince Aemon,*
the *Lady of Silk* and her sister *Lady's Shame,
Wildwind, Kingslander, White Hart, Lance, Seaflower.*
But where was the *Lionstar*? Where was the beautiful
Lady Lyanna that King Robert had named in honor of
the maid he'd loved and lost? And where was *King
Robert's Hammer*? She was the largest war galley in the
royal fleet, four hundred oars, the only warship the boy
king owned capable of overmatching *Fury.* By rights she
should have formed the heart of any defense.

Davos tasted a trap, yet he saw no sign of any foes
sweeping in behind them, only the great fleet of Stannis

Baratheon in their ordered ranks, stretching back to the watery horizon. *Will they raise the chain and cut us in two?* He could not see what good that would serve. The ships left out in the bay could still land men north of the city; a slower crossing, but safer.

A flight of flickering orange birds took wing from the castle, twenty or thirty of them; pots of burning pitch, arcing out over the river trailing threads of flame. The waters ate most, but a few found the decks of galleys in the first line of battle, spreading flame when they shattered. Men-at-arms were scrambling on *Queen Alysanne*'s deck, and he could see smoke rising from three different spots on *Dragonsbane*, nearest the bank. By then a second flight was on its way, and arrows were falling as well, hissing down from the archers' nests that studded the towers above. A soldier tumbled over *Cat*'s gunwale, crashed off the oars, and sank. *The first man to die today*, Davos thought, *but he will not be the last.*

Atop the Red Keep's battlements streamed the boy king's banners: the crowned stag of Baratheon on its gold field, the lion of Lannister on crimson. More pots of pitch came flying. Davos heard men shriek as fire spread across *Courageous*. Her oarsmen were safe below, protected from missiles by the half deck that sheltered them, but the men-at-arms crowded topside were not so fortunate. The starboard wing was taking all the damage, as he had feared. *It will be our turn soon*, he reminded himself, uneasy. *Black Betha* was well in range of the firepots, being the sixth ship out from the north bank. To starboard, she had only Allard's *Lady Marya*, the ungainly *Swordfish*—so far behind now that she was nearer the third line than the second—and *Piety*, *Prayer*, and *Devotion*, who would need all the godly intervention they could get, placed as vulnerably as they were.

As the second line swept past the twin towers, Davos took a closer look. He could see three links of a huge chain snaking out from a hole no bigger than a man's head and disappearing under the water. The towers had a single door, set a good twenty feet off the ground. Bowmen on the roof of the northern tower were firing down at *Prayer* and *Devotion*. The archers on *Devotion* fired back, and Davos heard a man scream as the arrows found him.

"Captain ser." His son Matthos was at his elbow. "Your helm." Davos took it with both hands and slid it over his head. The pothelm was visorless; he hated having his vision impeded.

By then the pitch pots were raining down around them. He saw one shatter on the deck of *Lady Marya*, but Allard's crew quickly beat it out. To port, warhorns sounded from the *Pride of Driftmark*. The oars flung up sprays of water with every stroke. The yard-long shaft of a scorpion came down not two feet from Matthos and sank into the wood of the deck, thrumming. Ahead, the first line was within bowshot of the enemy; flights of arrows flew between the ships, hissing like striking snakes.

South of the Blackwater, Davos saw men dragging crude rafts toward the water while ranks and columns formed up beneath a thousand streaming banners. The fiery heart was everywhere, though the tiny black stag imprisoned in the flames was too small to make out. *We should be flying the crowned stag,* he thought. *The stag was King Robert's sigil, the city would rejoice to see it. This stranger's standard serves only to set men against us.*

He could not behold the fiery heart without thinking of the shadow Melisandre had birthed in the gloom beneath Storm's End. *At least we fight this battle in the light, with the weapons of honest men,* he told himself. The red woman and her dark children would have no part of it. Stannis had shipped her back to Dragonstone with his bastard nephew Edric Storm. His captains and bannermen had insisted that a battlefield was no place for a woman. Only the queen's men had dissented, and then not loudly. All the same, the king had been on the point of refusing them until Lord Bryce Caron said, "Your Grace, if the sorceress is with us, afterward men will say it was her victory, not yours. They will say you owe your crown to her spells." That had turned the tide. Davos himself had held his tongue during the arguments, but if truth be told, he had not been sad to see the back of her. He wanted no part of Melisandre or her god.

To starboard, *Devotion* drove toward shore, sliding out a plank. Archers scrambled into the shallows, holding their bows high over their heads to keep the strings dry. They splashed ashore on the narrow strand beneath the bluffs. Rocks came bouncing down from the castle to crash among them, and arrows and spears as well, but the angle was steep and the missiles seemed to do little damage.

Prayer landed two dozen yards upstream and *Piety* was slanting toward the bank when the defenders came pounding down the riverside, the hooves of their warhorses sending up gouts of water from the shallows. The knights fell among the archers like wolves among chickens, driving them back toward the ships and into the river before most could notch an arrow. Men-at-arms rushed to defend them with spear and axe, and in three heartbeats the scene had turned to blood-soaked chaos. Davos recognized the dog's-head helm of the Hound. A white cloak streamed from his shoulders as he rode his horse up the plank onto the deck of *Prayer*, hacking down anyone who blundered within reach.

Beyond the castle, King's Landing rose on its hills behind the encircling walls. The riverfront was a blackened desolation; the Lannisters had burned everything and pulled back within the Mud Gate. The charred spars of sunken hulks sat in the shallows, forbidding access to the long stone quays. *We shall have no landing there.* He could see the tops of three huge trebuchets behind the Mud Gate. High on Visenya's Hill, sunlight blazed off the seven crystal towers of the Great Sept of Baelor.

Davos never saw the battle joined, but he heard it; a great rending crash as two galleys came together. He could not say which two. Another impact echoed over

the water an instant later, and then a third. Beneath the
screech of splintering wood, he heard the deep *thrum-
thump* of the *Fury*'s fore catapult. *Stag of the Sea* split
one of Joffrey's galleys clean in two, but *Dog's Nose* was
afire and *Queen Alysanne* was locked between *Lady of
Silk* and *Lady's Shame*, her crew fighting the boarders
rail-to-rail.

Directly ahead, Davos saw the enemy's *Kingslander*
drive between *Faithful* and *Sceptre*. The former slid her
starboard oars out of the way before impact, but *Sceptre*'s portside oars snapped like so much kindling as
Kingslander raked along her side. "Loose," Davos commanded, and his bowmen sent a withering rain of shafts
across the water. He saw *Kingslander*'s captain fall, and
tried to recall the man's name.

Ashore, the arms of the great trebuchets rose one,
two, three, and a hundred stones climbed high into the
yellow sky. Each one was as large as a man's head; when
they fell they sent up great gouts of water, smashed
through oak planking, and turned living men into bone
and pulp and gristle. All across the river the first line
was engaged. Grappling hooks were flung out, iron rams
crashed through wooden hulls, boarders swarmed,
flights of arrows whispered through each other in the
drifting smoke, and men died . . . but so far, none of
his.

Black Betha swept upriver, the sound of her
oarmaster's drum thundering in her captain's head as he
looked for a likely victim for her ram. The beleaguered
Queen Alysanne was trapped between two Lannister
warships, the three made fast by hooks and lines.

"Ramming speed!" Davos shouted.

The drumbeats blurred into a long fevered hammering, and *Black Betha* flew, the water turning white as
milk as it parted for her prow. Allard had seen the same
chance; *Lady Marya* ran beside them. The first line had
been transformed into a confusion of separate struggles.
The three tangled ships loomed ahead, turning, their
decks a red chaos as men hacked at each other with
sword and axe. *A little more*, Davos Seaworth be-

seeched the Warrior, *bring her around a little more, show me her broadside.*

The Warrior must have been listening. *Black Betha* and *Lady Marya* slammed into the side of *Lady's Shame* within an instant of each other, ramming her fore and aft with such force that men were thrown off the deck of *Lady of Silk* three boats away. Davos almost bit his tongue off when his teeth jarred together. He spat out blood. *Next time close your mouth, you fool.* Forty years at sea, and yet this was the first time he'd rammed another ship. His archers were loosing arrows at will.

"Back water," he commanded. When *Black Betha* reversed her oars, the river rushed into the splintered hole she left, and *Lady's Shame* fell to pieces before his eyes, spilling dozens of men into the river. Some of the living swam; some of the dead floated; the ones in heavy mail and plate sank to the bottom, the quick and the dead alike. The pleas of drowning men echoed in his ears.

A flash of green caught his eye, ahead and off to port, and a nest of writhing emerald serpents rose burning and hissing from the stern of *Queen Alysanne.* An instant later Davos heard the dread cry of *"Wildfire!"*

He grimaced. Burning pitch was one thing, wildfire quite another. Evil stuff, and well-nigh unquenchable. Smother it under a cloak and the cloak took fire; slap at a fleck of it with your palm and your hand was aflame. "Piss on wildfire and your cock burns off," old seamen liked to say. Still, Ser Imry had warned them to expect a taste of the alchemists' vile *substance.* Fortunately, there were few true pyromancers left. *They will soon run out,* Ser Imry had assured them.

Davos reeled off commands; one bank of oars pushed off while the other backed water, and the galley came about. *Lady Marya* had won clear too, and a good thing; the fire was spreading over *Queen Alysanne* and her foes faster than he would have believed possible. Men wreathed in green flame leapt into the water, shrieking like nothing human. On the walls of King's Landing, spitfires were belching death, and the great trebuchets behind the Mud Gate were throwing boulders. One the size of an ox crashed down between *Black Betha* and *Wraith*, rocking both ships and soaking every man on deck. Another, not much smaller, found *Bold Laughter*. The Velaryon galley exploded like a child's toy dropped from a tower, spraying splinters as long as a man's arm.

Through black smoke and swirling green fire, Davos glimpsed a swarm of small boats bearing downriver: a confusion of ferries and wherries, barges, skiffs, rowboats, and hulks that looked too rotten to float. It stank of desperation; such driftwood could not turn the tide of a fight, only get in the way. The lines of battle were hopelessly ensnarled, he saw. Off to port, *Lord Steffon*, *Ragged Jenna*, and *Swift Sword* had broken through and were sweeping upriver. The starboard wing was heavily engaged, however, and the center had shattered under the stones of those trebuchets, some captains turning downstream, others veering to port, anything to escape that crushing rain. *Fury* had swung her aft catapult to fire back at the city, but she lacked the range; the barrels of pitch were shattering under the walls. *Sceptre* had lost most of her oars, and *Faithful* had been rammed and was starting to list. He took *Black Betha* between them, and struck a glancing blow at Queen Cersei's ornate carved-and-gilded pleasure barge, laden with soldiers instead of sweetmeats now. The collision spilled a dozen of them into the river, where *Betha*'s archers picked them off as they tried to stay afloat.

Matthos's shout alerted him to the danger from port; one of the Lannister galleys was coming about to ram. "Hard to starboard," Davos shouted. His men used their oars to push free of the barge, while others turned the galley so her prow faced the onrushing *White Hart*. For a moment he feared he'd been too slow, that he was about to be sunk, but the current helped swing *Black Betha*, and when the impact came it was only a glancing blow, the two hulls scraping against each other, both ships snapping oars. A jagged piece of wood flew past his head, sharp as any spear. Davos flinched.

"Board her!" he shouted. Grappling lines were flung. He drew his sword and led them over the rail himself.

The crew of the White Hart met them at the rail, but *Black Betha's* men-at-arms swept over them in a screaming steel tide. Davos fought through the press, looking for the other captain, but the man was dead before he reached him. As he stood over the body, someone caught him from behind with an axe, but his helm turned the blow, and his skull was left ringing when it might have been split. Dazed, it was all he could do to roll. His attacker charged screaming. Davos grasped his sword in both hands and drove it up point first into the man's belly.

One of his crewmen pulled him back to his feet. "Captain ser, the *Hart* is ours." It was true, Davos saw. Most of the enemy were dead, dying, or yielded. He took off his helm, wiped blood from his face, and made his way back to his own ship, treading carefully on boards slimy with men's guts. Matthos lent him a hand to help him back over the rail.

For those few instants, *Black Betha* and *White Hart* were the calm eye in the midst of the storm. *Queen Alysanne* and *Lady of Silk*, still locked together, were a ranging green inferno, drifting downriver and dragging pieces of *Lady's Shame*. One of the Myrish galleys had slammed into them and was now afire as well. Cat was taking on men from the fast-sinking *Courageous*. The captain of *Dragonsbane* had driven her between two quays, ripping out her bottom; her crew poured ashore with the archers and men-at-arms to join the assault on the walls. *Red Raven*, rammed, was slowly listing. *Stag of the Sea* was fighting fires and boarders both, but the fiery heart had been raised over Joffrey's *Loyal Man*. *Fury*, her proud bow smashed in by a boulder, was engaged with *Godsgrace*. He saw Lord Velaryon's *Pride of Driftmark* crash between two Lannister river runners, overturning one and lighting the other up with fire arrows. On the south bank, knights were leading their mounts aboard the cogs, and some of the smaller galleys were already making their way across, laden with men-at-arms. They had to thread cautiously between sinking ships and patches of drifting wildfire. The whole of King Stannis's fleet was in the river now, save for Salladhor Saan's Lyseni. Soon enough they would control the Blackwater. *Ser Imry will have his victory*, Davos thought, *and Stannis will bring his host across, but gods be good, the cost of this . . .*

"Captain ser!" Matthos touched his shoulder.

It was *Swordfish*, her two banks of oars lifting and falling. She had never brought down her sails, and some burning pitch had caught in her rigging. The flames spread as Davos watched, creeping out over ropes and sails until she trailed a head of yellow flame. Her ungainly iron ram, fashioned after the likeness of the fish from which she took her name, parted the surface of the river before her. Directly ahead, drifting toward her and swinging around to present a tempting plump target, was one of the Lannister hulks, floating low in the water. Slow green blood was leaking out between her boards.

When he saw that, Davos Seaworth's heart stopped beating.

"No," he said. "No, *NOOOOOO!*" Above the roar and crash of battle, no one heard him but Matthos. Certainly the captain of the *Swordfish* did not, intent as he was on finally spearing something with his ungainly fat sword. The *Swordfish* went to battle speed. Davos lifted his maimed hand to clutch at the leather pouch that held his fingerbones.

With a grinding, splintering, tearing crash, *Swordfish* split the rotted hulk asunder. She burst like an overripe fruit, but no fruit had ever screamed that shattering wooden scream. From inside her Davos saw green gushing from a thousand broken jars, poison from the entrails of a dying beast, glistening, shining, spreading across the surface of the river . . .

"Back water," he roared. "Away. Get us off her, back water, back water!" The grappling lines were cut, and Davos felt the deck move under his feet as *Black Betha* pushed free of *White Hart*. Her oars slid down into the water.

Then he heard a short sharp *woof*, as if someone had blown in his ear. Half a heartbeat later came the roar. The deck vanished beneath him, and black water smashed him across the face, filling his nose and mouth. He was choking, drowning. Unsure which way was up, Davos wrestled the river in blind panic until suddenly he broke the surface. He spat out water, sucked in air, grabbed hold of the nearest chunk of debris, and held on.

Swordfish and the hulk were gone, blackened bodies were floating downstream beside him, and choking men clinging to bits of smoking wood. Fifty feet high, a swirling demon of green flame danced upon the river. It had a dozen hands, in each a whip, and whatever they touched burst into fire. He saw *Black Betha* burning, and *White Hart* and *Loyal Man* to either side. *Piety*, *Cat*, *Courageous*, *Sceptre*, *Red Raven*, *Harridan*, *Faithful*, *Fury*, they had all gone up, *Kingslander* and *Godsgrace* as well, the demon was eating his own. Lord Velaryon's shining *Pride of Driftmark* was trying to turn, but the demon ran a lazy green finger across her silvery oars and they flared up like so many tapers. For an instant she seemed to be stroking the river with two banks of long bright torches.

The current had him in its teeth by then, spinning him around and around. He kicked to avoid a floating patch of wildfire. *My sons*, Davos thought, but there was no way to look for them amidst the roaring chaos. Another hulk heavy with wildfire went up behind him. The Blackwater itself seemed to boil in its bed, and burning spars and burning men and pieces of broken ships filled the air.

I'm being swept out into the bay. It wouldn't be as bad there; he ought to be able to make shore, he was a strong swimmer. Salladhor Saan's galleys would be out in the bay as well, Ser Imry had commanded them to stand off . . .

And then the current turned him about again, and Davos saw what awaited him downstream.

The chain. Gods save us, they've raised the chain.

Where the river broadened out into Blackwater Bay, the boom stretched taut, a bare two or three feet above the water. Already a dozen galleys had crashed into it, and the current was pushing others against them. Almost all were aflame, and the rest soon would be. Davos could make out the striped hulls of Salladhor Saan's ships beyond, but he knew he would never reach them. A wall of red-hot steel, blazing wood, and swirling green flame stretched before him. The mouth of the Blackwater Rush had turned into the mouth of hell.

TYRION

Motionless as a gargoyle, Tyrion Lannister
hunched on one knee atop a merlon. Beyond
the Mud Gate and the desolation that had
once been the fishmarket and wharves, the river itself
seemed to have taken fire. Half of Stannis's fleet was
ablaze, along with most of Joffrey's. The kiss of wildfire
turned proud ships into funeral pyres and men into living torches. The air was full of smoke and arrows and
screams.

Downstream, commoners and highborn captains
alike could see the hot green death swirling toward
their rafts and carracks and ferries, borne on the current
of the Blackwater. The long white oars of the Myrish
galleys flashed like the legs of maddened centipedes as
they fought to come about, but it was no good. The
centipedes had no place to run.

A dozen great fires raged under the city walls, where
casks of burning pitch had exploded, but the wildfire
reduced them to no more than candles in a burning
house, their orange and scarlet pennons fluttering insig-

nificantly against the jade holocaust. The low clouds caught the color of the burning river and roofed the sky in shades of shifting green, eerily beautiful. *A terrible beauty. Like dragonfire.* Tyrion wondered if Aegon the Conqueror had felt like this as he flew above his Field of Fire.

The furnace wind lifted his crimson cloak and beat at his bare face, yet he could not turn away. He was dimly aware of the gold cloaks cheering from the hoardings. He had no voice to join them. It was a half victory. *It will not be enough.*

He saw another of the hulks he'd stuffed full of King Aerys's fickle fruits engulfed by the hungry flames. A fountain of burning jade rose from the river, the blast so bright he had to shield his eyes. Plumes of fire thirty and forty feet high danced upon the waters, crackling and hissing. For a few moments they washed out the screams. There were hundreds in the water, drowning or burning or doing a little of both.

Do you hear them shrieking, Stannis? Do you see them burning? This is your work as much as mine. Somewhere in that seething mass of men south of the Blackwater, Stannis was watching too, Tyrion knew. He'd never had his brother Robert's thirst for battle. He would command from the rear, from the reserve, much as Lord Tywin Lannister was wont to do. Like as not, he was sitting a warhorse right now, clad in bright armor, his crown upon his head. *A crown of red gold, Varys says, its points fashioned in the shapes of flames.*

"My ships." Joffrey's voice cracked as he shouted up from the wallwalk, where he huddled with his guards behind the ramparts. The golden circlet of kingship adorned his battle helm. "My *Kingslander*'s burning, *Queen Cersei, Loyal Man*. Look, that's *Seaflower*, there." He pointed with his new sword, out to where the green flames were licking at *Seaflower*'s golden hull and creeping up her oars. Her captain had turned her upriver, but not quickly enough to evade the wildfire.

She was doomed, Tyrion knew. *There was no other way. If we had not come forth to meet them, Stannis would have sensed the trap.* An arrow could be aimed, and a spear, even the stone from a catapult, but wildfire had a will of its own. Once loosed, it was beyond the control of mere men. "It could not be helped," he told his nephew. "Our fleet was doomed in any case."

Even from atop the merlon—he had been too short to see over the ramparts, so he'd had them boost him up— the flames and smoke and chaos of battle made it impossible for Tyrion to see what was happening down-river under the ·castle, but he had seen it a thousand times in his mind's eye. Bronn would have whipped the oxen into motion the moment Stannis's flagship passed under the Red Keep; the chain was ponderous heavy, and the great winches turned but slowly, creaking and rumbling. The whole of the usurper's fleet would have passed by the time the first glimmer of metal could be seen beneath the water. The links would emerge dripping wet, some glistening with mud, link by link by link, until the whole great chain stretched taut. King Stannis had rowed his fleet up the Blackwater, but he would not row out again.

Even so, some were getting away. A river's current was a tricky thing, and the wildfire was not spreading as evenly as he had hoped. The main channel was all aflame, but a good many of the Myrmen had made for the south bank and looked to escape unscathed, and at least eight ships had landed under the city walls. *Landed or wrecked, but it comes to the same thing, they've put men ashore.* Worse, a good part of the south wing of the enemy's first two battle lines had been well upstream of the inferno when the hulks went up. Stannis would be left with thirty or forty galleys, at a guess; more than enough to bring his whole host across, once they had regained their courage.

That might take a bit of time; even the bravest would be dismayed after watching a thousand or so of his fellows consumed by wildfire. Hallyne said that sometimes the substance burned so hot that flesh melted like tallow. Yet even so . . .

Tyrion had no illusions where his own men were concerned. *If the battle looks to be going sour they'll break, and they'll break bad,* Jacelyn Bywater had warned him, so the only way to win was to make certain the battle stayed sweet, start to finish.

He could see dark shapes moving through the charred ruins of the riverfront wharfs. *Time for another sortie,* he thought. Men were never so vulnerable as when they first staggered ashore. He must not give the foe time to form up on the north bank.

He scrambled down off the merlon. "Tell Lord Jacelyn we've got enemy on the riverfront," he said to one of the runners Bywater had assigned him. To another he said, "Bring my compliments to Ser Arneld and ask him to swing the Whores thirty degrees west." The angle would allow them to throw farther, if not as far out into the water.

"Mother promised I could have the Whores," Joffrey said. Tyrion was annoyed to see that the king had lifted the visor of his helm again. Doubtless the boy was cooking inside all that heavy steel . . . but the last thing he needed was some stray arrow punching through his nephew's eye.

He clanged the visor shut. "Keep that closed, Your Grace; your sweet person is precious to us all." *And you don't want to spoil that pretty face, either.* "The Whores are yours." It was as good a time as any; flinging more firepots down onto burning ships seemed pointless. Joff had the Antler Men trussed up naked in the square below, antlers nailed to their heads. When they'd been brought before the Iron Throne for justice, he had promised to send them to Stannis. A man was not as heavy as a boulder or a cask of burning pitch, and could be thrown a deal farther. Some of the gold cloaks had been wagering on whether the traitors would fly all the way across the Blackwater. "Be quick about it, Your Grace," he told Joffrey. "We'll want the trebuchets throwing stones again soon enough. Even wildfire does not burn forever."

Joffrey hurried off happy, escorted by Ser Meryn, but

Tyrion caught Ser Osmund by the wrist before he could follow. "Whatever happens, keep him safe and *keep him there,* is that understood?"

"As you command." Ser Osmund smiled amiably.

Tyrion had warned Trant and Kettleblack what would happen to them should any harm come to the king. And Joffrey had a dozen veteran gold cloaks waiting at the foot of the steps. *I'm protecting your wretched bastard as well as I can, Cersei,* he thought bitterly. *See you do the same for Alayaya.*

No sooner was Joff off than a runner came panting up the steps. "My lord, hurry!" He threw himself to one knee. "They've landed men on the tourney grounds, hundreds! They're bringing a ram up to the King's Gate."

Tyrion cursed and made for the steps with a rolling waddle. Podrick Payne waited below with their horses. They galloped off down River Row, Pod and Ser Mandon Moore coming hard behind him. The shuttered houses were steeped in green shadow, but there was no traffic to get in their way; Tyrion had commanded that the street be kept clear, so the defenders could move quickly from one gate to the next. Even so, by the time they reached the King's Gate, he could hear a booming crash of wood on wood that told him the battering ram had been brought into play. The groaning of the great hinges sounded like the moans of a dying giant. The gatehouse square was littered with the wounded, but he saw lines of horses as well, not all of them hurt, and sellswords and gold cloaks enough to form a strong column. "Form up," he shouted as he leapt to the ground. The gate moved under the impact of another blow. "Who commands here? You're going out."

"No." A shadow detached itself from the shadow of the wall, to become a tall man in dark grey armor. Sandor Clegane wrenched off his helm with both hands and let it fall to the ground. The steel was scorched and dented, the left ear of the snarling hound sheared off. A gash above one eye had sent a wash of blood down across the Hound's old burn scars, masking half his face.

"Yes." Tyrion faced him.

Clegane's breath came ragged. "Bugger that. And you."

A sellsword stepped up beside him. "We been out. Three times. Half our men are killed or hurt. Wildfire bursting all around us, horses screaming like men and men like horses—"

"Did you think we hired you to fight in a tourney? Shall I bring you a nice iced milk and a bowl of raspberries? No? Then get on your fucking horse. You too, dog."

The blood on Clegane's face glistened red, but his eyes showed white. He drew his longsword.

He is afraid, Tyrion realized, shocked. *The Hound is frightened.* He tried to explain their need. "They've taken a ram to the gate, you can hear them, we need to disperse them—"

"Open the gates. When they rush inside, surround them and kill them." The Hound thrust the point of his longsword into the ground and leaned upon the pommel, swaying. "I've lost half my men. Horse as well. I'm not taking more into that fire."

Ser Mandon Moore moved to Tyrion's side, immaculate in his enameled white plate. "The King's Hand commands you."

"Bugger the King's Hand." Where the Hound's face was not sticky with blood, it was pale as milk. "Someone bring me a drink." A gold cloak officer handed him a cup. Clegane took a swallow, spit it out, flung the cup away. "Water? Fuck your water. Bring me wine."

He is dead on his feet. Tyrion could see it now. *The wound, the fire . . . he's done, I need to find someone else, but who? Ser Mandon?* He looked at the men and knew it would not do. Clegane's fear had shaken them. Without a leader, they would refuse as well, and Ser Mandon . . . a dangerous man, Jaime said, yes, but not a man other men would follow.

In the distance Tyrion heard another great crash.

Above the walls, the darkening sky was awash with sheets of green and orange light. How long could the gate hold?

This is madness, he thought, *but sooner madness than defeat. Defeat is death and shame.* "Very well, *I'll* lead the sortie."

If he thought that would shame the Hound back to valor, he was wrong. Clegane only laughed. *"You?"*

Tyrion could see the disbelief on their faces. "Me. Ser Mandon, you'll bear the king's banner. Pod, my helm." The boy ran to obey. The Hound leaned on that notched and blood-streaked sword and looked at him with those wide white eyes. Ser Mandon helped Tyrion mount up again. *"Form up!"* he shouted.

His big red stallion wore crinet and chamfron. Crimson silk draped his hindquarters, over a coat of mail. The high saddle was gilded. Podrik Payne handed up helm and shield, heavy oak emblazoned with a golden hand on red, surrounded by small golden lions. He walked his horse in a circle, looking at the little force of men. Only a handful had responded to his command, no more than twenty. They sat their horses with eyes as white as the Hound's. He looked contemptuously at the others, the knights and sellswords who had ridden with Clegane. "They say I'm half a man," he said. "What does that make the lot of you?"

That shamed them well enough. A knight mounted, helmetless, and rode to join the others. A pair of sellswords followed. Then more. The King's Gate shuddered again. In a few moments the size of Tyrion's command had doubled. He had them trapped. *If I fight, they must do the same, or they are less than dwarfs.*

"You won't hear me shout out Joffrey's name," he told them. "You won't hear me yell for Casterly Rock either. This is your city Stannis means to sack, and that's your gate he's bringing down. So come with me and kill the son of a bitch!" Tyrion unsheathed his axe, wheeled the stallion around, and trotted toward the sally port. He *thought* they were following, but never dared to look.

SANSA

The torches shimmered brightly against the hammered metal of the wall sconces, filling the Queen's Ballroom with silvery light. Yet there was still darkness in that hall. Sansa could see it in the pale eyes of Ser Ilyn Payne, who stood by the back door still as stone, taking neither food nor wine. She could hear it in Lord Gyles's racking cough, and the whispered voice of Osney Kettleblack when he slipped in to bring Cersei the tidings.

Sansa was finishing her broth when he came the first time, entering through the back. She glimpsed him talking to his brother Osfryd. Then he climbed the dais and knelt beside the high seat, smelling of horse, four long thin scratches on his cheek crusted with scabs, his hair falling down past his collar and into his eyes. For all his whispering, Sansa could not help but hear. "The fleets are locked in battle. Some archers got ashore, but the Hound's cut them to pieces, Y'Grace. Your brother's raising his chain, I heard the signal. Some drunkards down to Flea Bottom are smashing doors and climbing through windows. Lord Bywater's sent the gold cloaks to deal with them. Baelor's Sept is jammed full, everyone praying."

"And my son?"

"The king went to Baelor's to get the High Septon's blessing. Now he's walking the walls with the Hand, telling the men to be brave, lifting their spirits as it were."

Cersei beckoned to her page for another cup of wine, a golden vintage from the Arbor, fruity and rich. The queen was drinking heavily, but the wine only seemed to make her more beautiful; her cheeks were flushed, and her eyes had a bright, feverish heat to them as she looked down over the hall. *Eyes of wildfire*, Sansa thought.

Musicians played. Jugglers juggled. Moon Boy lurched about the hall on stilts making mock of everyone, while Ser Dontos chased serving girls on his broomstick horse. The guests laughed, but it was a joyless laughter, the sort of laughter that can turn into sobbing in half a heartbeat. *Their bodies are here, but their thoughts are on the city walls, and their hearts as well.*

After the broth came a salad of apples, nuts, and raisins. At any other time, it might have made a tasty dish, but tonight all the food was flavored with fear. Sansa was not the only one in the hall without an appetite. Lord Gyles was coughing more than he was eating, Lollys Stokeworth sat hunched and shivering, and the young bride of one of Ser Lancel's knights began to weep uncontrollably. The queen commanded Maester Frenken to put her to bed with a cup of dreamwine. "Tears," she said scornfully to Sansa as the woman was led from the hall. "The woman's weapon, my lady mother used to call them. The man's weapon is a sword. And that tells us all you need to know, doesn't it?"

"Men must be very brave, though," said Sansa. "To ride out and face swords and axes, everyone trying to kill you . . ."

"Jaime told me once that he only feels truly alive in

battle and in bed." She lifted her cup and took a long swallow. Her salad was untouched. "I would sooner face any number of swords than sit helpless like this, pretending to enjoy the company of this flock of frightened hens."

"You asked them here, Your Grace."

"Certain things are expected of a queen. They will be expected of you should you ever wed Joffrey. Best learn." The queen studied the wives, daughters, and mothers who filled the benches. "Of themselves the hens are nothing, but their cocks are important for one reason or another, and some may survive this battle. So it behooves me to give their women my protection. If my wretched dwarf of a brother should somehow manage to prevail, they will return to their husbands and fathers full of tales about how brave I was, how my courage inspired them and lifted their spirits, how I never doubted our victory even for a moment."

"And if the castle should fall?"

"You'd like that, wouldn't you?" Cersei did not wait for a denial. "If I'm not betrayed by my own guards, I may be able to hold here for a time. Then I can go to the walls and offer to yield to Lord Stannis in person. That will spare us the worst. But if Maegor's Holdfast should fall before Stannis can come up, why then, most of my guests are in for a bit of rape, I'd say. And you should never rule out mutilation, torture, and murder at times like these."

Sansa was horrified. "These are women, unarmed, and gently born."

"Their birth protects them," Cersei admitted, "though not as much as you'd think. Each one's worth a good ransom, but after the madness of battle, soldiers often seem to want flesh more than coin. Even so, a golden shield is better than none. Out in the streets, the women won't be treated near as tenderly. Nor will our servants. Pretty things like that serving wench of Lady Tanda's could be in for a lively night, but don't imagine the old and the infirm and the ugly will be spared.

Enough drink will make blind washerwomen and reeking pig girls seem as comely as you, sweetling."

"*Me?*"

"*Try* not to sound so like a mouse, Sansa. You're a woman now, remember? And betrothed to my firstborn." The queen sipped at her wine. "Were it anyone else outside the gates, I might hope to beguile him. But this is Stannis Baratheon. I'd have a better chance of seducing his horse." She noticed the look on Sansa's face, and laughed. "Have I shocked you, my lady?" She leaned close. "You little fool. Tears are not a woman's *only* weapon. You've got another one between your legs, and you'd best learn to use it. You'll find men use their swords freely enough. Both kinds of swords."

Sansa was spared the need to reply when two Kettleblacks reentered the hall. Ser Osmund and his brothers had become great favorites about the castle; they were always ready with a smile and a jest, and got on with grooms and huntsmen as well as they did with knights and squires. With the serving wenches they got on best of all, it was gossiped. Of late Ser Osmund had taken Sandor Clegane's place by Joffrey's side, and Sansa had heard the women at the washing well saying he was as strong as the Hound, only younger and faster. If that was so, she wondered why she had never once heard of these Kettleblacks before Ser Osmund was named to the Kingsguard.

Osney was all smiles as he knelt beside the queen. "The hulks have gone up, Y'Grace. The whole Blackwater's awash with wildfire. A hundred ships burning, maybe more."

"And my son?"

"He's at the Mud Gate with the Hand and the Kingsguard, Y'Grace. He spoke to the archers on the hoardings before, and gave them a few tips on handling a crossbow, he did. All agree, he's a right brave boy."

"He'd best remain a right *live* boy." Cersei turned to his brother Osfryd, who was taller, sterner, and wore a drooping black mustache. "Yes?"

Osfryd had donned a steel halfhelm over his long

black hair, and the look on his face was grim. "Y'Grace," he said quietly, "the boys caught a groom and two maidservants trying to sneak out a postern with three of the king's horses."

"The night's first traitors," the queen said, "but not the last, I fear. Have Ser Ilyn see to them, and put their heads on pikes outside the stables as a warning." As they left, she turned to Sansa. "Another lesson you should learn, if you hope to sit beside my son. Be gentle on a night like this and you'll have treasons popping up all about you like mushrooms after a hard rain. The only way to keep your people loyal is to make certain they fear you more than they do the enemy."

"I will remember, Your Grace," said Sansa, though she had always heard that love was a surer route to the people's loyalty than fear. *If I am ever a queen, I'll make them love me.*

Crabclaw pies followed the salad. Then came mutton roasted with leeks and carrots, served in trenchers of hollowed bread. Lollys ate too fast, got sick, and retched all over herself and her sister. Lord Gyles coughed, drank, coughed, drank, and passed out. The queen gazed down in disgust to where he sprawled with his face in his trencher and his hand in a puddle of wine. "The gods must have been mad to waste manhood on the likes of him, and I must have been mad to demand his release."

Osfryd Kettleblack returned, crimson cloak swirling. "There's folks gathering in the square, Y'Grace, asking to take refuge in the castle. Not a mob, rich merchants and the like."

"Command them to return to their homes," the queen said. "If they won't go, have our crossbowmen kill a few. No sorties; I won't have the gates opened for any reason."

"As you command." He bowed and moved off.

The queen's face was hard and angry. "Would that I could take a sword to their necks myself." Her voice was starting to slur. "When we were little, Jaime and I were so much alike that even our lord father could not tell us apart. Sometimes as a lark we would dress in each other's clothes and spend a whole day each as the other. Yet even so, when Jaime was given his first sword, there was none for me. 'What do *I* get?' I remember asking. We were so much alike, I could never understand why they treated us so *differently*. Jaime learned to fight with sword and lance and mace, while I was taught to smile and sing and please. He was heir to Casterly Rock, while I was to be sold to some stranger like a horse, to be ridden whenever my new owner liked, beaten whenever he liked, and cast aside in time for a younger filly. Jaime's lot was to be glory and power, while mine was birth and moonblood."

"But you were queen of all the Seven Kingdoms," Sansa said.

"When it comes to swords, a queen is only a woman after all." Cersei's wine cup was empty. The page moved to fill it again, but she turned it over and shook her head. "No more. I must keep a clear head."

The last course was goat cheese served with baked apples. The scent of cinnamon filled the hall as Osney Kettleblack slipped in to kneel once more between them. "Y'Grace," he murmured. "Stannis has landed men on the tourney grounds, and there's more coming across. The Mud Gate's under attack, and they've brought a ram to the King's Gate. The Imp's gone out to drive them off."

"That will fill them with fear," the queen said dryly. "He hasn't taken Joff, I hope."

"No, Y'Grace, the king's with my brother at the Whores, flinging Antler Men into the river."

"With the Mud Gate under assault? Folly. Tell Ser Osmund I want him out of there at once, it's too dangerous. Fetch him back to the castle."

"The Imp said—"

"It's what *I* said that ought concern you." Cersei's eyes narrowed. "Your brother will do as he's told, or I'll see to it that he leads the next sortie himself, and you'll go with him."

After the meal had been cleared away, many of the guests asked leave to go to the sept. Cersei graciously granted their request. Lady Tanda and her daughters were among those who fled. For those who remained, a singer was brought forth to fill the hall with the sweet music of the high harp. He sang of Jonquil and Florian, of Prince Aemon the-Dragonknight and his love for his brother's queen, of Nymeria's ten thousand ships. They were beautiful songs, but terribly sad. Several of the women began to weep, and Sansa felt her own eyes growing moist.

"Very good, dear." The queen leaned close. "You want to practice those tears. You'll need them for King Stannis."

Sansa shifted nervously. "Your Grace?"

"Oh, spare me your hollow courtesies. Matters must have reached a desperate strait out there if they need a dwarf to lead them, so you might as well take off your mask. I know all about your little treasons in the godswood."

"The godswood?" *Don't look at Ser Dontos, don't, don't, Sansa told herself. She doesn't know, no one knows, Dontos promised me, my Florian would never fail me.* "I've done no treasons. I only visit the godswood to pray."

"For Stannis. Or your brother, it's all the same. Why else seek your father's gods? You're praying for our defeat. What would you call that, if not treason?"

"I pray for Joffrey," she insisted nervously.

"Why, because he treats you so sweetly?" The queen took a flagon of sweet plum wine from a passing serving girl and filled Sansa's cup. "Drink," she commanded coldly. "Perhaps it·will give you the courage to deal with truth for a change."

Sansa lifted the cup to her lips and took a sip. The wine was cloyingly sweet, but very strong.

"You can do better than that," Cersei said. "Drain the cup, Sansa. Your queen commands you."

It almost gagged her, but Sansa emptied the cup, gulping down the thick sweet wine until her head was swimming.

"More?" Cersei asked.

"No. Please."

The queen looked displeased. "When you asked about Ser Ilyn earlier, I lied to you. Would you like to hear the truth, Sansa? Would you like to know why he's really here?"

She did not dare answer, but it did not matter. The queen raised a hand and beckoned, never waiting for a reply. Sansa had not even seen Ser Ilyn return to the hall, but suddenly there he was, striding from the shadows behind the dais as silent as a cat. He carried Ice unsheathed. Her father had always cleaned the blade in the godswood after he took a man's head, Sansa recalled, but Ser Ilyn was not so fastidious. There was blood drying on the rippling steel, the red already fading to brown. "Tell Lady Sansa why I keep you by us," said Cersei.

Ser Ilyn opened his mouth and emitted a choking rattle. His pox-scarred face had no expression.

"He's here for us, he says," the queen said. "Stannis may take the city and he may take the throne, but I will not suffer him to judge me. I do not mean for him to have us alive."

"Us?"

"You heard me. So perhaps you had best pray again, Sansa, and for a different outcome. The Starks will have no joy from the fall of House Lannister, I promise you." She reached out and touched Sansa's hair, brushing it lightly away from her neck.

TYRION

The slot in his helm limited Tyrion's vision to what was before him, but when he turned his head he saw three galleys beached on the tourney grounds, and a fourth, larger than the others, standing well out into the river, firing barrels of burning pitch from a catapult.

"Wedge," Tyrion commanded as his men streamed out of the sally port. They formed up in spearhead, with him at the point. Ser Mandon Moore took the place to his right, flames shimmering against the white enamel of his armor, his dead eyes shining passionlessly through his helm. He rode a coal-black horse barded all in white, with the pure white shield of the Kingsguard strapped to his arm. On the left, Tyrion was surprised to see Podrick Payne, a sword in his hand. "You're too young," he said at once. "Go back."

"I'm your squire, my lord."

Tyrion could spare no time for argument. "With me, then. Stay close." He kicked his horse into motion.

They rode knee to knee, following the line of the

looming walls. Joffrey's standard streamed crimson and gold from Ser Mandon's staff, stag and lion dancing hoof to paw. They went from a walk to a trot, wheeling wide around the base of the tower. Arrows darted from the city walls while stones spun and tumbled overhead, crashing down blindly onto earth and water, steel and flesh. Ahead loomed the King's Gate and a surging mob of soldiers wrestling with a huge ram, a shaft of black oak with an iron head. Archers off the ships surrounded them, loosing their shafts at whatever defenders showed themselves on the gatehouse walls. "Lances," Tyrion commanded. He sped to a canter.

The ground was sodden and slippery, equal parts mud and blood. His stallion stumbled over a corpse, his hooves sliding and churning the earth, and for an instant Tyrion feared his charge would end with him tumbling from the saddle before he even reached the foe, but somehow he and his horse both managed to keep their balance. Beneath the gate men were turning, hurriedly trying to brace for the shock. Tyrion lifted his axe and shouted, *"King's Landing!"* Other voices took up the cry, and now the arrowhead flew, a long scream of steel and silk, pounding hooves and sharp blades kissed by fire.

Ser Mandon dropped the point of his lance at the last possible instant, and drove Joffrey's banner through the chest of a man in a studded jerkin, lifting him full off his feet before the shaft snapped. Ahead of Tyrion was a knight whose surcoat showed a fox peering through a ring of flowers. *Florent* was his first thought, but *helmless* ran a close second. He smashed the man in the face with all the weight of axe and arm and charging horse, taking off half his head. The shock of impact numbed his shoulder. *Shagga would laugh at me,* he thought, riding on.

A spear thudded against his shield. Pod galloped beside him, slashing down at every foe they passed. Dimly, he heard cheers from the men on the walls. The battering ram crashed down into the mud, forgotten in an instant as its handlers fled or turned to fight. Tyrion rode down an archer, opened a spearman from shoulder to armpit, glanced a blow off a swordfish-crested helm. At the ram his big red reared but the black stallion leapt the obstacle smoothly and Ser Mandon flashed past him, death in snow-white silk. His sword sheared off limbs, cracked heads, broke shields asunder—though few enough of the enemy had made it across the river with shields intact.

Tyrion urged his mount over the ram. Their foes were fleeing. He moved his head right to left and back again, but saw no sign of Podrick Payne. An arrow clattered against his cheek, missing his eye slit by an inch. His jolt of fear almost unhorsed him. *If I'm to sit here like a stump, I had as well paint a target on my breastplate.*

He spurred his horse back into motion, trotting over and around a scatter of corpses. Downriver, the Blackwater was jammed with the hulks of burning galleys. Patches of wildfire still floated atop the water, sending fiery green plumes swirling twenty feet into the air. They had dispersed the men on the battering ram, but he could see fighting all along the riverfront. Ser Balon Swann's men, most like, or Lancel's, trying to throw the enemy back into the water as they swarmed ashore off the burning ships. "We'll ride for the Mud Gate," he commanded.

Ser Mandon shouted, *"The Mud Gate!"* And they were off again. *"King's Landing!"* his men cried raggedly, and *"Halfman! Halfman!"* He wondered who had taught them that. Through the steel and padding of his helm, he heard anguished screams, the hungry crackle of flame, the shuddering of warhorns, and the brazen blast of trumpets. Fire was everywhere. *Gods be good, no wonder the Hound was frightened. It's the flames he fears . . .*

A splintering crash rang across the Blackwater as a stone the size of a horse landed square amidships on one of the galleys. *Ours or theirs?* Through the roiling smoke, he could not tell. His wedge was gone; every man was his own battle now. *I should have turned back*, he thought, riding on.

The axe was heavy in his fist. A handful still followed him, the rest dead or fled. He had to wrestle his stallion to keep his head to the east. The big destrier liked fire no more than Sandor Clegane had, but the horse was easier to cow.

Men were crawling from the river, men burned and bleeding, coughing up water, staggering, most dying. He led his troop among them, delivering quicker cleaner deaths to those strong enough to stand. The war shrank to the size of his eye slit. Knights twice his size fled from him, or stood and died. They seemed little things, and fearful. *"Lannister!"* he shouted, slaying. His arm was red to the elbow, glistening in the light off the river. When his horse reared again, he shook his axe at the stars and heard them call out *"Halfman! Halfman!"* Tyrion felt drunk.

The battle fever. He had never thought to experience it himself, though Jaime had told him of it often enough. How time seemed to blur and slow and even stop, how the past and the future vanished until there was nothing but the instant, how fear fled, and thought fled, and even your body. "You don't feel your wounds then, or the ache in your back from the weight of the armor, or the sweat running down into your eyes. You stop feeling, you stop thinking, you stop being *you*, there is only the fight, the foe, this man and then the next and the next and the next, and you know they are afraid and tired but you're not, you're alive, and death is all around you but their swords move so slowly, you can dance through them laughing." *Battle fever. I am half a man and drunk with slaughter, let them kill me if they can!*

They tried. Another spearman ran at him. Tyrion lopped off the head of his spear, then his hand, then his arm, trotting around him in a circle. An archer, bowless, thrust at him with an arrow, holding it as if it were a knife. The destrier kicked at the man's thigh to send him sprawling, and Tyrion barked laughter. He rode past a banner planted in the mud, one of Stannis's fiery hearts, and chopped the staff in two with a swing of his axe. A knight rose up from nowhere to hack at his shield with a two-handed greatsword, again and again, until someone thrust a dagger under his arm. One of Tyrion's men, perhaps. He never saw.

"I yield, ser," a different knight called out, farther down the river. "Yield. Ser knight, I yield to you. My pledge, here, here." The man lay in a puddle of black water, offering up a lobstered gauntlet in token of submission. Tyrion had to lean down to take it from him. As he did, a pot of wildfire burst overhead, spraying green flame. In the sudden stab of light he saw that the puddle was not black but red. The gauntlet still had the knight's hand in it. He flung it back. "Yield," the man sobbed hopelessly, helplessly. Tyrion reeled away.

A man-at-arms grabbed the bridle of his horse and thrust at Tyrion's face with a dagger. He knocked the blade aside and buried the axe in the nape of the man's neck. As he was wresting it free, a blaze of white appeared at the edge of his vision. Tyrion turned, thinking to find Ser Mandon Moore beside him again, but this was a different white knight. Ser Balon Swann wore the same armor, but his horse trappings bore the battling black-and-white swans of his House. *He's more a spotted knight than a white one*, Tyrion thought inanely. Every bit of Ser Balon was spattered with gore and smudged by smoke. He raised his mace to point downriver. Bits of brain and bone clung to its head. "My lord, look."

Tyrion swung his horse about to peer down the Blackwater. The current still flowed black and strong beneath, but the surface was a roil of blood and flame. The sky was red and orange and garish green. "What?" he said. Then he saw.

Steel-clad men-at-arms were clambering off a broken galley that had smashed into a pier. *So many, where are they coming from?* Squinting into the smoke and glare, Tyrion followed them back out into the river. Twenty galleys were jammed together out there, maybe more, it was hard to count. Their oars were crossed, their hulls locked together with grappling lines, they were impaled on each other's rams, tangled in webs of fallen rigging. One great hulk floated hull up between two smaller ships. Wrecks, but packed so closely that it was possible to leap from one deck to the other and so cross the Blackwater.

Hundreds of Stannis Baratheon's boldest were doing just that. Tyrion saw one great fool of a knight trying to ride across, urging a terrified horse over gunwales and oars, across tilting decks slick with blood and crackling with green fire. *We made them a bloody bridge,* he thought in dismay. Parts of the bridge were sinking and other parts were afire and the whole thing was creaking and shifting and like to burst asunder at any moment, but that did not seem to stop them. "Those are brave men," he told Ser Balon in admiration. "Let's go kill them."

He led them through the guttering fires and the soot and ash of the riverfront, pounding down a long stone quay with his own men and Ser Balon's behind him. Ser Mandon fell in with them, his shield a ragged ruin. Smoke and cinders swirled through the air, and the foe broke before their charge, throwing themselves back into the water, knocking over other men as they fought to climb up. The foot of the bridge was a half-sunken enemy galley with *Dragonsbane* painted on her prow, her bottom ripped out by one of the sunken hulks Tyrion had placed between the quays. A spearman wearing the red crab badge of House Celtigar drove the point of his weapon up through the chest of Balon Swann's horse before he could dismount, spilling the knight from the saddle. Tyrion hacked at the man's head as he flashed by, and by then it was too late to rein up. His stallion leapt from the end of the quay and over a splintered gunwale, landing with a splash and a scream in ankle-deep water. Tyrion's axe went spinning, followed by Tyrion himself, and the deck rose up to give him a wet smack.

Madness followed. His horse had broken a leg and was screaming horribly. Somehow he managed to draw his dagger, and slit the poor creature's throat. The blood gushed out in a scarlet fountain, drenching his arms and chest. He found his feet again and lurched to the rail, and then he was fighting, staggering and splashing across crooked decks awash with water. Men came at him. Some he killed, some he wounded, and some went away, but always there were more. He lost his knife and gained a broken spear, he could not have said how. He clutched it and stabbed, shrieking curses. Men ran from him and he ran after them, clambering up over the rail to the next ship and then the next. His two white shadows were always with him; Balon Swann and Mandon Moore, beautiful in their pale plate. Surrounded by a circle of Velaryon spearmen, they fought back to back; they made battle as graceful as a dance.

His own killing was a clumsy thing. He stabbed one man in the kidney when his back was turned, and grabbed another by the leg and upended him into the river. Arrows hissed past his head and clattered off his armor; one lodged between shoulder and breastplate, but he never felt it. A naked man fell from the sky and landed on the deck, body bursting like a melon dropped from a tower. His blood spattered through the slit of Tyrion's helm. Stones began to plummet down, crashing through the decks and turning men to pulp, until the whole bridge gave a shudder and twisted violently underfoot, knocking him sideways.

Suddenly the river was pouring into his helm. He ripped it off and crawled along the listing deck until the water was only neck deep. A groaning filled the air, like the death cries of some enormous beast. *The ship*, he had time to think, *the ship's about to tear loose*. The broken galleys were ripping apart, the bridge breaking apart. No sooner had he come to that realization than he heard a sudden *crack*, loud as thunder, the deck lurched beneath him, and he slid back down into the water.

The list was so steep he had to climb back up, hauling himself along a snapped line inch by bloody inch. Out of the corner of his eye, he saw the hulk they'd been tangled with drifting downstream with the current, spinning slowly as men leapt over her side. Some wore Stannis's flaming heart, some Joffrey's stag-and-lion, some other badges, but it seemed to make no matter. Fires were burning upstream and down. On one side of him was a raging battle, a great confusion of bright banners waving above a sea of struggling men, shield walls forming and breaking, mounted knights cutting through the press, dust and mud and blood and smoke. On the other side, the Red Keep loomed high on its hill, spitting fire. They were on the wrong sides, though. For a moment Tyrion thought he was going mad, that Stannis and the castle had traded places. *How could Stannis cross to the north bank?* Belatedly he realized that the deck was turning, and somehow he had gotten spun about, so castle and battle had changed sides. *Battle, what battle, if Stannis hasn't crossed who is he fighting?* Tyrion was too tired to make sense of it. His shoulder ached horribly, and when he reached up to rub it he saw the arrow, and remembered. *I have to get off this ship.* Downstream was nothing but a wall of fire, and if the wreck broke loose the current would take him right into it.

Someone was calling his name faintly through the din of battle. Tyrion tried to shout back. "Here! Here, I'm here, help me!" His voice sounded so thin he could scarcely hear himself. He pulled himself up the slanting deck, and grabbed for the rail. The hull slammed into the next galley over and rebounded so violently he was almost knocked into the water. Where had all his strength gone? It was all he could do to hang on.

"MY LORD! TAKE MY HAND! MY LORD TYRION!"

There on the deck of the next ship, across a widening gulf of black water, stood Ser Mandon Moore, a hand extended. Yellow and green fire shone against the white of his armor, and his lobstered gauntlet was sticky with blood, but Tyrion reached for it all the same, wishing his arms were longer. It was only at the very last, as their fingers brushed across the gap, that something niggled at him . . . Ser Mandon was holding out his *left* hand, why . . .

Was that why he reeled backward, or did he see the sword after all? He would never know. The point slashed just beneath his eyes, and he felt its cold hard touch and then a blaze of pain. His head spun around as if he'd been slapped. The shock of the cold water was a second slap more jolting than the first. He flailed for something to grab on to, knowing that once he went down he was not like to come back up. Somehow his hand found the splintered end of a broken oar. Clutching it tight as a desperate lover, he shinnied up foot by foot. His eyes were full of water, his mouth was full of blood, and his head throbbed horribly. *Gods give me strength to reach the deck* . . . There was nothing else, only the oar, the water, the deck.

Finally he rolled over the side and lay breathless and exhausted, flat on his back. Balls of green and orange flame crackled overhead, leaving streaks between the stars. He had a moment to think how pretty it was before Ser Mandon blocked out the view. The knight was a white steel shadow, his eyes shining darkly behind his helm. Tyrion had no more strength than a rag doll. Ser Mandon put the point of his sword to the hollow of his throat and curled both hands around the hilt.

And suddenly he lurched to the left, staggering into the rail. Wood split, and Ser Mandon Moore vanished with a shout and a splash. An instant later, the hulls came slamming together again, so hard the deck seemed to jump. Then someone was kneeling over him. "Jaime?" he croaked, almost choking on the blood that filled his mouth. Who else would save him, if not his brother?

"Be still, my lord, you're hurt bad." *A boy's voice, that makes no sense,* thought Tyrion. It sounded almost like Pod.

SANSA

When Ser Lancel Lannister told the queen that the battle was lost, she turned her empty wine cup in her hands and said, "Tell my brother, ser." Her voice was distant, as if the news were of no great interest to her.

"Your brother's likely dead." Ser Lancel's surcoat was soaked with the blood seeping out under his arm. When he had arrived in the hall, the sight of him had made some of the guests scream. "He was on the bridge of boats when it broke apart, we think. Ser Mandon's likely gone as well, and no one can find the Hound. Gods be damned, Cersei, *why* did you have them fetch Joffrey back to the castle? The gold cloaks are throwing down their spears and running, hundreds of them. When they saw the king leaving, they lost all heart. The whole Blackwater's awash with wrecks and fire and corpses, but we could have held if—"

Osney Kettleblack pushed past him. "There's fighting on both sides of the river now, Y'Grace. It may be that some of Stannis's lords are fighting each other, no one's sure, it's all confused over there. The Hound's gone, no one knows where, and Ser Balon's fallen back inside the city. The riverside's theirs. They're ramming at the King's Gate again, and Ser Lancel's right, your men are deserting the walls and killing their own officers. There's mobs at the Iron Gate and the Gate of the Gods fighting to get out, and Flea Bottom's one great drunken riot."

Gods be good, Sansa thought, *it is happening, Joffrey's lost his head and so have I.* She looked for Ser Ilyn, but the King's Justice was not to be seen. *I can feel him, though. He's close, I'll not escape him, he'll have my head.*

Strangely calm, the queen turned to his brother Osfryd. "Raise the drawbridge and bar the doors. No one enters or leaves Maegor's without my leave."

"What about them women who went to pray?"

"They chose to leave my protection. Let them pray; perhaps the gods will defend them. Where's my son?"

"The castle gatehouse. He wanted to command the crossbowmen. There's a mob howling outside, half of them gold cloaks who came with him when we left the Mud Gate."

"Bring him inside Maegor's *now.*"

"*No!*" Lancel was so angry he forgot to keep his voice down. Heads turned toward them as he shouted, "We'll have the Mud Gate all over again. Let him stay where he is, he's the *king*—"

"He's my son." Cersei Lannister rose to her feet. "You claim to be a Lannister as well, cousin, prove it. Osfryd, why are you standing there? *Now* means today."

Osfryd Kettleblack hurried from the hall, his brother with him. Many of the guests were rushing out as well. Some of the women were weeping, some praying. Others simply remained at the tables and called for more wine. "Cersei," Ser Lancel pleaded, "if we lose the castle, Joffrey will be killed in any case, you know that. Let him stay, I'll keep him by me, I swear—"

"Get out of my way." Cersei slammed her open palm

into his wound. Ser Lancel cried out in pain and almost fainted as the queen swept from the room. She spared Sansa not so much as a glance. *She's forgotten me. Ser Ilyn will kill me and she won't even think about it.*

"Oh, gods," an old woman wailed. "We're lost, the battle's lost, she's running." Several children were crying. *They can smell the fear.* Sansa found herself alone on the dais. Should she stay here, or run after the queen and plead for her life?

She never knew why she got to her feet, but she did. "Don't be afraid," she told them loudly. "The queen has raised the drawbridge. This is the safest place in the city. There's thick walls, the moat, the spikes . . ."

"What's happened?" demanded a woman she knew slightly, the wife of a lesser lordling. "What did Osney tell her? Is the king hurt, has the city fallen?"

"Tell us," someone else shouted. One woman asked about her father, another her son.

Sansa raised her hands for quiet. "Joffrey's come back to the castle. He's not hurt. They're still fighting, that's all I know, they're fighting bravely. The queen will be back soon." The last was a lie, but she had to soothe them. She noticed the fools standing under the galley. "Moon Boy, make us laugh."

Moon Boy did a cartwheel, and vaulted on top of a table. He grabbed up four wine cups and began to juggle them. Every so often one of them would come down and smash him in the head. A few nervous laughs echoed through the hall. Sansa went to Ser Lancel and knelt beside him. His wound was bleeding afresh where the queen had struck him. "Madness," he gasped. "Gods, the Imp was right, was right . . ."

"Help him," Sansa commanded two of the serving men. One just looked at her and ran, flagon and all. Other servants were leaving the hall as well, but she could not help that. Together, Sansa and the serving man got the wounded knight back on his feet. "Take him to Maester Frenken." Lancel was one of *them*, yet somehow she still could not bring herself to wish him dead. *I am soft and weak and stupid, just as Joffrey says. I should be killing him, not helping him.*

The torches had begun to burn low, and one or two had flickered out. No one troubled to replace them. Cersei did not return. Ser Dontos climbed the dais while all eyes were on the other fool. "Go back to your bedchamber, sweet Jonquil," he whispered. "Lock yourself in, you'll be safer there. I'll come for you when the battle's done."

Someone will come for me, Sansa thought, *but will it be you, or will it be Ser Ilyn?* For a mad moment she thought of begging Dontos to defend her. He had been a knight too, trained with the sword and sworn to defend the weak. *No. He has not the courage, or the skill. I would only be killing him as well.*

It took all the strength she had in her to walk slowly from the Queen's Ballroom when she wanted so badly to run. When she reached the steps, she *did* run, up and around until she was breathless and dizzy. One of the guards knocked into her on the stair. A jeweled wine cup and a pair of silver candlesticks spilled out of the crimson cloak he'd wrapped them in and went clattering down the steps. He hurried after them, paying Sansa no mind once he decided she was not going to try and take his loot.

Her bedchamber was black as pitch. Sansa barred the door and fumbled through the dark to the window. When she ripped back the drapes, her breath caught in her throat.

The southern sky was aswirl with glowing, shifting colors, the reflections of the great fires that burned below. Baleful green tides moved against the bellies of the clouds, and pools of orange light spread out across the heavens. The reds and yellows of common flame warred against the emeralds and jades of wildfire, each color flaring and then fading, birthing armies of short-lived shadows to die again an instant later. Green dawns gave way to orange dusks in half a heartbeat. The air itself smelled *burnt,* the way a soup kettle sometimes smelled if it was left on the fire too long and all the soup boiled away. Embers drifted through the night air like swarms of fireflies.

Sansa backed away from the window, retreating toward the safety of her bed. *I'll go to sleep,* she told herself, *and when I wake it will be a new day, and the sky will be blue again. The fighting will be done and someone will tell me whether I'm to live or die.* "Lady," she whimpered softly, wondering if she would meet her wolf again when she was dead.

Then something stirred behind her, and a hand reached out of the dark and grabbed her wrist.

Sansa opened her mouth to scream, but another hand clamped down over her face, smothering her. His fingers were rough and callused, and sticky with blood. "Little bird. I knew you'd come." The voice was a drunken rasp.

Outside, a swirling lance of jade light spit at the stars, filling the room with green glare. She saw him for a moment, all black and green, the blood on his face dark as tar, his eyes glowing like a dog's in the sudden glare. Then the light faded and he was only a hulking darkness in a stained white cloak.

"If you scream I'll kill you. Believe that." He took his hand from her mouth. Her breath was coming ragged. The Hound had a flagon of wine on her bedside table. He took a long pull. "Don't you want to ask who's winning the battle, little bird?"

"Who?" she said, too frightened to defy him.

The Hound laughed. "I only know who's lost. Me."

He is drunker than I've ever seen him. He was sleeping in my bed. What does he want here? "What have you lost?"

"All." The burnt half of his face was a mask of dried blood. "Bloody dwarf. Should have killed him. Years ago."

"He's dead, they say."

"Dead? No. Bugger that. I don't want him dead." He cast the empty flagon aside. "I want him *burned.* If the gods are good, they'll burn him, but I won't be here to see. I'm going."

"Going?" She tried to wriggle free, but his grasp was iron.

"The little bird repeats whatever she hears. *Going*, yes."

"Where will you go?"

"Away from here. Away from the fires. Go out the Iron Gate, I suppose. North somewhere, anywhere."

"You won't get out," Sansa said. "The queen's closed up Maegor's, and the city gates are shut as well."

"Not to me. I have the white cloak. And I have *this*." He patted the pommel of his sword. "The man who tries to stop me is a dead man. Unless he's on fire." He laughed bitterly.

"Why did you come here?"

"You promised me a song, little bird. Have you forgotten?"

She didn't know what he meant. She couldn't sing for him now, here, with the sky aswirl with fire and men dying in their hundreds and their thousands. "I can't," she said. "Let me go, you're scaring me."

"Everything scares you. Look at me. *Look* at me."

The blood masked the worst of his scars, but his eyes were white and wide and terrifying. The burnt corner of his mouth twitched and twitched again. Sansa could smell him; a stink of sweat and sour wine and stale vomit, and over it all the reek of blood, blood, blood.

"I could keep you safe," he rasped. "They're all afraid of me. No one would hurt you again, or I'd kill them." He yanked her closer, and for a moment she thought he meant to kiss her. He was too strong to fight. She closed her eyes, wanting it to be over, but nothing happened. "Still can't bear to look, can you?" she heard him say. He gave her arm a hard wrench, pulling her around and shoving her down onto the bed. "I'll have that song. Florian and Jonquil, you said." His dagger was out, poised at her throat. "Sing, little bird. Sing for your little life."

Her throat was dry and tight with fear, and every song she had ever known had fled from her mind. *Please don't kill me*, she wanted to scream, *please don't*. She could feel him twisting the point, pushing it into her throat, and she almost closed her eyes again, but then she remembered. It was not the song of Florian and Jonquil, but it was a song. Her voice sounded small and thin and tremulous in her ears.

> Gentle Mother, font of mercy,
> save our sons from war, we pray,
> stay the swords and stay the arrows,
> let them know a better day.
> Gentle Mother, strength of women,
> help our daughters through this fray,
> soothe the wrath and tame the fury,
> teach us all a kinder way.

She had forgotten the other verses. When her voice trailed off, she feared he might kill her, but after a moment the Hound took the blade from her throat, never speaking.

Some instinct made her lift her hand and cup his cheek with her fingers. The room was too dark for her to see him, but she could feel the stickiness of the blood, and a wetness that was not blood. "Little bird," he said once more, his voice raw and harsh as steel on stone. Then he rose from the bed. Sansa heard cloth ripping, followed by the softer sound of retreating footsteps.

When she crawled out of bed, long moments later, she was alone. She found his cloak on the floor, twisted up tight, the white wool stained by blood and fire. The sky outside was darker by then, with only a few pale green ghosts dancing against the stars. A chill wind was blowing, banging the shutters. Sansa was cold. She shook out the torn cloak and huddled beneath it on the floor, shivering.

How long she stayed there she could not have said, but after a time she heard a bell ringing, far off across the city. The sound was a deep-throated bronze booming, coming faster with each knell. Sansa was wondering what it might mean when a second bell

joined in, and a third, their voices calling across the
hills and hollows, the alleys and towers, to every corner
of King's Landing. She threw off the cloak and went to
her window.

The first faint hint of dawn was visible in the east,
and the Red Keep's own bells were ringing now, joining
in the swelling river of sound that flowed from the
seven crystal towers of the Great Sept of Baelor. They
had rung the bells when King Robert died, she remembered, but this was different, no slow dolorous death
knell but a joyful thunder. She could hear men shouting
in the streets as well, and something that could only be
cheers.

It was Ser Dontos who brought her the word. He staggered through her open door, wrapped her in his flabby
arms, and whirled her around and around the room,
whooping so incoherently that Sansa understood not a
word of it. He was as drunk as the Hound had been, but
in him it was a dancing happy drunk. She was breathless and dizzy when he let her down. "What is it?" She
clutched at a bedpost. "What's happened? Tell me!"

"It's done! Done! Done! The city is saved. Lord
Stannis is dead, Lord Stannis is fled, no one knows, no
one cares, his host is broken, the danger's done. Slaughtered, scattered, or gone over, they say. Oh, the bright
banners! The banners, Jonquil, the banners! Do you
have any wine? We ought to drink to this day, yes. It
means you're safe, don't you see?"

"Tell me what's happened!" Sansa shook him.

Ser Dontos laughed and hopped from one leg to the
other, almost falling. "They came up through the ashes
while the river was burning. The river, Stannis was
neck deep in the river, and they took him from the rear.
Oh, to be a knight again, to have been part of it! His
own men hardly fought, they say. Some ran but more
bent the knee and went over, shouting for Lord Renly!
What must Stannis have thought when he heard that? I
had it from Osney Kettleblack who had it from Ser Osmund, but Ser Balon's back now and his men say the
same, and the gold cloaks as well. We're delivered,

sweetling! They came up the roseroad and along the riverbank, through all the fields Stannis had burned, the ashes puffing up around their boots and turning all their armor grey, but oh! the *banners* must have been bright, the golden rose and golden lion and all the others, the Marbrand tree and the Rowan, Tarly's huntsman and Redwyne's grapes and Lady Oakheart's leaf. All the westermen, all the power of Highgarden and Casterly Rock! Lord Tywin himself had their right wing on the north side of the river, with Randyll Tarly commanding the center and Mace Tyrell the left, but the vanguard won the fight. They plunged through Stannis like a lance through a pumpkin, every man of them howling like some demon in steel. And do you know who led the vanguard? Do you? Do you? *Do you!*"

"Robb?" It was too much to be hoped, but . . .

"It was *Lord Renly!* Lord Renly in his green armor, with the fires shimmering off his golden antlers! Lord Renly with his tall spear in his hand! They say he killed Ser Guyard Morrigen himself in single combat, and a dozen other great knights as well. It was Renly, it was Renly, it was Renly! Oh! the banners, darling Sansa! Oh! to be a knight!"

DAENERYS

She was breaking her fast on a bowl of cold shrimp-and-persimmon soup when Irri brought her a Qartheen gown, an airy confection of ivory samite patterned with seed pearls. "Take it away," Dany said. "The docks are no place for lady's finery."

If the Milk Men thought her such a savage, she would dress the part for them. When she went to the stables, she wore faded sandsilk pants and woven grass sandals. Her small breasts moved freely beneath a painted Dothraki vest, and a curved dagger hung from her medallion belt. Jhiqui had braided her hair Dothraki fashion, and fastened a silver bell to the end of the braid. "I have won no victories," she tried telling her handmaid when the bell tinkled softly.

Jhiqui disagreed. "You burned the *maegi* in their house of dust and sent their souls to hell."

That was Drogon's victory, not mine, Dany wanted to say, but she held her tongue. The Dothraki would esteem her all the more for a few bells in her hair. She chimed as she mounted her silver mare, and again with every stride, but neither Ser Jorah nor her bloodriders made mention of it. To guard her people and her dragons in her absence, she chose Rakharo. Jhogo and Aggo would ride with her to the waterfront.

They left the marble palaces and fragrant gardens behind and made their way through a poorer part of the city where modest brick houses turned blind walls to the street. There were fewer horses and camels to be seen, and a dearth of palanquins, but the streets teemed with children, beggars, and skinny dogs the color of sand. Pale men in dusty linen skirts stood beneath arched doorways to watch them pass. *They know who I am, and they do not love me.* Dany could tell from the way they looked at her.

Ser Jorah would sooner have tucked her inside her palanquin, safely hidden behind silken curtains, but she refused him. She had reclined too long on satin cushions, letting oxen bear her hither and yon. At least when she rode she felt as though she was getting somewhere.

It was not by choice that she sought the waterfront. She was fleeing again. Her whole life had been one long flight, it seemed. She had begun running in her mother's womb, and never once stopped. How often had she and Viserys stolen away in the black of night, a bare step ahead of the Usurper's hired knives? But it was run or die. Xaro had learned that Pyat Pree was gathering the surviving warlocks together to work ill on her.

Dany had laughed when he told her. "Was it not you who told me warlocks were no more than old soldiers, vainly boasting of forgotten deeds and lost prowess?"

Xaro looked troubled. "And so it was, then. But now? I am less certain. It is said that the glass candles are burning in the house of Urrathon Night-Walker, that have not burned in a hundred years. Ghost grass grows in the Garden of Gehane, phantom tortoises have been seen carrying messages between the windowless houses on Warlock's Way, and all the rats in the city are chewing off their tails. The wife of Mathos Mallarawan, who once mocked a warlock's drab moth-eaten robe, has gone mad and will wear no clothes at all. Even fresh-washed silks make her feel as though a thousand insects were crawling on her skin. And Blind Sybassion the Eater of Eyes can see again, or so his slaves do swear. A man must wonder." He sighed. "These are strange times in Qarth. And strange times are bad for trade. It grieves me to say so, yet it might be best if you left Qarth entirely, and sooner rather than later." Xaro stroked her fingers reassuringly. "You need not go alone, though. You have seen dark visions in the Palace of Dust, but Xaro has dreamed brighter dreams. I see you happily abed, with our child at your breast. Sail with me around the Jade Sea, and we can yet make it so! It is not too late. Give me a son, my sweet song of joy!"

Give you a dragon, you mean. "I will not wed you, Xaro."

His face had grown cold at that. "Then go."

"But where?"

"Somewhere far from here."

Well, perhaps it was time. The people of her *khalasar* had welcomed the chance to recover from the ravages of the red waste, but now that they were plump and rested once again, they began to grow unruly. Dothraki were not accustomed to staying long in one place. They were a warrior people, not made for cities. Perhaps she had lingered in Qarth too long, seduced by its comforts and its beauties. It was a city that always promised more than it would give you, it seemed to her, and her welcome here had turned sour since the House of the Undying had collapsed in a great gout of smoke and flame. Overnight the Qartheen had come to remember that dragons were *dangerous.* No longer did they vie with each other to give her gifts. Instead the Tourmaline Brotherhood had called openly for her expulsion, and the Ancient Guild of Spicers for her death. It was all Xaro could do to keep the Thirteen from joining them.

But where am I to go? Ser Jorah proposed that they journey farther east, away from her enemies in the Seven Kingdoms. Her bloodriders would sooner have returned to their great grass sea, even if it meant braving the red waste again. Dany herself had toyed with the idea of settling in Vaes Tolorro until her dragons grew great and strong. But her heart was full of doubts. Each of these felt wrong, somehow . . . and even when she decided where to go, the question of how she would get there remained troublesome.

Xaro Xhoan Daxos would be no help to her, she knew that now. For all his professions of devotion, he was playing his own game, not unlike Pyat Pree. The night he asked her to leave, Dany had begged one last favor of him. "An army, is it?" Xaro asked. "A kettle of gold? A galley, perhaps?"

Dany blushed. She hated begging. "A ship, yes."

Xaro's eyes had glittered as brightly as the jewels in his nose. "I am a trader, *Khaleesi*. So perhaps we should speak no more of giving, but rather of trade. For one of your dragons, you shall have ten of the finest ships in my fleet. You need only say that one sweet word."

"No," she said.

"Alas," Xaro sobbed, "that was not the word I meant."

"Would you ask a mother to sell one of her children?"

"Whyever not? They can always make more. Mothers sell their children every day."

"Not the Mother of Dragons."

"Not even for twenty ships?"

"Not for a hundred."

His mouth curled downward. "I do not have a hundred. But you have three dragons. Grant me one, for all my kindnesses. You will still have two, and thirty ships as well."

Thirty ships would be enough to land a small army on the shore of Westeros. *But I do not have a small army.* "How many ships do you own, Xaro?"

"Eighty-three, if one does not count my pleasure barge."

"And your colleagues in the Thirteen?"

"Among us all, perhaps a thousand."

"And the Spicers and the Tourmaline Brotherhood?"

"Their trifling fleets are of no account."

"Even so," she said, "tell me."

"Twelve or thirteen hundred for the Spicers. No more than eight hundred for the Brotherhood."

"And the Asshai'i, the Braavosi, the Summer Islanders, the Ibbenese, and all the other peoples who sail the great salt sea, how many ships do they have? All together?"

"Many and more," he said irritably. "What does this matter?"

"I am trying to set a price on one of the three living dragons in the world." Dany smiled at him sweetly. "It seems to me that one-third of all the ships in the world would be fair."

Xaro's tears ran down his cheeks on either side of his jewel-encrusted nose. "Did I not warn you not to enter the Palace of Dust? This is the very thing I feared. The whispers of the warlocks have made you as mad as Mallarawan's wife. A third of all the ships in the world? Pah. Pah, I say. Pah."

Dany had not seen him since. His seneschal brought her messages, each cooler than the last. She must quit his house. He was done feeding her and her people. He demanded the return of his gifts, which she had accepted in bad faith. Her only consolation was that at least she'd had the great good sense not to marry him.

The warlocks whispered of three treasons . . . once for blood and once for gold and once for love. The first traitor was surely Mirri Maz Duur, who had murdered Khal Drogo and their unborn son to avenge her people. Could Pyat Pree and Xaro Xhoan Daxos be the second and the third? She did not think so. What Pyat did was not for gold, and Xaro had never truly loved her.

The streets grew emptier as they passed through a district given over to gloomy stone warehouses. Aggo went before her and Jhogo behind, leaving Ser Jorah Mormont at her side. Her bell rang softly, and Dany found her thoughts returning to the Palace of Dust once more, as the tongue returns to a space left by a missing tooth. *Child of three,* they had called her, *daughter of death, slayer of lies, bride of fire.* So many threes. Three fires, three mounts to ride, three treasons. "The dragon has three heads," she sighed. "Do you know what that means, Jorah?"

"Your Grace? The sigil of House Targaryen is a three-headed dragon, red on black."

"I know that. But there are no three-headed dragons."

"The three heads were Aegon and his sisters."

"Visenya and Rhaenys," she recalled. "I am descended from Aegon and Rhaenys through their son Aenys and their grandson Jaehaerys."

"Blue lips speak only lies, isn't that what Xaro told you? Why do you care what the warlocks whispered? All they wanted was to suck the life from you, you know that now."

"Perhaps," she said reluctantly. "Yet the things I saw . . ."

"A dead man in the prow of a ship, a blue rose, a banquet of blood . . . what does any of it mean, *Khaleesi*? A mummer's dragon, you said. What *is* a mummer's dragon, pray?"

"A cloth dragon on poles," Dany explained. "Mummers use them in their follies, to give the heroes something to fight."

Ser Jorah frowned.

Dany could not let it go. *"His is the song of ice and fire*, my brother said. I'm certain it was my brother. Not Viserys, Rhaegar. He had a harp with silver strings."

Ser Jorah's frown deepened until his eyebrows came together. "Prince Rhaegar played such a harp," he conceded. "You saw him?"

She nodded. "There was a woman in a bed with a babe at her breast. My brother said the babe was the prince that was promised and told her to name him Aegon."

"Prince Aegon was Rhaegar's heir by Elia of Dorne," Ser Jorah said. "But if he was this prince that was promised, the promise was broken along with his skull when the Lannisters dashed his head against a wall."

"I remember," Dany said sadly. "They murdered Rhaegar's daughter as well, the little princess. Rhaenys, she was named, like Aegon's sister. There was no Visenya, but he said the dragon has three heads. What is the song of ice and fire?"

"It's no song I've ever heard."

"I went to the warlocks hoping for answers, but instead they've left me with a hundred new questions."

By then there were people in the streets once more. "Make way," Aggo shouted, while Jhogo sniffed at the air suspiciously. "I smell it, *Khaleesi*," he called. "The poison water." The Dothraki distrusted the sea and all that moved upon it. Water that a horse could not drink was water they wanted no part of. *They will learn*, Dany resolved. *I braved their sea with Khal Drogo. Now they can brave mine.*

Qarth was one of the world's great ports, its great sheltered harbor a riot of color and clangor and strange smells. Winesinks, warehouses, and gaming dens lined the streets, cheek by jowl with cheap brothels and the temples of peculiar gods. Cutpurses, cutthroats, spell-sellers, and moneychangers mingled with every crowd. The waterfront was one great marketplace where the buying and selling went on all day and all night, and goods might be had for a fraction of what they cost at the bazaar, if a man did not ask where they came from. Wizened old women bent like hunchbacks sold flavored waters and goat's milk from glazed ceramic jugs strapped to their shoulders. Seamen from half a hundred nations wandered amongst the stalls, drinking spiced liquors and trading jokes in queer-sounding tongues. The air smelled of salt and frying fish, of hot tar and honey, of incense and oil and sperm.

Aggo gave an urchin a copper for a skewer of honey-roasted mice and nibbled them as he rode. Jhogo bought a handful of fat white cherries. Elsewhere they saw beautiful bronze daggers for sale, dried squids and carved onyx, a potent magical elixir made of virgin's milk and shade of the evening, even dragon's eggs which looked suspiciously like painted rocks.

As they passed the long stone quays reserved for the ships of the Thirteen, she saw chests of saffron, frankincense, and pepper being off-loaded from Xaro's ornate *Vermillion Kiss*. Beside her, casks of wine, bales of sourleaf, and pallets of striped hides were being trundled up the gangplank onto the *Bride in Azure*, to sail on the evening tide. Farther along, a crowd had gathered around the Spicer galley *Sunblaze* to bid on slaves. It was well known that the cheapest place to buy a slave was right off the ship, and the banners floating from her masts proclaimed that the *Sunblaze* had just arrived from Astapor on Slaver's Bay.

Dany would get no help from the Thirteen, the Tourmaline Brotherhood, or the Ancient Guild of Spicers. She rode her silver past several miles of their quays, docks, and storehouses, all the way out to the far end of the horseshoe-shaped harbor where the ships from the Summer Islands, Westeros, and the Nine Free Cities were permitted to dock.

She dismounted beside a gaming pit where a basilisk was tearing a big red dog to pieces amidst a shouting ring of sailors. "Aggo, Jhogo, you will guard the horses while Ser Jorah and I speak to the captains."

"As you say, *Khaleesi*. We will watch you as you go."

It was good to hear men speaking Valyrian once more, and even the Common Tongue, Dany thought as they approached the first ship. Sailors, dockworkers, and merchants alike gave way before her, not knowing what to make of this slim young girl with silver-gold hair who dressed in the Dothraki fashion and walked with a knight at her side. Despite the heat of the day, Ser Jorah wore his green wool surcoat over chainmail, the black bear of Mormont sewn on his chest.

But neither her beauty nor his size and strength would serve with the men whose ships they needed.

"You require passage for a hundred Dothraki, all their horses, yourself and this knight, and three *dragons*?" said the captain of the great cog *Ardent Friend* before he walked away laughing. When she told a Lyseni on the *Trumpeteer* that she was Daenerys Stormborn, Queen of the Seven Kingdoms, he gave her a deadface look and said, "Aye, and I'm Lord Tywin Lannister and shit gold

every night." The cargomaster of the Myrish galley
Silken Spirit opined that dragons were too dangerous at
sea, where any stray breath of flame might set the rigging afire. The owner of *Lord Faro's Belly* would risk
dragons, but not Dothraki. "I'll have no such godless
savages in my *Belly*, I'll not." The two brothers who
captained the sister ships *Quicksilver* and *Greyhound*
seemed sympathetic and invited them into the cabin for
a glass of Arbor red. They were so courteous that Dany
was hopeful for a time, but in the end the price they
asked was far beyond her means, and might have been
beyond Xaro's. *Pinchbottom Petto* and *Sloe-Eyed Maid*
were too small for her needs, *Bravo* was bound for the
Jade Sea, and *Magister Manolo* scarce looked seaworthy.

As they made their way toward the next quay, Ser
Jorah laid a hand against the small of her back. "Your
Grace. You are being followed. No, do not turn." He
guided her gently toward a brass-seller's booth. "This is
a noble work, my queen," he proclaimed loudly, lifting
a large platter for her inspection. "See how it shines in
the sun?"

The brass was polished to a high sheen. Dany could
see her face in it . . . and when Ser Jorah angled it to
the right, she could see behind her. "I see a fat brown
man and an older man with a staff. Which is it?"

"Both of them," Ser Jorah said. "They have been following us since we left *Quicksilver*."

The ripples in the brass stretched the strangers
queerly, making one man seem long and gaunt, the
other immensely squat and broad. "A most excellent
brass, great lady," the merchant exclaimed. "Bright as
the sun! And for the Mother of Dragons, only thirty
honors."

The platter was worth no more than three. "Where
are my guards?" Dany declared. "This man is trying to
rob me!" For Jorah, she lowered her voice and spoke in
the Common Tongue. "They may not mean me ill. Men
have looked at women since time began, perhaps it is
no more than that."

The brass-seller ignored their whispers. "Thirty? Did

I say thirty? Such a fool I am. The price is twenty honors."

"All the brass in this booth is not worth twenty honors," Dany told him as she studied the reflections. The old man had the look of Westeros about him, and the brown-skinned one must weigh twenty stone. *The Usurper offered a lordship to the man who kills me, and these two are far from home. Or could they be creatures of the warlocks, meant to take me unawares?*

"Ten, *Khaleesi*, because you are so lovely. Use it for a looking glass. Only brass this fine could capture such beauty."

"It might serve to carry nightsoil. If you threw it away, I might pick it up, so long as I did not need to stoop. But *pay* for it?" Dany shoved the platter back into his hands. "Worms have crawled up your nose and eaten your wits."

"Eight honors," he cried. "My wives will beat me and call me fool, but I am a helpless child in your hands. Come, eight, that is less than it is worth."

"What do I need with dull brass when Xaro Xhoan Daxos feeds me off plates of gold?" As she turned to walk off, Dany let her glance sweep over the strangers. The brown man was near as wide as he'd looked in the platter, with a gleaming bald head and the smooth cheeks of a eunuch. A long curving *arakh* was thrust through the sweat-stained yellow silk of his bellyband. Above the silk, he was naked but for an absurdly tiny iron-studded vest. Old scars crisscrossed his tree-trunk arms, huge chest, and massive belly, pale against his nut-brown skin.

The other man wore a traveler's cloak of undyed wool, the hood thrown back. Long white hair fell to his shoulders, and a silky white beard covered the lower half of his face. He leaned his weight on a hardwood staff as tall as he was. *Only fools would stare so openly if they meant me harm.* All the same, it might be prudent to head back toward Jhogo and Aggo. "The old man does not wear a sword," she said to Jorah in the Common Tongue as she drew him away.

The brass merchant came hopping after them. "Five honors, for five it is yours, it was meant for you."

Ser Jorah said, "A hardwood staff can crack a skull as well as any mace."

"Four! I know you want it!" He danced in front of them, scampering backward as he thrust the platter at their faces.

"Do they follow?"

"Lift that up a little higher," the knight told the merchant. "Yes. The old man pretends to linger at a potter's stall, but the brown one has eyes only for you."

"Two honors! Two! Two!" The merchant was panting heavily from the effort of running backward.

"Pay him before he kills himself," Dany told Ser Jorah, wondering what she was going to do with a huge brass platter. She turned back as he reached for his coins, intending to put an end to this mummer's farce. The blood of the dragon would not be herded through the bazaar by an old man and a fat eunuch.

A Qartheen stepped into her path. "Mother of Dragons, for you." He knelt and thrust a jewel box into her face.

Dany took it almost by reflex. The box was carved wood, its mother-of-pearl lid inlaid with jasper and chalcedony. "You are too generous." She opened it. Within was a glittering green scarab carved from onyx and emerald. *Beautiful,* she thought. *This will help pay for our passage.* As she reached inside the box, the man said, "I am so sorry," but she hardly heard.

The scarab unfolded with a hiss.

Dany caught a glimpse of a malign black face, almost human, and an arched tail dripping venom . . . and then the box flew from her hand in pieces, turning end over end. Sudden pain twisted her fingers. As she cried out and clutched her hand, the brass merchant let out a shriek, a woman screamed, and suddenly the Qartheen were shouting and pushing each other aside. Ser Jorah slammed past her, and Dany stumbled to one knee. She heard the *hiss* again. The old man drove the butt of his staff into the ground, Aggo came riding through an egg-seller's stall and vaulted from his saddle, Jhogo's whip cracked overhead, Ser Jorah slammed the eunuch over the head with the brass platter, sailors and whores and merchants were fleeing or shouting or both . . .

"Your Grace, a thousand pardons." The old man knelt. "It's dead. Did I break your hand?"

She closed her fingers, wincing. "I don't think so."

"I had to knock it away," he started, but her blood-riders were on him before he could finish. Aggo kicked his staff away and Jhogo seized him round the shoulders, forced him to his knees, and pressed a dagger to his throat. "*Khaleesi*, we saw him strike you. Would you see the color of his blood?"

"Release him." Dany climbed to her feet. "Look at the bottom of his staff, blood of my blood." Ser Jorah had been shoved off his feet by the eunuch. She ran between them as *arakh* and longsword both came flashing from their sheaths. "Put down your steel! Stop it!"

"Your Grace?" Mormont lowered his sword only an inch. "These men attacked you."

"They were defending me." Dany snapped her hand to shake the sting from her fingers. "It was the other one, the Qartheen." When she looked around he was gone. "He was a Sorrowful Man. There was a manticore in that jewel box he gave me. This man knocked it out of my hand." The brass merchant was still rolling on the ground. She went to him and helped him to his feet. "Were you stung?"

"No, good lady," he said, shaking, "or else I would be dead. But it touched me, *aieeee*, when it fell from the box it landed on my arm." He had soiled himself, she saw, and no wonder.

She gave him a silver for his trouble and sent him on his way before she turned back to the old man with the white beard. "Who is it that I owe my life to?"

"You owe me nothing, Your Grace. I am called Arstan, though Belwas named me Whitebeard on the voyage here." Though Jhogo had released him, the old man remained on one knee. Aggo picked up his staff, turned it over, cursed softly in Dothraki, scraped the remains of the manticore off on a stone, and handed it back.

"And who is Belwas?" she asked.

The huge brown eunuch swaggered forward, sheathing his *arakh.* "I am Belwas. Strong Belwas they name me in the fighting pits of Meereen. Never did I lose." He slapped his belly, covered with scars. "I let each man cut me once, before I kill him. Count the cuts and you will know how many Strong Belwas has slain."

Dany had no need to count his scars; there were many, she could see at a glance. "And why are you here, Strong Belwas?"

"From Meereen I am sold to Qohor, and then to Pentos and the fat man with sweet stink in his hair. He it was who send Strong Belwas back across the sea, and old Whitebeard to serve him."

The fat man with sweet stink in his hair . . . "Illyrio?" she said. "You were sent by Magister Illyrio?"

"We were, Your Grace," old Whitebeard replied. "The Magister begs your kind indulgence for sending us in his stead, but he cannot sit a horse as he did in his youth, and sea travel upsets his digestion." Earlier he had spoken in the Valyrian of the Free Cities, but now he changed to the Common Tongue. "I regret if we caused you alarm. If truth be told, we were not certain, we expected someone more . . . more . . . ."

"Regal?" Dany laughed. She had no dragon with her, and her raiment was hardly queenly. "You speak the Common Tongue well, Arstan. Are you of Westeros?"

"I am. I was born on the Dornish Marches, Your Grace. As a boy I squired for a knight of Lord Swann's household." He held the tall staff upright beside him like a lance in need of a banner. "Now I squire for Belwas."

"A bit old for such, aren't you?" Ser Jorah had shouldered his way to her side, holding the brass platter awkwardly under his arm. Belwas's hard head had left it badly bent.

"Not too old to serve my liege, Lord Mormont."

"You know me as well?"

"I saw you fight a time or two. At Lannisport where you near unhorsed the Kingslayer. And on Pyke, there as well. You do not recall, Lord Mormont?"

Ser Jorah frowned. "Your face seems familiar, but there were hundreds at Lannisport and thousands on Pyke. And I am no lord. Bear Island was taken from me. I am but a knight."

"A knight of my Queensguard." Dany took his arm. "And my true friend and good counselor." She studied Arstan's face. He had a great dignity to him, a quiet strength she liked. "Rise, Arstan Whitebeard. Be welcome, Strong Belwas. Ser Jorah you know. Ko Aggo and Ko Jhogo are blood of my blood. They crossed the red waste with me, and saw my dragons born."

"Horse boys." Belwas grinned toothily. "Belwas has killed many horse boys in the fighting pits. They jingle when they die."

Aggo's *arakh* leapt to his hand. "Never have I killed a fat brown man. Belwas will be the first."

"Sheath your steel, blood of my blood," said Dany, "this man comes to serve me. Belwas, you will accord all respect to my people, or you will leave my service sooner than you'd wish, and with more scars than when you came."

The gap-toothed smile faded from the giant's broad brown face, replaced by a confused scowl. Men did not often threaten Belwas, it would seem, and less so girls a third his size.

Dany gave him a smile, to take a bit of the sting from the rebuke. "Now tell me, what would Magister Illyrio have of me, that he would send you all the way from Pentos?"

"He would have dragons," said Belwas gruffly, "and the girl who makes them. He would have you."

"Belwas has the truth of us, Your Grace," said Arstan. "We were told to find you and bring you back to Pentos. The Seven Kingdoms have need of you. Robert the Usurper is dead, and the realm bleeds. When we set sail from Pentos there were four kings in the land, and no justice to be had."

Joy bloomed in her heart, but Dany kept it from her face. "I have three dragons," she said, "and more than a hundred in my *khalasar*, with all their goods and horses."

"It is no matter," boomed Belwas. "We take all. The fat man hires three ships for his little silverhair queen."

"It is so, Your Grace," Arstan Whitebeard said. "The great cog *Saduleon* is berthed at the end of the quay, and the galleys *Summer Sun* and *Joso's Prank* are anchored beyond the breakwater."

Three heads has the dragon, Dany thought, wondering. "I shall tell my people to make ready to depart at once. But the ships that bring me home must bear different names."

"As you wish," said Arstan. "What names would you prefer?"

"*Vhagar*," Daenerys told him. "*Meraxes*. And *Balerion*. Paint the names on their hulls in golden letters three feet high, Arstan. I want every man who sees them to know the dragons are returned."

ARYA

The heads had been dipped in tar to slow the rot. Every morning when Arya went to the well to draw fresh water for Roose Bolton's basin, she had to pass beneath them. They faced outward, so she never saw their faces, but she liked to pretend that one of them was Joffrey's. She tried to picture how his pretty face would look dipped in tar. *If I was a crow I could fly down and peck off his stupid fat pouty lips.*

The heads never lacked for attendants. The carrion crows wheeled about the gatehouse in raucous unkindness and quarreled upon the ramparts over every eye, screaming and cawing at each other and taking to the air whenever a sentry passed along the battlements. Sometimes the maester's ravens joined the feast as well, flapping down from the rookery on wide black wings. When the ravens came the crows would scatter, only to return the moment the larger birds were gone.

Do the ravens remember Maester Tothmure? Arya wondered. *Are they sad for him? When they quork at him, do they wonder why he doesn't answer?* Perhaps the dead could speak to them in some secret tongue the living could not hear.

Tothmure had been sent to the axe for dispatching birds to Casterly Rock and King's Landing the night Harrenhal had fallen, Lucan the armorer for making weapons for the Lannisters, Goodwife Harra for telling Lady Whent's household to serve them, the steward for giving Lord Tywin the keys to the treasure vault. The cook was spared (some said because he'd made the weasel soup), but stocks were hammered together for pretty Pia and the other women who'd shared their favors with Lannister soldiers. Stripped and shaved, they were left in the middle ward beside the bear pit, free for the use of any man who wanted them.

Three Frey men-at-arms were using them that morning as Arya went to the well. She tried not to look, but she could hear the men laughing. The pail was very heavy once full. She was turning to bring it back to Kingspyre when Goodwife Amabel seized her arm. The water went sloshing over the side onto Amabel's legs. "You did that on purpose," the woman screeched.

"What do you want?" Arya squirmed in her grasp. Amabel had been half-crazed since they'd cut Harra's head off.

"See there?" Amabel pointed across the yard at Pia. "When this northman falls you'll be where she is."

"Let me go." She tried to wrench free, but Amabel only tightened her fingers.

"He *will* fall too, Harrenhal pulls them all down in the end. Lord Tywin's won now, he'll be marching back with all his power, and then it will be his turn to punish the disloyal. And don't think he won't know what you did!" The old woman laughed. "I may have a turn at you myself. Harra had an old broom, I'll save it for you. The handle's cracked and splintery—"

Arya swung the bucket. The weight of the water made it turn in her hands, so she didn't smash Amabel's head in as she wanted, but the woman let go of her anyway when the water came out and drenched her.

"Don't *ever* touch me," Arya shouted, "or I'll *kill* you. You get *away*."

Sopping, Goodwife Amabel jabbed a thin finger at the flayed man on the front of Arya's tunic. "You think you're safe with that little bloody man on your teat, but you're not! The Lannisters are coming! See what happens when they get here."

Three-quarters of the water had splashed out on the ground, so Arya had to return to the well. *If I told Lord Bolton what she said, her head would be up next to Harra's before it got dark,* she thought as she drew up the bucket again. She wouldn't, though.

Once, when there had been only half as many heads, Gendry had caught Arya looking at them. "Admiring your work?" he asked.

He was angry because he'd liked Lucan, she knew, but it still wasn't fair. "It's Steelshanks Walton's work," she said defensively. "And the Mummers, and Lord Bolton."

"And who gave us all them? You and your weasel soup."

Arya punched his arm. "It was just hot broth. You hated Ser Amory too."

"I hate this lot worse. Ser Amory was fighting for his lord, but the Mummers are sellswords and turncloaks. Half of them can't even speak the Common Tongue. Septon Utt likes little boys, Qyburn does black magic, and your friend Biter *eats* people."

The worst thing was, she couldn't even say he was wrong. The Brave Companions did most of the foraging for Harrenhal, and Roose Bolton had given them the task of rooting out Lannisters. Vargo Hoat had divided them into four bands, to visit as many villages as possible. He led the largest group himself, and gave the others to his most trusted captains. She had heard Rorge laughing over Lord Vargo's way of finding traitors. All he did was return to places he had visited before under Lord Tywin's banner and seize those who had helped him. Many had been bought with Lannister silver, so the Mummers often returned with bags of coin as well as baskets of heads. "A riddle!" Shagwell would shout gleefully. "If Lord Bolton's goat eats the men who fed Lord Lannister's goat, how many goats are there?"

"One," Arya said when he asked her.

"Now there's a weasel clever as a goat!" the fool tittered.

Rorge and Biter were as bad as the others. Whenever Lord Bolton took a meal with the garrison, Arya would see them there among the rest. Biter gave off a stench like bad cheese, so the Brave Companions made him sit down near the foot of the table where he could grunt and hiss to himself and tear his meat apart with fingers and teeth. He would *sniff* at Arya when she passed, but it was Rorge who scared her most. He sat up near Faithful Ursywck, but she could feel his eyes crawling over her as she went about her duties.

Sometimes she wished she had gone off across the narrow sea with Jaqen H'ghar. She still had the stupid coin he'd given her, a piece of iron no larger than a penny and rusted along the rim. One side had writing on it, queer words she could not read. The other showed a man's head, but so worn that all his features had rubbed off. *He said it was of great value, but that was probably a lie too, like his name and even his face.* That made her so angry that she threw the coin away, but after an hour she got to feeling bad and went and found it again, even though it wasn't worth anything.

She was thinking about the coin as she crossed the Flowstone Yard, struggling with the weight of the water in her pail. "Nan," a voice called out. "Put down that pail and come help me."

Elmar Frey was no older than she was, and short for his age besides. He had been rolling a barrel of sand across the uneven stone, and was red-faced from exertion. Arya went to help him. Together they pushed the barrel all the way to the wall and back again, then stood it upright. She could hear the sand shifting around inside as Elmar pried open the lid and pulled out a chainmail hauberk. "Do you think it's clean enough?"

As Roose Bolton's squire, it was his task to keep his mail shiny bright.

"You need to shake out the sand. There's still spots of rust. See?" She pointed. "You'd best do it again."

"You do it." Elmar could be friendly when he needed help, but afterward he would always remember that he was a squire and she was only a serving girl. He liked to boast how he was the son of the Lord of the Crossing, not a nephew or a bastard or a grandson but a trueborn *son*, and on account of that he was going to marry a princess.

Arya didn't care about his precious princess, and didn't like him giving her commands. "I have to bring m'lord water for his basin. He's in his bedchamber being leeched. Not the regular black leeches but the big pale ones."

Elmar's eyes got as big as boiled eggs. Leeches terrified him, especially the big pale ones that looked like jelly until they filled up with blood. "I forgot, you're too skinny to push such a heavy barrel."

"I forgot, you're stupid." Arya picked up the pail. "Maybe you should get leeched too. There's leeches in the Neck as big as pigs." She left him there with his barrel.

The lord's bedchamber was crowded when she entered. Qyburn was in attendance, and dour Walton in his mail shirt and greaves, plus a dozen Freys, all brothers, half brothers, and cousins. Roose Bolton lay abed, naked. Leeches clung to the inside of his arms and legs and dotted his pallid chest, long translucent things that turned a glistening pink as they fed. Bolton paid them no more mind than he did Arya.

"We must not allow Lord Tywin to trap us here at Harrenhal," Ser Aenys Frey was saying as Arya filled the washbasin. A grey stooped giant of a man with watery red eyes and huge gnarled hands, Ser Aenys had brought fifteen hundred Frey swords south to Harrenhal, yet it often seemed as if he were helpless to command even his own brothers. "The castle is so large it requires an army to hold it, and once surrounded we cannot *feed* an army. Nor can we hope to lay in sufficient supplies. The country is ash, the villages given over to wolves, the harvest burnt or stolen. Autumn is on us, yet there is no food in store and none being planted. We live on forage, and if the Lannisters deny that to us, we will be down to rats and shoe leather in a moon's turn."

"I do not mean to be besieged here." Roose Bolton's voice was so soft that men had to strain to hear it, so his chambers were always strangely hushed.

"What, then?" demanded Ser Jared Frey, who was lean, balding, and pockmarked. "Is Edmure Tully so drunk on his victory that he thinks to give Lord Tywin battle in the open field?"

If he does he'll beat them, Arya thought. *He'll beat them as he did on the Red Fork, you'll see.* Unnoticed, she went to stand by Qyburn.

"Lord Tywin is many leagues from here," Bolton said calmly. "He has many matters yet to settle at King's Landing. He will not march on Harrenhal for some time."

Ser Aenys shook his head stubbornly. "You do not know the Lannisters as we do, my lord. King Stannis thought that Lord Tywin was a thousand leagues away as well, and it undid him."

The pale man in the bed smiled faintly as the leeches nursed of his blood. "I am not a man to be undone, ser."

"Even if Riverrun marshals all its strength and the Young Wolf wins back from the west, how can we hope to match the numbers Lord Tywin can send against us? When he comes, he will come with far more power than he commanded on the Green Fork. Highgarden has joined itself to Joffrey's cause, I remind you!"

"I had not forgotten."

"I have been Lord Tywin's captive once," said Ser Hosteen, a husky man with a square face who was said to be the strongest of the Freys. "I have no wish to enjoy Lannister hospitality again."

Ser Harys Haigh, who was a Frey on his mother's side, nodded vigorously. "If Lord Tywin could defeat a seasoned man like Stannis Baratheon, what chance will our boy king have against him?" He looked round to his brothers and cousins for support, and several of them muttered agreement.

"Someone must have the courage to say it," Ser Hosteen said. "The war is lost. King Robb must be made to see that."

Roose Bolton studied him with pale eyes. "His Grace has defeated the Lannisters every time he has faced them in battle."

"He has lost the north," insisted Hosteen Frey. "He has lost *Winterfell*! His brothers are dead . . ."

For a moment Arya forgot to breathe. *Dead? Bran and Rickon, dead? What does he mean? What does he mean about Winterfell, Joffrey could never take Winterfell, never, Robb would never let him.* Then she remembered that Robb was not at Winterfell. He was away in the west, and Bran was crippled, and Rickon only four. It took all her strength to remain still and silent, the way Syrio Forel had taught her, to stand there like a stick of furniture. She felt tears gathering in her eyes, and willed them away. *It's not true, it can't be true, it's just some Lannister lie.*

"Had Stannis won, all might have been different," Ronel Rivers said wistfully. He was one of Lord Walder's bastards.

"Stannis lost," Ser Hosteen said bluntly. "Wishing it were otherwise will not make it so. King Robb must make his peace with the Lannisters. He must put off his crown and bend the knee, little as he may like it."

"And who will tell him so?" Roose Bolton smiled. "It is a fine thing to have so many valiant brothers in such troubled times. I shall think on all you've said."

His smile was dismissal. The Freys made their courtesies and shuffled out, leaving only Qyburn, Steelshanks Walton, and Arya. Lord Bolton beckoned her closer. "I am bled sufficiently. Nan, you may remove the leeches."

"At once, my lord." It was best never to make Roose Bolton ask twice. Arya wanted to ask him what Ser

Hosteen had meant about Winterfell, but she dared not. *I'll ask Elmar*, she thought. *Elmar will tell me.* The leeches wriggled slowly between her fingers as she plucked them carefully from the lord's body, their pale bodies moist to the touch and distended with blood. *They're only leeches*, she reminded herself. *If I closed my hand, they'd squish between my fingers.*

"There is a letter from your lady wife." Qyburn pulled a roll of parchment from his sleeve. Though he wore maester's robes, there was no chain about his neck; it was whispered that he had lost it for dabbling in necromancy.

"You may read it," Bolton said.

The Lady Walda wrote from the Twins almost every day, but all the letters were the same. "I pray for you morn, noon, and night, my sweet lord," she wrote, "and count the days until you share my bed again. Return to me soon, and I will give you many trueborn sons to take the place of your dear Domeric and rule the Dreadfort after you." Arya pictured a plump pink baby in a cradle, covered with plump pink leeches.

She brought Lord Bolton a damp washcloth to wipe down his soft hairless body. "I will send a letter of my own," he told the onetime maester.

"To the Lady Walda?"

"To Ser Helman Tallhart."

A rider from Ser Helman had come two days past. Tallhart men had taken the castle of the Darrys, accepting the surrender of its Lannister garrison after a brief siege.

"Tell him to put the captives to the sword and the castle to the torch, by command of the king. Then he is to join forces with Robett Glover and strike east toward Duskendale. Those are rich lands, and hardly touched by the fighting. It is time they had a taste. Glover has lost a castle, and Tallhart a son. Let them take their vengeance on Duskendale."

"I shall prepare the message for your seal, my lord."

Arya was glad to hear that the castle of the Darrys would be burned. That was where they'd brought her when she'd been caught after her fight with Joffrey, and where the queen had made her father kill Sansa's wolf. *It deserves to burn.* She wished that Robett Glover and Ser Helman Tallhart would come back to Harrenhal, though; they had marched too quickly, before she'd been able to decide whether to trust them with her secret.

"I will hunt today," Roose Bolton announced as Qyburn helped him into a quilted jerkin.

"Is it safe, my lord?" Qyburn asked. "Only three days past, Septon Utt's men were attacked by wolves. They came right into his camp, not five yards from the fire, and killed two horses."

"It is wolves I mean to hunt. I can scarcely sleep at night for the howling." Bolton buckled on his belt, adjusting the hang of sword and dagger. "It's said that direwolves once roamed the north in great packs of a hundred or more, and feared neither man nor mammoth, but that was long ago and in another land. It is queer to see the common wolves of the south so bold."

"Terrible times breed terrible things, my lord."

Bolton showed his teeth in something that might have been a smile. "Are these times so terrible, Maester?"

"Summer is gone and there are four kings in the realm."

"One king may be terrible, but four?" He shrugged. "Nan, my fur cloak." She brought it to him. "My chambers will be clean and orderly upon my return," he told her as she fastened it. "And tend to Lady Walda's letter."

"As you say, my lord."

The lord and maester swept from the room, giving her not so much as a backward glance. When they were gone, Arya took the letter and carried it to the hearth, stirring the logs with a poker to wake the flames anew. She watched the parchment twist, blacken, and flare up. *If the Lannisters hurt Bran and Rickon, Robb will kill them every one. He'll never bend the knee, never, never, never. He's not afraid of any of them.* Curls of ash floated up the chimney. Arya squatted beside the fire, watching them rise through a veil of hot tears. *If Winterfell is truly gone, is this my home now? Am I still Arya, or only Nan the serving girl, for forever and forever and forever?*

She spent the next few hours tending to the lord's chambers. She swept out the old rushes and scattered fresh sweet-smelling ones, laid a fresh fire in the hearth, changed the linens and fluffed the featherbed, emptied the chamber pots down the privy shaft and scrubbed them out, carried an armload of soiled clothing to the washerwomen, and brought up a bowl of crisp autumn pears from the kitchen. When she was done with the bedchamber, she went down half a flight of stairs to do the same in the great solar, a spare drafty room as large as the halls of many a smaller castle. The candles were down to stubs, so Arya changed them out. Under the windows was a huge oaken table where the lord wrote his letters. She stacked the books, changed the candles, put the quills and inks and sealing wax in order.

A large ragged sheepskin was tossed across the papers. Arya had started to roll it up when the colors caught her eye: the blue of lakes and rivers, the red dots where castles and cities could be found, the green of woods. She spread it out instead. THE LANDS OF THE TRIDENT, said the ornate script beneath the map. The drawing showed everything from the Neck to the Blackwater Rush. *There's Harrenhal at the top of the big lake,* she realized, *but where's Riverrun?* Then she saw. *It's not so far . . .*

The afternoon was still young by the time she was done, so Arya took herself off to the godswood. Her duties were lighter as Lord Bolton's cupbearer than they had been under Weese or even Pinkeye, though they required dressing like a page and washing more than she liked. The hunt would not return for hours, so she had a little time for her needlework.

She slashed at birch leaves till the splintery point of the broken broomstick was green and sticky. "Ser Gregor," she breathed. "Dunsen, Polliver, Raff the

Sweetling." She spun and leapt and balanced on the balls of her feet, darting this way and that, knocking pinecones flying. "The Tickler," she called out one time, "the Hound," the next. "Ser Ilyn, Ser Meryn, Queen Cersei." The bole of an oak loomed before her, and she lunged to drive her point through it, grunting "Joffrey, Joffrey, Joffrey." Her arms and legs were dappled by sunlight and the shadows of leaves. A sheen of sweat covered her skin by the time she paused. The heel of her right foot was bloody where she'd skinned it, so she stood one-legged before the heart tree and raised her sword in salute. *"Valar morghulis,"* she told the old gods of the north. She liked how the words sounded when she said them.

As Arya crossed the yard to the bathhouse, she spied a raven circling down toward the rookery, and wondered where it had come from and what message it carried. *Might be it's from Robb, come to say it wasn't true about Bran and Rickon.* She chewed on her lip, hoping. *If I had wings I could fly back to Winterfell and see for myself. And if it was true, I'd just fly away, fly up past the moon and the shining stars, and see all the things in Old Nan's stories, dragons and sea monsters and the Titan of Braavos, and maybe I wouldn't ever fly back unless I wanted to.*

The hunting party returned near evenfall with nine dead wolves. Seven were adults, big grey-brown beasts, savage and powerful, their mouths drawn back over long yellow teeth by their dying snarls. But the other two had only been pups. Lord Bolton gave orders for the skins to be sewn into a blanket for his bed. "Cubs still have that soft fur, my lord," one of his men pointed out. "Make you a nice warm pair of gloves."

Bolton glanced up at the banners waving above the gatehouse towers. "As the Starks are wont to remind us, winter is coming. Have it done." When he saw Arya looking on, he said, "Nan, I'll want a flagon of hot spice wine, I took a chill in the woods. See that it doesn't get cold. I'm of a mind to sup alone. Barley bread, butter, and boar."

"At once, my lord." That was always the best thing to say.

Hot Pie was making oatcakes when she entered the kitchen. Three other cooks were boning fish, while a spit boy turned a boar over the flames. "My lord wants his supper, and hot spice wine to wash it down," Arya announced, "and he doesn't want it cold." One of the cooks washed his hands, took out a kettle, and filled it with a heavy, sweet red. Hot Pie was told to crumble in the spices as the wine heated. Arya went to help.

"I can do it," he said sullenly. "I don't need you to show me how to spice wine."

He hates me too, or else he's scared of me. She backed away, more sad than angry. When the food was ready, the cooks covered it with a silver cover and wrapped the flagon in a thick towel to keep it warm. Dusk was settling outside. On the walls the crows muttered round the heads like courtiers round a king. One of the guards held the door to Kingspyre. "Hope that's not weasel soup," he jested.

Roose Bolton was seated by the hearth reading from a thick leatherbound book when she entered. "Light some candles," he commanded her as he turned a page. "It grows gloomy in here."

She placed the food at his elbow and did as he bid her, filling the room with flickering light and the scent of cloves. Bolton turned a few more pages with his finger, then closed the book and placed it carefully in the fire. He watched the flames consume it, pale eyes shining with reflected light. The old dry leather went up with a *whoosh*, and the yellow pages stirred as they burned, as if some ghost were reading them. "I will have no further need of you tonight," he said, never looking at her.

She should have gone, silent as a mouse, but something had hold of her. "My lord," she asked, "will you take me with you when you leave Harrenhal?"

He turned to stare at her, and from the look in his eyes it was as if his supper had just spoken to him. "Did I give you leave to question me, Nan?"

"No, my lord." She lowered her eyes.

"You should not have spoken, then. Should you?"

"No. My lord."

For a moment he looked amused. "I will answer you, just this once. I mean to give Harrenhal to Lord Vargo when I return to the north. You will remain here, with him."

"But I don't—" she started.

He cut her off. "I am not in the habit of being questioned by servants, Nan. Must I have your tongue out?"

He would do it as easily as another man might cuff a dog, she knew. "No, my lord."

"Then I'll hear no more from you?"

"No, my lord."

"Go, then. I shall forget this insolence."

Arya went, but not to her bed. When she stepped out into the darkness of the yard, the guard on the door nodded at her and said, "Storm coming. Smell the air?" The wind was gusting, flames swirling off the torches mounted atop the walls beside the rows of heads. On her way to the godswood, she passed the Wailing Tower where once she had lived in fear of Weese. The Freys had taken it for their own since Harrenhal's fall. She could hear angry voices coming from a window, many men talking and arguing all at once. Elmar was sitting on the steps outside, alone.

"What's wrong?" Arya asked him when she saw the tears shining on his cheeks.

"My princess," he sobbed. "We've been dishonored, Aenys says. There was a bird from the Twins. My lord father says I'll need to marry someone else, or be a septon."

A stupid princess, she thought, *that's nothing to cry over.* "My brothers might be dead," she confided.

Elmar gave her a scornful look. "No one cares about a serving girl's brothers."

It was hard not to hit him when he said that. "I hope your princess dies," she said, and ran off before he could grab her.

In the godswood she found her broomstick sword where she had left it, and carried it to the heart tree.

There she knelt. Red leaves rustled. Red eyes peered inside her. *The eyes of the gods.* "Tell me what to do, you gods," she prayed.

For a long moment there was no sound but the wind and the water and the creak of leaf and limb. And then, far far off, beyond the godswood and the haunted towers and the immense stone walls of Harrenhal, from somewhere out in the world, came the long lonely howl of a wolf. Gooseprickles rose on Arya's skin, and for an instant she felt dizzy. Then, so faintly, it seemed as if she heard her father's voice. "When the snows fall and the white winds blow, the lone wolf dies, but the pack survives," he said.

"But there is no pack," she whispered to the weirwood. Bran and Rickon were dead, the Lannisters had Sansa, Jon had gone to the Wall. "I'm not even me now, I'm Nan."

"You are Arya of Winterfell, daughter of the north. You told me you could be strong. You have the wolf blood in you."

"The wolf blood." Arya remembered now. "I'll be as strong as Robb. I said I would." She took a deep breath, then lifted the broomstick in both hands and brought it down across her knee. It broke with a loud *crack,* and she threw the pieces aside. *I am a direwolf, and done with wooden teeth.*

That night she lay in her narrow bed upon the scratchy straw, listening to the voices of the living and the dead whisper and argue as she waited for the moon to rise. They were the only voices she trusted anymore. She could hear the sound of her own breath, and the wolves as well, a great pack of them now. *They are closer than the one I heard in the godswood,* she thought. *They are calling to me.*

Finally she slipped from under the blanket, wriggled into a tunic, and padded barefoot down the stairs. Roose Bolton was a cautious man, and the entrance to Kingspyre was guarded day and night, so she had to slip out of a narrow cellar window. The yard was still, the great castle lost in haunted dreams. Above, the wind keened through the Wailing Tower.

At the forge she found the fires extinguished and the doors closed and barred. She crept in a window, as she had once before. Gendry shared a mattress with two other apprentice smiths. She crouched in the loft for a long time before her eyes adjusted enough for her to be sure that he was the one on the end. Then she put a hand over his mouth and pinched him. His eyes opened. He could not have been very deeply asleep. *"Please,"* she whispered. She took her hand off his mouth and pointed.

For a moment she did not think he understood, but then he slid out from under the blankets. Naked, he padded across the room, shrugged into a loose rough-spun tunic, and climbed down from the loft after her. The other sleepers did not stir. "What do you want now?" Gendry said in a low angry voice.

"A sword."

"Blackthumb keeps all the blades locked up, I told you that a hundred times. Is this for Lord Leech?"

"For me. Break the lock with your hammer."

"They'll break my hand," he grumbled. "Or worse."

"Not if you run off with me."

"Run, and they'll catch you and kill you."

"They'll do you worse. Lord Bolton is giving Harrenhal to the Bloody Mummers, he told me so."

Gendry pushed black hair out of his eyes. "So?"

She looked right at him, fearless. "So when Vargo Hoat's the lord, he's going to cut off the feet of all the servants to keep them from running away. The smiths too."

"That's only a story," he said scornfully.

"No, it's true, I heard Lord Vargo say so," she lied. "He's going to cut one foot off everyone. The left one. Go to the kitchens and wake Hot Pie, he'll do what you say. We'll need bread or oakcakes or something. You get the swords and I'll do the horses. We'll meet near the postern in the east wall, behind the Tower of Ghosts. No one ever comes there."

"I know that gate. It's guarded, same as the rest."

"So? You won't forget the swords?"

"I never said I'd come."

"No. But if you do, you won't forget the swords?"

He frowned. "No," he said at last. "I guess I won't."

Arya reentered Kingspyre the same way she had left it, and stole up the winding steps listening for footfalls. In her cell, she stripped to the skin and dressed herself carefully, in two layers of smallclothes, warm stockings, and her cleanest tunic. It was Lord Bolton's livery. On the breast was sewn his sigil, the flayed man of the Dreadfort. She tied her shoes, threw a wool cloak over her skinny shoulders, and knotted it under her throat. Quiet as a shadow, she moved back down the stairs. Outside the lord's solar she paused to listen at the door, easing it open slowly when she heard only silence.

The sheepskin map was on the table, beside the remains of Lord Bolton's supper. She rolled it up tight and thrust it through her belt. He'd left his dagger on the table as well, so she took that too, just in case Gendry lost his courage.

A horse neighed softly as she slipped into the darkened stables. The grooms were all asleep. She prodded one with her toe until he sat up groggily and said, "Eh? Whas?"

"Lord Bolton requires three horses saddled and bridled."

The boy got to his feet, pushing straw from his hair. "Wha, at this hour? Horses, you say?" He blinked at the sigil on her tunic. "Whas he want horses for, in the dark?"

"Lord Bolton is not in the habit of being questioned by servants." She crossed her arms.

The stableboy was still looking at the flayed man. He knew what it meant. "Three, you say?"

"One two three. Hunting horses. Fast and surefoot." Arya helped him with the bridles and saddles, so he would not need to wake any of the others. She hoped they would not hurt him afterward, but she knew they probably would.

Leading the horses across the castle was the worst part. She stayed in the shadow of the curtain wall whenever she could, so the sentries walking their rounds on the ramparts above would have needed to look almost straight down to see her. *And if they do, what of it? I'm my lord's own cupbearer.* It was a chill dank autumn night. Clouds were blowing in from the west, hiding the stars, and the Wailing Tower screamed mournfully at every gust of wind. *It smells like rain.* Arya did not know whether that would be good or bad for their escape.

No one saw her, and she saw no one, only a grey and white cat creeping along atop the godswood wall. It stopped and spit at her, waking memories of the Red Keep and her father and Syrio Forel. "I could catch you if I wanted," she called to it softly, "but I have to go, cat." The cat hissed again and ran off.

The Tower of Ghosts was the most ruinous of Harrenhal's five immense towers. It stood dark and desolate behind the remains of a collapsed sept where only rats had come to pray for near three hundred years. It was there she waited to see if Gendry and Hot Pie would come. It seemed as though she waited a long time. The horses nibbled at the weeds that grew up between the broken stones while the clouds swallowed the last of the stars. Arya took out the dagger and sharpened it to keep her hands busy. Long smooth strokes, the way Syrio had taught her. The sound calmed her.

She heard them coming long before she saw them. Hot Pie was breathing heavily, and once he stumbled in the dark, barked his shin, and cursed loud enough to wake half of Harrenhal. Gendry was quieter, but the swords he was carrying rang together as he moved. "Here I am." She stood. "Be quiet or they'll hear you."

The boys picked their way toward her over tumbled stones. Gendry was wearing oiled chainmail under his cloak, she saw, and he had his blacksmith's hammer slung across his back. Hot Pie's red round face peered out from under a hood. He had a sack of bread dangling from his right hand and a big wheel of cheese under his left arm. "There's a guard on that postern," said Gendry quietly. "I told you there would be."

"You stay here with the horses," said Arya. "I'll get rid of him. Come quick when I call."

Gendry nodded. Hot Pie said, "Hoot like an owl when you want us to come."

"I'm not an owl," said Arya. "I'm a wolf. I'll howl."

Alone, she slid through the shadow of the Tower of Ghosts. She walked fast, to keep ahead of her fear, and it felt as though Syrio Forel walked beside her, and Yoren, and Jaqen H'ghar, and Jon Snow. She had not taken the sword Gendry had brought her, not yet. For this the dagger would be better. It was good and sharp. This postern was the least of Harrenhal's gates, a narrow door of stout oak studded with iron nails, set in an angle of the wall beneath a defensive tower. Only one man was set to guard it, but she knew there would be sentries up in that tower as well, and others nearby walking the walls. Whatever happened, she must be quiet as a shadow. *He must not call out.* A few scattered raindrops had begun to fall. She felt one land on her brow and run slowly down her nose.

She made no effort to hide, but approached the guard openly, as if Lord Bolton himself had sent her. He watched her come, curious as to what might bring a page here at this black hour. When she got closer, she saw that he was a northman, very tall and thin, huddled in a ragged fur cloak. That was bad. She might have been able to trick a Frey or one of the Brave Companions, but the Dreadfort men had served Roose Bolton their whole life, and they knew him better than she did. *If I tell him I am Arya Stark and command him to stand aside . . .* No, she dare not. He was a northman, but not a Winterfell man. He belonged to Roose Bolton.

When she reached him she pushed back her cloak so he would see the flayed man on her breast. "Lord Bolton sent me."

"At this hour? Why for?"

She could see the gleam of steel under the fur, and she did not know if she was strong enough to drive the point of the dagger through chainmail. *His throat, it must be his throat, but he's too tall, I'll never reach it.* For a moment she did not know what to say. For a moment she was a little girl again, and scared, and the rain on her face felt like tears.

"He told me to give all his guards a silver piece, for their good service." The words seemed to come out of nowhere.

"Silver, you say?" He did not believe her, but he *wanted* to; silver was silver, after all. "Give it over, then."

Her fingers dug down beneath her tunic and came out clutching the coin Jaqen had given her. In the dark the iron could pass for tarnished silver. She held it out . . . and let it slip through her fingers.

Cursing her softly, the man went to a knee to grope for the coin in the dirt, and there was his neck right in front of her. Arya slid her dagger out and drew it across his throat, as smooth as summer silk. His blood covered her hands in a hot gush and he tried to shout but there was blood in his mouth as well.

"Valar morghulis," she whispered as he died.

When he stopped moving, she picked up the coin. Outside the walls of Harrenhal, a wolf howled long and loud. She lifted the bar, set it aside, and pulled open the heavy oak door. By the time Hot Pie and Gendry came up with the horses, the rain was falling hard. "You *killed* him!" Hot Pie gasped.

"What did you think I would do?" Her fingers were sticky with blood, and the smell was making her mare skittish. *It's no matter,* she thought, swinging up into the saddle. *The rain will wash them clean again.*

SANSA

The throne room was a sea of jewels, furs, and bright fabrics. Lords and ladies filled the back of the hall and stood beneath the high windows, jostling like fishwives on a dock.

The denizens of Joffrey's court had striven to outdo each other today. Jalabhar Xho was all in feathers, a plumage so fantastic and extravagant that he seemed like to take flight. The High Septon's crystal crown fired rainbows through the air every time he moved his head. At the council table, Queen Cersei shimmered in a cloth-of-gold gown slashed in burgundy velvet, while beside her Varys fussed and simpered in a lilac brocade. Moon Boy and Ser Dontos wore new suits of motley, clean as a spring morning. Even Lady Tanda and her daughters looked pretty in matching gowns of turquoise silk and vair, and Lord Gyles was coughing into a square of scarlet silk trimmed with golden lace. King Joffrey sat above them all, amongst the blades and barbs of the Iron Throne. He was in crimson samite, his black mantle studded with rubies, on his head his heavy golden crown.

Squirming through a press of knights, squires, and rich townfolk, Sansa reached the front of the gallery just as a blast of trumpets announced the entry of Lord Tywin Lannister.

He rode his warhorse down the length of the hall and dismounted before the Iron Throne. Sansa had never seen such armor; all burnished red steel, inlaid with golden scrollwork and ornamentation. His rondels were sunbursts, the roaring lion that crowned his helm had ruby eyes, and a lioness on each shoulder fastened a cloth-of-gold cloak so long and heavy that it draped the hindquarters of his charger. Even the horse's armor was gilded, and his bardings were shimmering crimson silk emblazoned with the lion of Lannister.

The Lord of Casterly Rock made such an impressive figure that it was a shock when his destrier dropped a load of dung right at the base of the throne. Joffrey had to step gingerly around it as he descended to embrace his grandfather and proclaim him Savior of the City. Sansa covered her mouth to hide a nervous smile.

Joff made a show of asking his grandfather to assume governance of the realm, and Lord Tywin solemnly accepted the responsibility, "until Your Grace does come of age." Then squires removed his armor and Joff fastened the Hand's chain of office around his neck. Lord Tywin took a seat at the council table beside the queen. After the destrier was led off and his homage removed, Cersei nodded for the ceremonies to continue.

A fanfare of brazen trumpets greeted each of the heroes as he stepped between the great oaken doors. Heralds cried his name and deeds for all to hear, and the noble knights and highborn ladies cheered as lustily as cutthroats at a cockfight. Pride of place was given to Mace Tyrell, the Lord of Highgarden, a once-powerful man gone to fat, yet still handsome. His sons followed him in; Ser Loras and his older brother Ser Garlan the Gallant. The three dressed alike, in green velvet trimmed with sable.

The king descended the throne once more to greet them, a great honor. He fastened about the throat of each a chain of roses wrought in soft yellow gold, from which hung a golden disc with the lion of Lannister picked out in rubies. "The roses support the lion, as the might of Highgarden supports the realm," proclaimed Joffrey. "If there is any boon you would ask of me, ask and it shall be yours."

And now it comes, thought Sansa.

"Your Grace," said Ser Loras, "I beg the honor of serving in your Kingsguard, to defend you against your enemies."

Joffrey drew the Knight of Flowers to his feet and kissed him on his cheek. "Done, brother."

Lord Tyrell bowed his head. "There is no greater pleasure than to serve the King's Grace. If I was deemed worthy to join your royal council, you would find none more loyal or true."

Joff put a hand on Lord Tyrell's shoulder and kissed him when he stood. "Your wish is granted."

Ser Garlan Tyrell, five years senior to Ser Loras, was a taller bearded version of his more famous younger brother. He was thicker about the chest and broader at the shoulders, and though his face was comely enough, he lacked Ser Loras's startling beauty. "Your Grace," Garlan said when the king approached him, "I have a maiden sister, Margaery, the delight of our House. She was wed to Renly Baratheon, as you know, but Lord Renly went to war before the marriage could be consummated, so she remains innocent. Margaery has heard tales of your wisdom, courage, and chivalry, and has come to love you from afar. I beseech you to send for her, to take her hand in marriage, and to wed your House to mine for all time."

King Joffrey made a show of looking surprised. "Ser Garlan, your sister's beauty is famed throughout the Seven Kingdoms, but I am promised to another. A king must keep his word."

Queen Cersei got to her feet in a rustle of skirts. "Your Grace, in the judgment of your small council, it would be neither proper nor wise for you to wed the daughter of a man beheaded for treason, a girl whose brother is in open rebellion against the throne even now. Sire, your councillors beg you, for the good of your realm, set Sansa Stark aside. The Lady Margaery will make you a far more suitable queen."

Like a pack of trained dogs, the lords and ladies in the hall began to shout their pleasure. *"Margaery,"* they called. "Give us Margaery!" and "No traitor queens! Tyrell! Tyrell!"

Joffrey raised a hand. "I would like to heed the wishes of my people, Mother, but I took a holy vow."

The High Septon stepped forward. "Your Grace, the gods hold bethrothal solemn, but your father, King Robert of blessed memory, made this pact before the Starks of Winterfell had revealed their falseness. Their crimes against the realm have freed you from any promise you might have made. So far as the Faith is concerned, there is no valid marriage contract 'twixt you and Sansa Stark."

A tumult of cheering filled the throne room, and cries of *"Margaery, Margaery"* erupted all around her. Sansa leaned forward, her hands tight around the gallery's wooden rail. She knew what came next, but she was still frightened of what Joffrey might say, afraid that he would refuse to release her even now, when his whole kingdom depended upon it. She felt as if she were back again on the marble steps outside the Great Sept of Baelor, waiting for her prince to grant her father mercy, and instead hearing him command Ilyn Payne to strike off his head. *Please,* she prayed fervently, *make him say it, make him say it.*

Lord Tywin was looking at his grandson. Joff gave him a sullen glance, shifted his feet, and helped Ser Garlan Tyrell to rise. "The gods are good. I am free to heed my heart. I will wed your sweet sister, and gladly, ser." He kissed Ser Garlan on a bearded cheek as the cheers rose all around them.

Sansa felt curiously light-headed. *I am free.* She could feel eyes upon her. *I must not smile,* she reminded herself. The queen had warned her; no matter what she felt inside, the face she showed the world must look distraught. "I will not have my son humiliated," Cersei said. "Do you hear me?"

"Yes. But if I'm not to be queen, what will become of me?"

"That will need to be determined. For the moment, you shall remain here at court, as our ward."

"I want to go home."

The queen was irritated by that. "You should have learned by now, none of us get the things we want."

I have, though, Sansa thought. *I am free of Joffrey. I will not have to kiss him, nor give him my maidenhood, nor bear him children. Let Margaery Tyrell have all that, poor girl.*

By the time the outburst died down, the Lord of Highgarden had been seated at the council table, and his sons had joined the other knights and lordlings beneath the windows. Sansa tried to look forlorn and abandoned as other heroes of the Battle of the Blackwater were summoned forth to receive their rewards.

Paxter Redwyne, Lord of the Arbor, marched down the length of the hall flanked by his twin sons Horror and Slobber, the former limping from a wound taken in the battle. After them followed Lord Mathis Rowan in a snowy doublet with a great tree worked upon the breast in gold thread; Lord Randyll Tarly, lean and balding, a greatsword across his back in a jeweled scabbard; Ser Kevan Lannister, a thickset balding man with a close-trimmed beard; Ser Addam Marbrand, coppery hair streaming to his shoulders; the great western lords Lydden, Crakehall, and Brax.

Next came four of lesser birth who had distinguished themselves in the fighting: the one-eyed knight Ser Philip Foote, who had slain Lord Bryce Caron in single combat; the freerider Lothor Brune, who'd cut his way through half a hundred Fossoway men-at-arms to capture Ser Jon of the green apple and kill Ser Bryan and Ser Edwyd of the red, thereby winning himself the name Lothor Apple-Eater; Willit, a grizzled man-at-arms in the service of Ser Harys Swyft, who'd pulled his master from beneath his dying horse and defended him against a dozen attackers; and a downy-cheeked squire named Josmyn Peckledon, who had killed two knights, wounded a third, and captured two more, though he could not have been more than fourteen. Willit was borne in on a litter, so grievous were his wounds.

Ser Kevan had taken a seat beside his brother Lord Tywin. When the heralds had finished telling of each hero's deeds, he rose. "It is His Grace's wish that these good men be rewarded for their valor. By his decree, Ser Philip shall henceforth be Lord Philip of House Foote, and to him shall go all the lands, rights, and incomes of House Caron. Lothor Brune to be raised to the estate of knighthood, and granted land and keep in the riverlands at war's end. To Josmyn Peckledon, a sword and suit of plate, his choice of any warhorse in the royal stables, and knighthood as soon as he shall come of age. And lastly, for Goodman Willit, a spear with a silver-banded haft, a hauberk of new-forged ringmail, and a full helm with visor. Further, the goodman's sons shall be taken into the service of House Lannister at Casterly Rock, the elder as a squire and the younger as a page, with the chance to advance to knighthood if they serve loyally and well. To all this, the King's Hand and the small council consent."

The captains of the king's warships *Wildwind*, *Prince Aemon*, and *River Arrow* were honored next, along with some under officers from *Godsgrace*, *Lance*, *Lady of Silk*, and *Ramshead*. As near as Sansa could tell, their chief accomplishment had been surviving the battle on the river, a feat that few enough could boast. Hallyne the Pyromancer and the masters of the Alchemists' Guild received the king's thanks as well, and Hallyne was raised to the style of lord, though Sansa noted that neither lands nor castle accompanied the title, which made the alchemist no more a *true* lord than Varys was. A more significant lordship by far was granted to Ser Lancel Lannister. Joffrey awarded him the lands, castle, and rights of House Darry, whose last child lord had perished during the fighting in the riverlands, "leaving no trueborn heirs of lawful Darry blood, but only a bastard cousin."

Ser Lancel did not appear to accept the title; the talk was, his wound might cost him his arm or even his life. The Imp was said to be dying as well, from a terrible cut to the head.

When the herald called, *"Lord Petyr Baelish,"* he came forth dressed all in shades of rose and plum, his cloak patterned with mockingbirds. She could see him smiling as he knelt before the Iron Throne. *He looks so pleased.* Sansa had not heard of Littlefinger doing anything especially heroic during the battle, but it seemed he was to be rewarded all the same.

Ser Kevan got back to his feet. "It is the wish of the King's Grace that his loyal councillor Petyr Baelish be rewarded for faithful service to crown and realm. Be it known that Lord Baelish is granted the castle of Harrenhal with all its attendant lands and incomes, there to make his seat and rule henceforth as Lord Paramount of the Trident. Petyr Baelish and his sons and grandsons shall hold and enjoy these honors until the end of time, and all the lords of the Trident shall do him homage as their rightful liege. The King's Hand and the small council consent."

On his knees, Littlefinger raised his eyes to King Joffrey. "I thank you humbly, Your Grace. I suppose this means I'll need to see about getting some sons and grandsons."

Joffrey laughed, and the court with him. *Lord Paramount of the Trident,* Sansa thought, *and Lord of Harrenhal as well.* She did not understand why that should make him so happy; the honors were as empty as the title granted to Hallyne the Pyromancer. Harrenhal was cursed, everyone knew that, and the Lannisters did not even hold it at present. Besides, the lords of the Trident were sworn to Riverrun and House Tully, and to the King in the North; they would never accept Littlefinger as their liege. *Unless they are made to. Unless my brother and my uncle and my grandfa-*

ther are all cast down and killed. The thought made Sansa anxious, but she told herself she was being silly. *Robb has beaten them every time. He'll beat Lord Baelish too, if he must.*

More than six hundred new knights were made that day. They had held their vigil in the Great Sept of Baelor all through the night and crossed the city barefoot that morning to prove their humble hearts. Now they came forward dressed in shifts of undyed wool to receive their knighthoods from the Kingsguard. It took a long time, since only three of the Brothers of the White Sword were on hand to dub them. Mandon Moore had perished in the battle, the Hound had vanished, Aerys Oakheart was in Dorne with Princess Myrcella, and Jaime Lannister was Robb's captive, so the Kingsguard had been reduced to Balon Swann, Meryn Trant, and Osmund Kettleblack. Once knighted, each man rose, buckled on his swordbelt, and stood beneath the windows. Some had bloody feet from their walk through the city, but they stood tall and proud all the same, it seemed to Sansa.

By the time all the new knights had been given their *ser*s the hall was growing restive, and none more so than Joffrey. Some of those in the gallery had begun to slip quietly away, but the notables on the floor were trapped, unable to depart without the king's leave. Judging by the way he was fidgeting atop the Iron Throne, Joff would willingly have granted it, but the day's work was far from done. For now the coin was turned over, and the captives were ushered in.

There were great lords and noble knights in that company too: sour old Lord Celtigar, the Red Crab; Ser Bonifer the Good; Lord Estermont, more ancient even than Celtigar; Lord Varner, who hobbled the length of the hall on a shattered knee, but would accept no help; Ser Mark Mullendore, grey-faced, his left arm gone to the elbow; fierce Red Ronnet of Griffin Roost; Ser Dermot of the Rainwood; Lord Willum and his sons Josua and Elyas; Ser Jon Fossoway; Ser Timon the

Scrapesword; Aurane, the bastard of Driftmark; Lord Staedmon, called Pennylover; hundreds of others.

Those who had changed their allegiance during the battle needed only to swear fealty to Joffrey, but the ones who had fought for Stannis until the bitter end were compelled to speak. Their words decided their fate. If they begged forgiveness for their treasons and promised to serve loyally henceforth, Joffrey welcomed them back into the king's peace and restored them to all their lands and rights. A handful remained defiant, however. "Do not imagine this is done, boy," warned one, the bastard son of some Florent or other. "The Lord of Light protects King Stannis, now and always. All your swords and all your scheming shall not save you when his hour comes."

"*Your* hour is come right now." Joffrey beckoned to Ser Ilyn Payne to take the man out and strike his head off. But no sooner had that one been dragged away than a knight of solemn mien with a fiery heart on his surcoat shouted out, "Stannis is the true king! A monster sits the Iron Throne, an abomination born of incest!"

"Be silent," Ser Kevan Lannister bellowed.

The knight raised his voice instead. "Joffrey is the black worm eating the heart of the realm! Darkness was his father, and death his mother! Destroy him before he corrupts you all! Destroy them all, queen whore and king worm, vile dwarf and whispering spider, the false flowers. Save yourselves!" One of the gold cloaks knocked the man off his feet, but he continued to shout. "The scouring fire will come! King Stannis will return!"

Joffrey lurched to his feet. "*I'm* king! Kill him! Kill him now! I command it." He chopped down with his hand, a furious, angry gesture . . . and screeched in pain when his arm brushed against one of the sharp metal fangs that surrounded him. The bright crimson samite of his sleeve turned a darker shade of red as his blood soaked through it. *"Mother!"* he wailed.

With every eye on the king, somehow the man on the floor wrested a spear away from one of the gold cloaks, and used it to push himself back to his feet. "The throne denies him!" he cried. *"He is no king!"*

Cersei was running toward the throne, but Lord Tywin remained still as stone. He had only to raise a finger, and Ser Meryn Trant moved forward with drawn sword. The end was quick and brutal. The gold cloaks seized the knight by the arms. *"No king!"* he cried again as Ser Meryn drove the point of his longsword through his chest.

Joff fell into his mother's arms. Three maesters came hurrying forward, to bundle him out through the king's door. Then everyone began talking at once. When the gold cloaks dragged off the dead man, he left a trail of bright blood across the stone floor. Lord Baelish stroked his beard while Varys whispered in his ear. *Will they dismiss us now?* Sansa wondered. A score of captives still waited, though whether to pledge fealty or shout curses, who could say?

Lord Tywin rose to his feet. "We continue," he said in a clear strong voice that silenced the murmurs. "Those who wish to ask pardon for their treasons may do so. We will have no more follies." He moved to the Iron Throne and there seated himself on a step, a mere three feet off the floor.

The light outside the windows was fading by the time the session drew to a close. Sansa felt limp with exhaustion as she made her way down from the gallery. She wondered how badly Joffrey had cut himself. *They say the Iron Throne can be perilous cruel to those who were not meant to sit it.*

Back in the safety of her own chambers, she hugged a pillow to her face to muffle a squeal of joy. *Oh, gods be good, he did it, he put me aside in front of everyone.* When a serving girl brought her supper, she almost kissed her. There was hot bread and fresh-churned butter, a thick beef soup, capon and carrots, and peaches in honey. *Even the food tastes sweeter*, she thought.

Come dark, she slipped into a cloak and left for the godswood. Ser Osmund Kettleblack was guarding the drawbridge in his white armor. Sansa tried her best to sound miserable as she bid him a good evening. From the way he leered at her, she was not sure she had been wholly convincing.

Dontos waited in the leafy moonlight. "Why so sadface?" Sansa asked him gaily. "You were there, you heard. Joff put me aside, he's done with me, he's . . ."

He took her hand. "Oh, Jonquil, my poor Jonquil, you do not understand. Done with you? They've scarcely begun."

Her heart sank. "What do you mean?"

"The queen will never let you go, never. You are too valuable a hostage. And Joffrey . . . sweetling, he is still king. If he wants you in his bed, he will have you, only now it will be bastards he plants in your womb instead of trueborn sons."

"No," Sansa said, shocked. "He let me go, he . . ."

Ser Dontos planted a slobbery kiss on her ear. "Be brave. I swore to see you home, and now I can. The day has been chosen."

"When?" Sansa asked. "When will we go?"

"The night of Joffrey's wedding. After the feast. All the necessary arrangements have been made. The Red Keep will be full of strangers. Half the court will be drunk and the other half will be helping Joffrey bed his bride. For a little while, you will be forgotten, and the confusion will be our friend."

"The wedding won't be for a moon's turn yet. Margaery Tyrell is at Highgarden, they've only now sent for her."

"You've waited so long, be patient awhile longer. Here, I have something for you." Ser Dontos fumbled in his pouch and drew out a silvery spiderweb, dangling it between his thick fingers.

It was a hair net of fine-spun silver, the strands so thin and delicate the net seemed to weigh no more than a breath of air when Sansa took it in her fingers. Small gems were set wherever two strands crossed, so dark they drank the moonlight. "What stones are these?"

"Black amethysts from Asshai. The rarest kind, a deep true purple by daylight."

"It's very lovely," Sansa said, thinking, *It is a ship I need, not a net for my hair.*

"Lovelier than you know, sweet child. It's magic, you see. It's justice you hold. It's vengeance for your father." Dontos leaned close and kissed her again. "It's *home.*"

THEON

Maester Luwin came to him when the first scouts were seen outside the walls. "My lord prince," he said, "you must yield."

Theon stared at the platter of oakcakes, honey, and blood sausage they'd brought him to break his fast. Another sleepless night had left his nerves raw, and the very sight of food sickened him. "There has been no reply from my uncle?"

"None," the maester said. "Nor from your father on Pyke."

"Send more birds."

"It will not serve. By the time the birds reach—"

"*Send them!*" Knocking the platter of food aside with a swipe of his arm, he pushed off the blankets and rose from Ned Stark's bed naked and angry. "Or do you want me dead? Is that it, Luwin? The truth now."

The small grey man was unafraid. "My order serves."

"Yes, but whom?"

"The realm," Maester Luwin said, "and Winterfell. Theon, once I taught you sums and letters, history and warcraft. And might have taught you more, had you wished to learn. I will not claim to bear you any great love, no, but I cannot hate you either. Even if I did, so long as you hold Winterfell I am bound by oath to give you counsel. So now I counsel you to *yield*."

Theon stooped to scoop a puddled cloak off the floor, shook off the rushes, and draped it over his shoulders. *A fire, I'll have a fire, and clean garb. Where's Wex? I'll not go to my grave in dirty clothes.*

"You have no hope of holding here," the maester went on. "If your lord father meant to send you aid, he would have done so by now. It is the Neck that concerns him. The battle for the north will be fought amidst the ruins of Moat Cailin."

"That may be so," said Theon. "And so long as I hold Winterfell, Ser Rodrik and Stark's lords bannermen cannot march south to take my uncle in the rear." *I am not so innocent of warcraft as you think, old man.* "I have food enough to stand a year's siege, if need be."

"There will be no siege. Perhaps they will spend a day or two fashioning ladders and tying grapnels to the ends of ropes. But soon enough they will come over your walls in a hundred places at once. You may be able to hold the keep for a time, but the castle will fall within the hour. You would do better to open your gates and ask for—"

"—*mercy*? I know what kind of mercy they have for me."

"There is a way."

"I am ironborn," Theon reminded him. "I have my own way. What choice have they left me? No, don't answer, I've heard enough of your *counsel*. Go and send those birds as I commanded, and tell Lorren I want to see him. And Wex as well. I'll have my mail scoured clean, and my garrison assembled in the yard."

For a moment he thought the maester was going to defy him. But finally Luwin bowed stiffly. "As you command."

They made a pitifully small assembly; the ironmen were few, the yard large. "The northmen will be on us before nightfall," he told them. "Ser Rodrik Cassel and all the lords who have come to his call. I will not run from them. I took this castle and I mean to hold it, to live or die as Prince of Winterfell. But I will not command any man to die with me. If you leave now, before Ser Rodrik's main force is upon us, there's still a chance you may win free." He unsheathed his longsword and drew a line in the dirt. "Those who would stay and fight, step forward."

No one spoke. The men stood in their mail and fur and boiled leather, as still as if they were made of stone. A few exchanged looks. Urzen shuffled his feet. Dykk Harlaw hawked and spat. A finger of wind ruffled Endehar's long fair hair.

Theon felt as though he were drowning. *Why am I surprised?* he thought bleakly. His father had forsaken him, his uncles, his sister, even that wretched creature Reek. Why should his men prove any more loyal? There was nothing to say, nothing to do. He could only stand there beneath the great grey walls and the hard white sky, sword in hand, waiting, waiting . . .

Wex was the first to cross the line. Three quick steps and he stood at Theon's side, slouching. Shamed by the boy, Black Lorren followed, all scowls. "Who else?" he demanded. Red Rolfe came forward. Kromm. Werlag. Tymor and his brothers. Ulf the Ill. Harrag Sheepstealer. Four Harlaws and two Botleys. Kenned the Whale was the last. Seventeen in all.

Urzen was among those who did not move, and Stygg, and every man of the ten that Asha had brought from Deepwood Motte. "Go, then," Theon told them. "Run to my sister. She'll give you all a warm welcome, I have no doubt."

Stygg had the grace at least to look ashamed. The rest moved off without a word. Theon turned to the seventeen who remained. "Back to the walls. If the gods should spare us, I shall remember every man of you."

Black Lorren stayed when the others had gone. "The castle folk will turn on us soon as the fight begins."

"I know that. What would you have me do?"

"Put them out," said Lorren. "Every one."

Theon shook his head. "Is the noose ready?"

"It is. You mean to use it?"

"Do you know a better way?"

"Aye. I'll take my axe and stand on that drawbridge, and let them come try me. One at a time, two, three, it makes no matter. None will pass the moat while I still draw breath."

He means to die, thought Theon. *It's not victory he wants, it's an end worthy of a song.* "We'll use the noose."

"As you say," Lorren replied, contempt in his eyes.

Wex helped garb him for battle. Beneath his black surcoat and golden mantle was a shirt of well-oiled ringmail, and under that a layer of stiff boiled leather. Once armed and armored, Theon climbed the watchtower at the angle where the eastern and southern walls came together to have a look at his doom. The northmen were spreading out to encircle the castle. It was hard to judge their numbers. A thousand at least; perhaps twice that many. *Against seventeen.* They'd brought catapults and scorpions. He saw no siege towers rumbling up the kingsroad, but there was timber enough in the wolfswood to build as many as were required.

Theon studied their banners through Maester Luwin's Myrish lens tube. The Cerwyn battle-axe flapped bravely wherever he looked, and there were Tallhart trees as well, and mermen from White Harbor. Less common were the sigils of Flint and Karstark. Here and there he even saw the bull moose of the Hornwoods. *But no Glovers, Asha saw to them, no Boltons from the Dreadfort, no Umbers come down from the shadow of the Wall.* Not that they were needed. Soon enough the boy Cley Cerwyn appeared before the gates carrying a peace banner on a tall staff, to announce that Ser Rodrik Cassel wished to parley with Theon Turncloak.

Turncloak. The name was bitter as bile. He had gone to Pyke to lead his father's longships against Lannisport, he remembered. "I shall be out shortly," he shouted down. "Alone."

Black Lorren disapproved. "Only blood can wash out blood," he declared. "Knights may keep their truces with other knights, but they are not so careful of their honor when dealing with those they deem outlaw."

Theon bristled. "I am the Prince of Winterfell and heir to the Iron Islands. Now go find the girl and do as I told you."

Black Lorren gave him a murderous look. "Aye, Prince."

He's turned against me too, Theon realized. Of late it seemed to him as if the very stones of Winterfell had turned against him. *If I die, I die friendless and abandoned.* What choice did that leave him, but to live?

He rode to the gatehouse with his crown on his head. A woman was drawing water from the well, and Gage the cook stood in the door of the kitchens. They hid their hatred behind sullen looks and faces blank as slate, yet he could feel it all the same.

When the drawbridge was lowered, a chill wind sighed across the moat. The touch of it made him shiver. *It is the cold, nothing more,* Theon told himself, *a shiver, not a tremble. Even brave men shiver.* Into the teeth of that wind he rode, under the portcullis, over the drawbridge. The outer gates swung open to let him pass. As he emerged beneath the walls, he could sense the boys watching from the empty sockets where their eyes had been.

Ser Rodrik waited in the market astride his dappled gelding. Beside him, the direwolf of Stark flapped from a staff borne by young Cley Cerwyn. They were alone in the square, though Theon could see archers on the roofs of surrounding houses, spearmen to his right, and to his left a line of mounted knights beneath the merman-and-trident of House Manderly. *Every one of them wants me dead.* Some were boys he'd drunk with, diced with, even wenched with, but that would not save him if he fell into their hands.

"Ser Rodrik." Theon reined to a halt. "It grieves me that we must meet as foes."

"My own grief is that I must wait a while to hang you." The old knight spat onto the muddy ground. "Theon Turncloak."

"I am a Greyjoy of Pyke," Theon reminded him. "The cloak my father swaddled me in bore a kraken, not a direwolf."

"For ten years you have been a ward of Stark."

"Hostage and prisoner, I call it."

"Then perhaps Lord Eddard should have kept you chained to a dungeon wall. Instead he raised you among his own sons, the sweet boys you have butchered, and to my undying shame I trained you in the arts of war. Would that I had thrust a sword through your belly instead of placing one in your hand."

"I came out to parley, not to suffer your insults. Say what you have to say, old man. What would you have of me?"

"Two things," the old man said. "Winterfell, and your life. Command your men to open the gates and lay down their arms. Those who murdered no children shall be free to walk away, but you shall be held for King Robb's justice. May the gods take pity on you when he returns."

"Robb will never look on Winterfell again," Theon promised. "He will break himself on Moat Cailin, as every southron army has done for ten thousand years. We hold the north now, ser."

"You hold three castles," replied Ser Rodrik, "and this one I mean to take back, Turncloak."

Theon ignored that. "Here are *my* terms. You have until evenfall to disperse. Those who swear fealty to Balon Greyjoy as their king and to myself as Prince of Winterfell will be confirmed in their rights and properties and suffer no harm. Those who defy us will be destroyed."

Young Cerwyn was incredulous. "Are you mad, Greyjoy?"

Ser Rodrik shook his head. "Only vain, lad. Theon

has always had too lofty an opinion of himself, I fear." The old man jabbed a finger at him. "Do not imagine that I need wait for Robb to fight his way up the Neck to deal with the likes of you. I have near two thousand men with me . . . and if the tales be true, you have no more than fifty."

Seventeen, in truth. Theon made himself smile. "I have something better than men." And he raised a fist over his head, the signal Black Lorren had been told to watch for.

The walls of Winterfell were behind him, but Ser Rodrik faced them squarely and could not fail to see. Theon watched his face. When his chin quivered under those stiff white whiskers, he knew just what the old man was seeing. *He is not surprised,* he thought with sadness, *but the fear is there.*

"This is craven," Ser Rodrik said. "To use a child so . . . this is despicable."

"Oh, I know," said Theon. "It's a dish I tasted myself, or have you forgotten? I was ten when I was taken from my father's house, to make certain he would raise no more rebellions."

"It is not the same!"

Theon's face was impassive. "The noose I wore was not made of hempen rope, that's true enough, but I felt it all the same. And it chafed, Ser Rodrik. It chafed me raw." He had never quite realized that until now, but as the words came spilling out he saw the truth of them.

"No harm was ever done you."

"And no harm will be done your Beth, so long as you—"

Ser Rodrik never gave him the chance to finish. *"Viper,"* the knight declared, his face red with rage beneath those white whiskers. "I gave you the chance to save your men and die with some small shred of honor, Turncloak. I should have known that was too much to ask of a childkiller." His hand went to the hilt of his sword. "I ought cut you down here and now and put an end to your lies and deceits. By the gods, I should."

Theon did not fear a doddering old man, but those

A CLASH OF KINGS

watching archers and that line of knights were a different matter. If the swords came out his chances of getting back to the castle alive were small to none. "Forswear your oath and murder me, and you will watch your little Beth strangle at the end of a rope."

Ser Rodrik's knuckles had gone white, but after a moment he took his hand off the swordhilt. "Truly, I have lived too long."

"I will not disagree, ser. Will you accept my terms?"

"I have a duty to Lady Catelyn and House Stark."

"And your own House? Beth is the last of your blood."

The old knight drew himself up straight. "I offer myself in my daughter's place. Release her, and take me as your hostage. Surely the castellan of Winterfell is worth more than a child."

"Not to me." *A valiant gesture, old man, but I am not that great a fool.* "Not to Lord Manderly or Leobald Tallhart either, I'd wager." *Your sorry old skin is worth no more to them than any other man's.* "No, I'll keep the girl . . . and keep her safe, so long as you do as I've commanded you. Her life is in your hands."

"Gods be good, Theon, how can you do this? You know I must attack, have *sworn* . . ."

"If this host is still in arms before my gate when the sun sets, Beth will hang," said Theon. "Another hostage will follow her to the grave at first light, and another at sunset. Every dawn and every dusk will mean a death, until you are gone. I have no lack of hostages." He did not wait for a reply, but wheeled Smiler around and rode back toward the castle. He went slowly at first, but the thought of those archers at his back soon drove him to a canter. The small heads watched him come from their spikes, their tarred and flayed faces looming larger with every yard; between them stood little Beth Cassel, noosed and crying. Theon put his heel into Smiler and broke into a hard gallop. Smiler's hooves clattered on the drawbridge, like drumbeats.

In the yard he dismounted and handed his reins to Wex. "It may stay them," he told Black Lorren. "We'll know by sunset. Take the girl in till then, and keep her somewhere safe." Under the layers of leather, steel, and wool, he was slick with sweat. "I need a cup of wine. A vat of wine would do even better."

A fire had been laid in Ned Stark's bedchamber. Theon sat beside it and filled a cup with a heavy-bodied red from the castle vaults, a wine as sour as his mood. *They will attack,* he thought gloomily, staring at the flames. *Ser Rodrik loves his daughter, but he is still castellan, and most of all a knight.* Had it been Theon with a noose around his neck and Lord Balon commanding the army without, the warhorns would already have sounded the attack, he had no doubt. He should thank the gods that Ser Rodrik was not ironborn. The men of the green lands were made of softer stuff, though he was not certain they would prove soft enough.

If not, if the old man gave the command to storm the castle regardless, Winterfell would fall; Theon entertained no delusions on that count. His seventeen might kill three, four, five times their own number, but in the end they would be overwhelmed.

Theon stared at the flames over the rim of his wine goblet, brooding on the injustice of it all. "I rode beside Robb Stark in the Whispering Wood," he muttered. He had been frightened that night, but not like this. It was one thing to go into battle surrounded by friends, and another to perish alone and despised. *Mercy,* he thought miserably.

When the wine brought no solace, Theon sent Wex to fetch his bow and took himself to the old inner ward. There he stood, loosing shaft after shaft at the archery butts until his shoulders ached and his fingers were bloody, pausing only long enough to pull the arrows from the targets for another round. *I saved Bran's life with this bow,* he reminded himself. *Would that I could save my own.* Women came to the well, but did not linger; whatever they saw on Theon's face sent them away quickly.

Behind him the broken tower stood, its summit as jagged as a crown where fire had collapsed the upper stories long ago. As the sun moved, the shadow of the tower moved as well, gradually lengthening, a black arm reaching out for Theon Greyjoy. By the time the sun touched the wall, he was in its grasp. *If I hang the girl, the northmen will attack at once,* he thought as he loosed a shaft. *If I do not hang her, they will know my threats are empty.* He nocked another arrow to his bow. *There is no way out, none.*

"If you had a hundred archers as good as yourself, you might have a chance to hold the castle," a voice said softly.

When he turned, Maester Luwin was behind him. "Go away," Theon told him. "I have had enough of your counsel."

"And life? Have you had enough of that, my lord prince?"

He raised the bow. "One more word and I'll put this shaft through your heart."

"You won't."

Theon bent the bow, drawing the grey goose feathers back to his cheek. "Care to make a wager?"

"I am your last hope, Theon."

I have no hope, he thought. Yet he lowered the bow half an inch and said, "I will not run."

"I do not speak of running. Take the black."

"The Night's Watch?" Theon let the bow unbend slowly and pointed the arrow at the ground.

"Ser Rodrik has served House Stark all his life, and House Stark has always been a friend to the Watch. He will not deny you. Open your gates, lay down your arms, accept his terms, and he *must* let you take the black."

A brother of the Night's Watch. It meant no crown, no sons, no wife . . . but it meant life, and life with honor. Ned Stark's own brother had chosen the Watch, and Jon Snow as well.

I have black garb aplenty, once I tear the krakens off. Even my horse is black. I could rise high in the Watch—chief of rangers, likely even Lord Commander. Let Asha keep the bloody islands, they're as dreary as she is. If I served at Eastwatch, I could command my own ship, and there's fine hunting beyond the Wall. As for women, what wildling woman wouldn't want a prince in her bed? A slow smile crept across his face. *A black cloak can't be turned. I'd be as good as any man . . .*

"PRINCE THEON!" The sudden shout shattered his daydream. Kromm was loping across the ward. "The northmen—"

He felt a sudden sick sense of dread. "Is it the attack?"

Maester Luwin clutched his arm. "There's still time. Raise a peace banner—"

"They're fighting," Kromm said urgently. "More men came up, hundreds of them, and at first they made to join the others. But now they've fallen on them!"

"Is it Asha?" Had she come to save him after all?

But Kromm gave a shake of his head. "No. These are *northmen,* I tell you. With a bloody man on their banner."

The flayed man of the Dreadfort. Reek had belonged to the Bastard of Bolton before his capture, Theon recalled. It was hard to believe that a vile creature like him could sway the Boltons to change their allegiance, but nothing else made sense. "I'll see this for myself," Theon said.

Maester Luwin trailed after him. By the time they reached the battlements, dead men and dying horses were strewn about the market square outside the gates. He saw no battle lines, only a swirling chaos of banners and blades. Shouts and screams rang through the cold autumn air. Ser Rodrik seemed to have the numbers, but the Dreadfort men were better led, and had taken the others unawares. Theon watched them charge and wheel and charge again, chopping the larger force to bloody pieces every time they tried to form up between the houses. He could hear the crash of iron axeheads on oaken shields over the terrified trumpeting of a maimed horse. The inn was burning, he saw.

Black Lorren appeared beside him and stood silently

for a time. The sun was low in the west, painting the fields and houses all a glowing red. A thin wavering cry of pain drifted over the walls, and a warhorn sounded off beyond the burning houses. Theon watched a wounded man drag himself painfully across the ground, smearing his life's blood in the dirt as he struggled to reach the well that stood at the center of the market square. He died before he got there. He wore a leather jerkin and conical halfhelm, but no badge to tell which side he'd fought on.

The crows came in the blue dusk, with the evening stars. "The Dothraki believe the stars are spirits of the valiant dead," Theon said. Maester Luwin had told him that, a long time ago.

"Dothraki?"

"The horselords across the narrow sea."

"Oh. Them." Black Lorren frowned through his beard. "Savages believe all manner of foolish things."

As the night grew darker and the smoke spread it was harder to make out what was happening below, but the din of steel gradually diminished to nothing, and the shouts and warhorns gave way to moans and piteous wailing. Finally a column of mounted men rode out of the drifting smoke. At their head was a knight in dark armor. His rounded helm gleamed a sullen red, and a pale pink cloak streamed from his shoulders. Outside the main gate he reined up, and one of his men shouted for the castle to open.

"Are you friend or foe?" Black Lorren bellowed down.

"Would a foe bring such fine gifts?" Red Helm waved a hand, and three corpses were dumped in front of the gates. A torch was waved above the bodies, so the defenders upon the walls might see the faces of the dead.

"The old castellan," said Black Lorren.

"With Leobald Tallhart and Cley Cerwyn." The boy lord had taken an arrow in the eye, and Ser Rodrik had lost his left arm at the elbow. Maester Luwin gave a wordless cry of dismay, turned away from the battlements, and fell to his knees sick.

"The great pig Manderly was too craven to leave

White Harbor, or we would have brought him as well," shouted Red Helm.

I am saved, Theon thought. So why did he feel so empty? This was victory, sweet victory, the deliverance he had prayed for. He glanced at Maester Luwin. *To think how close I came to yielding, and taking the black . . .*

"Open the gates for our friends." Perhaps tonight Theon would sleep without fear of what his dreams might bring.

The Dreadfort men made their way across the moat and through the inner gates. Theon descended with Black Lorren and Maester Luwin to meet them in the yard. Pale red pennons trailed from the ends of a few lances, but many more carried battle-axes and great-swords and shields hacked half to splinters. "How many men did you lose?" Theon asked Red Helm as he dismounted.

"Twenty or thirty." The torchlight glittered off the chipped enamel of his visor. His helm and gorget were wrought in the shape of a man's face and shoulders, skinless and bloody, mouth open in a silent howl of anguish.

"Ser Rodrik had you five-to-one."

"Aye, but he thought us friends. A common mistake. When the old fool gave me his hand, I took half his arm instead. Then I let him see my face." The man put both hands to his helm and lifted it off his head, holding it in the crook of his arm.

"Reek," Theon said, disquieted. *How did a serving man get such fine armor?*

The man laughed. "The wretch is dead." He stepped closer. "The girl's fault. If she had not run so far, his horse would not have lamed, and we might have been able to flee. I gave him mine when I saw the riders from the ridge. I was done with her by then, and he liked to take his turn while they were still warm. I had to pull him off her and shove my clothes into his hands—calf-skin boots and velvet doublet, silver-chased swordbelt, even my sable cloak. Ride for the Dreadfort, I told him, bring all the help you can. Take my horse, he's swifter, and here, wear the ring my father gave me, so they'll know you came from me. He'd learned better than to question me. By the time they put that arrow through his back, I'd smeared myself with the girl's filth and dressed in his rags. They might have hanged me anyway, but it was the only chance I saw." He rubbed the back of his hand across his mouth. "And now, my sweet prince, there was a woman promised me, if I brought two hundred men. Well, I brought three times as many, and no green boys nor fieldhands neither, but my father's own garrison."

Theon had given his word. This was not the time to flinch. *Pay him his pound of flesh and deal with him later.* "Harrag," he said, "go to the kennels and bring Palla out for . . . ?"

"Ramsay." There was a smile on his plump lips, but none in those pale pale eyes. "Snow, my wife called me before she ate her fingers, but I say Bolton." His smile curdled. "So you'd offer me a kennel girl for my good service, is that the way of it?"

There was a tone in his voice Theon did not like, no more than he liked the insolent way the Dreadfort men were looking at him. "She was what was promised."

"She smells of dogshit. I've had enough of bad smells, as it happens. I think I'll have your bedwarmer instead. What do you call her? Kyra?"

"Are you mad?" Theon said angrily. "I'll have you—"

The Bastard's backhand caught him square, and his cheekbone shattered with a sickening crunch beneath the lobstered steel. The world vanished in a red roar of pain.

Sometime later, Theon found himself on the ground. He rolled onto his stomach and swallowed a mouthful of blood. *Close the gates!* he tried to shout, but it was too late. The Dreadfort men had cut down Red Rolfe and Kenned, and more were pouring through, a river of mail and sharp swords. There was a ringing in his ears, and horror all around him. Black Lorren had his sword out, but there were already four of them pressing in on him. He saw Ulf go down with a crossbow bolt through the belly as he ran for the Great Hall. Maester Luwin was trying to reach him when a knight on a warhorse planted a spear between his shoulders, then swung back to ride over him. Another man whipped a torch round and round his head and then lofted it toward the thatched roof of the stables. *"Save me the Freys,"* the Bastard was shouting as the flames roared upward, *"and burn the rest. Burn it, burn it all."*

The last thing Theon Greyjoy saw was Smiler, kicking free of the burning stables with his mane ablaze, screaming, rearing . . .

TYRION

He dreamed of a cracked stone ceiling and the smells of blood and shit and burnt flesh. The air was full of acrid smoke. Men were groaning and whimpering all around him, and from time to time a scream would pierce the air, thick with pain. When he tried to move, he found that he had fouled his own bedding. The smoke in the air made his eyes water. *Am I crying?* He must not let his father see. He was a Lannister of Casterly Rock. *A lion, I must be a lion, live a lion, die a lion.* He hurt so much, though. Too weak to groan, he lay in his own filth and shut his eyes. Nearby someone was cursing the gods in a heavy, monotonous voice. He listened to the blasphemies and wondered if he was dying. After a time the room faded.

He found himself outside the city, walking through a world without color. Ravens soared through a grey sky on wide black wings, while carrion crows rose from their feasts in furious clouds wherever he set his steps. White maggots burrowed through black corruption. The wolves were grey, and so were the silent sisters; together they stripped the flesh from the fallen. There were corpses strewn all over the tourney fields. The sun was a hot white penny, shining down upon the grey river as it rushed around the charred bones of sunken ships. From the pyres of the dead rose black columns of smoke and white-hot ashes. *My work*, thought Tyrion Lannister. *They died at my command.*

At first there was no sound in the world, but after a time he began to hear the voices of the dead, soft and terrible. They wept and moaned, they begged for an end to pain, they cried for help and wanted their mothers. Tyrion had never known his mother. He wanted Shae, but she was not there. He walked alone amidst grey shadows, trying to remember . . .

The silent sisters were stripping the dead men of their armor and clothes. All the bright dyes had leached out from the surcoats of the slain; they were garbed in shades of white and grey, and their blood was black and crusty. He watched their naked bodies lifted by arm and leg, to be carried swinging to the pyres to join their fellows. Metal and cloth were thrown in the back of a white wooden wagon, pulled by two tall black horses.

So many dead, so very many. Their corpses hung limply, their faces slack or·stiff or swollen with gas, unrecognizable, hardly human. The garments the sisters took from them were decorated with black hearts, grey lions, dead flowers, and pale ghostly stags. Their armor was all dented and gashed, the chainmail riven, broken, slashed. *Why did I kill them all?* He had known once, but somehow he had forgotten.

He would have asked one of the silent sisters, but when he tried to speak he found he had no mouth. Smooth seamless skin covered his teeth. The discovery terrified him. How could he live without a mouth? He began to run. The city was not far. He would be safe inside the city, away from all these dead. He did not belong with the dead. He had no mouth, but he was still a living man. *No, a lion, a lion, and alive.* But when he reached the city walls, the gates were shut against him.

It was dark when he woke again. At first he could see

nothing, but after a time the vague outlines of a bed appeared around him. The drapes were drawn, but he could see the shape of carved bedposts, and the droop of the velvet canopy over his head. Under him was the yielding softness of a featherbed, and the pillow beneath his head was goose down. *My own bed, I am in my own bed, in my own bedchamber.*

It was warm inside the drapes, under the great heap of furs and blankets that covered him. He was sweating. *Fever,* he thought groggily. He felt so weak, and the pain stabbed through him when he struggled to lift his hand. He gave up the effort. His head felt enormous, as big as the bed, too heavy to raise from the pillow. His body he could scarcely feel at all. *How did I come here?* He tried to remember. The battle came back in fits and flashes. The fight along the river, the knight who'd offered up his gauntlet, the bridge of ships . . .

Ser Mandon. He saw the dead empty eyes, the reaching hand, the green fire shining against the white enamel plate. Fear swept over him in a cold rush; beneath the sheets he could feel his bladder letting go. He would have cried out, if he'd had a mouth. *No, that was the dream,* he thought, his head pounding. *Help me, someone help me. Jaime, Shae, Mother, someone . . . Tysha . . .*

No one heard. No one came. Alone in the dark, he fell back into piss-scented sleep. He dreamed his sister was standing over his bed, with their lord father beside her, frowning. It had to be a dream, since Lord Tywin was a thousand leagues away, fighting Robb Stark in the west. Others came and went as well. Varys looked down on him and sighed, but Littlefinger made a quip. *Bloody treacherous bastard,* Tyrion thought venomously, *we sent you to Bitterbridge and you never came back.* Sometimes he could hear them talking to one another, but he did not understand the words. Their voices buzzed in his ears like wasps muffled in thick felt.

He wanted to ask if they'd won the battle. *We must have, else I'd be a head on a spike somewhere. If I live, we won.* He did not know what pleased him more: the

victory, or the fact he had been able to reason it out. His
wits were coming back to him, however slowly. That
was good. His wits were all he had.

The next time he woke, the draperies had been pulled
back, and Podrick Payne stood over him with a candle.
When he saw Tyrion open his eyes he ran off. *No, don't
go, help me, help,* he tried to call, but the best he could
do was a muffled moan. *I have no mouth.* He raised a
hand to his face, his every movement pained and fumbling. His fingers found stiff cloth where they should
have found flesh, lips, teeth. *Linen.* The lower half of
his face was bandaged tightly, a mask of hardened plaster with holes for breathing and feeding.

A short while later Pod reappeared. This time a
stranger was with him, a maester chained and robed.
"My lord, you must be still," the man murmured. "You
are grievous hurt. You will do yourself great injury. Are
you thirsty?"

He managed an awkward nod. The maester inserted a
curved copper funnel through the feeding hole over his
mouth and poured a slow trickle down his throat.
Tyrion swallowed, scarcely tasting. Too late he realized
the liquid was milk of the poppy. By the time the
maester removed the funnel from his mouth, he was
already spiraling back to sleep.

This time he dreamed he was at a feast, a victory feast
in some great hall. He had a high seat on the dais, and
men were lifting their goblets and hailing him as hero.
Marillion was there, the singer who'd journeyed with
them through the Mountains of the Moon. He played
his woodharp and sang of the Imp's daring deeds. Even
his father was smiling with approval. When the song
was over, Jaime rose from his place, commanded Tyrion
to kneel, and touched him first on one shoulder and
then on the other with his golden sword, and he rose up
a knight. Shae was waiting to embrace him. She took
him by the hand, laughing and teasing, calling him her
giant of Lannister.

He woke in darkness to a cold empty room. The draperies had been drawn again. Something felt wrong,

turned around, though he could not have said what. He was alone once more. Pushing back the blankets, he tried to sit, but the pain was too much and he soon subsided, breathing raggedly. His face was the least part of it. His right side was one huge ache, and a stab of pain went through his chest whenever he lifted his arm. *What's happened to me?* Even the battle seemed half a dream when he tried to think back on it. *I was hurt more badly than I knew. Ser Mandon . . .*

The memory frightened him, but Tyrion made himself hold it, turn it in his head, stare at it hard. *He tried to kill me, no mistake. That part was not a dream. He would have cut me in half if Pod had not . . . Pod, where's Pod?*

Gritting his teeth, he grabbed hold of the bed hangings and yanked. The drapes ripped free of the canopy overhead and tumbled down, half on the rushes and half on him. Even that small effort had dizzied him. The room whirled around him, all bare walls and dark shadows, with a single narrow window. He saw a chest he'd owned, an untidy pile of his clothing, his battered armor. *This is not my bedchamber*, he realized. *Not even the Tower of the Hand.* Someone had moved him. His shout of anger came out as a muffled moan. *They have moved me here to die*, he thought as he gave up the struggle and closed his eyes once more. The room was dank and cold, and he was burning.

He dreamed of a better place, a snug little cottage by the sunset sea. The walls were lopsided and cracked and the floor had been made of packed earth, but he had always been warm there, even when they let the fire go out. *She used to tease me about that*, he remembered. *I never thought to feed the fire, that had always been a servant's task.* "We have no servants," she would remind me, and I would say, "You have me, I'm your servant," and she would say, "A lazy servant. What do they do with lazy servants in Casterly Rock, my lord?" and he would tell her, "They kiss them." That would always make her giggle. "They do not neither. They beat them, I bet," she would say, but he would insist,

"No, they kiss them, just like this." He would show her how. "They kiss their fingers first, every one, and they kiss their wrists, yes, and inside their elbows. Then they kiss their funny ears, all our servants have funny ears. Stop laughing! And they kiss their cheeks and they kiss their noses with the little bump in them, there, so, like that, and they kiss their sweet brows and their hair and their lips, their . . . mmmm . . . mouths . . . so . . ."

They would kiss for hours, and spend whole days doing no more than lolling in bed, listening to the waves, and touching each other. Her body was a wonder to him, and she seemed to find delight in his. Sometimes she would sing to him. *I loved a maid as fair as summer, with sunlight in her hair.* "I love you, Tyrion," she would whisper before they went to sleep at night. "I love your lips. I love your voice, and the words you say to me, and how you treat me gentle. I love your face."

"*My* face?"

"Yes. Yes. I love your hands, and how you touch me. Your cock, I love your cock, I love how it feels when it's in me."

"It loves you too, my lady."

"I love to say your name. Tyrion Lannister. It goes with mine. Not the Lannister, t'other part. Tyrion and Tysha. Tysha and Tyrion. Tyrion. My lord Tyrion . . ."

Lies, he thought, *all feigned, all for gold, she was a whore, Jaime's whore, Jaime's gift, my lady of the lie.* Her face seemed to fade away, dissolving behind a veil of tears, but even after she was gone he could still hear the faint, far-off sound of her voice, calling his name. ". . . my lord, can you hear me? My lord? Tyrion? My lord? My lord?"

Through a haze of poppied sleep, he saw a soft pink face leaning over him. He was back in the dank room with the torn bed hangings, and the face was wrong, not hers, too round, with a brown fringe of beard. "Do you thirst, my lord? I have your milk, your good milk. You must not fight, no, don't try to move, you need your rest." He had the copper funnel in one damp pink hand and a flask in the other.

As the man leaned close, Tyrion's fingers slid underneath his chain of many metals, grabbed, pulled. The maester dropped the flask, spilling milk of the poppy all over the blanket. Tyrion twisted until he could feel the links digging into the flesh of the man's fat neck. *"No. More,"* he croaked, so hoarse he was not certain he had even spoken. But he must have, for the maester choked out a reply. "Unhand, please, my lord . . . need your milk, the pain . . . the chain, don't, unhand, no . . ."

The pink face was beginning to purple when Tyrion let go. The maester reeled back, sucking in air. His reddened throat showed deep white gouges where the links had pressed. His eyes were white too. Tyrion raised a hand to his face and made a ripping motion over the hardened mask. And again. And again.

"You . . . you want the bandages off, is that it?" the maester said at last. "But I'm not to . . . that would be . . . be most unwise, my lord. You are not yet healed, the queen would . . ."

The mention of his sister made Tyrion growl. *Are you one of hers, then?* He pointed a finger at the maester, then coiled his hand into a fist. Crushing, choking, a promise, unless the fool did as he was bid.

Thankfully, he understood. "I . . . I will do as my lord commands, to be sure, but . . . this is unwise, your wounds . . ."

"Do. It." Louder that time.

Bowing, the man left the room, only to return a few moments later, bearing a long knife with a slender sawtooth blade, a basin of water, a pile of soft cloths, and several flasks. By then Tyrion had managed to squirm backward a few inches, so he was half sitting against his pillow. The maester bade him be very still as he slid the tip of the knife in under his chin, beneath the mask. *A slip of the hand here, and Cersei will be free of me,* he thought. He could feel the blade sawing through the stiffened linen, only inches above his throat.

Fortunately this soft pink man was not one of his

sister's braver creatures. After a moment he felt cool air on his cheeks. There was pain as well, but he did his best to ignore that. The maester discarded the bandages, still crusty with potion. "Be still now, I must wash out the wound." His touch was gentle, the water warm and soothing. *The wound*, Tyrion thought, remembering a sudden flash of bright silver that seemed to pass just below his eyes. "This is like to sting some," the maester warned as he wet a cloth with wine that smelled of crushed herbs. It did more than sting. It traced a line of fire all the way across Tyrion's face, and twisted a burning poker up his nose. His fingers clawed the bedclothes and he sucked in his breath, but somehow he managed not to scream. The maester was clucking like an old hen. "It would have been wiser to leave the mask in place until the flesh had knit, my lord. Still, it looks clean, good, good. When we found you down in that cellar among the dead and dying, your wounds were filthy. One of your ribs was broken, doubtless you can feel it, the blow of some mace perhaps, or a fall, it's hard to say. And you took an arrow in the arm, there where it joins the shoulder. It showed signs of mortification, and for a time I feared you might lose the limb, but we treated it with boiling wine and maggots, and now it seems to be healing clean . . ."

"Name," Tyrion breathed up at him. *"Name."*

The maester blinked. "Why, you are Tyrion Lannister, my lord. Brother to the queen. Do you remember the battle? Sometimes with head wounds—"

"Your name." His throat was raw, and his tongue had forgotten how to shape the words.

"I am Maester Ballabar."

"Ballabar," Tyrion repeated. "Bring me. Looking glass."

"My lord," the maester said, "I would not counsel . . . that might be, ah, unwise, as it were . . . your wound . . ."

"Bring it," he had to say. His mouth was stiff and sore, as if a punch had split his lip. "And drink. *Wine.* No poppy."

The maester rose flush-faced and hurried off. He came back with a flagon of pale amber wine and a small silvered looking glass in an ornate golden frame. Sitting on the edge of the bed, he poured half a cup of wine and held it to Tyrion's swollen lips. The trickle went down cool, though he could hardly taste it. *"More,"* he said when the cup was empty. Maester Ballabar poured again. By the end of the second cup, Tyrion Lannister felt strong enough to face his face.

He turned over the glass, and did not know whether he ought to laugh or cry. The gash was long and crooked, starting a hair under his left eye and ending on the right side of his jaw. Three-quarters of his nose was gone, and a chunk of his lip. Someone had sewn the torn flesh together with catgut, and their clumsy stitches were still in place across the seam of raw, red, half-healed flesh. *"Pretty,"* he croaked, flinging the glass aside.

He remembered now. The bridge of boats, Ser Mandon Moore, a hand, a sword coming at his face. *If I had not pulled back, that cut would have taken off the top of my head.* Jaime had always said that Ser Mandon was the most dangerous of the Kingsguard, because his dead empty eyes gave no hint to his intentions. *I should never have trusted any of them.* He'd known that Ser Meryn and Ser Boros were his sister's, and Ser Osmund later, but he had let himself believe that the others were not wholly lost to honor. *Cersei must have paid him to see that I never came back from the battle. Why else? I never did Ser Mandon any harm that I know of.* Tyrion touched his face, plucking at the proud flesh with blunt thick fingers. *Another gift from my sweet sister.*

The maester stood beside the bed like a goose about to take flight. "My lord, there, there will most like be a scar . . ."

"Most like?" His snort of laughter turned into a wince of pain. There would be a scar, to be sure. Nor was it likely that his nose would be growing back anytime soon. It was not as if his face had ever been fit to look at. "Teach me, not to, play with, axes." His grin

felt tight. "Where, are we? What, what place?" It hurt to talk, but Tyrion had been too long in silence.

"Ah, you are in Maegor's Holdfast, my lord. A chamber over the Queen's Ballroom. Her Grace wanted you kept close, so she might watch over you herself."

I'll wager she did. "Return me," Tyrion commanded. "Own bed. Own chambers." *Where I will have my own men about me, and my own maester too, if I find one I can trust.*

"Your own . . . my lord, that would not be possible. The King's Hand has taken up residence in your former chambers."

"I. *Am.* King's Hand." He was growing exhausted by the effort of speaking, and confused by what he was hearing.

Maester Ballabar looked distressed. "No, my lord, I . . . you were wounded, near death. Your lord father has taken up those duties now. Lord Tywin, he . . ."

"Here?"

"Since the night of the battle. Lord Tywin saved us all. The smallfolk say it was King Renly's ghost, but wiser men know better. It was your father and Lord Tyrell, with the Knight of Flowers and Lord Littlefinger. They rode through the ashes and took the usurper Stannis in the rear. It was a great victory, and now Lord Tywin has settled into the Tower of the Hand to help His Grace set the realm to rights, gods be praised."

"Gods be praised," Tyrion repeated hollowly. His bloody father *and* bloody Littlefinger and *Renly's ghost?* "I want . . ." *Who do I want?* He could not tell pink Ballabar to fetch him Shae. Who could he send for, who could he trust? Varys? Bronn? Ser Jacelyn? ". . . my squire," he finished. "Pod. Payne." *It was Pod on the bridge of boats, the lad saved my life.*

"The boy? The odd boy?"

"Odd boy. Podrick. Payne. You go. Send *him.*"

"As you will, my lord." Maester Ballabar bobbed his head and hurried out. Tyrion could feel the strength seeping out of him as he waited. He wondered how long he had been here, asleep. *Cersei would have me sleep forever, but I won't be so obliging.*

Podrick Payne entered the bedchamber timid as a mouse. "My lord?" He crept close to the bed. *How can a boy so bold in battle be so frightened in a sickroom?* Tyrion wondered. "I meant to stay by you, but the maester sent me away."

"Send *him* away. Hear me. Talk's hard. Need dreamwine. *Dreamwine,* not milk of the poppy. Go to Frenken. *Frenken,* not Ballabar. Watch him make it. Bring it here." Pod stole a glance at Tyrion's face, and just as quickly averted his eyes. *Well, I cannot blame him for that.* "I want," Tyrion went on, "mine own. Guard. Bronn. Where's Bronn?"

"They made him a knight."

Even frowning hurt. "Find him. Bring him."

"As you say. My lord. Bronn."

Tyrion seized the lad's wrist. "Ser Mandon?"

The boy flinched. "I n-never meant to k-k-k-k-"

"*Dead?* You're, certain? *Dead?*"

He shuffled his feet, sheepish. "Drowned."

"Good. Say nothing. Of him. Of me. Any of it. *Nothing.*"

By the time his squire left, the last of Tyrion's strength was gone as well. He lay back and closed his eyes. Perhaps he would dream of Tysha again. *I wonder how she'd like my face now,* he thought bitterly.

JON

When Qhorin Halfhand told him to find some brush for a fire, Jon knew their end was near.

It will be good to feel warm again, if only for a little while, he told himself while he hacked bare branches from the trunk of a dead tree. Ghost sat on his haunches watching, silent as ever. *Will he howl for me when I'm dead, as Bran's wolf howled when he fell?* Jon wondered. *Will Shaggydog howl, far off in Winterfell, and Grey Wind and Nymeria, wherever they might be?*

The moon was rising behind one mountain and the sun sinking behind another as Jon struck sparks from flint and dagger, until finally a wisp of smoke appeared. Qhorin came and stood over him as the first flame rose up flickering from the shavings of bark and dead dry pine needles. "As shy as a maid on her wedding night," the big ranger said in a soft voice, "and near as fair. Sometimes a man forgets how pretty a fire can be."

He was not a man you'd expect to speak of maids and wedding nights. So far as Jon knew, Qhorin had spent his whole life in the Watch. *Did he ever love a maid or have a wedding?* He could not ask. Instead he fanned the fire. When the blaze was all acrackle, he peeled off his stiff gloves to warm his hands, and sighed, wondering if ever a kiss had felt as good. The warmth spread through his fingers like melting butter.

The Halfhand eased himself to the ground and sat cross-legged by the fire, the flickering light playing across the hard planes of his face. Only the two of them remained of the five rangers who had fled the Skirling Pass, back into the blue-grey wilderness of the Frostfangs.

At first Jon had nursed the hope that Squire Dalbridge would keep the wildlings bottled up in the pass. But when they'd heard the call of a far-off horn every man of them knew the squire had fallen. Later they spied the eagle soaring through the dusk on great blue-grey wings and Stonesnake unslung his bow, but the bird flew out of range before he could so much as string it. Ebben spat and muttered darkly of wargs and skinchangers.

They glimpsed the eagle twice more the day after, and heard the hunting horn behind them echoing against the mountains. Each time it seemed a little louder, a little closer. When night fell, the Halfhand told Ebben to take the squire's garron as well as his own, and ride east for Mormont with all haste, back the way they had come. The rest of them would draw off the pursuit. "Send Jon," Ebben had urged. "He can ride as fast as me."

"Jon has a different part to play."

"He is half a boy still."

"No," said Qhorin, "he is a man of the Night's Watch."

When the moon rose, Ebben parted from them. Stonesnake went east with him a short way, then doubled back to obscure their tracks, and the three who remained set off toward the southwest.

After that the days and nights blurred one into the other. They slept in their saddles and stopped only long enough to feed and water the garrons, then mounted up again. Over bare rock they rode, through gloomy pine forests and drifts of old snow, over icy ridges and across shallow rivers that had no names. Sometimes Qhorin or Stonesnake would loop back to sweep away their tracks, but it was a futile gesture. They were watched. At every dawn and every dusk they saw the eagle soaring between the peaks, no more than a speck in the vastness of the sky.

They were scaling a low ridge between two snow-capped peaks when a shadowcat came snarling from its lair, not ten yards away. The beast was gaunt and half-starved, but the sight of it sent Stonesnake's mare into a panic; she reared and ran, and before the ranger could get her back under control she had stumbled on the steep slope and broken a leg.

Ghost ate well that day, and Qhorin insisted that the rangers mix some of the garron's blood with their oats, to give them strength. The taste of that foul porridge almost choked Jon, but he forced it down. They each cut a dozen strips of raw stringy meat from the carcass to chew on as they rode, and left the rest for the shadowcats.

There was no question of riding double. Stonesnake offered to lay in wait for the pursuit and surprise them when they came. Perhaps he could take a few of them with him down to hell. Qhorin refused. "If any man in the Night's Watch can make it through the Frostfangs alone and afoot, it is you, brother. You can go over mountains that a horse must go around. Make for the Fist. Tell Mormont what Jon saw, and how. Tell him that the old powers are waking, that he faces giants and wargs and worse. Tell him that the trees have eyes again."

He has no chance, Jon thought when he watched Stonesnake vanish over a snow-covered ridge, a tiny black bug crawling across a rippling expanse of white.

After that, every night seemed colder than the night before, and more lonely. Ghost was not always with them, but he was never far either. Even when they were apart, Jon sensed his nearness. He was glad for that. The Halfhand was not the most companionable of men. Qhorin's long grey braid swung slowly with the motion of his horse. Often they would ride for hours without a word spoken, the only sounds the soft scrape of horse-shoes on stone and the keening of the wind, which blew endlessly through the heights. When he slept, he did not dream; not of wolves, nor his brothers, nor anything. *Even dreams cannot live up here,* he told himself.

"Is your sword sharp, Jon Snow?" asked Qhorin Half-hand across the flickering fire.

"My sword is Valyrian steel. The Old Bear gave it to me."

"Do you remember the words of your vow?"

"Yes." They were not words a man was like to forget. Once said, they could never be unsaid. They changed your life forever.

"Say them again with me, Jon Snow."

"If you like." Their voices blended as one beneath the rising moon, while Ghost listened and the mountains themselves bore witness. "Night gathers, and now my watch begins. It shall not end until my death. I shall take no wife, hold no lands, father no children. I shall wear no crowns and win no glory. I shall live and die at my post. I am the sword in the darkness. I am the watcher on the walls. I am the fire that burns against the cold, the light that brings the dawn, the horn that wakes the sleepers, the shield that guards the realms of men. I pledge my life and honor to the Night's Watch, for this night and all the nights to come."

When they were done, there was no sound but the faint crackle of the flames and a distant sigh of wind. Jon opened and closed his burnt fingers, holding tight to the words in his mind, praying that his father's gods would give him the strength to die bravely when his hour came. It would not be long now. The garrons were near the end of their strength. Qhorin's mount would not last another day, Jon suspected.

The flames were burning low by then, the warmth

fading. "The fire will soon go out," Qhorin said, "but if the Wall should ever fall, all the fires will go out."

There was nothing Jon could say to that. He nodded.

"We may escape them yet," the ranger said. "Or not."

"I'm not afraid to die." It was only half a lie.

"It may not be so easy as that, Jon."

He did not understand. "What do you mean?"

"If we are taken, you must yield."

"Yield?" He blinked in disbelief. The wildlings did not make captives of the men they called the crows. They killed them, except for . . . "They only spare oathbreakers. Those who join them, like Mance Rayder."

"And you."

"No." He shook his head. "Never. I won't."

"You will. I command it of you."

"*Command* it? But . . ."

"Our honor means no more than our lives, so long as the realm is safe. Are you a man of the Night's Watch?"

"Yes, but—"

"There is no *but*, Jon Snow. You are, or you are not."

Jon sat up straight. "I am."

"Then hear me. If we are taken, you will go over to them, as the wildling girl you captured once urged you. They may demand that you cut your cloak to ribbons, that you swear them an oath on your father's grave, that you curse your brothers and your Lord Commander. You must not balk, whatever is asked of you. Do as they bid you . . . but in your heart, remember who and what you are. Ride with them, eat with them, fight with them, for as long as it takes. And *watch*."

"For what?" Jon asked.

"Would that I knew," said Qhorin. "Your wolf saw their diggings in the valley of the Milkwater. What did they seek, in such a bleak and distant place? Did they find it? That is what you must learn, before you return to Lord Mormont and your brothers. That is the duty I lay on you, Jon Snow."

"I'll do as you say," Jon said reluctantly, "but . . .

you will tell them, won't you? The Old Bear, at least? You'll tell him that I never broke my oath."

Qhorin Halfhand gazed at him across the fire, his eyes lost in pools of shadow. "When I see him next. I swear it." He gestured at the fire. "More wood. I want it bright and hot."

Jon went to cut more branches, snapping each one in two before tossing it into the flames. The tree had been dead a long time, but it seemed to live again in the fire, as fiery dancers woke within each stick of wood to whirl and spin in their glowing gowns of yellow, red, and orange.

"Enough," Qhorin said abruptly. "Now we ride."

"Ride?" It was dark beyond the fire, and the night was cold. "Ride where?"

"Back." Qhorin mounted his weary garron one more time. "The fire will draw them past, I hope. Come, brother."

Jon pulled on his gloves again and raised his hood. Even the horses seemed reluctant to leave the fire. The sun was long gone, and only the cold silver shine of the half-moon remained to light their way over the treacherous ground that lay behind them. He did not know what Qhorin had in mind, but perhaps it was a chance. He hoped so. *I do not want to play the oathbreaker, even for good reason.*

They went cautiously, moving as silent as man and horse could move, retracing their steps until they reached the mouth of a narrow defile where an icy little stream emerged from between two mountains. Jon remembered the place. They had watered the horses here before the sun went down.

"The water's icing up," Qhorin observed as he turned aside, "else we'd ride in the streambed. But if we break the ice, they are like to see. Keep close to the cliffs. There's a crook a half mile on that will hide us." He rode into the defile. Jon gave one last wistful look to their distant fire, and followed.

The farther in they went, the closer the cliffs pressed

to either side. They followed the moonlit ribbon of stream back toward its source. Icicles bearded its stony banks, but Jon could still hear the sound of rushing water beneath the thin hard crust.

A great jumble of fallen rock blocked their way partway up, where a section of the cliff face had fallen, but the surefooted little garrons were able to pick their way through. Beyond, the walls pinched in sharply, and the stream led them to the foot of a tall twisting waterfall. The air was full of mist, like the breath of some vast cold beast. The tumbling waters shone silver in the moonlight. Jon looked about in dismay. *There is no way out.* He and Qhorin might be able to climb the cliffs, but not with the horses. He did not think they would last long afoot.

"Quickly now," the Halfhand commanded. The big man on the small horse rode over the ice-slick stones, right into the curtain of water, and vanished. When he did not reappear, Jon put his heels into his horse and went after. His garron did his best to shy away. The falling water slapped at them with frozen fists, and the shock of the cold seemed to stop Jon's breath.

Then he was through; drenched and shivering, but through.

The cleft in the rock was barely large enough for man and horse to pass, but beyond, the walls opened up and the floor turned to soft sand. Jon could feel the spray freezing in his beard. Ghost burst through the waterfall in an angry rush, shook droplets from his fur, sniffed at the darkness suspiciously, then lifted a leg against one rocky wall. Qhorin had already dismounted. Jon did the same. "You knew this place was here."

"When I was no older than you, I heard a brother tell how he followed a shadowcat through these falls." He unsaddled his horse, removed her bit and bridle, and ran his fingers through her shaggy mane. "There is a way through the heart of the mountain. Come dawn, if they have not found us, we will press on. The first watch is mine, brother." Qhorin seated himself on the sand, his back to a wall, no more than a vague black shadow in the gloom of the cave. Over the rush of falling waters, Jon heard a soft sound of steel on leather that could only mean that the Halfhand had drawn his sword.

He took off his wet cloak, but it was too cold and damp here to strip down any further. Ghost stretched out beside him and licked his glove before curling up to sleep. Jon was grateful for his warmth. He wondered if the fire was still burning outside, or if it had gone out by now. *If the Wall should ever fall, all the fires will go out.* The moon shone through the curtain of falling water to lay a shimmering pale stripe across the sand, but after a time that too faded and went dark.

Sleep came at last, and with it nightmares. He dreamed of burning castles and dead men rising unquiet from their graves. It was still dark when Qhorin woke him. While the Halfhand slept, Jon sat with his back to the cave wall, listening to the water and waiting for the dawn.

At break of day, they each chewed a half-frozen strip of horsemeat, then saddled their garrons once again, and fastened their black cloaks around their shoulders. During his watch the Halfhand had made a half-dozen torches, soaking bundles of dry moss with the oil he carried in his saddlebag. He lit the first one now and led the way down into the dark, holding the pale flame up before him. Jon followed with the horses. The stony path twisted and turned, first down, then up, then down more steeply. In spots it grew so narrow it was hard to convince the garrons they could squeeze through. *By the time we come out we will have lost them,* he told himself as they went. *Not even an eagle can see through solid stone. We will have lost them, and we will ride hard for the Fist, and tell the Old Bear all we know.*

But when they emerged back into the light long hours later, the eagle was waiting for them, perched on a dead tree a hundred feet up the slope. Ghost went bounding up the rocks after it, but the bird flapped its wings and took to the air.

Qhorin's mouth tightened as he followed its flight with his eyes. "Here is as good a place as any to make a stand," he declared. "The mouth of the cave shelters us from above, and they cannot get behind us without passing through the mountain. Is your sword sharp, Jon Snow?"

"Yes," he said.

"We'll feed the horses. They've served us bravely, poor beasts."

Jon gave his garron the last of the oats and stroked his shaggy mane while Ghost prowled restlessly amongst the rocks. He pulled his gloves on tighter and flexed his burnt fingers. *I am the shield that guards the realms of men.*

A hunting horn echoed through the mountains, and a moment later Jon heard the baying of hounds. "They will be with us soon," announced Qhorin. "Keep your wolf in hand."

"Ghost, to me," Jon called. The direwolf returned reluctantly to his side, tail held stiffly behind him.

The wildlings came boiling over a ridge not half a mile away. Their hounds ran before them, snarling greybrown beasts with more than a little wolf in their blood. Ghost bared his teeth, his fur bristling. "Easy," Jon murmured. "Stay." Overhead he heard a rustle of wings. The eagle landed on an outcrop of rock and screamed in triumph.

The hunters approached warily, perhaps fearing arrows. Jon counted fourteen, with eight dogs. Their large round shields were made of skins stretched over woven wicker and painted with skulls. About half of them hid their faces behind crude helms of wood and boiled leather. On either wing, archers notched shafts to the strings of small wood-and-horn bows, but did not loose. The rest seemed to be armed with spears and mauls. One had a chipped stone axe. They wore only what bits of armor they had looted from dead rangers or stolen during raids. Wildlings did not mine or smelt, and there were few smiths and fewer forges north of the Wall.

Qhorin drew his longsword. The tale of how he had taught himself to fight with his left hand after losing half of his right was part of his legend; it was said that he handled a blade better now than he ever had before. Jon stood shoulder to shoulder with the big ranger and pulled Longclaw from its sheath. Despite the chill in the air, sweat stung his eyes.

Ten yards below the cave mouth the hunters halted. Their leader came on alone, riding a beast that seemed more goat than horse, from the surefooted way it climbed the uneven slope. As man and mount grew nearer Jon could hear them clattering; both were armored in bones. Cow bones, sheep bones, the bones of goats and aurochs and elk, the great bones of the hairy mammoths . . . and human bones as well.

"Rattleshirt," Qhorin called down, icy-polite.

"To crows I be the Lord o' Bones." The rider's helm was made from the broken skull of a giant, and all up and down his arms bearclaws had been sewn to his boiled leather.

Qhorin snorted. "I see no lord. Only a dog dressed in chickenbones, who rattles when he rides."

The wildling hissed in anger, and his mount reared. He *did* rattle, Jon could hear it; the bones were strung together loosely, so they clacked and clattered when he moved. "It's *your* bones I'll be rattling soon, Halfhand. I'll boil the flesh off you and make a byrnie from your ribs. I'll carve your teeth to cast me runes, and eat me oaten porridge from your skull."

"If you want my bones, come get them."

That, Rattleshirt seemed reluctant to do. His numbers meant little in the close confines of the rocks where the black brothers had taken their stand; to winkle them out of the cave the wildlings would need to come up two at a time. But another of his company edged a horse up beside him, one of the fighting women called *spearwives*. "We are four-and-ten to two, crows, and eight dogs to your wolf," she called. "Fight or run, you are ours."

"Show them," commanded Rattleshirt.

The woman reached into a bloodstained sack and drew out a trophy. Ebben had been bald as an egg, so she dangled the head by an ear. "He died brave," she said.

"But he died," said Rattleshirt, "same like you." He freed his battle-axe, brandishing it above his head. Good steel it was, with a wicked gleam to both blades; Ebben was never a man to neglect his weapons. The other wildlings crowded forward beside him, yelling taunts. A few chose Jon for their mockery. "Is that your wolf, boy?" a skinny youth called, unlimbering a stone flail. "He'll be my cloak before the sun is down." On the other side of the line, another spearwife opened her ragged furs to show Jon a heavy white breast. "Does the baby want his momma? Come, have a suck o' this, boy." The dogs were barking too.

"They would shame us into folly." Qhorin gave Jon a long look. "Remember your orders."

"Belike we need to flush the crows," Rattleshirt bellowed over the clamor. "Feather them!"

"No!" The word burst from Jon's lips before the bowmen could loose. He took two quick steps forward. "We yield!"

"They warned me bastard blood was craven," he heard Qhorin Halfhand say coldly behind him. "I see it is so. Run to your new masters, coward."

Face reddening, Jon descended the slope to where Rattleshirt sat his horse. The wildling stared at him through the eyeholes of his helm, and said, "The free folk have no need of cravens."

"He is no craven." One of the archers pulled off her sewn sheepskin helm and shook out a head of shaggy red hair. "This is the Bastard o' Winterfell, who spared me. Let him live."

Jon met Ygritte's eyes, and had no words.

"Let him die," insisted the Lord of Bones. "The black crow is a tricksy bird. I trust him not."

On a rock above them, the eagle flapped its wings and split the air with a scream of fury.

"The bird hates you, Jon Snow," said Ygritte. "And well he might. He was a man, before you killed him."

"I did not know," said Jon truthfully, trying to remember the face of the man he had slain in the pass. "You told me Mance would take me."

"And he will," Ygritte said.

"Mance is not here," said Rattleshirt. "Ragwyle, gut him."

The big spearwife narrowed her eyes and said, "If the crow would join the free folk, let him show us his prowess and prove the truth of him."

"I'll do whatever you ask." The words came hard, but Jon said them.

Rattleshirt's bone armor clattered loudly as he laughed. "Then kill the Halfhand, bastard."

"As if he could," said Qhorin. "*Turn, Snow, and die.*"

And then Qhorin's sword was coming at him and somehow Longclaw leapt upward to block. The force of impact almost knocked the bastard blade from Jon's hand, and sent him staggering backward. *You must not balk, whatever is asked of you.* He shifted to a two-hand grip, quick enough to deliver a stroke of his own, but the big ranger brushed it aside with contemptuous ease. Back and forth they went, black cloaks swirling, the youth's quickness against the savage strength of Qhorin's left-hand cuts. The Halfhand's longsword seemed to be everywhere at once, raining down from one side and then the other, driving him where he would, keeping him off balance. Already he could feel his arms growing numb.

Even when Ghost's teeth closed savagely around the ranger's calf, somehow Qhorin kept his feet. But in that instant, as he twisted, the opening was there. Jon planted and pivoted. The ranger was leaning away, and for an instant it seemed that Jon's slash had not touched him. Then a string of red tears appeared across the big man's throat, bright as a ruby necklace, and the blood gushed out of him, and Qhorin Halfhand fell.

Ghost's muzzle was dripping red, but only the point of the bastard blade was stained, the last half inch. Jon pulled the direwolf away and knelt with one arm around him. The light was already fading in Qhorin's eyes. ". . . sharp," he said, lifting his maimed fingers. Then his hand fell, and he was gone.

He knew, he thought numbly. *He knew what they would ask of me.* He thought of Samwell Tarly then, of Grenn and Dolorous Edd, of Pyp and Toad back at Castle Black. Had he lost them all, as he had lost Bran and Rickon and Robb? Who was he now? What was he?

"Get him up." Rough hands dragged him to his feet. Jon did not resist. "Do you have a name?"

Ygritte answered for him. "His name is Jon Snow. He is Eddard Stark's blood, of Winterfell."

Ragwyle laughed. "Who would have thought it? Qhorin Halfhand slain by some lordling's byblow."

"Gut him." That was Rattleshirt, still ahorse. The eagle flew to him and perched atop his bony helm, screeching.

"He yielded," Ygritte reminded them.

"Aye, and slew his brother," said a short homely man in a rust-eaten iron halfhelm.

Rattleshirt rode closer, bones clattering. "The wolf did his work for him. It were foully done. The Halfhand's death was mine."

"We all saw how eager you were to take it," mocked Ragwyle.

"He is a warg," said the Lord of Bones, "and a crow. I like him not."

"A warg he may be," Ygritte said, "but that has never frightened us." Others shouted agreement. Behind the eyeholes of his yellowed skull Rattleshirt's stare was malignant, but he yielded grudgingly. *These are a free folk indeed,* thought Jon.

They burned Qhorin Halfhand where he'd fallen, on a pyre made of pine needles, brush, and broken branches. Some of the wood was still green, and it burned slow and smoky, sending a black plume up into the bright hard blue of the sky. Afterward Rattleshirt claimed some charred bones, while the others threw dice for the ranger's gear. Ygritte won his cloak.

"Will we return by the Skirling Pass?" Jon asked her. He did not know if he could face those heights again, or if his garron could survive a second crossing.

"No," she said. "There's nothing behind us." The look she gave him was sad. "By now Mance is well down the Milkwater, marching on your Wall."

BRAN

The ashes fell like a soft grey snow.

He padded over dry needles and brown leaves, to the edge of the wood where the pines grew thin. Beyond the open fields he could see the great piles of man-rock stark against the swirling flames. The wind blew hot and rich with the smell of blood and burnt meat, so strong he began to slaver.

Yet as one smell drew them onward, others warned them back. He sniffed at the drifting smoke. *Men, many men, many horses, and fire, fire, fire.* No smell was more dangerous, not even the hard cold smell of iron, the stuff of man-claws and hardskin. The smoke and ash clouded his eyes, and in the sky he saw a great winged snake whose roar was a river of flame. He bared his teeth, but then the snake was gone. Behind the cliffs tall fires were eating up the stars.

All through the night the fires crackled, and once there was a great roar and a crash that made the earth jump under his feet. Dogs barked and whined and horses screamed in terror. Howls shuddered through the night; the howls of the man-pack, wails of fear and wild shouts, laughter and screams. No beast was as noisy as man. He pricked up his ears and listened, and his brother growled at every sound. They prowled under the trees as a piney wind blew ashes and embers through the sky. In time the flames began to dwindle, and then they were gone. The sun rose grey and smoky that morning.

Only then did he leave the trees, stalking slow across the fields. His brother ran with him, drawn to the smell of blood and death. They padded silent through the dens the men had built of wood and grass and mud. Many and more were burned and many and more were collapsed; others stood as they had before. Yet nowhere did they see or scent a living man. Crows blanketed the bodies and leapt into the air screeching when his brother and he came near. The wild dogs slunk away before them.

Beneath the great grey cliffs a horse was dying noisily, struggling to rise on a broken leg and screaming when he fell. His brother circled round him, then tore out his throat while the horse kicked feebly and rolled his eyes. When he approached the carcass his brother snapped at him and laid back his ears, and he cuffed him with a forepaw and bit his leg. They fought amidst the grass and dirt and falling ashes beside the dead horse, until his brother rolled on his back in submission, tail tucked low. One more bite at his upturned throat; then he fed, and let his brother feed, and licked the blood off his black fur.

The dark place was pulling at him by then, the house of whispers where all men were blind. He could feel its cold fingers on him. The stony smell of it was a whisper up the nose. He struggled against the pull. He did not like the darkness. He was wolf. He was hunter and stalker and slayer, and he belonged with his brothers and sisters in the deep woods, running free beneath a starry sky. He sat on his haunches, raised his head, and howled. *I will not go*, he cried. *I am wolf, I will not go.* Yet even so the darkness thickened, until it covered his eyes and filled his nose and stopped his ears, so he could not see or smell or hear or run, and the grey cliffs were gone and the dead horse was gone and his brother was gone and all was black and still and black and cold and black and dead and black . . .

"Bran," a voice was whispering softly. "Bran, come back. Come back now, Bran. Bran . . ."

He closed his third eye and opened the other two, the old two, the blind two. In the dark place all men were blind. But someone was holding him. He could feel arms around him, the warmth of a body snuggled close. He could hear Hodor singing "Hodor, hodor, hodor," quietly to himself.

"Bran?" It was Meera's voice. "You were thrashing, making terrible noises. What did you see?"

"Winterfell." His tongue felt strange and thick in his mouth. *One day when I come back I won't know how to talk anymore.* "It was Winterfell. It was all on fire. There were horse smells, and steel, and blood. They killed everyone, Meera."

He felt her hand on his face, stroking back his hair. "You're all sweaty," she said. "Do you need a drink?"

"A drink," he agreed. She held a skin to his lips, and Bran swallowed so fast the water ran out of the corner of his mouth. He was always weak and thirsty when he came back. And hungry too. He remembered the dying horse, the taste of blood in his mouth, the smell of burnt flesh in the morning air. "How long?"

"Three days," said Jojen. The boy had come up softfoot, or perhaps he had been there all along; in this blind black world, Bran could not have said. "We were afraid for you."

"I was with Summer," Bran said.

"Too long. You'll starve yourself. Meera dribbled a little water down your throat, and we smeared honey on your mouth, but it is not enough."

"I ate," said Bran. "We ran down an elk and had to drive off a treecat that tried to steal him." The cat had been tan-and-brown, only half the size of the direwolves, but fierce. He remembered the musky smell of him, and the way he had snarled down at them from the limb of the oak.

"The wolf ate," Jojen said. "Not you. Take care, Bran. Remember who you are."

He remembered who he was all too well; Bran the boy, Bran the broken. *Better Bran the beastling.* Was it any wonder he would sooner dream his Summer dreams, his wolf dreams? Here in the chill damp darkness of the tomb his third eye had finally opened. He could reach Summer whenever he wanted, and once he had even touched Ghost and talked to Jon. Though maybe he had only dreamed that. He could not understand why Jojen was always trying to pull him back now. Bran used the strength of his arms to squirm to a sitting position. "I have to tell Osha what I saw. Is she here? Where did she go?"

The wildling woman herself gave answer. "Nowhere, m'lord. I've had my fill o' blundering in the black." He heard the scrape of a heel on stone, turned his head toward the sound, but saw nothing. He thought he could smell her, but he wasn't sure. All of them stank alike, and he did not have Summer's nose to tell one from the other. "Last night I pissed on a king's foot," Osha went on. "Might be it was morning, who can say? I was sleeping, but now I'm not." They all slept a lot, not only Bran. There was nothing else to do. Sleep and eat and sleep again, and sometimes talk a little . . . but not too much, and only in whispers, just to be safe. Osha might have liked it better if they had never talked at all, but there was no way to quiet Rickon, or to stop Hodor from muttering, "Hodor, hodor, hodor," endlessly to himself.

"Osha," Bran said, "I saw Winterfell burning." Off to his left, he could hear the soft sound of Rickon's breathing.

"A dream," said Osha.

"A wolf dream," said Bran. "I *smelled* it too. Nothing smells like fire, or blood."

"Whose blood?"

"Men, horses, dogs, everyone. We have to go *see*."

"This scrawny skin of mine's the only one I got," said Osha. "That squid prince catches hold o' me, they'll strip it off my back with a whip."

Meera's hand found Bran's in the darkness and gave his fingers a squeeze. "I'll go if you're afraid."

Bran heard fingers fumbling at leather, followed by the sound of steel on flint. Then again. A spark flew, caught. Osha blew softly. A long pale flame awoke, stretching upward like a girl on her toes. Osha's face floated above it. She touched the flame with the head of a torch. Bran had to squint as the pitch began to burn, filling the world with orange glare. The light woke Rickon, who sat up yawning.

When the shadows moved, it looked for an instant as if the dead were rising as well. Lyanna and Brandon, Lord Rickard Stark their father, Lord Edwyle his father, Lord Willam and his brother Artos the Implacable, Lord Donnor and Lord Beron and Lord Rodwell, one-eyed Lord Jonnel, Lord Barth and Lord Brandon and Lord Cregan who had fought the Dragonknight. On their stone chairs they sat with stone wolves at their feet. This was where they came when the warmth had seeped out of their bodies; this was the dark hall of the dead, where the living feared to tread.

And in the mouth of the empty tomb that waited for Lord Eddard Stark, beneath his stately granite likeness, the six fugitives huddled round their little cache of bread and water and dried meat. "Little enough left," Osha muttered as she blinked down on their stores. "I'd need to go up soon to steal food in any case, or we'd be down to eating Hodor."

"Hodor," Hodor said, grinning at her.

"Is it day or night up there?" Osha wondered. "I've lost all count o' such."

"Day," Bran told her, "but it's dark from all the smoke."

"M'lord is certain?"

Never moving his broken body, he reached out all the same, and for an instant he was seeing double. There stood Osha holding the torch, and Meera and Jojen and

Hodor, and the double row of tall granite pillars and long dead lords behind them stretching away into darkness . . . but there was Winterfell as well, grey with drifting smoke, the massive oak-and-iron gates charred and askew, the drawbridge down in a tangle of broken chains and missing planks. Bodies floated in the moat, islands for the crows.

"Certain," he declared.

Osha chewed on that a moment. "I'll risk a look then. I want the lot o' you close behind. Meera, get Bran's basket."

"Are we going home?" Rickon asked excitedly. "I want my horse. And I want applecakes and butter and honey, and Shaggy. Are we going where Shaggydog is?"

"Yes," Bran promised, "but you have to be quiet."

Meera strapped the wicker basket to Hodor's back and helped lift Bran into it, easing his useless legs through the holes. He had a queer flutter in his belly. He knew what awaited them above, but that did not make it any less fearful. As they set off, he turned to give his father one last look, and it seemed to Bran that there was a sadness in Lord Eddard's eyes, as if he did not want them to go. *We have to*, he thought. *It's time.*

Osha carried her long oaken spear in one hand and the torch in the other. A naked sword hung down her back, one of the last to bear Mikken's mark. He had forged it for Lord Eddard's tomb, to keep his ghost at rest. But with Mikken slain and the ironmen guarding the armory, good steel had been hard to resist, even if it meant grave-robbing. Meera had claimed Lord Rickard's blade, though she complained that it was too heavy. Brandon took his namesake's, the sword made for the uncle he had never known. He knew he would not be much use in a fight, but even so the blade felt good in his hand.

But it was only a game, and Bran knew it.

Their footsteps echoed through the cavernous crypts. The shadows behind them swallowed his father as the shadows ahead retreated to unveil other statues; no mere lords, these, but the old Kings in the North. On their brows they wore stone crowns. Torrhen Stark, the King Who Knelt. Edwyn the Spring King. Theon Stark, the Hungry Wolf. Brandon the Burner and Brandon the Shipwright. Jorah and Jonos, Brandon the Bad, Walton the Moon King, Edderion the Bridegroom, Eyron, Benjen the Sweet and Benjen the Bitter, King Edrick Snowbeard. Their faces were stern and strong, and some of them had done terrible things, but they were Starks every one, and Bran knew all their tales. He had never feared the crypts; they were part of his home and who he was, and he had always known that one day he would lie here too.

But now he was not so certain. *If I go up, will I ever come back down? Where will I go when I die?*

"Wait," Osha said when they reached the twisting stone stairs that led up to the surface, and down to the deeper levels where kings more ancient still sat their dark thrones. She handed Meera the torch. "I'll grope my way up." For a time they could hear the sound of her footfalls, but they grew softer and softer until they faded away entirely. "Hodor," said Hodor nervously.

Bran had told himself a hundred times how much he hated hiding down here in the dark, how much he wanted to see the sun again, to ride his horse through wind and rain. But now that the moment was upon him, he was afraid. He'd felt safe in the darkness; when you could not even find your own hand in front of your face, it was easy to believe that no enemies could ever find you either. And the stone lords had given him courage. Even when he could not see them, he had known they were there.

It seemed a long while before they heard anything again. Bran had begun to fear that something had happened to Osha. His brother was squirming restlessly. "I want to *go home!*" he said loudly. Hodor bobbed his head and said, "Hodor." Then they heard the footsteps again, growing louder, and after a few minutes Osha emerged into the light, looking grim. "Something is blocking the door. I can't move it."

"Hodor can move anything," said Bran.

Osha gave the huge stableboy an appraising look. "Might be he can. Come on, then."

The steps were narrow, so they had to climb in single file. Osha led. Behind came Hodor, with Bran crouched low on his back so his head wouldn't hit the ceiling. Meera followed with the torch, and Jojen brought up the rear, leading Rickon by the hand. Around and around they went, and up and up. Bran thought he could smell smoke now, but perhaps that was only the torch.

The door to the crypts was made of ironwood. It was old and heavy, and lay at a slant to the ground. Only one person could approach it at a time. Osha tried once more when she reached it, but Bran could see that it was not budging. "Let Hodor try."

They had to pull Bran from his basket first, so he would not get squished. Meera squatted beside him on the steps, one arm thrown protectively across his shoulders, as Osha and Hodor traded places. "Open the door, Hodor," Bran said.

The huge stableboy put both hands flat on the door, pushed, and grunted. "Hodor?" He slammed a fist against the wood, and it did not so much as jump. "Hodor."

"Use your back," urged Bran. "And your legs."

Turning, Hodor put his back to the wood and shoved. Again. Again. "Hodor!" He put one foot on a higher step so he was bent under the slant of the door and tried to rise. This time the wood groaned and creaked. *"Hodor!"* The other foot came up a step, and Hodor spread his legs apart, braced, and straightened. His face turned red, and Bran could see cords in his neck bulging as he strained against the weight above him. *"Hodor hodor hodor hodor hodor HODOR!"* From above came a dull rumble. Then suddenly the door jerked upward and a shaft of daylight fell across Bran's face, blinding him for a moment. Another shove brought the sound of shifting stone, and then the way was open. Osha poked her spear through and slid out after it, and Rickon squirmed through Meera's legs to follow. Hodor shoved the door open all the way and stepped to the surface. The Reeds had to carry Bran up the last few steps.

The sky was a pale grey, and smoke eddied all around them. They stood in the shadow of the First Keep, or what remained of it. One whole side of the building had torn loose and fallen away. Stone and shattered gargoyles lay strewn across the yard. *They fell just where I did*, Bran thought when he saw them. Some of the gargoyles had broken into so many pieces it made him wonder how he was alive at all. Nearby some crows were pecking at a body crushed beneath the tumbled stone, but he lay facedown and Bran could not say who he was.

The First Keep had not been used for many hundreds of years, but now it was more of a shell than ever. The floors had burned inside it, and all the beams. Where the wall had fallen away, they could see right into the rooms, even into the privy. Yet behind, the broken tower still stood, no more burned than before. Jojen Reed was coughing from the smoke. "Take me home!" Rickon demanded. "I want to be *home!*" Hodor stomped in a circle. "Hodor," he whimpered in a small voice. They stood huddled together with ruin and death all around them.

"We made noise enough to wake a dragon," Osha said, "but there's no one come. The castle's dead and burned, just as Bran dreamed, but we had best—" She broke off suddenly at a noise behind them, and whirled with her spear at the ready.

Two lean dark shapes emerged from behind the broken tower, padding slowly through the rubble. Rickon gave a happy shout of *"Shaggy!"* and the black direwolf came bounding toward him. Summer advanced more slowly, rubbed his head up against Bran's arm, and licked his face.

"We should go," said Jojen. "So much death will bring other wolves besides Summer and Shaggydog, and not all on four feet."

"Aye, soon enough," Osha agreed, "but we need food,

and there may be some survived this. Stay together. Meera, keep your shield up and guard our backs."

It took the rest of the morning to make a slow circuit of the castle. The great granite walls remained, blackened here and there by fire but otherwise untouched. But within, all was death and destruction. The doors of the Great Hall were charred and smoldering, and inside the rafters had given way and the whole roof had crashed down onto the floor. The green and yellow panes of the glass gardens were all in shards, the trees and fruits and flowers torn up or left exposed to die. Of the stables, made of wood and thatch, nothing remained but ashes, embers, and dead horses. Bran thought of his Dancer, and wanted to weep. There was a shallow steaming lake beneath the Library Tower, and hot water gushing from a crack in its side. The bridge between the Bell Tower and the rookery had collapsed into the yard below, and Maester Luwin's turret was gone. They saw a dull red glow shining up through the narrow cellar windows beneath the Great Keep, and a second fire still burning in one of the storehouses.

Osha called softly through the blowing smoke as they went, but no one answered. They saw one dog worrying at a corpse, but he ran when he caught the scents of the direwolves; the rest had been slain in the kennels. The maester's ravens were paying court to some of the corpses, while the crows from the broken tower attended others. Bran recognized Poxy Tym, even though someone had taken an axe to his face. One charred corpse, outside the ashen shell of Mother's sept, sat with his arms drawn up and his hands balled into hard black fists, as if to punch anyone who dared approach him. "If the gods are good," Osha said in a low angry voice, "the Others will take them that did this work."

"It was Theon," Bran said blackly.

"No. Look." She pointed across the yard with her spear. "That's one of his ironmen. And there. And that's Greyjoy's warhorse, see? The black one with the arrows in him." She moved among the dead, frowning. "And here's Black Lorren." He had been hacked and cut so badly that his beard looked a reddish-brown now. "Took a few with him, he did." Osha turned over one of the other corpses with her foot. "There's a badge. A little man, all red."

"The flayed man of the Dreadfort," said Bran.

Summer howled, and darted away.

"The godswood." Meera Reed ran after the direwolf, her shield and frog spear to hand. The rest of them trailed after, threading their way through smoke and fallen stones. The air was sweeter under the trees. A few pines along the edge of the wood had been scorched, but deeper in the damp soil and green wood had defeated the flames. "There is a power in living wood," said Jojen Reed, almost as if he knew what Bran was thinking, "a power strong as fire."

On the edge of the black pool, beneath the shelter of the heart tree, Maester Luwin lay on his belly in the dirt. A trail of blood twisted back through damp leaves where he had crawled. Summer stood over him, and Bran thought he was dead at first, but when Meera touched his throat, the maester moaned. "Hodor?" Hodor said mournfully. "Hodor?"

Gently, they eased Luwin onto his back. He had grey eyes and grey hair, and once his robes had been grey as well, but they were darker now where the blood had soaked through. "Bran," he said softly when he saw him sitting tall on Hodor's back. "And Rickon too." He smiled. "The gods are good. I knew . . ."

"Knew?" said Bran uncertainly.

"The legs, I could tell . . . the clothes fit, but the muscles in his legs . . . poor lad . . ." He coughed, and blood came up from inside him. "You vanished . . . in the woods . . . how, though?"

"We never went," said Bran. "Well, only to the edge, and then doubled back. I sent the wolves on to make a trail, but we hid in Father's tomb."

"The crypts." Luwin chuckled, a froth of blood on his lips. When the maester tried to move, he gave a sharp gasp of pain.

Tears filled Bran's eyes. When a man was hurt you

took him to the maester, but what could you do when your maester was hurt?

"We'll need to make a litter to carry him," said Osha.

"No use," said Luwin. "I'm dying, woman."

"You *can't*," said Rickon angrily. "No you can't." Beside him, Shaggydog bared his teeth and growled.

The maester smiled. "Hush now, child, I'm much older than you. I can . . . die as I please."

"Hodor, down," said Bran. Hodor went to his knees beside the maester.

"Listen," Luwin said to Osha, "the princes . . . Robb's heirs. Not . . . not together . . . do you hear?"

The wildling woman leaned on her spear. "Aye. Safer apart. But where to take them? I'd thought, might be these Cerwyns . . ."

Maester Luwin shook his head, though it was plain to see what the effort cost him. "Cerwyn boy's dead. Ser Rodrik, Leobald Tallhart, Lady Hornwood . . . all slain. Deepwood fallen, Moat Cailin, soon Torrhen's Square. Ironmen on the Stony Shore. And east, the Bastard of Bolton."

"Then where?" asked Osha.

"White Harbor . . . the Umbers . . . I do not know . . . war everywhere . . . each man against his neighbor, and winter coming . . . such folly, such black mad folly . . ." Maester Luwin reached up and grasped Bran's forearm, his fingers closing with a desperate strength. "You must be strong now. *Strong.*"

"I will be," Bran said, though it was hard. *Ser Rodrik killed and Maester Luwin, everyone, everyone* . . .

"Good," the maester said. "A good boy. Your . . . your father's son, Bran. Now *go.*"

Osha gazed up at the weirwood, at the red face carved in the pale trunk. "And leave you for the gods?"

"I beg . . ." The maester swallowed. ". . . a . . . a drink of water, and . . . another boon. If you would . . ."

"Aye." She turned to Meera. "Take the boys."

Jojen and Meera led Rickon out between them. Hodor followed. Low branches whipped at Bran's face as they pushed between the trees, and the leaves brushed away his tears. Osha joined them in the yard a few moments later. She said no word of Maester Luwin. "Hodor must stay with Bran, to be his legs," the wildling woman said briskly. "I will take Rickon with me."

"We'll go with Bran," said Jojen Reed.

"Aye, I thought you might," said Osha. "Believe I'll try the East Gate, and follow the kingsroad a ways."

"We'll take the Hunter's Gate," said Meera.

"Hodor," said Hodor.

They stopped at the kitchens first. Osha found some loaves of burned bread that were still edible, and even a cold roast fowl that she ripped in half. Meera unearthed a crock of honey and a big sack of apples. Outside, they made their farewells. Rickon sobbed and clung to Hodor's leg until Osha gave him a smack with the butt end of her spear. Then he followed her quick enough. Shaggydog stalked after them. The last Bran saw of them was the direwolf's tail as it vanished behind the broken tower.

The iron portcullis that closed the Hunter's Gate had been warped so badly by heat it could not be raised more than a foot. They had to squeeze beneath its spikes, one by one.

"Will we go to your lord father?" Bran asked as they crossed the drawbridge between the walls. "To Greywater Watch?"

Meera looked to her brother for the answer. "Our road is north," Jojen announced.

At the edge of the wolfswood, Bran turned in his basket for one last glimpse of the castle that had been his life. Wisps of smoke still rose into the grey sky, but no more than might have risen from Winterfell's chimneys on a cold autumn afternoon. Soot stains marked some of the arrow loops, and here and there a crack or a missing merlon could be seen in the curtain wall, but it seemed little enough from this distance. Beyond, the tops of the keeps and towers still stood as they had for hundreds of years, and it was hard to tell that the castle had been sacked and burned at all. *The stone is strong,*

Bran told himself, *the roots of the trees go deep, and under the ground the Kings of Winter sit their thrones.* So long as those remained, Winterfell remained. It was not dead, just broken. *Like me*, he thought. *I'm not dead either.*

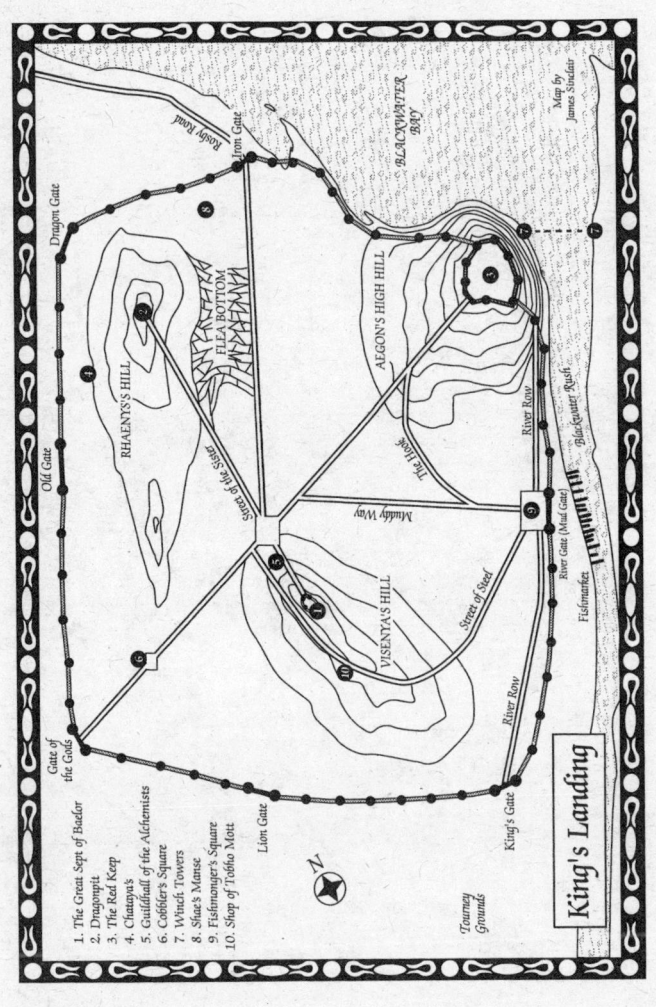

King's Landing

Map by James Sinclair

1. The Great Sept of Baelor
2. Dragonpit
3. The Red Keep
4. Chataya's
5. Guildhall of the Alchemists
6. Cobbler's Square
7. Winch Towers
8. Shae's Manse
9. Fishmonger's Square
10. Shop of Tobho Mott

BLACKWATER BAY

Rosby Road
Iron Gate
Dragon Gate
Old Gate
Gate of the Gods
Lion Gate
King's Gate
River Gate (Mud Gate)
River Row
Muddy Way
Tun Hook
Street of Steel
Street of the Sisters
Blackwater Rush
Fishmarket
Tourney Grounds

RHAENYS'S HILL
AEGON'S HIGH HILL
VISENYA'S HILL
FLEA BOTTOM

APPENDIX

THE KINGS AND THEIR COURTS

THE KING ON THE IRON THRONE

JOFFREY BARATHEON, the First of His Name, a boy of thirteen years, the eldest son of King Robert I Baratheon and Queen Cersei of House Lannister,

—his mother, QUEEN CERSEI, Queen Regent and Protector of the Realm,

—his sister, PRINCESS MYRCELLA, a girl of nine,

—his brother, PRINCE TOMMEN, a boy of eight, heir to the Iron Throne,

—his uncles, on his father's side:

—STANNIS BARATHEON, Lord of Dragonstone, styling himself King Stannis the First,

—RENLY BARATHEON, Lord of Storm's End, styling himself King Renly the First,

—his uncles, on his mother's side:

—SER JAIME LANNISTER, the Kingslayer, Lord Commander of the Kingsguard, a captive at Riverrun,

—TYRION LANNISTER, acting Hand of the King,

—Tyrion's squire, PODRICK PAYNE,

—Tyrion's guards and sworn swords:

—BRONN, a sellsword, black of hair and heart,

—SHAGGA SON OF DOLF, of the Stone Crows,

—TIMETT SON OF TIMETT, of the Burned Men,

—CHELLA DAUGHTER OF CHEYK, of the Black Ears,

—CRAWN SON OF CALOR, of the Moon Brothers,

—Tyrion's concubine, SHAE, a camp follower, eighteen,

—his small council:

—GRAND MAESTER PYCELLE,

—LORD PETYR BAELISH, called LITTLEFINGER, master of coin,

—LORD JANOS SLYNT, Commander of the City Watch of King's Landing (the "gold cloaks"),

—VARYS, a eunuch, called the SPIDER, master of whisperers,

—his Kingsguard:

—SER JAIME LANNISTER, called the KINGSLAYER, Lord Commander, a captive at Riverrun,

—SANDOR CLEGANE, called the HOUND,

—SER BOROS BLOUNT,

—SER MERYN TRANT,

—SER ARYS OAKHEART,

—SER PRESTON GREENFIELD,

—SER MANDON MOORE,

—his court and retainers:

—SER ILYN PAYNE, the King's Justice, a headsman,

—VYLARR, captain of the Lannister household guards at King's Landing (the "red cloaks"),

—SER LANCEL LANNISTER, formerly squire to King Robert, recently knighted,

—TYREK LANNISTER, formerly squire to King Robert,

—SER ARON SANTAGAR, master-at-arms,

—SER BALON SWANN, second son to Lord Gulian Swann of Stonehelm,

—LADY ERMESANDE HAYFORD, a babe at the breast,

—SER DONTOS HOLLARD, called the RED, a drunk,

—JALABHAR XHO, an exiled prince from the Summer Isles,

—MOON BOY, a jester and fool,

—LADY TANDA STOKEWORTH,

—FALYSE, her elder daughter,

—LOLLYS, her younger daughter, a maiden of thirty-three years,

—LORD GYLES ROSBY,

—SER HORAS REDWYNE and his twin SER HOBBER REDWYNE, sons of the Lord of the Arbor,

—the people of King's Landing:

—the City Watch (the "gold cloaks"):

—JANOS SLYNT, Lord of Harrenhal, Lord Commander,
— —MORROS, his eldest son and heir,
—ALLAR DEEM, Slynt's chief sergeant,
—SER JACELYN BYWATER, called IRONHAND, captain of the River Gate,
—HALLYNE THE PYROMANCER, a Wisdom of the Guild of Alchemists,
—CHATAYA, owner of an expensive brothel,
— —ALAYAYA, DANCY, MAREI, some of her girls,
—TOBHO MOTT, a master armorer,
—SALLOREON, a master armorer,
—IRONBELLY, a blacksmith,
—LOTHAR BRUNE, a freerider,
—SER OSMUND KETTLEBLACK, a hedge knight of unsavory reputation,
— —OSFRYD and OSNEY KETTLEBLACK, his brothers,
—SYMON SILVER TONGUE, a singer.

King Joffrey's banner shows the crowned stag of Baratheon, black on gold, and the lion of Lannister, gold on crimson, combatant.

THE KING IN THE NARROW SEA

STANNIS BARATHEON, the First of His Name, the older of King Robert's brothers, formerly Lord of Dragonstone, secondborn son of Lord Steffon Baratheon and Lady Cassana of House Estermont,
- —his wife, LADY SELYSE of House Florent,
  - —SHIREEN, their only child, a girl of ten,
- —his uncle and cousins:
  - —SER LOMAS ESTERMONT, an uncle,
    - —his son, SER ANDREW ESTERMONT, a cousin,
- —his court and retainers:
  - —MAESTER CRESSEN, healer and tutor, an old man,
  - —MAESTER PYLOS, his young successor,
  - —SEPTON BARRE,
  - —SER AXELL FLORENT, castellan of Dragonstone, and uncle to Queen Selyse,
  - —PATCHFACE, a lackwit fool,
  - —LADY MELISANDRE OF ASSHAI, called the RED WOMAN, a priestess of R'hllor, the Heart of Fire,
  - —SER DAVOS SEAWORTH, called the ONION KNIGHT and sometimes SHORTHAND, once a smuggler, captain of *Black Betha*,
    - —his wife MARYA, a carpenter's daughter,
      - —their seven sons:
        - —DALE, captain of the *Wraith*,
        - —ALLARD, captain of the *Lady Marya*,
        - —MATTHOS, second of *Black Betha*,
        - —MARIC, oarmaster of *Fury*,
        - —DEVAN, squire to King Stannis,
        - —STANNIS, a boy of nine years,

—STEFFON, a boy of six years,
—BRYEN FARRING, squire to King Stannis,
—his lords bannermen and sworn swords,
  —ARDRIAN CELTIGAR, Lord of Claw Isle, an old man,
  —MONFORD VELARYON, Lord of the Tides and Master of Driftmark,
  —DURAM BAR EMMON, Lord of Sharp Point, a boy of fourteen years,
  —GUNCER SUNGLASS, Lord of Sweetport Sound,
  —SER HUBARD RAMBTON,
  —SALLADHOR SAAN, of the Free City of Lys, styled Prince of the Narrow Sea,
  —MOROSH THE MYRMAN, a sellsail admiral.

King Stannis has taken for his banner the fiery heart of the Lord of Light; a red heart surrounded by orange flames upon a bright yellow field. Within the heart is pictured the crowned stag of House Baratheon, in black.

THE KING IN HIGHGARDEN

RENLY BARATHEON, the First of His Name, the younger of King Robert's brothers, formerly Lord of Storm's End, thirdborn son of Lord Steffon Baratheon and Lady Cassana of House Estermont,
- —his new bride, LADY MARGAERY of House Tyrell, a maid of fifteen years,
- —his uncle and cousins:
  - —SER ELDON ESTERMONT, an uncle,
    - —Ser Eldon's son, SER AEMON ESTERMONT, a cousin,
      - —Ser Aemon's son, SER ALYN ESTERMONT,
- —his lords bannermen:
  - —MACE TYRELL, Lord of Highgarden and Hand of the King,
  - —RANDYLL TARLY, Lord of Horn Hill,
  - —MATHIS ROWAN, Lord of Goldengrove,
  - —BRYCE CARON, Lord of the Marches,
  - —SHYRA ERROL, Lady of Haystack Hall,
  - —ARWYN OAKHEART, Lady of Old Oak,
  - —ALESTER FLORENT, Lord of Brightwater Keep,
  - —LORD SELWYN OF TARTH, called the EVENSTAR,
  - —LEYTON HIGHTOWER, Voice of Oldtown, Lord of the Port,
  - —LORD STEFFON VARNER,
- —his Rainbow Guard:
  - —SER LORAS TYRELL, the Knight of Flowers, Lord Commander,
  - —LORD BRYCE CARON, the Orange,
  - —SER GUYARD MORRIGEN, the Green,
  - —SER PARMEN CRANE, the Purple,

—SER ROBAR ROYCE, the Red,

—SER EMMON CUY, the Yellow,

—BRIENNE OF TARTH, the Blue, also called BRIENNE THE BEAUTY, daughter to Lord Selwyn the Evenstar,

—his knights and sworn swords:

—SER CORTNAY PENROSE, castellan of Storm's End,

—Ser Cortnay's ward, EDRIC STORM, a bastard son of King Robert by Lady Delena of House Florent,

—SER DONNEL SWANN, heir to Stonehelm,

—SER JON FOSSOWAY, of the green-apple Fossoways,

—SER BRYAN FOSSOWAY, SER TANTON FOSSOWAY, and SER EDWYD FOSSOWAY, of the red-apple Fossoways,

—SER COLEN OF GREENPOOLS,

—SER MARK MULLENDORE,

—RED RONNET, the Knight of Griffin's Roost,

—his household,

—MAESTER JURNE, counselor, healer, and tutor.

King Renly's banner is the crowned stag of House Baratheon of Storm's End, black upon a gold field, the same banner flown by his brother King Robert.

THE KING IN THE NORTH

ROBB STARK, Lord of Winterfell and King in the North, eldest son of Eddard Stark, Lord of Winterfell, and Lady Catelyn of House Tully, a boy of fifteen years,
—his direwolf, GREY WIND,
—his mother, LADY CATELYN, of House Tully,
—his siblings:
   —PRINCESS SANSA, a maid of twelve,
      —Sansa's direwolf, {LADY}, killed at Castle Darry,
   —PRINCESS ARYA, a girl of ten,
      —Arya's direwolf, NYMERIA, driven off a year past,
   —PRINCE BRANDON, called Bran, heir to Winterfell and the North, a boy of eight,
      —Bran's direwolf, SUMMER,
   —PRINCE RICKON, a boy of four,
      —Rickon's direwolf, SHAGGYDOG,
      —his half brother, JON SNOW, a bastard of fifteen years, a man of the Night's Watch,
      —Jon's direwolf, GHOST,
      —his uncles and aunts:
—{BRANDON STARK}, Lord Eddard's elder brother, slain at the command of King Aerys II Targaryen,
—BENJEN STARK, Lord Eddard's younger brother, a man of the Night's Watch, lost beyond the Wall,
—LYSA ARRYN, Lady Catelyn's younger sister, widow of {Lord Jon Arryn}, Lady of the Eyrie,
—SER EDMURE TULLY, Lady Catelyn's younger brother, heir to Riverrun,
—SER BRYNDEN TULLY, called the BLACKFISH, Lady Catelyn's uncle,

—his sworn swords and battle companions:

    —THEON GREYJOY, Lord Eddard's ward, heir to Pyke and the Iron Islands,

    —HALLIS MOLLEN, captain of guards for Winterfell,

      —JACKS, QUENT, SHADD, guardsmen under Mollen's command,

    —SER WENDEL MANDERLY, second son to the Lord of White Harbor,

    —PATREK MALLISTER, heir to Seagard,

    —DACEY MORMONT, eldest daughter of Lady Maege and heir to Bear Island,

    —JON UMBER, called the SMALLJON,

    —ROBIN FLINT, SER PERWYN FREY, LUCAS BLACKWOOD,

    —his squire, OLYVAR FREY, eighteen,

      —the household at Riverrun:

    —MAESTER VYMAN, counselor, healer, and tutor,

    —SER DESMOND GRELL, master-at-arms,

    —SER ROBIN RYGER, captain of the guard,

    —UTHERYDES WAYN, steward of Riverrun,

    —RYMUND THE RHYMER, a singer,

      —the household at Winterfell:

    —MAESTER LUWIN, counselor, healer, and tutor,

    —SER RODRIK CASSEL, master-at-arms,

      —BETH, his young daughter,

    —WALDER FREY, called BIG WALDER, a ward of Lady Catelyn, eight years of age,

    —WALDER FREY, called LITTLE WALDER, a ward of Lady Catelyn, also eight,

    —SEPTON CHAYLE, keeper of the castle sept and library,

    —JOSETH, master of horse,

      —BANDY and SHYRA, his twin daughters,

    —FARLEN, kennelmaster,

      —PALLA, a kennel girl,

    —OLD NAN, storyteller, once a wet nurse, now very aged,

      —HODOR, her great-grandson, a simpleminded stableboy,

    —GAGE, the cook,

      —TURNIP, a pot girl and scullion,

—OSHA, a wildling woman taken captive in the wolfswood, serving as kitchen drudge,

—MIKKEN, smith and armorer,

—HAYHEAD, SKITTRICK, POXY TYM, ALEBELLY, guardsmen,

—CALON, TOM, children of guardsmen,

—his lords bannermen and commanders:

—(with Robb at Riverrun)

—JON UMBER, called the GREATJON,

—RICKARD KARSTARK, Lord of Karhold,

—GALBART GLOVER, of Deepwood Motte,

—MAEGE MORMONT, Lady of Bear Island,

—SER STEVRON FREY, eldest son of Lord Walder Frey and heir to the Twins,

    —Ser Stevron's eldest son, SER RYMAN FREY,

      —Ser Ryman's son, BLACK WALDER FREY,

—MARTYN RIVERS, a bastard son of Lord Walder Frey,

—(with Roose Bolton's host at the Twins),

—ROOSE BOLTON, Lord of the Dreadfort, commanding the larger part of the northern host,

—ROBETT GLOVER, of Deepwood Motte,

—WALDER FREY, Lord of the Crossing,

—SER HELMAN TALLHART, of Torrhen's Square,

—SER AENYS FREY,

—(prisoners of Lord Tywin Lannister),

—LORD MEDGER CERWYN,

—HARRION KARSTARK, sole surviving son of Lord Rickard,

—SER WYLIS MANDERLY, heir to White Harbor,

—SER JARED FREY, SER HOSTEEN FREY, SER DANWELL FREY, and their bastard half brother, RONEL RIVERS,

—(in the field or at their own castles),

—LYMAN DARRY, a boy of eight,

—SHELLA WHENT, Lady of Harrenhal, dispossessed of her castle by Lord Tywin Lannister,

—JASON MALLISTER, Lord of Seagard,

—JONOS BRACKEN, Lord of the Stone Hedge,

—TYTOS BLACKWOOD, Lord of Raventree,

—LORD KARYL VANCE,

—SER MARQ PIPER,

—SER HALMON PAEGE,

—his lord bannermen and castellans in the north:

—WYMAN MANDERLY, Lord of White Harbor,

—HOWLAND REED of Greywater Watch, a crannogman,

  —Howland's daughter, MEERA, a maid of fifteen,

  —Howland's son, JOJEN, a boy of thirteen,

—LADY DONELLA HORNWOOD, a widow and grieving mother,

—CLEY CERWYN, Lord Medger's heir, a boy of fourteen,

—LEOBALD TALLHART, younger brother to Ser Helman, castellan at Torrhen's Square,

  —Leobald's wife, BERENA of House Hornwood,

  —Leobald's son, BRANDON, a boy of fourteen,

  —Leobald's son, BEREN, a boy of ten,

  —Ser Helman's son, BENFRED, heir to Torrhen's Square,

  —Ser Helman's daughter, EDDARA, a maid of nine,

—LADY SYBELLE, wife to Robett Glover, holding Deepwood Motte in his absence,

  —Robett's son, GAWEN, three, heir to Deepwood,

  —Robett's daughter, ERENA, a babe of one,

  —LARENCE SNOW, a bastard son of Lord Hornwood, aged twelve, ward of Galbart Glover,

—MORS CROWFOOD and HOTHER WHORESBANE of House Umber, uncles to the Greatjon,

—LADY LYESSA FLINT, mother to Robin,

—ONDREW LOCKE, Lord of Oldcastle, an old man.

The banner of the King in the North remains as it has for thousands of years: the grey direwolf of the Starks of Winterfell, running across an ice-white field.

THE QUEEN ACROSS THE WATER

DAENERYS TARGARYEN, called Daenerys Stormborn, the Unburnt, Mother of Dragons, *Khaleesi* of the Dothraki,
and First of Her Name, sole surviving child of King
Aerys II Targaryen by his sister/wife, Queen Rhaella, a
widow at fourteen years,
  —her new-hatched dragons, DROGON, VISERION, RHAEGAL,
  —her brothers:
    —{RHAEGAR}, Prince of Dragonstone and heir to the
      Iron Throne, slain by King Robert on the Trident,
      —{RHAENYS}, Rhaegar's daughter by Elia of Dorne,
        murdered during the Sack of King's Landing,
      —{AEGON}, Rhaegar's son by Elia of Dorne, mur-
        dered during the Sack of King's Landing,
    —{VISERYS}, styling himself King Viserys, the Third
      of His Name, called the Beggar King, slain in
      Vaes Dothrak by the hand of Khal Drogo,
  —her husband {DROGO}, a *khal* of the Dothraki, died of
    wounds gone bad,
    —{RHAEGO}, stillborn son of Daenerys and Khal
      Drogo, slain in the womb by Mirri Maz Duur,
  —her Queensguard:
    —SER JORAH MORMONT, an exile knight, once Lord of
      Bear Island,
    —JHOGO, *ko* and bloodrider, the whip,
    —AGGO, *ko* and bloodrider, the bow,
    —RAKHARO, *ko* and bloodrider, the *arakh*,
  —her handmaids:
    —IRRI, a Dothraki girl,
    —JHIQUI, a Dothraki girl,

—DOREAH, a Lyseni slave, formerly a whore,
—the three seekers:
—XARO XHOAN DAXOS, a merchant prince of Qarth,
—PYAT PREE, a warlock of Qarth,
—QUAITHE, a masked shadowbinder of Asshai,
—ILLYRIO MOPATIS, a magister of the Free City of Pentos, who arranged to wed Daenerys to Khal Drogo and conspired to restore Viserys to the Iron Throne.

The banner of the Targaryens is the banner of Aegon the Conqueror, who conquered six of Seven Kingdoms, founded the dynasty, and made the Iron Throne from the swords of his conquered enemies: a three-headed dragon, red on black.

OTHER HOUSES GREAT AND SMALL

CONCLUSIONS: LEGAL AND SOCIAL

HOUSE ARRYN

House Arryn declared for none of the rival claimants at the outbreak of the war, and kept its strength back to protect the Eyrie and the Vale of Arryn. The Arryn sigil is the moon-and-falcon, white, upon a sky-blue field. Their Arryn words are *As High As Honor*.

ROBERT ARRYN, Lord of the Eyrie, Defender of the Vale, Warden of the East, a sickly boy of eight years,
  —his mother, LADY LYSA, of House Tully, third wife and widow of {Lord Jon Arryn}, late Hand of the King, and sister to Catelyn Stark,
  —his household:
    —MAESTER COLEMON, counselor, healer, and tutor,
    —SER MARWYN BELMORE, captain of guards,
    —LORD NESTOR ROYCE, High Steward of the Vale,
      —Lord Nestor's son, SER ALBAR,
      —MYA STONE, a bastard girl in his service, natural daughter of King Robert,
    —MORD, a brutal gaoler,
    —MARILLION, a young singer,
  —his lords bannermen, suitors, and retainers:
    —LORD YOHN ROYCE, called BRONZE YOHN,
      —Lord Yohn's eldest son, SER ANDAR,
      —Lord Yohn's second son, SER ROBAR, in service to King Renly, Robar the Red of the Rainbow Guard,
      —Lord Yohn's youngest son, {SER WAYMAR}, a man of the Night's Watch, lost beyond the Wall,

—LORD NESTOR ROYCE, cousin of Lord Yohn, High
    Steward of the Vale,
    —Lord Nestor's son and heir, SER ALBAR,
    —Lord Nestor's daughter, MYRANDA,
—SER LYN CORBRAY, a suitor to Lady Lysa,
    —MYCHEL REDFORT, his squire,
—LADY ANYA WAYNWOOD,
    —Lady Anya's eldest son and heir, SER MORTON, a
    suitor to Lady Lysa,
    —Lady Anya's second son, SER DONNEL, the Knight
    of the Gate,
—EON HUNTER, Lord of Longbow Hall, an old man,
    and a suitor to Lady Lysa.

HOUSE FLORENT

The Florents of Brightwater Keep are sworn bannermen to Highgarden, and followed the Tyrells in declaring for King Renly. They also kept a foot in the other camp, however, since Stannis's queen is a Florent, and her uncle the castellan of Dragonstone. The sigil of House Florent shows a fox head in a circle of flowers.

ALESTER FLORENT, Lord of Brightwater,
—his wife, LADY MELARA, of House Crane,
—their children:
  —ALEKYNE, heir to Brightwater,
  —MELESSA, wed to Lord Randyll Tarly,
  —RHEA, wed to Lord Leyton Hightower,
—his siblings:
  —SER AXELL, castellan of Dragonstone,
  —{SER RYAM}, died in a fall from a horse,
    —Ser Ryam's daughter, QUEEN SELYSE, wed to King Stannis,
    —Ser Ryam's eldest son and heir, SER IMRY,
    —Ser Ryam's second son, SER ERREN,
  —SER COLIN,
    —Colin's daughter, DELENA, wed to SER HOSMAN NORCROSS,
      —Delena's son, EDRIC STORM, a bastard fathered by King Robert,
      —Delena's son, ALESTER NORCROSS,

    —Delena's son, RENLY NORCROSS,
—Colin's son, MAESTER OMER, in service at Old Oak,
—Colin's son, MERRELL, a squire on the Arbor,
—his sister, RYLENE, wed to Ser Rycherd Crane.

HOUSE FREY

Powerful, wealthy, and numerous, the Freys are bannermen to House Tully, their swords sworn to the service of Riverrun, but they have not always been diligent in performing their duty. When Robert Baratheon met Rhaegar Targaryen on the Trident, the Freys did not arrive until the battle was done, and thereafter Lord Hoster Tully always called Lord Walder "the Late Lord Frey." Lord Frey agreed to support the cause of the King in the North only after Robb Stark agreed to a betrothal, promising to marry one of his daughters or granddaughters after the war was done. Lord Walder has known ninety-one name days, but only recently took his eighth wife, a girl seventy years his junior. It is said of him that he is the only lord in the Seven Kingdoms who could field an army out of his breeches.

WALDER FREY, Lord of the Crossing,
—by his first wife, {LADY PERRA, of House Royce}:
——SER STEVRON, heir to the Twins,
———m. {Corenna Swann, died of a wasting illness},
———Stevron's eldest son, SER RYMAN,
————Ryman's son, EDWYN, wed to Janyce Hunter,
—————Edwyn's daughter, WALDA, a girl of eight,
————Ryman's son, WALDER, called BLACK WALDER,
————Ryman's son, PETYR, called PETYR PIMPLE,
—————m. Mylenda Caron,
—————Petyr's daughter, PERRA, a girl of five,
———m. {Jeyne Lydden, died in a fall from a horse},
———Stevron's son, AEGON, a halfwit called JINGLEBELL,

—Stevron's daughter, {MAEGELLE, died in childbed},
  —m. Ser Dafyn Vance,
    —Maegelle's daughter, MARIANNE, a maiden,
    —Maegelle's son, WALDER VANCE, a squire,
    —Maegelle's son, PATREK VANCE,
  —m. {Marsella Waynwood, died in childbed},
—Stevron's son, WALTON, w. Deana Hardyng,
  —Walton's son, STEFFON, called THE SWEET,
  —Walton's daughter, WALDA, called FAIR WALDA,
  —Walton's son, BRYAN, a squire,
—SER EMMON, m. Genna of House Lannister,
  —Emmon's son, SER CLEOS, m. Jeyne Darry,
    —Cleos's son, TYWIN, a squire of eleven,
    —Cleos's son, WILLEM, a page at Ashemark,
  —Emmon's son, SER LYONEL, m. Melesa Crakehall,
  —Emmon's son, TION, a squire captive at River-
    run,
  —Emmon's son, WALDER, called RED WALDER, a page
    at Casterly Rock,
—SER AENYS, m. {Tyana Wylde, died in childbed},
  —Aenys's son, AEGON BLOODBORN, an outlaw,
  —Aenys's son, RHAEGAR, m. Jeyne Beesbury,
    —Rhaegar's son, ROBERT, a boy of thirteen,
    —Rhaegar's daughter, WALDA, a girl of ten,
    called WHITE WALDA,
    —Rhaegar's son, JONOS, a boy of eight,
—PERRIANE, m. Ser Leslyn Haigh,
  —Perriane's son, SER HARYS HAIGH,
    —Harys's son, WALDER HAIGH, a boy of four,
  —Perriane's son, SER DONNEL HAIGH,
  —Perriane's son, ALYN HAIGH, a squire,
—by his second wife, {LADY CYRENNA, of House Swann}:
—SER JARED, their eldest son, m. {Alys Frey},
  —Jared's son, SER TYTOS, m. Zhoe Blanetree,
    —Tytos's daughter, ZIA, a maid of fourteen,
    —Tytos's son, ZACHERY, a boy of twelve, training
    at the Sept of Oldtown,
  —Jared's daughter, KYRA, m. Ser Garse
    Goodbrook,
    —Kyra's son, WALDER GOODBROOK, a boy of nine,

  —Kyra's daughter, JEYNE GOODBROOK, six,
 —SEPTON LUCEON, in service at the Great Sept of
  Baelor in King's Landing,
—by his third wife, {LADY AMAREI of House Crakehall}:
—SER HOSTEEN, their eldest son, m. Bellena Hawick,
 —Hosteen's son, SER ARWOOD, m. Ryella Royce,
  —Arwood's daughter, RYELLA, a girl of five,
  —Arwood's twin sons, ANDROW and ALYN, three,
—LADY LYTHENE, m. Lord Lucias Vypren,
 —Lythene's daughter, ELYANA, m. Ser Jon Wylde,
  —Elyana's son, RICKARD WYLDE, four,
 —Lythene's son, SER DAMON VYPREN,
—SYMOND, m. Betharios of Braavos,
 —Symond's son, ALESANDER, a singer,
 —Symond's daughter, ALYX, a maid of seventeen,
 —Symond's son, BRADAMAR, a boy of ten, fostered
  on Braavos as a ward of Oro Tendyris, a mer-
  chant of that city,
—SER DANWELL, m. Wynafrei Whent,
 —{many stillbirths and miscarriages},
—MERRETT, m. Mariya Darry,
 —Merrett's daughter, AMEREI, called AMI, a widow
  of sixteen, m. {Ser Pate of the Blue Fork},
 —Merrett's daughter, WALDA, called FAT WALDA, a
  maid of fifteen years,
 —Merrett's daughter, MARISSA, a maid of thirteen,
 —Merrett's son, WALDER, called LITTLE WALDER, a
  boy of eight, fostered at Winterfell as a ward of
  Lady Catelyn Stark,
—{SER GEREMY, drowned}, m. Carolei Waynwood,
 —Geremy's son, SANDOR, a boy of twelve, a squire
  to Ser Donnel Waynwood,
 —Geremy's daughter, CYNTHEA, a girl of nine, a
  ward of Lady Anya Waynwood,
—SER RAYMUND, m. Beony Beesbury,
 —Raymund's son, ROBERT, sixteen, in training at
  the Citadel in Oldtown,
 —Raymund's son, MALWYN, fifteen, apprenticed to
  an alchemist in Lys,

—Raymund's twin daughters, SERRA and SARRA, maiden girls of fourteen,

—Raymund's daughter, CERSEI, six, called LITTLE BEE,

—by his fourth wife, {LADY ALYSSA, of House Blackwood}:

—LOTHAR, their eldest son, called LAME LOTHAR, m. Leonella Lefford,

—Lothar's daughter, TYSANE, a girl of seven,

—Lothar's daughter, WALDA, a girl of four,

—Lothar's daughter, EMBERLEI, a girl of two,

—SER JAMMOS, m. Sallei Paege,

—Jammos's son, WALDER, called BIG WALDER, a boy of eight, fostered at Winterfell as a ward of Lady Catelyn Stark,

—Jammos's twin sons, DICKON and MATHIS, five,

—SER WHALEN, m. Sylwa Paege,

—Whalen's son, HOSTER, a boy of twelve, a squire to Ser Damon Paege,

—Whalen's daughter, MERIANNE, called MERRY, a girl of eleven,

—LADY MORYA, m. Ser Flement Brax,

—Morya's son, ROBERT BRAX, nine, fostered at Casterly Rock as a page,

—Morya's son, WALDER BRAX, a boy of six,

—Morya's son, JON BRAX, a babe of three,

—TYTA, called TYTA THE MAID, a maid of twenty-nine,

—by his fifth wife, {LADY SARYA of House Whent}:

—no progeny,

—by his sixth wife, {LADY BETHANY of House Rosby}:

—SER PERWYN, their eldest son,

—SER BENFREY, m. Jyanna Frey, a cousin,

—Benfrey's daughter, DELLA, called DEAF DELLA, a girl of three,

—Benfrey's son, OSMUND, a boy of two,

—MAESTER WILLAMEN, in service at Longbow Hall,

—OLYVAR, a squire in the service of Robb Stark,

—ROSLIN, a maid of sixteen,

—by his seventh wife, {LADY ANNARA of House Farring}:

—ARWYN, a maid of fourteen,

—WENDEL, their eldest son, a boy of thirteen, fostered at Seagard as a page,

—COLMAR, promised to the Faith, eleven,

—WALTYR, called TYR, a boy of ten,

—ELMAR, betrothed to Arya Stark, a boy of nine,

—SHIREI, a girl of six,

—his eighth wife, LADY JOYEUSE of House Erenford,

—no progeny as yet,

—Lord Walder's natural children, by sundry mothers,

—WALDER RIVERS, called BASTARD WALDER,

—Bastard Walder's son, SER AEMON RIVERS,

—Bastard Walder's daughter, WALDA RIVERS,

—MAESTER MELWYS, in service at Rosby,

—JEYNE RIVERS, MARTYN RIVERS, RYGER RIVERS, RONEL RIVERS, MELLARA RIVERS, others.

HOUSE GREYJOY

Balon Greyjoy, Lord of the Iron Islands, previously led a rebellion against the Iron Throne, put down by King Robert and Lord Eddard Stark. Though his son Theon, raised at Winterfell, was one of Robb Stark's supporters and closest companions, Lord Balon did not join the northmen when they marched south into the riverlands.

The Greyjoy sigil is a golden kraken upon a black field. Their words are *We Do Not Sow*.

BALON GREYJOY, Lord of the Iron Islands, King of Salt and Rock, Son of the   Sea Wind, Lord Reaper of Pyke, captain of the *Great Kraken*,

—his wife, LADY ALANNYS, of House Harlaw,
——their children:
——{RODRIK}, slain at Seagard during Greyjoy's Rebellion,
——{MARON}, slain at Pyke during Greyjoy's Rebellion,
——ASHA, captain of the *Black Wind*,
——THEON, a ward of Lord Eddard Stark at Winterfell,
—his brothers:
——EURON, called CROW'S EYE, captain of the *Silence*, an outlaw, pirate, and raider,
——VICTARION, Lord Captain of the Iron Fleet, master of the *Iron Victory*,
——AERON, called DAMPHAIR, a priest of the Drowned God,
—his household on Pyke:

—DAGMER called CLEFTJAW, master-at-arms, captain of the *Foamdrinker,*

—MAESTER WENDAMYR, healer and counselor,

—HELYA, keeper of the castle,

—people of Lordsport:

—SIGRIN, a shipwright,

—his lords bannermen,

—LORD BOTLEY, of Lordsport,

—LORD WYNCH, of Iron Holt,

—LORD HARLAW, of Harlaw,

—STONEHOUSE, of Old Wyk,

—DRUMM, of Old Wyk,

—GOODBROTHER, of Old Wyk,

—GOODBROTHER, of Great Wyk,

—LORD MERLYN, of Great Wyk,

—SPARR, of Great Wyk,

—LORD BLACKTYDE, of Blacktyde,

—LORD SALTCLIFFE, of Saltcliffe,

—LORD SUNDERLY, of Saltcliffe.

HOUSE LANNISTER

The Lannisters of Casterly Rock remain the principal support of King Joffrey's claim to the Iron Throne. Their sigil is a golden lion upon a crimson field. The Lannister words are *Hear Me Roar!*

TYWIN LANNISTER, Lord of Casterly Rock, Warden of the West, Shield of Lannisport, and Hand of the King, commanding the Lannister host at Harrenhal,
—his wife, {LADY JOANNA}, a cousin, died in childbed,
  —their children:
  —SER JAIME, called the Kingslayer, Warden of the East and Lord Commander of the Kingsguard, a twin to Queen Cersei,
  —QUEEN CERSEI, widow of King Robert, twin to Jaime, Queen Regent and Protector of the Realm,
  —TYRION, called the IMP, a dwarf,
—his siblings:
  —SER KEVAN, his eldest brother,
    —Ser Kevan's wife, DORNA, of House Swyft,
      —Lady Dorna's father, SER HARYS SWYFT,
    —their children:
  —SER LANCEL, formerly a squire to King Robert, knighted after his death,
  —WILLEM, twin to Martyn, a squire, taken captive at the Whispering Wood,
  —MARTYN, twin to Willem, a squire,
  —JANEI, a girl of two,
  —GENNA, his sister, wed to Ser Emmon Frey,

—Genna's son, SER CLEOS FREY, taken captive at the Whispering Wood,

—Genna's son, TION FREY, a squire, taken captive at the Whispering Wood,

—{SER TYGETT}, his second brother, died of a pox,

—Tygett's widow, DARLESSA, of House Marbrand,

—Tygett's son, TYREK, squire to the king,

—{GERION}, his youngest brother, lost at sea,

—Gerion's bastard daughter, JOY, eleven,

—his cousin, SER STAFFORD LANNISTER, brother to the late Lady Joanna,

—Ser Stafford's daughters, CERENNA and MYRIELLE,

—Ser Stafford's son, SER DAVEN,

—his lord bannermen, captains, and commanders:

—SER ADDAM MARBRAND, heir to Ashemark, commander of Lord Tywin's outriders and scouts,

—SER GREGOR CLEGANE, the Mountain That Rides,

—POLLIVER, CHISWYCK, RAFF THE SWEETLING, DUNSEN, and THE TICKLER, soldiers in his service,

—LORD LEO LEFFORD,

—SER AMORY LORCH, a captain of foragers,

—LEWYS LYDDEN, Lord of the Deep Den,

—GAWEN WESTERLING, Lord of the Crag, taken captive in the Whispering Wood and held at Seagard,

—SER ROBERT BRAX, and his brother, SER FLEMENT BRAX,

—SER FORLEY PRESTER, of the Golden Tooth,

—VARGO HOAT, of the Free City of Qohor, captain of the sellsword company called the Brave Companions,

—MAESTER CREYLEN, his counselor.

HOUSE MARTELL

DORNE was the last of the Seven Kingdoms to swear fealty to the Iron Throne. Blood, custom, and history all set the Dornishmen apart from the other kingdoms. When the war of succession broke out, the Prince of Dorne kept his silence and took no part.

The Martell banner is a red sun pierced by a golden spear. Their words are *Unbowed, Unbent, Unbroken.*

DORAN NYMEROS MARTELL, Lord of Sunspear, Prince of Dorne,
—his wife, MELLARIO, of the Free City of Norvos,
—their children:
—PRINCESS ARIANNE, their eldest daughter, heir to Sunspear,
—PRINCE QUENTYN, their eldest son,
—PRINCE TRYSTANE, their younger son,
—his siblings:
—his sister, {PRINCESS ELIA}, wed to Prince Rhaegar Targaryen, slain during the Sack of King's Landing,
—Elia's daughter, {PRINCESS RHAENYS}, a young girl murdered during the Sack of King's Landing,
—Elia's son, {PRINCE AEGON}, a babe, murdered during the Sack of King's Landing,
—his brother, PRINCE OBERYN, the Red Viper,
—his household:
—AREO HOTAH, a Norvoshi sellsword, captain of guards,

—MAESTER CALEOTTE, counselor, healer, and tutor,
—his lords bannermen:
—EDRIC DAYNE, Lord of Starfall.

The principal houses sworn to Sunspear include Jordayne, Santagar, Allyrion, Toland, Yronwood, Wyl, Fowler, and Dayne.

HOUSE TYRELL

Lord Tyrell of Highgarden declared his support for King Renly after Renly's marriage to his daughter Margaery, and brought most of his principal bannermen to Renly's cause. The Tyrell sigil is a golden rose on a grass-green field. Their words are *Growing Strong*.

MACE TYRELL, Lord of Highgarden, Warden of the South, Defender of the   Marches, High Marshal of the Reach, and Hand of the King,
 —his wife, LADY ALERIE, of House Hightower of Oldtown,
 —their children:
  —WILLAS, their eldest son, heir to Highgarden,
  —SER GARLAN, called the GALLANT, their second son,
  —SER LORAS, the Knight of Flowers, their youngest son, Lord Commander of the Rainbow Guard,
  —MARGAERY, their daughter, a maid of fifteen years, recently wed to Renly Baratheon,
 —his widowed mother, LADY OLENNA of House Redwyne, called the QUEEN OF THORNS,
 —his sisters:
  —MINA, wed to Paxter Redwyne, Lord of the Arbor,
   —their children:
   —SER HORAS REDWYNE, twin to Hobber, mocked as HORROR,
   —SER HOBBER REDWYNE, twin to Horas, mocked as SLOBBER,
   —DESMERA REDWYNE, a maid of sixteen,
  —JANNA, wed to Ser Jon Fossoway,

—his uncles:
  —GARTH, called the GROSS, Lord Seneschal of High-
    garden,
    —Garth's bastard sons, GARSE and GARRETT FLOWERS,
  —SER MORYN, Lord Commander of the City Watch of
    Oldtown,
  —MAESTER GORMON, a scholar of the Citadel,
—his household:
  —MAESTER LOMYS, counselor, healer, and tutor,
  —IGON VYRWEL, captain of the guard,
  —SER VORTIMER CRANE, master-at-arms,
  —BUTTERBUMPS, fool and jester, hugely fat.

THE MEN OF THE NIGHT'S WATCH

The Night's Watch protects the realm, and is sworn to take no part in civil wars and contests for the throne. Traditionally, in times of rebellion, they do honor to all kings and obey none.

At Castle Black

JEOR MORMONT, Lord Commander of the Night's Watch, called the OLD BEAR,
- —his steward and squire, JON SNOW, the bastard of Winterfell, called LORD SNOW,
  - —Jon's white direwolf, GHOST,
- —MAESTER AEMON (TARGARYEN), counselor and healer,
  - —SAMWELL TARLY and CLYDAS, his stewards,
- —BENJEN STARK, First Ranger, lost beyond the Wall,
  - —THOREN SMALLWOOD, a senior ranger,
  - —JARMEN BUCKWELL, a senior ranger,
  - —SER OTTYN WYTHERS, SER ALADALE WYNCH, GRENN, PYPAR, MATTHAR, ELRON, LARK called the SISTERMAN, rangers,
- —OTHELL YARWYCK, First Builder,
  - —HALDER, ALBETT, builders,
- —BOWEN MARSH, Lord Steward
  - —CHETT, steward and dog handler,
  - —EDDISON TOLLETT, called DOLOROUS EDD, a dour squire,
- —SEPTON CELLADAR, a drunken devout,
- —SER ENDREW TARTH, master-at-arms,
- —brothers of Castle Black:
  - —DONAL NOYE, armorer and smith, one-armed,
  - —THREE-FINGER HOBB, cook,

—JEREN, RAST, CUGEN, recruits still in training,

—CONWY, GUEREN, "wandering crows," recruiters who collect orphan boys and criminals for the Wall,

—YOREN, the senior of the "wandering crows,"

—PRAED, CUTJACK, WOTH, REYSEN, QYLE, recruits bound for the Wall,

—KOSS, GERREN, DOBBER, KURZ, BITER, RORGE, JAQEN H'GHAR, criminals bound for the Wall,

—LOMMY GREENHANDS, GENDRY, TARBER, HOT PIE, ARRY, orphan boys bound for the Wall.

At Eastwatch-by-the-Sea

COTTER PYKE, Commander, Eastwatch,

—SER ALLISER THORNE, master-at-arms,

—brothers of Eastwatch:

—DAREON, steward and singer.

At the Shadow Tower

SER DENYS MALLISTER, Commander, Shadow Tower,

—QHORIN called HALFHAND, a senior ranger,

—DALBRIDGE, an elderly squire and senior ranger,

—EBBEN, STONESNAKE, rangers.

ACKNOWLEDGMENTS

More details, more devils.

This time around, the angels who helped me put them to rest included Walter Jon Williams, Sage Walker, Melinda Snodgrass, and Carl Keim.

Thanks as well to my patient editors and publishers: Anne Groell, Nita Taublib, Joy Chamberlain, Jane Johnson, and Malcolm Edwards.

And finally, a tip o' the tilting helm to Parris for her Magic Coffee, the fuel that built the Seven Kingdoms.

George R. R. Martin's
epic fantasy saga
A Song of Ice and Fire

begins with
A GAME OF THRONES

and continues in
A CLASH OF KINGS

A STORM OF SWORDS

A FEAST FOR CROWS

and

A DANCE WITH DRAGONS

Don't miss any volume in the series!

Now, here's a special preview of
the next book in

George R. R. Martin's

landmark series

A STORM OF SWORDS

the riveting sequel to

A GAME OF THRONES

and

A CLASH OF KINGS

On sale now

SANSA

The invitation seemed innocent enough, but every time Sansa read it, her tummy tightened into a knot. *She's to be queen now, she's beautiful and rich and everyone loves her, why would Margaery Tyrell want to sup with a traitor's daughter?* It could be simple curiosity, she supposed; perhaps Margaery wanted to get the measure of the rival she'd displaced. *Does she resent me, I wonder? Does she think I bear her ill-will . . .*

Three days before, Sansa had watched from the castle walls as Margaery Tyrell and her escort had entered the city and made their way up Aegon's High Hill. Joffrey had met his new bride-to-be at the King's Gate to welcome her to the city, and they rode side by side through cheering crowds, Joff glittering in gilded armor and the Tyrell girl splendid in green silk with a cloak of autumn flowers blowing from her shoulders. She was sixteen, brown-haired and brown-eyed, slender and beautiful. The people called out her name as she passed, held up their children for her blessing, and scattered flowers under the hooves of her horse. Her mother and grandmother followed close behind, riding in a tall wheelhouse whose sides were carved into the shape of a hundred twining roses, every one gilded and shining. The smallfolk cheered them as well.

They pulled me from my horse and would have killed me, if not for the Hound, Sansa remembered, resentful. She had done nothing to make the commons hate her, no more than Margaery Tyrell had done to win their love.

Does she want me to love her too? Sansa studied the invitation, which looked to be written in Margaery's own hand. *Does she want my blessing?* She wondered if Joffrey knew of this supper. The king might not be pleased by the thought of his betrothed breaking bread with the woman she had supplanted. *Unless it is his doing.* That thought made her fearful. If Joff was behind the invitation, he would have some cruel jape planned to shame her in the older girl's eyes. Would he command his Kingsguard to strip her naked once again? The last time he had done that his uncle Tyrion had stopped him, but the Imp could not save her now.

No one can save me but my Florian. Ser Dontos had promised he would help her escape, but not until the night of Joffrey's wedding. The plans had been well laid, her dear devoted knight-turned-fool assured her; there was nothing to do until then but endure, and count the days.

And sup with my replacement . . .

Perhaps she was doing Margaery Tyrell an injustice. Perhaps the invitation was no more than a simple kindness, an act of courtesy. *It might be just a supper.* But this was the Red Keep, this was King's Landing, this was the court of King Joffrey Baratheon, the First of His Name, and if there was one thing that Sansa Stark had learned here, it was mistrust.

Even so, she must accept. She was nothing now, the discarded daughter of a traitor and disgraced sister of a rebel lord. She could scarcely refuse Joffrey's queen-to-be.

I wish the Hound were still here. The night of the battle, Sandor Clegane had come to her chambers and offered to take her from the city, but Sansa had refused. Sometimes she lay awake at night, wondering if she'd been wise. She had his stained white cloak hidden in a cedar chest beneath her summer silks. She could not say why she'd kept it. The Hound had turned craven, she heard it said; at the height of the battle, he got so drunk the Imp had to take his men. But Sansa understood. She knew the secret of his burned face. *It was only the fire he feared.* That night, the wildfire had set the river itself ablaze, and filled the very air with green flame. Even in the safety of the castle, Sansa had been afraid. Outside . . . she could scarcely imagine it.

Sighing, Sansa got out quill and ink, and wrote Margaery Tyrell a gracious note of acceptance.

When the appointed night arrived, another of the Kingsguard came for her, a man as different from Sandor Clegane as . . . *well, as a flower from a dog.* The sight of Ser Loras Tyrell standing on her threshold made Sansa's heart beat a little faster. This was the first time she had been so close to him since he had returned to King's Landing, leading the vanguard of his father's host. For a moment she did know what to say. "Ser Loras," she finally managed, "you . . . you look so lovely."

He gave her a puzzled smile. "My lady is too kind. And beautiful besides. My sister awaits you eagerly."

"I have so looked forward to our supper."

"As has Margaery, and my lady grandmother as well." He took her arm and led her toward the steps.

"Your grandmother?" Sansa was finding it hard to walk and talk and think all at the same time, with Ser Loras touching her arm. She could feel the warmth of his hand through the silk.

"Lady Olenna. She is to sup with you as well."

"Oh," said Sansa. *I am talking to him, and he's touching me, he's holding my arm and touching me.* "The Queen of Thorns, she's called. Isn't that right?"

"It is." Ser Loras laughed. *He has the warmest laugh,* she thought, as he went on, "You'd best not use that name in her presence, though, or you're like to get pricked."

Sansa reddened. Any fool would have realized that no woman would be happy about being called 'the Queen of Thorns.' *Maybe I truly am as stupid as Cersei Lannister says.* Desperately she tried to think of something clever and charming to say to him, but her wits had deserted her. She almost told him how beautiful he was, until she remembered that she'd already done that.

He *was* beautiful, though. He seemed taller than he'd been when she'd first met him, but still so lithe and graceful, and Sansa had never seen another boy with such wonderful eyes. *He's no boy, though, he's a man grown, a knight of the Kingsguard.* She thought he looked even finer in white than in the greens and golds of House Tyrell. The only spot of color on him now was the brooch that clasped his cloak; the rose of Highgarden wrought in soft yellow gold, nestled in a bed of delicate green jade leaves.

Ser Balon Swann held the door of Maegor's for them to

pass. He was all in white as well, though he did not wear it half so well as Ser Loras. Beyond the spiked moat, two dozen men were taking their practice with sword and shield. With the castle so crowded, the outer ward had been given over to guests to raise their tents and pavilions, leaving only the smaller inner yards for training. One of the Redwyne twins was being driven backwards by Ser Tallad, with the eyes on his shield. Chunky Ser Kennos of Kayce, who chuffed and puffed every time he raised his longsword, seemed to be holding his own against Osney Kettleblack, but Osney's brother Ser Osfryd was savagely punishing the frog-faced squire Morros Slynt. Blunted swords or no, Slynt would have a rich crop of bruises by the morrow. It made Sansa wince just to watch. *They have scarcely finished burying the dead from the last battle, and already they are practicing for the next one.*

On the edge of the yard, a lone knight with a pair of golden roses on his shield was holding off three foes. Even as they watched, he caught one of them alongside the head, knocking him senseless. "Is that your brother?" Sansa asked.

"It is, my lady," said Ser Loras. "Garlan often trains against three men, or even four. In battle it is seldom one against one, he says, so he likes to be prepared."

"He must be very brave."

"He is a great knight," Ser Loras replied. "A better sword than me, in truth, though I'm the better lance."

"I remember," said Sansa. "You ride wonderfully, ser."

"My lady is gracious to say so. When has she seen me ride?"

"At the Hand's tourney, don't you remember? You rode a white courser, and your armor was a hundred different kinds of flowers. You gave me a rose. A *red* rose. You threw white roses to the other girls that day." It made her flush to speak of it. "You said no victory was half as beautiful as me."

Ser Loras gave her a modest smile. "I spoke only a simple truth, that any man with eyes could see."

He doesn't remember, Sansa realized, startled. *He is only being kind to me, he doesn't remember me or the rose or any of it.* She had been so certain that it meant something, that it meant *everything*. A *red* rose, not a white. "It was after you unhorsed Ser Robar Royce," she said, desperately.

He took his hand from her arm. "I slew Robar at Storm's End, my lady." It was not a boast; he sounded sad. *Him, and another of King Renly's Rainbow Guard as well, yes.* Sansa had heard the women talking of it round the well, but for a moment she'd forgotten. "That was when Lord Renly was killed, wasn't it? How terrible for your poor sister."

"For Margaery?" His voice was tight. "To be sure. She was at Bitterbridge, though. She did not see."

"Even so, when she heard . . ."

Ser Loras brushed the hilt of his sword lightly with his hand. Its grip was white leather, its pommel a rose in alabaster. "Renly is dead. Robar as well. What use to speak of them?"

The sharpness in his tone took her aback. "I . . . my lord, I . . . I did not mean to give offense, ser."

"Nor could you, Lady Sansa," Ser Loras replied, but all the warmth had gone from his voice. Nor did he take her arm again.

They ascended the serpentine steps in a deepening silence. *Oh, why did I have to mention Ser Robar?* Sansa thought. *I've ruined everything. He is angry with me now.* She tried to think of something she might say to make amends, but all the words that came to her were lame and weak. *Be quiet, or you will only make it worse,* she told herself.

Lord Mace Tyrell and his entourage had been housed behind the royal sept, in the long slate-roofed keep that had been called the Maidenvault since King Baelor the Blessed had confined his sisters therein, so the sight of them might not tempt him into carnal thoughts. Outside its tall carved doors stood two guards in gilded halfhelms and green cloaks edged in gold satin, the golden rose of Highgarden sewn on their breasts. Both were seven-footers, wide of shoulder and narrow of waist, magnificently muscled. When Sansa got close enough to see their faces, she could not tell one from the other. They had the same strong jaws, the same deep blue eyes, the same thick, red mustaches. "Who are they?" she asked Ser Loras, her discomfit forgotten for a moment.

"My grandmother's personal guard," he told her. "Their mother named them Erryk and Arryk, but grandmother can't tell them apart, so she calls them Left and Right."

Left and Right opened the doors, and Margaery Tyrell herself emerged and swept down the short flight of steps to greet them. "Lady Sansa," she called, "I'm so pleased you came. Be welcome."

Sansa knelt at the feet of her future queen. "You do me great honor, Your Grace."

"Won't you call me Margaery? Please, rise. Loras, help the Lady Sansa to her feet. Might I call you Sansa?"

"If it please you." Ser Loras helped her up.

Margaery dismissed him with a sisterly kiss, and took Sansa by the hand. "Come, my grandmother awaits, and she is not the most patient of ladies."

A fire was crackling in the hearth, and sweet-swelling rushes had been scattered on the floor. Around the long trestle table a dozen women were seated.

Sansa recognized only Lord Tyrell's tall, dignified wife, Lady Alerie, whose long silvery braid was bound with jeweled rings. Margaery performed the other introductions. There were three Tyrell cousins, Megga and Alla and Elinor, all close to Sansa's age. Buxom Lady Janna was Lord Tyrell's sister, and wed to one of the red-apple Fossoways; dainty, bright-eyed Lady Leonette was of the green-apple Fossoways, and wed to Ser Garlan. Septa Nysterica had a homely pox-scarred face but seemed jolly. Pale, elegant Lady Graceford was with child, and Lady Bulwer *was* a child, no more than eight. And "Merry" was what she was to call boisterous plump Meredyth Crane, but most definitely *not* Lady Merryweather, a sultry black-eyed Myrish beauty.

Last of all, Margaery brought her before the wizened white-haired doll of a woman at the head of the table. "I am honored to present my grandmother the Lady Olenna, widow to the late Luthor Tyrell, Lord of Highgarden, whose memory is a comfort to us all."

The old woman smelled of rosewater. *Why, she's just the littlest bit of a thing.* There was nothing the least bit thorny about her. "Kiss me, child," Lady Olenna said, tugging at Sansa's wrist with a soft spotted hand. "It is so kind of you to sup with me and my foolish flock of hens."

Dutifully, Sansa kissed the old woman on the cheek. "It is kind of you to have me, my lady."

"I knew your grandfather, Lord Rickard, though not well."

"He died before I was born."

"I am aware of that, child. It's said that your Tully grandfather is dying too. Lord Hoster, surely they told you? An old man, though not so old as me. Still, night falls for all of us in the end, and too soon for some. You would know that more than most, poor child. You've had your share of grief, I know. We are sorry for your losses."

Sansa glanced at Margaery. "I was saddened when I heard of Lord Renly's death, Your Grace. He was very gallant."

"You are kind to say so," answered Margaery.

Her grandmother snorted. "Gallant, yes, and charming, and very clean. He knew how to dress and he knew how to smile and he knew how to bathe, and somehow he got the notion that this made him fit to be king. The Baratheons have always had some queer notions, to be sure. It comes from their Targaryen blood, I should think." She sniffed. "They tried to marry me to a Targaryen once, but I soon put an end to that."

"Renly was brave and gentle, grandmother," said Margaery. "Father liked him as well, and so did Loras."

"Loras is young," Lady Olenna said crisply, "and very good at knocking men off horses with a stick. That does not make him wise. As to your father, would that I'd been born a peasant woman with a big wooden spoon, I might have been able to beat some sense into his fat head."

"*Mother*," Lady Alerie scolded.

"Hush, Alerie, don't take that tone with me. And don't call me mother. If I'd given birth to you, I'm sure I'd remember. I'm only to blame for your husband, the lord oaf of Highgarden."

"Grandmother," Margaery said, "mind your words, or what will Sansa think of us?"

"She might think we have some wits about us. One of us, at any rate." The old woman turned back to Sansa. "It's treason, I warned them, Robert has two sons, and

Renly has an older brother, how can he *possibly* have any claim to that ugly iron chair? Tut-tut, says my son, don't you want your sweetling to be queen? You Starks were kings once, the Arryns and the Lannisters as well, and even the Baratheons through the female line, but the Tyrells were no more than stewards until Aegon the Dragon came along and cooked the rightful King of the Reach on the Field of Fire. If truth be told, even our claim to Highgarden is a bit dodgy, just as those dreadful Florents are always claiming. 'What does it matter?' you ask, and of course it doesn't, except to oafs like my son. The thought that one day he may see his grandson with his arse on the Iron Throne makes Mace puff up like . . . now, what do you call it? Margaery, you're clever, be a dear and tell your poor old half-daft grandmother the name of that queer fish from the Summer Isles that puffs up to ten times its own size when you poke it."

"They call them puff fish, grandmother."

"Of course they do. Summer Islanders have no imagina-tion. My son ought to take the puff fish for his sigil, if truth be told. He could put a crown on it, the way the Baratheons do their stag, mayhaps that would make him happy. We should have stayed well out of all this bloody foolishness if you ask me, but once the cow's been milked there's no squirting the cream back up her udder. After Lord Puff Fish put that crown on Renly's head, we were into the pudding up to our knees, so here we are to see things through. And what do you say to that, Sansa?"

Sansa's mouth opened and closed. She felt very like a puff fish herself. "The Tyrells can trace their descent back to Garth Greenhand," was the best she could manage at short notice.

The Queen of Thorns snorted. "So can the Florents, the Rowans, the Oakhearts and half the other noble houses of the south. Garth liked to plant his seed in fertile ground, they say. I shouldn't wonder that more than his hands were green."

"*Sansa,*" Lady Alerie broke in, "you must be very hun-gry. Shall we have a bite of boar together, and some lemon cakes?"

"Lemon cakes are my favorite," Sansa admitted.

"So we have been told," declared Lady Olenna, who

obviously had no intention of being hushed. "That Varys creature seemed to think we should be grateful for the information. I've never been quite sure what the *point* of a eunuch is, if truth be told. It seems to me they're only men with the useful bits cut off. Alerie, will you have them bring the food, or do you mean to starve me to death? Here, Sansa, sit here next to me, I'm much less boring than these others. I hope that you're fond of fools."

Sansa smoothed down her skirts and sat. "I think . . . fools, my lady? You mean . . . the sort in motley?"

"Feathers, in this case. What did you imagine I was speaking of? My son? Or these lovely ladies? No, don't blush, with your hair it makes you look like a pomegranate. All men are fools, if truth be told, but the ones in motley are more amusing than ones with crowns. Margaery, child, summon Butterbumps, let us see if we can't make Lady Sansa smile. The rest of you be seated, do I have to tell you everything? Sansa must think that my granddaughter is attended by a flock of sheep."

Butterbumps arrived before the food, dressed in a jester's suit of green and yellow feathers with a floppy coxcomb. An immense round fat man, as big as three Moon Boys, he came cartwheeling into the hall, vaulted onto the table, and laid a gigantic egg right in front of Sansa. "Break it, my lady," he commanded. When she did, a dozen yellow chicks escaped and began running in all directions. *"Catch them!"* Butterbumps exclaimed. Little Lady Bulwer snagged one and handed to him, whereby he tilted back his head, popped it into his huge rubbery mouth, and seemed to swallow it whole. When he belched, tiny yellow feathers flew out his nose. Lady Bulwer began to wail in distress, but her tears turned into a sudden squeal of delight when the chick came squirming out of the sleeve of her gown and ran down her arm.

As the servants brought out a broth of leeks and mushrooms, Butterbumps began to juggle and Lady Olenna pushed herself forward to rest her elbows on the table. "Do you know my son, Sansa? Lord Puff Fish of Highgarden?"

"A great lord," Sansa answered politely.

"A great oaf," said the Queen of Thorns. "His father was an oaf as well. My husband, the late Lord Luthor. Oh,

I loved him well enough, don't mistake me. A kind man, and not unskilled in the bedchamber, but an appalling oaf all the same. He managed to ride off a cliff whilst hawking. They say he was looking up at the sky and paying no mind to where his horse was taking him.

"And now my oaf son is doing the same, only he's riding a lion instead of a palfrey. It is easy to mount a lion and not so easy to get off, I warned him, but he only chuckles. Should you ever have a son, Sansa, beat him frequently so he learns to mind you. I only had the one boy and I hardly beat him at all, so now he pays more heed to Butterbumps than he does to me. A lion is not a lap cat, I told him, and he gives me a tut-tut-mother. There is entirely too much tut-tutting in this realm, if you ask me. All these kings would do a deal better if they would put down their swords and listen to their mothers."

Sansa realized that her mouth was open again. She filled it with a spoon of broth while Lady Alerie and the other women were giggling at the spectacle of Butterbumps bouncing oranges off his head, his elbows, and his ample rump.

"I want you to tell me the truth about this royal boy," said Lady Olenna abruptly. "This Joffrey."

Sansa's fingers tightened round her spoon. *The truth? I can't. Don't ask it, please, I can't.* "I . . . I . . . I . . ."

"You, yes. Who would know better? The lad seems kingly enough, I'll grant you. A bit full of himself, but that would be his Lannister blood. We have heard some troubling tales, however. Is there any truth to them? Has this boy mistreated you?"

Sansa glanced about nervously. Butterbumps popped a whole orange into his mouth, chewed and swallowed, slapped his cheek, and blew seeds out of his nose. The women giggled and laughed. Servants were coming and going, and the Maidenvault echoed to the clatter of spoons and plates. One of the chicks hopped back onto the table and ran through Lady Graceford's broth. No one seemed to be paying them any mind, but even so, she was frightened.

Lady Olenna was growing impatient. "Why are you gaping at Butterbumps? I asked a question, I expect an answer. Have the Lannisters stolen your tongue, child?"

Ser Dontos had warned her to speak freely only in the godswood. "Joff . . . King Joffrey, he's . . . His Grace is very fair and handsome, and . . . and as brave as a lion."

"Yes, all the Lannisters are lions, and when a Tyrell breaks wind it smells just like a rose," the old woman snapped. "But how *kind* is he? How clever? Has he a good heart, a gentle hand? Is he chivalrous as befits a king? Will he cherish Margaery and treat her tenderly, protect her honor as he would his own?"

"He will," Sansa lied. "He is very . . . very comely."

"You said that. You know, child, some say that you are as big a fool as Butterbumps here, and I am starting to believe them. *Comely!* I have taught my Margaery what comely is worth, I hope. Somewhat less than a mummer's fart. Aerion Brightflame was comely enough, but he was a monster all the same. The question is, what is Joffrey?" She reached to snag a passing servant. "I am not fond of leeks. Take this broth away, and bring me some cheese."

"The cheese will be served after the cakes, my lady."

"The cheese will be served when I want it served, and I want it served now." The old woman turned back to Sansa. "Are you frightened, child? No need for that, we're only women here. Tell me the truth, no harm will come to you?"

"My father always told the truth." Sansa spoke quietly, but even so, it was hard to get the words out.

"Lord Eddard, yes, he had that reputation, but they named him traitor and took his head off all the same." The old woman's eyes bore into her, sharp and bright as the points of swords.

"Joffrey," Sansa said. "Joffrey did that. He promised me he would be merciful, and cut my father's head off. He said *that* was mercy, and he took me up on the walls and made me look at it. The head. He wanted me to weep, but . . ." She stopped abruptly, and covered her mouth. *I've said too much, oh gods be good, they'll know, they'll hear, someone will tell on me.*

"Go on." It was Margaery who urged. Joffrey's own queen-to-be. Sansa did not know how much she had heard.

"I can't." *What if she tells him, what if she tells? He'll kill me for certain then, or give me to Ser Ilyn.* "I never meant . . . my father was a traitor, my brother as well, I have the traitor's blood, please, don't make me say more."

"Calm yourself, child," the Queen of Thorns commanded.

"She's terrified, grandmother, just look at her."

The old woman called to Butterbumps. *"Fool!* Give us a song. A long one, I should think. 'The Bear and the Maiden Fair' will do nicely."

"It will!" the huge jester replied. "It will do nicely indeed! Shall I sing it standing my head, my lady?"

"Will that make it sound better?"

"No."

"Stand on your feet, then. We wouldn't want your hat to fall off. As I recall, you never wash your hair."

"As my lady commands." Butterbumps bowed low, let loose of an enormous belch, then straightened, threw out his belly, and bellowed. *"A bear there was, a bear, a BEAR! All black and brown, and covered with hair . . ."*

Lady Olenna squirmed forward. "Even when I was a girl younger than you, it was well known that in the Red Keep the very walls have ears. Well, they will be the better for a song, and meanwhile we girls shall speak freely."

"But," Sansa said, "Varys . . . he *knows,* he always . . ."

"Sing louder!" the Queen of Thorns shouted at Butterbumps. "These old ears are almost deaf, you know. Are you whispering at me, you fat fool? I don't pay you for whispers. *Sing!"*

". . . THE BEAR!" thundered Butterbumps, his great deep voice echoing off the rafters. *"OH, COME, THEY SAID, OH COME TO THE FAIR! THE FAIR! SAID HE, BUT I'M A BEAR! ALL BLACK AND BROWN, AND COVERED WITH HAIR!"*

The wrinkled old lady smiled. "At Highgarden we have many spiders amongst the flowers. So long as they keep to themselves we let them spin their little webs, but if they get underfoot we step on him." She patted Sansa on the back of the hand. "Now, child, the truth. What sort of man is this Joffrey, who calls himself Baratheon but looks so very Lannister?"

"AND DOWN THE ROAD FROM HERE TO THERE. FROM HERE! TO THERE! THREE BOYS, A GOAT, AND A DANCING BEAR!"

Sansa felt as though her heart had lodged in her throat. The Queen of Thorns was so close she could smell the old woman's sour breath. Her gaunt thin fingers were pinching her wrist. To her other side, Margaery was listening as well. A shiver went through her. "A monster," she whispered, so tremulously she could scarcely hear her own voice. "Joffrey is a monster. He lied about the butcher's boy and made Father kill my wolf. When I displease him, he has the Kingsguard beat me. He's evil and cruel, my lady, it's so. And the queen as well."

Lady Olenna Tyrell and her granddaughter exchanged a look. "Ah," said the old woman, "that's a pity."

Oh, gods, thought Sansa, horrified. *Now Margaery won't marry him, and Joff will know that I'm to blame.* "Please," she blurted, "don't stop the wedding . . ."

"Have no fear, Lord Puff Fish is determined that Margaery shall be queen. And the word of a Tyrell is worth more than all the gold in Casterly Rock. At least it was in my day. Even so, we thank you for the truth, child."

". . . DANCED AND SPUN, ALL THE WAY TO THE FAIR! THE FAIR! THE FAIR!" Butterbumps hopped and roared and stomped his feet.

"Sansa, would you like to visit Highgarden?" When Margaery Tyrell smiled, she looked very like her brother Loras. "All the autumn flowers are in bloom just now, and there are groves and fountains, shady courtyards, marble colonnades. My lord father always keeps singers at court, sweeter ones than Butters here, and pipes and fiddlers and harpers as well. We have the best horses, and pleasure boats to sail along the Mander. Do you hawk, Sansa?"

"A little," she admitted.

"OH, SWEET SHE WAS, AND PURE, AND FAIR! THE MAID WITH HONEY IN HER HAIR!"

"You will love Highgarden as I do, I know it." Margaery brushed back a loose strand of Sansa's hair. "Once you see it, you'll never want to leave. And perhaps you won't have to."

"HER HAIR! HER HAIR! THE MAID WITH HONEY IN HER HAIR!"

"Shush, child," the Queen of Thorns said sharply. "Sansa hasn't even told us that she would like to come for a visit."

"Oh, but I would," Sansa said. Highgarden sounded like the place she had always dreamed of, like the beautiful magical court she had once hoped to find at King's Landing.

". . . SMELLED THE SCENT ON THE SUMMER AIR. THE BEAR! THE BEAR! ALL BLACK AND BROWN AND COVERED WITH HAIR."

"But the queen," Sansa went on, "she won't let me go . . ."

"She will. Without Highgarden, the Lannisters have no hope of keeping Joffrey on his throne. If my son the lord oaf asks, she will have no choice but to grant his request."

"Will he?" asked Sansa. "Will he ask?"

Lady Olenna frowned. "I see no need to give him a choice. Of course, he has no hint of our true purpose."

"HE SMELLED THE SCENT ON THE SUMMER AIR!"

Sansa wrinkled her brow. "Our true purpose, my lady?"

"HE SNIFFED AND ROARED AND SMELLED IT THERE! HONEY ON THE SUMMER AIR!"

"To see you safely wed, child," the old woman said, as Butterbumps bellowed out the old, old song, "to my grandson."

Wed to Ser Loras, oh . . . Sansa's breath caught in her throat. She remembered Ser Loras in his sparkling sapphire armor, tossing her a rose. Ser Loras in white silk, so pure, innocent, beautiful. The dimples at the corner of his mouth when he smiled. The sweetness of his laugh, the warmth of his hand. She could only imagine what it would be like to pull up his tunic and caress the smooth skin underneath, to stand on her toes and kiss him, to run her fingers through those thick brown curls and drown in his deep brown eyes. A flush crept up her neck.

"OH, I'M A MAID, AND I'M PURE AND FAIR! I'LL NEVER DANCE WITH A HAIRY BEAR! A BEAR! A BEAR! I'LL NEVER DANCE WITH A HAIRY BEAR!"

"Would you like that, Sansa?" asked Margaery. "I've

never had a sister, only brothers. Oh, please say yes, please say that you will consent to marry my brother."

The words came tumbling out her. "Yes. I will. I would like that more than anything. To wed Ser Loras, to love him . . ."

"*Loras?*" Lady Olenna sounded annoyed. "Don't be foolish, child. Kingsguard never wed. Didn't they teach you anything in Winterfell? We were speaking of my grandson Willas. He is a bit old for you, to be sure, but a dear boy for all that. Not the least bit oafish, and heir to Highgarden besides."

Sansa felt dizzy; one instant her head was full of dreams of Loras, and the next they had all been snatched away. *Willas! Willas!* "I," she said stupidly. *Courtesy is a lady's armor. You must not offend them, be careful what you say.* "I do not know Ser Willas. I have never had the pleasure, my lady. Is he . . . is he as great a knight as his brothers?"

"*. . . LIFTED HER HIGH INTO THE AIR! THE BEAR! THE BEAR!*"

"No," Margaery said. "He has never taken vows."

Her grandmother frowned. "Tell the girl the truth. The poor lad is crippled, and that's the way of it."

"He was hurt as a squire, riding in his first tourney," Margaery confided. "His horse fell and crushed his leg."

"That snake of a Dornishman was to blame, that Oberyn Martell. And his maester as well."

"*I CALLED FOR A KNIGHT, BUT YOU'RE A BEAR! A BEAR! A BEAR! ALL BLACK AND BROWN AND COVERED WITH HAIR!*"

"Willas has a bad leg but a good heart," said Margaery. "He used to read to me when I was a little girl, and draw me pictures of the stars. You will love him as much as we do, Sansa."

"*SHE KICKED AND WAILED, THE MAID SO FAIR, BUT HE LICKED THE HONEY FROM HER HAIR. HER HAIR! HER HAIR! HE LICKED THE HONEY FROM HER HAIR!*"

"When might I meet him?" asked Sansa, hesitantly.

"Soon," promised Margaery. "When you come to Highgarden, after Joffrey and I are wed. My grandmother will take you."

"I will," said the old woman, patting Sansa's hand and smiling a soft wrinkly smile. "I will indeed."

"THEN SHE SIGHED AND SQUEALED AND KICKED THE AIR! MY BEAR! SHE SANG. MY BEAR SO FAIR! AND OFF THEY WENT, FROM HERE TO THERE, THE BEAR, THE BEAR, AND THE MAIDEN FAIR." Butterbumps roared the last line, leapt into the air, and came down on both feet with a crash that shook the wine cups on the table. The women laughed and clapped.

"I thought that dreadful song would never end," said the Queen of Thorns. "But look, here comes my cheese."

Also by
GEORGE R. R. MARTIN

Novels

The
Armageddon Rag

Fevre Dream

Windhaven

Dying of the Light

Short Stories

Dreamsongs:
Volume I

Dreamsongs:
Volume II

Also available in Audio and eBook

THE RANDOM HOUSE PUBLISHING GROUP
www.GeorgeRRMartin.com

GAME OF THRONES™

THE COMPLETE FIRST SEASON

INCLUDES HOURS OF BONUS CONTENT INCLUDING INTERACTIVE GUIDES, SEVEN AUDIO COMMENTARIES, AND NEVER-BEFORE-SEEN FOOTAGE FROM THE SET.

NOW AVAILABLE
ON BLU-RAY™, DVD
AND DIGITAL DOWNLOAD

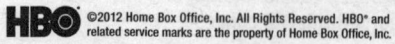

Praise for
GEORGE R. R. MARTIN
and
A SONG OF ICE AND FIRE

A FEAST FOR CROWS

"Of those who work in the grand epic-fantasy tradition, Martin is by far the best. In fact . . . this is as good a time as any to proclaim him the American Tolkien. . . . What really distinguishes Martin, and what marks him as a major force for evolution in fantasy, is his refusal to embrace a vision of the world as a Manichaean struggle between Good and Evil. Tolkien's work has enormous imaginative force, but you have to go elsewhere for moral complexity. Martin's wars are multifaceted and ambiguous, as are the men and women who wage them and the gods who watch them and chortle, and somehow that makes them mean more. *A Feast for Crows* isn't pretty elves against gnarly orcs. It's men and women slugging it out in the muck, for money and power and lust and love." —*Time*

"The complicated machinations as various characters jockey for power and position are only half of the reason to pick up this immensely entertaining series. With his introduction of characters that aren't as black and white as those typical of the genre, Martin has brought depth and believability to the usually cartoonish fantasy genre. . . . Martin's A Song of Ice and Fire series is that rare, once-in-a-generation work of fiction that manages to entertain readers while elevating an entire genre to fine literature."
—*Milwaukee Journal Sentinel*

"Martin's command of English and of characterization and setting remains equal to the task of the fantasy megasaga. . . . Good news for readers of robust appetite."
—*Booklist*

"What's A Song of Ice and Fire? It's the only fantasy series I'd put on a level with J.R.R. Tolkien's The Lord of the Rings. It's way better than the Harry Potter books and definitely not for children. It's a fantasy series for hip, smart people, even those who don't read fantasy."
—*Detroit Free Press/Chicago Tribune*

"A Song of Ice and Fire is firmly at the top of the bestseller lists, probably because it's the best fantasy series out there." —*Detroit Free Press*

"George R. R. Martin has created the unlikely genre of the realpolitik fantasy novel. Complete with warring kings, noble heroes and backroom dealings, it's addictive reading and reflects our current world a lot better than The Lord of the Rings." —*Rolling Stone*

"Martin has created a full, rich and interesting world filled with colorful characters. Some are heroic, some funny, some sinister, and alliances and betrayals come fast and frequently. Beautiful faces as often as not hide ugly minds, and few people are what they seem at first glance. One is just as likely to be tortured and killed at the hands of a priest or nun as a knight or bandit. . . . The plots and subplots are too tangled to try and unravel here; the intrigue is thick, the action brutal and the sex and violence worthy of at least an 'R' rating. This is a series for adults, not children, and readers expecting clean-cut Harry Potter will find themselves less than comfortable in

Martin's world. But if you're looking for a thick and delicious book to curl up with on rainy and cold fall evenings, this is just the ticket."—*Portland Oregonian*

"Mainstream readers . . . have a great treat ahead of them in Martin. *A Feast for Crows* is a fast-paced, emotionally complex, masterfully written adventure. . . . Most fantasy writers follow the battle-of-good-and-evil model of their great predecessor, J.R.R. Tolkien. Not Martin. He draws his protagonists from several warring families and shows what's happening through their eyes, switching with each chapter and telling their stories so compellingly that we root for them all to win—even though if any of them does, it will be a disaster for the others. . . . Martin's writing is as good as ever: His imaginary places are as vivid and thoroughly imagined, his characters as consistent and believable, his blood as wet and red. As for the missing characters, like the long, looming winter, they're coming soon." —*Newsday*

"Another splendid installment." —*Time Out London*

"Featuring a large, well-fleshed-out cast of characters, excellent writing (of the sort that made T.H. White's *Once and Future King* a classic), gritty details and a page-turning plot, Martin's latest novel in his A Song of Ice and Fire fantasy series continues to do the genre proud."
—STL today.com

"For a succinct summation of Martin's medieval fantasy series, imagine a mix of the literary quality of T.H. White's *Once and Future King,* the in-your-face, you-are-there grittiness of a movie like *Braveheart* and the sort of intricate character development found in a quality tele-

vision show like *Lost*. . . . Vast, complex and undeniably
entertaining. . . . Once in a while, there are books and
writers that manage to elevate an entire genre. Stephen
King did so with horror. George R. R. Martin's A Song of
Ice and Fire series has taken fantasy out of the two-
dimensional, black and white realm where it once happily
existed and dragged it kicking and screaming into a land
of believable characters, ambiguous situations, and
bloody, sometimes uncertain denouements.—*Denver Post*

"Martin doesn't disappoint. . . . A Song of Ice and Fire is
a thrilling fantasy series. . . . Martin's world and characters are so complex that one wonders whether there can
ever be an answer to all the riddles." —*Daily Californian*

A STORM OF SWORDS

"One of the more rewarding examples of gigantism in
contemporary fantasy . . . richly imagined."
—*Publishers Weekly* (starred review)

"George R. R. Martin continues to take epic fantasy to
new levels of insight and sophistication, resonant with the
turmoils and stress of the world we call our own."—*Locus*

"Martin creates a gorgeously and intricately textured
world, peopled with absolutely believable and fascinating
characters." —*Cleveland Plain Dealer*

"High fantasy doesn't get any better than this."
—*Portland Oregonian*

"A riveting continuation of a series whose brilliance continues to dazzle."—*Patriot News*

A CLASH OF KINGS

"Martin amply fulfills the first volume's promise and continues what seems destined to be one of the best fantasy series ever written." —*Denver Post*

"High fantasy with a vengeance."
—*San Diego Union-Tribune*

"Rivals T. H. White's *Once and Future King*."
—*Des Moines Register*

"So complex, fascinating and well-rendered, readers will almost certainly be hooked by the whole series."
—*Oregonian*

"The richness of this invented world and its cultures lends Mr. Martin's novels the feeling of medieval history rather than fiction—except, of course, that he knows how to entertain."
—*Dallas Morning News*

A GAME OF THRONES

"Reminiscent of T. H. White's *The Once and Future King*, this novel is an absorbing combination of the mythic, the sweepingly historical, and the intensely personal."
—*Chicago Sun-Times*

"I always expect the best from George R. R. Martin, and he always delivers. *A Game of Thrones* grabs hold and won't let go. It's brilliant." —Robert Jordan

"Such a splendid tale and such a fantistorical! I read my eyes out." —Anne McCaffrey

BY GEORGE R. R. MARTIN

A SONG OF ICE AND FIRE
Book One: *A Game of Thrones*
Book Two: *A Clash of Kings*
Book Three: *A Storm of Swords*
Book Four: *A Feast for Crows*
Book Five: *A Dance with Dragons*

Dying of the Light
Windhaven (with Lisa Tuttle)
Fevre Dream
The Armageddon Rag
Dead Man's Hand (with John J. Miller)

SHORT STORY COLLECTIONS
Dreamsongs, Volume I
Dreamsongs, Volume II
A Song of Lya and Other Stories
Songs of Stars and Shadows
Sandkings
Songs the Dead Men Sing
Nightflyers
Tuf Voyaging
Portraits of His Children
Quartet

EDITED BY GEORGE R. R. MARTIN
New Voices in Science Fiction, Volumes 1–4
The Science Fiction Weight-Loss Book
(with Isaac Asimov and Martin Harry Greenberg)
The John W. Campbell Awards, Volume 5
Night Visions 3
Wild Card I–XXI

A FEAST
FOR
CROWS

BOOK FOUR OF

A SONG OF ICE AND FIRE

GEORGE R. R. MARTIN

BANTAM BOOKS • NEW YORK

2011 Bantam Books Mass Market Edition

Copyright © 2005 by George R. R. Martin
Excerpt from *A Dance with Dragons* copyright © 2011 by George R. R. Martin

Published in the United States by Bantam Books, an imprint of The Random House Publishing Group, a division of Random House, Inc., New York.

BANTAM BOOKS and the rooster colophon are registered trademarks of Random House, Inc.

Originally published in hardcover in the United States by Bantam Spectra, a division of Random House, Inc., in 2005.

This book contains an excerpt from the forthcoming book *A Dance with Dragons* by George R. R. Martin. This excerpt has been set for this edition only and may not reflect the final content of the forthcoming edition.

ISBN 978-0-553-58202-4
eBook ISBN 978-0-553-90032-3

Cover art copyright © 2011 by Larry Rostant
Cover design by David Stevenson

Maps by James Sinclair
Heraldic crests by Virginia Norey

Printed in the United States of America

www.bantamdell.com

40 39

for Stephen Boucher
wizard of Windows, dragon of DOS
without whom this book would have
been written in crayon

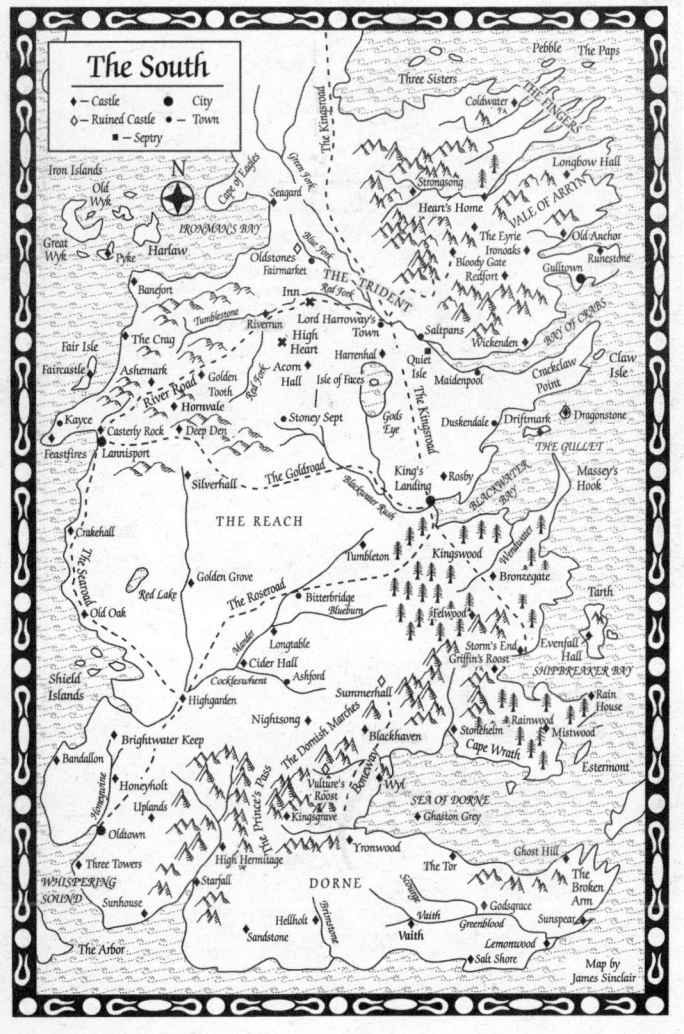

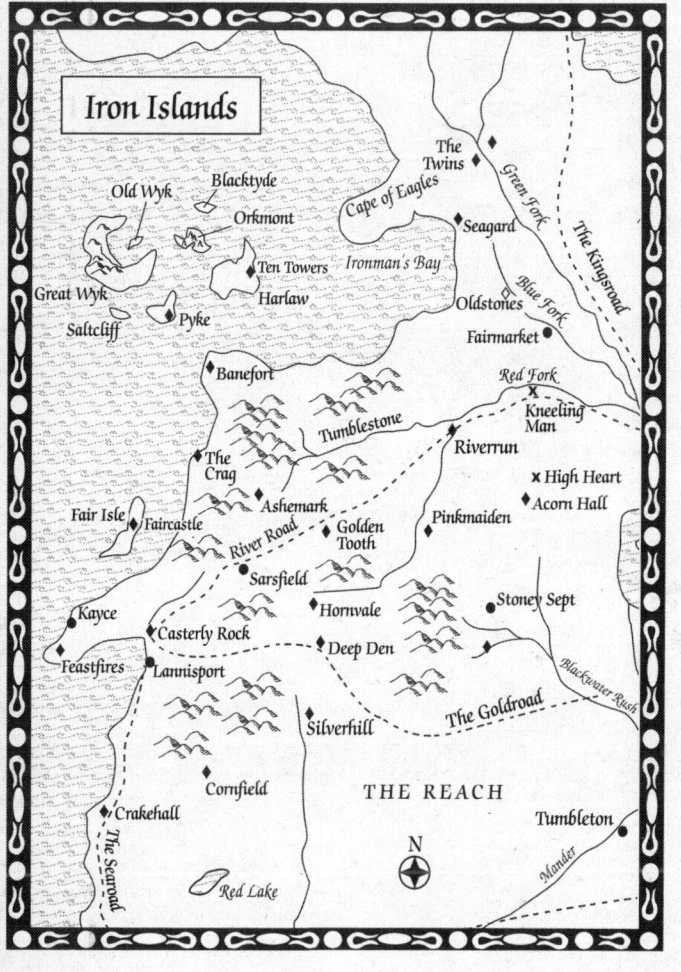

PROLOGUE

Dragons," said Mollander. He snatched a withered apple off the ground and tossed it hand to hand. "Throw the apple," urged Alleras the Sphinx. He slipped an arrow from his quiver and nocked it to his bowstring.

"I should like to see a dragon." Roone was the youngest of them, a chunky boy still two years shy of manhood. "I should like that very much."

And I should like to sleep with Rosey's arms around me, Pate thought. He shifted restlessly on the bench. By the morrow the girl could well be his. *I will take her far from Oldtown, across the narrow sea to one of the Free Cities.* There were no maesters there, no one to accuse him.

He could hear Emma's laughter coming through a shuttered window overhead, mingled with the deeper voice of the man she was entertaining. She was the oldest of the serving wenches at the Quill and Tankard, forty if she was a day, but still pretty in a fleshy sort of way. Rosey was her daughter, fifteen and freshly flowered. Emma had decreed that Rosey's maidenhead would cost a golden dragon. Pate had saved nine silver stags and a pot of copper stars and pennies, for all the good that would do him. He would have stood a better chance of hatching a real dragon than saving up enough coin to make a golden one.

"You were born too late for dragons, lad," Armen the Acolyte told Roone. Armen wore a leather thong about his neck, strung with links of pewter, tin, lead, and copper, and like most acolytes he seemed to believe that novices had turnips growing from their shoulders in place of heads. "The last one perished during the reign of King Aegon the Third."

"The last dragon in *Westeros*," insisted Mollander.

"Throw the apple," Alleras urged again. He was a comely youth, their Sphinx. All the serving wenches doted on him. Even Rosey would sometimes touch him on the arm when she brought him wine, and Pate had to gnash his teeth and pretend not to see.

"The last dragon in Westeros *was* the last dragon," said Armen doggedly. "That is well known."

"The *apple*," Alleras said. "Unless you mean to eat it."

"Here." Dragging his clubfoot, Mollander took a short hop, whirled, and whipped the apple sidearm into the mists that hung above the Honeywine. If not for his foot, he would have been a knight like his father. He had the strength for it in those thick arms and broad shoulders. Far and fast the apple flew . . .

. . . but not as fast as the arrow that whistled after it, a yard-long shaft of golden wood fletched with scarlet feathers. Pate did not see the arrow catch the apple, but he heard it. A soft *chunk* echoed back across the river, followed by a splash.

Mollander whistled. "You cored it. Sweet."

Not half as sweet as Rosey. Pate loved her hazel eyes and budding breasts, and the way she smiled every time she saw him. He loved the dimples in her cheeks. Sometimes she went barefoot as she served, to feel the grass beneath her feet. He loved that too. He loved the clean fresh smell of her, the way her hair curled behind her ears. He even loved her toes. One night she'd let him rub her feet and play with them, and he'd made up a funny tale for every toe to keep her giggling.

Perhaps he would do better to remain on this side of the narrow sea. He could buy a donkey with the coin he'd saved, and he and Rosey could take turns riding it as they wandered Westeros. Ebrose might not think him worthy of the silver, but Pate knew how to set a bone and leech a fever. The smallfolk would be grateful for his help. If he could learn to cut hair and shave beards, he might even be a barber. *That would be enough,* he told himself, *so long as I had Rosey.* Rosey was all that he wanted in the world.

That had not always been so. Once he had dreamed of being a maester in a castle, in service to some open-handed lord who would honor him for his wisdom and bestow a fine white horse on him to thank him for his service. How high he'd ride, how nobly, smiling down at the smallfolk when he passed them on the road . . .

One night in the Quill and Tankard's common room, after his second tankard of fearsomely strong cider, Pate had boasted that he would not always be a novice. "Too true," Lazy Leo had called out. "You'll be a former novice, herding swine."

He drained the dregs of his tankard. The torchlit terrace of the Quill and Tankard was an island of light in a sea of mist this morning. Downriver, the distant beacon of the Hightower floated in the damp of night like a hazy orange moon, but the light did little to lift his spirits.

The alchemist should have come by now. Had it all been some cruel jape, or had something happened to the man? It would not have been the first time that good fortune had turned sour on Pate. He had once counted himself lucky to be chosen to help old Archmaester Walgrave with the ravens, never dreaming that before long he would also be fetching the man's meals, sweeping out his chambers, and dressing him every morning. Everyone said that Walgrave had forgotten more of ravencraft than most maesters ever knew, so Pate assumed a black iron link was the least that he could hope for, only to find that Walgrave could not grant him one. The old man remained an archmaester only by courtesy. As great a maester as once he'd been, now his robes concealed soiled smallclothes oft as not, and half a year ago some acolytes found him weeping in the Library, unable to find his way back to his chambers. Maester Gormon sat below the iron mask in Walgrave's place, the same Gormon who had once accused Pate of theft.

In the apple tree beside the water, a nightingale began to sing. It was a sweet sound, a welcome respite from the harsh screams and endless *quork*ing of the ravens he had tended all day long. The white ravens knew his name, and would mutter it to each other whenever they caught sight of him, *"Pate, Pate, Pate,"* until he wanted to scream. The big white birds were Archmaester Walgrave's pride. He wanted them to eat him when he died, but Pate half suspected that they meant to eat him too.

Perhaps it was the fearsomely strong cider—he had not come here to drink, but Alleras had been buying to celebrate his copper link, and guilt had made him thirsty—but it almost sounded as if the nightingale were trilling *gold for iron, gold for iron, gold for iron*. Which was passing strange, because that was what the stranger had said the night Rosey brought the two of them together. "Who are you?" Pate had demanded of him, and the man had replied, "An alchemist. I can change iron into gold." And then the coin was in his hand, dancing across his knuckles, the soft yellow gold shining in the candlelight. On one side was a three-headed dragon, on the other the head of some dead king. *Gold for iron,* Pate remembered, *you won't do better. Do you want her? Do you love her?* "I am no thief," he had told the man who called himself the alchemist, "I am a novice of the Citadel." The alchemist had bowed his head, and said, "If you should reconsider, I shall return here three days hence, with my dragon."

Three days had passed. Pate had returned to the Quill and Tankard, still uncertain what he was, but instead of the alchemist he'd found Mollander and Armen and the Sphinx, with Roone in tow. It would have raised suspicions not to join them.

The Quill and Tankard never closed. For six hundred years it had been standing on its island in the Honeywine, and never once had its doors been shut to trade. Though the tall, timbered building leaned toward the south the way novices sometimes leaned after a tankard, Pate expected that the inn would go on standing for another six hundred years, selling wine and ale and fearsomely strong cider to rivermen and seamen, smiths and singers, priests and princes, and the novices and acolytes of the Citadel.

"Oldtown is not the world," declared Mollander, too loudly. He was a knight's son, and drunk as drunk could be. Since they brought him word of his father's death upon the Blackwater, he got drunk most every night. Even in Oldtown, far from the fighting and safe behind its walls, the War of the Five Kings had touched them all . . . although Archmaester Benedict insisted that there had never been a war of five kings, since Renly Baratheon had been slain before Balon Greyjoy had crowned himself.

"My father always said the world was bigger than any lord's castle," Mollander went on. "Dragons must be the least of the things a man might find in Qarth and Asshai and Yi Ti. These sailors' stories . . ."

". . . are stories told by sailors," Armen interrupted. "*Sailors,* my dear Mollander. Go back down to the docks, and I wager you'll find sailors who'll tell you of the mermaids that they bedded, or how they spent a year in the belly of a fish."

"How do you know they didn't?" Mollander thumped through the grass, looking for more apples. "You'd need to be down the belly yourself to swear they weren't. One sailor with a story, aye, a man might laugh at that, but when oarsmen off four different ships tell the same tale in four different tongues . . ."

"The tales are *not* the same," insisted Armen. "Dragons in Asshai, dragons in Qarth, dragons in Meereen, Dothraki dragons, dragons freeing slaves . . . each telling differs from the last."

"Only in details." Mollander grew more stubborn when he drank, and even when sober he was bullheaded. "All speak of *dragons,* and a beautiful young queen."

The only dragon Pate cared about was made of yellow gold. He wondered what had happened to the alchemist. *The third day. He said he'd be here.*

"There's another apple near your foot," Alleras called to Mollander, "and I still have two arrows in my quiver."

"Fuck your quiver." Mollander scooped up the windfall. "This one's wormy," he complained, but he threw it anyway. The arrow caught the apple as it began to fall and sliced it clean in two. One half landed on a turret roof, tumbled to a lower roof, bounced, and missed Armen by a foot. "If you cut a worm in two, you make two worms," the acolyte informed them.

"If only it worked that way with apples, no one would ever need go hungry," said Alleras with one of his soft smiles. The Sphinx was always smiling, as if he knew some secret jape. It gave him a wicked look that went well with his pointed chin, widow's peak, and dense mat of close-cropped jet-black curls.

Alleras would make a maester. He had only been at the Citadel for a year, yet already he had forged three links of his maester's chain. Armen might have more, but each of his had taken him a year to earn. Still, he would make a maester too. Roone and Mollander remained pink-necked novices, but Roone was very young and Mollander preferred drinking to reading.

Pate, though . . .

He had been five years at the Citadel, arriving when he was no more than three-and-ten, yet his neck remained as pink as it had been on the day he first arrived from the westerlands. Twice had he believed himself ready. The first time he had gone before Archmaester Vaellyn to demonstrate his knowledge of the heavens. Instead he learned how Vinegar Vaellyn had earned that name. It took Pate two years to summon up the courage to try again. This time he submitted himself to kindly old Archmaester Ebrose, renowned for his soft voice and gentle hands, but Ebrose's sighs had somehow proved just as painful as Vaellyn's barbs.

"One last apple," promised Alleras, "and I will tell you what I suspect about these dragons."

"What could you know that I don't?" grumbled Mollander. He spied an apple on a branch, jumped up, pulled it down, and threw. Alleras drew his bowstring back to his ear, turning gracefully to follow the target in flight. He loosed his shaft just as the apple began to fall.

"You always miss your last shot," said Roone.

The apple splashed down into the river, untouched.

"See?" said Roone.

"The day you make them all is the day you stop improving." Alleras unstrung his longbow and eased it into its leather case. The bow was carved from goldenheart, a rare and fabled wood from the Summer Isles. Pate had tried to bend it once, and failed. *The Sphinx looks slight, but there's strength in those slim arms,* he reflected, as Alleras threw a leg across the bench and reached for his wine cup. "The dragon has three heads," he announced in his soft Dornish drawl.

"Is this a riddle?" Roone wanted to know. "Sphinxes always speak in riddles in the tales."

"No riddle." Alleras sipped his wine. The rest of them were quaffing tankards of the fearsomely strong cider that the Quill and Tankard was renowned for, but he preferred the strange, sweet wines of his mother's country. Even in Oldtown such wines did not come cheap.

It had been Lazy Leo who dubbed Alleras "the Sphinx." A sphinx is a bit of this, a bit of that: a human face, the body of a lion, the wings of a hawk. Alleras was the same: his father was a Dornishman, his mother a black-skinned Summer Islander. His own skin was dark as teak. And like the green marble sphinxes that flanked the Citadel's main gate, Alleras had eyes of onyx.

"No dragon has ever had three heads except on shields and banners," Armen the Acolyte said firmly. "That was a heraldic charge, no more. Furthermore, the Targaryens are all dead."

"Not all," said Alleras. "The Beggar King had a sister."

"I thought her head was smashed against a wall," said Roone.

"No," said Alleras. "It was Prince Rhaegar's young son Aegon whose head was dashed against the wall by the Lion of Lannister's brave men. We speak of Rhaegar's sister, born on Dragonstone before its fall. The one they called Daenerys."

"The *Stormborn*. I recall her now." Mollander lifted his tankard high, sloshing the cider that remained. "Here's to her!" He gulped, slammed his empty tankard down, belched, and wiped his mouth with the back of his hand. "Where's Rosey? Our rightful queen deserves another round of cider, wouldn't you say?"

Armen the Acolyte looked alarmed. "Lower your voice, fool. You should not even jape about such things. You never know who could be listening. The Spider has ears everywhere."

"Ah, don't piss your breeches, Armen. I was proposing a drink, not a rebellion."

Pate heard a chuckle. A soft, sly voice called out from behind him. "I always knew you were a traitor, Hopfrog." Lazy Leo was slouching by the foot of the old plank bridge, draped in satin striped in green and gold, with a black silk half cape pinned to his shoulder by a rose of jade. The wine he'd dribbled down his front had been a robust red, judging from the color of the spots. A lock of his ash-blond hair fell down across one eye.

Mollander bristled at the sight of him. "Bugger that. Go away. You are not welcome here." Alleras laid a hand upon his arm to calm him, whilst Armen frowned. "Leo. My lord. I had understood that you were still confined to the Citadel for . . ."

". . . three more days." Lazy Leo shrugged. "Perestan says the world is forty thousand years old. Mollos says five hundred thousand. What are three days, I ask you?" Though there were a dozen empty tables on the terrace, Leo sat himself at theirs. "Buy me a cup of Arbor gold, Hopfrog, and perhaps I won't inform my father of your toast. The tiles turned against me at the Checkered Hazard, and I wasted my last stag on supper. Suckling pig in plum sauce, stuffed with chestnuts and white truffles. A man must eat. What did you lads have?"

"Mutton," muttered Mollander. He sounded none too pleased about it. "We shared a haunch of boiled mutton."

"I'm certain it was filling." Leo turned to Alleras. "A lord's son should be open-handed, Sphinx. I understand you won your copper link. I'll drink to that."

Alleras smiled back at him. "I only buy for friends. And I am no lord's son, I've told you that. My mother was a trader."

Leo's eyes were hazel, bright with wine and malice. "Your mother was a monkey from the Summer Isles. The Dornish will fuck anything with a hole between its legs. Meaning no offense. You may be brown as a nut, but at least you bathe. Unlike our spotted pig boy." He waved a hand toward Pate.

If I hit him in the mouth with my tankard, I could knock out half his teeth, Pate thought. Spotted Pate the pig boy was the hero of a thousand ribald stories: a good-hearted, empty-headed lout who always managed to best the fat lordlings, haughty knights, and pompous septons who beset him. Somehow his stupidity would turn out to have been a sort of uncouth cunning; the tales always ended with Spotted Pate sitting on a lord's high seat or bedding some knight's daughter. But those were stories. In the real world pig boys never fared so well. Pate sometimes thought his mother must have hated him to have named him as she did.

Alleras was no longer smiling. "You will apologize."

"Will I?" said Leo. "How can I, with my throat so dry . . ."

"You shame your House with every word you say," Alleras told him. "You shame the Citadel by being one of us."

"I know. So buy me some wine, that I might drown my shame."

Mollander said, "I would tear your tongue out by the roots."

"Truly? Then how would I tell you about the dragons?" Leo shrugged again. "The mongrel has the right of it. The Mad King's daughter is alive, and she's hatched herself three dragons."

"Three?" said Roone, astonished.

Leo patted his hand. "More than two and less than four. I would not try for my golden link just yet if I were you."

"You leave him be," warned Mollander.

"Such a chivalrous Hopfrog. As you wish. Every man off every ship that's sailed within a hundred leagues of Qarth is speaking of these dragons. A few will even tell you that they've seen them. The Mage is inclined to believe them."

Armen pursed his lips in disapproval. "Marwyn is unsound. Archmaester Perestan would be the first to tell you that."

"Archmaester Ryam says so too," said Roone.

Leo yawned. "The sea is wet, the sun is warm, and the menagerie hates the mastiff."

He has a mocking name for everyone, thought Pate, but he could not deny that Marwyn looked more a mastiff than a maester. *As if he wants to bite you.* The Mage was not like other maesters. People said that he kept company with whores and hedge wizards, talked with hairy Ibbenese and pitch-black Summer Islanders in their own tongues, and sacrificed to queer gods at the little sailors' temples down by the wharves. Men spoke of seeing him down in the undercity, in rat pits and black brothels, consorting with mummers, singers, sellswords, even beggars. Some even whispered that once he had killed a man with his fists.

When Marwyn had returned to Oldtown, after spending eight years in the east mapping distant lands, searching for lost books, and studying with warlocks and shadowbinders, Vinegar Vaellyn had dubbed him "Marwyn the Mage." The name was soon all over Oldtown, to Vaellyn's vast annoyance. "Leave spells and prayers to priests and septons and bend your wits to learning truths a man can trust in," Archmaester Ryam had once counseled Pate, but Ryam's ring and rod and mask were yellow gold, and his maester's chain had no link of Valyrian steel.

Armen looked down his nose at Lazy Leo. He had the perfect nose for it, long and thin and pointed. "Archmaester Marwyn believes in many curious things," he said, "but he has no more proof of dragons than Mollander. Just more sailors' stories."

"You're wrong," said Leo. "There is a glass candle burning in the Mage's chambers."

A hush fell over the torchlit terrace. Armen sighed and shook his head. Mollander began to laugh. The Sphinx studied Leo with his big black eyes. Roone looked lost.

Pate knew about the glass candles, though he had never seen one burn. They were the worst-kept secret of the Citadel. It was said that they had been brought to Oldtown from Valyria a thousand years before the Doom. He had heard there were four; one was green and three were black, and all were tall and twisted.

"What are these glass candles?" asked Roone.

Armen the Acolyte cleared his throat. "The night before an acolyte says his vows, he must stand a vigil in the vault. No lantern is permitted him, no torch, no lamp, no taper . . . only a candle of obsidian. He must spend the night in darkness, unless he can light that candle. Some will try. The foolish and the stubborn, those who have made a study of these so-called higher mysteries. Often they cut their fingers, for the ridges on the candles are said to be as sharp as razors. Then, with bloody hands, they must wait upon the dawn, brooding on their failure. Wiser men simply go to sleep, or spend their night in prayer, but every year there are always a few who must try."

"Yes." Pate had heard the same stories. "But what's the *use* of a candle that casts no light?"

"It is a lesson," Armen said, "the last lesson we must learn before we don our maester's chains. The glass candle is meant to represent truth and learning, rare and beautiful and fragile things. It is made in the shape of a candle to remind us that a maester must cast light wherever he serves, and it is sharp to remind us that knowledge can be dangerous. Wise men may grow arrogant in their wisdom, but a maester must always remain humble. The glass candle reminds us of that as well. Even after he has said his vow and donned his chain and gone forth to serve, a maester will think back on the darkness of his vigil and remember how nothing that he did could make the candle burn . . . for even with knowledge, some things are not possible."

Lazy Leo burst out laughing. "Not possible for you, you mean. I saw the candle burning with my own eyes."

"You saw *some* candle burning, I don't doubt," said Armen. "A candle of black wax, perhaps."

"I know what I saw. The light was queer and bright, much brighter than any beeswax or tallow candle. It cast strange shadows and the flame never flickered, not even when a draft blew through the open door behind me."

Armen crossed his arms. "Obsidian does not burn."

"Dragonglass," Pate said. "The smallfolk call it drag-onglass." Somehow that seemed important.

"They do," mused Alleras, the Sphinx, "and if there are dragons in the world again . . ."

"Dragons and darker things," said Leo. "The grey sheep have closed their eyes, but the mastiff sees the truth. Old powers waken. Shadows stir. An age of wonder and terror will soon be upon us, an age for gods and heroes." He stretched, smiling his lazy smile. "That's worth a round, I'd say."

"We've drunk enough," said Armen. "Morn will be upon us sooner than we'd like, and Archmaester Ebrose will be speaking on the properties of urine. Those who mean to forge a silver link would do well not to miss his talk."

"Far be it from me to keep you from the piss tasting," said Leo. "Myself, I prefer the taste of Arbor gold."

"If the choice is piss or you, I'll drink piss." Mollander pushed back from the table. "Come, Roone."

The Sphinx reached for his bowcase. "It's bed for me as well. I expect I'll dream of dragons and glass candles."

"All of you?" Leo shrugged. "Well, Rosey will remain. Perhaps I'll wake our little sweetmeat and make a woman of her."

Alleras saw the look on Pate's face. "If he does not have a copper for a cup of wine, he cannot have a dragon for the girl."

"Aye," said Mollander. "Besides, it takes a man to make a woman. Come with us, Pate. Old Walgrave will wake when the sun comes up. He'll be needing you to help him to the privy."

If he remembers who I am today. Archmaester Walgrave had no trouble telling one raven from another, but he was not so good with people. Some days he seemed to think

Pate was someone named Cressen. "Not just yet," he told his friends. "I'm going to stay awhile." Dawn had not broken, not quite. The alchemist might still be coming, and Pate meant to be here if he did.

"As you wish," said Armen. Alleras gave Pate a lingering look, then slung his bow over one slim shoulder and followed the others toward the bridge. Mollander was so drunk he had to walk with a hand on Roone's shoulder to keep from falling. The Citadel was no great distance as the raven flies, but none of them were ravens and Oldtown was a veritable labyrinth of a city, all wynds and crisscrossing alleys and narrow crookback streets. "Careful," Pate heard Armen say as the river mists swallowed up the four of them, "the night is damp, and the cobbles will be slippery."

When they were gone, Lazy Leo considered Pate sourly across the table. "How sad. The Sphinx has stolen off with all his silver, abandoning me to Spotted Pate the pig boy." He stretched, yawning. "How is our lovely little Rosey, pray?"

"She's sleeping," Pate said curtly.

"Naked, I don't doubt." Leo grinned. "Do you think she's truly worth a dragon? One day I suppose I must find out."

Pate knew better than to reply to that.

Leo needed no reply. "I expect that once I've broken in the wench, her price will fall to where even pig boys will be able to afford her. You ought to thank me."

I ought to kill you, Pate thought, but he was not near drunk enough to throw away his life. Leo had been trained to arms, and was known to be deadly with bravo's blade and dagger. And if Pate should somehow kill him, it would mean his own head too. Leo had two names where Pate had only one, and his second was *Tyrell.* Ser Moryn Tyrell, commander of the City Watch of Oldtown, was Leo's

father. Mace Tyrell, Lord of Highgarden and Warden of
the South, was Leo's cousin. And Oldtown's Old Man,
Lord Leyton of the Hightower, who numbered "Protector
of the Citadel" amongst his many titles, was a sworn bannerman of House Tyrell. *Let it go,* Pate told himself. *He
says these things just to wound me.*

The mists were lightening to the east. *Dawn,* Pate realized. *Dawn has come, and the alchemist has not.* He did
not know whether he should laugh or cry. *Am I still a thief
if I put it all back and no one ever knows?* It was another
question that he had no answer for, like those that Ebrose
and Vaellyn had once asked him.

When he pushed back from the bench and got to his
feet, the fearsomely strong cider all went to his head at
once. He had to put a hand on the table to steady himself.
"Leave Rosey be," he said, by way of parting. "Just leave
her be, or I may kill you."

Leo Tyrell flicked the hair back from his eye. "I do not
fight duels with pig boys. Go away."

Pate turned and crossed the terrace. His heels rang
against the weathered planks of the old bridge. By the
time he reached the other side, the eastern sky was turning
pink. *The world is wide,* he told himself. *If I bought that
donkey, I could still wander the roads and byways of the
Seven Kingdoms, leeching the smallfolk and picking nits
out of their hair. I could sign on to some ship, pull an oar,
and sail to Qarth by the Jade Gates to see these bloody
dragons for myself. I do not need to go back to old
Walgrave and the ravens.*

Yet somehow his feet turned back toward the Citadel.

When the first shaft of sunlight broke through the
clouds to the east, morning bells began to peal from the
Sailor's Sept down by the harbor. The Lord's Sept joined
in a moment later, then the Seven Shrines from their gar-

dens across the Honeywine, and finally the Starry Sept that had been the seat of the High Septon for a thousand years before Aegon landed at King's Landing. They made a mighty music. *Though not so sweet as one small nightingale.*

He could hear singing too, beneath the pealing of the bells. Each morning at first light the red priests gathered to welcome the sun outside their modest wharfside temple. *For the night is dark and full of terrors.* Pate had heard them cry those words a hundred times, asking their god R'hllor to save them from the darkness. The Seven were gods enough for him, but he had heard that Stannis Baratheon worshiped at the nightfires now. He had even put the fiery heart of R'hllor on his banners in place of the crowned stag. *If he should win the Iron Throne, we'll all need to learn the words of the red priests' song,* Pate thought, but that was not likely. Tywin Lannister had smashed Stannis and R'hllor upon the Blackwater, and soon enough he would finish them and mount the head of the Baratheon pretender on a spike above the gates of King's Landing.

As the night's mists burned away, Oldtown took form around him, emerging ghostlike from the predawn gloom. Pate had never seen King's Landing, but he knew it was a daub-and-wattle city, a sprawl of mud streets, thatched roofs, and wooden hovels. Oldtown was built in stone, and all its streets were cobbled, down to the meanest alley. The city was never more beautiful than at break of day. West of the Honeywine, the Guildhalls lined the bank like a row of palaces. Upriver, the domes and towers of the Citadel rose on both sides of the river, connected by stone bridges crowded with halls and houses. Downstream, below the black marble walls and arched windows of the Starry

Sept, the manses of the pious clustered like children gathered round the feet of an old dowager.

And beyond, where the Honeywine widened into Whispering Sound, rose the Hightower, its beacon fires bright against the dawn. From where it stood atop the bluffs of Battle Island, its shadow cut the city like a sword. Those born and raised in Oldtown could tell the time of day by where that shadow fell. Some claimed a man could see all the way to the Wall from the top. Perhaps that was why Lord Leyton had not made the descent in more than a decade, preferring to rule his city from the clouds.

A butcher's cart rumbled past Pate down the river road, five piglets in the back squealing in distress. Dodging from its path, he just avoided being spattered as a townswoman emptied a pail of night soil from a window overhead. *When I am a maester in a castle I will have a horse to ride,* he thought. Then he tripped upon a cobble and wondered who he was fooling. There would be no chain for him, no seat at a lord's high table, no tall white horse to ride. His days would be spent listening to ravens *quork* and scrubbing shit stains off Archmaester Walgrave's smallclothes.

He was on one knee, trying to wipe the mud off his robes, when a voice said, "Good morrow, Pate."

The alchemist was standing over him.

Pate rose. "The third day . . . you said you would be at the Quill and Tankard."

"You were with your friends. It was not my wish to intrude upon your fellowship." The alchemist wore a hooded traveler's cloak, brown and nondescript. The rising sun was peeking over the rooftops behind his shoulder, so it was hard to make out the face beneath his hood. "Have you decided what you are?"

Must he make me say it? "I suppose I am a thief."

"I thought you might be."

The hardest part had been getting down on his hands and knees to pull the strongbox from underneath Archmaester Walgrave's bed. Though the box was stoutly made and bound with iron, its lock was broken. Maester Gormon had suspected Pate of breaking it, but that wasn't true. Walgrave had broken the lock himself, after losing the key that opened it.

Inside, Pate had found a bag of silver stags, a lock of yellow hair tied up in a ribbon, a painted miniature of a woman who resembled Walgrave (even to her mustache), and a knight's gauntlet made of lobstered steel. The gauntlet had belonged to a prince, Walgrave claimed, though he could no longer seem to recall which one. When Pate shook it, the key fell out onto the floor.

If I pick that up, I am a thief, he remembered thinking. The key was old and heavy, made of black iron; supposedly it opened every door at the Citadel. Only the archmaesters had such keys. The others carried theirs upon their person or hid them away in some safe place, but if Walgrave had hidden his, no one would ever have seen it again. Pate snatched up the key and had been halfway to the door before turning back to take the silver too. A thief was a thief, whether he stole a little or a lot. *"Pate,"* one of the white ravens had called after him, *"Pate, Pate, Pate."*

"Do you have my dragon?" he asked the alchemist.

"If you have what I require."

"Give it here. I want to see." Pate did not intend to let himself be cheated.

"The river road is not the place. Come."

He had no time to think about it, to weigh his choices. The alchemist was walking away. Pate had to follow or lose Rosey and the dragon both, forever. He followed. As they walked, he slipped his hand up into his sleeve. He could feel the key, safe inside the hidden pocket he had sewn there. Maester's robes were full of pockets. He had known that since he was a boy.

He had to hurry to keep pace with the alchemist's longer strides. They went down an alley, around a corner, through the old Thieves Market, along Ragpicker's Wynd. Finally, the man turned into another alley, narrower than the first. "This is far enough," said Pate. "There's no one about. We'll do it here."

"As you wish."

"I want my dragon."

"To be sure." The coin appeared. The alchemist made it walk across his knuckles, the way he had when Rosey brought the two of them together. In the morning light the dragon glittered as it moved, and gave the alchemist's fingers a golden glow.

Pate grabbed it from his hand. The gold felt warm against his palm. He brought it to his mouth and bit down on it the way he'd seen men do. If truth be told, he wasn't sure what gold should taste like, but he did not want to look a fool.

"The key?" the alchemist inquired politely.

Something made Pate hesitate. "Is it some book you want?" Some of the old Valyrian scrolls down in the locked vaults were said to be the only surviving copies in the world.

"What I want is none of your concern."

"No." *It's done,* Pate told himself. *Go. Run back to the Quill and Tankard, wake Rosey with a kiss, and tell her she belongs to you.* Yet still he lingered. "Show me your face."

"As you wish." The alchemist pulled his hood down.

He was just a man, and his face was just a face. A young man's face, ordinary, with full cheeks and the shadow of a beard. A scar showed faintly on his right cheek. He had a hooked nose, and a mat of dense black hair that curled tightly around his ears. It was not a face Pate recognized. "I do not know you."

"Nor I you."

"Who are you?"

"A stranger. No one. Truly."

"Oh." Pate had run out of words. He drew out the key and put it in the stranger's hand, feeling light-headed, almost giddy. *Rosey,* he reminded himself. "We're done, then."

He was halfway down the alley when the cobblestones began to move beneath his feet. *The stones are slick and wet,* he thought, but that was not it. He could feel his heart hammering in his chest. "What's happening?" he said. His legs had turned to water. "I don't understand."

"And never will," a voice said sadly.

The cobblestones rushed up to kiss him. Pate tried to cry for help, but his voice was failing too.

His last thought was of Rosey.

THE PROPHET

The prophet was drowning men on Great Wyk when they came to tell him that the king was dead.

It was a bleak, cold morning, and the sea was as leaden as the sky. The first three men had offered their lives to the Drowned God fearlessly, but the fourth was weak in faith and began to struggle as his lungs cried out for air. Standing waist-deep in the surf, Aeron seized the naked boy by the shoulders and pushed his head back down as he tried to snatch a breath. "Have courage," he said. "We came from the sea, and to the sea we must return. Open your mouth and drink deep of god's blessing. Fill your lungs with water, that you may die and be reborn. It does no good to fight."

Either the boy could not hear him with his head beneath the waves, or else his faith had utterly deserted him. He began to kick and thrash so wildly that Aeron had to call for help. Four of his drowned men waded out to seize the wretch and hold him underwater. "Lord God who drowned for us," the priest prayed, in a voice as deep as the sea, "let Emmond your servant be reborn from the sea, as you were. Bless him with salt, bless him with stone, bless him with steel."

Finally, it was done. No more air was bubbling from his mouth, and all the strength had gone out of his limbs. Facedown in the shallow sea floated Emmond, pale and cold and peaceful.

That was when the Damphair realized that three horsemen had joined his drowned men on the pebbled shore. Aeron knew the Sparr, a hatchet-faced old man with watery eyes whose quavery voice was law on this part of Great Wyk. His son Steffarion accompanied him, with another youth whose dark red fur-lined cloak was pinned at the shoulder with an ornate brooch that showed the black-and-gold warhorn of the Goodbrothers. *One of Gorold's sons,* the priest decided at a glance. Three tall sons had been born to Goodbrother's wife late in life, after a dozen daughters, and it was said that no man could tell one son from the others. Aeron Damphair did not deign to try. Whether this be Greydon or Gormond or Gran, the priest had no time for him.

He growled a brusque command, and his drowned men seized the dead boy by his arms and legs to carry him above the tideline. The priest followed, naked but for a sealskin clout that covered his private parts. Goosefleshed and dripping, he splashed back onto land, across cold wet sand and sea-scoured pebbles. One of his drowned men handed him a robe of heavy roughspun dyed in mottled greens and blues and greys, the colors of the sea and the Drowned God. Aeron donned the robe and pulled his hair free. Black and wet, that hair; no blade had touched it since the sea had raised him up. It draped his shoulders like a ragged, ropy cloak, and fell down past his waist. Aeron wove strands of seaweed through it, and through his tangled, uncut beard.

His drowned men formed a circle around the dead boy, praying. Norjen worked his arms whilst Rus knelt astride him, pumping on his chest, but all moved aside for Aeron. He pried apart the boy's cold lips with his fingers and gave Emmond the kiss of life, and again, and again, until the sea came gushing from his mouth. The boy began to cough and spit, and his eyes blinked open, full of fear.

Another one returned. It was a sign of the Drowned God's favor, men said. Every other priest lost a man from time to time, even Tarle the Thrice-Drowned, who had once been thought so holy that he was picked to crown a king. But never Aeron Greyjoy. He was the Damphair, who had seen the god's own watery halls and returned to tell of it. "Rise," he told the sputtering boy as he slapped him on his naked back. "You have drowned and been returned to us. What is dead can never die."

"But rises." The boy coughed violently, bringing up more water. "Rises again." Every word was bought with pain, but that was the way of the world; a man must fight to live. "Rises again." Emmond staggered to his feet. "Harder. And stronger."

"You belong to the god now," Aeron told him. The other drowned men gathered round and each gave him a punch and a kiss to welcome him to the brotherhood. One helped him don a roughspun robe of mottled blue and green and grey. Another presented him with a driftwood cudgel. "You belong to the sea now, so the sea has armed you," Aeron said. "We pray that you shall wield your cudgel fiercely, against all the enemies of our god."

Only then did the priest turn to the three riders,

watching from their saddles. "Have you come to be drowned, my lords?"

The Sparr coughed. "I was drowned as a boy," he said, "and my son upon his name day."

Aeron snorted. That Steffarion Sparr had been given to the Drowned God soon after birth he had no doubt. He knew the manner of it too, a quick dip into a tub of seawater that scarce wet the infant's head. Small wonder the ironborn had been conquered, they who once held sway everywhere the sound of waves was heard. "That is no true drowning," he told the riders. "He that does not die in truth cannot hope to rise from death. Why have you come, if not to prove your faith?"

"Lord Gorold's son came seeking you, with news." The Sparr indicated the youth in the red cloak.

The boy looked to be no more than six-and-ten. "Aye, and which are you?" Aeron demanded.

"Gormond. Gormond Goodbrother, if it please my lord."

"It is the Drowned God we must please. Have you been drowned, Gormond Goodbrother?"

"On my name day, Damphair. My father sent me to find you and bring you to him. He needs to see you."

"Here I stand. Let Lord Gorold come and feast his eyes." Aeron took a leather skin from Rus, freshly filled with water from the sea. The priest pulled out the cork and took a swallow.

"I am to bring you to the keep," insisted young Gormond, from atop his horse.

He is afraid to dismount, lest he get his boots wet. "I have the god's work to do." Aeron Greyjoy was a prophet. He did not suffer petty lords ordering him about like some thrall.

"Gorold's had a bird," said the Sparr.

"A maester's bird, from Pyke," Gormond confirmed.

Dark wings, dark words. "The ravens fly o'er salt and stone. If there are tidings that concern me, speak them now."

"Such tidings as we bear are for your ears alone, Damphair," the Sparr said. "These are not matters I would speak of here before these others."

"*These others* are my drowned men, god's servants, just as I am. I have no secrets from them, nor from our god, beside whose holy sea I stand."

The horsemen exchanged a look. "Tell him," said the Sparr, and the youth in the red cloak summoned up his courage. "The king is dead," he said, as plain as that. Four small words, yet the sea itself trembled when he uttered them.

Four kings there were in Westeros, yet Aeron did not need to ask which one was meant. Balon Greyjoy ruled the Iron Islands, and no other. *The king is dead. How can that be?* Aeron had seen his eldest brother not a moon's turn past, when he had returned to the Iron Islands from harrying the Stony Shore. Balon's grey hair had gone half-white whilst the priest had been away, and the stoop in his shoulders was more pronounced than when the longships sailed. Yet all in all the king had not seemed ill.

Aeron Greyjoy had built his life upon two mighty pillars. Those four small words had knocked one down. *Only the Drowned God remains to me. May he make me as strong and tireless as the sea.* "Tell me the manner of my brother's death."

"His Grace was crossing a bridge at Pyke when he fell and was dashed upon the rocks below."

The Greyjoy stronghold stood upon a broken headland, its keeps and towers built atop massive stone stacks that thrust up from the sea. Bridges knotted Pyke together; arched bridges of carved stone and swaying spans of hempen rope and wooden planks. "Was the storm raging when he fell?" Aeron demanded of them.

"Aye," the youth said, "it was."

"The Storm God cast him down," the priest announced. For a thousand thousand years sea and sky had been at war. From the sea had come the ironborn, and the fish that sustained them even in the depths of winter, but storms brought only woe and grief. "My brother Balon made us great again, which earned the Storm God's wrath. He feasts now in the Drowned God's watery halls, with mermaids to attend his every want. It shall be for us who remain behind in this dry and dismal vale to finish his great work." He pushed the cork back into his waterskin. "I shall speak with your lord father. How far from here to Hammerhorn?"

"Six leagues. You may ride pillion with me."

"One can ride faster than two. Give me your horse, and the Drowned God will bless you."

"Take my horse, Damphair," offered Steffarion Sparr.

"No. His mount is stronger. Your horse, boy."

The youth hesitated half a heartbeat, then dismounted and held the reins for the Damphair. Aeron shoved a bare black foot into a stirrup and swung himself onto the saddle. He was not fond of horses—they were creatures from the green lands and helped to make men weak—but necessity required that he ride. *Dark wings, dark words.* A storm was brewing, he could hear it in the waves, and storms brought naught but evil. "Meet with me at Pebbleton beneath Lord Merlyn's tower," he told his drowned men, as he turned the horse's head.

The way was rough, up hills and woods and stony defiles, along a narrow track that oft seemed to disappear beneath the horse's hooves. Great Wyk was the largest of the Iron Islands, so vast that some of its lords had holdings that did not front upon the holy sea. Gorold Goodbrother was one such. His keep was in the Hardstone Hills, as far from the Drowned God's realm as any place in the isles. Gorold's folk toiled down in Gorold's mines, in the stony dark beneath the earth. Some lived and died without setting eyes upon salt water. *Small wonder that such folk are crabbed and queer.*

As Aeron rode, his thoughts turned to his brothers.

Nine sons had been born from the loins of Quellon Greyjoy, the Lord of the Iron Islands. Harlon, Quenton, and Donel had been born of Lord Quellon's first wife, a woman of the Stonetrees. Balon, Euron, Victarion, Urrigon, and Aeron were the sons of his second, a Sunderly of Saltcliffe. For a third wife Quellon took a girl from the green lands, who gave him a sickly idiot boy named Robin, the brother best forgotten. The priest had no memory of Quenton or Donel, who had died as infants. Harlon he recalled but dimly, sitting grey-faced and still in a windowless tower room and speaking in whispers that grew fainter every day as the greyscale turned his tongue and lips to stone. *One day we shall feast on fish together in the Drowned God's watery halls, the four of us and Urri too.*

Nine sons had been born from the loins of Quellon Greyjoy, but only four had lived to manhood. That was the way of this cold world, where men fished the sea and dug in the ground and died, whilst women brought forth short-lived children from beds of blood and pain. Aeron had been the last and least of the four krakens, Balon the eldest and boldest, a fierce and fearless boy who lived only to restore the ironborn to their ancient glory. At ten he scaled the Flint Cliffs to the Blind Lord's haunted tower. At thirteen he could run a longship's oars and dance the finger dance as well as any man in the isles. At fifteen he had sailed with Dagmer Cleftjaw to the Stepstones and spent a summer reaving. He slew his first man there and took his first two salt wives. At seventeen Balon captained his own ship. He was all that an elder brother ought to be, though he had never shown Aeron aught but scorn. *I was weak and full of sin, and scorn was more than I deserved. Better to be scorned by Balon the Brave than beloved of Euron Crow's Eye.* And if age and grief had turned Balon bitter with the years, they had also made him more determined than any man alive. *He was born a lord's son and died a king, murdered by a jealous god,* Aeron thought, *and now the storm is coming, a storm such as these isles have never known.*

It was long after dark by the time the priest espied the spiky iron battlements of the Hammerhorn clawing at the crescent moon. Gorold's keep was hulking and blocky, its great stones quarried from the cliff that loomed behind it. Below its walls, the entrances of caves and ancient mines yawned like toothless black mouths. The Hammerhorn's iron gates had been closed and barred for the night. Aeron beat on them with a rock until the clanging woke a guard.

The youth who admitted him was the image of Gormond, whose horse he'd taken. "Which one are you?" Aeron demanded.

"Gran. My father awaits you within."

The hall was dank and drafty, full of shadows. One of Gorold's daughters offered the priest a horn of ale. Another poked at a sullen fire that was giving off more smoke than heat. Gorold Goodbrother himself was talking quietly with a slim man in fine grey robes, who wore about his neck a chain of many metals that marked him for a maester of the Citadel.

"Where is Gormond?" Gorold asked when he saw Aeron.

"He returns afoot. Send your women away, my lord.

And the maester as well." He had no love of maesters. Their ravens were creatures of the Storm God, and he did not trust their healing, not since Urri. *No proper man would choose a life of thralldom, nor forge a chain of servitude to wear about his throat.*

"Gysella, Gwin, leave us," Goodbrother said curtly. "You as well, Gran. Maester Murenmure will stay."

"He will go," insisted Aeron.

"This is my hall, Damphair. It is not for you to say who must go and who remains. The maester stays."

The man lives too far from the sea, Aeron told himself. "Then I shall go," he told Goodbrother. Dry rushes rustled underneath the cracked soles of his bare black feet as he turned and stalked away. It seemed he had ridden a long way for naught.

Aeron was almost at the door when the maester cleared his throat, and said, "Euron Crow's Eye sits the Seastone Chair."

The Damphair turned. The hall had suddenly grown colder. *The Crow's Eye is half a world away. Balon sent him off two years ago, and swore that it would be his life if he returned.* "Tell me," he said hoarsely.

"He sailed into Lordsport the day after the king's death, and claimed the castle and the crown as Balon's eldest brother," said Gorold Goodbrother. "Now he sends forth ravens, summoning the captains and the kings from every isle to Pyke, to bend their knees and do him homage as their king."

"No." Aeron Damphair did not weigh his words. "Only a godly man may sit the Seastone Chair. The Crow's Eye worships naught but his own pride."

"You were on Pyke not long ago, and saw the king," said Goodbrother. "Did Balon say aught to you of the succession?"

Aye. They had spoken in the Sea Tower, as the wind howled outside the windows and the waves crashed restlessly below. Balon had shaken his head in despair when he heard what Aeron had to tell him of his last remaining son. "The wolves have made a weakling of him, as I feared," the king had said. "I pray god that they killed him, so he cannot stand in Asha's way." That was Balon's blindness; he saw himself in his wild, headstrong daughter, and believed she could succeed him. He was wrong in that, and Aeron tried to tell him so. "No woman will ever rule the ironborn, not even a woman such as Asha," he insisted, but Balon could be deaf to things he did not wish to hear.

Before the priest could answer Gorold Goodbrother, the maester's mouth flapped open once again. "By rights the Seastone Chair belongs to Theon, or Asha if the prince is dead. That is the law."

"Green land law," said Aeron with contempt. "What is that to us? We are ironborn, the sons of the sea, chosen of the Drowned God. No woman may rule over us, nor any godless man."

"And Victarion?" asked Gorold Goodbrother. "He has the Iron Fleet. Will Victarion make a claim, Damphair?"

"Euron is the elder brother . . ." began the maester.

Aeron silenced him with a look. In little fishing towns and great stone keeps alike such a look from Damphair would make maids feel faint and send children shrieking to their mothers, and it was more than sufficient to quell the chain-neck thrall. "Euron is elder," the priest said, "but Victarion is more godly."

"Will it come to war between them?" asked the maester.

"Ironborn must not spill the blood of ironborn."

"A pious sentiment, Damphair," said Goodbrother, "but not one that your brother shares. He had Sawane Botley drowned for saying that the Seastone Chair by rights belonged to Theon."

"If he was drowned, no blood was shed," said Aeron.

The maester and the lord exchanged a look. "I must send word to Pyke, and soon," said Gorold Goodbrother. "Damphair, I would have your counsel. What shall it be, homage or defiance?"

Aeron tugged his beard, and thought. *I have seen the storm, and its name is Euron Crow's Eye.* "For now, send only silence," he told the lord. "I must pray on this."

"Pray all you wish," the maester said. "It does not change the law. Theon is the rightful heir, and Asha next."

"Silence!" Aeron roared. "Too long have the ironborn listened to you chain-neck maesters prating of the green lands and their laws. It is time we listened to the sea again. It is time we listened to the voice of god." His own voice rang in that smoky hall, so full of power that neither Gorold Goodbrother nor his maester dared a reply. *The Drowned God is with me,* Aeron thought. *He has shown me the way.*

Goodbrother offered him the comforts of the castle for the night, but the priest declined. He seldom slept beneath a castle roof, and never so far from the sea. "Comforts I shall know in the Drowned God's watery halls beneath the waves. We are born to suffer, that our sufferings might make us strong. All that I require is a fresh horse to carry me to Pebbleton."

That Goodbrother was pleased to provide. He sent his son Greydon as well, to show the priest the shortest way through the hills down to the sea. Dawn was still an hour off when they set forth, but their mounts were hardy and surefooted, and they made good time despite the darkness. Aeron closed his eyes and said a silent prayer, and after a while began to drowse in the saddle.

The sound came softly, the scream of a rusted hinge. "Urri," he muttered, and woke, fearful. *There is no hinge here, no door, no Urri.* A flying axe took off half of Urri's hand when he was ten-and-four, playing at the finger dance whilst his father and his elder brothers were away at war. Lord Quellon's third wife had been a Piper of Pinkmaiden Castle, a girl with big soft breasts and brown doe's eyes. Instead of healing Urri's hand the Old Way, with fire and seawater, she gave him to her green land maester, who swore that he could sew back the missing fingers. He did that, and later he used potions and poltices and herbs, but the hand mortified and Urri took a fever. By the time the maester sawed his arm off, it was too late.

Lord Quellon never returned from his last voyage; the Drowned God in his goodness granted him a death at sea. It was Lord Balon who came back, with his brothers Euron and Victarion. When Balon heard what had befallen Urri, he removed three of the maester's fingers with a cook's cleaver and sent his father's Piper wife to sew them back on. Poltices and potions worked as well for the maester as they had for Urrigon. He died raving, and Lord Quellon's third wife followed soon thereafter, as the midwife drew a stillborn daughter from her womb. Aeron had been glad. It had been his axe that sheared off Urri's hand, whilst they danced the finger dance together, as friends and brothers will.

It shamed him still to recall the years that followed Urri's death. At six-and-ten he called himself a man, but in truth he had been a sack of wine with legs. He would sing, he would dance (but not the finger dance, never again), he would jape and jabber and make mock. He played the pipes, he juggled, he rode horses, and could drink more than all the Wynches and the Botleys, and half the Harlaws too. The Drowned God gives every man a gift, even him; no man could piss longer or farther than Aeron Greyjoy, as he proved at every feast. Once he bet his new longship against a herd of goats that he could quench a hearthfire with no more than his cock. Aeron feasted on goat for a year, and named the longship *Golden Storm,* though Balon threatened to hang him from her mast when he heard what sort of ram his brother proposed to mount upon her prow.

In the end the *Golden Storm* went down off Fair Isle during Balon's first rebellion, cut in half by a towering war galley called *Fury* when Stannis Baratheon caught Victarion in his trap and smashed the Iron Fleet. Yet the god was not done with Aeron, and carried him to shore. Some fishermen took him captive and marched him down to Lannisport in chains, and he spent the rest of the war in the bowels of Casterly Rock, proving that krakens can piss farther and longer than lions, boars, or chickens.

That man is dead. Aeron had drowned and been reborn from the sea, the god's own prophet. No mortal man could frighten him, no more than the darkness could . . . nor memories, the bones of the soul. *The sound of a door opening, the scream of a rusted iron hinge. Euron has come again.* It did not matter. He was the Damphair priest, beloved of the god.

"Will it come to war?" asked Greydon Goodbrother as the sun was lightening the hills. "A war of brother against brother?"

"If the Drowned God wills it. No godless man may sit the Seastone Chair." *The Crow's Eye will fight, that is certain.* No woman could defeat him, not even Asha; women were made to fight their battles in the birthing bed. And Theon, if he lived, was just as hopeless, a boy of sulks and smiles. At Winterfell he proved his worth, such that it was, but the Crow's Eye was no crippled boy. The decks of

Euron's ship were painted red, to better hide the blood that soaked them. *Victarion. The king must be Victarion, or the storm will slay us all.*

Greydon left him when the sun was up, to take the news of Balon's death to his cousins in their towers at Downdelving, Crow Spike Keep, and Corpse Lake. Aeron continued on alone, up hills and down vales along a stony track that drew wider and more traveled as he neared the sea. In every village he paused to preach, and in the yards of petty lords as well. "We were born from the sea, and to the sea we all return," he told them. His voice was as deep as the ocean, and thundered like the waves. "The Storm God in his wrath plucked Balon from his castle and cast him down, and now he feasts beneath the waves in the Drowned God's watery halls." He raised his hands. *"Balon is dead! The king is dead!* Yet a king will come again! For what is dead may never die, but rises again, harder and stronger! *A king will rise!"*

Some of those who heard him threw down their hoes and picks to follow, so by the time he heard the crash of waves a dozen men walked behind his horse, touched by god and desirous of drowning.

Pebbleton was home to several thousand fisherfolk, whose hovels huddled round the base of a square tower-house with a turret at each corner. Twoscore of Aeron's drowned men there awaited him, camped along a grey sand beach in sealskin tents and shelters built of driftwood. Their hands were roughened by brine, scarred by nets and lines, callused from oars and picks and axes, but now those hands gripped driftwood cudgels hard as iron, for the god had armed them from his arsenal beneath the sea.

They had built a shelter for the priest just above the tideline. Gladly he crawled into it, after he had drowned his newest followers. *My god,* he prayed, *speak to me in the rumble of the waves, and tell me what to do. The captains and the kings await your word. Who shall be our king in Balon's place? Sing to me in the language of leviathan, that I may know his name. Tell me, O Lord beneath the waves, who has the strength to fight the storm on Pyke?*

Though his ride to Hammerhorn had left him weary, Aeron Damphair was restless in his driftwood shelter, roofed over with black weeds from the sea. The clouds rolled in to cloak the moon and stars, and the darkness lay as thick upon the sea as it did upon his soul. *Balon favored Asha, the child of his body, but a woman cannot rule the ironborn. It must be Victarion.* Nine sons had been born from the loins of Quellon Greyjoy, and Victarion was the strongest of them, a bull of a man, fearless and dutiful. *And therein lies our danger.* A younger brother owes obedience to an elder, and Victarion was not a man to sail against tradition. *He has no love for Euron, though. Not since the woman died.*

Outside, beneath the snoring of his drowned men and the keening of the wind, he could hear the pounding of the waves, the hammer of his god calling him to battle. Aeron crept from his little shelter into the chill of the night. Naked he stood, pale and gaunt and tall, and naked he walked into the black salt sea. The water was icy cold, yet he did not flinch from his god's caress. A wave smashed against his chest, staggering him. The next broke over his head. He could taste the salt on his lips and feel the god around him, and his ears rang with the glory of his song. *Nine sons were born from the loins of Quellon Greyjoy, and I was the least of them, as weak and frightened as a girl. But no longer. That man is drowned, and the god has made me strong.* The cold salt sea surrounded him, embraced him, reached down through his weak man's flesh and touched his bones. *Bones,* he thought. *The bones of the soul. Balon's bones, and Urri's. The truth is in our bones, for flesh decays and bone endures. And on the hill of Nagga, the bones of the Grey King's Hall . . .*

And gaunt and pale and shivering, Aeron Damphair struggled back to the shore, a wiser man than he had been when he stepped into the sea. For he had found the answer in his bones, and the way was plain before him. The night was so cold that his body seemed to steam as he stalked back toward his shelter, but there was a fire burning in his heart, and sleep came easily for once, unbroken by the scream of iron hinges.

When he woke the day was bright and windy. Aeron broke his fast on a broth of clams and seaweed cooked above a driftwood fire. No sooner had he finished than the Merlyn descended from his towerhouse with half a dozen guards to seek him out. "The king is dead," the Damphair told him.

"Aye. I had a bird. And now another." The Merlyn was a bald round fleshy man who styled himself "Lord" in the manner of the green lands, and dressed in furs and velvets. "One raven summons me to Pyke, another to Ten Towers. You krakens have too many arms, you pull a man to pieces. What say you, priest? Where should I send my longships?"

Aeron scowled. "Ten Towers, do you say? What kraken calls you there?" Ten Towers was the seat of the Lord of Harlaw.

"The Princess Asha. She has set her sails for home. The Reader sends out ravens, summoning all her friends to Harlaw. He says that Balon meant for her to sit the Seastone Chair."

"The Drowned God shall decide who sits the Seastone

Chair," the priest said. "Kneel, that I might bless you." Lord Merlyn sank to his knees, and Aeron uncorked his skin and poured a stream of seawater on his bald pate. "Lord God who drowned for us, let Meldred your servant be born again from the sea. Bless him with salt, bless him with stone, bless him with steel." Water ran down Merlyn's fat cheeks to soak his beard and fox-fur mantle. "What is dead may never die," Aeron finished, "but rises again, harder and stronger." But when Merlyn rose, he told him, "Stay and listen, that you may spread god's word."

Three feet from the water's edge the waves broke around a rounded granite boulder. It was there that Aeron Damphair stood, so all his school might see him, and hear the words he had to say.

"We were born from the sea, and to the sea we all return," he began, as he had a hundred times before. "The Storm God in his wrath plucked Balon from his castle and cast him down, and now he feasts beneath the waves." He raised his hands. "*The iron king is dead!* Yet a king will come again! For what is dead may never die, but rises again, harder and stronger!"

"A king shall rise!" the drowned men cried.

"He shall. He must. But who?" The Damphair listened a moment, but only the waves gave answer. *"Who shall be our king?"*

The drowned men began to slam their driftwood cudgels one against the other. *"Damphair!"* they cried. *"Damphair King! Aeron King! Give us Damphair!"*

Aeron shook his head. "If a father has two sons and gives to one an axe and to the other a net, which does he intend should be the warrior?"

"The axe is for the warrior," Rus shouted back, "the net for a fisher of the seas."

"Aye," said Aeron. "The god took me deep beneath the

waves and drowned the worthless thing I was. When he cast me forth again he gave me eyes to see, ears to hear, and a voice to spread his word, that I might be his prophet and teach his truth to those who have forgotten. I was not made to sit upon the Seastone Chair . . . no more than Euron Crow's Eye. For I have heard the god, who says, *No godless man may sit my Seastone Chair!*"

The Merlyn crossed his arms against his chest. "Is it Asha, then? Or Victarion? Tell us, priest!"

"The Drowned God will tell you, but not here." Aeron pointed at the Merlyn's fat white face. "Look not to me, nor to the laws of men, but to the sea. Raise your sails and unship your oars, my lord, and take yourself to Old Wyk. You, and all the captains and the kings. Go not to Pyke, to bow before the godless, nor to Harlaw, to consort with scheming women. Point your prow toward Old Wyk, where stood the Grey King's Hall. In the name of the Drowned God I summon you. *I summon all of you!* Leave your halls and hovels, your castles and your keeps, and return to Nagga's hill to make a kingsmoot!"

The Merlyn gaped at him. "A kingsmoot? There has not been a true kingsmoot in . . ."

"*. . . too long a time!*" Aeron cried in anguish. "Yet in the dawn of days the ironborn chose their own kings, raising up the worthiest amongst them. It is time we returned to the Old Way, for only that shall make us great again. It was a kingsmoot that chose Urras Ironfoot for High King, and placed a driftwood crown upon his brows. Sylas Flatnose, Harrag Hoare, the Old Kraken, the kingsmoot raised them all. And from *this* kingsmoot shall emerge a man to finish the work King Balon has begun and win us back our freedoms. Go *not* to Pyke, nor to the Ten Towers of Harlaw, but to Old Wyk, I say again. Seek the hill of Nagga and the bones of the Grey King's Hall, for in that holy place when the moon has drowned and come again we shall make ourselves a worthy king, a *godly* king." He raised his bony hands on high again. "*Listen!* Listen to the waves! Listen to the god! He is speaking to us, and he says, *We shall have no king but from the kingsmoot!*"

A roar went up at that, and the drowned men beat their cudgels one against the other. "A *kingsmoot!*" they shouted. *"A kingsmoot, a kingsmoot. No king but from the kingsmoot!"* And the clamor that they made was so thunderous that surely the Crow's Eye heard the shouts on Pyke, and the vile Storm God in his cloudy hall. And Aeron Damphair knew he had done well.

THE CAPTAIN OF GUARDS

T he blood oranges are well past ripe," the prince observed in a weary voice, when the captain rolled him onto the terrace.

After that he did not speak again for hours.

It was true about the oranges. A few had fallen to burst open on the pale pink marble. The sharp sweet smell of them filled Hotah's nostrils each time he took a breath. No doubt the prince could smell them too, as he sat beneath the trees in the rolling chair Maester Caleotte had made for him, with its goose-down cushions and rumbling wheels of ebony and iron.

For a long while the only sounds were the children splashing in the pools and fountains, and once a soft *plop* as another orange dropped onto the terrace to burst. Then, from the far side of the palace, the captain heard the faint drumbeat of boots on marble.

Obara. He knew her stride; long-legged, hasty, angry. In the stables by the gates, her horse would be lathered, and bloody from her spurs. She always rode stallions, and had been heard to boast that she could master any horse in Dorne . . . and any man as well. The captain could hear other footsteps as well, the quick soft scuffing of Maester Caleotte hurrying to keep up.

Obara Sand always walked too fast. *She is chasing after something she can never catch,* the prince had told his daughter once, in the captain's hearing.

When she appeared beneath the triple arch, Areo Hotah swung his longaxe sideways to block the way. The head was on a shaft of mountain ash six feet long, so she could not go around. "My lady, no farther." His voice was a bass grumble thick with the accents of Norvos. "The prince does not wish to be disturbed."

Her face had been stone before he spoke; then it hardened. "You are in my way, Hotah." Obara was the eldest Sand Snake, a big-boned woman near to thirty, with the close-set eyes and rat-brown hair of the Oldtown whore who'd birthed her. Beneath a mottled sandsilk cloak of dun and gold, her riding clothes were old brown leather, worn and supple. They were the softest things about her. On one hip she wore a coiled whip, across her back a round shield of steel and copper. She had left her spear outside. For that, Areo Hotah gave thanks. Quick and strong as she was, the woman was no match for him, he knew . . . but *she* did not, and he had no wish to see her blood upon the pale pink marble.

Maester Caleotte shifted his weight from foot to foot. "Lady Obara, I tried to tell you . . ."

"Does he know that my father is dead?" Obara asked

the captain, paying the maester no more mind than she would a fly, if any fly had been foolish enough to buzz about her head.

"He does," the captain said. "He had a bird."

Death had come to Dorne on raven wings, writ small and sealed with a blob of hard red wax. Caleotte must have sensed what was in that letter, for he'd given it Hotah to deliver. The prince thanked him, but for the longest time he would not break the seal. All afternoon he'd sat with the parchment in his lap, watching the children at their play. He watched until the sun went down and the evening air grew cool enough to drive them inside; then he watched the starlight on the water. It was moonrise before he sent Hotah to fetch a candle, so he might read his letter beneath the orange trees in the dark of night.

Obara touched her whip. "Thousands are crossing the sands afoot to climb the Boneway, so they may help Ellaria bring my father home. The septs are packed to bursting, and the red priests have lit their temple fires. In the pillow houses women are coupling with every man who comes to them, and refusing any coin. In Sunspear, on the Broken Arm, along the Greenblood, in the mountains, out in the deep sand, everywhere, *everywhere,* women tear their hair and men cry out in rage. The same question is heard on every tongue—what will Doran do? *What will his brother do to avenge our murdered prince?*" She moved closer to the captain. "And you say, *he does not wish to be disturbed!*"

"He does not wish to be disturbed," Areo Hotah said again.

The captain of guards knew the prince he guarded. Once, long ago, a callow youth had come from Norvos, a big broad-shouldered boy with a mop of dark hair. That hair was white now, and his body bore the scars of many battles . . . but his strength remained, and he kept his long axe sharp, as the bearded priests had taught him. *She shall not pass,* he told himself, and said, "The prince is watching the children at their play. He is *never* to be disturbed when he is watching the children at their play."

"Hotah," said Obara Sand, "you will remove yourself from my path, else I shall take that longaxe and—"

"Captain," came the command, from behind. "Let her pass. I will speak with her." The prince's voice was hoarse.

Areo Hotah jerked his longaxe upright and stepped to one side. Obara gave him a lingering last look and strode past, the maester hurrying at her heels. Caleotte was no more than five feet tall and bald as an egg. His face was so smooth and fat that it was hard to tell his age, but he had been here before the captain, had even served the prince's mother. Despite his age and girth, he was still nimble enough, and clever as they came, but meek. *He is no match for any Sand Snake,* the captain thought.

In the shade of the orange trees, the prince sat in his chair with his gouty legs propped up before him, and heavy bags beneath his eyes . . . though whether it was grief or gout that kept him sleepless, Hotah could not say. Below, in the fountains and the pools, the children were still at their play. The youngest were no more than five, the oldest nine and ten. Half were girls and half were boys. Hotah could hear them splashing and shouting at each other in high, shrill voices. "It was not so long ago that you were one of the children in those pools, Obara," the prince said, when she took one knee before his rolling chair.

She snorted. "It has been twenty years, or near enough to make no matter. And I was not here long. I am the whore's whelp, or had you forgotten?" When he did not answer, she rose again and put her hands upon her hips. "My father has been murdered."

"He was slain in single combat during a trial by battle," Prince Doran said. "By law, that is no murder."

"He was your *brother.*"

"He was."

"What do you mean to do about his death?"

The prince turned his chair laboriously to face her. Though he was but two-and-fifty, Doran Martell seemed much older. His body was soft and shapeless beneath his linen robes, and his legs were hard to look upon. The gout had swollen and reddened his joints grotesquely; his left knee was an apple, his right a melon, and his toes had turned to dark red grapes, so ripe it seemed as though a touch would burst them. Even the weight of a coverlet could make him shudder, though he bore the pain without complaint. *Silence is a prince's friend,* the captain had heard him tell his daughter once. *Words are like arrows, Arianne. Once loosed, you cannot call them back.* "I have written to Lord Tywin—"

"*Written?* If you were half the man my father was—"

"I am not your father."

"That I knew." Obara's voice was thick with contempt.

"You would have me go to war."

"I know better. You need not even leave your chair. Let *me* avenge my father. You have a host in the Prince's Pass. Lord Yronwood has another in the Boneway. Grant me the one and Nym the other. Let her ride the kingsroad, whilst I turn the marcher lords out of their castles and hook round to march on Oldtown."

"And how could you hope to hold Oldtown?"

"It will be enough to sack it. The wealth of Hightower—"

"Is it gold you want?"

"It is blood I want."

"Lord Tywin shall deliver us the Mountain's head."

"And who will deliver us Lord Tywin's head? The Mountain has always been his pet."

The prince gestured toward the pools. "Obara, look at the children, if it please you."

"It does not please me. I'd get more pleasure from driving my spear into Lord Tywin's belly. I'll make him sing 'The Rains of Castamere' as I pull his bowels out and look for gold."

"Look," the prince repeated. "I command you."

A few of the older children lay facedown upon the smooth pink marble, browning in the sun. Others paddled in the sea beyond. Three were building a sand castle with a great spike that resembled the Spear Tower of the Old Palace. A score or more had gathered in the big pool, to watch the battles as smaller children rode through the waist-deep shallows on the shoulders of the larger and tried to shove each other into the water. Every time a pair went down, the splash was followed by a roar of laughter. They watched a nut-brown girl yank a towheaded boy off his brother's shoulders to tumble him headfirst into the pool.

"Your father played that same game once, as I did before him," said the prince. "We had ten years between us, so I had left the pools by the time he was old enough to play, but I would watch him when I came to visit Mother. He was so fierce, even as a boy. Quick as a water snake. I oft saw him topple boys much bigger than himself. He reminded me of that the day he left for King's Landing. He swore that he would do it one more time, else I would never have let him go."

"Let him go?" Obara laughed. "As if you could have stopped him. The Red Viper of Dorne went where he would."

"He did. I wish I had some word of comfort to—"

"I did not come to you for *comfort*." Her voice was full of scorn. "The day my father came to claim me, my mother did not wish for me to go. 'She is a girl,' she said, 'and I do not think that she is yours. I had a thousand other men.' He tossed his spear at my feet and gave my mother the back of his hand across the face, so she began to weep. 'Girl or boy, we fight our battles,' he said, 'but the gods let us choose our weapons.' He pointed to the spear, then to my mother's tears, and I picked up the spear. 'I told you she was mine,' my father said, and took me. My mother drank herself to death within the year. They say that she was weeping as she died." Obara edged closer to the prince in his chair. "Let me use the spear; I ask no more."

"It is a deal to ask, Obara. I shall sleep on it."

"You have slept too long already."

"You may be right. I will send word to you at Sunspear."

"So long as the word is war." Obara turned upon her heel and strode off as angrily as she had come, back to the stables for a fresh horse and another headlong gallop down the road.

Maester Caleotte remained behind. "My prince?" the little round man asked. "Do your legs hurt?"

The prince smiled faintly. "Is the sun hot?"

"Shall I fetch a draught for the pain?"

"No. I need my wits about me."

The maester hesitated. "My prince, is it . . . is it prudent to allow Lady Obara to return to Sunspear? She is certain to inflame the common people. They loved your brother well."

"So did we all." He pressed his fingers to his temples. "No. You are right. I must return to Sunspear as well."

The little round man hesitated. "Is that wise?"

"Not wise, but necessary. Best send a rider to Ricasso,

and have him open my apartments in the Tower of the Sun. Inform my daughter Arianne that I will be there on the morrow."

My little princess. The captain had missed her sorely.

"You will be seen," the maester warned.

The captain understood. Two years ago, when they had left Sunspear for the peace and isolation of the Water Gardens, Prince Doran's gout had not been half so bad. In those days he had still walked, albeit slowly, leaning on a stick and grimacing with every step. The prince did not wish his enemies to know how feeble he had grown, and the Old Palace and its shadow city were full of eyes. *Eyes,* the captain thought, *and steps he cannot climb. He would need to fly to sit atop the Tower of the Sun.*

"I *must* be seen. Someone must pour oil on the waters. Dorne must be reminded that it still has a prince." He smiled wanly. "Old and gouty though he is."

"If you return to Sunspear, you will need to give audience to Princess Myrcella," Caleotte said. "Her white knight will be with her . . . and you *know* he sends letters to his queen."

"I suppose he does."

The white knight. The captain frowned. Ser Arys had come to Dorne to attend his own princess, as Areo Hotah had once come with his. Even their names sounded oddly alike: Areo and Arys. Yet there the likeness ended. The captain had left Norvos and its bearded priests, but Ser Arys Oakheart still served the Iron Throne. Hotah had felt a certain sadness whenever he saw the man in the long snowy cloak, the times the prince had sent him down to Sunspear. One day, he sensed, the two of them would fight; on that day Oakheart would die, with the captain's longaxe crashing through his skull. He slid his hand along the smooth ashen shaft of his axe and wondered if that day was drawing nigh.

"The afternoon is almost done," the prince was saying. "We will wait for morn. See that my litter is ready by first light."

"As you command." Caleotte bobbed a bow. The captain stood aside to let him pass, and listened to his footsteps dwindle.

"Captain?" The prince's voice was soft.

Hotah strode forward, one hand wrapped about his longaxe. The ash felt as smooth as a woman's skin against his palm. When he reached the rolling chair he thumped its butt down hard to announce his presence, but the prince had eyes only for the children. "Did you have brothers, captain?" he asked. "Back in Norvos, when you were young? Sisters?"

"Both," Hotah said. "Two brothers, three sisters. I was the youngest." *The youngest, and unwanted. Another mouth to feed, a big boy who ate too much and soon outgrew his clothes.* Small wonder they had sold him to the bearded priests.

"I was the oldest," the prince said, "and yet I am the last. After Mors and Olyvar died in their cradles, I gave up hope of brothers. I was nine when Elia came, a squire in service at Salt Shore. When the raven arrived with word that my mother had been brought to bed a month too soon, I was old enough to understand that meant the child would not live. Even when Lord Gargalen told me that I had a sister, I assured him that she must shortly die. Yet she lived, by the Mother's mercy. And a year later Oberyn arrived, squalling and kicking. I was a man grown when they were playing in these pools. Yet here I sit, and they are gone."

Areo Hotah did not know what to say to that. He was

only a captain of guards, and still a stranger to this land and its seven-faced god, even after all these years. *Serve. Obey. Protect.* He had sworn those vows at six-and-ten, the day he wed his axe. *Simple vows for simple men,* the bearded priests had said. He had not been trained to counsel grieving princes.

He was still groping for some words to say when another orange fell with a heavy splat, no more than a foot from where the prince was seated. Doran winced at the sound, as if somehow it had hurt him. "Enough," he sighed, "it is enough. Leave me, Areo. Let me watch the children for a few more hours."

When the sun set the air grew cool and the children went inside in search of supper, still the prince remained beneath his orange trees, looking out over the still pools and the sea beyond. A serving man brought him a bowl of purple olives, with flatbread, cheese, and chickpea paste. He ate a bit of it, and drank a cup of the sweet, heavy strongwine that he loved. When it was empty, he filled it once again. Sometimes in the deep black hours of the morning sleep found him in his chair. Only then did the captain roll him down the moonlit gallery, past a row of fluted pillars and through a graceful archway, to a great bed with crisp cool linen sheets in a chamber by the sea. Doran groaned as the captain moved him, but the gods were good and he did not wake.

The captain's sleeping cell adjoined his prince's. He sat upon the narrow bed and found his whetstone and oilcloth in their niche, and set to work. *Keep your longaxe sharp,* the bearded priests had told him, the day they branded him. He always did.

As he honed the axe, Hotah thought of Norvos, the high city on the hill and the low beside the river. He could still recall the sounds of the three bells, the way that Noom's deep peals set his very bones to shuddering, the proud strong voice of Narrah, sweet Nyel's silvery laughter. The taste of wintercake filled his mouth again, rich with ginger and pine nuts and bits of cherry, with *nahsa* to wash it down, fermented goat's milk served in an iron cup and laced with honey. He saw his mother in her dress with the squirrel collar, the one she wore but once each year, when they went to see the bears dance down the Sinner's Steps. And he smelled the stench of burning hair as the bearded priest touched the brand to the center of his chest. The pain had been so fierce that he thought his heart might stop, yet Areo Hotah had not flinched. The hair had never grown back over the axe.

Only when both edges were sharp enough to shave with did the captain lay his ash-and-iron wife down on the bed. Yawning, he pulled off his soiled clothes, tossed them on the floor, and stretched out on his straw-stuffed mattress. Thinking of the brand had made it itch, so he had to scratch himself before he closed his eyes. *I should have gathered up the oranges that fell,* he thought, and went to sleep dreaming of the tart sweet taste of them, and the sticky feel of the red juice on his fingers.

Dawn came too soon. Outside the stables the smallest of the three horse litters stood ready, the cedarwood litter with the red silk draperies. The captain chose twenty spears to accompany it, out of the thirty who were posted at the Water Gardens; the rest would stay to guard the grounds and children, some of whom were the sons and daughters of great lords and wealthy merchants.

Although the prince had spoken of departing at first light, Areo Hotah knew that he would dawdle. Whilst the maester helped Doran Martell to bathe and bandaged up his swollen joints in linen wraps soaked with soothing lotions, the captain donned a shirt of copper scales as befit his rank, and a billowing cloak of dun-and-yellow sandsilk to keep the sun off the copper. The day promised to be hot, and the captain had long ago discarded the heavy horse-hair cape and studded leather tunic he had worn in Norvos, which were like to cook a man in Dorne. He had kept his iron halfhelm, with its crest of sharpened spikes, but now he wore it wrapped in orange silk, weaving the cloth in and around the spikes. Elsewise the sun beating down on the metal would have his head pounding before they saw the palace.

The prince was still not ready to depart. He had decided to break his fast before he went, with a blood orange and a plate of gull's eggs diced with bits of ham and fiery peppers. Then nought would do but he must say farewell to several of the children who had become especial favorites: the Dalt boy and Lady Blackmont's brood and the round-faced orphan girl whose father had sold cloth and spices up and down the Greenblood. Doran kept a splendid Myrish blanket over his legs as he spoke with them, to spare the young ones the sight of his swollen, bandaged joints.

It was midday before they got under way; the prince in his litter, Maester Caleotte riding on a donkey, the rest afoot. Five spearmen walked ahead and five behind, with five more flanking the litter to either side. Areo Hotah himself took his familiar place at the left hand of the prince, resting his longaxe on a shoulder as he walked. The road from Sunspear to the Water Gardens ran beside the sea, so they had a cool fresh breeze to soothe them as they made their way across a sparse red-brown land of stone and sand and twisted stunted trees.

Halfway there, the second Sand Snake caught them.

She appeared suddenly upon a dune, mounted on a golden sand steed with a mane like fine white silk. Even ahorse, the Lady Nym looked graceful, dressed all in shimmering lilac robes and a great silk cape of cream and copper that lifted at every gust of wind, and made her look as if she might take flight. Nymeria Sand was five-and-twenty, and slender as a willow. Her straight black hair, worn in a long braid bound up with red-gold wire, made a widow's peak above her dark eyes, just as her father's had. With her high cheekbones, full lips, and milk-pale skin, she had all the beauty that her elder sister lacked . . . but Obara's mother had been an Oldtown whore, whilst Nym was born from the noblest blood of old Volantis. A dozen mounted spearmen tailed her, their round shields gleaming in the sun. They followed her down the dune.

The prince had tied back the curtains on his litter, the better to enjoy the breeze blowing off the sea. Lady Nym fell in beside him, slowing her pretty golden mare to match the litter's pace. "Well met, Uncle," she sang out, as if it had been chance that brought her here. "May I ride with you to Sunspear?" The captain was on the opposite side of the litter from Lady Nym, yet he could hear every word she said.

"I would be glad of it," Prince Doran replied, though he did not *sound* glad to the captain's ears. "Gout and grief make poor companions on the road." By which the captain knew him to mean that every pebble drove a spike through his swollen joints.

"The gout I cannot help," she said, "but my father had no use for grief. Vengeance was more to his taste. Is it true that Gregor Clegane admitted slaying Elia and her children?"

"He roared out his guilt for all the court to hear," the prince admitted. "Lord Tywin has promised us his head."

"And a Lannister always pays his debts," said Lady Nym, "yet it seems to me that Lord Tywin means to pay us with our own coin. I had a bird from our sweet Ser Daemon, who swears my father tickled that monster more than once as they fought. If so, Ser Gregor is as good as dead, and no thanks to Tywin Lannister."

The prince grimaced. Whether it was from the pain of gout or his niece's words, the captain could not say. "It may be so."

"May be? I say 'tis."

"Obara would have me go to war."

Nym laughed. "Yes, she wants to set the torch to Oldtown. She hates that city as much as our little sister loves it."

"And you?"

Nym glanced over a shoulder, to where her companions rode a dozen lengths behind. "I was abed with the Fowler twins when the word reached me," the captain heard her say. "You know the Fowler words? *Let Me Soar!* That is all I ask of you. Let me soar, Uncle. I need no mighty host, only one sweet sister."

"Obara?"

"Tyene. Obara is too loud. Tyene is so sweet and gentle that no man will suspect her. Obara would make Oldtown our father's funeral pyre, but I am not so greedy. Four lives will suffice for me. Lord Tywin's golden twins, as payment for Elia's children. The old lion, for Elia herself. And last of all the little king, for my father."

"The boy has never wronged us."

"The boy is a bastard born of treason, incest, and adultery, if Lord Stannis can be believed." The playful tone had vanished from her voice, and the captain found himself watching her through narrowed eyes. Her sister Obara wore her whip upon her hip and carried a spear where any man could see it. Lady Nym was no less deadly, though she kept her knives well hidden. "Only royal blood can wash out my father's murder."

"Oberyn died during single combat, fighting in a matter that was none of his concern. I do not call that murder."

"Call it what you will. We sent them the finest man in Dorne, and they are sending back a bag of bones."

"He went beyond anything I asked of him. 'Take the measure of this boy king and his council, and make note of their strengths and weaknesses,' I told him, on the terrace. We were eating oranges. 'Find us friends, if there are any to be found. Learn what you can of Elia's end, but see that you do not provoke Lord Tywin unduly,' those were my words to him. Oberyn laughed, and said, 'When have I provoked any man . . . *unduly*? You would do better to warn the Lannisters against provoking me.' He wanted justice for Elia, but he would not wait—"

"He waited ten-and-seven years," the Lady Nym broke in. "Were it you they'd killed, my father would have led his banners north before your corpse was cold. Were it you, the spears would be falling thick as rain upon the marches now."

"I do not doubt it."

"No more should you doubt this, my prince—my sisters and I shall not wait ten-and-seven years for *our* vengeance." She put her spurs into the mare and she was off, galloping toward Sunspear with her tail in hot pursuit.

The prince leaned back against his pillows and closed his eyes, but Hotah knew he did not sleep. *He is in pain.* For a moment he considered calling Maester Caleotte up to the litter, but if Prince Doran had wanted him, he would have called himself.

The shadows of the afternoon were long and dark and the sun was as red and swollen as the prince's joints before they glimpsed the towers of Sunspear to the east. First the slender Spear Tower, a hundred-and-a-half feet tall and crowned with a spear of gilded steel that added another thirty feet to its height; then the mighty Tower of the Sun, with its dome of gold and leaded glass; last the dun-colored Sandship, looking like some monstrous dromond that had washed ashore and turned to stone.

Only three leagues of coast road divided Sunspear from the Water Gardens, yet they were two different worlds. There children frolicked naked in the sun, music played in tiled courtyards, and the air was sharp with the smell of lemons and blood oranges. Here the air smelled of dust, sweat, and smoke, and the nights were alive with the bab-ble of voices. In place of the pink marble of the Water Gardens, Sunspear was built from mud and straw, and col-ored brown and dun. The ancient stronghold of House Martell stood at the easternmost end of a little jut of stone and sand, surrounded on three sides by the sea. To the west, in the shadows of Sunspear's massive walls, mud-brick shops and windowless hovels clung to the castle like barnacles to a galley's hull. Stables and inns and winesinks and pillow houses had grown up west of those, many en-closed by walls of their own, and yet more hovels had risen beneath *those* walls. *And so and so and so, as the bearded priests would say.* Compared to Tyrosh or Myr or Great Norvos, the shadow city was no more than a town, yet it was the nearest thing to a true city that these Dornish had.

Lady Nym's arrival had preceded theirs by some hours, and no doubt she had warned the guards of their coming, for the Threefold Gate was open when they reached it. Only here were the gates lined up one behind the other to allow visitors to pass beneath all three of the Winding Walls directly to the Old Palace, without first making their way through miles of narrow alleys, hidden courts, and noisy bazaars.

Prince Doran had closed the draperies of his litter as soon as the Spear Tower came in sight, yet still the small-folk shouted out to him as the litter passed. *The Sand Snakes have stirred them to a boil,* the captain thought uneasily. They crossed the squalor of the outer crescent and went through the second gate. Beyond, the wind stank of tar and salt water and rotting seaweed, and the crowd grew thicker with every step. *"Make way for Prince Doran!"* Areo Hotah boomed out, thumping the butt of his longaxe on the bricks. *"Make way for the Prince of Dorne!"*

"The prince is dead!" a woman shrilled behind him.

"To spears!" a man bellowed from a balcony.

"Doran!" called some highborn voice. "To the spears!"

Hotah gave up looking for the speakers; the press was too thick, and a third of them were shouting. *"To spears! Vengeance for the Viper!"* By the time they reached the third gate, the guards were shoving people aside to clear a path for the prince's litter, and the crowd was throwing things. One ragged boy darted past the spearmen with a half-rotten pomegranate in one hand, but when he saw Areo Hotah in his path, with longaxe at the ready, he let the fruit fall unthrown and beat a quick retreat. Others farther back let fly with lemons, limes, and oranges, crying *"War! War! To the spears!"* One of the guards was hit in the eye with a lemon, and the captain himself had an orange splatter off his foot.

No answer came from within the litter. Doran Martell stayed cloaked within his silken walls until the thicker walls of the castle swallowed all of them, and the portcullis came down behind them with a rattling crunch. The sounds of shouting dwindled away slowly. Princess Arianne was waiting in the outer ward to greet her father, with half the court about her: the old blind seneschal Ricasso, Ser Manfrey Martell the castellan, young Maester Myles with his grey robes and silky perfumed beard, twoscore of Dornish knights in flowing linen of half a hundred hues. Little Myrcella Baratheon stood with her septa and Ser Arys of the Kingsguard, sweltering in his white-enameled scales.

Princess Arianne strode to the litter on snakeskin sandals laced up to her thighs. Her hair was a mane of jet-black ringlets that fell to the small of her back, and around her brow was a band of copper suns. *She is still a little thing,* the captain thought. Where the Sand Snakes were tall, Arianne took after her mother, who stood but five foot two. Yet beneath her jeweled girdle and loose layers of flowing purple silk and yellow samite she had a woman's body, lush and roundly curved. "Father," she announced as the curtains opened, "Sunspear rejoices at your return."

"Yes, I heard the joy." The prince smiled wanly and cupped his daughter's cheek with a reddened, swollen hand. "You look well. Captain, be so good as to help me down from here."

Hotah slid his longaxe into its sling across his back and gathered the prince into his arms, tenderly so as not to jar his swollen joints. Even so, Doran Martell bit back a gasp of pain.

"I have commanded the cooks to prepare a feast for this evening," Arianne said, "with all your favorite dishes."

"I fear I could not do them justice." The prince glanced slowly around the yard. "I do not see Tyene."

"She begs a private word. I sent her to the throne room to await your coming."

The prince sighed. "Very well. Captain? The sooner I am done with this, the sooner I may rest."

Hotah bore him up the long stone steps of the Tower of

the Sun, to the great round chamber beneath the dome, where the last light of the afternoon was slanting down through thick windows of many-colored glass to dapple the pale marble with diamonds of half a hundred colors. There the third Sand Snake awaited them.

She was sitting cross-legged on a pillow beneath the raised dais where the high seats stood, but she rose as they entered, dressed in a clinging gown of pale blue samite with sleeves of Myrish lace that made her look as innocent as the Maid herself. In one hand was a piece of embroidery she had been working on, in the other a pair of golden needles. Her hair was gold as well, and her eyes were deep blue pools . . . and yet somehow they reminded the captain of her father's eyes, though Oberyn's had been as black as night. *All of Prince Oberyn's daughters have his viper eyes,* Hotah realized suddenly. *The color does not matter.*

"Uncle," said Tyene Sand, "I have been waiting for you."

"Captain, help me to the high seat."

There were two seats on the dais, near twin to one another, save that one had the Martell spear inlaid in gold upon its back, whilst the other bore the blazing Rhoynish sun that had flown from the masts of Nymeria's ships when first they came to Dorne. The captain placed the prince beneath the spear and stepped away.

"Does it hurt so much?" Lady Tyene's voice was gentle, and she looked as sweet as summer strawberries. Her mother had been a septa, and Tyene had an air of almost otherworldy innocence about her. "Is there aught that I might do to ease your pain?"

"Say what you would and let me rest. I am weary, Tyene."

"I made this for you, Uncle." Tyene unfolded the piece she'd been embroidering. It showed her father, Prince

Oberyn, mounted on a sand steed and armored all in red, smiling. "When I finish, it is yours, to help you remember him."

"I am not like to forget your father."

"That is good to know. Many have wondered."

"Lord Tywin has promised us the Mountain's head."

"He is *so* kind . . . but a headsman's sword is no fit end for brave Ser Gregor. We have prayed so long for his death, it is only fair that he pray for it as well. I know the poison that my father used, and there is none slower or more agonizing. Soon we may hear the Mountain screaming, even here in Sunspear."

Prince Doran sighed. "Obara cries to me for war. Nym will be content with murder. And you?"

"War," said Tyene, "though not my sister's war. Dornishmen fight best at home, so I say let us hone our spears and wait. When the Lannisters and the Tyrells come down on us, we shall bleed them in the passes and bury them beneath the blowing sands, as we have a hundred times before."

"*If* they should come down on us."

"Oh, but they must, or see the realm riven once more, as it was before we wed the dragons. Father told me so. He said we had the Imp to thank, for sending us Princess Myrcella. She is so pretty, don't you think? I wish that I had curls like hers. She was made to be a queen, just like her mother." Dimples bloomed in Tyene's cheeks. "I would be honored to arrange the wedding, and to see to the making of the crowns as well. Trystane and Myrcella are so innocent, I thought perhaps white gold . . . with emeralds, to match Myrcella's eyes. Oh, diamonds and pearls would serve as well, so long as the children are wed and crowned. Then we need only hail Myrcella as the First of Her Name, Queen of the Andals, the Rhoynar, and the

First Men, and lawful heir to the Seven Kingdoms of Westeros, and wait for the lions to come."

"The *lawful* heir?" The prince snorted.

"She is older than her brother," explained Tyene, as if he were some fool. "By law the Iron Throne should pass to her."

"By *Dornish* law."

"When good King Daeron wed Princess Myriah and brought us into his kingdom, it was agreed that Dornish law would always rule in Dorne. And *Myrcella* is in Dorne, as it happens."

"So she is." His tone was grudging. "Let me think on it."

Tyene grew cross. "You think too much, Uncle."

"Do I?"

"Father said so."

"Oberyn thought too little."

"Some men *think* because they are afraid to *do.*"

"There is a difference between fear and caution."

"Oh, I must pray that I never see you *frightened,* Uncle. You might forget to breathe." She raised a hand . . .

The captain brought the butt of his longaxe down upon the marble with a thump. "My lady, you presume. Step from the dais, if it please you."

"I meant no harm, Captain. I love my uncle, as I know he loved my father." Tyene went to one knee before the prince. "I have said all I came to say, Uncle. Forgive me if I gave offense; my heart is broken all to pieces. Do I still have your love?"

"Always."

"Give me your blessing, then, and I shall go."

Doran hesitated half a heartbeat before placing his hand on his niece's head. "Be brave, child."

"Oh, how not? I am *his* daughter."

No sooner had she taken her leave than Maester

Caleotte hurried to the dais. "My prince, she did not . . . here, let me see your hand." He examined the palm first, then gently turned it upside down to sniff at the back of the prince's fingers. "No, good. That is good. There are no scratches, so . . ."

The prince withdrew his hand. "Maester, could I trouble you for some milk of the poppy? A thimble cup will suffice."

"The poppy. Yes, to be sure."

"Now, I think," Doran Martell urged gently, and Caleotte scurried to the stairs.

Outside the sun had set. The light within the dome was the blue of dusk, and all the diamonds on the floor were dying. The prince sat in his high seat beneath the Martell spear, his face pale with pain. After a long silence he turned to Areo Hotah. "Captain," he said, "how loyal are my guards?"

"Loyal." The captain did not know what else to say.

"All of them? Or some?"

"They are good men. Good *Dornishmen*. They will do as I command." He thumped his longaxe on the floor. "I will bring the head of any man who would betray you."

"I want no heads. I want obedience."

"You have it." *Serve. Obey. Protect. Simple vows for a simple man.* "How many men are needed?"

"I will leave that for you to decide. It may be that a few good men will serve us better than a score. I want this done as quickly and as quietly as possible, with no blood spilled."

"Quick and quiet and bloodless, aye. What is your command?"

"You will find my brother's daughters, take them into custody, and confine them in the cells atop the Spear Tower."

"The Sand Snakes?" The captain's throat was dry. "All . . . all eight, my prince? The little ones, also?"

The prince considered. "Ellaria's girls are too young to be a danger, but there are those who might seek to use them against me. It would be best to keep them safe in hand. Yes, the little ones as well . . . but first secure Tyene, Nymeria, and Obara."

"As my prince commands." His heart was troubled. *My little princess will mislike this.* "What of Sarella? She is a woman grown, almost twenty."

"Unless she returns to Dorne, there's naught I can do about Sarella save pray that she shows more sense than her sisters. Leave her to her . . . game. Gather up the others. I shall not sleep until I know that they are safe and under guard."

"It will be done." The captain hesitated. "When this is known in the streets, the common folk will howl."

"All Dorne will howl," said Doran Martell in a tired voice. "I only pray Lord Tywin hears them in King's Landing, so he might know what a loyal friend he has in Sunspear."

CERSEI

She dreamt she sat the Iron Throne, high above them all.

The courtiers were brightly colored mice below. Great lords and proud ladies knelt before her. Bold young knights laid their swords at her feet and pleaded for her favors, and the queen smiled down at them. Until the dwarf appeared as if from nowhere, pointing at her and howling with laughter. The lords and ladies began to chuckle too, hiding their smiles behind their hands. Only then did the queen realize she was naked.

Horrified, she tried to cover herself with her hands. The barbs and blades of the Iron Throne bit into her flesh as she crouched to hide her shame. Blood ran red down her legs, as steel teeth gnawed at her buttocks. When she tried to stand, her foot slipped through a gap in the twisted metal. The more she struggled the more the throne engulfed her, tearing chunks of flesh from her breasts and belly, slicing at her arms and legs until they were slick and red, glistening.

And all the while her brother capered below, laughing.

His merriment still echoed in her ears when she felt a light touch on her shoulder, and woke suddenly. For half a heartbeat the hand seemed part of the nightmare, and Cersei cried out, but it was only Senelle. The maid's face was white and frightened.

We are not alone, the queen realized. Shadows loomed around her bed, tall shapes with chainmail glimmering beneath their cloaks. Armed men had no business here. *Where are my guards?* Her bedchamber was dark, but for the lantern one of the intruders held on high. *I must show no fear.* Cersei pushed back sleep-tousled hair, and said, "What do you want of me?" A man stepped into the lantern light, and she saw his cloak was white. "Jaime?" *I dreamt of one brother, but the other has come to wake me.*

"Your Grace." The voice was not her brother's. "The Lord Commander said come get you." His hair curled, as Jaime's did, but her brother's hair was beaten gold, like hers, where this man's was black and oily. She stared at him, confused, as he muttered about a privy and a crossbow, and said her father's name. *I am dreaming still,* Cersei thought. *I have not woken, nor has my nightmare ended. Tyrion will creep out from under the bed soon and begin to laugh at me.*

But that was folly. Her dwarf brother was down in the black cells, condemned to die this very day. She looked down at her hands, turning them over to make certain all her fingers were still there. When she ran a hand down her arm the skin was covered with gooseprickles, but unbroken. There were no cuts on her legs, no gashes on the soles of her feet. *A dream, that's all it was, a dream. I drank too much last night, these fears are only humors born of wine. I will be the one laughing, come dusk. My children will be safe, Tommen's throne will be secure, and my twisted little* valonqar *will be short a head and rotting.*

Jocelyn Swyft was at her elbow, pressing a cup on her. Cersei took a sip: water, mixed with lemon squeezings, so tart she spit it out. She could hear the night wind rattling the shutters, and she saw with a strange sharp clarity. Jocelyn was trembling like a leaf, as frightened as Senelle. Ser Osmund Kettleblack loomed over her. Behind him stood Ser Boros Blount, with a lantern. At the door were Lannister guardsmen with gilded lions shining on the crests of their helmets. They looked afraid as well. *Can it be?* the queen wondered. *Can it be true?*

She rose, and let Senelle slip a bedrobe over her shoulders to hide her nakedness. Cersei belted it herself, her fingers stiff and clumsy. "My lord father keeps guards about him, night and day," she said. Her tongue felt thick. She took another swallow of lemon water and sloshed it round her mouth to freshen her breath. A moth had gotten into the lantern Ser Boros was holding; she could hear it buzzing and see the shadow of its wings as it beat against the glass.

"The guards were at their posts, Your Grace," said Osmund Kettleblack. "We found a hidden door behind the hearth. A secret passage. The Lord Commander's gone down to see where it goes."

"Jaime?" Terror seized her, sudden as a storm. "Jaime should be with the *king* . . ."

"The lad's not been harmed. Ser Jaime sent a dozen men to look in on him. His Grace is sleeping peaceful."

Let him have a sweeter dream than mine, and a kinder waking. "Who is with the king?"

"Ser Loras has that honor, if it please you."

It did not please her. The Tyrells were only stewards that the dragon-kings had upjumped far above their station. Their vanity was exceeded only by their ambition. Ser Loras might be as pretty as a maiden's dream, but underneath his white cloak he was Tyrell to the bone. For all she knew, this night's foul fruit had been planted and nurtured in Highgarden.

But that was a suspicion she dare not speak aloud. "Allow me a moment to dress. Ser Osmund, you shall accompany me to the Tower of the Hand. Ser Boros, roust the gaolers and make certain the dwarf is still in his cell." She would not say his name. *He would never have found the courage to lift a hand against Father,* she told herself, but she had to be certain.

"As Your Grace commands." Blount surrendered the lantern to Ser Osmund. Cersei was not displeased to see the back of him. *Father should never have restored him to the white.* The man had proved himself a craven.

By the time they left Maegor's Holdfast, the sky had turned a deep cobalt blue, though the stars still shone. *All but one,* Cersei thought. *The bright star of the west has fallen, and the nights will be darker now.* She paused upon the drawbridge that spanned the dry moat, gazing down at the spikes below. *They would not dare lie to me about such a thing.* "Who found him?"

"One of his guards," said Ser Osmund. "Lum. He felt a call of nature, and found his lordship in the privy."

No, that cannot be. That is not the way a lion dies. The queen felt strangely calm. She remembered the first time she had lost a tooth, when she was just a little girl. It hadn't hurt, but the hole in her mouth felt so odd she could not stop touching it with her tongue. *Now there is a hole in the world where Father stood, and holes want filling.*

If Tywin Lannister was truly dead, no one was safe . . .

least of all her son upon his throne. When the lion falls the lesser beasts move in: the jackals and the vultures and the feral dogs. They would try to push her aside, as they always had. She would need to move quickly, as she had when Robert died. This might be the work of Stannis Baratheon, through some catspaw. It could well be the prelude to another attack upon the city. She hoped it was. *Let him come. I will smash him, just as Father did, and this time he will die.* Stannis did not frighten her, no more than Mace Tyrell did. No one frightened her. She was a daughter of the Rock, a lion. *There will be no more talk of forcing me to wed again.* Casterly Rock was hers now, and all the power of House Lannister. No one would ever disregard her again. Even when Tommen had no further need of a regent, the Lady of Casterly Rock would remain a power in the land.

The rising sun had painted the tower tops a vivid red, but beneath the walls the night still huddled. The outer castle was so hushed that she could have believed all its people dead. *They should be. It is not fitting for Tywin Lannister to die alone. Such a man deserves a retinue to attend his needs in hell.*

Four spearmen in red cloaks and lion-crested helms were posted at the door of the Tower of the Hand. "No one is to enter or leave without my permission," she told them. The command came easily to her. *My father had steel in his voice as well.*

Within the tower, the smoke from the torches irritated her eyes, but Cersei did not weep, no more than her father would have. *I am the only true son he ever had.* Her heels scraped against the stone as she climbed, and she could still hear the moth fluttering wildly inside Ser Osmund's lantern. *Die,* the queen thought at it, in irritation, *fly into the flame and be done with it.*

Two more red-cloaked guardsmen stood atop the steps. Red Lester muttered a condolence as she passed. The queen's breath was coming fast and short, and she could feel her heart fluttering in her chest. *The steps,* she told herself, *this cursed tower has too many steps.* She had half a mind to tear it down.

The hall was full of fools speaking in whispers, as if Lord Tywin were asleep and they were afraid to wake him. Guards and servants alike shrank back before her, mouths flapping. She saw their pink gums and waggling tongues, but their words made no more sense than the buzzing of the moth. *What are they doing here? How did they know?* By rights they should have called her first. She was the Queen Regent, had they forgotten that?

Before the Hand's bedchamber stood Ser Meryn Trant in his white armor and cloak. The visor of his helm was open, and the bags beneath his eyes made him look still half-asleep. "Clear these people away," Cersei told him. "Is my father in the privy?"

"They carried him back to his bed, m'lady." Ser Meryn pushed the door open for her to enter.

Morning light slashed through the shutters to paint golden bars upon the rushes strewn across the floor of the bedchamber. Her uncle Kevan was on his knees beside the bed, trying to pray, but he could scarcely get the words out. Guardsmen clustered near the hearth. The secret door that Ser Osmund had spoken of gaped open behind the ashes, no bigger than an oven. A man would need to crawl. *But Tyrion is only half a man.* The thought made her angry. *No, the dwarf is locked in a black cell.* This could not be his work. *Stannis,* she told herself, *Stannis was behind it. He still has adherents in the city. Him, or the Tyrells . . .*

There had always been talk of secret passages within the Red Keep. Maegor the Cruel was supposed to have killed the men who built the castle to keep the knowledge of them secret. *How many other bedchambers have hidden doors?* Cersei had a sudden vision of the dwarf crawling out from behind a tapestry in Tommen's bedchamber with blade in hand. *Tommen is well guarded,* she told herself. But Lord Tywin had been well guarded too.

For a moment she did not recognize the dead man. He had hair like her father, yes, but this was some other man, surely, a smaller man, and much older. His bedrobe was hiked up around his chest, leaving him naked below the waist. The quarrel had taken him in his groin between his navel and his manhood, and was sunk so deep that only the fletching showed. His pubic hair was stiff with dried blood. More was congealing in his navel.

The smell of him made her wrinkle her nose. "Take the quarrel out of him," she commanded. "This is the King's Hand!" *And my father. My lord father. Should I scream and tear my hair?* They said Catelyn Stark had clawed her own face to bloody ribbons when the Freys slew her precious Robb. *Would you like that, Father?* she wanted to ask him. *Or would you want me to be strong? Did you weep for your own father?* Her grandfather had died when she was only a year old, but she knew the story. Lord Tytos had grown very fat, and his heart burst one day when he was climbing the steps to his mistress. Her father was off in King's Landing when it happened, serving as the Mad King's Hand. Lord Tywin was often away in King's Landing when she and Jaime were young. If he wept when they brought him word of his father's death, he did it where no one could see the tears.

The queen could feel her nails digging into her palms. "How could you leave him like this? My father was Hand to three kings, as great a man as ever strode the Seven Kingdoms. The bells must ring for him, as they rang for

Robert. He must be bathed and dressed as befits his stature, in ermine and cloth-of-gold and crimson silk. Where is Pycelle? *Where is Pycelle?*" She turned to the guardsmen. "Puckens, bring Grand Maester Pycelle. He must see to Lord Tywin."

"He's seen him, Your Grace," said Puckens. "He came and saw and went, to summon the silent sisters."

They sent for me last. The realization made her almost too angry for words. *And Pycelle runs off to send a message rather than soil his soft, wrinkled hands. The man is useless.* "Find Maester Ballabar," she commanded. "Find Maester Frenken. Any of them." Puckens and Shortear ran to obey. "Where is my brother?"

"Down the tunnel. There's a shaft, with iron rungs set in the stone. Ser Jaime went to see how deep it goes."

He has only one hand, she wanted to shout at them. *One of you should have gone. He has no business climbing ladders. The men who murdered Father might be down there, waiting for him.* Her twin had always been too rash, and it would seem that even losing a hand had not taught him caution. She was about to command the guards to go down after him and bring him back when Puckens and Shortear returned with a grey-haired man between them. "Your Grace," said Shortear, "this here claims he was a maester."

The man bowed low. "How may I serve Your Grace?"

His face was vaguely familiar, though Cersei could not place him. *Old, but not so old as Pycelle. This one has some strength in him still.* He was tall, though slightly stooped, with crinkles around his bold blue eyes. *His throat is naked.* "You wear no maester's chain."

"It was taken from me. My name is Qyburn, if it please Your Grace. I treated your brother's hand."

"His stump, you mean." She remembered him now. He had come with Jaime from Harrenhal.

"I could not save Ser Jaime's hand, it is true. My arts saved his arm, however, mayhaps his very life. The Citadel took my chain, but they could not take my knowledge."

"You may suffice," she decided. "If you fail me you will lose more than a chain, I promise you. Remove the quarrel from my father's belly and make him ready for the silent sisters."

"As my queen commands." Qyburn went to the bedside, paused, looked back. "And how shall I deal with the girl, Your Grace?"

"Girl?" Cersei had overlooked the second body. She strode to the bed, flung aside the heap of bloody coverlets, and there she was, naked, cold, and pink . . . save for her face, which had turned as black as Joff's had at his wedding feast. A chain of linked golden hands was half-buried in the flesh of her throat, twisted so tight that it had broken the skin. Cersei hissed like an angry cat. "What is *she* doing here?"

"We found her there, Your Grace," said Shortear. "It's the Imp's whore." As if that explained why she was here.

My lord father had no use for whores, she thought. *After our mother died he never touched a woman.* She gave the guardsman a chilly look. "This is not . . . when Lord Tywin's father died he returned to Casterly Rock to find a . . . a woman of this sort . . . bedecked in his lady mother's jewels, wearing one of her gowns. He stripped them off her, and all else as well. For a fortnight she was paraded naked through the streets of Lannisport, to confess to every man she met that she was a thief and a harlot. That was how Lord Tywin Lannister dealt with whores. He never . . . this woman was here for some other purpose, not for . . ."

"Perhaps his lordship was questioning the girl about her mistress," Qyburn suggested. "Sansa Stark vanished the night the king was murdered, I have heard."

"That's so." Cersei seized on the suggestion eagerly. "He was questioning her, to be sure. There can be no doubt." She could see Tyrion leering, his mouth twisted into a monkey's grin beneath the ruin of his nose. *And what better way to question her than naked, with her legs well spread?* the dwarf whispered. *That's how I like to question her too.*

The queen turned away. *I will not look at her.* Suddenly it was too much even to be in the same room as the dead woman. She pushed past Qyburn, out into the hall.

Ser Osmund had been joined by his brothers Osney and Osfryd. "There is a dead woman in the Hand's bedchamber," Cersei told the three Kettleblacks. "No one is ever to know that she was here."

"Aye, m'lady." Ser Osney had faint scratches on his cheek where another of Tyrion's whores had clawed him. "And what shall we do with her?"

"Feed her to your dogs. Keep her for a bedmate. What do I care? *She was never here.* I'll have the tongue of any man who dares to say she was. Do you understand me?"

Osney and Osfryd exchanged a look. "Aye, Your Grace."

She followed them back inside and watched as they bundled the girl up in her father's bloody blankets. *Shae, her name was Shae.* They had last spoken the night before the dwarf's trial by combat, after that smiling Dornish snake offered to champion him. Shae had been asking about some jewels Tyrion had given her, and certain promises Cersei might have made, a manse in the city and a knight to marry her. The queen made it plain that the whore would have nothing of her until she told them where Sansa Stark had gone. "You were her maid. Do you expect me to believe that you knew nothing of her plans?" she had said. Shae left in tears.

Ser Osfryd slung the bundled corpse up over his shoulder. "I want that chain," Cersei said. "See that you do not scratch the gold." Osfryd nodded and started toward the door. "No, not through the yard." She gestured toward the secret passage. "There's a shaft down to the dungeons. That way."

As Ser Osfryd went down on one knee before the hearth, the light brightened within, and the queen heard noises. Jaime emerged bent over like an old woman, his boots kicking up puffs of soot from Lord Tywin's last fire. "Get out of my way," he told the Kettleblacks.

Cersei rushed toward him. "Did you find them? Did you find the killers? How many were there?" Surely there had been more than one. One man alone could not have killed her father.

Her twin's face had a haggard look. "The shaft goes down to a chamber where half a dozen tunnels meet. They're closed off by iron gates, chained and locked. I need to find keys." He glanced around the bedchamber. "Whoever did this might still be lurking in the walls. It's a maze back there, and dark."

She imagined Tyrion creeping between the walls like some monstrous rat. *No. You are being silly. The dwarf is in his cell.* "Take hammers to the walls. Knock this tower down, if you must. I want them found. Whoever did this. I want them killed."

Jaime hugged her, his good hand pressing against the small of her back. He smelled of ash, but the morning sun was in his hair, giving it a golden glow. She wanted to draw his face to hers for a kiss. *Later,* she told herself, *later he will come to me, for comfort.* "We are his heirs, Jaime," she whispered. "It will be up to us to finish his work. You must take Father's place as Hand. You see that now, surely. Tommen will need you . . ."

He pushed away from her and raised his arm, forcing his stump into her face. "A Hand without a hand? A bad jape, sister. Don't ask me to rule."

Their uncle heard the rebuff. Qyburn as well, and the Kettleblacks, wrestling their bundle through the ashes. Even the guardsmen heard, Puckens and Hoke the Horseleg and Shortear. *It will be all over the castle by nightfall.* Cersei felt the heat rising up her cheeks. "Rule? I said naught of ruling. I shall rule until my son comes of age."

"I don't know who I pity more," her brother said. "Tommen, or the Seven Kingdoms."

She slapped him. Jaime's arm rose to catch the blow, cat-quick . . . but this cat had a cripple's stump in place of a right hand. Her fingers left red marks on his cheek.

The sound brought their uncle to his feet. "Your father lies here *dead.* Have the decency to take your quarrel outside."

Jaime inclined his head in apology. "Forgive us, Uncle. My sister is sick with grief. She forgets herself."

She wanted to slap him again for that. *I must have been mad to think he could be Hand.* She would sooner abolish the office. When had a Hand ever brought her anything but grief? Jon Arryn put Robert Baratheon in her bed, and before he died he'd begun sniffing about her and Jaime as well. Eddard Stark took up right where Arryn had left off; his meddling had forced her to rid herself of Robert sooner than she would have liked, before she could deal with his pestilential brothers. Tyrion sold Myrcella to the Dornishmen, made one of her sons his hostage, and murdered the other. And when Lord Tywin returned to King's Landing . . .

The next Hand will know his place, she promised herself. It would have to be Ser Kevan. Her uncle was tireless, prudent, unfailingly obedient. She could rely on him, as her father had. *The hand does not argue with the head.* She had a realm to rule, but she would need new men to help her rule it. Pycelle was a doddering lickspittle, Jaime had lost his courage with his sword hand, and Mace Tyrell and his cronies Redwyne and Rowan could not be trusted. For all she knew they might have had a part in this. Lord Tyrell had to know that he would never rule the Seven Kingdoms so long as Tywin Lannister lived.

I will need to move carefully with that one. The city was full of his men, and he'd even managed to plant one of his sons in the Kingsguard, and meant to plant his daughter in Tommen's bed. It still made her furious to think that Father had agreed to betroth Tommen to Margaery Tyrell. *The girl is twice his age and twice widowed.* Mace Tyrell claimed his daughter was still virgin, but Cersei had her doubts. Joffrey had been murdered before he could bed the girl, but she had been wed to Renly first . . . *A man may prefer the taste of hippocras, yet if you set a tankard of ale before him, he will quaff it quick enough.* She must command Lord Varys to find out what he could.

That stopped her where she stood. She had forgotten about Varys. *He should be here. He is always here.* Whenever anything of import happened in the Red Keep, the eunuch appeared as if from nowhere. *Jaime is here, and Uncle Kevan, and Pycelle has come and gone, but not Varys.* A cold finger touched her spine. *He was part of this. He must have feared that Father meant to have his head, so he struck first.* Lord Tywin had never had any love for the simpering master of whisperers. And if any man knew the Red Keep's secrets, it was surely the master of whisperers. *He must have made common cause with*

Lord Stannis. They served together on Robert's council, after all . . .

Cersei strode to the door of the bedchamber, to Ser Meryn Trant. "Trant, bring me Lord Varys. Squealing and squirming if need be, but unharmed."

"As Your Grace commands."

But no sooner had one Kingsguard departed than another one returned. Ser Boros Blount was red-faced and puffing from his headlong rush up the steps. "Gone," he panted, when he saw the queen. He sank to one knee. "The Imp . . . his cell's open, Your Grace . . . no sign of him anywhere . . ."

The dream was true. "I gave orders," she said. "He was to be kept under guard, night and day . . ."

Blount's chest was heaving. "One of the gaolers has gone missing too. Rugen, his name was. Two other men we found asleep."

It was all she could do not to scream. "I hope you did not wake them, Ser Boros. Let them sleep."

"Sleep?" He looked up, jowly and confused. "Aye, Your Grace. How long shall—"

"Forever. See that they sleep forever, ser. I will not suffer guards to sleep on watch." *He is in the walls. He killed Father as he killed Mother, as he killed Joff.* The dwarf would come for her as well, the queen knew, just as the old woman had promised her in the dimness of that tent. *I laughed in her face, but she had powers. I saw my future in a drop of blood. My doom.* Her legs were weak as water. Ser Boros tried to take her by the arm, but the queen recoiled from his touch. For all she knew he might be one of Tyrion's creatures. "Get away from me," she said. *"Get away!"* She staggered to a settle.

"Your Grace?" said Blount. "Shall I fetch a cup of water?"

It is blood I need, not water. Tyrion's blood, the blood of the valonqar. The torches spun around her. Cersei closed her eyes, and saw the dwarf grinning at her. *No*, she thought, *no, I was almost rid of you.* But his fingers had closed around her neck, and she could feel them beginning to tighten.

BRIENNE

I am looking for a maid of three-and-ten," she told the grey-haired goodwife beside the village well. "A highborn maid and very beautiful, with blue eyes and auburn hair. She may have been traveling with a portly knight of forty years, or perhaps with a fool. Have you seen her?"

"Not as I recall, ser," the goodwife said, knuckling her forehead. "But I'll keep my eye out, that I will."

The blacksmith had not seen her either, nor the septon in the village sept, the swineherd with his pigs, the girl pulling up onions from her garden, nor any of the other simple folk that the Maid of Tarth found amongst the daub-and-wattle huts of Rosby. Still, she persisted. *This is the shortest road to Duskendale,* Brienne told herself. *If Sansa came this way, someone must have seen her.* At the castle gates she posed her question to two spearmen whose badges showed three red chevronels on ermine, the arms of House Rosby. "If she's on the roads these days she won't be no maid for long," said the older man. The younger wanted to know if the girl had that auburn hair between her legs as well.

I will find no help here. As Brienne mounted up again, she glimpsed a skinny boy atop a piebald horse at the far end of the village. *I have not talked with that one,* she thought, but he vanished behind the sept before she could seek him out. She did not trouble to chase after him. Most like he knew no more than the others had. Rosby was scarce more than a wide place in the road; Sansa would have had no reason to linger here. Returning to the road, Brienne headed north and east past apple orchards and fields of barley, and soon left the village and its castle well behind. It was at Duskendale that she would find her quarry, she told herself. *If she came this way at all.*

"I will find the girl and keep her safe," Brienne had promised Ser Jaime, back at King's Landing. "For her lady mother's sake. And for yours." Noble words, but words were easy. Deeds were hard. She had lingered too long and learned too little in the city. *I should have set out earlier . . . but to where?* Sansa Stark had vanished on the night King Joffrey died, and if anyone had seen her since, or had any inkling where she might have gone, they were not talking. *Not to me, at least.*

Brienne believed the girl had left the city. If she were still in King's Landing, the gold cloaks would have turned her up. She had to have gone elsewhere . . . but elsewhere is a big place. *If I were a maiden newly flowered, alone and afraid, in desperate danger, what would I do?* she had asked herself. *Where would I go?* For her, the answer came easy. She would make her way back to Tarth, to her father. Sansa's father had been beheaded whilst she watched, however. Her lady mother was dead too, murdered at the Twins, and Winterfell, the great Stark stronghold, had been sacked and burned, its people put to the sword. *She has no home to run to, no father, no mother, no brothers.* She might be in the next town, or on a ship to Asshai; one seemed as likely as the other.

Even if Sansa Stark had wanted to go home, how would she get there? The kingsroad was not safe; even a child would know that. The ironborn held Moat Cailin athwart the Neck, and at the Twins sat the Freys, who had murdered Sansa's brother and lady mother. The girl could go by sea if she had the coin, but the harbor at King's Landing was still in ruins, the river a jumble of broken quays and burned and sunken galleys. Brienne had asked along the docks, but no one could remember a ship leaving on the night King Joffrey died. A few trading ships were anchoring in the bay and off-loading by boat, one man told her, but more were continuing up the coast to Duskendale, where the port was busier than ever.

Brienne's mare was sweet to look upon and kept a pretty pace. There were more travelers than she would have thought. Begging brothers trundled by with their bowls dangling on thongs about their necks. A young septon galloped past upon a palfrey as fine as any lord's, and later she met a band of silent sisters who shook their heads when Brienne put her question to them. A train of oxcarts lumbered south with grain and sacks of wool, and later she passed a swineherd driving pigs, and an old woman in a horse litter with an escort of mounted guards. She asked all of them if they had seen a highborn girl of three-and-ten years with blue eyes and auburn hair. None had. She asked about the road ahead as well. "'Twixt here and Duskendale is safe enough," one man told her, "but past

Duskendale there's outlaws, and broken men in the woods."

Only the soldier pines and sentinels still showed green; the broadleaf trees had donned mantles of russet and gold, or else uncloaked themselves to scratch against the sky with branches brown and bare. Every gust of wind drove swirling clouds of dead leaves across the rutted road. They made a rustling sound as they scuttled past the hooves of the big bay mare that Jaime Lannister had bestowed on her. *As easy to find one leaf in the wind as one girl lost in Westeros.* She found herself wondering whether Jaime had given her this task as some cruel jape. Perhaps Sansa Stark was dead, beheaded for her part in King Joffrey's death, buried in some unmarked grave. How better to conceal her murder than by sending some big stupid wench from Tarth to find her?

Jaime would not do that. He was sincere. He gave me the sword, and called it Oathkeeper. Anyway, it made no matter. She had promised Lady Catelyn that she would bring back her daughters, and no promise was as solemn as one sworn to the dead. The younger girl was long dead, Jaime claimed; the Arya the Lannisters sent north to marry Roose Bolton's bastard was a fraud. That left only Sansa. Brienne had to find her.

Near dusk she saw a campfire burning by a brook. Two men sat beside it grilling trout, their arms and armor stacked beneath a tree. One was old and one was somewhat younger, though far from young. The younger rose to greet her. He had a big belly straining at the laces of his spotted doeskin jerkin. A shaggy untrimmed beard covered his cheeks and chin, the color of old gold. "We have trout enough for three, ser," he called out.

It was not the first time Brienne had been mistaken for a man. She pulled off her greathelm, letting her hair spill free. It was yellow, the color of dirty straw, and near as brittle. Long and thin, it blew about her shoulders. "I thank you, ser."

The hedge knight squinted at her so earnestly that she realized he must be nearsighted. "A lady, is it? Armed and armored? Illy, gods be good, the *size* of her."

"I took her for a knight as well," the older knight said, turning the trout.

Had Brienne been a man, she would have been called big; for a woman, she was huge. *Freakish* was the word she had heard all her life. She was broad in the shoulder and broader in the hips. Her legs were long, her arms thick. Her chest was more muscle than bosom. Her hands were big, her feet enormous. And she was ugly besides, with a freckled, horsey face and teeth that seemed almost too big for her mouth. She did not need to be reminded of any of that. "Sers," she said, "have you seen a maid of three-and-ten upon the road? She has blue eyes and auburn hair, and may have been in company with a portly red-faced man of forty years."

The nearsighted hedge knight scratched his head. "I recall no such maid. What sort of hair is auburn?"

"Browny red," said the older man. "No, we saw her not."

"We saw her not, m'lady," the younger told her. "Come, dismount, the fish is almost done. Are you hungry?"

She was, as it happened, but she was wary as well. Hedge knights had an unsavory reputation. "A hedge knight and a robber knight are two sides of the same sword," it was said. *These two do not look too dangerous.* "Might I know your names, sers?"

"I have the honor to be Ser Creighton Longbough, of whom the singers sing," said the big-bellied one. "You will have heard of my deeds on the Blackwater, mayhaps. My companion is Ser Illifer the Penniless."

If there was a song about Creighton Longbough, it was not one Brienne had heard. Their names meant no more to her than did their arms. Ser Creighton's green shield showed only a brown chief, and a deep gouge made by some battle-axe. Ser Illifer bore gold and ermine gyronny, though everything about him suggested that painted gold and painted ermine were the only sorts he'd ever known. He was sixty if he was a day, his face pinched and narrow beneath the hood of a patched roughspun mantle. Mail-clad he went, but flecks of rust spotted the iron like freckles. Brienne stood a head taller than either of them, and was better mounted and better armed in the bargain. *If I fear the likes of these, I had as well swap my longsword for a pair of knitting needles.*

"I thank you, good sers," she said. "I will gladly share your trout." Swinging down, Brienne unsaddled her mare and watered her before hobbling her to graze. She stacked her arms and shield and saddlebags beneath an elm. By then the trout was crisply done. Ser Creighton brought her a fish, and she sat cross-legged on the ground to eat it.

"We are bound for Duskendale, m'lady," Longbough told her, as he pulled apart his own trout with his fingers. "You would do well to ride with us. The roads are perilous."

Brienne could have told him more about the perils of the roads than he might have cared to know. "I thank you, ser, but I have no need of your protection."

"I insist. A true knight must defend the gentler sex."

She touched her sword hilt. "This will defend me, ser."

"A sword is only as good as the man who wields it."

"I wield it well enough."

"As you will. It would not be courteous to argue with a lady. We will see you safe to Duskendale. Three together may ride more safely than one alone."

We were three when we set out from Riverrun, yet Jaime lost his hand and Cleos Frey his life. "Your mounts could not keep up with mine." Ser Creighton's brown gelding was an old swaybacked creature with rheumy eyes, and Ser Illifer's horse looked weedy and half-starved.

"My steed served me well enough on the Blackwater," Ser Creighton insisted. "Why, I did great carnage there and won a dozen ransoms. Was m'lady familiar with Ser Herbert Bolling? You shall never meet him now. I slew him where he stood. When swords clash, you shall ne'er find Ser Creighton Longbough to the rear."

His companion gave a dry chuckle. "Creigh, leave off. The likes o' her has no need for the likes o' us."

"The likes of me?" Brienne was uncertain what he meant.

Ser Illifer crooked a bony finger at her shield. Though its paint was cracked and peeling, the device it bore showed plain: a black bat on a field divided bendwise, silver and gold. "You bear a liar's shield, to which you have no right. My grandfather's grandfather helped kill the last o' Lothston. None since has dared to show that bat, black as the deeds of them that bore it."

The shield was the one Ser Jaime had taken from the armory at Harrenhal. Brienne had found it in the stables with her mare, along with much else; saddle and bridle, chainmail hauberk and visored greathelm, purses of gold and silver and a parchment more valuable than either. "I lost mine own shield," she explained.

"A true knight is the only shield a maiden needs," declared Ser Creighton stoutly.

Ser Illifer paid him no mind. "A barefoot man looks for a boot, a chilly man a cloak. But who would cloak themselves in shame? Lord Lucas bore that bat, the Pander, and Manfryd o' the Black Hood, his son. Why wear such arms,

I ask myself, unless your own sin is fouler still . . . and *fresher*." He unsheathed his dagger, an ugly piece of cheap iron. "A woman freakish big and freakish strong who hides her own true colors. Creigh, behold the Maid o' Tarth, who opened Renly's royal throat for him."

"That is a lie." Renly Baratheon had been more than a king to her. She had loved him since first he came to Tarth on his leisurely lord's progress, to mark his coming of age. Her father welcomed him with a feast and commanded her to attend; elsewise she would have hidden in her room like some wounded beast. She had been no older than Sansa, more afraid of sniggers than of swords. *They will know about the rose,* she told Lord Selwyn, *they will laugh at me.* But the Evenstar would not relent.

And Renly Baratheon had shown her every courtesy, as if she were a proper maid, and pretty. He even danced with her, and in his arms she'd felt graceful, and her feet had floated across the floor. Later others begged a dance of her, because of his example. From that day forth, she wanted only to be close to Lord Renly, to serve him and protect him. But in the end she failed him. *Renly died in my arms, but I did not kill him,* she thought, but these hedge knights would never understand. "I would have given my life for King Renly, and died happy," she said. "I did no harm to him. I swear it by my sword."

"A knight swears by his sword," Ser Creighton said.

"Swear it by the Seven," urged Ser Illifer the Penniless.

"By the Seven, then. I did no harm to King Renly. I swear it by the Mother. May I never know her mercy if I lie. I swear it by the Father, and ask that he might judge me justly. I swear it by the Maiden and Crone, by the Smith and the Warrior. And I swear it by the Stranger, may he take me now if I am false."

"She swears well, for a maid," Ser Creighton allowed.

"Aye." Ser Illifer the Penniless gave a shrug. "Well, if she's lied, the gods will sort her out." He slipped his dagger back away. "The first watch is yours."

As the hedge knights slept, Brienne paced restlessly around the little camp, listening to the crackle of the fire. *I should ride on whilst I can.* She did not know these men, yet she could not bring herself to leave them undefended. Even in the black of night, there were riders on the road, and noises in the woods that might or might not have been owls and prowling foxes. So Brienne paced, and kept her blade loose in its scabbard.

Her watch was easy, all in all. It was *after* that was hard, when Ser Illifer woke and said he would relieve her. Brienne spread a blanket on the ground, and curled up to close her eyes. *I will not sleep,* she told herself, bone weary though she was. She had never slept easily in the presence of men. Even in Lord Renly's camps, the risk of rape was always there. It was a lesson she had learned beneath the walls of Highgarden, and again when she and Jaime had fallen into the hands of the Brave Companions.

The cold in the earth seeped through Brienne's blankets to soak into her bones. Before long every muscle felt clenched and cramped, from her jaw down to her toes. She wondered whether Sansa Stark was cold as well, wherever she might be. Lady Catelyn had said that Sansa was a gentle soul who loved lemon cakes, silken gowns, and songs of chivalry, yet the girl had seen her father's head lopped off and been forced to marry one of his killers afterward. If half the tales were true, the dwarf was the cruelest Lannister of all. *If she did poison King Joffrey, the Imp surely forced her hand. She was alone and friendless at that court.* In King's Landing, Brienne had hunted down a certain Brella, who had been one of Sansa's maids. The woman told her that there was little warmth between

Sansa and the dwarf. Perhaps she had been fleeing him as well as Joffrey's murder.

Whatever dreams Brienne dreamed were gone when dawn awoke her. Her legs were stiff as wood from the cold ground, but no one had molested her, and her goods remained untouched. The hedge knights were up and about. Ser Illifer was cutting up a squirrel for breakfast, while Ser Creighton stood facing a tree, having himself a good long piss. *Hedge knights,* she thought, *old and vain and plump and nearsighted, yet decent men for all that.* It cheered her to know that there were still decent men in the world.

They broke their fast on roast squirrel, acorn paste, and pickles, whilst Ser Creighton regaled her with his exploits on the Blackwater, where he had slain a dozen fearsome knights that she had never heard of. "Oh, it was a rare fight, m'lady," he said, "a rare and bloody fray." He allowed that Ser Illifer had fought nobly in the battle as well. Illifer himself said little.

When time came to resume their journey, the knights fell in on either side of her, like guards protecting some great lady . . . though this lady dwarfed both of her protectors and was better armed and armored in the nonce. "Did anyone pass by during your watches?" Brienne asked them.

"Such as a maid of three-and-ten, with auburn hair?" said Ser Illifer the Penniless. "No, my lady. No one."

"I had a few," Ser Creighton put in. "Some farm boy on a piebald horse went by, and an hour later half a dozen men afoot with staves and scythes. They caught sight of our fire, and stopped for a long look at our horses, but I showed them a glimpse of my steel and told them to be along their way. Rough fellows, by the look o' them, and desperate too, but ne'er so desperate as to trifle with Ser Creighton Longbough."

No, Brienne thought, *not so desperate as that.* She turned away to hide her smile. Thankfully, Ser Creighton was too intent on the tale of his epic battle with the Knight of the Red Chicken to make note of the maiden's mirth. It felt good to have companions on the road, even such companions as these two.

It was midday when Brienne heard chanting drifting through the bare brown trees. "What is that sound?" Ser Creighton asked.

"Voices, raised in prayer." Brienne knew the chant. *They are beseeching the Warrior for protection, asking the Crone to light their way.*

Ser Illifer the Penniless bared his battered blade and reined in his horse to wait their coming. "They are close now."

The chanting filled the woods like pious thunder. And suddenly the source of the sound appeared in the road ahead. A group of begging brothers led the way, scruffy bearded men in roughspun robes, some barefoot and some in sandals. Behind them marched threescore ragged men, women, and children, a spotted sow, and several sheep. Several of the men had axes, and more had crude wooden clubs and cudgels. In their midst there rolled a two-wheeled wayn of grey and splintered wood, piled high with skulls and broken bits of bone. When they saw the hedge knights, the begging brothers halted, and the chanting died away. "Good knights," one said, "the Mother loves you."

"And you, brother," said Ser Illifer. "Who are you?"

"Poor fellows," said a big man with an axe. Despite the chill of the autumnal wood, he was shirtless, and on his breast was carved a seven-pointed star. Andal warriors had carved such stars in their flesh when first they crossed the narrow sea to overwhelm the kingdoms of the First Men.

"We are marching to the city," said a tall woman in the traces of the wayn, "to bring these holy bones to Blessed Baelor, and seek succor and protection from the king."

"Join us, friends," urged a spare small man in a threadbare septon's robe, who wore a crystal on a thong about his neck. "Westeros has need of every sword."

"We were bound for Duskendale," declared Ser Creighton, "but mayhaps we could see you safely to King's Landing."

"If you have the coin to pay us for this escort," added Ser Illifer, who seemed practical as well as penniless.

"Sparrows need no gold," the septon said.

Ser Creighton was lost. "Sparrows?"

"The sparrow is the humblest and most common of birds, as we are the humblest and most common of men." The septon had a lean sharp face and a short beard, grizzled grey and brown. His thin hair was pulled back and knotted behind his head, and his feet were bare and black, gnarled and hard as tree roots. "These are the bones of holy men, murdered for their faith. They served the Seven even unto death. Some starved, some were tortured. Septs have been despoiled, maidens and mothers raped by godless men and demon worshipers. Even silent sisters have been molested. Our Mother Above cries out in her anguish. It is time for all anointed knights to forsake their worldly masters and defend our Holy Faith. Come with us to the city, if you love the Seven."

"I love them well enough," said Illifer, "yet I must eat."

"So must all the Mother's children."

"We are bound for Duskendale," Ser Illifer said flatly.

One of the begging brothers spat, and a woman gave a moan. "You are false knights," said the big man with the star carved on his chest. Several others brandished their cudgels.

The barefoot septon calmed them with a word. "Judge not, for judgment is the Father's. Let them pass in peace. They are poor fellows too, lost upon the earth."

Brienne edged her mare forward. "My sister is lost as well. A girl of three-and-ten with auburn hair, fair to look upon."

"All the Mother's children are fair to look upon. May the Maiden watch over this poor girl . . . and you as well, I think." The septon lifted one of the traces of the wayn upon his shoulder, and began to pull. The begging brothers took up the chant once more. Brienne and the hedge knights sat upon their horses as the procession moved slowly past, following the rutted road toward Rosby. The sound of their chanting slowly dwindled away and died.

Ser Creighton lifted one cheek off the saddle to scratch his arse. "What sort of man would slay a holy septon?"

Brienne knew what sort. Near Maidenpool, she recalled, the Brave Companions had strung a septon up by his heels from the limb of a tree and used his corpse for archery practice. She wondered if his bones were piled in that wayn with all the rest.

"A man would need to be a fool to rape a silent sister," Ser Creighton was saying. "Even to lay hands upon one . . . it's said they are the Stranger's wives, and their female parts are cold and wet as ice." He glanced at Brienne. "Uh . . . beg pardon."

Brienne spurred her mare toward Duskendale. After a moment, Ser Illifer followed, and Ser Creighton came bringing up the rear.

Three hours later they came up upon another party struggling toward Duskendale; a merchant and his serving men, accompanied by yet another hedge knight. The merchant rode a dappled grey mare, whilst his servants took turns pulling his wagon. Four labored in the traces as the other two walked beside the wheels, but when they heard the sound of horses they formed up around the wagon with quarterstaffs of ash at the ready. The merchant produced a crossbow, the knight a blade. "You will forgive me if I am suspicious," called the merchant, "but the times are troubled, and I have only good Ser Shadrich to defend me. Who are you?"

"Why," Ser Creighton said, affronted, "I am the famous Ser Creighton Longbough, fresh from battle on the Blackwater, and this is my companion, Ser Illifer the Penniless."

"We mean you no harm," said Brienne.

The merchant considered her doubtfully. "My lady, you should be safe at home. Why do you wear such unnatural garb?"

"I am searching for my sister." She dared not mention Sansa's name, with her accused of regicide. "She is a high-born maid and beautiful, with blue eyes and auburn hair. Perhaps you saw her with a portly knight of forty years, or a drunken fool."

"The roads are full of drunken fools and despoiled maidens. As to portly knights, it is hard for any honest man to keep his belly round when so many lack for food . . . though your Ser Creighton has not hungered, it would seem."

"I have big bones," Ser Creighton insisted. "Shall we ride together for a time? I do not doubt Ser Shadrich's valor, but he seems small, and three blades are better than one."

Four blades, thought Brienne, but she held her tongue.

The merchant looked to his escort. "What say you, ser?"

"Oh, these three are nought to fear." Ser Shadrich was a

wiry, fox-faced man with a sharp nose and a shock of orange hair, mounted on a rangy chestnut courser. Though
he could not have been more than five foot two, he had a
cocksure manner. "The one is old, t'other fat, and the big
one is a woman. Let them come."

"As you say." The merchant lowered his crossbow.

As they resumed their journey, the hired knight
dropped back and looked her up and down as if she were a
side of good salt pork. "You're a strapping healthy wench,
I'd say."

Ser Jaime's mockery had cut her deep; the little man's
words hardly touched her. "A giant, compared to some."

He laughed. "I am big enough where it counts, wench."

"The merchant called you Shadrich."

"Ser Shadrich of the Shady Glen. Some call me the
Mad Mouse." He turned his shield to show her his sigil, a
large white mouse with fierce red eyes, on bendy brown
and blue. "The brown is for the lands I've roamed, the blue
for the rivers that I've crossed. The mouse is me."

"And are you mad?"

"Oh, quite. Your common mouse will run from blood
and battle. The mad mouse seeks them out."

"It would seem he seldom finds them."

"I find enough. 'Tis true, I am no tourney knight. I save
my valor for the battlefield, woman."

Woman was marginally better than *wench,* she supposed. "You and good Ser Creighton have much in common, then."

Ser Shadrich laughed. "Oh, I doubt that, but it may be
that you and I share a quest. A little lost sister, is it? With
blue eyes and auburn hair?" He laughed again. "You are
not the only hunter in the woods. I seek for Sansa Stark as
well."

Brienne kept her face a mask, to hide her dismay. "Who is this Sansa Stark, and why do you seek her?"

"For love, why else?"

She furrowed her brow. "Love?"

"Aye, love of gold. Unlike your good Ser Creighton, I did fight upon the Blackwater, but on the losing side. My ransom ruined me. You know who Varys is, I trust? The eunuch has offered a plump bag of gold for this girl you've never heard of. I am not a greedy man. If some oversized wench would help me find this naughty child, I would split the Spider's coin with her."

"I thought you were in this merchant's hire."

"Only so far as Duskendale. Hibald is as niggardly as he is fearful. And he is *very* fearful. What say you, wench?"

"I know no Sansa Stark," she insisted. "I am searching for my sister, a highborn girl . . ."

". . . with blue eyes and auburn hair, aye. Pray, who is this knight who travels with your sister? Or did you name him fool?" Ser Shadrich did not wait for her answer, which was good, since she had none. "A certain fool vanished from King's Landing the night King Joffrey died, a stout fellow with a nose full of broken veins, one Ser Dontos the Red, formerly of Duskendale. I pray your sister and *her* drunken fool are not mistaken for the Stark girl and Ser Dontos. That could be most unfortunate." He put his heels into his courser and trotted on ahead.

Even Jaime Lannister had seldom made Brienne feel such a fool. *You are not the only hunter in the woods.* The woman Brella had told her how Joffrey had stripped Ser Dontos of his spurs, how Lady Sansa begged Joffrey for his life. *He helped her flee,* Brienne had decided, when she heard the tale. *Find Ser Dontos, and I will find Sansa.* She should have known there would be others who would see it too. *Some may even be less savory than Ser*

Shadrich. She could only hope that Ser Dontos had hidden Sansa well. *But if so, how will I ever find her?*

She hunched her shoulders down and rode on, frowning.

Night was gathering by the time their party came upon the inn, a tall, timbered building that stood beside a river junction, astride an old stone bridge. That was the inn's name, Ser Creighton told them: the Old Stone Bridge. The innkeep was a friend of his. "Not a bad cook, and the rooms have no more fleas than most," he vouched. "Who's for a warm bed tonight?"

"Not us, unless your friend is giving them away," said Ser Illifer the Penniless. "We have no coin for rooms."

"I can pay for the three of us." Brienne did not lack for coin; Jaime had seen to that. In her saddlebags she'd found a purse fat with silver stags and copper stars, a smaller one stuffed with golden dragons, and a parchment commanding all loyal subjects of the king to assist the bearer, Brienne of House Tarth, who was about His Grace's business. It was signed in a childish hand by Tommen, the First of His Name, King of the Andals, the Rhoynar, and the First Men, and Lord of the Seven Kingdoms.

Hibald was for stopping too, and bid his men to leave the wagon near the stables. Warm yellow light shone through the diamond-shaped panes of the inn's windows, and Brienne heard a stallion trumpet at the scent of her mare. She was loosening the saddle when a boy came out the stable door, and said, "Let me do that, ser."

"I am no *ser,*" she told him, "but you may take the horse. See that she is fed and brushed and watered."

The boy reddened. "Beg pardons, m'lady. I thought . . ."

"It is a common mistake." Brienne gave him the reins and followed the others into the inn, with her saddlebags across a shoulder and her bedroll tucked up beneath one arm.

Sawdust covered the plank floor of the common room,

and the air smelled of hops and smoke and meat. A roast was spitting and crackling over the fire, unattended for the moment. Six locals sat about a table, talking, but they broke off when the strangers entered. Brienne could feel their eyes. Despite chainmail, cloak, and jerkin, she felt naked. When one man said, "Have a look at that," she knew he was not speaking of Ser Shadrich.

The innkeep appeared, clutching three tankards in each hand and slopping ale at every step.

"Do you have rooms, good man?" the merchant asked him.

"I might," the innkeep said, "for them as has coin."

Ser Creighton Longbough looked offended. "Naggle, is that how you would greet an old friend? 'Tis me, Longbough."

"'Tis you indeed. You owe me seven stags. Show me some silver and I'll show you a bed." The innkeep set the tankards down one by one, slopping more ale on the table in the process.

"I will pay for one room for myself, and a second for my two companions." Brienne indicated Ser Creighton and Ser Illifer.

"I shall take a room as well," said the merchant, "for myself and good Ser Shadrich. My serving men will bed down in your stables, if it please you."

The innkeep looked them over. "It don't please me, but might be I'll allow it. Will you be wanting supper? That's good goat on the spit, that is."

"I shall judge its goodness for myself," Hibald announced. "My men will content themselves with bread and drippings."

And so they supped. Brienne tried the goat herself, after following the innkeep up the steps, pressing some coins into his hand, and stashing her goods in the second room he showed her. She ordered goat for Ser Creighton and Ser Illifer as well, since they had shared their trout with her. The hedge knights and the septon washed down the meat with ale, but Brienne drank a cup of goat's milk. She listened to the table talk, hoping against hope that she might hear something that would help her find Sansa.

"You come from King's Landing," one of the locals said to Hibald. "Is it true that the Kingslayer's been crippled?"

"True enough," Hibald said. "He's lost his sword hand."

"Aye," Ser Creighton said, "chewed off by a direwolf, I hear, one of them monsters come down from the north. Nought that's good ever come from the north. Even their gods are queer."

"It was not a wolf," Brienne heard herself say. "Ser Jaime lost his hand to a Qohorik sellsword."

"It is no easy thing to fight with your off hand," observed the Mad Mouse.

"Bah," said Ser Creighton Longbough. "As it happens, I fight as well with either hand."

"Oh, I have no doubt of that." Ser Shadrich lifted his tankard in salute.

Brienne remembered her fight with Jaime Lannister in the woods. It had been all that she could do to keep his blade at bay. *He was weak from his imprisonment, and chained at the wrists. No knight in the Seven Kingdoms could have stood against him at his full strength, with no chains to hamper him.* Jaime had done many wicked things, but the man could *fight*! His maiming had been monstrously cruel. It was one thing to slay a lion, another to hack his paw off and leave him broken and bewildered.

Suddenly the common room was too loud to endure a moment longer. She muttered her good-nights and took herself up to bed. The ceiling in her room was low; entering with a taper in her hand, Brienne had to duck or crack her head. The only furnishings were a bed wide enough to sleep six, and the stub of a tallow candle on the sill. She lit it with the taper, barred the door, and hung her sword belt from a bedpost. Her scabbard was a plain thing, wood wrapped in cracked brown leather, and her sword was plainer still. She had bought it in King's Landing, to replace the blade the Brave Companions had stolen. *Renly's sword.* It still hurt, knowing she had lost it.

But she had another longsword hidden in her bedroll. She sat on the bed and took it out. Gold glimmered yellow in the candlelight and rubies smoldered red. When she slid Oathkeeper from the ornate scabbard, Brienne's breath caught in her throat. Black and red the ripples ran, deep within the steel. *Valyrian steel, spell-forged.* It was a sword fit for a hero. When she was small, her nurse had filled her ears with tales of valor, regaling her with the noble exploits of Ser Galladon of Morne, Florian the Fool, Prince Aemon the Dragonknight, and other champions. Each man bore a famous sword, and surely Oathkeeper belonged in their company, even if she herself did not. "You'll be defending Ned Stark's daughter with Ned Stark's own steel," Jaime had promised.

Kneeling between the bed and wall, she held the blade and said a silent prayer to the Crone, whose golden lamp showed men the way through life. *Lead me,* she prayed, *light the way before me, show me the path that leads to Sansa.* She had failed Renly, had failed Lady Catelyn. She must not fail Jaime. *He trusted me with his sword. He trusted me with his honor.*

Afterward she stretched out on the bed as best she could. For all its width it was not long enough, so Brienne lay across it sideways. She could hear the clatter of tankards from below, and voices drifting up the steps. The fleas that Longbough had spoken of put in their appearance. Scratching helped keep her awake.

She heard Hibald mount the stairs, and sometime later the knights as well. ". . . I never knew his name," Ser Creighton was saying as he went by, "but upon his shield he bore a blood-red chicken, and his blade was dripping gore . . ." His voice faded, and somewhere up above, a door opened and closed.

Her candle burned out. Darkness settled over the Old Stone Bridge, and the inn grew so still that she could hear the murmur of the river. Only then did Brienne rise to gather up her things. She eased the door open, listened, made her way barefoot down the steps. Outside she donned her boots and hurried to the stables to saddle her bay mare, asking a silent pardon of Ser Creighton and Ser Illifer as she mounted. One of Hibald's serving men woke when she rode past him, but made no move to stop her. Her mare's hooves rang upon the old stone bridge. Then the trees closed in around her, black as pitch and full of ghosts and memories. *I am coming for you, Lady Sansa,* she thought as she rode into the darkness. *Be not afraid. I shall not rest until I've found you.*

SAMWELL

S am was reading about the Others when he saw the mouse.

His eyes were red and raw. *I ought not rub them so much,* he always told himself as he rubbed them. The dust made them itch and water, and the dust was everywhere down here. Little puffs of it filled the air every time a page was turned, and it rose in grey clouds whenever he shifted a stack of books to see what might be hiding on the bottom.

Sam did not know how long it had been since last he'd slept, but scarce an inch remained of the fat tallow candle he'd lit when starting on the ragged bundle of loose pages that he'd found tied up in twine. He was beastly tired, but it was hard to stop. *One more book,* he had told himself, *then I'll stop. One more folio, just one more. One more page, then I'll go up and rest and get a bite to eat.* But there was always another page after that one, and another after that, and another book waiting underneath the pile. *I'll just take a quick peek to see what this one is about,* he'd think, and before he knew he would be halfway through it. He had not eaten since that bowl of bean-and-bacon soup with Pyp and Grenn. *Well, except for the bread and cheese, but that was only a nibble,* he thought. That was when he took a quick glance at the empty platter, and spied the mouse feasting on the bread crumbs.

The mouse was half as long as his pinky finger, with black eyes and soft grey fur. Sam knew he ought to kill it. Mice might prefer bread and cheese, but they ate paper too. He had found plenty of mouse droppings amongst the shelves and stacks, and some of the leather covers on the books showed signs of being gnawed.

It is such a little thing, though. And hungry. How could he begrudge it a few crumbs? *It's eating books, though . . .*

After hours in the chair Sam's back was stiff as a board, and his legs were half-asleep. He knew he was not quick enough to catch the mouse, but it might be he could squash it. By his elbow rested a massive leather-bound copy of *Annals of the Black Centaur,* Septon Jorquen's exhaustively detailed account of the nine years that Orbert Caswell had served as Lord Commander of the Night's Watch. There was a page for each day of his term, every one of which seemed to begin, "Lord Orbert rose at dawn and moved his bowels," except for the last, which said, "Lord Orbert was found to have died during the night."

No mouse is a match for Septon Jorquen. Very slowly, Sam took hold of the book with his left hand. It was thick and heavy, and when he tried to lift it one-handed, it slipped from his plump fingers and thumped back down. The mouse was gone in half a heartbeat, skittery-quick. Sam was relieved. Squishing the poor little thing would have given him nightmares. "You shouldn't eat the books, though," he said aloud. Maybe he should bring more cheese the next time he came down here.

He was surprised at how low the candle had burned. Had the bean-and-bacon soup been today or yesterday? *Yesterday. It must have been yesterday.* The realization made him yawn. Jon would be wondering what had become of him, though Maester Aemon would no doubt understand. Before he had lost his sight, the maester had loved books as much as Samwell Tarly did. He understood the way that you could sometimes fall right into them, as if each page was a hole into another world.

Pushing himself to his feet, Sam grimaced at the pins and needles in his calves. The chair was very hard and cut into the back of his thighs when he bent over a book. *I need to remember to bring a cushion.* It would be even better if he could sleep down here, in the cell he'd found half-hidden behind four chests full of loose pages that had gotten separated from the books they belonged to, but he did not want to leave Maester Aemon alone for so long. He had not been strong of late and required help, especially with the ravens. Aemon had Clydas, to be sure, but Sam was younger, and better with the birds.

With a stack of books and scrolls under his left arm and the candle in his right hand, Sam made his way through the tunnels the brothers called the wormways. A pale shaft of light illuminated the steep stone steps that led up to the surface, so he knew that day had come up top. He left the candle burning in a wall niche and began the climb. By the fifth step he was puffing. At the tenth he stopped to shift the books to his right arm.

He emerged beneath a sky the color of white lead. *A snow sky,* Sam thought, squinting up. The prospect made him uneasy. He remembered that night on the Fist of the

First Men when the wights and the snows had come together. *Don't be so craven,* he thought. *You have your
Sworn Brothers all around you, not to mention Stannis
Baratheon and all his knights.* Castle Black's keeps and
towers rose about him, dwarfed by the icy immensity of
the Wall. A small army was crawling over the ice a quarter
of the way up, where a new switchback stair was creeping
upward to meet the remnants of the old one. The sounds of
their saws and hammers echoed off the ice. Jon had the
builders working night and day on the task. Sam had heard
some of them complaining about it over supper, insisting
that Lord Mormont never worked them half so hard.
Without the great stair there was no way to reach the top
of the Wall except by the chain winch, however. And as
much as Samwell Tarly hated steps, he hated the winch
cage more. He always closed his eyes when he was riding
it, convinced that the chain was about to break. Every time
the iron cage scraped against the ice his heart stopped
beating for an instant.

There were dragons here two hundred years ago, Sam
found himself thinking, as he watched the cage making a
slow descent. *They would just have flown to the top of the
Wall.* Queen Alysanne had visited Castle Black on her
dragon, and Jaehaerys, her king, had come after her on his
own. Could Silverwing have left an egg behind? Or had
Stannis found one egg on Dragonstone? *Even if he has an
egg, how can he hope to quicken it?* Baelor the Blessed
had prayed over his eggs, and other Targaryens had sought
to hatch theirs with sorcery. All they got for it was farce
and tragedy.

"Samwell," said a glum voice, "I was coming to fetch
you. I was told to bring you to the Lord Commander."

A snowflake landed on Sam's nose. "Jon wants to see me?"

"As to that, I could not say," said Dolorous Edd Tollett.

"I never wanted to see half the things I've seen, and I've never seen half the things I wanted to. I don't think wanting comes into it. You'd best go all the same. Lord Snow wishes to speak with you as soon as he is done with Craster's wife."

"Gilly."

"That's the one. If my wet nurse had looked like her, I'd still be on the teat. Mine had whiskers."

"Most goats do," called Pyp, as he and Grenn emerged from around the corner, with longbows in hand and quivers of arrows on their backs. "Where have you been, Slayer? We missed you last night at supper. A whole roast ox went uneaten."

"Don't call me Slayer." Sam ignored the gibe about the ox. That was just Pyp. "I was reading. There was a mouse . . ."

"Don't mention mice to Grenn. He's terrified of mice."

"I am not," Grenn declared with indignation.

"You'd be too scared to eat one."

"I'd eat more mice than you would."

Dolorous Edd Tollett gave a sigh. "When I was a lad, we only ate mice on special feast days. I was the youngest, so I always got the tail. There's no meat on the tail."

"Where's your longbow, Sam?" asked Grenn. Ser Alliser used to call him *Aurochs,* and every day he seemed to grow into the name a little more. He had come to the Wall big but slow, thick of neck, thick of waist, red of face, and clumsy. Though his neck still reddened when Pyp twisted him around into some folly, hours of work with sword and shield had flattened his belly, hardened his arms, broadened his chest. He was *strong,* and shaggy as an aurochs too. "Ulmer was expecting you at the butts."

"Ulmer," Sam said, abashed. Almost the first thing Jon Snow had done as Lord Commander was institute daily archery drill for the entire garrison, even stewards and cooks. The Watch had been placing too much emphasis on the sword and too little on the bow, he had said, a relic of the days when one brother in every ten had been a knight, instead of one in every hundred. Sam saw the sense in the decree, but he hated longbow practice almost as much as he hated climbing steps. When he wore his gloves he could never hit anything, but when he took them off he got blisters on his fingers. Those bows were *dangerous.* Satin had torn off half his thumbnail on a bowstring. "I forgot."

"You broke the heart of the wildling princess, Slayer," said Pyp. Of late, Val had taken to watching them from the window of her chamber in the King's Tower. "She was looking for you."

"She was not! Don't say that!" Sam had only spoken to Val twice, when Maester Aemon called upon her to make sure the babes were healthy. The princess was so pretty that he oft found himself stammering and blushing in her presence.

"Why not?" asked Pyp. "She wants to have your children. Maybe we should call you Sam the Seducer."

Sam reddened. King Stannis had plans for Val, he knew; she was the mortar with which he meant to seal the peace between the northmen and the free folk. "I don't have time for archery today, I need to go see Jon."

"Jon? Jon? Do we know anyone named Jon, Grenn?"

"He means the Lord Commander."

"*Ohhh.* The Great Lord Snow. To be sure. Why do you want to see him? He can't even wiggle his ears." Pyp wiggled his, to show he could. They were large ears, and red from cold. "He's *Lord* Snow for true now, too bloody highborn for the likes of us."

"Jon has duties," Sam said in his defense. "The Wall is his, and all that goes with it."

"A man has duties to his friends as well. If not for us, Janos Slynt might be our lord commander. Lord Janos would have sent Snow ranging naked on a mule. 'Scamper on up to Craster's Keep,' he would have said, 'and fetch me back the Old Bear's cloak and boots.' We saved him from that, but now he has too many *duties* to drink a cup of mulled wine by the fire?"

Grenn agreed. "His duties don't keep him from the yard. More days than not, he's out there fighting someone."

That was true, Sam had to admit. Once, when Jon came to consult with Maester Aemon, Sam had asked him why he spent so much time at swordplay. "The Old Bear never trained much when he was Lord Commander," he had pointed out. In answer, Jon had pressed Longclaw into Sam's hand. He let him feel the lightness, the balance, had him turn the blade so that ripples gleamed in the smoke-dark metal. "Valyrian steel," he said, "spell-forged and razor-sharp, nigh on indestructible. A swordsman should be as good as his sword, Sam. Longclaw is Valyrian steel, but I'm not. The Halfhand could have killed me as easy as you swat a bug."

Sam handed back the sword. "When I try to swat a bug, it always flies away. All I do is slap my arm. It stings."

That made Jon laugh. "As you will. Qhorin could have killed me as easy as you eat a bowl of porridge." Sam was fond of porridge, especially when it was sweetened with honey.

"I don't have time for this." Sam left his friends and made his way toward the armory, clutching his books to his chest. *I am the shield that guards the realms of men,* he remembered. He wondered what those men would say if they realized their realms were being guarded by the likes of Grenn, Pyp, and Dolorous Edd.

The Lord Commander's Tower had been gutted by fire,

and Stannis Baratheon had claimed the King's Tower for his own residence, so Jon Snow had established himself in Donal Noye's modest quarters behind the armory. Gilly was leaving as Sam arrived, wrapped up in the old cloak he'd given her when they were fleeing Craster's Keep. She almost rushed right past him, but Sam caught her arm, spilling two books as he did. "Gilly."

"Sam." Her voice sounded raw. Gilly was dark-haired and slim, with the big brown eyes of a doe. She was swallowed by the folds of Sam's old cloak, her face half-hidden by its hood, but shivering all the same. Her face looked wan and frightened.

"What's wrong?" Sam asked her. "How are the babes?"

Gilly pulled loose from him. "They're good, Sam. Good."

"Between the two of them it's a wonder you can sleep," Sam said pleasantly. "Which one was it that I heard crying last night? I thought he'd never stop."

"Dalla's boy. He cries when he wants the teat. Mine . . . mine hardly ever cries. Sometimes he gurgles, but . . ." Her eyes filled with tears. "I have to go. It's past time that I fed them. I'll be leaking all over myself if I don't go." She rushed across the yard, leaving Sam perplexed behind her.

He had to get down on his knees to gather up the books he'd dropped. *I should not have brought so many,* he told himself as he brushed the dirt off Colloquo Votar's *Jade Compendium,* a thick volume of tales and legends from the east that Maester Aemon had commanded him to find. The book appeared undamaged. Maester Thomax's *Dragonkin, Being a History of House Targaryen from Exile to Apotheosis, with a Consideration of the Life and Death of Dragons* had not been so fortunate. It had come open as it fell, and a few pages had gotten muddy, including one with a rather nice picture of Balerion the Black Dread done in colored inks. Sam cursed himself for a clumsy oaf as he smoothed the pages down and brushed them off. Gilly's presence always flustered him and gave rise to . . . well, *risings*. A Sworn Brother of the Night's Watch should not be feeling the sorts of things that Gilly made him feel, especially when she would talk about her breasts and . . .

"Lord Snow is waiting." Two guards in black cloaks and iron halfhelms stood by the doors of the armory, leaning on their spears. Hairy Hal was the one who'd spoken. Mully helped Sam back to his feet. He blurted out thanks and hurried past them, clutching desperately at the stack of books as he made his way past the forge with its anvil and bellows. A shirt of ringmail rested on his workbench, half-completed. Ghost was stretched out beneath the anvil, gnawing on the bone of an ox to get at the marrow. The big white direwolf looked up when Sam went by, but made no sound.

Jon's solar was back beyond the racks of spears and shields. He was reading a parchment when Sam entered. Lord Commander Mormont's raven was on his shoulder, peering down as if it were reading too, but when the bird spied Sam it spread its wings and flapped toward him crying, *"Corn, corn!"*

Shifting the books, Sam thrust his arm into the sack beside the door and came out with a handful of kernels. The raven landed on his wrist and took one from his palm, pecking so hard that Sam yelped and snatched his hand back. The raven took to the air again, and yellow and red kernels went everywhere.

"Close the door, Sam." Faint scars still marked Jon's cheek, where an eagle had once tried to rip his eye out. "Did that wretch break the skin?"

Sam eased the books down and peeled off his glove. "He did." He felt faint. "I'm *bleeding*."

"We all shed our blood for the Watch. Wear thicker gloves." Jon shoved a chair toward him with a foot. "Sit, and have a look at this." He handed him the parchment.

"What is it?" asked Sam. The raven began to hunt out corn kernels amongst the rushes.

"A paper shield."

Sam sucked at the blood on his palm as he read. He knew Maester Aemon's hand on sight. His writing was small and precise, but the old man could not see where the ink had blotted, and sometimes he left unsightly smears. "A letter to King Tommen?"

"At Winterfell Tommen fought my brother Bran with wooden swords. He wore so much padding he looked like a stuffed goose. Bran knocked him to the ground." Jon went to the window. "Yet Bran's dead, and pudgy pink-faced Tommen is sitting on the Iron Throne, with a crown nestled amongst his golden curls."

Bran's not dead, Sam wanted to say. *He's gone beyond the Wall with Coldhands.* The words caught in his throat. *I swore I would not tell.* "You haven't signed the letter."

"The Old Bear begged the Iron Throne for help a hundred times. They sent him Janos Slynt. No letter will make the Lannisters love us better. Not once they hear that we've been helping Stannis."

"Only to defend the Wall, not in his rebellion." Sam read the letter quickly once again. "That's what it *says* here."

"The distinction may escape Lord Tywin." Jon took the letter back. "Why would he help us now? He never did before."

"Well," said Sam, "he will not want it said that Stannis rode to the defense of the realm whilst King Tommen was playing with his toys. That would bring scorn down upon House Lannister."

"It's death and destruction I want to bring down upon House Lannister, not scorn." Jon lifted up the letter. *"The Night's Watch takes no part in the wars of the Seven Kingdoms,"* he read. *"Our oaths are sworn to the realm, and the realm now stands in dire peril. Stannis Baratheon aids us against our foes from beyond the Wall, though we are not his men . . ."*

"Well," said Sam, squirming, "we're *not*. Are we?"

"I gave Stannis food, shelter, and the Nightfort, plus leave to settle some free folk in the Gift. That's all."

"Lord Tywin will say it was too much."

"Stannis says it's not enough. The more you give a king the more he wants. We are walking on a bridge of ice with an abyss on either side. Pleasing one king is difficult enough. Pleasing two is hardly possible."

"Yes, but . . . if the Lannisters should prevail and Lord Tywin decides that we betrayed the king by aiding Stannis, it could mean the end of the Night's Watch. He has the Tyrells behind him, with all the strength of Highgarden. And he did defeat Lord Stannis on the Blackwater." The sight of blood might make Sam faint, but he knew how wars were won. His own father had seen to that.

"The Blackwater was one battle. Robb won all his battles and still lost his head. If Stannis can raise the north . . ."

He's trying to convince himself, Sam realized, *but he can't.* The ravens had gone forth from Castle Black in a storm of black wings, summoning the lords of the north to declare for Stannis Baratheon and join their strength to his. Sam had sent out most of them himself. Thusfar only one bird had returned, the one they'd sent to Karhold. Elsewise the silence had been thunderous.

Even if he should somehow win the northmen to his side, Sam did not see how Stannis could hope to match the combined powers of Casterly Rock, Highgarden, and the

Twins. Yet without the north, his cause was surely doomed. *As doomed as the Night's Watch, if Lord Tywin marks us down as traitors.* "The Lannisters have northmen of their own. Lord Bolton and his bastard."

"Stannis has the Karstarks. If he can win White Harbor . . ."

"If," Sam stressed. "If not . . . my lord, even a paper shield is better than none."

Jon rattled the letter. "I suppose so." He sighed, then took up a quill and scrawled a signature across the bottom of the letter. "Get the sealing wax." Sam heated a stick of black wax over a candle and dribbled some onto the parchment, then watched as Jon pressed the Lord Commander's seal down firmly on the puddle. "Take this to Maester Aemon when you leave," he commanded, "and tell him to dispatch a bird to King's Landing."

"I will." Sam hesitated. "My lord, if I might ask . . . I saw Gilly leaving. She was almost crying."

"Val sent her to plead for Mance again."

"Oh." Val was the sister of the woman the King-beyond-the-Wall had taken for his queen. *The wildling princess* was what Stannis and his men were calling her. Her sister Dalla had died during the battle, though no blade had ever touched her; she had perished giving birth to Mance Rayder's son. Rayder himself would soon follow her to the grave, if the whispers Sam had heard had any truth to them. "What did you tell her?"

"That I would speak to Stannis, though I doubt my words will sway him. A king's first duty is to defend the realm, and Mance attacked it. His Grace is not like to forget that. My father used to say that Stannis Baratheon was a just man. No one has ever said he was forgiving." Jon paused, frowning. "I would sooner take off Mance's head myself. He was a man of the Night's Watch, once. By rights, his life belongs to us."

"Pyp says that Lady Melisandre means to give him to the flames, to work some sorcery."

"Pyp should learn to hold his tongue. I have heard the same from others. King's blood, to wake a dragon. Where Melisandre thinks to find a sleeping dragon, no one is quite sure. It's nonsense. Mance's blood is no more royal than mine own. He has never worn a crown nor sat a throne. He's a brigand, nothing more. There's no power in brigand's blood."

The raven looked up from the floor. *"Blood,"* it screamed.

Jon paid no mind. "I am sending Gilly away."

"Oh." Sam bobbed his head. "Well, that's . . . that's good, my lord." It would be the best thing for her, to go somewhere warm and safe, well away from the Wall and the fighting.

"Her and the boy. We will need to find another wet nurse for his milk brother."

"Goat's milk might serve, until you do. It's better for a babe than cow's milk." Sam had read that somewhere. He shifted in his seat. "My lord, when I was looking through the annals I came on another boy commander. Four hundred years before the Conquest. Osric Stark was ten when he was chosen, but he served for sixty years. That's four, my lord. You're not even close to being the youngest ever chosen. You're fifth youngest, so far."

"The younger four all being sons, brothers, or bastards of the King in the North. Tell me something useful. Tell me of our enemy."

"The Others." Sam licked his lips. "They are mentioned in the annals, though not as often as I would have thought. The annals I've found and looked at, that is. There's more I haven't found, I know. Some of the older books are falling to pieces. The pages crumble when I try and turn them. And the *really* old books . . . either they have crumbled all away or they are buried somewhere that I haven't looked yet or . . . well, it could be that there are no such books, and never were. The oldest histories we have were written after the Andals came to Westeros. The First Men only left us runes on rocks, so everything we think we know about the Age of Heroes and the Dawn Age and the Long Night comes from accounts set down by septons thousands of years later. There are archmaesters at the Citadel who question all of it. Those old histories are full of kings who reigned for hundreds of years, and knights riding around a thousand years before there *were* knights. You know the tales, Brandon the Builder, Symeon Star-Eyes, Night's King . . . we say that you're the nine hundred and ninety-eighth Lord Commander of the Night's Watch, but the oldest list I've found shows six hundred seventy-four commanders, which suggests that it was written during . . ."

"Long ago," Jon broke in. "What about the Others?"

"I found mention of dragonglass. The children of the forest used to give the Night's Watch a hundred obsidian daggers every year, during the Age of Heroes. The Others come when it is cold, most of the tales agree. Or else it gets cold when they come. Sometimes they appear during snowstorms and melt away when the skies clear. They hide from the light of the sun and emerge by night . . . or else night falls when they emerge. Some stories speak of them riding the corpses of dead animals. Bears, direwolves, mammoths, horses, it makes no matter, so long as the beast is dead. The one that killed Small Paul was riding a dead horse, so that part's plainly true. Some accounts speak of giant ice spiders too. I don't know what those are.

Men who fall in battle against the Others must be burned, or else the dead will rise again as their thralls."

"We knew all this. The question is, how do we fight them?"

"The armor of the Others is proof against most ordinary blades, if the tales can be believed," said Sam, "and their own swords are so cold they shatter steel. Fire will dismay them, though, and they are vulnerable to obsidian." He remembered the one he had faced in the haunted forest, and how it had seemed to melt away when he stabbed it with the dragonglass dagger Jon had made for him. "I found one account of the Long Night that spoke of the last hero slaying Others with a blade of dragonsteel. Supposedly they could not stand against it."

"Dragonsteel?" Jon frowned. "*Valyrian* steel?"

"That was my first thought as well."

"So if I can just convince the lords of the Seven Kingdoms to give us their Valyrian blades, all is saved? That won't be hard." His laugh had no mirth in it. "Did you find who the Others are, where they come from, what they want?"

"Not yet, my lord, but it may be that I've just been reading the wrong books. There are hundreds I have not looked at yet. Give me more time and I will find whatever there is to be found."

"There is no more time." Jon sounded sad. "You need to get your things together, Sam. You're going with Gilly."

"Going?" For a moment Sam did not understand. "I'm going? To Eastwatch, my lord? Or . . . where am I . . ."

"Oldtown."

"Oldtown?" It came out in a squeak. Horn Hill was close to Oldtown. *Home.* The notion made him lightheaded. *My father.*

"Aemon as well."

"Aemon? *Maester* Aemon? But . . . he's one hundred and two years old, my lord, he can't . . . you're sending him *and* me? Who will tend the ravens? If they're sick or wounded, who . . ."

"Clydas. He's been with Aemon for years."

"Clydas is only a steward, and his eyes are going bad. You need a *maester.* Maester Aemon is so frail, a sea voyage . . ." He thought of the Arbor and the *Arbor Queen,* and almost choked on his tongue. "It might . . . he's old, and . . ."

"His life will be at risk. I am aware of that, Sam, but the risk is greater here. Stannis knows who Aemon is. If the red woman requires king's blood for her spells . . ."

"Oh." Sam paled.

"Dareon will join you at Eastwatch. My hope is that his songs will win some men for us in the south. The *Blackbird* will deliver you to Braavos. From there you'll arrange your own passage to Oldtown. If you still mean to claim Gilly's babe as your bastard, send her and the child on to Horn Hill. Elsewise, Aemon will find a servant's place for her at the Citadel."

"My b-b-bastard." He had said that, yes, but . . . *All that water. I could drown. Ships sink all the time, and autumn is a stormy season.* Gilly would be with him, though, and the babe would grow up safe. "Yes, I . . . my mother and my sisters will help Gilly with the child." *I can send a letter, I won't need to go to Horn Hill myself.* "Dareon could see her to Oldtown just as well as me. I'm . . . I've been working at my archery every afternoon with Ulmer, as you commanded . . . well, except when I'm in the vaults, but you told me to find out about the Others. The longbow makes my shoulders ache and raises blisters on my fingers." He showed Jon where one had burst. "I still do it, though. I can hit the target more often than not now, but I'm still the worst archer who ever bent a bow. I like Ulmer's stories, though. Someone needs to write them down and put them in a book."

"You do it. They have parchment and ink at the Citadel, as well as longbows. I will expect you to continue with your practice. Sam, the Night's Watch has hundreds of men who can loose an arrow, but only a handful who can read or write. I need you to become my new maester."

The word made him flinch. *No, Father, please, I won't speak of it again, I swear it by the Seven. Let me out, please let me out.* "My lord, I . . . my work is here, the books . . ."

". . . will be here when you return to us."

Sam put a hand to his throat. He could almost feel the chain there, choking him. "My lord, the Citadel . . . they make you cut up corpses there." *They make you wear a chain about your neck. If it is chains you want, come with me.* For three days and three nights Sam had sobbed himself to sleep, manacled hand and foot to a wall. The chain around his throat was so tight it broke the skin, and whenever he rolled the wrong way in his sleep it would cut off his breath. "I cannot wear a chain."

"You can. You will. Maester Aemon is old and blind. His strength is leaving him. Who will take his place when he dies? Maester Mullin at the Shadow Tower is more fighter than scholar, and Maester Harmune of Eastwatch is drunk more than he's sober."

"If you ask the Citadel for more maesters . . ."

"I mean to. We'll have need of every one. Aemon Targaryen is not so easily replaced, however." Jon seemed puzzled. "I was certain this would please you. There are so many books at the Citadel that no man can hope to read them all. You would do well there, Sam. I know you would."

"No. I could read the books, but . . . a m-maester must be a healer and b-b-blood makes me faint." He held out a shaky hand for Jon to see. "I'm Sam the Scared, not Sam the Slayer."

"Scared? Of what? The chidings of old men? Sam, you saw the wights come swarming up the Fist, a tide of living dead men with black hands and bright blue eyes. You slew an Other."

"It was the d-d-d-dragonglass, not me."

"Be quiet. You lied and schemed and plotted to make me Lord Commander. You *will* obey me. You'll go to the Citadel and forge a chain, and if you have to cut up corpses, so be it. At least in Oldtown the corpses won't object."

He doesn't understand. "My lord," Sam said, "my f-f-f-father, Lord Randyll, he, he, he, he, he . . . the life of a maester is a life of *servitude.*" He was babbling, he knew. "No son of House Tarly will ever wear a chain. The men of Horn Hill do not bow and scrape to petty lords." *If it is chains you want, come with me.* "Jon, I cannot disobey my *father.*"

Jon, he'd said, but Jon was gone. It was Lord Snow who faced him now, grey eyes as hard as ice. "You have no father," said Lord Snow. "Only brothers. Only us. Your life belongs to the Night's Watch, so go and stuff your small-clothes into a sack, along with anything else you care to take to Oldtown. You leave an hour before sunrise. And here's another order. From this day forth, you will *not* call yourself a craven. You've faced more things this past year than most men face in a lifetime. You can face the Citadel, but you'll face it as a Sworn Brother of the Night's Watch. I can't command you to be brave, but I *can* command you to hide your fears. You said the words, Sam. Remember?"

I am the sword in the darkness. But he was wretched with a sword, and the darkness scared him. "I . . . I'll try."

"You won't try. You will obey."

"Obey." Mormont's raven flapped its great black wings.

"As my lord commands. Does . . . does Maester Aemon know?"

"It was as much his idea as mine." Jon opened the door for him. "No farewells. The fewer folk who know of this, the better. An hour before first light, by the lichyard."

Sam did not recall leaving the armory. The next thing he knew he was stumbling through mud and patches of old snow, toward Maester Aemon's chambers. *I could hide,* he told himself. *I could hide in the vaults amongst the books. I could live down there with the mouse and sneak up at night to steal food.* Crazed thoughts, he knew, as futile as they were desperate. The vaults were the first place they would look for him. The *last* place they would look for him was beyond the Wall, but that was even madder. *The wildlings would catch me and kill me slowly. They might burn me alive, the way the red woman means to burn Mance Rayder.*

When he found Maester Aemon in the rookery, he gave him Jon's letter and blurted out his fears in a great green gush of words. "He does not *understand.*" Sam felt as if he might throw up. "If I don a chain, my lord f-f-f-father . . . he, he, he . . ."

"My own father raised the same objections when I chose a life of service," the old man said. "It was *his* father who sent me to the Citadel. King Daeron had sired four sons, and three had sons of their own. *Too many dragons are as dangerous as too few,* I heard His Grace tell my lord father, the day they sent me off." Aemon raised a spotted hand to the chain of many metals that dangled loose about his thin neck. "The chain is heavy, Sam, but my grandsire had the right of it. So does your Lord Snow."

"*Snow,*" a raven muttered. "*Snow,*" another echoed. All of them picked it up then. "*Snow, snow, snow, snow, snow.*" Sam had taught them that word. There was no help here, he saw. Maester Aemon was as trapped as he was. *He will die at sea,* he thought, despairing. *He is too old to survive such a voyage. Gilly's little son may die as well, he's not as large and strong as Dalla's boy. Does Jon mean to kill us all?*

The next morning, Sam found himself saddling the mare he'd ridden from Horn Hill and leading her toward the lichyard beside the eastern road. Her saddlebags bulged with cheese and sausages and hard-cooked eggs, and half a salted ham that Three-Finger Hobb had given him on his name day. "You're a man who *appreciates* cooking, Slayer," the cook had said. "We need more o' your sort." The ham would help, no doubt. Eastwatch was a long cold ride away, and there were no towns nor inns in the shadow of the Wall.

The hour before dawn was dark and still. Castle Black seemed strangely hushed. At the lichyard, a pair of two-wheeled wayns awaited him, along with Black Jack Bulwer and a dozen seasoned rangers, tough as the garrons they rode. Kedge Whiteye cursed loudly when his one good eye spied Sam. "Don't mind him, Slayer," said Black Jack. "He lost a wager, said we'd need to drag you out squealing from beneath some bed."

Maester Aemon was too frail to ride a horse, so a wayn had been made ready for him, its bed heaped high with furs, and a leather awning fastened overhead to keep off the rain and snow. Gilly and her child would ride with him. The second wayn would carry their clothing and possessions, along with a chest of rare old books that Aemon thought the Citadel might lack. Sam had spent half the night searching for them, though he'd found only one in four. *And a good thing, or we'd need another wayn.*

When the maester appeared, he was bundled up in a bearskin three times his size. As Clydas led him toward the wayn, a gust of wind came up, and the old man staggered. Sam hurried to his side and put an arm about him. *Another gust like that could blow him over the Wall.* "Keep hold of my arm, maester. It's not far."

The blind man nodded as the wind pushed back their hoods. "It is always warm in Oldtown. There is an inn on an island in the Honeywine where I used to go when I was a young novice. It will be pleasant to sit there once again, sipping cider."

By the time they got the maester into the wayn, Gilly had appeared, the child bundled in her arms. Beneath her hood her eyes were red from crying. Jon turned up at the same time, with Dolorous Edd. "Lord Snow," Maester Aemon called, "I left a book for you in my chambers. The *Jade Compendium*. It was written by the Volantene adventurer Colloquo Votar, who traveled to the east and visited all the lands of the Jade Sea. There is a passage you may find of interest. I've told Clydas to mark it for you."

"I'll be sure to read it," Jon Snow replied.

A line of pale snot ran from Maester Aemon's nose. He wiped it away with the back of his glove. "Knowledge is a weapon, Jon. Arm yourself well before you ride forth to battle."

"I will." A light snow had begun to fall, the big soft flakes drifting down lazily from the sky. Jon turned to Black Jack Bulwer. "Make as good a time as you can, but take no foolish risks. You have an old man and a suckling babe with you. See that you keep them warm and well fed."

"You do the same, m'lord," said Gilly. "You do the

same for t'other. Find another wet nurse, like you said. You promised me you would. The boy . . . Dalla's boy . . . the little prince, I mean . . . you find him some good woman, so he grows up big and strong."

"You have my word," Jon Snow said solemnly.

"Don't you name him. Don't you do that till he's past two years. It's ill luck to name them when they're still on the breast. You crows may not know that, but it's true."

"As you command, my lady."

A spasm of anger flashed across Gilly's face. "Don't you call me that. I'm a mother, not a lady. I'm Craster's wife and Craster's daughter, and a *mother*."

Dolorous Edd took the babe as Gilly climbed into the wayn and covered her legs with some musty pelts. By then the eastern sky was more grey than black. Left Hand Lew was anxious to be off. Edd handed the infant up and Gilly put him to her breast. *This may be the last I ever see of Castle Black,* thought Sam as he hoisted himself atop his mare. As much as he had once hated Castle Black, it was tearing him apart to leave it.

"Let's do this," Bulwer commanded. A whip snapped, and the wayns began to rumble slowly down the rutted road as the snow came down around them. Sam lingered beside Clydas and Dolorous Edd and Jon Snow. "Well," he said, "farewell."

"And to you, Sam," said Dolorous Edd. "Your boat's not like to sink, I don't think. Boats only sink when I'm aboard."

Jon was watching the wayns. "The first time I saw Gilly," he said, "she was pressed back against the wall of Craster's Keep, this skinny dark-haired girl with her big belly, cringing away from Ghost. He had gotten in among her rabbits, and I think she was frightened that he would tear her open and devour the babe . . . but it was not the wolf she should have been afraid of, was it?"

No, Sam thought. *Craster was the danger, her own father.*

"She has more courage than she knows."

"So do you, Sam. Have a swift, safe voyage, and take care of her and Aemon and the child." Jon smiled a strange, sad smile. "And pull your hood up. The snowflakes are melting in your hair."

ARYA

Faint and far away the light burned, low on the horizon, shining through the sea mists.

"It looks like a star," said Arya.

"The star of home," said Denyo.

His father was shouting orders. Sailors scrambled up and down the three tall masts and moved along the rigging, reefing the heavy purple sails. Below, oarsmen heaved and strained over two great banks of oars. The decks tilted, creaking, as the galleas *Titan's Daughter* heeled to starboard and began to come about.

The star of home. Arya stood at the prow, one hand resting on the gilded figurehead, a maiden with a bowl of fruit. For half a heartbeat she let herself pretend that it *was* her home ahead.

But that was *stupid.* Her home was gone, her parents dead, and all her brothers slain but Jon Snow on the Wall.

That was where she had wanted to go. She *told* the captain as much, but even the iron coin did not sway him. Arya never seemed to find the places she set out to reach. Yoren had sworn to deliver her to Winterfell, only she had ended up in Harrenhal and Yoren in his grave. When she escaped Harrenhal for Riverrun, Lem and Anguy and Tom o' Sevens took her captive and dragged her to the hollow hill instead. Then the Hound had stolen her and dragged her to the Twins. Arya had left him dying by the river and gone ahead to Saltpans, hoping to take passage for Eastwatch-by-the-Sea, only . . .

Braavos might not be so bad. Syrio was from Braavos, and Jaqen might be there as well. It was Jaqen who had given her the iron coin. He hadn't truly been her friend, the way that Syrio had, but what good had friends ever done her? *I don't need any friends, so long as I have Needle.* She brushed the ball of her thumb across the sword's smooth pommel, wishing, wishing . . .

If truth be told, Arya did not know what to wish for, any more than she knew what awaited her beneath that distant light. The captain had given her passage but he had no time to speak with her. Some of the crew shunned her, but others gave her gifts—a silver fork, fingerless gloves, a floppy woolen hat patched with leather. One man showed her how to tie sailor's knots. Another poured her thimble cups of fire wine. The friendly ones would tap their chests, repeating their names over and over until Arya said them back, though none ever thought to ask *her* name. They called her Salty, since she'd come aboard at Saltpans, near the mouth of the Trident. It was as good a name as any, she supposed.

The last of the night's stars had vanished . . . all but the pair dead ahead. "It's *two* stars now."

"Two eyes," said Denyo. "The Titan sees us."

The Titan of Braavos. Old Nan had told them stories of the Titan back in Winterfell. He was a giant as tall as a mountain, and whenever Braavos stood in danger he would wake with fire in his eyes, his rocky limbs grinding and groaning as he waded out into the sea to smash the enemies. "The Braavosi feed him on the juicy pink flesh of little highborn girls," Nan would end, and Sansa would give a stupid squeak. But Maester Luwin said the Titan was only a statue, and Old Nan's stories were only stories.

Winterfell is burned and fallen, Arya reminded herself. Old Nan and Maester Luwin were both dead, most like, and Sansa too. It did no good to think of them. *All men must die.* That was what the words meant, the words that Jaqen H'ghar had taught her when he gave her the worn iron coin. She had learned more Braavosi words since they left Saltpans, the words for *please* and *thank you* and *sea* and *star* and *fire wine,* but she came to them knowing that *all men must die.* Most of the *Daughter's* crew had a smattering of the Common Tongue from nights ashore in Oldtown and King's Landing and Maidenpool, though only the captain and his sons spoke it well enough to talk to her. Denyo was the youngest of those sons, a plump, cheerful boy of twelve who kept his father's cabin and helped his eldest brother do his sums.

"I hope your Titan isn't hungry," Arya told him.

"Hungry?" Denyo said, confused.

"It takes no matter." Even if the Titan *did* eat juicy pink girl flesh, Arya would not fear him. She was a scrawny thing, no proper meal for a giant, and almost eleven, practically a woman grown. *And Salty isn't highborn, either.* "Is the Titan the god of Braavos?" she asked. "Or do you have the Seven?"

"All gods are honored in Braavos." The captain's son loved to talk about his city almost as much as he loved to talk about his father's ship. "Your Seven have a sept here, the Sept-Beyond-the-Sea, but only Westerosi sailors worship there."

They are not my Seven. They were my mother's gods, and they let the Freys murder her at the Twins. She wondered whether she would find a godswood in Braavos, with a weirwood at its heart. Denyo might know, but she could not ask him. Salty was from Saltpans, and what would a girl from Saltpans know about the old gods of the north? *The old gods are dead,* she told herself, *with Mother and Father and Robb and Bran and Rickon, all dead.* A long time ago, she remembered her father saying that when the cold winds blow the lone wolf dies and the pack survives. *He had it all backwards.* Arya, the lone wolf, still lived, but the wolves of the pack had been taken and slain and skinned.

"The Moonsingers led us to this place of refuge, where the dragons of Valyria could not find us," Denyo said. "Theirs is the greatest temple. We esteem the Father of Waters as well, but his house is built anew whenever he takes his bride. The rest of the gods dwell together on an isle in the center of the city. That is where you will find the . . . the Many-Faced God."

The Titan's eyes seemed brighter now, and farther apart. Arya did not know any Many-Faced God, but if he answered prayers, he might be the god she sought. *Ser Gregor,* she thought, *Dunsen, Raff the Sweetling, Ser Ilyn, Ser Meryn, Queen Cersei. Only six now.* Joffrey was dead, the Hound had slain Polliver, and she'd stabbed the Tickler herself, and that stupid squire with the pimple. *I wouldn't have killed him if he hadn't grabbed me.* The Hound had been dying when she left him on the banks of the Trident, burning up with fever from his wound. *I should have given him the gift of mercy and put a knife into his heart.*

"Salty, look!" Denyo took her by the arm and turned her. "Can you see? *There.*" He pointed.

The mists gave way before them, ragged grey curtains parted by their prow. The *Titan's Daughter* cleaved through the grey-green waters on billowing purple wings. Arya could hear the cries of seabirds overhead. There, where Denyo pointed, a line of stony ridges rose sudden from the sea, their steep slopes covered with soldier pines and black spruce. But dead ahead the sea had broken through, and there above the open water the Titan towered, with his eyes blazing and his long green hair blowing in the wind.

His legs bestrode the gap, one foot planted on each mountain, his shoulders looming tall above the jagged crests. His legs were carved of solid stone, the same black granite as the sea monts on which he stood, though around his hips he wore an armored skirt of greenish bronze. His breastplate was bronze as well, and his head in his crested halfhelm. His blowing hair was made of hempen ropes dyed green, and huge fires burned in the caves that were his eyes. One hand rested atop the ridge to his left, bronze fingers coiled about a knob of stone; the other thrust up into the air, clasping the hilt of a broken sword.

He is only a little bigger than King Baelor's statue in King's Landing, she told herself when they were still well off to sea. As the galleas drove closer to where the breakers smashed against the ridgeline, however, the Titan grew larger still. She could hear Denyo's father bellowing commands in his deep voice, and up in the rigging men were bringing in the sails. *We are going to row beneath the Titan's legs.* Arya could see the arrow slits in the great bronze breastplate, and stains and speckles on the Titan's arms and shoulders where the seabirds nested. Her neck craned upward. *Baelor the Blessed would not reach his knee. He could step right over the walls of Winterfell.*

Then the Titan gave a mighty roar.

The sound was as huge as he was, a terrible groaning and grinding, so loud it drowned out even the captain's voice and the crash of the waves against those pine-clad ridges. A thousand seabirds took to the air at once, and Arya flinched until she saw that Denyo was laughing. "He warns the Arsenal of our coming, that is all," he shouted. "You must not be afraid."

"I never *was*," Arya shouted back. "It was loud, is all."

Wind and wave had the *Titan's Daughter* hard in hand now, driving her swiftly toward the channel. Her double bank of oars stroked smoothly, lashing the sea to white foam as the Titan's shadow fell upon them. For a moment it seemed as though they must surely smash up against the stones beneath his legs. Huddled by Denyo at the prow, Arya could taste salt where the spray had touched her face. She had to look straight up to see the Titan's head. "The Braavosi feed him on the juicy pink flesh of little highborn girls," she heard Old Nan say again, but she was *not* a little girl, and she would not be frightened of a stupid *statue.*

Even so, she kept one hand on Needle as they slipped between his legs. More arrow slits dotted the insides of those great stone thighs, and when Arya craned her neck around to watch the crow's nest slip through with a good ten yards to spare, she spied murder holes beneath the Titan's armored skirts, and pale faces staring down at them from behind the iron bars.

And then they were past.

The shadow lifted, the pine-clad ridges fell away to either side, the winds dwindled, and they found themselves moving through a great lagoon. Ahead rose another sea mont, a knob of rock that pushed up from the water like a spiked fist, its stony battlements bristling with scorpions, spitfires, and trebuchets. "The Arsenal of Braavos," Denyo named it, as proud as if he'd built it. "They can build a war galley there in a day." Arya could see dozens of galleys tied up at quays and perched on launching slips. The painted prows of others poked from innumerable wooden sheds along the stony shores, like hounds in a kennel, lean and mean and hungry, waiting for a hunter's horn to call them forth. She tried to count them, but there were too many, and more docks and sheds and quays where the shoreline curved away.

Two galleys had come out to meet them. They seemed to skim upon the water like dragonflies, their pale oars flashing. Arya heard the captain shouting to them and their own captains shouting back, but she did not understand the words. A great horn sounded. The galleys passed to either side of them, so close that she could hear the muffled sound of drums from within their purple hulls, *bom bom bom bom bom bom bom bom,* like the beat of living hearts.

Then the galleys were behind them, and the Arsenal as well. Ahead stretched a broad expanse of pea-green water rippled like a sheet of colored glass. From its wet heart arose the city proper, a great sprawl of domes and towers and bridges, grey and gold and red. *The hundred isles of Braavos in the sea.*

Maester Luwin had taught them about Braavos, but Arya had forgotten much of what he'd said. It was a flat city, she could see that even from afar, not like King's Landing on its three high hills. The only hills here were the ones that men had raised of brick and granite, bronze and marble. Something else was missing as well, though it took her a few moments to realize what it was. *The city has no walls.* But when she said as much to Denyo, he laughed at her. "Our walls are made of wood and painted purple," he told her. "Our *galleys* are our walls. We need no other."

The deck creaked behind them. Arya turned to find Denyo's father looming over them in his long captain's coat of purple wool. Tradesman-Captain Ternesio Terys wore no whiskers and kept his grey hair cut short and neat, framing his square, windburnt face. On the crossing she had oft seen him jesting with his crew, but when he frowned men ran from him as if before a storm. He was frowning now. "Our voyage is at an end," he told Arya. "We make for the Chequy Port, where the Sealord's customs officers will come aboard to inspect our holds. They will be half a day at it, they always are, but there is no need for you to wait upon their pleasure. Gather your belongings. I shall lower a boat, and Yorko will put you ashore."

Ashore. Arya bit her lip. She had crossed the narrow sea to get here, but if the captain had asked she would have told him she wanted to stay aboard the *Titan's Daughter.* Salty was too small to man an oar, she knew that now, but she could learn to splice ropes and reef the sails and steer a course across the great salt seas. Denyo had taken her up to the crow's nest once, and she hadn't been afraid at all, though the deck had seemed a tiny thing below her. *I can do sums too, and keep a cabin neat.*

But the galleas had no need of a second boy. Besides, she had only to look at the captain's face to know how anxious he was to be rid of her. So Arya only nodded. "Ashore," she said, though ashore meant only strangers.

"Valar dohaeris." He touched two fingers to his brow. "I beg you remember Ternesio Terys and the service he has done you."

"I will," Arya said in a small voice. The wind tugged at her cloak, insistent as a ghost. It was time she was away.

Gather your belongings, the captain had said, but there were few enough of those. Only the clothes she was wearing, her little pouch of coins, the gifts the crew had given her, the dagger on her left hip and Needle on her right.

The boat was ready before she was, and Yorko was at the oars. He was the captain's son as well, but older than Denyo and less friendly. *I never said farewell to Denyo,* she thought as she clambered down to join him. She wondered if she would ever see the boy again. *I should have said farewell.*

The *Titan's Daughter* dwindled in their wake, while the city grew larger with every stroke of Yorko's oars. A harbor was visible off to her right, beyond a sinking point of land where the tops of half-drowned buildings thrust themselves above the water: a tangle of piers and quays crowded with big-bellied whalers out of Ibben, swan ships from the Summer Isles, and more galleys than a girl could count. Another harbor, more distant, was off to her left. Arya had never seen so many big buildings all together in one place. King's Landing had the Red Keep and the Great Sept of Baelor and the Dragonpit, but Braavos seemed to boast a score of temples and towers and palaces that were as large or even larger. *I will be a mouse again,* she thought glumly, *the way I was in Harrenhal before I ran away.*

The city had seemed like one big island from where the Titan stood, but as Yorko rowed them closer she saw that it was many small islands close together, linked by arched stone bridges that spanned innumerable canals. Beyond the harbor she glimpsed streets of grey stone houses, built so close they leaned one upon the other. To Arya's eyes they were queer-looking, four and five stories tall and very skinny, with sharp-peaked tile roofs like pointed hats. She saw no thatch, and only a few timbered houses of the sort she knew in Westeros. *They have no trees,* she realized. *Braavos is all stone, a grey city in a green sea.*

Yorko swung them north of the docks and down the gullet of a great canal, a broad green waterway that ran straight into the heart of the city. They passed under the arches of a carved stone bridge, decorated with half a hundred kinds of fish and crabs and squids. A second bridge appeared ahead, this one carved in lacy leafy vines, and beyond that a third, gazing down on them from a thousand painted eyes. The mouths of lesser canals opened to either side, and others still smaller off of those. Some of the houses were built *above* the waterways, she saw, turning the canals into a sort of tunnel. Slender boats slid in and out among them, wrought in the shapes of water serpents with painted heads and upraised tails. Those were not rowed but poled, she saw, by men who stood at their sterns in cloaks of grey and brown and deep moss green. She saw huge flat-bottomed barges too, heaped high with crates and barrels and pushed along by twenty polemen to a side, and fancy floating houses with lanterns of colored glass, velvet drapes, and brazen figureheads. Off in the far distance, looming above canals and houses both, was a massive grey stone roadway of some kind, supported by three tiers of mighty arches marching away south into the haze. "What's that?" Arya asked Yorko, pointing. "The sweetwater river," he told her. "It brings fresh water from the mainland, across the mudflats and the briny shallows. Good sweet water for the fountains."

When she looked behind her, the harbor and lagoon were lost to sight. Ahead, a row of mighty statues stood along both sides of the channel, solemn stone men in long bronze robes, spattered with the droppings of the seabirds. Some held books, some daggers, some hammers. One clutched a golden star in his upraised hand. Another was upending a stone flagon to send an endless stream of water splashing down into the canal. "Are they gods?" asked Arya.

"Sealords," said Yorko. "The Isle of the Gods is farther on. See? Six bridges down, on the right bank. That is the Temple of the Moonsingers."

It was one of those that Arya had spied from the lagoon, a mighty mass of snow-white marble topped by a huge silvered dome whose milk-glass windows showed all the phases of the moon. A pair of marble maidens flanked its gates, tall as the Sealords, supporting a crescent-shaped lintel.

Beyond it stood another temple, a red stone edifice as stern as any fortress. Atop its great square tower a fire blazed in an iron brazier twenty feet across, whilst smaller fires flanked its brazen doors. "The red priests love their fires," Yorko told her. "The Lord of Light is their god, red R'hllor."

I know. Arya remembered Thoros of Myr in his bits of old armor, worn over robes so faded that he had seemed more a pink priest than a red one. Yet his kiss had brought Lord Beric back from death. She watched the red god's house drift by, wondering whether these Braavosi priests of his could do the same.

Next came a huge brick structure festooned with lichen. Arya might have taken it for a storehouse had not Yorko said, "That is the Holy Refuge, where we honor the small gods the world has forgotten. You will hear it called the Warren too." A small canal ran between the Warren's looming lichen-covered walls, and there he swung them right. They passed through a tunnel and out again into the light. More shrines loomed up to either side.

"I never knew there were so many gods," Arya said.

Yorko grunted. They went around a bend and beneath

another bridge. On their left appeared a rocky knoll with a windowless temple of dark grey stone at its top. A flight of stone steps led from its doors down to a covered dock.

Yorko backed the oars, and the boat bumped gently against stone pilings. He grasped an iron ring set to hold them for a moment. "Here I leave you."

The dock was shadowed, the steps steep. The temple's black tile roof came to a sharp peak, like the houses along the canals. Arya chewed her lip. *Syrio came from Braavos. He might have visited this temple. He might have climbed those steps.* She grabbed a ring and pulled herself up onto the dock.

"You know my name," said Yorko from the boat.

"Yorko Terys."

"Valar dohaeris." He pushed off with his oar and drifted back off into the deeper water. Arya watched him row back the way they'd come, until he vanished in the shadows of the bridge. As the swish of oars faded, she could almost hear the beating of her heart. Suddenly she was somewhere else . . . back in Harrenhal with Gendry, maybe, or with the Hound in the woods along the Trident. *Salty is a stupid child,* she told herself. *I am a wolf, and will not be afraid.* She patted Needle's hilt for luck and plunged into the shadows, taking the steps two at a time so no one could ever say she'd been afraid.

At the top she found a set of carved wooden doors twelve feet high. The left-hand door was made of weirwood pale as bone, the right of gleaming ebony. In their center was a carved moon face; ebony on the weirwood side, weirwood on the ebony. The look of it reminded her somehow of the heart tree in the godswood at Winterfell. *The doors are watching me,* she thought. She pushed upon both doors at once with the flat of her gloved hands, but neither one would budge. *Locked and barred.* "Let me in, you stupid," she said. "I crossed the narrow sea." She made a fist and pounded. "Jaqen told me to come. I have the iron coin." She pulled it from her pouch and held it up. "See? *Valar morghulis.*"

The doors made no reply, except to open.

They opened inward all in silence, with no human hand to move them. Arya took a step forward, and another. The doors closed behind her, and for a moment she was blind. Needle was in her hand, though she did not remember drawing it.

A few candles burned along the walls, but gave so little light that Arya could not see her own feet. Someone was whispering, too softly for her to make out words. Someone else was weeping. She heard light footfalls, leather sliding over stone, a door opening and closing. *Water, I hear water too.*

Slowly her eyes adjusted. The temple seemed much larger within than it had without. The septs of Westeros were seven-sided, with seven altars for the seven gods, but here there were more gods than seven. Statues of them stood along the walls, massive and threatening. Around their feet red candles flickered, as dim as distant stars. The nearest was a marble woman twelve feet tall. Real tears were trickling from her eyes, to fill the bowl she cradled in her arms. Beyond her was a man with a lion's head seated on a throne, carved of ebony. On the other side of the doors, a huge horse of bronze and iron reared up on two great legs. Farther on she could make out a great stone face, a pale infant with a sword, a shaggy black goat the size of an aurochs, a hooded man leaning on a staff. The rest were only looming shapes to her, half-seen through the gloom. Between the gods were hidden alcoves thick with shadows, with here and there a candle burning.

Silent as a shadow, Arya moved between rows of long

stone benches, her sword in hand. The floor was made of stone, her feet told her; not polished marble like the floor of the Great Sept of Baelor, but something rougher. She passed some women whispering together. The air was warm and heavy, so heavy that she yawned. She could smell the candles. The scent was unfamiliar, and she put it down to some queer incense, but as she got deeper into the temple, they seemed to smell of snow and pine needles and hot stew. *Good smells,* Arya told herself, and felt a little braver. Brave enough to slip Needle back into its sheath.

In the center of the temple she found the water she had heard; a pool ten feet across, black as ink and lit by dim red candles. Beside it sat a young man in a silvery cloak, weeping softly. She watched him dip a hand in the water, sending scarlet ripples racing across the pool. When he drew his fingers back he sucked them, one by one. *He must be thirsty.* There were stone cups along the rim of the pool. Arya filled one and brought it to him, so he could drink. The young man stared at her for a long moment when she offered it to him. *"Valar morghulis,"* he said.

"Valar dohaeris," she replied.

He drank deep, and dropped the cup into the pool with a soft *plop.* Then he pushed himself to his feet, swaying, holding his belly. For a moment Arya thought he was going to fall. It was only then that she saw the dark stain below his belt, spreading as she watched. "You're stabbed," she blurted, but the man paid her no mind. He lurched unsteadily toward the wall and crawled into an alcove onto a hard stone bed. When Arya peered around, she saw other alcoves too. On some there were old people sleeping.

No, a half-remembered voice seemed to whisper in her head. *They are dead, or dying. Look with your eyes.*

A hand touched her arm.

Arya spun away, but it was only a little girl: a pale little girl in a cowled robe that seemed to engulf her, black on the right side and white on the left. Beneath the cowl was a gaunt and bony face, hollow cheeks, and dark eyes that looked as big as saucers. "Don't grab me," Arya warned the waif. "I killed the boy who grabbed me last."

The girl said some words that Arya did not know.

She shook her head. "Don't you know the Common Tongue?"

A voice behind her said, "I do."

Arya did not like the way they kept surprising her. The hooded man was tall, enveloped in a larger version of the black-and-white robe the girl was wearing. Beneath his cowl all she could see was the faint red glitter of candle-light reflecting off his eyes. "What place is this?" she asked him.

"A place of peace." His voice was gentle. "You are safe here. This is the House of Black and White, my child. Though you are young to seek the favor of the Many-Faced God."

"Is he like the southron god, the one with seven faces?"

"Seven? No. He has faces beyond count, little one, as many faces as there are stars in the sky. In Braavos, men worship as they will . . . but at the end of every road stands Him of Many Faces, waiting. He will be there for you one day, do not fear. You need not rush to his embrace."

"I only came to find Jaqen H'ghar."

"I do not know this name."

Her heart sank. "He was from Lorath. His hair was white on one side and red on the other. He said he'd teach me secrets, and gave me this." The iron coin was clutched in her fist. When she opened her fingers, it clung to her sweaty palm.

The priest studied the coin, though he made no move to

touch it. The waif with the big eyes was looking at it too. Finally, the cowled man said, "Tell me your name, child."

"Salty. I come from Saltpans, by the Trident."

Though she could not see his face, somehow she could feel him smiling. "No," he said. "Tell me your name."

"Squab," she answered this time.

"Your true name, child."

"My mother named me Nan, but they call me Weasel—"

"Your name."

She swallowed. "Arry. I'm *Arry.*"

"Closer. And now the truth?"

Fear cuts deeper than swords, she told herself. "Arya." She whispered the word the first time. The second time she threw it at him. "I am *Arya,* of House Stark."

"You are," he said, "but the House of Black and White is no place for Arya, of House Stark."

"Please," she said. "I have no place to go."

"Do you fear death?"

She bit her lip. "No."

"Let us see." The priest lowered his cowl. Beneath he had no face; only a yellowed skull with a few scraps of skin still clinging to the cheeks, and a white worm wriggling from one empty eye socket. "Kiss me, child," he croaked, in a voice as dry and husky as a death rattle.

Does he think to scare me? Arya kissed him where his nose should be and plucked the grave worm from his eye to eat it, but it melted like a shadow in her hand.

The yellow skull was melting too, and the kindliest old man that she had ever seen was smiling down at her. "No one has ever tried to eat my worm before," he said. "Are you hungry, child?"

Yes, she thought, *but not for food.*

CERSEI

A cold rain was falling, turning the walls and ramparts of the Red Keep dark as blood. The queen held the king's hand and led him firmly across the muddy yard to where her litter waited with its escort. "Uncle Jaime said I could ride my horse and throw pennies to the smallfolk," the boy objected.

"Do you want to catch a chill?" She would not risk it; Tommen had never been as robust as Joffrey. "Your grandfather would want you to look a proper king at his wake. We will not appear at the Great Sept wet and bedraggled." *Bad enough I must wear mourning again.* Black had never been a happy color on her. With her fair skin, it made her look half a corpse herself. Cersei had risen an hour before dawn to bathe and fix her hair, and she did not intend to let the rain destroy her efforts.

Inside the litter, Tommen settled back against his pillows and peered out at the falling rain. "The gods are weeping for grandfather. Lady Jocelyn says the raindrops are their tears."

"Jocelyn Swyft is a fool. If the gods could weep, they would have wept for your brother. Rain is rain. Close the curtain before you let any more in. That mantle is sable, would you have it soaked?"

Tommen did as he was bid. His meekness troubled her. A king had to be strong. *Joffrey would have argued. He was never easy to cow.* "Don't slump so," she told Tommen. "Sit like a king. Put your shoulders back and straighten your crown. Do you want it to tumble off your head in front of all your lords?"

"No, Mother." The boy sat straight and reached up to fix the crown. Joff's crown was too big for him. Tommen had always inclined to plumpness, but his face seemed thinner now. *Is he eating well?* She must remember to ask the steward. She could not risk Tommen growing ill, not with Myrcella in the hands of the Dornishmen. *He will grow into Joff's crown in time.* Until he did, a smaller one might be needed, one that did not threaten to swallow his head. She would take it up with the goldsmiths.

The litter made its slow way down Aegon's High Hill. Two Kingsguard rode before them, white knights on white horses with white cloaks hanging sodden from their shoulders. Behind came fifty Lannister guardsmen in gold and crimson.

Tommen peered through the drapes at the empty streets. "I thought there would be more people. When Father died, all the people came out to watch us go by."

"This rain has driven them inside." King's Landing had never loved Lord Tywin. *He never wanted love, though. "You cannot eat love, nor buy a horse with it, nor warm your halls on a cold night,"* she heard him tell Jaime once, when her brother had been no older than Tommen.

At the Great Sept of Baelor, that magnificence in marble atop Visenya's Hill, the little knot of mourners were outnumbered by the gold cloaks that Ser Addam Marbrand had drawn up across the plaza. *More will turn out later,* the queen told herself as Ser Meryn Trant helped her from the litter. Only the highborn and their retinues were to be admitted to the morning service; there would be another in the afternoon for the commons, and the evening prayers were open to all. Cersei would need to return for that, so that the smallfolk might see her mourn. *The mob must have its show.* It was a nuisance. She had offices to fill, a war to win, a realm to rule. Her father would have understood that.

The High Septon met them at the top of the steps. A bent old man with a wispy grey beard, he was so stooped by the weight of his ornate embroidered robes that his eyes were on a level with the queen's breasts . . . though his crown, an airy confection of cut crystal and spun gold, added a good foot and a half to his height.

Lord Tywin had given him that crown to replace the one that was lost when the mob killed the previous High Septon. They had pulled the fat fool from his litter and torn him apart, the day Myrcella sailed for Dorne. *That one was a great glutton, and biddable. This one . . .* This High Septon was of Tyrion's making, Cersei recalled suddenly. It was a disquieting thought.

The old man's spotted hand looked like a chicken claw as it poked from a sleeve encrusted with golden scrollwork and small crystals. Cersei knelt on the wet marble and kissed his fingers, and bid Tommen to do the same. *What does he know of me? How much did the dwarf tell him?* The High Septon smiled as he escorted her into the sept.

But was it a threatening smile full of unspoken knowledge, or just some vacuous twitch of an old man's wrinkled lips? The queen could not be certain.

They made their way through the Hall of Lamps beneath colored globes of leaded glass, Tommen's hand in hers. Trant and Kettleblack flanked them, water dripping from their wet cloaks to puddle on the floor. The High Septon walked slowly, leaning on a weirwood staff topped by a crystal orb. Seven of the Most Devout attended him, shimmering in cloth-of-silver. Tommen wore cloth-of-gold beneath his sable mantle, the queen an old gown of black velvet lined with ermine. There'd been no time to have a new one made, and she could not wear the same dress she had worn for Joffrey, nor the one she'd buried Robert in.

At least I will not be expected to don mourning for Tyrion. I shall dress in crimson silk and cloth-of-gold for that, and wear rubies in my hair. The man who brought her the dwarf's head would be raised to lordship, she had proclaimed, no matter how mean and low his birth or station. Ravens were carrying her promise to every part of the Seven Kingdoms, and soon enough word would cross the narrow sea to the Nine Free Cities and the lands beyond. *Let the Imp run to the ends of the earth, he will not escape me.*

The royal procession passed through the inner doors into the cavernous heart of the Great Sept, and down a wide aisle, one of seven that met beneath the dome. To right and left, highborn mourners sank to their knees as the king and queen went by. Many of her father's bannermen were here, and knights who had fought beside Lord Tywin in half a hundred battles. The sight of them made her feel more confident. *I am not without friends.*

Under the Great Sept's lofty dome of glass and gold

and crystal, Lord Tywin Lannister's body rested upon a stepped marble bier. At its head Jaime stood at vigil, his one good hand curled about the hilt of a tall golden greatsword whose point rested on the floor. The hooded cloak he wore was as white as freshly fallen snow, and the scales of his long hauberk were mother-of-pearl chased with gold. *Lord Tywin would have wanted him in Lannister gold and crimson,* she thought. *It always angered him to see Jaime all in white.* Her brother was growing his beard again as well. The stubble covered his jaw and cheeks, and gave his face a rough, uncouth look. *He might at least have waited till Father's bones were interred beneath the Rock.*

Cersei led the king up three short steps, to kneel beside the body. Tommen's eyes were filled with tears. "Weep quietly," she told him, leaning close. "You are a king, not a squalling child. Your lords are watching you." The boy swiped the tears away with the back of his hand. He had her eyes, emerald green, as large and bright as Jaime's eyes had been when he was Tommen's age. Her brother had been such a *pretty* boy . . . but fierce as well, as fierce as Joffrey, a true lion cub. The queen put her arm around Tommen and kissed his golden curls. *He will need me to teach him how to rule and keep him safe from his enemies.* Some of them stood around them even now, pretending to be friends.

The silent sisters had armored Lord Tywin as if to fight some final battle. He wore his finest plate, heavy steel enameled a deep, dark crimson, with gold inlay on his gauntlets, greaves, and breastplate. His rondels were golden sunbursts; a golden lioness crouched upon each shoulder; a maned lion crested the greathelm beside his head. Upon his chest lay a longsword in a gilded scabbard studded with rubies, his hands folded about its hilt in gloves of gilded mail. *Even in death his face is noble,* she thought, *although the mouth . . .* The corners of her father's lips curved upward ever so slightly, giving him a look of vague bemusement. *That should not be.* She blamed Pycelle; he should have told the silent sisters that Lord Tywin Lannister never smiled. *The man is as useless as nipples on a breastplate.* That half smile made Lord Tywin seem less fearful, somehow. That, and the fact that his eyes were closed. Her father's eyes had always been unsettling; pale green, almost luminous, flecked with gold. His eyes could see inside you, could see how weak and worthless and ugly you were down deep. *When he looked at you, you knew.*

Unbidden, a memory came to her, of the feast King Aerys had thrown when Cersei first came to court, a girl as green as summer grass. Old Merryweather had been nattering about raising the duty on wine when Lord Rykker said, "If we need gold, His Grace should sit Lord Tywin on his chamber pot." Aerys and his lickspittles laughed loudly, whilst Father stared at Rykker over his wine cup. Long after the merriment had died that gaze had lingered. Rykker turned away, turned back, met Father's eyes, then ignored them, drank a tankard of ale, and stalked off red-faced, defeated by a pair of unflinching eyes.

Lord Tywin's eyes are closed forever now, Cersei thought. *It is my look they will flinch from now, my frown that they must fear. I am a lion too.*

It was gloomy within the sept with the sky so grey outside. If the rain ever stopped, the sun would slant down through the hanging crystals to drape the corpse in rainbows. The Lord of Casterly Rock deserved rainbows. He had been a great man. *I shall be greater, though. A thousand years from now, when the maesters write about*

*this time, you shall be remembered only as Queen Cersei's
sire.*

"Mother." Tommen tugged her sleeve. "What smells so
bad?"

My lord father. "Death." She could smell it too; a faint
whisper of decay that made her want to wrinkle her
nose. Cersei paid it no mind. The seven septons in the silver robes stood behind the bier, beseeching the Father
Above to judge Lord Tywin justly. When they were done,
seventy-seven septas gathered before the altar of the
Mother and began to sing to her for mercy. Tommen was
fidgeting by then, and even the queen's knees had begun to
ache. She glanced at Jaime. Her twin stood as if he had
been carved from stone, and would not meet her eyes.

On the benches, their uncle Kevan knelt with his shoulders slumped, his son beside him. *Lancel looks worse than
Father.* Though only seventeen, he might have passed for
seventy; grey-faced, gaunt, with hollow cheeks, sunken
eyes, and hair as white and brittle as chalk. *How can
Lancel be among the living when Tywin Lannister is dead?
Have the gods taken leave of their wits?*

Lord Gyles was coughing more than usual and covering his nose with a square of red silk. *He can smell it too.*
Grand Maester Pycelle had his eyes closed. *If he has
fallen asleep, I swear I will have him whipped.* To the right
of the bier knelt the Tyrells: the Lord of Highgarden, his
hideous mother and vapid wife, his son Garlan and his
daughter Margaery. *Queen Margaery,* she reminded herself; Joff's widow and Tommen's wife-to-be. Margaery
looked very like her brother, the Knight of Flowers. The
queen wondered if they had other things in common. *Our
little rose has a good many ladies waiting attendance on
her, night and day.* They were with her now, almost a
dozen of them. Cersei studied their faces, wondering. *Who*

is the most fearful, the most wanton, the hungriest for favor? Who has the loosest tongue? She would need to make a point of finding out.

It was a relief when the singing finally ended. The smell coming off her father's corpse seemed to have grown stronger. Most of the mourners had the decency to pretend that nothing was amiss, but Cersei saw two of Lady Margaery's cousins wrinkling their little Tyrell noses. As she and Tommen were walking back down the aisle the queen thought she heard someone mutter "privy" and chortle, but when she turned her head to see who had spoken a sea of solemn faces gazed at her blankly. *They would never have dared make japes about him when he was still alive. He would have turned their bowels to water with a look.*

Back out in the Hall of Lamps, the mourners buzzed about them thick as flies, eager to shower her with useless condolences. The Redwyne twins both kissed her hand, their father her cheeks. Hallyne the Pyromancer promised her that a flaming hand would burn in the sky above the city on the day her father's bones went west. Between coughs, Lord Gyles told her that he had hired a master stonecarver to make a statue of Lord Tywin, to stand eternal vigil beside the Lion Gate. Ser Lambert Turnberry appeared with a patch over his right eye, swearing that he would wear it until he could bring her the head of her dwarf brother.

No sooner had the queen escaped the clutches of that fool than she found herself cornered by Lady Falyse of Stokeworth and her husband, Ser Balman Byrch. "My lady mother sends her regrets, Your Grace," Falyse burbled at her. "Lollys has been taken to bed with the child and she felt the need to stay with her. She begs that you forgive her, and said I should ask you . . . my mother admired your late father above all other men. Should my sister have a little boy, it is her wish that we might name him Tywin, if . . . if it please you."

Cersei stared at her, aghast. "Your lackwit sister gets herself raped by half of King's Landing, and Tanda thinks to honor the bastard with my lord father's name? I think not."

Falyse flinched back as if she'd been slapped, but her husband only stroked his thick blond mustache with a thumb. "I told Lady Tanda as much. We shall find a more, ah . . . a more fitting name for Lollys's bastard, you have my word."

"See that you do." Cersei showed them a shoulder and moved away. Tommen had fallen into the clutches of Margaery Tyrell and her grandmother, she saw. The Queen of Thorns was so short that for an instant Cersei took her for another child. Before she could rescue her son from the roses, the press brought her face-to-face with her uncle. When the queen reminded him of their meeting later, Ser Kevan gave a weary nod and begged leave to withdraw. But Lancel lingered, the very picture of a man with one foot in the grave. *But is he climbing in or climbing out?*

Cersei forced herself to smile. "Lancel, I am happy to see you looking so much stronger. Maester Ballabar brought us such dire reports, we feared for your life. But I would have thought you on your way to Darry by now, to take up your lordship." Her father had made Lancel a lord after the Battle of the Blackwater, as a sop to his brother Kevan.

"Not as yet. There are outlaws in my castle." Her cousin's voice was as wispy as the mustache on his upper lip. Though his hair had gone white, his mustache fuzz remained a sandy color. Cersei had often gazed up at it while the boy was inside her, pumping dutifully away. *It looks like a smudge of dirt on his lip.* She used to threaten to scrub it off with a little spit. "The riverlands have need of a strong hand, my father says."

A pity that they're getting yours, she wanted to say. Instead she smiled. "And you are to be wed as well."

A gloomy look passed across the young knight's ravaged face. "A Frey girl, and not of my choosing. She is not even maiden. A widow, of Darry blood. My father says that will help me with the peasants, but the peasants are all dead." He reached for her hand. "It is cruel, Cersei. Your Grace knows that I love—"

"—House Lannister," she finished for him. "No one can doubt that, Lancel. May your wife give you strong sons." *Best not let her lord grandfather host the wedding, though.* "I know you will do many noble deeds in Darry."

Lancel nodded, plainly miserable. "When it seemed that I might die, my father brought the High Septon to pray for me. He is a good man." Her cousin's eyes were wet and shiny, a child's eyes in an old man's face. "He says the Mother spared me for some holy purpose, so I might atone for my sins."

Cersei wondered how he intended to atone for her. *Knighting him was a mistake, and bedding him a bigger one.* Lancel was a weak reed, and she liked his newfound piety not at all; he had been much more amusing when he was trying to be Jaime. *What has this mewling fool told the High Septon? And what will he tell his little Frey when they lie together in the dark?* If he confessed to bedding Cersei, well, she could weather that. Men were always lying about women; she would put it down as the braggadocio of a callow boy smitten by her beauty. *If he sings of Robert and the strongwine, though . . .* "Atonement is best achieved through prayer," Cersei told him. "*Silent* prayer."

She left him to think about that and girded herself to face the Tyrell host.

Margaery embraced her like a sister, which the queen found presumptuous, but this was not the place to reproach her. Lady Alerie and the cousins contented themselves with kissing fingers. Lady Graceford, who was large with child, asked the queen's leave to name it Tywin if it were a boy, or Lanna if it were a girl. *Another one?* she almost groaned. *The realm will drown in Tywins.* She gave consent as graciously as she could, feigning delight.

It was Lady Merryweather who truly pleased her. "Your Grace," that one said, in her sultry Myrish tones, "I have sent word to my friends across the narrow sea, asking them to seize the Imp at once should he show his ugly face in the Free Cities."

"Do you have many friends across the water?"

"In Myr, many. In Lys as well, and Tyrosh. Men of power."

Cersei could well believe it. The Myrish woman was too beautiful by half; long-legged and full-breasted, with smooth olive skin, ripe lips, huge dark eyes, and thick black hair that always looked as if she'd just come from bed. *She even smells of sin, like some exotic lotus.* "Lord Merryweather and I wish only to serve Your Grace and the little king," the woman purred, with a look that was as pregnant as Lady Graceford.

This one is ambitious, and her lord is proud but poor. "We must speak again, my lady. Taena, is it? You are most kind. I know that we shall be great friends."

Then the Lord of Highgarden descended on her.

Mace Tyrell was no more than ten years older than Cersei, yet she thought of him as her father's age, not her own. He was not quite so tall as Lord Tywin had been, but elsewise he was bigger, with a thick chest and a gut grown even thicker. His hair was chestnut-colored, but there were specks of white and grey in his beard. His face was often red. "Lord Tywin was a great man, an *extraordinary* man," he declared ponderously after he had kissed both her cheeks. "We shall never see his like again, I fear."

You are looking at his like, fool, Cersei thought. *It is his daughter standing here before you.* But she needed Tyrell and the strength of Highgarden to keep Tommen on his throne, so all she said was, "He will be greatly missed."

Tyrell put a hand upon her shoulder. "No man alive is fit to don Lord Tywin's armor, that is plain. Still, the realm goes on, and must be ruled. If there is aught that I might do to serve in this dark hour, Your Grace need only ask."

If you want to be the King's Hand, my lord, have the courage to say it plainly. The queen smiled. *Let him read into that as much as he likes.* "Surely my lord is needed in the Reach?"

"My son Willas is an able lad," the man replied, refusing to take her perfectly good hint. "His leg may be twisted but he has no want of wits. And Garlan will soon take Brightwater. Between them the Reach will be in good hands, if it happens that I am needed elsewhere. The governance of the realm must come first, Lord Tywin often said. And I am pleased to bring Your Grace good tidings in that regard. My uncle Garth has agreed to serve as master of coin, as your lord father wished. He is making his way to Oldtown to take ship. His sons will accompany him. Lord Tywin mentioned something about finding places for the two of them as well. Perhaps in the City Watch."

The queen's smile had frozen so hard she feared her teeth might crack. *Garth the Gross on the small council and his two bastards in the gold cloaks . . . do the Tyrells think I will just serve the realm up to them on a gilded platter?* The arrogance of it took her breath away.

"Garth has served me well as Lord Seneschal, as he served my father before me," Tyrell was going on. "Littlefinger had a nose for gold, I grant you, but Garth—"

"My lord," Cersei broke in, "I fear there has been some misunderstanding. I have asked Lord Gyles Rosby to serve as our new master of coin, and he has done me the honor of accepting."

Mace gaped at her. "Rosby? That . . . *cougher*? But . . . the matter was agreed, Your Grace. Garth is on his way to Oldtown."

"Best send a raven to Lord Hightower and ask him to make certain your uncle does not take ship. We would hate for Garth to brave an autumn sea for nought." She smiled pleasantly.

A flush crept up Tyrell's thick neck. "This . . . your lord father assured me . . ." He began to sputter.

Then his mother appeared and slid her arm through his own. "It would seem that Lord Tywin did not share his plans with our regent, I can't *imagine* why. Still, there 'tis, no use hectoring Her Grace. She is quite right, you must write Lord Leyton before Garth boards a ship. You know the sea will sicken him and make his farting worse." Lady Olenna gave Cersei a toothless smile. "Your council chambers will smell sweeter with Lord Gyles, though I daresay that coughing would drive me to distraction. We all adore dear old uncle Garth, but the man is flatulent, that cannot be gainsaid. I do abhor foul smells." Her wrinkled face wrinkled up even more. "I caught a whiff of something unpleasant in the holy sept, in truth. Mayhaps you smelled it too?"

"No," Cersei said coldly. "A scent, you say?"

"More like a stink."

"Perhaps you miss your autumn roses. We have kept you here too long." The sooner she rid the court of Lady

Olenna the better. Lord Tyrell would doubtless dispatch a goodly number of knights to see his mother safely home, and the fewer Tyrell swords in the city, the more soundly the queen would sleep.

"I do long for the fragrances of Highgarden, I confess it," said the old lady, "but of course I cannot leave until I have seen my sweet Margaery wed to your precious little Tommen."

"I await that day eagerly as well," Tyrell put in. "Lord Tywin and I were on the point of setting a date, as it happens. Perhaps you and I might take up that discussion, Your Grace."

"Soon."

"Soon will serve," said Lady Olenna with a sniff. "Now come along, Mace, let Her Grace get on with her . . . grief."

I will see you dead, old woman, Cersei promised herself as the Queen of Thorns tottered off between her towering guardsmen, a pair of seven-footers that it amused her to call Left and Right. *We'll see how sweet a corpse you make.* The old woman was twice as clever as her lord son, that was plain.

The queen rescued her son from Margaery and her cousins, and made for the doors. Outside, the rain had finally stopped. The autumn air smelled sweet and fresh. Tommen took his crown off. "Put that back on," Cersei commanded him.

"It makes my neck hurt," the boy said, but he did as he was bid. "Will I be married soon? Margaery says that as soon as we're wed we can go to Highgarden."

"You are not going to Highgarden, but you can ride back to the castle." Cersei beckoned to Ser Meryn Trant. "Bring His Grace a mount, and ask Lord Gyles if he would do me the honor of sharing my litter." Things were moving more quickly than she had anticipated; there was no time to be squandered.

Tommen was happy at the prospect of a ride, and of course Lord Gyles was honored by her invitation . . . though when she asked him to be her master of coin, he began coughing so violently that she feared he might die right then and there. But the Mother was merciful, and Gyles eventually recovered sufficiently to accept, and even began coughing out the names of men he wanted to replace, customs officers and wool factors appointed by Littlefinger, even one of the keepers of the keys.

"Name the cow what you will, so long as the milk flows. And should the question arise, you joined the council yesterday."

"Yester—" A fit of coughing bent him over. "Yesterday. To be sure." Lord Gyles coughed into a square of red silk, as if to hide the blood in his spittle. Cersei pretended not to notice.

When he dies I will find someone else. Perhaps she would recall Littlefinger. The queen could not imagine that Petyr Baelish would be allowed to remain Lord Protector of the Vale for very long, with Lysa Arryn dead. The Vale lords were already stirring, if what Pycelle said was true. *Once they take that wretched boy away from him, Lord Petyr will come crawling back.*

"Your Grace?" Lord Gyles coughed, and dabbed his mouth. "Might I . . ." He coughed again. ". . . ask who . . ." Another series of coughs racked him. ". . . who will be the King's Hand?"

"My uncle," she replied absently.

It was a relief to see the gates of the Red Keep looming large before her. She gave Tommen over to the charge of his squires and retired gratefully to her own chambers to rest.

No sooner had she eased off her shoes than Jocelyn entered timidly to say that Qyburn was without and craved audience. "Send him in," the queen commanded. *A ruler gets no rest.*

Qyburn was old, but his hair still had more ash than snow in it, and the laugh lines around his mouth made him look like some little girl's favorite grandfather. *A rather shabby grandfather, though.* The collar of his robe was frayed, and one sleeve had been torn and badly sewn. "I must beg Your Grace's pardon for my appearance," he said. "I have been down in the dungeons making inquiries into the Imp's escape, as you commanded."

"And what have you discovered?"

"The night that Lord Varys and your brother disappeared, a third man also vanished."

"Yes, the gaoler. What of him?"

"Rugen was the man's name. An undergaoler who had charge of the black cells. The chief undergaoler describes him as portly, unshaven, gruff of speech. He held his appointment of the old king, Aerys, and came and went as he pleased. The black cells have not oft been occupied in recent years. The other turnkeys were afraid of him, it seems, but none knew much about him. He had no friends, no kin. Nor did he drink or frequent brothels. His sleeping cell was damp and dreary, and the straw he slept upon was mildewed. His chamber pot was overflowing."

"I know all this." Jaime had examined Rugen's cell, and Ser Addam's gold cloaks had examined it again.

"Aye, Your Grace," said Qyburn, "but did you know that under that stinking chamber pot was a loose stone, which opened on a small hollow? The sort of place where a man might hide valuables that he did not wish to be discovered?"

"Valuables?" This was new. "Coin, you mean?" She

had suspected all along that Tyrion had somehow bought this gaoler.

"Beyond a doubt. To be sure, the hole was empty when I found it. No doubt Rugen took his ill-gotten treasure with him when he fled. But as I crouched over the hole with my torch, I saw something glitter, so I scratched in the dirt until I dug it out." Qyburn opened his palm. "A gold coin."

Gold, yes, but the moment Cersei took it she could tell that it was wrong. *Too small,* she thought, *too thin.* The coin was old and worn. On one side was a king's face in profile, on the other side the imprint of a hand. "This is no dragon," she said.

"No," Qyburn agreed. "It dates from before the Conquest, Your Grace. The king is Garth the Twelfth, and the hand is the sigil of House Gardener."

Of Highgarden. Cersei closed her hand around the coin. *What treachery is this?* Mace Tyrell had been one of Tyrion's judges, and had called loudly for his death. *Was that some ploy? Could he have been plotting with the Imp all the while, conspiring at Father's death?* With Tywin Lannister in his grave, Lord Tyrell was an obvious choice to be King's Hand, but even so . . . "You will not speak of this with anyone," she commanded.

"Your Grace may trust in my discretion. Any man who rides with a sellsword company learns to hold his tongue, else he does not keep it long."

"In my company as well." The queen put the coin away. She would think about it later. "What of the other matter?"

"Ser Gregor." Qyburn shrugged. "I have examined him, as you commanded. The poison on the Viper's spear was manticore venom from the east, I would stake my life on that."

"Pycelle says no. He told my lord father that manticore venom kills the instant it reaches the heart."

"And so it does. But this venom has been *thickened* somehow, so as to draw out the Mountain's dying."

"Thickened? Thickened *how?* With some other substance?"

"It may be as Your Grace suggests, though in most cases adulterating a poison only lessens its potency. It may be that the cause is . . . less natural, let us say. A spell, I think."

Is this one as big a fool as Pycelle? "So are you telling me that the Mountain is dying of some black *sorcery?*"

Qyburn ignored the mockery in her voice. "He is dying of the venom, but slowly, and in exquisite agony. My efforts to ease his pain have proved as fruitless as Pycelle's. Ser Gregor is overly accustomed to the poppy, I fear. His squire tells me that he is plagued by blinding headaches and oft quaffs the milk of the poppy as lesser men quaff ale. Be that as it may, his veins have turned black from head to heel, his water is clouded with pus, and the venom has eaten a hole in his side as large as my fist. It is a wonder that the man is still alive, if truth be told."

"His size," the queen suggested, frowning. "Gregor is a very large man. Also a very stupid one. Too stupid to know when he should die, it seems." She held out her cup, and Senelle filled it once again. "His screaming frightens Tommen. It has even been known to wake me of a night. I would say it is past time we summoned Ilyn Payne."

"Your Grace," said Qyburn, "mayhaps I might move Ser Gregor to the dungeons? His screams will not disturb you there, and I will be able to tend to him more freely."

"Tend to him?" She laughed. "Let Ser Ilyn tend to him."

"If that is Your Grace's wish," Qyburn said, "but this

poison . . . it would be useful to know more about it, would it not? Send a knight to slay a knight and an archer to kill an archer, the smallfolk often say. To combat the black arts . . ." He did not finish the thought, but only smiled at her.

He is not Pycelle, that much is plain. The queen weighed him, wondering. "Why did the Citadel take your chain?"

"The archmaesters are all craven at heart. The grey sheep, Marwyn calls them. I was as skilled a healer as Ebrose, but aspired to surpass him. For hundreds of years the men of the Citadel have opened the bodies of the dead, to study the nature of life. I wished to understand the nature of death, so I opened the bodies of the living. For that crime the grey sheep shamed me and forced me into exile . . . but I understand the nature of life and death better than any man in Oldtown."

"Do you?" That intrigued her. "Very well. The Mountain is yours. Do what you will with him, but confine your studies to the black cells. When he dies, bring me his head. My father promised it to Dorne. Prince Doran would no doubt prefer to kill Gregor himself, but we all must suffer disappointments in this life."

"Very good, Your Grace." Qyburn cleared his throat. "I am not so well provided as Pycelle, however. I must needs equip myself with certain . . ."

"I shall instruct Lord Gyles to provide you with gold sufficient for your needs. Buy yourself some new robes as well. You look as though you've wandered up from Flea Bottom." She studied his eyes, wondering how far she dared trust this one. "Need I say that it will go ill for you if any word of your . . . labors . . . should pass beyond these walls?"

"No, Your Grace." Qyburn gave her a reassuring smile. "Your secrets are safe with me."

When he was gone, Cersei poured herself a cup of strongwine and drank it by the window, watching the shadows lengthen across the yard and thinking about the coin. *Gold from the Reach. Why would an undergaoler in King's Landing have gold from the Reach, unless he were paid to help bring about Father's death?*

Try as she might, she could not seem to bring Lord Tywin's face to mind without seeing that silly little half smile and remembering the foul smell coming off his corpse. She wondered whether Tyrion was somehow behind that as well. *It is small and cruel, like him.* Could Tyrion have made Pycelle his catspaw? *He sent the old man to the black cells, and this Rugen had charge of those cells,* she remembered. All the strings were tangled up together in ways she did not like. *This High Septon is Tyrion's creature too,* Cersei recalled suddenly, *and Father's poor body was in his care from dark till dawn.*

Her uncle arrived promptly at sunset, wearing a quilted doublet of charcoal-colored wool as somber as his face. Like all the Lannisters, Ser Kevan was fair-skinned and blond, though at five-and-fifty he had lost most of his hair. No one would ever call him comely. Thick of waist, round of shoulder, with a square jutting chin that his close-cropped yellow beard did little to conceal, he reminded her of some old mastiff . . . but a faithful old mastiff was the very thing that she required.

They ate a simple supper of beets and bread and bloody beef with a flagon of Dornish red to wash it all down. Ser Kevan said little and scarce touched his wine cup. *He broods too much,* she decided. *He needs to be put to work to get beyond his grief.*

She said as much, when the last of the food had been

cleared away and the servants had departed. "I know how much my father relied on you, Uncle. Now I must do the same."

"You need a Hand," he said, "and Jaime has refused you."

He is blunt. Very well. "Jaime . . . I felt so lost with Father dead, I scarce knew what I was saying. Jaime is gallant, but a bit of a fool, let us be frank. Tommen needs a more seasoned man. Someone older . . ."

"Mace Tyrell is older."

Her nostrils flared. "Never." Cersei pushed a lock of hair off her brow. "The Tyrells overreach themselves."

"You would be a fool to make Mace Tyrell your Hand," Ser Kevan admitted, "but a bigger fool to make him your foe. I've heard what happened in the Hall of Lamps. Mace should have known better than to broach such matters in public, but even so, you were unwise to shame him in front of half the court."

"Better that than suffer another Tyrell on the council." His reproach annoyed her. "Rosby will make an adequate master of coin. You've seen that litter of his, with its carvings and silk draperies. His horses are better dressed than most knights. A man that rich should have no problem finding gold. As for Handship . . . who better to finish my father's work than the brother who shared all his counsels?"

"Every man needs someone he can trust. Tywin had me, and once your mother."

"He loved her very much." Cersei refused to think about the dead whore in his bed. "I know they are together now."

"So I pray." Ser Kevan studied her face for a long moment before he replied. "You ask much of me, Cersei."

"No more than my father did."

"I am tired." Her uncle reached for his wine cup and

took a swallow. "I have a wife I have not seen in two years, a dead son to mourn, another son about to marry and assume a lordship. Castle Darry must be made strong again, its lands protected, its burned fields plowed and planted anew. Lancel needs my help."

"As does Tommen." Cersei had not expected Kevan to require coaxing. *He never played coy with Father.* "The realm needs you."

"The realm. Aye. And House Lannister." He sipped his wine again. "Very well. I will remain and serve His Grace . . ."

"Very good," she started to say, but Ser Kevan raised his voice and bulled right over her.

". . . so long as you name me regent as well as Hand and take yourself back to Casterly Rock."

For half a heartbeat Cersei could only stare at him. "*I* am the regent," she reminded him.

"You were. Tywin did not intend that you continue in that role. He told me of his plans to send you back to the Rock and find a new husband for you."

Cersei could feel her anger rising. "He spoke of such, yes. And I told him it was not my wish to wed again."

Her uncle was unmoved. "If you are resolved against another marriage, I will not force it on you. As to the other, though . . . you are the Lady of Casterly Rock now. Your place is there."

How dare you? she wanted to scream. Instead, she said, "I am also the Queen Regent. My place is with my son."

"Your father thought not."

"My father is dead."

"To my grief, and the woe of all the realm. Open your eyes and look about you, Cersei. The kingdom is in ruins. Tywin might have been able to set matters aright, but . . ."

"*I* shall set matters aright!" Cersei softened her tone.

"With your help, Uncle. If you will serve me as faithfully as you served my father—"

"You are not your father. And Tywin always regarded Jaime as his rightful heir."

"*Jaime* . . . Jaime has taken vows. Jaime never thinks, he laughs at everything and everyone and says whatever comes into his head. Jaime is a handsome fool."

"And yet he was your first choice to be the King's Hand. What does that make you, Cersei?"

"I told you, I was sick with grief, I did not think—"

"No," Ser Kevan agreed. "Which is why you should return to Casterly Rock and leave the king with those who do."

"The king is my son!" Cersei rose to her feet.

"Aye," her uncle said, "and from what I saw of Joffrey, you are as unfit a mother as you are a ruler."

She threw the contents of her wine cup full in his face.

Ser Kevan rose with a ponderous dignity. "Your Grace." Wine trickled down his cheeks and dripped from his close-cropped beard. "With your leave, might I withdraw?"

"By what right do you presume to give *me* terms? You are no more than one of my father's household knights."

"I hold no lands, that is true. But I have certain incomes, and chests of coin set aside. My own father forgot none of his children when he died, and Tywin knew how to reward good service. I feed two hundred knights and can double that number if need be. There are freeriders who will follow my banner, and I have the gold to hire sellswords. You would be wise not to take me lightly, Your Grace . . . and wiser still not to make of me a foe."

"Are you *threatening* me?"

"I am counseling you. If you will not yield the regency to me, name me your castellan for Casterly Rock and make either Mathis Rowan or Randyll Tarly the Hand of the King."

Tyrell bannermen, both of them. The suggestion left her speechless. *Is he bought?* she wondered. *Has he taken Tyrell gold to betray House Lannister?*

"Mathis Rowan is sensible, prudent, well liked," her uncle went on, oblivious. "Randyll Tarly is the finest soldier in the realm. A poor Hand for peacetime, but with Tywin dead there's no better man to finish this war. Lord Tyrell cannot take offense if you choose one of his own bannermen as Hand. Both Tarly and Rowan are able men . . . and *loyal*. Name either one, and you make him yours. You strengthen yourself and weaken Highgarden, yet Mace will likely thank you for it." He gave a shrug. "That is my counsel, take it or no. You may make Moon Boy your Hand for all I care. My brother is dead, woman. I am going to take him home."

Traitor, she thought. *Turncloak.* She wondered how much Mace Tyrell had given him. "You would abandon your king when he needs you most," she told him. "You would abandon Tommen."

"Tommen has his mother." Ser Kevan's green eyes met her own, unblinking. A last drop of wine trembled wet and red beneath his chin, and finally fell. "Aye," he added softly, after a pause, "and his father too, I think."

JAIME

Ser Jaime Lannister, all in white, stood beside his father's bier, five fingers curled about the hilt of a golden greatsword.

At dusk, the interior of the Great Sept of Baelor turned dim and eerie. The last light of day slanted down through the high windows, washing the towering likenesses of the Seven in a red gloom. Around their altars, scented candles flickered whilst deep shadows gathered in the transepts and crept silently across the marble floors. The echoes of the evensongs died away as the last mourners were departing.

Balon Swann and Loras Tyrell remained when the rest had gone. "No man can stand a vigil for seven days and seven nights," Ser Balon said. "When did you last sleep, my lord?"

"When my lord father was alive," said Jaime.

"Allow me to stand tonight in your stead," Ser Loras offered.

"He was not your father." *You did not kill him. I did. Tyrion may have loosed the crossbow bolt that slew him, but I loosed Tyrion.* "Leave me."

"As my lord commands," said Swann. Ser Loras looked as if he might have argued further, but Ser Balon took his arm and drew him off. Jaime listened to the echoes of their footfalls die away. And then he was alone again with his lord father, amongst the candles and the crystals and the sickly sweet smell of death. His back ached from the weight of his armor, and his legs felt almost numb. He shifted his stance a bit and tightened his fingers around the golden greatsword. He could not wield a sword, but he could hold one. His missing hand was throbbing. That was almost funny. He had more feeling in the hand he'd lost than in the rest of the body that remained to him.

My hand is hungry for a sword. I need to kill someone. Varys, for a start, but first I'd need to find the rock he's hiding under. "I commanded the eunuch to take him to a ship, not to your bedchamber," he told the corpse. "The blood is on his hands as much as . . . as Tyrion's." *The blood is on his hands as much as mine,* he meant to say, but the words stuck in his throat. *Whatever Varys did, I made him do.*

He had waited in the eunuch's chambers that night, when at last he had decided not to let his little brother die. As he waited, he had sharpened his dagger with one hand, taking a queer comfort from the *scrape-scrape-scrape* of steel on stone. At the sound of footsteps he stood beside the door. Varys entered in a wash of powder and lavender. Jaime stepped out behind him, kicked him in the back of the knee, knelt on his chest, and shoved the knife up under his soft white chin, forcing his head up. "Why, Lord Varys," he'd said pleasantly, "fancy meeting you here."

"Ser Jaime?" Varys panted. "You frightened me."

"I meant to." When he twisted the dagger, a trickle of blood ran down the blade. "I was thinking you might help me pluck my brother from his cell before Ser Ilyn lops his head off. It is an ugly head, I grant you, but he only has the one."

"Yes . . . well . . . if you would . . . remove the blade . . . yes, gently, as it please my lord, gently, oh, I'm pricked . . ." The eunuch touched his neck and gaped at the blood on his fingers. "I have always abhorred the sight of my own blood."

"You'll have more to abhor shortly, unless you help me."

Varys struggled to a sitting position. "Your brother . . . if the Imp should vanish unaccountably from his cell, q-questions would be asked. I would f-fear for my life . . ."

"Your life is mine. I do not care what secrets you know. If Tyrion dies, you will not long outlive him, I promise you."

"Ah." The eunuch sucked the blood off his fingers. "You ask a dreadful thing . . . to loose the Imp who slew our lovely king. Or is it that you believe him innocent?"

"Innocent or guilty," Jaime had said, like the fool he was, "a Lannister pays his debts." The words had come so easy.

He had not slept since. He could see his brother now, the way the dwarf had grinned beneath the stub of his nose as the torchlight licked his face. "You poor stupid blind crippled fool," he'd snarled, in a voice thick with malice. "Cersei is a lying whore, she's been fucking Lancel and Osmund Kettleblack and probably Moon Boy for all I know. And I am the monster they all say I am. Yes, I killed your vile son."

He never said he meant to kill our father. If he had, I

would have stopped him. Then I would be the kinslayer, not him.

Jaime wondered where Varys was hiding. Wisely, the master of whisperers had not returned to his own chambers, nor had a search of the Red Keep turned him up. It might be that the eunuch had taken ship with Tyrion, rather than remain to answer awkward questions. If so, the two of them were well out to sea by now, sharing a flagon of Arbor gold in the cabin of a galley.

Unless my brother murdered Varys too, and left his corpse to rot beneath the castle. Down there, it might be years before his bones were found. Jaime had led a dozen guards below, with torches and ropes and lanterns. For hours they had groped through twisting passages, narrow crawl spaces, hidden doors, secret steps, and shafts that plunged down into utter blackness. Seldom had he felt so utterly a cripple. A man takes much for granted when he has two hands. Ladders, for an instance. Even crawling did not come easy; not for nought do they speak of *hands* and knees. Nor could he hold a torch and climb, as others could.

And all for naught. They found only darkness, dust, and rats. *And dragons, lurking down below.* He remembered the sullen orange glow of the coals in the iron dragon's mouth. The brazier warmed a chamber at the bottom of a shaft where half a dozen tunnels met. On the floor he'd found a scuffed mosaic of the three-headed dragon of House Targaryen done in tiles of black and red. *I know you, Kingslayer,* the beast seemed to be saying. *I have been here all the time, waiting for you to come to me.* And it seemed to Jaime that he knew that voice, the iron tones that had once belonged to Rhaegar, Prince of Dragonstone.

The day had been windy when he said farewell to

Rhaegar, in the yard of the Red Keep. The prince had donned his night-black armor, with the three-headed dragon picked out in rubies on his breastplate. "Your Grace," Jaime had pleaded, "let Darry stay to guard the king this once, or Ser Barristan. Their cloaks are as white as mine."

Prince Rhaegar shook his head. "My royal sire fears your father more than he does our cousin Robert. He wants you close, so Lord Tywin cannot harm him. I dare not take that crutch away from him at such an hour."

Jaime's anger had risen up in his throat. "I am not a crutch. I am a knight of the Kingsguard."

"Then guard the king," Ser Jon Darry snapped at him. "When you donned that cloak, you promised to obey."

Rhaegar had put his hand on Jaime's shoulder. "When this battle's done I mean to call a council. Changes will be made. I meant to do it long ago, but . . . well, it does no good to speak of roads not taken. We shall talk when I return."

Those were the last words Rhaegar Targaryen ever spoke to him. Outside the gates an army had assembled, whilst another descended on the Trident. So the Prince of Dragonstone mounted up and donned his tall black helm, and rode forth to his doom.

He was more right than he knew. When the battle was done, there were changes made. "Aerys thought no harm could come to him if he kept me near," he told his father's corpse. "Isn't that amusing?" Lord Tywin seemed to think so; his smile was wider than before. *He seems to enjoy being dead.*

It was queer, but he felt no grief. *Where are my tears? Where is my rage?* Jaime Lannister had never lacked for rage. "Father," he told the corpse, "it was you who told me that tears were a mark of weakness in a man, so you cannot expect that I should cry for you."

A thousand lords and ladies had come that morning to file past the bier, and several thousand smallfolk after noon. They wore somber clothes and solemn faces, but Jaime suspected that many and more were secretly delighted to see the great man brought low. Even in the west, Lord Tywin had been more respected than beloved, and King's Landing still remembered the Sack.

Of all the mourners, Grand Maester Pycelle had seemed the most distraught. "I have served six kings," he told Jaime after the second service, whilst sniffing doubtfully about the corpse, "but here before us lies the greatest man I ever knew. Lord Tywin wore no crown, yet he was all a king should be."

Without his beard, Pycelle looked not only old, but feeble. *Shaving him was the cruelest thing Tyrion could have done,* thought Jaime, who knew what it was to lose a part of yourself, the part that made you who you were. Pycelle's beard had been magnificent, white as snow and soft as lambswool, a luxuriant growth that covered cheeks and chin and flowed down almost to his belt. The Grand Maester had been wont to stroke it when he pontificated. It had given him an air of wisdom, and concealed all manner of unsavory things: the loose skin dangling beneath the old man's jaw, the small querulous mouth and missing teeth, warts and wrinkles and age spots too numerous to count. Though Pycelle was trying to regrow what he had lost, he was failing. Only wisps and tufts sprouted from his wrinkled cheeks and weak chin, so thin that Jaime could see the splotchy pink skin beneath.

"Ser Jaime, I have seen terrible things in my time," the old man said. "Wars, battles, murders most foul . . . I was a boy in Oldtown when the grey plague took half the city and three-quarters of the Citadel. Lord Hightower burned every ship in port, closed the gates, and commanded his guards to slay all those who tried to flee, be they men, women, or babes in arms. They killed him when the plague had run its course. On the very day he reopened the port, they dragged him from his horse and slit his throat, and his young son's as well. To this day the ignorant in Oldtown will spit at the sound of his name, but Quenton Hightower did what was needed. Your father was that sort of man as well. A man who did what was needed."

"Is that why he looks so pleased with himself?"

The vapors rising from the corpse were making Pycelle's eyes water. "The flesh . . . as the flesh dries, the muscles grow taut and pull his lips upward. That is no smile, only a . . . a *drying,* that is all." He blinked back tears. "You must excuse me. I am so very tired." Leaning heavily on his cane, Pycelle tottered slowly from the sept. *That one is dying too,* Jaime realized. Small wonder Cersei called him useless.

To be sure, his sweet sister seemed to think half the court was either useless or treasonous; Pycelle, the Kingsguard, the Tyrells, Jaime himself . . . even Ser Ilyn Payne, the silent knight who served as headsman. As King's Justice, the dungeons were his responsibility. Since he lacked a tongue, Payne had largely left the running of those dungeons to his underlings, but Cersei held him to blame for Tyrion's escape all the same. *It was my work, not his,* Jaime almost told her. Instead he had promised to find what answers he could from the chief undergaoler, a bent-back old man named Rennifer Longwaters.

"I see you wonder, what sort of name is that?" the man had cackled when Jaime went to question him. "It is an old name, 'tis true. I am not one to boast, but there is royal blood in my veins. I am descended from a princess. My father told me the tale when I was a tad of a lad." Longwaters had not been a tad of a lad for many a year, to judge from his spotted head and the white hairs growing from his chin. "She was the fairest treasure of the Maidenvault. Lord Oakenfist the great admiral lost his heart to her, though he was married to another. She gave their son the bastard name of 'Waters' in honor of his father, and he grew to be a great knight, as did his own son, who put the 'Long' before the 'Waters' so men might know that he was not basely born himself. So I have a little dragon in me."

"Yes, I almost mistook you for Aegon the Conqueror," Jaime had answered. "Waters" was a common bastard name about Blackwater Bay; old Longwaters was more like to be descended from some minor household knight than from a princess. "As it matters, though, I have more pressing concerns than your lineage."

Longwaters inclined his head. "The lost prisoner."

"And the missing gaoler."

"Rugen," the old man supplied. "An undergaoler. He had charge of the third level, the black cells."

"Tell me of him," Jaime had to say. *A bloody farce.* He knew who Rugen was, even if Longwaters did not.

"Unkempt, unshaven, coarse of speech. I misliked the man, 'tis true, I do confess it. Rugen was here when I first came, twelve years past. He held his appointment from King Aerys. The man was seldom here, it must be said. I made note of it in my reports, my lord. I most suredly did, I give you my word upon it, the word of a man with royal blood."

Mention that royal blood once more and I may spill some of it, thought Jaime. "Who saw these reports?"

"Certain of them went to the master of coin, others to the master of whisperers. All to the chief gaoler and the

King's Justice. It has always been so in the dungeons."
Longwaters scratched his nose. "Rugen was here when
need be, my lord. That must be said. The black cells are little used. Before your lordship's little brother was sent
down, we had Grand Maester Pycelle for a time, and before him Lord Stark the traitor. There were three others,
common men, but Lord Stark gave them to the Night's
Watch. I did not think it good to free those three, but the
papers were in proper order. I made note of that in a report
as well, you may be certain of it."

"Tell me of the two gaolers who went to sleep."

"Gaolers?" Longwaters sniffed. "Those were no gaolers. They were merely *turnkeys*. The crown pays wages for
twenty turnkeys, my lord, a full score, but during my time
we have never had more than twelve. We are supposed to
have six undergaolers as well, two on each level, but there
are only the three."

"You and two others?"

Longwaters sniffed again. "I am the *chief* undergaoler,
my lord. I am *above* the undergaolers. I am charged with
keeping the counts. If my lord would like to look over my
books, he will see that all the figures are exact."
Longwaters had consulted the great leather-bound book
spread out before him. "At present, we have four prisoners
on the first level and one on the second, in addition to your
lordship's brother." The old man frowned. "Who is fled, to
be sure. 'Tis true. I will strike him out." He took up a quill
and began to sharpen it.

Six prisoners, Jaime thought sourly, *while we pay
wages for twenty turnkeys, six undergaolers, a chief undergaoler, a gaoler, and a King's Justice.* "I want to question these two turnkeys."

Rennifer Longwaters let up sharpening his quill and
peered doubtfully up at Jaime. "Question them, my lord?"

"You heard me."

"I did, my lord, I suredly did, and yet . . . my lord may question who he pleases, 'tis true, it is not my place to say that he may not. But, ser, if I may be so bold, I do not think them like to answer. They are dead, my lord."

"*Dead?* By whose command?"

"Your own, I thought, or . . . the king's, mayhaps? I did not ask. It . . . it is not my place to question the Kingsguard."

That was salt for his wound; Cersei had used his own men to do her bloody work, them and her precious Kettleblacks.

"You witless fools," Jaime had snarled at Boros Blount and Osmund Kettleblack later, in a dungeon that stank of blood and death. "What did you imagine you were doing?"

"No more'n we was told, my lord." Ser Boros was shorter than Jaime, but heavier. "Her Grace commanded it. Your sister."

Ser Osmund hooked a thumb through his swordbelt. "She said they were to sleep forever. So my brothers and me, we saw to it."

That you did. One corpse sprawled facedown upon the table, like a man passed out at a feast, but it was a puddle of blood beneath his head, not a puddle of wine. The second turnkey had managed to push back from the bench and draw his dagger before someone shoved a longsword through his ribs. His had been the longer, messier end. *I told Varys no one was to be harmed in this escape,* Jaime thought, *but I should have told my brother and my sister.* "This was ill done, ser."

Ser Osmund shrugged. "They won't be missed. I'll wager they was part of it, along with the one who's gone missing."

No, Jaime could have told him. *Varys dosed their wine*

to make them sleep. "If so, we might have coaxed the truth from them." . . . *she's been fucking Lancel and Osmund Kettleblack and Moon Boy for all I know* . . . "If I had a suspicious nature I might wonder why you were in such haste to make certain these two were never put to the question. Did you need to silence them to conceal your own part in this?"

"Us?" Kettleblack choked on that. "All we done was what the queen commanded. On my word as your Sworn Brother."

Jaime's phantom fingers twitched as he said, "Get Osney and Osfryd down here and clean up this mess you've made. And the next time my sweet sister commands you to kill a man, come to me first. Elsewise, stay out of my sight, ser."

The words echoed in his head in the dimness of Baelor's Sept. Above him, all the windows had gone black, and he could see the faint light of distant stars. The sun had set for good and all. The stench of death was growing stronger, despite the scented candles. The smell reminded Jaime Lannister of the pass below the Golden Tooth, where he had won a glorious victory in the first days of the war. On the morning after the battle, the crows had feasted on victors and vanquished alike, as once they had feasted on Rhaegar Targaryen after the Trident. *How much can a crown be worth, when a crow can dine upon a king?*

There were crows circling the seven towers and great dome of Baelor's Sept even now, Jaime suspected, their black wings beating against the night air as they searched for a way inside. *Every crow in the Seven Kingdoms should pay homage to you, Father. From Castamere to the Blackwater, you fed them well.* That notion pleased Lord Tywin; his smile widened further. *Bloody hell, he's grinning like a bridegroom at his bedding.*

That was so grotesque it made Jaime laugh aloud.

The sound echoed through the transepts and crypts and chapels, as if the dead interred within the walls were laughing too. *Why not? This is more absurd than a mummer's farce, me standing vigil for a father I helped to slay, sending men forth to capture the brother I helped to free* . . . He had commanded Ser Addam Marbrand to search the Street of Silk. "Look under every bed, you know how fond my brother is of brothels." The gold cloaks would find more of interest beneath the whores' skirts than beneath their beds. He wondered how many bastard children would be born of the pointless search.

Unbidden, his thoughts went to Brienne of Tarth. *Stupid stubborn ugly wench.* He wondered where she was. *Father, give her strength.* Almost a prayer . . . but was it the god he was invoking, the Father Above whose towering gilded likeness glimmered in the candlelight across the sept? Or was he praying to the corpse that lay before him? *Does it matter? They never listened, either one.* The Warrior had been Jaime's god since he was old enough to hold a sword. Other men might be fathers, sons, husbands, but never Jaime Lannister, whose sword was as golden as his hair. He was a warrior, and that was all he would ever be.

I should tell Cersei the truth, admit that it was me who freed our little brother from his cell. The truth had worked so splendidly with Tyrion, after all. *I killed your vile son, and now I'm off to kill your father too.* Jaime could hear the Imp laughing in the gloom. He turned his head to look, but the sound was only his own laughter coming back at him. He closed his eyes, and just as quickly snapped them open. *I must not sleep.* If he slept, he might dream. Oh, how Tyrion was sniggering. . . . *a lying whore . . . fucking Lancel and Osmund Kettleblack* . . .

At midnight the hinges on the Father's Doors gave a

groan as several hundred septons filed in for their devotions. Some were clad in the cloth-of-silver vestments and crystal coronals that marked the Most Devout; their humbler brethren wore their crystals on thongs about their necks and cinched white robes with seven-stranded belts, each plait a different color. Through the Mother's Doors marched white septas from their cloister, seven abreast and singing softly, while the silent sisters came single file down the Stranger's Steps. Death's handmaidens were garbed in soft grey, their faces hooded and shawled so only their eyes could be seen. A host of brothers appeared as well, in robes of brown and butternut and dun and even undyed roughspun, belted with lengths of hempen rope. Some hung the iron hammer of the Smith about their necks, whilst others carried begging bowls.

None of the devout paid Jaime any mind. They made a circuit of the sept, worshiping at each of the seven altars to honor the seven aspects of the deity. To each god they made sacrifice, to each they sang a hymn. Sweet and solemn rose their voices. Jaime closed his eyes to listen, but opened them again when he began to sway. *I am more weary than I knew.*

It had been years since his last vigil. *And I was younger then, a boy of fifteen years.* He had worn no armor then, only a plain white tunic. The sept where he'd spent the night was not a third as large as any of the Great Sept's seven transepts. Jaime had laid his sword across the Warrior's knees, piled his armor at his feet, and knelt upon the rough stone floor before the altar. When dawn came his knees were raw and bloody. "All knights must bleed, Jaime," Ser Arthur Dayne had said, when he saw. "Blood is the seal of our devotion." With dawn he tapped him on the shoulder; the pale blade was so sharp that even that light touch cut through Jaime's tunic, so he bled anew. He never felt it. A boy knelt; a knight rose. *The Young Lion, not the Kingslayer.*

But that was long ago, and the boy was dead.

He could not have said when the devotions ended. Perhaps he slept, still standing. When the devout had filed out, the Great Sept grew still once more. The candles were a wall of stars burning in the darkness, though the air was rank with death. Jaime shifted his grip upon the golden greatsword. Perhaps he should have let Ser Loras relieve him after all. *Cersei would have hated that.* The Knight of Flowers was still half a boy, arrogant and vain, but he had it in him to be great, to perform deeds worthy of the White Book.

The White Book would be waiting when this vigil was done, his page open in dumb reproach. *I'll hack the bloody book to pieces before I'll fill it full of lies.* Yet if he would not lie, what could he write but truth?

A woman stood before him.

It is raining again, he thought when he saw how wet she was. The water was trickling down her cloak to puddle round her feet. *How did she get here? I never heard her enter.* She was dressed like a tavern wench in a heavy roughspun cloak, badly dyed in mottled browns and fraying at the hem. A hood concealed her face, but he could see the candles dancing in the green pools of her eyes, and when she moved he knew her.

"Cersei." He spoke slowly, like a man waking from a dream, still wondering where he was. "What hour is it?"

"The hour of the wolf." His sister lowered her hood, and made a face. "The drowned wolf, perhaps." She smiled for him, so sweetly. "Do you remember the first time I came to you like this? It was some dismal inn off Weasel Alley, and I put on servant's garb to get past Father's guards."

"I remember. It was Eel Alley." *She wants something of me.* "Why are you here, at this hour? What would you have of me?" His last word echoed up and down the sept, *memememememememememe,* fading to a whisper. For a moment he dared to hope that all she wanted was the comfort of his arms.

"Speak softly." Her voice sounded strange . . . breathless, almost frightened. "Jaime, Kevan has refused me. He will not serve as Hand, he . . . he knows about us. He said as much."

"Refused?" That surprised him. "How could he know? He will have read what Stannis wrote, but there is no . . ."

"*Tyrion* knew," she reminded him. "Who can say what tales that vile dwarf may have told, or to whom? Uncle Kevan is the least of it. The High Septon . . . Tyrion raised him to the crown, when the fat one died. He may know as well." She moved closer. "You *must* be Tommen's Hand. I do not trust Mace Tyrell. What if he had a hand in Father's death? He may have been conspiring with Tyrion. The Imp could be on his way to Highgarden . . ."

"He's not."

"Be my Hand," she pleaded, "and we'll rule the Seven Kingdoms together, like a king and his queen."

"You were Robert's queen. And yet you won't be mine."

"I would, if I dared. But our son—"

"Tommen is no son of mine, no more than Joffrey was." His voice was hard. "You made them Robert's too."

His sister flinched. "You swore that you would always love me. It is not loving to make me beg."

Jaime could smell the fear on her, even through the rank stench of the corpse. He wanted to take her in his arms and kiss her, to bury his face in her golden curls and promise her that no one would ever hurt her . . . *not here,* he thought, *not here in front of the gods, and Father.* "No," he said. "I cannot. Will not."

"I *need* you. I need my other half." He could hear the rain pattering against the windows high above. "You are me, I am you. I need you with me. *In* me. Please, Jaime. *Please.*"

Jaime looked to make certain Lord Tywin was not rising from his bier in wrath, but his father lay still and cold, rotting. "I was made for a battlefield, not a council chamber. And now it may be that I am unfit even for that."

Cersei wiped her tears away on a ragged brown sleeve. "Very well. If it is battlefields you want, battlefields I shall give you." She jerked her hood up angrily. "I was a fool to come. I was a fool ever to love you." Her footsteps echoed loudly in the quiet, and left damp splotches on the marble floor.

Dawn caught Jaime almost unawares. As the glass in the dome began to lighten, suddenly there were rainbows shimmering off the walls and floors and pillars, bathing Lord Tywin's corpse in a haze of many-colored light. The King's Hand was rotting visibly. His face had taken on a greenish tinge, and his eyes were deeply sunken, two black pits. Fissures had opened in his cheeks, and a foul white fluid was seeping through the joints of his splendid gold-and-crimson armor to pool beneath his body.

The septons were the first to see, when they returned for their dawn devotions. They sang their songs and prayed their prayers and wrinkled up their noses, and one of the Most Devout grew so faint he had to be helped from the sept. Shortly after, a flock of novices came swinging censers, and the air grew so thick with incense that the bier seemed cloaked in smoke. All the rainbows vanished in that perfumed mist, yet the stench persisted, a sweet rotten smell that made Jaime want to gag.

When the doors were opened the Tyrells were amongst the first to enter, as befit their rank. Margaery had brought a great bouquet of golden roses. She placed them ostentatiously at the foot of Lord Tywin's bier but kept one back and held it beneath her nose as she took her seat. *So the girl is as clever as she is pretty. Tommen could do a deal worse for a queen. Others have.* Margaery's ladies followed her example.

Cersei waited until the rest were in their places to make her entrance, with Tommen at her side. Ser Osmund Kettleblack paced beside them in his white enamel plate and white wool cloak.

". . . she's been fucking Lancel and Osmund Kettleblack and Moon Boy for all I know . . ."

Jaime had seen Kettleblack naked in the bathhouse, had seen the black hair on his chest, and the coarser thatch between his legs. He pictured that chest pressed against his sister's, that hair scratching the soft skin of her breasts. *She would not do that. The Imp lied.* Spun gold and black wire tangled, sweaty. Kettleblack's narrow cheeks clenching each time he thrust. Jaime could hear his sister moan. *No. A lie.*

Red-eyed and pale, Cersei climbed the steps to kneel above their father, drawing Tommen down beside her. The boy recoiled at the sight, but his mother seized his wrist before he could pull away. *"Pray,"* she whispered, and Tommen tried. But he was only eight and Lord Tywin was a horror. One desperate breath of air, then the king began to sob. *"Stop that!"* Cersei said. Tommen turned his head and doubled over, retching. His crown fell off and rolled across the marble floor. His mother pulled back in disgust, and all at once the king was running for the doors, as fast as his eight-year-old legs could carry him.

"Ser Osmund, relieve me," Jaime said sharply, as

Kettleblack turned to chase the crown. He handed the man the golden sword and went after his king. In the Hall of Lamps he caught him, beneath the eyes of two dozen startled septas. "I'm sorry," Tommen wept. "I will do better on the morrow. Mother says a king must show the way, but the smell made me sick."

This will not do. Too many eager ears and watching eyes. "Best we go outside, Your Grace." Jaime led the boy out to where the air was as fresh and clean as King's Landing ever got. Twoscore gold cloaks had been posted around the plaza to guard the horses and the litters. He took the king off to the side, well away from everyone, and sat him down upon the marble steps. "I wasn't scared," the boy insisted. "The smell made me sick. Didn't it make you sick? How could you bear it, Uncle, ser?"

I have smelled my own hand rotting, when Vargo Hoat made me wear it for a pendant. "A man can bear most anything, if he must," Jaime told his son. *I have smelled a man roasting, as King Aerys cooked him in his own armor.* "The world is full of horrors, Tommen. You can fight them, or laugh at them, or look without seeing . . . go away inside."

Tommen considered that. "I . . . I used to go away inside sometimes," he confessed, "when Joffy . . ."

"Joffrey." Cersei stood over them, the wind whipping her skirts around her legs. "Your brother's name was *Joffrey.* He would never have shamed me so."

"I never meant to. I wasn't frightened, Mother. It was only that your lord father smelled so bad . . ."

"Do you think he smelled any sweeter to me? I have a nose too." She caught his ear and pulled him to his feet. "Lord Tyrell has a nose. Did you see him retching in the holy sept? Did you see Lady Margaery bawling like a baby?"

Jaime got to his feet. "Cersei, enough."

Her nostrils flared. "Ser? Why are you here? You swore to stand vigil over Father until the wake was done, as I recall."

"It *is* done. Go look at him."

"No. Seven days and seven nights, you said. Surely the Lord Commander remembers how to count to seven. Take the number of your fingers, then add two."

Others had begun to stream out onto the plaza, fleeing the noxious odors in the sept. "Cersei, keep your voice down," Jaime warned. "Lord Tyrell is approaching."

That reached her. The queen drew Tommen to her side. Mace Tyrell bowed before them. "His Grace is not unwell, I hope?"

"The king was overwhelmed by grief," said Cersei.

"As are we all. If there is aught that I can do . . ."

High above, a crow screamed loudly. He was perched on the statue of King Baelor, shitting on his holy head. "There is much and more you can do for Tommen, my lord," Jaime said. "Perhaps you would do Her Grace the honor of supping with her, after the evening services?"

Cersei threw him a withering look, but for once she had the sense to bite her tongue.

"Sup?" Tyrell seemed taken aback. "I suppose . . . of course, we should be honored. My lady wife and I."

The queen forced a smile and made pleasant noises. But when Tyrell had taken his leave and Tommen had been sent off with Ser Addam Marbrand, she turned on Jaime angrily. "Are you drunk or dreaming, ser? Pray tell, why am I having supper with that grasping fool and his puerile wife?" A gust of wind stirred her golden hair. "I will *not* name him Hand, if that's what—"

"You need Tyrell," Jaime broke in, "but not *here*. Ask him to capture Storm's End for Tommen. Flatter him, and tell him you need him in the field, to replace Father. Mace fancies himself a mighty warrior. Either he will deliver Storm's End to you, or he will muck it up and look a fool. Either way, you win."

"Storm's End?" Cersei looked thoughtful. "Yes, but . . . Lord Tyrell has made it tediously plain that he will not leave King's Landing till Tommen marries Margaery."

Jaime sighed. "Then let them wed. It will be years before Tommen is old enough to consummate the marriage. And until he does, the union can always be set aside. Give Tyrell his wedding and send him off to play at war."

A wary smile crept across his sister's face. "Even sieges have their dangers," she murmured. "Why, our Lord of Highgarden might even lose his life in such a venture."

"There is that risk," conceded Jaime. "Especially if his patience runs thin this time, and he elects to storm the gate."

Cersei gave him a lingering look. "You know," she said, "for a moment you sounded quite like Father."

BRIENNE

The gates of Duskendale were closed and barred. Through the predawn gloom the town walls shimmered palely. On their ramparts, wisps of fog moved like ghostly sentinels. A dozen wayns and oxcarts had drawn up outside the gates, waiting for the sun to rise. Brienne took her place behind some turnips. Her calves ached, and it felt good to dismount and stretch her legs. Before long another wayn came rumbling from the woods. By the time the sky began to lighten, the queue stretched back a quarter mile.

The farm folk gave her curious glances, but no one spoke to her. *It is for me to talk to them,* Brienne told herself, but she had always found it hard to speak with strangers. Even as a girl she had been shy. Long years of scorn had only made her shyer. *I must ask after Sansa. How else will I find her?* She cleared her throat.

"Goodwife," she said to the woman on the turnip cart, "perhaps you saw my sister on the road? A young maid, three-and-ten and fair of face, with blue eyes and auburn hair. She may be riding with a drunken knight."

The woman shook her head, but her husband said, "Then she's no maid, I'll wager. Does the poor girl have a name?"

Brienne's head was empty. *I should have made up some name for her.* Any name would do, but none came to her.

"No name? Well, the roads are full of nameless girls."

"The lichyard's even fuller," said his wife.

As dawn broke, guardsmen appeared on the parapets. The farmers climbed onto their wagons and shook the reins. Brienne mounted as well and took a glance behind her. Most of the queue waiting to enter Duskendale were farm folk with loads of fruits and vegetables to sell. A pair of wealthy townsmen sat on well-bred palfreys a dozen places behind her, and farther back she spied a skinny boy on a piebald rounsey. There was no sign of the two knights, nor Ser Shadrich the Mad Mouse.

The guards were waving through the wayns with scarce a look, but when Brienne reached the gate she gave them pause. "Halt, you!" the captain cried. A pair of men in chainmail hauberks crossed their spears to bar her way. "State your purpose here."

"I seek the Lord of Duskendale, or his maester."

The captain's eyes lingered on her shield. "The black bat of Lothston. Those are arms of ill repute."

"They are not mine. I mean to have the shield re-painted."

"Aye?" The captain rubbed his stubbled chin. "My sister does such work, as it happens. You'll find her at the house with the painted doors, across from the Seven

Swords." He gestured to the guards. "Let her pass, lads. It's a wench."

The gatehouse opened on a market square, where those who had entered before her were unloading to hawk their turnips, yellow onions, and sacks of barleycorn. Others were selling arms and armor, and very cheaply to judge from the prices they shouted out as she rode by. *The looters come with the carrion crows after every battle.* Brienne walked her horse past mail shirts still caked with brown blood, dinted helms, notched longswords. There was clothing to be had as well: leather boots, fur cloaks, stained surcoats with suspicious rents. She knew many of the badges. The mailed fist, the moose, the white sun, the double-bladed axe, all those were northern sigils. Tarly men had perished here as well, though, and many from the stormlands. She saw red and green apples, a shield that bore the three thunderbolts of Leygood, horse trappings patterned with the ants of Ambrose. Lord Tarly's own striding huntsman appeared on many a badge and brooch and doublet. *Friend or foe, the crows care not.*

There were pine and linden shields to be had for pennies, but Brienne rode past them. She meant to keep the heavy oaken shield Jaime had given her, the one he'd borne himself from Harrenhal to King's Landing. A pine shield had its advantages. It was lighter, and therefore easier to bear, and the soft wood was more like to trap a foeman's axe or sword. But oak gave more protection, if you were strong enough to bear its weight.

Duskendale was built around its harbor. North of town the chalk cliffs rose; to the south a rocky headland shielded the ships at anchor from storms coming up the narrow sea. The castle overlooked the port, its square keep and big drum towers visible from every part of town. In the crowded cobbled streets, it was easier to walk than ride, so Brienne put her mare up in a stable and continued on afoot, with her shield slung across her back and her bedroll tucked up beneath one arm.

The captain's sister was not hard to find. The Seven Swords was the largest inn in town, a four-story structure that towered over its neighbors, and the double doors on the house across the way were painted gorgeously. They showed a castle in an autumn wood, the trees done up in shades of gold and russet. Ivy crawled up the trunks of ancient oaks, and even the acorns had been done with loving care. When Brienne peered more closely, she saw creatures in the foliage: a sly red fox, two sparrows on a branch, and behind those leaves the shadow of a boar.

"Your door is very pretty," she told the dark-haired woman who answered when she knocked. "What castle is that meant to be?"

"All castles," said the captain's sister. "The only one I know is the Dun Fort by the harbor. I made t'other in my head, what a castle ought to look like. I never seen a dragon neither, nor a griffin, nor a unicorn." She had a cheerful manner, but when Brienne showed her the shield her face went dark. "My old ma used to say that giant bats flew out from Harrenhal on moonless nights, to carry bad children to Mad Danelle for her cookpots. Sometimes I'd hear them scrabbling at the shutters." She sucked her teeth a moment, thoughtful. "What goes in its place?"

The arms of Tarth were quartered rose and azure, and bore a yellow sun and crescent moon. But so long as men believed her to be a murderess, Brienne dare not carry them. "Your door reminded me of an old shield I once saw in my father's armory." She described the arms as best she could recall them.

The woman nodded. "I can paint it straightaway, but the

paint will need to dry. Take a room at the Seven Swords, if it please you. I'll bring the shield to you by morning."

Brienne had not meant to overnight in Duskendale, but it might be for the best. She did not know if the lord of the castle was in residence, or whether he would consent to see her. She thanked the painter and crossed the cobblestones to the inn. Above its door, seven wooden swords swung beneath an iron spike. The whitewash that covered them was cracked and peeling, but Brienne knew their meaning. They stood for the seven sons of Darklyn who had worn the white cloaks of the Kingsguard. No other house in all the realm could claim as many. *They were the glory of their House. And now they are a sign above an inn.* She pushed into the common room and asked the innkeep for a room and a bath.

He put her on the second floor, and a woman with a liver-colored birthmark on her face brought up a wooden tub, and then the water, pail by pail. "Do any Darklyns remain in Duskendale?" Brienne asked as she climbed into the tub.

"Well, there's Darkes, I'm one myself. My husband says I was Darke before we wed, and darker afterward." She laughed. "Can't throw a stone in Duskendale without you hit some Darke or Darkwood or Dargood, but the lordly Darklyns are all gone. Lord Denys was the last o' them, the sweet young fool. Did you know the Darklyns were kings in Duskendale before the Andals come? You'd never know t'look at me, but I got me royal blood. Can you see it? 'Your Grace, another cup of ale,' I ought to make them say. 'Your Grace, the chamber pot needs emptying, and fetch in some fresh faggots, Your Bloody Grace, the fire's going out.'" She laughed again and shook the last drops from the pail. "Well, there you are. Is that water hot enough for you?"

"It will serve." The water was lukewarm.

"I'd bring up more, but it'd just slop over. A girl the size o' you, you fill a tub."

Only a cramped small tub like this one. At Harrenhal the tubs had been huge, and made of stone. The bathhouse had been thick with the steam rising off the water, and Jaime had come walking through that mist naked as his name day, looking half a corpse and half a god. *He climbed into the tub with me,* she remembered, blushing. She seized a chunk of hard lye soap and scrubbed under her arms, trying to call up Renly's face again.

By the time the water had gone cold, Brienne was as clean as she was like to get. She put on the same clothes she had taken off and girded her swordbelt tight around her hips, but her mail and helm she left behind, so as not to seem so threatening at the Dun Fort. It felt good to stretch her legs. The guards at the castle gates wore leather jacks with a badge that showed crossed warhammers upon a white saltire. "I would speak with your lord," Brienne told them.

One laughed. "Best shout out loud, then."

"Lord Rykker rode to Maidenpool with Randyll Tarly," the other said. "He left Ser Rufus Leek as castellan, to look after Lady Rykker and the young ones."

It was to Leek that they escorted her. Ser Rufus was a short, stout greybeard whose left leg ended in a stump. "You will forgive me if I do not rise," he said. Brienne offered him her letter, but Leek could not read, so he sent her to the maester, a bald man with a freckled scalp and a stiff red mustache.

When he heard the name Hollard, the maester frowned with irritation. "How often must I sing this song?" Her face must have given her away. "Did you think you were the first to come seeking after Dontos? More like the twenty-first. The gold cloaks were here within days of the king's murder, with Lord Tywin's warrant. And what do you have, pray?"

Brienne showed him the letter, with Tommen's seal and childish signature. The maester *hmmmm*ed and *hrrrr*ed, picked at the wax, and finally gave it back. "It seems in order." He climbed onto a stool and gestured Brienne to another. "I never knew Ser Dontos. He was a boy when he left Duskendale. The Hollards were a noble House once, 'tis true. You know their arms? Barry red and pink, with three golden crowns upon a blue chief. The Darklyns were petty kings during the Age of Heroes, and three took Hollard wives. Later their little realm was swallowed up by larger kingdoms, yet the Darklyns endured and the Hollards served them . . . aye, even in defiance. You know of that?"

"A little." Her own maester used to say that it was the Defiance of Duskendale that had driven King Aerys mad.

"In Duskendale they love Lord Denys still, despite the woe he brought them. 'Tis Lady Serala that they blame, his Myrish wife. The Lace Serpent, she is called. If Lord Darklyn had only wed a Staunton or a Stokeworth . . . well, you know how smallfolk will go on. The Lace Serpent filled her husband's ear with Myrish poison, they say, until Lord Denys rose against his king and took him captive. In the taking, his master-at-arms Ser Symon Hollard cut down Ser Gwayne Gaunt of the Kingsguard. For half a year Aerys was held within these very walls, whilst the King's Hand sat outside Duskendale with a mighty host. Lord Tywin had sufficient strength to storm the town any time he wished, but Lord Denys sent word that at the first sign of assault he'd kill the king."

Brienne remembered what came next. "The king was rescued," she said. "Barristan the Bold brought him out."

"He did," the maester said. "Once Lord Denys lost his hostage, he opened his gates and ended his defiance rather than let Lord Tywin take the town. He bent the knee and begged for mercy, but the king was not of a forgiving mind. Lord Denys lost his head, as did his brothers and his sister, uncles, cousins, all the lordly Darklyns. The Lace Serpent was burned alive, poor woman, though her tongue was torn out first, and her female parts, with which it was said that she had enslaved her lord. Half of Duskendale will still tell you that Aerys was too kind to her."

"And the Hollards?"

"Attainted and destroyed," said the maester. "I was forging my chain at the Citadel when this happened, but I have read the accounts of their trials and punishments. Ser Jon Hollard the Steward was wed to Lord Denys's sister and died with his wife, as did their young son, who was half-Darklyn. Robin Hollard was a squire, and when the king was seized he danced around him and pulled his beard. He died upon the rack. Ser Symon Hollard was slain by Ser Barristan during the king's escape. The Hollard lands were taken, their castle torn down, their villages put to the torch. As with the Darklyns, House Hollard was extinguished."

"Save for Dontos."

"True enough. Young Dontos was the son of Ser Steffon Hollard, the twin brother of Ser Symon, who had died of a fever some years before and had no part in the Defiance. Aerys would have taken the boy's head off nonetheless, but Ser Barristan asked that his life be spared. The king could not refuse the man who'd saved him, so Dontos was taken to King's Landing as a squire. To my knowledge he never returned to Duskendale, and why should he? He held no lands here, had neither kin nor castle. If Dontos and this northern girl helped murder our sweet king, it seems to me that they would want to put as many leagues as they could betwixt themselves and justice. Look for them in Oldtown, if you must, or across the narrow sea. Look for them in Dorne, or on the Wall. Look *elsewhere*." He rose. "I hear my ravens calling. You will forgive me if I bid you good morrow."

The walk back to the inn seemed longer than the walk to the Dun Fort, though perhaps that was only her mood. She would not find Sansa Stark in Duskendale, that seemed plain. If Ser Dontos had taken her to Oldtown or across the narrow sea, as the maester seemed to think, Brienne's quest was hopeless. *What was there for her in Oldtown?* she asked herself. *The maester never knew her, no more than he knew Hollard. She would not have gone to strangers.*

In King's Landing, Brienne had found one of Sansa's former maids doing washing in a brothel. "I served with Lord Renly before m'lady Sansa, and both turned traitor," the woman Brella complained bitterly. "No lord will touch me now, so I have to wash for whores." But when Brienne asked about Sansa, she said, "I'll tell you what I told Lord Tywin. That girl was always praying. She'd go to sept and light her candles like a proper lady, but near every night she went off to the godswood. She's gone back north, she has. That's where her *gods* are."

The north was huge, though, and Brienne had no notion which of her father's bannermen Sansa might have been most inclined to trust. *Or would she seek her own blood instead?* Though all of her siblings had been slain, Brienne knew that Sansa still had an uncle and a bastard half brother on the Wall, serving in the Night's Watch. Another uncle, Edmure Tully, was a captive at the Twins, but *his* uncle Ser Brynden still held Riverrun. And Lady Catelyn's younger sister ruled the Vale. *Blood calls to blood.* Sansa might well have run to one of them. Which one, though?

The Wall was too far, surely, and a bleak and bitter place besides. And to reach Riverrun the girl would need to cross the war-torn riverlands and pass through the Lannister siege lines. The Eyrie would be simpler, and Lady Lysa would surely welcome her sister's daughter . . .

Ahead, the alley bent. Somehow Brienne had taken a wrong turn. She found herself in a dead end, a small muddy yard where three pigs were rooting round a low stone well. One squealed at the sight of her, and an old woman drawing water looked her up and down suspiciously. "What would you be wanting?"

"I was looking for the Seven Swords."

"Back the way you come. Left at the sept."

"I thank you." Brienne turned to retrace her steps, and walked headfirst into someone hurrying round the bend. The collision knocked him off his feet, and he landed on his arse in the mud. "Pardons," she murmured. He was only a boy; a scrawny lad with straight, thin hair and a sty beneath one eye. "Are you hurt?" She offered a hand to help him up, but the boy squirmed back away from her on heels and elbows. He could not have been more than ten or twelve, though he wore a chainmail byrnie and had a longsword in a leather sheath slung across his back. "Do I know you?" Brienne asked. His face seemed vaguely familiar, though she could not think from where.

"No. You don't. You never . . ." He scrambled to his feet. "F-f-forgive me. My lady. I wasn't looking. I mean, I was, but down. I was looking down. At my feet." The boy took to his heels, plunging headlong back the way he'd come.

Something about him roused all of Brienne's suspicions, but she was not about to chase him through the streets of Duskendale. *Outside the gates this morning, that was where I saw him,* she realized. *He was riding a piebald rounsey.* And it seemed as if she had seen him somewhere else as well, but where?

By the time Brienne found the Seven Swords again, the common room was crowded. Four septas sat closest to the fire, in robes stained and dusty from the road. Elsewhere locals filled the benches, sopping up bowls of hot crab stew with chunks of bread. The smell made her stomach rumble, but she saw no empty seats. Then a voice behind her said, "M'lady, here, have my place." Not until he hopped off the bench did Brienne realize that the speaker was a dwarf. The little man was not quite five feet tall. His nose was veined and bulbous, his teeth red from sourleaf, and he was dressed in the brown roughspun robes of a holy brother, with the iron hammer of the Smith dangling down about his thick neck.

"Keep your seat," she said. "I can stand as well as you."

"Aye, but my head is not so apt to knock upon the ceiling." The dwarf's speech was coarse but courteous. Brienne could see the crown of his scalp where he had shaved it. Many holy brothers wore such tonsures. Septa Roelle once told her that it was meant to show that they had nothing to hide from the Father. "Can't the Father see through hair?" Brienne had asked. *A stupid thing to say.* She had been a slow child; Septa Roelle often told her so. She felt near as stupid now, so she took the little man's place at the end of the bench, signaled for stew, and turned to thank the dwarf. "Do you serve some holy house in Duskendale, brother?"

"'Twas nearer Maidenpool, m'lady, but the wolves burned us out," the man replied, gnawing on a heel of bread. "We rebuilt as best we could, until some sellswords come. I could not say whose men they were, but they took our pigs and killed the brothers. I squeezed inside a hollow log and hid, but t'others were too big. It took me a long time to bury them all, but the Smith, he gave me strength. When that was done I dug up a few coins the elder brother had hid by and set off by myself."

"I met some other brothers going to King's Landing."

"Aye, there's hundreds on the roads. Not only brothers. Septons too, and smallfolk. Sparrows all. Might be I'm a sparrow too. The Smith, he made me small enough." He chuckled. "And what's your sad tale, m'lady?"

"I am looking for my sister. She's highborn, only three-and-ten, a pretty maid with blue eyes and auburn hair. You may have seen her traveling with a man. A knight, perhaps a fool. There's gold for the man who helps me find her."

"Gold?" The brother gave her a red smile. "A bowl of that crab stew would be enough reward for me, but I fear I cannot help you. Fools I've met, and plenty, but not so many pretty maids." He cocked his head and thought a moment. "There was a fool at Maidenpool, now that I think of it. He was clad in rags and dirt, as near as I could tell, but under the dirt was motley."

Did Dontos Hollard wear motley? No one had told Brienne that he did . . . but no one had ever said he didn't, either. Why would the man be in rags, though? Had some misfortune overtaken him and Sansa after they fled King's Landing? That could well be, with the roads so dangerous. *It might not have been him at all.* "Did this fool have a red nose, full of broken veins?"

"I could not swear to that. I confess, I paid him little heed. I'd gone to Maidenpool after burying my brothers, thinking that I might find a ship to take me to King's Landing. I first glimpsed the fool down by the docks. He had a furtive air to him and took care to avoid Lord Tarly's soldiers. Later, I encountered him again, at the Stinking Goose."

"The Stinking Goose?" she said, uncertain.

"An unsavory place," the dwarf admitted. "Lord Tarly's men patrol the port at Maidenpool, but the Goose is always full of sailors, and sailors have been known to smuggle men aboard their ships, if the price is right. This fool was seeking passage for three across the narrow sea. I oft saw him there, talking with oarsmen off the galleys. Sometimes he would sing a funny song."

"Seeking passage for *three*? Not two?"

"Three, m'lady. That I'd swear to, by the Seven." *Three,* she thought. *Sansa, Ser Dontos . . . but who would be the third? The Imp?* "Did the fool find his ship?"

"That I could not say," the dwarf told her, "but one night some of Lord Tarly's soldiers visited the Goose looking for him, and a few days later I heard another man boasting that he'd fooled a fool and had the gold to prove it. He was drunk, and buying ale for everyone."

"'Fooled a fool,'" she said. "What did he mean by that?"

"I could not tell you. His name was Nimble Dick, though, that I do recall." The dwarf spread his hands. "I fear that's all that I can offer you, aside from a small man's prayers."

True to her word, Brienne bought him his bowl of hot crab stew . . . and some hot fresh bread and a cup of wine as well. As he ate it, standing by her side, she mulled what he had told her. *Could the Imp have joined them?* If Tyrion Lannister were behind Sansa's disappearance, and not Dontos Hollard, it stood to reason that they would need to flee across the narrow sea.

When the little man was done with his bowl of stew, he finished what was left of hers as well. "You should eat more," he said. "A woman big as you needs t' keep her strength up. It is not far to Maidenpool, but the road is perilous these days."

I know. It was on that very road that Ser Cleos Frey had died, and she and Ser Jaime had been taken by the Bloody Mummers. *Jaime tried to kill me,* she remembered, *though he was gaunt and weak, and his wrists were chained.* It had been a close thing, even so, but that was before Zollo hacked his hand off. Zollo and Rorge and Shagwell would have raped her half a hundred times if Ser Jaime had not told them she was worth her weight in sapphires.

"M'lady? You look sad. Are you thinking of your sister?" The dwarf patted her on the hand. "The Crone will light your way to her, never fear. The Maiden will keep her safe."

"I pray that you are right."

"I am." He bowed. "But now I must be on my way. I've a long way yet to go to reach King's Landing."

"Do you have a horse? A mule?"

"Two mules." The little man laughed. "There they are, at the bottom of my legs. They get me where I want t' go." He bowed, and waddled to the door, swaying with each step.

She remained at the table after he had gone, lingering over a cup of watered wine. Brienne did not oft drink wine, but once in a great while she found it helped to settle her belly. *And where do I want to go?* she asked herself. *To Maidenpool, to look for a man named Nimble Dick in a place called the Stinking Goose?*

When last she had seen Maidenpool, the town had been a desolation, its lord shut up inside his castle, its smallfolk dead or fled or hiding. She remembered burned houses and empty streets, smashed and broken gates. Feral dogs had skulked along behind their horses, whilst swollen corpses floated like huge pale water lilies atop the spring-fed pool that gave the town its name. *Jaime sang "Six Maids in a Pool," and laughed when I begged him to be quiet.* And Randyll Tarly was at Maidenpool as well, another reason for her to avoid the town. She might do better to take ship for Gulltown or White Harbor. *I could do both, though. Pay a call on the Stinking Goose and talk to this Nimble Dick, then find a ship at Maidenpool to take me farther north.*

The common room had begun to empty. Brienne tore a chunk of bread in half, listening to the talk at the other tables. Most of it concerned the death of Lord Tywin Lannister. "Murdered by his own son, they say," a local man was saying, a cobbler by the look of him, "that vile little dwarf."

"And the king is just a boy," said the oldest of the four septas. "Who is to rule us till he comes of age?"

"Lord Tywin's brother," said a guardsman. "Or that Lord Tyrell, might be. Or the Kingslayer."

"Not him," declared the innkeep. "Not that oath-breaker." He spat into the fire. Brienne let the bread fall from her hands and wiped the crumbs off on her breeches. She'd heard enough.

That night she dreamed herself in Renly's tent again. All the candles were guttering out, and the cold was thick around her. Something was moving through green darkness, something foul and horrible was hurtling toward her king. She wanted to protect him, but her limbs felt stiff and frozen, and it took more strength than she had just to lift her hand. And when the shadow sword sliced through the green steel gorget and the blood began to flow, she saw that the dying king was not Renly after all but Jaime Lannister, and she had failed him.

The captain's sister found her in the common room,

drinking a cup of milk and honey with three raw eggs mixed in. "You did beautifully," she said, when the woman showed her the freshly painted shield. It was more a picture than a proper coat of arms, and the sight of it took her back through the long years, to the cool dark of her father's armory. She remembered how she'd run her fingertips across the cracked and fading paint, over the green leaves of the tree, and along the path of the falling star.

Brienne paid the captain's sister half again the sum they had agreed, and slung the shield across one shoulder when she left the inn, after buying some hardbread, cheese, and flour from the cook. She left the town by the north gate, riding slowly through the fields and farms where the worst of the fighting had been, when the wolves came down on Duskendale.

Lord Randyll Tarly had commanded Joffrey's army, made up of westermen and stormlanders and knights from the Reach. Those men of his who had died here had been carried back inside the walls, to rest in heroes' tombs beneath the septs of Duskendale. The northern dead, far more numerous, were buried in a common grave beside the sea. Above the cairn that marked their resting place, the victors had raised a rough-hewn wooden marker. HERE LIE THE WOLVES was all it said. Brienne stopped beside it and said a silent prayer for them, and for Catelyn Stark and her son Robb and all the men who'd died with them as well.

She remembered the night that Lady Catelyn had learned her sons were dead, the two young boys she'd left at Winterfell to keep them safe. Brienne had known that something was terribly amiss. She had asked her if there had been news of her sons. "I have no sons but Robb," Lady Catelyn had replied. She had sounded as if a knife were twisting her belly. Brienne had reached across the table to give her comfort, but she stopped before her fingers brushed the older woman's, for fear that she would flinch away. Lady Catelyn had turned over her hands, to show Brienne the scars on her palms and fingers where a knife once bit deep into her flesh. Then she had begun to talk about her daughters. "Sansa was a little lady," she had said, "always courteous and eager to please. She loved tales of knightly valor. She will grow into a woman far more beautiful than I, you can see that. I would often brush her hair myself. She had auburn hair, thick and soft . . . the red in it would shine like copper in the light of the torches."

She had spoken of Arya too, her younger daughter, but Arya was lost, most likely dead by now. Sansa, though . . . *I will find her, my lady,* Brienne swore to Lady Catelyn's restless shade. *I will never stop looking. I will give up my life if need be, give up my honor, give up all my dreams, but I will find her.*

Beyond the battleground the road ran beside the shore, between the surging grey-green sea and a line of low limestone hills. Brienne was not the only traveler on the road. There were fishing villages up along the coast for many leagues, and the fisherfolk used this road to take their fish to market. She rode past a fishwife and her daughters, walking home with empty baskets on their shoulders. In her armor, they took her for a knight until they saw her face. Then the girls whispered to one another and gave her looks. "Have you seen a maid of three-and-ten along the road?" she asked them. "A highborn maid with blue eyes and auburn hair?" Ser Shadrich had made her wary, but she had to keep on trying. "She may have been traveling with a fool." But they only shook their heads and giggled at her behind their hands.

In the first village she came to, barefoot boys ran along

beside her horse. She had donned her helm, stung by the giggles of the fisherfolk, so they took her for a man. One boy offered to sell her clams, one offered crabs, and one offered her his sister.

Brienne bought three crabs from the second boy. By the time she left the village it had begun to rain, and the wind was rising. *Storm coming,* she thought, glancing out to sea. The raindrops pinged against the steel of her helm, making her ears ring as she rode, but it was better than being out there in a boat.

An hour farther north, the road divided at a pile of tumbled stones that marked the ruins of a small castle. The right-hand fork followed the coast, meandering up along the shore toward Crackclaw Point, a dismal land of bogs and pine barrens; the left-hand ran through hills and fields and woods to Maidenpool. The rain was falling more heavily by then. Brienne dismounted and led her mare off the road to take shelter amongst the ruins. The course of the castle walls could still be discerned amongst the brambles, weeds, and wild elms, but the stones that had made them up were strewn like a child's blocks between the roads. Part of the main keep still stood, however. Its triple towers were grey granite, like the broken walls, but their merlons were yellow sandstone. *Three crowns,* she realized, as she gazed at them through the rain. *Three golden crowns.* This had been a Hollard castle. Ser Dontos had been born here, like as not.

She led her mare through the rubble to the keep's main entrance. Of the door only rusted iron hinges remained, but the roof was still sound, and it was dry within. Brienne tied her mare to a wall sconce, took off her helm, and shook out her hair. She was searching for some dry wood to light a fire when she heard the sound of another horse, coming closer. Some instinct made her step back into the shadows, where she could not be seen from the road. This was the very road where she and Ser Jaime had been captured. She did not intend to suffer that again.

The rider was a small man. *The Mad Mouse,* she thought, at her first sight of him. *Somehow he's followed me.* Her hand went to her sword hilt, and she found herself wondering if Ser Shadrich would think her easy prey just because she was a woman. Lord Grandison's castellan had once made that error. Humfrey Wagstaff was his name; a proud old man of five-and-sixty, with a nose like a hawk and a spotted head. The day they were betrothed, he warned Brienne that he would expect her to be a proper woman once they'd wed. "I will not have my lady wife cavorting about in man's mail. On this you shall obey me, lest I be forced to chastise you."

She was sixteen and no stranger to a sword, but still shy despite her prowess in the yard. Yet somehow she had found the courage to tell Ser Humfrey that she would accept chastisement only from a man who could outfight her. The old knight purpled, but agreed to don his own armor to teach her a woman's proper place. They fought with blunted tourney weapons, so Brienne's mace had no spikes. She broke Ser Humfrey's collarbone, two ribs, and their betrothal. He was her third prospective husband, and her last. Her father did not insist again.

If it *was* Ser Shadrich dogging her heels, she might well have a fight on her hands. She did not intend to partner with the man or let him follow her to Sansa. *He had the sort of easy arrogance that comes with skill at arms,* she thought, *but he was small. I'll have the reach on him, and I should be stronger too.*

Brienne was as strong as most knights, and her old master-at-arms used to say that she was quicker than any woman her size had any right to be. The gods had given her stamina too, which Ser Goodwin deemed a noble gift. Fighting with sword and shield was a wearisome business, and victory oft went to the man with most endurance. Ser Goodwin had taught her to fight cautiously, to conserve her strength while letting her foes spend theirs in furious attacks. "Men will always underestimate you," he said, "and their pride will make them want to vanquish you quickly, lest it be said that a woman tried them sorely." She had learned the truth of that once she went into the world. Even Jaime Lannister had come at her that way, in the woods by Maidenpool. If the gods were good, the Mad Mouse would make the same mistake. *He may be a seasoned knight,* she thought, *but he is no Jaime Lannister.* She slid her sword out of its scabbard.

But it was not Ser Shadrich's chestnut courser that drew up where the road forked, but a broken-down old piebald rounsey with a skinny boy upon his back. When Brienne saw the horse she drew back in confusion. *Only some boy,* she thought, until she glimpsed the face beneath his hood. *The boy in Duskendale, the one who bumped into me. It's him.*

The boy never gave the ruined castle a glance, but looked down one road, then the other. After a moment's hesitation, he turned the rounsey toward the hills and plodded on. Brienne watched him vanish through the falling rain, and suddenly it came to her that she had seen this same boy in Rosby. *He is stalking me,* she realized, *but that's a game that two can play.* She untied her mare, climbed back into the saddle, and went after him.

The boy was staring at the ground as he rode, watching the ruts in the road fill up with water. The rain muffled the sound of her approach, and no doubt his hood played a part as well. He never looked back once, until Brienne trotted up behind him and gave the rounsey a whack across the rump with the flat of her longsword.

The horse reared, and the skinny boy went flying, his cloak flapping like a pair of wings. He landed in the mud and came up with dirt and dead brown grass between his teeth to find Brienne standing over him. It was the same boy, beyond a doubt. She recognized the sty. "Who are you?" she demanded.

The boy's mouth worked soundlessly. His eyes were big as eggs. "Puh," was all he could manage. "Puh." His chainmail byrnie made a rattling sound when he shivered. "Puh. Puh."

"Please?" said Brienne. "Are you saying *please*?" She laid the point of her sword on the apple of his throat. "Please tell me who you are, and why you're following me."

"Not puh-puh-*please*." He stuck a finger in his mouth, and flicked away a clump of mud, spitting. "Puh-puh-*Pod*. My name. Puh-puh-*Podrick*. Puh-Payne."

Brienne lowered her sword. She felt a rush of sympathy for the boy. She remembered a day at Evenfall, and a young knight with a rose in his hand. *He brought the rose to give to me.* Or so her septa told her. All she had to do was welcome him to her father's castle. He was eighteen, with long red hair that tumbled to his shoulders. She was twelve, tightly laced into a stiff new gown, its bodice bright with garnets. The two of them were of a height, but she could not look him in the eye, nor say the simple words her septa had taught her. *Ser Ronnet. I welcome you to my lord father's hall. It is good to look upon your face at last.*

"Why are you following me?" she demanded of the boy. "Were you told to spy upon me? Do you belong to Varys, or the queen?"

"No. Not neither. No one."

Brienne put his age at ten, but she was terrible at judging how old a child was. She always thought they were younger than they were, perhaps because she had always been big for her age. *Freakish big,* Septa Roelle used to say, *and mannish.* "This road is too dangerous for a boy alone."

"Not for a *squire*. I'm his squire. The Hand's squire."

"Lord Tywin?" Brienne sheathed her blade.

"No. Not that Hand. The one before. His son. I fought with him in the battle. I shouted '*Halfman! Halfman!*'"

The Imp's squire. Brienne had not even known he had one. Tyrion Lannister was no knight. He might have been expected to have a serving boy or two to attend him, she supposed, a page and a cupbearer, someone to help dress him. But a *squire*? "Why are you stalking after me?" she said. "What do you want?"

"To find her." The boy got to his feet. "His lady. You're looking for her. Brella told me. She's his wife. Not Brella, Lady Sansa. So I thought, if you found her . . ." His face twisted in sudden anguish. "I'm his *squire*," he repeated, as the rain ran down his face, "but he *left* me."

SANSA

Once, when she was just a little girl, a wandering singer had stayed with them at Winterfell for half a year. An old man he was, with white hair and windburnt cheeks, but he sang of knights and quests and ladies fair, and Sansa had cried bitter tears when he left them, and begged her father not to let him go. "The man has played us every song he knows thrice over," Lord Eddard told her gently. "I cannot keep him here against his will. You need not weep, though. I promise you, other singers will come."

They hadn't, though, not for a year or more. Sansa had prayed to the Seven in their sept and old gods of the heart tree, asking them to bring the old man back, or better still to send another singer, young and handsome. But the gods never answered, and the halls of Winterfell stayed silent.

But that was when she was a little girl, and foolish. She

was a maiden now, three-and-ten and flowered. All her nights were full of song, and by day she prayed for silence.

If the Eyrie had been made like other castles, only rats and gaolers would have heard the dead man singing. Dungeon walls were thick enough to swallow songs and screams alike. But the sky cells had a wall of empty air, so every chord the dead man played flew free to echo off the stony shoulders of the Giant's Lance. And the songs he chose . . . He sang of the Dance of the Dragons, of fair Jonquil and her fool, of Jenny of Oldstones and the Prince of Dragonflies. He sang of betrayals, and murders most foul, of hanged men and bloody vengeance. He sang of grief and sadness.

No matter where she went in the castle, Sansa could not escape the music. It floated up the winding tower steps, found her naked in her bath, supped with her at dusk, and stole into her bedchamber even when she latched the shutters tight. It came in on the cold thin air, and like the air, it chilled her. Though it had not snowed upon the Eyrie since the day that Lady Lysa fell, the nights had all been bitter cold.

The singer's voice was strong and sweet. Sansa thought he sounded better than he ever had before, his voice richer somehow, full of pain and fear and longing. She did not understand why the gods would have given such a voice to such a wicked man. *He would have taken me by force on the Fingers if Petyr had not set Ser Lothor to watch over me,* she had to remind herself. *And he played to drown out my cries when Aunt Lysa tried to kill me.*

That did not make the songs any easier to hear. "Please," she begged Lord Petyr, "can't you make him stop?"

"I gave the man my word, sweetling." Petyr Baelish, Lord of Harrenhal, Lord Paramount of the Trident, and

Lord Protector of the Eyrie and the Vale of Arryn, looked up from the letter he was writing. He had written a hundred letters since Lady Lysa's fall. Sansa had seen the ravens coming and going from the rookery. "I'd sooner suffer his singing than listen to his sobbing."

It is better that he sings, yes, but . . . "Must he play all night, my lord? Lord Robert cannot sleep. He cries . . ."

". . . for his mother. That cannot be helped, the wench is dead." Petyr shrugged. "It will not be much longer. Lord Nestor is making his ascent on the morrow."

Sansa had met Lord Nestor Royce once before, after Petyr's wedding to her aunt. Royce was the Keeper of the Gates of the Moon, the great castle that stood at the base of the mountain and guarded the steps up to the Eyrie. The wedding party had guested with him overnight before beginning their ascent. Lord Nestor had scarce looked at her twice, but the prospect of him coming here terrified her. He was High Steward of the Vale as well, Jon Arryn's trusted liege man, and Lady Lysa's. "He won't . . . you won't let Lord Nestor see Marillion, will you?"

Her horror must have shown on her face, since Petyr put down his quill. "On the contrary. I shall insist on it." He beckoned her to take the seat beside him. "We have come to an agreement, Marillion and I. Mord can be most persuasive. And if our singer disappoints us and sings a song we do not care to hear, why, you and I need only say he lies. Whom do you imagine Lord Nestor will believe?"

"Us?" Sansa wished she could be certain.

"Of course. Our lies will profit him."

The solar was warm, the fire crackling merrily, but Sansa shivered all the same. "Yes, but . . . but what if . . ."

"What if Lord Nestor values honor more than profit?" Petyr put his arm around her. "What if it is truth he wants, and justice for his murdered lady?" He smiled. "I know

Lord Nestor, sweetling. Do you imagine I'd ever let him harm my daughter?"

I am not your daughter, she thought. *I am Sansa Stark, Lord Eddard's daughter and Lady Catelyn's, the blood of Winterfell.* She did not say it, though. If not for Petyr Baelish it would have been *Sansa* who went spinning through a cold blue sky to stony death six hundred feet below, instead of Lysa Arryn. *He is so bold.* Sansa wished she had his courage. She wanted to crawl back into bed and hide beneath her blanket, to sleep and sleep. She had not slept a whole night through since Lysa Arryn's death. "Couldn't you tell Lord Nestor that I am . . . indisposed, or . . ."

"He will want to hear your account of Lysa's death."

"My lord, if . . . if Marillion tells what truly . . ."

"If he lies, you mean?"

"Lies? Yes . . . if he lies, if it is my tale against his, and Lord Nestor looks in my eyes and sees how scared I am . . ."

"A touch of fear will not be out of place, Alayne. You've seen a fearful thing. Nestor will be moved." Petyr studied her eyes, as if seeing them for the first time. "You have your mother's eyes. Honest eyes, and innocent. Blue as a sunlit sea. When you are a little older, many a man will drown in those eyes."

Sansa did not know what to say to that.

"All you need do is tell Lord Nestor the same tale that you told Lord Robert," Petyr went on.

Robert is only a sick little boy, she thought, *Lord Nestor is a man grown, stern and suspicious.* Robert was not strong and had to be protected, even from the truth. "Some lies are love," Petyr had assured her. She reminded him of that. "When we lied to Lord Robert, that was just to spare him," she said.

"And this lie may spare *us.* Else you and I must leave the Eyrie by the same door Lysa used." Petyr picked up his quill again. "We shall serve him lies and Arbor gold, and he'll drink them down and ask for more, I promise you."

He is serving me lies as well, Sansa realized. They were comforting lies, though, and she thought them kindly meant. *A lie is not so bad if it is kindly meant.* If only she believed them . . .

The things her aunt had said just before she fell still troubled Sansa greatly. "Ravings," Petyr called them. "My wife was mad, you saw that for yourself." And so she had. *All I did was build a snow castle, and she meant to push me out the Moon Door. Petyr saved me. He loved my mother well, and . . .*

And her? How could she doubt it? He had saved her.

He saved Alayne, his daughter, a voice within her whispered. But she was Sansa too . . . and sometimes it seemed to her that the Lord Protector was two people as well. He was Petyr, her protector, warm and funny and gentle . . . but he was also Littlefinger, the lord she'd known at King's Landing, smiling slyly and stroking his beard as he whispered in Queen Cersei's ear. And Littlefinger was no friend of hers. When Joff had her beaten, the Imp defended her, not Littlefinger. When the mob sought to rape her, the Hound carried her to safety, not Littlefinger. When the Lannisters wed her to Tyrion against her will, Ser Garlan the Gallant gave her comfort, not Littlefinger. Littlefinger never lifted so much as his little finger for her.

Except to get me out. He did that for me. I thought it was Ser Dontos, my poor old drunken Florian, but it was Petyr all the while. Littlefinger was only a mask he had to wear. Only sometimes Sansa found it hard to tell where the man ended and the mask began. Littlefinger and Lord Petyr looked so very much alike. She would have fled them both, perhaps, but there was nowhere for her to go. Winterfell was burned and desolate, Bran and Rickon dead and cold. Robb had been betrayed and murdered at the Twins, along with their lady mother. Tyrion had been put to death for killing Joffrey, and if she ever returned to King's Landing the queen would have her head as well. The aunt she'd hoped would keep her safe had tried to murder her instead. Her uncle Edmure was a captive of the Freys, while her great-uncle the Blackfish was under siege at Riverrun. *I have no place but here,* Sansa thought miserably, *and no true friend but Petyr.*

That night the dead man sang "The Day They Hanged Black Robin," "The Mother's Tears," and "The Rains of Castamere." Then he stopped for a while, but just as Sansa began to drift off he started to play again. He sang "Six Sorrows," "Fallen Leaves," and "Alysanne." *Such sad songs,* she thought. When she closed her eyes she could see him in his sky cell, huddled in a corner away from the cold black sky, crouched beneath a fur with his woodharp cradled against his chest. *I must not pity him,* she told herself. *He was vain and cruel, and soon he will be dead.* She could not save him. And why should she want to? Marillion tried to rape her, and Petyr had saved her life not once but twice. *Some lies you have to tell.* Lies had been all that kept her alive in King's Landing. If she had not lied to Joffrey, his Kingsguard would have beat her bloody.

After "Alysanne" the singer stopped again, long enough for Sansa to snatch an hour's rest. But as the first light of dawn was prying at her shutters, she heard the soft strains of "On a Misty Morn" drifting up from below, and woke at once. That was more properly a woman's song, a lament sung by a mother on the dawn after some terrible battle, as she searches amongst the dead for the body of her only son. *The mother sings her grief for her dead son,* Sansa thought, *but Marillion grieves for his fingers, for his eyes.* The words rose like arrows and pierced her in the darkness.

Oh, have you seen my boy, good ser?
His hair is chestnut brown
He promised he'd come back to me
Our home's in Wendish Town.

Sansa covered her ears with a goose down pillow to shut out the rest of it, but it was no good. Day had come and she had woken, and Lord Nestor Royce was coming up the mountain.

The High Steward and his party reached the Eyrie in the late afternoon, with the valley gold and red beneath them and the wind rising. He brought his son Ser Albar, along with a dozen knights and a score of men-at-arms. *So many strangers.* Sansa looked at their faces anxiously, wondering if they were friends or foes.

Petyr welcomed his visitors in a black velvet doublet with grey sleeves that matched his woolen breeches and lent a certain darkness to his grey-green eyes. Maester Colemon stood beside him, his chain of many metals hanging loose about his long, skinny neck. Although the maester was much the taller of the two men, it was the Lord Protector who drew the eye. He had put away his smiles for the day, it seemed. He listened solemnly as Royce introduced the knights who had accompanied him, then said, "My lords are welcome here. You know our Maester Colemon, of course. Lord Nestor, you will recall Alayne, my natural daughter?"

"To be sure." Lord Nestor Royce was a bullnecked, barrel-chested, balding man with a grey-shot beard and a stern look. He inclined his head a whole half inch in greeting.

Sansa curtsied, too frightened to speak for fear she might misspeak. Petyr drew her to her feet. "Sweetling, be a good girl and bring Lord Robert to the High Hall to receive his guests."

"Yes, Father." Her voice sounded thin and strained. *A liar's voice,* she thought as she hurried up the steps and across the gallery to the Moon Tower. *A guilty voice.*

Gretchel and Maddy were helping Robert Arryn squirm into his breeches when Sansa stepped into his bedchamber. The Lord of the Eyrie had been crying again. His eyes were red and raw, his lashes crusty, his nose swollen and runny. A trail of snot glistened underneath one nostril, and his lower lip was bloody where he'd bitten it. *Lord Nestor must not see him like this,* Sansa thought, despairing. "Gretchel, fetch me the washbasin." She took the boy by the hand and drew him to the bed. "Did my Sweetrobin sleep well last night?"

"No." He sniffed. "I never slept one bit, Alayne. He was *singing* again, and my *door* was locked. I called for them to let me out, but no one ever came. Someone locked me in my room."

"That was wicked of them." Dipping a soft cloth into the warm water, she began to clean his face . . . gently, oh so gently. If you scrubbed Robert too briskly, he might begin to shake. The boy was frail, and terribly small for his age. He was eight, but Sansa had known bigger five-year-olds.

Robert's lip quivered. "I was going to come sleep with you."

I know you were. Sweetrobin had been accustomed to crawling in beside his mother, until she wed Lord Petyr. Since Lady Lysa's death he had taken to wandering the Eyrie in quest of other beds. The one he liked best was Sansa's . . . which was why she had asked Ser Lothor

Brune to lock his door last night. She would not have minded if he only slept, but he was always trying to nuzzle at her breasts, and when he had his shaking spells he often wet the bed.

"Lord Nestor Royce has come up from the Gates to see you." Sansa wiped beneath his nose.

"I don't want to see *him*," he said. "I want a story. A story of the Winged Knight."

"After," Sansa said. "First you must see Lord Nestor."

"Lord Nestor has a mole," he said, squirming. Robert was afraid of men with moles. "Mommy said he was *dreadful*."

"My poor Sweetrobin." Sansa smoothed his hair back. "You miss her, I know. Lord Petyr misses her too. He loved her just as you do." That was a lie, though kindly meant. The only woman Petyr ever loved was Sansa's murdered mother. He had confessed as much to Lady Lysa just before he pushed her out the Moon Door. *She was mad and dangerous. She murdered her own lord husband, and would have murdered me if Petyr had not come along to save me.*

Robert did not need to know that, though. He was only a sick little boy who'd loved his mother. "There," Sansa said, "you look a proper lord now. Maddy, fetch his cloak." It was lambswool, soft and warm, a handsome sky-blue that set off the cream color of his tunic. She fastened it about his shoulders with a silver brooch in the shape of a crescent moon, and took him by the hand. Robert came meekly for once.

The High Hall had been closed since Lady Lysa's fall, and it gave Sansa a chill to enter it again. The hall was long and grand and beautiful, she supposed, but she did not like it here. It was a pale cold place at the best of times. The slender pillars looked like fingerbones, and the blue veins in the white marble brought to mind the veins in an old crone's legs. Though fifty silver sconces lined the walls, less than a dozen torches had been lit, so shadows danced upon the floors and pooled in every corner. Their footsteps echoed off the marble, and Sansa could hear the wind rattling at the Moon Door. *I must not look at it,* she told herself, *else I'll start to shake as badly as Robert.*

With Maddy's help, she got Robert seated on his weirwood throne with a stack of pillows underneath him and sent word that his lordship would receive his guests. Two guards in sky-blue cloaks opened the doors at the lower end of the hall, and Petyr ushered them in and down the long blue carpet that ran between the rows of bone-white pillars.

The boy greeted Lord Nestor with squeaky courtesy and made no mention of his mole. When the High Steward asked about his lady mother, Robert's hands began to tremble ever so slightly. "Marillion hurt my mother. He threw her out the Moon Door."

"Did your lordship see this happen?" asked Ser Marwyn Belmore, a lanky ginger-headed knight who had been Lysa's captain of guards till Petyr had put Ser Lothor Brune in his place.

"Alayne saw it," the boy said. "And my lord stepfather."

Lord Nestor looked at her. Ser Albar, Ser Marwyn, Maester Colemon, all of them were looking. *She was my aunt but she wanted to kill me,* Sansa thought. *She dragged me to the Moon Door and tried to push me out. I never wanted a kiss, I was building a castle in the snow.* She hugged herself to keep from shaking.

"Forgive her, my lords," Petyr Baelish said softly. "She still has nightmares of that day. Small wonder if she cannot bear to speak of it." He came up behind her and put his hands gently on her shoulders. "I know how hard this is for you, Alayne, but our friends must hear the truth."

"Yes." Her throat felt so dry and tight it almost hurt to speak. "I saw . . . I was with the Lady Lysa when . . ." A tear rolled down her cheek. *That's good, a tear is good.* ". . . when Marillion . . . pushed her." And she told the tale again, hardly hearing the words as they spilled out of her.

Before she was half-done Robert began to cry, the pillows shifting perilously beneath him. "He killed my *mother.* I want him to fly!" The trembling in his hands had grown worse, and his arms were shaking too. The boy's head jerked and his teeth began to chatter. *"Fly!"* he shrieked. *"Fly, fly."* His arms and legs flailed wildly. Lothor Brune strode to the dais in time to catch the boy as he slipped from his throne. Maester Colemon was just a step behind, though there was naught that he could do.

Helpless as the rest, Sansa could only stand and watch as the shaking spell ran its course. One of Robert's legs kicked Ser Lothor in the face. Brune cursed, but still held on as the boy twitched and flailed and wet himself. Their visitors said not a word; Lord Nestor at least had seen these fits before. It was long moments before Robert's spasms began to subside, and seemed even longer. By the end, the little lordling was so weak he could not stand. "Best take his lordship back to bed and bleed him," Lord Petyr said. Brune lifted the boy in his arms and carried him from the hall. Maester Colemon followed, grim-faced.

When their footsteps died away there was no sound in the High Hall of the Eyrie. Sansa could hear the night wind moaning outside and scratching at the Moon Door. She was very cold and very tired. *Must I tell the tale again?* she wondered.

But she must have told it well enough. Lord Nestor

cleared his throat. "I misliked that singer from the first," he grumbled. "I urged Lady Lysa to send him away. Many a time I urged her."

"You always gave her good counsel, my lord," Petyr said.

"She took no heed of it," Royce complained. "She heard me grudgingly and took no heed."

"My lady was too trusting for this world." Petyr spoke so tenderly that Sansa would have believed he'd loved his wife. "Lysa could not see the evil in men, only the good. Marillion sang sweet songs, and she mistook that for his nature."

"He called us pigs," Ser Albar Royce said. A blunt broad-shouldered knight who shaved his chin but cultivated thick black side-whiskers that framed his homely face like hedgerows, Ser Albar was a younger version of his father. "He made a song about two pigs snuffling round a mountain, eating a falcon's leavings. That was meant to be us, but when I said so he laughed at me. 'Why, ser, 'tis a song about some pigs,' he said."

"He made mock of me as well," Ser Marwyn Belmore said. "Ser Ding-Dong, he named me. When I vowed I'd cut his tongue out, he ran to Lady Lysa and hid behind her skirts."

"As oft he did," Lord Nestor said. "The man was craven, but the favor Lady Lysa showed him made him insolent. She dressed him like a lord, gave him gold rings and a moonstone belt."

"Even Lord Jon's favorite falcon." The knight's doublet showed the six white candles of Waxley. "His lordship loved that bird. King Robert gave it to him."

Petyr Baelish sighed. "It was unseemly," he agreed, "and I put an end to it. Lysa agreed to send him away. That was why she met him here, that day. I should have been with her, but I never dreamt . . . if I had not insisted . . . it was I who killed her."

No, Sansa thought, *you mustn't say that, you mustn't tell them, you mustn't.* But Albar Royce was shaking his head. "No, my lord, you must not blame yourself," he said.

"This was the singer's work," his father agreed. "Bring him up, Lord Petyr. Let us write an end to this sorry business."

Petyr Baelish composed himself, and said, "As you wish, my lord." He turned to his guardsmen and spoke a command, and the singer was fetched up from the dungeons. The gaoler Mord came with him, a monstrous man with small black eyes and a lopsided, scarred face. One ear and part of his cheek had been cleaved off in some battle, but twenty stone of pallid white flesh remained. His clothes fit poorly and had a rank, ripe smell.

Marillion by contrast looked almost elegant. Someone had bathed him and dressed him in a pair of sky-blue breeches and a loose-fitting white tunic with puffed sleeves, belted with a silvery sash that had been a gift from Lady Lysa. White silk gloves covered his hands, while a white silk bandage spared the lords the sight of his eyes.

Mord stood behind him with a lash. When the gaoler prodded him in the ribs, the singer went to one knee. "Good lords, I beg your forgiveness."

Lord Nestor scowled. "You confess your crime?"

"If I had eyes I should weep." The singer's voice, so strong and sure by night, was cracked and whispery now. "I loved her so, I could not bear to see her in another's arms, to know she shared his bed. I meant no harm to my sweet lady, I swear it. I barred the door so no one could disturb us whilst I declared my passion, but Lady Lysa was so cold . . . when she told that she was carrying Lord Petyr's child, a . . . a madness seized me . . ."

Sansa stared at his hands while he spoke. Fat Maddy claimed that Mord had taken off three of his fingers, both pinkies and a ring finger. His little fingers did appear somewhat stiffer than the others, but with those gloves it was hard to be certain. *It might have been no more than a story. How would Maddy know?*

"Lord Petyr has been kind enough to let me keep my harp," the blind singer said. "My harp and . . . my tongue . . . so I may sing my songs. Lady Lysa dearly loved my singing . . ."

"Take this creature away, or I'm like to kill him myself," Lord Nestor growled. "It sickens me to look at him."

"Mord, take him back to his sky cell," said Petyr.

"Yes, m'lord." Mord grabbed Marillion roughly by the collar. "No more mouth." When he spoke, Sansa saw to her astonishment that the gaoler's teeth were made of gold. They watched as he half dragged half shoved the singer toward the doors.

"The man must die," Ser Marwyn Belmore declared when they were gone. "He should have followed Lady Lysa out the Moon Door."

"Without his tongue," Ser Albar Royce added. "Without that lying, mocking tongue."

"I have been too gentle with him, I know," Petyr Baelish said in an apologetic tone. "If truth be told, I pity him. He killed for love."

"For love or hate," said Belmore, "he must die."

"Soon enough," Lord Nestor said gruffly. "No man lingers long in the sky cells. The blue will call to him."

"It may," said Petyr Baelish, "but whether Marillion will answer, only he can say." He gestured, and his guardsmen opened the doors at the far end of the hall.

"Sers, I know you must be weary after your ascent. Rooms have been prepared for all of you to spend the night, and food and wine await you in the Lower Hall. Oswell, show them the way, and see that they have all they need." He turned to Nestor Royce. "My lord, will you join me in the solar for a cup of wine? Alayne, sweetling, come pour for us."

A low fire burned in the solar, where a flagon of wine awaited them. *Arbor gold.* Sansa filled Lord Nestor's cup whilst Petyr prodded at the logs with an iron poker.

Lord Nestor seated himself beside the fire. "This will not be the end of it," he said to Petyr, as if Sansa were not there. "My cousin means to question the singer himself."

"Bronze Yohn mistrusts me." Petyr pushed a log aside.

"He means to come in force. Symond Templeton will join him, do not doubt it. And Lady Waynwood too, I fear."

"And Lord Belmore, Young Lord Hunter, Horton Redfort. They will bring Strong Sam Stone, the Tolletts, the Shetts, the Coldwaters, some Corbrays."

"You are well-informed. Which Corbrays? Not Lord Lyonel?"

"No, his brother. Ser Lyn mislikes me, for some reason."

"Lyn Corbray is a dangerous man," Lord Nestor said doggedly. "What do you intend to do?"

"What *can* I do but make them welcome if they come?" Petyr gave the flames another stir and set the poker down.

"My cousin means to remove you as Lord Protector."

"If so, I cannot stop him. I keep a garrison of twenty men. Lord Royce and his friends can raise twenty thousand." Petyr went to the oaken chest that sat beneath the window. "Bronze Yohn will do what he will do," he said, kneeling. He opened the chest, drew out a roll of parchment, and brought it to Lord Nestor. "My lord. This is a token of the love my lady bore you."

Sansa watched Royce unroll the parchment. "This . . . this is unexpected, my lord." She was startled to see tears in his eyes.

"Unexpected, but not undeserved. My lady valued you above all her other bannermen. You were her rock, she told me."

"Her rock." Lord Nestor reddened. "She said that?"

"Often. And this"—Petyr gestured at the parchment—"is the proof of it."

"That . . . that is good to know. Jon Arryn valued my service, I know, but Lady Lysa . . . she scorned me when I came to court her, and I feared . . ." Lord Nestor furrowed his brow. "It bears the Arryn seal, I see, but the signature . . ."

"Lysa was murdered before the document could be presented for her signature, so I signed as Lord Protector. I knew that would have been her wish."

"I see." Lord Nestor rolled the parchment. "You are . . . dutiful, my lord. Aye, and not without courage. Some will call this grant unseemly, and fault you for making it. The Keeper's post has never been hereditary. The Arryns raised the Gates, in the days when they still wore the Falcon Crown and ruled the Vale as kings. The Eyrie was their summer seat, but when the snows began to fall the court would make its descent. Some would say the Gates were as royal as the Eyrie."

"There has been no king in the Vale for three hundred years," Petyr Baelish pointed out.

"The dragons came," Lord Nestor agreed. "But even after, the Gates remained an Arryn castle. Jon Arryn himself was Keeper of the Gates whilst his father lived. After his ascent, he named his brother Ronnel to the honor, and later his cousin Denys."

"Lord Robert has no brothers, and only distant cousins."

"True." Lord Nestor clutched the parchment tightly. "I will not say I had not hoped for this. Whilst Lord Jon ruled the realm as Hand, it fell to me to rule the Vale for him. I did all that he required of me and asked nothing for myself. But by the gods, I earned this!"

"You did," said Petyr, "and Lord Robert sleeps more easily knowing that you are always there, a staunch friend at the foot of his mountain." He raised a cup. "So . . . a toast, my lord. To House Royce, Keepers of the Gates of the Moon . . . now and forever."

"Now and forever, aye!" The silver cups crashed together.

Later, much later, after the flagon of Arbor gold was dry, Lord Nestor took his leave to rejoin his company of knights. Sansa was asleep on her feet by then, wanting only to crawl off to her bed, but Petyr caught her by the wrist. "You see the wonders that can be worked with lies and Arbor gold?"

Why did she feel like weeping? It was good that Nestor Royce was with them. "Were they all lies?"

"Not *all*. Lysa often called Lord Nestor a rock, though I do not think she meant it as a compliment. She called his son a clod. She knew Lord Nestor dreamed of holding the Gates in his own right, a lord in truth as well as name, but Lysa dreamed of other sons and meant the castle to go to Robert's little brother." He stood. "Do you understand what happened here, Alayne?"

Sansa hesitated a moment. "You gave Lord Nestor the Gates of the Moon to be certain of his support."

"I did," Petyr admitted, "but our rock is a Royce, which is to say he is overproud and prickly. Had I asked him his price, he would have swelled up like an angry toad at the slight upon his honor. But this way . . . the man is not *utterly* stupid, but the lies I served him were sweeter than the truth. He *wants* to believe that Lysa valued him above her other bannermen. One of those others is Bronze Yohn, after all, and Nestor is very much aware that he was born of the *lesser* branch of House Royce. He wants more for his son. Men of honor will do things for their children that they would never consider doing for themselves."

She nodded. "The signature . . . you might have had Lord Robert put his hand and seal to it, but instead . . ."

". . . I signed myself, as Lord Protector. Why?"

"So . . . if you are removed, or . . . or killed . . ."

". . . Lord Nestor's claim to the Gates will suddenly be called into question. I promise you, that is not lost on him. It was clever of you to see it. Though no more than I'd expect of mine own daughter."

"Thank you." She felt absurdly proud for puzzling it out, but confused as well. "I'm not, though. Your daughter. Not truly. I mean, I pretend to be Alayne, but *you* know . . ."

Littlefinger put a finger to her lips. "I know what I know, and so do you. Some things are best left unsaid, sweetling."

"Even when we are alone?"

"*Especially* when we are alone. Elsewise a day will come when a servant walks into a room unannounced, or a guardsman at the door chances to hear something he should not. Do you want more blood on your pretty little hands, my darling?"

Marillion's face seemed to float before her, the bandage

pale across his eyes. Behind him she could see Ser Dontos, the crossbow bolts still in him. "No," Sansa said. "Please."

"I am tempted to say this is no game we play, daughter, but of course it is. The game of thrones."

I never asked to play. The game was too dangerous. *One slip and I am dead.* "Oswell . . . my lord, Oswell rowed me from King's Landing the night that I escaped. He must know who I am."

"If he's half as clever as a sheep pellet, you would think so. Ser Lothor knows as well. But Oswell has been in my service a long time, and Brune is close-mouthed by nature. Kettleblack watches Brune for me, and Brune watches Kettleblack. *Trust no one,* I once told Eddard Stark, but he would not listen. You are Alayne, and you must be Alayne *all the time.*" He put two fingers on her left breast. "Even here. In your heart. Can you do that? Can you be my daughter in your heart?"

"I . . ." *I do not know, my lord,* she almost said, but that was not what he wanted to hear. *Lies and Arbor gold,* she thought. "I am Alayne, Father. Who else would I be?"

Lord Littlefinger kissed her cheek. "With my wits and Cat's beauty, the world will be yours, sweetling. Now off to bed."

Gretchel had laid a fire in her hearth and plumped her featherbed. Sansa undressed and slipped beneath the blankets. *He will not sing tonight,* she prayed, *not with Lord Nestor and the others in the castle. He would not dare.* She closed her eyes.

Sometime during the night she woke, as little Robert climbed up into her bed. *I forgot to tell Lothor to lock him in again,* she realized. There was nothing to be done for it, so she put her arm around him. "Sweetrobin? You can stay, but try not to squirm around. Just close your eyes and sleep, little one."

"I will." He cuddled close and laid his head between her breasts. "Alayne? Are you my mother now?"

"I suppose I am," she said. If a lie was kindly meant, there was no harm in it.

THE KRAKEN'S DAUGHTER

The hall was loud with drunken Harlaws, distant cousins all. Each lord had hung his banner behind the benches where his men were seated. *Too few,* thought Asha Greyjoy, looking down from the gallery, *too few by far.* The benches were three-quarters empty.

Qarl the Maid had said as much, when the *Black Wind* was approaching from the sea. He had counted the long-ships moored beneath her uncle's castle, and his mouth had tightened. "They have not come," he observed, "or not enough of them." He was not wrong, but Asha could not agree with him, out where her crew might hear. She did not doubt their devotion, but even ironborn will hesitate to give their lives for a cause that's plainly lost.

Do I have so few friends as this? Amongst the banners, she saw the silver fish of Botley, the stone tree of the

Stonetrees, the black leviathan of Volmark, the nooses of the Myres. The rest were Harlaw scythes. Boremund placed his upon a pale blue field, Hotho's was girdled within an embattled border, and the Knight had quartered his with the gaudy peacock of his mother's House. Even Sigfryd Silverhair showed two scythes counterchanged on a field divided bendwise. Only *the* Lord Harlaw displayed the silver scythe plain upon a night-black field, as it had flown in the dawn of days: Rodrik, called the Reader, Lord of the Ten Towers, Lord of Harlaw, Harlaw of Harlaw . . . her favorite uncle.

Lord Rodrik's high seat was vacant. Two scythes of beaten silver crossed above it, so huge that even a giant would have difficulty wielding them, but beneath were only empty cushions. Asha was not surprised. The feast was long concluded. Only bones and greasy platters remained upon the trestle tables. The rest was drinking, and her uncle Rodrik had never been partial to the company of quarrelsome drunks.

She turned to Three-Tooth, an old woman of fearful age who had been her uncle's steward since she was known as Twelve-Tooth. "My uncle is with his books?"

"Aye, where else?" The woman was so old that a septon had once said she must have nursed the Crone. That was when the Faith was still tolerated on the isles. Lord Rodrik had kept septons at Ten Towers, not for his soul's sake but for his books. "With the books, and Botley. He was with him too."

Botley's standard hung in the hall, a shoal of silver fish upon a pale green field, though Asha had not seen his *Swiftfin* amongst the other longships. "I had heard my nuncle Crow's Eye had old Sawane Botley drowned."

"Lord *Tristifer* Botley, this one is."

Tris. She wondered what had happened to Sawane's

elder son, Harren. *I will find out soon enough, no doubt.
This should be awkward.* She had not seen Tris Botley
since . . . no, she ought not dwell on it. "And my lady
mother?"

"Abed," said Three-Tooth, "in the Widow's Tower."

Aye, where else? The widow the tower was named after
was her aunt. Lady Gwynesse had come home to mourn
after her husband had died off Fair Isle during Balon
Greyjoy's first rebellion. "I will only stay until my grief
has passed," she had told her brother, famously, "though
by rights Ten Towers should be mine, for I am seven years
your elder." Long years had passed since then, but still the
widow lingered, grieving, and muttering from time to time
that the castle should be hers. *And now Lord Rodrik has a
second half-mad widowed sister beneath his roof,* Asha reflected. *Small wonder if he seeks solace in his books.*

Even now, it was hard to credit that frail, sickly Lady
Alannys had outlived her husband Lord Balon, who had
seemed so hard and strong. When Asha had sailed away to
war, she had done so with a heavy heart, fearing that her
mother might well die before she could return. Not once
had she thought that her father might perish instead. *The
Drowned God plays savage japes upon us all, but men are
crueler still.* A sudden storm and a broken rope had sent
Balon Greyjoy to his death. *Or so they claim.*

Asha had last seen her mother when she stopped at Ten
Towers to take on fresh water, on her way north to strike at
Deepwood Motte. Alannys Harlaw never had the sort of
beauty the singers cherished, but her daughter had loved
her fierce strong face and the laughter in her eyes. On that
last visit, though, she had found Lady Alannys in a window seat huddled beneath a pile of furs, staring out across
the sea. *Is this my mother, or her ghost?* she remembered
thinking as she'd kissed her cheek.

Her mother's skin had been parchment thin, her long hair white. Some pride remained in the way she held her head, but her eyes were dim and cloudy, and her mouth had trembled when she asked after Theon. "Did you bring my baby boy?" she had asked. Theon had been ten years old when he was carried off to Winterfell a hostage, and so far as Lady Alannys was concerned he would always be ten years old, it seemed. "Theon could not come," Asha had to tell her. "Father sent him reaving along the Stony Shore." Lady Alannys had naught to say to that. She only nodded slowly, yet it was plain to see how deep her daughter's words had cut her.

And now I must tell her that Theon is dead, and drive yet another dagger through her heart. There were two knives buried there already. On the blades were writ the words *Rodrik* and *Maron,* and many a time they twisted cruelly in the night. *I will see her on the morrow,* Asha vowed to herself. Her journey had been long and wearisome, she could not face her mother now.

"I must speak with Lord Rodrik," she told Three-Tooth. "See to my crew, once they're done unloading *Black Wind.* They'll bring captives. I want them to have warm beds and a hot meal."

"There's cold beef in the kitchens. And mustard in a big stone jar, from Oldtown." The thought of that mustard made the old woman smile. A single long brown tooth poked from her gums.

"That will not serve. We had a rough crossing. I want something hot in their bellies." Asha hooked a thumb through the studded belt about her hips. "Lady Glover and the children should not want for wood nor warmth. Put them in some tower, not the dungeons. The babe is sick."

"Babes are often sick. Most die, and folks are sorry. I shall ask my lord where to put these wolf folk."

She caught the woman's nose between thumb and fore-finger and pinched. "You will do as I say. And if *this* babe dies, no one will be sorrier than you." Three-Tooth squealed and promised to obey, till Asha let her loose and went to find her uncle.

It was good to walk these halls again. Ten Towers had always felt like home to Asha, more so than Pyke. *Not one castle, ten castles squashed together,* she had thought, the first time she had seen it. She remembered breathless races up and down the steps and along wallwalks and cov-ered bridges, fishing off the Long Stone Quay, days and nights lost amongst her uncle's wealth of books. His grandfather's grandfather had raised the castle, the newest on the isles. Lord Theomore Harlaw had lost three sons in the cradle and laid the blame upon the flooded cellars, damp stones, and festering nitre of ancient Harlaw Hall. Ten Towers was airier, more comfortable, better sited . . . but Lord Theomore was a changeable man, as any of his wives might have testified. He'd had six of those, as dis-similar as his ten towers.

The Book Tower was the fattest of the ten, octagonal in shape and made with great blocks of hewn stone. The stair was built within the thickness of the walls. Asha climbed quickly, to the fifth story and the room where her uncle read. *Not that there are any rooms where he does not read.* Lord Rodrik was seldom seen without a book in hand, be it in the privy, on the deck of his *Sea Song,* or whilst hold-ing audience. Asha had oft seen him reading on his high seat beneath the silver scythes. He would listen to each case as it was laid before him, pronounce his judgment . . . and read a bit whilst his captain-of-guards went to bring in the next supplicant.

She found him hunched over a table by a window, sur-rounded by parchment scrolls that might have come from

Valyria before its Doom, and heavy leather-bound books with bronze-and-iron hasps. Beeswax candles as thick and tall as a man's arm burned on either side of where he sat, on ornate iron holders. Lord Rodrik Harlaw was neither fat nor slim; neither tall nor short; neither ugly nor handsome. His hair was brown, as were his eyes, though the short, neat beard he favored had gone grey. All in all, he was an ordinary man, distinguished only by his love of written words, which so many ironborn found unmanly and perverse.

"Nuncle." She closed the door behind her. "What reading was so urgent that you leave your guests without a host?"

"Archmaester Marwyn's *Book of Lost Books.*" He lifted his gaze from the page to study her. "Hotho brought me a copy from Oldtown. He has a daughter he would have me wed." Lord Rodrik tapped the book with a long nail. "See here? Marwyn claims to have found three pages of *Signs and Portents,* visions written down by the maiden daughter of Aenar Targaryen before the Doom came to Valyria. Does Lanny know that you are here?"

"Not as yet." *Lanny* was his pet name for her mother; only the Reader called her that. "Let her rest." Asha moved a stack of books off a stool and seated herself. "Three-Tooth seems to have lost two more of her teeth. Do you call her One-Tooth now?"

"I seldom call her at all. The woman frightens me. What hour is it?" Lord Rodrik glanced out the window, at the moonlit sea. "Dark, so soon? I had not noticed. You come late. We looked for you some days ago."

"The winds were against us, and I had captives to concern me. Robett Glover's wife and children. The youngest is still at the breast, and Lady Glover's milk dried up during our crossing. I had no choice but to beach *Black Wind* upon the Stony Shore and send my men out to find a wet nurse. They found a goat instead. The girl does not thrive. Is there a nursing mother in the village? Deepwood is important to my plans."

"Your plans must change. You come too late."

"Late and hungry." She stretched her long legs out beneath the table and turned the pages of the nearest book, a septon's discourse on Maegor the Cruel's war against the Poor Fellows. "Oh, and thirsty too. A horn of ale would go down well, Nuncle."

Lord Rodrik pursed his lips. "You know I do not permit food nor drink in my library. The books—"

"—might suffer harm." Asha laughed.

Her uncle frowned. "You do like to provoke me."

"Oh, don't look so aggrieved. I have never met a man I didn't provoke, you should know that well enough by now. But enough of me. You are well?"

He shrugged. "Well enough. My eyes grow weaker. I have sent to Myr for a lens to help me read."

"And how fares my aunt?"

Lord Rodrik sighed. "Still seven years my elder, and convinced Ten Towers should be hers. Gwynesse grows forgetful, but *that* she does not forget. She mourns for her dead husband as deeply as she did the day he died, though she cannot always recall his name."

"I am not certain she ever knew his name." Asha closed the septon's book with a *thump*. "Was my father murdered?"

"So your mother believes."

There were times when she would gladly have murdered him herself, she thought. "And what does my nuncle believe?"

"Balon fell to his death when a rope bridge broke beneath him. A storm was rising, and the bridge was swaying and twisting with each gust of wind." Rodrik shrugged. "Or so we are told. Your mother had a bird from Maester Wendamyr."

Asha slid her dirk out of its sheath and began to clean the dirt from beneath her fingernails. "Three years away, and the Crow's Eye returns the very day my father dies."

"The day after, we had heard. *Silence* was still out to sea when Balon died, or so it is claimed. Even so, I will agree that Euron's return was . . . timely, shall we say?"

"That is not how I would say it." Asha slammed the point of the dirk into the table. "*Where are my ships?* I counted twoscore longships moored below, not near enough to throw the Crow's Eye off my father's chair."

"I sent the summons. In your name, for the love I bear you and your mother. House Harlaw has gathered. Stonetree as well, and Volmark. Some Myres . . ."

"All from the isle of Harlaw . . . one isle out of seven. I saw one lonely Botley banner in the hall, from Pyke. Where are the ships from Saltcliffe, from Orkwood, from the Wyks?"

"Baelor Blacktyde came from Blacktyde to consult with me, and just as soon set sail again." Lord Rodrik closed *The Book of Lost Books*. "He is on Old Wyk by now."

"Old Wyk?" Asha had feared he was about to say that they all had gone to Pyke, to do homage to the Crow's Eye. "Why Old Wyk?"

"I thought you would have heard. Aeron Damphair has called a kingsmoot."

Asha threw back her head and laughed. "The Drowned God must have shoved a pricklefish up Uncle Aeron's arse. A *kingsmoot*? Is this some jape, or does he mean it truly?"

"The Damphair has not japed since he was drowned. And the other priests have taken up the call. Blind Beron Blacktyde, Tarle the Thrice-Drowned . . . even the Old

Grey Gull has left that rock he lives on to preach this kingsmoot all across Harlaw. The captains are gathering on Old Wyk as we speak."

Asha was astonished. "Has the Crow's Eye agreed to attend this holy farce and abide by its decision?"

"The Crow's Eye does not confide in me. Since he summoned me to Pyke to do him homage, I have had no word from Euron."

A kingsmoot. This is something new . . . or rather, something very old. "And my uncle Victarion? What does he make of the Damphair's notion?"

"Victarion was sent word of your father's death. And of this kingsmoot too, I do not doubt. Beyond that, I cannot say."

Better a kingsmoot than a war. "I believe I'll kiss the Damphair's smelly feet and pluck the seaweed from out between his toes." Asha wrenched loose her dirk and sheathed it once again. "A bloody *kingsmoot*!"

"On Old Wyk," confirmed Lord Rodrik. "Though I pray it is not bloody. I have been consulting Haereg's *History of the Ironborn.* When last the salt kings and the rock kings met in kingsmoot, Urron of Orkmont let his axemen loose among them, and Nagga's ribs turned red with gore. House Greyiron ruled unchosen for a thousand years from that dark day, until the Andals came."

"You must lend me Haereg's book, Nuncle." She would need to learn all she could of kingsmoots before she reached Old Wyk.

"You may read it here. It is old and fragile." He studied her, frowning. "Archmaester Rigney once wrote that history is a wheel, for the nature of man is fundamentally unchanging. What has happened before will perforce happen again, he said. I think of that whenever I contemplate the Crow's Eye. Euron Greyjoy sounds queerly like Urron

Greyiron to these old ears. I shall not go to Old Wyk. Nor should you."

Asha smiled. "And miss the first kingsmoot called in . . . how long *has* it been, Nuncle?"

"Four thousand years, if Haereg can be believed. Half that, if you accept Maester Denestan's arguments in *Questions*. Going to Old Wyk serves no purpose. This dream of kingship is a madness in our blood. I told your father so the first time he rose, and it is more true now than it was then. It's land we need, not crowns. With Stannis Baratheon and Tywin Lannister contending for the Iron Throne, we have a rare chance to improve our lot. Let us take one side or the other, help them to victory with our fleets, and claim the lands we need from a grateful king."

"That might be worth some thought, once I sit the Seastone Chair," said Asha.

Her uncle sighed. "You will not want to hear this, Asha, but you will not be chosen. No woman has ever ruled the ironborn. Gwynesse *is* seven years my elder, but when our father died the Ten Towers came to me. It will be the same for you. You are Balon's daughter, not his son. And you have three uncles."

"Four."

"Three kraken uncles. I do not count."

"You do with me. So long as I have my nuncle of Ten Towers, I have Harlaw." Harlaw was not the largest of the Iron Islands, but it was the richest and most populous, and Lord Rodrik's power was not to be despised. On Harlaw, Harlaw had no rival. The Volmarks and Stonetrees had large holdings on the isle and boasted famous captains and fierce warriors of their own, but even the fiercest bent beneath the scythe. The Kennings and the Myres, once bitter foes, had long ago been beaten down to vassals.

"My cousins do me fealty, and in war I should command

their swords and sails. In kingsmoot, though . . ." Lord Rodrik shook his head. "Beneath the bones of Nagga every captain stands as equal. Some may shout your name, I do not doubt it. But not enough. And when the shouts ring out for Victarion or the Crow's Eye, some of those now drinking in my hall will join the rest. I say again, do not sail into this storm. Your fight is hopeless."

"No fight is hopeless till it has been fought. I have the best claim. I am the heir of Balon's body."

"You are still a willful child. Think of your poor mother. You are all that Lanny has left to her. I will put a torch to *Black Wind* if need be, to keep you here."

"What, and make me swim to Old Wyk?"

"A long cold swim, for a crown you cannot keep. Your father had more courage than sense. The Old Way served the isles well when we were one small kingdom amongst many, but Aegon's Conquest put an end to that. Balon refused to see what was plain before him. The Old Way died with Black Harren and his sons."

"I know that." Asha had loved her father, but she did not delude herself. Balon had been blind in some respects. *A brave man but a bad lord.* "Does that mean we must live and die as thralls to the Iron Throne? If there are rocks to starboard and a storm to port, a wise captain steers a third course."

"Show me this third course."

"I shall . . . at my queensmoot. Nuncle, how can you even think of not attending? This will be history, alive . . ."

"I prefer my history dead. Dead history is writ in ink, the living sort in blood."

"Do you want to die old and craven in your bed?"

"How else? Though not till I'm done reading." Lord Rodrik went to the window. "You have not asked about your lady mother."

I was afraid. "How is she?"

"Stronger. She may yet outlive us all. She will certainly outlive you, if you persist in this folly. She eats more than she did when she first came here, and oft sleeps through the night."

"Good." In her final years on Pyke, Lady Alannys could not sleep. She would wander the halls at night with a candle, looking for her sons. *"Maron?"* she would call shrilly. *"Rodrik, where are you? Theon, my baby, come to Mother."* Many a time Asha had watched the maester draw splinters from her mother's heels of a morning, after she had crossed the swaying plank bridge to the Sea Tower on bare feet. "I will see her in the morning."

"She will ask for word of Theon."

The Prince of Winterfell. "What have you told her?"

"Little and less. There was naught to tell." He hesitated. "You are certain that he is dead?"

"I am certain of nothing."

"You found a body?"

"We found parts of many bodies. The wolves were there before us . . . the four-legged sort, but they showed scant reverence for their two-legged kin. The bones of the slain were scattered, cracked open for their marrow. I confess, it was hard to know what happened there. It seemed as though the northmen fought amongst themselves."

"Crows will fight over a dead man's flesh and kill each other for his eyes." Lord Rodrik stared across the sea, watching the play of moonlight on the waves. "We had one king, then five. Now all I see are crows, squabbling over the corpse of Westeros." He fastened the shutters. "Do not go to Old Wyk, Asha. Stay with your mother. We shall not have her long, I fear."

Asha shifted in her seat. "My mother raised me to be

bold. If I do not go, I will spend the rest of my life wondering what might have happened if I had."

"If you do go, the rest of your life may be too short for wondering."

"Better that than fill the remainder of my days complaining that the Seastone Chair by rights was mine. I am no Gwynesse."

That made him wince. "Asha, my two tall sons fed the crabs of Fair Isle. I am not like to wed again. Stay, and I shall name you heir to the Ten Towers. Be content with that."

"Ten Towers?" *Would that I could.* "Your cousins will not like that. The Knight, old Sigfryd, Hotho Humpback . . ."

"They have lands and seats of their own."

True enough. Damp, decaying Harlaw Hall belonged to old Sigfryd Harlaw the Silverhair; humpbacked Hotho Harlaw had his seat at the Tower of Glimmering, on a crag above the western coast. The Knight, Ser Harras Harlaw, kept court at Grey Garden; Boremund the Blue ruled atop Harridan Hill. But each was subject to Lord Rodrik. "Boremund has three sons, Sigfryd Silverhair has grandsons, and Hotho has ambitions," Asha said. "They all mean to follow you, even Sigfryd. That one intends to live forever."

"The Knight will be the Lord of Harlaw after me," her uncle said, "but he can rule from Grey Garden as easily as from here. Do fealty to him for the castle and Ser Harras will protect you."

"I can protect myself. Nuncle, I am a kraken. Asha, of House *Greyjoy.*" She pushed to her feet. "It's my father's seat I want, not yours. Those scythes of yours look perilous. One could fall and slice my head off. No, I'll sit the Seastone Chair."

"Then you are just another crow, screaming for carrion." Rodrik sat again behind his table. "Go. I wish to return to Archmaester Marwyn and his search."

"Let me know if he should find another page." Her uncle was her uncle. He would never change. *But he will come to Old Wyk, no matter what he says.*

By now her crew would be eating in the hall. Asha knew she ought to join them, to speak of this gathering on Old Wyk and what it meant for them. Her own men would be solidly behind her, but she would need the rest as well, her Harlaw cousins, the Volmarks, and the Stonetrees. *Those are the ones I must win.* Her victory at Deepwood Motte would serve her in good stead, once her men began to boast of it, as she knew they would. The crew of her *Black Wind* took a perverse pride in the deeds of their woman captain. Half of them loved her like a daughter, and other half wanted to spread her legs, but either sort would die for her. *And I for them,* she was thinking as she shouldered through the door at the bottom of the steps, into the moonlit yard.

"Asha?" A shadow stepped out from behind the well.

Her hand went to her dirk at once . . . until the moonlight transformed the dark shape into a man in a sealskin cloak. *Another ghost.* "Tris. I'd thought to find you in the hall."

"I wanted to see you."

"What part of me, I wonder?" She grinned. "Well, here I stand, all grown up. Look all you like."

"A woman." He moved closer. "And beautiful."

Tristifer Botley had filled out since last she'd seen him, but he had the same unruly hair that she remembered, and eyes as large and trusting as a seal's. *Sweet eyes, truly.* That was the trouble with poor Tristifer; he was too sweet for the Iron Islands. *His face has grown comely,* she thought. As a boy Tris had been much troubled by pimples. Asha had suffered the same affliction; perhaps that had been what drew them together.

"I was sorry to hear about your father," she told him.

"I grieve for yours."

Why? Asha almost asked. It was Balon who'd sent the boy away from Pyke, to be a ward of Baelor Blacktyde's. "Is it true you are Lord Botley now?"

"In name, at least. Harren died at Moat Cailin. One of the bog devils shot him with a poisoned arrow. But I am the lord of nothing. When my father denied his claim to the Seastone Chair, the Crow's Eye drowned him and made my uncles swear him fealty. Even after that he gave half my father's lands to Iron Holt. Lord Wynch was the first man to bend his knee and call him king."

House Wynch was strong on Pyke, but Asha took care not to let her dismay show. "Wynch never had your father's courage."

"Your uncle bought him," Tris said. "The *Silence* returned with holds full of treasure. Plate and pearls, emeralds and rubies, sapphires big as eggs, bags of coin so heavy that no man can lift them . . . the Crow's Eye has been buying friends at every hand. My uncle Germund calls himself Lord Botley now, and rules in Lordsport as your uncle's man."

"You are the rightful Lord Botley," she assured him. "Once I hold the Seastone Chair, your father's lands shall be restored."

"If you like. It's nought to me. You look so lovely in the moonlight, Asha. A woman grown now, but I remember when you were a skinny girl with a face all full of pimples."

Why must they always mention the pimples? "I remember that as well." *Though not as fondly as you do.* Of the five boys her mother had brought to Pyke to foster after

Ned Stark had taken her last living son as hostage, Tris had been closest to Asha in age. He had not been the first boy she had ever kissed, but he was the first to undo the laces of her jerkin and slip a sweaty hand beneath to feel her budding breasts.

I would have let him feel more than that if he'd been bold enough. Her first flowering had come upon her during the war and wakened her desire, but even before that Asha had been curious. *He was there, he was mine own age, and he was willing, that was all it was . . . that, and the moon blood.* Even so, she'd called it love, till Tris began to go on about the children she would bear him; a dozen sons at least, and oh, some daughters too. "I don't want to have a dozen sons," she had told him, appalled. "I want to have *adventures.*" Not long after, Maester Qalen found them at their play, and young Tristifer Botley was sent away to Blacktyde.

"I wrote you letters," he said, "but Maester Joseran would not send them. Once I gave a stag to an oarsman on a trader bound for Lordsport, who promised to put my letter in your hands."

"Your oarsman winkled you and threw your letter in the sea."

"I feared as much. They never gave me your letters either."

I wrote none. In truth, she had been relieved when Tris was sent away. By then his fumblings had begun to bore her. That was not something he would care to hear, however. "Aeron Damphair has called a kingsmoot. Will you come and speak for me?"

"I will go anywhere with you, but . . . Lord Blacktyde says this kingsmoot is a dangerous folly. He thinks your uncle will descend on them and kill them all, as Urron did."

He's mad enough. "He lacks the strength."

"You do not know his strength. He's been gathering men on Pyke. Orkwood of Orkmont brought him twenty longships, and Pinchface Jon Myre a dozen. Left-Hand Lucas Codd is with them. And Harren Half-Hoare, the Red Oarsman, Kemmett Pyke the Bastard, Rodrik Freeborn, Torwold Browntooth . . ."

"Men of small account." Asha knew them, every one. "The sons of salt wives, the grandsons of thralls. The Codds . . . do you know their *words*?"

"Though All Men Do Despise Us," Tris said, "but if they catch you in those nets of theirs, you'll be as dead as if they had been dragonlords. And there's worse. The Crow's Eye brought back monsters from the east . . . aye, and *wizards* too."

"Nuncle always had a fondness for freaks and fools," said Asha. "My father used to fight with him about it. Let the wizards call upon their gods. The Damphair will call on ours, and drown them. Will I have your voice at the queensmoot, Tris?"

"You shall have all of me. I am your man, forever. Asha, I would wed you. Your lady mother has given her consent."

She stifled a groan. *You might have asked me first . . . though you might not have liked the answer half so well.*

"I am no second son now," he went on. "I am the rightful Lord Botley, as you said yourself. And you are—"

"What I am will be settled on Old Wyk. Tris, we are no longer children fumbling at each other and trying to see what fits where. You think you want to wed me, but you don't."

"I do. All I dream about is you. Asha, I swear upon the bones of Nagga, I have never touched another woman."

"Go touch one . . . or two, or ten. I have touched more

men than I can count. Some with my lips, more with my axe." She had surrendered her virtue at six-and-ten, to a beautiful blond-haired sailor on a trading galley up from Lys. He only knew six words of the Common Tongue, but "fuck" was one of them—the very word she'd hoped to hear. Afterward, Asha had the sense to find a woods witch, who showed her how to brew moon tea to keep her belly flat.

Botley blinked, as if he did not quite understand what she had said. "You . . . I thought you would wait. Why . . ." He rubbed his mouth. "Asha, were you *forced*?"

"So forced I tore his tunic. You do not want to wed me, take my word on that. You are a sweet boy and always were, but I am no sweet girl. If we wed, soon enough you'd come to hate me."

"Never. Asha, I have *ached* for you."

She had heard enough of this. A sickly mother, a murdered father, and a plague of uncles were enough for any woman to contend with; she did not require a lovesick puppy too. "Find a brothel, Tris. They'll cure you of that ache."

"I could never . . ." Tristifer shook his head. "You and I were meant to be, Asha. I have always known you would be my wife, and the mother of my sons." He seized her upper arm.

In a blink her dirk was at his throat. "Take your hand away or you won't live long enough to breed a son. *Now.*" When he did, she lowered the blade. "You want a woman, well and good. I'll put one in your bed tonight. Pretend she's me, if that will give you pleasure, but do not presume to grab at me again. I am your queen, not your wife. Remember that." Asha sheathed her dirk and left him standing there, with a fat drop of blood slowly creeping down his neck, black in the pale light of the moon.

CERSEI

Oh, I pray the Seven will not let it rain upon the king's wedding," Jocelyn Swyft said as she laced up the queen's gown.

"No one wants rain," said Cersei. For herself, she wanted sleet and ice, howling winds, thunder to shake the very stones of the Red Keep. She wanted a storm to match her rage. To Jocelyn she said, "Tighter. Cinch it *tighter,* you simpering little fool."

It was the wedding that enraged her, though the slow-witted Swyft girl made a safer target. Tommen's hold upon the Iron Throne was not secure enough for her to risk offending Highgarden. Not so long as Stannis Baratheon held Dragonstone and Storm's End, so long as Riverrun continued in defiance, so long as ironmen prowled the seas like wolves. So Jocelyn must needs eat the meal

Cersei would sooner have served to Margaery Tyrell and her hideous wrinkled grandmother.

To break her fast the queen sent to the kitchens for two boiled eggs, a loaf of bread, and a pot of honey. But when she cracked the first egg and found a bloody half-formed chick inside, her stomach roiled. "Take this away and bring me hot spiced wine," she told Senelle. The chill in the air was settling in her bones, and she had a long nasty day ahead of her.

Nor did Jaime help her mood when he turned up all in white and still unshaven, to tell her how he meant to keep her son from being poisoned. "I will have men in the kitchens watching as each dish is prepared," he said. "Ser Addam's gold cloaks will escort the servants as they bring the food to table, to make certain no tampering takes place along the way. Ser Boros will be tasting every course before Tommen puts a bite into his mouth. And if all that should fail, Maester Ballabar will be seated in the back of the hall, with purges and antidotes for twenty common poisons on his person. Tommen will be safe, I promise you."

"Safe." The word tasted bitter on her tongue. Jaime did not understand. No one understood. Only Melara had been in the tent to hear the old hag's croaking threats, and Melara was long dead. "Tyrion will not kill the same way twice. He is too cunning for that. He could be under the floor even now, listening to every word we say and making plans to open Tommen's throat."

"Suppose he was," said Jaime. "Whatever plans he makes, he will still be small and stunted. Tommen will be surrounded by the finest knights in Westeros. The Kingsguard will protect him."

Cersei glanced at where the sleeve of her brother's white silk tunic had been pinned up over his stump. "I remember how well they guarded Joffrey, these splendid knights of yours. I want you to remain with Tommen all night, is that understood?"

"I will have a guardsman outside his door."

She seized his arm. "Not a guardsman. You. And *inside* his bedchamber."

"In case Tyrion crawls out of the hearth? He won't."

"So you say. Will you tell me that you found all the hidden tunnels in these walls?" They both knew better. "I will *not* have Tommen alone with Margaery, not for so much as half a heartbeat."

"They will not be alone. Her cousins will be with them."

"As will you. I command it, in the king's name." Cersei had not wanted Tommen and his wife to share a bed at all, but the Tyrells had insisted. "Husband and wife should sleep together," the Queen of Thorns had said, "even if they do no more than sleep. His Grace's bed is big enough for two, surely." Lady Alerie had echoed her good-mother. "Let the children warm each other in the night. It will bring them closer. Margaery oft shares her blankets with her cousins. They sing and play games and whisper secrets to each other when the candles are snuffed out."

"How delightful," Cersei had said. "Let them continue, by all means. In the Maidenvault."

"I am sure Her Grace knows best," Lady Olenna had said to Lady Alerie. "She is the boy's own mother, after all, of *that* we are all sure. And surely we can agree about the wedding night? A man should not sleep apart from his wife on the night of their wedding. It is ill luck for their marriage if they do."

Someday I will teach you the meaning of "ill luck," the queen had vowed. "Margaery may share Tommen's bedchamber for that one night," she had been forced to say. "No longer."

"Your Grace is so gracious," the Queen of Thorns had replied, and everyone had exchanged smiles.

Cersei's fingers were digging into Jaime's arm hard enough to leave bruises. "I need *eyes* inside that room," she said.

"To see *what*?" he said. "There can be no danger of a consummation. Tommen is much too young."

"And Ossifer Plumm was much too dead, but that did not stop him fathering a child, did it?"

Her brother looked lost. "Who was Ossifer Plumm? Was he Lord Philip's father, or . . . who?"

He is near as ignorant as Robert. All his wits were in his sword hand. "Forget Plumm, just remember what I told you. Swear to me that you will stay by Tommen's side until the sun comes up."

"As you command," he said, as if her fears were groundless. "Do you still mean to go ahead and burn the Tower of the Hand?"

"After the feast." It was the only part of the day's festivities that Cersei thought she might enjoy. "Our lord father was murdered in that tower. I cannot bear to look at it. If the gods are good, the fire may smoke a few rats from the rubble."

Jaime rolled his eyes. "Tyrion, you mean."

"Him, and Lord Varys, and this gaoler."

"If any of them were hiding in the tower, we would have found them. I've had a small army going at it with picks and hammers. We've knocked through walls and ripped up floors and uncovered half a hundred secret passages."

"And for all you know there may be half a hundred more." Some of the secret crawlways had turned out to be so small that Jaime had needed pages and stableboys to explore them. A passage to the black cells had been found, and a stone well that seemed to have no bottom. They had found a chamber full of skulls and yellowed bones, and four sacks of tarnished silver coins from the reign of the first King Viserys. They had found a thousand rats as well . . . but neither Tyrion nor Varys had been amongst them, and Jaime had finally insisted on putting an end to the search. One boy had gotten stuck in a narrow passage and had to be pulled out by his feet, shrieking. Another fell down a shaft and broke his legs. And two guardsmen vanished exploring a side tunnel. Some of the other guards swore they could hear them calling faintly through the stone, but when Jaime's men tore down the wall they found only earth and rubble on the far side. "The Imp is small and cunning. He may still be in the walls. If he is, the fire will smoke him out."

"Even if Tyrion were still hiding in the castle, he won't be in the Tower of the Hand. We've reduced it to a shell."

"Would that we could do the same to the rest of this foul castle," said Cersei. "After the war I mean to build a new palace beyond the river." She had dreamed of it the night before last, a magnificent white castle surrounded by woods and gardens, long leagues from the stinks and noise of King's Landing. "This city is a cesspit. For half a groat I would move the court to Lannisport and rule the realm from Casterly Rock."

"That would be an even greater folly than burning the Tower of the Hand. So long as Tommen sits the Iron Throne, the realm sees him as the true king. Hide him under the Rock and he becomes just another claimant to the throne, no different than Stannis."

"I am aware of that," the queen said sharply. "I said that I *wanted* to move the court to Lannisport, not that I would. Were you always this slow, or did losing a hand make you stupid?"

Jaime ignored that. "If these flames spread beyond the tower, you may end up burning down the castle whether you mean to or not. Wildfire is treacherous."

"Lord Hallyne has assured me that his pyromancers can control the fire." The Guild of Alchemists had been brewing fresh wildfire for a fortnight. "Let all of King's Landing see the flames. It will be a lesson to our enemies."

"Now you sound like Aerys."

Her nostrils flared. "Guard your tongue, ser."

"I love you too, sweet sister."

How could I ever have loved that wretched creature? she wondered after he had gone. *He was your twin, your shadow, your other half,* another voice whispered. *Once, perhaps,* she thought. *No longer. He has become a stranger to me.*

Compared to the magnificence of Joffrey's nuptials, the wedding of King Tommen was a modest affair, and small. No one wanted another lavish ceremony, least of all the queen, and no one wanted to pay for one, least of all the Tyrells. So the young king took Margaery Tyrell to wife in the Red Keep's royal sept, with fewer than a hundred guests looking on in place of the thousands who had seen his brother joined to the same woman.

The bride was fair and gay and beautiful, the groom still baby-faced and plump. He recited his vows in a high, childish voice, promising his love and devotion to Mace Tyrell's twice-widowed daughter. Margaery wore the same gown she had worn to marry Joffrey, an airy confection of sheer ivory silk, Myrish lace, and seed pearls. Cersei herself was still in black, as a sign of mourning for her murdered firstborn. His widow might be pleased to laugh and drink and dance and put all memory of Joff aside, but his mother would not forget him so easily.

This is wrong, she thought. *It is too soon. A year, two*

years, that would have been time enough. Highgarden should have been content with a betrothal. Cersei stared back to where Mace Tyrell stood between his wife and mother. *You forced me into this travesty of a wedding, my lord, and I shall not soon forget it.*

When it was time for the changing of the cloaks, the bride sank gracefully to her knees and Tommen covered her with the heavy cloth-of-gold monstrosity that Robert had cloaked Cersei in on their own wedding day, with the crowned stag of Baratheon worked upon its back in beads of onyx. Cersei had wanted to use the fine red silk cloak Joffrey had used. "It was the cloak my lord father used when he wed my lady mother," she explained to the Tyrells, but the Queen of Thorns had balked her in that as well. "That old thing?" the crone had said. "It looks a bit threadbare to me . . . and dare I say, unlucky? And wouldn't a *stag* be more fitting for King Robert's trueborn son? In my day a bride donned her *husband's* colors, not his lady mother's."

Thanks to Stannis and his filthy letter, there were already too many rumors concerning Tommen's parentage. Cersei dared not fan the fires by insisting that he drape his bride in Lannister crimson, so she yielded as gracefully as she could. But the sight of all that gold and onyx still filled her with resentment. *The more we give these Tyrells, the more they demand of us.*

When all the vows were spoken, the king and his new queen stepped outside the sept to accept congratulations. "Westeros has two queens now, and the young one is as beautiful as the old one," boomed Lyle Crakehall, an oaf of a knight who oft reminded Cersei of her late and unlamented husband. She could have slapped him. Gyles Rosby made to kiss her hand, and only succeeded in coughing on her fingers. Lord Redwyne kissed her on one cheek and Mace Tyrell on both. Grand Maester Pycelle told Cersei that she had not lost a son, but rather gained a daughter. At least she was spared Lady Tanda's tearful embraces. None of the Stokeworth women had appeared, and for that much the queen was grateful.

Amongst the last was Kevan Lannister. "I understand you mean to leave us for another wedding," the queen said to him.

"Hardstone has cleared the broken men from Darry castle," he replied. "Lancel's bride awaits us there."

"Will your lady wife be joining you for the nuptials?"

"The riverlands are still too dangerous. Vargo Hoat's scum remain abroad, and Beric Dondarrion has been hanging Freys. Is it true that Sandor Clegane has joined him?"

How does he know that? "Some say. Reports are confused." The bird had come last night, from a septry on an island hard by the mouth of the Trident. The nearby town of Saltpans had been savagely raided by a band of outlaws, and some of the survivors claimed a roaring brute in a hound's head helm was amongst the raiders. Supposedly he'd killed a dozen men and raped a girl of twelve. "No doubt Lancel will be eager to hunt down Clegane and Lord Beric both, to restore the king's peace to the riverlands."

Ser Kevan stared into her eyes for a moment. "My son is not the man to deal with Sandor Clegane."

We agree on that much, at least. "His father might be."

Her uncle's mouth grew hard. "If my service is not required at the Rock . . ."

Your service was required here. Cersei had named her cousin Damion Lannister her castellan for the Rock, and another cousin, Ser Daven Lannister, the Warden of the West. *Insolence has its price, Uncle.* "Bring us Sandor's head, and I know His Grace will be most grateful. Joff may have liked the man, but Tommen was always afraid of him . . . with good reason, it would seem."

"When a dog goes bad, the fault lies with his master," Ser Kevan said. Then he turned and walked away.

Jaime escorted her to the Small Hall, where the feast was being readied. "I blame you for all this," she whispered as they walked. "*Let them wed*, you said. Margaery should be mourning Joffrey, not marrying his brother. She should be as sick with grief as I am. I do not believe she is a maid. Renly had a cock, didn't he? He was Robert's brother, he *surely* had a cock. If that disgusting old crone thinks that I will allow my son to—"

"You will be rid of Lady Olenna soon enough," Jaime broke in quietly. "She's returning to Highgarden on the morrow."

"So she says." Cersei did not trust any Tyrell promise.

"She's leaving," he insisted. "Mace is taking half the Tyrell strength to Storm's End, and the other half will be going back to the Reach with Ser Garlan to make good his claim on Brightwater. A few more days, and the only roses left in King's Landing will be Margaery and her ladies and a few guardsmen."

"And Ser Loras. Or have you forgotten your *Sworn Brother*?"

"Ser Loras is a knight of the Kingsguard."

"Ser Loras is so Tyrell he pisses rosewater. He should never have been given a white cloak."

"He would not have been my choice, I'll grant you. No one troubled to consult me. Loras will do well enough, I think. Once a man puts on that cloak, it changes him."

"It certainly changed *you*, and not for the better."

"I love you too, sweet sister." He held the door for her, and walked her to the high table and her seat beside the king. Margaery was on the other side of Tommen, in the place of honor. When she entered, arm in arm with the little king, she made a point of stopping to kiss Cersei on the cheeks and throw her arms around her. "Your Grace," the girl said, bold as polished brass, "I feel as though I have a second mother now. I pray that we shall be very close, united by our love for your sweet son."

"I loved both my sons."

"Joffrey is in my prayers as well," said Margaery. "I loved him dearly, though I never had the chance to know him."

Liar, the queen thought. *If you had loved him even for an instant, you would not have been in such unseemly haste to wed his brother. His crown was all you ever wanted.* For half a groat she would have slapped the blushing bride right there upon the dais, in view of half the court.

Like the service, the wedding feast was modest. Lady Alerie had made all the arrangements; Cersei had not had the stomach to face that daunting task again, after the way Joffrey's wedding had ended. Only seven courses were served. Butterbumps and Moon Boy entertained the guests between dishes, and musicians played as they ate. They listened to pipers and fiddlers, a lute and a flute, a high harp. The only singer was some favorite of Lady Margaery's, a dashing young cock-a-whoop clad all in shades of azure who called himself the Blue Bard. He sang a few love songs and retired. "What a disappointment," Lady Olenna complained loudly. "I was hoping for 'The Rains of Castamere.'"

Whenever Cersei looked at the old crone, the face of Maggy the Frog seemed to float before her eyes, wrinkled and terrible and wise. *All old women look alike,* she tried to tell herself, *that's all it is.* In truth, the bent-back sorceress had looked nothing like the Queen of Thorns, yet somehow the sight of Lady Olenna's nasty little smile was enough to put her back in Maggy's tent again. She could still remember the smell of it, redolent with queer eastern spices, and the softness of Maggy's gums as she sucked the blood from Cersei's finger. *Queen you shall be,* the old woman had promised, with her lips still wet and red and glistening, *until there comes another, younger and more beautiful, to cast you down and take all that you hold dear.*

Cersei glanced past Tommen, to where Margaery sat laughing with her father. *She is pretty enough,* she had to admit, *but most of that is youth. Even peasant girls are pretty at a certain age, when they are still fresh and innocent and unspoiled, and most of them have the same brown hair and brown eyes as she does. Only a fool would ever claim she was more beautiful than I.* The world was full of fools, however. So was her son's court.

Her mood was not improved when Mace Tyrell arose to lead the toasts. He raised a golden goblet high, smiling at his pretty little daughter, and in a booming voice said, "To the king and queen!" The other sheep all *baaaaaa*ed along with him. *"The king and queen!"* they cried, smashing their cups together. *"The king and queen!"* She had no choice but to drink along with them, all the time wishing that the guests had but a single face, so she could throw her wine into their eyes and remind them that *she* was the true queen. The only one of Tyrell's lickspittles who seemed to remember her at all was Paxter Redwyne, who rose to make his own toast, swaying slightly. *"To both our queens!"* he chirruped. *"To the young queen and the old!"*

Cersei drank several cups of wine and pushed her food around a golden plate. Jaime ate even less, and seldom deigned to occupy his seat upon the dais. *He is as anxious as I am,* the queen realized as she watched him prowl the hall, twitching aside the tapestries with his good hand to assure himself that no one was hiding behind them. There were Lannister spearmen posted around the building, she knew. Ser Osmund Kettleblack guarded one door, Ser Meryn Trant the other. Balon Swann stood behind the king's chair, Loras Tyrell behind the queen's. No swords had been allowed inside the feast save for those the white knights bore.

My son is safe, Cersei told herself. *No harm can come to him, not here, not now.* Yet every time she looked at Tommen, she saw Joffrey clawing at his throat. And when the boy began to cough the queen's heart stopped beating for a moment. She knocked aside a serving girl in her haste to reach him.

"Only a little wine that went down the wrong way," Margaery Tyrell assured her, smiling. She took Tommen's hand in her own and kissed his fingers. "My little love needs to take smaller sips. See, you scared your lady mother half to death."

"I'm sorry, Mother," Tommen said, abashed.

It was more than Cersei could stand. *I cannot let them see me cry,* she thought, when she felt the tears welling in her eyes. She walked past Ser Meryn Trant and out into the back passage. Alone beneath a tallow candle, she allowed herself a shuddering sob, then another. *A woman may weep, but not a queen.*

"Your Grace?" said a voice behind her. "Do I intrude?"

It was a woman's voice, flavored with the accents of the east. For an instant she feared that Maggy the Frog was speaking to her from the grave. But it was only Merryweather's wife, the sloe-eyed beauty Lord Orton had wed during his exile and fetched home with him to Longtable. "The Small Hall is so stuffy," Cersei heard herself say. "The smoke was making my eyes water."

"And mine, Your Grace." Lady Merryweather was as tall as the queen, but dark instead of fair, raven-haired and olive-skinned and younger by a decade. She offered the queen a pale blue handkerchief of silk and lace. "I have a son as well. I know that I shall weep rivers on the day he weds."

Cersei wiped her cheeks, furious that she had let her tears be seen. "My thanks," she said stiffly.

"Your Grace, I . . ." The Myrish woman lowered her voice. "There is something you must know. Your maid is bought and paid for. She tells Lady Margaery everything you do."

"Senelle?" Sudden fury twisted in the queen's belly. Was there no one she could trust? "You are certain of this?"

"Have her followed. Margaery never meets with her directly. Her cousins are her ravens, they bring her messages. Sometimes Elinor, sometimes Alla, sometimes Megga. All of them are as close to Margaery as sisters. They meet in the sept and pretend to pray. Put your own man in the gallery on the morrow, and he will see Senelle whispering to Megga beneath the altar of the Maiden."

"If this is true, why tell me? You are one of Margaery's companions. Why would you betray her?" Cersei had learned suspicion at her father's knee; this could well be some trap, a lie meant to sow discord between the lion and the rose.

"Longtable may be sworn to Highgarden," the woman replied, with a toss of her black hair, "but I am of Myr, and my loyalty is to my husband and my son. I want all that is best for them."

"I see." In the closeness of the passage, the queen could smell the other woman's perfume, a musky scent that spoke of moss and earth and wildflowers. Under it, she smelled ambition. *She gave testimony at Tyrion's trial,* Cersei recalled suddenly. *She saw the Imp put the poison in Joff's cup and was not afraid to say so.* "I shall look into this," she promised. "If what you say is true, you will be rewarded." *And if you've lied to me, I'll have your tongue, and your lord husband's lands and gold as well.*

"Your Grace is kind. And beautiful." Lady Merryweather smiled. Her teeth were white, her lips full and dark.

When the queen returned to the Small Hall, she found her brother pacing restlessly. "It was only a gulp of wine that went down the wrong way. Though it startled me as well."

"My belly is such a knot that I cannot eat," she growled at him. "The wine tastes of bile. This wedding was a mistake."

"This wedding was necessary. The boy is safe."

"Fool. No one who wears a crown is ever safe." She looked about the hall. Mace Tyrell laughed amongst his knights. Lords Redwyne and Rowan were talking furtively. Ser Kevan sat brooding over his wine at the back of the hall, whilst Lancel whispered something to a septon. Senelle was moving down the table, filling the cups of the bride's cousins with wine as red as blood. Grand Maester Pycelle had fallen asleep. *There is no one I can rely upon, not even Jaime,* she realized grimly. *I will need to sweep them all away and surround the king with mine own people.*

Later, after sweets and nuts and cheese had been served and cleared away, Margaery and Tommen began the dancing, looking more than a bit ridiculous as they whirled about the floor. The Tyrell girl stood a good foot and a half taller than her little husband, and Tommen was a clumsy dancer at best, with none of Joffrey's easy grace. He did his earnest best, though, and seemed oblivious to the spectacle he was making of himself. And no sooner was Maid Margaery done with him than her cousins swooped in, one after the other, insisting that His Grace must dance with them as well. *They will have him stumbling and shuffling like a fool by the time they're done,* Cersei thought resentfully as she watched. *Half the court will be laughing at him behind his back.*

Whilst Alla, Elinor, and Megga took their turns with Tommen, Margaery took a turn around the floor with her father, then another with her brother Loras. The Knight of Flowers was in white silk, with a belt of golden roses about his waist and a jade rose fastening his cloak. *They could be twins,* Cersei thought as she watched them. Ser Loras was a year older than his sister, but they had the same big brown eyes, the same thick brown hair falling in lazy ringlets to their shoulders, the same smooth unblemished skin. *A ripe crop of pimples would teach them some humility.* Loras was taller and had a few wisps of soft brown fuzz on his face, and Margaery had a woman's shape, but elsewise they were more alike than she and Jaime. That annoyed her too.

Her own twin interrupted her musings. "Would Your Grace honor her white knight with a dance?"

She gave him a withering look. "And have you fumbling at me with that stump? No. I will let you fill my wine cup for me, though. If you think you can manage it without spilling."

"A cripple like me? Not likely." He moved away and made another circuit of the hall. She had to fill her own cup.

Cersei refused Mace Tyrell as well, and later Lancel. The others took the hint, and no one else approached her. *Our fast friends and loyal lords.* She could not even trust the westermen, her father's sworn swords and bannermen. Not if her own uncle was conspiring with her enemies . . .

Margaery was dancing with her cousin Alla, Megga with Ser Tallad the Tall. The other cousin, Elinor, was sharing a cup of wine with the handsome young Bastard of Driftmark, Aurane Waters. It was not the first time the queen had made note of Waters, a lean young man with grey-green eyes and long silver-gold hair. The first time she had seen him, for half a heartbeat she had almost thought Rhaegar Targaryen had returned from the ashes. *It is his hair,* she told herself. *He is not half as comely as Rhaegar was. His face is too narrow, and he has that cleft in his chin.* The Velaryons came from old Valyrian stock, however, and some had the same silvery hair as the dragon-kings of old.

Tommen returned to his seat to nibble at an applecake. Her uncle's place was empty. The queen finally found him in a corner, talking intently with Mace Tyrell's son Garlan. *What do they have to talk about?* The Reach might call Ser Garlan gallant, but she trusted him no more than Margaery or Loras. She had not forgotten the gold coin that Qyburn had discovered beneath the gaoler's chamber pot. *A golden hand from Highgarden. And Margaery is spying on me.* When Senelle appeared to fill her wine cup, the queen had to resist an urge to take her by the throat and throttle her. *Do not presume to smile at me, you treacherous little bitch. You will be begging me for mercy before I'm done with you.*

"I think Her Grace has had enough wine for one night," she heard her brother Jaime say.

No, the queen thought. *All the wine in the world would not be enough to see me through this wedding.* She rose so fast she almost fell. Jaime caught her by the arm and steadied her. She wrenched free and clapped her hands together. The music died, the voices stilled. *"Lords and ladies,"* Cersei called out loudly, "if you will be so good as to come outside with me, we shall light a candle to celebrate the union of Highgarden and Casterly Rock, and a new age of peace and plenty for our Seven Kingdoms."

Dark and forlorn stood the Tower of the Hand, with only gaping holes where oaken doors and shuttered windows had once been. Yet even ruined and slighted, it loomed above the outer ward. As the wedding guests filed out of the Small Hall, they passed beneath its shadow. When Cersei looked up she saw the tower's crenellated battlements gnawing at a hunter's moon, and wondered for a moment how many Hands of how many kings had made their home there over the past three centuries.

A hundred yards from the tower, she took a breath to stop her head from spinning. "Lord Hallyne! You may commence."

Hallyne the pyromancer said *"Hmmmmmm"* and waved the torch he was holding, and the archers on the walls bent their bows and sent a dozen flaming arrows through the gaping windows.

The tower went up with a *whoosh*. In half a heartbeat its interior was alive with light, red, yellow, orange . . . and green, an ominous dark green, the color of bile and jade and pyromancer's piss. "The substance," the alchemists named it, but common folk called it *wildfire*. Fifty pots had been placed inside the Tower of the Hand, along with logs and casks of pitch and the greater part of the worldly possessions of a dwarf named Tyrion Lannister.

The queen could feel the heat of those green flames. The pyromancers said that only three things burned hotter than their substance: dragonflame, the fires beneath the earth, and the summer sun. Some of the ladies gasped when the first flames appeared in the windows, licking up the outer walls like long green tongues. Others cheered, and made toasts.

It is beautiful, she thought, *as beautiful as Joffrey, when they laid him in my arms.* No man had ever made her feel as good as she had felt when he took her nipple in his mouth to nurse.

Tommen stared wide-eyed at the fires, as fascinated as he was frightened, until Margaery whispered something in his ear that made him laugh. Some of the knights began to make wagers on how long it would be before the tower collapsed. Lord Hallyne stood humming to himself and rocking on his heels.

Cersei thought of all the King's Hands that she had known through the years: Owen Merryweather, Jon Connington, Qarlton Chelsted, Jon Arryn, Eddard Stark, her brother Tyrion. And her father, Lord Tywin Lannister, her father most of all. *All of them are burning now,* she told herself, savoring the thought. *They are dead and burning, every one, with all their plots and schemes and betrayals. It is my day now. It is my castle and my kingdom.*

The Tower of the Hand gave out a sudden groan, so loud that all the conversation stopped abruptly. Stone cracked and split, and part of the upper battlements fell away and landed with a crash that shook the hill, sending up a cloud of dust and smoke. As fresh air rushed in through the broken masonry, the fire surged upward. Green flames leapt into the sky and whirled around each other. Tommen shied away, till Margaery took his hand and said, "Look, the flames are dancing. Just as we did, my love."

"They are." His voice was filled with wonder. "Mother, look, they're dancing."

"I see them. Lord Hallyne, how long will the fires burn?"

"All night, Your Grace."

"It makes a pretty candle, I grant you," said Lady Olenna Tyrell, leaning on her cane between Left and Right. "Bright enough to see us safe to sleep, I think. Old bones grow weary, and these young ones have had enough excitement for one night. It is time the king and queen were put to bed."

"Yes." Cersei beckoned to Jaime. "Lord Commander, escort His Grace and his little queen to their pillows, if you would."

"As you command. And you as well?"

"No need." Cersei felt too alive for sleep. The wildfire was cleansing her, burning away all her rage and fear, filling her with resolve. "The flames are so pretty. I want to watch them for a while."

Jaime hesitated. "You should not stay alone."

"I will not be alone. Ser Osmund can remain with me and keep me safe. Your Sworn Brother."

"If it please Your Grace," said Kettleblack.

"It does." Cersei slid her arm through his, and side by side they watched the fire rage.

THE SOILED KNIGHT

The night was unseasonably cool, even for autumn. A brisk wet wind was swirling down the alleys, stirring up the day's dust. *A north wind, and full of chill.* Ser Arys Oakheart pulled up his hood to cover his face. It would not do for him to be recognized. A fortnight past, a trader had been butchered in the shadow city, a harmless man who'd come to Dorne for fruit and found death instead of dates. His only crime was being from King's Landing.

The mob would find a sterner foe in me. He would almost have welcomed an attack. His hand drifted down to brush lightly over the hilt on the longsword that hung half-hidden amongst the folds of his layered linen robes, the outer with its turquoise stripes and rows of golden suns, and the lighter orange one beneath. The Dornish garb was comfortable, but his father would have been aghast had he lived to see his son so dressed. He was a man of the Reach, and the Dornish were his ancient foes, as the tapestries at Old Oak bore witness. Arys only had to close his eyes to see them still. Lord Edgerran the Open-Handed, seated in splendor with the heads of a hundred Dornishmen piled round his feet. The Three Leaves in the Prince's Pass, pierced by Dornish spears, Alester sounding his warhorn with his last breath. Ser Olyvar the Green Oak all in white, dying at the side of the Young Dragon. *Dorne is no fit place for any Oakheart.*

Even before Prince Oberyn had died, the knight had been ill at ease whenever he left the grounds of Sunspear to walk the alleys of the shadow city. He could feel eyes upon him everywhere he went, small black Dornish eyes regarding him with thinly veiled hostility. The shopkeepers did their best to cheat him at every turn, and sometimes he wondered whether the taverners were spitting in his drinks. Once a group of ragged boys began pelting him with stones, until he drew his sword and ran them off. The Red Viper's death had inflamed the Dornish even more, though the streets had quieted a bit since Prince Doran had confined the Sand Snakes to a tower. Even so, to wear his white cloak openly in the shadow city would be asking for attack. He had brought three with him: two of wool, one light and one heavy, the third of fine white silk. He felt naked without one hanging from his shoulders.

Better naked than dead, he told himself. *I am a Kingsguard still, even uncloaked. She must respect that. I must make her understand.* He should never have let himself be drawn into this, but the singer said that love can make a fool of any man.

Sunspear's shadow city oft seemed deserted in the heat of the day, when only buzzing flies moved down the dusty streets, but once evening fell the same streets came to life.

Ser Arys heard faint music drifting through louvered windows as he passed below, and somewhere finger drums were beating out the quick rhythm of a spear dance, giving the night a pulse. Where three alleys met beneath the second of the Winding Walls, a pillow girl called down from a balcony. She was dressed in jewels and oil. He took a look at her, hunched his shoulders, and pushed on, into the teeth of the wind. *We men are so weak. Our bodies betray even the noblest of us.* He thought of King Baelor the Blessed, who would fast to the point of fainting to tame the lusts that shamed him. Must he do the same?

A short man stood in an arched doorway grilling chunks of snake over a brazier, turning them with wooden tongs as they crisped. The pungent smell of his sauces brought tears to the knight's eyes. The best snake sauce had a drop of venom in it, he had heard, along with mustard seeds and dragon peppers. Myrcella had taken to Dornish food as quick as she had to her Dornish prince, and from time to time Ser Arys would try a dish or two to please her. The food seared his mouth and made him gasp for wine, and burned even worse coming out than it did going in. His little princess loved it, though.

He had left her in her chambers, bent over a gaming table opposite Prince Trystane, pushing ornate pieces across squares of jade and carnelian and lapis lazuli. Myrcella's full lips had been slightly parted, her green eyes narrowed with concentration. *Cyvasse,* the game was called. It had come to the Planky Town on a trading galley from Volantis, and the orphans had spread it up and down the Greenblood. The Dornish court was mad for it.

Ser Arys just found it maddening. There were ten different pieces, each with its own attributes and powers, and the board would change from game to game, depending on how the players arrayed their home squares. Prince

Trystane had taken to the game at once, and Myrcella had learned it so she could play with him. She was not quite one-and-ten, her betrothed three-and-ten; even so, she had been winning more oft than not of late. Trystane did not seem to mind. The two children could not have looked more different, him with his olive skin and straight black hair, her pale as milk with a mop of golden curls; light and dark, like Queen Cersei and King Robert. He prayed Myrcella would find more joy in her Dornish boy than her mother had found with her storm lord.

It made him feel uneasy to leave her, though she should be safe enough within the castle. There were only two doors that gave access to Myrcella's chambers in the Tower of the Sun, and Ser Arys kept two men on each; Lannister household guards, men who had come with them from King's Landing, battle-tested, tough, and loyal to the bone. Myrcella had her maids and Septa Eglantine as well, and Prince Trystane was attended by his sworn shield, Ser Gascoyne of the Greenblood. *No one will trouble her,* he told himself, *and in a fortnight we shall be safely away.*

Prince Doran had promised as much. Though Arys had been shocked to see how aged and infirm the Dornish prince appeared, he did not doubt the prince's word. "I am sorry I could not see you until now, or meet Princess Myrcella," Martell had said when Arys was admitted to his solar, "but I trust that my daughter Arianne has made you welcome here in Dorne, ser."

"She has, my prince," he'd answered, and prayed that no blush would dare betray him.

"Ours is a harsh land, and poor, yet not without its beauties. It grieves us that you have seen no more of Dorne than Sunspear, but I fear that neither you nor your princess would be safe beyond these walls. We Dornish are a hot-blooded people, quick to anger and slow to forgive. It would gladden my heart if I could assure you that the Sand Snakes were alone in wanting war, but I will not tell you lies, ser. You have heard my smallfolk in the streets, crying out for me to call my spears. Half my lords agree with them, I fear."

"And you, my prince?" the knight had dared to ask.

"My mother taught me long ago that only madmen fight wars they cannot win." If the bluntness of the question had offended him, Prince Doran hid it well. "Yet this peace is fragile . . . as fragile as your princess."

"Only a beast would harm a little girl."

"My sister Elia had a little girl as well. Her name was Rhaenys. She was a princess too." The prince sighed. "Those who would plunge a knife into Princess Myrcella do not bear her any malice, no more than Ser Amory Lorch did when he killed Rhaenys, if indeed he did. They seek only to force my hand. For if Myrcella should be slain in Dorne whilst under my protection, who would believe my denials?"

"No one shall ever harm Myrcella whilst I live."

"A noble vow," said Doran Martell with a faint smile, "but you are only one man, ser. I had hoped that imprisoning my headstrong nieces would help to calm the waters, but all we've done is drive the roaches back beneath the rushes. Every night I hear them whispering and sharpening their knives."

He is afraid, Ser Arys realized then. *Look, his hand is shaking. The Prince of Dorne is terrified.* Words failed him.

"My apologies, ser," Prince Doran said. "I am frail and failing, and sometimes . . . Sunspear wearies me, with its noise and dirt and smells. As soon as my duty allows, I mean to return to the Water Gardens. When I do I shall take Princess Myrcella with me." Before the knight could protest, the prince raised a hand, its knuckles red and swollen. "You shall go as well. And her septa, her maids, her guards. Sunspear's walls are strong, but beneath them is the shadow city. Even within the castle hundreds come and go each day. The Gardens are my haven. Prince Maron raised them as a gift for his Targaryen bride, to mark Dorne's marriage to the Iron Throne. Autumn is a lovely season there . . . hot days, cool nights, the salt breeze off the sea, the fountains and the pools. And there are other children, boys and girls of high and gentle birth. Myrcella will have friends of her own age to play with. She will not be lonely."

"As you say." The prince's words pounded in his head. *She will be safe there.* Only why had Doran Martell urged him not to write King's Landing about the move? *Myrcella will be safest if no one knows just where she is.* Ser Arys had agreed, but what choice did he have? He was a knight of the Kingsguard, but only one man for all that, just as the prince had said.

The alley opened suddenly onto a moonlit courtyard. *Past the candlemaker's shop,* she wrote, *a gate and a short flight of exterior steps.* He pushed through the gate and climbed the worn steps to an unmarked door. *Should I knock?* He pushed the door open instead, and found himself in a large, dim room with a low ceiling, lit by a pair of scented candles that flickered in niches cut from the thick earthen walls. He saw patterned Myrish carpets underneath his sandals, a tapestry upon one wall, a bed. "My lady?" he called. "Where are you?"

"Here." She stepped out from the shadow behind the door.

An ornate snake coiled around her right forearm, its

copper and gold scales glimmering when she moved. It was all she wore.

No, he meant to tell her, *I only came to tell you I must go,* but when he saw her shining in the candlelight he seemed to lose the power of speech. His throat felt as dry as the Dornish sands. Silent he stood, drinking in the glories of her body, the hollow of her throat, the round ripe breasts with their huge dark nipples, the lush curves at waist and hip. And then somehow he was holding her, and she was pulling off his robes. When she reached his undertunic she seized it by the shoulders and ripped the silk down to his navel, but Arys was past caring. Her skin was smooth beneath his fingers, as warm to the touch as sand baked by the Dornish sun. He raised her head and found her lips. Her mouth opened under his, and her breasts filled his hands. He felt her nipples stiffen as his thumbs brushed over them. Her hair was black and thick and smelled of orchids, a dark and earthy smell that made him so hard it almost hurt.

"Touch me, ser," the woman whispered in his ear. His hand slipped down her rounded belly to find the sweet wet place beneath the thicket of black hair. "Yes, there," she murmured as he slipped a finger up inside her. She made a whimpering sound, drew him to the bed, and pushed him down. "More, oh more, yes, sweet, my knight, my knight, my sweet white knight, yes you, you, I want you." Her hands guided him inside her, then slipped around his back to pull him closer. "Deeper," she whispered. "Yes, oh." When she wrapped her legs around him, they felt as strong as steel. Her nails raked his back as he drove into her, again and again and again, until she screamed and arched her back beneath him. As she did, her fingers found his nipples, pinching till he spent his seed within her. *I could die now, happy,* the knight thought, and for a dozen heart-beats at least he was at peace.

He did not die.

His desire was as deep and boundless as the sea, but when the tide receded, the rocks of shame and guilt thrust up as sharp as ever. Sometimes the waves would cover them, but they remained beneath the waters, hard and black and slimy. *What am I doing?* he asked himself. *I am a knight of the Kingsguard.* He rolled off of her to sprawl staring at the ceiling. A great crack ran across it, from one wall to the other. He had not noticed that before, no more than he had noticed the picture on the tapestry, a scene of Nymeria and her ten thousand ships. *I see only her. A dragon might have been peering in the window, and I would never have seen anything but her breasts, her face, her smile.*

"There is wine," she murmured against his neck. She slid a hand across his chest. "Are you thirsty?"

"No." He rolled away, and sat on the edge of the bed. The room was hot, and yet he shivered.

"You bleed," she said. "I scratched too hard."

When she touched his back, he flinched as if her fingers were afire. "Don't." Naked, he stood. "No more."

"I have balm. For the scratches."

But none for my shame. "The scratches are nothing. Forgive me, my lady, I must go . . ."

"So soon?" She had a husky voice, a wide mouth made for whispers, full lips ripe for kissing. Her hair tumbled down across her bare shoulders to the tops of her full breasts, black and thick. It curled in big soft lazy ringlets. Even the hair upon her mound was soft and curly. "Stay with me tonight, ser. I still have much to teach you."

"I have learned too much from you already."

"You seemed glad enough for the lessons at the time,

ser. Are you certain you are not off to some other bed, some other woman? Tell me who she is. I will fight her for you, bare-breasted, knife to knife." She smiled. "Unless she is a Sand Snake. If so, we can share you. I love my cousins well."

"You know I have no other woman. Only . . . duty."

She rolled onto one elbow to look up at him, her big black eyes shining in the candlelight. "That poxy bitch? I know her. Dry as dust between the legs, and her kisses leave you bleeding. Let duty sleep alone for once, and stay with me tonight."

"My place is at the palace."

She sighed. "With your other princess. You will make me jealous. I think you love her more than me. The maid is much too young for you. You need a woman, not a little girl, but I can play the innocent if that excites you."

"You should not say such things." *Remember, she is Dornish.* In the Reach men said it was the food that made Dornishmen so hot-tempered and their women so wild and wanton. *Fiery peppers and strange spices heat the blood, she cannot help herself.* "I love Myrcella as a daughter." He could never have a daughter of his own, no more than he could have a wife. He had a fine white cloak instead. "We are going to the Water Gardens."

"Eventually," she agreed, "though with my father, everything takes four times as long as it should. If he says he means to leave upon the morrow, you will certainly set out within a fortnight. You will be lonely in the Gardens, I promise you. And where is the brave young gallant who said he wished to spend the rest of his life in my arms?"

"I was drunk when I said that."

"You'd had three cups of watered wine."

"I was drunk on you. It had been ten years since . . . I never touched a woman until you, not since I took the white. I never knew what love could be, yet now . . . I am afraid."

"What would frighten my white knight?"

"I fear for my honor," he said, "and for yours."

"I can tend to my own honor." She touched a finger to her breast, drawing it slowly round her nipple. "And to my own pleasures, if need be. I am a woman grown."

She was that, beyond a doubt. Seeing her there upon the featherbed, smiling that wicked smile, toying with her breast . . . was there ever a woman with nipples so large or so responsive? He could hardly look at them without wanting to grab them, to suckle them until they were hard and wet and shiny . . .

He looked away. His smallclothes were strewn on the carpets. The knight bent to pick them up.

"Your hands are shaking," she pointed out. "They would sooner be caressing me, I think. Must you be in such haste to don your clothes, ser? I prefer you as you are. Abed, unclad, we are our truest selves, a man and a woman, lovers, one flesh, as close as two can be. Our clothes make us different people. I would sooner be flesh and blood than silks and jewels, and you . . . you are not your white cloak, ser."

"I am," Ser Arys said. "I *am* my cloak. And this must end, for your sake as well as mine. If we should be discovered . . ."

"Men will think you fortunate."

"Men will think me an oathbreaker. What if someone were to go to your father and tell him how I'd dishonored you?"

"My father is many things, but no one has ever said he was a fool. The Bastard of Godsgrace had my maidenhead when we were both fourteen. Do you know what my father did when he learned of it?" She gathered the bedclothes in her fist and pulled them up under her chin, to hide her nakedness. "Nothing. My father is very good at doing nothing. He calls it *thinking*. Tell me true, ser, is it my dishonor that concerns you, or your own?"

"Both." Her accusation stung. "That is why this must be our last time."

"So you have said before."

I did, and meant it too. But I am weak, else I would not be here now. He could not tell her that; she was the sort of woman who despised weakness, he could sense that. *She has more of her uncle in her than her father.* He turned away and found his striped silk undertunic on a chair. She had ripped the fabric to the navel when she pulled it down over his arms. "This is ruined," he complained. "How can I wear it now?"

"Backwards," she suggested. "Once you don your robes, no one will see the tear. Perhaps your little princess will sew it up for you. Or shall I send a new one to the Water Gardens?"

"Send me no gifts." That would only draw attention. He shook out the undertunic and pulled it over his head, backwards. The silk felt cool against his skin, though it clung to his back where she'd scratched him. It would serve to get him back to the palace, at the least. "All I want is to end this . . . this . . ."

"Is that gallant, ser? You hurt me. I begin to think that all your words of love were lies."

I could never lie to you. Ser Arys felt as if she'd slapped him. "Why else would I have forsaken all my honor, but for love? When I am with you I . . . I can scarcely think, you are all I ever dreamt of, but . . ."

"Words are wind. If you love me, do not leave me."

"I swore a *vow* . . ."

". . . not to wed or father children. Well, I have drunk

my moon tea, and you know I cannot marry you." She smiled. "Though I might be persuaded to keep you for my paramour."

"Now you mock me."

"Perhaps a little. Do you think you are the only Kingsguard who ever loved a woman?"

"There have always been men who found it easier to speak vows than to keep them," he admitted. Ser Boros Blount was no stranger to the Street of Silk, and Ser Preston Greenfield used to call at a certain draper's house whenever the draper was away, but Arys would not shame his Sworn Brothers by speaking of their failings. "Ser Terrence Toyne was found abed with his king's mistress," he said instead. "'Twas love, he swore, but it cost his life and hers, and brought about the downfall of his House and the death of the noblest knight who ever lived."

"Yes, and what of Lucamore the Lusty, with his three wives and sixteen children? The song always makes me laugh."

"The truth is not so funny. He was never called Lucamore the Lusty whilst he lived. His name was Ser Lucamore Strong, and his whole life was a lie. When his deceit was discovered, his own Sworn Brothers gelded him, and the Old King sent him to the Wall. Those sixteen children were left weeping. He was no true knight, no more than Terrence Toyne . . ."

"And the Dragonknight?" She flung the bedclothes aside and swung her legs to the floor. "The noblest knight who ever lived, you said, and he took his queen to bed and got her with child."

"I will not believe that," he said, offended. "The tale of Prince Aemon's treason with Queen Naerys was only that, a tale, a lie his brother told when he wished to set his true-born son aside in favor of his bastard. Aegon was not called the Unworthy without cause." He found his sword-belt and buckled it around his waist. Though it looked queer against the silken Dornish undertunic, the familiar weight of longsword and dagger reminded him of who and what he was. "I will not be remembered as Ser Arys the Unworthy," he declared. "I will not soil my cloak."

"Yes," she said, "that fine white cloak. You forget, my great-uncle wore the same cloak. He died when I was little, yet I still remember him. He was as tall as a tower and used to tickle me until I could not breathe for laughing."

"I never had the honor to know Prince Lewyn," Ser Arys said, "but all agree that he was a great knight."

"A great knight with a paramour. She is an old woman now, but she was a rare beauty in her youth, men say."

Prince Lewyn? That tale Ser Arys had not heard. It shocked him. Terrence Toyne's treason and the deceits of Lucamore the Lusty were recorded in the White Book, but there was no hint of a woman on Prince Lewyn's page.

"My uncle always said that it was the sword in a man's hand that determined his worth, not the one between his legs," she went on, "so spare me all your pious talk of soiled cloaks. It is not our love that has dishonored you, it is the monsters you have served and the brutes you've called your brothers."

That cut too close to the bone. "Robert was no monster."

"He climbed onto his throne over the corpses of children," she said, "though I will grant you he was no Joffrey."

Joffrey. He had been a handsome lad, tall and strong for his age, but that was all the good that could be said of him. It still shamed Ser Arys to remember all the times he'd struck that poor Stark girl at the boy's command. When Tyrion had chosen him to go with Myrcella to Dorne, he lit a candle to the Warrior in thanks. "Joffrey is dead, poisoned by the Imp." He would never have thought the dwarf capable of such enormity. "Tommen is king now, and he is not his brother."

"Nor is he his sister."

It was true. Tommen was a good-hearted little man who always tried his best, but the last time Ser Arys saw him he had been weeping on the quay. Myrcella never shed a tear, though it was she who was leaving hearth and home to seal an alliance with her maidenhood. The truth was, the princess was braver than her brother, and brighter and more confident as well. Her wits were quicker, her courtesies more polished. Nothing ever daunted her, not even Joffrey. *The women are the strong ones, truly.* He was thinking not only of Myrcella, but of her mother and his own, of the Queen of Thorns, of the Red Viper's pretty, deadly Sand Snakes. And of Princess Arianne Martell, her most of all. "I will not say that you are wrong." His voice was hoarse.

"Will not? *Cannot!* Myrcella is more fit for rule . . ."

"A son comes before a daughter."

"*Why?* What god has made it so? I am my father's heir. Should I give up my rights to my brothers?"

"You twist my words. I never said . . . Dorne is different. The Seven Kingdoms have never had a ruling queen."

"The first Viserys intended his daughter Rhaenyra to follow him, do you deny it? But as the king lay dying the Lord Commander of his Kingsguard decided that it should be otherwise."

Ser Criston Cole. Criston the Kingmaker had set brother against sister and divided the Kingsguard against itself, bringing on the terrible war the singers named the Dance of the Dragons. Some claimed he acted from ambition, for Prince Aegon was more tractable than his willful older sister. Others allowed him nobler motives, and argued that he was defending ancient Andal custom. A few whispered that Ser Criston had been Princess Rhaenyra's lover before he took the white and wanted vengeance on the woman who had spurned him. "The Kingmaker wrought grave harm," Ser Arys said, "and gravely did he pay for it, but . . ."

". . . but perhaps the Seven sent you here so that one white knight might make right what another set awry. You do know that when my father returns to the Water Gardens he plans to take Myrcella with him?"

"To keep her safe from those who would do her harm."

"No. To keep her away from those who'd seek to *crown* her. Prince Oberyn Viper would have placed the crown upon her head himself if he had lived, but my father lacks the courage." She got to her feet. "You say you love the girl as you would a daughter of your own blood. Would you let your daughter be despoiled of her rights and locked away in prison?"

"The Water Gardens are no prison," he protested feebly.

"A prison does not have fountains and fig trees, is that what you think? Yet once the girl is there, she will not be allowed to leave. No more than you will. Hotah will see to that. You do not know him as I do. He is terrible when aroused."

Ser Arys frowned. The big Norvoshi captain with the scarred face had always made him feel profoundly uneasy. *They say he sleeps with that great axe beside him.* "What would you have me do?"

"No more than you have sworn. Protect Myrcella with your life. Defend her . . . *and* her rights. Set a crown upon her head."

"I swore an *oath*!"

"To Joffrey, not to Tommen."

"Aye, but Tommen is a good-hearted boy. He will be a better king than Joffrey."

"But not better than Myrcella. She loves the boy as well. I know she will not let him come to any harm. Storm's End is his by rights, since Lord Renly left no heir and Lord Stannis is attainted. In time, Casterly Rock will pass to the boy as well, through his lady mother. He will be as great a lord as any in the realm . . . but Myrcella by rights should sit the Iron Throne."

"The law . . . I do not know . . ."

"I do." When she stood, the long black tangle of her hair fell down to the small of her back. "Aegon the Dragon made the Kingsguard and its vows, but what one king does another can undo, or change. Formerly the Kingsguard served for life, yet Joffrey dismissed Ser Barristan so his dog could have a cloak. Myrcella would want you to be happy, and she is fond of me as well. She will give us leave to marry if we ask." Arianne put her arms around him and laid her face against his chest. The top of her head came to just beneath his chin. "You can have me and your white cloak both, if that is what you want."

She is tearing me apart. "You know I do, but . . ."

"I am a princess of Dorne," she said in her husky voice, "and it is not meet that you should make me beg."

Ser Arys could smell the perfume in her hair and feel her heart beating as she pressed against him. His body was responding to her closeness, and he did not doubt that she could feel it too. When he put his arms upon her shoulders, he realized she was trembling. "Arianne? My princess? What is it, my love?"

"Must I say it, ser? I am afraid. You call me *love,* yet you refuse me, when I have most desperate need of you. Is it so wrong of me to want a knight to keep me safe?"

He had never heard her sound so vulnerable. "No," he

said, "but you have your father's guards to keep you safe, why—"

"It is my father's guards I fear." For a moment she sounded younger than Myrcella. "It was my father's guards who dragged my sweet cousins off in chains."

"Not in chains. I have heard that they have every comfort."

She gave a bitter laugh. "Have you seen them? He will not permit me to see them, did you know that?"

"They were speaking treason, fomenting war . . ."

"Loreza is six, Dorea eight. What wars could they foment? Yet my father has imprisoned them with their sisters. You have seen him. Fear makes even strong men do things they might never do otherwise, and my father was never strong. Arys, my heart, hear me for the love you say you bear me. I have never been as fearless as my cousins, for I was made with weaker seed, but Tyene and I are of an age and have been close as sisters since we were little girls. We have no secrets between us. If she can be imprisoned, so can I, and for the same cause . . . this of Myrcella."

"Your father would never do that."

"You do not know my father. I have been disappointing him since I first arrived in this world without a cock. Half a dozen times he has tried to marry me to toothless greybeards, each more contemptible than the last. He never *commanded* me to wed them, I grant you, but the offers alone prove how little he regards me."

"Even so, you are his heir."

"Am I?"

"He left you to rule in Sunspear when he took himself off to his Water Gardens, did he not?"

"To *rule*? No. He left his cousin Ser Manfrey as castellan, old blind Ricasso as seneschal, his bailiffs to collect duties and taxes for his treasurer Alyse Ladybright to count, his shariffs to police the shadow city, his justiciars to sit in judgment, and Maester Myles to deal with any letters not requiring the prince's own attention. Above them all he placed the Red Viper. My charge was feasts and frolics, and the entertainment of distinguished guests. Oberyn would visit the Water Gardens twice a fortnight. Me, he summoned twice a year. I am not the heir my father wants, he has made that plain. Our laws constrain him, but he would sooner have my brother follow him, I know it."

"Your brother?" Ser Arys put his hand beneath her chin and raised her head, the better to look her in the eyes. "You cannot mean Trystane, he is just a boy."

"Not Trys. Quentyn." Her eyes were bold and black as sin, unflinching. "I have known the truth since I was four-and-ten, since the day that I went to my father's solar to give him a good night kiss, and found him gone. My mother had sent for him, I learned later. He'd left a candle burning. When I went to blow it out, I found a letter lying incomplete beside it, a letter to my brother Quentyn, off at Yronwood. My father told Quentyn that he must do all that his maester and his master-at-arms required of him, because *'one day you will sit where I sit and rule all Dorne, and a ruler must be strong of mind and body.'*" A tear crept down Arianne's soft cheek. "My father's words, written in his own hand. They burned themselves into my memory. I cried myself to sleep that night, and many nights thereafter."

Ser Arys had yet to meet Quentyn Martell. The prince had been fostered by Lord Yronwood from a tender age, had served him as a page, then a squire, had even taken knighthood at his hands in preference to the Red Viper's. *If I were a father, I would want my son to follow me as well,* he thought, but he could hear the hurt in her voice, and he knew that if he said what he was thinking, he would lose her. "Perhaps you misunderstood," he said. "You were only a child. Perhaps the prince was only saying that to encourage your brother to be more diligent."

"You think so? Then tell me, where is Quentyn now?"

"The prince is with Lord Yronwood's host in the Boneway," Ser Arys said cautiously. That was what Sunspear's ancient castellan had told him, when first he came to Dorne. The maester with the silky beard said the same.

Arianne demurred. "So my father wishes us to believe, but I have friends who tell me otherwise. My brother has crossed the narrow sea in secret, posing as a common merchant. Why?"

"How would I know? There could be a hundred reasons."

"Or one. Are you aware that the Golden Company has broken its contract with Myr?"

"Sellswords break their contracts all the time."

"Not the Golden Company. *Our word is good as gold* has been their boast since the days of Bittersteel. Myr is on the point of war with Lys and Tyrosh. Why break a contract that offered them the prospect of good wages and good plunder?"

"Perhaps Lys offered them better wages. Or Tyrosh."

"No," she said. "I would believe it of any of the other free companies, yes. Most of them would change sides for half a groat. The Golden Company is different. A brotherhood of exiles and the sons of exiles, united by the dream of Bittersteel. It's home they want, as much as gold. Lord Yronwood knows that as well as I do. His forebears rode with Bittersteel during three of the Blackfyre Rebellions." She took Ser Arys by the hand, and wove her fingers through his own. "Have you ever seen the arms of House Toland of Ghost Hill?"

He had to think a moment. "A dragon eating its own tail?"

"The dragon is time. It has no beginning and no ending, so all things come round again. Anders Yronwood is Criston Cole reborn. He whispers in my brother's ear that *he* should rule after my father, that it is not right for men to kneel to women . . . that Arianne especially is unfit to rule, being the willful wanton that she is." She tossed her hair defiantly. "So your two princesses share a common cause, ser . . . and they share as well a knight who claims to love them both, but will not fight for them."

"I will." Ser Arys sank to one knee. "Myrcella *is* the elder, and better suited to the crown. Who will defend her rights if not her Kingsguard? My sword, my life, my honor, all belong to her . . . and to you, my heart's delight. I swear, no man will steal your birthright whilst I still have the strength to lift a sword. I am yours. What would you have of me?"

"All." She knelt to kiss his lips. "*All,* my love, my true love, my sweet love, and forever. But first . . ."

"Ask, and it is yours."

". . . Myrcella."

BRIENNE

The stone wall was old and crumbling, but the sight of it across the field made the hairs on Brienne's neck stand up.

That was where the archers hid and slew poor Cleos Frey, she thought . . . but half a mile farther on she passed another wall that looked much like the first and found herself uncertain. The rutted road turned and twisted, and the bare brown trees looked different from the green ones she remembered. Had she ridden past the place where Ser Jaime had snatched his cousin's sword from its scabbard? Where were the woods they'd fought in? The stream where they'd splashed and slashed at one another until they drew the Brave Companions down upon them?

"My lady? Ser?" Podrick never seemed certain what to call her. "What are you looking for?"

Ghosts. "A wall I rode by once. It does not matter." *It*

was when Ser Jaime still had both his hands. How I loathed him, with all his taunts and smiles. "Stay quiet, Podrick. There may still be outlaws in these woods."

The boy looked at the bare brown trees, the wet leaves, the muddy road ahead. "I have a longsword. I can fight."

Not well enough. Brienne did not doubt the boy's courage, only his training. A squire he might be, in name at least, but the men he'd squired for had served him ill.

She had gotten his story out of him in fits and starts on the road from Duskendale. His was a lesser branch of House Payne, an impoverished offshoot sprouted from the loins of a younger son. His father had spent his life squiring for richer cousins and had sired Podrick upon a chandler's daughter he'd wed before going off to die in the Greyjoy Rebellion. His mother had abandoned him with one of those cousins when he was four, so she could run after a wandering singer who had put another baby in her belly. Podrick did not remember what she looked like. Ser Cedric Payne had been the nearest thing to a parent the boy had ever known, though from his stammered stories it seemed to Brienne that cousin Cedric had treated Podrick more like a servant than a son. When Casterly Rock called its banners, the knight had taken him along to tend his horse and clean his mail. Then Ser Cedric had been slain in the riverlands whilst fighting in Lord Tywin's host.

Far from home, alone, and penniless, the boy had attached himself to a fat hedge knight named Ser Lorimer the Belly, who was part of Lord Lefford's contingent, charged with protecting the baggage train. "The boys who guard the foodstuffs always eat the best," Ser Lorimer liked to say, until he was discovered with a salted ham he'd stolen from Lord Tywin's personal stores. Tywin Lannister chose to hang him as a lesson to other looters. Podrick had shared the ham and might have shared the rope as well, but his name had saved him. Ser Kevan Lannister took charge of him, and sometime later sent the boy to squire for his nephew Tyrion.

Ser Cedric had taught Podrick how to groom a horse and check his shoes for stones, and Ser Lorimer had taught him how to steal, but neither had given him much training with a sword. The Imp at least had dispatched him to the Red Keep's master-at-arms when they came to court. But during the bread riots Ser Aron Santagar had been amongst those slain, and that had been the end of Podrick's training.

Brienne cut two wooden swords from fallen branches to get a sense of Podrick's skills. The boy was slow of speech but not of hand, she was pleased to learn. Though fearless and attentive, he was also underfed and skinny, and not near strong enough. If he had survived the Battle of the Blackwater as he claimed, it could only be because no one thought him worth the killing. "You may call yourself a squire," she told him, "but I've seen pages half your age who could have beat you bloody. If you stay with me, you'll go to sleep with blisters on your hands and bruises on your arms most every night, and you'll be so stiff and sore you'll hardly sleep. You don't want that."

"I do," the boy insisted. "I want that. The bruises and the blisters. I mean, I don't, but I do. Ser. My lady."

So far he had been true to his word, and Brienne had been true to hers. Podrick had not complained. Every time he raised a new blister on his sword hand, he felt the need to show it to her proudly. He took good care of their horses too. *He is still no squire,* she reminded herself, *but I am no knight, no matter how many times he calls me "ser."* She would have sent him on his way, but he had nowhere to go. Besides, though Podrick said he did not know where Sansa Stark had gone, it might be that he knew more than he realized. Some chance remark, half-remembered, might hold the key to Brienne's quest.

"Ser? My lady?" Podrick pointed. "There's a cart ahead."

Brienne saw it: a wooden oxcart, two-wheeled and high-sided. A man and a woman were laboring in the traces, pulling the cart along the ruts toward Maidenpool. *Farm folk, by the look of them.* "Slowly now," she told the boy. "They may take us for outlaws. Say no more than you must and be courteous."

"I will, ser. Be courteous. My lady." The boy seemed almost pleased by the prospect of being taken for an outlaw.

The farm folk watched them warily as they came trotting up, but once Brienne made it plain that she meant them no harm, they let her ride beside them. "We used to have an ox," the old man told her as they made their way through the weed-choked fields, lakes of soft mud, and burnt and blackened trees, "but the wolves made off with him." His face was red from the effort of pulling the cart. "They took off our daughter too and had their way with her, but she come wandering back after the battle down at Duskendale. The ox never did. The wolves ate him, I expect."

The woman had little to add. She was younger than the man by twenty years, but never spoke a word, only looked at Brienne the same way she might have looked at a two-headed calf. The Maid of Tarth had seen such eyes before. Lady Stark had been kind to her, but most women were just as cruel as men. She could not have said which she found most hurtful, the pretty girls with their waspish tongues and brittle laughter or the cold-eyed ladies who hid their disdain behind a mask of courtesy. And common women could be worse than either. "Maidenpool was all in ruins when last I saw it," she said. "The gates were broken and half the town was burned."

"They rebuilt it some. This Tarly, he's a hard man, but a braver lord than Mooton. There's still outlaws in the woods, but not so many as there was. Tarly hunted down the worst o' them and shortened them with that big sword o' his." He turned his head and spat. "You've seen no outlaws on the road?"

"None." *Not this time.* The farther they had come from Duskendale, the emptier the road had been. The only travelers they'd glimpsed had melted away into the woods before they reached them, save for a big, bearded septon they met walking south with twoscore footsore followers. Such inns as they passed had either been sacked and abandoned or turned into armed camps. Yesterday they had encountered one of Lord Randyll's patrols, bristling with longbows and lances. The horsemen had surrounded them while their captain questioned Brienne, but in the end he'd let them continue on their way. "Be wary, woman. The next men you meet may not be as honest as my lads. The Hound has crossed the Trident with a hundred outlaws, and it's said they're raping every wench they come upon and cutting off their teats for trophies."

Brienne felt obligated to pass along that warning to the farmer and his wife. The man nodded as she told him, but when she was done he spat again and said, "Dogs and wolves and lions, may the Others take them all. These outlaws won't dare come too near to Maidenpool. Not so long as Lord Tarly has the rule there."

Brienne knew Lord Randyll Tarly from her time with King Renly's host. Though she could not find it in herself to like the man, she could not forget the debt she owed him either. *If the gods are good, we will pass Maidenpool before he knows that I am there.* "The town will be restored to Lord Mooton once the fighting's done," she told the farmer. "His lordship has been pardoned by the king."

"Pardoned?" The old man laughed. "For what? Sitting on his arse in his bloody castle? He sent men off to Riverrun to fight but never went himself. Lions sacked his town, then wolves, then sellswords, and his lordship just sat safe behind his walls. His brother 'ud never have hid like that. Ser Myles was bold as brass till that Robert killed him."

More ghosts, Brienne thought. "I am looking for my sister, a fair maid of three-and-ten. Perhaps you've seen her?"

"I've not seen no maids, fair nor foul."

No one has. But she had to keep asking.

"Mooton's daughter, she's a maid," the man went on. "Till the bedding, anyways. These eggs, they're for her wedding. Her and Tarly's son. The cooks will need eggs for cakes."

"They will." *Lord Tarly's son. Young Dickon's to be wed.* She tried to recall how old he was; eight or ten, she thought. Brienne had been betrothed at seven, to a boy three years her senior, Lord Caron's younger son, a shy boy with a mole above his lip. They had only met the once, on the occasion of their betrothal. Two years later he was dead, carried off by the same chill that took Lord and Lady Caron and their daughters. Had he lived, they would have been wed within a year of her first flowering, and her whole life would have been different. She would not be here now, dressed in man's mail and carrying a sword, hunting for a dead woman's child. More like she'd be at Nightsong, swaddling a child of her own and nursing another. It was not a new thought for Brienne. It always made her feel a little sad, but a little relieved as well.

The sun was half-hidden behind a bank of clouds when they emerged from the blackened trees to find Maidenpool before them, with the deep waters of the bay beyond. The town's gates had been rebuilt and strengthened, Brienne saw at once, and crossbowmen walked its pink stone walls once more. Above the gatehouse floated King Tommen's royal banner, a black stag and golden lion combatant on a field divided gold and crimson. Other banners displayed the Tarly huntsman, but the red salmon of House Mooton flew only from their castle on its hill.

At the portcullis they came upon a dozen guards armed with halberds. Their badges marked them for soldiers of Lord Tarly's host, though none was Tarly's own. She saw two centaurs, a thunderbolt, a blue beetle and a green arrow, but not the striding huntsman of Horn Hill. Their serjeant had a peacock on his breast, its bright tail faded by the sun. When the farmers drew their cart up he gave a whistle. "What's this now? Eggs?" He tossed one up, caught it, and grinned. "We'll take them."

The old man squawked. "Our eggs is for Lord Mooton. For the wedding cakes and such."

"Have your hens lay more. I haven't had an egg in half a year. Here, don't say you weren't paid." He flung a handful of pennies at the old man's feet.

The farmer's wife spoke up. "That's not enough," she said. "Not near enough."

"I say it is," said the serjeant. "For them eggs, and you as well. Bring her here, boys. She's too young for that old man." Two of the guards leaned their halberds against the wall and pulled the woman away from the cart, struggling. The farmer watched grey-faced, but dared not move.

Brienne spurred her mare forward. "Release her."

Her voice made the guards hesitate long enough for the farmer's wife to wrench free of their grasp. "This is none of your concern," one man said. "You mind your mouth, wench."

Brienne drew her sword instead.

"Well now," the serjeant said, "naked steel. Seems to me I smell an outlaw. You know what Lord Tarly does with outlaws?" He still held the egg he'd taken from the cart. His hand closed, and the yolk oozed through his fingers.

"I know what Lord Randyll does with outlaws," Brienne said. "I know what he does with rapers too."

She had hoped the name might cow them, but the serjeant only flicked egg off his fingers and signaled to his men to spread out. Brienne found herself surrounded by steel points. "What was it you was saying, wench? What is it that Lord Tarly does to . . ."

". . . rapers," a deeper voice finished. "He gelds them or sends them to the Wall. Sometimes both. And he cuts fingers off thieves." A languid young man stepped from the gatehouse, a swordbelt buckled at his waist. The surcoat he wore above his steel had once been white, and here and there still was, beneath the grass stains and dried blood. His sigil was displayed across his chest: a brown deer, dead and bound and slung beneath a pole.

Him. His voice was a punch in her stomach, his face a blade in her bowels. "Ser Hyle," she said stiffly.

"Best let her by, lads," warned Ser Hyle Hunt. "This is Brienne the Beauty, the Maid of Tarth, who slew King Renly and half his Rainbow Guard. She's as mean as she is ugly, and there's no one uglier . . . except perhaps for you, Pisspot, but your father was the rear end of an aurochs, so you have a good excuse. *Her* father is the Evenstar of Tarth."

The guards laughed, but the halberds parted. "Shouldn't we seize her, ser?" the serjeant asked. "For killing Renly?"

"Why? Renly was a rebel. So were we all, rebels to a man, but now we're Tommen's loyal lads." The knight waved the farm folk through the gate. "His lordship's steward will be pleased to see those eggs. You'll find him in the market."

The old man knuckled his forehead. "My thanks, m'lord. You're a true knight, it's plain to see. Come, wife." They put their shoulders to the cart again and rumbled through the gate.

Brienne trotted after them, with Podrick at her heels. *A true knight,* she thought, frowning. Inside the town she reined up. The ruins of a stable could be seen off to her left, fronting on a muddy alley. Across from it three half-dressed whores stood on the balcony of a brothel, whispering to one another. One looked a bit like a camp follower who had once come up to Brienne to ask if she had a cunt or a cock inside her breeches.

"That rounsey may be the most hideous horse I've ever seen," said Ser Hyle of Podrick's mount. "I am surprised that you're not riding it, my lady. Do you plan to thank me for my help?"

Brienne swung down off her mare. She stood a head taller than Ser Hyle. "One day I'll thank you in a mêlée, ser."

"The way you thanked Red Ronnet?" Hunt laughed. He had a full, rich laugh, though his face was plain. An honest face, she'd thought once, before she learned better; shaggy brown hair, hazel eyes, a little scar by his left ear. His chin had a cleft and his nose was crooked, but he did laugh well, and often.

"Shouldn't you be watching your gate?"

He made a wry face at her. "My cousin Alyn is off hunting outlaws. Doubtless he'll return with the Hound's head, gloating and covered in glory. Meanwhile, I am condemned to guard this gate, thanks to you. I hope you're pleased, my beauty. What is it that you're looking for?"

"A stable."

"Over by the east gate. This one burned."

I can see that. "What you said to those men . . . I was with King Renly when he died, but it was some sorcery that slew him, ser. I swear it on my sword." She put her hand upon her hilt, ready to fight if Hunt named her a liar to her face.

"Aye, and it was the Knight of Flowers who carved up the Rainbow Guard. On a good day you might have been able to defeat Ser Emmon. He was a rash fighter, and he tired easily. Royce, though? No. Ser Robar was twice the swordsman that you are . . . though you're *not* a swordsman, are you? Is there such a word as swordswench? What quest brings the Maid to Maidenpool, I wonder?"

Searching for my sister, a maid of three-and-ten, she almost said, but Ser Hyle would know she had no sisters. "There's a man I seek, at a place called the Stinking Goose."

"I thought Brienne the Beauty had no use for men." There was a cruel edge to his smile. "The Stinking Goose. An apt name, that . . . the stinking part, at least. It's by the harbor. First you will come with me to see his lordship."

Brienne did not fear Ser Hyle, but he was one of Randyll Tarly's captains. A whistle, and a hundred men would come running to defend him. "Am I to be arrested?"

"What, for Renly? Who was he? We've changed kings since then, some of us twice. No one cares, no one remembers." He laid a hand lightly on her arm. "This way, if you please."

She wrenched away. "I would thank you not to touch me."

"Thanks at last," he said, with a wry smile.

When last she had seen Maidenpool, the town had been a desolation, a grim place of empty streets and burned homes. Now the streets were full of pigs and children, and most of the burned buildings had been pulled down. Vegetables had been planted in the lots where some once stood; merchants' tents and knights' pavilions took the place of others. Brienne saw new houses going up, a stone inn rising where a wooden inn had burned, a new slate roof on the town sept. The cool autumn air rang to the sounds of saw and hammer. Men carried timber through the streets, and quarrymen drove their wagons down muddy lanes. Many wore the striding huntsman on their breasts. "The soldiers are rebuilding the town," she said, surprised.

"They would sooner be dicing, drinking, and fucking, I don't doubt, but Lord Randyll believes in putting idle men to work."

She had expected to be taken to the castle. Instead, Hunt led them toward the busy harbor. The traders had returned to Maidenpool, she was pleased to see. A galley, a galleas, and a big two-masted cog were in port, along with a score of little fishing boats. More fishermen were visible out on the bay. *If the Stinking Goose yields nothing, I will take passage on a ship,* she decided. Gulltown was only a short voyage away. From there she could make her way to the Eyrie easily enough.

They found Lord Tarly in the fishmarket, doing justice.

A platform had been thrown up beside the water, from which his lordship could look down upon the men accused of crimes. To his left stood a long gallows, with ropes enough for twenty men. Four corpses swung beneath it. One looked fresh, but the other three had plainly been there for some time. A crow was pulling strips of flesh from the ripe ruins of one of the dead men. The other crows had scattered, wary of the crowd of townsfolk who'd gathered in hopes of someone's being hanged.

Lord Randyll shared the platform with Lord Mooton, a

pale, soft, fleshy man in a white doublet and red breeches, his ermine cloak pinned at the shoulder by a red-gold brooch in the shape of a salmon. Tarly wore mail and boiled leather, and a breastplate of grey steel. The hilt of a greatsword poked up above his left shoulder. *Heartsbane,* it was named, the pride of his House.

A stripling in a roughspun cloak and soiled jerkin was being heard when they came up. "I never hurt no one, m'lord," Brienne heard him say. "I only took what the septons left when they run off. If you got to take my finger for that, do it."

"It is customary to take a finger from a thief," Lord Tarly replied in a hard voice, "but a man who steals from a sept is stealing from the gods." He turned to his captain of guards. "Seven fingers. Leave his thumbs."

"Seven?" The thief paled. When the guards seized hold of him he tried to fight, but feebly, as if he were already maimed. Watching him, Brienne could not help think of Ser Jaime, and the way he'd screamed when Zollo's *arakh* came flashing down.

The next man was a baker, accused of mixing sawdust in his flour. Lord Randyll fined him fifty silver stags. When the baker swore he did not have that much silver, his lordship declared that he could have a lash for every stag that he was short. He was followed by a haggard grey-faced whore, accused of giving the pox to four of Tarly's soldiers. "Wash out her private parts with lye and throw her in a dungeon," Tarly commanded. As the whore was dragged off sobbing, his lordship saw Brienne on the edge of the crowd, standing between Podrick and Ser Hyle. He frowned at her, but his eyes betrayed not a flicker of recognition.

A sailor off the galleas came next. His accuser was an archer of Lord Mooton's garrison, with a bandaged hand

and a salmon on his breast. "If it please m'lord, this bastid put his dagger through my hand. He said I was cheating him at dice."

Lord Tarly took his gaze away from Brienne to consider the men before him. "Were you?"

"No, m'lord. I never."

"For theft, I will take a finger. Lie to me and I will hang you. Shall I ask to see these dice?"

"The dice?" The archer looked to Mooton, but his lordship was gazing at the fishing boats. The bowman swallowed. "Might be I . . . them dice, they're lucky for me, 's true, but I . . ."

Tarly had heard enough. "Take his little finger. He can choose which hand. A nail through the palm for the other." He stood. "We're done. March the rest of them back to the dungeon, I'll deal with them on the morrow." He turned to beckon Ser Hyle forward. Brienne followed. "My lord," she said, when she stood before him. She felt eight years old again.

"My lady. To what do we owe this . . . honor?"

"I have been sent to look for . . . for . . ." She hesitated.

"How will you find him if you do not know his name? Did you slay Lord Renly?"

"No."

Tarly weighed the word. *He is judging me, as he judged those others.* "No," he said at last, "you only let him die."

He had died in her arms, his life's blood drenching her. Brienne flinched. "It was sorcery. I never . . ."

"You *never*?" His voice became a whip. "Aye. You never should have donned mail, nor buckled on a sword. You never should have left your father's hall. This is a war, not a harvest ball. By all the gods, I ought to ship you back to Tarth."

"Do that and answer to the throne." Her voice sounded

high and girlish, when she wanted to sound fearless. "Podrick. In my bag you'll find a parchment. Bring it to his lordship."

Tarly took the letter and unrolled it, scowling. His lips moved as he read. "The king's business. What sort of business?"

Lie to me and I will hang you. "S-sansa Stark."

"If the Stark girl were here, I'd know it. She's run back north, I'll wager. Hoping to find refuge with one of her father's bannermen. She had best hope she chooses the right one."

"She might have gone to the Vale instead," Brienne heard herself blurt out, "to her mother's sister."

Lord Randyll gave her a contemptuous look. "Lady Lysa is dead. Some singer pushed her off a mountain. Littlefinger holds the Eyrie now . . . though not for long. The lords of the Vale are not the sort to bend their knees to some upjumped jackanapes whose only skill is counting coppers." He handed her back her letter. "Go where you want and do as you will . . . but when you're raped don't look to me for justice. You will have earned it with your folly." He glanced at Ser Hyle. "And you, ser, should be at your gate. I gave you the command there, did I not?"

"You did, my lord," said Hyle Hunt, "but I thought—"

"You think too much." Lord Tarly strode away.

Lysa Tully is dead. Brienne stood beneath the gallows, the precious parchment in her hand. The crowd had dispersed, and the crows had returned to resume their feast. *A singer pushed her off a mountain.* Had the crows dined on Lady Catelyn's sister too?

"You spoke of the Stinking Goose, my lady," said Ser Hyle. "If you want me to show you—"

"Go back to your gate."

A look of annoyance flashed across his face. *A plain face, not an honest one.* "If that's your wish."

"It is."

"It was only a game to pass the time. We meant no harm." He hesitated. "Ben died, you know. Cut down on the Blackwater. Farrow too, and Will the Stork. And Mark Mullendore took a wound that cost him half his arm."

Good, Brienne wanted to say. *Good, he deserved it.* But she remembered Mullendore sitting outside his pavilion with his monkey on his shoulder in a little suit of chainmail, the two of them making faces at each other. What was it Catelyn Stark had called them, that night at Bitterbridge? *The knights of summer.* And now it was autumn and they were falling like leaves. . . .

She turned her back on Hyle Hunt. "Podrick, come."

The boy trotted after her, leading their horses. "Are we going to find the place? The Stinking Goose?"

"I am. You are going to the stables, by the east gate. Ask the stableman if there's an inn where we can spend the night."

"I will, ser. My lady." Podrick stared at the ground as they went, kicking stones from time to time. "Do you know where it is? The Goose? The Stinking Goose, I mean."

"No."

"He said he'd show us. That knight. Ser Kyle."

"Hyle."

"Hyle. What did he do to you, ser? I mean, my lady."

The boy may be a stumbletongue, but he's not stupid. "At Highgarden, when King Renly called his banners, some men played a game with me. Ser Hyle was one of them. It was a cruel game, hurtful and unchivalrous." She stopped. "The east gate is that way. Wait for me there."

"As you say, my lady. Ser."

No sign marked the Stinking Goose. It took her most of an hour to find it, down a flight of wooden steps beneath a knacker's barn. The cellar was dim and the ceiling low, and Brienne thumped her head on a beam as she entered. No geese were in evidence. A few stools were scattered about, and a bench had been shoved up against one earthen wall. The tables were old wine casks, grey and wormholed. The promised stink pervaded everything. Mostly it was wine and damp and mildew, her nose told her, but there was a little of the privy too, and something of the lichyard.

The only drinkers were three Tyroshi seamen in a corner, growling at each other through green and purple beards. They gave her a brief inspection, and one said something that made the others laugh. The proprietor stood behind a plank that had been placed across two barrels. She was a woman, round and pale and balding, with huge soft breasts swaying beneath a soiled smock. She looked as though the gods had made her out of uncooked dough.

Brienne did not dare to ask for water here. She bought a cup of wine and said, "I am looking for a man called Nimble Dick."

"Dick Crabb. Comes in most every night." The woman eyed Brienne's mail and sword. "If you're going to cut him, do it somewheres else. We don't want no trouble with Lord Tarly."

"I want to talk with him. Why would I do him harm?"

The woman shrugged.

"If you would nod when he comes in I'd be thankful."

"How thankful?"

Brienne put a copper star on the plank between them and found a place in the shadows with a good view of the steps.

She tried the wine. It was oily on the tongue and there was a hair floating in it. *A hair as slender as my hopes of finding Sansa,* she thought as she plucked it out. Chasing after Ser Dontos had been fruitless, and with Lady Lysa dead the Vale no longer seemed a likely refuge. *Where are you, Lady Sansa? Did you run home to Winterfell, or are you with your husband, as Podrick seems to think?* Brienne did not want to chase the girl across the narrow sea, where even the language would be strange to her. *I will be even more a freak there, grunting and gesturing to make myself understood. They will laugh at me, as they laughed at Highgarden.* A blush stole up her cheeks as she remembered.

When Renly donned his crown, the Maid of Tarth had ridden all the way across the Reach to join him. The king himself had greeted her courteously and welcomed her to his service. Not so his lords and knights. Brienne had not expected a warm welcome. She was prepared for coldness, for mockery, for hostility. She had supped upon such meat before. It was not the scorn of the many that left her confused and vulnerable, but the kindness of the few. The Maid of Tarth had been betrothed three times, but she had never been courted until she came to Highgarden.

Big Ben Bushy was the first, one of the few men in Renly's camp who overtopped her. He sent his squire to her to clean her mail, and made her a gift of a silver drinking horn. Ser Edmund Ambrose went him one better, bringing flowers and asking her to ride with him. Ser Hyle Hunt outdid them both. He gave her a book, beautifully illuminated and filled with a hundred tales of knightly valor. He brought apples and carrots for her horses, and a blue silk plume for her helm. He told her the gossip of the camp and said clever, cutting things that made her smile.

He even trained with her one day, which meant more than all the rest.

She thought it was because of him that the others started being courteous. *More than courteous.* At table men fought for the place beside her, offering to fill her wine cup or fetch her sweetbreads. Ser Richard Farrow played love songs on his lute outside her pavilion. Ser Hugh Beesbury brought her a pot of honey "as sweet as the maids of Tarth." Ser Mark Mullendore made her laugh with the antics of his monkey, a curious little black-and-white creature from the Summer Islands. A hedge knight called Will the Stork offered to rub the knots from her shoulders.

Brienne refused him. She refused them all. When Ser Owen Inchfield seized her one night and pressed a kiss upon her, she knocked him arse-backwards into a cookfire. Afterward she looked at herself in a glass. Her face was as broad and bucktoothed and freckled as ever, big-lipped, thick of jaw, so ugly. All she wanted was to be a knight and serve King Renly, yet now . . .

It was not as if she were the only woman there. Even the camp followers were prettier than she was, and up in the castle Lord Tyrell feasted King Renly every night, whilst highborn maids and lovely ladies danced to the music of pipe and horn and harp. *Why are you being kind to me?* she wanted to scream, every time some strange knight paid her a compliment. *What do you want?*

Randyll Tarly solved the mystery the day he sent two of his men-at-arms to summon her to his pavilion. His young son Dickon had overheard four knights laughing as they saddled up their horses, and had told his lord father what they said.

They had a wager.

Three of the younger knights had started it, he told her:

Ambrose, Bushy, and Hyle Hunt, of his own household. As word spread through the camp, however, others had joined the game. Each man was required to buy into the contest with a golden dragon, the whole sum to go to whoever claimed her maidenhead.

"I have put an end to their sport," Tarly told her. "Some of these . . . challengers . . . are less honorable than others, and the stakes were growing larger every day. It was only a matter of time before one of them decided to claim the prize by force."

"They were knights," she said, stunned, "anointed knights."

"And honorable men. The blame is yours."

The accusation made her flinch. "I would never . . . my lord, I did nought to encourage them."

"Your being here encouraged them. If a woman will behave like a camp follower, she cannot object to being treated like one. A war host is no place for a maiden. If you have any regard for your virtue or the honor of your House, you will take off that mail, return home, and beg your father to find a husband for you."

"I came to fight," she insisted. "To be a knight."

"The gods made men to fight, and women to bear children," said Randyll Tarly. "A woman's war is in the birthing bed."

Someone was coming down the cellar steps. Brienne pushed her wine aside as a ragged, scrawny, sharp-faced man with dirty brown hair stepped into the Goose. He gave the Tyroshi sailors a quick look and Brienne a longer one, then went up to the plank. "Wine," he said, "and none o' your horse piss in it, thank'e."

The woman gave Brienne a look and nodded.

"I'll buy your wine," she called out, "for a word."

The man looked her over, his eyes wary. "A word? I

know a lot o' words." He sat down on the stool across from her. "Tell me which m'lady wants t' hear, and Nimble Dick will say it."

"I heard you fooled a fool."

The ragged man sipped his wine, thinking. "Mighten be I did. Or not." He wore a faded, torn doublet from which some lord's badge had been ripped. "Who is it wants t' know?"

"King Robert." She put a silver stag on the barrel between them. Robert's head was on one side, the stag on the other.

"Does he now?" The man took the coin and spun it, smiling. "I like to see a king dance, hey-nonny hey-nonny hey-nonny-ho. Mighten be I saw this fool of yours."

"Was there a girl with him?"

"Two girls," he said at once.

"*Two* girls?" *Could the other one be Arya?*

"Well," the man said, "I never seen the little sweets, mind you, but he was wanting passage for three."

"Passage where?"

"T'other side o' the sea, as I recall."

"Do you remember what he looked like?"

"A fool." He snatched the spinning coin off the table as it began to slow, and made it vanish. "A frightened fool."

"Frightened why?"

He shrugged. "He never said, but old Nimble Dick knows the smell o' fear. He come here most every night, buying drinks for sailors, making japes, singing little songs. Only one night some men come in with that hunter on their teats, and your fool went white as milk and got quiet till they left." He edged his stool closer to hers. "That Tarly's got soldiers crawling over the docks, watching every ship that comes or goes. Man wants a deer, he goes t' the woods. He wants a ship, he goes t' the docks. Your fool didn't dare. So I offered him some help."

"What sort of help?"

"The sort that costs more than one silver stag."

"Tell me, and you'll have another."

"Let's see it," he said. She put another stag on the barrel. He spun it, smiled, scooped it up. "A man who can't go t' the ships need for the ships t' come t' him. I told him I knew a place where that might happen. A hidden place, like."

Gooseprickles rose along Brienne's arms. "A smugglers' cove. You sent the fool to smugglers."

"Him and them two girls." He chuckled. "Only thing, well, the place I sent them, been no ships there for a while. Thirty years, say." He scratched his nose. "What's this fool to you?"

"Those two girls are my sisters."

"Are they, now? Poor little things. Had a sister once meself. Skinny girl with knobby knees, but then she grew a pair o' teats and a knight's son got between her legs. Last I saw her she was off for King's Landing t' make a living on her back."

"Where did you send them?"

Another shrug. "As t' that, I can't recall."

"Where?" Brienne slapped another silver stag down.

He flicked the coin back at her with his forefinger. "Someplace no stag ever found . . . though a dragon might."

Silver would not get the truth from him, she sensed. *Gold might, or it might not. Steel would be more certain.* Brienne touched her dagger, then reached into her purse instead. She found a golden dragon and put in on the barrel. "Where?"

The ragged man snatched up the coin and bit it. "Sweet.

Puts me in mind o' Crackclaw Point. Up north o' here, 'tis a wild land o' hills and bogs, but it happens I was born and bred there. Dick Crabb, I'm named, though most call me Nimble Dick."

She did not offer her own name. "*Where* in Crackclaw Point?"

"The Whispers. You heard o' Clarence Crabb, o' course."

"No."

That seemed to surprise him. "*Ser* Clarence Crabb, I said. I got his blood in me. He was eight foot tall, and so strong he could uproot pine trees with one hand and chuck them half a mile. No horse could bear his weight, so he rode an aurochs."

"What does he have to do with this smugglers' cove?"

"His wife was a woods witch. Whenever Ser Clarence killed a man, he'd fetch his head back home and his wife would kiss it on the lips and bring it back t' life. Lords, they were, and wizards, and famous knights and pirates. One was king o' Duskendale. They gave old Crabb good counsel. Being they was just heads, they couldn't talk real loud, but they never shut up neither. When you're a head, talking's all you got to pass the day. So Crabb's keep got named the Whispers. Still is, though it's been a ruin for a thousand years. A lonely place, the Whispers." The man walked the coin deftly across his knuckles. "One dragon by hisself gets lonely. Ten, now . . ."

"Ten dragons are a fortune. Do you take me for a fool?"

"No, but I can take you to one." The coin danced one way, and back the other. "Take you to the Whispers, m'lady."

Brienne did not like the way his fingers played with that gold coin. Still . . . "Six dragons if we find my sister. Two if we only find the fool. Nothing if nothing is what we find."

Crabb shrugged. "Six is good. Six will serve."

Too quick. She caught his wrist before he could tuck the gold away. "Do not play me false. You'll not find me easy meat."

When she let go, Crabb rubbed his wrist. "Bloody piss," he muttered. "You hurt my hand."

"I am sorry for that. My sister is a girl of three-and-ten. I need to find her before—"

"—before some knight gets in her slit. Aye, I hear you. She's good as saved. Nimble Dick is with you now. Meet me by east gate at first light. I need t' see this man about a horse."

SAMWELL

The sea made Samwell Tarly greensick.

It was not all his fear of drowning, though that was surely some of it. It was the motion of the ship as well, the way the decks rolled beneath his feet. "I have a queasy belly," he confessed to Dareon the day they sailed from Eastwatch-by-the-Sea. The singer slapped him on the back and said, "With a belly big as yours, Slayer, that is a lot of quease."

Sam tried to keep a brave face on him, for Gilly's sake if little else. She had never seen the sea before. When they were struggling through the snows after fleeing Craster's Keep, they had come on several lakes, and even those had been a wonder to her. As *Blackbird* slipped away from shore the girl began to tremble, and big salt tears rolled down her cheeks. "Gods be good," Sam heard her whisper. Eastwatch vanished first, and the Wall grew smaller and smaller in the distance, until it finally disappeared. The wind was coming up by then. The sails were the faded grey of a black cloak that had been washed too often, and Gilly's face was white with fear. "This is a good ship," Sam tried to tell her. "You don't have to be afraid." But she only looked at him, held her baby tighter, and fled below.

Sam soon found himself clutching tightly to the gunwale and watching the sweep of the oars. The way they all moved together was somehow beautiful to behold, and better than looking at the water. Looking at the water only made him think of drowning. When he was small his lord father had tried to teach him how to swim by throwing him into the pond beneath Horn Hill. The water had gotten in his nose and in his mouth and in his lungs, and he coughed and wheezed for hours after Ser Hyle pulled him out. After that he never dared go in any deeper than his waist.

The Bay of Seals was a *lot* deeper than his waist, and not so friendly as that little fishpond below his father's castle. Its waters were grey and green and choppy, and the wooded shore they followed was a snarl of rocks and whirlpools. Even if he could kick and crawl that far somehow, the waves were like to smash him up against some stone and break his head to pieces.

"Looking for mermaids, Slayer?" asked Dareon when he saw Sam staring off across the bay. Fair-haired and hazel-eyed, the handsome young singer out of Eastwatch looked more like some dark prince than a black brother.

"No." Sam did not know what he was looking for, or what he was doing on this boat. *Going to the Citadel to forge a chain and be a maester, to be of better service to the Watch,* he told himself, but the thought just made him weary. He did not want to be a maester, with a heavy chain wrapped around his neck, cold against his skin. He did not want to leave his brothers, the only friends he'd ever had.

And he certainly did not want to face the father who had sent him to the Wall to die.

It was different for the others. For them, the voyage would have a happy ending. Gilly would be safe at Horn Hill, with all the width of Westeros between her and the horrors she had known in the haunted forest. As a serving maid in his father's castle, she would be warm and well fed, a small part of a great world she could never have dreamed of as Craster's wife. She would watch her son grow up big and strong, and become a huntsman or a stablehand or a smith. If the boy showed any aptitude for arms, some knight might even take him as a squire.

Maester Aemon was going to a better place as well. It was pleasant to think of him spending whatever time remained him bathed by the warm breezes of Oldtown, conversing with his fellow maesters and sharing his wisdom with acolytes and novices. He had earned his rest, a hundred times over.

Even Dareon would be happier. He had always claimed to be innocent of the rape that sent him to the Wall, insisting that he belonged at some lord's court, singing for his supper. Now he would have that chance. Jon had named him a recruiter, to take the place of a man named Yoren, who had vanished and was presumed dead. His task would be to travel the Seven Kingdoms, singing of the valor of the Night's Watch, and from time to time returning to the Wall with new recruits.

The voyage would be long and rough, no one could deny that, but for the others at least there would be a happy end. That was Sam's solace. *I am going for them,* he told himself, *for the Night's Watch, and for the happy ending.* The longer he looked at the sea, though, the colder and deeper it appeared.

But *not* looking at the water was even worse, Sam realized in the cramped cabin beneath the sterncastle that the passengers were sharing. He tried to take his mind off the roiling in his stomach by talking with Gilly as she nursed her son. "This ship will take us as far as Braavos," he said. "We'll find another ship to carry us to Oldtown. I read a book about Braavos when I was small. The whole city is built in a lagoon on a hundred little islands, and they have a titan there, a stone man hundreds of feet high. They have boats instead of horses, and their mummers play out written stories instead of just making up the usual stupid farces. The food is very good too, especially the fish. They have all kinds of clams and eels and oysters, fresh from their lagoon. We ought to have a few days between ships. If we do, we can go and see a mummer show, and have some oysters."

He thought that would excite her. He could not have been more wrong. Gilly peered at him with flat, dull eyes, looking through some strands of unwashed hair. "If you want, m'lord."

"What do *you* want?" Sam asked her.

"Nothing." She turned away from him and moved her son from one breast to the other.

The motion of the boat was stirring up the eggs and bacon and fried bread that Sam had eaten before the ship set out. All at once he could not stand the cabin one more instant. He pushed himself back to his feet and clambered up the ladder to give his breakfast to the sea. The sickness came on Sam so strongly that he did not stop to gauge which way the wind was blowing, so he retched from the wrong rail and ended up spattering himself. Even so, he felt much better afterward . . . though not for long.

The ship was *Blackbird,* the largest of the Watch's galleys. *Storm Crow* and *Talon* were faster, Cotter Pyke told Maester Aemon back at Eastwatch-by-the-Sea, but they

were fighting ships, lean, swift birds of prey where the
rowers sat on open decks. *Blackbird* was a better choice
for the rough waters of the narrow sea beyond Skagos.
"There have been storms," Pyke warned them. "Winter
storms are worse, but autumn's are more frequent."

The first ten days were calm enough, as *Blackbird* crept
across the Bay of Seals, never out of sight of land. It was
cold when the wind was blowing, but there was something
bracing about the salt smell in the air. Sam could hardly
eat, and when he did force something down it did not stay
down for long, but aside from that he did not do too badly.
He tried to bolster Gilly's courage and give her what cheer
he could, but that proved hard. She would not come up on
deck, no matter what he said, and seemed to prefer to huddle in the dark with her son. The babe liked the ship no
more than his mother did, it seemed. When he was not
squalling, he was retching up his mother's milk. His bowels were loose and always moving, staining the furs that
Gilly wrapped him in to keep him warm and filling the air
with a brown stench. No matter how many tallow candles
Sam lit, the smell of shit persisted.

It was more pleasant out in the open air, especially
when Dareon was singing. The singer was known to
Blackbird's oarsmen, and would play for them as they
rowed. He knew all their favorite songs: sad ones like
"The Day They Hanged Black Robin," "The Mermaid's
Lament," and "Autumn of My Day," rousing ones like
"Iron Lances" and "Seven Swords for Seven Sons," bawdy
ones like "Milady's Supper," "Her Little Flower," and
"Meggett Was a Merry Maid, a Merry Maid Was She."
When he sang "The Bear and the Maiden Fair," all the
oarsmen joined in, and *Blackbird* seemed to fly across the
water. Dareon had not been much of a swordsman, Sam
knew from their days training under Alliser Thorne, but he

had a beautiful voice. "Honey poured over thunder," Maester Aemon had once called it. He played woodharp and fiddle too, and even wrote his own songs . . . though Sam did not think them very good. Still, it was good to sit and listen, though the chest was so hard and splintery that Sam was almost grateful for his fleshy buttocks. *Fat men take a cushion with them wherever they go,* he thought.

Maester Aemon preferred to spend his days on deck as well, huddled beneath a pile of furs and gazing out across the water. "What is he looking at?" Dareon wondered one day. "For him it's as dark up here as it is down in the cabin."

The old man heard him. Though Aemon's eyes had dimmed and gone dark, there was nothing wrong with his ears. "I was not born blind," he reminded them. "When last I passed this way, I saw every rock and tree and white-cap, and watched the grey gulls flying in our wake. I was five-and-thirty and had been a maester of the chain for six-teen years. Egg wanted me to help him rule, but I knew my place was here. He sent me north aboard the *Golden Dragon,* and insisted that his friend Ser Duncan see me safe to Eastwatch. No recruit had arrived at the Wall with so much pomp since Nymeria sent the Watch six kings in golden fetters. Egg emptied out the dungeons too, so I would not need to say my vows alone. My honor guard, he called them. One was no less a man than Brynden Rivers. Later he was chosen lord commander."

"Bloodraven?" said Dareon. "I know a song about him. 'A Thousand Eyes, and One,' it's called. But I thought he lived a hundred years ago."

"We all did. Once I was as young as you." That seemed to make him sad. He coughed, and closed his eyes, and went to sleep, swaying in his furs whenever some wave rocked the ship.

Beneath grey skies they sailed, east and south and east again, as the Bay of Seals widened about them. The captain, a grizzled brother with a belly like a keg of ale, wore blacks so stained and faded that the crew called him Old Tattersalt. He seldom said a word. His mate made up for him, blistering the salt air with curses whenever the wind died or the oarsmen seemed to flag. They ate oaten porridge in the mornings, pease porridge in the afternoons, and salt beef, salt cod, and salt mutton at night, and washed it down with ale. Dareon sang, Sam retched, Gilly cried and nursed her babe, Maester Aemon slept and shivered, and the winds grew colder and more blustery with every passing day.

Even so, it was a better voyage than the last one Sam had taken. He had been no more than ten when he set sail on Lord Redwyne's galleas, the *Arbor Queen*. Five times as large as *Blackbird* and magnificent to behold, she had three great burgundy sails and banks of oars that flashed gold and white in the sunlight. The way they rose and fell as the ship departed Oldtown had made Sam hold his breath . . . but that was the last good memory he had of the Redwyne Straits. Then as now the sea had made him sick, to his lord father's disgust.

And when they reached the Arbor, things had gone from bad to worse. Lord Redwyne's twin sons had despised Sam on first sight. Every morn they found some fresh way to shame him in the practice yard. On the third day Horas Redwyne made him squeal like a pig when he begged for quarter. On the fifth his brother Hobber clad a kitchen girl in his own armor and let her beat Sam with a wooden sword until he began to cry. When she revealed herself, all the squires and pages and stableboys howled with laughter.

"The boy needs a bit of seasoning, that's all," his father

had told Lord Redwyne that night, but Redwyne's fool rattled his rattle and replied, "Aye, a pinch of pepper, a few nice cloves, and an apple in his mouth." Thereafter, Lord Randyll forbade Sam to eat apples so long as they remained beneath Paxter Redwyne's roof. He had been seasick on their voyage home as well, but so relieved to be going that he almost welcomed the taste of vomit at the back of his throat. It was not until they were back at Horn Hill that his mother told Sam that his father had never meant for him to return. "Horas was to come with us in your place, whilst you remained on the Arbor as Lord Paxter's page and cupbearer. If you had pleased him, you would have been betrothed to his daughter." Sam could still recall the soft touch of his mother's hand as she washed the tears off his face with a bit of lace, dampened with her spit. "My poor Sam," she murmured. "My poor poor Sam."

It will be good to see her again, he thought, as he clung to *Blackbird*'s rail and watched waves breaking on the stony shore. *If she saw me in my blacks, it might even make her proud. "I am a man now, Mother," I could tell her, "a steward, and a man of the Night's Watch. My brothers call me Sam the Slayer sometimes."* He would see his brother Dickon too, and his sisters. *"See," I could tell them, "see, I was good for something after all."*

If he went to Horn Hill, though, his father might be there.

The thought made his belly heave again. Sam bent over the gunwale and retched, but not into the wind. He had gone to the right rail this time. He was getting good at retching.

Or so he thought, until *Blackbird* left the land behind and struck east across the bay for the shores of Skagos.

The island sat at the mouth of the Bay of Seals, massive

and mountainous, a stark and forbidding land peopled by savages. They lived in caves and grim mountain fastnesses, Sam had read, and rode great shaggy unicorns to war. *Skagos* meant "stone" in the Old Tongue. The Skagosi named themselves the stoneborn, but their fellow northmen called them Skaggs and liked them little. Only a hundred years ago Skagos had risen in rebellion. Their revolt had taken years to quell and claimed the life of the Lord of Winterfell and hundreds of his sworn swords. Some songs said the Skaggs were cannibals; supposedly their warriors ate the hearts and livers of the men they slew. In ancient days, the Skagosi had sailed to the nearby isle of Skane, seized its women, slaughtered its men, and ate them on a pebbled beach in a feast that lasted for a fortnight. Skane remained unpeopled to this day.

Dareon knew the songs as well. When the bleak grey peaks of Skagos rose up from the sea, he joined Sam at *Blackbird*'s prow, and said, "If the gods are good, we may catch a glimpse of a unicorn."

"If the captain is good, we won't come that close. The currents are treacherous around Skagos, and there are rocks that can crack a ship's hull like an egg. But don't you mention that to Gilly. She's scared enough."

"Her and that squalling whelp of hers. I don't know which of them is noisier. The only time he ever stops crying is when she shoves a nipple in his mouth, and then *she* starts to sob."

Sam had noticed that as well. "Maybe the babe is hurting her," he said, feebly. "If his teeth are coming in . . ."

Dareon plucked at his lute with one finger, sending up a derisive note. "I'd heard that wildlings were braver than that."

"She *is* brave," Sam insisted, though even he had to admit that he had never seen Gilly in such a wretched state.

Though she hid her face more oft than not and kept the cabin dark, he could see that her eyes were always red, her cheeks wet with tears. When he asked her what was wrong, though, she only shook her head, leaving him to find answers of his own. "The sea scares her, that's all," he told Dareon. "Before she came to the Wall, all she knew was Craster's Keep and the woods around it. I don't know that she went more than half a league from the place that she was born. She knows streams and rivers, but she had never seen a lake until we came on one, and the sea . . . the sea is a scary thing."

"We've never been out of sight of land."

"We will be." Sam did not relish that part himself.

"Surely a little water does not frighten the Slayer."

"No," Sam lied, "not me. But Gilly . . . maybe if you played some lullabies for them, it would help the babe to sleep."

Dareon's mouth twisted in disgust. "Only if she shoves a plug up his arse. I cannot abide the smell."

The next day the rains began, and the seas grew rougher. "We had best go below, where it's dry," Sam said to Aemon, but the old maester only smiled, and said, "The rain feels good against my face, Sam. It feels like tears. Let me stay a while longer, I pray you. It has been a long time since last I wept."

If Maester Aemon meant to stay on deck, old and frail as he was, Sam had no choice but to do the same. He stayed beside the old man for nigh unto an hour, huddled in his cloak as a soft, steady rain soaked him to his skin. Aemon hardly seemed to feel it. He sighed and closed his eyes, and Sam moved closer to him, to shield him from the worst of the wind. *He will ask me to help him to the cabin soon,* he told himself. *He must.* But he never did, and finally thunder began to rumble in the distance, off to the east. "We *have* to get below," Sam said, shivering. Maester Aemon did not reply. It was only then that Sam realized the old man had gone to sleep. "Maester," he said, shaking him gently by one shoulder. "Maester Aemon, wake up."

Aemon's blind white eyes came open. "Egg?" he said, as the rain streamed down his cheeks. "Egg, I dreamed that I was old."

Sam did not know what to do. He knelt and scooped the old man up and carried him below. No one had ever called him strong, and the rain had soaked through Maester Aemon's blacks and made him twice as heavy, but even so, he weighed no more than a child.

When he shoved into the cabin with Aemon in his arms, he found that Gilly had let all the candles gutter out. The babe was asleep and she was curled up in a corner, sobbing softly in the folds of the big black cloak that Sam had given her. "Help me," he said urgently. "Help me dry him off and get him warm."

She rose at once, and together they got the old maester out of his wet clothes and buried him beneath a pile of furs. His skin was damp and cold, though, clammy to the touch. "You get in with him," Sam told Gilly. "Hold him. Warm him with your body. We have to warm him up." She did that too, never saying a word, all the while still sniffling. "Where's Dareon?" asked Sam. "We'd all be warmer if we were together. He needs to be here too." He was headed back up top to find the singer when the deck rose up beneath him, then fell away beneath his feet. Gilly wailed, Sam slammed down hard and lost his legs, and the babe woke screaming.

The next roll of the ship came as he was struggling back to his feet. It threw Gilly into his arms, and the wildling girl clung to him so fiercely that Sam could hardly breathe. "Don't you be frightened," he told her.

"This is just an adventure. One day you'll tell your son this tale." That only made her dig her nails into his arm. She shuddered, her whole body shaking with the violence of her sobs. *Whatever I say just makes her worse.* He held her tightly, uncomfortably aware of her breasts pressing up against him. As frightened as he was, somehow that was enough to make him stiff. *She'll feel it,* he thought, ashamed, but if she did, she gave no sign, only clung to him the harder.

The days ran together after that. They never saw the sun. The days were grey and the nights black, except when lightning lit the sky above the peaks of Skagos. All of them were starved yet none could eat. The captain broached a cask of firewine to fortify the oarsmen. Sam tried a cup and sighed as hot snakes wriggled down his throat and through his chest. Dareon took a liking to the drink as well, and was seldom sober thereafter.

The sails went up, the sails came down, and one ripped free of the mast and flew away like a great grey bird. As *Blackbird* rounded the south coast of Skagos, they spotted the wreckage of a galley on the rocks. Some of her crew had washed up on the shore, and the rooks and crabs had gathered to pay them homage. "Too bloody close," grumbled Old Tattersalt when he saw. "One good blow, and we'll be breaking up aside them." Exhausted as they were, his rowers bent to their oars again, and the ship clawed south toward the narrow sea, till Skagos dwindled to no more than a few dark shapes in the sky that might have been thunderheads, or the tops of tall black mountains, or both. After that, they had eight days and seven nights of clear, smooth sailing.

Then came more storms, worse than before.

Was it three storms, or only one, broken up by lulls? Sam never knew, though he tried desperately to care.

"What does it matter?" Dareon screamed at him once, when all of them were huddled in the cabin. *It doesn't,* Sam wanted to tell him, *but so long as I'm thinking about that I'm not thinking about drowning or being sick or Maester Aemon's shivering.* "It doesn't," he managed to squeak, but the thunder drowned out all the rest of it, and the deck lurched and knocked him sideways. Gilly was sobbing. The babe was shrieking. And up top he could hear Old Tattersalt bellowing at his crew, the ragged captain who never spoke at all.

I hate the sea, Sam thought, *I hate the sea, I hate the sea, I hate the sea.* The next lightning flash was so bright it lit the cabin through the seams in the planking overhead. *This is a good sound ship, a good sound ship, a good ship,* he told himself. *It will not sink. I am not afraid.*

During one of the lulls between the gales, as Sam clung white-knuckled to the rail wanting desperately to retch, he heard some of the crew muttering that this was what came of bringing a woman aboard ship, and a wildling woman at that. "Fucked her own father," Sam heard one man say, as the wind was rising once again. "Worse than whoring, that. Worse than *anything*. We'll all drown unless we get rid of her, and that abomination that she whelped."

Sam dared not confront them. They were older men, hard and sinewy, their arms and shoulders thickened by years at the oars. But he made certain that his knife was sharp, and whenever Gilly left the cabin to make water, he went with her.

Even Dareon had no good to say about the wildling girl. Once, at Sam's urging, the singer played a lullaby to soothe the babe, but partway through the first verse Gilly began to sob inconsolably. "Seven bloody hells," Dareon snapped, "can't you even stop weeping long enough to hear a *song*?"

"Just play," Sam pleaded, "just sing the song for her."

"She doesn't need a song," said Dareon. "She needs a good spanking, or maybe a hard fuck. Get out of my way, Slayer." He shoved Sam aside and went from the cabin to find some solace in a cup of firewine and the rough brotherhood of the oars.

Sam was at his wit's end by then. He had almost gotten used to the smells, but between the storms and Gilly's sobbing he had not slept for days. "Isn't there something you can give her?" he asked Maester Aemon very softly, when he saw that the old man was awake. "Some herb or potion, so she won't be so afraid?"

"It is not fear you hear," the old man told him. "That is the sound of grief, and there is no potion for that. Let her tears run their course, Sam. You cannot stem the flow."

Sam had not understood. "She's going to a safe place. A *warm* place. Why should she be grieving?"

"Sam," the old man whispered, "you have two good eyes, and yet you do not see. She is a mother grieving for her child."

"He's greensick, that's all. We're all greensick. Once we make port in Braavos . . ."

". . . the babe will still be Dalla's son, and not the child of her body."

It took Sam a moment to grasp what Aemon was suggesting. "That couldn't . . . she wouldn't . . . of course he's hers. Gilly would never have left the Wall without her *son*. She loves him."

"She nursed them both and loved them both," said Aemon, "but not alike. No mother loves all her children the same, not even the Mother Above. Gilly did not leave the child willingly, I am certain. What threats the Lord

Commander made, what promises, I can only guess . . . but threats and promises there surely were."

"No. No, that's wrong. Jon would never . . ."

"Jon would never. Lord Snow did. Sometimes there is no happy choice, Sam, only one less grievous than the others."

No happy choice. Sam thought of all the trials that he and Gilly suffered, Craster's Keep and the death of the Old Bear, snow and ice and freezing winds, days and days and days of walking, the wights at Whitetree, Coldhands and the tree of ravens, the Wall, the Wall, the Wall, the Black Gate beneath the earth. What had it all been for? *No happy choices and no happy endings.*

He wanted to scream. He wanted to howl and sob and shake and curl up in a little ball and whimper. *He switched the babes,* he told himself. *He switched the babes to protect the little prince, to keep him away from Lady Melisandre's fires, away from her red god. If she burns Gilly's boy, who will care? No one but Gilly. He was only Craster's whelp, an abomination born of incest, not the son of the King-beyond-the-Wall. He's no good for a hostage, no good for a sacrifice, no good for anything, he doesn't even have a name.*

Wordless, Sam staggered up onto the deck to retch, but there was nothing in his belly to bring up. Night had come upon them, a strange still night such as they had not seen for many days. The sea was black as glass. At the oars, the rowers rested. One or two were sleeping where they sat. The wind was in the sails, and to the north Sam could even see a scattering of stars, and the red wanderer the free folk called the Thief. *That ought to be my star,* Sam thought miserably. *I helped to make Jon Lord Commander, and I brought him Gilly and the babe. There are no happy endings.*

"Slayer." Dareon appeared beside him, oblivious to Sam's pain. "A sweet night, for once. Look, the stars are coming out. We might even get a bit of moon. Might be the worst is done."

"No." Sam wiped his nose, and pointed south with a fat finger, toward the gathering darkness. "There," he said. No sooner had he spoken than lightning flashed, sudden and silent and blinding bright. The distant clouds glowed for half a heartbeat, mountains heaped on mountains, purple and red and yellow, taller than the world. "The worst isn't done. The worst is just beginning, and there are no happy endings."

"Gods be good," said Dareon, laughing. "Slayer, you are *such* a craven."

JAIME

Lord Tywin Lannister had entered the city on a stallion, his enameled crimson armor polished and gleaming, bright with gems and goldwork. He left it in a tall wagon draped with crimson banners, with six silent sisters riding attendance on his bones.

The funeral procession departed King's Landing through the Gate of the Gods, wider and more splendid than the Lion Gate. The choice felt wrong to Jaime. His father had been a lion, that no one could deny, but even Lord Tywin never claimed to be a god.

An honor guard of fifty knights surrounded Lord Tywin's wagon, crimson pennons fluttering from their lances. The lords of the west followed close behind them. The winds snapped at their banners, making their charges dance and flutter. As he trotted up the column, Jaime passed boars, badgers, and beetles, a green arrow and a red ox, crossed halberds, crossed spears, a treecat, a straw-berry, a maunch, four sunbursts counterchanged.

Lord Brax was wearing a pale grey doublet slashed with cloth-of-silver, an amethyst unicorn pinned above his heart. Lord Jast was armored in black steel, three gold lion's heads inlaid on his breastplate. The rumors of his death had not been far wrong, to look at him; wounds and imprisonment had left him a shadow of the man he'd been. Lord Banefort had weathered battle better, and looked ready to return to war at once. Plumm wore purple, Prester ermine, Moreland russet and green, but each had donned a cloak of crimson silk, in honor of the man they were es-corting home.

Behind the lords came a hundred crossbowmen and three hundred men-at-arms, and crimson flowed from their shoulders as well. In his white cloak and white scale armor, Jaime felt out of place amongst that river of red.

Nor did his uncle make him more at ease. "Lord Commander," Ser Kevan said, when Jaime trotted up beside him at the head of the column. "Does Her Grace have some last command for me?"

"I am not here for Cersei." A drum began to beat behind them, slow, measured, funereal. *Dead,* it seemed to say, *dead, dead.* "I came to make my farewells. He was my father."

"And hers."

"I am not Cersei. I have a beard, and she has breasts. If you are still confused, nuncle, count our hands. Cersei has two."

"Both of you have a taste for mockery," his uncle said. "Spare me your japes, ser, I have no taste for them."

"As you will." *This is not going as well as I might have hoped.* "Cersei would have wanted to see you off, but she has many pressing duties."

Ser Kevan snorted. "So do we all. How fares your king?" His tone made the question a reproach.

"Well enough," Jaime said defensively. "Balon Swann is with him during the mornings. A good and valiant knight."

"Once that went without saying when men spoke of those who wore the white cloak."

No man can choose his brothers, Jaime thought. *Give me leave to pick my own men, and the Kingsguard will be great again.* Put that baldly, though, it sounded feeble; an empty boast from a man the realm called Kingslayer. *A man with shit for honor.* Jaime let it go. He had not come to argue with his uncle. "Ser," he said, "you need to make your peace with Cersei."

"Are we at war? No one told me."

Jaime ignored that. "Strife between Lannister and Lannister can only help the enemies of our House."

"If there is strife, it will not be my doing. Cersei wants to rule. Well and good. The realm is hers. All I ask is to be left in peace. My place is at Darry with my son. The castle must needs be restored, the lands planted and protected." He gave a bark of bitter laughter. "And your sister has left me little else to occupy my time. I had as well see Lancel wed. His bride has grown impatient waiting for us to make our way to Darry."

His widow from the Twins. His cousin Lancel was riding ten yards behind them. With his hollow eyes and dry white hair, he looked older than Lord Jast. Jaime could feel his phantom fingers itching at the sight of him. ... *fucking Lancel and Osmund Kettleblack and Moon Boy for all I know* ... He had tried to speak with Lancel more times than he could count, but never found him alone. If his father was not with him, some septon was. *He may be*

Kevan's son, but he has milk in his veins. Tyrion was lying to me. His words were meant to wound.

Jaime put his cousin from his thoughts and turned back to his uncle. "Will you remain at Darry after the wedding?"

"For a while, mayhaps. Sandor Clegane is raiding along the Trident, it would seem. Your sister wants his head. It may be that he has joined Dondarrion."

Jaime had heard about Saltpans. By now half the realm had heard. The raid had been exceptionally savage. Women raped and mutilated, children butchered in their mothers' arms, half the town put to the torch. "Randyll Tarly is at Maidenpool. Let him deal with the outlaws. I would sooner have you go to Riverrun."

"Ser Daven has command there. The Warden of the West. He has no need of me. Lancel does."

"As you say, uncle." Jaime's head was pounding to the same beat as the drum. *Dead, dead, dead.* "You would do well to keep your knights around you."

His uncle gave him a cool stare. "Is that a threat, ser?"

A threat? The suggestion took him aback. "A caution. I only meant . . . Sandor is dangerous."

"I was hanging outlaws and robber knights when you were still shitting in your swaddling clothes. I am not like to go off and face Clegane and Dondarrion by myself, if that is what you fear, ser. Not every Lannister is a fool for glory."

Why, nuncle, I believe you are talking about me. "Addam Marbrand could deal with these outlaws just as well as you. So could Brax, Banefort, Plumm, any of these others. But none would make a good King's Hand."

"Your sister knows my terms. They have not changed. Tell her that, the next time you are in her bedchamber." Ser

Kevan put his heels into his courser and galloped ahead, putting an abrupt end to their conversation.

Jaime let him go, his missing sword hand twitching. He had hoped against hope that Cersei had somehow misunderstood, but plainly that was wrong. *He knows about the two of us. About Tommen and Myrcella. And Cersei knows he knows.* Ser Kevan was a Lannister of Casterly Rock. He could not believe that she would ever do him harm, but . . . *I was wrong about Tyrion, why not about Cersei?* When sons were killing fathers, what was there to stop a niece from ordering an uncle slain? *An inconvenient uncle, who knows too much.* Though perhaps Cersei was hoping that the Hound might do her work for her. If Sandor Clegane cut down Ser Kevan, she would not need to bloody her own hands. *And he will, if they should meet.* Kevan Lannister had once been a stout man with a sword, but he was no longer young, and the Hound . . .

The column had caught up to him. As his cousin rode past, flanked by his two septons, Jaime called out to him. "Lancel. Coz. I wanted to congratulate you upon your marriage. I only regret that my duties do not permit me to attend."

"His Grace must be protected."

"And will be. Still, I hate to miss your bedding. It is your first marriage and her second, I understand. I'm sure my lady will be pleased to show you what goes where."

The bawdy remark drew a laugh from several nearby lords and a disapproving look from Lancel's septons. His cousin squirmed uncomfortably in the saddle. "I know enough to do my duty as a husband, ser."

"That's just the thing a bride wants on her wedding night," said Jaime. "A husband who knows how to do his *duty.*"

A flush crept up Lancel's cheeks. "I pray for you,

cousin. And for Her Grace the queen. May the Crone lead
her to her wisdom and the Warrior defend her."

"Why would Cersei need the Warrior? She has me."
Jaime turned his horse about, his white cloak snapping in
the wind. *The Imp was lying. Cersei would sooner have
Robert's corpse between her legs than a pious fool like
Lancel. Tyrion, you evil bastard, you should have lied
about someone more likely.* He galloped past his lord father's funeral wayn toward the city in the distance.

The streets of King's Landing seemed almost deserted
as Jaime Lannister made his way back to the Red Keep
atop Aegon's High Hill. The soldiers who had crowded the
city's gambling dens and pot shops were largely gone now.
Garlan the Gallant had taken half the Tyrell strength back
to Highgarden, and his lady mother and grandmother had
gone with him. The other half had marched south with
Mace Tyrell and Mathis Rowan to invest Storm's End.

As for the Lannister host, two thousand seasoned veterans remained encamped outside the city walls, awaiting
the arrival of Paxter Redwyne's fleet to carry them across
Blackwater Bay to Dragonstone. Lord Stannis appeared to
have left only a small garrison behind him when he sailed
north, so two thousand men would be more than sufficient,
Cersei had judged.

The rest of the westermen had gone back to their wives
and children, to rebuild their homes, plant their fields, and
bring in one last harvest. Cersei had taken Tommen round
their camps before they marched, to let them cheer their
little king. She had never looked more beautiful than she
did that day, with a smile on her lips and the autumn sunlight shining on her golden hair. Whatever else one might
say about his sister, she did know how to make men love
her when she cared enough to try.

As Jaime trotted through the castle gates, he came upon

two dozen knights riding at a quintain in the outer yard. *Something else I can no longer do,* he thought. A lance was heavier and more cumbersome than a sword, and swords were proving trial enough. He supposed he might try holding the lance with his left hand, but that would mean shifting his shield to his right arm. In a tilt, a man's foe was always to the left. A shield on his right arm would prove about as useful as nipples on his breastplate. *No, my jousting days are done,* he thought as he dismounted . . . but all the same, he stopped to watch a while.

Ser Tallad the Tall lost his mount when the sandbag came around and thumped him in the head. Strongboar struck the shield so hard he cracked it. Kennos of Kayce finished the destruction. A new shield was hung for Ser Dermot of the Rainwood. Lambert Turnberry only struck a glancing blow, but Beardless Jon Bettley, Humfrey Swyft, and Alyn Stackspear all scored solid hits, and Red Ronnet Connington broke his lance clean. Then the Knight of Flowers mounted up and put the others all to shame.

Jousting was three-quarters horsemanship, Jaime had always believed. Ser Loras rode superbly, and handled a lance as if he'd been born holding one . . . which no doubt accounted for his mother's pinched expression. *He puts the point just where he means to put it, and seems to have the balance of a cat. Perhaps it was not such a fluke that he unhorsed me.* It was a shame that he would never have the chance to try the boy again. He left the whole men to their sport.

Cersei was in her solar in Maegor's Holdfast, with Tommen and Lord Merryweather's dark-haired Myrish wife. The three of them were laughing at Grand Maester Pycelle. "Did I miss some clever jape?" Jaime said, as he shoved through the door.

"Oh, look," purred Lady Merryweather, "your brave brother has returned, Your Grace."

"Most of him." The queen was in her cups, Jaime realized. Of late, Cersei always seemed to have a flagon of wine to hand, she who had once scorned Robert Baratheon for his drinking. He misliked that, but these days he seemed to mislike everything his sister did. "Grand Maester," she said, "share the tidings with the Lord Commander, if you would."

Pycelle looked desperately uncomfortable. "There has been a bird," he said. "From Stokeworth. Lady Tanda sends word that her daughter Lollys has been delivered of a strong, healthy son."

"And you will never guess what they have named the little bastard, brother."

"They wanted to name him Tywin, I recall."

"Yes, but I forbade it. I told Falyse that I would not have our father's noble name bestowed upon the ill-gotten spawn of some pig boy and a feeble-witted sow."

"Lady Stokeworth insists the child's name was not her doing," Grand Maester Pycelle put in. Perspiration dotted his wrinkled forehead. "Lollys's husband made the choice, she writes. This man Bronn, he . . . it would seem that he . . ."

"Tyrion," ventured Jaime. "He named the child *Tyrion.*"

The old man gave a tremulous nod, mopping at his brow with the sleeve of his robe.

Jaime had to laugh. "There you are, sweet sister. You have been looking everywhere for Tyrion, and all the time he's been hiding in Lollys's womb."

"Droll. You and Bronn are both so droll. No doubt the bastard is sucking on one of Lollys Lackwit's dugs even as we speak, whilst this sellsword looks on, smirking at his little insolence."

"Perhaps this child bears some resemblance to your brother," suggested Lady Merryweather. "He might have been born deformed, or without a nose." She laughed a throaty laugh.

"We shall have to send the darling boy a gift," the queen declared. "Won't we, Tommen?"

"We could send him a kitten."

"A lion cub," said Lady Merryweather. *To rip his little throat out,* her smile suggested.

"I had a different sort of gift in mind," said Cersei.

A new stepfather, most like. Jaime knew the look in his sister's eyes. He had seen it before, most recently on the night of Tommen's wedding, when she burned the Tower of the Hand. The green light of the wildfire had bathed the face of the watchers, so they looked like nothing so much as rotting corpses, a pack of gleeful ghouls, but some of the corpses were prettier than others. Even in the baleful glow, Cersei had been beautiful to look upon. She'd stood with one hand on her breast, her lips parted, her green eyes shining. *She is crying,* Jaime had realized, but whether it was from grief or ecstasy he could not have said.

The sight had filled him with disquiet, reminding him of Aerys Targ-aryen and the way a burning would arouse him. A king has no secrets from his Kingsguard. Relations between Aerys and his queen had been strained during the last years of his reign. They slept apart and did their best to avoid each other during the waking hours. But whenever Aerys gave a man to the flames, Queen Rhaella would have a visitor in the night. The day he burned his mace-and-dagger Hand, Jaime and Jon Darry had stood at guard outside her bedchamber whilst the king took his pleasure. "You're hurting me," they had heard Rhaella cry through the oaken door. "You're *hurting* me." In some queer way, that had been worse than Lord Chelsted's screaming. "We are sworn to protect her as well," Jaime had finally been driven to say. "We are," Darry allowed, "but not from him."

Jaime had only seen Rhaella once after that, the morning of the day she left for Dragonstone. The queen had been cloaked and hooded as she climbed inside the royal wheelhouse that would take her down Aegon's High Hill to the waiting ship, but he heard her maids whispering after she was gone. They said the queen looked as if some beast had savaged her, clawing at her thighs and chewing on her breasts. *A crowned beast,* Jaime knew.

By the end the Mad King had become so fearful that he would allow no blade in his presence, save for the swords his Kingsguard wore. His beard was matted and unwashed, his hair a silver-gold tangle that reached his waist, his fingernails cracked yellow claws nine inches long. Yet still the blades tormented him, the ones he could never escape, the blades of the Iron Throne. His arms and legs were always covered with scabs and half-healed cuts.

Let him be king over charred bones and cooked meat, Jaime remembered, studying his sister's smile. *Let him be the king of ashes.* "Your Grace," he said, "might we have a private word?"

"As you wish. Tommen, it is past time you had your lesson for the day. Go with the Grand Maester."

"Yes, Mother. We are learning about Baelor the Blessed."

Lady Merryweather took her leave as well, kissing the queen on both cheeks. "Shall I return for supper, Your Grace?"

"I shall be very cross with you if you do not."

Jaime could not help but note the way the Myrish woman moved her hips as she walked. *Every step is a seduction.* When the door closed behind her, he cleared his throat and said, "First these Kettleblacks, then Qyburn, now her. It's a queer menagerie you are keeping these days, sweet sister."

"I am growing very fond of Lady Taena. She amuses me."

"She is one of Margaery Tyrell's companions," Jaime reminded her. "She's informing on you to the little queen."

"Of course she is." Cersei went to the sideboard to fill her cup anew. "Margaery was thrilled when I asked her leave to take Taena on as my companion. You should have heard her. '*She will be a sister to you, as she's been to me. Of course you must have her! I have my cousins and my other ladies.*' Our little queen does not want me to be lonely."

"If you know she is a spy, why take her on?"

"Margaery is not half so clever as she thinks. She has no notion what a sweet serpent she has in that Myrish slut. I use Taena to feed the little queen what I want her to know. Some of it is even true." Cersei's eyes were bright with mischief. "And Taena tells me everything Maid Margaery is doing."

"Does she? How much do you know about this woman?"

"I know she is a mother, with a young son that she wants to rise high in this world. She will do whatever is required to see that he does. Mothers are all the same. Lady Merryweather may be a serpent, but she is far from stupid. She knows I can do more for her than Margaery, so she makes herself useful to me. You would be surprised at all the interesting things she's told me."

"What sorts of things?"

Cersei sat beneath the window. "Did you know that the Queen of Thorns keeps a chest of coins in her wheelhouse? Old gold from before the Conquest. Should any tradesman be so unwise as to name a price in golden coins, she pays him with hands from Highgarden, each half the weight of one of our dragons. What merchant would dare complain of being cheated by Mace Tyrell's lady mother?" She sipped her wine, and said, "Did you enjoy your little ride?"

"Our uncle remarked upon your absence."

"Our uncle's remarks do not concern me."

"They should. You could make good use of him. If not at Riverrun or the Rock, then in the north against Lord Stannis. Father always relied upon Kevan when—"

"Roose Bolton is our Warden of the North. He will deal with Stannis."

"Lord Bolton is trapped below the Neck, cut off from the north by the ironmen at Moat Cailin."

"Not for long. Bolton's bastard son will soon remove that little obstacle. Lord Bolton will have two thousand Freys to augment his own strength, under Lord Walder's sons Hosteen and Aenys. That should be more than enough to deal with Stannis and a few thousand broken men."

"Ser Kevan—"

"—will have his hands full at Darry, teaching Lancel how to wipe his arse. Father's death has unmanned him. He is an old done man. Daven and Damion will serve us better."

"They'll suffice." Jaime had no quarrel with his cousins. "You still require a Hand, however. If not our uncle, who?"

His sister laughed. "Not you. Have no fear on that count. Perhaps Taena's husband. His grandfather was Hand under Aerys."

The horn-of-plenty Hand. Jaime remembered Owen Merryweather well enough; an amiable man, but ineffectual. "As I recall, he did so well that Aerys exiled him and seized his lands."

"Robert gave them back. Some, at least. Taena would be pleased if Orton could recover the rest."

"Is this about pleasing some Myrish whore? Here I thought it was about governing the realm."

"*I* govern the realm."

Seven save us all, you do. His sister liked to think of herself as Lord Tywin with teats, but she was wrong. Their father had been as relentless and implacable as a glacier, where Cersei was all wildfire, especially when thwarted. She had been giddy as a maiden when she learned that Stannis had abandoned Dragonstone, certain that he had finally given up the fight and sailed away to exile. When word came down from the north that he had turned up again at the Wall, her fury had been fearful to behold. *She does not lack for wits, but she has no judgment, and no patience.* "You need a strong Hand to help you."

"A *weak* ruler needs a strong Hand, as Aerys needed Father. A strong ruler requires only a diligent servant to carry out his orders." She swirled her wine. "Lord Hallyne might suit. He would not be the first pyromancer to serve as the King's Hand."

No. I killed the last one. "There is talk that you mean to make Aurane Waters the master of ships."

"Has someone been informing on me?" When he did not answer, Cersei tossed her hair back, and said, "Waters is well suited to the office. He has spent half his life on ships."

"Half his life? He cannot be more than twenty."

"Two-and-twenty, and what of it? Father was not even one-and-twenty when Aerys Targaryen named him Hand. It is past time Tommen had some young men about him in place of all these wrinkled greybeards. Aurane is strong and vigorous."

Strong and vigorous and handsome, Jaime thought. . . .

she's been fucking Lancel and Osmund Kettleblack and Moon Boy for all I know . . . "Paxter Redwyne would be a better choice. He commands the largest fleet in Westeros. Aurane Waters could command a skiff, but only if you bought him one."

"You are a child, Jaime. Redwyne is Tyrell's bannerman, and nephew to that hideous grandmother of his. I want none of Lord Tyrell's creatures on my council."

"Tommen's council, you mean."

"You know what I mean."

Too well. "I know that Aurane Waters is a bad idea, and Hallyne is a worse one. As for Qyburn . . . gods be good, Cersei, he rode with *Vargo Hoat.* The Citadel *stripped him of his chain!*"

"The grey sheep. Qyburn has made himself most useful to me. And he is loyal, which is more than I can say of mine own kin."

The crows will feast upon us all if you go on this way, sweet sister. "Cersei, listen to yourself. You are seeing dwarfs in every shadow and making foes of friends. Uncle Kevan is not your enemy. *I* am not your enemy."

Her face twisted in fury. "I begged you for your help. I went down on my knees to you, and *you refused me!*"

"My vows . . ."

". . . did not stop you slaying Aerys. Words are wind. You could have had me, but you chose a cloak instead. Get out."

"Sister . . ."

"*Get out,* I said. I am sick of looking at that ugly stump of yours. *Get out!*" To speed him on his way, she heaved her wine cup at his head. She missed, but Jaime took the hint.

Evenfall found him sitting alone in the common room of White Sword Tower, with a cup of Dornish red and the

White Book. He was turning pages with the stump of his
sword hand when the Knight of Flowers entered, removed
his cloak and swordbelt and hung them on a wall peg next
to Jaime's.

"I saw you in the yard today," said Jaime. "You rode
well."

"Better than *well*, surely." Ser Loras poured himself a
cup of wine, and took a seat across the half-moon table.

"A more modest man might have answered 'My lord is
too kind,' or 'I had a good mount.'"

"The horse was adequate, and my lord is as kind as I
am modest." Loras waved at the book. "Lord Renly always
said that books were for maesters."

"This one is for us. The history of every man who has
ever worn a white cloak is written here."

"I have glanced at it. The shields are pretty. I prefer
books with more illuminations. Lord Renly owned a few
with drawings that would turn a septon blind."

Jaime had to smile. "There's none of that here, ser, but
the histories will open your eyes. You would do well to
know about the lives of those who went before."

"I do. Prince Aemon the Dragonknight, Ser Ryam
Redwyne, the Greatheart, Barristan the Bold . . ."

". . . Gwayne Corbray, Alyn Connington, the Demon of
Darry, aye. You will have heard of Lucamore Strong as
well."

"Ser Lucamore the Lusty?" Ser Loras seemed amused.
"Three wives and thirty children, was it? They cut his
cock off. Shall I sing the song for you, my lord?"

"And Ser Terrence Toyne?"

"Bedded the king's mistress and died screaming. The
lesson is, men who wear white breeches need to keep them
tightly laced."

"Gyles Greycloak? Orivel the Open-Handed?"

"Gyles was a traitor, Orivel a coward. Men who shamed the white cloak. What is my lord suggesting?"

"Little and less. Don't take offense where none was meant, ser. How about Long Tom Costayne?"

Ser Loras shook his head.

"He was a Kingsguard knight for sixty years."

"When was that? I've never—"

"Ser Donnel of Duskendale, then?"

"I may have heard the name, but—"

"Addison Hill? The White Owl, Michael Mertyns? Jeffory Norcross? They called him Neveryield. Red Robert Flowers? What can you tell me of them?"

"Flowers is a bastard name. So is Hill."

"Yet both men rose to command the Kingsguard. Their tales are in the book. Rolland Darklyn is in here too. The youngest man ever to serve in the Kingsguard, until me. He was given his cloak on a battlefield and died within an hour of donning it."

"He can't have been very good."

"Good enough. He died, but his king lived. A lot of brave men have worn the white cloak. Most have been forgotten."

"Most deserve to be forgotten. The heroes will always be remembered. The best."

"The best and the worst." *So one of us is like to live in song.* "And a few who were a bit of both. Like him." He tapped the page he had been reading.

"Who?" Ser Loras craned his head around to see. "Ten black pellets on a scarlet field. I do not know those arms."

"They belonged to Criston Cole, who served the first Viserys and the second Aegon." Jaime closed the White Book. "They called him Kingmaker."

CERSEI

Three wretched fools with a leather sack, the queen thought as they sank to their knees before her. The look of them did not encourage her. *I suppose there is always a chance.*

"Your Grace," said Qyburn quietly, "the small council . . ."

". . . will await my pleasure. It may be that we can bring them word of a traitor's death." Off across the city, the bells of Baelor's Sept sang their song of mourning. *No bells will ring for you, Tyrion,* Cersei thought. *I shall dip your head in tar and give your twisted body to the dogs.* "Off your knees," she told the would-be lords. "Show me what you've brought me."

They rose; three ugly men, and ragged. One had a boil on his neck, and none had washed in half a year. The prospect of raising such to lordship amused her. *I could seat them next to Margaery at feasts.* When the chief fool undid the drawstring on the sack and plunged his hand inside, the smell of decay filled her audience chamber like some rank rose. The head he pulled out was grey-green and crawling with maggots. *It smells like Father.* Dorcas gasped, and Jocelyn covered her mouth and retched.

The queen considered her prize, unflinching. "You've killed the wrong dwarf," she said at last, grudging every word.

"We never did," one of the fools dared to say. "This is got to be him, ser. A dwarf, see. He's rotted some, is all."

"He has also grown a new nose," Cersei observed. "A rather bulbous one, I'd say. Tyrion's nose was hacked off in a battle."

The three fools exchanged a look. "No one told us," said the one with head in hand. "This one come walking along as bold as you please, some ugly dwarf, so we thought . . ."

"He *said* he were a sparrow," the one with the boil added, "and *you* said he was lying." That was directed at the third man.

The queen was angry to think that she had kept her small council waiting for this mummer's farce. "You have wasted my time and slain an innocent man. I should have your own heads off." But if she did, the next man might hesitate and let the Imp slip the net. She would pile dead dwarfs ten feet high before she let that happen. "Remove yourselves from my sight."

"Aye, Your Grace," said the boil. "We beg your pardons."

"Do you want the head?" asked the man who held it.

"Give it to Ser Meryn. No, *in* the sack, you lackwit. Yes. Ser Osmund, see them out."

Trant removed the head and Kettleblack the headsmen, leaving only Lady Jocelyn's breakfast as evidence of their visit. "Clean that up at once," the queen commanded her. This was the third head that had been delivered to her. *At least this one was a dwarf.* The last had simply been an ugly child.

"Someone will find the dwarf, never fear," Ser Osmund assured her. "And when they do, we'll kill him good."

Will you? Last night Cersei had dreamed of the old woman, with her pebbly jowls and croaking voice. Maggy the Frog, they had called her in Lannisport. *If Father had known what she said to me, he would have had her tongue out.* Cersei had never told anyone, though, not even Jaime. *Melara said that if we never spoke about her prophecies, we would forget them. She said that a forgotten prophecy couldn't come true.*

"I have informers sniffing after the Imp everywhere, Your Grace," said Qyburn. He had garbed himself in something very like maester's robes, but white instead of grey, immaculate as the cloaks of the Kingsguard. Whorls of gold decorated his hem, sleeves, and stiff high collar, and a golden sash was tied about his waist. "Oldtown, Gulltown, Dorne, even the Free Cities. Wheresoever he might run, my whisperers will find him."

"You assume he left King's Landing. He could be hiding in Baelor's Sept for all we know, swinging on the bell ropes to make that awful din." Cersei made a sour face and let Dorcas help her to her feet. "Come, my lord. My council awaits." She took Qyburn by the arm as they made their way down the stairs. "Have you attended to that little task I set you?"

"I have, Your Grace. I am sorry that it took so long. Such a large head. It took the beetles many hours to clean the flesh. By way of pardon, I have lined a box of ebony and silver with felt, to make a fitting presentation for the skull."

"A cloth sack would serve as well. Prince Doran wants his head. He won't give a fig what sort of box it comes in."

The pealing of the bells was louder in the yard. *He was only a High Septon. How long must we endure this?* The ringing was more melodious than the Mountain's screams had been, but . . .

Qyburn seemed to sense what she was thinking. "The bells will stop at sunset, Your Grace."

"That will be a great relief. How can you know?"

"Knowing is the nature of my service."

Varys had all of us believing he was irreplaceable. What fools we were. Once the queen let it become known that Qyburn had taken the eunuch's place, the usual vermin had wasted no time in making themselves known to him, to trade their whispers for a few coins. *It was the silver all along, not the Spider. Qyburn will serve us just as well.* She was looking forward to the look on Pycelle's face when Qyburn took his seat.

A knight of the Kingsguard was always posted outside the doors of the council chambers when the small council was in session. Today it was Ser Boros Blount. "Ser Boros," the queen said pleasantly, "you look quite grey this morning. Something you ate, perchance?" Jaime had made him the king's food taster. *A tasty task, but shameful for a knight.* Blount hated it. His sagging jowls quivered as he held the door for them.

The councillors quieted as she entered. Lord Gyles coughed by way of greeting, loud enough to wake Pycelle. The others rose, mouthing pleasantries. Cersei allowed herself the faintest of smiles. "My lords, I know you will forgive my lateness."

"We are here to serve Your Grace," said Ser Harys Swyft. "It is our pleasure to anticipate your coming."

"You all know Lord Qyburn, I am sure."

Grand Maester Pycelle did not disappoint her. "*Lord* Qyburn?" he managed, purpling. "Your Grace, this . . . a maester swears sacred vows, to hold no lands or lordships . . ."

"Your Citadel took away his chain," Cersei reminded him. "If he is not a maester, he cannot be held to a maester's vows. We called the eunuch *lord* as well, you may recall."

Pycelle sputtered. "This man is . . . he is unfit . . ."

"Do not presume to speak to me of *fitness*. Not after the stinking mockery you made of my lord father's corpse."

"Your Grace cannot think . . ." He raised a spotted hand, as if to ward off a blow. "The silent sisters removed Lord Tywin's bowels and organs, drained his blood . . . every care was taken . . . his body was stuffed with salts and fragrant herbs . . ."

"Oh, spare me the disgusting details. I smelled the results of your *care*. Lord Qyburn's healing arts saved my brother's life, and I do not doubt that he will serve the king more ably than that simpering eunuch. My lord, you know your fellow councillors?"

"I would be a poor informer if I did not, Your Grace." Qyburn seated himself between Orton Merryweather and Gyles Rosby.

My councillors. Cersei had uprooted every rose, and all those beholden to her uncle and her brothers. In their places were men whose loyalty would be to her. She had even given them new styles, borrowed from the Free Cities; the queen would have no "masters" at court beside herself. Orton Merryweather was her justiciar, Gyles Rosby her lord treasurer. Aurane Waters, the dashing young Bastard of Driftmark, would be her grand admiral.

And for her Hand, Ser Harys Swyft.

Soft, bald, and obsequious, Swyft had an absurd little

white puff of beard where most men had a chin. The blue bantam rooster of his House was worked across the front of his plush yellow doublet in beads of lapis. Over that he wore a mantle of blue velvet decorated with a hundred golden hands. Ser Harys had been thrilled by his appointment, too dim to realize that he was more hostage than Hand. His daughter was her uncle's wife, and Kevan loved his chinless lady, flat-chested and chicken-legged as she was. So long as she had Ser Harys in hand, Kevan Lannister must needs think twice about opposing her. *To be sure, a good-father is not the ideal hostage, but better a flimsy shield than none.*

"Will the king be joining us?" asked Orton Merryweather.

"My son is playing with his little queen. For the moment, his idea of kingship is stamping papers with the royal seal. His Grace is still too young to comprehend affairs of state."

"And our valiant Lord Commander?"

"Ser Jaime is at his armorer's being fitted for a hand. I know we were all tired of that ugly stump. And I daresay he would find these proceedings as tiresome as Tommen." Aurane Waters chuckled at that. *Good,* Cersei thought, *the more they laugh, the less he is a threat. Let them laugh.* "Do we have wine?"

"We do, Your Grace." Orton Merryweather was not a comely man, with his big lumpish nose and shock of unruly reddish-orange hair, but he was never less than courteous. "We have Dornish red and Arbor gold, and a fine sweet hippocras from Highgarden."

"The gold, I think. I find Dornish wines as sour as the Dornish." As Merryweather filled her cup, Cersei said, "I suppose we had as well begin with them."

Grand Maester Pycelle's lips were still quivering, yet

somehow he found his tongue. "As you command. Prince Doran has taken his brother's unruly bastards into custody, yet Sunspear still seethes. The prince writes that he cannot hope to calm the waters until he receives the justice that was promised him."

"To be sure." *A tiresome creature, this prince.* "His long wait is almost done. I am sending Balon Swann to Sunspear, to deliver him the head of Gregor Clegane." Ser Balon would have another task as well, but that part was best left unsaid.

"Ah." Ser Harys Swyft fumbled at his funny little beard with thumb and forefinger. "He is dead then? Ser Gregor?"

"I would think so, my lord," Aurane Waters said dryly. "I am told that removing the head from the body is often mortal."

Cersei favored him with a smile; she liked a bit of wit, so long as she was not its target. "Ser Gregor perished of his wounds, just as Grand Maester Pycelle foretold."

Pycelle *harrumph*ed and eyed Qyburn sourly. "The spear was poisoned. No man could have saved him."

"So you said. I recall it well." The queen turned to her Hand. "What were you speaking of when I arrived, Ser Harys?"

"Sparrows, Your Grace. Septon Raynard says there may be as many as two thousand in the city, and more arriving every day. Their leaders preach of doom and demon worship . . ."

Cersei took a taste of wine. *Very nice.* "And long past time, wouldn't you agree? What would you call this red god that Stannis worships, if not a demon? The Faith should oppose such evil." Qyburn had reminded her of that, the clever man. "Our late High Septon let too much pass, I fear. Age had dimmed his sight and sapped his strength."

"He was an old done man, Your Grace." Qyburn smiled at Pycelle. "His passing should not have surprised us. No man can ask for more than to die peacefully in his sleep, full of years."

"No," said Cersei, "but we must hope that his successor is more vigorous. My friends upon the other hill tell me that it will most like be Torbert or Raynard."

Grand Maester Pycelle cleared his throat. "I have friends among the Most Devout as well, and they speak of Septon Ollidor."

"Do not discount this man Luceon," Qyburn said. "Last night he feted thirty of the Most Devout on suckling pig and Arbor gold, and by day he hands out hardbread to the poor to prove his piety."

Aurane Waters seemed as bored as Cersei by all this prattle about septons. Seen up close, his hair was more silvery than gold, and his eyes were grey-green where Prince Rhaegar's had been purple. Even so, the resemblance . . . She wondered if Waters would shave his beard for her. Though he was ten years her junior, he wanted her; Cersei could see it in the way he looked at her. Men had been looking at her that way since her breasts began to bud. *Because I was so beautiful, they said, but Jaime was beautiful as well, and they never looked at him that way.* When she was small she would sometimes don her brother's clothing as a lark. She was always startled by how differently men treated her when they thought that she was Jaime. Even Lord Tywin himself . . .

Pycelle and Merryweather were still quibbling about who the new High Septon was like to be. "One will serve as well as another," the queen announced abruptly, "but whosoever dons the crystal crown must pronounce an anathema upon the Imp." This last High Septon had been conspicuously silent regarding Tyrion. "As for these pink sparrows, so long as they preach no treason they are the Faith's problem, not ours."

Lord Orton and Ser Harys murmured agreement. Gyles Rosby's attempt to do the same dissolved into a fit of coughing. Cersei turned away in distaste as he was hacking up a gob of bloody phlegm. "Maester, have you brought the letter from the Vale?"

"I have, Your Grace." Pycelle plucked it from his pile of papers and smoothed it out. "It is a declaration, rather than a letter. Signed at Runestone by Bronze Yohn Royce, Lady Waynwood, Lords Hunter, Redfort, and Belmore, and Symond Templeton, the Knight of Ninestars. All have affixed their seals. They write—"

A deal of rubbish. "My lords may read the letter if they wish. Royce and these others are massing men below the Eyrie. They mean to remove Littlefinger as Lord Protector of the Vale, forcibly if need be. The question is, ought we allow this?"

"Does Lord Baelish seek our help?" asked Harys Swyft.

"Not as yet. In truth, he seems quite unconcerned. His last letter mentions the rebels only briefly before beseeching me to ship him some old tapestries of Robert's."

Ser Harys fingered his chin beard. "And these lords of the declaration, do *they* appeal to the king to take a hand?"

"They do not."

"Then . . . mayhaps we need do nothing."

"A war in the Vale would be most tragic," said Pycelle.

"War?" Orton Merryweather laughed. "Lord Baelish is a most amusing man, but one does not fight a war with witticisms. I doubt there will be bloodshed. And does it matter who is regent for little Lord Robert, so long as the Vale remits its taxes?"

No, Cersei decided. If truth be told, Littlefinger had

been more use at court. *He had a gift for finding gold, and never coughed.* "Lord Orton has convinced me. Maester Pycelle, instruct these Lords Declarant that no harm must come to Petyr. Elsewise, the crown is content with whatever dispositions they might make for the governance of the Vale during Robert Arryn's minority."

"Very good, Your Grace."

"Might we discuss the fleet?" asked Aurane Waters. "Fewer than a dozen of our ships survived the inferno on the Blackwater. We must needs restore our strength at sea."

Harys Swyft nodded. "Strength at sea is most essential."

"Could we make use of the ironmen?" asked Orton Merryweather. "The enemy of our enemy? What would the Seastone Chair want of us as the price of an alliance?"

"They want the north," Grand Maester Pycelle said, "which our queen's noble father promised to House Bolton."

"How inconvenient," said Merryweather. "Still, the north is large. The lands could be divided. It need not be a permanent arrangement. Bolton might consent, so long as we assure him that our strength will be his once Stannis is destroyed."

"Balon Greyjoy is dead, I had heard," said Ser Harys Swyft. "Do we know who rules the isles now? Did Lord Balon have a son?"

"Leo?" coughed Lord Gyles. "Theo?"

"Theon Greyjoy was raised at Winterfell, a ward of Eddard Stark," Qyburn said. "He is not like to be a friend of ours."

"I had heard he was slain," said Merryweather.

"Was there only one son?" Ser Harys Swyft tugged

upon his chin beard. "Brothers. There were brothers. Were there not?"

Varys would have known, Cersei thought with irritation. "I do not propose to climb in bed with that sorry pack of squids. Their turn will come, once we have dealt with Stannis. What we require is our own fleet."

"I propose we build new dromonds," said Aurane Waters. "Ten, to start with."

"Where is the coin to come from?" asked Pycelle.

Lord Gyles took that as an invitation to begin coughing again. He brought up more pink spittle and dabbed it away with a square of red silk. "There is no . . ." he managed, before the coughing ate his words. ". . . no . . . we do not . . ."

Ser Harys proved swift enough at least to grasp the meaning between the coughs. "The crown incomes have never been greater," he objected. "Ser Kevan told me so himself."

Lord Gyles coughed. ". . . expenses . . . gold cloaks . . ."

Cersei had heard his objections before. "Our lord treasurer is trying to say that we have too many gold cloaks and too little gold." Rosby's coughing had begun to vex her. *Perhaps Garth the Gross would not have been so ill.* "Though large, the crown incomes are not large enough to keep abreast of Robert's debts. Accordingly, I have decided to defer our repayment of the sums owed the Holy Faith and the Iron Bank of Braavos until war's end." The new High Septon would doubtless wring his holy hands, and the Braavosi would squeak and squawk at her, but what of it? "The monies saved will be used for the building of our new fleet."

"Your Grace is prudent," said Lord Merryweather. "This is a wise measure. And needed, until the war is done. I concur."

"And I," said Ser Harys.

"Your Grace," Pycelle said in a quavering voice, "this will cause more trouble than you know, I fear. The Iron Bank . . ."

". . . remains on Braavos, far across the sea. They shall have their gold, maester. A Lannister pays his debts."

"The Braavosi have a saying too." Pycelle's jeweled chain clinked softly. "*The Iron Bank will have its due,* they say."

"The Iron Bank will have its due when I say they will. Until such time, the Iron Bank will wait respectfully. Lord Waters, commence the building of your dromonds."

"Very good, Your Grace."

Ser Harys shuffled through some papers. "The next matter . . . we have had a letter from Lord Frey putting forth some claims . . ."

"How many lands and honors does that man want?" snapped the queen. "His mother must have had three teats."

"My lords may not know," said Qyburn, "but in the winesinks and pot shops of this city, there are those who suggest that the crown might have been somehow complicit in Lord Walder's crime."

The other councillors stared at him uncertainly. "Do you refer to the Red Wedding?" asked Aurane Waters. "Crime?" said Ser Harys. Pycelle cleared his throat noisily. Lord Gyles coughed.

"These sparrows are especially outspoken," warned Qyburn. "The Red Wedding was an affront to all the laws of gods and men, they say, and those who had a hand in it are damned."

Cersei was not slow to take his meaning. "Lord Walder must soon face the Father's judgment. He is very old. Let the sparrows spit upon his memory. It has nought to do with us."

"No," said Ser Harys. "No," said Lord Merryweather. "No one could think so," said Pycelle. Lord Gyles coughed.

"A little spittle on Lord Walder's tomb is not like to disturb the grave worms," Qyburn agreed, "but it would also be useful if someone were to be *punished* for the Red Wedding. A few Frey heads would do much to mollify the north."

"Lord Walder will never sacrifice his own," said Pycelle.

"No," mused Cersei, "but his heirs may be less squeamish. Lord Walder will soon do us the courtesy of dying, we can hope. What better way for the new Lord of the Crossing to rid himself of inconvenient half brothers, disagreeable cousins, and scheming sisters than by naming them the culprits?"

"Whilst we await Lord Walder's death, there is another matter," said Aurane Waters. "The Golden Company has broken its contract with Myr. Around the docks I've heard men say that Lord Stannis has hired them and is bringing them across the sea."

"What would he pay them with?" asked Merryweather. "Snow? They are called the *Golden* Company. How much gold does Stannis have?"

"Little enough," Cersei assured him. "Lord Qyburn has spoken to the crew of that Myrish galley in the bay. They claim the Golden Company is making for Volantis. If they mean to cross to Westeros, they are marching in the wrong direction."

"Perhaps they grew weary of fighting on the losing side," suggested Lord Merryweather.

"There is that as well," agreed the queen. "Only a blind man could fail to see our war is all but won. Lord Tyrell has Storm's End invested. Riverrun is besieged by the Freys and my cousin Daven, our new Warden of the West.

Lord Redwyne's ships have passed through the Straits of Tarth and are moving swiftly up the coast. Only a few fishing boats remain on Dragonstone to oppose Redwyne's landing. The castle may hold for some time, but once we have the port we can cut the garrison off from the sea. Then only Stannis himself will remain to vex us."

"If Lord Janos can be believed, he is trying to make common cause with the wildlings," warned Grand Maester Pycelle.

"Savages in skins," declared Lord Merryweather. "Lord Stannis must be desperate indeed, to seek such allies."

"Desperate and foolish," the queen agreed. "The northmen hate the wildlings. Roose Bolton should have no trouble winning them to our cause. A few have already joined up with his bastard son to help him clear the wretched ironmen from Moat Cailin and clear the way for Lord Bolton to return. Umber, Ryswell . . . I forget the other names. Even White Harbor is on the point of joining us. Its lord has agreed to marry both his granddaughters to our friends of Frey and open his port to our ships."

"I thought we had no ships," Ser Harys said, confused.

"Wyman Manderly was a loyal bannerman to Eddard Stark," said Grand Maester Pycelle. "Can such a man be trusted?

No one can be trusted. "He's a fat old man, and frightened. However, he is proving stubborn on one point. He insists that he will not bend the knee until his heir has been returned to him."

"Do we have this heir?" asked Ser Harys.

"He will be at Harrenhal, if he is still alive. Gregor Clegane took him captive." The Mountain had not always been gentle with his prisoners, even those worth a goodly ransom. "If he is dead, I suppose we will need to send Lord Manderly the heads of those who killed him, with our most sincere apologies." If one head was enough to appease a prince of Dorne, a bag of them should be more than adequate for a fat northman wrapped in sealskins.

"Will not Lord Stannis seek to win the allegiance of White Harbor as well?" asked Grand Maester Pycelle.

"Oh, he has tried. Lord Manderly has sent his letters on to us and replied with evasions. Stannis demands White Harbor's swords and silver, for which he offers . . . well, *nothing*." One day she must light a candle to the Stranger for carrying Renly off and leaving Stannis. If it had been the other way around, her life would have been harder. "Just this morning there was another bird. Stannis has sent his onion smuggler to treat with White Harbor on his behalf. Manderly has clapped the wretch inside a cell. He asks us what he should do with him."

"Send him here, that we might question him," suggested Lord Merryweather. "The man might know much of value."

"Let him die," said Qyburn. "His death will be a lesson to the north, to show them what becomes of traitors."

"I quite agree," the queen said. "I have instructed Lord Manderly to have his head off forthwith. That should put an end to any chance of White Harbor supporting Stannis."

"Stannis will need another Hand," observed Aurane Waters with a chuckle. "The turnip knight, perhaps?"

"A turnip knight?" said Ser Harys Swyft, confused. "Who is this man? I have not heard of him."

Waters did not reply, except to roll his eyes.

"What if Lord Manderly should refuse?" asked Merryweather.

"He dare not. The onion knight's head is the coin he'll need to buy his son's life." Cersei smiled. "The fat old fool may have been loyal to the Starks in his own way, but with the wolves of Winterfell extinguished—"

"Your Grace has forgotten the Lady Sansa," said Pycelle.

The queen bristled. "I most certainly have *not* forgotten that little she-wolf." She refused to say the girl's name. "I ought to have shown her to the black cells as the daughter of a traitor, but instead I made her part of mine own household. She shared my hearth and hall, played with my own children. I fed her, dressed her, tried to make her a little less ignorant about the world, and how did she repay me for my kindness? She helped murder my son. When we find the Imp, we will find the Lady Sansa too. She is not dead . . . but before I am done with her, I promise you, she will be singing to the Stranger, begging for his kiss."

An awkward silence followed. *Have they all swallowed their tongues?* Cersei thought, with irritation. It was enough to make her wonder why she bothered with a council.

"In any case," the queen went on, "Lord Eddard's *younger* daughter is with Lord Bolton, and will be wed to his son Ramsay as soon as Moat Cailin has fallen." So long as the girl played her role well enough to cement their claim to Winterfell, neither of the Boltons would much care that she was actually some steward's whelp tricked up by Littlefinger. "If the north must have a Stark, we'll give them one." She let Lord Merryweather fill her cup once again. "Another problem has arisen on the Wall, however. The brothers of the Night's Watch have taken leave of their wits and chosen Ned Stark's bastard son to be their Lord Commander."

"Snow, the boy is called," Pycelle said unhelpfully.

"I glimpsed him once at Winterfell," the queen said, "though the Starks did their best to hide him. He looks very like his father." Her husband's by-blows had his look as well, though at least Robert had the grace to keep them out of sight. Once, after that sorry business with the cat, he had made some noises about bringing some baseborn daughter of his to court. "Do as you please," she'd told him, "but you may find that the city is not a healthy place for a growing girl." The bruise those words had won her had been hard to hide from Jaime, but they heard no more about the bastard girl. *Catelyn Tully was a mouse, or she would have smothered this Jon Snow in his cradle. Instead, she's left the filthy task to me.* "Snow shares Lord Eddard's taste for treason too," she said. "The father would have handed the realm to Stannis. The son has given him lands and castles."

"The Night's Watch is sworn to take no part in the wars of the Seven Kingdoms," Pycelle reminded them. "For thousands of years the black brothers have upheld that tradition."

"Until now," said Cersei. "The bastard boy has written us to avow that the Night's Watch takes no side, but his actions give the lie to his words. He has given Stannis food and shelter, yet has the insolence to plead with us for arms and men."

"An outrage," declared Lord Merryweather. "We cannot allow the Night's Watch to join its strength to that of Lord Stannis."

"We must declare this Snow a traitor and a rebel," agreed Ser Harys Swyft. "The black brothers must remove him."

Grand Maester Pycelle nodded ponderously. "I propose that we inform Castle Black that no more men will be sent to them until such time as Snow is gone."

"Our new dromonds will need oarsmen," said Aurane Waters. "Let us instruct the lords to send their poachers and thieves to me henceforth, instead of to the Wall."

Qyburn leaned forward with a smile. "The Night's

Watch defends us all from snarks and grumkins. My lords, I say that we must *help* the brave black brothers."

Cersei gave him a sharp look. "What are you saying?"

"This," Qyburn said. "For years now, the Night's Watch has begged for men. Lord Stannis has answered their plea. Can King Tommen do less? His Grace should send the Wall a hundred men. To take the black, ostensibly, but in truth . . ."

". . . to remove Jon Snow from the command," Cersei finished, delighted. *I knew I was right to want him on my council.* "That is just what we shall do." She laughed. *If this bastard boy is truly his father's son, he will not suspect a thing. Perhaps he will even thank me, before the blade slides between his ribs.* "It will need to be done carefully, to be sure. Leave the rest to me, my lords." This was how an enemy should be dealt with: with a dagger, not a declaration. "We have done good work today, my lords. I thank you. Is there aught else?"

"One last thing, Your Grace," said Aurane Waters, in an apologetic tone. "I hesitate to take up the council's time with trifles, but there has been some queer talk heard along the docks of late. Sailors from the east. They speak of dragons . . ."

". . . and manticores, no doubt, and bearded snarks?" Cersei chuckled. "Come back to me when you hear talk of *dwarfs,* my lord." She stood, to signal that the meeting was at an end.

A blustery autumn wind was blowing when Cersei left the council chambers, and bells of Blessed Baelor still sang their song of mourning off across the city. In the yard twoscore knights were hammering each other with sword and shield, adding to the din. Ser Boros Blount escorted the queen back to her apartments, where she found Lady

Merryweather chuckling with Jocelyn and Dorcas. "What is it you all find so amusing?"

"The Redwyne twins," said Taena. "Both of them have fallen in love with Lady Margaery. They used to fight over which would be the next Lord of the Arbor. Now both of them want to join the Kingsguard, just to be near the little queen."

"The Redwynes have always had more freckles than wits." It was a useful thing to know, though. *If Horror or Slobber were to be found abed with Margaery . . .* Cersei wondered if the little queen liked freckles. "Dorcas, fetch me Ser Osney Kettleblack."

Dorcas blushed. "As you command."

When the girl was gone, Taena Merryweather gave the queen a quizzical look. "Why did she turn so red?"

"Love." It was Cersei's turn to laugh. "She fancies our Ser Osney." He was the youngest Kettleblack, the clean-shaved one. Though he had the same black hair, hooked nose, and easy smile as his brother Osmund, one cheek bore three long scratches, courtesy of one of Tyrion's whores. "She likes his scars, I think."

Lady Merryweather's dark eyes shone with mischief. "Just so. Scars make a man look dangerous, and danger is exciting."

"You shock me, my lady," the queen said, teasing. "If danger excites you so, why wed Lord Orton? We all love him, it is true, but still . . ." Petyr had once remarked that the horn of plenty that adorned House Merryweather's arms suited Lord Orton admirably, since he had carrot-colored hair, a nose as bulbous as a beetroot, and pease porridge for wits.

Taena laughed. "My lord is more bountiful than danger-ous, this is so. Yet . . . I hope Your Grace will not think the less of me, but I did not come a maid entire to Orton's bed."

You are all whores in the Free Cities, aren't you? That was good to know; one day, she might be able to make use of it. "And pray, who was this lover who was so . . . full of danger?"

Taena's olive skin turned even darker as she blushed. "Oh, I should not have spoken. Your Grace will keep my secret, yes?"

"Men have scars, women mysteries." Cersei kissed her cheek. *I will have his name out of you soon enough.*

When Dorcas returned with Ser Osney Kettleblack, the queen dismissed her ladies. "Come sit with me by the window, Ser Osney. Will you take a cup of wine?" She poured for them herself. "Your cloak is threadbare. I have a mind to put you in a new one."

"What, a white one? Who's died?"

"No one, as yet," the queen said. "Is that your wish, to join your brother Osmund in our Kingsguard?"

"I'd rather be the *queen's* guard, if it please Your Grace." When Osney grinned, the scars on his cheek turned bright red.

Cersei's fingers traced their path across his cheek. "You have a bold tongue, ser. You will make me forget myself again."

"Good." Ser Osney caught her hand and kissed her fingers roughly. "My sweet queen."

"You are a wicked man," the queen whispered, "and no true knight, I think." She let him touch her breasts through the silk of her gown. "Enough."

"It isn't. I want you."

"You've had me."

"Only once." He grabbed her left breast again and gave it a clumsy squeeze that reminded her of Robert.

"One good night for one good knight. You did me valiant service, and you had your reward." Cersei walked her fingers up his laces. She could feel him stiffening through his breeches. "Was that a new horse you were riding in the yard yestermorn?"

"The black stallion? Aye. A gift from my brother Osfryd. Midnight, I call him."

How wonderfully original. "A fine mount for a battle. For pleasure, though, there is nothing to compare to a gallop on a spirited young filly." She gave him a smile and a squeeze. "Tell me true. Do you think our little queen is pretty?"

Ser Osney drew back, wary. "I suppose. For a girl. I'd sooner have a woman."

"Why not both?" she whispered. "Pluck the little rose for me, and you will not find me to be ungrateful."

"The little . . . Margaery, you mean?" Ser Osney's ardor was wilting in his breeches. "She's the king's wife. Wasn't there some Kingsguard who lost his head for bedding the king's wife?"

"Ages ago." *She was his king's mistress, not his wife, and his head was the only thing he did not lose. Aegon dismembered him piece by piece, and made the woman watch.* Cersei did not want Osney dwelling on that ancient unpleasantness, however. "Tommen is not Aegon the Unworthy. Have no fear, he will do as I bid him. I mean for Margaery to lose her head, not you."

That gave him pause. "Her maidenhead, you mean?"

"That too. Assuming she has still one." She traced his scars again. "Unless you think Margaery would prove unresponsive to your . . . charms?"

Osney gave her a wounded look. "She likes me well enough. Them cousins of hers are always teasing with me about my nose. How big it is, and all. The last time Megga did that, Margaery told them to stop and said I had a lovely face."

"There you are, then."

"There I am," the man agreed, in a doubtful tone, "but where am I going to be if she . . . if I . . . after we . . . ?"

". . . do the deed?" Cersei gave him a barbed smile. "Lying with a queen is treason. Tommen would have no choice but to send you to the Wall."

"The Wall?" he said with dismay.

It was all she could do not to laugh. *No, best not. Men hate being laughed at.* "A black cloak would go well with your eyes, and that black hair of yours."

"No one returns from the Wall."

"You will. All you need to do is kill a boy."

"What boy?"

"A bastard boy in league with Stannis. He's young and green, and you'll have a hundred men."

Kettleblack was afraid, she could smell it on him, but he was too proud to own up to that fear. *Men are all alike.* "I've killed more boys than I can count," he insisted. "Once this boy is dead, I'd get my pardon from the king?"

"That, and a lordship." *Unless Snow's brothers hang you first.* "A queen must have a consort. One who knows no fear."

"Lord Kettleblack?" A slow smile spread across his face, and his scars flamed red. "Aye, I like the sound o' that. A lordly lord . . ."

". . . and fit to bed a queen."

He frowned. "The Wall is cold."

"And I am warm." Cersei put her arms about his neck. "Bed a girl and kill a boy and I am yours. Do you have the courage?"

Osney thought a moment before he nodded. "I am your man."

"You are, ser." She kissed him, and let him have a little

taste of tongue before she broke away. "Enough for now. The rest must wait. Will you dream of me tonight?"

"Aye." His voice was hoarse.

"And when you're abed with our Maid Margaery?" she asked him, teasing. "When you're in her, will you dream of me then?"

"I will," swore Osney Kettleblack.

"Good."

After he was gone, Cersei summoned Jocelyn to brush her hair out whilst she slipped off her shoes and stretched like a cat. *I was made for this,* she told herself. It was the sheer elegance of it that pleased her most. Even Mace Tyrell would not dare defend his darling daughter if she was caught in the act with the likes of Osney Kettleblack, and neither Stannis Baratheon nor Jon Snow would have cause to wonder why Osney was being sent to the Wall. She would see to it that Ser Osmund was the one to discover his brother with the little queen; that way the loyalty of the other two Kettleblacks need not be impugned. *If Father could only see me now, he would not be so quick to speak of marrying me off again. A pity he's so dead. Him and Robert, Jon Arryn, Ned Stark, Renly Baratheon, all dead. Only Tyrion remains, and not for long.*

That night the queen summoned Lady Merryweather to her bedchamber. "Will you take a cup of wine?" she asked her.

"A small one." The Myrish woman laughed. "A big one."

"On the morrow I want you to pay a call on my good-daughter," Cersei said as Dorcas was dressing her for bed.

"Lady Margaery is always happy to see me."

"I know." The queen did not fail to note the style that Taena used when referring to Tommen's little wife. "Tell her I've sent seven beeswax candles to the Baelor's Sept in memory of our dear High Septon."

Taena laughed. "If so, she will send seven-and-seventy candles of her own, so as not to be outmourned."

"I will be very cross if she does not," the queen said, smiling. "Tell her also that she has a secret admirer, a knight so smitten with her beauty that he cannot sleep at night."

"Might I ask Your Grace which knight?" Mischief sparkled in Taena's big dark eyes. "Could it be Ser Osney?"

"It could be," the queen said, "but do not offer up that name freely. Make her worm it out of you. Will you do that?"

"If it please you. That is all I wish, Your Grace."

Outside a cold wind was rising. They stayed up late into the morning, drinking Arbor gold and telling one another tales. Taena got quite drunk and Cersei pried the name of her secret lover from her. He was a Myrish sea captain, half a pirate, with black hair to the shoulders and a scar that ran across his face from chin to ear. "A hundred times I told him no, and he said yes," the other woman told her, "until finally I was saying yes as well. He was not the sort of man to be denied."

"I know the sort," the queen said with a wry smile.

"Has Your Grace ever known a man like that, I wonder?"

"Robert," she lied, thinking of Jaime.

Yet when she closed her eyes, it was the other brother that she dreamt of, and the three wretched fools with whom she had begun her day. In the dream it was Tyrion's head they brought her in their sack. She had it bronzed, and kept it in her chamber pot.

THE IRON CAPTAIN

The wind was blowing from the north as the *Iron Victory* came round the point and entered the holy bay called Nagga's Cradle.

Victarion joined Nute the Barber at her prow. Ahead loomed the sacred shore of Old Wyk and the grassy hill above it, where the ribs of Nagga rose from the earth like the trunks of great white trees, as wide around as a dromond's mast and twice as tall.

The bones of the Grey King's Hall. Victarion could feel the magic of this place. "Balon stood beneath those bones, when first he named himself a king," he recalled. "He swore to win us back our freedoms, and Tarle the Thrice-Drowned placed a driftwood crown upon his head. '*BALON!*' they cried. '*BALON! BALON KING!*'"

"They will shout your name as loud," said Nute.

Victarion nodded, though he did not share the Barber's

certainty. *Balon had three sons, and a daughter he loved well.*

He had said as much to his captains at Moat Cailin, when first they urged him to claim the Seastone Chair. "Balon's sons are dead," Red Ralf Stonehouse had argued, "and Asha is a woman. You were your brother's strong right arm, you must pick up the sword that he let fall." When Victarion reminded them that Balon had commanded him to hold the Moat against the northmen, Ralf Kenning said, "The wolves are broken, lord. What good to win this swamp and lose the isles?" And Ralf the Limper added, "The Crow's Eye has been too long away. He knows us not."

Euron Greyjoy, King of the Isles and the North. The thought woke an old rage in his heart, but still . . .

"Words are wind," Victarion told them, "and the only good wind is that which fills our sails. Would you have me fight the Crow's Eye? Brother against brother, ironborn against ironborn?" Euron was still his elder, no matter how much bad blood might be between them. *No man is as accursed as the kinslayer.*

But when the Damphair's summons came, the call to kingsmoot, then all was changed. *Aeron speaks with the Drowned God's voice,* Victarion reminded himself, *and if the Drowned God wills that I should sit the Seastone Chair* . . . The next day he gave command of Moat Cailin to Ralf Kenning and set off overland for the Fever River where the Iron Fleet lay amongst the reeds and willows. Rough seas and fickle winds had delayed him, but only one ship had been lost, and he was home.

Grief and *Iron Vengeance* were close behind as *Iron Victory* passed the headland. Behind came *Hardhand, Iron Wind, Grey Ghost, Lord Quellon, Lord Vickon, Lord Dagon,* and the rest, nine-tenths of the Iron Fleet, sailing on the evening tide in a ragged column that extended back long leagues. The sight of their sails filled Victarion Greyjoy with content. No man had ever loved his wives half as well as the Lord Captain loved his ships.

Along the sacred strand of Old Wyk, longships lined the shore as far as the eye could see, their masts thrust up like spears. In the deeper waters rode prizes: cogs, carracks, and dromonds won in raid or war, too big to run ashore. From prow and stern and mast flew familiar banners.

Nute the Barber squinted toward the strand. "Is that Lord Harlaw's *Sea Song*?" The Barber was a thickset man with bandy legs and long arms, but his eyes were not so keen as they had been when he was young. In those days he could throw an axe so well that men said he could shave you with it.

"*Sea Song,* aye." Rodrik the Reader had left his books, it would seem. "And there's old Drumm's *Thunderer,* with Blacktyde's *Nightflyer* beside her." Victarion's eyes were as sharp as they had ever been. Even with their sails furled and their banners hanging limp, he knew them, as befit the Lord Captain of the Iron Fleet. "*Silverfin* too. Some kin of Sawane Botley." The Crow's Eye had drowned Lord Botley, Victarion had heard, and his heir had died at Moat Cailin, but there had been brothers, and other sons as well. *How many? Four? No, five, and none with any cause to love the Crow's Eye.*

And then he saw her: a single-masted galley, lean and low, with a dark red hull. Her sails, now furled, were black as a starless sky. Even at anchor *Silence* looked both cruel and fast. On her prow was a black iron maiden with one arm outstretched. Her waist was slender, her breasts high and proud, her legs long and shapely. A windblown mane

of black iron hair streamed from her head, and her eyes
were mother-of-pearl, but she had no mouth.

Victarion's hands closed into fists. He had beaten four
men to death with those hands, and one wife as well.
Though his hair was flecked with hoarfrost, he was as
strong as he had ever been, with a bull's broad chest and a
boy's flat belly. *The kinslayer is accursed in the eyes of
gods and men,* Balon had reminded him on the day he sent
the Crow's Eye off to sea.

"He is here," Victarion told the Barber. "Drop sail. We
proceed on oars alone. Command *Grief* and *Iron
Vengeance* to stand between *Silence* and the sea. The rest
of the fleet to seal the bay. None is to leave save at my
command, neither man nor crow."

The men upon the shore had spied their sails. Shouts
echoed across the bay as friends and kin called out greetings. But not from *Silence.* On her decks a motley crew
of mutes and mongrels spoke no word as the *Iron Victory*
drew nigh. Men black as tar stared out at him, and others
squat and hairy as the apes of Sothoryos. *Monsters,*
Victarion thought.

They dropped anchor twenty yards from *Silence.*
"Lower a boat. I would go ashore." He buckled on his
swordbelt as the rowers took their places; his longsword
rested on one hip, a dirk upon the other. Nute the Barber
fastened the Lord Captain's cloak about his shoulders. It
was made of nine layers of cloth-of-gold, sewn in the
shape of the kraken of Greyjoy, arms dangling to his
boots. Beneath he wore heavy grey chainmail over boiled
black leather. In Moat Cailin he had taken to wearing mail
day and night. Sore shoulders and an aching back were
easier to bear than bloody bowels. The poisoned arrows of
the bog devils need only scratch a man, and a few hours
later he would be squirting and screaming as his life ran

down his legs in gouts of red and brown. *Whoever wins the Seastone Chair, I shall deal with the bog devils.*

Victarion donned a tall black warhelm, wrought in the shape of an iron kraken, its arms coiled down around his cheeks to meet beneath his jaw. By then the boat was ready. "I put the chests into your charge," he told Nute as he climbed over the side. "See that they are strongly guarded." Much depended on the chests.

"As you command, Your Grace."

Victarion returned a sour scowl. "I am no king as yet." He clambered down into the boat.

Aeron Damphair was waiting for him in the surf with his waterskin slung beneath one arm. The priest was gaunt and tall, though shorter than Victarion. His nose rose like a shark's fin from a bony face, and his eyes were iron. His beard reached to his waist, and tangled ropes of hair slapped at the back of his legs when the wind blew. "Brother," he said as the waves broke white and cold around their ankles, "what is dead can never die."

"But rises again, harder and stronger." Victarion lifted off his helm and knelt. The bay filled his boots and soaked his breeches as Aeron poured a stream of salt water down upon his brow. And so they prayed.

"Where is our brother Crow's Eye?" the Lord Captain demanded of Aeron Damphair when the prayers were done.

"His is the great tent of cloth-of-gold, there where the din is loudest. He surrounds himself with godless men and monsters, worse than before. In him our father's blood went bad."

"Our mother's blood as well." Victarion would not speak of kinslaying, here in this godly place beneath the bones of Nagga and the Grey King's Hall, but many a night he dreamed of driving a mailed fist into Euron's smiling face, until the flesh split and his bad blood ran red and free. *I must not. I pledged my word to Balon.* "All have come?" he asked his priestly brother.

"All who matter. The captains and the kings." On the Iron Islands they were one and the same, for every captain was a king on his own deck, and every king must be a captain. "Do you mean to claim our father's crown?"

Victarion imagined himself seated on the Seastone Chair. "If the Drowned God wills it."

"The waves will speak," said Aeron Damphair as he turned away. "Listen to the waves, brother."

"Aye." He wondered how his name would sound whispered by waves and shouted by the captains and the kings. *If the cup should pass to me, I will not set it by.*

A crowd had gathered round to wish him well and seek his favor. Victarion saw men from every isle: Blacktydes, Tawneys, Orkwoods, Stonetrees, Wynches, and many more. The Goodbrothers of Old Wyk, the Goodbrothers of Great Wyk, and the Goodbrothers of Orkmont all had come. The Codds were there, though every decent man despised them. Humble Shepherds, Weavers, and Netleys rubbed shoulders with men from Houses ancient and proud; even humble Humbles, the blood of thralls and salt wives. A Volmark clapped Victarion on the back; two Sparrs pressed a wineskin into his hands. He drank deep, wiped his mouth, and let them bear him off to their cook-fires, to listen to their talk of war and crowns and plunder, and the glory and the freedom of his reign.

That night the men of the Iron Fleet raised a huge sail-cloth tent above the tideline, so Victarion might feast half a hundred famous captains on roast kid, salted cod, and lobster. Aeron came as well. He ate fish and drank water, whilst the captains quaffed enough ale to float the Iron Fleet. Many promised him their voices: Fralegg the

Strong, clever Alvyn Sharp, humpbacked Hotho Harlaw. Hotho offered him a daughter for his queen. "I have no luck with wives," Victarion told him. His first wife died in childbed, giving him a stillborn daughter. His second had been stricken by a pox. And his third . . .

"A king must have an heir," Hotho insisted. "The Crow's Eye brings three sons to show before the kingsmoot."

"Bastards and mongrels. How old is this daughter?"

"Twelve," said Hotho. "Fair and fertile, newly flowered, with hair the color of honey. Her breasts are small as yet, but she has good hips. She takes after her mother, more than me."

Victarion knew that to mean the girl did not have a hump. Yet when he tried to picture her, he only saw the wife he'd killed. He had sobbed each time he struck her, and afterward carried her down to the rocks to give her to the crabs. "I will gladly look at the girl once I am crowned," he said. That was as much as Hotho dared hope for, and he shambled off, content.

Baelor Blacktyde was more difficult to please. He sat by Victarion's elbow in his lambswool tunic of black-and-green vairy, smooth-faced and comely. His cloak was sable, and pinned with a silver seven-pointed star. He had been eight years a hostage in Oldtown, and had returned a worshiper of the seven green land gods. "Balon was mad, Aeron is madder, and Euron is maddest of them all," Lord Baelor said. "What of you, Lord Captain? If I shout your name, will you make an end of this mad war?"

Victarion frowned. "Would you have me bend the knee?"

"If need be. We cannot stand alone against all Westeros. King Robert proved that, to our grief. Balon would pay the iron price for freedom, he said, but our women bought

Balon's crowns with empty beds. My mother was one such. The Old Way is dead."

"What is dead can never die, but rises harder and stronger. In a hundred years men will sing of Balon the Bold."

"Balon the Widowmaker, call him. I will gladly trade his freedom for a father. Have you one to give me?" When Victarion did not answer, Blacktyde snorted and moved off.

The tent grew hot and smoky. Two of Gorold Goodbrother's sons knocked a table over fighting; Will Humble lost a wager and had to eat his boot; Little Lenwood Tawney fiddled whilst Romny Weaver sang "The Bloody Cup" and "Steel Rain" and other old reaving songs. Qarl the Maid and Eldred Codd danced the finger dance. A roar of laughter went up when one of Eldred's fingers landed in Ralf the Limper's wine cup.

A woman was amongst those laughing. Victarion rose and saw her by the tent flap, whispering something in the ear of Qarl the Maid that made him laugh as well. He had hoped she would not be fool enough to come here, yet the sight of her made him smile all the same. *"Asha,"* he called in a commanding voice. *"Niece."*

She made her way to his side, lean and lithe in high boots of salt-stained leather, green woolen breeches, and brown quilted tunic, a sleeveless leather jerkin half-unlaced. "Nuncle." Asha Greyjoy was tall for a woman, yet she had to stand on her toes to kiss his cheek. "I am pleased to see you at my queensmoot."

"Queensmoot?" Victarion laughed. "Are you drunk, niece? Sit. I did not spy your *Black Wind* on the strand."

"I beached her beneath Norne Goodbrother's castle and rode across the island." She sat upon a stool and helped herself unasked to Nute the Barber's wine. Nute raised no objection; he had passed out drunk some time ago. "Who holds the Moat?"

"Ralf Kenning. With the Young Wolf dead, only the bog devils remain to plague us."

"The Starks were not the only northmen. The Iron Throne has named the Lord of the Dreadfort as Warden of the North."

"Would you lesson me in warfare? I was fighting battles when you were sucking mother's milk."

"And losing battles too." Asha took a drink of wine.

Victarion did not like to be reminded of Fair Isle. "Every man should lose a battle in his youth, so he does not lose a war when he is old. You have not come to make a claim, I hope."

She teased him with a smile. "And if I have?"

"There are men who remember when you were a little girl, swimming naked in the sea and playing with your doll."

"I played with axes too."

"You did," he had to grant, "but a woman wants a husband, not a crown. When I am king I'll give you one."

"My nuncle is so good to me. Shall I find a pretty wife for you, when I am queen?"

"I have no luck with wives. How long have you been here?"

"Long enough to see that Uncle Damphair has woken more than he intended. The Drumm means to make a claim, and Tarle the Thrice-Drowned was heard to say that Maron Volmark is the true heir of the black line."

"The king must be a kraken."

"The Crow's Eye is a kraken. The elder brother comes before the younger." Asha leaned close. "But I am the child of King Balon's body, so I come before you both. Hear me, nuncle . . ."

But then a sudden silence fell. The singing died, Little Lenwood Tawney lowered his fiddle, men turned their heads. Even the clatter of plates and knives was hushed.

A dozen newcomers had entered the feast tent. Victarion saw Pinchface Jon Myre, Torwold Browntooth, Left-Hand Lucas Codd. Germund Botley crossed his arms against the gilded breastplate he had taken off a Lannister captain during Balon's first rebellion. Orkwood of Orkmont stood beside him. Behind them were Stonehand, Quellon Humble, and the Red Oarsman with his fiery hair in braids. Ralf the Shepherd too, and Ralf of Lordsport, and Qarl the Thrall.

And the Crow's Eye, Euron Greyjoy.

He looks unchanged, Victarion thought. *He looks the same as he did the day he laughed at me and left.* Euron was the most comely of Lord Quellon's sons, and three years of exile had not changed that. His hair was still black as a midnight sea, with never a whitecap to be seen, and his face was still smooth and pale beneath his neat dark beard. A black leather patch covered Euron's left eye, but his right was blue as a summer sky.

His smiling eye, thought Victarion. "Crow's Eye," he said.

"*King* Crow's Eye, brother." Euron smiled. His lips looked very dark in the lamplight, bruised and blue.

"We shall have no king but from the kingsmoot." The Damphair stood. "No godless man—"

"—may sit the Seastone Chair, aye." Euron glanced about the tent. "As it happens I have oft sat upon the Seastone Chair of late. It raises no objections." His smiling eye was glittering. "Who knows more of gods than I? Horse gods and fire gods, gods made of gold with gemstone eyes, gods carved of cedar wood, gods chiseled into mountains, gods of empty air . . . I know them all. I have seen their peoples garland them with flowers, and shed the blood of goats and bulls and children in their names. And I have heard the prayers, in half a hundred tongues. Cure my withered leg, make the maiden love me, grant me a healthy son. Save me, succor me, make me wealthy . . . *protect* me! Protect me from mine enemies, protect me from the darkness, protect me from the crabs inside my belly, from the horselords, from the slavers, from the sellswords at my door. Protect me from the *Silence*." He laughed. "*Godless?* Why, Aeron, I am the godliest man ever to raise sail! You serve one god, Damphair, but I have served ten thousand. From Ib to Asshai, when men see *my* sails, they pray."

The priest raised a bony finger. "They pray to trees and golden idols and goat-headed abominations. False gods . . ."

"Just so," said Euron, "and for that sin I kill them all. I spill their blood upon the sea and sow their screaming women with my seed. Their little gods cannot stop me, so plainly they are false gods. I am more devout than even you, Aeron. Perhaps it should be you who kneels to me for blessing."

The Red Oarsman laughed loudly at that, and the others took their lead from him.

"*Fools,*" said the priest, "fools and thralls and blind men, that is what you are. Do you not see what stands before you?"

"A king," said Quellon Humble.

The Damphair spat, and strode out into the night.

When he was gone, the Crow's Eye turned his smiling eye upon Victarion. "Lord Captain, have you no greeting for a brother long away? Nor you, Asha? How fares your lady mother?"

"Poorly," Asha said. "Some man made her a widow."

Euron shrugged. "I had heard the Storm God swept Balon to his death. Who is this man who slew him? Tell me his name, niece, so I might revenge myself on him."

Asha got to her feet. "You know his name as well as I. Three years you were gone from us, and yet *Silence* returns within a day of my lord father's death."

"Do you accuse me?" Euron asked mildly.

"Should I?" The sharpness in Asha's voice made Victarion frown. It was dangerous to speak so to the Crow's Eye, even when his smiling eye was shining with amusement.

"Do I command the winds?" the Crow's Eye asked his pets.

"No, Your Grace," said Orkwood of Orkmont.

"No man commands the winds," said Germund Botley.

"Would that you did," the Red Oarsman said. "You would sail wherever you liked and never be becalmed."

"There you have it, from the mouths of three brave men," Euron said. "The *Silence* was at sea when Balon died. If you doubt an uncle's word, I give you leave to ask my crew."

"A crew of mutes? Aye, that would serve me well."

"A husband would serve you well." Euron turned to his followers again. "Torwold, I misremember, do you have a wife?"

"Only the one." Torwold Browntooth grinned, and showed how he had won his name.

"I am unwed," announced Left-Hand Lucas Codd.

"And for good reason," Asha said. "All *women* do despise the Codds as well. Don't look at me so mournful, Lucas. You still have your famous hand." She made a pumping motion with her fist.

Codd cursed, till the Crow's Eye put a hand upon his

chest. "Was that courteous, Asha? You have wounded Lucas to the quick."

"Easier than wounding him in the prick. I throw an axe as well as any man, but when the target is so small . . ."

"This girl forgets herself," snarled Pinchface Jon Myre. "Balon let her believe she was a man."

"Your father made the same mistake with you," said Asha.

"Give her to me, Euron," suggested the Red Oarsman. "I'll spank her till her arse is as red as my hair."

"Come try," said Asha, "and hereafter we can call you the Red Eunuch." A throwing axe was in her hand. She tossed it in the air and caught it deftly. "Here is my husband, Nuncle. Any man who wants me should take it up with him."

Victarion slammed his fist upon the table. "I'll have no blood shed here. Euron, take your . . . pets . . . and go."

"I had looked for a warmer welcome from you, brother. I *am* your elder . . . and soon, your rightful king."

Victarion's face darkened. "When the kingsmoot speaks, we shall see who wears the driftwood crown."

"On that we can agree." Euron lifted two fingers to the patch that covered his left eye, and took his leave. The others followed at his heels like mongrel dogs. Silence lingered behind them, till Little Lenwood Tawney took up his fiddle. The wine and ale began to flow again, but several guests had lost their thirst. Eldred Codd slipped out, cradling his bloody hand. Then Will Humble, Hotho Harlaw, a goodly lot of Goodbrothers.

"Nuncle." Asha put a hand upon his shoulder. "Walk with me, if you would."

Outside the tent the wind was rising. Clouds raced across the moon's pale face. They looked a bit like galleys, stroking hard to ram. The stars were few and faint. All along the strand the longships rested, tall masts rising like a forest from the surf. Victarion could hear their hulls creaking as they settled on the sand. He heard the keening of their lines, the sound of banners flapping. Beyond, in the deeper waters of the bay, larger ships bobbed at anchor, grim shadows wreathed in mist.

They walked along the strand together just above the surf, far from the camps and the cookfires. "Tell me true, nuncle," Asha said, "why did Euron go away so suddenly?"

"The Crow's Eye oft went reaving."

"Never for so long."

"He took the *Silence* east. A lengthy voyage."

"I asked *why* he went, not where." When he did not answer, Asha said, "I was away when *Silence* sailed. I had taken *Black Wind* around the Arbor to the Stepstones, to steal a few trinkets from the Lyseni pirates. When I came home, Euron was gone and your new wife was dead."

"She was only a salt wife." He had not touched another woman since he gave her to the crabs. *I will need to take a wife when I am king. A true wife, to be my queen and bear me sons. A king must have an heir.*

"My father refused to speak of her," said Asha.

"It does no good to speak of things no man can change." He was weary of the subject. "I saw the Reader's longship."

"It took all my charm to winkle him out of his Book Tower."

She has the Harlaws, then. Victarion's frown grew deeper. "You cannot hope to rule. You are a woman."

"Is that why I always lose the pissing contests?" Asha laughed. "Nuncle, it grieves me to say so, but you may be right. For four days and four nights, I have been drinking with the captains and the kings, listening to what they say . . . and what they will not say. Mine own are with me, and many Harlaws. I have Tris Botley too, and some few others. Not enough." She kicked a rock, and sent it splashing into the water between two longships. "I am of a mind to shout my nuncle's name."

"Which uncle?" he demanded. "You have three."

"Four. Nuncle, hear me. I will place the driftwood crown upon your brow myself . . . if you will agree to share the rule."

"*Share* the rule? How could that be?" The woman was not making sense. *Does she want to be my queen?* Victarion found himself looking at Asha in a way he had never looked at her before. He could feel his manhood beginning to stiffen. *She is Balon's daughter,* he reminded himself. He remembered her as a little girl, throwing axes at a door. He crossed his arms against his chest. "The Seastone Chair seats but one."

"Then let my nuncle sit," Asha said. "I will stand behind you, to guard your back and whisper in your ear. No king can rule alone. Even when the dragons sat the Iron Throne, they had men to help them. The King's Hands. Let me be your Hand, Nuncle."

No King of the Isles had ever needed a Hand, much less one who was a woman. *The captains and the kings would mock me in their cups.* "Why would you wish to be my Hand?"

"To end this war before this war ends us. We have won all that we are like to win . . . and stand to lose all just as quick, unless we make a peace. I have shown Lady Glover every courtesy, and she swears her lord will treat with me. If we hand back Deepwood Motte, Torrhen's Square, and Moat Cailin, she says, the northmen will cede us Sea Dragon Point and all the Stony Shore. Those lands are thinly peopled, yet ten times larger than all the isles put together. An exchange of hostages will seal the pact, and each side will agree to make common cause with the other should the Iron Throne—"

Victarion chuckled. "This Lady Glover plays you for a fool, niece. Sea Dragon Point and the Stony Shore are ours. Why hand back anything? Winterfell is burnt and broken, and the Young Wolf rots headless in the earth. We will have *all* the north, as your lord father dreamed."

"When longships learn to row through trees, perhaps. A fisherman may hook a grey leviathan, but it will drag him down to death unless he cuts it loose. The north is too large for us to hold, and too full of northmen."

"Go back to your dolls, niece. Leave the winning of wars to warriors." Victarion showed her his fists. "I have two hands. No man needs three."

"I know a man who needs House Harlaw, though."

"Hotho Humpback has offered me his daughter for my queen. If I take her, I will have the Harlaws."

That took the girl aback. "Lord Rodrik rules House Harlaw."

"Rodrik has no daughters, only books. Hotho will be his heir, and I will be the king." Once he had said the words aloud, they sounded true. "The Crow's Eye has been too long away."

"Some men look larger at a distance," Asha warned. "Walk amongst the cookfires if you dare, and listen. They are not telling tales of your strength, nor of my famous beauty. They talk only of the Crow's Eye; the far places he has seen, the women he has raped and the men he's killed, the cities he has sacked, the way he burnt Lord Tywin's fleet at Lannisport . . ."

"*I* burnt the lion's fleet," Victarion insisted. "With mine own hands I flung the first torch onto his flagship."

"The Crow's Eye hatched the scheme." Asha put her

hand upon his arm. "And killed your wife as well . . . did he not?"

Balon had commanded them not to speak of it, but Balon was dead. "He put a baby in her belly and made me do the killing. I would have killed him too, but Balon would have no kinslaying in his hall. He sent Euron into exile, never to return . . ."

". . . so long as Balon lived?"

Victarion looked at his fists. "She gave me horns. I had no choice." *Had it been known, men would have laughed at me, as the Crow's Eye laughed when I confronted him. "She came to me wet and willing," he had boasted. "It seems Victarion is big everywhere but where it matters."* But he could not tell her that.

"I am sorry for you," said Asha, "and sorrier for her . . . but you leave me small choice but to claim the Seastone Chair myself."

You cannot. "Your breath is yours to waste, woman."

"It is," she said, and left him.

THE DROWNED MAN

Only when his arms and legs were numb from the cold did Aeron Greyjoy struggle back to shore and don his robes again.

He had run before the Crow's Eye as if he were still the weak thing he had been, but when the waves broke over his head they reminded once more that that man was dead. *I was reborn from the sea, a harder man and stronger.* No mortal man could frighten him, no more than the darkness could, nor the bones of his soul, the grey and grisly bones of his soul. *The sound of a door opening, the scream of a rusted iron hinge.*

The priest's robes crackled as he pulled them down, still stiff with salt from their last washing a fortnight past. The wool clung to his wet chest, drinking the brine that ran down from his hair. He filled his waterskin and slung it over his shoulder.

As he strode across the strand, a drowned man returning from a call of nature stumbled into him in the darkness. "Damphair," he murmured. Aeron laid a hand upon his head, blessed him, and moved on. The ground rose beneath his feet, gently at first, then more steeply. When he felt scrub grass between his toes, he knew that he had left the strand behind. Slowly he climbed, listening to the waves. *The sea is never weary. I must be as tireless.*

On the crown of the hill four-and-forty monstrous stone ribs rose from the earth like the trunks of great pale trees. The sight made Aeron's heart beat faster. Nagga had been the first sea dragon, the mightiest ever to rise from the waves. She fed on krakens and leviathans and drowned whole islands in her wrath, yet the Grey King had slain her and the Drowned God had changed her bones to stone so that men might never cease to wonder at the courage of the first of kings. Nagga's ribs became the beams and pillars of his longhall, just as her jaws became his throne. *For a thousand years and seven he reigned here,* Aeron recalled. *Here he took his mermaid wife and planned his wars against the Storm God. From here he ruled both stone and salt, wearing robes of woven seaweed and a tall pale crown made from Nagga's teeth.*

But that was in the dawn of days, when mighty men still dwelt on earth and sea. The hall had been warmed by Nagga's living fire, which the Grey King had made his thrall. On its walls hung tapestries woven from silver seaweed most pleasing to the eyes. The Grey King's warriors had feasted on the bounty of the sea at a table in the shape of a great starfish, whilst seated upon thrones carved from mother-of-pearl. *Gone, all the glory gone.* Men were smaller now. Their lives had grown short. The Storm God drowned Nagga's fire after the Grey King's death, the chairs and tapestries had been stolen, the roof and walls had rotted away. Even the Grey King's great throne of fangs had been swallowed by the sea. Only Nagga's bones endured to remind the ironborn of all the wonder that had been.

It is enough, thought Aeron Greyjoy.

Nine wide steps had been hewn from the stony hilltop. Behind rose the howling hills of Old Wyk, with mountains in the distance black and cruel. Aeron paused where the doors once stood, pulled the cork from his waterskin, took a swallow of salt water, and turned to face the sea. *We were born from the sea, and to the sea we must return.* Even here he could hear the ceaseless rumble of the waves and feel the power of the god who lurked below the waters. Aeron went to his knees. *You have sent your people to me,* he prayed. *They have left their halls and hovels, their castles and their keeps, and come here to Nagga's bones, from every fishing village and every hidden vale. Now grant to them the wisdom to know the true king when he stands before them, and the strength to shun the false.* All night he prayed, for when the god was in him Aeron Greyjoy had no need of sleep, no more than the waves did, nor the fishes of the sea.

Dark clouds ran before the wind as the first light stole into the world. The black sky went grey as slate; the black sea turned grey-green; the black mountains of Great Wyk across the bay put on the blue-green hues of soldier pines. As color stole back into the world, a hundred banners lifted and began to flap. Aeron beheld the silver fish of Botley, the bloody moon of Wynch, the dark green trees of Orkwood. He saw warhorns and leviathans and scythes, and everywhere the krakens great and golden. Beneath them, thralls and salt wives began to move about, stirring coals into new life and gutting fish for the captains and the kings to break their fasts. The dawnlight touched the stony strand, and he watched men wake from sleep, throwing aside their sealskin blankets as they called for their first horn of ale. *Drink deep,* he thought, *for we have god's work to do today.*

The sea was stirring too. The waves grew larger as the wind rose, sending plumes of spray to crash against the longships. *The Drowned God wakes,* thought Aeron. He could hear his voice welling from the depths of the sea. *I shall be with you here this day, my strong and faithful servant,* the voice said. *No godless man will sit my Seastone Chair.*

It was there beneath the arch of Nagga's ribs that his drowned men found him, standing tall and stern with his long black hair blowing in the wind. "Is it time?" Rus asked. Aeron gave a nod, and said, "It is. Go forth and sound the summons."

The drowned men took up their driftwood cudgels and began to beat them one against the other as they walked back down the hill. Others joined them, and the clangor spread along the strand. Such a fearful clacking and a clattering it made, as if a hundred trees were pummeling one another with their limbs. Kettledrums began to beat as well, *boom-boom-boom-boom-boom, boom-boom-boom-boom-boom.* A warhorn bellowed, then another. *AAAAAAooooooooooooooooooooooooooo.*

Men left their fires to make their way toward the bones of the Grey King's Hall; oarsmen, steersmen, sailmakers, shipwrights, the warriors with their axes and the fishermen with their nets. Some had thralls to serve them; some had salt wives. Others, who had sailed too often to the green lands, were attended by maesters and singers and knights. The common men crowded together in a crescent around the base of the knoll, with the thralls, children, and women toward the rear. The captains and the kings made their way up the slopes. Aeron Damphair saw cheerful Sigfry Stonetree, Andrik the Unsmiling, the knight Ser Harras Harlaw. Lord Baelor Blacktyde in his sable cloak stood beside The Stonehouse in ragged sealskin. Victarion loomed above all of them save Andrik. His brother wore no helm, but elsewise he was all in armor, his kraken cloak hanging golden from his shoulders. *He shall be our king. What man could look on him and doubt it?*

When the Damphair raised his bony hands the kettle-drums and the warhorns fell silent, the drowned men lowered their cudgels, and all the voices stilled. Only the sound of the waves pounding remained, a roar no man could still. "We were born from the sea, and to the sea we all return," Aeron began, softly at first, so men would strain to hear. "The Storm God in his wrath plucked Balon from his castle and cast him down, yet now he feasts beneath the waves in the Drowned God's watery halls." He lifted his eyes to the sky. *"Balon is dead! The iron king is dead!"*

"The king is dead!" his drowned men shouted.

"Yet what is dead may never die, but rises again, harder and stronger!" he reminded them. "Balon has fallen, Balon my brother, who honored the Old Way and paid the iron price. Balon the Brave, Balon the Blessed, Balon Twice-Crowned, who won us back our freedoms and our god. Balon is dead . . . but an iron king shall rise again, to sit upon the Seastone Chair and rule the isles."

"A king shall rise!" they answered. *"He shall rise!"*

"He shall. He must." Aeron's voice thundered like the waves. "But who? Who shall sit in Balon's place? Who shall rule these holy isles? Is he here among us now?" The priest spread his hands wide. *"Who shall be king over us?"*

A seagull screamed back at him. The crowd began to stir, like men waking from a dream. Each man looked at his neighbors, to see which of them might presume to claim a crown. *The Crow's Eye was never patient,* Aeron Damphair told himself. *Mayhaps he will speak first.* If so, it would be his undoing. The captains and the kings had come a long way to this feast and would not choose the first dish set before them. *They will want to taste and sample, a bite of him, a nibble of the other, until they find the one that suits them best.*

Euron must have known that as well. He stood with his arms crossed amongst his mutes and monsters. Only the wind and the waves answered Aeron's call.

"The ironborn must have a king," the priest insisted, after a long silence. "I ask again. *Who shall be king over us?*"

"I will," came the answer from below.

At once a ragged cry of "Gylbert! Gylbert King!" went up. The captains gave way to let the claimant and his champions ascend the hill to stand at Aeron's side beneath the ribs of Nagga.

This would-be king was a tall spare lord with a melancholy visage, his lantern jaw shaved clean. His three champions took up their position two steps below him, bearing his sword and shield and banner. They shared a certain look with the tall lord, and Aeron took them for his sons. One unfurled his banner, a great black longship against a setting sun. "I am Gylbert Farwynd, Lord of the Lonely Light," the lord told the kingsmoot.

Aeron knew some Farwynds, a queer folk who held lands on the westernmost shores of Great Wyk and the scattered isles beyond, rocks so small that most could support but a single household. Of those, the Lonely Light was the most distant, eight days' sail to the northwest amongst rookeries of seals and sea lions and the boundless grey oceans. The Farwynds there were even queerer than the rest. Some said they were skinchangers, unholy creatures who could take on the forms of sea lions, walruses, even spotted whales, the wolves of the wild sea.

Lord Gylbert began to speak. He told of a wondrous land beyond the Sunset Sea, a land without winter or want, where death had no dominion. "Make me your king, and I shall lead you there," he cried. "We will build ten thousand ships as Nymeria once did and take sail with all our people to the land beyond the sunset. There every man shall be a king and every wife a queen."

His eyes, Aeron saw, were now grey, now blue, as changeable as the seas. *Mad eyes,* he thought, *fool's eyes.* The vision he spoke of was doubtless a snare set by the Storm God to lure the ironborn to destruction. The offerings that his men spilled out before the kingsmoot included sealskins and walrus tusks, arm rings made of whalebone, warhorns banded in bronze. The captains looked and turned away, leaving lesser men to help themselves to the gifts. When the fool was done talking and his champions began to shout his name, only the Farwynds took up the cry, and not even all of them. Soon enough the cries of "Gylbert! Gylbert King!" faded away to silence. The gull screamed loudly above them, and landed atop one of Nagga's ribs as the Lord of the Lonely Light made his way back down the hill.

Aeron Damphair stepped forward once more. "I ask again. *Who shall be king over us?*"

"Me!" a deep voice boomed, and once more the crowd parted.

The speaker was borne up the hill in a carved driftwood chair carried on the shoulders of his grandsons. A great ruin of a man, twenty stones heavy and ninety years old, he was cloaked in a white bearskin. His own hair was snow white as well, and his huge beard covered him like a blanket from cheeks to thighs, so it was hard to tell where the beard ended and the pelt began. Though his grandsons were great strapping men, they struggled with his weight on the steep stone steps. Before the Grey King's Hall they set him down, and three remained below him as his champions.

Sixty years ago, this one might well have won the favor of the moot, Aeron thought, *but his hour is long past.*

"Aye, me!" the man roared from where he sat, in a voice as huge as he was. "Why not? Who better? I am Erik Ironmaker, for them who's blind. Erik the Just. Erik Anvil-Breaker. Show them my hammer, Thormor." One of his champions lifted it up for all to see; a monstrous thing it was, its haft wrapped in old leather, its head a brick of steel as large as a loaf of bread. "I can't count how many hands I've smashed to pulp with that hammer," Erik said, "but might be some thief could tell you. I can't say how many heads I've crushed against my anvil neither, but there's some widows could. I could tell you all the deeds I've done in battle, but I'm eight-and-eighty and won't live long enough to finish. If old is wise, no one is wiser than me. If big is strong, no one's stronger. You want a king with heirs? I've more'n I can count. King Erik, aye, I like the sound o' that. Come, say it with me. *ERIK! ERIK ANVIL-BREAKER! ERIK KING!*"

As his grandsons took up the cry, their own sons came forward with chests upon their shoulders. When they up-ended them at the base of the stone steps, a torrent of silver, bronze, and steel spilled forth; arm rings, collars, daggers, dirks, and throwing axes. A few captains snatched up the choicest items and added their voices to the swelling chant. But no sooner had the cry begun to build than a woman's voice cut through it. *"Erik!"* Men moved aside to let her through. With one foot on the lowest step, she said, "Erik, stand up."

A hush fell. The wind blew, waves broke against the shore, men murmured in each other's ears. Erik Ironmaker stared down at Asha Greyjoy. "Girl. Thrice-damned girl. What did you say?"

"Stand up, Erik," she called. "Stand up and I'll shout your name with all the rest. Stand up and I'll be the first to follow you. You want a crown, aye. Stand up and take it."

Elsewhere in the press, the Crow's Eye laughed. Erik glared at him. The big man's hands closed tight around the arms of his driftwood throne. His face went red, then purple. His arms trembled with effort. Aeron could see a thick blue vein pulsing in his neck as he struggled to rise. For a moment it seemed as though he might do it, but the breath went out of him all at once, and he groaned and sank back onto his cushion. Euron laughed all the louder. The big man hung his head and grew old, all in the blink of an eye. His grandsons carried him back down the hill.

"Who shall rule the ironborn?" Aeron Damphair called again. "Who shall be king over us?"

Men looked at one another. Some looked at Euron, some at Victarion, a few at Asha. Waves broke green and white against the longships. The gull cried once more, a raucous scream, forlorn. "Make your claim, Victarion," the Merlyn called. "Let us have done with this mummer's farce."

"When I am ready," Victarion shouted back.

Aeron was pleased. *It is better if he waits.*

The Drumm came next, another old man, though not so old as Erik. He climbed the hill on his own two legs, and on his hip rode Red Rain, his famous sword, forged of Valyrian steel in the days before the Doom. His champions were men of note: his sons Denys and Donnel, both stout fighters, and between them Andrik the Unsmiling, a giant of a man with arms as thick as trees. It spoke well of the Drumm that such a man would stand for him.

"Where is it written that our king must be a kraken?" Drumm began. "What right has Pyke to rule us? Great Wyk is the largest isle, Harlaw the richest, Old Wyk the most holy. When the black line was consumed by dragonfire, the ironborn gave the primacy to Vickon Greyjoy, aye . . . but as *lord,* not king."

It was a good beginning. Aeron heard shouts of approval, but they dwindled as the old man began to tell of the glory of the Drumms. He spoke of Dale the Dread, Roryn the Reaver, the hundred sons of Gormond Drumm the Oldfather. He drew Red Rain and told them how Hilmar Drumm the Cunning had taken the blade from an armored knight with wits and a wooden cudgel. He spoke of ships long lost and battles eight hundred years forgotten, and the crowd grew restive. He spoke and spoke, and then he spoke still more.

And when Drumm's chests were thrown open, the captains saw the niggard's gifts he'd brought them. *No throne was ever bought with bronze,* the Damphair thought. The truth of that was plain to hear, as the cries of *"Drumm! Drumm! Dunstan King!"* died away.

Aeron could feel a tightness in his belly, and it seemed to him that the waves were pounding louder than before. *It is time,* he thought. *It is time for Victarion to make his claim.* "Who shall be king over us?" the priest cried once more, but this time his fierce black eyes found his brother in the crowd. "Nine sons were born from the loins of Quellon Greyjoy. One was mightier than all the rest, and knew no fear."

Victarion met his eyes, and nodded. The captains parted before him as he climbed the steps. "Brother, give me blessing," he said when he reached the top. He knelt and bowed his head. Aeron uncorked his waterskin and poured a stream of seawater down upon his brow. *"What is dead can never die,"* the priest said, and Victarion replied, *"but rises again, harder and stronger."*

When Victarion rose, his champions arrayed themselves beneath him; Ralf the Limper, Red Ralf Stonehouse, and Nute the Barber, noted warriors all. Stonehouse bore the Greyjoy banner; the golden kraken on a field as black as the midnight sea. As soon as it unfurled, the captains and the kings began to shout out the Lord Captain's name. Victarion waited till they quieted, then said, "You all know me. If you want sweet words, look elsewhere. I have no singer's tongue. I have an axe, and I have these." He raised his huge mailed hands up to show them, and Nute the Barber displayed his axe, a fearsome piece of steel. "I was a loyal brother," Victarion went on. "When Balon was wed, it was me he sent to Harlaw to bring him back his bride. I led his longships into many a battle, and never lost but one. The first time Balon took a crown, it was me sailed into Lannisport to singe the lion's tail. The second time, it was me he sent to skin the Young Wolf should he come howling home. All you'll get from me is more of what you got from Balon. That's all I have to say."

With that his champions began to chant: *"VICTARION! VICTARION! VICTARION KING!"* Below, his men were spilling out his chests, a cascade of silver, gold, and gems, a wealth of plunder. Captains scrambled to seize the richest pieces, shouting as they did so. *"VICTARION! VICTAR-ION! VICTARION KING!"* Aeron watched the Crow's Eye. *Will he speak now, or let the kingsmoot run its course?* Orkwood of Orkmont was whispering in Euron's ear.

But it was not Euron who put an end to the shouting, it was the *woman.* She put two fingers in her mouth and *whistled,* a sharp shrill sound that cut through the tumult like a knife through curds. "Nuncle! *Nuncle!*" Bending, she snatched up a twisted golden collar and bounded up the steps. Nute seized her by the arm, and for half a heart-beat Aeron was hopeful that his brother's champions would keep her silent, but Asha wrenched free of the Barber's hand and said something to Red Ralf that made him step aside. As she pushed past, the cheering died away. She was Balon Greyjoy's daughter, and the crowd was curious to hear her speak.

"It was good of you to bring such gifts to my queensmoot, Nuncle," she told Victarion, "but you need not have worn so much armor. I promise not to hurt you." Asha turned to face the captains. "There's no one braver than my nuncle, no one stronger, no one fiercer in a fight. And he counts to ten as quick as any man, I have seen him do it . . . though when he needs to go to twenty he does take off his boots." That made them laugh. "He has no sons, though. His wives keep dying. The Crow's Eye is his elder and has a better claim . . ."

"He does!" the Red Oarsman shouted from below.

"Ah, but my claim is better still." Asha set the collar on her head at a jaunty angle, so the gold gleamed against her dark hair. "Balon's brother cannot come before Balon's son!"

"Balon's sons are dead," cried Ralf the Limper. "All I see is Balon's little daughter!"

"Daughter?" Asha slipped a hand beneath her jerkin. "Oho! What's this? Shall I show you? Some of you have not seen one since they weaned you." They laughed again. "Teats on a king are a terrible thing, is that the song? Ralf, you have me, I *am* a woman . . . though not an *old* woman like you. Ralf the Limper . . . shouldn't that be Ralf the Limp?" Asha drew a dirk from between her breasts. "I'm a mother too, and here's my suckling babe!" She held it up. "And here, my champions." They pushed past Victarion's three to stand below her: Qarl the Maid, Tristifer Botley, and the knight Ser Harras Harlaw, whose sword Nightfall was as storied as Dunstan Drumm's Red Rain. "My nuncle said you know him. You know me too—"

"I want to know you better!" someone shouted.

"Go home and know your wife," Asha shot back. "Nuncle says he'll give you more of what my father gave you. Well, what was that? Gold and glory, some will say. *Freedom,* ever sweet. Aye, it's so, he gave us that . . . and widows too, as Lord Blacktyde will tell you. How many of you had your homes put to the torch when Robert came? How many had daughters raped and despoiled? Burnt towns and broken castles, my father gave you that. *Defeat* was what he gave you. Nuncle here will give you more. Not me."

"What will you give us?" asked Lucas Codd. "Knitting?"

"Aye, Lucas. I'll knit us all a kingdom." She tossed her dirk from hand to hand. "We need to take a lesson from the Young Wolf, who won every battle . . . and lost all."

"A wolf is not a kraken," Victarion objected. "What the kraken grasps it does not lose, be it longship or leviathan."

"And what *have* we grasped, Nuncle? The north? What is that, but leagues and leagues of leagues and leagues, far from the sound of the sea? We have taken Moat Cailin, Deepwood Motte, Torrhen's Square, even *Winterfell.* What do we have to show for it?" She beckoned, and her *Black Wind* men pushed forward, chests of oak and iron on their shoulders. "I give you the wealth of the Stony Shore," Asha said as the first was upended. An avalanche of pebbles clattered forth, cascading down the steps; pebbles grey and black and white, worn smooth by the sea. "I give you the riches of Deepwood," she said, as the second chest was opened. Pinecones came pouring out, to roll and bounce down into the crowd. "And last, the gold of Winterfell." From the third chest came yellow turnips, round and hard and big as a man's head. They landed amidst the pebbles and the pinecones. Asha stabbed one with her dirk. "Harmund Sharp," she shouted, "your son Harrag died at Winterfell, for this." She pulled the turnip off her blade and tossed it to him. "You have other sons, I think. If you'd trade their lives for turnips, shout my nuncle's name!"

"And if I shout *your* name?" Harmund demanded. "What then?"

"Peace," said Asha. "Land. Victory. I'll give you Sea Dragon Point and the Stony Shore, black earth and tall trees and stones enough for every younger son to build a hall. We'll have the northmen too . . . as friends, to stand with us against the Iron Throne. Your choice is simple. Crown me, for peace and victory. Or crown my nuncle, for more war and more defeat." She sheathed her dirk again. "What will you have, ironmen?"

"VICTORY!" shouted Rodrik the Reader, his hands cupped about his mouth. *"Victory, and Asha!"*

"ASHA!" Lord Baelor Blacktyde echoed. *"ASHA QUEEN!"*

Asha's own crew took up the cry. *"ASHA! ASHA! ASHA QUEEN!"* They stamped their feet and shook their fists and yelled, as the Damphair listened in disbelief. *She would leave her father's work undone!* Yet Tristifer Botley was shouting for her, with many Harlaws, some Goodbrothers, red-faced Lord Merlyn, more men than the priest would ever have believed . . . for a *woman!*

But others were holding their tongues, or muttering asides to their neighbors. *"No craven's peace!"* Ralf the Limper roared. Red Ralf Stonehouse swirled the Greyjoy banner and bellowed, *"Victarion! VICTARION! VICTARION!"* Men began to shove at one another. Someone flung a pinecone at Asha's head. When she ducked, her makeshift crown fell off. For a moment it seemed to the priest as if he stood atop a giant anthill, with a thousand ants in a boil at his feet. Shouts of *"Asha!"* and *"Victarion!"* surged back and forth, and it seemed as though some savage storm was about to engulf them all. *The Storm God is amongst us,* the priest thought, *sowing fury and discord.*

Sharp as a swordthrust, the sound of a horn split the air.

Bright and baneful was its voice, a shivering hot scream that made a man's bones seem to *thrum* within him. The cry lingered in the damp sea air: *aaaaRREEEE eeeeeeeeeeeeeeeeeeeeeeee.*

All eyes turned toward the sound. It was one of Euron's mongrels winding the call, a monstrous man with a shaved head. Rings of gold and jade and jet glistened on his arms, and on his broad chest was tattooed some bird of prey, talons dripping blood.

aaaaRRREEEEeeeeeeeeeeeeeeeeeeeeeeeeeeee.

The horn he blew was shiny black and twisted, and taller than a man as he held it with both hands. It was bound about with bands of red gold and dark steel, incised with ancient Valyrian glyphs that seemed to glow redly as the sound swelled.

aaaaaaaRRREEEEEEEEEEEEEeeeeeeeeeeeeeeeeeeeeee eeeeeeeeeee.

It was a terrible sound, a wail of pain and fury that seemed to burn the ears. Aeron Damphair covered his, and prayed for the Drowned God to raise a mighty wave and smash the horn to silence, yet still the shriek went on and on. *It is the horn of hell,* he wanted to scream, though no man would have heard him. The cheeks of the tattooed man were so puffed out they looked about to burst, and the muscles in his chest twitched in a way that it made it seem as if the bird were about to rip free of his flesh and take wing. And now the glyphs were burning brightly, every line and letter shimmering with white fire. On and on and on the sound went, echoing amongst the howling hills behind them and across the waters of Nagga's Cradle to ring against the mountains of Great Wyk, on and on and on until it filled the whole wet world.

And when it seemed the sound would never end, it did.

The hornblower's breath failed at last. He staggered and almost fell. The priest saw Orkwood of Orkmont catch him by one arm to hold him up, whilst Left-Hand Lucas Codd took the twisted black horn from his hands. A thin wisp of smoke was rising from the horn, and the priest saw blood and blisters upon the lips of the man who'd sounded it. The bird on his chest was bleeding too.

Euron Greyjoy climbed the hill slowly, with every eye upon him. Above the gull screamed and screamed again. *No godless man may sit the Seastone Chair,* Aeron thought, but he knew that he must let his brother speak. His lips moved silently in prayer.

Asha's champions stepped aside, and Victarion's as well. The priest took a step backward and put one hand upon the cold rough stone of Nagga's ribs. The Crow's Eye stopped atop the steps, at the doors of the Grey King's Hall, and turned his smiling eye upon the captains and the kings, but Aeron could feel his other eye as well, the one that he kept hidden.

"IRONMEN," said Euron Greyjoy, "you have heard my horn. Now hear my words. I am Balon's brother, Quellon's eldest living son. Lord Vickon's blood is in my veins, and the blood of the Old Kraken. Yet I have sailed farther than any of them. Only one living kraken has never known defeat. Only one has never bent his knee. Only one has sailed

to Asshai by the Shadow, and seen wonders and terrors beyond imagining . . ."

"If you liked the Shadow so well, go back there," called out pink-cheeked Qarl the Maid, one of Asha's champions.

The Crow's Eye ignored him. "My little brother would finish Balon's war, and claim the north. My sweet niece would give us peace and pinecones." His blue lips twisted in a smile. "Asha prefers victory to defeat. Victarion wants a kingdom, not a few scant yards of earth. From me, you shall have both.

"Crow's Eye, you call me. Well, who has a keener eye than the crow? After every battle the crows come in their hundreds and their thousands to feast upon the fallen. A crow can espy death from afar. And I say that all of Westeros is dying. Those who follow me will feast until the end of their days.

"We are the ironborn, and once we were conquerors. Our writ ran everywhere the sound of the waves was heard. My brother would have you be content with the cold and dismal north, my niece with even less . . . but I shall give you Lannisport. Highgarden. The Arbor. Oldtown. The riverlands and the Reach, the kingswood and the rainwood, Dorne and the marches, the Mountains of the Moon and the Vale of Arryn, Tarth and the Stepstones. I say we take it *all*! I say, we take *Westeros*." He glanced at the priest. "All for the greater glory of our Drowned God, to be sure."

For half a heartbeat even Aeron was swept away by the boldness of his words. The priest had dreamed the same dream, when first he'd seen the red comet in the sky. *We shall sweep over the green lands with fire and sword, root out the seven gods of the septons and the white trees of the northmen . . .*

"Crow's Eye," Asha called, "did you leave your wits at

Asshai? If we cannot hold the north—and we cannot—how can we win the whole of the Seven Kingdoms?"

"Why, it has been done before. Did Balon teach his girl so little of the ways of war? Victarion, our brother's daughter has never heard of Aegon the Conqueror, it would seem."

"Aegon?" Victarion crossed his arms against his armored chest. "What has the Conqueror to do with us?"

"I know as much of war as you do, Crow's Eye," Asha said. "Aegon Targaryen conquered Westeros with *dragons.*"

"And so shall we," Euron Greyjoy promised. "That horn you heard I found amongst the smoking ruins that were Valyria, where no man has dared to walk but me. You heard its call, and felt its power. It is a dragon horn, bound with bands of red gold and Valyrian steel graven with enchantments. The dragonlords of old sounded such horns, before the Doom devoured them. With this horn, ironmen, I can bind *dragons* to my will."

Asha laughed aloud. "A horn to bind goats to your will would be of more use, Crow's Eye. There are no more dragons."

"Again, girl, you are wrong. There are three, and I know where to find them. Surely that is worth a driftwood crown."

"EURON!" shouted Left-Hand Lucas Codd.

"EURON! CROW'S EYE! EURON!" cried the Red Oarsman.

The mutes and mongrels from the *Silence* threw open Euron's chests and spilled out his gifts before the captains and the kings. Then it was Hotho Harlaw the priest heard, as he filled his hands with gold. Gorold Goodbrother shouted out as well, and Erik Anvil-Breaker. *"EURON! EURON! EURON!"* The cry swelled, became a roar. *"EURON! EURON! CROW'S EYE! EURON KING!"*

It rolled up Nagga's hill, like the Storm God rattling the clouds. *"EURON! EURON! EURON! EURON! EURON! EURON!"*

Even a priest may doubt. Even a prophet may know terror. Aeron Damphair reached within himself for his god and discovered only silence. As a thousand voices shouted out his brother's name, all he could hear was the scream of a rusted iron hinge.

BRIENNE

East of Maidenpool the hills rose wild, and the pines closed in about them like a host of silent grey-green soldiers.

Nimble Dick said the coast road was the shortest way, and the easiest, so they were seldom out of sight of the bay. The towns and villages along the shore grew smaller as they went, and less frequent. At nightfall they would seek an inn. Crabb would share the common bed with other travelers, whilst Brienne took a room for her and Podrick. "Cheaper if we all shared the same bed, m'lady," Nimble Dick would say. "You could lay your sword between us. Old Dick's a harmless fellow. Chivalrous as a knight, and honest as the day is long."

"The days are growing shorter," Brienne pointed out.

"Well, that may be. If you don't trust me in the bed, I could just curl up on the floor, m'lady."

"Not on my floor."

"A man might think you don't trust me none."

"Trust is earned. Like gold."

"As you say, m'lady," said Crabb, "but up north where the road gives out, you'll need t' trust Dick then. If I wanted t' take your gold at swordpoint, who's to stop me?"

"You don't own a sword. I do."

She shut the door between them and stood there listening until she was certain he had moved away. However nimble he might be, Dick Crabb was no Jaime Lannister, no Mad Mouse, not even a Humfrey Wagstaff. He was scrawny and ill fed, his only armor a dinted halfhelm spotted with rust. In place of a sword, he carried an old, nicked dagger. So long as she was awake, he posed no danger to her. "Podrick," she said, "there will come a time when there are no more inns to shelter us. I do not trust our guide. When we make camp, can you watch over me as I sleep?"

"Stay awake, my lady? Ser." He thought. "I have a sword. If Crabb tries to hurt you, I could kill him."

"No," she said sternly. "You are not to try and fight him. All I ask is that you watch him as I sleep, and wake me if he does anything suspicious. I wake quickly, you will find."

Crabb showed his true colors the next day, when they stopped to water the horses. Brienne had to step behind some bushes to empty her bladder. As she was squatting, she heard Podrick say, "What are you doing? You get away from there." She finished her business, hiked up her breeches, and returned to the road to find Nimble Dick wiping flour off his fingers. "You won't find any dragons in my saddlebags," she told him. "I keep my gold upon my person." Some of it was in the pouch at her belt, the rest hidden in a pair of pockets sewn inside her clothing. The fat purse inside her saddlebag was filled with coppers large and small, pennies and halfpennies, groats and stars . . . and fine white flour, to make it fatter still. She had bought the flour from the cook at the Seven Swords the morning she rode out from Duskendale.

"Dick meant no harm, m'lady." He wriggled his flour-spotted fingers to show he held no weapon. "I was only looking to see if you had these dragons what you promised me. The world's full o' liars, ready to cheat an honest man. Not that *you're* one."

Brienne hoped he was a better guide than he was a thief. "We had best be going." She mounted up again.

Dick would oft sing as they rode along together; never a whole song, only a snatch of this and a verse of that. She suspected that he meant to charm her, to put her off her guard. Sometimes he would try to get her and Podrick to sing along with him, to no avail. The boy was too shy and tongue-tied, and Brienne did not sing. *Did you sing for your father?* Lady Stark had asked her once, at Riverrun. *Did you sing for Renly?* She had not, not ever, though she had wanted . . . she had wanted . . .

When he was not singing, Nimble Dick would talk, regaling them with tales of Crackclaw Point. Every gloomy valley had its lord, he said, the lot of them united only by their mistrust of outsiders. In their veins the blood of the First Men ran dark and strong. "The Andals tried t' take Crackclaw, but we bled them in the valleys and drowned them in the bogs. Only what their sons couldn't win with swords, their pretty daughters won with kisses. They married into the houses they couldn't conquer, aye."

The Darklyn kings of Duskendale had tried to impose their rule on Crackclaw Point; the Mootons of Maidenpool had tried as well, and later the haughty Celtigars of Crab Isle. But the Crackclaws knew their bogs and forests as no outsider could, and if hard pressed would vanish into the caverns that honeycombed their hills. When not fighting would-be conquerors, they fought each other. Their blood feuds were as deep and dark as the bogs between their hills. From time to time some champion would bring peace to the Point, but it never lasted longer than his lifetime. Lord Lucifer Hardy, he was a great one, and the Brothers Brune as well. Old Crackbones even more so, but the Crabbs were the mightiest of all. Dick still refused to believe that Brienne had never heard of Ser Clarence Crabb and his exploits.

"Why would I lie?" she asked him. "Every place has its local heroes. Where I come from, the singers sing of Ser Galladon of Morne, the Perfect Knight."

"Ser Gallawho of What?" He snorted. "Never heard o' him. Why was he so bloody perfect?"

"Ser Galladon was a champion of such valor that the Maiden herself lost her heart to him. She gave him an enchanted sword as a token of her love. The Just Maid, it was called. No common sword could check her, nor any shield withstand her kiss. Ser Galladon bore the Just Maid proudly, but only thrice did he unsheathe her. He would not use the Maid against a mortal man, for she was so potent as to make any fight unfair."

Crabb thought that was hilarious. "The Perfect Knight? The Perfect Fool, he sounds like. What's the point o' having some magic sword if you don't bloody well use it?"

"Honor," she said. "The point is honor."

That only made him laugh the louder. "Ser Clarence Crabb would have wiped his hairy arse with your Perfect Knight, m'lady. If they'd ever have met, there'd be one more bloody head sitting on the shelf at the Whispers, you ask me. 'I should have used the magic sword,' it'd be saying to all the other heads. 'I should have used the bloody sword.'"

Brienne could not help but smile. "Perhaps," she allowed, "but Ser Galladon was no fool. Against a foe eight feet tall mounted on an aurochs, he might well have unsheathed the Just Maid. He used her once to slay a dragon, they say."

Nimble Dick was unimpressed. "Crackbones fought a dragon too, but he didn't need no magic sword. He just tied its neck in a knot, so every time it breathed fire it roasted its own arse."

"And what did Crackbones do when Aegon and his sisters came?" Brienne asked him.

"He was dead. M'lady must know that." Crabb gave her a sideways look. "Aegon sent his sister up to Crackclaw, that Visenya. The lords had heard o' Harren's end. Being no fools, they laid their swords at her feet. The queen took them as her own men, and said they'd owe no fealty to Maidenpool, Crab Isle, or Duskendale. Don't stop them bloody Celtigars from sending men to t' eastern shore to collect his taxes. If he sends enough, a few come back to him . . . elsewise, we bow only to our own lords, and the king. The *true* king, not Robert and his ilk." He spat. "There was Crabbs and Brunes and Boggses with Prince Rhaegar on the Trident, and in the Kingsguard too. A Hardy, a Cave, a Pyne, and *three* Crabbs, Clement and Rupert and Clarence the Short. Six foot tall, he was, but short compared to the *real* Ser Clarence. We're all good dragon men, up Crackclaw way."

The traffic continued to dwindle as they moved north and east, until finally there were no inns to be found. By then the bayside road was more weeds than ruts. That night they took shelter in a fishing village. Brienne paid the villagers a few coppers to allow them to bed down in a hay barn. She claimed the loft for Podrick and herself, and pulled the ladder up after them.

"You leave me down here alone, I could bloody well steal your horses," Crabb called up from below. "Best you get them up the ladder too, m'lady." When she ignored him, he went on to say, "It's going to rain tonight. A cold hard rain. You and Pods will sleep all snug and warm, and poor old Dick will be shivering down here by myself." He shook his head, muttering, as he made a bed on a pile of hay. "I never knew such a mistrustful maid as you."

Brienne curled up beneath her cloak, with Podrick yawning at her side. *I was not always wary,* she might have shouted down at Crabb. *When I was a little girl I believed that all men were as noble as my father.* Even the men who told her what a pretty girl she was, how tall and bright and clever, how graceful when she danced. It was Septa Roelle who had lifted the scales from her eyes. "They only say those things to win your lord father's favor," the woman had said. "You'll find truth in your looking glass, not on the tongues of men." It was a harsh lesson, one that left her weeping, but it had stood her in good stead at Harrenhal when Ser Hyle and his friends had played their game. *A maid has to be mistrustful in this world, or she will not be a maid for long,* she was thinking, as the rain began to fall.

In the mêlée at Bitterbridge she had sought out her suitors and battered them one by one, Farrow and Ambrose and Bushy, Mark Mullendore and Raymond Nayland and Will the Stork. She had ridden over Harry Sawyer and broken Robin Potter's helm, giving him a nasty scar. And when the last of them had fallen, the Mother had delivered Connington to her. This time Ser Ronnet held a sword and not a rose. Every blow she dealt him was sweeter than a kiss.

Loras Tyrell had been the last to face her wroth that day. He'd never courted her, had hardly looked at her at all, but he bore three golden roses on his shield that day, and Brienne hated roses. The sight of them had given her a furious strength. She went to sleep dreaming of the fight they'd had, and of Ser Jaime fastening a rainbow cloak about her shoulders.

It was still raining the next morning. As they broke their fast, Nimble Dick suggested that they wait for it to stop.

"When will that be? On the morrow? In a fortnight? When summer comes again? No. We have cloaks, and leagues to ride."

It rained all that day. The narrow track they followed soon turned to mud beneath them. What trees they saw were naked, and the steady rain had turned their fallen leaves into a sodden brown mat. Despite its squirrel-skin lining, Dick's cloak soaked through, and she could see him shivering. Brienne felt a moment's pity for the man. *He has not eaten well, that's plain.* She wondered if there truly was a smugglers' cove, or a ruined castle called the Whispers. Hungry men do desperate things. This all might be some ploy to cozen her. Suspicion soured her stomach.

For a time it seemed as though the steady wash of rain was the only sound in the world. Nimble Dick plowed on, heedless. She watched closely, noting how he bent his back, as if huddling low in the saddle would keep him dry. This time there was no village close at hand when darkness came upon them. Nor were there any trees to give them shelter. They were forced to camp amongst some rocks, fifty yards above the tideline. The rocks at least would keep the wind off. "Best we keep a watch tonight, m'lady," Crabb told her, as she was struggling to get a driftwood fire lit. "A place like this, there might be squishers."

"Squishers?" Brienne gave him a suspicious look.

"Monsters," Nimble Dick said, with relish. "They look like men till you get close, but their heads is too big, and they got scales where a proper man's got hair. Fish-belly white they are, with webs between their fingers. They're always damp and fishy-smelling, but behind these blubbery lips they got rows of green teeth sharp as needles. Some say the First Men killed them all, but don't you believe it. They come by night and steal bad little children, padding along on them webbed feet with a little *squish-squish* sound. The girls they keep to breed with, but the boys they eat, tearing at them with those sharp green teeth." He grinned at Podrick. "They'd eat you, boy. They'd eat you *raw*."

"If they try, I'll kill them." Podrick touched his sword.

"You try that. You just try. Squishers don't die easy." He winked at Brienne. "You a bad little girl, m'lady?"

"No." *Just a fool.* The wood was too damp to light, no matter how many sparks Brienne struck off her flint and steel. The kindling sent up some smoke, but that was all. Disgusted, she settled down with her back to a rock, pulled her cloak over herself, and resigned herself to a cold, wet night. Dreaming of a hot meal, she gnawed on a strip of hard salt beef whilst Nimble Dick talked about the time Ser Clarence Crabb had fought the squisher king. *He tells a lively tale,* she had to admit, *but Mark Mullendore was amusing too, with his little monkey.*

It was too wet to see the sun go down, too grey to see the moon come up. The night was black and starless. Crabb ran out of tales and went to sleep. Podrick was soon snoring too. Brienne sat with her back to the rock, listening to the waves. *Are you near the sea, Sansa?* she wondered. *Are you waiting at the Whispers for a ship that will never come? Who do you have with you? Passage for*

*three, he said. Has the Imp joined you and Ser Dontos, or
did you find your little sister?*

The day had been a long one, and Brienne was tired.
Even sitting up against the rock, with rain pattering softly
all around her, she found her eyelids growing heavy. Twice
she dozed. The second time she woke all at once, heart
pounding, convinced that someone was looming over her.
Her limbs were stiff, and her cloak had gotten tangled
round her ankles. She kicked free of it and stood. Nimble
Dick was curled against a rock, half-buried in wet, heavy
sand, asleep. *A dream. It was a dream.*

Perhaps she had made a mistake in abandoning Ser
Creighton and Ser Illifer. They had seemed like honest
men. *Would that Jaime had come with me,* she thought . . .
but he was a knight of the Kingsguard, his rightful place
was with his king. Besides, it was Renly that she wanted. *I
swore I would protect him, and I failed. Then I swore I
would avenge him, and I failed at that as well. I ran off
with Lady Catelyn instead, and failed her too.* The wind
had shifted, and the rain was running down her face.

The next day the road dwindled to a pebbled thread,
and finally to a mere suggestion. Near midday, it came to
an abrupt end at the foot of a wind-carved cliff. Above, a
small castle stood frowning over the waves, its three
crooked towers outlined against a leaden sky. "Is that the
Whispers?" Podrick asked.

"That look a bloody ruin t' you?" Crabb spat. "That's
the Dyre Den, where old Lord Brune keeps his seat. Road
ends here, though. It's the pines for us from here on."

Brienne studied the cliff. "How do we get up there?"

"Easy." Nimble Dick turned his horse. "Stay close t'
Dick. The squishers are apt t' take the laggards."

The way up proved to be a steep stony path hidden
within a cleft in the rock. Most of it was natural, but here

and there steps had been carved to ease the climb. Sheer walls of rock, eaten away by centuries of wind and spray, hemmed them in to either side. In some places they had assumed fantastic shapes. Nimble Dick pointed out a few as they climbed. "There's an ogre's head, see?" he said, and Brienne smiled when she saw it. "And that there's a stone dragon. T'other wing fell off when my father was a boy. Above it, that's the dugs drooping down, like some hag's teats." He glanced back at her own chest.

"Ser? My lady?" said Podrick. "There's a rider."

"Where?" None of the rocks suggested a rider to her.

"On the road. Not a rock rider. A real rider. Following us. Down there." He pointed.

Brienne twisted in her saddle. They had climbed high enough to see for leagues along the shore. The horse was coming up the same road they had taken, two or three miles behind them. *Again?* She glanced at Nimble Dick suspiciously.

"Don't squint at me," Crabb said. "He's naught t' do with old Nimble Dick, whoever he is. Some man o' Brune's, most like, come back from the wars. Or one o' them singers, wandering from place to place." He turned his head and spat. "He's no squisher, that's bloody certain. Their sort don't ride horses."

"No," said Brienne. On that, at least, they could agree.

The last hundred feet of the climb proved the steepest and most treacherous. Loose pebbles rolled beneath their horse's hooves and went rattling down the stony path behind them. When they emerged from the cleft in the rock, they found themselves under the castle walls. On a parapet above, a face peered down at them, then vanished. Brienne thought it might have been a woman, and said as much to Nimble Dick.

He agreed. "Brune's too old to go climbing wallwalks,

and his sons and grandsons went off to the wars. No one left in there but wenches, and a snot-nosed babe or three."

It was on her lips to ask her guide which king Lord Brune had espoused, but it made no matter any longer. Brune's sons were gone; some might not be coming back. *We will have no hospitality here tonight.* A castle full of old men, women, and children was not like to open its doors to armed strangers. "You speak of Lord Brune as if you know him," she said to Nimble Dick.

"Might be I did, once."

She glanced at the breast of his doublet. Loose threads and a ragged patch of darker fabric showed where some badge had been torn away. Her guide was a deserter, she did not doubt. Could the rider behind them be one of his brothers-in-arms?

"We should ride on," he urged, "before Brune starts to wonder why we're here beneath his walls. Even a wench can wind a bloody crossbow." Dick gestured toward the limestone hills that rose beyond the castle, with their wooded slopes. "No more roads from here on, only streams and game trails, but m'lady need not fear. Nimble Dick knows these parts."

That was what Brienne was afraid of. The wind was gusting along the top of the cliff, but all she could smell was a trap. "What about that rider?" Unless his horse could walk on waves, he would soon be coming up the cliff.

"What about him? If he's some fool from Maidenpool, he might not even find the bloody path. And if he does, we'll lose him in the woods. He won't have no road to follow there."

Only our tracks. Brienne wondered if it wouldn't be better to meet the rider here, with her blade in hand. *I'll look an utter fool if it is a wandering singer or one of Lord*

Brune's sons. Crabb had the right of it, she supposed. *If he is still behind us on the morrow, I can deal with him then.* "As you will," she said, turning her mare toward the trees.

Lord Brune's castle dwindled at their backs, and soon was lost to sight. Sentinels and soldier pines rose all around them, towering green-clad spears thrusting toward the sky. The forest floor was a bed of fallen needles as thick as a castle wall, littered with pinecones. The hooves of their horses seemed to make no sound. It rained a bit, stopped for a time, then started once again, but amongst the pines they scarce felt a drop.

The going was much slower in the woods. Brienne prodded her mare through the green gloom, weaving in and out amongst the trees. It would be very easy to get lost here, she realized. Every way she looked appeared the same. The very air seemed grey and green and still. Pine boughs scratched against her arms and scraped noisily against her newly painted shield. The eerie stillness grated on her more with every passing hour.

It bothered Nimble Dick as well. Late that day, as dusk was coming on, he tried to sing. *"A bear there was, a bear, a bear, all black and brown, and covered with hair,"* he sang, his voice as scratchy as a pair of woolen breeches. The pines drank his song, as they drank the wind and rain. After a little while he stopped.

"It's bad here," Podrick said. "This is a bad place."

Brienne felt the same, but it would not serve to admit it. "A pine wood is a gloomy place, but in the end it's just a wood. There's naught here that we need fear."

"What about the squishers? And the heads?"

"There's a clever lad," said Nimble Dick, laughing.

Brienne gave him a look of annoyance. "There are no squishers," she told Podrick, "and no heads."

The hills went up, the hills went down. Brienne found

herself praying that Nimble Dick was honest, and knew where he was taking them. By herself, she was not even certain she could have found the sea again. Day or night, the sky was solid grey and overcast, with neither sun nor stars to help her find her way.

They made camp early that night, after they came down a hill and found themselves on the edge of a glistening green bog. In the grey-green light, the ground ahead looked solid enough, but when they'd ridden out it had swallowed their horses up to their withers. They had to turn and fight their way back onto more solid footing. "It's no matter," Crabb assured them. "We'll go back up the hill and come down another way."

The next day was the same. They rode through pines and bogs, under dark skies and intermittent rain, past sinkholes and caves and the ruins of ancient strongholds whose stones were blanketed in moss. Every heap of stones had a story, and Nimble Dick told them all. To hear him tell it, the men of Crackclaw Point had watered their pine trees with blood. Brienne's patience soon began to fray. "How much longer?" she demanded finally. "We must have seen every tree in Crackclaw Point by now."

"Not hardly," said Crabb. "We're close now. See, the woods is thinning out. We're near the narrow sea."

This fool he promised me is like to be my own reflection in a pond, Brienne thought, but it seemed pointless to turn back when she had come so far. She was weary, though, she could not deny that. Her thighs were hard as iron from the saddle, and of late she had been sleeping only four hours a night, whilst Podrick watched over her. If Nimble Dick meant to try and murder them, she was convinced it would happen here, on ground that he knew well. He could be taking them to some robbers' den where he had kin as treacherous as he was. Or perhaps he was just leading them in circles, waiting for that rider to catch up. They had not seen any sign of the man since leaving Lord Brune's castle, but that did not mean he had given up the hunt.

It may be that I will need to kill him, she told herself one night as she paced about the camp. The notion made her queasy. Her old master-at-arms had always questioned whether she was hard enough for battle. "You have a man's strength in your arms," Ser Goodwin had said to her, more than once, "but your heart is as soft as any maid's. It is one thing to train in the yard with a blunted sword in hand, and another to drive a foot of sharpened steel into a man's gut and see the light go out of his eyes." To toughen her, Ser Goodwin used to send her to her father's butcher to slaughter lambs and suckling pigs. The piglets squealed and the lambs screamed like frightened children. By the time the butchering was done Brienne had been blind with tears, her clothes so bloody that she had given them to her maid to burn. But Ser Goodwin still had doubts. "A piglet is a piglet. It is different with a man. When I was a squire young as you, I had a friend who was strong and quick and agile, a champion in the yard. We all knew that one day he would be a splendid knight. Then war came to the Stepstones. I saw my friend drive his foeman to his knees and knock the axe from his hand, but when he might have finished he held back for half a heartbeat. In battle half a heartbeat is a lifetime. The man slipped out his dirk and found a chink in my friend's armor. His strength, his speed, his valor, all his hard-won skill . . . it was worth less than a mummer's fart, *because he flinched from killing.* Remember that, girl."

I will, she promised his shade, there in the piney wood. She sat down on a rock, took out her sword, and began to hone its edge. *I will remember, and I pray I will not flinch.*

The next day dawned bleak and cold and overcast. They never saw the sun come up, but when the blackness turned to grey Brienne knew it was time to saddle up again. With Nimble Dick leading the way, they rode back into the pines. Brienne followed close behind him, with Podrick bringing up the rear upon his rounsey.

The castle came upon them without warning. One moment they were in the depths of the forest, with nothing but pines to see for leagues and leagues. Then they rode around a boulder, and a gap appeared ahead. A mile farther on, the forest ended abruptly. Beyond was sky and sea . . . and an ancient, tumbledown castle, abandoned and overgrown on the edge of a cliff. "The Whispers," said Nimble Dick. "Have a listen. You can hear the heads."

Podrick's mouth gaped open. "I hear them."

Brienne heard them too. A faint, soft murmuring that seemed to be coming from the ground as much as from the castle. The sound grew louder as she neared the cliffs. It was the sea, she realized suddenly. The waves had eaten holes in the cliffs below and were rumbling through caves and tunnels beneath the earth. "There are no heads," she said. "It's the waves you hear whispering."

"Waves don't whisper. It's heads."

The castle was built of old, unmortared stones, no two the same. Moss grew thick in clefts between the rocks, and trees were growing up from the foundations. Most old castles had a godswood. By the look of it, the Whispers had little else. Brienne walked her mare to the cliff's edge, where the curtain wall had collapsed. Mounds of poisonous red ivy grew over the heap of broken stones. She tied the horse to a tree and edged as close to the precipice as she dared. Fifty feet below, the waves were swirling in and over the remnants of a shattered tower. Behind it, she glimpsed the mouth of a large cavern.

"That's the old beacon tower," said Nimble Dick as he came up behind her. "It fell when I was half as old as Pods here. Used to be steps down to the cove, but when the cliff collapsed they went too. The smugglers stopped landing here after that. Time was, they could row their boats into the cave, but no more. See?" He put one hand on her back, and pointed with the other.

Brienne's flesh prickled. *One shove, and I'll be down there with the tower.* She stepped back. "Keep your hands off me."

Crabb made a face. "I was only . . ."

"I don't care what you were *only*. Where's the gate?"

"Around t'other side." He hesitated. "This fool o' yours, he's not a man to hold a grudge, is he?" he said nervously. "I mean, last night I got to thinking that he might be angry at old Nimble Dick, on account o' that map I sold him, and how I left out that the smugglers don't land here no more."

"With the gold that you've got coming, you can give him back whatever he paid you for your *help*." Brienne could not imagine Dontos Hollard posing a threat. "That is, if he's even here."

They made a circuit of the walls. The castle had been triangular, with square towers at each corner. Its gates were badly rotted. When Brienne tugged at one, the wood cracked and peeled away in long wet splinters, and half the gate came down on her. She could see more green gloom inside. The forest had breached the walls, and swallowed keep and bailey. But there was a portcullis behind the gate, its teeth sunk deep into the soft muddy ground. The iron was red with rust, but it held when Brienne rattled it. "No one's used this gate for a long time."

"I could climb over," offered Podrick. "By the cliff. Where the wall fell down."

"It's too dangerous. Those stones looked loose to me, and that red ivy's poisonous. There has to be a postern gate."

They found it on the north side of the castle, half-hidden behind a huge blackberry bramble. The berries had all been picked, and half the bush had been hacked down to cut a path to the door. The sight of the broken branches filled Brienne with disquiet. "Someone's been through here, and recently."

"Your fool and those girls," said Crabb. "I told you."

Sansa? Brienne could not believe it. Even a wine-soaked sot like Dontos Hollard would have better sense than to bring her to this bleak place. Something about the ruins filled her with unease. She would not find the Stark girl here . . . but she had to have a look. *Someone was here,* she thought. *Someone who needed to stay hidden.* "I'm going in," she said. "Crabb, you'll come with me. Podrick, I want you to watch the horses."

"I want to come too. I'm a squire. I can fight."

"That's why I want you to stay here. There may be outlaws in these woods. We dare not leave the horses unprotected."

Podrick scuffed at a rock with his boot. "As you say."

She shouldered through the blackberries and pulled at a rusted iron ring. The postern door resisted for a moment, then jerked open, its hinges screaming protest. The sound made the hairs on the back of Brienne's neck stand up. She drew her sword. Even in mail and boiled leather, she felt naked.

"Go on, m'lady," urged Nimble Dick, behind her. "What are you waiting for? Old Crabb's been dead a thousand years."

What *was* she waiting for? Brienne told herself that she was being foolish. The sound was just the sea, echoing endlessly through the caverns beneath the castle, rising and falling with each wave. It *did* sound like whispering, though, and for a moment she could almost see the heads, sitting on their shelves and muttering to one another. *"I should have used the sword"* one of them was saying. *"I should have used the magic sword."*

"Podrick," said Brienne. "There's a sword and scabbard wrapped up in my bedroll. Bring them here to me."

"Yes, ser. My lady. I will." The boy went running off.

"A sword?" Nimble Dick scratched behind his ear. "You got a sword in your hand. What do you need another for?"

"This one's for you." Brienne offered him the hilt.

"For true?" Crabb reached out hesitantly, as if the blade might bite him. "The mistrustful maid's giving old Dick a sword?"

"You do know how to use one?"

"I'm a Crabb." He snatched the longsword from her hand. "I got the same blood as old Ser Clarence." He slashed the air and grinned at her. "It's the sword that makes the lord, some say."

When Podrick Payne returned, he held Oathkeeper as gingerly as if it were a child. Nimble Dick gave a whistle at the sight of the ornate scabbard with its row of lion's heads, but grew quiet when she drew the blade and tried a cut. *Even the sound of it is sharper than an ordinary sword.* "With me," she told Crabb. She slipped sideways through the postern, ducking her head to pass beneath the doorway's arch.

The bailey opened up before her, overgrown. To her left was the main gate, and the collapsed shell of what might have been a stable. Saplings were poking out of half the stalls and growing up through the dry brown thatch of its roof. To her right she saw rotted wooden steps descending into the darkness of a dungeon or a root cellar. Where the keep had been was a pile of collapsed stones, overgrown with green and purple moss. The yard was all weeds and pine needles. Soldier pines were everywhere, drawn up in solemn ranks. In their midst was a pale stranger; a slender young weirwood with a trunk as white as a cloistered maid. Dark red leaves sprouted from its reaching branches. Beyond was the emptiness of sky and sea where the wall had collapsed . . .

. . . and the remnants of a fire.

The whispers nibbled at her ears, insistent. Brienne knelt beside the fire. She picked up a blackened stick, sniffed at it, stirred the ashes. *Someone was trying to keep warm last night. Or else they were trying to send a signal to a passing ship.*

"Halloooooo," called Nimble Dick. "Anyone here?"

"Be quiet," Brienne told him.

"Someone might be hiding. Wanting to get a look at us before they show themself." He walked to where the steps went down beneath the ground, and peered down into the darkness. *"Hallooooo,"* he called again. "Anyone down there?"

Brienne saw a sapling sway. From the bushes slid a man, so caked with dirt that he looked as if he had sprouted from the earth. A broken sword was in his hand, but it was his face that gave her pause, the small eyes and wide flat nostrils.

She knew that nose. She knew those eyes. *Pyg,* his friends had called him.

Everything seemed to happen in a heartbeat. A second man slipped over the lip of the well, making no more noise than a snake might make slithering across a pile of wet leaves. He wore an iron halfhelm wrapped in stained red silk, and had a short, thick throwing spear in hand.

Brienne knew him too. From behind her came a rustling as a head poked down through the red leaves. Crabb was standing underneath the weirwood. He looked up and saw the face. "Here," he called to Brienne. "It's your fool."

"Dick," she called urgently, "to me."

Shagwell dropped from the weirwood, braying laughter. He was garbed in motley, but so faded and stained that it showed more brown than grey or pink. In place of a jester's flail he had a triple morningstar, three spiked balls chained to a wooden haft. He swung it hard and low, and one of Crabb's knees exploded in a spray of blood and bone. "*That's* funny," Shagwell crowed as Dick fell. The sword she'd given him went flying from his hand and vanished in the weeds. He writhed on the ground, screaming and clutching at the ruins of his knee. "Oh, look," said Shagwell, "it's Smuggler Dick, the one who made the map for us. Did you come all this way to give us back our gold?"

"*Please,*" Dick whimpered, "please don't, my leg . . ."

"Does it hurt? I can make it stop."

"Leave him be," said Brienne.

"*DON'T!*" shrieked Dick, lifting bloody hands to shield his head. Shagwell whirled the spiked ball once around his head and brought it down in the middle of Crabb's face. There was a sickening crunch. In the silence that followed, Brienne could hear the sound of her own heart.

"Bad Shags," said the man who'd come creeping from the well. When he saw Brienne's face, he laughed. "You again, woman? What, come to hunt us down? Or did you miss our friendly faces?"

Shagwell danced from foot to foot and spun his flail. "It's me she come for. She dreams of me every night, when she sticks her fingers up her slit. She wants me, lads, the big horse missed her merry Shags! I'm going to fuck her up the arse and pump her full of motley seed, until she whelps a little me."

"You need to use a different hole for that, Shags," said Timeon, in his Dornish drawl.

"I best use all her holes, then. Just to make certain." He moved to her right as Pyg was circling around to her left, forcing her back toward the ragged edge of the cliff. *Passage for three,* Brienne remembered. "There are only three of you."

Timeon shrugged. "We all went our own ways, after we left Harrenhal. Urswyck and his lot rode south for Oldtown. Rorge thought he might slip out at Saltpans. Me and my lads made for Maidenpool, but we couldn't get near a ship." The Dornishman hefted his spear. "You did for Vargo with that bite, you know. His ear turned black and started leaking pus. Rorge and Urswyck were for leaving, but the Goat says we got to hold his castle. Lord of Harrenhal, he says he is, no one was going to take it off him. He said it slobbery, the way he always talked. We heard the Mountain killed him piece by piece. A hand one day, a foot the next, lopped off neat and clean. They bandaged up the stumps so Hoat didn't die. He was saving his cock for last, but some bird called him to King's Landing, so he finished it and rode off."

"I am not here for you. I am looking for my . . ." She almost said *my sister.* ". . . for a fool."

"*I'm* a fool," Shagwell announced happily.

"The wrong fool," blurted Brienne. "The one I want is with a highborn girl, the daughter of Lord Stark of Winterfell."

"Then it's the Hound you want," said Timeon. "He's not here neither, as it happens. Just us."

"Sandor Clegane?" said Brienne. "What do you mean?"

"He's the one that's got the Stark girl. The way I hear it, she was making for Riverrun, and he stole her. Damned dog."

Riverrun, thought Brienne. *She was making for Riverrun. For her uncles.* "How do you know?"

"Had it from one of Beric's bunch. The lightning lord is looking for her too. He's sent his men all up and down the Trident, sniffing after her. We chanced on three of them after Harrenhal, and winkled the tale from one before he died."

"He might have lied."

"He might have, but he didn't. Later on, we heard how the Hound slew three of his brother's men at an inn by the crossroads. The girl was with him there. The innkeep swore to it before Rorge killed him, and the whores said the same. An ugly bunch, they were. Not so ugly as you, mind you, but still . . ."

He is trying to distract me, Brienne realized, *to lull me with his voice.* Pyg was edging closer. Shagwell took a hop toward her. She backed away from them. *They will back me off the cliff if I let them.* "Stay away," she warned them.

"I think I'm going to fuck you up the nose, wench," Shagwell announced. "Won't that be amusing?"

"He has a very small cock," Timeon explained. "Drop that pretty sword and might be we'll go gentle on you, woman. We need gold to pay these smugglers, that's all."

"And if I give you gold, you'll let us go?"

"We will." Timeon smiled. "Once you've fucked the lot of us. We'll pay you like a proper whore. A silver for each fuck. Or else we'll take the gold and rape you anyway, and do you like the Mountain did Lord Vargo. What's your choice?"

"This." Brienne threw herself toward Pyg.

He jerked his broken blade up to protect his face, but as he went high she went low. Oathkeeper bit through leather, wool, skin, and muscle, into the sellsword's thigh. Pyg cut back wildly as his leg went out from under him. His broken sword scraped against her chainmail before he landed on his back. Brienne stabbed him through the throat, gave the blade a hard turn, and slid it out, whirling just as Timeon's spear came flashing past her face. *I did not flinch,* she thought, as blood ran red down her cheek. *Did you see, Ser Goodwin?* She hardly felt the cut.

"Your turn," she told Timeon, as the Dornishman pulled out a second spear, shorter and thicker than the first. "Throw it."

"So you can dance away and charge me? I'd end up dead as Pyg. No. Get her, Shags."

"You get her," Shagwell said. "Did you see what she did to Pyg? She's mad with moon blood." The fool was behind her, Timeon in front. No matter how she turned, one was at her back.

"Get her," urged Timeon, "and you can fuck her corpse."

"Oh, you *do* love me." The morningstar was whirling. *Choose one,* Brienne told herself. *Choose one and kill him quickly.* Then a stone came out of nowhere, and hit Shagwell in the head. Brienne did not hesitate. She flew at Timeon.

He was better than Pyg, but he had only a short throwing spear, and she had a Valyrian steel blade. Oathkeeper was alive in her hands. She had never been so quick. The blade became a grey blur. He wounded her in the shoulder as she came at him, but she slashed off his ear and half his cheek, hacked the head off his spear, and put a foot of rippled steel into his belly through the links of the chainmail byrnie he was wearing.

Timeon was still trying to fight as she pulled her blade from him, its fullers running red with blood. He clawed at his belt and came up with a dagger, so Brienne cut his hand off. *That one was for Jaime.* "Mother have mercy," the Dornishman gasped, the blood bubbling from his mouth and spurting from his wrist. "Finish it. Send me back to Dorne, you bloody bitch."

She did.

Shagwell was on his knees when she turned, looking dazed as he fumbled for the morningstar. As he staggered to his feet, another stone slammed him in the ear. Podrick had climbed the fallen wall and was standing amongst the ivy glowering, a fresh rock in his hand. "I *told* you I could fight!" he shouted down.

Shagwell tried to crawl away. "I yield," the fool cried, "I *yield*. You mustn't hurt sweet Shagwell, I'm too droll to die."

"You are no better than the rest of them. You have robbed and raped and murdered."

"Oh, I have, I have, I shan't deny it . . . but I'm *amusing,* with all my japes and capers. I make men laugh."

"And women weep."

"Is that my fault? Women have no sense of humor."

Brienne lowered Oathkeeper. "Dig a grave. There, beneath the weirwood." She pointed with her blade.

"I have no spade."

"You have two hands." *One more than you left Jaime.*

"Why bother? Leave them for the crows."

"Timeon and Pyg can feed the crows. Nimble Dick will have a grave. He was a Crabb. This is his place."

The ground was soft from rain, but even so it took the fool the rest of the day to dig down deep enough. Night was falling by the time he was done, and his hands were bloody and blistered. Brienne sheathed Oathkeeper, gathered up

Dick Crabb, and carried him to the hole. His face was hard to look on. "I'm sorry that I never trusted you. I don't know how to do that anymore."

As she knelt to lay the body down, she thought, *The fool will make his try now, whilst my back is turned.*

She heard his ragged breathing half a heartbeat before Podrick cried out his warning. Shagwell had a jagged chunk of rock clutched in one hand. Brienne had her dagger up her sleeve.

A dagger will beat a rock almost every time.

She knocked aside his arm and punched the steel into his bowels. "Laugh," she snarled at him. He moaned instead. "Laugh," she repeated, grabbing his throat with one hand and stabbing at his belly with the other. *"Laugh!"* She kept saying it, over and over, until her hand was red up to the wrist and the stink of the fool's dying was like to choke her. But Shagwell never laughed. The sobs that Brienne heard were all her own. When she realized that, she threw down her knife and shuddered.

Podrick helped her lower Nimble Dick into his hole. By the time they were done the moon was rising. Brienne rubbed the dirt from her hands and tossed two dragons down into the grave.

"Why did you do that, my lady? Ser?" asked Pod.

"It was the reward I promised him for finding me the fool."

Laughter sounded from behind them. She ripped Oathkeeper from her sheath and whirled, expecting more Bloody Mummers . . . but it was only Hyle Hunt atop the crumbling wall, his legs crossed. "If there are brothels down in hell, the wretch will thank you," the knight called down. "Elsewise, that's a waste of good gold."

"I keep my promises. What are *you* doing here?"

"Lord Randyll bid me follow you. If by some freak's

chance you stumbled onto Sansa Stark, he told me to bring her back to Maidenpool. Have no fear, I was commanded not to harm you."

Brienne snorted. "As if you could."

"What will you do now, my lady?"

"Cover him."

"About the girl, I meant. The Lady Sansa."

Brienne thought a moment. "She was making for Riverrun, if Timeon told it true. Somewhere along the way she was taken by the Hound. If I find him . . ."

". . . he'll kill you."

"Or I'll kill him," she said stubbornly. "Will you help me cover up poor Crabb, ser?"

"No true knight could refuse such beauty." Ser Hyle climbed down from the wall. Together, they shoved the dirt on top of Nimble Dick as the moon rose higher in the sky, and down below the ground the heads of forgotten kings whispered secrets.

THE QUEENMAKER

Beneath the burning sun of Dorne, wealth was measured as much in water as in gold, so every well was zealously guarded. The well at Shandystone had gone dry a hundred years before, however, and its guardians had departed for some wetter place, abandoning their modest holdfast with its fluted columns and triple arches. Afterward the sands had crept back in to reclaim their own.

Arianne Martell arrived with Drey and Sylva just as the sun was going down, with the west a tapestry of gold and purple and the clouds all glowing crimson. The ruins seemed aglow as well; the fallen columns glimmered pinkly, red shadows crept across the cracked stone floors, and the sands themselves turned from gold to orange to purple as the light faded. Garin had arrived a few hours earlier, and the knight called Darkstar the day before.

"It is lovely here," Drey observed as he was helping Garin water the horses. They had carried their own water with them. The sand steeds of Dorne were swift and tireless, and would keep going for long leagues after other horses had given out, but even such as they could not run dry. "How did you know of this place?"

"My uncle brought me here, with Tyene and Sarella." The memory made Arianne smile. "He caught some vipers and showed Tyene the safest way to milk them for their venom. Sarella turned over rocks, brushed sand off the mosaics, and wanted to know everything there was to know about the people who had lived here."

"And what did you do, princess?" asked Spotted Sylva.

I sat beside the well and pretended that some robber knight had brought me here to have his way with me, she thought, *a tall hard man with black eyes and a widow's peak.* The memory made her uneasy. "I dreamed," she said, "and when the sun went down I sat cross-legged at my uncle's feet and begged him for a story."

"Prince Oberyn was full of stories." Garin had been with them as well that day; he was Arianne's milk brother, and they had been inseparable since before they learned to walk. "He told about Prince Garin, I remember, the one that I was named for."

"Garin the Great," offered Drey, "the wonder of the Rhoyne."

"That's the one. He made Valyria tremble."

"They trembled," said Ser Gerold, "then they killed him. If I led a quarter of a million men to death, would they call me Gerold the Great?" He snorted. "I shall remain Darkstar, I think. At least it is mine own." He unsheathed his longsword, sat upon the lip of the dry well, and began to hone the blade with an oilstone.

Arianne watched him warily. *He is highborn enough to*

make a worthy consort, she thought. *Father would question my good sense, but our children would be as beautiful as dragonlords.* If there was a handsomer man in Dorne, she did not know him. Ser Gerold Dayne had an aquiline nose, high cheekbones, a strong jaw. He kept his face clean-shaven, but his thick hair fell to his collar like a silver glacier, divided by a streak of midnight black. *He has a cruel mouth, though, and a crueler tongue.* His eyes seemed black as he sat outlined against the dying sun, sharpening his steel, but she had looked at them from a closer vantage and she knew that they were purple. *Dark purple. Dark and angry.*

He must have felt her gaze upon him, for he looked up from his sword, met her eyes, and smiled. Arianne felt heat rushing to her face. *I should never have brought him. If he gives me such a look when Arys is here, we will have blood on the sand.* Whose, she could not say. By tradition the Kingsguard were the finest knights in all the Seven Kingdoms . . . but Darkstar was Darkstar.

The Dornish nights grow cold out upon the sands. Garin gathered wood for them, bleached white branches from trees that had withered up and died a hundred years ago. Drey built a fire, whistling as he struck sparks off his flint.

Once the kindling caught, they sat around the flames and passed a skin of summerwine from hand to hand . . . all but Darkstar, who preferred to drink unsweetened lemonwater. Garin was in a lively mood and entertained them with the latest tales from the Planky Town at the mouth of the Greenblood, where the orphans of the river came to trade with the carracks, cogs, and galleys from across the narrow sea. If the sailors could be believed, the east was seething with wonders and terrors: a slave revolt in Astapor, dragons in Qarth, grey plague in Yi Ti. A new corsair king had risen in the Basilisk Isles and raided Tall Trees Town, and in Qohor followers of the red priests had rioted and tried to burn down the Black Goat. "And the Golden Company broke its contract with Myr, just as the Myrmen were about to go to war with Lys."

"The Lyseni bought them off," suggested Sylva.

"Clever Lyseni," Drey said. "Clever, craven Lyseni."

Arianne knew better. *If Quentyn has the Golden Company behind him . . .* "Beneath the gold the bitter steel," was their cry. *You will need bitter steel and more, brother, if you think to set me aside.* Arianne was loved in Dorne, Quentyn little known. No company of sellswords could change that.

Ser Gerold rose. "I believe I'll have a piss."

"Watch where you set your feet," Drey cautioned. "It has been a while since Prince Oberyn milked the local vipers."

"I was weaned on venom, Dalt. Any viper takes a bite of me will rue it." Ser Gerold vanished through a broken arch.

When he was gone, the others exchanged glances. "Forgive me, princess," said Garin softly, "but I do not like that man."

"A pity," Drey said. "I believe he's half in love with you."

"We need him," Arianne reminded them. "It may be that we will need his sword, and we will surely need his castle."

"High Hermitage is not the only castle in Dorne," Spotted Sylva pointed out, "and you have other knights who love you well. Drey is a knight."

"I am," he affirmed. "I have a wonderful horse and a very fine sword, and my valor is second to . . . well, several, actually."

"More like several hundred, ser," said Garin.

Arianne left them to their banter. Drey and Spotted Sylva were her dearest friends, aside from her cousin Tyene, and Garin had been teasing her since both of them were drinking from his mother's teats, but just now she was in no mood for japery. The sun was gone, and the sky was full of stars. *So many.* She leaned her back against a fluted pillar and wondered if her brother was looking at the same stars tonight, wherever he might be. *Do you see the white one, Quentyn? That is Nymeria's star, burning bright, and that milky band behind her, those are ten thousand ships. She burned as bright as any man, and so shall I. You will not rob me of my birthright!*

Quentyn had been very young when he was sent to Yronwood; too young, according to their mother. Norvoshi did not foster out their children, and Lady Mellario had never forgiven Prince Doran for taking her son away from her. "I like it no more than you do," Arianne had overheard her father say, "but there is a blood debt, and Quentyn is the only coin Lord Ormond will accept."

"Coin?" her mother had screamed. "He is your *son.* What sort of father uses his own flesh and blood to pay his debts?"

"The princely sort," Doran Martell had answered.

Prince Doran was still pretending that her brother was with Lord Yronwood, but Garin's mother had seen him at the Planky Town, posing as a merchant. One of his companions had a lazy eye, the same as Cletus Yronwood, Lord Anders's randy son. A maester traveled with them too, a maester skilled in tongues. *My brother is not as clever as he thinks. A clever man would have left from Oldtown, even if it meant a longer voyage. In Oldtown he might have gone unrecognized.* Arianne had friends amongst the orphans of the Planky Town, and some had grown curious as to why a prince and a lord's son might be traveling under false names and seeking passage across the narrow sea. One of them had crept through a window of a night, tickled the lock on Quentyn's little strongbox, and found the scrolls within.

Arianne would have given much and more to know that this secret trip across the narrow sea was Quentyn's own doing, and his alone . . . but parchments he had carried had been sealed with the sun and spear of Dorne. Garin's cousin had not dared break the seal to read them, but . . .

"Princess." Ser Gerold Dayne stood behind her, half in starlight and half in shadow.

"How was your piss?" Arianne inquired archly.

"The sands were duly grateful." Dayne put a foot upon the head of a statue that might have been the Maiden till the sands had scoured her face away. "It occurred to me as I was pissing that this plan of yours may not yield you what you want."

"And what is it I want, ser?"

"The Sand Snakes freed. Vengeance for Oberyn and Elia. Do I know the song? You want a little taste of lion blood."

That, and my birthright. I want Sunspear, and my father's seat. I want Dorne. "I want justice."

"Call it what you will. Crowning the Lannister girl is a hollow gesture. She will never sit the Iron Throne. Nor will you get the war you want. The lion is not so easily provoked." Ser Gerold drew his sword. It glimmered in the starlight, sharp as lies. "This is how you start a war. Not with a crown of gold, but with a blade of steel."

I am no murderer of children. "Put that away. Myrcella is under my protection. And Ser Arys will permit no harm to come to his precious princess, you know that."

"No, my lady. What I know is that Daynes have been killing Oakhearts for several thousand years."

His arrogance took her breath away. "It seems to me that Oakhearts have been killing Daynes for just as long."

"We all have our family traditions." Darkstar sheathed his sword. "The moon is rising, and I see your paragon approaching."

His eyes were sharp. The horseman on the tall grey palfrey did indeed prove to be Ser Arys, white cloak fluttering bravely as he spurred across the sand. Princess Myrcella rode pillion behind him, swaddled in a cowled robe that hid her golden curls.

As Ser Arys helped her from the saddle, Drey went to one knee before her. "Your Grace."

"My lady liege." Spotted Sylva knelt beside him.

"My queen, I am your man." Garin dropped to both knees.

Confused, Myrcella clutched Arys Oakheart by the arm. "Why do they call me Grace?" she asked in a plaintive voice. "Ser Arys, what is this place, and who are they?"

Has he told her nought? Arianne moved forward in a swirl of silk, smiling to put the child at ease. "They are my true and loyal friends, Your Grace . . . and would be your friends as well."

"Princess Arianne?" The girl threw her arms around her. "Why do they call me queen? Did something bad happen to Tommen?"

"He fell in with evil men, Your Grace," Arianne said, "and I fear they have conspired with him to steal your throne."

"My throne? You mean, the *Iron* Throne?" The girl was more confused than ever. "He never stole that, Tommen is . . ."

". . . younger than you, surely?"

"I am older by a year."

"That means the Iron Throne by rights is yours," Arianne said. "Your brother is only a little boy, you must not blame him. He has bad counselors . . . but *you* have friends. May I have the honor of presenting them?" She took the child by the hand. "Your Grace, I give you Ser Andrey Dalt, the heir to Lemonwood."

"My friends call me Drey," he said, "and I should be greatly honored if Your Grace would do the same."

Though Drey had an open face and an easy smile, Myrcella regarded him warily. "Until I know you I must call you *ser.*"

"Whatever name Your Grace prefers, I am her man."

Sylva cleared her throat, till Arianne said, "Might I present Lady Sylva Santagar, my queen? My dearest Spotted Sylva."

"Why do they call you that?" Myrcella asked.

"For my freckles, Your Grace," Sylva answered, "though they all pretend it is because I am the heir to Spottswood."

Garin was next, a loose-limbed, swarthy, long-nosed fellow with a jade stud in one ear. "Here is gay Garin of the orphans, who makes me laugh," said Arianne. "His mother was my wet nurse."

"I am sorry she is dead," Myrcella said.

"She's not, sweet queen." Garin flashed the golden tooth Arianne had bought him to replace the one she'd broken. "I'm of the orphans of the Greenblood, is what my lady means."

Myrcella would have time enough to learn the history of the orphans on her voyage up the river. Arianne led her queen-to-be to the final member of her little band. "Last, but first in valor, I give you Ser Gerold Dayne, a knight of Starfall."

Ser Gerold went to one knee. The moonlight shone in his dark eyes as he studied the child coolly.

"There was an Arthur Dayne," Myrcella said. "He was a knight of the Kingsguard in the days of Mad King Aerys."

"He was the Sword of the Morning. He is dead."

"Are you the Sword of the Morning now?"

"No. Men call me Darkstar, and I am of the night."

Arianne drew the child away. "You must be hungry. We have dates and cheese and olives, and lemonsweet to drink. You ought not eat or drink too much, though. After a little rest, we must ride. Out here on the sands it is always best to travel by night, before the sun ascends the sky. It is kinder to the horses."

"And the riders," Spotted Sylva said. "Come, Your Grace, warm yourself. I should be honored if you'd let me serve you."

As she led the princess to the fire, Arianne found Ser Gerold behind her. "My House goes back ten thousand years, unto the dawn of days," he complained. "Why is it that my cousin is the only Dayne that anyone remembers?"

"He was a great knight," Ser Arys Oakheart put in.

"He had a great sword," Darkstar said.

"And a great heart." Ser Arys took Arianne by the arm. "Princess, I beg a moment's word."

"Come." She led Ser Arys deeper into the ruins. Beneath his cloak, the knight wore a cloth-of-gold doublet embroidered with the three green oak leaves of his House. On his head was a light steel helm topped by a jagged spike, wound about with a yellow scarf in the Dornish fashion. He might have passed for any knight, but for the cloak. Of shimmering white silk it was, pale as moonlight and airy as a breeze. *A Kingsguard cloak beyond all doubt, the gallant fool.* "How much does the child know?"

"Little enough. Before we left King's Landing, her uncle reminded her that I was her protector and that any commands that I might give her were meant to keep her safe. She has heard them in the streets as well, shouting out for vengeance. She knew this was no game. The girl is brave, and wise beyond her years. She did all I asked of her, and never asked a question." The knight took her arm, glanced about, lowered his voice. "There are other tidings you should hear. Tywin Lannister is dead."

That was a shock. "Dead?"

"Murdered by the Imp. The queen has assumed the regency."

"Has she?" *A woman on the Iron Throne?* Arianne thought about that for a moment and decided it was all to the good. If the lords of the Seven Kingdoms grew accustomed to Queen Cersei's rule, it would be that much easier for them to bend their knees to Queen Myrcella. And Lord Tywin had been a dangerous foe; without him, Dorne's enemies would be much weaker. *Lannisters are killing Lannisters, how sweet.* "What became of the dwarf?"

"He's fled," Ser Arys said. "Cersei is offering a lordship to whosoever delivers her his head." In a tiled inner courtyard half-buried by the drifting sands, he pushed her back against a column to kiss her, and his hand went to her breast. He kissed her long and hard and would have pushed her skirts up, but Arianne broke free of him, laughing. "I see that queenmaking excites you, ser, but we have no time for this. Later, I promise you." She touched his cheek. "Did you meet with any problems?"

"Only Trystane. He wanted to sit beside Myrcella's bedside and play *cyvasse* with her."

"He had redspots when he was four, I told you. You can only get it once. You should have put out that Myrcella was suffering from greyscale, that would have kept him well away."

"The boy perhaps, but not your father's maester."

"Caleotte," she said. "Did he try to see her?"

"Not once I described the red spots on her face. He said that nothing could be done until the disease had run its course, and gave me a pot of salve to soothe her itching."

No one under ten ever died of redspots, but it could be mortal in adults, and Maester Caleotte had never suffered it as a child. Arianne learned that when she suffered her own spots, at eight. "Good," she said. "And the handmaid? Is she convincing?"

"From a distance. The Imp picked her for this purpose, over many girls of nobler birth. Myrcella helped her curl her hair, and painted the dots on her face herself. They are distant kin. Lannisport teems with Lannys, Lannetts, Lantells, and lesser Lannisters, and half of them have that yellow hair. Dressed in Myrcella's bedrobe with the maester's salve smeared across her face . . . she might even have fooled me, in a dim light. It was a deal harder to find a man to take my place. Dake is closest to my height, but he's too fat, so I put Rolder in my armor and told him to keep his visor down. The man is three inches shorter than I am, but perhaps no one will notice if I'm not there to stand beside him. He'll keep to Myrcella's chambers in any case."

"All we need is a few days. By that time the princess will be beyond my father's reach."

"Where?" He drew her close and nuzzled at her neck. "It's time you told me the rest of the plan, don't you think?"

She laughed, pushing him away. "No, it's time we rode."

The moon had crowned the Moonmaid as they set out from the dust-dry ruins of Shandystone, striking south and west. Arianne and Ser Arys took the lead, with Myrcella on a frisky mare between them. Garin followed close behind with Spotted Sylva, whilst her two Dornish knights took the rear. *We are seven,* Arianne realized as they rode. She had not thought of that before, but it seemed a good omen for their cause. *Seven riders on their way to glory. One day the singers will make all of us immortal.* Drey had wanted a larger party, but that might have attracted unwelcome attention, and every additional man doubled the risk of betrayal. *That much my father taught me, at the least.* Even when he was younger and stronger, Doran Martell had been a cautious man much given to silences and secrets. *It is time he put his burdens down, but I will suffer no slights to his honor or his person.* She would return him to his Water Gardens, to live out what years remained him surrounded by laughing children and the smell of limes and oranges. *Yes, and Quentyn can keep him company. Once I crown Myrcella and free the Sand Snakes, all Dorne will rally to my banners.* The Yronwoods might declare for Quentyn, but alone they were no threat. If they went over to Tommen and the Lannisters, she would have Darkstar destroy them root and branch.

"I am tired," Myrcella complained, after several hours in the saddle. "Is it much farther? Where are we going?"

"Princess Arianne is taking Your Grace to a place where you'll be safe," Ser Arys assured her.

"It is a long journey," Arianne said, "but it will go easier once we reach the Greenblood. Some of Garin's people will meet us there, the orphans of the river. They live on boats, and pole them up and down the Greenblood and its vassals, fishing and picking fruit and doing whatever work needs doing."

"Aye," Garin called out cheerfully, "and we sing and play and dance on water, and know much and more of healing. My mother is the best midwife in Westeros, and my father can cure warts."

"How can you be orphans if you have mothers and fathers?" the girl asked.

"They are the Rhoynar," Arianne explained, "and their Mother was the river Rhoyne."

Myrcella did not understand. "I thought *you* were the Rhoynar. You Dornishmen, I mean."

"We are in part, Your Grace. Nymeria's blood is in me, along with that of Mors Martell, the Dornish lord she married. On the day they wed, Nymeria fired her ships, so her people would understand that there could be no going back. Most were glad to see those flames, for their voyagings had been long and terrible before they came to Dorne, and many and more had been lost to storm, disease, and slavery. There were a few who mourned, however. They did not love this dry red land or its seven-faced god, so they clung to their old ways, hammered boats together from the hulks of the burned ships, and became the orphans of the Greenblood. The Mother in their songs is not *our* Mother, but Mother Rhoyne, whose waters nourished them from the dawn of days."

"I'd heard the Rhoynar had some turtle god," said Ser Arys.

"The Old Man of the River is a lesser god," said Garin. "He was born from Mother River too, and fought the Crab King to win dominion over all who dwell beneath the flowing waters."

"Oh," said Myrcella.

"I understand you've fought some mighty battles too, Your Grace," said Drey in his most cheerful voice. "It is said you show our brave Prince Trystane no mercy at the *cyvasse* table."

"He always sets his squares up the same way, with all the mountains in the front and his elephants in the passes," said Myrcella. "So I send my dragon through to eat his elephants."

"Does your handmaid play the game as well?" asked Drey.

"Rosamund?" asked Myrcella. "No. I tried to teach her, but she said the rules were too hard."

"She is a Lannister as well?" said Lady Sylva.

"A Lannister of *Lannisport,* not a Lannister of Casterly Rock. Her hair is the same color as mine, but straight instead of curly. Rosamund doesn't truly favor me, but when she dresses up in my clothes people who don't know us think she's me."

"You have done this before, then?"

"Oh, yes. We traded places on the *Seaswift,* on the way to Braavos. Septa Eglantine put brown dye in my hair. She said we were doing it as a game, but it was meant to keep me safe in case the ship was taken by my uncle Stannis."

The girl was plainly growing tired, so Arianne called a halt. They watered the horses once again, rested for a bit, and had some cheese and fruit. Myrcella split an orange with Spotted Sylva, whilst Garin ate olives and spit the stones at Drey.

Arianne had hoped to reach the river before the sun came up, but they had started much later than she'd planned, so they were still in the saddle when the eastern sky turned red. Darkstar cantered up beside her. "Princess," he said, "I'd set a faster pace, unless you mean to kill the child after all. We have no tents, and by day the sands are cruel."

"I know the sands as well as you do, ser," she told him. All the same, she did as he suggested. It was hard on their mounts, but better she should lose six horses than one princess.

Soon enough the wind came gusting from the west, hot and dry and full of grit. Arianne drew her veil across her face. It was made of shimmering silk, pale green above and yellow below, the colors blending into one another. Small green pearls gave it weight, and rattled softly against each other as she rode.

"I know why my princess wears a veil," Ser Arys said as she was fastening it to the temples of her copper helm. "Elsewise her beauty would outshine the sun above."

She had to laugh. "No, your princess wears a veil to keep the glare out of her eyes and the sand out of her mouth. You should do the same, ser." She wondered how long her white knight had been polishing his ponderous gallantry. Ser Arys was pleasant company abed, but wit and he were strangers.

Her Dornishmen covered their faces as she did, and Spotted Sylva helped veil the little princess from the sun, but Ser Arys stayed stubborn. Before long the sweat was running down his face, and his cheeks had taken on a rosy blush. *Much longer and he will cook in those heavy clothes,* she reflected. He would not be the first. In centuries past, many a host had come down from the Prince's Pass with banners streaming, only to wither and broil on the hot red Dornish sands. "The arms of House Martell display the sun and spear, the Dornishman's two favored weapons," the Young Dragon had once written in his boastful *Conquest of Dorne*, "but of the two, the sun is the more deadly."

Thankfully, they did not need to cross the deep sands but only a sliver of the drylands. When Arianne spied a hawk wheeling high above them against a cloudless sky, she knew the worst was behind them. Soon they came upon a tree. It was a gnarled and twisted thing with as many thorns as leaves, of the sort called sandbeggars, but it meant that they were not far from water.

"We're almost there, Your Grace," Garin told Myrcella cheerfully when they spied more sandbeggars up ahead, a thicket of them growing all around the dry bed of a stream. The sun was beating down like a fiery hammer, but it did not matter with their journey at its end. They stopped to water the horses again, drank deep from their skins and wet their veils, then mounted for the last push. Within half a league they were riding over devilgrass and past olive groves. Beyond a line of stony hills the grass grew greener and more lush, and there were lemon orchards watered by a spider's web of old canals. Garin was the first to spy the river glimmering green. He gave a shout and raced ahead.

Arianne Martell had crossed the Mander once, when she had gone with three of the Sand Snakes to visit Tyene's mother. Compared to that mighty waterway, the Greenblood was scarce worthy of the name of river, yet it remained the life of Dorne. It took its name from the murky green of its sluggish waters; but as they approached, the sunlight seemed to turn those waters gold. She had seldom seen a sweeter sight. *The next part should be slow and simple,* she thought, *up the Greenblood and onto the Vaith, as far as a poleboat can go.* That would give her time enough to prepare Myrcella for all that was to come. Beyond Vaith the deep sands waited. They would need help from Sandstone and the Hellholt to make that crossing, but she did not doubt that it would be forthcoming. The Red Viper had been fostered at Sandstone, and Prince Oberyn's paramour Ellaria Sand was Lord Uller's natural daughter; four of the Sand Snakes were his grand-daughters. *I will crown Myrcella at the Hellholt and raise my banners there.*

They found the boat half a league downstream, hidden beneath the drooping branches of a great green willow. Low of roof and wide abeam, the poleboats had hardly any draft to speak of; the Young Dragon had disparaged them as "hovels built on rafts," but that was hardly fair. All but the poorest orphan boats were wonderfully carved and painted. This one was done in shades of green, with a curved wooden tiller shaped like a mermaid, and fish faces peering through her rails. Poles and ropes and jars of olive oil cluttered her decks, and iron lanterns swung fore and aft. Arianne saw no orphans. *Where is her crew?* she wondered.

Garin reined up beneath the willow. "Wake up, you fish-eyed lagabeds," he called as he leapt down from the saddle. "Your *queen* is here, and wants her royal welcome. Come up, come out, we'll have some songs and sweet-wine. My mouth is set for—"

The door on the poleboat slammed open. Out into the sunlight stepped Areo Hotah, longaxe in hand.

Garin jerked to a halt. Arianne felt as though an axe had caught her in the belly. *It was not supposed to end this way. This was not supposed to happen.* When she heard Drey say, "There's the last face I'd hoped to see," she knew she had to act. *"Away!"* she cried, vaulting back into the saddle. "Arys, protect the princess—"

Hotah thumped the butt of his longaxe upon the deck. Behind the ornate rails of the poleboat, a dozen guards-men rose, armed with throwing spears or crossbows. Still more appeared atop the cabin. "Yield, my princess," the captain called, "else we must slay all but the child and yourself, by your father's word."

Princess Myrcella sat motionless upon her mount. Garin backed slowly from the poleboat, his hands in the air. Drey unbuckled his swordbelt. "Yielding seems the wisest course," he called to Arianne, as his sword thumped to the ground.

"No!" Ser Arys Oakheart put his horse between Arianne and the crossbows, his blade shining silver in his hand. He had unslung his shield and slipped his left arm through the straps. "You will not take her whilst I still draw breath."

You reckless fool, was all that Arianne had time to think, *what do you think you're doing?*

Darkstar's laughter rang out. "Are you blind or stupid, Oakheart? There are too many. Put up your sword."

"Do as he says, Ser Arys," Drey urged.

We are taken, ser, Arianne might have called out. *Your death will not free us. If you love your princess, yield.* But when she tried to speak, the words caught in her throat.

Ser Arys Oakheart gave her one last longing look, then put his golden spurs into his horse and charged.

He rode headlong for the poleboat, his white cloak streaming behind him. Arianne Martell had never seen anything half so gallant, or half so stupid. *"Noooo,"* she shrieked, but she had found her tongue too late. A crossbow *thrumm*ed, then another. Hotah bellowed a command. At such close range, the white knight's armor had as well been made of parchment. The first bolt punched right through his heavy oaken shield, pinning it to his shoulder. The second grazed his temple. A thrown spear took Ser Arys's mount in the flank, yet still the horse came on, staggering as he hit the gangplank. *"No,"* some girl was shouting, some foolish little girl, *"no, please, this was not* *supposed to happen."* She could hear Myrcella shrieking too, her voice shrill with fear.

Ser Arys's longsword slashed right and left, and two spearmen went down. His horse reared, and kicked a crossbowman in the face as he was trying to reload, but the other crossbows were firing, feathering the big courser with their quarrels. The bolts hit home so hard they knocked the horse sideways. His legs went out from under him and sent him crashing down the deck. Somehow Arys Oakheart leapt free. He even managed to keep hold of his sword. He struggled to his knees beside his dying horse . . .

. . . and found Areo Hotah standing over him.

The white knight raised his blade, too slowly. Hotah's longaxe took his right arm off at the shoulder, spun away spraying blood, and came flashing back again in a terrible two-handed slash that removed the head of Arys Oakheart and sent it spinning through the air. It landed amongst the reeds, and the Greenblood swallowed the red with a soft splash.

Arianne did not remember climbing from her horse. Perhaps she'd fallen. She did not remember that either. Yet she found herself on her hands and feet in the sand, shaking and sobbing and retching up her supper. *No,* was all that she could think, *no, no one was to be hurt, it was all planned, I was so careful.* She heard Areo Hotah roar, "After him. He must not escape. *After him!*" Myrcella was on the ground, wailing, shaking, her pale face in her hands, blood streaming through her fingers. Arianne did not understand. Men were scrambling onto horses whilst others swarmed over her and her companions, but none of it made sense. She had fallen into a dream, some terrible red nightmare. *This cannot be real. I will wake soon, and laugh at my night terrors.*

When they sought to bind her hands behind her back, she did not resist. One of the guardsmen jerked her to her feet. He wore her father's colors. Another bent and seized the throwing knife inside her boot, a gift from her cousin Lady Nym.

Areo Hotah took it from the man and frowned at it. "The prince said I must bring you back to Sunspear," he announced. His cheeks and brow were freckled with the blood of Arys Oakheart. "I am sorry, little princess."

Arianne raised a tear-streaked face. "How could he know?" she asked the captain. "I was so careful. How could he know?"

"Someone told." Hotah shrugged. "Someone always tells."

ARYA

Each night before sleep, she murmured her prayer into her pillow. "Ser Gregor," it went. "Dunsen, Raff the Sweetling, Ser Ilyn, Ser Meryn, Queen Cersei." She would have whispered the names of the Freys of the Crossing too, if she had known them. *One day I'll know,* she told herself, *and then I'll kill them all.*

No whisper was too faint to be heard in the House of Black and White. "Child," said the kindly man one day, "what are those names you whisper of a night?"

"I don't whisper any names," she said.

"You lie," he said. "All men lie when they are afraid. Some tell many lies, some but a few. Some have only one great lie they tell so often that they almost come to believe it . . . though some small part of them will always know that it is still a lie, and that will show upon their faces. Tell me of these names."

She chewed her lip. "The names don't matter."

"They do," the kindly man insisted. "Tell me, child."

Tell me, or we will turn you out, she heard. "They're people I hate. I want them to die."

"We hear many such prayers in this House."

"I know," said Arya. Jaqen H'ghar had granted three of her prayers once. *All I had to do was whisper . . .*

"Is that why you have come to us?" the kindly man went on. "To learn our arts, so you may kill these men you hate?"

Arya did not know how to answer that. "Maybe."

"Then you have come to the wrong place. It is not for you to say who shall live and who shall die. That gift belongs to Him of Many Faces. We are but his servants, sworn to do his will."

"Oh." Arya glanced at the statues that stood along the walls, candles glimmering round their feet. "Which god is he?"

"Why, all of them," said the priest in black and white.

He never told her his name. Neither did the waif, the little girl with the big eyes and hollow face who reminded her of another little girl, named Weasel. Like Arya, the waif lived below the temple, along with three acolytes, two serving men, and a cook called Umma. Umma liked to talk as she worked, but Arya could not understand a word she said. The others had no names, or did not choose to share them. One serving man was very old, his back bent like a bow. The second was red-faced, with hair growing from his ears. She took them both for mutes until she heard them praying. The acolytes were younger. The eldest was her father's age; the other two could not have been much older than Sansa, who had been her sister. The acolytes wore black and white too, but their robes had no cowls, and were black on the left side and white on the right. With the kindly man and the waif, it was the opposite. Arya was given servant's garb: a tunic of undyed wool, baggy breeches, linen smallclothes, cloth slippers for her feet.

Only the kindly man knew the Common Tongue. "Who are you?" he would ask her every day.

"No one," she would answer, she who had been Arya of House Stark, Arya Underfoot, Arya Horseface. She had been Arry and Weasel too, and Squab and Salty, Nan the cupbearer, a grey mouse, a sheep, the ghost of Harrenhal . . . but not for true, not in her heart of hearts. In there she was Arya of Winterfell, the daughter of Lord Eddard Stark and Lady Catelyn, who had once had brothers named Robb and Bran and Rickon, a sister named Sansa, a direwolf called Nymeria, a half brother named Jon Snow. In there she was someone . . . but that was not the answer that he wanted.

Without a common language, Arya had no way of talking to the others. She listened to them, though, and repeated the words she heard to herself as she went about her work. Though the youngest acolyte was blind, he had charge of the candles. He would walk the temple in soft slippers, surrounded by the murmurings of the old women who came each day to pray. Even without eyes, he always knew which candles had gone out. "He has the scent to guide him," the kindly man explained, "and the air is warmer where a candle burns." He told Arya to close her eyes and try it for herself.

They prayed at dawn before they broke their fast, kneeling around the still, black pool. Some days the kindly man led the prayer. Other days it was the waif. Arya only knew a few words of Braavosi, the ones that were the same in High Valyrian. So she prayed her own prayer to the Many-Faced God, the one that went, "Ser Gregor, Dunsen,

Raff the Sweetling, Ser Ilyn, Ser Meryn, Queen Cersei."
She prayed in silence. If the Many-Faced God was a
proper god, he would hear her.

Worshipers came to the House of Black and White
every day. Most came alone and sat alone; they lit candles
at one altar or another, prayed beside the pool, and sometimes wept. A few drank from the black cup and went to
sleep; more did not drink. There were no services, no
songs, no paeans of praise to please the god. The temple
was never full. From time to time, a worshiper would ask
to see a priest, and the kindly man or the waif would take
him down into the sanctum, but that did not happen often.

Thirty different gods stood along the walls, surrounded
by their little lights. The Weeping Woman was the favorite
of old women, Arya saw; rich men preferred the Lion of
Night, poor men the Hooded Wayfarer. Soldiers lit candles
to Bakkalon, the Pale Child, sailors to the Moon-Pale
Maiden and the Merling King. The Stranger had his shrine
as well, though hardly anyone ever came to him. Most of
the time only a single candle stood flickering at his feet.
The kindly man said it did not matter. "He has many faces,
and many ears to hear."

The knoll on which the temple stood was honeycombed
with passageways hewn from the rock. The priests and
acolytes had their sleeping cells on the first level, Arya
and the servants on the second. The lowest level was forbidden to all save the priests. That was where the holy
sanctum lay.

When she was not working, Arya was free to wander as
she would amongst the vaults and storerooms, so long as
she did not leave the temple, nor descend to the third cellar. She found a room full of weapons and armor: ornate
helms and curious old breastplates, longswords, daggers,
and dirks, crossbows and tall spears with leaf-shaped

heads. Another vault was crammed with clothing, thick
furs and splendid silks in half a hundred colors, next to
piles of foul-smelling rags and threadbare roughspuns.
There must be treasure chambers too, Arya decided. She
pictured stacks of golden plates, bags of silver coins, sapphires blue as the sea, ropes of fat green pearls.

One day the kindly man came on her unexpectedly and
asked what she was doing. She told him that she had gotten lost.

"You lie. Worse, you lie *poorly.* Who are you?"

"No one."

"Another lie." He sighed.

Weese would have beaten her bloody if he had caught
her in a lie, but it was different in the House of Black and
White. When she was helping in the kitchen, Umma
would sometimes smack her with her spoon if she got in
the way, but no one else ever raised a hand to her. *They
only raise their hands to kill,* she thought.

She got along well enough with the cook. Umma would
slap a knife into her hand and point at an onion, and Arya
would chop it. Umma would shove her toward a mound of
dough, and Arya would knead it until the cook said stop
(*stop* was the first Braavosi word she learned). Umma
would hand her a fish, and Arya would bone it and fillet it
and roll it in the nuts the cook was crushing. The brackish
waters that surrounded Braavos teemed with fish and
shellfish of every sort, the kindly man explained. A slow
brown river entered the lagoon from the south, wandering
through a wide expanse of reeds, tidal pools, and mudflats. Clams and cockles abounded hereabouts; mussels
and muskfish, frogs and turtles, mud crabs and leopard
crabs and climber crabs, red eels, black eels, striped eels,
lampreys, and oysters; all made frequent appearances on
the carved wooden table where the servants of the Many-

Faced God took their meals. Some nights Umma spiced the fish with sea salt and cracked peppercorns, or cooked the eels with chopped garlic. Once in a great while the cook would even use some saffron. *Hot Pie would have liked it here,* Arya thought.

Supper was her favorite time. It had been a long while since Arya had gone to sleep every night with a full belly. Some nights the kindly man would allow her to ask him questions. Once she asked him why the people who came to the temple always seemed so peaceful; back home, people were scared to die. She remembered how that pimply squire had wept when she stabbed him in the belly, and the way Ser Amory Lorch had begged when the Goat had him thrown in the bear pit. She remembered the village by the God's Eye, and the way the villagers shrieked and screamed and whimpered whenever the Tickler started asking after gold.

"Death is not the worst thing," the kindly man replied. "It is His gift to us, an end to want and pain. On the day that we are born the Many-Faced God sends each of us a dark angel to walk through life beside us. When our sins and our sufferings grow too great to be borne, the angel takes us by the hand to lead us to the nightlands, where the stars burn ever bright. Those who come to drink from the black cup are looking for their angels. If they are afraid, the candles soothe them. When you smell our candles burning, what does it make you think of, my child?"

Winterfell, she might have said. *I smell snow and smoke and pine needles. I smell the stables. I smell Hodor laughing, and Jon and Robb battling in the yard, and Sansa singing about some stupid lady fair. I smell the crypts where the stone kings sit, I smell hot bread baking, I smell the godswood. I smell my wolf, I smell her fur, almost as if she were still beside me.* "I don't smell anything," she said, to see what he would say.

"You lie," he said, "but you may keep your secrets if you wish, Arya of House Stark." He only called her that when she displeased him. "You know that you may leave this place. You are not one of us, not yet. You may go home anytime you wish."

"You told me that if I left, I couldn't come back."

"Just so."

Those words made her sad. *Syrio used to say that too,* Arya remembered. *He said it all the time.* Syrio Forel had taught her needlework and died for her. "I don't want to leave."

"Then stay . . . but remember, the House of Black and White is not a home for orphans. All men must serve beneath this roof. *Valar dohaeris* is how we say it here. Remain if you will, but know that we shall require your obedience. At all times and in all things. If you cannot obey, you must depart."

"I can obey."

"We shall see."

She had other tasks besides helping Umma. She swept the temple floors; she served and poured at meals; she sorted piles of dead men's clothing, emptied their purses, and counted out stacks of queer coins. Every morning she walked beside the kindly man as he made his circuit of the temple to find the dead. *Silent as a shadow,* she would tell herself, remembering Syrio. She carried a lantern with thick iron shutters. At each alcove, she would open the shutter a crack, to look for corpses.

The dead were never hard to find. They came to the House of Black and White, prayed for an hour or a day or a year, drank sweet dark water from the pool, and stretched out on a stone bed behind one god or another.

They closed their eyes, and slept, and never woke. "The gift of the Many-Faced God takes myriad forms," the kindly man told her, "but here it is always gentle." When they found a body he would say a prayer and make certain life had fled, and Arya would fetch the serving men, whose task it was to carry the dead down to the vaults. There acolytes would strip and wash the bodies. The dead men's clothes and coins and valuables went into a bin for sorting. Their cold flesh would be taken to the lower sanctum where only the priests could go; what happened in there Arya was not allowed to know. Once, as she was eating her supper, a terrible suspicion seized hold of her, and she put down her knife and stared suspiciously at a slice of pale white meat. The kindly man saw the horror on her face. "It is pork, child," he told her, "only pork."

Her bed was stone, and reminded her of Harrenhal and the bed she'd slept in when scrubbing steps for Weese. The mattress was stuffed with rags instead of straw, which made it lumpier than the one she'd had at Harrenhal, but less scratchy too. She was allowed as many blankets as she wished; thick woolen blankets, red and green and plaid. And her cell was hers alone. She kept her treasures there: the silver fork and floppy hat and fingerless gloves given her by the sailors on the *Titan's Daughter,* her dagger, boots, and belt, her small store of coins, the clothes she had been wearing . . .

And Needle.

Though her duties left her little time for needlework, she practiced when she could, dueling with her shadow by the light of a blue candle. One night the waif happened to be passing and saw Arya at her swordplay. The girl did not say a word, but the next day, the kindly man walked Arya back to her cell. "You need to rid yourself of all this," he said of her treasures.

Arya felt stricken. "They're mine."

"And who are you?"

"No one."

He picked up her silver fork. "This belongs to Arya of House Stark. All these things belong to her. There is no place for them here. There is no place for her. Hers is too proud a name, and we have no room for pride. We are servants here."

"I serve," she said, wounded. She liked the silver fork.

"You play at being a servant, but in your heart you are a lord's daughter. You have taken other names, but you wore them as lightly as you might wear a gown. Under them was always Arya."

"I don't wear *gowns*. You can't fight in a stupid *gown*."

"Why would you wish to fight? Are you some bravo, strutting through the alleys, spoiling for blood?" He sighed. "Before you drink from the cold cup, you must offer up all you are to Him of Many Faces. Your body. Your soul. *Yourself.* If you cannot bring yourself to do that, you must leave this place."

"The iron coin—"

"—has paid your passage here. From this point you must pay your own way, and the cost is dear."

"I don't have any gold."

"What we offer cannot be bought with gold. The cost is all of you. Men take many paths through this vale of tears and pain. Ours is the hardest. Few are made to walk it. It takes uncommon strength of body and spirit, and a heart both hard and strong."

I have a hole where my heart should be, she thought, *and nowhere else to go.* "I'm strong. As strong as you. I'm hard."

"You believe this is the only place for you." It was as if he'd heard her thoughts. "You are wrong in that. You would find softer service in the household of some merchant. Or would you sooner be a courtesan, and have songs sung of your beauty? Speak the word, and we will send you to the Black Pearl or the Daughter of the Dusk. You will sleep on rose petals and wear silken skirts that rustle when you walk, and great lords will beggar themselves for your maiden's blood. Or if it is marriage and children you desire, tell me, and we shall find a husband for you. Some honest apprentice boy, a rich old man, a seafarer, whatever you desire."

She wanted none of that. Wordless, she shook her head.

"Is it Westeros you dream of, child? Luco Prestayn's *Lady Bright* leaves upon the morrow, for Gulltown, Duskendale, King's Landing, and Tyrosh. Shall we find you passage on her?"

"I only just *came* from Westeros." Sometimes it seemed a thousand years since she had fled King's Landing, and sometimes it seemed like only yesterday, but she knew she could not go back. "I'll go if you don't want me, but I won't go *there.*"

"My wants do not matter," said the kindly man. "It may be that the Many-Faced God has led you here to be His instrument, but when I look at you I see a child . . . and worse, a girl child. Many have served Him of Many Faces through the centuries, but only a few of His servants have been women. Women bring life into the world. We bring the gift of death. No one can do both."

He is trying to scare me away, Arya thought, *the way he did with the worm.* "I don't care about that."

"You should. Stay, and the Many-Faced God will take your ears, your nose, your tongue. He will take your sad grey eyes that have seen so much. He will take your hands, your feet, your arms and legs, your private parts. He will take your hopes and dreams, your loves and hates. Those who enter His service must give up all that makes them who they are. Can you do that?" He cupped her chin and gazed deep into her eyes, so deep it made her shiver. "No," he said, "I do not think you can."

Arya knocked his hand away. "I could if I *wanted* to."

"So says Arya of House Stark, eater of grave worms."

"I can give up *anything* I want!"

He gestured at her treasures. "Then start with these."

That night after supper, Arya went back to her cell and took off her robe and whispered her names, but sleep refused to take her. She tossed on her mattress stuffed with rags, gnawing on her lip. She could feel the hole inside her where her heart had been.

In the black of night she rose again, donned the clothes she'd worn from Westeros, and buckled on her swordbelt. Needle hung from one hip, her dagger from the other. With her floppy hat on her head, her fingerless gloves tucked into her belt, and her silver fork in one hand, she went stealing up the steps. *There is no place here for Arya of House Stark,* she was thinking. Arya's place was Winterfell, only Winterfell was gone. *When the snows fall and the white winds blow, the lone wolf dies, but the pack survives.* She had no pack, though. They had killed her pack, Ser Ilyn and Ser Meryn and the queen, and when she tried to make a new one all of them ran off, Hot Pie and Gendry and Yoren and Lommy Greenhands, even Harwin, who had been her father's man. She shoved through the doors, out into the night.

It was the first time she had been outside since entering the temple. The sky was overcast, and fog covered the ground like a frayed grey blanket. Off to her right she heard paddling from the canal. *Braavos, the Secret City,* she thought. The name seemed very apt. She crept down the steep steps to the covered dock, the mists swirling round her feet. It was so foggy she could not see the water, but she heard it lapping softly at stone pilings. In the distance, a light glowed through the gloom: the nightfire at the temple of the red priests, she thought.

At the water's edge she stopped, the silver fork in hand. It was real silver, solid through and through. *It's not my fork. It was Salty that he gave it to.* She tossed it underhand, heard the soft *plop* as it sank below the water.

Her floppy hat went next, then the gloves. They were Salty's too. She emptied her pouch into her palm; five silver stags, nine copper stars, some pennies and halfpennies and groats. She scattered them across the water. Next her boots. They made the loudest splashes. Her dagger followed, the one she'd gotten off the archer who had begged the Hound for mercy. Her swordbelt went into the canal. Her cloak, tunic, breeches, smallclothes, all of it. All but Needle.

She stood on the end of the dock, pale and goosefleshed and shivering in the fog. In her hand, Needle seemed to whisper to her. *Stick them with the pointy end,* it said, and, *don't tell Sansa!* Mikken's mark was on the blade. *It's just a sword.* If she needed a sword, there were a hundred under the temple. Needle was too small to be a *proper* sword, it was hardly more than a toy. She'd been a stupid little girl when Jon had it made for her. "It's just a sword," she said, aloud this time . . .

. . . but it wasn't.

Needle was Robb and Bran and Rickon, her mother and her father, even Sansa. Needle was Winterfell's grey walls, and the laughter of its people. Needle was the summer snows, Old Nan's stories, the heart tree with its red leaves and scary face, the warm earthy smell of the glass gardens, the sound of the north wind rattling the shutters of her room. Needle was Jon Snow's smile. *He used to mess my hair and call me "little sister,"* she remembered, and suddenly there were tears in her eyes.

Polliver had stolen the sword from her when the Mountain's men took her captive, but when she and the Hound walked into the inn at the crossroads, there it was. *The gods wanted me to have it.* Not the Seven, nor Him of Many Faces, but her father's gods, the old gods of the north. *The Many-Faced God can have the rest,* she thought, *but he can't have this.*

She padded up the steps as naked as her name day, clutching Needle. Halfway up, one of the stones rocked beneath her feet. Arya knelt and dug around its edges with her fingers. It would not move at first, but she persisted, picking at the crumbling mortar with her nails. Finally, the stone shifted. She grunted and got both hands in and pulled. A crack opened before her.

"You'll be safe here," she told Needle. "No one will know where you are but me." She pushed the sword and sheath behind the step, then shoved the stone back into place, so it looked like all the other stones. As she climbed back to the temple, she counted steps, so she would know where to find the sword again. One day she might have need of it. "One day," she whispered to herself.

She never told the kindly man what she had done, yet he knew. The next night he came to her cell after supper. "Child," he said, "come sit with me. I have a tale to tell you."

"What kind of tale?" she asked, wary.

"The tale of our beginnings. If you would be one of us, you had best know who we are and how we came to be. Men may whisper of the Faceless Men of Braavos, but we are older than the Secret City. Before the Titan rose, before the Unmasking of Uthero, before the Founding, we were. We have flowered in Braavos amongst these northern fogs, but we first took root in Valyria, amongst the wretched slaves who toiled in the deep mines beneath the Fourteen Flames that lit the Freehold's nights of old. Most mines are dank and chilly places, cut from cold dead stone, but the Fourteen Flames were living mountains with veins of molten rock and hearts of fire. So the mines of old Valyria were always hot, and they grew hotter as the shafts were driven deeper, ever deeper. The slaves toiled in an oven. The rocks around them were too hot to touch. The air stank of brimstone and would sear their lungs as they breathed it. The soles of their feet would burn and blister, even through the thickest sandals. Sometimes, when they broke through a wall in search of gold, they would find steam instead, or boiling water, or molten rock. Certain shafts were cut so low that the slaves could not stand upright, but had to crawl or bend. And there were wyrms in that red darkness too."

"Earthworms?" she asked, frowning.

"Firewyrms. Some say they are akin to dragons, for wyrms breathe fire too. Instead of soaring through the sky, they bore through stone and soil. If the old tales can be believed, there were wyrms amongst the Fourteen Flames even before the dragons came. The young ones are no larger than that skinny arm of yours, but they can grow to monstrous size and have no love for men."

"Did they kill the slaves?"

"Burnt and blackened corpses were oft found in shafts where the rocks were cracked or full of holes. Yet still the mines drove deeper. Slaves perished by the score, but their masters did not care. Red gold and yellow gold and silver were reckoned to be more precious than the lives of slaves, for slaves were cheap in the old Freehold. During war, the Valyrians took them by the thousands. In times of peace they bred them, though only the worst were sent down to die in the red darkness."

"Didn't the slaves rise up and fight?"

"Some did," he said. "Revolts were common in the mines, but few accomplished much. The dragonlords of the old Freehold were strong in sorcery, and lesser men defied them at their peril. The first Faceless Man was one who did."

"Who was he?" Arya blurted, before she stopped to think.

"No one," he answered. "Some say he was a slave himself. Others insist he was a freeholder's son, born of noble stock. Some will even tell you he was an overseer who took pity on his charges. The truth is, no one knows. Whoever he was, he moved amongst the slaves and would hear them at their prayers. Men of a hundred different nations labored in the mines, and each prayed to his own god in his own tongue, yet all were praying for the same thing. It was release they asked for, an end to pain. A small thing, and simple. Yet their gods made no answer, and their suffering went on. *Are their gods all deaf?* he wondered . . . until a realization came upon him, one night in the red darkness.

"All gods have their instruments, men and women who serve them and help to work their will on earth. The slaves were not crying out to a hundred different gods, as it seemed, but to one god with a hundred different faces . . . and *he* was that god's instrument. That very night he chose the most wretched of the slaves, the one who had prayed most earnestly for release, and freed him from his bondage. The first gift had been given."

Arya drew back from him. "He killed the *slave*?" That did not sound right. "He should have killed the *masters*!"

"He would bring the gift to them as well . . . but that is

a tale for another day, one best shared with no one." He cocked his head. "And who are you, child?"

"No one."

"A lie."

"How do you *know*? Is it magic?"

"A man does not need to be a wizard to know truth from falsehood, not if he has eyes. You need only learn to read a face. Look at the eyes. The mouth. The muscles here, at the corners of the jaw, and here, where the neck joins the shoulders." He touched her lightly with two fingers. "Some liars blink. Some stare. Some look away. Some lick their lips. Many cover their mouths just before they tell a lie, as if to hide their deceit. Other signs may be more subtle, but they are always there. A false smile and a true one may look alike, but they are as different as dusk from dawn. Can you tell dusk from dawn?"

Arya nodded, though she was not certain that she could.

"Then you can learn to see a lie . . . and once you do, no secret will be safe from you."

"Teach me." She would be no one if that was what it took. No one had no holes inside her.

"*She* will teach you," said the kindly man as the waif appeared outside her door. "Starting with the tongue of Braavos. What use are you if you cannot speak or understand? And you shall teach her your own tongue. The two of you shall learn together, each from the other. Will you do this?"

"Yes," she said, and from that moment she was a novice in the House of Black and White. Her servant's garb was taken away, and she was given a robe to wear, a robe of black and white as buttery soft as the old red blanket she'd once had at Winterfell. Beneath it she wore smallclothes of fine white linen, and a black undertunic that hung down past her knees.

Thereafter she and the waif spent their time together touching things and pointing, as each tried to teach the other a few words of her own tongue. Simple words at first, cup and candle and shoe; then harder words; then sentences. Once Syrio Forel used to make Arya stand on one leg until she was trembling. Later he sent her chasing after cats. She had danced the water dance on the limbs of trees, a stick sword in her hand. Those things had all been hard, but this was harder.

Even sewing was more fun than tongues, she told herself, after a night when she had forgotten half the words she thought she knew, and pronounced the other half so badly that the waif had laughed at her. *My sentences are as crooked as my stitches used to be.* If the girl had not been so small and starved, Arya would have smashed her stupid face. Instead she gnawed her lip. *Too stupid to learn and too stupid to give up.*

The Common Tongue came to the waif more quickly. One day at supper she turned to Arya, and asked, "Who are you?"

"No one," Arya answered, in Braavosi.

"You lie," said the waif. "You must lie gooder."

Arya laughed. "Gooder? You mean *better,* stupid."

"Better stupid. I will show you."

The next day they began the lying game, asking questions of one another, taking turns. Sometimes they would answer truly, sometimes they would lie. The questioner had to try and tell what was true and what was false. The waif always seemed to know. Arya had to guess. Most of the time she guessed wrong.

"How many years have you?" the waif asked her once, in the Common Tongue. "Ten," said Arya, and raised ten fingers. She *thought* she was still ten, though it was hard to know for certain. The Braavosi counted days differently than they did in Westeros. For all she knew her name day had come and gone.

The waif nodded. Arya nodded back, and in her best Braavosi said, "How many years have *you*?"

The waif showed ten fingers. Then ten again, and yet again. Then six. Her face remained as smooth as still water. *She can't be six-and-thirty,* Arya thought. *She's a little girl.* "You're lying," she said. The waif shook her head and showed her once again: ten and ten and ten and six. She said the words for six-and-thirty, and made Arya say them too.

The next day she told the kindly man what the waif had claimed. "She did not lie," the priest said, chuckling. "The one you call *waif* is a woman grown who has spent her life serving Him of Many Faces. She gave Him all she was, all she ever might have been, all the lives that were within her."

Arya bit her lip. "Will I be like her?"

"No," he said, "not unless you wish it. It is the poisons that have made her as you see her."

Poisons. She understood then. Every evening after prayer the waif emptied a stone flagon into the waters of the black pool.

The waif and kindly man were not the only servants of the Many-Faced God. From time to time others would visit the House of Black and White. The fat fellow had fierce black eyes, a hook nose, and a wide mouth full of yellow teeth. The stern face never smiled; his eyes were pale, his lips full and dark. The handsome man had a beard of a different color every time she saw him, and a different nose, but he was never less than comely. Those three came most often, but there were others: the squinter, the lordling, the starved man. One time the fat fellow and the squinter came together. Umma sent Arya to pour for them. "When you are not pouring, you must stand as still as if you had been carved of stone," the kindly man told her. "Can you do that?"

"Yes." *Before you can learn to move you must learn to be still,* Syrio Forel had taught her long ago at King's Landing, and she had. She had served as Roose Bolton's cupbearer at Harrenhal, and he would flay you if you spilled his wine.

"Good," the kindly man said. "It would be best if you were blind and deaf as well. You may hear things, but you must let them pass in one ear and out the other. Do not listen."

Arya heard much and more that night, but almost all of it was in the tongue of Braavos, and she hardly understood one word in ten. *Still as stone,* she told herself. The hardest part was struggling not to yawn. Before the night was done, her wits were wandering. Standing there with the flagon in her hands, she dreamed she was a wolf, running free through a moonlit forest with a great pack howling at her heels.

"Are the other men all priests?" she asked the kindly man the next morning. "Were those their real faces?"

"What do you think, child?"

She thought *no.* "Is Jaqen H'ghar a priest too? Do you know if Jaqen will be coming back to Braavos?"

"Who?" he said, all innocence.

"Jaqen *H'ghar.* He gave me the iron coin."

"I know no one by this name, child."

"I asked him how he changed his face, and he said it was no harder than taking a new name, if you knew the way."

"Did he?"

"Will you show me how to change my face?"

"If you wish." He cupped her chin in his hand and turned her head. "Puff up your cheeks and stick out your tongue."

Arya puffed up her cheeks and stuck out her tongue.

"There. Your face is changed."

"That's not how I meant. Jaqen used magic."

"All sorcery comes at a cost, child. Years of prayer and sacrifice and study are required to work a proper glamor."

"Years?" she said, dismayed.

"If it were easy all men would do it. You must walk before you run. Why use a spell, where mummer's tricks will serve?"

"I don't know any mummer's tricks either."

"Then practice making faces. Beneath your skin are muscles. Learn to use them. It is your face. Your cheeks, your lips, your ears. Smiles and scowls should not come upon you like sudden squalls. A smile should be a servant, and come only when you call it. Learn to *rule* your face."

"Show me how."

"Puff up your cheeks." She did. "Lift your eyebrows. No, higher." She did that too. "Good. See how long you can hold that. It will not be long. Try it again on the morrow. You will find a Myrish mirror in the vaults. Train before it for an hour every day. Eyes, nostrils, cheeks, ears, lips, learn to rule them all." He cupped her chin. "Who are you?"

"No one."

"A lie. A sad little lie, child."

She found the Myrish mirror the next day, and every morn and every night she sat before it with a candle on each side of her, making faces. *Rule your face,* she told herself, *and you can lie.*

Soon thereafter the kindly man commanded her to help the other acolytes prepare the corpses. The work was not near as hard as scrubbing steps for Weese. Sometimes if the corpse was big or fat she would struggle with the weight, but most of the dead were old dry bones in wrinkled skins. Arya would look at them as she washed them, wondering what brought them to the black pool. She remembered a tale she had heard from Old Nan, about how sometimes during a long winter men who'd lived beyond their years would announce that they were going hunting. *And their daughters would weep and their sons would turn their faces to the fire,* she could hear Old Nan saying, *but no one would stop them, or ask what game they meant to hunt, with the snows so deep and the cold wind howling.* She wondered what the old Braavosi told their sons and daughters, before they set off for the House of Black and White.

The moon turned and turned again, though Arya never saw it. She served, washed the dead, made faces at the mirrors, learned the Braavosi tongue, and tried to remember that she was no one.

One day the kindly man sent for her. "Your accent is a horror," he said, "but you have enough words to make your wants understood after a fashion. It is time that you left us for a while. The only way you will ever truly master our tongue is if you speak it every day from dawn to dusk. You must go."

"When?" she asked him. "Where?"

"Now," he answered. "Beyond these walls you will find the hundred isles of Braavos in the sea. You have been taught the words for mussels, cockles, and clams, have you not?"

"Yes." She repeated them, in her best Braavosi.

Her best Braavosi made him smile. "It will serve. Along the wharves below the Drowned Town you will find a fishmonger named Brusco, a good man with a bad back.

He has need of a girl to push his barrow and sell his cockles, clams, and mussels to the sailors off the ships. You shall be that girl. Do you understand?"

"Yes."

"And when Brusco asks, who are you?"

"No one."

"No. That will not serve, outside this House."

She hesitated. "I could be Salty, from Saltpans."

"Salty is known to Ternesio Terys and the men of the *Titan's Daughter*. You are marked by the way you speak, so you must be some girl of Westeros . . . but a different girl, I think."

She bit her lip. "Could I be Cat?"

"Cat." He considered. "Yes. Braavos is full of cats. One more will not be noticed. You are Cat, an orphan of . . ."

"King's Landing." She had visited White Harbor with her father twice, but she knew King's Landing better.

"Just so. Your father was oarmaster on a galley. When your mother died, he took you off to sea with him. Then he died as well, and his captain had no use for you, so he put you off the ship in Braavos. And what was the name of the ship?"

"Nymeria," she said at once.

That night she left the House of Black and White. A long iron knife rode on her right hip, hidden by her cloak, a patched and faded thing of the sort an orphan might wear. Her shoes pinched her toes and her tunic was so threadbare that the wind cut right through it. But Braavos lay before her. The night air smelled of smoke and salt and fish. The canals were crooked, the alleys crookeder. Men gave her curious looks as she went past, and beggar children called out words she could not understand. Before long she was completely lost.

"Ser Gregor," she chanted, as she crossed a stone

bridge supported by four arches. From the center of its span she could see the masts of ships in the Ragman's Harbor. "Dunsen, Raff the Sweetling, Ser Ilyn, Ser Meryn, Queen Cersei." Rain began to fall. Arya turned her face up to let the raindrops wash her cheeks, so happy she could dance. *"Valar morghulis,"* she said, *"valar morghulis, valar morghulis."*

ALAYNE

As the rising sun came streaming through the
windows, Alayne sat up in bed and stretched.
Gretchel heard her stir and rose at once to fetch
her bedrobe. The rooms had grown chilly during the night.
It will be worse when winter has us in its grip, she
thought. *Winter will make this place as cold as any tomb.*
Alayne slipped into the robe and belted it about her waist.
"The fire's almost out," she observed. "Put another log on,
if you would."

"As my lady wishes," the old woman said.

Alayne's apartments in the Maiden's Tower were larger
and more lavish than the little bedchamber where she'd
been kept when Lady Lysa was alive. She had a dressing
room and a privy of her own now, and a balcony of carved
white stone that looked off across the Vale. While Gretchel
was tending to the fire, Alayne padded barefoot across the

room and slipped outside. The stone was cold beneath her feet, and the wind was blowing fiercely, as it always did up here, but the view made her forget all that for half a heart-beat. Maiden's was the easternmost of the Eyrie's seven slender towers, so she had the Vale before her, its forests and rivers and fields all hazy in the morning light. The way the sun was hitting the mountains made them look like solid gold.

So lovely. The snow-clad summit of the Giant's Lance loomed above her, an immensity of stone and ice that dwarfed the castle perched upon its shoulder. Icicles twenty feet long draped the lip of the precipice where Alyssa's Tears fell in summer. A falcon soared above the frozen waterfall, blue wings spread wide against the morning sky. *Would that I had wings as well.*

She rested her hands on the carved stone balustrade and made herself peer over the edge. She could see Sky six hundred feet below, and the stone steps carved into the mountain, the winding way that led past Snow and Stone all the way down to the valley floor. She could see the tow-ers and keeps of the Gates of the Moon, as small as a child's toys. Around the walls the hosts of Lords Declarant were stirring, emerging from their tents like ants from an anthill. *If only they were truly ants,* she thought, *we could step on them and crush them.*

Young Lord Hunter and his levies had joined the others two days past. Nestor Royce had closed the Gates against them, but he had fewer than three hundred men in his gar-rison. Each of the Lords Declarant had brought a thou-sand, and there were six of them. Alayne knew their names as well as her own. Benedar Belmore, Lord of Strongsong. Symond Templeton, the Knight of Ninestars. Horton Redfort, Lord of Redfort. Anya Waynwood, Lady of Ironoaks. Gilwood Hunter, called Young Lord Hunter by all and sundry, Lord of Longbow Hall. And Yohn Royce, mightiest of them all, the redoubtable Bronze Yohn, Lord of Runestone, Nestor's cousin and the chief of the senior branch of House Royce. The six had gathered at Runestone after Lysa Arryn's fall, and there made a pact together, vowing to defend Lord Robert, the Vale, and one another. Their declaration made no mention of the Lord Protector, but spoke of "misrule" that must be ended, and of "false friends and evil counselors" as well.

A cold gust of wind blew up her legs. She went inside to choose a gown to break her fast in. Petyr had given her his late wife's wardrobe, a wealth of silks, satins, velvets, and furs far beyond anything she had ever dreamed, though the great bulk of it was far too large for her; Lady Lysa had grown very stout during her long succession of pregnancies, stillbirths, and miscarriages. A few of the oldest gowns had been made for young Lysa Tully of Riverrun, however, and others Gretchel had been able to alter to fit Alayne, who was almost as long of leg at three-and-ten as her aunt had been at twenty.

This morning her eye was caught by a parti-colored gown of Tully red and blue, lined with vair. Gretchel helped her slide her arms into the belled sleeves and laced her back, then brushed and pinned her hair. Alayne had darkened it again last night before she went to bed. The wash her aunt had given her changed her own rich auburn into Alayne's burnt brown, but it was seldom long before the red began creeping back at the roots. *And what must I do when the dye runs out?* The wash had come from Tyrosh, across the narrow sea.

As she went down to break her fast, Alayne was struck again by the stillness of the Eyrie. There was no quieter castle in all the Seven Kingdoms. The servants here were few and old and kept their voices down so as not to excite the young lord. There were no horses on the mountain, no hounds to bark and growl, no knights training in the yard. Even the footsteps of the guards seemed strangely muffled as they walked the pale stone halls. She could hear the wind moaning and sighing round the towers, but that was all. When she had first come to Eyrie, there had been the murmur of Alyssa's Tears as well, but the waterfall was frozen now. Gretchel said it would stay silent till the spring.

She found Lord Robert alone in the Morning Hall above the kitchens, pushing a wooden spoon listlessly through a big bowl of porridge and honey. "I wanted eggs," he complained when he saw her. "I wanted *three* eggs boiled soft, and some back bacon."

They had no eggs, no more than they had bacon. The Eyrie's granaries held sufficient oats and corn and barley to feed them for a year, but they depended on a bastard girl named Mya Stone to bring fresh foodstuffs up from the valley floor. With the Lords Declarant encamped at the foot of the mountain there was no way for Mya to get through. Lord Belmore, first of the six to reach the Gates, had sent a raven to tell Littlefinger that no more food would go up to the Eyrie until he sent Lord Robert down. It was not quite a siege, not as yet, but it was the next best thing.

"You can have eggs when Mya comes, as many as you like," Alayne promised the little lordling. "She'll bring eggs and butter and melons, all sorts of tasty things."

The boy was unappeased. "I wanted eggs *today.*"

"Sweetrobin, there are no eggs, you know that. Please, eat your porridge, it's very nice." She ate a spoonful of her own.

Robert pushed his spoon across the bowl and back, but never brought it to his lips. "I am not hungry," he decided.

"I want to go back to bed. I never slept last night. I heard *singing*. Maester Colemon gave me dreamwine but I could still hear it."

Alayne put down her spoon. "If there had been singing, I should have heard it too. You had a bad dream, that's all."

"No, it *wasn't* a dream." Tears filled his eyes. "Marillion was singing again. Your father says he's dead, but he *isn't*."

"He is." It frightened her to hear him talk like this. *Bad enough that he is small and sickly, what if he is mad as well?* "Sweetrobin, he *is*. Marillion loved your lady mother too much and could not live with what he'd done to her, so he walked into the sky." Alayne had not seen the body, no more than Robert had, but she did not doubt the fact of the singer's death. "He's gone, truly."

"But I hear him every night. Even when I close the shutters and put a *pillow* on my head. Your father should have cut his tongue out. I *told* him to, but he wouldn't."

He needed a tongue to confess. "Be a good boy and eat your porridge," Alayne pleaded. "Please? For me?"

"I don't want porridge." Robert flung his spoon across the hall. It bounced off a hanging tapestry, and left a smear of porridge upon a white silk moon. "The *lord* wants *eggs*!"

"The lord shall eat porridge and be thankful for it," said Petyr's voice, behind them.

Alayne turned, and saw him in the doorway arch with Maester Colemon at his side. "You should heed the Lord Protector, my lord," the maester said. "Your lord's bannermen are coming up the mountain to pay you homage, so you will need all your strength."

Robert rubbed at his left eye with a knuckle. "Send them away. I don't *want* them. If they come, I'll make them fly."

"You tempt me sorely, my lord, but I fear I promised them safe conduct," said Petyr. "In any case, it is too late to turn them back. By now they may have climbed as far as Stone."

"Why won't they leave us be?" wailed Alayne. "We never did them any harm. What do they *want* of us?"

"Just Lord Robert. Him, and the Vale." Petyr smiled. "There will be eight of them. Lord Nestor is showing them up, and they have Lyn Corbray with them. Ser Lyn is not the sort of man to stay away when blood is in the offing."

His words did little to soothe her fears. Lyn Corbray had slain almost as many men in duels as he had in battle. He had won his spurs during Robert's Rebellion, she knew, fighting first against Lord Jon Arryn at the gates of Gulltown, and later beneath his banners on the Trident, where he had cut down Prince Lewyn of Dorne, a white knight of the Kingsguard. Petyr said that Prince Lewyn had been sorely wounded by the time the tide of battle swept him to his final dance with Lady Forlorn, but added, "That's not a point you'll want to raise with Corbray, though. Those who do are soon given the chance to ask Martell himself the truth of it, down in the halls of hell." If even half of what she had heard from Lord Robert's guards was true, Lyn Corbray was more dangerous than all six of the Lords Declarant put together. "Why is *he* coming?" she asked. "I thought the Corbrays were for you."

"Lord Lyonel Corbray is well disposed toward my rule," said Petyr, "but his brother goes his own way. On the Trident, when their father fell wounded, it was Lyn who snatched up Lady Forlorn and slew the man who'd cut him down. Whilst Lyonel was carrying the old man back to the maesters in the rear, Lyn led his charge against the Dornishmen threatening Robert's left, broke their lines to pieces, and slew Lewyn Martell. So when old Lord

Corbray died, he bestowed the Lady upon his younger son. Lyonel got his lands, his title, his castle, and all his coin, yet still feels he was cheated of his birthright, whilst Ser Lyn . . . well, he loves Lyonel as much as he loves me. He wanted Lysa's hand for himself."

"I don't like Ser Lyn," Robert insisted. "I won't have him here. You send him back down. I never said that he could come. Not *here*. The Eyrie is im*preg*nable, Mother said."

"Your mother is dead, my lord. Until your sixteenth name day, *I* rule the Eyrie." Petyr turned to the stoop-backed serving woman hovering near the kitchen steps. "Mela, fetch his lordship a new spoon. He wants to eat his porridge."

"I do *not*! Let my porridge *fly*!" This time Robert flung the bowl, porridge and honey and all. Petyr Baelish ducked aside nimbly, but Maester Colemon was not so quick. The wooden bowl caught him square in the chest, and its contents exploded upward over his face and shoulders. He yelped in a most unmaesterlike fashion, while Alayne turned to soothe the little lordling, but too late. The fit was on him. A pitcher of milk went flying as his hand caught it, flailing. When he tried to rise he knocked his chair backwards and fell on top of it. One foot caught Alayne in the belly, so hard it knocked the wind from her. "Oh, gods be good," she heard Petyr say, disgusted.

Globs of porridge dotted Maester Colemon's face and hair as he knelt over his charge, murmuring soothing words. One gobbet crept slowly down his right cheek, like a lumpy grey-brown tear. *It is not so bad a spell as the last one,* Alayne thought, trying to be hopeful. By the time the shaking stopped, two guards in sky-blue cloaks and silvery mail shirts had come at Petyr's summons. "Take him back to bed and leech him," the Lord Protector said, and the taller guardsman scooped the boy up in his arms. *I could carry him myself,* Alayne thought. *He is no heavier than a doll.*

Colemon lingered a moment before following. "My lord, this parley might best be left for another day. His lordship's spells have grown worse since Lady Lysa's death. More frequent and more violent. I bleed the child as often as I dare, and mix him dreamwine and milk of the poppy to help him sleep, but . . ."

"He sleeps twelve hours a day," Petyr said. "I require him awake from time to time."

The maester combed his fingers through his hair, dribbling globs of porridge on the floor. "Lady Lysa would give his lordship her breast whenever he grew overwrought. Archmaester Ebrose claims that mother's milk has many heathful properties."

"Is that your counsel, maester? That we find a wet nurse for the Lord of the Eyrie and Defender of the Vale? When shall we wean him, on his wedding day? That way he can move directly from his nurse's nipples to his wife's." Lord Petyr's laugh made it plain what he thought of that. "No, I think not. I suggest you find another way. The boy is fond of sweets, is he not?"

"Sweets?" said Colemon.

"Sweets. Cakes and pies, jams and jellies, honey on the comb. Perhaps a pinch of sweetsleep in his milk, have you tried that? Just a pinch, to calm him and stop his wretched shaking."

"A pinch?" The apple in the maester's throat moved up and down as he swallowed. "One small pinch . . . perhaps, perhaps. Not too much, and not too often, yes, I might try . . ."

"A pinch," Lord Petyr said, "before you bring him forth to meet the lords."

"As you command, my lord." The maester hurried out, his chain clinking softly with every step.

"Father," Alayne asked when he was gone, "will you have a bowl of porridge to break your fast?"

"I despise porridge." He looked at her with Little-finger's eyes. "I'd sooner break my fast with a kiss."

A true daughter would not refuse her sire a kiss, so Alayne went to him and kissed him, a quick dry peck upon the cheek, and just as quickly stepped away.

"How . . . dutiful." Littlefinger smiled with his mouth, but not his eyes. "Well, I have other duties for you, as it happens. Tell the cook to mull some red wine with honey and raisins. Our guests will be cold and thirsty after their long climb. You are to meet them when they arrive, and offer them refreshment. Wine, bread, and cheese. What sort of cheese is left to us?"

"The sharp white and the stinky blue."

"The white. And you'd best change as well."

Alayne looked down at her dress, the deep blue and rich dark red of Riverrun. "Is it too—"

"It is too *Tully.* The Lords Declarant will not be pleased by the sight of my bastard daughter prancing about in my dead wife's clothes. Choose something else. Need I remind you to avoid sky blue and cream?"

"No." Sky blue and cream were the colors of House Arryn. "Eight, you said . . . Bronze Yohn is one of them?"

"The only one who matters."

"Bronze Yohn *knows* me," she reminded him. "He was a guest at Winterfell when his son rode north to take the black." She had fallen wildly in love with Ser Waymar, she remembered dimly, but that was a lifetime ago, when she was a stupid little girl. "And that was not the only time. Lord Royce saw . . . he saw Sansa Stark again at King's Landing, during the Hand's tourney."

Petyr put a finger under her chin. "That Royce glimpsed this pretty face I do not doubt, but it was one face in a thousand. A man fighting in a tourney has more to concern him than some child in the crowd. And at Winterfell, Sansa was a little girl with auburn hair. My daughter is a maiden tall and fair, and her hair is chestnut. Men see what they expect to see, Alayne." He kissed her nose. "Have Maddy lay a fire in the solar. I shall receive our Lords Declarant there."

"Not the High Hall?"

"No. Gods forbid they glimpse me near the high seat of the Arryns, they might think that I mean to sit in it. Cheeks born so low as mine must never aspire to such lofty cushions."

"The solar." She should have stopped with that, but the words came tumbling out of her. "If you gave them Robert . . ."

". . . and the Vale?"

"They *have* the Vale."

"Oh, much of it, that's true. Not all, however. I am well loved in Gulltown, and have some lordly friends of mine own as well. Grafton, Lynderly, Lyonel Corbray . . . though I'll grant you, they are no match for the Lords Declarant. Still, where would you have us go, Alayne? Back to my mighty stronghold on the Fingers?"

She had thought about that. "Joffrey gave you Harrenhal. You are lord in your own right there."

"By title. I needed a great seat to marry Lysa, and the Lannisters were not about to grant me Casterly Rock."

"Yes, but the castle is *yours*."

"Ah, and what a castle it is. Cavernous halls and ruined towers, ghosts and draughts, ruinous to heat, impossible to garrison . . . and there's that small matter of a curse."

"Curses are only in songs and stories."

That seemed to amuse him. "Has someone made a song about Gregor Clegane dying of a poisoned spear thrust? Or about the sellsword before him, whose limbs Ser Gregor removed a joint at a time? That one took the castle from Ser Amory Lorch, who received it from Lord Tywin. A bear killed one, your dwarf the other. Lady Whent's died as well, I hear. Lothstons, Strongs, Harroways, . . . Harrenhal has withered every hand to touch it."

"Then give it to Lord Frey."

Petyr laughed. "Perhaps I shall. Or better still, to our sweet Cersei. Though I should not speak harshly of her, she is sending me some splendid tapestries. Isn't that kind of her?"

The mention of the queen's name made her stiffen. "She's *not* kind. She scares me. If she should learn where I am—"

"—I might have to remove her from the game sooner than I'd planned. Provided she does not remove herself first." Petyr teased her with a little smile. "In the game of thrones, even the humblest pieces can have wills of their own. Sometimes they refuse to make the moves you've planned for them. Mark that well, Alayne. It's a lesson that Cersei Lannister still has yet to learn. Now, don't you have some duties to perform?"

She did indeed. She saw to the mulling of the wine first, found a suitable wheel of sharp white cheese, and commanded the cook to bake bread enough for twenty, in case the Lords Declarant brought more men than expected. *Once they eat our bread and salt they are our guests and cannot harm us.* The Freys had broken all the laws of hospitality when they'd murdered her lady mother and her brother at the Twins, but she could not believe that a lord as noble as Yohn Royce would ever stoop to do the same.

The solar next. Its floor was covered by a Myrish carpet,

so there was no need to lay down rushes. Alayne asked two serving men to erect the trestle table and bring up eight of the heavy oak-and-leather chairs. For a feast she would have placed one at the head of the table, one at the foot, and three along each side, but this was no feast. She had the men arrange six chairs on one side of the table, two on the other. By now the Lords Declarant might have climbed as far as Snow. It took most of a day to make the climb, even on muleback. Afoot, most men took several days.

It might be that the lords would talk late into the night. They would need fresh candles. After Maddy laid the fire, she sent her down to find the scented beeswax candles Lord Waxley had given Lady Lysa when he sought to win her hand. Then she visited the kitchens once again, to make certain of the wine and bread. All seemed well in hand, and there was still time enough for her to bathe and wash her hair and change.

There was a gown of purple silk that gave her pause, and another of dark blue velvet slashed with silver that would have woken all the color in her eyes, but in the end she remembered that Alayne was after all a bastard, and must not presume to dress above her station. The dress she picked was lambswool, dark brown and simply cut, with leaves and vines embroidered around the bodice, sleeves, and hem in golden thread. It was modest and becoming, though scarce richer than something a serving girl might wear. Petyr had given her all of Lady Lysa's jewels as well, and she tried on several necklaces, but they all seemed ostentatious. In the end she chose a simple velvet ribbon in autumn gold. When Gretchel fetched her Lysa's silvered looking glass, the color seemed just perfect with Alayne's mass of dark brown hair. *Lord Royce will never know me,* she thought. *Why, I hardly know myself.*

Feeling near as bold as Petyr Baelish, Alayne Stone donned her smile and went down to meet their guests.

The Eyrie was the only castle in the Seven Kingdoms where the main entrance was underneath the dungeons. Steep stone steps crept up the mountainside past the way-castles Stone and Snow, but they came to an end at Sky. The final six hundred feet of the ascent were vertical, forcing would-be visitors to dismount their mules and make a choice. They could ride the swaying wooden basket that was used to lift supplies, or clamber up a rocky chimney using handholds carved into the rock.

Lord Redfort and Lady Waynwood, the most elderly of the Lords Declarant, chose to be drawn up by the winch, after which the basket was lowered once more for fat Lord Belmore. The other lords made the climb. Alayne met them in the Crescent Chamber beside a warming fire, where she welcomed them in Lord Robert's name and served them bread and cheese and cups of hot mulled wine in silver cups.

Petyr had given her a roll of arms to study, so she knew their heraldry if not their faces. The red castle was Redfort, plainly; a short man with a neat grey beard and mild eyes. Lady Anya was the only woman amongst the Lords Declarant, and wore a deep green mantle with the broken wheel of Waynwood picked out in beads of jet. Six silver bells on purple, that was Belmore, pear-bellied and round of shoulder. His beard was a ginger-grey horror sprouting from a multiplicity of chins. Symond Templeton's, by contrast, was black and sharply pointed. A beak of a nose and icy blue eyes made the Knight of Ninestars look like some elegant bird of prey. His doublet displayed nine black stars within a golden saltire. Young Lord Hunter's ermine cloak confused her till she spied the brooch that pinned it, five silver arrows fanned. Alayne would have put his age closer to fifty than to forty. His father had ruled at Longbow Hall for nigh on sixty years, only to die so abruptly that some whispered the new lord had hastened his inheritance. Hunter's cheeks and nose were red as apples, which bespoke a certain fondness for the grape. She made certain to fill his cup as often as he emptied it.

The youngest man in the party had three ravens on his chest, each clutching a blood-red heart in its talons. His brown hair was shoulder length; one stray lock curled down across his forehead. *Ser Lyn Corbray,* Alayne thought, with a wary glance at his hard mouth and restless eyes.

Last of all came the Royces, Lord Nestor and Bronze Yohn. The Lord of Runestone stood as tall as the Hound. Though his hair was grey and his face lined, Lord Yohn still looked as though he could break most younger men like twigs in those huge gnarled hands. His seamed and solemn face brought back all of Sansa's memories of his time at Winterfell. She remembered him at table, speaking quietly with her mother. She heard his voice booming off the walls when he rode back from a hunt with a buck behind his saddle. She could see him in the yard, a practice sword in hand, hammering her father to the ground and turning to defeat Ser Rodrik as well. *He will know me. How could he not?* She considered throwing herself at his feet to beg for his protection. *He never fought for Robb, why should he fight for me? The war is finished and Winterfell is fallen.* "Lord Royce," she asked timidly, "will you have a cup of wine, to take the chill off?"

Bronze Yohn had slate-grey eyes, half-hidden beneath the bushiest eyebrows she had ever seen. They crinkled when he looked down at her. "Do I know you, girl?"

Alayne felt as though she had swallowed her tongue,

but Lord Nestor rescued her. "Alayne is the Lord Protector's natural daughter," he told his cousin gruffly.

"Littlefinger's little finger has been busy," said Lyn Corbray, with a wicked smile. Belmore laughed, and Alayne could feel the color rising in her cheeks.

"How old are you, child?" asked Lady Waynwood.

"Four-fourteen, my lady." For a moment she forgot how old Alayne should be. "And I am no child, but a maiden flowered."

"But not *de*flowered, one can hope." Young Lord Hunter's bushy mustache hid his mouth entirely.

"Yet," said Lyn Corbray, as if she were not there. "But ripe for plucking soon, I'd say."

"Is that what passes for courtesy at Heart's Home?" Anya Waynwood's hair was greying and she had crow's-feet around her eyes and loose skin beneath her chin, but there was no mistaking the air of nobility about her. "The girl is young and gently bred, and has suffered enough horrors. Mind your tongue, ser."

"My tongue is my concern," Corbray replied. "Your ladyship should take care to mind her own. I have never taken kindly to chastisement, as any number of dead men could tell you."

Lady Waynwood turned away from him. "Best take us to your father, Alayne. The sooner we are done with this, the better."

"The Lord Protector awaits you in the solar. If my lords would follow me." From the Crescent Chamber they climbed a steep flight of marble steps that bypassed both undercrofts and dungeons and passed beneath three murder holes, which the Lords Declarant pretended not to notice. Belmore was soon puffing like a bellows, and Redfort's face turned as grey as his hair. The guards atop the stairs raised the portcullis at their coming. "This way, if it please my lords." Alayne led them down the arcade past a dozen splendid tapestries. Ser Lothor Brune stood outside the solar. He opened the door for them and followed them inside.

Petyr was seated at the trestle table with a cup of wine to hand, looking over a crisp white parchment. He glanced up as the Lords Declarant filed in. "My lords, be welcome. And you as well, my lady. The ascent is wearisome, I know. Please be seated. Alayne, my sweet, more wine for our noble guests."

"As you say, Father." The candles had been lighted, she was pleased to see; the solar smelled of nutmeg and other costly spices. She went to fetch the flagon whilst the visitors arranged themselves side by side . . . all save Nestor Royce, who hesitated before walking around the table to take the empty chair beside Lord Petyr, and Lyn Corbray, who went to stand beside the hearth instead. The heart-shaped ruby in the pommel of his sword shone redly as he warmed his hands. Alayne saw him smile at Ser Lothor Brune. *Ser Lyn is very handsome, for an older man,* she thought, *but I do not like the way he smiles.*

"I have been reading this remarkable declaration of yours," Petyr began. "Splendid. Whatever maester wrote this has a gift for words. I only wish you had invited me to sign as well."

That took them unawares. "You?" said Belmore. "Sign?"

"I wield a quill as well as any man, and no one loves Lord Robert more than I do. As for these false friends and evil counselors, by all means let us root them out. My lords, I am with you, heart and hand. Show me where to sign, I beg you."

Alayne, pouring, heard Lyn Corbray chuckle. The others seemed at a loss till Bronze Yohn Royce cracked his knuckles, and said, "We did not come for your signature. Nor do we mean to bandy words with you, Littlefinger."

"What a pity. I do so love a nicely bandied word." Petyr set the parchment to one side. "As you wish. Let us be blunt. What would you have of me, my lords and lady?"

"We will have naught of you." Symond Templeton fixed the Lord Protector with his cold blue stare. "We will have you gone."

"Gone?" Petyr feigned surprise. "Where would I go?"

"The crown has made you Lord of Harrenhal," Young Lord Hunter pointed out. "That should be enough for any man."

"The riverlands have need of a lord," old Horton Redfort said. "Riverrun stands besieged, Bracken and Blackwood are at open war, and outlaws roam freely on both sides of the Trident, stealing and killing as they will. Unburied corpses litter the landscape everywhere you go."

"You make it sound so wonderfully attractive, Lord Redfort," Petyr answered, "but as it happens I have pressing duties here. And there is Lord Robert to consider. Would you have me drag a sickly child into the midst of such carnage?"

"His lordship will remain in the Vale," declared Yohn Royce.

"I mean to take the boy with me to Runestone, and raise him up to be a knight that Jon Arryn would be proud of."

"Why Runestone?" Petyr mused. "Why not Ironoaks or the Redfort? Why not Longbow Hall?"

"Any of these would serve as well," declared Lord Belmore, "and his lordship will visit each in turn, in due time."

"Will he?" Petyr's tone seemed to hint at doubts.

Lady Waynwood sighed. "Lord Petyr, if you think to set us one against the other, you may spare yourself the effort.

484 GEORGE R. R. MARTIN

We speak with one voice here. Runestone suits us all. Lord Yohn raised three fine sons of his own, there is no man more fit to foster his young lordship. Maester Helliweg is a good deal older and more experienced than your own Maester Colemon, and better suited to treat Lord Robert's frailties. In Runestone the boy will learn the arts of war from Strong Sam Stone. No man could hope for a finer master-at-arms. Septon Lucos will instruct him in matters of the spirit. At Runestone he will also find other boys his own age, more suitable companions than the old women and sellswords that presently surround him."

Petyr Baelish fingered his beard. "His lordship needs companions, I do not disagree. Alayne is hardly an old woman, though. Lord Robert loves my daughter dearly, he will be glad to tell you so himself. And as it happens, I have asked Lord Grafton and Lord Lynderly to send me each a son to ward. Each of them has a boy of an age with Robert."

Lyn Corbray laughed. "Two pups from a pair of lapdogs."

"Robert should have an older boy about him too. A promising young squire, say. Someone he could admire and try to emulate." Petyr turned to Lady Waynwood. "You have such a boy at Ironoaks, my lady. Perhaps you might agree to send me Harrold Hardyng."

Anya Waynwood seemed amused. "Lord Petyr, you are as bold a thief as I'd ever care to meet."

"I do not wish to steal the boy," said Petyr, "but he and Lord Robert should be friends."

Bronze Yohn Royce leaned forward. "It is meet and proper that Lord Robert should befriend young Harry, and he shall . . . at Runestone, under my care, as my ward and squire."

"Give us the boy," said Lord Belmore, "and you may

depart the Vale unmolested for your proper seat at Harrenhal."

Petyr gave him a look of mild reproach. "Are you suggesting that elsewise I might come to harm, my lord? I cannot think why. My late wife seemed to think *this* was my proper seat."

"Lord Baelish," Lady Waynwood said, "Lysa Tully was Jon Arryn's widow and the mother of his child, and ruled here as his regent. You . . . let us be frank, you are no Arryn, and Lord Robert is no blood of yours. By what right do you presume to rule us?"

"Lysa named me Lord Protector, I do seem to recall."

Young Lord Hunter said, "Lysa Tully was never truly of the Vale, nor had she the right to dispose of us."

"And Lord Robert?" Petyr asked. "Will your lordship also claim that Lady Lysa had no right to dispose of her own son?"

Nestor Royce had been silent all this while, but now he spoke up loudly. "I once hoped to wed Lady Lysa myself. As did Lord Hunter's father and Lady Anya's son. Corbray scarce left her side for half a year. Had she chosen any one of us, no man here would dispute his right to be the Lord Protector. It happens that she chose Lord Littlefinger, and entrusted her son to his care."

"He was Jon Arryn's son as well, cousin," Bronze Yohn said, frowning at the Keeper. "He belongs to the Vale."

Petyr feigned puzzlement. "The Eyrie is as much a part of the Vale as Runestone. Unless someone has moved it?"

"Jape all you like, Littlefinger," Lord Belmore blustered. "The boy shall come with us."

"I am loath to disappoint you, Lord Belmore, but my stepson will be remaining here with me. He is not a robust child, as all of you know well. The journey would tax him sorely. As his stepfather and Lord Protector, I cannot permit it."

Symond Templeton cleared his throat, and said, "Each of us has a thousand men at the foot of this mountain, Littlefinger."

"What a splendid place for them."

"If need be, we can summon many more."

"Are you threatening me with war, ser?" Petyr did not sound the least afraid.

Bronze Yohn said, "We *shall* have Lord Robert."

For a moment it seemed as though they had come to an impasse, until Lyn Corbray turned from the fire. "All this talk makes me ill. Littlefinger will talk you out of your smallclothes if you listen long enough. The only way to settle his sort is with steel." He drew his longsword.

Petyr spread his hands. "I wear no sword, ser."

"Easily remedied." Candlelight rippled along the smoke-grey steel of Corbray's blade, so dark that it put Sansa in mind of Ice, her father's greatsword. "Your apple-eater holds a blade. Tell him to give it to you, or draw that dagger."

She saw Lothor Brune reach for his own sword, but before the blades could meet Bronze Yohn rose in wrath. "*Put up your steel, ser!* Are you a Corbray or a *Frey?* We are guests here."

Lady Waynwood pursed her lips, and said, "This is unseemly."

"Sheathe your sword, Corbray," Young Lord Hunter echoed. "You shame us all with this."

"Come, Lyn," chided Redfort in a softer tone. "This will serve for nought. Put Lady Forlorn to bed."

"My lady has a thirst," Ser Lyn insisted. "Whenever she comes out to dance, she likes a drop of red."

"Your lady must go thirsty." Bronze Yohn put himself squarely in Corbray's path.

"The Lords Declarant." Lyn Corbray snorted. "You should have named yourselves the Six Old Women." He slid the dark sword back into its scabbard and left them, shouldering Brune aside as if he were not there. Alayne listened to his footsteps recede.

Anya Waynwood and Horton Redfort exchanged a look. Hunter drained his wine cup and held it out to be re-filled. "Lord Baelish," Ser Symond said, "you must forgive us that display."

"Must I?" Littlefinger's voice had grown cold. "You brought him here, my lords."

Bronze Yohn said, "It was never our intent—"

"*You brought him here.* I would be well within my rights to call my guards and have all of you arrested."

Hunter lurched to his feet so wildly that he almost knocked the flagon out of Alayne's hands. "You gave us safe conduct!"

"Yes. Be grateful that I have more honor than some." Petyr sounded as angry as she had ever heard him. "I have read your *declaration* and heard your demands. Now hear mine. Remove your armies from this mountain. Go home and leave my son in peace. Misrule there has been, I will not deny it, but that was Lysa's work, not mine. Grant me but a year, and with Lord Nestor's help I promise that none of you shall have any cause for grievance."

"So you say," said Belmore. "Yet how shall we trust you?"

"You dare call *me* untrustworthy? It was not me who bared steel at a parley. You write of defending Lord Robert even as you deny him food. That must end. I am no war-rior, but I *will* fight you if you do not lift this siege. There are other lords besides you in the Vale, and King's

Landing will send men as well. If it is war you want, say so now and the Vale will bleed."

Alayne could see the doubt blooming in the eyes of the Lords Declarant. "A year is not so long a time," Lord Redfort said uncertainly. "Mayhaps . . . if you gave assurances . . ."

"None of us wants war," acknowledged Lady Waynwood. "Autumn wanes, and we must gird ourselves for winter."

Belmore cleared his throat. "At the end of this year . . ."

". . . if I have not set the Vale to rights, I shall willingly step down as Lord Protector," Petyr promised them.

"I call that more than fair," Lord Nestor Royce put in.

"There must be no reprisals," insisted Templeton. "No talk of treason or rebellion. You must swear to that as well."

"Gladly," said Petyr. "It is friends I want, not foes. I shall pardon all of you, in writing if you wish. Even Lyn Corbray. His brother is a good man, there is no need to bring down shame upon a noble House."

Lady Waynwood turned to her fellow Lords Declarant. "My lords, perhaps we might confer?"

"There is no need. It is plain that he has won." Bronze Yohn's grey eyes considered Petyr Baelish. "I like it not, but it would seem you have your year. Best use it well, my lord. Not all of us are fooled." He opened the door so forcefully that he all but wrenched it off its hinges.

Later there was a feast of sorts, though Petyr was forced to make apologies for the humble fare. Robert was trotted out in a doublet of cream and blue, and played the little lord quite graciously. Bronze Yohn was not there to see; he had already departed from the Eyrie to begin the long descent, as had Ser Lyn Corbray before him. The other lords remained with them till morn.

He bewitched them, Alayne thought as she lay abed that night listening to the wind howl outside her windows. She could not have said where the suspicion came from, but once it crossed her mind it would not let her sleep. She tossed and turned, worrying at it like a dog at some old bone. Finally, she rose and dressed herself, leaving Gretchel to her dreams.

Petyr was still awake, scratching out a letter. "Alayne," he said. "My sweet. What brings you here so late?"

"I had to know. What will happen in a year?"

He put down his quill. "Redfort and Waynwood are old. One or both of them may die. Gilwood Hunter will be murdered by his brothers. Most likely by young Harlan, who arranged Lord Eon's death. In for a penny, in for a stag, I always say. Belmore is corrupt and can be bought. Templeton I shall befriend. Bronze Yohn Royce will continue to be hostile, I fear, but so long as he stands alone he is not so much a threat."

"And Ser Lyn Corbray?"

The candlelight was dancing in his eyes. "Ser Lyn will remain my implacable enemy. He will speak of me with scorn and loathing to every man he meets, and lend his sword to every secret plot to bring me down."

That was when her suspicion turned to certainty. "And how shall you reward him for this service?"

Littlefinger laughed aloud. "With gold and boys and promises, of course. Ser Lyn is a man of simple tastes, my sweetling. All he likes is gold and boys and killing."

CERSEI

The king was pouting. "I want to sit on the Iron Throne," he told her. "You always let Joff sit up there."

"Joffrey was twelve."

"But I'm the *king*. The throne *belongs* to me."

"Who told you that?" Cersei took a deep breath, so Dorcas could lace her up more tightly. She was a big girl, much stronger than Senelle, though clumsier as well.

Tommen's face turned red. "No one told me."

"*No one?* Is that what you call your lady wife?" The queen could smell Margaery Tyrell all over this rebellion. "If you lie to me, I will have no choice but to send for Pate and have him beaten till he bleeds." Pate was Tommen's whipping boy, as he had been Joffrey's. "Is that what you want?"

"No," the king muttered sullenly.

"Who told you?"

He shuffled his feet. "Lady Margaery." He knew better than to call her *queen* in his mother's hearing.

"That is better. Tommen, I have grave matters to decide, matters that you are far too young to understand. I do not need a silly little boy fidgeting on the throne behind me and distracting me with childish questions. I suppose Margaery thinks you ought to be at my council meetings too?"

"Yes," he admitted. "She says I have to learn to be king."

"When you are older, you can attend as many councils as you wish," Cersei told him. "I promise you, you will soon grow sick of them. Robert used to doze through the sessions." *When he troubled to attend at all.* "He preferred to hunt and hawk, and leave the tedium to old Lord Arryn. Do you remember him?"

"He died of a bellyache."

"So he did, poor man. As you are so eager to learn, perhaps you should learn the names of all the kings of Westeros *and* the Hands who served them. You may recite them to me on the morrow."

"Yes, Mother," he said meekly.

"That's my good boy." The rule was hers; Cersei did not mean to give it up until Tommen came of age. *I waited, so can he. I waited half my life.* She had played the dutiful daughter, the blushing bride, the pliant wife. She had suffered Robert's drunken groping, Jaime's jealousy, Renly's mockery, Varys with his titters, Stannis endlessly grinding his teeth. She had contended with Jon Arryn, Ned Stark, and her vile, treacherous, murderous dwarf brother, all the while promising herself that one day it would be her turn. *If Margaery Tyrell thinks to cheat me of my hour in the sun, she had bloody well think again.*

Still, it was an ill way to break her fast, and Cersei's day did not soon improve. She spent the rest of the morning with Lord Gyles and his ledger books, listening to him cough about stars and stags and dragons. After him Lord Waters arrived, to report that the first three dromonds were nearing completion and beg for more gold to finish them in the splendor they deserved. The queen was pleased to grant him his request. Moon Boy capered as she took her midday meal with members of the merchant guilds and listened to them complain about sparrows wandering the streets and sleeping in the squares. *I may need to use the gold cloaks to chase these sparrows from the city,* she was thinking, when Pycelle intruded.

The Grand Maester had been especially querulous in council of late. At the last session he had complained bitterly about the men that Aurane Waters had chosen to captain her new dromonds. Waters meant to give the ships to younger men, whilst Pycelle argued for experience, insisting that the commands should go to those captains who had survived the fires of the Blackwater. "Seasoned men of proven loyalty," he called them. Cersei called them old, and sided with Lord Waters. "The only thing these captains proved was that they know how to swim," she'd said. "No mother should outlive her children, and no captain should outlive his ship." Pycelle had taken the rebuke with ill grace.

He seemed less choleric today, and even managed a sort of tremulous smile. "Your Grace, glad tidings," he announced. "Wyman Manderly has done as you commanded, and beheaded Lord Stannis's onion knight."

"We know this for a certainty?"

"The man's head and hands have been mounted above the walls of White Harbor. Lord Wyman avows this, and the Freys confirm. They have seen the head there, with an onion in its mouth. And the hands, one marked by his shortened fingers."

"Very good," said Cersei. "Send a bird to Manderly and inform him that his son will be returned forthwith, now that he has demonstrated his loyalty." White Harbor would soon return to the king's peace, and Roose Bolton and his bastard son were closing in on Moat Cailin from south and north. Once the Moat was theirs, they would join their strength and clear the ironmen out of Torrhen's Square and Deepwood Motte as well. That should win them the allegiance of Ned Stark's remaining bannermen when the time came to march against Lord Stannis.

To the south, meanwhile, Mace Tyrell had raised a city of tents outside Storm's End and had two dozen mangonels flinging stones against the castle's massive walls, thus far to small effect. *Lord Tyrell the warrior,* the queen mused. *His sigil ought to be a fat man sitting on his arse.*

That afternoon the dour Braavosi envoy turned up for his audience. Cersei had put him off for a fortnight and would have gladly put him off another year, but Lord Gyles claimed he could no longer deal with the man . . . though the queen was starting to wonder if Gyles was capable of doing *anything* but coughing.

Noho Dimittis, the Braavosi named himself. *An irritating name for an irritating man.* His voice was irritating too. Cersei shifted in her seat as he went on, wondering how long she must endure his hectoring. Behind her loomed the Iron Throne, its barbs and blades throwing twisted shadows across the floor. Only the king or his Hand could sit upon the throne itself. Cersei sat by its foot, in a seat of gilded wood piled with crimson cushions.

When the Braavosi paused for breath, she saw her chance. "This is more properly a matter for our lord treasurer."

That answer did not please the noble Noho, it would seem. "I have spoken with Lord Gyles six times. He coughs at me and makes excuses, Your Grace, but the gold is not forthcoming."

"Speak to him a seventh time," Cersei suggested pleasantly. "The number seven is sacred to our gods."

"It pleases Your Grace to make a jest, I see."

"When I make a jest I smile. Do you see me smiling? Do you hear laughter? I assure you, when I make a jest, men laugh."

"King Robert—"

"—is dead," she said sharply. "The Iron Bank will have its gold when this rebellion has been put down."

He had the insolence to scowl at her. "Your Grace—"

"This audience is at an end." Cersei had suffered quite enough for one day. "Ser Meryn, show the noble Noho Dimittis to the door. Ser Osmund, you may escort me back to my apartments." Her guests would soon arrive, and she had to bathe and change. Supper promised to be a tedious affair as well. It was hard work to rule a kingdom, much less seven of them.

Ser Osmund Kettleblack fell in beside her on the steps, tall and lean in his Kingsguard whites. When Cersei was certain they were quite alone, she slid her arm through his. "How is your little brother faring, pray?"

Ser Osmund looked uneasy. "Ah . . . well enough, only . . ."

"*Only?*" The queen let a hint of anger edge her words. "I must confess, I am running short of patience with dear Osney. It is past time he broke in that little filly. I named him Tommen's sworn shield so he could spend part of every day in Margaery's company. He should have plucked the rose by now. Is the little queen blind to his charms?"

"His charms is fine. He's a Kettleblack, ain't he? Begging your pardon." Ser Osmund ran his fingers through his oily black hair. "It's her that's the trouble."

"And why is that?" The queen had begun to nurse doubts about Ser Osney. Perhaps another man would have been more to Margaery's liking. *Aurane Waters, with that silvery hair, or a big strapping fellow like Ser Tallad.* "Would the maid prefer someone else? Does your brother's face displease her?"

"She likes his face. She touched his scars two days ago, he told me. 'What woman gave you these?' she asked. Osney never said it was a woman, but she knew. Might be someone told her. She's always touching him when they talk, he says. Straightening the clasp on his cloak, brushing back his hair, and like that. One time at the archery butts she had him show her how to hold a longbow, so he had to put his arms around her. Osney tells her bawdy jests, and she laughs and comes back with ones that are even bawdier. No, she wants him, that's plain, but . . ."

"But?" Cersei prompted.

"They are never alone. The king's with them most all the time, and when he's not, there's someone else. Two of her ladies share her bed, different ones every night. Two others bring her breakfast and help her dress. She prays with her septa, reads with her cousin Elinor, sings with her cousin Alla, sews with her cousin Megga. When she's not off hawking with Janna Fossoway and Merry Crane, she's playing come-into-my-castle with that little Bulwer girl. She never goes riding but she takes a tail, four or five companions and a dozen guards at least. And there's always men about her, even in the Maidenvault."

"Men." That was something. That had possibilities. "What men are these, pray tell?"

Ser Osmund shrugged. "Singers. She's a fool for

singers and jugglers and such. Knights, come round to moon over her cousins. Ser Tallad's the worst, Osney says. That big oaf don't seem to know if it's Elinor or Alla he wants, but he knows he wants her awful bad. The Redwyne twins come calling too. Slobber brings flowers and fruit, and Horror's taken up the lute. To hear Osney tell it, you could make a sweeter sound strangling a cat. The Summer Islander's always underfoot as well."

"Jalabhar Xho?" Cersei gave a derisive snort. "Begging her for gold and swords to win his homeland back, most like." Beneath his jewels and feathers, Xho was little more than a wellborn beggar. Robert could have put an end to his importuning for good with one firm "No," but the notion of conquering the Summer Isles had appealed to her drunken lout of a husband. No doubt he dreamt of brown-skinned wenches naked beneath feathered cloaks, with nipples black as coal. So instead of "No," Robert always told Xho, "Next year," though somehow next year never came.

"I couldn't say if he was begging, Your Grace," Ser Osmund answered. "Osney says he's teaching them the Summer Tongue. Not Osney, the quee—the filly and her cousins."

"A horse that speaks the Summer Tongue would make a great sensation," the queen said dryly. "Tell your brother to keep his spurs well honed. I shall find some way for him to mount his filly soon, you may rely on that."

"I'll tell him, Your Grace. He's eager for that ride, don't think he ain't. She's a pretty little thing, that filly."

It is me he's eager for, fool, the queen thought. *All he wants of Margaery is the lordship between her legs.* As fond as she was of Osmund, at times he seemed as slow as Robert. *I hope his sword is quicker than his wits. The day may come that Tommen has some need of it.*

They were crossing beneath the shadow of the broken Tower of the Hand when the sound of cheers swept over them. Across the yard, some squire had made a pass at the quintain and sent the crossarm spinning. The cheers were being led by Margaery Tyrell and her hens. *A lot of uproar for very little. You would think the boy had won a tourney.* Then she was startled to see that it was Tommen on the courser, clad all in gilded plate.

The queen had little choice but to don a smile and go to see her son. She reached him as the Knight of Flowers was helping him from his horse. The boy was breathless with excitement. "Did you see?" he was asking everyone. "I did it just the way Ser Loras said. Did you see, Ser Osney?"

"I did," said Osney Kettleblack. "A pretty sight."

"You have a better seat than me, sire," put in Ser Dermot.

"I broke the lance too. Ser Loras, did you hear it?"

"As loud as a crack of thunder." A rose of jade and gold clasped Ser Loras's white cloak at the shoulder, and the wind was riffling artfully through his brown locks. "You rode a splendid course, but once is not enough. You must do it again upon the morrow. You must ride every day, until every blow lands true and straight, and your lance is as much a part of you as your arm."

"I want to."

"You were glorious." Margaery went to one knee, kissed the king upon his cheek, and put an arm around him. "Brother, take care," she warned Loras. "My gallant husband will be unhorsing you in a few more years, I think." Her three cousins all agreed, and the wretched little Bulwer girl began to hop about, chanting, "Tommen will be the *champion,* the *champion,* the *champion.*"

"When he is a man grown," said Cersei.

Their smiles withered like roses kissed by frost. The

pock-faced old septa was the first to bend her knee. The rest followed, save for the little queen and her brother.

Tommen did not seem to notice the sudden chill in the air. "Mother, did you see me?" he burbled happily. "I broke my lance on the shield, and the bag never hit me!"

"I was watching from across the yard. You did very well, Tommen. I would expect no less of you. Jousting is in your blood. One day you shall rule the lists, as your father did."

"No man will stand before him." Margaery Tyrell gave the queen a coy smile. "But I never knew that King Robert was so accomplished at the joust. Pray tell us, Your Grace, what tourneys did he win? What great knights did he unseat? I know the king should like to hear about his father's victories."

A flush crept up Cersei's neck. The girl had caught her out. Robert Baratheon had been an indifferent jouster, in truth. During tourneys he had much preferred the mêlée, where he could beat men bloody with blunted axe or hammer. It had been Jaime she had been thinking of when she spoke. *It is not like me to forget myself.* "Robert won the tourney of the Trident," she had to say. "He overthrew Prince Rhaegar and named me his queen of love and beauty. I am surprised you do not know that story, good-daughter." She gave Margaery no time to frame a reply. "Ser Osmund, help my son from his armor, if you would be so good. Ser Loras, walk with me. I need a word with you."

The Knight of Flowers had no recourse but to follow at her heels like the puppy he was. Cersei waited until they were on the serpentine steps before she said, "Whose notion was that, pray?"

"My sister's," he admitted. "Ser Tallad, Ser Dermot,

and Ser Portifer were riding at the quintain, and the queen suggested that His Grace might like to have a turn."

He calls her that to irk me. "And your part?"

"I helped His Grace to don his armor and showed him how to couch his lance," he answered.

"That horse was much too large for him. What if he had fallen off? What if the sandbag had smashed his head in?"

"Bruises and bloody lips are all part of being a knight."

"I begin to understand why your brother is a cripple." That wiped the smile off his pretty face, she was pleased to see. "Perhaps my brother failed to explain your duties to you, ser. You are here to protect my son from his enemies. Training him for knighthood is the province of the master-at-arms."

"The Red Keep has had no master-at-arms since Aron Santagar was slain," Ser Loras said, with a hint of reproach in his voice. "His Grace is almost nine, and eager to learn. At his age he should be a squire. Someone has to teach him."

Someone will, but it will not be you. "Pray, who did you squire for, ser?" she asked sweetly. "Lord Renly, was it not?"

"I had that honor."

"Yes, I thought as much." Cersei had seen how tight the bonds grew between squires and the knights they served. She did not want Tommen growing close to Loras Tyrell. The Knight of Flowers was no sort of man for any boy to emulate. "I have been remiss. With a realm to rule, a war to fight, and a father to mourn, somehow I overlooked the crucial matter of naming a new master-at-arms. I shall rectify that error at once."

Ser Loras pushed back a brown curl that had fallen across his forehead. "Your Grace will not find any man half so skilled with sword and lance as I."

Humble, aren't we? "Tommen is your king, not your squire. You are to fight for him and die for him, if need be. No more."

She left him on the drawbridge that spanned the dry moat with its bed of iron spikes and entered Maegor's Holdfast alone. *Where am I to find a master-at-arms?* she wondered as she climbed to her apartments. Having refused Ser Loras, she dare not turn to any of the Kingsguard knights; that would be salt in the wound, certain to anger Highgarden. *Ser Tallad? Ser Dermot? There must be someone.* Tommen was growing fond of his new sworn shield, but Osney was proving himself less capable than she had hoped in the matter of Maid Margaery, and she had a different office in mind for his brother Osfryd. It was rather a pity that the Hound had gone rabid. Tommen had always been frightened of Sandor Clegane's harsh voice and burned face, and Clegane's scorn would have been the perfect antidote to Loras Tyrell's simpering chivalry.

Aron Santagar was Dornish, Cersei recalled. *I could send to Dorne.* Centuries of blood and war lay between Sunspear and Highgarden. *Yes, a Dornishman might suit my needs admirably. There must be some good swords in Dorne.*

When she entered her solar, Cersei found Lord Qyburn reading in a window seat. "If it please Your Grace, I have reports."

"More plots and treasons?" Cersei asked. "I have had a long and tiring day. Tell me quickly."

He smiled sympathetically. "As you wish. There is talk that the Archon of Tyrosh has offered terms to Lys, to end their present trade war. It had been rumored that Myr was about to enter the war on the Tyroshi side, but without the Golden Company the Myrish did not believe they . . ."

"What the Myrish believe does not concern me." The Free Cities were always fighting one another. Their endless betrayals and alliances meant little and less to Westeros. "Do you have any news of more import?"

"The slave revolt in Astapor has spread to Meereen, it would seem. Sailors off a dozen ships speak of dragons . . ."

"Harpies. It is harpies in Meereen." She remembered that from somewhere. Meereen was at the far end of the world, out east beyond Valyria. "Let the slaves revolt. Why should I care? We keep no slaves in Westeros. Is that all you have for me?"

"There is some news from Dorne that Your Grace may find of more interest. Prince Doran has imprisoned Ser Daemon Sand, a bastard who once squired for the Red Viper."

"I recall him." Ser Daemon had been amongst the Dornish knights who had accompanied Prince Oberyn to King's Landing. "What did he do?"

"He demanded that Prince Oberyn's daughters be set free."

"More fool him."

"Also," Lord Qyburn said, "the daughter of the Knight of Spottswood was betrothed quite unexpectedly to Lord Estermont, our friends in Dorne inform us. She was sent to Greenstone that very night, and it is said she and Estermont have already wed."

"A bastard in the belly would explain that." Cersei toyed with a lock of her hair. "How old is the blushing bride?"

"Three-and-twenty, Your Grace. Whereas Lord Estermont—"

"—must be seventy. I am aware of that." The Estermonts were her good-kin through Robert, whose father had taken one of them to wife in what must have been a fit of lust or madness. By the time Cersei wed the king, Robert's lady mother was long dead, though both of her brothers had turned up for the wedding and stayed for half a year. Robert had later insisted on returning the courtesy with a visit to Estermont, a mountainous little island off Cape Wrath. The dank and dismal fortnight Cersei spent at Greenstone, the seat of House Estermont, was the longest of her young life. Jaime dubbed the castle *"Greenshit"* at first sight, and soon had Cersei doing it too. Elsewise she passed her days watching her royal husband hawk, hunt, and drink with his uncles, and bludgeon various male cousins senseless in Greenshit's yard.

There had been a female cousin too, a chunky little widow with breasts as big as melons whose husband and father had both died at Storm's End during the siege. "Her father was good to me," Robert told her, "and she and I would play together when the two of us were small." It did not take him long to start playing with her again. As soon as Cersei closed her eyes, the king would steal off to console the poor lonely creature. One night she had Jaime follow him, to confirm her suspicions. When her brother returned he asked her if she wanted Robert dead. "No," she had replied, "I want him horned." She liked to think that was the night when Joffrey was conceived.

"Eldon Estermont has taken a wife fifty years his junior," she said to Qyburn. "Why should that concern me?"

He shrugged. "I do not say it should . . . but Daemon Sand and this Santagar girl were both close to Prince Doran's own daughter, Arianne, or so the Dornishmen would have us believe. Perhaps it means little or less, but I thought Your Grace should know."

"Now I do." She was losing patience. "Do you have more?"

"One more thing. A trifling matter." He gave her an

apologetic smile and told her of a puppet show that had recently become popular amongst the city's smallfolk; a puppet show wherein the kingdom of the beasts was ruled by a pride of haughty lions. "The puppet lions grow greedy and arrogant as this treasonous tale proceeds, until they begin to devour their own subjects. When the noble stag makes objection, the lions devour him as well, and roar that it is their right as the mightiest of beasts."

"And is that the end of it?" Cersei asked, amused. Looked at in the right light, it could be seen as a salutary lesson.

"No, Your Grace. At the end a dragon hatches from an egg and devours all of the lions."

The ending took the puppet show from simple insolence to treason. "Witless fools. Only cretins would hazard their heads upon a wooden dragon." She considered a moment. "Send some of your whisperers to these shows and make note of who attends. If any of them should be men of note, I would know their names."

"What will be done with them, if I may be so bold?"

"Any men of substance shall be fined. Half their worth should be sufficient to teach them a sharp lesson and refill our coffers, without quite ruining them. Those too poor to pay can lose an eye, for watching treason. For the puppeteers, the axe."

"There are four. Perhaps Your Grace might allow me two of them for mine own purposes. A woman would be especially . . ."

"I gave you Senelle," the queen said sharply.

"Alas. The poor girl is quite . . . exhausted."

Cersei did not like to think about that. The girl had come with her unsuspecting, thinking she was along to serve and pour. Even when Qyburn clapped the chain around her wrist, she had not seemed to understand. The memory still made the queen queasy. *The cells were bitter cold. Even the torches shivered. And that foul thing screaming in the darkness . . .* "Yes, you may take a woman. Two, if it please you. But first I will have names."

"As you command." Qyburn withdrew.

Outside, the sun was setting. Dorcas had prepared a bath for her. The queen was soaking pleasantly in the warm water and contemplating what she would say to her supper guests when Jaime came bursting through the door and ordered Jocelyn and Dorcas from the room. Her brother looked rather less than immaculate and had a smell of horse about him. He had Tommen with him too. "Sweet sister," he said, "the king requires a word."

Cersei's golden tresses floated in the bathwater. The room was steamy. A drop of sweat trickled down her cheek. "Tommen?" she said, in a dangerously soft voice. "What is it now?"

The boy knew that tone. He shrank back.

"His Grace wants his white courser on the morrow," Jaime said. "For his jousting lesson."

She sat up in the tub. "There will be no jousting."

"Yes, there will." Tommen puffed out his lower lip. "I have to ride *every day.*"

"And you shall," the queen declared, "once we have a proper master-at-arms to supervise your training."

"I don't *want* a proper master-at-arms. I want Ser Loras."

"You make too much of that boy. Your little wife has filled your head with foolish notions of his prowess, I know, but Osmund Kettleblack is thrice the knight that Loras is."

Jaime laughed. "Not the Osmund Kettleblack I know."

She could have throttled him. *Perhaps I need to command Ser Loras to allow Ser Osmund to unhorse him.* That might chase the stars from Tommen's eyes. *Salt a slug and shame a hero, and they shrink right up.* "I am sending for a Dornishman to train you," she said. "The Dornish are the finest jousters in the realm."

"They are not," said Tommen. "Anyway, I don't want any stupid Dornishman, I want *Ser Loras*. I *command* it."

Jaime laughed. *He is no help at all. Does he think this is amusing?* The queen slapped the water angrily. "Must I send for Pate? You do *not* command me. I am your mother."

"Yes, but I'm the *king*. Margaery says that everyone has to do what the king says. I want my white courser saddled on the morrow so Ser Loras can teach me how to joust. I want a kitten too, and I don't want to eat beets." He crossed his arms.

Jaime was still laughing. The queen ignored him. "Tommen, come here." When he hung back, she sighed. "Are you afraid? A king should not show fear." The boy approached the tub, his eyes downcast. She reached out and stroked his golden curls. "King or no, you are a little boy. Until you come of age, the rule is mine. You *will* learn to joust, I promise you. But not from Loras. The knights of the Kingsguard have more important duties than playing with a child. Ask the Lord Commander. Isn't that so, ser?"

"Very important duties." Jaime smiled thinly. "Riding round the city walls, for an instance."

Tommen looked close to tears. "Can I still have a kitten?"

"Perhaps," the queen allowed. "So long as I hear no more nonsense about jousting. Can you promise me that?"

He shuffled his feet. "Yes."

"Good. Now run along. My guests will be here shortly." Tommen ran along, but before he left he turned back to say, "When I'm king in my own right, I'm going to *outlaw* beets."

Her brother shoved the door shut with his stump. "Your Grace," he said, when he and Cersei were alone, "I was wondering. Are you drunk, or merely stupid?"

She slapped the water once again, sending up another splash to wash across his feet. "Guard your tongue, or—"

"—or what? Will you send me to inspect the city walls again?" He sat and crossed his legs. "Your bloody walls are fine. I've crawled over every inch of them and had a look at all seven of the gates. The hinges on the Iron Gate are rusted, and the King's Gate and Mud Gate need to be replaced after the pounding Stannis gave them with his rams. The walls are as strong as they have ever been . . . but perchance Your Grace has forgotten that our friends of Highgarden are *inside* the walls?"

"I forget nothing," she told him, thinking of a certain gold coin, with a hand on one face and the head of a forgotten king on the other. *How did some miserable wretch of a gaoler come to have such a coin hidden beneath his chamber pot? How does a man like Rugen come to have old gold from Highgarden?*

"This is the first I have heard of a new master-at-arms. You'll need to look long and hard to find a better jouster than Loras Tyrell. Ser Loras is—"

"I know what he is. I won't have him near my son. You had best remind him of his duties." Her bath was growing cool.

"He knows his duties, and there's no better lance—"

"*You* were better, before you lost your hand. Ser Barristan, when he was young. Arthur Dayne was better, and Prince Rhaegar was a match for even him. Do not prate at me about how fierce the Flower is. He's just a boy." She was tired of Jaime balking her. No one had ever balked her lord father. When Tywin Lannister spoke, men obeyed. When Cersei spoke, they felt free to counsel her, to contradict her, even *refuse* her. *It is all because I am a woman. Because I cannot fight them with a sword. They gave Robert more respect than they give me, and Robert was a witless sot.* She would not suffer it, especially not from Jaime. *I need to rid myself of him, and soon.* Once upon a time she had dreamt that the two of them might rule the Seven Kingdoms side by side, but Jaime had become more of a hindrance than a help.

Cersei rose from the bath. Water ran down her legs and trickled from her hair. "When I want your counsel I will ask for it. Leave me, ser. I must needs dress."

"Your supper guests, I know. What plot is this, now? There are so many I lose track." His glance fell to the water beading in the golden hair between her legs.

He still wants me. "Pining for what you've lost, brother?"

Jaime raised his eyes. "I love you too, sweet sister. But you're a fool. A beautiful golden fool."

The words stung. *You called me kinder words at Greenstone, the night you planted Joff inside me,* Cersei thought. "Get out." She turned her back to him and listened to him leave, fumbling at the door with his stump.

Whilst Jocelyn was making certain that all was in readiness for the supper, Dorcas helped the queen into her new gown. It had stripes of shiny green satin alternating with stripes of plush black velvet, and intricate black Myrish lace above the bodice. Myrish lace was costly, but it was necessary for a queen to look her best at all times, and her wretched washerwomen had shrunk several of her old gowns so they no longer fit. She would have whipped them for their carelessness, but Taena had urged her to be merciful. "The smallfolk will love you more if you are kind," she had said, so Cersei had ordered the value of the gowns deducted from the women's wages, a much more elegant solution.

Dorcas put a silver looking glass into her hand. *Very good,* the queen thought, smiling at her reflection. It was pleasant to be out of mourning. Black made her look too pale. *A pity I am not supping with Lady Merryweather,* the queen reflected. It had been a long day, and Taena's wit always cheered her. Cersei had not had a friend she so enjoyed since Melara Hetherspoon, and Melara had turned out to be a greedy little schemer with ideas above her station. *I should not think ill of her. She's dead and drowned, and she taught me never to trust anyone but Jaime.*

By the time she joined them in the solar, her guests had made a good start on the hippocras. *Lady Falyse not only looks like a fish, she drinks like one,* she reflected, when she made note of the half-empty flagon. "Sweet Falyse," she exclaimed, kissing the woman's cheek, "and brave Ser Balman. I was so distraught when I heard about your dear, dear mother. How fares our Lady Tanda?"

Lady Falyse looked as if she were about to cry. "Your Grace is good to ask. Mother's hip was shattered by the fall, Maester Frenken says. He did what he could. Now we pray, but . . ."

Pray all you like, she will still be dead before the moon turns. Women as old as Tanda Stokeworth did not survive a broken hip. "I shall add my prayers to your own," said Cersei. "Lord Qyburn tells me that Tanda was thrown from her horse."

"Her saddle girth burst whilst she was riding," said Ser Balman Byrch. "The stableboy should have seen the strap was worn. He has been chastised."

"Severely, I hope." The queen seated herself and indicated that her guests should sit as well. "Will you have another cup of hippocras, Falyse? You were always fond of it, I seem to recall."

"It is so good of you to remember, Your Grace."

How could I have forgotten? Cersei thought. *Jaime said it was a wonder you did not piss the stuff.* "How was your journey?"

"Uncomfortable," complained Falyse. "It rained most of the day. We thought to spend the night at Rosby, but that young ward of Lord Gyles refused us hospitality." She sniffed. "Mark my word, when Gyles dies that ill-born wretch will make off with his gold. He may even try and claim the lands and lordship, though by rights Rosby should come to us when Gyles passes. My lady mother was aunt to his second wife, third cousin to Gyles himself."

Is your sigil a lamb, my lady, or some sort of grasping monkey? Cersei thought. "Lord Gyles has been threatening to die for as long as I have known him, but he is still with us, and will be for many years, I do hope." She smiled pleasantly. "No doubt he will cough the whole lot of us into our graves."

"Like as not," Ser Balman agreed. "Rosby's ward was not the only one to vex us, Your Grace. We encountered ruffians on the road as well. Filthy, unkempt creatures, with leather shields and axes. Some had stars sewn on their jerkins, sacred stars of seven points, but they had an evil look about them all the same."

"They were lice-ridden, I am certain," added Falyse.

"They call themselves *sparrows*," said Cersei. "A plague upon the land. Our new High Septon will need to deal with them, once he is crowned. If not, I shall deal with them myself."

"Has His High Holiness been chosen yet?" asked Falyse.

"No," the queen had to confess. "Septon Ollidor was on the verge of being chosen, until some of these sparrows followed him to a brothel and dragged him naked out into the street. Luceon seems the likely choice now, though our friends on the other hill say that he is still a few votes short of the required number."

"May the Crone guide the deliberations with her golden lamp of wisdom," said Lady Falyse, most piously.

Ser Balman shifted in his seat. "Your Grace, an awkward matter, but . . . lest bad feeling fester between us, you should know that neither my good wife nor her mother had any hand in the naming of this bastard child. Lollys is a simple creature, and her husband is given to black humors. I told him to choose a more fitting name for the boy. He laughed."

The queen sipped her wine and studied him. Ser Balman had been a noted jouster once, and one of the handsomest knights in the Seven Kingdoms. He could still boast a handsome mustache; elsewise, he had not aged well. His wavy blond hair had retreated, whilst his belly advanced inexorably against his doublet. *As a catspaw he leaves much to be desired,* she reflected. *Still, he should serve.* "Tyrion was a king's name before the dragons came. The Imp has despoiled it, but perhaps this child can restore the name to honor." *If the bastard lives so long.* "I know you are not to blame. Lady Tanda is the sister that I never had, and you . . ." Her voice broke. "Forgive me. I live in fear."

Falyse opened and closed her mouth, which made her look like some especially stupid fish. "In . . . in fear, Your Grace?"

"I have not slept a whole night through since Joffrey died." Cersei filled the goblets with hippocras. "My friends . . . you *are* my friends, I hope? And King Tommen's?"

"That sweet lad," Ser Balman declared. "Your Grace, the very words of House Stokeworth are *Proud to Be Faithful.*"

"Would that there were more like you, good ser. I tell you truly, I have grave doubts about Ser Bronn of the Blackwater."

Husband and wife exchanged a look. "The man is insolent, Your Grace," Falyse said. "Uncouth and foul-mouthed."

"He is no true knight," Ser Balman said.

"No." Cersei smiled, all for him. "And you are a man who would know true knighthood. I remember watching you joust in . . . which tourney was it where you fought so brilliantly, ser?"

He smiled modestly. "That affair at Duskendale six years ago? No, you were not there, else you would surely have been crowned the queen of love and beauty. Was it the tourney at Lannisport after Greyjoy's Rebellion? I unhorsed many a good knight in that one . . ."

"That was the one." Her face grew somber. "The Imp vanished the night my father died, leaving two honest gaolers behind in pools of blood. Some claim he fled across the narrow sea, but I wonder. The dwarf is cunning. Perhaps he still lurks near, planning more murders. Perhaps some friend is hiding him."

"Bronn?" Ser Balman stroked his bushy mustache.

"He was ever the Imp's creature. Only the Stranger knows how many men he's sent to hell at Tyrion's behest."

"Your Grace, I think I should have noticed a dwarf skulking about our lands," said Ser Balman.

"My brother is small. He was made for skulking." Cersei let her hand shake. "A child's name is a small thing . . . but insolence unpunished breeds rebellion. And this man Bronn has been gathering sellswords to him, Qyburn has told me."

"He has taken four knights into his household," said Falyse.

Ser Balman snorted. "My good wife flatters them, to call them knights. They're upjumped sellswords, with not a thimble of chivalry to be found amongst the four of them."

"As I feared. Bronn is gathering swords for the dwarf. May the Seven save my little son. The Imp will kill him as he killed his brother." She sobbed. "My friends, I put my honor in your hands . . . but what is a queen's honor against a mother's fears?"

"Say on, Your Grace," Ser Balman assured her. "Your words shall ne'er leave this room."

Cersei reached across the table and gave his hand a squeeze. "I . . . I would sleep more easily of a night if I were to hear that Ser Bronn had suffered a . . . a mishap . . . whilst hunting, perhaps."

Ser Balman considered a moment. "A *mortal* mishap?"

No, I desire you to break his little toe. She had to bite her lip. *My enemies are everywhere and my friends are fools.* "I beg you, ser," she whispered, "do not make me say it . . ."

"I understand." Ser Balman raised a finger.

A turnip would have grasped it quicker. "You are a true knight indeed, ser. The answer to a frightened mother's prayers." Cersei kissed him. "Do it quickly, if you would. Bronn has only a few men about him now, but if we do not act, he will surely gather more." She kissed Falyse. "I shall never forget this, my friends. My *true* friends of Stokeworth. *Proud to Be Faithful.* You have my word, we shall find Lollys a better husband when this is done." *A Kettleblack, perhaps.* "We Lannisters pay our debts."

The rest was hippocras and buttered beets, hot-baked bread, herb-crusted pike, and ribs of wild boar. Cersei had become very fond of boar since Robert's death. She did not even mind the company, though Falyse simpered and Balman preened from soup to sweet. It was past midnight before she could rid herself of them. Ser Balman proved a great one for suggesting yet another flagon, and the queen did not think it prudent to refuse. *I could have hired a Faceless Man to kill Bronn for half of what I've spent on hippocras,* she reflected when they were gone at last.

At that hour, her son was fast asleep, but Cersei looked in upon him before seeking her own bed. She was surprised to find three black kittens cuddled up beside him. "Where did those come from?" she asked Ser Meryn Trant, outside the royal bedchamber.

"The little queen gave them to him. She only meant to give him one, but he couldn't decide which one he liked the best."

Better than cutting them out of their mother with a dagger, I suppose. Margaery's clumsy attempts at seduction were so obvious as to be laughable. *Tommen is too young for kisses, so she gives him kittens.* Cersei rather wished they were not black, though. Black cats brought ill luck, as Rhaegar's little girl had discovered in this very castle. *She would have been my daughter, if the Mad King had not played his cruel jape on Father.* It had to have been the madness that led Aerys to refuse Lord Tywin's daughter and take his son instead, whilst marrying his own son to a feeble Dornish princess with black eyes and a flat chest.

The memory of the rejection still rankled, even after all these years. Many a night she had watched Prince Rhaegar in the hall, playing his silver-stringed harp with those long, elegant fingers of his. Had any man ever been so beautiful? *He was more than a man, though. His blood was the blood of old Valyria, the blood of dragons and gods.* When she was just a little girl, her father had promised her that she would marry Rhaegar. She could not have been more than six or seven. "Never speak of it, child," he had told her, smiling his secret smile that only Cersei ever saw. "Not until His Grace agrees to the betrothal. It must remain our secret for now." And so it had, though once she had drawn a picture of herself flying behind Rhaegar on a dragon, her arms wrapped tight about his chest. When Jaime had discovered it she told him it was Queen Alysanne and King Jaehaerys.

She was ten when she finally saw her prince in the flesh, at the tourney her lord father had thrown to welcome King Aerys to the west. Viewing stands had been raised beneath the walls of Lannisport, and the cheers of the smallfolk had echoed off Casterly Rock like rolling thunder. *They cheered Father twice as loudly as they cheered the king,* the queen recalled, *but only half as loudly as they cheered Prince Rhaegar.*

Seventeen and new to knighthood, Rhaegar Targaryen had worn black plate over golden ringmail when he cantered onto the lists. Long streamers of red and gold and orange silk had floated behind his helm, like flames. Two of her uncles fell before his lance, along with a dozen of her father's finest jousters, the flower of the west. By night the prince played his silver harp and made her weep. When she had been presented to him, Cersei had almost drowned in the depths of his sad purple eyes. *He has been wounded,* she recalled thinking, *but I will mend his hurt when we are wed.* Next to Rhaegar, even her beautiful Jaime had seemed no more than a callow boy. *The prince is going to be my husband,* she had thought, giddy with excitement, *and when the old king dies I'll be the queen.*

Her aunt had confided that truth to her before the tourney. "You must be especially beautiful," Lady Genna told her, fussing with her dress, "for at the final feast it shall be announced that you and Prince Rhaegar are betrothed."

Cersei had been so happy that day. Elsewise she would never have dared visit the tent of Maggy the Frog. She had only done it to show Jeyne and Melara that the lioness fears nothing. *I was going to be a queen. Why should a queen be afraid of some hideous old woman?* The memory of that foretelling still made her flesh crawl a lifetime later. *Jeyne ran shrieking from the tent in fear,* the queen remembered, *but Melara stayed and so did I. We let her taste our blood, and laughed at her stupid prophecies. None of them made the least bit of sense.* She was going to be Prince Rhaegar's wife, no matter what the woman said. Her *father* had promised it, and Tywin Lannister's word was gold.

Her laughter died at tourney's end. There had been no final feast, no toasts to celebrate her betrothal to Prince Rhaegar. Only cold silences and chilly looks between the king and her father. Later, when Aerys and his son and all his gallant knights had departed for King's Landing, the girl had gone to her aunt in tears, not understanding. "Your father proposed the match," Lady Genna told her, "but Aerys refused to hear of it. 'You are my most able servant, Tywin,' the king said, 'but a man does not marry his heir to his servant's daughter.' Dry those tears, little one. Have you ever seen a lion weep? Your father will find another man for you, a better man than Rhaegar."

Her aunt had lied, though, and her father had failed her, just as Jaime was failing her now. *Father found no better man. Instead he gave me Robert, and Maggy's curse bloomed like some poisonous flower.* If she had only married Rhaegar as the gods intended, he would never have looked twice at the wolf girl. *Rhaegar would be our king today and I would be his queen, the mother of his sons.*

She had never forgiven Robert for killing him.

But then, lions were not good at forgiving. As Ser Bronn of the Blackwater would shortly learn.

BRIENNE

I t was Hyle Hunt who insisted that they take the heads. "Tarly will want them for the walls," he said.

"We have no tar," Brienne pointed out. "The flesh will rot. Leave them." She did not want to travel through the green gloom of the piney woods with the heads of the men she'd killed.

Hunt would not listen. He hacked through the dead men's necks himself, tied the three heads together by the hair, and slung them from his saddle. Brienne had no choice but to try and pretend they were not there, but sometimes, especially at night, she could feel their dead eyes on her back, and once she dreamed she heard them whispering to one another.

It was cold and wet on Crackclaw Point as they retraced their steps. Some days it rained and some days it threatened rain. They were never warm. Even when they made camp, it was hard to find enough dry wood for a fire.

By the time they reached the gates of Maidenpool, a host of flies attended them, a crow had eaten Shagwell's eyes, and Pyg and Timeon were crawling with maggots. Brienne and Podrick had long since taken to riding a hundred yards ahead, to keep the smell of rot well behind them. Ser Hyle claimed to have lost all sense of smell by then. "Bury them," she told him every time they made camp for a night, but Hunt was nothing if not stubborn. *He will most like tell Lord Randyll that he slew all three of them.*

To his honor, though, the knight did nothing of the sort.

"The stammering squire threw a rock," he said, when he and Brienne were ushered into Tarly's presence in the yard of Mooton's castle. The heads had been presented to a serjeant of the guard, who was told to have them cleaned and tarred and mounted above the gate. "The swordswench did the rest."

"All three?" Lord Randyll was incredulous.

"The way she fought, she could have killed three more."

"And did you find the Stark girl?" Tarly demanded of her.

"No, my lord."

"Instead you slew some rats. Did you enjoy it?"

"No, my lord."

"A pity. Well, you've had your taste of blood. Proved whatever it is you meant to prove. It's time you took off that mail and donned proper clothes again. There are ships in port. One's bound to stop at Tarth. I'll have you on it."

"Thank you, my lord, but no."

Lord Tarly's face suggested he would have liked nothing better than to stick her own head on a spike and mount it above the gates of Maidenpool with Timeon, Pyg, and Shagwell. "You mean to continue with this folly?"

"I mean to find the Lady Sansa."

"If it please my lord," Ser Hyle said, "I watched her fight the Mummers. She is stronger than most men, and quick—"

"The *sword* is quick," Tarly snapped. "That is the nature of Valyrian steel. Stronger than most men? Aye. She's a freak of nature, far be it from me to deny it."

His sort will never love me, Brienne thought, *no matter what I do.* "My lord, it may be that Sandor Clegane has some knowledge of the girl. If I could find him . . ."

"Clegane's turned outlaw. He rides with Beric Dondarrion now, it would seem. Or not, the tales vary. Show me where they're hiding, I will gladly slit their bellies open, pull their entrails out, and burn them. We've hanged dozens of outlaws, but the leaders still elude us. Clegane, Dondarrion, the red priest, and now this woman Stoneheart . . . how do *you* propose to find them, when I cannot?"

"My lord, I : . ." She had no good answer for him. "All I can do is try."

"Try, then. You have your letter, you do not need my leave, but I'll give it nonetheless. If you're fortunate, all you'll get for your trouble are saddle sores. If not, perhaps Clegane will let you live after he and his pack are done raping you. You can crawl back to Tarth with some dog's bastard in your belly."

Brienne ignored that. "If it please my lord, how many men ride with the Hound?"

"Six or sixty or six hundred. It would seem to depend on whom we ask." Randyll Tarly had plainly had enough of the conversation. He started to turn away.

"If my squire and I might beg your hospitality until—"

"Beg all you want. I will not suffer you beneath my roof."

Ser Hyle Hunt stepped forward. "If it please my lord, I had understood that it was still Lord Mooton's roof."

Tarly gave the knight a venomous look. "Mooton has the courage of a worm. You will not speak to me of Mooton. As for you, my lady, it is said that your father is a good man. If so, I pity him. Some men are blessed with sons, some with daughters. No man deserves to be cursed with such as you. Live or die, Lady Brienne, do not return to Maidenpool whilst I rule here."

Words are wind, Brienne told herself. *They cannot hurt you. Let them wash over you.* "As you command, my lord," she tried to say, but Tarly had gone before she got it out. She walked from the yard like one asleep, not knowing where she was going.

Ser Hyle fell in beside her. "There are inns."

She shook her head. She did not want words with Hyle Hunt.

"Do you recall the Stinking Goose?"

Her cloak still smelled of it. "Why?"

"Meet me there on the morrow, at midday. My cousin Alyn was one of those sent out to find the Hound. I'll speak with him."

"Why would you do that?"

"Why not? If you succeed where Alyn failed, I shall be able to taunt him with that for years."

There were still inns in Maidenpool; Ser Hyle had not been wrong. Some had burned during one sack or the other, however, and had yet to be rebuilt, and those that remained were full to bursting with men from Lord Tarly's host. She and Podrick visited all of them that afternoon, but there were no beds to be had anywhere.

"Ser? My lady?" Podrick said as the sun was going down. "There are ships. Ships have beds. Hammocks. Or bunks."

Lord Randyll's men still prowled the docks, as thick as the flies had been on the heads of the three Bloody Mummers, but their serjeant knew Brienne by sight and let her pass. The local fisherfolk were tying up for the night and crying the day's catch, but her interest was in the larger ships that plied the stormy waters of the narrow sea. Half a dozen were in port, though one, a galleas called the *Titan's Daughter,* was casting off her lines to ride out on the evening tide. She and Podrick Payne made the rounds of the ships that remained. The master of the *Gulltown Girl* took Brienne for a whore and told them that his ship was not a bawdy house, and a harpooner on the Ibbenese whaler offered to buy her boy, but they had better fortune elsewhere. She purchased Podrick an orange on the *Seastrider,* a cog just in from Oldtown by way of Tyrosh, Pentos, and Duskendale. "Gulltown next," her captain told her, "thence around the Fingers to Sisterton and White Harbor, if the storms allow. She's a clean ship, *'Strider,* not so many rats as most, and we'll have fresh eggs and new-churned butter aboard. Is m'lady seeking passage north?"

"No." *Not yet.* She was tempted, but . . .

As they were making their way to the next pier, Podrick shuffled his feet, and said, "Ser? My lady? What if my lady did go home? My other lady, I mean. Ser. Lady Sansa."

"They burned her home."

"Still. That's where her *gods* are. And gods can't die."

Gods cannot die, but girls can. "Timeon was a cruel man and a murderer, but I do not think he lied about the Hound. We cannot go north until we know for certain. There will be other ships."

At the east end of the harbor they finally found shelter for the night, aboard a storm-wracked trading galley

called the *Lady of Myr*. She was listing badly, having lost
her mast and half her crew in a storm, but her master did
not have the coin he needed to refit her, so he was glad to
take a few pennies from Brienne and allow her and Pod to
share an empty cabin.

They had a restless night. Thrice Brienne woke. Once
when the rain began, and once at a creak that made her
think Nimble Dick was creeping in to kill her. The second
time, she woke with knife in hand, but it was nothing. In
the darkness of the cramped little cabin, it took her a moment to remember that Nimble Dick was dead. When she
finally drifted back to sleep, she dreamed about the men
she'd killed. They danced around her, mocking her, pinching at her as she slashed at them with her sword. She cut
them all to bloody ribbons, yet still they swarmed around
her . . . Shagwell, Timeon, and Pyg, aye, but Randyll Tarly
too, and Vargo Hoat, and Red Ronnet Connington. Ronnet
had a rose between his fingers. When he held it out to her,
she cut his hand off.

She woke sweating, and spent the rest of the night huddled under her cloak, listening to rain pound against the
deck over her head. It was a wild night. From time to time
she heard the sound of distant thunder, and thought of the
Braavosi ship that had sailed upon the evening tide.

The next morning she found the Stinking Goose again,
woke its slatternly proprietor, and paid her for some
greasy sausages, fried bread, half a cup of wine, a flagon
of boiled water, and two clean cups. The woman squinted
at Brienne as she was putting the water on to boil. "You're
the big one went off with Nimble Dick. I remember. He
cheat you?"

"No."

"Rape you?"

"No."

"Steal your horse?"

"No. He was slain by outlaws."

"Outlaws?" The woman seemed more curious than upset. "I always figured Dick would hang, or get sent off to that Wall."

They ate the fried bread and half the sausages. Podrick Payne washed his down with wine-flavored water whilst Brienne nursed a cup of watered wine and wondered why she'd come. Hyle Hunt was no true knight. His honest face was just a mummer's mask. *I do not need his help, I do not need his protection, and I do not need him,* she told herself. *He is probably not even coming. Telling me to meet him here was just another jape.*

She was getting up to go when Ser Hyle arrived. "My lady. Podrick." He glanced at the cups and plates and the half-eaten sausages cooling in a puddle of grease, and said, "Gods, I hope you did not eat the food here."

"What we ate is no concern of yours," Brienne said. "Did you find your cousin? What did he tell you?"

"Sandor Clegane was last seen in Saltpans, the day of the raid. Afterward he rode west, along the Trident."

She frowned. "The Trident is a long river."

"Aye, but I don't think our dog will have wandered too far from its mouth. Westeros has lost its charm for him, it would seem. At Saltpans he was looking for a *ship.*" Ser Hyle drew a roll of sheepskin from his boot, pushed the sausages aside, and unrolled it. It proved to be a map. "The Hound butchered three of his brother's men at the old inn by the crossroads, here. He led the raid on Saltpans, here." He tapped Saltpans with his finger. "He may be trapped. The Freys are up here at the Twins, Darry and Harrenhal are south across the Trident, west he's got the Blackwoods and the Brackens fighting, and Lord Randyll's here at Maidenpool. The high road to the Vale is closed by snow, even if he could get past the mountain clans. Where's a dog to go?"

"If he is with Dondarrion . . . ?"

"He's not. Alyn is certain of that. Dondarrion's men are looking for him too. They have put out word that they mean to hang him for what he did at Saltpans. They had no part of that. Lord Randyll is putting it about that they did in hopes of turning the commons against Beric and his brotherhood. He will never take the lightning lord so long as the smallfolk are protecting him. And there's this other band, led by this woman Stoneheart . . . Lord Beric's lover, according to one tale. Supposedly she was hanged by the Freys, but Dondarrion kissed her and brought her back to life, and now she cannot die, no more than he can." Brienne considered the map. "If Clegane was last seen at Saltpans, that would be the place to find his trail."

"There is no one left at Saltpans but an old knight hiding in his castle, Alyn said."

"Still, it would be a place to start."

"There's a man," Ser Hyle said. "A septon. He came in through my gate the day before you turned up. Meribald, his name is. River-born and river-bred and he's served here all his life. He's departing on the morrow to make his circuit, and he always calls at Saltpans. We should go with him."

Brienne looked up sharply. *"We?"*

"I am going with you."

"You're not."

"Well, I'm going with Septon Meribald to Saltpans. You and Podrick can go wherever you bloody well like."

"Did Lord Randyll command you to follow me again?"

"He commanded me to stay away from you. Lord Randyll is of the view that you might benefit from a good hard raping."

"Then why would you come with me?"

"It was that, or return to gate duty."

"If your lord commanded—"

"He is no longer my lord."

That took her aback. "You left his service?"

"His lordship informed me that he had no further need of my sword, or my insolence. It amounts to the same thing. Henceforth I shall enjoy the adventuresome life of a hedge knight . . . though if we do find Sansa Stark, I imagine we will be well rewarded."

Gold and land, that's what he sees in this. "I mean to save the girl, not sell her. I swore a vow."

"I don't recall that I did."

"That is why you will not be coming with me."

They left the next morning, as the sun was coming up.

It was a queer procession: Ser Hyle on a chestnut courser and Brienne on her tall grey mare, Podrick Payne astride his swayback stot, and Septon Meribald walking beside them with his quarterstaff, leading a small donkey and a large dog. The donkey carried such a heavy load that Brienne was half afraid its back would break. "Food for the poor and hungry of the riverlands," Septon Meribald told them at the gates of Maidenpool. "Seeds and nuts and dried fruit, oaten porridge, flour, barley bread, three wheels of yellow cheese from the inn by the Fool's Gate, salt cod for me, salt mutton for Dog . . . oh, and salt. Onions, carrots, turnips, two sacks of beans, four of barley, and nine of oranges. I have a weakness for the orange, I confess. I got these from a sailor, and I fear they will be the last I'll taste till spring."

Meribald was a septon without a sept, only one step up from a begging brother in the hierarchy of the Faith. There were hundreds like him, a ragged band whose humble task it was to trudge from one flyspeck of a village to the next, conducting holy services, performing marriages, and for-giving sins. Those he visited were expected to feed and shelter him, but most were as poor as he was, so Meribald could not linger in one place too long without causing hardship to his hosts. Kindly innkeeps would sometimes allow him to sleep in their kitchens or their stables, and there were septries and holdfasts and even a few castles where he knew he would be given hospitality. Where no such places were at hand, he slept beneath the trees or un-der hedges. "There are many fine hedges in the river-lands," Meribald said. "The old ones are the best. There's nothing beats a hundred-year-old hedge. Inside one of those a man can sleep as snug as at an inn, and with less fear of fleas."

The septon could neither read nor write, as he cheer-fully confessed along the road, but he knew a hundred dif-ferent prayers and could recite long passages from *The Seven-Pointed Star* from memory, which was all that was required in the villages. He had a seamed, windburnt face, a shock of thick grey hair, wrinkles at the corners of his eyes. Though a big man, six feet tall, he had a way of hunching forward as he walked that made him seem much shorter. His hands were large and leathery, with red knuckles and dirt beneath the nails, and he had the biggest feet that Brienne had ever seen, bare and black and hard as horn.

"I have not worn a shoe in twenty years," he told Brienne. "The first year, I had more blisters than I had toes, and my soles would bleed like pigs whenever I trod on a hard stone, but I prayed and the Cobbler Above turned my skin to leather."

"There is no cobbler above," Podrick protested.

"There is, lad . . . though you may call him by another name. Tell me, which of the seven gods do you love best?"

"The Warrior," said Podrick without a moment's hesitation.

Brienne cleared her throat. "At Evenfall my father's septon always said that there was but one god."

"One god with seven aspects. That's so, my lady, and you are right to point it out, but the mystery of the Seven Who Are One is not easy for simple folk to grasp, and I am nothing if not simple, so I speak of seven gods." Meribald turned back to Podrick. "I have never known a boy who did not love the Warrior. I am old, though, and being old, I love the Smith. Without his labor, what would the Warrior defend? Every town has a smith, and every castle. They make the plows we need to plant our crops, the nails we use to build our ships, iron shoes to save the hooves of our faithful horses, the bright swords of our lords. No one could doubt the value of a smith, and so we name one of the Seven in his honor, but we might as easily have called him the Farmer or the Fisherman, the Carpenter or the Cobbler. What he works at makes no matter. What matters is, he works. The Father rules, the Warrior fights, the Smith labors, and together they perform all that is rightful for a man. Just as the Smith is one aspect of the godhead, the Cobbler is one aspect of the Smith. It was he who heard my prayer and healed my feet."

"The gods are good," Ser Hyle said in a dry voice, "but why trouble them, when you might just have kept your shoes?"

"Going barefoot was my penance. Even holy septons can be sinners, and my flesh was weak as weak could be. I was young and full of sap, and the girls . . . a septon can seem as gallant as a prince if he is the only man you know who has ever been more than a mile from your village. I would recite to them from *The Seven-Pointed Star.* The Maiden's Book worked best. Oh, I was a wicked man, before I threw away my shoes. It shames me to think of all the maidens I deflowered."

Brienne shifted in the saddle uncomfortably, thinking back to the camp below the walls of Highgarden and the wager Ser Hyle and the others had made to see who could bed her first.

"We're looking for a maiden," confided Podrick Payne. "A highborn girl of three-and-ten, with auburn hair."

"I had understood that you were seeking outlaws."

"Them too," Podrick admitted.

"Most travelers do all they can to avoid such men," said Septon Meribald, "yet you would seek them out."

"We only seek one outlaw," Brienne said. "The Hound."

"So Ser Hyle told me. May the Seven save you, child. It's said he leaves a trail of butchered babes and ravished maids behind him. The Mad Dog of Saltpans, I have heard him called. What would good folk want with such a creature?"

"The maid that Podrick spoke of may be with him."

"Truly? Then we must pray for the poor girl."

And for me, thought Brienne, *a prayer for me as well. Ask the Crone to raise her lamp and lead me to the Lady Sansa, and the Warrior to give strength to my arm so that I might defend her.* She did not say the words aloud, though; not where Hyle Hunt might hear her and mock her for her woman's weakness.

With Septon Meribald afoot and his donkey bearing such a heavy load, the going was slow all that day. They did not take the main road west, the road that Brienne had once ridden with Ser Jaime when they came the other way to find Maidenpool sacked and full of corpses. Instead they struck off toward the northwest, following the shore of the Bay of Crabs on a crooked track so small that it did not appear on either of Ser Hyle's precious sheepskin maps. The steep hills, black bogs, and piney woods of Cracklaw Point were nowhere to be found this side of Maidenpool. The lands they traveled through were low and wet, a wilderness of sandy dunes and salt marshes beneath a vast blue-grey vault of sky. The road was prone to vanishing amongst the reeds and tidal pools, only to appear again a mile farther on; without Meribald, Brienne knew, they surely would have lost their way. The ground was often soft, so in places the septon would walk ahead, tapping with his quarterstaff to make certain of the footing. There were no trees for leagues around, just sea and sky and sand.

No land could have been more different from Tarth, with its mountains and waterfalls, its high meadows and shadowed vales, yet this place had its own beauty, Brienne thought. They crossed a dozen slow-flowing streams alive with frogs and crickets, watched terns floating high above the bay, heard the sandpipers calling from amongst the dunes. Once a fox crossed their path, and set Meribald's dog to barking wildly.

And there were people too. Some lived amongst the reeds in houses built of mud and straw, whilst others fished the bay in leather coracles and built their homes on rickety wooden stilts above the dunes. Most seemed to live alone, out of sight of any human habitation but their own. They seemed a shy folk for the most part, but near midday the dog began to bark again, and three women emerged from the reeds to give Meribald a woven basket full of clams. He gave each of them an orange in return, though clams were as common as mud in this world, and oranges were rare and costly. One of the women was very old, one was heavy with child, and one was a girl as fresh and pretty as a flower in spring. When Meribald took them off to hear their sins, Ser Hyle chuckled, and said, "It would seem the gods walk with us . . . at least the Maiden, the Mother, and the Crone." Podrick looked so astonished that Brienne had to tell him no, they were only three marsh women.

Afterward, when they resumed their journey, she turned to the septon, and said, "These people live less than a day's ride from Maidenpool, and yet the fighting has not touched them."

"They have little to touch, my lady. Their treasures are shells and stones and leather boats, their finest weapons knives of rusted iron. They are born, they live, they love, they die. They know Lord Mooton rules their lands, but few have ever seen him, and Riverrun and King's Landing are only names to them."

"And yet they know the gods," said Brienne. "That is your work, I think. How long have you walked the river-lands?"

"It will be forty years soon," the septon said, and his dog gave a loud bark. "From Maidenpool to Maidenpool, my circuit takes me half a year and ofttimes more, but I will not say I know the Trident. I glimpse the castles of the great lords only at a distance, but I know the market towns and holdfasts, the villages too small to have a name, the hedges and the hills, the rills where a thirsty man can drink and the caves where he can shelter. And the roads the smallfolk use, the crooked muddy tracks that do not appear on parchment maps, I know them too." He chuckled. "I should. My feet have trod every mile of them, ten times over."

The back roads are the ones the outlaws use, and the caves would make fine places for hunted men to hide. A prickle of suspicion made Brienne wonder just how well Ser Hyle knew this man. "It must make for a lonely life, septon."

"The Seven are always with me," said Meribald, "and I have my faithful servant, and Dog."

"Does your dog have a name?" asked Podrick Payne.

"He must," said Meribald, "but he is not my dog. Not him."

The dog barked and wagged his tail. He was a huge, shaggy creature, ten stone of dog at least, but friendly.

"Who does he belong to?" asked Podrick.

"Why, to himself, and to the Seven. As to his name, he has not told me what it is. I call him Dog."

"Oh." Podrick did not know what to make of a dog named Dog, plainly. The boy chewed on that a while, then said, "I used to have a dog when I was little. I called him Hero."

"Was he?"

"Was he what?"

"A hero."

"No. He was a good dog, though. He died."

"Dog keeps me safe upon the roads, even in such trying times as these. Neither wolf nor outlaw dare molest me when Dog is at my side." The septon frowned. "The wolves have grown terrible of late. There are places where a man alone would do well to find a tree to sleep in. In all my years the biggest pack I ever saw had fewer than a dozen wolves in it, but the great pack that prowls along the Trident now numbers in the hundreds."

"Have you come on them yourself?" Ser Hyle asked.

"I have been spared that, Seven save me, but I have heard them in the night, and more than once. So many voices . . . a sound to curdle a man's blood. It even set Dog to shivering, and Dog has killed a dozen wolves." He ruffled the dog's head. "Some will tell you that they are demons. They say the pack is led by a monstrous she-wolf, a stalking shadow grim and grey and huge. They will tell you that she has been known to bring aurochs down all by herself, that no trap nor snare can hold her, that she fears neither steel nor fire, slays any wolf that tries to mount her, and devours no other flesh but man."

Ser Hyle Hunt laughed. "Now you've done it, septon. Poor Podrick's eyes are big as boiled eggs."

"They're not," said Podrick, indignant. Dog barked.

That night they made a cold camp in the dunes. Brienne sent Podrick walking by the shore to find some driftwood for a fire, but he came back empty-handed, with mud up to his knees. "The tide's out, ser. My lady. There's no water, only mudflats."

"Stay off the mud, child," counseled Septon Meribald. "The mud is not fond of strangers. If you walk in the wrong place, it will open up and swallow you."

"It's only *mud*," insisted Podrick.

"Until it fills your mouth and starts creeping up your nose. Then it's death." He smiled to take the chill off his words. "Wipe off that mud and have a slice of orange, lad."

The next day was more of the same. They broke their fast on salt cod and more orange slices, and were on their way before the sun was wholly risen, with a pink sky behind them and a purple sky ahead. Dog led the way, sniffing at every clump of reeds and stopping every now and then to piss on one; he seemed to know the road as well as Meribald. The cries of terns shivered through the morning air as the tide came rushing in.

Near midday they stopped at a tiny village, the first they had encountered, where eight of the stilt-houses loomed above a small stream. The men were out fishing in their coracles, but the women and young boys clambered down dangling rope ladders and gathered around Septon Meribald to pray. After the service he absolved their sins and left them with some turnips, a sack of beans, and two of his precious oranges.

Back on the road, the septon said, "We would do well to keep a watch tonight, my friends. The villagers say they've seen three broken men skulking round the dunes, west of the old watchtower."

"Only three?" Ser Hyle smiled. "Three is honey to our swordswench. They're not like to trouble armed men."

"Unless they're starving," the septon said. "There is food in these marshes, but only for those with the eyes to find it, and these men are strangers here, survivors from some battle. If they should accost us, ser, I beg you, leave them to me."

"What will you do with them?"

"Feed them. Ask them to confess their sins, so that I might forgive them. Invite them to come with us to the Quiet Isle."

"That's as good as inviting them to slit our throats as we sleep," Hyle Hunt replied. "Lord Randyll has better ways to deal with broken men—steel and hempen rope."

"Ser? My lady?" said Podrick. "Is a broken man an outlaw?"

"More or less," Brienne answered.

Septon Meribald disagreed. "More less than more. There are many sorts of outlaws, just as there are many sorts of birds. A sandpiper and a sea eagle both have wings, but they are not the same. The singers love to sing of good men forced to go outside the law to fight some wicked lord, but most outlaws are more like this ravening Hound than they are the lightning lord. They are evil men, driven by greed, soured by malice, despising the gods and caring only for themselves. Broken men are more deserving of our pity, though they may be just as dangerous. Almost all are common-born, simple folk who had never been more than a mile from the house where they were born until the day some lord came round to take them off to war. Poorly shod and poorly clad, they march away beneath his banners, ofttimes with no better arms than a sickle or a sharpened hoe, or a maul they made themselves by lashing a stone to a stick with strips of hide. Brothers march with brothers, sons with fathers, friends with friends. They've heard the songs and stories, so they go off with eager hearts, dreaming of the wonders they will see, of the wealth and glory they will win. War seems a fine adventure, the greatest most of them will ever know.

"Then they get a taste of battle.

"For some, that one taste is enough to break them. Others go on for years, until they lose count of all the battles they have fought in, but even a man who has survived a hundred fights can break in his hundred-and-first. Brothers watch their brothers die, fathers lose their sons, friends see their friends trying to hold their entrails in after they've been gutted by an axe.

"They see the lord who led them there cut down, and some other lord shouts that they are his now. They take a wound, and when that's still half-healed they take another. There is never enough to eat, their shoes fall to pieces from the marching, their clothes are torn and rotting, and half of them are shitting in their breeches from drinking bad water.

"If they want new boots or a warmer cloak or maybe a rusted iron halfhelm, they need to take them from a corpse, and before long they are stealing from the living too, from the smallfolk whose lands they're fighting in, men very like the men they used to be. They slaughter their sheep and steal their chickens, and from there it's just a short step to carrying off their daughters too. And one day they look around and realize all their friends and kin are gone, that they are fighting beside strangers beneath a banner that they hardly recognize. They don't know where they are or how to get back home and the lord they're fighting for does not know their names, yet here he comes, shouting for them to form up, to make a line with their spears and scythes and sharpened hoes, to stand their ground. And the knights come down on them, faceless men clad all in steel, and the iron thunder of their charge seems to fill the world . . .

"And the man breaks.

"He turns and runs, or crawls off afterward over the corpses of the slain, or steals away in the black of night, and he finds someplace to hide. All thought of home is gone by then, and kings and lords and gods mean less to him than a haunch of spoiled meat that will let him live another day, or a skin of bad wine that might drown his fear for a few hours. The broken man lives from day to day, from meal to meal, more beast than man. Lady Brienne is not wrong. In times like these, the traveler must beware of broken men, and fear them . . . but he should pity them as well."

When Meribald was finished a profound silence fell upon their little band. Brienne could hear the wind rustling through a clump of pussywillows, and farther off the faint cry of a loon. She could hear Dog panting softly as he loped along beside the septon and his donkey, tongue lolling from his mouth. The quiet stretched and stretched, until finally she said, "How old were you when they marched you off to war?"

"Why, no older than your boy," Meribald replied. "Too young for such, in truth, but my brothers were all going, and I would not be left behind. Willam said I could be his squire, though Will was no knight, only a potboy armed with a kitchen knife he'd stolen from the inn. He died upon the Stepstones, and never struck a blow. It was fever did for him, and for my brother Robin. Owen died from a mace that split his head apart, and his friend Jon Pox was hanged for rape."

"The War of the Ninepenny Kings?" asked Hyle Hunt.

"So they called it, though I never saw a king, nor earned a penny. It was a war, though. That it was."

SAMWELL

S am stood before the window, rocking nervously as he watched the last light of the sun vanish behind a row of sharp-peaked rooftops. *He must have gotten drunk again,* he thought glumly. *Or else he's met another girl.* He did not know whether to curse or weep. Dareon was supposed to be his brother. *Ask him to sing, and no one could be better. Ask him to do aught else . . .*

The mists of evening had begun to rise, sending grey fingers up the walls of the buildings that lined the old canal. "He promised he'd be back," Sam said. "You heard him too."

Gilly looked at him with eyes red-rimmed and puffy. Her hair hung about her face, unwashed and tangled. She looked like some wary animal peering through a bush. It had been days since they'd last had a fire, yet the wildling girl liked to huddle near the hearth, as if the cold ashes still held some lingering warmth. "He doesn't like it here with us," she said, whispering so as not to wake the babe. "It's sad here. He likes it where the wine is, and the smiles."

Yes, thought Sam, *and the wine is everywhere but here.* Braavos was full of inns, alehouses, and brothels. And if Dareon preferred a fire and a cup of mulled wine to stale bread and the company of a weeping woman, a fat craven, and a sick old man, who could blame him? *I could blame him. He said he would be back before the gloaming; he said he would bring us wine and food.*

He looked out the window once more, hoping against hope to see the singer hurrying home. Darkness was falling across the secret city, creeping through the alleys and down the canals. The good folk of Braavos would soon be shuttering their windows and sliding bars across their doors. Night belonged to the bravos and the courtesans. *Dareon's new friends,* Sam thought bitterly. They were all the singer could talk about of late. He was trying to write a song about one courtesan, a woman called the Moonshadow who had heard him singing beside the Moon Pool and rewarded him with a kiss. "You should have asked her for silver," Sam had said. "It's coin we need, not kisses." But the singer only smiled. "Some kisses are worth more than yellow gold, Slayer."

That made him angry too. Dareon was not supposed to be making up songs about courtesans. He was supposed to be singing about the Wall and the valor of the Night's Watch. Jon had hoped that perhaps his songs might persuade a few young men to take the black. Instead he sang of golden kisses, silvery hair, and red, red lips. No one ever took the black for red, red lips.

Sometimes his playing would wake the babe too. Then the child would begin to wail, Dareon would shout at him to be quiet, Gilly would weep, and the singer would storm out and not return for days. "All that weeping makes me want to slap her," he complained, "and I can scarce sleep for her sobbing."

You would weep as well if you had a son and lost him, Sam almost said. He could not blame Gilly for her grief. Instead, he blamed Jon Snow and wondered when Jon's heart had turned to stone. Once he asked Maester Aemon that very question, when Gilly was down at the canal fetching water for them. "When you raised him up to be the lord commander," the old man answered.

Even now, rotting here in this cold room beneath the eaves, part of Sam did not want to believe that Jon had done what Maester Aemon thought. *It must be true, though. Why else would Gilly weep so much?* All he had to do was ask her whose child she was nursing at her breast, but he did not have the courage. He was afraid of the answer he might get. *I am still a craven, Jon.* No matter where he went in this wide world, his fears went with him.

A hollow rumbling echoed off the roofs of Braavos, like the sound of distant thunder; the Titan, sounding nightfall from across the lagoon. The noise was loud enough to wake the babe, and his sudden wail woke Maester Aemon. As Gilly went to give the boy the breast, the old man's eyes opened, and he stirred feebly in his narrow bed. "Egg? It's dark. Why is it so dark?"

Because you're blind. Aemon's wits were wandering more and more since they arrived at Braavos. Some days he did not seem to know where he was. Some days he would lose his way when saying something and begin to ramble on about his father or his brother. *He is one hundred and two,* Sam reminded himself, but he had been just as old at Castle Black and his wits had never wandered there.

"It's me," he had to say. "Samwell Tarly. Your steward."

"Sam." Maester Aemon licked his lips, and blinked. "Yes. And this is Braavos. Forgive me, Sam. Is morning come?"

"No." Sam felt the old man's brow. His skin was damp with sweat, cool and clammy to the touch, his every breath a soft wheeze. "It's night, maester. You've been asleep."

"Too long. It's cold in here."

"We have no wood," Sam told him, "and the innkeep will not give us more unless we have the coin." It was the fourth or fifth time they'd had this same conversation. *I should have used our coin for wood,* Sam chided himself every time. *I should have had the sense to keep him warm.*

Instead he had squandered the last of their silver on a healer from the House of the Red Hands, a tall pale man in robes embroidered with swirling stripes of red and white. All that the silver bought him was half a flask of dreamwine. "This may help gentle his passing," the Braavosi had said, not unkindly. When Sam asked if there wasn't any more that he could do, he shook his head. "Ointments I have, potions and infusions, tinctures and venoms and poultices. I might bleed him, purge him, leech him . . . but why? No leech can make him young again. This is an old man, and death is in his lungs. Give him this and let him sleep."

And so he had, all night and all day, but now the old man was struggling to sit. "We must go down to the ships."

The ships again. "You're too weak to go out," he had to say. A chill had gotten inside Maester Aemon during the voyage and settled in his chest. By the time they got to Braavos, he had been so weak they'd had to carry him ashore. They'd still had a fat bag of silver then, so Dareon had asked for the inn's biggest bed. The one they'd gotten was large enough to sleep eight, so the innkeep insisted on charging them for that many.

"On the morrow we can go to the docks," Sam promised. "You can ask about and find which ship is departing next for Oldtown." Even in autumn, Braavos was still a busy port. Once Aemon was strong enough to travel, they should have no trouble finding a suitable vessel to take them where they had to go. Paying for their passage would prove more difficult. A ship from the Seven Kingdoms would be their best hope. *A trader out of Oldtown, maybe, with kin in the Night's Watch. There must still be some who honor the men who walk the Wall.*

"Oldtown," Maester Aemon wheezed. "Yes. I dreamt of Oldtown, Sam. I was young again and my brother Egg was with me, with that big knight he served. We were drinking in the old inn where they make the fearsomely strong cider." He tried to rise again, but the effort proved too much for him. After a moment he settled back. "The ships," he said again. "We will find our answer there. About the dragons. I need to know."

No, thought Sam, *it's food and warmth you need, a full belly and a hot fire crackling in the hearth.* "Are you hungry, maester? We have some bread left, and a bit of cheese."

"Not just now, Sam. Later, when I'm feeling stronger."

"How will you get stronger unless you eat?" None of them had eaten much at sea, not after Skagos. The autumn gales had hounded them all across the narrow sea. Sometimes they came up from the south, roiling with thunder and lightning and black rains that fell for days. Sometimes they came down from the north, cold and grim, with savage winds that cut right through a man. Once it got so cold that Sam had woken to find the whole ship coated in ice, shining as white as pearl. The captain had taken down their mast and tied it to the deck, to finish the crossing on oars alone. No one had been eating by the time they saw the Titan.

Once safe ashore, though, Sam had found himself ravenously hungry. It was the same for Dareon and Gilly. Even the babe had begun to suck more lustily. Aemon, though . . .

"The bread's gone stale, but I can beg some gravy from the kitchens to soak it in," Sam told the old man. The innkeep was a hard man, cold-eyed and suspicious of these black-clad strangers beneath his roof, but his cook was kinder.

"No. Perhaps a sip of wine, though?"

They had no wine. Dareon had promised to buy some with the coin from his singing. "We'll have wine later," Sam had to say. "There's water, but it's not the good water." The good water came over the arches of the great brick aqueduct the Braavosi called the sweetwater river. Rich men had it piped into their homes; the poor filled their pails and buckets at public fountains. Sam had sent Gilly out to get some, forgetting that the wildling girl had lived her whole life in sight of Craster's Keep and never seen so much as a market town. The stony maze of islands and canals that was Braavos, devoid of grass and trees and teeming with strangers who spoke to her in words she could not understand, frightened her so badly that she lost the map and soon herself. Sam found her weeping at the stony feet of some long-dead sealord. "All we have is canal water," he told Maester Aemon, "but the cook gave it a boil. There's dreamwine too, if you need more of that."

"I have dreamt enough for now. Canal water will suffice. Help me, if you would."

Sam eased the old man up and held the cup to his dry, cracked lips. Even so, half the water dribbled down the maester's chest. "Enough," Aemon coughed, after a few sips. "You'll drown me." He shivered in Sam's arms. "Why is the room so cold?"

"There's no more wood." Dareon had paid the innkeep double for a room with a hearth, but none of them had realized that wood would be so costly here. Trees did not grow on Braavos, save in the courts and gardens of the mighty. Nor would the Braavosi cut the pines that covered the outlying islands around their great lagoon and acted as windbreaks to shield them from storms. Instead, firewood was brought in by barge, up the rivers and across the lagoon. Even dung was dear here; the Braavosi used boats in place of horses. None of that would have mattered if they had departed as planned for Oldtown, but that had proved impossible with Maester Aemon so weak. Another voyage on the open sea would kill him.

Aemon's hand crept across the blankets, groping for Sam's arm. "We must go to the docks, Sam."

"When you are stronger." The old man was in no state to brave the salt spray and wet winds along the waterfront, and Braavos was all waterfront. To the north was the Purple Harbor, where Braavosi traders tied up beneath the domes and towers of the Sealord's Palace. To the west lay the Ragman's Harbor, crowded with ships from the other Free Cities, from Westeros and Ibben and the fabled, far-off lands of the east. And everywhere else were little piers and ferry berths and old grey wharves where shrimpers and crabbers and fisherfolk moored after working the mudflats and river mouths. "It would be too great a strain on you."

"Then go in my stead," Aemon urged, "and bring me someone who has seen these dragons."

"Me?" Sam was dismayed by the suggestion. "Maester, it was only a story. A sailor's story." Dareon was to blame for this as well. The singer had been bringing back all manner of queer tales from the alehouses and brothels. Unfortunately, he had been in his cups when he heard the one about the dragons and could not recall the details. "Dareon may have made up the whole story. Singers do that. They make things up."

"They do," said Maester Aemon, "but even the most fanciful song may hold a kernel of truth. Find that truth for me, Sam."

"I wouldn't know who to ask, or how to ask him. I only have a little High Valyrian, and when they speak to me in Braavosi I cannot understand half of what they're saying. You speak more tongues than I do, once you are stronger you can . . ."

"When will I be stronger, Sam? Tell me that."

"Soon. If you rest and eat. When we reach Oldtown . . ."

"I shall not see Oldtown again. I know that now." The old man tightened his grip on Sam's arm. "I will be with my brothers soon. Some were bound to me by vows and some by blood, but they were all my brothers. And my father . . . he never thought the throne would pass to him, and yet it did. He used to say that was his punishment for the blow that slew his brother. I pray he found the peace in death that he never knew in life. The septons sing of sweet surcease, of laying down our burdens and voyaging to a far sweet land where we may laugh and love and feast until the end of days . . . but what if there is no land of light and honey, only cold and dark and pain beyond the wall called death?"

He is afraid, Sam realized. "You are not dying. You're ill, that's all. It will pass."

"Not this time, Sam. I dreamed . . . in the black of night a man asks all the questions he dare not ask by daylight. For me, these past years, only one question has remained.

Why would the gods take my eyes and my strength, yet condemn me to linger on so long, frozen and forgotten? What use could they have for an old done man like me?" Aemon's fingers trembled, twigs sheathed in spotted skin. "I remember, Sam. I still remember."

He was not making sense. "Remember what?"

"Dragons," Aemon whispered. "The grief and glory of my House, they were."

"The last dragon died before you were born," said Sam. "How could you remember them?"

"I see them in my dreams, Sam. I see a red star bleeding in the sky. I still remember red. I see their shadows on the snow, hear the crack of leathern wings, feel their hot breath. My brothers dreamed of dragons too, and the dreams killed them, every one. Sam, we tremble on the cusp of half-remembered prophecies, of wonders and terrors that no man now living could hope to comprehend . . . or . . ."

"Or?" said Sam.

". . . or not." Aemon chuckled softly. "Or I am an old man, feverish and dying." He closed his white eyes wearily, then forced them open once again. "I should not have left the Wall. Lord Snow could not have known, but *I* should have seen it. Fire consumes, but cold preserves. The Wall . . . but it is too late to go running back. The Stranger waits outside my door and will not be denied. Steward, you have served me faithfully. Do this one last brave thing for me. Go down to the ships, Sam. Learn all you can about these dragons."

Sam eased his arm out of the old man's grasp. "I will. If you want. I only . . ." He did not know what else to say. *I cannot refuse him.* He could look for Dareon as well, along the docks and wharves of the Ragman's Harbor. *I will find Dareon first, and we'll go to the ships together.*

And when we come back, we'll bring food and wine and wood. We'll have a fire and a good hot meal. He rose. "Well. I should go, then. If I am going. Gilly will be here. Gilly, bar the door when I am gone." *The Stranger waits outside the door.*

Gilly nodded, cradling the babe against her breast, her eyes welling full of tears. *She is going to weep again,* Sam realized. It was more than he could take. His swordbelt hung from a peg on the wall, beside the old cracked horn that Jon had given him. He ripped it down and buckled it about him, then swept his black wool cloak about his rounded shoulders, slumped through the door, and clattered down a wooden stair whose steps creaked beneath his weight. The inn had two front doors, one opening on a street and one on a canal. Sam went out through the former, to avoid the common room where the innkeep was sure to give him the sour eye that he reserved for guests who had overstayed their welcome.

There was a chill in the air, but the night was not half so foggy as some. Sam was grateful for that much. Sometimes the mists covered the ground so thick that a man could not see his own feet. Once he had come within a step of walking into a canal.

As a boy Sam had read a history of Braavos and dreamed of one day coming here. He wanted to behold the Titan rising stern and fearsome from the sea, glide down the canals in a serpent boat past all the palaces and temples, and watch the bravos do their water dance, blades flashing in the starlight. But now that he was here, all he wanted was to leave and go to Oldtown.

With his hood up and his cloak flapping, he made his way along the cobblestones toward the Ragman's Harbor. His swordbelt kept threatening to fall down about his ankles, so he had to keep tugging it back up as he went. He stayed to the smaller, darker streets, where he was less likely to encounter anyone, yet every passing cat still made his heart thump . . . and Braavos crawled with cats. *I need to find Dareon,* he thought. *He is a man of the Night's Watch, my Sworn Brother; he and I will puzzle out what to do.* Maester Aemon's strength was gone, and Gilly would have been lost here even if she had not been grief-stricken, but Dareon . . . *I should not think ill of him. He could be hurt, perhaps that is why he did not come back. He could be dead, lying in some alley in a pool of blood, or floating facedown in one of the canals.* At night the bravos swaggered through the city in their parti-colored finery, spoiling to prove their skill with those slender swords they wore. Some would fight for any cause, some for none at all, and Dareon had a loose tongue and quick temper, especially when he'd been drinking. *Just because a man can sing about battles doesn't mean he's fit to fight one.*

The best alehouses, inns, and brothels were near the Purple Harbor or the Moon Pool, but Dareon preferred the Ragman's Harbor, where the patrons were more apt to speak the Common Tongue. Sam began his search at the Inn of the Green Eel, the Black Bargeman, and Moroggo's, places where Dareon had played before. He was not to be found at any of them. Outside the Foghouse several serpent boats were tied up awaiting patrons, and Sam tried to ask the polemen if they had seen a singer all in black, but none of the polemen understood his High Valyrian. *That, or they do not chose to understand.* Sam peered into the dingy winesink beneath the second arch of Nabbo's Bridge, barely large enough to accommodate ten people. Dareon was not one of them. He tried the Outcast Inn, the House of Seven Lamps, and the brothel called the Cattery, where he got strange looks but no help.

Leaving, he almost bumped into two young men beneath

the Cattery's red lantern. One was dark and one was fair. The dark-haired one said something in Braavosi. "I am sorry," Sam had to say. "I do not understand." He edged away from them, afraid. In the Seven Kingdoms nobles draped themselves in velvets, silks, and samites of a hundred hues whilst peasants and smallfolk wore raw wool and dull brown roughspun. In Braavos it was otherwise. The bravos swaggered about like peacocks, fingering their swords, whilst the mighty dressed in charcoal grey and purple, blues that were almost black and blacks as dark as a moonless night.

"My friend Terro says you are so fat you make him sick," said the fair-haired bravo, whose jacket was green velvet on one side and cloth-of-silver on the other. "My friend Terro says that the rattle of your sword makes his head ache." He was speaking in the Common Tongue. The other one, the dark-haired bravo in the burgundy brocade and yellow cloak whose name would appear to have been Terro, made some comment in Braavosi, and his fair-haired friend laughed, and said, "My friend Terro says you dress above your station. Are you some great lord, to wear the black?"

Sam wanted to run, but if he did was like to trip over his own swordbelt. *Do not touch your sword,* he told himself. Even a finger on the hilt might be enough for one or the other of the bravos to take as a challenge. He tried to think of words that might appease them. "I'm not—" was all he managed.

"He is not a lord," a child's voice put in. "He's in the Night's Watch, stupid. From *Westeros.*" A girl edged into the light, pushing a barrow full of seaweed; a scruffy, skinny creature in big boots, with ragged unwashed hair. "There's another one down at the Happy Port, singing songs to the Sailor's Wife," she informed the two bravos.

To Sam she said, "If they ask who is the most beautiful woman in the world, say the Nightingale or else they'll challenge you. Do you want to buy some clams? I sold all my oysters."

"I have no coin," Sam said.

"He has no coin," mocked the fair-haired bravo. His dark-haired friend grinned and said something in Braavosi. "My friend Terro is chilly. Be our good fat friend and give him your cloak."

"Don't do that either," said the barrow girl, "or else they'll ask for your boots next, and before long you'll be naked."

"Little cats who howl too loud get drowned in the canals," warned the fair-haired bravo.

"Not if they have claws." And suddenly there was a knife in the girl's left hand, a blade as skinny as she was. The one called Terro said something to his fair-haired friend and the two of them moved off, chuckling at one another.

"Thank you," Sam told the girl when they were gone.

Her knife vanished. "If you wear a sword at night it means you can be challenged. Did you *want* to fight them?"

"No." It came out in a squeak that made Sam wince.

"Are you truly in the Night's Watch? I never saw a black brother like you before." The girl gestured at the barrow. "You can have the last clams if you want. It's dark, no one will buy them now. Are you sailing to the Wall?"

"To Oldtown." Sam took one of the baked clams and wolfed it down. "We're between ships." The clam was good. He ate another.

"The bravos never bother anyone without a sword. Not even stupid camel cunts like Terro and Orbelo."

"Who are you?"

"No one." She stank of fish. "I used to be someone, but now I'm not. You can call me Cat, if you like. Who are you?"

"Samwell, of House Tarly. You speak the Common Tongue."

"My father was the oarmaster on *Nymeria*. A bravo killed him for saying that my mother was more beautiful than the Nightingale. Not one of those camel cunts you met, a real bravo. Someday I'll slit his throat. The captain said *Nymeria* had no need of little girls, so he put me off. Brusco took me in and gave me a barrow." She looked up at him. "What ship will you be sailing on?"

"We bought passage on the *Lady Ushanora*."

The girl squinted at him suspiciously. "She's gone. Don't you know? She left days and days ago."

I know, Sam might have said. He and Dareon had stood on the dock watching the rise and fall of her oars as she beat for the Titan and the open sea. "Well," the singer said, "that's done." If Sam had been a braver man, he would have shoved him into the water. When it came to talking girls out of their clothes Dareon had a honeyed tongue, yet in the captain's cabin somehow Sam had done all the talking, trying to persuade the Braavosi to wait for them. "Three days I have waited for this old man," the captain had said. "My holds are full, and my men have fucked their wives farewell. With you or without, my *Lady* leaves on the tide."

"Please," Sam had pleaded. "Just a few more days, that's all I ask. So Maester Aemon can recover his strength."

"He has no strength." The captain had visited the inn the night before to see Maester Aemon for himself. "He is old and ill and I will not have him dying on my *Lady*. Stay with him or leave him, it matters not to me. I sail." Even worse, he had refused to return the passage money they had paid him, the silver that was meant to see them safe to Oldtown. "You bought my finest cabin. It is there, awaiting you. If you do not choose to occupy it, that is no fault of mine. Why should I bear the loss?"

By now we might be at Duskendale, Sam thought mournfully. *We might even have reached Pentos, if the winds were kind.*

But none of that would matter to the barrow girl. "You said you saw a singer . . ."

"At the Happy Port. He's going to wed the Sailor's Wife."

"Wed?"

"She only beds the ones who marry her."

"Where is this Happy Port?"

"Across from the Mummer's Ship. I can show you the way."

"I know the way." Sam had seen the Mummer's Ship. *Dareon cannot wed! He said the words!* "I have to go."

He ran. It was a long way over slick cobbles. Before long he was puffing, his big black cloak flapping noisily behind him. He had to keep one hand on his swordbelt as he ran. What few people he encountered gave him curious looks, and once a cat reared up and hissed at him. By the time he reached the ship he was staggering. The Happy Port was just across the alley.

No sooner had he entered, flushed and out of breath, than a one-eyed woman threw her arms around his neck. "Don't," Sam told her, "I'm not here for that." She answered in Braavosi. "I do not speak that tongue," Sam said in High Valyrian. There were candles burning and a fire crackling in the hearth. Someone was sawing on a fiddle, and he saw two girls dancing around a red priest, holding hands. The one-eyed woman pressed her breasts against his chest. "Don't do that! I'm not here for that!"

"Sam!" Dareon's familiar voice rang out. "Yna, let him go, that's Sam the Slayer. My Sworn Brother!"

The one-eyed woman peeled away, though she kept one hand on his arm. One of the dancers called out, "He can slay me if he likes," and the other said, "Do you think he'd let me touch his sword?" Behind them a purple galleas had been painted on the wall, crewed by women clad in thigh-high boots and nothing else. A Tyroshi sailor was passed out in a corner, snoring into his huge scarlet beard. Elsewhere an older woman with huge breasts was turning tiles with a massive Summer Islander in black-and-scarlet feathers. In the center of it all sat Dareon, nuzzling at the neck of the woman in his lap. She was wearing his black cloak.

"Slayer," the singer called out drunkenly, "come meet my lady wife." His hair was sand and honey, his smile warm. "I sang her love songs. Women melt like butter when I sing. How could I resist this face?" He kissed her nose. "Wife, give Slayer a kiss, he's my brother." When the girl got to her feet, Sam saw that she was naked underneath the cloak. "Don't go fondling my wife now, Slayer," said Dareon, laughing. "But if you want one of her sisters, you feel free. I still have coin enough, I think."

Coin that might have bought us food, Sam thought, *coin that might have bought wood, so Maester Aemon could keep warm.* "What have you done? You can't *marry*. You said the words, the same as me. They could have your head for this."

"We're only wed for this one night, Slayer. Even in Westeros no one takes your head for that. Haven't you ever gone to Mole's Town to dig for buried treasure?"

"No." Sam reddened. "I would never . . ."

"What about your wildling wench? You must have fucked her a time or three. All those nights in the woods, huddled together under your cloak, don't you tell me that you never stuck it in her." He waved a hand toward a chair. "Sit down, Slayer. Have a cup of wine. Have a whore. Have both."

Sam did not want a cup of wine. "You promised to come back before the gloaming. To bring back wine and food."

"Is this how you killed that Other? Scolding him to death?" Dareon laughed. "*She*'s my wife, not you. If you will not drink to my marriage, go away."

"Come with me," said Sam. "Maester Aemon's woken up and wants to hear about these dragons. He's talking about bleeding stars and white shadows and dreams and . . . if we could find out more about these dragons, it might help give him ease. Help me."

"On the morrow. Not on my wedding night." Dareon pushed himself to his feet, took his bride by the hand, and started toward the stairs, pulling her behind him.

Sam blocked his way. "You *promised,* Dareon. You said the words. You're supposed to be my brother."

"In Westeros. Does this look like Westeros to you?"

"Maester Aemon—"

"—is dying. That stripey healer you wasted all our silver on said as much." Dareon's mouth had turned hard. "Have a girl or go away, Sam. You're ruining my wedding."

"I'll go," said Sam, "but you'll come with me."

"No. I'm done with you. I'm done with *black.*" Dareon tore his cloak off his naked bride and tossed it in Sam's face. "Here. Throw that rag on the old man, it may keep him a little warmer. I shan't be needing it. I'll be clad in velvet soon. Next year I'll be wearing furs and eating—"

Sam hit him.

He did not think about it. His hand came up, curled into a fist, and crashed into the singer's mouth. Dareon cursed and his naked wife gave a shriek and Sam threw himself onto the singer and knocked him backwards over a low table. They were almost of a height, but Sam weighed twice as much, and for once he was too angry to be afraid. He punched the singer in the face and in the belly, then began to pummel him about the shoulders with both hands. When Dareon grabbed his wrists, Sam butted him with his head and broke his lip. The singer let go and he smashed him in the nose. Somewhere a man was laughing, a woman cursing. The fight seemed to slow, as if they were two black flies struggling in amber. Then someone dragged Sam off the singer's chest. He hit that person too, and something hard crashed into his head.

The next he knew he was outside, flying headfirst through the fog. For half a heartbeat he saw black water underneath him. Then the canal came up and smashed him in the face.

Sam sank like a stone, like a boulder, like a mountain. The water got into his eyes and up his nose, dark and cold and salty. When he tried to shout for help he swallowed more. Kicking and gasping, he rolled over, bubbles bursting from his nose. *Swim,* he told himself, *swim.* The brine stung his eyes when he opened them, blinding him. He popped to the surface for just an instant, sucked down air, and slapped desperately with one hand whilst the other scrabbled at the wall of the canal. But the stones were slick and slimy and he could not get a grasp. He sank again.

Sam could feel the cold against his skin as the water soaked through his clothes. His swordbelt slipped down his legs and tangled round his ankles. *I'm going to drown,* he thought, in a blind black panic. He thrashed, trying to claw his way back to the surface, but instead his face bumped the bottom of the canal. *I'm upside down,* he realized, *I'm drowning.* Something moved beneath one flailing hand, an eel or a fish, slithering through his fingers. *I can't drown, Maester Aemon will die without me, and Gilly will have no one. I have to swim, I have to . . .*

There was a huge splash, and something coiled around him, under his arms and around his chest. *The eel,* was his first thought, *the eel has got me, it's going to pull me down.* He opened his mouth to scream, and swallowed more water. *I'm drowned,* was his last thought. *Oh, gods be good, I'm drowned.*

When he opened his eyes he was on his back and a big black Summer Islander was pounding on his belly with fists the size of hams. *Stop that, you're hurting me,* Sam tried to scream. Instead of words he retched out water, and gasped. He was sodden and shivering, lying on the cobbles in a puddle of canal water. The Summer Islander punched him in the belly again, and more water came squirting out his nose. "Stop that," Sam gasped. "I haven't drowned. I haven't drowned."

"No." His rescuer leaned over him, huge and black and dripping. "You owe Xhondo many feathers. The water ruined Xhondo's fine cloak."

It had, Sam saw. The feathered cloak clung to the black man's huge shoulders, sodden and soiled. "I never meant . . ."

". . . to be swimming? Xhondo saw. Too much splashing. Fat men should float." He grabbed Sam's doublet with a huge black fist and hauled him to his feet. "Xhondo mates on *Cinnamon Wind*. Many tongues he speaks, a little. Inside Xhondo laughs, to see you punch the singer. And Xhondo hears." A broad white smile spread across his face. "Xhondo knows these dragons."

JAIME

I had hoped that by now you would have grown tired
of that wretched beard. All that hair makes you look
like Robert." His sister had put aside her mourning
for a jade-green gown with sleeves of silver Myrish lace.
An emerald the size of a pigeon's egg hung on a golden
chain about her neck.

"Robert's beard was black. Mine is gold."

"Gold? Or silver?" Cersei plucked a hair from beneath
his chin and held it up. It was grey. "All the color is drain-
ing out of you, brother. You've become a ghost of what
you were, a pale crippled thing. And so bloodless, always
in white." She flicked the hair away. "I prefer you garbed
in crimson and gold."

*I prefer you dappled in sunlight, with water beading on
your naked skin.* He wanted to kiss her, carry her to her
bedchamber, throw her on the bed . . . *she's been fucking*

Lancel and Osmund Kettleblack and Moon Boy . . . "I will make a bargain with you. Relieve me of this duty, and my razor is yours to command."

Her mouth tightened. She had been drinking hot spiced wine and smelled of nutmeg. "You presume to dicker with me? Need I remind you, you are sworn to obey."

"I am sworn to protect the king. My place is at his side."

"Your place is wherever he sends you."

"Tommen puts his seal on every paper that you put in front of him. This is your doing, and it's folly. Why name Daven your Warden of the West if you have no faith in him?"

Cersei took a seat beneath the window. Behind her Jaime could see the blackened ruin of the Tower of the Hand. "Why so reluctant, ser? Did you lose your courage with your hand?"

"I swore an oath to Lady Stark, never again to take up arms against the Starks or Tullys."

"A drunken promise made with a sword at your throat."

"How can I defend Tommen if I am not with him?"

"By defeating his enemies. Father always said that a swift sword stroke is a better defense than any shield. Admittedly, most sword strokes require a hand. Still, even a crippled lion may inspire fear. I want Riverrun. I want Brynden Tully chained or dead. And someone needs to set Harrenhal to rights. We have urgent need of Wylis Manderly, assuming he is still alive and captive, but the garrison has not replied to any of our ravens."

"Those are Gregor's men at Harrenhal," Jaime reminded her. "The Mountain liked them cruel and stupid. Most like they ate your ravens, messages and all."

"That's why I'm sending you. They may eat you as well, brave brother, but I trust you'll give them indigestion." Cersei smoothed her skirt. "I want Ser Osmund to command the Kingsguard in your absence."

. . . she's been fucking Lancel and Osmund Kettleblack and Moon Boy for all I know . . . "That's not your choice. If I must go, Ser Loras will command here in my stead."

"Is that a jape? You know how I feel about Ser Loras."

"If you had not sent Balon Swann to Dorne—"

"I need him there. These Dornishmen cannot be trusted. That red snake championed Tyrion, have you forgotten that? I will not leave my daughter to their mercy. And I will *not* have Loras Tyrell commanding the Kingsguard."

"Ser Loras is thrice the man Ser Osmund is."

"Your notions of manhood have changed somewhat, brother."

Jaime felt his anger rising. "True, Loras does not leer at your teats the way Ser Osmund does, but I hardly think—"

"Think about this." Cersei slapped his face.

Jaime made no attempt to block the blow. "I see I need a thicker beard, to cushion me against my queen's caresses." He wanted to rip her gown off and turn her blows to kisses. He'd done it before, back when he had two good hands.

The queen's eyes were green ice. "You had best go, ser."

. . . Lancel, Osmund Kettleblack, and Moon Boy . . .

"Are you deaf as well as maimed? You'll find the door behind you, ser."

"As you command." Jaime turned on his heel and left her.

Somewhere the gods were laughing. Cersei had never taken kindly to being balked, he *knew* that. Softer words might have swayed her, yet of late the very sight of her made him angry.

Part of him would be glad to put King's Landing behind him. He had no taste for the company of the lickspittles and fools who surrounded Cersei. "The smallest council," they were calling them in Flea Bottom, according to Addam Marbrand. And Qyburn . . . he might have saved Jaime's life, but he was still a Bloody Mummer. "Qyburn stinks of secrets," he warned Cersei. That only made her laugh. "We all have secrets, brother," she replied.

    . . . *she's been fucking Lancel and Osmund Kettleblack and Moon Boy for all I know* . . .

Forty knights and as many esquires awaited him outside the Red Keep's stables. Half were westermen sworn to House Lannister, the others recent foes turned doubtful friends. Ser Dermot of the Rainwood would carry Tommen's standard, Red Ronnet Connington the white banner of the Kingsguard. A Paege, a Piper, and a Peckledon would share the honor of squiring for the Lord Commander. "Keep friends at your back and foes where you can see them," Sumner Crakehall had once counseled him. Or had that been Father?

His palfrey was a blood bay, his destrier a magnificent grey stallion. It had been long years since Jaime had named any of his horses; he had seen too many die in battle, and that was harder when you named them. But when the Piper boy started calling them Honor and Glory, he laughed and let the names stand. Glory wore trappings of Lannister crimson; Honor was barded in Kingsguard white. Josmyn Peckledon held the palfrey's reins as Ser Jaime mounted. The squire was skinny as a spear, with long arms and legs, greasy mouse-brown hair, and cheeks soft with peach fuzz. His cloak was Lannister crimson, but his surcoat showed the ten purple mullets of his own House arrayed upon a yellow field. "My lord," the lad asked, "will you be wanting your new hand?"

"Wear it, Jaime," urged Ser Kennos of Kayce. "Wave at the smallfolk and give them a tale to tell their children."

"I think not." Jaime would not show the crowds a golden lie. *Let them see the stump. Let them see the cripple.* "But feel free to make up for my lack, Ser Kennos. Wave with both hands, and waggle your feet if it please you." He gathered the reins in his left hand and wheeled his horse around. "Payne," he called as the rest were forming up, "you'll ride beside me."

Ser Ilyn Payne made his way to Jaime's side, looking like the beggar at the ball. His ringmail was old and rusted, worn over a stained jack of boiled leather. Neither the man nor his mount showed any heraldry; his shield was so hacked and battered it was hard to say what color paint might once have covered it. With his grim face and deep-sunk hollow eyes, Ser Ilyn might have passed for death himself . . . as he had, for years.

No longer, though. Ser Ilyn had been half of Jaime's price, for swallowing his boy king's command like a good little Lord Commander. The other half had been Ser Addam Marbrand. "I need them," he had told his sister, and Cersei had not put up a fight. *Most like she's pleased to rid herself of them.* Ser Addam was a boyhood friend of Jaime's, and the silent headsman had belonged to their father, if he belonged to anyone. Payne had been the captain of the Hand's guard when he had been heard boasting that it was Lord Tywin who ruled the Seven Kingdoms and told King Aerys what to do. Aerys Targaryen took his tongue for that.

"Open the gates," said Jaime, and Strongboar, in his booming voice, called out, *"OPEN THE GATES!"*

When Mace Tyrell had marched out through the Mud Gate to the sound of drums and fiddles, thousands lined the streets to cheer him off. Little boys had joined the march, striding along beside the Tyrell soldiers with heads held high and legs pumping, whilst their sisters threw down kisses from the windows.

Not so today. A few whores called out invitations as they passed, and a meat pie man cried his wares. In Cobbler's Square two threadbare sparrows were haranguing several hundred smallfolk, crying doom upon the heads of godless men and demon worshipers. The crowd parted for the column. Sparrows and cobblers alike looked on with dull eyes. "They like the smell of roses but have no love for lions," Jaime observed. "My sister would be wise to take note of that." Ser Ilyn made no reply. *The perfect companion for a long ride. I will enjoy his conversation.*

The greater part of his command awaited him beyond the city walls; Ser Addam Marbrand with his outriders, Ser Steffon Swyft and the baggage train, the Holy Hundred of old Ser Bonifer the Good, Sarsfield's mounted archers, Maester Gulian with four cages full of ravens, two hundred heavy horse under Ser Flement Brax. Not a great host, all in all; fewer than a thousand men in total. Numbers were the last thing needed at Riverrun. A Lannister army already invested the castle, and an even larger force of Freys; the last bird they'd received suggested that the besiegers were having difficulty keeping themselves fed. Brynden Tully had scoured the land clean before retiring behind his walls.

Not that it required much scouring. From what Jaime had seen of the riverlands, scarce a field remained unburnt, a town unsacked, a maiden undespoiled. *And now my sweet sister sends me to finish the work that Amory Lorch and Gregor Clegane began.* It left a bitter taste in his mouth.

This near to King's Landing, the kingsroad was as safe as any road could be in such times, yet Jaime sent

Marbrand and his outriders ahead to scout. "Robb Stark took me unawares in the Whispering Wood," he said. "That will never happen again."

"You have my word on it." Marbrand seemed visibly relieved to be ahorse again, wearing the smoke-grey cloak of his own House instead of the gold wool of the City Watch. "If any foe should come within a dozen leagues, you will know of them beforehand."

Jaime had given stern commands that no man was to depart the column without his leave. Elsewise, he knew he would have bored young lordlings racing through the fields, scattering livestock and trampling down the crops. There were still cows and sheep to be seen near the city; apples on the trees and berries in the brush, stands of barleycorn and oats and winter wheat, wayns and oxcarts on the road. Farther afield, things would not be so rosy.

Riding at the front of the host with Ser Ilyn silent by his side, Jaime felt almost content. The sun was warm on his back and the wind riffled through his hair like a woman's fingers. When Little Lew Piper came galloping up with a helm full of blackberries, Jaime ate a handful and told the boy to share the rest with his fellow squires and Ser Ilyn Payne.

Payne seemed as comfortable in his silence as in his rusted ringmail and boiled leather. The clop of his gelding's hooves and the rattle of sword in scabbard whenever he shifted his seat were the only sounds he made. Though his pox-scarred face was grim and his eyes as cold as ice on a winter lake, Jaime sensed that he was glad he'd come. *I gave the man a choice,* he reminded himself. *He could have refused me and remained King's Justice.*

Ser Ilyn's appointment had been a wedding gift from Robert Baratheon to the father of his bride, a sinecure to compensate Payne for the tongue he'd lost in the service of

House Lannister. He made a splendid headsman. He had never botched an execution, and seldom required as much as a second stroke. And there was something about his silence that inspired terror. Seldom had a King's Justice seemed so well fitted for his office.

When Jaime decided to take him, he had sought out Ser Ilyn's chambers at the end of Traitor's Walk. The upper floor of the squat, half-round tower was divided into cells for prisoners who required some measure of comfort, captive knights or lordlings awaiting ransom or exchange. The entrance to the dungeons proper was at ground level, behind a door of hammered iron and a second of splintery grey wood. On the floors between were rooms set aside for the use of the Chief Gaoler, the Lord Confessor, and the King's Justice. The Justice was a headsman, but by tradition he also had charge of the dungeons and the men who kept them.

And for that task, Ser Ilyn Payne was singularly ill suited. As he could neither read, nor write, nor speak, Ser Ilyn had left the running of the dungeons to his underlings, such as they were. The realm had not had a Lord Confessor since the second Daeron, however, and the last Chief Gaoler had been a cloth merchant who purchased the office from Littlefinger during Robert's reign. No doubt he'd had good profit from it for a few years, until he made the error of conspiring with some other rich fools to give the Iron Throne to Stannis. They called themselves "Antler Men," so Joff had nailed antlers to their heads before flinging them over the city walls. So it had been left to Rennifer Longwaters, the head undergaoler with the twisted back who claimed at tedious length to have a "drop of dragon" in him, to unlock the dungeon doors for Jaime and conduct him up the narrow steps inside the walls to the place where Ilyn Payne had lived for fifteen years.

The chambers stank of rotted food, and the rushes were crawling with vermin. As Jaime entered, he almost trod upon a rat. Payne's greatsword rested on a trestle table, beside a whetstone and a greasy oilcloth. The steel was immaculate, the edge glimmering blue in the pale light, but elsewhere piles of soiled clothing were strewn about the floors, and the bits of mail and armor scattered here and there were red with rust. Jaime could not count the broken wine jars. *The man cares for naught but killing,* he thought, as Ser Ilyn emerged from a bedchamber that reeked of overflowing chamber pots. "His Grace bids me win back his riverlands," Jaime told him. "I would have you with me . . . if you can bear to give up all of this."

Silence was his answer, and a long, unblinking stare. But just as he was about to turn and take his leave, Payne had given him a nod. *And here he rides.* Jaime glanced at his companion. *Perhaps there is yet hope for the both of us.*

That night they made camp beneath the hilltop castle of the Hayfords. As the sun went down, a hundred tents sprouted beneath the hill, along the banks of the stream that ran beside it. Jaime set the sentries himself. He did not expect trouble this close to the city, but his uncle Stafford had once thought himself safe on the Oxcross too. It was best to take no chances.

When the invitation came down from the castle for him to sup with Lady Hayford's castellan, Jaime took Ser Ilyn with him, along with Ser Addam Marbrand, Ser Bonifer Hasty, Red Ronnet Connington, Strongboar, and a dozen other knights and lordlings. "I suppose I ought to wear the hand," he said to Peck before making his ascent.

The lad fetched it straightaway. The hand was wrought

of gold, very lifelike, with inlaid nails of mother-of-pearl, its fingers and thumb half closed so as to slip around a goblet's stem. *I cannot fight, but I can drink,* Jaime reflected as the lad was tightening the straps that bound it to his stump. "Men shall name you Goldenhand from this day forth, my lord," the armorer had assured him the first time he'd fitted it onto Jaime's wrist. *He was wrong. I shall be the Kingslayer till I die.*

The golden hand was the occasion for much admiring comment over supper, at least until Jaime knocked over a goblet of wine. Then his temper got the best of him. "If you admire the bloody thing so much, lop off your own sword hand and you can have it," he told Flement Brax. After that there was no more talk about his hand, and he managed to drink some wine in peace.

The lady of the castle was a Lannister by marriage, a plump toddler who had been wed to his cousin Tyrek before she was a year old. Lady Ermesande was duly trotted out for their approval, all trussed up in a little gown of cloth-of-gold, with the green fretty and green pale wavy of House Hayford rendered in tiny beads of jade. But soon enough the girl began to squall, whereupon she was promptly whisked off to bed by her wet nurse.

"Has there been no word of our Lord Tyrek?" her castellan asked as a course of trout was served.

"None." Tyrek Lannister had vanished during the riots in King's Landing whilst Jaime himself was still captive at Riverrun. The boy would be fourteen by now, assuming he was still alive.

"I led a search myself, at Lord Tywin's command," offered Addam Marbrand as he boned his fish, "but I found no more than Bywater had before me. The boy was last seen ahorse, when the press of the mob broke the line of gold cloaks. Afterward . . . well, his palfrey was found, but not the rider. Most like they pulled him down and slew him. But if that's so, where is his body? The mob let the other corpses lie, why not his?"

"He would be of more value alive," suggested Strongboar. "Any Lannister would bring a hefty ransom."

"No doubt," Marbrand agreed, "yet no ransom demand was ever made. The boy is simply gone."

"The boy is dead." Jaime had drunk three cups of wine, and his golden hand seemed to be growing heavier and clumsier by the moment. *A hook would serve me just as well.* "If they realized whom they'd killed, no doubt they threw him in the river for fear of my father's wrath. They know the taste of that in King's Landing. Lord Tywin always paid his debts."

"Always," Strongboar agreed, and that was the end of that.

Yet afterward, alone in the tower room he had been offered for the night, Jaime found himself wondering. Tyrek had served King Robert as a squire, side by side with Lancel. Knowledge could be more valuable than gold, more deadly than a dagger. It was Varys he thought of then, smiling and smelling of lavender. The eunuch had agents and informers all over the city. It would have been a simple matter for him to arrange to have Tyrek snatched during the confusion . . . provided he knew beforehand that the mob was like to riot. *And Varys knew all, or so he would have us believe. Yet he gave Cersei no warning of that riot. Nor did he ride down to the ships to see Myrcella off.*

He opened the shutters. The night was growing cold, and a horned moon rode the sky. His hand shone dully in its light. *No good for throttling eunuchs, but heavy enough to smash that slimy smile into a fine red ruin.* He wanted to hit someone.

Jaime found Ser Ilyn honing his greatsword. "It's time," he told the man. The headsman rose and followed, his cracked leather boots scraping against the steep stone steps as they went down the stair. A small courtyard opened off the armory. Jaime found two shields there, two halfhelms, and a pair of blunted tourney swords. He offered one to Payne and took the other in his left hand as he slid his right through the loops of the shield. His golden fingers were curved enough to hook, but could not grasp, so his hold upon the shield was loose. "You were a knight once, ser," Jaime said. "So was I. Let us see what we are now."

Ser Ilyn raised his blade in reply, and Jaime moved at once to the attack. Payne was as rusty as his ringmail, and not so strong as Brienne, yet he met every cut with his own blade, or interposed his shield. They danced beneath the horned moon as the blunted swords sang their steely song. The silent knight was content to let Jaime lead the dance for a while, but finally he began to answer stroke for stroke. Once he shifted to the attack, he caught Jaime on the thigh, on the shoulder, on the forearm. Thrice he made his head ring with cuts to the helm. One slash ripped the shield off his right arm, and almost burst the straps that bound his golden hand to his stump. By the time they lowered their swords he was bruised and battered, but the wine had burned away and his head was clear. "We will dance again," he promised Ser Ilyn. "On the morrow, and the morrow. Every day we'll dance, till I am as good with my left hand as ever I was with the right."

Ser Ilyn opened his mouth and made a clacking sound. *A laugh,* Jaime realized. Something twisted in his gut.

Come morning, none of the others was so bold as to make mention of his bruises. Not one of them had heard the sound of swordplay in the night, it would seem. Yet when they climbed back down to camp, Little Lew Piper voiced the question the knights and lordlings dared not ask. Jaime grinned at him. "They have lusty wenches in House Hayford. These are love bites, lad."

Another bright and blustery day was followed by a cloudy one, then three days of rain. Wind and water made no matter. The column kept its pace, north along the kingsroad, and each night Jaime found some private place to win himself more love bites. They fought inside a stable as a one-eyed mule looked on, and in the cellar of an inn amongst the casks of wine and ale. They fought in the blackened shell of a big stone barn, on a wooded island in a shallow stream, and in an open field as the rain pattered softly against their helms and shields.

Jaime made excuses for his nightly forays, but he was not so foolish as to think that they were believed. Addam Marbrand knew what he was about, surely, and some of his other captains must have suspected. But no one spoke of it in his hearing . . . and since the only witness lacked a tongue, he need not fear anyone learning just how inept a swordsman the Kingslayer had become.

Soon the signs of war could be seen on every hand. Weeds and thorns and brushy trees grew high as a horse's head in fields where autumn wheat should be ripening, the kingsroad was bereft of travelers, and wolves ruled the weary world from dusk till dawn. Most of the animals were wary enough to keep their distance, but one of Marbrand's outriders had his horse run off and killed when he dismounted for a piss. "No beast would be so bold," declared Ser Bonifer the Good, of the stern sad face. "These are demons in the skins of wolves, sent to chastise us for our sins."

"This must have been an uncommonly sinful horse," Jaime said, standing over what remained of the poor animal. He gave orders for the rest of the carcass to be cut apart and salted down; it might be they would need the meat.

At a place called Sow's Horn they found a tough old knight named Ser Roger Hogg squatting stubbornly in his towerhouse with six men-at-arms, four crossbowmen, and a score of peasants. Ser Roger was as big and bristly as his name and Ser Kennos suggested that he might be some lost Crakehall, since their sigil was a brindled boar. Strongboar seemed to believe it and spent an earnest hour questioning Ser Roger about his ancestors.

Jaime was more interested in what Hogg had to say of wolves. "We had some trouble with a band of them white star wolves," the old knight told him. "They come round sniffing after you, my lord, but we saw them off, and buried three down by the turnips. Before them there was a pack of bloody lions, begging your pardon. The one who led them had a manticore on his shield."

"Ser Amory Lorch," Jaime offered. "My lord father commanded him to harry the riverlands."

"Which we're no part of," Ser Roger Hogg said stoutly. "My fealty's owed to House Hayford, and Lady Ermesande bends her little knee at King's Landing, or will when she's old enough to walk. I told him that, but this Lorch wasn't much for listening. He slaughtered half my sheep and three good milk goats, and tried to roast me in my tower. My walls are solid stone and eight feet thick, though, so after his fire burned out he rode off bored. The wolves come later, the ones on four legs. They ate the sheep the manticore left me. I got a few good pelts in recompense, but fur don't fill your belly. What should we do, my lord?"

"Plant," said Jaime, "and pray for one last harvest." It was not a hopeful answer, but it was the only one he had.

The next day, the column crossed the stream that formed the boundary between the lands that did fealty to King's Landing and those beholden to Riverrun. Maester Gulian consulted a map and announced that these hills were held by the brothers Wode, a pair of landed knights sworn to Harrenhal . . . but *their* halls had been earth and timber, and only blackened beams remained of them.

No Wodes appeared, nor any of their smallfolk, though some outlaws had taken shelter in the root cellar beneath the second brother's keep. One of them wore the ruins of a crimson cloak, but Jaime hanged him with the rest. It felt good. This was justice. *Make a habit of it, Lannister, and one day men might call you Goldenhand after all. Goldenhand the Just.*

The world grew ever greyer as they drew near to Harrenhal. They rode beneath slate skies, beside waters that shone old and cold as a sheet of beaten steel. Jaime found himself wondering if Brienne might have passed this way before him. *If she thought that Sansa Stark had made for Riverrun . . .* Had they encountered other travelers, he might have stopped to ask if any of them had chanced to see a pretty maid with auburn hair, or a big ugly one with a face that would curdle milk. But there was no one on the roads but wolves, and their howling held no answers.

Across the pewter waters of the lake the towers of Black Harren's folly appeared at last, five twisted fingers of black, misshapen stone grasping for the sky. Though Littlefinger had been named the Lord of Harrenhal, he seemed in no great haste to occupy his new seat, so it had fallen to Jaime Lannister to "sort out" Harrenhal on his way to Riverrun.

That it needed sorting out he did not doubt. Gregor Clegane had wrested the immense, gloomy castle away from the Bloody Mummers before Cersei recalled him to King's Landing. No doubt the Mountain's men were still rattling around inside like so many dried peas in a suit of plate, but they were not ideally suited to restore the king's peace to the Trident. The only peace Ser Gregor's lot had ever given anyone was the peace of the grave.

Ser Addam's outriders had reported that the gates of Harrenhal were closed and barred. Jaime drew his men up before them and commanded Ser Kennos of Kayce to sound the Horn of Herrock, black and twisted and banded in old gold.

When three blasts had echoed off the walls, they heard the groan of iron hinges and the gates swung slowly open. So thick were the walls of Black Harren's folly that Jaime passed beneath a dozen murder holes before emerging into sudden sunlight in the yard where he'd bid farewell to the Bloody Mummers, not so long ago. Weeds were sprouting from the hard-packed earth, and flies buzzed about the carcass of a horse.

A handful of Ser Gregor's men emerged from the towers to watch him dismount; hard-eyed, hard-mouthed men, the lot of them. *They would have to be, to ride beside the Mountain.* About the best that could be said for Gregor's men was that they were not quite as vile and violent a bunch as the Brave Companions. "Fuck me, Jaime Lannister," blurted one grey and grizzled man-at-arms. "It's the bleeding Kingslayer, boys. Fuck me with a spear!"

"Who might you be?" Jaime asked.

"Ser used to call me Shitmouth, if it please m'lord." He spit in his hands and wiped his cheeks with them, as if that would somehow make him more presentable.

"Charming. Do you command here?"

"Me? Shit, no. M'lord. Bugger me with a bloody

spear." Shitmouth had enough crumbs in his beard to feed
the garrison. Jaime had to laugh. The man took that for encouragement. "Bugger me with a bloody spear," he said
again, and started laughing too.

"You heard the man," Jaime said to Ilyn Payne. "Find a
nice long spear, and shove it up his arse."

Ser Ilyn did not have a spear, but Beardless Jon Bettley was
glad to toss him one. Shitmouth's drunken laughter stopped
abruptly. "You keep that bloody thing away from me."

"Make up your mind," said Jaime. "Who has the command here? Did Ser Gregor name a castellan?"

"Polliver," another man said, "only the Hound killed
him, m'lord. Him and the Tickler both, and that Sarsfield
boy."

The Hound again. "You know it was Sandor? You saw
him?"

"Not us, m'lord. That innkeep told us."

"It happened at the crossroads inn, my lord." The
speaker was a younger man with a mop of sandy hair. He
wore the chain of coins that had once belonged to Vargo
Hoat; coins from half a hundred distant cities, silver and
gold, copper and bronze, square coins and round coins,
triangles and rings and bits of bone. "The innkeep swore
the man had one side of his face all burned. His whores
told the same tale. Sandor had some boy with him, a
ragged peasant lad. They hacked Polly and the Tickler to
bloody bits and rode off down the Trident, we were told."

"Did you send men after them?"

Shitmouth frowned, as if the thought were painful. "No,
m'lord. Fuck us all, we never did."

"When a dog goes mad you cut his throat."

"Well," the man said, rubbing his mouth, "I never
much liked Polly, that shit, and the dog, he were Ser's
brother, so . . ."

"We're bad, m'lord," broke in the man who wore the coins, "but you'd need to be mad to face the Hound."

Jaime looked him over. *Bolder than the rest, and not as drunk as Shitmouth.* "You were afraid of him."

"I wouldn't say *afraid*, m'lord. I'd say we was leaving him for our betters. Someone like Ser. Or you."

Me, when I had two hands. Jaime did not delude himself. Sandor would make short work of him now. "You have a name?"

"Rafford, if it pleases. Most call me Raff."

"Raff, gather the garrison together in the Hall of a Hundred Hearths. Your captives as well. I'll want to see them. Those whores from the crossroads too. Oh, and Hoat. I was distraught to hear that he had died. I'd like to look upon his head."

When they brought it to him, he found that the Goat's lips had been sliced off, along with his ears and most of his nose. The crows had supped upon his eyes. It was still recognizably Hoat, however. Jaime would have known his beard anywhere; an absurd rope of hair two feet long, dangling from a pointed chin. Elsewise, only a few leathery strips of flesh still clung to the Qohorik's skull. "Where is the rest of him?" he asked.

No one wanted to tell him. Finally, Shitmouth lowered his eyes, and muttered, "Rotted, ser. And et."

"One of the captives was always begging food," Rafford admitted, "so Ser said to give him roast goat. The Qohorik didn't have much meat on him, though. Ser took his hands and feet first, then his arms and legs."

"The fat bugger got most, m'lord," Shitmouth offered, "but Ser, he said to see that all the captives had a taste. And Hoat too, his own self. That whoreson 'ud slobber when we fed him, and the grease'd run down into that skinny beard o' his."

Father, Jaime thought, *your dogs have both gone mad.* He found himself remembering tales he had first heard as a child at Casterly Rock, of mad Lady Lothston who bathed in tubs of blood and presided over feasts of human flesh within these very walls.

Somehow revenge had lost its savor. "Take this and throw it in the lake." Jaime tossed Hoat's head to Peck, and turned to address the garrison. "Until such time as Lord Petyr arrives to claim his seat, Ser Bonifer Hasty shall hold Harrenhal in the name of the crown. Those of you who wish may join him, if he'll have you. The rest will ride with me to Riverrun."

The Mountain's men looked at one another. "We're owed," said one. "Ser promised us. Rich rewards, he said."

"His very words," Shitmouth agreed. *"Rich rewards, for them as rides with me."* A dozen others began to yammer their assent.

Ser Bonifer raised a gloved hand. "Any man who remains with me shall have a hide of land to work, a second hide when he takes a wife, a third at the birth of his first child."

"Land, ser?" Shitmouth spat. "Piss on that. If we wanted to grub in the bloody dirt, we could have bloody well stayed home, begging your pardon, ser. *Rich rewards,* Ser said. Meaning gold."

"If you have a grievance, go to King's Landing and take it up with my sweet sister." Jaime turned to Rafford. "I'll see those captives now. Starting with Ser Wylis Manderly."

"He the fat one?" asked Rafford.

"I devoutly hope so. And tell me no sad stories of how he died, or the lot of you are apt to do the same."

Any hopes he might have nursed of finding Shagwell, Pyg, or Zollo languishing in the dungeons were sadly disappointed. The Brave Companions had abandoned Vargo Hoat to a man, it would seem. Of Lady Whent's people, only three remained—the cook who had opened the postern gate for Ser Gregor, a bent-back armorer called Ben Blackthumb, and a girl named Pia, who was not near as pretty as she had been when Jaime saw her last. Someone had broken her nose and knocked out half her teeth. The girl fell at Jaime's feet when she saw him, sobbing and clinging to his leg with hysterical strength till Strongboar pulled her off. "No one will hurt you now," he told her, but that only made her sob the louder.

The other captives had been better treated. Ser Wylis Manderly was amongst them, along with several other highborn northmen taken prisoner by the Mountain That Rides in the fighting at the fords of the Trident. Useful hostages, all worth a goodly ransom. They were ragged, filthy, and shaggy to a man, and some had fresh bruises, cracked teeth, and missing fingers, but their wounds had been washed and bandaged, and none of them had gone hungry. Jaime wondered if they had any inkling what they'd been eating, and decided it was better not to inquire.

None had any defiance left; especially not Ser Wylis, a bushy-faced tub of suet with dull eyes and sallow, sagging jowls. When Jaime told him that he would be escorted to Maidenpool and there put on a ship for White Harbor, Ser Wylis collapsed into a puddle on the floor and sobbed longer and louder than Pia had. It took four men to lift him back onto his feet. *Too much roast goat,* Jaime reflected. *Gods, but I hate this bloody castle.* Harrenhal had seen more horror in its three hundred years than Casterly Rock had witnessed in three thousand.

Jaime commanded that fires be lit in the Hall of a Hundred Hearths and sent the cook hobbling back to the kitchens to prepare a hot meal for the men of his column. "Anything but goat."

He took his own supper in Hunter's Hall with Ser Bonifer Hasty, a solemn stork of a man prone to salting his speech with appeals to the Seven. "I want none of Ser Gregor's followers," he declared as he was cutting up a pear as withered as he was, so as to make certain that its nonexistent juice did not stain his pristine purple doublet, embroidered with the white bend cotised of his House. "I will not have such sinners in my service."

"My septon used to say all men were sinners."

"He was not wrong," Ser Bonifer allowed, "but some sins are blacker than others, and fouler in the nostrils of the Seven."

And you have no more nose than my little brother, or my own sins would have you choking on that pear. "Very well. I'll take Gregor's lot off your hands." He could always find a use for fighters. If nothing else, he could send them up the ladders first, should he need to storm the walls of Riverrun.

"Take the whore as well," Ser Bonifer urged. "You know the one. The girl from the dungeons."

"Pia." The last time he had been here, Qyburn had sent the girl to his bed, thinking that would please him. But the Pia they had brought up from the dungeons was a different creature from the sweet, simple, giggly creature who'd crawled beneath his blankets. She had made the mistake of speaking when Ser Gregor wanted quiet, so the Mountain had smashed her teeth to splinters with a mailed fist and broken her pretty little nose as well. He would have done worse, no doubt, if Cersei had not called him down to King's Landing to face the Red Viper's spear. Jaime would not mourn him. "Pia was born in this castle," he told Ser Bonifer. "It is the only home she has ever known."

"She is a font of corruption," said Ser Bonifer. "I won't have her near my men, flaunting her . . . parts."

"I expect her flaunting days are done," he said, "but if you find her that objectionable, I'll take her." He could make her a washerwoman, he supposed. His squires did not mind raising his tent, grooming his horse, or cleaning his armor, but the task of caring for his clothes struck them as unmanly. "Can you hold Harrenhal with just your Holy Hundred?" Jaime asked. They should actually be called the Holy Eighty-Six, having lost fourteen men upon the Blackwater, but no doubt Ser Bonifer would fill up his ranks again as soon as he found some sufficiently pious recruits.

"I anticipate no difficulty. The Crone will light our way, and the Warrior will give strength to our arms."

Or else the Stranger will turn up for the whole holy lot of you. Jaime could not be certain who had convinced his sister that Ser Bonifer should be named castellan of Harrenhal, but the appointment smelled of Orton Merryweather. Hasty had once served Merryweather's grandsire, he seemed to recall dimly. And the carrot-haired justiciar was just the sort of simpleminded fool to assume that someone called "the Good" was the very potion the riverlands required to heal the wounds left by Roose Bolton, Vargo Hoat, and Gregor Clegane.

But he might not be wrong. Hasty hailed from the stormlands, so had neither friends nor foes along the Trident; no blood feuds, no debts to pay, no cronies to reward. He was sober, just, and dutiful, and his Holy Eighty-Six were as well disciplined as any soldiers in the Seven Kingdoms, and made a lovely sight as they wheeled and pranced their tall grey geldings. Littlefinger had once quipped that Ser Bonifer must have gelded the riders too, so spotless was their repute.

All the same, Jaime wondered about any soldiers who were better known for their lovely horses than for the foes they'd slain. *They pray well, I suppose, but can they fight?* They had not disgraced themselves on the Blackwater, so far as he knew, but they had not distinguished themselves either. Ser Bonifer himself had been a promising knight in his youth, but something had happened to him, a defeat or a disgrace or a near brush with death, and afterward he had decided that jousting was an empty vanity and put away his lance for good and all.

Harrenhal must be held, though, and Baelor Butthole here is the man that Cersei chose to hold it. "This castle has an ill repute," he warned him, "and one that's well deserved. It's said that Harren and his sons still walk the halls by night, afire. Those who look upon them burst into flame."

"I fear no shade, ser. It is written in *The Seven-Pointed Star* that spirits, wights, and revenants cannot harm a pious man, so long as he is armored in his faith."

"Then armor yourself in faith, by all means, but wear a suit of mail and plate as well. Every man who holds this castle seems to come to a bad end. The Mountain, the Goat, even my father . . ."

"If you will forgive my saying so, they were not godly men, as we are. The Warrior defends us, and help is always near, if some dread foe should threaten. Maester Gulian will be remaining with his ravens, Lord Lancel is nearby at Darry with his garrison, and Lord Randyll holds Maidenpool. Together we three shall hunt down and destroy whatever outlaws prowl these parts. Once that is done, the Seven will guide the goodfolk back to their villages to plow and plant and build anew."

The ones the Goat didn't kill, at least. Jaime hooked his golden fingers round the stem of his wine goblet. "If any of Hoat's Brave Companions fall into your hands, send word to me at once." The Stranger might have made off with the Goat before Jaime could get around to him, but fat Zollo was still out there, with Shagwell, Rorge, Faithful Urswyck, and the rest.

"So you can torture them and kill them?"

"I suppose you would forgive them, in my place?"

"If they made sincere repentance for their sins . . . yes, I would embrace them all as brothers and pray with them before I sent them to the block. Sins may be forgiven. Crimes require punishment." Hasty folded his hands before him like a steeple, in a way that reminded Jaime uncomfortably of his father. "If it is Sandor Clegane that we encounter, what would you have me do?"

Pray hard, Jaime thought, *and run.* "Send him to join his beloved brother and be glad the gods made seven hells. One would never be enough to hold both of the Cleganes." He pushed himself awkwardly to his feet. "Beric Dondarrion is a different matter. Should you capture him, hold him for my return. I'll want to march him back to King's Landing with a rope about his neck, and have Ser Ilyn take his head off where half the realm can see."

"And this Myrish priest who runs with him? It is said he spreads his false faith everywhere."

"Kill him, kiss him, or pray with him, as you please."

"I have no wish to kiss the man, my lord."

"No doubt he'd say the same of you." Jaime's smile turned into a yawn. "My pardons. I shall take my leave of you, if you have no objections."

"None, my lord," said Hasty. No doubt he wished to pray.

Jaime wished to fight. He took the steps two at a time, out to where the night air was cold and crisp. In the torchlit yard Strongboar and Ser Flement Brax were having at each other whilst a ring of men-at-arms cheered them on. *Ser Lyle will have the best of that one,* he knew. *I need to find Ser Ilyn.* His fingers had the itch again. His footsteps took him away from the noise and the light. He passed beneath the covered bridge and through the Flowstone Yard before he realized where he was headed.

As he neared the bear pit, he saw the glow of a lantern, its pale wintry light washing over the tiers of steep stone seats. *Someone has come before me, it would seem.* The pit would be a fine place to dance; perhaps Ser Ilyn had anticipated him.

But the knight standing over the pit was bigger; a husky, bearded man in a red-and-white surcoat adorned with griffins. *Connington. What's he doing here?* Below, the carcass of the bear still sprawled upon the sands, though only bones and ragged fur remained, half-buried. Jaime felt a pang of pity for the beast. *At least he died in battle.* "Ser Ronnet," he called, "have you lost your way? It is a large castle, I know."

Red Ronnet raised his lantern. "I wished to see where the bear danced with the maiden not-so-fair." His beard shone in the light as if it were afire. Jaime could smell wine on his breath. "Is it true the wench fought naked?"

"Naked? No." He wondered how that wrinkle had been added to the story. "The Mummers put her in a pink silk gown and shoved a tourney sword into her hand. The Goat wanted her death to be *amuthing.* Elsewise . . ."

". . . the sight of Brienne naked might have made the bear flee in terror." Connington laughed.

Jaime did not. "You speak as if you know the lady."

"I was betrothed to her."

That took him by surprise. Brienne had never mentioned a betrothal. "Her father made a match for her . . ."

"Thrice," said Connington. "I was the second. My father's

notion. I had heard the wench was ugly, and I told him so, but he said all women were the same once you blew the candle out."

"Your father." Jaime eyed Red Ronnet's surcoat, where two griffins faced each other on a field of red and white. *Dancing griffins.* "Our late Hand's . . . brother, was he?"

"Cousin. Lord Jon had no brothers."

"No." It all came back to him. Jon Connington had been Prince Rhaegar's friend. When Merryweather failed so dismally to contain Robert's Rebellion and Prince Rhaegar could not be found, Aerys had turned to the next best thing, and raised Connington to the Handship. But the Mad King was always chopping off his Hands. He had chopped Lord Jon after the Battle of the Bells, stripping him of honors, lands, and wealth, and packing him off across the sea to die in exile, where he soon drank himself to death. The cousin, though—Red Ronnet's father—had joined the rebellion and been rewarded with Griffin's Roost after the Trident. He only got the castle, though; Robert kept the gold, and bestowed the greater part of the Connington lands on more fervent supporters.

Ser Ronnet was a landed knight, no more. For any such, the Maid of Tarth would have been a sweet plum indeed. "How is it that you did not wed?" Jaime asked him.

"Why, I went to Tarth and saw her. I had six years on her, yet the wench could look me in the eye. She was a sow in silk, though most sows have bigger teats. When she tried to talk she almost choked on her own tongue. I gave her a rose and told her it was all that she would ever have from me." Connington glanced into the pit. "The bear was less hairy than that freak, I'll—"

Jaime's golden hand cracked him across the mouth so hard the other knight went stumbling down the steps. His lantern fell and smashed, and the oil spread out, burning.

"You are speaking of a highborn lady, ser. Call her by her name. Call her Brienne."

Connington edged away from the spreading flames on his hands and knees. "Brienne. If it please my lord." He spat a glob of blood at Jaime's foot. "Brienne the Beauty."

CERSEI

I t was a slow climb to the top of Visenya's Hill. As the horses labored upward, the queen leaned back against a plump red cushion. From outside came the voice of Ser Osmund Kettleblack. *"Make way. Clear the street. Make way for Her Grace the queen."*

"Margaery *does* keep a lively court," Lady Merryweather was saying. "We have jugglers, mummers, poets, puppets . . ."

"Singers?" prompted Cersei.

"Many and more, Your Grace. Hamish the Harper plays for her once a fortnight, and sometimes Alaric of Eysen will entertain us of an evening, but the Blue Bard is her favorite."

Cersei recalled the bard from Tommen's wedding. *Young, and fair to look upon. Could there be something there?* "There are other men as well, I hear. Knights and courtiers. Admirers. Tell me true, my lady. Do you think Margaery is still a maiden?"

"She says she is, Your Grace."

"So she does. What do you say?"

Taena's black eyes sparkled with mischief. "When she wed Lord Renly at Highgarden, I helped disrobe him for the bedding. His lordship was a well-made man, and lusty. I saw the proof when we tumbled him into the wedding bed where his bride awaited him as naked as her name day, blushing prettily beneath the coverlets. Ser Loras had carried her up the steps himself. Margaery may say that the marriage was never consummated, that Lord Renly had drunk too much wine at the wedding feast, but I promise you, the bit between his legs was anything but weary when last I saw it."

"Did you chance to see the marriage bed the morning after?" Cersei asked. "Did she bleed?"

"No sheet was shown, Your Grace."

A pity. Still, the absence of a bloody sheet meant little, by itself. Common peasant girls bled like pigs upon their wedding nights, she had heard, but that was less true of highborn maids like Margaery Tyrell. A lord's daughter was more like to give her maidenhead to a horse than a husband, it was said, and Margaery had been riding since she was old enough to walk. "I understand the little queen has many admirers amongst our household knights. The Redwyne twins, Ser Tallad . . . who else, pray tell?"

Lady Merryweather gave a shrug. "Ser Lambert, the fool who hides a good eye behind a patch. Bayard Norcross. Courtenay Greenhill. The brothers Woodwright, sometimes Portifer and often Lucantine. Oh, and Grand Maester Pycelle is a frequent visitor."

"Pycelle? Truly?" Had that doddering old worm forsaken the lion for the rose? *If so, he will regret it.* "Who else?"

"The Summer Islander in his feathered cloak. How could I have forgotten him, with his skin as black as ink? Others come to pay court to her cousins. Elinor is promised to the Ambrose boy, but loves to flirt, and Megga has a new suitor every fortnight. Once she kissed a potboy in the kitchen. I have heard talk of her marrying Lady Bulwer's brother, but if Megga were to choose for herself, she would sooner have Mark Mullendore, I am certain."

Cersei laughed. "The butterfly knight who lost his arm on the Blackwater? What good is half a man?"

"Megga thinks him sweet. She has asked Lady Margaery to help her find a monkey for him."

"A monkey." The queen did not know what to say to that. *Sparrows and monkeys. Truly, the realm is going mad.* "What of our brave Ser Loras? How often does he call upon his sister?"

"More than any of the others." When Taena frowned, a tiny crease appeared between her dark eyes. "Every morn and every night he visits, unless duty interferes. Her brother is devoted to her, they share everything with . . . oh . . ." For a moment, the Myrish woman looked almost shocked. Then a smile spread across her face. "I have had a most *wicked* thought, Your Grace."

"Best keep it to yourself. The hill is thick with sparrows, and we all know how sparrows abhor wickedness."

"I have heard they abhor soap and water too, Your Grace."

"Perhaps too much prayer robs a man of his sense of smell. I shall be sure to ask His High Holiness."

The draperies swayed back and forth in a wash of crimson silk. "Orton told me that the High Septon has no name," Lady Taena said. "Can that be true? In Myr we all have names."

"Oh, he had a name *once*. They all do." The queen waved a hand dismissively. "Even septons born of noble blood go only by their given names once they have taken their vows. When one of them is elevated to *High* Septon, he puts aside that name as well. The Faith will tell you he no longer has any need of a man's name, for he has become the avatar of the gods."

"How do you distinguish one High Septon from another?"

"With difficulty. One has to say, 'the fat one,' or 'the one before the fat one,' or 'the old one who died in his sleep.' You can always winkle out their birth names if you like, but they take umbrage if you use them. It reminds them that they were born ordinary men, and they do not like that."

"My lord husband tells me this new one was born with filth beneath his fingernails."

"So I suspect. As a rule the Most Devout elevate one of their own, but there have been exceptions." Grand Maester Pycelle had informed her of the history, at tedious length. "During the reign of King Baelor the Blessed a simple stonemason was chosen as High Septon. He worked stone so beautifully that Baelor decided he was the Smith reborn in mortal flesh. The man could neither read nor write, nor recall the words of the simplest of prayers." Some still claimed that Baelor's Hand had the man poisoned to spare the realm embarrassment. "After that one died, an eight-year-old boy was elevated, once more at King Baelor's urging. The boy worked miracles, His Grace declared, though even his little healing hands could not save Baelor during his final fast."

Lady Merryweather gave a laugh. "Eight years old?

Perhaps my son could be High Septon. He is almost seven."

"Does he pray a lot?" the queen asked.

"He prefers to play with swords."

"A real boy, then. Can he name all seven gods?"

"I think so."

"I shall have to take him under consideration." Cersei did not doubt that there were any number of boys who would do more honor to the crystal crown than the wretch on whom the Most Devout had chosen to bestow it. *This is what comes of letting fools and cowards rule themselves. Next time, I will choose their master for them.* And the next time might not be long in coming, if the new High Septon continued to annoy her. Baelor's Hand had little to teach Cersei Lannister where such matters were concerned.

"Clear the way!" Ser Osmund Kettleblack was shouting. *"Make way for the Queen's Grace!"*

The litter began to slow, which could only mean that they were near the top of the hill. "You should bring this son of yours to court," Cersei told Lady Merryweather. "Six is not too young. Tommen needs other boys about him. Why not your son?" Joffrey had never had a close friend of his own age, that she recalled. *The poor boy was always alone. I had Jaime when I was a child . . . and Melara, until she fell into the well.* Joff had been fond of the Hound, to be sure, but that was not friendship. He was looking for the father he never found in Robert. *A little foster brother might be just what Tommen needs to wean him away from Margaery and her hens.* In time they might grow as close as Robert and his boyhood friend Ned Stark. *A fool, but a loyal fool. Tommen will have need of loyal friends to watch his back.*

"Your Grace is kind, but Russell has never known any

home but Longtable. I fear he would be lost in this great city."

"In the beginning," the queen allowed, "but he will soon outgrow that, as I did. When my father sent for me to court I wept and Jaime raged, until my aunt sat me down in the Stone Garden and told me there was no one in King's Landing that I need ever fear. 'You are a lioness,' she said, 'and it is for all the lesser beasts to fear you.' Your son will find his courage too. Surely you would prefer to have him close at hand, where you could see him every day? He is your only child, is he not?"

"For the present. My lord husband has asked the gods to bless us with another son, in case . . ."

"I know." She thought of Joffrey, clawing at his neck. In his last moments he had looked to her in desperate appeal, and a sudden memory had stopped her heart; a drop of red blood hissing in a candle flame, a croaking voice that spoke of crowns and shrouds, of death at the hands of the *valonqar.*

Outside the litter, Ser Osmund was shouting something, and someone was shouting back. The litter jerked to a halt. "Are you all dead?" roared Kettleblack. *"Get out of the bloody way!"*

The queen pulled back a corner of the curtain and beckoned to Ser Meryn Trant. "What seems to be the trouble?"

"The sparrows, Your Grace." Ser Meryn wore white scale armor beneath his cloak. His helm and shield were slung from his saddle. "Camping in the street. We'll make them move."

"Do that, but gently. I do not care to be caught up in another riot." Cersei let the curtain fall. "This is absurd."

"It is, Your Grace," Lady Merryweather agreed. "The

High Septon should have come to you. And these wretched sparrows . . ."

"He feeds them, coddles them, *blesses* them. Yet will not bless the king." The blessing was an empty ritual, she knew, but rituals and ceremonies had power in the eyes of the ignorant. Aegon the Conqueror himself had dated the start of his realm from the day the High Septon anointed him in Oldtown. "This wretched priest will obey, or learn how weak and human he still is."

"Orton says it is the gold he really wants. That he means to withhold his blessing until the crown resumes its payments."

"The Faith will have its gold as soon as we have peace." Septon Torbert and Septon Raynard had been most understanding of her plight . . . unlike the wretched Braavosi, who had hounded poor Lord Gyles so mercilessly that he had taken to his bed, coughing up blood. *We had to have those ships.* She could not rely upon the Arbor for her navy; the Redwynes were too close to the Tyrells. She needed her own strength at sea.

The dromonds rising on the river would give her that. Her flagship would dip twice as many oars as *King Robert's Hammer.* Aurane had asked her leave to name her *Lord Tywin,* which Cersei had been pleased to grant. She looked forward to hearing men speak of her father as a "she." Another of the ships would be named *Sweet Cersei,* and would bear a gilded figurehead carved in her likeness, clad in mail and lion helm, with spear in hand. *Brave Joffrey, Lady Joanna,* and *Lioness* would follow her to sea, along with *Queen Margaery, Golden Rose, Lord Renly, Lady Olenna,* and *Princess Myrcella.* The queen had made the mistake of telling Tommen he might name the last five. He had actually chosen *Moon Boy* for one. Only when Lord Aurane suggested that men might not want to serve on a ship named for a fool had the boy reluctantly agreed to honor his sister instead.

"If this ragged septon thinks to make me *buy* Tommen's blessing, he will soon learn better," she told Taena. The queen did not intend to truckle to a pack of priests.

The litter halted yet again, so suddenly that Cersei jerked. "Oh, this is infuriating." She leaned out once more, and saw that they had reached the top of Visenya's Hill. Ahead loomed the Great Sept of Baelor, with its magnificent dome and seven shining towers, but between her and the marble steps lay a sullen sea of humanity, brown and ragged and unwashed. *Sparrows,* she thought, sniffing, though no sparrows had ever smelled so rank.

Cersei was appalled. Qyburn had brought her reports of their numbers, but hearing about them was one thing and seeing them another. Hundreds were encamped upon the plaza, hundreds more in the gardens. Their cookfires filled the air with smoke and stinks. Roughspun tents and miserable hovels made of mud and scrap wood besmirched the pristine white marble. They were even huddled on the steps, beneath the Great Sept's towering doors.

Ser Osmund came trotting back to her. Beside him rode Ser Osfryd, mounted on a stallion as golden as his cloak. Osfryd was the middle Kettleblack, quieter than his siblings, more apt to scowl than smile. *And crueler as well, if the tales are true. Perhaps I should have sent him to the Wall.*

Grand Maester Pycelle had wanted an older man "more seasoned in the ways of war" to command the gold cloaks, and several of her other councillors had agreed with him. "Ser Osfryd is seasoned quite sufficiently," she had told them, but even that did not shut them up. *They yap at me like a pack of small, annoying dogs.* Her patience with Pycelle had all but run its course. He had even had the temerity to object to her sending to Dorne for a master-at-arms, on the grounds that it might offend the Tyrells. "Why do you think I'm *doing* it?" she had asked him scornfully.

"Beg pardon, Your Grace," said Ser Osmund. "My brother's summoning more gold cloaks. We'll clear a path, never fear."

"I do not have the time. I will continue on afoot."

"Please, Your Grace." Taena caught her arm. "They frighten me. There are hundreds of them, and so dirty."

Cersei kissed her cheek. "The lion does not fear the sparrow . . . but it is good of you to care. I know you love me well, my lady. Ser Osmund, kindly help me down."

If I had known I was going to have to walk, I would have dressed for it. She wore a white gown slashed with cloth-of-gold, lacy but demure. It had been several years since the last time she had donned it, and the queen found it uncomfortably tight about the middle. "Ser Osmund, Ser Meryn, you will accompany me. Ser Osfryd, see that my litter comes to no harm." Some of the sparrows looked gaunt and hollow-eyed enough to eat her horses.

As she made her way through the ragged throng, past their cookfires, wagons, and crude shelters, the queen found herself remembering another crowd that had once gathered on this plaza. The day she wed Robert Baratheon, thousands had turned out to cheer for them. All the women wore their best, and half the men had children on their shoulders. When she had emerged from inside the sept, hand in hand with the young king, the crowd sent up a roar so loud it could be heard in Lannisport. "They like you well, my lady," Robert whispered in her ear. "See, every face is smiling." For that one short moment she had been happy in her marriage . . . until she chanced to glance at

Jaime. *No*, she remembered thinking, *not every face, my lord.*

No one was smiling now. The looks the sparrows gave her were dull, sullen, hostile. They made way but reluctantly. *If they were truly sparrows, a shout would send them flying. A hundred gold cloaks with staves and swords and maces could clear this rabble quick enough.* That was what Lord Tywin would have done. *He would have ridden over them instead of walking through.*

When she saw what they had done to Baelor the Beloved, the queen had cause to rue her soft heart. The great marble statue that had smiled serenely over the plaza for a hundred years was waist-deep in a heap of bones and skulls. Some of the skulls had scraps of flesh still clinging to them. A crow sat atop one such, enjoying a dry, leathery feast. Flies were everywhere. "What is the meaning of this?" Cersei demanded of the crowd. "Do you mean to bury Blessed Baelor in a mountain of carrion?"

A one-legged man stepped forward, leaning on a wooden crutch. "Your Grace, these are the bones of holy men and women, murdered for their faith. Septons, septas, brothers brown and dun and green, sisters white and blue and grey. Some were hanged, some disemboweled. Septs have been despoiled, maidens and mothers raped by godless men and demon worshipers. Even silent sisters have been molested. The Mother Above cries out in her anguish. We have brought their bones here from all over the realm, to bear witness to the agony of the Holy Faith."

Cersei could feel the weight of eyes upon her. "The king shall know of these atrocities," she answered solemnly. "Tommen will share your outrage. This is the work of Stannis and his red witch, and the savage northmen who worship trees and wolves." She raised her voice. *"Good people, your dead shall be avenged!"*

A few cheered, but only a few. "We ask no vengeance for our dead," said the one-legged man, "only protection for the living. For the septs and holy places."

"The Iron Throne must defend the Faith," growled a hulking lout with a seven-pointed star painted on his brow. "A king who does not protect his people is no king at all." Mutters of assent went up from those around him. One man had the temerity to grasp Ser Meryn by the wrist, and say, "It is time for all anointed knights to forsake their worldly masters and defend our Holy Faith. Stand with us, ser, if you love the Seven."

"Unhand me," said Ser Meryn, wrenching free.

"I hear you," Cersei said. "My son is young, but he loves the Seven well. You shall have his protection, and mine own."

The man with the star upon his brow was not appeased. "The Warrior will defend us," he said, "not this fat boy king."

Meryn Trant reached for his sword, but Cersei stopped him before he could unsheathe it. She had only two knights amidst a sea of sparrows. She saw staves and scythes, cudgels and clubs, several axes. "I will have no blood shed in this holy place, ser." *Why are all men such children? Cut him down, and the rest will tear us limb from limb.* "We are all the Mother's children. Come, His High Holiness awaits us." But as she made her way through the press to the steps of the sept, a gaggle of armed men stepped out to block the doors. They wore mail and boiled leather, with here and there a bit of dinted plate. Some had spears and some had longswords. More favored axes, and had sewn red stars upon their bleached white surcoats. Two had the insolence to cross their spears and bar her way.

"Is this how you receive your queen?" she demanded of

them. "Pray, where are Raynard and Torbert?" It was not like those two to miss a chance to fawn on her. Torbert always made a show of getting down on his knees to wash her feet.

"I do not know the men you speak of," said one of the men with a red star on his surcoat, "but if they are of the Faith, no doubt the Seven had need of their service."

"Septon Raynard and Septon Torbert are of the *Most Devout*," Cersei said, "and will be furious to learn that you obstructed me. Do you mean to deny me entrance to Baelor's holy sept?"

"Your Grace," said a greybeard with a stooped shoulder. "You are welcome here, but your men must leave their swordbelts. No weapons are allowed within, by command of the High Septon."

"Knights of the Kingsguard do not set aside their swords, not even in the presence of the king."

"In the king's house, the king's word must rule," replied the aged knight, "but this is the house of the gods."

Color rose to her cheeks. One word to Meryn Trant, and the stoop-backed greybeard would be meeting his gods sooner than he might have liked. *Not here, though. Not now.* "Wait for me," she told the Kingsguard curtly. Alone, she climbed the steps. The spearmen uncrossed their spears. Two other men put their weight against the doors, and with a great groan they swung apart.

In the Hall of Lamps, Cersei found a score of septons on their knees, but not in prayer. They had pails of soap and water, and were scrubbing at the floor. Their rough-spun robes and sandals led Cersei to take them for sparrows, until one raised his head. His face was red as a beet, and there were broken blisters on his hands, bleeding. "Your Grace."

"Septon Raynard?" The queen could scarce believe

what she was seeing. "What are you doing on your knees?"

"He is cleaning the floor." The speaker was shorter than the queen by several inches and as thin as a broom handle. "Work is a form of prayer, most pleasing to the Smith." He stood, scrub brush in hand. "Your Grace. We have been expecting you."

The man's beard was grey and brown and closely trimmed, his hair tied up in a hard knot behind his head. Though his robes were clean, they were frayed and patched as well. He had rolled his sleeves up to his elbows as he scrubbed, but below the knees the cloth was soaked and sodden. His face was sharply pointed, with deep-set eyes as brown as mud. *His feet are bare,* she saw with dismay. They were hideous as well, hard and horny things, thick with callus. "You are His High Holiness?"

"We are."

Father, give me strength. The queen knew that she should kneel, but the floor was wet with soap and dirty water and she did not wish to ruin her gown. She glanced over at the old men on their knees. "I do not see my friend Septon Torbert."

"Septon Torbert has been confined to a penitent's cell on bread and water. It is sinful for any man to be so plump when half the realm is starving."

Cersei had suffered quite enough for one day. She let him see her anger. "Is this how you greet me? With a scrub brush in your hand, dripping water? Do you know who I am?"

"Your Grace is the Queen Regent of the Seven Kingdoms," the man said, "but in *The Seven-Pointed Star* it is written that as men bow to their lords, and lords to their kings, so kings and queens must bow before the Seven Who Are One."

Is he telling me to kneel? If so, he did not know her very well. "By rights you should have met me on the steps in your finest robes, with the crystal crown upon your head."

"We have no crown, Your Grace."

Her frown deepened. "My lord father gave your predecessor a crown of rare beauty, wrought in crystal and spun gold."

"And for that gift we honor him in our prayers," the High Septon said, "but the poor need food in their bellies more than we need gold and crystal on our head. That crown has been sold. So have the others in our vaults, and all our rings, and our robes of cloth-of-gold and cloth-of-silver. Wool will keep a man as warm. That is why the Seven gave us sheep."

He is utterly mad. The Most Devout must have been mad as well, to elevate this creature . . . mad, or terrified of the beggars at their doors. Qyburn's whisperers claimed that Septon Luceon had been nine votes from elevation when those doors had given way, and the sparrows came pouring into the Great Sept with their leader on their shoulders and their axes in their hands.

She fixed the small man with an icy stare. "Is there someplace where we may speak more privily, Your Holiness?"

The High Septon surrendered his scrub brush to one of the Most Devout. "If Your Grace will follow us?"

He led her through the inner doors, into the sept proper. Their footsteps echoed off the marble floor. Dust motes swam in the beams of colored light slanting down through the leaded glass of the great dome. Incense sweetened the air, and beside the seven altars candles shone like stars. A thousand twinkled for the Mother and near as many for the Maid, but you could count the Stranger's candles on two hands and still have fingers left.

Even here the sparrows had invaded. A dozen scruffy hedge knights were kneeling before the Warrior, beseeching him to bless the swords they had piled at his feet. At the Mother's altar, a septon was leading a hundred sparrows in prayer, their voices as distant as waves upon the shore. The High Septon led Cersei to where the Crone raised her lantern. When he knelt before the altar, she had no choice but to kneel beside him. Mercifully, this High Septon was not as long-winded as the fat one had been. *I should be grateful for that much, I suppose.*

His High Holiness made no move to rise when his prayer was done. It would seem they must confer upon their knees. *A small man's ploy,* she thought, amused. "High Holiness," she said, "these sparrows are frightening the city. I want them gone."

"Where should they go, Your Grace?"

There are seven hells, any one of them will serve. "Back where they came from, I would imagine."

"They came from everywhere. As the sparrow is the humblest and most common of the birds, they are the humblest and most common of men."

They are common, we agree on that much. "Have you seen what they have done to Blessed Baelor's statue? They befoul the plaza with their pigs and goats and night soil."

"Night soil can be washed away more easily than blood, Your Grace. If the plaza was befouled, it was befouled by the execution that was done here."

He dares throw Ned Stark in my face? "We all regret that. Joffrey was young, and not as wise as he might have been. Lord Stark should have been beheaded elsewhere, out of respect for Blessed Baelor . . . but the man *was* a traitor, let us not forget."

"King Baelor forgave those who conspired against him."

King Baelor imprisoned his own sisters, whose only crime was being beautiful. The first time Cersei heard that tale, she had gone to Tyrion's nursery and pinched the little monster till he cried. *I should have pinched his nose shut and stuffed my sock into his mouth.* She forced herself to smile. "King Tommen will forgive the sparrows too, once they have returned to their homes."

"Most have lost their homes. Suffering is everywhere . . . and grief, and death. Before coming to King's Landing, I tended to half a hundred little villages too small to have a septon of their own. I walked from each one to the next, performing marriages, absolving sinners of their sins, naming newborn children. Those villages are no more, Your Grace. Weeds and thorns grow where gardens once flourished, and bones litter the roadsides."

"War is a dreadful thing. These atrocities are the work of the northmen, and of Lord Stannis and his demon-worshipers."

"Some of my sparrows speak of bands of lions who despoiled them . . . and of the Hound, who was your own sworn man. At Saltpans he slew an aged septon and despoiled a girl of twelve, an innocent child promised to the Faith. He wore his armor as he raped her and her tender flesh was torn and crushed by his iron mail. When he was done he gave her to his men, who cut off her nose and nipples."

"His Grace cannot be held responsible for the crimes of every man who ever served House Lannister. Sandor Clegane is a traitor and a brute. Why do you think I dismissed him from our service? He fights for the outlaw Beric Dondarrion now, not for King Tommen."

"As you say. Yet it must be asked—where were the king's knights when these things were being done? Did not Jaehaerys the Conciliator once swear upon the Iron

Throne itself that the crown would always protect and defend the Faith?"

Cersei had no idea what Jaehaerys the Conciliator might have sworn. "He did," she agreed, "and the High Septon blessed him and anointed him as king. It is traditional for every new High Septon to give the king his blessing . . . and yet you have refused to bless King Tommen."

"Your Grace is mistaken. We have not refused."

"You have not come."

"The hour is not yet ripe."

Are you a priest or a greengrocer? "And what might I do to make it . . . riper?" *If he dares mention gold, I will deal with this one as I did the last and find a pious eight-year-old to wear the crystal crown.*

"The realm is full of kings. For the Faith to exalt one above the rest we must be certain. Three hundred years ago, when Aegon the Dragon landed beneath this very hill, the High Septon locked himself within the Starry Sept of Oldtown and prayed for seven days and seven nights, taking no nourishment but bread and water. When he emerged he announced that the Faith would not oppose Aegon and his sisters, for the Crone had lifted up her lamp to show him what lay ahead. If Oldtown took up arms against the Dragon, Oldtown would burn, and the Hightower and the Citadel and the Starry Sept would be cast down and destroyed. Lord Hightower was a godly man. When he heard the prophecy, he kept his strength at home and opened the city gates to Aegon when he came. And His High Holiness anointed the Conqueror with the seven oils. I must do as he did, three hundred years ago. I must pray, and fast."

"For seven days and seven nights?"

"For as long as need be."

Cersei itched to slap his solemn, pious face. *I could help you fast,* she thought. *I could shut you up in some tower and see that no one brings you food until the gods have spoken.* "These false kings espouse false gods," she reminded him. "Only King Tommen defends the Holy Faith."

"Yet everywhere septs are burned and looted. Even silent sisters have been raped, crying their anguish to the sky. Your Grace has seen the bones and skulls of our holy dead?"

"I have," she had to say. "Give Tommen your blessing, and he shall put an end to these outrages."

"And how shall he do that, Your Grace? Will he send a knight to walk the roads with every begging brother? Will he give us men to guard our septas against the wolves and lions?"

I will pretend you did not mention lions. "The realm is at war. His Grace has need of every man." Cersei did not intend to squander Tommen's strength playing wet nurse to sparrows, or guarding the wrinkled cunts of a thousand sour septas. *Half of them are probably praying for a good raping.* "Your sparrows have clubs and axes. Let them defend themselves."

"King Maegor's laws prohibit that, as Your Grace must know. It was by his decree that the Faith laid down its swords."

"Tommen is king now, not Maegor." What did she care what Maegor the Cruel had decreed three hundred years ago? *Instead of taking the swords out of the hands of the faithful, he should have used them for his own ends.* She pointed to where the Warrior stood above his altar of red marble. "What is that he holds?"

"A sword."

"Has he forgotten how to use it?"

"Maegor's laws—"

"—could be undone." She let that hang there, waiting for the High Sparrow to rise to the bait.

He did not disappoint her. "The Faith Militant reborn . . . that would be the answer to three hundred years of prayer, Your Grace. The Warrior would lift his shining sword again and cleanse this sinful realm of all its evil. If His Grace were to allow me to restore the ancient blessed orders of the Sword and Star, every godly man in the Seven Kingdoms would know him to be our true and rightful lord."

That was sweet to hear, but Cersei took care not to seem too eager. "Your High Holiness spoke of forgiveness earlier. In these troubled times, King Tommen would be most grateful if you could see your way to forgiving the crown's debt. It seems to me we owe the Faith some nine hundred thousand dragons."

"Nine hundred thousand six hundred and seventy-four dragons. Gold that could feed the hungry and rebuild a thousand septs."

"Is it gold you want?" the queen asked. "Or do you want these dusty laws of Maegor's set aside?"

The High Septon pondered that a moment. "As you wish. This debt shall be forgiven, and King Tommen will have his blessing. The Warrior's Sons shall escort me to him, shining in the glory of their Faith, whilst my sparrows go forth to defend the meek and humble of the land, reborn as Poor Fellows as of old."

The queen got to her feet and smoothed her skirts. "I shall have the papers drawn up, and His Grace will sign them and affix them with the royal seal." If there was one part of kingship that Tommen loved, it was playing with his seal.

"Seven save His Grace. Long may he reign." The High

Septon made a steeple of his hands and raised his eyes to heaven. "Let the wicked tremble!"

Do you hear that, Lord Stannis? Cersei could not help but smile. Even her lord father could have done no better. At a stroke, she had rid King's Landing of the plague of sparrows, secured Tommen's blessing, and lessened the crown's debt by close to a million dragons. Her heart was soaring as she allowed the High Septon to escort her back to the Hall of Lamps.

Lady Merryweather shared the queen's delight, though she had never heard of the Warrior's Sons or the Poor Fellows. "They date from before Aegon's Conquest," Cersei explained to her. "The Warrior's Sons were an order of knights who gave up their lands and gold and swore their swords to His High Holiness. The Poor Fellows . . . they were humbler, though far more numerous. Begging brothers of a sort, though they carried axes instead of bowls. They wandered the roads, escorting travelers from sept to sept and town to town. Their badge was the seven-pointed star, red on white, so the smallfolk named them Stars. The Warrior's Sons wore rainbow cloaks and inlaid silver armor over hair shirts, and bore star-shaped crystals in the pommels of their longswords. They were the Swords. Holy men, ascetics, fanatics, sorcerers, dragon-slayers, demonhunters . . . there were many tales about them. But all agree that they were implacable in their hatred for all enemies of the Holy Faith."

Lady Merryweather understood at once. "Enemies such as Lord Stannis and his red sorceress, perhaps?"

"Why, yes, as it happens," said Cersei, giggling like a girl. "Shall we broach a flagon of hippocras and drink to the fervor of the Warrior's Sons on our way home?"

"To the fervor of the Warrior's Sons and the brilliance of the Queen Regent. To Cersei, the First of Her Name!"

The hippocras was as sweet and savory as Cersei's triumph, and the queen's litter seemed almost to float back across the city. But at the base of Aegon's High Hill, they encountered Margaery Tyrell and her cousins returning from a ride. *She dogs me everywhere I go,* Cersei thought with annoyance when she laid eyes on the little queen.

Behind Margaery came a long tail of courtiers, guards, and servants, many of them laden with baskets of fresh flowers. Each of her cousins had an admirer in thrall; the gangly squire Alyn Ambrose rode with Elinor, to whom he was betrothed, Ser Tallad with shy Alla, one-armed Mark Mullendore with Megga, plump and laughing. The Redwyne twins were escorting two of Margaery's other ladies, Meredyth Crane and Janna Fossoway. The women all wore flowers in their hair. Jalabhar Xho had attached himself to the party too, as had Ser Lambert Turnberry with his eye patch, and the handsome singer known as the Blue Bard.

And of course a knight of the Kingsguard must accompany the little queen, and of course it is the Knight of Flowers. In white scale armor chased with gold, Ser Loras glittered. Though he no longer presumed to train Tommen at arms, the king still spent far too much time in his company. Every time the boy returned from an afternoon with his little wife, he had some new tale to tell about something that Ser Loras had said or done.

Margaery hailed them when the two columns met and fell in beside the queen's litter. Her cheeks were flushed, her brown ringlets tumbling loosely about her shoulders, stirred by every puff of wind. "We have been picking autumn flowers in the kingswood," she told them.

I know where you were, the queen thought. Her informers were very good about keeping her apprised of Margaery's movements. *Such a restless girl, our little queen.* She seldom let more than three days pass without going off for a ride. Some days they would ride along the Rosby road to hunt for shells and eat beside the sea. Other times she would take her entourage across the river for an afternoon of hawking. The little queen was fond of going out on boats as well, sailing up and down the Blackwater Rush to no particular purpose. When she was feeling pious she would leave the castle to pray at Baelor's Sept. She gave her custom to a dozen different seamstresses, was well-known amongst the city's goldsmiths, and had even been known to visit the fish market by the Mud Gate for a look at the day's catch. Wherever she went, the smallfolk fawned on her, and Lady Margaery did all she could to fan their ardor. She was forever giving alms to beggars, buying hot pies off bakers' carts, and reining up to speak to common tradesmen.

Had it been up to her, she would have had Tommen doing all these things as well. She was forever inviting him to accompany her and her hens on their adventures, and the boy was forever pleading with his mother for leave to go along. The queen had given her consent a few times, if only to allow Ser Osney to spend a few more hours in Margaery's company. *For all the good it has done. Osney has proved a grievous disappointment.* "Do you remember the day your sister sailed for Dorne?" Cersei asked her son. "Do you recall the mob howling on our way back to the castle? The stones, the curses?"

But the king was deaf to sense, thanks to his little queen. "If we mingle with the commons, they will love us better."

"The mob loved the fat High Septon so well they tore him limb from limb, and him a holy man," she reminded him. All it did was make him sullen with her. *Just as Margaery wants, I wager. Every day in every way she tries to steal him from me.* Joffrey would have seen through her schemer's smile and let her know her place, but Tommen was more gullible. *She knew Joff was too strong for her,* Cersei thought, remembering the gold coin Qyburn had found. *For House Tyrell to hope to rule, he had to be removed.* It came back to her that Margaery and her hideous grandmother had once plotted to marry Sansa Stark to the little queen's crippled brother Willas. Lord Tywin had forestalled that by stealing a march on them and wedding Sansa to Tyrion, but the link had been there. *They are all in it together,* she realized with a start. *The Tyrells bribed the gaolers to free Tyrion, and whisked him down the roseroad to join his vile bride. By now the both of them are safe in Highgarden, hidden away behind a wall of roses.*

"You should have come along with us, Your Grace," the little schemer prattled on as they climbed the slope of Aegon's High Hill. "We could have had such a lovely time together. The trees are gowned in gold and red and orange, and there are flowers everywhere. Chestnuts too. We roasted some on our way home."

"I have no time for riding through the woods and picking flowers," Cersei said. "I have a kingdom to rule."

"Only one, Your Grace? Who rules the other six?" Margaery laughed a merry little laugh. "You will forgive me my jest, I hope. I know what a burden you bear. You should let me share the load. There must be some things I could do to help you. It would put to rest all this talk that you and I are rivals for the king."

"Is that what they say?" Cersei smiled. "How foolish. I have never looked upon you as a rival, not even for a moment."

"I am so pleased to hear that." The girl did not seem to realize that she had been cut. "You and Tommen must come with us the next time. I know His Grace would love it. The Blue Bard played for us, and Ser Tallad showed us how to fight with a staff the way the smallfolk do. The woods are so beautiful in autumn."

"My late husband loved the forest too." In the early years of their marriage, Robert was forever imploring her to hunt with him, but Cersei had always begged off. His hunting trips allowed her time with Jaime. *Golden days and silver nights.* It was a dangerous dance that they had danced, to be sure. Eyes and ears were everywhere within the Red Keep, and one could never be certain when Robert would return. Somehow the peril had only served to make their times together that much more thrilling. "Still, beauty can sometimes mask deadly danger," she warned the little queen. "Robert lost his life in the woods."

Margaery smiled at Ser Loras; a sweet sisterly smile, full of fondness. "Your Grace is kind to fear for me, but my brother keeps me well protected."

Go and hunt, Cersei had urged Robert, half a hundred times. *My brother keeps me well protected.* She recalled what Taena had told her earlier, and a laugh came bursting from her lips.

"Your Grace laughs so prettily." Lady Margaery gave her a quizzical smile. "Might we share the jest?"

"You will," the queen said. "I promise you, you will."

THE REAVER

The drums were pounding out a battle beat as the *Iron Victory* swept forward, her ram cutting through the choppy green waters. The smaller ship ahead was turning, oars slapping at the sea. Roses streamed upon her banners; fore and aft a white rose upon a red escutcheon, atop her mast a golden one on a field as green as grass. The *Iron Victory* raked her side so hard that half the boarding party lost their feet. Oars snapped and splintered, sweet music to the captain's ears.

He vaulted over the gunwale, landing on the deck below with his golden cloak billowing behind him. The white roses drew back, as men always did at the sight of Victarion Greyjoy armed and armored, his face hidden behind his kraken helm. They were clutching swords and spears and axes, but nine of every ten wore no armor, and the tenth had only a shirt of sewn scales. *These are no ironmen,* Victarion thought. *They still fear drowning.*

"Get him!" one man shouted. "He's alone!"

"COME!" he roared back. *"Come kill me, if you can."*

From all sides the rosey warriors converged, with grey steel in their hands and terror behind their eyes. Their fear was so ripe Victarion could taste it. Left and right he laid about, hewing off the first man's arm at the elbow, cleaving through the shoulder of the second. The third buried his own axehead in the soft pine of Victarion's shield. He slammed it into the fool's face, knocked him off his feet, and slew him when he tried to rise again. As he was struggling to free his axe from the dead man's rib cage, a spear jabbed him between the shoulder blades. It felt as though someone had slapped him on the back. Victarion spun and slammed his axe down onto the spearman's head, feeling the impact in his arm as the steel went crunching through helm and hair and skull. The man swayed for half a heartbeat, till the iron captain wrenched the steel free and sent his corpse staggering loose-limbed across the deck, looking more drunk than dead.

By then his ironborn had followed him down onto the deck of the broken longship. He heard Wulfe One-Ear let out a howl as he went to work, glimpsed Ragnor Pyke in his rusted mail, saw Nute the Barber send a throwing axe spinning through the air to catch a man in the chest. Victarion slew another man, and another. He would have killed a third, but Ragnor cut him down first. "Well struck," Victarion bellowed at him.

When he turned to find the next victim for his axe, he spied the other captain across the deck. His white surcoat was spotted with blood and gore, but Victarion could make out the arms upon his breast, the white rose within its red escutcheon. The man bore the same device upon his shield, on a white field with a red embattled border. *"You!"* the iron captain called across the carnage. *"You of the rose! Be you the lord of Southshield?"*

The other raised his visor to show a beardless face. "His son and heir. Ser Talbert Serry. And who are you, kraken?"

"Your death." Victarion bulled toward him.

Serry leapt to meet him. His longsword was good castle-forged steel, and the young knight made it sing. His first cut was low, and Victarion deflected it off his axe. His second caught the iron captain on the helm before he got his shield up. Victarion answered with a sidearm blow of his axe. Serry's shield got in the way. Wooden splinters flew, and the white rose split lengthwise with a sweet sharp *crack.* The young knight's longsword hammered at his thigh, once, twice, thrice, screaming against the steel. *This boy is quick,* the iron captain realized. He smashed his shield in Serry's face and sent him staggering back against the gunwale. Victarion raised his axe and put all his weight behind his cut, to open the boy from neck to groin, but Serry spun away. The axehead crashed through the rail, sending splinters flying, and lodged there when he tried to pull it free. The deck moved under his feet, and he stumbled to one knee.

Ser Talbert cast away his broken shield and slashed down with his longsword. Victarion's own shield had twisted half around when he stumbled. He caught Serry's blade in an iron fist. Lobstered steel crunched, and a stab of pain made him grunt, yet Victarion held on. "I am quick as well, boy," he said as he ripped the sword from the knight's hand and flung it into the sea.

Ser Talbert's eyes went wide. "My sword . . ."

Victarion caught the lad about the throat with a bloody

fist. "Go and get it," he said, forcing him backwards over the side into the bloodstained waters.

That won him a respite to pull his axe loose. The white roses were falling back before the iron tide. Some tried to flee belowdecks, as others cried for quarter. Victarion could feel warm blood trickling down his fingers beneath the mail and leather and lobstered plate, but that was nothing. Around the mast a thick knot of foemen fought on, standing shoulder to shoulder in a ring. *These few are men, at least. They would sooner die than yield.* Victarion would grant some of them that wish. He beat his axe against his shield and charged them.

The Drowned God had not shaped Victarion Greyjoy to fight with words at kingsmoots, nor struggle against furtive sneaking foes in endless bogs. *This* was why he had been put on earth; to stand steel-clad with an axe red and dripping in his hand, dealing death with every blow.

They hacked at him from front and back, but their swords might have been willow switches for all the harm they did him. No blade could cut through Victarion Greyjoy's heavy plate, nor did he give his foes the time to find the weak points at the joints, where only mail and leather warded him. Let three men assail him, or four, or five; it made no matter. He slew them one at a time, trusting in his steel to protect him from the others. As each foe fell he turned his wroth upon the next.

The last man to face him must have been a smith; he had shoulders like a bull, and one much more muscular than the other. His armor was a studded brigandine and a cap of boiled leather. The only blow he landed completed the ruin of Victarion's shield, but the cut the captain dealt in answer split his head in two. *Would that I could deal with the Crow's Eye as simply.* When he jerked his axehead free again, the smith's skull seemed to burst. Bone and blood and brain went everywhere, and the corpse fell forward, up against his legs. *Too late to plead for quarter now,* Victarion thought as he untangled himself from the dead man.

By then the deck was slick beneath his feet, and the dead and the dying lay in heaps on every side. He threw his shield away and sucked in air. "Lord Captain," he heard the Barber say beside him, "the day is ours."

All around the sea was full of ships. Some were burning, some were sinking, some had been smashed to splinters. Between the hulls the water was thick as stew, full of corpses, broken oars, and men clinging to the wreckage. In the distance, half a dozen of southron longships were racing back toward the Mander. *Let them go,* Victarion thought, *let them tell the tale.* Once a man had turned his tail and run from battle he ceased to be a man.

His eyes were stinging from the sweat that had run down into them during the fight. Two of his oarsmen helped undo his kraken helm so he might lift it off. Victarion mopped at his brow. "That knight," he grumbled, "the knight of the white rose. Did any of you pull him out?" A lord's son would be worth a goodly ransom; from his father, if Lord Serry had survived the day. From his liege at Highgarden, if not.

None of his men had seen what became of the knight after he went over the side, however. Most like the man had drowned. "May he feast as he fought, in the Drowned God's watery halls." Though the men of the Shield Islands called themselves sailors, they crossed the seas in dread and went lightly clad in battle for fear of drowning. Young Serry had been different. *A brave man,* thought Victarion. *Almost ironborn.*

He gave the captured ship to Ragnor Pyke, named a dozen men to crew her, and clambered back up onto his own *Iron Victory.* "Strip the captives of arms and armor and have their wounds bound up," he told Nute the Barber. "Throw the dying in the sea. If any beg for mercy, cut their throats first." He had only contempt for such; better to drown on seawater than on blood. "I want a count of the ships we won and all the knights and lordlings we took captive. I want their banners too." One day he would hang them in his hall, so when he grew old and feeble he could remember all the foes he had slain when he was young and strong.

"It will be done." Nute grinned. "It is a great victory."

Aye, he thought, *a great victory for the Crow's Eye and his wizards.* The other captains would shout his brother's name anew when the tidings reached Oakenshield. Euron had seduced them with his glib tongue and smiling eye and bound them to his cause with the plunder of half a hundred distant lands; gold and silver, ornate armor, curved swords with gilded pommels, daggers of Valyrian steel, striped tiger pelts and the skins of spotted cats, jade manticores and ancient Valyrian sphinxes, chests of nutmeg, cloves, and saffron, ivory tusks and the horns of unicorns, green and orange and yellow feathers from the Summer Sea, bolts of fine silk and shimmering samite . . . and yet all that was little and less, compared to this. *Now he has given them conquest, and they are his for good and all,* the captain thought. The taste was bitter on his tongue. *This was my victory, not his. Where was he? Back on Oakenshield, lazing in a castle. He stole my wife and he stole my throne, and now he steals my glory.*

Obedience came naturally to Victarion Greyjoy; he had been born to it. Growing to manhood in the shadow of his brothers, he had followed Balon dutifully in everything he did. Later, when Balon's sons were born, he had grown to accept that one day he would kneel to them as well, when one of them took his father's place upon the Seastone Chair. But the Drowned God had summoned Balon and his sons down to his watery halls, and Victarion could not call Euron "king" without tasting bile in his throat.

The wind was freshening, and his thirst was raging. After a battle he always wanted wine. He gave the deck to Nute and went below. In his cramped cabin aft, he found the dusky woman wet and ready; perhaps the battle had warmed her blood as well. He took her twice, in quick succession. When they were done there was blood smeared across her breasts and thighs and belly, but it was his blood, from the gash in his palm. The dusky woman washed it out for him with boiled vinegar.

"The plan was good, I grant him," Victarion said as she knelt beside him. "The Mander is open to us now, as it was of old." It was a lazy river, wide and slow and treacherous with snags and sandbars. Most seagoing vessels dared not sail beyond Highgarden, but longships with their shallow draughts could navigate as far upstream as Bitterbridge. In ancient days, the ironborn had boldly sailed the river road and plundered all along the Mander and its vassal streams . . . until the kings of the green hand had armed the fisherfolk on the four small islands off the Mander's mouth and named them his shields.

Two thousand years had passed, but in the watchtowers along their craggy shores, greybeards still kept the ancient vigil. At the first glimpse of longships the old men would light their beacon fires, and the call would leap from hill to hill and island to island. *Fear! Foes! Raiders! Raiders!* When the fisherfolk saw the fires burning on the high places they would put their nets and plows aside and take up their swords and axes. Their lords would rush from their castles, attended by their knights and men-at-arms. Warhorns would echo across the waters, from Greenshield and Greyshield, Oakenshield and Southshield, and their longships would come sliding out from moss-covered stone pens along the shores, oars flashing as they swarmed across the straits to seal the Mander and hound and harry the raiders upriver to their doom.

Euron had sent Torwold Browntooth and the Red Oarsman up the Mander with a dozen swift longships, so the lords of the Shield Islands would spill forth in pursuit. By the time his main fleet arrived, only a handful of fighting men remained to defend the isles themselves. The ironborn had come in on the evening tide, so the glare of the setting sun would keep them hidden from the greybeards in the watchtowers until it was too late. The wind was at their backs, as it had been all the way down from Old Wyk. It was whispered about the fleet that Euron's wizards had much and more to do with that, that the Crow's Eye appeased the Storm God with blood sacrifice. How else would he have dared sail so far to the west, instead of following the shoreline as was the custom?

The ironborn ran their longships up onto the stony shingles and spilled out into the purple dusk with steel glimmering in their hands. By then the fires were burning in the high places, but few remained to take up arms. Greyshield, Greenshield, and Southshield fell before the sun came up. Oakenshield lasted half a day longer. And when the men of the Four Shields broke off their pursuit of Torwold and the Red Oarsman and turned downriver, they found the Iron Fleet waiting at the Mander's mouth.

"All fell out as Euron said it would," Victarion told the dusky woman as she bound up his hand with linen. "His wizards must have seen it." He had three aboard the *Silence,* Quellon Humble had confided in a whisper. Queer men and terrible, they were, but the Crow's Eye had made them slaves. "He still needs me to fight his battles, though," Victarion insisted. "Wizards may be well and good, but blood and steel win wars." The vinegar made his wound hurt worse than ever. He shoved the woman away and closed his fist, glowering. "Bring me wine."

He drank in the darkness, brooding on his brother. *If I do not strike the blow with mine own hand, am I still a kinslayer?* Victarion feared no man, but the Drowned God's curse gave him pause. *If another strikes him down at my command, will his blood still stain my hands?* Aeron Damphair would know the answer, but the priest was somewhere back on the Iron Islands, still hoping to raise the ironborn against their new-crowned king. *Nute the Barber can shave a man with a thrown axe from twenty yards away. And none of Euron's mongrels could stand against Wulfe One-Ear or Andrik the Unsmiling. Any of them could do it.* But what a man *can* do and what a man *will* do are two different things, he knew.

"Euron's blasphemies will bring down the Drowned God's wroth upon us all," Aeron had prophesied, back on Old Wyk. "We must stop him, brother. We are still of Balon's blood, are we not?"

"So is he," Victarion had said. "I like it no more than you, but Euron is the king. Your kingsmoot raised him up, and you put the driftwood crown upon his head yourself!"

"I placed the crown upon his head," said the priest, seaweed dripping in his hair, "and gladly will I wrest it off again and crown you in his stead. Only you are strong enough to fight him."

"The Drowned God raised him up," Victarion complained. "Let the Drowned God cast him down."

Aeron gave him a baleful look, the look that had been known to sour wells and make women barren. "It was not the god who spoke. Euron is known to keep wizards and foul sorcerers on that red ship of his. They sent some spell among us, so we could not hear the sea. The captains and the kings were drunk with all this talk of dragons."

"Drunk, and fearful of that horn. You heard the sound it made. It makes no matter. Euron is our king."

"Not mine," the priest declared. "The Drowned God helps bold men, not those who cower below their decks when the storm is rising. If you will not bestir yourself to remove the Crow's Eye from the Seastone Chair, I must take the task upon myself."

"How? You have no ships, no swords."

"I have my voice," the priest replied, "and the god is with me. Mine is the strength of the sea, a strength the Crow's Eye cannot hope to withstand. The waves may break upon the mountain, yet still they come, wave upon wave, and in the end only pebbles remain where once the mountain stood. And soon even the pebbles are swept away, to be ground beneath the sea for all eternity."

"Pebbles?" Victarion grumbled. "You are mad if you think to bring the Crow's Eye down with talk of waves and pebbles."

"The ironborn shall be waves," the Damphair said. "Not the great and lordly, but the simple folk, tillers of the soil and fishers of the sea. The captains and the kings raised Euron up, but the common folk shall tear him down. I shall go to Great Wyk, to Harlaw, to Orkmont, to Pyke itself. In every town and village shall my words be heard. *No godless man may sit the Seastone Chair!*" He shook his shaggy head and stalked back out into the night. When the sun came up the next day, Aeron Greyjoy had vanished from Old Wyk. Even his drowned men knew not where. They said the Crow's Eye only laughed when he was told.

But though the priest was gone, his dire warnings lingered. Victarion found himself remembering Baelor

Blacktyde's words as well. *"Balon was mad, Aeron is madder, and Euron is maddest of them all."* The young lord had tried to sail home after the kingsmoot, refusing to accept Euron as his liege. But the Iron Fleet had closed the bay, the habit of obedience was rooted deep in Victarion Greyjoy, and Euron wore the driftwood crown. *Nightflyer* was seized, Lord Blacktyde delivered to the king in chains. Euron's mutes and mongrels had cut him into seven parts, to feed the seven green land gods he worshiped.

As a reward for his leal service, the new-crowned king had given Victarion the dusky woman, taken off some slaver bound for Lys. "I want none of your leavings," he had told his brother scornfully, but when the Crow's Eye said that the woman would be killed unless he took her, he had weakened. Her tongue had been torn out, but elsewise she was undamaged, and beautiful besides, with skin as brown as oiled teak. Yet sometimes when he looked at her, he found himself remembering the first woman his brother had given him, to make a man of him.

Victarion wanted to use the dusky woman once again, but found himself unable. "Fetch me another skin of wine," he told her, "then get out." When she returned with a skin of sour red, the captain took it up on deck, where he could breathe the clean sea air. He drank half the skin and poured the rest into the sea for all the men who'd died.

The *Iron Victory* lingered for hours off the mouth of the Mander. As the greater part of the Iron Fleet got under way for Oakenshield, Victarion kept *Grief, Lord Dagon, Iron Wind,* and *Maiden's Bane* about him as a rear guard. They pulled survivors from the sea, and watched *Hardhand* sink slowly, dragged under by the wreck that she had rammed. By the time she vanished beneath the waters Victarion had the count he'd asked for. He had lost six ships, and captured eight-and-thirty. "It will serve," he told Nute. "To the oars. We return to Lord Hewett's Town."

His oarsmen bent their backs toward Oakenshield, and the iron captain went belowdecks once again. "I could kill him," he told the dusky woman. "Though it is a great sin to kill your king, and a worse one to kill your brother." He frowned. "Asha should have given me her voice." How could she have ever hoped to win the captains and the kings, her with her pinecones and her turnips? *Balon's blood is in her, but she is still a woman.* She had run after the kingsmoot. The night the driftwood crown was placed on Euron's head, she and her crew had melted away. Some small part of Victarion was glad she had. *If the girl keeps her wits about her, she will wed some northern lord and live with him in his castle, far from the sea and Euron Crow's Eye.*

"Lord Hewett's Town, Lord Captain," a crewman called.

Victarion rose. The wine had dulled the throbbing in his hand. Perhaps he would have Hewett's maester look at it, if the man had not been killed. He returned to deck as they came around a headland. The way Lord Hewett's castle sat above the harbor reminded him of Lordsport, though this town was twice as big. A score of longships prowled the waters beyond the port, the golden kraken writhing on their sails. Hundreds more were beached along the shingles and drawn up to the piers that lined the harbor. At a stone quay stood three great cogs and a dozen smaller ones, taking on plunder and provisions. Victarion gave orders for the *Iron Victory* to drop anchor. "Have a boat made ready."

The town seemed strangely still as they approached. Most of the shops and houses had been looted, as their smashed doors and broken shutters testified, but only the sept had been put to the torch. The streets were strewn with corpses, each with a small flock of carrion crows in attendance. A gang of sullen survivors moved amongst them, chasing off the black birds and tossing the dead into the back of a wagon for burial. The notion filled Victarion with disgust. No true son of the sea would want to rot beneath the ground. How would he ever find the Drowned God's watery halls, to drink and feast for all eternity?

The *Silence* was amongst the ships they passed. Victarion's gaze was drawn to the iron figurehead at her prow, the mouthless maiden with the windblown hair and outstretched arm. Her mother-of-pearl eyes seemed to follow him. *She had a mouth like any other woman, till the Crow's Eye sewed it shut.*

As they neared the shore, he noticed a line of women and children herded up onto the deck of one of the great cogs. Some had their hands bound behind their backs, and all wore loops of hempen rope about their necks. "Who are they?" he asked the men who helped tie up their boat.

"Widows and orphans. They're to be sold as slaves."

"Sold?" There were no slaves in the Iron Islands, only thralls. A thrall was bound to service, but he was not chattel. His children were born free, so long as they were given to the Drowned God. And thralls were never bought nor sold for gold. A man paid the iron price for thralls, or else had none. "They should be thralls, or salt wives," Victarion complained.

"It's by the king's decree," the man said.

"The strong have always taken from the weak," said Nute the Barber. "Thralls or slaves, it makes no matter. Their men could not defend them, so now they are ours, to do with as we will."

It is not the Old Way, he might have said, but there was no time. His victory had preceded him, and men were gathering round to offer congratulations. Victarion let them fawn, until one began to praise Euron's daring. "It is daring to sail out of sight of land, so no word of our coming could reach these islands before us," he growled, "but crossing half the world to hunt for dragons, that is something else." He did not wait for a reply, but shouldered through the press and on up to the keep.

Lord Hewett's castle was small but strong, with thick walls and studded oaken gates that evoked his House's ancient arms, an oak escutcheon studded with iron upon a field of undy blue and white. But it was the kraken of House Greyjoy that flew atop his green-roofed towers now, and they found the great gates burned and broken. On the ramparts walked ironborn with spears and axes, and some of Euron's mongrels too.

In the yard Victarion came on Gorold Goodbrother and old Drumm, speaking quietly with Rodrik Harlaw. Nute the Barber gave a hoot at the sight of them. "Reader," he called out, "why is your face so long? Your misgivings were for nought. The day is ours, and ours the prize!"

Lord Rodrik's mouth puckered. "These rocks, you mean? All four together wouldn't make Harlaw. We have won some stones and trees and trinkets, and the enmity of House Tyrell."

"The roses?" Nute laughed. "What rose can harm the krakens of the deep? We have taken their shields from them, and smashed them all to pieces. Who will protect them now?"

"Highgarden," replied the Reader. "Soon enough all the power of the Reach will be marshaled against us, Barber, and then you may learn that some roses have steel thorns."

Drumm nodded, one hand on the hilt of his Red Rain. "Lord Tarly bears the greatsword Heartsbane, forged of Valyrian steel, and he is always in Lord Tyrell's van."

Victarion's hunger flared. "Let him come. I will take his sword for mine own, as your own forebear took Red Rain. Let them all come, and bring the Lannisters as well. A lion may be fierce enough on land, but at sea the kraken rules supreme." He would give half his teeth for the chance to try his axe against the Kingslayer or the Knight of Flowers. That was the sort of battle that he understood. The kinslayer was accursed in the eyes of gods and men, but the warrior was honored and revered.

"Have no fear, Lord Captain," said the Reader. "They will come. His Grace desires it. Why else would he have commanded us to let Hewett's ravens fly?"

"You read too much and fight too little," Nute said. "Your blood is milk." But the Reader made as if he had not heard.

A riotous feast was in progress when Victarion entered the hall. Ironborn filled the tables, drinking and shouting and jostling each other, boasting of the men that they had slain, the deeds that they had done, the prizes they had won. Many were bedecked with plunder. Left-Hand Lucas Codd and Quellon Humble had torn tapestries off the walls to serve as cloaks. Germund Botley wore a rope of pearls and garnets over his gilded Lannister breastplate. Andrik the Unsmiling staggered by with a woman under each arm; though he remained unsmiling, he had rings on every finger. Instead of trenchers carved from old stale bread, the captains were eating off solid silver platters.

Nute the Barber's face grew dark with anger as he looked about. "The Crow's Eye sends us forth to face the longships, whilst his own men take the castles and the villages and grab all the loot and women. What has he left for us?"

"We have the glory."

"Glory is good," said Nute, "but gold is better."

Victarion shrugged. "The Crow's Eye says we shall have all of Westeros. The Arbor, Oldtown, Highgarden . . . that's where you'll find your gold. But enough talk. I'm hungry."

By right of blood Victarion might have claimed a seat on the dais, but he did not care to eat with Euron and his creatures. Instead, he chose a place by Ralf the Limper, the captain of the *Lord Quellon*. "A great victory, Lord Captain," said the Limper. "A victory worthy of a lordship. You should have an island."

Lord Victarion. Aye, and why not? It might not be the Seastone Chair, but it would be something.

Hotho Harlaw was across the table, sucking meat off a bone. He flicked it aside and hunched forward. "The Knight's to have Greyshield. My cousin. Did you hear?"

"No." Victarion looked across the hall, to where Ser Harras Harlaw sat drinking wine from a golden cup; a tall man, long-faced and austere. "Why would Euron give that one an island?"

Hotho held out his empty wine cup, and a pale young woman in a gown of blue velvet and gilt lace refilled it for him. "The Knight took Grimston by himself. He planted his standard beneath the castle and defied the Grimms to face him. One did, and then another, and another. He slew them all . . . well, near enough, two yielded. When the seventh man went down, Lord Grimm's septon decided the gods had spoken and surrendered the castle." Hotho laughed. "He'll be the Lord of Greyshield, and welcome to it. With him gone, I am the Reader's heir." He thumped his wine cup against his chest. "Hotho the Humpback, Lord of Harlaw."

"Seven, you say." Victarion wondered how Nightfall would fare against his axe. He had never fought a man armed with a Valyrian steel blade, though he had thrashed young Harras Harlaw many a time when both of them were young. As a boy Harlaw had been fast friends with Balon's eldest son, Rodrik, who had died beneath the walls of Seagard.

The feast was good. The wine was of the best, and there was roast ox, rare and bloody, and stuffed ducks as well, and buckets of fresh crabs. The serving wenches wore fine woolens and plush velvets, the Lord Captain did not fail to note. He took them for scullions dressed up in the clothes of Lady Hewett and her ladies, until Hotho told him they *were* Lady Hewett and her ladies. It amused the Crow's Eye to make them wait and pour. There were eight of them: her ladyship herself, still handsome though grown somewhat stout, and seven younger women aged from twenty-five to ten, her daughters and good-daughters.

Lord Hewett himself sat in his accustomed place upon the dais, dressed in all his heraldic finery. His arms and legs had been tied to his chair, and a huge white radish shoved between his teeth so he could not speak . . . though he could see and hear. The Crow's Eye had claimed the place of honor at his lordship's right hand. A pretty, buxom girl of seventeen or eighteen years was in his lap, barefoot and disheveled, her arms around his neck. "Who is that?" Victarion asked the men around him.

"His lordship's bastard daughter," laughed Hotho. "Before Euron took the castle, she was made to wait at table on the rest and take her own meals with the servants."

Euron put his blue lips to her throat, and the girl giggled and whispered something in his ear. Smiling, he kissed her throat again. Her white skin was covered with red marks where his mouth had been; they made a rosy necklace about her neck and shoulders. Another whisper in his ear, and this time the Crow's Eye laughed aloud, then slammed his wine cup down for silence. "Good ladies," he called out to his highborn serving women, "Falia is concerned for your fine gowns. She would not have them stained with grease and wine and dirty groping fingers, since I have promised that she may choose her own clothes from your wardrobes after the feast. So you had best disrobe."

A roar of laughter washed over the great hall, and Lord Hewett's face turned so red that Victarion thought his head might burst. The women had no choice but to obey. The youngest one cried a little, but her mother comforted her and helped undo the laces down her back. Afterward, they continued to serve as before, moving along the tables with flagons full of wine to fill each empty cup, only now they did so naked.

He shames Hewett as he once shamed me, the captain thought, remembering how his wife had sobbed as he was beating her. The men of the Four Shields oft married one another, he knew, just as the ironborn did. One of these naked serving wenches might well be Ser Talbert Serry's wife. It was one thing to kill a foe, another to dishonor him. Victarion made a fist. His hand was bloody where his wound had soaked through the linen.

On the dais, Euron pushed aside his slattern and climbed upon the table. The captains began to bang their cups and stamp their feet upon the floor. *"EURON!"* they shouted. *"EURON! EURON! EURON!"* It was kingsmoot come again.

"I swore to give you Westeros," the Crow's Eye said when the tumult died away, "and here is your first taste. A morsel, nothing more . . . but we shall feast before the fall of night!" The torches along the walls were burning bright, and so was he, blue lips, blue eye, and all. "What the kraken grasps it does not loose. These isles were once ours, and now they are again . . . but we need strong men to hold them. So rise, Ser Harras Harlaw, Lord of Greyshield." The Knight stood, one hand upon Nightfall's moonstone pommel. "Rise, Andrik the Unsmiling, Lord of Southshield." Andrik shoved away his women and lurched to his feet, like a mountain rising sudden from the sea. "Rise, Maron Volmark, Lord of Greenshield." A beardless boy of six-and-ten years, Volmark stood hesitantly, looking like the lord of rabbits. "And rise, Nute the Barber, Lord of Oakenshield."

Nute's eyes grew wary, as if he feared he was the butt of some cruel jape. "A lord?" he croaked.

Victarion had expected the Crow's Eye to give the lordships to his own creatures, Stonehand and the Red Oarsman and Left-Hand Lucas Codd. *A king must needs be open-handed,* he tried to tell himself, but another voice whispered, *Euron's gifts are poisoned.* When he turned it over in his head, he saw it plain. *The Knight was the Reader's chosen heir, and Andrik the Unsmiling the strong right arm of Dunstan Drumm. Volmark is a callow boy, but he has Black Harren's blood in him through his mother. And the Barber . . .*

Victarion grabbed him by the forearm. "Refuse him!"

Nute looked at him as if he had gone mad. "Refuse him? Lands and lordship? Will *you* make me a lord?" He wrenched his arm away and stood, basking in the cheers.

And now he steals my men away, Victarion thought.

King Euron called to Lady Hewett for a fresh cup of wine and raised it high above his head. "Captains and kings, lift your cups to the Lords of the Four Shields!" Victarion drank with the rest. *There is no wine so sweet as wine taken from a foe.* Someone had told him that once. His father, or his brother Balon. *One day I shall drink your wine, Crow's Eye, and take from you all that you hold dear.* But was there anything Euron held dear?

"On the morrow we prepare once more to sail," the king was saying. "Fill our casks anew with spring water, take every sack of grain and cask of beef, and as many sheep and goats as we can carry. The wounded who are still hale enough to pull an oar will row. The rest shall remain here, to help hold these isles for their new lords. Torwold and the Red Oarsman will soon be back with more provisions. Our decks will stink of pigs and chickens on the voyage east, but we'll return with dragons."

"When?" The voice was Lord Rodrik's. "When shall we return, Your Grace? A year? Three years? Five? Your dragons are a world away, and autumn is upon us." The Reader walked forward, sounding all the hazards. "Galleys guard the Redwyne Straits. The Dornish coast is dry and bleak, four hundred leagues of whirlpools, cliffs, and hidden shoals with hardly a safe landing anywhere. Beyond wait the Stepstones, with their storms and their nests of Lysene and Myrish pirates. If a thousand ships set sail, three hundred may reach the far side of the narrow sea . . . and then what? Lys will not welcome us, nor will Volantis. Where will you find fresh water, food? The first storm will scatter us across half the earth."

A smile played across Euron's blue lips. "I *am* the storm, my lord. The first storm, and the last. I have taken the *Silence* on longer voyages than this, and ones far more hazardous. Have you forgotten? I have sailed the Smoking Sea and seen Valyria."

Every man there knew that the Doom still ruled Valyria. The very sea there boiled and smoked, and the land was overrun with demons. It was said that any sailor who so much as glimpsed the fiery mountains of Valyria rising above the waves would soon die a dreadful death, yet the Crow's Eye had been there, and returned.

"Have you?" the Reader asked, so softly.

Euron's blue smile vanished. "Reader," he said into the quiet, "you would do well to keep your nose in your books."

Victarion could feel the unease in the hall. He pushed himself to his feet. "Brother," he boomed. "You have not answered Harlaw's questions."

Euron shrugged. "The price of slaves is rising. We will sell our slaves in Lys and Volantis. That, and the plunder we have taken here, will give us sufficient gold to buy provisions."

"Are we slavers now?" asked the Reader. "And for what? Dragons that no man here has seen? Shall we chase some drunken sailor's fancy to the far ends of the earth?"

His words drew mutters of assent. "Slaver's Bay is too far," called out Ralf the Limper. "And too close to Valyria," shouted Quellon Humble. Fralegg the Strong said, "Highgarden's close. I say, look for dragons there. The *golden* kind!" Alvyn Sharp said, "Why sail the world, when the Mander lies before us?" Red Ralf Stonehouse bounded to his feet. "Oldtown is richer, and the Arbor richer still. Redwyne's fleet is off away. We need only reach out our hand to pluck the ripest fruit in Westeros."

"Fruit?" The king's eye looked more black than blue. "Only a craven would steal a fruit when he could take the orchard."

"It is the Arbor we want," said Red Ralf, and other men took up the cry. The Crow's Eye let the shouts wash over him. Then he leapt down from the table, grabbed his slattern by the arm, and pulled her from the hall.

Fled, like a dog. Euron's hold upon the Seastone Chair suddenly did not seem as secure as it had a few moments before. *They will not follow him to Slaver's Bay. Perhaps they are not such dogs and fools as I had feared.* That was such a merry thought that Victarion had to wash it down. He drained a cup with the Barber, to show him that he did not begrudge him his lordship, even if it came from Euron's hand.

Outside the sun went down. Darkness gathered beyond the walls, but inside the torches burned with a ruddy orange glow, and their smoke gathered under the rafters like a grey cloud. Drunken men began to dance the finger dance. At some point Left-Hand Lucas Codd decided he wanted one of Lord Hewett's daughters, so he took her on a table whilst her sisters screamed and sobbed.

Victarion felt a tap upon his shoulder. One of Euron's mongrel sons stood behind him, a boy of ten with woolly hair and skin the color of mud. "My father wishes words with you."

Victarion rose unsteadily. He was a big man, with a large capacity for wine, but even so, he had drunk too much. *I beat her to death with mine own hands,* he thought, *but the Crow's Eye killed her when he shoved himself inside her. I had no choice.* He followed the bastard boy from the hall and up a winding stone stair. The sounds of rape and revelry diminished as they climbed, until there was only the soft scrape of boots on stone.

The Crow's Eye had taken Lord Hewett's bedchamber along with his bastard daughter. When he entered, the girl was sprawled naked on the bed, snoring softly. Euron stood by the window, drinking from a silver cup. He wore the sable cloak he took from Blacktyde, his red leather eye patch, and nothing else. "When I was a boy, I dreamt that I could fly," he announced. "When I woke, I couldn't . . . or so the maester said. But what if he lied?"

Victarion could smell the sea through the open window,

though the room stank of wine and blood and sex. The cold salt air helped to clear his head. "What do you mean?"

Euron turned to face him, his bruised blue lips curled in a half smile. "Perhaps we can fly. All of us. How will we ever know unless we leap from some tall tower?" The wind came gusting through the window and stirred his sable cloak. There was something obscene and disturbing about his nakedness. "No man ever truly knows what he can do unless he dares to leap."

"There is the window. Leap." Victarion had no patience for this. His wounded hand was troubling him. "What do you want?"

"The world." Firelight glimmered in Euron's eye. *His smiling eye.* "Will you take a cup of Lord Hewett's wine? There's no wine half so sweet as wine taken from a beaten foe."

"No." Victarion glanced away. "Cover yourself."

Euron seated himself and gave his cloak a twitch, so it covered his private parts. "I had forgotten what a small and noisy folk they are, my ironborn. I would bring them dragons, and they shout out for grapes."

"Grapes are real. A man can gorge himself on grapes. Their juice is sweet, and they make wine. What do dragons make?"

"Woe." The Crow's Eye sipped from his silver cup. "I once held a dragon's egg in this hand, brother. This Myrish wizard swore he could hatch it if I gave him a year and all the gold that he required. When I grew bored with his excuses, I slew him. As he watched his entrails sliding through his fingers he said, '*But it has not been a year.*'" He laughed. "Cragorn's died, you know."

"Who?"

"The man who blew my dragon horn. When the

maester cut him open, his lungs were charred as black as soot."

Victarion shuddered. "Show me this dragon's egg."

"I threw it in the sea during one of my dark moods." Euron gave a shrug. "It comes to me that the Reader was not wrong. Too large a fleet could never hold together over such a distance. The voyage is too long, too perilous. Only our finest ships and crews could hope to sail to Slaver's Bay and back. The Iron Fleet."

The Iron Fleet is mine, Victarion thought. He said nothing.

The Crow's Eye filled two cups with a strange black wine that flowed as thick as honey. "Drink with me, brother. Have a taste of this." He offered one of the cups to Victarion.

The captain took the cup Euron had not offered, sniffed at its contents suspiciously. Seen up close, it looked more blue than black. It was thick and oily, with a smell like rotted flesh. He tried a small swallow, and spit it out at once. "Foul stuff. Do you mean to poison me?"

"I mean to open your eyes." Euron drank deep from his own cup, and smiled. "*Shade-of-the-evening,* the wine of the warlocks. I came upon a cask of it when I captured a certain galleas out of Qarth, along with some cloves and nutmeg, forty bolts of green silk, and four warlocks who told a curious tale. One presumed to threaten me, so I killed him and fed him to the other three. They refused to eat of their friend's flesh at first, but when they grew hungry enough they had a change of heart. Men are meat."

Balon was mad, Aeron is madder, and Euron is maddest of them all. Victarion was turning to go when the Crow's Eye said, "A king must have a wife, to give him heirs. Brother, I have need of you. Will you go to Slaver's Bay and bring my love to me?"

I had a love once too. Victarion's hands coiled into fists, and a drop of blood fell to patter on the floor. *I should beat you raw and red and feed you to the crabs, the same as I did her.* "You have sons," he told his brother.

"Baseborn mongrels, born of whores and weepers."

"They are of your body."

"So are the contents of my chamber pot. None is fit to sit the Seastone Chair, much less the Iron Throne. No, to make an heir that's worthy of him, I need a different woman. When the kraken weds the dragon, brother, let all the world beware."

"What dragon?" said Victarion, frowning.

"The last of her line. They say she is the fairest woman in the world. Her hair is silver-gold, and her eyes are amethysts . . . but you need not take my word for it, brother. Go to Slaver's Bay, behold her beauty, and bring her back to me."

"Why should I?" Victarion demanded.

"For love. For duty. Because your king commands it." Euron chuckled. "And for the Seastone Chair. It is yours, once I claim the Iron Throne. You shall follow me as I followed Balon . . . and your own trueborn sons shall one day follow you."

My own sons. But to have a trueborn son a man must first have a wife. Victarion had no luck with wives. *Euron's gifts are poisoned,* he reminded himself, *but still . . .*

"The choice is yours, brother. Live a thrall or die a king. Do you dare to fly? Unless you take the leap, you'll never know."

Euron's smiling eye was bright with mockery. "Or do I ask too much of you? It is a fearsome thing to sail beyond Valyria."

"I could sail the Iron Fleet to hell if need be." When

Victarion opened his hand, his palm was red with blood. "I'll go to Slaver's Bay, aye. I'll find this dragon woman, and I'll bring her back." *But not for you. You stole my wife and despoiled her, so I'll have yours. The fairest woman in the world, for me.*

JAIME

The fields outside the walls of Darry were being tilled once more. The burned crops had been plowed under, and Ser Addam's scouts reported seeing women in the furrows pulling weeds, whilst a team of oxen broke new ground on the edge of a nearby wood. A dozen bearded men with axes stood guard over them as they worked.

By the time Jaime and his column reached the castle, all of them had fled within the walls. He found Darry closed to him, just as Harrenhal had been. *A chilly welcome from mine own blood.*

"Sound the horn," he commanded. Ser Kennos of Kayce unslung the Horn of Herrock and let it wind. As he waited for a response from the castle, Jaime eyed the banner floating brown and crimson above his cousin's barbican. Lancel had taken to quartering the lion of Lannister

with the Darry plowman, it would seem. He saw his uncle's hand in that, as in Lancel's choice of bride. House
Darry had ruled these lands since the Andals cast down
the First Men. No doubt Ser Kevan realized that his son
would have an easier time of it if the peasants saw him as a
continuation of the old line, holding these lands by right of
marriage rather than royal decree. *Kevan should be
Tommen's Hand. Harys Swyft is a toad, and my sister is a
fool if she thinks elsewise.*

The castle gates swung open slowly. "My coz will not
have room to accommodate a thousand men," Jaime told
Strongboar. "We'll make camp beneath the western wall. I
want the perimeters ditched and staked. There are still
bands of outlaws in these parts."

"They'd need to be mad to attack a force as strong as
ours."

"Mad or starving." Until he had a better notion of these
outlaws and their strength, Jaime was not inclined to take
any risks with his defenses. "Ditched and staked," he said
again, before spurring Honor toward the gate. Ser Dermot
rode beside him with the royal stag and lion, and Ser Hugo
Vance with the white standard of the Kingsguard. Jaime
had charged Red Ronnet with the task of delivering Wylis
Manderly to Maidenpool, so he would not need to look on
him henceforth.

Pia rode with Jaime's squires, on the gelding Peck had
found for her. "It's like some toy castle," Jaime heard her
say. *She's known no home but Harrenhal,* he reflected.
*Every castle in the realm will seem small to her, except the
Rock.*

Josmyn Peckleton was saying the same thing. "You
must not judge by Harrenhal. Black Harren built too big."
Pia listened as solemnly as a girl of five being lessoned by
her septa. *That's all she is, a little girl in a woman's body,*

scarred and scared. Peck was taken with her, though. Jaime suspected that the boy had never known a woman, and Pia was still pretty enough, so long as she kept her mouth closed. *There's no harm in him bedding her, I suppose, so long as she's willing.*

One of the Mountain's men had tried to rape the girl at Harrenhal, and had seemed honestly perplexed when Jaime commanded Ilyn Payne to take his head off. "I had her before, a hunnerd times," he kept saying as they forced him to his knees. "A hunnerd times, m'lord. We all had her." When Ser Ilyn presented Pia with his head, she had smiled through her ruined teeth.

Darry had changed hands several times during the fighting, and its castle had been burned once and sacked at least twice, but Lancel had seemingly wasted little time setting things to rights. The castle gates were newly hung, raw oaken planks reinforced with iron studs. A new stable was going up where an older one had been put to the torch. The steps to the keep had been replaced, and the shutters on many of the windows. Blackened stones showed where the flames had licked, but time and rain would fade those.

Within the walls, crossbowmen walked the ramparts, some in crimson cloaks and lion-crested helms, others in the blue and grey of House Frey. As Jaime trotted across the yard, chickens ran out from under Honor's hooves, sheep bleated, and peasants stared at him with sullen eyes. *Armed peasants,* he did not fail to note. Some had scythes, some staves, some hoes sharpened to cruel points. There were axes in evidence as well, and he spied several bearded men with red, seven-pointed stars sewn onto ragged, filthy tunics. *More bloody sparrows. Where do they all come from?*

Of his uncle Kevan he saw no sign. Nor of Lancel. Only a maester emerged to greet him, with a grey robe flapping about his skinny legs. "Lord Commander, Darry is honored by this . . . unexpected visit. You must forgive our lack of preparations. We had been given to understand that you were bound for Riverrun."

"Darry was on my way," lied Jaime. *Riverrun will keep.* And if perchance the siege had ended before he reached the castle, he would be spared the need to take up arms against House Tully.

Dismounting, he handed Honor to a stableboy. "Will I find my uncle here?" He did not supply a name. Ser Kevan was the only uncle he had left, the last surviving son of Tytos Lannister.

"No, my lord. Ser Kevan took his leave of us after the wedding." The maester pulled at the chain collar, as if it had grown too tight for him. "I know Lord Lancel will be pleased to see you and . . . and all your gallant knights. Though it pains me to confess that Darry cannot feed so many."

"We have our own provisions. You are?"

"Maester Ottomore, if it please my lord. Lady Amerei wished to welcome you herself, but she is seeing to the preparation of a feast in your honor. It is her hope that you and your chief knights and captains will join us at table this evening."

"A hot meal would be most welcome. The days have been cold and wet." Jaime glanced about the yard, at the bearded faces of the sparrows. *Too many. And too many Freys as well.* "Where will I find Hardstone?"

"We had a report of outlaws beyond the Trident. Ser Harwyn took five knights and twenty archers and went to deal with them."

"And Lord Lancel?"

"He is at his prayers. His lordship has commanded us never to disturb him when he is praying."

He and Ser Bonifer should get on well. "Very well." There would be time enough to talk with his cousin later. "Show me to my chambers and have a bath brought up."

"If it please my lord, we have put you in the Plowman's Keep. I will show you there."

"I know the way." Jaime was no stranger to this castle. He and Cersei had been guests here twice before, once on their way to Winterfell with Robert, and again on the way back to King's Landing. Though small as castles went, it was larger than an inn, with good hunting along the river. Robert Baratheon had never been loath to impose upon the hospitality of his subjects.

The keep was much as he recalled it. "The walls are still bare," Jaime observed as the maester led him down a gallery.

"Lord Lancel hopes one day to cover them with hangings," said Ottomore. "Scenes of piety and devotion."

Piety and devotion. It was all he could do not to laugh. The walls had been bare on his first visit too. Tyrion had pointed out the squares of darker stone where tapestries had once hung. Ser Raymun could remove the hangings, but not the marks they'd left. Later, the Imp had slipped a handful of stags to one of Darry's serving men for the key to the cellar where the missing tapestries were hidden. He showed them to Jaime by the light of a candle, grinning; woven portraits of all the Targaryen kings, from the first Aegon to the second Aerys. "If I tell Robert, mayhaps he'll make *me* Lord of Darry," the dwarf said, chortling.

Maester Ottomore led Jaime to the top of the keep. "I trust you will be comfortable here, my lord. There is a privy, when nature calls. Your window looks out upon the godswood. The bedchamber adjoins her ladyship's, with a servant's cell between."

"These were Lord Darry's own apartments."

"Yes, my lord."

"My cousin is too kind. I did not intend to put Lancel out of his own bedchamber."

"Lord Lancel has been sleeping in the sept."

Sleeping with the Mother and the Maiden, when he has a warm wife just through that door? Jaime did not know whether to laugh or weep. *Maybe he is praying for his cock to harden.* In King's Landing it had been rumored that Lancel's wounds had left him incapable. *Still, he ought to have sense enough to try.* His cousin's hold on his new lands would not be secure until he fathered a son on his half-Darry wife. Jaime had begun to rue the impulse that had brought him here. He gave thanks to Ottomore, reminded him about the bath, and had Peck see him out.

The lord's bedchamber had changed since his last visit, and not for the better. Old stale rushes covered the floor in place of the fine Myrish carpet that had been there previously, and all the furnishings were new and crudely made. Ser Raymun Darry's bed had been large enough to sleep six, with brown velvet draperies and oakwood posts carved with vines and leaves; Lancel's was a lumpy straw pallet, placed beneath the window where the first light of day would be sure to wake him. The other bed had no doubt been burned or smashed or stolen, but even so . . .

When the tub arrived, Little Lew pulled off Jaime's boots and helped remove his golden hand. Peck and Garrett hauled water, and Pia found him something clean to sup in. The girl glanced at him shyly as she shook his doublet out. Jaime was uncomfortably aware of the curve of hip and breast beneath her roughspun brown dress. He found himself remembering the things that Pia had whispered to him at Harrenhal, the night that Qyburn sent her to his bed. *Sometimes when I'm with some man,* she'd said, *I close my eyes and pretend it's you on top of me.*

He was grateful when the bath was deep enough to conceal his arousal. As he lowered himself into the steaming water, he recalled another bath, the one he'd shared with Brienne. He had been feverish and weak from loss of blood, and the heat had made him so dizzy he found himself saying things better left unsaid. This time he had no such excuse. *Remember your vows. Pia is more fit for Tyrion's bed than yours.* "Fetch me soap and a stiff brush," he told Peck. "Pia, you may leave us."

"Aye, m'lord. Thank you, m'lord." She covered her mouth when she spoke, to hide her broken teeth.

"Do you want her?" Jaime asked Peck, when she was gone.

The squire turned beet red.

"If she'll have you, take her. She'll teach you a few things you'll find useful on your wedding night, I don't doubt, and you're not like to get a bastard by her." Pia had spread her legs for half his father's army and never quickened; most like the girl was barren. "If you bed her, though, be kind to her."

"Kind, my lord? How . . . how would I . . . ?"

"Sweet words. Gentle touches. You don't want to wed her, but so long as you're abed treat her as you would your bride."

The lad nodded. "My lord, I . . . where should I take her? There's never a place to . . . to . . ."

". . . to be alone?" Jaime grinned. "We'll be at supper several hours. The straw looks lumpy, but it should serve."

Peck's eyes grew wide. "His lordship's bed?"

"You'll feel a lord yourself when you're done, if Pia knows her business." *And someone ought to make some use of that miserable straw mattress.*

When he descended for the feast that night, Jaime Lannister wore a doublet of red velvet slashed with cloth-of-gold, and a golden chain studded with black diamonds. He had strapped on his golden hand as well, polished to a fine bright sheen. This was no fit place to wear his whites. His duty awaited him at Riverrun; a darker need had brought him here.

Darry's great hall was great only by courtesy. Trestle tables crowded it from wall to wall, and the ceiling rafters were black with smoke. Jaime had been seated on the dais, to the right of Lancel's empty chair. "Will my cousin not be joining us for supper?" he asked as he sat down.

"My lord prefers to fast," said Lancel's wife, the Lady Amerei. "He's sick with grief for the poor High Septon." She was a long-legged, full-breasted, strapping girl of some eight-and-ten years; a healthy wench to look at her, though her pinched, chinless face reminded Jaime of his late and unlamented cousin Cleos, who had always looked somewhat like a weasel.

Fasting? He is an even bigger fool than I suspected. His cousin should be busy fathering a little weasel-faced heir on his widow instead of starving himself to death. He wondered what Ser Kevan might have had to say about his son's new fervor. Could that be the reason for his uncle's abrupt departure?

Over bowls of bean-and-bacon soup Lady Amerei told Jaime how her first husband had been slain by Ser Gregor Clegane when the Freys were still fighting for Robb Stark. "I begged him not to go, but my Pate was oh so *very* brave, and swore he was the man to slay that monster. He wanted to make a great name for himself."

We all do. "When I was a squire I told myself I'd be the man to slay the Smiling Knight."

"The Smiling Knight?" She sounded lost. "Who was that?"

The Mountain of my boyhood. Half as big but twice as mad.

"An outlaw, long dead. No one who need concern your ladyship."

Amerei's lip trembled. Tears rolled from her brown eyes.

"You must forgive my daughter," said an older woman. Lady Amerei had brought a score of Freys to Darry with her; a sister, an uncle, a half uncle, various cousins . . . and her mother, who had been born a Darry. "She still grieves for her father."

"Outlaws *killed* him," sobbed Lady Amerei. "Father had only gone out to ransom Petyr Pimple. He brought them the gold they asked for, but they hung him anyway."

"*Hanged,* Ami. Your father was not a tapestry." Lady Mariya turned back to Jaime. "I believe you knew him, ser."

"We were squires together once, at Crakehall." He would not go so far as to claim they had been friends. When Jaime had arrived, Merrett Frey had been the castle bully, lording it over all the younger boys. *Then he tried to bully me.* "He was . . . very strong." It was the only praise that came to mind. Merrett had been slow and clumsy and stupid, but he *was* strong.

"You fought against the Kingswood Brotherhood together," sniffed Lady Amerei. "Father used to tell me stories."

Father used to boast and lie, you mean. "We did." Frey's chief contributions to the fight had consisted of contracting the pox from a camp follower and getting himself captured by the White Fawn. The outlaw queen burned her sigil into his arse before ransoming him back to Sumner Crakehall. Merrett had not been able to sit down for a fortnight, though Jaime doubted that the red-hot iron was half so nasty as the kettles of shit his fellow squires made him eat once he was returned. *Boys are the cruelest creatures on the earth.* He slipped his golden hand around his wine cup and raised it up. "To Merrett's memory," he said. It was easier to drink to the man than to talk of him.

After the toast Lady Amerei stopped weeping and the table talk turned to wolves, of the four-footed kind. Ser Danwell Frey claimed there were more of them about than even his grandfather could remember. "They've lost all fear of men. Packs of them attacked our baggage train on our way down from the Twins. Our archers had to feather a dozen before the others fled." Ser Addam Marbrand confessed that their own column had faced similar troubles on their way up from King's Landing.

Jaime concentrated on the fare before him, tearing off chunks of bread with his left hand and fumbling at his wine cup with his right. He watched Addam Marbrand charm the girl beside him, watched Steffon Swyft refight the battle for King's Landing with bread and nuts and carrots. Ser Kennos pulled a serving girl into his lap, urging her to stroke his horn, whilst Ser Dermot regaled some squires with tales of knight errantry in the rainwood. Farther down the table Hugo Vance had closed his eyes. *Brooding on the mysteries of life,* thought Jaime. *That, or napping between courses.* He turned back to Lady Mariya. "The outlaws who killed your husband . . . was it Lord Beric's band?"

"So we thought, at first." Though Lady Mariya's hair was streaked with grey, she was still a handsome woman. "The killers scattered when they left Oldstones. Lord Vypren tracked one band to Fairmarket, but lost them there. Black Walder led hounds and hunters into Hag's Mire after the others. The peasants denied seeing them, but when questioned sharply they sang a different song.

They spoke of a one-eyed man and another who wore a yellow cloak . . . and a woman, cloaked and hooded."

"A woman?" He would have thought that the White Fawn would have taught Merrett to stay clear of outlaw wenches. "There was a woman in the Kingswood Brotherhood as well."

"I know of her." *How not,* her tone suggested, *when she left her mark upon my husband?* "The White Fawn was young and fair, they say. This hooded woman is neither. The peasants would have us believe that her face was torn and scarred, and her eyes terrible to look upon. They claim she led the outlaws."

"Led them?" Jaime found that hard to believe. "Beric Dondarrion and the red priest . . ."

". . . were not seen." Lady Mariya sounded certain.

"Dondarrion's dead," said Strongboar. "The Mountain drove a knife through his eye, we have men with us who saw it."

"That's one tale," said Addam Marbrand. "Others will tell you that Lord Beric can't be killed."

"Ser Harwyn says those tales are lies." Lady Amerei wound a braid around her finger. "He has promised me Lord Beric's head. He's very gallant." She was blushing beneath her tears.

Jaime thought back on the head he'd given to Pia. He could almost hear his little brother chuckle. *Whatever became of giving women flowers?* Tyrion might have asked. He would have had a few choice words for Harwyn Plumm as well, though *gallant* would not have been one of them. Plumm's brothers were big, fleshy fellows with thick necks and red faces; loud and lusty, quick to laugh, quick to anger, quick to forgive. Harwyn was a different sort of Plumm; hard-eyed and taciturn, unforgiving . . . and deadly, with his hammer in his hand. A good man to command a garrison, but not a man to love. *Although . . .* Jaime gazed at Lady Amerei.

The serving men were bringing out the fish course, a river pike baked in a crust of herbs and crushed nuts. Lancel's lady tasted it, approved, and commanded that the first portion be served to Jaime. As they set the fish before him, she leaned across her husband's place to touch his golden hand. "*You* could kill Lord Beric, Ser Jaime. You slew the Smiley Knight. Please, my lord, I beg you, stay and help us with Lord Beric and the Hound." Her pale fingers caressed his golden ones.

Does she think that I can feel that? "The Sword of the Morning slew the Smiling Knight, my lady. Ser Arthur Dayne, a better knight than me." Jaime pulled back his golden fingers and turned once more to Lady Mariya. "How far did Black Walder track this hooded woman and her men?"

"His hounds picked up their scent again north of Hag's Mire," the older woman told him. "He swears that he was no more than half a day behind them when they vanished into the Neck."

"Let them rot there," declared Ser Kennos cheerfully. "If the gods are good, they'll be swallowed up in quicksand or gobbled down by lizard-lions."

"Or taken in by frogeaters," said Ser Danwell Frey. "I would not put it past the crannogmen to shelter outlaws."

"Would that it were only them," said Lady Mariya. "Some of the river lords are hand in glove with Lord Beric's men as well."

"The smallfolk too," sniffed her daughter. "Ser Harwyn says they hide them and feed them, and when he asks where they've gone, they lie. They *lie* to their own lords!"

"Have their tongues out," urged Strongboar.

"Good luck getting answers then," said Jaime. "If you

want their help, you need to make them love you. That was how Arthur Dayne did it, when we rode against the Kingswood Brotherhood. He paid the smallfolk for the food we ate, brought their grievances to King Aerys, expanded the grazing lands around their villages, even won them the right to fell a certain number of trees each year and take a few of the king's deer during the autumn. The forest folk had looked to Toyne to defend them, but Ser Arthur did more for them than the Brotherhood could ever hope to do, and won them to our side. After that, the rest was easy."

"The Lord Commander speaks wisely," said Lady Mariya. "We shall never be rid of these outlaws until the smallfolk come to love Lancel as much as they once loved my father and grandfather."

Jaime glanced at his cousin's empty place. *Lancel will never win their love by praying, though.*

Lady Amerei put on a pout. "Ser Jaime, I pray you, do not abandon us. My lord has need of you, and so do I. These are such fearful times. Some nights I can hardly sleep, for fear."

"My place is with the king, my lady."

"I'll come," offered Strongboar. "Once we're done at Riverrun, I'll be itching for another fight. Not that Beric Dondarrion is like to give me one. I recall the man from tourneys past. A comely lad in a pretty cloak, he was. Slight and callow."

"That was before he died," said young Ser Arwood Frey. "Death changed him, the smallfolk say. You can kill him, but he won't stay dead. How do you fight a man like that? And there's the Hound as well. He slew twenty men at Saltpans."

Strongboar guffawed. "Twenty fat innkeeps, maybe. Twenty serving men pissing in their breeches. Twenty begging brothers armed with bowls. Not twenty knights. Not *me*."

"There is a knight at Saltpans," Ser Arwood insisted. "He hid behind his walls whilst Clegane and his mad dogs ravaged through his town. You have not seen the things he did, ser. I have. When the reports reached the Twins, I rode down with Harys Haigh and his brother Donnel and half a hundred men, archers and men-at-arms. We thought it was Lord Beric's work, and hoped to find his trail. All that remains of Saltpans is the castle, and old Ser Quincy so frightened he would not open his gates, but shouted down at us from his battlements. The rest is bones and ashes. A whole town. The Hound put the buildings to the torch and the people to the sword and rode off laughing. The women . . . you would not believe what he did to some of the women. I will not speak of it at table. It made me sick to see."

"I cried when I heard," said Lady Amerei.

Jaime sipped his wine. "What makes you certain it was the Hound?" What they were describing sounded more like Gregor's work than Sandor's. Sandor had been hard and brutal, yes, but it was his big brother who was the real monster in House Clegane.

"He was seen," Ser Arwood said. "That helm of his is not easily mistaken, nor forgotten, and there were a few who survived to tell the tale. The girl he raped, some boys who hid, a woman we found trapped beneath a blackened beam, the fisherfolk who watched the butchery from their boats . . ."

"Do not call it butchery," Lady Mariya said softly. "That gives insult to honest butchers everywhere. Saltpans was the work of some fell beast in human skin."

This is a time for beasts, Jaime reflected, *for lions and wolves and angry dogs, for ravens and carrion crows.*

"Evil work." Strongboar filled his cup again. "Lady Mariya, Lady Amerei, your distress has moved me. You have my word, once Riverrun has fallen I shall return to hunt down the Hound and kill him for you. Dogs do not frighten me."

This one should. Both men were large and powerful, but Sandor Clegane was much quicker, and fought with a savagery that Lyle Crakehall could not hope to match.

Lady Amerei was thrilled, however. "You are a true knight, Ser Lyle, to help a lady in distress."

At least she did not call herself "a maiden." Jaime reached for his cup and knocked it over. The linen tablecloth drank the wine. As the red stain spread, his companions all pretended not to notice. *High table courtesy,* he told himself, but it tasted just like pity. He rose abruptly. "My lady. Pray excuse me."

Lady Amerei looked stricken. "Would you leave us? There's venison to come, and capons stuffed with leeks and mushrooms."

"Very fine, no doubt, but I could not eat another bite. I need to see my cousin." Bowing, Jaime left them to their food.

Men were eating in the yard as well. The sparrows had gathered round a dozen cookfires to warm their hands against the chill of dusk and watch fat sausages spit and sizzle above the flames. There had to be a hundred of them. *Useless mouths.* Jaime wondered how many sausages his cousin had laid by and how he intended to feed the sparrows once they were gone. *They will be eating rats by winter, unless they can get a harvest in.* This late in autumn, the chances of another harvest were not good.

He found the sept off the castle's inner ward; a windowless, seven-sided, half-timbered building with carved wood doors and a tiled roof. Three sparrows sat upon its steps. When Jaime approached, they rose. "Where you going, m'lord?" asked one. He was the smallest of the three, but he had the biggest beard.

"Inside."

"His lordship's in there, praying."

"His lordship is my cousin."

"Well, then, m'lord," said a different sparrow, a huge bald man with a seven-pointed star painted over one eye, "you won't want to bother your cousin at his prayers."

"Lord Lancel is asking the Father Above for guidance," said the third sparrow, the beardless one. A boy, Jaime had thought, but her voice marked her for a woman, dressed in shapeless rags and a shirt of rusted mail. "He is praying for the soul of the High Septon and all the others who have died."

"They'll still be dead tomorrow," Jaime told her. "The Father Above has more time than I do. Do you know who I am?"

"Some lord," said the big man with the starry eye.

"Some cripple," said the small one with the big beard.

"The Kingslayer," said the woman, "but we're no kings, just Poor Fellows, and you can't go in unless his lordship says you can." She hefted a spiked club, and the small man raised an axe.

The doors behind them opened. "Let my cousin pass in peace, friends," Lancel said softly. "I have been expecting him."

The sparrows moved aside.

Lancel looked even thinner than he had at King's Landing. He was barefoot, and dressed in a plain, rough-spun tunic of undyed wool that made him look more like a beggar than a lord. The crown of his head had been shaved smooth, but his beard had grown out a little. To call it peach fuzz would have given insult to the peach. It went queerly with the white hair around his ears.

"Cousin," said Jaime when they were alone within the sept, "have you lost your bloody wits?"

"I prefer to say I've found my faith."

"Where is your father?"

"Gone. We quarreled." Lancel knelt before the altar of his other Father. "Will you pray with me, Jaime?"

"If I pray nicely, will the Father give me a new hand?"

"No. But the Warrior will give you courage, the Smith will lend you strength, and the Crone will give you wisdom."

"It's a hand I need." The seven gods loomed above carved altars, the dark wood gleaming in the candlelight. A faint smell of incense hung in the air. "You sleep down here?"

"Each night I make my bed beneath a different altar, and the Seven send me visions."

Baelor the Blessed once had visions too. *Especially when he was fasting.* "How long has it been since you've eaten?"

"My faith is all the nourishment I need."

"Faith is like porridge. Better with milk and honey."

"I dreamed that you would come. In the dream you knew what I had done. How I'd sinned. You killed me for it."

"You're more like to kill yourself with all this fasting. Didn't Baelor the Blessed fast himself onto a bier?"

"Our lives are candle flames, says *The Seven-Pointed Star.* Any errant puff of wind can snuff us out. Death is never far in this world, and seven hells await sinners who do not repent their sins. Pray with me, Jaime."

"If I do, will you eat a bowl of porridge?" When his coz did not answer, Jaime sighed. "You should be sleeping with your wife, not with the Maid. You need a son with Darry blood if you want to keep this castle."

"A pile of cold stones. I never asked for it. I never wanted it. I only wanted . . ." Lancel shuddered. "Seven save me, but I wanted to be you."

Jaime had to laugh. "Better me than Blessed Baelor. Darry needs a lion, coz. So does your little Frey. She gets moist between the legs every time someone mentions Hardstone. If she hasn't bedded him yet, she will soon."

"If she loves him, I wish them joy of one another."

"A lion shouldn't have horns. You took the girl to wife."

"I said some words and gave her a red cloak, but only to please Father. Marriage requires consummation. King Baelor was made to wed his sister Daena, but they never lived as man and wife, and he put her aside as soon as he was crowned."

"The realm would have been better served if he had closed his eyes and fucked her. I know enough history to know that. In any case, you're not like to be taken for Baelor the Blessed."

"No," Lancel allowed. "He was a rare spirit, pure and brave and innocent, untouched by all the evils of the world. I am a sinner, with much and more to atone for."

Jaime put his hand on his cousin's shoulder. "What do you know of sin, coz? I killed my king."

"The brave man slays with a sword, the craven with a wineskin. We are both kingslayers, ser."

"Robert was no true king. Some might even say that a stag is a lion's natural prey." Jaime could feel the bones beneath his cousin's skin . . . and something else as well. Lancel was wearing a hair shirt underneath his tunic. "What else did you do, to require so much atonement? Tell me."

His cousin bowed his head, tears running down his cheeks.

Those tears were all the answer Jaime needed. "You killed the king," he said, "then you fucked the queen."

"I never . . ."

". . . lay with my sweet sister?" *Say it. Say it!*

"Never spilled my seed in . . . in her . . ."

". . . cunt?" suggested Jaime.

". . . womb," Lancel finished. "It is not treason unless you finish inside. I gave her comfort, after the king died. You were a captive, your father was in the field, and your brother . . . she was afraid of him, and with good reason. He made me betray her."

"Did he?" *Lancel and Ser Osmund and how many more? Was the part about Moon Boy just a gibe?* "Did you force her?"

"*No!* I loved her. I wanted to protect her."

You wanted to be me. His phantom fingers itched. The day his sister had come to White Sword Tower to beg him to renounce his vows, she had laughed after he refused her and boasted of having lied to him a thousand times. Jaime had taken that for a clumsy attempt to hurt him as he'd hurt her. *It may have been the only true thing that she ever said to me.*

"Do not think ill of the queen," Lancel pleaded. "All flesh is weak, Jaime. No harm came of our sin. No . . . no bastard."

"No. Bastards are seldom made upon the belly." He wondered what his cousin would say if he were to confess his own sins, the three treasons Cersei had named Joffrey, Tommen, and Myrcella.

"I was angry with Her Grace after the battle, but the High Septon said I must forgive her."

"You confessed your sins to His High Holiness, did you?"

"He prayed for me when I was wounded. He was a good man."

He's a dead man. They rang the bells for him. He wondered if his cousin had any notion what fruit his words had borne. "Lancel, you're a bloody fool."

"You are not wrong," said Lancel, "but my folly is behind me, ser. I have asked the Father Above to show me the way, and he has. I am renouncing this lordship and this wife. Hardstone is welcome to the both of them, if he likes. On the morrow I will return to King's Landing and swear my sword to the new High Septon and the Seven. I mean to take vows and join the Warrior's Sons."

The boy was not making sense. "The Warrior's Sons were proscribed three hundred years ago."

"The new High Septon has revived them. He's sent out a call for worthy knights to pledge their lives and swords to the service of the Seven. The Poor Fellows are to be restored as well."

"Why would the Iron Throne allow that?" One of the early Targaryen kings had fought for years to suppress the two military orders, Jaime recalled, though he did not remember which. Maegor, perhaps, or the first Jaehaerys. *Tyrion would have known.*

"His High Holiness writes that King Tommen has given his consent. I will show you the letter, if you like."

"Even if this is true . . . you are a lion of the Rock, a *lord.* You have a wife, a castle, lands to defend, people to protect. If the gods are good, you will have sons of your blood to follow you. Why would you throw all that away for . . . for some vow?"

"Why did you?" asked Lancel softly.

For honor, Jaime might have said. *For glory.* That

would have been a lie, though. Honor and glory had
played their parts, but most of it had been for Cersei. A
laugh escaped his lips. "Is it the High Septon you're running to, or my sweet sister? Pray on that one, coz. Pray
hard."

"Will you pray with me, Jaime?"

He glanced about the sept, at the gods. The Mother, full
of mercy. The Father, stern in judgment. The Warrior, one
hand upon his sword. The Stranger in the shadows, his
half-human face concealed beneath a hooded mantle. *I
thought that I was the Warrior and Cersei was the Maid,
but all the time she was the Stranger, hiding her true face
from my gaze.* "Pray for me, if you like," he told his
cousin. "I've forgotten all the words."

The sparrows were still fluttering about the steps when
Jaime stepped back out into the night. "Thank you," he
told them. "I feel ever so much holier now."

He went and found Ser Ilyn and a pair of swords.

The castle yard was full of eyes and ears. To escape
them, they sought out Darry's godswood. There were no
sparrows there, only trees bare and brooding, their black
branches scratching at the sky. A mat of dead leaves
crunched beneath their feet.

"Do you see that window, ser?" Jaime used a sword to
point. "That was Raymun Darry's bedchamber. Where
King Robert slept, on our return from Winterfell. Ned
Stark's daughter had run off after her wolf savaged Joff,
you'll recall. My sister wanted the girl to lose a hand. The
old penalty, for striking one of the blood royal. Robert told
her she was cruel and mad. They fought for half the
night . . . well, Cersei fought, and Robert drank. Past midnight, the queen summoned me inside. The king was
passed out snoring on the Myrish carpet. I asked my sister
if she wanted me to carry him to bed. She told me I should

carry her to bed, and shrugged out of her robe. I took her on Raymun Darry's bed after stepping over Robert. If His Grace had woken I would have killed him there and then. He would not have been the first king to die upon my sword . . . but you know that story, don't you?" He slashed at a tree branch, shearing it in half. "As I was fucking her, Cersei cried, 'I *want.*' I thought that she meant me, but it was the Stark girl that she wanted, maimed or dead." *The things I do for love.* "It was only by chance that Stark's own men found the girl before me. If I had come on her first . . ."

The pockmarks on Ser Ilyn's face were black holes in the torchlight, as dark as Jaime's soul. He made that clacking sound.

He is laughing at me, realized Jaime Lannister. "For all I know you fucked my sister too, you pock-faced bastard," he spat out. "Well, shut your bloody mouth and kill me if you can."

BRIENNE

The septry stood upon an upthrust island half a mile from the shore, where the wide mouth of the Trident widened further still to kiss the Bay of Crabs. Even from shore its prosperity was apparent. Its slope was covered with terraced fields, with fishponds down below and a windmill above, its wood-and-sailcloth blades turning slowly in the breeze off the bay. Brienne could see sheep grazing on the hillside and storks wading in the shallow waters around the ferry landing.

"Saltpans is just across the water," said Septon Meribald, pointing north across the bay. "The brothers will ferry us over on the morning tide, though I fear what we shall find there. Let us enjoy a good hot meal before we face that. The brothers always have a bone to spare for Dog." Dog barked and wagged his tail.

The tide was going out now, and swiftly. The water that

separated the island from the shore was receding, leaving behind a broad expanse of glistening brown mudflats dotted by tidal pools that glittered like golden coins in the afternoon sun. Brienne scratched the back of her neck, where an insect had bitten her. She had pinned her hair up, and the sun had warmed her skin.

"Why do they call it the Quiet Isle?" asked Podrick.

"Those who dwell here are penitents, who seek to atone for their sins through contemplation, prayer, and silence. Only the Elder Brother and his proctors are permitted to speak, and the proctors only for one day of every seven."

"The silent sisters never speak," said Podrick. "I heard they don't have any tongues."

Septon Meribald smiled. "Mothers have been cowing their daughters with that tale since I was your age. There was no truth to it then and there is none now. A vow of silence is an act of contrition, a sacrifice by which we prove our devotion to the Seven Above. For a mute to take a vow of silence would be akin to a legless man giving up the dance." He led his donkey down the slope, beckoning them to follow. "If you would sleep beneath a roof tonight, you must climb off your horses and cross the mud with me. The path of faith, we call it. Only the faithful may cross safely. The wicked are swallowed by the quicksands, or drowned when the tide comes rushing in. None of you are wicked, I hope? Even so, I would be careful where I set my feet. Walk only where I walk, and you shall reach the other side."

The path of faith was a crooked one, Brienne could not help but note. Though the island seemed to rise to the northeast of where they left the shore, Septon Meribald did not make directly for it. Instead, he started due east, toward the deeper waters of the bay, which shimmered blue and silver in the distance. The soft brown mud squished up between his toes. As he walked he paused from time to time, to probe ahead with his quarterstaff. Dog stayed near his heels, sniffing at every rock, shell, and clump of seaweed. For once he did not bound ahead or stray.

Brienne followed, taking care to keep close to the line of prints left by the dog, the donkey, and the holy man. Then came Podrick, and last of all Ser Hyle. A hundred yards out, Meribald turned abruptly toward the south, so his back was almost to the septry. He proceeded in that direction for another hundred yards, leading them between two shallow tidal pools. Dog stuck his nose in one and yelped when a crab pinched it with his claw. A brief but furious struggle ensued before the dog came trotting back, wet and mud-spattered, with the crab between his jaws.

"Isn't *that* where we want to go?" Ser Hyle called out from behind them, pointing at the septry. "We seem to be walking every way but toward it."

"Faith," urged Septon Meribald. "Believe, persist, and follow, and we shall find the peace we seek."

The flats shimmered wetly all about them, mottled in half a hundred hues. The mud was such a dark brown it appeared almost black, but there were swathes of golden sand as well, upthrust rocks both grey and red, and tangles of black and green seaweed. Storks stalked through the tidal pools and left their footprints all around them, and crabs scuttled across the surface of shallow waters. The air smelled of brine and rot, and the ground sucked at their feet and let them go only reluctantly, with a pop and a squelchy sigh. Septon Meribald turned and turned again and yet again. His footprints filled up with water as soon as he moved on. By the time the ground grew firmer and began to rise beneath the feet, they had walked at least a mile and a half.

Three men were waiting for them as they clambered up the broken stones that ringed the isle's shoreline. They were clad in the brown-and-dun robes of brothers, with wide bell sleeves and pointed cowls. Two had wound lengths of wool about the lower halves of their faces as well, so all that could be seen of them were their eyes. The third brother was the one to speak. "Septon Meribald," he called. "It has been nigh upon a year. You are welcome. Your companions as well."

Dog wagged his tail, and Meribald shook mud from his feet. "Might we beg your hospitality for a night?"

"Yes, of course. There's to be fish stew this evening. Will you require the ferry in the morning?"

"If it is not too much to ask." Meribald turned to his fellow travelers. "Brother Narbert is a proctor of the order, so he is allowed to speak one day of every seven. Brother, these good folk helped me on my way. Ser Hyle Hunt is a gallant from the Reach. The lad is Podrick Payne, late of the westerland. And this is Lady Brienne, known as the Maid of Tarth."

Brother Narbert drew up short. "A woman."

"Yes, brother." Brienne unpinned her hair and shook it out. "Do you have no women here?"

"Not at present," said Narbert. "Those women who do visit come to us sick or hurt, or heavy with child. The Seven have blessed our Elder Brother with healing hands. He has restored many a man to health that even the maesters could not cure, and many a woman too."

"I am not sick or hurt or heavy with child."

"Lady Brienne is a warrior maid," confided Septon Meribald, "hunting for the Hound."

"Aye?" Narbert seemed taken aback. "To what end?"

Brienne touched Oathkeeper's hilt. "His," she said.

The proctor studied her. "You are . . . brawny for a

woman, it is true, but . . . mayhaps I should take you up to
Elder Brother. He will have seen you crossing the mud.
Come."

Narbert led them along a pebbled path and through a
grove of apple trees to a whitewashed stable with a peaked
thatch roof. "You may leave your animals here. Brother
Gillam will see that they are fed and watered."

The stable was more than three-quarters empty. At one
end were half a dozen mules, being tended by a bandy-
legged little brother whom Brienne took for Gillam. Way
down at the far end, well away from the other animals, a
huge black stallion trumpeted at the sound of their voices
and kicked at the door of his stall.

Ser Hyle gave the big horse an admiring look as he was
handing his reins to Brother Gillam. "A handsome beast."

Brother Narbert sighed. "The Seven send us blessings,
and the Seven send us trials. Handsome he may be, but
Driftwood was surely whelped in hell. When we sought to
harness him to a plow he kicked Brother Rawney and
broke his shinbone in two places. We had hoped gelding
might improve the beast's ill temper, but . . . Brother
Gillam, will you show them?"

Brother Gillam lowered his cowl. Underneath he had a
mop of blond hair, a tonsured scalp, and a bloodstained
bandage where he should have had an ear.

Podrick gasped. "The horse bit off your *ear*?"

Gillam nodded, and covered his head again.

"Forgive me, brother," said Ser Hyle, "but I might take
the other ear, if you approached me with a pair of shears."

The jest did not sit well with Brother Narbert. "You
are a knight, ser. Driftwood is a beast of burden. The
Smith gave men horses to help them in their labors." He
turned away. "If you will. Elder Brother will no doubt be
waiting."

The slope was steeper than it had looked from across the mudflats. To ease it, the brothers had erected a flight of wooden steps that wandered back and forth across the hillside and amongst the buildings. After a long day in the saddle Brienne was glad for a chance to stretch her legs.

They passed a dozen brothers of the order on their way up; cowled men in dun-and-brown who gave them curious looks as they went by, but spoke no word of greeting. One was leading a pair of milk cows toward a low barn roofed in sod; another worked a butter churn. On the upper slopes they saw three boys driving sheep, and higher still they passed a lichyard where a brother bigger than Brienne was struggling to dig a grave. From the way he moved, it was plain to see that he was lame. As he flung a spadeful of the stony soil over one shoulder, some chanced to spatter against their feet. "Be more watchful there," chided Brother Narbert. "Septon Meribald might have gotten a mouthful of dirt." The gravedigger lowered his head. When Dog went to sniff him he dropped his spade and scratched his ear.

"A novice," explained Narbert.

"Who is the grave for?" asked Ser Hyle, as they resumed their climb up the wooden steps.

"Brother Clement, may the Father judge him justly."

"Was he old?" asked Podrick Payne.

"If you consider eight-and-forty old, aye, but it was not the years that killed him. He died of wounds he got at Saltpans. He had taken some of our mead to the market there, on the day the outlaws descended on the town."

"The Hound?" said Brienne.

"Another, just as brutal. He cut poor Clement's tongue out when he would not speak. Since he had taken a vow of silence, the raider said he had no need of it. The Elder Brother will know more. He keeps the worst of the tidings from outside to himself, so as not to disturb the tranquillity of the septry. Many of our brothers came here to escape the horrors of the world, not to dwell upon them. Brother Clement was not the only wounded man amongst us. Some wounds do not show." Brother Narbert gestured to their right. "There lies our summer arbor. The grapes are small and tart, but make a drinkable wine. We brew our own ale as well, and our mead and cider are far famed."

"The war has never come here?" Brienne said.

"Not this war, praise the Seven. Our prayers protect us."

"And your tides," suggested Meribald. Dog barked agreement.

The brow of the hill was crowned by a low wall of unmortared stone, encircling a cluster of large buildings; the windmill, its sails creaking as they turned, the cloisters where the brothers slept and the common hall where they took their meals, a wooden sept for prayer and meditation. The sept had windows of leaded glass, wide doors carved with likenesses of the Mother and the Father, and a seven-sided steeple with a walk on top. Behind it was a vegetable garden where some older brothers were pulling weeds. Brother Narbert led the visitors around a chestnut tree to a wooden door set in the side of the hill.

"A cave with a door?" Ser Hyle said, surprised.

Septon Meribald smiled. "It is called the Hermit's Hole. The first holy man to find his way here lived therein, and worked such wonders that others came to join him. That was two thousand years ago, they say. The door came somewhat later."

Perhaps two thousand years ago the Hermit's Hole had been a damp, dark place, floored with dirt and echoing to the sounds of dripping water, but no longer. The cave that Brienne and her companions entered had been turned into a warm, snug sanctum. Woolen carpets covered the ground, tapestries the walls. Tall beeswax candles gave more than ample light. The furnishings were strange but simple; a long table, a settle, a chest, several tall cases full of books, and chairs. All were made from driftwood, oddly shaped pieces cunningly joined together and polished till they shone a deep gold in the candlelight.

The Elder Brother was not what Brienne had expected. He could hardly be called *elder,* for a start; whereas the brothers weeding in the garden had had the stooped shoulders and bent backs of old men, he stood straight and tall, and moved with the vigor of a man in the prime of his years. Nor did he have the gentle, kindly face she expected of a healer. His head was large and square, his eyes shrewd, his nose veined and red. Though he wore a tonsure, his scalp was as stubbly as his heavy jaw.

He looks more like a man made to break bones than to heal one, thought the Maid of Tarth, as the Elder Brother strode across the room to embrace Septon Meribald and pat Dog. "It is always a glad day when our friends Meribald and Dog honor us with another visit," he announced, before turning to his other guests. "And new faces are always welcome. We see so few of them."

Meribald performed the customary courtesies before seating himself upon the settle. Unlike Septon Narbert, the Elder Brother did not seem dismayed by Brienne's sex, but his smile did flicker and fade when the septon told him why she and Ser Hyle had come. "I see," was all he said, before he turned away with, "You must be thirsty. Please, have some of our sweet cider to wash the dust of travel from your throats." He poured for them himself. The cups were carved from driftwood too, no two the same. When Brienne complimented them, he said, "My lady is too kind. All we do is cut and polish the wood. We are blessed here. Where the river meets the bay, the currents and the tides wrestle one against the other, and many strange and wondrous things are pushed toward us, to wash up on our shores. Driftwood is the least of it. We have found silver cups and iron pots, sacks of wool and bolts of silk, rusted helms and shining swords . . . aye, and rubies."

That interested Ser Hyle. "Rhaegar's rubies?"

"It may be. Who can say? The battle was long leagues from here, but the river is tireless and patient. Six have been found. We are all waiting for the seventh."

"Better rubies than bones." Septon Meribald was rubbing his foot, the mud flaking off beneath his finger. "Not all the river's gifts are pleasant. The good brothers collect the dead as well. Drowned cows, drowned deer, dead pigs swollen up to half the size of horses. Aye, and corpses."

"Too many corpses, these days." The Elder Brother sighed. "Our gravedigger knows no rest. Rivermen, westermen, northmen, all wash up here. Knights and knaves alike. We bury them side by side, Stark and Lannister, Blackwood and Bracken, Frey and Darry. That is the duty the river asks of us in return for all its gifts, and we do it as best we can. Sometimes we find a woman, though . . . or worse, a little child. Those are the cruelest gifts." He turned to Septon Meribald. "I hope that you have time to absolve us of our sins. Since the raiders slew old Septon Bennet, we have had no one to hear confession."

"I shall make time," said Meribald, "though I hope you have some better sins than the last time I came through." Dog barked. "You see? Even Dog was bored."

Podrick Payne was puzzled. "I thought no one could talk. Well, not no one. The brothers. The other brothers, not you."

"We are allowed to break silence when confessing,"

said the Elder Brother. "It is hard to speak of sin with signs and nods."

"Did they burn the sept at Saltpans?" asked Hyle Hunt.

The smile vanished. "They burned everything at Saltpans, save the castle. Only that was made of stone . . . though it had as well been made of suet for all the good it did the town. It fell to me to treat some of the survivors. The fisherfolk brought them across the bay to me after the flames had gone out and they deemed it safe to land. One poor woman had been raped a dozen times, and her breasts . . . my lady, you wear man's mail, so I shall not spare you these horrors . . . her breasts had been torn and chewed and *eaten*, as if by some . . . cruel beast. I did what I could for her, though that was little enough. As she lay dying, her worst curses were not for the men who had raped her, nor the monster who devoured her living flesh, but for Ser Quincy Cox, who barred his gates when the outlaws entered the town and sat safe behind stone walls as his people screamed and died."

"Ser Quincy is an old man," said Septon Meribald gently. "His sons and good-sons are far away or dead, his grandsons are still boys, and he has two daughters. What could he have done, one man against so many?"

He could have tried, Brienne thought. *He could have died. Old or young, a true knight is sworn to protect those who are weaker than himself, or die in the attempt.*

"True words, and wise," the Elder Brother said to Septon Meribald. "When you cross to Saltpans, no doubt Ser Quincy will ask you for forgiveness. I am glad that you are here to give it. I could not." He put aside the driftwood cup, and stood. "The supper bell will sound soon. My friends, will you come with me to the sept, to pray for the souls of the good folk of Saltpans before we sit down to break bread and share some meat and mead?"

"Gladly," said Meribald. Dog barked.

Their supper in the septry was as strange a meal as Brienne had ever eaten, though not at all unpleasant. The food was plain, but very good; there were loaves of crusty bread still warm from the ovens, crocks of fresh-churned butter, honey from the septry's hives, and a thick stew of crabs, mussels, and at least three different kinds of fish. Septon Meribald and Ser Hyle drank the mead the brothers made, and pronounced it excellent, whilst she and Podrick contented themselves with more sweet cider. Nor was the meal a somber one. Meribald pronounced a prayer before the food was served, and whilst the brothers ate at four long trestle tables, one of their number played for them on the high harp, filling the hall with soft sweet sounds. When the Elder Brother excused the musician to take his own meal, Brother Narbert and another proctor took turns reading from *The Seven-Pointed Star.*

By the time the readings were completed, the last of the food had been cleared away by the novices whose task it was to serve. Most were boys near Podrick's age, or younger, but there were grown men as well, amongst them the big gravedigger they had encountered on the hill, who walked with the awkward lurching gait of one half-crippled. As the hall emptied, the Elder Brother asked Narbert to show Podrick and Ser Hyle to their pallets in the cloisters. "You will not mind sharing a cell, I hope? It is not large, but you will find it comfortable."

"I want to stay with ser," said Podrick. "I mean, my lady."

"What you and Lady Brienne may do elsewhere is between you and the Seven," said Brother Narbert, "but on the Quiet Isle, men and women do not sleep beneath the same roof unless they are wed."

"We have some modest cottages set aside for the

women who visit us, be they noble ladies or common village girls," said the Elder Brother. "They are not oft used, but we keep them clean and dry. Lady Brienne, would you allow me to show you the way?"

"Yes, thank you. Podrick, go with Ser Hyle. We are guests of the holy brothers here. Beneath their roof, their rules."

The women's cottages were on the east side of the isle, looking out over a broad expanse of mud and the distant waters of the Bay of Crabs. It was colder here than on the sheltered side, and wilder. The hill was steeper, and the path meandered back and forth through weeds and briars, wind-carved rocks, and twisted, thorny trees that clung tenaciously to the stony hillside. The Elder Brother brought a lantern to light their way down. At one turn he paused. "On a clear night you could see the fires of Saltpans from here. Across the bay, just there." He pointed.

"There's nothing," Brienne said.

"Only the castle remains. Even the fisherfolk are gone, the fortunate few who were out on the water when the raiders came. They watched their houses burn and listened to screams and cries float across the harbor, too fearful to land their boats. When at last they came ashore, it was to bury friends and kin. What is there for them at Saltpans now but bones and bitter memories? They have moved to Maidenpool or other towns." He gestured with the lantern, and they resumed their descent. "Saltpans was never an important port, but ships did call there from time to time. That was what the raiders wanted, a galley or a cog to carry them across the narrow sea. When none was at hand, they took their rage and desperation out upon the townsfolk. I wonder, my lady . . . what do you hope to find there?"

"A girl," she told him. "A highborn maid of three-and-ten, with a fair face and auburn hair."

"Sansa Stark." The name was softly said. "You believe this poor child is with the Hound?"

"The Dornishman said that she was on her way to Riverrun. Timeon. He was a sellsword, one of the Brave Companions, a killer and a raper and a liar, but I do not think he lied about this. He said that the Hound stole her and carried her away."

"I see." The path turned, and there were the cottages ahead of them. The Elder Brother had called them modest. That they were. They looked like beehives made of stone, low and rounded, windowless. "This one," he said, indicating the nearest cottage, the only one with smoke rising from the smokehole in the center of its roof. Brienne had to duck when entering to keep from banging her head against the lintel. Inside she found a dirt floor, a straw pallet, furs and blankets to keep her warm, a basin of water, a flagon of cider, some bread and cheese, a small fire, and two low chairs. The Elder Brother sat in one, and put the lantern down. "May I stay a while? I feel that we should talk."

"If you wish." Brienne undid her swordbelt and hung it from the second chair, then sat cross-legged on the pallet.

"Your Dornishman did not lie," the Elder Brother began, "but I fear you did not understand him. You are chasing the wrong wolf, my lady. Eddard Stark had two daughters. It was the other one that Sandor Clegane made off with, the younger one."

"*Arya* Stark?" Brienne stared open-mouthed, astonished. "You know this? Lady Sansa's sister is alive?"

"Then," said the Elder Brother. "Now . . . I do not know. She may have been amongst the children slain at Saltpans."

The words were a knife in her belly. *No,* Brienne thought. *No, that would be too cruel.* "*May* have been . . . meaning that you are not certain . . . ?"

"I am certain that the child was with Sandor Clegane at the inn beside the crossroads, the one old Masha Heddle used to keep, before the lions hanged her. I am certain they were on their way to Saltpans. Beyond that . . . no. I do not know where she is, or even if she lives. There is one thing I do know, however. The man you hunt is dead."

That was another shock. "How did he die?"

"By the sword, as he had lived."

"You know this for a certainty?"

"I buried him myself. I can tell you where his grave lies, if you wish. I covered him with stones to keep the carrion eaters from digging up his flesh, and set his helm atop the cairn to mark his final resting place. That was a grievous error. Some other wayfarer found my marker and claimed it for himself. The man who raped and killed at Saltpans was not Sandor Clegane, though he may be as dangerous. The riverlands are full of such scavengers. I will not call them wolves. Wolves are nobler than that . . . and so are dogs, I think.

"I know a little of this man, Sandor Clegane. He was Prince Joffrey's sworn shield for many a year, and even here we would hear tell of his deeds, both good and ill. If even half of what we heard was true, this was a bitter, tormented soul, a sinner who mocked both gods and men. He served, but found no pride in service. He fought, but took no joy in victory. He drank, to drown his pain in a sea of wine. He did not love, nor was he loved himself. It was hate that drove him. Though he committed many sins, he never sought forgiveness. Where other men dream of love, or wealth, or glory, this man Sandor Clegane dreamed of slaying his own brother, a sin so terrible it makes me shudder just to speak of it. Yet that was the bread that nourished him, the fuel that kept his fires burning. Ignoble as it was, the hope of seeing his brother's blood upon his blade was all this sad and angry creature lived for . . . and even that was taken from him, when Prince Oberyn of Dorne stabbed Ser Gregor with a poisoned spear."

"You sound as if you pity him," said Brienne.

"I did. You would have pitied him as well, if you had seen him at the end. I came upon him by the Trident, drawn by his cries of pain. He begged me for the gift of mercy, but I am sworn not to kill again. Instead, I bathed his fevered brow with river water, and gave him wine to drink and a poultice for his wound, but my efforts were too little and too late. The Hound died there, in my arms. You may have seen a big black stallion in our stables. That was his warhorse, Stranger. A blasphemous name. We prefer to call him Driftwood, as he was found beside the river. I fear he has his former master's nature."

The horse. She had seen the stallion, had heard it kicking, but she had not understood. Destriers were trained to kick and bite. In war they were a weapon, like the men who rode them. *Like the Hound.* "It is true, then," she said dully. "Sandor Clegane is dead."

"He is at rest." The Elder Brother paused. "You are young, child. I have counted four-and-forty name days . . . which makes me more than twice your age, I think. Would it surprise you to learn that I was once a knight?"

"No. You look more like a knight than you do a holy man." It was written in his chest and shoulders, and across that thick square jaw. "Why would you give up knighthood?"

"I never chose it. My father was a knight, and his before him. So were my brothers, every one. I was trained for battle since the day they deemed me old enough to hold a wooden sword. I saw my share of them, and did not disgrace myself. I had women too, and there I did disgrace myself, for some I took by force. There was a girl I wished to marry, the younger daughter of a petty lord, but I was my father's thirdborn son and had neither land nor wealth to offer her . . . only a sword, a horse, a shield. All in all, I was a sad man. When I was not fighting, I was drunk. My life was writ in red, in blood and wine."

"When did it change?" asked Brienne.

"When I died in the Battle of the Trident. I fought for Prince Rhaegar, though he never knew my name. I could not tell you why, save that the lord I served served a lord who served a lord who had decided to support the dragon rather than the stag. Had he decided elsewise, I might have been on the other side of the river. The battle was a bloody thing. The singers would have us believe it was all Rhaegar and Robert struggling in the stream for a woman both of them claimed to love, but I assure you, other men were fighting too, and I was one. I took an arrow through the thigh and another through the foot, and my horse was killed from under me, yet I fought on. I can still remember how desperate I was to find another horse, for I had no coin to buy one, and without a horse I would no longer be a knight. That was all that I was thinking of, if truth be told. I never saw the blow that felled me. I heard hooves behind my back and thought, *a horse!* but before I could turn something slammed into my head and knocked me back into the river, where by rights I should have drowned.

"Instead I woke here, upon the Quiet Isle. The Elder Brother told me I had washed up on the tide, naked as my name day. I can only think that someone found me in the shallows, stripped me of my armor, boots, and breeches, and pushed me back out into the deeper water. The river did the rest. We are all born naked, so I suppose it was only fitting that I come into my second life the same way. I spent the next ten years in silence."

"I see." Brienne did not know why he was telling her all of this, or what else she ought to say.

"Do you?" He leaned forward, his big hands on his knees. "If so, give up this quest of yours. The Hound is dead, and in any case he never had your Sansa Stark. As for this beast who wears his helm, he will be found and hanged. The wars are ending, and these outlaws cannot survive the peace. Randyll Tarly is hunting them from Maidenpool and Walder Frey from the Twins, and there is a new young lord in Darry, a pious man who will surely set his lands to rights. Go home, child. You *have* a home, which is more than many can say in these dark days. You have a noble father who must surely love you. Consider his grief if you should never return. Perhaps they will bring your sword and shield to him, after you have fallen. Perhaps he will even hang them in his hall and look on them with pride . . . but if you were to ask him, I know he would tell you that he would sooner have a living daughter than a shattered shield."

"A daughter." Brienne's eyes filled with tears. "He deserves that. A daughter who could sing to him and grace his hall and bear him grandsons. He deserves a son too, a strong and gallant son to bring honor to his name. Galladon drowned when I was four and he was eight, though, and Alysanne and Arianne died still in the cradle. I am the only child the gods let him keep. The freakish one, not fit to be a son *or* daughter." All of it came pouring out of Brienne then, like black blood from a wound; the betrayals and betrothals, Red Ronnet and his rose, Lord Renly dancing with her, the wager for her maidenhead, the bitter tears she shed the night her king wed Margaery Tyrell, the mêlée at Bitterbridge, the rainbow cloak that she had been so proud of, the shadow in the king's pavilion, Renly dying in her arms, Riverrun and Lady Catelyn, the voyage down the Trident, dueling Jaime in the woods, the Bloody Mummers, Jaime crying *"Sapphires,"* Jaime in the tub at Harrenhal with steam rising from his body, the taste of Vargo Hoat's blood when she bit down on his ear, the bear pit, Jaime leaping down onto the sand, the long ride to King's Landing, Sansa Stark, the vow she'd sworn to Jaime, the vow she'd sworn to Lady Catelyn, Oathkeeper, Duskendale, Maidenpool, Nimble Dick and Crackclaw and the Whispers, the men she'd killed . . .

"I *have* to find her," she finished. "There are others looking, all wanting to capture her and sell her to the queen. I have to find her first. I promised Jaime. *Oathkeeper,* he named the sword. I have to try to save her . . . or die in the attempt."

CERSEI

A thousand ships!" The little queen's brown hair was tousled and uncombed, and the torchlight made her cheeks look flushed, as if she had just come from some man's embrace. "Your Grace, this must be answered *fiercely*!" Her last word rang off the rafters and echoed through the cavernous throne room.

Seated on her gold-and-crimson high seat beneath the Iron Throne, Cersei could feel a growing tightness in her neck. *Must,* she thought. *She dares say "must" to me.* She itched to slap the Tyrell girl across the face. *She should be on her knees, begging for my help. Instead, she presumes to tell her rightful queen what she must do.*

"A thousand ships?" Ser Harys Swyft was wheezing. "Surely not. No lord commands a thousand ships."

"Some frightened fool has counted double," agreed Orton Merryweather. "That, or Lord Tyrell's bannermen are lying to us, puffing up the numbers of the foe so we will not think them lax."

The torches on the back wall threw the long, barbed shadow of the Iron Throne halfway to the doors. The far end of the hall was lost in darkness, and Cersei could not but feel that the shadows were closing around her too. *My enemies are everywhere, and my friends are useless.* She had only to glance at her councillors to know that; only Lord Qyburn and Aurane Waters seemed awake. The others had been roused from bed by Margaery's messengers pounding on their doors, and stood there rumpled and confused. Outside the night was black and still. The castle and the city slept. Boros Blount and Meryn Trant seemed to be sleeping too, albeit on their feet. Even Osmund Kettleblack was yawning. *Not Loras, though. Not our Knight of Flowers.* He stood behind his little sister, a pale shadow with a longsword on his hip.

"Half as many ships would still be five hundred, my lord," Waters pointed out to Orton Merryweather. "Only the Arbor has enough strength at sea to oppose a fleet that size."

"What of your new dromonds?" asked Ser Harys. "The longships of the ironmen cannot stand before our dromonds, surely? *King Robert's Hammer* is the mightiest warship in all Westeros."

"She was," said Waters. "*Sweet Cersei* will be her equal, once complete, and *Lord Tywin* will be twice the size of either. Only half are fitted out, however, and none is fully crewed. Even when they are, the numbers would be greatly against us. The common longship is small compared to our galleys, this is true, but the ironmen have larger ships as well. Lord Balon's *Great Kraken* and the warships of the Iron Fleet were made for battle, not for raids. They are the equal of our lesser war galleys in speed and strength, and most are better crewed and captained. The ironmen live their whole lives at sea."

Robert should have scoured the isles after Balon Greyjoy rose against him, Cersei thought. *He smashed their fleet, burned their towns, and broke their castles, but when he had them on their knees he let them up again. He should have made another island of their skulls.* That was what her father would have done, but Robert never had the stomach that a king requires if he hopes to keep peace in the realm. "The ironmen have not dared raid the Reach since Dagon Greyjoy sat the Seastone Chair," she said. "Why would they do so now? What has emboldened them?"

"Their new king." Qyburn stood with his hands hidden up his sleeves. "Lord Balon's brother. The Crow's Eye, he is called."

"Carrion crows make their feasts upon the carcasses of the dead and dying," said Grand Maester Pycelle. "They do not descend upon hale and healthy animals. Lord Euron will gorge himself on gold and plunder, aye, but as soon as we move against him he will back to Pyke, as Lord Dagon was wont to do in his day."

"You are wrong," said Margaery Tyrell. "Reavers do not come in such strength. *A thousand ships!* Lord Hewett and Lord Chester are slain, as well as Lord Serry's son and heir. Serry has fled to Highgarden with what few ships remain him, and Lord Grimm is a prisoner in his own castle. Willas says that the iron king has raised up four lords of his own in their places."

Willas, Cersei thought, *the cripple. He is to blame for this. That oaf Mace Tyrell left the defense of the Reach in the hands of a hapless weakling.* "It is a long voyage from the Iron Isles to the Shields," she pointed out. "How could a thousand ships come all that way without being seen?"

"Willas believes that they did not follow the coast," said Margaery. "They made the voyage out of sight of land, sailing far out into the Sunset Sea and swooping back in from the west."

More like the cripple did not have his watchtowers manned, and now he fears to have us know it. The little queen is making excuses for her brother. Cersei's mouth was dry. *I need a cup of Arbor gold.* If the ironmen decided to take the Arbor next, the whole realm might soon be going thirsty. "Stannis may have had a hand in this. Balon Greyjoy offered my lord father an alliance. Perhaps his son has offered one to Stannis."

Pycelle frowned. "What would Lord Stannis gain by . . ."

"He *gains* another foothold. And plunder, that as well. Stannis needs gold to pay his sellswords. By raiding in the west, he hopes he can distract us from Dragonstone and Storm's End."

Lord Merryweather nodded. "A diversion. Stannis is more cunning than we knew. Your Grace is clever to have seen through his ploy."

"Lord Stannis is striving to win the northmen to his cause," said Pycelle. "If he befriends the ironborn, he cannot hope . . ."

"The northmen will not have him," said Cersei, wondering how such a learned man could be so stupid. "Lord Manderly hacked the head and hands off the onion knight, we have that from the Freys, and half a dozen other northern lords have rallied to Lord Bolton. *The enemy of my enemy is my friend.* Where else can Stannis turn, but to the ironmen and the wildlings, the enemies of the north? But if he thinks that I am going to walk into his trap, he is a bigger fool than you." She turned back to the little queen. "The Shield Islands belong to the Reach. Grimm and

Serry and the rest are sworn to Highgarden. It is for Highgarden to answer this."

"Highgarden shall answer," said Margaery Tyrell. "Willas has sent word to Leyton Hightower in Oldtown, so he can see to his own defenses. Garlan is gathering men to retake the isles. The best part of our power remains with my lord father, though. We must send word to him at Storm's End. At once."

"And lift the siege?" Cersei did not care for Margaery's presumption. *She says "at once" to me. Does she take me for her handmaid?* "I have no doubt that Lord Stannis would be pleased by that. Have you been listening, my lady? If he can draw our eyes away from Dragonstone and Storm's End to these rocks . . ."

"Rocks?" gasped Margaery. "Did Your Grace say *rocks*?"

The Knight of Flowers put a hand upon his sister's shoulder. "If it please Your Grace, from those *rocks* the ironmen threaten Oldtown and the Arbor. From strongholds on the Shields, raiders can sail up the Mander into the very heart of the Reach, as they did of old. With enough men they might even threaten Highgarden."

"Truly?" said the queen, all innocence. "Why then, your brave brothers had best roust them off those rocks, and quickly."

"How would the queen suggest they accomplish that, without sufficient ships?" asked Ser Loras. "Willas and Garlan can raise ten thousand men within a fortnight and twice that in a moon's turn, but they cannot walk on water, Your Grace."

"Highgarden sits above the Mander," Cersei reminded him. "You and your vassals command a thousand leagues of coast. Are there no fisherfolk along your shores? Do you have no pleasure barges, no ferries, no river galleys, no skiffs?"

"Many and more," Ser Loras admitted.

"Such should be more than sufficient to carry a host across a little stretch of water, I would think."

"And when the longships of the ironborn descend upon our ragtag fleet as it is making its way across this 'little stretch of water,' what would Your Grace have us do then?"

Drown, thought Cersei. "Highgarden has gold as well. You have my leave to hire sellsails from beyond the narrow sea."

"Pirates out of Myr and Lys, you mean?" Loras said with contempt. "The scum of the Free Cities?"

He is as insolent as his sister. "Sad to say, all of us must deal with scum from time to time," she said with poisonous sweetness. "Perhaps you have a better notion?"

"Only the Arbor has sufficient galleys to retake the mouth of the Mander from the ironmen and protect my brothers from their longships during their crossing. I beg Your Grace, send word to Dragonstone and command Lord Redwyne to raise his sails at once."

At least he has the sense to beg. Paxter Redwyne owned two hundred warships, and five times as many merchant carracks, wine cogs, trading galleys, and whalers. Redwyne was encamped beneath the walls of Dragonstone, however, and the greater part of his fleet was engaged in ferrying men across Blackwater Bay for the assault on that island stronghold. The remainder prowled Shipbreaker Bay to the south, where only their presence prevented Storm's End from being resupplied by sea.

Aurane Waters bristled at Ser Loras's suggestion. "If Lord Redwyne sails his ships away, how are we to supply our men on Dragonstone? Without the Arbor's galleys, how will we maintain the siege of Storm's End?"

"The siege can be resumed later, after—"

Cersei cut him off. "Storm's End is a hundred times

more valuable than the Shields, and Dragonstone . . . so long as Dragonstone remains in the hands of Stannis Baratheon, it is a knife at my son's throat. We will release Lord Redwyne and his fleet when the castle falls." The queen pushed herself to her feet. "This audience is at an end. Grand Maester Pycelle, a word."

The old man started, as if her voice had woken him from some dream of youth, but before he could answer, Loras Tyrell strode forward, so swiftly that the queen drew back in alarm. She was about to shout for Ser Osmund to defend her when the Knight of Flowers sank to one knee. "Your Grace, let me take Dragonstone."

His sister's hand went to her mouth. "Loras, no."

Ser Loras ignored her plea. "It will take half a year or more to starve Dragonstone into submission, as Lord Paxter means to do. Give me the command, Your Grace. The castle will be yours within a fortnight if I have to tear it down with my bare hands."

No one had given Cersei such a lovely gift since Sansa Stark had run to her to divulge Lord Eddard's plans. She was pleased to see that Margaery had gone pale. "Your courage takes my breath away, Ser Loras," Cersei said. "Lord Waters, are any of the new dromonds fit to put to sea?"

"*Sweet Cersei* is, Your Grace. A swift ship, and as strong as the queen she's named for."

"Splendid. Let *Sweet Cersei* carry our Knight of Flowers to Dragonstone at once. Ser Loras, the command is yours. Swear to me that you shall not return until Dragonstone is Tommen's."

"I shall, Your Grace." He rose.

Cersei kissed him on both cheeks. She kissed his sister too, and whispered, "You have a gallant brother." Either

Margaery did not have the grace to answer or fear had stolen all her words.

Dawn was still several hours away when Cersei slipped out the king's door behind the Iron Throne. Ser Osmund went before her with a torch and Qyburn strolled along beside her. Pycelle had to struggle to keep up. "If it please Your Grace," he puffed, "young men are overbold, and think only of the glory of battle and never of its dangers. Ser Loras . . . this plan of his is fraught with peril. To storm the very walls of Dragonstone . . ."

". . . is *very* brave."

". . . brave, yes, but . . ."

"I have no doubt that our Knight of Flowers will be the first man to gain the battlements." *And perhaps the first to fall.* The pox-scarred bastard that Stannis had left to hold his castle was no callow tourney champion but a seasoned killer. If the gods were good, he would give Ser Loras the glorious end he seemed to want. *Assuming the boy does not drown on the way.* There had been another storm last night, a savage one. The rain had come down in black sheets for hours. *And wouldn't that be sad?* the queen mused. *Drowning is ordinary. Ser Loras lusts for glory as real men lust for women, the least the gods can do is grant him a death worthy of a song.*

No matter what befell the boy on Dragonstone, however, the queen would be the winner. If Loras took the castle, Stannis would suffer a grievous blow, and the Redwyne fleet could sail off to meet the ironmen. If he failed, she would see to it that he had the lion's share of the blame. Nothing tarnishes a hero as much as failure. *And if he should come home on his shield, covered in blood and glory, Ser Osney will be there to console his grieving sister.*

The laugh would not be contained any longer. It burst from Cersei's lips, and echoed down the hall.

"Your Grace?" Grand Maester Pycelle blinked, his mouth sagging open. "Why . . . why would you laugh?"

"Why," she had to say, "elsewise I might weep. My heart is bursting with love for our Ser Loras and his valor."

She left the Grand Maester on the serpentine steps. *That one has outlived any usefulness he ever had,* the queen decided. All Pycelle ever seemed to do of late was plague her with cautions and objections. He had even objected to the understanding she had reached with the High Septon, gaping at her with dim and rheumy eyes when she commanded him to prepare the necessary papers and babbling about old dead history until Cersei cut him off. "King Maegor's day is done, and so are his decrees," she said firmly. "This is King Tommen's day, and mine." *I would have done better to let him perish in the black cells.*

"Should Ser Loras fall, Your Grace will need to find another worthy for the Kingsguard," Lord Qyburn said as they crossed over the spiked moat that girded Maegor's Holdfast.

"Someone splendid," she agreed. "Someone so young and swift and strong that Tommen will forget all about Ser Loras. A bit of gallantry would not be amiss, but his head should not be full of foolish notions. Do you know of such a man?"

"Alas, no," said Qyburn. "I had another sort of champion in mind. What he lacks in gallantry he will give you tenfold in devotion. He will protect your son, kill your enemies, and keep your secrets, and no living man will be able to withstand him."

"So you say. Words are wind. When the hour is ripe, you may produce this paragon of yours and we will see if he is all that you have promised."

"They will sing of him, I swear it." Lord Qyburn's eyes crinkled with amusement. "Might I ask about the armor?"

"I have placed your order. The armorer thinks that I am mad. He assures me that no man is strong enough to move and fight in such a weight of plate." Cersei gave the chainless maester a warning look. "Play me for a fool, and you'll die screaming. You are aware of that, I trust?"

"Always, Your Grace."

"Good. Say no more of this."

"The queen is wise. These walls have ears."

"So they do." At night Cersei sometimes heard soft sounds, even in her own apartments. *Mice in the walls,* she would tell herself, *no more than that.*

A candle was burning by her bedside, but the hearthfire had gone out and there was no other light. The room was cold as well. Cersei undressed and slipped beneath the blankets, leaving her gown to puddle on the floor. Across the bed, Taena stirred. "Your Grace," she murmured softly. "What hour is it?"

"The hour of the owl," the queen replied.

Though Cersei often slept alone, she had never liked it. Her oldest memories were of sharing a bed with Jaime, when they had still been so young that no one could tell the two of them apart. Later, after they were separated, she'd had a string of bedmaids and companions, most of them girls of an age with her, the daughters of her father's household knights and bannermen. None had pleased her, and few lasted very long. *Little sneaks, the lot of them. Vapid, weepy creatures, always telling tales and trying to worm their way between me and Jaime.* Still, there had been nights deep within the black bowels of the Rock when she had welcomed their warmth beside her. An empty bed was a cold bed.

Here most of all. There were chills in this room, and her

wretched royal husband had died beneath this canopy. *Robert Baratheon, the First of His Name, may there never be a second. A dim, drunken brute of a man. Let him weep in hell.* Taena warmed the bed as well as Robert ever had, and never tried to force Cersei's legs apart. Of late she had shared the queen's bed more often than Lord Merryweather's. Orton did not seem to mind . . . or if he did, he knew better than to say so.

"I was concerned when I woke and found you gone," murmured Lady Merryweather, sitting up against the pillows, the coverlets tangled about her waist. "Is aught amiss?"

"No," said Cersei, "all is well. On the morrow Ser Loras will sail for Dragonstone, to win the castle, loose the Redwyne fleet, and prove his manhood to us all." She told the Myrish woman all that had occurred beneath the shifting shadow of the Iron Throne. "Without her valiant brother, our little queen is next to naked. She has her guards, to be sure, but I have their captain here and there about the castle. A garrulous old man with a squirrel on his surcoat. Squirrels run from lions. He does not have it in him to defy the Iron Throne."

"Margaery has other swords about her," cautioned Lady Merryweather. "She has made many friends about the court, and she and her young cousins all have admirers."

"A few suitors do not concern me," Cersei said. "The army at Storm's End, however . . ."

"What do you mean to do, Your Grace?"

"Why do you ask?" The question was a little too pointed for Cersei's taste. "I do hope you are not thinking of sharing my idle musings with our poor little queen?"

"Never. I am not that girl Senelle."

Cersei did not care to think about Senelle. *She repaid my kindness with betrayal.* Sansa Stark had done the same.

So had Melara Hetherspoon and fat Jeyne Farman when the three of them were girls. *I would never have gone into that tent if not for them. I would never have allowed Maggy the Frog to taste my morrows in a drop of blood.* "I would be very sad if you ever betrayed my trust, Taena. I would have no choice but to give you to Lord Qyburn, but I know that I should weep."

"I will never give you cause to weep, Your Grace. If I do, say the word, and I will give myself to Qyburn. I want only to be close to you. To serve you, however you require."

"And for this service, what reward will you expect?"

"Nothing. It pleases me to please you." Taena rolled onto her side, her olive skin shining in the candlelight. Her breasts were larger than the queen's and tipped with huge nipples, black as horn. *She is younger than I am. Her breasts have not begun to sag.* Cersei wondered what it would feel like to kiss another woman. Not lightly on the cheek, as was common courtesy amongst ladies of high birth, but full upon the lips. Taena's lips were very full. She wondered what it would feel like to suckle on those breasts, to lay the Myrish woman on her back and push her legs apart and use her as a man would use her, the way Robert would use *her* when the drink was in him, and she was unable to bring him off with hand or mouth.

Those had been the worst nights, lying helpless underneath him as he took his pleasure, stinking of wine and grunting like a boar. Usually he rolled off and went to sleep as soon as it was done, and was snoring before his seed could dry upon her thighs. She was always sore afterward, raw between the legs, her breasts painful from the mauling he would give them. The only time he'd ever made her wet was on their wedding night.

Robert had been handsome enough when they first

married, tall and strong and powerful, but his hair was black and heavy, thick on his chest and coarse around his sex. *The wrong man came back from the Trident,* the queen would sometimes think as he was plowing her. In the first few years, when he mounted her more often, she would close her eyes and pretend that he was Rhaegar. She could not pretend that he was Jaime; he was too different, too unfamiliar. Even the *smell* of him was wrong.

For Robert, those nights never happened. Come morning he remembered nothing, or so he would have had her believe. Once, during the first year of their marriage, Cersei had voiced her displeasure the next day. "You hurt me," she complained. He had the grace to look ashamed. "It was not me, my lady," he said in a sulky sullen tone, like a child caught stealing apple cakes from the kitchen. "It was the wine. I drink too much wine." To wash down his admission, he reached for his horn of ale. As he raised it to his mouth, she smashed her own horn in his face, so hard she chipped a tooth. Years later at a feast, she heard him telling a serving wench how he'd cracked the tooth in a mêlée. *Well, our marriage was a mêlée,* she reflected, *so he did not lie.*

The rest had all been lies, though. He *did* remember what he did to her at night, she was convinced of that. She could see it in his eyes. He only pretended to forget; it was easier to do that than to face his shame. Deep down Robert Baratheon was a coward. In time the assaults did grow less frequent. During the first year he took her at least once a fortnight; by the end it was not even once a year. He never stopped completely, though. Sooner or later there would always come a night when he would drink too much and want to claim his rights. What shamed him in the light of day gave him pleasure in the darkness.

"My queen?" said Taena Merryweather. "You have a strange look in your eyes. Are you unwell?"

"I was just . . . remembering." Her throat was dry. "You are a good friend, Taena. I have not had a true friend in . . ."

Someone hammered at the door.

Again? The urgency of the sound made her shiver. *Have another thousand ships descended on us?* She slipped into a bedrobe and went to see who it was. "Beg pardon for disturbing you, Your Grace," the guardsman said, "but Lady Stokeworth is below, begging audience."

"At this hour?" snapped Cersei. "Has Falyse lost her wits? Tell her I have retired. Tell her that smallfolk on the Shields are being slaughtered. Tell her that I have been awake for half the night. I will see her on the morrow."

The guard hesitated. "If it please Your Grace, she's . . . she's not in a good way, if you take my meaning."

Cersei frowned. She had assumed Falyse was here to tell her that Bronn was dead. "Very well. I shall need to dress. Take her to my solar and have her wait." When Lady Merryweather made to rise and come with her, the queen demurred. "No, stay. One of us should get some rest, at least. I shan't be long."

Lady Falyse's face was bruised and swollen, her eyes red from her tears. Her lower lip was broken, her clothing soiled and torn. "Gods be good," Cersei said as she ushered her into the solar and closed the door. "What has happened to your face?"

Falyse did not seem to hear the question. "He *killed* him," she said in a quavery voice. "Mother have mercy, he . . . he . . ." She broke down sobbing, her whole body trembling.

Cersei poured a cup of wine and took it to the weeping woman. "Drink this. The wine will calm you. That's it. A little more now. Stop that weeping and tell me why you're here."

It took the rest of the flagon before the queen was finally able to coax the whole sad tale out of Lady Falyse. Once she had, she did not know whether to laugh or rage. "Single combat," she repeated. *Is there no one in the Seven Kingdoms that I can rely upon? Am I the only one in Westeros with a pinch of wits?* "You are telling me Ser Balman challenged Bronn to *single combat?*"

"He said it would be s-s-simple. The lance is a kn-knight's weapon, he said, and B-Bronn was no true knight. Balman said he would unhorse him and finish him as he lay st-st-stunned."

Bronn was no knight, that was true. Bronn was a battle-hardened killer. *Your cretin of a husband wrote his own death warrant.* "A splendid plan. Dare I ask how it went awry?"

"B-Bronn drove his lance through the chest of Balman's poor *h-h-h-horse.* Balman, he . . . his legs were crushed when the beast fell. He screamed so piteously . . ."

Sellswords have no pity, Cersei might have said. "I asked you to arrange a hunting mishap. An arrow gone astray, a fall from a horse, an angry boar . . . there are so many ways a man can die in the woods. None of them involving *lances.*"

Falyse did not seem to hear her. "When I tried to run to my Balman, he, he, he *struck* me in the face. He made my lord c-c-confess. Balman was crying out for Maester Frenken to attend him, but the sellsword, he, he, he . . ."

"Confess?" Cersei did not like that word. "I trust our brave Ser Balman held his tongue."

"Bronn put a dagger in his *eye,* and told me I had best be gone from Stokeworth before the sun went down or I'd get the same. He said he'd pass me around to the g-g-garrison, if any of them would have me. When I ordered Bronn seized, one of his knights had the insolence to say that I should do as Lord Stokeworth said. He called him *Lord Stokeworth*!" Lady Falyse clutched at the queen's hand. "Your Grace must give me knights. A hundred knights! And crossbowmen, to take my castle back. Stokeworth is mine! They would not even permit me to gather up my *clothes*! Bronn said they were his wife's clothes now, all my s-silks and velvets."

Your rags are the least of your concern. The queen pulled her fingers free of the other woman's clammy grasp. "I asked you to snuff out a candle to help protect the king. Instead you heaved a pot of wildfire at it. Did your witless Balman bring my name into this? Tell me he did not."

Falyse licked her lips. "He . . . he was in pain, his legs were broken. Bronn said he would show him mercy, but . . . What will happen to my poor m-m-mother?"

I imagine she will die. "What do you think?" Lady Tanda might well be dead already. Bronn did not seem the sort of man who would expend much effort nursing an old woman with a broken hip.

"You have to help me. Where am I to go? What will I do?"

Perhaps you might wed Moon Boy, Cersei almost said. *He is nigh as big a fool as your late husband.* She could not risk a war on the very doorstep of King's Landing, not now. "The silent sisters are always glad to welcome widows," she said. "Theirs is a serene life, a life of prayer and contemplation and good works. They bring solace to the living and peace to the dead." *And they do not talk.* She could not have the woman running about the Seven Kingdoms spreading dangerous tales.

Falyse was deaf to good sense. "All we did, we did in service to Your Grace. *Proud to Be Faithful.* You said . . ."

"I recall." Cersei forced a smile. "You shall stay here with us, my lady, until such time as we find a way to win your castle back. Let me pour you another cup of wine. It will help you sleep. You are weary and sick of heart, that's plain to see. My poor dear Falyse. That's it, drink up."

As her guest was working on the flagon, Cersei went to the door and called her maids. She told Dorcas to find Lord Qyburn for her and bring him here at once. Jocelyn Swyft she dispatched to the kitchens. "Bring bread and cheese, a meat pie and some apples. And wine. We have a thirst."

Qyburn arrived before the food. Lady Falyse had put down three more cups by then, and was beginning to nod, though from time to time she would rouse and give another sob. The queen took Qyburn aside and told him of Ser Balman's folly. "I cannot have Falyse spreading tales about the city. Her grief has made her witless. Do you still need women for your . . . work?"

"I do, Your Grace. The puppeteers are quite used up."

"Take her and do with her as you will, then. But once she goes down into the black cells . . . need I say more?"

"No, Your Grace. I understand."

"Good." The queen donned her smile once again. "Sweet Falyse, Maester Qyburn's here. He'll help you rest."

"Oh," said Falyse vaguely. "Oh, good."

When the door closed behind them Cersei poured herself another cup of wine. "I am surrounded by enemies and imbeciles," she said. She could not even trust to her own blood and kin, nor Jaime, who had once been her other half. *He was meant to be my sword and shield, my strong right arm. Why does he insist on vexing me?*

Bronn was no more than an annoyance, to be sure. She had never truly believed that he was harboring the Imp. Her twisted little brother was too clever to allow Lollys to name her wretched ill-begotten bastard after him, knowing it was sure to draw the queen's wroth down upon her. Lady Merryweather had pointed that out, and she was right. The mockery was almost certainly the sellsword's doing. She could picture him watching his wrinkled red stepson sucking on one of Lollys's swollen dugs, a cup of wine in his hand and an insolent smile on his face. *Grin all you wish, Ser Bronn, you'll be screaming soon enough. Enjoy your lackwit lady and your stolen castle whilst you can. When the time comes, I shall swat you as if you were a fly.* Perhaps she would send Loras Tyrell to do the swatting, if the Knight of Flowers should somehow return alive from Dragonstone. *That would be delicious. If the gods were good, each of them would kill the other, like Ser Arryk and Ser Erryk.* As for Stokeworth . . . no, she was sick of thinking about Stokeworth.

Taena had drifted back to sleep by the time the queen returned to the bedchamber, her head spinning. *Too much wine and too little sleep,* she told herself. It was not every night that she was awakened twice with such desperate tidings. *At least I could awaken. Robert would have been too drunk to rise, let alone rule. It would have fallen to Jon Arryn to deal with all of this.* It pleased her to think that she made a better king than Robert.

The sky outside the window was already beginning to lighten. Cersei sat on the bed beside Lady Merryweather, listening to her soft breathing, watching her breasts rise and fall. *Does she dream of Myr?* she wondered. *Or is it her lover with the scar, the dangerous dark-haired man who would not be refused?* She was quite certain Taena was not dreaming of Lord Orton.

Cersei cupped the other woman's breast. Softly at first, hardly touching, feeling the warmth of it beneath her palm, the skin as smooth as satin. She gave it a gentle squeeze, then ran her thumbnail lightly across the big dark nipple, back and forth and back and forth until she felt it stiffen. When she glanced up, Taena's eyes were open. "Does that feel good?" she asked.

"Yes," said Lady Merryweather.

"And this?" Cersei pinched the nipple now, pulling on it hard, twisting it between her fingers.

The Myrish woman gave a gasp of pain. "You're hurting me."

"It's just the wine. I had a flagon with my supper, and another with the widow Stokeworth. I had to drink to keep her calm." She twisted Taena's other nipple too, pulling until the other woman gasped. "I am the queen. I mean to claim my rights."

"Do what you will." Taena's hair was as black as Robert's, even down between her legs, and when Cersei touched her there she found her hair all sopping wet, where Robert's had been coarse and dry. "Please," the Myrish woman said, "go on, my queen. Do as you will with me. I'm yours."

But it was no good. She could not feel it, whatever Robert felt on the nights he took her. There was no pleasure in it, not for her. For Taena, yes. Her nipples were two black diamonds, her sex slick and steamy. *Robert would have loved you, for an hour.* The queen slid a finger into that Myrish swamp, then another, moving them in and out, *but once he spent himself inside you, he would have been hard-pressed to recall your name.*

She wanted to see if it would be as easy with a woman as it had always been with Robert. *Ten thousand of your children perished in my palm, Your Grace,* she thought, slipping a third finger into Myr. *Whilst you snored, I would lick your sons off my face and fingers one by one, all those pale sticky princes. You claimed your rights, my lord, but in the darkness I would eat your heirs.* Taena gave a shudder. She gasped some words in a foreign tongue, then shuddered again and arched her back and screamed. *She sounds as if she is being gored,* the queen thought. For a moment she let herself imagine that her fingers were a bore's tusks, ripping the Myrish woman apart from groin to throat.

It was still no good.

It had never been any good with anyone but Jaime.

When she tried to take her hand away, Taena caught it and kissed her fingers. "Sweet queen, how shall I pleasure you?" She slid her hand down Cersei's side and touched her sex. "Tell me what you would have of me, my love."

"Leave me." Cersei rolled away and pulled up the bed-clothes to cover herself, shivering. Dawn was breaking. It would be morning soon, and all of this would be forgotten.

It had never happened.

JAIME

The trumpets made a brazen blare, and cut the still blue air of dusk. Josmyn Peckledon was on his feet at once, scrambling for his master's swordbelt.

The boy has good instincts. "Outlaws don't blow trumpets to herald their arrival," Jaime told him. "I shan't need my sword. That will be my cousin, the Warden of the West."

The riders were dismounting when he emerged from his tent; half a dozen knights, and twoscore mounted archers and men-at-arms. *"Jaime!"* roared a shaggy man clad in gilded ringmail and a fox-fur cloak. "So gaunt, and all in white! And bearded too!"

"This? Mere stubble, against that mane of yours, coz." Ser Daven's bristling beard and bushy mustache grew into sidewhiskers as thick as a hedgerow, and those into the tangled yellow thicket atop his head, matted down by the helm he was removing. Somewhere in the midst of all that hair lurked a pug nose and a pair of lively hazel eyes. "Did some outlaw steal your razor?"

"I vowed I would not let my hair be cut until my father was avenged." For a man who looked so leonine, Daven Lannister sounded oddly sheepish. "The Young Wolf got to Karstark first, though. Robbed me of my vengeance." He handed his helm to a squire and pushed his fingers through his hair where the weight of the steel had crushed it down. "I like a bit of hair. The nights grow colder, and a little foliage helps to keep your face warm. Aye, and Aunt Genna always said I had a brick for a chin." He clasped Jaime by the arms. "We feared for you after the Whispering Wood. Heard Stark's direwolf tore out your throat."

"Did you weep bitter tears for me, coz?"

"Half of Lannisport was mourning. The female half." Ser Daven's gaze went to Jaime's stump. "So it's true. The bastards took your sword hand."

"I have a new one, made of gold. There's much to be said for being one-handed. I drink less wine for fear of spilling and am seldom inclined to scratch my arse at court."

"Aye, there's that. Maybe I should have mine off as well." His cousin laughed. "Was it Catelyn Stark who took it?"

"Vargo Hoat." *Where do these tales come from?*

"The Qohorik?" Ser Daven spat. "That's for him and all his Brave Companions. I told your father I would forage for him, but he refused me. Some tasks are fit for lions, he said, but foraging is best left for goats and dogs."

Lord Tywin's very words, Jaime knew; he could almost

hear his father's voice. "Come inside, coz. We need to talk."

Garrett had lit the braziers, and their glowing coals filled Jaime's tent with a ruddy heat. Ser Daven shrugged out of his cloak and tossed it at Little Lew. "You a Piper, boy?" he growled. "You have a runty look to you."

"I'm Lewys Piper, if it please my lord."

"I beat your brother bloody in a mêlée once. The runty little fool took offense when I asked him if that was his sister dancing naked on his shield."

"She's the sigil of our House. We don't have a sister."

"More's the pity. Your sigil has nice teats. What sort of man hides behind a naked woman, though? Every time I thumped your brother's shield, I felt unchivalrous."

"Enough," said Jaime, laughing. "Leave him be." Pia was mulling wine for them, stirring the kettle with a spoon. "I need to know what I can expect to find at Riverrun."

His cousin shrugged. "The siege drags on. The Blackfish sits inside the castle, we sit outside in our camps. Bloody boring, if you want the truth." Ser Daven seated himself upon a camp stool. "Tully ought to make a sortie, to remind us all we're still at war. Be nice if he culled some Freys too. Ryman, for a start. The man's drunk more oft than not. Oh, and Edwyn. Not as thick as his father, but as full of hate as a boil's full of pus. And our own Ser Emmon . . . no, *Lord* Emmon, Seven save us, must not forget his new title . . . our Lord of Riverrun does nought but try to tell me how to run the siege. He wants me to take the castle without *damaging* it, since it is now his lordly seat."

"Is that wine hot yet?" Jaime asked Pia.

"Yes, m'lord." The girl covered her mouth when she spoke. Peck served the wine on a golden platter. Ser

Daven pulled off his gloves and took a cup. "Thank you, boy. Who might you be?"

"Josmyn Peckledon, if it please my lord."

"Peck was a hero on the Blackwater," Jaime said. "He slew two knights and captured two more."

"You must be more dangerous than you look, lad. Is that a beard, or did you forget to wash the dirt off your face? Stannis Baratheon's wife has a thicker mustache. How old are you?"

"Fifteen, ser."

Ser Daven snorted. "You know the best thing about heroes, Jaime? They all die young and leave more women for the rest of us." He tossed the cup back to the squire. "Fill that full again, and I'll call you hero too. I have a thirst."

Jaime lifted his own cup left-handed and took a swallow. The warmth spread through his chest. "You were speaking of the Freys you wanted dead. Ryman, Edwyn, Emmon . . ."

"And Walder Rivers," Daven said, "that whoreson. Hates that he's a bastard, and hates everyone who's not. Ser Perwyn seems a decent fellow, though, might as well spare him. The women too. I'm to marry one, I hear. Your father might have seen fit to consult with me about this marriage, by the bye. My own father was treating with Paxter Redwyne before Oxcross, did you know? Redwyne has a nicely dowered daughter . . ."

"Desmera?" Jaime laughed. "How well do you like freckles?"

"If my choice is Freys or freckles, well . . . half of Lord Walder's brood look like stoats."

"Only half? Be thankful. I saw Lancel's bride at Darry."

"Gatehouse Ami, gods be good. I couldn't believe that Lancel picked that one. What's wrong with that boy?"

"He's grown pious," said Jaime, "but it wasn't him who

did the picking. Lady Amerei's mother is a Darry. Our uncle thought she'd help Lancel win the Darry smallfolk."

"How, by fucking them? You know why they call her Gatehouse Ami? She raises her portcullis for every knight who happens by. Lancel had best find an armorer to make him a horned helm."

"That won't be necessary. Our coz is off to King's Landing to take vows as one of the High Septon's swords."

Ser Daven could not have looked more astonished if Jaime had told him that Lancel had decided to become a mummer's monkey. "Not truly? You are japing with me. Gatehouse Ami must be more stoatish than I'd heard if she could drive the boy to *that*."

When Jaime had taken his leave of Lady Amerei, she had been weeping softly at the dissolution of her marriage whilst letting Lyle Crakehall console her. Her tears had not troubled him half so much as the hard looks on the faces of her kin as they stood about the yard. "I hope you do not intend to take vows as well, coz," he said to Daven. "The Freys are prickly where marriage contracts are concerned. I would hate to disappoint them again."

Ser Daven snorted. "I'll wed and bed my stoat, never fear. I know what happened to Robb Stark. From what Edwyn tells me, though, I'd best pick one who hasn't flowered yet, or I'm like to find that Black Walder has been there first. I'll wager he's had Gatehouse Ami, and more than thrice. Maybe that explains Lancel's godliness, and his father's mood."

"You have seen Ser Kevan?"

"Aye. He passed here on his way west. I asked him to help us take the castle, but Kevan would have none of it. He brooded the whole time he was here. Courteous enough, but chilly. I swore to him that I never asked to be made Warden of the West, that the honor should have gone to him, and he declared that he held no grudge against me, but you would never have known it from his tone. He stayed three days and hardly said three words to me. Would that he'd remained, I could have used his counsel. Our friends of Frey would not have dared vex Ser Kevan the way that they've been vexing me."

"Tell me," said Jaime.

"I would, but where to begin? Whilst I've been building rams and siege towers, Ryman Frey has raised a gibbet. Every day at dawn he brings forth Edmure Tully, drapes a noose around his neck, and threatens to hang him unless the castle yields. The Blackfish pays his mummer's show no mind, so come evenfall Lord Edmure is taken down again. His wife's with child, did you know?"

He hadn't. "Edmure bedded her, after the Red Wedding?"

"He was bedding her *during* the Red Wedding. Roslin's a pretty little thing, hardly stoatish at all. And fond of Edmure, queerly. Perwyn tells me she's praying for a girl."

Jaime considered that a moment. "Once Edmure's son is born, Lord Walder will have no more need of Edmure."

"That's how I see it too. Our good-uncle Emm . . . ah, *Lord* Emmon, that is . . . he wants Edmure hanged at once. The presence of a Tully Lord of Riverrun distresses him almost as much as the prospective birth of yet another. Daily he beseeches me to *make* Ser Ryman dangle Tully, never mind how. Meanwhile, I have Lord Gawen Westerling tugging at my other sleeve. The Blackfish has his lady wife inside the castle, along with three of his snot-nosed whelps. His lordship fears Tully will kill them if the Freys hang Edmure. One of them is the Young Wolf's little queen."

Jaime had met Jeyne Westerling, he thought, though he could not recall what she looked like. *She must be fair indeed, to have been worth a kingdom.* "Ser Brynden won't kill children," he assured his cousin. "He's not as black a fish as that." He was beginning to grasp why Riverrun had not yet fallen. "Tell me of your dispositions, coz."

"We have the castle well encircled. Ser Ryman and the Freys are north of the Tumblestone. South of Red Fork sits Lord Emmon, with Ser Forley Prester and with what remains of your old host, plus the river lords who came over to us after the Red Wedding. A sullen lot, I don't mind saying. Good for sulking in their tents, but not much more. Mine own camp is between the rivers, facing the moat and Riverrun's main gates. We've thrown a boom across the Red Fork, downstream of the castle. Manfryd Yew and Raynard Ruttiger have charge of its defense, so no one can escape by boat. I gave them nets as well, to fish. It helps keep us fed."

"Can we starve the castle out?"

Ser Daven shook his head. "The Blackfish expelled all the useless mouths from Riverrun and picked this country clean. He has enough stores to keep man and horse alive for two full years."

"And how well are we provisioned?"

"So long as there are fish in the rivers, we won't starve, though I don't know how we're going to feed the horses. The Freys are hauling food and fodder down from the Twins, but Ser Ryman claims he does not have enough to share, so we must forage for ourselves. Half the men I send off to look for food do not return. Some are deserting. Others we find ripening under trees, with ropes about their necks."

"We came on some, the day before last," said Jaime. Addam Marbrand's scouts had found them, hanging black-faced beneath a crabapple tree. The corpses had been stripped naked, and each man had a crabapple shoved between his teeth. None bore any wounds; plainly, they had yielded. Strongboar had grown furious at that, vowing bloody vengeance on the heads of any men who would truss up warriors to die like suckling pigs.

"It might have been outlaws," Ser Daven said, when Jaime told the tale, "or not. There are still bands of northmen about. And these Lords of the Trident may have bent their knees, but methinks their hearts are still . . . wolfish."

Jaime glanced at his two younger squires, who were hovering near the braziers pretending not to listen. Lewys Piper and Garrett Paege were both the sons of river lords. He had grown fond of both of them and would hate to have to give them to Ser Ilyn. "The ropes suggest Dondarrion to me."

"Your lightning lord's not the only man who knows how to tie a noose. Don't get me started on Lord Beric. He's here, he's there, he's everywhere, but when you send men after him, he melts away like dew. The river lords are helping him, never doubt it. A bloody marcher lord, if you can believe it. One day you hear the man is dead, the next they're saying how he can't be killed." Ser Daven put his wine cup down. "My scouts report fires in the high places at night. Signal fires, they think . . . as if there were a ring of watchers all around us. And there are fires in the villages as well. Some new god . . ."

No, an old one. "Thoros is with Dondarrion, the fat Myrish priest who used to drink with Robert." His golden hand was on the table. Jaime touched it and watched the gold glimmer in the sullen light of the braziers. "We'll deal with Dondarrion if we have to, but the Blackfish must come first. He has to know his cause is hopeless. Have you tried to treat with him?"

"Ser Ryman did. Rode up to the castle gates half-drunk and blustering, making threats. The Blackfish appeared on the ramparts long enough to say that he would not waste fair words on foul men. Then he put an arrow in the rump of Ryman's palfrey. The horse reared, Frey fell into the mud, and I laughed so hard I almost pissed myself. If it had been me inside the castle, I would have put that arrow through Ryman's lying throat."

"I'll wear a gorget when I treat with them," said Jaime, with a half smile. "I mean to offer him generous terms." If he could end this siege without bloodshed, then it could not be said that he had taken up arms against House Tully.

"You are welcome to try, my lord, but I doubt that words will win the day. We need to storm the castle."

There had been a time, not so long ago, when Jaime would doubtless have urged the same course. He knew he could not sit here for two years to starve the Blackfish out. "Whatever we do needs to be done quickly," he told Ser Daven. "My place is back at King's Landing, with the king."

"Aye," his cousin said. "I don't doubt your sister needs you. Why did she send off Kevan? I thought she'd make him Hand."

"He would not take it." *He was not as blind as I was.*

"Kevan should be the Warden of the West. Or you. It's not that I'm not grateful for the honor, mind you, but our uncle's twice my age and has more experience of command. I hope he knows I never asked for this."

"He knows."

"How is Cersei? As beautiful as ever?"

"Radiant." *Fickle.* "Golden." *False as fool's gold.* Last night he dreamed he'd found her fucking Moon Boy. He'd killed the fool and smashed his sister's teeth to splinters with his golden hand, just as Gregor Clegane had done to poor Pia. In his dreams Jaime always had two hands; one was made of gold, but it worked just like the other. "The sooner we are done with Riverrun, the sooner I'll be back at Cersei's side." What Jaime would do then he did not know.

He talked with his cousin for another hour before the Warden of the West finally took his leave. When he was gone, Jaime donned his gold hand and brown cloak to walk amongst the tents.

If truth be told, he liked this life. He felt more comfortable amongst soldiers in the field than he ever had at court. And his men seemed comfortable with him as well. At one cookfire three crossbowmen offered him a share of a hare they'd caught. At another a young knight asked his counsel on the best way to defend against a warhammer. Down beside the river, he watched two washerwomen jousting in the shallows, mounted on the shoulders of a pair of men-at-arms. The girls were half-drunk and half-naked, laughing and snapping rolled-up cloaks at one another as a dozen other men urged them on. Jaime bet a copper star on the blond girl riding Raff the Sweetling, and lost it when the two of them went down splashing amongst the reeds.

Across the river wolves were howling, and the wind was gusting through a stand of willows, making their branches writhe and whisper. Jaime found Ser Ilyn Payne alone outside his tent, honing his greatsword with a whetstone. "Come," he said, and the silent knight rose, smiling thinly. *He enjoys this,* he realized. *It pleases him to humiliate me nightly. It might please him even more to kill me.* He liked to believe that he was getting better, but the improvement was slow and not without cost. Underneath his steel and wool and boiled leather Jaime Lannister was a tapestry of cuts and scabs and bruises.

A sentry challenged them as they led their horses from the camp. Jaime clapped the man's shoulder with his golden hand. "Stay vigilant. There are wolves about."

They rode back along the Red Fork to the ruins of a burned village they had passed that afternoon. It was there they danced their midnight dance, amongst blackened stones and old cold cinders. For a little while Jaime had the better of it. Perhaps his old skill *was* coming back, he allowed himself to think. Perhaps tonight it would be Payne who went to sleep bruised and bloody.

It was as if Ser Ilyn heard his thoughts. He parried Jaime's last cut lazily and launched a counterattack that drove Jaime back into the river, where his boot slipped out from under him in the mud. He ended on his knees, with the silent knight's sword at his throat and his own lost in the reeds. In the moonlight the pockmarks on Payne's face were large as craters. He made that clacking sound that might have been a laugh and drew his sword up Jaime's throat till the point came to rest between his lips. Only then did he step back and sheathe his steel.

I would have done better to challenge Raff the Sweetling, with a whore upon my back, Jaime thought as he shook mud off his gilded hand. Part of him wanted to tear the thing off and fling it in the river. It was good for nothing, and the left was not much better. Ser Ilyn had gone back to the horses, leaving him to find his own feet. *At least I still have two of those.*

The last day of their journey was cold and gusty. The wind rattled amongst the branches in the bare brown woods and made the river reeds bow low along the Red Fork. Even mantled in the winter wool of the Kingsguard, Jaime could feel the iron teeth of that wind as he rode beside his cousin Daven. It was late afternoon when they sighted Riverrun, rising from the narrow point where the Tumblestone joined the Red Fork. The Tully castle looked like a great stone ship with its prow pointed downriver. Its sandstone walls were drenched in red-gold light, and seemed higher and thicker than Jaime had remembered. *This nut will not crack easily,* he thought gloomily. If the Blackfish would not listen, he would have no choice but to break the vow he'd made to Catelyn Stark. The vow he'd sworn his king came first.

The boom across the river and the three great camps of the besieging army were just as his cousin had described. Ser Ryman Frey's encampment north of the Tumblestone was the largest, and the most disorderly. A great grey gallows loomed above the tents, as tall as any trebuchet. On it stood a solitary figure with a rope about his neck. *Edmure Tully.* Jaime felt a stab of pity. *To keep him standing there day after day, with that noose around his neck . . . better to have his head off and be done with it.*

Behind the gallows, tents and cookfires spread out in ragged disarray. The Frey lordlings and their knights had raised their pavilions comfortably upstream of the latrine trenches; downstream were muddy hovels, wayns, and oxcarts. "Ser Ryman don't want his boys getting bored, so he gives them whores and cockfights and boar baiting," Ser Daven said. "He's even got himself a bloody *singer.* Our aunt brought Whitesmile Wat from Lannisport, if you can believe it, so Ryman had to have a singer too. Couldn't we just dam the river and drown the whole lot of them, coz?"

Jaime could see archers moving behind the merlons on the castle ramparts. Above them streamed the banners of House Tully, the silver trout defiant on its striped field of red and blue. But the highest tower flew a different flag; a long white standard emblazoned with the direwolf of Stark. "The first time I saw Riverrun, I was a squire green as summer grass," Jaime told his cousin. "Old Sumner Crakehall sent me to deliver a message, one he swore could not be entrusted to a raven. Lord Hoster kept me for a fortnight whilst mulling his reply, and sat me beside his daughter Lysa at every meal."

"Small wonder you took the white. I'd have done the same."

"Oh, Lysa was not so fearsome as all that." She had been a pretty girl, in truth; dimpled and delicate, with long auburn hair. *Timid, though. Prone to tongue-tied silences and fits of giggles, with none of Cersei's fire.* Her older sister had seemed more interesting, though Catelyn was promised to some northern boy, the heir of Winterfell . . . but at that age, no girl interested Jaime half so much as Hoster's famous brother, who had won renown fighting the Ninepenny Kings upon the Stepstones. At table he had ignored poor Lysa, whilst pressing Brynden Tully for tales of Maelys the Monstrous and the Ebon Prince. *Ser Brynden was younger then than I am now,* Jaime reflected, *and I was younger than Peck.*

The nearest ford across the Red Fork was upstream of the castle. To reach Ser Daven's camp they had to ride through Emmon Frey's, past the pavilions of the river lords who had bent their knees and been accepted back into the king's peace. Jaime noted the banners of Lychester and Vance, of Roote and Goodbrook, the acorns of House Smallford and Lord Piper's dancing maiden, but the banners he did *not* see gave him pause. The silver eagle of Mallister was nowhere in evidence; nor the red horse of Bracken, the willow of the Rygers, the twining snakes of Paege. Though all had renewed their fealty to the Iron Throne, none had come to join the siege. The Brackens were fighting the Blackwoods, Jaime knew, which accounted for their absence, but as for the rest . . .

Our new friends are no friends at all. Their loyalty goes no deeper than their skins. Riverrun had to be taken, and soon. The longer the siege dragged on, the more it would hearten other recalcitrants, like Tytos Blackwood.

At the ford, Ser Kennos of Kayce blew the Horn of Herrock. *That should bring the Blackfish to the battlements.* Ser Hugo and Ser Dermot led Jaime's way across the river, splashing through the muddy red-brown waters with the white standard of the Kingsguard and Tommen's stag and lion streaming in the wind. The rest of the column followed hard behind them.

The Lannister camp rang to the sound of wooden hammers where a new siege tower was rising. Two other towers stood completed, half-covered with raw horsehide. Between them sat a rolling ram; a tree trunk with a fire-hardened point suspended on chains beneath a wooden roof. *My coz has not been idle, it would seem.*

"My lord," Peck asked, "where do you want your tent?"

"There, upon that rise." He pointed with his golden hand, though it was not well suited to that task. "Baggage there, horse lines there. We'll use the latrines my cousin has so kindly dug for us. Ser Addam, inspect our perimeter with an eye for any weaknesses." Jaime did not anticipate an attack, but he had not anticipated the Whispering Wood either.

"Shall I summon the stoats for a war council?" Daven asked.

"Not until I've spoken to the Blackfish." Jaime beckoned to Beardless Jon Bettley. "Shake out a peace banner and bear a message to the castle. Inform Ser Brynden Tully that I would have words with him, at first light on the morrow. I will come to the edge of the moat and meet him on his drawbridge."

Peck looked alarmed. "My lord, the bowmen could . . ."

"They won't." Jaime dismounted. "Raise my tent and

plant my standards." *And we'll see who comes running, and how quickly.*

It did not require long. Pia was fussing at a brazier, trying to light the coals. Peck went to help her. Of late, Jaime oft went to sleep to the sound of them fucking in a corner of the tent. As Garrett was undoing the clasps on Jaime's greaves, the tent flapped open. "Here at last, are you?" boomed his aunt. She filled the door, with her Frey husband peering out from behind her. "Past time. Have you no hug for your old fat aunt?" She held out her arms and left him no choice but to embrace her.

Genna Lannister had been a shapely woman in her youth, always threatening to overflow her bodice. Now the only shape she had was square. Her face was broad and smooth, her neck a thick pink pillar, her bosom enormous. She carried enough flesh to make two of her husband. Jaime hugged her dutifully and waited for her to pinch his ear. She had been pinching his ear for as long as he could remember, but today she forbore. Instead, she planted soft and sloppy kisses on his cheeks. "I am sorry for your loss."

"I had a new hand made, of gold." He showed her.

"Very nice. Will they make you a gold father too?" Lady Genna's voice was sharp. "Tywin was the loss I meant."

"A man such as Tywin Lannister comes but once in a thousand years," declared her husband. Emmon Frey was a fretful man with nervous hands. He might have weighed ten stone . . . but only wet, and clad in mail. He was a weed in wool, with no chin to speak of, a flaw that the prominence of the apple in his throat made even more absurd. Half his hair had been gone before he turned thirty. Now he was sixty and only a few white wisps remained.

"Some queer tales have been reaching us of late," Lady

Genna said, after Jaime dismissed Pia and his squires. "A woman hardly knows what to believe. Can it be true that Tyrion slew Tywin? Or is that some calumny your sister put about?"

"It's true enough." The weight of his golden hand had grown irksome. He fumbled at the straps that secured it to his wrist.

"For a son to raise his hand against a father," Ser Emmon said. "Monstrous. These are dark days in Westeros. I fear for us all with Lord Tywin gone."

"You feared for us all when he was here." Genna settled her ample rump upon a camp stool, which creaked alarmingly beneath her weight. "Nephew, speak to us of our son Cleos and the manner of his death."

Jaime undid the last fastening and set his hand aside. "We were set upon by outlaws. Ser Cleos scattered them, but it cost his life." The lie came easy; he could see that it pleased them.

"The boy had courage, I always said so. It was in his blood." A pinkish froth glistened on Ser Emmon's lips when he spoke, courtesy of the sourleaf he liked to chew.

"His bones should be interred beneath the Rock, in the Hall of Heroes," Lady Genna declared. "Where was he laid to rest?"

Nowhere. The Bloody Mummers stripped his corpse and left his flesh to feast the carrion crows. "Beside a stream," he lied. "When this war is done, I will find the place and send him home." Bones were bones; these days, nothing was easier to come by.

"This war . . ." Lord Emmon cleared his throat, the apple in his throat moving up and down. "You will have seen the siege machines. Rams, trebuchets, towers. It will not serve, Jaime. Daven means to break my walls, smash in my gates. He talks of burning pitch, of setting the castle afire. *My* castle." He reached up one sleeve, brought out a parchment, and thrust it at Jaime's face. "I have the decree. Signed by the king, by Tommen, see, the royal seal, the stag and lion. I am the lawful lord of Riverrun, and I will not have it reduced to a smoking ruin."

"Oh, put that fool thing away," his wife snapped. "So long as the Blackfish sits inside Riverrun you can wipe your arse with that paper for all the good it does us." Though she had been a Frey for fifty years, Lady Genna remained very much a Lannister. *Quite a lot of Lannister.* "Jaime will deliver you the castle."

"To be sure," Lord Emmon said. "Ser Jaime, your lord father's faith in me was well placed, you shall see. I mean to be firm but fair with my new vassals. Blackwood and Bracken, Jason Mallister, Vance and Piper, they shall learn that they have a just overlord in Emmon Frey. My father as well, yes. He is the Lord of the Crossing, but *I* am the Lord of Riverrun. A son has a duty to obey his father, true, but a bannerman must obey his overlord."

Oh, gods be good. "You are not his overlord, ser. Read your parchment. You were granted Riverrun with its lands and incomes, no more. Petyr Baelish is the Lord Paramount of the Trident. Riverrun will be subject to the rule of Harrenhal."

That did not please Lord Emmon. "Harrenhal is a ruin, haunted and accursed," he objected, "and Baelish . . . the man is a coin counter, no proper lord, his birth . . ."

"If you are unhappy with the arrangements, go to King's Landing and take it up with my sweet sister." Cersei would devour Emmon Frey and pick her teeth with his bones, he did not doubt. *That is, if she's not too busy fucking Osmund Kettleblack.*

Lady Genna gave a snort. "There is no need to trouble

Her Grace with such nonsense. Emm, why don't you step outside and have a breath of air?"

"A breath of air?"

"Or a good long piss, if you prefer. My nephew and I have *family* matters to discuss."

Lord Emmon flushed. "Yes, it is warm in here. I will wait outside, my lady. Ser." His lordship rolled up his parchment, sketched a bow toward Jaime, and tottered from the tent.

It was hard not to feel contemptuous of Emmon Frey. He had arrived at Casterly Rock in his fourteenth year to wed a lioness half his age. Tyrion used to say that Lord Tywin had given him a nervous belly for a wedding gift. *Genna has played her part as well.* Jaime remembered many a feast where Emmon sat poking at his food sullenly whilst his wife made ribald jests with whatever household knight had been seated to her left, their conversations punctuated by loud bursts of laughter. *She gave Frey four sons, to be sure. At least she says they are his.* No one in Casterly Rock had the courage to suggest otherwise, least of all Ser Emmon.

No sooner was he gone than his lady wife rolled her eyes. "My lord and master. What *was* your father thinking, to name him Lord of Riverrun?"

"I imagine he was thinking of your sons."

"I think of them as well. Emm will make a wretched lord. Ty may do better, if he has the sense to learn from me and not his father." She looked about the tent. "Do you have wine?"

Jaime found a flagon and poured for her, one-handed. "Why are you here, my lady? You should have remained at Casterly Rock until the fighting's done."

"Once Emm heard he was a lord, he had to come at once to claim his seat." Lady Genna took a drink and wiped her mouth on her sleeve. "Your father should have granted us Darry. Cleos married one of the plowman's daughters, you will recall. His grieving widow is furious that her sons were not granted her lord father's lands. Gatehouse Ami is Darry only on her mother's side. My good-daughter Jeyne is her aunt, a full sister to Lady Mariya."

"A younger sister," Jaime reminded her, "and Ty will have Riverrun, a greater prize than Darry."

"A poisoned prize. House Darry is extinguished in the male line, House Tully is not. That muttonhead Ser Ryman puts a noose round Edmure's neck, but will not hang him. And Roslin Frey has a trout growing in her belly. My grandsons will never be secure in Riverrun so long as any Tully heir remains alive."

She was not wrong, Jaime knew. "If Roslin has a girl—"

"—she can wed Ty, provided old Lord Walder will consent. Yes, I've thought of that. A boy is just as likely, though, and his little cock would cloud the issue. And if Ser Brynden should survive this siege, he might be inclined to claim Riverrun in his own name . . . or in the name of young Robert Arryn."

Jaime remembered little Robert from King's Landing, still sucking on his mother's teats at four. "Arryn won't live long enough to breed. And why should the Lord of the Eyrie need Riverrun?"

"Why does a man with one pot of gold need another? Men are greedy. Tywin should have granted Riverrun to Kevan and Darry to Emm. I would have told him so if he had troubled to ask me, but when did your father ever consult with anyone but Kevan?" She sighed deeply. "I do not blame Kevan for wanting the safer seat for his own boy, mind you. I know him too well."

"What Kevan wants and what Lancel wants appear to

be two different things." He told her of Lancel's decision to renounce wife and lands and lordship to fight for the Holy Faith. "If you still want Darry, write to Cersei and make your case."

Lady Genna waved her cup in dismissal. "No, that horse has left the yard. Emm has it in his pointed head that he will rule the riverlands. And Lancel . . . I suppose we should have seen this coming from afar. A life protecting the High Septon is not so different from a life protecting the king, after all. Kevan will be wroth, I fear. As wroth as Tywin was when you got it in your head to take the white. At least Kevan still has Martyn for an heir. He can marry him to Gatehouse Ami in Lancel's place. Seven save us all." His aunt gave a sigh. "And speaking of the Seven, why would Cersei permit the Faith to arm again?"

Jaime shrugged. "I am certain she had reasons."

"Reasons?" Lady Genna made a rude noise. "They had best be *good* reasons. The Swords and Stars troubled even the Targaryens. The Conqueror himself tread carefully with the Faith, so they would not oppose him. And when Aegon died and the lords rose up against his sons, both orders were in the thick of that rebellion. The more pious lords supported them, and many of the smallfolk. King Maegor finally had to put a bounty on them. He paid a dragon for the head of any unrepentant Warrior's Son, and a silver stag for the scalp of a Poor Fellow, if I recall my history. Thousands were slain, but nigh as many still roamed the realm, defiant, until the Iron Throne slew Maegor and King Jaehaerys agreed to pardon all those who would set aside their swords."

"I'd forgotten most of that," Jaime confessed.

"You and your sister both." She took another swallow of her wine. "Is it true that Tywin was smiling on his bier?"

"He was rotting on his bier. It made his mouth twist."

"Was that all it was?" That seemed to sadden her. "Men say that Tywin never smiled, but he smiled when he wed your mother, and when Aerys made him Hand. When Tarbeck Hall came crashing down on Lady Ellyn, that scheming bitch, Tyg claimed he smiled then. And he smiled at your birth, Jaime, I saw that with mine own eyes. You and Cersei, pink and perfect, as alike as two peas in a pod . . . well, except between the legs. What *lungs* you had!"

"Hear us roar." Jaime grinned. "Next you'll be telling me how much he liked to laugh."

"No. Tywin mistrusted laughter. He heard too many people laughing at your grandsire." She frowned. "I promise you, this mummer's farce of a siege would not have amused him. How do you mean to end it, now that you're here?"

"Treat with the Blackfish."

"That won't work."

"I mean to offer him good terms."

"Terms require trust. The Freys murdered guests beneath their roof, and you, well . . . I mean no offense, my love, but you *did* kill a certain king you had sworn to protect."

"And I'll kill the Blackfish if he does not yield." His tone was harsher than he'd intended, but he was in no mood for having Aerys Targaryen thrown in his face.

"How, with your tongue?" Her voice was scornful. "I may be an old fat woman, but I do not have cheese between my ears, Jaime. Neither does the Blackfish. Empty threats won't daunt him."

"What would you counsel?"

She gave a ponderous shrug. "Emm wants Edmure's head off. For once, he may be right. Ser Ryman has made us a laughingstock with that gibbet of his. You need to show Ser Brynden that your threats have teeth."

"Killing Edmure might harden Ser Brynden's resolve."

"Resolve is one thing Brynden Blackfish never lacked for. Hoster Tully could have told you that." Lady Genna finished her wine. "Well, I would never presume to tell you how to fight a war. I know my place . . . unlike your sister. Is it true that Cersei burned the Red Keep?"

"Only the Tower of the Hand."

His aunt rolled her eyes. "She would have done better to leave the tower and burn her Hand. Harys *Swyft*? If ever a man deserved his arms, it is Ser Harys. And Gyles Rosby, Seven save us, I thought he died years ago. Merryweather . . . your father used to call his grandsire 'the Chuckler,' I'll have you know. Tywin claimed the only thing Merryweather was good for was chuckling at the king's witticisms. His lordship chuckled himself right into exile, as I recall. Cersei has put some bastard on the council too, and a kettle in the Kingsguard. She has the Faith arming and the Braavosi calling in loans all over Westeros. None of which would be happening if she'd had the simple sense to make your uncle the King's Hand."

"Ser Kevan refused the office."

"So he said. He did not say why. There was much he did not say. *Would* not say." Lady Genna made a face. "Kevan *always* did what was asked of him. It is not like him to turn away from any duty. Something is awry here, I can smell it."

"He said that he was tired." *He knows,* Cersei had said, as they stood above their father's corpse. *He knows about us.*

"Tired?" His aunt pursed her lips. "I suppose he has a right to be. It has been hard for Kevan, living all his life in Tywin's shadow. It was hard for all my brothers. That shadow Tywin cast was long and black, and each of them had to struggle to find a little sun. Tygett tried to be his own man, but he could never match your father, and that just made him angrier as the years went by. Gerion made japes. Better to mock the game than to play and lose. But Kevan saw how things stood early on, so he made himself a place by your father's side."

"And you?" Jaime asked her.

"It was not a game for girls. I was my father's precious princess . . . and Tywin's too, until I disappointed him. My brother never learned to like the taste of disappointment." She pushed herself to her feet. "I've said what I came to say, I shan't take any more of your time. Do what Tywin would have done."

"Did you love him?" Jaime heard himself ask.

His aunt looked at him strangely. "I was seven when Walder Frey persuaded my lord father to give my hand to Emm. His *second* son, not even his heir. Father was himself a thirdborn son, and younger children crave the approval of their elders. Frey sensed that weakness in him, and Father agreed for no better reason than to please him. My betrothal was announced at a feast with half the west in attendance. Ellyn Tarbeck laughed and the Red Lion went angry from the hall. The rest sat on their tongues. Only Tywin dared speak against the match. A boy of ten. Father turned as white as mare's milk, and Walder Frey was *quivering*." She smiled. "How could I not love him, after that? That is not to say that I approved of all he did, or much enjoyed the company of the man that he became . . . but every little girl needs a big brother to protect her. Tywin was big even when he was little." She gave a sigh. "Who will protect us now?"

Jaime kissed her cheek. "He left a son."

"Aye, he did. That is what I fear the most, in truth."

That was a queer remark. "Why should you fear?"

"Jaime," she said, tugging on his ear, "sweetling, I have known you since you were a babe at Joanna's breast. You smile like Gerion and fight like Tyg, and there's some of Kevan in you, else you would not wear that cloak . . . but *Tyrion* is Tywin's son, not you. I said so once to your father's face, and he would not speak to me for half a year. Men are such thundering great fools. Even the sort who come along once in a thousand years."

CAT OF THE CANALS

She woke before the sun came up, in the little room beneath the eaves that she shared with Brusco's daughters.

Cat was always the first to awaken. It was warm and snug under the blankets with Talea and Brea. She could hear the soft sounds of their breath. When she stirred, sitting up and fumbling for her slippers, Brea muttered a sleepy complaint and rolled over. The chill off the grey stone walls gave Cat gooseprickles. She dressed quickly in the darkness. As she was slipping her tunic over her head, Talea opened her eyes and called out, "Cat, be a sweet and bring my clothes for me." She was a gawky girl, all skin and bones and elbows, always complaining she was cold.

Cat fetched her clothes for her, and Talea squirmed into them underneath the blankets. Together they pulled her big sister from the bed, as Brea muttered sleepy threats.

By the time the three of them climbed down the ladder from the room beneath the eaves, Brusco and his sons were out in the boat on the little canal behind the house. Brusco barked at the girls to hurry, as he did every morning. His sons helped Talea and Brea onto the boat. It was Cat's task to untie them from the piling, toss the rope to Brea, and shove the boat away from the dock with a booted foot. Brusco's sons leaned into their poles. Cat ran and leapt across the widening gap between dock and deck.

After that, she had nothing to do but sit and yawn for a long while as Brusco and his sons pushed them through the predawn gloom, wending down a confusion of small canals. The day looked to be a rare one, crisp and clear and bright. Braavos only had three kinds of weather; fog was bad, rain was worse, and freezing rain was worst. But every so often would come a morning when the dawn broke pink and blue and the air was sharp and salty. Those were the days that Cat loved best.

When they reached the broad straight waterway that was the Long Canal, they turned south for the fishmarket. Cat sat with her legs crossed, fighting a yawn and trying to recall the details of her dream. *I dreamed I was a wolf again.* She could remember the smells best of all: trees and earth, her pack brothers, the scents of horse and deer and man, each different from the others, and the sharp acrid tang of fear, always the same. Some nights the wolf dreams were so vivid that she could hear her brothers howling even as she woke, and once Brea had claimed that she was growling in her sleep as she thrashed beneath the covers. She thought that was some stupid lie till Talea said it too.

I should not be dreaming wolf dreams, the girl told herself. *I am a cat now, not a wolf. I am Cat of the Canals.* The wolf dreams belonged to Arya of House Stark. Try as she might, though, she could not rid herself of Arya. It made no difference whether she slept beneath the temple or in the little room beneath the eaves with Brusco's daughters, the wolf dreams still haunted her by night . . . and sometimes other dreams as well.

The wolf dreams were the good ones. In the wolf dreams she was swift and strong, running down her prey with her pack at her heels. It was the other dream she hated, the one where she had two feet instead of four. In that one she was always looking for her mother, stumbling through a wasted land of mud and blood and fire. It was always raining in that dream, and she could hear her mother screaming, but a monster with a dog's head would not let her go save her. In that dream she was always weeping, like a frightened little girl. *Cats never weep,* she told herself, *no more than wolves do. It's just a stupid dream.*

The Long Canal took Brusco's boat beneath the green copper domes of the Palace of Truth and the tall square towers of the Prestayns and Antaryons before passing under the immense grey arches of the sweetwater river to the district known as Silty Town, where the buildings were smaller and less grand. Later in the day the canal would be choked with serpent boats and barges, but in the predawn darkness they had the waterway almost to themselves. Brusco liked to reach the fishmarket just as the Titan roared to herald the coming of the sun. The sound would boom across the lagoon, faint with distance but still loud enough to wake the sleeping city.

By the time Brusco and his sons tied up by the fishmarket, it was swarming with herring sellers and cod wives, oystermen, clam diggers, stewards, cooks, smallwives, and sailors off the galleys, all haggling loudly with one another as they inspected the morning catch. Brusco would walk from boat to boat, having a look at all the shellfish, and from time to time tapping a cask or crate with his cane. "This one," he would say. "Yes." *Tap tap.* "This one." *Tap tap.* "No, not that. Here." *Tap.* He was not much one for talking. Talea said her father was as grudging with his words as with his coins. Oysters, clams, crabs, mussels, cockles, sometimes prawns . . . Brusco bought it all, depending on what looked best each day. It was for them to carry the crates and casks that he tapped back to the boat. Brusco had a bad back, and could not lift anything heavier than a tankard of brown ale.

Cat always stank of brine and fish by the time they pushed off for home again. She had grown so used to it that she hardly even smelled it anymore. She did not mind the work. When her muscles ached from lifting, or her back got sore from the weight of a cask, she told herself that she was getting stronger.

Once all the casks were loaded, Brusco shoved them off again, and his sons poled them back up the Long Canal. Brea and Talea sat at the front of the boat whispering to one another. Cat knew that they were talking about Brea's boy, the one she climbed up on the roof to meet, after her father was asleep.

"Learn three new things before you come back to us," the kindly man had commanded Cat, when he sent her forth into the city. She always did. Sometimes it was no more than three new words of the Braavosi tongue. Sometimes she brought back sailor's tales, of strange and wondrous happenings from the wide wet world beyond the isles of Braavos, wars and rains of toads and dragons hatching. Sometimes she learned three new japes or three new riddles, or tricks of this trade or the other. And every so often, she would learn some secret.

Braavos was a city made for secrets, a city of fogs and masks and whispers. Its very existence had been a secret for a century, the girl had learned; its location had been hidden thrice that long. "The Nine Free Cities are the daughters of Valyria that was," the kindly man taught her, "but Braavos is the bastard child who ran away from home. We are a mongrel folk, the sons of slaves and whores and thieves. Our forebears came from half a hundred lands to this place of refuge, to escape the dragonlords who had enslaved them. Half a hundred gods came with them, but there is one god all of them shared in common."

"Him of Many Faces."

"And many names," the kindly man had said. "In Qohor he is the Black Goat, in Yi Ti the Lion of Night, in Westeros the Stranger. All men must bow to him in the end, no matter if they worship the Seven or the Lord of Light, the Moon Mother or the Drowned God or the Great Shepherd. All mankind belongs to him . . . else somewhere in the world would be a folk who lived forever. Do you know of any folk who live forever?"

"No," she would answer. "All men must die."

Cat would always find the kindly man waiting for her when she went creeping back to the temple on the knoll on the night the moon went black. "What do you know that you did not know when you left us?" he would always ask her.

"I know what Blind Beqqo puts in the hot sauce he uses on his oysters," she would say. "I know the mummers at the Blue Lantern are going to do *The Lord of the Woeful Countenance* and the mummers at the Ship mean to answer with *Seven Drunken Oarsmen*. I know the bookseller Lotho Lornel sleeps in the house of Tradesman-Captain Moredo Prestayn whenever the honorable tradesman-captain is away on a voyage, and moves out whenever the *Vixen* comes home."

"It is good to know these things. And who are you?"

"No one."

"You lie. You are Cat of the canals, I know you well. Go and sleep, child. On the morrow you must serve."

"All men must serve." And so she did, three days of every thirty. When the moon was black she was no one, a servant of the Many-Faced God in a robe of black and white. She walked beside the kindly man through the fragrant darkness, carrying her iron lantern. She washed the dead, went through their clothes, and counted out their coins. Some days she still helped Umma cook, chopping big white mushrooms and boning fish. But only when the moon was black. The rest of the time she was an orphan girl in a pair of battered boots too big for her feet and a brown cloak with a ragged hem, crying *"Mussels and cockles and clams"* as she wheeled her barrow through the Ragman's Harbor.

The moon would be black tonight, she knew; last night it had been no more than a sliver. "What do you know that you did not know when you left us?" the kindly man would ask as soon as he saw her. *I know that Brusco's daughter Brea meets a boy on the roof when her father is asleep,* she thought. *Brea lets him touch her, Talea says, even though he's just a roof rat and all the roof rats are supposed to be thieves.* That was only one thing, though. Cat would need two more. She was not concerned. There were always new things to learn, down by the ships.

When they returned to the house Cat helped Brusco's sons unload the boat. Brusco and his daughters divided the shellfish amongst three barrows, arranging them on layered beds of seaweed. "Come back when all is sold," Brusco told the girls, just as he did every morning, and they set forth to cry the catch. Brea would wheel her barrow to the Purple Harbor, to sell to the Braavosi sailors whose ships were anchored there. Talea would try the alleys round the Moon Pool, or sell amongst the temples on the Isle of the Gods. Cat headed for the Ragman's Harbor, as she did nine days of every ten.

Only Braavosi were permitted use of the Purple Harbor, from the Drowned Town and the Sealord's Palace; ships from her sister cities and the rest of the wide world had to use the Ragman's Harbor, a poorer, rougher, dirtier port than the Purple. It was noisier as well, as sailors and traders from half a hundred lands crowded its wharves and alleys, mingling with those who served and preyed on them. Cat liked it best of any place in Braavos. She liked the noise and the strange smells, and seeing what ships had come in on the evening tide and what ships had departed. She liked the sailors too; the boisterous Tyroshi with their booming voices and dyed whiskers; the fair-haired Lyseni, always trying to niggle down her prices; the squat, hairy sailors from the Port of Ibben, growling curses in low, raspy voices. Her favorites were the Summer Islanders, with their skins as smooth and dark as teak. They wore feathered cloaks of red and green and yellow, and the tall masts and white sails of their swan ships were magnificent.

And sometimes there were Westerosi too, oarsmen and sailors off carracks out of Oldtown, trading galleys out of Duskendale, King's Landing, and Gulltown, big-bellied wine cogs from the Arbor. Cat knew the Braavosi words for mussels and cockles and clams, but along the Ragman's Harbor she cried her wares in the trade tongue, the language of the wharves and docks and sailor's taverns, a coarse jumble of words and phrases from a dozen languages, accompanied by hand signs and gestures, most of them insulting. Those were the ones that Cat liked best. Any man who bothered her was apt to see the fig, or hear himself described as an ass's pizzle or a camel's cunt. "Maybe I never saw a camel," she would tell them, "but I know a camel's cunt when I smell one."

Once in a great while that would make somebody angry, but when it did she had her finger knife. She kept it very sharp, and knew how to use it too. Red Roggo showed her one afternoon at the Happy Port, while he was waiting for Lanna to come free. He taught her how to hide it up her sleeve and slip it out when she had need of it, and how to slice a purse so smooth and quick the coins would all be spent before their owner ever missed them. That was good to know, even the kindly man agreed; especially at night, when the bravos and roof rats were abroad.

Cat had made friends along the wharves; porters and mummers, ropemakers and sailmenders, taverners, brewers and bakers and beggars and whores. They bought clams and cockles from her, told her true tales of Braavos and lies about their lives, and laughed at the way she talked when she tried to speak Braavosi. She never let that trouble her. Instead, she showed them all the fig, and told them they were camel cunts, which made them roar with laughter. Gyloro Dothare taught her filthy songs, and his brother Gyleno told her the best places to catch eels. The mummers off the Ship showed her how a hero stands, and taught her speeches from *The Song of the Rhoyne, The Conqueror's Two Wives,* and *The Merchant's Lusty Lady.* Quill, the sad-eyed little man who made up all the bawdy farces for the Ship, offered to teach her how a woman kisses, but Tagganaro smacked him with a codfish and put an end to that. Cossomo the Conjurer instructed her in sleight of hand. He could swallow mice and pull them from her ears. "It's magic," he'd say. "It's not," Cat said. "The mouse was up your sleeve the whole time. I could see it moving."

"Oysters, clams, and cockles" were Cat's magic words, and like all good magic words they could take her almost anywhere. She had boarded ships from Lys and Oldtown and the Port of Ibben and sold her oysters right on deck. Some days she rolled her barrow past the towers of the mighty to offer baked clams to the guardsmen at their gates. Once she cried her catch on the steps of the Palace of Truth, and when another peddler tried to run her off she turned his cart over and sent his oysters skittering across the cobbles. Customs officers from the Chequy Port would buy from her, and paddlers from the Drowned Town, whose sunken domes and towers poked up from the green waters of the lagoon. One time, when Brea took to her bed with her moon blood, Cat had pushed her barrow to the Purple Harbor to sell crabs and prawns to oarsmen off the Sealord's pleasure barge, covered stem to stern with laughing faces. Other days she followed the sweetwater river to the Moon Pool. She sold to swaggering bravos in striped satin, and to keyholders and justiciars in drab coats of brown and grey. But she always returned to the Ragman's Harbor.

"Oysters, clams, and cockles," the girl shouted as she pushed her barrow along the wharves. *"Mussels, prawns, and cockles."* A dirty orange cat came padding after her, drawn by the sound of her call. Farther on, a second cat appeared, a sad, bedraggled grey thing with a stub tail. Cats liked the smell of Cat. Some days she would have a dozen trailing after her before the sun went down. From time to time the girl would throw an oyster at them and watch to see who came away with it. The biggest toms would seldom win, she noticed; oft as not, the prize went to some smaller, quicker animal, thin and mean and hungry. *Like me,* she told herself. Her favorite was a scrawny old tom with a chewed ear who reminded her of a cat that

she'd once chased all around the Red Keep. *No, that was some other girl, not me.*

Two of the ships that had been here yesterday were gone, Cat saw, but five new ones had docked; a small carrack called the *Brazen Monkey,* a huge Ibbenese whaler that reeked of tar and blood and whale oil, two battered cogs from Pentos, and a lean green galley up from Old Volantis. Cat stopped at the foot of every gangplank to cry her clams and oysters, once in the trade talk and again in the Common Tongue of Westeros. A crewman on the whaler cursed at her so loudly that he scared away her cats and one of the Pentoshi oarsman asked how much she wanted for the clam between her legs, but she fared better at the other ships. A mate on the green galley wolfed half a dozen oysters and told her how his captain had been killed by the Lysene pirates who had tried to board them near the Stepstones. "That bastard Saan it was, with *Old Mother's Son* and his big *Valyrian.* We got away, but just."

The little *Brazen Monkey* proved to be from Gulltown, with a Westerosi crew who were glad to talk to someone in the Common Tongue. One asked how a girl from King's Landing came to be selling mussels on the docks of Braavos, so she had to tell her tale. "We're here four days, and four long nights," another told her. "Where's a man to go to find a bit of sport?"

"The mummers at the Ship are doing *Seven Drunken Oarsmen,*" Cat told them, "and there's eel fights in the Spotted Cellar, down by the gates of Drowned Town. Or if you want you can go by the Moon Pool, where the bravos duel at night."

"Aye, that's good," another sailor said, "but what Wat was really wanting was a woman."

"The best whores are at the Happy Port, down by where the mummers' Ship is moored." She pointed. Some of the dockside whores were vicious, and sailors fresh from the sea never knew which ones. S'vrone was the worst. Everyone said she had robbed and killed a dozen men, rolling the bodies into the canals to feed the eels. The Drunken Daughter could be sweet when sober, but not with wine in her. And Canker Jeyne was really a man. "Ask for Merry. Meralyn is her true name, but everyone calls her Merry, and she is." Merry bought a dozen oysters every time Cat came by the brothel and shared them with her girls. She had a good heart, everyone agreed. "That, and the biggest pair of teats in all of Braavos," Merry herself was fond of boasting.

Her girls were nice as well; Blushing Bethany and the Sailor's Wife, one-eyed Yna who could tell your fortune from a drop of blood, pretty little Lanna, even Assadora, the Ibbenese woman with the mustache. They might not be beautiful, but they were kind to her. "The Happy Port is where all the porters go," Cat assured the men of the *Brazen Monkey*. "'The boys unload the ships,' Merry says, 'and my girls unload the lads who sail them.'"

"What about them fancy whores the singers sing about?" asked the youngest monkey, a red-haired boy with freckles who could not have been much more than six-and-ten. "Are they as pretty as they say? Where would I get one o' them?"

His shipmates looked at him and laughed. "Seven hells, boy," said one of them. "Might be the captain could get hisself a courty-san, but only if he sold the bloody ship. That sort o' cunt's for lords and such, not for the likes o' us."

The courtesans of Braavos were famed across the world. Singers sang of them, goldsmiths and jewelers showered them with gifts, craftsmen begged for the honor of their custom, merchant princes paid royal ransoms to have them on their arms at balls and feasts and mummer shows, and bravos slew each other in their names. As she pushed her barrow along the canals, Cat would sometimes glimpse one of them floating by, on her way to an evening with some lover. Every courtesan had her own barge, and servants to pole her to her trysts. The Poetess always had a book to hand, the Moonshadow wore only white and silver, and the Merling Queen was never seen without her Mermaids, four young maidens in the blush of their first flowering who held her train and did her hair. Each courtesan was more beautiful than the last. Even the Veiled Lady was beautiful, though only those she took as lovers ever saw her face.

"I sold three cockles to a courtesan," Cat told the sailors. "She called to me as she was stepping off her barge." Brusco had made it plain to her that she was never to speak to a courtesan unless she was spoken to first, but the woman had smiled at her and paid her in silver, ten times what the cockles had been worth.

"Which one was this, now? The Queen o' Cockles, was it?"

"The Black Pearl," she told them. Merry claimed the Black Pearl was the most famous courtesan of all. "She's descended from the dragons, that one," the woman had told Cat. "The first Black Pearl was a pirate queen. A Westerosi prince took her for a lover and got a daughter on her, who grew up to be a courtesan. Her own daughter followed her, and *her* daughter after her, until you get to this one. What did she say to you, Cat?"

"She said '*I'll take three cockles*,' and '*Do you have some hot sauce, little one?*'" the girl had answered.

"And what did you say?"

"I said, '*No, my lady,*' and, '*Don't call me little one. My name is Cat.'* I should have hot sauce. Beqqo does, and he sells three times as many oysters as Brusco."

Cat told the kindly man about the Black Pearl too. "Her true name is Bellegere Otherys," she informed him. It was one of the three things that she had learned.

"It is," the priest said softly. "Her mother was Bellonara, but the first Black Pearl was a Bellegere as well."

Cat knew that the men off the *Brazen Monkey* would not care about the name of a courtesan's mother, though. Instead, she asked them for tidings of the Seven Kingdoms, and the war.

"War?" laughed one of them. "What war? There is no war."

"Not in Gulltown," said another. "Not in the Vale. The little lord's kept us out of it, same as his mother did."

Same as his mother did. The lady of the Vale was her own mother's sister. "Lady Lysa," she said, "is she . . . ?"

". . . dead?" finished the freckled boy whose head was full of courtesans. "Aye. Murdered by her own singer."

"Oh." *It's nought to me. Cat of the Canals never had an aunt. She never did.* Cat lifted her barrow and wheeled away from the *Brazen Monkey,* bumping over cobblestones. *"Oysters, clams, and cockles,"* she called. *"Oysters, clams, and cockles."* She sold most of her clams to the porters off-loading the big wine cog from the Arbor, and the rest to the men repairing a Myrish trading galley that had been savaged by the storms.

Farther down the docks she came on Tagganaro sitting with his back against a piling, next to Casso, King of Seals. He bought some mussels from her, and Casso barked and let her shake his flipper. "You come work with me, Cat," urged Tagganaro as he was sucking mussels from their shells. He had been looking for a new partner ever since the Drunken Daughter put her knife through Little Narbo's hand. "I give you more than Brusco, and you would not smell like fish."

"Casso likes the way I smell," she said. The King of Seals barked, as if to agree. "Is Narbo's hand no better?"

"Three fingers do not bend," complained Tagganaro, between mussels. "What good is a cutpurse who cannot use his fingers? Narbo was good at picking pockets, not so good at picking whores."

"Merry says the same." Cat was sad. She liked Little Narbo, even if he was a thief. "What will he do?"

"Pull an oar, he says. Two fingers are enough for that, he thinks, and the Sealord's always looking for more oarsmen. I tell him, 'Narbo, no. That sea is colder than a maiden and crueler than a whore. Better you should cut off the hand, and beg.' Casso knows I am right. Don't you, Casso?"

The seal barked, and Cat had to smile. She tossed another cockle his way before she went off on her own.

The day was nearly done by the time Cat reached the Happy Port, across the alley from where the Ship was anchored. Some of the mummers sat up atop the listing hulk, passing a skin of wine from hand to hand, but when they saw Cat's barrow they came down for some oysters. She asked them how it went with *Seven Drunken Oarsmen*. Joss the Gloom shook his head. "Quence finally came on Allaquo abed with Sloey. They went at one another with mummer swords, and both of them have left us. We'll only be five drunken oarsmen tonight, it would seem."

"We shall strive to make up in drunkenness what we lack in oarsmen," declared Myrmello. "I for one am equal to the task."

"Little Narbo wants to be an oarsman," Cat told them. "If you got him, you'd have six."

"You had best go see Merry," Joss told her. "You know how sour she gets without her oysters."

When Cat slipped inside the brothel, though, she found Merry sitting in the common room with her eyes shut, listening to Dareon play his woodharp. Yna was there too, braiding Lanna's fine long golden hair. *Another stupid love song.* Lanna was always begging the singer to play her stupid love songs. She was the youngest of the whores, only ten-and-four. Merry asked three times as much for her as for any of the other girls, Cat knew.

It made her angry to see Dareon sitting there so brazen, making eyes at Lanna as his fingers danced across the harp strings. The whores called him the black singer, but there was hardly any black about him now. With the coin his singing brought him, the crow had transformed himself into a peacock. Today he wore a plush purple cloak lined with vair, a striped white-and-lilac tunic, and the parti-colored breeches of a bravo, but he owned a silken cloak as well, and one made of burgundy velvet that was lined with cloth-of-gold. The only black about him was his boots. Cat had heard him tell Lanna that he'd thrown all the rest in a canal. "I am done with darkness," he had announced.

He is a man of the Night's Watch, she thought, as he sang about some stupid lady throwing herself off some stupid tower because her stupid prince was dead. *The lady should go kill the ones who killed her prince. And the singer should be on the Wall.* When Dareon had first appeared at the Happy Port, Arya had almost asked if he would take her with him back to Eastwatch, until she heard him telling Bethany that he was never going back. "Hard beds, salt cod, and endless watches, that's the Wall," he'd said. "Besides, there's no one half as pretty as you at Eastwatch. How could I ever leave you?" He had said the same thing to Lanna, Cat had heard, and to one of the whores at the Cattery, and even to the Nightingale the night he played at the House of Seven Lamps.

I wish I had been here the night the fat one hit him. Merry's whores still laughed about that. Yna said the fat boy had gone red as a beet every time she touched him, but when he started trouble Merry had him dragged outside and thrown in the canal.

Cat was thinking about the fat boy, remembering how she had saved him from Terro and Orbelo, when the Sailor's Wife appeared beside her. "He sings a pretty song," she murmured softly, in the Common Tongue of Westeros. "The gods must have loved him to give him such a voice, and that fair face as well."

He is fair of face and foul of heart, thought Arya, but she did not say it. Dareon had once wed the Sailor's Wife, who would only bed with men who married her. The Happy Port sometimes had three or four weddings a night. Often the cheerful wine-soaked red priest Ezzelyno performed the rites. Elsewise it was Eustace, who had once been a septon at the Sept-Beyond-the-Sea. If neither priest nor septon was on hand, one of the whores would run to the Ship and fetch back a mummer. Merry always claimed the mummers made much better priests than priests, especially Myrmello.

The weddings were loud and jolly, with a lot of drinking. Whenever Cat happened by with her barrow, the Sailor's Wife would insist that her new husband buy some oysters, to stiffen him for the consummation. She was good that way, and quick to laugh as well, but Cat thought there was something sad about her too.

The other whores said that the Sailor's Wife visited the Isle of the Gods on the days when her flower was in bloom, and knew all the gods who lived there, even the ones that Braavos had forgotten. They said she went to pray for her first husband, her true husband, who had been lost at sea when she was a girl no older than Lanna. "She thinks that if she finds the right god, maybe he will send the winds and blow her old love back to her," said one-eyed Yna, who had known her longest, "but I pray it never happens. Her love is dead, I could taste that in her blood. If he ever should come back to her, it will be a corpse."

Dareon's song was finally ending. As the last notes faded in the air, Lanna gave a sigh and the singer put his harp aside and pulled her up into his lap. He had just started to tickle her when Cat said loudly, "There's oysters, if anyone is wanting some," and Merry's eyes popped open. "Good," the woman said. "Bring them in, child. Yna, fetch some bread and vinegar."

The swollen red sun hung in the sky behind the row of masts when Cat took her leave of the Happy Port, with a plump purse of coins and a barrow empty but for salt and seaweed. Dareon was leaving too. He had promised to sing at the Inn of the Green Eel this evening, he told her as they strolled along together. "Every time I play the Eel I come away with silver," he boasted, "and some nights there are captains there, and owners." They crossed a little bridge, and made their way down a crooked back street as the shadows of the day grew longer. "Soon I will be playing in the Purple, and after that the Sealord's Palace," Dareon went on. Cat's empty barrow clattered over the cobblestones, making its own sort of rattling music. "Yesterday I ate herring with the whores, but within the year I'll be having emperor crab with courtesans."

"What happened to your brother?" Cat asked. "The fat one. Did he ever find a ship to Oldtown? He said he was supposed to sail on the *Lady Ushanora*."

"We all were. Lord Snow's command. I told Sam, leave

the old man, but the fat fool would not listen." The last light of the setting sun shone in his hair. "Well, it's too late now."

"Just so," said Cat as they stepped into the gloom of a twisty little alley.

By the time Cat returned to Brusco's house, an evening fog was gathering above the small canal. She put away her barrow, found Brusco in his counting room, and thumped her purse down on the table in front of him. She thumped the boots down too.

Brusco gave the purse a pat. "Good. But what's this?"

"Boots."

"Good boots are hard to find," said Brusco, "but these are too small for my feet." He picked one up to squint at it.

"The moon will be black tonight," she reminded him.

"Best you pray, then." Brusco shoved the boots aside and poured out the coins to count them. *"Valar dohaeris."*

Valar morghulis, she thought.

Fog rose all around as she walked through the streets of Braavos. She was shivering a little by the time she pushed through the weirwood door into the House of Black and White. Only a few candles burned this evening, flickering like fallen stars. In the darkness all the gods were strangers.

Down in the vaults, she untied Cat's threadbare cloak, pulled Cat's fishy brown tunic over her head, kicked off Cat's salt-stained boots, climbed out of Cat's smallclothes, and bathed in lemonwater to wash away the very smell of Cat of the Canals. When she emerged, soaped and scrubbed pink with her brown hair plastered to her cheeks, Cat was gone. She donned clean robes and a pair of soft cloth slippers, and padded to the kitchens to beg some food of Umma. The priests and acolytes had already eaten, but the cook had saved a piece of nice fried cod for her, and some mashed yellow turnips. She wolfed it down, washed the dish, then went to help the waif prepare her potions.

Her part was mostly fetching, scrambling up ladders to find the herbs and leaves the waif required. "Sweetsleep is the gentlest of poisons," the waif told her, as she was grinding some with a mortar and pestle. "A few grains will slow a pounding heart and stop a hand from shaking, and make a man feel calm and strong. A pinch will grant a night of deep and dreamless sleep. Three pinches will produce that sleep that does not end. The taste is very sweet, so it is best used in cakes and pies and honeyed wines. Here, you can smell the sweetness." She let her have a whiff, then sent her up the ladders to find a red glass bottle. "This is a crueler poison, but tasteless and odorless, hence easier to hide. The tears of Lys, men call it. Dissolved in wine or water, it eats at a man's bowels and belly, and kills as a sickness of those parts. Smell." Arya sniffed, and smelled nothing. The waif put the tears to one side and opened a fat stone jar. "This paste is spiced with basilisk blood. It will give cooked flesh a savory smell, but if eaten it produces violent madness, in beasts as well as men. A mouse will attack a lion after a taste of basilisk blood."

Arya chewed her lip. "Would it work on dogs?"

"On any animal with warm blood." The waif slapped her.

She raised her hand to her cheek, more surprised than hurt. "Why did you do that?"

"It is Arya of House Stark who chews on her lip whenever she is thinking. Are you Arya of House Stark?"

"I am no one." She was angry. "Who are *you*?"

She did not expect the waif to answer, but she did. "I was born the only child of an ancient House, my noble father's heir," the waif replied. "My mother died when I was little, I have no memory of her. When I was six my father wed again. His new wife treated me kindly until she gave birth to a daughter of her own. Then it was her wish that I should die, so her own blood might inherit my father's wealth. She should have sought the favor of the Many-Faced God, but she could not bear the sacrifice he would ask of her. Instead, she thought to poison me herself. It left me as you see me now, but I did not die. When the healers in the House of the Red Hands told my father what she had done, he came here and made sacrifice, offering up all his wealth and me. Him of Many Faces heard his prayer. I was brought to the temple to serve, and my father's wife received the gift."

Arya considered her warily. "Is that true?"

"There is truth in it."

"And lies as well?"

"There is an untruth, and an exaggeration."

She had been watching the waif's face the whole time she told her story, but the other girl had shown her no signs. "The Many-Faced God took two-thirds of your father's wealth, not all."

"Just so. That was my exaggeration."

Arya grinned, realized she was grinning, and gave her cheek a pinch. *Rule your face,* she told herself. *My smile is my servant, he should come at my command.* "What part was the lie?"

"No part. I lied about the lie."

"Did you? Or are you lying now?"

But before the waif could answer, the kindly man stepped into the chamber, smiling. "You have returned to us."

"The moon is black."

"It is. What three new things do you know, that you did not know when last you left us?"

I know thirty new things, she almost said. "Three of Little Narbo's fingers will not bend. He means to be an oarsman."

"It is good to know this. And what else?"

She thought back on her day. "Quence and Alaquo had a fight and left the Ship, but I think that they'll come back."

"Do you only think, or do you *know*?"

"I only think," she had to confess, even though she was certain of it. Mummers had to eat the same as other men, and Quence and Alaquo were not good enough for the Blue Lantern.

"Just so," said the kindly man. "And the third thing?"

This time she did not hesitate. "Dareon is dead. The black singer who was sleeping at the Happy Port. He was really a deserter from the Night's Watch. Someone slit his throat and pushed him into a canal, but they kept his boots."

"Good boots are hard to find."

"Just so." She tried to keep her face still.

"Who could have done this thing, I wonder?"

"Arya of House Stark." She watched his eyes, his mouth, the muscles of his jaw.

"That girl? I thought she had left Braavos. Who are you?"

"No one."

"You lie." He turned to the waif. "My throat is dry. Do me a kindness and bring a cup of wine for me and warm milk for our friend Arya, who has returned to us so unexpectedly."

On her way across the city Arya had wondered what the kindly man would say when she told him about Dareon.

Maybe he would be angry with her, or maybe he would be pleased that she had given the singer the gift of the Many-Faced God. She had played this talk out in her head half a hundred times, like a mummer in a show. But she had never thought *warm milk.*

When the milk came, Arya drank it down. It smelled a little burnt and had a bitter aftertaste. "Go to bed now, child," the kindly man said. "On the morrow you must serve."

That night she dreamed she was a wolf again, but it was different from the other dreams. In this dream she had no pack. She prowled alone, bounding over rooftops and padding silently beside the banks of a canal, stalking shadows through the fog.

When she woke the next morning, she was blind.

SAMWELL

The *Cinnamon Wind* was a swan ship out of Tall Trees Town on the Summer Isles, where men were black, women were wanton, and even the gods were strange. She had no septon aboard her to lead them in the prayers of passing, so the task fell to Samwell Tarly, somewhere off the sun-scorched southern coast of Dorne.

Sam donned his blacks to say the words, though the afternoon was warm and muggy, with nary a breath of wind. "He was a good man," he began . . . but as soon as he had said the words he knew that they were wrong. "No. He was a *great* man. A maester of the Citadel, chained and sworn, and Sworn Brother of the Night's Watch, ever faithful. When he was born they named him for a hero who had died too young, but though he lived a long long time, his own life was no less heroic. No man was wiser, or gentler, or kinder. At the Wall, a dozen lords commander came and went during his years of service, but he was always there to counsel them. He counseled kings as well. He could have been a king himself, but when they offered him the crown he told them they should give it to his younger brother. How many men would do that?" Sam felt the tears welling in his eyes, and knew he could not go on much longer. "He was the blood of the dragon, but now his fire has gone out. He was Aemon Targaryen. And now his watch is ended."

"And now his watch is ended," Gilly murmured after him, rocking the babe in her arms. Kojja Mo echoed her in the Common Tongue of Westeros, then repeated the words in the Summer Tongue for Xhondo and her father and the rest of the assembled crew. Sam hung his head and began to weep, his sobs so loud and wrenching that they made his whole body shake. Gilly came and stood beside him and let him cry upon her shoulder. There were tears in her eyes as well.

The air was moist and warm and dead calm, and the *Cinnamon Wind* was adrift upon a deep blue sea far beyond the sight of land. "Black Sam said good words," Xhondo said. "Now we drink his life." He shouted something in the Summer Tongue, and a cask of spiced rum was rolled up onto the afterdeck and breached, so those on watch might down a cup in the memory of the old blind dragon. The crew had known him only a short while, but Summer Islanders revered the elderly and celebrated their dead.

Sam had never drunk rum before. The liquor was strange and heady; sweet at first, but with a fiery aftertaste that burned his tongue. He was tired, so tired. Every muscle he had was aching, and there were other aches in places where Sam hadn't known he had muscles. His knees were stiff, his hands covered with fresh new blisters and raw, sticky patches of skin where the old blisters had burst. Yet between them, rum and sadness seemed to wash his hurts away. "If only we could have gotten him to Oldtown, the archmaesters might have saved him," he told Gilly, as they sipped their rum on the *Cinnamon Wind*'s high forecastle. "The healers of the Citadel are the best in the Seven Kingdoms. For a while I thought . . . I hoped . . ."

On Braavos, it had seemed possible that Aemon might recover. Xhondo's talk of dragons had almost seemed to restore the old man to himself. That night he ate every bite Sam put before him. "No one ever looked for a girl," he said. "It was a prince that was promised, not a princess. Rhaegar, I thought . . . the smoke was from the fire that devoured Summerhall on the day of his birth, the salt from the tears shed for those who died. He shared my belief when he was young, but later he became persuaded that it was his own son who fulfilled the prophecy, for a comet had been seen above King's Landing on the night Aegon was conceived, and Rhaegar was certain the bleeding star had to be a comet. What fools we were, who thought ourselves so wise! The error crept in from the translation. Dragons are neither male nor female, Barth saw the truth of that, but now one and now the other, as changeable as flame. The language misled us all for a thousand years. *Daenerys* is the one, born amidst salt and smoke. The dragons prove it." Just talking of her seemed to make him stronger. "I must go to her. I *must*. Would that I was even ten years younger."

The old man had been so determined that he had even walked up the plank onto the *Cinnamon Wind* on his own two legs, after Sam made arrangements for their passage. He had already given his sword and scabbard to Xhondo, to repay the big mate for the feathered cloak he'd ruined saving Sam from drowning. The only things of value that still remained to them were the books they had brought from the vaults of Castle Black. Sam parted with them glumly. "They were meant for the Citadel," he said, when Xhondo asked him what was wrong. When the mate translated those words, the captain laughed. "Quhuru Mo says the grey men will be having these books still," Xhondo told him, "only they will be buying them from Quhuru Mo. The maesters give good silver for books they are not having, and sometimes red and yellow gold."

The captain wanted Aemon's chain as well, but there Sam had refused. It was a great shame for any maester to surrender his chain, he had explained. Xhondo had to go over that part three times before Quhuru Mo accepted it. By the time the dealing was done, Sam was down to his boots and blacks and smallclothes, and the broken horn Jon Snow had found on the Fist of First Men. *I had no choice,* he told himself. *We could not stay on Braavos, and short of theft or beggary, there was no other way to pay for passage.* He would have counted it cheap at thrice the price if only they had gotten Maester Aemon safe to Oldtown.

Their passage south had been a stormy one, however, and every gale took its toll on the old man's strength and spirits. At Pentos he asked to be brought up onto deck so Sam might paint a picture of the city for him with words, but that was the last time he left the captain's bed. Soon after that, his wits began to wander once again. By the time the *Cinnamon Wind* swept past the Bleeding Tower into Tyrosh harbor, Aemon no longer spoke of trying to find a ship to take him east. Instead his talk turned back to Oldtown, and the archmaesters of the Citadel.

"You must tell them, Sam," he said. "The archmaesters. You must make them understand. The men who were at the Citadel when I was have been dead for fifty years. These others never knew me. My letters . . . in Oldtown, they must have read like the ravings of an old man whose wits had fled. You must convince them, where I could not. Tell them, Sam . . . tell them how it is upon the Wall . . . the wights and the white walkers, the creeping cold . . ."

"I will," Sam promised. "I will add my voice to yours, maester. We will both tell them, the two of us together."

"No," the old man said. "It must be you. Tell them. The prophecy . . . my brother's dream . . . Lady Melisandre has misread the signs. Stannis . . . Stannis has some of the dragon blood in him, yes. His brothers did as well. Rhaelle, Egg's little girl, she was how they came by it . . . their father's mother . . . she used to call me Uncle Maester when she was a little girl. I remembered that, so I allowed myself to hope . . . perhaps I wanted to . . . we all deceive ourselves, when we want to believe. Melisandre most of all, I think. The sword is wrong, she has to know that . . . light without heat . . . an empty glamor . . . the sword is *wrong*, and the false light can only lead us deeper into darkness, Sam. *Daenerys* is our hope. Tell them that, at the Citadel. Make them listen. They must send her a maester. Daenerys must be counseled, taught, *protected*. For all these years I've lingered, waiting, watching, and now that the day has dawned I am too old. I am dying, Sam." Tears ran from his blind white eyes at that admission. "Death should hold no fear for a man as old as me, but it does. Isn't that silly? It is always dark where I am, so why should I fear the darkness? Yet I cannot help but wonder what will follow, when the last warmth leaves my body. Will I feast forever in the Father's golden hall as the septons say? Will I talk with Egg again, find Dareon whole and happy, hear my sisters singing to their children? What if the horselords have the truth of it? Will I ride through the night sky forever on a stallion made of flame? Or must I return again to this vale of sorrow? Who can say, truly? Who has been beyond the wall of death to see? Only the wights, and we know what they are like. We know."

There was little and less that Sam could say to that, but he had given the old man what little comfort he could. And Gilly came in afterward and sang a song for him, a nonsense song thing that she learned from some of Craster's other wives. It made the old man smile and helped him go to sleep.

That had been one of his last good days. After that the old man spent more time sleeping than awake, curled up beneath a pile of furs in the captain's cabin. Sometimes he would mutter in his sleep. When he woke he'd call for Sam, insisting that he had to tell him something, but oft as not he would have forgotten what he meant to say by the time that Sam arrived. Even when he did recall, his talk was all a jumble. He spoke of dreams and never named the dreamer, of a glass candle that could not be lit and eggs that would not hatch. He said the sphinx was the riddle, not the riddler, whatever that meant. He asked Sam to read for him from a book by Septon Barth, whose writings had been burned during the reign of Baelor the Blessed. Once he woke up weeping. "The dragon must have three heads," he wailed, "but I am too old and frail to be one of them. I should be with her, showing her the way, but my body has betrayed me."

As the *Cinnamon Wind* made her way through the Stepstones, Maester Aemon forgot Sam's name oft as not. Some days he took him for one of his dead brothers. "He was too frail for such a long voyage," Sam told Gilly on the forecastle, after another sip of the rum. "Jon should have seen that. Aemon was a hundred and two years old, he should never have been sent to sea. If he had stayed at Castle Black, he might have lived another ten years."

"Or else she might have burned him. The red woman." Even here, a thousand leagues from the Wall, Gilly was reluctant to say Lady Melisandre's name aloud. "She wanted king's blood for her fires. Val knew she did. Lord Snow too. That was why they made me take Dalla's babe away and leave my own behind in his place. Maester Aemon went to sleep and didn't wake up, but if he had stayed, she would have burned him."

He will still burn, Sam thought miserably, *only now I have to do it.* The Targaryens always gave their fallen to the flames. Quhuru Mo would not allow a funeral pyre aboard the *Cinnamon Wind,* so Aemon's corpse had been stuffed inside a cask of blackbelly rum to preserve it until the ship reached Oldtown.

"The night before he died, he asked if he might hold the babe," Gilly went on. "I was afraid he might drop him, but he never did. He rocked him and hummed a song for him, and Dalla's boy reached up and touched his face. The way he pulled his lip I thought he might be hurting him, but it only made the old man laugh." She stroked Sam's hand. "We could name the little one Maester, if you like. When he's old enough, not now. We could."

"*Maester* is not a name. You could call him Aemon, though."

Gilly thought about that. "Dalla brought him forth during battle, as the swords sang all around her. That should be his name. Aemon Battleborn. Aemon Steelsong."

A name even my lord father might like. A warrior's name. The boy was Mance Rayder's son and Craster's grandson, after all. He had none of Sam's craven blood. "Yes. Call him that."

"When he is two," she promised, "not before."

"Where is the boy?" Sam thought to ask. Between rum and sorrow, it had taken him that long to realize that Gilly did not have the babe with her.

"Kojja has him. I asked her to take him for a while."

"Oh." Kojja Mo was the captain's daughter, taller than Sam and slender as a spear, with skin as black and smooth as polished jet. She captained the ship's red archers too, and pulled a double-curved goldenheart bow that could send a shaft four hundred yards. When the pirates had attacked them in the Stepstones, Kojja's arrows had slain a dozen of them whilst Sam's own shafts were falling in the water. The only thing Kojja Mo loved better than her bow was bouncing Dalla's boy upon her knee and singing to him in the Summer Tongue. The wildling prince had become the darling of all the women in the crew, and Gilly seemed to trust them with him as she had never trusted any man.

"That was kind of Kojja," Sam said.

"I was afraid of her at first," said Gilly. "She was so black, and her teeth were so big and white, I was afraid she was a beastling or a monster, but she's not. She's good. I like her."

"I know you do." For most of her life the only man Gilly had known had been the terrifying Craster. The rest of her world had been female. *Men frighten her, but women don't,* Sam realized. He could understand that. Back at Horn Hill he had preferred the company of girls as well. His sisters had been kind to him, and though the other girls would sometimes taunt him, cruel words were easier to shrug off than the blows and buffets he got from the other castle boys. Even now, on the *Cinnamon Wind,* Sam felt more comfortable with Kojja Mo than with her father, though that might be because she spoke the Common Tongue and he did not.

"I like you too, Sam," whispered Gilly. "And I like this drink. It tastes like fire."

Yes, Sam thought, *a drink for dragons.* Their cups were empty, so he went over to the cask and filled them once again. The sun was low in the west, he saw, swollen to thrice its proper size. Its ruddy light made Gilly's face seem flushed and red. They drank a cup to Kojja Mo, and one to Dalla's boy, and one to Gilly's babe back on the Wall. And after that nothing would do but to drink two cups for Aemon of House Targaryen. "May the Father judge him justly," Sam said, sniffing. The sun was almost gone by the time they were done with Maester Aemon. Only a long thin line of red still glowed upon the western horizon, like a slash across the sky. Gilly said that the drink was making the ship spin round, so Sam helped her down the ladder to the women's quarters in the bow of the ship.

There was a lantern hanging just inside the cabin, and he managed to bang his head on it going in. "Ow," he said, and Gilly said, "Are you hurt? Let me see." She leaned close . . .

. . . and kissed his mouth.

Sam found himself kissing her back. *I said the words,* he thought, but her hands were tugging at his blacks, pulling at the laces of his breeches. He broke off the kiss long enough to say, "We can't," but Gilly said, "We can," and covered his mouth with her own again. The *Cinnamon Wind* was spinning all around them and he could taste the rum on Gilly's tongue and the next thing her breasts were bare and he was touching them. *I said the words,* Sam thought again, but one of her nipples found its way between his lips. It was pink and hard and when he sucked on it her milk filled his mouth, mingling with the taste of rum, and he had never tasted anything so fine and sweet and good. *If I do this I am no better than Dareon,* Sam thought, but it felt too good to stop. And suddenly his cock was out, jutting upward from his breeches like a fat pink mast. It looked so silly standing there that he might have laughed, but Gilly pushed him back onto her pallet, hiked her skirts up around her thighs, and lowered herself onto him with a little whimpery sound. That was even better than her nipples. *She's so wet,* he thought, gasping. *I never knew a woman could get so wet down there.* "I am your wife now," she whispered, sliding up and down on him. And Sam groaned and thought, *No, no, you can't be, I said the words, I said the words,* but the only word he said was, "Yes."

Afterward she went to sleep with her arms around him and her face across his chest. Sam needed sleep as well, but he was drunk on rum and mother's milk and Gilly. He knew he ought to crawl back to his own hammock in the men's cabin, but she felt so good curled up against him that somehow he could not move.

Others came in, men and women both, and he listened to them kissing and laughing and mating with one another. *Summer Islanders. That's how they mourn. They answer death with life.* Sam had read that somewhere, a long time ago. He wondered if Gilly knew, if Kojja Mo had told her what to do.

He breathed the fragrance of her hair and stared at the lantern swinging overhead. *Even the Crone herself could not lead me safely out of this.* The best thing he could do would be to slip away and jump into the sea. *If I'm drowned, no one need ever know that I shamed myself and broke my vows, and Gilly can find herself a better man, one who is not some big fat coward.*

He awoke the next morning in his own hammock in the men's cabin, with Xhondo bellowing about the wind.

"Wind is up," the mate kept shouting. *"Wake and work, Black Sam. Wind is up."* What Xhondo lacked in vocabulary he made up for in volume. Sam rolled from his hammock to his feet, and regretted it at once. His head was fit to split, one of the blisters on his palm had torn open in the night, and he felt as if he were about to retch.

Xhondo had no mercy, though, so all that Sam could do was struggle back into his blacks. He found them on the deck beneath his hammock, all bundled up in one damp heap. He sniffed at them to see how foul they were, and inhaled the smell of salt and sea and tar, wet canvas and mildew, fruit and fish and blackbelly rum, strange spices and exotic woods, and a heady bouquet of his own dried sweat. But Gilly's smell was on them too, the clean smell of her hair and the sweet smell of her milk, and that made him glad to wear them. He would have given much and more for warm dry socks, though. Some sort of fungus had begun to grow between his toes.

The chest of books had not been near enough to buy passage for four from Braavos to Oldtown. The *Cinnamon Wind* was shorthanded, however, so Quhuru Mo had agreed that he would take them, provided that they worked their way. When Sam had protested that Maester Aemon was too weak, the boy a babe in arms, and Gilly terrified of the sea, Xhondo only laughed, "Black Sam is big fat man. Black Sam will work for four."

If truth be told, Sam was so fumble-fingered that he doubted he was even doing the work of one good man, but he did try. He scrubbed decks and rubbed them smooth with stones, he hauled on anchor chains, he coiled rope and hunted rats, he sewed up torn sails, patched leaks with bubbling hot tar, boned fish and chopped fruit for the cook. Gilly tried as well. She was better in the rigging than

Sam was, though from time to time the sight of so much empty water still made her close her eyes.

Gilly, Sam thought, *what am I going to do with Gilly?*

It was a long hot sticky day, made longer by his pounding head. Sam busied himself with ropes and sails and the other tasks that Xhondo set him, and tried not to let his eyes wander to the cask of rum that held old Maester Aemon's body . . . or to Gilly. He could not face the wildling girl right now, not after what they'd done last night. When she came up on deck he went below. When she went forward he went aft. When she smiled at him he turned away, feeling wretched. *I should have jumped into the sea whilst she was still asleep,* he thought. *I have always been a craven, but I was never an oathbreaker till now.*

If Maester Aemon had not died, Sam could have asked him what to do. If Jon Snow had been aboard, or even Pyp and Grenn, he might have turned to them. Instead he had Xhondo. *Xhondo would not understand what I was saying. Or if he did, he'd just tell me to fuck the girl again.* "Fuck" had been the first word of the Common Tongue that Xhondo had learned, and he was very fond of it.

He was fortunate that the *Cinnamon Wind* was so big. Aboard the *Blackbird* Gilly could have run him down in hardly any time at all. "Swan ships," the great vessels from the Summer Isles were called in the Seven Kingdoms, for their billowing white sails and for their figureheads, most of which depicted birds. Large as they were, they rode the waves with a grace that was all their own. With a good brisk wind behind them, the *Cinnamon Wind* could outrun any galley, though she was helpless when becalmed. And she offered plenty of places for a craven to hide.

Near the end of Sam's watch, he was finally cornered. He was climbing down a ladder when Xhondo seized him by the collar. *"Black Sam come with Xhondo,"* he said, dragging him across the deck and dumping him at the feet of Kojja Mo.

Far off to the north, a haze was visible low on the horizon. Kojja pointed at it. "There is the coast of Dorne. Sand and rocks and scorpions, and no good anchorage for hundreds of leagues. You can swim there if you like, and walk to Oldtown. You will need to cross the deep desert and climb some mountains and swim the Torentine. Or else you could go to Gilly."

"You do not understand. Last night we . . ."

". . . honored your dead, and the gods who made you both. Xhondo did the same. I had the child, else I would have been with him. All you Westerosi make a shame of loving. There is no shame in loving. If your septons say there is, your seven gods must be demons. In the isles we know better. Our gods gave us legs to run with, noses to smell with, hands to touch and feel. What mad cruel god would give a man eyes and tell him he must forever keep them shut, and never look at all the beauty in the world? Only a monster god, a demon of the darkness." Kojja put her hand between Sam's legs. "The gods gave you this for a reason too, for . . . what is your Westerosi word?"

"Fucking," Xhondo offered helpfully.

"Yes, for fucking. For the giving of pleasure and the making of children. There is no shame in that."

Sam backed away from her. "I took a vow. *I will take no wife, and father no children.* I said the words."

"She knows the words you said. She is a child in some ways, but she is not blind. She knows why you wear the black, why you go to Oldtown. She knows she cannot keep you. She wants you for a little while, is all. She lost her father and her husband, her mother and her sisters, her home, her *world*. All she has is you, and the babe. So you go to her, or swim."

Sam looked despairingly at the haze that marked the distant shoreline. He could never swim so far, he knew.

He went to Gilly. "What we did . . . if I could take a wife, I would sooner have you than any princess or high-born maiden, but I can't. I am still a crow. I said the words, Gilly. I went with Jon into the woods and said the words before a heart tree."

"The trees watch over us," Gilly whispered, brushing the tears from his cheeks. "In the forest, they see all . . . but there are no trees here. Only water, Sam. Only water."

CERSEI

The day had been cold and grey and wet. It had poured all morning, and even when the rain stopped that afternoon the clouds refused to part. They never saw the sun. Such wretched weather was enough to discourage even the little queen. Instead of riding with her hens and their retinue of guardsmen and admirers, she spent all day in the Maidenvault with her hens, listening to the Blue Bard sing.

Cersei's own day was little better, till evenfall. As the grey sky began to fade to black, they told her that the *Sweet Cersei* had come in on the evening tide, and that Aurane Waters was without, begging audience.

The queen sent for him at once. As soon as he strode into her solar, she knew his tidings were good. "Your Grace," he said with a broad smile, "Dragonstone is yours."

"How splendid." She took his hands and kissed him on the cheeks. "I know Tommen will be pleased as well. This will mean that we can release Lord Redwyne's fleet, and drive the ironmen from the Shields." The news from the Reach seemed to grow more dire with every raven. The ironmen had not been content with their new rocks, it seemed. They were raiding up the Mander in strength, and had gone so far as to attack the Arbor and the smaller islands that surrounded it. The Redwynes had kept no more than a dozen warships in their home waters, and all those had been overwhelmed, taken, or sunk. And now there were reports that this madman who called himself Euron Crow's Eye was even sending longships up Whispering Sound toward Oldtown.

"Lord Paxter was taking on provisions for the voyage home when *Sweet Cersei* raised sail," Lord Waters reported. "I would imagine that by now his main fleet has put to sea."

"Let us hope they enjoy a swift voyage, and better weather than today." The queen drew Waters down into the window seat beside her. "Do we have Ser Loras to thank for this triumph?"

His smile vanished. "Some will say so, Your Grace."

"Some?" She gave him a quizzical look. "Not you?"

"I never saw a braver knight," Waters said, "but he turned what could have been a bloodless victory into a slaughter. A thousand men are dead, or near enough to make no matter. Most of them our own. And not just common men, Your Grace, but knights and young lords, the best and the bravest."

"And Ser Loras himself?"

"He will make a thousand and one. They carried him inside the castle after the battle, but his wounds are grievous.

He has lost so much blood that the maesters will not even leech him."

"Oh, how sad. Tommen will be heartbroken. He did so admire our gallant Knight of Flowers."

"The smallfolk too," her admiral said. "We'll have maidens weeping into their wine all across the realm when Loras dies."

He was not wrong, the queen knew. Three thousand smallfolk had crowded through the Mud Gate to see Ser Loras off the day he sailed, and three of every four were women. The sight had only served to fill her with contempt. She had wanted to scream at them that they were sheep, to tell them that all that they could ever hope to get from Loras Tyrell was a smile and a flower. Instead she had proclaimed him the boldest knight in the Seven Kingdoms, and smiled as Tommen presented him with a jeweled sword to carry into battle. The king had given him a hug as well, which had not been part of Cersei's plans, but it made no matter now. She could afford to be generous. Loras Tyrell was dying.

"Tell me," Cersei commanded. "I want to know all of it, from the beginning to the end."

The room had grown dark by the time that he was done. The queen lit some candles and sent Dorcas to the kitchens to bring them up some bread and cheese and a bit of boiled beef with horseradish. As they supped, she bid Aurane to tell the tale again, so she would remember all the details correctly. "I do not want our precious Margaery to hear these tidings from a stranger, after all," she said. "I will tell her myself."

"Your Grace is kind," said Waters with a smile. *A wicked smile,* the queen thought. Aurane did not resemble Prince Rhaegar as much as she had thought. *He has the hair, but so do half the whores in Lys, if the tales are true.*

Rhaegar was a man. This is a sly boy, no more. Useful in his way, though.

Margaery was in the Maidenvault, sipping wine and trying to puzzle out some new game from Volantis with her three cousins. Though the hour was late, the guards admitted Cersei at once. "Your Grace," she began, "it is best you hear the news from me. Aurane is back from Dragonstone. Your brother is a hero."

"I always knew he was." Margaery did not seem surprised. *Why should she? She expected this, from the moment Loras begged for the command.* Yet by the time Cersei had finished with her tale, tears glistened on the cheeks of the younger queen. "Redwyne had miners working to drive a tunnel underneath the castle walls, but that was too slow for the Knight of Flowers. No doubt he was thinking of your lord father's people suffering on the Shields. Lord Waters says he ordered the assault not half a day after taking command, after Lord Stannis's castellan refused his offer to settle the siege between them in single combat. Loras was the first one through the breach when the ram broke the castle gates. He rode straight into the dragon's mouth, they say, all in white and swinging his morningstar about his head, slaying left and right."

Megga Tyrell was sobbing openly by then. "How did he die?" she asked. "Who killed him?"

"No one man has that honor," said Cersei. "Ser Loras took a quarrel through the thigh and another through the shoulder, but he fought on gallantly, though the blood was streaming from him. Later he suffered a mace blow that broke some ribs. After that . . . but no, I would spare you the worst of it."

"Tell me," said Margaery. "I command it."

Command it? Cersei paused a moment, then decided she would let that pass. "The defenders fell back to an inner keep once the curtain wall was taken. Loras led the attack there as well. He was doused with boiling oil."

Lady Alla turned white as chalk, and ran from the room.

"The maesters are doing all they can, Lord Waters assures me, but I fear your brother is too badly burned." Cersei took Margaery in her arms to comfort her. "He saved the realm." When she kissed the little queen upon the cheek, she could taste the salt of her tears. "Jaime will enter all his deeds in the White Book, and the singers will sing of him for a thousand years."

Margaery wrenched free of her embrace, so violently that Cersei almost fell. "Dying is not dead," she said.

"No, but the maesters say—"

"Dying is not dead!"

"I only want to spare you—"

"I know what you want. Get out."

Now you know how I felt, the night my Joffrey died. She bowed, her face a mask of cool courtesy. "Sweet daughter. I am so sad for you. I will leave you with your grief."

Lady Merryweather did not appear that night, and Cersei found herself too restless to sleep. *If Lord Tywin could see me now, he would know he had his heir, an heir worthy of the Rock,* she thought as she lay abed with Jocelyn Swyft snoring softly into the other pillow. Margaery would soon be weeping the bitter tears she should have wept for Joffrey. Mace Tyrell might weep as well, but she had given him no cause to break with her. What had she done, after all, but honor Loras with her trust? He had requested the command on bended knee whilst half her court looked on.

When he dies I must raise a statue of him somewhere, and give him a funeral such as King's Landing has never seen. The smallfolk would like that. So would Tommen.

Mace may even thank me, poor man. As for his lady mother, if the gods are good this news will kill her.

The sunrise was the prettiest that Cersei had seen in years. Taena appeared soon thereafter, and confessed to having spent the night consoling Margaery and her ladies, drinking wine and crying and telling tales of Loras. "Margaery is still convinced he will not die," she reported, as the queen was dressed for court. "She plans to send her own maester to look after him. The cousins are praying for the Mother's mercy."

"I shall pray as well. On the morrow, come with me to Baelor's Sept, and we will light a hundred candles for our gallant Knight of Flowers." She turned to her handmaid. "Dorcas, bring my crown. The new one, if you please." It was lighter than the old, pale spun gold set with emeralds that sparkled when she turned her head.

"There are four come about the Imp this morning," Ser Osmund said, when Jocelyn admitted him.

"Four?" The queen was pleasantly surprised. A steady stream of informers had been making their way to the Red Keep, claiming knowledge of Tyrion, but four in one day was unusual.

"Aye," said Osmund. "One brought a head for you."

"I will see him first. Bring him to my solar." *This time, let there be no mistakes. Let me be avenged at long last, so Joff can rest in peace.* The septons said that the number seven was sacred to the gods. If so, perhaps this seventh head would bring her the balm her soul desired.

The man proved to be Tyroshi; short and stout and sweaty, with an unctuous smile that reminded her of Varys and a forked beard dyed green and pink. Cersei misliked him on sight, but was willing to overlook his flaws if he actually had Tyrion's head inside the chest he carried. It was cedar, inlaid with ivory in a pattern of vines and flowers, with hinges and clasps of white gold. A lovely thing, but the queen's only interest lay in what might be within. *It is big enough, at least. Tyrion had a grotesquely large head, for one so small and stunted.*

"Your Grace," the Tyroshi murmured, bowing low, "I see you are as lovely as the tales. Even beyond the narrow sea we have heard of your great beauty, and the grief that tears your gentle heart. No man can restore your brave young son to you, but it is my hope I can at least offer you some balm for your pain." He laid his hand upon his chest. "I bring you justice. I bring you the head of your *valonqar.*"

The old Valyrian word sent a chill through her, though it also gave her a tingle of hope. "The Imp is no longer my brother, if he ever was," she declared. "Nor will I say his name. It was a proud name once, before he dishonored it."

"In Tyrosh we name him Redhands, for the blood running from his fingers. A king's blood, and a father's. Some say he slew his mother too, ripping his way from her womb with savage claws."

What nonsense, Cersei thought. "'Tis true," she said. "If the Imp's head is in that chest, I shall raise you to lord-ship and grant you rich lands and keeps." Titles were cheaper than dirt, and the riverlands were full of ruined castles, standing desolate amidst untended fields and burned villages. "My court awaits. Open the box and let us see."

The Tyroshi threw open the box with a flourish, and stepped back smiling. Within, the head of a dwarf reposed upon a bed of soft blue velvet, staring up at her.

Cersei took a long look. "That is not my brother." There was a sour taste in her mouth. *I suppose it was too much to hope for, especially after Loras. The gods are never that good.* "This man has brown eyes. Tyrion had one black eye and one green."

"The eyes, just so . . . Your Grace, your brother's own eyes had . . . somewhat decayed. I took the liberty of re-placing them with glass . . . but of the wrong color, as you say."

That only annoyed her further. "Your head may have glass eyes, but I do not. There are gargoyles on Dragonstone that look more like the Imp than this crea-ture. He's *bald,* and twice my brother's age. What hap-pened to his teeth?"

The man shrank before the fury in her voice. "He had a fine set of gold teeth, Your Grace, but we . . . I regret . . ."

"Oh, not yet. But you will." *I ought to have him stran-gled. Let him gasp for breath until his face turns black, the way my sweet son did.* The words were on her lips.

"An honest mistake. One dwarf looks so much like an-other, and . . . Your Grace will observe, he has no nose . . ."

"He has no nose because you *cut it off.*"

"No!" The sweat on his brow gave the lie to his denial.

"Yes." A poisonous sweetness crept into Cersei's tone. "At least you had that much sense. The last fool tried to tell me that a hedge wizard had regrown it. Still, it seems to me that you owe this dwarf a nose. House Lannister pays its debts, and so shall you. Ser Meryn, take this fraud to Qyburn."

Ser Meryn Trant took the Tyroshi by the arm and hauled him off, still protesting. When they were gone, Cersei turned to Osmund Kettleblack. "Ser Osmund, get this thing out of my sight, and bring in the other three who claim knowledge of the Imp."

"Aye, Your Grace."

Sad to say, the three would-be informers proved no more useful than the Tyroshi. One said that the Imp was hiding in an Oldtown brothel, pleasuring men with his mouth. It made for a droll picture, but Cersei did not believe it for an instant. The second claimed to have seen the dwarf in a mummer's show in Braavos. The third insisted Tyrion had become a hermit in the riverlands, living on some haunted hill. The queen made the same response to each. "If you will be so good as to lead some of my brave knights to this dwarf, you shall be richly rewarded," she promised. "Provided that it *is* the Imp. If not . . . well, my knights have little patience for deception, nor fools who send them chasing after shadows. A man could lose his tongue." And quick as that, all three informers suddenly lost faith, and allowed that perhaps it might have been some other dwarf they saw.

Cersei had never realized there were so many dwarfs. "Is the whole world overrun with these twisted little monsters?" she complained, whilst the last of the informers was being ushered out. "How many of them can there be?"

"Fewer than there were," said Lady Merryweather. "May I have the honor of accompanying Your Grace to court?"

"If you can bear the tedium," said Cersei. "Robert was a fool about most things, but he was right in one regard. It is wearisome work to rule a kingdom."

"It saddens me to see Your Grace so careworn. I say, run off and play and leave the King's Hand to hear these tiresome petitions. We could dress as serving girls and spend the day amongst the smallfolk, to hear what they are saying of the fall of Dragonstone. I know the inn where the Blue Bard plays when he is not singing attendance on the little queen, and a certain cellar where a conjurer turns lead into gold, water into wine, and girls into boys. Perhaps he would work his spells on the two of us. Would it amuse Your Grace to be a man one night?"

If I were a man I would be Jaime, the queen thought. *If I were a man I could rule this realm in my own name in place of Tommen's.* "Only if you remained a woman," she said, knowing that was what Taena wanted to hear. "You are a wicked thing to tempt me so, but what sort of queen would I be if I put my realm in the trembling hands of Harys Swyft?"

Taena pouted. "Your Grace is too diligent."

"I am," Cersei allowed, "and by day's end I shall rue it." She slipped her arm through Lady Merryweather's. "Come."

Jalabhar Xho was the first to petition her that day, as befit his rank as a prince in exile. Splendid as he looked in his bright feathered cloak, he had only come to beg. Cersei let him make his usual plea for men and arms to help him regain Red Flower Vale, then said, "His Grace is fighting his own war, Prince Jalabhar. He has no men to spare for yours just now. Next year, perhaps." That was what Robert always told him. Next year she would tell him *never*, but not today. Dragonstone was hers.

Lord Hallyne of the Guild of Alchemists presented himself, to ask that his pyromancers be allowed to hatch any dragon's eggs that might turn up upon Dragonstone, now that the isle was safely back in royal hands. "If any such eggs remained, Stannis would have sold them to pay for his rebellion," the queen told him. She refrained from saying that the plan was mad. Ever since the last Targaryen dragon had died, all such attempts had ended in death, disaster, or disgrace.

A group of merchants appeared before her to beg the throne to intercede for them with the Iron Bank of Braavos. The Braavosi were demanding repayment of their outstanding debts, it seemed, and refusing all new loans. *We need our own bank,* Cersei decided, *the Golden*

Bank of Lannisport. Perhaps when Tommen's throne was secure, she could make that happen. For the nonce, all she could do was tell the merchants to pay the Braavosi usurers their due.

The delegation from the Faith was headed by her old friend Septon Raynard. Six of the Warrior's Sons escorted him across the city; together they were seven, a holy and propitious number. The new High Septon—or High Sparrow, as Moon Boy had dubbed him—did everything by sevens. The knights wore swordbelts striped in the seven colors of the Faith. Crystals adorned the pommels of their longswords and the crests of their greathelms. They carried kite shields of a style not common since the Conquest, displaying a device not seen in the Seven Kingdoms for centuries: a rainbow sword shining bright upon a field of darkness. Close to a hundred knights had already come forth to pledge their lives and swords to the Warrior's Sons, Qyburn claimed, and more turned up every day. *Drunk on the gods, the lot of them. Who would have thought the realm contained so many of them?*

Most had been household knights and hedge knights, but a handful were of high birth; younger sons, petty lords, old men wanting to atone for the old sins. And then there was Lancel. She had thought Qyburn must be japing when he had told her that her mooncalf cousin had forsaken castle, lands, and wife and wandered back to the city to join the Noble and Puissant Order of the Warrior's Sons, yet there he stood with the other pious fools.

Cersei liked that not at all. Nor was she pleased by the High Sparrow's endless truculence and ingratitude. "Where is the High Septon?" she demanded of Raynard. "It was him I summoned."

Septon Raynard assumed a regretful tone. "His High

Holiness sent me in his stead, and bade me tell Your Grace that the Seven have sent him forth to battle wickedness."

"How? By preaching chastity along the Street of Silk? Does he think praying over whores will turn them back to virgins?"

"Our bodies were shaped by our Father and Mother so we might join male to female and beget trueborn children," Raynard replied. "It is base and sinful for women to sell their holy parts for coin."

The pious sentiment would have been more convincing if the queen had not known that Septon Raynard had special friends in every brothel on the Street of Silk. No doubt he had decided that echoing the High Sparrow's twitterings was preferable to scrubbing floors. "Do not presume to preach at me," she told him. "The brothel keepers have been complaining, and rightly so."

"If sinners speak, why should the righteous listen?"

"These sinners feed the royal coffers," the queen said bluntly, "and their pennies help pay the wages of my gold cloaks and build galleys to defend our shores. There is trade to be considered as well. If King's Landing had no brothels, the ships would go to Duskendale or Gulltown. His High Holiness promised me peace in my streets. Whoring helps to keep that peace. Common men deprived of whores are apt to turn to rape. Henceforth let His High Holiness do his praying in the sept where it belongs."

The queen had expected to hear from Lord Gyles as well, but instead Grand Maester Pycelle appeared, greyfaced and apologetic, to tell her that Rosby was too weak to leave his bed. "Sad to say, I fear Lord Gyles must join his noble forebears soon. May the Father judge him justly."

If Rosby dies, Mace Tyrell and the little queen will try and force Garth the Gross on me again. "Lord Gyles has had that cough for *years,* and it never killed him before," she complained. "He coughed through half of Robert's reign and all of Joffrey's. If he is dying now, it can only be because someone wants him dead."

Grand Maester Pycelle blinked in disbelief. "Your Grace? Wh-who would want Lord Gyles dead?"

"His heir, perhaps." *Or the little queen.* "Some woman he once scorned." *Margaery and Mace and the Queen of Thorns, why not? Gyles is in their way.* "An old enemy. A new one. You."

The old man blanched. "Y-your Grace japes. I . . . I have purged his lordship, bled him, treated him with poultices and infusions . . . the mists give him some relief and sweetsleep helps with the violence of his coughing, but he is bringing up bits of lung with the blood now, I fear."

"Be that as it may. You will return to Lord Gyles and inform him that he does not have my leave to die."

"If it please Your Grace." Pycelle bowed stiffly.

There was more, and more, and more, each petitioner more boring than the last. And that evening, when the last of them had finally gone and she was eating a simple supper with her son, she told him, "Tommen, when you say your prayers before bed, tell the Mother and the Father that you are thankful you are still a child. Being king is hard work. I promise you, you will not like it. They peck at you like a murder of crows. Every one wants a piece of your flesh."

"Yes, Mother," said Tommen, in a sad tone. The little queen had told him of Ser Loras, she understood. Ser Osmund said the boy had wept. *He is young. By the time he is Joff's age he will not recall what Loras looked like.* "I wouldn't mind them pecking, though," her son went on to say. "I should go to court with you every day, to listen. Margaery says—"

"—a deal too much," Cersei snapped. "For half a groat I'd gladly have her tongue torn out."

"Don't you say that," Tommen shouted suddenly, his round little face turning red. "You leave her tongue alone. Don't you touch her. I'm the king, not you."

She stared at him, incredulous. "What did you say?"

"I'm the king. I get to say who has their tongues torn out, not you. I won't let you hurt Margaery. I *won't.* I forbid it."

Cersei took him by the ear and dragged him squealing to the door, where she found Ser Boros Blount standing guard. "Ser Boros, His Grace has forgotten himself. Kindly escort him to his bedchamber and bring up Pate. This time I want Tommen to whip the boy himself. He is to continue until the boy is bleeding from both cheeks. If His Grace refuses, or says one word of protest, summon Qyburn and tell him to remove Pate's tongue, so His Grace can learn the cost of insolence."

"As you command," Ser Boros huffed, glancing at the king uneasily. "Your Grace, please come with me."

As night fell over the Red Keep, Jocelyn kindled a fire in the queen's hearth whilst Dorcas lit the bedside candles. Cersei opened the window for a breath of air, and found that the clouds had rolled back in to hide the stars. "Such a dark night, Your Grace," murmured Dorcas.

Aye, she thought, *but not so dark as in the Maidenvault, or on Dragonstone where Loras Tyrell lies burned and bleeding, or down in the black cells beneath the castle.* The queen did not know why that occurred to her. She had resolved not to give Falyse another thought. *Single combat. Falyse should have known better than to marry such a fool.* The word from Stokeworth was that Lady Tanda had died of a chill in the chest, brought on by her broken hip. Lollys Lackwit had been proclaimed Lady Stokeworth, with Ser Bronn her lord. *Tanda dead and Gyles dying. It is well that we have Moon Boy, or the court would be entirely bereft of fools.* The queen smiled as she lay her head upon the pillow. *When I kissed her cheek, I could taste the salt of her tears.*

She dreamt an old dream, of three girls in brown cloaks, a wattled crone, and a tent that smelled of death.

The crone's tent was dark, with a tall peaked roof. She did not want to go in, no more than she had wanted to at ten, but the other girls were watching her, so she could not turn away. They were three in the dream, as they had been in life. Fat Jeyne Farman hung back as she always did. It was a wonder she had come this far. Melara Hetherspoon was bolder, older, and prettier, in a freckly sort of way. Wrapped in roughspun cloaks with their hoods pulled up, the three of them had stolen from their beds and crossed the tourney grounds to seek the sorceress. Melara had heard the serving girls whispering how she could curse a man or make him fall in love, summon demons and foretell the future.

In life the girls had been breathless and giddy, whispering to each other as they went, as excited as they were afraid. The dream was different. In the dream the pavilions were shadowed, and the knights and serving men they passed were made of mist. The girls wandered for a long while before they found the crone's tent. By the time they did all the torches were guttering out. Cersei watched the girls huddling, whispering to one another. *Go back,* she tried to tell them. *Turn away. There is nothing here for you.* But though she moved her mouth, no words came out.

Lord Tywin's daughter was the first through the flap, with Melara close behind her. Jeyne Farman came last, and tried to hide behind the other two, the way she always did.

The inside of the tent was full of smells. Cinnamon and

nutmeg. Pepper, red and white and black. Almond milk and onions. Cloves and lemongrass and precious saffron, and stranger spices, rarer still. The only light came from an iron brazier shaped like a basilisk's head, a dim green light that made the walls of the tent look cold and dead and rotten. Had it been that way in life as well? Cersei could not seem to remember.

The sorceress was sleeping in the dream, as once she'd slept in life. *Leave her be,* the queen wanted to cry out. *You little fools, never wake a sleeping sorceress.* Without a tongue, she could only watch as the girl threw off her cloak, kicked the witch's bed, and said, "Wake up, we want our futures told."

When Maggy the Frog opened her eyes, Jeyne Farman gave a frightened squeak and fled the tent, plunging headlong back into the night. Plump stupid timid little Jeyne, pasty-faced and fat and scared of every shadow. *She was the wise one, though.* Jeyne lived on Fair Isle still. She had married one of her lord brother's bannermen and whelped a dozen children.

The old woman's eyes were yellow, and crusted all about with something vile. In Lannisport it was said that she had been young and beautiful when her husband had brought her back from the east with a load of spices, but age and evil had left their marks on her. She was short, squat, and warty, with pebbly greenish jowls. Her teeth were gone and her dugs hung down to her knees. You could smell sickness on her if you stood too close, and when she spoke her breath was strange and strong and foul. "Begone," she told the girls, in a croaking whisper.

"We came for a foretelling," young Cersei told her.

"Begone," croaked the old woman, a second time.

"We heard that you can see into the morrow," said

Melara. "We just want to know what men we're going to marry."

"Begone," croaked Maggy, a third time.

Listen to her, the queen would have cried if she had her tongue. *You still have time to flee. Run, you little fools!*

The girl with the golden curls put her hands upon her hips. "Give us our foretelling, or I'll go to my lord father and have you whipped for insolence."

"Please," begged Melara. "Just tell us our futures, then we'll go."

"Some are here who have no futures," Maggy muttered in her terrible deep voice. She pulled her robe about her shoulders and beckoned the girls closer. "Come, if you will not go. Fools. Come, yes. I must taste your blood."

Melara paled, but not Cersei. A lioness does not fear a frog, no matter how old and ugly she might be. She should have gone, she should have listened, she should have run away. Instead she took the dagger Maggy offered her, and ran the twisted iron blade across the ball of her thumb. Then she did Melara too.

In the dim green tent, the blood seemed more black than red. Maggy's toothless mouth trembled at the sight of it. "Here," she whispered, "give it here." When Cersei offered her hand, she sucked away the blood with gums as soft as a newborn babe's. The queen could still remember how queer and cold her mouth had been.

"Three questions may you ask," the crone said, once she'd had her drink. "You will not like my answers. Ask, or begone with you."

Go, the dreaming queen thought, *hold your tongue, and flee.* But the girl did not have sense enough to be afraid.

"When will I wed the prince?" she asked.

"Never. You will wed the king."

Beneath her golden curls, the girl's face wrinkled up in

puzzlement. For years after, she took those words to mean that she would not marry Rhaegar until after his father Aerys had died. "I *will* be queen, though?" asked the younger her.

"Aye." Malice gleamed in Maggy's yellow eyes. "Queen you shall be . . . until there comes another, younger and more beautiful, to cast you down and take all that you hold dear."

Anger flashed across the child's face. "If she tries I will have my brother kill her." Even then she would not stop, willful child as she was. She still had one more question due her, one more glimpse into her life to come. "Will the king and I have children?" she asked.

"Oh, aye. Six-and-ten for him, and three for you."

That made no sense to Cersei. Her thumb was throbbing where she'd cut it, and her blood was dripping on the carpet. *How could that be?* she wanted to ask, but she was done with her questions.

The old woman was not done with her, however. "Gold shall be their crowns and gold their shrouds," she said. "And when your tears have drowned you, the *valonqar* shall wrap his hands about your pale white throat and choke the life from you."

"What is a *valonqar*? Some monster?" The golden girl did not like that foretelling. "You're a liar and a warty frog and a smelly old savage, and I don't believe a word of what you say. Come away, Melara. She is not worth hearing."

"I get three questions too," her friend insisted. And when Cersei tugged upon her arm, she wriggled free and turned back to the crone. "Will I marry Jaime?" she blurted out.

You stupid girl, the queen thought, angry even now. *Jaime does not even know you are alive.* Back then her brother lived only for swords and dogs and horses . . . and for her, his twin.

"Not Jaime, nor any other man," said Maggy. "Worms will have your maidenhead. Your death is here tonight, little one. Can you smell her breath? She is very close."

"The only breath we smell is yours," said Cersei. There was a jar of some thick potion by her elbow, sitting on a table. She snatched it up and threw it into the old woman's eyes. In life the crone had screamed at them in some queer foreign tongue, and cursed them as they fled her tent. But in the dream her face dissolved, melting away into ribbons of grey mist until all that remained were two squinting yellow eyes, the eyes of death.

The valonqar *shall wrap his hands about your throat,* the queen heard, but the voice did not belong to the old woman. The hands emerged from the mists of her dream and coiled around her neck; thick hands, and strong. Above them floated his face, leering down at her with his mismatched eyes. *No,* the queen tried to cry out, but the dwarf's fingers dug deep into her neck, choking off her protests. She kicked and screamed to no avail. Before long she was making the same sound her son had made, the terrible thin sucking sound that marked Joff's last breath on earth.

She woke gasping in the dark with her blanket wound about her neck. Cersei wrenched it off so violently that it tore, and sat up with her breasts heaving. *A dream,* she told herself, *an old dream and a tangled coverlet, that's all it was.*

Taena was spending the night with the little queen again, so it was Dorcas asleep beside her. The queen shook the girl roughly by the shoulder. "Wake up, and find Pycelle. He'll be with Lord Gyles, I expect. Fetch him here at once." Still half asleep, Dorcas stumbled from the bed and went scampering across the chamber for her clothing, her bare feet rustling on the rushes.

Ages later, Grand Maester Pycelle entered shuffling, and stood before her with bowed head, blinking his heavy-lidded eyes and struggling not to yawn. He looked as if the weight of the huge maester's chain about his wattled neck was dragging him down to the floor. Pycelle had been old as far back as Cersei could remember, but there was a time when he had also been magnificent: richly clad, dignified, exquisitely courteous. His immense white beard had given him an air of wisdom. Tyrion had shaved his beard off, though, and what had grown back was pitiful, a few patchy tufts of thin, brittle hair that did little to hide the loose pink flesh beneath his sagging chin. *This is no man,* she thought, *only the ruins of one. The black cells robbed him of whatever strength he had. That, and the Imp's razor.*

"How old are you?" Cersei asked, abruptly.

"Four-and-eighty, if it please Your Grace."

"A younger man would please me more."

His tongue flicked across his lips. "I was but two-and-forty when the Conclave called me. Kaeth was eighty when they chose him, and Ellendor was nigh on ninety. The cares of office crushed them, and both were dead within a year of being raised. Merion came next, only six-and-sixty, but he died of a chill on his way to King's Landing. Afterward King Aegon asked the Citadel to send a younger man. He was the first king I served."

And Tommen shall be the last. "I need a potion from you. Something to help me sleep."

"A cup of wine before bed will oft—"

"I *drink* wine, you witless cretin. I require something stronger. Something that will not let me dream."

"You . . . Your Grace does not wish to dream?"

"What did I just say? Have your ears grown as feeble as

your cock? Can you make me such a potion, or must I command Lord Qyburn to rectify another of your failures?"

"No. There is no need to involve that . . . to involve Qyburn. Dreamless sleep. You shall have your potion."

"Good. You may go." As he turned toward the door, though, she called him back. "One more thing. What does the Citadel teach concerning prophecy? Can our morrows be foretold?"

The old man hesitated. One wrinkled hand groped blindly at his chest, as if to stroke the beard that was not there. "Can our morrows be foretold?" he repeated slowly. "Mayhaps. There are certain spells in the old books . . . but Your Grace might ask instead, '*Should* our morrows be foretold?' And to that I should answer, 'No.' Some doors are best left closed."

"See that you close mine as you leave." She should have known that he would give her an answer as useless as he was.

The next morning she broke her fast with Tommen. The boy seemed much subdued; ministering to Pate had served its purpose, it would seem. They ate fried eggs, fried bread, bacon, and some blood oranges newly come by ship from Dorne. Her son was attended by his kittens. As she watched the cats frolic about his feet, Cersei felt a little better. *No harm will ever come to Tommen whilst I still live.* She would kill half the lords in Westeros and all the common people, if that was what it took to keep him safe. "Go with Jocelyn," she told the boy after they had eaten.

Then she sent for Qyburn. "Is Lady Falyse still alive?"

"Alive, yes. Perhaps not entirely . . . comfortable."

"I see." Cersei considered a moment. "This man Bronn . . . I cannot say I like the notion of an enemy so close. His power all derives from Lollys. If we were to produce her elder sister . . ."

"Alas," said Qyburn. "I fear that Lady Falyse is no longer capable of ruling Stokeworth. Or, indeed, of feeding herself. I have learned a great deal from her, I am pleased to say, but the lessons have not been entirely without cost. I hope I have not exceeded Your Grace's instructions."

"No." Whatever she had intended, it was too late. There was no sense dwelling on such things. *It is better if she dies*, she told herself. *She would not want to go on living without her husband. Oaf that he was, the fool seemed fond of him.* "There is another matter. Last night I had a dreadful dream."

"All men are so afflicted, from time to time."

"This dream concerned a witch woman I visited as a child."

"A woods witch? Most are harmless creatures. They know a little herb-craft and some midwifery, but elsewise . . ."

"She was more than that. Half of Lannisport used to go to her for charms and potions. She was mother to a petty lord, a wealthy merchant upjumped by my grandsire. This lord's father had found her whilst trading in the east. Some say she cast a spell on him, though more like the only charm she needed was the one between her thighs. She was not always hideous, or so they said. I don't recall the woman's name. Something long and eastern and outlandish. The smallfolk used to call her Maggy."

"Maegi?"

"Is that how you say it? The woman would suck a drop of blood from your finger, and tell you what your morrows held."

"Bloodmagic is the darkest kind of sorcery. Some say it is the most powerful as well."

Cersei did not want to hear that. "This *maegi* made certain prophecies. I laughed at them at first, but . . . she foretold the death of one of my bedmaids. At the time she made the prophecy, the girl was one-and-ten, healthy as a little horse and safe within the Rock. Yet she soon fell down a well and drowned." Melara had begged her never to speak of the things they heard that night in the *maegi's* tent. *If we never talk about it we'll soon forget, and then it will be just a bad dream we had,* Melara had said. *Bad dreams never come true.* The both of them had been so young, that had sounded almost wise.

"Do you still grieve for this friend of your childhood?" Qyburn asked. "Is that what troubles you, Your Grace?"

"Melara? No. I can hardly recall what she looked like. It is just . . . the *maegi* knew how many children I would have, and she knew of Robert's bastards. Years before he'd sired even the first of them, she knew. She promised me I should be queen, but said another queen would come . . ." *Younger and more beautiful, she said.* ". . . another queen, who would take from me all I loved."

"And you wish to forestall this prophecy?"

More than anything, she thought. "*Can* it be forestalled?"

"Oh, yes. Never doubt that."

"How?"

"I think Your Grace knows how."

She did. *I knew it all along,* she thought. *Even in the tent. "If she tries I will have my brother kill her."*

Knowing what needed to be done was one thing, though; knowing how to do it was another. Jaime could no longer be relied on. A sudden sickness would be best, but the gods were seldom so obliging. *How then? A knife, a pillow, a cup of heart's bane?* All of those posed problems. When an old man died in his sleep no one thought twice of it, but a girl of six-and-ten found dead in bed was certain to raise awkward questions. Besides, Margaery never slept alone. Even with Ser Loras dying, there were swords about her night and day.

Swords have two edges, though. The very men who guard her could be used to bring her down. The evidence would need to be so overwhelming that even Margaery's own lord father would have no choice but to consent to her execution. That would not be easy. *Her lovers are not like to confess, knowing it would mean their heads as well as hers. Unless . . .*

The next day the queen came on Osmund Kettleblack in the yard, as he was sparring with one of the Redwyne twins. Which one she could not say; she had never been able to tell the two of them apart. She watched the sword-play for a while, then called Ser Osmund aside. "Walk with me a bit," she said, "and tell me true. I want no empty boasting now, no talk of how a Kettleblack is thrice as good as any other knight. Much may ride upon your answer. Your brother Osney. How good a sword is he?"

"Good. You've seen him. He's not as strong as me nor Osfryd, but he's quick to the kill."

"If it came to it, could he defeat Ser Boros Blount?"

"Boros the Belly?" Ser Osmund chortled. "He's what, forty? Fifty? Half-drunk half the time, fat even when he's sober. If he ever had a taste for battle, he's lost it. Aye, Your Grace, if Ser Boros wants for killing, Osney could do it easy enough. Why? Has Boros done some treason?"

"No," she said. *But Osney has.*

BRIENNE

They came upon the first corpse a mile from the crossroads.

He swung beneath the limb of a dead tree whose blackened trunk still bore the scars of the lightning that had killed it. The carrion crows had been at work on his face, and wolves had feasted on his lower legs where they dangled near the ground. Only bones and rags remained below his knees . . . along with one well-chewed shoe, half-covered by mud and mold.

"What does he have in his mouth?" asked Podrick.

Brienne had to steel herself to look. His face was grey and green and ghastly, his mouth open and distended. Someone had shoved a jagged white rock between his teeth. A rock, or . . .

"Salt," said Septon Meribald.

Fifty yards farther on they spied the second body. The

scavengers had torn him down, so what remained of him was strewn on the ground beneath a frayed rope looped about the limb of an elm. Brienne might have ridden past him, unawares, if Dog had not sniffed him out and loped into the weeds for a closer smell.

"What do you have there, Dog?" Ser Hyle dismounted, strode after the dog, and came up with a halfhelm. The dead man's skull was still inside it, along with some worms and beetles. "Good steel," he pronounced, "and not too badly dinted, though the lion's lost his head. Pod, would you like a helm?"

"Not that one. It's got worms in it."

"Worms wash out, lad. You're squeamish as a girl."

Brienne scowled at him. "It is too big for him."

"He'll grow into it."

"I don't want to," said Podrick. Ser Hyle shrugged, and tossed the broken helm back into the weeds, lion crest and all. Dog barked and went to lift his leg against the tree.

After that, hardly a hundred yards went by without a corpse. They dangled under ash and alder, beech and birch, larch and elm, hoary old willows and stately chestnut trees. Each man wore a noose around his neck, and swung from a length of hempen rope, and each man's mouth was packed with salt. Some wore cloaks of grey or blue or crimson, though rain and sun had faded them so badly that it was hard to tell one color from another. Others had badges sewn on their breasts. Brienne spied axes, arrows, several salmon, a pine tree, an oak leaf, beetles, bantams, a boar's head, half a dozen tridents. *Broken men,* she realized, *dregs from a dozen armies, the leavings of the lords.*

Some of the dead men had been bald and some bearded, some young and some old, some short, some tall, some fat, some thin. Swollen in death, with faces gnawed and rotten, they all looked the same. *On the gallows tree, all men are brothers.* Brienne had read that in a book, though she could not recall which one.

It was Hyle Hunt who finally put words to what all of them had realized. "These are the men who raided Saltpans."

"May the Father judge them harshly," said Meribald, who had been a friend to the town's aged septon.

Who they were did not concern Brienne half so much as who had hanged them. The noose was the preferred method of execution for Beric Dondarrion and his band of outlaws, it was said. If so, the so-called lightning lord might well be near.

Dog barked, and Septon Meribald glanced about and frowned. "Shall we keep a brisker pace? The sun will soon be setting, and corpses make poor company by night. These were dark and dangerous men, alive. I doubt that death will have improved them."

"There we disagree," said Ser Hyle. "These are just the sort of fellows who are most improved by death." All the same, he put his heels into his horse, and they moved a little faster.

Farther on the trees began to thin, though not the corpses. The woods gave way to muddy fields, tree limbs to gibbets. Clouds of crows rose screeching from the bodies as the travelers came near, and settled again once they had passed. *These were evil men,* Brienne reminded herself, yet the sight still made her sad. She forced herself to look at every man in turn, searching for familiar faces. A few she thought she recognized from Harrenhal, but their condition made it hard to be certain. None had a hound's head helm, but few had helms of any sort. Most had been stripped of arms, armor, and boots before they were strung up.

When Podrick asked the name of the inn where they hoped to spend the night, Septon Meribald seized upon the question eagerly, perhaps to take their minds off the grisly sentinels along the roadside. "The Old Inn, some call it. There has been an inn there for many hundreds of years, though *this* inn was only raised during the reign of the first Jaehaerys, the king who built the kingsroad. Jaehaerys and his queen slept there during their journeys, it is said. For a time the inn was known as the Two Crowns in their honor, until one innkeep built a bell tower, and changed it to the Bellringer Inn. Later it passed to a crippled knight named Long Jon Heddle, who took up ironworking when he grew too old to fight. He forged a new sign for the yard, a three-headed dragon of black iron that he hung from a wooden post. The beast was so big it had to be made in a dozen pieces, joined with rope and wire. When the wind blew it would clank and clatter, so the inn became known far and wide as the Clanking Dragon."

"Is the dragon sign still there?" asked Podrick.

"No," said Septon Meribald. "When the smith's son was an old man, a bastard son of the fourth Aegon rose up in rebellion against his trueborn brother and took for his sigil a black dragon. These lands belonged to Lord Darry then, and his lordship was fiercely loyal to the king. The sight of the black iron dragon made him wroth, so he cut down the post, hacked the sign into pieces, and cast them into the river. One of the dragon's heads washed up on the Quiet Isle many years later, though by that time it was red with rust. The innkeep never hung another sign, so men forgot the dragon and took to calling the place the River Inn. In those days, the Trident flowed beneath its back door, and half its rooms were built out over the water. Guests could throw a line out their window and catch trout, it's said. There was a ferry landing here as well, so travelers could cross to Lord Harroway's Town and Whitewalls."

"We left the Trident south of here, and have been riding north and west . . . not toward the river but away from it."

"Aye, my lady," the septon said. "The river moved. Seventy years ago, it was. Or was it eighty? It was when old Masha Heddle's grandfather kept the place. It was her who told me all this history. A kindly woman, Masha, fond of sourleaf and honey cakes. When she did not have a room for me, she would let me sleep beside the hearth, and she never sent me on my way without some bread and cheese and a few stale cakes."

"Is she the innkeep now?" asked Podrick.

"No. The lions hanged her. After they moved on, I heard that one of her nephews tried opening the inn again, but the wars had made the roads too dangerous for common folk to travel, so there was little custom. He brought in whores, but even that could not save him. Some lord killed him as well, I hear."

Ser Hyle made a wry face. "I never dreamed that keeping an inn could be so deadly dangerous."

"It is being common-born that is dangerous, when the great lords play their game of thrones," said Septon Meribald. "Isn't that so, Dog?" Dog barked agreement.

"So," said Podrick, "does the inn have a name *now*?"

"The smallfolk call it the crossroads inn. Elder Brother told me that two of Masha Heddle's nieces have opened it to trade once again." He raised his staff. "If the gods are good, that smoke rising beyond the hanged men will be from its chimneys."

"They could call the place the Gallows Inn," Ser Hyle said.

By any name the inn was large, rising three stories above the muddy roads, its walls and turrets and chimneys made of fine white stone that glimmered pale and ghostly against the grey sky. Its south wing had been built upon heavy wooden pilings above a cracked and sunken expanse of weeds and dead brown grass. A thatch-roofed stable and a bell tower were attached to the north side. The whole sprawl was surrounded by a low wall of broken white stones overgrown by moss.

At least no one has burned it down. At Saltpans, they had found only death and desolation. By the time Brienne and her companions were ferried over from the Quiet Isle, the survivors had fled and the dead had been given to the ground, but the corpse of the town itself remained, ashen and unburied. The air still smelled of smoke, and the cries of the seagulls floating overhead sounded almost human, like the lamentations of lost children. Even the castle had seemed forlorn and abandoned. Grey as the ashes of the town around it, the castle consisted of a square keep girded by a curtain wall, built so as to overlook the harbor. It was closed tight as Brienne and the others led their horses off the ferry, nothing moving on its battlements but banners. It took a quarter hour of Dog barking and Septon Meribald knocking on the front gate with his quarterstaff before a woman appeared above them to demand their business.

By that time the ferry had departed and it had begun to rain. "I am a holy septon, good lady," Meribald had shouted up, "and these are honest travelers. We seek shelter from the rain, and a place by your fire for the night." The woman had been unmoved by his appeals. "The closest inn is at the crossroads, to the west," she replied. "We want no strangers here. Begone." Once she vanished, neither Meribald's prayers, Dog's barks, nor Ser Hyle's curses could bring her back. In the end they had spent the night in the woods, beneath a shelter made of woven branches.

There was life at the crossroads inn, though. Even before they reached the gate, Brienne heard the sound: a hammering, faint but steady. It had a steely ring.

"A forge," Ser Hyle said. "Either they have themselves a smith, or the old innkeep's ghost is making another iron dragon." He put his heels into his horse. "I hope they have a ghostly cook as well. A crisp roast chicken would set the world aright."

The inn's yard was a sea of brown mud that sucked at the hooves of the horses. The clang of steel was louder here, and Brienne saw the red glow of the forge down past the far end of the stables, behind an oxcart with a broken wheel. She could see horses in the stables too, and a small boy was swinging from the rusted chains of the weathered gibbet that loomed above the yard. Four girls stood on the inn's porch, watching him. The youngest was no more than two, and naked. The oldest, nine or ten, stood with her arms protectively about the little one. "Girls," Ser Hyle called to them, "run and fetch your mother."

The boy dropped from the chain and dashed off toward the stables. The four girls stood fidgeting. After a moment one said, "We have no mothers," and another added, "I had one but they killed her." The oldest of the four stepped forward, pushing the little one behind her skirts. "Who are you?" she demanded.

"Honest travelers seeking shelter. My name is Brienne, and this is Septon Meribald, who is well-known through the riverlands. The boy is my squire, Podrick Payne, the knight Ser Hyle Hunt."

The hammering stopped suddenly. The girl on the porch looked them over, wary as only a ten-year-old can be. "I'm Willow. Will you be wanting beds?"

"Beds, and ale, and hot food to fill our bellies," said Ser Hyle Hunt as he dismounted. "Are you the innkeep?"

She shook her head. "That's my sister Jeyne. She's not here. All we have to eat is horse meat. If you come for whores, there are none. My sister run them off. We have beds, though. Some featherbeds, but more are straw."

"And all have fleas, I don't doubt," said Ser Hyle.

"Do you have coin to pay? Silver?"

Ser Hyle laughed. "Silver? For a night's bed and a haunch of horse? Do you mean to rob us, child?"

"We'll have silver. Else you can sleep in the woods with the dead men." Willow glanced toward the donkey, and the casks and bundles on his back. "Is that food? Where did you get it?"

"Maidenpool," said Meribald. Dog barked.

"Do you question all your guests this way?" asked Ser Hyle.

"We don't have so many guests. Not like before the war. It's mostly sparrows on the roads these days, or worse."

"Worse?" Brienne asked.

"Thieves," said a boy's voice from the stables. "Robbers."

Brienne turned, and saw a ghost.

Renly. No hammerblow to the heart could have felled her half so hard. "My lord?" she gasped.

"Lord?" The boy pushed back a lock of black hair that had fallen across his eyes. "I'm just a smith."

He is not Renly, Brienne realized. *Renly is dead. Renly died in my arms, a man of one-and-twenty. This is a only a boy.* A boy who looked as Renly had, the first time he came to Tarth. *No, younger. His jaw is squarer, his brows bushier.* Renly had been lean and lithe, whereas this boy had the heavy shoulders and muscular right arm so often seen on smiths. He wore a long leather apron, but under it his chest was bare. A dark stubble covered his cheeks and chin, and his hair was a thick black mop that grew down past his ears. King Renly's hair had been that same coal black, but his had always been washed and brushed and combed. Sometimes he cut it short, and sometimes he let it fall loose to his shoulders, or tied it back behind his head with a golden ribbon, but it was never tangled or matted with sweat. And though his eyes had been that same deep blue, Lord Renly's eyes had always been warm and welcoming, full of laughter, whereas this boy's eyes brimmed with anger and suspicion.

Septon Meribald saw it too. "We mean no harm, lad. When Masha Heddle owned this inn she always had a honey cake for me. Sometimes she even let me have a bed, if the inn was not full."

"She's dead," the boy said. "The lions hanged her."

"Hanging seems your favorite sport in these parts," said Ser Hyle Hunt. "Would that I had some land hereabouts. I'd plant hemp, sell rope, and make my fortune."

"All these children," Brienne said to the girl Willow. "Are they your . . . sisters? Brothers? Kin and cousins?"

"No." Willow was staring at her, in a way that she knew well. "They're just . . . I don't know . . . the sparrows bring them here, sometimes. Others find their own way. If you're a woman, why are you dressed up like a man?"

Septon Meribald answered. "Lady Brienne is a warrior maid upon a quest. Just now, though, she is in need of a dry bed and a warm fire. As are we all. My old bones say it's going to rain again, and soon. Do you have rooms for us?"

"No," said the boy smith. "Yes," said the girl Willow.

They glared at one another. Then Willow stomped her foot. "They have *food,* Gendry. The little ones are hungry." She whistled, and more children appeared as if by magic; ragged boys with unshorn locks crept from under the porch, and furtive girls appeared in the windows overlooking the yard. Some clutched crossbows, wound and loaded.

"They could call it Crossbow Inn," Ser Hyle suggested.

Orphan Inn would be more apt, thought Brienne.

"Wat, you help them with those horses," said Willow. "Will, put down that rock, they've not come to hurt us. Tansy, Pate, run get some wood to feed the fire. Jon Penny, you help the septon with those bundles. I'll show them to some rooms."

In the end they took three rooms adjoining one another, each boasting a featherbed, a chamber pot, and a window. Brienne's room had a hearth as well. She paid a few pennies more for some wood. "Will I sleep in your room, or Ser Hyle's?" Podrick asked as she was opening the shutters. "This is not the Quiet Isle," she told him. "You can stay with me." Come the morrow she meant for the two of them to strike out on their own. Septon Meribald was going on to Nutten, Riverbend, and Lord Harroway's Town, but Brienne saw no sense in following him any farther. He had Dog to keep him company, and the Elder Brother had persuaded her that she would not find Sansa Stark along the Trident. "I mean to rise before the sun comes up, whilst Ser Hyle is still sleeping." Brienne had not forgiven him for Highgarden . . . and as he himself had said, Hunt had sworn no vows concerning Sansa.

"Where will we go, ser? I mean, my lady?"

Brienne had no ready answer for him. They had come to the crossroads, quite literally; the place where the kingsroad, the river road, and the high road all came together. The high road would take them east through the mountains to the Vale of Arryn, where Lady Sansa's aunt had ruled until her death. West ran the river road, which followed the course of the Red Fork to Riverrun and

Sansa's great-uncle, who was besieged but still alive. Or they could ride the kingsroad north, past the Twins and through the Neck with its bogs and marshes. If she could find a way past Moat Cailin and whoever held it now, the kingsroad would bring them all the way to Winterfell.

Or I could take the kingsroad south, Brienne thought. *I could slink back to King's Landing, confess my failure to Ser Jaime, give him back his sword, and find a ship to carry me home to Tarth, as the Elder Brother urged.* The thought was a bitter one, yet there was part of her that yearned for Evenfall and her father, and another part that wondered if Jaime would comfort her should she weep upon his shoulder. That was what men wanted, wasn't it? Soft helpless women that they needed to protect?

"Ser? My lady? I asked, where are we going?"

"Down to the common room, to supper."

The common room was crawling with children. Brienne tried to count them, but they would not stand still even for an instant, so she counted some of them twice or thrice and others not at all, until she finally gave it up. They had pushed the tables together in three long rows, and the older boys were wrestling benches from the back. *Older* here meant ten or twelve. Gendry was the closest thing to a man grown, but it was Willow shouting all the orders, as if she were a queen in her castle and the other children were no more than servants.

If she were highborn, command would come naturally to her, and deference to them. Brienne wondered whether Willow might be more than she appeared. The girl was too young and too plain to be Sansa Stark, but she was of the right age to be the younger sister, and even Lady Catelyn had said that Arya lacked her sister's beauty. *Brown hair, brown eyes, skinny . . . could it be?* Arya Stark's hair was brown, she recalled, but Brienne was not sure of the color of her eyes. *Brown and brown, was that it? Could it be that she did not die at Saltpans after all?*

Outside, the last light of day was fading. Inside, Willow had four greasy tallow candles lit and told the girls to keep the hearthfire burning high and hot. The boys helped Podrick Payne unpack the donkey and carried in the salt cod, mutton, vegetables, nuts, and wheels of cheese, whilst Septon Meribald repaired to the kitchens to take charge of the porridge. "Alas, my oranges are gone, and I doubt that I shall see another till the spring," he told one small boy. "Have you ever had an orange, lad? Squeezed one and sucked down that fine juice?" When the boy shook his head no, the septon mussed his hair. "Then I'll bring you one, come spring, if you will be a good lad and help me stir the porridge."

Ser Hyle pulled off his boots to warm his feet by the fire. When Brienne sat down next to him, he nodded at the far end of the room. "There are bloodstains on the floor over there where Dog is sniffing. They've been scrubbed, but the blood soaked deep into the wood, and there's no getting it out."

"This is the inn where Sandor Clegane killed three of his brother's men," she reminded him.

"'Tis that," Hunt agreed, "but who is to say that they were the first to die here . . . or that they'll be the last."

"Are you afraid of a few children?"

"Four would be a few. Ten would be a surfeit. This is a cacophony. Children should be wrapped in swaddling clothes and hung upon the wall until the girls grow breasts and the boys are old enough to shave."

"I feel sorry for them. All of them have lost their mothers and fathers. Some have seen them slain."

Hunt rolled his eyes. "I forgot that I was talking to a woman. Your heart is as mushy as our septon's porridge.

Can it be? Somewhere inside our swordswench is a mother just squirming to give birth. What you really want is a sweet pink babe to suckle at your teat." Ser Hyle grinned. "You need a man for that, I hear. A husband, preferably. Why not me?"

"If you still hope to win your wager—"

"What I want to win is you, Lord Selwyn's only living child. I've known men to wed lackwits and suckling babes for prizes a tenth the size of Tarth. I am not Renly Baratheon, I confess it, but I have the virtue of being still amongst the living. Some would say that is my only virtue. Marriage would serve the both of us. Lands for me, and a castle full of these for you." He waved his hand at the children. "I am capable, I assure you. I've sired at least one bastard that I know of. Have no fear, I shan't inflict her upon you. The last time I went to see her, her mother doused me with a kettle of soup."

A flush crept up her neck. "My father's only four-and-fifty. Not too old to wed again and get a son by his new wife."

"That's a risk . . . *if* your father weds again and *if* his bride proves fertile and *if* the babe's a boy. I've made worse wagers."

"And lost them. Play your game with someone else, ser."

"So speaks a maid who has never played the game with anyone. Once you do you'll take a different view. In the dark you'd be as beautiful as any other woman. Your lips were made for kissing."

"They are lips," said Brienne. "All lips are the same."

"And all lips are made for kissing," Hunt agreed pleasantly. "Leave your chamber door unbarred tonight, and I will steal into your bed and prove the truth of what I say."

"If you do, you'll be a eunuch when you leave." Brienne got up and walked away from him.

Septon Meribald asked if he might lead the children in a grace, ignoring the small girl crawling naked across the table. "Aye," said Willow, snatching up the crawler before she reached the porridge. So they bowed their heads together and thanked the Father and the Mother for their bounty . . . all but the black-haired boy from the forge, who crossed his arms against his chest and sat glowering as the others prayed. Brienne was not the only one to notice. When the prayer was done Septon Meribald looked across the table, and said, "Do you have no love for the gods, son?"

"Not for your gods." Gendry stood abruptly. "I have work to do." He stalked out without a bite of food.

"Is there some other god he loves?" asked Hyle Hunt.

"The Lord of Light," piped one scrawny boy, nigh to six.

Willow hit him with her spoon. "Ben Big Mouth. There's *food*. You should be eating it, not bothering m'lords with talk."

The children fell upon the supper like wolves upon a wounded deer, quarreling over codfish, tearing the barley bread to pieces, and getting porridge everywhere. Even the huge wheel of cheese did not long survive. Brienne contented herself with fish and bread and carrots, whilst Septon Meribald fed two morsels to Dog for every one he ate himself. Outside, a rain began to fall. Inside, the fire crackled, and the common room was filled by the sounds of chewing, and Willow smacking children with her spoon. "One day that little girl will make some man a frightful wife," Ser Hyle observed. "That poor 'prentice boy, most like."

"Someone should take him some food before it's all gone."

"You're someone."

She wrapped a wedge of cheese, a heel of bread, a dried

apple, and two chunks of flaky fried cod in a square of cloth. When Podrick got up to follow her outside, she told him to sit back down and eat. "I will not be long."

The rain was coming down heavy in the yard. Brienne covered the food with a fold of her cloak. Some of the horses whinnied at her as she made her way past the stables. *They are hungry too.*

Gendry was at his forge, bare-chested beneath his leather apron. He was beating on a sword as if he wished it were a foe, his sweat-soaked hair falling across his brow. She watched him for a moment. *He has Renly's eyes and Renly's hair, but not his build. Lord Renly was more lithe than brawny . . . not like his brother Robert, whose strength was fabled.*

It was not until he stopped to wipe his brow that Gendry saw her standing there. "What do *you* want?"

"I brought supper." She opened the cloth for him to see.

"If I wanted food, I would have eaten some."

"A smith needs to eat to keep his strength up."

"Are you my mother?"

"No." She put down the food. "Who was your mother?"

"What's that to you?"

"You were born in King's Landing." The way he spoke made her certain of it.

"Me and many more." He plunged the sword into a tub of rainwater to quench it. The hot steel hissed angrily.

"How old are you?" Brienne asked. "Is your mother still alive? And your father, who was he?"

"You ask too many questions." He set down the sword. "My mother's dead and I never knew my father."

"You're a bastard."

He took it for an insult. "I'm a *knight*. That sword will be mine own, once it's done."

What would a knight be doing working at a smithy?

"You have black hair and blue eyes, and you were born in the shadow of the Red Keep. Has no one ever remarked upon your face?"

"What's wrong with my face? It's not as ugly as yours."

"In King's Landing you must have seen King Robert."

He shrugged. "Sometimes. At tourneys, from afar. Once at Baelor's Sept. The gold cloaks shoved us aside so he could pass. Another time I was playing near the Mud Gate when he come back from a hunt. He was so drunk he almost rode me down. A big fat sot, he was, but a better king than these sons of his."

They are not his sons. Stannis told it true, that day he met with Renly. Joffrey and Tommen were never Robert's sons. This boy, though . . . "Listen to me," Brienne began. Then she heard Dog barking, loud and frantic. "Someone is coming."

"Friends," said Gendry, unconcerned.

"What sort of friends?" Brienne moved to the door of the smithy to peer out through the rain.

He shrugged. "You'll meet them soon enough."

I may not want to meet them, Brienne thought, as the first riders came splashing through the puddles into the yard. Beneath the patter of the rain and Dog's barking, she could hear the faint clink of swords and mail from beneath their ragged cloaks. She counted them as they came. *Two, four, six, seven.* Some of them were wounded, judging from the way they rode. The last man was massive and hulking, as big as two of the others. His horse was blown and bloody, staggering beneath his weight. All the riders had their hoods up against the lashing rain, save him alone. His face was broad and hairless, maggot white, his round cheeks covered with weeping sores.

Brienne sucked in her breath and drew Oathkeeper. *Too many,* she thought, with a start of fear, *they are too many.*

"Gendry," she said in a low voice, "you'll want a sword, and armor. These are not your friends. They're no one's friends."

"What are you talking about?" The boy came and stood beside her, his hammer in his hand.

Lightning cracked to the south as the riders swung down off their horses. For half a heartbeat darkness turned to day. An axe gleamed silvery blue, light shimmered off mail and plate, and beneath the dark hood of the lead rider Brienne glimpsed an iron snout and rows of steel teeth, snarling.

Gendry saw it too. "Him."

"Not him. His helm." Brienne tried to keep the fear from her voice, but her mouth was dry as dust. She had a pretty good notion who wore the Hound's helm. *The children,* she thought.

The door to the inn banged open. Willow stepped out into the rain, a crossbow in her hands. The girl was shouting at the riders, but a clap of thunder rolled across the yard, drowning out her words. As it faded, Brienne heard the man in the Hound's helm say, "Loose a quarrel at me and I'll shove that crossbow up your cunt and fuck you with it. Then I'll pop your fucking eyes out and make you eat them." The fury in the man's voice drove Willow back a step, trembling.

Seven, Brienne thought again, despairing. She had no chance against seven, she knew. *No chance, and no choice.*

She stepped out into the rain, Oathkeeper in hand. *"Leave her be.* If you want to rape someone, try me."

The oulaws turned as one. One laughed, and another said something in a tongue Brienne did not know. The huge one with the broad white face gave a malevolent *hisssssssssssssssss.* The man in the Hound's helm began to laugh. "You're even uglier than I remembered. I'd sooner rape your horse."

"Horses, that's what we want," one of the wounded men said. "Fresh horses, and some food. There are outlaws after us. Give us your horses and we'll be gone. We won't do you harm."

"Fuck that." The outlaw in the Hound's helm yanked a battle axe off his saddle. "I want to cut her bloody legs off. I'll set her on her stumps so she can watch me fuck the crossbow girl."

"With what?" taunted Brienne. "Shagwell said they cut your manhood off when they took your nose."

She meant it to provoke him, and it did. Bellowing curses, he came at her, his feet sending up splashes of black water as he charged. The others stood back to watch the show, as she had prayed they might. Brienne stayed as still as stone, waiting. The yard was dark, the mud slippery underfoot. *Better to let him come to me. If the gods are good, he'll slip and fall.*

The gods were not that good, but her sword was. *Five steps, four steps, now,* Brienne counted, and Oathkeeper swept up to meet his rush. Steel crashed against steel as her blade bit through his rags and opened a gash in his chainmail, even as his axe came crashing down at her. She twisted aside, slashing at his chest again as she retreated.

He followed, staggering and bleeding, roaring rage. *"Whore!"* he boomed. *"Freak! Bitch! I'll give you to my dog to fuck, you bloody bitch!"* His axe whirled in murderous arcs, a brutal black shadow that turned silver every time the lightning flashed. Brienne had no shield to catch the blows. All she could do was slide back away from him, darting this way and that as the axehead flew at her. Once the mud gave way under her heel and she almost fell, but somehow she recovered herself, though the axe grazed her left shoulder that time and left a blaze of pain in its wake. "You got the bitch!" one of the others called, and another said, "Let's see her dance away from that one."

Dance she did, relieved that they were watching. Better that than have them interfere. She could not fight seven, not alone, even if one or two were wounded. Old Ser Goodwin was long in his grave, yet she could hear him whispering in her ear. *Men will always underestimate you,* he said, *and their pride will make them want to vanquish you quickly, lest it be said that a woman tried them sorely. Let them spend their strength in furious attacks, whilst you conserve your own. Wait and watch, girl, wait and watch.* She waited, watching, moving sideways, then backwards, then sideways again, slashing now at his face, now at his legs, now at his arm. His blows came more slowly as his axe grew heavier. Brienne turned him so the rain was in his eyes, and stepped back two quick steps. He wrenched his axe up once more, cursing, and lurched after her, one foot sliding in the mud . . .

. . . and she leapt to meet his rush, both hands on her sword hilt. His headlong charge brought him right onto her point, and Oathkeeper punched through cloth and mail and leather and more cloth, deep into his bowels and out his back, rasping as it scraped along his spine. His axe fell from limp fingers, and the two of them slammed together, Brienne's face mashed up against the dog's head helm. She felt the cold wet metal against her cheek. Rain ran down the steel in rivers, and when the lightning flashed again she saw pain and fear and rank disbelief through the eye slits. *"Sapphires,"* she whispered at him, as she gave her blade a hard twist that made him shudder. His weight sagged heavily against her, and all at once it was a corpse that she embraced, there in the black rain. She stepped back and let him fall . . .

. . . and Biter crashed into her, shrieking.

He fell on her like an avalanche of wet wool and milk-white flesh, lifting her off her feet and slamming her down into the ground. She landed in a puddle with a splash that sent water up her nose and into her eyes. All the air was driven out of her, and her head snapped down against some half-buried stone with a *crack.* "No," was all that she had time to say before he fell on top of her, his weight driving her deeper into the mud. One of his hands was in her hair, pulling her head back. The other groped for her throat. Oathkeeper was gone, torn from her grasp. She had only her hands to fight him off, but when she slammed a fist into his face it was like punching a ball of wet white dough. He *hissed* at her.

She hit him again, again, *again,* smashing the heel of her hand into his eye, but he did not seem to feel her blows. She clawed at his wrists, but his grip just grew tighter, though blood ran from the gouges where she scratched him. He was crushing her, smothering her. She pushed at his shoulders to get him off her, but he was heavy as a horse, impossible to move. When she tried to knee him in the groin, all she did was drive her knee into his belly. Grunting, Biter tore out a handful of her hair.

My dagger. Brienne clutched at the thought, desperate. She worked her hand down between them, fingers squirming under his sour, suffocating flesh, searching until they finally found the hilt. Biter locked both his hands about her neck and began to slam her head against the ground. The lightning flashed again, this time inside her skull, yet somehow her fingers tightened, pulled the dagger from its sheath. With him on top of her, she could not raise the blade to stab, so she drew it hard across his belly. Something warm and wet gushed between her fingers. Biter *hissed* again, louder than before, and let go of her throat just long enough to smash her in the face. She heard bones crack, and the pain blinded her for an instant. When she tried to slash at him again, he wrenched the dagger from her fingers and slammed a knee down onto her forearm, breaking it. Then he seized her head again and resumed trying to tear it off her shoulders.

Brienne could hear Dog barking, and men were shouting all about her, and between the claps of thunder she heard the clash of steel on steel. *Ser Hyle,* she thought, *Ser Hyle has joined the fight,* but all that seemed far away and unimportant. Her world was no larger than the hands at her throat and the face that loomed above her. The rain ran off his hood as he leaned closer. His breath stank like cheese gone rotten.

Brienne's chest was burning, and the storm was behind her eyes, blinding her. Bones ground against each other inside of her. Biter's mouth gaped open, impossibly wide. She saw his teeth, yellow and crooked, filed into points. When they closed on the soft meat of her cheek, she hardly felt it. She could feel herself spiraling down into the dark. *I cannot die yet,* she told herself, *there is something I still need to do.*

Biter's mouth tore free, full of blood and flesh. He spat, grinned, and sank his pointed teeth into her flesh again. This time he chewed and swallowed. *He is eating me,* she realized, but she had no strength left to fight him any longer. She felt as if she were floating above herself, watching the horror as if it were happening to some other woman, to some stupid girl who thought she was a knight. *It will be finished soon,* she told herself. *Then it will not matter if he eats me.* Biter threw back his head and opened his mouth again, howling, and stuck his tongue out at her. It was sharply pointed, dripping blood, longer than any tongue should be. Sliding from his mouth, out and out and out, red and wet and glistening, it made a hideous sight, obscene. *His tongue is a foot long,* Brienne thought, just before the darkness took her. *Why, it looks almost like a sword.*

JAIME

The brooch that fastened Ser Brynden Tully's cloak was a black fish, wrought in jet and gold. His ringmail was grim and grey. Over it he wore greaves, gorget, gauntlets, pauldron, and poleyns of blackened steel, none half so dark as the look upon his face as he waited for Jaime Lannister at the end of the drawbridge, alone atop a chestnut courser caparisoned in red and blue.

He loves me not. Tully had a craggy face, deeply lined and windburnt beneath a shock of stiff grey hair, but Jaime could still see the great knight who had once enthralled a squire with tales of the Ninepenny Kings. Honor's hooves clattered against the planks of the drawbridge. Jaime had thought long and hard about whether to wear his gold armor or his white to this meeting; in the end, he'd chosen a leather jack and a crimson cloak.

He drew up a yard from Ser Brynden, and inclined his head to the older man. "Kingslayer," said Tully.

That he would make that name the first word from his mouth spoke volumes, but Jaime was resolved to keep his temper. "Blackfish," he responded. "Thank you for coming."

"I assume you have returned to fulfill the oaths you swore my niece," Ser Brynden said. "As I recall, you promised Catelyn her daughters in return for your freedom." His mouth tightened. "Yet I do not see the girls. Where are they?"

Must he make me say it? "I do not have them."

"Pity. Do you wish to resume your captivity? Your old cell is still available. We have put fresh rushes on the floor."

And a nice new pail for me to shit in, I don't doubt. "That was thoughtful of you, ser, but I fear I must decline. I prefer the comforts of my pavilion."

"Whilst Catelyn enjoys the comforts of her grave."

I had no hand in Lady Catelyn's death, he might have said, *and her daughters were gone before I reached King's Landing.* It was on his tongue to speak of Brienne and the sword he'd given her, but the Blackfish was looking at him the way that Eddard Stark had looked at him when he'd found him on the Iron Throne with the Mad King's blood upon his blade. "I came to speak of the living, not the dead. Of those who need not die, but shall . . ."

". . . unless I hand you Riverrun. Is this where you threaten to hang Edmure?" Beneath his bushy brows, Tully's eyes were stone. "My nephew is marked for death no matter what I do. So hang him and be done with it. I expect that Edmure is as weary of standing on those gallows as I am of seeing him there."

Ryman Frey is a bloody fool. His mummer's show with

Edmure and the gallows had only made the Blackfish more obdurate, that was plain. "You hold Lady Sybelle Westerling and three of her children. I'll return your nephew in exchange for them."

"As you returned Lady Catelyn's daughters?"

Jaime did not allow himself to be provoked. "An old woman and three children for your liege lord. That's a better bargain than you could have hoped for."

Ser Brynden smiled a hard smile. "You do not lack for gall, Kingslayer. Bargaining with oathbreakers is like building on quicksand, though. Cat should have known better than to trust the likes of you."

It was Tyrion she trusted in, Jaime almost said. *The Imp deceived her too.* "The promises I made to Lady Catelyn were wrung from me at swordpoint."

"And the oath you swore to Aerys?"

He felt his phantom fingers twitching. "Aerys is no part of this. Will you exchange the Westerlings for Edmure?"

"No. My king entrusted his queen to my keeping, and I swore to keep her safe. I will not hand her over to a Frey noose."

"The girl has been pardoned. No harm will come to her. You have my word on that."

"Your word of *honor*?" Ser Brynden raised an eyebrow. "Do you even know what honor is?"

A horse. "I will swear any oath that you require."

"Spare me, Kingslayer."

"I want to. Strike your banners and open your gates and I'll grant your men their lives. Those who wish to remain at Riverrun in service to Lord Emmon may do so. The rest shall be free to go where they will, though I will require them to surrender their arms and armor."

"I wonder, how far will they get, unarmed, before 'outlaws' set upon them? You dare not allow them to join Lord

Beric, we both know that. And what of me? Will I be paraded through King's Landing to die like Eddard Stark?"

"I will permit you to take the black. Ned Stark's bastard is the Lord Commander on the Wall."

The Blackfish narrowed his eyes. "Did your father arrange for that as well? Catelyn never trusted the boy, as I recall, no more than she ever trusted Theon Greyjoy. It would seem she was right about them both. No, ser, I think not. I'll die warm, if you please, with a sword in hand running red with lion blood."

"Tully blood runs just as red," Jaime reminded him. "If you will not yield the castle, I must storm it. Hundreds will die."

"Hundreds of mine. Thousands of yours."

"Your garrison will perish to a man."

"I know that song. Do you sing it to the tune of 'The Rains of Castamere'? My men would sooner die upon their feet fighting than on their knees beneath a headsman's axe."

This is not going well. "This defiance serves no purpose, ser. The war is done, and your Young Wolf is dead."

"Murdered in breach of all the sacred laws of hospitality."

"Frey's work, not mine."

"Call it what you will. It stinks of Tywin Lannister."

Jaime could not deny that. "My father is dead as well."

"May the Father judge him justly."

Now, there's an awful prospect. "I would have slain Robb Stark in the Whispering Wood, if I could have reached him. Some fools got in my way. Does it matter how the boy perished? He's no less dead, and his kingdom died when he did."

"You must be blind as well as maimed, ser. Lift your eyes, and you will see that the direwolf still flies above our walls."

"I've seen him. He looks lonely. Harrenhal has fallen. Seagard and Maidenpool. The Brackens have bent the knee, and they've got Tytos Blackwood penned up in Raventree. Piper, Vance, Mooton, all your bannermen have yielded. Only Riverrun remains. We have twenty times your numbers."

"Twenty times the men require twenty times the food. How well are you provisioned, my lord?"

"Well enough to sit here till the end of days if need be, whilst you starve inside your walls." He told the lie as boldly as he could and hoped his face did not betray him.

The Blackfish was not deceived. "The end of your days, perhaps. Our own supplies are ample, though I fear we did not leave much in the fields for visitors."

"We can bring food down from the Twins," said Jaime, "or over the hills from the west, if it comes to that."

"If you say so. Far be it from me to question the word of such an honorable knight."

The scorn in his voice made Jaime bristle. "There is a quicker way to decide the matter. A single combat. My champion against yours."

"I was wondering when you would get to that." Ser Brynden laughed. "Who will it be? Strongboar? Addam Marbrand? Black Walder Frey?" He leaned forward. "Why not you and me, ser?"

That would have been a sweet fight once, Jaime thought, *fine fodder for the singers.* "When Lady Catelyn freed me, she made me swear not to take arms again against the Starks or Tullys."

"A most convenient oath, ser."

His face darkened. "Are you calling me a coward?"

"No. I am calling you a cripple." The Blackfish nodded at Jaime's golden hand. "We both know you cannot fight with that."

"I had two hands." *Would you throw your life away for pride?* a voice inside him whispered. "Some might say a cripple and an old man are well matched. Free me from my vow to Lady Catelyn and I will meet you sword to sword. If I win, Riverrun is ours. If you slay me, we'll lift the siege."

Ser Brynden laughed again. "Much as I would welcome the chance to take that golden sword away from you and cut out your black heart, your promises are worthless. I would gain nothing from your death but the pleasure of killing you, and I will not risk my own life for that . . . as small a risk as that may be."

It was a good thing that Jaime wore no sword; elsewise he would have ripped his blade out, and if Ser Brynden did not slay him, the archers on the walls most surely would. "Are there any terms you will accept?" he demanded of the Blackfish.

"From you?" Ser Brynden shrugged. "No."

"Why did you even come to treat with me?"

"A siege is deadly dull. I wanted to see this stump of yours and hear whatever excuses you cared to offer up for your latest enormities. They were feebler than I'd hoped. You always disappoint, Kingslayer." The Blackfish wheeled his mare and trotted back toward Riverrun. The portcullis descended with a rush, its iron spikes biting deep into the muddy ground.

Jaime turned Honor's head about for the long ride back to the Lannister siege lines. He could feel the eyes on him; the Tully men upon their battlements, the Freys across the river. *If they are not blind, they'll all know he threw my offer in my teeth.* He would need to storm the castle. *Well, what's one more broken vow to the Kingslayer? Just more shit in the bucket.* Jaime resolved to be the first man on the battlements. *And with this golden hand of mine, most like the first to fall.*

Back at camp, Little Lew held his bridle whilst Peck gave him a hand down from the saddle. *Do they think I'm such a cripple that I cannot dismount by myself?* "How did you fare, my lord?" asked his cousin Ser Daven.

"No one put an arrow in my horse's rump. Elsewise, there was little to distinguish me from Ser Ryman." He grimaced. "So now he must needs turn the Red Fork redder." *Blame yourself for that, Blackfish. You left me little choice.* "Assemble a war council. Ser Addam, Strongboar, Forley Prester, those river lords of ours . . . and our friends of Frey. Ser Ryman, Lord Emmon, whoever else they care to bring."

They gathered quickly. Lord Piper and both Lords Vance came to speak for the repentant lords of the Trident, whose loyalties would shortly be put to the test. The west was represented by Ser Daven, Strongboar, Addam Marbrand, and Forley Prester. Lord Emmon Frey joined them, with his wife. Lady Genna claimed her stool with a look that dared any man there to question her presence. None did. The Freys sent Ser Walder Rivers, called "Bastard Walder," and Ser Ryman's firstborn Edwyn, a pallid, slender man with a pinched nose and lank dark hair. Under a blue lambswool cloak, Edwyn wore a jerkin of finely tooled grey calfskin with ornate scrollwork worked into the leather. "I speak for House Frey," he announced. "My father is indisposed this morning."

Ser Daven gave a snort. "Is he drunk, or just greensick from last night's wine?"

Edwyn had the hard mean mouth of a miser. "Lord Jaime," he said, "must I suffer such discourtesy?"

"Is it true?" Jaime asked him. "Is your father drunk?"

Frey pressed his lips together and eyed Ser Ilyn Payne,

who was standing beside by the tent flap in his rusted mail, his sword poking up above one bony shoulder. "He . . . my father has a bad belly, my lord. Red wine helps with his digestion."

"He must be digesting a bloody mammoth," said Ser Daven. Strongboar laughed, and Lady Genna chuckled.

"Enough," said Jaime. "We have a castle to win." When his father sat in council, he let his captains speak first. He was resolved to do the same. "How shall we proceed?"

"*Hang* Edmure Tully, for a start," urged Lord Emmon Frey. "That will teach Ser Brynden that we mean what we say. If we send Ser Edmure's head to his uncle, it may move him to yield."

"Brynden Blackfish is not moved so easily." Karyl Vance, the Lord of Wayfarer's Rest, had a melancholy look. A winestain birthmark covered half his neck and one side of his face. "His own brother could not move him to a marriage bed."

Ser Daven shook his shaggy head. "We have to storm the walls, as I've been saying all along. Siege towers, scaling ladders, a ram to break the gate, that's what's needed here."

"I will lead the assault," said Strongboar. "Give the fish a taste of steel and fire, that's what I say."

"They are *my* walls," protested Lord Emmon, "and that is my gate you would break." He drew his parchment out of his sleeve again. "King Tommen himself has granted me—"

"We've all seen your paper, nuncle," snapped Edwyn Frey. "Why don't you go wave it at the Blackfish for a change?"

"Storming the walls will be a bloody business," said Addam Marbrand. "I propose we wait for a moonless night and send a dozen picked men across the river in a boat with muffled oars. They can scale the walls with ropes and grapnels, and open the gates from the inside. I will lead them, if the council wishes."

"Folly," declared the bastard, Walder Rivers. "Ser Brynden is no man to be cozened by such tricks."

"The Blackfish is the obstacle," agreed Edwyn Frey. "His helm bears a black trout on its crest that makes him easy to pick out from afar. I propose that we move our siege towers close, fill them full of bowmen, and feign an attack upon the gates. That will bring Ser Brynden to the battlements, crest and all. Let every archer smear his shafts with night soil, and make that crest his mark. Once Ser Brynden dies, Riverrun is ours."

"Mine," piped Lord Emmon. "Riverrun is *mine*."

Lord Karyl's birthmark darkened. "Will the night soil be your own contribution, Edwyn? A mortal poison, I don't doubt."

"The Blackfish deserves a nobler death, and I'm the man to give it to him." Strongboar thumped his fist on the table. "I will challenge him to single combat. Mace or axe or longsword, makes no matter. The old man will be my meat."

"Why would he deign to accept your challenge, ser?" asked Ser Forley Prester. "What could he gain from such a duel? Will we lift the siege if he should win? I do not believe that. Nor will he. A single combat would accomplish nought."

"I have known Brynden Tully since we were squires together, in service to Lord Darry," said Norbert Vance, the blind Lord of Atranta. "If it please my lords, let me go and speak with him and try to make him understand the hopelessness of his position."

"He understands that well enough," said Lord Piper. He was a short, rotund, bowlegged man with a bush of wild red hair, the father of one of Jaime's squires; the resemblance to the boy was unmistakeable. "The man's not bloody *stupid,* Norbert. He has eyes . . . and too much sense to yield to such as these." He made a rude gesture in the direction of Edwyn Frey and Walder Rivers.

Edwyn bristled. "If my lord of Piper means to imply—"

"I don't *imply,* Frey. I say what I mean straight out, like an honest man. But what would *you* know of the ways of honest men? You're a treacherous lying weasel, like all your kin. I'd sooner drink a pint of piss than take the word of any Frey." He leaned across the table. "Where is Marq, answer me that? What have you done with my son? He was a *guest* at your bloody wedding."

"And our honored guest he shall remain," said Edwyn, "until you prove your loyalty to His Grace, King Tommen."

"Five knights and twenty men-at-arms went with Marq to the Twins," said Piper. "Are they your guests as well, Frey?"

"Some of the knights, perhaps. The others were served no more than they deserved. You'd do well to guard your traitor's tongue, Piper, unless you want your heir returned in pieces."

My father's councils never went like this, Jaime thought, as Piper came lurching to his feet. "Say that with a sword in your hand, Frey," the small man snarled. "Or do you only fight with smears of shit?"

Frey's pinched face went pale. Beside him Walder Rivers rose. "Edwyn is no man of the sword . . . but I am, Piper. If you have more remarks to make, come outside and make them."

"This is a war council, not a war," Jaime reminded them. "Sit down, the both of you." Neither man moved. *"Now!"*

Walder Rivers seated himself. Lord Piper was not so easy to cow. He muttered a curse and strode from the tent. "Shall I send men after him to drag him back, my lord?" Ser Daven asked Jaime.

"Send Ser Ilyn," urged Edwyn Frey. "We only need his head."

Karyl Vance turned to Jaime. "Lord Piper spoke from grief. Marq is his firstborn son. Those knights who accompanied him to the Twins were nephews and cousins all."

"Traitors and rebels all, you mean," said Edwyn Frey.

Jaime gave him a cold look. "The Twins took up the Young Wolf's cause as well," he reminded the Freys. "Then you betrayed him. That makes you twice as treacherous as Piper." He enjoyed seeing Edwyn's thin smile curdle up and die. *I have endured sufficient counsel for one day,* he decided. "We're done. See to your preparations, my lords. We attack at first light."

The wind was blowing from the north as the lords filed from the tent. Jaime could smell the stink of the Frey encampments beyond the Tumblestone. Across the water Edmure Tully stood forlorn atop the tall grey gallows, with a rope around his neck.

His aunt departed last, her husband at her heels. "Lord nephew," Emmon protested, "this assault on my seat . . . you must not do this." When he swallowed, the apple in his throat moved up and down. "You must *not*. I . . . I forbid it." He had been chewing sourleaf again; pinkish froth glistened on his lips. "The castle is mine, I have the parchment. Signed by the king, by little Tommen. I am the lawful lord of Riverrun, and . . ."

"Not so long as Edmure Tully lives," said Lady Genna. "He is soft of heart and soft of head, I know, but alive, the man is still a danger. What do you mean to do about that, Jaime?"

It's the Blackfish who is the danger, not Edmure. "Leave Edmure to me. Ser Lyle, Ser Ilyn. Attend me, if you would. It's time I paid a visit to those gallows."

The Tumblestone was deeper and swifter than the Red Fork, and the nearest ford was leagues upstream. The ferry had just started across with Walder Rivers and Edwyn Frey when Jaime and his men arrived at the river. As they awaited its return, Jaime told them what he wanted. Ser Ilyn spat into the river.

When the three of them stepped off the ferry on the north bank, a drunken camp follower offered to pleasure Strongboar with her mouth. "Here, pleasure my friend," Ser Lyle said, shoving her toward Ser Ilyn. Laughing, the woman moved to kiss Payne on the lips, then saw his eyes and shrank away.

The paths between the cookfires were raw brown mud, mixed with horse dung and torn up by hooves and boots alike. Everywhere Jaime saw the twin towers of House Frey displayed on shield and banners, blue on grey, along with the arms of lesser Houses sworn to the Crossing: the heron of Erenford, the pitchfork of Haigh, Lord Charlton's three sprigs of mistletoe. The arrival of the Kingslayer did not go unnoticed. An old woman selling piglets from a basket stopped to stare at him, a knight with a half-familiar face went to one knee, and two men-at-arms pissing in a ditch turned and sprayed each other. "Ser Jaime," someone called after him, but he strode on without turning. Around him he glimpsed the faces of men he'd done his best to kill in the Whispering Wood, where the Freys had fought beneath the direwolf banners of Robb Stark. His golden hand hung heavy at his side.

Ryman Frey's great rectangular pavilion was the largest in the camp; its grey canvas walls were made of sewn squares to resemble stonework, and its two peaks evoked the Twins. Far from being indisposed, Ser Ryman was enjoying some entertainment. The sound of a woman's drunken laughter drifted from within the tent, mingled with the strains of a woodharp and a singer's voice. *I will deal with you later, ser,* Jaime thought. Walder Rivers stood before his own modest tent, talking with two men-at-arms. His shield bore the arms of House Frey with the colors reversed, and a red bend sinister across the towers. When the bastard saw Jaime, he frowned. *There's a cold suspicious look if ever I saw one. That one is more dangerous than any of his trueborn brothers.*

The gallows had been raised ten feet off the ground. Two spearmen were posted at the foot of the steps. "You can't go up without Ser Ryman's leave," one told Jaime.

"This says I can." Jaime tapped his sword hilt with a finger. "The question is, will I need to step over your corpse?"

The spearmen moved aside.

Atop the gallows, the Lord of Riverrun stood staring at the trap beneath him. His feet were black and caked with mud, his legs bare. Edmure wore a soiled silken tunic striped in Tully red and blue, and a noose of hempen rope. At the sound of Jaime's footsteps, he raised his head and licked his dry, cracked lips. *"Kingslayer?"* The sight of Ser Ilyn widened his eyes. "Better a sword than a rope. Do it, Payne."

"Ser Ilyn," said Jaime. "You heard Lord Tully. Do it."

The silent knight gripped his greatsword with both hands. Long and heavy it was, sharp as common steel could be. Edmure's cracked lips moved soundlessly. As Ser Ilyn drew the blade back, he closed his eyes. The stroke had all Payne's weight behind it.

"No! Stop. NO!" Edwyn Frey came panting into view. "My father comes. Fast as he can. Jaime, you must . . ."

"*My lord* would suit me better, Frey," said Jaime. "And you would do well to omit *must* from any speech directed at me."

Ser Ryman came stomping up the gallows steps in company with a straw-haired slattern as drunk as he was. Her gown laced up the front, but someone had undone the laces to the navel, so her breasts were spilling out. They were large and heavy, with big brown nipples. On her head a circlet of hammered bronze sat askew, graven with runes and ringed with small black swords. When she saw Jaime, she laughed. "Who in seven hells is this one?"

"The Lord Commander of the Kingsguard," Jaime returned with cold courtesy. "I might ask the same of you, my lady."

"Lady? I'm no lady. I'm the queen."

"My sister will be surprised to hear that."

"Lord Ryman crowned me his very self." She gave a shake of her ample hips. "I'm the queen o' whores."

No, Jaime thought, *my sweet sister holds that title too.*

Ser Ryman found his tongue. "Shut your mouth, slut, Lord Jaime doesn't want to hear some harlot's nonsense." This Frey was a thickset man with a broad face, small eyes, and a soft fleshy set of chins. His breath stank of wine and onions.

"Making queens, Ser Ryman?" Jaime asked softly. "Stupid. As stupid as this business with Lord Edmure."

"I gave the Blackfish warning. I told him Edmure would die unless the castle yielded. I had this gallows built, to show them that Ser Ryman Frey does not make idle threats. At Seagard my son Walder did the same with Patrek Mallister and Lord Jason bent the knee, but . . . the Blackfish is a cold man. He refused us, so . . ."

". . . you hanged Lord Edmure?"

The man reddened. "My lord grandfather . . . if we

hang the man we have no *hostage,* ser. Have you considered that?"

"Only a fool makes threats he's not prepared to carry out. If I were to threaten to hit you unless you shut your mouth, and you presumed to speak, what do you think I'd do?"

"Ser, you do not unders—"

Jaime hit him. It was a backhand blow delivered with his golden hand, but the force of it sent Ser Ryman stumbling backward into the arms of his whore. "You have a fat head, Ser Ryman, and a thick neck as well. Ser Ilyn, how many strokes would it take you to cut through that neck?"

Ser Ilyn laid a single finger against his nose.

Jaime laughed. "An empty boast. I say three."

Ryman Frey went to his knees. "I have done nothing . . ."

". . . but drink and whore. I know."

"I am heir to the Crossing. You can't . . ."

"I warned you about talking." Jaime watched the man turn white. *A sot, a fool, and a craven. Lord Walder had best outlive this one, or the Freys are done.* "You are dismissed, ser."

"Dismissed?"

"You heard me. Go away."

"But . . . where should I go?"

"To hell or home, as you prefer. See that you are not in camp when the sun comes up. You may take your queen of whores, but not that crown of hers." Jaime turned from Ser Ryman to his son. "Edwyn, I am giving you your father's command. Try not to be so stupid as your sire."

"That ought not pose much difficulty, my lord."

"Send word to Lord Walder. The crown requires all his prisoners." Jaime waved his golden hand. "Ser Lyle, bring him."

Edmure Tully had collapsed facedown on the scaffold

when Ser Ilyn's blade sheared the rope in two. A foot of hemp still dangled from the noose about his neck. Strongboar grabbed the end of it and pulled him to his feet. "A fish on a leash," he said, chortling. "There's a sight I never saw before."

The Freys stepped aside to let them pass. A crowd had gathered below the scaffold, including a dozen camp followers in various states of disarray. Jaime noticed one man holding a woodharp. "You. Singer. Come with me."

The man doffed his hat. "As my lord commands."

No one said a word as they walked back to the ferry, with Ser Ryman's singer trailing after them. But as they shoved off from the riverbank and made for the south side of the Tumblestone, Edmure Tully grabbed Jaime by the arm. *"Why?"*

A Lannister pays his debts, he thought, *and you're the only coin that's left to me.* "Consider it a wedding gift."

Edmure stared at him with wary eyes. "A . . . wedding gift?"

"I am told your wife is pretty. She'd have to be, for you to bed her while your sister and your king were being murdered."

"I never knew." Edmure licked his cracked lips. "There were fiddlers outside the bedchamber . . ."

"And Lady Roslin was distracting you."

"She . . . they made her do it, Lord Walder and the rest. Roslin never wanted . . . she wept, but I thought it was . . ."

"The sight of your rampant manhood? Aye, that would make any woman weep, I'm sure."

"She is carrying my child."

No, Jaime thought, *that's your death she has growing in her belly.* Back at his pavilion, he dismissed Strongboar and Ser Ilyn, but not the singer. "I may have need of a song shortly," he told the man. "Lew, heat some bathwater for my guest. Pia, find him some clean clothing. Nothing with lions on it, if you please. Peck, wine for Lord Tully. Are you hungry, my lord?"

Edmure nodded, but his eyes were still suspicious.

Jaime settled on a stool while Tully had his bath. The filth came off in grey clouds. "Once you've eaten, my men will escort you to Riverrun. What happens after that is up to you."

"What do you mean?"

"Your uncle is an old man. Valiant, yes, but the best part of his life is done. He has no bride to grieve for him, no children to defend. A good death is all the Blackfish can hope for . . . but you have years remaining, Edmure. And *you* are the rightful lord of House Tully, not him. Your uncle serves at your pleasure. The fate of Riverrun is in your hands."

Edmure stared. "The fate of Riverrun . . ."

"Yield the castle and no one dies. Your smallfolk may go in peace or stay to serve Lord Emmon. Ser Brynden will be allowed to take the black, along with as many of the garrison as choose to join him. You as well, if the Wall appeals to you. Or you may go to Casterly Rock as my captive and enjoy all the comforts and courtesy that befits a hostage of your rank. I'll send your wife to join you, if you like. If her child is a boy, he will serve House Lannister as a page and a squire, and when he earns his knighthood we'll bestow some lands upon him. Should Roslin give you a daughter, I'll see her well dowered when she's old enough to wed. You yourself may even be granted parole, once the war is done. All you need do is yield the castle."

Edmure raised his hands from the tub and watched the water run between his fingers. "And if I will not yield?"

Must you make me say the words? Pia was standing by

the flap of the tent with her arms full of clothes. His squires were listening as well, and the singer. *Let them hear,* Jaime thought. *Let the world hear. It makes no matter.* He forced himself to smile, "You've seen our numbers, Edmure. You've seen the ladders, the towers, the trebuchets, the rams. If I speak the command, my coz will bridge your moat and break your gate. Hundreds will die, most of them your own. Your former bannermen will make up the first wave of attackers, so you'll start your day by killing the fathers and brothers of men who died for you at the Twins. The second wave will be Freys, I have no lack of those. My westermen will follow when your archers are short of arrows and your knights so weary they can hardly lift their blades. When the castle falls, all those inside will be put to the sword. Your herds will be butchered, your godswood will be felled, your keeps and towers will burn. I'll pull your walls down, and divert the Tumblestone over the ruins. By the time I'm done no man will ever know that a castle once stood here." Jaime got to his feet. "Your wife may whelp before that. You'll want your child, I expect. I'll send him to you when he's born. With a trebuchet."

Silence followed his speech. Edmure sat in his bath. Pia clutched the clothing to her breasts. The singer tightened a string on his harp. Little Lew hollowed out a loaf of stale bread to make a trencher, pretending that he had not heard. *With a trebuchet,* Jaime thought. If his aunt had been there, would she still say Tyrion was Tywin's son?

Edmure Tully finally found his voice. "I could climb out of this tub and kill you where you stand, Kingslayer."

"You could try." Jaime waited. When Edmure made no move to rise, he said, "I'll leave you to enjoy your food. Singer, play for our guest whilst he eats. You know the song, I trust."

"The one about the rain? Aye, my lord. I know it."

Edmure seemed to see the man for the first time. "No. Not him. Get him away from me."

"Why, it's just a song," said Jaime. "He cannot have *that* bad a voice."

CERSEI

Grand Maester Pycelle had been old for as long as she had known him, but he seemed to have aged another hundred years in the past three nights. It took him an eternity to bend his creaky knee before her, and once he had he could not rise again until Ser Osmund jerked him to his feet.

Cersei studied him with displeasure. "Lord Qyburn informs me that Lord Gyles has coughed his last."

"Yes, Your Grace. I did my best to ease his passing."

"Did you?" The queen turned to Lady Merryweather. "I *did* say I wanted Rosby alive, did I not?"

"You did, Your Grace."

"Ser Osmund, what is your recollection of the conversation?"

"You commanded Grand Maester Pycelle to save the man, Your Grace. We all heard."

Pycelle's mouth opened and closed. "Your Grace must know, I did all that could be done for the poor man."

"As you did for Joffrey? And his father, my own beloved husband? Robert was as strong as any man in the Seven Kingdoms, yet you lost him to a boar. Oh, and let us not forget Jon Arryn. No doubt you would have killed Ned Stark as well, if I had let you keep him longer. Tell me, maester, was it at the Citadel that you learned to wring your hands and make excuses?"

Her voice made the old man flinch. "No man could have done more, Your Grace. I . . . I have always given leal service."

"When you counseled King Aerys to open his gates as my father's host approached, was that your notion of leal service?"

"That . . . I misjudged the . . ."

"Was that good counsel?"

"Your Grace must surely know . . ."

"What I *know* is that when my son was poisoned you proved to be of less use than Moon Boy. What I *know* is that the crown has desperate need of gold, and our lord treasurer is dead."

The old fool seized upon that. "I . . . I shall draw up a list of men suitable to take Lord Gyles's place upon the council."

"A list." Cersei was amused by his presumption. "I can well imagine the sort of list you would provide me. Greybeards and grasping fools and Garth the Gross." Her lips tightened. "You have been much in Lady Margaery's company of late."

"Yes. Yes, I . . . Queen Margaery has been most distraught about Ser Loras. I provide Her Grace with sleeping draughts and . . . other sorts of potions."

"No doubt. Tell me, was it our little queen who commanded you to kill Lord Gyles?"

"K-kill?" Grand Maester Pycelle's eyes grew as big as boiled eggs. "Your Grace cannot believe . . . it was his cough, by all the gods, I . . . Her Grace would not . . . she bore Lord Gyles no ill will, why would Queen Margaery want him . . ."

". . . dead? Why, to plant another rose on Tommen's council. Are you blind or bought? Rosby stood in her way, so she put him in his grave. With your connivance."

"Your Grace, I swear to you, Lord Gyles perished from his cough." His mouth was quivering. "My loyalty has always been to the crown, to the realm . . . t-to House Lannister."

In that order? Pycelle's fear was palpable. *He is ripe enough. Time to squeeze the fruit and taste the juice.* "If you are as leal as you claim, why are you lying to me? Do not trouble to deny it. You began to dance attendance on Maid Margaery *before* Ser Loras went to Dragonstone, so spare me further fables about how you want only to console our good-daughter in her grief. What brings you to the Maidenvault so often? Not Margaery's vapid conversation, surely? Are you courting that pox-faced septa of hers? Diddling little Lady Bulwer? Do you play the spy for her, informing on me to serve her plots?"

"I . . . I obey. A maester takes an oath of service . . ."

"A grand maester swears to serve the *realm*."

"Your Grace, she . . . she is the queen . . ."

"*I* am the queen."

"I meant . . . she is the king's wife, and . . ."

"I know who she is. What I want to know is why she has need of *you*. Is my good-daughter unwell?"

"Unwell?" The old man plucked at the thing he called a beard, that patched growth of thin white hair sprouting from the loose pink wattles under his chin. "N-not unwell, Your Grace, not as such. My oaths forbid me to divulge . . ."

"Your oaths will be of small comfort in the black cells," she warned him. "I'll hear the truth, or you'll wear chains."

Pycelle collapsed to his knees. "I beg you . . . I was your lord father's man, and a friend to you in the matter of Lord Arryn. I could not survive the dungeons, not again . . ."

"Why does Margaery send for you?"

"She desires . . . she . . . she . . ."

"Say it!"

He cringed. "Moon tea," he whispered. "Moon tea, for . . ."

"I know what moon tea is for." *There it is.* "Very well. Get off those saggy knees and try to remember what it was to be a man." Pycelle struggled to rise, but took so long about it that she had to tell Osmund Kettleblack to give him another yank. "As to Lord Gyles, no doubt our Father Above will judge him justly. He left no children?"

"No children of his body, but there is a ward . . ."

". . . not of his blood." Cersei dismissed that annoyance with a flick of her hand. "Gyles knew of our dire need for gold. No doubt he told you of his wish to leave all his lands and wealth to Tommen." Rosby's gold would help refresh their coffers, and Rosby's lands and castle could be bestowed upon one of her own as a reward for leal service. *Lord Waters, perhaps.* Aurane had been hinting at his need for a seat; his lordship was only an empty honor without one. He had his eye on Dragonstone, Cersei knew, but there he aimed too high. Rosby would be more suitable to his birth and station.

"Lord Gyles loved His Grace with all his heart," Pycelle was saying, "but . . . his ward . . ."

". . . will doubtless understand, once he hears you speak of Lord Gyles's dying wish. Go, and see it done."

"If it please Your Grace." Grand Maester Pycelle almost tripped over his own robes in his haste to leave.

Lady Merryweather closed the door behind him. "Moon tea," she said, as she turned back to the queen. "How foolish of her. Why would she do such a thing, take such a risk?"

"The little queen has appetites that Tommen is as yet too young to satisfy." That was always a danger, when a grown woman was married to a child. *Even more so with a widow. She may claim that Renly never touched her, but I will not believe it.* Women only drank moon tea for one reason; maidens had no need for it at all. "My son has been betrayed. Margaery has a lover. That is high treason, punishable by death." She could only hope that Mace Tyrell's prune-faced harridan of a mother lived long enough to see the trial. By insisting that Tommen and Margaery be wed at once, Lady Olenna had condemned her precious rose to a headsman's sword. "Jaime made off with Ser Ilyn Payne. I suppose I shall need to find a new King's Justice to snick her head off."

"I'll do it," offered Osmund Kettleblack, with an easy grin. "Margaery's got a pretty little neck. A good sharp sword will go right through it."

"It would," said Taena, "but there is a Tyrell army at Storm's End and another at Maidenpool. They have sharp swords as well."

I am awash in roses. It was vexing. She still had need of Mace Tyrell, if not his daughter. *At least until such time as Stannis is defeated. Then I shan't need any of them.* But how could she rid herself of the daughter without losing the father? "Treason is treason," she said, "but we must have proof, something more substantial than moon tea. If she is *proved* to be untrue, even her own lord father must condemn her, or her shame becomes his own."

Kettleblack chewed on one end of his mustache. "We need to catch them during the deed."

"How? Qyburn has eyes on her day and night. Her serving men take my coin, but bring us only trifles. Yet no one has seen this lover. The ears outside her door hear singing, laughter, gossip, nothing of any use."

"Margaery is too shrewd to be caught so easily," said Lady Merryweather. "Her women are her castle walls. They sleep with her, dress her, pray with her, read with her, sew with her. When she is not hawking or riding she is playing come-into-my-castle with little Alysanne Bulwer. Whenever men are about, her septa will be with her, or her cousins."

"She must rid herself of her hens *sometime,*" the queen insisted. A thought struck her. "Unless her ladies are part of it as well . . . not all of them, perhaps, but some."

"The cousins?" Even Taena sounded doubtful. "All three are younger than the little queen, and more innocent."

"Wantons clad in maiden's white. That only makes their sins more shocking. Their names will live in shame." Suddenly the queen could almost taste it. "Taena, your lord husband is my justiciar. The two of you must sup with me, this very night." She wanted this done quickly, before Margaery took it in her little head to return to Highgarden, or sail to Dragonstone to be with her wounded brother at death's door. "I shall command the cooks to roast a boar for us. And of course we must have some music, to help with our digestion."

Taena was very quick. "Music. Just so."

"Go and tell your lord husband and make arrangements for the singer," Cersei urged. "Ser Osmund, you may remain. We have much and more to discuss. I shall have need of Qyburn too."

Sad to say, the kitchens proved to have no wild boar on hand, and there was not time enough to send out hunters. Instead, the cooks butchered one of the castle sows, and served them ham studded with cloves and basted with honey and dried cherries. It was not what Cersei wanted, but she made do. Afterward they had baked apples with a sharp white cheese. Lady Taena savored every bite. Not so Orton Merryweather, whose round face remained blotched and pale from broth to cheese. He drank heavily and kept stealing glances at the singer.

"A great pity about Lord Gyles," Cersei said at last. "I daresay none of us will miss his coughing, though."

"No. No, I'd think not."

"We shall have need of a new lord treasurer. If the Vale were not so unsettled, I would bring back Petyr Baelish, but . . . I am minded to try Ser Harys in the office. He can do no worse than Gyles, and at least he does not cough."

"Ser Harys is the King's Hand," said Taena.

Ser Harys is a hostage, and feeble even at that. "It is time that Tommen had a more forceful Hand."

Lord Orton lifted his gaze from his wine cup. "Forceful. To be sure." He hesitated. "Who . . . ?"

"You, my lord. It is in your blood. Your grandsire took my own father's place as Hand to Aerys." Replacing Tywin Lannister with Owen Merryweather had proved to be akin to replacing a destrier with a donkey, to be sure, but Owen had been an old done man when Aerys raised him, amiable if ineffectual. His grandson was younger, and . . . *Well, he has a strong wife.* It was a pity Taena could not serve as Hand. She was thrice the man her husband was, and far more amusing. She was also Myrish-born and female, however, so Orton must needs suffice. "I have no doubt that you are more able than Ser Harys." *The contents of my chamber pot are more able than Ser Harys.* "Will you consent to serve?"

"I . . . yes, of course. Your Grace does me great honor."

A greater one than you deserve. "You have served me ably as justiciar, my lord. And will continue to do so through these . . . trying times ahead." When she saw that Merryweather had grasped her meaning, the queen turned to smile at the singer. "And you must be rewarded as well, for all the sweet songs you have played for us whilst we ate. The gods have given you a gift."

The singer bowed. "Your Grace is kind to say so."

"Not kind," said Cersei, "merely truthful. Taena tells me that you are called the Blue Bard."

"I am, Your Grace." The singer's boots were supple blue calfskin, his breeches fine blue wool. The tunic he wore was pale blue silk slashed with shiny blue satin. He had even gone so far as to dye his hair blue, in the Tyroshi fashion. Long and curly, it fell to his shoulders and smelled as if it had been washed in rosewater. *From blue roses, no doubt. At least his teeth are white.* They were good teeth, not the least bit crooked.

"You have no other name?"

A hint of pink suffused his cheeks. "As a boy, I was called Wat. A fine name for a plowboy, less fitting for a singer."

The Blue Bard's eyes were the same color as Robert's. For that alone, she hated him. "It is easy to see why you are Lady Margaery's favorite."

"Her Grace is kind. She says I give her pleasure."

"Oh, I'm certain of it. Might I see your lute?"

"If it please Your Grace." Beneath the courtesy, there was a faint hint of unease, but he handed her the lute all the same. One does not refuse the queen's request.

Cersei plucked a string and smiled at the sound. "Sweet and sad as love. Tell me, Wat . . . the first time you took Margaery to bed, was that before she wed my son, or after?"

For a moment he did not seem to understand. When he did, his eyes grew large. "Your Grace has been misinformed. I swear to you, I never—"

"Liar!" Cersei smashed the lute across the singer's face so hard the painted wood exploded into shards and splinters. "Lord Orton, summon my guards and take this creature to the dungeons."

Orton Merryweather's face was damp with fear. "This . . . oh, infamy . . . he dared seduce *the queen*?"

"I fear it was the other way around, but he is a traitor all the same. Let him sing for Lord Qyburn."

The Blue Bard went white. "No." Blood dripped from his lip where the lute had torn it. "I never . . ." When Merryweather seized him by the arm, he screamed, *"Mother have mercy, no."*

"I am not your mother," Cersei told him.

Even in the black cells, all they got from him were denials, prayers, and pleas for mercy. Before long, blood was streaming down his chin from all his broken teeth, and he wet his dark blue breeches three times over, yet still the man persisted in his lies. "Is it possible we have the wrong singer?" Cersei asked.

"All things are possible, Your Grace. Have no fear. The man will confess before the night is done." Down here in the dungeons, Qyburn wore roughspun wool and a blacksmith's leather apron. To the Blue Bard he said, "I am sorry if the guards were rough with you. Their courtesies are sadly lacking." His voice was kind, solicitous. "All we want from you is the truth."

"I've told you the truth," the singer sobbed. Iron shackles held him hard against the cold stone wall.

"We know better." Qyburn had a razor in his hand, its edge gleaming faintly in the torchlight. He cut away the Blue Bard's clothing, until the man was naked but for his high blue boots. The hair between his legs was brown, Cersei was amused to see. "Tell us how you pleasured the little queen," she commanded.

"I never . . . I sang, was all, I sang and played. Her ladies will tell you. They were always with us. Her cousins."

"How many of them did you have carnal knowledge of?"

"None of them. I'm just a singer. Please."

Qyburn said, "Your Grace, mayhaps this poor man only played for Margaery whilst she entertained other lovers."

"No. *Please.* She never . . . I *sang,* I only *sang . . .*"

Lord Qyburn ran a hand up the Blue Bard's chest. "Does she take your nipples in her mouth during your love play?" He took one between his thumb and forefinger, and twisted. "Some men enjoy that. Their nipples are as sensitive as a woman's." The razor flashed, the singer shrieked. On his chest a wet red eye wept blood. Cersei felt ill. Part of her wanted to close her eyes, to turn away, to make it stop. But she was the queen and this was treason. *Lord Tywin would not have turned away.*

In the end the Blue Bard told them his whole life, back to his first name day. His father had been a chandler and Wat was raised to that trade, but as a boy he found he had more skill at making lutes than barrels. When he was twelve he ran off to join a troupe of musicians he had heard performing at a fair. He had wandered half the Reach before coming to King's Landing in hopes of finding favor at court.

"Favor?" Qyburn chuckled. "Is that what women call it

now? I fear you found too much of it, my friend . . . and from the wrong queen. The true one stands before you."

Yes. Cersei blamed Margaery Tyrell for this. If not for her, Wat might have lived a long and fruitful life, singing his little songs and bedding pig girls and crofter's daughters. *Her scheming forced this on me. She has soiled me with her treachery.*

By dawn the singer's high blue boots were full of blood, and he had told them how Margaery would fondle herself as she watched her cousins pleasuring him with their mouths. At other times he would sing for her whilst she sated her lusts with other lovers. "Who were they?" the queen demanded, and the wretched Wat named Ser Tallad the Tall, Lambert Turnberry, Jalabhar Xho, the Redwyne twins, Osney Kettleblack, Hugh Clifton, and the Knight of Flowers.

That displeased her. She dare not besmirch the name of the hero of Dragonstone. Besides, no one who knew Ser Loras would ever believe it. The Redwynes could not be a part of it either. Without the Arbor and its fleet, the realm could never hope to rid itself of this Euron Crow's Eye and his accursed ironmen. "All you are doing is spitting up the names of men you saw about her chambers. We want the *truth*!"

"The truth." Wat looked at her with the one blue eye that Qyburn had left him. Blood bubbled through the holes where his front teeth had been. "I might have . . . misremembered."

"Horas and Hobber had no part of this, did they?"

"No," he admitted. "Not them."

"As for Ser Loras, I am certain Margaery took pains to hide what she was doing from her brother."

"She did. I remember now. Once I had to hide under the

bed when Ser Loras came to see her. *He must never know,* she said."

"I prefer this song to the other." Leave the great lords out of it, that was for the best. The others, though . . . Ser Tallad had been a hedge knight, Jalabhar Xho was an exile and a beggar, Clifton was the only one of the little queen's guardsmen. *And Osney is the plum that makes the pudding.* "I know you feel better for having told the truth. You will want to remember that when Margaery comes to trial. If you were to start lying again . . ."

"I won't. I'll tell it true. And after . . ."

". . . you will be allowed to take the black. You have my word on that." Cersei turned to Qyburn. "See that his wounds are cleaned and dressed, and give him milk of the poppy for the pain."

"Your Grace is good." Qyburn dropped the bloody razor into a pail of vinegar. "Margaery may wonder where her bard has gone."

"Singers come and go, they are infamous for it."

The climb up the dark stone steps from the black cells left Cersei feeling breathless. *I must rest.* Getting to the truth was wearisome work, and she dreaded what must follow. *I must be strong. What I must do I do for Tommen and the realm.* It was a pity that Maggy the Frog was dead. *Piss on your prophecy, old woman. The little queen may be younger than I, but she has never been more beautiful, and soon she will be dead.*

Lady Merryweather was waiting in her bedchamber. It was the black of night, closer to dawn than to dusk. Jocelyn and Dorcas were both asleep, but not Taena. "Was it terrible?" she asked.

"You cannot know. I need to sleep, but fear to dream."

Taena stroked her hair. "It was all for Tommen."

"It was. I know it was." Cersei shuddered. "My throat is raw. Be a sweet and pour me some wine."

"If it please you. That is all that I desire."

Liar. She knew what Taena desired. So be it. If the woman was besotted with her, that would help ensure that she and her husband remained loyal. In a world so full of treachery, that was worth a few kisses. *She is no worse than most men. At least there is no danger of her ever getting me with child.*

The wine helped, but not enough. "I feel soiled," the queen complained as she stood beside her window, cup in hand.

"A bath will set you right, my sweet." Lady Merryweather woke Dorcas and Jocelyn and sent them for hot water. As the tub was filled, she helped the queen disrobe, undoing her laces with deft fingers and easing the gown off her shoulders. Then she slipped out of her own dress and let it puddle on the floor.

The two of them shared the bath together, with Cersei lying back in Taena's arms. "Tommen must be spared the worst of this," she told the Myrish woman. "Margaery still takes him to the sept every day, so they can ask the gods to heal her brother." Ser Loras still clung to life, annoyingly. "He is fond of her cousins as well. It will go hard on him, to lose them all."

"All three may not be guilty," suggested Lady Merryweather. "Why, it might well be that one of them took no part. If she was shamed and sickened by the things she saw . . ."

". . . she might be persuaded to bear witness against the others. Yes, very good, but which one is the innocent?"

"Alla."

"The shy one?"

"So she seems, but there is more of *sly* than *shy* in her. Leave her to me, my sweet."

"Gladly." Alone, the Blue Bard's confession would never suffice. Singers lied for their living, after all. Alla Tyrell would be of great help, if Taena could deliver her. "Ser Osney shall confess as well. The others must be made to understand that only through confession can they earn the king's forgiveness, and the Wall." Jalabhar Xho would find the truth attractive. About the rest she was less certain, but Qyburn was persuasive . . .

Dawn was breaking over King's Landing when they climbed from the tub. The queen's skin was white and wrinkled from her long immersion. "Stay with me," she told Taena. "I do not want to sleep alone." She even said a prayer before she crawled beneath her coverlet, beseeching the Mother for sweet dreams.

It proved a waste of breath; as ever, the gods were deaf. Cersei dreamt that she was down in the black cells once again, only this time it was her chained to the wall in place of the singer. She was naked, and blood dripped from the tips of her breasts where the Imp had torn off her nipples with his teeth. "Please," she begged, "please, not my children, do not harm my children." Tyrion only leered at her. He was naked too, covered with coarse hair that made him look more like a monkey than a man. "You shall see them crowned," he said, "and you shall see them die." Then he took her bleeding breast into his mouth and began to suck, and pain sawed through her like a hot knife.

She woke shuddering in Taena's arms. "A bad dream," she said weakly. "Did I scream? I'm sorry."

"Dreams turn to dust in light of day. Was it the dwarf again? Why does he frighten you so, this silly little man?"

"He is going to kill me. It was foreseen when I was ten. I wanted to know who I would marry, but she said . . ."

"She?"

"The *maegi*." The words came tumbling out of her. She could still hear Melara Hetherspoon insisting that if they never spoke about the prophecies, they would not come true. *She was not so silent in the well, though. She screamed and shouted.* "Tyrion is the *valonqar*," she said. "Do you use that word in Myr? It's High Valyrian, it means *little brother*." She had asked Septa Saranella about the word, after Melara drowned.

Taena took her hand and stroked it. "This was a hateful woman, old and sick and ugly. You were young and beautiful, full of life and pride. She lived in Lannisport, you said, so she would have known of the dwarf and how he killed your lady mother. This creature dared not strike you, because of who you were, so she sought to wound you with her viper's tongue."

Could it be? Cersei wanted to believe it. "Melara died, though, just as she foretold. I never wed Prince Rhaegar. And Joffrey . . . the dwarf killed my son before my eyes."

"One son," said Lady Merryweather, "but you have another, sweet and strong, and no harm will ever come to *him*."

"Never, whilst I live." Saying it helped her believe that it was so. *Dreams turn to dust in light of day, yes.* Outside the morning sun was shining through a haze of cloud. Cersei slipped out from under the blankets. "I will break my fast with the king this morning. I want to see my son." *All I do, I do for him.*

Tommen helped restore her to herself. He had never been more precious to her than he was that morning, chattering about his kittens as he dribbled honey onto a chunk of hot black bread fresh from the ovens. "Ser Pounce caught a mouse," he told her, "but Lady Whiskers stole it from him."

I was never so sweet and innocent, Cersei thought. *How can he ever hope to rule in this cruel realm?* The mother in her wanted only to protect him; the queen in her knew he must grow harder, or the Iron Throne was certain to devour him. "Ser Pounce must learn to defend his rights," she told him. "In this world the weak are always the victims of the strong."

The king considered that, licking honey off his fingers. "When Ser Loras comes back I'm going to learn to fight with lance and sword and morningstar, the same way he does."

"You will learn to fight," the queen promised, "but not from Ser Loras. He will not be coming back, Tommen."

"Margaery says he will. We pray for him. We ask for the Mother's mercy, and for the Warrior to give him strength. Elinor says that this is Ser Loras's hardest battle."

She smoothed his hair back, the soft golden curls that reminded her so much of Joff. "Will you be spending the afternoon with your wife and her cousins?"

"Not today. She has to fast and purify herself, she said."

Fast and purify . . . oh, for Maiden's Day. It had been years since Cersei had been required to observe that particular holy day. *Thrice wed, yet she still would have us believe she is a maid.* Demure in white, the little queen would lead her hens to Baelor's Sept to light tall white candles at the Maiden's feet and hang parchment garlands about her holy neck. *A few of her hens, at least.* On Maiden's Day widows, mothers, and whores alike were barred from the septs, along with men, lest they profane the sacred songs of innocence. Only virgin maids could . . .

"Mother? Did I say something wrong?"

Cersei kissed her son's brow. "You said something very

wise, sweetling. Now run along and play with your kittens."

Afterward she summoned Ser Osney Kettleblack to her solar. He came in sweaty from the yard and swaggering, and as he took a knee he undressed her with his eyes, the way he always did.

"Rise, ser, and sit here next to me. You did me a valiant service once, but now I have a harder task for you."

"Aye, and I have something hard for you."

"That must wait." She traced his scars lightly with the tips of her fingers. "Do you recall the whore who gave these to you? I'll give her to you when you come back from the Wall. Would you like that?"

"It's you I want."

That was the right answer. "First you must confess your treason. A man's sins can poison his soul if left to fester. I know it must be hard for you to live with what you've done. It is past time that you rid yourself of your shame."

"Shame?" Osney sounded baffled. "I told Osmund, Margaery just teases. She never lets me do any more than . . ."

"It is chivalrous of you to protect her," Cersei broke in, "but you are too good a knight to go on living with your crime. No, you must take yourself to the Great Sept of Baelor this very night and speak with the High Septon. When a man's sins are so black, only His High Holiness himself can save him from hell's torments. Tell him how you bedded Margaery and her cousins."

Osney blinked. "What, the cousins too?"

"Megga and Elinor," she decided, "never Alla." That little detail would make the whole story more plausible. "Alla would sit weeping, and plead with the others to stop their sinning."

"Just Megga and Elinor? Or Margaery too?"

"Margaery, most certainly. She was the one behind it all."

She told him all she had in mind. As Osney listened, apprehension slowly spread across his face. When she finished he said, "After you cut her head off, I want to take that kiss she never gave me."

"You may take all the kisses you like."

"And then the Wall?"

"For just a little while. Tommen is a forgiving king."

Osney scratched at his scarred cheek. "Usually if I lie about some woman, it's me saying how I never fucked them and them saying how I did. This . . . I never lied to no *High Septon* before. I think you go to some hell for that. One o' the bad ones."

The queen was taken aback. The last thing she expected was piety from a Kettleblack. "Are you refusing to obey me?"

"No." Osney touched her golden hair. "The thing is, the best lies have some truth in 'em . . . to give 'em flavor, as it were. And you want me to go tell how I fucked a queen . . ."

She almost slapped his face. Almost. But she had gone too far, and too much was at stake. *All I do, I do for Tommen.* She turned her head and caught Ser Osney's hand with her own, kissing his fingers. They were rough and hard, callused from the sword. *Robert had hands like that,* she thought.

Cersei wrapped her arms about his neck. "I would not want it said I made a liar of you," she whispered in a husky voice. "Give me an hour, and meet me in my bedchamber."

"We waited long enough." He thrust his fingers inside

the bodice of her gown and yanked, and the silk parted with a ripping sound so loud that Cersei was afraid that half of the Red Keep must have heard it. "Take off the rest before I tear that too," he said. "You can keep the crown on. I like you in the crown."

THE PRINCESS IN
THE TOWER

Hers was a gentle prison.

Arianne took solace from that. Why would her father go to such great pains to provide for her comfort in captivity if he had marked her for a traitor's death? *He cannot mean to kill me,* she told herself a hundred times. *He does not have it in him to be so cruel. I am his blood and seed, his heir, his only daughter.* If need be, she would throw herself beneath the wheels of his chair, admit her fault, and beg him for his pardon. And she would weep. When he saw tears rolling down her face, he would forgive her.

She was less certain whether she would forgive herself.

"Areo," she had pleaded with her captor during the long dry ride from the Greenblood back to Sunspear, "I never wanted the girl to come to harm. You must believe me."

Hotah made no reply, except to grunt. Arianne could feel his anger. Darkstar had escaped him, the most dangerous of all her little group of plotters. He had outraced all his pursuers and vanished into the deep desert, with blood upon his blade.

"You know me, captain," Arianne had said, as the leagues rolled past. "You have known me since I was little. You always kept me safe, as you kept my lady mother safe when you came with her from Great Norvos to be her shield in a strange land. I need you now. I need your help. I never meant—"

"What you meant does not matter, little princess," Areo Hotah said. "Only what you did." His countenance was stony. "I am sorry. It is for my prince to command, for Hotah to obey."

Arianne expected to be brought before her father's high seat beneath the dome of leaded glass in the Tower of the Sun. Instead, Hotah delivered her to the Spear Tower, and the custody of her father's seneschal Ricasso and Ser Manfrey Martell, the castellan. "Princess," Ricasso said, "you will forgive an old blind man if he does not make the climb with you. These legs are not equal to so many steps. A chamber has been prepared for you. Ser Manfrey shall escort you there, to await the prince's pleasure."

"The prince's displeasure, you mean. Will my friends be confined here as well?" Arianne had been parted from Garin, Drey, and the others after capture, and Hotah had refused to say what would be done with them. "That is for the prince to decide," was all the captain had to say upon the subject. Ser Manfrey proved a bit more forthcoming. "They were taken to the Planky Town and will be conveyed by ship to Ghaston Grey, until such time as Prince Doran decides their fate."

Ghaston Grey was a crumbling old castle perched on a

rock in the Sea of Dorne, a drear and dreadful prison where the vilest of criminals were sent to rot and die. "Does my father mean to *kill* them?" Arianne could not believe it. "All they did they did for love for me. If my father must have blood, it should be mine."

"As you say, princess."

"I want to speak with him."

"He thought you might." Ser Manfrey took her arm and marched her up the steps, up and up until her breath grew short. The Spear Tower stood a hundred and a half feet high, and her cell was nearly at the top. Arianne eyed every door they passed, wondering if one of the Sand Snakes might be locked within.

When her own door had been closed and barred, Arianne explored her new home. Her cell was large and airy, and did not lack for comforts. There were Myrish carpets on the floor, red wine to drink, books to read. In one corner stood an ornate *cyvasse* table with pieces carved of ivory and onyx, though she had no one to play with even if she had been so inclined. She had a featherbed to sleep in, and a privy with a marble seat, sweetened by a basketful of herbs. This high up, the views were splendid. One window opened to the east, so she could watch the sun rise above the sea. The other allowed her to look down upon the Tower of the Sun, and the Winding Walls and Threefold Gate beyond.

The exploration took less time than it would have taken her to lace a pair of sandals, but at least it served to keep the tears at bay for a time. Arianne found a basin and a flagon of cool water and washed her hands and face, but no amount of scrubbing could cleanse her of her grief. *Arys*, she thought, *my white knight*. Tears filled her eyes, and suddenly she was weeping, her whole body wracked by sobs. She remembered how Hotah's heavy axe had cleaved through his flesh and bone, the way his head had gone spinning through the air. *Why did you do it? Why throw your life away? I never told you to, I never wanted that, I only wanted . . . I wanted . . . I wanted . . .*

That night she cried herself to sleep . . . for the first time, if not the last. Even in her dreams she found no peace. She dreamt of Arys Oakheart caressing her, smiling at her, telling her that he loved her . . . but all the while the quarrels were in him and his wounds were weeping, turning his whites to red. Part of her knew it was a nightmare, even as she dreamt it. *Come morning all of this will vanish,* the princess told herself, but when morning came, she was still in her cell, Ser Arys was still dead, and Myrcella . . . *I never wanted that, never. I meant the girl no harm. All I wanted was for her to be a queen. If we had not been betrayed . . .*

"Someone told," Hotah had said. The memory still made her angry. Arianne clung to that, feeding the flame within her heart. Anger was better than tears, better than grief, better than guilt. Someone told, someone she had trusted. Arys Oakheart had died because of that, slain by the traitor's whisper as much as by the captain's axe. The blood that had streamed down Myrcella's face, that was the betrayer's work as well. Someone told, someone she had loved. That was the cruelest cut of all.

She found a cedar chest full of her clothes at the foot of her bed, so she stripped out of the travel-stained garb she had slept in and donned the most revealing garments she could find, wisps of silk that covered everything and hid nothing. Prince Doran might treat her like a child, but she refused to dress like one. She knew such garb would discomfit her father when he came to chastise her for making off with Myrcella. She counted on it. *If I must crawl and weep, let him be uncomfortable as well.*

She expected him that day, but when the door finally opened it proved to be only the servants with her midday meal. "When might I see my father?" she asked, but none of them would answer. The kid had been roasted with lemon and honey. With it were grape leaves stuffed with a mélange of raisins, onions, mushrooms, and fiery dragon peppers. "I am not hungry," Arianne said. Her friends would be eating ship's biscuits and salt beef on their way to Ghaston Grey. "Take this away and bring me Prince Doran." But they left the food, and her father did not come. After a while, hunger weakened her resolve, so she sat and ate.

Once the food was gone, there was nothing else for Arianne to do. She paced around her tower, twice and thrice and three times thrice. She sat beside the *cyvasse* table and idly moved an elephant. She curled up in the window seat and tried to read a book, until the words became a blur and she realized that she was crying again. *Arys, my sweet, my white knight, why did you do it? You should have yielded. I tried to tell you, but the words caught in my mouth. You gallant fool, I never meant for you to die, or for Myrcella . . . oh, gods be good, that little girl . . .*

Finally, she crawled back onto the featherbed. The world had grown dark, and there was little she could do but sleep. *Someone told,* she thought. *Someone told.* Garin, Drey, and Spotted Sylva were friends of her girlhood, as dear to her as her cousin Tyene. She could not believe they would inform on her . . . but that left only Darkstar, and if he was the betrayer, why had he turned his sword on poor Myrcella? *He wanted to kill her instead of crowning her, he said as much at Shandystone. He said that was how I'd get the war I wanted.* But it made no sense for Dayne to be the traitor. If Ser Gerold had been the worm in the apple, why would he have turned his sword upon Myrcella?

Someone told. Could it have been Ser Arys? Had the white knight's guilt won out over his lust? Had he loved Myrcella more than her and betrayed his new princess to atone for his betrayal of the old? Was he so ashamed of what he'd done that he threw his life away at the Greenblood rather than live to face dishonor?

Someone told. When her father came to see her, she would learn which one. Prince Doran did not come the next day, though. Nor the day after. The princess was left alone to pace, and weep, and nurse her wounds. During the daylight hours she would try to read, but the books that they had given her were deadly dull: ponderous old histories and geographies, annotated maps, a dry-as-dust study of the laws of Dorne, *The Seven-Pointed Star* and *Lives of the High Septons,* a huge tome about dragons that somehow made them about as interesting as newts. Arianne would have given much and more for a copy of *Ten Thousand Ships* or *The Loves of Queen Nymeria,* anything to occupy her thoughts and let her escape her tower for an hour or two, but such amusements were denied her.

From her window seat, she had only to glance out to see the great dome of gold and colored glass below her, where her father sat in state. *He will summon me soon,* she told herself.

No visitors were permitted her beyond the servants; Bors with his stubbly jaw, tall Timoth dripping dignity, the sisters Morra and Mellei, pretty little Cedra, old Belandra who had been her mother's bedmaid. They brought her meals, changed her bed, and emptied the chamber pot beneath her privy, but none would speak with her. When she required more wine, Timoth would fetch it. If she desired some favorite food, figs or olives or peppers stuffed with cheese, she need only tell Belandra, and it would appear. Morra and Mellei took away her dirty clothes and returned them clean and fresh. Every second day a bath was brought for her, and shy little Cedra would soap her back and help her brush her hair.

Yet none of them had a word for her, nor would they deign to tell her what was happening in the world outside her sandstone cage. "Has Darkstar been captured?" she asked Bors one day. "Are they still hunting for him?" The man only turned his back on her and walked away. "Have you gone deaf?" Arianne snapped at him. "Come back here and answer me. I command it." Her only reply was the sound of a door closing.

"Timoth," she tried, another day, "what has become of Princess Myrcella? I never meant for harm to come to her." The last she had seen of the other princess had been on their ride back to Sunspear. Too weak to sit a horse, Myrcella had traveled in a litter, her head bound up in silken bandages where Darkstar slashed at her, her green eyes bright with fever. "Tell me that she has not died, I beg you. What harm could come of my knowing that? Tell me how she fares." Timoth would not.

"Belandra," Arianne said, a few days later, "if you ever loved my lady mother, take pity on her poor daughter and tell me when my father means to come and see me. Please. Please." But Belandra had lost her tongue as well.

Is this my father's notion of torment? Not hot irons or the rack, but simple silence? That was so very like Doran Martell that Arianne had to laugh. *He thinks he is being subtle when he is only being feeble.* She resolved to enjoy the quiet, to use the time to heal and fortify herself for what must come.

It was no good dwelling endlessly on Ser Arys, she knew. Instead, she made herself think about the Sand

Snakes, Tyene especially. Arianne loved all her bastard cousins, from prickly, hot-tempered Obara to little Loreza, the youngest, only six years old. Tyene had always been the one she loved the most, though; the sweet sister that she never had. The princess had never been close to her brothers; Quentyn was off at Yronwood, and Trystane was too young. No, it had always been her and Tyene, with Garin and Drey and Spotted Sylva. Nym would sometimes join them in their sport, and Sarella was forever pushing in where she didn't belong, but for the most part they had been a company of five. They splashed in the pools and fountains of the Water Gardens, and rode into battle perched on one another's naked backs. She and Tyene had learned to read together, learned to ride together, learned to dance together. When they were ten Arianne had stolen a flagon of wine, and the two of them had gotten drunk together. They shared meals and beds and jewelry. They would have shared their first man as well, but Drey got too excited and spurted all over Tyene's fingers the moment she drew him from his breeches. *Her hands are dangerous.* The memory made her smile.

The more she thought about her cousins, the more the princess missed them. *For all I know, they might be right below me.* That night Arianne tried pounding on the floor with the heel of her sandal. When no one answered, she leaned out a window and peered down. She could see other windows below, smaller than her own, some no more than arrow loops. *"Tyene!"* she called. *"Tyene, are you there? Obara, Nym? Can you hear me? Ellaria? Anyone? TYENE?"* The princess spent half the night hanging out the window, calling till her throat was raw, but no answering shouts came back to her. That frightened her more than she could say. If the Sand Snakes were imprisoned in the Spear Tower, they surely would have heard her shouting. Why didn't they answer? *If Father has done them harm, I will never forgive him, never,* she told herself.

By the time a fortnight had passed, her patience had worn paper-thin. "I will speak with my father now," she told Bors, in her most commanding voice. "You will take me to him." He did not take her to him. "I am ready to see the prince," she told Timoth, but he turned away as if he had not heard. The next morning, Arianne was waiting beside the door when it opened. She bolted past Belandra, sending a platter of spiced eggs to crash against the wall, but the guards caught her before she'd gone three yards. She knew them too, but they were deaf to her entreaties. They dragged her back to her cell, kicking and squirming.

Arianne decided that she must needs be more subtle. Cedra was her best hope; the girl was young, naive, and gullible. Garin had boasted of bedding her once, the princess recalled. The next time she bathed, as Cedra soaped her shoulders, she began to talk of everything and nothing. "I know you have been commanded not to speak to me," she said, "but no one told me not to speak to you." She spoke about the heat of the day, and what she'd had last night for supper, and how slow and stiff poor Belandra was becoming. Prince Oberyn had armed each of *his* daughters so they need never be defenseless, but Arianne Martell had no weapon but her guile. And so she smiled and charmed, and asked nothing in return of Cedra, neither word nor nod.

The next day at supper, she nattered at the girl again as she was serving. This time she contrived to mention Garin. Cedra glanced up shyly at his name and almost spilled the wine that she was pouring. *So it is that way, is it?* thought Arianne.

During her next bath, she spoke of her imprisoned

friends, especially Garin. "He's the one I fear for most," she confided to the serving girl. "The orphans are free spirits, they live to wander. Garin needs sunshine and fresh air. If they lock him away in some dank stone cell, how will he survive? He will not last a year at Ghaston Grey." Cedra did not reply, but her face was pale when Arianne rose from the water, and she was squeezing the sponge so tightly that soap was dripping on the Myrish carpet.

Even so, it was four more days and two more baths before the girl was hers. "Please," Cedra finally whispered, after Arianne had painted a vivid picture of Garin throwing himself from the window of his cell, to taste freedom one last time before he died. "You have to help him. Please don't let him die."

"I can do little and less so long as I am locked up here," she whispered back. "My father will not see me. *You* are the only one who can save Garin. Do you love him?"

"Yes," Cedra whispered, blushing. "But how can I help?"

"You can smuggle out a letter for me," said the princess. "Will do you that? Will you take the risk . . . for Garin?"

Cedra's eyes got big. She nodded.

I have a raven, Arianne thought, triumphantly, *but who to send her to?* The only one of her conspirators to escape her father's net was Darkstar. By now Ser Gerold might well have been taken, however; if not, he would surely have fled Dorne. Her next thought was of Garin's mother and the orphans of the Greenblood. *No, not them. It must be someone with real power, someone who had no part of our plot yet might have reason to be sympathetic to us.* She considered appealing to her own mother, but Lady Mellario was far away in Norvos. Besides, Prince Doran had not listened to his lady wife for many years. *Not her either. I need a lord, one great enough to cow my father into releasing me.*

The most powerful of the Dornish lords was Anders Yronwood, the Bloodroyal, Lord of Yronwood and Warden of the Stone Way, but Arianne knew better than to look for help from the man who had fostered her brother Quentyn. *No.* Drey's brother Ser Deziel Dalt had once aspired to marry her, but he was much too dutiful to go against his prince. Besides, whilst the Knight of Lemonwood might intimidate a petty lord, he did not have the strength to sway the Prince of Dorne. *No.* The same was true of Spotted Sylva's father. *No.* Arianne finally decided that she had but two real hopes: Harmen Uller, Lord of Hellholt, and Franklyn Fowler, Lord of Skyreach and Warden of the Prince's Pass.

Half of the Ullers are half-mad, the saying went, *and the other half are worse.* Ellaria Sand was Lord Harmen's natural daughter. She and her little ones had been locked away with the rest of the Sand Snakes. That would have made Lord Harmen wroth, and the Ullers were dangerous when wroth. *Too dangerous, perhaps.* The princess did not want to put any more lives in danger.

Lord Fowler might be a safer choice. The Old Hawk, he was called. He had never gotten on with Anders Yronwood; there was bad blood between their Houses going back a thousand years, from when the Fowlers had chosen Martell over Yronwood during Nymeria's War. The Fowler twins were famous friends of Lady Nym as well, but how much weight would that carry with the Old Hawk?

For days Arianne wavered as she composed her secret letter. "Give the man who brings this to you a hundred silver stags," she began. That should ensure that the message was delivered. She wrote where she was, and pleaded for rescue. "Whoever shall deliver me from this cell, he shall not be forgotten when I wed." *That should bring the heroes running.* Unless Prince Doran had attainted her, she remained the lawful heir to Sunspear; the man who married her would one day rule Dorne by her side. Arianne could only pray that her rescuer would prove younger than the greybeards her father had offered her over the years. "I want a consort with teeth," she had told him when she refused the last.

She dare not ask for parchment for fear of rousing the suspicions of her captors, so she wrote the letter on the bottom of a page torn from *The Seven-Pointed Star,* and pressed it into Cedra's hand on her next bath day. "There's a place beside the Threefold Gate where the caravans take on supplies before crossing the deep sand," Arianne told her. "Find some traveler headed for the Prince's Pass, and promise him a hundred silver stags if he will put this in Lord Fowler's hand."

"I will." Cedra hid the message in her bodice. "I'll find someone before the sun goes down, princess."

"Good," she said. "Tell me how it went on the morrow."

The girl did not return upon the morrow, however. Nor on the day that followed. When it was time for Arianne to bathe, it was Morra and Mellei who filled her tub, and stayed to wash her back and brush her hair. "Has Cedra taken ill?" the princess asked them, but neither would reply. *She has been caught* was all that she could think. *What else could it be?* That night she hardly slept, for fear of what might come next.

When Timoth brought her breakfast the next morning, Arianne asked to see Ricasso rather than her father. Plainly she could not compel Prince Doran to attend her, but surely a mere seneschal would not ignore a summons from the rightful heir to Sunspear.

He did, though. "Did you tell Ricasso what I said?" she demanded the next time she saw Timoth. "Did you tell him I had need of him?" When the man refused to answer her, Arianne seized a flagon of red wine and upended it over his head. The serving man retreated dripping, his face a mask of wounded dignity. *My father means to leave me here to rot,* the princess decided. *Or else he is making plans to marry me off to some disgusting old fool and intends to keep me locked away until the bedding.*

Arianne Martell had grown up expecting that one day she would wed some great lord of her father's choosing. That was what princesses were for, she had been taught . . . though, admittedly, her uncle Oberyn had taken a different view of matters. "If you would wed, wed," the Red Viper had told his own daughters. "If not, take your pleasure where you find it. There's little enough of it in this world. Choose well, though. If you saddle yourself with a fool or a brute, don't look to me to rid you of him. I gave you the tools to do that for yourself."

The freedom that Prince Oberyn allowed his bastard daughters had never been shared by Prince Doran's lawful heir. Arianne must wed; she had accepted that. Drey had wanted her, she knew; so had his brother Deziel, the Knight of Lemonwood. Daemon Sand had gone so far as to ask for her hand. Daemon was bastard-born, however, and Prince Doran did not mean for her to wed a Dornishman.

Arianne had accepted that as well. One year King Robert's brother came to visit and she did her best to seduce him, but she was half a girl and Lord Renly seemed more bemused than inflamed by her overtures. Later, when Hoster Tully asked her to come to Riverrun and meet his heir, she lit candles to the Maid in thanks, but Prince Doran had declined the invitation. The princess might even have considered Willas Tyrell, crippled leg and all, but her father refused to send her to Highgarden to meet him. She tried to go despite him, with Tyene's help . . . but Prince Oberyn caught them at Vaith and brought them back. That same year, Prince Doran tried to betroth her to Ben Beesbury, a minor lordling who was eighty if he was a day, and as blind as he was toothless.

Beesbury died a few years later. That gave her some small comfort in her present pass; she could not be forced to marry him if he was dead. And the Lord of the Crossing had wed again, so she was safe from him as well. *Elden Estermont is still alive and unwed, though. Lord Rosby and Lord Grandison as well.* Grandison was called the Greybeard, but by the time she'd met him his beard had gone snow white. At the welcoming feast, he had gone to sleep between the fish course and the meat. Drey called that apt, since his sigil was a sleeping lion. Garin challenged her to see if she could tie a knot in his beard without waking him, but Arianne refrained. Grandison had seemed a pleasant fellow, less querulous than Estermont and more robust than Rosby. She would never marry him, however. *Not even if Hotah stands behind me with his axe.*

No one came to marry her the next day, nor the day after. Nor did Cedra return. Arianne tried to win Morra and Mellei the same way, but it was no good. If she had been able to get either one alone she might have some hope, but together the sisters were a wall. By that time, the princess would have welcomed a touch of a hot iron, or an evening on the rack. The loneliness was like to drive her mad. *I deserve a headsman's axe for what I did, but he will not even give me that. He would sooner shut me away and forget I ever lived.* She wondered if Maester Caleotte was drawing a proclamation to name her brother Quentyn heir to Dorne.

Days came and went, one after the other, so many that Arianne lost count of how long she had been imprisoned. She found herself spending more and more time abed, until she reached the point where she did not rise at all except to use her privy. The meals the servants brought grew cold, untouched. Arianne slept and woke and slept again, and still felt too weary to rise. She prayed to the Mother for mercy and to the Warrior for courage, then slept some more. Fresh meals replaced the old ones, but she did not eat them either. Once, when she felt especially strong, she carried all the food to the window and flung it out into the yard, so it would not tempt her. The effort exhausted her, so afterward she crawled back into bed and slept for half a day.

Then came a day when a rough hand woke her, shaking her by the shoulder. "Little princess," said a voice she'd known from childhood. "Up and dress. The prince has called for you." Areo Hotah stood over her, her old friend and protector. He was *talking* to her. Arianne smiled sleepily. It was good to see that seamed, scarred face, and hear his gruff, deep voice and thick Norvoshi accent. "What did you do with Cedra?"

"The prince sent her to the Water Gardens," Hotah said. "He will tell you. First you must wash, and eat."

She must look a wretched creature. Arianne crawled from the bed, weak as a kitten. "Have Morra and Mellei prepare a bath," she told him, "and tell Timoth to bring me up some food. Nothing heavy. Some cold broth and a bit of bread and fruit."

"Aye," said Hotah. Never had she heard a sweeter sound.

The captain waited without whilst the princess bathed

and brushed her hair and ate sparingly of the cheese and fruit they'd brought her. She drank a little wine to settle her stomach. *I am frightened,* she realized, *for the first time in my life, I am frightened of my father.* That made her laugh until the wine came out her nose. When it was time to dress, she chose a simple gown of ivory linen, with vines and purple grapes embroidered around the sleeves and bodice. She wore no jewels. *I must be chaste and humble and contrite. I must throw myself at his feet and beg forgiveness, or I may never hear another human voice again.*

By the time she was ready, dusk had fallen. Arianne had thought that Hotah would escort her to the Tower of the Sun to hear her father's judgment. Instead he delivered her to the prince's solar, where they found Doran Martell seated behind a *cyvasse* table, his gouty legs supported by a cushioned footstool. He was toying with an onyx elephant, turning it in his reddened, swollen hands. The prince looked worse than she had ever seen him. His face was pale and puffy, his joints so inflamed that it hurt her just to look at them. Seeing him this way made Arianne's heart go out to him . . . yet somehow she could not bring herself to kneel and beg, as she had planned. "Father," she said instead.

When he raised his head to look at her, his dark eyes were clouded with pain. *Is that the gout?* Arianne wondered. *Or is it me?* "A strange and subtle folk, the Volantenes," he muttered, as he put the elephant aside. "I saw Volantis once, on my way to Norvos, where I first met Mellario. The bells were ringing, and the bears danced down the steps. Areo will recall the day."

"I remember," echoed Areo Hotah in his deep voice. "The bears danced and the bells rang, and the prince wore red and gold and orange. My lady asked me who it was who shone so bright."

Prince Doran smiled wanly. "Leave us, captain."

Hotah stamped the butt of his longaxe on the floor, turned on his heel, and took his leave.

"I told them to place a *cyvasse* table in your chambers," her father said when the two of them were alone.

"Who was I supposed to play with?" *Why is he talking about a game? Has the gout robbed him of his wits?*

"Yourself. Sometimes it is best to study a game before you attempt to play it. How well do you know the game, Arianne?"

"Well enough to play."

"But not to win. My brother loved the fight for its own sake, but I only play such games as I can win. *Cyvasse* is not for me." He studied her face for a long moment before he said, "Why? Tell me that, Arianne. Tell me why."

"For the honor of our House." Her father's voice made her angry. He sounded so sad, so exhausted, so *weak. You are a prince!* she wanted to shout. *You should be raging!* "Your meekness shames all Dorne, Father. Your brother went to King's Landing in your place, and *they killed him*!"

"Do you think I do not know that? Oberyn is with me every time I close my eyes."

"Telling you to open them, no doubt." She seated herself across the *cyvasse* table from her father.

"I did not give you leave to sit."

"Then call Hotah back and whip me for my insolence. You are the Prince of Dorne. You can do that." She touched one of the *cyvasse* pieces, the heavy horse. "Have you caught Ser Gerold?"

He shook his head. "Would that we had. You were a fool to make him part of this. Darkstar is the most dangerous man in Dorne. You and he have done us all great harm."

Arianne was almost afraid to ask. "Myrcella. Is she . . . ?"

". . . dead? No, though Darkstar did his best. All eyes were on your white knight so no one seems quite certain just what happened, but it would appear that her horse shied away from his at the last instant, else he would have taken off the top of the girl's skull. As it is, the slash opened her cheek down to the bone and sliced off her right ear. Maester Caleotte was able to save her life, but no poultice nor potion will ever restore her face. She was my *ward,* Arianne. Betrothed to your own brother and under my protection. You have dishonored all of us."

"I never meant her harm," Arianne insisted. "If Hotah had not interfered . . ."

". . . you would have crowned Myrcella queen, to raise a rebellion against her brother. Instead of an ear, she would have lost her life."

"Only if we lost."

"*If?* The word is *when.* Dorne is the least populous of the Seven Kingdoms. It pleased the Young Dragon to make all our armies larger when he wrote that book of his, so as to make his conquest that much more glorious, and it has pleased us to water the seed he planted and let our foes think us more powerful than we are, but a princess ought to know the truth. Valor is a poor substitute for numbers. Dorne cannot hope to win a war against the Iron Throne, not alone. And yet that may well be what you have given us. Are you proud?" The prince did not allow her time to answer. "What am I to do with you, Arianne?"

Forgive me, part of her wanted to say, but his words had cut her too deeply. "Why, do what you always do. Do nothing."

"You make it difficult for a man to swallow his anger."

"Best stop swallowing, you're like to choke on it." The prince did not answer. "Tell me how you knew my plans."

"I am the Prince of Dorne. Men seek my favor."

Someone told. "You knew, and yet you still allowed us to make off with Myrcella. Why?"

"That was my mistake, and it has proved a grievous one. You are my daughter, Arianne. The little girl who used to run to me when she skinned her knee. I found it hard to believe that you would conspire against me. I had to learn the truth."

"Now you have. I want to know who informed on me."

"I would as well, in your place."

"Will you tell me?"

"I can think of no reason why I should."

"You think I cannot discover the truth on my own?"

"You are welcome to try. Until such time you must mistrust them all . . . and a little mistrust is a good thing in a princess." Prince Doran sighed. "You disappoint me, Arianne."

"Said the crow to the raven. You have been disappointing me for years, Father." She had not meant to be so blunt with him, but the words came spilling out. *There, now I have said it.*

"I know. I am too meek and weak and cautious, too lenient to our enemies. Just now, though, you are in need of some of that leniency, it seems to me. You ought to be pleading for my forgiveness rather than seeking to provoke me further."

"I ask leniency only for my friends."

"How noble of you."

"What they did they did for love for me. They do not deserve to die on Ghaston Grey."

"As it happens, I agree. Aside from Darkstar, your fellow plotters were no more than foolish children. Still, this was no harmless game of *cyvasse*. You and your friends were playing at treason. I might have had their heads off."

"You might have, but you didn't. Dayne, Dalt, Santagar . . . no, you would never dare make enemies of such Houses."

"I dare more than you dream . . . but leave that for the nonce. Ser Andrey has been sent to Norvos to serve your lady mother for three years. Garin will spend his next two years in Tyrosh. From his kin amongst the orphans, I took coin and hostages. Lady Sylva received no punishment from me, but she was of an age to marry. Her father has shipped her to Greenstone to wed Lord Estermont. As for Arys Oakheart, he chose his own fate and met it bravely. A knight of the Kingsguard . . . what did you *do* to him?"

"I fucked him, Father. You did command me to entertain our noble visitors, as I recall."

His face grew flushed. "Was that all that was required?"

"I told him that once Myrcella was the queen she would give us leave to marry. He wanted me for his wife."

"You did everything you could to stop him from dishonoring his vows, I am certain," her father said.

It was her turn to flush. Her seduction of Ser Arys had required half a year. Though he claimed to have known other women before taking the white, she would never have known that from the way he acted. His caresses had been clumsy, his kisses nervous, and the first time they were abed together he spent his seed on her thigh as she was guiding him inside her with her hand. Worse, he had been consumed by shame. If she only had a dragon for every time he had whispered, "We should not be doing this," she would be richer than the Lannisters. *Did he charge at Areo Hotah in hopes of saving me?* Arianne wondered. *Or did he do it to escape me, to wash out his dishonor with his life's blood?* "He did love me," she heard herself say. "He died for me."

"If so, he may well be but the first of many. You and your cousins wanted war. You may get your wish. Another Kingsguard knight creeps toward Sunspear even as we speak. Ser Balon Swann is bringing me the Mountain's head. My bannermen have been delaying him, to purchase me some time. The Wyls kept him hunting and hawking for eight days on the Boneway, and Lord Yronwood feasted him for a fortnight when he emerged from the mountains. At present he is at the Tor, where Lady Jordayne has arranged games in his honor. When he reaches Ghost Hill he will find Lady Toland intent on out-doing her. Soon or late, however, Ser Balon must arrive at Sunspear, and when he does he will expect to see Princess Myrcella . . . and Ser Arys, his Sworn Brother. What shall we tell him, Arianne? Shall I say that Oakheart perished in a hunting accident, or from a tumble down some slip-pery steps? Perhaps Arys went swimming at the Water Gardens, slipped upon the marble, hit his head, and drowned?"

"No," Arianne said. "Say that he died defending his lit-tle princess. Tell Ser Balon that Darkstar tried to kill her and Ser Arys stepped between them and saved her life." That was how the white knights of the Kingsguard were supposed to die, giving up their own lives for those that they had sworn to protect. "Ser Balon may be suspicious, as you were when the Lannisters killed your sister and her children, but he will have no proof . . ."

". . . until he speaks with Myrcella. Or must that brave child suffer a tragic accident as well? If so, it will mean war. No lie will save Dorne from the queen's wroth if her daughter should perish whilst in my care."

He needs me, Arianne realized. *That's why he sent for me.*

"I could tell Myrcella what to say, but why should I?"

A spasm of anger rippled across her father's face. "I warn you, Arianne, I am out of patience."

"With me?" *That is so like him.* "For Lord Tywin and the Lannisters you always had the forbearance of Baelor the Blessed, but for your own blood, none."

"You mistake patience for forbearance. I have worked at the downfall of Tywin Lannister since the day they told me of Elia and her children. It was my hope to strip him of all that he held most dear before I killed him, but it would seem his dwarf son has robbed me of that pleasure. I take some small solace in knowing that he died a cruel death at the hands of the monster that he himself begot. Be that as it may. Lord Tywin is howling down in hell . . . where thousands more will soon be joining him, if your folly turns to war." Her father grimaced, as if the very word were painful to him. "Is that what you want?"

The princess refused to be cowed. "I want my cousins freed. I want my uncle avenged. I want my rights."

"Your *rights*?"

"Dorne."

"You will have Dorne after I am dead. Are you so anxious to be rid of me?"

"I should turn that question back on you, Father. You have been trying to rid yourself of me for years."

"That is not true."

"No? Shall we ask my brother?"

"Trystane?"

"Quentyn."

"What of him?"

"Where is he?"

"He is with Lord Yronwood's host in the Boneway."

"You do lie well, Father, I will grant you that. You did not so much as blink. Quentyn has gone to Lys."

"Where did you get that notion?"

"A friend told me." She could have secrets too.

"Your friend lied. You have my word, your brother has not gone to Lys. I swear it by sun and spear and Seven."

Arianne could not be fooled so easily. "Is it Myr, then? Tyrosh? I know he is somewhere across the narrow sea, hiring sellswords to steal away my birthright."

Her father's face darkened. "This mistrust does you no honor, Arianne. Quentyn should be the one conspiring against me. I sent him away when he was just a child, too young to understand the needs of Dorne. Anders Yronwood has been more a father to him than I have, yet your brother remains faithful and obedient."

"Why not? You favor him and always have. He looks like you, he thinks like you, and you mean to give him Dorne, don't trouble to deny it. I read your letter." The words still burned as bright as fire in her memory. "'*One day you will sit where I sit and rule all Dorne,*' you wrote him. Tell me, Father, when did you decide to disinherit me? Was it the day that Quentyn was born, or the day that *I* was born? What did I ever do to make you hate me so?" To her fury, there were tears in her eyes.

"I never hated you." Prince Doran's voice was parchment-thin, and full of grief. "Arianne, you do not understand."

"Do you deny you wrote those words?"

"No. That was when Quentyn first went to Yronwood. I did intend for him to follow me, yes. I had other plans for you."

"Oh, yes," she said scornfully, "such plans. Gyles Rosby. Blind Ben Beesbury. Greybeard Grandison. They were your *plans*."

She gave him no chance to reply. "I know it is my duty to provide an heir for Dorne, I have *never* been forgetful of that. I would have wed, and gladly, but the matches that you brought to me were insults. With every one you spit on me. If you ever felt any love for me at all, why offer me to *Walder Frey*?"

"Because I knew that you would spurn him. I had to be seen to *try* to find a consort for you once you'd reached a certain age, else it would have raised suspicions, but I dared not bring you any man you might accept. You were promised, Arianne."

Promised? Arianne stared at him incredulously. "What are you saying? Is this another lie? You never said . . ."

"The pact was sealed in secret. I meant to tell you when you were old enough . . . when you came of age, I thought, but . . ."

"I am three-and-twenty, for seven years a woman grown."

"I know. If I kept you ignorant too long, it was only to protect you. Arianne, your nature . . . to you, a secret was only a choice tale to whisper to Garin and Tyene in your bed of a night. Garin gossips as only the orphans can, and Tyene keeps nothing from Obara and the Lady Nym. And if they knew . . . Obara is too fond of wine, and Nym is too close to the Fowler twins. And who might the Fowler twins confide in? *I could not take the risk.*"

She was lost, confounded. *Promised. I was promised.* "Who is it? Who have I been betrothed to, all these years?"

"It makes no matter. He is dead."

That left her more baffled than ever. "The old ones are so frail. Was it a broken hip, a chill, the gout?"

"It was a pot of molten gold. We princes make our care-ful plans and the gods smash them all awry." Prince Doran made a weary gesture with a chafed red hand. "Dorne will be yours. You have my word on that, if my word still has any meaning for you. Your brother Quentyn has a harder road to walk."

"What road?" Arianne regarded him suspiciously. "What are you holding back? Seven save me, but I am sick of secrets. Tell me the rest, Father . . . or else name Quentyn your heir and send for Hotah and his axe, and let me die beside my cousins."

"Do you truly believe I would harm my brother's children?" Her father grimaced. "Obara, Nym, and Tyene lack for nothing but their freedom, and Ellaria and her daughters are happily ensconced at the Water Gardens. Dorea stalks about knocking oranges off the trees with her morningstar, and Elia and Obella have become the terror of the pools." He sighed. "It has not been so long since you were playing in those pools. You used to ride the shoulders of an older girl . . . a tall girl with wispy yellow hair . . ."

"Jeyne Fowler, or her sister Jennelyn." It had been years since Arianne had thought of that. "Oh, and Frynne, her father was a smith. Her hair was brown. Garin was my favorite, though. When I rode Garin no one could defeat us, not even Nym and that green-haired Tyroshi girl."

"That green-haired girl was the Archon's daughter. I was to have sent you to Tyrosh in her place. You would have served the Archon as a cupbearer and met with your betrothed in secret, but your mother threatened to harm herself if I stole another of her children, and I . . . I could not do that to her."

His tale grows ever stranger. "Is that where Quentyn's gone? To Tyrosh, to court the Archon's green-haired daughter?"

Her father plucked up a *cyvasse* piece. "I must know how you learned that Quentyn was abroad. Your brother went with Cletus Yronwood, Maester Kedry, and three of Lord Yronwood's best young knights on a long and perilous voyage, with an uncertain welcome at its end. He has gone to bring us back our heart's desire."

She narrowed her eyes. "What is our heart's desire?"

"Vengeance." His voice was soft, as if he were afraid that someone might be listening. "Justice." Prince Doran pressed the onyx dragon into her palm with his swollen, gouty fingers, and whispered, *"Fire and blood."*

ALAYNE

She turned the iron ring and pushed the door open, just a crack. "Sweetrobin?" she called. "May I enter?"

"Have a care, m'lady," warned old Gretchel, wringing her hands. "His lordship threw his chamber pot at the maester."

"Then he has none to throw at me. Isn't there some work you should be doing? And you, Maddy . . . are all the windows closed and shuttered? Have all the furnishings been covered?"

"All of them, m'lady," said Maddy.

"Best make certain of it." Alayne slipped into the darkened bedchamber. "It's only me, Sweetrobin."

Someone sniffled in the darkness. "Are you alone?"

"I am, my lord."

"Come close, then. Just you."

Alayne shut the door firmly behind her. It was solid oak, four inches thick; Maddy and Gretchel might listen all they wished, but they would hear nothing. That was just as well. Gretchel could hold her tongue, but Maddy gossiped shamelessly.

"Did Maester Colemon send you?" the boy asked.

"No," she lied. "I heard my Sweetrobin was ailing." After his encounter with the chamber pot the maester had come running to Ser Lothor, and Brune had come to her. "If m'lady can talk him out of bed nice," the knight said, "I won't have to drag him out."

We can't have that, she told herself. When Robert was handled roughly he was apt to go into a shaking fit. "Are you hungry, my lord?" she asked the little lord. "Shall I send Maddy down for berries and cream, or some warm bread and butter?" Too late she remembered that there was no warm bread; the kitchens were closed, the ovens cold. *If it gets Robert out of bed, it would be worth the bother of lighting a fire,* she told herself.

"I don't want food," the little lord said, in a reedy, petulant voice. "I'm going to stay in bed today. You could read to me if you want."

"It is too dark in here for reading." The heavy curtains drawn across the windows made the bedchamber black as night. "Has my Sweetrobin forgotten what day this is?"

"No," he said, "but I'm not going. I want to stay in bed. You could read to me about the Winged Knight."

The Winged Knight was Ser Artys Arryn. Legend said that he had driven the First Men from the Vale and flown to the top of the Giant's Lance on a huge falcon to slay the Griffin King. There were a hundred tales of his adventures. Little Robert knew them all so well he could have recited them from memory, but he liked to have them read to him all the same. "Sweetling, we have to go," she told the boy, "but I promise, I'll read you *two* tales of the Winged Knight when we reach the Gates of the Moon."

"Three," he said at once. No matter what you offered him, Robert always wanted more.

"Three," she agreed. "Might I let some sun in?"

"No. The light hurts my eyes. Come to bed, Alayne."

She went to the windows anyway, edging around the broken chamber pot. She could smell it better than she saw it. "I shan't open them very wide. Only enough to see my Sweetrobin's face."

He sniffled. "If you must."

The curtains were of plush blue velvet. She pulled one back a finger's length and tied it off. Dust motes danced in a shaft of pale morning light. The small diamond-shaped panes of the window were obscured by frost. Alayne rubbed at one with the heel of her hand, enough to glimpse a brilliant blue sky and a blaze of white from the mountainside. The Eyrie was wrapped in an icy mantle, the Giant's Lance above buried in waist-deep snows.

When she turned back, Robert Arryn was propped up against the pillows looking at her. *The Lord of the Eyrie and Defender of the Vale.* A woolen blanket covered him below the waist. Above it he was naked, a pasty boy with hair as long as any girl's. Robert had spindly arms and legs, a soft concave chest and little belly, and eyes that were always red and runny. *He cannot help the way he is. He was born small and sickly.* "You look very strong this morning, my lord." He loved to be told how strong he was. "Shall I have Maddy and Gretchel fetch hot water for your bath? Maddy will scrub your back for you and wash your hair, to make you clean and lordly for your journey. Won't that be nice?"

"No. I hate Maddy. She has a wart on her eye, and she

scrubs so hard it hurts. My mommy never hurt me scrubbing."

"I will tell Maddy not to scrub my Sweetrobin so hard. You'll feel better when you're fresh and clean."

"No bath, I *told* you, my head hurts most awfully."

"Shall I bring you a warm cloth for your brow? Or a cup of dreamwine? Only a little one, though. Mya Stone is waiting down at Sky, and she'll be hurt if you go to sleep on her. You know how much she loves you."

"I don't love *her*. She's just the mule girl." Robert sniffled. "Maester Colemon put something vile in my milk last night, I could taste it. I told him I wanted sweetmilk, but he wouldn't bring me any. Not even when I *commanded* him. I am the lord, he should do what I say. No one does what I *say*."

"I'll speak to him," Alayne promised, "but only if you get up out of bed. It's beautiful outside, Sweetrobin. The sun is shining bright, a perfect day for going down the mountain. The mules are waiting down at Sky with Mya . . ."

His mouth quivered. "I hate those smelly mules. One tried to bite me once! You tell that Mya that I'm staying here." He sounded as if he were about to cry. "No one can hurt me so long as I stay here. The Eyrie is im*preg*nable."

"Who would want to hurt my Sweetrobin? Your lords and knights adore you, and the smallfolk cheer your name." *He is afraid,* she thought, *and with good reason.* Since his lady mother had fallen, the boy would not even stand upon a balcony, and the way from the Eyrie to the Gates of the Moon was perilous enough to daunt anyone. Alayne's heart had been in her throat when she made her own ascent with Lady Lysa and Lord Petyr, and everyone agreed that the descent was even more harrowing, since you were looking down the whole time. Mya could tell of great lords and bold knights who had gone pale and wet their smallclothes on the mountain. *And none of them had the shaking sickness either.*

Still, it would not serve. On the valley floor autumn still lingered, warm and golden, but winter had closed around the mountain peaks. They had weathered three snow-storms, and an ice storm that transformed the castle into crystal for a fortnight. The Eyrie might be impregnable, but it would soon be inaccessible as well, and the way down grew more hazardous every day. Most of the castle's servants and soldiers had already made the descent. Only a dozen still lingered up here, to attend Lord Robert.

"Sweetrobin," she said gently, "the descent will be ever so jolly, you'll see. Ser Lothor will be with us, and Mya. Her mules have gone up and down this old mountain a thousand times."

"I hate mules," he insisted. "Mules are nasty. I *told* you, one tried to bite me when I was little."

Robert had never learned to ride properly, she knew. Mules, horses, donkeys, it made no matter; to him they were all fearsome beasts, as terrifying as dragons or griffins. He had been brought to the Vale at six, riding with his head cradled between his mother's milky breasts, and had never left the Eyrie since.

Still, they had to go, before the ice closed about the castle for good. There was no telling how long the weather would hold. "Mya will keep the mules from biting," Alayne said, "and I'll be riding just behind you. I'm only a girl, not as brave or strong as you. If I can do it, I know you can, Sweetrobin."

"I *could* do it," Lord Robert said, "but I don't choose to." He swiped at his runny nose with the back of his hand. "Tell Mya I am going to stay abed. Perhaps I will come down on the morrow, if I feel better. Today is too cold out, and my head hurts. You can have some sweetmilk too, and

I'll tell Gretchel to bring us some honeycombs to eat. We'll sleep and kiss and play games, and you can read me about the Winged Knight."

"I will. Three tales, as I promised . . . when we reach the Gates of the Moon." Alayne was running short of patience. *We have to go,* she reminded herself, *or we'll still be above the snow line when the sun goes down.* "Lord Nestor has prepared a feast to welcome you, mushroom soup and venison and cakes. You don't want to disappoint him, do you?"

"Will they be lemon cakes?" Lord Robert loved lemon cakes, perhaps because Alayne did.

"Lemony lemony lemon cakes," she assured him, "and you can have as many as you like."

"A hundred?" he wanted to know. "Could I have a *hundred*?"

"If it please you." She sat on the bed and smoothed his long, fine hair. *He does have pretty hair.* Lady Lysa had brushed it herself every night, and cut it when it wanted cutting. After she had fallen Robert had suffered terrible shaking fits whenever anyone came near him with a blade, so Petyr had commanded that his hair be allowed to grow. Alayne wound a lock around her finger, and said, "Now, will you get out of bed and let us dress you?"

"I want a hundred lemon cakes and *five* tales!"

I'd like to give you a hundred spankings and five slaps. You would not dare behave like this if Petyr were here. The little lord had a good healthy fear of his stepfather. Alayne forced a smile. "As my lord desires. But nothing till you're washed and dressed and on your way. Come, before the morning's gone." She took him firmly by the hand, and drew him out of bed.

Before she could summon the servants, however, Sweetrobin threw his skinny arms around her and kissed her. It was a little boy's kiss, and clumsy. Everything Robert Arryn did was clumsy. *If I close my eyes I can pretend he is the Knight of Flowers.* Ser Loras had given Sansa Stark a red rose once, but he had never kissed her . . . and no Tyrell would ever kiss Alayne Stone. Pretty as she was, she had been born on the wrong side of the blanket.

As the boy's lips touched her own she found herself thinking of another kiss. She could still remember how it felt, when his cruel mouth pressed down on her own. He had come to Sansa in the darkness as green fire filled the sky. *He took a song and a kiss, and left me nothing but a bloody cloak.*

It made no matter. That day was done, and so was Sansa.

Alayne pushed her little lord away. "That's enough. You can kiss me again when we reach the Gates, if you keep your word."

Maddy and Gretchel were waiting outside with Maester Colemon. The maester had washed the night soil from his hair and changed his robe. Robert's squires had turned up as well. Terrance and Gyles could always sniff out trouble.

"Lord Robert is feeling stronger," Alayne told the serving women. "Fetch hot water for his bath, but see you don't scald him. And do not pull on his hair when you brush out the tangles, he hates that." One of the squires sniggered, until she said, "Terrance, lay out his lordship's riding clothes and his warmest cloak. Gyles, you may clean up that broken chamber pot."

Gyles Grafton made a face. "I'm no scrubwoman."

"Do as Lady Alayne commands, or Lothor Brune will hear of it," said Maester Colemon. He followed her along the hallway and down the twisting stairs. "I am grateful for your intercession, my lady. You have a way with him." He hesitated. "Did you observe any shaking while you were with him?"

"His fingers trembled a little bit when I held his hand, that's all. He says you put something vile in his milk."

"Vile?" Colemon blinked at her, and the apple in his throat moved up and down. "I merely . . . is he bleeding from the nose?"

"No."

"Good. That is good." His chain clinked softly as he bobbed his head, atop a ridiculously long and skinny neck. "This descent . . . my lady, it might be safest if I mixed his lordship some milk of the poppy. Mya Stone could lash him over the back of her most surefooted mule whilst he slumbered."

"The Lord of the Eyrie cannot descend from his mountain tied up like a sack of barleycorn." Of that Alayne was certain. They dare not let the full extent of Robert's frailty and cowardice become too widely known, her father had warned her. *I wish he were here. He would know what to do.*

Petyr Baelish was clear across the Vale, though, attending Lord Lyonel Corbray at his wedding. A widower of forty-odd years, and childless, Lord Lyonel was to wed the strapping sixteen-year-old daughter of a rich Gulltown merchant. Petyr had brokered the match himself. The bride's dower was said to be staggering; it had to be, since she was of common birth. Corbray's vassals would be there, with the Lords Waxley, Grafton, Lynderly, some petty lords and landed knights . . . and Lord Belmore, who had lately reconciled with her father. The other Lords Declarant were expected to shun the nuptials, so Petyr's presence was essential.

Alayne understood all that well enough, but it meant that the burden of getting Sweetrobin safely down the mountain fell on her. "Give his lordship a cup of sweet-milk," she told the maester. "That will stop him from shaking on the journey down."

"He had a cup not three days past," Colemon objected.

"And wanted another last night, which you refused him."

"It was too soon. My lady, you do not understand. As I've told the Lord Protector, a pinch of sweetsleep will prevent the shaking, but it does not leave the flesh, and in time . . ."

"Time will not matter if his lordship has a shaking fit and falls off the mountain. If my father were here, I know he would tell you to keep Lord Robert calm at all costs."

"I try, my lady, yet his fits grow ever more violent, and his blood is so thin I dare not leech him any more. Sweetsleep . . . you are *certain* he was not bleeding from the nose?"

"He was sniffling," Alayne admitted, "but I saw no blood."

"I must speak to the Lord Protector. This feast . . . is that wise, I wonder, after the strain of the descent?"

"It will not be a large feast," she assured him. "No more than forty guests. Lord Nestor and his household, the Knight of the Gate, a few lesser lords and their retainers . . ."

"Lord Robert mislikes strangers, you know that, and there will be drinking, noise . . . *music*. Music frightens him."

"Music soothes him," she corrected, "the high harp especially. It's *singing* he can't abide, since Marillion killed his mother." Alayne had told the lie so many times that she remembered it that way more oft than not; the other seemed no more than a bad dream that sometimes troubled her sleep. "Lord Nestor will have no singers at the feast, only flutes and fiddles for the dancing." What would she do when the music began to play? It was a vexing question, to which her heart and head gave different answers. Sansa loved to dance, but Alayne . . . "Just give him a cup of the sweetmilk before we go, and another at the feast, and there should be no trouble."

"Very well." They paused at the foot of the stairs. "But this must be the last. For half a year, or longer."

"You had best take that up with the Lord Protector." She pushed through the door and crossed the yard. Colemon only wanted the best for his charge, Alayne knew, but what was best for Robert the boy and what was best for Lord Arryn were not always the same. Petyr had said as much, and it was true. *Maester Colemon cares only for the boy, though. Father and I have larger concerns.*

Old snow cloaked the courtyard, and icicles hung down like crystal spears from the terraces and towers. The Eyrie was built of fine white stone, and winter's mantle made it whiter still. *So beautiful,* Alayne thought, *so impregnable.* She could not love this place, no matter how she tried. Even before the guards and serving men had made their descent, the castle had seemed as empty as a tomb, and more so when Petyr Baelish was away. No one sang up there, not since Marillion. No one ever laughed too loud. Even the gods were silent. The Eyrie boasted a sept, but no septon; a godswood, but no heart tree. *No prayers are answered here,* she often thought, though some days she felt so lonely she had to try. Only the wind answered her, sighing endlessly around the seven slim white towers and rattling the Moon Door every time it gusted. *It will be even worse in winter,* she knew. *In winter this will be a cold white prison.*

And yet the thought of leaving frightened her almost as much as it frightened Robert. She only hid it better. Her father said there was no shame in being afraid, only in showing your fear. "All men live with fear," he said. Alayne was not certain she believed that. Nothing frightened Petyr Baelish. *He only said that to make me brave.* She would need to be brave down below, where the chance of being unmasked was so much greater. Petyr's friends at court had sent him word that the queen had men out looking for the Imp and Sansa Stark. *It will mean my head if I am found,* she reminded herself as she descended a flight of icy stone steps. *I must be Alayne all the time, inside and out.*

Lothor Brune was in the winch room, helping the gaoler Mord and two serving men wrestle chests of clothes and bales of cloth into six huge oaken buckets, each big enough around to hold three men. The great chain winches were the easiest way to reach the waycastle Sky, six hundred feet below them; elsewise you had to descend the natural stone chimney from the undercellar. *Or go the way Marillion went, and Lady Lysa before him.*

"Boy out of bed?" Ser Lothor asked.

"They're bathing him. He will be ready within the hour."

"We best hope he is. Mya won't wait past midday." The winch room was unheated, so his breath misted with every word.

"She'll wait," Alayne said. "She has to wait."

"Don't be so certain, m'lady. She's half mule herself, that one. I think she'd leave us all to starve before she'd put those animals at risk." He smiled when he said it. *He always smiles when he speaks of Mya Stone.* Mya was much younger than Ser Lothor, but when her father had been brokering the marriage between Lord Corbray and his merchant's daughter, he'd told her that young girls were always happiest with older men. "Innocence and experience make for a perfect marriage," he had said.

Alayne wondered what Mya made of Ser Lothor. With his squashed nose, square jaw, and nap of woolly grey hair, Brune could not be called comely, but he was not *ugly* either. *It is a common face but an honest one.* Though he had risen to knighthood, Ser Lothor's birth had been very low. One night he had told her that he was kin to the Brunes of Brownhollow, an old knightly family from Crackclaw Point. "I went to them when my father died," he confessed, "but they shat on me, and said I was no blood of theirs." He would not speak of what happened after that, except to say that he had learned all he knew of arms the hard way. Sober, he was a quiet man, but a strong one. *And Petyr says he's loyal. He trusts him as much as he trusts anyone.* Brune would be a good match for a bastard girl like Mya Stone, she thought. *It might be different if her father had acknowledged her, but he never did. And Maddy says that she's no maid either.*

Mord took up his whip and cracked it, and the first pair of oxen began to lumber in a circle, turning the winch. The chain uncoiled, rattling as it scraped across the stone, the oaken bucket swaying as it began its long descent to Sky. *Poor oxen,* thought Alayne. Mord would cut their throats and butcher them before he left, and leave them for the falcons. Whatever part remained when the Eyrie was re-opened would be roasted up for the spring feast, if it had not spoiled. A good supply of hard frozen meat foretold a summer of plenty, old Gretchel claimed.

"M'lady," Ser Lothor said, "you'd best know. Mya didn't come up alone. Lady Myranda's with her."

"Oh." *Why would she ride all the way up the mountain, just to ride back down again?* Myranda Royce was the Lord Nestor's daughter. The one time that Sansa had visited the

Gates of the Moon, on the way up to the Eyrie with her aunt Lysa and Lord Petyr, she had been away, but Alayne had heard much of her since from the Eyrie's soldiers and serving girls. Her mother was long dead, so Lady Myranda kept her father's castle for him; it was a much livelier court when she was home than when she was away, according to rumor. "Soon or late you must meet Myranda Royce," Petyr had warned her. "When you do, be careful. She likes to play the merry fool, but underneath she's shrewder than her father. Guard your tongue around her."

I will, she thought, *but I did not know I'd need to start so soon.* "Robert will be pleased." He liked Myranda Royce. "You must excuse me, ser. I need to finish packing." Alone, she climbed the steps back to her room for one last time. The windows had been sealed and shuttered, the furnishings covered. A few of her things had already been removed, the rest stored away. All of Lady Lysa's silks and samites were to be left behind. Her sheerest linens and plushest velvets, the rich embroidery and fine Myrish lace; all would remain. Down below, Alayne must dress modestly, as befit a girl of modest birth. *It makes no matter,* she told herself. *I dared not wear the best clothes even here.*

Gretchel had stripped the bed and laid out the rest of her clothing. Alayne was already wearing woolen hose beneath her skirts, over a double layer of smallclothes. Now she donned a lambswool overtunic and a hooded fur cloak, fastening it with an enameled mockingbird that had been a gift from Petyr. There was a scarf as well, and a pair of leather gloves lined with fur to match her riding boots. When she'd donned it all, she felt as fat and furry as a bear cub. *I will be glad of it on the mountain,* she had to remind herself. She took one last look at her room before she left. *I was safe here,* she thought, *but down below . . .*

When Alayne returned to the winch room, she found Mya Stone waiting impatiently with Lothor Brune and Mord. *She must have come up in the bucket to see what was taking us so long.* Slim and sinewy, Mya looked as tough as the old riding leathers she wore beneath her silvery ringmail shirt. Her hair was black as a raven's wing, so short and shaggy that Alayne suspected that she cut it with a dagger. Mya's eyes were her best feature, big and blue. *She could be pretty, if she would dress up like a girl.* Alayne found herself wondering whether Ser Lothor liked her best in her iron and leather, or dreamed of her gowned in lace and silk. Mya liked to say that her father had been a goat and her mother an owl, but Alayne had gotten the true story from Maddy. *Yes,* she thought, looking at her now, *those are his eyes, and she has his hair too, the thick black hair he shared with Renly.*

"Where is he?" the bastard girl demanded.

"His lordship is being bathed and dressed."

"He needs to make some haste. It's getting colder, can't you feel it? We need to get below Snow before the sun goes down."

"How bad is the wind?" Alayne asked her.

"It could be worse . . . and will be, after dark." Mya pushed a lock of hair from her eyes. "If he bathes much longer, we'll be trapped up here all winter with nothing to eat except each other."

Alayne did not know what to say to that. Thankfully, she was spared by the arrival of Robert Arryn. The little lord wore sky-blue velvet, a chain of gold and sapphires, and a white bearskin cloak. His squires each held an end, to keep the cloak from dragging on the floor. Maester

Colemon accompanied them, in a threadbare grey cloak lined with squirrel fur. Gretchel and Maddy were not far behind.

When he felt the cold wind on his face, Robert quailed, but Terrance and Gyles were behind him, so he could not flee. "My lord," said Mya, "will you ride down with me?"

Too brusque, Alayne thought. *She should have greeted him with a smile, told him how strong and brave he looks.*

"I want Alayne," Lord Robert said. "I'll only go with her."

"The bucket can hold all three of us."

"I just want Alayne. You smell all stinky, like a mule."

"As you wish." Mya's face showed no emotion.

Some of the winch chains were fixed to wicker baskets, others to stout oaken buckets. The largest of those was taller than Alayne, with iron bands girding its dark brown staves. Even so, her heart was in her throat as she took Robert's hand and helped him in. Once the hatch was closed behind them, the wood surrounded them on all sides. Only the top was open. *It is best that way,* she told herself, *we can't look down.* Below them was only Sky and sky. Six hundred feet of sky. For a moment she found herself wondering how long it had taken her aunt to fall that distance, and what her last thought had been as the mountain rushed up to meet her. *No, I mustn't think of that. I mustn't!*

"AWAY!" came Ser Lothor's shout. Someone shoved the bucket hard. It swayed and tipped, scraped against the floor, then swung free. She heard the *crack* of Mord's whip and the rattle of the chain. They began to descend, by jerks and starts at first, then more smoothly. Robert's face was pale and his eyes puffy, but his hands were still. The Eyrie shrank above them. The sky cells on the lower levels made the castle look something like a honeycomb from below. *A honeycomb made of ice,* Alayne thought, *a castle made of snow.* She could hear the wind whistling round the bucket.

A hundred feet down, a sudden gust caught hold of them. The bucket swayed sideways, spinning in the air, then bumped hard against the rock face behind them. Shards of ice and snow rained down on them, and the oak creaked and strained. Robert gave a gasp and clung to her, burying his face between her breasts.

"My lord is brave," Alayne said, when she felt him shaking. "I'm so frightened I can hardly talk, but not you."

She felt him nod. "The Winged Knight was brave, and so am I," he boasted to her bodice. "I'm an *Arryn.*"

"Will my Sweetrobin hold me tight?" she asked, though he was already holding her so tightly that she could scarcely breathe.

"If you like," he whispered. And clinging hard to one another, they continued on straight down to Sky.

Calling this a castle is like calling a puddle on a privy floor a lake, Alayne thought, when the bucket was opened so they might emerge within the waycastle. Sky was no more than a crescent-shaped wall of old unmortared stone, enclosing a stony ledge and the yawning mouth of a cavern. Inside were storehouses and stables, a long natural hall, and the chiseled handholds that led up to the Eyrie. Outside, the ground was strewn by broken stones and boulders. Earthen ramps gave access to the wall. Six hundred feet above, the Eyrie was so small she could hide it with her hand, but far below the Vale stretched green and golden.

Twenty mules awaited them within the waycastle, along with two mule-walkers and the Lady Myranda Royce. Lord Nestor's daughter proved to be a short, fleshy woman, of an age with Mya Stone, but where Mya was slim and sinewy, Myranda was soft-bodied and sweet-smelling, broad of hip, thick of waist, and extremely buxom. Her thick chestnut curls framed round red cheeks, a small mouth, and a pair of lively brown eyes. When Robert climbed gingerly from the bucket, she knelt in a patch of snow to kiss his hand and cheeks. "My lord," she said, "you've grown so *big*!"

"Have I?" said Robert, pleased.

"You will be taller than me soon," the lady lied. She got to her feet and brushed the snow from her skirts. "And you must be the Lord Protector's daughter," she added, as the bucket went rattling back up to the Eyrie. "I had heard that you were beautiful. I see that it is true."

Alayne curtsied. "My lady is kind to say so."

"Kind?" The older girl gave a laugh. "How boring that would be. I aspire to be wicked. You must tell me all your secrets on the ride down. May I call you Alayne?"

"If you wish, my lady." *But you'll get no secrets from me.*

"I am 'my lady' at the Gates, but up here on the mountain you may call me Randa. How many years have you, Alayne?"

"Four-and-ten, my lady." She had decided that Alayne Stone should be older than Sansa Stark.

"*Randa.* It seems a hundred years since I was four-and-ten. How innocent I was. Are you still innocent, Alayne?"

She blushed. "You should not . . . yes, of course."

"Saving yourself for Lord Robert?" Lady Myranda teased. "Or is there some ardent squire dreaming of your favors?"

"No," said Alayne, even as Robert said, "She's *my* friend. Terrance and Gyles can't have her."

A second bucket had arrived by then, thumping down softly on a mound of frozen snow. Maester Colemon emerged with the squires Terrance and Gyles. The next winch delivered Maddy and Gretchel, who rode with Mya

Stone. The bastard girl wasted no time taking charge. "We don't want to get bunched up on the mountain," she told the other mule handlers. "I'll take Lord Robert and his companions. Ossy, you'll bring down Ser Lothor and the rest, but give me an hour's lead. Carrot, you'll have charge of their chests and boxes." She turned to Robert Arryn, her black hair blowing. "Which mule will you ride today, my lord?"

"They're all stinky. I'll have the grey one, with the ear chewed off. I want Alayne to ride with me. And Myranda too."

"Where the way is wide enough. Come, my lord, let's get you on your mule. There's a smell of snow in the air."

It was another half hour before they were ready to set out. When all of them were mounted up, Mya Stone gave a crisp command, and two of Sky's men-at-arms swung the gates open. Mya led them out, with Lord Robert just behind her, swaddled in his bearskin cloak. Alayne and Myranda Royce followed, then Gretchel and Maddy, then Terrance Lynderly and Gyles Grafton. Maester Colemon brought up the rear, leading a second mule laden with his chests of herbs and potions.

Beyond the walls, the wind picked up sharply. They were above the tree line here, exposed to the elements. Alayne was thankful that she'd dressed so warmly. Her cloak was flapping noisily behind her, and a sudden gust blew back her hood. She laughed, but a few yards ahead Lord Robert squirmed, and said, "It's too cold. We should go back and wait until it's warmer."

"It will be warmer on the valley floor, my lord," said Mya. "You'll see when we get down there."

"I don't *want* to see," said Robert, but Mya paid no mind.

Their road was a crooked series of stone steps carved

into the mountainside, but the mules knew every inch of it. Alayne was glad of that. Here and there the stone was shattered from the strain of countless seasons, with all their thaws and freezes. Patches of snow clung to the rock on either side of the path, blinding white. The sun was bright, the sky was blue, and there were falcons circling overhead, riding on the wind.

Up here where the slope was steepest, the steps wound back and forth rather than plunging straight down. *Sansa Stark went up the mountain, but Alayne Stone is coming down.* It was a strange thought. Coming up, Mya had warned her to keep her eyes on the path ahead, she remembered. "Look up, not down," she said . . . but that was not possible on the descent. *I could close my eyes. The mule knows the way, he has no need of me.* But that seemed more something Sansa would have done, that frightened girl. Alayne was an older woman, and bastard brave.

At first they rode in single file, but farther down the path widened enough for two to ride abreast, and Myranda Royce came up beside her. "We have had a letter from your father," she said, as casually as if they were sitting with their septa, doing needlework. "He is on his way home, he says, and hopes to see his darling daughter soon. He writes that Lyonel Corbray seems well pleased with his bride, and even more so with her dowry. I *do* hope Lord Lyonel remembers which one he needs to bed. Lady Waynwood turned up with the Knight of Ninestars for the wedding feast, Lord Petyr says, to everyone's astonishment."

"Anya Waynwood? Truly?" The Lords Declarant were down from six to three, it would seem. The day he'd departed the mountain, Petyr Baelish had been confident of winning Symond Templeton to his side, but not so Lady Waynwood. "Was there more?" she asked. The Eyrie was such a lonely place that she was eager for any bit of news from the world beyond, however trivial or insignificant.

"Not from your father, no, but we've had other birds. The war goes on, everywhere but here. Riverrun has yielded, but Dragonstone and Storm's End still hold for Lord Stannis."

"Lady Lysa was so wise, to keep us out of it."

Myranda gave her a shrewd little smile. "Yes, she was the very soul of wisdom, that good lady." She shifted her seat. "Why must mules be so bony and ill-tempered? Mya does not feed them enough. A nice fat mule would be more comfortable to ride. There's a new High Septon, did you know? Oh, and the Night's Watch has a boy commander, some bastard son of Eddard Stark's."

"Jon Snow?" she blurted out, surprised.

"Snow? Yes, it would be Snow, I suppose."

She had not thought of Jon in ages. He was only her half brother, but still . . . with Robb and Bran and Rickon dead, Jon Snow was the only brother that remained to her. *I am a bastard too now, just like him. Oh, it would be so sweet, to see him once again.* But of course that could never be. Alayne Stone had no brothers, baseborn or otherwise.

"Our cousin Bronze Yohn had himself a mêlée at Runestone," Myranda Royce went on, oblivious, "a small one, just for squires. It was meant for Harry the Heir to win the honors, and so he did."

"Harry the Heir?"

"Lady Waynwood's ward. Harrold Hardyng. I suppose we must call him *Ser* Harry now. Bronze Yohn knighted him."

"Oh." Alayne was confused. Why should Lady Waynwood's ward be her heir? She had sons of her own blood. One was the Knight of the Bloody Gate, Ser

Donnel. She did not want to look stupid, though, so all she said was, "I pray he proves a worthy knight."

Lady Myranda snorted. "I pray he gets the pox. He has a bastard daughter by some common girl, you know. My lord father had hoped to marry me to Harry, but Lady Waynwood would not hear of it. I do not know whether it was me she found unsuitable, or just my dowry." She gave a sigh. "I do need another husband. I had one once, but I killed him."

"You did?" Alayne said, shocked.

"Oh, yes. He died on top of me. *In* me, if truth be told. You do know what goes on in a marriage bed, I hope?"

She thought of Tyrion, and of the Hound and how he'd kissed her, and gave a nod. "That must have been dreadful, my lady. Him dying. *There,* I mean, whilst . . . whilst he was . . ."

". . . fucking me?" She shrugged. "It was disconcerting, certainly. Not to mention discourteous. He did not even have the common decency to plant a child in me. Old men have weak seed. So here I am, a widow, but scarce used. Harry could have done much worse. I daresay that he will. Lady Waynwood will most like marry him to one of her granddaughters, or one of Bronze Yohn's."

"As you say, my lady." Alayne remembered Petyr's warning.

"*Randa.* Come now, you can say it. Ran. Da."

"Randa."

"Much better. I fear I must apologize to you. You will think me a dreadful slut, I know, but I bedded that pretty boy Marillion. I did not know he was a monster. He sang beautifully, and could do the sweetest things with his fingers. I would never have taken him to bed if I had known he was going to push Lady Lysa through the Moon Door. I do not bed monsters, as a rule." She studied Alayne's face and chest. "You are prettier than me, but my breasts are larger. The maesters say large breasts produce no more milk than small ones, but I do not believe it. Have you ever known a wet nurse with small teats? Yours are ample for a girl your age, but as they are bastard breasts, I shan't concern myself with them." Myranda edged her mule closer. "You know our Mya's not a maid, I trust?"

She did. Fat Maddy had whispered it to her, one time when Mya brought up their supplies. "Maddy told me."

"Of course she did. She has a mouth as big as her thighs, and her thighs are *enormous*. Mychel Redfort was the one. He used to be Lyn Corbray's squire. A *real* squire, not like that loutish lad Ser Lyn's got squiring for him now. He only took that one on for coin, they say. Mychel was the best young swordsman in the Vale, and gallant . . . or so poor Mya thought, till he wed one of Bronze Yohn's daughters. Lord Horton gave him no choice in the matter, I am sure, but it was still a cruel thing to do to Mya."

"Ser Lothor is fond of her." Alayne glanced down at the mule girl, twenty steps below. "More than fond."

"Lothor *Brune*?" Myranda raised an eyebrow. "Does she know?" She did not wait for an answer. "He has no hope, poor man. My father's tried to make a match for Mya, but she'll have none of them. She *is* half mule, that one."

Despite herself, Alayne found herself warming to the older girl. She had not had a friend to gossip with since poor Jeyne Poole. "Do you think Ser Lothor likes her as she is, in mail and leather?" she asked the older girl, who seemed so worldly-wise. "Or does he dream of her draped in silks and velvets?"

"He's a man. He dreams of her naked."

She is trying to make me blush again.

Lady Myranda must have heard her thoughts. "You do turn such a pretty shade of pink. When I blush I look quite like an apple. I have not blushed for years, though." She leaned closer. "Does your father plan to wed again?"

"My father?" Alayne had never considered that. Somehow the notion made her squirm. She found herself remembering the look on Lysa Arryn's face as she'd tumbled through the Moon Door.

"We all know how devoted he was to Lady Lysa," said Myranda, "but he cannot mourn forever. He needs a pretty young wife to wash away his grief. I imagine he could have his pick of half the noble maidens in the Vale. Who could be a better husband than our own bold Lord Protector? Though I do wish he had a better name than *Littlefinger*. How little is it, do you know?"

"His finger?" She blushed again. "I don't . . . I never . . ."

Lady Myranda laughed so loud that Mya Stone glanced back at them. "Never you mind, Alayne, I'm sure it's large enough."

They passed beneath a wind-carved arch, where long icicles clung to the pale stone, dripping down on them. On the far side the path narrowed and plunged down sharply for a hundred feet or more. Myranda was forced to drop back. Alayne gave the mule his head. The steepness of this part of the descent made her cling tightly to her saddle. The steps here had been worn smooth by the iron-shod hooves of all the mules who'd passed this way, until they resembled a series of shallow stone bowls. Water filled the bottoms of the bowls, glimmering golden in the afternoon sun. *It is water now,* Alayne thought, *but come dark, all of it will turn to ice.* She realized that she was holding her breath, and let it out. Mya Stone and Lord Robert had almost reached the rock spire where the slope leveled off again. She tried to look at them, and only them. *I will not fall,* she told herself. *Mya's mule will see me through.* The wind skirled around her, as she bumped and scraped her way down step by step. It seemed to take a lifetime.

Then all at once she was at the bottom with Mya and her little lord, huddled beneath a twisted, rocky spire. Ahead stretched a high stone saddle, narrow and icy. Alayne could hear the wind shrieking, and feel it plucking at her cloak. She remembered this place from her ascent. It had frightened her then, and it frightened her now. "It is wider than it looks," Mya was telling Lord Robert in a cheerful voice. "A yard across, and no more than eight yards long, that's nothing."

"Nothing," Robert said. His hand was shaking.

Oh, no, Alayne thought. *Please. Not here. Not now.*

"It's best to lead the mules across," Mya said. "If it please my lord, I'll take mine over first, then come back for yours." Lord Robert did not answer. He was staring at the narrow saddle with his reddened eyes. "I shan't be long, my lord," Mya promised, but Alayne doubted that the boy could even hear her.

When the bastard girl led her mule out from beneath the shelter of the spire, the wind caught her in its teeth. Her cloak lifted, twisting and flapping in the air. Mya staggered, and for half a heartbeat it seemed as if she would be blown over the precipice, but somehow she regained her balance and went on.

Alayne took Robert's gloved hand in her own to stop his shaking. "Sweetrobin," she said, "I'm scared. Hold my hand, and help me get across. I know *you're* not afraid."

He looked at her, his pupils small dark pinpricks in eyes as big and white as eggs. "I'm not?"

"Not you. You're my winged knight, Ser Sweetrobin."

"The Winged Knight could fly," Robert whispered.

"Higher than the mountains." She gave his hand a squeeze.

Lady Myranda had joined them by the spire. "He could," she echoed, when she saw what was happening.

"Ser Sweetrobin," Lord Robert said, and Alayne knew that she dare not wait for Mya to return. She helped the boy dismount, and hand in hand they walked out onto the bare stone saddle, their cloaks snapping and flapping behind them. All around was empty air and sky, the ground falling away sharply to either side. There was ice underfoot, and broken stones just waiting to turn an ankle, and the wind was howling fiercely. *It sounds like a wolf,* thought Sansa. *A ghost wolf, big as mountains.*

And then they were on the other side, and Mya Stone was laughing and lifting Robert for a hug. "Be careful," Alayne told her. "He can hurt you, flailing. You wouldn't think so, but he can." They found a place for him, a cleft in the rock to keep him out of the cold wind. Alayne tended him until the shaking passed, whilst Mya went back to help the others cross.

Fresh mules awaited them at Snow, and a hot meal of stewed goat and onions. She ate with Mya and Myranda. "So you're brave as well as beautiful," Myranda said to her.

"No." The compliment made her blush. "I'm not. I was so scared. I don't think I could have crossed without Lord Robert." She turned to Mya Stone. "You almost fell."

"You're mistaken. I never fall." Mya's hair had tumbled across her cheek, hiding one eye.

"Almost, I said. I saw you. Weren't you afraid?"

Mya shook her head. "I remember a man throwing me in the air when I was very little. He stands as tall as the sky, and he throws me up so high it feels as though I'm flying. We're both laughing, laughing so much that I can hardly catch a breath, and finally I laugh so hard I wet myself, but that only makes him laugh the louder. I was never afraid when he was throwing me. I knew that he would always be there to catch me." She pushed her hair back. "Then one day he wasn't. Men come and go. They lie, or die, or leave you. A mountain is not a man, though, and a stone is a mountain's daughter. I trust my father, and I trust my mules. I won't fall." She put her hand on a jagged spur of rock, and got to her feet. "Best finish. We have a long way yet to go, and I can smell a storm."

The snow began to fall as they were leaving Stone, the largest and lowest of the three waycastles that defended the approaches to the Eyrie. Dusk was settling by then. Lady Myranda suggested that perhaps they might turn back, spend the night at Stone, and resume their descent when the sun came up, but Mya would not hear of it. "The snow might be five feet deep by then, and the steps treacherous even for my mules," she said. "We will do better to press on. We'll take it slow."

And so they did. Below Stone the steps were broader and less steep, winding in and out of the tall pines and grey-green sentinels that cloaked the lower slopes of the Giant's Lance. Mya's mules knew every root and rock on the way down, it seemed, and any they forgot the bastard girl remembered. Half the night was gone before they sighted the lights of the Gates of the Moon through the falling snow. The last part of their journey was the most peaceful. The snow fell steadily, cloaking all the world in white. Sweetrobin drifted to sleep in the saddle, swaying back and forth with the motion of his mule. Even Lady Myranda began to yawn and complain of being weary. "We have apartments prepared for all of you," she told Alayne, "but if you like you may share my bed tonight. It's large enough for four."

"I should be honored, my lady."

"Randa. Count yourself fortunate that I'm so tired. All I

want to do is curl up and go to sleep. Usually when ladies share my bed they have to pay a pillow tax and tell me all about the wicked things they've done."

"What if they haven't done any wicked things?"

"Why, then they must confess all the wicked things they *want* to do. Not you, of course. I can see how virtuous you are just by looking at those rosy cheeks and big blue eyes of yours." She yawned again. "I hope your feet are warm. I do hate bedmaids with cold feet."

By the time they finally reached her father's castle, Lady Myranda was drowsing too, and Alayne was dreaming of her bed. *It will be a featherbed,* she told herself, *soft and warm and deep, piled high with furs. I will dream a sweet dream, and when I wake there will be dogs barking, women gossiping beside the well, swords ringing in the yard. And later there will be a feast, with music and dancing.* After the deathly silence of the Eyrie, she yearned for shouts and laughter.

As the riders were climbing off their mules, however, one of Petyr's guardsmen emerged from within the keep. "Lady Alayne," he said, "the Lord Protector has been waiting for you."

"He's back?" she said, startled.

"At evenfall. You'll find him in the west tower."

The hour was closer to dawn than to dusk, and most of the castle was asleep, but not Petyr Baelish. Alayne found him seated by a crackling fire, drinking hot mulled wine with three men she did not know. They all rose when she entered, and Petyr smiled warmly. "Alayne. Come, give your father a kiss."

She hugged him dutifully and kissed him on the cheek. "I am sorry to intrude, Father. No one told me you had company."

"You are never an intrusion, sweetling. I was just now telling these good knights what a dutiful daughter I had."

"Dutiful and beautiful," said an elegant young knight whose thick blond mane cascaded down well past his shoulders.

"Aye," said the second knight, a burly fellow with a thick salt-and-pepper beard, a red nose bulbous with broken veins, and gnarled hands as large as hams. "You left out that part, m'lord."

"I would do the same if she were my daughter," said the last knight, a short, wiry man with a wry smile, pointed nose, and bristly orange hair. "Particularly around louts like us."

Alayne laughed. "Are you louts?" she said, teasing. "Why, I took the three of you for gallant knights."

"Knights they are," said Petyr. "Their gallantry has yet to be demonstrated, but we may hope. Allow me to present Ser Byron, Ser Morgarth, and Ser Shadrich. Sers, the Lady Alayne, my natural and very clever daughter . . . with whom I must needs confer, if you will be so good as to excuse us."

The three knights bowed and withdrew, though the tall one with the blond hair kissed her hand before taking his leave.

"Hedge knights?" said Alayne, when the door had closed.

"Hungry knights. I thought it best that we have a few more swords about us. The times grow ever more interesting, my sweet, and when the times are interesting you can never have too many swords. The *Merling King*'s returned to Gulltown, and old Oswell had some tales to tell."

She knew better than to ask what sort of tales. If Petyr had wanted her to know, he would have told her. "I did not expect you back so soon," she said. "I am glad you've come."

"I would never have known it from the kiss you gave me." He pulled her closer, caught her face between his hands, and kissed her on the lips for a long time. "Now that's the sort of kiss that says *welcome home*. See that you do better next time."

"Yes, Father." She could feel herself blushing.

He did not hold her kiss against her. "You would not believe half of what is happening in King's Landing, sweetling. Cersei stumbles from one idiocy to the next, helped along by her council of the deaf, the dim, and the blind. I always anticipated that she would beggar the realm and destroy herself, but I never expected she would do it quite so *fast*. It is quite vexing. I had hoped to have four or five quiet years to plant some seeds and allow some fruits to ripen, but now . . . it is a good thing that I thrive on chaos. What little peace and order the five kings left us will not long survive the three queens, I fear."

"Three queens?" She did not understand.

Nor did Petyr choose to explain. Instead, he smiled and said, "I have brought my sweet girl back a gift."

Alayne was as pleased as she was surprised. "Is it a gown?" She had heard there were fine seamstresses in Gulltown, and she was so tired of dressing drably.

"Something better. Guess again."

"Jewels?"

"No jewels could hope to match my daughter's eyes."

"Lemons? Did you find some lemons?" She had promised Sweetrobin lemon cake, and for lemon cake you needed lemons.

Petyr Baelish took her by the hand and drew her down onto his lap. "I have made a marriage contract for you."

"A marriage . . ." Her throat tightened. She did not

want to wed again, not now, perhaps not ever. "I do not . . . I cannot marry. Father, I . . ." Alayne looked to the door, to make certain it was closed. "I *am* married," she whispered. "You know."

Petyr put a finger to her lips to silence her. "The dwarf wed Ned Stark's daughter, not mine. Be that as it may. This is only a betrothal. The marriage must needs wait until Cersei is done and Sansa's safely widowed. And you must meet the boy and win his approval. Lady Waynwood will not make him marry against his will, she was quite firm on that."

"Lady *Waynwood*?" Alayne could hardly believe it. "Why would she marry one of her sons to . . . to a . . ."

". . . bastard? For a start, you are the *Lord Protector*'s bastard, never forget. The Waynwoods are very old and very proud, but not as rich as one might think, as I discovered when I began buying up their debt. Not that Lady Anya would ever sell a son for gold. A ward, however . . . young Harry's only a cousin, and the dower that I offered her ladyship was even larger than the one that Lyonel Corbray just collected. It had to be, for her to risk Bronze Yohn's wroth. This will put all his plans awry. You are promised to Harrold Hardyng, sweetling, provided you can win his boyish heart . . . which should not be hard, for you."

"Harry the Heir?" Alayne tried to recall what Myranda had told her about him on the mountain. "He was just knighted. And he has a bastard daughter by some common girl."

"And another on the way by a different wench. Harry can be a beguiling one, no doubt. Soft sandy hair, deep blue eyes, and dimples when he smiles. And *very* gallant, I am told." He teased her with a smile. "Bastard-born or no, sweetling, when this match is announced you will be the envy of every highborn maiden in the Vale, and a few from the riverlands and the Reach as well."

"Why?" Alayne was lost. "Is Ser Harrold . . . how could he be Lady Waynwood's heir? Doesn't she have sons of her own blood?"

"Three," Petyr allowed. She could smell the wine on his breath, the cloves and nutmeg. "Daughters too, and grandsons."

"Won't they come before Harry? I don't understand."

"You will. Listen." Petyr took her hand in his own and brushed his finger lightly down the inside of her palm. "Lord Jasper Arryn, begin with him. Jon Arryn's father. He begot three children, two sons and a daughter. Jon was the eldest, so the Eyrie and the lordship passed to him. His sister Alys wed Ser Elys Waynwood, uncle to the present Lady Waynwood." He made a wry face. "Elys and Alys, isn't that precious? Lord Jasper's younger son, Ser Ronnel Arryn, wed a Belmore girl, but only rang her once or twice before dying of a bad belly. Their son Elbert was being born in one bed even as poor Ronnel was dying in another down the hall. Are you paying close attention, sweetling?"

"Yes. There was Jon and Alys and Ronnel, but Ronnel died."

"Good. Now, Jon Arryn married thrice, but his first two wives gave him no children, so for long years his nephew Elbert was his heir. Meantime, Elys was plowing Alys quite dutifully, and she was whelping once a year. She gave him nine children, eight girls and one precious little boy, another Jasper, after which she died exhausted. Boy Jasper, inconsiderate of the heroic efforts that had gone into begetting him, got himself kicked in the head by a horse when he was three years old. A pox took two of his sisters soon after, leaving six. The eldest married Ser

Denys Arryn, a distant cousin to the Lords of the Eyrie. There are several branches of House Arryn scattered across the Vale, all as proud as they are penurious, save for the Gulltown Arryns, who had the rare good sense to marry merchants. They're rich, but less than couth, so no one talks about them. Ser Denys hailed from one of the poor, proud branches . . . but he was also a renowned jouster, handsome and gallant and brimming with courtesy. And he had that magic Arryn name, which made him ideal for the eldest Waynwood girl. Their children would be Arryns, and the next heirs to the Vale should any ill befall Elbert. Well, as it happened, Mad King Aerys befell Elbert. You know that story?"

She did. "The Mad King murdered him."

"He did indeed. And soon after, Ser Denys left his pregnant Waynwood wife to ride to war. He died during the Battle of the Bells, of an excess of gallantry and an axe. When they told his lady of his death she perished of grief, and her newborn son soon followed. No matter. Jon Arryn had gotten himself a young wife during the war, one he had reason to believe fertile. He was very hopeful, I'm sure, but you and I know that all he ever got from Lysa were stillbirths, miscarriages, and poor Sweetrobin.

"Which brings us back to the five remaining daughters of Elys and Alys. The eldest had been left terribly scarred by the same pox that killed her sisters, so she became a septa. Another was seduced by a sellsword. Ser Elys cast her out, and she joined the silent sisters after her bastard died in infancy. The third wed the Lord of the Paps, but proved barren. The fourth was on her way to the riverlands to marry some Bracken when Burned Men carried her off. That left the youngest, who wed a landed knight sworn to the Waynwoods, gave him a son that she named Harrold, and perished." He turned her hand over and lightly kissed her wrist. "So tell me, sweetling—why is Harry the Heir?"

Her eyes widened. "He is not Lady Waynwood's heir. He's *Robert*'s heir. If Robert were to die . . ."

Petyr arched an eyebrow. "*When* Robert dies. Our poor brave Sweetrobin is such a sickly boy, it is only a matter of time. *When* Robert dies, Harry the Heir becomes Lord Harrold, Defender of the Vale and Lord of the Eyrie. Jon Arryn's bannermen will never love me, nor our silly, shaking Robert, but they will love their Young Falcon . . . and when they come together for his wedding, and you come out with your long auburn hair, clad in a maiden's cloak of white and grey with a direwolf emblazoned on the back . . . why, every knight in the Vale will pledge his sword to win you back your birthright. So those are your gifts from me, my sweet Sansa . . . Harry, the Eyrie, and Winterfell. That's worth another kiss now, don't you think?"

BRIENNE

This is an evil dream, she thought. But if she were dreaming, why did it hurt so much?

The rain had stopped falling, but all the world was wet. Her cloak felt as heavy as her mail. The ropes that bound her wrists were soaked through, but that only made them tighter. No matter how Brienne turned her hands, she could not slip free. She did not understand who had bound her, or why. She tried to ask the shadows, but they did not answer. Perhaps they did not hear her. Perhaps they were not real. Under her layers of wet wool and rusting mail, her skin was flushed and feverish. She wondered whether all of this was just a fever dream.

She had a horse beneath her, though she could not remember mounting. She lay facedown across his hindquarters, like a sack of oats. Her wrists and ankles had been lashed together. The air was damp, the ground cloaked in mist. Her head pounded with every step. She could hear voices, but all she could see was the earth beneath the horse's hooves. There were things broken inside of her. Her face felt swollen, her cheek was sticky with blood, and every jounce and bounce send a stab of agony through her arm. She could hear Podrick calling her, as if from far away. "Ser?" he kept saying. "Ser? My lady? Ser? My lady?" His voice was faint and hard to hear. Finally, there was only silence.

She dreamt she was at Harrenhal, down in the bear pit once again. This time it was Biter facing her, huge and bald and maggot-white, with weeping sores upon his cheeks. Naked he came, fondling his member, gnashing his filed teeth together. Brienne fled from him. "My sword," she called. "Oathkeeper. Please." The watchers did not answer. Renly was there, with Nimble Dick and Catelyn Stark. Shagwell, Pyg, and Timeon had come, and the corpses from the trees with their sunken cheeks, swollen tongues, and empty eye sockets. Brienne wailed in horror at the sight of them, and Biter grabbed her arm and yanked her close and tore a chunk from her face. "Jaime," she heard herself scream, *"Jaime."*

Even in the depths of dream the pain was there. Her face throbbed. Her shoulder bled. Breathing hurt. The pain crackled up her arm like lightning. She cried out for a maester.

"We have no maester," said a girl's voice. "Only me."

I am looking for a girl, Brienne remembered. *A highborn maid of three-and-ten, with blue eyes and auburn hair.* "My lady?" she said. "Lady Sansa?"

A man laughed. "She thinks you're Sansa Stark."

"She can't go much farther. She'll die."

"One less lion. I won't weep."

Brienne heard the sound of someone praying. She

thought of Septon Meribald, but all the words were wrong. *The night is dark and full of terrors, and so are dreams.*

They were riding through a gloomy wood, a dank, dark, silent place where the pines pressed close. The ground was soft beneath her horse's hooves, and the tracks she left behind filled up with blood. Beside her rode Lord Renly, Dick Crabb, and Vargo Hoat. Blood ran from Renly's throat. The Goat's torn ear oozed pus. "Where are we going?" Brienne asked. "Where are you taking me?" None of them would answer. *How can they answer? All of them are dead.* Did that mean that she was dead as well?

Lord Renly was ahead of her, her sweet smiling king. He was leading her horse through the trees. Brienne called out to tell him how much she loved him, but when he turned to scowl at her, she saw that he was not Renly after all. Renly never scowled. *He always had a smile for me,* she thought . . . except . . .

"Cold," her king said, puzzled, and a shadow moved without a man to cast it, and her sweet lord's blood came washing through the green steel of his gorget to drench her hands. He had been a warm man, but his blood was cold as ice. *This is not real,* she told herself. *This is another bad dream, and soon I'll wake.*

Her mount came to a sudden halt. Rough hands seized hold of her. She saw shafts of red afternoon light slanting through the branches of a chestnut tree. A horse rooted amongst the dead leaves after chestnuts, and men moved nearby, talking in quiet voices. Ten, twelve, maybe more. Brienne did not recognize their faces. She was stretched out on the ground, her back against a tree trunk. "Drink this, m'lady," said the girl's voice. She lifted a cup to Brienne's lips. The taste was strong and sour. Brienne spat it out. "Water," she gasped. "Please. Water."

"Water won't help the pain. This will. A little." The girl put the cup to Brienne's lips again.

It even hurt to drink. Wine ran down her chin and dribbled on her chest. When the cup was empty the girl filled it from a skin. Brienne sucked it down until she sputtered. "No more."

"More. You have a broken arm, and some of your ribs is cracked. Two, maybe three."

"Biter," Brienne said, remembering the weight of him, the way his knee had slammed into her chest.

"Aye. A real monster, that one."

It all came back to her; lightning above and mud below, the rain *pinging* softly against the dark steel of the Hound's helm, the terrible strength in Biter's hands. Suddenly she could not stand being bound. She tried to wrench free of her ropes, but all that did was chafe her worse. Her wrists were tied too tightly. There was dried blood on the hemp. "Is he dead?" She trembled. "Biter. *Is he dead?*" She remembered his teeth tearing into the flesh of her face. The thought that he might still be out there somewhere, breathing, made Brienne want to scream.

"He's dead. Gendry shoved a spearpoint through the back of his neck. Drink, m'lady, or I'll pour it down your throat."

She drank. "I am looking for a girl," she whispered, between swallows. She almost said *my sister.* "A highborn maid of three-and-ten. She has blue eyes and auburn hair."

"I'm not her."

No. Brienne could see that. The girl was thin to the point of looking starved. She wore her brown hair in a braid, and her eyes were older than her years. *Brown hair, brown eyes, plain. Willow, six years older.* "You're the sister. The innkeep."

"I might be." The girl squinted. "What if I am?"

"Do you have a name?" Brienne asked. Her stomach gurgled. She was afraid that she might retch.

"Heddle. Same as Willow. Jeyne Heddle."

"Jeyne. Untie my hands. Please. Have pity. The ropes are chafing my wrists. I'm bleeding."

"It's not allowed. You're to stay bound, till . . ."

". . . till you stand before m'lady." Renly stood behind the girl, pushing his black hair out of his eyes. *Not Renly. Gendry.* "M'lady means for you to answer for your crimes."

"M'lady." The wine was making her head spin. It was hard to think. "Stoneheart. Is that who you mean?" Lord Randyll had spoken of her, back at Maidenpool. "Lady Stoneheart."

"Some call her that. Some call her other things. The Silent Sister. Mother Merciless. The Hangwoman."

The Hangwoman. When Brienne closed her eyes, she saw the corpses swaying underneath the bare brown limbs, their faces black and swollen. Suddenly she was desperately afraid. "Podrick. My squire. Where is Podrick? And the others . . . Ser Hyle, Septon Meribald. Dog. What did you do with Dog?"

Gendry and the girl exchanged a look. Brienne fought to rise, and managed to get one knee under her before the world began to spin. "It was you killed the dog, m'lady," she heard Gendry say, just before the darkness swallowed her again.

Then she was back at the Whispers, standing amongst the ruins and facing Clarence Crabb. He was huge and fierce, mounted on an aurochs shaggier than he was. The beast pawed the ground in fury, tearing deep furrows in the earth. Crabb's teeth had been filed into points. When Brienne went to draw her sword, she found her scabbard empty. "No," she cried, as Ser Clarence charged. It wasn't fair. She could not fight without her magic sword. Ser Jaime had given it to her. The thought of failing him as she had failed Lord Renly made her want to weep. "My sword. Please, I have to find my sword."

"The wench wants her sword back," a voice declared.

"And I want Cersei Lannister to suck my cock. So what?"

"Jaime called it Oathkeeper. *Please.*" But the voices did not listen, and Clarence Crabb thundered down on her and swept off her head. Brienne spiraled down into a deeper darkness.

She dreamed that she was lying in a boat, her head pillowed on someone's lap. There were shadows all around them, hooded men in mail and leather, paddling them across a foggy river with muffled oars. She was drenched in sweat, burning, yet somehow shivering too. The fog was full of faces. *"Beauty,"* whispered the willows on the bank, but the reeds said, *"freak, freak."* Brienne shuddered. "Stop," she said. "Someone make them stop."

The next time she woke, Jeyne was holding a cup of hot soup to her lips. *Onion broth,* Brienne thought. She drank as much of it as she could, until a bit of carrot caught in her throat and made her choke. Coughing was agony. "Easy," the girl said.

"Gendry," she wheezed. "I have to talk with Gendry."

"He turned back at the river, m'lady. He's gone back to his forge, to Willow and the little ones, to keep them safe."

No one can keep them safe. She began to cough again. "Ah, let her choke. Save us a rope." One of the shadow men shoved the girl aside. He was clad in rusted rings and a studded belt. At his hip hung longsword and dirk. A yellow greatcloak was plastered to his shoulders, sodden and filthy. From his shoulders rose a steel dog's head, its teeth bared in a snarl.

"No," Brienne moaned. "No, you're dead, I killed you."

The Hound laughed. "You got that backwards. It'll be me killing you. I'd do it now, but m'lady wants to see you hanged."

Hanged. The word sent a jolt of fear through her. She looked at the girl, Jeyne. *She is too young to be so hard.* "Bread and salt," Brienne gasped. "The inn . . . Septon Meribald fed the children . . . we broke bread with your sister . . ."

"Guest right don't mean so much as it used to," said the girl. "Not since m'lady come back from the wedding. Some o' them swinging down by the river figured they was guests too."

"We figured different," said the Hound. "They wanted beds. We gave 'em trees."

"We got more trees, though," put in another shadow, one-eyed beneath a rusty pothelm. "We always got more trees."

When it was time to mount again, they yanked a leather hood down over her face. There were no eyeholes. The leather muffled the sounds around her. The taste of onions lingered on her tongue, sharp as the knowledge of her failure. *They mean to hang me.* She thought of Jaime, of Sansa, of her father back on Tarth, and was glad for the hood. It helped hide the tears welling in her eyes. From time to time she heard the outlaws talking, but she could not make out their words. After a while she gave herself up to weariness and the slow, steady motion of her horse.

This time she dreamed that she was home again, at Evenfall. Through the tall arched windows of her lord father's hall she could see the sun just going down. *I was safe here. I was safe.*

She was dressed in silk brocade, a quartered gown of blue and red decorated with golden suns and silver crescent moons. On another girl it might have been a pretty gown, but not on her. She was twelve, ungainly and uncomfortable, waiting to meet the young knight her father had arranged for her to marry, a boy six years her senior, sure to be a famous champion one day. She dreaded his arrival. Her bosom was too small, her hands and feet too big. Her hair kept sticking up, and there was a pimple nestled in the fold beside her nose. "He will bring a rose for you," her father promised her, but a rose was no good, a rose could not keep her safe. It was a sword she wanted. *Oathkeeper. I have to find the girl. I have to find his honor.*

Finally the doors opened, and her betrothed strode into her father's hall. She tried to greet him as she had been instructed, only to have blood come pouring from her mouth. She had bitten her tongue off as she waited. She spat it at the young knight's feet, and saw the disgust on his face. "Brienne the Beauty," he said in a mocking tone. "I have seen sows more beautiful than you." He tossed the rose in her face. As he walked away, the griffins on his cloak rippled and blurred and changed to lions. *Jaime!* she wanted to cry. *Jaime, come back for me!* But her tongue lay on the floor by the rose, drowned in blood.

Brienne woke suddenly, gasping.

She did not know where she was. The air was cold and heavy, and smelled of earth and worms and mold. She was lying on a pallet beneath a mound of sheepskins, with rock above her head and roots poking through the walls. The only light came from a tallow candle, smoking in a pool of melted wax.

She pushed aside the sheepskins. Someone had stripped her of her clothes and armor, she saw. She was clad in a brown woolen shift, thin but freshly washed. Her forearm had been splinted and bound up with linen, though. One side of her face felt wet and stiff. When she touched herself, she found some sort of damp poultice covering her cheek and jaw and ear. *Biter . . .*

Brienne got to her feet. Her legs felt weak as water, her head as light as air. "Is anyone there?"

Something moved in one of the shadowed alcoves behind the candle; an old grey man clad in rags. The blankets that had covered him slipped to the floor. He sat up and rubbed his eyes. "Lady Brienne? You gave me a fright. I was dreaming."

No, she thought, *that was me.* "What place is this? Is this a dungeon?"

"A cave. Like rats, we must run back to our holes when the dogs come sniffing after us, and there are more dogs every day." He was clad in the ragged remains of an old robe, pink and white. His hair was long and grey and tangled, the loose skin of his cheeks and chin was covered with coarse stubble. "Are you hungry? Could you keep down a cup of milk? Perhaps some bread and honey?"

"I want my clothes. My sword." She felt naked without her mail, and she wanted Oathkeeper at her side. "The way out. Show me the way out." The floor of the cave was dirt and stone, rough beneath the soles of her feet. Even now she felt light-headed, as if she were floating. The flickering light cast queer shadows. *Spirits of the slain,* she thought, *dancing all about me, hiding when I turn to look at them.* Everywhere she saw holes and cracks and crevices, but there was no way to know which passages led out, which would take her deeper into the cave, and which went nowhere. All were black as pitch.

"Might I feel your brow, my lady?" Her gaoler's hand was scarred and hard with callus, yet strangely gentle. "Your fever has broken," he announced, in a voice flavored with the accents of the Free Cities. "Well and good. Just yesterday your flesh felt as if it were on fire. Jeyne feared that we might lose you."

"Jeyne. The tall girl?"

"The very one. Though she is not so tall as you, my lady. Long Jeyne, the men call her. It was she who set your arm and splinted it, as well as any maester. She did what she could for your face as well, washing out the wounds with boiled ale to stop the mortification. Even so . . . a human bite is a filthy thing. That is where the fever came from, I am certain." The grey man touched her bandaged face. "We had to cut away some of the flesh. Your face will not be pretty, I fear."

It has never been pretty. "Scars, you mean?"

"My lady, that creature chewed off half your cheek."

Brienne could not help but flinch. *Every knight has battle scars,* Ser Goodwin had warned her, when she asked him to teach her the sword. *Is that what you want, child?* Her old master-at-arms had been talking about sword cuts, though; he could never have anticipated Biter's pointed teeth. "Why set my bones and wash my wounds if you only mean to hang me?"

"Why indeed?" He glanced at the candle, as if he could no longer bear to look at her. "You fought bravely at the inn, they tell me. Lem should not have left the crossroads. He was told to stay close, hidden, to come at once if he saw smoke rising from the chimney . . . but when word reached him that the Mad Dog of Saltpans had been seen making his way north along the Green Fork, he took the bait. We have been hunting that lot for so long . . . still, he ought to have known better. As it was, it was half a day before he realized that the mummers had used a stream to hide their tracks and doubled back behind him, and then he lost more time circling around a column of Frey knights. If not for you, only corpses might have remained at the inn by the time that Lem and his men got back. *That* was why Jeyne dressed your wounds, mayhaps. Whatever else you may have done, you won those wounds honorably, in the best of causes."

Whatever else you may have done. "What is it that you think I've done?" she said. *"Who are you?"*

"We were king's men when we began," the man told her, "but king's men must have a king, and we have none. We were brothers too, but now our brotherhood is broken. I do not know who we are, if truth be told, nor where we might be going. I only know the road is dark. The fires have not shown me what lies at its end."

I know where it ends. I have seen the corpses in the trees. "Fires," Brienne repeated. All at once she understood. "You are the Myrish priest. The red wizard."

He looked down at his ragged robes, and smiled ruefully. "The pink pretender, rather. I am Thoros, late of Myr, aye . . . a bad priest and a worse wizard."

"You ride with the Dondarrion. The lightning lord."

"Lightning comes and goes and then is seen no more. So too with men. Lord Beric's fire has gone out of this world, I fear. A grimmer shadow leads us in his place."

"The Hound?"

The priest pursed his lips. "The Hound is dead and buried."

"I saw him. In the woods."

"A fever dream, my lady."

"He said that he would hang me."

"Even dreams can lie. My lady, how long has it been since you have eaten? Surely you are famished?"

She was, she realized. Her belly felt hollow. "Food . . . food would be welcome, thank you."

"A meal, then. Sit. We will talk more, but first a meal. Wait here." Thoros lit a taper from the sagging candle, and vanished into a black hole beneath a ledge of rock. Brienne found herself alone in the small cave. *For how long, though?*

She prowled the chamber, looking for a weapon. Any sort of weapon would have served; a staff, a club, a dagger. She found only rocks. One fit her fist nicely . . . but she remembered the Whispers, and what happened when Shagwell tried to pit a stone against a knife. When she heard the priest's returning footsteps, she let the rock fall to the cavern floor and resumed her seat.

Thoros had bread and cheese and a bowl of stew. "I am sorry," he said. "The last of the milk had soured, and the honey is all gone. Food grows scant. Still, this will fill you."

The stew was cold and greasy, the bread hard, the cheese harder. Brienne had never eaten anything half so good. "Are my companions here?" she asked the priest, as she was spooning up the last of the stew.

"The septon was set free to go upon his way. There was no harm in him. The others are here, awaiting judgment."

"Judgment?" She frowned. "Podrick Payne is just a boy."

"He says he is a squire."

"You know how boys will boast."

"The Imp's squire. He has fought in battles, by his own admission. He has even killed, to hear him tell it."

"A boy," she said again. "Have pity."

"My lady," Thoros said, "I do not doubt that kindness and mercy and forgiveness can still be found somewhere in these Seven Kingdoms, but do not look for them here. This is a cave, not a temple. When men must live like rats in the dark beneath the earth, they soon run out of pity, as they do of milk and honey."

"And justice? Can that be found in caves?"

"Justice." Thoros smiled wanly. "I remember justice. It

had a pleasant taste. Justice was what we were about when Beric led us, or so we told ourselves. We were king's men, knights, and heroes . . . but some knights are dark and full of terror, my lady. War makes monsters of us all."

"Are you saying you are monsters?"

"I am saying we are human. You are not the only one with wounds, Lady Brienne. Some of my brothers were good men when this began. Some were . . . less good, shall we say? Though there are those who say it does not matter how a man begins, but only how he ends. I suppose it is the same for women." The priest got to his feet. "Our time together is at an end, I fear. I hear my brothers coming. Our lady sends for you."

Brienne heard their footsteps and saw torchlight flickering in the passage. "You told me she had gone to Fairmarket."

"And so she had. She returned whilst we were sleeping. She never sleeps herself."

I will not be afraid, she told herself, but it was too late for that. *I will not let them see my fear,* she promised herself instead. There were four of them, hard men with haggard faces, clad in mail and scale and leather. She recognized one of them; the man with one eye, from her dreams.

The biggest of the four wore a stained and tattered yellow cloak. "Enjoy the food?" he asked. "I hope so. It's the last food you're ever like to eat." He was brown-haired, bearded, brawny, with a broken nose that had healed badly. *I know this man,* Brienne thought. "You are the Hound."

He grinned. His teeth were awful; crooked, and streaked brown with rot. "I suppose I am. Seeing as how m'lady went and killed the last one." He turned his head and spat.

She remembered lightning flashing, the mud beneath

her feet. "It was Rorge I killed. He took the helm from Clegane's grave, and you stole it off his corpse."

"I didn't hear him objecting."

Thoros sucked in his breath in dismay. "Is this true? A dead man's helm? Have we fallen that low?"

The big man scowled at him. "It's good steel."

"There is nothing good about that helm, nor the men who wore it," said the red priest. "Sandor Clegane was a man in torment, and Rorge a beast in human skin."

"I'm not them."

"Then why show the world their face? Savage, snarling, twisted . . . is that who you would be, Lem?"

"The sight of it will make my foes afraid."

"The sight of it makes me afraid."

"Close your eyes, then." The man in the yellow cloak made a sharp gesture. "Bring the whore."

Brienne did not resist. There were four of them, and she was weak and wounded, naked beneath the woolen shift. She had to bend her neck to keep from hitting her head as they marched her through the twisting passage. The way ahead rose sharply, turning twice before emerging in a much larger cavern full of outlaws.

A fire pit had been dug into the center of the floor, and the air was blue with smoke. Men clustered near the flames, warming themselves against the chill of the cave. Others stood along the walls or sat cross-legged on straw pallets. There were women too, and even a few children peering out from behind their mothers' skirts. The one face Brienne knew belonged to Long Jeyne Heddle.

A trestle table had been set up across the cave, in a cleft in the rock. Behind it sat a woman all in grey, cloaked and hooded. In her hands was a crown, a bronze circlet ringed by iron swords. She was studying it, her fingers stroking the blades as if to test their sharpness. Her eyes glimmered under her hood.

Grey was the color of the silent sisters, the handmaidens of the Stranger. Brienne felt a shiver climb her spine. *Stoneheart.*

"M'lady," said the big man. "Here she is."

"Aye," added the one-eyed man. "The Kingslayer's whore."

She flinched. "Why would you call me that?"

"If I had a silver stag for every time you said his name, I'd be as rich as your friends the Lannisters."

"That was only . . . you do not understand . . ."

"Don't we, though?" The big man laughed. "I think we might. There's a stink of *lion* about you, lady."

"That's not so."

Another of the outlaws stepped forward, a younger man in a greasy sheepskin jerkin. In his hand was Oathkeeper. "This says it is." His voice was frosted with the accents of the north. He slid the sword from its scabbard and placed it in front of Lady Stoneheart. In the light from the firepit the red and black ripples in the blade almost seemed to move, but the woman in grey had eyes only for the pommel: a golden lion's head, with ruby eyes that shone like two red stars.

"There is this as well." Thoros of Myr drew a parchment from his sleeve, and put it down next to the sword. "It bears the boy king's seal and says the bearer is about his business."

Lady Stoneheart set the sword aside to read the letter.

"The sword was given me for a good purpose," said Brienne. "Ser Jaime swore an oath to Catelyn Stark . . ."

". . . before his friends cut her throat for her, that must have been," said the big man in the yellow cloak. "We all know about the Kingslayer and his oaths."

It is no good, Brienne realized. *No words of mine will sway them.* She plunged ahead despite that. "He promised Lady Catelyn her daughters, but by the time we reached King's Landing they were gone. Jaime sent me out to seek the Lady Sansa . . ."

". . . and if you had found the girl," asked the young northman, "what were you to do with her?"

"Protect her. Take her somewhere safe."

The big man laughed. "Where's that? Cersei's dungeon?"

"No."

"Deny it all you want. That sword says you're a liar. Are we supposed to believe the Lannisters are handing out gold and ruby swords to *foes*? That the Kingslayer meant for you to hide the girl from *his own twin*? I suppose the paper with the boy king's seal was just in case you needed to wipe your arse? And then there's the company you keep . . ." The big man turned and beckoned, the ranks of outlaws parted, and two more captives were brought forth. "The boy was the Imp's own squire, m'lady," he said to Lady Stoneheart. "T'other is one of Randyll Bloody Tarly's bloody household knights."

Hyle Hunt had been beaten so badly that his face was swollen almost beyond recognition. He stumbled as they shoved him, and almost fell. Podrick caught him by the arm. "Ser," the boy said miserably, when he saw Brienne. "My lady, I mean. Sorry."

"You have nothing to be sorry for." Brienne turned to Lady Stoneheart. "Whatever treachery you think I may have done, my lady, Podrick and Ser Hyle were no part of it."

"They're lions," said the one-eyed man. "That's enough. I say they hang. Tarly's hanged a score o' ours, past time we strung up some o' his."

Ser Hyle gave Brienne a faint smile. "My lady," he said, "you should have wed me when I made my offer. Now I fear you're doomed to die a maid, and me a poor man."

"Let them go," Brienne pleaded.

The woman in grey gave no answer. She studied the sword, the parchment, the bronze-and-iron crown. Finally she reached up under her jaw and grasped her neck, as if she meant to throttle herself. Instead she spoke . . . Her voice was halting, broken, tortured. The sound seemed to come from her throat, part croak, part wheeze, part death rattle. *The language of the damned,* thought Brienne. "I don't understand. What did she say?"

"She asked the name of this blade of yours," said the young northman in the sheepskin jerkin.

"Oathkeeper," Brienne answered.

The woman in grey *hissed* through her fingers. Her eyes were two red pits burning in the shadows. She spoke again.

"No, she says. Call it Oathbreaker, she says. It was made for treachery and murder. She names it *False Friend.* Like you."

"To whom have I been false?"

"To her," the northman said. "Can it be that my lady has forgotten that you once swore her your service?"

There was only one woman that the Maid of Tarth had ever sworn to serve. "That cannot be," she said. "She's dead."

"Death and guest right," muttered Long Jeyne Heddle. "They don't mean so much as they used to, neither one."

Lady Stoneheart lowered her hood and unwound the grey wool scarf from her face. Her hair was dry and brittle, white as bone. Her brow was mottled green and grey, spotted with the brown blooms of decay. The flesh of her face clung in ragged strips from her eyes down to her jaw.

Some of the rips were crusted with dried blood, but others gaped open to reveal the skull beneath.

Her face, Brienne thought. *Her face was so strong and handsome, her skin so smooth and soft.* "Lady Catelyn?" Tears filled her eyes. "They said . . . they said that you were dead."

"She is," said Thoros of Myr. "The Freys slashed her throat from ear to ear. When we found her by the river she was three days dead. Harwin begged me to give her the kiss of life, but it had been too long. I would not do it, so Lord Beric put his lips to hers instead, and the flame of life passed from him to her. And . . . she rose. May the Lord of Light protect us. She *rose.*"

Am I dreaming still? Brienne wondered. *Is this another nightmare born from Biter's teeth?* "I never betrayed her. Tell her that. I swear it by the Seven. I swear it by my *sword.*"

The thing that had been Catelyn Stark took hold of her throat again, fingers pinching at the ghastly long slash in her neck, and choked out more sounds. "Words are wind, she says," the northman told Brienne. "She says that you must prove your faith."

"How?" asked Brienne.

"With your sword. *Oathkeeper,* you call it? Then keep your oath to her, milady says."

"What does she want of me?"

"She wants her son alive, or the men who killed him dead," said the big man. "She wants to feed the crows, like they did at the Red Wedding. Freys and Boltons, aye. We'll give her those, as many as she likes. All she asks from you is Jaime Lannister."

Jaime. The name was a knife, twisting in her belly. "Lady Catelyn, I . . . you do not understand, Jaime . . . he saved me from being raped when the Bloody Mummers took us, and later he came back for me, he leapt into the bear pit empty-handed . . . I swear to you, he is not the man he was. He sent me after Sansa to keep her safe, he could not have had a part in the Red Wedding."

Lady Catelyn's fingers dug deep into her throat, and the words came rattling out, choked and broken, a stream as cold as ice. The northman said, "She says that you must choose. Take the sword and slay the Kingslayer, or be hanged for a betrayer. The sword or the noose, she says. Choose, she says. *Choose.*"

Brienne remembered her dream, waiting in her father's hall for the boy she was to marry. In the dream she had bitten off her tongue. *My mouth was full of blood.* She took a ragged breath and said, "I will not make that choice."

There was a long silence. Then Lady Stoneheart spoke again. This time Brienne understood her words. There were only two. *"Hang them,"* she croaked.

"As you command, m'lady," said the big man.

They bound Brienne's wrists with rope again and led her from the cavern, up a twisting stony path to the surface. It was morning outside, she was surprised to see. Shafts of pale dawn light were slanting through the trees. *So many trees to choose from,* she thought. *They will not need to take us far.*

Nor did they. Beneath a crooked willow, the outlaws slipped a noose about her neck, jerked it tight, and tossed the other end of the rope over a limb. Hyle Hunt and Podrick Payne were given elms. Ser Hyle was shouting that he would kill Jaime Lannister, but the Hound cuffed him across the face and shut him up. He had donned the helm again. "If you got crimes to confess to your gods, this would be the time to say them."

"Podrick has never harmed you. My father will ransom him. Tarth is called the sapphire isle. Send Podrick with my bones to Evenfall, and you'll have sapphires, silver, whatever you want."

"I want my wife and daughter back," said the Hound. "Can your father give me that? If not, he can get buggered. The boy will rot beside you. Wolves will gnaw your bones."

"Do you mean to hang her, Lem?" asked the one-eyed man. "Or do you figure to talk the bitch to death?"

The Hound snatched the end of the rope from the man holding it. "Let's see if she can dance," he said, and gave a yank.

Brienne felt the hemp constricting, digging into her skin, jerking her chin upward. Ser Hyle was cursing them eloquently, but not the boy. Podrick never lifted his eyes, not even when his feet were jerked up off the ground. *If this is another dream, it is time for me to awaken. If this is real, it is time for me to die.* All she could see was Podrick, the noose around his thin neck, his legs twitching. Her mouth opened. Pod was kicking, choking, *dying.* Brienne sucked the air in desperately, even as the rope was strangling her. Nothing had ever hurt so much.

She screamed a word.

CERSEI

Septa Moelle was a white-haired harridan with a face as sharp as an axe and lips pursed in perpetual disapproval. *This one still has her maidenhead, I'll wager,* Cersei thought, *though by now it's hard and stiff as boiled leather.* Six of the High Sparrow's knights escorted her, with the rainbow sword of their reborn order emblazoned on their kite shields.

"Septa." Cersei sat beneath the Iron Throne, clad in green silk and golden lace. "Tell his High Holiness that we are vexed with him. He presumes too much." Emeralds glimmered on her fingers and in her golden hair. The eyes of court and city were upon her, and she meant for them to see Lord Tywin's daughter. By the time this mummer's farce was done they would know they had but one true queen. *But first we must dance the dance and never miss a step.* "Lady Margaery is my son's true and gentle wife, his helpmate and consort. His High Holiness had no cause to lay his hands upon her person, or to confine her and her young cousins, who are so dear to all of us. I demand that he release them."

Septa Moelle's stern expression did not flicker. "I shall convey Your Grace's words to His High Holiness, but it grieves me to say that the young queen and her ladies cannot be released until and unless their innocence has been proved."

"*Innocence?* Why, you need only look upon their sweet young faces to see how innocent they are."

"A sweet face oft hides a sinner's heart."

Lord Merryweather spoke up from the council table. "What offense have these young maids been accused of, and by whom?"

The septa said, "Megga Tyrell and Elinor Tyrell stand accused of lewdness, fornication, and conspiracy to commit high treason. Alla Tyrell has been charged with witnessing their shame and helping them conceal it. All this Queen Margaery has also been accused of, as well as adultery and high treason."

Cersei put a hand to her breast. "Tell me who is spreading such calumnies about my good-daughter! I do not believe a word of this. My sweet son loves Lady Margaery with all his heart, she could never have been so cruel as to play him false."

"The accuser is a knight of your own household. Ser Osney Kettleblack has confessed his carnal knowledge of the queen to the High Septon himself, before the altar of the Father."

At the council table Harys Swyft gasped, and Grand Maester Pycelle turned away. A buzz filled the air, as if a thousand wasps were loose in the throne room. Some of the ladies in the galleries began to slip away, followed by a stream of petty lords and knights from the back of the hall. The gold cloaks let them go, but the queen had instructed Ser Osfryd to make note of all who fled. *Suddenly the Tyrell rose does not smell so sweet.*

"Ser Osney is young and lusty, I will grant you," the queen said, "but a faithful knight for all that. If he says that he was part of this . . . no, it cannot be. Margaery is a maiden!"

"She is not. I examined her myself, at the behest of His High Holiness. Her maidenhead is not intact. Septa Aglantine and Septa Melicent will say the same, as will Queen Margaery's own septa, Nysterica, who has been confined to a penitent's cell for her part in the queen's shame. Lady Megga and Lady Elinor were examined as well. Both were found to have been broken."

The wasps were growing so loud that the queen could hardly hear herself think. *I do hope the little queen and her cousins enjoyed those rides of theirs.*

Lord Merryweather thumped his fist on the table. "Lady Margaery had sworn solemn oaths attesting to her maidenhood, to Her Grace the queen and her late father. Many here bore witness. Lord Tyrell has also testified to her innocence, as has the Lady Olenna, whom we all know to be above reproach. Would you have us believe that all of these noble people *lied* to us?"

"Perhaps they were deceived as well, my lord," said Septa Moelle. "I cannot speak to this. I can only swear to the truth of what I discovered for myself when I examined the queen."

The picture of this sour old crone poking her wrinkled fingers up Margaery's little pink cunt was so droll that Cersei almost laughed. "We insist that His High Holiness allow our own maesters to examine my good-daughter, to determine if there is any shred of truth to these slanders.

Grand Maester Pycelle, you shall accompany Septa Moelle back to Beloved Baelor's Sept, and return to us with the truth about our Margaery's maidenhead."

Pycelle had gone the color of curdled white. *At council meetings the wretched old fool cannot say enough, but now that I need a few words from him he has lost the power of speech,* the queen thought, before the old man finally came out with, "There is no need for me to examine her . . . her privy parts." His voice was a quaver. "I grieve to say . . . Queen Margaery is no maiden. She has required me to make her moon tea, not once, but many times."

The uproar that followed that was all that Cersei Lannister could ever have hoped for.

Even the royal herald beating on the floor with his staff did little to quell the noise. The queen let it wash over her for a few heartbeats, savoring the sounds of the little queen's disgrace. When it had gone on long enough, she rose stone-faced and commanded that the gold cloaks clear the hall. *Margaery Tyrell is done,* she thought, exulting. Her white knights fell in around her as she made her exit through the king's door behind the Iron Throne; Boros Blount, Meryn Trant, and Osmund Kettleblack, the last of the Kingsguard still remaining in the city.

Moon Boy was standing beside the door, holding his rattle in his hand and gaping at the confusion with his big round eyes. *A fool he may be, but he wears his folly honestly. Maggy the Frog should have been in motley too, for all she knew about the morrow.* Cersei prayed the old fraud was screaming down in hell. The younger queen whose coming she'd foretold was finished, and if that prophecy could fail, so could the rest. *No golden shrouds, no* valonqar, *I am free of your croaking malice at last.*

The remnants of her small council followed her out. Harys Swyft appeared dazed. He stumbled at the door and might have fallen if Aurane Waters had not caught him by the arm. Even Orton Merryweather seemed anxious. "The smallfolk are fond of the little queen," he said. "They will not take well to this. I fear what might happen next, Your Grace."

"Lord Merryweather is right," said Lord Waters. "If it please Your Grace, I will launch the rest of our new dromonds. The sight of them upon the Blackwater with King Tommen's banner flying from their masts will remind the city who rules here, and keep them safe should the mobs decide to run riot again."

He left the rest unspoken; once on the Blackwater, his dromonds could stop Mace Tyrell from bringing his army back across the river, just as Tyrion had once stopped Stannis. Highgarden had no sea power of its own this side of Westeros. They relied upon the Redwyne fleet, presently on its way back to the Arbor.

"A prudent measure," the queen announced. "Until this storm has passed, I want your ships crewed and on the water."

Ser Harys Swyft was so pale and damp he looked about to faint. "When word of this reaches Lord Tyrell, his fury will know no bounds. There will be blood in the streets . . ."

The knight of the yellow chicken, Cersei mused. *You ought to take a worm for your sigil, ser. A chicken is too bold for you. If Mace Tyrell will not even assault Storm's End, how do you imagine that he would ever dare attack the gods?* When he was done blathering she said, "It must not come to blood, and I mean to see that it does not. I will go to Baelor's Sept myself to speak to Queen Margaery and the High Septon. Tommen loves them both, I know, and would want me to make peace between them."

"Peace?" Ser Harys dabbed at his brow with a velvet sleeve. "If peace is possible . . . that is very brave of you."

"Some sort of trial may be necessary," said the queen, "to disprove these base calumnies and lies and show the world that our sweet Margaery is the innocent we all know her to be."

"Aye," said Merryweather, "but this High Septon may want to try the queen himself, as the Faith once tried men of old."

I hope so, Cersei thought. Such a court was not like to look with favor on treasonous queens who spread their legs for singers and profaned the Maiden's holy rites to hide their shame. "The important thing is to find the truth, I am sure we all agree," she said. "And now, my lords, you must excuse me. I must go see the king. He should not be alone at such a time."

Tommen was fishing for cats when his mother returned to him. Dorcas had made him a mouse with scraps of fur and tied it on a long string at the end of an old fishing pole. The kittens loved to chase it, and the boy liked nothing better than jerking it about the floor as they pounced after it. He seemed surprised when Cersei gathered him up in her arms and kissed him on his brow. "What's that for, Mother? Why are you crying?"

Because you're safe, she wanted to tell him. *Because no harm will ever come to you.* "You are mistaken. A lion never cries." There would be time later to tell him about Margaery and her cousins. "There are some warrants that I need you to sign."

For the king's sake, the queen had left the names off the arrest warrants. Tommen signed them blank, and pressed his seal into the warm wax happily, as he always did. Afterward she sent him off with Jocelyn Swyft.

Ser Osfryd Kettleblack arrived as the ink was drying.

Cersei had written in the names herself: Ser Tallad the Tall, Jalabhar Xho, Hamish the Harper, Hugh Clifton, Mark Mullendore, Bayard Norcross, Lambert Turnberry, Horas Redwyne, Hobber Redwyne, and a certain churl named Wat, who called himself the Blue Bard.

"So many." Ser Osfryd shuffled through the warrants, as wary of the words as if they had been roaches crawling across the parchment. None of the Kettleblacks could read.

"Ten. You have six thousand gold cloaks. Sufficient for ten, I would think. Some of the clever ones may have fled, if the rumors reached their ears in time. If so, it makes no matter, their absence only makes them look that much more guilty. Ser Tallad is a bit of an oaf and may try to resist you. See that he does not die before confessing, and do no harm to any of the others. A few may well be innocent." It was important that the Redwyne twins be found to have been falsely accused. That would demonstrate the fairness of the judgments against the others.

"We'll have them all before the sun comes up, Your Grace." Ser Osfryd hesitated. "There's a crowd gathering outside the door of Baelor's Sept."

"What sort of crowd?" Anything unexpected made her wary. She remembered what Lord Waters had said about the riots. *I had not considered how the smallfolk might react to this. Margaery has been their little pet.* "How many?"

"A hundred or so. They're shouting for the High Septon to release the little queen. We can send them running, if you like."

"No. Let them shout until they're hoarse, it will not sway the Sparrow. He only listens to the gods." There was a certain irony in His High Holiness having an angry mob encamped upon his doorstep, since just such a mob had raised him to the crystal crown. *Which he promptly sold.* "The Faith has its own knights now. Let them defend the sept. Oh, and close the city gates as well. No one is to enter or leave King's Landing without my leave, until all this is done and settled."

"As you command, Your Grace." Ser Osfryd bowed and went off to find someone to read the warrants to him.

By the time the sun went down that day, all of the accused traitors were in custody. Hamish the Harper had collapsed when they came for him, and Ser Tallad the Tall had wounded three gold cloaks before the others overwhelmed him. Cersei ordered that the Redwyne twins be given comfortable chambers in a tower. The rest went down to the dungeons.

"Hamish is having difficulty breathing," Qyburn informed her when he came to call that night. "He is calling for a maester."

"Tell him he can have one as soon as he confesses." She thought a moment. "He is too old to have been amongst the lovers, but no doubt he was made to play and sing for Margaery whilst she was entertaining other men. We will need details."

"I shall help him to remember them, Your Grace."

The next day, Lady Merryweather helped Cersei dress for their visit to the little queen. "Nothing too rich or colorful," she said. "Something suitably devout and drab for the High Septon. He's like to make me pray with him."

In the end, she chose a soft woolen dress that covered her from throat to ankle, with only a few small vines embroidered on the bodice and the sleeves in golden thread to soften the severity of its lines. Even better, brown would help conceal the dirt if she was made to kneel. "Whilst I am comforting my good-daughter you shall speak with the three cousins," she told Taena. "Win Alla if you can, but be careful what you say. The gods may not be the only ones listening."

Jaime always said that the hardest part of any battle is just before, waiting for the carnage to begin. When she stepped outside, Cersei saw that the sky was grey and bleak. She could not take the risk of being caught in a downpour and arriving at Baelor's Sept soaked and bedraggled. That meant the litter. For her escort, she took ten Lannister house guards and Boros Blount. "Margaery's mob may not have the wit to tell one Kettleblack from another," she told Ser Osmund, "and I cannot have you cutting through the commons. Best we keep you out of sight for a time."

As they made their way across King's Landing, Taena had a sudden doubt. "This trial," she said, in a quiet voice, "what if Margaery demands that her guilt or innocence be determined by wager of battle?"

A smile brushed Cersei's lips. "As queen, her honor must be defended by a knight of the Kingsguard. Why, every child in Westeros knows how Prince Aemon the Dragonknight championed his sister Queen Naerys against Ser Morghil's accusations. With Ser Loras so gravely wounded, though, I fear Prince Aemon's part must fall to one of his Sworn Brothers." She shrugged. "Who, though? Ser Arys and Ser Balon are far away in Dorne, Jaime is off at Riverrun, and Ser Osmund is the brother of the man accusing her, which leaves only . . . oh, dear . . ."

"Boros Blount and Meryn Trant." Lady Taena laughed.

"Yes, and Ser Meryn has been feeling ill of late. Remind me to tell him that when we return to the castle."

"I shall, my sweet." Taena took her hand and kissed it. "I pray that I never offend you. You are terrible when roused."

"Any mother would do the same to protect her children,"

said Cersei. "When do you mean to bring that boy of yours to court? Russell, was that his name? He could train with Tommen."

"That would thrill the boy, I know . . . but things are so uncertain just now, I thought it best to wait until the danger passed."

"Soon enough," promised Cersei. "Send word to Longtable and have Russell pack his best doublet and his wooden sword. A new young friend will be just the thing to help Tommen forget his loss, after Margaery's little head has rolled."

They descended from the litter under Blessed Baelor's statue. The queen was pleased to see that the bones and filth had been cleaned away. Ser Osfryd had told it true; the crowd was neither as numerous nor as unruly as the sparrows had been. They stood about in small clumps, gazing sullenly at the doors of the Great Sept, where a line of novice septons had been drawn up with quarterstaffs in their hands. *No steel,* Cersei noted. That was either very wise or very stupid, she was not sure which.

No one made any attempt to hinder her. Smallfolk and novices alike parted as they passed. Once inside the doors, they were met by three knights in the Hall of Lamps, each clad in the rainbow-striped robes of the Warrior's Sons. "I am here to see my good-daughter," Cersei told them.

"His High Holiness has been expecting you. I am Ser Theodan the True, formerly Ser Theodan Wells. If Your Grace will come with me."

The High Sparrow was on his knees, as ever. This time he was praying before the Father's altar. Nor did he break off his prayer when the queen approached, but made her wait impatiently until he had finished. Only then did he rise and bow to her. "Your Grace. This is a sad day."

"Very sad. Do we have your leave to speak with

Margaery and her cousins?" She chose a meek and humble manner; with this man, that was like to work the best.

"If that is your wish. Come to me afterward, my child. We must pray together, you and I."

The little queen had been confined atop one of the Great Sept's slender towers. Her cell was eight feet long and six feet wide, with no furnishings but a straw-stuffed pallet and a bench for prayer, a ewer of water, a copy of *The Seven-Pointed Star,* and a candle to read it by. The only window was hardly wider than an arrow slit.

Cersei found Margaery barefoot and shivering, clad in the roughspun shift of a novice sister. Her locks were all a tangle, and her feet were filthy. "They took my *clothes* from me," the little queen told her once they were alone. "I wore a gown of ivory lace, with freshwater pearls on the bodice, but the septas laid their *hands* on me and stripped me to the skin. My cousins too. Megga sent one septa crashing into the candles and set her robe afire. I fear for Alla, though. She went as white as milk, too frightened even to cry."

"Poor child." There were no chairs, so Cersei sat beside the little queen on her pallet. "Lady Taena has gone to speak with her, to let her know that she is not forgotten."

"He will not even let me see them," fumed Margaery. "He keeps each of us apart from the others. Until you came, I was allowed no visitors but septas. One comes every hour to ask if I wish to confess my fornications. They will not even let me sleep. They wake me to demand confessions. Last night I confessed to Septa Unella that I wished to scratch her eyes out."

A shame you did not do it, Cersei thought. *Blinding some poor old septa would certainly persuade the High Sparrow of your guilt.* "They are questioning your cousins the same way."

"Damn them, then," said Margaery. "Damn them all to seven hells. Alla is gentle and shy, how can they do this to her? And Megga . . . she laughs as loud as a dockside whore, I know, but inside she's still just a little girl. I love them all, and they love me. If this sparrow thinks to make them lie about me . . ."

"They stand accused as well, I fear. All three."

"My *cousins*?" Margaery paled. "Alla and Megga are hardly more than children. Your Grace, this . . . this is obscene. Will you take us out of here?"

"Would that I could." Her voice was full of sorrow. "His High Holiness has his new knights guarding you. To free you I would need to send the gold cloaks and profane this holy place with killing." Cersei took Margaery's hand in hers. "I have not been idle, though. I have gathered up all those that Ser Osney named as your lovers. They will tell His High Holiness of your innocence, I am certain, and swear to it at your trial."

"Trial?" There was real fear in the girl's voice now. "Must there be a trial?"

"How else will you prove your innocence?" Cersei gave Margaery's hand a reassuring squeeze. "It is your right to decide the manner of the trial, to be sure. You are the queen. The knights of the Kingsguard are sworn to defend you."

Margaery understood at once. "A trial by battle? Loras is hurt, though, elsewise he . . ."

"He has six brothers."

Margaery stared at her, then pulled her hand away. "Is that a jape? Boros is a craven, Meryn is old and slow, your brother is maimed, the other two are off in Dorne, and Osmund is a bloody *Kettleblack*. Loras has *two* brothers, not six. If there's to be a trial by battle, I want Garlan as my champion."

"Ser Garlan is not a member of the Kingsguard," the queen said. "When the queen's honor is at issue, law and custom require that her champion be one of the king's sworn seven. The High Septon will insist, I fear." *I will make certain of it.*

Margaery did not answer at once, but her brown eyes narrowed in suspicion. "Blount or Trant," she said at last. "It would have to be one of them. You'd like that, wouldn't you? Osney Kettleblack would cut either one to pieces."

Seven hells. Cersei donned a look of hurt. "You wrong me, daughter. All I want—"

"—is your son, all for yourself. He will never have a wife that you don't hate. And I am *not* your daughter, thank the gods. Leave me."

"You are being foolish. I am only here to help you."

"To help me to my grave. I asked for you to leave. Will you make me call my gaolers and have you dragged away, you vile, scheming, evil bitch?"

Cersei gathered up her skirts and dignity. "This must be very frightening for you. I shall forgive those words." Here, as at court, one never knew who might be listening. "I would be afraid as well, in your place. Grand Maester Pycelle has admitted providing you with moon tea, and your Blue Bard . . . if I were you, my lady, I would pray to the Crone for wisdom and to the Mother for her mercy. I fear you may soon be in dire need of both."

Four shriveled septas escorted the queen down the tower steps. Each of the crones seemed more feeble than the last. When they reached the ground they continued down, into the heart of Visenya's Hill. The steps ended well below the earth, where a line of flickering torches lit a long hallway.

She found the High Septon waiting for her in a small seven-sided audience chamber. The room was sparse and plain, with bare stone walls, a rough-hewn table, three chairs, and a prayer bench. The faces of the Seven had been carved into the walls. Cersei thought the carvings crude and ugly, but there was a certain power to them, especially about the eyes, orbs of onyx, malachite, and yellow moonstone that somehow made the faces come alive.

"You spoke with the queen," the High Septon said.

She resisted the urge to say, *I am the queen.* "I did."

"All men sin, even kings and queens. I have sinned myself, and been forgiven. Without confession, though, there can be no forgiveness. The queen will not confess."

"Perhaps she is innocent."

"She is not. Holy septas have examined her, and testify that her maidenhead is broken. She has drunk of moon tea, to murder the fruit of her fornications in her womb. An anointed knight has sworn upon his sword to having carnal knowledge of her and two of her three cousins. Others have lain with her as well, he says, and names many names of men both great and humble."

"My gold cloaks have taken all of them to the dungeons," Cersei assured him. "Only one has yet been questioned, a singer called the Blue Bard. What he had to say was disturbing. Even so, I pray that when my good-daughter is brought to trial, her innocence may yet be proved." She hesitated. "Tommen loves his little queen so much, Your Holiness, I fear it might be hard for him or his lords to judge her justly. Perhaps the Faith should conduct the trial?"

The High Sparrow steepled his thin hands. "I have had the selfsame thought, Your Grace. Just as Maegor the Cruel once took the swords from the Faith, so Jaehaerys the Conciliator deprived us of the scales of judgment. Yet who is truly fit to judge a queen, save the Seven Above and the godsworn below? A sacred court of seven judges shall sit upon this case. Three shall be of your female sex. A maiden, a mother, and a crone. Who could be more suited to judge the wickedness of women?"

"That would be for the best. To be sure, Margaery does have the right to demand that her guilt or innocence be proven by wager of battle. If so, her champion must be one of Tommen's Seven."

"The knights of the Kingsguard have served as the rightful champions of king and queen since the days of Aegon the Conqueror. Crown and Faith speak as one on this."

Cersei covered her face with her hands, as if in grief. When she raised her head again, a tear glistened in one eye. "These are sad days indeed," she said, "but I am pleased to find us so much in agreement. If Tommen were here I know he would thank you. Together you and I must find the truth."

"We shall."

"I must return to the castle. With your leave, I will take Ser Osney Kettleblack back with me. The small council will want to question him, and hear his accusations for themselves."

"No," said the High Septon.

It was only a word, one little word, but to Cersei it felt like a splash of icy water in the face. She blinked, and her certainty flickered, just a little. "Ser Osney will be held securely, I promise you."

"He is held securely here. Come. I will show you."

Cersei could feel the eyes of the Seven staring at her, eyes of jade and malachite and onyx, and a sudden shiver of fear went through her, cold as ice. *I am the queen,* she told herself. *Lord Tywin's daughter.* Reluctantly, she followed.

Ser Osney was not far. The chamber was dark, and

closed by a heavy iron door. The High Septon produced the key to open it, and took a torch down from the wall to light the room within. "After you, Your Grace."

Within, Osney Kettleblack hung naked from the ceiling, swinging from a pair of heavy iron chains. He had been whipped. His back and shoulders had been laid almost bare, and cuts and welts crisscrossed his legs and arse as well.

The queen could hardly stand to look at him. She turned back to the High Septon. "What have you *done*?"

"We have sought after the truth, most earnestly."

"He told you the truth. He came to you of his own free will and confessed his sins."

"Aye. He did that. I have heard many men confess, Your Grace, but seldom have I heard a man so pleased to be so guilty."

"You *whipped* him!"

"There can be no penance without pain. No man should spare himself the scourge, as I told Ser Osney. I seldom feel so close to god as when I am being whipped for mine own wickedness, though my darkest sins are no wise near as black as his."

"B-but," she sputtered, "you preach the Mother's mercy . . ."

"Ser Osney shall taste of that sweet milk in the afterlife. In *The Seven-Pointed Star* it is written that all sins may be forgiven, but crimes must still be punished. Osney Kettleblack is guilty of treason and murder, and the wages of treason are death."

He is just a priest, he cannot do this. "It is not for the Faith to condemn a man to death, whatever his offense."

"Whatever his offense." The High Septon repeated the words slowly, weighing them. "Strange to say, Your Grace, the more diligently we applied the scourge, the more Ser

Osney's offenses seemed to change. He would now have us believe that he never touched Margaery Tyrell. Is that not so, Ser Osney?"

Osney Kettleblack opened his eyes. When he saw the queen standing there before him he ran his tongue across his swollen lips, and said, "The Wall. You promised me the Wall."

"He is mad," said Cersei. "You have driven him mad."

"Ser Osney," said the High Septon, in a firm, clear voice, "did you have carnal knowledge of the queen?"

"Aye." The chains rattled softly as Osney twisted in his shackles. "That one there. She's the queen I fucked, the one sent me to kill the old High Septon. He never had no guards. I just come in when he was sleeping and pushed a pillow down across his face."

Cersei whirled, and ran.

The High Septon tried to seize her, but he was some old sparrow and she was a lioness of the Rock. She pushed him aside and burst through the door, slamming it behind her with a *clang. The Kettleblacks, I need the Kettleblacks, I will send in Osfryd with the gold cloaks and Osmund with the Kingsguard, Osney will deny it all once they cut him free, and I'll rid myself of this High Septon just as I did the other.* The four old septas blocked her way and clutched at her with wrinkled hands. She knocked one to the floor and clawed another across the face, and gained the steps. Halfway up, she remembered Taena Merryweather. It made her stumble, panting. *Seven save me,* she prayed. *Taena knows it all. If they take her too, and whip her . . .*

She ran as far as the sept, but no farther. There were women waiting for her there, more septas and silent sisters too, younger than the four old crones below. "I am the *queen,*" she shouted, backing away from them. "I will have your heads for this, I will have all your heads. Let me pass." Instead, they laid hands upon her. Cersei ran to the altar of the Mother, but they caught her there, a score of them, and dragged her kicking up the tower steps. Inside the cell three silent sisters held her down as a septa named Scolera stripped her bare. She even took her smallclothes. Another septa tossed a roughspun shift at her. "You cannot do this," the queen kept screaming at them. "I am a Lannister, unhand me, my brother will kill you, Jaime will slice you open from throat to cunt, *unhand me*! I am *the queen*!"

"The queen should pray," said Septa Scolera, before they left her naked in the cold bleak cell.

She was not meek Margaery Tyrell, to don her little shift and submit to such captivity. *I will teach them what it means to put a lion in a cage,* Cersei thought. She tore the shift into a hundred pieces, found a ewer of water and smashed it against the wall, then did the same with the chamber pot. When no one came, she began to pound on the door with her fists. Her escort was below, on the plaza: ten Lannister guardsmen and Ser Boros Blount. *Once they hear they'll come free me, and we'll drag the bloody High Sparrow back to the Red Keep in chains.*

She screamed and kicked and howled until her throat was raw, at the door and at the window. No one shouted back, nor came to rescue her. The cell began to darken. It was growing cold as well. Cersei began to shiver. *How can they leave me like this, without so much as a fire? I am their queen.* She began to regret tearing apart the shift they'd given her. There was a blanket on the pallet in the corner, a threadbare thing of thin brown wool. It was rough and scratchy, but it was all she had. Cersei huddled underneath to keep from shivering, and before long she had fallen into an exhausted sleep.

The next she knew, a heavy hand was shaking her awake. It was black as pitch inside the cell, and a huge ugly woman was kneeling over her, a candle in her hand. "Who are you?" the queen demanded. "Are you come to set me free?"

"I am Septa Unella. I am come to hear you tell of all your murders and fornications."

Cersei knocked her hand aside. "I will have your head. Do not presume to touch me. Get away."

The woman rose. "Your Grace. I will be back in an hour. Mayhaps by then you will be ready to confess."

An hour and an hour and an hour. So passed the longest night that Cersei Lannister had ever known, save for the night of Joffrey's wedding. Her throat was so raw from shouting that she could hardly swallow. The cell turned freezing cold. She had smashed the chamber pot, so she had to squat in a corner to make her water and watch it trickle across the floor. Every time she closed her eyes, Unella was looming over her again, shaking her and asking her if she wanted to confess her sins.

Day brought no relief. Septa Moelle brought her a bowl of some waterly grey gruel as the sun was coming up. Cersei flung it at her head. When they brought a fresh ewer of water, though, she was so thirsty that she had no choice but to drink. When they brought another shift, grey and thin and smelling of mildew, she put it on over her nakedness. And that evening when Moelle appeared again she ate the bread and fish and demanded wine to wash it down. No wine appeared, only Septa Unella, making her hourly visit to ask if the queen was ready to confess.

What can be happening? Cersei wondered, as the thin slice of sky outside her window began to darken once again. *Why has no one come to pry me out of here?* She could not believe that the Kettleblacks would abandon their brother. What was her council doing? *Cravens and traitors. When I get out of here I will have the lot of them beheaded and find better men to take their place.*

Thrice that day she heard the sound of distant shouting drifting up from the plaza, but it was Margaery's name that the mob was calling, not hers.

It was near dawn on the second day and Cersei was licking the last of the porridge from the bottom of the bowl when her cell door swung open unexpectedly to admit Lord Qyburn. It was all she could do not to throw herself at him. "Qyburn," she whispered, "oh, gods, I am so glad to see your face. Take me home."

"That will not be allowed. You are to be tried before a holy court of seven, for murder, treason, and fornication."

Cersei was so exhausted that the words seemed nonsensical to her at first. "Tommen. Tell me of my son. Is he still king?"

"He is, Your Grace. He is safe and well, secure within the walls of Maegor's Holdfast, protected by the Kingsguard. He is lonely, though. Fretful. He asks for you, and for his little queen. As yet, no one has told him of your . . . your . . ."

". . . difficulties?" she suggested. "What of Margaery?"

"She is to be tried as well, by the same court that conducts your trial. I had the Blue Bard delivered to the High Septon, as Your Grace commanded. He is here now, somewhere down below us. My whisperers tell me that they are whipping him, but so far he is still singing the same sweet song we taught him."

The same sweet song. Her wits were dull for want of sleep. *Wat, his real name is Wat.* If the gods were good, Wat might die beneath the lash, leaving Margaery with no way to disprove his testimony. "Where are my knights? Ser Osfryd . . . the High Septon means to kill his brother Osney, his gold cloaks must . . ."

"Osfryd Kettleblack no longer commands the City Watch. The king has removed him from office and raised the captain of the Dragon Gate in his place, a certain Humfrey Waters."

Cersei was so tired, none of this made any sense. "Why would Tommen do that?"

"The boy is not to blame. When his council puts a decree in front of him, he signs his name and stamps it with his seal."

"*My* council . . . who? Who would do that? Not you?"

"Alas, I have been dismissed from the council, although for the nonce they allow me to continue my work with the eunuch's whisperers. The realm is being ruled by Ser Harys Swyft and Grand Maester Pycelle. They have dispatched a raven to Casterly Rock, inviting your uncle to return to court and assume the regency. If he means to accept, he had best make haste. Mace Tyrell has abandoned his siege of Storm's End and is marching back to the city with his army, and Randyll Tarly is reported on his way down from Maidenpool as well."

"Has Lord Merryweather agreed to this?"

"Merryweather has resigned his seat on the council and fled back to Longtable with his wife, who was the first to bring us news of the . . . accusations . . . against Your Grace."

"They let Taena go." That was the best thing she had heard since the High Sparrow had said *no*. Taena could have doomed her. "What of Lord Waters? His ships . . . if he brings his crews ashore, he should have enough men to . . ."

"As soon as word of Your Grace's present troubles reached the river, Lord Waters raised sail, unshipped his oars, and took his fleet to sea. Ser Harys fears he means to join Lord Stannis. Pycelle believes that he is sailing to the Stepstones, to set himself up as a pirate."

"All my lovely dromonds." Cersei almost laughed. "My lord father used to say that bastards are treacherous by nature. Would that I had listened." She shivered. "I am lost, Qyburn."

"No." He took her hand. "Hope remains. Your Grace has the right to prove your innocence by battle. My queen, your champion stands ready. There is no man in all the Seven Kingdoms who can hope to stand against him. If you will only give the command . . ."

This time she did laugh. It was funny, terribly funny, *hideously* funny. "The gods make japes of all our hopes and plans. I have a champion no man can defeat, but I am forbidden to make use of him. I am the *queen,* Qyburn. My honor can only be defended by a Sworn Brother of the Kingsguard."

"I see." The smile died on Qyburn's face. "Your Grace, I am at a loss. I do not know how to counsel you . . ."

Even in her exhausted, frightened state, the queen knew she dare not trust her fate to a court of sparrows. Nor could she count on Ser Kevan to intervene, after the words that had passed between them at their last meeting. *It will have to be a trial by battle. There is no other way.* "Qyburn, for the love you bear me, I beg you, send a message for me. A raven if you can. A rider, if not. You must send to Riverrun, to my brother. Tell him what has happened, and write . . . write . . ."

"Yes, Your Grace?"

She licked her lips, shivering. "Come at once. Help me. Save me. I need you now as I have never needed you before. I love you. I love you. I love you. *Come at once.*"

"As you command. '*I love you*' thrice?"

"Thrice." She had to reach him. "He will come. I know he will. He must. Jaime is my only hope."

"My queen," said Qyburn, "have you . . . forgotten? Ser Jaime has no sword hand. If he should champion you and lose . . ."

We will leave this world together, as we once came into it. "He will not lose. Not Jaime. Not with my life at stake."

JAIME

The new Lord of Riverrun was so angry that he was shaking. "We have been deceived," he said. "This man has played us false!" Pink spittle flew from his lips as he jabbed a finger at Edmure Tully. "I will have his head off! I rule in Riverrun, by the king's own decree, I—"

"Emmon," said his wife, "the Lord Commander knows about the king's decree. Ser Edmure knows about the king's decree. The stableboys know about the king's decree."

"I am the lord, and I will have his head!"

"For what crime?" Thin as he was, Edmure still looked more lordly than Emmon Frey. He wore a quilted doublet of red wool with a leaping trout embroidered on its chest. His boots were black, his breeches blue. His auburn hair had been washed and barbered, his red beard neatly trimmed. "I did all that was asked of me."

"Oh?" Jaime Lannister had not slept since Riverrun had opened its gates, and his head was pounding. "I do not recall asking you to let Ser Brynden escape."

"You required me to surrender my castle, not my uncle. Am I to blame if your men let him slip through their siege lines?"

Jaime was not amused. *"Where is he?"* he said, letting his irritation show. His men had searched Riverrun thrice over, and Brynden Tully was nowhere to be found.

"He never told me where he meant to go."

"And you never asked. How did he get out?"

"Fish swim. Even black ones." Edmure smiled.

Jaime was sorely tempted to crack him across the mouth with his golden hand. A few missing teeth would put an end to his smiles. For a man who was going to spend the rest of his life a prisoner, Edmure was entirely too pleased with himself. "We have oubliettes beneath the Casterly Rock that fit a man as tight as a suit of armor. You can't turn in them, or sit, or reach down to your feet when the rats start gnawing at your toes. Would you care to re-consider that answer?"

Lord Edmure's smile went away. "You gave me your word that I would be treated honorably, as befits my rank."

"So you shall," said Jaime. "Nobler knights than you have died whimpering in those oubliettes, and many a high lord too. Even a king or two, if I recall my history. Your wife can have the one beside you, if you like. I would not want to part you."

"He did swim," said Edmure, sullenly. He had the same blue eyes as his sister Catelyn, and Jaime saw the same loathing there that he'd once seen in hers. "We raised the portcullis on the Water Gate. Not all the way, just three feet or so. Enough to leave a gap under the water, though the gate still appeared to be closed. My uncle is a strong swimmer. After dark, he pulled himself beneath the spikes."

And he slipped under our boom the same way, no doubt. A moonless night, bored guards, a black fish in a black river floating quietly downstream. If Ruttiger or Yew or any of their men heard a splash, they would put it down to a turtle or a trout. Edmure had waited most of the day before hauling down the direwolf of Stark in token of surrender. In the confusion of the castle changing hands, it had been the next morning before Jaime had been informed that the Blackfish was not amongst the prisoners.

He went to the window and gazed out over the river. It was a bright autumn day, and the sun was shining on the waters. *By now the Blackfish could be ten leagues downstream.*

"You have to find him," insisted Emmon Frey.

"He'll be found." Jaime spoke with a certainty he did not feel. "I have hounds and hunters sniffing after him even now." Ser Addam Marbrand was leading the search on the south side of the river, Ser Dermot of the Rainwood on the north. He had considered enlisting the riverlords as well, but Vance and Piper and their ilk were more like to help the Blackfish escape than clap him into fetters. All in all, he was not hopeful. "He may elude us for a time," he said, "but eventually he must surface."

"What if he should try and take my castle back?"

"You have a garrison of two hundred." Too large a garrison, in truth, but Lord Emmon had an anxious disposition. At least he would have no trouble feeding them; the Blackfish had left Riverrun amply provisioned, just as he had claimed. "After the trouble Ser Brynden took to leave us, I doubt that he'll come skulking back." *Unless it is at the head of a band of outlaws.* He did not doubt that the Blackfish meant to continue the fight.

"This is your seat," Lady Genna told her husband. "It is for you to hold it. If you cannot do that, put it to the torch and run back to the Rock."

Lord Emmon rubbed his mouth. His hand came away red and slimy from the sourleaf. "To be sure. Riverrun is mine, and no man shall ever take it from me." He gave Edmure Tully one last suspicious look, as Lady Genna drew him from the solar.

"Is there any more that you would care to tell me?" Jaime asked Edmure when the two of them were alone.

"This was my father's solar," said Tully. "He ruled the riverlands from here, wisely and well. He liked to sit beside that window. The light was good there, and whenever he looked up from his work he could see the river. When his eyes were tired he would have Cat read to him. Littlefinger and I built a castle out of wooden blocks once, there beside the door. You will never know how sick it makes me to see you in this room, Kingslayer. You will never know how much I despise you."

He was wrong about that. "I have been despised by better men than you, Edmure." Jaime called for a guard. "Take his lordship back to his tower and see that he's fed."

The Lord of Riverrun went silently. On the morrow, he would start west. Ser Forley Prester would command his escort; a hundred men, including twenty knights. *Best double that. Lord Beric may try to free Edmure before they reach the Golden Tooth.* Jaime did not want to have to capture Tully for a third time.

He returned to Hoster Tully's chair, pulled over the map of the Trident, and flattened it beneath his golden hand. *Where would I go, if I were the Blackfish?*

"Lord Commander?" A guardsman stood in the open

door. "Lady Westerling and her daughter are without, as you commanded."

Jaime shoved the map aside. "Show them in." *At least the girl did not vanish too.* Jeyne Westerling had been Robb Stark's queen, the girl who cost him everything. With a wolf in her belly, she could have proved more dangerous than the Blackfish.

She did not look dangerous. Jeyne was a willowy girl, no more than fifteen or sixteen, more awkward than graceful. She had narrow hips, breasts the size of apples, a mop of chestnut curls, and the soft brown eyes of a doe. *Pretty enough for a child,* Jaime decided, *but not a girl to lose a kingdom for.* Her face was puffy, and there was a scab on her forehead, half-hidden by a lock of brown hair. "What happened there?" he asked her.

The girl turned her head away. "It is nothing," insisted her mother, a stern-faced woman in a gown of green velvet. A necklace of golden seashells looped about her long, thin neck. "She would not give up the little crown the rebel gave her, and when I tried to take it from her head the willful child fought me."

"It was mine." Jeyne sobbed. "You had no right. Robb had it made for me. I *loved* him."

Her mother made to slap her, but Jaime stepped between them. "None of that," he warned Lady Sybell. "Sit down, both of you." The girl curled up in her chair like a frightened animal, but her mother sat stiffly, her head high. "Will you have wine?" he asked them. The girl did not answer. "No, thank you," said her mother.

"As you will." Jaime turned to the daughter. "I am sorry for your loss. The boy had courage, I'll give him that. There is a question I must ask you. Are you carrying his child, my lady?"

Jeyne burst from her chair and would have fled the

room if the guard at the door had not seized her by the arm. "She is not," said Lady Sybell, as her daughter struggled to escape. "I made certain of that, as your lord father bid me."

Jaime nodded. Tywin Lannister was not a man to overlook such details. "Unhand the girl," he said, "I'm done with her for now." As Jeyne fled sobbing down the stairs, he considered her mother. "House Westerling has its pardon, and your brother Rolph has been made Lord of Castamere. What else would you have of us?"

"Your lord father promised me worthy marriages for Jeyne and her younger sister. Lords or heirs, he swore to me, not younger sons nor household knights."

Lords or heirs. To be sure. The Westerlings were an old House, and proud, but Lady Sybell herself had been born a Spicer, from a line of upjumped merchants. Her grandmother had been some sort of half-mad witch woman from the east, he seemed to recall. And the Westerlings were impoverished. Younger sons would have been the best that Sybell Spicer's daughters could have hoped for in the ordinary course of events, but a nice fat pot of Lannister gold would make even a dead rebel's widow look attractive to some lord. "You'll have your marriages," said Jaime, "but Jeyne must wait two full years before she weds again." If the girl took another husband too soon and had a child by him, inevitably there would come whispers that the Young Wolf was the father.

"I have two sons as well," Lady Westerling reminded him. "Rollam is with me, but Raynald was a knight and went with the rebels to the Twins. If I had known what was to happen there, I would never have allowed that." There was a hint of reproach in her voice. "Raynald knew nought of any . . . of the understanding with your lord father. He may be a captive at the Twins."

Or he may be dead. Walder Frey would not have known of *the understanding* either. "I will make inquiries. If Ser Raynald is still a captive, we'll pay his ransom for you."

"Mention was made of a match for him as well. A bride from Casterly Rock. Your lord father said that Raynald should have joy of him, if all went as we hoped."

Even from the grave, Lord Tywin's dead hand moves us all. "Joy is my late uncle Gerion's natural daughter. A betrothal can be arranged, if that is your wish, but any marriage will need to wait. Joy was nine or ten when last I saw her."

"His *natural* daughter?" Lady Sybell looked as if she had swallowed a lemon. "You want a Westerling to wed a *bastard*?"

"No more than I want Joy to marry the son of some scheming turncloak bitch. She deserves better." Jaime would happily have strangled the woman with her seashell necklace. Joy was a sweet child, albeit a lonely one; her father had been Jaime's favorite uncle. "Your daughter is worth ten of you, my lady. You'll leave with Edmure and Ser Forley on the morrow. Until then, you would do well to stay out of my sight." He shouted for a guardsman, and Lady Sybell went off with her lips pressed primly together. Jaime had to wonder how much Lord Gawen knew about his wife's scheming. *How much do we men ever know?*

When Edmure and the Westerlings departed, four hundred men rode with them; Jaime had doubled the escort again at the last moment. He rode with them a few miles, to talk with Ser Forley Prester. Though he bore a bull's head upon his surcoat and horns upon his helm, Ser Forley could not have been less bovine. He was a short, spare, hard-bitten man. With his pinched nose, bald pate, and grizzled brown beard, he looked more like an innkeep than a knight. "We don't know where the Blackfish is," Jaime reminded him, "but if he can cut Edmure free, he will."

"That will not happen, my lord." Like most innkeeps, Ser Forley was no man's fool. "Scouts and outriders will screen our march, and we'll fortify our camps by night. I have picked ten men to stay with Tully day and night, my best longbowmen. If he should ride so much as a foot off the road, they will loose so many shafts at him that his own mother would take him for a goose."

"Good." Jaime would as lief have Tully reach Casterly Rock safely, but better dead than fled. "Best keep some archers near Lord Westerling's daughter as well."

Ser Forley seemed taken aback. "Gawen's girl? She's—"

"—the Young Wolf's widow," Jaime finished, "and twice as dangerous as Edmure if she were ever to escape us."

"As you say, my lord. She will be watched."

Jaime had to canter past the Westerlings as he rode down the column on his way back to Riverrun. Lord Gawen nodded gravely as he passed, but Lady Sybell looked through him with eyes like chips of ice. Jeyne never saw him at all. The widow rode with downcast eyes, huddled beneath a hooded cloak. Underneath its heavy folds, her clothes were finely made, but torn. *She ripped them herself, as a mark of mourning,* Jaime realized. *That could not have pleased her mother.* He found himself wondering if Cersei would tear her gown if she should ever hear that he was dead.

He did not go straight back to the castle but crossed the Tumblestone once more to call on Edwyn Frey and discuss the transfer of his great-grandfather's prisoners. The Frey host had begun to break up within hours of Riverrun's surrender, as Lord Walder's bannermen and freeriders pulled up stakes to make for home. The Freys who still remained were striking camp, but he found Edwyn with his bastard uncle in the latter's pavilion.

The two of them were huddled over a map, arguing heatedly, but they broke off when Jaime entered. "Lord Commander," Rivers said with cold courtesy, but Edwyn blurted out, "My father's blood is on your hands, ser."

That took Jaime a bit aback. "How so?"

"You were the one who sent him home, were you not?"

Someone had to. "Has some ill befallen Ser Ryman?"

"Hanged with all his party," said Walder Rivers. "The outlaws caught them two leagues south of Fairmarket."

"Dondarrion?"

"Him, or Thoros, or this woman Stoneheart."

Jaime frowned. Ryman Frey had been a fool, a craven, and a sot, and no one was like to miss him much, least of all his fellow Freys. If Edwyn's dry eyes were any clue, even his own sons would not mourn him long. *Still . . . these outlaws are growing bold, if they dare hang Lord Walder's heir not a day's ride from the Twins.* "How many men did Ser Ryman have with him?" he asked.

"Three knights and a dozen men-at-arms," said Rivers. "It is almost as if they knew that he would be returning to the Twins, and with a small escort."

Edwyn's mouth twisted. "My brother had a hand in this, I'll wager. He allowed the outlaws to escape after they murdered Merrett and Petyr, and this is why. With our father dead, there's only me left between Black Walder and the Twins."

"You have no proof of this," said Walder Rivers.

"I do not need proof. I know my brother."

"Your brother is at Seagard," Rivers insisted. "How could he have known that Ser Ryman was returning to the Twins?"

"Someone told him," said Edwyn in a bitter tone. "He has his spies in our camp, you can be sure."

And you have yours at Seagard. Jaime knew that the enmity between Edwyn and Black Walder ran deep, but cared not a fig which of them succeeded their great-grandfather as Lord of the Crossing.

"If you will pardon me for intruding on your grief," he said, in a dry tone, "we have other matters to consider. When you return to the Twins, please inform Lord Walder that King Tommen requires all the captives you took at the Red Wedding."

Ser Walder frowned. "These prisoners are valuable, ser."

"His Grace would not ask for them if they were worthless."

Frey and Rivers exchanged a look. Edwyn said, "My lord grandfather will expect recompense for these prisoners."

And he'll have it, as soon as I grow a new hand, thought Jaime. "We all have expectations," he said mildly. "Tell me, is Ser Raynald Westerling amongst these captives?"

"The knight of seashells?" Edwyn sneered. "You'll find that one feeding the fish at the bottom of the Green Fork."

"He was in the yard when our men came to put the direwolf down," said Walder Rivers. "Whalen demanded his sword and he gave it over meek enough, but when the crossbowmen began feathering the wolf he seized Whalen's axe and cut the monster loose of the net they'd thrown over him. Whalen says he took a quarrel in his shoulder and another in the gut, but still managed to reach the wallwalk and throw himself into the river."

"He left a trail of blood on the steps," said Edwyn.

"Did you find his corpse afterward?" asked Jaime.

"We found a thousand corpses afterward. Once they've spent a few days in the river they all look much the same."

"I've heard the same is true of hanged men," said Jaime, before he took his leave.

By the next morning little remained of the Frey encampment but flies, horse dung, and Ser Ryman's gallows, standing forlorn beside the Tumblestone. His coz wanted to know what should be done with it, and with the siege equipment he had built, his rams and sows and towers and trebuchets. Daven proposed that they drag it all to Raventree and use it there. Jaime told him to put everything to the torch, starting with the gallows. "I mean to deal with Lord Tytos myself. It won't require a siege tower."

Daven grinned through his bushy beard. "Single combat, coz? Scarce seems fair. Tytos is an old grey man."

An old grey man with two hands.

That night he and Ser Ilyn fought for three hours. It was one of his better nights. If they had been in earnest, Payne only would have killed him twice. Half a dozen deaths were more the rule, and some nights were worse than that. "If I keep at this for another year, I may be as good as Peck," Jaime declared, and Ser Ilyn made that clacking sound that meant he was amused. "Come, let's drink some more of Hoster Tully's good red wine."

Wine had become a part of their nightly ritual. Ser Ilyn made the perfect drinking companion. He never interrupted, never disagreed, never complained or asked for favors or told long pointless stories. All he did was drink and listen.

"I should have the tongues removed from all my friends," said Jaime as he filled their cups, "and from my kin as well. A silent Cersei would be sweet. Though I'd miss her tongue when we kissed." He drank. The wine was a deep red, sweet and heavy. It warmed him going down. "I can't remember when we first began to kiss. It was innocent at first. Until it wasn't." He finished the wine and set his cup aside. "Tyrion once told me that most whores will not kiss you. They'll fuck you blind, he said, but you'll never feel their lips on yours. Do you think my sister kisses Kettleblack?"

Ser Ilyn did not answer.

"I don't think it would be proper for me to slay mine own Sworn Brother. What I need to do is geld him and send him to the Wall. That's what they did with Lucamore the Lusty. Ser Osmund may not take kindly to the gelding, to be sure. And there are his brothers to consider. Brothers can be dangerous. After Aegon the Unworthy put Ser Terrence Toyne to death for sleeping with his mistress, Toyne's brothers did their best to kill him. Their best was not quite good enough, thanks to the Dragonknight, but it was not for want of trying. It's written down in the White Book. All of it, save what to do with Cersei."

Ser Ilyn drew a finger across his throat.

"No," said Jaime. "Tommen has lost a brother, and the man he thought of as his father. If I were to kill his mother, he would hate me for it . . . and that sweet little wife of his would find a way to turn that hatred to the benefit of Highgarden."

Ser Ilyn smiled in a way Jaime did not like. *An ugly smile. An ugly soul.* "You talk too much," he told the man.

The next day Ser Dermot of the Rainwood returned to the castle, empty-handed. When asked what he'd found, he answered, "Wolves. Hundreds of the bloody beggars." He'd lost two sentries to them. The wolves had come out of the dark to savage them. "Armed men in mail and boiled leather, and yet the beasts had no fear of them. Before he died, Jate said the pack was led by a she-wolf of monstrous size. A direwolf, to hear him tell it. The wolves got in amongst our horse lines too. The bloody bastards killed my favorite bay."

"A ring of fires round your camp might keep them off," said Jaime, though he wondered. Could Ser Dermot's direwolf be the same beast that had mauled Joffrey near the crossroads?

Wolves or no, Ser Dermot took fresh horses and more men and went out again the next morning, to resume the search for Brynden Tully. That same afternoon, the lords of the Trident came to Jaime asking his leave to return to their own lands. He granted it. Lord Piper also wanted to know about his son Marq. "All the captives will be ransomed," Jaime promised. As the riverlords took their leave, Lord Karyl Vance lingered to say, "Lord Jaime, you must go to Raventree. So long as it is Jonos at his gates Tytos will never yield, but I know he will bend his knee for you." Jaime thanked him for his counsel.

Strongboar was the next to depart. He wanted to return to Darry as he'd promised and fight the outlaws. "We rode across half the bloody realm and for what? So you could make Edmure Tully piss his breeches? There's no song in that. I need a *fight*. I want the Hound, Jaime. Him, or the marcher lord."

"The Hound's head is yours if you can take it," Jaime said, "but Beric Dondarrion is to be captured alive, so he can be brought back to King's Landing. A thousand people need to see him die, or else he won't stay dead." Strongboar grumbled at that, but finally agreed. The next day he departed with his squire and men-at-arms, plus Beardless Jon Bettley, who had decided that hunting outlaws was preferable to returning to his famously homely wife. Supposedly she had the beard that Bettley lacked.

Jaime still had the garrison to deal with. To a man, they

swore that they knew nothing of Ser Brynden's plans or where he might have gone. "They are lying," Emmon Frey insisted, but Jaime thought not. "If you share your plans with no one, no one can betray you," he pointed out. Lady Genna suggested that a few of the men might be put to the question. He refused. "I gave Edmure my word that if he yielded, the garrison could leave unharmed."

"That was chivalrous of you," his aunt said, "but it's strength that's needed here, not chivalry."

Ask Edmure how chivalrous I am, thought Jaime. *Ask him about the trebuchet.* Somehow he did not think the maesters were like to confuse him with Prince Aemon the Dragonknight when they wrote their histories. Still, he felt curiously content. The war was all but won. Dragonstone had fallen and Storm's End would soon enough, he could not doubt, and Stannis was welcome to the Wall. The northmen would love him no more than the storm lords had. If Roose Bolton did not destroy him, winter would.

And he had done his own part here at Riverrun without actually ever taking up arms against the Starks or Tullys. Once he found the Blackfish, he would be free to return to King's Landing, where he belonged. *My place is with my king. With my son.* Would Tommen want to know that? The truth could cost the boy his throne. *Would you sooner have a father or a chair, lad?* Jaime wished he knew the answer. *He does like stamping papers with his seal.* The boy might not even believe him, to be sure. Cersei would say it was a lie. *My sweet sister, the deceiver.* He would need to find some way to winkle Tommen from her clutches before the boy became another Joffrey. And whilst at that, he should find the lad a new small council too. *If Cersei can be put aside, Ser Kevan may agree to serve as Tommen's Hand.* And if not, well, the Seven Kingdoms did not lack for able men. Forley Prester would make a good choice, or Roland

Crakehall. If someone other than a westerman was needed to appease the Tyrells, there was always Mathis Rowan . . . or even Petyr Baelish. Littlefinger was as amiable as he was clever, but too lowborn to threaten any of the great lords, with no swords of his own. *The perfect Hand.*

The Tully garrison departed the next morning, stripped of all their arms and armor. Each man was allowed three days' food and the clothing on his back, after he swore a solemn oath never to take up arms against Lord Emmon or House Lannister. "If you're fortunate, one man in ten may keep that vow," Lady Genna said.

"Good. I'd sooner face nine men than ten. The tenth might have been the one who would have killed me."

"The other nine will kill you just as quick."

"Better that than die in bed." *Or on the privy.*

Two men did not choose to depart with the others. Ser Desmond Grell, Lord Hoster's old master-at-arms, preferred to take the black. So did Ser Robin Ryger, Riverrun's captain of guards. "This castle's been my home for forty years," said Grell. "You say I'm free to go, but where? I'm too old and too stout to make a hedge knight. But men are always welcome at the Wall."

"As you wish," said Jaime, though it was a bloody nuisance. He allowed them to keep their arms and armor, and assigned a dozen of Gregor Clegane's men to escort the two of them to Maidenpool. The command he gave to Rafford, the one they called the Sweetling. "See to it that the prisoners reach Maidenpool unspoiled," he told the man, "or what Ser Gregor did to the Goat will seem a jolly lark compared to what I'll do to you."

More days passed. Lord Emmon assembled all of Riverrun in the yard, Lord Edmure's people and his own, and spoke to them for close on three hours about what would be expected of them now that he was their lord and master. From time to time he waved his parchment, as stableboys and serving girls and smiths listened in a sullen silence and a light rain fell down upon them all.

The singer was listening too, the one that Jaime had taken from Ser Ryman Frey. Jaime came upon him standing inside an open door, where it was dry. "His lordship should have been a singer," the man said. "This speech is longer than a marcher ballad, and I don't think he's stopped for breath."

Jaime had to laugh. "Lord Emmon does not need to breathe, so long as he can chew. Are you going to make a song of it?"

"A funny one. I'll call it 'Talking to the Fish.'"

"Just don't play it where my aunt can hear." Jaime had never paid the man much mind before. He was a small fellow, garbed in ragged green breeches and a frayed tunic of a lighter shade of green, with brown leather patches covering the holes. His nose was long and sharp, his smile big and loose. Thin brown hair fell to his collar, snaggled and unwashed. *Fifty if he's a day,* thought Jaime, *a hedge harp, and hard used by life.* "Weren't you Ser Ryman's man when I found you?" he asked.

"Only for a fortnight."

"I would have expected you to depart with the Freys."

"That one up there's a Frey," the singer said, nodding at Lord Emmon, "and this castle seems a nice snug place to pass the winter. Whitesmile Wat went home with Ser Forley, so I thought I'd see if I could win his place. Wat's got that high sweet voice that the likes o' me can't hope to match. But I know twice as many bawdy songs as he does. Begging my lord's pardon."

"You should get on famously with my aunt," said Jaime. "If you hope to winter here, see that your playing pleases Lady Genna. She's the one that matters."

"Not you?"

"My place is with the king. I shall not stay here long."

"I'm sorry to hear that, my lord. I know better songs than 'The Rains of Castamere.' I could have played you . . . oh, all sorts o' things."

"Some other time," said Jaime. "Do you have a name?"

"Tom of Sevenstreams, if it please my lord." The singer doffed his hat. "Most call me Tom o' Sevens, though."

"Sing sweetly, Tom o' Sevens."

That night he dreamt that he was back in the Great Sept of Baelor, still standing vigil over his father's corpse. The sept was still and dark, until a woman emerged from the shadows and walked slowly to the bier. "Sister?" he said.

But it was not Cersei. She was all in grey, a silent sister. A hood and veil concealed her features, but he could see the candles burning in the green pools of her eyes. "Sister," he said, "what would you have of me?" His last word echoed up and down the sept, *memememememe mememememe.*

"I am not your sister, Jaime." She raised a pale soft hand and pushed her hood back. "Have you forgotten me?"

Can I forget someone I never knew? The words caught in his throat. He *did* know her, but it had been so long . . .

"Will you forget your own lord father too? I wonder if you ever knew him, truly." Her eyes were green, her hair spun gold. He could not tell how old she was. *Fifteen,* he thought, *or fifty.* She climbed the steps to stand above the bier. "He could never abide being laughed at. That was the thing he hated most."

"Who are you?" He had to hear her say it.

"The question is, who are you?"

"This is a dream."

"Is it?" She smiled sadly. "Count your hands, child."

One. One hand, clasped tight around the sword hilt.

Only one. "In my dreams I always have two hands." He raised his right arm and stared uncomprehending at the ugliness of his stump.

"We all dream of things we cannot have. Tywin dreamed that his son would be a great knight, that his daughter would be a queen. He dreamed they would be so strong and brave and beautiful that no one would ever laugh at them."

"I am a knight," he told her, "and Cersei is a queen."

A tear rolled down her cheek. The woman raised her hood again and turned her back on him. Jaime called after her, but already she was moving away, her skirt whispering lullabies as it brushed across the floor. *Don't leave me,* he wanted to call, but of course she'd left them long ago.

He woke in darkness, shivering. The room had grown cold as ice. Jaime flung aside the covers with the stump of his sword hand. The fire in the hearth had died, he saw, and the window had blown open. He crossed the pitch-dark chamber to fumble with the shutters, but when he reached the window his bare foot came down in something wet. Jaime recoiled, startled for a moment. His first thought was of blood, but blood would not have been so cold.

It was snow, drifting through the window.

Instead of closing the shutters he threw them wide. The yard below was covered by a thin white blanket, growing thicker even as he watched. The merlons on the battlements wore white cowls. The flakes fell silently, a few drifting in the window to melt upon his face. Jaime could see his own breath.

Snow in the riverlands. If it was snowing here, it could well be snowing on Lannisport as well, and on King's Landing. *Winter is marching south, and half our granaries are empty.* Any crops still in the fields were doomed. There would be no more plantings, no more hopes of one last harvest. He found himself wondering what his father would do to feed the realm, before he remembered that Tywin Lannister was dead.

When morning broke the snow was ankle deep, and deeper in the godswood, where drifts had piled up under the trees. Squires, stableboys, and highborn pages turned to children again under its cold white spell, and fought a snowball war up and down the wards and all along the battlements. Jaime heard them laughing. There was a time, not long ago, when he might have been out making snowballs with the best of them, to fling at Tyrion when he waddled by, or slip down the back of Cersei's gown. *You need two hands to make a decent snowball, though.*

There was a rap upon his door. "See who that is, Peck."

It was Riverrun's old maester, with a message clutched in his lined and wrinkled hand. Vyman's face was as pale as the new-fallen snow. "I know," Jaime said, "there has been a white raven from the Citadel. Winter has come."

"No, my lord. The bird was from King's Landing. I took the liberty . . . I did not know . . ." He held the letter out.

Jaime read it in the window seat, bathed in the light of that cold white morning. Qyburn's words were terse and to the point, Cersei's fevered and fervent. *Come at once,* she said. *Help me. Save me. I need you now as I have never needed you before. I love you. I love you. I love you. Come at once.*

Vyman was hovering by the door, waiting, and Jaime sensed that Peck was watching too. "Does my lord wish to answer?" the maester asked, after a long silence.

A snowflake landed on the letter. As it melted, the ink began to blur. Jaime rolled the parchment up again, as tight as one hand would allow, and handed it to Peck. "No," he said. "Put this in the fire."

SAMWELL

The most perilous part of the voyage was the last. The Redwyne Straits were swarming with long-ships, as they had been warned in Tyrosh. With the main strength of the Arbor's fleet on the far side of Westeros, the ironmen had sacked Ryamsport and taken Vinetown and Starfish Harbor for their own, using them as bases to prey on shipping bound for Oldtown.

Thrice longships were sighted by the crow's nest. Two were well astern, however, and the *Cinnamon Wind* soon outdistanced them. The third appeared near sunset, to cut them off from Whispering Sound. When they saw her oars rising and falling, lashing the copper waters white, Kojja Mo sent her archers to the castles with their great bows of goldenheart that could send a shaft farther and truer than even Dornish yew. She waited till the longship came within two hundred yards before she gave the command to loose. Sam loosed with them, and this time he thought his arrow reached the ship. One volley was all it took. The longship veered south in search of tamer prey.

A deep blue dusk was falling as they entered Whispering Sound. Gilly stood beside the prow with the babe, gazing up at a castle on the cliffs. "Three Towers," Sam told her, "the seat of House Costayne." Etched against the evening stars with torchlight flickering from its windows, the castle made a splendid sight, but he was sad to see it. Their voyage was almost at its end.

"It's very tall," said Gilly.

"Wait until you see the Hightower."

Dalla's babe began to cry. Gilly pulled open her tunic and gave the boy her breast. She smiled as he nursed, and stroked his soft brown hair. *She has come to love this one as much as the one she left behind,* Sam realized. He hoped that the gods would be kind to both of the children.

The ironmen had penetrated even to the sheltered waters of Whispering Sound. Come morning, as the *Cinnamon Wind* continued on toward Oldtown, she began to bump up against corpses drifting down to the sea. Some of the bodies carried complements of crows, who rose into the air complaining noisily when the swan ship disturbed their grotesquely swollen rafts. Scorched fields and burned villages appeared on the banks, and the shallows and sandbars were strewn with shattered ships. Merchanters and fishing boats were the most common, but they saw abandoned longships too, and the wreckage of two big dromonds. One had been burned down to the waterline, whilst the other had a gaping splintered hole in her side where her hull had been rammed.

"Battle here," said Xhondo. "Not so long."

"Who would be so mad as to raid this close to Oldtown?"

Xhondo pointed at a half-sunken longship in the shallows. The remnants of a banner drooped from her stern, smoke-stained and ragged. The charge was one Sam had never seen before: a red eye with a black pupil, beneath a black iron crown supported by two crows. "Whose banner is that?" Sam asked. Xhondo only shrugged.

The next day was cold and misty. As the *Cinnamon Wind* was creeping past another plundered fishing village, a war galley came sliding from the fog, stroking slowly toward them. *Huntress* was the name she bore, behind a figurehead of a slender maiden clad in leaves and brandishing a spear. A heartbeat later, two smaller galleys appeared on either side of her, like a pair of matched greyhounds stalking at their master's heels. To Sam's relief, they flew King Tommen's stag-and-lion banner above the stepped white tower of Oldtown, with its crown of flame.

The captain of the *Huntress* was a tall man in a smoke-grey cloak with a border of red satin flames. He brought his galley in alongside the *Cinnamon Wind,* raised his oars, and shouted that he was coming aboard. As his crossbowmen and Kojja Mo's archers eyed each other across the narrow span of water, he crossed over with half a dozen knights, gave Quhuru Mo a nod, and asked to see his holds. Father and daughter conferred briefly, then agreed.

"My apologies," the captain said when his inspection was complete. "It grieves me that honest men must suffer such discourtesy, but sooner that than ironmen in Oldtown. Only a fortnight ago some of those bloody bastards captured a Tyroshi merchantman in the straits. They killed her crew, donned their clothes, and used the dyes they found to color their whiskers half a hundred colors. Once inside the walls they meant to set the port ablaze and open a gate from within whilst we fought the fire. Might have worked, but they ran afoul of the *Lady of the Tower,* and her oarsmaster has a Tyroshi wife. When he saw all the green and purple beards he hailed them in the tongue of Tyrosh, and not one of them had the words to hail him back."

Sam was aghast. "They cannot mean to raid *Oldtown.*"

The captain of the *Huntress* gave him a curious look. "These are no mere reavers. The ironmen have always raided where they could. They would strike sudden from the sea, carry off some gold and girls, and sail away, but there were seldom more than one or two longships, and never more than half a dozen. Hundreds of their ships afflict us now, sailing out of the Shield Islands and some of the rocks around the Arbor. They have taken Stonecrab Cay, the Isle of Pigs, and the Mermaid's Palace, and there are other nests on Horseshoe Rock and Bastard's Cradle. Without Lord Redwyne's fleet, we lack the ships to come to grips with them."

"What is Lord Hightower doing?" Sam blurted. "My father always said he was as wealthy as the Lannisters, and could command thrice as many swords as any of Highgarden's other bannermen."

"More, if he sweeps the cobblestones," the captain said, "but swords are no good against the ironmen, unless the men who wield them know how to walk on water."

"The Hightower must be doing *something.*"

"To be sure. Lord Leyton's locked atop his tower with the Mad Maid, consulting books of spells. Might be he'll raise an army from the deeps. Or not. Baelor's building galleys, Gunthor has charge of the harbor, Garth is training new recruits, and Humfrey's gone to Lys to hire sellsails. If he can winkle a proper fleet out of his whore of a sister, we can start paying back the ironmen with some of their own coin. Till then, the best we can do is guard the sound and wait for the bitch queen in King's Landing to let Lord Paxter off his leash."

The bitterness of the captain's final words shocked Sam as much as the things he said. *If King's Landing loses Oldtown and the Arbor, the whole realm will fall to pieces,* he thought as he watched the *Huntress* and her sisters moving off.

It made him wonder if even Horn Hill was truly safe. The Tarly lands lay inland amidst thickly wooded foothills, a hundred leagues northeast of Oldtown and a long way from any coast. They should be well beyond the reach of ironmen and longships, even with his lord father off fighting in the riverlands and the castle lightly held. The Young Wolf had no doubt thought the same was true of Winterfell until the night that Theon Turncloak scaled his walls. Sam could not bear the thought that he might have brought Gilly and her babe all this long way to keep them out of harm, only to abandon them in the midst of war.

He wrestled with his doubts through the rest of the voyage, wondering what to do. He could keep Gilly with him in Oldtown, he supposed. The city's walls were much more formidable than those of his father's castle, and had thousands of men to defend them, as opposed to the handful Lord Randyll would have left at Horn Hill when he marched to Highgarden to answer his liege lord's summons. If he did, though, he would need to hide her somehow; the Citadel did not permit its novices to keep wives or paramours, at least not openly. *Besides, if I stay with Gilly very much longer, how will I ever find the strength to leave her?* He *had* to leave her, or desert. *I said the words,* Sam reminded himself. *If I desert, it will mean my head, and how will that help Gilly?*

He considered begging Kojja Mo and her father to take the wildling girl with them to the Summer Isles. That path had its perils too, however. When the *Cinnamon Wind* left Oldtown, she would need to cross the Redwyne Straits again, and this time she might not be so fortunate. What if the wind died, and the Summer Islanders found themselves becalmed? If the tales he'd heard were true, Gilly would be carried off for a thrall or salt wife, and the babe was like to be chucked into the sea as a nuisance.

It has to be Horn Hill, Sam finally decided. *Once we reach Oldtown I'll hire a wagon and some horses and take her there myself.* That way he could make certain of the castle and its garrison, and if any part of what he saw or heard gave him pause, he could just turn around and bring Gilly back to Oldtown.

They reached Oldtown on a cold damp morning, when the fog was so thick that the beacon of the Hightower was the only part of the city to be seen. A boom stretched across the harbor, linking two dozen rotted hulks. Just behind it stood a line of warships, anchored by three big dromonds and Lord Hightower's towering four-decked banner ship, the *Honor of Oldtown.* Once again the *Cinnamon Wind* had to submit to inspection. This time it was Lord Leyton's son Gunthor who came aboard, in a cloth-of-silver cloak and a suit of grey enameled scales. Ser Gunthor had studied at the Citadel for several years and spoke the Summer Tongue, so he and Qurulu Mo adjourned to the captain's cabin for a privy conference.

Sam used the time to explain his plans to Gilly. "First the Citadel, to present Jon's letters and tell them of Maester Aemon's death. I expect the archmaesters will send a cart for his body. Then I will arrange for horses and a wagon to take you to my mother at Horn Hill. I will be back as soon as I can, but it may not be until the morrow."

"The morrow," she repeated, and gave him a kiss for luck.

At length Ser Gunthor reemerged and gave the signal for the chain to be opened so the *Cinnamon Wind* could slip through the boom to dock. Sam joined Kojja Mo and three of her archers near the gangplank as the swan ship was tying up, the Summer Islanders resplendent in the feathered cloaks they only wore ashore. He felt a shabby thing beside them in his baggy blacks, faded cloak, and salt-stained boots. "How long will you remain in port?"

"Two days, ten days, who can say? However long it takes to empty our holds and fill them again." Kojja grinned. "My father must visit the grey maesters as well. He has books to sell."

"Can Gilly stay aboard till I return?"

"Gilly can stay as long as she likes." She poked Sam in the belly with a finger. "She does not eat so much as some."

"I'm not so fat as I was before," Sam said defensively. The passage south had seen to that. All those watches, and nothing to eat but fruit and fish. Summer Islanders loved fruit and fish.

Sam followed the archers across the plank, but once ashore they parted company and went their separate ways. He hoped he still remembered the way to the Citadel. Oldtown was a maze, and he had no time for getting lost.

The day was damp, so the cobblestones were wet and slippery underfoot, the alleys shrouded in mist and mystery. Sam avoided them as best he could and stayed on the river road that wound along beside the Honeywine through the heart of the old city. It felt good to have solid ground beneath his feet again instead of a rolling deck, but the walk made him feel uncomfortable all the same. He could feel eyes on him, peering down from balconies and windows, watching him from the darkened doorways. On the *Cinnamon Wind* he had known every face. Here, everywhere he turned he saw another stranger. Even worse was the thought of being seen by someone who knew him. Lord Randyll Tarly was known in Oldtown, but little loved. Sam did not know which would be worse: to be recognized by one of his lord father's enemies or by one of his friends. He pulled his cloak up and quickened his pace.

The gates of the Citadel were flanked by a pair of towering green sphinxes with the bodies of lions, the wings of eagles, and the tails of serpents. One had a man's face, one a woman's. Just beyond stood Scribe's Hearth, where Oldtowners came in search of acolytes to write their wills and read their letters. Half a dozen bored scribes sat in open stalls, waiting for some custom. At other stalls books were being bought and sold. Sam stopped at one that offered maps, and looked over a hand-drawn map of Citadel to ascertain the shortest way to the Seneschal's Court.

The path divided where the statue of King Daeron the First sat astride his tall stone horse, his sword lifted toward Dorne. A seagull was perched on the Young Dragon's head, and two more on the blade. Sam took the left fork, which ran beside the river. At the Weeping Dock, he watched two acolytes help an old man into a boat for the short voyage to the Bloody Isle. A young mother climbed in after him, a babe not much older than Gilly's squalling in her arms. Beneath the dock, some cook's boys waded in the shallows, gathering frogs. A stream of pink-cheeked novices hurried by him toward the septry. *I should have come here when I was their age,* Sam thought. *If I had run off and taken a false name, I could have disappeared amongst the other novices. Father could have pretended that Dickon was his only son. I doubt he would even have troubled to search for me, unless I took a mule to ride.*

Then he would have hunted me down, but only for the mule.

Outside the Seneschal's Court, the rectors were locking an older novice into the stocks. "Stealing food from the kitchens," one explained to the acolytes who were waiting to pelt the captive with rotting vegetables. They all gave Sam curious looks as he strode past, his black cloak billowing behind him like a sail.

Beyond the doors he found a hall with a stone floor and high, arched windows. At the far end a man with a pinched face sat upon a raised dais, scratching in a ledger with a quill. Though the man was clad in a maester's robe, there was no chain about his neck. Sam cleared his throat. "Good morrow."

The man glanced up and did not appear to approve of what he saw. "You smell of novice."

"I hope to be one soon." Sam drew out the letters Jon Snow had given him. "I came from the Wall with Maester Aemon, but he died during the voyage. If I could speak with the Seneschal . . ."

"Your name?"

"Samwell. Samwell Tarly."

The man wrote the name in his ledger and waved his quill at a bench along the wall. "Sit. You'll be called when wanted."

Sam took a seat on the bench.

Others came and went. Some delivered messages and took their leave. Some spoke to the man on the dais and were sent through the door behind him and up a turnpike stair. Some joined Sam on the benches, waiting for their names to be called. A few of those who were summoned had come in after him, he was almost certain. After the fourth or fifth time that happened, he rose and crossed the room again. "How much longer will it be?"

"The Seneschal is an important man."

"I came all the way from the Wall."

"Then you will have no trouble going a bit farther." He waved his quill. "To that bench just there, beneath the window."

Sam returned to the bench. Another hour passed. Others entered, spoke to the man on the dais, waited a few moments, and were ushered onward. The gatekeeper did not so much as glance at Sam in all that time. The fog outside grew thinner as the day wore on, and pale sunlight slanted down through the windows. He found himself watching dust motes dance in the light. A yawn escaped him, then another. He picked at a broken blister on his palm, then leaned his head back and closed his eyes.

He must have drowsed. The next he knew, the man behind the dais was calling out a name. Sam came lurching to his feet, then sat back down again when he realized it was not his name.

"You need to slip Lorcas a penny, or you'll be waiting here three days," a voice beside him said. "What brings the Night's Watch to the Citadel?"

The speaker was a slim, slight, comely youth, clad in doeskin breeches and a snug green brigandine with iron studs. He had skin the color of a light brown ale and a cap of tight black curls that came to a widow's peak above his big black eyes. "The Lord Commander is restoring the abandoned castles," Sam explained. "We need more maesters, for the ravens . . . did you say, a penny?"

"A penny will serve. For a silver stag Lorcas will carry you up to the Seneschal on his back. He has been fifty years an acolyte. He hates novices, particularly novices of noble birth."

"How could you tell I was of noble birth?"

"The same way you can tell that I'm half Dornish." The

statement was delivered with a smile, in a soft Dornish drawl.

Sam fumbled for a penny. "Are you a novice?"

"An acolyte. Alleras, by some called Sphinx."

The name gave Sam a jolt. "The sphinx is the riddle, not the riddler," he blurted. "Do you know what that means?"

"No. Is it a riddle?"

"I wish I knew. I'm Samwell Tarly. Sam."

"Well met. And what business does Samwell Tarly have with Archmaester Theobald?"

"Is he the Seneschal?" said Sam, confused. "Maester Aemon said his name was Norren."

"Not for the past two turns. There is a new one every year. They fill the office by lot from amongst the archmaesters, most of whom regard it as a thankless task that takes them away from their true work. This year the black stone was drawn by Archmaester Walgrave, but Walgrave's wits are prone to wander, so Theobald stepped up and said he'd serve his term. He's a gruff man, but a good one. Did you say Maester *Aemon*?"

"Aye."

"Aemon *Targaryen*?"

"Once. Most just called him Maester Aemon. He died during our voyage south. How is it that you know of him?"

"How not? He was more than just the oldest living maester. He was the oldest man in Westeros, and lived through more history than Archmaester Perestan has ever learned. He could have told us much and more about his father's reign, and his uncle's. How old was he, do you know?"

"One hundred and two."

"What was he doing at sea, at his age?"

Sam chewed on the question for a moment, wondering

how much he ought to say. *The sphinx is the riddle, not the riddler.* Could Maester Aemon have meant *this* Sphinx? It seemed unlikely. "Lord Commander Snow sent him away to save his life," he began, hesitantly. He spoke awkwardly of King Stannis and Melisandre of Asshai, intending to stop at that, but one thing led to another and he found himself speaking of Mance Rayder and his wildlings, king's blood and dragons, and before he knew what was happening, all the rest came spilling out; the wights at the Fist of First Men, the Other on his dead horse, the murder of the Old Bear at Craster's Keep, Gilly and their flight, Whitetree and Small Paul, Coldhands and the ravens, Jon's becoming lord commander, the *Blackbird,* Dareon, Braavos, the dragons Xhondo saw in Qarth, the *Cinnamon Wind* and all that Maester Aemon whispered toward the end. He held back only the secrets that he was sworn to keep, about Bran Stark and his companions and the babes Jon Snow had swapped. "Daenerys is the only hope," he concluded. "Aemon said the Citadel must send her a maester at once, to bring her home to Westeros before it is too late."

Alleras listened intently. He blinked from time to time, but he never laughed and never interrupted. When Sam was done he touched him lightly on the forearm with a slim brown hand and said, "Save your penny, Sam. Theobald will not believe half of that, but there are those who might. Will you come with me?"

"Where?"

"To speak with an archmaester."

You must tell them, Sam, Maester Aemon had said. *You must tell the archmaesters.* "Very well." He could always return to the Seneschal on the morrow, with a penny in his hand. "How far do we have to go?"

"Not far. The Isle of Ravens."

They did not need a boat to reach the Isle of Ravens; a weathered wooden drawbridge linked it to the eastern bank. "The Ravenry is the oldest building at the Citadel," Alleras told him, as they crossed over the slow-flowing waters of the Honeywine. "In the Age of Heroes it was supposedly the stronghold of a pirate lord who sat here robbing ships as they came down the river."

Moss and creeping vines covered the walls, Sam saw, and ravens walked its battlements in place of archers. The drawbridge had not been raised in living memory.

It was cool and dim inside the castle walls. An ancient weirwood filled the yard, as it had since these stones had first been raised. The carved face on its trunk was grown over by the same purple moss that hung heavy from the tree's pale limbs. Half of the branches seemed dead, but elsewhere a few red leaves still rustled, and it was there the ravens liked to perch. The tree was full of them, and there were more in the arched windows overhead, all around the yard. The ground was speckled by their droppings. As they crossed the yard, one flapped overhead and he heard the others *quork*ing to each other. "Archmaester Walgrave has his chambers in the west tower, below the white rookery," Alleras told him. "The white ravens and the black ones quarrel like Dornishmen and Marchers, so they keep them apart."

"Will Archmaester Walgrave understand what I am telling him?" wondered Sam. "You said his wits were prone to wander."

"He has good days and bad ones," said Alleras, "but it is not Walgrave you're going to see." He opened the door to the north tower and began to climb. Sam clambered up the steps behind him. There were flutterings and mutterings from above, and here and there an angry scream, as the ravens complained of being woken.

At the top of the steps, a pale blond youth about Sam's age sat outside a door of oak and iron, staring intently into a candle flame with his right eye. His left was hidden beneath a fall of ash blond hair. "What are you looking for?" Alleras asked him. "Your destiny? Your death?"

The blond youth turned from the candle, blinking. "Naked women," he said. "Who's this now?"

"Samwell. A new novice, come to see the Mage."

"The Citadel is not what it was," complained the blond. "They will take anything these days. Dusky dogs and Dornishmen, pig boys, cripples, cretins, and now a black-clad whale. And here I thought leviathans were grey." A half cape striped in green and gold draped one shoulder. He was very handsome, though his eyes were sly and his mouth cruel.

Sam knew him. "Leo Tyrell." Saying the name made him feel as if he were still a boy of seven, about to wet his smallclothes. "I am Sam, from Horn Hill. Lord Randyll Tarly's son."

"Truly?" Leo gave him another look. "I suppose you are. Your father told us all that you were dead. Or was it only that he wished you were?" He grinned. "Are you still a craven?"

"No," lied Sam. Jon had made it a command. "I went beyond the Wall and fought in battles. They call me Sam the Slayer." He did not know why he said it. The words just tumbled out.

Leo laughed, but before he could reply the door behind him opened. "Get in here, Slayer," growled the man in the doorway. "And you, Sphinx. Now."

"Sam," said Alleras, "this is Archmaester Marwyn."

Marwyn wore a chain of many metals around his bull's neck. Save for that, he looked more like a dockside thug than a maester. His head was too big for his body, and the way it thrust forward from his shoulders, together with that slab of jaw, made him look as if he were about to tear off someone's head. Though short and squat, he was heavy in the chest and shoulders, with a round, rock-hard ale belly straining at the laces of the leather jerkin he wore in place of robes. Bristly white hair sprouted from his ears and nostrils. His brow beetled, his nose had been broken more than once, and sourleaf had stained his teeth a mottled red. He had the biggest hands that Sam had ever seen.

When Sam hesitated, one of those hands grabbed him by the arm and yanked him through the door. The room beyond was large and round. Books and scrolls were everywhere, strewn across the tables and stacked up on the floor in piles four feet high. Faded tapestries and ragged maps covered the stone walls. A fire was burning in the hearth, beneath a copper kettle. Whatever was inside of it smelled burned. Aside from that, the only light came from a tall black candle in the center of the room.

The candle was unpleasantly bright. There was something queer about it. The flame did not flicker, even when Archmaester Marwyn closed the door so hard that papers blew off a nearby table. The light did something strange to colors too. Whites were bright as fresh-fallen snow, yellow shone like gold, reds turned to flame, but the shadows were so black they looked like holes in the world. Sam found himself staring. The candle itself was three feet tall and slender as a sword, ridged and twisted, glittering black. "Is that . . . ?"

". . . obsidian," said the other man in the room, a pale, fleshy, pasty-faced young fellow with round shoulders, soft hands, close-set eyes, and food stains on his robes.

"Call it dragonglass." Archmaester Marwyn glanced at the candle for a moment. "It burns but is not consumed."

"What feeds the flame?" asked Sam.

"What feeds a dragon's fire?" Marwyn seated himself upon a stool. "All Valyrian sorcery was rooted in blood or fire. The sorcerers of the Freehold could see across mountains, seas, and deserts with one of these glass candles. They could enter a man's dreams and give him visions, and speak to one another half a world apart, seated before their candles. Do you think that might be useful, Slayer?"

"We would have no more need of ravens."

"Only after battles." The archmaester peeled a sourleaf off a bale, shoved it in his mouth, and began to chew it. "Tell me all you told our Dornish sphinx. I know much of it and more, but some small parts may have escaped my notice."

He was not a man to be refused. Sam hesitated a moment, then told his tale again as Marywn, Alleras, and the other novice listened. "Maester Aemon believed that Daenerys Targaryen was the fulfillment of a prophecy . . . her, not Stannis, nor Prince Rhaegar, nor the princeling whose head was dashed against the wall."

"Born amidst salt and smoke, beneath a bleeding star. I know the prophecy." Marwyn turned his head and spat a gob of red phlegm onto the floor. "Not that I would trust it. Gorghan of Old Ghis once wrote that a prophecy is like a treacherous woman. She takes your member in her mouth, and you moan with the pleasure of it and think, how sweet, how fine, how good this is . . . and then her teeth snap shut and your moans turn to screams. That is the nature of prophecy, said Gorghan. Prophecy will bite your prick off every time." He chewed a bit. "Still . . ."

Alleras stepped up next to Sam. "Aemon would have gone to her if he had the strength. He wanted us to send a maester to her, to counsel her and protect her and fetch her safely home."

"Did he?" Archmaester Marwyn shrugged. "Perhaps

it's good that he died before he got to Oldtown. Elsewise the grey sheep might have had to kill him, and that would have made the poor old dears wring their wrinkled hands."

"Kill him?" Sam said, shocked. "Why?"

"If I tell you, they may need to kill you too." Marywn smiled a ghastly smile, the juice of the sourleaf running red between his teeth. "Who do you think killed all the dragons the last time around? Gallant dragonslayers armed with swords?" He spat. "The world the Citadel is building has no place in it for sorcery or prophecy or glass candles, much less for dragons. Ask yourself why Aemon Targaryen was allowed to waste his life upon the Wall, when by rights he should have been raised to archmaester. His *blood* was why. He could not be trusted. No more than I can."

"What will you do?" asked Alleras, the Sphinx.

"Get myself to Slaver's Bay, in Aemon's place. The swan ship that delivered Slayer should serve my needs well enough. The grey sheep will send their man on a galley, I don't doubt. With fair winds I should reach her first." Marwyn glanced at Sam again, and frowned. "You . . . you should stay and forge your chain. If I were you, I would do it quickly. A time will come when you'll be needed on the Wall." He turned to the pasty-faced novice. "Find Slayer a dry cell. He'll sleep here, and help you tend the ravens."

"B-b-but," Sam sputtered, "the other archmaesters . . . the Seneschal . . . what should I tell them?"

"Tell them how wise and good they are. Tell them that Aemon commanded you to put yourself into their hands. Tell them that you have always dreamed that one day you might be allowed to wear the chain and serve the greater good, that service is the highest honor, and obedience the highest virtue. But say nothing of prophecies or dragons, unless you fancy poison in your porridge." Marwyn snatched a stained leather cloak off a peg near the door and tied it tight. "Sphinx, look after this one."

"I will," Alleras answered, but the archmaester was already gone. They heard his boots stomping down the steps.

"Where has he gone?" asked Sam, bewildered.

"To the docks. The Mage is not a man who believes in wasting time." Alleras smiled. "I have a confession. Ours was no chance encounter, Sam. The Mage sent me to snatch you up before you spoke to Theobald. He knew that you were coming."

"How?"

Alleras nodded at the glass candle.

Sam stared at the strange pale flame for a moment, then blinked and looked away. Outside the window it was growing dark.

"There's an empty sleeping cell under mine in the west tower, with steps that lead right up to Walgrave's chambers," said the pasty-faced youth. "If you don't mind the ravens *quork*ing, there's a good view of the Honeywine. Will that serve?"

"I suppose." He had to sleep somewhere.

"I will bring you some woolen coverlets. Stone walls turn cold at night, even here."

"My thanks." There was something about the pale, soft youth that he misliked, but he did not want to seem discourteous, so he added, "My name's not Slayer, truly. I'm Sam. Samwell Tarly."

"I'm Pate," the other said, "like the pig boy."

MEANWHILE, BACK ON THE WALL . . .

Hey, wait a minute!" some of you may be saying about now. "Wait a minute, wait a minute! Where's Dany and the dragons? Where's Tyrion? We hardly saw Jon Snow. That can't be all of it. . . ."

Well, no. There's more to come. Another book as big as this one.

I did not forget to write about the other characters. Far from it. I wrote lots about them. Pages and pages and pages. Chapters and more chapters. I was still writing when it dawned on me that the book had become too big to publish in a single volume . . . and I wasn't close to finished yet. To tell all of the story that I wanted to tell, I was going to have to cut the book in two.

The simplest way to do that would have been to take what I had, chop it in half around the middle, and end with

"To Be Continued." The more I thought about that, however, the more I felt that the readers would be better served by a book that told all the story for half the characters, rather than half the story for all the characters. So that's the route I chose to take.

Tyrion, Jon, Dany, Stannis and Melisandre, Davos Seaworth, and all the rest of the characters you love or love to hate will be along next year (I devoutly hope) in *A Dance with Dragons*, which will focus on events along the Wall and across the sea, just as the present book focused on King's Landing.

—George R. R. Martin
June 2005

APPENDIX

THE KINGS AND THEIR COURTS

THE QUEEN REGENT

CERSEI LANNISTER, the First of Her Name, widow of {King Robert I Baratheon}, Queen Dowager, Protector of the Realm, Lady of Casterly Rock, and Queen Regent,

—Queen Cersei's children:
    —{KING JOFFREY I BARATHEON}, poisoned at his wedding feast, a boy of twelve,
    —PRINCESS MYRCELLA BARATHEON, a girl of nine, a ward of Prince Doran Martell at Sunspear,
    —KING TOMMEN I BARATHEON, a boy king of eight years,
        —his kittens, SER POUNCE, LADY WHISKERS, BOOTS,
—Queen Cersei's brothers:
    —SER JAIME LANNISTER, her twin, called THE KINGSLAYER, Lord Commander of the Kingsguard,
    —TYRION LANNISTER, called THE IMP, a dwarf, accused and condemned for regicide and kinslaying,
        —PODRICK PAYNE, Tyrion's squire, a boy of ten,
—Queen Cersei's uncles, aunt, and cousins:
    —SER KEVAN LANNISTER, her uncle,

—SER LANCEL, Ser Kevan's son, her cousin, formerly King Robert's squire and Cersei's lover, newly raised to Lord of Darry,

—{WILLEM}, Ser Kevan's son, murdered at Riverrun,

—MARTYN, twin to Willem, a squire,

—JANEI, Ser Kevan's daughter, a girl of three,

—LADY GENNA LANNISTER, Cersei's aunt, m. Ser Emmon Frey,

—{SER CLEOS FREY}, Genna's son, killed by outlaws,

    —SER TYWIN FREY, called TY, Cleos's son,

    —WILLEM FREY, Cleos's son, a squire,

—SER LYONEL FREY, Lady Genna's second son,

—{TION FREY}, Genna's son, murdered at Riverrun,

—WALDER FREY, called RED WALDER, Lady Genna's youngest son, a page at Casterly Rock,

—TYREK LANNISTER, Cersei's cousin, son of her father's late brother Tygett,

—LADY ERMESANDE HAYFORD, Tyrek's child wife,

—JOY HILL, bastard daughter of Queen Cersei's lost uncle Gerion, a girl of eleven,

—CERENNA LANNISTER, Cersei's cousin, daughter of her late uncle Stafford, her mother's brother,

—MYRIELLE LANNISTER, Cersei's cousin and Cerenna's sister, daughter of her uncle Stafford,

—SER DAVEN LANNISTER, her cousin, Stafford's son,

—SER DAMION LANNISTER, a more distant cousin, m. Shiera Crakehall,

—SER LUCION LANNISTER, their son,

—LANNA, their daughter, m. Lord Antario Jast,

—LADY MARGOT, a cousin still more distant, m. Lord Titus Peake,

—King Tommen's small council:

  —{LORD TYWIN LANNISTER}, Hand of the King,

  —SER JAIME LANNISTER, Lord Commander of the Kingsguard,

  —SER KEVAN LANNISTER, master of laws,

  —VARYS, a eunuch, master of whisperers,

  —GRAND MAESTER PYCELLE, counselor and healer,

  —LORD MACE TYRELL, LORD MATHIS ROWAN, LORD PAXTER REDWYNE, counselors,

—Tommen's Kingsguard:

  —SER JAIME LANNISTER, Lord Commander,

  —SER MERYN TRANT,

  —SER BOROS BLOUNT, removed and thence restored,

  —SER BALON SWANN,

  —SER OSMUND KETTLEBLACK,

  —SER LORAS TYRELL, the Knight of Flowers,

  —SER ARYS OAKHEART, with Princess Myrcella in Dorne,

—Cersei's household at King's Landing:

  —LADY JOCELYN SWYFT, her companion,

  —SENELLE and DORCAS, her bedmaids and servingwomen,

—LUM, RED LESTER, HOKE, called HORSELEG, SHORT-EAR, and PUCKENS, guardsmen,

—QUEEN MARGAERY of House Tyrell, a maid of sixteen, widowed bride of King Joffrey I Baratheon and of Lord Renly Baratheon before him,
  —Margaery's court at King's Landing:
    —MACE TYRELL, Lord of Highgarden, her father,
    —LADY ALERIE of House Hightower, her mother,
    —LADY OLENNA TYRELL, her grandmother, an aged widow called THE QUEEN OF THORNS,
      —ARRYK and ERRYK, Lady Olenna's guards, twins seven feet tall called LEFT and RIGHT,
    —SER GARLAN TYRELL, Margaery's brother, THE GALLANT,
      —his wife, LADY LEONETTE of House Fossoway,
    —SER LORAS TYRELL, her youngest brother, the Knight of Flowers, a Sworn Brother of the Kingsguard,
  —Margaery's lady companions:
    —her cousins, MEGGA, ALLA, and ELINOR TYRELL,
      —Elinor's betrothed, ALYN AMBROSE, squire,
    —LADY ALYSANNE BULWER, a girl of eight,
    —MEREDYTH CRANE, called MERRY,
    —LADY TAENA MERRYWEATHER,
    —LADY ALYCE GRACEFORD,

—SEPTA NYSTERICA, a sister of the Faith,
—PAXTER REDWYNE, Lord of the Arbor,
  —his twin sons, SER HORAS and SER HOBBER,
  —MAESTER BALLABAR, his healer and counselor,
—MATHIS ROWAN, Lord of Goldengrove,
—SER WILLAM WYTHERS, Margaery's captain of guards,
  —HUGH CLIFTON, a handsome young guardsman,
—SER PORTIFER WOODWRIGHT and his brother, SER LUCANTINE,

—Cersei's court at King's Landing:
  —SER OSFRYD KETTLEBLACK and SER OSNEY KETTLEBLACK, younger brothers to Ser Osmund Kettleblack,
  —SER GREGOR CLEGANE, called THE MOUNTAIN THAT RIDES, dying painfully of a poisoned wound,
  —SER ADDAM MARBRAND, Commander of the City Watch of King's Landing (the "gold cloaks"),
  —JALABHAR XHO, Prince of the Red Flower Vale, an exile from the Summer Isles,
  —GYLES ROSBY, Lord of Rosby, troubled by a cough,
  —ORTON MERRYWEATHER, Lord of Longtable,
    —TAENA, his wife, a woman of Myr,
  —LADY TANDA STOKEWORTH,
    —LADY FALYSE, her elder daughter and heir,
      —SER BALMAN BYRCH, Lady Falyse's husband,

—LADY LOLLYS, her younger daughter, great
  with child but weak of wit,
  —SER BRONN OF THE BLACKWATER,
    Lady Lollys's husband, a former sellsword,
  —{SHAE}, a camp follower serving as Lollys's
    bedmaid, strangled in Lord Tywin's bed,
  —MAESTER FRENKEN, in Lady Tanda's
    service,
—SER ILYN PAYNE, the King's Justice, a headsman,
—RENNIFER LONGWATERS, chief undergaoler of
  the Red Keep's dungeons,
  —RUGEN, undergaoler for the black cells,
—LORD HALLYNE THE PYROMANCER, a
  Wisdom of the Guild of Alchemists,
—NOHO DIMITTIS, envoy from the Iron Bank of
  Braavos,
—QYBURN, a necromancer, once a maester of the
  Citadel, more recently of the Brave Companions,
—MOON BOY, the royal jester and fool,
—PATE, a lad of eight, King Tommen's whipping
  boy,
—ORMOND OF OLDTOWN, the royal harper and
  bard,
—SER MARK MULLENDORE, who lost a monkey
  and half an arm in the Battle of the Blackwater,
—AURANE WATERS, the Bastard of Driftmark,
—LORD ALESANDER STAEDMON, called
  PENNYLOVER,
—SER RONNET CONNINGTON, called RED
  RONNET, the Knight of Griffin's Roost,
—SER LAMBERT TURNBERRY, SER DERMOT
  OF THE RAINWOOD, SER TALLAD called THE
  TALL, SER BAYARD NORCROSS, SER
  BONIFER HASTY called BONIFER THE

GOOD, SER HUGO VANCE, knights sworn to the Iron Throne,

—SER LYLE CRAKEHALL called STRONGBOAR, SER ALYN STACKSPEAR, SER JON BETTLEY called BEARDLESS JON, SER STEFFON SWYFT, SER HUMFREY SWYFT, knights sworn to Casterly Rock,

—JOSMYN PECKLEDON, a squire and hero of the Blackwater,

—GARRETT PAEGE and LEW PIPER, squires and hostages,

—the people of King's Landing:
   —THE HIGH SEPTON, Father of the Faithful, Voice of the Seven on Earth, an old man and frail,
      —SEPTON TORBERT, SEPTON RAYNARD, SEPTON LUCEON, SEPTON OLLIDOR, of the Most Devout, serving the Seven at the Great Sept of Baelor,
      —SEPTA MOELLE, SEPTA AGLANTINE, SEPTA HELICENT, SEPTA UNELLA, of the Most Devout, serving the Seven at the Great Sept of Baelor,
      —the "sparrows," the humblest of men, fierce in their piety,
   —CHATAYA, proprietor of an expensive brothel,
      —ALAYAYA, her daughter,
      —DANCY, MAREI, two of Chataya's girls,
   —BRELLA, a servingwoman, lately in the service of Lady Sansa Stark,
   —TOBHO MOTT, a master armorer,
   —HAMISH THE HARPER, an aged singer,
   —ALARIC OF EYSEN, a singer, far-traveled,
   —WAT, a singer, styling himself THE BLUE BARD,

—SER THEODAN WELLS, a pious knight, later
called SER THEODAN THE TRUE.

King Tommen's banner shows the crowned stag of
Baratheon, black on gold, and the lion of Lannister, gold on
crimson, combatant.

THE KING AT THE WALL

STANNIS BARATHEON, the First of His Name, second son of Lord Steffon Baratheon and Lady Cassana of House Estermont, Lord of Dragonstone, styling himself King of Westeros,

—QUEEN SELYSE of House Florent, his wife, presently at Eastwatch-by-the-Sea,
—PRINCESS SHIREEN, their daughter, a girl of eleven,
—PATCHFACE, Shireen's lackwit fool,
—EDRIC STORM, his bastard nephew, King Robert's son by Lady Delena Florent, a boy of twelve, sailing the narrow sea on the *Mad Prendos*,
—SER ANDREW ESTERMONT, King Stannis's cousin, a king's man, commanding Edric's escort,
—SER GERALD GOWER, LEWYS called THE FISHWIFE, SER TRISTON OF TALLY HILL, OMER BLACKBERRY, king's men, Edric's guards and protectors,

—Stannis's court at Castle Black:
—LADY MELISANDRE OF ASSHAI, called THE RED WOMAN, a priestess of R'hllor, the Lord of Light,

—MANCE RAYDER, King-Beyond-the-Wall, a
  captive condemned to death,
    —Rayder's son by his wife {DALLA}, a newborn
      as yet unnamed, "the wildling prince,"
        —GILLY, the babe's wet nurse, a wildling girl,
          —her son, another newborn as yet unnamed,
            fathered by her father {CRASTER},
—SER RICHARD HORPE, SER JUSTIN MASSEY,
  SER CLAYTON SUGGS, SER GODRY
  FARRING, called GIANTSLAYER, LORD
  HARWOOD FELL, SER CORLISS PENNY,
  queen's men and knights,
—DEVAN SEAWORTH and BRYEN FARRING,
  royal squires,

—Stannis's court at Eastwatch-by-the-Sea:
  —SER DAVOS SEAWORTH, called THE ONION
    KNIGHT, Lord of the Rainwood, Admiral of the
    Narrow Sea, and Hand of the King,
  —SER AXELL FLORENT, Queen Selyse's uncle,
    foremost of the queen's men,
  —SALLADHAR SAAN of Lys, a pirate and sellsail,
    master of the *Valyrian* and a fleet of galleys,

—Stannis's garrison at Dragonstone:
  —SER ROLLAND STORM, called THE BASTARD
    OF NIGHTSONG, a king's man, castellan of
    Dragonstone,
    —MAESTER PYLOS, healer, tutor, counselor,
    —"PORRIDGE" and "LAMPREY," two gaolers,

—lords sworn to Dragonstone:
  —MONTERYS VELARYON, Lord of the Tides and
    Master of Driftmark, a boy of six,

—DURAM BAR EMMON, Lord of Sharp Point, a
  boy of fifteen years,

—Stannis's garrison at Storm's End:
  —SER GILBERT FARRING, castellan of Storm's
    End,
    —LORD ELWOOD MEADOWS, Ser Gilbert's
      second,
    —MAESTER JURNE, Ser Gilbert's counselor and
      healer,

—lords sworn to Storm's End:
  —ELDON ESTERMONT, Lord of Greenstone, uncle
    to King Stannis, great uncle to King Tommen, a
    cautious friend to both,
    —SER AEMON, Lord Eldon's son and heir, with
      King Tommen in King's Landing,
      —SER ALYN, Ser Aemon's son, likewise with
        King Tommen in King's Landing,
    —SER LOMAS, brother of Lord Eldon, uncle and
      supporter of King Stannis, at Storm's End,
      —SER ANDREW, Ser Lomas's son, protecting
        Edric Storm upon the narrow sea,
  —LESTER MORRIGEN, Lord of Crows Nest,
  —LORD LUCOS CHYTTERING, called LITTLE
    LUCOS, a youth of sixteen,
  —DAVOS SEAWORTH, Lord of the Rainwood,
    —MARYA, his wife, a carpenter's daughter,
      —{DALE, ALLARD, MATTHOS, MARIC},
        their four eldest sons, lost in the Battle of the
        Blackwater,
      —DEVAN, a squire with King Stannis at Castle
        Black,

—STANNIS, a boy of ten years, with Lady
    Marya on Cape Wrath,
—STEFFON, a boy of six years, with Lady
    Marya on Cape Wrath.

Stannis has taken for his banner the fiery heart of the Lord
of Light; a red heart surrounded by orange flames upon a
yellow field. Within the heart is the crowned stag of House
Baratheon, in black.

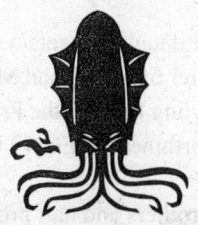

KING OF THE ISLES AND THE NORTH

The Greyjoys of Pyke claim descent from the Grey King of the Age of Heroes. Legend says the Grey King ruled the sea itself and took a mermaid to wife. Aegon the Dragon ended the line of the last King of the Iron Islands, but allowed the ironborn to revive their ancient custom and choose who should have the primacy among them. They chose Lord Vickon Greyjoy of Pyke. The Greyjoy sigil is a golden kraken upon a black field. Their words are *We Do Not Sow.*

Balon Greyjoy's first rebellion against the Iron Throne was put down by King Robert I Baratheon and Lord Eddard Stark of Winterfell, but in the chaos following Robert's death Lord Balon named himself king once more, and sent his ships to attack the north.

{BALON GREYJOY}, the Ninth of His Name Since the Grey King, King of the Iron Islands and the North, King of Salt and Rock, Son of the Sea Wind, and Lord Reaper of Pyke, killed in a fall,
—King Balon's widow, QUEEN ALANNYS, of House Harlaw,
—their children:
—{RODRIK}, slain during Balon's first rebellion,
—{MARON}, slain during Balon's first rebellion,

—ASHA, their daughter, captain of the *Black Wind*
    and conquerer of Deepwood Motte,
—THEON, styling himself the Prince of Winterfell,
    called by northmen THEON TURNCLOAK,

—King Balon's brothers and half brothers:
    —{HARLON}, died of greyscale in his youth,
    —{QUENTON}, died in infancy,
    —{DONEL}, died in infancy,
    —EURON, called Crow's Eye, captain of the *Silence,*
    —VICTARION, Lord Captain of the Iron Fleet,
        master of the *Iron Victory,*
    —{URRIGON}, died of a wound gone bad,
    —AERON, called DAMPHAIR, a priest of the
        Drowned God,
        —RUS and NORJEN, two of his acolytes, the
            "drowned men,"
    —{ROBIN}, died in infancy,

—King Balon's household on Pyke:
    —MAESTER WENDAMYR, healer and counselor,
    —HELYA, keeper of the castle,

—King Balon's warriors and sworn swords:
    —DAGMER called CLEFTJAW, captain of
        Foamdrinker, commanding the ironborn at
        Torrhen's Square,
    —BLUETOOTH, a longship captain,
    —ULLER, SKYTE, oarsmen and warriors,

—CLAIMANTS TO THE SEASTONE CHAIR AT THE
    KINGSMOOT ON OLD WYK

GYLBERT FARWYND, Lord of the Lonely Light,
—Gylbert's champions: his sons GYLES, YGON, YOHN,

ERIK IRONMAKER, called ERIK ANVIL-BREAKER and ERIK THE JUST, an old man, once a famed captain and raider,
—Erik's champions: his grandsons UREK, THORMOR, DAGON,

DUNSTAN DRUMM, The Drumm, the Bone Hand, Lord of Old Wyk,
—Dunstan's champions: his sons DENYS and DONNEL, and ANDRIK THE UNSMILING, a giant of a man,

ASHA GREYJOY, only daughter of Balon Greyjoy, captain of the *Black Wind*,
—Asha's champions: QARL THE MAID, TRISTIFER BOTLEY, and SER HARRAS HARLAW
—Asha's captains and supporters: LORD RODRIK HARLAW, LORD BAELOR BLACKTYDE, LORD MELDRED MERLYN, HARMUND SHARP,

VICTARION GREYJOY, brother to Balon Greyjoy, master of the *Iron Victory* and Lord Captain of the Iron Fleet,
—Victarion's champions: RED RALF STONEHOUSE, RALF THE LIMPER, and NUTE THE BARBER,
—Victarion's captains and supporters: HOTHO HARLAW, ALVYN SHARP, FRALEGG THE

STRONG, ROMNY WEAVER, WILL HUMBLE, LITTLE LENWOOD TAWNEY, RALF KENNING, MARON VOLMARK, GOROLD GOODBROTHER,
—Victarion's crewmen: WULF ONE-EAR, RAGNOR PYKE
—Victarion's bedmate, a certain dusky woman, mute and tongueless, a gift from his brother Euron,

EURON GREYJOY, called THE CROW'S EYE, brother to Balon Greyjoy and captain of the *Silence*,
—Euron's champions: GERMUND BOTLEY, LORD ORKWOOD OF ORKMONT, DONNOR SALTCLIFFE
—Euron's captains and supporters: TORWOLD BROWNTOOTH, PINCHFACE JON MYRE, RODRIK FREEBORN, THE RED OARSMAN, LEFT-HAND LUCAS CODD, QUELLON HUMBLE, HARREN HALF-HOARE, KEMMETT PYKE THE BASTARD, QARL THE THRALL, STONEHAND, RALF THE SHEPHERD, RALF OF LORDSPORT
—Euron's crewmen: CRAGORN,

—Balon's bannermen, the Lords of the Iron Islands:

ON PYKE
—{SAWANE BOTLEY}, Lord of Lordsport, drowned by Euron Crow's Eye,
—{HARREN}, his eldest son, killed at Moat Cailin,
—TRISTIFER, his second son and rightful heir, dispossessed by his uncle,

—SYMOND, HARLON, VICKON, and
    BENNARION, his younger sons, likewise
    dispossessed,
—GERMUND, his brother, made Lord of
    Lordsport,
    —Germund's sons, BALON and QUELLON,
—SARGON and LUCIMORE, Sawane's half
    brothers,
        —WEX, a mute boy of twelve years, bastard
        son of Sargon, squire to Theon Greyjoy,
—WALDON WYNCH, Lord of Iron Holt,

ON HARLAW
—RODRIK HARLAW, called THE READER, Lord
    of Harlaw, Lord of Ten Towers, Harlaw of Harlaw,
    —LADY GWYNESSE, his elder sister,
    —LADY ALANNYS, his younger sister, widow of
        King Balon Greyjoy,
    —SIGFRYD HARLAW, called SIGFRYD
        SILVERHAIR, his great uncle, master of
        Harlaw Hall,
    —HOTHO HARLAW, called HOTHO
        HUMPBACK, of the Tower of Glimmering, a
        cousin,
    —SER HARRAS HARLAW, called THE
        KNIGHT, the Knight of Grey Garden, a cousin,
    —BOREMUND HARLAW, called BOREMUND
        THE BLUE, master of Harridan Hill, a cousin,
    —Lord Rodrik's bannermen and sworn swords:
        —MARON VOLMARK, Lord of Volmark,
        —MYRE, STONETREE, and KENNING,
    —Lord Rodrik's household:
        —THREE-TOOTH, his steward, a crone,

ON BLACKTYDE
—BAELOR BLACKTYDE, Lord of Blacktyde, captain of the *Nightflyer*,
—BLIND BEN BLACKTYDE, a priest of the Drowned God,

ON OLD WYK
—DUNSTAN DRUMM, The Drumm, captain of *Thunderer*,
—NORNE GOODBROTHER, of Shatterstone,
—THE STONEHOUSE,
—TARLE, called TARLE THE THRICE-DROWNED, a priest of the Drowned God,

ON GREAT WYK
—GOROLD GOODBROTHER, Lord of the Hammerhorn,
—his sons, GREYDON, GRAN, and GORMOND, triplets,
—his daughters, GYSELLA and GWIN,
—MAESTER MURENMURE, tutor, healer, and counselor,
—TRISTON FARWYND, Lord of Sealskin Point,
—THE SPARR,
—his son and heir, STEFFARION,
—MELDRED MERLYN, Lord of Pebbleton,

ON ORKMONT
—ORKWOOD OF ORKMONT,
—LORD TAWNEY,

ON SALTCLIFFE
—LORD DONNOR SALTCLIFFE,
—LORD SUNDERLY

ON THE LESSER ISLANDS AND ROCKS
  —GYLBERT FARWYND, Lord of the Lonely Light,
  —THE OLD GREY GULL, a priest of the Drowned
  God.

OTHER HOUSES
GREAT AND SMALL

HOUSE ARRYN

The Arryns are descended from the Kings of Mountain and
Vale. Their sigil is a white moon-and-falcon upon a sky-blue
field. House Arryn has taken no part in the War of the Five
Kings. Their Arryn words are *As High as Honor*.

ROBERT ARRYN, Lord of the Eyrie, Defender of the
Vale, styled by his mother True Warden of the East, a
sickly boy of eight years, sometimes called
SWEETROBIN,
—his mother, {LADY LYSA of House Tully}, widow
of Lord Jon Arryn, pushed from the Moon Door to
her death,
—his stepfather, PETYR BAELISH, called
LITTLEFINGER, Lord of Harrenhal, Lord
Paramount of the Trident, and Lord Protector of
the Vale,
—ALAYNE STONE, Lord Petyr's natural daughter, a
maid of three-and-ten, actually Sansa Stark,
—SER LOTHOR BRUNE, a sellsword in Lord
Petyr's service, the Eyrie's captain of guards,
—OSWELL, a grizzled man-at-arms in Lord Petyr's
service, sometimes called KETTLEBLACK,

—Lord Robert's household at the Eyrie:

—MARILLION, a handsome young singer much favored by Lady Lysa and accused of her murder,

—MAESTER COLEMON, counselor, healer, and tutor,

—MORD, a brutal gaoler with teeth of gold,

—GRETCHEL, MADDY, and MELA, servingwomen,

—Lord Robert's bannermen, the Lords of the Vale:

—LORD NESTOR ROYCE, High Steward of the Vale and castellan of the Gates of the Moon,

　　—SER ALBAR, Lord Nestor's son and heir,

　　—MYRANDA, called RANDA, Lord Nestor's daughter, a widow, but scarce used,

　　—Lord Nestor's household:

　　　　—SER MARWYN BELMORE, captain of guards,

　　　　—MYA STONE, a mule tender and guide, bastard daughter of King Robert I Baratheon,

　　　　—OSSY and CARROT, mule tenders,

—LYONEL CORBRAY, Lord of Heart's Home,

　　—SER LYN CORBRAY, his brother and heir, who wields the famed blade Lady Forlorn,

　　—SER LUCAS CORBRAY, his younger brother,

—JON LYNDERLY, Lord of the Snakewood,

　　—TERRANCE, his son and heir, a young squire,

—EDMUND WAXLEY, the Knight of Wickenden,

—GEROLD GRAFTON, the Lord of Gulltown,

　　—GYLES, his youngest son, a squire,

—TRISTON SUNDERLAND, Lord of the Three Sisters,

　　—GODRIC BORRELL, Lord of Sweetsister,

—ROLLAND LONGTHORPE, Lord of
Longsister,
—ALESANDOR TORRENT, Lord of Littlesister,

—the Lords Declarant, bannermen of House Arryn
joined together in defense of young Lord Robert:
—YOHN ROYCE, called BRONZE YOHN, Lord of
Runestone, of the senior branch of House Royce,
—SER ANDAR, Bronze Yohn's sole surviving
son, and heir to Runestone,
—Bronze Yohn's household:
—MAESTER HELLIWEG, tutor, healer,
counselor,
—SEPTON LUCOS,
—SER SAMWELL STONE, called STRONG
SAM STONE, master-at-arms,
—Bronze Yohn's bannermen and sworn swords:
—ROYCE COLDWATER, Lord of Coldwater
Burn,
—SER DAMON SHETT, Knight of Gull
Tower,
—UTHOR TOLLETT, Lord of the Grey Glen,
—ANYA WAYNWOOD, Lady of Ironoaks Castle,
—SER MORTON, her eldest son and heir,
—SER DONNEL, her second son, the Knight of
the Gate,
—WALLACE, her youngest son,
—HARROLD HARDYNG, her ward, a squire oft
called HARRY THE HEIR,
—BENEDAR BELMORE, Lord of Strongsong,
—SER SYMOND TEMPLETON, the Knight of
Ninestars,
—{EON HUNTER}, Lord of Longbow Hall, recently
deceased,

—SER GILWOOD, Lord Eon's eldest son and
   heir, now called YOUNG LORD HUNTER,
—SER EUSTACE, Lord Eon's second son,
—SER HARLAN, Lord Eon's youngest son,
—Young Lord Hunter's household:
   —MAESTER WILLAMEN, counselor, healer,
      tutor,
—HORTON REDFORT, Lord of Redfort, thrice wed,
   —SER JASPER, SER CREIGHTON, SER JON,
      his sons,
   —SER MYCHEL, his youngest son, a new-made
      knight, m. Ysilla Royce of Runestone,

—clan chiefs from the Mountains of the Moon,
   —SHAGGA SON OF DOLF, OF THE STONE
      CROWS, presently leading a band in the
      kingswood,
   —TIMETT SON OF TIMETT, OF THE BURNED
      MEN,
   —CHELLA DAUGHTER OF CHEYK, OF THE
      BLACK EARS,
   —CRAWN SON OF CALOR, OF THE MOON
      BROTHERS.

HOUSE FLORENT

The Florents of Brightwater Keep are bannermen of Highgarden. At the outset of the War of the Five Kings, Lord Alester Florent followed his liege lord in declaring for King Renly while his brother Ser Axell chose Stannis, husband to his niece Selyse. After Renly's death, Lord Alester went over to Stannis as well, with all the strength of Brightwater. Stannis made Lord Alester his Hand, and gave command of his fleet to Ser Imry Florent, his wife's brother. The fleet and Ser Imry both were lost in the Battle of Blackwater, and Lord Alester's efforts to negotiate a peace after the defeat were regarded by King Stannis as treason. He was given to the red priestess Melisandre, who burned him as a sacrifice to R'hllor.

The Iron Throne has also named the Florents traitors for their support of Stannis and his rebellion. They were attainted, and Brightwater Keep and its lands were awarded to Ser Garlan Tyrell.

The sigil of House Florent shows a fox head in a circle of flowers.

{ALESTER FLORENT}, Lord of Brightwater, burned
    as a traitor,
    —his wife, LADY MELARA, of House Crane,
    —their children:

—ALEKYNE, attainted Lord of Brightwater, fled to Oldtown to seek refuge at the Hightower,

—LADY MELESSA, wed to Lord Randyll Tarly,

—LADY RHEA, wed to Lord Leyton Hightower,

—his siblings:

—SER AXELL, a queen's man, in service to his niece Queen Selyse at Eastwatch-by-the-Sea,

—{SER RYAM}, died in a fall from a horse,

—SELYSE, his daughter, wife and queen to King Stannis I Baratheon,

—SHIREEN BARATHEON, her only child,

—{SER IMRY}, his eldest son, killed in the Battle of the Blackwater,

—SER ERREN, his second son, a captive at Highgarden,

—SER COLIN, castellan at Brightwater Keep,

—DELENA, his daughter, m. SER HOSMAN NORCROSS,

—her natural son, EDRIC STORM, fathered by King Robert I Baratheon,

—ALESTER NORCROSS, her eldest trueborn son, a boy of nine,

—RENLY NORCROSS, her second trueborn son, a boy of three,

—MAESTER OMER, Ser Colin's eldest son, in service at Old Oak,

—MERRELL, Ser Colin's youngest son, a squire on the Arbor,

—RYLENE, Lord Alester's sister, m. Ser Rycherd Crane.

HOUSE FREY

The Freys are bannermen to House Tully, but have not always been diligent in their duty. At the onset of the War of the Five Kings, Robb Stark won Lord Walder's allegiance by pledging to marry one of his daughters or granddaughters. When he wed Lady Jeyne Westerling instead, the Freys conspired with Roose Bolton and murdered the Young Wolf and his followers at what became known as the Red Wedding.

WALDER FREY, Lord of the Crossing,
—by his first wife, {LADY PERRA, of House Royce}:
—{SER STEVRON}, died after the Battle of Oxcross,
  —m. {Corenna Swann}, died of a wasting illness,
  —Stevron's eldest son, SER RYMAN, heir to the Twins,
    —Ryman's son, EDWYN, wed to Janyce Hunter,
      —Edwyn's daughter, WALDA, a girl of nine,
    —Ryman's son, WALDER, called BLACK WALDER,
    —Ryman's son, {PETYR}, called PETYR PIMPLE, hanged at Oldstones, m. Mylenda Caron,
      —Petyr's daughter, PERRA, a girl of five,
  —m. {Jeyne Lydden}, died in a fall from a horse,
  —Stevron's son, {AEGON}, called JINGLEBELL, killed at the Red Wedding by Catelyn Stark,

—Stevron's daughter, {MAEGELLE}, died in
childbed, m. Ser Dafyn Vance,
  —Maegelle's daughter, MARIANNE VANCE, a
    maiden,
  —Maegelle's son, WALDER VANCE, a squire,
  —Maegelle's son, PATREK VANCE,
—m. {Marsella Waynwood}, died in childbed,
—Stevron's son, WALTON, m. Deana Hardyng,
  —Walton's son, STEFFON, called THE SWEET,
  —Walton's daughter, WALDA, called FAIR
    WALDA,
  —Walton's son, BRYAN, a squire,

—SER EMMON, Lord Walder's second son, m. Genna
  Lannister,
  —Emmon's son, {SER CLEOS}, killed by outlaws
    near Maidenpool, m. Jeyne Darry,
    —Cleos's son, TYWIN, a squire of twelve,
    —Cleos's son, WILLEM, a page at Ashemark, ten,
  —Emmon's son, SER LYONEL, m. Melesa
    Crakehall,
  —Emmon's son, {TION}, a squire, murdered by
    Rickard Karstark while a captive at Riverrun,
  —Emmon's son, WALDER, called RED WALDER,
    fourteen, a page at Casterly Rock,

—SER AENYS, Lord Walder's third son, m. {Tyana
  Wylde}, died in childbed,
  —Aenys's son, AEGON BLOODBORN, an outlaw,
  —Aenys's son, RHAEGAR, m. {Jeyne Beesbury},
    died of a wasting illness,
    —Rhaegar's son, ROBERT, a boy of thirteen,
    —Rhaegar's daughter, WALDA, a girl of eleven,
      called WHITE WALDA,

—Rhaegar's son, JONOS, a boy of eight,

—PERRIANE, Lord Walder's daughter, m. Ser Leslyn
Haigh,
  —Perriane's son, SER HARYS HAIGH,
    —Harys's son, WALDER HAIGH, a boy of five,
  —Perriane's son, SER DONNEL HAIGH,
  —Perriane's son, ALYN HAIGH, a squire,

—by his second wife, {LADY CYRENNA, of House
Swann}:
—SER JARED, Lord Walder's fourth son, m. {Alys
Frey},
  —Jared's son, {SER TYTOS}, slain by Sandor
    Clegane during the Red Wedding, m. Zhoe
    Blanetree,
      —Tytos's daughter, ZIA, a maid of fourteen,
      —Tytos's son, ZACHERY, a boy of twelve sworn
        to the Faith, training at the Sept of Oldtown,
  —Jared's daughter, KYRA, m. {Ser Garse
    Goodbrook}, slain during the Red Wedding,
      —Kyra's son, WALDER GOODBROOK, a boy of
        nine,
      —Kyra's daughter, JEYNE GOODBROOK, six,
—SEPTON LUCEON, in service at the Great Sept of
Baelor,

—by his third wife, {LADY AMAREI of House
Crakehall}:
—SER HOSTEEN, m. Bellena Hawick,
  —Hosteen's son, SER ARWOOD, m. Ryella Royce,
    —Arwood's daughter, RYELLA, a girl of five,
    —Arwood's twin sons, ANDROW and ALYN,
      four,

　　　　—Arwood's daughter, HOSTELLA, a newborn
　　　　　　babe,
　　—LYENTHE, Lord Walder's daughter, m. Lord Lucias
　　　　Vypren,
　　　　—Lyenthe's daughter, ELYANA, m. Ser Jon Wylde,
　　　　　　—Elyana's son, RICKARD WYLDE, four,
　　　　—Lyenthe's son, SER DAMON VYPREN,
　　—SYMOND, m. Betharios of Braavos,
　　　　—Symond's son, ALESANDER, a singer,
　　　　—Symond's daughter, ALYX, a maid of seventeen,
　　　　—Symond's son, BRADAMAR, a boy of ten, a ward
　　　　　　of Oro Tendyris, a merchant of Braavos,
　　—SER DANWELL, Lord Walder's eighth son, m.
　　　　Wynafrei Whent,
　　　　—{many stillbirths and miscarriages},
　　—{MERRETT}, hanged at Oldstones, m. Mariya Darry,
　　　　—Merrett's daughter, AMEREI, called AMI, m. {Ser
　　　　　　Pate of the Blue Fork, slain by Ser Gregor
　　　　　　Clegane},
　　　　—Merrett's daughter, WALDA, called FAT WALDA,
　　　　　　m. Roose Bolton, Lord of the Dreadfort,
　　　　—Merrett's daughter, MARISSA, a maid of thirteen,
　　　　—Merrett's son, WALDER, called LITTLE
　　　　　　WALDER, eight, a squire in service to Ramsay
　　　　　　Bolton,
　　—{SER GEREMY}, drowned, m. Carolei Waynwood,
　　　　—Geremy's son, SANDOR, a boy of twelve, a squire,
　　　　—Geremy's daughter, CYNTHEA, a girl of nine, a
　　　　　　ward of Lady Anya Waynwood,
　　—SER RAYMUND, m. Beony Beesbury,
　　　　—Raymund's son, ROBERT, an acolyte at the
　　　　　　Citadel,
　　　　—Raymund's son, MALWYN, serving with alchemist
　　　　　　in Lys,

—Raymund's twin daughters, SERRA and SARRA,
—Raymund's daughter, CERSEI, called LITTLE
  BEE,
—Raymund's twin sons, JAIME and TYWIN,
  newborn,

—by his fourth wife, {LADY ALYSSA, of House
  Blackwood}:
—LOTHAR, Lord Walder's twelfth son, called LAME
  LOTHAR, m. Leonella Lefford,
    —Lothar's daughter, TYSANE, a girl of seven,
    —Lothar's daughter, WALDA, a girl of five,
    —Lothar's daughter, EMBERLEI, a girl of three,
    —Lothar's daughter, LEANA, a newborn babe,
—SER JAMMOS, Lord Walder's thirteenth son, m.
  Sallei Paege,
    —Jammos's son, WALDER, called BIG WALDER,
      eight, a squire in service to Ramsey Bolton,
    —Jammos's twin sons, DICKON and MATHIS, five,
—SER WHALEN, Lord Walder's fourteenth son, m.
  Sylwa Paege,
—Whalen's son, HOSTER, a squire of twelve, in service
  to Ser Damon Paege,
    —Whalen's daughter, MERIANNE, called MERRY,
      eleven,
—MORYA, Lord Walder's daughter, m. Ser Flement
  Brax,
    —Morya's son, ROBERT BRAX, nine, a page at
      Casterly Rock,
    —Morya's son, WALDER BRAX, a boy of six,
    —Morya's son, JON BRAX, a babe of three,
—TYTA, Lord Walder's daughter, called TYTA THE
  MAID,

—by his fifth wife, {LADY SARYA of House Whent}:
  —no progeny,

—by his sixth wife, {LADY BETHANY of House Rosby}:
—SER PERWYN, Lord Walder's fifteenth son,
—{SER BENFREY}, Lord Walder's sixteenth son, died of a wound received at the Red Wedding, m. Jyanna Frey, a cousin,
  —Benfrey's daughter, DELLA, called DEAF DELLA, a girl of three,
  —Benfrey's son, OSMUND, a boy of two,
—MAESTER WILLAMEN, Lord Walder's seventeenth son, in service at Longbow Hall,
—OLYVAR, Lord Walder's eighteenth son, formerly a squire to Robb Stark,
—ROSLIN, sixteen, m. Lord Edmure Tully at the Red Wedding,

—by his seventh wife, {LADY ANNARA of House Farring}:
—ARWYN, Lord Walder's daughter, a maid of fourteen,
—WENDEL, Lord Walder's nineteenth son, thirteen, a page at Seagard,
—COLMAR, Lord Walder's twentieth son, eleven and promised to the Faith,
—WALTYR, called TYR, Lord Walder's twenty-first son, ten,
—ELMAR, Lord Walder's lastborn son, a boy of nine briefly betrothed to Arya Stark,
—SHIREI, Lord Walder's youngest child, a girl of seven,

—his eighth wife, LADY JOYEUSE of House Erenford,
  —presently with child,

　—Lord Walder's natural children, by sundry mothers,
　　—WALDER RIVERS, called BASTARD WALDER,
　　　—Bastard Walder's son, SER AEMON RIVERS,
　　　—Bastard Walder's daughter, WALDA RIVERS,
　　—MAESTER MELWYS, in service at Rosby,
　　—JEYNE RIVERS, MARTYN RIVERS, RYGER
　　　RIVERS, RONEL RIVERS, MELLARA
　　　RIVERS, others.

HOUSE HIGHTOWER

The Hightowers of Oldtown are among the oldest and proudest of the Great Houses of Westeros, tracing their descent back to the First Men. Once kings, they have ruled Oldtown and its environs since the Dawn of Days, welcoming the Andals rather than resisting them, and later bending the knee to the Kings of the Reach and giving up their crowns whilst retaining all their ancient privileges. Though powerful and immensely wealthy, the Lords of the High Tower have traditionally preferred trade to battle, and have seldom played a large part in the wars of Westeros. The Hightowers were instrumental in the founding of the Citadel and continue to protect it to this day. Subtle and sophisticated, they have always been great patrons of learning and the Faith, and it is said that certain of them have also dabbled in alchemy, necromancy, and other sorcerous arts.

The arms of House Hightower show a stepped white tower crowned with fire on a smoke-grey field. The House words are *We Light the Way*.

LEYTON HIGHTOWER, Voice of Oldtown, Lord of the Port, Lord of the High Tower, Defender of the Citadel, Beacon of the South, called THE OLD MAN OF OLDTOWN,
—LADY RHEA of House Hightower, his fourth wife,
—Lord Leyton's eldest son and heir, SER BAELOR,

called BAELOR BRIGHTSMILE, m. Rhonda
Rowan,
—Lord Leyton's daughter, MALORA, called THE MAD
MAID,
—Lord Leyton's daughter, ALERIE, m. Lord Mace
Tyrell,
—Lord Leyton's son SER GARTH, called
GREYSTEEL,
—Lord Leyton's daughter, DENYSE, m. Ser Desmond
Redwyne,
——her son, DENYS, a squire,
—Lord Leyton's daughter, LEYLA, m. Ser Jon Cupps,
—Lord Leyton's daughter, ALYSANNE, m. Lord Arthur
Ambrose,
—Lord Leyton's daughter, LYNESSE, m. Lord Jorah
Mormont, presently chief concubine to Tregar
Ormollen of Lys,
—Lord Leyton's son, SER GUNTHOR, m. Jeyne
Fossoway, of the green apple Fossoways,
—Lord Leyton's youngest son, SER HUMFREY,

—Lord Leyton's bannermen:
——TOMMEN COSTAYNE, Lord of the Three Towers,
——ALYSANNE BULWER, Lady of Blackcrown, a
girl of eight,
——MARTYN MULLENDORE, Lord of Uplands,
——WARRYN BEESBURY, Lord of Honeyholt,
——BRANSTON CUY, Lord of Sunflower Hall,

—the people of Oldtown:
——EMMA, a serving wench at the Quill and Tankard,
where the women are willing and the cider is
fearsomely strong,

—ROSEY, her daughter, a girl of five-and-ten
whose maidenhead will cost a golden dragon,

—the Archmaesters of the Citadel:
—ARCHMAESTER NORREN, Seneschal for the
waning year, whose ring and rod and mask are
electrum,
—ARCHMAESTER THEOBALD, Seneschal for the
coming year, whose ring and rod and mask are
lead,
—ARCHMAESTER EBROSE, the healer, whose
ring and rod and mask are silver,
—ARCHMAESTER MARWYN, called MARWYN
THE MAGE, whose ring and rod and mask are
Valyrian steel,
—ARCHMAESTER PERESTAN, the historian,
whose ring and rod and mask are copper,
—ARCHMAESTER VAELLYN, called VINEGAR
VAELLYN, the stargazer, whose ring and rod and
mask are bronze,
—ARCHMAESTER RYAM, whose ring and rod and
mask are yellow gold,
—ARCHMAESTER WALGRAVE, an old man of
uncertain wit, whose ring and rod and mask are
black iron,
—GALLARD, CASTOS, ZARABELO, BENEDICT,
GARIZON, NYMOS, CETHERES, WILLIFER,
MOLLOS, HARODON, GUYNE, AGRIVANE,
OCLEY, archmaesters all,

—maesters, acolytes, and novices of the Citadel:
—MAESTER GORMON, who oft serves in
Walgrave's stead,

—ARMEN, an acolyte of four links, called THE
   ACOLYTE,
—ALLERAS, called THE SPHINX, an acolyte of
   three links, a devoted archer,
—ROBERT FREY, sixteen, an acolyte of two links,
—LORCAS, an acolyte of nine links, in service to the
   Seneschal,
—LEO TYRELL, called LAZY LEO, a highborn
   novice,
—MOLLANDER, a novice, born with a club foot,
—PATE, who tends Archmaester Walgrave's ravens, a
   novice of little promise,
—ROONE, a young novice.

HOUSE LANNISTER

The Lannisters of Casterly Rock remain the principal support of King Tommen's claim to the Iron Throne. They boast of descent from Lann the Clever, the legendary trickster of the Age of Heroes. The gold of Casterly Rock and the Golden Tooth has made them the wealthiest of the Great Houses. The Lannister sigil is a golden lion upon a crimson field. Their words are *Hear Me Roar!*

{TYWIN LANNISTER}, Lord of Casterly Rock,
   Shield of Lannisport, Warden of the West, and Hand
   of the King, murdered by his dwarf son in his privy,
—Lord Tywin's children:
   —CERSEI, twin to Jaime, now Lady of Casterly
      Rock,
   —SER JAIME, twin to Cersei, called THE
      KINGSLAYER,
   —TYRION, called THE IMP, dwarf and kinslayer,

—Lord Tywin's siblings and their offspring:
   —SER KEVAN LANNISTER, m. Dorna of House
      Swyft,
   —LADY GENNA, m. Ser Emmon Frey, now Lord of
      Riverrun,
      —Genna's eldest son, {SER CLEOS FREY}, m.
         Jeyne of House Darry, killed by outlaws,

—Cleos's eldest son, SER TYWIN FREY, called TY, now heir to Riverrun,

—Cleos's second son, WILLEM FREY, a squire,

—Genna's second son, SER LYONEL FREY,

—Genna's third son, {TION FREY}, a squire, murdered while a captive at Riverrun,

—Genna's youngest son, WALDER FREY, called RED WALDER, a page at Casterly Rock,

—WHITESMILE WAT, a singer in service to Lady Genna,

—{SER TYGETT LANNISTER}, died of a pox,

—TYREK, Tygett's son, missing and feared dead,

—LADY ERMESANDE HAYFORD, Tyrek's child wife,

—{GERION LANNISTER}, lost at sea,

—JOY HILL, Gerion's bastard daughter, eleven,

—Lord Tywin's other close kin:

—{SER STAFFORD LANNISTER}, a cousin and brother to Lord Tywin's wife, slain in battle at Oxcross,

—CERENNA and MYRIELLE, Stafford's daughters,

—SER DAVEN LANNISTER, Stafford's son,

—SER DAMION LANNISTER, a cousin, m. Lady Shiera Crakehall,

—their son, SER LUCION,

—their daughter, LANNA, m. Lord Antario Jast,

—LADY MARGOT, a cousin, m. Lord Titus Peake,

—the household at Casterly Rock:

—MAESTER CREYLEN, healer, tutor, and counselor,

—VYLARR, captain of guards,
—SER BENEDICT BROOM, master-at-arms,
—WHITESMILE WAT, a singer,

—bannermen and sworn swords, Lords of the West:
—DAMON MARBRAND, Lord of Ashemark,
  —SER ADDAM MARBRAND, his son and heir,
    Commander of the City Watch of King's
    Landing,
—ROLAND CRAKEHALL, Lord of Crakehall,
  —Roland's brother, {SER BURTON}, slain by
    outlaws,
  —Roland's son and heir, SER TYBOLT,
  —Roland's son, SER LYLE, called
    STRONGBOAR,
  —Roland's youngest son, SER MERLON,
—SEBASTON FARMAN, Lord of Fair Isle,
  —JEYNE, his sister, m. Ser Gareth Clifton,
—TYTOS BRAX, Lord of Hornvale,
  —SER FLEMENT BRAX, his brother and heir,
—QUENTEN BANEFORT, Lord of Banefort,
—SER HARYS SWYFT, good-father to Ser Kevan
Lannister,
  —Ser Harys's son, SER STEFFON SWYFT,
    —Ser Steffon's daughter, JOANNA,
  —Ser Harys's daughter, SHIERLE, m. Ser
    Melwyn Sarsfield,
—REGENARD ESTREN, Lord of Wyndhall,
—GAWEN WESTERLING, Lord of the Crag,
  —his wife, LADY SYBELL, of House Spicer,
    —her brother, SER ROLPH SPICER, newly raised
    to Lord of Castamere,
    —her cousin, SER SAMWELL SPICER,

—their children:
  —SER RAYNALD WESTERLING,
  —JEYNE, widowed wife of Robb Stark,
  —ELEYNA, a girl of twelve,
  —ROLLAM, a boy of nine,
—LORD SELMOND STACKSPEAR,
  —his son, SER STEFFON STACKSPEAR,
  —his younger son, SER ALYN STACKSPEAR,
—TERRENCE KENNING, Lord of Kayce,
  —SER KENNOS OF KAYCE, a knight in his
    service,
—LORD ANTARIO JAST,
—LORD ROBIN MORELAND,
—LADY ALYSANNE LEFFORD,
—LEWYS LYDDEN, Lord of the Deep Den,
—LORD PHILIP PLUMM,
  —his sons, SER DENNIS PLUMM, SER PETER
    PLUMM, and SER HARWYN PLUMM, called
    HARDSTONE,
—LORD GARRISON PRESTER,
  —SER FORLEY PRESTER, his cousin,
—SER GREGOR CLEGANE, called THE MOUNTAIN
  THAT RIDES,
  —SANDOR CLEGANE, his brother,
—SER LORENT LORCH, a landed knight,
—SER GARTH GREENFIELD, a landed knight,
—SER LYMOND VIKARY, a landed knight,
—SER RAYNARD RUTTIGER, a landed knight,
—SER MANFRYD YEW, a landed knight,
—SER TYBOLT HETHERSPOON, a landed knight,
  —{MELARA HETHERSPOON}, his daughter,
    drowned in a well while a ward at Casterly Rock.

HOUSE MARTELL

Dorne was the last of the Seven Kingdoms to swear fealty to the Iron Throne. Blood, custom, geography, and history all helped to set the Dornishmen apart from the other kingdoms. At the outbreak of the War of the Five Kings Dorne took no part, but when Myrcella Baratheon was betrothed to Prince Trystane, Sunspear declared its support for King Joffrey. The Martell banner is a red sun pierced by a golden spear. Their words are *Unbowed, Unbent, Unbroken*.

DORAN NYMEROS MARTELL, Lord of Sunspear,
    Prince of Dorne,
    —his wife, MELLARIO, of the Free City of Norvos,
    —their children:
        —PRINCESS ARIANNE, heir to Sunspear,
        —GARIN, Arianne's milk brother and companion,
            of the orphans of the Greenblood,
        —PRINCE QUENTYN, a new-made knight, long
            fostered by Lord Yronwood of Yronwood,
        —PRINCE TRYSTANE, betrothed to Myrcella
            Baratheon,
    —Prince Doran's siblings:
        —{PRINCESS ELIA, raped and murdered during
            the Sack of King's Landing},
        —{RHAENYS TARGARYEN}, her young

daughter, murdered during the Sack of King's
Landing,
—{AEGON TARGARYEN}, a babe at the breast,
murdered during the Sack of King's Landing,
—{PRINCE OBERYN}, called THE RED VIPER,
slain by Ser Gregor Clegane during a trial by
combat,
—ELLARIA SAND, Prince Oberyn's paramour,
natural daughter of Lord Harmen Uller,
—THE SAND SNAKES, Oberyn's bastard
daughters:
—OBARA, eight-and-twenty, Oberyn's
daughter by an Oldtown whore,
—NYMERIA, called LADY NYM, five-and-
twenty, his daughter by a noblewoman of
Volantis,
—TYENE, three-and-twenty, Oberyn's
daughter by a septa,
—SARELLA, nineteen, his daughter by a
trader, captain of the *Feathered Kiss,*
—ELIA, fourteen, his daughter by Ellaria Sand,
—OBELLA, twelve, his daughter by Ellaria
Sand,
—DOREA, eight, his daughter by Ellaria Sand,
—LOREZA, six, his daughter by Ellaria Sand,

—Prince Doran's court, at the Water Gardens:
—AREO HOTAH, of Norvos, captain of the guards,
—MAESTER CALEOTTE, counselor, healer, and
tutor,
—threescore children of both high and common birth,
sons and daughters of lords, knights, orphans,
merchants, craftsmen, and peasants, his wards,

—Prince Doran's court, at Sunspear:
   —PRINCESS MYRCELLA BARATHEON, his
      ward, betrothed to Prince Trystane,
         —SER ARYS OAKHEART, Myrcella's sworn
            shield,
         —ROSAMUND LANNISTER, Myrcella's
            bedmaid and companion, a distant cousin,
         —SEPTA EGLANTINE, Myrcella's confessor,
   —MAESTER MYLES, counselor, healer, and tutor,
   —RICASSO, Seneschal at Sunspear, old and blind,
   —SER MANFREY MARTELL, castellan at
      Sunspear
   —LADY ALYSE LADYBRIGHT, lord treasurer,
   —SER GASCOYNE of the Greenblood, Prince
      Trystane's sworn shield,
   —BORS and TIMOTH, serving men at Sunspear,
   —BELANDRA, CEDRA, the sisters MORRA and
      MELLEI, servingwomen at Sunspear,

—Prince Doran's bannermen, the Lords of Dorne:
   —ANDERS YRONWOOD, Lord of Yronwood,
      Warden of the Stone Way, the Bloodroyal,
         —SER CLETUS, his son, known for a lazy eye,
         —MAESTER KEDRY, healer, tutor, and
            counselor,
   —HARMEN ULLER, Lord of Hellholt,
         —ELLARIA SAND, his natural daughter,
         —SER ULWYCK ULLER, his brother,
   —DELONNE ALLYRION, Lady of Godsgrace,
         —SER RYON, her son and heir,
            —SER DAEMON SAND, Ryon's natural son,
               the Bastard of Godsgrace,
   —DAGOS MANWOODY, Lord of Kingsgrave,
         —MORS and DICKON, his sons,

—SER MYLES, his brother,

—LARRA BLACKMONT, Lady of Blackmont,
  —JYNESSA, her daughter and heir,
  —PERROS, her son, a squire,
—NYMELLA TOLAND, Lady of Ghost Hill,
—QUENTYN QORGYLE, Lord of Sandstone,
  —SER GULIAN, his eldest son and heir
  —SER ARRON, his second son,
—SER DEZIEL DALT, the Knight of Lemonwood,
  —SER ANDREY, his brother and heir, called
    DREY,
—FRANKLYN FOWLER, Lord of Skyreach, called
  THE OLD HAWK, the Warden of the Prince's
  Pass,
  —JEYNE and JENNELYN, his twin daughters,
—SER SYMON SANTAGAR, the Knight of
  Spottswood,
  —SYLVA, his daughter and heir, called SPOTTED
    SYLVA for her freckles,
—EDRIC DAYNE, Lord of Starfall, a squire,
  —SER GEROLD DAYNE, called DARKSTAR,
    the Knight of High Hermitage, his cousin and
    bannerman,
—TREBOR JORDAYNE, Lord of the Tor,
  —MYRIA, his daughter and heir,
—TREMOND GARGALEN, Lord of Salt Shore,
—DAERON VAITH, Lord of the Red Dunes.

HOUSE STARK

The Starks trace their descent from Brandon the Builder and the Kings of Winter. For thousands of years, they ruled from Winterfell as Kings in the North, until Torrhen Stark, the King Who Knelt, chose to swear fealty to Aegon the Dragon rather than give battle. When Lord Eddard Stark of Winterfell was executed by King Joffrey, the northmen foreswore their loyalty to the Iron Throne and proclaimed Lord Eddard's son Robb as King in the North. During the War of the Five Kings, he won every battle, but was betrayed and murdered by the Freys and Boltons at the Twins during his uncle's wedding.

{ROBB STARK}, King in the North, King of the Trident, Lord of Winterfell, eldest son of Lord Eddard Stark and Lady Catelyn of House Tully, a youth of sixteen called THE YOUNG WOLF, murdered at the Red Wedding,
—{GREY WIND}, his direwolf, killed at the Red Wedding,
—his trueborn siblings:
—SANSA, his sister, m. Tyrion of House Lannister,
—{LADY}, her direwolf, killed at Castle Darry,
—ARYA, a girl of eleven, missing and thought dead,
—NYMERIA, her direwolf, prowling the riverlands,

—BRANDON, called BRAN, a crippled boy of nine, heir to Winterfell, believed dead,
  —SUMMER, his direwolf,
  —Bran's companions and protectors:
    —MEERA REED, a maid of sixteen, daughter of Lord Howland Reed of Greywater Watch,
    —JOJEN REED, her brother, thirteen,
    —HODOR, a simple boy, seven feet tall,
—RICKON, a boy of four, believed dead,
  —SHAGGYDOG, his direwolf, black and savage,
  —Rickon's companion, OSHA, a wildling once captive at Winterfell,
—his bastard half brother, JON SNOW, of the Night's Watch,
  —GHOST, Jon's direwolf, white and silent,
—Robb's sworn swords:
  —{DONNEL LOCKE, OWEN NORREY, DACEY MORMONT, SER WENDEL MANDERLY, ROBIN FLINT}, slain at the Red Wedding,
  —HALLIS MOLLEN, captain of the guards, escorting Eddard Stark's bones back to Winterfell,
    —JACKS, QUENT, SHADD, guardsmen,
—Robb's uncles and cousins:
  —BENJEN STARK, his father's younger brother, lost ranging beyond the Wall, presumed dead,
  —{LYSA ARRYN}, his mother's sister, Lady of the Eyrie, m. Lord Jon Arryn, slain with a shove,
    —their son, ROBERT ARRYN, Lord of the Eyrie and Defender of the Vale, a sickly boy,
  —EDMURE TULLY, Lord of Riverrun, his mother's brother, taken captive at the Red Wedding,
    —LADY ROSLIN, of House Frey, Edmure's bride,
  —SER BRYNDEN TULLY, called THE

BLACKFISH, his mother's uncle, castellan of Riverrun,

—the Young Wolf's bannermen, the Lords of the North:

—ROOSE BOLTON, Lord of the Dreadfort, the turncloak,
  —{DOMERIC}, his trueborn son and heir, died of a bad belly,
  —RAMSAY BOLTON (formerly RAMSAY SNOW), Roose's natural son, called THE BASTARD OF BOLTON, castellan of the Dreadfort,
    —WALDER FREY and WALDER FREY, called BIG WALDER and LITTLE WALDER, Ramsay's squires,
    —{REEK}, a man-at-arms infamous for his stench, slain while posing as Ramsay,
  —"ARYA STARK," Lord Roose's captive, a feigned girl betrothed to Ramsay,
  —WALTON called STEELSHANKS, Roose's captain,
  —BETH CASSELL, KYRA, TURNIP, PALLA, BANDY, SHYRA, PALLA, and OLD NAN, women of Winterfell held captive at the Dreadfort,

—JON UMBER, called THE GREATJON, Lord of the Last Hearth, a captive at the Twins,
  —{JON}, called THE SMALLJON, the Greatjon's eldest son and heir, slain at the Red Wedding,
  —MORS called CROWFOOD, uncle to the Greatjon, castellan at the Last Hearth,

—HOTHER called WHORESBANE, uncle to the
Greatjon, likewise castellan at the Last Hearth,

—{RICKARD KARSTARK}, Lord of Karhold,
beheaded for treason and murder of prisoner,
—{EDDARD}, his son, slain in the Whispering
Wood,
—{TORRHEN} his son, slain in the Whispering
Wood,
—HARRION, his son, a captive at Maidenpool,
—ALYS, Lord Rickard's daughter, a maid of
fifteen,
—Rickard's uncle, ARNOLF, castellan of Karhold,

—GALBART GLOVER, Master of Deepwood
Motte, unwed,
—ROBETT GLOVER, his brother and heir,
—Robett's wife, SYBELLE of House Locke,
—their children:
—GAWEN, a boy of three,
—ERENA, a babe at the breast,
—Galbart's ward, LARENCE SNOW, natural son
of {Lord Halys Hornwood}, a boy of thirteen,

—HOWLAND REED, Lord of Greywater Watch, a
crannogman,
—his wife, JYANA, of the crannogmen,
—their children:
—MEERA, a young huntress,
—JONJEN, a boy blessed with green sight,

—WYMAN MANDERLY, Lord of White Harbor,
vastly fat,

—SER WYLIS MANDERLY, his eldest son and heir, very fat, a captive at Harrenhal,
—Wylis's wife, LEONA of House Woolfield,
    —WYNAFRYD, their daughter, a maid of nineteen years,
    —WYLLA, their daughter, a maid of fifteen,
—{SER WENDEL MANDERLY}, his second son, slain at the Red Wedding,
—SER MARLON MANDERLY, his cousin, commander of the garrison at White Harbor,
—MAESTER THEOMORE, counselor, tutor, healer,

—MAEGE MORMONT, Lady of Bear Island,
    —{DACEY}, her eldest daughter and heir, slain at the Red Wedding,
    —ALYSANE, LYRA, JORELLE, LYANNA, her daughters,
    —{JEOR MORMONT}, her brother, Lord Commander of the Night's Watch, slain by own men,
        —SER JORAH MORMONT, Lord Jeor's son, once Lord of Bear Island in his own right, a knight condemned and exiled,

—{SER HELMAN TALLHART}, Master of Torrhen's Square, slain at Duskendale,
    —{BENFRED}, his son and heir, slain by ironmen on the Stony Shore,
    —EDDARA, his daughter, captive at Torrhen's Square,
    —{LEOBALD}, his brother, killed at Winterfell,
        —Leobald's wife, BERENA of House Hornwood, captive at Torrhen's Square,

——their sons, BRANDON and BEREN,
    likewise captives at Torrhen's Square,

—RODRIK RYSWELL, Lord of the Rills,
    —BARBREY DUSTIN, his daughter, Lady of
        Barrowton, widow of {Lord Willam Dustin},
        —HARWOOD STOUT, her liege man, a petty
            lord at Barrowton,
    —{BETHANY BOLTON}, his daughter, second
        wife of Lord Roose Bolton, died of a fever,
    —ROGER RYSWELL, RICKARD RYSWELL,
        ROOSE RYSWELL, his quarrelsome cousins
        and bannermen,

—{CLEY CERWYN}, Lord of Cerwyn, killed at
    Winterfell,
    —JONELLE, his sister, a maid of two-and-thirty,
—LYESSA FLINT, Lady of Widow's Watch,
—ONDREW LOCKE, Lord of Oldcastle, an old
    man,
—HUGO WULL, called BIG BUCKET, chief of his
    clan,
—BRANDON NORREY, called THE NORREY,
    chief of his clan,
—TORREN LIDDLE, called THE LIDDLE, chief of
    his clan.

The Stark arms show a grey direwolf racing across an ice-
white field. The Stark words are *Winter Is Coming*.

HOUSE TULLY

Lord Edmyn Tully of Riverrun was one of the first of the river lords to swear fealty to Aegon the Conquerer. King Aegon rewarded him by raising House Tully to dominion over all the lands of the Trident. The Tully sigil is a leaping trout, silver, on a field of rippling blue and red. The Tully words are *Family, Duty, Honor.*

EDMURE TULLY, Lord of Riverrun, taken captive at his wedding and held prisoner by the Freys,
—LADY ROSLIN of House Frey, Edmure's young bride,
—{LADY CATELYN STARK}, his sister, widow of Lord Eddard Stark of Winterfell, slain at the Red Wedding,
—{LADY LYSA ARRYN}, his sister, widow of Lord Jon Arryn of the Vale, pushed to her death from the Eyrie,
—SER BRYNDEN TULLY, called THE BLACKFISH, Edmure's uncle, castellan of Riverrun,
—Lord Edmure's household at Riverrun:
—MAESTER VYMAN, counselor, healer, and tutor,
—SER DESMOND GRELL, master-at-arms,
—SER ROBIN RYGER, captain of the guard,

—LONG LEW, ELWOOD, DELP, guardsmen,
—UTHERYDES WAYN, steward of Riverrun,

—Edmure's bannermen, the Lords of the Trident:
  —TYTOS BLACKWOOD, Lord of Raventree Hall,
    —{LUCAS}, his son, slain at the Red Wedding,
  —JONOS BRACKEN, Lord of the Stone Hedge,
  —JASON MALLISTER, Lord of Seagard, a prisoner
    in his own castle,
    —PATREK, his son, imprisoned with his father,
    —SER DENYS MALLISTER, Lord Jason's
      uncle, a man of the Night's Watch,
  —CLEMENT PIPER, Lord of Pinkmaiden Castle,
    —his son and heir, SER MARQ PIPER, taken
      captive at the Red Wedding,
  —KARYL VANCE, Lord of Wayfarer's Rest,
    —his elder daughter and heir, LIANE,
    —his younger daughters, RHIALTA and
      EMPHYRIA,
  —NORBERT VANCE, the blind Lord of Atranta,
    —his eldest son and heir, SER RONALD VANCE,
      called THE BAD,
    —his younger sons, SER HUGO, SER ELLERY,
      SER KIRTH, and MAESTER JON,
  —THEOMAR SMALLWOOD, Lord of Acorn Hall,
    —his wife, LADY RAVELLA, of House Swann,
    —their daughter, CARELLEN,
  —WILLIAM MOOTON, Lord of Maidenpool,
  —SHELLA WHENT, dispossessed Lady of
    Harrenhal,
    —SER WILLIS WODE, a knight in her service,
  —SER HALMON PAEGE,
  —LORD LYMOND GOODBROOK.

HOUSE TYRELL

The Tyrells rose to power as stewards to the Kings of the Reach, though they claim descent from Garth Greenhand, gardener king of the First Men. When the last king of House Gardener was slain on the Field of Fire, his steward Harlen Tyrell surrendered Highgarden to Aegon the Conquerer. Aegon granted him the castle and dominion over the Reach. Mace Tyrell declared his support for Renly Baratheon at the onset of the War of the Five Kings, and gave him the hand of his daughter Margaery. Upon Renly's death, Highgarden made alliance with House Lannister, and Margaery was betrothed to King Joffrey.

MACE TYRELL, Lord of Highgarden, Warden of the South, Defender of the Marches, and High Marshal of the Reach,
—his wife, LADY ALERIE, of House Hightower of Oldtown,
—their children:
——WILLAS, their eldest son, heir to Highgarden,
——SER GARLAN, called THE GALLANT, their second son, newly raised to Lord of Brightwater,
———Garlan's wife, LADY LEONETTE of House Fossoway,
——SER LORAS, the Knight of Flowers, their youngest son, a Sworn Brother of the Kingsguard,

—MARGAERY, their daughter, twice wed and twice widowed,
  —Margaery's companions and ladies-in-waiting:
  —her cousins, MEGGA, ALLA, and ELINOR TYRELL,
    —Elinor's betrothed, ALYN AMBROSE, squire,
  —LADY ALYSANNE BULWER, LADY ALYCE GRACEFORD, LADY TAENA MERRYWEATHER, MEREDYTH CRANE called MERRY, SEPTA NYSTERICA, her companions,
—Mace's widowed mother, LADY OLENNA of House Redwyne, called THE QUEEN OF THORNS,
  —ARRYK and ERRYK, her guardsmen, twins seven feet tall called LEFT and RIGHT,
—Mace's sisters:
  —LADY MINA, wed to Paxter Redwyne, Lord of the Arbor,
    —their children:
    —SER HORAS REDWYNE, twin to Hobber, called HORROR,
    —SER HOBBER REDWYNE, twin to Horas, called SLOBBER,
    —DESMERA REDWYNE, a maid of sixteen,
  —LADY JANNA, wed to Ser Jon Fossoway,
—Mace's uncles and cousins:
  —Mace's uncle, GARTH, called THE GROSS, Lord Seneschal of Highgarden,
    —Garth's bastard sons, GARSE and GARRETT FLOWERS,
  —Mace's uncle, SER MORYN, Lord Commander of the City Watch of Oldtown,

—Moryn's son, {SER LUTHOR}, m. Lady Elyn
Norridge,
—Luthor's son, SER THEODORE, m. Lady
Lia Serry,
—Theodore's daughter, ELINOR,
—Theodore's son, LUTHOR, a squire,
—Luthor's son, MAESTER MEDWICK,
—Luthor's daughter, OLENE, m. Ser Leo
Blackbar,
—Moryn's son, LEO, called LEO THE LAZY, a
novice at the Citadel of Oldtown,
—Mace's uncle, MAESTER GORMON, serving at the
Citadel,
—Mace's cousin, {SER QUENTIN}, died at Ashford,
—Quentin's son, SER OLYMER, m. Lady Lysa
Meadows,
—Olymer's sons, RAYMUND and RICKARD,
—Olymer's daughter, MEGGA,
—Mace's cousin, MAESTER NORMUND, in service
at Blackcrown,
—Mace's cousin, {SER VICTOR}, slain by the
Smiling Knight of the Kingswood Brotherhood,
—Victor's daughter, VICTARIA, m. {Lord Jon
Bulwer}, died of a summer fever,
—their daughter, LADY ALYSANNE
BULWER, eight,
—Victor's son, SER LEO, m. Lady Alys Beesbury,
—Leo's daughters, ALLA and LEONA,
—Leo's sons, LYONEL, LUCAS, and
LORENT,

—Mace's household at Highgarden:
—MAESTER LOMYS, counselor, healer, and tutor,
—IGON VYRWEL, captain of the guard,

—SER VORTIMER CRANE, master-at-arms,
—BUTTERBUMPS, fool and jester, hugely fat,

—his bannermen, the Lords of the Reach:
  —RANDYLL TARLY, Lord of Horn Hill,
  —PAXTER REDWYNE, Lord of the Arbor,
    —SER HORAS and SER HOBBER, his twin sons,
    —Lord Paxter's healer, MAESTER BALLABAR,
  —ARWYN OAKHEART, Lady of Old Oak,
    —Lady Arwyn's youngest son, SER ARYS, a
      Sworn Brother of the Kingsguard,
  —MATHIS ROWAN, Lord of Goldengrove, m.
  Bethany of House Redwyne,
  —LEYTON HIGHTOWER, Voice of Oldtown, Lord
  of the Port,
  —HUMFREY HEWETT, Lord of Oakenshield,
    —FALIA FLOWERS, his bastard daughter,
  —OSBERT SERRY, Lord of Southshield,
    —SER TALBERT, his son and heir,
  —GUTHOR GRIMM, Lord of Greyshield,
  —MORIBALD CHESTER, Lord of Greenshield,
  —ORTON MERRYWEATHER, Lord of Longtable,
    —LADY TAENA, his wife, a woman of Myr,
      —RUSSELL, her son, a boy of eight,
  —LORD ARTHUR AMBROSE, m. Lady Alysanne
  Hightower,

—his knights and sworn swords:
  —SER JON FOSSOWAY, of the green-apple Fossoways,
  —SER TANTON FOSSOWAY, of the red-apple
  Fossoways.

The Tyrell sigil is a golden rose on a grass-green field. Their words are *Growing Strong*.

REBELS AND ROGUES

SMALLFOLK AND SWORN BROTHERS

BEYOND THE NARROW SEA

—RANDYLL TARLY, Lord of Horn Hill, commanding King Tommen's forces along the Trident,
—DICKON, his son and heir, a young squire,
—SER HYLE HUNT, sworn to the service of House Tarly,
—SER ALYN HUNT, Ser Hyle's cousin, likewise in Lord Randyll's service,
—DICK CRABB, called NIMBLE DICK, a Crabb of Crackclaw Point,
—EUSTACE BRUNE, Lord of the Dyre Den,
—BENNARD BRUNE, the Knight of Brownhollow, his cousin,
—SER ROGER HOGG, the Knight of Sow's Horn,
—SEPTON MERIBALD, a barefoot septon,
—his dog, DOG,
—THE ELDER BROTHER, of the Quiet Isle,
—BROTHER NARBERT, BROTHER GILLAM, BROTHER RAWNEY, pentitent brothers of the Quiet Isle,
—SER QUINCY COX, the Knight of Saltpans, an old man in his dotage,

—at the old crossroads inn:
—JEYNE HEDDLE, called LONG JEYNE, innkeep, a tall young wench of eighteen years,
—WILLOW, her sister, stern with a spoon,
—TANSY, PATE, JON PENNY, BEN, orphans at the inn,
—GENDRY, an apprentice smith and bastard son of King Robert I Baratheon, ignorant of his birth,

—at Harrenhal,
—RAFFORD called RAFF THE SWEETLING, SHITMOUTH, DUNSEN, men of the garrison,

—BEN BLACKTHUMB, a smith and armorer,
—PIA, a serving wench, once pretty,
—MAESTER GULIAN, healer, tutor, and counselor,

—at Darry,
  —LADY AMEREI FREY, called GATEHOUSE
    AMI, an amorous young widow betrothed to Lord
    Lancel Lannister,
    —Lady Amerei's mother, LADY MARIYA of
      House Darry, widowed wife of Merrett Frey,
    —Lady Amerei's sister, MARISSA, a maid of
      thirteen,
  —SER HARWYN PLUMM, called HARDSTONE,
    commander of the garrison,
  —MAESTER OTTOMORE, healer, tutor, and
    advisor,

—at the Inn of the Kneeling Man:
  —SHARNA, the innkeep, a cook and midwife,
    —her husband, called HUSBAND,
    —BOY, an orphan of the war,
    —HOT PIE, a baker's boy, now orphaned.

OUTLAWS AND BROKEN MEN

{BERIC DONDARRION}, once Lord of Blackhaven,
  six times slain,
—EDRIC DAYNE, Lord of Starfall, a boy of twelve,
  Lord Beric's squire,
—THE MAD HUNTSMAN of Stoney Sept, his
  sometime ally,
—GREENBEARD, a Tyroshi sellsword, his uncertain
  friend,
—ANGUY THE ARCHER, a bowman from the Dornish
  Marches,
—MERRIT O' MOONTOWN, WATTY THE MILLER,
  SWAMPY MEG, JON O' NUTTEN, outlaws in his
  band,

LADY STONEHEART, a hooded woman, sometimes
  called MOTHER MERCY, THE SILENT SISTER,
  and THE HANGWOMAN,
—LEM, called LEM LEMONCLOAK, a onetime
  soldier,
—THOROS OF MYR, a red priest,
—HARWIN, son of Hullén, a northman once in service
  to Lord Eddard Stark of Winterfell,
—JACK-BE-LUCKY, a wanted man, short an eye,

—TOM OF SEVENSTREAMS, a singer of dubious
   report, called TOM SEVENSTRINGS and TOM O'
   SEVENS,
—LIKELY LUKE, NOTCH, MUDGE, BEARDLESS
   DICK, outlaws,

SANDOR CLEGANE, called THE HOUND, once King
   Joffrey's sworn shield, later a Sworn Brother of the
   Kingsguard, last seen feverish and dying beside the
   Trident,

{VARGO HOAT} of the Free City of Qohor, called
   THE GOAT, a sellsword captain of slobbery speech,
   slain at Harrenhal by Ser Gregor Clegane,
—his Brave Companions, also called the Bloody
   Mummers:
   —URSWYCK called FAITHFUL, his lieutenant,
   —{SEPTON UTT}, hanged by Lord Beric
      Dondarrion,
   —TIMEON OF DORNE, FAT ZOLLO, RORGE,
      BITER, PYG, SHAGWELL THE FOOL, TOGG
      JOTH of Ibben, THREE TOES, scattered and
      running,

—at the Peach, a brothel in Stoney Sept:
   —TANSY, the red-haired proprietor,
      —ALYCE, CASS, LANNA, JYZENE, HELLY,
         BELLA, some of her peaches,
—at Acorn Hall, the seat of House Smallwood:
   —LADY RAVELLA, formerly of House Swann, wife
      to Lord Theomar Smallwood,
—here and there and elsewhere:
   —LORD LYMOND LYCHESTER, an old man of

wandering wit, who once held Ser Maynard at the bridge,
—his young caretaker, MAESTER ROONE,
—the ghost of High Heart,
—the Lady of the Leaves,
—the septon at Sallydance.

THE SWORN BROTHERS OF THE NIGHT'S WATCH

JON SNOW, the Bastard of Winterfell, nine-hundred-and-ninety-eighth Lord Commander of the Night's Watch,
—GHOST, his white direwolf,
—his steward, EDDISON TOLLETT called DOLOROUS EDD,

the men of Castle Black
—BENJEN STARK, First Ranger, long missing, presumed dead,
　—SER WYNTON STOUT, an aged ranger, feeble of wit,
　—KEDGE WHITEYE, BEDWYCK called GIANT, MATTHAR, DYWEN, GARTH GREYFEATHER, ULMER OF THE KINGSWOOD, ELRON, PYPAR called PYP, GRENN called AUROCHS, BERNARR called BLACK BERNARR, GOADY, TIM STONE, BLACK JACK BULWER, GEOFF called THE SQUIRREL, BEARDED BEN, rangers,
—BOWEN MARSH, Lord Steward,
　—THREE-FINGER HOBB, steward and chief cook,
　—{DONAL NOYE}, one-armed armorer and smith, slain at the gate by Mag the Mighty,

—OWEN called THE OAF, TIM TANGLETONGUE,
 MULLY, CUGEN, DONNEL HILL called
 SWEET DONNEL, LEFT HAND LEW, JEREN,
 WICK WHITTLESTICK, stewards,
—OTHELL YARWYCK, First Builder,
 —SPARE BOOT, HALDER, ALBETT, KEGS,
 builders,
—CONWY, GUEREN, wandering recruiters,
—SEPTON CELLADOR, a drunken devout,
—SER ALLISER THORNE, former master-at-arms,
—LORD JANOS SLYNT, former commander of the
 City Watch of King's Landing, briefly Lord of
 Harrenhal,
—MAESTER AEMON (TARGARYEN), healer and
 counselor, a blind man, one hundred and two years
 old,
 —Aemon's steward, CLYDAS,
 —Aemon's steward, SAMWELL TARLY, fat and
 bookish,
—IRON EMMETT, formerly of Eastwatch, master-at-
 arms,
 —HARETH called HORSE, the twins ARRON
 and EMRICK, SATIN, HOP-ROBIN, recruits
 in training,

the men of the Shadow Tower
 SER DENYS MALLISTER, Commander, Shadow
 Tower,
—his steward and squire, WALLACE MASSEY,
—MAESTER MULLIN, healer and counselor,
—{QHORIN HALFHAND}, chief ranger, slain by Jon
 Snow beyond the Wall,
—brothers of the Shadow Tower:

—{SQUIRE DALBRIDGE, EGGEN}, rangers, slain in the Skirling Pass,

—STONESNAKE, a ranger, lost afoot in Skirling Pass,

the men of Eastwatch-by-the-Sea
 COTTER PYKE, Commander,

—MAESTER HARMUNE, healer and counselor,

—OLD TATTERSALT, captain of the *Blackbird*,

—SER GLENDON HEWETT, master-at-arms,

—brothers of Eastwatch:

  —DAREON, steward and singer,

at Craster's Keep (the betrayers)

—DIRK, who murdered Craster, his host,

—OLLO LOPHAND, who slew his lord commander, Jeor Mormont,

—GARTH OF GREENAWAY, MAWNEY, GRUBBS, ALAN OF ROSBY, former rangers

—CLUBFOOT KARL, ORPHAN OSS, MUTTERING BILL, former stewards.

the WILDLINGS, or THE FREE FOLK

MANCE RAYDER, King-beyond-the-Wall, a captive at
  Castle Black,
—his wife, {DALLA}, died in childbirth,
—their newborn son, born in battle, not yet named,
    —VAL, Dalla's younger sister, "the wildling
      princess," a captive at Castle Black,

—wildling chiefs and captains:
  —{HARMA}, called DOGSHEAD, slain beneath the
    Wall,
      —HALLECK, her brother,
—THE LORD OF BONES, mocked as RATTLESHIRT,
  a raider and leader of a war band, captive at Castle
  Black,
    —{YGRITTE}, a young spearwife, Jon Snow's lover,
      killed during the attack on Castle Black,
    —RYK, called LONGSPEAR, a member of his band,
    —RAGWYLE, LENYL, members of his band,
—{STYR}, Magnar of Thenn, slain attacking Castle
  Black,
    —SIGORN, Styr's son, the new Magnar of Thenn,
—TORMUND, Mead-King of Ruddy Hall, called
  GIANTSBANE, TALL-TALKER, HORN-BLOWER,
  and BREAKER OF ICE, also THUNDERFIST,

HUSBAND TO BEARS, SPEAKER TO GODS, and
FATHER OF HOSTS,
—Tormund's sons, TOREGG THE TALL,
    TORWYRD THE TAME, DORMUND, and
    DRYN, his daughter MUNDA,
—THE WEEPER, a raider and leader of a war band,
—{ALFYN CROWKILLER}, a raider, slain by
    Qhorin Halfhand of the Night's Watch,
—{ORELL}, called ORELL THE EAGLE, a
    skinchanger slain by Jon Snow in the Skirling
    Pass,
—{MAG MAR TUN DOH WEG}, called MAG THE
    MIGHTY, a giant, slain by Donal Noye at the gate
    of Castle Black,
—VARAMYR called SIXSKINS, a skinchanger,
    master of three wolves, a shadowcat, and snow
    bear,
—{JARL}, a young raider, Val's lover, killed in a fall
    from the Wall,
    —GRIGG THE GOAT, ERROK, BODGER, DEL,
        BIG BOIL, HEMPEN DAN, HENK THE
        HELM, LENN, TOEFINGER, wildlings and
        raiders,

{CRASTER}, master of Craster's Keep, slain by Dirk of
    the Night's Watch, a guest beneath his roof,
—GILLY, his daughter and wife,
    —Gilly's newborn son, not yet named,
—DYAH, FERNY, NELLA, three of Craster's
    nineteen wives.

BEYOND THE NARROW SEA

IN BRAAVOS

FERREGO ANTARYON, Sealord of Braavos,
  —QARRO VOLENTIN, First Sword of Braavos, his
  protector,
  —BELLEGERE OTHERYS called THE BLACK
  PEARL, a courtesan descended from the pirate
  queen of the same name,
  —THE VEILED LADY, THE MERLING QUEEN,
  THE MOONSHADOW, THE DAUGHTER OF
  THE DUSK, THE NIGHTINGALE, THE
  POETESS, famous courtesans,
  —TERNESIO TERYS, Merchant-Captain of the
  Titan's Daughter,
  —YORKO and DENYO, two of his sons,
  —MOREDO PRESTAYN, Merchant-Captain of the
  Vixen,
  —LOTHO LORNEL, a dealer in old books and
  scrolls,
  —EZZELYNO, a red priest, oft drunk,
  —SEPTON EUSTACE, disgraced and defrocked,
  —TERRO and ORBELO, a pair of bravos,
  —BLIND BEQQO, a fishmonger,
  —BRUSCO, a fishmonger,
    —his daughters, TALEA and BREA,
  —MERALYN, called MERRY, proprietor of the
  Happy Port, a brothel near the Ragman's Harbor,

—THE SAILOR'S WIFE, a whore at the Happy
  Port,
—LANNA, her daughter, a young whore,
—BLUSHING BETHANY, YNA ONE-EYE,
  ASSADORA OF IBBEN, the whores of the Happy
  Port,
—RED ROGGO, GYLORO DOTHARE, GYLENO
  DOTHARE, a scribbler called QUILL,
  COSSOMO THE CONJURER, patrons of the
  Happy Port,
—TAGGANARO, a dockside cutpurse and thief,
  —CASSO, KING OF THE SEALS, his trained seal,
  —LITTLE NARBO, his sometime partner,
—MYRMELLO, JOSS THE GLOOM, QUENCE,
  ALLAQUO, SLOEY, mummers performing nightly
  on the Ship,
—S'VRONE, a dockside whore of a murderous bent,
—THE DRUNKEN DAUGHTER, a whore of uncertain
  temper,
—CANKER JEYNE, a whore of uncertain sex,
—THE KINDLY MAN and THE WAIF, servants of the
  Many-Faced God at the House of Black and White,
  —UMMA, the temple cook,
  —THE HANDSOME MAN, THE FAT FELLOW,
    THE LORDLING, THE STERN FACE, THE
    SQUINTER, and THE STARVED MAN, secret
    servants of Him of Many Faces,
—ARYA of House Stark, a girl with an iron coin, also
  known as ARRY, NAN, WEASEL, SQUAB, SALTY,
  and CAT,
—QUHURU MO, of Tall Trees Town in the Summer
  Isles, master of the merchantman *Cinnamon Wind*,
  —KOJJA MO, his daughter, the red archer,
  —XHONDO DHORU, mate on the *Cinnamon Wind*.

ACKNOWLEDGMENTS

This one was a bitch.

My thanks and appreciation go out once again to those stalwart souls, my editors: Nita Taublib, Joy Chamberlain, Jane Johnson, and especially Anne Lesley Groell, for her counsel, her good humor, and her vast forbearance.

Thanks also to my readers, for all their kind and supportive e-mails, and for their patience. A special tip of the helm to Lodey of the Three Fists, Pod the Devil Bunny, Trebla and Daj the Trivial Kings, sweet Caress of the Wall, Lannister the Squirrel Slayer, and the rest of the Brotherhood Without Banners, that half-mad drunken fellowship of brave knights and lovely ladies who throw the best parties at worldcon, year after year after year. And let me sound a fanfare too for Elio and Linda, who seem to know the Seven Kingdoms better than I do, and help me keep my continuity straight. Their Westeros website and concordance is a joy and a wonder.

And thanks to Walter Jon Williams for guiding me across more salty seas, to Sage Walker for leeches and fevers and broken bones, to Pati Nagle for HTML and spinning shields and getting all my news up quickly, and to Melinda Snodgrass and Daniel Abraham for service that was truly above and beyond the call of duty. I get by with a little help from my friends.

No words could suffice for Parris, who has been there on the good days and the bad ones for every bloody page. All that needs be said is that I could not sing this Song without her.

ABOUT THE AUTHOR

GEORGE R. R. MARTIN sold his first story in 1971 and hasn't stopped. As a writer/producer, he worked on *The Twilight Zone, Beauty and the Beast,* and various feature films and pilots that were never made. In the mid '90s he returned to prose and began work on A Song of Ice and Fire. He has been in the Seven Kingdoms ever since. He lives in Santa Fe, New Mexico, with the lovely Parris.

And coming soon

A DANCE WITH DRAGONS

BY

GEORGE R. R. MARTIN

The epic continuation of his landmark series

A SONG OF ICE AND FIRE

Here's a special preview:

DAENERYS

She could hear the dead man coming up the steps. The slow, measured sound of footsteps went before him, echoing amongst the purple pillars of her hall. Daenerys Targaryen awaited him upon the ebon bench that she had made her throne. Her eyes were soft with sleep, her silver-gold hair all tousled.

"Your Grace," said Ser Barristan Selmy, the Lord Commander of her Queensguard, "there is no need for you to see this."

"He died for me." Dany clutched her lion pelt to her chest. Underneath, a sheer white linen tunic covered her to mid-thigh. She had been dreaming of a house with a red door when Missandei woke her. There had been no time to dress.

"Khaleesi," whispered Irri, "you must not touch the dead man. It is bad luck to touch the dead."

"Unless you killed them yourself." Jhiqui was bigger-boned than Irri, with wide hips and heavy breasts. "That is known."

"It is known," Irri agreed.

Dany paid no heed. Dothraki were wise where horses were concerned, but could be utter fools about much else. *They are only girls, besides.* Her handmaids were of an age with her; women grown to look at them, with their black hair, copper skin, and almond-shaped eyes, but children all the same. Khal Drogo had given them to her, who was her sun-and-stars. Drogo had given her the pelt too, the head and hide of a *hrakkar,* the white lion of the Dothraki sea. It was too big for her and had a musty smell, but it made her feel as if Drogo were still near her.

Grey Worm appeared atop the steps first, a torch in hand. His bronze cap was crested with three spikes. Behind him followed four of his Unsullied, bearing the dead man on their shoulders. Their caps had only one spike, and their faces showed so little they might have been cast of bronze as well. They laid the corpse down at her feet. Ser Barristan pulled back the blood-stained shroud. Grey Worm lowered the torch, so she might see.

The dead man's face was smooth and hairless, though his cheeks had been slashed open almost ear to ear. He had been a tall man, blue-eyed and fair of face. *Some child of Lys or old Volantis, snatched off a ship by corsairs and sold into bondage in red Astapor.* Though his eyes were open, it was his wounds that wept. There were more wounds than she could count.

"Your Grace," Ser Barristan said, "there was a harpy drawn on the bricks in the alley where he was found . . ."

". . . drawn in his own blood." Daenerys knew the way of it by now. The Sons of the Harpy did their butchery by night, and over each kill they left their mark. "Grey Worm, why was this man alone? Had he no partner?" When the Unsullied walked the streets of Meereen by night, they always walked in pairs.

"My queen," replied the captain, "your servant Stalwart

Shield had no duty last night. He had gone to a . . . a certain place . . . to drink, and have companionship."

"A certain place? What do you mean?"

"A house of pleasure, Your Grace." Beneath the spiked bronze cap, Grey Worm's face might have been made of stone.

A brothel. Half of her freedmen were from Yunkai, where the Wise Masters had been famed for training bed slaves. *The way of the seven sighs.* Brothels had sprouted up like mushrooms all over Meereen. *It is all they know. They need to survive.* Food grew more costly every day, whilst the pleasures of the flesh got cheaper. In the poorer districts between the stepped pyramids of Meereen's slaver nobility, there were brothels catering to every conceivable erotic taste, she knew. *Even so . . .*

"What could a eunuch hope to find in a brothel?" she asked.

"Even those who lack a man's parts may still have a man's heart, Your Grace," said Grey Worm. "This one has been told that your servant Stalwart Shield sometimes gave coin to the women of the brothels, to lay with him and hold him."

The blood of the dragon does not weep. "Stalwart Shield," she said, dry-eyed. "That was his name?"

"If it please Your Grace."

"It is a fine name." The Good Masters of Astapor had not allowed their slave soldiers even names. Some of her Unsullied reclaimed their birth names after she had freed them; others chose new names for themselves. "Is it known how many attackers fell upon Stalwart Shield?"

"This one does not know. Many."

"Six or more," said Ser Barristan. "From the look of his wounds, they swarmed him from all sides. He was found with an empty scabbard. It may be that he wounded some of his attackers."

Dany said a silent prayer that somewhere one of them was dying even now, clutching at his belly and writhing in pain. "Why did they cut open his cheeks like that?"

"Gracious queen," said Grey Worm, "his killers had forced the genitals of a goat down the throat of your servant Stalwart Shield. This one removed them before bringing him here."

They could not feed him his own genitals. The Astapori left him neither root nor stem. "The Sons grow bolder," Dany observed. Until now, they had limited their attacks to unarmed freedmen, cutting them down in the streets or breaking into their homes under the cover of darkness to murder them in their beds. "This is the first of my soldiers they have slain."

"The first," Ser Barristan warned, "but not the last."

I am still at war, Dany realized, *only now I am fighting shadows.* She had hoped to have a respite from the killing, some time to build and heal. Shrugging off the lion pelt, she knelt beside the corpse and closed the dead man's eyes, ignoring Jhiqui's gasp. "Stalwart Shield shall not be forgotten. Have him washed and dressed for battle, and bury him with cap and shield and spears."

"It shall be as Your Grace commands," said Grey Worm.

She stood. "Send a dozen men to the Temple of the Graces, and ask the Blue Graces if any man has come to them seeking treatment for a sword wound. And spread the word that we will pay good gold for the short sword of Stalwart Shield. Inquire of the butchers and the herdsmen too, and learn who has been gelding goats of late." Perhaps they would be fortunate, and some frightened goatherd would confess. "Henceforth, see that no man of mine walks alone after dark, whether he has the duty or no."

"These ones shall obey."

Daenerys pushed her hair back. "Find these cowards for me," she said fiercely. "Find them, so that I might teach the Harpy's Sons what it means to wake the dragon."

Grey Worm saluted her. His Unsullied closed the shroud once more, lifted the dead man onto their shoulders, and bore him from the hall. Ser Barristan Selmy remained behind. His hair was white, and there were crow's feet at the corners of his pale blue eyes. Yet his back was still unbent, and the years had not yet robbed him of his skill at arms. "Your Grace," he said, "I fear your eunuchs are ill-suited for the tasks you set them."

Dany settled on her bench and wrapped her pelt about her shoulders once again. "The Unsullied are my finest warriors."

"Soldiers, not warriors, if it please Your Grace. They were made for the battlefield, to stand shoulder to shoulder behind their shields, with their spears thrust out before them. Their training teaches them to obey, fearlessly, perfectly, without thought or hesitation . . . not to unravel secrets or ask questions."

"Would knights serve me any better?" Selmy was training knights for her, teaching the sons of slaves to fight with lance and longsword in the Westerosi fashion . . . but what good would lances do, against cowards who killed from the shadows?

"Not in this," the old man admitted. "And Your Grace has no knights, save me. It will be years before the boys are ready."

"Then who, if not Unsullied? Dothraki would be even worse." Her *khalasar* was tiny, and largely of green boys and old men. And Dothraki fought from horseback. Mounted men were of more use in open fields and hills than in the narrow streets and alleys of the city. Beyond Meereen's walls of many-colored brick her rule was tenuous at best. Thousands of slaves still toiled on vast estates in the hills, growing wheat and olives, herding sheep and goats, and mining salt and copper. Meereen's storehouses still held ample supplies of grain, oil, olives, dried fruit, and salted meat, but the stores were dwindling. So Dany had dispatched her *khalasar* to subdue the hinterlands, under the command of her three bloodriders, whilst Brown Ben Plumm took his Second Sons south to guard against Yunkish incursions.

The most crucial task of all she had entrusted to Daario Naharis, glib-tongued Daario with his gold tooth and trident beard, smiling his wicked smile through purple whiskers.

Beyond the eastern hills was a range of rounded sandstone mountains, the Khyzai Pass, and Lhazar. If Daario could convince the Lhazarene to reopen the overland trade routes, grains could be brought down the river or over the hills at need . . . but the Lamb Men had no reason to love Meereen. "When the Stormcrows return from Lhazar, perhaps I can use them in the streets," she told Ser Barristan, "but until then I have only the Unsullied."

Dany wondered if Daario had reached Lhazar. *Daario will not fail me . . . but if he does, I will find another way. That is what queens do. They find a way, a way that does not involve taking plows across the river.* Even famine might be preferable to sending plows across the Skahazadhan. It was known. "You must excuse me, ser," she said. "The petitioners will soon be at my gates. I must don my floppy ears and become their queen again. Summon Reznak and the Shavepate; I'll see them when I'm dressed."

"As Your Grace commands." Selmy bowed.

The Great Pyramid shouldered eight hundred feet into the sky, from its huge square base to the lofty apex where the queen kept her private chambers, surrounded by greenery and fragrant pools. As a cool blue dawn broke over the city, Dany walked out onto the terrace. To the west sunlight blazed off the golden domes of the Temple of the Graces, and etched deep shadows behind the stepped pyramids of the mighty. *In some of those pyramids, the Sons of the Harpy are plotting new murders even now,* she thought, *and I am powerless to stop them.* Viserion sensed her disquiet. The white dragon lay coiled around a pear tree, his head resting on his tail. When Dany passed his eyes came open, two pools of molten gold. His horns were gold as well, and the scales that ran down his back from head to tail. "You're lazy," she told him, scratching under his jaw. His scales were hot to the touch, like armor left cooking too long in the sun. *Dragons are fire made flesh.* She had read that in one of the books Ser Jorah had given her as a wedding gift. "You should be hunting with your brothers. Have you been fighting Drogon again?" Her dragons had grown wilder of late. Rhaegal had snapped at Irri, and Viserion had set Reznak's *tokar* ablaze the last time the Seneschal had called. *I have left them too much to themselves, but where am I to find the time for them?*

Viserion's tail lashed sideways, thumping the trunk of the tree so hard that a pear came tumbling down to land at Dany's feet. His wings unfolded, and he half-flew, half-hopped onto the parapet. *He is growing,* she thought, as the dragon launched himself into the sky. *They are all three growing. Soon they will be large enough to bear my weight.* Then she would fly as Aegon the Conquerer had flown, up and up, until Meereen was so small that she could blot it out with her thumb.

She watched Viserion climb in widening circles, until he was lost to sight beyond muddy waters of the Skahazadhan. Only then did Dany go back inside the pyramid, where Irri and Jhiqui were waiting to brush the tangles from her hair and garb her as befit the Queen of Meereen, in a Ghiscari *tokar*.

The garment was a clumsy thing, a long loose shapeless sheet that had to be wound around her hips and under an arm and over a shoulder, its dangling fringes carefully layered and displayed. Wound too loose, it was like to fall off; wound too tight, it would tangle, trip, and bind. Even wound properly, the *tokar* required its wearer to hold it in place with the left hand. Walking in a *tokar* demanded small, mincing steps and exquisite balance, lest one tread upon those heavy trailing fringes. It was not a garment meant for any man who had to work. The *tokar* was a *master's* garment, a sign of wealth and power.

Dany had wanted to ban the *tokar* when she took Meereen, but her council had convinced her otherwise. "The Mother of Dragons must don the *tokar* or be forever hated," warned the Green Grace, Galazza Galare. "In the wools of Westeros or a gown of Myrish lace, Your Radiance shall forever remain a stranger amongst us, a grotesque outlander, a barbarian conquerer. Meereen's queen must be a lady of Old Ghis." Brown Ben Plumm, the captain of the Second Sons, had put it more succinctly. "Man wants to be the king o' the rabbits, he best wear a pair o' floppy ears."

The floppy ears she chose today were made of sheer white linen, with a fringe of golden tassels. With Jhiqui's help, she wound the *tokar* about herself correctly on her third attempt. Irri fetched her crown, wrought in the shape of the three-headed dragon of her House. Its coils were gold, its wings silver, its three heads ivory, onyx, and jade. Dany's neck and shoulders would be stiff and sore from the weight of it before the day was done. *A crown should not sit easy on the head.* One of her royal forebears had said that, once. *An Aegon, but which one?*

Five Aegons had ruled the Seven Kingdoms of Westeros, and there might have been a sixth if the Usurper's dogs had not murdered her brother's son when he was still a babe at the breast. *If he had lived I might have married him. Aegon would have been closer to my age than Viserys.* Dany had scarcely been conceived when Aegon and his sister were murdered. Their father had perished even earlier, slain by the Usurper on the Trident. Her other brother, Viserys, had died screaming in Vaes Dothrak with a crown of molten gold upon his head. *They will kill me too, if I allow it. The knives that slew my Stalwart Shield were meant for me.*

She had not forgotten the slave children the Great Masters had nailed up along the road from Yunkai. They had numbered one hundred sixty-three, a child every mile, nailed to mileposts with one arm outstetched to point her way. After Meereen had fallen, Dany nailed up a like number of Great Masters. Swarms of flies had attended their slow dying, and the stench had lingered long in the plaza. Yet some days she feared that she had not gone nearly far enough. These Meereenese were a sly and stubborn people who resisted her at every turn. They had freed their slaves, yes . . . only to hire them back as servants at wages so meager that most could scarce afford to eat. Freedmen too old or young to be of use had been cast into the streets, along with the infirm and the crippled. And still the

Great Masters gathered atop their lofty pyramids to complain of how the dragon queen had filled their noble city with hordes of unwashed beggars, thieves, and whores.

To rule Meereen I must win the Meereenese, however much I may despise them. "I am ready," she told Irri.

Reznak and Skahaz waited atop the marble steps. "Great queen," declared Reznak mo Reznak, "you are so radiant today I fear to look on you." The Seneschal wore a *tokar* of maroon silk with a golden fringe. A small, damp man, he smelled as if he had bathed in perfume and spoke a bastard form of High Valyrian, much corrupted and flavored with a thick Ghiscari growl.

"You are kind to say so," Dany answered, in a purer form of the same tongue.

"My queen," growled Skahaz mo Kandaq, of the shaven head. Ghiscari hair was dense and wiry; it had long been the fashion for the men of the Slaver Cities to tease it into horns and spikes and wings. By shaving, Skahaz had put old Meereen behind him to accept the new. His Kandaq kin had done the same after his example. Others followed, though whether from fear, fashion, or ambition, Dany could not say; shavepates, they were called. Skahaz was *the* Shavepate . . . and the vilest of traitors to the Sons of the Harpy and their ilk. "We were told about the eunuch."

"His name was Stalwart Shield."

"More will die, unless the murderers are punished." Even with his shaven scalp, Skahaz had an odious face; a beetled brow, small eyes with heavy bags beneath them, a big nose dark with blackheads, oily skin that looked more yellow than the usual amber of Ghiscari. It was a blunt, brutal, angry face. She could only pray it was an honest one as well.

"How can I punish them when I do not know who they are?" Dany demanded of him. "Tell me that, bold Skahaz."

"You have no lack of enemies, Your Grace. You can see their pyramids from your terrace. Zhak, Hazkar, Ghazeen, Merreq, Loraq, all the old slaving families. Pahl. Pahl, most of all. A house of women now. Bitter old women with a taste for blood. Women do not forget. Women do not forgive."

No, Dany thought, *and the Usurper's dogs will learn that, when I return to Westeros.* It was true that there was blood between her and the house of Pahl. Oznak zo Pahl had been Meereen's hero until Strong Belwas slew him. His father, commander of the city watch, had died defending the gates when Joso's Cock smashed them into splinters. His uncle had been one of the hundred sixty-three on the plaza.

"How much gold have we offered for information concerning the Sons of the Harpy?" Dany asked of Reznak.

"One hundred honors, if it please Your Radiance."

"One thousand honors would please us more. Make it so."

"Your Grace has not asked for my counsel," said Skahaz Shavepate, "but I say that blood must pay for blood. Take one man from each of the families I have named and kill him. The next time one of yours is slain, take two from each great house and kill them both. There will not be a third murder."

Reznak squealed in distress. "Noooo . . . gentle queen, such savagery would bring down the ire of the gods. We will find the murderers, I promise you, and when we do they will prove to be baseborn filth, you shall see."

The Seneschal was as bald as Skahaz, though in his case the gods were responsible. "Should any hair be so insolent as to appear, my barber stands with razor ready," he had said when she raised him up. There were times when Dany wondered if that razor might not be better used on Reznak's throat. He was a useful man, but she liked him little and trusted him less. She had not forgotten the *maegi* Mirri Maz Duur, who had repaid her kindness by murdering her sun-and-stars and unborn child.

The Undying had told her she would be thrice betrayed. The *maegi* had been the first, Ser Jorah the second. *Will Reznak be the third, or the Shavepate, or Daario? Or will it be someone I would never suspect, Ser Barristan or Grey Worm or Missandei?*

"Skahaz," she told the Shavepate, "I thank you for your counsel. Reznak, see what one thousand honors may accomplish." Clutching her *tokar*, Daenerys swept past them down the broad marble stair. She took one step at a time, lest she trip over her fringe and go tumbling headfirst into court.

Missandei announced her. The little scribe had a sweet, strong voice. *"All kneel for Daenerys Stormborn, the Unburnt, Queen of Meereen, Queen of the Andals and the Rhoynar and the First Men, Khaleesi of Great Grass Sea, Breaker of Shackles and Mother of Dragons,"* she cried as Dany made her slow descent.

The hall had filled. Unsullied stood with their backs to the pillars, holding their shields and spears, the spikes on their caps jutting upward like a row of knives. The Meereenese had gathered beneath the eastern windows, in a throng of shaven pates and hairy horns and hands and spirals. Her freedmen stood well apart from their former masters. *Until they stand together, Meereen will know no peace.* "Arise." Dany settled onto her bench. The hall rose. *That at least they do as one.*

Reznak mo Reznak had a list. Custom demanded that the queen begin with the Astapori envoy, a former slave who called himself Lord Ghael, though no one seemed to know what he was lord of.

Lord Ghael had a mouth of brown and rotten teeth and the pointed yellow face of a weasel. He also had a gift. "Cleon the Great sends these slippers as a token of his love for Daenerys Stormborn, the Mother of Dragons," he announced.

Irri fetched the slippers for her and put them on Dany's feet. They were gilded leather, decorated with green freshwater pearls. *Does the butcher king believe a pair of pretty slippers will win my hand?* "King Cleon is most generous," she said. "You may thank him for his lovely gift." *Lovely, but made for a child.* Dany had small feet, yet the slippers mashed her toes together.

"Great Cleon will be pleased to know they pleased you," said Lord Ghael. "His Magnificence bids me say that he stands ready to defend the Mother of Dragons from all her foes."

If he proposes that I marry Cleon again, I'll throw a slipper at his head, Dany thought, but for once the Astapori envoy made no mention of a marriage.

Instead he said, "The time has come for Astapor and Meereen to end the savage reign of the Wise Masters of Yunkai, sworn foes to all those who live in freedom. Great Cleon bids me tell you that he and his new Unsullied will soon march."

His new Unsullied are an obscene jape. "King Cleon would be wise to tend his own gardens and let the Yunkai'i tend theirs." It was not that she harbored any love for Yunkai. More and more she was coming to regret leaving the Yellow City untaken after defeating its army in the field. The Wise Masters had returned to slaving as soon as she'd moved on, and were busy raising levies, hiring sellswords, and making alliances against her. Cleon the self-styled Great was little better, however. The Butcher King had restored slavery to Astapor, the only change being that the former slaves were now the masters and the former masters were now the slaves. *He is still a butcher, and his hands are bloody.* "I am only a young girl and know little of the ways of war," she went on, "but it is said that Astapor is starving. Let King Cleon feed his people before he leads them out to battle." She made a gesture of dismissal, and Ghael withdrew.

"Magnificence," prompted Reznak mo Reznak, "will you hear the noble Hizdahr zo Loraq?"

Again? Dany nodded, and Hizdahr strode forth; a tall man, very slender, with flawless amber skin. He bowed on the same spot where Stalwart Shield had lain in death not long before. *I need this man,* Dany reminded herself. Hizdahr was a weathly merchant with many friends in Meereen, and more across the seas. He had visited Volantis, Lys, and Qarth, had kin in Tolos and Elyria, and was even said to wield some influence in New Ghis, where the Yunkai'i were trying to stir up enmity against Dany and her rule.

And he was rich. Famously and fabulously rich . . .

And like to grow richer, if I grant his petition. When Dany had closed the city's fighting pits, the value of pit shares had plummeted. Hizdahr zo Loraq had grabbed them up with both hands, and now owned most of the pits in Meereen.

The nobleman had wings of hair sprouting from his temples as if his head were about to take flight. His long face was made even longer by a beard of wiry red-black hair bound with rings of gold. His purple *tokar* was fringed with amethysts and pearls. "Your Radiance will know the reason I am here."

"Why," she said, "it must be because you have no other purpose but to plague me. How many times have I refused you?"

"Five times, Your Magnificence."

"Six, now. I will not have the fighting pits reopened."

"If Your Majesty will hear my arguments . . ."

"I have. Five times. Have you brought new arguments?"

"Old arguments," Hizdahr admitted, "new words. Lovely words, and courteous, more apt to move a queen."

"It is your cause I find wanting, not your courtesies. I have heard your arguments so often I could plead your case myself. Shall I?" She leaned forward. "The fighting pits have been a part of Meereen since the city was founded. The combats are profoundly religious in nature, a blood sacrifice to the gods of Ghis. The *mortal art* of Ghis is not mere butchery, but a display of courage, skill, and strength most pleasing to the gods. Victorious fighters are well fed, pampered, and acclaimed, and the heroic slain are honored and remembered. By reopening the pits I would show the people of Meereen that I respect their ways and customs. The pits are far-famed across the world. They draw trade to Meereen, and fill the city's coffers with coin from the far ends of the earth.

All men share a taste for blood, a taste the pits help slake. In that way they make Meereen more tranquil. For criminals condemned to die upon the sands, the pits represent a judgment by battle, a last chance for a man to prove his innocence." Dany tossed her hair. "There. How have I done?"

"Your Radiance has stated the case much better than I could have hoped to do myself. I see that you are eloquent as well as beautiful. I am quite persuaded."

She had to laugh. "Very good . . . but I am not."

"Your Magnificence," whispered Reznak mo Reznak in her ear, "if I might remind you, it is customary for the city to claim one-tenth of all the profits from the fighting pits, after expenses, as a tax. That coin might be put to many noble uses."

"It might," she agreed, "though if we *were* to reopen the pits, we should take our tenth before expenses. I am only a young girl and know little of trade, but I dwelled with Illyrio Mopatis and Xaro Xhoan Daxos long enough to know that much. It makes no matter. Hizdahr, if you could marshal armies as you marshal arguments, you could conquer the world . . . but my answer is still no. For the sixth time."

He bowed again, as deeply as before. His pearls and amethysts clattered softly against the marble floor. A very limber man was Hizdahr zo Loraq. "The queen has spoken."

He might be handsome, but for that silly hair. Reznak and the Green Grace had been urging Dany to take a Meereenese noble for her husband, to reconcile the city to her rule. If it came to that, Hizdahr zo Loraq might be worth a careful look. *Sooner him than Skahaz.* The Shavepate had offered to set aside his wife for her, but the notion made her shudder. Hizdahr at least knew how to smile, though when Dany tried to imagine what it would be like to share a bed with him, she almost laughed aloud.

"Magnificence," said Reznak, consulting his list, "the noble Grazdan zo Galare would address you. Will you hear him?"

"It would be my pleasure," said Dany, admiring the glimmer of the gold and the sheen of the green pearls on Cleon's slippers while doing her best to ignore the pinching in her toes. Grazdan, she had been forewarned, was a cousin of the Green Grace, whose support she had found invaluable. The priestess was a voice for peace, acceptance, and obedience to lawful authority. *I can give her cousin a respectful hearing, whatever he desires.*

What he desired turned out to be gold. Dany had refused to compensate any of the Great Masters for the value of the slaves that she had freed, but the Meereenese kept devising other ways to try to squeeze coin from her. The noble Grazdan was one such. He had once owned a slave woman who was a very fine weaver, he told her; the fruits of her loom were greatly valued, not only in Meereen, but in New Ghis and Astapor and Qarth. When this woman had grown old, Grazdan had purchased half a dozen young girls and commanded the crone to instruct them in the secrets of her craft. The old woman was dead now. The young ones, freed, had opened a shop by the harbor wall to sell their weavings. Grazdan zo Galare asked that he be granted a portion of their earnings. "They owe their skill to me," he insisted. "I plucked them from the auction bloc and gave them to the loom."

Dany listened quietly, her face still. When he was done, she said, "What was the name of the old weaver?"

"The slave?" Grazdan shifted his weight, frowning. "She was . . . Elza, it might have been. Or Ella. It was six years ago she died. I have owned so many slaves, Your Grace."

"Let us say Elza." Dany raised a hand. "Here is our ruling. From the girls, you shall have nothing. It was Elza who taught them weaving, not you. From you, the girls shall have a new loom, the finest coin can buy. That is for forgetting the name of the old woman. You may go."

Reznak would have summoned another *tokar* next, but Dany insisted that he call upon one of the freedmen instead. From that point on she alternated between the former masters and the former slaves. Many and more of the matters brought before her involved redress. Meereen had been sacked savagely after its fall. The stepped pyramids of the mighty had been spared the worst of the ravages, but the humbler parts of the city had been given over to an orgy of looting and killing as the city's slaves rose up and the starving hordes who had followed her from Yunkai and Astapor came pouring through the broken gates. Her Unsullied had finally restored order, but the sack had left a plague of problems in its wake, and no one was quite certain which laws still held true. And so they came to see the queen.

A rich woman came, whose husband and sons had died defending the city walls. During the sack she had fled to her brother in fear. When she returned, she found her house had been turned into a brothel. The whores had bedecked themselves in her jewels and clothes. She wanted her house back, and her jewels. "They can keep the clothes," she allowed. Dany granted her the jewels, but ruled the house was lost when she abandoned it.

A former slave came, to accuse a certain noble of the Zhak. The man had recently taken to wife a freedwoman who had been the noble's bedwarmer before the city fell. The noble had taken her maidenhood, used her for his pleasure, and gotten her with child. Her new husband wanted the noble gelded for the crime of rape, and he wanted a purse of gold as well, to pay him for raising the noble's bastard as his own. Dany granted him the gold, but not the gelding. "When he lay with her, your wife was his property, to do with as he would. By law, there was no rape." Her decision did not please him, she could see, but if she gelded every man who ever forced a bedslave, she would soon rule a city of eunuchs.

A boy came, younger than Dany, slight and scarred, dressed up in a frayed grey *tokar* trailing silver fringe. His voice broke when he told of how two of his father's household slaves had risen up the night the gate broke. One had slain his father, the other his elder brother. Both had raped his mother before killing her as well. The boy had escaped with no more than the scar upon his face, but one of the murderers was still living in his father's house, and the other had joined the queen's soldiers as one of the Mother's Men. He wanted them both hanged.

I am queen over a city built on dust and death. Dany had no choice but to deny him. She had declared a blanket pardon for all crimes committed during the sack. Nor would she punish slaves for rising up against their masters.

When she told him, the boy rushed at her, but his feet tangled in his *tokar* and he went sprawling headlong on the purple marble. Strong Belwas was on him at once. The huge brown eunuch yanked him up one-handed and shook him like a mastiff with a rat. "Enough, Belwas," Dany called. "Release him." To the boy she said, "Treasure that *tokar,* for it saved your life. Had you laid a hand on us in anger, you would have lost that hand. You are only a boy, so we will forget what happened here. You should do the same." But as he left, the boy looked back over his shoulder, and when she saw his eyes Dany thought, *The harpy has another son.*

And so her day crept by, tedious and terrifying by turns. By midday Daenerys was feeling the weight of the crown upon her head, and the hardness of the bench beneath her. With so many still waiting on her pleasure, she did not stop to eat. Instead she dispatched Jhiqui to the kitchens for a platter of flatbread, olives, figs, and cheese. She nibbled whilst she listened, and sipped from a cup of watered wine. The figs were fine, the olives even finer, but the wine left a tart metallic aftertaste in her mouth. The small, pale yellow grapes native to these regions produced a notably inferior vintage. *We shall have no trade in wine,* Dany realized as she sipped. Besides, the Great Masters had burned the best arbors along with the olive trees.

In the afternoon a sculptor came, proposing to replace the head of the great bronze harpy in the Plaza of Purification with one cast in Dany's image. She denied him with as much courtesy as she could muster, struggling not to shudder. A pike of unprecedented size had been caught in the Skahazadhan, and the fisherman wished to give it to the queen. She admired the fish extravagantly, rewarded the fisherman with a plump purse of silver, and sent the pike down to her kitchens. A coppersmith had fashioned her a suit of burnished rings to wear to war. She accepted it with fulsome thanks; it was lovely to behold, and all that burnished copper would flash prettily in the sun, though if actual battle threatened she would sooner be clad in steel. Even a young girl who knew nothing of the ways of war knew *that*.

The slippers the Butcher King had sent her had grown too uncomfortable. Dany kicked them off, and sat with one foot tucked beneath her and the other swinging back and forth. It was not a very regal pose, but she was tired of being regal. The crown had given her a headache, and her buttocks had gone to sleep. "Ser Barristan," she called, "I know what quality a king needs most."

"Courage, Your Grace?"

"No," she teased, "cheeks like iron. All I do is sit."

"Your Grace takes too much on herself. You should allow your councillors to shoulder more of your burdens."

"I have too many councillors. What I need is cushions." Dany turned to Reznak. "How many more?"

"Three and twenty, if it please Your Magnificence. With as many claims." The seneschal consulted some papers. "One calf and three goats. The rest will be sheep or lambs, no doubt."

"Three and twenty." Dany sighed. "My dragons have developed a prodigious taste for mutton since we began to pay the shepherds for their kills. Have these claims been proven?"

"Some men have brought burnt bones."

"Men make fires. Men cook mutton. Burnt bones prove nothing. Brown Ben says there are red wolves in the hills outside the city, and jackals and wild dogs. Must we pay good silver for every lamb that goes astray between Yunkai and the Skahazadhan?"

"No, Magnificence." Reznak bowed. "Shall I send these rascals away, or will you want them scourged?"

Daenerys shifted on the bench. The ebony felt hard beneath her. "No man should ever fear to come to me. Pay them." Some claims were false, she did not doubt, but more were genuine. Her dragons had grown too large to be content with rats and cats and dogs, as before. *The more they eat the larger they will grow,* Ser Barristan had warned her, *and the larger they grow, the more they'll eat.* Drogon especially ranged far afield and could easily devour a sheep a day. "Pay them for the value of their animals," she told Reznak, "but henceforth claimants must present themselves at the Temple of the Graces, and swear a holy oath before the gods of Ghis."

"It shall be done." Reznak turned to the petitioners. "Her Magnificence the Queen has consented to compensate each of you for the animals you have lost," he told them in the Ghiscari tongue. "Present yourselves to my factors on the morrow, and you shall be paid in coin or kind, as you prefer."

The pronouncement was received in sullen silence. *You would think they might be happier,* Dany thought, annoyed. *They have what they came for. Is there no way to please these people?*

One man lingered behind as the rest were filing out; a squat man with a windburnt face, shabbily dressed. His hair was a cap of coarse red-black wire cropped about his ears, and in one hand he held a sad cloth sack. He stood with his head down, gazing at the marble floor as if he had quite forgotten where he was. *And what does this one want?* Dany wondered, frowning.

"All kneel for Daenerys Stormborn, the Unburnt, Queen of Meereen, Queen of the Andals and the Rhoynar and the First Men, Khaleesi of Great Grass Sea, Breaker of Shackles and Mother of Dragons," cried Missandei in her high, sweet voice.

As Dany stood, her *tokar* began to slip. She caught it and tugged it back into place. "You with the sack," she called, "did you wish to speak with us? You may approach."

When he raised his head, his eyes were red and raw as open sores. Dany glimpsed Ser Barristan sliding closer, a white shadow at her side. The man approached in a stumbling shuffle, one step and then another, clutching his sack. *Is he drunk, or ill?* she wondered. There was dirt beneath his cracked yellow fingernails.

"What is it?" she demanded. "Do you have some grievance to lay before us, some petition? What would you have of us?"

His tongue flicked nervously over chapped, cracked lips. "I . . . I brought . . ."

"Bones?" she said, impatiently. "Burnt bones?"

He lifted the sack, and spilled its contents on the marble.

Bones they were, broken bones and blackened. The longer ones had been cracked open for their marrow.

"It were the black one," the man said, in a Ghiscari growl, "the winged shadow. He come down from the sky and . . . and . . ."

No. Dany shivered. *No, no, oh no.*

"Are you deaf, fool?" Reznak mo Reznak demanded of the man. "Did you not hear my pronouncement? See my factors on the morrow, and you shall be paid for your sheep."

"Reznak," Ser Barristan said quietly, "hold your tongue and open your eyes. Those are no sheep bones."

No, Dany thought, *those are the bones of a child.*

Also by
GEORGE R. R. MARTIN

— Novels —

The
Armageddon Rag

Fevre Dream

Windhaven

Dying of the Light

— Short Stories —

Dreamsongs:
Volume I

Dreamsongs:
Volume II

Also available in Audio and eBook

THE RANDOM HOUSE PUBLISHING GROUP

www.GeorgeRRMartin.com

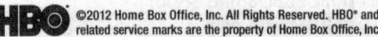

PRAISE FOR
A GAME OF THRONES

"We have been invited to a grand feast and pageant: George R. R. Martin has unveiled for us an intensely realized, romantic but realistic world...if the next two volumes are as good as this one, it will be a wonderful feast indeed."
—*Chicago Sun-Times*

"I would be very surprised if this is not the major fantasy publishing event of 1996, and I'm already impatient for the next installment." —*Science Fiction Chronicle*

"A colorful, majestic tapestry of characters, action and plot that deserves a spot on any reader's wall...the pages seem to pass in a blur as you read." —*Albuquerque Journal*

"George Martin is assuredly a new master craftsman in the guild of heroic fantasy." —Katharine Kerr

"*A Game of Thrones* offers the rich tapestry that the very best fantasy demands: iron and steel within the silk, grandeur within the wonder, and characters torn between deep love and loyalty. Few created worlds are as imaginative and diverse. George R. R. Martin is to be applauded."
—Janny Wurts

"A dazzling fantasy adventure...with a great cast of characters that weave a tapestry of court intrigue, skullduggery, vicious betrayal and greathearted sacrifice." —Julian May

"Terrific, incredibly powerful, with phenomenal characterizations and exquisite writing." —Teresa Medeiros

"The characterization was superb, the story vivid and heartbreaking...when is the next one coming out?"
—Linda Howard

A CLASH OF KINGS

"A truly epic fantasy set in a world bedecked with 8,000 years of history, beset by an imminent winter that will last ten years and bedazzled by swords and spells wielded to devastating effect...here he provides a banquet for fantasy lovers with large appetites."
—*Publishers Weekly* (starred review)

"Martin amply fulfills the first volume's promise and continues what seems destined to be one of the best fantasy series ever written." —*The Denver Post*

"High fantasy with a vengeance."
—*The San Diego Union-Tribune*

"Rivals T. H. White's *The Once and Future King*."
—*The Des Moines Register*

"So complex, fascinating and well-rendered, readers will almost certainly be hooked by the whole series."
—*The Oregonian*

A STORM OF SWORDS

"One of the more rewarding examples of gigantism in contemporary fantasy...richly imagined."
—*Publishers Weekly* (starred review)

"George R. R. Martin continues to take epic fantasy to new levels of insight and sophistication, resonant with the turmoils and stress of the world we call our own."
—*Locus Magazine*

"Martin creates a gorgeously and intricately textured world, peopled with absolutely believable and fascinating characters." —*The Plain Dealer* (Cleveland)

"High fantasy doesn't get any better than this."
—*The Oregonian*

"A riveting continuation of a series whose brilliance continues to dazzle." —*The Patriot News*

"Enough grit and action to please even the most macho... a page-turner." —*The Dallas Morning News*

"The latest and the best in a powerful...cycle that delivers real people and a page-turning plot." —*Contra Costa Times*

"Martin's epic advances his series with gritty characterizations, bold plot moves and plenty of action."
—*St. Louis Post-Dispatch*

BY GEORGE R. R. MARTIN

A SONG OF ICE AND FIRE
Book One: *A Game of Thrones*
Book Two: *A Clash of Kings*
Book Three: *A Storm of Swords*
Book Four: *A Feast for Crows*
Book Five: *A Dance with Dragons*

Dying of the Light
Windhaven (with Lisa Tuttle)
Fevre Dream
The Armageddon Rag
Dead Man's Hand (with John J. Miller)

SHORT STORY COLLECTIONS
Dreamsongs, Volume I
Dreamsongs, Volume II
A Song of Lya and Other Stories
Songs of Stars and Shadows
Sandkings
Songs the Dead Men Sing
Nightflyers
Tuf Voyaging
Portraits of His Children
Quartet

EDITED BY GEORGE R. R. MARTIN
New Voices in Science Fiction, Volumes 1–4
The Science Fiction Weight-Loss Book
(with Isaac Asimov and Martin Harry Greenberg)
The John W. Campbell Awards, Volume 5
Night Visions 3
Wild Card I–XXI

A STORM OF SWORDS

BOOK THREE OF

A SONG OF ICE AND FIRE

GEORGE R. R. MARTIN

BANTAM BOOKS • NEW YORK

2011 Bantam Books Mass Market Edition

Published in the United States by Bantam Books, an imprint of The Random House Publishing Group, a division of Random House, Inc., New York.

BANTAM BOOKS and the rooster colophon are registered trademarks of Random House, Inc.

Originally published in hardcover in the United States by Bantam Spectra, a division of Random House, Inc., in 2000.

ISBN 978-0-553-57342-8
eBook ISBN 978-0-553-89787-6

Cover art copyright © 2011 by Larry Rostant
Cover design by David Stevenson

Maps by James Sinclair
Heraldic crests by Virginia Norey

Printed in the United States of America

www.bantamdell.com

50 49 48 47 46

A NOTE ON CHRONOLOGY

A Song of Ice and Fire is told through the eyes of characters who are sometimes hundreds or even thousands of miles apart from one another. Some chapters cover a day, some only an hour; others might span a fortnight, a month, half a year. With such a structure, the narrative cannot be strictly sequential; sometimes important things are happening simultaneously, a thousand leagues apart.

In the case of the volume now in hand, the reader should realize that the opening chapters of *A Storm of Swords* do not follow the closing chapters of *A Clash of Kings* so much as overlap them. I open with a look at some of the things that were happening on the Fist of the First Men, at Riverrun, Harrenhal, and on the Trident while the Battle of the Blackwater was being fought at King's Landing, and during its aftermath...

George R. R. Martin

for Phyllis
who made me put the dragons in

The North

- ♦ — Castle
- ◇ — Ruined Castle
- ● — City
- • — Town

N

The Frostfangs

The Haunted Forest

THE FROZEN SHORE

THE WALL

The Shadow Tower   Castle Black   Eastwatch by the Sea

Queenscrown   THE GIFT

BAY OF ICE

BAY OF SEALS

Skagos

Bear Island

Last Hearth

Karhold

Sea Dragon Point

The Last River

Deepwood Motte

Wolfswood

The Dreadfort

Stony Shore

Winterfell

White Knife

Torrhen's Square

THE RILLS

BARROWLANDS

White Harbor

Widow's Watch

The Kingsroad

SALTSPEAR

Moat Cailin

BLAZEWATER BAY

Flint's Finger

THE NECK

THE BITE

Pebble

The Paps

Cape Kraken

The Flint Cliffs

Greywater Watch

Three Sisters

Iron Islands

Old Wyk

The Twins

Great Wyk

Harlow

Cape of Eagles

Seagard

BRONSMAN'S BAY

Oldstones

Green Fork

Blue Fork

The Eyrie

Bloody Gate

VALE OF ARRYN

THE FINGERS

Tumblestone

Red Fork

Map by James Sinclair

The South

- ◆ — Castle
- ◇ — Ruined Castle
- ● — City
- ● — Town

N

The Paps

Three Sisters

THE FINGERS

Iron Islands

Old Wyk

Longbow Hall

VALE OF ARRYN

Cape of Eagles

Green Fork

Seagard

Heart's Home

The Eyrie

Bloody Gate

Gulltown

Great Wyk

Pyke

Harlaw

IRONMAN'S BAY

Oldstones

Blue Fork

THE TRIDENT

Red Fork

Inn

Lord Harroway's Town

Saltpans

BAY OF CRABS

Fair Isle

Faircastle

Tumbleton

Riverrun

High Heart

Harrenhal

Crackclaw Point

Claw Isle

The Crag

Ashemark

Golden Tooth

Acorn Hall

Isle of Faces

Maidenpool

Duskendale

Driftmark

Dragonstone

Kayce

Casterly Rock

Red Fork

Stoney Sept

Gods Eye

King's Landing

Rosby

THE GULLET

Feastfires

Lannisport

The Goldroad

Blackwater Rush

BLACKWATER BAY

Massey's Hook

THE REACH

Kingswood

Wendwater

Bronzegate

Tarth

The Searoad

The Roseroad

Bitterbridge

Cider Hall

Mander

Evenfall Hall

Storm's End

SHIPBREAKER BAY

Shield Islands

Ashford

Summerhall

Highgarden

Nightsong

Blackhaven

Rainwood

Greenstone

Brightwater Keep

The Prince's Pass

The Dornish Marches

Cape Wrath

Honeywine

Honeyholt

Boneway

SEA OF DORNE

Oldtown

WHISPERING SOUND

Yronwood

Starfall

DORNE

Scourge

The Broken Arm

Vaith

Sunspear

The Arbor

Brimstone

Greenblood

Map by James Sinclair

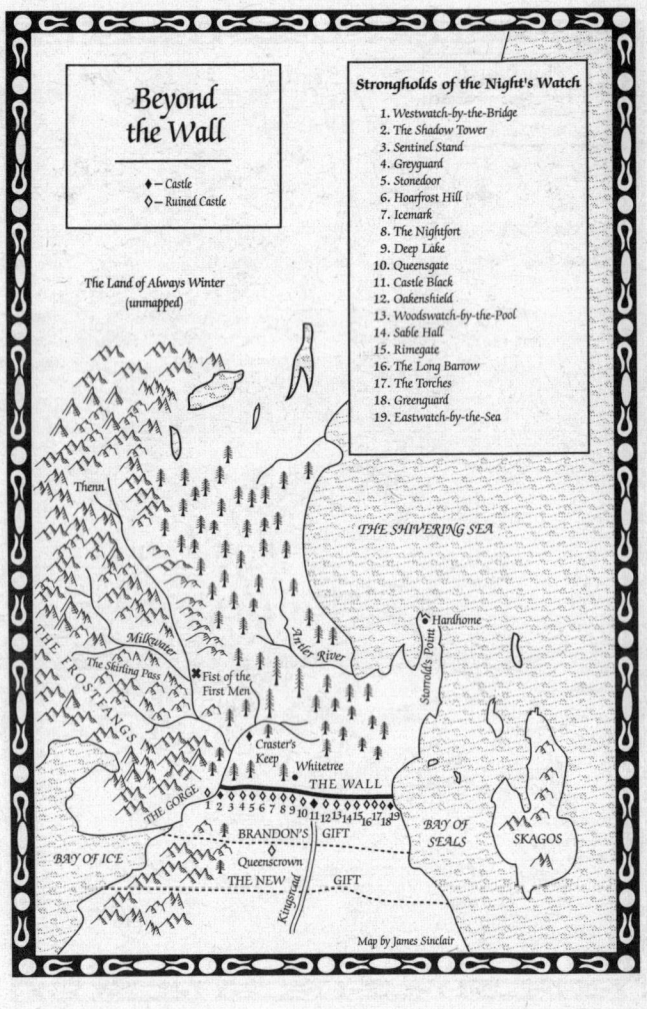

Beyond the Wall

♦ — Castle
◇ — Ruined Castle

The Land of Always Winter
(unmapped)

Strongholds of the Night's Watch

1. Westwatch-by-the-Bridge
2. The Shadow Tower
3. Sentinel Stand
4. Greyguard
5. Stonedoor
6. Hoarfrost Hill
7. Icemark
8. The Nightfort
9. Deep Lake
10. Queensgate
11. Castle Black
12. Oakenshield
13. Woodswatch-by-the-Pool
14. Sable Hall
15. Rimegate
16. The Long Barrow
17. The Torches
18. Greenguard
19. Eastwatch-by-the-Sea

Thenn

THE SHIVERING SEA

Milkwater

THE FROSTFANGS

The Skirling Pass

Fist of the First Men

Antler River

Hardhome

Starrod's Point

Craster's Keep

Whitetree

THE WALL

THE GORGE

1 2 3 4 5 6 7 8 9 10 11 12 13 14 15 16 17 18 19

BRANDON'S GIFT

BAY OF SEALS

SKAGOS

BAY OF ICE

Queenscrown

THE NEW GIFT

Kingsroad

Map by James Sinclair

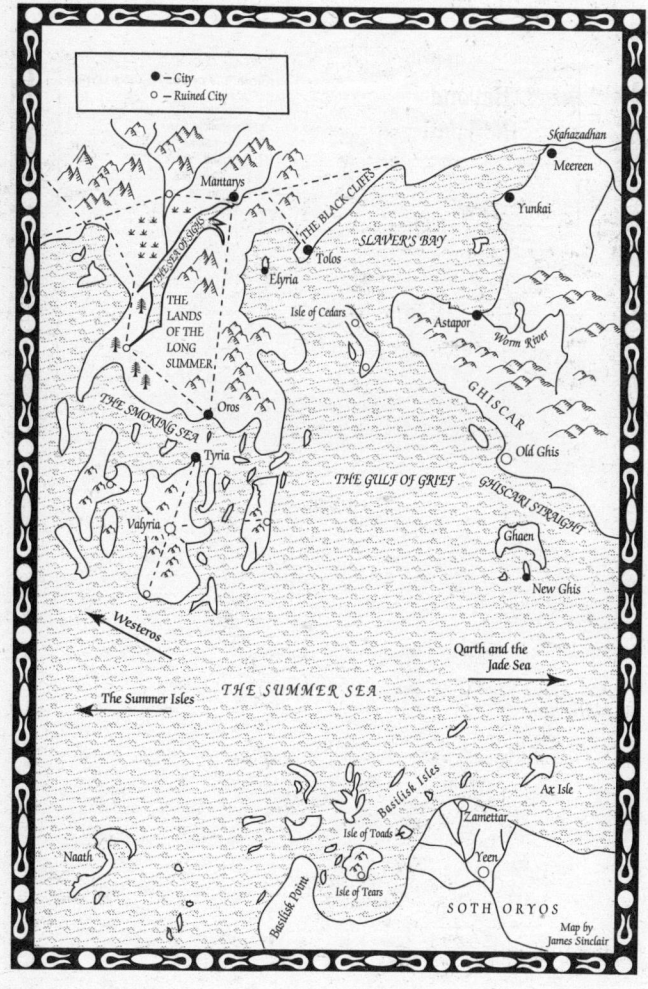

A Storm
of Swords

PROLOGUE

T he day was grey and bitter cold, and the dogs would not take the scent.

The big black bitch had taken one sniff at the bear tracks, backed off, and skulked back to the pack with her tail between her legs. The dogs huddled together miserably on the riverbank as the wind snapped at them. Chett felt it too, biting through his layers of black wool and boiled leather. It was too bloody cold for man or beast, but here they were. His mouth twisted, and he could almost feel the boils that covered his cheeks and neck growing red and angry. *I should be safe back at the Wall, tending the bloody ravens and making fires for old Maester Aemon.* It was the bastard Jon Snow who had taken that from him, him and his fat friend Sam Tarly. It was their fault he was here, freezing his bloody balls off with a pack of hounds deep in the haunted forest.

"Seven hells." He gave the leashes a hard yank to get the dogs' attention. "*Track*, you bastards. That's a bear print. You want some meat or no? *Find!*" But the hounds only huddled closer, whining. Chett snapped his short lash above their heads, and the black bitch snarled at him. "Dog meat would taste as good as bear," he warned her, his breath frosting with every word.

Lark the Sisterman stood with his arms crossed over his chest and his hands tucked up into his armpits. He wore black wool gloves, but he was always complaining how his fingers were frozen. "It's too bloody cold to hunt," he said. "Bugger this bear, he's not worth freezing over."

"We can't go back emptyhand, Lark," rumbled Small Paul through the brown whiskers that covered most of his face. "The Lord Commander wouldn't like that." There was ice under the big man's squashed pug nose, where his snot had frozen. A huge hand in a thick fur glove clenched tight around the shaft of a spear.

"Bugger that Old Bear too," said the Sisterman, a thin man with sharp features and nervous eyes. "Mormont will be dead before daybreak, remember? Who cares what he likes?"

Small Paul blinked his black little eyes. Maybe he *had* forgotten, Chett thought; he was stupid enough to forget most anything. "Why do we have to kill the Old Bear? Why don't we just go off and let him be?"

"You think he'll let *us* be?" said Lark. "He'll hunt us down. You want to be hunted, you great muttonhead?"

"No," said Small Paul. "I don't want that. I don't."

"So you'll kill him?" said Lark.

"Yes." The huge man stamped the butt of his spear on the frozen riverbank. "I will. He shouldn't hunt us."

The Sisterman took his hands from his armpits and turned to Chett. "We need to kill *all* the officers, I say."

Chett was sick of hearing it. "We been over this. The Old Bear dies, and Blane from the Shadow Tower. Grubbs and Aethan as well, their ill luck for drawing the watch, Dywen and Bannen for their tracking, and Ser Piggy for the ravens. That's *all*. We kill them quiet, while they sleep. One scream and we're wormfood, every one of us." His boils were red with rage. "Just do your bit and see that your cousins do theirs. And Paul, try and remember, it's *third* watch, not second."

"Third watch," the big man said, through hair and frozen snot. "Me and Softfoot. I remember, Chett."

The moon would be black tonight, and they had jiggered

the watches so as to have eight of their own standing sentry, with two more guarding the horses. It wasn't going to get much riper than that. Besides, the wildlings could be upon them any day now. Chett meant to be well away from here before that happened. He meant to live.

Three hundred sworn brothers of the Night's Watch had ridden north, two hundred from Castle Black and another hundred from the Shadow Tower. It was the biggest ranging in living memory, near a third of the Watch's strength. They meant to find Ben Stark, Ser Waymar Royce, and the other rangers who'd gone missing, and discover why the wildlings were leaving their villages. Well, they were no closer to Stark and Royce than when they'd left the Wall, but they'd learned where all the wildlings had gone—up into the icy heights of the godsforsaken Frostfangs. They could squat up there till the end of time and it wouldn't prick Chett's boils none.

But no. They were coming down. Down the Milkwater.

Chett raised his eyes and there it was. The river's stony banks were bearded by ice, its pale milky waters flowing endlessly down out of the Frostfangs. And now Mance Rayder and his wildlings were flowing down the same way. Thoren Smallwood had returned in a lather three days past. While he was telling the Old Bear what his scouts had seen, his man Kedge Whiteye told the rest of them. "They're still well up the foothills, but they're coming," Kedge said, warming his hands over the fire. "Harma the Dogshead has the van, the poxy bitch. Goady crept up on her camp and saw her plain by the fire. That fool Tumberjon wanted to pick her off with an arrow, but Smallwood had better sense."

Chett spat. "How many were there, could you tell?"

"Many and more. Twenty, thirty thousand, we didn't stay to count. Harma had five hundred in the van, every one ahorse."

The men around the fire exchanged uneasy looks. It was a rare thing to find even a dozen mounted wildlings, and *five hundred* . . .

"Smallwood sent Bannen and me wide around the van to catch a peek at the main body," Kedge went on. "There was no end of them. They're moving slow as a frozen river, four, five miles a day, but they don't look like they mean to go back to their villages neither. More'n half were women and children, and they were driving their animals before them, goats, sheep, even aurochs dragging sledges. They'd loaded up with bales of fur and sides of meat, cages of chickens, butter churns and spinning wheels, every damn thing they own. The mules and garrons was so heavy laden you'd think their backs would break. The women as well."

"And they follow the Milkwater?" Lark the Sisterman asked.

"I said so, didn't I?"

The Milkwater would take them past the Fist of the First Men, the ancient ringfort where the Night's Watch had made its camp. Any man with a thimble of sense could see that it was time to pull up stakes and fall back on the Wall. The Old Bear had strengthened the Fist with spikes and pits and caltrops, but against such a host all that was pointless. If they stayed here, they would be engulfed and overwhelmed.

And Thoren Smallwood wanted to *attack*. Sweet Donnel Hill was squire to Ser Mallador Locke, and the night before last Smallwood had come to Locke's tent. Ser Mallador had been of the same mind as old Ser Ottyn Wythers, urging a retreat on the Wall, but Smallwood wanted to convince him otherwise. "This King-beyond-the-Wall will never look for us so far north," Sweet Donnel reported him saying. "And this great host of his is a shambling horde, full of useless mouths who won't know what end of a sword to hold. One blow will take all the fight out of them and send them howling back to their hovels for another fifty years."

Three hundred against thirty thousand. Chett called that rank madness, and what was madder still was that Ser Mallador had been persuaded, and the two of them together were on the point of persuading the Old Bear. "If we wait too long, this chance may be lost, never to come again," Smallwood was saying to anyone who would listen. Against that, Ser Ottyn Wythers said, "We are the shield that guards the realms of men. You do not throw away your shield for no good purpose," but to that Thoren Smallwood said, "In a swordfight, a man's surest defense is the swift stroke that slays his foe, not cringing behind a shield."

Neither Smallwood nor Wythers had the command,

though. Lord Mormont did, and Mormont was waiting for his other scouts, for Jarman Buckwell and the men who'd climbed the Giant's Stair, and for Qhorin Halfhand and Jon Snow, who'd gone to probe the Skirling Pass. Buckwell and the Halfhand were late in returning, though. *Dead, most like.* Chett pictured Jon Snow lying blue and frozen on some bleak mountaintop with a wildling spear up his bastard's arse. The thought made him smile. *I hope they killed his bloody wolf as well.*

"There's no bear here," he decided abruptly. "Just an old print, that's all. Back to the Fist." The dogs almost yanked him off his feet, as eager to get back as he was. Maybe they thought they were going to get fed. Chett had to laugh. He hadn't fed them for three days now, to turn them mean and hungry. Tonight, before slipping off into the dark, he'd turn them loose among the horse lines, after Sweet Donnel Hill and Clubfoot Karl cut the tethers. *They'll have snarling hounds and panicked horses all over the Fist, running through fires, jumping the ringwall, and trampling down tents.* With all the confusion, it might be hours before anyone noticed that fourteen brothers were missing.

Lark had wanted to bring in twice that number, but what could you expect from some stupid fishbreath Sisterman? Whisper a word in the wrong ear and before you knew it you'd be short a head. No, fourteen was a good number, enough to do what needed doing but not so many that they couldn't keep the secret. Chett had recruited most of them himself. Small Paul was one of his; the strongest man on the Wall, even if he was slower than a dead snail. He'd once broken a wildling's back with a hug. They had Dirk as well, named for his favorite weapon, and the little grey man the brothers called Softfoot, who'd raped a hundred women in his youth, and liked to boast how none had ever seen nor heard him until he shoved it up inside them.

The plan was Chett's. He was the clever one; he'd been steward to old Maester Aemon for four good years before that bastard Jon Snow had done him out so his job could be handed to his fat pig of a friend. When he killed Sam Tarly tonight, he planned to whisper, "Give my love to Lord Snow," right in his ear before he sliced Ser Piggy's throat open to let the blood come bubbling out through all those layers of suet. Chett knew the ravens, so he wouldn't have no trouble there, no more than he would with Tarly. One touch of the knife and that craven would piss his pants and start blubbering for his life. *Let him beg, it won't do him no good.* After he opened his throat, he'd open the cages and shoo the birds away, so no messages reached the Wall. Softfoot and Small Paul would kill the Old Bear, Dirk would do Blane, and Lark and his cousins would silence Bannen and old Dywen, to keep them from sniffing after their trail. They'd been caching food for a fortnight, and Sweet Donnel and Clubfoot Karl would have the horses ready. With Mormont dead, command would pass to Ser Ottyn Wythers, an old done man, and failing. *He'll be running for the Wall before sundown, and he won't waste no men sending them after us neither.*

The dogs pulled at him as they made their way through the trees. Chett could see the Fist punching its way up through the green. The day was so dark that the Old Bear had the torches lit, a great circle of them burning all along the ringwall that crowned the top of the steep stony hill. The three of them waded across a brook. The water was icy cold, and patches of ice were spreading across its surface. "I'm going to make for the coast," Lark the Sisterman confided. "Me and my cousins. We'll build us a boat, sail back home to the Sisters."

And at home they'll know you for deserters and lop off your fool heads, thought Chett. There was no leaving the Night's Watch, once you said your words. Anywhere in the Seven Kingdoms, they'd take you and kill you.

Ollo Lophand now, he was talking about sailing back to Tyrosh, where he claimed men didn't lose their hands for a bit of honest thievery, nor get sent off to freeze their life away for being found in bed with some knight's wife. Chett had weighed going with him, but he didn't speak their wet girly tongue. And what could he do in Tyrosh? He had no trade to speak of, growing up in Hag's Mire. His father had spent his life grubbing in other men's fields and collecting leeches. He'd strip down bare but for a thick leather clout, and go wading in the murky waters. When he climbed out he'd be covered from nipple to ankle. Sometimes he made Chett help pull the leeches off. One had attached itself to his palm once, and he'd smashed it against a wall in revul-

sion. His father beat him bloody for that. The maesters
bought the leeches at twelve-for-a-penny.

Lark could go home if he liked, and the damn Tyroshi
too, but not Chett. If he never saw Hag's Mire again, it
would be too bloody soon. He had liked the look of
Craster's Keep, himself. Craster lived high as a lord there,
so why shouldn't he do the same? That would be a laugh.
Chett the leechman's son, a lord with a keep. His banner
could be a dozen leeches on a field of pink. But why stop at
lord? Maybe he should be a king. *Mance Rayder started
out a crow. I could be a king same as him, and have me
some wives.* Craster had nineteen, not even counting the
young ones, the daughters he hadn't gotten around to bedding yet. Half them wives were as old and ugly as Craster,
but that didn't matter. The old ones Chett could put to
work cooking and cleaning for him, pulling carrots and
slopping pigs, while the young ones warmed his bed and
bore his children. Craster wouldn't object, not once Small
Paul gave him a hug.

The only women Chett had ever known were the
whores he'd bought in Mole's Town. When he'd been
younger, the village girls took one look at his face, with its
boils and its wen, and turned away sickened. The worst
was that slattern Bessa. She'd spread her legs for every boy
in Hag's Mire so he'd figured why not him too? He even
spent a morning picking wildflowers when he heard she
liked them, but she'd just laughed in his face and told him
she'd crawl in a bed with his father's leeches before she'd
crawl in one with him. She stopped laughing when he put
his knife in her. That was sweet, the look on her face, so he
pulled the knife out and put it in her again. When they
caught him down near Sevenstreams, old Lord Walder Frey
hadn't even bothered to come himself to do the judging.
He'd sent one of his *bastards*, that Walder Rivers, and the
next thing Chett had known he was walking to the Wall
with that foul-smelling black devil Yoren. To pay for his
one sweet moment, they took his whole life.

But now he meant to take it back, and Craster's women
too. *That twisted old wildling has the right of it. If you
want a woman to wife you take her, and none of this giving her flowers so that maybe she don't notice your bloody
boils.* Chett didn't mean to make *that* mistake again.

It would work, he promised himself for the hundredth time. *So long as we get away clean.* Ser Ottyn would strike south for the Shadow Tower, the shortest way to the Wall. *He won't bother with us, not Wythers, all he'll want is to get back whole.* Thoren Smallwood now, he'd want to press on with the attack, but Ser Ottyn's caution ran too deep, and he was senior. *It won't matter anyhow. Once we're gone, Smallwood can attack anyone he likes. What do we care? If none of them ever returns to the Wall, no one will ever come looking for us, they'll think we died with the rest.* That was a new thought, and for a moment it tempted him. But they would need to kill Ser Ottyn and Ser Mallador Locke as well to give Smallwood the command, and both of them were well-attended day and night . . . no, the risk was too great.

"Chett," said Small Paul as they trudged along a stony game trail through sentinels and soldier pines, "what about the bird?"

"What bloody bird?" The last thing he needed now was some mutton-head going on about a bird.

"The Old Bear's raven," Small Paul said. "If we kill him, who's going to feed his bird?"

"Who bloody well cares? Kill the bird too if you like."

"I don't want to hurt no bird," the big man said. "But that's a talking bird. What if it tells what we did?"

Lark the Sisterman laughed. "Small Paul, thick as a castle wall," he mocked.

"You shut up with that," said Small Paul dangerously.

"Paul," said Chett, before the big man got too angry, "when they find the old man lying in a pool of blood with his throat slit, they won't need no bird to tell them someone killed him."

Small Paul chewed on that a moment. "That's true," he allowed. "Can I keep the bird, then? I like that bird."

"He's yours," said Chett, just to shut him up.

"We can always eat him if we get hungry," offered Lark.

Small Paul clouded up again. "Best not try and eat *my* bird, Lark. Best not."

Chett could hear voices drifting through the trees. "Close your bloody mouths, both of you. We're almost to the Fist."

They emerged near the west face of the hill, and walked

around south where the slope was gentler. Near the edge of the forest a dozen men were taking archery practice. They had carved outlines on the trunks of trees, and were loosing shafts at them. "Look," said Lark. "A pig with a bow."

Sure enough, the nearest bowman was Ser Piggy himself, the fat boy who had stolen his place with Maester Aemon. Just the sight of Samwell Tarly filled him with anger. Stewarding for Maester Aemon had been as good a life as he'd ever known. The old blind man was undemanding, and Clydas had taken care of most of his wants anyway. Chett's duties were easy: cleaning the rookery, a few fires to build, a few meals to fetch . . . and Aemon never once hit him. *Thinks he can just walk in and shove me out, on account of being highborn and knowing how to read. Might be I'll ask him to read my knife before I open his throat with it.* "You go on," he told the others, "I want to watch this." The dogs were pulling, anxious to go with them, to the food they thought would be waiting at the top. Chett kicked the bitch with the toe of his boot, and that settled them down some.

He watched from the trees as the fat boy wrestled with a longbow as tall as he was, his red moon face screwed up with concentration. Three arrows stood in the ground before him. Tarly nocked and drew, held the draw a long moment as he tried to aim, and let fly. The shaft vanished into the greenery. Chett laughed loudly, a snort of sweet disgust.

"We'll never find that one, and I'll be blamed," announced Edd Tollett, the dour grey-haired squire everyone called Dolorous Edd. "Nothing ever goes missing that they don't look at me, ever since that time I lost my horse. As if that could be helped. He was white and it was snowing, what did they expect?"

"The wind took that one," said Grenn, another friend of Lord Snow's. "Try to hold the bow steady, Sam."

"It's heavy," the fat boy complained, but he pulled the second arrow all the same. This one went high, sailing through the branches ten feet above the target.

"I believe you knocked a leaf off that tree," said Dolorous Edd. "Fall is falling fast enough, there's no need to help it." He sighed. "And we all know what follows fall. Gods, but I am cold. Shoot the last arrow, Samwell, I believe my tongue is freezing to the roof of my mouth."

Ser Piggy lowered the bow, and Chett thought he was going to start bawling. "It's too hard."

"Notch, draw, and loose," said Grenn. "Go on."

Dutifully, the fat boy plucked his final arrow from the earth, notched it to his longbow, drew, and released. He did it quickly, without squinting along the shaft painstakingly as he had the first two times. The arrow struck the charcoal outline low in the chest and hung quivering. "I *hit* him." Ser Piggy sounded shocked. "Grenn, did you see? Edd, look, I hit him!"

"Put it between his ribs, I'd say," said Grenn.

"Did I kill him?" the fat boy wanted to know.

Tollett shrugged. "Might have punctured a lung, if he had a lung. Most trees don't, as a rule." He took the bow from Sam's hand. "I've seen worse shots, though. Aye, and made a few."

Ser Piggy was beaming. To look at him you'd think he'd actually *done* something. But when he saw Chett and the dogs, his smile curled up and died squeaking.

"You hit a tree," Chett said. "Let's see how you shoot when it's Mance Rayder's lads. They won't stand there with their arms out and their leaves rustling, oh no. They'll come right at you, screaming in your face, and I bet you'll piss those breeches. One o' them will plant his axe right between those little pig eyes. The last thing you'll hear will be the *thunk* it makes when it bites into your skull."

The fat boy was shaking. Dolorous Edd put a hand on his shoulder. "Brother," he said solemnly, "just because it happened that way for you doesn't mean Samwell will suffer the same."

"What are you talking about, Tollett?"

"The axe that split your skull. Is it true that half your wits leaked out on the ground and your dogs ate them?"

The big lout Grenn laughed, and even Samwell Tarly managed a weak little smile. Chett kicked the nearest dog, yanked on their leashes, and started up the hill. *Smile all you want, Ser Piggy. We'll see who laughs tonight.* He only wished he had time to kill Tollett as well. *Gloomy horsefaced fool, that's what he is.*

The climb was steep, even on this side of the Fist, which had the gentlest slope. Partway up the dogs started barking and pulling at him, figuring that they'd get fed soon. He gave them a taste of his boot instead, and a crack of the whip for the big ugly one that snapped at him. Once they were tied up, he went to report. "The prints were there like Giant said, but the dogs wouldn't track," he told Mormont in front of his big black tent. "Down by the river like that, could be old prints."

"A pity." Lord Commander Mormont had a bald head and a great shaggy grey beard, and sounded as tired as he looked. "We might all have been better for a bit of fresh meat." The raven on his shoulder bobbed its head and echoed, "*Meat. Meat. Meat.*"

We could cook the bloody dogs, Chett thought, but he kept his mouth shut until the Old Bear sent him on his way. *And that's the last time I'll need to bow my head to that one*, he thought to himself with satisfaction. It seemed to him that it was growing even colder, which he would have sworn wasn't possible. The dogs huddled together miserably in the hard frozen mud, and Chett was half tempted to crawl in with them. Instead he wrapped a black wool scarf round the lower part of his face, leaving a slit for his mouth between the winds. It was warmer if he kept moving, he found, so he made a slow circuit of the perimeter with a wad of sourleaf, sharing a chew or two with the black brothers on guard and hearing what they had to say. None of the men on the day watch were part of his scheme; even so, he figured it was good to have some sense of what they were thinking.

Mostly what they were thinking was that it was bloody cold.

The wind was rising as the shadows lengthened. It made a high thin sound as it shivered through the stones of the ringwall. "I hate that sound," little Giant said. "It sounds like a babe in the brush, wailing away for milk."

When he finished the circuit and returned to the dogs, he found Lark waiting for him. "The officers are in the Old Bear's tent again, talking something fierce."

"That's what they do," said Chett. "They're highborn, all but Blane, they get drunk on words instead of wine."

Lark sidled closer. "Cheese-for-wits keeps going on about the bird," he warned, glancing about to make certain no one was close. "Now he's asking if we cached any seed for the damn thing."

"It's a raven," said Chett. "It eats corpses."

Lark grinned. "His, might be?"

Or yours. It seemed to Chett that they needed the big man more than they needed Lark. "Stop fretting about Small Paul. You do your part, he'll do his."

Twilight was creeping through the woods by the time he rid himself of the Sisterman and sat down to edge his sword. It was bloody hard work with his gloves on, but he wasn't about to take them off. Cold as it was, any fool that touched steel with a bare hand was going to lose a patch of skin.

The dogs whimpered when the sun went down. He gave them water and curses. "Half a night more, and you can find your own feast." By then he could smell supper.

Dywen was holding forth at the cookfire as Chett got his heel of hardbread and a bowl of bean and bacon soup from Hake the cook. "The wood's too silent," the old forester was saying. "No frogs near that river, no owls in the dark. I never heard no deader wood than this."

"Them teeth of yours sound pretty dead," said Hake.

Dywen clacked his wooden teeth. "No wolves neither. There was, before, but no more. Where'd they go, you figure?"

"Someplace warm," said Chett.

Of the dozen odd brothers who sat by the fire, four were his. He gave each one a hard squinty look as he ate, to see if any showed signs of breaking. Dirk seemed calm enough, sitting silent and sharpening his blade, the way he did every night. And Sweet Donnel Hill was all easy japes. He had white teeth and fat red lips and yellow locks that he wore in an artful tumble about his shoulders, and he claimed to be the bastard of some Lannister. Maybe he was at that. Chett had no use for pretty boys, nor for bastards neither, but Sweet Donnel seemed like to hold his own.

He was less certain about the forester the brothers called Sawwood, more for his snoring than for anything to do with trees. Just now he looked so restless he might never snore again. And Maslyn was worse. Chett could see sweat trickling down his face, despite the frigid wind. The beads of moisture sparkled in the firelight, like so many little wet jewels. Maslyn wasn't eating neither, only staring at his soup as if the smell of it was about to make him sick. *I'll need to watch that one,* Chett thought.

"Assemble!" The shout came suddenly, from a dozen throats, and quickly spread to every part of the hilltop camp. "Men of the Night's Watch! Assemble at the central fire!"

Frowning, Chett finished his soup and followed the rest.

The Old Bear stood before the fire with Smallwood, Locke, Wythers, and Blane ranged behind him in a row. Mormont wore a cloak of thick black fur, and his raven perched upon his shoulder, preening its black feathers. *This can't be good.* Chett squeezed between Brown Bernarr and some Shadow Tower men. When everyone was gathered, save for the watchers in the woods and the guards on the ringwall, Mormont cleared his throat and spat. The spittle was frozen before it hit the ground. "Brothers," he said, "men of the Night's Watch."

"*Men!*" his raven screamed. "*Men! Men!*"

"The wildlings are on the march, following the course of the Milkwater down out of the mountains. Thoren believes their van will be upon us ten days hence. Their most seasoned raiders will be with Harma Dogshead in that van. The rest will likely form a rearguard, or ride in close company with Mance Rayder himself. Elsewhere their fighters will be spread thin along the line of march. They have oxen, mules, horses . . . but few enough. Most will be afoot, and ill-armed and untrained. Such weapons as they carry are more like to be stone and bone than steel. They are burdened with women, children, herds of sheep and goats, and all their worldly goods besides. In short, though they are numerous, they are vulnerable . . . and *they do not know that we are here.* Or so we must pray."

They know, thought Chett. *You bloody old pus bag, they know, certain as sunrise. Qhorin Halfhand hasn't come back, has he? Nor Jarman Buckwell. If any of them got caught, you know damned well the wildlings will have wrung a song or two out of them by now.*

Smallwood stepped forward. "Mance Rayder means to break the Wall and bring red war to the Seven Kingdoms. Well, that's a game two can play. On the morrow we'll bring the war to him."

"We ride at dawn with all our strength," the Old Bear said as a murmur went through the assembly. "We will ride north, and loop around to the west. Harma's van will

be well past the Fist by the time we turn. The foothills of
the Frostfangs are full of narrow winding valleys made for
ambush. Their line of march will stretch for many miles.
We shall fall on them in several places at once, and make
them swear we were three thousand, not three hundred."

"We'll hit hard and be away before their horsemen can
form up to face us," Thoren Smallwood said. "If they pursue, we'll lead them a merry chase, then wheel and hit
again farther down the column. We'll burn their wagons,
scatter their herds, and slay as many as we can. Mance
Rayder himself, if we find him. If they break and return to
their hovels, we've won. If not, we'll harry them all the
way to the Wall, and see to it that they leave a trail of
corpses to mark their progress."

"*There are thousands,*" someone called from behind
Chett.

"*We'll die.*" That was Maslyn's voice, green with fear.

"*Die,*" screamed Mormont's raven, flapping its black
wings. "*Die, die, die.*"

"Many of us," the Old Bear said. "Mayhaps even all of
us. But as another Lord Commander said a thousand years
ago, that is why they dress us in black. Remember your
words, brothers. For we are the swords in the darkness, the
watchers on the walls . . ."

"The fire that burns against the cold." Ser Mallador
Locke drew his longsword.

"The light that brings the dawn," others answered, and
more swords were pulled from scabbards.

Then all of them were drawing, and it was near three
hundred upraised swords and as many voices crying, "*The
horn that wakes the sleepers! The shield that guards the
realms of men!*" Chett had no choice but to join his voice
to the others. The air was misty with their breath, and firelight glinted off the steel. He was pleased to see Lark and
Softfoot and Sweet Donnel Hill joining in, as if they were
as big fools as the rest. That was good. No sense to draw attention, when their hour was so close.

When the shouting died away, once more he heard the
sound of the wind picking at the ringwall. The flames
swirled and shivered, as if they too were cold, and in the
sudden quiet the Old Bear's raven cawed loudly and once
again said, "*Die.*"

Clever bird, thought Chett as the officers dismissed them, warning everyone to get a good meal and a long rest tonight. Chett crawled under his furs near the dogs, his head full of things that could go wrong. What if that bloody oath gave one of his a change of heart? Or Small Paul forgot and tried to kill Mormont during the second watch in place of the third? Or Maslyn lost his courage, or someone turned informer, or . . .

He found himself listening to the night. The wind did sound like a wailing child, and from time to time he could hear men's voices, a horse's whinny, a log spitting in the fire. But nothing else. *So quiet.*

He could see Bessa's face floating before him. *It wasn't the knife I wanted to put in you*, he wanted to tell her. *I picked you flowers, wild roses and tansy and goldencups, it took me all morning.* His heart was thumping like a drum, so loud he feared it might wake the camp. Ice caked his beard all around his mouth. *Where did that come from, with Bessa?* Whenever he'd thought of her before, it had only been to remember the way she'd looked, dying. What was wrong with him? He could hardly breathe. Had he gone to sleep? He got to his knees, and something wet and cold touched his nose. Chett looked up.

Snow was falling.

He could feel tears freezing to his cheeks. *It isn't fair*, he wanted to scream. Snow would ruin everything he'd worked for, all his careful plans. It was a heavy fall, thick white flakes coming down all about him. How would they find their food caches in the snow, or the game trail they meant to follow east? *They won't need Dywen nor Bannen to hunt us down neither, not if we're tracking through fresh snow.* And snow hid the shape of the ground, especially by night. A horse could stumble over a root, break a leg on a stone. *We're done*, he realized. *Done before we began. We're lost.* There'd be no lord's life for the leechman's son, no keep to call his own, no wives nor crowns. Only a wildling's sword in his belly, and then an unmarked grave. *The snow's taken it all from me . . . the bloody snow . . .*

Snow had ruined him once before. Snow and his pet pig.

Chett got to his feet. His legs were stiff, and the falling snowflakes turned the distant torches to vague orange glows. He felt as though he were being attacked by a cloud of pale cold bugs. They settled on his shoulders, on his head, they flew at his nose and his eyes. Cursing, he brushed them off. *Samwell Tarly*, he remembered. *I can still deal with Ser Piggy.* He wrapped his scarf around his face, pulled up his hood, and went striding through the camp to where the coward slept.

The snow was falling so heavily that he got lost among the tents, but finally he spotted the snug little windbreak the fat boy had made for himself between a rock and the raven cages. Tarly was buried beneath a mound of black wool blankets and shaggy furs. The snow was drifting in to cover him. He looked like some kind of soft round mountain. Steel whispered on leather faint as hope as Chett eased his dagger from its sheath. One of the ravens *quorked.* "Snow," another muttered, peering through the bars with black eyes. The first added a "Snow" of its own. He edged past them, placing each foot carefully. He would clap his left hand down over the fat boy's mouth to muffle his cries, and then . . .

Uuuuuuuhooooooooooo.

He stopped midstep, swallowing his curse as the sound of the horn shuddered through the camp, faint and far, yet unmistakable. *Not now. Gods be damned, not NOW!* The Old Bear had hidden far-eyes in a ring of trees around the Fist, to give warning of any approach. *Jarman Buckwell's back from the Giant's Stair*, Chett figured, *or Qhorin Halfhand from the Skirling Pass.* A single blast of the horn meant brothers returning. If it was the Halfhand, Jon Snow might be with him, alive.

Sam Tarly sat up puffy-eyed and stared at the snow in confusion. The ravens were cawing noisily, and Chett could hear his dogs baying. *Half the bloody camp's awake.* His gloved fingers clenched around the dagger's hilt as he waited for the sound to die away. But no sooner had it gone than it came again, louder and longer.

Uuuuuuuuuuuuuhooooooooooooooooo.

"Gods," he heard Sam Tarly whimper. The fat boy lurched to his knees, his feet tangled in his cloak and blankets. He kicked them away and reached for a chainmail hauberk he'd hung on the rock nearby. As he slipped the huge tent of a garment down over his head and wriggled into it, he spied Chett standing there. "Was it two?" he asked. "I dreamed I heard two blasts . . ."

"No dream," said Chett. "Two blasts to call the Watch to arms. Two blasts for foes approaching. There's an axe out there with *Piggy* writ on it, fat boy. Two blasts means *wildlings*." The fear on that big moon face made him want to laugh. "Bugger them all to seven hells. Bloody Harma. Bloody Mance Rayder. Bloody Smallwood, he said they wouldn't be on us for another—"

Uuuuuuuuuuuuuuuuhoooooooooooooooooooooooooooo.

The sound went on and on and on, until it seemed it would never die. The ravens were flapping and screaming, flying about their cages and banging off the bars, and all about the camp the brothers of the Night's Watch were rising, donning their armor, buckling on swordbelts, reaching for battleaxes and bows. Samwell Tarly stood shaking, his face the same color as the snow that swirled down all around them. "Three," he squeaked to Chett, "that was three, I heard three. They never blow three. Not for hundreds and thousands of years. Three means—"

"—*Others*." Chett made a sound that was half a laugh and half a sob, and suddenly his smallclothes were wet, and he could feel the piss running down his leg, see steam rising off the front of his breeches.

JAIME

An east wind blew through his tangled hair, as soft and fragrant as Cersei's fingers. He could hear birds singing, and feel the river moving beneath the boat as the sweep of the oars sent them toward the pale pink dawn. After so long in darkness, the world was so sweet that Jaime Lannister felt dizzy. *I am alive, and drunk on sunlight.* A laugh burst from his lips, sudden as a quail flushed from cover.

"Quiet," the wench grumbled, scowling. Scowls suited her broad homely face better than a smile. Not that Jaime had ever seen her smiling. He amused himself by picturing her in one of Cersei's silken gowns in place of her studded leather jerkin. *As well dress a cow in silk as this one.*

But the cow could row. Beneath her roughspun brown breeches were calves like cords of wood, and the long muscles of her arms stretched and tightened with each stroke of the oars. Even after rowing half the night, she showed no signs of tiring, which was more than could be said for his cousin Ser Cleos, laboring on the other oar. *A big strong peasant wench to look at her, yet she speaks like one highborn and wears longsword and dagger. Ah, but can she use them!* Jaime meant to find out, as soon as he rid himself of these fetters.

He wore iron manacles on his wrists and a matching pair about his ankles, joined by a length of heavy chain no more than a foot long. "You'd think my word as a Lannister was not good enough," he'd japed as they bound him. He'd been very drunk by then, thanks to Catelyn Stark. Of their escape from Riverrun, he recalled only bits and pieces. There had been some trouble with the gaoler, but the big wench had overcome him. After that they had climbed an endless stair, around and around. His legs were weak as grass, and he'd stumbled twice or thrice, until the wench lent him an arm to lean on. At some point he was bundled into a traveler's cloak and shoved into the bottom of a skiff. He remembered listening to Lady Catelyn command someone to raise the portcullis on the Water Gate. She was sending Ser Cleos Frey back to King's Landing with new terms for the queen, she'd declared in a tone that brooked no argument.

He must have drifted off then. The wine had made him sleepy, and it felt good to stretch, a luxury his chains had not permitted him in the cell. Jaime had long ago learned to snatch sleep in the saddle during a march. This was no harder. *Tyrion is going to laugh himself sick when he hears how I slept through my own escape.* He was awake now, though, and the fetters were irksome. "My lady," he called out, "if you'll strike off these chains, I'll spell you at those oars."

She scowled again, her face all horse teeth and glowering suspicion. "You'll wear your chains, Kingslayer."

"You figure to row all the way to King's Landing, wench?"

"You will call me Brienne. Not *wench*."

"My name is Ser Jaime. Not Kingslayer."

"Do you deny that you slew a king?"

"No. Do you deny your sex? If so, unlace those breeches and show me." He gave her an innocent smile. "I'd ask you to open your bodice, but from the look of you that wouldn't prove much."

Ser Cleos fretted. "Cousin, remember your courtesies."

The Lannister blood runs thin in this one. Cleos was his Aunt Genna's son by that dullard Emmon Frey, who had lived in terror of Lord Tywin Lannister since the day he wed his sister. When Lord Walder Frey had brought the Twins into the war on the side of Riverrun, Ser Emmon had chosen his wife's allegiance over his father's. *Casterly Rock got the worst of that bargain*, Jaime reflected. Ser Cleos looked like a weasel, fought like a goose, and had the courage of an especially brave ewe. Lady Stark had promised him release if he delivered her message to Tyrion, and Ser Cleos had solemnly vowed to do so.

They'd all done a deal of vowing back in that cell, Jaime most of all. That was Lady Catelyn's price for loosing him. She had laid the point of the big wench's sword against his heart and said, "Swear that you will never again take up arms against Stark nor Tully. Swear that you will compel your brother to honor his pledge to return my daughters safe and unharmed. Swear on your honor as a knight, on your honor as a Lannister, on your honor as a Sworn Brother of the Kingsguard. Swear it by your sister's life, and your father's, and your son's, by the old gods and the new, and I'll send you back to your sister. Refuse, and I will have your blood." He remembered the prick of the steel through his rags as she twisted the point of the sword.

I wonder what the High Septon would have to say about the sanctity of oaths sworn while dead drunk, chained to a wall, with a sword pressed to your chest? Not that Jaime was truly concerned about that fat fraud, or the gods he claimed to serve. He remembered the pail Lady Catelyn had kicked over in his cell. A strange woman, to trust her girls to a man with shit for honor. Though she was trusting him as little as she dared. *She is putting her hope in Tyrion, not in me.* "Perhaps she is not so stupid after all," he said aloud.

His captor took it wrong. "I am not stupid. Nor deaf."

He was gentle with her; mocking this one would be so easy there would be no sport to it. "I was speaking to myself, and not of you. It's an easy habit to slip into in a cell."

She frowned at him, pushing the oars forward, pulling them back, pushing them forward, saying nothing.

As glib of tongue as she is fair of face. "By your speech, I'd judge you nobly born."

"My father is Selwyn of Tarth, by the grace of the gods Lord of Evenfall." Even that was given grudgingly.

"Tarth," Jaime said. "A ghastly large rock in the narrow sea, as I recall. And Evenfall is sworn to Storm's End. How is it that you serve Robb of Winterfell?"

"It is Lady Catelyn I serve. And she commanded me to deliver you safe to your brother Tyrion at King's Landing, not to bandy words with you. Be silent."

"I've had a bellyful of silence, woman."

"Talk with Ser Cleos then. I have no words for monsters."

Jaime hooted. "Are there monsters hereabouts? Hiding beneath the water, perhaps? In that thick of willows? And me without my sword!"

"A man who would violate his own sister, murder his king, and fling an innocent child to his death deserves no other name."

Innocent! The wretched boy was spying on us. All Jaime had wanted was an hour alone with Cersei. Their journey north had been one long torment; seeing her every day, unable to touch her, knowing that Robert stumbled drunkenly into her bed every night in that great creaking wheelhouse. Tyrion had done his best to keep him in a good humor, but it had not been enough. "You will be courteous as concerns Cersei, wench," he warned her.

"My name is Brienne, not *wench*."

"What do you care what a monster calls you?"

"My name is Brienne," she repeated, dogged as a hound.

"Lady Brienne?" She looked so uncomfortable that Jaime sensed a weakness. "Or would *Ser* Brienne be more to your taste?" He laughed. "No, I fear not. You can trick out a milk cow in crupper, crinet, and chamfron, and bard her all in silk, but that doesn't mean you can ride her into battle."

"Cousin Jaime, please, you ought not speak so roughly." Under his cloak, Ser Cleos wore a surcoat quartered with the twin towers of House Frey and the golden lion of Lannister. "We have far to go, we should not quarrel amongst ourselves."

"When I quarrel I do it with a sword, coz. I was speaking to the lady. Tell me, wench, are all the women on Tarth as homely as you? I pity the men, if so. Perhaps they do not know what real women look like, living on a dreary mountain in the sea."

"Tarth is beautiful," the wench grunted between strokes. "The Sapphire Isle, it's called. Be quiet, monster, unless you mean to make me gag you."

"She's rude as well, isn't she, coz?" Jaime asked Ser Cleos. "Though she has steel in her spine, I'll grant you. Not many men dare name me monster to my face." *Though behind my back they speak freely enough, I have no doubt.*

Ser Cleos coughed nervously. "Lady Brienne had those lies from Catelyn Stark, no doubt. The Starks cannot hope to defeat you with swords, ser, so now they make war with poisoned words."

They did defeat me with swords, you chinless cretin. Jaime smiled knowingly. Men will read all sorts of things into a knowing smile, if you let them. *Has cousin Cleos truly swallowed this kettle of dung, or is he striving to ingratiate himself? What do we have here, an honest muttonhead or a lickspittle?*

Ser Cleos prattled blithely on. "Any man who'd believe that a Sworn Brother of the Kingsguard would harm a child does not know the meaning of honor."

Lickspittle. If truth be told, Jaime had come to rue heaving Brandon Stark out that window. Cersei had given him no end of grief afterward, when the boy refused to die. "He was *seven*, Jaime," she'd berated him. "Even if he understood what he saw, we should have been able to frighten him into silence."

"I didn't think you'd want—"

"You *never* think. If the boy should wake and tell his father what he saw—"

"If if if." He had pulled her into his lap. "If he wakes we'll say he was dreaming, we'll call him a liar, and should worse come to worst I'll kill Ned Stark."

"And then what do you imagine *Robert* will do?"

"Let Robert do as he pleases. I'll go to war with him if I must. The War for Cersei's Cunt, the singers will call it."

"Jaime, let go of me!" she raged, struggling to rise.

Instead he had kissed her. For a moment she resisted, but then her mouth opened under his. He remembered the taste of wine and cloves on her tongue. She gave a shudder. His hand went to her bodice and yanked, tearing the silk so her breasts spilled free, and for a time the Stark boy had been forgotten.

Had Cersei remembered him afterward and hired this man Lady Catelyn spoke of, to make sure the boy never woke? *If she wanted him dead she would have sent me. And it is not like her to chose a catspaw who would make such a royal botch of the killing.*

Downriver, the rising sun shimmered against the wind-whipped surface of the river. The south shore was red clay, smooth as any road. Smaller streams fed into the greater, and the rotting trunks of drowned trees clung to the banks. The north shore was wilder. High rocky bluffs rose twenty feet above them, crowned by stands of beech, oak, and chestnut. Jaime spied a watchtower on the heights ahead, growing taller with every stroke of the oars. Long before they were upon it, he knew that it stood abandoned, its weathered stones overgrown with climbing roses.

When the wind shifted, Ser Cleos helped the big wench run up the sail, a stiff triangle of striped red-and-blue canvas. Tully colors, sure to cause them grief if they encountered any Lannister forces on the river, but it was the only sail they had. Brienne took the rudder. Jaime threw out the leeboard, his chains rattling as he moved. After that, they made better speed, with wind and current both favoring their flight. "We could save a deal of traveling if you delivered me to my father instead of my brother," he pointed out.

"Lady Catelyn's daughters are in King's Landing. I will return with the girls or not at all."

Jaime turned to Ser Cleos. "Cousin, lend me your knife."

"No." The woman tensed. "I will not have you armed." Her voice was as unyielding as stone.

She fears me, even in irons. "Cleos, it seems I must ask you to shave me. Leave the beard, but take the hair off my head."

"You'd be shaved bald?" asked Cleos Frey.

"The realm knows Jaime Lannister as a beardless knight with long golden hair. A bald man with a filthy yellow beard may pass unnoticed. I'd sooner not be recognized while I'm in irons."

The dagger was not as sharp as it might have been. Cleos hacked away manfully, sawing and ripping his way through the mats and tossing the hair over the side. The golden curls floated on the surface of the water, gradually falling astern. As the tangles vanished, a louse went crawling down his neck. Jaime caught it and crushed it against his thumbnail. Ser Cleos picked others from his scalp and flicked them into the water. Jaime doused his head and made Ser Cleos whet the blade before he let him scrape away the last inch of yellow stubble. When that was done, they trimmed back his beard as well.

The reflection in the water was a man he did not know. Not only was he bald, but he looked as though he had aged five years in that dungeon; his face was thinner, with hollows under his eyes and lines he did not remember. *I don't look as much like Cersei this way. She'll hate that.*

By midday, Ser Cleos had fallen asleep. His snores sounded like ducks mating. Jaime stretched out to watch the world flow past; after the dark cell, every rock and tree was a wonder.

A few one-room shacks came and went, perched on tall poles that made them look like cranes. Of the folk who lived there they saw no sign. Birds flew overhead, or cried out from the trees along the shore, and Jaime glimpsed silvery fish knifing through the water. *Tully trout, there's a bad omen*, he thought, until he saw a worse—one of the floating logs they passed turned out to be a dead man, bloodless and swollen. His cloak was tangled in the roots of a fallen tree, its color unmistakably Lannister crimson. He wondered if the corpse had been someone he knew.

The forks of the Trident were the easiest way to move goods or men across the riverlands. In times of peace, they would have encountered fisherfolk in their skiffs, grain barges being poled downstream, merchants selling needles and bolts of cloth from floating shops, perhaps even a gaily painted mummer's boat with quilted sails of half a hundred colors, making its way upriver from village to village and castle to castle.

But the war had taken its toll. They sailed past villages, but saw no villagers. An empty net, slashed and torn and hanging from some trees, was the only sign of fisherfolk. A young girl watering her horse rode off as soon as she glimpsed their sail. Later they passed a dozen peasants digging in a field beneath the shell of a burnt towerhouse. The men gazed at them with dull eyes, and went back to their labors once they decided the skiff was no threat.

The Red Fork was wide and slow, a meandering river of loops and bends dotted with tiny wooded islets and frequently choked by sandbars and snags that lurked just below the water's surface. Brienne seemed to have a keen eye for the dangers, though, and always seemed to find the channel. When Jaime complimented her on her knowledge of the river, she looked at him suspiciously and said, "I do not know the river. Tarth is an island. I learned to manage oars and sail before I ever sat a horse."

Ser Cleos sat up and rubbed at his eyes. "Gods, my arms are sore. I hope the wind lasts." He sniffed at it. "I smell rain."

Jaime would welcome a good rain. The dungeons of Riverrun were not the cleanest place in the Seven Kingdoms. By now he must smell like an overripe cheese.

Cleos squinted downriver. "Smoke."

A thin grey finger crooked them on. It was rising from the south bank several miles on, twisting and curling. Below, Jaime made out the smouldering remains of a large building, and a live oak full of dead women.

The crows had scarcely started on their corpses. The thin ropes cut deeply into the soft flesh of their throats, and when the wind blew they twisted and swayed. "This was not chivalrously done," said Brienne when they were close enough to see it clearly. "No true knight would condone such wanton butchery."

"True knights see worse every time they ride to war, wench," said Jaime. "And *do* worse, yes."

Brienne turned the rudder toward the shore. "I'll leave no innocents to be food for crows."

"A heartless wench. Crows need to eat as well. Stay to the river and leave the dead alone, woman."

They landed upstream of where the great oak leaned out over the water. As Brienne lowered the sail, Jaime climbed out, clumsy in his chains. The Red Fork filled his boots and soaked through the ragged breeches. Laughing, he dropped to his knees, plunged his head under the water, and came up drenched and dripping. His hands were caked with dirt, and when he rubbed them clean in the current they seemed thinner and paler than he remembered. His legs were stiff as well, and unsteady when he put his weight upon them. *I was too bloody long in Hoster Tully's dungeon.*

Brienne and Cleos dragged the skiff onto the bank. The corpses hung above their heads, ripening in death like foul fruit. "One of us will need to cut them down," the wench said.

"I'll climb." Jaime waded ashore, clanking. "Just get these chains off."

The wench was staring up at one of the dead women. Jaime shuffled closer with small stutter steps, the only kind the foot-long chain permitted. When he saw the crude sign hung about the neck of the highest corpse, he smiled. "*They Lay With Lions,*" he read. "Oh, yes, woman, this was most *unchivalrously* done . . . but by your side, not mine. I wonder who they were, these women?"

"Tavern wenches," said Ser Cleos Frey. "This was an inn, I remember it now. Some men of my escort spent the night here when we last returned to Riverrun." Nothing remained of the building but the stone foundation and a tangle of collapsed beams, charred black. Smoke still rose from the ashes.

Jaime left brothels and whores to his brother Tyrion; Cersei was the only woman he had ever wanted. "The girls pleasured some of my lord father's soldiers, it would seem. Perhaps served them food and drink. That's how they earned their traitors' collars, with a kiss and a cup of ale." He glanced up and down the river, to make certain they were quite alone. "This is Bracken land. Lord Jonos might have ordered them killed. My father burned his castle, I fear he loves us not."

"It might be Marq Piper's work," said Ser Cleos. "Or that wisp o' the wood Beric Dondarrion, though I'd heard he kills only soldiers. Perhaps a band of Roose Bolton's northmen?"

"Bolton was defeated by my father on the Green Fork."

"But not broken," said Ser Cleos. "He came south again when Lord Tywin marched against the fords. The word at Riverrun was that he'd taken Harrenhal from Ser Amory Lorch."

Jaime liked the sound of that not at all. "Brienne," he said, granting her the courtesy of the name in the hopes that she might listen, "if Lord Bolton holds Harrenhal, both the Trident and the kingsroad are likely watched."

He thought he saw a touch of uncertainty in her big

blue eyes. "You are under my protection. They'd need to kill me."

"I shouldn't think that would trouble them."

"I am as good a fighter as you," she said defensively. "I was one of King Renly's chosen seven. With his own hands, he cloaked me with the striped silk of the Rainbow Guard."

"The *Rainbow* Guard? You and six other girls, was it? A singer once said that all maids are fair in silk . . . but he never met you, did he?"

The woman turned red. "We have graves to dig." She went to climb the tree.

The lower limbs of the oak were big enough for her to stand upon once she'd gotten up the trunk. She walked amongst the leaves, dagger in hand, cutting down the corpses. Flies swarmed around the bodies as they fell, and the stench grew worse with each one she dropped. "This is a deal of trouble to take for whores," Ser Cleos complained. "What are we supposed to dig with? We have no spades, and I will not use my sword, I—"

Brienne gave a shout. She jumped down rather than climbing. "To the boat. Be quick. There's a sail."

They made what haste they could, though Jaime could hardly run, and had to be pulled back up into the skiff by his cousin. Brienne shoved off with an oar and raised sail hurriedly. "Ser Cleos, I'll need you to row as well."

He did as she bid. The skiff began to cut the water a bit faster; current, wind, and oars all worked for them. Jaime sat chained, peering upriver. Only the top of the other sail was visible. With the way the Red Fork looped, it looked to be across the fields, moving north behind a screen of trees while they moved south, but he knew that was deceptive. He lifted both hands to shade his eyes. "Mud red and watery blue," he announced.

Brienne's big mouth worked soundlessly, giving her the look of a cow chewing its cud. "Faster, ser."

The inn soon vanished behind them, and they lost sight of the top of the sail as well, but that meant nothing. Once the pursuers swung around the loop they would become visible again. "We can hope the noble Tullys will stop to bury the dead whores, I suppose." The prospect of returning to his cell did not appeal to Jaime. *Tyrion could think of something clever now, but all that occurs to me is to go at them with a sword.*

For the good part of an hour they played peek-and-seek with the pursuers, sweeping around bends and between small wooded isles. Just when they were starting to hope that somehow they might have left behind the pursuit, the distant sail became visible again. Ser Cleos paused in his stroke. "The Others take them." He wiped sweat from his brow.

"*Row!*" Brienne said.

"That is a river galley coming after us," Jaime announced after he'd watched for a while. With every stroke, it seemed to grow a little larger. "Nine oars on each side, which means eighteen men. More, if they crowded on fighters as well as rowers. And larger sails than ours. We cannot outrun her."

Ser Cleos froze at his oars. "Eighteen, you said?"

"Six for each of us. I'd want eight, but these bracelets hinder me somewhat." Jaime held up his wrists. "Unless the Lady Brienne would be so kind as to unshackle me?"

She ignored him, putting all her effort into her stroke.

"We had half a night's start on them," Jaime said. "They've been rowing since dawn, resting two oars at a time. They'll be exhausted. Just now the sight of our sail has given them a burst of strength, but that will not last. We ought to be able to kill a good many of them."

Ser Cleos gaped. "But . . . there are *eighteen*."

"At the least. More likely twenty or twenty-five."

His cousin groaned. "We can't hope to defeat eighteen."

"Did I say we could? The best we can hope for is to die with swords in our hands." He was perfectly sincere. Jaime Lannister had never been afraid of death.

Brienne broke off rowing. Sweat had stuck strands of her flax-colored hair to her forehead, and her grimace made her look homelier than ever. "You are under my protection," she said, her voice so thick with anger that it was almost a growl.

He had to laugh at such fierceness. *She's the Hound with teats,* he thought. *Or would be, if she had any teats to speak of.* "Then protect me, wench. Or free me to protect myself."

The galley was skimming downriver, a great wooden

dragonfly. The water around her was churned white by the furious action of her oars. She was gaining visibly, the men on her deck crowding forward as she came on. Metal glinted in their hands, and Jaime could see bows as well. *Archers.* He hated archers.

At the prow of the onrushing galley stood a stocky man with a bald head, bushy grey eyebrows, and brawny arms. Over his mail he wore a soiled white surcoat with a weeping willow embroidered in pale green, but his cloak was fastened with a silver trout. *Riverrun's captain of guards.* In his day Ser Robin Ryger had been a notably tenacious fighter, but his day was done; he was of an age with Hoster Tully, and had grown old with his lord.

When the boats were fifty yards apart, Jaime cupped his hands around his mouth and shouted back over the water. *"Come to wish me godspeed, Ser Robin?"*

"Come to take you back, Kingslayer," Ser Robin Ryger bellowed. *"How is it that you've lost your golden hair?"*

"I hope to blind my enemies with the sheen off my head. It's worked well enough for you."

Ser Robin was unamused. The distance between skiff and galley had shrunk to forty yards. *"Throw your oars and your weapons into the river, and no one need be harmed."*

Ser Cleos twisted around. "Jaime, tell him we were freed by Lady Catelyn . . . an exchange of captives, lawful . . ."

Jaime told him, for all the good it did. *"Catelyn Stark does not rule in Riverrun,"* Ser Robin shouted back. Four archers crowded into position on either side of him, two standing and two kneeling. *"Cast your swords into the water."*

"I have no sword," he returned, *"but if I did, I'd stick it through your belly and hack the balls off those four cravens."*

A flight of arrows answered him. One thudded into the mast, two pierced the sail, and the fourth missed Jaime by a foot.

Another of the Red Fork's broad loops loomed before them. Brienne angled the skiff across the bend. The yard swung as they turned, their sail cracking as it filled with wind. Ahead a large island sat in midstream. The main channel flowed right. To the left a cutoff ran between the

island and the high bluffs of the north shore. Brienne
moved the tiller and the skiff sheared left, sail rippling.
Jaime watched her eyes. *Pretty eyes*, he thought, *and calm*.
He knew how to read a man's eyes. He knew what fear
looked like. *She is determined, not desperate*.

Thirty yards behind, the galley was entering the bend.
"Ser Cleos, take the tiller," the wench commanded.
"Kingslayer, take an oar and keep us off the rocks."

"As my lady commands." An oar was not a sword, but
the blade could break a man's face if well swung, and the
shaft could be used to parry.

Ser Cleos shoved the oar into Jaime's hand and scrambled aft. They crossed the head of the island and turned
sharply down the cutoff, sending a wash of water against
the face of the bluff as the boat tilted. The island was
densely wooded, a tangle of willows, oaks, and tall pines
that cast deep shadows across the rushing water, hiding
snags and the rotted trunks of drowned trees. To their left
the bluff rose sheer and rocky, and at its foot the river
foamed whitely around broken boulders and tumbles of
rock fallen from the cliff face.

They passed from sunlight into shadow, hidden from
the galley's view between the green wall of the trees
and the stony grey-brown bluff. *A few moments' respite
from the arrows*, Jaime thought, pushing them off a half-
submerged boulder.

The skiff rocked. He heard a soft splash, and when he
glanced around, Brienne was gone. A moment later he
spied her again, pulling herself from the water at the base
of the bluff. She waded through a shallow pool, scrambled
over some rocks, and began to climb. Ser Cleos goggled,
mouth open. *Fool*, thought Jaime. "Ignore the wench," he
snapped at his cousin. "Steer."

They could see the sail moving behind the trees. The
river galley came into full view at the top of the cutoff,
twenty-five yards behind. Her bow swung hard as she came
around, and a half-dozen arrows took flight, but all went
well wide. The motion of the two boats was giving the
archers difficulty, but Jaime knew they'd soon enough
learn to compensate. Brienne was halfway up the cliff face,
pulling herself from handhold to handhold. *Ryger's sure to
see her, and once he does he'll have those bowmen bring*

her down. Jaime decided to see if the old man's pride would make him stupid. *"Ser Robin,"* he shouted, *"hear me for a moment."*

Ser Robin raised a hand, and his archers lowered their bows. *"Say what you will, Kingslayer, but say it quickly."*

The skiff swung through a litter of broken stones as Jaime called out, *"I know a better way to settle this—single combat. You and I."*

"I was not born this morning, Lannister."

"No, but you're like to die this afternoon." Jaime raised his hands so the other could see the manacles. *"I'll fight you in chains. What could you fear?"*

"Not you, ser. If the choice were mine, I'd like nothing better, but I am commanded to bring you back alive if possible. Bowmen." He signaled them on. *"Notch. Draw. Loo—"*

The range was less than twenty yards. The archers could scarcely have missed, but as they pulled on their longbows a rain of pebbles cascaded down around them. Small stones rattled on their deck, bounced off their helms, and made splashes on both sides of the bow. Those who had wits enough to understand raised their eyes just as a boulder the size of a cow detached itself from the top of the bluff. Ser Robin shouted in dismay. The stone tumbled through the air, struck the face of the cliff, cracked in two, and smashed down on them. The larger piece snapped the mast, tore through the sail, sent two of the archers flying into the river, and crushed the leg of a rower as he bent over his oar. The rapidity with which the galley began to fill with water suggested that the smaller fragment had punched right through her hull. The oarsman's screams echoed off the bluff while the archers flailed wildly in the current. From the way they were splashing, neither man could swim. Jaime laughed.

By the time they emerged from the cutoff, the galley was foundering amongst pools, eddies, and snags, and Jaime Lannister had decided that the gods were good. Ser Robin and his thrice-damned archers would have a long wet walk back to Riverrun, and he was rid of the big homely wench as well. *I could not have planned it better myself. Once I'm free of these irons . . .*

Ser Cleos raised a shout. When Jaime looked up, Brienne was lumbering along the clifftop well ahead of them, having cut across a finger of land while they were following the bend in the river. She threw herself off the rock, and looked almost graceful as she folded into a dive. It would have been ungracious to hope that she would smash her head on a stone. Ser Cleos turned the skiff toward her. Thankfully, Jaime still had his oar. *One good swing when she comes paddling up and I'll be free of her.*

Instead he found himself stretching the oar out over the water. Brienne grabbed hold, and Jaime pulled her in. As he helped her into the skiff, water ran from her hair and dripped from her sodden clothing to pool on the deck. *She's even uglier wet. Who would have thought it possible?* "You're a bloody stupid wench," he told her. "We could have sailed on without you. I suppose you expect me to thank you?"

"I want none of your thanks, Kingslayer. I swore an oath to bring you safe to King's Landing."

"And you actually mean to keep it?" Jaime gave her his brightest smile. "Now there's a wonder."

CATELYN

Ser Desmond Grell had served House Tully all his life. He had been a squire when Catelyn was born, a knight when she learned to walk and ride and swim, master-at-arms by the day that she was wed. He had seen Lord Hoster's little Cat become a young woman, a great lord's lady, mother to a king. *And now he has seen me become a traitor as well.*

Her brother Edmure had named Ser Desmond castellan of Riverrun when he rode off to battle, so it fell to him to deal with her crime. To ease his discomfort he brought her father's steward with him, dour Utherydes Wayn. The two men stood and looked at her; Ser Desmond stout, red-faced, embarrassed, Utherydes grave, gaunt, melancholy. Each waited for the other to speak. *They have given their lives to my father's service, and I have repaid them with disgrace,* Catelyn thought wearily.

"Your sons," Ser Desmond said at last. "Maester Vyman told us. The poor lads. Terrible. Terrible. But . . ."

"We share your grief, my lady," said Utherydes Wayn. "All Riverrun mourns with you, but . . ."

"The news must have driven you mad," Ser Desmond broke in, "a madness of grief, a *mother's* madness, men will understand. You did not know . . ."

"I did," Catelyn said firmly. "I understood what I was doing and knew it was treasonous. If you fail to punish me, men will believe that we connived together to free Jaime Lannister. It was mine own act and mine alone, and I alone must answer for it. Put me in the Kingslayer's empty irons, and I will wear them proudly, if that is how it must be."

"Fetters?" The very word seemed to shock poor Ser Desmond. "For the king's mother, my lord's own daughter? Impossible."

"Mayhaps," said the steward Utherydes Wayn, "my lady would consent to be confined to her chambers until Ser Edmure returns. A time alone, to pray for her murdered sons?"

"Confined, aye," Ser Desmond said. "Confined to a tower cell, that would serve."

"If I am to be confined, let it be in my father's chambers, so I might comfort him in his last days."

Ser Desmond considered a moment. "Very well. You shall lack no comfort nor courtesy, but freedom of the castle is denied you. Visit the sept as you need, but elsewise remain in Lord Hoster's chambers until Lord Edmure returns."

"As you wish." Her brother was no lord while their father lived, but Catelyn did not correct him. "Set a guard on me if you must, but I give you my pledge that I shall attempt no escape."

Ser Desmond nodded, plainly glad to be done with his distasteful task, but sad-eyed Utherydes Wayn lingered a moment after the castellan took his leave. "It was a grave thing you did, my lady, but for naught. Ser Desmond has sent Ser Robin Ryger after them, to bring back the Kingslayer . . . or failing that, his head."

Catelyn had expected no less. *May the Warrior give strength to your sword arm, Brienne,* she prayed. She had done all she could; nothing remained but to hope.

Her things were moved into her father's bedchamber, dominated by the great canopied bed she had been born in, its pillars carved in the shapes of leaping trout. Her father himself had been moved half a turn down the stair, his sickbed placed to face the triangular balcony that opened off his solar, from whence he could see the rivers that he had always loved so well.

Lord Hoster was sleeping when Catelyn entered. She went out to the balcony and stood with one hand on the rough stone balustrade. Beyond the point of the castle the swift Tumblestone joined the placid Red Fork, and she could see a long way downriver. *If a striped sail comes from the east, it will be Ser Robin returning.* For the moment the surface of the waters was empty. She thanked the gods for that, and went back inside to sit with her father.

Catelyn could not say if Lord Hoster knew that she was there, or if her presence brought him any comfort, but it gave her solace to be with him. *What would you say if you knew my crime, Father?* she wondered. *Would you have done as I did, if it were Lysa and me in the hands of our enemies? Or would you condemn me too, and call it mother's madness?*

There was a smell of death about that room; a heavy smell, sweet and foul, clinging. It reminded her of the sons that she had lost, her sweet Bran and her little Rickon, slain at the hand of Theon Greyjoy, who had been Ned's ward. She still grieved for Ned, she would always grieve for Ned, but to have her babies taken as well . . . "It is a monstrous cruel thing to lose a child," she whispered softly, more to herself than to her father.

Lord Hoster's eyes opened. "*Tansy,*" he husked in a voice thick with pain.

He does not know me. Catelyn had grown accustomed to him taking her for her mother or her sister Lysa, but Tansy was a name strange to her. "It's Catelyn," she said. "It's Cat, Father."

"Forgive me . . . the blood . . . oh, please . . . Tansy . . ."

Could there have been another woman in her father's life? Some village maiden he had wronged when he was young, perhaps? *Could he have found comfort in some serving wench's arms after Mother died?* It was a queer thought, unsettling. Suddenly she felt as though she had not known her father at all. "Who is Tansy, my lord? Do you want me to send for her, Father? Where would I find the woman? Does she still live?"

Lord Hoster groaned. "*Dead.*" His hand groped for hers. "You'll have others . . . sweet babes, and trueborn."

Others? Catelyn thought. *Has he forgotten that Ned is gone? Is he still talking to Tansy, or is it me now, or Lysa, or Mother?*

When he coughed, the sputum came up bloody. He clutched her fingers. ". . . be a good wife and the gods will bless you . . . sons . . . trueborn sons . . . *aaahhh.*" The sudden spasm of pain made Lord Hoster's hand tighten. His nails dug into her hand, and he gave a muffled scream.

Maester Vyman came quickly, to mix another dose of milk of the poppy and help his lord swallow it down. Soon enough, Lord Hoster Tully had fallen back into a heavy sleep.

"He was asking after a woman," said Cat. "Tansy."

"Tansy?" The maester looked at her blankly.

"You know no one by that name? A serving girl, a woman from some nearby village? Perhaps someone from years past?" Catelyn had been gone from Riverrun for a very long time.

"No, my lady. I can make inquiries, if you like. Utherydes Wayn would surely know if any such person ever served at Riverrun. Tansy, did you say? The smallfolk often name their daughters after flowers and herbs." The maester looked thoughtful. "There was a widow, I recall, she used to come to the castle looking for old shoes in need of new soles. Her name was Tansy, now that I think on it. Or was it Pansy? Some such. But she has not come for many years . . ."

"Her name was Violet," said Catelyn, who remembered the old woman very well.

"Was it?" The maester looked apologetic. "My pardons, Lady Catelyn, but I may not stay. Ser Desmond has decreed that we are to speak to you only so far as our duties require."

"Then you must do as he commands." Catelyn could not blame Ser Desmond; she had given him small reason to trust her, and no doubt he feared that she might use the loyalty that many of the folk of Riverrun would still feel toward their lord's daughter to work some further mischief. *I am free of the war, at least,* she told herself, *if only for a little while.*

After the maester had gone, she donned a woolen cloak and stepped out onto the balcony once more. Sunlight shimmered on the rivers, gilding the surface of the waters as they rolled past the castle. Catelyn shaded her eyes against the glare, searching for a distant sail, dreading the sight of one. But there was nothing, and nothing meant that her hopes were still alive.

All that day she watched, and well into the night, until her legs ached from the standing. A raven came to the castle in late afternoon, flapping down on great black wings to the rookery. *Dark wings, dark words*, she thought, remembering the last bird that had come and the horror it had brought.

Maester Vyman returned at evenfall to minister to Lord Tully and bring Catelyn a modest supper of bread, cheese, and boiled beef with horseradish. "I spoke to Utherydes Wayn, my lady. He is quite certain that no woman by the name of Tansy has ever been at Riverrun during his service."

"There was a raven today, I saw. Has Jaime been taken again?" *Or slain, gods forbid?*

"No, my lady, we've had no word of the Kingslayer."

"Is it another battle, then? Is Edmure in difficulty? Or Robb? Please, be kind, put my fears at rest."

"My lady, I should not . . ." Vyman glanced about, as if to make certain no one else was in the room. "Lord Tywin has left the riverlands. All's quiet on the fords."

"Whence came the raven, then?"

"From the west," he answered, busying himself with Lord Hoster's bedclothes and avoiding her eyes.

"Was it news of Robb?"

He hesitated. "Yes, my lady."

"Something is wrong." She knew it from his manner. He was hiding something from her. "Tell me. Is it Robb? Is he hurt?" *Not dead, gods be good, please do not tell me that he is dead.*

"His Grace took a wound storming the Crag," Maester Vyman said, still evasive, "but writes that it is no cause for concern, and that he hopes to return soon."

"A wound? What sort of wound? How serious?"

"No cause for concern, he writes."

"All wounds concern me. Is he being cared for?"

"I am certain of it. The maester at the Crag will tend to him, I have no doubt."

"Where was he wounded?"

"My lady, I am commanded not to speak with you. I am sorry." Gathering up his potions, Vyman made a hurried exit, and once again Catelyn was left alone with her father. The milk of the poppy had done its work, and Lord Hoster was sunk in heavy sleep. A thin line of spittle ran down from one corner of his open mouth to dampen his pillow. Catelyn took a square of linen and wiped it away gently. When she touched him, Lord Hoster moaned. "Forgive me," he said, so softly she could scarcely hear the words. "Tansy . . . blood . . . the blood . . . gods be kind . . ."

His words disturbed her more than she could say, though she could make no sense of them. *Blood*, she thought. *Must it all come back to blood? Father, who was this woman, and what did you do to her that needs so much forgiveness?*

That night Catelyn slept fitfully, haunted by formless dreams of her children, the lost and the dead. Well before the break of day, she woke with her father's words echoing in her ears. *Sweet babes, and trueborn . . . why would he say that, unless . . . could he have fathered a bastard on this woman Tansy?* She could not believe it. Her brother Edmure, yes; it would not have surprised her to learn that Edmure had a dozen natural children. But not her father, not Lord Hoster Tully, never.

Could Tansy be some pet name he called Lysa, the way he called me Cat? Lord Hoster had mistaken her for her sister before. *You'll have others*, he said. *Sweet babes, and trueborn.* Lysa had miscarried five times, twice in the Eyrie, thrice at King's Landing . . . but never at Riverrun, where Lord Hoster would have been at hand to comfort her. *Never, unless . . . unless she was with child, that first time . . .*

She and her sister had been married on the same day, and left in their father's care when their new husbands had ridden off to rejoin Robert's rebellion. Afterward, when their moon blood did not come at the accustomed time, Lysa had gushed happily of the sons she was certain they carried. "Your son will be heir to Winterfell and mine to the Eyrie. Oh, they'll be the best of friends, like your Ned and Lord Robert. They'll be more brothers than cousins, truly, I just know it." *She was so happy.*

But Lysa's blood had come not long after, and all the joy had gone out of her. Catelyn had always thought that Lysa had simply been a little late, but if she *had* been with child . . .

She remembered the first time she gave her sister Robb to hold; small, red-faced, and squalling, but strong even then, full of life. No sooner had Catelyn placed the babe in her sister's arms than Lysa's face dissolved into tears. Hurriedly she had thrust the baby back at Catelyn and fled.

If she had lost a child before, that might explain Father's words, and much else besides . . . Lysa's match with Lord Arryn had been hastily arranged, and Jon was an old man even then, older than their father. *An old man without an heir.* His first two wives had left him childless, his brother's son had been murdered with Brandon Stark in King's Landing, his gallant cousin had died in the Battle of the Bells. He needed a young wife if House Arryn was to continue . . . *a young wife known to be fertile.*

Catelyn rose, threw on a robe, and descended the steps to the darkened solar to stand over her father. A sense of helpless dread filled her. "Father," she said, "Father, I know what you did." She was no longer an innocent bride with a head full of dreams. She was a widow, a traitor, a grieving mother, and wise, wise in the ways of the world. "You made him take her," she whispered. "Lysa was the price Jon Arryn had to pay for the swords and spears of House Tully."

Small wonder her sister's marriage had been so loveless. The Arryns were proud, and prickly of their honor. Lord Jon might wed Lysa to bind the Tullys to the cause of the rebellion, and in hopes of a son, but it would have been hard for him to love a woman who came to his bed soiled and unwilling. He would have been kind, no doubt; dutiful, yes; but Lysa needed warmth.

The next day, as she broke her fast, Catelyn asked for quill and paper and began a letter to her sister in the Vale of Arryn. She told Lysa of Bran and Rickon, struggling with the words, but mostly she wrote of their father. *His thoughts are all of the wrong he did you, now that his time grows short. Maester Vyman says he dare not make the milk of the poppy any stronger. It is time for Father to lay down his sword and shield. It is time for him to rest. Yet he fights on grimly, will not yield. It is for your sake, I think. He needs your forgiveness. The war has made the road from the Eyrie to Riverrun dangerous to travel, I know, but surely a strong force of knights could see you safely through the Mountains of the Moon? A hundred men, or a thousand? And if you cannot come, will you not write him at least? A few words of love, so he might die in peace? Write what you will, and I shall read it to him, and ease his way.*

Even as she set the quill aside and asked for sealing wax, Catelyn sensed that the letter was like to be too little and too late. Maester Vyman did not believe Lord Hoster would linger long enough for a raven to reach the Eyrie and return. *Though he has said much the same before . . .* Tully men did not surrender easily, no matter the odds. After she entrusted the parchment to the maester's care, Catelyn went to the sept and lit a candle to the Father Above for her own father's sake, a second to the Crone, who had let the first raven into the world when she peered through the door of death, and a third to the Mother, for Lysa and all the children they had both lost.

Later that day, as she sat at Lord Hoster's bedside with a book, reading the same passage over and over, she heard the sound of loud voices and a trumpet's blare. *Ser Robin,* she thought at once, flinching. She went to the balcony, but there was nothing to be seen out on the rivers, but she could hear the voices more clearly from outside, the sound of many horses, the clink of armor, and here and there a cheer. Catelyn made her way up the winding stairs to the roof of the keep. *Ser Desmond did not forbid me the roof,* she told herself as she climbed.

The sounds were coming from the far side of the castle, by the main gate. A knot of men stood before the portcullis as it rose in jerks and starts, and in the fields beyond, outside the castle, were several hundred riders. When the wind blew, it lifted their banners, and she trembled in relief at the sight of the leaping trout of Riverrun. *Edmure.*

It was two hours before he saw fit to come to her. By then the castle rang to the sound of noisy reunions as men embraced the women and children they had left behind.

Three ravens had risen from the rookery, black wings beating at the air as they took flight. Catelyn watched them from her father's balcony. She had washed her hair, changed her clothing, and prepared herself for her brother's reproaches . . . but even so, the waiting was hard.

When at last she heard sounds outside her door, she sat and folded her hands in her lap. Dried red mud spattered Edmure's boots, greaves, and surcoat. To look at him, you would never know he had won his battle. He was thin and drawn, with pale cheeks, unkempt beard, and too-bright eyes.

"Edmure," Catelyn said, worried, "you look unwell. Has something happened? Have the Lannisters crossed the river?"

"I threw them back. Lord Tywin, Gregor Clegane, Addam Marbrand, I turned them away. Stannis, though . . ." He grimaced.

"Stannis? What of Stannis?"

"He lost the battle at King's Landing," Edmure said unhappily. "His fleet was burned, his army routed."

A Lannister victory was ill tidings, but Catelyn could not share her brother's obvious dismay. She still had nightmares about the shadow she had seen slide across Renly's tent and the way the blood had come flowing out through the steel of his gorget. "Stannis was no more a friend than Lord Tywin."

"You do not understand. Highgarden has declared for Joffrey. Dorne as well. All the south." His mouth tightened. "And *you* see fit to loose the Kingslayer. You had no right."

"I had a mother's right." Her voice was calm, though the news about Highgarden was a savage blow to Robb's hopes. She could not think about that now, though.

"No right," Edmure repeated. "He was Robb's captive, your *king's* captive, and Robb charged me to keep him safe."

"Brienne will keep him safe. She swore it on her sword."

"That *woman*?"

"She will deliver Jaime to King's Landing, and bring Arya and Sansa back to us safely."

"Cersei will never give them up."

"Not Cersei. Tyrion. He swore it, in open court. And the Kingslayer swore it as well."

"Jaime's word is worthless. As for the Imp, it's said he took an axe in the head during the battle. He'll be dead before your Brienne reaches King's Landing, if she ever does."

"Dead?" *Could the gods truly be so merciless!* She had made Jaime swear a hundred oaths, but it was his brother's promise she had pinned her hopes on.

Edmure was blind to her distress. "Jaime was *my* charge, and I mean to have him back. I've sent ravens—"

"Ravens to whom? How many?"

"Three," he said, "so the message will be certain to reach Lord Bolton. By river or road, the way from Riverrun to King's Landing must needs take them close by Harrenhal."

"Harrenhal." The very word seemed to darken the room. Horror thickened her voice as she said, "Edmure, do you know what you have done?"

"Have no fear, I left your part out. I wrote that Jaime had escaped, and offered a thousand dragons for his recapture."

Worse and worse, Catelyn thought in despair. *My brother is a fool.* Unbidden, unwanted, tears filled her eyes. "If this was an escape," she said softly, "and not an exchange of hostages, why should the Lannisters give my daughters to Brienne?"

"It will never come to that. The Kingslayer will be returned to us, I have made certain of it."

"All you have made certain is that I shall never see my daughters again. Brienne might have gotten him to King's Landing safely . . . *so long as no one was hunting for them.* But now . . ." Catelyn could not go on. "Leave me, Edmure." She had no right to command him, here in the castle that would soon be his, yet her tone would brook no argument. "Leave me to Father and my grief, I have no more to say to you. Go. *Go.*" All she wanted was to lie down, to close her eyes and sleep, and pray no dreams would come.

ARYA

The sky was as black as the walls of Harrenhal behind them, and the rain fell soft and steady, muffling the sound of their horses' hooves and running down their faces.

They rode north, away from the lake, following a rutted farm road across the torn fields and into the woods and streams. Arya took the lead, kicking her stolen horse to a brisk heedless trot until the trees closed in around her. Hot Pie and Gendry followed as best they could. Wolves howled off in the distance, and she could hear Hot Pie's heavy breathing. No one spoke. From time to time Arya glanced over her shoulder, to make sure the two boys had not fallen too far behind, and to see if they were being pursued.

They would be, she knew. She had stolen three horses from the stables and a map and a dagger from Roose Bolton's own solar, and killed a guard on the postern gate, slitting his throat when he knelt to pick up the worn iron coin that Jaqen H'ghar had given her. Someone would find him lying dead in his own blood, and then the hue and cry would go up. They would wake Lord Bolton and search Harrenhal from crenel to cellar, and when they did they would find the map and the dagger missing, along with some swords from the armory, bread and cheese from the kitchens, a baker boy, a 'prentice smith, and a cupbearer called Nan . . . or Weasel, or Arry, depending on who you asked.

The Lord of the Dreadfort would not come after them himself. Roose Bolton would stay abed, his pasty flesh dotted with leeches, giving commands in his whispery soft voice. His man Walton might lead the hunt, the one they called Steelshanks for the greaves he always wore on his long legs. Or perhaps it would be slobbery Vargo Hoat and his sellswords, who named themselves the Brave Companions. Others called them Bloody Mummers (though never to their faces), and sometimes the Footmen, for Lord Vargo's habit of cutting off the hands and feet of men who displeased him.

If they catch us, he'll cut off our hands and feet, Arya thought, *and then Roose Bolton will peel the skin off us.* She was still dressed in her page's garb, and on the breast over her heart was sewn Lord Bolton's sigil, the flayed man of the Dreadfort.

Every time she looked back, she half expected to see a blaze of torches pouring out the distant gates of Harrenhal or rushing along the tops of its huge high walls, but there was nothing. Harrenhal slept on, until it was lost in darkness and hidden behind the trees.

When they crossed the first stream, Arya turned her horse aside and led them off the road, following the twisting course of the water for a quarter-mile before finally scrambling out and up a stony bank. If the hunters brought dogs, that might throw them off the scent, she hoped. They could not stay on the road. *There is death on the road*, she told herself, *death on all the roads.*

Gendry and Hot Pie did not question her choice. She had the map, after all, and Hot Pie seemed almost as terrified of her as of the men who might be coming after them. He had seen the guard she'd killed. *It's better if he's scared of me*, she told herself. *That way he'll do like I say, instead of something stupid.*

She should be more frightened herself, she knew. She

was only ten, a skinny girl on a stolen horse with a dark forest ahead of her and men behind who would gladly cut off her feet. Yet somehow she felt calmer than she ever had in Harrenhal. The rain had washed the guard's blood off her fingers, she wore a sword across her back, wolves were prowling through the dark like lean grey shadows, and Arya Stark was unafraid. *Fear cuts deeper than swords,* she whispered under her breath, the words that Syrio Forel had taught her, and Jaqen's words too, *valar morghulis.*

The rain stopped and started again and stopped once more and started, but they had good cloaks to keep the water off. Arya kept them moving at a slow steady pace. It was too black beneath the trees to ride any faster; the boys were no horsemen, neither one, and the soft broken ground was treacherous with half-buried roots and hidden stones. They crossed another road, its deep ruts filled with runoff, but Arya shunned it. Up and down the rolling hills she took them, through brambles and briars and tangles of underbrush, along the bottoms of narrow gullies where branches heavy with wet leaves slapped at their faces as they passed.

Gendry's mare lost her footing in the mud once, going down hard on her hindquarters and spilling him from the saddle, but neither horse nor rider was hurt, and Gendry got that stubborn look on his face and mounted right up again. Not long after, they came upon three wolves devouring the corpse of a fawn. When Hot Pie's horse caught the scent, he shied and bolted. Two of the wolves fled as well, but the third raised his head and bared his teeth, prepared to defend his kill. "Back off," Arya told Gendry. "Slow, so you don't spook him." They edged their mounts away, until the wolf and his feast were no longer in sight. Only then did she swing about to ride after Hot Pie, who was clinging desperately to the saddle as he crashed through the trees.

Later they passed through a burned village, threading their way carefully between the shells of blackened hovels and past the bones of a dozen dead men hanging from a row of apple trees. When Hot Pie saw them he began to pray, a thin whispered plea for the Mother's mercy, repeated over and over. Arya looked up at the fleshless dead in their wet rotting clothes and said her own prayer. *Ser Gregor,* it went, *Dunsen, Polliver, Raff the Sweetling. The Tickler and the Hound. Ser Ilyn, Ser Meryn, King Joffrey, Queen Cersei.* She ended it with *valar morghulis*, touched Jaqen's coin where it nestled under her belt, and then reached up and plucked an apple from among the dead men as she rode beneath them. It was mushy and overripe, but she ate it worms and all.

That was the day without a dawn. Slowly the sky lightened around them, but they never saw the sun. Black turned to grey, and colors crept timidly back into the world. The soldier pines were dressed in somber greens, the broadleafs in russets and faded golds already beginning to brown. They stopped long enough to water the horses and eat a cold, quick breakfast, ripping apart a loaf of the bread that Hot Pie had stolen from the kitchens and passing chunks of hard yellow cheese from hand to hand.

"Do you know where we're going?" Gendry asked her.

"North," said Arya.

Hot Pie peered around uncertainly. "Which way is north?"

She used her cheese to point. "That way."

"But there's no sun. How do you know?"

"From the moss. See how it grows mostly on one side of the trees? That's south."

"What do we want with the north?" Gendry wanted to know.

"The Trident." Arya unrolled the stolen map to show them. "See? Once we reach the Trident, all we need to do is follow it upstream till we come to Riverrun, here." Her finger traced the path. "It's a long way, but we can't get lost so long as we keep to the river."

Hot Pie blinked at the map. "Which one is Riverrun?"

Riverrun was painted as a castle tower, in the fork between the flowing blue lines of two rivers, the Tumblestone and the Red Fork. "There." She touched it. "*Riverrun*, it reads."

"You can read writing?" he said to her, wonderingly, as if she'd said she could walk on water.

She nodded. "We'll be safe once we reach Riverrun."

"We will? Why?"

Because Riverrun is my grandfather's castle, and my brother Robb will be there, she wanted to say. She bit her lip and rolled up the map. "We just will. But only if we get there." She was the first one back in the saddle. It made her feel bad to hide the truth from Hot Pie, but she did not trust him with her secret. Gendry knew, but that was different. Gendry had his own secret, though even he didn't seem to know what it was.

That day Arya quickened their pace, keeping the horses to a trot as long as she dared, and sometimes spurring to a gallop when she spied a flat stretch of field before them. That was seldom enough, though; the ground was growing hillier as they went. The hills were not high, nor especially steep, but there seemed to be no end of them, and they soon grew tired of climbing up one and down the other, and found themselves following the lay of the land, along streambeds and through a maze of shallow wooded valleys where the trees made a solid canopy overhead.

From time to time she sent Hot Pie and Gendry on while she doubled back to try to confuse their trail, listening all the while for the first sign of pursuit. *Too slow*, she thought to herself, chewing her lip, *we're going too slow, they'll catch us for certain*. Once, from the crest of a ridge, she spied dark shapes crossing a stream in the valley behind them, and for half a heartbeat she feared that Roose Bolton's riders were on them, but when she looked again she realized they were only a pack of wolves. She cupped her hands around her mouth and howled down at them, "*Ahooooooooo, ahooooooooo*." When the largest of the wolves lifted its head and howled back, the sound made Arya shiver.

By midday Hot Pie had begun to complain. His arse was sore, he told them, and the saddle was rubbing him raw inside his legs, and besides he had to get some sleep. "I'm so tired I'm going to fall off the horse."

Arya looked at Gendry. "If he falls off, who do you think will find him first, the wolves or the Mummers?"

"The wolves," said Gendry. "Better noses."

Hot Pie opened his mouth and closed it. He did not fall off his horse. The rain began again a short time later. They still had not seen so much as a glimpse of the sun. It was growing colder, and pale white mists were threading between the pines and blowing across the bare burned fields.

Gendry was having almost as bad a time of it as Hot Pie, though he was too stubborn to complain. He sat awkwardly in the saddle, a determined look on his face beneath his shaggy black hair, but Arya could tell he was no horseman. *I should have remembered*, she thought to herself. She had been riding as long as she could remember, ponies when she was little and later horses, but Gendry and Hot Pie were city-born, and in the city smallfolk walked. Yoren had given them mounts when he took them from King's Landing, but sitting on a donkey and plodding up the kingsroad behind a wagon was one thing. Guiding a hunting horse through wild woods and burned fields was something else.

She would make much better time on her own, Arya knew, but she could not leave them. They were her pack, her friends, the only living friends that remained to her, and if not for her they would still be safe at Harrenhal, Gendry sweating at his forge and Hot Pie in the kitchens. *If the Mummers catch us, I'll tell them that I'm Ned Stark's daughter and sister to the King in the North. I'll command them to take me to my brother, and to do no harm to Hot Pie and Gendry.* They might not believe her, though, and even if they did . . . Lord Bolton was her brother's bannerman, but he frightened her all the same. *I won't let them take us,* she vowed silently, reaching back over her shoulder to touch the hilt of the sword that Gendry had stolen for her. *I won't.*

Late that afternoon, they emerged from beneath the trees and found themselves on the banks of a river. Hot Pie gave a whoop of delight. "The *Trident*! Now all we have to do is go upstream, like you said. We're almost there!"

Arya chewed her lip. "I don't think this is the Trident." The river was swollen by the rain, but even so it couldn't be much more than thirty feet across. She remembered the Trident as being much wider. "It's too little to be the Trident," she told them, "and we didn't come far enough."

"Yes we did," Hot Pie insisted. "We rode all day, and hardly stopped at all. We must have come a long way."

"Let's have a look at that map again," said Gendry.

Arya dismounted, took out the map, unrolled it. The rain pattered against the sheepskin and ran off in rivulets. "We're someplace here, I think," she said, pointing, as the boys peered over her shoulders.

"But," said Hot Pie, "that's hardly any ways at all. See,

Harrenhal's there by your finger, you're almost *touching* it. And we rode all day!"

"There's miles and miles before we reach the Trident," she said. "We won't be there for *days*. This must be some different river, one of these, see." She showed him some of the thinner blue lines the mapmaker had painted in, each with a name painted in fine script beneath it. "The Darry, the Greenapple, the Maiden . . . here, this one, the Little Willow, it might be that."

Hot Pie looked from the line to the river. "It doesn't look so little to me."

Gendry was frowning as well. "The one you're pointing at runs into that other one, see."

"The Big Willow," she read.

"The Big Willow, then. See, and the Big Willow runs into the Trident, so we could follow the one to the other, but we'd need to go downstream, not up. Only if this river *isn't* the Little Willow, if it's this other one here . . ."

"Rippledown Rill," Arya read.

"See, it loops around and flows down toward the lake, back to Harrenhal." He traced the line with a finger.

Hot Pie's eyes grew wide. "*No!* They'll kill us for sure."

"We have to know which river this is," declared Gendry, in his stubbornest voice. "We have to know."

"Well, we *don't*." The map might have names written beside the blue lines, but no one had written a name on the riverbank. "We won't go up *or* downstream," she decided, rolling up the map. "We'll cross and keep going north, like we were."

"Can horses swim?" asked Hot Pie. "It looks *deep*, Arry. What if there are snakes?"

"Are you sure we're going north?" asked Gendry. "All these hills . . . if we got turned around . . ."

"The moss on the trees—"

He pointed to a nearby tree. "That tree's got moss on three sides, and that next one has no moss at all. We could be lost, just riding around in a circle."

"We could be," said Arya, "but I'm going to cross the river anyway. You can come or you can stay here." She climbed back into the saddle, ignoring the both of them. If they didn't want to follow, they could find Riverrun on their own, though more likely the Mummers would just find them.

She had to ride a good half mile along the bank before she finally found a place where it looked as though it might be safe to cross, and even then her mare was reluctant to enter the water. The river, whatever its name, was running brown and fast, and the deep part in the middle came up past the horse's belly. Water filled her boots, but she pressed in her heels all the same and climbed out on the far bank. From behind she heard splashing, and a mare's nervous whinny. *They followed, then. Good.* She turned to watch as the boys struggled across and emerged dripping beside her. "It wasn't the Trident," she told them. "It *wasn't.*"

The next river was shallower and easier to ford. That one wasn't the Trident either, and no one argued with her when she told them they would cross it.

Dusk was settling as they stopped to rest the horses once more and share another meal of bread and cheese. "I'm cold and wet," Hot Pie complained. "We're a long way from Harrenhal now, for sure. We could have us a fire—"

"*NO!*" Arya and Gendry both said, at the exact same instant. Hot Pie quailed a little. Arya gave Gendry a sideways look. *He said it with me, like Jon used to do, back in Winterfell.* She missed Jon Snow the most of all her brothers.

"Could we sleep at least?" Hot Pie asked. "I'm so tired, Arry, and my arse is sore. I think I've got blisters."

"You'll have more than that if you're caught," she said. "We've got to keep going. We've *got* to."

"But it's almost dark, and you can't even see the moon."

"Get back on your horse."

Plodding along at a slow walking pace as the light faded around them, Arya found her own exhaustion weighing heavy on her. She needed sleep as much as Hot Pie, but they dare not. If they slept, they might open their eyes to find Vargo Hoat standing over them with Shagwell the Fool and Faithful Urswyck and Rorge and Biter and Septon Utt and all his other monsters.

Yet after a while the motion of her horse became as soothing as the rocking of a cradle, and Arya found her eyes growing heavy. She let them close, just for an instant, then snapped them wide again. *I can't go to sleep*, she screamed at herself silently, *I can't, I can't.* She knuckled at her eye and rubbed it hard to keep it open, clutching the reins tightly and kicking her mount to a canter. But neither she nor the horse could sustain the pace, and it was only a few moments before they fell back to a walk again, and a few more until her eyes closed a second time. This time they did not open quite so quickly.

When they did, she found that her horse had come to a stop and was nibbling at a tuft of grass, while Gendry was shaking her arm. "You fell asleep," he told her.

"I was just resting my eyes."

"You were resting them a long while, then. Your horse was wandering in a circle, but it wasn't till she stopped that I realized you were sleeping. Hot Pie's just as bad, he rode into a tree limb and got knocked off, you should have heard him yell. Even *that* didn't wake you up. You need to stop and sleep."

"I can keep going as long as you can." She yawned.

"Liar," he said. "You keep going if you want to be stupid, but I'm stopping. I'll take the first watch. You sleep."

"What about Hot Pie?"

Gendry pointed. Hot Pie was already on the ground, curled up beneath his cloak on a bed of damp leaves and snoring softly. He had a big wedge of cheese in one fist, but it looked as though he had fallen asleep between bites.

It was no good arguing, Arya realized; Gendry had the right of it. *The Mummers will need to sleep too*, she told herself, hoping it was true. She was so weary it was a struggle even to get down from the saddle, but she remembered to hobble her horse before finding a place beneath a beech tree. The ground was hard and damp. She wondered how long it would be before she slept in a bed again, with hot food and a fire to warm her. The last thing she did before closing her eyes was unsheathe her sword and lay it down beside her. "Ser Gregor," she whispered, yawning. "Dunsen, Polliver, Raff the Sweetling. The Tickler and . . . the Tickler . . . the Hound . . ."

Her dreams were red and savage. The Mummers were in them, four at least, a pale Lyseni and a dark brutal axeman from Ib, the scarred Dothraki horse lord called Iggo and a Dornishman whose name she never knew. On and on they came, riding through the rain in rusting mail and wet leather, swords and axe clanking against their saddles. They thought they were hunting her, she knew with all the strange sharp certainty of dreams, but they were wrong. She was hunting them.

She was no little girl in the dream; she was a wolf, huge and powerful, and when she emerged from beneath the trees in front of them and bared her teeth in a low rumbling growl, she could smell the rank stench of fear from horse and man alike. The Lyseni's mount reared and screamed in terror, and the others shouted at one another in mantalk, but before they could act the other wolves came hurtling from the darkness and the rain, a great pack of them, gaunt and wet and silent.

The fight was short but bloody. The hairy man went down as he unslung his axe, the dark one died stringing an arrow, and the pale man from Lys tried to bolt. Her brothers and sisters ran him down, turning him again and again, coming at him from all sides, snapping at the legs of his horse and tearing the throat from the rider when he came crashing to the earth.

Only the belled man stood his ground. His horse kicked in the head of one of her sisters, and he cut another almost in half with his curved silvery claw as his hair tinkled softly.

Filled with rage, she leapt onto his back, knocking him head-first from his saddle. Her jaws locked on his arm as they fell, her teeth sinking through the leather and wool and soft flesh. When they landed she gave a savage jerk with her head and ripped the limb loose from his shoulder. Exulting, she shook it back and forth in her mouth, scattering the warm red droplets amidst the cold black rain.

TYRION

He woke to the creak of old iron hinges.

"Who?" he croaked. At least he had his voice back, raw and hoarse though it was. The fever was still on him, and Tyrion had no notion of the hour. How long had he slept this time? He was so weak, so damnably weak. "Who?" he called again, more loudly. Torchlight spilled through the open door, but within the chamber the only light came from the stub of a candle beside his bed.

When he saw a shape moving toward him, Tyrion shivered. Here in Maegor's Holdfast, every servant was in the queen's pay, so any visitor might be another of Cersei's catspaws, sent to finish the work Ser Mandon had begun.

Then the man stepped into the candlelight, got a good look at the dwarf's pale face, and chortled. "Cut yourself shaving, did you?"

Tyrion's fingers went to the great gash that ran from above one eye down to his jaw, across what remained of his nose. The proud flesh was still raw and warm to the touch. "With a fearful big razor, yes."

Bronn's coal-black hair was freshly washed and brushed

straight back from the hard lines of his face, and he was dressed in high boots of soft, tooled leather, a wide belt studded with nuggets of silver, and a cloak of pale green silk. Across the dark grey wool of his doublet, a burning chain was embroidered diagonally in bright green thread.

"Where have you been?" Tyrion demanded of him. "I sent for you . . . it must have been a fortnight ago."

"Four days ago, more like," the sellsword said, "and I've been here twice, and found you dead to the world."

"Not dead. Though my sweet sister did try." Perhaps he should not have said that aloud, but Tyrion was past caring. Cersei was behind Ser Mandon's attempt to kill him, he knew that in his gut. "What's that ugly thing on your chest?"

Bronn grinned. "My knightly sigil. A flaming chain, green, on a smoke-grey field. By your lord father's command, I'm Ser Bronn of the Blackwater now, Imp. See you don't forget it."

Tyrion put his hands on the featherbed and squirmed back a few inches, against the pillows. "I was the one who promised you knighthood, remember?" He had liked that *"by your lord father's command"* not at all. Lord Tywin had wasted little time. Moving his son from the Tower of the Hand to claim it for himself was a message anyone could read, and this was another. "I lose half my nose and you gain a knighthood. The gods have a deal to answer for." His voice was sour. "Did my father dub you himself?"

"No. Them of us as survived the fight at the winch towers got ourselves dabbed by the High Septon and dubbed by the Kingsguard. Took half the bloody day, with only three of the White Swords left to do the honors."

"I knew Ser Mandon died in the battle." *Shoved into the river by Pod, half a heartbeat before the treacherous bastard could drive his sword through my heart.* "Who else was lost?"

"The Hound," said Bronn. "Not dead, only gone. The gold cloaks say he turned craven and you led a sortie in his place."

Not one of my better notions. Tyrion could feel the scar tissue pull tight when he frowned. He waved Bronn toward a chair. "My sister has mistaken me for a mushroom. She keeps me in the dark and feeds me shit. Pod's a good lad, but the knot in his tongue is the size of Casterly Rock, and I don't trust half of what he tells me. I sent him to bring Ser Jacelyn and he came back and told me he's dead."

"Him, and thousands more." Bronn sat.

"How?" Tyrion demanded, feeling that much sicker.

"During the battle. Your sister sent the Kettleblacks to fetch the king back to the Red Keep, the way I hear it. When the gold cloaks saw him leaving, half of them decided they'd leave with him. Ironhand put himself in their path and tried to order them back to the walls. They say Bywater was blistering them good and almost had 'em ready to turn when someone put an arrow through his neck. He didn't seem so fearsome then, so they dragged him off his horse and killed him."

Another debt to lay at Cersei's door. "My nephew," he said, "Joffrey. Was he in any danger?"

"No more'n some, and less than most."

"Had he suffered any harm? Taken a wound? Mussed his hair, stubbed his toe, cracked a nail?"

"Not as I heard."

"I warned Cersei what would happen. Who commands the gold cloaks now?"

"Your lord father's given them to one of his westermen, some knight named Addam Marbrand."

In most cases the gold cloaks would have resented having an outsider placed over them, but Ser Addam Marbrand was a shrewd choice. Like Jaime, he was the sort of man other men liked to follow. *I have lost the City Watch.* "I sent Pod looking for Shagga, but he's had no luck."

"The Stone Crows are still in the kingswood. Shagga seems to have taken a fancy to the place. Timett led the Burned Men home, with all the plunder they took from Stannis's camp after the fighting. Chella turned up with a dozen Black Ears at the River Gate one morning, but your father's red cloaks chased them off while the Kingslanders threw dung and cheered."

Ingrates. The Black Ears died for them. Whilst Tyrion lay drugged and dreaming, his own blood had pulled his claws out, one by one. "I want you to go to my sister. Her precious son made it through the battle unscathed, so Cersei has no more need of a hostage. She swore to free Alayaya once—"

"She did. Eight, nine days ago, after the whipping."

Tyrion shoved himself up higher, ignoring the sudden stab of pain through his shoulder. *"Whipping?"*

"They tied her to a post in the yard and scourged her, then shoved her out the gate naked and bloody."

She was learning to read, Tyrion thought, absurdly. Across his face the scar stretched tight, and for a moment it felt as though his head would burst with rage. Alayaya was a whore, true enough, but a sweeter, braver, more innocent girl he had seldom met. Tyrion had never touched her; she had been no more than a veil, to hide Shae. In his carelessness, he had never thought what the role might cost her. "I promised my sister I would treat Tommen as she treated Alayaya," he remembered aloud. He felt as though he might retch. "How can I scourge an eight-year-old boy?" *But if I don't, Cersei wins.*

"You don't have Tommen," Bronn said bluntly. "Once she learned that Ironhand was dead, the queen sent the Kettleblacks after him, and no one at Rosby had the balls to say them nay."

Another blow; yet a relief as well, he must admit it. He was fond of Tommen. "The Kettleblacks were supposed to be ours," he reminded Bronn with more than a touch of irritation.

"They were, so long as I could give them two of your pennies for every one they had from the queen, but now she's raised the stakes. Osney and Osfryd were made knights after the battle, same as me. Gods know what for, no one saw them do any fighting."

My hirelings betray me, my friends are scourged and shamed, and I lie here rotting, Tyrion thought. *I thought I won the bloody battle. Is this what triumph tastes like?* "Is it true that Stannis was put to rout by Renly's ghost?"

Bronn smiled thinly. "From the winch towers, all we saw was banners in the mud and men throwing down their spears to run, but there's hundreds in the pot shops and brothels who'll tell you how they saw Lord Renly kill this one or that one. Most of Stannis's host had been Renly's to start, and they went right back over at the sight of him in that shiny green armor."

After all his planning, after the sortie and the bridge of ships, after getting his face slashed in two, Tyrion had been eclipsed by a dead man. *If indeed Renly is dead.* Something else he would need to look into. "How did Stannis escape?"

"His Lyseni kept their galleys out in the bay, beyond your chain. When the battle turned bad, they put in along the bay shore and took off as many as they could. Men were killing each other to get aboard, toward the end."

"What of Robb Stark, what has he been doing?"

"There's some of his wolves burning their way down toward Duskendale. Your father's sending this Lord Tarly to sort them out. I'd half a mind to join him. It's said he's a good soldier, and openhanded with the plunder."

The thought of losing Bronn was the final straw. "No. Your place is here. You're the captain of the Hand's guard."

"You're not the Hand," Bronn reminded him sharply. "Your father is, and he's got his own bloody guard."

"What happened to all the men you hired for me?"

"Some died at the winch towers. That uncle of yours, Ser Kevan, he paid the rest of us and tossed us out."

"How good of him," Tyrion said acidly. "Does that mean you've lost your taste for gold?"

"Not bloody likely."

"Good," said Tyrion, "because as it happens, I still have need of you. What do you know of Ser Mandon Moore?"

Bronn laughed. "I know he's bloody well drowned."

"I owe him a great debt, but how to pay it?" He touched his face, feeling the scar. "I know precious little of the man, if truth be told."

"He had eyes like a fish and he wore a white cloak. What else do you need to know?"

"Everything," said Tyrion, "for a start." What he wanted was proof that Ser Mandon had been Cersei's, but he dare not say so aloud. In the Red Keep a man did best to hold his tongue. There were rats in the walls, and little birds who talked too much, and spiders. "Help me up," he said, struggling with the bedclothes. "It's time I paid a call on my father, and past time I let myself be seen again."

"Such a pretty sight," mocked Bronn.

"What's half a nose, on a face like mine? But speaking of pretty, is Margaery Tyrell in King's Landing yet?"

"No. She's coming, though, and the city's mad with love for her. The Tyrells have been carting food up from Highgarden and giving it away in her name. Hundreds of wayns each day. There's thousands of Tyrell men swaggering about with little golden roses sewn on their doublets, and not a one is buying his own wine. Wife, widow, or whore, the women are all giving up their virtue to every peach-fuzz boy with a gold rose on his teat."

They spit on me, and buy drinks for the Tyrells. Tyrion slid from the bed to the floor. His legs turned wobbly beneath him, the room spun, and he had to grasp Bronn's arm to keep from pitching headlong into the rushes. "*Pod!*" he shouted. "Podrick Payne! Where in the seven hells are you?" Pain gnawed at him like a toothless dog. Tyrion hated weakness, especially his own. It shamed him, and shame made him angry. "Pod, *get in here!*"

The boy came running. When he saw Tyrion standing and clutching Bronn's arm, he gaped at them. "My lord. You stood. Is that . . . do you . . . do you need wine? Dreamwine? Should I get the maester? He said you must stay. Abed, I mean."

"I have stayed abed too long. Bring me some clean garb."

"Garb?"

How the boy could be so clearheaded and resourceful in battle and so confused at all other times Tyrion could never comprehend. "Clothing," he repeated. "Tunic, doublet, breeches, hose. For me. To dress in. So I can leave this bloody cell."

It took all three of them to clothe him. Hideous though his face might be, the worst of his wounds was the one at the juncture of shoulder and arm, where his own mail had been driven back into his armpit by an arrow. Pus and blood still seeped from the discolored flesh whenever Maester Frenken changed his dressing, and any movement sent a stab of agony through him.

In the end, Tyrion settled for a pair of breeches and an oversized bed robe that hung loosely about his shoulders. Bronn yanked his boots onto his feet while Pod went in search of a stick for him to lean on. He drank a cup of dreamwine to fortify himself. The wine was sweetened with honey, with just enough of the poppy to make his wounds bearable for a time.

Even so, he was dizzy by the time he turned the latch, and the descent down the twisting stone steps made his legs tremble. He walked with the stick in one hand and the other on Pod's shoulder. A serving girl was coming up as they were going down. She stared at them with wide white eyes, as if she were looking at a ghost. *The dwarf has risen from the dead*, Tyrion thought. *And look, he's uglier than ever, run tell your friends.*

Maegor's Holdfast was the strongest place in the Red Keep, a castle within the castle, surrounded by a deep dry moat lined with spikes. The drawbridge was up for the night when they reached the door. Ser Meryn Trant stood before it in his pale armor and white cloak. "Lower the bridge," Tyrion commanded him.

"The queen's orders are to raise the bridge at night." Ser Meryn had always been Cersei's creature.

"The queen's asleep, and I have business with my father."

There was magic in the name of Lord Tywin Lannister. Grumbling, Ser Meryn Trant gave the command, and the drawbridge was lowered. A second Kingsguard knight stood sentry across the moat. Ser Osmund Kettleblack managed a smile when he saw Tyrion waddling toward him. "Feeling stronger, m'lord?"

"Much. When's the next battle? I can scarcely wait."

When Pod and he reached the serpentine steps, however, Tyrion could only gape at them in dismay. *I will never climb those by myself*, he confessed to himself. Swallowing his dignity, he asked Bronn to carry him, hoping against hope that at this hour there would be no one to see and smile, no one to tell the tale of the dwarf being carried up the steps like a babe in arms.

The outer ward was crowded with tents and pavilions, dozens of them. "Tyrell men," Podrick Payne explained as they threaded their way through a maze of silk and canvas. "Lord Rowan's too, and Lord Redwyne's. There wasn't room enough for all. In the castle, I mean. Some took rooms. Rooms in the city. In inns and all. They're here for the wedding. The king's wedding, King Joffrey's. Will you be strong enough to attend, my lord?"

"Ravening weasels could not keep me away." There was this to be said for weddings over battles, at least; it was less likely that someone would cut off your nose.

Lights still burned dimly behind shuttered windows in the Tower of the Hand. The men on the door wore the crimson cloaks and lion-crested helms of his father's household guard. Tyrion knew them both, and they admitted him on sight . . . though neither could bear to look long at his face, he noted.

Within, they came upon Ser Addam Marbrand, descending the turnpike stair in the ornate black breastplate and cloth-of-gold cloak of an officer in the City Watch. "My lord," he said, "how good to see you on your feet. I'd heard—"

"—rumors of a small grave being dug? Me too. Under the circumstances it seemed best to get up. I hear you're commander of the City Watch. Shall I offer congratulations or condolences?"

"Both, I fear." Ser Addam smiled. "Death and desertion have left me with some forty-four hundred. Only the gods and Littlefinger know how we are to go on paying wages for so many, but your sister forbids me to dismiss any."

Still anxious, Cersei? The battle's done, the gold cloaks won't help you now. "Do you come from my father?" he asked.

"Aye. I fear I did not leave him in the best of moods. Lord Tywin feels forty-four hundred guardsmen more than sufficient to find one lost squire, but your cousin Tyrek remains missing."

Tyrek was the son of his late Uncle Tygett, a boy of thirteen. He had vanished in the riot, not long after wedding the Lady Ermesande, a suckling babe who happened to be the last surviving heir of House Hayford. *And likely the first bride in the history of the Seven Kingdoms to be widowed before she was weaned.* "I couldn't find him either," confessed Tyrion.

"He's feeding worms," said Bronn with his usual tact. "Ironhand looked for him, and the eunuch rattled a nice fat purse. They had no more luck than we did. Give it up, ser."

Ser Addam gazed at the sellsword with distaste. "Lord Tywin is stubborn where his blood is concerned. He will have the lad, alive or dead, and I mean to oblige him." He looked back to Tyrion. "You will find your father in his solar."

My solar, thought Tyrion. "I believe I know the way."

The way was up more steps, but this time he climbed under his own power, with one hand on Pod's shoulder.

Bronn opened the door for him. Lord Tywin Lannister was seated beneath the window, writing by the glow of an oil lamp. He raised his eyes at the sound of the latch. "Tyrion." Calmly, he laid his quill aside.

"I'm pleased you remember me, my lord." Tyrion released his grip on Pod, leaned his weight on the stick, and waddled closer. *Something is wrong,* he knew at once.

"Ser Bronn," Lord Tywin said, "Podrick. Perhaps you had best wait without until we are done."

The look Bronn gave the Hand was little less than insolent; nonetheless, he bowed and withdrew, with Pod on his heels. The heavy door swung shut behind them, and Tyrion Lannister was alone with his father. Even with the windows of the solar shuttered against the night, the chill in the room was palpable. *What sort of lies has Cersei been telling him?*

The Lord of Casterly Rock was as lean as a man twenty years younger, even handsome in his austere way. Stiff blond whiskers covered his cheeks, framing a stern face, a bald head, a hard mouth. About his throat he wore a chain of golden hands, the fingers of each clasping the wrist of the next. "That's a handsome chain," Tyrion said. *Though it looked better on me.*

Lord Tywin ignored the sally. "You had best be seated. Is it wise for you to be out of your sickbed?"

"I am sick of my sickbed." Tyrion knew how much his father despised weakness. He claimed the nearest chair. "Such pleasant chambers you have. Would you believe it, while I was dying, someone moved me to a dark little cell in Maegor's?"

"The Red Keep is overcrowded with wedding guests. Once they depart, we will find you more suitable accommodations."

"I rather liked *these* accommodations. Have you set a date for this great wedding?"

"Joffrey and Margaery shall marry on the first day of the new year, which as it happens is also the first day of the new century. The ceremony will herald the dawn of a new era."

A new Lannister era, thought Tyrion. "Oh, bother, I fear I've made other plans for that day."

"Did you come here just to complain of your bedchamber and make your lame japes? I have important letters to finish."

"*Important* letters. To be sure."

"Some battles are won with swords and spears, others with quills and ravens. Spare me these coy reproaches, Tyrion. I visited your sickbed as often as Maester Ballabar would allow it, when you seemed like to die." He steepled his fingers under his chin. "Why did you dismiss Ballabar?"

Tyrion shrugged. "Maester Frenken is not so determined to keep me insensate."

"Ballabar came to the city in Lord Redwyne's retinue. A gifted healer, it's said. It was kind of Cersei to ask him to look after you. She feared for your life."

Feared that I might keep it, you mean. "Doubtless that's why she's never once left my bedside."

"Don't be impertinent. Cersei has a royal wedding to plan, I am waging a war, and you have been out of danger for at least a fortnight." Lord Tywin studied his son's disfigured face, his pale green eyes unflinching. "Though the wound is ghastly enough, I'll grant you. What madness possessed you?"

"The foe was at the gates with a battering ram. If Jaime had led the sortie, you'd call it valor."

"Jaime would never be so foolish as to remove his helm in battle. I trust you killed the man who cut you?"

"Oh, the wretch is dead enough." Though it had been Podrick Payne who'd killed Ser Madon, shoving him into the river to drown beneath the weight of his armor. "A dead enemy is a joy forever," Tyrion said blithely, though Ser Mandon was not his true enemy. The man had no reason to want him dead. *He was only a catspaw, and I believe I know the cat. She told him to make certain I did not survive the battle.* But without proof Lord Tywin would never listen to such a charge. "Why are you here in the city, Father?" he asked. "Shouldn't you be off fighting Lord Stannis or Robb Stark or someone?" *And the sooner the better.*

"Until Lord Redwyne brings his fleet up, we lack the ships to assail Dragonstone. It makes no matter. Stannis Baratheon's sun set on the Blackwater. As for Stark, the boy is still in the west, but a large force of northmen under

Helman Tallhart and Robett Glover are descending toward Duskendale. I've sent Lord Tarly to meet them, while Ser Gregor drives up the kingsroad to cut off their retreat. Tallhart and Glover will be caught between them, with a third of Stark's strength."

"Duskendale?" There was nothing at Duskendale worth such a risk. Had the Young Wolf finally blundered?

"It's nothing you need trouble yourself with. Your face is pale as death, and there's blood seeping through your dressings. Say what you want and take yourself back to bed."

"What I want . . ." His throat felt raw and tight. What *did* he want? *More than you can ever give me, Father.* "Pod tells me that Littlefinger's been made Lord of Harrenhal."

"An empty title, so long as Roose Bolton holds the castle for Robb Stark, yet Lord Baelish was desirous of the honor. He did us good service in the matter of the Tyrell marriage. A Lannister pays his debts."

The Tyrell marriage had been Tyrion's notion, in point of fact, but it would seem churlish to try to claim that now. "That title may not be as empty as you think," he warned. "Littlefinger does nothing without good reason. But be that as it may. You said something about paying debts, I believe?"

"And you want your own reward, is that it? Very well. What is it you would have of me? Lands, castle, some office?"

"A little bloody gratitude would make a nice start."

Lord Tywin stared at him, unblinking. "Mummers and monkeys require applause. So did Aerys, for that matter. You did as you were commanded, and I am sure it was to the best of your ability. No one denies the part you played."

"That *part* I played?" What nostrils Tyrion had left must surely have flared. "I saved your bloody city, it seems to me."

"Most people seem to feel that it was my attack on Lord Stannis's flank that turned the tide of battle. Lords Tyrell, Rowan, Redwyne, and Tarly fought nobly as well, and I'm told it was your sister Cersei who set the pyromancers to making the wildfire that destroyed the Baratheon fleet."

"While all I did was get my nosehairs trimmed, is that it?" Tyrion could not keep the bitterness out of his voice.

"Your chain was a clever stroke, and crucial to our victory. Is that what you wanted to hear? I am told we have you to thank for our Dornish alliance as well. You may be pleased to learn that Myrcella has arrived safely at Sunspear. Ser Arys Oakheart writes that she has taken a great liking to Princess Arianne, and that Prince Trystane is enchanted with her. I mislike giving House Martell a hostage, but I suppose that could not be helped."

"We'll have our own hostage," Tyrion said. "A council seat was also part of the bargain. Unless Prince Doran brings an army when he comes to claim it, he'll be putting himself in our power."

"Would that a council seat were all Martell came to claim," Lord Tywin said. "You promised him vengeance as well."

"I promised him justice."

"Call it what you will. It still comes down to blood."

"Not an item in short supply, surely? I splashed through lakes of it during the battle." Tyrion saw no reason not to cut to the heart of the matter. "Or have you grown so fond of Gregor Clegane that you cannot bear to part with him?"

"Ser Gregor has his uses, as did his brother. Every lord has need of a beast from time to time . . . a lesson you seem to have learned, judging from Ser Bronn and those clansmen of yours."

Tyrion thought of Timett's burned eye, Shagga with his axe, Chella in her necklace of dried ears. And Bronn. Bronn most of all. "The woods are full of beasts," he reminded his father. "The alleyways as well."

"True. Perhaps other dogs would hunt as well. I shall think on it. If there is nothing else . . ."

"You have important letters, yes." Tyrion rose on unsteady legs, closed his eyes for an instant as a wave of dizziness washed over him, and took a shaky step toward the door. Later, he would reflect that he should have taken a second, and then a third. Instead he turned. "What do I want, you ask? I'll tell you what I want. I want what is mine by rights. I want Casterly Rock."

His father's mouth grew hard. "Your brother's birthright?"

"The knights of the Kingsguard are forbidden to marry, to father children, and to hold land, you know that as well as I. The day Jaime put on that white cloak, he gave up his claim to Casterly Rock, but never once have you acknowledged it. It's past time. I want you to stand up before the realm and proclaim that I am your son and your lawful heir."

Lord Tywin's eyes were a pale green flecked with gold, as luminous as they were merciless. "Casterly Rock," he declared in a flat cold dead tone. And then, "Never."

The word hung between them, huge, sharp, poisoned.

I knew the answer before I asked, Tyrion said. *Eighteen years since Jaime joined the Kingsguard, and I never once raised the issue. I must have known. I must always have known.* "Why?" he made himself ask, though he knew he would rue the question.

"You ask that? You, who killed your mother to come into the world? You are an ill-made, devious, disobedient, spiteful little creature full of envy, lust, and low cunning. Men's laws give you the right to bear my name and display my colors, since I cannot prove that you are not mine. To teach me humility, the gods have condemned me to watch you waddle about wearing that proud lion that was my father's sigil and his father's before him. But neither gods nor men shall ever compel me to let you turn Casterly Rock into your whorehouse."

"My *whorehouse*?" The dawn broke; Tyrion understood all at once where this bile had come from. He ground his teeth together and said, "Cersei told you about Alayaya."

"Is that her name? I confess, I cannot remember the names of all your whores. Who was the one you married as a boy?"

"Tysha." He spat out the answer, defiant.

"And that camp follower on the Green Fork?"

"Why do you care?" he asked, unwilling even to speak Shae's name in his presence.

"I don't. No more than I care if they live or die."

"It was *you* who had Yaya whipped." It was not a question.

"Your sister told me of your threats against my grandsons." Lord Tywin's voice was colder than ice. "Did she lie?"

Tyrion would not deny it. "I made threats, yes. To keep Alayaya safe. So the Kettleblacks would not misuse her."

"To save a whore's virtue, you threatened your own House, your own kin? Is that the way of it?"

"You were the one who taught me that a good threat is often more telling than a blow. Not that Joffrey hasn't tempted me sore a few hundred times. If you're so anxious to whip people, start with him. But Tommen . . . why would I harm Tommen? He's a good lad, and mine own blood."

"As was your mother." Lord Tywin rose abruptly, to tower over his dwarf son. "Go back to your bed, Tyrion, and speak to me no more of *your rights* to Casterly Rock. You shall have your reward, but it shall be one I deem appropriate to your service and station. And make no mistake—this was the last time I will suffer you to bring shame onto House Lannister. You are *done* with whores. The next one I find in your bed, I'll hang."

DAVOS

He watched the sail grow for a long time, trying to decide whether he would sooner live or die.

Dying would be easier, he knew. All he had to do was crawl inside his cave and let the ship pass by, and death would find him. For days now the fever had been burning through him, turning his bowels to brown water and making him shiver in his restless sleep. Each morning found him weaker. *It will not be much longer*, he had taken to telling himself.

If the fever did not kill him, thirst surely would. He had no fresh water here, but for the occasional rainfall that pooled in hollows on the rock. Only three days past (or had it been four? On his rock, it was hard to tell the days apart) his pools had been dry as old bone, and the sight of the bay rippling green and grey all around him had been almost more than he could bear. Once he began to drink seawater the end would come swiftly, he knew, but all the same he had almost taken that first swallow, so parched was his throat. A sudden squall had saved him. He had grown so feeble by then that it was all he could do to lie in the rain with his eyes closed and his mouth open, and let the water splash down on his cracked lips and swollen tongue. But afterward he felt a little stronger, and the island's pools and cracks and crevices once more had brimmed with life.

But that had been three days ago (or maybe four), and most of the water was gone now. Some had evaporated, and he had sucked up the rest. By the morrow he would be tasting the mud again, and licking the damp cold stones at the bottom of the depressions.

And if not thirst or fever, starvation would kill him. His island was no more than a barren spire jutting up out of the immensity of Blackwater Bay. When the tide was low, he could sometimes find tiny crabs along the stony strand where he had washed ashore after the battle. They nipped his fingers painfully before he smashed them apart on the rocks to suck the meat from their claws and the guts from their shells.

But the strand vanished whenever the tide came rushing in, and Davos had to scramble up the rock to keep from being swept out into the bay once more. The point of the spire was fifteen feet above the water at high tide, but when the bay grew rough the spray went even higher, so there was no way to keep dry, even in his cave (which was really no more than a hollow in the rock beneath an overhang). Nothing grew on the rock but lichen, and even the seabirds shunned the place. Now and again some gulls would land atop the spire and Davos would try to catch one, but they were too quick for him to get close. He took to flinging stones at them, but he was too weak to throw with much force, so even when his stones hit, the gulls would only scream at him in annoyance and then take to the air.

There were other rocks visible from his refuge, distant stony spires taller than his own. The nearest stood a good forty feet above the water, he guessed, though it was hard to be sure at this distance. A cloud of gulls swirled about it constantly, and often Davos thought of crossing over to raid their nests. But the water was cold here, the currents strong and treacherous, and he knew he did not have the strength for such a swim. That would kill him as sure as drinking seawater.

Autumn in the narrow sea could often be wet and rainy,

he remembered from years past. The days were not bad so long as the sun was shining, but the nights were growing colder and sometimes the wind would come gusting across the bay, driving a line of whitecaps before it, and before long Davos would be soaked and shivering. Fever and chills assaulted him in turn, and of late he had developed a persistent racking cough.

His cave was all the shelter he had, and that was little enough. Driftwood and bits of charred debris would wash up on the strand during low tide, but he had no way to strike a spark or start a fire. Once, in desperation, he had tried rubbing two pieces of driftwood against each other, but the wood was rotted, and his efforts earned him only blisters. His clothes were sodden as well, and he had lost one of his boots somewhere in the bay before he washed up here.

Thirst; hunger; exposure. They were his companions, with him every hour of every day, and in time he had come to think of them as his friends. Soon enough, one or the other of his friends would take pity on him and free him from this endless misery. Or perhaps he would simply walk into the water one day, and strike out for the shore that he knew lay somewhere to the north, beyond his sight. It was too far to swim, as weak as he was, but that did not matter. Davos had always been a sailor; he was meant to die at sea. *The gods beneath the waters have been waiting for me*, he told himself. *It's past time I went to them.*

But now there was a sail; only a speck on the horizon, but growing larger. *A ship where no ship should be.* He knew where his rock lay, more or less; it was one of a series of sea monts that rose from the floor of Blackwater Bay. The tallest of them jutted a hundred feet above the tide, and a dozen lesser monts stood thirty to sixty feet high. Sailors called them *spears of the merling king*, and knew that for every one that broke the surface, a dozen lurked treacherously just below it. Any captain with sense kept his course well away from them.

Davos watched the sail swell through pale red-rimmed eyes, and tried to hear the sound of the wind caught in the canvas. *She is coming this way.* Unless she changed course soon, she would pass within hailing distance of his meager refuge. It might mean life. If he wanted it. He was not sure he did.

Why should I live? he thought as tears blurred his vision. *Gods be good, why? My sons are dead, Dale and Allard, Maric and Matthos, perhaps Devan as well. How can a father outlive so many strong young sons? How would I go on? I am a hollow shell, the crab's died, there's nothing left inside. Don't they know that?*

They had sailed up the Blackwater Rush flying the fiery heart of the Lord of Light. Davos and *Black Betha* had been in the second line of battle, between Dale's *Wraith* and Allard on *Lady Marya*. Maric his third-born was oarmaster on *Fury*, at the center of the first line, while Matthos served as his father's second. Beneath the walls of the Red Keep Stannis Baratheon's galleys had joined in battle with the boy king Joffrey's smaller fleet, and for a few moments the river had rung to the thrum of bowstrings and the crash of iron rams shattering oars and hulls alike.

And then some vast beast had let out a roar, and green flames were all around them: wildfire, pyromancer's piss, the jade demon. Matthos had been standing at his elbow on the deck of *Black Betha* when the ship seemed to lift from the water. Davos found himself in the river, flailing as the current took him and spun him around and around. Upstream, the flames had ripped at the sky, fifty feet high. He had seen *Black Betha* afire, and *Fury*, and a dozen other ships, had seen burning men leaping into the water to drown. *Wraith* and *Lady Marya* were gone, sunk or shattered or vanished behind a veil of wildfire, and there was no time to look for them, because the mouth of the river was almost upon him, and across the mouth of the river the Lannisters had raised a great iron chain. From bank to bank there was nothing but burning ships and wildfire. The sight of it seemed to stop his heart for a moment, and he could still remember the sound of it, the crackle of flames, the hiss of steam, the shrieks of dying men, and the beat of that terrible heat against his face as the current swept him down toward hell.

All he needed to do was nothing. A few moments more, and he would be with his sons now, resting in the cool green mud on the bottom of the bay, with fish nibbling at his face.

Instead he sucked in a great gulp of air and dove, kicking for the bottom of the river. His only hope was to pass under the chain and the burning ships and the wildfire that floated on the surface of the water, to swim hard for the safety of the bay beyond. Davos had always been a strong swimmer, and he'd worn no steel that day, but for the helm he'd lost when he'd lost *Black Betha*. As he knifed through the green murk, he saw other men struggling beneath the water, pulled down to drown beneath the weight of plate and mail. Davos swam past them, kicking with all the strength left in his legs, giving himself up to the current, the water filling his eyes. Deeper he went, and deeper, and deeper still. With every stroke it grew harder to hold his breath. He remembered seeing the bottom, soft and dim, as a stream of bubbles burst from his lips. Something touched his leg . . . a snag or a fish or a drowning man, he could not tell.

He needed air by then, but he was afraid. Was he past the chain yet, was he out in the bay? If he came up under a ship he would drown, and if he surfaced amidst the floating patches of wildfire his first breath would sear his lungs to ash. He twisted in the water to look up, but there was nothing to see but green darkness and then he spun too far and suddenly he could no longer tell up from down. Panic took hold of him. His hands flailed against the bottom of the river and sent up a cloud of mud that blinded him. His chest was growing tighter by the instant. He clawed at the water, kicking, pushing himself, turning, his lungs screaming for air, kicking, kicking, lost now in the river murk, kicking, kicking, kicking until he could kick no longer. When he opened his mouth to scream, the water came rushing in, tasting of salt, and Davos Seaworth knew that he was drowning.

The next he knew the sun was up, and he lay upon a stony strand beneath a spire of naked stone, with the empty bay all around and a broken mast, a burned sail, and a swollen corpse beside him. The mast, the sail, and the dead man vanished with the next high tide, leaving Davos alone on his rock amidst the spears of the merling king.

His long years as a smuggler had made the waters around King's Landing more familiar to him than any home he'd ever had, and he knew his refuge was no more than a speck on the charts, in a place that honest sailors steered away from, not toward ... though Davos himself had come by it once or twice in his smuggling days, the better to stay unseen. *When they find me dead here, if ever they do, perhaps they will name the rock for me,* he thought. *Onion Rock, they'll call it; it will be my tombstone and my legacy.* He deserved no more. *The Father protects his children,* the septons taught, but Davos had led his boys into the fire. Dale would never give his wife the child they had prayed for, and Allard, with his girl in Oldtown and his girl in King's Landing and his girl in Braavos, they would all be weeping soon. Matthos would never captain his own ship, as he'd dreamed. Maric would never have his knighthood.

How can I live when they are dead? So many brave knights and mighty lords have died, better men than me, and highborn. Crawl inside your cave, Davos. Crawl inside and shrink up small and the ship will go away, and no one will trouble you ever again. Sleep on your stone pillow, and let the gulls peck out your eyes while the crabs feast on your flesh. You've feasted on enough of them, you owe them. Hide, smuggler. Hide, and be quiet, and die.

The sail was almost on him. A few moments more, and the ship would be safely past, and he could die in peace.

His hand reached for his throat, fumbling for the small leather pouch he always wore about his neck. Inside he kept the bones of the four fingers his king had shortened for him, on the day he made Davos a knight. *My luck.* His shortened fingers patted at his chest, groping, finding nothing. The pouch was gone, and the fingerbones with them. Stannis could never understand why he'd kept the bones. "To remind me of my king's justice," he whispered through cracked lips. But now they were gone. *The fire took my luck as well as my sons.* In his dreams the river was still aflame and demons danced upon the waters with fiery whips in their hands, while men blackened and burned beneath the lash. "Mother, have mercy," Davos prayed. "Save me, gentle Mother, save us all. My luck is gone, and my sons." He was weeping freely now, salt tears streaming down his cheeks. "The fire took it all ... the fire ..."

Perhaps it was only wind blowing against the rock, or

the sound of the sea on the shore, but for an instant Davos
Seaworth heard her answer. "You called the fire," she
whispered, her voice as faint as the sound of waves in a
seashell, sad and soft. "You burned us . . . burned us . . .
burrrrned usssssss."

"It was *her*!" Davos cried. "Mother, don't forsake us. It
was her who burned you, the red woman, Melisandre,
her!" He could see her; the heart-shaped face, the red eyes,
the long coppery hair, her red gowns moving like flames as
she walked, a swirl of silk and satin. She had come from
Asshai in the east, she had come to Dragonstone and won
Selsye and her queen's men for her alien god, and then the
king, Stannis Baratheon himself. He had gone so far as to
put the fiery heart on his banners, the fiery heart of R'hllor,
Lord of Light and God of Flame and Shadow. At
Melisandre's urging, he had dragged the Seven from their
sept at Dragonstone and burned them before the castle
gates, and later he had burned the godswood at Storm's End
as well, even the heart tree, a huge white weirwood with a
solemn face.

"It was her work," Davos said again, more weakly. *Her
work, and yours, onion knight. You rowed her into Storm's
End in the black of night, so she might loose her shadow
child. You are not guiltless, no. You rode beneath her banner and flew it from your mast. You watched the Seven
burn at Dragonstone, and did nothing. She gave the
Father's justice to the fire, and the Mother's mercy, and the
wisdom of the Crone. Smith and Stranger, Maid and
Warrior, she burnt them all to the glory of her cruel god,
and you stood and held your tongue. Even when she killed
old Maester Cressen, even then, you did nothing.*

The sail was a hundred yards away and moving fast
across the bay. In a few more moments it would be past
him, and dwindling.

Ser Davos Seaworth began to climb his rock.

He pulled himself up with trembling hands, his head
swimming with fever. Twice his maimed fingers slipped on
the damp stone and he almost fell, but somehow he managed to cling to his perch. If he fell he was dead, and he had
to live. For a little while more, at least. There was something he had to do.

The top of the rock was too small to stand on safely, as

weak as he was, so he crouched and waved his fleshless arms. "*Ship*," he screamed into the wind. "Ship, here, *here!*" From up here, he could see her more clearly; the lean striped hull, the bronze figurehead, the billowing sail. There was a name painted on her hull, but Davos had never learned to read. "*Ship*," he called again, "*help me, HELP ME!*"

A crewman on her forecastle saw him and pointed. He watched as other sailors moved to the gunwale to gape at him. A short while later the galley's sail came down, her oars slid out, and she swept around toward his refuge. She was too big to approach the rock closely, but thirty yards away she launched a small boat. Davos clung to his rock and watched it creep toward him. Four men were rowing, while a fifth sat in the prow. "You," the fifth man called out when they were only a few feet from his island, "you up on the rock. Who are you?"

A smuggler who rose above himself, thought Davos, *a fool who loved his king too much, and forgot his gods.* "I . . ." His throat was parched, and he had forgotten how to talk. The words felt strange on his tongue and sounded stranger in his ears. "I was in the battle. I was . . . a captain, a . . . a knight, I was a knight."

"Aye, ser," the man said, "and serving which king?"

The galley might be Joffrey's, he realized suddenly. If he spoke the wrong name now, she would abandon him to his fate. But no, her hull was striped. She was Lysene, she was Salladhor Saan's. The Mother sent her here, the Mother in her mercy. She had a task for him. *Stannis lives*, he knew then. *I have a king still. And sons, I have other sons, and a wife loyal and loving.* How could he have forgotten? The Mother was merciful indeed.

"Stannis," he shouted back at the Lyseni. "Gods be good, I serve King Stannis."

"Aye," said the man in the boat, "and so do we."

SANSA

The invitation seemed innocent enough, but every time Sansa read it her tummy tightened into a knot. *She's to be queen now, she's beautiful and rich and everyone loves her, why would she want to sup with a traitor's daughter?* It could be curiosity, she supposed; perhaps Margaery Tyrell wanted to get the measure of the rival she'd displaced. *Does she resent me, I wonder? Does she think I bear her ill will . . .*

Sansa had watched from the castle walls as Margaery Tyrell and her escort made their way up Aegon's High Hill. Joffrey had met his new bride-to-be at the King's Gate to welcome her to the city, and they rode side by side through cheering crowds, Joff glittering in gilded armor and the Tyrell girl splendid in green with a cloak of autumn flowers blowing from her shoulders. She was sixteen, brown-haired and brown-eyed, slender and beautiful. The people called out her name as she passed, held up their children for her blessing, and scattered flowers under the hooves of her horse. Her mother and grandmother followed close behind, riding in a tall wheelhouse whose sides were carved into the shape of a hundred twining roses, every one gilded and shining. The smallfolk cheered them as well.

The same smallfolk who pulled me from my horse and would have killed me, if not for the Hound. Sansa had done nothing to make the commons hate her, no more than Margaery Tyrell had done to win their love. *Does she want me to love her too?* She studied the invitation, which looked to be written in Margaery's own hand. *Does she want my blessing?* Sansa wondered if Joffrey knew of this supper. For all she knew, it might be his doing. That thought made her fearful. If Joff was behind the invitation, he would have some cruel jape planned to shame her in the older girl's eyes. Would he command his Kingsguard to strip her naked once again? The last time he had done that his uncle Tyrion had stopped him, but the Imp could not save her now.

No one can save me but my Florian. Ser Dontos had promised he would help her escape, but not until the night of Joffrey's wedding. The plans had been well laid, her dear devoted knight-turned-fool assured her; there was nothing to do until then but endure, and count the days.

And sup with my replacement . . .

Perhaps she was doing Margaery Tyrell an injustice. Perhaps the invitation was no more than a simple kindness, an act of courtesy. *It might be just a supper.* But this was the Red Keep, this was King's Landing, this was the court of King Joffrey Baratheon, the First of His Name, and if there was one thing that Sansa Stark had learned here, it was mistrust.

Even so, she must accept. She was nothing now, the discarded daughter of a traitor and disgraced sister of a rebel lord. She could scarcely refuse Joffrey's queen-to-be.

I wish the Hound were here. The night of the battle, Sandor Clegane had come to her chambers to take her from the city, but Sansa had refused. Sometimes she lay awake at night, wondering if she'd been wise. She had his stained white cloak hidden in a cedar chest beneath her summer silks. She could not say why she'd kept it. The Hound had turned craven, she heard it said; at the height of the battle, he got so drunk the Imp had to take his men. But Sansa understood. She knew the secret of his burned face. *It was only the fire he feared.* That night, the wildfire had set the river itself ablaze, and filled the very air with green flame. Even in the castle, Sansa had been afraid. Outside . . . she could scarcely imagine it.

Sighing, she got out quill and ink, and wrote Margaery Tyrell a gracious note of acceptance.

When the appointed night arrived, another of the Kingsguard came for her, a man as different from Sandor Clegane as . . . *well, as a flower from a dog.* The sight of Ser Loras Tyrell standing on her threshold made Sansa's heart beat a little faster. This was the first time she had been so close to him since he had returned to King's Landing, leading the vanguard of his father's host. For a moment she did not know what to say. "Ser Loras," she finally managed, "you . . . you look so lovely."

He gave her a puzzled smile. "My lady is too kind. And beautiful besides. My sister awaits you eagerly."

"I have so looked forward to our supper."

"As has Margaery, and my lady grandmother as well." He took her arm and led her toward the steps.

"Your grandmother?" Sansa was finding it hard to walk and talk and think all at the same time, with Ser Loras touching her arm. She could feel the warmth of his hand through the silk.

"Lady Olenna. She is to sup with you as well."

"Oh," said Sansa. *I am talking to him, and he's touching me, he's holding my arm and touching me.* "The Queen of Thorns, she's called. Isn't that right?"

"It is." Ser Loras laughed. *He has the warmest laugh,* she thought as he went on, "You'd best not use that name in her presence, though, or you're like to get pricked."

Sansa reddened. Any fool would have realized that no woman would be happy about being called "the Queen of Thorns." *Maybe I truly am as stupid as Cersei Lannister says.* Desperately she tried to think of something clever and charming to say to him, but her wits had deserted her. She almost told him how beautiful he was, until she remembered that she'd already done that.

He *was* beautiful, though. He seemed taller than he'd been when she'd first met him, but still so lithe and graceful, and Sansa had never seen another boy with such wonderful eyes. *He's no boy, though, he's a man grown, a knight of the Kingsguard.* She thought he looked even finer in white than in the greens and golds of House Tyrell. The only spot of color on him now was the brooch that clasped his cloak; the rose of Highgarden wrought in soft yellow gold, nestled in a bed of delicate green jade leaves.

Ser Balon Swann held the door of Maegor's for them to pass. He was all in white as well, though he did not wear it half so well as Ser Loras. Beyond the spiked moat, two dozen men were taking their practice with sword and shield. With the castle so crowded, the outer ward had been given over to guests to raise their tents and pavilions, leaving only the smaller inner yards for training. One of the Redwyne twins was being driven backward by Ser Tallad, with the eyes on his shield. Chunky Ser Kennos of Kayce, who chuffed and puffed every time he raised his longsword, seemed to be holding his own against Osney Kettleblack, but Osney's brother Ser Osfryd was savagely punishing the frog-faced squire Morros Slynt. Blunted swords or no, Slynt would have a rich crop of bruises by the morrow. It made Sansa wince just to watch. *They have scarcely finished burying the dead from the last battle, and already they are practicing for the next one.*

On the edge of the yard, a lone knight with a pair of golden roses on his shield was holding off three foes. Even as they watched, he caught one of them alongside the head, knocking him senseless. "Is that your brother?" Sansa asked.

"It is, my lady," said Ser Loras. "Garlan often trains against three men, or even four. In battle it is seldom one against one, he says, so he likes to be prepared."

"He must be very brave."

"He is a great knight," Ser Loras replied. "A better sword than me, in truth, though I'm the better lance."

"I remember," said Sansa. "You ride wonderfully, ser."

"My lady is gracious to say so. When has she seen me ride?"

"At the Hand's tourney, don't you remember? You rode a white courser, and your armor was a hundred different kinds of flowers. You gave me a rose. A *red* rose. You threw white roses to the other girls that day." It made her flush to speak of it. "You said no victory was half as beautiful as me."

Ser Loras gave her a modest smile. "I spoke only a simple truth, that any man with eyes could see."

He doesn't remember, Sansa realized, startled. *He is only being kind to me, he doesn't remember me or the rose or any of it.* She had been so certain that it meant something, that it meant *everything.* A *red* rose, not a white. "It was after you unhorsed Ser Robar Royce," she said, desperately.

He took his hand from her arm. "I slew Robar at Storm's End, my lady." It was not a boast; he sounded sad.

Him, and another of King Renly's Rainbow Guard as well, yes. Sansa had heard the women talking of it round the well, but for a moment she'd forgotten. "That was when Lord Renly was killed, wasn't it? How terrible for your poor sister."

"For Margaery?" His voice was tight. "To be sure. She was at Bitterbridge, though. She did not see."

"Even so, when she heard . . ."

Ser Loras brushed the hilt of his sword lightly with his hand. Its grip was white leather, its pommel a rose in alabaster. "Renly is dead. Robar as well. What use to speak of them?"

The sharpness in his tone took her aback. "I . . . my lord, I . . . I did not mean to give offense, ser."

"Nor could you, Lady Sansa," Ser Loras replied, but all the warmth had gone from his voice. Nor did he take her arm again.

They ascended the serpentine steps in a deepening silence.

Oh, why did I have to mention Ser Robar? Sansa thought. *I've ruined everything. He is angry with me now.* She tried to think of something she might say to make amends, but all the words that came to her were lame and weak. *Be quiet, or you will only make it worse,* she told herself.

Lord Mace Tyrell and his entourage had been housed behind the royal sept, in the long slate-roofed keep that had been called the Maidenvault since King Baelor the Blessed had confined his sisters therein, so the sight of them might not tempt him into carnal thoughts. Outside its tall carved doors stood two guards in gilded halfhelms and green cloaks edged in gold satin, the golden rose of Highgarden sewn on their breasts. Both were seven-footers, wide of shoulder and narrow of waist, magnificently muscled.

When Sansa got close enough to see their faces, she could not tell one from the other. They had the same strong jaws, the same deep blue eyes, the same thick red mustaches. "Who are they?" she asked Ser Loras, her discomfit forgotten for a moment.

"My grandmother's personal guard," he told her. "Their mother named them Erryk and Arryk, but Grandmother can't tell them apart, so she calls them Left and Right."

Left and Right opened the doors, and Margaery Tyrell herself emerged and swept down the short flight of steps to greet them. "Lady Sansa," she called, "I'm so pleased you came. Be welcome."

Sansa knelt at the feet of her future queen. "You do me great honor, Your Grace."

"Won't you call me Margaery? Please, rise. Loras, help the Lady Sansa to her feet. Might I call you Sansa?"

"If it please you." Ser Loras helped her up.

Margaery dismissed him with a sisterly kiss, and took Sansa by the hand. "Come, my grandmother awaits, and she is not the most patient of ladies."

A fire was crackling in the hearth, and sweet-swelling rushes had been scattered on the floor. Around the long trestle table a dozen women were seated.

Sansa recognized only Lord Tyrell's tall, dignified wife, Lady Alerie, whose long silvery braid was bound with jeweled rings. Margaery performed the other introductions. There were three Tyrell cousins, Megga and Alla and Elinor, all close to Sansa's age. Buxom Lady Janna was Lord Tyrell's sister, and wed to one of the green-apple Fossoways; dainty, bright-eyed Lady Leonette was a Fossoway as well, and wed to Ser Garlan. Septa Nysterica had a homely pox-scarred face but seemed jolly. Pale, elegant Lady Graceford was with child, and Lady Bulwer *was* a child, no more than eight. And "Merry" was what she was to call boisterous plump Meredyth Crane, but most definitely *not* Lady Merryweather, a sultry black-eyed Myrish beauty.

Last of all, Margaery brought her before the wizened white-haired doll of a woman at the head of the table. "I am honored to present my grandmother the Lady Olenna, widow to the late Luthor Tyrell, Lord of Highgarden, whose memory is a comfort to us all."

The old woman smelled of rosewater. *Why, she's just the littlest bit of a thing.* There was nothing the least bit thorny about her. "Kiss me, child," Lady Olenna said, tugging at Sansa's wrist with a soft spotted hand. "It is so kind of you to sup with me and my foolish flock of hens."

Dutifully, Sansa kissed the old woman on the cheek. "It is kind of you to have me, my lady."

"I knew your grandfather, Lord Rickard, though not well."

"He died before I was born."

"I am aware of that, child. It's said that your Tully grandfather is dying too. Lord Hoster, surely they told you? An old man, though not so old as me. Still, night falls for all of us in the end, and too soon for some. You would know that more than most, poor child. You've had your share of grief, I know. We are sorry for your losses."

Sansa glanced at Margaery. "I was saddened when I heard of Lord Renly's death, Your Grace. He was very gallant."

"You are kind to say so," answered Margaery.

Her grandmother snorted. "Gallant, yes, and charming, and very clean. He knew how to dress and he knew how to smile and he knew how to bathe, and somehow he got the notion that this made him fit to be king. The Baratheons have always had some queer notions, to be sure. It comes from their Targaryen blood, I should think." She sniffed. "They tried to marry me to a Targaryen once, but I soon put an end to that."

"Renly was brave and gentle, Grandmother," said Margaery. "Father liked him as well, and so did Loras."

"Loras is young," Lady Olenna said crisply, "and very good at knocking men off horses with a stick. That does not make him wise. As to your father, would that I'd been born a peasant woman with a big wooden spoon, I might have been able to beat some sense into his fat head."

"*Mother*," Lady Alerie scolded.

"Hush, Alerie, don't take that tone with me. And don't call me Mother. If I'd given birth to you, I'm sure I'd remember. I'm only to blame for your husband, the lord oaf of Highgarden."

"Grandmother," Margaery said, "mind your words, or what will Sansa think of us?"

"She might think we have some wits about us. One of us, at any rate." The old woman turned back to Sansa. "It's treason, I warned them, Robert has two sons, and Renly has an older brother, how can he *possibly* have any claim to that ugly iron chair? Tut-tut, says my son, don't you want your sweetling to be queen? You Starks were kings once, the Arryns and the Lannisters as well, and even the Baratheons through the female line, but the Tyrells were no more than stewards until Aegon the Dragon came along and cooked the rightful King of the Reach on the Field of Fire. If truth be told, even our claim to Highgarden is a bit dodgy, just as those dreadful Florents are always whining. 'What does it matter?' you ask, and of course it doesn't, except to oafs like my son. The thought that one day he may see his grandson with his arse on the Iron Throne makes Mace puff up like . . . now, what do you call it? Margaery, you're clever, be a dear and tell your poor old half-daft grandmother the name of that queer fish from the Summer Isles that puffs up to ten times its own size when you poke it."

"They call them puff fish, Grandmother."

"Of course they do. Summer Islanders have no imagination. My son ought to take the puff fish for his sigil, if truth be told. He could put a crown on it, the way the Baratheons do their stag, mayhap that would make him happy. We should have stayed well out of all this bloody foolishness if you ask me, but once the cow's been milked there's no squirting the cream back up her udder. After Lord Puff Fish put that crown on Renly's head, we were into the pudding up to our knees, so here we are to see things through. And what do you say to that, Sansa?"

Sansa's mouth opened and closed. She felt very like a puff fish herself. "The Tyrells can trace their descent back to Garth Greenhand," was the best she could manage at short notice.

The Queen of Thorns snorted. "So can the Florents, the Rowans, the Oakhearts, and half the other noble houses of the south. Garth liked to plant his seed in fertile ground, they say. I shouldn't wonder that more than his hands were green."

"*Sansa*," Lady Alerie broke in, "you must be very hungry. Shall we have a bite of boar together, and some lemon cakes?"

"Lemon cakes are my favorite," Sansa admitted.

"So we have been told," declared Lady Olenna, who obviously had no intention of being hushed. "That Varys creature seemed to think we should be grateful for the information. I've never been quite sure what the *point* of a eunuch is, if truth be told. It seems to me they're only men with the useful bits cut off. Alerie, will you have them bring the food, or do you mean to starve me to death? Here, Sansa, sit here next to me, I'm much less boring than these others. I hope that you're fond of fools."

Sansa smoothed down her skirts and sat. "I think . . . fools, my lady? You mean . . . the sort in motley?"

"Feathers, in this case. What did you imagine I was speaking of? My son? Or these lovely ladies? No, don't blush, with your hair it makes you look like a pomegranate. All men are fools, if truth be told, but the ones in motley are more amusing than ones with crowns. Margaery, child, summon Butterbumps, let us see if we can't make Lady Sansa smile. The rest of you be seated, do I have to tell you everything? Sansa must think that my granddaughter is attended by a flock of sheep."

Butterbumps arrived before the food, dressed in a jester's suit of green and yellow feathers with a floppy coxcomb. An immense round fat man, as big as three Moon Boys, he came cartwheeling into the hall, vaulted onto the table, and laid a gigantic egg right in front of Sansa. "Break it, my lady," he commanded. When she did, a dozen yellow chicks escaped and began running in all directions. "*Catch them!*" Butterbumps exclaimed. Little Lady Bulwer snagged one and handed it to him, whereby he tilted back his head, popped it into his huge rubbery mouth, and seemed to swallow it whole. When he belched, tiny yellow feathers flew out his nose. Lady Bulwer began to wail in distress, but her tears turned into a sudden squeal of delight when the chick came squirming out of the sleeve of her gown and ran down her arm.

As the servants brought out a broth of leeks and mushrooms, Butterbumps began to juggle and Lady Olenna pushed herself forward to rest her elbows on the table. "Do you know my son, Sansa? Lord Puff Fish of Highgarden?"

"A great lord," Sansa answered politely.

"A great oaf," said the Queen of Thorns. "His father was

an oaf as well. My husband, the late Lord Luthor. Oh, I loved him well enough, don't mistake me. A kind man, and not unskilled in the bedchamber, but an appalling oaf all the same. He managed to ride off a cliff whilst hawking. They say he was looking up at the sky and paying no mind to where his horse was taking him.

"And now my oaf son is doing the same, only he's riding a lion instead of a palfrey. It is easy to mount a lion and not so easy to get off, I warned him, but he only chuckles. Should you ever have a son, Sansa, beat him frequently so he learns to mind you. I only had the one boy and I hardly beat him at all, so now he pays more heed to Butterbumps than he does to me. A lion is not a lap cat, I told him, and he gives me a 'tut-tut-Mother.' There is entirely too much tut-tutting in this realm, if you ask me. All these kings would do a deal better if they would put down their swords and listen to their mothers."

Sansa realized that her mouth was open again. She filled it with a spoon of broth while Lady Alerie and the other women were giggling at the spectacle of Butterbumps bouncing oranges off his head, his elbows, and his ample rump.

"I want you to tell me the truth about this royal boy," said Lady Olenna abruptly. "This Joffrey."

Sansa's fingers tightened round her spoon. *The truth? I can't. Don't ask it, please, I can't.* "I . . . I . . . I . . ."

"You, yes. Who would know better? The lad seems kingly enough, I'll grant you. A bit full of himself, but that would be his Lannister blood. We have heard some troubling tales, however. Is there any truth to them? Has this boy mistreated you?"

Sansa glanced about nervously. Butterbumps popped a whole orange into his mouth, chewed and swallowed, slapped his cheek, and blew seeds out of his nose. The women giggled and laughed. Servants were coming and going, and the Maidenvault echoed to the clatter of spoons and plates. One of the chicks hopped back onto the table and ran through Lady Graceford's broth. No one seemed to be paying them any mind, but even so, she was frightened.

Lady Olenna was growing impatient. "Why are you gaping at Butterbumps? I asked a question, I expect an answer. Have the Lannisters stolen your tongue, child?"

Ser Dontos had warned her to speak freely only in the godswood. "Joff . . . King Joffrey, he's . . . His Grace is very fair and handsome, and . . . and as brave as a lion."

"Yes, all the Lannisters are lions, and when a Tyrell breaks wind it smells just like a rose," the old woman snapped. "But how *kind* is he? How clever? Has he a good heart, a gentle hand? Is he chivalrous as befits a king? Will he cherish Margaery and treat her tenderly, protect her honor as he would his own?"

"He will," Sansa lied. "He is very . . . very comely."

"You said that. You know, child, some say that you are as big a fool as Butterbumps here, and I am starting to believe them. *Comely?* I have taught my Margaery what comely is worth, I hope. Somewhat less than a mummer's fart. Aerion Brightfire was comely enough, but a monster all the same. The question is, what is Joffrey?" She reached to snag a passing servant. "I am not fond of leeks. Take this broth away, and bring me some cheese."

"The cheese will be served after the cakes, my lady."

"The cheese will be served when I want it served, and I want it served now." The old woman turned back to Sansa. "Are you frightened, child? No need for that, we're only women here. Tell me the truth, no harm will come to you."

"My father always told the truth." Sansa spoke quietly, but even so, it was hard to get the words out.

"Lord Eddard, yes, he had that reputation, but they named him traitor and took his head off even so." The old woman's eyes bore into her, sharp and bright as the points of swords.

"Joffrey," Sansa said. "Joffrey did that. He promised me he would be merciful, and cut my father's head off. He said *that* was mercy, and he took me up on the walls and made me look at it. The head. He wanted me to weep, but . . ." She stopped abruptly, and covered her mouth. *I've said too much, oh gods be good, they'll know, they'll hear, someone will tell on me.*

"Go on." It was Margaery who urged. Joffrey's own queen-to-be. Sansa did not know how much she had heard.

"I can't." *What if she tells him, what if she tells? He'll kill me for certain then, or give me to Ser Ilyn.* "I never meant . . . my father was a traitor, my brother as well, I have the traitor's blood, please, don't make me say more."

"Calm yourself, child," the Queen of Thorns commanded.

"She's terrified, Grandmother, just look at her."

The old woman called to Butterbumps. "*Fool!* Give us a song. A long one, I should think. 'The Bear and the Maiden Fair' will do nicely."

"It will!" the huge jester replied. "It will do nicely indeed! Shall I sing it standing on my head, my lady?"

"Will that make it sound better?"

"No."

"Stand on your feet, then. We wouldn't want your hat to fall off. As I recall, you never wash your hair."

"As my lady commands." Butterbumps bowed low, let loose of an enormous belch, then straightened, threw out his belly, and bellowed. "*A bear there was, a bear, a BEAR! All black and brown, and covered with hair . . .*"

Lady Olenna squirmed forward. "Even when I was a girl younger than you, it was well known that in the Red Keep the very walls have ears. Well, they will be the better for a song, and meanwhile we girls shall speak freely."

"But," Sansa said, "Varys . . . he *knows*, he always . . ."

"*Sing louder!*" the Queen of Thorns shouted at Butterbumps. "These old ears are almost deaf, you know. Are you whispering at me, you fat fool? I don't pay you for whispers. *Sing!*"

"*. . . THE BEAR!*" thundered Butterbumps, his great deep voice echoing off the rafters. "*OH, COME, THEY SAID, OH COME TO THE FAIR! THE FAIR! SAID HE, BUT I'M A BEAR! ALL BLACK AND BROWN, AND COVERED WITH HAIR!*"

The wrinkled old lady smiled. "At Highgarden we have many spiders amongst the flowers. So long as they keep to themselves we let them spin their little webs, but if they get underfoot we step on them." She patted Sansa on the back of the hand. "Now, child, the truth. What sort of man is this Joffrey, who calls himself Baratheon but looks so very Lannister?"

"*AND DOWN THE ROAD FROM HERE TO THERE. FROM HERE! TO THERE! THREE BOYS, A GOAT, AND A DANCING BEAR!*"

Sansa felt as though her heart had lodged in her throat. The Queen of Thorns was so close she could smell the old woman's sour breath. Her gaunt thin fingers were pinching her wrist. To her other side, Margaery was listening as well. A shiver went through her. "A monster," she whispered, so tremulously she could scarcely hear her own voice. "Joffrey is a monster. He lied about the butcher's boy and made Father kill my wolf. When I displease him, he has the Kingsguard beat me. He's evil and cruel, my lady, it's so. And the queen as well."

Lady Olenna Tyrell and her granddaughter exchanged a look. "Ah," said the old woman, "that's a pity."

Oh, gods, thought Sansa, horrified. *If Margaery won't marry him, Joff will know that I'm to blame.* "Please," she blurted, "don't stop the wedding . . ."

"Have no fear, Lord Puff Fish is determined that Margaery shall be queen. And the word of a Tyrell is worth more than all the gold in Casterly Rock. At least it was in my day. Even so, we thank you for the truth, child."

"*. . . DANCED AND SPUN, ALL THE WAY TO THE FAIR! THE FAIR! THE FAIR!*" Butterbumps hopped and roared and stomped his feet.

"Sansa, would you like to visit Highgarden?" When Margaery Tyrell smiled, she looked very like her brother Loras. "All the autumn flowers are in bloom just now, and there are groves and fountains, shady courtyards, marble colonnades. My lord father always keeps singers at court, sweeter ones than Butters here, and pipers and fiddlers and harpers as well. We have the best horses, and pleasure boats to sail along the Mander. Do you hawk, Sansa?"

"A little," she admitted.

"*OH, SWEET SHE WAS, AND PURE, AND FAIR! THE MAID WITH HONEY IN HER HAIR!*"

"You will love Highgarden as I do, I know it." Margaery brushed back a loose strand of Sansa's hair. "Once you see it, you'll never want to leave. And perhaps you won't have to."

"*HER HAIR! HER HAIR! THE MAID WITH HONEY IN HER HAIR!*"

"Shush, child," the Queen of Thorns said sharply. "Sansa hasn't even told us that she would like to come for a visit."

"Oh, but I would," Sansa said. Highgarden sounded like the place she had always dreamed of, like the beautiful magical court she had once hoped to find at King's Landing.

". . . SMELLED THE SCENT ON THE SUMMER AIR. THE BEAR! THE BEAR! ALL BLACK AND BROWN AND COVERED WITH HAIR."

"But the queen," Sansa went on, "she won't let me go . . ."

"She will. Without Highgarden, the Lannisters have no hope of keeping Joffrey on his throne. If my son the lord oaf asks, she will have no choice but to grant his request."

"Will he?" asked Sansa. "Will he ask?"

Lady Olenna frowned. "I see no need to give him a choice. Of course, he has no hint of our true purpose."

"HE SMELLED THE SCENT ON THE SUMMER AIR!"

Sansa wrinkled her brow. "Our true purpose, my lady?"

"HE SNIFFED AND ROARED AND SMELLED IT THERE! HONEY ON THE SUMMER AIR!"

"To see you safely wed, child," the old woman said, as Butterbumps bellowed out the old, old song, "to my grandson."

Wed to Ser Loras, oh . . . Sansa's breath caught in her throat. She remembered Ser Loras in his sparkling sapphire armor, tossing her a rose. Ser Loras in white silk, so pure, innocent, beautiful. The dimples at the corner of his mouth when he smiled. The sweetness of his laugh, the warmth of his hand. She could only imagine what it would be like to pull up his tunic and caress the smooth skin underneath, to stand on her toes and kiss him, to run her fingers through those thick brown curls and drown in his deep brown eyes. A flush crept up her neck.

"OH, I'M A MAID, AND I'M PURE AND FAIR! I'LL NEVER DANCE WITH A HAIRY BEAR! A BEAR! A BEAR! I'LL NEVER DANCE WITH A HAIRY BEAR!"

"Would you like that, Sansa?" asked Margaery. "I've never had a sister, only brothers. Oh, please say yes, please say that you will consent to marry my brother."

The words came tumbling out of her. "Yes. I will. I would like that more than anything. To wed Ser Loras, to love him . . ."

"Loras?" Lady Olenna sounded annoyed. "Don't be foolish, child. Kingsguard never wed. Didn't they teach you anything in Winterfell? We were speaking of my grandson Willas. He is a bit old for you, to be sure, but a dear boy for all that. Not the least bit oafish, and heir to Highgarden besides."

Sansa felt dizzy; one instant her head was full of dreams of Loras, and the next they had all been snatched away. *Willas? Willas?* "I," she said stupidly. *Courtesy is a lady's armor. You must not offend them, be careful what you say.* "I do not know Ser Willas. I have never had the pleasure, my lady. Is he . . . is he as great a knight as his brothers?"

". . . LIFTED HER HIGH INTO THE AIR! THE BEAR! THE BEAR!"

"No," Margaery said. "He has never taken vows."

Her grandmother frowned. "Tell the girl the truth. The poor lad is crippled, and that's the way of it."

"He was hurt as a squire, riding in his first tourney," Margaery confided. "His horse fell and crushed his leg."

"That snake of a Dornishman was to blame, that Oberyn Martell. And his maester as well."

"I CALLED FOR A KNIGHT, BUT YOU'RE A BEAR! A BEAR! A BEAR! ALL BLACK AND BROWN AND COVERED WITH HAIR!"

"Willas has a bad leg but a good heart," said Margaery. "He used to read to me when I was a little girl, and draw me pictures of the stars. You will love him as much as we do, Sansa."

"SHE KICKED AND WAILED, THE MAID SO FAIR, BUT HE LICKED THE HONEY FROM HER HAIR. HER HAIR! HER HAIR! HE LICKED THE HONEY FROM HER HAIR!"

"When might I meet him?" asked Sansa, hesitantly.

"Soon," promised Margaery. "When you come to Highgarden, after Joffrey and I are wed. My grandmother will take you."

"I will," said the old woman, patting Sansa's hand and smiling a soft wrinkly smile. "I will indeed."

"THEN SHE SIGHED AND SQUEALED AND KICKED THE AIR! MY BEAR! SHE SANG. MY BEAR SO FAIR! AND OFF THEY WENT, FROM HERE TO THERE, THE BEAR, THE BEAR, AND THE MAIDEN FAIR."

Butterbumps roared the last line, leapt into the air, and came down on both feet with a crash that shook the wine cups on the table. The women laughed and clapped.

"I thought that dreadful song would never end," said the Queen of Thorns. "But look, here comes my cheese."

JON

The world was grey darkness, smelling of pine and moss and cold. Pale mists rose from the black earth as the riders threaded their way through the scatter of stones and scraggly trees, down toward the welcoming fires strewn like jewels across the floor of the river valley below. There were more fires than Jon Snow could count, hundreds of fires, thousands, a second river of flickery lights along the banks of the icy white Milkwater. The fingers of his sword hand opened and closed.

They descended the ridge without banners or trumpets, the quiet broken only by the distant murmur of the river, the clop of hooves, and the clacking of Rattleshirt's bone armor. Somewhere above an eagle soared on great blue-grey wings, while below came men and dogs and horses and one white direwolf.

A stone bounced down the slope, disturbed by a passing hoof, and Jon saw Ghost turn his head at the sudden sound. He had followed the riders at a distance all day, as was his custom, but when the moon rose over the soldier pines he'd come bounding up, red eyes aglow. Rattleshirt's dogs greeted him with a chorus of snarls and growls and wild barking, as ever, but the direwolf paid them no mind. Six days ago, the largest hound had attacked him from behind as the wildlings camped for the night, but Ghost had turned and lunged, sending the dog fleeing with a bloody haunch. The rest of the pack maintained a healthy distance after that.

Jon Snow's garron whickered softly, but a touch and a soft word soon quieted the animal. Would that his own fears could be calmed so easily. He was all in black, the black of the Night's Watch, but the enemy rode before and behind. *Wildlings, and I am with them.* Ygritte wore the cloak of Qhorin Halfhand. Lenyl had his hauberk, the big spearwife Ragwyle his gloves, one of the bowmen his boots. Qhorin's helm had been won by the short homely man called Longspear Ryk, but it fit poorly on his narrow head, so he'd given that to Ygritte as well. And Rattleshirt had Qhorin's bones in his bag, along with the bloody head of Ebben, who set out with Jon to scout the Skirling Pass. *Dead, all dead but me, and I am dead to the world.*

Ygritte rode just behind him. In front was Longspear Ryk. The Lord of Bones had made the two of them his guards. "If the crow flies, I'll boil your bones as well," he warned them when they had set out, smiling through the crooked teeth of the giant's skull he wore for a helm.

Ygritte hooted at him. "*You* want to guard him? If you want us to do it, leave us be and we'll do it."

These are a free folk indeed, Jon saw. Rattleshirt might lead them, but none of them were shy in talking back to him.

The wildling leader fixed him with an unfriendly stare. "Might be you fooled these others, crow, but don't think you'll be fooling Mance. He'll take one look a' you and know you're false. And when he does, I'll make a cloak o' your wolf there, and open your soft boy's belly and sew a weasel up inside."

Jon's sword hand opened and closed, flexing the burned fingers beneath the glove, but Longspear Ryk only laughed. "And where would you find a weasel in the snow?"

That first night, after a long day ahorse, they made camp in a shallow stone bowl atop a nameless mountain, huddling close to the fire while the snow began to fall. Jon watched the flakes melt as they drifted over the flames. Despite his layers of wool and fur and leather, he'd felt cold to the bone. Ygritte sat beside him after she had eaten, her hood pulled up and her hands tucked into her sleeves for warmth. "When Mance hears how you did for Halfhand, he'll take you quick enough," she told him.

"Take me for what?"

The girl laughed scornfully. "For one o' us. D'ya think you're the first crow ever flew down off the Wall? In your hearts you all want to fly free."

"And when I'm free," he said slowly, "will I be free to go?"

"Sure you will." She had a warm smile, despite her crooked teeth. "And we'll be free to kill you. It's *dangerous* being free, but most come to like the taste o' it." She put her gloved hand on his leg, just above the knee. "You'll see."

I will, thought Jon. *I will see, and hear, and learn, and when I have I will carry the word back to the Wall.* The wildlings had taken him for an oathbreaker, but in his heart he was still a man of the Night's Watch, doing the last duty that Qhorin Halfhand had laid on him. *Before I killed him.*

At the bottom of the slope they came upon a little stream flowing down from the foothills to join the Milkwater. It looked all stones and glass, though they could hear the sound of water running beneath the frozen surface. Rattleshirt led them across, shattering the thin crust of ice.

Mance Rayder's outriders closed in as they emerged. Jon took their measure with a glance: eight riders, men and women both, clad in fur and boiled leather, with here and there a helm or bit of mail. They were armed with spears and fire-hardened lances, all but their leader, a fleshy blond man with watery eyes who bore a great curved scythe of sharpened steel. *The Weeper,* he knew at once. The black brothers told tales of this one. Like Rattleshirt and Harma Dogshead and Alfyn Crowkiller, he was a known raider.

"The Lord o' Bones," the Weeper said when he saw them. He eyed Jon and his wolf. "Who's this, then?"

"A crow come over," said Rattleshirt, who preferred to be called the Lord of Bones, for the clattering armor he wore.

"He was afraid I'd take his bones as well as Halfhand's." He shook his sack of trophies at the other wildlings.

"He slew Qhorin Halfhand," said Longspear Ryk. "Him and that wolf o' his."

"And did for Orell too," said Rattleshirt.

"The lad's a warg, or close enough," put in Ragwyle, the big spearwife. "His wolf took a piece o' Halfhand's leg."

The Weeper's red rheumy eyes gave Jon another look. "Aye? Well, he has a wolfish cast to him, now as I look close. Bring him to Mance, might be he'll keep him." He wheeled his horse around and galloped off, his riders hard behind him.

The wind was blowing wet and heavy as they crossed the valley of the Milkwater and rode singlefile through the river camp. Ghost kept close to Jon, but the scent of him went before them like a herald, and soon there were wildling dogs all around them, growling and barking. Lenyl screamed at them to be quiet, but they paid him no heed. "They don't much care for that beast o' yours," Longspear Ryk said to Jon.

"They're dogs and he's a wolf," said Jon. "They know he's not their kind." *No more than I am yours.* But he had his duty to be mindful of, the task Qhorin Halfhand had laid upon him as they shared that final fire—to play the part of turncloak, and find whatever it was that the wildlings had been seeking in the bleak cold wilderness of the Frostfangs. "Some *power*," Qhorin had named it to the Old Bear, but he had died before learning what it was, or whether Mance Rayder had found it with his digging.

There were cookfires all along the river, amongst wayns and carts and sleds. Many of the wildlings had thrown up tents, of hide and skin and felted wool. Others sheltered behind rocks in crude lean-tos, or slept beneath their wagons. At one fire Jon saw a man hardening the points of long wooden spears and tossing them in a pile. Elsewhere two bearded youths in boiled leather were sparring with staffs, leaping at each other over the flames, grunting each time one landed a blow. A dozen women sat nearby in a circle, fletching arrows.

Arrows for my brothers, Jon thought. *Arrows for my father's folk, for the people of Winterfell and Deepwood Motte and the Last Hearth. Arrows for the north.*

But not all he saw was warlike. He saw women dancing as well, and heard a baby crying, and a little boy ran in front of his garron, all bundled up in fur and breathless from play. Sheep and goats wandered freely, while oxen plodded along the riverbank in search of grass. The smell of roast mutton drifted from one cookfire, and at another he saw a boar turning on a wooden spit.

In an open space surrounded by tall green soldier pines, Rattleshirt dismounted. "We'll make camp here," he told Lenyl and Ragwyle and the others. "Feed the horses, then the dogs, then yourself. Ygritte, Longspear, bring the crow so Mance can have his look. We'll gut him after."

They walked the rest of the way, past more cookfires and more tents, with Ghost following at their heels. Jon had never seen so many wildlings. He wondered if anyone ever had. *The camp goes on forever,* he reflected, *but it's more a hundred camps than one, and each more vulnerable than the last.* Stretched out over long leagues, the wildlings had no defenses to speak of, no pits nor sharpened stakes, only small groups of outriders patrolling their perimeters. Each group or clan or village had simply stopped where they wanted, as soon as they saw others stopping or found a likely spot. *The free folk.* If his brothers were to catch them in such disarray, many of them would pay for that freedom with their life's blood. They had numbers, but the Night's Watch had discipline, and in battle discipline beats numbers nine times of every ten, his father had once told him.

There was no doubting which tent was the king's. It was thrice the size of the next largest he'd seen, and he could hear music drifting from within. Like many of the lesser tents it was made of sewn hides with the fur still on, but Mance Rayder's hides were the shaggy white pelts of snow bears. The peaked roof was crowned with a huge set of antlers from one of the giant elks that had once roamed freely throughout the Seven Kingdoms, in the times of the First Men.

Here at least they found defenders; two guards at the flap of the tent, leaning on tall spears with round leather shields strapped to their arms. When they caught sight of Ghost, one of them lowered his spearpoint and said, "That beast stays here."

"Ghost, stay," Jon commanded. The direwolf sat.

"Longspear, watch the beast." Rattleshirt yanked open the tent and gestured Jon and Ygritte inside.

The tent was hot and smoky. Baskets of burning peat stood in all four corners, filling the air with a dim reddish light. More skins carpeted the ground. Jon felt utterly alone as he stood there in his blacks, awaiting the pleasure of the turncloak who called himself King-beyond-the-Wall. When his eyes had adjusted to the smoky red gloom, he saw six people, none of whom paid him any mind. A dark young man and a pretty blonde woman were sharing a horn of mead. A pregnant woman stood over a brazier cooking a brace of hens, while a grey-haired man in a tattered cloak of black and red sat crosslegged on a pillow, playing a lute and singing:

> *The Dornishman's wife was as fair as the sun,*
> *and her kisses were warmer than spring.*
> *But the Dornishman's blade was made of black steel,*
> *and its kiss was a terrible thing.*

Jon knew the song, though it was strange to hear it here, in a shaggy hide tent beyond the Wall, ten thousand leagues from the red mountains and warm winds of Dorne.

Rattleshirt took off his yellowed helm as he waited for the song to end. Beneath his bone-and-leather armor he was a small man, and the face under the giant's skull was ordinary, with a knobby chin, thin mustache, and sallow, pinched cheeks. His eyes were close-set, one eyebrow creeping all the way across his forehead, dark hair thinning back from a sharp widow's peak.

> *The Dornishman's wife would sing as she bathed,*
> *in a voice that was sweet as a peach,*
> *But the Dornishman's blade had a song of its own,*
> *and a bite sharp and cold as a leech.*

Beside the brazier, a short but immensely broad man sat on a stool, eating a hen off a skewer. Hot grease was running down his chin and into his snow-white beard, but he smiled happily all the same. Thick gold bands graven with runes bound his massive arms, and he wore a heavy shirt of black ringmail that could only have come from a dead ranger. A few feet away, a taller, leaner man in a leather shirt sewn with bronze scales stood frowning over a map, a two-handed greatsword slung across his back in a leather sheath. He was straight as a spear, all long wiry muscle, clean-shaved, bald, with a strong straight nose and deepset grey eyes. He might even have been comely if he'd had ears, but he had lost both along the way, whether to frost-bite or some enemy's knife Jon could not tell. Their lack made the man's head seem narrow and pointed.

Both the white-bearded man and the bald one were war-riors, that was plain to Jon at a glance. *These two are more dangerous than Rattleshirt by far*. He wondered which was Mance Rayder.

> *As he lay on the ground with the darkness around,*
> *and the taste of his blood on his tongue,*
> *His brothers knelt by him and prayed him a prayer,*
> *and he smiled and he laughed and he sung,*
> *"Brothers, oh brothers, my days here are done,*
> *the Dornishman's taken my life,*
> *But what does it matter, for all men must die,*
> *and I've tasted the Dornishman's wife!"*

As the last strains of "The Dornishman's Wife" faded, the bald earless man glanced up from his map and scowled ferociously at Rattleshirt and Ygritte, with Jon between them. "What's this?" he said. "A crow?"

"The black bastard what gutted Orell," said Rattleshirt, "and a bloody warg as well."

"You were to kill them all."

"This one come over," explained Ygritte. "He slew Qhorin Halfhand with his own hand."

"This *boy*?" The earless man was angered by the news. "The Halfhand should have been mine. Do you have a name, crow?"

"Jon Snow, Your Grace." He wondered whether he was expected to bend the knee as well.

"Your Grace?" The earless man looked at the big white-bearded one. "You see. He takes me for a king."

The bearded man laughed so hard he sprayed bits of chicken everywhere. He rubbed the grease from his mouth with the back of a huge hand. "A blind boy, must be. Who ever heard of a king without ears? Why, his crown would fall straight down to his neck! Har!" He grinned at Jon, wiping his fingers clean on his breeches. "Close your beak, crow. Spin yourself around, might be you'd find who you're looking for."

Jon turned.

The singer rose to his feet. "I'm Mance Rayder," he said as he put aside the lute. "And you are Ned Stark's bastard, the Snow of Winterfell."

Stunned, Jon stood speechless for a moment, before he recovered enough to say, "How . . . how could you know . . ."

"That's a tale for later," said Mance Rayder. "How did you like the song, lad?"

"Well enough. I'd heard it before."

"*But what does it matter, for all men must die,*" the King-beyond-the-Wall said lightly, "*and I've tasted the Dornishman's wife.* Tell me, does my Lord of Bones speak truly? Did you slay my old friend the Halfhand?"

"I did." *Though it was his doing more than mine.*

"The Shadow Tower will never again seem as fearsome," the king said with sadness in his voice. "Qhorin was my enemy. But also my brother, once. So . . . shall I thank you for killing him, Jon Snow? Or curse you?" He gave Jon a mocking smile.

The King-beyond-the-Wall looked nothing like a king, nor even much a wildling. He was of middling height, slender, sharp-faced, with shrewd brown eyes and long brown hair that had gone mostly to grey. There was no crown on his head, no gold rings on his arms, no jewels at his throat, not even a gleam of silver. He wore wool and leather, and his only garment of note was his ragged black wool cloak, its long tears patched with faded red silk.

"You ought to thank me for killing your enemy," Jon said finally, "and curse me for killing your friend."

"*Har!*" boomed the white-bearded man. "Well answered!"

"Agreed." Mance Rayder beckoned Jon closer. "If you would join us, you'd best know us. The man you took for me is Styr, Magnar of Thenn. *Magnar* means 'lord' in the Old Tongue." The earless man stared at Jon coldly as

Mance turned to the white-bearded one. "Our ferocious chicken-eater here is my loyal Tormund. The woman—"

Tormund rose to his feet. "Hold. You gave Styr his style, give me mine."

Mance Rayder laughed. "As you wish. Jon Snow, before you stands Tormund Giantsbane, Tall-talker, Horn-blower, and Breaker of Ice. And here also Tormund Thunderfist, Husband to Bears, the Mead-king of Ruddy Hall, Speaker to Gods and Father of Hosts."

"That sounds more like me," said Tormund. "Well met, Jon Snow. I am fond o' wargs, as it happens, though not o' Starks."

"The good woman at the brazier," Mance Rayder went on, "is Dalla." The pregnant woman smiled shyly. "Treat her like you would any queen, she is carrying my child." He turned to the last two. "This beauty is her sister Val. Young Jarl beside her is her latest pet."

"I am no man's pet," said Jarl, dark and fierce.

"And Val's no man," white-bearded Tormund snorted. "You ought to have noticed that by now, lad."

"So there you have us, Jon Snow," said Mance Rayder. "The King-beyond-the-Wall and his court, such as it is. And now some words from you, I think. Where did you come from?"

"Winterfell," he said, "by way of Castle Black."

"And what brings you up the Milkwater, so far from the fires of home?" He did not wait for Jon's answer, but looked at once to Rattleshirt. "How many were they?"

"Five. Three's dead and the boy's here. T'other went up a mountainside where no horse could follow."

Rayder's eyes met Jon's again. "Was it only the five of you? Or are more of your brothers skulking about?"

"We were four and the Halfhand. Qhorin was worth twenty common men."

The King-beyond-the-Wall smiled at that. "Some thought so. Still . . . a boy from Castle Black with rangers from the Shadow Tower? How did that come to be?"

Jon had his lie all ready. "The Lord Commander sent me to the Halfhand for seasoning, so he took me on his ranging."

Styr the Magnar frowned at that. "Ranging, you call it . . . why would crows come ranging up the Skirling Pass?"

"The villages were deserted," Jon said, truthfully. "It was as if all the free folk had vanished."

"Vanished, aye," said Mance Rayder. "And not just the free folk. Who told you where we were, Jon Snow?"

Tormund snorted. "It were Craster, or I'm a blushing maid. I told you, Mance, that creature needs to be shorter by a head."

The king gave the older man an irritated look. "Tormund, some day try thinking before you speak. I know it was Craster. I asked Jon to see if he would tell it true."

"Har." Tormund spat. "Well, I stepped in that!" He grinned at Jon. "See, lad, that's why he's king and I'm not. I can outdrink, outfight, and outsing him, and my member's thrice the size o' his, but Mance has cunning. He was raised a crow, you know, and the crow's a tricksy bird."

"I would speak with the lad alone, my Lord of Bones," Mance Rayder said to Rattleshirt. "Leave us, all of you."

"What, me as well?" said Tormund.

"No, you especially," said Mance.

"I eat in no hall where I'm not welcome." Tormund got to his feet. "Me and the hens are leaving." He snatched another chicken off the brazier, shoved it into a pocket sewn in the lining of his cloak, said "Har," and left licking his fingers. The others followed him out, all but the woman Dalla.

"Sit, if you like," Rayder said when they were gone. "Are you hungry? Tormund left us two birds at least."

"I would be pleased to eat, Your Grace. And thank you."

"Your Grace?" The king smiled. "That's not a style one often hears from the lips of free folk. I'm Mance to most, *The* Mance to some. Will you take a horn of mead?"

"Gladly," said Jon.

The king poured himself as Dalla cut the well-crisped hens apart and brought them each a half. Jon peeled off his gloves and ate with his fingers, sucking every morsel of meat off the bones.

"Tormund spoke truly," said Mance Rayder as he ripped apart a loaf of bread. "The black crow is a tricksy bird, that's so . . . but I was a crow when you were no bigger than the babe in Dalla's belly, Jon Snow. So take care not to play tricksy with me."

"As you say, Your—Mance."

The king laughed. "Your Mance! Why not? I promised you a tale before, of how I knew you. Have you puzzled it out yet?"

Jon shook his head. "Did Rattleshirt send word ahead?"

"By wing? We have no trained ravens. No, I knew your face. I've seen it before. Twice."

It made no sense at first, but as Jon turned it over in his mind, dawn broke. "When you were a brother of the Watch . . ."

"Very good! Yes, that was the first time. You were just a boy, and I was all in black, one of a dozen riding escort to old Lord Commander Qorgyle when he came down to see your father at Winterfell. I was walking the wall around the yard when I came on you and your brother Robb. It had snowed the night before, and the two of you had built a great mountain above the gate and were waiting for some-one likely to pass underneath."

"I remember," said Jon with a startled laugh. A young black brother on the wallwalk, yes . . . "You swore not to tell."

"And kept my vow. That one, at least."

"We dumped the snow on Fat Tom. He was Father's slowest guardsman." Tom had chased them around the yard afterward, until all three were red as autumn apples. "But you said you saw me twice. When was the other time?"

"When King Robert came to Winterfell to make your fa-ther Hand," the King-beyond-the-Wall said lightly.

Jon's eyes widened in disbelief. "That can't be so."

"It was. When your father learned the king was coming, he sent word to his brother Benjen on the Wall, so he might come down for the feast. There is more commerce between the black brothers and the free folk than you know, and soon enough word came to my ears as well. It was too choice a chance to resist. Your uncle did not know me by sight, so I had no fear from that quarter, and I did not think your father was like to remember a young crow he'd met briefly years before. I wanted to see this Robert with my own eyes, king to king, and get the measure of your uncle Benjen as well. He was First Ranger by then, and the bane of all my people. So I saddled my fleetest horse, and rode."

"But," Jon objected, "the Wall . . ."

"The Wall can stop an army, but not a man alone. I took a lute and a bag of silver, scaled the ice near Long Barrow, walked a few leagues south of the New Gift, and bought a horse. All in all I made much better time than Robert, who was traveling with a ponderous great wheelhouse to keep his queen in comfort. A day south of Winterfell I came up on him and fell in with his company. Freeriders and hedge knights are always attaching themselves to royal processions, in hopes of finding service with the king, and my lute gained me easy acceptance." He laughed. "I know every bawdy song that's ever been made, north or south of the Wall. So there you are. The night your father feasted Robert, I sat in the back of his hall on a bench with the other freeriders, listening to Orland of Oldtown play the high harp and sing of dead kings beneath the sea. I betook of your lord father's meat and mead, had a look at Kingslayer and Imp . . . and made passing note of Lord Eddard's children and the wolf pups that ran at their heels."

"Bael the Bard," said Jon, remembering the tale that Ygritte had told him in the Frostfangs, the night he'd almost killed her.

"Would that I were. I will not deny that Bael's exploit inspired mine own . . . but I did not steal either of your sisters that I recall. Bael wrote his own songs, and lived them. I only sing the songs that better men have made. More mead?"

"No," said Jon. "If you had been discovered . . . taken . . ."

"Your father would have had my head off." The king gave a shrug. "Though once I had eaten at his board I was protected by guest right. The laws of hospitality are as old as the First Men, and sacred as a heart tree." He gestured at the board between them, the broken bread and chicken bones. "Here you are the guest, and safe from harm at my hands . . . this night, at least. So tell me truly, Jon Snow. Are you a craven who turned your cloak from fear, or is there another reason that brings you to my tent?"

Guest right or no, Jon Snow knew he walked on rotten ice here. One false step and he might plunge through, into water cold enough to stop his heart. *Weigh every word before you speak it*, he told himself. He took a long draught of mead to buy time for his answer. When he set the horn aside he said, "Tell me why you turned your cloak, and I'll tell you why I turned mine."

Mance Rayder smiled, as Jon had hoped he would. The king was plainly a man who liked the sound of his own voice. "You will have heard stories of my desertion, I have no doubt."

"Some say it was for a crown. Some say for a woman. Others that you had the wildling blood."

"The wildling blood is the blood of the First Men, the same blood that flows in the veins of the Starks. As to a crown, do you see one?"

"I see a woman." He glanced at Dalla.

Mance took her by the hand and pulled her close. "My lady is blameless. I met her on my return from your father's castle. The Halfhand was carved of old oak, but I am made of flesh, and I have a great fondness for the charms of women . . . which makes me no different from three-quarters of the Watch. There are men still wearing black who have had ten times as many women as this poor king. You must guess again, Jon Snow."

Jon considered a moment. "The Halfhand said you had a passion for wildling music."

"I did. I do. That's closer to the mark, yes. But not a hit." Mance Rayder rose, unfastened the clasp that held his cloak, and swept it over the bench. "It was for this."

"A cloak?"

"The black wool cloak of a Sworn Brother of the Night's Watch," said the King-beyond-the-Wall. "One day on a ranging we brought down a fine big elk. We were skinning it when the smell of blood drew a shadow-cat out of its lair. I drove it off, but not before it shredded my cloak to ribbons. Do you see? Here, here, and here?" He chuckled. "It shredded my arm and back as well, and I bled worse than the elk. My brothers feared I might die before they got me back to Maester Mullin at the Shadow Tower, so they carried me to a wildling village where we knew an old wise-woman did some healing. She was dead, as it happened, but her daughter saw to me. Cleaned my wounds, sewed me up, and fed me porridge and potions until I was strong enough to ride again. And she sewed up the rents in my cloak as well, with some scarlet silk from Asshai that her grandmother had pulled from the wreck of a cog washed up on the Frozen Shore. It was the greatest treasure she had, and her gift to me." He swept the cloak back over his shoulders. "But at the Shadow Tower, I was given a new wool cloak from stores, black and black, and trimmed with black, to go with my black breeches and black boots, my black doublet and black mail. The new cloak had no frays nor rips nor tears . . . and most of all, no red. The men of the Night's Watch dressed in *black*, Ser Denys Mallister reminded me sternly, as if I had forgotten. My old cloak was fit for burning now, he said.

"I left the next morning . . . for a place where a kiss was not a crime, and a man could wear any cloak he chose." He closed the clasp and sat back down again. "And you, Jon Snow?"

Jon took another swallow of mead. *There is only one tale that he might believe.* "You say you were at Winterfell, the night my father feasted King Robert."

"I did say it, for I was."

"Then you saw us all. Prince Joffrey and Prince Tommen, Princess Myrcella, my brothers Robb and Bran and Rickon, my sisters Arya and Sansa. You saw them walk the center aisle with every eye upon them and take their seats at the table just below the dais where the king and queen were seated."

"I remember."

"And did you see where I was seated, Mance?" He leaned forward. "Did you see where they put the bastard?"

Mance Rayder looked at Jon's face for a long moment. "I think we had best find you a new cloak," the king said, holding out his hand.

DAENERYS

Across the still blue water came the slow steady beat of drums and the soft swish of oars from the galleys. The great cog groaned in their wake, the heavy lines stretched taut between. *Balerion's* sails hung limp, drooping forlorn from the masts. Yet even so, as she stood upon the forecastle watching her dragons chase each other across a cloudless blue sky, Daenerys Targaryen was as happy as she could ever remember being.

Her Dothraki called the sea *the poison water*, distrusting any liquid that their horses could not drink. On the day the three ships had lifted anchor at Quarth, you would have thought they were sailing to hell instead of Pentos. Her brave young bloodriders had stared off at the dwindling coastline with huge white eyes, each of the three determined to show no fear before the other two, while her handmaids Irri and Jhiqui clutched the rail desperately and retched over the side at every little swell. The rest of Dany's tiny *khalasar* remained below decks, preferring the company of their nervous horses to the terrifying landless world about the ships. When a sudden squall had enveloped them six days into the voyage, she heard them through the hatches; the horses kicking and screaming, the riders praying in thin quavery voices each time *Balerion* heaved or swayed.

No squall could frighten Dany, though. *Daenerys Stormborn*, she was called, for she had come howling into the world on distant Dragonstone as the greatest storm in the memory of Westeros howled outside, a storm so fierce that it ripped gargoyles from the castle walls and smashed her father's fleet to kindling.

The narrow sea was often stormy, and Dany had crossed it half a hundred times as a girl, running from one Free City to the next half a step ahead of the Usurper's hired knives. She loved the sea. She liked the sharp salty smell of the air, and the vastness of horizons bounded only by a vault of azure sky above. It made her feel small, but free as well. She liked the dolphins that sometimes swam along beside *Balerion*, slicing through the waves like silvery spears, and the flying fish they glimpsed now and again. She even liked the sailors, with all their songs and stories. Once on a voyage to Braavos, as she'd watched the crew wrestle down a great green sail in a rising gale, she had even thought how fine it would be to be a sailor. But when she told her brother, Viserys had twisted her hair until she cried. "You are blood of the dragon," he had screamed at her. "A *dragon*, not some smelly fish."

He was a fool about that, and so much else, Dany thought. *If he had been wiser and more patient, it would be him sailing west to take the throne that was his by rights.* Viserys had been stupid and vicious, she had come to realize, yet sometimes she missed him all the same. Not the cruel weak man he had become by the end, but the brother who had sometimes let her creep into his bed, the boy who told her tales of the Seven Kingdoms, and talked of how much better their lives would be once he claimed his crown.

The captain appeared at her elbow. "Would that this *Balerion* could soar as her namesake did, Your Grace," he said in bastard Valyrian heavily flavored with accents of Pentos. "Then we should not need to row, nor tow, nor pray for wind."

"Just so, Captain," she answered with a smile, pleased

to have won the man over. Captain Groleo was an old Pentoshi like his master, Illyrio Mopatis, and he had been nervous as a maiden about carrying three dragons on his ship. Half a hundred buckets of seawater still hung from the gunwales, in case of fires. At first Groleo had wanted the dragons caged and Dany had consented to put his fears at ease, but their misery was so palpable that she soon changed her mind and insisted they be freed.

Even Captain Groleo was glad of that, now. There had been one small fire, easily extinguished; against that, *Balerion* suddenly seemed to have far fewer rats than she'd had before, when she sailed under the name *Saduleon*. And her crew, once as fearful as they were curious, had begun to take a queer fierce pride in "their" dragons. Every man of them, from captain to cook's boy, loved to watch the three fly . . . though none so much as Dany.

They are my children, she told herself, *and if the* maegi *spoke truly, they are the only children I am ever like to have.*

Viserion's scales were the color of fresh cream, his horns, wing bones, and spinal crest a dark gold that flashed bright as metal in the sun. Rhaegal was made of the green of summer and the bronze of fall. They soared above the ships in wide circles, higher and higher, each trying to climb above the other.

Dragons always preferred to attack from above, Dany had learned. Should either get between the other and the sun, he would fold his wings and dive screaming, and they would tumble from the sky locked together in a tangled scaly ball, jaws snapping and tails lashing. The first time they had done it, she feared that they meant to kill each other, but it was only sport. No sooner would they splash into the sea than they would break apart and rise again, shrieking and hissing, the salt water steaming off them as their wings clawed at the air. Drogon was aloft as well, though not in sight; he would be miles ahead, or miles behind, hunting.

He was always hungry, her Drogon. *Hungry and growing fast. Another year, or perhaps two, and he may be large enough to ride. Then I shall have no need of ships to cross the great salt sea.*

But that time was not yet come. Rhaegal and Viserion

were the size of small dogs, Drogon only a little larger, and any dog would have out-weighed them; they were all wings and neck and tail, lighter than they looked. And so Daenerys Targaryen must rely on wood and wind and canvas to bear her home.

The wood and the canvas had served her well enough so far, but the fickle wind had turned traitor. For six days and six nights they had been becalmed, and now a seventh day had come, and still no breath of air to fill their sails. Fortunately, two of the ships that Magister Illyrio had sent after her were trading galleys, with two hundred oars apiece and crews of strong-armed oarsmen to row them. But the great cog *Balerion* was a song of a different key; a ponderous broad-beamed sow of a ship with immense holds and huge sails, but helpless in a calm. *Vhagar* and *Meraxes* had let out lines to tow her, but it made for painfully slow going. All three ships were crowded, and heavily laden.

"I cannot see Drogon," said Ser Jorah Mormont as he joined her on the forecastle. "Is he lost again?"

"We are the ones who are lost, ser. Drogon has no taste for this wet creeping, no more than I do." Bolder than the other two, her black dragon had been the first to try his wings above the water, the first to flutter from ship to ship, the first to lose himself in a passing cloud . . . and the first to kill. The flying fish no sooner broke the surface of the water than they were enveloped in a lance of flame, snatched up, and swallowed. "How big will he grow?" Dany asked curiously. "Do you know?"

"In the Seven Kingdoms, there are tales of dragons who grew so huge that they could pluck giant krakens from the seas."

Dany laughed. "That would be a wondrous sight to see."

"It is only a tale, *Khaleesi*," said her exile knight. "They talk of wise old dragons living a thousand years as well."

"Well, how long *does* a dragon live?" She looked up as Viserion swooped low over the ship, his wings beating slowly and stirring the limp sails.

Ser Jorah shrugged. "A dragon's natural span of days is many times as long as a man's, or so the songs would have us believe . . . but the dragons the Seven Kingdoms knew best were those of House Targaryen. They were bred for war, and in war they died. It is no easy thing to slay a dragon, but it can be done."

The squire Whitebeard, standing by the figurehead with one lean hand curled about his tall hardwood staff, turned toward them and said, "Balerion the Black Dread was two hundred years old when he died during the reign of Jaehaerys the Conciliator. He was so large he could swallow an aurochs whole. A dragon never stops growing, Your Grace, so long as he has food and freedom." His name was Arstan, but Strong Belwas had named him Whitebeard for his pale whiskers, and most everyone called him that now. He was taller than Ser Jorah, though not so muscular; his eyes were a pale blue, his long beard as white as snow and as fine as silk.

"Freedom?" asked Dany, curious. "What do you mean?"

"In King's Landing, your ancestors raised an immense domed castle for their dragons. The Dragonpit, it is called. It still stands atop the Hill of Rhaenys, though all in ruins now. That was where the royal dragons dwelt in days of yore, and a cavernous dwelling it was, with iron doors so wide that thirty knights could ride through them abreast. Yet even so, it was noted that none of the pit dragons ever reached the size of their ancestors. The maesters say it was because of the walls around them, and the great dome above their heads."

"If walls could keep us small, peasants would all be tiny and kings as large as giants," said Ser Jorah. "I've seen huge men born in hovels, and dwarfs who dwelt in castles."

"Men are men," Whitebeard replied. "Dragons are dragons."

Ser Jorah snorted his disdain. "How profound." The exile knight had no love for the old man, he'd made that plain from the first. "What do you know of dragons, anyway?"

"Little enough, that's true. Yet I served for a time in King's Landing in the days when King Aerys sat the Iron Throne, and walked beneath the dragonskulls that looked down from the walls of his throne room."

"Viserys talked of those skulls," said Dany. "The Usurper took them down and hid them away. He could not bear them looking down on him upon his stolen throne." She beckoned Whitebeard closer. "Did you ever meet my royal father?" King Aerys II had died before his daughter was born.

"I had that great honor, Your Grace."

"Did you find him good and gentle?"

Whitebeard did his best to hide his feelings, but they were there, plain on his face. "His Grace was . . . often pleasant."

"Often?" Dany smiled. "But not always?"

"He could be very harsh to those he thought his enemies."

"A wise man never makes an enemy of a king," said Dany. "Did you know my brother Rhaegar as well?"

"It was said that no man ever knew Prince Rhaegar, truly. I had the privilege of seeing him in tourney, though, and often heard him play his harp with its silver strings."

Ser Jorah snorted. "Along with a thousand others at some harvest feast. Next you'll claim you squired for him."

"I make no such claim, ser. Myles Mooton was Prince Rhaegar's squire, and Richard Lonmouth after him. When they won their spurs, he knighted them himself, and they remained his close companions. Young Lord Connington was dear to the prince as well, but his oldest friend was Arthur Dayne."

"The Sword of the Morning!" said Dany, delighted. "Viserys used to talk about his wondrous white blade. He said Ser Arthur was the only knight in the realm who was our brother's peer."

Whitebeard bowed his head. "It is not my place to question the words of Prince Viserys."

"King," Dany corrected. "He was a king, though he never reigned. Viserys, the Third of His Name. But what do you mean?" His answer had not been one that she'd expected. "Ser Jorah named Rhaegar the last dragon once. He had to have been a peerless warrior to be called that, surely?"

"Your Grace," said Whitebeard, "the Prince of Dragonstone was a most puissant warrior, but . . ."

"Go on," she urged. "You may speak freely to me."

"As you command." The old man leaned upon his hardwood staff, his brow furrowed. "A warrior without peer . . . those are fine words, Your Grace, but words win no battles."

"Swords win battles," Ser Jorah said bluntly. "And Prince Rhaegar knew how to use one."

"He did, ser, but . . . I have seen a hundred tournaments and more wars than I would wish, and however strong or fast or skilled a knight may be, there are others who can match him. A man will win one tourney, and fall quickly in the next. A slick spot in the grass may mean defeat, or what you ate for supper the night before. A change in the wind may bring the gift of victory." He glanced at Ser Jorah. "Or a lady's favor knotted round an arm."

Mormont's face darkened. "Be careful what you say, old man."

Arstan had seen Ser Jorah fight at Lannisport, Dany knew, in the tourney Mormont had won with a lady's favor knotted round his arm. He had won the lady too; Lynesse of House Hightower, his second wife, highborn and beautiful . . . but she had ruined him, and abandoned him, and the memory of her was bitter to him now. "Be gentle, my knight." She put a hand on Jorah's arm. "Arstan had no wish to give offense, I'm certain."

"As you say, *Khaleesi.*" Ser Jorah's voice was grudging.

Dany turned back to the squire. "I know little of Rhaegar. Only the tales Viserys told, and he was a little boy when our brother died. What was he truly like?"

The old man considered a moment. "Able. That above all. Determined, deliberate, dutiful, single-minded. There is a tale told of him . . . but doubtless Ser Jorah knows it as well."

"I would hear it from you."

"As you wish," said Whitebeard. "As a young boy, the Prince of Dragonstone was bookish to a fault. He was reading so early that men said Queen Rhaella must have swallowed some books and a candle whilst he was in her womb. Rhaegar took no interest in the play of other children. The maesters were awed by his wits, but his father's knights would jest sourly that Baelor the Blessed had been born again. Until one day Prince Rhaegar found something in his scrolls that changed him. No one knows what it might have been, only that the boy suddenly appeared early one morning in the yard as the knights were donning their steel. He walked up to Ser Willem Darry, the master-at-arms, and said, 'I will require sword and armor. It seems I must be a warrior.' "

"And he was!" said Dany, delighted.

"He was indeed." Whitebeard bowed. "My pardons, Your Grace. We speak of warriors, and I see that Strong Belwas has arisen. I must attend him."

Dany glanced aft. The eunuch was climbing through the hold amidships, nimble for all his size. Belwas was squat but broad, a good fifteen stone of fat and muscle, his great brown gut crisscrossed by faded white scars. He wore baggy pants, a yellow silk bellyband, and an absurdly tiny leather vest dotted with iron studs. "Strong Belwas is hungry!" he roared at everyone and no one in particular. "Strong Belwas will eat now!" Turning, he spied Arstan on the forecastle. "Whitebeard! You will bring food for Strong Belwas!"

"You may go," Dany told the squire. He bowed again, and moved off to tend the needs of the man he served.

Ser Jorah watched with a frown on his blunt honest face. Mormont was big and burly, strong of jaw and thick of shoulder. Not a handsome man by any means, but as true a friend as Dany had ever known. "You would be wise to take that old man's words well salted," he told her when Whitebeard was out of earshot.

"A queen must listen to all," she reminded him. "The highborn and the low, the strong and the weak, the noble and the venal. One voice may speak you false, but in many there is always truth to be found." She had read that in a book.

"Hear my voice then, Your Grace," the exile said. "This Arstan Whitebeard is playing you false. He is too old to be a squire, and too well spoken to be serving that oaf of a eunuch."

That does seem queer, Dany had to admit. Strong Belwas was an ex-slave, bred and trained in the fighting pits of Meereen. Magister Illyrio had sent him to guard her, or so Belwas claimed, and it was true that she needed guarding. The Usurper on his Iron Throne had offered land and lordship to any man who killed her. One attempt had been made already, with a cup of poisoned wine. The closer she came to Westeros, the more likely another attack became. Back in Qarth, the warlock Pyat Pree had sent a Sorrowful Man after her to avenge the Undying she'd burned in their House of Dust. Warlocks never forgot a wrong, it was said, and the Sorrowful Men never failed to kill. Most of the Dothraki would be against her as well. Khal Drogo's *kos* led *khalasars* of their own now, and none of them would hesitate to attack her own little band on sight, to slay and slave her people and drag Dany herself back to Vaes Dothrak to take her proper place among the withered crones of the *dosh khaleen*. She *hoped* that Xaro Xhoan Daxos was not an enemy, but the Quartheen merchant had coveted her dragons. And there was Quaithe of the Shadow, that strange woman in the red lacquer mask with all her cryptic counsel. Was she an enemy too, or only a dangerous friend? Dany could not say.

Ser Jorah saved me from the poisoner, and Arstan Whitebeard from the manticore. Perhaps Strong Belwas will save me from the next. He was huge enough, with arms like small trees and a great curved *arakh* so sharp he might have shaved with it, in the unlikely event of hair sprouting on those smooth brown cheeks. Yet he was childlike as well. *As a protector, he leaves much to be desired. Thankfully, I have Ser Jorah and my bloodriders. And my dragons, never forget.* In time, the dragons would be her most formidable guardians, just as they had been for Aegon the Conqueror and his sisters three hundred years ago. Just now, though, they brought her more danger than protection. In all the world there were but three living dragons, and those were hers; they were a wonder, and a terror, and beyond price.

She was pondering her next words when she felt a cool breath on the back of her neck, and a loose strand of her silver-gold hair stirred against her brow. Above, the canvas creaked and moved, and suddenly a great cry went up from all over *Balerion*. "Wind!" the sailors shouted. "The wind returns, the *wind!*"

Dany looked up to where the great cog's sails rippled and belled as the lines thrummed and tightened and sang the sweet song they had missed so for six long days. Captain Groleo rushed aft, shouting commands. The Pentoshi were scrambling up the masts, those that were not cheering. Even Strong Belwas let out a great bellow and did a little dance. "The gods are good!" Dany said. "You see, Jorah? We are on our way once more."

"Yes," he said, "but to what, my queen?"

All day the wind blew, steady from the east at first, and then in wild gusts. The sun set in a blaze of red. *I am still half a world from Westeros*, Dany reminded herself, *but every hour brings me closer.* She tried to imagine what it would feel like, when she first caught sight of the land she was born to rule. *It will be as fair a shore as I have ever seen, I know it. How could it be otherwise?*

But later that night, as *Balerion* plunged onward through the dark and Dany sat crosslegged on her bunk in the captain's cabin, feeding her dragons—"Even upon the sea," Groleo had said, so graciously, "queens take precedence over captains"—a sharp knock came upon the door.

Irri had been sleeping at the foot of her bunk (it was too narrow for three, and tonight was Jhiqui's turn to share the soft featherbed with her *khaleesi*), but the handmaid roused at the knock and went to the door. Dany pulled up a coverlet and tucked it in under her arms. She was naked, and had not expected a caller at this hour. "Come," she said when she saw Ser Jorah standing without, beneath a swaying lantern.

The exile knight ducked his head as he entered. "Your Grace. I am sorry to disturb your sleep."

"I was not sleeping, ser. Come and watch." She took a chunk of salt pork out of the bowl in her lap and held it up for her dragons to see. All three of them eyed it hungrily. Rhaegal spread green wings and stirred the air, and Viserion's neck swayed back and forth like a long pale snake's as he followed the movement of her hand. "Drogon," Dany said softly, "*dracarys*." And she tossed the pork in the air.

Drogon moved quicker than a striking cobra. Flame roared from his mouth, orange and scarlet and black, searing the meat before it began to fall. As his sharp black teeth snapped shut around it, Rhaegal's head darted close, as if to steal the prize from his brother's jaws, but Drogon swallowed and screamed, and the smaller green dragon could only *hiss* in frustration.

"Stop that, Rhaegal," Dany said in annoyance, giving his head a swat. "You had the last one. I'll have no greedy dragons." She smiled at Ser Jorah. "I won't need to char their meat over a brazier any longer."

"So I see. *Dracarys?*"

All three dragons turned their heads at the sound of that word, and Viserion let loose with a blast of pale gold flame that made Ser Jorah take a hasty step backward. Dany giggled. "Be careful with that word, ser, or they're like to singe your beard off. It means 'dragonfire' in High Valyrian. I wanted to choose a command that no one was like to utter by chance."

Mormont nodded. "Your Grace," he said, "I wonder if I might have a few private words?"

"Of course. Irri, leave us for a bit." She put a hand on Jhiqui's bare shoulder and shook the other handmaid awake. "You as well, sweetling. Ser Jorah needs to talk to me."

"Yes, *Khaleesi.*" Jhiqui tumbled from the bunk, naked and yawning, her thick black hair tumbled about her head. She dressed quickly and left with Irri, closing the door behind them.

Dany gave the dragons the rest of the salt pork to squabble over, and patted the bed beside her. "Sit, good ser, and tell me what is troubling you."

"Three things." Ser Jorah sat. "Strong Belwas. This Arstan Whitebeard. And Illyrio Mopatis, who sent them."

Again? Dany pulled the coverlet higher and tugged one end over her shoulder. "And why is that?"

"The warlocks in Qarth told you that you would be betrayed three times," the exile knight reminded her, as Viserion and Rhaegal began to snap and claw at each other.

"Once for blood and once for gold and once for love." Dany was not like to forget. "Mirri Maz Duur was the first."

"Which means two traitors yet remain . . . and now these two appear. I find that troubling, yes. Never forget, Robert offered a lordship to the man who slays you."

Dany leaned forward and yanked Viserion's tail, to pull him off his green brother. Her blanket fell away from her chest as she moved. She grabbed it hastily and covered herself again. "The Usurper is dead," she said.

"But his son rules in his place." Ser Jorah lifted his gaze, and his dark eyes met her own. "A dutiful son pays his father's debts. Even blood debts."

"This boy Joffrey might want me dead . . . if he recalls

that I'm alive. What has that to do with Belwas and Arstan Whitebeard? The old man does not even wear a sword. You've seen that."

"Aye. And I have seen how deftly he handles that staff of his. Recall how he killed that manticore in Qarth? It might as easily have been your throat he crushed."

"Might have been, but was not," she pointed out. "It was a stinging manticore meant to slay me. He saved my life."

"*Khaleesi*, has it occurred to you that Whitebeard and Belwas might have been in league with the assassin? It might all have been a ploy to win your trust."

Her sudden laughter made Drogon *hiss*, and sent Viserion flapping to his perch above the porthole. "The ploy worked well."

The exile knight did not return her smile. "These are Illyrio's ships, Illyrio's captains, Illyrio's sailors . . . and Strong Belwas and Arstan are his men as well, not yours."

"Magister Illyrio has protected me in the past. Strong Belwas says that he wept when he heard my brother was dead."

"Yes," said Mormont, "but did he weep for Viserys, or for the plans he had made with him?"

"His plans need not change. Magister Illyrio is a friend to House Targaryen, and wealthy . . ."

"He was not born wealthy. In the world as I have seen it, no man grows rich by kindness. The warlocks said the second treason would be for *gold*. What does Illyrio Mopatis love more than gold?"

"His skin." Across the cabin Drogon stirred restlessly, steam rising from his snout. "Mirri Maz Duur betrayed me. I burned her for it."

"Mirri Maz Duur was in your power. In Pentos, you shall be in Illyrio's power. It is not the same. I know the magister as well as you. He is a devious man, and clever—"

"I need clever men about me if I am to win the Iron Throne."

Ser Jorah snorted. "That wineseller who tried to poison you was a clever man as well. Clever men hatch ambitious schemes."

Dany drew her legs up beneath the blanket. "You will protect me. You, and my bloodriders."

"Four men? *Khaleesi*, you believe you know Illyrio Mopatis, very well. Yet you insist on surrounding yourself with men you do *not* know, like this puffed-up eunuch and the world's oldest squire. Take a lesson from Pyat Pree and Xaro Xhoan Daxos."

He means well, Dany reminded herself. *He does all he does for love.* "It seems to me that a queen who trusts no one is as foolish as a queen who trusts everyone. Every man I take into my service is a risk, I understand that, but how am I to win the Seven Kingdoms without such risks? Am I to conquer Westeros with one exile knight and three Dothraki bloodriders?"

His jaw set stubbornly. "Your path is dangerous, I will not deny that. But if you blindly trust in every liar and schemer who crosses it, you will end as your brothers did."

His obstinacy made her angry. *He treats me like some child.* "Strong Belwas could not scheme his way to break-fast. And what lies has Arstan Whitebeard told me?"

"He is not what he pretends to be. He speaks to you more boldly than any squire would dare."

"He spoke frankly at my command. He knew my brother."

"A great many men knew your brother. Your Grace, in Westeros the Lord Commander of the Kingsguard sits on the small council, and serves the king with his wits as well as his steel. If I am the first of your Queensguard, I pray you, hear me out. I have a plan to put to you."

"What plan? Tell me."

"Illyrio Mopatis wants you back in Pentos, under his roof. Very well, go to him . . . but in your own time, and not alone. Let us see how loyal and obedient these new subjects of yours truly are. Command Groleo to change course for Slaver's Bay."

Dany was not certain she liked the sound of that at all. Everything she'd ever heard of the flesh marts in the great slave cities of Yunkai, Meereen, and Astapor was dire and frightening. "What is there for me in Slaver's Bay?"

"An army," said Ser Jorah. "If Strong Belwas is so much to your liking you can buy hundreds more like him out of the fighting pits of Meereen . . . but it is Astapor I'd set my sails for. In Astapor you can buy Unsullied."

"The slaves in the spiked bronze hats?" Dany had seen

Unsullied guards in the Free Cities, posted at the gates of magisters, archons, and dynasts. "Why should I want Unsullied? They don't even ride horses, and most of them are fat."

"The Unsullied you may have seen in Pentos and Myr were household guards. That's soft service, and eunuchs tend to plumpness in any case. Food is the only vice allowed them. To judge all Unsullied by a few old household slaves is like judging all squires by Arstan Whitebeard, Your Grace. Do you know the tale of the Three Thousand of Qohor?"

"No." The coverlet slipped off Dany's shoulder, and she tugged it back into place.

"It was four hundred years ago or more, when the Dothraki first rode out of the east, sacking and burning every town and city in their path. The *khal* who led them was named Temmo. His *khalasar* was not so big as Drogo's, but it was big enough. Fifty thousand, at the least. Half of them braided warriors with bells ringing in their hair.

"The Qohorik knew he was coming. They strengthened their walls, doubled the size of their own guard, and hired two free companies besides, the Bright Banners and the Second Sons. And almost as an afterthought, they sent a man to Astapor to buy three thousand Unsullied. It was a long march back to Qohor, however, and as they approached they saw the smoke and dust and heard the distant din of battle.

"By the time the Unsullied reached the city the sun had set. Crows and wolves were feasting beneath the walls on what remained of the Qohorik heavy horse. The Bright Banners and Second Sons had fled, as sellswords are wont to do in the face of hopeless odds. With dark falling, the Dothraki had retired to their own camps to drink and dance and feast, but none doubted that they would return on the morrow to smash the city gates, storm the walls, and rape, loot, and slave as they pleased.

"But when dawn broke and Temmo and his bloodriders led their *khalasar* out of camp, they found three thousand Unsullied drawn up before the gates with the Black Goat standard flying over their heads. So small a force could easily have been flanked, but you know Dothraki. These were men on foot, and men on foot are fit only to be ridden down.

"The Dothraki charged. The Unsullied locked their shields, lowered their spears, and stood firm. Against twenty thousand screamers with bells in their hair, they stood firm.

"Eighteen times the Dothraki charged, and broke themselves on those shields and spears like waves on a rocky shore. Thrice Temmo sent his archers wheeling past and arrows fell like rain upon the Three Thousand, but the Unsullied merely lifted their shields above their heads until the squall had passed. In the end only six hundred of them remained . . . but more than twelve thousand Dothraki lay dead upon that field, including Khal Temmo, his bloodriders, his *kos*, and all his sons. On the morning of the fourth day, the new *khal* led the survivors past the city gates in a stately procession. One by one, each man cut off his braid and threw it down before the feet of the Three Thousand.

"Since that day, the city guard of Qohor has been made up solely of Unsullied, every one of whom carries a tall spear from which hangs a braid of human hair.

"*That* is what you will find in Astapor, Your Grace. Put ashore there, and continue on to Pentos overland. It will take longer, yes . . . but when you break bread with Magister Illyrio, you will have a thousand swords behind you, not just four."

There is wisdom in this, yes, Dany thought, *but . . .* "How am I to buy a thousand slave soldiers? All I have of value is the crown the Tourmaline Brotherhood gave me."

"Dragons will be as great a wonder in Astapor as they were in Qarth. It may be that the slavers will shower you with gifts, as the Qartheen did. If not . . . these ships carry more than your Dothraki and their horses. They took on trade goods at Qarth, I've been through the holds and seen for myself. Bolts of silk and bales of tiger skin, amber and jade carvings, saffron, myrrh . . . slaves are cheap, Your Grace. Tiger skins are costly."

"Those are *Illyrio's* tiger skins," she objected.

"And Illyrio is a friend to House Targaryen."

"All the more reason not to steal his goods."

"What use are wealthy friends if they will not put their

wealth at your disposal, my queen? If Magister Illyrio would deny you, he is only Xaro Xhoan Daxos with four chins. And if he is sincere in his devotion to your cause, he will not begrudge you three shiploads of trade goods. What better use for his tiger skins than to buy you the beginnings of an army?"

That's true. Dany felt a rising excitement. "There will be dangers on such a long march . . ."

"There are dangers at sea as well. Corsairs and pirates hunt the southern route, and north of Valyria the Smoking Sea is demon-haunted. The next storm could sink or scatter us, a kraken could pull us under . . . or we might find ourselves becalmed again, and die of thirst as we wait for the wind to rise. A march will have different dangers, my queen, but none greater."

"What if Captain Groleo refuses to change course, though? And Arstan, Strong Belwas, what will they do?"

Ser Jorah stood. "Perhaps it's time you found that out."

"Yes," she decided. "I'll do it!" Dany threw back the coverlets and hopped from the bunk. "I'll see the captain at once, command him to set course for Astapor." She bent over her chest, threw open the lid, and seized the first garment to hand, a pair of loose sandsilk trousers. "Hand me my medallion belt," she commanded Jorah as she pulled the sandsilk up over her hips. "And my vest—" she started to say, turning.

Ser Jorah slid his arms around her.

"Oh," was all Dany had time to say as he pulled her close and pressed his lips down on hers. He smelled of sweat and salt and leather, and the iron studs on his jerkin dug into her naked breasts as he crushed her hard against him. One hand held her by the shoulder while the other slid down her spine to the small of her back, and her mouth opened for his tongue, though she never told it to. *His beard is scratchy*, she thought, *but his mouth is sweet.* The Dothraki wore no beards, only long mustaches, and only Khal Drogo had ever kissed her before. *He should not be doing this. I am his queen, not his woman.*

It was a long kiss, though how long Dany could not have said. When it ended, Ser Jorah let go of her, and she took a quick step backward. "You . . . you should not have . . ."

"I should not have waited so long," he finished for her.

"I should have kissed you in Qarth, in Vaes Tolorru. I should have kissed you in the red waste, every night and every day. You were made to be kissed, often and well." His eyes were on her breasts.

Dany covered them with her hands, before her nipples could betray her. "I . . . that was not fitting. I am your queen."

"My queen," he said, "and the bravest, sweetest, and most beautiful woman I have ever seen. Daenerys—"

"*Your Grace!*"

"Your Grace," he conceded, "*the dragon has three heads*, remember? You have wondered at that, ever since you heard it from the warlocks in the House of Dust. Well, here's your meaning: Balerion, Meraxes, and Vhagar, ridden by Aegon, Rhaenys, and Visenya. The three-headed dragon of House Targaryen—three dragons, and *three riders.*"

"Yes," said Dany, "but my brothers are dead."

"Rhaenys and Visenya were Aegon's wives as well as his sisters. You have no brothers, but you can take husbands. And I tell you truly, Daenerys, there is no man in all the world who will ever be half so true to you as me."

BRAN

The ridge slanted sharply from the earth, a long fold of stone and soil shaped like a claw. Trees clung to its lower slopes, pines and hawthorn and ash, but higher up the ground was bare, the ridgeline stark against the cloudy sky.

He could feel the high stone calling him. Up he went, loping easy at first, then faster and higher, his strong legs eating up the incline. Birds burst from the branches overhead as he raced by, clawing and flapping their way into the sky. He could hear the wind sighing up amongst the leaves, the squirrels chittering to one another, even the sound a pinecone made as it tumbled to the forest floor. The smells were a song around him, a song that filled the good green world.

Gravel flew from beneath his paws as he gained the last few feet to stand upon the crest. The sun hung above the tall pines huge and red, and below him the trees and hills went on and on as far as he could see or smell. A kite was circling far above, dark against the pink sky.

Prince. The man-sound came into his head suddenly,

yet he could feel the rightness of it. *Prince of the green, prince of the wolfswood.* He was strong and swift and fierce, and all that lived in the good green world went in fear of him.

Far below, at the base of the woods, something moved amongst the trees. A flash of grey, quick-glimpsed and gone again, but it was enough to make his ears prick up. Down there beside a swift green brook, another form slipped by, running. *Wolves,* he knew. His little cousins, chasing down some prey. Now the prince could see more of them, shadows on fleet grey paws. *A pack.*

He had a pack as well, once. Five they had been, and a sixth who stood aside. Somewhere down inside him were the sounds the men had given them to tell one from the other, but it was not by their sounds he knew them. He remembered their scents, his brothers and his sisters. They all had smelled alike, had smelled of *pack,* but each was different too.

His angry brother with the hot green eyes was near, the prince felt, though he had not seen him for many hunts. Yet with every sun that set he grew more distant, and he had been the last. The others were far scattered, like leaves blown by the wild wind.

Sometimes he could sense them, though, as if they were still with him, only hidden from his sight by a boulder or a stand of trees. He could not smell them, nor hear their howls by night, yet he felt their presence at his back . . . all but the sister they had lost. His tail drooped when he remembered her. *Four now, not five. Four and one more, the white who has no voice.*

These woods belonged to them, the snowy slopes and stony hills, the great green pines and the golden leaf oaks, the rushing streams and blue lakes fringed with fingers of white frost. But his sister had left the wilds, to walk in the halls of man-rock where other hunters ruled, and once within those halls it was hard to find the path back out. The wolf prince remembered.

The wind shifted suddenly.

Deer, and fear, and blood. The scent of prey woke the hunger in him. The prince sniffed the air again, turning, and then he was off, bounding along the ridgetop with jaws half-parted. The far side of the ridge was steeper than the one he'd come up, but he flew surefoot over stones and roots and rotting leaves, down the slope and through the trees, long strides eating up the ground. The scent pulled him onward, ever faster.

The deer was down and dying when he reached her, ringed by eight of his small grey cousins. The heads of the pack had begun to feed, the male first and then his female, taking turns tearing flesh from the red underbelly of their prey. The others waited patiently, all but the tail, who paced in a wary circle a few strides from the rest, his own tail tucked low. He would eat the last of all, whatever his brothers left him.

The prince was downwind, so they did not sense him until he leapt up upon a fallen log six strides from where they fed. The tail saw him first, gave a piteous whine, and slunk away. His pack brothers turned at the sound and bared their teeth, snarling, all but the head male and female.

The direwolf answered the snarls with a low warning growl and showed them his own teeth. He was bigger than his cousins, twice the size of the scrawny tail, half again as large as the two pack heads. He leapt down into their midst, and three of them broke, melting away into the brush. Another came at him, teeth snapping. He met the attack head on, caught the wolf's leg in his jaws when they met, and flung him aside yelping and limping.

And then there was only the head wolf to face, the great grey male with his bloody muzzle fresh from the prey's soft belly. There was white on his muzzle as well, to mark him as an old wolf, but when his mouth opened, red slaver ran from his teeth.

He has no fear, the prince thought, *no more than me*. It would be a good fight. They went for each other.

Long they fought, rolling together over roots and stones and fallen leaves and the scattered entrails of the prey, tearing at each other with tooth and claw, breaking apart, circling each round the other, and bolting in to fight again. The prince was larger, and much the stronger, but his cousin had a pack. The female prowled around them closely, snuffing and snarling, and would interpose herself whenever her mate broke off bloodied. From time to time the other wolves would dart in as well, to snap at a leg or an ear when the prince was turned the other way. One angered him so much that he whirled in a black fury and tore out the attacker's throat. After that the others kept their distance.

And as the last red light was filtering through green boughs and golden, the old wolf lay down weary in the dirt, and rolled over to expose his throat and belly. It was submission.

The prince sniffed at him and licked the blood from fur and torn flesh. When the old wolf gave a soft whimper, the direwolf turned away. He was very hungry now, and the prey was his.

"Hodor."

The sudden sound made him stop and snarl. The wolves regarded him with green and yellow eyes, bright with the last light of day. None of them had heard it. It was a queer wind that blew only in his ears. He buried his jaws in the deer's belly and tore off a mouthful of flesh.

"Hodor, hodor."

No, he thought. *No, I won't*. It was a boy's thought, not a direwolf's. The woods were darkening all about him, until only the shadows of the trees remained, and the glow of his cousins' eyes. And *through* those and behind those eyes, he saw a big man's grinning face, and a stone vault whose walls were spotted with niter. The rich warm taste of blood faded on his tongue. *No, don't, don't, I want to eat, I want to, I want* . . .

"Hodor, hodor, hodor, hodor, hodor," Hodor chanted as he shook him softly by the shoulders, back and forth and back and forth. He was trying to be gentle, he always tried, but Hodor was seven feet tall and stronger than he knew, and his huge hands rattled Bran's teeth together. "*NO!*" he shouted angrily. "Hodor, leave off, I'm here, I'm *here*."

Hodor stopped, looking abashed. "Hodor?"

The woods and wolves were gone. Bran was back again, down in the damp vault of some ancient watchtower that must have been abandoned thousands of years before. It wasn't much of a tower now. Even the tumbled stones were so overgrown with moss and ivy that you could hardly see them until you were right on top of them. "Tumbledown Tower," Bran had named the place; it was Meera who found the way down into the vault, however.

"You were gone too long." Jojen Reed was thirteen, only four years older than Bran. Jojen wasn't much bigger either, no more than two inches or maybe three, but he had a solemn way of talking that made him seem older and wiser than he really was. At Winterfell, Old Nan had dubbed him "little grandfather."

Bran frowned at him. "I wanted to eat."

"Meera will be back soon with supper."

"I'm sick of frogs." Meera was a frogeater from the Neck, so Bran couldn't really *blame* her for catching so many frogs, he supposed, but even so . . . "I wanted to eat the deer." For a moment he remembered the taste of it, the blood and the raw rich meat, and his mouth watered. *I won the fight for it. I won.*

"Did you mark the trees?"

Bran flushed. Jojen was always telling him to do things when he opened his third eye and put on Summer's skin. To claw the bark of a tree, to catch a rabbit and bring it back in his jaws uneaten, to push some rocks in a line. *Stupid things.* "I forgot," he said.

"You always forget."

It was true. He *meant* to do the things that Jojen asked, but once he was a wolf they never seemed important. There were always things to see and things to smell, a whole green world to hunt. And he could *run!* There was nothing better than running, unless it was running after prey. "I was a prince, Jojen," he told the older boy. "I was the prince of the woods."

"You are a prince," Jojen reminded him softly. "You remember, don't you? Tell me who you are."

"You *know*." Jojen was his friend and his teacher, but sometimes Bran just wanted to hit him.

"I want you to say the words. Tell me who you are."

"Bran," he said sullenly. *Bran the Broken.* "Brandon Stark." *The cripple boy.* "The Prince of Winterfell." Of Winterfell burned and tumbled, its people scattered and slain. The glass gardens were smashed, and hot water gushed from the cracked walls to steam beneath the sun. *How can you be the prince of someplace you might never see again?*

"And who is Summer?" Jojen prompted.

"My direwolf." He smiled. "Prince of the green."

"Bran the boy and Summer the wolf. You are two, then?"

"Two," he sighed, "and one." He hated Jojen when he got stupid like this. *At Winterfell he wanted me to dream my wolf dreams, and now that I know how he's always calling me back.*

"Remember that, Bran. Remember *yourself*, or the wolf will consume you. When you join, it is not enough to run and hunt and howl in Summer's skin."

It is for me, Bran thought. He liked Summer's skin better than his own. *What good is it to be a skinchanger if you can't wear the skin you like?*

"Will you remember? And next time, mark the tree. Any tree, it doesn't matter, so long as you do it."

"I will. I'll remember. I could go back and do it now, if you like. I won't forget this time." *But I'll eat my deer first, and fight with those little wolves some more.*

Jojen shook his head. "No. Best stay, and eat. With your own mouth. A warg cannot live on what his beast consumes."

How would you know? Bran thought resentfully. *You've never been a warg, you don't know what it's like.*

Hodor jerked suddenly to his feet, almost hitting his head on the barrel-vaulted ceiling. "HODOR!" he shouted, rushing to the door. Meera pushed it open just before he reached it, and stepped through into their refuge. "Hodor, hodor," the huge stableboy said, grinning.

Meera Reed was sixteen, a woman grown, but she stood no higher than her brother. All the crannogmen were small, she told Bran once when he asked why she wasn't taller. Brown-haired, green-eyed, and flat as a boy, she walked with a supple grace that Bran could only watch and envy. Meera wore a long sharp dagger, but her favorite way to fight was with a slender three-pronged frog spear in one hand and a woven net in the other.

"Who's hungry?" she asked, holding up her catch: two small silvery trout and six fat green frogs.

"I am," said Bran. *But not for frogs.* Back at Winterfell before all the bad things had happened, the Walders used to say that eating frogs would turn your teeth green and make moss grow under your arms. He wondered if the Walders were dead. He hadn't seen their corpses at Winterfell . . .

but there had been a *lot* of corpses, and they hadn't looked inside the buildings.

"We'll just have to feed you, then. Will you help me clean the catch, Bran?"

He nodded. It was hard to sulk with Meera. She was much more cheerful than her brother, and always seemed to know how to make him smile. Nothing ever scared her or made her angry. *Well, except Jojen, sometimes . . .* Jojen Reed could scare most anyone. He dressed all in green, his eyes were murky as moss, and he had green dreams. What Jojen dreamed came true. *Except he dreamed me dead, and I'm not.* Only he was, in a way.

Jojen sent Hodor out for wood and built them a small fire while Bran and Meera were cleaning the fish and frogs. They used Meera's helm for a cooking pot, chopping up the catch into little cubes and tossing in some water and some wild onions Hodor had found to make a froggy stew. It wasn't as good as deer, but it wasn't bad either, Bran decided as he ate. "Thank you, Meera," he said. "My lady."

"You are most welcome, Your Grace."

"Come the morrow," Jojen announced, "we had best move on."

Bran could see Meera tense. "Have you had a green dream?"

"No," he admitted.

"Why leave, then?" his sister demanded. "Tumbledown Tower's a good place for us. No villages near, the woods are full of game, there's fish and frogs in the streams and lakes . . . and who is ever going to find us here?"

"This is not the place we are meant to be."

"It is safe, though."

"It *seems* safe, I know," said Jojen, "but for how long? There was a battle at Winterfell, we saw the dead. Battles mean wars. If some army should take us unawares . . ."

"It might be Robb's army," said Bran. "Robb will come back from the south soon, I know he will. He'll come back with all his banners and chase the ironmen away."

"Your maester said naught of Robb when he lay dying," Jojen reminded him. "*Ironmen on the Stony Shore,* he said, and, *east, the Bastard of Bolton.* Moat Cailin and Deepwood Motte fallen, the heir to Cerwyn dead, and the castellan of Torrhen's Square. *War everywhere*, he said, *each man against his neighbor*."

"We have plowed this field before," his sister said. "You want to make for the Wall, and your three-eyed crow. That's well and good, but the Wall is a very long way and Bran has no legs but Hodor. If we were mounted . . ."

"If we were eagles we might fly," said Jojen sharply, "but we have no wings, no more than we have horses."

"There are horses to be had," said Meera. "Even in the deep of the wolfswood there are foresters, crofters, hunters. Some will have horses."

"And if they do, should we steal them? Are we thieves? The last thing we need is men hunting us."

"We could buy them," she said. "Trade for them."

"Look at us, Meera. A crippled boy with a direwolf, a simpleminded giant, and two crannogmen a thousand leagues from the Neck. *We will be known*. And word will spread. So long as Bran remains dead, he is safe. Alive, he becomes prey for those who want him dead for good and true." Jojen went to the fire to prod the embers with a stick. "Somewhere to the north, the three-eyed crow awaits us. Bran has need of a teacher wiser than me."

"How, Jojen?" his sister asked. "*How?*"

"Afoot," he answered. "A step at a time."

"The road from Greywater to Winterfell went on forever, and we were mounted then. You want us to travel a longer road on foot, without even knowing where it ends. Beyond the Wall, you say. I haven't been there, no more than you, but I know that Beyond the Wall's a big place, Jojen. Are there many three-eyed crows, or only one? How do we find him?"

"Perhaps he will find us."

Before Meera could find a reply to that, they heard the sound; the distant howl of a wolf, drifting through the night. "Summer?" asked Jojen, listening.

"No." Bran knew the voice of his direwolf.

"Are you certain?" said the little grandfather.

"Certain." Summer had wandered far afield today, and would not be back till dawn. *Maybe Jojen dreams green, but he can't tell a wolf from a direwolf*. He wondered why they all listened to Jojen so much. He was not a prince like Bran, nor big and strong like Hodor, nor as good a hunter as

Meera, yet somehow it was always Jojen telling them what to do. "We should steal horses like Meera wants," Bran said, "and ride to the Umbers up at Last Hearth." He thought a moment. "Or we could steal a boat and sail down the White Knife to White Harbor town. That fat Lord Manderly rules there, he was friendly at the harvest feast. He wanted to build ships. Maybe he built some, and we could sail to Riverrun and bring Robb home with all his army. Then it wouldn't matter who knew I was alive. Robb wouldn't let anyone hurt us."

"Hodor!" burped Hodor. "Hodor, hodor."

He was the only one who liked Bran's plan, though. Meera just smiled at him and Jojen frowned. They never listened to what he wanted, even though Bran was a Stark and a prince besides, and the Reeds of the Neck were Stark bannermen.

"Hooooodor," said Hodor, swaying. "Hooooooodor, hoooooodor, hoDOR, hoDOR, hoDOR." Sometimes he liked to do this, just saying his name different ways, over and over and over. Other times, he would stay so quiet you forgot he was there. There was never any knowing with Hodor. "*HODOR, HODOR, HODOR!*" he shouted.

He is not going to stop, Bran realized. "Hodor," he said, "why don't you go outside and train with your sword?"

The stableboy had forgotten about his sword, but now he remembered. "Hodor!" he burped. He went for his blade. They had three tomb swords taken from the crypts of Winterfell where Bran and his brother Rickon had hidden from Theon Greyjoy's ironmen. Bran claimed his uncle Brandon's sword, Meera the one she found upon the knees of his grandfather Lord Rickard. Hodor's blade was much older, a huge heavy piece of iron, dull from centuries of neglect and well spotted with rust. He could swing it for hours at a time. There was a rotted tree near the tumbled stones that he had hacked half to pieces.

Even when he went outside they could hear him through the walls, bellowing "HODOR!" as he cut and slashed at his tree. Thankfully the wolfswood was huge, and there was not like to be anyone else around to hear.

"Jojen, what did you mean about a teacher?" Bran asked.

"*You're* my teacher. I know I never marked the tree, but I

will the next time. My third eye is open like you
wanted . . ."

"So wide open that I fear you may fall through it, and
live all the rest of your days as a wolf of the woods."

"I won't, I promise."

"The boy promises. Will the wolf remember? You run
with Summer, you hunt with him, kill with him . . . but
you bend to his will more than him to yours."

"I just forget," Bran complained. "I'm only nine. I'll be
better when I'm older. Even Florian the Fool and Prince
Aemon the Dragonknight weren't great knights when they
were *nine*."

"That is true," said Jojen, "and a wise thing to say, if the
days were still growing longer . . . but they aren't. You are a
summer child, I know. Tell me the words of House Stark."

"*Winter is coming.*" Just saying it made Bran feel cold.

Jojen gave a solemn nod. "I dreamed of a winged wolf
bound to earth by chains of stone, and came to Winterfell
to free him. The chains are off you now, yet still you do not
fly."

"Then *you* teach me." Bran still feared the three-eyed
crow who haunted his dreams sometimes, pecking endlessly at the skin between his eyes and telling him to fly.
"You're a greenseer."

"No," said Jojen, "only a boy who dreams. The
greenseers were more than that. They were wargs as well,
as *you* are, and the greatest of them could wear the skins of
any beast that flies or swims or crawls, and could look
through the eyes of the weirwoods as well, and see the
truth that lies beneath the world.

"The gods give many gifts, Bran. My sister is a hunter. It
is given to her to run swiftly, and stand so still she seems to
vanish. She has sharp ears, keen eyes, a steady hand with
net and spear. She can breathe mud and fly through trees. I
could not do these things, no more than you could. To me
the gods gave the green dreams, and to you . . . you could
be more than me, Bran. You are the winged wolf, and there
is no saying how far and high you might fly . . . if you had
someone to teach you. How can I help you master a gift I do
not understand? We remember the First Men in the Neck,
and the children of the forest who were their friends . . .
but so much is forgotten, and so much we never knew."

Meera took Bran by the hand. "If we stay here, troubling no one, you'll be safe until the war ends. You will not learn, though, except what my brother can teach you, and you've heard what he says. If we leave this place to seek refuge at Last Hearth or beyond the Wall, we risk being taken. You are only a boy, I know, but you are our prince as well, our lord's son and our king's true heir. We have sworn you our faith by earth and water, bronze and iron, ice and fire. The risk is yours, Bran, as is the gift. The choice should be yours too, I think. We are your servants to command." She grinned. "At least in this."

"You mean," Bran said, "you'll do what *I* say? Truly?"

"Truly, my prince," the girl replied, "so consider well."

Bran tried to think it through, the way his father might have. The Greatjon's uncles Hother Whoresbane and Mors Crowfood were fierce men, but he thought they would be loyal. And the Karstarks, them too. Karhold was a strong castle, Father always said. *We would be safe with the Umbers or the Karstarks.*

Or they could go south to fat Lord Manderly. At Winterfell, he'd laughed a lot, and never seemed to look at Bran with so much pity as the other lords. Castle Cerwyn was closer than White Harbor, but Maester Luwin had said that Cley Cerwyn was dead. *The Umbers and the Karstarks and the Manderlys may all be dead as well*, he realized. As he would be, if he was caught by the ironmen or the Bastard of Bolton.

If they stayed here, hidden down beneath Tumbledown Tower, no one would find them. He would stay alive. *And crippled.*

Bran realized he was crying. *Stupid baby*, he thought at himself. No matter where he went, to Karhold or White Harbor or Greywater Watch, he'd be a cripple when he got there. He balled his hands into fists. "I want to fly," he told them. "Please. Take me to the crow."

DAVOS

When he came up on deck, the long point of Driftmark was dwindling behind them while Dragonstone rose from the sea ahead. A pale grey wisp of smoke blew from the top of the mountain to mark where the island lay. *Dragonmont is restless this morning,* Davos thought, *or else Melisandre is burning someone else.*

Melisandre had been much in his thoughts as *Shayala's Dance* made her way across Blackwater Bay and through the Gullet, tacking against perverse contrary winds. The great fire that burned atop the Sharp Point watchtower at the end of Massey's Hook reminded him of the ruby she wore at her throat, and when the world turned red at dawn and sunset the drifting clouds turned the same color as the silks and satins of her rustling gowns.

She would be waiting on Dragonstone as well, waiting in all her beauty and all her power, with her god and her shadows and his king. The red priestess had always seemed loyal to Stannis, until now. *She has broken him, as a man breaks a horse. She would ride him to power if she could, and for that she gave my sons to the fire. I will cut the living heart from her breast and see how it burns.* He touched the hilt of the fine long Lysene dirk that the captain had given him.

The captain had been very kind to him. His name was Khorane Sathmantes, a Lyseni like Salladhor Saan, whose ship this was. He had the pale blue eyes you often saw on Lys, set in a bony weatherworn face, but he had spent many years trading in the Seven Kingdoms. When he learned that the man he had plucked from the sea was the celebrated onion knight, he gave him the use of his own cabin and his own clothes, and a pair of new boots that almost fit. He insisted that Davos share his provisions as well, though that turned out badly. His stomach could not tolerate the snails and lampreys and other rich food Captain Khorane so relished, and after his first meal at the captain's table he spent the rest of the day with one end or the other dangling over the rail.

Dragonstone loomed larger with every stroke of the oars. Davos could see the shape of the mountain now, and on its side the great black citadel with its gargoyles and dragon towers. The bronze figurehead at the bow of *Shayala's Dance* sent up wings of salt spray as it cut the waves. He leaned his weight against the rail, grateful for its support. His ordeal had weakened him. If he stood too long his legs shook, and sometimes he fell prey to uncontrollable fits of coughing and brought up gobs of bloody phlegm. *It is nothing,* he told himself. *Surely the gods did not bring me safe through fire and sea only to kill me with a flux.*

As he listened to the pounding of the oarmaster's drum, the thrum of the sail, and the rhythmic swish and creak of the oars, he thought back to his younger days, when these same sounds woke dread in his heart on many a misty morn. They heralded the approach of old Ser Tristimun's sea watch, and the sea watch was death to smugglers when Aerys Targaryen sat the Iron Throne.

But that was another lifetime, he thought. *That was before the onion ship, before Storm's End, before Stannis shortened my fingers. That was before the war or the red comet, before I was a Seaworth or a knight. I was a different man in those days, before Lord Stannis raised me high.*

Captain Khorane had told him of the end of Stannis's hopes, on the night the river burned. The Lannisters had taken him from the flank, and his fickle bannermen had abandoned him by the hundreds in the hour of his greatest need. "King Renly's shade was seen as well," the captain said, "slaying right and left as he led the lion lord's van. It's said his green armor took a ghostly glow from the wildfire, and his antlers ran with golden flames."

Renly's shade. Davos wondered if his sons would return as shades as well. He had seen too many queer things on the sea to say that ghosts did not exist. "Did none keep faith?" he asked.

"Some few," the captain said. "The queen's kin, them in chief. We took off many who wore the fox-and-flowers, though many more were left ashore, with all manner of badges. Lord Florent is the King's Hand on Dragonstone now."

The mountain grew taller, crowned all in pale smoke. The sail sang, the drum beat, the oars pulled smoothly, and before very long the mouth of the harbor opened before them. *So empty,* Davos thought, remembering how it had been before, with the ships crowding every quay and rocking at anchor off the breakwater. He could see Salladhor Saan's flagship *Valyrian* moored at the quay where *Fury* and her sisters had once tied up. The ships on either side of her had striped Lysene hulls as well. In vain he looked for any sign of *Lady Marya* or *Wraith*.

They pulled down the sail as they entered the harbor, to dock on oars alone. The captain came to Davos as they were tying up. "My prince will wish to see you at once."

A fit of coughing seized Davos as he tried to answer. He clutched the rail for support and spat over the side. "The king," he wheezed. "I must go to the king." *For where the king is, I will find Melisandre.*

"No one goes to the king," Khorane Sathmantes replied firmly. "Salladhor Saan will tell you. Him first."

Davos was too weak to defy him. He could only nod.

Salladhor Saan was not aboard his *Valyrian*. They found him at another quay a quarter mile distant, down in the hold of a big-bellied Pentoshi cog named *Bountiful Harvest*, counting cargo with two eunuchs. One held a lantern, the other a wax tablet and stylus. "Thirty-seven, thirty-eight, thirty-nine," the old rogue was saying when

Davos and the captain came down the hatch. Today he wore a wine-colored tunic and high boots of bleached white leather inlaid with silver scrollwork. Pulling the stopper from a jar, he sniffed, sneezed, and said, "A coarse grind, and of the second quality, my nose declares. The bill of lading is saying forty-three jars. Where have the others gotten to, I am wondering? These Pentoshi, do they think I am not counting?" When he saw Davos he stopped suddenly. "Is it pepper stinging my eyes, or tears? Is this the knight of the onions who stands before me? No, how can it be, my dear friend Davos died on the burning river, all agree. Why has he come to haunt me?"

"I am no ghost, Salla."

"What else? My onion knight was never so thin or so pale as you." Salladhor Saan threaded his way between the jars of spice and bolts of cloth that filled the hold of the merchanter, wrapped Davos in a fierce embrace, then kissed him once on each cheek and a third time on his forehead. "You are still warm, ser, and I feel your heart thumpety-thumping. Can it be true? The sea that swallowed you has spit you up again."

Davos was reminded of Patchface, Princess Shireen's lackwit fool. He had gone into the sea as well, and when he came out he was mad. *Am I mad as well?* He coughed into a gloved hand and said, "I swam beneath the chain and washed ashore on a spear of the merling king. I would have died there, if *Shayala's Dance* had not come upon me."

Salladhor Saan threw an arm around the captain's shoulders. "This was well done, Khorane. You will be having a fine reward, I am thinking. Meizo Mahr, be a good eunuch and take my friend Davos to the owner's cabin. Fetch him some hot wine with cloves, I am misliking the sound of that cough. Squeeze some lime in it as well. And bring white cheese and a bowl of those cracked green olives we counted earlier! Davos, I will join you soon, once I have bespoken our good captain. You will be forgiving me, I know. Do not eat all the olives, or I must be cross with you!"

Davos let the elder of the two eunuchs escort him to a large and lavishly furnished cabin at the stern of the ship. The carpets were deep, the windows stained glass, and any of the great leather chairs would have seated three of Davos quite comfortably. The cheese and olives arrived shortly, and a cup of steaming hot red wine. He held it between his hands and sipped it gratefully. The warmth felt soothing as it spread through his chest.

Salladhor Saan appeared not long after. "You must be forgiving me for the wine, my friend. These Pentoshi would drink their own water if it were purple."

"It will help my chest," said Davos. "Hot wine is better than a compress, my mother used to say."

"You shall be needing compresses as well, I am thinking. Sitting on a spear all this long time, oh my. How are you finding that excellent chair? He has fat cheeks, does he not?"

"Who?" asked Davos, between sips of hot wine.

"Illyrio Mopatis. A whale with whiskers, I am telling you truly. These chairs were built to his measure, though he is seldom bestirring himself from Pentos to sit in them. A fat man always sits comfortably, I am thinking, for he takes his pillow with him wherever he goes."

"How is it you come by a Pentoshi ship?" asked Davos. "Have you gone pirate again, my lord?" He set his empty cup aside.

"Vile calumny. Who has suffered more from pirates than Salladhor Saan? I ask only what is due me. Much gold is owed, oh yes, but I am not without reason, so in place of coin I have taken a handsome parchment, very crisp. It bears the name and seal of Lord Alester Florent, the Hand of the King. I am made Lord of Blackwater Bay, and no vessel may be crossing my lordly waters without my lordly leave, no. And when these outlaws are trying to steal past me in the night to avoid my lawful duties and customs, why, they are no better than smugglers, so I am well within my rights to seize them." The old pirate laughed. "I cut off no man's fingers, though. What good are bits of fingers? The ships I am taking, the cargoes, a few ransoms, nothing unreasonable." He gave Davos a sharp look. "You are unwell, my friend. That cough . . . and so thin, I am seeing your bones through your skin. And yet I am not seeing your little bag of fingerbones . . ."

Old habit made Davos reach for the leather pouch that was no longer there. "I lost it in the river." *My luck.*

"The river was terrible," Salladhor Saan said solemnly. "Even from the bay, I was seeing, and shuddering."

Davos coughed, spat, and coughed again. "I saw *Black*

Betha burning, and *Fury* as well," he finally managed, hoarsely. "Did none of our ships escape the fire?" Part of him still hoped.

"*Lord Steffon, Ragged Jenna, Swift Sword, Laughing Lord*, and some others were upstream of the pyromancers' pissing, yes. They did not burn, but with the chain raised, neither could they be flying. Some few were surrendering. Most rowed far up the Blackwater, away from the battling, and then were sunk by their crews so they would not be falling into Lannister hands. *Ragged Jenna* and *Laughing Lord* are still playing pirate on the river, I have heard, but who can say if it is so?"

"*Lady Marya?*" Davos asked. "*Wraith?*"

Salladhor Saan put a hand on Davos's forearm and gave a squeeze. "No. Of them, no. I am sorry, my friend. They were good men, your Dale and Allard. But this comfort I can give you—your young Devan was among those we took off at the end. The brave boy never once left the king's side, or so they say."

For a moment he felt almost dizzy, his relief was so palpable. He had been afraid to ask about Devan. "The Mother is merciful. I must go to him, Salla. I must see him."

"Yes," said Salladhor Saan. "And you will be wanting to sail to Cape Wrath, I know, to see your wife and your two little ones. You must be having a new ship, I am thinking.".

"His Grace will give me a ship," said Davos.

The Lyseni shook his head. "Of ships, His Grace has none, and Salladhor Saan has many. The king's ships burned up on the river, but not mine. You shall have one, old friend. You will sail for me, yes? You will dance into Braavos and Myr and Volantis in the black of night, all unseen, and dance out again with silks and spices. We will be having fat purses, yes."

"You are kind, Salla, but my duty's to my king, not your purse. The war will go on. Stannis is still the rightful heir by all the laws of the Seven Kingdoms."

"All the laws are not helping when all the ships burn up, I am thinking. And your king, well, you will be finding him changed, I am fearing. Since the battle, he sees no one, but broods in his Stone Drum. Queen Selyse keeps court for him with her uncle the Lord Alester, who is naming himself the Hand. The king's seal she has given to this uncle, to fix to the letters he writes, even to my pretty parchment. But it is a little kingdom they are ruling, poor and rocky, yes. There is no gold, not even a little bit to pay faithful Salladhor Saan what is owed him, and only those knights that we took off at the end, and no ships but my little brave few."

A sudden racking cough bent Davos over. Salladhor Saan moved to help him, but he waved him off, and after a moment he recovered. "No one?" he wheezed. "What do you mean, he sees no one?" His voice sounded wet and thick, even in his own ears, and for a moment the cabin swam dizzily around him.

"No one but *her*," said Salladhor Saan, and Davos did not have to ask who he meant. "My friend, you tire yourself. It is a bed you are needing, not Salladhor Saan. A bed and many blankets, with a hot compress for your chest and more wine and cloves."

Davos shook his head. "I will be fine. Tell me, Salla, I must know. No one but Melisandre?"

The Lyseni gave him a long doubtful look, and continued reluctantly. "The guards keep all others away, even his queen and his little daughter. Servants bring meals that no one eats." He leaned forward and lowered his voice. "Queer talking I have heard, of hungry fires within the mountain, and how Stannis and the red woman go down together to watch the flames. There are shafts, they say, and secret stairs down into the mountain's heart, into hot places where only *she* may walk unburned. It is enough and more to give an old man such terrors that sometimes he can scarcely find the strength to eat."

Melisandre. Davos shivered. "The red woman did this to him," he said. "She sent the fire to consume us, to punish Stannis for setting her aside, to teach him that he could not hope to win without her sorceries."

The Lyseni chose a plump olive from the bowl between them. "You are not the first to be saying this, my friend. But if I am you, I am not saying it so loudly. Dragonstone crawls with these queen's men, oh yes, and they have sharp ears and sharper knives." He popped the olive into his mouth.

"I have a knife myself. Captain Khorane made me a gift of

it." He pulled out the dirk and laid it on the table between them. "A knife to cut out Melisandre's heart. If she has one."

Salladhor Saan spit out an olive pit. "Davos, good Davos, you must not be saying such things, even in jest."

"No jest. I mean to kill her." *If she can be killed by mortal weapons.* Davos was not certain that she could. He had seen old Maester Cressen slip poison into her wine, with his own eyes he had seen it, but when they both drank from the poisoned cup it was the maester who died, not the red priestess. *A knife in the heart, though . . . even demons can be killed by cold iron, the singers say.*

"These are dangerous talkings, my friend," Salladhor Saan warned him. "I am thinking you are still sick from the sea. The fever has cooked your wits, yes. Best you are taking to your bed for a long resting, until you are stronger."

Until my resolve weakens, you mean. Davos got to his feet. He did feel feverish and a little dizzy, but it did not matter. "You are a treacherous old rogue, Salladhor Saan, but a good friend all the same."

The Lyseni stroked his pointed silver beard. "So with this great friend you will be staying, yes?"

"No, I will be going." He coughed.

"Go! Look at you! You cough, you tremble, you are thin and weak. Where will you be going?"

"To the castle. My bed is there, and my son."

"And the red woman," Salladhor Saan said suspiciously. "She is in the castle also."

"Her too." Davos slid the dirk back into its sheath.

"You are an onion smuggler, what do you know of skulkings and stabbings? And you are ill, you cannot even hold the dirk. Do you know what will be happening to you, if you are caught? While we were burning on the river, the queen was burning traitors. *Servants of the dark,* she named them, poor men, and the red woman sang as the fires were lit."

Davos was unsurprised. *I knew,* he thought, *I knew before he told me.* "She took Lord Sunglass from the dungeons," he guessed, "and Hubard Rambton's sons."

"Just so, and burned them, as she will burn you. If you kill the red woman, they will burn you for revenge, and if you fail to kill her, they will burn you for the trying. She will sing and you will scream, and then you will die. And you have only just come back to life!"

"And this is why," said Davos. "To do this thing. To make an end of Melisandre of Asshai and all her works. Why else would the sea have spit me out? You know Blackwater Bay as well as I do, Salla. No sensible captain would ever take his ship through the spears of the merling king and risk ripping out his bottom. *Shayala's Dance* should never have come near me."

"A wind," insisted Salladhor Saan loudly, "an ill wind, is all. A wind drove her too far to the south."

"And who sent the wind? Salla, the Mother spoke to me."

The old Lyseni blinked at him. "Your mother is dead . . ."

"*The* Mother. She blessed me with seven sons, and yet I let them burn her. She spoke to me. We *called* the fire, she said. We called the shadows too. I rowed Melisandre into the bowels of Storm's End and watched her birth a horror." He saw it still in his nightmares, the gaunt black hands pushing against her thighs as it wriggled free of her swollen womb. "She killed Cressen and Lord Renly and a brave man named Cortnay Penrose, and she killed my sons as well. Now it is time someone killed her."

"*Someone*," said Salladhor Saan. "Yes, just so, someone. But not you. You are weak as a child, and no warrior. Stay, I beg you, we will talk more and you will eat, and perhaps we will sail to Braavos and hire a Faceless Man to do this thing, yes? But you, no, you must sit and eat."

He is making this much harder, thought Davos wearily, *and it was perishingly hard to begin with*. "I have vengeance in my belly, Salla. It leaves no room for food. Let me go now. For our friendship, wish me luck and let me go."

Salladhor Saan pushed himself to his feet. "You are no true friend, I am thinking. When you are dead, who will be bringing your ashes and bones back to your lady wife and telling her that she has lost a husband and four sons? Only sad old Salladhor Saan. But so be it, brave ser knight, go rushing to your grave. I will gather your bones in a sack and give them to the sons you leave behind, to wear in little bags around their necks." He waved an angry hand, with rings on every finger. "Go, go, go, go, go."

Davos did not want to leave like this. "Salla—"

"*GO*. Or stay, better, but if you are going, go."

He went.

His walk up from the *Bountiful Harvest* to the gates of Dragonstone was long and lonely. The dockside streets where soldiers and sailors and smallfolk had thronged were empty and deserted. Where once he had stepped around squealing pigs and naked children, rats scurried. His legs felt like pudding beneath him, and thrice the coughing racked him so badly that he had to stop and rest. No one came to help him, nor even peered through a window to see what was the matter. The windows were shuttered, the doors barred, and more than half the houses displayed some mark of mourning. *Thousands sailed up the Blackwater Rush, and hundreds came back*, Davos reflected. *My sons did not die alone. May the Mother have mercy on them all.*

When he reached the castle gates, he found them shut as well. Davos pounded on the iron-studded wood with his fist. When there was no answer, he kicked at it, again and again. Finally a crossbowman appeared atop the barbican, peering down between two towering gargoyles. "Who goes there?"

He craned his head back and cupped his hands around his mouth. "Ser Davos Seaworth, to see His Grace."

"Are you drunk? Go away and stop that pounding."

Salladhor Saan had warned him. Davos tried a different tack. "Send for my son, then. Devan, the king's squire."

The guard frowned. "Who did you say you were?"

"Davos," he shouted. "The onion knight."

The head vanished, to return a moment later. "Be off with you. The onion knight died on the river. His ship burned."

"His ship burned," Davos agreed, "but he lived, and here he stands. Is Jate still captain of the gate?"

"Who?"

"Jate Blackberry. He knows me well enough."

"I never heard of him. Most like he's dead."

"Lord Chyttering, then."

"That one I know. He burned on the Blackwater."

"Hookface Will? Hal the Hog?"

"Dead and dead," the crossbowman said, but his face betrayed a sudden doubt. "You wait there." He vanished again.

Davos waited. *Gone, all gone,* he thought dully, remembering how fat Hal's white belly always showed beneath his grease-stained doublet, the long scar the fish hook had left across Will's face, the way Jate always doffed his cap at the women, be they five or fifty, highborn or low. *Drowned or burned, with my sons and a thousand others, gone to make a king in hell.*

Suddenly the crossbowman was back. "Go round to the sally port and they'll admit you."

Davos did as he was bid. The guards who ushered him inside were strangers to him. They carried spears, and on their breasts they wore the fox-and-flowers sigil of House Florent. They escorted him not to the Stone Drum, as he'd expected, but under the arch of the Dragon's Tail and down to Aegon's Garden. "Wait here," their sergeant told him.

"Does His Grace know that I've returned?" asked Davos.

"Bugger all if I know. Wait, I said." The man left, taking his spearmen with him.

Aegon's Garden had a pleasant piney smell to it, and tall dark trees rose on every side. There were wild roses as well, and towering thorny hedges, and a boggy spot where cranberries grew.

Why have they brought me here? Davos wondered.

Then he heard a faint ringing of bells, and a child's giggle, and suddenly the fool Patchface popped from the bushes, shambling along as fast as he could go with the Princess Shireen hot on his heels. "You come back now," she was shouting after him. "Patches, you come back."

When the fool saw Davos, he jerked to a sudden halt, the bells on his antlered tin helmet going *ting-a-ling, ting-a-ling.* Hopping from one foot to the other, he sang, *"Fool's blood, king's blood, blood on the maiden's thigh, but chains for the guests and chains for the bridegroom, aye aye aye."* Shireen almost caught him then, but at the last instant he hopped over a patch of bracken and vanished among the trees. The princess was right behind him. The sight of them made Davos smile.

He had turned to cough into his gloved hand when

another small shape crashed out of the hedge and bowled right into him, knocking him off his feet.

The boy went down as well, but he was up again almost at once. "What are you doing here?" he demanded as he brushed himself off. Jet-black hair fell to his collar, and his eyes were a startling blue. "You shouldn't get in my way when I'm running."

"No," Davos agreed. "I shouldn't." Another fit of coughing seized him as he struggled to his knees.

"Are you unwell?" The boy took him by the arm and pulled him to his feet. "Should I summon the maester?"

Davos shook his head. "A cough. It will pass."

The boy took him at his word. "We were playing monsters and maidens," he explained. "I was the monster. It's a childish game but my cousin likes it. Do you have a name?"

"Ser Davos Seaworth."

The boy looked him up and down dubiously. "Are you certain? You don't look very knightly."

"I am the knight of the onions, my lord."

The blue eyes blinked. "The one with the black ship?"

"You know that tale?"

"You brought my uncle Stannis fish to eat before I was born, when Lord Tyrell had him under siege." The boy drew himself up tall. "I am Edric Storm," he announced. "King Robert's son."

"Of course you are." Davos had known that almost at once. The lad had the prominent ears of a Florent, but the hair, the eyes, the jaw, the cheekbones, those were all Baratheon.

"Did you know my father?" Edric Storm demanded.

"I saw him many a time while calling on your uncle at court, but we never spoke."

"My father taught me to fight," the boy said proudly. "He came to see me almost every year, and sometimes we trained together. On my last name day he sent me a warhammer just like his, only smaller. They made me leave it at Storm's End, though. Is it true my uncle Stannis cut off your fingers?"

"Only the last joint. I still have fingers, only shorter."

"Show me."

Davos peeled his glove off. The boy studied his hand carefully. "He did not shorten your thumb?"

"No." Davos coughed. "No, he left me that."

"He should not have chopped any of your fingers," the lad decided. "That was ill done."

"I was a smuggler."

"Yes, but you smuggled him fish and onions."

"Lord Stannis knighted me for the onions, and took my fingers for the smuggling." He pulled his glove back on.

"My father would not have chopped your fingers."

"As you say, my lord." *Robert was a different man than Stannis, true enough. The boy is like him. Aye, and like Renly as well.* That thought made him anxious.

The boy was about to say something more when they heard steps. Davos turned. Ser Axell Florent was coming down the garden path with a dozen guards in quilted jerkins. On their breasts they wore the fiery heart of the Lord of Light. *Queen's men,* Davos thought. A cough came on him suddenly.

Ser Axell was short and muscular, with a barrel chest, thick arms, bandy legs, and hair growing from his ears. The queen's uncle, he had served as castellan of Dragonstone for a decade, and had always treated Davos courteously, knowing he enjoyed the favor of Lord Stannis. But there was neither courtesy nor warmth in his tone as he said, "Ser Davos, and undrowned. How can that be?"

"Onions float, ser. Have you come to take me to the king?"

"I have come to take you to the dungeon." Ser Axell waved his men forward. "Seize him, and take his dirk. He means to use it on our lady."

JAIME

Jaime was the first to spy the inn. The main building
hugged the south shore where the river bent, its long
low wings outstretched along the water as if to embrace travelers sailing downstream. The lower story was
grey stone, the upper whitewashed wood, the roof slate. He
could see stables as well, and an arbor heavy with vines.
"No smoke from the chimneys," he pointed out as they approached. "Nor lights in the windows."

"The inn was still open when last I passed this way,"
said Ser Cleos Frey. "They brewed a fine ale. Perhaps there
is still some to be had in the cellars."

"There may be people," Brienne said. "Hiding. Or
dead."

"Frightened of a few corpses, wench?" Jaime said.

She glared at him. "My name is—"

"—Brienne, yes. Wouldn't you like to sleep in a bed for a
night, Brienne? We'd be safer than on the open river, and it
might be prudent to find what's happened here."

She gave no answer, but after a moment she pushed at
the tiller to angle the skiff in toward the weathered wooden

dock. Ser Cleos scrambled to take down the sail. When they bumped softly against the pier, he climbed out to tie them up. Jaime clambered after him, made awkward by his chains.

At the end of the dock, a flaking shingle swung from an iron post, painted with the likeness of a king upon his knees, his hands pressed together in the gesture of fealty. Jaime took one look and laughed aloud. "We could not have found a better inn."

"Is this some special place?" the wench asked, suspicious.

Ser Cleos answered. "This is the Inn of the Kneeling Man, my lady. It stands upon the very spot where the last King in the North knelt before Aegon the Conqueror to offer his submission. That's him on the sign, I suppose."

"Torrhen had brought his power south after the fall of the two kings on the Field of Fire," said Jaime, "but when he saw Aegon's dragon and the size of his host, he chose the path of wisdom and bent his frozen knees." He stopped at the sound of a horse's whinny. "Horses in the stable. One at least." *And one is all I need to put the wench behind me.* "Let's see who's home, shall we?" Without waiting for an answer, Jaime went clinking down the dock, put a shoulder to the door, shoved it open . . .

. . . and found himself eye to eye with a loaded crossbow. Standing behind it was a chunky boy of fifteen. "Lion, fish, or wolf?" the lad demanded.

"We were hoping for capon." Jaime heard his companions entering behind him. "The crossbow is a coward's weapon."

"It'll put a bolt through your heart all the same."

"Perhaps. But before you can wind it again my cousin here will spill your entrails on the floor."

"Don't be scaring the lad, now," Ser Cleos said.

"We mean no harm," the wench said. "And we have coin to pay for food and drink." She dug a silver piece from her pouch.

The boy looked suspiciously at the coin, and then at Jaime's manacles. "Why's this one in irons?"

"Killed some crossbowmen," said Jaime. "Do you have ale?"

"Yes." The boy lowered the crossbow an inch. "Undo

your swordbelts and let them fall, and might be we'll feed you." He edged around to peer through the thick, diamond-shaped windowpanes and see if any more of them were outside. "That's a Tully sail."

"We come from Riverrun." Brienne undid the clasp on her belt and let it clatter to the floor. Ser Cleos followed suit.

A sallow man with a pocked doughy face stepped through the cellar door, holding a butcher's heavy cleaver. "Three, are you? We got horsemeat enough for three. The horse was old and tough, but the meat's still fresh."

"Is there bread?" asked Brienne.

"Hardbread and stale oatcakes."

Jaime grinned. "Now there's an honest innkeep. They'll all serve you stale bread and stringy meat, but most don't own up to it so freely."

"I'm no innkeep. I buried him out back, with his women."

"Did you kill them?"

"Would I tell you if I did?" The man spat. "Likely it were wolves' work, or maybe lions, what's the difference? The wife and I found them dead. The way we see it, the place is ours now."

"Where is this wife of yours?" Ser Cleos asked.

The man gave him a suspicious squint. "And why would you be wanting to know that? She's not here . . . no more'n you three will be, unless I like the taste of your silver."

Brienne tossed the coin to him. He caught it in the air, bit it, and tucked it away.

"She's got more," the boy with the crossbow announced.

"So she does. Boy, go down and find me some onions."

The lad raised the crossbow to his shoulder, gave them one last sullen look, and vanished into the cellar.

"Your son?" Ser Cleos asked.

"Just a boy the wife and me took in. We had two sons, but the lions killed one and the other died of the flux. The boy lost his mother to the Bloody Mummers. These days, a man needs someone to keep watch while he sleeps." He waved the cleaver at the tables. "Might as well sit."

The hearth was cold, but Jaime picked the chair nearest

the ashes and stretched out his long legs under the table.
The clink of his chains accompanied his every movement.
*An irritating sound. Before this is done, I'll wrap these
chains around the wench's throat, see how she likes them
then.*

The man who wasn't an innkeep charred three huge
horse steaks and fried the onions in bacon grease, which almost made up for the stale oatcakes. Jaime and Cleos drank
ale, Brienne a cup of cider. The boy kept his distance,
perching atop the cider barrel with his crossbow across his
knees, cocked and loaded. The cook drew a tankard of ale
and sat with them. "What news from Riverrun?" he asked
Ser Cleos, taking him for their leader.

Ser Cleos glanced at Brienne before answering. "Lord
Hoster is failing, but his son holds the fords of the Red Fork
against the Lannisters. There have been battles."

"Battles everywhere. Where are you bound, ser?"

"King's Landing." Ser Cleos wiped grease off his lips.

Their host snorted. "Then you're three fools. Last I
heard, King Stannis was outside the city walls. They say he
has a hundred thousand men and a magic sword."

Jaime's hands wrapped around the chain that bound his
wrists, and he twisted it taut, wishing for the strength to
snap it in two. *Then I'd show Stannis where to sheathe his
magic sword.*

"I'd stay well clear of that kingsroad, if I were you," the
man went on. "It's worse than bad, I hear. Wolves and lions
both, and bands of broken men preying on anyone they can
catch."

"Vermin," declared Ser Cleos with contempt. "Such
would never dare to trouble armed men."

"Begging your pardon, ser, but I see one armed man,
traveling with a woman and a prisoner in chains."

Brienne gave the cook a dark look. *The wench does hate
being reminded that she's a wench,* Jaime reflected, twisting at the chains again. The links were cold and hard
against his flesh, the iron implacable. The manacles had
chafed his wrists raw.

"I mean to follow the Trident to the sea," the wench
told their host. "We'll find mounts at Maidenpool and ride
by way of Duskendale and Rosby. That should keep us well
away from the worst of the fighting."

Their host shook his head. "You'll never reach Maidenpool by river. Not thirty miles from here a couple boats burned and sank, and the channel's been silting up around them. There's a nest of outlaws there preying on anyone tries to come by, and more of the same downriver around the Skipping Stones and Red Deer Island. And the lightning lord's been seen in these parts as well. He crosses the river wherever he likes, riding this way and that way, never still."

"And who is this lightning lord?" demanded Ser Cleos Frey.

"Lord Beric, as it please you, ser. They call him that 'cause he strikes so sudden, like lightning from a clear sky. It's said he cannot die."

They all die when you shove a sword through them, Jaime thought. "Does Thoros of Myr still ride with him?"

"Aye. The red wizard. I've heard tell he has strange powers."

Well, he had the power to match Robert Baratheon drink for drink, and there were few enough who could say that. Jaime had once heard Thoros tell the king that he became a red priest because the robes hid the winestains so well. Robert had laughed so hard he'd spit ale all over Cersei's silken mantle. "Far be it from me to make objection," he said, "but perhaps the Trident is not our safest course."

"I'd say that's so," their cook agreed. "Even if you get past Red Deer Island and don't meet up with Lord Beric and the red wizard, there's still the ruby ford before you. Last I heard, it was the Leech Lord's wolves held the ford, but that was some time past. By now it could be lions again, or Lord Beric, or anyone."

"Or no one," Brienne suggested.

"If m'lady cares to wager her skin on that I won't stop her . . . but if I was you, I'd leave this here river, cut overland. If you stay off the main roads and shelter under the trees of a night, hidden as it were . . . well, I still wouldn't want to go with you, but you might stand a mummer's chance."

The big wench was looking doubtful. "We would need horses."

"There are horses here," Jaime pointed out. "I heard one in the stable."

"Aye, there are," said the innkeep, who wasn't an innkeep. "Three of them, as it happens, but they're not for sale."

Jaime had to laugh. "Of course not. But you'll show them to us anyway."

Brienne scowled, but the man who wasn't an innkeep met her eyes without blinking, and after a moment, reluctantly, she said, "Show me," and they all rose from the table.

The stables had not been mucked out in a long while, from the smell of them. Hundreds of fat black flies swarmed amongst the straw, buzzing from stall to stall and crawling over the mounds of horse dung that lay everywhere, but there were only the three horses to be seen. They made an unlikely trio; a lumbering brown plow horse, an ancient white gelding blind in one eye, and a knight's palfrey, dapple grey and spirited. "They're not for sale at any price," their alleged owner announced.

"How did you come by these horses?" Brienne wanted to know.

"The dray was stabled here when the wife and me come on the inn," the man said, "along with the one you just ate. The gelding come wandering up one night, and the boy caught the palfrey running free, still saddled and bridled. Here, I'll show you."

The saddle he showed them was decorated with silver inlay. The saddlecloth had originally been checkered pink and black, but now it was mostly brown. Jaime did not recognize the original colors, but he recognized bloodstains easily enough. "Well, her owner won't be coming to claim her anytime soon." He examined the palfrey's legs, counted the gelding's teeth. "Give him a gold piece for the grey, if he'll include the saddle," he advised Brienne. "A silver for the plow horse. He ought to pay us for taking the white off his hands."

"Don't speak discourteously of your horse, ser." The wench opened the purse Lady Catelyn had given her and took out three golden coins. "I will pay you a dragon for each."

He blinked and reached for the gold, then hesitated and

drew his hand back. "I don't know. I can't ride no golden dragon if I need to get away. Nor eat one if I'm hungry."

"You can have our skiff as well," she said. "Sail up the river or down, as you like."

"Let me have a taste o' that gold." The man took one of the coins from her palm and bit it. "Hm. Real enough, I'd say. Three dragons *and* the skiff?"

"He's robbing you blind, wench," Jaime said amiably.

"I'll want provisions too," Brienne told their host, ignoring Jaime. "Whatever you have that you can spare."

"There's more oatcakes." The man scooped the other two dragons from her palm and jingled them in his fist, smiling at the sound they made. "Aye, and smoked salt fish, but that will cost you silver. My beds will be costing as well. You'll be wanting to stay the night."

"No," Brienne said at once.

The man frowned at her. "Woman, you don't want to go riding at night through strange country on horses you don't know. You're like to blunder into some bog or break your horse's leg."

"The moon will be bright tonight," Brienne said. "We'll have no trouble finding our way."

Their host chewed on that. "If you don't have the silver, might be some coppers would buy you them beds, and a coverlet or two to keep you warm. It's not like I'm turning travelers away, if you get my meaning."

"That sounds more than fair," said Ser Cleos.

"The coverlets is fresh washed, too. My wife saw to that before she had to go off. Not a flea to be found neither, you have my word on that." He jingled the coins again, smiling.

Ser Cleos was plainly tempted. "A proper bed would do us all good, my lady," he said to Brienne. "We'd make better time on the morrow once refreshed." He looked to his cousin for support.

"No, coz, the wench is right. We have promises to keep, and long leagues before us. We ought ride on."

"But," said Cleos, "you said yourself—"

"Then." *When I thought the inn deserted.* "Now I have a full belly, and a moonlight ride will be just the thing." He smiled for the wench. "But unless you mean to throw me over the back of that plow horse like a sack of flour, someone had best do something about these irons. It's difficult to ride with your ankles chained together."

Brienne frowned at the chain. The man who wasn't an innkeep rubbed his jaw. "There's a smithy round back of the stable."

"Show me," Brienne said.

"Yes," said Jaime, "and the sooner the better. There's far too much horse shit about here for my taste. I would hate to step in it." He gave the wench a sharp look, wondering if she was bright enough to take his meaning.

He hoped she might strike the irons off his wrists as well, but Brienne was still suspicious. She split the ankle chain in the center with a half-dozen sharp blows from the smith's hammer delivered to the blunt end of a steel chisel. When he suggested that she break the wrist chain as well, she ignored him.

"Six miles downriver you'll see a burned village," their host said as he was helping them saddle the horses and load their packs. This time he directed his counsel at Brienne. "The road splits there. If you turn south, you'll come on Ser Warren's stone towerhouse. Ser Warren went off and died, so I couldn't say who holds it now, but it's a place best shunned. You'd do better to follow the track through the woods, south by east."

"We shall," she answered. "You have my thanks."

More to the point, he has your gold. Jaime kept the thought to himself. He was tired of being disregarded by this huge ugly cow of a woman.

She took the plow horse for herself and assigned the palfrey to Ser Cleos. As threatened, Jaime drew the one-eyed gelding, which put an end to any thoughts he might have had of giving his horse a kick and leaving the wench in his dust.

The man and the boy came out to watch them leave. The man wished them luck and told them to come back in better times, while the lad stood silent, his crossbow under his arm. "Take up the spear or maul," Jaime told him, "they'll serve you better." The boy stared at him distrustfully. *So much for friendly advice.* He shrugged, turned his horse, and never looked back.

Ser Cleos was all complaints as they rode out, still in mourning for his lost featherbed. They rode east, along the bank of the moonlit river. The Red Fork was very broad here, but shallow, its banks all mud and reeds. Jaime's mount plodded along placidly, though the poor old thing had a tendency to want to drift off to the side of his good eye. It felt good to be mounted once more. He had not been on a horse since Robb Stark's archers had killed his destrier under him in the Whispering Wood.

When they reached the burned village, a choice of equally unpromising roads confronted them; narrow tracks, deeply rutted by the carts of farmers hauling their grain to the river. One wandered off toward the southeast and soon vanished amidst the trees they could see in the distance, while the other, straighter and stonier, arrowed due south. Brienne considered them briefly, and then swung her horse onto the southern road. Jaime was pleasantly surprised; it was the same choice he would have made.

"But this is the road the innkeep warned us against," Ser Cleos objected.

"He was no innkeep." She hunched gracelessly in the saddle, but seemed to have a sure seat nonetheless. "The man took too great an interest in our choice of route, and those woods . . . such places are notorious haunts of outlaws. He may have been urging us into a trap."

"Clever wench." Jaime smiled at his cousin. "Our host has friends down that road, I would venture. The ones whose mounts gave that stable such a memorable aroma."

"He may have been lying about the river as well, to put us on these horses," the wench said, "but I could not take the risk. There will be soldiers at the ruby ford and the crossroads."

Well, she may be ugly but she's not entirely stupid. Jaime gave her a grudging smile.

The ruddy light from the upper windows of the stone towerhouse gave them warning of its presence a long way off, and Brienne led them off into the fields. Only when the stronghold was well to the rear did they angle back and find the road again.

Half the night passed before the wench allowed that it might be safe to stop. By then all three of them were drooping in their saddles. They sheltered in a small grove of oak and ash beside a sluggish stream. The wench would allow no fire, so they shared a midnight supper of stale oatcakes and salt fish. The night was strangely peaceful. The half-moon sat overhead in a black felt sky, surrounded by stars. Off in the distance, some wolves were howling. One of their horses whickered nervously. There was no other sound. *The war has not touched this place*, Jaime thought. He was glad to be here, glad to be alive, glad to be on his way back to Cersei.

"I'll take the first watch," Brienne told Ser Cleos, and Frey was soon snoring softly.

Jaime sat against the bole of an oak and wondered what Cersei and Tyrion were doing just now. "Do you have any siblings, my lady?" he asked.

Brienne squinted at him suspiciously. "No. I was my father's only s—child."

Jaime chuckled. "*Son*, you meant to say. Does he think of you as a son? You make a queer sort of daughter, to be sure."

Wordless, she turned away from him, her knuckles tight on her sword hilt. *What a wretched creature this one is.* She reminded him of Tyrion in some queer way, though at first blush two people could scarcely be any more dissimilar. Perhaps it was that thought of his brother that made him say, "I did not intend to give offense, Brienne. Forgive me."

"Your crimes are past forgiving, Kingslayer."

"That name again." Jaime twisted idly at his chains. "Why do I enrage you so? I've never done you harm that I know of."

"You've harmed others. Those you were sworn to protect. The weak, the innocent . . ."

". . . the king?" It always came back to Aerys. "Don't presume to judge what you do not understand, wench."

"My name is—"

"—Brienne, yes. Has anyone ever told you that you're as tedious as you are ugly?"

"You will not provoke me to anger, Kingslayer."

"Oh, I might, if I cared enough to try."

"Why did you take the oath?" she demanded. "Why don the white cloak if you meant to betray all it stood for?"

Why? What could he say that she might possibly understand? "I was a boy. Fifteen. It was a great honor for one so young."

"That is no answer," she said scornfully.

You would not like the truth. He had joined the Kingsguard for love, of course.

Their father had summoned Cersei to court when she was twelve, hoping to make her a royal marriage. He refused every offer for her hand, preferring to keep her with him in the Tower of the Hand while she grew older and more womanly and ever more beautiful. No doubt he was waiting for Prince Viserys to mature, or perhaps for Rhaegar's wife to die in childbed. Elia of Dorne was never the healthiest of women.

Jaime, meantime, had spent four years as squire to Ser Sumner Crake-hall and earned his spurs against the Kingswood Brotherhood. But when he made a brief call at King's Landing on his way back to Casterly Rock, chiefly to see his sister, Cersei took him aside and whispered that Lord Tywin meant to marry him to Lysa Tully, had gone so far as to invite Lord Hoster to the city to discuss dower. But if Jaime took the white, he could be near her always. Old Ser Harlan Grandison had died in his sleep, as was only appropriate for one whose sigil was a sleeping lion. Aerys would want a young man to take his place, so why not a roaring lion in place of a sleepy one?

"Father will never consent," Jaime objected.

"The king won't ask him. And once it's done, Father can't object, not openly. Aerys had Ser Ilyn Payne's tongue torn out just for boasting that it was the Hand who truly ruled the Seven Kingdoms. The captain of the Hand's guard, and yet Father dared not try and stop it! He won't stop this, either."

"But," Jaime said, "there's Casterly Rock . . ."

"Is it a rock you want? Or me?"

He remembered that night as if it were yesterday. They spent it in an old inn on Eel Alley, well away from watchful eyes. Cersei had come to him dressed as a simple serving wench, which somehow excited him all the more. Jaime had never seen her more passionate. Every time he went to sleep, she woke him again. By morning Casterly Rock seemed a small price to pay to be near her always. He gave his consent, and Cersei promised to do the rest.

A moon's turn later, a royal raven arrived at Casterly Rock to inform him that he had been chosen for the

Kingsguard. He was commanded to present himself to the king during the great tourney at Harrenhal to say his vows and don his cloak.

Jaime's investiture freed him from Lysa Tully. Elsewise, nothing went as planned. His father had never been more furious. He could not object openly—Cersei had judged that correctly—but he resigned the Handship on some thin pretext and returned to Casterly Rock, taking his daughter with him. Instead of being together, Cersei and Jaime just changed places, and he found himself alone at court, guarding a mad king while four lesser men took their turns dancing on knives in his father's ill-fitting shoes. So swiftly did the Hands rise and fall that Jaime remembered their heraldry better than their faces. The horn-of-plenty Hand and the dancing griffins Hand had both been exiled, the mace-and-dagger Hand dipped in wildfire and burned alive. Lord Rossart had been the last. His sigil had been a burning torch; an unfortunate choice, given the fate of his predecessor, but the alchemist had been elevated largely because he shared the king's passion for fire. *I ought to have drowned Rossart instead of gutting him.*

Brienne was still awaiting his answer. Jaime said, "You are not old enough to have known Aerys Targaryen . . ."

She would not hear it. "Aerys was mad and cruel, no one has ever denied that. He was still king, crowned and anointed. And you had sworn to protect him."

"I know what I swore."

"And what you did." She loomed above him, six feet of freckled, frowning, horse-toothed disapproval.

"Yes, and what *you* did as well. We're both kingslayers here, if what I've heard is true."

"I never harmed Renly. I'll kill the man who says I did."

"Best start with Cleos, then. And you'll have a deal of killing to do after that, the way he tells the tale."

"*Lies.* Lady Catelyn was there when His Grace was murdered, she saw. There was a shadow. The candles guttered and the air grew cold, and there was blood—"

"Oh, very good." Jaime laughed. "Your wits are quicker than mine, I confess it. When they found me standing over my dead king, I never thought to say, 'No, no, it wasn't me, it was a shadow, a terrible cold shadow.'" He laughed again. "Tell me true, one kingslayer to another—did the

Starks pay you to slit his throat, or was it Stannis? Had Renly spurned you, was that the way of it? Or perhaps your moon's blood was on you. Never give a wench a sword when she's bleeding."

For a moment Jaime thought Brienne might strike him. *A step closer, and I'll snatch that dagger from her sheath and bury it up her womb.* He gathered a leg under him, ready to spring, but the wench did not move. "It is a rare and precious gift to be a knight," she said, "and even more so a knight of the Kingsguard. It is a gift given to few, a gift you scorned and soiled."

A gift you want desperately, wench, and can never have. "I earned my knighthood. Nothing was given to me. I won a tourney mêlée at thirteen, when I was yet a squire. At fifteen, I rode with Ser Arthur Dayne against the Kingswood Brotherhood, and he knighted me on the battlefield. It was that white cloak that soiled me, not the other way around. So spare me your envy. It was the gods who neglected to give you a cock, not me."

The look Brienne gave him then was full of loathing. *She would gladly hack me to pieces, but for her precious vow,* he reflected. *Good. I've had enough of feeble pieties and maidens' judgments.* The wench stalked off without saying a word. Jaime curled up beneath his cloak, hoping to dream of Cersei.

But when he closed his eyes, it was Aerys Targaryen he saw, pacing alone in his throne room, picking at his scabbed and bleeding hands. The fool was always cutting himself on the blades and barbs of the Iron Throne. Jaime had slipped in through the king's door, clad in his golden armor, sword in hand. *The golden armor, not the white, but no one ever remembers that. Would that I had taken off that damned cloak as well.*

When Aerys saw the blood on his blade, he demanded to know if it was Lord Tywin's. "I want him dead, the traitor. I want his head, you'll bring me his head, or you'll burn with all the rest. All the traitors. Rossart says they are *inside the walls!* He's gone to make them a warm welcome. Whose blood? *Whose?"*

"Rossart's," answered Jaime.

Those purple eyes grew huge then, and the royal mouth drooped open in shock. He lost control of his bowels, turned, and ran for the Iron Throne. Beneath the empty eyes of the skulls on the walls, Jaime hauled the last dragon-king bodily off the steps, squealing like a pig and smelling like a privy. A single slash across his throat was all it took to end it. *So easy*, he remembered thinking. *A king should die harder than this.* Rossart at least had tried to make a fight of it, though if truth be told he fought like an al-chemist. *Queer that they never ask who killed Rossart . . . but of course, he was no one, lowborn, Hand for a fort-night, just another mad fancy of the Mad King.*

Ser Elys Westerling and Lord Crakehall and others of his father's knights burst into the hall in time to see the last of it, so there was no way for Jaime to vanish and let some braggart steal the praise or blame. It would be blame, he knew at once when he saw the way they looked at him . . . though perhaps that was fear. Lannister or no, he was one of Aerys's seven.

"The castle is ours, ser, and the city," Roland Crakehall told him, which was half true. Targaryen loyalists were still dying on the serpentine steps and in the armory, Gregor Clegane and Amory Lorch were scaling the walls of Maegor's Holdfast, and Ned Stark was leading his north-men through the King's Gate even then, but Crakehall could not have known that. He had not seemed surprised to find Aerys slain; Jaime had been Lord Tywin's son long before he had been named to the Kingsguard.

"Tell them the Mad King is dead," he commanded. "Spare all those who yield and hold them captive."

"Shall I proclaim a new king as well?" Crakehall asked, and Jaime read the question plain: Shall it be your father, or Robert Baratheon, or do you mean to try to make a new dragonking? He thought for a moment of the boy Viserys, fled to Dragonstone, and of Rhaegar's infant son Aegon, still in Maegor's with his mother. *A new Targaryen king, and my father as Hand. How the wolves will howl, and the storm lord choke with rage.* For a moment he was tempted, until he glanced down again at the body on the floor, in its spreading pool of blood. *His blood is in both of them*, he thought. "Proclaim who you bloody well like," he told Crakehall. Then he climbed the Iron Throne and seated himself with his sword across his knees, to see who would come to claim the kingdom. As it happened, it had been Eddard Stark.

You had no right to judge me either, Stark.

In his dreams the dead came burning, gowned in swirling green flames. Jaime danced around them with a golden sword, but for every one he struck down two more arose to take his place.

Brienne woke him with a boot in the ribs. The world was still black, and it had begun to rain. They broke their fast on oatcakes, salt fish, and some blackberries that Ser Cleos had found, and were back in the saddle before the sun came up.

TYRION

The eunuch was humming tunelessly to himself as he came through the door, dressed in flowing robes of peach-colored silk and smelling of lemons. When he saw Tyrion seated by the hearth, he stopped and grew very still. "My lord Tyrion," came out in a squeak, punctuated by a nervous giggle.

"So you *do* remember me? I had begun to wonder."

"It is so *very* good to see you looking so strong and well." Varys smiled his slimiest smile. "Though I confess, I had not thought to find you in mine own humble chambers."

"They are humble. Excessively so, in truth." Tyrion had waited until Varys was summoned by his father before slipping in to pay him a visit. The eunuch's apartments were sparse and small, three snug windowless chambers under the north wall. "I'd hoped to discover bushel baskets of juicy secrets to while away the waiting, but there's not a paper to be found." He'd searched for hidden passages too, knowing the Spider must have ways of coming and going unseen, but those had proved equally elusive. "There was *water* in your flagon, gods have mercy," he went on, "your sleeping cell is no wider than a coffin, and that bed . . . is it actually made of stone, or does it only feel that way?"

Varys closed the door and barred it. "I am plagued with backaches, my lord, and prefer to sleep upon a hard surface."

"I would have taken you for a featherbed man."

"I am full of surprises. Are you cross with me for abandoning you after the battle?"

"It made me think of you as one of my family."

"It was not for want of love, my good lord. I have such a delicate disposition, and your scar is so dreadful to look upon . . ." He gave an exaggerated shudder. "Your poor nose . . ."

Tyrion rubbed irritably at the scab. "Perhaps I should have a new one made of gold. What sort of nose would you suggest, Varys? One like yours, to smell out secrets? Or should I tell the goldsmith that I want my father's nose?" He smiled. "My noble father labors so diligently that I scarce see him anymore. Tell me, is it true that he's restoring Grand Maester Pycelle to the small council?"

"It is, my lord."

"Do I have my sweet sister to thank for that?" Pycelle had been his sister's creature; Tyrion had stripped the man of office, beard, and dignity, and flung him down into a black cell.

"Not at all, my lord. Thank the archmaesters of Oldtown, those who wished to insist on Pycelle's restoration on the grounds that only the Conclave may make or unmake a Grand Maester."

Bloody fools, thought Tyrion. "I seem to recall that Maegor the Cruel's headsman unmade three with his axe."

"Quite true," Varys said. "And the second Aegon fed Grand Maester Gerardys to his dragon."

"Alas, I am quite dragonless. I suppose I could have dipped Pycelle in wildfire and set him ablaze. Would the Citadel have preferred that?"

"Well, it would have been more in keeping with tradition." The eunuch tittered. "Thankfully, wiser heads prevailed, and the Conclave accepted the fact of Pycelle's dismissal and set about choosing his successor. After giving due consideration to Maester Turquin the cordwainer's son and Maester Erreck the hedge knight's bastard, and thereby demonstrating to their own satisfaction that ability counts for more than birth in their order, the Conclave was on the verge of sending us Maester Gormon, a Tyrell of Highgarden. When I told your lord father, he acted at once."

The Conclave met in Oldtown behind closed doors, Tyrion knew; its deliberations were supposedly a secret. *So Varys has little birds in the Citadel too.* "I see. So my father decided to nip the rose before it bloomed." He had to chuckle. "Pycelle is a toad. But better a Lannister toad than a Tyrell toad, no?"

"Grand Maester Pycelle has always been a good friend to your House," Varys said sweetly. "Perhaps it will console you to learn that Ser Boros Blount is also being restored."

Cersei had stripped Ser Boros of his white cloak for failing to die in the defense of Prince Tommen when Bronn had seized the boy on the Rosby road. The man was no friend of Tyrion's, but after that he likely hated Cersei almost as much. *I suppose that's something.* "Blount is a blustering coward," he said amiably.

"Is he? Oh dear. Still, the knights of the Kingsguard *do* serve for life, traditionally. Perhaps Ser Boros will prove braver in future. He will no doubt remain very loyal."

"To my father," said Tyrion pointedly.

"While we are on the subject of the Kingsguard . . . I wonder, could this delightfully unexpected visit of yours happen to concern Ser Boros's fallen brother, the gallant Ser Mandon Moore?" The eunuch stroked a powdered cheek. "Your man Bronn seems most interested in him of late."

Bronn had turned up all he could on Ser Mandon, but no doubt Varys knew a deal more . . . should he choose to share it. "The man seems to have been quite friendless," Tyrion said carefully.

"Sadly," said Varys, "oh, sadly. You might find some kin if you turned over enough stones back in the Vale, but here . . . Lord Arryn brought him to King's Landing and Robert gave him his white cloak, but neither loved him much, I fear. Nor was he the sort the smallfolk cheer in tourneys, despite his undoubted prowess. Why, even his brothers of the Kingsguard never warmed to him. Ser Barristan was once heard to say that the man had no friend but his sword and no life but duty . . . but you know, I do not think Selmy meant it altogether as praise. Which is queer when you consider it, is it not? Those are the very qualities we seek in our Kingsguard, it could be said—men who live not for themselves, but for their king. By those lights, our brave Ser Mandon was the perfect white knight. And he died as a knight of the Kingsguard ought, with sword in hand, defending one of the king's own blood." The eunuch gave him a slimy smile and watched him sharply.

Trying to murder one of the king's own blood, you mean. Tyrion wondered if Varys knew rather more than he was saying. Nothing he'd just heard was new to him; Bronn had brought back much the same reports. He needed a link to Cersei, some sign that Ser Mandon had been his sister's catspaw. *What we want is not always what we get*, he reflected bitterly, which reminded him . . .

"It is not Ser Mandon who brings me here."

"To be sure." The eunuch crossed the room to his flagon of water. "May I serve you, my lord?" he asked as he filled a cup.

"Yes. But not with water." He folded his hands together. "I want you to bring me Shae."

Varys took a drink. "Is that wise, my lord? The dear sweet child. It would be such a shame if your father hanged her."

It did not surprise him that Varys knew. "No, it's not wise, it's bloody madness. I want to see her one last time, before I send her away. I cannot abide having her so close."

"I understand."

How could you? Tyrion had seen her only yesterday, climbing the serpentine steps with a pail of water. He had watched as a young knight had offered to carry the heavy pail. The way she had touched his arm and smiled for him had tied Tyrion's guts into knots. They passed within inches of each other, him descending and her climbing, so close that he could smell the clean fresh scent of her hair. "M'lord," she'd said to him, with a little curtsy, and he wanted to reach out and grab her and kiss her right there, but all he could do was nod stiffly and waddle on past. "I have seen her several times," he told Varys, "but I dare not speak to her. I suspect that all my movements are being watched."

"You are wise to suspect so, my good lord."

"Who?" He cocked his head.

"The Kettleblacks report frequently to your sweet sister."

"When I think of how much coin I paid those wretched . . . do you think there's any chance that more gold might win them away from Cersei?"

"There is always a chance, but I should not care to wager on the likelihood. They are knights now, all three, and your sister has promised them further advancement." A wicked little titter burst from the eunuch's lips. "And the eldest, Ser Osmund of the Kingsguard, dreams of certain other . . . *favors* . . . as well. You can match the queen coin for coin, I have no doubt, but she has a second purse that is quite inexhaustible."

Seven hells, thought Tyrion. "Are you suggesting that Cersei's fucking Osmund Kettleblack?"

"Oh, dear me, no, that would be dreadfully dangerous, don't you think? No, the queen only *hints* . . . perhaps on the morrow, or when the wedding's done . . . and then a smile, a whisper, a ribald jest . . . a breast brushing lightly against his sleeve as they pass . . . and yet it seems to serve. But what would a eunuch know of such things?" The tip of his tongue ran across his lower lip like a shy pink animal.

If I could somehow push them beyond sly fondling, arrange for Father to catch them abed together . . . Tyrion fingered the scab on his nose. He did not see how it could be done, but perhaps some plan would come to him later. "Are the Kettleblacks the only ones?"

"Would that were true, my lord. I fear there are many eyes upon you. You are . . . how shall we say? *Conspicuous?* And not well loved, it grieves me to tell you. Janos Slynt's sons would gladly inform on you to avenge their father, and our sweet Lord Petyr has friends in half the brothels of King's Landing. Should you be so unwise as to visit any of them, he will know at once, and your lord father soon thereafter."

It's even worse than I feared. "And my father? Who does he have spying on me?"

This time the eunuch laughed aloud. "Why, me, my lord."

Tyrion laughed as well. He was not so great a fool as to trust Varys any further than he had to—but the eunuch already knew enough about Shae to get her well and thoroughly hanged. "You will bring Shae to me through the walls, hidden from all these eyes. As you have done before."

Varys wrung his hands. "Oh, my lord, nothing would please me more, but . . . King Maegor wanted no rats in his own walls, if you take my meaning. He did require a means of secret egress, should he ever be trapped by his enemies, but that door does not connect with any other passages. I can steal your Shae away from Lady Lollys for a time, to be sure, but I have no way to bring her to your bedchamber without us being seen."

"Then bring her somewhere else."

"But where? There is no safe place."

"There is." Tyrion grinned. "Here. It's time to put that rock-hard bed of yours to better use, I think."

The eunuch's mouth opened. Then he giggled. "Lollys tires easily these days. She is great with child. I imagine she will be safely asleep by moonrise."

Tyrion hopped down from the chair. "Moonrise, then. See that you lay in some wine. And two clean cups."

Varys bowed. "It shall be as my lord commands."

The rest of the day seemed to creep by as slow as a worm in molasses. Tyrion climbed to the castle library and tried to distract himself with Beldecar's *History of the Rhoynish Wars*, but he could hardly see the elephants for imagining Shae's smile. Come the afternoon, he put the book aside and called for a bath. He scrubbed himself until the water grew cool, and then had Pod even out his whiskers. His beard was a trial to him; a tangle of yellow, white, and black hairs, patchy and coarse, it was seldom less than unsightly, but it did serve to conceal some of his face, and that was all to the good.

When he was as clean and pink and trimmed as he was like to get, Tyrion looked over his wardrobe, and chose a pair of tight satin breeches in Lannister crimson and his best doublet, the heavy black velvet with the lion's head studs. He would have donned his chain of golden hands as well, if his father hadn't stolen it while he lay dying. It was not until he was dressed that he realized the depths of his folly. *Seven hells, dwarf, did you lose all your sense along with your nose? Anyone who sees you is going to wonder why you've put on your court clothes to visit the eunuch.* Cursing, Tyrion stripped and dressed again, in simpler garb; black woolen breeches, an old white tunic, and a faded brown leather jerkin. *It doesn't matter*, he told himself as he waited for moonrise. *Whatever you wear, you're still a dwarf. You'll never be as tall as that knight on the steps, him with his long straight legs and hard stomach and wide manly shoulders.*

The moon was peeping over the castle wall when he told Podrick Payne that he was going to pay a call on Varys. "Will you be long, my lord?" the boy asked.

"Oh, I hope so."

With the Red Keep so crowded, Tyrion could not hope to go unnoticed. Ser Balon Swann stood guard on the door, and Ser Loras Tyrell on the drawbridge. He stopped to exchange pleasantries with both of them. It was strange to see the Knight of Flowers all in white when before he had always been as colorful as a rainbow. "How old are you, Ser Loras?" Tyrion asked him.

"Seventeen, my lord."

Seventeen, and beautiful, and already a legend. Half the girls in the Seven Kingdoms want to bed him, and all the boys want to be him. "If you will pardon my asking, ser—why would anyone choose to join the Kingsguard at seventeen?"

"Prince Aemon the Dragonknight took his vows at seventeen," Ser Loras said, "and your brother Jaime was younger still."

"I know their reasons. What are yours? The honor of serving beside such paragons as Meryn Trant and Boros Blount?" He gave the boy a mocking grin. "To guard the king's life, you surrender your own. You give up your lands and titles, give up hope of marriage, children . . ."

"House Tyrell continues through my brothers," Ser Loras said. "It is not necessary for a third son to wed, or breed."

"Not necessary, but some find it pleasant. What of love?"

"When the sun has set, no candle can replace it."

"Is that from a song?" Tyrion cocked his head, smiling. "Yes, you are seventeen, I see that now."

Ser Loras tensed. "Do you mock me?"

A prickly lad. "No. If I've given offense, forgive me. I had my own love once, and we had a song as well." *I loved a maid as fair as summer, with sunlight in her hair.* He bid Ser Loras a good evening and went on his way.

Near the kennels a group of men-at-arms were fighting a pair of dogs. Tyrion stopped long enough to see the smaller dog tear half the face off the larger one, and earned a few coarse laughs by observing that the loser now resembled Sandor Clegane. Then, hoping he had disarmed their suspicions, he proceeded to the north wall and down the short flight of steps to the eunuch's meager abode. The door opened as he was lifting his hand to knock.

"Varys?" Tyrion slipped inside. "Are you there?" A single candle lit the gloom, spicing the air with the scent of jasmine.

"My lord." A woman sidled into the light; plump, soft, matronly, with a round pink moon of a face and heavy dark curls. Tyrion recoiled. "Is something amiss?" she asked.

Varys, he realized with annoyance. "For one horrid moment I thought you'd brought me Lollys instead of Shae. Where is she?"

"Here, m'lord." She put her hands over his eyes from behind. "Can you guess what I'm wearing?"

"Nothing?"

"Oh, you're so *smart,*" she pouted, snatching her hands away. "How did you know?"

"You're very beautiful in nothing."

"Am I?" she said. "Am I truly?"

"Oh yes."

"Then shouldn't you be fucking me instead of talking?"

"We need to rid ourselves of Lady Varys first. I am not the sort of dwarf who likes an audience."

"He's gone," Shae said.

Tyrion turned to look. It was true. The eunuch had vanished, skirts and all. *The hidden doors are here somewhere, they have to be.* That was as much as he had time to think, before Shae turned his head to kiss him. Her mouth was wet and hungry, and she did not even seem to see his scar, or the raw scab where his nose had been. Her skin was warm silk beneath his fingers. When his thumb brushed against her left nipple, it hardened at once. "Hurry," she urged, between kisses, as his fingers went to his laces, "oh, hurry, hurry, I want you in me, in me, in me." He did not even have time to undress properly. Shae pulled his cock out of his breeches, then pushed him down onto the floor and climbed atop him. She screamed as he pushed past her lips, and rode him wildly, moaning, "My giant, my giant, my giant," every time she slammed down on him. Tyrion was so eager that he exploded on the fifth stroke, but Shae did not seem to mind. She smiled wickedly when she felt him spurting, and leaned forward to kiss the sweat from his brow. "My giant of Lannister," she murmured. "Stay inside me, please. I like to feel you there."

So Tyrion did not move, except to put his arms around her. *It feels so good to hold her, and to be held,* he thought. *How can something this sweet be a crime worth hanging her for?* "Shae," he said, "sweetling, this must be our last time together. The danger is too great. If my lord father should find you . . ."

"I like your scar." She traced it with her finger. "It makes you look very fierce and strong."

He laughed. "Very ugly, you mean."

"M'lord will never be ugly in my eyes." She kissed the scab that covered the ragged stub of his nose.

"It's not my face that need concern you, it's my father—"

"He does not frighten me. Will m'lord give me back my jewels and silks now? I asked Varys if I could have them when you were hurt in the battle, but he wouldn't give them to me. What would have become of them if you'd died?"

"I didn't die. Here I am."

"I know." Shae wriggled atop him, smiling. "Just where you belong." Her mouth turned pouty. "But how long must I go on with Lollys, now that you're well?"

"Have you been listening?" Tyrion said. "You can stay with Lollys if you like, but it would be best if you left the city."

"I don't want to leave. You promised you'd move me

into a manse again after the battle." Her cunt gave him a little squeeze, and he started to stiffen again inside her. "A Lannister always pays his debts, you said."

"Shae, gods be damned, stop that. *Listen* to me. You have to go away. The city's full of Tyrells just now, and I am closely watched. You don't understand the dangers."

"Can I come to the king's wedding feast? Lollys won't go. I told her no one's like to rape her in the king's own throne room, but she's so *stupid.*" When Shae rolled off, his cock slid out of her with a soft wet sound. "Symon says there's to be a singers' tourney, and tumblers, even a fools' joust."

Tyrion had almost forgotten about Shae's thrice-damned singer. "How is it you spoke to Symon?"

"I told Lady Tanda about him, and she hired him to play for Lollys. The music calms her when the baby starts to kick. Symon says there's to be a dancing bear at the feast, and wines from the Arbor. I've never seen a bear dance."

"They do it worse than I do." It was the singer who concerned him, not the bear. One careless word in the wrong ear, and Shae would hang.

"Symon says there's to be seventy-seven courses and a hundred doves baked into a great pie," Shae gushed. "When the crust's opened, they'll all burst out and fly."

"After which they will roost in the rafters and rain down birdshit on the guests." Tyrion had suffered such wedding pies before. The doves liked to shit on *him* especially, or so he had always suspected.

"Couldn't I dress in my silks and velvets and go as a lady instead of a maidservant? No one would know I wasn't."

Everyone would know you weren't, thought Tyrion. "Lady Tanda might wonder where Lollys's bedmaid found so many jewels."

"There's to be a thousand guests, Symon says. She'd never even see me. I'd find a place in some dark corner below the salt, but whenever you got up to go to the privy I could slip out and meet you." She cupped his cock and stroked it gently. "I won't wear any smallclothes under my gown, so m'lord won't even need to unlace me." Her fingers teased him, up and down. "Or if he liked, I could do this for him." She took him in her mouth.

Tyrion was soon ready again. This time he lasted much

longer. When he finished Shae crawled back up him and curled up naked under his arm. "You'll let me come, won't you?"

"Shae," he groaned, "it *is not safe.*"

For a time she said nothing at all. Tyrion tried to speak of other things, but he met a wall of sullen courtesy as icy and unyielding as the Wall he'd once walked in the north. *Gods be good*, he thought wearily as he watched the candle burn down and begin to gutter, *how could I let this happen again, after Tysha? Am I as great a fool as my father thinks?* Gladly would he have given her the promise she wanted, and gladly walked her back to his own bedchamber on his arm to let her dress in the silks and velvets she loved so much. Had the choice been his, she could have sat beside him at Joffrey's wedding feast, and danced with all the bears she liked. But he could not see her hang.

When the candle burned out, Tyrion disentangled himself and lit another. Then he made a round of the walls, tapping on each in turn, searching for the hidden door. Shae sat with her legs drawn up and her arms wrapped around them, watching him. Finally she said, "They're under the bed. The secret steps."

He looked at her, incredulous. "The bed? The bed is solid stone. It weighs half a ton."

"There's a place where Varys pushes, and it floats right up. I asked him how, and he said it was magic."

"Yes." Tyrion had to grin. "A counterweight spell."

Shae stood. "I should go back. Sometimes the baby kicks and Lollys wakes and calls for me."

"Varys should return shortly. He's probably listening to every word we say." Tyrion set the candle down. There was a wet spot on the front of his breeches, but in the darkness it ought to go unnoticed. He told Shae to dress and wait for the eunuch.

"I will," she promised. "You are my lion, aren't you? My giant of Lannister?"

"I am," he said. "And you're—"

"—your whore." She laid a finger to his lips. "I know. I'd be your lady, but I never can. Else you'd take me to the feast. It doesn't matter. I like being a whore for you, Tyrion. Just keep me, my lion, and keep me safe."

"I shall," he promised. *Fool, fool*, the voice inside him

screamed. *Why did you say that? You came here to send her away!* Instead he kissed her once more.

The walk back seemed long and lonely. Podrick Payne was asleep in his trundle bed at the foot of Tyrion's, but he woke the boy. "Bronn," he said.

"Ser Bronn?" Pod rubbed the sleep from his eyes. "Oh. Should I get him? My lord?"

"Why no, I woke you up so we could have a little chat about the way he dresses," said Tyrion, but his sarcasm was wasted. Pod only gaped at him in confusion until he threw up his hands and said, "Yes, get him. Bring him. Now."

The lad dressed hurriedly and all but ran from the room. *Am I really so terrifying?* Tyrion wondered, as he changed into a bedrobe and poured himself some wine.

He was on his third cup and half the night was gone before Pod finally returned, with the sellsword knight in tow. "I hope the boy had a damn good reason dragging me out of Chataya's," Bronn said as he seated himself.

"*Chataya's?*" Tyrion said, annoyed.

"It's good to be a knight. No more looking for the cheaper brothels down the street." Bronn grinned. "Now it's Alayaya and Marei in the same featherbed, with Ser Bronn in the middle."

Tyrion had to bite back his annoyance. Bronn had as much right to bed Alayaya as any other man, but still . . . *I never touched her, much as I wanted to, but Bronn could not know that. He should have kept his cock out of her.* He dare not visit Chataya's himself. If he did, Cersei would see that his father heard of it, and 'Yaya would suffer more than a whipping. He'd sent the girl a necklace of silver and jade and a pair of matching bracelets by way of apology, but other than that . . .

This is fruitless. "There is a singer who calls himself Symon Silver Tongue," Tyrion said wearily, pushing his guilt aside. "He plays for Lady Tanda's daughter sometimes."

"What of him?"

Kill him, he might have said, but the man had done nothing but sing a few songs. *And fill Shae's sweet head with visions of doves and dancing bears.* "Find him," he said instead. "Find him before someone else does."

ARYA

She was grubbing for vegetables in a dead man's garden when she heard the singing.

Arya stiffened, still as stone, listening, the three stringy carrots in her hand suddenly forgotten. She thought of the Bloody Mummers and Roose Bolton's men, and a shiver of fear went down her back. *It's not fair, not when we finally found the Trident, not when we thought we were almost safe.*

Only why would the Mummers be singing?

The song came drifting up the river from somewhere beyond the little rise to the east. *"Off to Gulltown to see the fair maid, heigh-ho, heigh-ho . . ."*

Arya rose, carrots dangling from her hand. It sounded like the singer was coming up the river road. Over among the cabbages, Hot Pie had heard it too, to judge by the look on his face. Gendry had gone to sleep in the shade of the burned cottage, and was past hearing anything.

"I'll steal a sweet kiss with the point of my blade, heigh-ho, heigh-ho." She thought she heard a woodharp too, beneath the soft rush of the river.

"Do you hear?" Hot Pie asked in a hoarse whisper, as he hugged an armful of cabbages. "Someone's coming."

"Go wake Gendry," Arya told him. "Just shake him by the shoulder, don't make a lot of noise." Gendry was easy to wake, unlike Hot Pie, who needed to be kicked and shouted at.

"*I'll make her my love and we'll rest in the shade, heigh-ho, heigh-ho.*" The song swelled louder with every word.

Hot Pie opened his arms. The cabbages fell to the ground with soft thumps. "We have to *hide.*"

Where? The burned cottage and its overgrown garden stood hard beside the banks of the Trident. There were a few willows growing along the river's edge and reed beds in the muddy shallows beyond, but most of the ground hereabouts was painfully open. *I knew we should never have left the woods,* she thought. They'd been so hungry, though, and the garden had been too much a temptation. The bread and cheese they had stolen from Harrenhal had given out six days ago, back in the thick of the woods. "Take Gendry and the horses behind the cottage," she decided. There was part of one wall still standing, big enough, maybe, to conceal two boys and three horses. *If the horses don't whinny, and that singer doesn't come poking around the garden.*

"What about you?"

"I'll hide by the tree. He's probably alone. If he bothers me, I'll kill him. *Go!*"

Hot Pie went, and Arya dropped her carrots and drew the stolen sword from over her shoulder. She had strapped the sheath across her back; the longsword was made for a man grown, and it bumped against the ground when she wore it on her hip. *It's too heavy besides,* she thought, missing Needle the way she did every time she took this clumsy thing in her hand. But it was a sword and she could kill with it, that was enough.

Lightfoot, she moved to the big old willow that grew beside the bend in the road and went to one knee in the grass and mud, within the veil of trailing branches. *You old gods,* she prayed as the singer's voice grew louder, *you tree gods, hide me, and make him go past.* Then a horse whickered, and the song broke off suddenly. *He's heard,* she knew, *but maybe he's alone, or if he's not, maybe they'll be as scared of us as we are of them.*

"Did you hear that?" a man's voice said. "There's something behind that wall, I would say."

"Aye," replied a second voice, deeper. "What do you think it might be, Archer?"

Two, then. Arya bit her lip. She could not see them from where she knelt, on account of the willow. But she could hear.

"A bear." A third voice, or the first one again?

"A lot of meat on a bear," the deep voice said. "A lot of fat as well, in fall. Good to eat, if it's cooked up right."

"Could be a wolf. Maybe a lion."

"With four feet, you think? Or two?"

"Makes no matter. Does it?"

"Not so I know. Archer, what do you mean to do with all them arrows?"

"Drop a few shafts over the wall. Whatever's hiding back there will come out quick enough, watch and see."

"What if it's some honest man back there, though? Or some poor woman with a little babe at her breast?"

"An honest man would come out and show us his face. Only an outlaw would skulk and hide."

"Aye, that's so. Go on and loose your shafts, then."

Arya sprang to her feet. *"Don't!"* She showed them her sword. There were three, she saw. *Only three.* Syrio could fight more than three, and she had Hot Pie and Gendry to stand with her, maybe. *But they're boys, and these are men.*

They were men afoot, travel-stained and mud-specked. She knew the singer by the woodharp he cradled against his jerkin, as a mother might cradle a babe. A small man, fifty from the look of him, he had a big mouth, a sharp nose, and thinning brown hair. His faded greens were mended here and there with old leather patches, and he wore a brace of throwing knives on his hip and a woodman's axe slung across his back.

The man beside him stood a good foot taller, and had the look of a soldier. A longsword and dirk hung from his studded leather belt, rows of overlapping steel rings were sewn onto his shirt, and his head was covered by a black iron halfhelm shaped like a cone. He had bad teeth and a bushy brown beard, but it was his hooded yellow cloak that drew the eye. Thick and heavy, stained here with grass and there with blood, frayed along the bottom and patched with deer-skin on the right shoulder, the greatcloak gave the big man the look of some huge yellow bird.

The last of the three was a youth as skinny as his long-bow, if not quite as tall. Red-haired and freckled, he wore a studded brigantine, high boots, fingerless leather gloves, and a quiver on his back. His arrows were fletched with grey goose feathers, and six of them stood in the ground before him, like a little fence.

The three men looked at her, standing there in the road with her blade in hand. Then the singer idly plucked a string. "Boy," he said, "put up that sword now, unless you're wanting to be hurt. It's too big for you, lad, and be-sides, Anguy here could put three shafts through you be-fore you could hope to reach us."

"He could not," Arya said, "and I'm a *girl*."

"So you are." The singer bowed. "My pardons."

"You go on down the road. Just walk right past here, and you keep on singing, so we'll know where you are. Go away and leave us be and I won't kill you."

The freckle-faced archer laughed. "Lem, she won't kill us, did you hear?"

"I heard," said Lem, the big soldier with the deep voice.

"Child," said the singer, "put up that sword, and we'll take you to a safe place and get some food in that belly. There are wolves in these parts, and lions, and worse things. No place for a little girl to be wandering alone."

"She's not alone." Gendry rode out from behind the cot-tage wall, and behind him Hot Pie, leading her horse. In his chainmail shirt with a sword in his hand, Gendry looked almost a man grown, and dangerous. Hot Pie looked like Hot Pie. "Do like she says, and leave us be," warned Gendry.

"Two and three," the singer counted, "and is that all of you? And horses too, lovely horses. Where did you steal them?"

"They're ours." Arya watched them carefully. The singer kept distracting her with his talk, but it was the archer who was the danger. *If he should pull an arrow from the ground . . .*

"Will you give us your names like honest men?" the singer asked the boys.

"I'm Hot Pie," Hot Pie said at once.

"Aye, and good for you." The man smiled. "It's not every day I meet a lad with such a tasty name. And what would your friends be called, Mutton Chop and Squab?"

Gendry scowled down from his saddle. "Why should I tell you my name? I haven't heard yours."

"Well, as to that, I'm Tom of Sevenstreams, but Tom Sevenstrings is what they call me, or Tom o' Sevens. This great lout with the brown teeth is Lem, short for Lemoncloak. It's yellow, you see, and Lem's a sour sort. And young fellow me lad over there is Anguy, or Archer as we like to call him."

"Now who are you?" demanded Lem, in the deep voice that Arya had heard through the branches of the willow.

She was not about to give up her true name as easy as that. "Squab, if you want," she said. "I don't care."

The big man laughed. "A squab with a sword," he said. "Now there's something you don't often see."

"I'm the Bull," said Gendry, taking his lead from Arya. She could not blame him for preferring Bull to Mutton Chop.

Tom Sevenstrings strummed his harp. "Hot Pie, Squab, and the Bull. Escaped from Lord Bolton's kitchen, did you?"

"How did you know?" Arya demanded, uneasy.

"You bear his sigil on your chest, little one."

She had forgotten that for an instant. Beneath her cloak, she still wore her fine page's doublet, with the flayed man of the Dreadfort sewn on her breast. "Don't call me little one!"

"Why not?" said Lem. "You're little enough."

"I'm bigger than I was. I'm not a *child*." Children didn't kill people, and she had.

"I can see that, Squab. You're none of you children, not if you were Bolton's."

"We never were." Hot Pie never knew when to keep quiet. "We were at Harrenhal before he came, that's all."

"So you're lion cubs, is that the way of it?" said Tom.

"Not that either. We're nobody's men. Whose men are you?"

Anguy the Archer said, "We're king's men."

Arya frowned. "Which king?"

"King Robert," said Lem, in his yellow cloak.

"That old drunk?" said Gendry scornfully. "He's dead, some boar killed him, everyone knows that."

"Aye, lad," said Tom Sevenstrings, "and more's the pity." He plucked a sad chord from his harp.

Arya didn't think they were king's men at all. They looked more like outlaws, all tattered and ragged. They didn't even have horses to ride. King's men would have had horses.

But Hot Pie piped up eagerly. "We're looking for Riverrun," he said. "How many days' ride is it, do you know?"

Arya could have killed him. "You be quiet, or I'll stuff rocks in your big stupid mouth."

"Riverrun is a long way upstream," said Tom. "A long hungry way. Might be you'd like a hot meal before you set out? There's an inn not far ahead kept by some friends of ours. We could share some ale and a bite of bread, instead of fighting one another."

"An inn?" The thought of hot food made Arya's belly rumble, but she didn't trust this Tom. Not everyone who spoke you friendly was really your friend. "It's near, you say?"

"Two miles upstream," said Tom. "A league at most."

Gendry looked as uncertain as she felt. "What do you mean, *friends?*" he asked warily.

"Friends. Have you forgotten what friends are?"

"Sharna is the innkeep's name," Tom put in. "She has a sharp tongue and a fierce eye, I'll grant you that, but her heart's a good one, and she's fond of little girls."

"I'm not a little girl," she said angrily. "Who else is there? You said *friends.*"

"Sharna's husband, and an orphan boy they took in. They won't harm you. There's ale, if you think you're old enough. Fresh bread and maybe a bit of meat." Tom glanced toward the cottage. "And whatever you stole from Old Pate's garden besides."

"We never stole," said Arya.

"Are you Old Pate's daughter, then? A sister? A wife? Tell me no lies, Squab. I buried Old Pate myself, right there under that willow where you were hiding, and you don't have his look." He drew a sad sound from his harp. "We've buried many a good man this past year, but we've no wish to bury you, I swear it on my harp. Archer, show her."

The archer's hand moved quicker than Arya would have believed. His shaft went hissing past her head within an inch of her ear and buried itself in the trunk of the willow behind her. By then the bowman had a second arrow notched and drawn. She'd thought she understood what Syrio meant by *quick as a snake* and *smooth as summer silk*, but now she knew she hadn't. The arrow thrummed behind her like a bee. "You missed," she said.

"More fool you if you think so," said Anguy. "They go where I send them."

"That they do," agreed Lem Lemoncloak.

There were a dozen steps between the archer and the point of her sword. *We have no chance*, Arya realized, wishing she had a bow like his, and the skill to use it. Glumly, she lowered her heavy longsword till the point touched the ground. "We'll come see this inn," she conceded, trying to hide the doubt in her heart behind bold words. "You walk in front and we'll ride behind, so we can see what you're doing."

Tom Sevenstrings bowed deeply and said, "Before, behind, it makes no matter. Come along, lads, let's show them the way. Anguy, best pull up those arrows, we won't be needing them here."

Arya sheathed her sword and crossed the road to where her friends sat on their horses, keeping her distance from the three strangers. "Hot Pie, get those cabbages," she said as she vaulted into her saddle. "And the carrots too."

For once he did not argue. They set off as she had wanted, walking their horses slowly down the rutted road a dozen paces behind the three on foot. But before very long, somehow they were riding right on top of them. Tom Sevenstrings walked slowly, and liked to strum his woodharp as he went. "Do you know any songs?" he asked them. "I'd dearly love someone to sing with, that I would. Lem can't carry a tune, and our longbow lad only knows marcher ballads, every one of them a hundred verses long."

"We sing real songs in the marches," Anguy said mildly.

"Singing is *stupid*," said Arya. "Singing makes noise. We heard you a long way off. We could have killed you."

Tom's smile said he did not think so. "There are worse things than dying with a song on your lips."

"If there were wolves hereabouts, we'd know it," groused Lem. "Or lions. These are our woods."

"You never knew we were there," said Gendry.

"Now, lad, you shouldn't be so certain of that," said Tom. "Sometimes a man knows more than he says."

Hot Pie shifted his seat. "I know the song about the bear," he said. "Some of it, anyhow."

Tom ran his fingers down his strings. "Then let's hear it, pie boy." He threw back his head and sang, *"A bear there was, a bear, a bear! All black and brown, and covered with hair . . ."*

Hot Pie joined in lustily, even bouncing in his saddle a little on the rhymes. Arya stared at him in astonishment. He had a good voice and he sang well. *He never did anything well, except bake,* she thought to herself.

A small brook flowed into the Trident a little farther on. As they waded across, their singing flushed a duck from among the reeds. Anguy stopped where he stood, unslung his bow, notched an arrow, and brought it down. The bird fell in the shallows not far from the bank. Lem took off his yellow cloak and waded in knee-deep to retrieve it, complaining all the while. "Do you think Sharna might have lemons down in that cellar of hers?" said Anguy to Tom as they watched Lem splash around, cursing. "A Dornish girl once cooked me duck with lemons." He sounded wistful.

Tom and Hot Pie resumed their song on the other side of the brook, with the duck hanging from Lem's belt beneath his yellow cloak. Somehow the singing made the miles seem shorter. It was not very long at all until the inn appeared before them, rising from the riverbank where the Trident made a great bend to the north. Arya squinted at it suspiciously as they neared. It did not *look* like an outlaws' lair, she had to admit; it looked friendly, even homey, with its whitewashed upper story and slate roof and the smoke curling up lazy from its chimney. Stables and other outbuildings surrounded it, and there was an arbor in back, and apple trees, a small garden. The inn even had its own dock, thrusting out into the river, and . . .

"Gendry," she called, her voice low and urgent. "They

have a boat. We could sail the rest of the way up to Riverrun. It would be faster than riding, I think."

He looked dubious. "Did you ever sail a boat?"

"You put up the sail," she said, "and the wind pushes it."

"What if the wind is blowing the wrong way?"

"Then there's oars to row."

"Against the current?" Gendry frowned. "Wouldn't that be slow? And what if the boat tips over and we fall into the water? It's not our boat anyway, it's the inn's."

We could take it. Arya chewed her lip and said nothing. They dismounted in front of stables. There were no other horses to be seen, but Arya noticed fresh manure in many of the stalls. "One of us should watch the horses," she said, wary.

Tom overheard her. "There's no need for that, Squab. Come eat, they'll be safe enough."

"I'll stay," Gendry said, ignoring the singer. "You can come get me after you've had some food."

Nodding, Arya set off after Hot Pie and Lem. Her sword was still in its sheath across her back, and she kept a hand close to the hilt of the dagger she had stolen from Roose Bolton, in case she didn't like whatever they found within.

The painted sign above the door showed a picture of some old king on his knees. Inside was the common room, where a very tall ugly woman with a knobby chin stood with her hands on her hips, glaring. "Don't just stand there, boy," she snapped. "Or are you a girl? Either one, you're blocking my door. Get in or get out. Lem, what did I tell you about my floor? You're all mud."

"We shot a duck." Lem held it out like a peace banner.

The woman snatched it from his hand. "Anguy shot a duck, is what you're meaning. Get your boots off, are you deaf or just stupid?" She turned away. *"Husband!"* she called loudly. "Get up here, the lads are back. *Husband!"*

Up the cellar steps came a man in a stained apron, grumbling. He was a head shorter than the woman, with a lumpy face and loose yellowish skin that still showed the marks of some pox. "I'm here, woman, quit your bellowing. What is it now?"

"Hang this," she said, handing him the duck.

Anguy shuffled his feet. "We were thinking we might eat it, Sharna. With lemons. If you had some."

"Lemons. And where would we get lemons? Does this look like Dorne to you, you freckled fool? Why don't you hop out back to the lemon trees and pick us a bushel, and some nice olives and pomegranates too." She shook a finger at him. "Now, I suppose I could cook it with Lem's cloak, if you like, but not till it's hung for a few days. You'll eat rabbit, or you won't eat. Roast rabbit on a spit would be quickest, if you've got a hunger. Or might be you'd like it stewed, with ale and onions."

Arya could almost taste the rabbit. "We have no coin, but we brought some carrots and cabbages we could trade you."

"Did you now? And where would they be?"

"Hot Pie, give her the cabbages," Arya said, and he did, though he approached the old woman as gingerly as if she were Rorge or Biter or Vargo Hoat.

The woman gave the vegetables a close inspection, and the boy a closer one. "Where is this *hot pie?*"

"Here. Me. It's my name. And she's . . . ah . . . Squab."

"Not under my roof. I give my diners and my dishes different names, so as to tell them apart. *Husband!*"

Husband had stepped outside, but at her shout he hurried back. "The duck's hung. What is it now, woman?"

"Wash these vegetables," she commanded. "The rest of you, sit down while I start the rabbits. The boy will bring you drink." She looked down her long nose at Arya and Hot Pie. "I am not in the habit of serving ale to children, but the cider's run out, there's no cows for milk, and the river water tastes of war, with all the dead men drifting downstream. If I served you a cup of soup full of dead flies, would you drink it?"

"Arry would," said Hot Pie. "I mean, Squab."

"So would Lem," offered Anguy with a sly smile.

"Never you mind about Lem," Sharna said. "It's ale for all." She swept off toward the kitchen.

Anguy and Tom Sevenstrings took the table near the hearth while Lem was hanging his big yellow cloak on a peg. Hot Pie plopped down heavily on a bench at the table by the door, and Arya wedged herself in beside him.

Tom unslung his harp. "*A lonely inn on a forest road,*" he sang, slowly picking out a tune to go with the words. "*The innkeep's wife was plain as a toad.*"

"Shut up with that now or we won't be getting no rabbit," Lem warned him. "You know how she is."

Arya leaned close to Hot Pie. "Can you sail a boat?" she asked. Before he could answer, a thickset boy of fifteen or sixteen appeared with tankards of ale. Hot Pie took his reverently in both hands, and when he sipped he smiled wider than Arya had ever seen him smile. "Ale," he whispered, "and *rabbit*."

"Well, here's to His Grace," Anguy the Archer called out cheerfully, lifting a toast. "Seven save the king!"

"All twelve o' them," Lem Lemoncloak muttered. He drank, and wiped the foam from his mouth with the back of his hand.

Husband came bustling in through the front door, with an apron full of washed vegetables. "There's strange horses in the stable," he announced, as if they hadn't known.

"Aye," said Tom, setting the woodharp aside, "and better horses than the three you gave away."

Husband dropped the vegetables on a table, annoyed. "I never gave them away. I *sold* them for a good price, and got us a skiff as well. Anyways, you lot were supposed to get them back."

I knew they were outlaws, Arya thought, listening. Her hand went under the table to touch the hilt of her dagger, and make sure it was still there. *If they try to rob us, they'll be sorry.*

"They never came our way," said Lem.

"Well, I sent them. You must have been drunk, or asleep."

"Us? Drunk?" Tom drank a long draught of ale. "Never."

"You could have taken them yourself," Lem told Husband.

"What, with only the boy here? I told you twice, the old woman was up to Lambswold helping that Fern birth her babe. And like as not it was one o' you planted the bastard in the poor girl's belly." He gave Tom a sour look. "You, I'd wager, with that harp o' yours, singing all them sad songs just to get poor Fern out of her smallclothes."

"If a song makes a maid want to slip off her clothes and feel the good warm sun kiss her skin, why, is that the singer's fault?" asked Tom. "And 'twas Anguy she fancied, besides. 'Can I touch your bow?' I heard her ask him. 'Ooohh, it feels so smooth and hard. Could I give it a little pull, do you think?' "

Husband snorted. "You and Anguy, makes no matter which. You're as much to blame as me for them horses. They was three, you know. What can one man do against three?"

"Three," said Lem scornfully, "but one a woman and t'other in chains, you said so yourself."

Husband made a face. "A *big* woman, dressed like a man. And the one in chains . . . I didn't fancy the look of his eyes."

Anguy smiled over his ale. "When I don't fancy a man's eyes, I put an arrow through one."

Arya remembered the shaft that had brushed by her ear. She wished she knew how to shoot arrows.

Husband was not impressed. "You be quiet when your elders are talking. Drink your ale and mind your tongue, or I'll have the old woman take a spoon to you."

"My elders talk too much, and I don't need you to tell me to drink my ale." He took a big swallow, to show that it was so.

Arya did the same. After days of drinking from brooks and puddles, and then the muddy Trident, the ale tasted as good as the little sips of wine her father used to allow her. A smell was drifting out from the kitchen that made her mouth water, but her thoughts were still full of that boat. *Sailing it will be harder than stealing it. If we wait until they're all asleep . . .*

The serving boy reappeared with big round loaves of bread. Arya broke off a chunk hungrily and tore into it. It was hard to chew, though, sort of thick and lumpy, and burned on the bottom.

Hot Pie made a face as soon as he tasted it. "That's bad bread," he said. "It's burned, and tough besides."

"It's better when there's stew to sop up," said Lem.

"No, it isn't," said Anguy, "but you're less like to break your teeth."

"You can eat it or go hungry," said Husband. "Do I look like some bloody baker? I'd like to see you make better."

"I could," said Hot Pie. "It's easy. You kneaded the dough too much, that's why it's so hard to chew." He took another sip of ale, and began talking lovingly of breads and pies and tarts, all the things he loved. Arya rolled her eyes.

Tom sat down across from her. "Squab," he said, "or Arry, or whatever your true name might be, this is for you." He placed a dirty scrap of parchment on the wooden tabletop between them.

She looked at it suspiciously. "What is it?"

"Three golden dragons. We need to buy those horses."

Arya looked at him warily. "They're *our* horses."

"Meaning you stole them yourselves, is that it? No shame in that, girl. War makes thieves of many honest folk." Tom tapped the folded parchment with his finger. "I'm paying you a handsome price. More than any horse is worth, if truth be told."

Hot Pie grabbed the parchment and unfolded it. "There's no gold," he complained loudly. "It's only writing."

"Aye," said Tom, "and I'm sorry for that. But after the war, we mean to make that good, you have my word as a king's man."

Arya pushed back from the table and got to her feet. "You're no king's men, you're robbers."

"If you'd ever met a true robber, you'd know they do not pay, not even in paper. It's not for us we take your horses, child, it's for the good of the realm, so we can get about more quickly and fight the fights that need fighting. The king's fights. Would you deny the king?"

They were all watching her; the Archer, big Lem, Husband with his sallow face and shifty eyes. Even Sharna, who stood in the door to the kitchen squinting. *They are going to take our horses no matter what I say*, she realized. *We'll need to walk to Riverrun, unless . . .* "We don't want paper." Arya slapped the parchment out of Hot Pie's hand. "You can have our horses for that boat outside. But only if you show us how to work it."

Tom Sevenstrings stared at her a moment, and then his wide homely mouth quirked into a rueful grin. He laughed aloud. Anguy joined in, and then they were all laughing, Lem Lemoncloak, Sharna and Husband, even the serving boy, who had stepped out from behind the casks with a crossbow under one arm. Arya wanted to scream at them, but instead she started to smile . . .

"*Riders!*" Gendry's shout was shrill with alarm. The

door burst open and there he was. *"Soldiers,"* he panted. "Coming down the river road, a dozen of them."

Hot Pie leapt up, knocking over his tankard, but Tom and the others were unpertubed. "There's no cause for spilling good ale on my floor," said Sharna. "Sit back down and calm yourself, boy, there's rabbit coming. You too, girl. Whatever harm's been done you, it's over and it's done and you're with king's men now. We'll keep you safe as best we can."

Arya's only answer was to reach over her shoulder for her sword, but before she had it halfway drawn Lem grabbed her wrist. "We'll have no more of that, now." He twisted her arm until her hand opened. His fingers were hard with callus and fearsomely strong. *Again!* Arya thought. *It's happening again, like it happened in the village, with Chiswyck and Raff and the Mountain That Rides.* They were going to steal her sword and turn her back into a mouse. Her free hand closed around her tankard, and she swung it at Lem's face. The ale sloshed over the rim and splashed into his eyes, and she heard his nose break and saw the spurt of blood. When he roared his hands went to his face, and she was free. *"Run!"* she screamed, bolting.

But Lem was on her again at once, with his long legs that made one of his steps equal to three of hers. She twisted and kicked, but he yanked her off her feet effortlessly and held her dangling while the blood ran down his face.

"Stop it, you little fool," he shouted, shaking her back and forth. "Stop it now!" Gendry moved to help her, until Tom Sevenstrings stepped in front of him with a dagger.

By then it was too late to flee. She could hear horses outside, and the sound of men's voices. A moment later came a man came swaggering through the open door, a Tyroshi even bigger than Lem with a great thick beard, bright green at the ends but growing out grey. Behind came a pair of crossbowmen helping a wounded man between them, and then others . . .

A more ragged band Arya had never seen, but there was nothing ragged about the swords, axes, and bows they carried. One or two gave her curious glances as they entered, but no one said a word. A one-eyed man in a rusty pothelm sniffed the air and grinned, while an archer with a head of stiff yellow hair was shouting for ale. After them came a spearman in a lion-crested helm, an older man with a limp, a Braavosi sellsword, a . . .

"Harwin?" Arya whispered. *It was!* Under the beard and the tangled hair was the face of Hullen's son, who used to lead her pony around the yard, ride at quintain with Jon and Robb, and drink too much on feast days. He was thinner, harder somehow, and at Winterfell he had never worn a beard, but it was him—her father's man. "*Harwin!*" Squirming, she threw herself forward, trying to wrench free of Lem's iron grip. "It's me," she shouted, "Harwin, it's me, don't you know me, don't you?" The tears came, and she found herself weeping like a baby, just like some stupid little girl. "Harwin, *it's me!*"

Harwin's eyes went from her face to the flayed man on her doublet. "How do you know me?" he said, frowning suspiciously. "The flayed man . . . who are you, some serving boy to Lord Leech?"

For a moment she did not know how to answer. She'd had so many names. Had she only dreamed Arya Stark? "I'm a girl," she sniffed. "I was Lord Bolton's cupbearer but he was going to leave me for the goat, so I ran off with Gendry and Hot Pie. You *have* to know me! You used to lead my pony, when I was little."

His eyes went wide, "Gods be good," he said in a choked voice. "Arya Underfoot? Lem, let go of her."

"She broke my nose." Lem dumped her unceremoniously to the floor. "Who in seven hells is she supposed to be?"

"The Hand's daughter." Harwin went to one knee before her. "Arya Stark, of Winterfell."

CATELYN

Robb, she knew, the moment she heard the kennels erupt.

Her son had returned to Riverrun, and Grey Wind with him. Only the scent of the great grey direwolf could send the hounds into such a frenzy of baying and barking. *He will come to me*, she knew. Edmure had not returned after his first visit, preferring to spend his days with Marq Piper and Patrek Mallister, listening to Rymund the Rhymer's verses about the battle at the Stone Mill. *Robb is not Edmure, though. Robb will see me.*

It had been raining for days now, a cold grey downpour that well suited Catelyn's mood. Her father was growing weaker and more delirious with every passing day, waking only to mutter, "Tansy," and beg forgiveness. Edmure shunned her, and Ser Desmond Grell still denied her freedom of the castle, however unhappy it seemed to make him. Only the return of Ser Robin Ryger and his men, footweary and drenched to the bone, served to lighten her spirits. They had walked back, it seemed. Somehow the Kingslayer had contrived to sink their galley and escape,

Maester Vyman confided. Catelyn asked if she might speak with Ser Robin to learn more of what had happened, but that was refused her.

Something else was wrong as well. On the day her brother returned, a few hours after their argument, she had heard angry voices from the yard below. When she climbed to the roof to see, there were knots of men gathered across the castle beside the main gate. Horses were being led from the stables, saddled and bridled, and there was shouting, though Catelyn was too far away to make out the words. One of Robb's white banners lay on the ground, and one of the knights turned his horse and trampled over the direwolf as he spurred toward the gate. Several others did the same. *Those are men who fought with Edmure on the fords*, she thought. *What could have made them so angry? Has my brother slighted them somehow, given them some insult?* She thought she recognized Ser Perwyn Frey, who had traveled with her to Bitterbridge and Storm's End and back, and his bastard half brother Martyn Rivers as well, but from this vantage it was hard to be certain. Close to forty men poured out through the castle gates, to what end she did not know.

They did not come back. Nor would Maester Vyman tell her who they had been, where they had gone, or what had made them so angry. "I am here to see to your father, and only that, my lady," he said. "Your brother will soon be Lord of Riverrun. What he wishes you to know, he must tell you."

But now Robb was returned from the west, returned in triumph. *He will forgive me*, Catelyn told herself. *He must forgive me, he is my own son, and Arya and Sansa are as much his blood as mine. He will free me from these rooms and then I will know what has happened.*

By the time Ser Desmond came for her, she had bathed and dressed and combed out her auburn hair. "King Robb has returned from the west, my lady," the knight said, "and commands that you attend him in the Great Hall."

It was the moment she had dreamt of and dreaded. *Have I lost two sons, or three?* She would know soon enough.

The hall was crowded when they entered. Every eye was on the dais, but Catelyn knew their backs: Lady Mormont's patched ringmail, the Greatjon and his son looming above every other head in the hall, Lord Jason Mallister white-haired with his winged helm in the crook of his arm, Tytos Blackwood in his magnificent raven-feather cloak ... *Half of them will want to hang me now. The other half may only turn their eyes away.* She had the uneasy feeling that someone was missing, too.

Robb stood on the dais. *He is a boy no longer,* she realized with a pang. *He is sixteen now, a man grown. Just look at him.* War had melted all the softness from his face and left him hard and lean. He had shaved his beard away, but his auburn hair fell uncut to his shoulders. The recent rains had rusted his mail and left brown stains on the white of his cloak and surcoat. Or perhaps the stains were blood. On his head was the sword crown they had fashioned him of bronze and iron. *He bears it more comfortably now. He bears it like a king.*

Edmure stood below the crowded dais, head bowed modestly as Robb praised his victory. "... fell at the Stone Mill shall never be forgotten. Small wonder Lord Tywin ran off to fight Stannis. He'd had his fill of northmen and rivermen both." That brought laughter and approving shouts, but Robb raised a hand for quiet. "Make no mistake, though. The Lannisters will march again, and there will be other battles to win before the kingdom is secure."

The Greatjon roared out, *"King in the North!"* and thrust a mailed fist into the air. The river lords answered with a shout of *"King of the Trident!"* The hall grew thunderous with pounding fists and stamping feet.

Only a few noted Catelyn and Ser Desmond amidst the tumult, but they elbowed their fellows, and slowly a hush grew around her. She held her head high and ignored the eyes. *Let them think what they will. It is Robb's judgment that matters.*

The sight of Ser Brynden Tully's craggy face on the dais gave her comfort. A boy she did not know seemed to be acting as Robb's squire. Behind him stood a young knight in a sand-colored surcoat blazoned with seashells, and an older one who wore three black pepperpots on a saffron bend, across a field of green and silver stripes. Between them were a handsome older lady and a pretty maid who looked to be her daughter. There was another girl as well, near Sansa's age. The seashells were the sigil of some lesser house, Catelyn knew; the older man's she did not recognize. *Prisoners?* Why would Robb bring captives onto the dais?

Utherydes Wayn banged his staff on the floor as Ser Desmond escorted her forward. *If Robb looks at me as Edmure did, I do not know what I will do.* But it seemed to her that it was not anger she saw in her son's eyes, but something else . . . apprehension, perhaps? No, that made no sense. What should *he* fear? He was the Young Wolf, King of the Trident and the North.

Her uncle was the first to greet her. As black a fish as ever, Ser Brynden had no care for what others might think. He leapt off the dais and pulled Catelyn into his arms. When he said, "It is good to see you home, Cat," she had to struggle to keep her composure. "And you," she whispered.

"Mother."

Catelyn looked up at her tall kingly son. "Your Grace, I have prayed for your safe return. I had heard you were wounded."

"I took an arrow through the arm while storming the Crag," he said. "It's healed well, though. I had the best of care."

"The gods are good, then." Catelyn took a deep breath. *Say it. It cannot be avoided.* "They will have told you what I did. Did they tell you my reasons?"

"For the girls."

"I had five children. Now I have three."

"Aye, my lady." Lord Rickard Karstark pushed past the Greatjon, like some grim specter with his black mail and long ragged grey beard, his narrow face pinched and cold. "And I have one son, who once had three. You have robbed me of my vengeance."

Catelyn faced him calmly. "Lord Rickard, the Kingslayer's dying would not have bought life for your children. His living may buy life for mine."

The lord was unappeased. "Jaime Lannister has played you for a fool. You've bought a bag of empty words, no more. My Torrhen and my Eddard deserved better of you."

"Leave off, Karstark," rumbled the Greatjon, crossing his huge arms against his chest. "It was a mother's folly. Women are made that way."

"A mother's folly?" Lord Karstark rounded on Lord Umber. "I name it treason."

"*Enough.*" For just an instant Robb sounded more like Brandon than his father. "No man calls my lady of Winterfell a traitor in my hearing, Lord Rickard." When he turned to Catelyn, his voice softened. "If I could wish the Kingslayer back in chains I would. You freed him without my knowledge or consent . . . but what you did, I know you did for love. For Arya and Sansa, and out of grief for Bran and Rickon. Love's not always wise, I've learned. It can lead us to great folly, but we follow our hearts . . . wherever they take us. Don't we, Mother?"

Is that what I did? "If my heart led me into folly, I would gladly make whatever amends I can to Lord Karstark and yourself."

Lord Rickard's face was implacable. "Will your *amends* warm Torrhen and Eddard in the cold graves where the Kingslayer laid them?" He shouldered between the Greatjon and Maege Mormont and left the hall.

Robb made no move to detain him. "Forgive him, Mother."

"If you will forgive me."

"I have. I know what it is to love so greatly you can think of nothing else."

Catelyn bowed her head. "Thank you." *I have not lost this child, at least.*

"We must talk," Robb went on. "You and my uncles. Of this and . . . other things. Steward, call an end."

Utherydes Wayn slammed his staff on the floor and shouted the dismissal, and river lords and northerners alike moved toward the doors. It was only then that Catelyn realized what was amiss. *The wolf. The wolf is not here. Where is Grey Wind?* She knew the direwolf had returned with Robb, she had heard the dogs, but he was not in the hall, not at her son's side where he belonged.

Before she could think to question Robb, however, she found herself surrounded by a circle of well-wishers. Lady Mormont took her hand and said, "My lady, if Cersei Lannister held two of my daughters, I would have done the same." The Greatjon, no respecter of proprieties, lifted her off her feet and squeezed her arms with his huge hairy hands. "Your wolf pup mauled the Kingslayer once, he'll do it again if need be." Galbart Glover and Lord Jason Mallister were cooler, and Jonos Bracken almost icy, but their words were courteous enough. Her brother was the last to approach her. "I pray for your girls as well, Cat. I hope you do not doubt that."

"Of course not." She kissed him. "I love you for it."

When all the words were done, the Great Hall of Riverrun was empty save for Robb, the three Tullys, and the six strangers Catelyn could not place. She eyed them curiously. "My lady, sers, are you new to my son's cause?"

"New," said the younger knight, him of the seashells, "but fierce in our courage and firm in our loyalties, as I hope to prove to you, my lady."

Robb looked uncomfortable. "Mother," he said, "may I present the Lady Sybell, the wife of Lord Gawen Westerling of the Crag." The older woman came forward with solemn mien. "Her husband was one of those we took captive in the Whispering Wood."

Westerling, yes, Catelyn thought. *Their banner is six seashells, white on sand. A minor house sworn to the Lannisters.*

Robb beckoned the other strangers forward, each in turn. "Ser Rolph Spicer, Lady Sybell's brother. He was castellan at the Crag when we took it." The pepperpot knight inclined his head. A square-built man with a broken nose and a close-cropped grey beard, he looked doughty enough. "The children of Lord Gawen and Lady Sybell. Ser Raynald Westerling." The seashell knight smiled beneath a bushy mustache. Young, lean, rough-hewn, he had good teeth and a thick mop of chestnut hair. "Elenya." The little girl did a quick curtsy. "Rollam Westerling, my squire." The boy started to kneel, saw no one else was kneeling, and bowed instead.

"The honor is mine," Catelyn said. *Can Robb have won the Crag's allegiance?* If so, it was no wonder the Westerlings were with him. Casterly Rock did not suffer such betrayals gently. Not since Tywin Lannister had been old enough to go to war . . .

The maid came forward last, and very shy. Robb took her hand. "Mother," he said, "I have the great honor to present you the Lady Jeyne Westerling. Lord Gawen's elder daughter, and my . . . ah . . . my lady wife."

The first thought that flew across Catelyn's mind was, *No, that cannot be, you are only a child.*

The second was, *And besides, you have pledged another.*

The third was, *Mother have mercy, Robb, what have you done?*

Only then came her belated remembrance. *Follies done for love? He has bagged me neat as a hare in a snare. I seem to have already forgiven him.* Mixed with her annoyance was a rueful admiration; the scene had been staged with the cunning worthy of a master mummer . . . or a king. Catelyn saw no choice but to take Jeyne Westerling's hands. "I have a new daughter," she said, more stiffly than she'd intended. She kissed the terrified girl on both cheeks. "Be welcome to our hall and hearth."

"Thank you, my lady. I shall be a good and true wife to Robb, I swear. And as wise a queen as I can."

Queen. Yes, this pretty little girl is a queen, I must remember that. She *was* pretty, undeniably, with her chestnut curls and heart-shaped face, and that shy smile. Slender, but with good hips, Catelyn noted. *She should have no trouble bearing children, at least.*

Lady Sybell took a hand before any more was said. "We are honored to be joined to House Stark, my lady, but we are also very weary. We have come a long way in a short time. Perhaps we might retire to our chambers, so you may visit with your son?"

"That would be best." Robb kissed his Jeyne. "The steward will find you suitable accommodations."

"I'll take you to him," Ser Edmure Tully volunteered.

"You are most kind," said Lady Sybell.

"Must I go too?" asked the boy, Rollam. "I'm your squire."

Robb laughed. "But I'm not in need of squiring just now."

"Oh."

"His Grace has gotten along for sixteen years without you, Rollam," said Ser Raynald of the seashells. "He will survive a few hours more, I think." Taking his little brother firmly by the hand, he walked him from the hall.

"Your wife is lovely," Catelyn said when they were out

of earshot, "and the Westerlings seem worthy . . . though Lord Gawen is Tywin Lannister's sworn man, is he not?"

"Yes. Jason Mallister captured him in the Whispering Wood and has been holding him at Seagard for ransom. Of course I'll free him now, though he may not wish to join me. We wed without his consent, I fear, and this marriage puts him in dire peril. The Crag is not strong. For love of me, Jeyne may lose all."

"And you," she said softly, "have lost the Freys."

His wince told all. She understood the angry voices now, why Perwyn Frey and Martyn Rivers had left in such haste, trampling Robb's banner into the ground as they went.

"Dare I ask how many swords come with your bride, Robb?"

"Fifty. A dozen knights." His voice was glum, as well it might be. When the marriage contract had been made at the Twins, old Lord Walder Frey had sent Robb off with a thousand mounted knights and near three thousand foot. "Jeyne is bright as well as beautiful. And kind as well. She has a gentle heart."

It is swords you need, not gentle hearts. How could you do this, Robb? How could you be so heedless, so stupid? How could you be so . . . so very . . . young. Reproaches would not serve here, however. All she said was, "Tell me how this came to be."

"I took her castle and she took my heart." Robb smiled. "The Crag was weakly garrisoned, so we took it by storm one night. Black Walder and the Smalljon led scaling parties over the walls, while I broke the main gate with a ram. I took an arrow in the arm just before Ser Rolph yielded us the castle. It seemed nothing at first, but it festered. Jeyne had me taken to her own bed, and she nursed me until the fever passed. And she was with me when the Greatjon brought me the news of . . . of Winterfell. Bran and Rickon." He seemed to have trouble saying his brothers' names. "That night, she . . . she comforted me, Mother."

Catelyn did not need to be told what sort of comfort Jeyne Westerling had offered her son. "And you wed her the next day."

He looked her in the eyes, proud and miserable all at

once. "It was the only honorable thing to do. She's gentle and sweet, Mother, she will make me a good wife."

"Perhaps. That will not appease Lord Frey."

"I know," her son said, stricken. "I've made a botch of everything but the battles, haven't I? I thought the battles would be the hard part, but . . . if I had listened to you and kept Theon as my hostage, I'd still rule the north, and Bran and Rickon would be alive and safe in Winterfell."

"Perhaps. Or not. Lord Balon might still have chanced war. The last time he reached for a crown, it cost him two sons. He might have thought it a bargain to lose only one this time." She touched his arm. "What happened with the Freys, after you wed?"

Robb shook his head. "With Ser Stevron, I might have been able to make amends, but Ser Ryman is dull-witted as a stone, and Black Walder . . . that one was not named for the color of his beard, I promise you. He went so far as to say that his sisters would not be loath to wed a widower. I would have killed him for that if Jeyne had not begged me to be merciful."

"You have done House Frey a grievous insult, Robb."

"I never meant to. Ser Stevron died for me, and Olyvar was as loyal a squire as any king could want. He asked to stay with me, but Ser Ryman took him with the rest. All their strength. The Greatjon urged me to attack them . . ."

"Fighting your own in the midst of your enemies?" she said. "It would have been the end of you."

"Yes. I thought perhaps we could arrange other matches for Lord Walder's daughters. Ser Wendel Manderly has offered to take one, and the Greatjon tells me his uncles wish to wed again. If Lord Walder will be reasonable—"

"He is *not* reasonable," said Catelyn. "He is proud, and prickly to a fault. You know that. He wanted to be grandfather to a king. You will not appease him with the offer of two hoary old brigands and the second son of the fattest man in the Seven Kingdoms. Not only have you broken your oath, but you've slighted the honor of the Twins by choosing a bride from a lesser house."

Robb bristled at that. "The Westerlings are better blood than the Freys. They're an ancient line, descended from the First Men. The Kings of the Rock sometimes wed Westerlings before the Conquest, and there was another

Jeyne Westerling who was queen to King Maegor three hundred years ago."

"All of which will only salt Lord Walder's wounds. It has always rankled him that older houses look down on the Freys as upstarts. This insult is not the first he's borne, to hear him tell it. Jon Arryn was disinclined to foster his grandsons, and my father refused the offer of one of his daughters for Edmure." She inclined her head toward her brother as he rejoined them.

"Your Grace," Brynden Blackfish said, "perhaps we had best continue this in private."

"Yes." Robb sounded tired. "I would kill for a cup of wine. The audience chamber, I think."

As they started up the steps, Catelyn asked the question that had been troubling her since she entered the hall. "Robb, where is Grey Wind?"

"In the yard, with a haunch of mutton. I told the kennelmaster to see that he was fed."

"You always kept him with you before."

"A hall is no place for a wolf. He gets restless, you've seen. Growling and snapping. I should never have taken him into battle with me. He's killed too many men to fear them now. Jeyne's anxious around him, and he terrifies her mother."

And there's the heart of it, Catelyn thought. "He is part of you, Robb. To fear him is to fear you."

"I am not a wolf, no matter what they call me." Robb sounded cross. "Grey Wind killed a man at the Crag, another at Ashemark, and six or seven at Oxcross. If you had seen—"

"I saw Bran's wolf tear out a man's throat at Winterfell," she said sharply, "and loved him for it."

"That's different. The man at the Crag was a knight Jeyne had known all her life. You can't blame her for being afraid. Grey Wind doesn't like her uncle either. He bares his teeth every time Ser Rolph comes near him."

A chill went through her. "Send Ser Rolph away. At once."

"Where? Back to the Crag, so the Lannisters can mount his head on a spike? Jeyne loves him. He's her uncle, and a fair knight besides. I need more men like Rolph Spicer, not fewer. I am not going to banish him just because my wolf doesn't seem to like the way he smells."

"Robb." She stopped and held his arm. "I told you once to keep Theon Greyjoy close, and you did not listen. Listen now. *Send this man away*. I am not saying you must banish him. Find some task that requires a man of courage, some honorable duty, what it is matters not . . . but *do not keep him near you*."

He frowned. "Should I have Grey Wind sniff all my knights? There might be others whose smell he mislikes."

"Any man Grey Wind mislikes is a man I do not want close to you. These wolves are more than wolves, Robb. You *must* know that. I think perhaps the gods sent them to us. Your father's gods, the old gods of the north. Five wolf pups, Robb, five for five Stark children."

"Six," said Robb. "There was a wolf for Jon as well. I found them, remember? I know how many there were and where they came from. I used to think the same as you, that the wolves were our guardians, our protectors, until . . ."

"Until?" she prompted.

Robb's mouth tightened. ". . . .until they told me that Theon had murdered Bran and Rickon. Small good their wolves did them. I am no longer a boy, Mother. I'm a king, and I can protect myself." He sighed. "I will find some duty for Ser Rolph, some pretext to send him away. Not because of his smell, but to ease your mind. You have suffered enough."

Relieved, Catelyn kissed him lightly on the cheek before the others could come around the turn of the stair, and for a moment he was her boy again, and not her king.

Lord Hoster's private audience chamber was a small room above the Great Hall, better suited to intimate discussions. Robb took the high seat, removed his crown, and set it on the floor beside him as Catelyn rang for wine. Edmure was filling his uncle's ear with the whole story of the fight at the Stone Mill. It was only after the servants had come and gone that the Blackfish cleared his throat and said, "I think we've all heard sufficient of your boasting, Nephew."

Edmure was taken aback. "Boasting? What do you mean?"

"I *mean*," said the Blackfish, "that you owe His Grace

your thanks for his forbearance. He played out that mummer's farce in the Great Hall so as not to shame you before your own people. Had it been me I would have flayed you for your stupidity rather than praising this folly of the fords."

"Good men died to defend those fords, Uncle." Edmure sounded outraged. "What, is no one to win victories but the Young Wolf? Did I steal some glory meant for you, Robb?"

"*Your Grace*," Robb corrected, icy. "You took me for your king, Uncle. Or have you forgotten that as well?"

The Blackfish said, "You were commanded to hold Riverrun, Edmure, no more."

"I held Riverrun, *and* I bloodied Lord Tywin's nose—"

"So you did," said Robb. "But a bloody nose won't win the war, will it? Did you ever think to ask yourself why we remained in the west so long after Oxcross? You knew I did not have enough men to threaten Lannisport or Casterly Rock."

"Why . . . there were other castles . . . gold, cattle . . ."

"You think we stayed for *plunder*?" Robb was incredulous. "Uncle, I wanted Lord Tywin to come west."

"We were all horsed," Ser Brynden said. "The Lannister host was mainly foot. We planned to run Lord Tywin a merry chase up and down the coast, then slip behind him to take up a strong defensive position athwart the gold road, at a place my scouts had found where the ground would have been greatly in our favor. If he had come at us there, he would have paid a grievous price. But if he did not attack, he would have been trapped in the west, a thousand leagues from where he needed to be. All the while we would have lived off his land, instead of him living off ours."

"Lord Stannis was about to fall upon King's Landing," Robb said. "He might have rid us of Joffrey, the queen, and the Imp in one red stroke. Then we might have been able to make a peace."

Edmure looked from uncle to nephew. "You never told me."

"I *told* you to hold Riverrun," said Robb. "What part of that command did you fail to comprehend?"

"When you stopped Lord Tywin on the Red Fork," said

the Blackfish, "you delayed him just long enough for riders out of Bitterbridge to reach him with word of what was happening to the east. Lord Tywin turned his host at once, joined up with Matthis Rowan and Randyll Tarly near the headwaters of the Blackwater, and made a forced march to Tumbler's Falls, where he found Mace Tyrell and two of his sons waiting with a huge host and a fleet of barges. They floated down the river, disembarked half a day's ride from the city, and took Stannis in the rear."

Catelyn remembered King Renly's court, as she had seen it at Bitterbridge. A thousand golden roses streaming in the wind, Queen Margaery's shy smile and soft words, her brother the Knight of Flowers with the bloody linen around his temples. *If you had to fall into a woman's arms, my son, why couldn't they have been Margaery Tyrell's?* The wealth and power of Highgarden could have made all the difference in the fighting yet to come. *And perhaps Grey Wind would have liked the smell of her as well.*

Edmure looked ill. "I never meant . . . *never*, Robb, you must let me make amends. I will lead the van in the next battle!"

For amends, Brother? Or for glory? Catelyn wondered.

"The next battle," Robb said. "Well, that will be soon enough. Once Joffrey is wed, the Lannisters will take the field against me once more, I don't doubt, and this time the Tyrells will march beside them. And I may need to fight the Freys as well, if Black Walder has his way . . ."

"So long as Theon Greyjoy sits in your father's seat with your brothers' blood on his hands, these other foes must wait," Catelyn told her son. "Your first duty is to defend your own people, win back Winterfell, and hang Theon in a crow's cage to die slowly. Or else put off that crown for good, Robb, for men will know that you are no true king at all."

From the way Robb looked at her, she could tell that it had been a long while since anyone had dared speak to him so bluntly. "When they told me Winterfell had fallen, I wanted to go north at once," he said, with a hint of defensiveness. "I wanted to free Bran and Rickon, but I thought . . . I never dreamed that Theon could harm them, truly. If I had . . ."

"It is too late for *ifs*, and too late for rescues," Catelyn said. "All that remains is vengeance."

"The last word we had from the north, Ser Rodrik had defeated a force of ironmen near Torrhen's Square, and was assembling a host at Castle Cerwyn to retake Winterfell," said Robb. "By now he may have done it. There has been no news for a long while. And what of the Trident, if I turn north? I can't ask the river lords to abandon their own people."

"No," said Catelyn. "Leave them to guard their own, and win back the north with northmen."

"How will you get the northmen to the north?" her brother Edmure asked. "The ironmen control the sunset sea. The Greyjoys hold Moat Cailin as well. No army has ever taken Moat Cailin from the south. Even to march against it is madness. We could be trapped on the causeway, with the ironborn before us and angry Freys at our backs."

"We must win back the Freys," said Robb. "With them, we still have some chance of success, however small. Without them, I see no hope. I am willing to give Lord Walder whatever he requires . . . apologies, honors, lands, gold . . . there must be *something* that would soothe his pride . . ."

"Not something," said Catelyn. "Some*one*."

JON

Big enough for you?" Snowflakes speckled Tormund's broad face, melting in his hair and beard.

The giants swayed slowly atop the mammoths as they rode past two by two. Jon's garron shied, frightened by such strangeness, but whether it was the mammoths or their riders that scared him it was hard to say. Even Ghost backed off a step, baring his teeth in a silent snarl. The direwolf was big, but the mammoths were a deal bigger, and there were many and more of them.

Jon took the horse in hand and held him still, so he could count the giants emerging from the blowing snow and pale mists that swirled along the Milkwater. He was well beyond fifty when Tormund said something and he lost the count. *There must be hundreds.* No matter how many went past, they just seemed to keep coming.

In Old Nan's stories, giants were outsized men who lived in colossal castles, fought with huge swords, and walked about in boots a boy could hide in. These were something else, more bearlike than human, and as wooly as the mammoths they rode. Seated, it was hard to say how big they truly were. *Ten feet tall maybe, or twelve,* Jon thought. *Maybe fourteen, but no taller.* Their sloping chests might have passed for those of men, but their arms hung down too far, and their lower torsos looked half again as wide as their upper. Their legs were shorter than their arms, but very thick, and they wore no boots at all; their feet were broad splayed things, hard and horny and black. Neckless, their huge heavy heads thrust forward from between their shoulder blades, and their faces were squashed and brutal. Rats' eyes no larger than beads were almost lost within folds of horny flesh, but they snuffled constantly, smelling as much as they saw.

They're not wearing skins, Jon realized. *That's hair.* Shaggy pelts covered their bodies, thick below the waist, sparser above. The stink that came off them was choking, but perhaps that was the mammoths. *And Joramun blew the Horn of Winter, and woke giants from the earth.* He looked for great swords ten feet long, but saw only clubs. Most were just the limbs of dead trees, some still trailing shattered branches. A few had stone balls lashed to the ends to make colossal mauls. *The song never says if the horn can put them back to sleep.*

One of the giants coming up on them looked older than the rest. His pelt was grey and streaked with white, and the mammoth he rode, larger than any of the others, was grey and white as well. Tormund shouted something up to him as he passed, harsh clanging words in a tongue that Jon did not comprehend. The giant's lips split apart to reveal a mouth full of huge square teeth, and he made a sound half belch and half rumble. After a moment Jon realized he was laughing. The mammoth turned its massive head to regard the two of them briefly, one huge tusk passing over the top of Jon's head as the beast lumbered by, leaving huge footprints in the soft mud and fresh snow along the river. The giant shouted down something in the same coarse tongue that Tormund had used.

"Was that their king?" asked Jon.

"Giants have no kings, no more'n mammoths do, nor snow bears, nor the great whales o' the grey sea. That was Mag Mar Tun Doh Weg. Mag the Mighty. You can kneel to him if you like, he won't mind. I know your kneeler's knees must be itching, for want of some king to bend to. Watch out he don't step on you, though. Giants have bad eyes, and might be he wouldn't see some little crow all the way down there by his feet."

"What did you say to him? Was that the Old Tongue?"

"Aye. I asked him if that was his father he was forking, they looked so much alike, except his father had a better smell."

"And what did he say to you?"

Tormund Thunderfist cracked a gap-toothed smile. "He asked me if that was my daughter riding there beside me, with her smooth pink cheeks." The wildling shook snow from his arm and turned his horse about. "It may be he never saw a man without a beard before. Come, we start back. Mance grows sore wroth when I'm not found in my accustomed place."

Jon wheeled and followed Tormund back toward the head of the column, his new cloak hanging heavy from his shoulders. It was made of unwashed sheepskins, worn fleece side in, as the wildlings suggested. It kept the snow off well enough, and at night it was good and warm, but he kept his black cloak as well, folded up beneath his saddle. "Is it true you killed a giant once?" he asked Tormund as they rode. Ghost loped silently beside them, leaving paw prints in the new-fallen snow.

"Now why would you doubt a mighty man like me? It was winter and I was half a boy, and stupid the way boys are. I went too far and my horse died and then a storm caught me. A *true* storm, not no little dusting such as this. Har! I knew I'd freeze to death before it broke. So I found me a sleeping giant, cut open her belly, and crawled up right inside her. Kept me warm enough, she did, but the stink near did for me. The worst thing was, she woke up when the spring come and took me for her babe. Suckled me for three whole moons before I could get away. Har! There's times I miss the taste o' giant's milk, though."

"If she nursed you, you couldn't have killed her."

"I never did, but see you don't go spreading that about. Tormund Giantsbane has a better ring to it than Tormund Giantsbabe, and that's the honest truth o' it."

"So how did you come by your other names?" Jon asked. "Mance called you the Horn-Blower, didn't he? Mead-king of Ruddy Hall, Husband to Bears, Father to Hosts?" It was the horn blowing he particularly wanted to hear about, but he dared not ask too plainly. *And Joramun blew the Horn of Winter, and woke giants from the earth.* Is that where they had come from, them and their mammoths? Had Mance Rayder found the Horn of Joramun, and given it to Tormund Thunderfist to blow?

"Are all crows so curious?" asked Tormund. "Well, here's a tale for you. It were another winter, colder even than the one I spent inside that giant, and snowing day and night, snowflakes as big as your head, not these little things. It snowed so hard the whole village was half buried. I was in me Ruddy Hall, with only a cask o' mead to keep me company and nothing to do but drink it. The more I drank the more I got to thinking about this woman lived close by, a fine strong woman with the biggest pair of teats you ever saw. She had a temper on her, that one, but oh, she could be warm too, and in the deep of winter a man needs his warmth.

"The more I drank the more I thought about her, and the more I thought the harder me member got, till I couldn't suffer it no more. Fool that I was, I bundled meself up in furs from head to heels, wrapped a winding wool around me face, and set off to find her. The snow was coming down so hard I got turned around once or twice, and the wind blew right through me and froze me bones, but finally I come on her, all bundled up like I was.

"The woman had a terrible temper, and she put up quite the fight when I laid hands on her. It was all I could do to carry her home and get her out o' them furs, but when I did, oh, she was hotter even than I remembered, and we had a fine old time, and then I went to sleep. Next morning when I woke the snow had stopped and the sun was shining, but I was in no fit state to enjoy it. All ripped and torn I was, and half me member bit right off, and there on me floor was a she-bear's pelt. And soon enough the free folk were telling tales o' this bald bear seen in the woods, with the queerest pair o' cubs behind her. Har!" He slapped a meaty thigh. "Would that I could find her again. She was fine to lay with, that bear. Never was a woman gave me such a fight, nor such strong sons neither."

"What could you do if you *did* find her?" Jon asked, smiling. "You said she bit your member off."

"Only half. And half me member is twice as long as any

other man's." Tormund snorted. "Now as to you . . . is it true they cut your members off when they take you for the Wall?"

"No," Jon said, affronted.

"I think it must be true. Else why refuse Ygritte? She'd hardly give you any fight at all, seems to me. The girl wants you in her, that's plain enough to see."

Too bloody plain, thought Jon, *and it seems that half the column has seen it*. He studied the falling snow so Tormund might not see him redden. *I am a man of the Night's Watch*, he reminded himself. So why did he feel like some blushing maid?

He spent most of his days in Ygritte's company, and most nights as well. Mance Rayder had not been blind to Rattleshirt's mistrust of the "crow-come-over," so after he had given Jon his new sheepskin cloak he had suggested that he might want to ride with Tormund Giantsbane instead. Jon had happily agreed, and the very next day Ygritte and Longspear Ryk left Rattleshirt's band for Tormund's as well. "Free folk ride with who they want," the girl told him, "and we had a bellyful of Bag o' Bones."

Every night when they made camp, Ygritte threw her sleeping skins down beside his own, no matter if he was near the fire or well away from it. Once he woke to find her nestled against him, her arm across his chest. He lay listening to her breathe for a long time, trying to ignore the tension in his groin. Rangers often shared skins for warmth, but warmth was not all Ygritte wanted, he suspected. After that he had taken to using Ghost to keep her away. Old Nan used to tell stories about knights and their ladies who would sleep in a single bed with a blade between them for honor's sake, but he thought this must be the first time where a direwolf took the place of the sword.

Even then, Ygritte persisted. The day before last, Jon had made the mistake of wishing he had hot water for a bath. "Cold is better," she had said at once, "if you've got someone to warm you up after. The river's only part ice yet, go on."

Jon laughed. "You'd freeze me to death."

"Are all crows afraid of gooseprickles? A little ice won't kill you. I'll jump in with you t'prove it so."

"And ride the rest of the day with wet clothes frozen to our skins?" he objected.

"Jon Snow, you know nothing. You don't go in with clothes."

"I don't go in at all," he said firmly, just before he heard Tormund Thunderfist bellowing for him (he hadn't, but never mind).

The wildlings seemed to think Ygritte a great beauty because of her hair; red hair was rare among the free folk, and those who had it were said to be kissed by fire, which was supposed to be lucky. Lucky it might be, and red it certainly was, but Ygritte's hair was such a tangle that Jon was tempted to ask her if she only brushed it at the changing of the seasons.

At a lord's court the girl would never have been considered anything but common, he knew. She had a round peasant face, a pug nose, and slightly crooked teeth, and her eyes were too far apart. Jon had noticed all that the first time he'd seen her, when his dirk had been at her throat. Lately, though, he was noticing some other things. When she grinned, the crooked teeth didn't seem to matter. And maybe her eyes were too far apart, but they were a pretty blue-grey color, and lively as any eyes he knew. Sometimes she sang in a low husky voice that stirred him. And sometimes by the cookfire when she sat hugging her knees with the flames waking echoes in her red hair, and looked at him, just smiling . . . well, *that* stirred some things as well.

But he was a man of the Night's Watch, he had taken a vow. *I shall take no wife, hold no lands, father no children.* He had said the words before the weirwood, before his father's gods. He could not unsay them . . . no more than he could admit the reason for his reluctance to Tormund Thunderfist, Father to Bears.

"Do you mislike the girl?" Tormund asked him as they passed another twenty mammoths, these bearing wildlings in tall wooden towers instead of giants.

"No, but I . . ." *What can I say that he will believe?* "I am still too young to wed."

"Wed?" Tormund laughed. "Who spoke of wedding? In the south, must a man wed every girl he beds?"

Jon could feel himself turning red again. "She spoke for me when Rattleshirt would have killed me. I would not dishonor her."

"You are a free man now, and Ygritte is a free woman. What dishonor if you lay together?"

"I might get her with child."

"Aye, I'd hope so. A strong son or a lively laughing girl kissed by fire, and where's the harm in that?"

Words failed him for a moment. "The boy . . . the child would be a bastard."

"Are bastards weaker than other children? More sickly, more like to fail?"

"No, but—"

"You're bastard-born yourself. And if Ygritte does not want a child, she will go to some woods witch and drink a cup o' moon tea. You do not come into it, once the seed is planted."

"I will *not* father a bastard."

Tormund shook his shaggy head. "What fools you kneelers be. Why did you steal the girl if you don't want her?"

"*Steal?* I never . . ."

"You did," said Tormund. "You slew the two she was with and carried her off, what do you call it?"

"I took her prisoner."

"You made her yield to you."

"Yes, but . . . Tormund, I swear, I've never touched her."

"Are you *certain* they never cut your member off?" Tormund gave a shrug, as if to say he would never understand such madness. "Well, you are a free man now, but if you will not have the girl, best find yourself a she-bear. If a man does not use his member it grows smaller and smaller, until one day he wants to piss and cannot find it."

Jon had no answer for that. Small wonder that the Seven Kingdoms thought the free folk scarcely human. *They have no laws, no honor, not even simple decency. They steal endlessly from each other, breed like beasts, prefer rape to marriage, and fill the world with baseborn children.* Yet he was growing fond of Tormund Giantsbane, great bag of wind and lies though he was. Longspear as well. *And Ygritte . . . no, I will not think about Ygritte.*

Along with the Tormunds and the Longspears rode other sorts of wildlings, though; men like Rattleshirt and the Weeper who would as soon slit you as spit on you. There was Harma Dogshead, a squat keg of a woman with cheeks like slabs of white meat, who hated dogs and killed one every fortnight to make a fresh head for her banner; earless Styr, Magnar of Thenn, whose own people thought him more god than lord; Varamyr Sixskins, a small mouse of a man whose steed was a savage white snow bear that stood thirteen feet tall on its hind legs. And wherever the bear and Varamyr went, three wolves and a shadowcat came following. Jon had been in his presence only once, and once had been enough; the mere sight of the man had made him bristle, even as the fur on the back of Ghost's neck had bristled at the sight of the bear and that long black-and-white 'cat.

And there were folks fiercer even than Varamyr, from the northernmost reaches of the haunted forest, the hidden valleys of the Frostfangs, and even queerer places: the men of the Frozen Shore who rode in chariots made of walrus bones pulled along by packs of savage dogs, the terrible ice-river clans who were said to feast on human flesh, the cave dwellers with their faces dyed blue and purple and green. With his own eyes Jon had beheld the Hornfoot men trotting along in column on bare soles as hard as boiled leather. He had not seen any snarks or grumpkins, but for all he knew Tormund would be having some to supper.

Half the wildling host had lived all their lives without so much as a glimpse of the Wall, Jon judged, and most of those spoke no word of the Common Tongue. It did not matter. Mance Rayder spoke the Old Tongue, even sang in it, fingering his lute and filling the night with strange wild music.

Mance had spent years assembling this vast plodding host, talking to this clan mother and that magnar, winning one village with sweet words and another with a song and a third with the edge of his sword, making peace between Harma Dogshead and the Lord o' Bones, between the Hornfoots and the Nightrunners, between the walrus men of the Frozen Shore and the cannibal clans of the great ice rivers, hammering a hundred different daggers into one great spear, aimed at the heart of the Seven Kingdoms. He had no crown nor scepter, no robes of silk and velvet, but it was plain to Jon that Mance Rayder *was* a king in more than name.

Jon had joined the wildlings at Qhorin Halfhand's command. "Ride with them, eat with them, fight with them," the ranger had told him, the night before he died. "And *watch*." But all his watching had learned him little. The Halfhand had suspected that the wildlings had gone up into the bleak and barren Frostfangs in search of some weapon, some power, some fell sorcery with which to break the Wall . . . but if they had found any such, no one was boasting of it openly, or showing it to Jon. Nor had Mance Rayder confided any of his plans or strategies. Since that first night, he had hardly seen the man save at a distance.

I will kill him if I must. The prospect gave Jon no joy; there would be no honor in such a killing, and it would mean his own death as well. Yet he could not let the wildlings breach the Wall, to threaten Winterfell and the north, the barrowlands and the Rills, White Harbor and the Stony Shore, even the Neck. For eight thousand years the men of House Stark had lived and died to protect their people against such ravagers and reavers . . . and bastard-born or no, the same blood ran in his veins. *Bran and Rickon are still at Winterfell besides. Maester Luwin, Ser Rodrik, Old Nan, Farlen the kennelmaster, Mikken at his forge and Gage by his ovens . . . everyone I ever knew, everyone I ever loved.* If Jon must slay a man he half admired and almost liked to save them from the mercies of Rattleshirt and Harma Dogshead and the earless Magnar of Thenn, that was what he meant to do.

Still, he prayed his father's gods might spare him that bleak task. The host moved but slowly, burdened as it was by all the wildlings' herds and children and mean little treasures, and the snows had slowed its progress even more. Most of the column was out of the foothills now, oozing down along the west bank of the Milkwater like honey on a cold winter's morning, following the course of the river into the heart of the haunted forest.

And somewhere close ahead, Jon knew, the Fist of the First Men loomed above the trees, home to three hundred black brothers of the Night's Watch, armed, mounted, and waiting. The Old Bear had sent out other scouts besides the Halfhand, and surely Jarman Buckwell or Thoren Smallwood would have returned by now with word of what was coming down out of the mountains.

Mormont will not run, Jon thought. *He is too old and he*

has come too far. He will strike, and damn the numbers. One day soon he would hear the sound of warhorns, and see a column of riders pounding down on them with black cloaks flapping and cold steel in their hands. Three hundred men could not hope to kill a hundred times their number, of course, but Jon did not think they would need to. *He need not slay a thousand, only one. Mance is all that keeps them together.*

The King-beyond-the-Wall was doing all he could, yet the wildlings remained hopelessly undisciplined, and that made them vulnerable. Here and there within the leagues-long snake that was their line of march were warriors as fierce as any in the Watch, but a good third of them were grouped at either end of the column, in Harma Dogshead's van and the savage rearguard with its giants, aurochs, and fire flingers. Another third rode with Mance himself near the center, guarding the wayns and sledges and dog carts that held the great bulk of the host's provisions and supplies, all that remained of the last summer harvest. The rest, divided into small bands under the likes of Rattleshirt, Jarl, Tormund Giantsbane, and the Weeper, served as outriders, foragers, and whips, galloping up and down the column endlessly to keep it moving in a more or less orderly fashion.

And even more telling, only one in a hundred wildlings was mounted. *The Old Bear will go through them like an axe through porridge.* And when that happened, Mance must give chase with his center, to try and blunt the threat. If he should fall in the fight that must follow, the Wall would be safe for another hundred years, Jon judged. *And if not . . .*

He flexed the burned fingers of his sword hand. Longclaw was slung to his saddle, the carved stone wolf's-head pommel and soft leather grip of the great bastard sword within easy reach.

The snow was falling heavily by the time they caught Tormund's band, several hours later. Ghost departed along the way, melting into the forest at the scent of prey. The direwolf would return when they made camp for the night, by dawn at the latest. However far he prowled, Ghost always came back . . . and so, it seemed, did Ygritte.

"So," the girl called when she saw him, "d'you believe

us now, Jon Snow? Did you see the giants on their mammoths?"

"Har!" shouted Tormund, before Jon could reply. "The crow's in love! He means to marry one!"

"A giantess?" Longspear Ryk laughed.

"No, a *mammoth*!" Tormund bellowed. "Har!"

Ygritte trotted beside Jon as he slowed his garron to a walk. She claimed to be three years older than him, though she stood half a foot shorter; however old she might be, the girl was a tough little thing. Stonesnake had called her a "spearwife" when they'd captured her in the Skirling Pass. She wasn't wed and her weapon of choice was a short curved bow of horn and weirwood, but "spearwife" fit her all the same. She reminded him a little of his sister Arya, though Arya was younger and probably skinnier. It was hard to tell how plump or thin Ygritte might be, with all the furs and skins she wore.

"Do you know 'The Last of the Giants'?" Without waiting for an answer Ygritte said, "You need a deeper voice than mine to do it proper." Then she sang, "*Ooooooh, I am the last of the giants, my people are gone from the earth.*"

Tormund Giantsbane heard the words and grinned. "*The last of the great mountain giants, who ruled all the world at my birth,*" he bellowed back through the snow.

Longspear Ryk joined in, singing, "*Oh, the smallfolk have stolen my forests, they've stolen my rivers and hills.*"

"*And they've built a great wall through my valleys, and fished all the fish from my rills,*" Ygritte and Tormund sang back at him in turn, in suitably gigantic voices.

Tormund's sons Toregg and Dormund added their deep voices as well, then his daughter Munda and all the rest. Others began to bang their spears on leathern shields to keep rough time, until the whole war band was singing as they rode.

In stone halls they burn their great fires,
in stone halls they forge their sharp spears.
Whilst I walk alone in the mountains,
with no true companion but tears.
They hunt me with dogs in the daylight,
they hunt me with torches by night.
For these men who are small can never stand tall,

whilst giants still walk in the light.
Oooooooh, I am the LAST of the giants,
so learn well the words of my song.
For when I am gone the singing will fade,
and the silence shall last long and long.

There were tears on Ygritte's cheeks when the song ended.

"Why are you weeping?" Jon asked. "It was only a song. There are hundreds of giants, I've just seen them."

"Oh, hundreds," she said furiously. "You know nothing, Jon Snow. You—*JON!*"

Jon turned at the sudden sound of wings. Blue-grey feathers filled his eyes, as sharp talons buried themselves in his face. Red pain lanced through him sudden and fierce as pinions beat round his head. He saw the beak, but there was no time to get a hand up or reach for a weapon. Jon reeled backward, his foot lost the stirrup, his garron broke in panic, and then he was falling. And still the eagle clung to his face, its talons tearing at him as it flapped and shrieked and pecked. The world turned upside down in a chaos of feathers and horseflesh and blood, and then the ground came up to smash him.

The next he knew, he was on his face with the taste of mud and blood in his mouth and Ygritte kneeling over him protectively, a bone dagger in her hand. He could still hear wings, though the eagle was not in sight. Half his world was black. "My eye," he said in sudden panic, raising a hand to his face.

"It's only blood, Jon Snow. He missed the eye, just ripped your skin up some."

His face was throbbing. Tormund stood over them bellowing, he saw from his right eye as he rubbed blood from his left. Then there were hoofbeats, shouts, and the clacking of old dry bones.

"Bag o' Bones," roared Tormund, "call off your hellcrow!"

"There's your hellcrow!" Rattleshirt pointed at Jon. "Bleeding in the mud like a faithless dog!" The eagle came flapping down to land atop the broken giant's skull that served him for his helm. "I'm here for him."

"Come take him then," said Tormund, "but best come

with sword in hand, for that's where you'll find mine. Might be I'll boil *your* bones, and use your skull to piss in. Har!"

"Once I prick you and let the air out, you'll shrink down smaller'n that girl. Stand aside, or Mance will hear o' this."

Ygritte stood. "What, is it *Mance* who wants him?"

"I said so, didn't I? Get him up on those black feet."

Tormund frowned down at Jon. "Best go, if it's the Mance who's wanting you."

Ygritte helped pull him up. "He's bleeding like a butchered boar. Look what Orell did t' his sweet face."

Can a bird hate? Jon had slain the wilding Orell, but some part of the man remained within the eagle. The golden eyes looked out on him with cold malevolence. "I'll come," he said. The blood kept running down into his right eye, and his cheek was a blaze of pain. When he touched it his black gloves came away stained with red. "Let me catch my garron." It was not the horse he wanted so much as Ghost, but the direwolf was nowhere to be seen. *He could be leagues away by now, ripping out the throat of some elk.* Perhaps that was just as well.

The garron shied away from him when he approached, no doubt frightened by the blood on his face, but Jon calmed him with a few quiet words and finally got close enough to take the reins. As he swung back into the saddle his head whirled. *I will need to get this tended,* he thought, *but not just now. Let the King-beyond-the-Wall see what his eagle did to me.* His right hand opened and closed, and he reached down for Longclaw and slung the bastard sword over a shoulder before he wheeled to trot back to where the Lord of Bones and his band were waiting.

Ygritte was waiting too, sitting on her horse with a fierce look on her face. "I am coming too."

"Be gone." The bones of Rattleshirt's breastplate clattered together. "I was sent for the crow-come-down, none other."

"A free woman rides where she will," Ygritte said.

The wind was blowing snow into Jon's eyes. He could feel the blood freezing on his face. "Are we talking or riding?"

"Riding," said the Lord of Bones.

It was a grim gallop. They rode two miles down the column through swirling snows, then cut through a tangle of baggage wayns to splash across the Milkwater where it took a great loop toward the east. A crust of thin ice covered the river shallows; with every step their horses' hooves crashed through, until they reached the deeper water ten yards out. The snow seemed be falling even faster on the eastern bank, and the drifts were deeper too. *Even the wind is colder.* And night was falling too.

But even through the blowing snow, the shape of the great white hill that loomed above the trees was unmistakable. *The Fist of the First Men.* Jon heard the scream of the eagle overhead. A raven looked down from a soldier pine and *quorked* as he went past. *Had the Old Bear made his attack?* Instead of the clash of steel and the thrum of arrows taking flight, Jon heard only the soft crunch of frozen crust beneath his garron's hooves.

In silence they circled round to the south slope, where the approach was easiest. It was there at the bottom that Jon saw the dead horse, sprawled at the base of the hill, half buried in the snow. Entrails spilled from the belly of the animal like frozen snakes, and one of its legs was gone. *Wolves,* was Jon's first thought, but that was wrong. Wolves eat their kill.

More garrons were strewn across the slope, legs twisted grotesquely, blind eyes staring in death. The wildlings crawled over them like flies, stripping them of saddles, bridles, packs, and armor, and hacking them apart with stone axes.

"Up," Rattleshirt told Jon. "Mance is up top."

Outside the ringwall they dismounted to squeeze through a crooked gap in the stones. The carcass of a shaggy brown garron was impaled upon the sharpened stakes the Old Bear had placed inside every entrance. *He was trying to get out, not in.* There was no sign of a rider.

Inside was more, and worse. Jon had never seen pink snow before. The wind gusted around him, pulling at his heavy sheepskin cloak. Ravens flapped from one dead horse to the next. *Are those wild ravens, or our own?* Jon could not tell. He wondered where poor Sam was now. And *what* he was.

A crust of frozen blood crunched beneath the heel of his boot. The wildlings were stripping the dead horses of every scrap of steel and leather, even prying the horseshoes off their hooves. A few were going through packs they'd turned up, looking for weapons and food. Jon passed one of Chett's dogs, or what remained of him, lying in a sludgy pool of half-frozen blood.

A few tents were still standing on the far side of the camp, and it was there they found Mance Rayder. Beneath his slashed cloak of black wool and red silk he wore black ringmail and shaggy fur breeches, and on his head was a great bronze-and-iron helm with raven wings at either temple. Jarl was with him, and Harma the Dogshead; Styr as well, and Varamyr Sixskins with his wolves and his shadowcat.

The look Mance gave Jon was grim and cold. "What happened to your face?"

Ygritte said, "Orell tried to take his eye out."

"It was him I asked. Has he lost his tongue? Perhaps he should, to spare us further lies."

Styr the Magnar drew a long knife. "The boy might see more clear with one eye, instead of two."

"Would you like to keep your eye, Jon?" asked the King-beyond-the-Wall. "If so, tell me how many they were. And try and speak the truth this time, Bastard of Winterfell."

Jon's throat was dry. "My lord . . . what . . ."

"I am not your lord," said Mance. "And the *what* is plain enough. Your brothers died. The question is, how many?"

Jon's face was throbbing, the snow kept coming down, and it was hard to think. *You must not balk, whatever is asked of you,* Qhorin had told him. The words stuck in his throat, but he made himself say, "There were three hundred of us."

"Us?" Mance said sharply.

"Them. Three hundred of them." *Whatever is asked,* the Halfhand said. *So why do I feel so craven?* "Two hundred from Castle Black, and one hundred from the Shadow Tower."

"There's a truer song than the one you sang in my tent." Mance looked to Harma Dogshead. "How many horses have we found?"

"More'n a hundred," that huge woman replied, "less than two. There's more dead to the east, under the snow, hard t' know how many." Behind her stood her banner bearer, holding a pole with a dog's head on it, fresh enough to still be leaking blood.

"You should never have lied to me, Jon Snow," said Mance.

"I . . . I know that." *What could he say?*

The wildling king studied his face. "Who had the command here? And tell me true. Was it Rykker? Smallwood? Not Wythers, he's too feeble. Whose tent was this?"

I have said too much. "You did not find his body?"

Harma snorted, her disdain frosting from her nostrils. "What fools these black crows be."

"The next time you answer me with a question, I will give you to my Lord of Bones," Mance Rayder promised Jon. He stepped closer. "Who led here?"

One more step, thought Jon. *Another foot.* He moved his hand closer to Longclaw's hilt. *If I hold my tongue . . .*

"Reach up for that bastard sword and I'll have your bastard head off before it clears the scabbard," said Mance. "I am fast losing patience with you, crow."

"Say it," Ygritte urged. "He's dead, whoever he was."

His frown cracked the blood on his cheek. *This is too hard*, Jon thought in despair. *How do I play the turncloak without becoming one?* Qhorin had not told him that. But the second step is always easier than the first. "The Old Bear."

"That old man?" Harma's tone said she did not believe it. "He came himself? Then who commands at Castle Black?"

"Bowen Marsh." This time Jon answered at once. *You must not balk, whatever is asked of you.*

Mance laughed. "If so, our war is won. Bowen knows a deal more about counting swords than he's ever known about using them."

"The Old Bear commanded," said Jon. "This place was high and strong, and he made it stronger. He dug pits and planted stakes, laid up food and water. He was ready for . . ."

". . . me?" finished Mance Rayder. "Aye, he was. Had I been fool enough to storm this hill, I might have lost five men for every crow I slew and still counted myself lucky." His mouth grew hard. "But when the dead walk, walls and stakes and swords mean nothing. You cannot fight the dead, Jon Snow. No man knows that half so well as me." He gazed up at the darkening sky and said, "The crows may have helped us more than they know. I'd wondered why we'd suffered no attacks. But there's still a hundred leagues to go, and the cold is rising. Varamyr, send your wolves sniffing after the wights, I won't have them taking us unawares. My Lord of Bones, double all the patrols, and make certain every man has torch and flint. Styr, Jarl, you ride at first light."

"Mance," Rattleshirt said, "I want me some crow bones."

Ygritte stepped in front of Jon. "You can't kill a man for lying to protect them as was his brothers."

"They are still his brothers," declared Styr.

"They're *not*," insisted Ygritte. "He never killed me, like they told him. And he slew the Halfhand, we all saw."

Jon's breath misted the air. *If I lie to him, he'll know.* He looked Mance Rayder in the eyes, opened and closed his burned hand. "I wear the cloak you gave me, Your Grace."

"A sheepskin cloak!" said Ygritte. "And there's many a night we dance beneath it, too!"

Jarl laughed, and even Harma Dogshead smirked. "Is that the way of it, Jon Snow?" asked Mance Rayder, mildly. "Her and you?"

It was easy to lose your way beyond the Wall. Jon did not know that he could tell honor from shame anymore, or right from wrong. *Father forgive me.* "Yes," he said.

Mance nodded. "Good. You'll go with Jarl and Styr on the morrow, then. Both of you. Far be it from me to separate two hearts that beat as one."

"Go where?" said Jon.

"Over the Wall. It's past time you proved your faith with something more than words, Jon Snow."

The Magnar was not pleased. "What do I want with a crow?"

"He knows the Watch and he knows the Wall," said Mance, "and he knows Castle Black better than any raider ever could. You'll find a use for him, or you're a fool."

Styr scowled. "His heart may still be black."

"Then cut it out." Mance turned to Rattleshirt. "My Lord of Bones, keep the column moving at all costs. If we reach the Wall before Mormont, we've won."

"They'll move." Rattleshirt's voice was thick and angry.

Mance nodded, and walked away, Harma and Sixskins beside him. Varamyr's wolves and shadowcat followed behind. Jon and Ygritte were left with Jarl, Rattleshirt, and the Magnar. The two older wildlings looked at Jon with ill-concealed rancor as Jarl said, "You heard, we ride at daybreak. Bring all the food you can, there'll be no time to hunt. And have your face seen to, crow. You look a bloody mess."

"I will," said Jon.

"You best not be lying, girl," Rattleshirt said to Ygritte, his eyes shiny behind the giant's skull.

Jon drew Longclaw. "Get away from us, unless you want what Qhorin got."

"You got no wolf to help you here, boy." Rattleshirt reached for his own sword.

"Sure o' that, are you?" Ygritte laughed.

Atop the stones of the ringwall, Ghost hunched with white fur bristling. He made no sound, but his dark red eyes spoke blood. The Lord of Bones moved his hand slowly away from his sword, backed off a step, and left them with a curse.

Ghost padded beside their garrons as Jon and Ygritte descended the Fist. It was not until they were halfway across the Milkwater that Jon felt safe enough to say, "I never asked you to lie for me."

"I never did," she said. "I left out part, is all."

"You said—"

"—that we fuck beneath your cloak many a night. I never said when we started, though." The smile she gave him was almost shy. "Find another place for Ghost to sleep tonight, Jon Snow. It's like Mance said. Deeds is truer than words."

SANSA

A new gown?" she said, as wary as she was astonished.

"More lovely than any you have worn, my lady," the old woman promised. She measured Sansa's hips with a length of knotted string. "All silk and Myrish lace, with satin linings. You will be very beautiful. The queen herself has commanded it."

"Which queen?" Margaery was not yet Joff's queen, but she had been Renly's. Or did she mean the Queen of Thorns? Or . . .

"The Queen Regent, to be sure."

"Queen *Cersei*?"

"None other. She has honored me with her custom for many a year." The old woman laid her string along the inside of Sansa's leg. "Her Grace said to me that you are a woman now, and should not dress like a little girl. Hold out your arm."

Sansa lifted her arm. She needed a new gown, that was true. She had grown three inches in the past year, and most of her old wardrobe had been ruined by the smoke when she'd tried to burn her mattress on the day of her first flowering

"Your bosom will be as lovely as the queen's," the old woman said as she looped her string around Sansa's chest. "You should not hide it so."

The comment made her blush. Yet the last time she'd gone riding, she could not lace her jerkin all the way to the top, and the stableboy gaped at her as he helped her mount. Sometimes she caught grown men looking at her chest as well, and some of her tunics were so tight she could scarce breathe in them.

"What color will it be?" she asked the seamstress.

"Leave the colors to me, my lady. You will be pleased, I know you will. You shall have smallclothes and hose as well, kirtles and mantles and cloaks, and all else befitting a . . . a lovely young lady of noble birth."

"Will they be ready in time for the king's wedding?"

"Oh, sooner, much sooner, Her Grace insists. I have six seamstresses and twelve apprentice girls, and we have set all our other work aside for this. Many ladies will be cross with us, but it was the queen's command."

"Thank Her Grace kindly for her thoughtfulness," Sansa said politely. "She is too good to me."

"Her Grace is most generous," the seamstress agreed, as she gathered up her things and took her leave.

But why? Sansa wondered when she was alone. It made her uneasy. *I'll wager this gown is Margaery's doing somehow, or her grandmother's.*

Margaery's kindness had been unfailing, and her presence changed everything. Her ladies welcomed Sansa as well. It had been so long since she had enjoyed the company of other women, she had almost forgotten how pleasant it could be. Lady Leonette gave her lessons on the high harp, and Lady Janna shared all the choice gossip. Merry Crane always had an amusing story, and little Lady Bulwer reminded her of Arya, though not so fierce.

Closest to Sansa's own age were the cousins Elinor, Alla, and Megga, Tyrells from junior branches of the House. "Roses from lower on the bush," quipped Elinor, who was witty and willowy. Megga was round and loud, Alla shy and pretty, but Elinor ruled the three by right of womanhood; she was a maiden flowered, whereas Megga and Alla were mere girls.

The cousins took Sansa into their company as if they had known her all their lives. They spent long afternoons doing needlework and talking over lemon cakes and honeyed wine, played at tiles of an evening, sang together in the castle sept . . . and often one or two of them would be chosen to share Margaery's bed, where they would whisper half the night away. Alla had a lovely voice, and when coaxed would play the woodharp and sing songs of chivalry and lost loves. Megga couldn't sing, but she was mad to be kissed. She and Alla played a kissing game sometimes, she confessed, but it wasn't the same as kissing a man, much less a king. Sansa wondered what Megga would think about kissing the Hound, as she had. He'd come to her the night of the battle stinking of wine and blood. *He kissed me and threatened to kill me, and made me sing him a song.*

"King Joffrey has such beautiful lips," Megga gushed, oblivious, "oh, poor Sansa, how your heart must have broken when you lost him. Oh, how you must have wept!"

Joffrey made me weep more often than you know, she wanted to say, but Butterbumps was not on hand to drown out her voice, so she pressed her lips together and held her tongue.

As for Elinor, she was promised to a young squire, a son of Lord Ambrose; they would be wed as soon as he won his spurs. He had worn her favor in the Battle of the Blackwater, where he'd slain a Myrish crossbowman and a Mullendore man-at-arms. "Alyn said her favor made him fearless," said Megga. "He says he shouted her name for his battle cry, isn't that ever so gallant? Someday I want some champion to wear my favor, and kill a hundred men." Elinor told her to hush, but looked pleased all the same.

They are children, Sansa thought. *They are silly little girls, even Elinor. They've never seen a battle, they've never seen a man die, they know nothing.* Their dreams were full of songs and stories, the way hers had been before Joffrey cut her father's head off. Sansa pitied them. Sansa envied them.

Margaery was different, though. Sweet and gentle, yet there was a little of her grandmother in her, too. The day

before last she'd taken Sansa hawking. It was the first time
she had been outside the city since the battle. The dead had
been burned or buried, but the Mud Gate was scarred and
splintered where Lord Stannis's rams had battered it, and
the hulls of smashed ships could be seen along both sides of
the Blackwater, charred masts poking from the shallows
like gaunt black fingers. The only traffic was the flat-
bottomed ferry that took them across the river, and when
they reached the kingswood they found a wilderness of ash
and charcoal and dead trees. But the waterfowl teemed in
the marshes along the bay, and Sansa's merlin brought
down three ducks while Margaery's peregrine took a heron
in full flight.

"Willas has the best birds in the Seven Kingdoms,"
Margaery said when the two of them were briefly alone.
"He flies an eagle sometimes. You will see, Sansa." She
took her by the hand and gave it a squeeze. "Sister."

Sister. Sansa had once dreamt of having a sister like
Margaery, beautiful and gentle, with all the world's graces
at her command. Arya had been entirely unsatisfactory as
sisters went. *How can I let my sister marry Joffrey?* she
thought, and suddenly her eyes were full of tears.
"Margaery, please," she said, "you mustn't." It was hard to
get the words out. "You *mustn't* marry him. He's not like
he seems, he's not. He'll hurt you."

"I shouldn't think so." Margaery smiled confidently.
"It's brave of you to warn me, but you need not fear. Joff's
spoiled and vain and I don't doubt that he's as cruel as you
say, but Father forced him to name Loras to his Kingsguard
before he would agree to the match. I shall have the finest
knight in the Seven Kingdoms protecting me night and
day, as Prince Aemon protected Naerys. So our little lion
had best behave, hadn't he?" She laughed, and said,
"Come, sweet sister, let's race back to the river. It will
drive our guards quite mad." And without waiting for an
answer, she put her heels into her horse and flew.

She is so brave, Sansa thought, galloping after her . . .
and yet, her doubts still gnawed at her. Ser Loras was a
great knight, all agreed. But Joffrey had other Kingsguard,
and gold cloaks and red cloaks besides, and when he was
older he would command armies of his own. Aegon the
Unworthy had never harmed Queen Naerys, perhaps for

fear of their brother the Dragonknight . . . but when another of his Kingsguard fell in love with one of his mistresses, the king had taken both their heads.

Ser Loras is a Tyrell, Sansa reminded herself. *That other knight was only a Toyne. His brothers had no armies, no way to avenge him but with swords.* Yet the more she thought about it all, the more she wondered. *Joff might restrain himself for a few turns, perhaps as long as a year, but soon or late he will show his claws, and when he does* . . . The realm might have a second Kingslayer, and there would be war *inside* the city, as the men of the lion and the men of the rose made the gutters run red.

Sansa was surprised that Margaery did not see it too. *She is older than me, she must be wiser. And her father, Lord Tyrell, he knows what he is doing, surely. I am just being silly.*

When she told Ser Dontos that she was going to Highgarden to marry Willas Tyrell, she thought he would be relieved and pleased for her. Instead he had grabbed her arm and said, "You *cannot!*" in a voice as thick with horror as with wine. "I tell you, these Tyrells are only Lannisters with flowers. I beg of you, forget this folly, give your Florian a kiss, and promise you'll go ahead as we have planned. The night of Joffrey's wedding, that's not so long, wear the silver hair net and do as I told you, and afterward we make our escape." He tried to plant a kiss on her cheek.

Sansa slipped from his grasp and stepped away from him. "I won't. I can't. Something would go wrong. When I *wanted* to escape you wouldn't take me, and now I don't need to."

Dontos stared at her stupidly. "But the arrangements are made, sweetling. The ship to take you home, the boat to take you to the ship, your Florian did it all for his sweet Jonquil."

"I am sorry for all the trouble I put you to," she said, "but I have no need of boats and ships now."

"But it's all to see you *safe.*"

"I will be safe in Highgarden. Willas will keep me safe."

"But he does not know you," Dontos insisted, "and he will not love you. Jonquil, Jonquil, open your sweet eyes, these Tyrells care nothing for you. It's your *claim* they mean to wed."

"My claim?" She was lost for a moment.

"Sweetling," he told her, "you are heir to Winterfell." He grabbed her again, pleading that she must not do this thing, and Sansa wrenched free and left him swaying beneath the heart tree. She had not visited the godswood since.

But she had not forgotten his words, either. *The heir to Winterfell*, she would think as she lay abed at night. *It's your claim they mean to wed.* Sansa had grown up with three brothers. She never thought to have a claim, but with Bran and Rickon dead . . . *It doesn't matter, there's still Robb, he's a man grown now, and soon he'll wed and have a son. Anyway, Willas Tyrell will have Highgarden, what would he want with Winterfell?*

Sometimes she would whisper his name into her pillow just to hear the sound of it. "Willas, Willas, Willas." Willas was as good a name as Loras, she supposed. They even sounded the same, a little. What did it matter about his leg? Willas would be Lord of Highgarden and she would be his lady.

She pictured the two of them sitting together in a garden with puppies in their laps, or listening to a singer strum upon a lute while they floated down the Mander on a pleasure barge. *If I give him sons, he may come to love me.* She would name them Eddard and Brandon and Rickon, and raise them all to be as valiant as Ser Loras. *And to hate Lannisters, too.* In Sansa's dreams, her children looked just like the brothers she had lost. Sometimes there was even a girl who looked like Arya.

She could never hold a picture of Willas long in her head, though; her imaginings kept turning him back into Ser Loras, young and graceful and beautiful. *You must not think of him like that*, she told herself. *Or else he may see the disappointment in your eyes when you meet, and how could he marry you then, knowing it was his brother you loved?* Willas Tyrell was twice her age, she reminded herself constantly, and lame as well, and perhaps even plump and red-faced like his father. But comely or no, he might be the only champion she would ever have.

Once she dreamed it was still her marrying Joff, not Margaery, and on their wedding night he turned into the headsman Ilyn Payne. She woke trembling. She did not want Margaery to suffer as she had, but she dreaded the thought that the Tyrells might refuse to go ahead with the wedding. *I warned her, I did, I told her the truth of him.* Perhaps Margaery did not believe her. Joff always played the perfect knight with her, as once he had with Sansa. *She will see his true nature soon enough. After the wedding if not before.* Sansa decided that she would light a candle to the Mother Above the next time she visited the sept, and ask her to protect Margaery from Joffrey's cruelty. And perhaps a candle to the Warrior as well, for Loras.

She would wear her new gown for the ceremony at the Great Sept of Baelor, she decided as the seamstress took her last measurement. *That must be why Cersei is having it made for me, so I will not look shabby at the wedding.* She really ought to have a different gown for the feast afterward but she supposed one of her old ones would do. She did not want to risk getting food or wine on the new one. *I must take it with me to Highgarden.* She wanted to look beautiful for Willas Tyrell. *Even if Dontos was right, and it is Winterfell he wants and not me, he still may come to love me for myself.* Sansa hugged herself tightly, wondering how long it would be before the gown was ready. She could scarcely wait to wear it.

ARYA

The rains came and went, but there was more grey sky than blue, and all the streams were running high. On the morning of the third day, Arya noticed that the moss was growing mostly on the wrong side of the trees. "We're going the wrong way," she said to Gendry, as they rode past an especially mossy elm. "We're going south. See how the moss is growing on the trunk?"

He pushed thick black hair from eyes and said, "We're following the road, that's all. The road goes south here."

We've been going south all day, she wanted to tell him. *And yesterday too, when we were riding along that streambed.* But she hadn't been paying close attention yesterday, so she couldn't be certain. "I think we're lost," she said in a low voice. "We shouldn't have left the river. All we had to do was follow it."

"The river bends and loops," said Gendry. "This is just a shorter way, I bet. Some secret outlaw way. Lem and Tom and them have been living here for years."

That was true. Arya bit her lip. "But the moss . . ."

"The way it's raining, we'll have moss growing from our ears before long," Gendry complained.

"Only from our *south* ear," Arya declared stubbornly. There was no use trying to convince the Bull of anything. Still, he was the only true friend she had, now that Hot Pie had left them.

"Sharna says she needs me to bake bread," he'd told her, the day they rode. "Anyhow I'm tired of rain and saddle-sores and being scared all the time. There's ale here, and rabbit to eat, and the bread will be better when I make it. You'll see, when you come back. You will come back, won't you? When the war's done?" He remembered who she was then, and added, "My lady," reddening.

Arya didn't know if the war would ever be done, but she had nodded. "I'm sorry I beat you that time," she said. Hot Pie was stupid and craven, but he'd been with her all the way from King's Landing and she'd gotten used to him. "I broke your nose."

"You broke Lem's too." Hot Pie grinned. "That was good."

"Lem didn't think so," Arya said glumly. Then it was time to go. When Hot Pie asked if he might kiss milady's hand, she punched his shoulder. "Don't call me that. You're Hot Pie, and I'm Arry."

"I'm not Hot Pie here. Sharna just calls me Boy. The same as she calls the other boy. It's going to be confusing."

She missed him more than she thought she would, but Harwin made up for it some. She had told him about his father Hullen, and how she'd found him dying by the stables in the Red Keep, the day she fled. "He always said he'd die in a stable," Harwin said, "but we all thought some bad-tempered stallion would be his death, not a pack of lions." Arya told of Yoren and their escape from King's Landing as well, and much that had happened since, but she left out the stableboy she'd stabbed with Needle, and the guard whose throat she'd cut to get out of Harrenhal. Telling Harwin would be almost like telling her father, and there were some things that she could not bear having her father know.

Nor did she speak of Jaqen H'ghar and the three deaths he'd owed and paid. The iron coin he'd given her Arya kept tucked away beneath her belt, but sometimes at night she would take it out and remember how his face had melted and changed when he ran his hand across it. "*Valar morghulis*," she would say under her breath. "Ser Gregor, Dunsen, Polliver, Raff the Sweetling. The Tickler and the Hound. Ser Ilyn, Ser Meryn, Queen Cersei, King Joffrey."

Only six Winterfell men remained of the twenty her father had sent west with Beric Dondarrion, Harwin told her, and they were scattered. "It was a trap, milady. Lord Tywin sent his Mountain across the Red Fork with fire and sword, hoping to draw your lord father. He planned for Lord Eddard to come west himself to deal with Gregor Clegane. If he had he would have been killed, or taken prisoner and traded for the Imp, who was your lady mother's captive at the time. Only the Kingslayer never knew Lord Tywin's plan, and when he heard about his brother's capture he attacked your father in the streets of King's Landing."

"I remember," said Arya. "He killed Jory." Jory had always smiled at her, when he wasn't telling her to get from underfoot.

"He killed Jory," Harwin agreed, "and your father's leg was broken when his horse fell on him. So Lord Eddard *couldn't* go west. He sent Lord Beric instead, with twenty of his own men and twenty from Winterfell, me among them. There were others besides. Thoros and Ser Raymun Darry and their men, Ser Gladden Wylde, a lord named Lothar Mallery. But Gregor was waiting for us at the Mummer's Ford, with men concealed on both banks. As we crossed he fell upon us from front and rear.

"I saw the Mountain slay Raymun Darry with a single blow so terrible that it took Darry's arm off at the elbow and killed the horse beneath him too. Gladden Wylde died there with him, and Lord Mallery was ridden down and drowned. We had lions on every side, and I thought I was doomed with the rest, but Alyn shouted commands and restored order to our ranks, and those still ahorse rallied around Thoros and cut our way free. Six score we'd been that morning. By dark no more than two score were left, and Lord Beric was gravely wounded. Thoros drew a foot of lance from his chest that night, and poured boiling wine into the hole it left.

"Every man of us was certain his lordship would be dead by daybreak. But Thoros prayed with him all night beside the fire, and when dawn came, he was still alive, and stronger than he'd been. It was a fortnight before he could mount a horse, but his courage kept us strong. He told us that our war had not ended at the Mummer's Ford, but only begun there, and that every man of ours who'd fallen would be avenged tenfold.

"By then the fighting had passed by us. The Mountain's men were only the van of Lord Tywin's host. They crossed the Red Fork in strength and swept up into the riverlands, burning everything in their path. We were so few that all we could do was harry their rear, but we told each other that we'd join up with King Robert when he marched west to crush Lord Tywin's rebellion. Only then we heard that Robert was dead, and Lord Eddard as well, and Cersei Lannister's whelp had ascended the Iron Throne.

"That turned the whole world on its head. We'd been sent out by the King's Hand to deal with outlaws, you see, but now we *were* the outlaws, and Lord Tywin was the Hand of the King. There was some wanted to yield then, but Lord Beric wouldn't hear of it. We were still king's men, he said, and these were the king's people the lions were savaging. If we could not fight for Robert, we would fight for them, until every man of us was dead. And so we did, but as we fought something queer happened. For every man we lost, two showed up to take his place. A few were knights or squires, of gentle birth, but most were common men—fieldhands and fiddlers and innkeeps, servants and shoemakers, even two septons. Men of all sorts, and women too, children, dogs . . ."

"*Dogs!*" said Arya.

"Aye." Harwin grinned. "One of our lads keeps the meanest dogs you'd ever want to see."

"I wish I had a good mean dog," said Arya wistfully. "A lion-killing dog." She'd had a direwolf once, Nymeria, but she'd thrown rocks at her until she fled, to keep the queen from killing her. *Could a direwolf kill a lion?* she wondered.

It rained again that afternoon, and long into the evening. Thankfully the outlaws had secret friends all over, so they did not need to camp out in the open or seek shelter beneath some leaky bower, as she and Hot Pie and Gendry had done so often.

That night they sheltered in a burned, abandoned village. At least it *seemed* to be abandoned, until Jack-Be-Lucky blew two short blasts and two long ones on his hunting horn. Then all sorts of people came crawling out of the ruins and up from secret cellars. They had ale and dried apples and some stale barley bread, and the outlaws had a goose that Anguy had brought down on the ride, so supper that night was almost a feast.

Arya was sucking the last bit of meat off a wing when one of the villagers turned to Lem Lemoncloak and said, "There were men through here not two days past, looking for the Kingslayer."

Lem snorted. "They'd do better looking in Riverrun. Down in the deepest dungeons, where it's nice and damp." His nose looked like a squashed apple, red and raw and swollen, and his mood was foul.

"No," another villager said. "He's escaped."

The Kingslayer. Arya could feel the hair on the back of her neck prickling. She held her breath to listen.

"Could that be true?" Tom o' Sevens said.

"I'll not believe it," said the one-eyed man in the rusty pothelm. The other outlaws called him Jack-Be-Lucky, though losing an eye didn't seem very lucky to Arya. "I've had me a taste o' them dungeons. How could he escape?"

The villagers could only shrug at that. Greenbeard stroked his thick grey-and-green whiskers and said, "The wolves will drown in blood if the Kingslayer's loose again. Thoros must be told. The Lord of Light will show him Lannister in the flames."

"There's a fine fire burning here," said Anguy, smiling.

Greenbeard laughed, and cuffed the archer's ear. "Do I look a priest to you, Archer? When Pello of Tyrosh peers into the fire, the cinders singe his beard."

Lem cracked his knuckles and said, "Wouldn't Lord Beric love to capture Jaime Lannister, though . . ."

"Would he hang him, Lem?" one of the village women asked. "It'd be half a shame to hang a man as pretty as that one."

"A trial first!" said Anguy. "Lord Beric always gives them a trial, you know that." He smiled. "*Then* he hangs them."

There was laughter all around. Then Tom drew his

fingers across the strings of his woodharp and broke into
soft song.

> The brothers of the Kingswood,
> they were an outlaw band.
> The forest was their castle,
> but they roamed across the land.
> No man's gold was safe from them,
> nor any maiden's hand.
> Oh, the brothers of the Kingswood,
> that fearsome outlaw band . . .

Warm and dry in a corner between Gendry and Harwin,
Arya listened to the singing for a time, then closed her eyes
and drifted off to sleep. She dreamt of home; not Riverrun,
but Winterfell. It was not a good dream, though. She was
alone outside the castle, up to her knees in mud. She could
see the grey walls ahead of her, but when she tried to reach
the gates every step seemed harder than the one before, and
the castle faded before her, until it looked more like smoke
than granite. And there were wolves as well, gaunt grey
shapes stalking through the trees all around her, their eyes
shining. Whenever she looked at them, she remembered
the taste of blood.

The next morning they left the road to cut across the
fields. The wind was gusting, sending dry brown leaves
swirling around the hooves of their horses, but for once it
did not rain. When the sun came out from behind a cloud,
it was so bright Arya had to pull her hood forward to keep
it out of her eyes.

She reined up very suddenly. "We *are* going the wrong
way!"

Gendry groaned. "What is it, moss again?"

"Look at the *sun*," she said. "We're going *south*!" Arya
rummaged in her saddlebag for the map, so she could show
them. "We should never have left the Trident. See." She
unrolled the map on her leg. All of them were looking at
her now. "See, there's Riverrun, between the rivers."

"As it happens," said Jack-Be-Lucky, "we know where
Riverrun is. Every man o' us."

"You're not going to Riverrun," Lem told her bluntly.

I was almost there, Arya thought. *I should have let*

them take our horses. I could have walked the rest of the way. She remembered her dream then, and bit her lip.

"Ah, don't look so hurt, child," said Tom Sevenstrings. "No harm will come to you, you have my word on that."

"The word of a *liar!*"

"No one lied," said Lem. "We made no promises. It's not for us to say what's to be done with you."

Lem was not the leader, though, no more than Tom; that was Greenbeard, the Tyroshi. Arya turned to face him. "Take me to Riverrun and you'll be rewarded," she said desperately.

"Little one," Greenbeard answered, "a peasant may skin a common squirrel for his pot, but if he finds a gold squirrel in his tree he takes it to his lord, or he will wish he did."

"I'm not a squirrel," Arya insisted.

"You are." Greenbeard laughed. "A little gold squirrel who's off to see the lightning lord, whether she wills it or not. He'll know what's to be done with you. I'll wager he sends you back to your lady mother, just as you wish."

Tom Sevenstrings nodded. "Aye, that's like Lord Beric. He'll do right by you, see if he don't."

Lord Beric Dondarrion. Arya remembered all she'd heard at Harrenhal, from the Lannisters and the Bloody Mummers alike. Lord Beric the wisp o' the wood. Lord Beric who'd been killed by Vargo Hoat and before that by Ser Amory Lorch, and twice by the Mountain That Rides. *If he won't send me home maybe I'll kill him too.* "Why do I have to see Lord Beric?" she asked quietly.

"We bring him all our highborn captives," said Anguy.

Captive. Arya took a breath to still her soul. *Calm as still water.* She glanced at the outlaws on their horses, and turned her horse's head. *Now, quick as a snake,* she thought, as she slammed her heels into the courser's flank. Right between Greenbeard and Jack-Be-Lucky she flew, and caught one glimpse of Gendry's startled face as his mare moved out of her way. And then she was in the open field, and running.

North or south, east or west, that made no matter now. She could find the way to Riverrun later, once she'd lost them. Arya leaned forward in the saddle and urged the horse to a gallop. Behind her the outlaws were cursing and shouting at her to come back. She shut her ears to the calls, but when she glanced back over her shoulder four of them were coming after her, Anguy and Harwin and Greenbeard racing side by side with Lem farther back, his big yellow cloak flapping behind him as he rode. "Swift as a deer," she told her mount. "Run, now, *run*."

Arya dashed across brown weedy fields, through waist-high grass and piles of dry leaves that flurried and flew when her horse galloped past. There were woods to her left, she saw. *I can lose them there.* A dry ditch ran along one side of the field, but she leapt it without breaking stride, and plunged in among the stand of elm and yew and birch trees. A quick peek back showed Anguy and Harwin still hard on her heels. Greenbeard had fallen behind, though, and she could not see Lem at all. "Faster," she told her horse, "you can, you *can*."

Between two elms she rode, and never paused to see which side the moss was growing on. She leapt a rotten log and swung wide around a monstrous deadfall, jagged with broken branches. Then up a gentle slope and down the other side, slowing and speeding up again, her horse's shoes striking sparks off the flintstones underfoot. At the top of the hill she glanced back. Harwin had pushed ahead of Anguy, but both were coming hard. Greenbeard had fallen further back and seemed to be flagging.

A stream barred her way. She splashed down into it, through water choked with wet brown leaves. Some clung to her horse's legs as they climbed the other side. The undergrowth was thicker here, the ground so full of roots and rocks that she had to slow, but she kept as good a pace as she dared. Another hill before her, this one steeper. Up she went, and down again. *How big are these woods?* she wondered. She had the faster horse, she knew that, she had stolen one of Roose Bolton's best from the stables at Harrenhal, but his speed was wasted here. *I need to find the fields again. I need to find a road.* Instead she found a game trail. It was narrow and uneven, but it was something. She raced along it, branches whipping at her face. One snagged her hood and yanked it back, and for half a heartbeat she feared they had caught her. A vixen burst from the brush as she passed, startled by the fury of her flight. The game trail brought her to another stream. Or was it the same one? Had she gotten turned around? There was no time to puzzle it out, she could hear their horses crashing through the trees behind her. Thorns scratched at her face like the cats she used to chase in King's Landing. Sparrows exploded from the branches of an alder. But the trees were thinning now, and suddenly she was out of them. Broad level fields stretched before her, all weeds and wild wheat, sodden and trampled. Arya kicked her horse back to a gallop. *Run*, she thought, *run for Riverrun, run for home.* Had she lost them? She took one quick look, and there was Harwin six yards back and gaining. *No*, she thought, *no, he can't, not him, it isn't fair.*

Both horses were lathered and flagging by the time he came up beside her, reached over, and grabbed her bridle. Arya was breathing hard herself then. She knew the fight was done. "You ride like a northman, milady," Harwin said when he'd drawn them to a halt. "Your aunt was the same. Lady Lyanna. But my father was master of horse, remember."

The look she gave him was full of hurt. "I thought you were my father's man."

"Lord Eddard's dead, milady. I belong to the lightning lord now, and to my brothers."

"What brothers?" Old Hullen had fathered no other sons that Arya could remember.

"Anguy, Lem, Tom o' Sevens, Jack and Greenbeard, all of them. We mean your brother Robb no ill, milady . . . but it's not him we fight for. He has an army all his own, and many a great lord to bend the knee. The smallfolk have only us." He gave her a searching look. "Can you understand what I am telling you?"

"Yes." That he was not Robb's man, she understood well enough. And that she was his captive. *I could have stayed with Hot Pie. We could have taken the little boat and sailed it up to Riverrun.* She had been better off as Squab. No one would take Squab captive, or Nan, or Weasel, or Arry the orphan boy. *I was a wolf*, she thought, *but now I'm just some stupid little lady again.*

"Will you ride back peaceful now," Harwin asked her, "or must I tie you up and throw you across your horse?"

"I'll ride peaceful," she said sullenly. *For now.*

SAMWELL

Sobbing, Sam took another step. *This is the last one, the very last, I can't go on, I can't.* But his feet moved again. One and then the other. They took a step, and then another, and he thought, *They're not my feet, they're someone else's, someone else is walking, it can't be me.*

When he looked down he could see them stumbling through the snow, shapeless things, and clumsy. His boots had been black, he seemed to remember, but the snow had caked around them, and now they were misshapen white balls. Like two clubfeet made of ice.

It would not stop, the snow. The drifts were up past his knees, and a crust covered his lower legs like a pair of white greaves. His steps were dragging, lurching. The heavy pack he carried made him look like some monstrous hunchback. And he was tired, so tired. *I can't go on. Mother have mercy, I can't.*

Every fourth or fifth step he had to reach down and tug up his swordbelt. He had lost the sword on the Fist, but the scabbard still weighed down the belt. He did have two knives; the dragonglass dagger Jon had given him and the steel one he cut his meat with. All that weight dragged heavy, and his belly was so big and round that if he forgot to tug the belt slipped right off and tangled round his ankles, no matter how tight he cinched it. He had tried belting it *above* his belly once, but then it came almost to his armpits. Grenn had laughed himself sick at the sight of it, and Dolorous Edd had said, "I knew a man once who wore his sword on a chain around his neck like that. One day he stumbled, and the hilt went up his nose."

Sam was stumbling himself. There were rocks beneath the snow, and the roots of trees, and sometimes deep holes in the frozen ground. Black Bernarr had stepped in one and broken his ankle three days past, or maybe four, or . . . he did not know how long it had been, truly. The Lord Commander had put Bernarr on a horse after that.

Sobbing, Sam took another step. It felt more like he was falling down than walking, falling endlessly but never hitting the ground, just falling forward and forward. *I have to stop, it hurts too much. I'm so cold and tired, I need to sleep, just a little sleep beside a fire, and a bite to eat that isn't frozen.*

But if he stopped he died. He knew that. They all knew that, the few who were left. They had been fifty when they fled the Fist, maybe more, but some had wandered off in the snow, a few wounded had bled to death . . . and sometimes Sam heard shouts behind him, from the rear guard, and once an *awful* scream. When he heard that he had run, twenty yards or thirty, as fast and as far as he could, his half-frozen feet kicking up the snow. He would be running still if his legs were stronger. *They are behind us, they are still behind us, they are taking us one by one.*

Sobbing, Sam took another step. He had been cold so long he was forgetting what it was like to feel warm. He wore three pairs of hose, two layers of smallclothes beneath a double lambswool tunic, and over that a thick quilted coat that padded him against the cold steel of his chainmail. Over the hauberk he had a loose surcoat, over *that* a triple-thick cloak with a bone button that fastened tight under his chins. Its hood flopped forward over his forehead. Heavy fur mitts covered his hands over thin wool-and-leather gloves, a scarf was wrapped snugly about the lower half of his face, and he had a tight-fitting fleece-lined cap to pull down over his ears beneath the hood. And still the cold was in him. His feet especially. He couldn't even feel them now, but only yesterday they had hurt so bad he could hardly bear to stand on them, let alone walk. Every step made him want to scream. Was that yesterday? He could not remember. He had not slept since the Fist, not once since the horn had blown. Unless it was while he was walking. Could a man walk while he was sleeping? Sam did not know, or else he had forgotten.

Sobbing, he took another step. The snow swirled down around him. Sometimes it fell from a white sky, and sometimes from a black, but that was all that remained of day and night. He wore it on his shoulders like a second cloak, and it piled up high atop the pack he carried and made it even heavier and harder to bear. The small of his back hurt abominably, as if someone had shoved a knife in there and was wiggling it back and forth with every step. His shoulders were in agony from the weight of the mail. He would have given most anything to take it off, but he was afraid to. Anyway he would have needed to remove his cloak and surcoat to get at it, and then the cold would have him.

If only I was stronger . . . He wasn't, though, and it was no good wishing. Sam was weak, and fat, so very fat, he could hardly bear his own weight, the mail was much too much for him. It felt as though it was rubbing his shoulders raw, despite the layers of cloth and quilt between the steel and skin. The only thing he could do was cry, and when he cried the tears froze on his cheeks.

Sobbing, he took another step. The crust was broken where he set his feet, otherwise he did not think he could have moved at all. Off to the left and right, half-seen through the silent trees, torches turned to vague orange haloes in the falling snow. When he turned his head he could see them, slipping silent through the wood, bobbing up and down and back and forth. *The Old Bear's ring of fire*, he reminded himself, *and woe to him who leaves it*. As he walked, it seemed as if he were chasing the torches ahead of him, but they had legs as well, longer and stronger than his, so he could never catch them.

Yesterday he begged for them to let him be one of the torchbearers, even if it meant walking outside of the column with the darkness pressing close. He wanted the fire, dreamed of the fire. *If I had the fire, I would not be cold.* But someone reminded him that he'd *had* a torch at the start, but he'd dropped it in the snow and snuffed the fire out. Sam didn't remember dropping any torch, but he supposed it was true. He was too weak to hold his arm up for long. Was it Edd who reminded him about the torch, or Grenn? He couldn't remember that either. *Fat and weak and useless, even my wits are freezing now.* He took another step.

He had wrapped his scarf over his nose and mouth, but it was covered with snot now, and so stiff he feared it must be frozen to his face. Even breathing was hard, and the air was so cold it hurt to swallow it. "Mother have mercy," he muttered in a hushed husky voice beneath the frozen mask. "Mother have mercy, Mother have mercy, Mother have mercy." With each prayer he took another step, dragging his legs through the snow. "Mother have mercy, Mother have mercy, Mother have mercy."

His own mother was a thousand leagues south, safe with his sisters and his little brother Dickon in the keep at Horn Hill. *She can't hear me, no more than the Mother Above.* The Mother was merciful, all the septons agreed, but the Seven had no power beyond the Wall. This was where the old gods ruled, the nameless gods of the trees and the wolves and the snows. "Mercy," he whispered then, to whatever might be listening, old gods or new, or demons too, "oh, mercy, mercy me, mercy me."

Maslyn screamed for mercy. Why had he suddenly remembered that? It was nothing he wanted to remember. The man had stumbled backward, dropping his sword, pleading, yielding, even yanking off his thick black glove and thrusting it up before him as if it were a gauntlet. He was still shrieking for quarter as the wight lifted him in the air by the throat and near ripped the head off him. *The dead have no mercy left in them, and the Others . . . no, I mustn't think of that, don't think, don't remember, just walk, just walk, just walk.*

Sobbing, he took another step.

A root beneath the crust caught his toe, and Sam tripped and fell heavily to one knee, so hard he bit his tongue. He could taste the blood in his mouth, warmer than anything he had tasted since the Fist. *This is the end,* he thought. Now that he had fallen he could not seem to find the strength to rise again. He groped for a tree branch and clutched it tight, trying to pull himself back to his feet, but his stiff legs would not support him. The mail was too heavy, and he was too fat besides, and too weak, and too tired.

"Back on your feet, Piggy," someone growled as he went past, but Sam paid him no mind. *I'll just lie down in the snow and close my eyes.* It wouldn't be so bad, dying here. He couldn't possibly be any colder, and after a little while he wouldn't be able to feel the ache in his lower back or the terrible pain in his shoulders, no more than he could feel his feet. *I won't be the first to die, they can't say I was.* Hundreds had died on the Fist, they had died all around him, and more had died after, he'd seen them. Shivering, Sam released his grip on the tree and eased himself down in the snow. It was cold and wet, he knew, but he could scarcely feel it through all his clothing. He stared upward at the pale white sky as snowflakes drifted down upon his stomach and his chest and his eyelids. *The snow will cover me like a thick white blanket. It will be warm under the snow, and if they speak of me they'll have to say I died a man of the Night's Watch. I did. I did. I did my duty. No one can say I forswore myself. I'm fat and I'm weak and I'm craven, but I did my duty.*

The ravens had been his responsibility. That was why they had brought him along. He hadn't wanted to go, he'd told them so, he'd told them all what a big coward he was. But Maester Aemon was very old and blind besides, so they had to send Sam to tend to the ravens. The Lord Commander had given him his orders when they made their camp on the Fist. "You're no fighter. We both know that, boy. If it happens that we're attacked, don't go trying to prove otherwise, you'll just get in the way. You're to send a message. And don't come running to ask what the letter should say. Write it out yourself, and send one bird to Castle Black and another to the Shadow Tower." The Old Bear pointed a gloved finger right in Sam's face. "I don't care if you're so scared you foul your breeches, and I don't care if a thousand wildlings are coming over the walls howling for your blood, *you get those birds off,* or I swear

I'll hunt you through all seven hells and make you damn sorry that you didn't." And Mormont's own raven had bobbed its head up and down and croaked, "*Sorry, sorry, sorry.*"

Sam *was* sorry; sorry he hadn't been braver, or stronger, or good with swords, that he hadn't been a better son to his father and a better brother to Dickon and the girls. He was sorry to die too, but better men had died on the Fist, good men and true, not squeaking fat boys like him. At least he would not have the Old Bear hunting him through hell, though. *I got the birds off. I did that right, at least.* He had written out the messages ahead of time, short messages and simple, telling of an attack on the Fist of the First Men, and then he had tucked them away safe in his parchment pouch, hoping he would never need to send them.

When the horns blew Sam had been sleeping. He thought he was dreaming them at first, but when he opened his eyes snow was falling on the camp and the black brothers were all grabbing bows and spears and running toward the ringwall. Chett was the only one nearby, Maester Aemon's old steward with the face full of boils and the big wen on his neck. Sam had never seen so much fear on a man's face as he saw on Chett's when that third blast came moaning through the trees. "Help me get the birds off," he pleaded, but the other steward had turned and run off, dagger in hand. *He has the dogs to care for*, Sam remembered. Probably the Lord Commander had given him some orders as well.

His fingers had been so stiff and clumsy in the gloves, and he was shaking from fear and cold, but he found the parchment pouch and dug out the messages he'd written. The ravens were shrieking furiously, and when he opened the Castle Black cage one of them flew right in his face. Two more escaped before Sam could catch one, and when he did it pecked him through his glove, drawing blood. Yet somehow he held on long enough to attach the little roll of parchment. The warhorn had fallen silent by then, but the Fist rang with shouted commands and the clatter of steel. "*Fly!*" Sam called as he tossed the raven into the air.

The birds in the Shadow Tower cage were screaming and fluttering about so madly that he was afraid to open the door, but he made himself do it anyway. This time he caught the first raven that tried to escape. A moment later, it was clawing its way up through the falling snow, bearing word of the attack.

His duty done, he finished dressing with clumsy, frightened fingers, donning his cap and surcoat and hooded cloak and buckling on his swordbelt, buckling it real tight so it wouldn't fall down. Then he found his pack and stuffed all his things inside, spare smallclothes and dry socks, the dragonglass arrowheads and spearhead Jon had given him and the old horn too, his parchments, inks, and quills, the maps he'd been drawing, and a rock-hard garlic sausage he'd been saving since the Wall. He tied it all up and shouldered the pack onto his back. *The Lord Commander said I wasn't to rush to the ringwall*, he recalled, *but he said I shouldn't come running to him either*. Sam took a deep breath and realized that he did not know what to do next.

He remembered turning in a circle, lost, the fear growing inside him as it always did. There were dogs barking and horses trumpeting, but the snow muffled the sounds and made them seem far away. Sam could see nothing beyond three yards, not even the torches burning along the low stone wall that ringed the crown of the hill. *Could the torches have gone out?* That was too scary to think about. *The horn blew thrice long, three long blasts means Others.* The white walkers of the wood, the cold shadows, the monsters of the tales that made him squeak and tremble as a boy, riding their giant ice-spiders, hungry for blood . . .

Awkwardly he drew his sword, and plodded heavily through the snow holding it. A dog ran past barking, and he saw some of the men from the Shadow Tower, big bearded men with longaxes and eight-foot spears. He felt safer for their company, so he followed them to the wall. When he saw the torches still burning atop the ring of stones a shudder of relief went through him.

The black brothers stood with swords and spears in hand, watching the snow fall, waiting. Ser Mallador Locke went by on his horse, wearing a snow-speckled helm. Sam stood well back behind the others, looking for Grenn or Dolorous Edd. *If I have to die, let me die beside my friends*, he remembered thinking. But all the men around him were strangers, Shadow Tower men under the command of the ranger named Blane.

"Here they come," he heard a brother say.

"Notch," said Blane, and twenty black arrows were pulled from as many quivers, and notched to as many bowstrings.

"Gods be good, there's hundreds," a voice said softly.

"Draw," Blane said, and then, "hold." Sam could not see and did not want to see. The men of the Night's Watch stood behind their torches, waiting with arrows pulled back to their ears, as *something* came up that dark, slippery slope through the snow. "Hold," Blane said again, "hold, hold." And then, "Loose."

The arrows whispered as they flew.

A ragged cheer went up from the men along the ring-wall, but it died quickly. "They're not stopping, m'lord," a man said to Blane, and another shouted, *"More!* Look there, coming from the trees," and yet another said, "Gods ha' mercy, they's crawling. They's almost here, *they's on us!"* Sam had been backing away by then, shaking like the last leaf on the tree when the wind kicks up, as much from cold as from fear. It had been very cold that night. *Even colder than now. The snow feels almost warm. I feel better now. A little rest was all I needed. Maybe in a little while I'll be strong enough to walk again. In a little while.*

A horse stepped past his head, a shaggy grey beast with snow in its mane and hooves crusted with ice. Sam watched it come and watched it go. Another appeared from out of the falling snow, with a man in black leading it. When he saw Sam in his path he cursed him and led the horse around. *I wish I had a horse,* he thought. *If I had a horse I could keep going. I could sit, and even sleep some in the saddle.* Most of their mounts had been lost at the Fist, though, and those that remained carried their food, their torches, and their wounded. Sam wasn't wounded. *Only fat and weak, and the greatest craven in the Seven Kingdoms.*

He was *such* a coward. Lord Randyll, his father, had always said so, and he had been right. Sam was his heir, but he had never been worthy, so his father had sent him away to the Wall. His little brother Dickon would inherit the Tarly lands and castle, and the greatsword Heartsbane that the lords of Horn Hill had borne so proudly for centuries. He wondered whether Dickon would shed a tear for his brother who died in the snow, somewhere off beyond the edge of the world. *Why should he? A coward's not worth weeping over.* He had heard his father tell his mother as much, half a hundred times. The Old Bear knew it too.

"Fire arrows," the Lord Commander roared that night on the Fist, when he appeared suddenly astride his horse, "give them flame." It was then he noticed Sam there quaking. *"Tarly!* Get out of here! Your place is with the ravens."

"I . . . I . . . I got the messages away."

"Good." On Mormont's shoulder his own raven echoed, *"Good, good."* The Lord Commander looked huge in fur and mail. Behind his black iron visor, his eyes were fierce. "You're in the way here. Go back to your cages. If I need to send another message, I don't want to have to find you first. See that the birds are ready." He did not wait for a response, but turned his horse and trotted around the ring, shouting, "Fire! Give them fire!"

Sam did not need to be told twice. He went back to the birds, as fast as his fat legs could carry him. *I should write the message ahead of time,* he thought, *so we can get the birds away as fast as need be.* It took him longer than it should have to light his little fire, to warm the frozen ink. He sat beside it on a rock with quill and parchment, and wrote his messages.

Attacked amidst snow and cold, but we've thrown them back with fire arrows, he wrote, as he heard Thoren Smallwood's voice ring out with a command of, "Notch, draw . . . loose." The flight of arrows made a sound as sweet as a mother's prayer. "Burn, you dead bastards, burn," Dywen sang out, cackling. The brothers cheered and cursed. *All safe,* he wrote. *We remain on the Fist of the First Men.* Sam hoped they were better archers than him.

He put that note aside and found another blank parchment. *Still fighting on the Fist, amidst heavy snow,* he wrote when someone shouted, "They're still coming." *Result uncertain.* "Spears," someone said. It might have been Ser Mallador, but Sam could not swear to it. *Wights attacked us on the Fist, in snow,* he wrote, *but we drove them off with fire.* He turned his head. Through the drifting snow, all he could see was the huge fire at the center of the camp, with mounted men moving restlessly around it. The reserve, he knew, ready to ride down anything that breached the ringwall. They had armed themselves with torches in place of swords, and were lighting them in the flames.

Wights all around us, he wrote, when he heard the shouts from the north face. *Coming up from north and south at once. Spears and swords don't stop them, only fire.* "Loose, loose, loose," a voice screamed in the night, and another shouted, "Bloody huge," and a third voice said, "A giant!" and a fourth insisted, "A bear, a *bear!*" A horse shrieked and the hounds began to bay, and there was so much shouting that Sam couldn't make out the voices anymore. He wrote faster, note after note. *Dead wildlings, and a giant, or maybe a bear, on us, all around.* He heard the crash of steel on wood, which could only mean one thing. *Wights over the ringwall. Fighting inside the camp.* A dozen mounted brothers pounded past him toward the east wall, burning brands streaming flames in each rider's hand. *Lord Commander Mormont is meeting them with fire. We've won. We're winning. We're holding our own. We're cutting our way free and retreating for the Wall. We're trapped on the Fist, hard pressed.*

One of the Shadow Tower men came staggering out of the darkness to fall at Sam's feet. He crawled within a foot of the fire before he died. *Lost*, Sam wrote, *the battle's lost. We're all lost.*

Why must he remember the fight at the Fist? He didn't want to remember. Not *that*. He tried to make himself remember his mother, or his little sister Talla, or that girl Gilly at Craster's Keep. Someone was shaking him by the shoulder. "Get up," a voice said. "Sam, you can't go to sleep here. Get up and keep walking."

I wasn't asleep, I was remembering. "Go away," he said, his words frosting in the cold air. "I'm well. I want to rest."

"Get up." Grenn's voice, harsh and husky. He loomed over Sam, his blacks crusty with snow. "There's no resting, the Old Bear said. You'll die."

"Grenn." He smiled. "No, truly, I'm good here. You just go on. I'll catch you after I've rested a bit longer."

"You won't." Grenn's thick brown beard was frozen all around his mouth. It made him look like some old man. "You'll freeze, or the Others will get you. Sam, *get up!*"

The night before they left the Wall, Pyp had teased Grenn the way he did, Sam remembered, smiling and saying how Grenn was a good choice for the ranging, since he was too stupid to be terrified. Grenn hotly denied it until he realized what he was saying. He was stocky and thick-necked and strong—Ser Alliser Thorne had called him "Aurochs," the same way he called Sam "Ser Piggy" and Jon "Lord Snow"—but he had always treated Sam nice enough. *That was only because of Jon, though. If it weren't for Jon, none of them would have liked me.* And now Jon was gone, lost in the Skirling Pass with Qhorin Halfhand, most likely dead. Sam would have cried for him, but those tears would only freeze as well, and he could scarcely keep his eyes open now.

A tall brother with a torch stopped beside them, and for a wonderful moment Sam felt the warmth on his face. "Leave him," the man said to Grenn. "If they can't walk, they're done. Save your strength for yourself, Grenn."

"He'll get up," Grenn replied. "He only needs a hand."

The man moved on, taking the blessed warmth with him. Grenn tried to pull Sam to his feet. "That hurts," he complained. "Stop it. Grenn, you're hurting my arm. Stop it."

"You're too bloody heavy." Grenn jammed his hands into Sam's armpits, gave a grunt, and hauled him upright. But the moment he let go, the fat boy sat back down in the snow. Grenn kicked him, a solid thump that cracked the crust of snow around his boot and sent it flying everywhere. "Get *up!*" He kicked him again. "Get up and walk. You have to walk."

Sam fell over sideways, curling up into a tight ball to protect himself from the kicks. He hardly felt them through all his wool and leather and mail, but even so, they hurt. *I thought Grenn was my friend. You shouldn't kick your friends. Why won't they let me be? I just need to rest, that's all, to rest and sleep some, and maybe die a little.*

"If you take the torch, I can take the fat boy."

Suddenly he was jerked up into the cold air, away from his sweet soft snow; he was floating. There was an arm under his knees, and another one under his back. Sam raised his head and blinked. A face loomed close, a broad brutal face with a flat nose and small dark eyes and a thicket of coarse brown beard. He had seen the face before, but it took him a moment to remember. *Paul. Small Paul.* Melting ice ran down into his eyes from the heat of the torch. "Can you carry him?" he heard Grenn ask.

"I carried a calf once was heavier than him. I carried him down to his mother so he could get a drink of milk."

Sam's head bobbed up and down with every step that Small Paul took. "Stop it," he muttered, "put me down, I'm not a baby. I'm a man of the Night's Watch." He sobbed. "Just let me die."

"Be quiet, Sam," said Grenn. "Save your strength. Think about your sisters and brother. Maester Aemon. Your favorite foods. Sing a song if you like."

"Aloud?"

"In your head."

Sam knew a hundred songs, but when he tried to think of one he couldn't. The words had all gone from his head. He sobbed again and said, "I don't know any songs, Grenn. I did know some, but now I don't."

"Yes you do," said Grenn. "How about 'The Bear and the Maiden Fair,' everybody knows that one. *A bear there was, a bear, a bear! All black and brown and covered with hair!*"

"No, not that one," Sam pleaded. The bear that had come up the Fist had no hair left on its rotted flesh. He didn't want to think about bears. "No songs. Please, Grenn."

"Think about your ravens, then."

"*They were never mine.*" *They were the Lord Commander's ravens, the ravens of the Night's Watch.* "They belonged to Castle Black and the Shadow Tower."

Small Paul frowned. "Chett said I could have the Old Bear's raven, the one that talks. I saved food for it and everything." He shook his head. "I forgot, though. I left the food where I hid it." He plodded onward, pale white breath coming from his mouth with every step, then suddenly said, "Could I have one of your ravens? Just the one. I'd never let Lark eat it."

"They're gone," said Sam. "I'm sorry." *So sorry.* "They're flying back to the Wall now." He had set the birds free when he'd heard the warhorns sound once more, calling the Watch to horse. *Two short blasts and a long one, that was the call to mount up.* But there was no reason to mount, unless to abandon the Fist, and that meant the battle was lost. The fear bit him so strong then that it was all Sam could do to open the cages. Only as he watched the last raven flap up into the snowstorm did he realize that he had forgotten to send any of the messages he'd written.

"No," he'd squealed, "oh, no, oh, no." The snow fell and the horns blew; *ahooo ahooo ahoooooooooooooooooooooo, they cried,* to horse, to horse, to horse. Sam saw two ravens perched on a rock and ran after them, but the birds flapped off lazily through the swirling snow, in opposite directions. He chased one, his breath puffing out his nose in thick white clouds, stumbled, and found himself ten feet from the ringwall.

After that . . . he remembered the dead coming over the stones with arrows in their faces and through their throats. Some were all in ringmail and some were almost naked . . . wildings, most of them, but a few wore faded blacks. He remembered one of the Shadow Tower men shoving his spear through a wight's pale soft belly and out his back, and how the thing staggered right up the shaft and reached out his black hands and twisted the brother's head around until blood came out his mouth. That was when his bladder let go the first time, he was almost sure.

He did not remember running, but he must have, because the next he knew he was near the fire half a camp away, with old Ser Ottyn Wythers and some archers. Ser Ottyn was on his knees in the snow, staring at the chaos around them, until a riderless horse came by and kicked him in the face. The archers paid him no mind. They were loosing fire arrows at shadows in the dark. Sam saw one wight hit, saw the flames engulf it, but there were a dozen more behind it, and a huge pale shape that must have been the bear, and soon enough the bowmen had no arrows.

And then Sam found himself on a horse. It wasn't his own horse, and he never recalled mounting up either. Maybe it was the horse that had smashed Ser Ottyn's face in. The horns were still blowing, so he kicked the horse and turned him toward the sound.

In the midst of carnage and chaos and blowing snow, he found Dolorous Edd sitting on his garron with a plain black banner on a spear. "Sam," Edd said when he saw him, "would you wake me, please? I am having this terrible nightmare."

More men were mounting up every moment. The warhorns called them back. *Ahooo ahooo ahooooooooooo-ooooooooo.* "They're over the west wall, m'lord," Thoren Smallwood screamed at the Old Bear, as he fought to control his horse. "I'll send reserves . . ."

"NO!" Mormont had to bellow at the top of his lungs to be heard over the horns. "Call them back, we have to cut our way out." He stood in his stirrups, his black cloak snapping in the wind, the fire shining off his armor. *"Spearhead!"* he roared. "Form wedge, we ride. Down the south face, then east!"

"My lord, the south slope's crawling with them!"

"The others are too steep," Mormont said. "We have—"

His garron screamed and reared and almost threw him as the bear came staggering through the snow. Sam pissed himself all over again. *I didn't think I had any more left inside me.* The bear was dead, pale and rotting, its fur and skin all sloughed off and half its right arm burned to bone, yet still it came on. Only its eyes lived. *Bright blue, just as Jon said.* They shone like frozen stars. Thoren Smallwood charged, his longsword shining all orange and red from the light of the fire. His swing near took the bear's head off. And then the bear took his.

"RIDE!" the Lord Commander shouted, wheeling.

They were at the gallop by the time they reached the ring. Sam had always been too frightened to jump a horse before, but when the low stone wall loomed up before him he knew he had no choice. He kicked and closed his eyes and whimpered, and the garron took him over, somehow, *somehow*, the garron took him over. The rider to his right came crashing down in a tangle of steel and leather and screaming horseflesh, and then the wights were swarming over him and the wedge was closing up. They plunged down the hillside at a run, through clutching black hands and burning blue eyes and blowing snow. Horses stumbled and rolled, men were swept from their saddles, torches spun through the air, axes and swords hacked at dead flesh, and Samwell Tarly sobbed, clutching desperately to his horse with a strength he never knew he had.

He was in the middle of the flying spearhead with brothers

on either side, and before and behind him as well. A dog ran with them for a ways, bounding down the snowy slope and in and out among the horses, but it could not keep up. The wights stood their ground and were ridden down and trampled underhoof. Even as they fell they clutched at swords and stirrups and the legs of passing horses. Sam saw one claw open a garron's belly with its right hand while it clung to the saddle with its left.

Suddenly the trees were all about them, and Sam was splashing through a frozen stream with the sounds of slaughter dwindling behind. He turned, breathless with relief . . . until a man in black leapt from the brush and yanked him out of the saddle. Who he was, Sam never saw; he was up in an instant, and galloping away the next. When he tried to run after the horse, his feet tangled in a root and he fell hard on his face and lay weeping like a baby until Dolorous Edd found him there.

That was his last coherent memory of the Fist of the First Men. Later, hours later, he stood shivering among the other survivors, half mounted and half afoot. They were miles from the Fist by then, though Sam did not remember how. Dywen had led down five packhorses, heavy laden with food and oil and torches, and three had made it this far. The Old Bear made them redistribute the loads, so the loss of any one horse and its provisions would not be such a catastrophe. He took garrons from the healthy men and gave them to the wounded, organized the walkers, and set torches to guard their flanks and rear. *All I need do is walk,* Sam told himself, as he took that first step toward home. But before an hour was gone he had begun to struggle, and to lag . . .

They were lagging now as well, he saw. He remembered Pyp saying once how Small Paul was the strongest man in the Watch. *He must be, to carry me.* Yet even so, the snow was growing deeper, the ground more treacherous, and Paul's strides had begun to shorten. More horsemen passed, wounded men who looked at Sam with dull incurious eyes. Some torch bearers went by as well. "You're falling behind," one told them. The next agreed. "No one's like to wait for you, Paul. Leave the pig for the dead men."

"He promised I could have a bird," Small Paul said, even

though Sam hadn't, not truly. *They aren't mine to give.* "I want me a bird that talks, and eats corn from my hand."

"Bloody fool," the torch man said. Then he was gone.

It was a while after when Grenn stopped suddenly. "We're alone," he said in a hoarse voice. "I can't see the other torches. Was that the rear guard?"

Small Paul had no answer for him. The big man gave a grunt and sank to his knees. His arms trembled as he lay Sam gently in the snow. "I can't carry you no more. I would, but I can't." He shivered violently.

The wind sighed through the trees, driving a fine spray of snow into their faces. The cold was so bitter that Sam felt naked. He looked for the other torches, but they were gone, every one of them. There was only the one Grenn carried, the flames rising from it like pale orange silks. He could see through them, to the black beyond. *That torch will burn out soon,* he thought, *and we are all alone, without food or friends or fire.*

But that was wrong. They weren't alone at all.

The lower branches of the great green sentinel shed their burden of snow with a soft wet *plop.* Grenn spun, thrusting out his torch. "Who goes there?" A horse's head emerged from the darkness. Sam felt a moment's relief, until he saw the horse. Hoarfrost covered it like a sheen of frozen sweat, and a nest of stiff black entrails dragged from its open belly. On its back was a rider pale as ice. Sam made a whimpery sound deep in his throat. He was so scared he might have pissed himself all over again, but the cold was in him, a cold so savage that his bladder felt frozen solid. The Other slid gracefully from the saddle to stand upon the snow. Sword-slim it was, and milky white. Its armor rippled and shifted as it moved, and its feet did not break the crust of the new-fallen snow.

Small Paul unslung the long-hafted axe strapped across his back. "Why'd you hurt that horse? That was Mawney's horse."

Sam groped for the hilt of his sword, but the scabbard was empty. He had lost it on the Fist, he remembered too late.

"Get away!" Grenn took a step, thrusting the torch out before him. "*Away*, or you burn." He poked at it with the flames.

The Other's sword gleamed with a faint blue glow. It moved toward Grenn, lightning quick, slashing. When the ice blue blade brushed the flames, a screech stabbed Sam's ears sharp as a needle. The head of the torch tumbled sideways to vanish beneath a deep drift of snow, the fire snuffed out at once. And all Grenn held was a short wooden stick. He flung it at the Other, cursing, as Small Paul charged in with his axe.

The fear that filled Sam then was worse than any fear he had ever felt before, and Samwell Tarly knew every kind of fear. "Mother have mercy," he wept, forgetting the old gods in his terror. "Father protect me, oh oh . . ." His fingers found his dagger and he filled his hand with that.

The wights had been slow clumsy things, but the Other was light as snow on the wind. It slid away from Paul's axe, armor rippling, and its crystal sword twisted and spun and slipped between the iron rings of Paul's mail, through leather and wool and bone and flesh. It came out his back with a *hissssssssssss* and Sam heard Paul say, "Oh," as he lost the axe. Impaled, his blood smoking around the sword, the big man tried to reach his killer with his hands and almost had before he fell. The weight of him tore the strange pale sword from the Other's grip.

Do it now. Stop crying and fight, you baby. Fight, craven. It was his father he heard, it was Alliser Thorne, it was his brother Dickon and the boy Rast. *Craven, craven, craven.* He giggled hysterically, wondering if they would make a wight of him, a huge fat white wight always tripping over its own dead feet. *Do it, Sam.* Was that Jon, now? Jon was dead. *You can do it, you can, just do it.* And then he was stumbling forward, falling more than running, really, closing his eyes and shoving the dagger blindly out before him with both hands. He heard a *crack*, like the sound ice makes when it breaks beneath a man's foot, and then a screech so shrill and sharp that he went staggering backward with his hands over his muffled ears, and fell hard on his arse.

When he opened his eyes the Other's armor was running down its legs in rivulets as pale blue blood hissed and steamed around the black dragonglass dagger in its throat. It reached down with two bone-white hands to pull out the knife, but where its fingers touched the obsidian they *smoked*.

Sam rolled onto his side, eyes wide as the Other shrank and puddled, dissolving away. In twenty heartbeats its flesh was gone, swirling away in a fine white mist. Beneath were bones like milkglass, pale and shiny, and they were melting too. Finally only the dragonglass dagger remained, wreathed in steam as if it were alive and sweating. Grenn bent to scoop it up and flung it down again at once. "Mother, that's *cold*."

"Obsidian." Sam struggled to his knees. "Dragonglass, they call it. Dragonglass. *Dragon* glass." He giggled, and cried, and doubled over to heave his courage out onto the snow.

Grenn pulled Sam to his feet, checked Small Paul for a pulse and closed his eyes, then snatched up the dagger again. This time he was able to hold it.

"You keep it," Sam said. "You're not craven like me."

"So craven you killed an Other." Grenn pointed with the knife. "Look there, through the trees. Pink light. Dawn, Sam. Dawn. That must be east. If we head that way, we should catch Mormont."

"If you say." Sam kicked his left foot against a tree, to knock off all the snow. Then the right. "I'll try." Grimacing, he took a step. "I'll try hard." And then another.

TYRION

Lord Tywin's chain of hands made a golden glitter against the deep wine velvet of his tunic. The Lords Tyrell, Redwyne, and Rowan gathered round him as he entered. He greeted each in turn, spoke a quiet word to Varys, kissed the High Septon's ring and Cersei's cheek, clasped the hand of Grand Maester Pycelle, and seated himself in the king's place at the head of the long table, between his daughter and his brother.

Tyrion had claimed Pycelle's old place at the foot, propped up by cushions so he could gaze down the length of the table. Dispossessed, Pycelle had moved up next to Cersei, about as far from the dwarf as he could get without claiming the king's seat. The Grand Maester was a shambling skeleton, leaning heavily on a twisted cane and shaking as he walked, a few white hairs sprouting from his long chicken's neck in place of his once-luxuriant white beard. Tyrion gazed at him without remorse.

The others had to scramble for seats: Lord Mace Tyrell, a heavy, robust man with curling brown hair and a spade-shaped beard well salted with white; Paxter Redwyne of the Arbor, stoop-shouldered and thin, his bald head fringed by tufts of orange hair; Mathis Rowan, Lord of Goldengrove, clean-shaven, stout, and sweating; the High Septon, a frail man with wispy white chin hair. *Too many strange faces*, Tyrion thought, *too many new players. The game changed while I lay rotting in my bed, and no one will tell me the rules.*

Oh, the lords had been courteous enough, though he could tell how uncomfortable it made them to look at him. "That chain of yours, that was cunning," Mace Tyrell had said in a jolly tone, and Lord Redwyne nodded and said, "Quite so, quite so, my lord of Highgarden speaks for all of us," and very cheerfully too.

Tell it to the people of this city, Tyrion thought bitterly. *Tell it to the bloody singers, with their songs of Renly's ghost.*

His uncle Kevan had been the warmest, going so far as to kiss his cheek and say, "Lancel has told me how brave you were, Tyrion. He speaks very highly of you."

He'd better, or I'll have a few things to say of him. He made himself smile and say, "My good cousin is too kind. His wound is healing, I trust?"

Ser Kevan frowned. "One day he seems stronger, the next . . . it is worrisome. Your sister often visits his sickbed, to lift his spirits and pray for him."

But is she praying that he lives, or dies? Cersei had made shameless use of their cousin, both in and out of bed; a little secret she no doubt hoped Lancel would carry to his grave now that Father was here and she no longer had need of him. *Would she go so far as to murder him, though?* To look at her today, you would never suspect Cersei was capable of such ruthlessness. She was all charm, flirting with Lord Tyrell as they spoke of Joffrey's wedding feast, complimenting Lord Redwyne on the valor of his twins, softening gruff Lord Rowan with jests and smiles, making pious noises at the High Septon. "Shall we begin with the wedding arrangements?" she asked as Lord Tywin took his seat.

"No," their father said. "With the war. Varys."

The eunuch smiled a silken smile. "I have such *delicious* tidings for you all, my lords. Yesterday at dawn our brave Lord Randyll caught Robett Glover outside Duskendale and trapped him against the sea. Losses were heavy on both sides, but in the end our loyal men prevailed. Ser Helman Tallhart is reported dead, with a thousand others. Robett Glover leads the survivors back toward Harrenhal in bloody disarray, little dreaming he will find valiant Ser Gregor and his stalwarts athwart his path."

"Gods be praised!" said Paxter Redwyne. "A great victory for King Joffrey!"

What did Joffrey have to do with it? thought Tyrion.

"And a terrible defeat for the north, certainly," observed Littlefinger, "yet one in which Robb Stark played no part. The Young Wolf remains unbeaten in the field."

"What do we know of Stark's plans and movements?" asked Mathis Rowan, ever blunt and to the point.

"He has run back to Riverrun with his plunder, abandoning the castles he took in the west," announced Lord Tywin. "Our cousin Ser Daven is reforming the remnants of his late father's army at Lannisport. When they are ready he shall join Ser Forley Prester at the Golden Tooth. As soon as the Stark boy starts north, Ser Forley and Ser Daven will descend on Riverrun."

"You are certain Lord Stark means to go north?" Lord Rowan asked. "Even with the ironmen at Moat Cailin?"

Mace Tyrell spoke up. "Is there anything as pointless as a king without a kingdom? No, it's plain, the boy must abandon the riverlands, join his forces to Roose Bolton's once more, and throw all his strength against Moat Cailin. That is what *I* would do."

Tyrion had to bite his tongue at that. Robb Stark had won more battles in a year than the Lord of Highgarden had in twenty. Tyrell's reputation rested on one indecisive victory over Robert Baratheon at Ashford, in a battle largely won by Lord Tarly's van before the main host had even arrived. The siege of Storm's End, where Mace Tyrell actually did hold the command, had dragged on a year to no result, and after the Trident was fought, the Lord of Highgarden had meekly dipped his banners to Eddard Stark.

"I ought to write Robb Stark a stern letter," Littlefinger was saying. "I understand his man Bolton is stabling goats in *my* high hall, it's really quite unconscionable."

Ser Kevan Lannister cleared his throat. "As regards the Starks . . . Balon Greyjoy, who now styles himself King of the Isles and the North, has written to us offering terms of alliance."

"He ought to be offering fealty," snapped Cersei. "By what right does he call himself king?"

"By right of conquest," Lord Tywin said. "King Balon has strangler's fingers round the Neck. Robb Stark's heirs are dead, Winterfell is fallen, and the ironmen hold Moat Cailin, Deepwood Motte, and most of the Stony Shore. King Balon's longships command the sunset sea, and are well placed to menace Lannisport, Fair Isle, and even Highgarden, should we provoke him."

"And if we accept this alliance?" inquired Lord Mathis Rowan. "What terms does he propose?"

"That we recognize his kingship and grant him everything north of the Neck."

Lord Redwyne laughed. "What is there north of the Neck that any sane man would want? If Greyjoy will trade swords and sails for stone and snow, I say do it, and count ourselves lucky."

"Truly," agreed Mace Tyrell. "That's what I would do. Let King Balon finish the northmen whilst we finish Stannis."

Lord Tywin's face gave no hint as to his feelings. "There is Lysa Arryn to deal with as well. Jon Arryn's widow, Hoster Tully's daughter, Catelyn Stark's sister . . . whose husband was conspiring with Stannis Baratheon at the time of his death."

"Oh," said Mace Tyrell cheerfully, "women have no stomach for war. Let her be, I say, she's not like to trouble us."

"I agree," said Redwyne. "The Lady Lysa took no part in the fighting, nor has she committed any overt acts of treason."

Tyrion stirred. "She did throw me in a cell and put me on trial for my life," he pointed out, with a certain amount of rancor. "Nor has she returned to King's Landing to swear fealty to Joff, as she was commanded. My lords, grant me the men, and I will sort out Lysa Arryn." He could think of nothing he would enjoy more, except perhaps strangling Cersei. Sometimes he still dreamed of the Eyrie's sky cells, and woke drenched in cold sweat.

Mace Tyrell's smile was jovial, but behind it Tyrion

sensed contempt. "Perhaps you'd best leave the fighting to fighters," said the Lord of Highgarden. "Better men than you have lost great armies in the Mountains of the Moon, or shattered them against the Bloody Gate. We know your worth, my lord, no need to tempt fate."

Tyrion pushed off his cushions, bristling, but his father spoke before he could lash back. "I have other tasks in mind for Tyrion. I believe Lord Petyr may hold the key to the Eyrie."

"Oh, I do," said Littlefinger, "I have it here between my legs." There was mischief in his grey-green eyes. "My lords, with your leave, I propose to travel to the Vale and there woo and win Lady Lysa Arryn. Once I am her consort, I shall deliver you the Vale of Arryn without a drop of blood being spilled."

Lord Rowan looked doubtful. "Would Lady Lysa have you?"

"She's had me a few times before, Lord Mathis, and voiced no complaints."

"Bedding," said Cersei, "is not wedding. Even a cow like Lysa Arryn might be able to grasp the difference."

"To be sure. It would not have been fitting for a daughter of Riverrun to marry one so far below her." Littlefinger spread his hands. "Now, though . . . a match between the Lady of the Eyrie and the Lord of Harrenhal is not so unthinkable, is it?"

Tyrion noted the look that passed between Paxter Redwyne and Mace Tyrell. "It might serve," Lord Rowan said, "if you are certain that you can keep the woman loyal to the King's Grace."

"My lords," pronounced the High Septon, "autumn is upon us, and all men of good heart are weary of war. If Lord Baelish can bring the Vale back into the king's peace without more shedding of blood, the gods will surely bless him."

"But can he?" asked Lord Redwyne. "Jon Arryn's son is Lord of the Eyrie now. The Lord Robert."

"Only a boy," said Littlefinger. "I will see that he grows to be Joffrey's most loyal subject, and a fast friend to us all."

Tyrion studied the slender man with the pointed beard and irreverent grey-green eyes. *Lord of Harrenhal an empty honor? Bugger that, Father. Even if he never sets foot in the castle, the title makes this match possible, as he's known all along.*

"We have no lack of foes," said Ser Kevan Lannister. "If the Eyrie can be kept out of the war, all to the good. I am of a mind to see what Lord Petyr can accomplish."

Ser Kevan was his brother's vanguard in council, Tyrion knew from long experience; he never had a thought that Lord Tywin had not had first. *It has all been settled beforehand*, he concluded, *and this discussion's no more than show.*

The sheep were bleating their agreement, unaware of how neatly they'd been shorn, so it fell to Tyrion to object. "How will the crown pay its debts without Lord Petyr? He is our wizard of coin, and we have no one to replace him."

Littlefinger smiled. "My little friend is too kind. All I do is count coppers, as King Robert used to say. Any clever tradesman could do as well . . . and a Lannister, blessed with the golden touch of Casterly Rock, will no doubt far surpass me."

"A Lannister?" Tyrion had a bad feeling about this.

Lord Tywin's gold-flecked eyes met his son's mismatched ones. "You are admirably suited to the task, I believe."

"Indeed!" Ser Kevan said heartily. "I've no doubt you'll make a splendid master of coin, Tyrion."

Lord Tywin turned back to Littlefinger. "If Lysa Arryn will take you for a husband and return to the king's peace, we shall restore the Lord Robert to the honor of Warden of the East. How soon might you leave?"

"On the morrow, if the winds permit. There's a Braavosi galley standing out past the chain, taking on cargo by boat. The *Merling King*. I'll see her captain about a berth."

"You will miss the king's wedding," said Mace Tyrell.

Petyr Baelish gave a shrug. "Tides and brides wait on no man, my lord. Once the autumn storms begin the voyage will be much more hazardous. Drowning would definitely diminish my charms as a bridegroom."

Lord Tyrell chuckled. "True. Best you do not linger."

"May the gods speed you on your way," the High Septon said. "All King's Landing shall pray for your success."

Lord Redwyne pinched at his nose. "May we return to

the matter of the Greyjoy alliance? In my view, there is much to be said for it. Greyjoy's longships will augment my own fleet and give us sufficient strength at sea to assault Dragonstone and end Stannis Baratheon's pretensions."

"King Balon's longships are occupied for the nonce," Lord Tywin said politely, "as are we. Greyjoy demands half the kingdom as the price of alliance, but what will he do to earn it? Fight the Starks? He is doing that already. Why should we pay for what he has given us for free? The best thing to do about our lord of Pyke is nothing, in my view. Granted enough time, a better option may well present itself. One that does not require the king to give up half his kingdom."

Tyrion watched his father closely. *There's something he's not saying.* He remembered those important letters Lord Tywin had been writing, the night Tyrion had demanded Casterly Rock. *What was it he said? Some battles are won with swords and spears, others with quills and ravens . . .* He wondered who the "better option" was, and what sort of price he was demanding.

"Perhaps we ought move on to the wedding," Ser Kevan said.

The High Septon spoke of the preparations being made at the Great Sept of Baelor, and Cersei detailed the plans she had been making for the feast. They would feed a thousand in the throne room, but many more outside in the yards. The outer and middle wards would be tented in silk, with tables of food and casks of ale for all those who could not be accommodated within the hall.

"Your Grace," said Grand Maester Pycelle, "in regard to the number of guests . . . we have had a raven from Sunspear. Three hundred Dornishmen are riding toward King's Landing as we speak, and hope to arrive before the wedding."

"How do they come?" asked Mace Tyrell gruffly. "They have not asked leave to cross *my* lands." His thick neck had turned a dark red, Tyrion noted. Dornishmen and Highgardeners had never had great love for one another; over the centuries, they had fought border wars beyond count, and raided back and forth across mountains and marches even when at peace. The enmity had waned a bit

after Dorne had become part of the Seven Kingdoms . . .
until the Dornish prince they called the Red Viper had crippled the young heir of Highgarden in a tourney. *This could
be ticklish*, the dwarf thought, waiting to see how his father would handle it.

"Prince Doran comes at my son's invitation," Lord
Tywin said calmly, "not only to join in our celebration, but
to claim his seat on this council, and the justice Robert denied him for the murder of his sister Elia and her children."

Tyrion watched the faces of the Lords Tyrell, Redwyne,
and Rowan, wondering if any of the three would be bold
enough to say, "But Lord Tywin, wasn't it *you* who presented the bodies to Robert, all wrapped up in Lannister
cloaks?" None of them did, but it was there on their faces
all the same. *Redwyne does not give a fig*, he thought, *but
Rowan looks fit to gag*.

"When the king is wed to your Margaery and Myrcella
to Prince Trystane, we shall all be one great House," Ser
Kevan reminded Mace Tyrell. "The enmities of the past
should remain there, would you not agree, my lord?"

"This is *my daughter's wedding*—"

"—and my grandson's," said Lord Tywin firmly. "No
place for old quarrels, surely?"

"I have no quarrel with *Doran* Martell," insisted Lord
Tyrell, though his tone was more than a little grudging. "If
he wishes to cross the Reach in peace, he need only ask my
leave."

Small chance of that, thought Tyrion. *He'll climb the
Boneway, turn east near Summerhall, and come up the
kingsroad.*

"Three hundred Dornishmen need not trouble our
plans," said Cersei. "We can feed the men-at-arms in the
yard, squeeze some extra benches into the throne room for
the lordlings and highborn knights, and find Prince Doran
a place of honor on the dais."

Not by me, was the message Tyrion saw in Mace
Tyrell's eyes, but the Lord of Highgarden made no reply but
a curt nod.

"Perhaps we can move to a more pleasant task," said
Lord Tywin. "The fruits of victory await division."

"What could be sweeter?" said Littlefinger, who had already swallowed his own fruit, Harrenhal.

Each lord had his own demands; this castle and that village, tracts of lands, a small river, a forest, the wardship of certain minors left fatherless by the battle. Fortunately, these fruits were plentiful, and there were orphans and castles for all. Varys had lists. Forty-seven lesser lordlings and six hundred nineteen knights had lost their lives beneath the fiery heart of Stannis and his Lord of Light, along with several thousand common men-at-arms. Traitors all, their heirs were disinherited, their lands and castles granted to those who had proved more loyal.

Highgarden reaped the richest harvest. Tyrion eyed Mace Tyrell's broad belly and thought, *He has a prodigious appetite, this one.* Tyrell demanded the lands and castles of Lord Alester Florent, his own bannerman, who'd had the singular ill judgment to back first Renly and then Stannis. Lord Tywin was pleased to oblige. Brightwater Keep and all its lands and incomes were granted to Lord Tyrell's second son, Ser Garlan, transforming him into a great lord in the blink of an eye. His elder brother, of course, stood to inherit Highgarden itself.

Lesser tracts were granted to Lord Rowan, and set aside for Lord Tarly, Lady Oakheart, Lord Hightower, and other worthies not present. Lord Redwyne asked only for thirty years' remission of the taxes that Littlefinger and his wine factors had levied on certain of the Arbor's finest vintages. When that was granted, he pronounced himself well satisfied and suggested that they send for a cask of Arbor gold, to toast good King Joffrey and his wise and benevolent Hand. At that Cersei lost patience. "It's swords Joff needs, not toasts," she snapped. "His realm is still plagued with would-be usurpers and self-styled kings."

"But not for long, I think," said Varys unctuously.

"A few more items remain, my lords." Ser Kevan consulted his papers. "Ser Addam has found some crystals from the High Septon's crown. It appears certain now that the thieves broke up the crystals and melted down the gold."

"Our Father Above knows their guilt and will sit in judgment on them all," the High Septon said piously.

"No doubt he will," said Lord Tywin. "All the same, you must be crowned at the king's wedding. Cersei, summon your goldsmiths, we must see to a replacement." He did not wait for her reply, but turned at once to Varys. "You have reports?"

The eunuch drew a parchment from his sleeve. "A kraken has been seen off the Fingers." He giggled. "Not a *Greyjoy*, mind you, a true kraken. It attacked an Ibbenese whaler and pulled it under. There is fighting on the Stepstones, and a new war between Tyrosh and Lys seems likely. Both hope to win Myr as ally. Sailors back from the Jade Sea report that a three-headed dragon has hatched in Qarth, and is the wonder of that city—"

"Dragons and krakens do not interest me, regardless of the number of their heads," said Lord Tywin. "Have your whisperers perchance found some trace of my brother's son?"

"Alas, our beloved Tyrek has quite vanished, the poor brave lad." Varys sounded close to tears.

"Tywin," Ser Kevan said, before Lord Tywin could vent his obvious displeasure, "some of the gold cloaks who deserted during the battle have drifted back to barracks, thinking to take up duty once again. Ser Addam wishes to know what to do with them."

"They might have endangered Joff with their cowardice," Cersei said at once. "I want them put to death."

Varys sighed. "They have surely earned death, Your Grace, none can deny it. And yet, perhaps we might be wiser to send them to the Night's Watch. We have had disturbing messages from the Wall of late. Of wildlings astir . . ."

"Wildlings, krakens, and dragons." Mace Tyrell chuckled. "Why, is there anyone *not* stirring?"

Lord Tywin ignored that. "The deserters serve us best as a lesson. Break their knees with hammers. They will not run again. Nor will any man who sees them begging in the streets." He glanced down the table to see if any of the other lords disagreed.

Tyrion remembered his own visit to the Wall, and the crabs he'd shared with old Lord Mormont and his officers. He remembered the Old Bear's fears as well. "Perhaps we might break the knees of a few to make our point. Those who killed Ser Jacelyn, say. The rest we can send to Marsh. The Watch is grievously under strength. If the Wall should fail . . ."

". . . the wildlings will flood the north," his father finished, "and the Starks and Greyjoys will have another enemy to contend with. They no longer wish to be subject to the Iron Throne, it would seem, so by what right do they look to the Iron Throne for aid? King Robb and King Balon both claim the north. Let *them* defend it, if they can. And if not, this Mance Rayder might even prove a useful ally." Lord Tywin looked to his brother. "Is there more?"

Ser Kevan shook his head. "We are done. My lords, His Grace King Joffrey would no doubt wish to thank you all for your wisdom and good counsel."

"I should like private words with my children," said Lord Tywin as the others rose to leave. "You as well, Kevan."

Obediently, the other councillors made their farewells, Varys the first to depart and Tyrell and Redwyne the last. When the chamber was empty but for the four Lannisters, Ser Kevan closed the door.

"*Master of coin?*" said Tyrion in a thin strained voice. "Whose notion was that, pray?"

"Lord Petyr's," his father said, "but it serves us well to have the treasury in the hands of a Lannister. You have asked for important work. Do you fear you might be incapable of the task?"

"No," said Tyrion, "I fear a trap. Littlefinger is subtle and ambitious. I do not trust him. Nor should you."

"He won Highgarden to our side . . ." Cersei began.

". . . and sold you Ned Stark, I know. He will sell us just as quick. A coin is as dangerous as a sword in the wrong hands."

His uncle Kevan looked at him oddly. "Not to us, surely. The gold of Casterly Rock . . ."

". . . is dug from the ground. Littlefinger's gold is made from thin air, with a snap of his fingers."

"A more useful skill than any of yours, sweet brother," purred Cersei, in a voice sweet with malice.

"Littlefinger is a liar—"

"—and black as well, said the raven of the crow."

Lord Tywin slammed his hand down on the table. "*Enough!* I will have no more of this unseemly squabbling. You are both Lannisters, and will comport yourselves as such."

Ser Kevan cleared his throat. "I would sooner have Petyr Baelish ruling the Eyrie than any of Lady Lysa's other suitors. Yohn Royce, Lyn Corbray, Horton Redfort . . . these are dangerous men, each in his own way. And proud. Littlefinger may be clever, but he has neither high birth nor skill at arms. The lords of the Vale will never accept such as their liege." He looked to his brother. When Lord Tywin nodded, he continued. "And there is this—Lord Petyr continues to demonstrate his loyalty. Only yesterday he brought us word of a Tyrell plot to spirit Sansa Stark off to Highgarden for a 'visit,' and there marry her to Lord Mace's eldest son, Willas."

"*Littlefinger* brought you word?" Tyrion leaned against the table. "Not our master of whisperers? How interesting."

Cersei looked at their uncle in disbelief. "Sansa is my hostage. She goes *nowhere* without my leave."

"Leave you must perforce grant, should Lord Tyrell ask," their father pointed out. "To refuse him would be tantamount to declaring that we did not trust him. He would take offense."

"Let him. What do we care?"

Bloody fool, thought Tyrion. "Sweet sister," he explained patiently, "offend Tyrell and you offend Redwyne, Tarly, Rowan, and Hightower as well, and perhaps start them wondering whether Robb Stark might not be more accommodating of their desires."

"I will not have the rose and the direwolf in bed together," declared Lord Tywin. "We must forestall him."

"How?" asked Cersei.

"By marriage. Yours, to begin with."

It came so suddenly that Cersei could only stare for a moment. Then her cheeks reddened as if she had been slapped. "No. Not again. I will not."

"Your Grace," said Ser Kevan, courteously, "you are a young woman, still fair and fertile. Surely you cannot wish to spend the rest of your days alone? And a new marriage would put to rest this talk of incest for good and all."

"So long as you remain unwed, you allow Stannis to spread his disgusting slander," Lord Tywin told his daughter. "You must have a new husband in your bed, to father children on you."

"Three children is quite sufficient. I am Queen of the Seven Kingdoms, not a brood mare! The Queen *Regent*!"

"You are my daughter, and will do as I command."

She stood. "I will not sit here and listen to this—"

"You will if you wish to have any voice in the choice of your next husband," Lord Tywin said calmly.

When she hesitated, then sat, Tyrion knew she was lost, despite her loud declaration of, "I will *not* marry again!"

"You will marry and you will breed. Every child you birth makes Stannis more a liar." Their father's eyes seemed to pin her to her chair. "Mace Tyrell, Paxter Redwyne, and Doran Martell are wed to younger women likely to outlive them. Balon Greyjoy's wife is elderly and failing, but such a match would commit us to an alliance with the Iron Islands, and I am still uncertain whether that would be our wisest course."

"No," Cersei said from between white lips. "No, no, no."

Tyrion could not quite suppress the grin that came to his lips at the thought of packing his sister off to Pyke. *Just when I was about to give up praying, some sweet god gives me this.*

Lord Tywin went on. "Oberyn Martell might suit, but the Tyrells would take that very ill. So we must look to the sons. I assume you do not object to wedding a man younger than yourself?"

"I object to wedding *any*—"

"I have considered the Redwyne twins, Theon Greyjoy, Quentyn Martell, and a number of others. But our alliance with Highgarden was the sword that broke Stannis. It should be tempered and made stronger. Ser Loras has taken the white and Ser Garlan is wed to one of the Fossoways, but there remains the eldest son, the boy they scheme to wed to Sansa Stark."

Willas Tyrell. Tyrion was taking a wicked pleasure in Cersei's helpless fury. "That would be the cripple," he said.

Their father chilled him with a look. "Willas is heir to Highgarden, and by all reports a mild and courtly young man, fond of reading books and looking at the stars. He has a passion for breeding animals as well, and owns the finest hounds, hawks, and horses in the Seven Kingdoms."

A perfect match, mused Tyrion. *Cersei also has a passion for breeding.* He pitied poor Willas Tyrell, and did not know whether he wanted to laugh at his sister or weep for her.

"The Tyrell heir would be my choice," Lord Tywin concluded, "but if you would prefer another, I will hear your reasons."

"That is so very kind of you, Father," Cersei said with icy courtesy. "It is such a difficult choice you give me. Who would I sooner take to bed, the old squid or the crippled dog boy? I shall need a few days to consider. Do I have your leave to go?"

You are the queen, Tyrion wanted to tell her. *He ought to be begging leave of you.*

"Go," their father said. "We shall talk again after you have composed yourself. Remember your duty."

Cersei swept stiffly from the room, her rage plain to see. *Yet in the end she will do as Father bid.* She had proved that with Robert. *Though there is Jaime to consider.* Their brother had been much younger when Cersei wed the first time; he might not acquiesce to a second marriage quite so easily. The unfortunate Willas Tyrell was like to contract a sudden fatal case of sword-through-bowels, which could rather sour the alliance between Highgarden and Casterly Rock. *I should say something, but what? Pardon me, Father, but it's our brother she wants to marry?*

"Tyrion."

He gave a resigned smile. "Do I hear the herald summoning me to the lists?"

"Your whoring is a weakness in you," Lord Tywin said without preamble, "but perhaps some share of the blame is mine. Since you stand no taller than a boy, I have found it easy to forget that you are in truth a man grown, with all of a man's baser needs. It is past time you were wed."

I was wed, or have you forgotten? Tyrion's mouth twisted, and the noise emerged that was half laugh and half snarl.

"Does the prospect of marriage amuse you?"

"Only imagining what a bugger-all handsome bridegroom I'll make." A wife might be the very thing he needed. If she brought him lands and a keep, it would give him a place in the world apart from Joffrey's court . . . and away from Cersei and their father.

On the other hand, there was Shae. *She will not like this, for all she swears that she is content to be my whore.*

That was scarcely a point to sway his father, however, so Tyrion squirmed higher in his seat and said, "You mean to wed me to Sansa Stark. But won't the Tyrells take the match as an affront, if they have designs on the girl?"

"Lord Tyrell will not broach the matter of the Stark girl until after Joffrey's wedding. If Sansa is wed before that, how can he take offense, when he gave us no hint of his intentions?"

"Quite so," said Ser Kevan, "and any lingering resentments should be soothed by the offer of Cersei for his Willas."

Tyrion rubbed at the raw stub of his nose. The scar tissue itched abominably sometimes. "His Grace the royal pustule has made Sansa's life a misery since the day her father died, and now that she is finally rid of Joffrey you propose to marry her to me. That seems singularly cruel. Even for you, Father."

"Why, do you plan to mistreat her?" His father sounded more curious than concerned. "The girl's happiness is not my purpose, nor should it be yours. Our alliances in the south may be as solid as Casterly Rock, but there remains the north to win, and the key to the north is Sansa Stark."

"She is no more than a child."

"Your sister swears she's flowered. If so, she is a woman, fit to be wed. You must needs take her maidenhead, so no man can say the marriage was not consummated. After that, if you prefer to wait a year or two before bedding her again, you would be within your rights as her husband."

Shae is all the woman I need just now, he thought, *and Sansa's a girl, no matter what you say.* "If your purpose here is to keep her from the Tyrells, why not return her to her mother? Perhaps that would convince Robb Stark to bend the knee."

Lord Tywin's look was scornful. "Send her to Riverrun and her mother will match her with a Blackwood or a Mallister to shore up her son's alliances along the Trident. Send her north, and she will be wed to some Manderly or Umber before the moon turns. Yet she is no less dangerous here at court, as this business with the Tyrells should prove. She must marry a Lannister, and soon."

"The man who weds Sansa Stark can claim Winterfell in her name," his uncle Kevan put in. "Had that not occurred to you?"

"If you will not have the girl, we shall give her to one of your cousins," said his father. "Kevan, is Lancel strong enough to wed, do you think?"

Ser Kevan hesitated. "If we bring the girl to his bedside, he could say the words . . . but to consummate, no . . . I would suggest one of the twins, but the Starks hold them both at Riverrun. They have Genna's boy Tion as well, else he might serve."

Tyrion let them have their byplay; it was all for his benefit, he knew. *Sansa Stark*, he mused. Soft-spoken sweet-smelling Sansa, who loved silks, songs, chivalry and tall gallant knights with handsome faces. He felt as though he was back on the bridge of boats, the deck shifting beneath his feet.

"You asked me to reward you for your efforts in the battle," Lord Tywin reminded him forcefully. "This is a chance for you, Tyrion, the best you are ever likely to have." He drummed his fingers impatiently on the table. "I once hoped to marry your brother to Lysa Tully, but Aerys named Jaime to his Kingsguard before the arrangements were complete. When I suggested to Lord Hoster that Lysa might be wed to you instead, he replied that he wanted a whole man for his daughter."

So he wed her to Jon Arryn, who was old enough to be her grandfather. Tyrion was more inclined to be thankful than angry, considering what Lysa Arryn had become.

"When I offered you to Dorne I was told that the suggestion was an insult," Lord Tywin continued. "In later years I had similar answers from Yohn Royce and Leyton Hightower. I finally stooped so low as to suggest you might take the Florent girl Robert deflowered in his brother's wedding bed, but her father preferred to give her to one of his own household knights.

"If you will not have the Stark girl, I shall find you another wife. Somewhere in the realm there is doubtless some little lordling who'd gladly part with a daughter to win the friendship of Casterly Rock. Lady Tanda has offered Lollys . . ."

Tyrion gave a shudder of dismay. "I'd sooner cut it off and feed it to the goats."

"Then open your eyes. The Stark girl is young, nubile, tractable, of the highest birth, and still a maid. She is not uncomely. Why would you hesitate?"

Why indeed? "A quirk of mine. Strange to say, I would prefer a wife who wants me in her bed."

"If you think your whores want you in their bed, you are an even greater fool than I suspected," said Lord Tywin. "You disappoint me, Tyrion. I had hoped this match would please you."

"Yes, we all know how important my pleasure is to you, Father. But there's more to this. The key to the north, you say? The Greyjoys hold the north now, and King Balon has a daughter. Why Sansa Stark, and not her?" He looked into his father's cool green eyes with their bright flecks of gold.

Lord Tywin steepled his fingers beneath his chin. "Balon Greyjoy thinks in terms of plunder, not rule. Let him enjoy an autumn crown and suffer a northern winter. He will give his subjects no cause to love him. Come spring, the northmen will have had a bellyful of krakens. When you bring Eddard Stark's grandson home to claim his birthright, lords and little folk alike will rise as one to place him on the high seat of his ancestors. You *are* capable of getting a woman with child, I hope?"

"I believe I am," he said, bristling. "I confess, I cannot prove it. Though no one can say I have not tried. Why, I plant my little seeds just as often as I can . . ."

"In the gutters and the ditches," finished Lord Tywin, "and in common ground where only bastard weeds take root. It is past time you kept your own garden." He rose to his feet. "You shall never have Casterly Rock, I promise you. But wed Sansa Stark, and it is just possible that you might win Winterfell."

Tyrion Lannister, Lord Protector of Winterfell. The prospect gave him a queer chill. "Very good, Father," he said slowly, "but there's a big ugly roach in your rushes. Robb Stark is as *capable* as I am, presumably, and sworn to marry one of those fertile Freys. And once the Young Wolf sires a litter, any pups that Sansa births are heirs to nothing."

Lord Tywin was unconcerned. "Robb Stark will father no children on his fertile Frey, you have my word. There is a bit of news I have not yet seen fit to share with the council, though no doubt the good lords will hear it soon enough. The Young Wolf has taken Gawen Westerling's eldest daughter to wife."

For a moment Tyrion could not believe he'd heard his father right. "He broke his sworn word?" he said, incredulous. "He threw away the Freys for . . ." Words failed him.

"A maid of sixteen years, named Jeyne," said Ser Kevan. "Lord Gawen once suggested her to me for Willem or Martyn, but I had to refuse him. Gawen is a good man, but his wife is Sybell Spicer. He should never have wed her. The Westerlings always did have more honor than sense. Lady Sybell's grandfather was a trader in saffron and pepper, almost as lowborn as that smuggler Stannis keeps. And the grandmother was some woman he'd brought back from the east. A frightening old crone, supposed to be a priestess. *Maegi*, they called her. No one could pronounce her real name. Half of Lannisport used to go to her for cures and love potions and the like." He shrugged. "She's long dead, to be sure. And Jeyne seemed a sweet child, I'll grant you, though I only saw her once. But with such doubtful blood . . ."

Having once married a whore, Tyrion could not entirely share his uncle's horror at the thought of wedding a girl whose great grandfather sold cloves. Even so . . . *A sweet child*, Ser Kevan had said, but many a poison was sweet as well. The Westerlings were old blood, but they had more pride than power. It would not surprise him to learn that Lady Sybell had brought more wealth to the marriage than her highborn husband. The Westerling mines had failed years ago, their best lands had been sold off or lost, and the Crag was more ruin than stronghold. *A romantic ruin, though, jutting up so brave above the sea.* "I am surprised," Tyrion had to confess. "I thought Robb Stark had better sense."

"He is a boy of sixteen," said Lord Tywin. "At that age, sense weighs for little, against lust and love and honor."

"He forswore himself, shamed an ally, betrayed a solemn promise. Where is the honor in that?"

Ser Kevan answered. "He chose the girl's honor over his own. Once he had deflowered her, he had no other course."

"It would have been kinder to leave her with a bastard

in her belly," said Tyrion bluntly. The Westerlings stood to lose everything here; their lands, their castle, their very lives. *A Lannister always pays his debts.*

"Jeyne Westerling is her mother's daughter," said Lord Tywin, "and Robb Stark is his father's son."

This Westerling betrayal did not seem to have enraged his father as much as Tyrion would have expected. Lord Tywin did not suffer disloyalty in his vassals. He had extinguished the proud Reynes of Castamere and the ancient Tarbecks of Tarbeck Hall root and branch when he was still half a boy. The singers had even made a rather gloomy song of it. Some years later, when Lord Farman of Faircastle grew truculent, Lord Tywin sent an envoy bearing a lute instead of a letter. But once he'd heard "The Rains of Castamere" echoing through his hall, Lord Farman gave no further trouble. And if the song were not enough, the shattered castles of the Reynes and Tarbecks still stood as mute testimony to the fate that awaited those who chose to scorn the power of Casterly Rock. "The Crag is not so far from Tarbeck Hall and Castamere," Tyrion pointed out. "You'd think the Westerlings might have ridden past and seen the lesson there."

"Mayhaps they have," Lord Tywin said. "They are well aware of Castamere, I promise you."

"Could the Westerlings and Spicers be such great fools as to believe the wolf can defeat the lion?"

Every once in a very long while, Lord Tywin Lannister would actually threaten to smile; he never did, but the threat alone was terrible to behold. "The greatest fools are ofttimes more clever than the men who laugh at them," he said, and then, "You will marry Sansa Stark, Tyrion. And soon."

CATELYN

They carried the corpses in upon their shoulders and laid them beneath the dais. A silence fell across the torchlit hall, and in the quiet Catelyn could hear Grey Wind howling half a castle away. *He smells the blood*, she thought, *through stone walls and wooden doors, through night and rain, he still knows the scent of death and ruin.*

She stood at Robb's left hand beside the high seat, and for a moment felt almost as if she were looking down at her own dead, at Bran and Rickon. These boys had been much older, but death had shrunken them. Naked and wet, they seemed such little things, so still it was hard to remember them living.

The blond boy had been trying to grow a beard. Pale yellow peach fuzz covered his cheeks and jaw above the red ruin the knife had made of his throat. His long golden hair was still wet, as if he had been pulled from a bath. By the look of him, he had died peacefully, perhaps in sleep, but his brown-haired cousin had fought for life. His arms bore slashes where he'd tried to block the blades, and red still trickled slowly from the stab wounds that covered his chest and belly and back like so many tongueless mouths, though the rain had washed him almost clean.

Robb had donned his crown before coming to the hall, and the bronze shone darkly in the torchlight. Shadows hid his eyes as he looked upon the dead. *Does he see Bran and Rickon as well?* She might have wept, but there were no tears left in her. The dead boys were pale from long imprisonment, and both had been fair; against their smooth white skin, the blood was shockingly red, unbearable to look upon. *Will they lay Sansa down naked beneath the Iron Throne after they have killed her? Will her skin seem as white, her blood as red?* From outside came the steady wash of rain and the restless howling of a wolf.

Her brother Edmure stood to Robb's right, one hand upon the back of his father's seat, his face still puffy from sleep. They had woken him as they had her, pounding on his door in the black of night to yank him rudely from his dreams. *Were they good dreams, brother? Do you dream of sunlight and laughter and a maiden's kisses? I pray you do.* Her own dreams were dark and laced with terrors.

Robb's captains and lords bannermen stood about the hall, some mailed and armed, others in various states of dishevelment and undress. Ser Raynald and his uncle Ser Rolph were among them, but Robb had seen fit to spare his queen this ugliness. *The Crag is not far from Casterly Rock*, Catelyn recalled. *Jeyne may well have played with these boys when all of them were children.*

She looked down again upon the corpses of the squires Tion Frey and Willem Lannister, and waited for her son to speak.

It seemed a very long time before Robb lifted his eyes from the bloody dead. "Smalljon," he said, "tell your father to bring them in." Wordless, Smalljon Umber turned to obey, his steps echoing in the great stone hall.

As the Greatjon marched his prisoners through the doors, Catelyn made note of how some other men stepped back to give them room, as if treason could somehow be passed by a touch, a glance, a cough. The captors and the captives looked much alike; big men, every one, with thick beards and long hair. Two of the Greatjon's men were wounded, and three of their prisoners. Only the fact that some had spears and others empty scabbards served to set them apart. All were clad in mail hauberks or shirts of sewn rings, with heavy boots and thick cloaks, some of wool and some of fur. *The north is hard and cold, and has no mercy*, Ned had told her when she first came to Winterfell a thousand years ago.

"Five," said Robb when the prisoners stood before him, wet and silent. "Is that all of them?"

"There were eight," rumbled the Greatjon. "We killed two taking them, and a third is dying now."

Robb studied the faces of the captives. "It required eight of you to kill two unarmed squires."

Edmure Tully spoke up. "They murdered two of my men as well, to get into the tower. Delp and Elwood."

"It was no murder, ser," said Lord Rickard Karstark, no more discomfited by the ropes about his wrists than by the blood that trickled down his face. "Any man who steps between a father and his vengeance asks for death."

His words rang against Catelyn's ears, harsh and cruel as the pounding of a war drum. Her throat was dry as bone. *I did this. These two boys died so my daughters might live.*

"I saw your sons die, that night in the Whispering Wood," Robb told Lord Karstark. "Tion Frey did not kill Torrhen. Willem Lannister did not slay Eddard. How then can you call this vengeance? This was folly, and bloody murder. Your sons died honorably on a battlefield, with swords in their hands."

"They *died*," said Rickard Karstark, yielding no inch of ground. "The Kingslayer cut them down. These two were of his ilk. Only blood can pay for blood."

"The blood of children?" Robb pointed at the corpses. "How old were they? Twelve, thirteen? *Squires.*"

"Squires die in every battle."

"Die fighting, yes. Tion Frey and Willem Lannister gave up their swords in the Whispering Wood. They were captives, locked in a cell, asleep, unarmed . . . boys. *Look at them!*"

Lord Karstark looked instead at Catelyn. "Tell your mother to look at them," he said. "She slew them, as much as I."

Catelyn put a hand on the back of Robb's seat. The hall

seemed to spin about her. She felt as though she might retch.

"My mother had naught to do with this," Robb said angrily. "This was your work. Your murder. Your *treason*."

"How can it be treason to kill Lannisters, when it is not treason to free them?" asked Karstark harshly. "Has Your Grace forgotten that we are at war with Casterly Rock? In war you kill your enemies. Didn't your father teach you that, boy?"

"*Boy?*" The Greatjon dealt Rickard Karstark a buffet with a mailed fist that sent the other lord to his knees.

"Leave him!" Robb's voice rang with command. Umber stepped back away from the captive.

Lord Karstark spit out a broken tooth. "Yes, Lord Umber, leave me to the king. He means to give me a scolding before he forgives me. That's how he deals with treason, our King in the North." He smiled a wet red smile. "Or should I call you the King Who Lost the North, Your Grace?"

The Greatjon snatched a spear from the man beside him and jerked it to his shoulder. "Let me spit him, sire. Let me open his belly so we can see the color of his guts."

The doors of the hall crashed open, and the Blackfish entered with water running from his cloak and helm. Tully men-at-arms followed him in, while outside lightning cracked across the sky and a hard black rain pounded against the stones of Riverrun. Ser Brynden removed his helm and went to one knee. "Your Grace," was all he said, but the grimness of his tone spoke volumes.

"I will hear Ser Brynden privily, in the audience chamber." Robb rose to his feet. "Greatjon, keep Lord Karstark here till I return, and hang the other seven."

The Greatjon lowered the spear. "Even the dead ones?"

"Yes. I will not have such fouling my lord uncle's rivers. Let them feed the crows."

One of the captives dropped to his knees. "Mercy, sire. I killed no one, I only stood at the door to watch for guards."

Robb considered that a moment. "Did you know what Lord Rickard intended? Did you see the knives drawn? Did you hear the shouts, the screams, the cries for mercy?"

"Aye, I did, but I took no part. I was only the watcher, I swear it . . ."

"Lord Umber," said Robb, "this one was only the watcher. Hang him last, so he may watch the others die. Mother, Uncle, with me, if you please." He turned away as the Greatjon's men closed upon the prisoners and drove them from the hall at spearpoint. Outside the thunder crashed and boomed, so loud it sounded as if the castle were coming down about their ears. *Is this the sound of a kingdom falling?* Catelyn wondered.

It was dark within the audience chamber, but at least the sound of the thunder was muffled by another thickness of wall. A servant entered with an oil lamp to light the fire, but Robb sent him away and kept the lamp. There were tables and chairs, but only Edmure sat, and he rose again when he realized that the others had remainded standing. Robb took off his crown and placed it on the table before him.

The Blackfish shut the door. "The Karstarks are gone."

"All?" Was it anger or despair that thickened Robb's voice like that? Even Catelyn was not certain.

"All the fighting men," Ser Brynden replied. "A few camp followers and serving men were left with their wounded. We questioned as many as we needed, to be certain of the truth. They started leaving at nightfall, stealing off in ones and twos at first, and then in larger groups. The wounded men and servants were told to keep the campfires lit so no one would know they'd gone, but once the rains began it didn't matter."

"Will they re-form, away from Riverrun?" asked Robb.

"No. They've scattered, hunting. Lord Karstark has sworn to give the hand of his maiden daughter to any man highborn or low who brings him the head of the Kingslayer."

Gods be good. Catelyn felt ill again.

"Near three hundred riders and twice as many mounts, melted away in the night." Robb rubbed his temples, where the crown had left its mark in the soft skin above his ears. "All the mounted strength of Karhold, lost."

Lost by me. By me, may the gods forgive me. Catelyn did not need to be a soldier to grasp the trap Robb was in. For the moment he held the riverlands, but his kingdom was surrounded by enemies to every side but east, where Lysa sat aloof on her mountaintop. Even the Trident was scarce secure so long as the Lord of the Crossing withheld his allegiance. *And now to lose the Karstarks as well . . .*

"No word of this must leave Riverrun," her brother Edmure said. "Lord Tywin would . . . the Lannisters pay their debts, they are always saying that. Mother have mercy, when he hears."

Sansa. Catelyn's nails dug into the soft flesh of her palms, so hard did she close her hand.

Robb gave Edmure a look that chilled. "Would you make me a liar as well as a murderer, Uncle?"

"We need speak no falsehood. Only say nothing. Bury the boys and hold our tongues till the war's done. Willem was son to Ser Kevan Lannister, and Lord Tywin's nephew. Tion was Lady Genna's, *and* a Frey. We must keep the news from the Twins as well, until . . ."

"Until we can bring the murdered dead back to life?" said Brynden Blackfish sharply. "The truth escaped with the Karstarks, Edmure. It is too late for such games."

"I owe their fathers truth," said Robb. "And justice. I owe them that as well." He gazed at his crown, the dark gleam of bronze, the circle of iron swords. "Lord Rickard defied me. Betrayed me. I have no choice but to condemn him. Gods know what the Karstark foot with Roose Bolton will do when they hear I've executed their liege for a traitor. Bolton must be warned."

"Lord Karstark's heir was at Harrenhal as well," Ser Brynden reminded him. "The eldest son, the one the Lannisters took captive on the Green Fork."

"Harrion. His name is Harrion." Robb laughed bitterly. "A king had best know the names of his enemies, don't you think?"

The Blackfish looked at him shrewdly. "You know that for a certainty? That this will make young Karstark your enemy?"

"What else would he be? I am about to kill his father, he's not like to thank me."

"He might. There are sons who hate their fathers, and in a stroke you will make him Lord of Karhold."

Robb shook his head. "Even if Harrion were that sort, he could never openly forgive his father's killer. His own men would turn on him. These are *northmen*, Uncle. The north remembers."

"Pardon him, then," urged Edmure Tully.

Robb stared at him in frank disbelief.

Under that gaze, Edmure's face reddened. "Spare his life, I mean. I don't like the taste of it any more than you, sire. He slew my men as well. Poor Delp had only just recovered from the wound Ser Jaime gave him. Karstark must be punished, certainly. Keep him in chains, I say."

"A hostage?" said Catelyn. *It might be best . . .*

"Yes, a hostage!" Her brother seized on her musing as agreement. "Tell the son that so long as he remains loyal, his father will not be harmed. Otherwise . . . we have no hope of the Freys now, not if I offered to marry *all* Lord Walder's daughters and carry his litter besides. If we should lose the Karstarks as well, what hope is there?"

"What hope . . ." Robb let out a breath, pushed his hair back from his eyes, and said, "We've had naught from Ser Rodrik in the north, no response from Walder Frey to our new offer, only silence from the Eyrie." He appealed to his mother. "Will your sister never answer us? How many times must I write her? I will not believe that *none* of the birds have reached her."

Her son wanted comfort, Catelyn realized; he wanted to hear that it would be all right. But her king needed truth. "The birds have reached her. Though she may tell you they did not, if it ever comes to that. Expect no help from that quarter, Robb.

"Lysa was never brave. When we were girls together, she would run and hide whenever she'd done something wrong. Perhaps she thought our lord father would forget to be wroth with her if he could not find her. It is no different now. She ran from King's Landing for fear, to the safest place she knows, and she sits on her mountain hoping everyone will forget her."

"The knights of the Vale could make all the difference in this war," said Robb, "but if she will not fight, so be it. I've asked only that she open the Bloody Gate for us, and provide ships at Gulltown to take us north. The high road would be hard, but not so hard as fighting our way up the Neck. If I could land at White Harbor I could flank Moat Cailin and drive the ironmen from the north in half a year."

"It will not happen, sire," said the Blackfish. "Cat is

right. Lady Lysa is too fearful to admit an army to the Vale.
Any army. The Bloody Gate will remain closed."

"The Others can take her, then," Robb cursed, in a fury
of despair. "Bloody Rickard Karstark as well. And Theon
Greyjoy, Walder Frey, Tywin Lannister, and all the rest of
them. Gods be good, why would any man ever want to be
king? When everyone was shouting *King in the North,
King in the North,* I told myself . . . *swore* to myself . . .
that I would be a good king, as honorable as Father, strong,
just, loyal to my friends and brave when I faced my enemies . . . now I can't even tell one from the other. How did
it all get so *confused?* Lord Rickard's fought at my side in
half a dozen battles. His sons died for me in the Whispering
Wood. Tion Frey and Willem Lannister were my *enemies.*
Yet now I have to kill my dead friends' father for their
sakes." He looked at them all. "Will the Lannisters thank
me for Lord Rickard's head? Will the Freys?"

"No," said Brynden Blackfish, blunt as ever.

"All the more reason to spare Lord Rickard's life and
keep him hostage," Edmure urged.

Robb reached down with both hands, lifted the heavy
bronze-and-iron crown, and set it back atop his head, and
suddenly he was a king again. "Lord Rickard dies."

"But *why?*" said Edmure. "You said yourself—"

"I know what I said, Uncle. It does not change what I
must do." The swords in his crown stood stark and black
against his brow. "In battle I might have slain Tion and
Willem myself, but this was no battle. They were asleep in
their beds, naked and unarmed, in a cell where I put them.
Rickard Karstark killed more than a Frey and a Lannister.
He killed my honor. I shall deal with him at dawn."

When day broke, grey and chilly, the storm had diminished to a steady, soaking rain, yet even so the godswood
was crowded. River lords and northmen, highborn and low,
knights and sellswords and stableboys, they stood amongst
the trees to see the end of the night's dark dance. Edmure
had given commands, and a headsman's block had been set
up before the heart tree. Rain and leaves fell all around
them as the Greatjon's men led Lord Rickard Karstark
through the press, hands still bound. His men already hung
from Riverrun's high walls, slumping at the end of long
ropes as the rain washed down their darkening faces.

Long Lew waited beside the block, but Robb took the poleaxe from his hand and ordered him to step aside. "This is my work," he said. "He dies at my word. He must die by my hand."

Lord Rickard Karstark dipped his head stiffly. "For that much, I thank you. But for naught else." He had dressed for death in a long black wool surcoat emblazoned with the white sunburst of his House. "The blood of the First Men flows in my veins as much as yours, boy. You would do well to remember that. I was named for your grandfather. I raised my banners against King Aerys for your father, and against King Joffrey for you. At Oxcross and the Whispering Wood and in the Battle of the Camps, I rode beside you, and I stood with Lord Eddard on the Trident. We are kin, Stark and Karstark."

"This kinship did not stop you from betraying me," Robb said. "And it will not save you now. Kneel, my lord."

Lord Rickard had spoken truly, Catelyn knew. The Karstarks traced their descent to Karlon Stark, a younger son of Winterfell who had put down a rebel lord a thousand years ago, and been granted lands for his valor. The castle he built had been named Karl's Hold, but that soon became Karhold, and over the centuries the Karhold Starks had become Karstarks.

"Old gods or new, it makes no matter," Lord Rickard told her son, "no man is so accursed as the kinslayer."

"Kneel, traitor," Robb said again. "Or must I have them force your head onto the block?"

Lord Karstark knelt. "The gods shall judge you, as you have judged me." He laid his head upon the block.

"Rickard Karstark, Lord of Karhold." Robb lifted the heavy axe with both hands. "Here in sight of gods and men, I judge you guilty of murder and high treason. In mine own name I condemn you. With mine own hand I take your life. Would you speak a final word?"

"Kill me, and be cursed. You are no king of mine."

The axe crashed down. Heavy and well-honed, it killed at a single blow, but it took three to sever the man's head from his body, and by the time it was done both living and dead were drenched in blood. Robb flung the poleaxe down in disgust, and turned wordless to the heart tree. He stood shaking with his hands half-clenched and the rain running down his cheeks. *Gods forgive him*, Catelyn prayed in silence. *He is only a boy, and he had no other choice.*

That was the last she saw of her son that day. The rain continued all through the morning, lashing the surface of the rivers and turning the godswood grass into mud and puddles. The Blackfish assembled a hundred men and rode out after Karstarks, but no one expected he would bring back many. "I only pray I do not need to hang them," he said as he departed. When he was gone, Catelyn retreated to her father's solar, to sit once more beside Lord Hoster's bed.

"It will not be much longer," Maester Vyman warned her, when he came that afternoon. "His last strength is going, though still he tries to fight."

"He was ever a fighter," she said. "A sweet stubborn man."

"Yes," the maester said, "but this battle he cannot win. It is time he lay down his sword and shield. Time to yield."

To yield, she thought, *to make a peace.* Was it her father the maester was speaking of, or her son?

At evenfall, Jeyne Westerling came to see her. The young queen entered the solar timidly. "Lady Catelyn, I do not mean to disturb you . . ."

"You are most welcome here, Your Grace." Catelyn had been sewing, but she put the needle aside now.

"Please. Call me Jeyne. I don't feel like a Grace."

"You are one, nonetheless. Please, come sit, Your Grace."

"Jeyne." She sat by the hearth and smoothed her skirt out anxiously.

"As you wish. How might I serve you, Jeyne?"

"It's Robb," the girl said. "He's so miserable, so . . . so angry and disconsolate. I don't know what to do."

"It is a hard thing to take a man's life."

"I know. I told him, he should use a headsman. When Lord Tywin sends a man to die, all he does is give the command. It's easier that way, don't you think?"

"Yes," said Catelyn, "but my lord husband taught his sons that killing should never be easy."

"Oh." Queen Jeyne wet her lips. "Robb has not eaten all day. I had Rollam bring him a nice supper, boar's ribs and stewed onions and ale, but he never touched a bite of it. He spent all morning writing a letter and told me not to disturb him, but when the letter was done he burned it. Now he is sitting and looking at maps. I asked him what he was looking for, but he never answered. I don't think he ever heard me. He wouldn't even change out of his clothes. They were damp all day, and bloody. I want to be a good wife to him, I do, but I don't know how to help. To cheer him, or comfort him. I don't know what he *needs*. Please, my lady, you're his mother, tell me what I should do."

Tell me what I should do. Catelyn might have asked the same, if her father had been well enough to ask. But Lord Hoster was gone, or near enough. Her Ned as well. *Bran and Rickon too, and Mother, and Brandon so long ago.* Only Robb remained to her, Robb and the fading hope of her daughters.

"Sometimes," Catelyn said slowly, "the best thing you can do is nothing. When I first came to Winterfell, I was hurt whenever Ned went to the godswood to sit beneath his heart tree. Part of his soul was in that tree, I knew, a part I would never share. Yet without that part, I soon realized, he would not have been Ned. Jeyne, child, you have wed the north, as I did . . . and in the north, the winters will come." She tried to smile. "Be patient. Be understanding. He loves you and he needs you, and he will come back to you soon enough. This very night, perhaps. Be there when he does. That is all I can tell you."

The young queen listened raptly. "I will," she said when Catelyn was done. "I'll be there." She got to her feet. "I should go back. He might have missed me. I'll see. But if he's still at his maps, I'll be patient."

"Do," said Catelyn, but when the girl was at the door, she thought of something else. "Jeyne," she called after, "there's one more thing Robb needs from you, though he may not know it yet himself. A king must have an heir."

The girl smiled at that. "My mother says the same. She makes a posset for me, herbs and milk and ale, to help make me fertile. I drink it every morning. I told Robb I'm sure to give him twins. An Eddard and a Brandon. He liked that, I think. We . . . we try most every day, my lady. Sometimes twice or more." The girl blushed very prettily. "I'll be with child soon, I promise. I pray to our Mother Above, every night."

"Very good. I will add my prayers as well. To the old gods *and* the new."

When the girl had gone, Catelyn turned back to her father and smoothed the thin white hair across his brow. "An Eddard and a Brandon," she sighed softly. "And perhaps in time a Hoster. Would you like that?" He did not answer, but she had never expected that he would. As the sound of the rain on the roof mingled with her father's breathing, she thought about Jeyne. The girl did seem to have a good heart, just as Robb had said. *And good hips, which might be more important.*

JAIME

Two days' ride to either side of the kingsroad, they passed through a wide swath of destruction, miles of blackened fields and orchards where the trunks of dead trees jutted into the air like archers' stakes. The bridges were burnt as well, and the streams swollen by autumn rains, so they had to range along the banks in search of fords. The nights were alive with howling of wolves, but they saw no people.

At Maidenpool, Lord Mooton's red salmon still flew above the castle on its hill, but the town walls were deserted, the gates smashed, half the homes and shops burned or plundered. They saw nothing living but a few feral dogs that went slinking away at the sound of their approach. The pool from which the town took its name, where legend said that Florian the Fool had first glimpsed Jonquil bathing with her sisters, was so choked with rotting corpses that the water had turned into a murky greygreen soup.

Jaime took one look and burst into song. *"Six maids there were in a spring-fed pool . . ."*

"What are you *doing?*" Brienne demanded.

"Singing. 'Six Maids in a Pool,' I'm sure you've heard it. And shy little maids they were, too. Rather like you. Though somewhat prettier, I'll warrant."

"Be quiet," the wench said, with a look that suggested she would love to leave him floating in the pool among the corpses.

"Please, Jaime," pleaded cousin Cleos. "Lord Mooton is sworn to Riverrun, we don't want to draw him out of his castle. And there may be other enemies hiding in the rubble . . ."

"Hers or ours? They are not the same, coz. I have a yen to see if the wench can use that sword she wears."

"If you won't be quiet, you leave me no choice but to gag you, Kingslayer."

"Unchain my hands and I'll play mute all the way to King's Landing. What could be fairer than that, wench?"

"*Brienne!* My name is *Brienne!*" Three crows went flapping into the air, startled at the sound.

"Care for a bath, Brienne?" He laughed. "You're a maiden and there's the pool. I'll wash your back." He used to scrub Cersei's back, when they were children together at Casterly Rock.

The wench turned her horse's head and trotted away. Jaime and Ser Cleos followed her out of the ashes of Maidenpool. A half mile on, green began to creep back into the world once more. Jaime was glad. The burned lands reminded him too much of Aerys.

"She's taking the Duskendale road," Ser Cleos muttered. "It would be safer to follow the coast."

"Safer but slower. I'm for Duskendale, coz. If truth be told, I'm bored with your company." *You may be half Lannister, but you're a far cry from my sister.*

He could never bear to be long apart from his twin. Even as children, they would creep into each other's beds and sleep with their arms entwined. *Even in the womb.* Long before his sister's flowering or the advent of his own manhood, they had seen mares and stallions in the fields and dogs and bitches in the kennels and played at doing the same. Once their mother's maid had caught them at it . . . he did not recall just what they had been doing, but whatever it was had horrified Lady Joanna. She'd sent the maid away, moved Jaime's bedchamber to the other side of Casterly Rock, set a guard outside Cersei's, and told them that they must *never* do that again or she would have no choice but to tell their lord father. They need not have feared, though. It was not long after that she died birthing Tyrion. Jaime barely remembered what his mother had looked like.

Perhaps Stannis Baratheon and the Starks had done him a kindness. They had spread their tale of incest all over the Seven Kingdoms, so there was nothing left to hide. *Why shouldn't I marry Cersei openly and share her bed every night? The dragons always married their sisters.* Septons, lords, and smallfolk had turned a blind eye to the Targaryens for hundreds of years, let them do the same for House Lannister. It would play havoc with Joffrey's claim to the crown, to be sure, but in the end it had been swords that had won the Iron Throne for Robert, and swords could keep Joffrey there as well, regardless of whose seed he was. *We could marry him to Myrcella, once we've sent Sansa Stark back to her mother. That would show the realm that the Lannisters are above their laws, like gods and Targaryens.*

Jaime had decided that he *would* return Sansa, and the younger girl as well if she could be found. It was not like to win him back his lost honor, but the notion of keeping faith when they all expected betrayal amused him more than he could say.

They were riding past a trampled wheatfield and a low stone wall when Jaime heard a soft *thrum* from behind, as if a dozen birds had taken flight at once. "*Down!*" he shouted, throwing himself against the neck of his horse. The gelding screamed and reared as an arrow took him in the rump. Other shafts went hissing past. Jaime saw Ser Cleos lurch from the saddle, twisting as his foot caught in the stirrup. His palfrey bolted, and Frey was dragged past shouting, head bouncing against the ground.

Jaime's gelding lumbered off ponderously, blowing and snorting in pain. He craned around to look for Brienne. She was still ahorse, an arrow lodged in her back and another in her leg, but she seemed not to feel them. He saw her pull her sword and wheel in a circle, searching for the bowmen. "*Behind the wall*," Jaime called, fighting to turn his half-blind mount back toward the fight. The reins were tangled in his damned chains, and the air was full of arrows again. *"At them!"* he shouted, kicking to show her how it was done. The old sorry horse found a burst of speed from somewhere. Suddenly they were racing across the wheatfield, throwing up clouds of chaff. Jaime had just enough time to think, *The wench had better follow before they realize they're being charged by an unarmed man in chains.* Then he heard her coming hard behind. "Evenfall!" she shouted as her plow horse thundered by. She brandished her longsword. "Tarth! Tarth!"

A few last arrows sped harmlessly past; then the bowmen broke and ran, the way unsupported bowmen always broke and ran before the charge of knights. Brienne reined up at the wall. By the time Jaime reached her, they had all melted into the wood twenty yards away. "Lost your taste for battle?"

"They were running."

"That's the best time to kill them."

She sheathed her sword. "Why did you charge?"

"Bowmen are fearless so long as they can hide behind walls and shoot at you from afar, but if you come at them, they run. They know what will happen when you reach them. You have an arrow in your back, you know. And another in your leg. You ought to let me tend them."

"You?"

"Who else? The last I saw of cousin Cleos, his palfrey was using his head to plow a furrow. Though I suppose we ought to find him. He *is* a Lannister of sorts."

They found Cleos still tangled in his stirrup. He had an arrow through his right arm and a second in his chest, but it was the ground that had done for him. The top of his head was matted with blood and mushy to the touch, pieces of broken bone moving under the skin beneath the pressure of Jaime's hand.

Brienne knelt and held his hand. "He's still warm."

"He'll cool soon enough. I want his horse and his clothes. I'm weary of rags and fleas."

"He was your cousin." The wench was shocked.

"Was," Jaime agreed. "Have no fear, I am amply provisioned in cousins. I'll have his sword as well. You need someone to share the watches."

"You can stand a watch without weapons." She rose.

"Chained to a tree? Perhaps I could. Or perhaps I could make my own bargain with the next lot of outlaws and let them slit that thick neck of yours, wench."

"I will not arm you. And my name is—"

"—Brienne, I know. I'll swear an oath not to harm you, if that will ease your girlish fears."

"Your oaths are worthless. You swore an oath to Aerys."

"You haven't cooked anyone in their armor so far as I know. And we both want me safe and whole in King's Landing, don't we?" He squatted beside Cleos and began to undo his swordbelt.

"Step away from him. Now. Stop that."

Jaime was tired. Tired of her suspicions, tired of her insults, tired of her crooked teeth and her broad spotty face and that limp thin hair of hers. Ignoring her protests, he grasped the hilt of his cousin's longsword with both hands, held the corpse down with his foot, and pulled. As the blade slid from the scabbard, he was already pivoting, bringing the sword around and up in a swift deadly arc. Steel met steel with a ringing, bone-jarring *clang*. Somehow Brienne had gotten her own blade out in time. Jaime laughed. "Very good, wench."

"Give me the sword, Kingslayer."

"Oh, I will." He sprang to his feet and drove at her, the longsword alive in his hands. Brienne jumped back, parrying, but he followed, pressing the attack. No sooner did she turn one cut than the next was upon her. The swords kissed and sprang apart and kissed again. Jaime's blood was singing. This was what he was meant for; he never felt so alive as when he was fighting, with death balanced on every stroke. *And with my wrists chained together, the wench may even give me a contest for a time.* His chains forced him to use a two-handed grip, though of course the weight and reach were less than if the blade had been a true two-handed greatsword, but what did it matter? His cousin's sword was long enough to write an end to this Brienne of Tarth.

High, low, overhand, he rained down steel upon her. Left, right, backslash, swinging so hard that sparks flew when the swords came together, upswing, sideslash, overhand, always attacking, moving into her, step and slide, strike and step, step and strike, hacking, slashing, faster, faster, faster . . .

. . . until, breathless, he stepped back and let the point of the sword fall to the ground, giving her a moment of respite. "Not half bad," he acknowledged. "For a wench."

She took a slow deep breath, her eyes watching him warily. "I would not hurt you, Kingslayer."

"As if you could." He whirled the blade back up above his head and flew at her again, chains rattling.

Jaime could not have said how long he pressed the attack. It might have been minutes or it might have been hours; time slept when swords woke. He drove her away from his cousin's corpse, drove her across the road, drove her into the trees. She stumbled once on a root she never saw, and for a moment he thought she was done, but she went to one knee instead of falling, and never lost a beat. Her sword leapt up to block a downcut that would have opened her from shoulder to groin, and then she cut at *him*, again and again, fighting her way back to her feet stroke by stroke.

The dance went on. He pinned her against an oak, cursed as she slipped away, followed her through a shallow brook half-choked with fallen leaves. Steel rang, steel sang, steel screamed and sparked and scraped, and the woman started grunting like a sow at every crash, yet somehow he could not reach her. It was as if she had an iron cage around her that stopped every blow.

"Not bad at all," he said when he paused for a second to catch his breath, circling to her right.

"For a wench?"

"For a squire, say. A green one." He laughed a ragged, breathless laugh. "Come on, come on, my sweetling, the music's still playing. Might I have this dance, my lady?"

Grunting, she came at him, blade whirling, and suddenly it was Jaime struggling to keep steel from skin. One of her slashes raked across his brow, and blood ran down into his right eye. *The Others take her, and Riverrun as well!* His skills had gone to rust and rot in that bloody dungeon, and the chains were no great help either. His eye closed, his shoulders were going numb from the jarring they'd taken, and his wrists ached from the weight of chains, manacles, and sword. His longsword grew heavier with every blow, and Jaime knew he was not swinging it as quickly as he'd done earlier, nor raising it as high.

She is stronger than I am.

The realization chilled him. Robert had been stronger than him, to be sure. The White Bull Gerold Hightower as well, in his heyday, and Ser Arthur Dayne. Amongst the living, Greatjon Umber was stronger, Strongboar of Crakehall most likely, both Cleganes for a certainty. The Mountain's strength was like nothing human. It did not matter. With speed and skill, Jaime could beat them all. But this was a *woman*. A huge cow of a woman, to be sure, but even so . . . by rights, she should be the one wearing down.

Instead she forced him back into the brook again, shouting, "Yield! Throw down the sword!"

A slick stone turned under Jaime's foot. As he felt himself falling, he twisted the mischance into a diving lunge. His point scraped past her parry and bit into her upper thigh. A red flower blossomed, and Jaime had an instant to savor the sight of her blood before his knee slammed into a rock. The pain was blinding. Brienne splashed into him and kicked away his sword. "*YIELD!*"

Jaime drove his shoulder into her legs, bringing her down on top of him. They rolled, kicking and punching until finally she was sitting astride him. He managed to jerk her dagger from its sheath, but before he could plunge it into her belly she caught his wrist and slammed his hands back on a rock so hard he thought she'd wrenched an arm from its socket. Her other hand spread across his face. "Yield!" She shoved his head down, held it under, pulled it up. "*Yield!*" Jaime spit water into her face. A shove, a splash, and he was under again, kicking uselessly, fighting to breathe. Up again. "*Yield, or I'll drown you!*"

"And break your oath?" he snarled. "Like me?"

She let him go, and he went down with a splash.

And the woods rang with coarse laughter.

Brienne lurched to her feet. She was all mud and blood below the waist, her clothing askew, her face red. *She looks as if they caught us fucking instead of fighting.* Jaime crawled over the rocks to shallow water, wiping the blood from his eye with his chained hands. Armed men lined both sides of the brook. *Small wonder, we were making enough noise to wake a dragon.* "Well met, friends," he called to them amiably. "My pardons if I disturbed you. You caught me chastising my wife."

"Seemed to me she was doing the *chastising.*" The man who spoke was thick and powerful, and the nasal bar of his iron halfhelm did not wholly conceal his lack of a nose.

These were not the outlaws who had killed Ser Cleos, Jaime realized suddenly. The scum of the earth surrounded them: swarthy Dornishmen and blond Lyseni, Dothraki with bells in their braids, hairy Ibbenese, coal-black Summer Islanders in feathered cloaks. He knew them. *The Brave Companions.*

Brienne found her voice. "I have a hundred stags—"

A cadaverous man in a tattered leather cloak said, "We'll take that for a start, m'lady."

"Then we'll have your cunt," said the noseless man. "It can't be as ugly as the rest of you."

"Turn her over and rape her arse, Rorge," urged a Dornish spearman with a red silk scarf wound about his helm. "That way you won't need to look at her."

"And rob her o' the pleasure o' looking at *me*?" Noseless said, and the others laughed.

Ugly and stubborn though she might be, the wench deserved better than to be gang raped by such refuse as these. "Who commands here?" Jaime demanded loudly.

"I have that honor, Ser Jaime." The cadaver's eyes were rimmed in red, his hair thin and dry. Dark blue veins could be seen through the pallid skin of his hands and face. "Urswyck I am. Called Urswyck the Faithful."

"You know who I am?"

The sellsword inclined his head. "It takes more than a beard and a shaved head to deceive the Brave Companions."

The Bloody Mummers, you mean. Jaime had no more use for these than he did for Gregor Clegane or Amory Lorch. *Dogs,* his father called them all, and he used them like dogs, to hound his prey and put fear in their hearts. "If you know me, Urswyck, you know you'll have your reward. A Lannister always pays his debts. As for the wench, she's highborn, and worth a good ransom."

The other cocked his head. "Is it so? How fortunate."

There was something sly about the way Urswyck was

smiling that Jaime did not like. "You heard me. Where's the goat?"

"A few hours distant. He will be pleased to see you, I have no doubt, but I would not call him a goat to his face. *Lord* Vargo grows prickly about his dignity."

Since when has that slobbering savage had dignity? "I'll be sure and remember that, when I see him. Lord of what, pray?"

"Harrenhal. It has been promised."

Harrenhal? Has my father taken leave of his senses? Jaime raised his hands. "I'll have these chains off."

Urswyck's chuckle was papery dry.

Something is very wrong here. Jaime gave no sign of his discomfiture, but only smiled. "Did I say something amusing?"

Noseless grinned. "You're the funniest thing I seen since Biter chewed that septa's teats off."

"You and your father lost too many battles," offered the Dornishman. "We had to trade our lion pelts for wolf-skins."

Urswyck spread his hands. "What Timeon means to say is that the Brave Companions are no longer in the hire of House Lannister. We now serve Lord Bolton, and the King in the North."

Jaime gave him a cold, contemptuous smile. "And men say *I* have shit for honor?"

Urswyck was unhappy with that comment. At his signal, two of the Mummers grasped Jaime by the arms and Rorge drove a mailed fist into his stomach. As he doubled over grunting, he heard the wench protesting, "Stop, he's not to be harmed! Lady Catelyn sent us, an exchange of captives, he's under my protection . . ." Rorge hit him again, driving the air from his lungs. Brienne dove for her sword beneath the waters of the brook, but the Mummers were on her before she could lay hands on it. Strong as she was, it took four of them to beat her into submission.

By the end the wench's face was as swollen and bloody as Jaime's must have been, and they had knocked out two of her teeth. It did nothing to improve her appearance. Stumbling and bleeding, the two captives were dragged back through the woods to the horses, Brienne limping from the thigh wound he'd given her in the brook. Jaime felt sorry for her. She would lose her maidenhood tonight, he had no doubt. That noseless bastard would have her for a certainty, and some of the others would likely take a turn.

The Dornishman bound them back to back atop Brienne's plow horse while the other Mummers were stripping Cleos Frey to his skin to divvy up his possessions. Rorge won the bloodstained surcoat with its proud Lannister and Frey quarterings. The arrows had punched holes through lions and towers alike.

"I hope you're pleased, wench," Jaime whispered at Brienne. He coughed, and spat out a mouthful of blood. "If you'd armed me, we'd never have been taken." She made no answer. *There's a pig-stubborn bitch*, he thought. *But brave, yes.* He could not take that from her. "When we make camp for the night, you'll be raped, and more than once," he warned her. "You'd be wise not to resist. If you fight them, you'll lose more than a few teeth."

He felt Brienne's back stiffen against his. "Is that what *you* would do, if you were a woman?"

If I were a woman I'd be Cersei. "If I were a woman, I'd make them kill me. But I'm not." Jaime kicked their horse to a trot. "*Urswyck!* A word!"

The cadaverous sellsword in the ragged leather cloak reined up a moment, then fell in beside him. "What would you have of me, ser? And mind your tongue, or I'll chastise you again."

"Gold," said Jaime. "You do like gold?"

Urswyck studied him through reddened eyes. "It has its uses, I do confess."

Jaime gave Urswyck a knowing smile. "All the gold in Casterly Rock. Why let the goat enjoy it? Why not take us to King's Landing, and collect my ransom for yourself? Hers as well, if you like. Tarth is called the Sapphire Isle, a maiden told me once." The wench squirmed at that, but said nothing.

"Do you take me for a turncloak?"

"Certainly. What else?"

For half a heartbeat Urswyck considered the proposition. "King's Landing is a long way, and your father is there. Lord Tywin may resent us for selling Harrenhal to Lord Bolton."

He's cleverer than he looks. Jaime had been been look-ing forward to hanging the wretch while his pockets bulged with gold. "Leave me to deal with my father. I'll get you a royal pardon for any crimes you have committed. I'll get you a knighthood."

"Ser Urswyck," the man said, savoring the sound. "How proud my dear wife would be to hear it. If only I hadn't killed her." He sighed. "And what of brave Lord Vargo?"

"Shall I sing you a verse of 'The Rains of Castamere'? The goat won't be quite so brave when my father gets hold of him."

"And how will he do that? Are your father's arms so long that they can reach over the walls of Harrenhal and pluck us out?"

"If need be." King Harren's monstrous folly had fallen before, and it could fall again. "Are you such a fool as to think the goat can outfight the lion?"

Urswyck leaned over and slapped him lazily across the face. The sheer casual *insolence* of it was worse than the blow itself. *He does not fear me,* Jaime realized, with a chill. "I have heard enough, Kingslayer. I would have to be a great fool indeed to believe the promises of an oath-breaker like you." He kicked his horse and galloped smartly ahead.

Aerys, Jaime thought resentfully. *It always turns on Aerys.* He swayed with the motion of his horse, wishing for a sword. *Two swords would be even better. One for the wench and one for me. We'd die, but we'd take half of them down to hell with us.* "Why did you tell him Tarth was the Sapphire Isle?" Brienne whispered when Urswyck was out of earshot. "He's like to think my father's rich in gemstones . . ."

"You best pray he does."

"Is every word you say a lie, Kingslayer? Tarth is called the Sapphire Isle for the blue of its waters."

"Shout it a little louder, wench, I don't think Urswyck heard you. The sooner they know how little you're worth in ransom, the sooner the rapes begin. Every man here will mount you, but what do you care? Just close your eyes, open your legs, and pretend they're all Lord Renly."

Mercifully, that shut her mouth for a time.

The day was almost done by the time they found Vargo

Hoat, sacking a small sept with another dozen of his Brave Companions. The leaded windows had been smashed, the carved wooden gods dragged out into the sunlight. The fattest Dothraki Jaime had ever seen was sitting on the Mother's chest when they rode up, prying out her chalcedony eyes with the point of his knife. Nearby, a skinny balding septon hung upside down from the limb of a spreading chestnut tree. Three of the Brave Companions were using his corpse for an archery butt. One of them must have been good; the dead man had arrows through both of his eyes.

When the sellswords spied Urswyck and the captives, a cry went up in half a dozen tongues. The goat was seated by a cookfire eating a half-cooked bird off a skewer, grease and blood running down his fingers into his long stringy beard. He wiped his hands on his tunic and rose. "*Kingthlayer,*" he slobbered. "You are my captifth."

"My lord, I am Brienne of Tarth," the wench called out. "Lady Catelyn Stark commanded me to deliver Ser Jaime to his brother at King's Landing."

The goat gave her a disinterested glance. "Thilence her."

"Hear me," Brienne entreated as Rorge cut the ropes that bound her to Jaime, "in the name of the King in the North, the king you serve, please, listen—"

Rorge dragged her off the horse and began to kick her. "See that you don't break any bones," Urswyck called out to him. "The horse-faced bitch is worth her weight in sapphires."

The Dornishman Timeon and a foul-smelling Ibbenese pulled Jaime down from the saddle and shoved him roughly toward the cookfire. It would not have been hard for him to have grasped one of their sword hilts as they manhandled him, but there were too many, and he was still in fetters. He might cut down one or two, but in the end he would die for it. Jaime was not ready to die just yet, and certainly not for the likes of Brienne of Tarth.

"Thith ith a thweet day," Vargo Hoat said. Around his neck hung a chain of linked coins, coins of every shape and size, cast and hammered, bearing the likenesses of kings, wizards, gods and demons, and all manner of fanciful beasts.

Coins from every land where he has fought, Jaime remembered. Greed was the key to this man. *If he was turned once, he can be turned again.* "Lord Vargo, you were foolish to leave my father's service, but it is not too late to make amends. He will pay well for me, you know it."

"Oh yeth," said Vargo Hoat. "Half the gold in Cathterly Rock, I thall have. But firth I mutht thend him a methage." He said something in his slithery goatish tongue.

Urswyck shoved him in the back, and a jester in green and pink motley kicked his legs out from under him. When he hit the ground one of the archers grabbed the chain between Jaime's wrists and used it to yank his arms out in front of him. The fat Dothraki put aside his knife to unsheathe a huge curved *arakh*, the wickedly sharp scythe-sword the horselords loved.

They mean to scare me. The fool hopped on Jaime's back, giggling, as the Dothraki swaggered toward him. *The goat wants me to piss my breeches and beg his mercy, but he'll never have that pleasure.* He was a Lannister of Casterly Rock, Lord Commander of the Kingsguard; no sellsword would make him scream.

Sunlight ran silver along the edge of the *arakh* as it came shivering down, almost too fast to see. And Jaime screamed.

ARYA

The small square keep was half a ruin, and so too the great grey knight who lived there. He was so old he did not understand their questions. No matter what was said to him, he would only smile and mutter, "I held the bridge against Ser Maynard. Red hair and a black temper, he had, but he could not move me. Six wounds I took before I killed him. Six!"

The maester who cared for him was a young man, thankfully. After the old knight had drifted to sleep in his chair, he took them aside and said, "I fear you seek a ghost. We had a bird, ages ago, half a year at least. The Lannisters caught Lord Beric near the Gods Eye. He was hanged."

"Aye, hanged he was, but Thoros cut him down before he died." Lem's broken nose was not so red or swollen as it had been, but it was healing crooked, giving his face a lopsided look. "His lordship's a hard man to kill, he is."

"And a hard man to find, it would seem," the maester said. "Have you asked the Lady of the Leaves?"

"We shall," said Greenbeard.

The next morning, as they crossed the little stone bridge

behind the keep, Gendry wondered if this was the bridge the old man had fought over. No one knew. "Most like it is," said Jack-Be-Lucky. "Don't see no other bridges."

"You'd know for certain if there was a song," said Tom Sevenstrings. "One good song, and we'd know who Ser Maynard used to be and why he wanted to cross this bridge so bad. Poor old Lychester might be as far famed as the Dragonknight if he'd only had sense enough to keep a singer."

"Lord Lychester's sons died in Robert's Rebellion," grumbled Lem. "Some on one side, some on t'other. He's not been right in the head since. No bloody song's like to help any o' that."

"What did the maester mean, about asking the Lady of the Leaves?" Arya asked Anguy as they rode.

The archer smiled. "Wait and see."

Three days later, as they rode through a yellow wood, Jack-Be-Lucky unslung his horn and blew a signal, a different one than before. The sounds had scarcely died away when rope ladders unrolled from the limbs of trees. "Hobble the horses and up we go," said Tom, half singing the words. They climbed to a hidden village in the upper branches, a maze of rope walkways and little moss-covered houses concealed behind walls of red and gold, and were taken to the Lady of the Leaves, a stick-thin white-haired woman dressed in roughspun. "We cannot stay here much longer, with autumn on us," she told them. "A dozen wolves went down the Hayford road nine days past, hunting. If they'd chanced to look up they might have seen us."

"You've not seen Lord Beric?" asked Tom Sevenstrings.

"He's dead." The woman sounded sick. "The Mountain caught him, and drove a dagger through his eye. A begging brother told us. He had it from the lips of a man who saw it happen."

"That's an old stale tale, and false," said Lem. "The lightning lord's not so easy to kill. Ser Gregor might have put his eye out, but a man don't die o' that. Jack could tell you."

"Well, I never did," said one-eyed Jack-Be-Lucky. "My father got himself good and hanged by Lord Piper's bailiff, my brother Wat got sent to the Wall, and the Lannisters killed my other brothers. An eye, that's nothing."

"You swear he's not dead?" The woman clutched Lem's arm. "Bless you, Lem, that's the best tidings we've had in half a year. May the Warrior defend him, and the red priest too."

The next night they found shelter beneath the scorched shell of a sept, in a burned village called Sallydance. Only shards remained of its windows of leaded glass, and the aged septon who greeted them said the looters had even made off with the Mother's costly robes, the Crone's gilded lantern, and the silver crown the Father had worn. "They hacked the Maiden's breasts off too, though those were only wood," he told them. "And the eyes, the eyes were jet and lapis and mother-of-pearl, they pried them out with their knives. May the Mother have mercy on them all."

"Whose work was this?" said Lem Lemoncloak. "Mummers?"

"No," the old man said. "Northmen, they were. Savages who worship trees. They wanted the Kingslayer, they said."

Arya heard him, and chewed her lip. She could feel Gendry looking at her. It made her angry and ashamed.

There were a dozen men living in the vault beneath the sept, amongst cobwebs and roots and broken wine casks, but they had no word of Beric Dondarrion either. Not even their leader, who wore soot-blackened armor and a crude lightning bolt on his cloak. When Greenbeard saw Arya staring at him, he laughed and said, "The lightning lord is everywhere and nowhere, skinny squirrel."

"I'm not a squirrel," she said. "I'll almost be a woman soon. I'll be one-and-ten."

"Best watch out I don't marry you, then!" He tried to tickle her under the chin, but Arya slapped his stupid hand away.

Lem and Gendry played tiles with their hosts that night, while Tom Sevenstrings sang a silly song about Big Belly Ben and the High Septon's goose. Anguy let Arya try his longbow, but no matter how hard she bit her lip she could not draw it. "You need a lighter bow, milady," the freckled bowman said. "If there's seasoned wood at Riverrun, might be I'll make you one."

Tom overheard him, and broke off his song. "You're a young fool, Archer. If we go to Riverrun it will only be to collect her ransom, won't be no time for you to sit about making bows. Be thankful if you get out with your hide. Lord Hoster was hanging outlaws before you were shaving. And that son of his . . . a man who hates music can't be trusted, I always say."

"It's not music he hates," said Lem. "It's you, fool."

"Well, he has no cause. The wench was willing to make a man of him, is it my fault he drank too much to do the deed?"

Lem snorted through his broken nose. "Was it you who made a song of it, or some other bloody arse in love with his own voice?"

"I only sang it the once," Tom complained. "And who's to say the song was about him? 'Twas a song about a fish."

"A floppy fish," said Anguy, laughing.

Arya didn't care what Tom's stupid songs were about. She turned to Harwin. "What did he mean about ransom?"

"We have sore need of horses, milady. Armor as well. Swords, shields, spears. All the things coin can buy. Aye, and seed for planting. Winter is coming, remember?" He touched her under the chin. "You will not be the first high-born captive we've ransomed. Nor the last, I'd hope."

That much was true, Arya knew. Knights were captured and ransomed all the time, and sometimes women were too. *But what if Robb won't pay their price?* She wasn't a famous knight, and kings were supposed to put the realm before their sisters. And her lady mother, what would she say? Would she still want her back, after all the things she'd done? Arya chewed her lip and wondered.

The next day they rode to a place called High Heart, a hill so lofty that from atop it Arya felt as though she could see half the world. Around its brow stood a ring of huge pale stumps, all that remained of a circle of once-mighty weirwoods. Arya and Gendry walked around the hill to count them. There were thirty-one, some so wide that she could have used them for a bed.

High Heart had been sacred to the children of the forest, Tom Sevenstrings told her, and some of their magic lingered here still. "No harm can ever come to those as sleep here," the singer said. Arya thought that must be true; the hill was so high and the surrounding lands so flat that no enemy could approach unseen.

The smallfolk hereabouts shunned the place, Tom told her; it was said to be haunted by the ghosts of the children of the forest who had died here when the Andal king named Erreg the Kinslayer had cut down their grove. Arya knew about the children of the forest, and about the Andals too, but ghosts did not frighten her. She used to hide in the crypts of Winterfell when she was little, and play games of come-into-my-castle and monsters and maidens amongst the stone kings on their thrones.

Yet even so, the hair on the back of her neck stood up that night. She had been asleep, but the storm woke her. The wind pulled the coverlet right off her and sent it swirling into the bushes. When she went after it she heard voices.

Beside the embers of their campfire, she saw Tom, Lem, and Greenbeard talking to a tiny little woman, a foot shorter than Arya and older than Old Nan, all stooped and wrinkled and leaning on a gnarled black cane. Her white hair was so long it came almost to the ground. When the wind gusted it blew about her head in a fine cloud. Her flesh was whiter, the color of milk, and it seemed to Arya that her eyes were red, though it was hard to tell from the bushes. "The old gods stir and will not let me sleep," she heard the woman say. "I dreamt I saw a shadow with a burning heart butchering a golden stag, aye. I dreamt of a man without a face, waiting on a bridge that swayed and swung. On his shoulder perched a drowned crow with sea-weed hanging from his wings. I dreamt of a roaring river and a woman that was a fish. Dead she drifted, with red tears on her cheeks, but when her eyes did open, *oh*, I woke from terror. All this I dreamt, and more. Do you have gifts for me, to pay me for my dreams?"

"Dreams," grumbled Lem Lemoncloak, "what good are dreams? Fish women and drowned crows. I had a dream myself last night. I was kissing this tavern wench I used to know. Are you going to pay me for that, old woman?"

"The wench is dead," the woman hissed. "Only worms may kiss her now." And then to Tom Sevenstrings she said, "I'll have my song or I'll have you gone."

So the singer played for her, so soft and sad that Arya only heard snatches of the words, though the tune was half-familiar. *Sansa would know it, I bet.* Her sister had known all the songs, and she could even play a little, and sing so sweetly. *All I could ever do was shout the words.*

The next morning the little white woman was nowhere to be seen. As they saddled their horses, Arya asked Tom Sevenstrings if the children of the forest still dwelled on High Heart. The singer chuckled. "Saw her, did you?"

"Was she a ghost?"

"Do ghosts complain of how their joints creak? No, she's only an old dwarf woman. A queer one, though, and evil-eyed. But she knows things she has no business knowing, and sometimes she'll tell you if she likes the look of you."

"Did she like the looks of *you*?" Arya asked doubtfully.

The singer laughed. "The sound of me, at least. She always makes me sing the same bloody song, though. Not a bad song, mind you, but I know others just as good." He shook his head. "What matters is, we have the scent now. You'll soon be seeing Thoros and the lightning lord, I'll wager."

"If you're their men, why do they hide from you?"

Tom Sevenstrings rolled his eyes at that, but Harwin gave her an answer. "I wouldn't call it hiding, milady, but it's true, Lord Beric moves about a lot, and seldom lets on what his plans are. That way no one can betray him. By now there must be hundreds of us sworn to him, maybe thousands, but it wouldn't do for us all to trail along behind him. We'd eat the country bare, or get butchered in a battle by some bigger host. The way we're scattered in little bands, we can strike in a dozen places at once, and be off somewhere else before they know. And when one of us is caught and put to the question, well, we can't tell them where to find Lord Beric no matter what they do to us." He hesitated. "You know what it means, to be put to the question?"

Arya nodded. "Tickling, they called it. Polliver and Raff and all." She told them about the village by the Gods Eye where she and Gendry had been caught, and the questions that the Tickler had asked. "Is there gold hidden in the village?" he would always begin. "Silver, gems? Is there food? Where is Lord Beric? Which of you village folk helped him? Where did he go? How many men did he have with him? How many knights? How many bowmen? How many were horsed? How are they armed? How many wounded? Where did they go, did you say?" Just thinking of it, she could hear the shrieks again, and smell the stench of blood and shit and burning flesh. "He always asked the same questions," she told the outlaws solemnly, "but he changed the tickling every day."

"No child should be made to suffer that," Harwin said when she was done. "The Mountain lost half his men at the Stone Mill, we hear. Might be this Tickler's floating down the Red Fork even now, with fish biting at his face. If not, well, it's one more crime they'll answer for. I've heard his lordship say this war began when the Hand sent him out to bring the king's justice to Gregor Clegane, and that's how he means for it to end." He gave her shoulder a reassuring pat. "You best mount up, milady. It's a long day's ride to Acorn Hall, but at the end of it we'll have a roof above our heads and a hot supper in our bellies."

It *was* a long day's ride, but as dusk was settling they forded a brook and came up on Acorn Hall, with its stone curtain walls and great oaken keep. Its master was away fighting in the retinue of *his* master, Lord Vance, the castle gates closed and barred in his absence. But his lady wife was an old friend of Tom Sevenstrings, and Anguy said they'd once been lovers. Anguy often rode beside her; he was closer to her in age than any of them but Gendry, and he told her droll tales of the Dornish Marches. He never fooled her, though. *He's not my friend. He's only staying close to watch me and make sure I don't ride off again.* Well, Arya could watch as well. Syrio Forel had taught her how.

Lady Smallwood welcomed the outlaws kindly enough, though she gave them a tongue lashing for dragging a young girl through the war. She became even more wroth when Lem let slip that Arya was highborn. "Who dressed the poor child in those Bolton rags?" she demanded of them. "That badge . . . there's many a man who would hang her in half a heartbeat for wearing a flayed man on her breast." Arya promptly found herself marched upstairs, forced into a tub, and doused with scalding hot water. Lady Smallwood's maidservants scrubbed her so hard it felt like they were flaying her themselves. They even dumped in some stinky-sweet stuff that smelled like flowers.

And afterward, they insisted she dress herself in girl's things, brown woolen stockings and a light linen shift, and over that a light green gown with acorns embroidered all over the bodice in brown thread, and more acorns border-ing the hem. "My great-aunt is a septa at a motherhouse in Oldtown," Lady Smallwood said as the women laced the gown up Arya's back. "I sent my daughter there when the war began. She'll have outgrown these things by the time she returns, no doubt. Are you fond of dancing, child? My Carellen's a lovely dancer. She sings beautifully as well. What do you like to do?"

She scuffed a toe amongst the rushes. "Needlework."

"Very restful, isn't it?"

"Well," said Arya, "not the way I do it."

"No? I have always found it so. The gods give each of us our little gifts and talents, and it is meant for us to use them, my aunt always says. Any act can be a prayer, if done as well as we are able. Isn't that a lovely thought? Remember that the next time you do your needlework. Do you work at it every day?"

"I did till I lost Needle. My new one's not as good."

"In times like these, we all must make do as best we can." Lady Smallwood fussed at the bodice of the gown. "Now you look a proper young lady."

I'm not a lady, Arya wanted to tell her, *I'm a wolf.*

"I do not know who you are, child," the woman said, "and it may be that's for the best. Someone important, I fear." She smoothed down Arya's collar. "In times like these, it is better to be insignificant. Would that I could keep you here with me. That would not be safe, though. I have walls, but too few men to hold them." She sighed.

Supper was being served in the hall by the time Arya was all washed and combed and dressed. Gendry took one look and laughed so hard that wine came out his nose, un-til Harwin gave him a *thwack* alongside his ear. The meal was plain but filling; mutton and mushrooms, brown bread, pease pudding, and baked apples with yellow cheese. When the food had been cleared and the servants sent away, Greenbeard lowered his voice to ask if her ladyship had word of the lightning lord.

"Word?" She smiled. "They were here not a fortnight past. Them and a dozen more, driving sheep. I could scarcely believe my eyes. Thoros gave me three as thanks. You've eaten one tonight."

"Thoros herding sheep?" Anguy laughed aloud.

"I grant you it was an odd sight, but Thoros claimed that as a priest he knew how to tend a flock."

"Aye, and shear them too," chuckled Lem Lemoncloak.

"Someone could make a rare fine song of that." Tom plucked a string on his woodharp.

Lady Smallwood gave him a withering look. "Someone who doesn't rhyme *carry on* with *Dondarrion*, perhaps. Or play 'Oh, Lay My Sweet Lass Down in the Grass' to every milkmaid in the shire and leave two of them with big bellies."

"It was 'Let Me Drink Your Beauty,' " said Tom defensively, "and milkmaids are always glad to hear it. As was a certain highborn lady I do recall. I play to please."

Her nostrils flared. "The riverlands are full of maids you've pleased, all drinking tansy tea. You'd think a man as old as you would know to spill his seed on their bellies. Men will be calling you Tom Sevensons before much longer."

"As it happens," said Tom, "I passed seven many years ago. And fine boys they are too, with voices sweet as nightingales." Plainly he did not care for the subject.

"Did his lordship say where he was bound, milady?" asked Harwin.

"Lord Beric never shares his plans, but there's hunger down near Stoney Sept and the Threepenny Wood. I should look for him there." She took a sip of wine. "You'd best know, I've had less pleasant callers as well. A pack of wolves came howling around my gates, thinking I might have Jaime Lannister in here."

Tom stopped his plucking. "Then it's true, the Kingslayer is loose again?"

Lady Smallwood gave him a scornful look. "I hardly think they'd be hunting him if he was chained up under Riverrun."

"What did m'lady tell them?" asked Jack-Be-Lucky.

"Why, that I had Ser Jaime naked in my bed, but I'd left him much too exhausted to come down. One of them had the effrontery to call me a liar, so we saw them off with a few quarrels. I believe they made for Blackbottom Bend."

Arya squirmed restlessly in her seat. "What northmen was it, who came looking after the Kingslayer?"

Lady Smallwood seemed surprised that she'd spoken.

"They did not give their names, child, but they wore black, with the badge of a white sun on the breast."

A white sun on black was the sigil of Lord Karstark, Arya thought. *Those were Robb's men.* She wondered if they were still close. If she could give the outlaws the slip and find them, maybe they would take her to her mother at Riverrun . . .

"Did they say how Lannister came to escape?" Lem asked.

"They did," said Lady Smallwood. "Not that I believe a word of it. They claimed that Lady Catelyn set him free."

That startled Tom so badly he snapped a string. "Go on with you," he said. "That's madness."

It's not true, thought Arya. *It couldn't be true.*

"I thought the same," said Lady Smallwood.

That was when Harwin remembered Arya. "Such talk is not for your ears, milady."

"No, I want to hear."

The outlaws were adamant. "Go on with you, skinny squirrel," said Greenbeard. "Be a good little lady and go play in the yard while we talk, now."

Arya stalked away angry, and would have slammed the door if it hadn't been so heavy. Darkness had settled over Acorn Hall. A few torches burned along the walls, but that was all. The gates of the little castle were closed and barred. She had promised Harwin that she would not try and run away again, she knew, but that was before they started telling lies about her mother.

"Arya?" Gendry had followed her out. "Lady Smallwood said there's a smithy. Want to have a look?"

"If you want." She had nothing else to do.

"This Thoros," Gendry said as they walked past the kennels, "is he the same Thoros who lived in the castle at King's Landing? A red priest, fat, with a shaved head?"

"I think so." Arya had never spoken to Thoros at King's Landing that she could recall, but she knew who he was. He and Jalabhar Xho had been the most colorful figures at Robert's court, and Thoros was a great friend of the king as well.

"He won't remember me, but he used to come to our forge." The Smallwood forge had not been used in some time, though the smith had hung his tools neatly on the wall. Gendry lit a candle and set it on the anvil while he took down a pair of tongs. "My master always scolded him about his flaming swords. It was no way to treat good steel, he'd say, but this Thoros never used good steel. He'd just dip some cheap sword in wildfire and set it alight. It was only an alchemist's trick, my master said, but it scared the horses and some of the greener knights."

She screwed up her face, trying to remember if her father had ever talked about Thoros. "He isn't very priestly, is he?"

"No," Gendry admitted. "Master Mott said Thoros could outdrink even King Robert. They were pease in a pod, he told me, both gluttons and sots."

"You shouldn't call the king a sot." Maybe King Robert had drunk a lot, but he'd been her father's friend.

"I was talking about Thoros." Gendry reached out with the tongs as if to pinch her face, but Arya swatted them away. "He liked feasts and tourneys, that was why King Robert was so fond of him. And this Thoros was brave. When the walls of Pyke crashed down, he was the first through the breach. He fought with one of his flaming swords, setting ironmen afire with every slash."

"I wish I had a flaming sword." Arya could think of lots of people she'd like to set on fire.

"It's only a trick, I told you. The wildfire ruins the steel. My master sold Thoros a new sword after every tourney. Every time they would have a fight about the price." Gendry hung the tongs back up and took down the heavy hammer. "Master Mott said it was time I made my first longsword. He gave me a sweet piece of steel, and I knew just how I wanted to shape the blade. Only Yoren came, and took me away for the Night's Watch."

"You can still make swords if you want," said Arya. "You can make them for my brother Robb when we get to Riverrun."

"Riverrun." Gendry put the hammer down and looked at her. "You look different now. Like a proper little girl."

"I look like an oak tree, with all these stupid acorns."

"Nice, though. A nice oak tree." He stepped closer, and *sniffed* at her. "You even smell nice for a change."

"You don't. You *stink*." Arya shoved him back against the anvil and made to run, but Gendry caught her arm. She stuck a foot between his legs and tripped him, but he yanked her down with him, and they rolled across the floor of the smithy. He was very strong, but she was quicker. Every time he tried to hold her still she wriggled free and punched him. Gendry only laughed at the blows, which made her mad. He finally caught both her wrists in one hand and started to tickle her with the other, so Arya slammed her knee between his legs, and wrenched free. Both of them were covered in dirt, and one sleeve was torn on her stupid acorn dress. "I bet I don't look so nice *now*," she shouted.

Tom was singing when they returned to the hall.

> *My featherbed is deep and soft,*
> *and there I'll lay you down,*
> *I'll dress you all in yellow silk,*
> *and on your head a crown.*
> *For you shall be my lady love,*
> *and I shall be your lord.*
> *I'll always keep you warm and safe,*
> *and guard you with my sword.*

Harwin took one look at them and burst out laughing, and Anguy smiled one of his stupid freckly smiles and said, "Are we *certain* this one is a highborn lady?" But Lem Lemoncloak gave Gendry a clout alongside the head. "You want to fight, fight with me! She's a girl, and half your age! You keep your hands off o' her, you hear me?"

"I started it," said Arya. "Gendry was just talking."

"Leave the boy, Lem," said Harwin. "Arya did start it, I have no doubt. She was much the same at Winterfell."

Tom winked at her as he sang:

> *And how she smiled and how she laughed,*
> *the maiden of the tree.*
> *She spun away and said to him,*
> *no featherbed for me.*
> *I'll wear a gown of golden leaves,*
> *and bind my hair with grass,*
> *But you can be my forest love,*
> *and me your forest lass.*

"I have no gowns of leaves," said Lady Smallwood with a small fond smile, "but Carellen left some other dresses that might serve. Come, child, let us go upstairs and see what we can find."

It was even worse than before; Lady Smallwood insisted that Arya take *another* bath, and cut and comb her hair besides; the dress she put her in this time was sort of lilac-colored, and decorated with little baby pearls. The only good thing about it was that it was so delicate that no one could expect her to ride in it. So the next morning as they broke their fast, Lady Smallwood gave her breeches, belt, and tunic to wear, and a brown doeskin jerkin dotted with iron studs. "They were my son's things," she said. "He died when he was seven."

"I'm sorry, my lady." Arya suddenly felt bad for her, and ashamed. "I'm sorry I tore the acorn dress too. It was pretty."

"Yes, child. And so are you. Be brave."

DAENERYS

In the center of the Plaza of Pride stood a red brick fountain whose waters smelled of brimstone, and in the center of the fountain a monstrous harpy made of hammered bronze. Twenty feet tall she reared. She had a woman's face, with gilded hair, ivory eyes, and pointed ivory teeth. Water gushed yellow from her heavy breasts. But in place of arms she had the wings of a bat or a dragon, her legs were the legs of an eagle, and behind she wore a scorpion's curled and venomous tail.

The harpy of Ghis, Dany thought. Old Ghis had fallen five thousand years ago, if she remembered true; its legions shattered by the might of young Valyria, its brick walls pulled down, its streets and buildings turned to ash and cinder by dragonflame, its very fields sown with salt, sulfur, and skulls. The gods of Ghis were dead, and so too its people; these Astapori were mongrels, Ser Jorah said. Even the Ghiscari tongue was largely forgotten; the slave cities spoke the High Valyrian of their conquerors, or what they had made of it.

Yet the symbol of the Old Empire still endured here,

though this bronze monster had a heavy chain dangling from her talons, an open manacle at either end. *The harpy of Ghis had a thunderbolt in her claws. This is the harpy of Astapor.*

"Tell the Westerosi whore to lower her eyes," the slaver Kraznys mo Nakloz complained to the slave girl who spoke for him. "I deal in meat, not metal. The bronze is not for sale. Tell her to look at the soldiers. Even the dim purple eyes of a sunset savage can see how magnificent my creatures are, surely."

Kraznys's High Valyrian was twisted and thickened by the characteristic growl of Ghis, and flavored here and there with words of slaver argot. Dany understood him well enough, but she smiled and looked blankly at the slave girl, as if wondering what he might have said.

"The Good Master Kraznys asks, are they not magnificent?" The girl spoke the Common Tongue well, for one who had never been to Westeros. No older than ten, she had the round flat face, dusky skin, and golden eyes of Naath. *The Peaceful People*, her folk were called. All agreed that they made the best slaves.

"They might be adequate to my needs," Dany answered. It had been Ser Jorah's suggestion that she speak only Dothraki and the Common Tongue while in Astapor. *My bear is more clever than he looks.* "Tell me of their training."

"The Westerosi woman is pleased with them, but speaks no praise, to keep the price down," the translator told her master. "She wishes to know how they were trained."

Kraznys mo Nakloz bobbed his head. He smelled as if he'd bathed in raspberries, this slaver, and his jutting red-black beard glistened with oil. *He has larger breasts than I do*, Dany reflected. She could see them through the thin sea-green silk of the gold-fringed *tokar* he wound about his body and over one shoulder. His left hand held the *tokar* in place as he walked, while his right clasped a short leather whip. "Are all Westerosi pigs so ignorant?" he complained. "All the world knows that the Unsullied are masters of spear and shield and shortsword." He gave Dany a broad smile. "Tell her what she would know, slave, and be quick about it. The day is hot."

That much at least is no lie. A matched pair of slave girls stood behind them, holding a striped silk awning over their heads, but even in the shade Dany felt light-headed, and Kraznys was perspiring freely. The Plaza of Pride had been baking in the sun since dawn. Even through the thickness of her sandals, she could feel the warmth of the red bricks underfoot. Waves of heat rose off them shimmering to make the stepped pyramids of Astapor around the plaza seem half a dream.

If the Unsullied felt the heat, however, they gave no hint of it. *They could be made of brick themselves, the way they stand there.* A thousand had been marched out of their barracks for her inspection; drawn up in ten ranks of one hundred before the fountain and its great bronze harpy, they stood stiffly at attention, their stony eyes fixed straight ahead. They wore nought but white linen clouts knotted about their loins, and conical bronze helms topped with a sharpened spike a foot tall. Kraznys had commanded them to lay down their spears and shields, and doff their swordbelts and quilted tunics, so the Queen of Westeros might better inspect the lean hardness of their bodies.

"They are chosen young, for size and speed and strength," the slave told her. "They begin their training at five. Every day they train from dawn to dusk, until they have mastered the shortsword, the shield, and the three spears. The training is most rigorous, Your Grace. Only one boy in three survives it. This is well known. Among the Unsullied it is said that on the day they win their spiked cap, the worst is done with, for no duty that will ever fall to them could be as hard as their training."

Kraznys mo Nakloz supposedly spoke no word of the Common Tongue, but he bobbed his head as he listened, and from time to time gave the slave girl a poke with the end of his lash. "Tell her that these have been standing here for a day and a night, with no food nor water. Tell her that they will stand until they drop if I should command it, and when nine hundred and ninety-nine have collapsed to die upon the bricks, the last will stand there still, and never move until his own death claims him. Such is their courage. Tell her that."

"I call that madness, not courage," said Arstan Whitebeard, when the solemn little scribe was done. He tapped the end of his hardwood staff against the bricks, *tap tap*, as if to tell his displeasure. The old man had not wanted to sail to Astapor; nor did he favor buying this slave army. A queen should hear all sides before reaching a decision. That was why Dany had brought him with her to the Plaza of Pride, not to keep her safe. Her bloodriders would do that well enough. Ser Jorah Mormont she had left aboard *Balerion* to guard her people and her dragons. Much against her inclination, she had locked the dragons belowdecks. It was too dangerous to let them fly freely over the city; the world was all too full of men who would gladly kill them for no better reason than to name themselves *dragonslayer*.

"What did the smelly old man say?" the slaver demanded of his translator. When she told him, he smiled and said, "Inform the savages that we call this *obedience*. Others may be stronger or quicker or larger than the Unsullied. Some few may even equal their skill with sword and spear and shield. But nowhere between the seas will you ever find any more obedient."

"Sheep are obedient," said Arstan when the words had been translated. He had some Valyrian as well, though not so much as Dany, but like her he was feigning ignorance.

Kraznys mo Nakloz showed his big white teeth when that was rendered back to him. "A word from me and these sheep would spill his stinking old bowels on the bricks," he said, "but do not say that. Tell them that these creatures are more dogs than sheep. Do they eat dogs or horse in these Seven Kingdoms?"

"They prefer pigs and cows, your worship."

"Beef. Pfag. Food for unwashed savages."

Ignoring them all, Dany walked slowly down the line of slave soldiers. The girls followed close behind with the silk awning, to keep her in the shade, but the thousand men before her enjoyed no such protection. More than half had the copper skins and almond eyes of Dothraki and Lhazerene, but she saw men of the Free Cities in the ranks as well, along with pale Qartheen, ebon-faced Summer Islanders, and others whose origins she could not guess. And some had skins of the same amber hue as Kraznys mo Nakloz, and the bristly red-black hair that marked the ancient folk of Ghis, who named themselves the harpy's sons. *They sell even their own kind.* It should not have surprised her. The Dothraki did the same, when *khalasar* met *khalasar* in the sea of grass.

Some of the soldiers were tall and some were short. They ranged in age from fourteen to twenty, she judged. Their cheeks were smooth, and their eyes all the same, be they black or brown or blue or grey or amber. *They are like one man*, Dany thought, until she remembered that they were no men at all. The Unsullied were eunuchs, every one of them. "Why do you cut them?" she asked Kraznys through the slave girl. "Whole men are stronger than eunuchs, I have always heard."

"A eunuch who is cut young will never have the brute strength of one of your Westerosi knights, this is true," said Kraznys mo Nakloz when the question was put to him. "A bull is strong as well, but bulls die every day in the fighting pits. A girl of nine killed one not three days past in Jothiel's Pit. The Unsullied have something better than strength, tell her. They have discipline. We fight in the fashion of the Old Empire, yes. They are the lockstep legions of Old Ghis come again, absolutely obedient, absolutely loyal, and utterly without fear."

Dany listened patiently to the translation.

"Even the bravest men fear death and maiming," Arstan said when the girl was done.

Kraznys smiled again when he heard that. "Tell the old man that he smells of piss, and needs a stick to hold him up."

"Truly, your worship?"

He poked her with his lash. "No, not truly, are you a girl or a goat, to ask such folly? Say that Unsullied are not men. Say that death means nothing to them, and maiming less than nothing." He stopped before a thickset man who had the look of Lhazar about him and brought his whip up sharply, laying a line of blood across one copper cheek. The eunuch blinked, and stood there, bleeding. "Would you like another?" asked Kraznys.

"If it please your worship."

It was hard to pretend not to understand. Dany laid a hand on Kraznys's arm before he could raise the whip again. "Tell the Good Master that I see how strong his Unsullied are, and how bravely they suffer pain."

Kraznys chuckled when he heard her words in Valyrian. "Tell this ignorant whore of a westerner that courage has nothing to do with it."

"The Good Master says that was not courage, Your Grace."

"Tell her to open those slut's eyes of hers."

"He begs you attend this carefully, Your Grace."

Kraznys moved to the next eunuch in line, a towering youth with the blue eyes and flaxen hair of Lys. "Your sword," he said. The eunuch knelt, unsheathed the blade, and offered it up hilt first. It was a short-sword, made more for stabbing than for slashing, but the edge looked razor-sharp. "Stand," Kraznys commanded.

"Your worship." The eunuch stood, and Kraznys mo Nakloz slid the sword slowly up his torso, leaving a thin red line across his belly and between his ribs. Then he jabbed the swordpoint in beneath a wide pink nipple and began to work it back and forth.

"What is he doing?" Dany demanded of the girl, as the blood ran down the man's chest.

"Tell the cow to stop her bleating," said Kraznys, without waiting for the translation. "This will do him no great harm. Men have no need of nipples, eunuchs even less so." The nipple hung by a thread of skin. He slashed, and sent it tumbling to the bricks, leaving behind a round red eye copiously weeping blood. The eunuch did not move, until Kraznys offered him back his sword, hilt first. "Here, I'm done with you."

"This one is pleased to have served you."

Kraznys turned back to Dany. "They feel no pain, you see."

"How can that be?" she demanded through the scribe.

"*The wine of courage,*" was the answer he gave her. "It is no true wine at all, but made from deadly nightshade, bloodfly larva, black lotus root, and many secret things. They drink it with every meal from the day they are cut, and with each passing year feel less and less. It makes them fearless in battle. Nor can they be tortured. Tell the savage her secrets are safe with the Unsullied. She may set them to guard her councils and even her bedchamber, and never a worry as to what they might overhear.

"In Yunkai and Meereen, eunuchs are often made by removing a boy's testicles, but leaving the penis. Such a creature is infertile, yet often still capable of erection. Only trouble can come of this. We remove the penis as well, leaving nothing. The Unsullied are the purest creatures on the earth." He gave Dany and Arstan another of his broad white smiles. "I have heard that in the Sunset Kingdoms men take solemn vows to keep chaste and father no children, but live only for their duty. Is it not so?"

"It is," Arstan said, when the question was put. "There are many such orders. The maesters of the Citadel, the septons and septas who serve the Seven, the silent sisters of the dead, the Kingsguard and the Night's Watch . . ."

"Poor things," growled the slaver, after the translation. "Men were not made to live thus. Their days are a torment of temptation, any fool must see, and no doubt most succumb to their baser selves. Not so our Unsullied. They are wed to their swords in a way that your Sworn Brothers cannot hope to match. No woman can ever tempt them, nor any man."

His girl conveyed the essence of his speech, more politely. "There are other ways to tempt men, besides the flesh," Arstan Whitebeard objected, when she was done.

"Men, yes, but not Unsullied. Plunder interests them no more than rape. They own nothing but their weapons. We do not even permit them names."

"No names?" Dany frowned at the little scribe. "Can that be what the Good Master said? They have no names?"

"It is so, Your Grace."

Kraznys stopped in front of a Ghiscari who might have been his taller fitter brother, and flicked his lash at a small bronze disk on the swordbelt at his feet. "There is his name. Ask the whore of Westeros whether she can read Ghiscari glyphs." When Dany admitted that she could not, the slaver turned to the Unsullied. "What is your name?" he demanded.

"This one's name is Red Flea, your worship."

The girl repeated their exchange in the Common Tongue.

"And yesterday, what was it?"

"Black Rat, your worship."

"The day before?"

"Brown Flea, your worship."

"Before that?"

"This one does not recall, your worship. Blue Toad, perhaps. Or Blue Worm."

"Tell her all their names are such," Kraznys commanded the girl. "It reminds them that by themselves they are vermin. The name disks are thrown in an empty cask at duty's end, and each dawn plucked up again at random."

"More madness," said Arstan, when he heard. "How can any man possibly remember a new name every day?"

"Those who cannot are culled in training, along with those who cannot run all day in full pack, scale a mountain in the black of night, walk across a bed of coals, or slay an infant."

Dany's mouth surely twisted at that. *Did he see, or is he blind as well as cruel?* She turned away quickly, trying to keep her face a mask until she heard the translation. Only then did she allow herself to say, "Whose infants do they slay?"

"To win his spiked cap, an Unsullied must go to the slave marts with a silver mark, find some wailing newborn, and kill it before its mother's eyes. In this way, we make certain that there is no weakness left in them."

She was feeling faint. *The heat,* she tried to tell herself. "You take a babe from its mother's arms, kill it as she watches, and pay for her pain with a silver coin?"

When the translation was made for him, Kraznys mo Nakloz laughed aloud. "What a soft mewling fool this one is. Tell the whore of Westeros that the mark is for the child's owner, not the mother. The Unsullied are not permitted to steal." He tapped his whip against his leg. "Tell her that few ever fail that test. The dogs are harder for them, it must be said. We give each boy a puppy on the day that he is cut. At the end of the first year, he is required to strangle it. Any who cannot are killed, and fed to the surviving dogs. It makes for a good strong lesson, we find."

Arstan Whitebeard tapped the end of his staff on the bricks as he listened to that. *Tap tap tap.* Slow and steady. *Tap tap tap.* Dany saw him turn his eyes away, as if he could not bear to look at Kraznys any longer.

"The Good Master has said that these eunuchs cannot be tempted with coin or flesh," Dany told the girl, "but if some enemy of mine should offer them *freedom* for betraying me . . ."

"They would kill him out of hand and bring her his head, tell her that," the slaver answered. "Other slaves may steal and hoard up silver in hopes of buying freedom, but an Unsullied would not take it if the little mare offered it as a gift. They have no life outside their duty. They are *soldiers*, and that is all."

"It is soldiers I need," Dany admitted.

"Tell her it is well she came to Astapor, then. Ask her how large an army she wishes to buy."

"How many Unsullied do you have to sell?"

"Eight thousand fully trained and available at present. We sell them only by the unit, she should know. By the thousand or the century. Once we sold by the ten, as household guards, but that proved unsound. Ten is too few. They mingle with other slaves, even freemen, and forget who and what they are." Kraznys waited for that to be rendered in the Common Tongue, and then continued. "This beggar queen must understand, such wonders do not come cheaply. In Yunkai and Meereen, slave swordsmen can be had for less than the price of their swords, but Unsullied are the finest foot in all the world, and each represents many years of training. Tell her they are like Valyrian steel, folded over and over and hammered for years on end, until they are stronger and more resilient than any metal on earth."

"I know of Valyrian steel," said Dany. "Ask the Good Master if the Unsullied have their own officers."

"You must set your own officers over them. We train them to obey, not to think. If it is wits she wants, let her buy scribes."

"And their gear?"

"Sword, shield, spear, sandals, and quilted tunic are included," said Kraznys. "And the spiked caps, to be sure. They will wear such armor as you wish, but you must provide it."

Dany could think of no other questions. She looked at Arstan. "You have lived long in the world, Whitebeard. Now that you have seen them, what do you say?"

"I say *no*, Your Grace," the old man answered at once.

"Why?" she asked. "Speak freely." Dany thought she

knew what he would say, but she wanted the slave girl to hear, so Kraznys mo Nakloz might hear later.

"My queen," said Arstan, "there have been no slaves in the Seven Kingdoms for thousands of years. The old gods and the new alike hold slavery to be an abomination. Evil. If you should land in Westeros at the head of a slave army, many good men will oppose you for no other reason than that. You will do great harm to your cause, and to the honor of your House."

"Yet I must have some army," Dany said. "The boy Joffrey will not give me the Iron Throne for asking politely."

"When the day comes that you raise your banners, half of Westeros will be with you," Whitebeard promised. "Your brother Rhaegar is still remembered, with great love."

"And my father?" Dany said.

The old man hesitated before saying, "King Aerys is also remembered. He gave the realm many years of peace. Your Grace, you have no need of slaves. Magister Illyrio can keep you safe while your dragons grow, and send secret envoys across the narrow sea on your behalf, to sound out the high lords for your cause."

"Those same high lords who abandoned my father to the Kingslayer and bent the knee to Robert the Usurper?"

"Even those who bent their knees may yearn in their hearts for the return of the dragons."

"*May*," said Dany. That was such a slippery word, *may*. In any language. She turned back to Kraznys mo Nakloz and his slave girl. "I must consider carefully."

The slaver shrugged. "Tell her to consider quickly. There are many other buyers. Only three days past I showed these same Unsullied to a corsair king who hopes to buy them all."

"The corsair wanted only a hundred, your worship," Dany heard the slave girl say.

He poked her with the end of the whip. "Consairs are all liars. He'll buy them all. Tell her that, girl."

Dany knew she would take more than a hundred, if she took any at all. "Remind your Good Master of who I am. Remind him that I am Daenerys Stormborn, Mother of Dragons, the Unburnt, trueborn queen of the Seven

Kingdoms of Westeros. My blood is the blood of Aegon the Conqueror, and of old Valyria before him."

Yet her words did not move the plump perfumed slaver, even when rendered in his own ugly tongue. "Old Ghis ruled an empire when the Valyrians were still fucking sheep," he growled at the poor little scribe, "and we are the sons of the harpy." He gave a shrug. "My tongue is wasted wagging at women. East or west, it makes no matter, they cannot decide until they have been pampered and flattered and stuffed with sweetmeats. Well, if this is my fate, so be it. Tell the whore that if she requires a guide to our sweet city, Kraznys mo Nakloz will gladly serve her . . . and service her as well, if she is more woman than she looks."

"Good Master Kraznys would be most pleased to show you Astapor while you ponder, Your Grace," the translator said.

"I will feed her jellied dog brains, and a fine rich stew of red octopus and unborn puppy." He wiped his lips.

"Many delicious dishes can be had here, he says."

"Tell her how pretty the pyramids are at night," the slaver growled. "Tell her I will lick honey off her breasts, or allow her to lick honey off mine if she prefers."

"Astapor is most beautiful at dusk, Your Grace," said the slave girl. "The Good Masters light silk lanterns on every terrace, so all the pyramids glow with colored lights. Pleasure barges ply the Worm, playing soft music and calling at the little islands for food and wine and other delights."

"Ask her if she wishes to view our fighting pits," Kraznys added. "Douquor's Pit has a fine folly scheduled for the evening. A bear and three small boys. One boy will be rolled in honey, one in blood, and one in rotting fish, and she may wager on which the bear will eat first."

Tap tap tap, Dany heard. Arstan Whitebeard's face was still, but his staff beat out his rage. *Tap tap tap*. She made herself smile. "I have my own bear on *Balerion*," she told the translator, "and he may well eat me if I do not return to him."

"See," said Kraznys when her words were translated. "It is not the woman who decides, it is this man she runs to. As ever!"

"Thank the Good Master for his patient kindness,"

Dany said, "and tell him that I will think on all I learned here." She gave her arm to Arstan Whitebeard, to lead her back across the plaza to her litter. Aggo and Jhogo fell in to either side of them, walking with the bowlegged swagger all the horselords affected when forced to dismount and stride the earth like common mortals.

Dany climbed into her litter frowning, and beckoned Arstan to climb in beside her. A man as old as him should not be walking in such heat. She did not close the curtains as they got under way. With the sun beating down so fiercely on this city of red brick, every stray breeze was to be cherished, even if it did come with a swirl of fine red dust. *Besides, I need to see.*

Astapor was a queer city, even to the eyes of one who had walked within the House of Dust and bathed in the Womb of the World beneath the Mother of Mountains. All the streets were made of the same red brick that had paved the plaza. So too were the stepped pyramids, the deep-dug fighting pits with their rings of descending seats, the sulfurous fountains and gloomy wine caves, and the ancient walls that encircled them. *So many bricks*, she thought, *and so old and crumbling.* Their fine red dust was everywhere, dancing down the gutters at each gust of wind. Small wonder so many Astapori women veiled their faces; the brick dust stung the eyes worse than sand.

"Make way!" Jhogo shouted as he rode before her litter. "Make way for the Mother of Dragons!" But when he uncoiled the great silver-handled whip that Dany had given him, and made to crack it in the air, she leaned out and told him nay. "Not in this place, blood of my blood," she said, in his own tongue. "These bricks have heard too much of the sound of whips."

The streets had been largely deserted when they had set out from the port that morning, and scarcely seemed more crowded now. An elephant lumbered past with a lattice-work litter on its back. A naked boy with peeling skin sat in a dry brick gutter, picking his nose and staring sullenly at some ants in the street. He lifted his head at the sound of hooves, and gaped as a column of mounted guards trotted by in a cloud of red dust and brittle laughter. The copper disks sewn to their cloaks of yellow silk glittered like so many suns, but their tunics were embroidered linen, and below the waist they wore sandals and pleated linen skirts. Bareheaded, each man had teased and oiled and twisted his stiff red-black hair into some fantastic shape, horns and wings and blades and even grasping hands, so they looked like some troupe of demons escaped from the seventh hell. The naked boy watched them for a bit, along with Dany, but soon enough they were gone, and he went back to his ants, and a knuckle up his nose.

An old city, this, she reflected, *but not so populous as it was in its glory, nor near so crowded as Qarth or Pentos or Lys.*

Her litter came to a sudden halt at the cross street, to allow a coffle of slaves to shuffle across her path, urged along by the crack of an overseer's lash. These were no Unsullied, Dany noted, but a more common sort of men, with pale brown skins and black hair. There were women among them, but no children. All were naked. Two Astapori rode behind them on white asses, a man in a red silk *tokar* and a veiled woman in sheer blue linen decorated with flakes of lapis lazuli. In her red-black hair she wore an ivory comb. The man laughed as he whispered to her, paying no more mind to Dany than to his slaves, nor the overseer with his twisted five-thonged lash, a squat broad Dothraki who had the harpy and chains tattooed proudly across his muscular chest.

"Bricks and blood built Astapor," Whitebeard murmured at her side, "and bricks and blood her people."

"What is that?" Dany asked him, curious.

"An old rhyme a maester taught me, when I was a boy. I never knew how true it was. The bricks of Astapor are red with the blood of the slaves who make them."

"I can well believe that," said Dany.

"Then leave this place before your heart turns to brick as well. Sail this very night, on the evening tide."

Would that I could, thought Dany. "When I leave Astapor it must be with an army, Ser Jorah says."

"Ser Jorah was a slaver himself, Your Grace," the old man reminded her. "There are sellswords in Pentos and Myr and Tyrosh you can hire. A man who kills for coin has no honor, but at least they are no slaves. Find your army there, I beg you."

"My brother visited Pentos, Myr, Braavos, near all the

Free Cities. The magisters and archons fed him wine and promises, but his soul was starved to death. A man cannot sup from the beggar's bowl all his life and stay a man. I had my taste in .Qarth, that was enough. I will not come to Pentos bowl in hand."

"Better to come a beggar than a slaver," Arstan said.

"There speaks one who has been neither." Dany's nostrils flared. "Do you know what it is like to be *sold*, squire? I do. My brother sold me to Khal Drogo for the promise of a golden crown. Well, Drogo crowned him in gold, though not as he had wished, and I . . . my sun-and-stars made a queen of me, but if he had been a different man, it might have been much otherwise. Do you think I have forgotten how it felt to be afraid?"

Whitebeard bowed his head. "Your Grace, I did not mean to give offense."

"Only lies offend me, never honest counsel." Dany patted Arstan's spotted hand to reassure him. "I have a dragon's temper, that's all. You must not let it frighten you."

"I shall try and remember." Whitebeard smiled.

He has a good face, and great strength to him, Dany thought. She could not understand why Ser Jorah mistrusted the old man so. *Could he be jealous that I have found another man to talk to?* Unbidden, her thoughts went back to the night on *Balerion* when the exile knight had kissed her. *He should never have done that. He is thrice my age, and of too low a birth for me, and I never gave him leave. No true knight would ever kiss a queen without her leave.* She had taken care never to be alone with Ser Jorah after that, keeping her handmaids with her aboard ship, and sometimes her bloodriders. *He wants to kiss me again, I see it in his eyes.*

What Dany wanted she could not begin to say, but Jorah's kiss had woken something in her, something that had been sleeping since Khal Drogo died. Lying abed in her narrow bunk, she found herself wondering how it would be to have a man squeezed in beside her in place of her handmaid, and the thought was more exciting than it should have been. Sometimes she would close her eyes and dream of him, but it was never Jorah Mormont she dreamed of;

her lover was always younger and more comely, though his face remained a shifting shadow.

Once, so tormented she could not sleep, Dany slid a hand down between her legs, and gasped when she felt how wet she was. Scarce daring to breathe, she moved her fingers back and forth between her lower lips, slowly so as not to wake Irri beside her, until she found one sweet spot and lingered there, touching herself lightly, timidly at first and then faster. Still, the relief she wanted seemed to recede before her, until her dragons stirred, and one screamed out across the cabin, and Irri woke and saw what she was doing.

Dany knew her face was flushed, but in the darkness Irri surely could not tell. Wordless, the handmaid put a hand on her breast, then bent to take a nipple in her mouth. Her other hand drifted down across the soft curve of belly, through the mound of fine silvery-gold hair, and went to work between Dany's thighs. It was no more than a few moments until her legs twisted and her breasts heaved and her whole body shuddered. She screamed then. Or perhaps that was Drogon. Irri never said a thing, only curled back up and went back to sleep the instant the thing was done.

The next day, it all seemed a dream. And what did Ser Jorah have to do with it, if anything? *It is Drogo I want, my sun-and-stars*, Dany reminded herself. *Not Irri, and not Ser Jorah, only Drogo*. Drogo was dead, though. She'd thought these feelings had died with him there in the red waste, but one treacherous kiss had somehow brought them back to life. *He should never have kissed me. He presumed too much, and I permitted it. It must never happen again*. She set her mouth grimly and gave her head a shake, and the bell in her braid chimed softly.

Closer to the bay, the city presented a fairer face. The great brick pyramids lined the shore, the largest four hundred feet high. All manner of trees and vines and flowers grew on their broad terraces, and the winds that swirled around them smelled green and fragrant. Another gigantic harpy stood atop the gate, this one made of baked red clay and crumbling visibly, with no more than a stub of her scorpion's tail remaining. The chain she grasped in her clay claws was old iron, rotten with rust. It was cooler down by the water, though. The lapping of the waves against the rotting pilings made a curiously soothing sound.

Aggo helped Dany down from her litter. Strong Belwas was seated on a massive piling, eating a great haunch of brown roasted meat. "Dog," he said happily when he saw Dany. "Good dog in Astapor, little queen. Eat?" He offered it with a greasy grin.

"That is kind of you, Belwas, but no." Dany had eaten dog in other places, at other times, but just now all she could think of was the Unsullied and their stupid puppies. She swept past the huge eunuch and up the plank onto the deck of *Balerion*.

Ser Jorah Mormont stood waiting for her. "Your Grace," he said, bowing his head. "The slavers have come and gone. Three of them, with a dozen scribes and as many slaves to lift and fetch. They crawled over every foot of our holds and made note of all we had." He walked her aft. "How many men do they have for sale?"

"None." Was it Mormont she was angry with, or this city with its sullen heat, its stinks and sweats and crumbling bricks? "They sell eunuchs, not men. Eunuchs made of brick, like the rest of Astapor. Shall I buy eight thousand brick eunuchs with dead eyes that never move, who kill suckling babes for the sake of a spiked hat and strangle their own dogs? They don't even have names. So don't call them *men*, ser."

"*Khaleesi*," he said, taken aback by her fury, "the Unsullied are chosen as boys, and trained—"

"I have heard all I care to of their *training*." Dany could feel tears welling in her eyes, sudden and unwanted. Her hand flashed up and cracked Ser Jorah hard across the face. It was either that, or cry.

Mormont touched the cheek she'd slapped. "If I have displeased my queen—"

"You *have*. You've displeased me greatly, ser. If you were my true knight, you would never have brought me to this vile sty." *If you were my true knight, you would never have kissed me, or looked at my breasts the way you did, or . . .*

"As Your Grace commands. I shall tell Captain Groleo to make ready to sail on the evening tide, for some sty less vile."

"No," said Dany. Groleo watched them from the fore-castle, and his crew was watching too. Whitebeard, her bloodriders, Jhiqui, every one had stopped what they were doing at the sound of the slap. "I want to sail *now*, not on the tide, I want to sail far and fast and never look back. But I can't, can I? There are eight thousand brick eunuchs for sale, and I must find some way to buy them." And with that she left him, and went below.

Behind the carved wooden door of the captain's cabin, her dragons were restless. Drogon raised his head and screamed, pale smoke venting from his nostrils, and Viserion flapped at her and tried to perch on her shoulder, as he had when he was smaller. "No," Dany said, trying to shrug him off gently. "You're too big for that now, sweet-ling." But the dragon coiled his white and gold tail around one arm and dug black claws into the fabric of her sleeve, clinging tightly. Helpless, she sank into Groleo's great leather chair, giggling.

"They have been wild while you were gone, *Khaleesi*," Irri told her. "Viserion clawed splinters from the door, do you see? And Drogon made to escape when the slaver men came to see them. When I grabbed his tail to hold him back, he turned and bit me." She showed Dany the marks of his teeth on her hand.

"Did any of them try to burn their way free?" That was the thing that frightened Dany the most.

"No, *Khaleesi*. Drogon breathed his fire, but in the empty air. The slaver men feared to come near him."

She kissed Irri's hand where Drogon had bitten it. "I'm sorry he hurt you. Dragons are not meant to be locked up in a small ship's cabin."

"Dragons are like horses in this," Irri said. "And riders, too. The horses scream below, *Khaleesi*, and kick at the wooden walls. I hear them. And Jhiqui says the old women and the little ones scream too, when you are not here. They do not like this water cart. They do not like the black salt sea."

"I know," Dany said. "I do, I know."

"My *khaleesi* is sad?"

"Yes," Dany admitted. *Sad and lost.*

"Should I pleasure the *khaleesi*?"

Dany stepped away from her. "No. Irri, you do not need

to do that. What happened that night, when you woke . . . you're no bed slave, I freed you, remember? You . . ."

"I am handmaid to the Mother of Dragons," the girl said. "It is great honor to please my *khaleesi*."

"I don't want that," she insisted. "I don't." She turned away sharply. "Leave me now. I want to be alone. To think."

Dusk had begun to settle over the waters of Slaver's Bay before Dany returned to the deck. She stood by the rail and looked out over Astapor. *From here it looks almost beautiful*, she thought. The stars were coming out above, and the silk lanterns below, just as Kraznys's translator had promised. The brick pyramids were all glimmery with light. *But it is dark below, in the streets and plazas and fighting pits. And it is darkest of all in the barracks, where some little boy is feeding scraps to the puppy they gave him when they took away his manhood.*

There was a soft step behind her. "*Khaleesi*." His voice. "Might I speak frankly?"

Dany did not turn. She could not bear to look at him just now. If she did, she might well slap him again. Or cry. Or kiss him. And never know which was right and which was wrong and which was madness. "Say what you will, ser."

"When Aegon the Dragon stepped ashore in Westeros, the kings of Vale and Rock and Reach did not rush to hand him their crowns. If you mean to sit his Iron Throne, you must win it as he did, with steel and dragonfire. And that will mean blood on your hands before the thing is done."

Blood and fire, thought Dany. The words of House Targaryen. She had known them all her life. "The blood of my enemies I will shed gladly. The blood of innocents is another matter. Eight thousand Unsullied they would offer me. Eight thousand dead babes. Eight thousand strangled dogs."

"Your Grace," said Jorah Mormont, "I saw King's Landing after the Sack. Babes were butchered that day as well, and old men, and children at play. More women were raped than you can count. There is a savage beast in every man, and when you hand that man a sword or spear and send him forth to war, the beast stirs. The scent of blood is all it takes to wake him. Yet I have never heard of these Unsullied raping, nor putting a city to the sword, nor even plundering, save at the express command of those who lead them. Brick they may be, as you say, but if you buy them henceforth the only dogs they'll kill are those *you* want dead. And you do have some dogs you want dead, as I recall."

The Usurper's dogs. "Yes." Dany gazed off at the soft colored lights and let the cool salt breeze caress her. "You speak of sacking cities. Answer me this, ser—why have the Dothraki never sacked *this* city?" She pointed. "Look at the walls. You can see where they've begun to crumble. There, and there. Do you see any guards on those towers? I don't. Are they hiding, ser? I saw these sons of the harpy today, all their proud highborn warriors. They dressed in linen skirts, and the fiercest thing about them was their hair. Even a modest *khalasar* could crack this Astapor like a nut and spill out the rotted meat inside. So tell me, why is that ugly harpy not sitting beside the godsway in Vaes Dothrak among the other stolen gods?"

"You have a dragon's eye, *Khaleesi*, that's plain to see."

"I wanted an answer, not a compliment."

"There are two reasons. Astapor's brave defenders are so much chaff, it's true. Old names and fat purses who dress up as Ghiscari scourges to pretend they still rule a vast empire. Every one is a high officer. On feastdays they fight mock wars in the pits to demonstrate what brilliant commanders they are, but it's the eunuchs who do the dying. All the same, any enemy wanting to sack Astapor would have to know that they'd be facing Unsullied. The slavers would turn out the whole garrison in the city's defense. The Dothraki have not ridden against Unsullied since they left their braids at the gates of Qohor."

"And the second reason?" Dany asked.

"Who would attack Astapor?" Ser Jorah asked. "Meereen and Yunkai are rivals but not enemies, the Doom destroyed Valyria, the folk of the eastern hinterlands are all Ghiscari, and beyond the hills lies Lhazar. The Lamb Men, as your Dothraki call them, a notably unwarlike people."

"Yes," she agreed, "but *north* of the slave cities is the Dothraki sea, and two dozen mighty *khals* who like nothing more than sacking cities and carrying off their people into slavery."

"Carrying them off *where?* What good are slaves once you've killed the slavers? Valyria is no more, Qarth lies beyond the red waste, and the Nine Free Cities are thousands of leagues to the west. And you may be sure the sons of the harpy give lavishly to every passing *khal*, just as the magisters do in Pentos and Norvos and Myr. They know that if they feast the horselords and give them gifts, they will soon ride on. It's cheaper than fighting, and a deal more certain."

Cheaper than fighting, Dany thought. *Yes, it might be.* If only it could be that easy for her. How pleasant it would be to sail to King's Landing with her dragons, and pay the boy Joffrey a chest of gold to make him go away.

"*Khaleesi!*" Ser Jorah prompted, when she had been silent for a long time. He touched her elbow lightly.

Dany shrugged him off. "Viserys would have bought as many Unsullied as he had the coin for. But you once said I was like Rhaegar . . ."

"I remember, Daenerys."

"*Your Grace*," she corrected. "Prince Rhaegar led free men into battle, not slaves. Whitebeard said he dubbed his squires himself, and made many other knights as well."

"There was no higher honor than to receive your knighthood from the Prince of Dragonstone."

"Tell me, then—when he touched a man on the shoulder with his sword, what did he say? 'Go forth and kill the weak'? Or 'Go forth and defend them'? At the Trident, those brave men Viserys spoke of who died beneath our dragon banners—did they give their lives because they *believed* in Rhaegar's cause, or because they had been bought and paid for?" Dany turned to Mormont, crossed her arms, and waited for an answer.

"My queen," the big man said slowly, "all you say is true. But Rhaegar lost on the Trident. He lost the battle, he lost the war, he lost the kingdom, and he lost his life. His blood swirled downriver with the rubies from his breastplate, and Robert the Usurper rode over his corpse to steal the Iron Throne. Rhaegar fought valiantly, Rhaegar fought nobly, Rhaegar fought honorably. And Rhaegar *died*."

BRAN

No roads ran through the twisted mountain valleys where they walked now. Between the grey stone peaks lay still blue lakes, long and deep and narrow, and the green gloom of endless piney woods. The russet and gold of autumn leaves grew less common when they left the wolfswood to climb amongst the old flint hills, and vanished by the time those hills had turned to mountains. Giant grey-green sentinels loomed above them now, and spruce and fir and soldier pines in endless profusion. The undergrowth was sparse beneath them, the forest floor carpeted in dark green needles.

When they lost their way, as happened once or twice, they need only wait for a clear cold night when the clouds did not intrude, and look up in the sky for the Ice Dragon. The blue star in the dragon's eye pointed the way north, as Osha told him once. Thinking of Osha made Bran wonder where she was. He pictured her safe in White Harbor with Rickon and Shaggydog, eating eels and fish and hot crab pie with fat Lord Manderly. Or maybe they were warming themselves at the Last Hearth before the Greatjon's fires.

But Bran's life had turned into endless chilly days on Hodor's back, riding his basket up and down the slopes of mountains.

"Up and down," Meera would sigh sometimes as they walked, "then down and up. Then up and down again. I hate these stupid mountains of yours, Prince Bran."

"Yesterday you said you loved them."

"Oh, I do. My lord father told me about mountains, but I never saw one till now. I love them more than I can say."

Bran made a face at her. "But you just said you hated them."

"Why can't it be both?" Meera reached up to pinch his nose.

"Because they're *different*," he insisted. "Like night and day, or ice and fire."

"If ice can burn," said Jojen in his solemn voice, "then love and hate can mate. Mountain or marsh, it makes no matter. The land is one."

"One," his sister agreed, "but over wrinkled."

The high glens seldom did them the courtesy of running north and south, so often they found themselves going long leagues in the wrong direction, and sometimes they were forced to double back the way they'd come. "If we took the kingsroad we could be at the Wall by now," Bran would remind the Reeds. He wanted to find the three-eyed crow, so he could learn to fly. Half a hundred times he said it if he said it once, until Meera started teasing by saying it along with him.

"If we took the kingsroad we wouldn't be so hungry either," he started saying then. Down in the hills they'd had no lack of food. Meera was a fine huntress, and even better at taking fish from streams with her three-pronged frog spear. Bran liked to watch her, admiring her quickness, the way she sent the spear lancing down and pulled it back with a silvery trout wriggling on the end of it. And they had Summer hunting for them as well. The direwolf vanished most every night as the sun went down, but he was always back again before dawn, most often with something in his jaws, a squirrel or a hare.

But here in the mountains, the streams were smaller and more icy, and the game scarcer. Meera still hunted and fished when she could, but it was harder, and some nights even Summer found no prey. Often they went to sleep with empty bellies.

But Jojen remained stubbornly determined to stay well away from roads. "Where you find roads you find travelers," he said in that way he had, "and travelers have eyes to see, and mouths to spread tales of the crippled boy, his giant, and the wolf that walks beside them." No one could get as stubborn as Jojen, so they struggled on through the wild, and every day climbed a little higher, and moved a little farther north.

Some days it rained, some days were windy, and once they were caught in a sleet storm so fierce that even Hodor bellowed in dismay. On the clear days, it often seemed as if they were the only living things in all the world. "Does no one live up here?" Meera Reed asked once, as they made their way around a granite upthrust as large as Winterfell.

"There's people," Bran told her. "The Umbers are mostly east of the kingsroad, but they graze their sheep in the high meadows in summer. There are Wulls west of the mountains along the Bay of Ice, Harclays back behind us in the hills, and Knotts and Liddles and Norreys and even some Flints up here in the high places." His father's mother's mother had been a Flint of the mountains. Old Nan once said that it was her blood in him that made Bran such a fool for climbing before his fall. She had died years and years and years before he was born, though, even before his father had been born.

"Wull?" said Meera. "Jojen, wasn't there a Wull who rode with Father during the war?"

"Theo Wull." Jojen was breathing hard from the climb. "Buckets, they used to call him."

"That's their sigil," said Bran. "Three brown buckets on a blue field, with a border of white and grey checks. Lord Wull came to Winterfell once, to do his fealty and talk with Father, and he had the buckets on his shield. He's no true lord, though. Well, he is, but they call him just *the Wull*, and there's the Knott and the Norrey and the Liddle too. At Winterfell we called them lords, but their own folk don't."

Jojen Reed stopped to catch his breath. "Do you think these mountain folk know we're here?"

"They know." Bran had seen them watching; not with his own eyes, but with Summer's sharper ones, that missed so little. "They won't bother us so long as we don't try and make off with their goats or horses."

Nor did they. Only once did they encounter any of the mountain people, when a sudden burst of freezing rain sent them looking for shelter. Summer found it for them, sniffing out a shallow cave behind the grey-green branches of a towering sentinel tree, but when Hodor ducked beneath the stony overhang, Bran saw the orange glow of fire farther back and realized they were not alone. "Come in and warm yourselves," a man's voice called out. "There's stone enough to keep the rain off all our heads."

He offered them oatcakes and blood sausage and a swallow of ale from a skin he carried, but never his name; nor did he ask theirs. Bran figured him for a Liddle. The clasp that fastened his squirrelskin cloak was gold and bronze and wrought in the shape of a pinecone, and the Liddles bore pinecones on the white half of their green-and-white shields.

"Is it far to the Wall?" Bran asked him as they waited for the rain to stop.

"Not so far as the raven flies," said the Liddle, if that was who he was. "Farther, for them as lacks wings."

Bran started, "I'd bet we'd be there if . . ."

". . . we took the kingsroad," Meera finished with him.

The Liddle took out a knife and whittled at a stick. "When there was a Stark in Winterfell, a maiden girl could walk the kingsroad in her name-day gown and still go unmolested, and travelers could find fire, bread, and salt at many an inn and holdfast. But the nights are colder now, and doors are closed. There's squids in the wolfswood, and flayed men ride the kingsroad asking after strangers."

The Reeds exchanged a look. "Flayed men?" said Jojen.

"The Bastard's boys, aye. He was dead, but now he's not. And paying good silver for wolfskins, a man hears, and maybe gold for word of certain other walking dead." He looked at Bran when he said that, and at Summer stretched out beside him. "As to that Wall," the man went on, "it's not a place that I'd be going. The Old Bear took the Watch into the haunted woods, and all that come back was his ravens, with hardly a message between them. *Dark wings, dark words*, me mother used to say, but when the birds fly silent, seems to me that's even darker." He poked at the fire with his stick. "It was different when there was a Stark in Winterfell. But the old wolf's dead and young one's gone south to play the game of thrones, and all that's left us is the ghosts."

"The wolves will come again," said Jojen solemnly.

"And how would you be knowing, boy?"

"I dreamed it."

"Some nights I dream of me mother that I buried nine years past," the man said, "but when I wake, she's not come back to us."

"There are dreams and dreams, my lord."

"Hodor," said Hodor.

They spent that night together, for the rain did not let up till well past dark, and only Summer seemed to want to leave the cave. When the fire had burned down to embers, Bran let him go. The direwolf did not feel the damp as people did, and the night was calling him. Moonlight painted the wet woods in shades of silver and turned the grey peaks white. Owls hooted through the dark and flew silently between the pines, while pale goats moved along the mountainsides. Bran closed his eyes and gave himself up to the wolf dream, to the smells and sounds of midnight.

When they woke the next morning, the fire had gone out and the Liddle was gone, but he'd left a sausage for them, and a dozen oatcakes folded up neatly in a green and white cloth. Some of the cakes had pinenuts baked in them and some had blackberries. Bran ate one of each, and still did not know which sort he liked the best. One day there would be Starks in Winterfell again, he told himself, and then he'd send for the Liddles and pay them back a hundredfold for every nut and berry.

The trail they followed was a little easier that day, and by noon the sun came breaking through the clouds. Bran sat in his basket up on Hodor's back and felt almost content. He dozed off once, lulled to sleep by the smooth swing of the big stableboy's stride and the soft humming sound he made sometimes when he walked. Meera woke him up with a light touch on his arm. "Look," she said, pointing at the sky with her frog spear, "an eagle."

Bran lifted his head and saw it, its grey wings spread and still as it floated on the wind. He followed it with his eyes as it circled higher, wondering what it would be like to soar

about the world so effortless. *Better than climbing, even.*
He tried to reach the eagle, to leave his stupid crippled
body and rise into the sky to join it, the way he joined with
Summer. *The greenseers could do it. I should be able to do
it too.* He tried and tried, until the eagle vanished in the
golden haze of the afternoon. "It's gone," he said, disappointed.

"We'll see others," said Meera. "They live up here."

"I suppose."

"Hodor," said Hodor.

"Hodor," Bran agreed.

Jojen kicked a pinecone. "Hodor likes it when you say
his name, I think."

"Hodor's not his true name," Bran explained. "It's just
some word he says. His real name is Walder, Old Nan told
me. She was his grandmother's grandmother or something." Talking about Old Nan made him sad. "Do you
think the ironmen killed her?" They hadn't seen her body
at Winterfell. He didn't remember seeing any women dead,
now that he thought back. "She never hurt no one, not
even Theon. She just told stories. Theon wouldn't hurt
someone like that. Would he?"

"Some people hurt others just because they can," said
Jojen.

"And it wasn't Theon who did the killing at Winterfell," said Meera. "Too many of the dead were ironmen."
She shifted her frog spear to her other hand. "Remember
Old Nan's stories, Bran. Remember the way she told them,
the sound of her voice. So long as you do that, part of her
will always be alive in you."

"I'll remember," he promised. They climbed without
speaking for a long time, following a crooked game trail
over the high saddle between two stony peaks. Scrawny
soldier pines clung to the slopes around them. Far ahead
Bran could see the icy glitter of a stream where it tumbled
down a mountainside. He found himself listening to Jojen's
breathing and the crunch of pine needles under Hodor's
feet. "Do you know any stories?" he asked the Reeds all of
a sudden.

Meera laughed. "Oh, a few."

"A few," her brother admitted.

"Hodor," said Hodor, humming.

"You could tell one," said Bran. "While we walked. Hodor likes stories about knights. I do, too."

"There are no knights in the Neck," said Jojen.

"Above the water," his sister corrected. "The bogs are full of dead ones, though."

"That's true," said Jojen. "Andals and ironmen, Freys and other fools, all those proud warriors who set out to conquer Greywater. Not one of them could find it. They ride into the Neck, but not back out. And sooner or later they blunder into the bogs and sink beneath the weight of all that steel and drown there in their armor."

The thought of drowned knights under the water gave Bran the shivers. He didn't object, though; he *liked* the shivers.

"There was one knight," said Meera, "in the year of the false spring. The Knight of the Laughing Tree, they called him. He might have been a crannogman, that one."

"Or not." Jojen's face was dappled with green shadows. "Prince Bran has heard that tale a hundred times, I'm sure."

"No," said Bran. "I haven't. And if I have it doesn't matter. Sometimes Old Nan would tell the same story she'd told before, but we never minded, if it was a good story. Old stories are like old friends, she used to say. You have to visit them from time to time."

"That's true." Meera walked with her shield on her back, pushing an occasional branch out of the way with her frog spear. Just when Bran began to think that she wasn't going to tell the story after all, she began, "Once there was a curious lad who lived in the Neck. He was small like all crannogmen, but brave and smart and strong as well. He grew up hunting and fishing and climbing trees, and learned all the magics of my people."

Bran was almost certain he had never heard this story. "Did he have green dreams like Jojen?"

"No," said Meera, "but he could breathe mud and run on leaves, and change earth to water and water to earth with no more than a whispered word. He could talk to trees and weave words and make castles appear and disappear."

"I wish I could," Bran said plaintively. "When does he meet the tree knight?"

Meera made a face at him. "Sooner if a certain prince would be quiet."

"I was just asking."

"The lad knew the magics of the crannogs," she continued, "but he wanted more. Our people seldom travel far from home, you know. We're a small folk, and our ways seem queer to some, so the big people do not always treat us kindly. But this lad was bolder than most, and one day when he had grown to manhood he decided he would leave the crannogs and visit the Isle of Faces."

"No one visits the Isle of Faces," objected Bran. "That's where the green men live."

"It was the green men he meant to find. So he donned a shirt sewn with bronze scales, like mine, took up a leathern shield and a three-pronged spear, like mine, and paddled a little skin boat down the Green Fork."

Bran closed his eyes to try and see the man in his little skin boat. In his head, the crannogman looked like Jojen, only older and stronger and dressed like Meera.

"He passed beneath the Twins by night so the Freys would not attack him, and when he reached the Trident he climbed from the river and put his boat on his head and began to walk. It took him many a day, but finally he reached the Gods Eye, threw his boat in the lake, and paddled out to the Isle of Faces."

"Did he meet the green men?"

"Yes," said Meera, "but that's another story, and not for me to tell. My prince asked for knights."

"Green men are good too."

"They are," she agreed, but said no more about them. "All that winter the crannogman stayed on the isle, but when the spring broke he heard the wide world calling and knew the time had come to leave. His skin boat was just where he'd left it, so he said his farewells and paddled off toward shore. He rowed and rowed, and finally saw the distant towers of a castle rising beside the lake. The towers reached ever higher as he neared shore, until he realized that this must be the greatest castle in all the world."

"Harrenhal!" Bran knew at once. "It was Harrenhal!"

Meera smiled. "Was it? Beneath its walls he saw tents of many colors, bright banners cracking in the wind, and knights in mail and plate on barded horses. He smelled roasting meats, and heard the sound of laughter and the blare of heralds' trumpets. A great tourney was about to commence, and champions from all over the land had come to contest it. The king himself was there, with his son the dragon prince. The White Swords had come, to welcome a new brother to their ranks. The storm lord was on hand, and the rose lord as well. The great lion of the rock had quarreled with the king and stayed away, but many of his bannermen and knights attended all the same. The crannogman had never seen such pageantry, and knew he might never see the like again. Part of him wanted nothing so much as to be part of it."

Bran knew that feeling well enough. When he'd been little, all he had ever dreamed of was being a knight. But that had been before he fell and lost his legs.

"The daughter of the great castle reigned as queen of love and beauty when the tourney opened. Five champions had sworn to defend her crown; her four brothers of Harrenhal, and her famous uncle, a white knight of the Kingsguard."

"Was she a fair maid?"

"She was," said Meera, hopping over a stone, "but there were others fairer still. One was the wife of the dragon prince, who'd brought a dozen lady companions to attend her. The knights all begged them for favors to tie about their lances."

"This isn't going to be one of those *love* stories, is it?" Bran asked suspiciously. "Hodor doesn't like those so much."

"Hodor," said Hodor agreeably.

"He likes the stories where the knights fight monsters."

"Sometimes the knights are the monsters, Bran. The little crannogman was walking across the field, enjoying the warm spring day and harming none, when he was set upon by three squires. They were none older than fifteen, yet even so they were bigger than him, all three. This was *their* world, as they saw it, and he had no right to be there. They snatched away his spear and knocked him to the ground, cursing him for a frogeater."

"Were they Walders?" It sounded like something Little Walder Frey might have done.

"None offered a name, but he marked their faces well so

he could revenge himself upon them later. They shoved him down every time he tried to rise, and kicked him when he curled up on the ground. But then they heard a roar. 'That's my father's man you're kicking,' howled the she-wolf."

"A wolf on four legs, or two?"

"Two," said Meera. "The she-wolf laid into the squires with a tourney sword, scattering them all. The crannog-man was bruised and bloodied, so she took him back to her lair to clean his cuts and bind them up with linen. There he met her pack brothers: the wild wolf who led them, the quiet wolf beside him, and the pup who was youngest of the four.

"That evening there was to be a feast in Harrenhal, to mark the opening of the tourney, and the she-wolf insisted that the lad attend. He was of high birth, with as much a right to a place on the bench as any other man. She was not easy to refuse, this wolf maid, so he let the young pup find him garb suitable to a king's feast, and went up to the great castle.

"Under Harren's roof he ate and drank with the wolves, and many of their sworn swords besides, barrowdown men and moose and bears and mermen. The dragon prince sang a song so sad it made the wolf maid sniffle, but when her pup brother teased her for crying she poured wine over his head. A black brother spoke, asking the knights to join the Night's Watch. The storm lord drank down the knight of skulls and kisses in a wine-cup war. The crannogman saw a maid with laughing purple eyes dance with a white sword, a red snake, and the lord of griffins, and lastly with the quiet wolf . . . but only after the wild wolf spoke to her on behalf of a brother too shy to leave his bench.

"Amidst all this merriment, the little crannogman spied the three squires who'd attacked him. One served a pitchfork knight, one a porcupine, while the last attended a knight with two towers on his surcoat, a sigil all crannog-men know well."

"The Freys," said Bran. "The Freys of the Crossing."

"Then, as now," she agreed. "The wolf maid saw them too, and pointed them out to her brothers. 'I could find you a horse, and some armor that might fit,' the pup offered. The little crannogman thanked him, but gave no answer.

His heart was torn. Crannogmen are smaller than most, but just as proud. The lad was no knight, no more than any of his people. We sit a boat more often than a horse, and our hands are made for oars, not lances. Much as he wished to have his vengeance, he feared he would only make a fool of himself and shame his people. The quiet wolf had offered the little crannogman a place in his tent that night, but before he slept he knelt on the lakeshore, looking across the water to where the Isle of Faces would be, and said a prayer to the old gods of north and Neck . . ."

"You never heard this tale from your father?" asked Jojen.

"It was Old Nan who told the stories. Meera, go on, you can't stop there."

Hodor must have felt the same. "Hodor," he said, and then, "Hodor hodor hodor hodor."

"Well," said Meera, "if you would hear the rest . . ."

"Yes. *Tell* it."

"Five days of jousting were planned," she said. "There was a great seven-sided mêlée as well, and archery and axe-throwing, a horse race and tourney of singers . . ."

"Never mind about all that." Bran squirmed impatiently in his basket on Hodor's back. "Tell about the jousting."

"As my prince commands. The daughter of the castle was the queen of love and beauty, with four brothers and an uncle to defend her, but all four sons of Harrenhal were defeated on the first day. Their conquerors reigned briefly as champions, until they were vanquished in turn. As it happened, the end of the first day saw the porcupine knight win a place among the champions, and on the morning of the second day the pitchfork knight and the knight of the two towers were victorious as well. But late on the afternoon of that second day, as the shadows grew long, a mystery knight appeared in the lists."

Bran nodded sagely. Mystery knights would oft appear at tourneys, with helms concealing their faces, and shields that were either blank or bore some strange device. Sometimes they were famous champions in disguise. The Dragonknight once won a tourney as the Knight of Tears, so he could name his sister the queen of love and beauty in place of the king's mistress. And Barristan the Bold twice donned a mystery knight's armor, the first time when he was only ten. "It was the little crannogman, I bet."

"No one knew," said Meera, "but the mystery knight was short of stature, and clad in ill-fitting armor made up of bits and pieces. The device upon his shield was a heart tree of the old gods, a white weirwood with a laughing red face."

"Maybe he came from the Isle of Faces," said Bran. "Was he green?" In Old Nan's stories, the guardians had dark green skin and leaves instead of hair. Sometimes they had antlers too, but Bran didn't see how the mystery knight could have worn a helm if he had antlers. "I bet the old gods sent him."

"Perhaps they did. The mystery knight dipped his lance before the king and rode to the end of the lists, where the five champions had their pavilions. You know the three he challenged."

"The porcupine knight, the pitchfork knight, and the knight of the twin towers." Bran had heard enough stories to know *that*. "He was the little crannogman, I told you."

"Whoever he was, the old gods gave strength to his arm. The porcupine knight fell first, then the pitchfork knight, and lastly the knight of the two towers. None were well loved, so the common folk cheered lustily for the Knight of the Laughing Tree, as the new champion soon was called. When his fallen foes sought to ransom horse and armor, the Knight of the Laughing Tree spoke in a booming voice through his helm, saying, '*Teach your squires honor, that shall be ransom enough.*' Once the defeated knights chastised their squires sharply, their horses and armor were returned. And so the little crannogman's prayer was answered . . . by the green men, or the old gods, or the children of the forest, who can say?"

It was a good story, Bran decided after thinking about it a moment or two. "Then what happened? Did the Knight of the Laughing Tree win the tourney and marry a princess?"

"No," said Meera. "That night at the great castle, the storm lord and the knight of skulls and kisses each swore they would unmask him, and the king himself urged men to challenge him, declaring that the face behind that helm was no friend of his. But the next morning, when the heralds blew their trumpets and the king took his seat, only two champions appeared. The Knight of the Laughing Tree had vanished. The king was wroth, and even sent his son the dragon prince to seek the man, but all they ever found was his painted shield, hanging abandoned in a tree. It was the dragon prince who won that tourney in the end."

"Oh." Bran thought about the tale awhile. "That was a good story. But it should have been the three bad knights who hurt him, not their squires. Then the little crannogman could have killed them all. The part about the ransoms was stupid. And the mystery knight should win the tourney, defeating every challenger, and name the wolf maid the queen of love and beauty."

"She was," said Meera, "but that's a sadder story."

"Are you certain you never heard this tale before, Bran?" asked Jojen. "Your lord father never told it to you?"

Bran shook his head. The day was growing old by then, and long shadows were creeping down the mountainsides to send black fingers through the pines. *If the little crannogman could visit the Isle of Faces, maybe I could too.* All the tales agreed that the green men had strange magic powers. Maybe they could help him walk again, even turn him into a knight. *They turned the little crannogman into a knight, even if it was only for a day,* he thought. *A day would be enough.*

DAVOS

The cell was warmer than any cell had a right to be.

It was dark, yes. Flickering orange light fell through the ancient iron bars from the torch in the sconce on the wall outside, but the back half of the cell remained drenched in gloom. It was dank as well, as might be expected on an isle such as Dragonstone, where the sea was never far. And there were rats, as many as any dungeon could expect to have and a few more besides.

But Davos could not complain of chill. The smooth stony passages beneath the great mass of Dragonstone were always warm, and Davos had often heard it said they grew warmer the farther down one went. He was well below the castle, he judged, and the wall of his cell often felt warm to his touch when he pressed a palm against it. Perhaps the old tales were true, and Dragonstone was built with the stones of hell.

He was sick when they first brought him here. The cough that had plagued him since the battle grew worse, and a fever took hold of him as well. His lips broke with blood blisters, and the warmth of the cell did not stop his shivering. *I will not linger long,* he remembered thinking. *I will die soon, here in the dark.*

Davos soon found that he was wrong about that, as about so much else. Dimly he remembered gentle hands and a firm voice, and young Maester Pylos looking down on him. He was given hot garlic broth to drink, and milk of the poppy to take away his aches and shivers. The poppy made him sleep and while he slept they leeched him to drain off the bad blood. Or so he surmised, by the leech marks on his arms when he woke. Before very long the coughing stopped, the blisters vanished, and his broth had chunks of whitefish in it, and carrots and onions as well. And one day he realized that he felt stronger than he had since *Black Betha* shattered beneath him and flung him in the river.

He had two gaolers to tend him. One was broad and squat, with thick shoulders and huge strong hands. He wore a leather brigantine dotted with iron studs, and once a day brought Davos a bowl of oaten porridge. Sometimes he sweetened it with honey or poured in a bit of milk. The other gaoler was older, stooped and sallow, with greasy unwashed hair and pebbled skin. He wore a doublet of white velvet with a ring of stars worked upon the breast in golden thread. It fit him badly, being both too short and too loose, and was soiled and torn besides. He would bring Davos plates of meat and mash, or fish stew, and once even half a lamprey pie. The lamprey was so rich he could not keep it down, but even so, it was a rare treat for a prisoner in a dungeon.

Neither sun nor moon shone in the dungeons; no windows pierced the thick stone walls. The only way to tell day from night was by his gaolers. Neither man would speak to him, though he knew they were no mutes; sometimes he heard them exchange a few brusque words as the watch was changing. They would not even tell him their names, so he gave them names of his own. The short strong one he called Porridge, the stooped sallow one Lamprey, for the pie. He marked the passage of days by the meals they brought, and by the changing of the torches in the sconce outside his cell.

A man grows lonely in the dark, and hungers for the sound of a human voice. Davos would talk to the gaolers whenever they came to his cell, whether to bring him food or change his slops pail. He knew they would be deaf to pleas for freedom or mercy; instead he asked them questions, hoping perhaps one day one might answer. "What news of the war?" he asked, and "Is the king well?" He asked after his son Devan, and the Princess Shireen, and Salladhor Saan. "What is the weather like?" he asked, and "Have the autumn storms begun yet? Do ships still sail the narrow sea?"

It made no matter what he asked; they never answered, though sometimes Porridge gave him a look, and for half a heartbeat Davos would think that he was about to speak. With Lamprey there was not even that much. *I am not a man to him*, Davos thought, *only a stone that eats and shits and speaks*. He decided after a while that he liked Porridge much the better. Porridge at least seemed to know he was alive, and there was a queer sort of kindness to the man. Davos suspected that he fed the rats; that was why there were so many. Once he thought he heard the gaoler talking to them as if they were children, but perhaps he'd only dreamed that.

They do not mean to let me die, he realized. *They are keeping me alive, for some purpose of their own*. He did not like to think what that might be. Lord Sunglass had been confined in the cells beneath Dragonstone for a time, as had Ser Hubard Rambton's sons; all of them had ended on the pyre. *I should have given myself to the sea*, Davos thought as he sat staring at the torch beyond the bars. *Or let the sail pass me by, to perish on my rock. I would sooner feed crabs than flames*.

Then one night as he was finishing his supper, Davos felt a queer flush come over him. He glanced up through the bars, and there she stood in shimmering scarlet with her great ruby at her throat, her red eyes gleaming as bright as the torch that bathed her. "Melisandre," he said, with a calm he did not feel.

"Onion Knight," she replied, just as calmly, as if the two of them had met on a stair or in the yard, and were exchanging polite greetings. "Are you well?"

"Better than I was."

"Do you lack for anything?"

"My king. My son. I lack for them." He pushed the bowl aside and stood. "Have you come to burn me?"

Her strange red eyes studied him through the bars. "This is a bad place, is it not? A dark place, and foul. The good sun does not shine here, nor the bright moon." She lifted a hand toward the torch in the wall sconce. "This is all that stands between you and the darkness, Onion Knight. This little fire, this gift of R'hllor. Shall I put it out?"

"No." He moved toward the bars. "Please." He did not think he could bear that, to be left alone in utter blackness with no one but the rats for company.

The red woman's lips curved upward in a smile. "So you have come to love the fire, it would seem."

"I need the torch." His hands opened and closed. *I will not beg her. I will not.*

"I am like this torch, Ser Davos. We are both instruments of R'hllor. We were made for a single purpose—to keep the darkness at bay. Do you believe that?"

"No." Perhaps he should have lied, and told her what she wanted to hear, but Davos was too accustomed to speaking truth. "You are the mother of darkness. I saw that under Storm's End, when you gave birth before my eyes."

"Is the brave Ser Onions so frightened of a passing shadow? Take heart, then. Shadows only live when given birth by light, and the king's fires burn so low I dare not draw off any more to make another son. It might well kill him." Melisandre moved closer. "With another man, though . . . a man whose flames still burn hot and high . . . if you truly wish to serve your king's cause, come to my chamber one night. I could give you pleasure such as you have never known, and with your life-fire I could make . . ."

". . . a horror." Davos retreated from her. "I want no part of you, my lady. Or your god. May the Seven protect me."

Melisandre sighed. "They did not protect Guncer Sunglass. He prayed thrice each day, and bore seven seven-pointed stars upon his shield, but when R'hllor reached out his hand his prayers turned to screams, and he burned. Why cling to these false gods?"

"I have worshiped them all my life."

"All your life, Davos Seaworth? As well say *it was so*

yesterday." She shook her head sadly. "You have never feared to speak the truth to kings, why do you lie to yourself? Open your eyes, ser knight."

"What is it you would have me see?"

"The way the world is made. The truth is all around you, plain to behold. The night is dark and full of terrors, the day bright and beautiful and full of hope. One is black, the other white. There is ice and there is fire. Hate and love. Bitter and sweet. Male and female. Pain and pleasure. Winter and summer. Evil and good." She took a step toward him. "*Death and life.* Everywhere, opposites. Everywhere, the war."

"The war?" asked Davos.

"The war," she affirmed. "*There are two,* Onion Knight. Not seven, not one, not a hundred or a thousand. *Two!* Do you think I crossed half the world to put yet another vain king on yet another empty throne? The war has been waged since time began, and before it is done, all men must choose where they will stand. On one side is R'hllor, the Lord of Light, the Heart of Fire, the God of Flame and Shadow. Against him stands the Great Other whose name may not be spoken, the Lord of Darkness, the Soul of Ice, the God of Night and Terror. Ours is not a choice between Baratheon and Lannister, between Greyjoy and Stark. It is death we choose, or life. Darkness, or light." She clasped the bars of his cell with her slender white hands. The great ruby at her throat seemed to pulse with its own radiance. "So tell me, Ser Davos Seaworth, and tell me truly—does your heart burn with the shining light of R'hllor? Or is it black and cold and full of worms?" She reached through the bars and laid three fingers upon his breast, as if to feel the truth of him through flesh and wool and leather.

"My heart," Davos said slowly, "is full of doubts."

Melisandre sighed. "Ahhhh, Davos. The good knight is honest to the last, even in his day of darkness. It is well you did not lie to me. I would have known. The Other's servants oft hide black hearts in gaudy light, so R'hllor gives his priests the power to see through falsehoods." She stepped lightly away from the cell. "Why did you mean to kill me?"

"I will tell you," said Davos, "if you will tell me who betrayed me." It could only have been Salladhor Saan, and yet even now he prayed it was not so.

The red woman laughed. "No one betrayed you, onion knight. I saw your purpose in my flames."

The flames. "If you can see the future in these flames, how is it that we burned upon the Blackwater? You gave my sons to the fire . . . my sons, my ship, my men, all burning . . ."

Melisandre shook her head. "You wrong me, onion knight. Those were no fires of mine. Had I been with you, your battle would have had a different ending. But His Grace was surrounded by unbelievers, and his pride proved stronger than his faith. His punishment was grievous, but he has learned from his mistake."

Were my sons no more than a lesson for a king, then? Davos felt his mouth tighten.

"It is night in your Seven Kingdoms now," the red woman went on, "but soon the sun will rise again. The war continues, Davos Seaworth, and some will soon learn that even an ember in the ashes can still ignite a great blaze. The old maester looked at Stannis and saw only a man. You see a king. You are both wrong. He is the Lord's chosen, the warrior of fire. I have seen him leading the fight against the dark, I have seen it in the flames. The flames do not lie, else you would not be here. It is written in prophecy as well. When the red star bleeds and the darkness gathers, Azor Ahai shall be born again amidst smoke and salt to wake dragons out of stone. The bleeding star has come and gone, and Dragonstone is the place of smoke and salt. Stannis Baratheon is Azor Ahai reborn!" Her red eyes blazed like twin fires, and seemed to stare deep into his soul. "You do not believe me. You doubt the truth of R'hllor even now . . . yet have served him all the same, and will serve him again. I shall leave you here to think on all that I have told you. And because R'hllor is the source of all good, I shall leave the torch as well."

With a smile and swirl of scarlet skirts, she was gone. Only her scent lingered after. That, and the torch. Davos lowered himself to the floor of the cell and wrapped his arms about his knees. The shifting torchlight washed over him. Once Melisandre's footsteps faded away, the only sound was the scrabbling of rats. *Ice and fire*, he thought.

Black and white. Dark and light. Davos could not deny the
power of her god. He had seen the shadow crawling from
Melisandre's womb, and the priestess knew things she had
no way of knowing. *She saw my purpose in her flames.* It
was good to learn that Salla had not sold him, but the
thought of the red woman spying out his secrets with her
fires disquieted him more than he could say. *And what did
she mean when she said that I had served her god and
would serve him again?* He did not like that either.

He lifted his eyes to stare up at the torch. He looked for
a long time, never blinking, watching the flames shift and
shimmer. He tried to see beyond them, to peer through the
fiery curtain and glimpse whatever lived back there . . . but
there was nothing, only fire, and after a time his eyes began
to water.

God-blind and tired, Davos curled up on the straw and
gave himself to sleep.

Three days later—well, Porridge had come thrice, and
Lamprey twice—Davos heard voices outside his cell. He
sat up at once, his back to the stone wall, listening to the
sounds of struggle. This was new, a change in his unchanging world. The noise was coming from the left, where the
steps led up to daylight. He could hear a man's voice, pleading and shouting.

". . . *madness!*" the man was saying as he came into
view, dragged along between two guardsmen with fiery
hearts on their breasts. Porridge went before them, jangling
a ring of keys, and Ser Axell Florent walked behind.
"Axell," the prisoner said desperately, "for the love you
bear me, *unhand me!* You cannot do this, I'm no traitor."
He was an older man, tall and slender, with silvery grey
hair, a pointed beard, and a long elegant face twisted in
fear. "Where is Selyse, where is the queen? I demand to see
her. The Others take you all! *Release me!*"

The guards paid no mind to his outcries. "Here?"
Porridge asked in front of the cell. Davos got to his feet. For
an instant he considered trying to rush them when the
door was opened, but that was madness. There were too
many, the guards wore swords, and Porridge was strong as a
bull.

Ser Axell gave the gaoler a curt nod. "Let the traitors enjoy each other's company."

"*I am no traitor!*" screeched the prisoner as Porridge was unlocking the door. Though he was plainly dressed, in grey wool doublet and black breeches, his speech marked him as highborn. *His birth will not serve him here,* thought Davos.

Porridge swung the bars wide, Ser Axell gave a nod, and the guards flung their charge in headlong. The man stumbled and might have fallen, but Davos caught him. At once he wrenched away and staggered back toward the door, only to have it slammed in his pale, pampered face. "*No,*" he shouted. "*Nooooo.*" All the strength suddenly left his legs, and he slid slowly to the floor, clutching at the iron bars. Ser Axell, Porridge, and the guards had already turned to leave. "You cannot do this," the prisoner shouted at their retreating backs. "*I am the King's Hand!*"

It was then that Davos knew him. "You are Alester Florent."

The man turned his head. "Who . . . ?"

"Ser Davos Seaworth."

Lord Alester blinked. "Seaworth . . . the onion knight. You tried to murder Melisandre."

Davos did not deny it. "At Storm's End you wore red-gold armor, with inlaid lapis flowers on your breastplate." He reached down a hand to help the other man to his feet.

Lord Alester brushed the filthy straw from his clothing. "I . . . I must apologize for my appearance, ser. My chests were lost when the Lannisters overran our camp. I escaped with no more than the mail on my back and the rings on my fingers."

He still wears those rings, noted Davos, who had lacked even all of his fingers.

"No doubt some cook's boy or groom is prancing around King's Landing just now in my slashed velvet doublet and jeweled cloak," Lord Alester went on, oblivious. "But war has its horrors, as all men know. No doubt you suffered your own losses."

"My ship," said Davos. "All my men. Four of my sons."

"May the . . . may the Lord of Light lead them through the darkness to a better world," the other man said.

May the Father judge them justly, and the Mother grant them mercy, Davos thought, but he kept his prayer to himself. The Seven had no place on Dragonstone now.

"My own son is safe at Brightwater," the lord went on, "but I lost a nephew on the *Fury*. Ser Imry, my brother Ryam's son."

It had been Ser Imry Florent who led them blindly up the Blackwater Rush with all oars pulling, paying no heed to the small stone towers at the mouth of the river. Davos was not like to forget him. "My son Maric was your nephew's oarmaster." He remembered his last sight of *Fury*, engulfed in wildfire. "Has there been any word of survivors?"

"The *Fury* burned and sank with all hands," his lordship said. "Your son and my nephew were lost, with countless other good men. The war itself was lost that day, ser."

This man is defeated. Davos remembered Melisandre's talk of embers in the ashes igniting great blazes. *Small wonder he ended here.* "His Grace will never yield, my lord."

"Folly, that's folly." Lord Alester sat on the floor again, as if the effort of standing for a moment had been too much for him. "Stannis Baratheon will never sit the Iron Throne. Is it treason to say the truth? A bitter truth, but no less true for that. His fleet is gone, save for the Lyseni, and Salladhor Saan will flee at the first sight of a Lannister sail. Most of the lords who supported Stannis have gone over to Joffrey or died . . ."

"Even the lords of the narrow sea? The lords sworn to Dragonstone?"

Lord Alester waved his hand feebly. "Lord Celtigar was captured and bent the knee. Monford Velaryon died with his ship, the red woman burned Sunglass, and Lord Bar Emmon is fifteen, fat, and feeble. Those are your lords of the narrow sea. Only the strength of House Florent is left to Stannis, against all the might of Highgarden, Sunspear, and Casterly Rock, and now most of the storm lords as well. The best hope that remains is to try and salvage something with a peace. That is all I meant to do. Gods be good, how can they call it *treason*?"

Davos stood frowning. "My lord, what did you do?"

"Not treason. Never treason. I love His Grace as much as any man. My own niece is his queen, and I remained loyal to him when wiser men fled. I am his *Hand*, the Hand of the King, how can I be a traitor? I only meant to save our lives, and . . . honor . . . yes." He licked his lips. "I penned a letter. Salladhor Saan swore that he had a man who could get it to King's Landing, to Lord Tywin. His lordship is a . . . a man of reason, and my terms . . . the terms were fair . . . more than fair."

"What terms were these, my lord?"

"It is filthy here," Lord Alester said suddenly. "And that odor . . . what is that odor?"

"The pail," said Davos, gesturing. "We have no privy here. What terms?"

His lordship stared at the pail in horror. "That Lord Stannis give up his claim to the Iron Throne and retract all he said of Joffrey's bastardy, on the condition that he be accepted back into the king's peace and confirmed as Lord of Dragonstone and Storm's End. I vowed to do the same, for the return of Brightwater Keep and all our lands. I thought . . . Lord Tywin would see the sense in my proposal. He still has the Starks to deal with, and the ironmen as well. I offered to seal the bargain by wedding Shireen to Joffrey's brother Tommen." He shook his head. "The terms . . . they are as good as we are ever like to get. Even you can see that, surely?"

"Yes," said Davos, "even me." Unless Stannis should father a son, such a marriage would mean that Dragonstone and Storm's End would one day pass to Tommen, which would doubtless please Lord Tywin. Meanwhile, the Lannisters would have Shireen as hostage to make certain Stannis raised no new rebellions. "And what did His Grace say when you proposed these terms to him?"

"He is always with the red woman, and . . . he is not in his right mind, I fear. This talk of a stone dragon . . . madness, I tell you, sheer madness. Did we learn nothing from Aerion Brightfire, from the nine mages, from the alchemists? Did we learn nothing from *Summerhall*? No good has ever come from these dreams of dragons, I told Axell as much. My way was better. Surer. And Stannis gave me his seal, he gave me leave to rule. The Hand speaks with the king's voice."

"Not in this." Davos was no courtier, and he did not even try to blunt his words. "It is not in Stannis to yield, so long as he knows his claim is just. No more than he can unsay his words against Joffrey, when he believes them true.

As for the marriage, Tommen was born of the same incest as Joffrey, and His Grace would sooner see Shireen dead than wed to such."

A vein throbbed in Florent's forehead. *"He has no choice."*

"You are wrong, my lord. He can choose to die a king."

"And us with him? Is that what you desire, Onion Knight?"

"No. But I am the king's man, and I will make no peace without his leave."

Lord Alester stared at him helplessly for a long moment, and then began to weep.

JON

The last night fell black and moonless, but for once the sky was clear. "I am going up the hill to look for Ghost," he told the Thenns at the cave mouth, and they grunted and let him pass.

So many stars, he thought as he trudged up the slope through pines and firs and ash. Maester Luwin had taught him his stars as a boy in Winterfell; he had learned the names of the twelve houses of heaven and the rulers of each; he could find the seven wanderers sacred to the Faith; he was old friends with the Ice Dragon, the Shadowcat, the Moonmaid, and the Sword of the Morning. All those he shared with Ygritte, but not some of the others. *We look up at the same stars, and see such different things.* The King's Crown was the Cradle, to hear her tell it; the Stallion was the Horned Lord; the red wanderer that septons preached was sacred to their Smith up here was called the Thief. And when the Thief was in the Moonmaid, that was a propitious time for a man to steal a woman, Ygritte insisted. "Like the night you stole me. The Thief was bright that night."

"I never meant to steal you," he said. "I never knew you were a girl until my knife was at your throat."

"If you kill a man, and never mean t', he's just as dead," Ygritte said stubbornly. Jon had never met anyone so stubborn, except maybe for his little sister Arya. *Is she still my sister?* he wondered. *Was she ever?* He had never truly been a Stark, only Lord Eddard's motherless bastard, with no more place at Winterfell than Theon Greyjoy. And even that he'd lost. When a man of the Night's Watch said his words, he put aside his old family and joined a new one, but Jon Snow had lost those brothers too.

He found Ghost atop the hill, as he thought he might. The white wolf never howled, yet something drew him to the heights all the same, and he would squat there on his hindquarters, hot breath rising in a white mist as his red eyes drank the stars.

"Do you have names for them as well?" Jon asked, as he went to one knee beside the direwolf and scratched the thick white fur on his neck. "The Hare? The Doe? The She-Wolf?" Ghost licked his face, his rough wet tongue rasping against the scabs where the eagle's talons had ripped Jon's cheek. *The bird marked both of us,* he thought. "Ghost," he said quietly, "on the morrow we go over. There's no steps here, no cage-and-crane, no way for me to get you to the other side. We have to part. Do you understand?"

In the dark, the direwolf's red eyes looked black. He nuzzled at Jon's neck, silent as ever, his breath a hot mist. The wildlings called Jon Snow a warg, but if so he was a poor one. He did not know how to put on a wolf skin, the way Orell had with his eagle before he'd died. Once Jon had dreamed that he was Ghost, looking down upon the valley of the Milkwater where Mance Rayder had gathered his people, and that dream had turned out to be true. But he was not dreaming now, and that left him only words.

"You cannot come with me," Jon said, cupping the wolf's head in his hands and looking deep into those eyes. "You have to go to Castle Black. Do you understand? *Castle Black.* Can you find it? The way home? Just follow the ice, east and east, into the sun, and you'll find it. They will know you at Castle Black, and maybe your coming will warn them." He had thought of writing out a warning for Ghost to carry, but he had no ink, no parchment, not even a writing quill, and the risk of discovery was too great. "I will meet you again at Castle Black, but you have to get there by yourself. We must each hunt alone for a time. *Alone.*"

The direwolf twisted free of Jon's grasp, his ears pricked up. And suddenly he was bounding away. He loped through a tangle of brush, leapt a deadfall, and raced down the hillside, a pale streak among the trees. *Off to Castle Black?* Jon wondered. *Or off after a hare?* He wished he knew. He feared he might prove just as poor a warg as a sworn brother and a spy.

A wind sighed through the trees, rich with the smell of pine needles, tugging at his faded blacks. Jon could see the Wall looming high and dark to the south, a great shadow blocking out the stars. The rough hilly ground made him think they must be somewhere between the Shadow Tower and Castle Black, and likely closer to the former. For days they had been wending their way south between deep lakes that stretched like long thin fingers along the floors of narrow valleys, while flint ridges and pine-clad hills jostled against one another to either side. Such ground made for slow riding, but offered easy concealment for those wishing to approach the Wall unseen.

For wildling raiders, he thought. *Like us. Like me.*

Beyond that Wall lay the Seven Kingdoms, and everything he had sworn to protect. He had said the words, had pledged his life and honor, and by rights he should be up there standing sentry. He should be raising a horn to his lips to rouse the Night's Watch to arms. He had no horn, though. It would not be hard to steal one from the wildlings, he suspected, but what would that accomplish? Even if he blew it, there was no one to hear. The Wall was a hundred leagues long and the Watch sadly dwindled. All but three of the strongholds had been abandoned; there might not be a brother within forty miles of here, but for Jon. If he was a brother still . . .

I should have tried to kill Mance Rayder on the Fist, even if it meant my life. That was what Qhorin Halfhand would have done. But Jon had hesitated, and the chance passed. The next day he had ridden off with Styr the Magnar, Jarl, and more than a hundred picked Thenns and raiders. He told himself that he was only biding his time, that when the moment came he would slip away and ride for Castle Black. The moment never came. They rested most nights in empty wildling villages, and Styr always set a dozen of his Thenns to guard the horses. Jarl watched him suspiciously. And Ygritte was never far, day or night.

Two hearts that beat as one. Mance Rayder's mocking words rang bitter in his head. Jon had seldom felt so confused. *I have no choice,* he'd told himself the first time, when she slipped beneath his sleeping skins. *If I refuse her, she will know me for a turncloak. I am playing the part the Halfhand told me to play.*

His body had played the part eagerly enough. His lips on hers, his hand sliding under her doeskin shirt to find a breast, his manhood stiffening when she rubbed her mound against it through their clothes. *My vows,* he'd thought, remembering the weirwood grove where he had said them, the nine great white trees in a circle, the carved red faces watching, listening. But her fingers were undoing his laces and her tongue was in his mouth and her hand slipped inside his smallclothes and brought him out, and he could not see the weirwoods anymore, only her. She bit his neck and he nuzzled hers, burying his nose in her thick red hair. *Lucky,* he thought, *she is lucky, fire-kissed.* "Isn't that good?" she whispered as she guided him inside her. She was sopping wet down there, and no maiden, that was plain, but Jon did not care. His vows, her maidenhood, none of it mattered, only the heat of her, the mouth on his, the finger that pinched at his nipple. "Isn't that sweet?" she said again. "Not so fast, oh, slow, yes, like that. There now, there now, yes, sweet, sweet. You know nothing, Jon Snow, but I can show you. Harder now. Yessss."

A part, he tried to remind himself afterward. *I am playing a part. I had to do it once, to prove I'd abandoned my vows. I had to make her trust me.* It need never happen again. He was still a man of the Night's Watch, and a son of Eddard Stark. He had done what needed to be done, proved what needed to be proven.

The proving had been so sweet, though, and Ygritte had gone to sleep beside him with her head against his chest, and that was sweet as well, dangerously sweet. He thought of the weirwoods again, and the words he'd said before them. *It was only once, and it had to be. Even my father stumbled once, when he forgot his marriage vows and sired a bastard.* Jon vowed to himself that it would be the same with him. *It will never happen again.*

It happened twice more that night, and again in the morning, when she woke to find him hard. The wildlings were stirring by then, and several could not help but notice what was going on beneath the pile of furs. Jarl told them to be quick about it, before he had to throw a pail of water over them. *Like a pair of rutting dogs,* Jon thought afterward. Was that what he'd become? *I am a man of the Night's Watch,* a small voice inside insisted, but every night it seemed a little fainter, and when Ygritte kissed his ears or bit his neck, he could not hear it at all. *Was this how it was for my father?* he wondered. *Was he as weak as I am, when he dishonored himself in my mother's bed?*

Something was coming up the hill behind him, he realized suddenly. For half a heartbeat he thought it might be Ghost come back, but the direwolf never made so much noise. Jon drew Longclaw in a single smooth motion, but it was only one of the Thenns, a broad man in a bronze helm. "Snow," the intruder said. "Come. Magnar wants." The men of Thenn spoke the Old Tongue, and most had only a few words of the Common.

Jon did not much care what the Magnar wanted, but there was no use arguing with someone who could scarcely understand him, so he followed the man back down the hill.

The mouth of the cave was a cleft in the rock barely wide enough for a horse, half concealed behind a soldier pine. It opened to the north, so the glows of the fires within would not be visible from the Wall. Even if by some mischance a patrol should happen to pass atop the Wall tonight, they would see nothing but hills and pines and the icy sheen of starlight on a half-frozen lake. Mance Rayder had planned his thrust well.

Within the rock, the passage descended twenty feet before it opened out onto a space as large as Winterfell's Great Hall. Cookfires burned amongst the columns, their smoke rising to blacken the stony ceiling. The horses had been hobbled along one wall, beside a shallow pool. A sinkhole in the center of the floor opened on what might have been an even greater cavern below, though the darkness made it hard to tell. Jon could hear the soft rushing sound of an underground stream somewhere below as well.

Jarl was with the Magnar; Mance had given them the joint command. Styr was none too pleased by that, Jon had noted early on. Mance Rayder had called the dark youth a "pet" of Val, who was sister to Dalla, his own queen, which made Jarl a sort of good brother once removed to the King-beyond-the-Wall. The Magnar plainly resented sharing his authority. He had brought a hundred Thenns, five times as many men as Jarl, and often acted as if he had the sole command. But it would be the younger man who got them over the ice, Jon knew. Though he could not have been older than twenty, Jarl had been raiding for eight years, and had gone over the Wall a dozen times with the likes of Alfyn Crowkiller and the Weeper, and more recently with his own band.

The Magnar was direct. "Jarl has warned me of crows, patrolling on high. Tell me all you know of these patrols."

Tell me, Jon noted, not *tell us*, though Jarl stood right beside him. He would have liked nothing better than to refuse the brusque demand, but he knew Styr would put him to death at the slightest disloyalty, and Ygritte as well, for the crime of being his. "There are four men in each patrol, two rangers and two builders," he said. "The builders are supposed to make note of cracks, melting, and other structural problems, while the rangers look for signs of foes. They ride mules."

"Mules?" The earless man frowned. "Mules are slow."

"Slow, but more surefooted on the ice. The patrols often ride atop the Wall, and aside from Castle Black, the paths up there have not been graveled for long years. The mules are bred at Eastwatch, and specially trained to their duty."

"They *often* ride atop the Wall? Not always?"

"No. One patrol in four follows the base instead, to search for cracks in the foundation ice or signs of tunneling."

The Magnar nodded. "Even in far Thenn we know the tale of Arson Iceaxe and his tunnel."

Jon knew the tale as well. Arson Iceaxe had been halfway through the Wall when his tunnel was found by rangers from the Nightfort. They did not trouble to disturb him at his digging, only sealed the way behind with ice and stone and snow. Dolorous Edd used to say that if you pressed your ear flat to the Wall, you could still hear Arson chipping away with his axe.

"When do these patrols go out? How often?"

Jon shrugged. "It changes. I've heard that Lord Commander Qorgyle used to send them out every third day from Castle Black to Eastwatch-by-the-Sea, and every second day from Castle Black to the Shadow Tower. The Watch had more men in his day, though. Lord Commander Mormont prefers to vary the number of patrols and the days of their departure, to make it more difficult for anyone to know their comings and goings. And sometimes the Old Bear will even send a larger force to one of the abandoned castles for a fortnight or a moon's turn." His uncle had originated that tactic, Jon knew. Anything to make the enemy unsure.

"Is Stonedoor manned at present?" asked Jarl. "Greyguard?"

So we're between those two, are we? Jon kept his face carefully blank. "Only Eastwatch, Castle Black, and the Shadow Tower were manned when I left the Wall. I can't speak to what Bowen Marsh or Ser Denys might have done since."

"How many crows remain within the castles?" asked Styr.

"Five hundred at Castle Black. Two hundred at Shadow Tower, perhaps three hundred at Eastwatch." Jon added three hundred men to the count. *If only it were that easy . . .*

Jarl was not fooled, however. "He's lying," he told Styr. "Or else including those they lost on the Fist."

"Crow," the Magnar warned, "do not take me for Mance Rayder. If you lie to me, I will have your tongue."

"I'm no crow, and won't be called a liar." Jon flexed the fingers of his sword hand.

The Magnar of Thenn studied Jon with his chilly grey eyes. "We shall learn their numbers soon enough," he said after a moment. "Go. I will send for you if I have further questions."

Jon bowed his head stiffly, and went. *If all the wildlings were like Styr, it would be easier to betray them.* The Thenns were not like other free folk, though. The Magnar claimed to be the last of the First Men, and ruled with an iron hand. His little land of Thenn was a high mountain valley hidden amongst the northernmost peaks of the Frostfangs, surrounded by cave dwellers, Hornfoot men, giants, and the cannibal clans of the ice rivers. Ygritte said the Thenns were savage fighters, and that their Magnar was a god to them. Jon could believe that. Unlike Jarl and Harma and Rattleshirt, Styr commanded absolute obedience from his men, and that discipline was no doubt part of why Mance had chosen him to go over the Wall.

He walked past the Thenns, sitting atop their rounded bronze helms about their cookfires. *Where did Ygritte get herself to?* He found her gear and his together, but no sign of the girl herself. "She took a torch and went off that way," Grigg the Goat told him, pointing toward the back of the cavern.

Jon followed his finger, and found himself in a dim back room wandering through a maze of columns and stalactites. *She can't be here,* he was thinking, when he heard her laugh. He turned toward the sound, but within ten paces he was in a dead end, facing a blank wall of rose and white flowstone. Baffled, he made his way back the way he'd come, and then he saw it: a dark hole under an outthrust of wet stone. He knelt, listened, heard the faint sound of water. "Ygritte?"

"In here," her voice came back, echoing faintly.

Jon had to crawl a dozen paces before the cave opened up around him. When he stood again, it took his eyes a moment to adjust. Ygritte had brought a torch, but there was no other light. She stood beside a little waterfall that fell from a cleft in the rock down into a wide dark pool. The orange and yellow flames shone against the pale green water.

"What are you doing here?" he asked her.

"I heard water. I wanted t'see how deep the cave went." She pointed with the torch. "There's a passage goes down further. I followed it a hundred paces before I turned back."

"A dead end?"

"You know nothing, Jon Snow. It went on and on and on. There are hundreds o' caves in these hills, and down deep they all connect. There's even a way under your Wall. Gorne's Way."

"Gorne," said Jon. "Gorne was King-beyond-the-Wall."

"Aye," said Ygritte. "Together with his brother Gendel, three thousand years ago. They led a host o' free folk through the caves, and the Watch was none the wiser. But when they come out, the wolves o' Winterfell fell upon them."

"There was a battle," Jon recalled. "Gorne slew the King in the North, but his son picked up his banner and took the crown from his head, and cut down Gorne in turn."

"And the sound o' swords woke the crows in their castles, and they rode out all in black to take the free folk in the rear."

"Yes. Gendel had the king to the south, the Umbers to the east, and the Watch to the north of him. He died as well."

"You know nothing, Jon Snow. Gendel did not die. He cut his way free, *through* the crows, and led his people back north with the wolves howling at their heels. Only Gendel did not know the caves as Gorne had, and took a wrong turn." She swept the torch back and forth, so the shadows jumped and moved. "Deeper he went, and deeper, and when he tried t' turn back the ways that seemed familiar ended in stone rather than sky. Soon his torches began t' fail, one by one, till finally there was naught but dark. Gendel's folk were never seen again, but on a still night you can hear their children's children's children sobbing under the hills, still looking for the way back up. Listen? Do you hear them?"

All Jon could hear was the falling water and the faint crackle of flames. "This way under the Wall was lost as well?"

"Some have searched for it. Them that go too deep find Gendel's children, and Gendel's children are always hungry." Smiling, she set the torch carefully in a notch of rock, and came toward him. "There's naught to eat in the dark but flesh," she whispered, biting at his neck.

Jon nuzzled her hair and filled his nose with the smell of her. "You sound like Old Nan, telling Bran a monster story."

Ygritte punched his shoulder. "An old woman, am I?"

"You're older than me."

"Aye, and wiser. You know nothing, Jon Snow." She

pushed away from him, and shrugged out of her rabbitskin vest.

"What are you doing?"

"Showing you how old I am." She unlaced her doeskin shirt, tossed it aside, pulled her three woolen undershirts up over her head all at once. "I want you should see me."

"We shouldn't—"

"We *should*." Her breasts bounced as she stood on one leg to pull one boot, then hopped onto her other foot to attend to the other. Her nipples were wide pink circles. "You as well," Ygritte said as she yanked down her sheepskin breeches. "If you want to look you have to show. You know nothing, Jon Snow."

"I know I want you," he heard himself say, all his vows and all his honor forgotten. She stood before him naked as her name day, and he was as hard as the rock around them. He had been in her half a hundred times by now, but always beneath the furs, with others all around them. He had never seen how beautiful she was. Her legs were skinny but well muscled, the hair at the juncture of her thighs a brighter red than that on her head. *Does that make it even luckier?* He pulled her close. "I love the smell of you," he said. "I love your red hair. I love your mouth, and the way you kiss me. I love your smile. I love your teats." He kissed them, one and then the other. "I love your skinny legs, and what's between them." He knelt to kiss her there, lightly on her mound at first, but Ygritte moved her legs apart a little, and he saw the pink inside and kissed that as well, and tasted her. She gave a little gasp. "If you love me all so much, why are you still dressed?" she whispered. "You know nothing, Jon Snow. *Noth—oh. Oh. OHHH.*"

Afterward, she was almost shy, or as shy as Ygritte ever got. "That thing you did," she said, when they lay together on their piled clothes. "With your . . . mouth." She hesitated. "Is that . . . is it what lords do to their ladies, down in the south?"

"I don't think so." No one had ever told Jon just what lords did with their ladies. "I only . . . wanted to kiss you there, that's all. You seemed to like it."

"Aye. I . . . I liked it some. No one taught you such?"

"There's been no one," he confessed. "Only you."

"A maid," she teased. "You were a maid."

He gave her closest nipple a playful pinch. "I was a man of the Night's Watch." *Was*, he heard himself say. What was he now? He did not want to look at that. "Were you a maid?"

Ygritte pushed herself onto an elbow. "I am nineteen, and a spearwife, and kissed by fire. How could I be maiden?"

"Who was he?"

"A boy at a feast, five years past. He'd come trading with his brothers, and he had hair like mine, kissed by fire, so I thought he would be lucky. But he was weak. When he came back t' try and steal me, Longspear broke his arm and ran him off, and he never tried again, not once."

"It wasn't Longspear, then?" Jon was relieved. He liked Longspear, with his homely face and friendly ways.

She punched him. "That's vile. Would you bed your sister?"

"Longspear's not your brother."

"He's of my village. You know nothing, Jon Snow. A true man steals a woman from afar, t' strengthen the clan. Women who bed brothers or fathers or clan kin offend the gods, and are cursed with weak and sickly children. Even monsters."

"Craster weds his daughters," Jon pointed out.

She punched him again. "Craster's more your kind than ours. His father was a crow who stole a woman out of Whitetree village, but after he had her he flew back t' his Wall. She went t' Castle Black once t' show the crow his son, but the brothers blew their horns and run her off. Craster's blood is black, and he bears a heavy curse." She ran her fingers lightly across his stomach. "I feared you'd do the same once. Fly back to the Wall. You never knew what t' do after you stole me."

Jon sat up. "Ygritte, I never stole you."

"Aye, you did. You jumped down the mountain and killed Orell, and afore I could get my axe you had a knife at my throat. I thought you'd have me then, or kill me, or maybe both, but you never did. And when I told you the tale o' Bael the Bard and how he plucked the rose o' Winterfell, I thought you'd know to pluck me then for certain, but you didn't. You know *nothing*, Jon Snow." She gave him a shy smile. "You might be learning some, though."

The light was shifting all about her, Jon noticed suddenly. He looked around. "We had best go up. The torch is almost done."

"Is the crow afeared o' Gendel's children?" she said, with a grin. "It's only a little way up, and I'm not done with you, Jon Snow." She pushed him back down on the clothes and straddled him. "Would you . . ." She hesitated.

"What?" he prompted, as the torch began to gutter.

"Do it again?" Ygritte blurted. "With your mouth? The lord's kiss? And I . . . I could see if you liked it any."

By the time the torch burned out, Jon Snow no longer cared.

His guilt came back afterward, but weaker than before. *If this is so wrong,* he wondered, *why did the gods make it feel so good?*

The grotto was pitch-dark by the time they finished. The only light was the dim glow of the passage back up to the larger cavern, where a score of fires burned. They were soon fumbling and bumping into each other as they tried to dress in the dark. Ygritte stumbled into the pool and screeched at the cold of the water. When Jon laughed, she pulled him in too. They wrestled and splashed in the dark, and then she was in his arms again, and it turned out they were not finished after all.

"Jon Snow," she told him, when he'd spent his seed inside her, "don't move now, sweet. I like the feel of you in there, I do. Let's not go back t' Styr and Jarl. Let's go down inside, and join up with Gendel's children. I don't ever want t' leave this cave, Jon Snow. Not ever."

DAENERYS

All?" The slave girl sounded wary. "Your Grace, did this one's worthless ears mishear you?"

Cool green light filtered down through the diamond-shaped panes of colored glass set in the sloping triangular walls, and a breeze was blowing gently through the terrace doors, carrying the scents of fruit and flowers from the garden beyond. "Your ears heard true," said Dany. "I want to buy them all. Tell the Good Masters, if you will."

She had chosen a Qartheen gown today. The deep violet silk brought out the purple of her eyes. The cut of it bared her left breast. While the Good Masters of Astapor conferred among themselves in low voices, Dany sipped tart persimmon wine from a tall silver flute. She could not quite make out all that they were saying, but she could hear the greed.

Each of the eight brokers was attended by two or three body slaves . . . though one Grazdan, the eldest, had six. So as not to seem a beggar, Dany had brought her own attendants; Irri and Jhiqui in their sandsilk trousers and painted vests, old Whitebeard and mighty Belwas, her bloodriders.

Ser Jorah stood behind her sweltering in his green surcoat with the black bear of Mormont embroidered upon it. The smell of his sweat was an earthy answer to the sweet perfumes that drenched the Astapori.

"All," growled Kraznys mo Nakloz, who smelled of peaches today. The slave girl repeated the word in the Common Tongue of Westeros. "Of thousands, there are eight. Is this what she means by *all*? There are also six centuries, who shall be part of a ninth thousand when complete. Would she have them too?"

"I would," said Dany when the question was put to her. "The eight thousands, the six centuries . . . and the ones still in training as well. The ones who have not earned the spikes."

Kraznys turned back to his fellows. Once again they conferred among themselves. The translator had told Dany their names, but it was hard to keep them straight. Four of the men seemed to be named Grazdan, presumably after Grazdan the Great who had founded Old Ghis in the dawn of days. They all looked alike; thick fleshy men with amber skin, broad noses, dark eyes. Their wiry hair was black, or a dark red, or that queer mixture of red and black that was peculiar to Ghiscari. All wrapped themselves in *tokars*, a garment permitted only to freeborn men of Astapor.

It was the fringe on the *tokar* that proclaimed a man's status, Dany had been told by Captain Groleo. In this cool green room atop the pyramid, two of the slavers wore *tokars* fringed in silver, five had gold fringes, and one, the oldest Grazdan, displayed a fringe of fat white pearls that clacked together softly when he shifted in his seat or moved an arm.

"We cannot sell half-trained boys," one of the silver-fringe Grazdans was saying to the others.

"We can, if her gold is good," said a fatter man whose fringe was gold.

"They are not Unsullied. They have not killed their sucklings. If they fail in the field, they will shame us. And even if we cut five thousand raw boys tomorrow, it would be ten years before they are fit for sale. What would we tell the next buyer who comes seeking Unsullied?"

"We will tell him that he must wait," said the fat man. "Gold in my purse is better than gold in my future."

Dany let them argue, sipping the tart persimmon wine and trying to keep her face blank and ignorant. *I will have them all, no matter the price*, she told herself. The city had a hundred slave traders, but the eight before her were the greatest. When selling bed slaves, fieldhands, scribes, craftsmen, and tutors, these men were rivals, but their ancestors had allied one with the other for the purpose of making and selling the Unsullied. *Brick and blood built Astapor, and brick and blood her people.*

It was Kraznys who finally announced their decision. "Tell her that the eight thousands she shall have, if her gold proves sufficient. And the six centuries, if she wishes. Tell her to come back in a year, and we will sell her another two thousand."

"In a year I shall be in Westeros," said Dany when she had heard the translation. "My need is *now*. The Unsullied are well trained, but even so, many will fall in battle. I shall need the boys as replacements to take up the swords they drop." She put her wine aside and leaned toward the slave girl. "Tell the Good Masters that I will want even the little ones who still have their puppies. Tell them that I will pay as much for the boy they cut yesterday as for an Unsullied in a spiked helm."

The girl told them. The answer was still no.

Dany frowned in annoyance. "Very well. Tell them I will pay double, so long as I get them all."

"Double?" The fat one in the gold fringe all but drooled.

"This little whore is a fool, truly," said Khaznys mo Nakloz. "Ask her for triple, I say. She is desperate enough to pay. Ask for ten times the price of every slave, yes."

The tall Grazdan with the spiked beard spoke in the Common Tongue, though not so well as the slave girl. "Your Grace," he growled, "Westeros is being wealthy, yes, but you are not being queen now. Perhaps will never being queen. Even Unsullied may be losing battles to savage steel knights of Seven Kingdoms. I am reminding, the Good Masters of Astapor are not selling flesh for promisings. Are you having gold and trading goods sufficient to be paying for all these eunuchs you are wanting?"

"You know the answer to that better than I, Good Master," Dany replied. "Your men have gone through my ships and tallied every bead of amber and jar of saffron. How much do I have?"

"Sufficient to be buying one of thousands," the Good Master said, with a contemptuous smile. "Yet you are paying double, you are saying. Five centuries, then, is all you buy."

"Your pretty crown might buy another century," said the fat one in Valyrian. "Your crown of the three dragons."

Dany waited for his words to be translated. "My crown is not for sale." When Viserys sold their mother's crown, the last joy had gone from him, leaving only rage. "Nor will I enslave my people, nor sell their goods and horses. But my ships you can have. The great cog *Balerion* and the galleys *Vhagar* and *Meraxes*." She had warned Groleo and the other captains it might come to this, though they had protested the necessity of it furiously. "Three good ships should be worth more than a few paltry eunuchs."

The fat Grazdan turned to the others. They conferred in low voices once again. "Two of the thousands," the one with the spiked beard said when he turned back. "It is too much, but the Good Masters are being generous and your need is being great."

Two thousand would never serve for what she meant to do. *I must have them all.* Dany knew what she must do now, though the taste of it was so bitter that even the persimmon wine could not cleanse it from her mouth. She had considered long and hard and found no other way. *It is my only choice.* "Give me all," she said, "and you may have a dragon."

There was the sound of indrawn breath from Jhiqui beside her. Kraznys smiled at his fellows. "Did I not tell you? Anything, she would give us."

Whitebeard stared in shocked disbelief. His hand trembled where it grasped the staff. "*No.*" He went to one knee before her. "Your Grace, I beg you, win your throne with dragons, not slaves. You must not do this thing—"

"*You* must not presume to instruct me. Ser Jorah, remove Whitebeard from my presence."

Mormont seized the old man roughly by an elbow, yanked him back to his feet, and marched him out onto the terrace.

"Tell the Good Masters I regret this interruption," said Dany to the slave girl. "Tell them I await their answer."

She knew the answer, though; she could see it in the glitter of their eyes and the smiles they tried so hard to hide. Astapor had thousands of eunuchs, and even more slave boys waiting to be cut, but there were only three living dragons in all the great wide world. *And the Ghiscari lust for dragons.* How could they not? Five times had Old Ghis contended with Valyria when the world was young, and five times gone down to bleak defeat. For the Freehold had dragons, and the Empire had none.

The oldest Grazdan stirred in his seat, and his pearls clacked together softly. "A dragon of our choice," he said in a thin, hard voice. "The black one is largest and healthiest."

"His name is Drogon." She nodded.

"All your goods, save your crown and your queenly raiment, which we will allow you to keep. The three ships. And Drogon."

"Done," she said, in the Common Tongue.

"Done," the old Grazdan answered in his thick Valyrian.

The others echoed that old man of the pearl fringe. "Done," the slave girl translated, "and done, and done, eight times done."

"The Unsullied will learn your savage tongue quick enough," added Kraznys mo Nakloz, when all the arrangements had been made, "but until such time you will need a slave to speak to them. Take this one as our gift to you, a token of a bargain well struck."

"I shall," said Dany.

The slave girl rendered his words to her, and hers to him. If she had feelings about being given for a token, she took care not to let them show.

Arstan Whitebeard held his tongue as well, when Dany swept by him on the terrace. He followed her down the steps in silence, but she could hear his hardwood staff *tap tapping* on the red bricks as they went. She did not blame him for his fury. It was a wretched thing she did. *The Mother of Dragons has sold her strongest child.* Even the thought made her ill.

Yet down in the Plaza of Pride, standing on the hot red

bricks between the slavers' pyramid and the barracks of the eunuchs, Dany turned on the old man. "Whitebeard," she said, "I want your counsel, and you should never fear to speak your mind with me . . . when we are alone. But *never* question me in front of strangers. Is that understood?"

"Yes, Your Grace," he said unhappily.

"I am not a child," she told him. "I am a queen."

"Yet even queens can err. The Astapori have cheated you, Your Grace. A dragon is worth more than any army. Aegon proved that three hundred years ago, upon the Field of Fire."

"I know what Aegon proved. I mean to prove a few things of my own." Dany turned away from him, to the slave girl standing meekly beside her litter. "Do you have a name, or must you draw a new one every day from some barrel?"

"That is only for Unsullied," the girl said. Then she realized the question had been asked in High Valyrian. Her eyes went wide. "Oh."

"Your name is Oh?"

"No. Your Grace, forgive this one her outburst. Your slave's name is Missandei, but . . ."

"Missandei is no longer a slave. I free you, from this instant. Come ride with me in the litter, I wish to talk." Rakharo helped them in, and Dany drew the curtains shut against the dust and heat. "If you stay with me you will serve as one of my handmaids," she said as they set off. "I shall keep you by my side to speak for me as you spoke for Kraznys. But you may leave my service whenever you choose, if you have father or mother you would sooner return to."

"This one will stay," the girl said. "This one . . . I . . . there is no place for me to go. This . . . I will serve you, gladly."

"I can give you freedom, but not safety," Dany warned. "I have a world to cross and wars to fight. You may go hungry. You may grow sick. You may be killed."

"*Valar morghulis*," said Missandei, in High Valyrian.

"All men must die," Dany agreed, "but not for a long while, we may pray." She leaned back on the pillows and took the girl's hand. "Are these Unsullied truly fearless?"

"Yes, Your Grace."

"You serve me now. Is it true they feel no pain?"

"The wine of courage kills such feelings. By the time they slay their sucklings, they have been drinking it for years."

"And they are obedient?"

"Obedience is all they know. If you told them not to breathe, they would find that easier than not to obey."

Dany nodded. "And when I am done with them?"

"Your Grace?"

"When I have won my war and claimed the throne that was my father's, my knights will sheathe their swords and return to their keeps, to their wives and children and mothers . . . to their *lives*. But these eunuchs have no lives. What am I to do with eight thousand eunuchs when there are no more battles to be fought?"

"The Unsullied make fine guards and excellent watch-men, Your Grace," said Missandei. "And it is never hard to find a buyer for such fine well-blooded troops."

"Men are not bought and sold in Westeros, they tell me."

"With all respect, Your Grace, Unsullied are not men."

"If I did resell them, how would I know they could not be used against me?" Dany asked pointedly. "Would they do that? Fight *against* me, even do me harm?"

"If their master commanded. They do not question, Your Grace. All the questions have been culled from them. They obey." She looked troubled. "When you are . . . when you are done with them . . . Your Grace might command them to fall upon their swords."

"And even that, they would do?"

"Yes." Missandei's voice had grown soft. "Your Grace."

Dany squeezed her hand. "You would sooner I did not ask it of them, though. Why is that? Why do you care?"

"This one does not . . . I . . . Your Grace . . ."

"Tell me."

The girl lowered her eyes. "Three of them were my brothers once, Your Grace."

Then I hope your brothers are as brave and clever as you. Dany leaned back into her pillow, and let the litter bear her onward, back to *Balerion* one last time to set her world in order. *And back to Drogon.* Her mouth set grimly.

It was a long, dark, windy night that followed. Dany fed her dragons as she always did, but found she had no appetite herself. She cried awhile, alone in her cabin, then dried her tears long enough for yet another argument with Groleo. "Magister Illyrio is not here," she finally had to tell him, "and if he was, he could not sway me either. I need the Unsullied more than I need these ships, and I will hear no more about it."

The anger burned the grief and fear from her, for a few hours at the least. Afterward she called her bloodriders to her cabin, with Ser Jorah. They were the only ones she truly trusted.

She meant to sleep afterward, to be well rested for the morrow, but an hour of restless tossing in the stuffy confines of the cabin soon convinced her that was hopeless. Outside her door she found Aggo fitting a new string to his bow by the light of a swinging oil lamp. Rakharo sat crosslegged on the deck beside him, sharpening his *arakh* with a whetstone. Dany told them both to keep on with what they were doing, and went up on deck for a taste of the cool night air. The crew left her alone as they went about their business, but Ser Jorah soon joined her by the rail. *He is never far*, Dany thought. *He knows my moods too well.*

"*Khaleesi*. You ought to be asleep. Tomorrow will be hot and hard, I promise you. You'll need your strength."

"Do you remember Eroeh?" she asked him.

"The Lhazareen girl?"

"They were raping her, but I stopped them and took her under my protection. Only when my sun-and-stars was dead Mago took her back, used her again, and killed her. Aggo said it was her fate."

"I remember," Ser Jorah said.

"I was alone for a long time, Jorah. All alone but for my brother. I was such a small scared thing. Viserys should have protected me, but instead he hurt me and scared me worse. He shouldn't have done that. He wasn't just my brother, he was my *king*. Why do the gods make kings and queens, if not to protect the ones who can't protect themselves?"

"Some kings make themselves. Robert did."

"He was no true king," Dany said scornfully. "He did no justice. Justice . . . that's what kings are *for*."

Ser Jorah had no answer. He only smiled, and touched her hair, so lightly. It was enough.

That night she dreamt that she was Rhaegar, riding to the Trident. But she was mounted on a dragon, not a horse. When she saw the Usurper's rebel host across the river they were armored all in ice, but she bathed them in drag-onfire and they melted away like dew and turned the Trident into a torrent. Some small part of her knew that she was dreaming, but another part exulted. *This is how it was meant to be. The other was a nightmare, and I have only now awakened.*

She woke suddenly in the darkness of her cabin, still flush with triumph. *Balerion* seemed to wake with her, and she heard the faint creak of wood, water lapping against the hull, a football on the deck above her head. And something else.

Someone was in the cabin with her.

"Irri? Jhiqui? Where are you?" Her handmaids did not respond. It was too black to see, but she could hear them breathing. "Jorah, is that you?"

"They sleep," a woman said. "They all sleep." The voice was very close. "Even dragons must sleep."

She is standing over me. "Who's there?" Dany peered into the darkness. She thought she could see a shadow, the faintest outline of a shape. "What do you want of me?"

"Remember. To go north, you must journey south. To reach the west, you must go east. To go forward you must go back, and to touch the light you must pass beneath the shadow."

"*Quaithe?*" Dany sprung from the bed and threw open the door. Pale yellow lantern light flooded the cabin, and Irri and Jhiqui sat up sleepily. "*Khaleesi?*" murmured Jhiqui, rubbing her eyes. Viserion woke and opened his jaws, and a puff of flame brightened even the darkest cor-ners. There was no sign of a woman in a red lacquer mask. "*Khaleesi*, are you unwell?" asked Jhiqui.

"A dream." Dany shook her head. "I dreamed a dream, no more. Go back to sleep. All of us, go back to sleep." Yet try as she might, sleep would not come again.

If I look back I am lost, Dany told herself the next morning as she entered Astapor through the harbor gates. She dared not remind herself how small and insignificant her following truly was, or she would lose all courage. Today she rode her silver, clad in horsehair pants and

376   **GEORGE R. R. MARTIN**

painted leather vest, a bronze medallion belt about her
waist and two more crossed between her breasts. Irri and
Jhiqui had braided her hair and hung it with a tiny silver
bell whose chime sang of the Undying of Qarth, burned in
their Palace of Dust.

The red brick streets of Astapor were almost crowded
this morning. Slaves and servants lined the ways, while the
slavers and their women donned their *tokars* to look down
from their stepped pyramids. *They are not so different
from Qartheen after all*, she thought. *They want a glimpse
of dragons to tell their children of, and their children's
children.* It made her wonder how many of them would
ever have children.

Aggo went before her with his great Dothraki bow.
Strong Belwas walked to the right of her mare, the girl
Missandei to her left. Ser Jorah Mormont was behind in
mail and surcoat, glowering at anyone who came too near.
Rakharo and Jhogo protected the litter. Dany had commanded that the top be removed, so her three dragons
might be chained to the platform. Irri and Jhiqui rode with
them, to try and keep them calm. Yet Viserion's tail lashed
back and forth, and smoke rose angry from his nostrils.
Rhaegal could sense something wrong as well. Thrice he
tried to take wing, only to be pulled down by the heavy
chain in Jhiqui's hand. Drogon coiled into a ball, wings and
tail tucked tight. Only his eyes remained to tell that he was
not asleep.

The rest of her people followed: Groleo and the other
captains and their crews, and the eighty-three Dothraki
who remained to her of the hundred thousand who had
once ridden in Drogo's *khalasar*. She put the oldest and
weakest on the inside of the column, with the nursing
women and those with child, and the little girls, and the
boys too young to braid their hair. The rest—her warriors,
such as they were—rode outside and moved their dismal
herd along, the hundred-odd gaunt horses that had survived both red waste and black salt sea.

I ought to have a banner sewn, she thought as she led
her tattered band up along Astapor's meandering river. She
closed her eyes to imagine how it would look: all flowing
black silk, and on it the red three-headed dragon of
Targaryen, breathing golden flames. *A banner such as*

Rhaegar might have borne. The river's banks were strangely tranquil. The Worm, the Astapori called the stream. It was wide and slow and crooked, dotted with tiny wooded islands. She glimpsed children playing on one of them, darting amongst elegant marble statues. On another island two lovers kissed in the shade of tall green trees, with no more shame than Dothraki at a wedding. Without clothing, she could not tell if they were slave or free.

The Plaza of Pride with its great bronze harpy was too small to hold all the Unsullied she had bought. Instead they had been assembled in the Plaza of Punishment, fronting on Astapor's main gate, so they might be marched directly from the city once Daenerys had taken them in hand. There were no bronze statues here; only a wooden platform where rebellious slaves were racked, and flayed, and hanged. "The Good Masters place them so they will be the first thing a new slave sees upon entering the city," Missandei told her as they came to the plaza.

At first glimpse, Dany thought their skin was striped like the zorses of the Jogos Nhai. Then she rode her silver nearer and saw the raw red flesh beneath the crawling black stripes. *Flies. Flies and maggots.* The rebellious slaves had been peeled like a man might peel an apple, in a long curling strip. One man had an arm black with flies from fingers to elbow, and red and white beneath. Dany reined in beneath him. "What did this one do?"

"He raised a hand against his owner."

Her stomach roiling, Dany wheeled her silver about and trotted toward the center of the plaza, and the army she had bought so dear. Rank on rank on rank they stood, her stone halfmen with their hearts of brick; eight thousand and six hundred in the spiked bronze caps of fully trained Unsullied, and five thousand odd behind them, bareheaded, yet armed with spears and shortswords. The ones farthest to the back were only boys, she saw, but they stood as straight and still as all the rest.

Kraznys mo Nakloz and his fellows were all there to greet her. Other well-born Astapori stood in knots behind them, sipping wine from silver flutes as slaves circulated among them with trays of olives and cherries and figs. The elder Grazdan sat in a sedan chair supported by four huge copper-skinned slaves. Half a dozen mounted lancers rode along the edges of the plaza, keeping back the crowds who had come to watch. The sun flashed blinding bright off the polished copper disks sewn to their cloaks, but she could not help but notice how nervous their horses seemed. *They fear the dragons. And well they might.*

Kraznys had a slave help her from her saddle. His own hands were full; one clutched his *tokar*, while the other held an ornate whip. "Here they are." He looked at Missandei. "Tell her they are hers . . . if she can pay."

"She can," the girl said.

Ser Jorah barked a command, and the trade goods were brought forward. Six bales of tiger skins, three hundred bolts of fine silk. Jars of saffron, jars of myrrh, jars of pepper and curry and cardamom, an onyx mask, twelve jade monkeys, casks of ink in red and black and green, a box of rare black amethysts, a box of pearls, a cask of pitted olives stuffed with maggots, a dozen casks of pickled cave fish, a great brass gong and a hammer to beat it with, seventeen ivory eyes, and a huge chest full of books written in tongues that Dany could not read. And more, and more, and more. Her people stacked it all before the slavers.

While the payment was being made, Kraznys mo Nakloz favored her with a few final words on the handling of her troops. "They are green as yet," he said through Missandei. "Tell the whore of Westeros she would be wise to blood them early. There are many small cities between here and there, cities ripe for sacking. Whatever plunder she takes will be hers alone. Unsullied have no lust for gold or gems. And should she take captives, a few guards will suffice to march them back to Astapor. We'll buy the healthy ones, and for a good price. And who knows? In ten years, some of the boys she sends us may be Unsullied in their turn. Thus all shall prosper."

Finally there were no more trade goods to add to the pile. Her Dothraki mounted their horses once more, and Dany said, "This was all we could carry. The rest awaits you on the ships, a great quantity of amber and wine and black rice. And you have the ships themselves. So all that remains is . . ."

". . . the dragon," finished the Grazdan with the spiked beard, who spoke the Common Tongue so thickly.

"And here he waits." Ser Jorah and Belwas walked beside her to the litter, where Drogon and his brothers lay basking in the sun. Jhiqui unfastened one end of the chain, and handed it down to her. When she gave a yank, the black dragon raised his head, hissing, and unfolded wings of night and scarlet. Kraznys mo Nakloz smiled broadly as their shadow fell across him.

Dany handed the slaver the end of Drogon's chain. In return he presented her with the whip. The handle was black dragonbone, elaborately carved and inlaid with gold. Nine long thin leather lashes trailed from it, each one tipped by a gilded claw. The gold pommel was a woman's head, with pointed ivory teeth. "The harpy's fingers," Kraznys named the scourge.

Dany turned the whip in her hand. *Such a light thing, to bear such weight.* "Is it done, then? Do they belong to me?"

"It is done," he agreed, giving the chain a sharp pull to bring Drogon down from the litter.

Dany mounted her silver. She could feel her heart thumping in her chest. She felt desperately afraid. *Was this what my brother would have done?* She wondered if Prince Rhaegar had been this anxious when he saw the Usurper's host formed up across the Trident with all their banners floating on the wind.

She stood in her stirrups and raised the harpy's fingers above her head for all the Unsullied to see. "*IT IS DONE!*" she cried at the top of her lungs. "*YOU ARE MINE!*" She gave the mare her heels and galloped along the first rank, holding the fingers high. "*YOU ARE THE DRAGON'S NOW! YOU'RE BOUGHT AND PAID FOR! IT IS DONE! IT IS DONE!*"

She glimpsed old Grazdan turn his grey head sharply. *He hears me speak Valyrian.* The other slavers were not listening. They crowded around Kraznys and the dragon, shouting advice. Though the Astapori yanked and tugged, Drogon would not budge off the litter. Smoke rose grey from his open jaws, and his long neck curled and straightened as he snapped at the slaver's face.

It is time to cross the Trident, Dany thought, as she wheeled and rode her silver back. Her bloodriders moved in close around her. "You are in difficulty," she observed.

"He will not come," Kraznys said.

"There is a reason. A dragon is no slave." And Dany swept the lash down as hard as she could across the slaver's face. Kraznys screamed and staggered back, the blood running red down his cheeks into his perfumed beard. The harpy's fingers had torn his features half to pieces with one slash, but she did not pause to contemplate the ruin. "Drogon," she sang out loudly, sweetly, all her fear forgotten. "*Dracarys*."

The black dragon spread his wings and roared.

A lance of swirling dark flame took Kraznys full in the face. His eyes melted and ran down his cheeks, and the oil in his hair and beard burst so fiercely into fire that for an instant the slaver wore a burning crown twice as tall as his head. The sudden stench of charred meat overwhelmed even his perfume, and his wail seemed to drown all other sound.

Then the Plaza of Punishment blew apart into blood and chaos. The Good Masters were shrieking, stumbling, shoving one another aside and tripping over the fringes of their *tokars* in their haste. Drogon flew almost lazily at Kraznys, black wings beating. As he gave the slaver another taste of fire, Irri and Jhiqui unchained Viserion and Rhaegal, and suddenly there were three dragons in the air. When Dany turned to look, a third of Astapor's proud demon-horned warriors were fighting to stay atop their terrified mounts, and another third were fleeing in a bright blaze of shiny copper. One man kept his saddle long enough to draw a sword, but Jhogo's whip coiled about his neck and cut off his shout. Another lost a hand to Rakharo's *arakh* and rode off reeling and spurting blood. Aggo sat calmly notching arrows to his bowstring and sending them at *tokars*. Silver, gold, or plain, he cared nothing for the fringe. Strong Belwas had his *arakh* out as well, and he spun it as he charged.

"*Spears!*" Dany heard one Astapori shout. It was Grazdan, old Grazdan in his tokar heavy with pearls. "*Unsullied!* Defend us, stop them, defend your masters! Spears! Swords!"

When Rakharo put an arrow through his mouth, the slaves holding his sedan chair broke and ran, dumping him unceremoniously on the ground. The old man crawled to the first rank of eunuchs, his blood pooling on the bricks.

The Unsullied did not so much as look down to watch him die. Rank on rank on rank, they stood.

And did not move. *The gods have heard my prayer.*

"Unsullied!" Dany galloped before them, her silver-gold braid flying behind her, her bell chiming with every stride. "Slay the Good Masters, slay the soldiers, slay every man who wears a *tokar* or holds a whip, but harm no child under twelve, and strike the chains off every slave you see." She raised the harpy's fingers in the air . . . and then she flung the scourge aside. "Freedom!" she sang out. *"Dracarys! Dracarys!"*

"Dracarys!" they shouted back, the sweetest word she'd ever heard. *"Dracarys! Dracarys!"* And all around them slavers ran and sobbed and begged and died, and the dusty air was filled with spears and fire.

SANSA

On the morning her new gown was to be ready, the serving girls filled Sansa's tub with steaming hot water and scrubbed her head to toe until she glowed pink. Cersei's own bedmaid trimmed her nails and brushed and curled her auburn hair so it fell down her back in soft ringlets. She brought a dozen of the queen's favorite scents as well. Sansa chose a sharp sweet fragrance with a hint of lemon in it under the smell of flowers. The maid dabbed some on her finger and touched Sansa behind each ear, and under her chin, and then lightly on her nipples.

Cersei herself arrived with the seamstress, and watched as they dressed Sansa in her new clothes. The smallclothes were all silk, but the gown itself was ivory samite and cloth-of-silver, and lined with silvery satin. The points of the long dagged sleeves almost touched the ground when she lowered her arms. And it was a woman's gown, not a little girl's, there was no doubt of that. The bodice was slashed in front almost to her belly, the deep vee covered over with a panel of ornate Myrish lace in dove-grey. The skirts were long and full, the waist so tight that Sansa had to hold her breath as they laced her into it. They brought her new shoes as well, slippers of soft grey doeskin that hugged her feet like lovers. "You are very beautiful, my lady," the seamstress said when she was dressed.

"I am, aren't I?" Sansa giggled, and spun, her skirts swirling around her. "Oh, I *am*." She could not wait for Willas to see her like this. *He will love me, he will, he must . . . he will forget Winterfell when he sees me, I'll see that he does.*

Queen Cersei studied her critically. "A few gems, I think. The moonstones Joffrey gave her."

"At once, Your Grace," her maid replied.

When the moonstones hung from Sansa's ears and about her neck, the queen nodded. "Yes. The gods have been kind to you, Sansa. You are a lovely girl. It seems almost obscene to squander such sweet innocence on that gargoyle."

"What gargoyle?" Sansa did not understand. Did she mean Willas? *How could she know?* No one knew, but her and Margaery and the Queen of Thorns . . . oh, and Dontos, but he didn't count.

Cersei Lannister ignored the question. "The cloak," she commanded, and the women brought it out: a long cloak of white velvet heavy with pearls. A fierce direwolf was embroidered upon it in silver thread. Sansa looked at it with sudden dread. "Your father's colors," said Cersei, as they fastened it about her neck with a slender silver chain.

A maiden's cloak. Sansa's hand went to her throat. She would have torn the thing away if she had dared.

"You're prettier with your mouth closed, Sansa," Cersei told her. "Come along now, the septon is waiting. And the wedding guests as well."

"No," Sansa blurted. "*No.*"

"Yes. You are a ward of the crown. The king stands in your father's place, since your brother is an attainted traitor. That means he has every right to dispose of your hand. You are to marry my brother Tyrion."

My claim, she thought, sickened. Dontos the Fool was not so foolish after all; he had seen the truth of it. Sansa backed away from the queen. "I won't." *I'm to marry Willas, I'm to be the lady of Highgarden, please . . .*

"I understand your reluctance. Cry if you must. In your

place, I would likely rip my hair out. He's a loathsome little imp, no doubt of it, but marry him you shall."

"You can't make me."

"Of course we can. You may come along quietly and say your vows as befits a lady, or you may struggle and scream and make a spectacle for the stableboys to titter over, but you will end up wedded and bedded all the same." The queen opened the door. Ser Meryn Trant and Ser Osmund Kettleblack were waiting without, in the white scale armor of the Kingsguard. "Escort Lady Sansa to the sept," she told them. "Carry her if you must, but try not to tear the gown, it was very costly."

Sansa tried to run, but Cersei's handmaid caught her before she'd gone a yard. Ser Meryn Trant gave her a look that made her cringe, but Kettleblack touched her almost gently and said, "Do as you're told, sweetling, it won't be so bad. Wolves are supposed to be brave, aren't they?"

Brave. Sansa took a deep breath. *I am a Stark, yes, I can be brave.* They were all looking at her, the way they had looked at her that day in the yard when Ser Boros Blount had torn her clothes off. It had been the Imp who saved her from a beating that day, the same man who was waiting for her now. *He is not so bad as the rest of them,* she told herself. "I'll go."

Cersei smiled. "I knew you would."

Afterward, she could not remember leaving the room or descending the steps or crossing the yard. It seemed to take all her attention just to put one foot down in front of the other. Ser Meryn and Ser Osmund walked beside her, in cloaks as pale as her own, lacking only the pearls and the direwolf that had been her father's. Joffrey himself was waiting for her on the steps of the castle sept. The king was resplendent in crimson and gold, his crown on his head. "I'm your father today," he announced.

"You're not," she flared. "You'll never be."

His face darkened. "I am. I'm your father, and I can marry you to whoever I like. To *anyone.* You'll marry the pig boy if I say so, and bed down with him in the sty." His green eyes glittered with amusement. "Or maybe I should give you to Ilyn Payne, would you like him better?"

Her heart lurched. "Please, Your Grace," she begged. "If

you ever loved me even a little bit, don't make me marry your—"

"—uncle?" Tyrion Lannister stepped through the doors of the sept. "Your Grace," he said to Joffrey. "Grant me a moment alone with Lady Sansa, if you would be so kind?"

The king was about to refuse, but his mother gave him a sharp look. They drew off a few feet.

Tyrion wore a doublet of black velvet covered with golden scrollwork, thigh-high boots that added three inches to his height, a chain of rubies and lions' heads. But the gash across his face was raw and red, and his nose was a hideous scab. "You are very beautiful, Sansa," he told her.

"It is good of you to say so, my lord." She did not know what else to say. *Should I tell him he is handsome? He'll think me a fool or a liar.* She lowered her gaze and held her tongue.

"My lady, this is no way to bring you to your wedding. I am sorry for that. And for making this so sudden, and so secret. My lord father felt it necessary, for reasons of state. Else I would have come to you sooner, as I wished." He waddled closer. "You did not ask for this marriage, I know. No more than I did. If I had refused you, however, they would have wed you to my cousin Lancel. Perhaps you would prefer that. He is nearer your age, and fairer to look upon. If that is your wish, say so, and I will end this farce."

I don't want any Lannister, she wanted to say. *I want Willas, I want Highgarden and the puppies and the barge, and sons named Eddard and Bran and Rickon.* But then she remembered what Dontos had told her in the godswood. *Tyrell or Lannister, it makes no matter, it's not me they want, only my claim.* "You are kind, my lord," she said, defeated. "I am a ward of the throne and my duty is to marry as the king commands."

He studied her with his mismatched eyes. "I know I am not the sort of husband young girls dream of, Sansa," he said softly, "but neither am I Joffrey."

"No," she said. "You were kind to me. I remember."

Tyrion offered her a thick, blunt-fingered hand. "Come, then. Let us do our duty."

So she put her hand in his, and he led her to the marriage altar, where the septon waited between the Mother and the Father to join their lives together. She saw Dontos in his fool's motley, looking at her with big round eyes. Ser Balon Swann and Ser Boros Blount were there in Kingsguard white, but not Ser Loras. *None of the Tyrells are here*, she realized suddenly. But there were other witnesses aplenty; the eunuch Varys, Ser Addam Marbrand, Lord Philip Foote, Ser Bronn, Jalabhar Xho, a dozen others. Lord Gyles was coughing, Lady Ermesande was at the breast, and Lady Tanda's pregnant daughter was sobbing for no apparent reason. *Let her sob*, Sansa thought. *Perhaps I shall do the same before this day is done.*

The ceremony passed as in a dream. Sansa did all that was required of her. There were prayers and vows and singing, and tall candles burning, a hundred dancing lights that the tears in her eyes transformed into a thousand. Thankfully no one seemed to notice that she was crying as she stood there, wrapped in her father's colors; or if they did, they pretended not to. In what seemed no time at all, they came to the changing of the cloaks.

As father of the realm, Joffrey took the place of Lord Eddard Stark. Sansa stood stiff as a lance as his hands came over her shoulders to fumble with the clasp of her cloak. One of them brushed her breast and lingered to give it a little squeeze. Then the clasp opened, and Joff swept her maiden's cloak away with a kingly flourish and a grin.

His uncle's part went less well. The bride's cloak he held was huge and heavy, crimson velvet richly worked with lions and bordered with gold satin and rubies. No one had thought to bring a stool, however, and Tyrion stood a foot and a half shorter than his bride. As he moved behind her, Sansa felt a sharp tug on her skirt. *He wants me to kneel*, she realized, blushing. She was mortified. It was not supposed to be this way. She had dreamed of her wedding a thousand times, and always she had pictured how her betrothed would stand behind her tall and strong, sweep the cloak of his protection over her shoulders, and tenderly kiss her cheek as he leaned forward to fasten the clasp.

She felt another tug at her skirt, more insistent. *I won't. Why should I spare his feelings, when no one cares about mine?*

The dwarf tugged at her a third time. Stubbornly she pressed her lips together and pretended not to notice. Someone behind them tittered. *The queen*, she thought, but it didn't matter. They were all laughing by then, Joffrey the loudest. "Dontos, down on your hands and knees," the king commanded. "My uncle needs a boost to climb his bride."

And so it was that her lord husband cloaked her in the colors of House Lannister whilst standing on the back of a fool.

When Sansa turned, the little man was gazing up at her, his mouth tight, his face as red as her cloak. Suddenly she was ashamed of her stubbornness. She smoothed her skirts and knelt in front of him, so their heads were on the same level. "With this kiss I pledge my love, and take you for my lord and husband."

"With this kiss I pledge my love," the dwarf replied hoarsely, "and take you for my lady and wife." He leaned forward, and their lips touched briefly.

He is so ugly, Sansa thought when his face was close to hers. *He is even uglier than the Hound.*

The septon raised his crystal high, so the rainbow light fell down upon them. "Here in the sight of gods and men," he said, "I do solemnly proclaim Tyrion of House Lannister and Sansa of House Stark to be man and wife, one flesh, one heart, one soul, now and forever, and cursed be the one who comes between them."

She had to bite her lip to keep from sobbing.

The wedding feast was held in the Small Hall. There were perhaps fifty guests; Lannister retainers and allies for the most part, joining those who had been at the wedding. And here Sansa found the Tyrells. Margaery gave her such a sad look, and when the Queen of Thorns tottered in between Left and Right, she never looked at her at all. Elinor, Alla, and Megga seemed determined not to know her. *My friends,* Sansa thought bitterly.

Her husband drank heavily and ate but little. He listened whenever someone rose to make a toast and sometimes nodded a curt acknowledgment, but otherwise his face might have been made of stone. The feast seemed to go on forever, though Sansa tasted none of the food. She wanted it to be done, and yet she dreaded its end. For after the feast would come the bedding. The men would carry her up to her wedding bed, undressing her on the way and making rude jokes about the fate that awaited her between

the sheets, while the women did Tyrion the same honors.
Only after they had been bundled naked into bed would
they be left alone, and even then the guests would stand
outside the bridal chamber, shouting ribald suggestions
through the door. The bedding had seemed wonderfully
wicked and exciting when Sansa was a girl, but now that
the moment was upon her she felt only dread. She did not
think she could bear for them to rip off her clothes, and she
was certain she would burst into tears at the first randy
jape.

When the musicians began to play, she timidly laid her
hand on Tyrion's and said, "My lord, should we lead the
dance?"

His mouth twisted. "I think we have already given them
sufficent amusement for one day, don't you?"

"As you say, my lord." She pulled her hand back.

Joffrey and Margaery led in their place. *How can a monster dance so beautifully?* Sansa wondered. She had often
daydreamed of how she would dance at her wedding, with
every eye upon her and her handsome lord. In her dreams
they had all been smiling. *Not even my husband is smiling.*

Other guests soon joined the king and his betrothed on
the floor. Elinor danced with her young squire, and Megga
with Prince Tommen. Lady Merryweather, the Myrish
beauty with the black hair and the big dark eyes, spun so
provocatively that every man in the hall was soon watching her. Lord and Lady Tyrell moved more sedately. Ser
Kevan Lannister begged the honor of Lady Janna Fossoway,
Lord Tyrell's sister. Merry Crane took the floor with the exile prince Jalabhar Xho, gorgeous in his feathered finery.
Cersei Lannister partnered first Lord Redwyne, then Lord
Rowan, and finally her own father, who danced with
smooth unsmiling grace.

Sansa sat with her hands in her lap, watching how the
queen moved and laughed and tossed her blonde curls. *She
charms them all*, she thought dully. *How I hate her*. She
looked away, to where Moon Boy danced with Dontos.

"Lady Sansa." Ser Garlan Tyrell stood beside the dais.
"Would you honor me? If your lord consents?"

The Imp's mismatched eyes narrowed. "My lady can
dance with whomever she pleases."

Perhaps she ought to have remained beside her husband,

but she wanted to dance so badly . . . and Ser Garlan was brother to Margaery, to Willas, to her Knight of Flowers. "I see why they name you Garlan the Gallant, ser," she said, as she took his hand.

"My lady is gracious to say so. My brother Willas gave me that name, as it happens. To protect me."

"To protect you?" She gave him a puzzled look.

Ser Garlan laughed. "I was a plump little boy, I fear, and we do have an uncle called Garth the Gross. So Willas struck first, though not before threatening me with Garlan the Greensick, Garlan the Galling, and Garlan the Gargoyle."

It was so sweet and silly that Sansa had to laugh, despite everything. Afterward she was absurdly grateful. Somehow the laughter made her hopeful again, if only for a little while. Smiling, she let the music take her, losing herself in the steps, in the sound of flute and pipes and harp, in the rhythm of the drum . . . and from time to time in Ser Garlan's arms, when the dance brought them together. "My lady wife is most concerned for you," he said quietly, one such time.

"Lady Leonette is too sweet. Tell her I am well."

"A bride at her wedding should be more than *well*." His voice was not unkind. "You seemed close to tears."

"Tears of joy, ser."

"Your eyes give the lie to your tongue." Ser Garlan turned her, drew her close to his side. "My lady, I have seen how you look at my brother. Loras is valiant and handsome, and we all love him dearly . . . but your Imp will make a better husband. He is a bigger man than he seems, I think."

The music spun them apart before Sansa could think of a reply. It was Mace Tyrell opposite her, red-faced and sweaty, and then Lord Merryweather, and then Prince Tommen. "I want to be married too," said the plump little princeling, who was all of nine. "I'm taller than my uncle!"

"I know you are," said Sansa, before the partners changed again. Ser Kevan told her she was beautiful, Jalabhar Xho said something she did not understand in the Summer Tongue, and Lord Redwyne wished her many fat children and long years of joy. And then the dance brought her face-to-face with Joffrey.

Sansa stiffened as his hand touched hers, but the king tightened his grip and drew her closer. "You shouldn't look so sad. My uncle is an ugly little thing, but you'll still have me."

"You're to marry Margaery!"

"A king can have other women. Whores. My father did. One of the Aegons did too. The third one, or the fourth. He had lots of whores and lots of bastards." As they whirled to the music, Joff gave her a moist kiss. "My uncle will bring you to my bed whenever I command it."

Sansa shook her head. "He won't."

"He will, or I'll have his head. That King Aegon, he had any woman he wanted, whether they were married or no."

Thankfully, it was time to change again. Her legs had turned to wood, though, and Lord Rowan, Ser Tallad, and Elinor's squire all must have thought her a very clumsy dancer. And then she was back with Ser Garlan once more, and soon, blessedly, the dance was over.

Her relief was short-lived. No sooner had the music died than she heard Joffrey say, "It's time to bed them! Let's get the clothes off her, and have a look at what the she-wolf's got to give my uncle!" Other men took up the cry, loudly.

Her dwarf husband lifted his eyes slowly from his wine cup. "I'll have no bedding."

Joffrey seized Sansa's arm. "You will if I command it."

The Imp slammed his dagger down in the table, where it stood quivering. "Then you'll service your own bride with a wooden prick. I'll geld you, I swear it."

A shocked silence fell. Sansa pulled away from Joffrey, but he had a grip on her, and her sleeve ripped. No one even seemed to hear. Queen Cersei turned to her father. "Did you hear him?"

Lord Tywin rose from his seat. "I believe we can dispense with the bedding. Tyrion, I am certain you did not mean to threaten the king's royal person."

Sansa saw a spasm of rage pass across her husband's face. "I misspoke," he said. "It was a bad jape, sire."

"You threatened to *geld* me!" Joffrey said shrilly.

"I did, Your Grace," said Tyrion, "but only because I envied your royal manhood. Mine own is so small and stunted." His face twisted into a leer. "And if you take my tongue, you will leave me no way at all to pleasure this sweet wife you gave me."

Laughter burst from the lips of Ser Osmund Kettleblack. Someone else sniggered. But Joff did not laugh, nor Lord Tywin. "Your Grace," he said, "my son is drunk, you can see that."

"I am," the Imp confessed, "but not so drunk that I cannot attend to my own bedding." He hopped down from the dais and grabbed Sansa roughly. "Come, wife, time to smash your portcullis. I want to play come-into-the-castle."

Red-faced, Sansa went with him from the Small Hall. *What choice do I have?* Tyrion waddled when he walked, especially when he walked as quickly as he did now. The gods were merciful, and neither Joffrey nor any of the others moved to follow.

For their wedding night, they had been granted the use of an airy bedchamber high in the Tower of the Hand. Tyrion kicked the door shut behind them. "There is a flagon of good Arbor gold on the sideboard, Sansa. Will you be so kind as to pour me a cup?"

"Is that wise, my lord?"

"Nothing was ever wiser. I am not truly drunk, you see. But I mean to be."

Sansa filled a goblet for each of them. *It will be easier if I am drunk as well.* She sat on the edge of the great curtained bed and drained half her cup in three long swallows. No doubt it was very fine wine, but she was too nervous to taste it. It made her head swim. "Would you have me undress, my lord?"

"Tyrion." He cocked his head. "My name is Tyrion, Sansa."

"Tyrion. My lord. Should I take off my gown, or do you want to undress me?" She took another swallow of wine.

The Imp turned away from her. "The first time I wed, there was us and a drunken septon, and some pigs to bear witness. We ate one of our witnesses at our wedding feast. Tysha fed me crackling and I licked the grease off her fingers, and we were laughing when we fell into bed."

"You were wed before? I . . . I had forgotten."

"You did not forget. You never knew."

"Who was she, my lord?" Sansa was curious despite herself.

"Lady Tysha." His mouth twisted. "Of House Silverfist.

Their arms have one gold coin and a hundred silver, upon a bloody sheet. Ours was a very short marriage . . . as befits a very short man, I suppose."

Sansa stared down at her hands and said nothing.

"How old are you, Sansa?" asked Tyrion, after a moment.

"Thirteen," she said, "when the moon turns."

"Gods have mercy." The dwarf took another swallow of wine. "Well, talk won't make you older. Shall we get on with this, my lady? If it please you?"

"It will please me to please my lord husband."

That seemed to anger him. "You hide behind courtesy as if it were a castle wall."

"Courtesy is a lady's armor," Sansa said. Her septa had always told her that.

"I am your husband. You can take off your armor now."

"And my clothing?"

"That too." He waved his wine cup at her. "My lord father has commanded me to consummate this marriage."

Her hands trembled as she began fumbling at her clothes. She had ten thumbs instead of fingers, and all of them were broken. Yet somehow she managed the laces and buttons, and her cloak and gown and girdle and undersilk slid to the floor, until finally she was stepping out of her smallclothes. Gooseprickles covered her arms and legs. She kept her eyes on the floor, too shy to look at him, but when she was done she glanced up and found him staring. There was hunger in his green eye, it seemed to her, and fury in the black. Sansa did not know which scared her more.

"You're a child," he said.

She covered her breasts with her hands. "I've flowered."

"A child," he repeated, "but I want you. Does that frighten you, Sansa?"

"Yes."

"Me as well. I know I am ugly—"

"No, my—"

He pushed himself to his feet. "Don't lie, Sansa. I am malformed, scarred, and small, but . . ." she could see him groping ". . . abed, when the candles are blown out, I am made no worse than other men. In the dark, I am the Knight of Flowers." He took a draught of wine. "I am gen-

erous. Loyal to those who are loyal to me. I've proven I'm
no craven. And I am cleverer than most, surely wits count
for something. I can even be kind. Kindness is not a habit
with us Lannisters, I fear, but I know I have some somewhere. I could be . . . I could be good to you."

He is as frightened as I am, Sansa realized. Perhaps that
should have made her feel more kindly toward him, but it
did not. All she felt was pity, and pity was death to desire.
He was looking at her, waiting for her to say something,
but all her words had withered. She could only stand there
trembling.

When he finally realized that she had no answer for him,
Tyrion Lannister drained the last of his wine. "I understand," he said bitterly. "Get in the bed, Sansa. We need to
do our duty."

She climbed onto the featherbed, conscious of his stare.
A scented beeswax candle burned on the bedside table and
rose petals had been strewn between the sheets. She had
started to pull up a blanket to cover herself when she heard
him say, "No."

The cold made her shiver, but she obeyed. Her eyes
closed, and she waited. After a moment she heard the
sound of her husband pulling off his boots, and the rustle of
clothing as he undressed himself. When he hopped up on
the bed and put his hand on her breast, Sansa could not
help but shudder. She lay with her eyes closed, every muscle tense, dreading what might come next. Would he touch
her again? Kiss her? Should she open her legs for him now?
She did not know what was expected of her.

"Sansa." The hand was gone. "Open your eyes."

She had promised to obey; she opened her eyes. He was
sitting by her feet, naked. Where his legs joined, his man's
staff poked up stiff and hard from a thicket of coarse yellow
hair, but it was the only thing about him that was straight.

"My lady," Tyrion said, "you are lovely, make no mistake, but . . . I cannot do this. My father be damned. We
will wait. The turn of a moon, a year, a season, however
long it takes. Until you have come to know me better, and
perhaps to trust me a little." His smile might have been
meant to be reassuring, but without a nose it only made
him look more grotesque and sinister.

Look at him, Sansa told herself, *look at your husband*,

*at all of him, Septa Mordane said all men are beautiful,
find his beauty, try.* She stared at the stunted legs, the
swollen brutish brow, the green eye and the black one, the
raw stump of his nose and crooked pink scar, the coarse
tangle of black and gold hair that passed for his beard. Even
his manhood was ugly, thick and veined, with a bulbous
purple head. *This is not right, this is not fair, how have I
sinned that the gods would do this to me, how?*

"On my honor as a Lannister," the Imp said, "I will not
touch you until you want me to."

It took all the courage that was in her to look in those
mismatched eyes and say, "And if I never want you to, my
lord?"

His mouth jerked as if she had slapped him. "Never?"

Her neck was so tight she could scarcely nod.

"Why," he said, "that is why the gods made whores for
imps like me." He closed his short blunt fingers into a fist,
and climbed down off the bed.

ARYA

Stoney Sept was the biggest town Arya had seen since King's Landing, and Harwin said her father had won a famous battle here.

"The Mad King's men had been hunting Robert, trying to catch him before he could rejoin your father," he told her as they rode toward the gate. "He was wounded, being tended by some friends, when Lord Connington the Hand took the town with a mighty force and started searching house by house. Before they could find him, though, Lord Eddard and your grandfather came down on the town and stormed the walls. Lord Connington fought back fierce. They battled in the streets and alleys, even on the rooftops, and all the septons rang their bells so the smallfolk would know to lock their doors. Robert came out of hiding to join the fight when the bells began to ring. He slew six men that day, they say. One was Myles Mooton, a famous knight who'd been Prince Rhaegar's squire. He would have slain the Hand too, but the battle never brought them together. Connington wounded your grandfather Tully sore, though, and killed Ser Denys Arryn, the darling of the Vale. But when he saw the day was lost, he flew off as fast as the griffins on his shield. The Battle of the Bells, they called it after. Robert always said your father won it, not him."

More recent battles had been fought here as well, Arya thought from the look of the place. The town gates were made of raw new wood; outside the walls a pile of charred planks remained to tell what had happened to the old ones.

Stoney Sept was closed up tight, but when the captain of the gate saw who they were, he opened a sally port for them. "How you fixed for food?" Tom asked as they entered.

"Not so bad as we were. The Huntsman brought in a flock o' sheep, and there's been some trading across the Blackwater. The harvest wasn't burned south o' the river. Course, there's plenty want to take what we got. Wolves one day, Mummers the next. Them that's not looking for food are looking for plunder, or women to rape, and them that's not out for gold or wenches are looking for the bloody Kingslayer. Talk is, he slipped right through Lord Edmure's fingers."

"*Lord* Edmure?" Lem frowned. "Is Lord Hoster dead, then?"

"Dead or dying. Think Lannister might be making for the Blackwater? It's the quickest way to King's Landing, the Huntsman swears." The captain did not wait for an answer. "He took his dogs out for a sniff round. If Ser Jaime's hereabouts, they'll find him. I've seen them dogs rip bears apart. Think they'll like the taste of lion blood?"

"A chewed-up corpse's no good to no one," said Lem. "The Huntsman bloody well knows that, too."

"When the westermen came through they raped the Huntsman's wife and sister, put his crops to the torch, ate half his sheep, and killed the other half for spite. Killed six dogs too, and threw the carcasses down his well. A chewed-up corpse would be plenty good enough for him, I'd say. Me as well."

"He'd best not," said Lem. "That's all I got to say. He'd best not, and you're a bloody fool."

Arya rode between Harwin and Anguy as the outlaws moved down the streets where her father once had fought. She could see the sept on its hill, and below it a stout strong holdfast of grey stone that looked much too small for such a big town. But every third house they passed was a blackened shell, and she saw no people. "Are all the townfolk dead?"

"Only shy." Anguy pointed out two bowmen on a roof, and some boys with sooty faces crouched in the rubble of an alehouse. Farther on, a baker threw open a shuttered window and shouted down to Lem. The sound of his voice brought more people out of hiding, and Stoney Sept slowly seemed to come to life around them.

In the market square at the town's heart stood a fountain in the shape of a leaping trout, spouting water into a shallow pool. Women were filling pails and flagons there. A few feet away, a dozen iron cages hung from creaking wooden posts. *Crow cages,* Arya knew. The crows were mostly outside the cages, splashing in the water or perched atop the bars; inside were men. Lem reined up scowling. "What's this, now?"

"Justice," answered a woman at the fountain.

"What, did you run short o' hempen rope?"

"Was this done at Ser Wilbert's decree?" asked Tom.

A man laughed bitterly. "The lions killed Ser Wilbert a year ago. His sons are all off with the Young Wolf, getting fat in the west. You think they give a damn for the likes of us? It was the Mad Huntsman caught these wolves."

Wolves. Arya went cold. *Robb's men, and my father's.* She felt drawn toward the cages. The bars allowed so little room that prisoners could neither sit nor turn; they stood naked, exposed to sun and wind and rain. The first three cages held dead men. Carrion crows had eaten out their eyes, yet the empty sockets seemed to follow her. The fourth man in the row stirred as she passed. Around his mouth his ragged beard was thick with blood and flies. They exploded when he spoke, buzzing around his head. "*Water.*" The word was a croak. "Please . . . water . . ."

The man in the next cage opened his eyes at the sound. "Here," he said. "Here, me." An old man, he was; his beard was grey and his scalp was bald and mottled brown with age.

There was another dead man beyond the old one, a big red-bearded man with a rotting grey bandage covering his left ear and part of his temple. But the worst thing was between his legs, where nothing remained but a crusted brown hole crawling with maggots. Farther down was a fat man. The crow cage was so cruelly narrow it was hard to see how they'd ever gotten him inside. The iron dug painfully into his belly, squeezing bulges out between the bars. Long days baking in the sun had burned him a painful red from head to heel. When he shifted his weight, his cage creaked and swayed, and Arya could see pale white stripes where the bars had shielded his flesh from the sun.

"Whose men were you?" she asked them.

At the sound of her voice, the fat man opened his eyes. The skin around them was so red they looked like boiled eggs floating in a dish of blood. "Water . . . a drink . . ."

"Whose?" she said again.

"Pay them no mind, boy," the townsman told her. "They're none o' your concern. Ride on by."

"What did they do?" she asked him.

"They put eight people to the sword at Tumbler's Falls," he said. "They wanted the Kingslayer, but he wasn't there so they did some rape and murder." He jerked a thumb toward the corpse with maggots where his manhood ought to be. "That one there did the raping. Now move along."

"A swallow," the fat one called down. "Ha' mercy, boy, a swallow." The old one slid an arm up to grasp the bars. The motion made his cage swing violently. "Water," gasped the one with the flies in his beard.

She looked at their filthy hair and scraggly beards and reddened eyes, at their dry, cracked, bleeding lips. *Wolves*, she thought again. *Like me.* Was this her pack? *How could they be Robb's men?* She wanted to hit them. She wanted to hurt them. She wanted to cry. They all seemed to be looking at her, the living and the dead alike. The old man had squeezed three fingers out between the bars. "Water," he said, "water."

Arya swung down from her horse. *They can't hurt me, they're dying.* She took her cup from her bedroll and went to the fountain. "What do you think you're doing, boy?" the townsman snapped. "They're no concern o' yours." She raised the cup to the fish's mouth. The water splashed across her fingers and down her sleeve, but Arya did not move until the cup was brimming over. When she turned back toward the cages, the townsman moved to stop her. "You get away from them, boy—"

"She's a girl," said Harwin. "Leave her be."

"Aye," said Lem. "Lord Beric don't hold with caging men to die of thirst. Why don't you hang them decent?"

"There was nothing decent 'bout them things they did at Tumbler's Falls," the townsman growled right back at him.

The bars were too narrow to pass a cup through, but Harwin and Gendry offered her a leg up. She planted a foot in Harwin's cupped hands, vaulted onto Gendry's shoulders, and grabbed the bars on top of the cage. The fat man turned his face up and pressed his cheek to the iron, and Arya poured the water over him. He sucked at it eagerly and let it run down over his head and cheeks and hands, and then he licked the dampness off the bars. He would have licked Arya's fingers if she hadn't snatched them back. By the time she served the other two the same, a crowd had gathered to watch her. "The Mad Huntsman will hear of this," a man threatened. "He won't like it. No, he won't."

"He'll like this even less, then." Anguy strung his long-bow, slid an arrow from his quiver, nocked, drew, loosed. The fat man shuddered as the shaft drove up between his chins, but the cage would not let him fall. Two more arrows ended the other two northmen. The only sound in the market square was the splash of falling water and the buzzing of flies.

Valar morghulis, Arya thought.

On the east side of the market square stood a modest inn with whitewashed walls and broken windows. Half its roof had burnt off recently, but the hole had been patched over. Above the door hung a wooden shingle painted as a peach, with a big bite taken out of it. They dismounted at the stables sitting catty-corner, and Greenbeard bellowed for grooms.

The buxom red-haired innkeep howled with pleasure at the sight of them, then promptly set to tweaking them. "Greenbeard, is it? Or Greybeard? Mother take mercy, when did you get so old? Lem, is that you? Still wearing the same ratty cloak, are you? I know why you never wash it, I do. You're afraid all the piss will wash out and we'll see you're really a knight o' the Kingsguard! And Tom o' Sevens, you randy old goat! You come to see that son o' yours? Well, you're too late, he's off riding with that bloody Huntsman. And don't tell me he's not yours!"

"He hasn't got my voice," Tom protested weakly.

"He's got your nose, though. Aye, and t'other parts as well, to hear the girls talk." She spied Gendry then, and pinched him on the cheek. "Look at this fine young ox. Wait till Alyce sees those arms. Oh, and he blushes like a maid, too. Well, Alyce will fix that for you, boy, see if she don't."

Arya had never seen Gendry turn so red. "Tansy, you leave the Bull alone, he's a good lad," said Tom Seven-strings. "All we need from you is safe beds for a night."

"Speak for yourself, singer." Anguy slid his arm around a strapping young serving girl as freckly as he was.

"Beds we got," said red-haired Tansy. "There's never been no lack o' beds at the Peach. But you'll all climb in a tub first. Last time you lot stayed under my roof you left your fleas behind." She poked Greenbeard in the chest. "And yours was green, too. You want food?"

"If you can spare it, we won't say no," Tom conceded.

"Now when did you ever say no to anything, Tom?" the woman hooted. "I'll roast some mutton for your friends, and an old dry rat for you. It's more than you deserve, but if you gargle me a song or three, might be I'll weaken. I always pity the afflicted. Come on, come on. Cass, Lanna, put some kettles on. Jyzene, help me get the clothes off them, we'll need to boil those too."

She made good on all her threats. Arya tried to tell them that she'd been bathed *twice* at Acorn Hall, not a fortnight past, but the red-haired woman was having none of it. Two serving wenches carried her up the stairs bodily, arguing about whether she was a girl or a boy. The one called Helly won, so the other had to fetch the hot water and scrub Arya's back with a stiff bristly brush that almost took her skin off. Then they stole all the clothes that Lady Smallwood had given her and dressed her up like one of Sansa's dolls in linen and lace. But at least when they were done she got to go down and eat.

As she sat in the common room in her stupid girl clothes, Arya remembered what Syrio Forel had told her, the trick of looking and seeing what was there. When she looked, she saw more serving wenches than any inn could want, and most of them young and comely. And come evenfall, lots of men started coming and going at the Peach. They did not linger long in the common room, not even when Tom took out his woodharp and began to sing "Six Maids in a Pool." The wooden steps were old and steep, and creaked something fierce whenever one of the men took a girl upstairs. "I bet this is a brothel," she whispered to Gendry.

"You don't even know what a brothel is."

"I do so," she insisted. "It's like an inn, with girls."

He was turning red again. "What are you doing here, then?" he demanded. "A brothel's no fit place for no bloody highborn lady, everybody knows that."

One of the girls sat down on the bench beside him. "Who's a highborn lady? The little skinny one?" She looked at Arya and laughed. "I'm a king's daughter myself."

Arya knew she was being mocked. "You are not."

"Well, I might be." When the girl shrugged, her gown slipped off one shoulder. "They say King Robert fucked my mother when he hid here, back before the battle. Not that he didn't have all the other girls too, but Leslyn says he liked my ma the best."

The girl *did* have hair like the old king's, Arya thought; a great thick mop of it, as black as coal. *That doesn't mean anything, though. Gendry has the same kind of hair too. Lots of people have black hair.*

"I'm named Bella," the girl told Gendry. "For the battle. I bet I could ring *your* bell, too. You want to?"

"No," he said gruffly.

"I bet you do." She ran a hand along his arm. "I don't cost nothing to friends of Thoros and the lightning lord."

"*No*, I said." Gendry rose abruptly and stalked away from the table out into the night.

Bella turned to Arya. "Don't he like girls?"

Arya shrugged. "He's just stupid. He likes to polish helmets and beat on swords with hammers."

"Oh." Bella tugged her gown back over her shoulder and went to talk with Jack-Be-Lucky. Before long she was sitting in his lap, giggling and drinking wine from his cup. Greenbeard had two girls, one on each knee. Anguy had vanished with his freckle-faced wench, and Lem was gone as well. Tom Sevenstrings sat by the fire, singing. "The Maids that Bloom in Spring." Arya sipped at the cup of watered wine the red-haired woman had allowed her, listening. Across the square the dead men were rotting in their crow cages, but inside the Peach everyone was jolly. Except it seemed to her that some of them were laughing too hard, somehow.

It would have been a good time to sneak away and steal a horse, but Arya couldn't see how that would help her. She could only ride as far as the city gates. *That captain would never let me pass, and if he did, Harwin would come after me, or that Huntsman with his dogs.* She wished she had her map, so she could see how far Stoney Sept was from Riverrun.

By the time her cup was empty, Arya was yawning. Gendry hadn't come back. Tom Sevenstrings was singing "Two Hearts that Beat as One," and kissing a different girl at the end of every verse. In the corner by the window Lem and Harwin sat talking to red-haired Tansy in low voices. ". . . spent the night in Jaime's cell," she heard the woman say. "Her and this other wench, the one who slew Renly. All three o' them together, and come the morn Lady Catelyn cut him loose for love." She gave a throaty chuckle.

It's not true, Arya thought. *She never would.* She felt sad and angry and lonely, all at once.

An old man sat down beside her. "Well, aren't you a pretty little peach?" His breath smelled near as foul as the dead men in the cages, and his little pig eyes were crawling up and down her. "Does my sweet peach have a name?"

For half a heartbeat she forgot who she was supposed to be. She wasn't any peach, but she couldn't be Arya Stark either, not here with some smelly drunk she did not know. "I'm . . ."

"She's my sister." Gendry put a heavy hand on the old man's shoulder, and squeezed. "Leave her be."

The man turned, spoiling for a quarrel, but when he saw Gendry's size he thought better of it. "Your sister, is she? What kind of brother are you? I'd never bring no sister of mine to the Peach, that I wouldn't." He got up from the bench and moved off muttering, in search of a new friend.

"Why did you say that?" Arya hopped to her feet. "You're not my brother."

"That's right," he said angrily. "I'm too bloody lowborn to be kin to m'lady high."

Arya was taken aback by the fury in his voice. "That's not the way I meant it."

"Yes it is." He sat down on the bench, cradling a cup of wine between his hands. "Go away. I want to drink this wine in peace. Then maybe I'll go find that black-haired girl and ring her bell for her."

"But . . ."

"I said, *go away*. M'lady."

Arya whirled and left him there. *A stupid bullheaded bastard boy, that's all he is.* He could ring all the bells he wanted, it was nothing to her.

Their sleeping room was at the top of the stairs, under the eaves. Maybe the Peach had no lack of beds, but there was only one to spare for the likes of them. It was a *big* bed, though. It filled the whole room, just about, and the musty straw-stuffed mattress looked large enough for all of them. Just now, though, she had it to herself. Her real clothes were hanging from a peg on the wall, between Gendry's stuff and Lem's. Arya took off the linen and lace, pulled her tunic over her head, climbed up into the bed, and burrowed under the blankets. "Queen Cersei," she whispered into the pillow. "King Joffrey, Ser Ilyn, Ser Meryn. Dunsen, Raff, and Polliver. The Tickler, the Hound, and Ser Gregor the Mountain." She liked to mix up the order of the names sometimes. It helped her remember who they were and what they'd done. *Maybe some of them are dead,* she thought. *Maybe they're in iron cages someplace, and the crows are picking out their eyes.*

Sleep came as quick as she closed her eyes. She dreamed of wolves that night, stalking through a wet wood with the smell of rain and rot and blood thick in the air. Only they were good smells in the dream, and Arya knew she had nothing to fear. She was strong and swift and fierce, and her pack was all around her, her brothers and her sisters. They ran down a frightened horse together, tore its throat out, and feasted. And when the moon broke through the clouds, she threw back her head and *howled.*

But when the day came, she woke to the barking of dogs.

Arya sat up yawning. Gendry was stirring on her left and Lem Lemoncloak snoring loudly to her right, but the baying outside all but drowned him out. *There must be half a hundred dogs out there.* She crawled from under the blankets and hopped over Lem, Tom, and Jack-Be-Lucky to the window. When she opened the shutters wide, wind and wet and cold all came flooding in together. The day was grey and overcast. Down below, in the square, the dogs were barking, running in circles, growling and howling. There was a pack of them, great black mastiffs and lean wolfhounds and black-and-white sheepdogs and kinds Arya did not know, shaggy brindled beasts with long yellow teeth. Between the inn and the fountain, a dozen riders sat astride their horses, watching the townsmen open the fat man's cage and tug his arm until his swollen corpse spilled out onto the ground. The dogs were at him at once, tearing chunks of flesh off his bones.

Arya heard one of the riders laugh. "Here's your new castle, you bloody Lannister bastard," he said. "A little snug for the likes o' you, but we'll squeeze you in, never fret." Beside him a prisoner sat sullen, with coils of hempen rope tight around his wrists. Some of the townsmen were throwing dung at him, but he never flinched. "You'll *rot* in them cages," his captor was shouting. "The crows will be picking out your eyes while we're spending all that good Lannister gold o' yours! And when them crows are done, we'll send what's left o' you to your bloody brother. Though I doubt he'll know you."

The noise had woken half the Peach. Gendry squeezed into the window beside Arya, and Tom stepped up behind them naked as his name day. "What's all that bloody shouting?" Lem complained from bed. "A man's trying to get some bloody sleep."

"Where's Greenbeard?" Tom asked him.

"Abed with Tansy," Lem said. "Why?"

"Best find him. Archer too. The Mad Huntsman's come back, with another man for the cages."

"Lannister," said Arya. "I heard him say *Lannister*."

"Have they caught the Kingslayer?" Gendry wanted to know.

Down in the square, a thrown stone caught the captive on the cheek, turning his head. *Not the Kingslayer*, Arya thought, when she saw his face. The gods had heard her prayers after all.

JON

Ghost was gone when the wildings led their horses from the cave. *Did he understand about Castle Black?* Jon took a breath of the crisp morning air and allowed himself to hope. The eastern sky was pink near the horizon and pale grey higher up. The Sword of the Morning still hung in the south, the bright white star in its hilt blazing like a diamond in the dawn, but the blacks and greys of the darkling forest were turning once again to greens and golds, reds and russets. And above the soldier pines and oaks and ash and sentinels stood the Wall, the ice pale and glimmering beneath the dust and dirt that pocked its surface.

The Magnar sent a dozen men riding west and a dozen more east, to climb the highest hills they could find and watch for any sign of rangers in the wood or riders on the high ice. The Thenns carried bronze-banded warhorns to give warning should the Watch be sighted. The other wildings fell in behind Jarl, Jon and Ygritte with the rest. This was to be the young raider's hour of glory.

The Wall was often said to stand seven hundred feet

high, but Jarl had found a place where it was both higher and lower. Before them, the ice rose sheer from out of the trees like some immense cliff, crowned by wind-carved battlements that loomed at least eight hundred feet high, perhaps nine hundred in spots. But that was deceptive, Jon realized as they drew closer. Brandon the Builder had laid his huge foundation blocks along the heights wherever feasible, and hereabouts the hills rose wild and rugged.

He had once heard his uncle Benjen say that the Wall was a sword east of Castle Black, but a snake to the west. It was true. Sweeping in over one huge humped hill, the ice dipped down into a valley, climbed the knife edge of a long granite ridgeline for a league or more, ran along a jagged crest, dipped again into a valley deeper still, and then rose higher and higher, leaping from hill to hill as far as the eye could see, into the mountainous west.

Jarl had chosen to assault the stretch of ice along the ridge. Here, though the top of the Wall loomed eight hundred feet above the forest floor, a good third of that height was earth and stone rather than ice; the slope was too steep for their horses, almost as difficult a scramble as the Fist of the First Men, but still vastly easier to ascend than the sheer vertical face of the Wall itself. And the ridge was densely wooded as well, offering easy concealment. Once brothers in black had gone out every day with axes to cut back the encroaching trees, but those days were long past, and here the forest grew right up to the ice.

The day promised to be damp and cold, and damper and colder by the Wall, beneath those tons of ice. The closer they got, the more the Thenns held back. *They have never seen the Wall before, not even the Magnar,* Jon realized. *It frightens them.* In the Seven Kingdoms it was said that the Wall marked the end of the world. *That is true for them as well.* It was all in where you stood.

And where do I stand? Jon did not know. To stay with Ygritte, he would need to become a wildling heart and soul. If he abandoned her to return to his duty, the Magnar might cut her heart out. And if he took her with him ... assuming she would go, which was far from certain ... well, he could scarcely bring her back to Castle Black to live among the brothers. A deserter and a wildling could expect no welcome anywhere in the Seven Kingdoms. *We could go look for Gendel's children, I suppose. Though they'd be more like to eat us than to take us in.*

The Wall did not awe Jarl's raiders, Jon saw. *They have done this before, every man of them.* Jarl called out names when they dismounted beneath the ridge, and eleven gathered round him. All were young. The oldest could not have been more than five-and-twenty, and two of the ten were younger than Jon. Every one was lean and hard, though; they had a look of sinewy strength that reminded him of Stonesnake, the brother the Halfhand had sent off afoot when Rattleshirt was hunting them.

In the very shadow of the Wall the wildlings made ready, winding thick coils of hempen rope around one shoulder and down across their chests, and lacing on queer boots of supple doeskin. The boots had spikes jutting from the toes; iron, for Jarl and two others, bronze for some, but most often jagged bone. Small stone-headed hammers hung from one hip, a leathern bag of stakes from the other. Their ice axes were antlers with sharpened tines, bound to wooden hafts with strips of hide. The eleven climbers sorted themselves into three teams of four; Jarl himself made the twelfth man. "Mance promises swords for every man of the first team to reach the top," he told them, his breath misting in the cold air. "Southron swords of castle-forged steel. And your name in the song he'll make of this, that too. What more could a free man ask? *Up*, and the Others take the hindmost!"

The Others take them all, thought Jon, as he watched them scramble up the steep slope of the ridge and vanish beneath the trees. It would not be the first time wildlings had scaled the Wall, not even the hundred and first. The patrols stumbled on climbers two or three times a year, and rangers sometimes came on the broken corpses of those who had fallen. Along the east coast the raiders most often built boats to slip across the Bay of Seals. In the west they would descend into the black depths of the Gorge to make their way around the Shadow Tower. But in between the only way to defeat the Wall was to go over it, and many a raider had. *Fewer come back, though*, he thought with a certain grim pride. Climbers must of necessity leave their mounts behind, and many younger, greener raiders began by taking the first horses they found. Then a hue and cry would go up, ravens would fly, and as often as not the Night's Watch would hunt them down and hang them before they could get back with their plunder and stolen women. Jarl would not make that mistake, Jon knew, but he wondered about Styr. *The Magnar is a ruler, not a raider. He may not know how the game is played.*

"There they are," Ygritte said, and Jon glanced up to see the first climber emerge above the treetops. It was Jarl. He had found a sentinel tree that leaned against the Wall, and led his men up the trunk to get a quicker start. *The wood should never have been allowed to creep so close. They're three hundred feet up, and they haven't touched the ice itself yet.*

He watched the wildling move carefully from wood to Wall, hacking out a handhold with short sharp blows of his ice axe, then swinging over. The rope around his waist tied him to the second man in line, still edging up the tree. Step by slow step, Jarl moved higher, kicking out toeholds with his spiked boots when there were no natural ones to be found. When he was ten feet above the sentinel, he stopped upon a narrow icy ledge, slung his axe from his belt, took out his hammer, and drove an iron stake into a cleft. The second man moved onto the Wall behind him while the third was scrambling to the top of the tree.

The other two teams had no happily placed trees to give them a leg up, and before long the Thenns were wondering whether they had gotten lost climbing the ridge. Jarl's party were all on the Wall and eighty feet up before the leading climbers from the other groups came into view. The teams were spaced a good twenty yards apart. Jarl's four were in the center. To the right of them was a team headed up by Grigg the Goat, whose long blond braid made him easy to spot from below. To the left a very thin man named Errok led the climbers.

"So slow," the Magnar complained loudly, as he watched them edge their way upward. "Has he forgotten the crows? He should climb faster, afore we are discovered."

Jon had to hold his tongue. He remembered the Skirling Pass all too well, and the moonlight climb he'd made with Stonesnake. He had swallowed his heart a half-dozen times that night, and by the end his arms and legs had been aching and his fingers were half frozen. *And that was stone, not ice.* Stone was solid. Ice was treacherous stuff at the best of times, and on a day like this, when the Wall was weeping, the warmth of a climber's hand might be enough to melt it. The huge blocks could be frozen rock-hard inside, but their outer surface would be slick, with runnels of water trickling down, and patches of rotten ice where the air had gotten in. *Whatever else the wildlings are, they're brave.*

All the same, Jon found himself hoping that Styr's fears proved well founded. *If the gods are good, a patrol will chance by and put an end to this.* "No wall can keep you safe," his father had told him once, as they walked the walls of Winterfall. "A wall is only as strong as the men who defend it." The wildlings might have a hundred and twenty men, but four defenders would be enough to see them off, with a few well-placed arrows and perhaps a pail of stones.

No defenders appeared, however; not four, not even one. The sun climbed the sky and the wildlings climbed the Wall. Jarl's four remained well ahead till noon, when they hit a pitch of bad ice. Jarl had looped his rope around a wind-carved pinnace and was using it to support his weight when the whole jagged thing suddenly crumbled and came crashing down, and him with it. Chunks of ice as big as a man's head bombarded the three below, but they clung to the handholds and the stakes held, and Jarl jerked to a sudden halt at the end of the rope.

By the time his team had recovered from that mischance, Grigg the Goat had almost drawn even with them. Errok's four remained well behind. The face where they were climbing looked smooth and unpitted, covered with a sheet of icemelt that glistened wetly where the sun brushed it. Grigg's section was darker to the eye, with more obvious features; long horizontal ledges where a block had been imperfectly positioned atop the block below, cracks and crevices, even chimneys along the vertical joins, where wind and water had eaten holes large enough for a man to hide in.

Jarl soon had his men edging upward again. His four and Grigg's moved almost side by side, with Errok's fifty feet below. Deerhorn axes chopped and hacked, sending showers of glittery shards cascading down onto the trees. Stone hammers pounded stakes deep into the ice to serve as anchors for the ropes; the iron stakes ran out before they were halfway up, and after that the climbers used horn and sharpened bone. And the men kicked, driving the spikes on their boots against the hard unyielding ice again and again and again and again to make one foothold. *Their legs must be numb*, Jon thought by the fourth hour. *How long can they keep on with that?* He watched as restless as the Magnar, listening for the distant moan of a Thenn warhorn. But the horns stayed silent, and there was no sign of the Night's Watch.

By the sixth hour, Jarl had moved ahead of Grigg the Goat again, and his men were widening the gap. "The Mance's pet must want a sword," the Magnar said, shading his eyes. The sun was high in the sky, and the upper third of the Wall was a crystalline blue from below, reflecting so brilliantly that it hurt the eyes to look on it. Jarl's four and Grigg's were all but lost in the glare, though Errok's team was still in shadow. Instead of moving upward they were edging their way sideways at about five hundred feet, making for a chimney. Jon was watching them inch along when he heard the sound—a sudden *crack* that seemed to roll along the ice, followed by a shout of alarm. And then the air was full of shards and shrieks and falling men, as a sheet of ice a foot thick and fifty feet square broke off from the Wall and came tumbling, crumbling, rumbling, sweeping all before it. Even down at the foot of the ridge, some chunks came spinning through the trees and rolling down the slope. Jon grabbed Ygritte and pulled her down to shield her, and one of the Thenns was struck in the face by a chunk that broke his nose.

And when they looked up Jarl and his team were gone. Men, ropes, stakes, all gone; nothing remained above six hundred feet. There was a wound in the Wall where the climbers had clung half a heartbeat before, the ice within as smooth and white as polished marble and shining in the sun. Far far below there was a faint red smear where someone had smashed against a frozen pinnace.

The Wall defends itself, Jon thought as he pulled Ygritte back to her feet.

They found Jarl in a tree, impaled upon a splintered

branch and still roped to the three men who lay broken beneath him. One was still alive, but his legs and spine were shattered, and most of his ribs as well. "Mercy," he said when they came upon him. One of the Thenns smashed his head in with a big stone mace. The Magnar gave orders, and his men began to gather fuel for a pyre.

The dead were burning when Grigg the Goat reached the top of the Wall. By the time Errok's four had joined them, nothing remained of Jarl and his team but bone and ash.

The sun had begun to sink by then, so the climbers wasted little time. They unwound the long coils of hemp they'd had looped around their chests, tied them all together, and tossed down one end. The thought of trying to climb five hundred feet up that rope filled Jon with dread, but Mance had planned better than that. The raiders Jarl had left below uncasked a huge ladder, with rungs of woven hemp as thick as a man's arm, and tied it to the climbers' rope. Errok and Grigg and their men grunted and heaved, pulled it up, staked it to the top, then lowered the rope again to haul up a second ladder. There were five altogether.

When all of them were in place, the Magnar shouted a brusque command in the Old Tongue, and five of his Thenns started up together. Even with the ladders, it was no easy climb. Ygritte watched them struggle for a while. "I hate this Wall," she said in a low angry voice. "Can you feel how *cold* it is?"

"It's made of ice," Jon pointed out.

"You know nothing, Jon Snow. This wall is made o' blood."

Nor had it drunk its fill. By sunset, two of the Thenns had fallen from the ladder to their deaths, but they were the last. It was near midnight before Jon reached the top. The stars were out again, and Ygritte was trembling from the climb. "I almost fell," she said, with tears in her eyes. "Twice. Thrice. The Wall was trying t' shake me off, I could feel it." One of the tears broke free and trickled slowly down her cheek.

"The worst is behind us." Jon tried to sound confident. "Don't be frightened." He tried to put an arm around her.

Ygritte slammed the heel of her hand into his chest, so hard it stung even through his layers of wool, mail, and boiled leather. "I wasn't *frightened*. You know nothing, Jon Snow."

"Why are you crying, then?"

"Not for fear!" She kicked savagely at the ice beneath her with a heel, chopping out a chunk. "I'm crying because we never found the Horn of Winter. We opened half a hundred graves and let all those shades loose in the world, and never found the Horn of Joramun to bring this cold thing down!"

JAIME

His hand burned.

Still, *still*, long after they had snuffed out the torch they'd used to sear his bloody stump, days after, he could still feel the fire lancing up his arm, and his fingers twisting in the flames, the fingers he no longer had.

He had taken wounds before, but never like this. He had never known there could be such pain. Sometimes, unbidden, old prayers bubbled from his lips, prayers he learned as a child and never thought of since, prayers he had first prayed with Cersei kneeling beside him in the sept at Casterly Rock. Sometimes he even wept, until he heard the Mummers laughing. Then he made his eyes go dry and his heart go dead, and prayed for his fever to burn away his tears. *Now I know how Tyrion has felt, all those times they laughed at him.*

After the second time he fell from the saddle, they bound him tight to Brienne of Tarth and made them share a horse again. One day, instead of back to front, they bound them face-to-face. "The lovers," Shagwell sighed loudly, "and what a lovely sight they are. 'Twould be cruel to separate the good knight and his lady." Then he laughed that high shrill laugh of his, and said, "Ah, but which one is the knight and which one is the lady?"

If I had my hand, you'd learn that soon enough, Jaime thought. His arms ached and his legs were numb from the ropes, but after a while none of that mattered. His world shrunk to the throb of agony that was his phantom hand, and Brienne pressed against him. *She's warm, at least*, he consoled himself, though the wench's breath was as foul as his own.

His hand was always between them. Urswyck had hung it about his neck on a cord, so it dangled down against his chest, slapping Brienne's breasts as Jaime slipped in and out of consciousness. His right eye was swollen shut, the wound inflamed where Brienne had cut him during their fight, but it was his hand that hurt the most. Blood and pus seeped from his stump, and the missing hand throbbed every time the horse took a step.

His throat was so raw that he could not eat, but he drank wine when they gave it to him, and water when that was all they offered. Once they handed him a cup and he quaffed it straight away, trembling, and the Brave Companions burst into laughter so loud and harsh it hurt his ears. "That's horse piss you're drinking, Kingslayer," Rorge told him. Jaime was so thirsty he drank it anyway, but afterward he retched it all back up. They made Brienne wash the vomit out of his beard, just as they made her clean him up when he soiled himself in the saddle.

One damp cold morning when he was feeling slightly stronger, a madness took hold of him and he reached for the Dornishman's sword with his left hand and wrenched it clumsily from its scabbard. *Let them kill me*, he thought, *so long as I die fighting, a blade in hand*. But it was no good. Shagwell came hopping from leg to leg, dancing nimbly aside when Jaime slashed at him. Unbalanced, he staggered forward, hacking wildly at the fool, but Shagwell spun and ducked and darted until all the Mummers were laughing at Jaime's futile efforts to land a blow. When he tripped over a rock and stumbled to his knees, the fool leapt in and planted a wet kiss atop his head.

Rorge finally flung him aside and kicked the sword from Jaime's feeble fingers as he tried to bring it up. "That wath amuthing, Kingthlayer," said Vargo Hoat, "but if you try it again, I thall take your other hand, or perhapth a foot."

Jaime lay on his back afterward, staring at the night sky, trying not to feel the pain that snaked up his right arm every time he moved it. The night was strangely beautiful. The moon was a graceful crescent, and it seemed as though he had never seen so many stars. The King's Crown was at the zenith, and he could see the Stallion rearing, and there the Swan. The Moonmaid, shy as ever, was half-hidden behind a pine tree. *How can such a night be beautiful?* he asked himself. *Why would the stars want to look down on such as me?*

"Jaime," Brienne whispered, so faintly he thought he was dreaming it. "Jaime, what are you doing?"

"Dying," he whispered back.

"No," she said, "no, you must live."

He wanted to laugh. "Stop telling me what do, wench. I'll die if it pleases me."

"Are you so craven?"

The word shocked him. He was Jaime Lannister, a knight of the Kingsguard, he was the Kingslayer. No man had ever called him craven. Other things they called him, yes; oathbreaker, liar, murderer. They said he was cruel, treacherous, reckless. But never craven. "What else can I do, but die?"

"Live," she said, "live, and fight, and take revenge." But she spoke too loudly. Rorge heard her voice, if not her words, and came over to kick her, shouting at her to hold her bloody tongue if she wanted to keep it.

Craven, Jaime thought, as Brienne fought to stifle her moans. *Can it be? They took my sword hand. Was that all I was, a sword hand? Gods be good, is it true?*

The wench had the right of it. He could not die. Cersei was waiting for him. She would have need of him. And Tyrion, his little brother, who loved him for a lie. And his enemies were waiting too; the Young Wolf who had beaten him in the Whispering Wood and killed his men around him, Edmure Tully who had kept him in darkness and chains, these Brave Companions.

When morning came, he made himself eat. They fed him a mush of oats, horse food, but he forced down every spoon. He ate again at evenfall, and the next day. *Live*, he told himself harshly, when the mush was like to gag him, *live for Cersei, live for Tyrion. Live for vengeance. A Lannister always pays his debts.* His missing hand throbbed and burned and stank. *When I reach King's Landing I'll have a new hand forged, a golden hand, and one day I'll use it to rip out Vargo Hoat's throat.*

The days and the nights blurred together in a haze of pain. He would sleep in the saddle, pressed against Brienne, his nose full of the stink of his rotting hand, and then at night he would lie awake on the hard ground, caught in a waking nightmare. Weak as he was, they always bound him to a tree. It gave him some cold consolation to know that they feared him that much, even now.

Brienne was always bound beside him. She lay there in her bonds like a big dead cow, saying not a word. *The wench has built a fortress inside herself. They will rape her soon enough, but behind her walls they cannot touch her.* But Jaime's walls were gone. They had taken his hand, they had taken his *sword hand,* and without it he was nothing. The other was no good to him. Since the time he could walk, his left arm had been his shield arm, no more. It was his right hand that made him a knight; his right arm that made him a man.

One day, he heard Urswyck say something about Harrenhal, and remembered that was to be their destination. That made him laugh aloud, and *that* made Timeon slash his face with a long thin whip. The cut bled, but beside his hand he scarcely felt it. "Why did you laugh?" the wench asked him that night, in a whisper.

"Harrenhal was where they gave me the white cloak," he whispered back. "Whent's great tourney. He wanted to show us all his big castle and his fine sons. I wanted to show them too. I was only fifteen, but no one could have beaten me that day. Aerys never let me joust." He laughed again. "He sent me away. But now I'm coming back."

They heard the laugh. That night it was Jaime who got the kicks and punches. He hardly felt them either, until Rorge slammed a boot into his stump, and then he fainted.

It was the next night when they finally came, three of the worst; Shagwell, noseless Rorge, and the fat Dothraki Zollo, the one who'd cut his hand off. Zollo and Rorge were arguing about who would go first as they approached; there seemed to be no question but that the fool would be going last. Shagwell suggested that they should both go first, and take her front and rear. Zollo and Rorge liked that notion, only then they began to fight about who would get the front and who the rear.

They will leave her a cripple too, but inside, where it does not show. "Wench," he whispered as Zollo and Rorge were cursing one another, "let them have the meat, and you go far away. It will be over quicker, and they'll get less pleasure from it."

"They'll get no pleasure from what I'll give them," she whispered back, defiant.

Stupid stubborn brave bitch. She was going to get herself good and killed, he knew it. *And what do I care if she does? If she hadn't been so pigheaded, I'd still have a hand.* Yet he heard himself whisper, "Let them do it, and go away inside." That was what he'd done, when the Starks had died before him, Lord Rickard cooking in his armor while his son Brandon strangled himself trying to save him. "Think of Renly, if you loved him. Think of Tarth, mountains and seas, pools, waterfalls, whatever you have on your Sapphire Isle, think . . ."

But Rorge had won the argument by then. "You're the ugliest woman I ever seen," he told Brienne, "but don't think I can't make you uglier. You want a nose like mine? Fight me, and you'll get one. And two eyes, that's too many. One scream out o' you, and I'll pop one out and make you eat it, and then I'll pull your fucking teeth out one by one."

"Oh, do it, Rorge," pleaded Shagwell. "Without her teeth, she'll look just like my dear old mother." He cackled. "And I *always* wanted to fuck my dear old mother up the arse."

Jaime chuckled. "There's a funny fool. I have a riddle for you, Shagwell. Why do you care if she screams? Oh, wait, I know." He shouted, "*SAPPHIRES,*" as loudly as he could.

Cursing, Rorge kicked at his stump again. Jaime howled. *I never knew there was such agony in the world,* was the last thing he remembered thinking. It was hard to say how long he was gone, but when the pain spit him out, Urswyck was there, and Vargo Hoat himself. "Thee'th not to be touched," the goat screamed, spraying spittle all over

Zollo. "Thee hath to be a maid, you foolth! Thee'th worth a bag of thapphireth!" And from then on, every night Hoat put guards on them, to protect them from his own.

Two nights passed in silence before the wench finally found the courage to whisper, "Jaime? Why did you shout out?"

"Why did I shout 'sapphires,' you mean? Use your wits, wench. Would this lot have cared if I shouted 'rape'?"

"You did not need to shout at all."

"You're hard enough to look at with a nose. Besides, I wanted to make the goat say 'thapphireth.'" He chuckled. "A good thing for you I'm such a liar. An honorable man would have told the truth about the Sapphire Isle."

"All the same," she said. "I thank you, ser."

His hand was throbbing again. He ground his teeth and said, "A Lannister pays his debts. That was for the river, and those rocks you dropped on Robin Ryger."

The goat wanted to make a show of parading him in, so Jaime was made to dismount a mile from the gates of Harrenhal. A rope was looped around his waist, a second around Brienne's wrists; the ends were tied to the pommel of Vargo Hoat's saddle. They stumbled along side by side behind the Qohorik's striped zorse.

Jaime's rage kept him walking. The linen that covered the stump was grey and stinking with pus. His phantom fingers screamed with every step. *I am stronger than they know*, he told himself. *I am still a Lannister. I am still a knight of the Kingsguard.* He would reach Harrenhal, and then King's Landing. He would live. *And I will pay this debt with interest.*

As they approached the clifflike walls of Black Harren's monstrous castle, Brienne squeezed his arm. "Lord Bolton holds this castle. The Boltons are bannermen to the Starks."

"The Boltons skin their enemies." Jaime remembered that much about the northman. Tyrion would have known all there was to know about the Lord of the Dreadfort, but Tyrion was a thousand leagues away, with Cersei. *I cannot die while Cersei lives*, he told himself. *We will die together as we were born together.*

The castleton outside the walls had been burned to ash and blackened stone, and many men and horses had re-

cently encamped beside the lakeshore, where Lord Whent
had staged his great tourney in the year of the false spring.
A bitter smile touched Jaime's lips as they crossed that
torn ground. Someone had dug a privy trench in the very
spot where he'd once knelt before the king to say his vows.
*I never dreamed how quick the sweet would turn to sour.
Aerys would not even let me savor that one night. He honored me, and then he spat on me.*

"The banners," Brienne observed. "Flayed man and
twin towers, see. King Robb's sworn men. There, above the
gatehouse, grey on white. They fly the direwolf."

Jaime twisted his head upward for a look. "That's your
bloody wolf, true enough," he granted her. "And those are
heads to either side of it."

Soldiers, servants, and camp followers gathered to hoot
at them. A spotted bitch followed them through the camps
barking and growling until one of the Lyseni impaled her
on a lance and galloped to the front of the column. "I am
bearing Kingslayer's banner," he shouted, shaking the dead
dog above Jaime's head.

The walls of Harrenhal were so thick that passing beneath them was like passing through a stone tunnel. Vargo
Hoat had sent two of his Dothraki ahead to inform Lord
Bolton of their coming, so the outer ward was full of the curious. They gave way as Jaime staggered past, the rope
around his waist jerking and pulling at him whenever he
slowed. "I give you the *Kingthlayer*," Vargo Hoat proclaimed in that thick slobbery voice of his. A spear jabbed
at the small of Jaime's back, sending him sprawling.

Instinct made him put out his hands to stop his fall.
When his stump smashed against the ground the pain was
blinding, yet somehow he managed to fight his way back to
one knee. Before him, a flight of broad stone steps led up to
the entrance of one of Harrenhal's colossal round towers.
Five knights and a northman stood looking down on him;
the one paleeyed in wool and fur, the five fierce in mail and
plate, with the twin towers sigil on their surcoats. "A fury
of Freys," Jaime declared. "Ser Danwell, Ser Aenys, Ser
Hosteen." He knew Lord Walder's sons by sight; his aunt
had married one, after all. "You have my condolences."

"For what, ser?" Ser Danwell Frey asked.

"Your brother's son, Ser Cleos," said Jaime. "He was

with us until outlaws filled him full of arrows. Urswyck and this lot took his goods and left him for the wolves."

"*My lords!*" Brienne wrenched herself free and pushed forward. "I saw your banners. Hear me for your oath!"

"Who speaks?" demanded Ser Aenys Frey.

"Lannither'th wet nurth."

"I am Brienne of Tarth, daughter to Lord Selwyn the Evenstar, and sworn to House Stark even as you are."

Ser Aenys spit at her feet. "That's for your oaths. We trusted the word of Robb Stark, and he repaid our faith with betrayal."

Now this is interesting. Jaime twisted to see how Brienne might take the accusation, but the wench was as singleminded as a mule with a bit between his teeth. "I know of no betrayal." She chafed at the ropes around her wrists. "Lady Catelyn commanded me to deliver Lannister to his brother at King's Landing—"

"She was trying to drown him when we found them," said Urswyck the Faithful.

She reddened. "In anger I forgot myself, but I would never have killed him. If he dies the Lannisters will put my lady's daughters to the sword."

Ser Aenys was unmoved. "Why should that trouble us?"

"Ransom him back to Riverrun," urged Ser Danwell.

"Casterly Rock has more gold," one brother objected.

"Kill him!" said another. "His head for Ned Stark's!"

Shagwell the Fool somersaulted to the foot of the steps in his grey and pink motley and began to sing. "*There once was a lion who danced with a bear, oh my, oh my . . .*"

"Thilenth, fool." Vargo Hoat cuffed the man. "The Kingthlayer ith not for the bear. He ith mine."

"He is no one's should he die." Roose Bolton spoke so softly that men quieted to hear him. "And pray recall, my lord, you are not master of Harrenhal till I march north."

Fever made Jaime as fearless as he was lightheaded. "Can this be the Lord of the Dreadfort? When last I heard, my father had sent you scampering off with your tail betwixt your legs. When did you stop running, my lord?"

Bolton's silence was a hundred times more threatening than Vargo Hoat's slobbering malevolence. Pale as morning mist, his eyes concealed more than they told. Jaime misliked those eyes. They reminded him of the day at King's

Landing when Ned Stark had found him seated on the Iron Throne. The Lord of the Dreadfort finally pursed his lips and said, "You have lost a hand."

"No," said Jaime, "I have it here, hanging round my neck."

Roose Bolton reached down, snapped the cord, and flung the hand at Hoat. "Take this away. The sight of it offends me."

"I will thend it to hith lord father. I will tell him he muth pay one hundred thouthand dragonth, or we thall return the Kingthlayer to him pieth by pieth. And when we hath hith gold, we thall deliver Ther Jaime to Karthark, and collect a maiden too!" A roar of laughter went up from the Brave Companions.

"A fine plan," said Roose Bolton, the same way he might say, "A fine wine," to a dinner companion, "though Lord Karstark will not be giving you his daughter. King Robb has shortened him by a head, for treason and murder. As to Lord Tywin, he remains at King's Landing, and there he will stay till the new year, when his grandson takes for bride a daughter of Highgarden."

"Winterfell," said Brienne. "You mean Winterfell. King Joffrey is betrothed to Sansa Stark."

"No longer. The Battle of the Blackwater changed all. The rose and the lion joined there, to shatter Stannis Baratheon's host and burn his fleet to ashes."

I warned you, Urswyck, Jaime thought, *and you, goat. When you bet against the lions, you lose more than your purse.* "Is there word of my sister?" he asked.

"She is well. As is your . . . nephew." Bolton paused before he said *nephew*, a pause that said *I know*. "Your brother also lives, though he took a wound in the battle." He beckoned to a dour northman in a studded brigantine. "Escort Ser Jaime to Qyburn. And unbind this woman's hands." As the rope between Brienne's wrists was slashed in two, he said, "Pray forgive us, my lady. In such troubled times it is hard to know friend from foe."

Brienne rubbed inside her wrist where the hemp had scraped her skin bloody. "My lord, these men tried to rape me."

"Did they?" Lord Bolton turned his pale eyes on Vargo

Hoat. "I am displeased. By that, and this of Ser Jaime's hand."

There were five northmen and as many Freys in the yard for every Brave Companion. The goat might not be as clever as some, but he could count that high at least. He held his tongue.

"They took my sword," Brienne said, "my armor . . ."

"You shall have no need of armor here, my lady," Lord Bolton told her. "In Harrenhal, you are under my protection. Amabel, find suitable rooms for the Lady Brienne. Walton, you will see to Ser Jaime at once." He did not wait for an answer, but turned and climbed the steps, his fur-trimmed cloak swirling behind. Jaime had only enough time to exchange a quick look with Brienne before they were marched away, separately.

In the maester's chambers beneath the rookery, a grey-haired, fatherly man named Qyburn sucked in his breath when he cut away the linen from the stump of Jaime's hand.

"That bad? Will I die?"

Qyburn pushed at the wound with a finger, and wrinkled his nose at the gush of pus. "No. Though in a few more days . . ." He sliced away Jaime's sleeve. "The corruption has spread. See how tender the flesh is? I must cut it all away. The safest course would be to take the arm off."

"Then *you'll* die," Jaime promised. "Clean the stump and sew it up. I'll take my chances."

Qyburn frowned. "I can leave you the upper arm, make the cut at your elbow, but . . ."

"Take any part of my arm, and you'd best chop off the other one as well, or I'll strangle you with it afterward."

Qyburn looked in his eyes. Whatever he saw there gave him pause. "Very well. I will cut away the rotten flesh, no more. Try to burn out the corruption with boiling wine and a poultice of nettle, mustard seed, and bread mold. Mayhaps that will suffice. It is on your head. You will want milk of the poppy—"

"No." Jaime dare not let himself be put to sleep; he might be short an arm when he woke, no matter what the man said.

Qyburn was taken aback. "There will be pain."

"I'll scream."

"A great deal of pain."

"I'll scream very loudly."

"Will you take some wine at least?"

"Does the High Septon ever pray?"

"Of that I am not certain. I shall bring the wine. Lie back, I must needs strap down your arm."

With a bowl and a sharp blade, Qyburn cleaned the stump while Jaime gulped down strongwine, spilling it all over himself in the process. His left hand did not seem to know how to find his mouth, but there was something to be said for that. The smell of wine in his sodden beard helped disguise the stench of pus.

Nothing helped when the time came to pare away the rotten flesh. Jaime did scream then, and pounded his table with his good fist, over and over and over again. He screamed again when Qyburn poured boiling wine over what remained of his stump. Despite all his vows and all his fears, he lost consciousness for a time. When he woke, the maester was sewing at his arm with needle and catgut. "I left a flap of skin to fold back over your wrist."

"You have done this before," muttered Jaime, weakly. He could taste blood in his mouth where he'd bitten his tongue.

"No man who serves with Vargo Hoat is a stranger to stumps. He makes them wherever he goes."

Qyburn did not look a monster, Jaime thought. He was spare and soft-spoken, with warm brown eyes. "How does a maester come to ride with the Brave Companions?"

"The Citadel took my chain." Qyburn put away his needle. "I should do something about that wound above your eye as well. The flesh is badly inflamed."

Jaime closed his eyes and let the wine and Qyburn do their work. "Tell me of the battle." As keeper of Harrenhal's ravens, Qyburn would have been the first to hear the news.

"Lord Stannis was caught between your father and the fire. It's said the Imp set the river itself aflame."

Jaime saw green flames reaching up into the sky higher than the tallest towers, as burning men screamed in the streets. *I have dreamed this dream before.* It was almost funny, but there was no one to share the joke.

"Open your eye." Qyburn soaked a cloth in warm water

and dabbed at the crust of dried blood. The eyelid was swollen, but Jaime found he could force it open halfway. Qyburn's face loomed above. "How did you come by this one?" the maester asked.

"A wench's gift."

"Rough wooing, my lord?"

"This wench is bigger than me and uglier than you. You'd best see to her as well. She's still limping on the leg I pricked when we fought."

"I will ask after her. What is this woman to you?"

"My protector." Jaime had to laugh, no matter how it hurt.

"I'll grind some herbs you can mix with wine to bring down your fever. Come back on the morrow and I'll put a leech on your eye to drain the bad blood."

"A leech. Lovely."

"Lord Bolton is very fond of leeches," Qyburn said primly.

"Yes," said Jaime. "He would be."

TYRION

Nothing remained beyond the King's Gate but mud and ashes and bits of burned bone, yet already there were people living in the shadow of the city walls, and others selling fish from barrows and barrels. Tyrion felt their eyes on him as he rode past; chilly eyes, angry and unsympathetic. No one dared speak to him, or try to bar his way; not with Bronn beside him in oiled black mail. *If I were alone, though, they would pull me down and smash my face in with a cobblestone, as they did for Preston Greenfield.*

"They come back quicker than the rats," he complained. "We burned them out once, you'd think they'd take that as a lesson."

"Give me a few dozen gold cloaks and I'll kill them all," said Bronn. "Once they're dead they don't come back."

"No, but others come in their places. Leave them be . . . but if they start throwing up hovels against the wall again, pull them down at once. The war's not done yet, no matter what these fools may think." He spied the Mud Gate up ahead. "I have seen enough for now. We'll return on the morrow with the guild masters to go over their plans." He sighed. *Well, I burned most of this, I suppose it's only just that I rebuild it.*

That task was to have been his uncle's, but solid, steady, tireless Ser Kevan Lannister had not been himself since the raven had come from Riverrun with word of his son's murder. Willem's twin Martyn had been taken captive by Robb Stark as well, and their elder brother Lancel was still abed, beset by an ulcerating wound that would not heal. With one son dead and two more in mortal danger, Ser Kevan was consumed by grief and fear. Lord Tywin had always relied on his brother, but now he had no choice but to turn again to his dwarf son.

The cost of rebuilding was going to be ruinous, but there was no help for that. King's Landing was the realm's principal harbor, rivaled only by Oldtown. The river had to be reopened, and the sooner the better. *And where am I going to find the bloody coin?* It was almost enough to make him miss Littlefinger, who had sailed north a fortnight past. *While he beds Lysa Arryn and rules the Vale beside her, I get to clean up the mess he left behind him.* Though at least his father was giving him significant work to do. *He won't name me heir to Casterly Rock, but he'll make use of me wherever he can,* Tyrion thought, as a captain of gold cloaks waved them through the Mud Gate.

The Three Whores still dominated the market square inside the gate, but they stood idle now, and the boulders and barrels of pitch had all been trundled away. There were children climbing the towering wooden structures, swarming up like monkeys in roughspun to perch on the throwing arms and hoot at each other.

"Remind me to tell Ser Addam to post some gold cloaks here," Tyrion told Bronn as they rode between two of the trebuchets. "Some fool boy's like to fall off and break his back." There was a shout from above, and a clod of manure exploded on the ground a foot in front of them. Tyrion's mare reared and almost threw him. "On second thoughts," he said when he had the horse in hand, "let the poxy brats splatter on the cobbles like overripe melons."

He was in a black mood, and not just because a few street urchins wanted to pelt him with dung. His marriage was a daily agony. Sansa Stark remained a maiden, and half the castle seemed to know it. When they had saddled up this morning, he'd heard two of the stableboys sniggering behind his back. He could almost imagine that the horses were sniggering as well. He'd risked his skin to avoid the bedding ritual, hoping to preserve the privacy of his bedchamber, but that hope had been dashed quick enough. Either Sansa had been stupid enough to confide in one of her bedmaids, every one of whom was a spy for Cersei, or Varys and his little birds were to blame.

What difference did it make? They were laughing at him all the same. The only person in the Red Keep who didn't seem to find his marriage a source of amusement was his lady wife.

Sansa's misery was deepening every day. Tyrion would gladly have broken through her courtesy to give her what solace he might, but it was no good. No words would ever make him fair in her eyes. *Or any less a Lannister.* This was the wife they had given him, for all the rest of his life, and she hated him.

And their nights together in the great bed were another source of torment. He could no longer bear to sleep naked, as had been his custom. His wife was too well trained ever to say an unkind word, but the revulsion in her eyes whenever she looked on his body was more than he could bear. Tyrion had commanded Sansa to wear a sleeping shift as well. *I want her,* he realized. *I want Winterfell, yes, but I want her as well, child or woman or whatever she is. I want to comfort her. I want to hear her laugh. I want her to come to me willingly, to bring me her joys and her sorrows and her lust.* His mouth twisted in a bitter smile. *Yes, and I want to be tall as Jaime and as strong as Ser Gregor the Mountain too, for all the bloody good it does.*

Unbidden, his thoughts went to Shae. Tyrion had not wanted her to hear the news from any lips but his own, so he had commanded Varys to bring her to him the night before his wedding. They met again in the eunuch's chambers, and when Shae began to undo the laces of his jerkin, he'd caught her by the wrist and pushed her away. "Wait," he said, "there is something you must hear. On the morrow I am to be wed . . ."

". . . to Sansa Stark. I know."

He was speechless for an instant. Even *Sansa* did not

know, not then. "How could you know? Did Varys tell you?"

"Some page was telling Ser Tallad about it when I took Lollys to the sept. He had it from this serving girl who heard Ser Kevan talking to your father." She wriggled free of his grasp and pulled her dress up over her head. As ever, she was naked underneath. "I don't care. She's only a little girl. You'll give her a big belly and come back to me."

Some part of him had hoped for less indifference. *Had hoped*, he jeered bitterly, *but now you know better, dwarf. Shae is all the love you're ever like to have.*

Muddy Way was crowded, but soldiers and townfolk alike made way for the Imp and his escort. Hollow-eyed children swarmed underfoot, some looking up in silent appeal whilst others begged noisily. Tyrion pulled a big fistful of coppers from his purse and tossed them in the air, and the children went running for them, shoving and shouting. The lucky ones might be able to buy a heel of stale bread tonight. He had never seen markets so crowded, and for all the food the Tyrells were bringing in, prices remained shockingly high. Six coppers for a melon, a silver stag for a bushel of corn, a dragon for a side of beef or six skinny piglets. Yet there seemed no lack of buyers. Gaunt men and haggard women crowded around every wagon and stall, while others even more ragged looked on sullenly from the mouths of alleys.

"This way," Bronn said, when they reached the foot of the Hook. "If you still mean to . . . ?"

"I do." The riverfront had made a convenient excuse, but Tyrion had another purpose today. It was not a task he relished, but it must be done. They turned away from Aegon's High Hill, into the maze of smaller streets that clustered around the foot of Visenya's. Bronn led the way. Once or twice Tyrion glanced back over his shoulder to see if they were being followed, but there was nothing to be seen except the usual rabble: a carter beating his horse, an old woman throwing nightsoil from her window, two little boys fighting with sticks, three gold cloaks escorting a captive . . . they all looked innocent, but any one of them could be his undoing. Varys had informers everywhere.

They turned at a corner, and again at the next, and rode slowly through a crowd of women at a well. Bronn led him along a curving wynd, through an alley, under a broken archway. They cut through the rubble where a house had burned and walked their horses up a shallow flight of stone steps. The buildings were close and poor. Bronn halted at the mouth of a crooked alley, too narrow for two to ride abreast. "There's two jags and then a dead end. The sink is in the cellar of the last building."

Tyrion swung down off his horse. "See that no one enters or leaves till I return. This won't take long." His hand went into his cloak, to make certain the gold was still there in the hidden pocket. Thirty dragons. *A bloody fortune, for a man like him.* He waddled up the alley quickly, anxious to be done with this.

The wine sink was a dismal place, dark and damp, walls pale with niter, the ceiling so low that Bronn would have had to duck to keep from hitting his head on the beams. Tyrion Lannister had no such problem. At this hour, the front room was empty but for a dead-eyed woman who sat on a stool behind a rough plank bar. She handed him a cup of sour wine and said, "In the back."

The back room was even darker. A flickering candle burned on a low table, beside a flagon of wine. The man behind it scarce looked a danger; a short man—though all men were tall to Tyrion—with thinning brown hair, pink cheeks, and a little pot pushing at the bone buttons of his doeskin jerkin. In his soft hands he held a twelve-stringed woodharp more deadly than a longsword.

Tyrion sat across from him. "Symon Silver Tongue."

The man inclined his head. He was bald on top. "My lord Hand," he said.

"You mistake me. My father is the King's Hand. I am no longer even a finger, I fear."

"You shall rise again, I am sure. A man like you. My sweet lady Shae tells me you are newly wed. Would that you had sent for me earlier. I should have been honored to sing at your feast."

"The last thing my wife needs is more songs," said Tyrion. "As for Shae, we both know she is no lady, and I would thank you never to speak her name aloud."

"As the Hand commands," Symon said.

The last time Tyrion had seen the man, a sharp word had been enough to set him sweating, but it seemed the singer had found some courage somewhere. *Most like in that flagon.* Or perhaps Tyrion himself was to blame for this new boldness. *I threatened him, but nothing ever came of the threat, so now he believes me toothless.* He sighed. "I am told you are a very gifted singer."

"You are most kind to say so, my lord."

Tyrion gave him a smile. "I think it is time you brought your music to the Free Cities. They are great lovers of song in Braavos and Pentos and Lys, and generous with those who please them." He took a sip of wine. It was foul stuff, but strong. "A tour of all nine cities would be best. You wouldn't want to deny anyone the joy of hearing you sing. A year in each should suffice." He reached inside his cloak, to where the gold was hidden. "With the port closed, you will need to go to Duskendale to take ship, but my man Bronn will find a horse for you, and I would be honored if you would let me pay your passage . . ."

"But my lord," the man objected, "you have never heard me sing. Pray listen a moment." His fingers moved deftly over the strings of the woodharp, and soft music filled the cellar. Symon began to sing.

> *He rode through the streets of the city,*
> *down from his hill on high,*
> *O'er the wynds and the steps and the cobbles,*
> *he rode to a woman's sigh.*
> *For she was his secret treasure,*
> *she was his shame and his bliss.*
> *And a chain and a keep are nothing,*
> *compared to a woman's kiss.*

"There's more," the man said as he broke off. "Oh, a good deal more. The refrain is especially nice, I think. *For hands of gold are always cold, but a woman's hands are warm . . .*"

"Enough." Tyrion slid his fingers from his cloak, empty. "That's not a song I would care to hear again. Ever."

"No?" Symon Silver Tongue put his harp aside and took a sip of wine. "A pity. Still, each man has his song, as my old master used to say when he was teaching me to play. Others might like my tune better. The queen, perhaps. Or your lord father."

Tyrion rubbed the scar over his nose, and said, "My father has no time for singers, and my sister is not as generous as one might think. A wise man could earn more from silence than from song." He could not put it much plainer than that.

Symon seemed to take his meaning quick enough. "You will find my price modest, my lord."

"That's good to know." This would not be a matter of thirty golden dragons, Tyrion feared. "Tell me."

"At King Joffrey's wedding feast," the man said, "there is to be a tournament of singers."

"And jugglers, and jesters, and dancing bears."

"Only one dancing bear, my lord," said Symon, who had plainly attended Cersei's arrangements with far more interest than Tyrion had, "but seven singers. Galyeon of Cuy, Bethany Fair-fingers, Aemon Costayne, Alaric of Eysen, Hamish the Harper, Collio Quaynis, and Orland of Oldtown will compete for a gilded lute with silver strings . . . yet unaccountably, no invitation has been forthcoming for one who is master of them all."

"Let me guess. Symon Silver Tongue?"

Symon smiled modestly. "I am prepared to prove the truth of my boast before king and court. Hamish is old, and oft forgets what he is singing. And Collio, with that absurd Tyroshi accent! If you understand one word in three, count yourself fortunate."

"My sweet sister has arranged the feast. Even if I could secure you this invitation, it might look queer. Seven kingdoms, seven vows, seven challenges, seventy-seven dishes . . . but *eight* singers? What would the High Septon think?"

"You did not strike me as a pious man, my lord."

"Piety is not the point. Certain forms must be observed."

Symon took a sip of wine. "Still . . . a singer's life is not without peril. We ply our trade in alehouses and wine sinks, before unruly drunkards. If one of your sister's seven should suffer some mishap, I hope you might consider me to fill his place." He smiled slyly, inordinately pleased with himself.

"Six singers would be as unfortunate as eight, to be sure. I will inquire after the health of Cersei's seven. If any of them should be indisposed, my man Bronn will find you."

"Very good, my lord." Symon might have left it at that, but flushed with triumph, he added, "I *shall* sing the night of King Joffrey's wedding. Should it happen that I am called to court, why, I will want to offer the king my very best compositions, songs I have sung a thousand times that are certain to please. If I should find myself singing in some dreary winesink, though . . . well, that would be an apt occasion to try my new song. *For hands of gold are always cold, but a woman's hands are warm.*"

"That will not be necessary," said Tyrion. "You have my word as a Lannister, Bronn will call upon you soon."

"Very *good*, my lord." The balding kettle-bellied singer took up his woodharp again.

Bronn was waiting with the horses at the mouth of the alley. He helped Tyrion into his saddle. "When do I take the man to Duskendale?"

"You don't." Tyrion turned his horse. "Give him three days, then inform him that Hamish the Harper has broken his arm. Tell him that his clothes will never serve for court, so he must be fitted for new garb at once. He'll come with you quick enough." He grimaced. "You may want his tongue, I understand it's made of silver. The rest of him should never be found."

Bronn grinned. "There's a pot shop I know in Flea Bottom makes a savory bowl of brown. All kinds of meat in it, I hear."

"Make certain I never eat there." Tyrion spurred to a trot. He wanted a bath, and the hotter the better.

Even that modest pleasure was denied him, however; no sooner had he returned to his chambers than Podrick Payne informed him that he had been summoned to the Tower of the Hand. "His lordship wants to see you. The Hand. Lord Tywin."

"I recall who the Hand is, Pod," Tyrion said. "I lost my nose, not my wits."

Bronn laughed. "Don't bite the boy's head off now."

"Why not? He never uses it." Tyrion wondered what he'd done now. *Or more like, what I have failed to do.* A summons from Lord Tywin always had teeth; his father never sent for him just to share a meal or a cup of wine, that was for certain.

As he entered his lord father's solar a few moments

later, he heard a voice saying, ". . . cherrywood for the scabbards, bound in red leather and ornamented with a row of lion's-head studs in pure gold. Perhaps with garnets for the eyes . . ."

"Rubies," Lord Tywin said. "Garnets lack the fire."

Tyrion cleared his throat. "My lord. You sent for me?"

His father glanced up. "I did. Come have a look at this." A bundle of oilcloth lay on the table between them, and Lord Tywin had a longsword in his hand. "A wedding gift for Joffrey," he told Tyrion. The light streaming through the diamond-shaped panes of glass made the blade shimmer black and red as Lord Tywin turned it to inspect the edge, while the pommel and crossguard flamed gold. "With this fool's jabber of Stannis and his magic sword, it seemed to me that we had best give Joffrey something extraordinary as well. A king should bear a kingly weapon."

"That's much too much sword for Joff," Tyrion said.

"He will grow into it. Here, feel the weight of it." He offered the weapon hilt first.

The sword was much lighter than he had expected. As he turned it in his hand he saw why. Only one metal could be beaten so thin and still have strength enough to fight with, and there was no mistaking those ripples, the mark of steel that has been folded back on itself many thousands of times. "Valyrian steel?"

"Yes," Lord Tywin said, in a tone of deep satisfaction.

At long last, Father! Valyrian steel blades were scarce and costly, yet thousands remained in the world, perhaps two hundred in the Seven Kingdoms alone. It had always irked his father that none belonged to House Lannister. The old Kings of the Rock had owned such a weapon, but the greatsword Brightroar had been lost when the second King Tommen carried it back to Valyria on his fool's quest. He had never returned; nor had Uncle Gery, the youngest and most reckless of his father's brothers, who had gone seeking after the lost sword some eight years past.

Thrice at least Lord Tywin had offered to buy Valyrian longswords from impoverished lesser houses, but his advances had always been firmly rebuffed. The little lordlings would gladly part with their daughters should a Lannister come asking, but they cherished their old family swords.

Tyrion wondered where the metal for this one had come from. A few master armorers could rework old Valyrian steel, but the secrets of its making had been lost when the Doom came to old Valyria. "The colors are strange," he commented as he turned the blade in the sunlight. Most Valyrian steel was a grey so dark it looked almost black, as was true here as well. But blended into the folds was a red as deep as the grey. The two colors lapped over one another without ever touching, each ripple distinct, like waves of night and blood upon some steely shore. "How did you get this patterning? I've never seen anything like it."

"Nor I, my lord," said the armorer. "I confess, these colors were not what I intended, and I do not know that I could duplicate them. Your lord father had asked for the crimson of your House, and it was that color I set out to infuse into the metal. But Valyrian steel is stubborn. These old swords remember, it is said, and they do not change easily. I worked half a hundred spells and brightened the red time and time again, but always the color would darken, as if the blade was drinking the sun from it. And some folds would not take the red at all, as you can see. If my lords of Lannister are displeased, I will of course try again, as many times as you should require, but—"

"No need," Lord Tywin said. "This will serve."

"A crimson sword might flash prettily in the sun, but if truth be told I like these colors better," said Tyrion. "They have an ominous beauty . . . and they make this blade unique. There is no other sword like it in all the world, I should think."

"There is one." The armorer bent over the table and unfolded the bundle of oilcloth, to reveal a second longsword.

Tyrion put down Joffrey's sword and took up the other. If not twins, the two were at least close cousins. This one was thicker and heavier, a half-inch wider and three inches longer, but they shared the same fine clean lines and the same distinctive color, the ripples of blood and night. Three fullers, deeply incised, ran down the second blade from hilt to point; the king's sword had only two. Joff's hilt was a good deal more ornate, the arms of its crossguard done as lions' paws with ruby claws unsheathed, but both swords had grips of finely tooled red leather and gold lions' heads for pommels.

"Magnificent." Even in hands as unskilled as Tyrion's, the blade felt alive. "I have never felt better balance."

"It is meant for my son."

No need to ask which son. Tyrion placed Jaime's sword back on the table beside Joffrey's, wondering if Robb Stark would let his brother live long enough to wield it. *Our father must surely think so, else why have this blade forged?*

"You have done good work, Master Mott," Lord Tywin told the armorer. "My steward will see to your payment. And remember, rubies for the scabbards."

"I shall, my lord. You are most generous." The man folded the swords up in the oilcloth, tucked the bundle under one arm, and went to his knee. "It is an honor to serve the King's Hand. I shall deliver the swords the day before the wedding."

"See that you do."

When the guards had seen the armorer out, Tyrion clambered up onto a chair. "So . . . a sword for Joff, a sword for Jaime, and not even a dagger for the dwarf. Is that the way of it, Father?"

"The steel was sufficient for two blades, not three. If you have need of a dagger, take one from the armory. Robert left a hundred when he died. Gerion gave him a gilded dagger with an ivory grip and a sapphire pommel for a wedding gift, and half the envoys who came to court tried to curry favor by presenting His Grace with jewel-encrusted knives and silver inlay swords."

Tyrion smiled. "They'd have pleased him more if they'd presented him with their daughters."

"No doubt. The only blade he ever used was the hunting knife he had from Jon Arryn, when he was a boy." Lord Tywin waved a hand, dismissing King Robert and all his knives. "What did you find at the riverfront?"

"Mud," said Tyrion, "and a few dead things no one's bothered to bury. Before we can open the port again, the Blackwater's going to have to be dredged, the sunken ships broken up or raised. Three-quarters of the quays need repair, and some may have to be torn down and rebuilt. The entire fish market is gone, and both the River Gate and the King's Gate are splintered from the battering Stannis gave them and should be replaced. I shudder to think of the cost." *If you do shit gold, Father, find a privy and get busy*, he wanted to say, but he knew better.

"You will find whatever gold is required."

"Will I? Where? The treasury is empty, I've told you that. We're not done paying the alchemists for all that wildfire, or the smiths for my chain, and Cersei's pledged the crown to pay half the costs of Joff's wedding—seventy-seven bloody courses, a thousand guests, a pie full of doves, singers, jugglers . . ."

"Extravagance has its uses. We must demonstrate the power and wealth of Casterly Rock for all the realm to see."

"Then perhaps Casterly Rock should pay."

"Why? I have seen Littlefinger's accounts. Crown incomes are ten times higher than they were under Aerys."

"As are the crown's expenses. Robert was as generous with his coin as he was with his cock. Littlefinger borrowed heavily. From you, amongst others. Yes, the incomes are considerable, but they are barely sufficient to cover the usury on Littlefinger's loans. Will you forgive the throne's debt to House Lannister?"

"Don't be absurd."

"Then perhaps seven courses would suffice. Three hundred guests instead of a thousand. I understand that a marriage can be just as binding *without* a dancing bear."

"The Tyrells would think us niggardly. I will have the wedding *and* the waterfront. If you cannot pay for them, say so, and I shall find a master of coin who can."

The disgrace of being dismissed after so short a time was not something Tyrion cared to suffer. "I will find your money."

"You will," his father promised, "and while you are about it, see if you can find your wife's bed as well."

So the talk has reached even him. "I have, thank you. It's that piece of furniture between the window and the hearth, with the velvet canopy and the mattress stuffed with goose down."

"I am pleased you know of it. Now perhaps you ought to try and know the woman who shares it with you."

Woman? Child, you mean. "Has a spider been whispering in your ear, or do I have my sweet sister to thank?" Considering the things that went on beneath Cersei's blankets, you would think she'd have the decency to keep her nose out of his. "Tell me, why is it that all of Sansa's maids are women in Cersei's service? I am sick of being spied upon in my own chambers."

"If you mislike your wife's servants, dismiss them and hire ones more to your liking. That is your right. It is your wife's maidenhood that concerns me, not her maids. This . . . delicacy puzzles me. You seem to have no difficulty bedding whores. Is the Stark girl made differently?"

"Why do you take so much bloody interest in where I put my cock?" Tyrion demanded. "Sansa is too young."

"She is old enough to be Lady of Winterfell once her brother is dead. Claim her maidenhood and you will be one step closer to claiming the north. Get her with child, and the prize is all but won. Do I need to remind you that a marriage that has not been consummated can be set aside?"

"By the High Septon or a Council of Faith. Our present High Septon is a trained seal who barks prettily on command. Moon Boy is more like to annul my marriage than he is."

"Perhaps I should have married Sansa Stark to Moon Boy. He might have known what to do with her."

Tyrion's hands clenched on the arms of his chair. "I have heard all I mean to hear on the subject of my wife's maidenhead. But so long as we are discussing marriage, why is it that I hear nothing of my sister's impending nuptials? As I recall—"

Lord Tywin cut him off. "Mace Tyrell has refused my offer to marry Cersei to his heir Willas."

"*Refused* our sweet Cersei?" That put Tyrion in a *much* better mood.

"When I first broached the match to him, Lord Tyrell seemed well enough disposed," his father said. "A day later, all was changed. The old woman's work. She hectors her son unmercifully. Varys claims she told him that your sister was too old and too *used* for this precious one-legged grandson of hers."

"Cersei must have loved that." He laughed.

Lord Tywin gave him a chilly look. "She does not know. Nor will she. It is better for all of us if the offer was never made. See that you remember that, Tyrion. *The offer was never made.*"

"What offer?" Tyrion rather suspected that Lord Tyrell might come to regret this rebuff.

"Your sister *will* be wed. The question is, to whom? I have several thoughts—" Before he could get to them, there was a rap at the door and a guardsman stuck in his head to announce Grand Maester Pycelle. "He may enter," said Lord Tywin.

Pycelle tottered in on a cane, and stopped long enough to give Tyrion a look that would curdle milk. His once-magnificent white beard, which someone had unaccountably shaved off, was growing back sparse and wispy, leaving him with unsightly pink wattles to dangle beneath his neck. "My lord Hand," the old man said, bowing as deeply as he could without falling, "there has been another bird from Castle Black. Mayhaps we could consult privily?"

"There's no need for that." Lord Tywin waved Grand Maester Pycelle to a seat. "Tyrion may stay."

Oooooh, may I? He rubbed his nose, and waited.

Pycelle cleared his throat, which involved a deal of coughing and hawking. "The letter is from the same Bowen Marsh who sent the last. The castellan. He writes that Lord Mormont has sent word of wildlings moving south in vast numbers."

"The lands beyond the Wall cannot support vast numbers," said Lord Tywin firmly. "This warning is not new."

"This last is, my lord. Mormont sent a bird from the haunted forest, to report that he was under attack. More ravens have returned since, but none with letters. This Bowen Marsh fears Lord Mormont slain, with all his strength."

Tyrion had rather liked old Jeor Mormont, with his gruff manner and talking bird. "Is this certain?" he asked.

"It is not," Pycelle admitted, "but none of Mormont's men have returned as yet. Marsh fears the wildlings have killed them, and that the Wall itself may be attacked next." He fumbled in his robe and found the paper. "Here is his letter, my lord, a plea to all five kings. He wants men, as many men as we can send him."

"Five kings?" His father was annoyed. "There is one king in Westeros. Those fools in black might try and remember that if they wish His Grace to heed them. When you reply, tell him that Renly is dead and the others are traitors and pretenders."

"No doubt they will be glad to learn it. The Wall is a world apart, and news oft reaches them late." Pycelle bobbed his head up and down. "What shall I tell Marsh concerning the men he begs for? Shall we convene the council . . ."

"There is no need. The Night's Watch is a pack of thieves, killers, and baseborn churls, but it occurs to me that they *could* prove otherwise, given proper discipline. If Mormont is indeed dead, the black brothers must choose a new Lord Commander."

Pycelle gave Tyrion a sly glance. "An excellent thought, my lord. I know the very man. Janos Slynt."

Tyrion liked that notion not at all. "The black brothers choose their own commander," he reminded them. "Lord Slynt is new to the Wall. I know, I sent him there. Why should they pick *him* over a dozen more senior men?"

"Because," his father said, in a tone that suggested Tyrion was quite the simpleton, "if they do not vote as they are told, their Wall will melt before it sees another man."

Yes, that would work. Tyrion hitched forward. "Janos Slynt is the wrong man, Father. We'd do better with the commander of the Shadow Tower. Or Eastwatch-by-the-Sea."

"The commander of the Shadow Tower is a Mallister of Seagard. Eastwatch is held by an ironman." Neither would serve his purposes, Lord Tywin's tone said clear enough.

"Janos Slynt is a butcher's son," Tyrion reminded his father forcefully. "You yourself told me—"

"I recall what I told you. Castle Black is not Harrenhal, however. The Night's Watch is not the king's council. There is a tool for every task, and a task for every tool."

Tyrion's anger flashed. "Lord Janos is a hollow suit of armor who will sell himself to the highest bidder."

"I count that a point in his favor. Who is like to bid higher than us?" He turned to Pycelle. "Send a raven. Write that King Joffrey was deeply saddened to hear of Lord Commander Mormont's death, but regrets that he can spare no men just now, whilst so many rebels and usurpers remain in the field. Suggest that matters might be quite different once the throne is secure . . . provided the king has full confidence in the leadership of the Watch. In closing, ask Marsh to pass along His Grace's fondest regards to his faithful friend and servant, Lord Janos Slynt."

"Yes, my lord." Pycelle bobbed his withered head once more. "I shall write as the Hand commands. With great pleasure."

I should have trimmed his head, not his beard, Tyrion reflected. *And Slynt should have gone for a swim with his dear friend Allar Deem.* At least he had not made the same foolish mistake with Symon Silver Tongue. *See there, Father?* he wanted to shout. *See how fast I learn my lessons?*

SAMWELL

Up in the loft a woman was giving birth noisily, while below a man lay dying by the fire. Samwell Tarly could not say which frightened him more.

They'd covered poor Bannen with a pile of furs and stoked the fire high, yet all he could say was, "I'm cold. Please. I'm so cold." Sam was trying to feed him onion broth, but he could not swallow. The broth dribbled over his lips and down his chin as fast as Sam could spoon it in.

"That one's dead." Craster eyed the man with indifference as he worried at a sausage. "Be kinder to stick a knife in his chest than that spoon down his throat, you ask me."

"I don't recall as we did." Giant was no more than five feet tall—his true name was Bedwyck—but a fierce little man for all that. "Slayer, did you ask Craster for his counsel?"

Sam cringed at the name, but shook his head. He filled another spoon, brought it to Bannen's mouth, and tried to ease it between his lips.

"Food and fire," Giant was saying, "that was all we asked of you. And you grudge us the food."

"Be glad I didn't grudge you fire too." Craster was a thick man made thicker by the ragged smelly sheepskins he wore day and night. He had a broad flat nose, a mouth that drooped to one side, and a missing ear. And though his matted hair and tangled beard might be grey going white, his hard knuckly hands still looked strong enough to hurt. "I fed you what I could, but you crows are always hungry. I'm a godly man, else I would have chased you off. You think I need the likes of him, dying on my floor? You think I need all your mouths, little man?" The wildling spat. "Crows. When did a black bird ever bring good to a man's hall, I ask you? Never. Never."

More broth ran from the corner of Bannen's mouth. Sam dabbed it away with a corner of his sleeve. The ranger's eyes were open but unseeing. "I'm cold," he said again, so faintly. A maester might have known how to save him, but they had no maester. Kedge Whiteye had taken Bannen's mangled foot off nine days past, in a gout of pus and blood that made Sam sick, but it was too little, too late. "I'm so cold," the pale lips repeated.

About the hall, a ragged score of black brothers squatted on the floor or sat on rough-hewn benches, drinking cups of the same thin onion broth and gnawing on chunks of hardbread. A couple were wounded worse than Bannen, to look at them. Fornio had been delirious for days, and Ser Byam's shoulder was oozing a foul yellow pus. When they'd left Castle Black, Brown Bernarr had been carrying bags of Myrish fire, mustard salve, ground garlic, tansy, poppy, kingscopper, and other healing herbs. Even sweetsleep, which gave the gift of painless death. But Brown Bernarr had died on the Fist and no one had thought to search for Maester Aemon's medicines. Hake had known some herblore as well, being a cook, but Hake was also lost. So it was left to the surviving stewards to do what they could for the wounded, which was little enough. *At least they are dry here, with a fire to warm them. They need more food, though.*

They all needed more food. The men had been grumbling for days. Clubfoot Karl kept saying how Craster had to have a hidden larder, and Garth of Oldtown had begun to echo him, when he was out of the Lord Commander's hearing. Sam had thought of begging for something more nourishing for the wounded men at least, but he did not have the courage. Craster's eyes were cold and mean, and whenever the wildling looked his way his hands twitched a little, as if they wanted to curl up into fists. *Does he know I spoke to Gilly, the last time we were here?* he wondered. *Did she tell him I said we'd take her? Did he beat it out of her?*

"I'm cold," said Bannen. "Please. I'm cold."

For all the heat and smoke in Craster's hall, Sam felt cold himself. *And tired, so tired.* He needed sleep, but whenever he closed his eyes he dreamed of blowing snow and dead men shambling toward him with black hands and bright blue eyes.

Up in the loft, Gilly let out a shuddering sob that echoed down the long low windowless hall. "Push," he heard one of Craster's older wives tell her. "Harder. *Harder.* Scream if it helps." She did, so loud it made Sam wince.

Craster turned his head to glare. "I've had a bellyful o' that shrieking," he shouted up. "Give her a rag to bite down on, or I'll come up there and give her a taste o' my hand."

He would too, Sam knew. Craster had nineteen wives, but none who'd dare interfere once he started up that ladder. No more than the black brothers had two nights past, when he was beating one of the younger girls. There had been mutterings, to be sure. "He's killing her," Garth of Greenaway had said, and Clubfoot Karl laughed and said, "If he don't want the little sweetmeat he could give her to me." Black Bernarr cursed in a low angry voice, and Alan of Rosby got up and went outside so he wouldn't have to hear. "His roof, his rule," the ranger Ronnel Harclay had reminded them. "Craster's a friend to the Watch."

A friend, thought Sam, as he listened to Gilly's muffled shrieks. Craster was a brutal man who ruled his wives and daughters with an iron hand, but his keep was a refuge all the same. "Frozen crows," Craster sneered when they straggled in, those few who had survived the snow, the wights, and the bitter cold. "And not so big a flock as went north, neither." Yet he had given them space on his floor, a roof to keep the snow off, a fire to dry them out, and his wives had brought them cups of hot wine to put some warmth in their bellies. "Bloody crows," he called them, but he'd fed them too, meager though the fare might be.

We are guests, Sam reminded himself. *Gilly is his. His daughter, his wife. His roof, his rule.*

The first time he'd seen Craster's Keep, Gilly had come begging for help, and Sam had lent her his black cloak to conceal her belly when she went to find Jon Snow. *Knights are supposed to defend women and children.* Only a few of the black brothers were knights, but even so . . . *We all say the words*, Sam thought. *I am the shield that guards the realms of men.* A woman was a woman, even a wildling woman. *We should help her. We should.* It was her child Gilly feared for; she was frightened that it might be a boy. Craster raised up his daughters to be his wives, but there were neither men nor boys to be seen about his compound. Gilly had told Jon that Craster gave his sons to the gods. *If the gods are good, they will send her a daughter*, Sam prayed.

Up in the loft, Gilly choked back a scream. "That's it," a woman said. "Another push, now. Oh, I see his head."

Hers, Sam thought miserably. *Her head, hers.*

"Cold," said Bannen, weakly. "Please. I'm so cold." Sam put the bowl and spoon aside, tossed another fur across the dying man, put another stick on the fire. Gilly gave a shriek, and began to pant. Craster gnawed on his hard black sausage. He had sausages for himself and his wives, he said, but none for the Watch. "Women," he complained. "The way they wail . . . I had me a fat sow once birthed a litter of eight with no more'n a grunt." Chewing, he turned his head to squint contemptuously at Sam. "She was near as fat as you, boy. Slayer." He laughed.

It was more than Sam could stand. He stumbled away from the firepit, stepping awkwardly over and around the men sleeping and squatting and dying upon the hard-packed earthen floor. The smoke and screams and moans were making him feel faint. Bending his head, he pushed through the hanging deerhide flaps that served Craster for a door and stepped out into the afternoon.

The day was cloudy, but still bright enough to blind him after the gloom of the hall. Some patches of snow weighed down the limbs of surrounding trees and blanketed the gold and russet hills, but fewer than there had been. The storm had passed on, and the days at Craster's Keep had been . . . well, not warm perhaps, but not so bitter cold.

Sam could hear the soft *drip-drip-drip* of water melting off the icicles that bearded the edge of the thick sod roof. He took a deep shuddering breath and looked around.

To the west Ollo Lophand and Tim Stone were moving through the horselines, feeding and watering the remaining garrons.

Downwind, other brothers were skinning and butchering the animals deemed too weak to go on. Spearmen and archers walked sentry behind the earthen dikes that were Craster's only defense against whatever hid in the wood beyond, while a dozen firepits sent up thick fingers of blue-grey smoke. Sam could hear the distant echoes of axes at work in the forest, where a work detail was harvesting enough wood to keep the blazes burning all through the night. Nights were the bad time. When it got dark. And *cold*.

There had been no attacks while they had been at Craster's, neither wights nor Others. Nor would there be, Craster said. "A godly man got no cause to fear such. I said as much to that Mance Rayder once, when he come sniffing round. He never listened, no more'n you crows with your swords and your bloody fires. That won't help you none when the white cold comes. Only the gods will help you then. You best get right with the gods."

Gilly had spoken of the white cold as well, and she'd told them what sort of offerings Craster made to his gods. Sam had wanted to kill him when he heard. *There are no laws beyond the Wall*, he reminded himself, *and Craster's a friend to the Watch*.

A ragged shout went up from behind the daub-and-wattle hall. Sam went to take a look. The ground beneath his feet was a slush of melting snow and soft mud that Dolorous Edd insisted was made of Craster's shit. It was thicker than shit, though; it sucked at Sam's boots so hard he felt one pull loose.

Back of a vegetable garden and empty sheepfold, a dozen black brothers were loosing arrows at a butt they'd built of hay and straw. The slender blond steward they called Sweet Donnel had laid a shaft just off the bull's eye at fifty yards. "Best that, old man," he said.

"Aye. I will." Ulmer, stooped and grey-bearded and loose of skin and limb, stepped to the mark and pulled an arrow from the quiver at his waist. In his youth he had been an outlaw, a member of the infamous Kingswood Brotherhood. He claimed he'd once put an arrow through the hand of the White Bull of the Kingsguard to steal a kiss from the lips of a Dornish princess. He had stolen her jewels too, and a chest of golden dragons, but it was the kiss he liked to boast of in his cups.

He notched and drew, all smooth as summer silk, then let fly. His shaft struck the butt an inch inside of Donnel Hill's. "Will that do, lad?" he asked, stepping back.

"Well enough," said the younger man, grudgingly. "The crosswind helped you. It blew more strongly when I loosed."

"You ought to have allowed for it, then. You have a good eye and a steady hand, but you'll need a deal more to best a man of the kingswood. Fletcher Dick it was who showed me how to bend the bow, and no finer archer ever lived. Have I told you about old Dick, now?"

"Only three hundred times." Every man at Castle Black had heard Ulmer's tales of the great outlaw band of yore; of Simon Toyne and the Smiling Knight, Oswyn Longneck the Thrice-Hanged, Wenda the White Fawn, Fletcher Dick, Big Belly Ben, and all the rest. Searching for escape, Sweet Donnel looked about and spied Sam standing in the muck. "*Slayer*," he called. "Come, show us how you slew the Other." He held out the tall yew longbow.

Sam turned red. "It wasn't an arrow, it was a dagger, dragonglass . . ." He knew what would happen if he took the bow. He would miss the butt and send the arrow sailing over the dike off into the trees. Then he'd hear the laughter.

"No matter," said Alan of Rosby, another fine bowman. "We're all keen to see the Slayer shoot. Aren't we, lads?"

He could not face them; the mocking smiles, the mean little jests, the contempt in their eyes. Sam turned to go back the way he'd come, but his right foot sank deep in the muck, and when he tried to pull it out his boot came off. He had to kneel to wrench it free, laughter ringing in his ears. Despite all his socks, the snowmelt had soaked through to his toes by the time he made his escape. *Useless*, he thought miserably. *My father saw me true. I have no right to be alive when so many brave men are dead.*

Grenn was tending the firepit south of the compound gate, stripped to the waist as he split logs. His face was red with exertion, the sweat steaming off his skin. But he grinned as Sam came chuffing up. "The Others get your boot, Slayer?"

Him too? "It was the mud. Please don't call me that."

"Why not?" Grenn sounded honestly puzzled. "It's a good name, and you came by it fairly."

Pyp always teased Grenn about being thick as a castle wall, so Sam explained patiently. "It's just a different way of calling me a coward," he said, standing on his left leg and wriggling back into his muddy boot. "They're mocking me, the same way they mock Bedwyck by calling him 'Giant.' "

"He's not a giant, though," said Grenn, "and Paul was never small. Well, maybe when he was a babe at the breast, but not after. You *did* slay the Other, though, so it's not the same."

"I just . . . I never . . . I was *scared!*"

"No more than me. It's only Pyp who says I'm too dumb to be frightened. I get as frightened as anyone." Grenn bent to scoop up a split log, and tossed it into the fire. "I used to be scared of Jon, whenever I had to fight him. He was so quick, and he fought like he meant to kill me." The green damp wood sat in the flames, smoking before it took fire. "I never said, though. Sometimes I think everyone is just pretending to be brave, and none of us really are. Maybe pretending is how you *get* brave, I don't know. Let them call you Slayer, who cares?"

"You never liked Ser Alliser to call you Aurochs."

"He was saying I was big and stupid." Grenn scratched at his beard. "If Pyp wanted to call me Aurochs, though, he could. Or you, or Jon. An aurochs is a fierce strong beast, so that's not so bad, and I *am* big, and getting bigger. Wouldn't you rather be Sam the Slayer than Ser Piggy?"

"Why can't I just be Samwell Tarly?" He sat down heavily on a wet log that Grenn had yet to split. "It was the dragonglass that slew it. Not me, the dragonglass."

He had told them. He had told them all. Some of them didn't believe him, he knew. Dirk had shown Sam his dirk and said, "I got iron, what do I want with glass?" Black Bernarr and the three Garths made it plain that they doubted his whole story, and Rolley of Sisterton came right out and said, "More like you stabbed some rustling bushes and it turned out to be Small Paul taking a shit, so you came up with a lie."

But Dywen listened, and Dolorous Edd, and they made Sam and Grenn tell the Lord Commander. Mormont frowned all through the tale and asked pointed questions, but he was too cautious a man to shun any possible advantage. He asked Sam for all the dragonglass in his pack, though that was little enough. Whenever Sam thought of the cache Jon had found buried beneath the Fist, it made him want to cry. There'd been dagger blades and spearheads, and two or three hundred arrowheads at least. Jon had made daggers for himself, Sam, and Lord Commander Mormont, and he'd given Sam a spearhead, an old broken horn, and some arrowheads. Grenn had taken a handful of arrowheads as well, but that was all.

So now all they had was Mormont's dagger and the one Sam had given Grenn, plus nineteen arrows and a tall hardwood spear with a black dragonglass head. The sentries passed the spear along from watch to watch, while Mormont had divided the arrows among his best bowmen. Muttering Bill, Garth Greyfeather, Ronnel Harclay, Sweet Donnel Hill, and Alan of Rosby had three apiece, and Ulmer had four. But even if they made every shaft tell, they'd soon be down to fire arrows like all the rest. They had loosed hundreds of fire arrows on the Fist, yet still the wights kept coming.

It will not be enough, Sam thought. Craster's sloping palisades of mud and melting snow would hardly slow the wights, who'd climbed the much steeper slopes of the Fist to swarm over the ringwall. And instead of three hundred brothers drawn up in disciplined ranks to meet them, the wights would find forty-one ragged survivors, nine too badly hurt to fight. Forty-four had come straggling into Craster's out of the storm, out of the sixty-odd who'd cut their way free of the Fist, but three of those had died of their wounds, and Bannen would soon make four.

"Do you think the wights are gone?" Sam asked Grenn. "Why don't they come finish us?"

"They only come when it's cold."

"Yes," said Sam, "but is it the cold that brings the wights, or the wights that bring the cold?"

"Who cares?" Grenn's axe sent wood chips flying. "They come together, that's what matters. Hey, now that we know that dragonglass kills them, maybe they won't come at all. Maybe they're frightened of *us* now!"

Sam wished he could believe that, but it seemed to him that when you were dead, fear had no more meaning than pain or love or duty. He wrapped his hands around his legs, sweating under his layers of wool and leather and fur. The dragonglass dagger had melted the pale thing in the woods, true . . . but Grenn was talking like it would do the same to the wights. *We don't know that*, he thought. *We don't know anything, really. I wish Jon was here.* He liked Grenn, but he couldn't talk to him the same way. *Jon wouldn't call me Slayer, I know. And I could talk to him about Gilly's baby.* Jon had ridden off with Qhorin Halfhand, though, and they'd had no word of him since. *He had a dragonglass dagger too, but did he think to use it? Is he lying dead and frozen in some ravine . . . or worse, is he dead and walking?*

He could not understand why the gods would want to take Jon Snow and Bannen and leave him, craven and clumsy as he was. He *should* have died on the Fist, where he'd pissed himself three times and lost his sword besides. And he *would* have died in the woods if Small Paul had not come along to carry him. *I wish it was all a dream. Then I could wake up.* How fine that would be, to wake back on the Fist of the First Men with all his brothers still around him, even Jon and Ghost. Or even better, to wake in Castle Black behind the Wall and go to the common room for a bowl of Three-Finger Hobb's thick cream of wheat, with a big spoon of butter melting in the middle and a dollop of honey besides. Just the thought of it made his empty stomach rumble.

"Snow."

Sam glanced up at the sound. Lord Commander Mormont's raven was circling the fire, beating the air with wide black wings.

"Snow," the bird cawed. *"Snow, snow."*

Wherever the raven went, Mormont soon followed. The Lord Commander emerged from beneath the trees, mounted on his garron between old Dywen and the fox-faced ranger Ronnel Harclay, who'd been raised to Thoren Smallwood's place. The spearmen at the gate shouted a challenge, and the Old Bear returned a gruff, "Who in seven hells do you *think* goes there? Did the Others take your eyes?" He rode between the gateposts, one bearing a ram's skull and the other the skull of a bear, then reined up, raised a fist, and whistled. The raven came flapping down at his call.

"My lord," Sam heard Ronnel Harclay say, "we have only twenty-two mounts, and I doubt half will reach the Wall."

"I know that," Mormont grumbled. "We must go all the same. Craster's made that plain." He glanced to the west, where a bank of dark clouds hid the sun. "The gods gave us a respite, but for how long?" Mormont swung down from the saddle, jolting his raven back into the air. He saw Sam then, and bellowed, "*Tarly!*"

"Me?" Sam got awkwardly to his feet.

"*Me?*" The raven landed on the old man's head. "*Me?*"

"Is your name Tarly? Do you have a brother hereabouts? Yes, you. Close your mouth and come with me."

"With you?" The words tumbled out in a squeak.

Lord Commander Mormont gave him a withering look. "You are a man of the Night's Watch. Try not to soil your smallclothes every time I look at you. Come, I said." His boots made squishing sounds in the mud, and Sam had to hurry to keep up. "I've been thinking about this dragonglass of yours."

"It's not *mine*," Sam said.

"Jon Snow's dragonglass, then. If dragonglass daggers are what we need, why do we have only two of them? Every man on the Wall should be armed with one the day he says his words."

"We never knew . . ."

"We *never knew!* But we must have known once. The Night's Watch has forgotten its true purpose, Tarly. You don't build a wall seven hundred feet high to keep savages in skins from stealing women. The Wall was made *to guard the realms of men* . . . and not against other men, which is all the wildlings are when you come right down to it. Too many years, Tarly, too many hundreds and thousands of years. We lost sight of the true enemy. And now he's here, but we don't know how to fight him. Is dragonglass made by dragons, as the smallfolk like to say?"

"The m-maesters think not," Sam stammered. "The maesters say it comes from the fires of the earth. They call it obsidian."

Mormont snorted. "They can call it lemon pie for all I care. If it kills as you claim, I want more of it."

Sam stumbled. "Jon found more, on the Fist. Hundreds of arrowheads, spearheads as well . . ."

"So you said. Small good it does us there. To reach the Fist again we'd need to be armed with the weapons we won't have until we reach the bloody Fist. And there are still the wildlings to deal with. We need to find dragonglass someplace else."

Sam had almost forgotten about the wildlings, so much had happened since. "The children of the forest used dragonglass blades," he said. "They'd know where to find obsidian."

"The children of the forest are all dead," said Mormont. "The First Men killed half of them with bronze blades, and the Andals finished the job with iron. Why a glass dagger should—"

The Old Bear broke off as Craster emerged from between the deerhide flaps of his door. The wildling smiled, revealing a mouth of brown rotten teeth. "I have a son."

"*Son*," cawed Mormont's raven. "*Son, son, son*."

The Lord Commander's face was stiff. "I'm glad for you."

"Are you, now? Me, I'll be glad when you and yours are gone. Past time, I'm thinking."

"As soon as our wounded are strong enough . . ."

"They're strong as they're like to get, old crow, and both of us know it. Them that's dying, you know them too, cut their bloody throats and be done with it. Or leave them, if you don't have the stomach, and I'll sort them out myself."

Lord Commander Mormont bristled. "Thoren Smallwood claimed you were a friend to the Watch—"

"Aye," said Craster. "I gave you all I could spare, but winter's coming on, and now the girl's stuck me with another squalling mouth to feed."

"We could take him," someone squeaked.

Craster's head turned. His eyes narrowed. He spat on Sam's foot. "What did you say, Slayer?"

Sam opened and closed his mouth. "I . . . I . . . I only meant . . . if you didn't want him . . . his mouth to feed . . . with winter coming on, we . . . we could take him, and . . ."

"My son. My blood. You think I'd give him to you crows?"

"I only thought . . ." *You have no sons, you expose them, Gilly said as much, you leave them in the woods, that's why you have only wives here, and daughters who grow up to be wives.*

"Be quiet, Sam," said Lord Commander Mormont. "You've said enough. Too much. Inside."

"M-my lord—"

"*Inside!*"

Red-faced, Sam pushed through the deerhides, back into the gloom of the hall. Mormont followed. "How great a fool are you?" the old man said within, his voice choked and angry. "Even if Craster gave us the child, he'd be dead before we reached the Wall. We need a newborn babe to care for near as much as we need more snow. Do you have milk to feed him in those big teats of yours? Or did you mean to take the mother too?"

"She wants to come," Sam said. "She begged me . . ."

Mormont raised a hand. "I will hear no more of this, Tarly. You've been told and *told* to stay well away from Craster's wives."

"She's his daughter," Sam said feebly.

"Go see to Bannen. Now. Before you make me wroth."

"Yes, my lord." Sam hurried off quivering.

But when he reached the fire, it was only to find Giant pulling a fur cloak up over Bannen's head. "He said he was cold," the small man said. "I hope he's gone someplace warm, I do."

"His wound . . ." said Sam.

"Bugger his wound." Dirk prodded the corpse with his foot. "His *foot* was hurt. I knew a man back in my village lost a foot. He lived to nine-and-forty."

"The cold," said Sam. "He was never warm."

"He was never *fed*," said Dirk. "Not proper. That bastard Craster starved him dead."

Sam looked around anxiously, but Craster had not returned to the hall. If he had, things might have grown ugly. The wildling hated bastards, though the rangers said he was baseborn himself, fathered on a wildling woman by some long-dead crow.

"Craster's got his own to feed," said Giant. "All these women. He's given us what he can."

"Don't you bloody believe it. The day we leave, he'll tap a keg o' mead and sit down to feast on ham and honey. And *laugh* at us, out starving in the snow. He's a bloody wildling, is all he is. There's none o' them friends of the Watch." He kicked at Bannen's corpse. "Ask him if you don't believe me."

They burned the ranger's corpse at sunset, in the fire that Grenn had been feeding earlier that day. Tim Stone and Garth of Oldtown carried out the naked corpse and swung him twice between them before heaving him into the flames. The surviving brothers divided up his clothes, his weapons, his armor, and everything else he owned. At Castle Black, the Night's Watch buried its dead with all due ceremony. They were not at Castle Black, though. *And bones do not come back as wights.*

"His name was Bannen," Lord Commander Mormont said, as the flames took him. "He was a brave man, a good ranger. He came to us from . . . where did he come from?"

"Down White Harbor way," someone called out.

Mormont nodded. "He came to us from White Harbor, and never failed in his duty. He kept his vows as best he could, rode far, fought fiercely. We shall never see his like again."

"*And now his watch is ended,*" the black brothers said, in solemn chant.

"And now his watch is ended," Mormont echoed.

"*Ended,*" cried his raven. "*Ended.*"

Sam was red-eyed and sick from the smoke. When he looked at the fire, he thought he saw Bannen sitting up, his hands coiling into fists as if to fight off the flames that were consuming him, but it was only for an instant, before the swirling smoke hid all. The worst thing was the *smell*, though. If it had been a foul unpleasant smell he might have stood it, but his burning brother smelled so much like roast pork that Sam's mouth began to water, and that was so horrible that as soon as the bird squawked *"Ended"* he ran behind the hall to throw up in the ditch.

He was there on his knees in the mud when Dolorous Edd came up. "Digging for worms, Sam? Or are you just sick?"

"Sick," said Sam weakly, wiping his mouth with the back of his hand. "The smell . . ."

"Never knew Bannen could smell so good." Edd's tone was as morose as ever. "I had half a mind to carve a slice off him. If we had some applesauce, I might have done it. Pork's always best with applesauce, I find." Edd undid his laces and pulled out his cock. "You best not die, Sam, or I fear I might succumb. There's bound to be more crackling on you than Bannen ever had, and I never could resist a bit of crackling." He sighed as his piss arced out, yellow and steaming. "We ride at first light, did you hear? Sun or snow, the Old Bear tells me."

Sun or snow. Sam glanced up anxiously at the sky. "Snow?" he squeaked. "We . . . ride? All of us?"

"Well, no, some will need to walk." He shook himself. "Dywen now, he says we need to learn to ride dead horses, like the Others do. He claims it would save on feed. How much could a dead horse eat?" Edd laced himself back up. "Can't say I fancy the notion. Once they figure a way to work a dead horse, we'll be next. Likely I'll be the first too. 'Edd,' they'll say, 'dying's no excuse for lying down no more, so get on up and take this spear, you've got the watch tonight.' Well, I shouldn't be so gloomy. Might be I'll die before they work it out."

Might be we'll all die, and sooner than we'd like, Sam thought, as he climbed awkwardly to his feet.

When Craster learned that his unwanted guests would be departing on the morrow, the wildling became almost amiable, or as close to amiable as Craster ever got. "Past time," he said, "you don't belong here, I told you that. All the same, I'll see you off proper, with a feast. Well, a feed. My wives can roast them horses you slaughtered, and I'll find some beer and bread." He smiled his brown smile. "Nothing better than beer and horsemeat. If you can't ride 'em, eat 'em, that's what I say."

His wives and daughters dragged out the benches and the long log tables, and cooked and served as well. Except for Gilly, Sam could hardly tell the women apart. Some were old and some were young and some were only girls, but a lot of them were Craster's daughters as well as his wives, and they all looked sort of alike. As they went about their work, they spoke in soft voices to each other, but never to the men in black.

Craster owned but one chair. He sat in it, clad in a sleeveless sheepskin jerkin. His thick arms were covered with white hair, and about one wrist was a twisted ring of gold. Lord Commander Mormont took the place at the top of the bench to his right, while the brothers crowded in knee to knee; a dozen remained outside to guard the gate and tend the fires.

Sam found a place between Grenn and Orphan Oss, his stomach rumbling. The charred horsemeat dripped with grease as Craster's wives turned the spits above the firepit, and the smell of it set his mouth to watering again, but that reminded him of Bannen. Hungry as he was, Sam knew he would retch if he so much as tried a bite. How could they eat the poor faithful garrons who had carried them so far? When Craster's wives brought onions, he seized one eagerly. One side was black with rot, but he cut that part off with his dagger and ate the good half raw. There was bread as well, but only two loaves. When Ulmer asked for more, the woman only shook her head. That was when the trouble started.

"Two loaves?" Clubfoot Karl complained from down the bench. "How stupid are you women? We need more bread than this!"

Lord Commander Mormont gave him a hard look. "Take what you're given, and be thankful. Would you sooner be out in the storm eating snow?"

"We'll be there soon enough." Clubfoot Karl did not flinch from the Old Bear's wrath. "I'd sooner eat what Craster's hiding, my lord."

Craster narrowed his eyes. "I gave you crows enough. I got me women to feed."

Dirk speared a chunk of horsemeat. "Aye. So you admit you got a secret larder. How else to make it through a winter?"

"I'm a godly man . . ." Craster started.

"You're a niggardly man," said Karl, "and a liar."

"Hams," Garth of Oldtown said, in a reverent voice. "There were pigs, last time we come. I bet he's got hams hid someplace. Smoked and salted hams, and bacon too."

"Sausage," said Dirk. "Them long black ones, they're like rocks, they keep for years. I bet he's got a hundred hanging in some cellar."

"Oats," suggested Ollo Lophand. "Corn. Barley."

"*Corn,*" said Mormont's raven, with a flap of the wings. "*Corn, corn, corn, corn, corn.*"

"*Enough,*" said Lord Commander Mormont over the bird's raucous calls. "Be quiet, all of you. This is folly."

"Apples," said Garth of Greenaway. "Barrels and barrels of crisp autumn apples. There are apple trees out there, I saw 'em."

"Dried berries. Cabbages. Pine nuts."

"*Corn. Corn. Corn.*"

"Salt mutton. There's a sheepfold. He's got casks and casks of mutton laid by, you know he does."

Craster looked fit to spit them all by then. Lord Commander Mormont rose. "*Silence.* I'll hear no more such talk."

"Then stuff bread in your ears, old man." Clubfoot Karl pushed back from the table. "Or did you swallow your bloody crumb already?"

Sam saw the Old Bear's face go red. "Have you forgotten who I am? Sit, eat, and be silent. That is a *command.*"

No one spoke. No one moved. All eyes were on the Lord Commander and the big clubfooted ranger, as the two of them stared at each other across the table. It seemed to Sam that Karl broke first, and was about to sit, though sullenly . . .

. . . but Craster stood, and his axe was in his hand. The big black steel axe that Mormont had given him as a guest gift. "No," he growled. "You'll not sit. No one who calls me niggard will sleep beneath my roof nor eat at my board. Out with you, cripple. And you and you and you." He jabbed the head of the axe toward Dirk and Garth and Garth in turn. "Go sleep in the cold with empty bellies, the lot o' you, or . . ."

"Bloody *bastard!*" Sam heard one of the Garths curse. He never saw which one.

"*Who calls me bastard?*" Craster roared, sweeping platter and meat and wine cups from the table with his left hand while lifting the axe with his right.

"It's no more than all men know," Karl answered.

Craster moved quicker than Sam would have believed possible, vaulting across the table with axe in hand. A woman screamed, Garth Greenaway and Orphan Oss drew knives, Karl stumbled back and tripped over Ser Byam lying wounded on the floor. One instant Craster was coming after him spitting curses. The next he was spitting blood. Dirk had grabbed him by the hair, yanked his head back, and opened his throat ear to ear with one long slash. Then he gave him a rough shove, and the wildling fell forward, crashing face first across Ser Byam. Byam screamed in agony as Craster drowned in his own blood, the axe slipping from his fingers. Two of Craster's wives were wailing, a third cursed, a fourth flew at Sweet Donnel and tried to scratch his eyes out. He knocked her to the floor. The Lord Commander stood over Craster's corpse, dark with anger. "The gods will curse us," he cried. "There is no crime so foul as for a guest to bring murder into a man's hall. By all the laws of the hearth, we—"

"There are no laws beyond the Wall, old man. Remember?" Dirk grabbed one of Craster's wives by the arm, and shoved the point of his bloody dirk up under her chin. "Show us where he keeps the food, or you'll get the same as he did, woman."

"Unhand her." Mormont took a step. "I'll have your head for this, you—"

Garth of Greenaway blocked his path, and Ollo Lophand yanked him back. They both had blades in hand. "Hold your tongue," Ollo warned. Instead the Lord Commander grabbed for his dagger. Ollo had only one hand, but that was quick. He twisted free of the old man's grasp, shoved the knife into Mormont's belly, and yanked it out again, all red. And then the world went mad.

Later, much later, Sam found himself sitting crosslegged on the floor, with Mormont's head in his lap. He did not remember how they'd gotten there, or much of anything else that had happened after the Old Bear was stabbed. Garth of Greenaway had killed Garth of Oldtown, he recalled, but not why. Rolley of Sisterton had fallen from the loft and broken his neck after climbing the ladder to have a taste of Craster's wives. Grenn . . .

Grenn had shouted and slapped him, and then he'd run away with Giant and Dolorous Edd and some others. Craster still sprawled across Ser Byam, but the wounded knight no longer moaned. Four men in black sat on the bench eating chunks of burned horsemeat while Ollo coupled with a weeping woman on the table.

"Tarly." When he tried to speak, the blood dribbled from the Old Bear's mouth down into his beard. "Tarly, go. *Go.*"

"Where, my lord?" His voice was flat and lifeless. *I am not afraid.* It was a queer feeling. "There's no place to go."

"The Wall. Make for the Wall. Now."

"*Now,*" squawked the raven. "*Now. Now.*" The bird walked up the old man's arm to his chest, and plucked a hair from his beard.

"You must. Must tell them."

"Tell them what, my lord?" Sam asked politely.

"All. The Fist. The wildlings. Dragonglass. This. *All.*" His breathing was very shallow now, his voice a whisper. "Tell my son. Jorah. Tell him, take the black. My wish. Dying wish."

"*Wish?*" The raven cocked its head, beady black eyes shining. "*Corn?*" the bird asked.

"No corn," said Mormont feebly. "Tell Jorah. Forgive him. My son. Please. Go."

"It's too far," said Sam. "I'll never reach the Wall, my lord." He was so very tired. All he wanted was to sleep, to sleep and sleep and never wake, and he knew that if he just stayed here soon enough Dirk or Ollo Lophand or Clubfoot Karl would get angry with him and grant his wish, just to see him die. "I'd sooner stay with you. See, I'm not frightened anymore. Of you, or . . . of anything."

"You should be," said a woman's voice.

Three of Craster's wives were standing over them. Two were haggard old women he did not know, but Gilly was between them, all bundled up in skins and cradling a bundle of brown and white fur that must have held her baby. "We're not supposed to talk to Craster's wives," Sam told them. "We have orders."

"That's done now," said the old woman on the right.

"The blackest crows are down in the cellar, gorging,"

said the old woman on the left, "or up in the loft with the young ones. They'll be back soon, though. Best you be gone when they do. The horses run off, but Dyah's caught two."

"You said you'd help me," Gilly reminded him.

"I said Jon would help you. Jon's brave, and he's a good fighter, but I think he's dead now. I'm a craven. And fat. Look how fat I am. Besides, Lord Mormont's hurt. Can't you see? I couldn't leave the Lord Commander."

"Child," said the other old woman, "that old crow's gone before you. Look."

Mormont's head was still in his lap, but his eyes were open and staring and his lips no longer moved. The raven cocked its head and squawked, then looked up at Sam. "*Corn?*"

"No corn. He has no corn." Sam closed the Old Bear's eyes and tried to think of a prayer, but all that came to mind was, "Mother have mercy. Mother have mercy. Mother have mercy."

"Your mother can't help you none," said the old woman on the left. "That dead old man can't neither. You take his sword and you take that big warm fur cloak o' his and you take his horse if you can find him. And you go."

"The girl don't lie," the old woman on the right said. "She's my girl, and I beat the lying out of her early on. You said you'd help her. Do what Ferny says, boy. Take the girl and be quick about it."

"*Quick,*" the raven said. "*Quick quick quick.*"

"Where?" asked Sam, puzzled. "Where should I take her?"

"Someplace warm," the two old women said as one.

Gilly was crying. "Me and the babe. Please. I'll be your wife, like I was Craster's. Please, ser crow. He's a boy, just like Nella said he'd be. If you don't take him, *they* will."

"They?" said Sam, and the raven cocked its black head and echoed, "*They. They. They.*"

"The boy's brothers," said the old woman on the left. "Craster's sons. The white cold's rising out there, crow. I can feel it in my bones. These poor old bones don't lie. They'll be here soon, the sons."

ARYA

Her eyes had grown accustomed to blackness. When Harwin pulled the hood off her head, the ruddy glare inside the hollow hill made Arya blink like some stupid owl.

A huge firepit had been dug in the center of the earthen floor, and its flames rose swirling and crackling toward the smoke-stained ceiling. The walls were equal parts stone and soil, with huge white roots twisting through them like a thousand slow pale snakes. People were emerging from between those roots as she watched; edging out from the shadows for a look at the captives, stepping from the mouths of pitch-black tunnels, popping out of crannies and crevices on all sides. In one place on the far side of the fire, the roots formed a kind of stairway up to a hollow in the earth where a man sat almost lost in the tangle of weirwood.

Lem unhooded Gendry. "What is this place?" he asked.

"An old place, deep and secret. A refuge where neither wolves nor lions come prowling."

Neither wolves nor lions. Arya's skin prickled. She remembered the dream she'd had, and the taste of blood when she tore the man's arm from his shoulder.

Big as the fire was, the cave was bigger; it was hard to tell where it began and where it ended. The tunnel mouths might have been two feet deep or gone on two miles. Arya saw men and women and little children, all of them watching her warily.

Greenbeard said, "Here's the wizard, skinny squirrel. You'll get your answers now." He pointed toward the fire, where Tom Sevenstrings stood talking to a tall thin man with oddments of old armor buckled on over his ratty pink robes. *That can't be Thoros of Myr.* Arya remembered the red priest as fat, with a smooth face and a shiny bald head. This man had a droopy face and a full head of shaggy grey hair. Something Tom said made him look at her, and Arya thought he was about to come over to her. Only then the Mad Huntsman appeared, shoving his captive down into the light, and she and Gendry were forgotten.

The Huntsman had turned out to be a stocky man in patched tan leathers, balding and weak-chinned and quarrelsome. At Stoney Sept she had thought that Lem and Greenbeard might be torn to pieces when they faced him at the crow cages to claim his captive for the lightning lord. The hounds had been all around them, sniffing and snarling. But Tom o' Sevens soothed them with his playing, Tansy marched across the square with her apron full of bones and fatty mutton, and Lem pointed out Anguy in the brothel window, standing with an arrow notched. The Mad Huntsman had cursed them all for lickspittles, but finally he had agreed to take his prize to Lord Beric for judgment.

They had bound his wrists with hempen rope, strung a noose around his neck, and pulled a sack down over his head, but even so there was danger in the man. Arya could feel it across the cave. Thoros—if that *was* Thoros—met captor and captive halfway to the fire. "How did you take him?" the priest asked.

"The dogs caught the scent. He was sleeping off a drunk under a willow tree, if you believe it."

"Betrayed by his own kind." Thoros turned to the prisoner and yanked his hood off. "Welcome to our humble hall, dog. It is not so grand as Robert's throne room, but the company is better."

The shifting flames painted Sandor Clegane's burned face with orange shadows, so he looked even more terrible than he did in daylight. When he pulled at the rope that bound his wrists, flakes of dry blood fell off. The Hound's mouth twitched. "I know you," he said to Thoros.

"You did. In mêlées, you'd curse my flaming sword, though thrice I overthrew you with it."

"Thoros of Myr. You used to shave your head."

"To betoken a humble heart, but in truth my heart was vain. Besides, I lost my razor in the woods." The priest slapped his belly. "I am less than I was, but more. A year in the wild will melt the flesh off a man. Would that I could find a tailor to take in my skin. I might look young again, and pretty maids would shower me with kisses."

"Only the blind ones, priest."

The outlaws hooted, none so loud as Thoros. "Just so. Yet I am not the false priest you knew. The Lord of Light has woken in my heart. Many powers long asleep are waking, and there are forces moving in the land. I have seen them in my flames."

The Hound was unimpressed. "Bugger your flames. And you as well." He looked around at the others. "You keep queer company for a holy man."

"These are my brothers," Thoros said simply.

Lem Lemoncloak pushed forward. He and Greenbeard were the only men there tall enough to look the Hound in the eye. "Be careful how you bark, dog. We hold your life in our hands."

"Best wipe the shit off your fingers, then." The Hound laughed. "How long have you been hiding in this hole?"

Anguy the Archer bristled at the suggestion of cowardice. "Ask the goat if we've hidden, Hound. Ask your brother. Ask the lord of leeches. We've bloodied them all."

"You lot? Don't make me laugh. You look more swineherds than soldiers."

"Some of us was swineherds," said a short man Arya did not know. "And some was tanners or singers or masons. But that was before the war come."

"When we left King's Landing we were men of Winterfell and men of Darry and men of Blackhaven, Mallery men and Wylde men. We were knights and squires and men-at-arms, lords and commoners, bound together only by our purpose." The voice came from the man seated amongst the weirwood roots halfway up the wall. "Six score of us set out to bring the king's justice to your brother." The speaker was descending the tangle of steps toward the floor. "Six score brave men and true, led by a fool in a starry cloak." A scarecrow of a man, he wore a ragged black cloak speckled with stars and an iron breast-plate dinted by a hundred battles. A thicket of red-gold hair hid most of his face, save for a bald spot above his left ear where his head had been smashed in. "More than eighty of our company are dead now, but others have taken up the swords that fell from their hands." When he reached the floor, the outlaws moved aside to let him pass. One of his eyes was gone, Arya saw, the flesh about the socket scarred and puckered, and he had a dark black ring all around his neck. "With their help, we fight on as best we can, for Robert and the realm."

"Robert?" rasped Sandor Clegane, incredulous.

"Ned Stark sent us out," said pothelmed Jack-Be-Lucky, "but he was sitting the Iron Throne when he gave us our commands, so we were never truly his men, but Robert's."

"Robert is the king of the worms now. Is that why you're down in the earth, to keep his court for him?"

"The king is dead," the scarecrow knight admitted, "but we are still king's men, though the royal banner we bore was lost at the Mummer's Ford when your brother's butchers fell upon us." He touched his breast with a fist. "Robert is slain, but his realm remains. And we defend her."

"*Her?*" The Hound snorted. "Is she your mother, Dondarrion? Or your whore?"

Dondarrion? Beric Dondarrion had been handsome; Sansa's friend Jeyne had fallen in love with him. Even Jeyne Poole was not so blind as to think this man was fair. Yet when Arya looked at him again, she saw it; the remains of a forked purple lightning bolt on the cracked enamel of his breastplate.

"Rocks and trees and rivers, that's what your realm is made of," the Hound was saying. "Do the rocks need defending? Robert wouldn't have thought so. If he couldn't fuck it, fight it, or drink it, it bored him, and so would you . . . you *brave companions.*"

Outrage swept the hollow hill. "Call us that name

again, dog, and you'll swallow that tongue." Lem drew his longsword.

The Hound stared at the blade with contempt. "Here's a brave man, baring steel on a bound captive. Untie me, why don't you? We'll see how brave you are then." He glanced at the Mad Huntsman behind him. "How about you? Or did you leave all your courage in your kennels?"

"No, but I should have left you in a crow cage." The Huntsman drew a knife. "I might still."

The Hound laughed in his face.

"We are brothers here," Thoros of Myr declared. "Holy brothers, sworn to the realm, to our god, and to each other."

"The brotherhood without banners." Tom Sevenstrings plucked a string. "The knights of the hollow hill."

"*Knights?*" Clegane made the word a sneer. "Dondarrion's a knight, but the rest of you are the sorriest lot of outlaws and broken men I've ever seen. I shit better men than you."

"Any knight can make a knight," said the scarecrow that was Beric Dondarrion, "and every man you see before you has felt a sword upon his shoulder. We are the forgotten fellowship."

"Send me on my way and I'll forget you too," Clegane rasped. "But if you mean to murder me, then bloody well get on with it. You took my sword, my horse, and my gold, so take my life and be done with it . . . but spare me this pious bleating."

"You will die soon enough, dog," promised Thoros, "but it shan't be murder, only justice."

"Aye," said the Mad Huntsman, "and a kinder fate than you deserve for all your kind have done. Lions, you call yourselves. At Sherrer and the Mummer's Ford, girls of six and seven years were raped, and babes still on the breast were cut in two while their mothers watched. No lion ever killed so cruel."

"I was not at Sherrer, nor the Mummer's Ford," the Hound told him. "Lay your dead children at some other door."

Thoros answered him. "Do you deny that House Clegane was built upon dead children? I saw them lay Prince Aegon and Princess Rhaenys before the Iron Throne.

By rights your arms should bear two bloody infants in place of those ugly dogs."

The Hound's mouth twitched. "Do you take me for my brother? Is being born Clegane a crime?"

"Murder is a crime."

"Who did I murder?"

"Lord Lothar Mallery and Ser Gladden Wylde," said Harwin.

"My brothers Lister and Lennocks," declared Jack-Be-Lucky.

"Goodman Beck and Mudge the miller's son, from Donnelwood," an old woman called from the shadows.

"Merriman's widow, who loved so sweet," added Greenbeard.

"Them septons at Sludgy Pond."

"Ser Andrey Charlton. His squire Lucas Roote. Every man, woman, and child in Fieldstone and Mousedown Mill."

"Lord and Lady Deddings, that was so rich."

Tom Sevenstrings took up the count. "Alyn of Winterfell, Joth Quick-bow, Little Matt and his sister Randa, Anvil Ryn. Ser Ormond. Ser Dudley. Pate of Mory, Pate of Lancewood, Old Pate, and Pate of Shermer's Grove. Blind Wyl the Whittler. Goodwife Maerie. Maerie the Whore. Becca the Baker. Ser Raymun Darry, Lord Darry, young Lord Darry. The Bastard of Bracken. Fletcher Will. Harsley. Goodwife Nolla—"

"*Enough.*" The Hound's face was tight with anger. "You're making noise. These names mean nothing. Who were they?"

"People," said Lord Beric. "People great and small, young and old. Good people and bad people, who died on the points of Lannister spears or saw their bellies opened by Lannister swords."

"It wasn't *my* sword in their bellies. Any man who says it was is a bloody liar."

"You serve the Lannisters of Casterly Rock," said Thoros.

"Once. Me and thousands more. Is each of us guilty of the crimes of the others?" Clegane spat. "Might be you *are* knights after all. You lie like knights, maybe you murder like knights."

Lem and Jack-Be-Lucky began to shout at him, but Dondarrion raised a hand for silence. "Say what you mean, Clegane."

"A knight's a sword with a horse. The rest, the vows and the sacred oils and the lady's favors, they're silk ribbons tied round the sword. Maybe the sword's prettier with ribbons hanging off it, but it will kill you just as dead. Well, bugger your ribbons, and shove your swords up your arses. I'm the same as you. The only difference is, I don't lie about what I am. So kill me, but don't call me a murderer while you stand there telling each other that your shit don't stink. *You hear me?*"

Arya squirted past Greenbeard so fast he never saw her. "You *are* a murderer!" she screamed. "You killed *Mycah*, don't say you never did. You *murdered* him!"

The Hound stared at her with no flicker of recognition. "And who was this Mycah, boy?"

"I'm not a boy! But Mycah was. He was a butcher's boy and you *killed* him. Jory said you cut him near in half, and he never even had a sword." She could feel them looking at her now, the women and the children and the men who called themselves the knights of the hollow hill. "Who's this now?" someone asked.

The Hound answered. "*Seven hells.* The little sister. The brat who tossed Joff's pretty sword in the river." He gave a bark of laughter. "Don't you know you're dead?"

"No, *you're* dead," she threw back at him.

Harwin took her arm to draw her back as Lord Beric said, "The girl has named you a murderer. Do you deny killing this butcher's boy, Mycah?"

The big man shrugged. "I was Joffrey's sworn shield. The butcher's boy attacked a prince of the blood."

"That's a *lie!*" Arya squirmed in Harwin's grip. "It was *me*. I hit Joffrey and threw Lion's Paw in the river. Mycah just ran away, like I told him."

"Did you see the boy attack Prince Joffrey?" Lord Beric Dondarrion asked the Hound.

"I heard it from the royal lips. It's not my place to question princes." Clegane jerked his hands toward Arya. "This one's own sister told the same tale when she stood before your precious Robert."

"Sansa's just a liar," Arya said, furious at her sister all over again. "It wasn't like she said. It *wasn't*."

Thoros drew Lord Beric aside. The two men stood talking in low whispers while Arya seethed. *They have to kill him. I prayed for him to die, hundreds and hundreds of times.*

Beric Dondarrion turned back to the Hound. "You stand accused of murder, but no one here knows the truth or falsehood of the charge, so it is not for us to judge you. Only the Lord of Light may do that now. I sentence you to trial by battle."

The Hound frowned suspiciously, as if he did not trust his ears. "Are you a fool or a madman?"

"Neither. I am a just lord. Prove your innocence with a blade, and you shall be free to go."

"No," Arya cried, before Harwin covered her mouth. *No, they can't, he'll go free.* The Hound was deadly with a sword, everyone knew that. *He'll laugh at them*, she thought.

And so he did, a long rasping laugh that echoed off the cave walls, a laugh choking with contempt. "So who will it be?" He looked at Lem Lemoncloak. "The brave man in the piss-yellow cloak? No? How about you, Huntsman? You've kicked dogs before, try me." He saw Greenbeard. "You're big enough, Tyrosh, step forward. Or do you mean to make the little girl fight me herself?" He laughed again. "Come on, who wants to die?"

"It's me you'll face," said Lord Beric Dondarrion.

Arya remembered all the tales. *He can't be killed*, she thought, hoping against hope. The Mad Huntsman sliced apart the ropes that bound Sandor Clegane's hands together. "I'll need sword and armor." The Hound rubbed a torn wrist.

"Your sword you shall have," declared Lord Beric, "but your innocence must be your armor."

Clegane's mouth twitched. "My innocence against your breastplate, is that the way of it?"

"Ned, help me remove my breastplate."

Arya got goosebumps when Lord Beric said her father's name, but this Ned was only a boy, a fair-haired squire no more than ten or twelve. He stepped up quickly to undo the clasps that fastened the battered steel about the

Marcher lord. The quilting beneath was rotten with age and sweat, and fell away when the metal was pulled loose. Gendry sucked in his breath. "Mother have mercy."

Lord Beric's ribs were outlined starkly beneath his skin. A puckered crater scarred his breast just above his left nipple, and when he turned to call for sword and shield, Arya saw a matching scar upon his back. *The lance went through him.* The Hound had seen it too. *Is he scared?* Arya wanted him to be scared before he died, as scared as Mycah must have been.

Ned fetched Lord Beric his swordbelt and a long black surcoat. It was meant to be worn over armor, so it draped his body loosely, but across it crackled the forked purple lightning of his House. He unsheathed his sword and gave the belt back to his squire.

Thoros brought the Hound his swordbelt. "Does a dog have honor?" the priest asked. "Lest you think to cut your way free of here, or seize some child for a hostage . . . Anguy, Dennet, Kyle, feather him at the first sign of treachery." Only when the three bowmen had notched their shafts did Thoros hand Clegane the belt.

The Hound ripped the sword free and threw away the scabbard. The Mad Huntsman gave him his oaken shield, all studded with iron and painted yellow, the three black dogs of Clegane emblazoned upon it. The boy Ned helped Lord Beric with his own shield, so hacked and battered that the purple lightning and the scatter of stars upon it had almost been obliterated.

But when the Hound made to step toward his foe, Thoros of Myr stopped him. "First we pray." He turned toward the fire and lifted his arms. "Lord of Light, look down upon us."

All around the cave, the brotherhood without banners lifted their own voices in response. *"Lord of Light, defend us."*

"Lord of Light, protect us in the darkness."

"Lord of Light, shine your face upon us."

"Light your flame among us, R'hllor," said the red priest. "Show us the truth or falseness of this man. Strike him down if he is guilty, and give strength to his sword if he is true. Lord of Light, give us wisdom."

"For the night is dark," the others chanted, Harwin and Anguy loud as all the rest, *"and full of terrors."*

"This cave is dark too," said the Hound, "but I'm the terror here. I hope your god's a sweet one, Dondarrion. You're going to meet him shortly."

Unsmiling, Lord Beric laid the edge of his longsword against the palm of his left hand, and drew it slowly down. Blood ran dark from the gash he made, and washed over the steel.

And then the sword took fire.

Arya heard Gendry whisper a prayer.

"Burn in seven hells," the Hound cursed. "You, and Thoros too." He threw a glance at the red priest. "When I'm done with him you'll be next, Myr."

"Every word you say proclaims your guilt, dog," answered Thoros, while Lem and Greenbeard and Jack-Be-Lucky shouted threats and curses. Lord Beric himself waited silent, calm as still water, his shield on his left arm and his sword burning in his right hand. *Kill him*, Arya thought, *please, you have to kill him*. Lit from below, his face was a death mask, his missing eye a red and angry wound. The sword was aflame from point to crossguard, but Dondarrion seemed not to feel the heat. He stood so still he might have been carved of stone.

But when the Hound charged him, he moved fast enough.

The flaming sword leapt up to meet the cold one, long streamers of fire trailing in its wake like the ribbons the Hound had spoken of. Steel rang on steel. No sooner was his first slash blocked than Clegane made another, but this time Lord Beric's shield got in the way, and wood chips flew from the force of the blow. Hard and fast the cuts came, from low and high, from right and left, and each one Dondarrion blocked. The flames swirled about his sword and left red and yellow ghosts to mark its passage. Each move Lord Beric made fanned them and made them burn the brighter, until it seemed as though the lightning lord stood within a cage of fire. "Is it wildfire?" Arya asked Gendry.

"No. This is different. This is . . ."

". . . magic?" she finished as the Hound edged back. Now it was Lord Beric attacking, filling the air with ropes of fire, driving the bigger man back on his heels. Clegane caught one blow high on his shield, and a painted dog lost a

head. He countercut, and Dondarrion interposed his own
shield and launched a fiery backslash. The outlaw brotherhood shouted on their leader. *"He's yours!"* Arya heard,
and *"At him! At him! At him!"* The Hound parried a cut at
his head, grimacing as the heat of the flames beat against
his face. He grunted and cursed and reeled away.

Lord Beric gave him no respite. Hard on the big man's
heels he followed, his arm never still. The swords clashed
and sprang apart and clashed again, splinters flew from the
lightning shield while swirling flames kissed the dogs
once, and twice, and thrice. The Hound moved to his right,
but Dondarrion blocked him with a quick sidestep and
drove him back the other way . . . toward the sullen red
blaze of the firepit. Clegane gave ground until he felt the
heat at his back. A quick glance over his shoulder showed
him what was behind him, and almost cost him his head
when Lord Beric attacked anew.

Arya could see the whites of Sandor Clegane's eyes as he
bulled his way forward again. Three steps up and two back,
a move to the left that Lord Beric blocked, two more forward and one back, *clang* and *clang*, and the big oaken
shields took blow after blow after blow. The Hound's lank
dark hair was plastered to his brow in a sheen of sweat.
Wine sweat, Arya thought, remembering that he'd been
taken drunk. She thought she could see the beginnings of
fear wake in his eyes. *He's going to lose,* she told herself,
exulting, as Lord Beric's flaming sword whirled and
slashed. In one wild flurry, the lightning lord took back all
the ground the Hound had gained, sending Clegane staggering to the very edge of the firepit once more. *He is, he is,
he's going to die.* She stood on her toes for a better look.

"Bloody bastard!" the Hound screamed as he felt the
fire licking against the back of his thighs. He charged,
swinging the heavy sword harder and harder, trying to
smash the smaller man down with brute force, to break
blade or shield or arm. But the flames of Dondarrion's parries snapped at his eyes, and when the Hound jerked away
from them, his foot went out from under him and he staggered to one knee. At once Lord Beric closed, his downcut
screaming through the air trailing pennons of fire. Panting
from exertion, Clegane jerked his shield up over his head

just in time, and the cave rang with the loud *crack* of splintering oak.

"His shield is afire," Gendry said in a hushed voice. Arya saw it in the same instant. The flames had spread across the chipped yellow paint, and the three black dogs were engulfed.

Sandor Clegane had fought his way back to his feet with a reckless counterattack. Not until Lord Beric retreated a pace did the Hound seem to realize that the fire that roared so near his face was his own shield, burning. With a shout of revulsion, he hacked down savagely on the broken oak, completing its destruction. The shield shattered, one piece of it spinning away, still afire, while the other clung stubbornly to his forearm. His efforts to free himself only fanned the flames. His sleeve caught, and now his whole left arm was ablaze. *"Finish him!"* Greenbeard urged Lord Beric, and other voices took up the chant of *"Guilty!"* Arya shouted with the rest. *"Guilty, guilty, kill him, guilty!"*

Smooth as summer silk, Lord Beric slid close to make an end of the man before him. The Hound gave a rasping scream, raised his sword in both hands and brought it crashing down with all his strength. Lord Beric blocked the cut easily . . .

"Noooooo," Arya shrieked.

. . . but the burning sword snapped in two, and the Hound's cold steel plowed into Lord Beric's flesh where his shoulder joined his neck and clove him clean down to the breastbone. The blood came rushing out in a hot black gush.

Sandor Clegane jerked backward, still burning. He ripped the remnants of his shield off and flung them away with a curse, then rolled in the dirt to smother the fire running along his arm.

Lord Beric's knees folded slowly, as if for prayer. When his mouth opened only blood came out. The Hound's sword was still in him as he toppled face forward. The dirt drank his blood. Beneath the hollow hill there was no sound but the soft crackling of flames and the whimper the Hound made when he tried to rise. Arya could only think of Mycah and all the stupid prayers she'd prayed for the Hound to die. *If there were gods, why didn't Lord Beric win?* She *knew* the Hound was guilty.

"Please," Sandor Clegane rasped, cradling his arm. "I'm burned. Help me. Someone. Help me." He was crying. "*Please.*"

Arya looked at him in astonishment. *He's crying like a little baby,* she thought.

"Melly, see to his burns," said Thoros. "Lem, Jack, help me with Lord Beric. Ned, you'd best come too." The red priest wrenched the Hound's sword from the body of his fallen lord and thrust the point of it down in the blood-soaked earth. Lem slid his big hands under Dondarrion's arms, while Jack-Be-Lucky took his feet. They carried him around the firepit, into the darkness of one of the tunnels. Thoros and the boy Ned followed after.

The Mad Huntsman spat. "I say we take him back to Stoney Sept and put him in a crow cage."

"Yes," Arya said. "He murdered Mycah. He *did.*"

"Such an angry squirrel," murmured Greenbeard.

Harwin sighed. "R'hllor has judged him innocent."

"Who's *Rulore?*" She couldn't even say it.

"The Lord of Light. Thoros has taught us—"

She didn't care what Thoros had taught them. She yanked Greenbeard's dagger from its sheath and spun away before he could catch her. Gendry made a grab for her as well, but she had always been too fast for Gendry.

Tom Sevenstrings and some woman were helping the Hound to his feet. The sight of his arm shocked her speechless. There was a strip of pink where the leather strap had clung, but above and below the flesh was cracked and red and bleeding from elbow to wrist. When his eyes met hers, his mouth twitched. "You want me dead that bad? Then do it, wolf girl. Shove it in. It's cleaner than fire." Clegane tried to stand, but as he moved a piece of burned flesh sloughed right off his arm, and his knees went out from under him. Tom caught him by his good arm and held him up.

His arm, Arya thought, and *his face.* But he was the Hound. He deserved to burn in a fiery hell. The knife felt heavy in her hand. She gripped it tighter. "You killed Mycah," she said once more, daring him to deny it. "Tell them. You did. You *did.*"

"I did." His whole face twisted. "I rode him down and cut him in half, and laughed. I watched them beat your sister bloody too, watched them cut your father's head off."

Lem grabbed her wrist and twisted, wrenching the dagger away. She kicked at him, but he would not give it back. "You go to hell, Hound," she screamed at Sandor Clegane in helpless empty-handed rage. *"You just go to hell!"*

"He has," said a voice scarce stronger than a whisper.

When Arya turned, Lord Beric Dondarrion was standing behind her, his bloody hand clutching Thoros by the shoulder.

CATELYN

Let the kings of winter have their cold crypt under the earth, Catelyn thought. The Tullys drew their strength from the river, and it was to the river they returned when their lives had run their course.

They laid Lord Hoster in a slender wooden boat, clad in shining silver armor, plate-and-mail. His cloak was spread beneath him, rippling blue and red. His surcoat was divided blue-and-red as well. A trout, scaled in silver and bronze, crowned the crest of the greathelm they placed beside his head. On his chest they placed a painted wooden sword, his fingers curled about its hilt. Mail gauntlets hid his wasted hands, and made him look almost strong again. His massive oak-and-iron shield was set by his left side, his hunting horn to his right. The rest of the boat was filled with driftwood and kindling and scraps of parchment, and stones to make it heavy in the water. His banner flew from the prow, the leaping trout of Riverrun.

Seven were chosen to push the funereal boat to the water, in honor of the seven faces of god. Robb was one, Lord Hoster's liege lord. With him were the Lords Bracken,

Blackwood, Vance, and Mallister, Ser Marq Piper . . . and Lame Lothar Frey, who had come down from the Twins with the answer they had awaited. Forty soldiers rode in his escort, commanded by Walder Rivers, the eldest of Lord Walder's bastard brood, a stern, grey-haired man with a formidable reputation as a warrior. Their arrival, coming within hours of Lord Hoster's passing, had sent Edmure into a rage. "Walder Frey should be flayed and quartered!" he'd shouted. "He sends a cripple and a bastard to treat with us, tell me there is no insult meant by that."

"I have no doubt that Lord Walder chose his envoys with care," she replied. "It was a peevish thing to do, a petty sort of revenge, but remember who we are dealing with. The Late Lord Frey, Father used to call him. The man is ill-tempered, envious, and above all *prideful*."

Blessedly, her son had shown better sense than her brother. Robb had greeted the Freys with every courtesy, found barracks space for the escort, and quietly asked Ser Desmond Grell to stand aside so Lothar might have the honor of helping to send Lord Hoster on his last voyage. *He has learned a rough wisdom beyond his years, my son.* House Frey might have abandoned the King in the North, but the Lord of the Crossing remained the most powerful of Riverrun's bannermen, and Lothar was here in his stead.

The seven launched Lord Hoster from the water stair, wading down the steps as the portcullis was winched upward. Lothar Frey, a soft-bodied portly man, was breathing heavily as they shoved the boat out into the current. Jason Mallister and Tytos Blackwood, at the prow, stood chest deep in the river to guide it on its way.

Catelyn watched from the battlements, waiting and watching as she had waited and watched so many times before. Beneath her, the swift wild Tumblestone plunged like a spear into the side of the broad Red Fork, its blue-white current churning the muddy red-brown flow of the greater river. A morning mist hung over the water, as thin as gossamer and the wisps of memory.

Bran and Rickon will be waiting for him, Catelyn thought sadly, *as once I used to wait.*

The slim boat drifted out from under the red stone arch of the Water Gate, picking up speed as it was caught in the headlong rush of the Tumblestone and pushed out into the tumult where the waters met. As the boat emerged from beneath the high sheltering walls of the castle, its square sail filled with wind, and Catelyn saw sunlight flashing on her father's helm. Lord Hoster Tully's rudder held true, and he sailed serenely down the center of the channel, into the rising sun.

"Now," her uncle urged. Beside him, her brother Edmure—*Lord* Edmure now in truth, and how long would that take to grow used to?—nocked an arrow to his bowstring. His squire held a brand to its point. Edmure waited until the flame caught, then lifted the great bow, drew the string to his ear, and let fly. With a deep *thrum*, the arrow sped upward. Catelyn followed its flight with her eyes and heart, until it plunged into the water with a soft *hiss*, well astern of Lord Hoster's boat.

Edmure cursed softly. "The wind," he said, pulling a second arrow. "Again." The brand kissed the oil-soaked rag behind the arrowhead, the flames went licking up, Edmure lifted, pulled, and released. High and far the arrow flew. Too far. It vanished in the river a dozen yards beyond the boat, its fire winking out in an instant. A flush was creeping up Edmure's neck, red as his beard. "Once more," he commanded, taking a third arrow from the quiver. *He is as tight as his bowstring,* Catelyn thought.

Ser Brynden must have seen the same thing. "Let me, my lord," he offered.

"I can do it," Edmure insisted. He let them light the arrow, jerked the bow up, took a deep breath, drew back the arrow. For a long moment he seemed to hesitate while the fire crept up the shaft, crackling. Finally he released. The arrow flashed up and up, and finally curved down again, falling, falling . . . and hissing past the billowing sail.

A narrow miss, no more than a handspan, and yet a miss. "The Others take it!" her brother swore. The boat was almost out of range, drifting in and out among the river mists. Wordless, Edmure thrust the bow at his uncle.

"Swiftly," Ser Brynden said. He nocked an arrow, held it steady for the brand, drew and released before Catelyn was quite sure that the fire had caught . . . but as the shot rose, she saw the flames trailing through the air, a pale orange pennon. The boat had vanished in the mists. Falling, the flaming arrow was swallowed up as well . . . but only for a heartbeat. Then, sudden as hope, they saw the red bloom flower. The sails took fire, and the fog glowed pink and orange. For a moment Catelyn saw the outline of the boat clearly, wreathed in leaping flames.

Watch for me, little cat, she could hear him whisper.

Catelyn reached out blindly, groping for her brother's hand, but Edmure had moved away, to stand alone on the highest point of the battlements. Her uncle Brynden took her hand instead, twining his strong fingers through hers. Together they watched the little fire grow smaller as the burning boat receded in the distance.

And then it was gone . . . drifting downriver still, perhaps, or broken up and sinking. The weight of his armor would carry Lord Hoster down to rest in the soft mud of the riverbed, in the watery halls where the Tullys held eternal court, with schools of fish their last attendants.

No sooner had the burning boat vanished from their sight than Edmure walked off. Catelyn would have liked to embrace him, if only for a moment; to sit for an hour or a night or the turn of a moon to speak of the dead and mourn. Yet she knew as well as he that this was not the time; he was Lord of Riverrun now, and his knights were falling in around him, murmuring condolences and promises of fealty, walling him off from something as small as a sister's grief. Edmure listened, hearing none of the words.

"It is no disgrace to miss your shot," her uncle told her quietly. "Edmure should hear that. The day my own lord father went downriver, Hoster missed as well."

"With his first shaft." Catelyn had been too young to remember, but Lord Hoster had often told the tale. "His second found the sail." She sighed. Edmure was not as strong as he seemed. Their father's death had been a mercy when it came at last, but even so her brother had taken it hard.

Last night in his cups he had broken down and wept, full of regrets for things undone and words unsaid. He ought never to have ridden off to fight his battle on the fords, he told her tearfully; he should have stayed at their father's bedside. "I should have been with him, as you were," he said. "Did he speak of me at the end? Tell me true, Cat. Did he ask for me?"

Lord Hoster's last word had been "*Tansy*," but Catelyn could not bring herself to tell him that. "He whispered

your name," she lied, and her brother had nodded gratefully and kissed her hand. *If he had not tried to drown his
grief and guilt, he might have been able to bend a bow*, she
thought to herself, sighing, but that was something else
she dare not say.

The Blackfish escorted her down from the battlements
to where Robb stood among his bannermen, his young
queen at his side. When he saw her, her son took her
silently in his arms.

"Lord Hoster looked as noble as a king, my lady," murmured Jeyne. "Would that I had been given the chance to
know him."

"And I to know him better," added Robb.

"He would have wished that too," said Catelyn. "There
were too many leagues between Riverrun and Winterfell."
*And too many mountains and rivers and armies between
Riverrun and the Eyrie, it would seem*. Lysa had made no
reply to her letter.

And from King's Landing came only silence as well. By
now she had hoped that Brienne and Ser Cleos would have
reached the city with their captive. It might even be that
Brienne was on her way back, and the girls with her. *Ser
Cleos swore he would make the Imp send a raven once the
trade was made. He swore it!* Ravens did not always win
through. Some bowman could have brought the bird down
and roasted him for supper. The letter that would have set
her heart at ease might even now be lying by the ashes of
some campfire beside a pile of raven bones.

Others were waiting to offer Robb their consolations, so
Catelyn stood aside patiently while Lord Jason Mallister, the
Greatjon, and Ser Rolph Spicer spoke to him each in turn.
But when Lothar Frey approached, she gave his sleeve a tug.
Robb turned, and waited to hear what Lothar would say.

"Your Grace." A plump man in his middle thirties,
Lothar Frey had close-set eyes, a pointed beard, and dark
hair that fell to his shoulders in ringlets. A leg twisted at
birth had earned him the name *Lame Lothar*. He had
served as his father's steward for the past dozen years. "We
are loath to intrude upon your grief, but perhaps you might
grant us audience tonight?"

"It would be my pleasure," said Robb. "It was never my
wish to sow enmity between us."

"Nor mine to be the cause of it," said Queen Jeyne.

Lothar Frey smiled. "I understand, as does my lord father. He instructed me to say that he was young once, and well remembers what it is like to lose one's heart to beauty."

Catelyn doubted very much that Lord Walder had said any such thing, or that he had ever lost his heart to beauty. The Lord of the Crossing had outlived seven wives and was now wed to his eighth, but he spoke of them only as bedwarmers and brood mares. Still, the words were fairly spoken, and she could scarce object to the compliment. Nor did Robb. "Your father is most gracious," he said. "I shall look forward to our talk."

Lothar bowed, kissed the queen's hand, and withdrew. By then a dozen others had gathered for a word. Robb spoke with them each, giving a thanks here, a smile there, as needed. Only when the last of them was done did he turn back to Catelyn. "There is something we must speak of. Will you walk with me?"

"As you command, Your Grace."

"That wasn't a command, Mother."

"It will be my pleasure, then." Her son had treated her kindly enough since returning to Riverrun, yet he seldom sought her out. If he was more comfortable with his young queen, she could scarcely blame him. *Jeyne makes him smile, and I have nothing to share with him but grief.* He seemed to enjoy the company of his bride's brothers, as well; young Rollam his squire and Ser Raynald his standard-bearer. *They are standing in the boots of those he's lost,* Catelyn realized when she watched them together. *Rollam has taken Bran's place, and Raynald is part Theon and part Jon Snow.* Only with the Westerlings did she see Robb smile, or hear him laugh like the boy he was. To the others he was always the King in the North, head bowed beneath the weight of the crown even when his brows were bare.

Robb kissed his wife gently, promised to see her in their chambers, and went off with his lady mother. His steps led them toward the godswood. "Lothar seemed amiable, that's a hopeful sign. We need the Freys."

"That does not mean we shall have them."

He nodded, and there was glumness to his face and a

slope to his shoulders that made her heart go out to him. *The crown is crushing him,* she thought. *He wants so much to be a good king, to be brave and honorable and clever, but the weight is too much for a boy to bear.* Robb was doing all he could, yet still the blows kept falling, one after the other, relentless. When they brought him word of the battle at Duskendale, where Lord Randyll Tarly had shattered Robett Glover and Ser Helman Tallhart, he might have been expected to rage. Instead he'd stared in dumb disbelief and said, "Duskendale, on the narrow sea? Why would they go to Duskendale?" He'd shook his head, bewildered. "A third of my foot, lost for *Duskendale?*"

"The ironmen have my castle and now the Lannisters hold my brother," Galbart Glover said, in a voice thick with despair. Robett Glover had survived the battle, but had been captured near the kingsroad not long after.

"Not for long," her son promised. "I will offer them Martyn Lannister in exchange. Lord Tywin will have to accept, for his brother's sake." Martyn was Ser Kevan's son, a twin to the Willem that Lord Karstark had butchered. Those murders still haunted her son, Catelyn knew. He had tripled the guard around Martyn, but still feared for his safety.

"I should have traded the Kingslayer for Sansa when you first urged it," Robb said as they walked the gallery. "If I'd offered to wed her to the Knight of Flowers, the Tyrells might be ours instead of Joffrey's. I should have thought of that."

"Your mind was on your battles, and rightly so. Even a king cannot think of everything."

"Battles," muttered Robb as he led her out beneath the trees. "I have won every battle, yet somehow I'm losing the war." He looked up, as if the answer might be written on the sky. "The ironmen hold Winterfell, and Moat Cailin too. Father's dead, and Bran and Rickon, maybe Arya. And now your father too."

She could not let him despair. She knew the taste of that draught too well herself. "My father has been dying for a long time. You could not have changed that. You have made mistakes, Robb, but what king has not? Ned would have been proud of you."

"Mother, there is something you must know."

Catelyn's heart skipped a beat. *This is something he hates. Something he dreads to tell me.* All she could think of was Brienne and her mission. "Is it the Kingslayer?"

"No. It's Sansa."

She's dead, Catelyn thought at once. *Brienne failed, Jaime is dead, and Cersei has killed my sweet girl in retribution.* For a moment she could barely speak. "Is . . . is she gone, Robb?"

"Gone?" He looked startled. "Dead? Oh, Mother, no, not that, they haven't harmed her, not that way, only . . . a bird came last night, but I couldn't bring myself to tell you, not until your father was sent to his rest." Robb took her hand. "They married her to Tyrion Lannister."

Catelyn's fingers clutched at his. "The Imp."

"Yes."

"He swore to trade her for his brother," she said numbly. "Sansa and Arya both. We would have them back if we returned his precious Jaime, he swore it before the whole court. How could he marry her, after saying that in sight of gods and men?"

"He's the Kingslayer's brother. Oathbreaking runs in their blood." Robb's fingers brushed the pommel of his sword. "If I could I'd take his ugly head off. Sansa would be a widow then, and free. There's no other way that I can see. They made her speak the vows before a septon and don a crimson cloak."

Catelyn remembered the twisted little man she had seized at the crossroads inn and carried all the way to the Eyrie. "I should have let Lysa push him out her Moon Door. My poor sweet Sansa . . . why would anyone do this to her?"

"For Winterfell," Robb said at once. "With Bran and Rickon dead, Sansa is my heir. If anything should happen to me . . ."

She clutched tight at his hand. "Nothing will happen to you. *Nothing.* I could not stand it. They took Ned, and your sweet brothers. Sansa is married, Arya is lost, my father's dead . . . if anything befell you, I would go mad, Robb. You are all I have left. You are all the *north* has left."

"I am not dead yet, Mother."

Suddenly Catelyn was full of dread. "Wars need not be fought until the last drop of blood." Even she could hear the desperation in her voice. "You would not be the first king to bend the knee, nor even the first Stark."

His mouth tightened. "No. Never."

"There is no shame in it. Balon Greyjoy bent the knee to Robert when his rebellion failed. Torrhen Stark bent the knee to Aegon the Conqueror rather than see his army face the fires."

"Did Aegon kill King Torrhen's father?" He pulled his hand from hers. "Never, I said."

He is playing the boy now, not the king. "The Lannisters do not need the north. They will require homage and hostages, no more . . . and the Imp will keep Sansa no matter what we do, so they have their hostage. The ironmen will prove a more implacable enemy, I promise you. To have any hope of holding the north, the Greyjoys must leave no single sprig of House Stark alive to dispute their right. Theon's murdered Bran and Rickon, so now all they need do is kill you . . . *and* Jeyne, yes. Do you think Lord Balon can afford to let her live to bear you heirs?"

Robb's face was cold. "Is that why you freed the Kingslayer? To make a peace with the Lannisters?"

"I freed Jaime for Sansa's sake . . . and Arya's, if she still lives. You know that. But if I nurtured some hope of buying peace as well, was that so ill?"

"Yes," he said. "The Lannisters killed my father."

"Do you think I have forgotten that?"

"I don't know. Have you?"

Catelyn had never struck her children in anger, but she almost struck Robb then. It was an effort to remind herself how frightened and alone he must feel. "You are King in the North, the choice is yours. I only ask that you think on what I've said. The singers make much of kings who die valiantly in battle, but your life is worth more than a song. To me at least, who gave it to you." She lowered her head. "Do I have your leave to go?"

"Yes." He turned away and drew his sword. What he meant to do with it, she could not say. There was no enemy there, no one to fight. Only her and him, amongst tall trees and fallen leaves. *There are fights no sword can win,* Catelyn wanted to tell him, but she feared the king was deaf to such words.

Hours later, she was sewing in her bedchamber when

young Rollam Westerling came running with the summons to supper. *Good*, Catelyn thought, relieved. She had not been certain that her son would want her there, after their quarrel. "A dutiful squire," she said to Rollam gravely. *Bran would have been the same.*

If Robb seemed cool at table and Edmure surly, Lame Lothar made up for them both. He was the model of courtesy, reminiscing warmly about Lord Hoster, offering Catelyn gentle condolences on the loss of Bran and Rickon, praising Edmure for the victory at Stone Mill, and thanking Robb for the "swift sure justice" he had meted out to Rickard Karstark. Lothar's bastard brother Walder Rivers was another matter; a harsh sour man with old Lord Walder's suspicious face, he spoke but seldom and devoted most of his attention to the meat and mead that was set before him.

When all the empty words were said, the queen and the other Westerlings excused themselves, the remains of the meal were cleared away, and Lothar Frey cleared his throat. "Before we turn to the business that brings us here, there is another matter," he said solemnly. "A grave matter, I fear. I had hoped it would not fall to me to bring you these tidings, but it seems I must. My lord father has had a letter from his grandsons."

Catelyn had been so lost in grief for her own that she had almost forgotten the two Freys she had agreed to foster. *No more*, she thought. *Mother have mercy, how many more blows can we bear?* Somehow she knew the next words she heard would plunge yet another blade into her heart. "The grandsons at Winterfell?" she made herself ask. "My wards?"

"Walder and Walder, yes. But they are presently at the Dreadfort, my lady. I grieve to tell you this, but there has been a battle. Winterfell is burned."

"*Burned*?" Robb's voice was incredulous.

"Your northern lords tried to retake it from the ironmen. When Theon Greyjoy saw that his prize was lost, he put the castle to the torch."

"We have heard naught of any battle," said Ser Brynden.

"My nephews are young, I grant you, but they were there. Big Walder wrote the letter, though his cousin signed as well. It was a bloody bit of business, by their account. Your castellan was slain. Ser Rodrik, was that his name?"

"Ser Rodrik Cassel," said Catelyn numbly. *That dear brave loyal old soul*. She could almost see him, tugging on his fierce white whiskers. "What of our other people?"

"The ironmen put many of them to the sword, I fear."

Wordless with rage, Robb slammed a fist down on the table and turned his face away, so the Freys would not see his tears.

But his mother saw them. *The world grows a little darker every day*. Catelyn's thoughts went to Ser Rodrik's little daughter Beth, to tireless Maester Luwin and cheerful Septon Chayle, Mikken at the forge, Farlen and Palla in the kennels, Old Nan and simple Hodor. Her heart was sick. "Please, not *all*."

"No," said Lame Lothar. "The women and children hid, my nephews Walder and Walder among them. With Winterfell in ruins, the survivors were carried back to the Dreadfort by this son of Lord Bolton's."

"Bolton's *son*?" Robb's voice was strained.

Walder Rivers spoke up. "A bastard son, I believe."

"Not Ramsay Snow? Does Lord Roose have another bastard?" Robb scowled. "This Ramsay was a monster and a murderer, and he died a coward. Or so I was told."

"I cannot speak to that. There is much confusion in any war. Many false reports. All I can tell you is that my nephews claim it was this bastard son of Bolton's who saved the women of Winterfell, and the little ones. They are safe at the Dreadfort now, all those who remain."

"Theon," Robb said suddenly. "What happened to Theon Greyjoy? Was he slain?"

Lame Lothar spread his hands. "That I cannot say, Your Grace. Walder and Walder made no mention of his fate. Perhaps Lord Bolton might know, if he has had word from this son of his."

Ser Brynden said, "We will be certain to ask him."

"You are all distraught, I see. I am sorry to have brought you such fresh grief. Perhaps we should adjourn until the morrow. Our business can wait until you have composed yourselves . . ."

"No," said Robb, "I want the matter settled."

Her brother Edmure nodded. "Me as well. Do you have an answer to our offer, my lord?"

"I do." Lothar smiled. "My lord father bids me tell Your Grace that he will agree to this new marriage alliance between our houses and renew his fealty to the King in the North, upon the condition that the King's Grace apologize for the insult done to House Frey, in his royal person, face to face."

An apology was a small enough price to pay, but Catelyn misliked this petty condition of Lord Walder's at once.

"I am pleased," Robb said cautiously. "It was never my wish to cause this rift between us, Lothar. The Freys have fought valiantly for my cause. I would have them at my side once more."

"You are too kind, Your Grace. As you accept these terms, I am then instructed to offer Lord Tully the hand of my sister, the Lady Roslin, a maid of sixteen years. Roslin is my lord father's youngest daughter by Lady Bethany of House Rosby, his sixth wife. She has a gentle nature and a gift for music."

Edmure shifted in his seat. "Might not it be better if I first met—"

"You'll meet when you're wed," said Walder Rivers curtly. "Unless Lord Tully feels a need to count her teeth first?"

Edmure kept his temper. "I will take your word so far as her teeth are concerned, but it would be pleasant if I might gaze upon her face before I espoused her."

"You must accept her now, my lord," said Walder Rivers. "Else my father's offer is withdrawn."

Lame Lothar spread his hands. "My brother has a soldier's bluntness, but what he says is true. It is my lord father's wish that this marriage take place at once."

"*At once?*" Edmure sounded so unhappy that Catelyn had the unworthy thought that perhaps he had been entertaining notions of breaking the betrothal after the fighting was done.

"Has Lord Walder forgotten that we are fighting a war?" Brynden Blackfish asked sharply.

"Scarcely," said Lothar. "That is why he insists that the marriage take place now, ser. Men die in war, even men who are young and strong. What would become of our alliance should Lord Edmure fall before he took Roslin to bride? And there is my father's age to consider as well. He is past ninety and not like to see the end of this struggle. It would put his noble heart at peace if he could see his dear Roslin safely wed before the gods take him, so he might die with the knowledge that the girl had a strong husband to cherish and protect her."

We all want Lord Walder to die happy. Catelyn was growing less and less comfortable with this arrangement. "My brother has just lost his own father. He needs time to mourn."

"Roslin is a cheerful girl," said Lothar. "She may be the very thing Lord Edmure needs to help him through his grief."

"And my grandfather has come to mislike lengthy betrothals," the bastard Walder Rivers added. "I cannot imagine why."

Robb gave him a chilly look. "I take your meaning, Rivers. Pray excuse us."

"As Your Grace commands." Lame Lothar rose, and his bastard brother helped him hobble from the room.

Edmure was seething. "They're as much as saying that my promise is worthless. Why should I let that old weasel choose my bride? Lord Walder has other daughters besides this Roslin. Granddaughters as well. I should be offered the same choice you were. I'm his liege lord, he should be overjoyed that I'm willing to wed *any* of them."

"He is a proud man, and we've wounded him," said Catelyn.

"The Others take his pride! I will not be shamed in my own hall. My answer is no."

Robb gave him a weary look. "I will not command you. Not in this. But if you refuse, Lord Frey will take it for another slight, and any hope of putting this arights will be gone."

"You cannot know that," Edmure insisted. "Frey has wanted me for one of his daughters since the day I was born. He will not let a chance like this slip between those grasping fingers of his. When Lothar brings him our answer, he'll come wheedling back and accept a betrothal . . . and to a daughter of *my* choosing."

"Perhaps, in time," said Brynden Blackfish. "But can we

wait, while Lothar rides back and forth with offers and counters?"

Robb's hands curled into fists. "I *must* get back to the north. My brothers dead, Winterfell burned, my smallfolk put to the sword . . . the gods only know what this bastard of Bolton's is about, or whether Theon is still alive and on the loose. I can't sit here waiting for a wedding that might or might not happen."

"It *must* happen," said Catelyn, though not gladly. "I have no more wish to suffer Walder Frey's insults and complaints than you do, Brother, but I see little choice here. Without this wedding, Robb's cause is lost. Edmure, we must accept."

"*We* must accept?" he echoed peevishly. "I don't see you offering to become the ninth Lady Frey, Cat."

"The eighth Lady Frey is still alive and well, so far as I know," she replied. *Thankfully.* Otherwise it might well have come to that, knowing Lord Walder.

The Blackfish said, "I am the last man in the Seven Kingdoms to tell anyone who they must wed, Nephew. Nonetheless, you *did* say something of making amends for your Battle of the Fords."

"I had in mind a different sort of amends. Single combat with the Kingslayer. Seven years of penance as a begging brother. Swimming the sunset sea with my legs tied." When he saw that no one was smiling, Edmure threw up his hands. "The Others take you all! Very well, I'll wed the wench. As *amends*."

DAVOS

Lord Alester looked up sharply. "Voices," he said. "Do you hear, Davos? Someone is coming for us."

"Lamprey," said Davos. "It's time for our supper, or near enough." Last night Lamprey had brought them half a beef-and-bacon pie, and a flagon of mead as well. Just the thought of it made his belly start to rumble.

"No, there's more than one."

He's right. Davos heard two voices at least, and footsteps, growing louder. He got to his feet and moved to the bars.

Lord Alester brushed the straw from his clothes. "The king has sent for me. Or the queen, yes, Selyse would never let me rot here, her own blood."

Outside the cell, Lamprey appeared with a ring of keys in hand. Ser Axell Florent and four guardsmen followed close behind him. They waited beneath the torch while Lamprey searched for the correct key.

"Axell," Lord Alester said. "Gods be good. Is it the king who sends for me, or the queen?"

"No one has sent for you, traitor," Ser Axell said.

Lord Alester recoiled as if he'd been slapped. "No, I swear to you, I committed no treason. Why won't you listen? If His Grace would only let me explain—"

Lamprey thrust a great iron key into the lock, turned it, and pulled open the cell. The rusted hinges screamed in protest. "You," he said to Davos. "Come."

"Where?" Davos looked to Ser Axell. "Tell me true, ser, do you mean to burn me?"

"You are sent for. Can you walk?"

"I can walk." Davos stepped from the cell. Lord Alester gave a cry of dismay as Lamprey slammed the door shut once more.

"Take the torch," Ser Axell commanded the gaoler. "Leave the traitor to the darkness."

"No," his brother said. "Axell, please, don't take the light . . . gods have mercy . . ."

"Gods? There is only R'hllor, and the Other." Ser Axell gestured sharply, and one of his guardsmen pulled the torch from its sconce and led the way to the stair.

"Are you taking me to Melisandre?" Davos asked.

"She will be there," Ser Axell said. "She is never far from the king. But it is His Grace himself who asked for you."

Davos lifted his hand to his chest, where once his luck had hung in a leather bag on a thong. *Gone now*, he remembered, *and the ends of four fingers as well*. But his hands were still long enough to wrap about a woman's throat, he thought, especially a slender throat like hers.

Up they went, climbing the turnpike stair in single file. The walls were rough dark stone, cool to the touch. The light of the torches went before them, and their shadows marched beside them on the walls. At the third turn they passed an iron gate that opened on blackness, and another at the fifth turn. Davos guessed that they were near the surface by then, perhaps even above it. The next door they came to was made of wood, but still they climbed. Now the walls were broken by arrow slits, but no shafts of sunlight pried their way through the thickness of the stone. It was night outside.

His legs were aching by the time Ser Axell thrust open a heavy door and gestured him through. Beyond, a high stone bridge arched over emptiness to the massive central tower called the Stone Drum. A sea wind blew restlessly through the arches that supported the roof, and Davos could smell the salt water as they crossed. He took a deep breath, filling his lungs with the clean cold air. *Wind and water, give me strength*, he prayed. A huge nightfire burned in the yard below, to keep the terrors of the dark at bay, and the queen's men were gathered around it, singing praises to their new red god.

They were in the center of the bridge when Ser Axell stopped suddenly. He made a brusque gesture with his hand, and his men moved out of earshot. "Were it my choice, I would burn you with my brother Alester," he told Davos. "You are both traitors."

"Say what you will. I would never betray King Stannis."

"You would. You will. I see it in your face. And I have seen it in the flames as well. R'hllor has blessed me with that gift. Like Lady Melisandre, he shows me the future in the fire. Stannis Baratheon *will* sit the Iron Throne. I have seen it. And I know what must be done. His Grace must make me his Hand, in place of my traitor brother. And you will tell him so."

Will I? Davos said nothing.

"The queen has urged my appointment," Ser Axell went on. "Even your old friend from Lys, the pirate Saan, he says the same. We have made a plan together, him and me. Yet His Grace does not act. The defeat gnaws inside him, a black worm in his soul. It is up to us who love him to show him what to do. If you are as devoted to his cause as you claim, smuggler, you will join your voice to ours. Tell him that I am the only Hand he needs. Tell him, and when we sail I shall see that you have a new ship."

A ship. Davos studied the other man's face. Ser Axell had big Florent ears, much like the queen's. Coarse hair grew from them, as from his nostrils; more sprouted in tufts and patches beneath his double chin. His nose was broad, his brow beetled, his eyes close-set and hostile. *He would sooner give me a pyre than a ship, he said as much, but if I do him this favor . . .*

"If you think to betray me," Ser Axell said, "pray remember that I have been castellan of Dragonstone a good long time. The garrison is mine. Perhaps I cannot burn you without the king's consent, but who is to say you might not suffer a fall." He laid a meaty hand on the back of Davos's neck and shoved him bodily against the waist-high side of the bridge, then shoved a little harder to force his face out over the yard. "Do you hear me?"

"I hear," said Davos. *And you dare name me traitor?*

Ser Axell released him. "Good." He smiled. "His Grace awaits. Best we do not keep him."

At the very top of Stone Drum, within the great round room called the Chamber of the Painted Table, they found Stannis Baratheon standing behind the artifact that gave the hall its name, a massive slab of wood carved and painted in the shape of Westeros as it had been in the time of Aegon the Conqueror. An iron brazier stood beside the king, its coals glowing a ruddy orange. Four tall pointed windows looked out to north, south, east, and west. Beyond was the night and the starry sky. Davos could hear the wind moving, and fainter, the sounds of the sea.

"Your Grace," Ser Axell said, "as it please you, I have brought the onion knight."

"So I see." Stannis wore a grey wool tunic, a dark red mantle, and a plain black leather belt from which his sword and dagger hung. A red-gold crown with flame-shaped points encircled his brows. The look of him was a shock. He seemed ten years older than the man that Davos had left at Storm's End when he set sail for the Blackwater and the battle that would be their undoing. The king's close-cropped beard was spiderwebbed with grey hairs, and he had dropped two stone or more of weight. He had never been a fleshy man, but now the bones moved beneath his skin like spears, fighting to cut free. Even his crown seemed too large for his head. His eyes were blue pits lost in deep hollows, and the shape of a skull could be seen beneath his face.

Yet when he saw Davos, a faint smile brushed his lips. "So the sea has returned me my knight of the fish and onions."

"It did, Your Grace." *Does he know that he had me in his dungeon?* Davos went to one knee.

"Rise, Ser Davos," Stannis commanded. "I have missed you, ser. I have need of good counsel, and you never gave me less. So tell me true—what is the penalty for treason?"

The word hung in the air. *A frightful word*, thought

Davos. Was he being asked to condemn his cellmate? Or himself, perchance? *Kings know the penalty for treason better than any man.* "Treason?" he finally managed, weakly.

"What else would you call it, to deny your king and seek to steal his rightful throne. I ask you again—what is the penalty for treason under the law?"

Davos had no choice but to answer. "Death," he said. "The penalty is death, Your Grace."

"It has always been so. I am *not* . . . I am not a cruel man, Ser Davos. You know me. Have known me long. This is not my decree. It has always been so, since Aegon's day and before. Daemon Blackfyre, the brothers Toyne, the Vulture King, Grand Maester Hareth . . . traitors have always paid with their lives . . . even Rhaenyra Targaryen. She was daughter to one king and mother to two more, yet she died a traitor's death for trying to usurp her brother's crown. It is law. *Law*, Davos. Not cruelty."

"Yes, Your Grace." *He does not speak of me.* Davos felt a moment's pity for his cellmate down in the dark. He knew he should keep silent, but he was tired and sick of heart, and he heard himself say, "Sire, Lord Florent meant no treason."

"Do smugglers have another name for it? I made him Hand, and he would have sold my rights for a bowl of pease porridge. He would even have given them Shireen. Mine only child, he would have wed to a bastard born of incest." The king's voice was thick with anger. "My brother had a gift for inspiring loyalty. Even in his foes. At Summerhall he won three battles in a single day, and brought Lords Grandison and Cafferen back to Storm's End as prisoners. He hung their banners in the hall as trophies. Cafferen's white fawns were spotted with blood and Grandison's sleeping lion was torn near in two. Yet they would sit beneath those banners of a night, drinking and feasting with Robert. He even took them hunting. 'These men meant to deliver you to Aerys to be burned,' I told him after I saw them throwing axes in the yard. 'You should not be putting axes in their hands.' Robert only laughed. I would have thrown Grandison and Cafferen into a dungeon, but he turned them into friends. Lord Cafferen died at Ashford Castle, cut down by Randyll Tarly whilst fighting *for*

Robert. Lord Grandison was wounded on the Trident and died of it a year after. My brother made them love him, but it would seem that I inspire only betrayal. Even in mine own blood and kin. Brother, grandfather, cousins, good uncle . . ."

"Your Grace," said Ser Axell, "I beg you, give me the chance to prove to you that not all Florents are so feeble."

"Ser Axell would have me resume the war," King Stannis told Davos. "The Lannisters think I am done and beaten, and my sworn lords have forsaken me, near every one. Even Lord Estermont, my own mother's father, has bent his knee to Joffrey. The few loyal men who remain to me are losing heart. They waste their days drinking and gambling, and lick their wounds like beaten curs."

"Battle will set their hearts ablaze once more, Your Grace," Ser Axell said. "Defeat is a disease, and victory is the cure."

"Victory." The king's mouth twisted. "There are victories and victories, ser. But tell your plan to Ser Davos. I would hear his views on what you propose."

Ser Axell turned to Davos, with a look on his face much like the look that proud Lord Belgrave must have worn, the day King Baelor the Blessed had commanded him to wash the beggar's ulcerous feet. Nonetheless, he obeyed.

The plan Ser Axell had devised with Salladhor Saan was simple. A few hours' sail from Dragonstone lay Claw Isle, ancient sea-girt seat of House Celtigar. Lord Ardrian Celtigar had fought beneath the fiery heart on the Blackwater, but once taken, he had wasted no time in going over to Joffrey. He remained in King's Landing even now. "Too frightened of His Grace's wrath to come near Dragonstone, no doubt," Ser Axell declared. "And wisely so. The man has betrayed his rightful king."

Ser Axell proposed to use Salladhor Saan's fleet and the men who had escaped the Blackwater—Stannis still had some fifteen hundred on Dragonstone, more than half of them Florents—to exact retribution for Lord Celtigar's defection. Claw Isle was but lightly garrisoned, its castle reputedly stuffed with Myrish carpets, Volantene glass, gold and silver plate, jeweled cups, magnificent hawks, an axe of Valyrian steel, a horn that could summon monsters from the deep, chests of rubies, and more wines than a man could drink in a hundred years. Though Celtigar had shown the world a niggardly face, he had never stinted on his own comforts. "Put his castle to the torch and his people to the sword, I say," Ser Axell concluded. "Leave Claw Isle a desolation of ash and bone, fit only for carrion crows, so the realm might see the fate of those who bed with Lannisters."

Stannis listened to Ser Axell's recitation in silence, grinding his jaw slowly from side to side. When it was done, he said, "It could be done, I believe. The risk is small. Joffrey has no strength at sea until Lord Redwyne sets sail from the Arbor. The plunder might serve to keep that Lysene pirate Salladhor Saan loyal for a time. By itself Claw Isle is worthless, but its fall would serve notice to Lord Tywin that my cause is not yet done." The king turned back to Davos. "Speak truly, ser. What do you make of Ser Axell's proposal?"

Speak truly, ser. Davos remembered the dark cell he had shared with Lord Alester, remembered Lamprey and Porridge. He thought of the promises that Ser Axell had made on the bridge above the yard. *A ship or a shove, what shall it be?* But this was Stannis asking. "Your Grace," he said slowly, "I make it folly . . . aye, and cowardice."

"*Cowardice?*" Ser Axell all but shouted. "No man calls me craven before my king!"

"Silence," Stannis commanded. "Ser Davos, speak on, I would hear your reasons."

Davos turned to face Ser Axell. "You say we ought show the realm we are not done. Strike a blow. Make war, aye . . . but on what enemy? You will find no Lannisters on Claw Isle."

"We will find *traitors*," said Ser Axell, "though it may be I could find some closer to home. Even in this very room."

Davos ignored the jibe. "I don't doubt Lord Celtigar bent the knee to the boy Joffrey. He is an old done man, who wants no more than to end his days in his castle, drinking his fine wine out of his jeweled cups." He turned back to Stannis. "Yet he came when you called, sire. Came, with his ships and swords. He stood by you at Storm's End when Lord Renly came down on us, and his ships sailed up the Blackwater. His men fought for you, killed for you, *burned* for you. Claw Isle is weakly held, yes. Held by women and children and old men. And why is that? Because their husbands and sons and fathers died on the Blackwater, that's why. Died at their oars, or with swords in their hands, fighting beneath our banners. Yet Ser Axell proposes we swoop down on the homes they left behind, to rape their widows and put their children to the sword. These smallfolk are no traitors . . ."

"They *are*," insisted Ser Axell. "Not all of Celtigar's men were slain on the Blackwater. Hundreds were taken with their lord, and bent the knee when he did."

"*When he did*," Davos repeated. "They were his men. His sworn men. What choice were they given?"

"Every man has choices. They might have refused to kneel. Some did, and died for it. Yet they died true men, and loyal."

"Some men are stronger than others." It was a feeble answer, and Davos knew it. Stannis Baratheon was a man of iron will who neither understood nor forgave weakness in others. *I am losing*, he thought, despairing.

"It is every man's duty to remain loyal to his rightful king, even if the lord he serves proves false," Stannis declared in a tone that brooked no argument.

A desperate folly took hold of Davos, a recklessness akin to madness. "As you remained loyal to King Aerys when your brother raised his banners?" he blurted.

Shocked silence followed, until Ser Axell cried, "*Treason!*" and snatched his dagger from its sheath. "Your Grace, he speaks his infamy to your face!"

Davos could hear Stannis grinding his teeth. A vein bulged, blue and swollen, in the king's brow. Their eyes met. "Put up your knife, Ser Axell. And leave us."

"As it please Your Grace—"

"It would please me for you to leave," said Stannis. "Take yourself from my presence, and send me Melisandre."

"As you command." Ser Axell slid the knife away, bowed, and hurried toward the door. His boots rang against the floor, angry.

"You have always presumed on my forbearance," Stannis warned Davos when they were alone. "I can shorten your tongue as easy as I did your fingers, smuggler."

"I am your man, Your Grace. So it is your tongue, to do with as you please."

"It is," he said, calmer. "And I would have it speak the truth. Though the truth is a bitter draught at times. *Aerys?* If you only knew . . . that was a hard choosing. My blood or my liege. My brother or my king." He grimaced. "Have you ever seen the Iron Throne? The barbs along the back, the ribbons of twisted steel, the jagged ends of swords and knives all tangled up and melted? It is not a *comfortable* seat, ser. Aerys cut himself so often men took to calling him King Scab, and Maegor the Cruel was murdered in that chair. *By* that chair, to hear some tell it. It is not a seat where a man can rest at ease. Ofttimes I wonder why my brothers wanted it so desperately."

"Why would *you* want it, then?" Davos asked him.

"It is not a question of wanting. The throne is mine, as Robert's heir. That is law. After me, it must pass to my daughter, unless Selyse should finally give me a son." He ran three fingers lightly down the table, over the layers of smooth hard varnish, dark with age. "I *am* king. Wants do not enter into it. I have a duty to my daughter. To the realm. Even to Robert. He loved me but little, I know, yet he was my brother. The Lannister woman gave him horns and made a motley fool of him. She may have murdered him as well, as she murdered Jon Arryn and Ned Stark. For such crimes there must be justice. Starting with Cersei and her abominations. But only starting. I mean to scour that court clean. As Robert should have done, after the Trident. Ser Barristan once told me that the rot in King Aerys's reign began with Varys. The eunuch should never have been pardoned. No more than the Kingslayer. At the least, Robert should have stripped the white cloak from Jaime and sent him to the Wall, as Lord Stark urged. He listened to Jon Arryn instead. I was still at Storm's End, under siege and unconsulted." He turned abruptly, to give Davos a hard shrewd look. "The truth, now. Why did you wish to murder Lady Melisandre?"

So he does know. Davos could not lie to him. "Four of my sons burned on the Blackwater. She gave them to the flames."

"You wrong her. Those fires were no work of hers. Curse the Imp, curse the pyromancers, curse that fool of Florent who sailed my fleet into the jaws of a trap. Or curse me for my stubborn pride, for sending her away when I needed her most. But not Melisandre. She remains my faithful servant."

"Maester Cressen was your faithful servant. She slew him, as she killed Ser Cortnay Penrose and your brother Renly."

"Now you sound a fool," the king complained. "She *saw* Renly's end in the flames, yes, but she had no more part in it than I did. The priestess was with me. Your Devan would tell you so. Ask him, if you doubt me. She would have spared Renly if she could. It was Melisandre who urged me to meet with him, and give him one last chance to amend his treason. And it was Melisandre who told me to send for you when Ser Axell wished to give you to R'hllor." He smiled thinly. "Does that surprise you?"

"Yes. She knows I am no friend to her or her red god."

"But you are a friend to me. She knows that as well." He beckoned Davos closer. "The boy is sick. Maester Pylos has been leeching him."

"The boy?" His thoughts went to his Devan, the king's squire. "My son, sire?"

"Devan? A good boy. He has much of you in him. It is Robert's bastard who is sick, the boy we took at Storm's End."

Edric Storm. "I spoke with him in Aegon's Garden."

"As she wished. As she saw." Stannis sighed. "Did the boy charm you?" *He has that gift. He got it from his father, with the blood. He knows he is a king's son, but chooses to forget that he is bastard-born. And he worships Robert, as Renly did when he was young. My royal brother played the fond father on his visits to Storm's End, and there were gifts . . . swords and ponies and fur-trimmed cloaks. The eunuch's work, every one. The boy would write the Red Keep full of thanks, and Robert would laugh and ask Varys what he'd sent this year. Renly was no better. He left the boy's upbringing to castellans and maesters, and every one fell victim to his charm. Penrose chose to die rather than give him up."* The king ground his teeth together. "It still angers me. How could he think I would hurt the boy? I chose Robert, did I not? When that hard day came. I chose blood over honor."

He does not use the boy's name. That made Davos very uneasy. "I hope young Edric will recover soon."

Stannis waved a hand, dismissing his concern. "It is a chill, no more. He coughs, he shivers, he has a fever. Maester Pylos will soon set him right. By himself the boy is nought, you understand, but in his veins flows my brother's blood. There is power in a king's blood, she says."

Davos did not have to ask who *she* was.

Stannis touched the Painted Table. "Look at it, onion knight. My realm, by rights. My Westeros." He swept a hand across it. "This talk of Seven Kingdoms is a folly. Aegon saw that three hundred years ago when he stood where we are standing. They painted this table at his command. Rivers and bays they painted, hills and mountains, castles and cities and market towns, lakes and swamps and forests . . . but no borders. *It is all one.* One realm, for one king to rule alone."

"One king," agreed Davos. "One king means peace."

"I shall bring justice to Westeros. A thing Ser Axell understands as little as he does war. Claw Isle would gain me naught . . . and it was evil, just as you said. Celtigar must pay the traitor's price himself, in his own person. And when I come into my kingdom, he shall. Every man shall reap what he has sown, from the highest lord to the lowest gutter rat. And some will lose more than the tips off their fingers, I promise you. They have made my kingdom bleed, and I do not forget that." King Stannis turned from the table. "On your knees, Onion Knight."

"Your Grace?"

"For your onions and fish, I made you a knight once. For this, I am of a mind to raise you to lord."

This? Davos was lost. "I am content to be your knight, Your Grace. I would not know how to begin being lordly."

"Good. To be lordly is to be false. I have learned that lesson hard. Now, *kneel*. Your king commands."

Davos knelt, and Stannis drew his longsword. *Lightbringer,* Melisandre had named it; the red sword of heroes, drawn from the fires where the seven gods were consumed. The room seemed to grow brighter as the blade slid from its scabbard. The steel had a glow to it; now orange, now yellow, now red. The air shimmered around it, and no jewel had ever sparkled so brilliantly. But when Stannis touched it to Davos's shoulder, it felt no different than any other longsword. "Ser Davos of House Seaworth," the king said, "are you my true and honest liege man, now and forever?"

"I am, Your Grace."

"And do you swear to serve me loyally all your days, to give me honest counsel and swift obedience, to defend my rights and my realm against all foes in battles great and small, to protect my people and punish my enemies?"

"I do, Your Grace."

"Then rise again, Davos Seaworth, and rise as Lord of the Rainwood, Admiral of the Narrow Sea, and Hand of the King."

For a moment Davos was too stunned to move. *I woke this morning in his dungeon.* "Your Grace, you cannot . . . I am no fit man to be a King's Hand."

"There is no man fitter." Stannis sheathed Lightbringer, gave Davos his hand, and pulled him to his feet.

"I am lowborn," Davos reminded him. "An upjumped smuggler. Your lords will never obey me."

"Then we will make new lords."

"But . . . I cannot read . . . nor write . . ."

"Maester Pylos can read for you. As to writing, my last Hand wrote the head off his shoulders. All I ask of you are the things you've always given me. Honesty. Loyalty. Service."

"Surely there is someone better . . . some great lord . . ."

Stannis snorted. "Bar Emmon, that boy? My faithless grandfather? Celtigar has abandoned me, the new Velaryon is six years old, and the new Sunglass sailed for Volantis after I burned his brother." He made an angry gesture. "A few good men remain, it's true. Ser Gilbert Farring holds Storm's End for me still, with two hundred loyal men. Lord Morrigen, the Bastard of Nightsong, young Chyttering, my cousin Andrew . . . but I trust none of them as I trust you, my lord of Rainwood. You will be my Hand. It is you I want beside me for the battle."

Another battle will be the end of all of us, thought Davos. *Lord Alester saw that much true enough.* "Your

Grace asked for honest counsel. In honesty then . . . we lack the strength for another battle against the Lannisters."

"It is the great battle His Grace is speaking of," said a woman's voice, rich with the accents of the east. Melisandre stood at the door in her red silks and shimmering satins, holding a covered silver dish in her hands. "These little wars are no more than a scuffle of children before what is to come. The one whose name may not be spoken is marshaling his power, Davos Seaworth, a power fell and evil and strong beyond measure. Soon comes the cold, and the night that never ends." She placed the silver dish on the Painted Table. "Unless true men find the courage to fight it. Men whose hearts are fire."

Stannis stared at the silver dish. "She has shown it to me, Lord Davos. In the flames."

"*You* saw it, sire?" It was not like Stannis Baratheon to lie about such a thing.

"With mine own eyes. After the battle, when I was lost to despair, the Lady Melisandre bid me gaze into the hearthfire. The chimney was drawing strongly, and bits of ash were rising from the fire. I stared at them, feeling half a fool, but she bid me look deeper, and . . . the ashes were white, rising in the updraft, yet all at once it seemed as if they were falling. *Snow*, I thought. Then the sparks in the air seemed to circle, to become a ring of torches, and I was looking *through* the fire down on some high hill in a forest. The cinders had become men in black behind the torches, and there were shapes moving through the snow. For all the heat of the fire, I felt a cold so terrible I shivered, and when I did the sight was gone, the fire but a fire once again. But what I saw was real, I'd stake my kingdom on it."

"And have," said Melisandre.

The conviction in the king's voice frightened Davos to the core. "A hill in a forest . . . shapes in the snow . . . I don't . . ."

"It means that the battle is begun," said Melisandre. "The sand is running through the glass more quickly now, and man's hour on earth is almost done. We must act boldly, or all hope is lost. Westeros must unite beneath her one true king, the prince that was promised, Lord of Dragonstone and chosen of R'hllor."

"R'hllor chooses queerly, then." The king grimaced, as

if he'd tasted something foul. "Why me, and not my brothers? Renly and his peach. In my dreams I see the juice running from his mouth, the blood from his throat. If he had done his duty by his brother, we would have smashed Lord Tywin. A victory even Robert could be proud of. Robert . . ." His teeth ground side to side. "He is in my dreams as well. Laughing. Drinking. Boasting. Those were the things he was best at. Those, and fighting. I never bested him at anything. The Lord of Light should have made Robert his champion. Why me?"

"Because you are a righteous man," said Melisandre.

"A righteous man." Stannis touched the covered silver platter with a finger. "With leeches."

"Yes," said Melisandre, "but I must tell you once more, this is not the way."

"You swore it would work." The king looked angry.

"It will . . . and it will not."

"Which?"

"Both."

"Speak sense to me, woman."

"When the fires speak more plainly, so shall I. There is truth in the flames, but it is not always easy to see." The great ruby at her throat drank fire from the glow of the brazier. "Give me the boy, Your Grace. It is the surer way. The better way. Give me the boy and I shall wake the stone dragon."

"I have told you, no."

"He is only one baseborn boy, against all the boys of Westeros, and all the girls as well. Against all the children that might ever be born, in all the kingdoms of the world."

"The boy is innocent."

"The boy defiled your marriage bed, else you would surely have sons of your own. He shamed you."

"*Robert* did that. Not the boy. My daughter has grown fond of him. And he is mine own blood."

"Your brother's blood," Melisandre said. "A king's blood. Only a king's blood can wake the stone dragon."

Stannis ground his teeth. "I'll hear no more of this. The dragons are done. The Targaryens tried to bring them back half a dozen times. And made fools of themselves, or corpses. Patchface is the only fool we need on this godsforsaken rock. You have the leeches. Do your work."

Melisandre bowed her head stiffly, and said, "As my king commands." Reaching up her left sleeve with her right hand, she flung a handful of powder into the brazier. The coals roared. As pale flames writhed atop them, the red woman retrieved the silver dish and brought it to the king. Davos watched her lift the lid. Beneath were three large black leeches, fat with blood.

The boy's blood, Davos knew. *A king's blood.*

Stannis stretched forth a hand, and his fingers closed around one of the leeches.

"Say the name," Melisandre commanded.

The leech was twisting in the king's grip, trying to attach itself to one of his fingers. "The usurper," he said. "Joffrey Baratheon." When he tossed the leech into the fire, it curled up like an autumn leaf amidst the coals, and burned.

Stannis grasped the second. "The usurper," he declared, louder this time. "Balon Greyjoy." He flipped it lightly onto the brazier, and its flesh split and cracked. The blood burst from it, hissing and smoking.

The last was in the king's hand. This one he studied a moment as it writhed between his fingers. "The usurper," he said at last. "Robb Stark." And he threw it on the flames.

JAIME

Harrenhal's bathhouse was a dim, steamy, low-ceilinged room filled with great stone tubs. When they led Jaime in, they found Brienne seated in one of them, scrubbing her arm almost angrily.

"Not so hard, wench," he called. "You'll scrub the skin off." She dropped her brush and covered her teats with hands as big as Gregor Clegane's. The pointy little buds she was so intent on hiding would have looked more natural on some ten-year-old than they did on her thick muscular chest.

"What are you doing here?" she demanded.

"Lord Bolton insists I sup with him, but he neglected to invite my fleas." Jaime tugged at his guard with his left hand. "Help me out of these stinking rags." One-handed, he could not so much as unlace his breeches. The man obeyed grudgingly, but he obeyed. "Now leave us," Jaime said when his clothes lay in a pile on the wet stone floor. "My lady of Tarth doesn't want the likes of you scum gaping at her teats." He pointed his stump at the hatchet-faced woman attending Brienne. "You too. Wait without. There's only the one door, and the wench is too big to try and shinny up a chimney."

The habit of obedience went deep. The woman followed his guard out, leaving the bathhouse to the two of them. The tubs were large enough to hold six or seven, after the fashion of the Free Cities, so Jaime climbed in with the wench, awkward and slow. Both his eyes were open, though the right remained somewhat swollen, despite Qyburn's leeches. Jaime felt a hundred and nine years old, which was a deal better than he had been feeling when he came to Harrenhal.

Brienne shrunk away from him. "There are other tubs."

"This one suits me well enough." Gingerly, he immersed himself up to the chin in the steaming water. "Have no fear, wench. Your thighs are purple and green, and I'm not interested in what you've got between them." He had to rest his right arm on the rim, since Qyburn had warned him to keep the linen dry. He could feel the tension drain from his legs, but his head spun. "If I faint, pull me out. No Lannister has ever drowned in his bath and I don't mean to be the first."

"Why should I care how you die?"

"You swore a solemn vow." He smiled as a red flush crept up the thick white column of her neck. She turned her back to him. "Still the shy maiden? What is it that you think I haven't seen?" He groped for the brush she had dropped, caught it with his fingers, and began to scrub himself desultorily. Even that was difficult, awkward. *My left hand is good for nothing.*

Still, the water darkened as the caked dirt dissolved off his skin. The wench kept her back to him, the muscles in her great shoulders hunched and hard.

"Does the sight of my stump distress you so?" Jaime asked. "You ought to be pleased. I've lost the hand I killed the king with. The hand that flung the Stark boy from that tower. The hand I'd slide between my sister's thighs to make her wet." He thrust his stump at her face. "No wonder Renly died, with you guarding him."

She jerked to her feet as if he'd struck her, sending a wash of hot water across the tub. Jaime caught a glimpse of the thick blonde bush at the juncture of her thighs as she climbed out. She was much hairier than his sister.

Absurdly, he felt his cock stir beneath the bathwater. *Now I know I have been too long away from Cersei.* He averted his eyes, troubled by his body's response. "That was unworthy," he mumbled. "I'm a maimed man, and bitter. Forgive me, wench. You protected me as well as any man could have, and better than most."

She wrapped her nakedness in a towel. "Do you mock me?"

That pricked him back to anger. "Are you as thick as a castle wall? That was an apology. I am tired of fighting with you. What say we make a truce?"

"Truces are built on trust. Would you have me trust—"

"The Kingslayer, yes. The oathbreaker who murdered poor sad Aerys Targaryen." Jaime snorted. "It's not Aerys I rue, it's Robert. 'I hear they've named you Kingslayer,' he said to me at his coronation feast. 'Just don't think to make it a habit.' And he laughed. Why is it that no one names Robert oathbreaker? He tore the realm apart, yet *I* am the one with shit for honor."

"Robert did all he did for love." Water ran down Brienne's legs and pooled beneath her feet.

"Robert did all he did for pride, a cunt, and a pretty face." He made a fist . . . or would have, if he'd had a hand. Pain lanced up his arm, cruel as laughter.

"He rode to save the realm," she insisted.

To save the realm. "Did you know that my brother set the Blackwater Rush afire? Wildfire will burn on water. Aerys would have bathed in it if he'd dared. The Targaryens were all mad for fire." Jaime felt light-headed. *It is the heat in here, the poison in my blood, the last of my fever. I am not myself.* He eased himself down until the water reached his chin. "Soiled my white cloak . . . I wore my gold armor that day, but . . ."

"Gold armor?" Her voice sounded far off, faint.

He floated in heat, in memory. "After dancing griffins lost the Battle of the Bells, Aerys exiled him." *Why am I telling this absurd ugly child?* "He had finally realized that Robert was no mere outlaw lord to be crushed at whim, but the greatest threat House Targaryen had faced since Daemon Blackfyre. The king reminded Lewyn Martell gracelessly that he held Elia and sent him to take command of the ten thousand Dornishmen coming up the kingsroad. Jon Darry and Barristan Selmy rode to Stoney Sept to rally what they could of griffins' men, and Prince Rhaegar returned from the south and persuaded his father to swallow his pride and summon my father. But no raven returned from Casterly Rock, and that made the king even more afraid. He saw traitors everywhere, and Varys was always there to point out any he might have missed. So His Grace commanded his alchemists to place caches of wildfire all over King's Landing. Beneath Baelor's Sept and the hovels of Flea Bottom, under stables and storehouses, at all seven gates, even in the cellars of the Red Keep itself.

"Everything was done in the utmost secrecy by a handful of master pyromancers. They did not even trust their own acolytes to help. The queen's eyes had been closed for years, and Rhaegar was busy marshaling an army. But Aerys's new mace-and-dagger Hand was not utterly stupid, and with Rossart, Belis, and Garigus coming and going night and day, he became suspicious. Chelsted, that was his name, Lord Chelsted." It had come back to him suddenly, with the telling. "I'd thought the man craven, but the day he confronted Aerys he found some courage somewhere. He did all he could to dissuade him. He reasoned, he jested, he threatened, and finally he begged. When that failed he took off his chain of office and flung it down on the floor. Aerys burnt him alive for that, and hung his chain about the neck of Rossart, his favorite pyromancer. The man who had cooked Lord Rickard Stark in his own armor. And all the time, I stood by the foot of the Iron Throne in my white plate, still as a corpse, guarding my liege and all his sweet secrets.

"My Sworn Brothers were all away, you see, but Aerys liked to keep me close. I was my father's son, so he did not trust me. He wanted me where Varys could watch me, day and night. So I heard it all." He remembered how Rossart's eyes would shine when he unrolled his maps to show where *the substance* must be placed. Garigus and Belis were the same. "Rhaegar met Robert on the Trident, and you know what happened there. When the word reached court, Aerys packed the queen off to Dragonstone with Prince Viserys. Princess Elia would have gone as well, but he forbade it. Somehow he had gotten it in his head that Prince Lewyn must have betrayed Rhaegar on the Trident, but he thought he could keep Dorne loyal so long as he kept Elia and Aegon by his side. *The traitors want my city*, I heard him tell Rossart, *but I'll give them naught but ashes. Let Robert be king over charred bones and cooked meat.* The Targaryens never bury their dead, they burn them. Aerys meant to have the greatest funeral pyre of them all. Though if truth be told, I do not believe he truly expected to die. Like Aerion Brightfire before him, Aerys thought the fire would transform him . . . that he would rise again, reborn as a dragon, and turn all his enemies to ash.

"Ned Stark was racing south with Robert's van, but my father's forces reached the city first. Pycelle convinced the king that his Warden of the West had come to defend him, so he opened the gates. The one time he *should* have heeded Varys, and he ignored him. My father had held back from the war, brooding on all the wrongs Aerys had done him and determined that House Lannister should be on the winning side. The Trident decided him.

"It fell to me to hold the Red Keep, but I knew we were lost. I sent to Aerys asking his leave to make terms. My man came back with a royal command. '*Bring me your father's head, if you are no traitor.*' Aerys would have no yielding. Lord Rossart was with him, my messenger said. I knew what *that* meant.

"When I came on Rossart, he was dressed as a common man-at-arms, hurrying to a postern gate. I slew him first. Then I slew Aerys, before he could find someone else to carry his message to the pyromancers. Days later, I hunted down the others and slew them as well. Belis offered me gold, and Garigus wept for mercy. Well, a sword's more merciful than fire, but I don't think Garigus much appreciated the kindness I showed him."

The water had grown cool. When Jaime opened his eyes, he found himself staring at the stump of his sword hand. *The hand that made me Kingslayer.* The goat had robbed him of his glory and his shame, both at once. *Leaving what? Who am I now?*

The wench looked ridiculous, clutching her towel to her meager teats with her thick white legs sticking out beneath. "Has my tale turned you speechless? Come, curse me or kiss me or call me a liar. *Something.*"

"If this is true, how is it no one knows?"

"The knights of the Kingsguard are sworn to keep the king's secrets. Would you have me break my oath?" Jaime laughed. "Do you think the noble Lord of Winterfell wanted to hear my feeble explanations? Such an *honorable* man. He only had to look at me to judge me guilty." Jaime lurched to his feet, the water running cold down his chest. "By what right does the wolf judge the lion? *By what right?*" A violent shiver took him, and he smashed his stump against the rim of the tub as he tried to climb out.

Pain shuddered through him . . . and suddenly the bathhouse was spinning. Brienne caught him before he could fall. Her arm was all gooseflesh, clammy and chilled, but she was strong, and gentler than he would have thought. *Gentler than Cersei*, he thought as she helped him from the tub, his legs wobbly as a limp cock. "*Guards!*" he heard the wench shout. "The Kingslayer!"

Jaime, he thought, *my name is Jaime.*

The next he knew, he was lying on the damp floor with the guards and the wench and Qyburn all standing over him looking concerned. Brienne was naked, but she seemed to have forgotten that for the moment. "The heat of the tubs will do it," Maester Qyburn was telling them. *No, he's not a maester, they took his chain.* "There's still poison in his blood as well, and he's malnourished. What have you been feeding him?"

"Worms and piss and grey vomit," offered Jaime.

"Hardbread and water and oat porridge," insisted the guard. "He don't hardly eat it, though. What should we do with him?"

"Scrub him and dress him and carry him to Kingspyre, if need be," Qyburn said. "Lord Bolton insists he will sup with him tonight. The time is growing short."

"Bring me clean garb for him," Brienne said, "I'll see that he's washed and dressed."

The others were all too glad to give her the task. They lifted him to his feet and sat him on a stone bench by the wall. Brienne went away to retrieve her towel, and returned with a stiff brush to finish scrubbing him. One of the guards gave her a razor to trim his beard. Qyburn returned with roughspun smallclothes, clean black woolen breeches, a loose green tunic, and a leather jerkin that laced up the front. Jaime was feeling less dizzy by then, though no less clumsy. With the wench's help he managed to dress himself. "Now all I need is a silver looking glass."

The Bloody Maester had brought fresh clothing for Brienne as well; a stained pink satin gown and a linen undertunic. "I am sorry, my lady. These were the only women's garments in Harrenhal large enough to fit you."

It was obvious at once that the gown had been cut for someone with slimmer arms, shorter legs, and much fuller breasts. The fine Myrish lace did little to conceal the bruising that mottled Brienne's skin. All in all, the garb made the wench look ludicrous. *She has thicker shoulders than I do, and a bigger neck,* Jaime thought. *Small wonder she prefers to dress in mail.* Pink was not a kind color for her either. A dozen cruel japes leaped into his head, but for once he kept them there. Best not to make her angry; he was no match for her one-handed.

Qyburn had brought a flask as well. "What is it?" Jaime demanded when the chainless maester pressed him to drink.

"Licorice steeped in vinegar, with honey and cloves. It will give you some strength and clear your head."

"Bring me the potion that grows new hands," said Jaime. "That's the one I want."

"Drink it," Brienne said, unsmiling, and he did.

It was half an hour before he felt strong enough to stand. After the dim wet warmth of the bathhouse, the air outside was a slap across the face. "M'lord will be looking for him by now," a guard told Qyburn. "Her too. Do I need to carry him?"

"I can still walk. Brienne, give me your arm."

Clutching her, Jaime let them herd him across the yard to a vast draughty hall, larger even than the throne room in King's Landing. Huge hearths lined the walls, one every ten feet or so, more than he could count, but no fires had been lit, so the chill between the walls went bone-deep. A dozen spearmen in fur cloaks guarded the doors and the steps that led up to the two galleries above. And in the center of that immense emptiness, at a trestle table surrounded by what seemed like acres of smooth slate floor, the Lord of the Dreadfort waited, attended only by a cupbearer.

"My lord," said Brienne, when they stood before him.

Roose Bolton's eyes were paler than stone, darker than

milk, and his voice was spider soft. "I am pleased that you are strong enough to attend me, ser. My lady, do be seated." He gestured at the spread of cheese, bread, cold meat, and fruit that covered the table. "Will you drink red or white? Of indifferent vintage, I fear. Ser Amory drained Lady Whent's cellars nearly dry."

"I trust you killed him for it." Jaime slid into the offered seat quickly, so Bolton could not see how weak he was. "White is for Starks. I'll drink red like a good Lannister."

"I would prefer water," said Brienne.

"Elmar, the red for Ser Jaime, water for the Lady Brienne, and hippocras for myself." Bolton waved a hand at their escort, dismissing them, and the men beat a silent retreat.

Habit made Jaime reach for his wine with his right hand. His stump rocked the goblet, spattering his clean linen bandages with bright red spots and forcing him to catch the cup with his left hand before it fell, but Bolton pretended not to notice his clumsiness. The northman helped himself to a prune and ate it with small sharp bites. "Do try these, Ser Jaime. They are most sweet, and help move the bowels as well. Lord Vargo took them from an inn before he burnt it."

"My bowels move fine, that goat's no lord, and your prunes don't interest me half so much as your intentions."

"Regarding you?" A faint smile touched Roose Bolton's lips. "You are a perilous prize, ser. You sow dissension wherever you go. Even here, in my happy house of Harrenhal." His voice was a whisker above a whisper. "And in Riverrun as well, it seems. Do you know, Edmure Tully has offered a thousand golden dragons for your recapture?"

Is that all? "My sister will pay ten times as much."

"Will she?" That smile again, there for an instant, gone as quick. "Ten thousand dragons is a formidable sum. Of course, there is Lord Karstark's offer to consider as well. He promises the hand of his daughter to the man who brings him your head."

"Leave it to your goat to get it backward," said Jaime.

Bolton gave a soft chuckle. "Harrion Karstark was captive here when we took the castle, did you know? I gave him all the Karhold men still with me and sent him off

with Glover. I do hope nothing ill befell him at Duskendale . . . else Alys Karstark would be all that remains of
Lord Rickard's progeny." He chose another prune. "Fortunately for you, I have no need of a wife. I wed the Lady
Walda Frey whilst I was at the Twins."

"Fair Walda?" Awkwardly, Jaime tried to hold the bread
with his stump while tearing it with his left hand.

"Fat Walda. My lord of Frey offered me my bride's
weight in silver for a dowry, so I chose accordingly. Elmar,
break off some bread for Ser Jaime."

The boy tore a fist-sized chunk off one end of the loaf
and handed it to Jaime. Brienne tore her own bread. "Lord
Bolton," she asked, "it's said you mean to give Harrenhal
to Vargo Hoat."

"That was his price," Lord Bolton said. "The Lannisters
are not the only men who pay their debts. I must take my
leave soon in any case. Edmure Tully is to wed the Lady
Roslin Frey at the Twins, and my king commands my attendance."

"*Edmure* weds?" said Jaime. "Not Robb Stark?"

"His Grace King Robb is wed." Bolton spit a prune pit
into his hand and put it aside. "To a Westerling of the Crag.
I am told her name is Jeyne. No doubt you know her, ser.
Her father is your father's bannerman."

"My father has a good many bannermen, and most of
them have daughters." Jaime groped one-handed for his
goblet, trying to recall this Jeyne. The Westerlings were an
old house, with more pride than power.

"This cannot be true," Brienne said stubbornly. "King
Robb was sworn to wed a Frey. He would never break faith,
he—"

"His Grace is a boy of sixteen," said Roose Bolton
mildly. "And I would thank you not to question my word,
my lady."

Jaime felt almost sorry for Robb Stark. *He won the war
on the battlefield and lost it in a bedchamber, poor fool.*
"How does Lord Walder relish dining on trout in place of
wolf?" he asked.

"Oh, trout makes for a tasty supper." Bolton lifted a pale
finger toward his cupbearer. "Though my poor Elmar is
bereft. He was to wed Arya Stark, but my good father of

Frey had no choice but to break the betrothal when King Robb betrayed him."

"Is there word of Arya Stark?" Brienne leaned forward. "Lady Catelyn had feared that . . . is the girl still alive?"

"Oh, yes," said the Lord of the Dreadfort.

"You have certain knowledge of that, my lord?"

Roose Bolton shrugged. "Arya Stark was lost for a time, it was true, but now she has been found. I mean to see her returned safely to the north."

"Her and her sister both," said Brienne. "Tyrion Lannister has promised us both girls for his brother."

That seemed to amuse the Lord of the Dreadfort. "My lady, has no one told you? Lannisters lie."

"Is that a slight on the honor of my House?" Jaime picked up the cheese knife with his good hand. "A rounded point, and dull," he said, sliding his thumb along the edge of the blade, "but it will go through your eye all the same." Sweat beaded his brow. He could only hope he did not look as feeble as he felt.

Lord Bolton's little smile paid another visit to his lips. "You speak boldly for a man who needs help to break his bread. My guards are all around us, I remind you."

"All around us, and half a league away." Jaime glanced down the vast length of the hall. "By the time they reach us, you'll be as dead as Aerys."

" 'Tis scarcely chivalrous to threaten your host over his own cheese and olives," the Lord of the Dreadfort scolded. "In the north, we hold the laws of hospitality sacred still."

"I'm a captive here, not a guest. Your goat cut off my hand. If you think some prunes will make me overlook that, you're bloody well mistaken."

That took Roose Bolton aback. "Perhaps I am. Perhaps I ought to make a wedding gift of you to Edmure Tully . . . or strike your head off, as your sister did for Eddard Stark."

"I would not advise it. Casterly Rock has a long memory."

"A thousand leagues of mountain, sea, and bog lie between my walls and your rock. Lannister enmity means little to Bolton."

"Lannister friendship could mean much." Jaime thought he knew the game they were playing now. *But does the wench know as well?* He dare not look to see.

"I am not certain you are the sort of friends a wise man would want." Roose Bolton beckoned to the boy. "Elmar, carve our guests a slice off the roast."

Brienne was served first, but made no move to eat. "My lord," she said, "Ser Jaime is to be exchanged for Lady Catelyn's daughters. You must free us to continue on our way."

"The raven that came from Riverrun told of an escape, not an exchange. And if you helped this captive slip his bonds, you are guilty of treason, my lady."

The big wench rose to her feet. "I serve Lady Stark."

"And I the King in the North. Or the King Who Lost the North, as some now call him. Who never wished to trade Ser Jaime back to the Lannisters."

"Sit down and eat, Brienne," Jaime urged, as Elmar placed a slice of roast before him, dark and bloody. "If Bolton meant to kill us, he wouldn't be wasting his precious prunes on us, at such peril to his bowels." He stared at the meat and realized there was no way to cut it, one-handed. *I am worth less than a girl now*, he thought. *The goat's evened the trade, though I doubt Lady Catelyn will thank him when Cersei returns her whelps in like condition.* The thought made him grimace. *I will get the blame for that as well, I'll wager.*

Roose Bolton cut his meat methodically, the blood running across his plate. "Lady Brienne, will you sit if I tell you that I hope to send Ser Jaime on, just as you and Lady Stark desire?"

"I . . . you'd send us on?" The wench sounded wary, but she sat. "That is good, my lord."

"It is. However, Lord Vargo has created me one small . . . difficulty." He turned his pale eyes on Jaime. "Do you know why Hoat cut off your hand?"

"He enjoys cutting off hands." The linen that covered Jaime's stump was spotted with blood and wine. "He enjoys cutting off feet as well. He doesn't seem to need a reason."

"Nonetheless, he had one. Hoat is more cunning than he appears. No man commands a company such as the Brave Companions for long unless he has some wits about him." Bolton stabbed a chunk of meat with the point of his dagger, put it in his mouth, chewed thoughtfully, swallowed. "Lord Vargo abandoned House Lannister because I offered him Harrenhal, a reward a thousand times greater than any he could hope to have from Lord Tywin. As a stranger to Westeros, he did not know the prize was poisoned."

"The curse of Harren the Black?" mocked Jaime.

"The curse of Tywin Lannister." Bolton held out his goblet and Elmar refilled it silently. "Our goat should have consulted the Tarbecks or the Reynes. They might have warned him how your lord father deals with betrayal."

"There are no Tarbecks or Reynes," said Jaime.

"My point precisely. Lord Vargo doubtless hoped that Lord Stannis would triumph at King's Landing, and thence confirm him in his possession of this castle in gratitude for his small part in the downfall of House Lannister." He gave a dry chuckle. "He knows little of Stannis Baratheon either, I fear. That one might have given him Harrenhal for his service . . . but he would have given him a noose for his crimes as well."

"A noose is kinder than what he'll get from my father."

"By now he has come to the same realization. With Stannis broken and Renly dead, only a Stark victory can save him from Lord Tywin's vengeance, but the chances of that grow perishingly slim."

"King Robb has won every battle," Brienne said stoutly, as stubbornly loyal of speech as she was of deed.

"Won every battle, while losing the Freys, the Karstarks, Winterfell, and the north. A pity the wolf is so young. Boys of sixteen always believe they are immortal and invincible. An older man would bend the knee, I'd think. After a war there is always a peace, and with peace there are pardons . . . for the Robb Starks, at least. Not for the likes of Vargo Hoat." Bolton gave him a small smile. "Both sides have made use of him, but neither will shed a tear at his passing. The Brave Companions did not fight in the Battle of the Blackwater, yet they died there all the same."

"You'll forgive me if I don't mourn?"

"You have no pity for our wretched doomed goat? Ah, but the gods must . . . else why deliver *you* into his hands?" Bolton chewed another chunk of meat. "Karhold is smaller and meaner than Harrenhal, but it lies well beyond the reach of the lion's claws. Once wed to Alys

Karstark, Hoat might be a lord in truth. If he could collect some gold from your father so much the better, but he would have delivered you to Lord Rickard no matter how much Lord Tywin paid. His price would be the maid, and safe refuge.

"But to sell you he must keep you, and the riverlands are full of those who would gladly steal you away. Glover and Tallhart were broken at Duskendale, but remnants of their host are still abroad, with the Mountain slaughtering the stragglers. A thousand Karstarks prowl the lands south and east of Riverrun, hunting you. Elsewhere are Darry men left lordless and lawless, packs of four-footed wolves, and the lightning lord's outlaw bands. Dondarrion would gladly hang you and the goat together from the same tree." The Lord of the Dreadfort sopped up some of the blood with a chunk of bread. "Harrenhal was the only place Lord Vargo could hope to hold you safe, but here his Brave Companions are much outnumbered by my own men, and by Ser Aenys and his Freys. No doubt he feared I might return you to Ser Edmure at Riverrun . . . or worse, send you on to your father.

"By maiming you, he meant to remove your sword as a threat, gain himself a grisly token to send to your father, and diminish your value to me. For he is my man, as I am King Robb's man. Thus his crime is mine, or may seem so in your father's eyes. And therein lies my . . . small difficulty." He gazed at Jaime, his pale eyes unblinking, expectant, chill.

I see. "You want me to absolve you of blame. To tell my father that this stump is no work of yours." Jaime laughed. "My lord, send me to Cersei, and I'll sing as sweet a song as you could want, of how gently you treated me." Any other answer, he knew, and Bolton would give him back to the goat. "Had I a hand, I'd write it out. How I was maimed by the sellsword my own father brought to Westeros, and saved by the noble Lord Bolton."

"I will trust to your word, ser."

There's something I don't often hear. "How soon might we be permitted to leave? And how do you mean to get me past all these wolves and brigands and Karstarks?"

"You will leave when Qyburn says you are strong enough, with a strong escort of picked men under the command of my captain, Walton. Steelshanks, he is called. A soldier of iron loyalty. Walton will see you safe and whole to King's Landing."

"Provided Lady Catelyn's daughters are delivered safe and whole as well," said the wench. "My lord, your man Walton's protection is welcome, but the girls are *my* charge."

The Lord of the Dreadfort gave her an uninterested glance. "The girls need not concern you any further, my lady. The Lady Sansa is the dwarf's wife, only the gods can part them now."

"His wife?" Brienne said, appalled. "The Imp? But . . . he swore, before the whole court, in sight of gods and men . . ."

She is such an innocent. Jaime was almost as surprised, if truth be told, but he hid it better. *Sansa Stark, that ought to put a smile on Tyrion's face.* He remembered how happy his brother had been with his little crofter's daughter . . . for a fortnight.

"What the Imp did or did nor swear scarcely matters now," said Lord Bolton. "Least of all to you." The wench looked almost wounded. Perhaps she finally felt the steel jaws of the trap when Roose Bolton beckoned to his guards. "Ser Jaime will continue on to King's Landing. I said nothing about you, I fear. It would be unconscionable of me to deprive Lord Vargo of both his prizes." The Lord of the Dreadfort reached out to pick another prune. "Were I you, my lady, I should worry less about Starks and rather more about sapphires."

TYRION

A horse whickered impatiently behind him, from amidst the ranks of gold cloaks drawn up across the road. Tyrion could hear Lord Gyles coughing as well. He had not asked for Gyles, no more than he'd asked for Ser Addam or Jalabhar Xho or any of the rest, but his lord father felt Doran Martell might take it ill if only a dwarf came out to escort him across the Blackwater.

Joffrey should have met the Dornishmen himself, he reflected as he sat waiting, *but he would have mucked it up, no doubt.* Of late the king had been repeating little jests about the Dornish that he'd picked up from Mace Tyrell's men-at-arms. *How many Dornishmen does it take to shoe a horse? Nine. One to do the shoeing, and eight to lift the horse up.* Somehow Tyrion did not think Doran Martell would find that amusing.

He could see their banners flying as the riders emerged from the green of the living wood in a long dusty column. From here to the river, only bare black trees remained, a legacy of his battle. *Too many banners,* he thought sourly, as he watched the ashes kick up under the hooves of the approaching horses, as they had beneath the hooves of the Tyrell van as it smashed Stannis in the flank. *Martell's brought half the lords of Dorne, by the look of it.* He tried to think of some good that might come of that, and failed. "How many banners do you count?" he asked Bronn.

The sellsword knight shaded his eyes. "Eight . . . no, nine."

Tyrion turned in his saddle. "Pod, come up here. Describe the arms you see, and tell me which houses they represent."

Podrick Payne edged his gelding closer. He was carrying the royal standard, Joffrey's great stag-and-lion, and struggling with its weight. Bronn bore Tyrion's own banner, the lion of Lannister gold on crimson.

He's getting taller, Tyrion realized as Pod stood in his stirrups for a better look. *He'll soon tower over me like all the rest.* The lad had been making a diligent study of Dornish heraldry, at Tyrion's command, but as ever he was nervous. "I can't see. The wind is flapping them."

"Bronn, tell the boy what you see."

Bronn looked very much the knight today, in his new doublet and cloak, the flaming chain across his chest. "A red sun on orange," he called, "with a spear through its back."

"Martell," Podrick Payne said at once, visibly relieved. "House Martell of Sunspear, my lord. The Prince of Dorne."

"My horse would have known that one," said Tyrion dryly. "Give him another, Bronn."

"There's a purple flag with yellow balls."

"Lemons?" Pod said hopefully. "A purple field strewn with lemons? For House Dalt? Of, of Lemonwood."

"Might be. Next's a big black bird on yellow. Something pink or white in its claws, hard to say with the banner flapping."

"The vulture of Blackmont grasps a baby in its talons," said Pod. "House Blackmont of Blackmont, ser."

Bronn laughed. "Reading books again? Books will ruin your sword eye, boy. I see a skull too. A black banner."

"The crowned skull of House Manwoody, bone and gold on black." Pod sounded more confident with every correct answer. "The Manwoodys of Kingsgrave."

"Three black spiders?"

"They're scorpions, ser. House Qorgyle of Sandstone, three scorpions black on red."

"Red and yellow, a jagged line between."

"The flames of Hellholt. House Uller."

Tyrion was impressed. *The boy's not half stupid, once he gets his tongue untied.* "Go on, Pod," he urged. "If you get them all, I'll make you a gift."

"A pie with red and black slices," said Bronn. "There's a gold hand in the middle."

"House Allyrion of Godsgrace."

"A red chicken eating a snake, looks like."

"The Gargalens of Salt Shore. A cockatrice. Ser. Pardon. Not a chicken. Red, with a black snake in its beak."

"Very good!" exclaimed Tyrion. "One more, lad."

Bronn scanned the ranks of the approaching Dornishmen. "The last's a golden feather on green checks."

"A golden quill, ser. Jordayne of the Tor."

Tyrion laughed. "Nine, and well done. I could not have named them all myself." That was a lie, but it would give the boy some pride, and that he badly needed.

Martell brings some formidable companions, it would seem. Not one of the houses Pod had named was small or insignificant. Nine of the greatest lords of Dorne were coming up the kingsroad, them or their heirs, and somehow Tyrion did not think they had come all this way just to see the dancing bear. There was a message here. *And not one I like.* He wondered if it had been a mistake to ship Myrcella down to Sunspear.

"My lord," Pod said, a little timidly, "there's no litter."

Tyrion turned his head sharply. The boy was right.

"Doran Martell always travels in a litter," the boy said. "A carved litter with silk hangings, and suns on the drapes."

Tyrion had heard the same talk. Prince Doran was past fifty, and gouty. *He may have wanted to make faster time,* he told himself. *He may have feared his litter would make too tempting a target for brigands, or that it would prove too cumbersome in the high passes of the Boneway. Perhaps his gout is better.*

So why did he have such a bad feeling about this?

This waiting was intolerable. "Banners forward," he snapped. "We'll meet them." He kicked his horse. Bronn and Pod followed, one to either side. When the Dornishmen saw them coming, they spurred their own mounts, banners rippling as they rode. From their ornate saddles were slung the round metal shields they favored, and many carried bundles of short throwing spears, or the double-curved Dornish bows they used so well from horseback.

There were three sorts of Dornishmen, the first King Daeron had observed. There were the salty Dornishmen who lived along the coasts, the sandy Dornishmen of the deserts and long river valleys, and the stony Dornishmen who made their fastnesses in the passes and heights of the Red Mountains. The salty Dornishmen had the most Rhoynish blood, the stony Dornishmen the least.

All three sorts seemed well represented in Doran's retinue. The salty Dornishmen were lithe and dark, with smooth olive skin and long black hair streaming in the wind. The sandy Dornishmen were even darker, their faces burned brown by the hot Dornish sun. They wound long bright scarfs around their helms to ward off sunstroke. The stony Dornishmen were biggest and fairest, sons of the Andals and the First Men, brown-haired or blond, with faces that freckled or burned in the sun instead of browning.

The lords wore silk and satin robes with jeweled belts and flowing sleeves. Their armor was heavily enameled and inlaid with burnished copper, shining silver, and soft red gold. They came astride red horses and golden ones and a few as pale as snow, all slim and swift, with long necks and narrow beautiful heads. The fabled sand steeds of Dorne were smaller than proper warhorses and could not bear such weight of armor, but it was said that they could run for a day and night and another day, and never tire.

The Dornish leader forked a stallion black as sin with a mane and tail the color of fire. He sat his saddle as if he'd been born there, tall, slim, graceful. A cloak of pale red silk fluttered from his shoulders, and his shirt was armored with overlapping rows of copper disks that glittered like a thousand bright new pennies as he rode. His high gilded helm displayed a copper sun on its brow, and the round shield slung behind him bore the sun-and-spear of House Martell on its polished metal surface.

A Martell sun, but ten years too young, Tyrion thought as he reined up, *too fit as well, and far too fierce.* He knew what he must deal with by then. *How many Dornishmen does it take to start a war?* he asked himself. *Only one.* Yet he had no choice but to smile. "Well met, my lords. We had word of your approach, and His Grace King Joffrey bid me ride out to welcome you in his name. My lord father the King's Hand sends his greetings as well." He feigned an amiable confusion. "Which of you is Prince Doran?"

"My brother's health requires he remain at Sunspear." The princeling removed his helm. Beneath, his face was lined and saturnine, with thin arched brows above large eyes as black and shiny as pools of coal oil. Only a few streaks of silver marred the lustrous black hair that receded from his brow in a widow's peak as sharply pointed as his nose. *A salty Dornishmen for certain.* "Prince Doran has sent me to join King Joffrey's council in his stead, as it please His Grace."

"His Grace will be most honored to have the counsel of a warrior as renowned as Prince Oberyn of Dorne," said Tyrion, thinking, *This will mean blood in the gutters.* "And your noble companions are most welcome as well."

"Permit me to acquaint you with them, my lord of Lannister. Ser Deziel Dalt, of Lemonwood. Lord Tremond Gargalen. Lord Harmen Uller and his brother Ser Ulwyck. Ser Ryon Allyrion and his natural son Ser Daemon Sand, the Bastard of Godsgrace. Lord Dagos Manwoody, his brother Ser Myles, his sons Mors and Dickon. Ser Arron Qorgyle. And never let it be thought that I would neglect the ladies. Myria Jordayne, heir to the Tor. Lady Larra Blackmont, her daughter Jynessa, her son Perros." He raised a slender hand toward a black-haired woman to the rear, beckoning her forward. "And this is Ellaria Sand, mine own paramour."

Tyrion swallowed a groan. *His paramour, and bastard-born, Cersei will pitch a holy fit if he wants her at the wedding.* If she consigned the woman to some dark corner below the salt, his sister would risk the Red Viper's wrath. Seat her beside him at the high table, and every other lady on the dais was like to take offense. *Did Prince Doran mean to provoke a quarrel?*

Prince Oberyn wheeled his horse about to face his fellow Dornishmen. "Ellaria, lords and ladies, sers, see how well King Joffrey loves us. His Grace has been so kind as to send his own Uncle Imp to bring us to his court."

Bronn snorted back laughter, and Tyrion perforce must feign amusement as well. "Not alone, my lords. That would be too enormous a task for a little man like me." His own party had come up on them, so it was his turn to name the names. "Let me present Ser Flement Brax, heir to Hornvale. Lord Gyles of Rosby. Ser Addam Marbrand, Lord Commander of the City Watch. Jalabhar Xho, Prince of the Red Flower Vale. Ser Harys Swyft, my uncle Kevan's good father by marriage. Ser Merlon Crakehall. Ser Philip Foote and Ser Bronn of the Blackwater, two heroes of our recent battle against the rebel Stannis Baratheon. And mine own squire, young Podrick of House Payne." The names had a nice ringing sound as Tyrion reeled them off, but the bearers were nowise near as distinguished nor formidable a company as those who accompanied Prince Oberyn, as both of them knew full well.

"My lord of Lannister," said Lady Blackmont, "we have come a long dusty way, and rest and refreshment would be most welcome. Might we continue on to the city?"

"At once, my lady." Tyrion turned his horse's head, and called to Ser Addam Marbrand. The mounted gold cloaks who formed the greatest part of his honor guard turned their horses crisply at Ser Addam's command, and the column set off for the river and King's Landing beyond.

Oberyn Nymeros Martell, Tyrion muttered under his breath as he fell in beside the man. *The Red Viper of Dorne. And what in the seven hells am I supposed to do with him?*

He knew the man only by reputation, to be sure . . . but the reputation was fearsome. When he was no more than sixteen, Prince Oberyn had been found abed with the paramour of old Lord Yronwood, a huge man of fierce repute and short temper. A duel ensued, though in view of the prince's youth and high birth, it was only to first blood. Both men took cuts, and honor was satisfied. Yet Prince Oberyn soon recovered, while Lord Yronwood's wounds

festered and killed him. Afterward men whispered that
Oberyn had fought with a poisoned sword, and ever thereafter friends and foes alike called him the Red Viper.

That was many years ago, to be sure. The boy of sixteen
was a man past forty now, and his legend had grown a deal
darker. He had traveled in the Free Cities, learning the poisoner's trade and perhaps arts darker still, if rumors could
be believed. He had studied at the Citadel, going so far as to
forge six links of a maester's chain before he grew bored.
He had soldiered in the Disputed Lands across the narrow
sea, riding with the Second Sons for a time before forming
his own company. His tourneys, his battles, his duels, his
horses, his carnality . . . it was said that he bedded men and
women both, and had begotten bastard girls all over Dorne.
The *sand snakes*, men called his daughters. So far as
Tyrion had heard, Prince Oberyn had never fathered a son.

And of course, he had crippled the heir to Highgarden.

*There is no man in the Seven Kingdoms who will be
less welcome at a Tyrell wedding*, thought Tyrion. To send
Prince Oberyn to King's Landing while the city still hosted
Lord Mace Tyrell, two of his sons, and thousands of their
men-at-arms was a provocation as dangerous as Prince
Oberyn himself. *A wrong word, an ill-timed jest, a look,
that's all it will take, and our noble allies will be at one
another's throats.*

"We have met before," the Dornish prince said lightly
to Tyrion as they rode side by side along the kingsroad, past
ashen fields and the skeletons of trees. "I would not expect
you to remember, though. You were even smaller than you
are now."

There was a mocking edge to his voice that Tyrion misliked, but he was not about to let the Dornishman provoke
him. "When was this, my lord?" he asked in tones of polite
interest.

"Oh, many and many a year ago, when my mother ruled
in Dorne and your lord father was Hand to a different
king."

Not so different as you might think, reflected Tyrion.

"It was when I visited Casterly Rock with my mother,
her consort, and my sister Elia. I was, oh, fourteen, fifteen,
thereabouts, Elia a year older. Your brother and sister were
eight or nine, as I recall, and you had just been born."

A queer time to come visiting. His mother had died giving him birth, so the Martells would have found the Rock deep in mourning. His father especially. Lord Tywin seldom spoke of his wife, but Tyrion had heard his uncles talk of the love between them. In those days, his father had been Aerys's Hand, and many people said that Lord Tywin Lannister ruled the Seven Kingdoms, but Lady Joanna ruled Lord Tywin. "He was not the same man after she died, Imp," his Uncle Gery told him once. "The best part of him died with her." Gerion had been the youngest of Lord Tytos Lannister's four sons, and the uncle Tyrion liked best.

But he was gone now, lost beyond the seas, and Tyrion himself had put Lady Joanna in her grave. "Did you find Casterly Rock to your liking, my lord?"

"Scarcely. Your father ignored us the whole time we were there, after commanding Ser Kevan to see to our entertainment. The cell they gave me had a featherbed to sleep in and Myrish carpets on the floor, but it was dark and windowless, much like a dungeon when you come down to it, as I told Elia at the time. Your skies were too grey, your wines too sweet, your women too chaste, your food too bland . . . and you yourself were the greatest disappointment of all."

"I had just been born. What did you expect of me?"

"*Enormity*," the black-haired prince replied. "You were small, but far-famed. We were in Oldtown at your birth, and all the city talked of was the monster that had been born to the King's Hand, and what such an omen might foretell for the realm."

"Famine, plague, and war, no doubt." Tyrion gave a sour smile. "It's always famine, plague, and war. Oh, and winter, and the long night that never ends."

"All that," said Prince Oberyn, "and your father's fall as well. Lord Tywin had made himself greater than King Aerys, I heard one begging brother preach, but only a god is meant to stand above a king. You were his curse, a punishment sent by the gods to teach him that he was no better than any other man."

"I try, but he refuses to learn." Tyrion gave a sigh. "But do go on, I pray you. I love a good tale."

"And well you might, since you were said to have one, a

stiff curly tail like a swine's. Your head was monstrous huge, we heard, half again the size of your body, and you had been born with thick black hair and a beard besides, an evil eye, and lion's claws. Your teeth were so long you could not close your mouth, and between your legs were a girl's privates as well as a boy's."

"Life would be much simpler if men could fuck themselves, don't you agree? And I can think of a few times when claws and teeth might have proved useful. Even so, I begin to see the nature of your complaint."

Bronn gave out with a chuckle, but Oberyn only smiled. "We might never have seen you at all but for your sweet sister. You were never seen at table or hall, though sometimes at night we could hear a baby howling down in the depths of the Rock. You did have a monstrous great voice, I must grant you that. You would wail for hours, and nothing would quiet you but a woman's teat."

"Still true, as it happens."

This time Prince Oberyn did laugh. "A taste we share. Lord Gargalen once told me he hoped to die with a sword in his hand, to which I replied that I would sooner go with a breast in mine."

Tyrion had to grin. "You were speaking of my sister?"

"Cersei promised Elia to show you to us. The day before we were to sail, whilst my mother and your father were closeted together, she and Jaime took us down to your nursery. Your wet nurse tried to send us off, but your sister was having none of that. 'He's mine,' she said, 'and you're just a milk cow, you can't tell me what to do. Be quiet or I'll have my father cut your tongue out. A cow doesn't need a tongue, only udders.' "

"Her Grace learned charm at an early age," said Tyrion, amused by the notion of his sister claiming him as hers. "She's never been in any rush to claim me since, the gods know.

"Cersei even undid your swaddling clothes to give us a better look," the Dornish prince continued. "You did have one evil eye, and some black fuzz on your scalp. Perhaps your head was larger than most . . . but there was no tail, no beard, neither teeth nor claws, and nothing between your legs but a tiny pink cock. After all the wonderful whispers, Lord Tywin's Doom turned out to be just a hideous red infant with stunted legs. Elia even made the noise that young girls make at the sight of infants, I'm sure you've heard it. The same noise they make over cute kittens and playful puppies. I believe she wanted to nurse you herself, ugly as you were. When I commented that you seemed a poor sort of monster, your sister said, 'He killed my mother,' and twisted your little cock so hard I thought she was like to pull it off. You shrieked, but it was only when your brother Jaime said, 'Leave him be, you're hurting him,' that Cersei let go of you. 'It doesn't matter,' she told us. 'Everyone says he's like to die soon. He shouldn't even have lived this long.' "

The sun was shining bright above them, and the day was pleasantly warm for autumn, but Tyrion Lannister went cold all over when he heard that. *My sweet sister.* He scratched at the scar of his nose and gave the Dornishman a taste of his "evil eye." *Now why would he tell such a tale? Is he testing me, or simply twisting my cock as Cersei did, so he can hear me scream?* "Be sure and tell that story to my father. It will delight him as much as it did me. The part about my tail, especially. I did have one, but he had it lopped off."

Prince Oberyn had a chuckle. "You've grown more amusing since last we met."

"Yes, but I *meant* to grow taller."

"While we are speaking of amusement, I heard a curious tale from Lord Buckler's steward. He claimed that you had put a tax on women's privy purses."

"It is a tax on whoring," said Tyrion, irritated all over again. *And it was my bloody father's notion.* "Only a penny for each, ah . . . act. The King's Hand felt it might help improve the morals of the city." *And pay for Joffrey's wedding besides.* Needless to say, as master of coin, Tyrion had gotten all the blame for it. Bronn said they were calling it *the dwarf's penny* in the streets. "Spread your legs for the Halfman, now," they were shouting in the brothels and wine sinks, if the sellsword could be believed.

"I will make certain to keep my pouch full of pennies. Even a prince must pay his taxes."

"Why should you need to go whoring?" He glanced back to where Ellaria Sand rode among the other women. "Did you tire of your paramour on the road?"

"Never. We share too much." Prince Oberyn shrugged. "We have never shared a beautiful blonde woman, however, and Ellaria is curious. Do you know of such a creature?"

"I am a man wedded." *Though not yet bedded.* "I no longer frequent whores." *Unless I want to see them hanged.*

Oberyn abruptly changed the subject. "It's said there are to be seventy-seven dishes served at the king's wedding feast."

"Are you hungry, my prince?"

"I have hungered for a long time. Though not for food. Pray tell me, when will the *justice* be served?"

"*Justice.*" *Yes, that is why he's here, I should have seen that at once.* "You were close to your sister?"

"As children Elia and I were inseparable, much like your own brother and sister."

Gods, I hope not. "Wars and weddings have kept us well occupied, Prince Oberyn. I fear no one has yet had the time to look into murders sixteen years stale, dreadful as they were. We shall, of course, just as soon as we may. Any help that Dorne might be able to provide to restore the king's peace would only hasten the beginning of my lord father's inquiry—"

"Dwarf," said the Red Viper, in a tone grown markedly less cordial, "spare me your Lannister lies. Is it sheep you take us for, or fools? My brother is not a bloodthirsty man, but neither has he been asleep for sixteen years. Jon Arryn came to Sunspear the year after Robert took the throne, and you can be sure that he was questioned closely. Him, and a hundred more. I did not come for some mummer's show of an *inquiry*. I came for justice for Elia and her children, and I will have it. Starting with this lummox Gregor Clegane . . . but not, I think, ending there. Before he dies, the Enormity That Rides will tell me whence came his orders, please assure your lord father of that." He smiled. "An old septon once claimed I was living proof of the goodness of the gods. Do you know why that is, Imp?"

"No," Tyrion admitted warily.

"Why, if the gods were cruel, they would have made me my mother's firstborn, and Doran her third. I *am* a bloodthirsty man, you see. And it is me you must contend with now, not my patient, prudent, and gouty brother."

Tyrion could see the sun shining on the Blackwater Rush half a mile ahead, and on the walls and towers and hills of King's Landing beyond. He glanced over his shoulder, at the glittering column following them up the kingsroad. "You speak like a man with a great host at his back," he said, "yet all I see are three hundred. Do you spy that city there, north of the river?"

"The midden heap you call King's Landing?"

"That's the very one."

"Not only do I see it, I believe I smell it now."

"Then take a good sniff, my lord. Fill up your nose. Half a million people stink more than three hundred, you'll find. Do you smell the gold cloaks? There are near five thousand of them. My father's own sworn swords must account for another twenty thousand. And then there are the roses. Roses smell so sweet, don't they? Especially when there are so *many* of them. Fifty, sixty, seventy thousand roses, in the city or camped outside it, I can't really say how many are left, but there's more than I care to count, anyway."

Martell gave a shrug. "In Dorne of old before we married Daeron, it was said that all flowers bow before the sun. Should the roses seek to hinder me I'll gladly trample them underfoot."

"As you trampled Willas Tyrell?"

The Dornishman did not react as expected. "I had a letter from Willas not half a year past. We share an interest in fine horseflesh. He has never borne me any ill will for what happened in the lists. I struck his breastplate clean, but his foot caught in a stirrup as he fell and his horse came down on top of him. I sent a maester to him afterward, but it was all he could do to save the boy's leg. The knee was far past mending. If any were to blame, it was his fool of a father. Willas Tyrell was green as his surcoat and had no business riding in such company. The Fat Flower thrust him into tourneys at too tender an age, just as he did with the other two. He wanted another Leo Longthorn, and made himself a cripple."

"There are those who say Ser Loras is better than Leo Longthorn ever was," said Tyrion.

"Renly's little rose? I doubt that."

"Doubt it all you wish," said Tyrion, "but Ser Loras has defeated many good knights, including my brother Jaime."

"By *defeated*, you mean *unhorsed*, in tourney. Tell me who he's slain in battle if you mean to frighten me."

"Ser Robar Royce and Ser Emmon Cuy, for two. And men say he performed prodigious feats of valor on the Blackwater, fighting beside Lord Renly's ghost."

"So these same men who saw the prodigious feats saw the ghost as well, yes?" The Dornishman laughed lightly.

Tyrion gave him a long look. "Chataya's on the Street of Silk has several girls who might suit your needs. Dancy has hair the color of honey. Marie's is pale white-gold. I would advise you to keep one or the other by your side at all times, my lord."

"At all times?" Prince Oberyn lifted a thin black eyebrow. "And why is that, my good Imp?"

"You want to die with a breast in hand, you said." Tyrion cantered on ahead to where the ferry barges waited on the south bank of the Blackwater. He had suffered all he meant to suffer of what passed for Dornish wit. *Father should have sent Joffrey after all. He could have asked Prince Oberyn if he knew how a Dornishman differed from a cowflop.* That made him grin despite himself. He would have to make a point of being on hand when the Red Viper was presented to the king.

ARYA

The man on the roof was the first to die. He was crouched down by the chimney two hundred yards away, no more than a vague shadow in the predawn gloom, but as the sky began to lighten he stirred, stretched, and stood. Anguy's arrow took him in the chest. He tumbled bonelessly down the steep slate pitch, and fell in front of the septry door.

The Mummers had posted two guards there, but their torch left them night blind, and the outlaws had crept in close. Kyle and Notch let fly together. One man went down with an arrow through his throat, the other through his belly. The second man dropped the torch, and the flames licked up at him. He screamed as his clothes took fire, and that was the end of stealth. Thoros gave a shout, and the outlaws attacked in earnest.

Arya watched from atop her horse, on the crest of the wooded ridge that overlooked the septry, mill, brewhouse, and stables and the desolation of weeds, burnt trees, and mud that surrounded them. The trees were mostly bare now, and the few withered brown leaves that still clung to the branches did little to obstruct her view. Lord Beric had left Beardless Dick and Mudge to guard them. Arya hated being left behind like she was some stupid *child*, but at least Gendry had been kept back as well. She knew better than to try and argue. This was battle, and in battle you had to obey.

The eastern horizon glowed gold and pink, and overhead a half moon peeked out through low scuttling clouds. The wind blew cold, and Arya could hear the rush of water and the creak of the mill's great wooden waterwheel. There was a smell of rain in the dawn air, but no drops were falling yet. Flaming arrows flew through the morning mists, trailing pale ribbons of fire, and thudded into the wooden walls of the septry. A few smashed through shuttered windows, and soon enough thin tendrils of smoke were rising between the broken shutters.

Two Mummers came bursting from the septry side by side, axes in their hands. Anguy and the other archers were waiting. One axeman died at once. The other managed to duck, so the shaft ripped through his shoulder. He staggered on, till two more arrows found him, so quickly it was hard to say which had struck first. The long shafts punched through his breastplate as if it had been made of silk instead of steel. He fell heavily. Anguy had arrows tipped with bodkins as well as broadheads. A bodkin could pierce even heavy plate. *I'm going to learn to shoot a bow*, Arya thought. She loved swordfighting, but she could see how arrows were good too.

Flames were creeping up the west wall of the septry, and thick smoke poured through a broken window. A Myrish crossbowman poked his head out a different window, got off a bolt, and ducked down to rewind. She could hear fighting from the stables as well, shouts well mingled with the screams of horses and the clang of steel. *Kill them all*, she thought fiercely. She bit her lip so hard she tasted blood. *Kill every single one.*

The crossbowman appeared again, but no sooner had he loosed than three arrows hissed past his head. One rattled off his helm. He vanished, bow and all. Arya could see flames in several of the second-story windows. Between the smoke and the morning mists, the air was a haze of blowing black and white. Anguy and the other bowmen were creeping closer, the better to find targets.

Then the septry erupted, the Mummers boiling out like angry ants. Two Ibbenese rushed through the door with shaggy brown shields held high before them, and behind them came a Dothraki with a great curved *arakh* and bells in his braid, and behind him three Volantene sellswords covered with fierce tattoos. Others were climbing out windows and leaping to the ground. Arya saw a man take an arrow through the chest with one leg across a windowsill, and heard his scream as he fell. The smoke was thickening. Quarrels and arrows sped back and forth. Watty fell with a grunt, his bow slipping from his hand. Kyle was trying to nock another shaft to his string when a man in black mail flung a spear through his belly. She heard Lord Beric shout. From out of the ditches and trees the rest of his band came pouring, steel in hand. Arya saw Lem's bright yellow cloak flapping behind him as he rode down the man who'd killed Kyle. Thoros and Lord Beric were everywhere, their swords swirling fire. The red priest hacked at a hide shield until it flew to pieces, while his horse kicked the man in the face. A Dothraki screamed and charged the lightning lord, and the flaming sword leapt out to meet his *arakh*. The blades kissed and spun and kissed again. Then the Dothraki's hair was ablaze, and a moment later he was dead. She spied Ned too, fighting at the lightning lord's side. *It's not fair, he's only a little older than me, they should have let me fight.*

The battle did not last very long. The Brave Companions still on their feet soon died, or threw down their swords. Two of the Dothraki managed to regain their horses and flee, but only because Lord Beric let them go. "Let them carry the word back to Harrenhal," he said, with flaming sword in hand. "It will give the Leech Lord and his goat a few more sleepless nights."

Jack-Be-Lucky, Harwin, and Merrit o' Moontown braved the burning septry to search for captives. They emerged from the smoke and flames a few moments later with eight brown brothers, one so weak that Merrit had to carry him across a shoulder. There was a septon with them as well, round-shouldered and balding, but he wore black chain-mail over his grey robes. "Found him hiding under the cellar steps," said Jack, coughing.

Thoros smiled to see him. "You are Utt."

"*Septon* Utt. A man of god."

"What god would want the likes o' you?" growled Lem.

"I have sinned," the septon wailed. "I know, I know. Forgive me, Father. Oh, grievously have I sinned."

Arya remembered Septon Utt from her time at Harrenhal. Shagwell the Fool said he always wept and prayed for forgiveness after he'd killed his latest boy. Sometimes he even made the other Mummers scourge him. They all thought that was very funny.

Lord Beric slammed his sword into its scabbard, quenching the flames. "Give the dying the gift of mercy and bind the others hand and foot for trial," he commanded, and it was done.

The trials went swiftly. Various of the outlaws came forward to tell of things the Brave Companions had done; towns and villages sacked, crops burned, women raped and murdered, men maimed and tortured. A few spoke of the boys that Septon Utt had carried off. The septon wept and prayed through it all. "I am a weak reed," he told Lord Beric. "I pray to the Warrior for strength, but the gods made me weak. Have mercy on my weakness. The boys, the sweet boys . . . I never mean to hurt them . . ."

Septon Utt soon dangled beneath a tall elm, swinging slowly by the neck, as naked as his name day. The other Brave Companions followed one by one. A few fought, kicking and struggling as the noose was tightened round their throats. One of the crossbowmen kept shouting, "I soldier, I soldier," in a thick Myrish accent. Another offered to lead his captors to gold; a third told them what a good outlaw he would make. Each was stripped and bound and hanged in turn. Tom Sevenstrings played a dirge for them on his woodharp, and Thoros implored the Lord of Light to roast their souls until the end of time.

A mummer tree, Arya thought as she watched them dangle, their pale skins painted a sullen red by the flames of the burning septry. Already the crows were coming, appearing out of nowhere. She heard them croaking and cackling at one another, and wondered what they were saying. Arya had not feared Septon Utt as much as she did Rorge and Biter and some of the others still at Harrenhal, but she was glad that he was dead all the same. *They should have hanged the Hound too, or chopped his head off.* Instead, to her disgust, the outlaws had treated Sandor Clegane's burned arm, restored his sword and horse and armor, and set him free a few miles from the hollow hill. All they'd taken was his gold.

The septry soon collapsed in a roar of smoke and flame, its walls no longer able to support the weight of its heavy slate roof. The eight brown brothers watched with resignation. They were all that remained, explained the eldest, who wore a small iron hammer on a thong about his neck to signify his devotion to the Smith. "Before the war we were four-and-forty, and this was a prosperous place. We had a dozen milk cows and a bull, a hundred beehives, a vineyard and an apple arbor. But when the lions came through they took all our wine and milk and honey, slaughtered the cows, and put our vineyard to the torch. After that . . . I have lost count of our visitors. This false septon was only the latest. There was one monster . . . we gave him all our silver, but he was certain we were hiding gold, so his men killed us one by one to make Elder Brother talk."

"How did the eight of you survive?" asked Anguy the Archer.

"I am ashamed," the old man said. "It was me. When it came my turn to die, I told them where our gold was hidden."

"Brother," said Thoros of Myr, "the only shame was not telling them at once."

The outlaws sheltered that night in the brewhouse beside the little river. Their hosts had a cache of food hidden beneath the floor of the stables, so they shared a simple supper; oaten bread, onions, and a watery cabbage soup tasting faintly of garlic. Arya found a slice of carrot floating in her bowl, and counted herself lucky. The brothers never asked the outlaws for names. *They know,* Arya thought. How could they not? Lord Beric wore the lightning bolt on breastplate, shield, and cloak, and Thoros his red robes, or what remained of them. One brother, a young novice, was bold enough to tell the red priest not to pray to his false god so long as he was under their roof. "Bugger that," said Lem Lemoncloak. "He's our god too, and you owe us for your bloody lives. And what's false about him? Might be your Smith can mend a broken sword, but can he heal a broken man?"

"Enough, Lem," Lord Beric commanded. "Beneath their roof we will honor their rules."

"The sun will not cease to shine if we miss a prayer or two," Thoros agreed mildly. "I am one who would know."

Lord Beric himself did not eat. Arya had never seen him eat, though from time to time he took a cup of wine. He did not seem to sleep, either. His good eye would often close, as if from weariness, but when you spoke to him it would flick open again at once. The Marcher lord was still clad in his ratty black cloak and dented breastplate with its chipped enamel lightning. He even slept in that breastplate. The dull black steel hid the terrible wound the Hound had given him, the same way his thick woolen scarf concealed the dark ring about his throat. But nothing hid his broken head, all caved in at the temple, or the raw red pit that was his missing eye, or the shape of the skull beneath his face.

Arya looked at him warily, remembering all the tales told of him in Harrenhal. Lord Beric seemed to sense her fear. He turned his head, and beckoned her closer. "Do I frighten you, child?"

"No." She chewed her lip. "Only . . . well . . . I thought the Hound had killed you, but . . ."

"A wound," said Lem Lemoncloak. "A grievous wound, aye, but Thoros healed it. There's never been no better healer."

Lord Beric gazed at Lem with a queer look in his good eye and no look at all in the other, only scars and dried blood. "No better healer," he agreed wearily. "Lem, past time to change the watch, I'd think. See to it, if you'd be so good."

"Aye, m'lord." Lem's big yellow cloak swirled behind him as he strode out into the windy night.

"Even brave men blind themselves sometimes, when they are afraid to see," Lord Beric said when Lem was gone. "Thoros, how many times have you brought me back now?"

The red priest bowed his head. "It is R'hllor who brings you back, my lord. The Lord of Light. I am only his instrument."

"How many times?" Lord Beric insisted.

"Six," Thoros said reluctantly. "And each time is harder. You have grown reckless, my lord. Is death so very sweet?"

"Sweet? No, my friend. Not sweet."

"Then do not court it so. Lord Tywin leads from the rear. Lord Stannis as well. You would be wise to do the same. A seventh death might mean the end of both of us."

Lord Beric touched the spot above his left ear where his temple was caved in. "Here is where Ser Burton Crakehall broke helm and head with a blow of his mace." He unwound his scarf, exposing the black bruise that encircled his neck. "Here the mark the manticore made at Rushing Falls. He seized a poor beekeeper and his wife, thinking they were mine, and let it be known far and wide that he would hang them both unless I gave myself up to him. When I did he hanged them anyway, and me on the gibbet between them." He lifted a finger to the raw red pit of his eye. "Here is where the Mountain thrust his dirk through my visor." A weary smile brushed his lips. "That's thrice I have died at the hands of House Clegane. You would think that I might have learned . . ."

It was a jest, Arya knew, but Thoros did not laugh. He put a hand on Lord Beric's shoulder. "Best not to dwell on it."

"Can I dwell on what I scarce remember? I held a castle on the Marches once, and there was a woman I was pledged to marry, but I could not find that castle today, nor tell you the color of that woman's hair. Who knighted me, old friend? What were my favorite foods? It all fades. Sometimes I think I was born on the bloody grass in that grove of ash, with the taste of fire in my mouth and a hole in my chest. Are you my mother, Thoros?"

Arya stared at the Myrish priest, all shaggy hair and pink rags and bits of old armor. Grey stubble covered his cheeks and the sagging skin beneath his chin. He did not look much like the wizards in Old Nan's stories, but even so . . .

"Could you bring back a man without a head?" Arya asked. "Just the once, not six times. Could you?"

"I have no magic, child. Only prayers. That first time, his lordship had a hole right through him and blood in his mouth, I knew there was no hope. So when his poor torn chest stopped moving, I gave him the good god's own kiss to send him on his way. I filled my mouth with fire and breathed the flames inside him, down his throat to lungs and heart and soul. The *last kiss* it is called, and many a time I saw the old priests bestow it on the Lord's servants as they died. I had given it a time or two myself, as all priests must. But never before had I felt a dead man shudder as the fire filled him, nor seen his eyes come open. It was not me who raised him, my lady. It was the Lord. R'hllor is not done with him yet. Life is warmth, and warmth is fire, and fire is God's and God's alone."

Arya felt tears well in her eyes. Thoros used a lot of words, but all they meant was *no*, that much she understood.

"Your father was a good man," Lord Beric said. "Harwin has told me much of him. For his sake, I would gladly forgo your ransom, but we need the gold too desperately."

She chewed her lip. *That's true, I guess.* He had given the Hound's gold to Greenbeard and the Huntsman to buy provisions south of the Mander, she knew. "The last harvest burned, this one is drowning, and winter will soon be on us," she had heard him say when he sent them off. "The smallfolk need grain and seed, and we need blades and horses. Too many of my men ride rounseys, drays, and mules against foes mounted on coursers and destriers."

Arya didn't know how much Robb would pay for her, though. He was a king now, not the boy she'd left at Winterfell with snow melting in his hair. And if he knew the things she'd done, the stableboy and the guard at Harrenhal and all . . . "What if my brother doesn't want to ransom me?"

"Why would you think that?" asked Lord Beric.

"Well," Arya said, "my hair's messy and my nails are dirty and my feet are all hard." Robb wouldn't care about that, probably, but her mother would. Lady Catelyn always wanted her to be like Sansa, to sing and dance and sew and mind her courtesies. Just thinking of it made Arya try to comb her hair with her fingers, but it was all tangles and mats, and all she did was tear some out. "I ruined that gown that Lady Smallwood gave me, and I don't sew so good." She chewed her lip. "I don't sew *very well*, I mean. Septa Mordane used to say I had a blacksmith's hands."

Gendry hooted. "Those soft little things?" he called out. "You couldn't even hold a hammer."

"I could if I wanted!" she snapped at him.

Thoros chuckled. "Your brother will pay, child. Have no fear on that count."

"Yes, but what if he *won't?*" she insisted.

Lord Beric sighed. "Then I will send you to Lady Smallwood for a time, or perhaps to mine own castle of Blackhaven. But that will not be necessary, I'm certain. I do not have the power to give you back your father, no more than Thoros does, but I can at least see that you are returned safely to your mother's arms."

"Do you *swear?*" she asked him. Yoren had promised to take her home too, only he'd gotten killed instead.

"On my honor as a knight," the lightning lord said solemnly.

It was raining when Lem returned to the brewhouse, muttering curses as water ran off his yellow cloak to puddle on the floor. Anguy and Jack-Be-Lucky sat by the door rolling dice, but no matter which game they played one-eyed Jack had no luck at all. Tom Sevenstrings replaced a string on his woodharp, and sang "The Mother's Tears," "When Willum's Wife Was Wet," "Lord Harte Rode Out on a Rainy Day," and then "The Rains of Castamere."

> *And who are you, the proud lord said,*
> *that I must bow so low?*
> *Only a cat of a different coat,*
> *that's all the truth I know.*
> *In a coat of gold or a coat of red,*
> *a lion still has claws,*
> *And mine are long and sharp, my lord,*
> *as long and sharp as yours.*
> *And so he spoke, and so he spoke,*
> *that lord of Castamere,*
> *But now the rains weep o'er his hall,*
> *with no one there to hear.*
> *Yes now the rains weep o'er his hall,*
> *and not a soul to hear.*

Finally Tom ran out of rain songs and put away his harp. Then there was only the sound of the rain itself beating down on the slate roof of the brewhouse. The dice game ended, and Arya stood on one leg and then the other listening to Merrit complain about his horse throwing a shoe.

"I could shoe him for you," said Gendry, all of a sudden. "I was only a 'prentice, but my master said my hand was made to hold a hammer. I can shoe horses, close up rents in mail, and beat the dents from plate. I bet I could make swords too."

"What are you saying, lad?" asked Harwin.

"I'll smith for you." Gendry went to one knee before Lord Beric. "If you'll have me, m'lord, I could be of use. I've made tools and knives and once I made a helmet that wasn't so bad. One of the Mountain's men stole it from me when we was taken."

Arya bit her lip. *He means to leave me too.*

"You would do better serving Lord Tully at Riverrun," said Lord Beric. "I cannot pay for your work."

"No one ever did. I want a forge, and food to eat, some place I can sleep. That's enough, m'lord."

"A smith can find a welcome most anywhere. A skilled armorer even more so. Why would you choose to stay with us?"

Arya watched Gendry screw up his stupid face, thinking. "At the hollow hill, what you said about being King Robert's men, and brothers, I liked that. I liked that you gave the Hound a trial. Lord Bolton just hanged folk or took off their heads, and Lord Tywin and Ser Amory were the same. I'd sooner smith for you."

"We got plenty of mail needs mending, m'lord," Jack reminded Lord Beric. "Most we took off the dead, and there's holes where the death came through."

"You must be a lackwit, boy," said Lem. "We're *outlaws.* Lowborn scum, most of us, excepting his lordship. Don't think it'll be like Tom's fool songs neither. You won't be stealing no kisses from a princess, nor riding in no tourneys in stolen armor. You join us, you'll end with your neck in a noose, or your head mounted up above some castle gate."

"It's no more than they'd do for you," said Gendry.

"Aye, that's so," said Jack-Be-Lucky cheerfully. "The crows await us all. M'lord, the boy seems brave enough, and we do have need of what he brings us. Take him, says Jack."

"And quick," suggested Harwin, chuckling, "before the fever passes and he comes back to his senses."

A wan smile crossed Lord Beric's lips. "Thoros, my sword."

This time the lightning lord did not set the blade afire, but merely laid it light on Gendry's shoulder. "Gendry, do you swear before the eyes of gods and men to defend those who cannot defend themselves, to protect all women and children, to obey your captains, your liege lord, and your king, to fight bravely when needed and do such other tasks as are laid upon you, however hard or humble or dangerous they may be?"

"I do, m'lord."

The marcher lord moved the sword from the right shoulder to the left, and said, "Arise Ser Gendry, knight of the hollow hill, and be welcome to our brotherhood."

From the door came rough, rasping laughter.

The rain was running off him. His burned arm was wrapped in leaves and linen and bound tight against his chest by a crude rope sling, but the older burns that marked his face glistened black and slick in the glow of their little fire. "Making more knights, Dondarrion?" the intruder said in a growl. "I ought to kill you all over again for that."

Lord Beric faced him coolly. "I'd hoped we'd seen the last of you, Clegane. How did you come to find us?"

"It wasn't hard. You made enough bloody smoke to be seen in Oldtown."

"What's become of the sentries I posted?"

Clegane's mouth twitched. "Those two blind men? Might be I killed them both. What would you do if I had?"

Anguy strung his bow. Notch was doing the same. "Do you wish to die so very much, Sandor?" asked Thoros. "You must be mad or drunk to follow us here."

"Drunk on rain? You didn't leave me enough gold to buy a cup of wine, you whoresons."

Anguy drew an arrow. "We're outlaws. Outlaws steal. It's in the songs, if you ask nice Tom may sing you one. Be thankful we didn't kill you."

"Come try it, Archer. I'll take that quiver off you and shove those arrows up your freckly little arse."

Anguy raised his longbow, but Lord Beric lifted a hand before he could loose. "Why did you come here, Clegane?"

"To get back what's mine."

"Your gold?"

"What else? It wasn't for the pleasure of looking at your face, Dondarrion, I'll tell you that. You're uglier than me now. And a robber knight besides, it seems."

"I gave you a note for your gold," Lord Beric said calmly. "A promise to pay, when the war's done."

"I wiped my arse with your paper. I want the gold."

"We don't have it. I sent it south with Greenbeard and the Huntsman, to buy grain and seed across the Mander."

"To feed all them whose crops you burned," said Gendry.

"Is that the tale, now?" Sandor Clegane laughed again. "As it happens, that's just what I meant to do with it. Feed a bunch of ugly peasants and their poxy whelps."

"You're lying," said Gendry.

"The boy has a mouth on him, I see. Why believe them and not me? Couldn't be my face, could it?" Clegane glanced at Arya. "You going to make her a knight too, Dondarrion? The first eight-year-old girl knight?"

"I'm *twelve*," Arya lied loudly, "and I could be a knight if I wanted. I could have killed you too, only Lem took my knife." Remembering that still made her angry.

"Complain to Lem, not me. Then tuck your tail between your legs and run. Do you know what dogs do to wolves?"

"Next time I *will* kill you. I'll kill your brother too!"

"No." His dark eyes narrowed. "That you won't." He turned back to Lord Beric. "Say, make my horse a knight. He never shits in the hall and doesn't kick more than most, he deserves to be knighted. Unless you meant to steal him too."

"Best climb on that horse and go," warned Lem.

"I'll go with my gold. Your own god said I'm guiltless—"

"The Lord of Light gave you back your life," declared Thoros of Myr. "He did not proclaim you Baelor the Blessed come again." The red priest unsheathed his sword, and Arya saw that Jack and Merrit had drawn as well. Lord Beric still held the blade he'd used to dub Gendry. *Maybe this time they'll kill him.*

The Hound's mouth gave another twitch. "You're no more than common thieves."

Lem glowered. "Your lion friends ride into some village, take all the food and every coin they find, and call it *foraging*. The wolves as well, so why not us? No one robbed you, dog. You just been good and *foraged*."

Sandor Clegane looked at their faces, every one, as if he were trying to commit them all to memory. Then he walked back out into the darkness and the pouring rain from whence he'd come, with never another word. The outlaws waited, wondering . . .

"I best go see what he did to our sentries." Harwin took a wary look out the door before he left, to make certain the Hound was not lurking just outside.

"How'd that bloody bastard get all that gold anyhow?" Lem Lemoncloak said, to break the tension.

Anguy shrugged. "He won the Hand's tourney. In King's Landing." The bowman grinned. "I won a fair fortune myself, but then I met Dancy, Jayde, and Alayaya. They taught me what roast swan tastes like, and how to bathe in Arbor wine."

"Pissed it all away, did you?" laughed Harwin.

"Not *all*. I bought these boots, and this excellent dagger."

"You ought t'have bought some land and made one o' them roast swan girls an honest woman," said Jack-Be-Lucky. "Raised yourself a crop o' turnips and a crop o' sons."

"Warrior defend me! What a waste that would have been, to turn my gold to turnips."

"I like turnips," said Jack, aggrieved. "I could do with some mashed turnips right now."

Thoros of Myr paid no heed to the banter. "The Hound has lost more than a few bags of coin," he mused. "He has lost his master and kennel as well. He cannot go back to the Lannisters, the Young Wolf would never have him, nor would his brother be like to welcome him. That gold was all he had left, it seems to me."

"Bloody hell," said Watty the Miller. "He'll come murder us in our sleep for sure, then."

"No." Lord Beric had sheathed his sword. "Sandor Clegane would kill us all gladly, but not in our sleep.

Anguy, on the morrow, take the rear with Beardless Dick. If you see Clegane still sniffing after us, kill his horse."

"That's a good horse," Anguy protested.

"Aye," said Lem. "It's the bloody rider we should be killing. We could use that horse."

"I'm with Lem," Notch said. "Let me feather the dog a few times, discourage him some."

Lord Beric shook his head. "Clegane won his life beneath the hollow hill. I will not rob him of it."

"My lord is wise," Thoros told the others. "Brothers, a trial by battle is a holy thing. You heard me ask R'hllor to take a hand, and you saw his fiery finger snap Lord Beric's sword, just as he was about to make an end of it. The Lord of Light is not yet done with Joffrey's Hound, it would seem."

Harwin soon returned to the brewhouse. "Puddingfoot was sound asleep, but unharmed."

"Wait till I get hold of him," said Lem. "I'll cut him a new bunghole. He could have gotten every one of us killed."

No one rested very comfortably that night, knowing that Sandor Clegane was out there in the dark, somewhere close. Arya curled up near the fire, warm and snug, yet sleep would not come. She took out the coin that Jaqen H'ghar had given her and curled her fingers around it as she lay beneath her cloak. It made her feel strong to hold it, remembering how she'd seen the ghost in Harrenhal. She could kill with a whisper then.

Jaqen was gone, though. He'd left her. *Hot Pie left me too, and now Gendry is leaving.* Lommy had died, Yoren had died, Syrio Forel had died, even her father had died, and Jaqen had given her a stupid iron penny and vanished. "*Valar morghulis,*" she whispered softly, tightening her fist so the hard edges of the coin dug into her palm. "Ser Gregor, Dunsen, Polliver, Raff the Sweetling. The Tickler and the Hound. Ser Ilyn, Ser Meryn, King Joffrey, Queen Cersei." Arya tried to imagine how they would look when they were dead, but it was hard to bring their faces to mind. The Hound she could see, and his brother the Mountain, and she would never forget Joffrey's face, or his mother's . . . but Raff and Dunsen and Polliver were all fading, and even the Tickler, whose looks had been so commonplace.

Sleep took her at last, but in the black of night Arya woke again, tingling. The fire had burned down to embers. Mudge stood by the door, and another guard was pacing outside. The rain had stopped, and she could hear wolves howling. *So close*, she thought, *and so many*. They sounded as if they were all around the stable, dozens of them, maybe hundreds. *I hope they eat the Hound*. She remembered what he'd said, about wolves and dogs.

Come morning, Septon Utt still swung beneath the tree, but the brown brothers were out in the rain with spades, digging shallow graves for the other dead. Lord Beric thanked them for the night's lodging and the meal, and gave them a bag of silver stags to help rebuild. Harwin, Likely Luke, and Watty the Miller went out scouting, but neither wolves nor hounds were found.

As Arya was cinching her saddle girth, Gendry came up to say that he was sorry. She put a foot in the stirrup and swung up into her saddle, so she could look down on him instead of up. *You could have made swords at Riverrun for my brother*, she thought, but what she said was, "If you want to be some stupid outlaw knight and get hanged, why should I care? I'll be at Riverrun, ransomed, with my brother."

There was no rain that day, thankfully, and for once they made good time.

BRAN

The tower stood upon an island, its twin reflected on the still blue waters. When the wind blew, ripples moved across the surface of the lake, chasing one another like boys at play. Oak trees grew thick along the lakeshore, a dense stand of them with a litter of fallen acorns on the ground beneath. Beyond them was the village, or what remained of it.

It was the first village they had seen since leaving the foothills. Meera had scouted ahead to make certain there was no one lurking amongst the ruins. Sliding in and amongst oaks and apple trees with her net and spear in hand, she startled three red deer and sent them bounding away through the brush. Summer saw the flash of motion and was after them at once. Bran watched the direwolf lope off, and for a moment wanted nothing so much as to slip his skin and run with him, but Meera was waving for them to come ahead. Reluctantly, he turned away from Summer and urged Hodor on, into the village. Jojen walked with them.

The ground from here to the Wall was grasslands, Bran

knew; fallow fields and low rolling hills, high meadows and lowland bogs. It would be much easier going than the mountains behind, but so much open space made Meera uneasy. "I feel naked," she confessed. "There's no place to hide."

"Who holds this land?" Jojen asked Bran.

"The Night's Watch," he answered. "This is the Gift. The New Gift, and north of that Brandon's Gift." Maester Luwin had taught him the history. "Brandon the Builder gave all the land south of the Wall to the black brothers, to a distance of twenty-five leagues. For their . . . for their *sustenance and support*." He was proud that he still remembered that part. "Some maesters say it was some other Brandon, not the Builder, but it's still Brandon's Gift. Thousands of years later, Good Queen Alysanne visited the Wall on her dragon Silverwing, and she thought the Night's Watch was so brave that she had the Old King double the size of their lands, to fifty leagues. So that was the New Gift." He waved a hand. "Here. All this."

No one had lived in the village for long years, Bran could see. All the houses were falling down. Even the inn. It had never been *much* of an inn, to look at it, but now all that remained was a stone chimney and two cracked walls, set amongst a dozen apple trees. One was growing up through the common room, where a layer of wet brown leaves and rotting apples carpeted the floor. The air was thick with the smell of them, a cloying cidery scent that was almost overwhelming. Meera stabbed a few apples with her frog spear, trying to find some still good enough to eat, but they were all too brown and wormy.

It was a peaceful spot, still and tranquil and lovely to behold, but Bran thought there was something sad about an empty inn, and Hodor seemed to feel it too. "Hodor?" he said in a confused sort of way. "Hodor? Hodor?"

"This is good land." Jojen picked up a handful of dirt, rubbing it between his fingers. "A village, an inn, a stout holdfast in the lake, all these apple trees . . . but where are the people, Bran? Why would they leave such a place?"

"They were afraid of the wildlings," said Bran. "Wildlings come over the Wall or through the mountains, to raid and steal and carry off women. If they catch you, they make your skull into a cup to drink blood, Old Nan used to say. The Night's Watch isn't so strong as it was in Brandon's day or Queen Alysanne's, so more get through. The places nearest the Wall got raided so much the small-folk moved south, into the mountains or onto the Umber lands east of the kingsroad. The Greatjon's people get raided too, but not so much as the people who used to live in the Gift."

Jojen Reed turned his head slowly, listening to music only he could hear. "We need to shelter here. There's a storm coming. A bad one."

Bran looked up at the sky. It had been a beautiful crisp clear autumn day, sunny and almost warm, but there were dark clouds off to the west now, that was true, and the wind seemed to be picking up. "There's no roof on the inn and only the two walls," he pointed out. "We should go out to the holdfast."

"Hodor," said Hodor. Maybe he agreed.

"We have no boat, Bran." Meera poked through the leaves idly with her frog spear.

"There's a causeway. A stone causeway, hidden under the water. We could walk out." *They* could, anyway; he would have to ride on Hodor's back, but at least he'd stay dry that way.

The Reeds exchanged a look. "How do you know that?" asked Jojen. "Have you been here before, my prince?"

"No. Old Nan told me. The holdfast has a golden crown, see?" He pointed across the lake. You could see patches of flaking gold paint up around the crenellations. "Queen Alysanne slept there, so they painted the merlons gold in her honor."

"A causeway?" Jojen studied the lake. "You are certain?"

"Certain," said Bran.

Meera found the foot of it easily enough, once she knew to look; a stone pathway three feet wide, leading right out into the lake. She took them out step by careful step, probing ahead with her frog spear. They could see where the path emerged again, climbing from the water onto the is-land and turning into a short flight of stone steps that led to the holdfast door.

Path, steps, and door were in a straight line, which made you think the causeway ran straight, but that wasn't so.

Under the lake it zigged and zagged, going a third of a way around the island before jagging back. The turns were treacherous, and the long path meant that anyone approaching would be exposed to arrow fire from the tower for a long time. The hidden stones were slimy and slippery too; twice Hodor almost lost his footing and shouted *"HODOR!"* in alarm before regaining his balance. The second time scared Bran badly. If Hodor fell into the lake with him in his basket, he could well drown, especially if the huge stableboy panicked and forgot that Bran was there, the way he did sometimes. *Maybe we should have stayed at the inn, under the apple tree,* he thought, but by then it was too late.

Thankfully there was no third time, and the water never got up past Hodor's waist, though the Reeds were in it up to their chests. And before long they were on the island, climbing the steps to the holdfast. The door was still stout, though its heavy oak planks had warped over the years and it could no longer be closed completely. Meera shoved it open all the way, the rusted iron hinges screaming. The lintel was low. "Duck down, Hodor," Bran said, and he did, but not enough to keep Bran from hitting his head. "That hurt," he complained.

"Hodor," said Hodor, straightening.

They found themselves in a gloomy strongroom, barely large enough to hold the four of them. Steps built into the inner wall of the tower curved away upward to their left, downward to their right, behind iron grates. Bran looked up and saw another grate just above his head. *A murder hole.* He was glad there was no one up there now to pour boiling oil down on them.

The grates were locked, but the iron bars were red with rust. Hodor grabbed hold of the lefthand door and gave it a pull, grunting with effort. Nothing happened. He tried pushing with no more success. He shook the bars, kicked, shoved against them and rattled them and punched the hinges with a huge hand until the air was filled with flakes of rust, but the iron door would not budge. The one down to the undervault was no more accommodating. "No way in," said Meera, shrugging.

The murder hole was just above Bran's head, as he sat in his basket on Hodor's back. He reached up and grabbed the bars to give them a try. When he pulled down the grating came out of the ceiling in a cascade of rust and crumbling stone. *"HODOR!"* Hodor shouted. The heavy iron grate gave Bran another bang in the head, and crashed down near Jojen's feet when he shoved it off of him. Meera laughed. "Look at that, my prince," she said, "you're stronger than Hodor." Bran blushed.

With the grate gone, Hodor was able to boost Meera and Jojen up through the gaping murder hole. The crannogmen took Bran by the arms and drew him up after them. Getting Hodor inside was the hard part. He was too heavy for the Reeds to lift the way they'd lifted Bran. Finally Bran told him to go look for some big rocks. The island had no lack of those, and Hodor was able to pile them high enough to grab the crumbling edges of the hole and climb through. "Hodor," he panted happily, grinning at all of them.

They found themselves in a maze of small cells, dark and empty, but Meera explored until she found the way back to the steps. The higher they climbed, the better the light; on the third story the thick outer wall was pierced by arrow slits, the fourth had actual windows, and the fifth and highest was one big round chamber with arched doors on three sides opening onto small stone balconies. On the fourth side was a privy chamber perched above a sewer chute that dropped straight down into the lake.

By the time they reached the roof the sky was completely overcast, and the clouds to the west were black. The wind was blowing so strong it lifted up Bran's cloak and made it flap and snap. "Hodor," Hodor said at the noise.

Meera spun in a circle. "I feel almost a giant, standing high above the world."

"There are trees in the Neck that stand twice as tall as this," her brother reminded her.

"Aye, but they have other trees around them just as high," said Meera. "The world presses close in the Neck, and the sky is so much smaller. Here . . . feel that wind, Brother? And look how large the world has grown."

It was true, you could see a long ways from up here. To the south the foothills rose, with the mountains grey and green beyond them. The rolling plains of the New Gift stretched away to all the other directions, as far as the eye could see. "I was hoping we could see the Wall from here," said Bran, disappointed. "That was stupid, we must still be fifty leagues away." Just speaking of it made him feel tired, and cold as well. "Jojen, what will we do when we reach the Wall? My uncle always said how big it was. Seven hundred feet high, and so thick at the base that the gates are more like tunnels through the ice. How are we going to get past to find the three-eyed crow?"

"There are abandoned castles along the Wall, I've heard," Jojen answered. "Fortresses built by the Night's Watch but now left empty. One of them may give us our way through."

The ghost castles, Old Nan had called them. Maester Luwin had once made Bran learn the names of every one of the forts along the Wall. That had been hard; there were nineteen of them all told, though no more than seventeen had ever been manned at any one time. At the feast in honor of King Robert's visit to Winterfell, Bran had recited the names for his uncle Benjen, east to west and then west to east. Benjen Stark had laughed and said, "You know them better than I do, Bran. Perhaps you should be First Ranger. I'll stay here in your place." That was before Bran fell, though. Before he was broken. By the time he'd woken crippled from his sleep, his uncle had gone back to Castle Black.

"My uncle said the gates were sealed with ice and stone whenever a castle had to be abandoned," said Bran.

"Then we'll have to open them again," said Meera.

That made him uneasy. "We shouldn't do that. Bad things might come through from the other side. We should just go to Castle Black and tell the Lord Commander to let us pass."

"Your Grace," said Jojen, "we must avoid Castle Black, just as we avoided the kingsroad. There are hundreds of men there."

"Men of the Night's Watch," said Bran. "They say vows, to take no part in wars and stuff."

"Aye," said Jojen, "but one man willing to forswear himself would be enough to sell your secret to the ironmen or the Bastard of Bolton. And we cannot be certain that the Watch would agree to let us pass. They might decide to hold us or send us back."

"But my father was a friend of the Night's Watch, and my uncle is First Ranger. He might know where the three-eyed crow lives. And Jon's at Castle Black too." Bran had been hoping to see Jon again, and their uncle too. The last black brothers to visit Winterfell said that Benjen Stark had vanished on a ranging, but surely he would have made his way back by *now*. "I bet the Watch would even give us horses," he went on.

"Quiet." Jojen shaded his eyes with a hand and gazed off toward the setting sun. "Look. There's something . . . a rider, I think. Do you see him?"

Bran shaded his eyes as well, and even so he had to squint. He saw nothing at first, till some movement made him turn. At first he thought it might be Summer, but no. *A man on a horse.* He was too far away to see much else.

"Hodor?" Hodor had put a hand over his eyes as well, only he was looking the wrong way. "Hodor?"

"He is in no haste," said Meera, "but he's making for this village, it seems to me."

"We had best go inside, before we're seen," said Jojen.

"Summer's near the village," Bran objected.

"Summer will be fine," Meera promised. "It's only one man on a tired horse."

A few fat wet drops began to patter against the stone as they retreated to the floor below. That was well timed; the rain began to fall in earnest a short time later. Even through the thick walls they could hear it lashing against the surface of the lake. They sat on the floor in the round empty room, amidst gathering gloom. The north-facing balcony looked out toward the abandoned village. Meera crept out on her belly to peer across the lake and see what had become of the horseman. "He's taken shelter in the ruins of the inn," she told them when she came back. "It looks as though he's making a fire in the hearth."

"I wish we could have a fire," Bran said. "I'm cold. There's broken furniture down the stairs, I saw it. We could have Hodor chop it up and get warm."

Hodor liked that idea. "Hodor," he said hopefully.

Jojen shook his head. "Fire means smoke. Smoke from this tower could be seen a long way off."

"If there were anyone to see," his sister argued.

"There's a man in the village."

"One man."

"One man would be enough to betray Bran to his enemies, if he's the wrong man. We still have half a duck from
yesterday. We should eat and rest. Come morning the man
will go on his way, and we will do the same."

Jojen had his way; he always did. Meera divided the
duck between the four of them. She'd caught it in her net
the day before, as it tried to rise from the marsh where
she'd surprised it. It wasn't as tasty cold as it had been hot
and crisp from the spit, but at least they did not go hungry.
Bran and Meera shared the breast while Jojen ate the thigh.
Hodor devoured the wing and leg, muttering "Hodor" and
licking the grease off his fingers after every bite. It was
Bran's turn to tell a story, so he told them about another
Brandon Stark, the one called Brandon the Shipwright, who
had sailed off beyond the Sunset Sea.

Dusk was settling by the time duck and tale were done,
and the rain still fell. Bran wondered how far Summer had
roamed and whether he had caught one of the deer.

Grey gloom filled the tower, and slowly changed to
darkness. Hodor grew restless and walked awhile, striding
round and round the walls and stopping to peer into the
privy on every circuit, as if he had forgotten what was in
there. Jojen stood by the north balcony, hidden by the shadows, looking out at the night and the rain. Somewhere to
the north a lightning bolt crackled across the sky, brighten-
ing the inside of the tower for an instant. Hodor jumped
and made a frightened noise. Bran counted to eight, waiting
for the thunder. When it came, Hodor shouted, "*Hodor!*"

I hope Summer isn't scared too, Bran thought. The dogs
in Winterfell's kennels had always been spooked by thun-
derstorms, just like Hodor. *I should go see, to calm him . . .*

The lightning flashed again, and this time the thunder
came at six. "Hodor!" Hodor yelled again. "HODOR!
HODOR!" He snatched up his sword, as if to fight the
storm.

Jojen said, "Be quiet, Hodor. Bran, tell him not to shout.
Can you get the sword away from him, Meera?"

"I can try."

"Hodor, *hush*," said Bran. "Be quiet now. No more stupid hodoring. Sit down."

"Hodor?" He gave the longsword to Meera meekly enough, but his face was a mask of confusion.

Jojen turned back to the darkness, and they all heard him suck in his breath. "What is it?" Meera asked.

"Men in the village."

"The man we saw before?"

"Other men. Armed. I saw an axe, and spears as well." Jojen had never sounded so much like the boy he was. "I saw them when the lightning flashed, moving under the trees."

"How many?"

"Many and more. Too many to count."

"Mounted?"

"No."

"Hodor." Hodor sounded frightened. "Hodor. Hodor."

Bran felt a little scared himself, though he didn't want to say so in front of Meera. "What if they come out here?"

"They won't." She sat down beside him. "Why should they?"

"For shelter." Jojen's voice was grim. "Unless the storm lets up. Meera, could you go down and bar the door?"

"I couldn't even close it. The wood's too warped. They won't get past those iron gates, though."

"They might. They could break the lock, or the hinges. Or climb up through the murder hole as we did."

Lightning slashed the sky, and Hodor whimpered. Then a clap of thunder rolled across the lake. "HODOR!" he roared, clapping his hands over his ears and stumbling in a circle through the darkness. "HODOR! HODOR! HODOR!"

"NO!" Bran shouted back. "NO HODORING!"

It did no good. "HOOOODOR!" moaned Hodor. Meera tried to catch him and calm him, but he was too strong. He flung her aside with no more than a shrug. "HOOOOOO-DOOOOOOOR!" the stableboy screamed as lightning filled the sky again, and even Jojen was shouting now, shouting at Bran and Meera to shut him up.

"Be *quiet!*" Bran said in a shrill scared voice, reaching up uselessly for Hodor's leg as he crashed past, reaching, *reaching*.

Hodor staggered, and closed his mouth. He shook his head slowly from side to side, sank back to the floor, and sat crosslegged. When the thunder boomed, he scarcely seemed to hear it. The four of them sat in the dark tower, scarce daring to breathe.

"Bran, what did you do?" Meera whispered.

"Nothing." Bran shook his head. "I don't know." But he did. *I reached for him, the way I reach for Summer.* He had *been* Hodor for half a heartbeat. It scared him.

"Something is happening across the lake," said Jojen. "I thought I saw a man pointing at the tower."

I won't be afraid. He was the Prince of Winterfell, Eddard Stark's son, almost a man grown and a warg too, not some little baby boy like Rickon. *Summer would not be afraid.* "Most like they're just some Umbers," he said. "Or they could be Knotts or Norreys or Flints come down from the mountains, or even brothers from the Night's Watch. Were they wearing black cloaks, Jojen?"

"By night all cloaks are black, Your Grace. And the flash came and went too fast for me to tell what they were wearing."

Meera was wary. "If they were black brothers, they'd be mounted, wouldn't they?"

Bran had thought of something else. "It doesn't matter," he said confidently. "They couldn't get out to us even if they wanted. Not unless they had a boat, or knew about the causeway."

"The causeway!" Meera mussed Bran's hair and kissed him on the forehead. "Our sweet prince! He's right, Jojen, they won't know about the causeway. Even if they did they could never find the way across at night in the rain."

"The night will end, though. If they stay till morning . . ." Jojen left the rest unsaid. After a few moments he said, "They are feeding the fire the first man started." Lightning crashed through the sky, and light filled the tower and etched them all in shadow. Hodor rocked back and forth, humming.

Bran could feel Summer's fear in that bright instant. He closed two eyes and opened a third, and his boy's skin slipped off him like a cloak as he left the tower behind . . .

. . . and found himself out in the rain, his belly full of deer, cringing in the brush as the sky broke and boomed above him. The smell of rotten apples and wet leaves almost drowned the scent of man, but it was there. He heard the clink and slither of hardskin, saw men moving under the trees. A man with a stick blundered by, a skin pulled up over his head to make him blind and deaf. The wolf went wide around him, behind a dripping thornbush and beneath the bare branches of an apple tree. He could hear them talking, and there beneath the scents of rain and leaves and horse came the sharp red stench of fear . . .

JON

The ground was littered with pine needles and blown leaves, a carpet of green and brown still damp from the recent rains. It squished beneath their feet. Huge bare oaks, tall sentinels, and hosts of soldier pines stood all around them. On a hill above them was another roundtower, ancient and empty, thick green moss crawling up its side almost to the summit. "Who built that, all of stone like that?" Ygritte asked him. "Some king?"

"No. Just the men who used to live here."

"What happened to them?"

"They died or went away." Brandon's Gift had been farmed for thousands of years, but as the Watch dwindled there were fewer hands to plow the fields, tend the bees, and plant the orchards, so the wild had reclaimed many a field and hall. In the New Gift there had been villages and holdfasts whose taxes, rendered in goods and labor, helped feed and clothe the black brothers. But those were largely gone as well.

"They were fools to leave such a castle," said Ygritte.

"It's only a towerhouse. Some little lordling lived there

once, with his family and a few sworn men. When raiders came he would light a beacon from the roof. Winterfell has towers three times the size of that."

She looked as if she thought he was making that up. "How could men build so high, with no giants to lift the stones?"

In legend, Brandon the Builder *had* used giants to help raise Winterfell, but Jon did not want to confuse the issue. "Men can build a lot higher than this. In Oldtown there's a tower taller than the Wall." He could tell she did not believe him. *If I could show her Winterfell . . . give her a flower from the glass gardens, feast her in the Great Hall, and show her the stone kings on their thrones. We could bathe in the hot pools, and love beneath the heart tree while the old gods watched over us.*

The dream was sweet . . . but Winterfell would never be his to show. It belonged to his brother, the King in the North. He was a Snow, not a Stark. *Bastard, oathbreaker, and turncloak . . .*

"Might be after we could come back here, and live in that tower," she said. "Would you want that, Jon Snow? After?"

After. The word was a spear thrust. *After the war. After the conquest. After the wildlings break the Wall . . .*

His lord father had once talked about raising new lords and settling them in the abandoned holdfasts as a shield against wildlings. The plan would have required the Watch to yield back a large part of the Gift, but his uncle Benjen believed the Lord Commander could be won around, so long as the new lordlings paid taxes to Castle Black rather than Winterfell. "It is a dream for spring, though," Lord Eddard had said. "Even the promise of land will not lure men north with a winter coming on."

If winter had come and gone more quickly and spring had followed in its turn, I might have been chosen to hold one of these towers in my father's name. Lord Eddard was dead, however, his brother Benjen lost; the shield they dreamt together would never be forged. "This land belongs to the Watch," Jon said.

Her nostrils flared. "No one lives here."

"Your raiders drove them off."

"They were cowards, then. If they wanted the land they should have stayed and fought."

"Maybe they were tired of fighting. Tired of barring their doors every night and wondering if Rattleshirt or someone like him would break them down to carry off their wives. Tired of having their harvests stolen, and any valuables they might have. It's easier to move beyond the reach of raiders." *But if the Wall should fail, all the north will lie within the reach of raiders.*

"You know nothing, Jon Snow. Daughters are taken, not wives. *You're* the ones who steal. You took the whole world, and built the Wall t' keep the free folk out."

"Did we?" Sometimes Jon forgot how wild she was, and then she would remind him. "How did that happen?"

"The gods made the earth for all men t' share. Only when the kings come with their crowns and steel swords, they claimed it was all theirs. *My trees*, they said, *you can't eat them apples. My stream, you can't fish here. My wood, you're not t' hunt. My earth, my water, my castle, my daughter, keep your hands away or I'll chop 'em off, but maybe if you kneel t' me I'll let you have a sniff.* You call us thieves, but at least a thief has t' be brave and clever and quick. A kneeler only has t' kneel."

"Harma and the Bag of Bones don't come raiding for fish and apples. They steal swords and axes. Spices, silks, and furs. They grab every coin and ring and jeweled cup they can find, casks of wine in summer and casks of beef in winter, and they take women in any season and carry them off beyond the Wall."

"And what if they do? I'd sooner be stolen by a strong man than be given t' some weakling by my father."

"You say that, but how can you know? What if you were stolen by someone you hated?"

"He'd have t' be quick and cunning and brave t' steal *me*. So his sons would be strong and smart as well. Why would I hate such a man as that?"

"Maybe he never washes, so he smells as rank as a bear."

"Then I'd push him in a stream or throw a bucket o' water on him. Anyhow, men shouldn't smell sweet like flowers."

"What's wrong with flowers?"

"Nothing, for a bee. For bed I want one o' these." Ygritte made to grab the front of his breeches.

Jon caught her wrist. "What if the man who stole you drank too much?" he insisted. "What if he was brutal or cruel?" He tightened his grip to make a point. "What if he was stronger than you, and liked to beat you bloody?"

"I'd cut his throat while he slept. You know nothing, Jon Snow." Ygritte twisted like an eel and wrenched away from him.

I know one thing. I know that you are wildling to the bone. It was easy to forget that sometimes, when they were laughing together, or kissing. But then one of them would say something, or do something, and he would suddenly be reminded of the wall between their worlds.

"A man can own a woman or a man can own a knife," Ygritte told him, "but no man can own both. Every little girl learns that from her mother." She raised her chin defiantly and gave her thick red hair a shake. "And men can't own the land no more'n they can own the sea or the sky. You kneelers think you do, but Mance is going t' show you different."

It was a fine brave boast, but it rang hollow. Jon glanced back to make certain the Magnar was not in earshot. Errok, Big Boil, and Hempen Dan were walking a few yards behind them, but paying no attention. Big Boil was complaining of his arse. "Ygritte," he said in a low voice, "Mance cannot win this war."

"He can!" she insisted. "You know nothing, Jon Snow. You have never seen the free folk fight!"

Wildlings fought like heroes or demons, depending on who you talked to, but it came down to the same thing in the end. *They fight with reckless courage, every man out for glory.* "I don't doubt that you're all very brave, but when it comes to battle, discipline beats valor every time. In the end Mance will fail as all the Kings-beyond-the-Wall have failed before him. And when he does, you'll die. All of you."

Ygritte had looked so angry he thought she was about to strike him. "All of *us*," she said. "You too. You're no crow now, Jon Snow. I swore you weren't, so you better not be." She pushed him back against the trunk of a tree and kissed him, full on the lips right there in the midst of the ragged column. Jon heard Grigg the Goat urging her on. Someone else laughed. He kissed her back despite all that. When they finally broke apart, Ygritte was flushed. "You're mine," she whispered. "Mine, as I'm yours. And if we die, we die. All men must die, Jon Snow. But first we'll live."

"Yes." His voice was thick. "First we'll live."

She grinned at that, showing Jon the crooked teeth that he had somehow come to love. *Wildling to the bone,* he thought again, with a sick sad feeling in the pit of his stomach. He flexed the fingers of his sword hand, and wondered what Ygritte would do if she knew his heart. Would she betray him if he sat her down and told her that he was still Ned Stark's son and a man of the Night's Watch? He hoped not, but he dare not take that risk. Too many lives depended on his somehow reaching Castle Black before the Magnar . . . assuming he found a chance to escape the wildlings.

They had descended the south face of the Wall at Greyguard, abandoned for two hundred years. A section of the huge stone steps had collapsed a century before, but even so the descent was a good deal easier than the climb. From there Styr marched them deep into the Gift, to avoid the Watch's customary patrols. Grigg the Goat led them past the few inhabited villages that remained in these lands. Aside from a few scattered roundtowers poking the sky like stone fingers, they saw no sign of man. Through cold wet hills and windy plains they marched, unwatched, unseen.

You must not balk, whatever is asked of you, the Halfhand had said. *Ride with them, eat with them, fight with them, for as long as it takes.* He'd ridden many leagues and walked for more, had shared their bread and salt, and Ygritte's blankets as well, but still they did not trust him. Day and night the Thenns watched him, alert for any signs of betrayal. He could not get away, and soon it would be too late.

Fight with them, Qhorin had said, before he surrendered his own life to Longclaw . . . but it had not come to that, till now. *Once I shed a brother's blood I am lost. I cross the Wall for good then, and there is no crossing back.*

After each day's march the Magnar summoned him to ask shrewd sharp questions about Castle Black, its garrison and defenses. Jon lied where he dared and feigned ignorance a few times, but Grigg the Goat and Errok listened as well, and they knew enough to make Jon careful. Too blatant a lie would betray him.

But the truth was terrible. Castle Black had no defenses, but for the Wall itself. It lacked even wooden palisades or earthen dikes. The "castle" was nothing more than a cluster of towers and keeps, two-thirds of them falling into ruin. As for the garrison, the Old Bear had taken two hundred on his ranging. Had any returned? Jon could not know. Perhaps four hundred remained at the castle, but most of those were builders or stewards, not rangers.

The Thenns were hardened warriors, and more disciplined than the common run of wildling; no doubt that was why Mance had chosen them. The defenders of Castle Black would include blind Maester Aemon and his half-blind steward Clydas, one-armed Donal Noye, drunken Septon Cellador, Deaf Dick Follard, Three-Finger Hobb the cook, old Ser Wynton Stout, as well as Halder and Toad and Pyp and Albett and the rest of the boys who'd trained with Jon. And commanding them would be red-faced Bowen Marsh, the plump Lord Steward who had been made castellan in Lord Mormont's absence. Dolorous Edd sometimes called Marsh "the Old Pomegranate," which fit him just as well as "the Old Bear" fit Mormont. "He's the man you want in front when the foes are in the field," Edd would say in his usual dour voice. "He'll count them right up for you. A regular demon for counting, that one."

If the Magnar takes Castle Black unawares, it will be red slaughter, boys butchered in their beds before they know they are under attack. Jon had to warn them, but how? He was never sent out to forage or hunt, nor allowed to stand a watch alone. And he feared for Ygritte as well. He could not take her, but if he left her, would the Magnar make her answer for his treachery? *Two hearts that beat as one . . .*

They shared the same sleeping skins every night, and he went to sleep with her head against his chest and her red hair tickling his chin. The smell of her had become a part of him. Her crooked teeth, the feel of her breast when he cupped it in his hand, the taste of her mouth . . . they were his joy and his despair. Many a night he lay with Ygritte warm beside him, wondering if his lord father had felt this confused about his mother, whoever she had been. *Ygritte set the trap and Mance Rayder pushed me into it.*

Every day he spent among the wildlings made what he had to do that much harder. He was going to have to find some way to betray these men, and when he did they would die. He did not want their friendship, any more than he wanted Ygritte's love. And yet . . . the Thenns spoke the Old Tongue and seldom talked to Jon at all, but it was different with Jarl's raiders, the men who'd climbed the Wall. Jon was coming to know them despite himself: gaunt, quiet Errok and gregarious Grigg the Goat, the boys Quort and Bodger, Hempen Dan the ropemaker. The worst of the lot was Del, a horsefaced youth near Jon's own age, who would talk dreamily of this wildling girl he meant to steal. "She's lucky, like your Ygritte. She's kissed by fire."

Jon had to bite his tongue. He didn't want to know about Del's girl or Bodger's mother, the place by the sea that Henk the Helm came from, how Grigg yearned to visit the green men on the Isle of Faces, or the time a moose had chased Toefinger up a tree. He didn't want to hear about the boil on Big Boil's arse, how much ale Stone Thumbs could drink, or how Quort's little brother had begged him not to go with Jarl. Quort could not have been older than fourteen, though he'd already stolen himself a wife and had a child on the way. "Might be he'll be born in some castle," the boy boasted. "Born in a castle like a lord!" He was very taken with the "castles" they'd seen, by which he meant watchtowers.

Jon wondered where Ghost was now. Had he gone to Castle Black, or was he running with some wolfpack in the woods? He had no sense of the direwolf, not even in his dreams. It made him feel as if part of himself had been cut off. Even with Ygritte sleeping beside him, he felt alone. He did not want to die alone.

By that afternoon the trees had begun to thin, and they marched east over gently rolling plains. Grass rose waist high around them, and stands of wild wheat swayed gently when the wind came gusting, but for the most part the day was warm and bright. Toward sunset, however, clouds began to threaten in the west. They soon engulfed the orange sun, and Lenn foretold a bad storm coming. His mother was a woods witch, so all the raiders agreed he had a gift for foretelling the weather. "There's a village close," Grigg the Goat told the Magnar. "Two miles, three. We could shelter there." Styr agreed at once.

It was well past dark and the storm was raging by the time they reached the place. The village sat beside a lake, and had been so long abandoned that most of the houses had collapsed. Even the small timber inn that must once have been a welcome sight for travelers stood half-fallen and roofless. *We will find scant shelter here,* Jon thought gloomily. Whenever the lightning flashed he could see a stone roundtower rising from an island out in the lake, but without boats they had no way to reach it.

Errok and Del had crept ahead to scout the ruins, but Del was back almost at once. Styr halted the column and sent a dozen of his Thenns trotting forward, spears in hand. By then Jon had seen it too: the glimmer of a fire, reddening the chimney of the inn. *We are not alone.* Dread coiled inside him like a snake. He heard a horse neigh, and then shouts. *Ride with them, eat with them, fight with them,* Qhorin had said.

But the fighting was done. "There's only one of them," Errok said when he came back. "An old man with a horse."

The Magnar shouted commands in the Old Tongue and a score of his Thenns spread out to establish a perimeter around the village, whilst others went prowling through the houses to make certain no one else was hiding amongst the weeds and tumbled stones. The rest crowded into the roofless inn, jostling each other to get closer to the hearth. The broken branches the old man had been burning seemed to generate more smoke than heat, but any warmth was welcome on such a wild rainy night. Two of the Thenns had thrown the man to the ground and were going through his things. Another held his horse, while three more looted his saddlebags.

Jon walked away. A rotten apple squished beneath his heel. *Styr will kill him.* The Magnar had said as much at Greyguard; any kneelers they met were to be put to death at once, to make certain they could not raise the alarm. *Ride with them, eat with them, fight with them.* Did that mean he must stand mute and helpless while they slit an old man's throat?

Near the edge of the village, Jon came face-to-face with one of the guards Styr had posted. The Thenn growled something in the Old Tongue and pointed his spear back toward the inn. *Get back where you belong*, Jon guessed. *But where is that?*

He walked towards the water, and discovered an almost dry spot beneath the leaning daub-and-wattle wall of a tumbledown cottage that had mostly tumbled down. That was where Ygritte found him sitting, staring off across the rain-whipped lake. "I know this place," he told her when she sat beside him. "That tower . . . look at the top of it the next time the lightning flashes, and tell me what you see."

"Aye, if you like," she said, and then, "Some o' the Thenns are saying they heard noises out there. Shouting, they say."

"Thunder."

"They say shouting. Might be it's ghosts."

The holdfast did have a grim haunted look, standing there black against the storm on its rocky island with the rain lashing at the lake all around it. "We could go out and take a look," he suggested. "I doubt we could get much wetter than we are."

"Swimming? In the storm?" She laughed at the notion. "Is this a trick t' get the clothes off me, Jon Snow?"

"Do I need a trick for that now?" he teased. "Or is that you can't swim a stroke?" Jon was a strong swimmer himself, having learned the art as a boy in Winterfell's great moat.

Ygritte punched his arm. "You know nothing, Jon Snow. I'm half a fish, I'll have you know."

"Half fish, half goat, half horse . . . there's too many halves to you, Ygritte." He shook his head. "We wouldn't need to swim, if this is the place I think. We could walk."

She pulled back and gave him a look. "Walk on water? What southron sorcery is that?"

"No sorc—" he began, as a huge bolt of lightning stabbed down from the sky and touched the surface of the lake. For half a heartbeat the world was noonday bright. The clap of thunder was so loud that Ygritte gasped and covered her ears.

"Did you look?" Jon asked, as the sound rolled away and the night turned black again. "Did you see?"

"Yellow," she said. "Is that what you meant? Some o' them standing stones on top were yellow."

"We call them merlons. They were painted gold a long time ago. This is Queenscrown."

Across the lake, the tower was black again, a dim shape dimly seen. "A queen lived there?" asked Ygritte.

"A queen stayed there for a night." Old Nan had told him the story, but Maester Luwin had confirmed most of it. "Alysanne, the wife of King Jaehaerys the Conciliator. He's called the Old King because he reigned so long, but he was young when he first came to the Iron Throne. In those days, it was his wont to travel all over the realm. When he came to Winterfell, he brought his queen, six dragons, and half his court. The king had matters to discuss with his Warden of the North, and Alysanne grew bored, so she mounted her dragon Silverwing and flew north to see the Wall. This village was one of the places where she stopped. Afterward the smallfolk painted the top of their holdfast to look like the golden crown she'd worn when she spent the night among them."

"I have never seen a dragon."

"No one has. The last dragons died a hundred years ago or more. But this was before that."

"Queen Alysanne, you say?"

"Good Queen Alysanne, they called her later. One of the castles on the Wall was named for her as well. Queensgate. Before her visit they called it Snowgate."

"If she was so good, she should have torn that Wall down."

No, he thought. *The Wall protects the realm. From the Others . . . and from you and your kind as well, sweetling.* "I had another friend who dreamed of dragons. A dwarf. He told me—"

"*JON SNOW!*" One of the Thenns loomed above them, frowning. "Magnar wants." Jon thought it might have been the same man who'd found him outside the cave, the night before they climbed the Wall, but he could not be sure. He got to his feet. Ygritte came with him, which always made Styr frown, but whenever he tried to dismiss her she would remind him that she was a free woman, not a kneeler. She came and went as she pleased.

They found the Magnar standing beneath the tree that

grew through the floor of the common room. His captive knelt before the hearth, encircled by wooden spears and bronze swords. He watched Jon approach, but did not speak. The rain was running down the walls and pattering against the last few leaves that still clung to the tree, while smoke swirled thick from the fire.

"He must die," Styr the Magnar said. "Do it, crow."

The old man said no word. He only looked at Jon, standing amongst the wildlings. Amidst the rain and smoke, lit only by the fire, he could not have seen that Jon was all in black, but for his sheepskin cloak. *Or could he?*

Jon drew Longclaw from its sheath. Rain washed the steel, and the firelight traced a sullen orange line along the edge. *Such a small fire, to cost a man his life.* He remembered what Qhorin Halfhand had said when they spied the fire in the Skirling Pass. *Fire is life up here,* he told them, *but it can be death as well.* That was high in the Frostfangs, though, in the lawless wild beyond the Wall. This was the Gift, protected by the Night's Watch and the power of Winterfell. A man should have been free to build a fire here, without dying for it.

"Why do you hesitate?" Styr said. "Kill him, and be done."

Even then the captive did not speak. "Mercy," he might have said, or "You have taken my horse, my coin, my food, let me keep my life," or "No, please, I have done you no harm." He might have said a thousand things, or wept, or called upon his gods. No words would save him now, though. Perhaps he knew that. So he held his tongue, and looked at Jon in accusation and appeal.

You must not balk, whatever is asked of you. Ride with them, eat with them, fight with them . . . But this old man had offered no resistance. He had been unlucky, that was all. Who he was, where he came from, where he meant to go on his sorry sway-backed horse . . . none of it mattered.

He is an old man, Jon told himself. *Fifty, maybe even sixty. He lived a longer life than most. The Thenns will kill him anyway, nothing I can say or do will save him.* Longclaw seemed heavier than lead in his hand, too heavy to lift. The man kept staring at him, with eyes as big and black as wells. *I will fall into those eyes and drown.* The Magnar was looking at him too, and he could almost taste the mistrust. *The man is dead. What matter if it is my hand that slays him?* One cut would do it, quick and clean. Longclaw was forged of Valyrian steel. *Like Ice.* Jon remembered another killing; the deserter on his knees, his head rolling, the brightness of blood on snow . . . his father's sword, his father's words, his father's face . . .

"Do it, Jon Snow," Ygritte urged. "You must. T' prove you are no crow, but one o' the free folk."

"An old man sitting by a fire?"

"Orell was sitting by a fire too. You killed him quick enough." The look she gave him then was hard. "You meant t' kill me too, till you saw I was a woman. And I was asleep."

"That was different. You were soldiers . . . sentries."

"Aye, and you crows didn't want t' be seen. No more'n we do, now. It's just the same. Kill him."

He turned his back on the man. "No."

The Magnar moved closer, tall, cold, and dangerous. "I say yes. I command here."

"You command Thenns," Jon told him, "not free folk."

"I see no free folk. I see a crow and a crow wife."

"I'm no crow wife!" Ygritte snatched her knife from its sheath. Three quick strides, and she yanked the old man's head back by the hair and opened his throat from ear to ear. Even in death, the man did not cry out. "You know *nothing*, Jon Snow!" she shouted at him, and flung the bloody blade at his feet.

The Magnar said something in the Old Tongue. He might have been telling the Thenns to kill Jon where he stood, but he would never know the truth of that. Lightning crashed down from the sky, a searing blue-white bolt that touched the top of the tower in the lake. They could smell the fury of it, and when the thunder came it seemed to shake the night.

And death leapt down amongst them.

The lightning flash left Jon night-blind, but he glimpsed the hurtling shadow half a heartbeat before he heard the shriek. The first Thenn died as the old man had, blood gushing from his torn throat. Then the light was gone and the shape was spinning away, snarling, and another man went down in the dark. There were curses, shouts, howls of pain. Jon saw Big Boil stumble backward and knock down three men behind him. *Ghost,* he thought for one mad instant. *Ghost leapt the Wall.* Then the lightning turned the night to day, and he saw the wolf standing on Del's chest, blood running black from his jaws. *Grey. He's grey.*

Darkness descended with the thunderclap. The Thenns were jabbing with their spears as the wolf darted between them. The old man's mare reared, maddened by the smell of slaughter, and lashed out with her hooves. Longclaw was still in his hand. All at once Jon Snow knew he would never get a better chance.

He cut down the first man as he turned toward the wolf, shoved past a second, slashed at a third. Through the madness he heard someone call his name, but whether it was Ygritte or the Magnar he could not say. The Thenn fighting to control the horse never saw him. Longclaw was feather-light. He swung at the back of the man's calf, and felt the steel bite down to the bone. When the wildling fell the mare bolted, but somehow Jon managed to grab her mane with his off hand and vault himself onto her back. A hand closed round his ankle, and he hacked down and saw Bodger's face dissolve in a welter of blood. The horse reared, lashing out. One hoof caught a Thenn in the temple, with a *crunch.*

And then they were running. Jon made no effort to guide the horse. It was all he could do to stay on her as they plunged through mud and rain and thunder. Wet grass whipped at his face and a spear flew past his ear. *If the horse stumbles and breaks a leg, they will run me down and kill me,* he thought, but the old gods were with him and the horse did not stumble. Lightning shivered through the black dome of sky, and thunder rolled across the plains. The shouts dwindled and died behind him.

Long hours later, the rain stopped. Jon found himself alone in a sea of tall black grass. There was a deep throbbing ache in his right thigh. When he looked down, he was surprised to see an arrow jutting out the back of it. *When did that happen?* He grabbed hold of the shaft and gave it a tug, but the arrowhead was sunk deep in the meat of his leg, and the pain when he pulled on it was excruciating. He tried to think back on the madness at the inn, but all he could remember was the beast, gaunt and grey and terrible. *It was too large to be a common wolf. A direwolf, then. It had to be.* He had never seen an animal move so fast. *Like a grey wind . . .* Could Robb have returned to the north?

Jon shook his head. He had no answers. It was too hard to think . . . about the wolf, the old man, Ygritte, any of it . . .

Clumsily, he slid down off the mare's back. His wounded leg buckled under him, and he had to swallow a scream. *This is going to be agony.* The arrow had to come out, though, and nothing good could come of waiting. Jon curled his hand around the fletching, took a deep breath, and shoved the arrow forward. He grunted, then cursed. It hurt so much he had to stop. *I am bleeding like a butchered pig,* he thought, but there was nothing to be done for it until the arrow was out. He grimaced and tried again . . . and soon stopped again, trembling. *Once more.* This time he screamed, but when he was done the arrowhead was poking through the front of his thigh. Jon pushed back his bloody breeches to get a better grip, grimaced, and slowly drew the shaft through his leg. How he got through that without fainting he never knew.

He lay on the ground afterward, clutching his prize and bleeding quietly, too weak to move. After a while, he realized that if he did not *make* himself move he was like to bleed to death. Jon crawled to the shallow stream where the mare was drinking, washed his thigh in the cold water, and bound it tight with a strip of cloth torn from his cloak. He washed the arrow too, turning it in his hands. Was the fletching grey, or white? Ygritte fletched her arrows with pale grey goose feathers. *Did she loose a shaft at me as I fled?* Jon could not blame her for that. He wondered if she'd been aiming for him or the horse. If the mare had gone down, he would have been doomed. "A lucky thing my leg got in the way," he muttered.

He rested for a while to let the horse graze. She did not wander far. That was good. Hobbled with a bad leg, he could never have caught her. It was all he could do to force himself back to his feet and climb onto her back. *How did I ever mount her before, without saddle or stirrups, and a sword in one hand?* That was another question he could not answer.

Thunder rumbled softly in the distance, but above him the clouds were breaking up. Jon searched the sky until he found the Ice Dragon, then turned the mare north for the Wall and Castle Black. The throb of pain in his thigh muscle made him wince as he put his heels into the old man's horse. *I am going home,* he told himself. But if that was true, why did he feel so hollow?

He rode till dawn, while the stars stared down like eyes.

DAENERYS

Her Dothraki scouts had told her how it was, but Dany wanted to see for herself. Ser Jorah Mormont rode with her through a birchwood forest and up a slanting sandstone ridge. "Near enough," he warned her at the crest.

Dany reined in her mare and looked across the fields, to where the Yunkish host lay athwart her path. Whitebeard had been teaching her how best to count the numbers of a foe. "Five thousand," she said after a moment.

"I'd say so." Ser Jorah pointed. "Those are sellswords on the flanks. Lances and mounted bowmen, with swords and axes for the close work. The Second Sons on the left wing, the Stormcrows to the right. About five hundred men apiece. See the banners?"

Yunkai's harpy grasped a whip and iron collar in her talons instead of a length of chain. But the sellswords flew their own standards beneath those of the city they served: on the right four crows between crossed thunderbolts, on the left a broken sword. "The Yunkai's hold the center themselves," Dany noted. Their officers looked indistinguishable from Astapor's at a distance; tall bright helms and cloaks sewn with flashing copper disks. "Are those slave soldiers they lead?"

"In large part. But not the equal of Unsullied. Yunkai is known for training bed slaves, not warriors."

"What say you? Can we defeat this army?"

"Easily," Ser Jorah said.

"But not bloodlessly." Blood aplenty had soaked into the bricks of Astapor the day that city fell, though little of it belonged to her or hers. "We might win a battle here, but at such cost we cannot take the city."

"That is ever a risk, *Khaleesi*. Astapor was complacent and vulnerable. Yunkai is forewarned."

Dany considered. The slaver host seemed small compared to her own numbers, but the sellswords were ahorse. She'd ridden too long with Dothraki not to have a healthy respect for what mounted warriors could do to foot. *The Unsullied could withstand their charge, but my freedmen will be slaughtered.* "The slavers like to talk," she said. "Send word that I will hear them this evening in my tent. And invite the captains of the sellsword companies to call on me as well. But not together. The Stormcrows at midday, the Second Sons two hours later."

"As you wish," Ser Jorah said. "But if they do not come—"

"They'll come. They will be curious to see the dragons and hear what I might have to say, and the clever ones will see it for a chance to gauge my strength." She wheeled her silver mare about. "I'll await them in my pavilion."

Slate skies and brisk winds saw Dany back to her host. The deep ditch that would encircle her camp was already half dug, and the woods were full of Unsullied lopping branches off birch trees to sharpen into stakes. The eunuchs could not sleep in an unfortified camp, or so Grey Worm insisted. He was there watching the work. Dany halted a moment to speak with him. "Yunkai has girded up her loins for battle."

"This is good, Your Grace. These ones thirst for blood."

When she had commanded the Unsullied to choose officers from amongst themselves, Grey Worm had been their overwhelming choice for the highest rank. Dany had put Ser Jorah over him to train him for command, and the exile knight said that so far the young eunuch was hard but fair, quick to learn, tireless, and utterly unrelenting in his attention to detail.

"The Wise Masters have assembled a slave army to meet us."

"A slave in Yunkai learns the way of seven sighs and the sixteen seats of pleasure, Your Grace. The Unsullied learn the way of the three spears. Your Grey Worm hopes to show you."

One of the first things Dany had done after the fall of Astapor was abolish the custom of giving the Unsullied new slave names every day. Most of those born free had returned to their birth names; those who still remembered them, at least. Others had called themselves after heroes or gods, and sometimes weapons, gems, and even flowers, which resulted in soldiers with some very peculiar names, to Dany's ears. Grey Worm had remained Grey Worm. When she asked him why, he said, "It is a lucky name. The name this one was born to was accursed. That was the name he had when he was taken for a slave. But Grey Worm is the name this one drew the day Daenerys Stormborn set him free."

"If battle is joined, let Grey Worm show wisdom as well as valor," Dany told him. "Spare any slave who runs or throws down his weapon. The fewer slain, the more remain to join us after."

"This one will remember."

"I know he will. Be at my tent by midday. I want you there with my other officers when I treat with the sellsword captains." Dany spurred her silver on to camp.

Within the perimeter the Unsullied had established, the tents were going up in orderly rows, with her own tall golden pavilion at the center. A second encampment lay close beyond her own; five times the size, sprawling and chaotic, this second camp had no ditches, no tents, no sentries, no horselines. Those who had horses or mules slept beside them, for fear they might be stolen. Goats, sheep, and half-starved dogs wandered freely amongst hordes of women, children, and old men. Dany had left Astapor in the hands of a council of former slaves led by a healer, a scholar, and a priest. Wise men all, she thought, and just. Yet even so, tens of thousands preferred to follow her to

Yunkai, rather than remain behind in Astapor. *I gave them the city, and most of them were too frightened to take it.*

The raggle-taggle host of freedmen dwarfed her own, but they were more burden than benefit. Perhaps one in a hundred had a donkey, a camel, or an ox; most carried weapons looted from some slaver's armory, but only one in ten was strong enough to fight, and none was trained. They ate the land bare as they passed, like locusts in sandals. Yet Dany could not bring herself to abandon them as Ser Jorah and her bloodriders urged. *I told them they were free. I cannot tell them now they are not free to join me.* She gazed at the smoke rising from their cookfires and swallowed a sigh. She might have the best footsoldiers in the world, but she also had the worst.

Arstan Whitebeard stood outside the entrance of her tent, while Strong Belwas sat crosslegged on the grass nearby, eating a bowl of figs. On the march, the duty of guarding her fell upon their shoulders. She had made Jhogo, Aggo, and Rakharo her *kos* as well as her bloodriders, and just now she needed them more to command her Dothraki than to protect her person. Her *khalasar* was tiny, some thirty-odd mounted warriors, and most of them braidless boys and bentback old men. Yet they were all the horse she had, and she dared not go without them. The Unsullied might be the finest infantry in all the world, as Ser Jorah claimed, but she needed scouts and outriders as well.

"Yunkai will have war," Dany told Whitebeard inside the pavilion. Irri and Jhiqui had covered the floor with carpets while Missandei lit a stick of incense to sweeten the dusty air. Drogon and Rhaegal were asleep atop some cushions, curled about each other, but Viserion perched on the edge of her empty bath. "Missandei, what language will these Yunkai'i speak, Valyrian?"

"Yes, Your Grace," the child said. "A different dialect than Astapor's, yet close enough to understand. The slavers name themselves the Wise Masters."

"Wise?" Dany sat crosslegged on a cushion, and Viserion spread his white-and-gold wings and flapped to her side. "We shall see how wise they are," she said as she scratched the dragon's scaly head behind the horns.

Ser Jorah Mormont returned an hour later, accompanied by three captains of the Stormcrows. They wore black feathers on their polished helms, and claimed to be all equal in honor and authority. Dany studied them as Irri and Jhiqui poured the wine. Prendahl na Ghezn was a thickset Ghiscari with a broad face and dark hair going grey; Sallor the Bald had a twisting scar across his pale Qartheen cheek; and Daario Naharis was flamboyant even for a Tyroshi. His beard was cut into three prongs and dyed blue, the same color as his eyes and the curly hair that fell to his collar. His pointed mustachios were painted gold. His clothes were all shades of yellow; a foam of Myrish lace the color of butter spilled from his collar and cuffs, his doublet was sewn with brass medallions in the shape of dandelions, and ornamental goldwork crawled up his high leather boots to his thighs. Gloves of soft yellow suede were tucked into a belt of gilded rings, and his fingernails were enameled blue.

But it was Prendahl na Ghezn who spoke for the sellswords. "You would do well to take your rabble elsewhere," he said. "You took Astapor by treachery, but Yunkai shall not fall so easily."

"Five hundred of your Stormcrows against ten thousand of my Unsullied," said Dany. "I am only a young girl and do not understand the ways of war, yet these odds seem poor to me."

"The Stormcrows do not stand alone," said Prendahl.

"Stormcrows do not stand at all. They fly, at the first sign of thunder. Perhaps you should be flying now. I have heard that sellswords are notoriously unfaithful. What will it avail you to be staunch, when the Second Sons change sides?"

"That will not happen," Prendahl insisted, unmoved. "And if it did, it would not matter. The Second Sons are nothing. We fight beside the stalwart men of Yunkai."

"You fight beside bed-boys armed with spears." When she turned her head, the twin bells in her braid rang softly. "Once battle is joined, do not think to ask for quarter. Join me now, however, and you shall keep the gold the Yunkai'i paid you and claim a share of the plunder besides, with greater rewards later when I come into my kingdom. Fight for the Wise Masters, and your wages will be death. Do you imagine that Yunkai will open its gates when my Unsullied are butchering you beneath the walls?"

"Woman, you bray like an ass, and make no more sense."

"*Woman?*" She chuckled. "Is that meant to insult me? I would return the slap, if I took you for a man." Dany met his stare. "I am Daenerys Stormborn of House Targaryen, the Unburnt, Mother of Dragons, *khaleesi* to Drogo's riders, and queen of the Seven Kingdoms of Westeros."

"What you are," said Prendahl na Ghezn, "is a horselord's whore. When we break you, I will breed you to my stallion."

Strong Belwas drew his *arakh*. "Strong Belwas will give his ugly tongue to the little queen, if she likes."

"No, Belwas. I have given these men my safe conduct." She smiled. "Tell me this—are the Stormcrows slave or free?"

"We are a brotherhood of free men," Sallor declared.

"Good." Dany stood. "Go back and tell your brothers what I said, then. It may be that some of them would sooner sup on gold and glory than on death. I shall want your answer on the morrow."

The Stormcrow captains rose in unison. "Our answer is no," said Prendahl na Ghezn. His fellows followed him out of the tent . . . but Daario Naharis glanced back as he left, and inclined his head in polite farewell.

Two hours later the commander of the Second Sons arrived alone. He proved to be a towering Braavosi with pale green eyes and a bushy red-gold beard that reached nearly to his belt. His name was Mero, but he called himself the Titan's Bastard.

Mero tossed down his wine straightaway, wiped his mouth with the back of his hand, and leered at Dany. "I believe I fucked your twin sister in a pleasure house back home. Or was it you?"

"I think not. I would remember a man of such magnificence, I have no doubt."

"Yes, that is so. No woman has ever forgotten the Titan's Bastard." The Braavosi held out his cup to Jhiqui. "What say you take those clothes off and come sit on my lap? If you please me, I might bring the Second Sons over to your side."

"If you bring the Second Sons over to my side, I might not have you gelded."

The big man laughed. "Little girl, another woman once tried to geld me with her teeth. She has no teeth now, but my sword is as long and thick as ever. Shall I take it out and show you?"

"No need. After my eunuchs cut it off, I can examine it at my leisure." Dany took a sip of wine. "It is true that I am only a young girl, and do not know the ways of war. Explain to me how you propose to defeat ten thousand Unsullied with your five hundred. Innocent as I am, these odds seem poor to me."

"The Second Sons have faced worse odds and won."

"The Second Sons have faced worse odds and run. At Qohor, when the Three Thousand made their stand. Or do you deny it?"

"That was many and more years ago, before the Second Sons were led by the Titan's Bastard."

"So it is from you they get their courage?" Dany turned to Ser Jorah. "When the battle is joined, kill this one first."

The exile knight smiled. "Gladly, Your Grace."

"Of course," she said to Mero, "you could run again. We will not stop you. Take your Yunkish gold and go."

"Had you ever seen the Titan of Braavos, foolish girl, you would know that it has no tail to turn."

"Then stay, and fight for me."

"You are worth fighting for, it is true," the Braavosi said, "and I would gladly let you kiss my sword, if I were free. But I have taken Yunkai's coin and pledged my holy word."

"Coins can be returned," she said. "I will pay you as much and more. I have other cities to conquer, and a whole kingdom awaiting me half a world away. Serve me faithfully, and the Second Sons need never seek hire again."

The Braavosi tugged on his thick red beard. "As much and more, and perhaps a kiss besides, eh? Or more than a kiss? For a man as magnificent as me?"

"Perhaps."

"I will like the taste of your tongue, I think."

She could sense Ser Jorah's anger. *My black bear does not like this talk of kissing.* "Think on what I've said tonight. Can I have your answer on the morrow?"

"You can." The Titan's Bastard grinned. "Can I have a flagon of this fine wine to take back to my captains?"

"You may have a tun. It is from the cellars of the Good Masters of Astapor, and I have wagons full of it."

"Then give me a wagon. A token of your good regard."

"You have a big thirst."

"I am big all over. And I have many brothers. The Titan's Bastard does not drink alone, *Khaleesi*."

"A wagon it is, if you promise to drink to my health."

"Done!" he boomed. "And done, and done! Three toasts we'll drink you, and bring you an answer when the sun comes up."

But when Mero was gone, Arstan Whitebeard said, "That one has an evil reputation, even in Westeros. Do not be misled by his manner, Your Grace. He will drink three toasts to your health tonight, and rape you on the morrow."

"The old man's right for once," Ser Jorah said. "The Second Sons are an old company, and not without valor, but under Mero they've turned near as bad as the Brave Companions. The man is as dangerous to his employers as to his foes. That's why you find him out here. None of the Free Cities will hire him any longer."

"It is not his reputation that I want, it's his five hundred horse. What of the Stormcrows, is there any hope there?"

"No," Ser Jorah said bluntly. "That Prendahl is Ghiscari by blood. Likely he had kin in Astapor."

"A pity. Well, perhaps we will not need to fight. Let us wait and hear what the Yunkai'i have to say."

The envoys from Yunkai arrived as the sun was going down; fifty men on magnificent black horses and one on a great white camel. Their helms were twice as tall as their heads, so as not to crush the bizarre twists and towers and shapes of their oiled hair beneath. They dyed their linen skirts and tunics a deep yellow, and sewed copper disks to their cloaks.

The man on the white camel named himself Grazdan mo Eraz. Lean and hard, he had a white smile such as Kraznys had worn until Drogon burned off his face. His hair was drawn up in a unicorn's horn that jutted from his brow, and his *tokar* was fringed with golden Myrish lace. "Ancient and glorious is Yunkai, the queen of cities," he said when Dany welcomed him to her tent. "Our walls are strong, our nobles proud and fierce, our common folk without fear. Ours is the blood of ancient Ghis, whose empire was old when Valyria was yet a squalling child. You were wise to sit and speak, *Khaleesi*. You shall find no easy conquest here."

"Good. My Unsullied will relish a bit of a fight." She looked to Grey Worm, who nodded.

Grazdan shrugged expansively. "If blood is what you wish, let it flow. I am told you have freed your eunuchs. Freedom means as much to an Unsullied as a hat to a haddock." He smiled at Grey Worm, but the eunuch might have been made of stone. "Those who survive we shall enslave again, and use to retake Astapor from the rabble. We can make a slave of you as well, do not doubt it. There are pleasure houses in Lys and Tyrosh where men would pay handsomely to bed the last Targaryen."

"It is good to see you know who I am," said Dany mildly.

"I pride myself on my knowledge of the savage senseless west." Grazdan spread his hands, a gesture of conciliation. "And yet, why should we speak thus harshly to one another? It is true that you committed savageries in Astapor, but we Yunkai'i are a most forgiving people. Your quarrel is not with us, Your Grace. Why squander your strength against our mighty walls when you will need every man to regain your father's throne in far Westeros? Yunkai wishes you only well in that endeavor. And to prove the truth of that, I have brought you a gift." He clapped his hands, and two of his escort came forward bearing a heavy cedar chest bound in bronze and gold. They set it at her feet. "Fifty thousand golden marks," Grazdan said smoothly. "Yours, as a gesture of friendship from the Wise Masters of Yunkai. Gold given freely is better than plunder bought with blood, surely? So I say to you, Daenerys Targaryen, take this chest, and go."

Dany pushed open the lid of the chest with a small slippered foot. It was full of gold coins, just as the envoy said. She grabbed a handful and let them run through her fingers. They shone brightly as they tumbled and fell; new minted, most of them, stamped with a stepped pyramid on one face and the harpy of Ghis on the other. "Very pretty. I wonder how many chests like this I shall find when I take your city?"

He chuckled. "None, for that you shall never do."

"I have a gift for you as well." She slammed the chest shut. "Three days. On the morning of the third day, send out your slaves. All of them. Every man, woman, and child shall be given a weapon, and as much food, clothing, coin, and goods as he or she can carry. These they shall be allowed to choose freely from among their masters' possessions, as payment for their years of servitude. When all the slaves have departed, you will open your gates and allow my Unsullied to enter and search your city, to make certain none remain in bondage. If you do this, Yunkai will not be burned or plundered, and none of your people shall be molested. The Wise Masters will have the peace they desire, and will have proved themselves wise indeed. What say you?"

"I say, you are mad."

"Am I?" Dany shrugged, and said, "*Dracarys.*"

The dragons answered. Rhaegal *hissed* and smoked, Viserion snapped, and Drogon spat swirling red-black flame. It touched the drape of Grazdan's *tokar*, and the silk caught in half a heartbeat. Golden marks spilled across the carpets as the envoy stumbled over the chest, shouting curses and beating at his arm until Whitebeard flung a flagon of water over him to douse the flames. "You swore I should have safe conduct!" the Yunkish envoy wailed.

"Do all the Yunkai'i whine so over a singed *tokar*? I shall buy you a new one . . . if you deliver up your slaves within three days. Elsewise, Drogon shall give you a warmer kiss." She wrinkled her nose. "You've soiled yourself. Take your gold and go, and see that the Wise Masters hear my message."

Grazdan mo Eraz pointed a finger. "You shall rue this arrogance, whore. These little lizards will not keep you safe, I promise you. We will fill the air with arrows if they come within a league of Yunkai. Do you think it is so hard to kill a dragon?"

"Harder than to kill a slaver. Three days, Grazdan. Tell them. By the end of the third day, I will be in Yunkai, whether you open your gates for me or no."

Full dark had fallen by the time the Yunkai'i departed from her camp. It promised to be a gloomy night; moonless, starless, with a chill wet wind blowing from the west. *A fine black night*, thought Dany. The fires burned all around her, small orange stars strewn across hill and field. "Ser Jorah," she said, "summon my bloodriders." Dany seated herself on a mound of cushions to await them, her dragons all about her. When they were assembled, she said, "An hour past midnight should be time enough."

"Yes, *Khaleesi*," said Rakharo. "Time for what?"

"To mount our attack."

Ser Jorah Mormont scowled. "You told the sell-swords—"

"—that I wanted their answers on the morrow. I made no promises about tonight. The Stormcrows will be arguing about my offer. The Second Sons will be drunk on the wine I gave Mero. And the Yunkai'i believe they have three days. We will take them under cover of this darkness."

"They will have scouts watching for us."

"And in the dark, they will see hundreds of campfires burning," said Dany. "If they see anything at all."

"*Khaleesi*," said Jhogo, "I will deal with these scouts. They are no riders, only slavers on horses."

"Just so," she agreed. "I think we should attack from three sides. Grey Worm, your Unsullied shall strike at them from right and left, while my *kos* lead my horse in wedge for a thrust through their center. Slave soldiers will never stand before mounted Dothraki." She smiled. "To be sure, I am only a young girl and know little of war. What do you think, my lords?"

"I think you are Rhaegar Targaryen's sister," Ser Jorah said with a rueful half smile.

"Aye," said Arstan Whitebeard, "and a queen as well."

It took an hour to work out all the details. *Now begins the most dangerous time*, Dany thought as her captains departed to their commands. She could only pray that the gloom of the night would hide her preparations from the foe.

Near midnight, she got a scare when Ser Jorah bulled his way past Strong Belwas. "The Unsullied caught one of the sellswords trying to sneak into the camp."

"A spy?" That frightened her. If they'd caught one, how many others might have gotten away?

"He claims to come bearing gifts. It's the yellow fool with the blue hair."

Daario Naharis. "That one. I'll hear him, then."

When the exile knight delivered him, she asked herself whether two men had ever been so different. The Tyroshi was fair where Ser Jorah was swarthy; lithe where the knight was brawny; graced with flowing locks where the other was balding, yet smooth-skinned where Mormont was hairy. And her knight dressed plainly while this other made a peacock look drab, though he had thrown a heavy black cloak over his bright yellow finery for this visit. He carried a heavy canvas sack slung over one shoulder.

"*Khaleesi,*" he cried, "I bring gifts and glad tidings. The Stormcrows are yours." A golden tooth gleamed in his mouth when he smiled. "And so is Daario Naharis!"

Dany was dubious. If this Tyroshi had come to spy, this declaration might be no more than a desperate plot to save his head. "What do Prendahl na Ghezn and Sallor say of this?"

"Little." Daario upended the sack, and the heads of Sallor the Bald and Prendahl na Ghezn spilled out upon her carpets. "My gifts to the dragon queen."

Viserion sniffed the blood leaking from Prendahl's neck, and let loose a gout of flame that took the dead man full in the face, blackening and blistering his bloodless cheeks. Drogon and Rhaegal stirred at the smell of roasted meat.

"You did this?" Dany asked queasily.

"None other." If her dragons discomfited Daario Naharis, he hid it well. For all the mind he paid them, they might have been three kittens playing with a mouse.

"Why?"

"Because you are so beautiful." His hands were large and strong, and there was something in his hard blue eyes and great curving nose that suggested the fierceness of some splendid bird of prey. "Prendahl talked too much and said too little." His garb, rich as it was, had seen hard wear; salt stains patterned his boots, the enamel of his nails was chipped, his lace was soiled by sweat, and she could see where the end of his cloak was fraying. "And Sallor picked his nose as if his snot was gold." He stood with his hands crossed at the wrists, his palms resting on the pommels of his blades; a curving Dothraki *arakh* on his left hip, a Myrish stiletto on his right. Their hilts were a matched pair of golden women, naked and wanton.

"Are you skilled in the use of those handsome blades?" Dany asked him.

"Prendahl and Sallor would tell you so, if dead men could talk. I count no day as lived unless I have loved a woman, slain a foeman, and eaten a fine meal . . . and the days that I have lived are as numberless as the stars in the sky. I make of slaughter a thing of beauty, and many a tumbler and fire dancer has wept to the gods that they might be half so quick, a quarter so graceful. I would tell you the names of all the men I have slain, but before I could finish your dragons would grow large as castles, the walls of Yunkai would crumble into yellow dust, and winter would come and go and come again."

Dany laughed. She liked the swagger she saw in this Daario Naharis. "Draw your sword and swear it to my service."

In a blink, Daario's *arakh* was free of its sheath. His submission was as outrageous as the rest of him, a great swoop that brought his face down to her toes. "My sword is yours. My life is yours. My love is yours. My blood, my body, my songs, you own them all. I live and die at your command, fair queen."

"Then live," Dany said, "and fight for me tonight."

"That would not be wise, my queen." Ser Jorah gave Daario a cold, hard stare. "Keep this one here under guard until the battle's fought and won."

She considered a moment, then shook her head. "If he can give us the Stormcrows, surprise is certain."

"And if he betrays you, surprise is lost."

Dany looked down at the sellsword again. He gave her such a smile that she flushed and turned away. "He won't."

"How can you know that?"

She pointed to the lumps of blackened flesh the dragons were consuming, bite by bloody bite. "I would call that proof of his sincerity. Daario Naharis, have your Stormcrows ready to strike the Yunkish rear when my attack begins. Can you get back safely?"

"If they stop me, I will say I have been scouting, and saw nothing." The Tyroshi rose to his feet, bowed, and swept out.

Ser Jorah Mormont lingered. "Your Grace," he said, too

bluntly, "that was a mistake. We know nothing of this man—"

"We know that he is a great fighter."

"A great talker, you mean."

"He brings us the Stormcrows." *And he has blue eyes.*

"Five hundred sellswords of uncertain loyalty."

"All loyalties are uncertain in such times as these," Dany reminded him. *And I shall be betrayed twice more, once for gold and once for love.*

"Daenerys, I am thrice your age," Ser Jorah said. "I have seen how false men are. Very few are worthy of trust, and Daario Naharis is not one of them. Even his beard wears false colors."

That angered her. "Whilst you have an honest beard, is that what you are telling me? You are the only man I should ever trust?"

He stiffened. "I did not say that."

"You say it every day. Pyat Pree's a liar, Xaro's a schemer, Belwas a braggart, Arstan an assassin . . . do you think I'm still some virgin girl, that I cannot hear the words behind the words?"

"Your Grace—"

She bulled over him. "You have been a better friend to me than any I have known, a better brother than Viserys ever was. You are the first of my Queensguard, the commander of my army, my most valued counselor, my good right hand. I honor and respect and cherish you—but I do not desire you, Jorah Mormont, and I am weary of your trying to push every other man in the world away from me, so I must needs rely on you and you alone. It will not serve, and it will not make me love you any better."

Mormont had flushed red when she first began, but by the time Dany was done his face was pale again. He stood still as stone. "If my queen commands," he said, curt and cold.

Dany was warm enough for both of them. "She does," she said. "She *commands.* Now go see to your Unsullied, ser. You have a battle to fight and win."

When he was gone, Dany threw herself down on her pillows beside her dragons. She had not meant to be so sharp with Ser Jorah, but his endless suspicion had finally woken her dragon.

He will forgive me, she told herself. *I am his liege.* Dany found herself wondering whether he was right about Daario. She felt very lonely all of a sudden. Mirri Maz Duur had promised that she would never bear a living child. *House Targaryen will end with me.* That made her sad. "You must be my children," she told the dragons, "my three fierce children. Arstan says dragons live longer than men, so you will go on after I am dead."

Drogon looped his neck around to nip at her hand. His teeth were very sharp, but he never broke her skin when they played like this. Dany laughed, and rolled him back and forth until he roared, his tail lashing like a whip. *It is longer than it was*, she saw, *and tomorrow it will be longer still. They grow quickly now, and when they are grown I shall have my wings.* Mounted on a dragon, she could lead her own men into battle, as she had in Astapor, but as yet they were still too small to bear her weight.

A stillness settled over her camp when midnight came and went. Dany remained in her pavilion with her maids, while Arstan Whitebeard and Strong Belwas kept the guard. *The waiting is the hardest part.* To sit in her tent with idle hands while her battle was being fought without her made Dany feel half a child again.

The hours crept by on turtle feet. Even after Jhiqui rubbed the knots from her shoulders, Dany was too restless for sleep. Missandei offered to sing her a lullaby of the Peaceful People, but Dany shook her head. "Bring me Arstan," she said.

When the old man came, she was curled up inside her *hrakkar* pelt, whose musty smell still reminded her of Drogo. "I cannot sleep when men are dying for me, Whitebeard," she said. "Tell me more of my brother Rhaegar, if you would. I liked the tale you told me on the ship, of how he decided that he must be a warrior."

"Your Grace is kind to say so."

"Viserys said that our brother won many tourneys."

Arstan bowed his white head respectfully. "It is not meet for me to deny His Grace's words . . ."

"But?" said Dany sharply. "Tell me. I command it."

"Prince Rhaegar's prowess was unquestioned, but he seldom entered the lists. He never loved the song of swords the way that Robert did, or Jaime Lannister. It was something he had to do, a task the world had set him. He did it well, for he did everything well. That was his nature. But he took no joy in it. Men said that he loved his harp much better than his lance."

"He won *some* tourneys, surely," said Dany, disappointed.

"When he was young, His Grace rode brilliantly in a tourney at Storm's End, defeating Lord Steffon Baratheon, Lord Jason Mallister, the Red Viper of Dorne, and a mystery knight who proved to be the infamous Simon Toyne, chief of the kingswood outlaws. He broke twelve lances against Ser Arthur Dayne that day."

"Was he the champion, then?"

"No, Your Grace. That honor went to another knight of the Kingsguard, who unhorsed Prince Rhaegar in the final tilt."

Dany did not want to hear about Rhaegar being unhorsed. "But what tourneys did my brother *win*?"

"Your Grace." The old man hesitated. "He won the greatest tourney of them all."

"Which was that?" Dany demanded.

"The tourney Lord Whent staged at Harrenhal beside the Gods Eye, in the year of the false spring. A notable event. Besides the jousting, there was a mêlée in the old style fought between seven teams of knights, as well as archery and axe-throwing, a horse race, a tournament of singers, a mummer show, and many feasts and frolics. Lord Whent was as open handed as he was rich. The lavish purses he proclaimed drew hundreds of challengers. Even your royal father came to Harrenhal, when he had not left the Red Keep for long years. The greatest lords and mightiest champions of the Seven Kingdoms rode in that tourney, and the Prince of Dragonstone bested them all."

"But that was the tourney when he crowned Lyanna Stark as queen of love and beauty!" said Dany. "Princess Elia was there, his wife, and yet my brother gave the crown to the Stark girl, and later stole her away from her betrothed. How could he do that? Did the Dornish woman treat him so ill?"

"It is not for such as me to say what might have been in your brother's heart, Your Grace. The Princess Elia was a

good and gracious lady, though her health was ever delicate."

Dany pulled the lion pelt tighter about her shoulders.
"Viserys said once that it was my fault, for being born too
late." She had denied it hotly, she remembered, going so far
as to tell Viserys that it was his fault for not being born a
girl. He beat her cruelly for that insolence. "If I had been
born more timely, he said, Rhaegar would have married me
instead of Elia, and it would all have come out different. If
Rhaegar had been happy in his wife, he would not have
needed the Stark girl."

"Perhaps so, Your Grace." Whitebeard paused a moment. "But I am not certain it was in Rhaegar to be happy."

"You make him sound so sour," Dany protested.

"Not sour, no, but . . . there was a melancholy to Prince
Rhaegar, a sense . . ." The old man hesitated again.

"Say it," she urged. "A sense . . . ?"

". . . of doom. He was born in grief, my queen, and that
shadow hung over him all his days."

Viserys had spoken of Rhaegar's birth only once.
Perhaps the tale saddened him too much. "It was the
shadow of Summerhall that haunted him, was it not?"

"Yes. And yet Summerhall was the place the prince
loved best. He would go there from time to time, with only
his harp for company. Even the knights of the Kingsguard
did not attend him there. He liked to sleep in the ruined
hall, beneath the moon and stars, and whenever he came
back he would bring a song. When you heard him play his
high harp with the silver strings and sing of twilights and
tears and the death of kings, you could not but feel that he
was singing of himself and those he loved."

"What of the Usurper? Did he play sad songs as well?"

Arstan chuckled. "Robert? Robert liked songs that
made him laugh, the bawdier the better. He only sang
when he was drunk, and then it was like to be 'A Cask of
Ale' or 'Fifty-Four Tuns' or 'The Bear and the Maiden Fair.'
Robert was much—"

As one, her dragons lifted their heads and roared.

"Horses!" Dany leapt to her feet, clutching the lion pelt.
Outside, she heard Strong Belwas bellow something, and
then other voices, and the sounds of many horses. "Irri, go
see who . . ."

The tent flap pushed open, and Ser Jorah Mormont entered. He was dusty, and spattered with blood, but otherwise none the worse for battle. The exile knight went to one knee before Dany and said, "Your Grace, I bring you victory. The Stormcrows turned their cloaks, the slaves broke, and the Second Sons were too drunk to fight, just as you said. Two hundred dead, Yunkai'i for the most part. Their slaves threw down their spears and ran, and their sellswords yielded. We have several thousand captives."

"Our own losses?"

"A dozen. If that many."

Only then did she allow herself to smile. "Rise, my good brave bear. Was Grazdan taken? Or the Titan's Bastard?"

"Grazdan went to Yunkai to deliver your terms." Ser Jorah got to his feet. "Mero fled, once he realized the Stormcrows had turned. I have men hunting him. He shouldn't escape us long."

"Very well," Dany said. "Sellsword or slave, spare all those who will pledge me their faith. If enough of the Second Sons will join us, keep the company intact."

The next day they marched the last three leagues to Yunkai. The city was built of yellow bricks instead of red; elsewise it was Astapor all over again, with the same crumbling walls and high stepped pyramids, and a great harpy mounted above its gates. The wall and towers swarmed with crossbowmen and slingers. Ser Jorah and Grey Worm deployed her men, Irri and Jhiqui raised her pavilion, and Dany sat down to wait.

On the morning of the third day, the city gates swung open and a line of slaves began to emerge. Dany mounted her silver to greet them. As they passed, little Missandei told them that they owed their freedom to Daenerys Stormborn, the Unburnt, Queen of the Seven Kingdoms of Westeros and Mother of Dragons.

"*Mhysa!*" a brown-skinned man shouted out at her. He had a child on his shoulder, a little girl, and she screamed the same word in her thin voice. "*Mhysa! Mhysa!*"

Dany looked at Missandei. "What are they shouting?"

"It is Ghiscari, the old pure tongue. It means 'Mother.' "

Dany felt a lightness in her chest. *I will never bear a living child*, she remembered. Her hand trembled as she raised it. Perhaps she smiled. She must have, because the man grinned and shouted again, and others took up the cry. *"Mhysa!"* they called. *"Mhysa! MHYSA!"* They were all smiling at her, reaching for her, kneeling before her. *"Maela,"* some called her, while others cried *"Aelalla"* or *"Qathei"* or *"Tato,"* but whatever the tongue it all meant the same thing. *Mother. They are calling me Mother.*

The chant grew, spread, swelled. It swelled so loud that it frightened her horse, and the mare backed and shook her head and lashed her silver-grey tail. It swelled until it seemed to shake the yellow walls of Yunkai. More slaves were streaming from the gates every moment, and as they came they took up the call. They were running toward her now, pushing, stumbling, wanting to touch her hand, to stroke her horse's mane, to kiss her feet. Her poor bloodriders could not keep them all away, and even Strong Belwas grunted and growled in dismay.

Ser Jorah urged her to go, but Dany remembered a dream she had dreamed in the House of the Undying. "They will not hurt me," she told him. "They are my children, Jorah." She laughed, put her heels into her horse, and rode to them, the bells in her hair ringing sweet victory. She trotted, then cantered, then broke into a gallop, her braid streaming behind. The freed slaves parted before her. "Mother," they called from a hundred throats, a thousand, ten thousand. "Mother," they sang, their fingers brushing her legs as she flew by. "Mother, Mother, Mother!"

ARYA

When Arya saw the shape of a great hill looming in the distance, golden in the afternoon sun, she knew it at once. They had come all the way back to High Heart.

By sunset they were at the top, making camp where no harm could come to them. Arya walked around the circle of weirwood stumps with Lord Beric's squire Ned, and they stood on top of one watching the last light fade in the west. From up here she could see a storm raging to the north, but High Heart stood *above* the rain. It wasn't above the wind, though; the gusts were blowing so strongly that it felt like someone was behind her, yanking on her cloak. Only when she turned, no one was there.

Ghosts, she remembered. *High Heart is haunted.*

They built a great fire atop the hill, and Thoros of Myr sat crosslegged beside it, gazing deep into the flames as if there was nothing else in all the world.

"What is he doing?" Arya asked Ned.

"Sometimes he sees things in the flames," the squire

told her. "The past. The future. Things happening far away."

Arya squinted at the fire to see if she could see what the red priest was seeing, but it only made her eyes water and before long she turned away. Gendry was watching the red priest as well. "Can you truly see the future there?" he asked suddenly.

Thoros turned from the fire, sighing. "Not here. Not now. But some days, yes, the Lord of Light grants me visions."

Gendry looked dubious. "My master said you were a sot and a fraud, as bad a priest as there ever was."

"That was unkind." Thoros chuckled. "True, but unkind. Who was this master of yours? Did I know you, boy?"

"I was 'prenticed to the master armorer Tobho Mott, on the Street of Steel. You used to buy your swords from him."

"Just so. He charged me twice what they were worth, then scolded me for setting them afire." Thoros laughed. "Your master had it right. I was no very holy priest. I was born youngest of eight, so my father gave me over to the Red Temple, but it was not the path I would have chosen. I prayed the prayers and I spoke the spells, but I would also lead raids on the kitchens, and from time to time they found girls in my bed. Such wicked girls, I never knew how they got there.

"I had a gift for tongues, though. And when I gazed into the flames, well, from time to time I saw things. Even so, I was more bother than I was worth, so they sent me finally to King's Landing to bring the Lord's light to seven-besotted Westeros. King Aerys so loved fire it was thought he might make a convert. Alas, his pyromancers knew better tricks than I did.

"King Robert was fond of me, though. The first time I rode into a mêlée with a flaming sword, Kevan Lannister's horse reared and threw him and His Grace laughed so hard I thought he might rupture." The red priest smiled at the memory. "It was no way to treat a blade, though, your master had the right of that too."

"Fire consumes." Lord Beric stood behind them, and there was something in his voice that silenced Thoros at once. "It *consumes*, and when it is done there is nothing left. *Nothing*."

"Beric. Sweet friend." The priest touched the lightning lord on the forearm. "What are you saying?"

"Nothing I have not said before. Six times, Thoros? Six times is too many." He turned away abruptly.

That night the wind was howling almost like a wolf and there were some real wolves off to the west giving it lessons. Notch, Anguy, and Merrit o' Moontown had the watch. Ned, Gendry, and many of the others were fast asleep when Arya spied the small pale shape creeping behind the horses, thin white hair flying wild as she leaned upon a gnarled cane. The woman could not have been more than three feet tall. The firelight made her eyes gleam as red as the eyes of Jon's wolf. *He was a ghost too.* Arya stole closer, and knelt to watch.

Thoros and Lem were with Lord Beric when the dwarf woman sat down uninvited by the fire. She squinted at them with eyes like hot coals. "The Ember and the Lemon come to honor me again, and His Grace the Lord of Corpses."

"An ill-omened name. I have asked you not to use it."

"Aye, you have. But the stink of death is fresh on you, my lord." She had but a single tooth remaining. "Give me wine or I will go. My bones are old. My joints ache when the winds do blow, and up here the winds are always blowing."

"A silver stag for your dreams, my lady," Lord Beric said, with solemn courtesy. "Another if you have news for us."

"I cannot eat a silver stag, nor ride one. A skin of wine for my dreams, and for my news a kiss from the great oaf in the yellow cloak." The little woman cackled. "Aye, a sloppy kiss, a bit of tongue. It has been too long, too long. His mouth will taste of lemons, and mine of bones. I am too old."

"Aye," Lem complained. "Too old for wine and kisses. All you'll get from me is the flat of my sword, crone."

"My hair comes out in handfuls and no one has kissed me for a thousand years. It is hard to be so old. Well, I will have a song then. A song from Tom o' Sevens, for my news."

"You will have your song from Tom," Lord Beric promised. He gave her the wineskin himself.

The dwarf woman drank deep, the wine running down her chin. When she lowered the skin, she wiped her mouth with the back of a wrinkled hand and said, "Sour wine for sour tidings, what could be more fitting? The king is dead, is that sour enough for you?"

Arya's heart caught in her throat.

"*Which* bloody king is dead, crone?" Lem demanded.

"The wet one. The kraken king, m'lords. I dreamt him dead and he died, and the iron squids now turn on one another. Oh, and Lord Hoster Tully's died too, but you know that, don't you? In the hall of kings, the goat sits alone and fevered as the great dog descends on him." The old woman took another long gulp of wine, squeezing the skin as she raised it to her lips.

The great dog. Did she mean the Hound? Or maybe his brother, the Mountain That Rides? Arya was not certain. They bore the same arms, three black dogs on a yellow field. Half the men whose deaths she prayed for belonged to Ser Gregor Clegane; Polliver, Dunsen, Raff the Sweetling, the Tickler, and Ser Gregor himself. *Maybe Lord Beric will hang them all.*

"I dreamt a wolf howling in the rain, but no one heard his grief," the dwarf woman was saying. "I dreamt such a clangor I thought my head might burst, drums and horns and pipes and screams, but the saddest sound was the little bells. I dreamt of a maid at a feast with purple serpents in her hair, venom dripping from their fangs. And later I dreamt that maid again, slaying a savage giant in a castle built of snow." She turned her head sharply and smiled through the gloom, right at Arya. "You cannot hide from me, child. Come closer, now."

Cold fingers walked down Arya's neck. *Fear cuts deeper than swords*, she reminded herself. She stood and approached the fire warily, light on the balls of her feet, poised to flee.

The dwarf woman studied her with dim red eyes. "I see you," she whispered. "I see you, wolf child. Blood child. I thought it was the lord who smelled of death . . ." She began to sob, her little body shaking. "You are cruel to come to my hill, cruel. I gorged on grief at Summerhall, I need none of yours. Begone from here, dark heart. *Begone!*"

There was such fear in her voice that Arya took a step

backward, wondering if the woman was mad. "Don't frighten the child," Thoros protested. "There's no harm in her."

Lem Lemoncloak's finger went to his broken nose. "Don't be so bloody sure of that."

"She will leave on the morrow, with us," Lord Beric assured the little woman. "We're taking her to Riverrun, to her mother."

"Nay," said the dwarf. "You're not. The black fish holds the rivers now. If it's the mother you want, seek her at the Twins. For there's to be a *wedding*." She cackled again. "Look in your fires, pink priest, and you will see. Not now, though, not here, you'll see nothing here. This place belongs to the old gods still . . . they linger here as I do, shrunken and feeble but not yet dead. Nor do they love the flames. For the oak recalls the acorn, the acorn dreams the oak, the stump lives in them both. And they remember when the First Men came with fire in their fists." She drank the last of the wine in four long swallows, flung the skin aside, and pointed her stick at Lord Beric. "I'll have my payment now. I'll have the song you promised me."

And so Lem woke Tom Sevenstrings beneath his furs, and brought him yawning to the fireside with his woodharp in hand. "The same song as before?" he asked.

"Oh, aye. My Jenny's song. Is there another?"

And so he sang, and the dwarf woman closed her eyes and rocked slowly back and forth, murmuring the words and crying. Thoros took Arya firmly by the hand and drew her aside. "Let her savor her song in peace," he said. "It is all she has left."

I wasn't going to hurt her, Arya thought. "What did she mean about the Twins? My mother's at Riverrun, isn't she?"

"She was." The red priest rubbed beneath his chin. "A wedding, she said. We shall see. Wherever she is, Lord Beric will find her, though."

Not long after, the sky opened. Lightning cracked and thunder rolled across the hills, and the rain fell in blinding sheets. The dwarf woman vanished as suddenly as she had appeared, while the outlaws gathered branches and threw up crude shelters.

It rained all through that night, and come morning Ned,

Lem, and Watty the Miller awoke with chills. Watty could not keep his breakfast down, and young Ned was feverish and shivering by turns, with skin clammy to the touch. There was an abandoned village half a day's ride to the north, Notch told Lord Beric; they'd find better shelter there, a place to wait out the worst of the rains. So they dragged themselves back into the saddles and urged their horses down the great hill.

The rains did not let up. They rode through woods and fields, fording swollen streams where the rushing water came up to the bellies of their horses. Arya pulled up the hood of her cloak and hunched down, sodden and shivering but determined not to falter. Merrit and Mudge were soon coughing as bad as Watty, and poor Ned seemed to grow more miserable with every mile. "When I wear my helm, the rain beats against the steel and gives me headaches," he complained. "But when I take it off, my hair gets soaked and sticks to my face and in my mouth."

"You have a knife," Gendry suggested. "If your hair annoys you so much, shave your bloody head."

He doesn't like Ned. The squire seemed nice enough to Arya; maybe a little shy, but good-natured. She had always heard that Dornishmen were small and swarthy, with black hair and small black eyes, but Ned had big blue eyes, so dark that they looked almost purple. And his hair was a pale blond, more ash than honey.

"How long have you been Lord Beric's squire?" she asked, to take his mind from his misery.

"He took me for his page when he espoused my aunt." He coughed. "I was seven, but when I turned ten he raised me to squire. I won a prize once, riding at rings."

"I never learned the lance, but I could beat you with a sword," said Arya. "Have you killed anyone?"

That seemed to startle him. "I'm only twelve."

I killed a boy when I was eight, Arya almost said, but she thought she'd better not. "You've been in battles, though."

"Yes." He did not sound very proud of it. "I was at the Mummer's Ford. When Lord Beric fell into the river, I dragged him up onto the bank so he wouldn't drown and stood over him with my sword. I never had to fight, though. He had a broken lance sticking out of him, so no one bothered us. When we regrouped, Green Gergen helped pull his lordship back onto a horse."

Arya was remembering the stableboy at King's Landing. After him there'd been that guard whose throat she cut at Harrenhal, and Ser Amory's men at that holdfast by the lake. She didn't know if Weese and Chiswyck counted, or the ones who'd died on account of the weasel soup . . . all of a sudden, she felt very sad. "My father was called Ned too," she said.

"I know. I saw him at the Hand's tourney. I wanted to go up and speak with him, but I couldn't think what to say." Ned shivered beneath his cloak, a sodden length of pale purple. "Were you at the tourney? I saw your sister there. Ser Loras Tyrell gave her a rose."

"She told me." It all seemed so long ago. "Her friend Jeyne Poole fell in love with your Lord Beric."

"He's promised to my aunt." Ned looked uncomfortable. "That was before, though. Before he . . ."

. . . *died?* she thought, as Ned's voice trailed off into an awkward silence. Their horses' hooves made sucking sounds as they pulled free of the mud.

"My lady?" Ned said at last. "You have a baseborn brother . . . Jon Snow?"

"He's with the Night's Watch on the Wall." *Maybe I should go to the Wall instead of Riverrun. Jon wouldn't care who I killed or whether I brushed my hair . . .* "Jon looks like me, even though he's bastard-born. He used to muss my hair and call me 'little sister.' " Arya missed Jon most of all. Just saying his name made her sad. "How do you know about Jon?"

"He is my milk brother."

"Brother?" Arya did not understand. "But you're from Dorne. How could you and Jon be blood?"

"*Milk* brothers. Not blood. My lady mother had no milk when I was little, so Wylla had to nurse me."

Arya was lost. "Who's Wylla?"

"Jon Snow's mother. He never told you? She's served us for years and years. Since before I was born."

"Jon never knew his mother. Not even her name." Arya gave Ned a wary look. "You know her? Truly?" *Is he making mock of me?* "If you lie I'll punch your face."

"Wylla was my wetnurse," he repeated solemnly. "I swear it on the honor of my House."

"You have a House?" That was stupid; he was a squire, of course he had a House. "Who *are* you?"

"My lady?" Ned looked embarrassed. "I'm Edric Dayne, the . . . the Lord of Starfall."

Behind them, Gendry groaned. "Lords and ladies," he proclaimed in a disgusted tone. Arya plucked a withered crabapple off a passing branch and whipped it at him, bouncing it off his thick bull head. "Ow," he said. "That hurt." He felt the skin above his eye. "What kind of lady throws crabapples at people?"

"The bad kind," said Arya, suddenly contrite. She turned back to Ned. "I'm sorry I didn't know who you were. My lord."

"The fault is mine, my lady." He was very polite.

Jon has a mother. Wylla, her name is Wylla. She would need to remember so she could tell him, the next time she saw him. She wondered if he would still call her "little sister." *I'm not so little anymore. He'd have to call me something else.* Maybe once she got to Riverrun she could write Jon a letter and tell him what Ned Dayne had said. "There was an Arthur Dayne," she remembered. "The one they called the Sword of the Morning."

"My father was Ser Arthur's elder brother. Lady Ashara was my aunt. I never knew her, though. She threw herself into the sea from atop the Palestone Sword before I was born."

"Why would she do that?" said Arya, startled.

Ned looked wary. Maybe he was afraid that she was going to throw something at him. "Your lord father never spoke of her?" he said. "The Lady Ashara Dayne, of Starfall?"

"No. Did he know her?"

"Before Robert was king. She met your father and his brothers at Harrenhal, during the year of the false spring."

"Oh." Arya did not know what else to say. "Why did she jump in the sea, though?"

"Her heart was broken."

Sansa would have sighed and shed a tear for true love, but Arya just thought it was stupid. She couldn't say that to Ned, though, not about his own aunt. "Did someone break it?"

He hesitated. "Perhaps it's not my place . . ."

"*Tell me.*"

He looked at her uncomfortably. "My aunt Allyria says Lady Ashara and your father fell in love at Harrenhal—"

"That's not so. He loved my lady mother."

"I'm sure he did, my lady, but—"

"She was the *only* one he loved."

"He must have found that bastard under a cabbage leaf, then," Gendry said behind them.

Arya wished she had another crabapple to bounce off his face. "My father had *honor*," she said angrily. "And we weren't talking to *you* anyway. Why don't you go back to Stoney Sept and ring that girl's stupid bells?"

Gendry ignored that. "At least your father *raised* his bastard, not like mine. I don't even know my father's name. Some smelly drunk, I'd wager, like the others my mother dragged home from the alehouse. Whenever she got mad at me, she'd say, 'If your father was here, he'd beat you bloody.' That's all I know of him." He spat. "Well, if he was here now, might be I'd beat *him* bloody. But he's dead, I figure, and your father's dead too, so what does it matter who he lay with?"

It mattered to Arya, though she could not have said why. Ned was trying to apologize for upsetting her, but she did not want to hear it. She pressed her heels into her horse and left them both. Anguy the Archer was riding a few yards ahead. When she caught up with him, she said, "Dornishmen lie, don't they?"

"They're famous for it." The bowman grinned. "Of course, they say the same of us marchers, so there you are. What's the trouble now? Ned's a good lad . . ."

"He's just a stupid liar." Arya left the trail, leapt a rotten log and splashed across a streambed, ignoring the shouts of the outlaws behind her. *They just want to tell me more lies.* She thought about trying to get away from them, but there were too many and they knew these lands too well. What was the use of running if they caught you?

It was Harwin who rode up beside her, in the end. "Where do you think you're going, milady? You shouldn't run off. There are wolves in these woods, and worse things."

"I'm not afraid," she said. "That boy Ned said . . ."

"Aye, he told me. Lady Ashara Dayne. It's an old tale, that one. I heard it once at Winterfell, when I was no older than you are now." He took hold of her bridle firmly and turned her horse around. "I doubt there's any truth to it. But if there is, what of it? When Ned met this Dornish lady, his brother Brandon was still alive, and it was him betrothed to Lady Catelyn, so there's no stain on your father's honor. There's nought like a tourney to make the blood run hot, so maybe some words were whispered in a tent of a night, who can say? Words or kisses, maybe more, but where's the harm in that? Spring had come, or so they thought, and neither one of them was pledged."

"She killed herself, though," said Arya uncertainly. "Ned says she jumped from a tower into the sea."

"So she did," Harwin admitted, as he led her back, "but that was for grief, I'd wager. She'd lost a brother, the Sword of the Morning." He shook his head. "Let it lie, my lady. They're dead, all of them. Let it lie . . . and please, when we come to Riverrun, say naught of this to your mother."

The village was just where Notch had promised it would be. They took shelter in a grey stone stable. Only half a roof remained, but that was half a roof more than any other building in the village. *It's not a village, it's only black stones and old bones.* "Did the Lannisters kill the people who lived here?" Arya asked as she helped Anguy dry the horses.

"No." He pointed. "Look at how thick the moss grows on the stones. No one's moved them for a long time. And there's a tree growing out of the wall there, see? This place was put to the torch a long time ago."

"Who did it, then?" asked Gendry.

"Hoster Tully." Notch was a stooped thin grey-haired man, born in these parts. "This was Lord Goodbrook's village. When Riverrun declared for Robert, Goodbrook stayed loyal to the king, so Lord Tully came down on him with fire and sword. After the Trident, Goodbrook's son made his peace with Robert and Lord Hoster, but that didn't help the dead none."

A silence fell. Gendry gave Arya a queer look, then turned away to brush his horse. Outside the rain came down and down. "I say we need a fire," Thoros declared.

"The night is dark and full of terrors. And wet too, eh? Too very wet."

Jack-Be-Lucky hacked some dry wood from a stall, while Notch and Merrit gathered straw for kindling. Thoros himself struck the spark, and Lem fanned the flames with his big yellow cloak until they roared and swirled. Soon it grew almost hot inside the stable. Thoros sat before it crosslegged, devouring the flames with his eyes just as he had atop High Heart. Arya watched him closely, and once his lips moved, and she thought she heard him mutter, "Riverrun." Lem paced back and forth, coughing, a long shadow matching him stride for stride, while Tom o' Sevens pulled off his boots and rubbed his feet. "I must be mad, to be going back to Riverrun," the singer complained. "The Tullys have never been lucky for old Tom. It was that Lysa sent me up the high road, when the moon men took my gold and my horse and all my clothes as well. There's knights in the Vale still telling how I came walking up to the Bloody Gate with only my harp to keep me modest. They made me sing 'The Name Day Boy' and 'The King Without Courage' before they opened that gate. My only solace was that three of them died laughing. I haven't been back to the Eyrie since, and I won't sing 'The King Without Courage' either, not for all the gold in Casterly—"

"*Lannisters*," Thoros said. "Roaring red and gold." He lurched to his feet and went to Lord Beric. Lem and Tom wasted no time joining them. Arya could not make out what they were saying, but the singer kept glancing at her, and one time Lem got so angry he pounded a fist against the wall. That was when Lord Beric gestured for her to come closer. It was the last thing she wanted to do, but Harwin put a hand in the small of her back and pushed her forward. She took two steps and hesitated, full of dread. "My lord." She waited to hear what Lord Beric would say.

"Tell her," the lightning lord commanded Thoros.

The red priest squatted down beside her. "My lady," he said, "the Lord granted me a view of Riverrun. An island in a sea of fire, it seemed. The flames were leaping lions with long crimson claws. And how they roared! A sea of Lannisters, my lady. Riverrun will soon come under attack."

Arya felt as though he'd punched her in the belly. "*No!*"

"Sweetling," said Thoros, "the flames do not lie. Sometimes I read them wrongly, blind fool that I am. But not this time, I think. The Lannisters will soon have Riverrun under siege."

"Robb will beat them." Arya got a stubborn look. "He'll beat them like he did before."

"Your brother may be gone," said Thoros. "Your mother as well. I did not see them in the flames. This wedding the old one spoke of, a wedding on the Twins . . . she has her own ways of knowing things, that one. The weirwoods whisper in her ear when she sleeps. If she says your mother is gone to the Twins . . ."

Arya turned on Tom and Lem. "If you hadn't caught me, I would have *been* there. I would have been *home*."

Lord Beric paid no heed to her outburst. "My lady," he said with weary courtesy, "would you know your grandfather's brother by sight? Ser Brynden Tully, called the Blackfish? Would he know you, perchance?"

Arya shook her head miserably. She had heard her mother speak of Ser Brynden Blackfish, but if she had ever met him herself it had been when she was too little to remember.

"Small chance the Blackfish will pay good coin for a girl he doesn't know," said Tom. "Those Tullys are a sour, suspicious lot, he's like to think we're selling him false goods."

"We'll convince him," Lem Lemoncloak insisted. "*She* will, or Harwin. Riverrun is closest. I say we take her there, get the gold, and be bloody well done with her."

"And if the lions catch us inside the castle?" said Tom. "They'd like nothing better than to hang his lordship in a cage from the top of Casterly Rock."

"I do not mean to be taken," said Lord Beric. A final word hung unspoken in the air. *Alive.* They all heard it, even Arya, though it never passed his lips. "Still, we dare not go blindly here. I want to know where the armies are, the wolves and lions both. Sharna will know something, and Lord Vance's maester will know more. Acorn Hall's not far. Lady Smallwood will shelter us for a time while we send scouts ahead to learn . . ."

His words beat at her ears like the pounding of a drum,

and suddenly it was more than Arya could stand. She wanted Riverrun, not Acorn Hall; she wanted her mother and her brother Robb, not Lady Smallwood or some uncle she never knew. Whirling, she broke for the door, and when Harwin tried to grab her arm she spun away from him quick as a snake.

Outside the stables the rain was still falling, and distant lightning flashed in the west. Arya ran as fast as she could. She did not know where she was going, only that she wanted to be alone, away from all the voices, away from their hollow words and broken promises. *All I wanted was to go to Riverrun.* It was her own fault, for taking Gendry and Hot Pie with her when she left Harrenhal. She would have been better alone. If she had been alone, the outlaws would never have caught her, and she'd be with Robb and her mother by now. *They were never my pack. If they had been, they wouldn't leave me.* She splashed through a puddle of muddy water. Someone was shouting her name, Harwin probably, or Gendry, but the thunder drowned them out as it rolled across the hills, half a heartbeat behind the lightning. *The lightning lord,* she thought angrily. Maybe he couldn't die, but he could lie.

Somewhere off to her left a horse whinnied. Arya couldn't have gone more than fifty yards from the stables, yet already she was soaked to the bone. She ducked around the corner of one of the tumbledown houses, hoping the mossy walls would keep the rain off, and almost bowled right into one of the sentries. A mailed hand closed hard around her arm.

"You're *hurting* me," she said, twisting in his grasp. "Let *go,* I was going to go back, I . . ."

"*Back?*" Sandor Clegane's laughter was iron scraping over stone. "Bugger that, wolf girl. You're *mine.*" He needed only one hand to yank her off her feet and drag her kicking toward his waiting horse. The cold rain lashed them both and washed away her shouts, and all that Arya could think of was the question he had asked her. *Do you know what dogs do to wolves?*

JAIME

Though his fever lingered stubbornly, the stump was healing clean, and Qyburn said his arm was no longer in danger. Jaime was anxious to be gone, to put Harrenhal, the Bloody Mummers, and Brienne of Tarth all behind him. A real woman waited for him in the Red Keep.

"I am sending Qyburn with you, to look after you on the way to King's Landing," Roose Bolton said on the morn of their departure. "He has a fond hope that your father will force the Citadel to give him back his chain, in gratitude."

"We all have fond hopes. If he grows me back a hand, my father will make him Grand Maester."

Steelshanks Walton commanded Jaime's escort; blunt, brusque, brutal, at heart a simple soldier. Jaime had served with his sort all his life. Men like Walton would kill at their lord's command, rape when their blood was up after battle, and plunder wherever they could, but once the war was done they would go back to their homes, trade their spears for hoes, wed their neighbors' daughters, and raise a pack of squalling children. Such men obeyed without question, but the deep malignant cruelty of the Brave Companions was not a part of their nature.

Both parties left Harrenhal the same morning, beneath a cold grey sky that promised rain. Ser Aenys Frey had marched three days before, striking northeast for the kingsroad. Bolton meant to follow him. "The Trident is in flood," he told Jaime. "Even at the ruby ford, the crossing will be difficult. You will give my warm regards to your father?"

"So long as you give mine to Robb Stark."

"That I shall."

Some Brave Companions had gathered in the yard to watch them leave. Jaime trotted over to where they stood. "Zollo. How kind of you to see me off. Pyg. Timeon. Will you miss me? No last jest to share, Shagwell? To lighten my way down the road? And Rorge, did you come to kiss me goodbye?"

"Bugger off, cripple," said Rorge.

"If you insist. Rest assured, though, I will be back. A Lannister always pays his debts." Jaime wheeled his horse around and rejoined Steelshanks Walton and his two hundred.

Lord Bolton had accoutred him as a knight, preferring to ignore the missing hand that made such warlike garb a travesty. Jaime rode with sword and dagger on his belt, shield and helm hung from his saddle, chainmail under a dark brown surcoat. He was not such a fool as to show the lion of Lannister on his arms, though, nor the plain white blazon that was his right as a Sworn Brother of the Kingsguard. He found an old shield in the armory, battered and splintered, the chipped paint still showing most of the great black bat of House Lothston upon a field of silver and gold. The Lothstons held Harrenhal before the Whents and had been a powerful family in their day, but they had died out ages ago, so no one was likely to object to him bearing their arms. He would be no one's cousin, no one's enemy, no one's sworn sword . . . in sum, no one.

They left through Harrenhal's smaller eastern gate, and took their leave of Roose Bolton and his host six miles farther on, turning south to follow along the lake road for a time. Walton meant to avoid the kingsroad as long as he could, preferring the farmer's tracks and game trails near the Gods Eye.

"The kingsroad would be faster." Jaime was anxious to return to Cersei as quickly as he could. If they made haste, he might even arrive in time for Joffrey's wedding.

"I want no trouble," said Steelshanks. "Gods know who we'd meet along that kingsroad."

"No one you need fear, surely? You have two hundred men."

"Aye. But others might have more. M'lord said to bring you safe to your lord father, and that's what I mean to do."

I have come this way before, Jaime reflected a few miles further on, when they passed a deserted mill beside the lake. Weeds now grew where once the miller's daughter had smiled shyly at him, and the miller himself had shouted out, "The tourney's back the other way, ser." *As if I had not known.*

King Aerys made a great show of Jaime's investiture. He said his vows before the king's pavilion, kneeling on the green grass in white armor while half the realm looked on. When Ser Gerold Hightower raised him up and put the white cloak about his shoulders, a roar went up that Jaime still remembered, all these years later. But that very night Aerys had turned sour, declaring that he had no need of *seven* Kingsguard here at Harrenhal. Jaime was commanded to return to King's Landing to guard the queen and little Prince Viserys, who'd remained behind. Even when the White Bull offered to take that duty himself, so Jaime might compete in Lord Whent's tourney, Aerys had refused. "He'll win no glory here," the king had said. "He's mine now, not Tywin's. He'll serve as I see fit. I am the king. I rule, and he'll obey."

That was the first time that Jaime understood. It was not his skill with sword and lance that had won him his white cloak, nor any feats of valor he'd performed against the Kingswood Brotherhood. Aerys had chosen him to spite his father, to rob Lord Tywin of his heir.

Even now, all these years later, the thought was bitter. And that day, as he'd ridden south in his new white cloak to guard an empty castle, it had been almost too much to stomach. He would have ripped the cloak off then and there if he could have, but it was too late. He had said the words whilst half the realm looked on, and a Kingsguard served for life.

Qyburn fell in beside him. "Is your hand troubling you?"

"The lack of my hand is troubling me." The mornings were the hardest. In his dreams Jaime was a whole man, and each dawn he would lie half-awake and feel his fingers move. *It was a nightmare*, some part of him would whisper, refusing to believe even now, *only a nightmare.* But then he would open his eyes.

"I understand you had a visitor last night," said Qyburn. "I trust that you enjoyed her?"

Jaime gave him a cool look. "She did not say who sent her."

The maester smiled modestly. "Your fever was largely gone, and I thought you might enjoy a bit of exercise. Pia is quite skilled, would you not agree? And so . . . willing."

She had been that, certainly. She had slipped in his door and out of her clothes so quickly that Jaime had thought he was still dreaming.

It hadn't been until the woman slid in under his blankets and put his good hand on her breast that he roused. *She was a pretty little thing, too.* "I was a slip of a girl when you came for Lord Whent's tourney and the king gave you your cloak," she confessed. "You were so handsome all in white, and everyone said what a brave knight you were. Sometimes when I'm with some man, I close my eyes and pretend it's you on top of me, with your smooth skin and gold curls. I never truly thought I'd have you, though."

Sending her away had not been easy after that, but Jaime had done it all the same. *I have a woman*, he reminded himself. "Do you send girls to everyone you leech?" he asked Qyburn.

"More often Lord Vargo sends them to me. He likes me to examine them, before . . . well, suffice it to say that once he loved unwisely, and he has no wish to do so again. But have no fear, Pia is quite healthy. As is your maid of Tarth."

Jaime gave him a sharp look. "Brienne?"

"Yes. A strong girl, that one. And her maidenhead is still intact. As of last night, at least." Qyburn gave a chuckle.

"He sent you to examine her?"

"To be sure. He is . . . fastidious, shall we say?"

"Does this concern the ransom?" Jaime asked. "Does her father require proof she is still maiden?"

"You have not heard?" Qyburn gave a shrug. "We had a bird from Lord Selwyn. In answer to mine. The Evenstar offers three hundred dragons for his daughter's safe return. I had told Lord Vargo there were no sapphires on Tarth, but he will not listen. He is convinced the Evenstar intends to cheat him."

"Three hundred dragons is a fair ransom for a knight. The goat should take what he can get."

"The goat is Lord of Harrenhal, and the Lord of Harrenhal does not haggle."

The news irritated him, though he supposed he should have seen it coming. *The lie spared you awhile, wench. Be grateful for that much.* "If her maidenhead's as hard as the rest of her, the goat will break his cock off trying to get in," he jested. Brienne was tough enough to survive a few rapes, Jaime judged, though if she resisted too vigorously Vargo Hoat might start lopping off her hands and feet. *And if he does, why should I care? I might still have a hand if she had let me have my cousin's sword without getting stupid.* He had almost taken off her leg himself with that first stroke of his, but after that she had given him more than he wanted. *Hoat may not know how freakish strong she is. He had best be careful, or she'll snap that skinny neck of his, and wouldn't that be sweet?*

Qyburn's companionship was wearing on him. Jaime trotted toward the head of the column. A round little tick of a northman name of Nage went before Steelshanks with the peace banner; a rainbow-striped flag with seven long tails, on a staff topped by a seven-pointed star. "Shouldn't you northmen have a different sort of peace banner?" he asked Walton. "What are the Seven to you?"

"Southern gods," the man said, "but it's a southron peace we need, to get you safe to your father."

My father. Jaime wondered whether Lord Tywin had received the goat's demand for ransom, with or without his rotted hand. *What is a swordsman worth without his sword hand? Half the gold in Casterly Rock? Three hundred dragons? Or nothing?* His father had never been unduly swayed by sentiment. Tywin Lannister's own father Lord Tytos had once imprisoned an unruly bannerman, Lord Tarbeck. The redoubtable Lady Tarbeck responded by capturing three Lannisters, including young Stafford, whose sister was betrothed to cousin Tywin. "Send back my lord and love, or these three shall answer for any harm that comes him," she had written to Casterly Rock. Young Tywin suggested his father oblige by sending back Lord Tarbeck in three pieces. Lord Tytos was a gentler sort of lion, however, so Lady Tarbeck won a few more years for her muttonheaded lord, and Stafford wed and bred and blundered on till Oxcross. But Tywin Lannister endured, eternal as Casterly Rock. *And now you have a cripple for a son as well as a dwarf, my lord. How you will hate that . . .*

The road led them through a burned village. It must have been a year or more since the place had been put to torch. The hovels stood blackened and roofless, but weeds were growing waist high in all the surrounding fields. Steelshanks called a halt to allow them to water the horses. *I know this place too*, Jaime thought as he waited by the well. There had been a small inn where only a few foundation stones and a chimney now stood, and he had gone in for a cup of ale. A dark-eyed serving wench brought him cheese and apples, but the innkeep had refused his coin. "It's an honor to have a knight of the Kingsguard under my roof, ser," the man had said. "It's a tale I'll tell my grandchildren." Jaime looked at the chimney poking out of the weeds and wondered whether he had ever gotten those grandchildren. *Did he tell them the Kingslayer once drank his ale and ate his cheese and apples, or was he ashamed to admit he fed the likes of me?* Not that he would ever know; whoever burned the inn had likely killed the grandchildren as well.

He could feel his phantom fingers clench. When Steelshanks said that perhaps they should have a fire and a bit of food, Jaime shook his head. "I mislike this place. We'll ride on."

By evenfall they had left the lake to follow a rutted track through a wood of oak and elm. Jaime's stump was throbbing dully when Steelshanks decided to make camp. Qyburn had brought a skin of dreamwine, thankfully. While Walton set the watches, Jaime stretched out near the fire and propped a rolled-up bearskin against a stump as a pillow for his head. The wench would have told him he had to eat before he slept, to keep his strength up, but he was more tired than hungry. He closed his eyes, and hoped to dream of Cersei. The fever dreams were all so vivid . . .

Naked and alone he stood, surrounded by enemies, with stone walls all around him pressing close. *The Rock*, he knew. He could feel the immense weight of it above his head. He was home. He was home and whole.

He held his right hand up and flexed his fingers to feel the strength in them. It felt as good as sex. As good as swordplay. *Four fingers and a thumb*. He had dreamed that he was maimed, but it wasn't so. Relief made him dizzy. *My hand, my good hand*. Nothing could hurt him so long as he was whole.

Around him stood a dozen tall dark figures in cowled robes that hid their faces. In their hands were spears. "Who are you?" he demanded of them. "What business do you have in Casterly Rock?"

They gave no answer, only prodded him with the points of their spears. He had no choice but to descend. Down a twisting passageway he went, narrow steps carved from the living rock, down and down. *I must go up*, he told himself. *Up, not down. Why am I going down?* Below the earth his doom awaited, he knew with the certainty of dream; something dark and terrible lurked there, something that wanted him. Jaime tried to halt, but their spears prodded him on. *If only I had my sword, nothing could harm me.*

The steps ended abruptly on echoing darkness. Jaime had the sense of vast space before him. He jerked to a halt, teetering on the edge of nothingness. A spearpoint jabbed at the small of the back, shoving him into the abyss. He shouted, but the fall was short. He landed on his hands and knees, upon soft sand and shallow water. There were watery caverns deep below Casterly Rock, but this one was strange to him. "What place is this?"

"Your place." The voice echoed; it was a hundred voices, a thousand, the voices of all the Lannisters since Lann the Clever, who'd lived at the dawn of days. But most of all it was his father's voice, and beside Lord Tywin stood his sister, pale and beautiful, a torch burning in her hand.

Joffrey was there as well, the son they'd made together, and behind them a dozen more dark shapes with golden hair.

"Sister, why has Father brought us here?"

"Us? This is your place, Brother. This is your darkness." Her torch was the only light in the cavern. Her torch was the only light in the world. She turned to go.

"Stay with me," Jaime pleaded. "Don't leave me here alone." But they were leaving. *Don't leave me in the dark!* Something terrible lived down here. "Give me a sword, at least."

"I gave you a sword," Lord Tywin said.

It was at his feet. Jaime groped under the water until his hand closed upon the hilt. *Nothing can hurt me so long as I have a sword.* As he raised the sword a finger of pale flame flickered at the point and crept up along the edge, stopping a hand's breadth from the hilt. The fire took on the color of the steel itself so it burned with a silvery-blue light, and the gloom pulled back. Crouching, listening, Jaime moved in a circle, ready for anything that might come out of the darkness. The water flowed into his boots, ankle deep and bitterly cold. *Beware the water*, he told himself. *There may be creatures living in it, hidden deeps . . .*

From behind came a great splash. Jaime whirled toward the sound . . . but the faint light revealed only Brienne of Tarth, her hands bound in heavy chains. "I swore to keep you safe," the wench said stubbornly. "I swore an oath." Naked, she raised her hands to Jaime. "Ser. Please. If you would be so good."

The steel links parted like silk. "A sword," Brienne begged, and there it was, scabbard, belt, and all. She buckled it around her thick waist. The light was so dim that Jaime could scarcely see her, though they stood a scant few feet apart. *In this light she could almost be a beauty*, he thought. *In this light she could almost be a knight.* Brienne's sword took flame as well, burning silvery blue. The darkness retreated a little more.

"The flames will burn so long as you live," he heard Cersei call. "When they die, so must you."

"*Sister!*" he shouted. "Stay with me. *Stay!*" There was no reply but the soft sound of retreating footsteps.

Brienne moved her longsword back and forth, watching

the silvery flames shift and shimmer. Beneath her feet, a reflection of the burning blade shone on the surface of the flat black water. She was as tall and strong as he remembered, yet it seemed to Jaime that she had more of a woman's shape now.

"Do they keep a bear down here?" Brienne was moving, slow and wary, sword to hand; step, turn, and listen. Each step made a little splash. "A cave lion? Direwolves? Some bear? Tell me, Jaime. What lives here? What lives in the darkness?"

"Doom." *No bear*, he knew. *No lion.* "Only doom."

In the cool silvery-blue light of the swords, the big wench looked pale and fierce. "I mislike this place."

"I'm not fond of it myself." Their blades made a little island of light, but all around them stretched a sea of darkness, unending. "My feet are wet."

"We could go back the way they brought us. If you climbed on my shoulders you'd have no trouble reaching that tunnel mouth."

Then I could follow Cersei. He could feel himself growing hard at the thought, and turned away so Brienne would not see.

"Listen." She put a hand on his shoulder, and he trembled at the sudden touch. *She's warm.* "Something comes." Brienne lifted her sword to point off to his left. "There."

He peered into the gloom until he saw it too. Something was moving through the darkness, he could not quite make it out . . .

"A man on a horse. No, two. Two riders, side by side."

"Down here, beneath the Rock?" It made no sense. Yet there came two riders on pale horses, men and mounts both armored. The destriers emerged from the blackness at a slow walk. *They make no sound*, Jaime realized. *No splashing, no clink of mail nor clop of hoof.* He remembered Eddard Stark, riding the length of Aerys's throne room wrapped in silence. Only his eyes had spoken; a lord's eyes, cold and grey and full of judgment.

"Is it you, Stark?" Jaime called. "Come ahead. I never feared you living, I do not fear you dead."

Brienne touched his arm. "There are more."

He saw them too. They were armored all in snow, it

seemed to him, and ribbons of mist swirled back from their shoulders. The visors of their helms were closed, but Jaime Lannister did not need to look upon their faces to know them.

Five had been his brothers. Oswell Whent and Jon Darry. Lewyn Martell, a prince of Dorne. The White Bull, Gerold Hightower. Ser Arthur Dayne, Sword of the Morning. And beside them, crowned in mist and grief with his long hair streaming behind him, rode Rhaegar Targaryen, Prince of Dragonstone and rightful heir to the Iron Throne.

"You don't frighten me," he called, turning as they split to either side of him. He did not know which way to face. "I will fight you one by one or all together. But who is there for the wench to duel? She gets cross when you leave her out."

"I swore an oath to keep him safe," she said to Rhaegar's shade. "I swore a holy oath."

"We all swore oaths," said Ser Arthur Dayne, so sadly.

The shades dismounted from their ghostly horses. When they drew their longswords, it made not a sound. "He was going to burn the city," Jaime said. "To leave Robert only ashes."

"He was your king," said Darry.

"You swore to keep him safe," said Whent.

"And the children, them as well," said Prince Lewyn.

Prince Rhaegar burned with a cold light, now white, now red, now dark. "I left my wife and children in your hands."

"I never thought he'd hurt them." Jaime's sword was burning less brightly now. "I was with the king . . ."

"Killing the king," said Ser Arthur.

"Cutting his throat," said Prince Lewyn.

"The king you had sworn to die for," said the White Bull.

The fires that ran along the blade were guttering out, and Jaime remembered what Cersei had said. *No.* Terror closed a hand about his throat. Then his sword went dark, and only Brienne's burned, as the ghosts came rushing in.

"No," he said, "no, no, no. *Noooooooooo!*"

Heart pounding, he jerked awake, and found himself in starry darkness amidst a grove of trees. He could taste bile in his mouth, and he was shivering with sweat, hot and cold at once. When he looked down for his sword hand, his wrist ended in leather and linen, wrapped snug around an ugly stump. He felt sudden tears well up in his eyes. *I felt it, I felt the strength in my fingers, and the rough leather of the sword's grip. My hand . . .*

"My lord." Qyburn knelt beside him, his fatherly face all crinkly with concern. "What is it? I heard you cry out."

Steelshanks Walton stood above them, tall and dour. "What is it? Why did you scream?"

"A dream . . . only a dream." Jaime stared at the camp around him, lost for a moment. "I was in the dark, but I had my hand back." He looked at the stump and felt sick all over again. *There's no place like that beneath the Rock*, he thought. His stomach was sour and empty, and his head was pounding where he'd pillowed it against the stump.

Qyburn felt his brow. "You still have a touch of fever."

"A fever dream." Jaime reached up. "Help me." Steelshanks took him by his good hand and pulled him to his feet.

"Another cup of dreamwine?" asked Qyburn.

"No. I've dreamt enough this night." He wondered how long it was till dawn. Somehow he knew that if he closed his eyes, he would be back in that dark wet place again.

"Milk of the poppy, then? And something for your fever? You are still weak, my lord. You need to sleep. To rest."

That is the last thing I mean to do. The moonlight glimmered pale upon the stump where Jaime had rested his head. The moss covered it so thickly he had not noticed before, but now he saw that the wood was white. It made him think of Winterfell, and Ned Stark's heart tree. *It was not him*, he thought. *It was never him.* But the stump was dead and so was Stark and so were all the others, Prince Rhaegar and Ser Arthur and the children. *And Aerys. Aerys is most dead of all.* "Do you believe in ghosts, Maester?" he asked Qyburn.

The man's face grew strange. "Once, at the Citadel, I came into an empty room and saw an empty chair. Yet I knew a woman had been there, only a moment before. The cushion was dented where she'd sat, the cloth was still warm, and her scent lingered in the air. If we leave our smells behind us when we leave a room, surely something of our souls must remain when we leave this life?" Qyburn spread his hands. "The archmaesters did not like my thinking, though. Well, Marwyn did, but he was the only one."

Jaime ran his fingers through his hair. "Walton," he said, "saddle the horses. I want to go back."

"Back?" Steelshanks regarded him dubiously.

He thinks I've gone mad. And perhaps I have. "I left something at Harrenhal."

"Lord Vargo holds it now. Him and his Bloody Mummers."

"You have twice the men he does."

"If I don't serve you up to your father as commanded, Lord Bolton will have my hide. We press on to King's Landing."

Once Jaime might have countered with a smile and a threat, but one-handed cripples do not inspire much fear. He wondered what his brother would do. *Tyrion would find a way.* "Lannisters lie, Steelshanks. Didn't Lord Bolton tell you that?"

The man frowned suspiciously. "What if he did?"

"Unless you take me back to Harrenhal, the song I sing my father may not be one the Lord of the Dreadfort would wish to hear. I might even say it was Bolton ordered my hand cut off, and Steelshanks Walton who swung the blade."

Walton gaped at him. "That isn't so."

"No, but who will my father believe?" Jaime made himself smile, the way he used to smile when nothing in the world could frighten him. "It will be so much easier if we just go back. We'd be on our way again soon enough, and I'd sing such a sweet song in King's Landing you'll never believe your ears. You'd get the girl, and a nice fat purse of gold as thanks."

"Gold?" Walton liked that well enough. "How much gold?"

I have him. "Why, how much would you want?"

And by the time the sun came up, they were halfway back to Harrenhal.

Jaime pushed his horse much harder than he had the day before, and Steelshanks and the northmen were forced to match his pace. Even so, it was midday before they reached the castle on the lake. Beneath a darkening sky that threatened rain, the immense walls and five great towers stood black and ominous. *It looks so dead.* The walls were empty, the gates closed and barred. But high above the barbican, a single banner hung limp. *The black goat of Qohor*, he knew. Jaime cupped his hands to shout. "You in there! Open your gates, or I'll kick them down!"

It was not until Qyburn and Steelshanks added their voices that a head finally appeared on the battlements above them. He goggled down at them, then vanished. A short time later, they heard the portcullis being drawn upward. The gates swung open, and Jaime Lannister spurred his horse through the walls, scarcely glancing at the murder holes as he passed beneath them. He had been worried that the goat might not admit them, but it seemed as if the Brave Companions still thought of them as allies. *Fools.*

The outer ward was deserted; only the long slate-roofed stables showed any signs of life, and it was not horses that interested Jaime just then. He reined up and looked about. He could hear sounds from somewhere behind the Tower of Ghosts, and men shouting in half a dozen tongues. Steelshanks and Qyburn rode up on either side. "Get what you came back for, and we'll be gone again," said Walton. "I want no trouble with the Mummers."

"Tell your men to keep their hands on their sword hilts, and the Mummers will want no trouble with you. Two to one, remember?" Jaime's head jerked round at the sound of a distant roar, faint but ferocious. It echoed off the walls of Harrenhal, and the laughter swelled up like the sea. All of a sudden, he knew what was happening. *Have we come too late?* His stomach did a lurch, and he slammed his spurs into his horse, galloping across the outer ward, beneath an arched stone bridge, around the Wailing Tower, and through the Flowstone Yard.

They had her in the bear pit.

King Harren the Black had wished to do even his bear-baiting in lavish style. The pit was ten yards across and five yards deep, walled in stone, floored with sand, and encircled by six tiers of marble benches. The Brave Companions filled only a quarter of the seats, Jaime saw as he swung down clumsily from his horse. The sellswords were so fixed on the spectacle beneath that only those across the pit noticed their arrival.

Brienne wore the same ill-fitting gown she'd worn to supper with Roose Bolton. No shield, no breastplate, no chainmail, not even boiled leather, only pink satin and Myrish lace. Maybe the goat thought she was more amusing when dressed as a woman. Half her gown was hanging off in tatters, and her left arm dripped blood where the bear had raked her.

At least they gave her a sword. The wench held it one-handed, moving sideways, trying to put some distance between her and the bear. *That's no good, the ring's too small.* She needed to attack, to make a quick end to it. Good steel was a match for any bear. But the wench seemed afraid to close. The Mummers showered her with insults and obscene suggestions.

"This is none of our concern," Steelshanks warned Jaime. "Lord Bolton said the wench was theirs, to do with as they liked."

"Her name's Brienne." Jaime descended the steps, past a dozen startled sellswords. Vargo Hoat had taken the lord's box in the lowest tier. "Lord Vargo," he called over the shouts.

The Qohorik almost spilt his wine. "*Kingthlayer?*" The left side of his face was bandaged clumsily, the linen over his ear spotted with blood.

"Pull her out of there."

"Thay out of thith, Kingthlayer, unleth you'd like another thump." He waved a wine cup. "Your thee-mooth bit oth my ear. Thmall wonder her father will not ranthom thuch a freak."

A roar turned Jaime back around. The bear was eight feet tall. *Gregor Clegane with a pelt*, he thought, *though likely smarter*. The beast did not have the reach the Mountain had with that monster greatsword of his, though.

Bellowing in fury, the bear showed a mouth full of great yellow teeth, then fell back to all fours and went straight at Brienne. *There's your chance*, Jaime thought. *Strike! Now!*

Instead, she poked out ineffectually with the point of her blade. The bear recoiled, then came on, rumbling.

Brienne slid to her left and poked again at the bear's face.
This time he lifted a paw to swat the sword aside.

He's wary, Jaime realized. *He's gone up against other
men. He knows swords and spears can hurt him. But that
won't keep him off her long.* "Kill him!" he shouted, but
his voice was lost amongst all the other shouts. If Brienne
heard, she gave no sign. She moved around the pit, keeping
the wall at her back. *Too close. If the bear pins her by the
wall . . .*

The beast turned clumsily, too far and too fast. Quick as
a cat, Brienne changed direction. *There's the wench I remember.* She leapt in to land a cut across the bear's back.
Roaring, the beast went up on his hind legs again. Brienne
scrambled back away. *Where's the blood?* Then suddenly
he understood. Jaime rounded on Hoat. "You gave her a
tourney sword."

The goat brayed laughter, spraying him with wine and
spittle. "Of courth."

"*I'll* pay her bloody ransom. Gold, sapphires, whatever
you want. Pull her out of there."

"You want her? Go get her."

So he did.

He put his good hand on the marble rail and vaulted
over, rolling as he hit the sand. The bear turned at the
thump, sniffing, watching this new intruder warily. Jaime
scrambled to one knee. *Well, what in seven hells do I do
now?* He filled his fist with sand. "Kingslayer?" he heard
Brienne say, astonished.

"Jaime." He uncoiled, flinging the sand at the bear's
face. The bear mauled the air and roared like blazes.

"What are you *doing* here?"

"Something stupid. Get behind me." He circled toward
her, putting himself between Brienne and the bear.

"*You* get behind. I have the sword."

"A sword with no point and no edge. *Get behind me!*"
He saw something half-buried in the sand, and snatched it
up with his good hand. It proved to be a human jawbone,
with some greenish flesh still clinging to it, crawling with
maggots. *Charming*, he thought, wondering whose face he
held. The bear was edging closer, so Jaime whipped his arm
around and flung bone, meat, and maggots at the beast's

head. He missed by a good yard. *I ought to lop my left hand off as well, for all the good it does me.*

Brienne tried to dart around, but he kicked her legs out from under her. She fell in the sand, clutching the useless sword. Jaime straddled her, and the bear came charging.

There was a deep *twang*, and a feathered shaft sprouted suddenly beneath the beast's left eye. Blood and slaver ran from his open mouth, and another bolt took him in the leg. The bear roared, reared. He saw Jaime and Brienne again and lumbered toward them. More crossbows fired, the quarrels ripping through fur and flesh. At such short range, the bowmen could hardly miss. The shafts hit as hard as maces, but the bear took another step. *The poor dumb brave brute.* When the beast swiped at him, he danced aside, shouting, kicking sand. The bear turned to follow his tormentor, and took another two quarrels in the back. He gave one last rumbling growl, settled back onto his haunches, stretched out on the bloodstained sand, and died.

Brienne got back to her knees, clutching the sword and breathing short ragged breaths. Steelshanks's archers were winding their crossbows and reloading while the Bloody Mummers shouted curses and threats at them. Rorge and Three Toes had swords out, Jaime saw, and Zollo was uncoiling his whip.

"You thlew my bear!" Vargo Hoat shrieked.

"And I'll serve you the same if you give me trouble," Steelshanks threw back. "We're taking the wench."

"Her name is Brienne," Jaime said. "Brienne, the maid of Tarth. You *are* still maiden, I hope?"

Her broad homely face turned red. "Yes."

"Oh, good," Jaime said. "I only rescue maidens." To Hoat he said, "You'll have your ransom. For both of us. A Lannister pays his debts. Now fetch some ropes and get us out of here."

"Bugger that," Rorge growled. "Kill them, Hoat. Or you'll bloody well wish you had!"

The Qohorik hesitated. Half his men were drunk, the northmen stone sober, and there were twice as many. Some of the crossbowmen had reloaded by now. "Pull them out," Hoat said, and then, to Jaime, "I hath chothen to be merthiful. Tell your lord father."

"I will, my lord." *Not that it will do you any good.*

Not until they were half a league from Harrenhal and out of range of archers on the walls did Steelshanks Walton let his anger show. "Are you *mad*, Kingslayer? Did you mean to die? No man can fight a bear with his bare hands!"

"One bare hand and one bare stump," Jaime corrected. "But I hoped you'd kill the beast before the beast killed me. Elsewise, Lord Bolton would have peeled you like an orange, no?"

Steelshanks cursed him roundly for a fool of Lannister, spurred his horse, and galloped away up the column.

"Ser Jaime?" Even in soiled pink satin and torn lace, Brienne looked more like a man in a gown than a proper woman. "I am grateful, but . . . you were well away. Why come back?"

A dozen quips came to mind, each crueler than the one before, but Jaime only shrugged. "I dreamed of you," he said.

CATELYN

Robb bid farewell to his young queen thrice. Once in the godswood before the heart tree, in sight of gods and men. The second time beneath the portcullis, where Jeyne sent him forth with a long embrace and a longer kiss. And finally an hour beyond the Tumblestone, when the girl came galloping up on a well-lathered horse to plead with her young king to take her along.

Robb was touched by that, Catelyn saw, but abashed as well. The day was damp and grey, a drizzle had begun to fall, and the last thing he wanted was to call a halt to his march so he could stand in the wet and console a tearful young wife in front of half his army. *He speaks her gently*, she thought as she watched them together, *but there is anger underneath.*

All the time the king and queen were talking, Grey Wind prowled around them, stopping only to shake the water from his coat and bare his teeth at the rain. When at last Robb gave Jeyne one final kiss, dispatched a dozen men to take her back to Riverrun, and mounted his horse once more, the direwolf raced off ahead as swift as an arrow loosed from a longbow.

"Queen Jeyne has a loving heart, I see," said Lame Lothar Frey to Catelyn. "Not unlike my own sisters. Why, I would wager a guess that even now Roslin is dancing round the Twins chanting 'Lady *Tully*, Lady *Tully*, Lady *Roslin* Tully.' By the morrow she'll be holding swatches of Riverrun red-and-blue to her cheek to picture how she'll look in her bride's cloak." He turned in the saddle to smile at Edmure. "But you are strangely quiet, Lord Tully. How do *you* feel, I wonder?"

"Much as I did at the Stone Mill just before the warhorns sounded," Edmure said, only half in jest.

Lothar gave a good-natured laugh. "Let us pray your marriage ends as happily, my lord."

And may the gods protect us if it does not. Catelyn pressed her heels into her horse, leaving her brother and Lame Lothar to each other's company.

It had been her who had insisted that Jeyne remain at Riverrun, when Robb would sooner have kept her by his side. Lord Walder might well construe the queen's absence from the wedding as another slight, yet her presence would have been a different sort of insult, salt in the old man's wound. "Walder Frey has a sharp tongue and a long memory," she had warned her son. "I do not doubt that you are strong enough to suffer an old man's rebukes as the price of his allegiance, but you have too much of your father in you to sit there while he insults Jeyne to her face."

Robb could not deny the sense of that. *Yet all the same, he resents me for it,* Catelyn thought wearily. *He misses Jeyne already, and some part of him blames me for her absence, though he knows it was good counsel.*

Of the six Westerlings who had come with her son from the Crag, only one remained by his side; Ser Raynald, Jeyne's brother, the royal banner-bearer. Robb had dispatched Jeyne's uncle Rolph Spicer to deliver young Martyn Lannister to the Golden Tooth the very day he received Lord Tywin's assent to the exchange of captives. It was deftly done. Her son was relieved of his fear for Martyn's safety, Galbart Glover was relieved to hear that his brother Robett had been put on a ship at Duskendale, Ser Rolph had important and honorable employment . . .

and Grey Wind was at the king's side once more. *Where he belongs.*

Lady Westerling had remained at Riverrun with her children; Jeyne, her little sister Eleyna, and young Rollam, Robb's squire, who complained bitterly about being left. Yet that was wise as well. Olyvar Frey had squired for Robb previously, and would doubtless be present for his sister's wedding; to parade his replacement before him would be as unwise as it was unkind. As for Ser Raynald, he was a cheerful young knight who swore that no insult of Walder Frey's could possibly provoke him. *And let us pray that insults are all we need to contend with.*

Catelyn had her fears on that score, though. Her lord father had never trusted Walder Frey after the Trident, and she was ever mindful of that. Queen Jeyne would be safest behind the high, strong walls of Riverrun, with the Blackfish to protect her. Robb had even created him a new title, Warden of the Southern Marches. Ser Brynden would hold the Trident if any man could.

All the same, Catelyn would miss her uncle's craggy face, and Robb would miss his counsel. Ser Brynden had played a part in every victory her son had won. Galbart Glover had taken command of the scouts and outriders in his place; a good man, loyal and steady, but without the Blackfish's brilliance.

Behind Glover's screen of scouts, Robb's line of march stretched several miles. The Greatjon led the van. Catelyn traveled in the main column, surrounded by plodding warhorses with steelclad men on their backs. Next came the baggage train, a procession of wayns laden with food, fodder, camp supplies, wedding gifts, and the wounded too weak to walk, under the watchful eye of Ser Wendel Manderly and his White Harbor knights. Herds of sheep and goats and scrawny cattle trailed behind, and then a little trail of footsore camp followers. Even farther back was Robin Flint and the rearguard. There was no enemy in back of them for hundreds of leagues, but Robb would take no chances.

Thirty-five hundred they were, thirty-five hundred who had been blooded in the Whispering Wood, who had reddened their swords at the Battle of the Camps, at Oxcross, Ashemark, and the Crag, and all through the gold-rich hills of the Lannister west. Aside from her brother Edmure's modest retinue of friends, the lords of the Trident had remained to hold the riverlands while the king retook the north. Ahead awaited Edmure's bride and Robb's next battle . . . *and for me, two dead sons, an empty bed, and a castle full of ghosts.* It was a cheerless prospect. *Brienne, where are you? Bring my girls back to me, Brienne. Bring them back safe.*

The drizzle that had sent them off turned into a soft steady rain by midday, and continued well past nightfall. The next day the northmen never saw the sun at all, but rode beneath leaden skies with their hoods pulled up to keep the water from their eyes. It was a heavy rain, turning roads to mud and fields to quagmires, swelling the rivers and stripping the trees of their leaves. The constant patter made idle chatter more bother than it was worth, so men spoke only when they had something to say, and that was seldom enough.

"We are stronger than we seem, my lady," Lady Maege Mormont said as they rode. Catelyn had grown fond of Lady Maege and her eldest daughter, Dacey; they were more understanding than most in the matter of Jaime Lannister, she had found. The daughter was tall and lean, the mother short and stout, but they dressed alike in mail and leather, with the black bear of House Mormont on shield and surcoat. By Catelyn's lights, that was queer garb for a lady, yet Dacey and Lady Maege seemed more comfortable, both as warriors and as women, than ever the girl from Tarth had been.

"I have fought beside the Young Wolf in every battle," Dacey Mormont said cheerfully. "He has not lost one yet."

No, but he has lost everything else, Catelyn thought, but it would not do to say it aloud. The northmen did not lack for courage, but they were far from home, with little enough to sustain them but for their faith in their young king. That faith must be protected, at all costs. *I must be stronger*, she told herself. *I must be strong for Robb. If I despair, my grief will consume me.* Everything would turn on this marriage. If Edmure and Roslin were happy in one another, if the Late Lord Frey could be appeased and his power once more wedded to Robb's . . . *Even then, what chance will we have, caught between Lannister and*

Greyjoy? It was a question Catelyn dared not dwell on, though Robb dwelt on little else. She saw how he studied his maps whenever they made camp, searching for some plan that might win back the north.

Her brother Edmure had other cares. "You don't suppose *all* Lord Walder's daughters look like him, do you?" he wondered, as he sat in his tall striped pavilion with Catelyn and his friends.

"With so many different mothers, a few of the maids are bound to turn up comely," said Ser Marq Piper, "but why should the old wretch give you a pretty one?"

"No reason at all," said Edmure in a glum tone.

It was more than Catelyn could stand. "Cersei Lannister is comely," she said sharply. "You'd be wiser to pray that Roslin is strong and healthy, with a good head and a loyal heart." And with that she left them.

Edmure did not take that well. The next day he avoided her entirely on the march, preferring the company of Marq Piper, Lymond Goodbrook, Patrek Mallister, and the young Vances. *They do not scold him, except in jest*, Catelyn told herself when they raced by her that afternoon with nary a word. *I have always been too hard with Edmure, and now grief sharpens my every word.* She regretted her rebuke. There was rain enough falling from the sky without her making more. And was it really such a terrible thing, to want a pretty wife? She remembered her own childish disappointment, the first time she had laid eyes on Eddard Stark. She had pictured him as a younger version of his brother Brandon, but that was wrong. Ned was shorter and plainer of face, and so somber. He spoke courteously enough, but beneath the words she sensed a coolness that was all at odds with Brandon, whose mirths had been as wild as his rages. Even when he took her maidenhood, their love had more of duty to it than of passion. *We made Robb that night, though; we made a king together. And after the war, at Winterfell, I had love enough for any woman, once I found the good sweet heart beneath Ned's solemn face. There is no reason Edmure should not find the same, with his Roslin.*

As the gods would have it, their route took them through the Whispering Wood where Robb had won his first great victory. They followed the course of the twisting stream on the floor of that pinched narrow valley, much as Jaime Lannister's men had done that fateful night. *It was warmer then*, Catelyn remembered, *the trees were still green, and the stream did not overflow its banks.* Fallen leaves choked the flow now and lay in sodden snarls among the rocks and roots, and the trees that had once hidden Robb's army had exchanged their green raiment for leaves of dull gold spotted with brown, and a red that reminded her of rust and dry blood. Only the spruce and the soldier pines still showed green, thrusting up at the belly of the clouds like tall dark spears.

More than the trees have died since then, she reflected. On the night of the Whispering Wood, Ned was still alive in his cell beneath Aegon's High Hill, Bran and Rickon were safe behind the walls of Winterfell. *And Theon Greyjoy fought at Robb's side, and boasted of how he had almost crossed swords with the Kingslayer. Would that he had. If Theon had died in place of Lord Karstark's sons, how much ill would have been undone?*

As they passed through the battleground, Catelyn glimpsed signs of the carnage that had been; an overturned helm filling with rain, a splintered lance, the bones of a horse. Stone cairns had been raised over some of the men who had fallen here, but scavengers had already been at them. Amidst the tumbles of rock, she spied brightly colored cloth and bits of shiny metal. Once she saw a face peering out at her, the shape of the skull beginning to emerge from beneath the melting brown flesh.

It made her wonder where Ned had come to rest. The silent sisters had taken his bones north, escorted by Hallis Mollen and a small honor guard. Had Ned ever reached Winterfell, to be interred beside his brother Brandon in the dark crypts beneath the castle? Or did the door slam shut at Moat Cailin before Hal and the sisters could pass?

Thirty-five hundred riders wound their way along the valley floor through the heart of the Whispering Wood, but Catelyn Stark had seldom felt lonelier. Every league she crossed took her farther from Riverrun, and she found herself wondering whether she would ever see the castle again. Or was it lost to her forever, like so much else?

Five days later, their scouts rode back to warn them that the rising waters had washed out the wooden bridge at

Fairmarket. Galbart Glover and two of his bolder men had tried swimming their mounts across the turbulent Blue Fork at Ramsford. Two of the horses had been swept under and drowned, and one of the riders; Glover himself managed to cling to a rock until they could pull him in. "The river hasn't run this high since spring," Edmure said. "And if this rain keeps falling, it will go higher yet."

"There's a bridge further upstream, near Oldstones," remembered Catelyn, who had often crossed these lands with her father. "It's older and smaller, but if it still stands—"

"It's gone, my lady," Galbart Glover said. "Washed away even before the one at Fairmarket."

Robb looked to Catelyn. "Is there another bridge?"

"No. And the fords will be impassable." She tried to remember. "If we cannot cross the Blue Fork, we'll have to go around it, through Sevenstreams and Hag's Mire."

"Bogs and bad roads, or none at all," warned Edmure. "The going will be slow, but we'll get there, I suppose."

"Lord Walder will wait, I'm sure," said Robb. "Lothar sent him a bird from Riverrun, he knows we are coming."

"Yes, but the man is prickly, and suspicious by nature," said Catelyn. "He may take this delay as a deliberate insult."

"Very well, I'll beg his pardon for our tardiness as well. A sorry king I'll be, apologizing with every second breath." Robb made a wry face. "I hope Bolton got across the Trident before the rains began. The kingsroad runs straight north, he'll have an easy march. Even afoot, he should reach the Twins before us."

"And when you've joined his men to yours and seen my brother married, what then?" Catelyn asked him.

"North." Robb scratched Grey Wind behind an ear.

"By the causeway? Against Moat Cailin?"

He gave her an enigmatic smile. "That's one way to go," he said, and she knew from his tone that he would say no more. *A wise king keeps his own counsel*, she reminded herself.

They reached Oldstones after eight more days of steady rain, and made their camp upon the hill overlooking the Blue Fork, within a ruined stronghold of the ancient river kings. Its foundations remained amongst the weeds to show where the walls and keeps had stood, but the local smallfolk had long ago made off with most of the stones to raise their barns and septs and holdfasts. Yet in the center of what once would have been the castle's yard, a great carved sepulcher still rested, half hidden in waist-high brown grass amongst a stand of ash.

The lid of the sepulcher had been carved into a likeness of the man whose bones lay beneath, but the rain and the wind had done their work. The king had worn a beard, they could see, but otherwise his face was smooth and feature-less, with only vague suggestions of a mouth, a nose, eyes, and the crown about the temples. His hands folded over the shaft of a stone warhammer that lay upon his chest. Once the warhammer would have been carved with runes that told its name and history, but all that the centuries had worn away. The stone itself was cracked and crumbling at the corners, discolored here and there by spreading white splotches of lichen, while wild roses crept up over the king's feet almost to his chest.

It was there that Catelyn found Robb, standing somber in the gathering dusk with only Grey Wind beside him. The rain had stopped for once, and he was bareheaded. "Does this castle have a name?" he asked quietly, when she came up to him.

"Oldstones, all the smallfolk called it when I was a girl, but no doubt it had some other name when it was still a hall of kings." She had camped here once with her father, on their way to Seagard. *Petyr was with us too . . .*

"There's a song," he remembered. " 'Jenny of Oldstones, with the flowers in her hair.' "

"We're all just songs in the end. If we are lucky." She had played at being Jenny that day, had even wound flowers in her hair. And Petyr had pretended to be her Prince of Dragonflies. Catelyn could not have been more than twelve, Petyr just a boy.

Robb studied the sepulcher. "Whose grave is this?"

"Here lies Tristifer, the Fourth of His Name, King of the Rivers and the Hills." Her father had told her his story once. "He ruled from the Trident to the Neck, thousands of years before Jenny and her prince, in the days when the kingdoms of the First Men were falling one after the other before the onslaught of the Andals. The Hammer of Justice, they called him. He fought a hundred battles and won nine-and-ninety, or so the singers say, and when he raised this castle it was the strongest in Westeros." She put a hand on her son's shoulder. "He died in his hundredth battle, when seven Andal kings joined forces against him. The fifth Tristifer was not his equal, and soon the kingdom was lost, and then the castle, and last of all the line. With Tristifer the Fifth died House Mudd, that had ruled the riverlands for a thousand years before the Andals came."

"His heir failed him." Robb ran a hand over the rough weathered stone. "I had hoped to leave Jeyne with child . . . we tried often enough, but I'm not certain . . ."

"It does not always happen the first time." *Though it did with you.* "Nor even the hundredth. You are very young."

"Young, and a king," he said. "A king must have an heir. If I should die in my next battle, the kingdom must not die with me. By law Sansa is next in line of succession, so Winterfell and the north would pass to her." His mouth tightened. "To her, and her lord husband. Tyrion Lannister. I cannot allow that. I *will* not allow that. That dwarf must never have the north."

"No," Catelyn agreed. "You must name another heir, until such time as Jeyne gives you a son." She considered a moment. "Your father's father had no siblings, but his father had a sister who married a younger son of Lord Raymar Royce, of the junior branch. They had three daughters, all of whom wed Vale lordlings. A Waynwood and a Corbray, for certain. The youngest . . . it might have been a Templeton, but . . ."

"Mother." There was a sharpness in Robb's tone. "You forget. My father had four sons."

She had not forgotten; she had not wanted to look at it, yet there it was. "A Snow is not a Stark."

"Jon's more a Stark than some lordlings from the Vale who have never so much as set eyes on Winterfell."

"Jon is a brother of the Night's Watch, sworn to take no wife and hold no lands. Those who take the black serve for life."

"So do the knights of the Kingsguard. That did not stop the Lannisters from stripping the white cloaks from Ser Barristan Selmy and Ser Boros Blount when they had no more use for them. If I send the Watch a hundred men in Jon's place, I'll wager they find some way to release him from his vows."

He is set on this. Catelyn knew how stubborn her son could be. "A bastard cannot inherit."

"Not unless he's legitimized by a royal decree," said Robb. "There is more precedent for that than for releasing a Sworn Brother from his oath."

"Precedent," she said bitterly. "Yes, Aegon the Fourth legitimized all his bastards on his deathbed. And how much pain, grief, war, and murder grew from that? I know you trust Jon. But can you trust his sons? Or *their* sons? The Blackfyre pretenders troubled the Targaryens for five generations, until Barristan the Bold slew the last of them on the Stepstones. If you make Jon legitimate, there is no way to turn him bastard again. Should he wed and breed, any sons you may have by Jeyne will never be safe."

"Jon would never harm a son of mine."

"No more than Theon Greyjoy would harm Bran or Rickon?"

Grey Wind leapt up atop King Tristifer's crypt, his teeth bared. Robb's own face was cold. "That is as cruel as it is unfair. Jon is no Theon."

"So you pray. Have you considered your sisters? What of *their* rights? I agree that the north must not be permitted to pass to the Imp, but what of Arya? By law, she comes after Sansa . . . your own sister, trueborn . . ."

". . . and *dead*. No one has seen or heard of Arya since they cut Father's head off. Why do you lie to yourself? Arya's gone, the same as Bran and Rickon, and they'll kill Sansa too once the dwarf gets a child from her. Jon is the only brother that remains to me. Should I die without issue, I want him to succeed me as King in the North. I had hoped you would support my choice."

"I cannot," she said. "In all else, Robb. In everything. But not in this . . . this folly. Do not ask it."

"I don't have to. I'm the king." Robb turned and walked off, Grey Wind bounding down from the tomb and loping after him.

What have I done? Catelyn thought wearily, as she stood alone by Tristifer's stone sepulcher. *First I anger Edmure, and now Robb, but all I have done is speak the truth. Are men so fragile they cannot bear to hear it?* She might have wept then, had not the sky begun to do it for her. It was all she could do to walk back to her tent, and sit there in the silence.

In the days that followed, Robb was everywhere and anywhere; riding at the head of the van with the Greatjon, scouting with Grey Wind, racing back to Robin Flint and the rearguard. Men said proudly that the Young Wolf was the first to rise each dawn and the last to sleep at night, but Catelyn wondered whether he was sleeping at all. *He grows as lean and hungry as his direwolf.*

"My lady," Maege Mormont said to her one morning as they rode through a steady rain, "you seem so somber. Is aught amiss?"

My lord husband is dead, as is my father. Two of my sons have been murdered, my daughter has been given to a faithless dwarf to bear his vile children, my other daughter is vanished and likely dead, and my last son and my only brother are both angry with me. What could possibly be amiss? That was more truth than Lady Maege would wish to hear, however. "This is an evil rain," she said instead. "We have suffered much, and there is more peril and more grief ahead. We need to face it boldly, with horns blowing and banners flying bravely. But this rain beats us down. The banners hang limp and sodden, and the men huddle under their cloaks and scarcely speak to one another. Only an evil rain would chill our hearts when most we need them to burn hot."

Dacey Mormont looked up at the sky. "I would sooner have water raining down on me than arrows."

Catelyn smiled despite herself. "You are braver than I am, I fear. Are all your Bear Island women such warriors?"

"She-bears, aye," said Lady Maege. "We have needed to be. In olden days the ironmen would come raiding in their longboats, or wildlings from the Frozen Shore. The men would be off fishing, like as not. The wives they left behind had to defend themselves and their children, or else be carried off."

"There's a carving on our gate," said Dacey. "A woman in a bearskin, with a child in one arm suckling at her breast. In the other hand she holds a battleaxe. She's no proper lady, that one, but I always loved her."

"My nephew Jorah brought home a proper lady once," said Lady Maege. "He won her in a tourney. How she hated that carving."

"Aye, and all the rest," said Dacey. "She had hair like spun gold, that Lynesse. Skin like cream. But her soft hands were never made for axes."

"Nor her teats for giving suck," her mother said bluntly.

Catelyn knew of whom they spoke; Jorah Mormont had brought his second wife to Winterfell for feasts, and once they had guested for a fortnight. She remembered how young the Lady Lynesse had been, how fair, and how unhappy. One night, after several cups of wine, she had confessed to Catelyn that the north was no place for a Hightower of Oldtown. "There was a Tully of Riverrun who felt the same once," she had answered gently, trying to console, "but in time she found much here she could love."

All lost now, she reflected. *Winterfell and Ned, Bran and Rickon, Sansa, Arya, all gone. Only Robb remains.* Had there been too much of Lynesse Hightower in her after all, and too little of the Starks? *Would that I had known how to wield an axe, perhaps I might have been able to protect them better.*

Day followed day, and still the rain kept falling. All the way up the Blue Fork they rode, past Sevenstreams where the river unraveled into a confusion of rills and brooks, then through Hag's Mire, where glistening green pools waited to swallow the unwary and the soft ground sucked at the hooves of their horses like a hungry babe at its mother's breast. The going was worse than slow. Half the wayns had to be abandoned to the muck, their loads distributed amongst mules and draft horses.

Lord Jason Mallister caught up with them amidst the bogs of Hag's Mire. There was more than an hour of daylight remaining when he rode up with his column, but Robb called a halt at once, and Ser Raynald Westerling came to escort Catelyn to the king's tent. She found her son seated beside a brazier, a map across his lap. Grey Wind slept at his feet. The Greatjon was with him, along with Galbart Glover, Maege Mormont, Edmure, and a man that Catelyn did not know, a fleshy balding man with a cringing look to him. *No lordling, this one,* she knew the moment she laid eyes on the stranger. *Not even a warrior.*

Jason Mallister rose to offer Catelyn his seat. His hair had almost as much white in it as brown, but the Lord of Seagard was still a handsome man; tall and lean, with a chiseled clean-shaven face, high cheekbones, and fierce blue-grey eyes. "Lady Stark, it is ever a pleasure. I bring good tidings, I hope."

"We are in sore need of some, my lord." She sat, listening to the rain patter down noisily against the canvas overhead.

Robb waited for Ser Raynald to close the tent flap. "The gods have heard our prayers, my lords. Lord Jason has brought us the captain of the *Myraham,* a merchanter out of Oldtown. Captain, tell them what you told me."

"Aye, Your Grace." He licked his thick lips nervously. "My last port of call afore Seagard, that was Lordsport on Pyke. The ironmen kept me there more'n half a year, they did. King Balon's command. Only, well, the long and the short of it is, he's dead."

"Balon Greyjoy?" Catelyn's heart skipped a beat. "You are telling us that Balon Greyjoy is dead?"

The shabby little captain nodded. "You know how Pyke's built on a headland, and part on rocks and islands off the shore, with bridges between? The way I heard it in Lordsport, there was a blow coming in from the west, rain and thunder, and old King Balon was crossing one of them bridges when the wind got hold of it and just tore the thing to pieces. He washed up two days later, all bloated and broken. Crabs ate his eyes, I hear."

The Greatjon laughed. "King crabs, I hope, to sup upon such royal jelly, eh?"

The captain bobbed his head. "Aye, but that's not all of it, no!" He leaned forward. "The *brother's* back."

"Victarion?" asked Galbart Glover, surprised.

"Euron. Crow's Eye, they call him, as black a pirate as ever raised a sail. He's been gone for years, but Lord Balon was no sooner cold than there he was, sailing into Lordsport in his *Silence.* Black sails and a red hull, and crewed by mutes. He'd been to Asshai and back, I heard. Wherever he was, though, he's home now, and he marched right into Pyke and sat his arse in the Seastone Chair, and drowned Lord Botley in a cask of seawater when he objected. That was when I ran back to *Myraham* and slipped anchor, hoping I could get away whilst things were confused. And so I did, and here I am."

"Captain," said Robb when the man was done, "you have my thanks, and you will not go unrewarded. Lord Jason will take you back to your ship when we are done. Pray wait outside."

"That I will, Your Grace. That I will."

No sooner had he left the king's pavilion than the Greatjon began to laugh, but Robb silenced him with a look. "Euron Greyjoy is no man's notion of a king, if half of what Theon said of him was true. Theon is the rightful heir, unless he's dead . . . but Victarion commands the Iron Fleet. I can't believe he would remain at Moat Cailin while Euron Crow's Eye holds the Seastone Chair. He *has* to go back."

"There's a daughter as well," Galbart Glover reminded him. "The one who holds Deepwood Motte, and Robett's wife and child."

"If she stays at Deepwood Motte that's *all* she can hope to hold," said Robb. "What's true for the brothers is even more true for her. She will need to sail home to oust Euron and press her own claim." Her son turned to Lord Jason Mallister. "You have a fleet at Seagard?"

"A fleet, Your Grace? Half a dozen longships and two war galleys. Enough to defend my own shores against raiders, but I could not hope to meet the Iron Fleet in battle."

"Nor would I ask it of you. The ironborn will be setting sail toward Pyke, I expect. Theon told me how his people think. Every captain a king on his own deck. They will all want a voice in the succession. My lord, I need two of your longships to sail around the Cape of Eagles and up the Neck to Greywater Watch."

Lord Jason hesitated. "A dozen streams drain the wetwood, all shallow, silty, and uncharted. I would not even call them rivers. The channels are ever drifting and changing. There are endless sandbars, deadfalls, and tangles of rotting trees. And Greywater Watch *moves*. How are my ships to find it?"

"Go upriver flying my banner. The crannogmen will find you. I want two ships to double the chances of my message reaching Howland Reed. Lady Maege shall go on one, Galbart on the second." He turned to the two he'd named. "You'll carry letters for those lords of mine who remain in the north, but all the commands within will be false, in case you have the misfortune to be taken. If that happens, you must tell them that you were sailing for the north. Back to Bear Island, or for the Stony Shore." He tapped a finger on the map. "Moat Cailin is the key. Lord Balon knew that, which is why he sent his brother Victarion there with the hard heart of the Greyjoy strength."

"Succession squabbles or no, the ironborn are not such fools as to abandon Moat Cailin," said Lady Maege.

"No," Robb admitted. "Victarion will leave the best part of his garrison, I'd guess. Every man he takes will be one less man we need to fight, however. And he *will* take many of his captains, count on that. The leaders. He will need such men to speak for him if he hopes to sit the Seastone Chair."

"You cannot mean to attack up the causeway, Your Grace," said Galbart Glover. "The approaches are too narrow. There is no way to deploy. No one has ever taken the Moat."

"From the south," said Robb. "But if we can attack from the north and west simultaneously, and take the ironmen in the rear while they are beating off what they think is my main thrust up the causeway, then we have a chance. Once I link up with Lord Bolton and the Freys, I will have more than twelve thousand men. I mean to divide them into three battles and start up the causeway a half-day apart. If the Greyjoys have eyes south of the Neck, they will see my whole strength rushing headlong at Moat Cailin.

"Roose Bolton will have the rearguard, while I command the center. Greatjon, you shall lead the van against Moat Cailin. Your attack must be so fierce that the ironborn have no leisure to wonder if anyone is creeping down on them from the north."

The Greatjon chuckled. "Your creepers best come fast, or my men will swarm those walls and win the Moat before you show your face. I'll make a gift of it to you when you come dawdling up."

"That's a gift I should be glad to have," said Robb.

Edmure was frowning. "You talk of attacking the ironmen in the rear, sire, but how do you mean to get north of them?"

"There are ways through the Neck that are not on any map, Uncle. Ways known only to the crannogmen—narrow trails between the bogs, and wet roads through the reeds that only boats can follow." He turned to his two messengers. "Tell Howland Reed that he is to send guides to me, two days after I have started up the causeway. To the *center* battle, where my own standard flies. Three hosts will leave the Twins, but only two will reach Moat Cailin. Mine own battle will melt away into the Neck, to reemerge on the Fever. If we move swiftly once my uncle's wed, we can all be in position by year's end. We will fall upon the Moat from three sides on the first day of the new century, as the ironmen are waking with hammers beating at their heads from the mead they'll quaff the night before."

"I like this plan," said the Greatjon. "I like it well."

Galbart Glover rubbed his mouth. "There are risks. If the crannogmen should fail you . . ."

"We will be no worse than before. But they will not fail. My father knew the worth of Howland Reed." Robb rolled up the map, and only then looked at Catelyn. "Mother."

She tensed. "Do you have some part in this for me?"

"Your part is to stay safe. Our journey through the Neck will be dangerous, and naught but battle awaits us in the north. But Lord Mallister has kindly offered to keep you safe at Seagard until the war is done. You will be comfortable there, I know."

Is this my punishment for opposing him about Jon Snow? Or for being a woman, and worse, a mother? It took her a moment to realize that they were all watching her. They had *known*, she realized. Catelyn should not have been surprised. She had won no friends by freeing the Kingslayer, and more than once she had heard the Greatjon say that women had no place on a battlefield.

Her anger must have blazed across her face, because Galbart Glover spoke up before she said a word. "My lady, His Grace is wise. It's best you do not come with us."

"Seagard will be brightened by your presence, Lady Catelyn," said Lord Jason Mallister.

"You would make me a prisoner," she said.

"An honored guest," Lord Jason insisted.

Catelyn turned to her son. "I mean no offense to Lord Jason," she said stiffly, "but if I cannot continue on with you, I would sooner return to Riverrun."

"I left my wife at Riverrun. I want my mother elsewhere. If you keep all your treasures in one purse, you only make it easier for those who would rob you. After the wedding, you shall go to Seagard, that is my royal command." Robb stood, and as quick as that, her fate was settled. He picked up a sheet of parchment. "One more matter. Lord Balon has left chaos in his wake, we hope. I would not do the same. Yet I have no son as yet, my brothers Bran and Rickon are dead, and my sister is wed to a Lannister. I've thought long and hard about who might follow me. I command you now as my true and loyal lords to fix your seals to this document as witnesses to my decision."

A king indeed, Catelyn thought, defeated. She could only hope that the trap he'd planned for Moat Cailin worked as well as the one in which he'd just caught her.

SAMWELL

Whitetree, Sam thought. *Please, let this be Whitetree.* He remembered Whitetree. Whitetree was on the maps he'd drawn, on their way north. If this village was Whitetree, he knew where they were. *Please, it has to be.* He wanted that so badly that he forgot his feet for a little bit, he forgot the ache in his calves and his lower back and the stiff frozen fingers he could scarcely feel. He even forgot about Lord Mormont and Craster and the wights and the Others. *Whitetree*, Sam prayed, to any god that might be listening.

All wildling villages looked much alike, though. A huge weirwood grew in the center of this one . . . but a white tree did not mean Whitetree, necessarily. Hadn't the weirwood at Whitetree been bigger than this one? Maybe he was remembering it wrong. The face carved into the bone pale trunk was long and sad; red tears of dried sap leaked from its eyes. *Was that how it looked when we came north?* Sam couldn't recall.

Around the tree stood a handful of one-room hovels with sod roofs, a longhall built of logs and grown over with moss, a stone well, a sheepfold . . . but no sheep, nor any people. The wildlings had gone to join Mance Rayder in the Frostfangs, taking all they owned except their houses. Sam was thankful for that. Night was coming on, and it would be good to sleep beneath a roof for once. He was so tired. It seemed as though he had been walking half his life. His boots were falling to pieces, and all the blisters on his feet had burst and turned to callus, but now he had new blisters *under* the callus, and his toes were getting frostbitten.

But it was either walk or die, Sam knew. Gilly was still weak from childbirth and carrying the babe besides; she needed the horse more than he did. The second horse had died on them three days out from Craster's Keep. It was a wonder she lasted that long, poor half-starved thing. Sam's weight had probably done for her. They might have tried riding double, but he was afraid the same thing would happen again. *It's better that I walk.*

Sam left Gilly in the longhall to make a fire while he poked his head into the hovels. She was better at making fires; he could never seem to get the kindling to catch, and the last time he'd tried to strike a spark off flint and steel he managed to cut himself on his knife. Gilly bound up the gash for him, but his hand was stiff and sore, even clumsier than it had been before. He knew he should wash the wound and change the binding, but he was afraid to look at it. Besides, it was so cold that he hated taking off his gloves.

Sam did not know what he hoped to find in the empty houses. Maybe the wildlings had left some food behind. He had to take a look. Jon had searched the huts at Whitetree, on their way north. Inside one hovel Sam heard a rustling of rats from a dark corner, but otherwise there was nothing in any of them but old straw, old smells, and some ashes beneath the smoke hole.

He turned back to the weirwood and studied the carved face a moment. *It is not the face we saw,* he admitted to himself. *The tree's not half as big as the one at Whitetree.* The red eyes wept blood, and he didn't remember that either. Clumsily, Sam sank to his knees. "Old gods, hear my prayer. The Seven were my father's gods but I said my words to you when I joined the Watch. Help us now. I fear we might be lost. We're hungry too, and so cold. I don't know what gods I believe in now, but . . . please, if you're there, help us. Gilly has a little son." That was all that he could think to say. The dusk was deepening, the leaves of the weirwood rustling softly, waving like a thousand blood-red hands. Whether Jon's gods had heard him or not he could not say.

By the time he returned to the longhall, Gilly had the fire going. She sat close to it with her furs opened, the babe at her breast. *He's as hungry as we are*, Sam thought. The old women had smuggled out food for them from Craster's, but they had eaten most of it by now. Sam had been a hopeless hunter even at Horn Hill, where game was plentiful and he had hounds and huntsmen to help him; here in this endless empty forest, the chances of him catching anything were remote. His efforts at fishing the lakes and half-frozen streams had been dismal failures as well.

"How much longer, Sam?" Gilly asked. "Is it far, still?"

"Not so far. Not so far as it was." Sam shrugged out of his pack, eased himself awkwardly to the floor, and tried to cross his legs. His back ached so abominably from the walking that he would have liked to lean up against one of the carved wooden pillars that supported the roof, but the fire was in the center of the hall beneath the smoke hole and he craved warmth even more than comfort. "Another few days should see us there."

Sam had his maps, but if this wasn't Whitetree then they weren't going to be much use. *We went too far east to get around that lake*, he fretted, *or maybe too far west when I tried to double back*. He was coming to hate lakes and rivers. Up here there was never a ferry or bridge, which meant walking all the way around the lakes and searching for places to ford the rivers. It was easier to follow a game trail than to struggle through the brush, easier to circle a ridge instead of climbing it. *If Bannen or Dywen were with us we'd be at Castle Black by now, warming our feet in the common room*. Bannen was dead, though, and Dywen gone with Grenn and Dolorous Edd and the others.

The Wall is three hundred miles long and seven hundred feet high, Sam reminded himself. If they kept going south, they *had* to find it, sooner or later. And he was certain that they had been going south. By day he took directions from the sun, and on clear nights they could follow the Ice Dragon's tail, though they hadn't traveled much by night since the second horse had died. Even when the moon was full it was too dark beneath the trees, and it would have been so easy for Sam or the last garron to break a leg. *We have to be well south by now, we have to be.*

What he wasn't so certain of was how far east or west they might have strayed. They would reach the Wall, yes . . . in a day or a fortnight, it couldn't be farther than that, surely, surely . . . but *where*? It was the gate at Castle Black they needed to find; the only way through the Wall for a hundred leagues.

"Is the Wall as big as Craster used to say?" Gilly asked.

"Bigger." Sam tried to sound cheerful. "So big you can't even see the castles hidden behind it. But they're there, you'll see. The Wall is all ice, but the castles are stone and wood. There are tall towers and deep vaults and a huge longhall with a great fire burning in the hearth, day and night. It's so hot in there, Gilly, you'll hardly believe it."

"Could I stand by the fire? Me and the boy? Not for a long time, just till we're good and warm?"

"You can stand by the fire as long as you like. You'll have food and drink, too. Hot mulled wine and a bowl of venison stewed with onions, and Hobb's bread right out of the oven, so hot it will burn your fingers." Sam peeled a glove off to wriggle his own fingers near the flames, and soon regretted it. They had been numb with cold, but as feeling returned they hurt so much he almost cried. "Sometimes one of the brothers will sing," he said, to take his mind off the pain. "Dareon sang best, but they sent him to Eastwatch. There's still Halder, though. And Toad. His real name is Todder, but he looks like a toad, so we call him that. He likes to sing, but he has an awful voice."

"Do you sing?" Gilly rearranged her furs, and she moved the babe from one breast to the other.

Sam blushed. "I . . . I know some songs. When I was little I liked to sing. I danced too, but my lord father never liked me to. He said if I wanted to prance around I should do it in the yard with a sword in my hand."

"Could you sing some southron song? For the babe?"

"If you like." Sam thought for a moment. "There's a song our septon used to sing to me and my sisters, when we were little and it was time for us to go to sleep. 'The Song of the Seven,' it's called." He cleared his throat and softly sang:

> The Father's face is stern and strong,
> he sits and judges right from wrong.
> He weighs our lives, the short and long,
> and loves the little children.

> The Mother gives the gift of life,
> and watches over every wife.
> Her gentle smile ends all strife,
> and she loves her little children.

> The Warrior stands before the foe,
> protecting us where e'er we go.
> With sword and shield and spear and bow,
> he guards the little children.

> The Crone is very wise and old,
> and sees our fates as they unfold.
> She lifts her lamp of shining gold,
> to lead the little children.

> The Smith, he labors day and night,
> to put the world of men to right.
> With hammer, plow, and fire bright,
> he builds for little children.

> The Maiden dances through the sky,
> she lives in every lover's sigh,
> Her smiles teach the birds to fly,
> and give dreams to little children.

> The Seven Gods who made us all,
> are listening if we should call.
> So close your eyes, you shall not fall,
> they see you, little children,
> Just close your eyes, you shall not fall,
> they see you, little children.

Sam remembered the last time he'd sung the song with his mother, to lull baby Dickon to sleep. His father had heard their voices and come barging in, angry. "I will have no more of that," Lord Randyll told his wife harshly. "You ruined one boy with those soft septon's songs, do you mean to do the same to this babe?" Then he looked at Sam and said, "Go sing to your sisters, if you must sing. I don't want you near my son."

Gilly's babe had gone to sleep. He was such a tiny thing, and so quiet that Sam feared for him. He didn't even have a name. He had asked Gilly about that, but she said it was bad luck to name a child before he was two. So many of them died.

She tucked her nipple back inside her furs. "That was pretty, Sam. You sing good."

"You should hear Dareon. His voice is sweet as mead."

"We drank the sweetest mead the day Craster made me a wife. It was summer then, and not so cold." Gilly gave him a puzzled look. "Did you only sing of six gods? Craster always told us you southrons had seven."

"Seven," he agreed, "but no one sings of the Stranger." The Stranger's face was the face of death. Even talking of him made Sam uncomfortable. "We should eat something. A bite or two."

Nothing was left but a few black sausages, as hard as wood. Sam sawed off a few thin slices for each of them. The effort made his wrist ache, but he was hungry enough to persist. If you chewed the slices long enough they softened up, and tasted good. Craster's wives seasoned them with garlic.

After they had finished, Sam begged her pardon and went out to relieve himself and look after the horse. A biting wind was blowing from the north, and the leaves in the trees rattled at him as he passed. He had to break the thin scum of ice on top of the stream so the horse could get a drink. *I had better bring her inside.* He did not want to wake up at break of day to find that their horse had frozen to death during the night. *Gilly would keep going even if that happened.* The girl was very brave, not like him. He wished he knew what he was going to do with her back at Castle Black. She kept saying how she'd be his wife if he wanted, but black brothers didn't keep wives; besides, he was a Tarly of Horn Hill, he could never wed a wildling. *I'll have to think of something. So long as we reach the Wall alive, the rest doesn't matter, it doesn't matter one little bit.*

Leading the horse to the longhall was simple enough. Getting her through the door was not, but Sam persisted.

Gilly was already dozing by the time he got the garron inside. He hobbled the horse in a corner, fed some fresh wood to the fire, took off his heavy cloak, and wriggled down under the furs beside the wildling woman. His cloak was big enough to cover all three of them and keep in the warmth of their bodies.

Gilly smelled of milk and garlic and musty old fur, but he was used to that by now. They were good smells, so far as Sam was concerned. He liked sleeping next to her. It made him remember times long past, when he had shared a huge bed at Horn Hill with two of his sisters. That had ended when Lord Randyll decided it was making him soft as a girl. *Sleeping alone in my own cold cell never made me any harder or braver, though.* He wondered what his father would say if he could see him now. *I killed one of the Others, my lord,* he imagined saying. *I stabbed him with an obsidian dagger, and my Sworn Brothers call me Sam the Slayer now.* But even in his fancies, Lord Randyll only scowled, disbelieving.

His dreams were strange that night. He was back at Horn Hill, at the castle, but his father was not there. It was Sam's castle now. Jon Snow was with him. Lord Mormont too, the Old Bear, and Grenn and Dolorous Edd and Pyp and Toad and all his other brothers from the Watch, but they wore bright colors instead of black. Sam sat at the high table and feasted them all, cutting thick slices off a roast with his father's greatsword Heartsbane. There were sweet cakes to eat and honeyed wine to drink, there was singing and dancing, and everyone was warm. When the feast was done he went up to sleep, not to the lord's bedchamber where his mother and father lived but to the room he had once shared with his sisters. Only instead of his sisters it was Gilly waiting in the huge soft bed, wearing nothing but a big shaggy fur, milk leaking from her breasts.

He woke suddenly, in cold and dread.

The fire had burned down to smouldering red embers. The air itself seemed frozen, it was so cold. In the corner the garron was whinnying and kicking the logs with her hind legs. Gilly sat beside the fire, hugging her babe. Sam sat up groggy, his breath puffing pale from his open mouth. The longhall was dark with shadows, black and blacker. The hair on his arms was standing up.

It's nothing, he told himself. *I'm cold, that's all.*

Then, by the door, one of the shadows moved. A big one.

This is still a dream, Sam prayed. *Oh, make it that I'm still asleep, make it a nightmare. He's dead, he's dead, I saw him die.* "He's come for the babe," Gilly wept. "He smells him. A babe fresh-born stinks o' life. He's come for the life."

The huge dark shape stooped under the lintel, into the hall, and shambled toward them. In the dim light of the fire, the shadow became Small Paul.

"Go away," Sam croaked. "We don't want you here."

Paul's hands were coal, his face was milk, his eyes shone a bitter blue. Hoarfrost whitened his beard, and on one shoulder hunched a raven, pecking at his cheek, eating the dead white flesh. Sam's bladder let go, and he felt the warmth running down his legs. "Gilly, calm the horse and lead her out. You do that."

"You—" she started.

"I have the knife. The dragonglass dagger." He fumbled it out as he got to his feet. He'd given the first knife to Grenn, but thankfully he'd remembered to take Lord Mormont's dagger before fleeing Craster's Keep. He clutched it tight, moving away from the fire, away from Gilly and the babe. "Paul?" He meant to sound brave, but it came out in a squeak. "Small Paul. Do you know me? I'm Sam, fat Sam, Sam the Scared, you saved me in the woods. You carried me when I couldn't walk another step. No one else could have done that, but you did." Sam backed away, knife in hand, sniveling. *I am such a coward.* "Don't hurt us, Paul. Please. Why would you want to hurt us?"

Gilly scrabbled backward across the hard dirt floor. The wight turned his head to look at her, but Sam shouted "*NO!*" and he turned back. The raven on his shoulder ripped a strip of flesh from his pale ruined cheek. Sam held the dagger before him, breathing like a blacksmith's bellows. Across the longhall, Gilly reached the garron. *Gods give me courage*, Sam prayed. *For once, give me a little courage. Just long enough for her to get away.*

Small Paul moved toward him. Sam backed off until he came up against a rough log wall. He clutched the dagger with both hands to hold it steady. The wight did not seem to fear the dragonglass. Perhaps he did not know what it was. He moved slowly, but Small Paul had never been quick even when he'd been alive. Behind him, Gilly murmured to calm the garron and tried to urge it toward the door. But the horse must have caught a whiff of the wight's queer cold scent. Suddenly she balked, rearing, her hooves lashing at the frosty air. Paul swung toward the sound, and seemed to lose all interest in Sam.

There was no time to think or pray or be afraid. Samwell Tarly threw himself forward and plunged the dagger down into Small Paul's back. Half-turned, the wight never saw him coming. The raven gave a shriek and took to the air. "You're dead!" Sam screamed as he stabbed. "You're dead, you're dead." He stabbed and screamed, again and again, tearing huge rents in Paul's heavy black cloak. Shards of dragonglass flew everywhere as the blade shattered on the iron mail beneath the wool.

Sam's wail made a white mist in the black air. He dropped the useless hilt and took a hasty step backwards as Small Paul twisted around. Before he could get out his other knife, the steel knife that every brother carried, the wight's black hands locked beneath his chins. Paul's fingers were so cold they seemed to burn. They burrowed deep into the soft flesh of Sam's throat. *Run, Gilly, run*, he wanted to scream, but when he opened his mouth only a choking sound emerged.

His fumbling fingers finally found the dagger, but when he slammed it up into the wight's belly the point skidded off the iron links, and the blade went spinning from Sam's hand. Small Paul's fingers tightened inexorably, and began to twist. *He's going to rip my head off*, Sam thought in despair. His throat felt frozen, his lungs on fire. He punched and pulled at the wight's wrists, to no avail. He kicked Paul between the legs, uselessly. The world shrank to two blue stars, a terrible crushing pain, and a cold so fierce that his tears froze over his eyes. Sam squirmed and pulled, desperate . . . and then he lurched forward.

Small Paul was big and powerful, but Sam still outweighed him, and the wights were clumsy, he had seen that on the Fist. The sudden shift sent Paul staggering back a step, and the living man and the dead one went crashing down together. The impact knocked one hand from Sam's throat, and he was able to suck in a quick breath of air before the icy black fingers returned. The taste of blood filled his mouth. He twisted his neck around, looking for his knife, and saw a dull orange glow. *The fire!* Only ember and ashes remained, but still . . . he could not breathe, or think . . . Sam wrenched himself sideways, pulling Paul with him . . . his arms flailed against the dirt floor, groping, reaching, scattering the ashes, until at last they found something hot . . . a chunk of charred wood, smouldering red and orange within the black . . . his fingers closed around it, and he smashed it into Paul's mouth, so hard he felt teeth shatter.

Yet even so the wight's grip did not loosen. Sam's last thoughts were for the mother who had loved him and the father he had failed. The longhall was spinning around him when he saw the wisp of smoke rising from between Paul's broken teeth. Then the dead man's face burst into flame, and the hands were gone.

Sam sucked in air, and rolled feebly away. The wight was burning, hoarfrost dripping from his beard as the flesh beneath blackened. Sam heard the raven shriek, but Paul himself made no sound. When his mouth opened, only flames came out. And his eyes . . . *It's gone, the blue glow is gone.*

He crept to the door. The air was so cold that it hurt to breathe, but such a fine sweet hurt. He ducked from the longhall. "Gilly?" he called. "Gilly, I killed it. Gil—"

She stood with her back against the weirwood, the boy in her arms. The wights were all around her. There were a dozen of them, a score, more . . . some had been wildlings once, and still wore skins and hides . . . but more had been his brothers. Sam saw Lark the Sisterman, Softfoot, Ryles. The wen on Chett's neck was black, his boils covered with a thin film of ice. And that one looked like Hake, though it was hard to know for certain with half his head missing. They had torn the poor garron apart, and were pulling out her entrails with dripping red hands. Pale steam rose from her belly.

Sam made a whimpery sound. "It's not fair . . ."

"*Fair.*" The raven landed on his shoulder. "*Fair, far, fear.*" It flapped its wings, and screamed along with Gilly. The wights were almost on her. He heard the dark red leaves of the weirwood rustling, whispering to one another in a tongue he did not know. The starlight itself seemed to

stir, and all around them the trees groaned and creaked.
Sam Tarly turned the color of curdled milk, and his eyes
went wide as plates. *Ravens!* They were in the weirwood,
hundreds of them, thousands, perched on the bone-white
branches, peering between the leaves. He saw their beaks
open as they screamed, saw them spread their black wings.
Shrieking, flapping, they descended on the wights in angry
clouds. They swarmed round Chett's face and pecked at his
blue eyes, they covered the Sisterman like flies, they
plucked gobbets from inside Hake's shattered head. There
were so many that when Sam looked up, he could not see
the moon.

   "*Go,*" said the bird on his shoulder. "*Go, go, go.*"

   Sam ran, puffs of frost exploding from his mouth. All
around him the wights flailed at the black wings and sharp
beaks that assailed them, falling in an eerie silence with
never a grunt nor cry. But the ravens ignored Sam. He took
Gilly by the hand and pulled her away from the weirwood.
"We have to go."

   "But where?" Gilly hurried after him, holding her baby.
"They killed our horse, how will we . . ."

   "*Brother!*" The shout cut through the night, through
the shrieks of a thousand ravens. Beneath the trees, a man
muffled head to heels in mottled blacks and greys sat
astride an elk. "*Here,*" the rider called. A hood shadowed
his face.

   He's wearing blacks. Sam urged Gilly toward him. The
elk was huge, a great elk, ten feet tall at the shoulder, with
a rack of antlers near as wide. The creature sank to his
knees to let them mount. "Here," the rider said, reaching
down with a gloved hand to pull Gilly up behind him.
Then it was Sam's turn. "My thanks," he puffed. Only
when he grasped the offered hand did he realize that the
rider wore no glove. His hand was black and cold, with fingers hard as stone.

ARYA

When they reached the top of the ridge and saw the river, Sandor Clegane reined up hard and cursed.

The rain was falling from a black iron sky, pricking the green and brown torrent with ten thousand swords. *It must be a mile across*, Arya thought. The tops of half a hundred trees poked up out the swirling waters, their limbs clutching for the sky like the arms of drowning men. Thick mats of sodden leaves choked the shoreline, and farther out in the channel she glimpsed something pale and swollen, a deer or perhaps a dead horse, moving swiftly downstream. There was a sound too, a low rumble at the edge of hearing, like the sound a dog makes just before he growls.

Arya squirmed in the saddle and felt the links of the Hound's mail digging into her back. His arms encircled her; on the left, the burned arm, he'd donned a steel vambrace for protection, but she'd seen him change the dressings, and the flesh beneath was still raw and seeping. If the burns pained him, though, Sandor Clegane gave no hint of it.

"Is this the Blackwater Rush?" They had ridden so far in rain and darkness, through trackless woods and nameless villages, that Arya had lost all sense of where they were.

"It's a river we need to cross, that's all you need to know." Clegane would answer her from time to time, but he had warned her not to talk back. He had given her a lot of warnings that first day. "The next time you hit me, I'll tie your hands behind your back," he'd said. "The next time you try and run off, I'll bind your feet together. Scream or shout or bite me again, and I'll gag you. We can ride double, or I can throw you across the back of the horse trussed up like a sow for slaughter. Your choice."

She had chosen to ride, but the first time they made camp she'd waited until she thought he was asleep, and found a big jagged rock to smash his ugly head in. *Quiet as a shadow*, she told herself as she crept toward him, but that wasn't quiet enough. The Hound hadn't been asleep after all. Or maybe he'd woken. Whichever it was, his eyes opened, his mouth twitched, and he took the rock away from her as if she were a baby. The best she could do was kick him. "I'll give you that one," he said, when he flung the rock into the bushes. "But if you're stupid enough to try again, I'll hurt you."

"Why don't you just *kill* me like you did Mycah?" Arya had screamed at him. She was still defiant then, more angry than scared.

He answered by grabbing the front of her tunic and yanking her within an inch of his burned face. "The next time you say that name I'll beat you so bad you'll *wish* I killed you."

After that, he rolled her in his horse blanket every night when he went to sleep, and tied ropes around her top and bottom so she was bound up as tight as a babe in swaddling clothes.

It has to be the Blackwater, Arya decided as she watched the rain lash the river. The Hound was Joffrey's dog; he was taking her back to the Red Keep, to hand to Joffrey and the queen. She wished that the sun would come out, so she could tell which way they were going. The more she looked at the moss on the trees the more confused she got. *The Blackwater wasn't so wide at King's Landing, but that was before the rains.*

"The fords will all be gone," Sandor Clegane said, "and I wouldn't care to try and swim over neither."

There's no way across, she thought. *Lord Beric will catch us for sure*. Clegane had pushed his big black stallion hard, doubling back thrice to throw off pursuit, once even riding half a mile up the center of a swollen stream . . . but Arya still expected to see the outlaws every time she looked back. She had tried to help them by scratching her name on the trunks of trees when she went in the bushes to make water, but the fourth time she did it he caught her, and that was the end of that. *It doesn't matter*, Arya told herself, *Thoros will find me in his flames*. Only he hadn't. Not yet, anyway, and once they crossed the river . . .

"Harroway town shouldn't be far," the Hound said. "Where Lord Roote stables Old King Andahar's two-headed water horse. Maybe we'll ride across."

Arya had never heard of Old King Andahar. She'd never seen a horse with two heads either, especially not one who could run on water, but she knew better than to ask. She held her tongue and sat stiff as the Hound turned the stallion's head and trotted along the ridgeline, following the river downstream. At least the rain was at their backs this way. She'd had enough of it stinging her eyes half-blind and washing down her cheeks like she was crying. *Wolves never cry*, she reminded herself again.

It could not have been much past noon, but the sky was dark as dusk. They had not seen the sun in more days than she could count. Arya was soaked to the bone, saddle-sore, sniffling, and achy. She had a fever too, and sometimes shivered uncontrollably, but when she'd told the Hound that she was sick he'd only snarled at her. "Wipe your nose and shut your mouth," he told her. Half the time he slept in the saddle now, trusting his stallion to follow whatever rutted farm track or game trail they were on. The horse was a heavy courser, almost as big as a destrier but much faster. *Stranger*, the Hound called him. Arya had tried to steal him once, when Clegane was taking a piss against a tree, thinking she could ride off before he could catch her. Stranger had almost bitten her face off. He was gentle as an old gelding with his master, but otherwise he had a temper as black as he was. She had never known a horse so quick to bite or kick.

They rode beside the river for hours, splashing across two muddy vassal streams before they reached the place that Sandor Clegane had spoken of. "Lord Harroway's Town," he said, and then, when he saw it, "*Seven hells!*" The town was drowned and desolate. The rising waters had overflowed the riverbanks. All that remained of Harroway town was the upper story of a daub-and-wattle inn, the seven-sided dome of a sunken sept, two-thirds of a stone roundtower, some moldy thatch roofs, and a forest of chimneys.

But there was smoke coming from the tower, Arya saw, and below one arched window a wide flat-bottomed boat was chained up tight. The boat had a dozen oarlocks and a pair of great carved wooden horse heads mounted fore and aft. *The two-headed horse*, she realized. There was a wooden house with a sod roof right in the middle of the deck, and when the Hound cupped his hands around his mouth and shouted two men came spilling out. A third appeared in the window of the roundtower, clutching a loaded crossbow. "*What do you want?*" he shouted across the swirling brown waters.

"*Take us over*," the Hound shouted back.

The men in the boat conferred with one another. One of them, a grizzled grey-haired man with thick arms and a bent back, stepped to the rail. "*It will cost you.*"

"*Then I'll pay.*"

With what? Arya wondered. The outlaws had taken Clegane's gold, but maybe Lord Beric had left him some silver and copper. A ferry ride shouldn't cost more than a few coppers . . .

The ferrymen were talking again. Finally the bent-backed one turned away and gave a shout. Six more men appeared, pulling up hoods to keep the rain off their heads. Still more squirmed out the holdfast window and leapt down onto the deck. Half of them looked enough like the bent-backed man to be his kin. Some of them undid the chains and took up long poles, while the others slid heavy wide-bladed oars through the locks. The ferry swung about and began to creep slowly toward the shallows, oars stroking smoothly on either side. Sandor Clegane rode down the hill to meet it.

When the aft end of the boat slammed into the hillside,

the ferrymen opened a wide door beneath the carved horse's head, and extended a heavy oaken plank. Stranger balked at the water's edge, but the Hound put his heels into the courser's flank and urged him up the gangway. The bent-backed man was waiting for them on deck. "Wet enough for you, ser?" he asked, smiling.

The Hound's mouth gave a twitch. "I need your boat, not your bloody wit." He dismounted, and pulled Arya down beside him. One of the boatmen reached for Stranger's bridle. "I wouldn't," Clegane said, as the horse kicked. The man leapt back, slipped on the rain-slick deck, and crashed onto his arse, cursing.

The ferryman with the bent back wasn't smiling any longer. "We can get you across," he said sourly. "It will cost you a gold piece. Another for the horse. A third for the boy."

"Three dragons?" Clegane gave a bark of laughter. "For three dragons I should own the bloody ferry."

"Last year, might be you could. But with this river, I'll need extra hands on the poles and oars just to see we don't get swept a hundred miles out to sea. Here's your choice. Three dragons, or you teach that hellhorse how to walk on water."

"I like an honest brigand. Have it your way. Three dragons . . . when you put us ashore safe on the north bank."

"I'll have them now, or we don't go." The man thrust out a thick, callused hand, palm up.

Clegane rattled his longsword to loosen the blade in the scabbard. "Here's *your* choice. Gold on the north bank, or steel on the south."

The ferryman looked up at the Hound's face. Arya could tell that he didn't like what he saw there. He had a dozen men behind him, strong men with oars and hardwood poles in their hands, but none of them were rushing forward to help him. Together they could overwhelm Sandor Clegane, though he'd likely kill three or four of them before they took him down. "How do I know you're good for it?" the bent-backed man asked, after a moment.

He's not, she wanted to shout. Instead she bit her lip.

"Knight's honor," the Hound said, unsmiling.

He's not even a knight. She did not say that either.

"That will do." The ferryman spat. "Come on then, we

can have you across before dark. Tie the horse up, I don't want him spooking when we're under way. There's a brazier in the cabin if you and your son want to get warm."

"I'm not his stupid son!" said Arya furiously. That was even worse than being taken for a boy. She was so angry that she might have told them who she *really* was, only Sandor Clegane grabbed her by the back of the collar and hoisted her one-handed off the deck. "How many times do I need to tell you to *shut your bloody mouth?*" He shook her so hard her teeth rattled, then let her fall. "Get in there and get dry, like the man said."

Arya did as she was told. The big iron brazier was glowing red, filling the room with a sullen suffocating heat. It felt pleasant to stand beside it, to warm her hands and dry off a little bit, but as soon as she felt the deck move under her feet she slipped back out through the forward door.

The two-headed horse eased slowly through the shallows, picking its way between the chimneys and rooftops of drowned Harroway. A dozen men labored at the oars while four more used the long poles to push off whenever they came too close to a rock, a tree, or a sunken house. The bent-backed man had the rudder. Rain pattered against the smooth planks of the deck and splashed off the tall carved horseheads fore and aft. Arya was getting soaked again, but she didn't care. She wanted to see. The man with the crossbow still stood in the window of the roundtower, she saw. His eyes followed her as the ferry slid by underneath. She wondered if he was this Lord Roote that the Hound had mentioned. *He doesn't look much like a lord.* But then, she didn't look much like a lady either.

Once they were beyond the town and out in the river proper, the current grew much stronger. Through the grey haze of rain Arya could make out a tall stone pillar on the far shore that surely marked the ferry landing, but no sooner had she seen it than she realized that they were being pushed away from it, downstream. The oarsmen were rowing more vigorously now, fighting the rage of the river. Leaves and broken branches swirled past as fast as if they'd been fired from a scorpion. The men with the poles leaned out and shoved away anything that came too close. It was windier out here, too. Whenever she turned to look upstream, Arya got a face full of blowing rain. Stranger was screaming and kicking as the deck moved underfoot.

If I jumped over the side, the river would wash me away before the Hound even knew that I was gone. She looked back over a shoulder, and saw Sandor Clegane struggling with his frightened horse, trying to calm him. She would never have a better chance to get away from him. *I might drown, though.* Jon used to say that she swam like a fish, but even a fish might have trouble in this river. Still, drowning might be better than King's Landing. She thought about Joffrey and crept up to the prow. The river was murky brown with mud and lashed by rain, looking more like soup than water. Arya wondered how cold it would be. *I couldn't get much wetter than I am now.* She put a hand on the rail.

But a sudden shout snapped her head about before she could leap. The ferrymen were rushing forward, poles in hand. For a moment she did not understand what was happening. Then she saw it: an uprooted tree, huge and dark, coming straight at them. A tangle of roots and limbs poked up out of the water as it came, like the reaching arms of a great kraken. The oarsmen were backing water frantically, trying to avoid a collision that could capsize them or stove their hull in. The old man had wrenched the rudder about, and the horse at the prow was swinging downstream, but too slowly. Glistening brown and black, the tree rushed toward them like a battering ram.

It could not have been more than ten feet from their prow when two of the boatmen somehow caught it with their long poles. One snapped, and the long splintering *craaaack* made it sound as if the ferry were breaking up beneath them. But the second man managed to give the trunk a hard shove, just enough to deflect it away from them. The tree swept past the ferry with inches to spare, its branches scrabbling like claws against the horsehead. Only just when it seemed as if they were clear, one of the monster's upper limbs dealt them a glancing thump. The ferry seemed to shudder, and Arya slipped, landing painfully on one knee. The man with the broken pole was not so lucky. She heard him shout as he stumbled over the side. Then the raging brown water closed over him, and he was gone in the time it took Arya to climb back to her feet. One of the other boatmen snatched up a coil of rope, but there was no one to throw it to.

Maybe he'll wash up someplace downstream, Arya tried to tell herself, but the thought had a hollow ring. She had lost all desire to go swimming. When Sandor Clegane shouted at her to get back inside before he beat her bloody, she went meekly. The ferry was fighting to turn back on course by then, against a river that wanted nothing more than to carry it down to the sea.

When they finally came ashore, it was a good two miles downriver of their usual landing. The boat slammed into the bank so hard that another pole snapped, and Arya almost lost her feet again. Sandor Clegane lifted her onto Stranger's back as if she weighed no more than a doll. The boatmen stared at them with dull, exhausted eyes, all but the bent-backed man, who held his hand out. "Six dragons," he demanded. "Three for the passage, and three for the man I lost."

Sandor Clegane rummaged in his pouch and shoved a crumpled wad of parchment into the boatman's palm. "There. Take ten."

"Ten?" The ferryman was confused. "What's this, now?"

"A dead man's note, good for nine thousand dragons or nearabouts." The Hound swung up into the saddle behind Arya, and smiled down unpleasantly. "Ten of it is yours. I'll be back for the rest one day, so see you don't go spending it."

The man squinted down at the parchment. "Writing. What good's writing? You promised gold. Knight's honor, you said."

"Knights have no bloody honor. Time you learned that, old man." The Hound gave Stranger the spur and galloped off through the rain. The ferrymen threw curses at their backs, and one or two threw stones. Clegane ignored rocks and words alike, and before long they were lost in the gloom of the trees, the river a dwindling roar behind them. "The ferry won't cross back till morning," he said, "and that lot won't be taking paper promises from the next fools to come along. If your friends are chasing us, they're going to need to be bloody strong swimmers."

Arya huddled down and held her tongue. *Valar morghulis,*

she thought sullenly. *Ser Ilyn, Ser Meryn, King Joffrey, Queen Cersei. Dunsen,* Poliver, Raff the Sweetling, Ser Gregor and the Tickler. And the Hound, the Hound, the Hound.

By the time the rain stopped and the clouds broke, she was shivering and sneezing so badly that Clegane called a halt for the night, and even tried to make a fire. The wood they gathered proved too wet, though. Nothing he tried was enough to make the spark catch. Finally he kicked it all apart in disgust. "Seven bloody hells," he swore. "I hate fires."

They sat on damp rocks beneath an oak tree, listening to the slow patter of water dripping from the leaves as they ate a cold supper of hardbread, moldy cheese, and smoked sausage. The Hound sliced the meat with his dagger, and narrowed his eyes when he caught Arya looking at the knife. "Don't even think about it."

"I wasn't," she lied.

He snorted to show what he thought of *that*, but he gave her a thick slice of sausage. Arya worried it with her teeth, watching him all the while. "I never beat your sister," the Hound said. "But I'll beat you if you make me. Stop trying to think up ways to kill me. None of it will do you a bit of good."

She had nothing to say to that. She gnawed on the sausage and stared at him coldly. *Hard as stone,* she thought.

"At least you look at my face. I'll give you that, you little she-wolf. How do you like it?"

"I don't. It's all burned and ugly."

Clegane offered her a chunk of cheese on the point of his dagger. "You're a little fool. What good would it do you if you *did* get away? You'd just get caught by someone worse."

"I would *not*," she insisted. "There is no one worse."

"You never knew my brother. Gregor once killed a man for snoring. His own man." When he grinned, the burned side of his face pulled tight, twisting his mouth in a queer unpleasant way. He had no lips on that side, and only the stump of an ear.

"I did so know your brother." Maybe the Mountain *was* worse, now that Arya thought about it. "Him and Dunsen and Polliver, and Raff the Sweetling and the Tickler."

The Hound seemed surprised. "And how would Ned Stark's precious little daughter come to know the likes of them? Gregor never brings his pet rats to court."

"I know them from the village." She ate the cheese, and reached for a hunk of hardbread. "The village by the lake where they caught Gendry, me, and Hot Pie. They caught Lommy Greenhands too, but Raff the Sweetling killed him because his leg was hurt."

Clegane's mouth twitched. "Caught you? My brother *caught* you?" That made him laugh, a sour sound, part rumble and part snarl. "Gregor never knew what he had, did he? He couldn't have, or he would have dragged you back kicking and screaming to King's Landing and dumped you in Cersei's lap. Oh, that's bloody sweet. I'll be sure and tell him that, before I cut his heart out."

It wasn't the first time he had talked of killing the Mountain. "But he's your brother," Arya said dubiously.

"Didn't you ever have a brother you wanted to kill?" He laughed again. "Or maybe a sister?" He must have seen something in her face then, for he leaned closer. "Sansa. That's it, isn't it? The wolf bitch wants to kill the pretty bird."

"No," Arya spat back at him. "I'd like to kill *you*."

"Because I hacked your little friend in two? I've killed a lot more than him, I promise you. You think that makes me some monster. Well, maybe it does, but I saved your sister's life too. The day the mob pulled her off her horse, I cut through them and brought her back to the castle, else she would have gotten what Lollys Stokeworth got. And she sang for me. You didn't know that, did you? Your sister sang me a sweet little song."

"You're lying," she said at once.

"You don't know half as much as you think you do. The *Blackwater?* Where in seven hells do you think we are? Where do you think we're going?"

The scorn in his voice made her hesitate. "Back to King's Landing," she said. "You're bringing me to Joffrey and the queen." That was wrong, she realized all of a sudden, just from the way he asked the questions. But she had to say *something*.

"Stupid blind little wolf bitch." His voice was rough and hard as an iron rasp. "Bugger Joffrey, bugger the queen, and bugger that twisted little gargoyle she calls a brother. I'm done with their city, done with their Kingsguard, done with Lannisters. What's a dog to do with lions, I ask you?" He reached for his waterskin, took a long pull. As he wiped his mouth, he offered the skin to Arya and said, "The river was the Trident, girl. The *Trident*, not the Blackwater. Make the map in your head, if you can. On the morrow we should reach the kingsroad. We'll make good time after that, straight up to the Twins. It's going to be me who hands you over to that mother of yours. Not the noble lightning lord or that flaming fraud of a priest, the monster." He grinned at the look on her face. "You think your outlaw friends are the only ones can smell a ransom? Dondarrion took my gold, so I took you. You're worth twice what they stole from me, I'd say. Maybe even more if I sold you back to the Lannisters like you fear, but I won't. Even a dog gets tired of being kicked. If this Young Wolf has the wits the gods gave a toad, he'll make me a lordling and beg me to enter his service. He *needs* me, though he may not know it yet. Maybe I'll even kill Gregor for him, he'd like that."

"He'll never take you," she spat back. "Not *you*."

"Then I'll take as much gold as I can carry, laugh in his face, and ride off. If he doesn't take me, he'd be wise to kill me, but he won't. Too much his father's son, from what I hear. Fine with me. Either way I win. And so do you, she-wolf. So stop whimpering and snapping at me, I'm sick of it. Keep your mouth shut and do as I tell you, and maybe we'll even be in time for your uncle's bloody wedding."

JON

The mare was blown, but Jon could not let up on her. He had to reach the Wall before the Magnar. He would have slept in the saddle if he'd had one; lacking that, it was hard enough to stay ahorse while awake. His wounded leg grew ever more painful. He dare not rest long enough to let it heal. Instead he ripped it open anew each time he mounted up.

When he crested a rise and saw the brown rutted kingsroad before him wending its way north through hill and plain, he patted the mare's neck and said, "Now all we need do is follow the road, girl. Soon the Wall." His leg had gone as stiff as wood by then, and fever had made him so light-headed that twice he found himself riding in the wrong direction.

Soon the Wall. He pictured his friends drinking mulled wine in the common hall. Hobb would be with his kettles, Donal Noye at his forge, Maester Aemon in his rooms beneath the rookery. *And the Old Bear? Sam, Grenn, Dolorous Edd, Dywen with his wooden teeth* . . . Jon could only pray that some had escaped the Fist.

Ygritte was much in his thoughts as well. He remembered the smell of her hair, the warmth of her body . . . and the look on her face as she slit the old man's throat. *You were wrong to love her*, a voice whispered. *You were wrong to leave her*, a different voice insisted. He wondered if his father had been torn the same way, when he'd left Jon's mother to return to Lady Catelyn. *He was pledged to Lady Stark, and I am pledged to the Night's Watch.*

He almost rode through Mole's Town, so feverish that he did not know where he was. Most of the village was hidden underground, only a handful of small hovels to be seen by the light of the waning moon. The brothel was a shed no bigger than a privy, its red lantern creaking in the wind, a bloodshot eye peering through the blackness. Jon dismounted at the adjoining stable, half-stumbling from the mare's back as he shouted two boys awake. "I need a fresh mount, with saddle and bridle," he told them, in a tone that brooked no argument. They brought him that; a skin of wine as well, and half a loaf of brown bread. "Wake the village," he told them. "Warn them. There are wildlings south of the Wall. Gather your goods and make for Castle Black." He pulled himself onto the black gelding they'd given him, gritting his teeth at the pain in his leg, and rode hard for the north.

As the stars began to fade in the eastern sky, the Wall appeared before him, rising above the trees and the morning mists. Moonlight glimmered pale against the ice. He urged the gelding on, following the muddy slick road until he saw the stone towers and timbered halls of Castle Black huddled like broken toys beneath the great cliff of ice. By then the Wall glowed pink and purple with the first light of dawn.

No sentries challenged him as he rode past the outbuildings. No one came forth to bar his way. Castle Black seemed as much a ruin as Greyguard. Brown brittle weeds grew between cracks in the stones of the courtyards. Old snow covered the roof of the Flint Barracks and lay in drifts against the north side of Hardin's Tower, where Jon used to sleep before being made the Old Bear's steward. Fingers of soot streaked the Lord Commander's Tower where the smoke had boiled from the windows. Mormont had moved to the King's Tower after the fire, but Jon saw no lights there either. From the ground he could not tell if there were sentries walking the Wall seven hundred feet above, but he saw no one on the huge switchback stair that climbed the south face of the ice like some great wooden thunderbolt.

There was smoke rising from the chimney of the armory, though; only a wisp, almost invisible against the grey northern sky, but it was enough. Jon dismounted and limped toward it. Warmth poured out the open door like the hot breath of summer. Within, one-armed Donal Noye was working his bellows at the fire. He looked up at the noise. "Jon Snow?"

"None else." Despite fever, exhaustion, his leg, the Magnar, the old man, Ygritte, Mance, despite it all, Jon smiled. It was good to be back, good to see Noye with his big belly and pinned-up sleeve, his jaw bristling with black stubble.

The smith released his grip on the bellows. "Your face . . ."

He had almost forgotten about his face. "A skinchanger tried to rip out my eye."

Noye frowned. "Scarred or smooth, it's a face I thought I'd seen the last of. We heard you'd gone over to Mance Rayder."

Jon grasped the door to stay upright. "Who told you that?"

"Jarman Buckwell. He returned a fortnight past. His scouts claim they saw you with their own eyes, riding along beside the wildling column and wearing a sheepskin cloak." Noye eyed him. "I see the last part's true."

"It's all true," Jon confessed. "As far as it goes."

"Should I be pulling down a sword to gut you, then?"

"No. I was acting on orders. Qhorin Halfhand's last command. Noye, where is the garrison?"

"Defending the Wall against your wildling friends."

"Yes, but *where*?"

"Everywhere. Harma Dogshead was seen at Woodswatch-by-the-Pool, Rattleshirt at Long Barrow, the Weeper near Icemark. All along the Wall . . . they're here, they're there, they're climbing near Queensgate, they're hacking at the gates of Greyguard, they're massing against

Eastwatch . . . but one glimpse of a black cloak and they're gone. Next day they're somewhere else."

Jon swallowed a groan. "Feints. Mance wants us to spread ourselves thin, don't you see? *And Bowen Marsh has obliged him.* "The gate is here. The attack is here."

Noye crossed the room. "Your leg is drenched in blood."

Jon looked down dully. It was true. His wound had opened again. "An arrow wound . . ."

"A wildling arrow." It was not a question. Noye had only one arm, but that was thick with muscle. He slid it under Jon's to help support him. "You're white as milk, and burning hot besides. I'm taking you to Aemon."

"There's no time. There are wildlings *south* of the Wall, coming up from Queenscrown to open the gate."

"How many?" Noye half-carried Jon out the door.

"A hundred and twenty, and well armed for wildlings. Bronze armor, some bits of steel. How many men are left here?"

"Forty odd," said Donal Noye. "The crippled and infirm, and some green boys still in training."

"If Marsh is gone, who did he name as castellan?"

The armorer laughed. "Ser Wynton, gods preserve him. Last knight in the castle and all. The thing is, Stout seems to have forgotten and no one's been rushing to remind him. I suppose I'm as much a commander as we have now. The meanest of the cripples."

That was for the good, at least. The one-armed armorer was hard headed, tough, and well seasoned in war. Ser Wynton Stout, on the other hand . . . well, he had been a good man once, everyone agreed, but he had been eighty years a ranger, and both strength and wits were gone. Once he'd fallen asleep at supper and almost drowned in a bowl of pea soup.

"Where's your wolf?" Noye asked as they crossed the yard.

"Ghost. I had to leave him when I climbed the Wall. I'd hoped he'd make his way back here."

"I'm sorry, lad. There's been no sign of him." They limped up to the maester's door, in the long wooden keep beneath the rookery. The armorer gave it a kick. "*Clydas!*"

After a moment a stooped, round-shouldered little man in black peered out. His small pink eyes widened at the sight of Jon. "Lay the lad down, I'll fetch the maester."

A fire was burning in the hearth, and the room was almost stuffy. The warmth made Jon sleepy. As soon as Noye eased him down onto his back, he closed his eyes to stop the world from spinning. He could hear the ravens *quork*ing and complaining in the rookery above. "*Snow*," one bird was saying. "*Snow, snow, snow*." That was Sam's doing, Jon remembered. Had Samwell Tarly made it home safely, he wondered, or only the birds?

Maester Aemon was not long in coming. He moved slowly, one spotted hand on Clydas's arm as he shuffled forward with small careful steps. Around his thin neck his chain hung heavy, gold and silver links glinting amongst iron, lead, tin, and other base metals. "Jon Snow," he said, "you must tell me all you've seen and done when you are stronger. Donal, put a kettle of wine on the fire, and my irons as well. I will want them red-hot. Clydas, I shall need that good sharp knife of yours." The maester was more than a hundred years old; shrunken, frail, hairless, and quite blind. But if his milky eyes saw nothing, his wits were still as sharp as they had ever been.

"There are wildlings coming," Jon told him, as Clydas ran a blade up the leg of his breeches, slicing the heavy black cloth, crusty with old blood and sodden with new. "From the south. We climbed the Wall . . ."

Maester Aemon gave Jon's crude bandage a sniff when Clydas cut it away. "We?"

"I was with them. Qhorin Halfhand commanded me to join them." Jon winced as the maester's finger explored his wound, poking and prodding. "The Magnar of Thenn—*aaaaah*, that hurts." He clenched his teeth. "Where is the Old Bear?"

"Jon . . . it grieves me to say, but Lord Commander Mormont was murdered at Craster's Keep, at the hands of his Sworn Brothers."

"Bro . . . *our own men?*" Aemon's words hurt a hundred times worse than his fingers. Jon remembered the Old Bear as last he'd seen him, standing before his tent with his raven on his arm croaking for corn. *Mormont gone?* He had feared it ever since he'd seen the aftermath of battle on the

Fist, yet it was no less a blow. "Who was it? Who turned on him?"

"Garth of Oldtown, Ollo Lophand, Dirk . . . thieves, cowards and killers, the lot of them. We should have seen it coming. The Watch is not what it was. Too few honest men to keep the rogues in line." Donal Noye turned the maester's blades in the fire. "A dozen true men made it back. Dolorous Edd, Giant, your friend the Aurochs. We had the tale from them."

Only a dozen? Two hundred men had left Castle Black with Lord Commander Mormont, two hundred of the Watch's best. "Does this mean Marsh is Lord Commander, then?" The Old Pomegranate was amiable, and a diligent First Steward, but he was woefully ill-suited to face a wildling host.

"For the nonce, until we can hold a choosing," said Maester Aemon. "Clydas, bring me the flask."

A choosing. With Qhorin Halfhand and Ser Jaremy Rykker both dead and Ben Stark still missing, who was there? Not Bowen Marsh or Ser Wynton Stout, that was certain. Had Thoren Smallwood survived the Fist, or Ser Ottyn Wythers? *No, it will be Cotter Pyke or Ser Denys Mallister. Which, though?* The commanders at the Shadow Tower and Eastwatch were good men, but very different; Ser Denys courtly and cautious, as chivalrous as he was elderly, Pyke younger, bastard-born, rough-tongued, and bold to a fault. Worse, the two men despised each other. The Old Bear had always kept them far apart, at opposite ends of the Wall. The Mallisters had a bone-deep mistrust of the ironborn, Jon knew.

A stab of pain reminded him of his own woes. The maester squeezed his hand. "Clydas is bringing milk of the poppy."

Jon tried to rise. "I don't need—"

"You do," Aemon said firmly. "This will hurt."

Donal Noye crossed the room and shoved Jon back onto his back. "Be still, or I'll tie you down." Even with only one arm, the smith handled him as if he were a child. Clydas returned with a green flask and a rounded stone cup. Maester Aemon poured it full. "Drink this."

Jon had bitten his lip in his struggles. He could taste

blood mingled with the thick, chalky potion. It was all he could do not to retch it back up.

Clydas brought a basin of warm water, and Maester Aemon washed the pus and blood from his wound. Gentle as he was, even the lightest touch made Jon want to scream. "The Magnar's men are disciplined, and they have bronze armor," he told them. Talking helped keep his mind off his leg.

"The Magnar's a lord on Skagos," Noye said. "There were Skagossons at Eastwatch when I first came to the Wall, I remember hearing them talk of him."

"Jon was using the word in its older sense, I think," Maester Aemon said, "not as a family name but as a title. It derives from the Old Tongue."

"It means lord," Jon agreed. "Styr is the Magnar of some place called Thenn, in the far north of the Frostfangs. He has a hundred of his own men, and a score of raiders who know the Gift almost as well as we do. Mance never found the horn, though, that's something. The Horn of Winter, that's what he was digging for up along the Milkwater."

Maester Aemon paused, washcloth in hand. "The Horn of Winter is an ancient legend. Does the King-beyond-the-Wall truly believe that such a thing exists?"

"They all do," said Jon. "Ygritte said they opened a hundred graves . . . graves of kings and heroes, all over the valley of the Milkwater, but they never . . ."

"Who is *Ygritte?*" Donal Noye asked pointedly.

"A woman of the free folk." How could he explain Ygritte to them? *She's warm and smart and funny and she can kiss a man or slit his throat.* "She's with Styr, but she's not . . . she's young, only a girl, in truth, wild, but she . . ." *She killed an old man for building a fire.* His tongue felt thick and clumsy. The milk of the poppy was clouding his wits. "I broke my vows with her. I never meant to, but . . ." *It was wrong. Wrong to love her, wrong to leave her . . .* "I wasn't strong enough. The Halfhand commanded me, ride with them, watch, I must not balk, I . . ." His head felt as if it were packed with wet wool.

Maester Aemon sniffed Jon's wound again. Then he put the bloody cloth back in the basin and said, "Donal, the hot knife, if you please. I shall need you to hold him still."

I will not scream, Jon told himself when he saw the blade glowing red hot. But he broke that vow as well. Donal Noye held him down, while Clydas helped guide the maester's hand. Jon did not move, except to pound his fist against the table, again and again and again. The pain was so huge he felt small and weak and helpless inside it, a child whimpering in the dark. *Ygritte*, he thought, when the stench of burning flesh was in his nose and his own shriek echoing in her ears. *Ygritte, I had to.* For half a heartbeat the agony started to ebb. But then the iron touched him once again, and he fainted.

When his eyelids fluttered open, he was wrapped in thick wool and floating. He could not seem to move, but that did not matter. For a time he dreamed that Ygritte was with him, tending him with gentle hands. Finally he closed his eyes and slept.

The next waking was not so gentle. The room was dark, but under the blankets the pain was back, a throbbing in his leg that turned into a hot knife at the least motion. Jon learned that the hard way when he tried to see if he still had a leg. Gasping, he swallowed a scream and made another fist.

"Jon?" A candle appeared, and a well-remembered face was looking down on him, big ears and all. "You shouldn't move."

"Pyp?" Jon reached up, and the other boy clasped his hand and gave it a squeeze. "I thought you'd gone . . ."

". . . with the Old Pomegranate? No, he thinks I'm too small and green. Grenn's here too."

"I'm here too." Grenn stepped to the other side of the bed. "I fell asleep."

Jon's throat was dry. "Water," he gasped. Grenn brought it, and held it to his lips. "I saw the Fist," he said, after a long swallow. "The blood, and the dead horses . . . Noye said a dozen made it back . . . who?"

"Dywen did. Giant, Dolorous Edd, Sweet Donnel Hill, Ulmer, Left Hand Lew, Garth Greyfeather. Four or five more. Me."

"Sam?"

Grenn looked away. "He killed one of the Others, Jon. I saw it. He stabbed him with that dragonglass knife you made him, and we started calling him Sam the Slayer. He hated that."

Sam the Slayer. Jon could hardly imagine a less likely warrior than Sam Tarly. "What happened to him?"

"We left him." Grenn sounded miserable. "I shook him and screamed at him, even slapped his face. Giant tried to drag him to his feet, but he was too heavy. Remember in training how he'd curl up on the ground and lie there whimpering? At Craster's he wouldn't even whimper. Dirk and Ollo were tearing up the walls looking for food, Garth and Garth were fighting, some of the others were raping Craster's wives. Dolorous Edd figured Dirk's bunch would kill all the loyal men to keep us from telling what they'd done, and they had us two to one. We left Sam with the Old Bear. He wouldn't *move*, Jon."

You were his brother, he almost said. *How could you leave him amongst wildlings and murderers?*

"He might still be alive," said Pyp. "He might surprise us all and come riding up tomorrow."

"With Mance Rayder's head, aye." Grenn was trying to sound cheerful, Jon could tell. "Sam the Slayer!"

Jon tried to sit again. It was as much a mistake as the first time. He cried out, cursing.

"Grenn, go wake Maester Aemon," said Pyp. "Tell him Jon needs more milk of the poppy."

Yes, Jon thought. "No," he said. "The Magnar . . ."

"We know," said Pyp. "The sentries on the Wall have been told to keep one eye on the south, and Donal Noye dispatched some men to Weatherback Ridge to watch the kingsroad. Maester Aemon's sent birds to Eastwatch and the Shadow Tower too."

Maester Aemon shuffled to the bedside, one hand on Grenn's shoulder. "Jon, be gentle with yourself. It is good that you have woken, but you must give yourself time to heal. We drowned the wound with boiling wine, and closed you up with a poultice of nettle, mustard seed and moldy bread, but unless you rest . . ."

"I can't." Jon fought through the pain to sit. "Mance will be here soon . . . thousands of men, giants, mammoths . . . has word been sent to Winterfell? To the king?" Sweat dripped off his brow. He closed his eyes a moment.

Grenn gave Pyp a strange look. "He doesn't know."

"Jon," said Maester Aemon, "much and more happened while you were away, and little of it good. Balon Greyjoy has crowned himself again and sent his longships against the north. Kings sprout like weeds at every hand and we have sent appeals to all of them, yet none will come. They have more pressing uses for their swords, and we are far off and forgotten. And Winterfell . . . Jon, be strong . . . Winterfell is no more . . ."

"No more?" Jon stared at Aemon's white eyes and wrinkled face. "My brothers are at Winterfell. Bran and Rickon . . ."

The maester touched his brow. "I am so very sorry, Jon. Your brothers died at the command of Theon Greyjoy, after he took Winterfell in his father's name. When your father's bannermen threatened to retake it, he put the castle to the torch."

"Your brothers were avenged," Grenn said. "Bolton's son killed all the ironmen, and it's said he's flaying Theon Greyjoy inch by inch for what he did."

"I'm sorry, Jon." Pyp squeezed his shoulder. "We are all."

Jon had never liked Theon Greyjoy, but he had been their father's ward. Another spasm of pain twisted up his leg, and the next he knew he was flat on his back again. "There's some mistake," he insisted. "At Queenscrown I saw a direwolf, a *grey* direwolf . . . grey . . . *it knew me.*" If Bran was dead, could some part of him live on in his wolf, as Orell lived within his eagle?

"Drink this." Grenn held a cup to his lips. Jon drank. His head was full of wolves and eagles, the sound of his brothers' laughter. The faces above him began to blur and fade. *They can't be dead. Theon would never do that. And Winterfell . . . grey granite, oak and iron, crows wheeling around the towers, steam rising off the hot pools in the godswood, the stone kings sitting on their thrones . . . how could Winterfell be gone?*

When the dreams took him, he found himself back home once more, splashing in the hot pools beneath a huge white weirwood that had his father's face. Ygritte was with him, laughing at him, shedding her skins till she was naked as her name day, trying to kiss him, but he couldn't, not with his father watching. He was the blood of

Winterfell, a man of the Night's Watch. *I will not father a bastard*, he told her. *I will not. I will not.* "You know nothing, Jon Snow," she whispered, her skin dissolving in the hot water, the flesh beneath sloughing off her bones until only skull and skeleton remained, and the pool bubbled thick and red.

CATELYN

They heard the Green Fork before they saw it, an endless susurrus, like the growl of some great beast. The river was a boiling torrent, half again as wide as it had been last year, when Robb had divided his army here and vowed to take a Frey to bride as the price of his crossing. *He needed Lord Walder and his bridge then, and he needs them even more now.* Catelyn's heart was full of misgivings as she watched the murky green waters swirl past. *There is no way we will ford this, nor swim across, and it could be a moon's turn before these waters fall again.*

As they neared the Twins, Robb donned his crown and summoned Catelyn and Edmure to ride beside him. Ser Raynald Westerling bore his banner, the direwolf of Stark on its ice-white field.

The gatehouse towers emerged from the rain like ghosts, hazy grey apparitions that grew more solid the closer they rode. The Frey stronghold was not one castle but two; mirror images in wet stone standing on opposite sides of the water, linked by a great arched bridge. From the center of its span rose the Water Tower, the river running straight and swift below. Channels had been cut from the banks, to form moats that made each twin an island. The rains had turned the moats to shallow lakes.

Across the turbulent waters, Catelyn could see several thousand men encamped around the eastern castle, their banners hanging like so many drowned cats from the lances outside their tents. The rain made it impossible to distinguish colors and devices. Most were grey, it seemed to her, though beneath such skies the whole world seemed grey.

"Tread lightly here, Robb," she cautioned her son. "Lord Walder has a thin skin and a sharp tongue, and some of these sons of his will doubtless take after their father. You must not let yourself be provoked."

"I know the Freys, Mother. I know how much I wronged them, and how much I *need* them. I shall be as sweet as a septon."

Catelyn shifted her seat uncomfortably. "If we are offered refreshment when we arrive, on no account refuse. Take what is offered, and eat and drink where all can see. If nothing is offered, ask for bread and cheese and a cup of wine."

"I'm more wet than hungry . . ."

"Robb, *listen to me*. Once you have eaten of his bread and salt, you have the guest right, and the laws of hospitality protect you beneath his roof."

Robb looked more amused than afraid. "I have an army to protect me, Mother, I don't need to trust in bread and salt. But if it pleases Lord Walder to serve me stewed crow smothered in maggots, I'll eat it and ask for a second bowl."

Four Freys rode out from the western gatehouse, wrapped in heavy cloaks of thick grey wool. Catelyn recognized Ser Ryman, son of the late Ser Stevron, Lord Walder's firstborn. With his father dead, Ryman was heir to the Twins. The face she saw beneath his hood was fleshy, broad, and stupid. The other three were likely his own sons, Lord Walder's great grandsons.

Edmure confirmed as much. "Edwyn is eldest, the pale slender man with the constipated look. The wiry one with the beard is Black Walder, a nasty bit of business. Petyr is on the bay, the lad with the unfortunate face. Petyr Pimple, his brothers call him. Only a year or two older than Robb, but Lord Walder married him off at ten to a woman thrice his age. Gods, I hope Roslin doesn't take after *him*."

They halted to let their hosts come to them. Robb's banner drooped on its staff, and the steady sound of rainfall mingled with the rush of the swollen Green Fork on their right. Grey Wind edged forward, tail stiff, watching through slitted eyes of dark gold. When the Freys were a half-dozen yards away Catelyn heard him growl, a deep rumble that seemed almost one with rush of the river. Robb looked startled. "Grey Wind, to me. To *me!*"

Instead the direwolf leapt forward, snarling.

Ser Ryman's palfrey shied off with a whinny of fear, and Petyr Pimple's reared and threw him. Only Black Walder kept his mount in hand. He reached for the hilt of his sword. "*No!*" Robb was shouting. "Grey Wind, here. *Here.*" Catelyn spurred between the direwolf and the horses. Mud spattered from the hooves of her mare as she cut in front of Grey Wind. The wolf veered away, and only then seemed to hear Robb calling.

"Is this how a Stark makes amends?" Black Walder shouted, with naked steel in hand. "A poor greeting I call it, to set your wolf upon us. Is this why you've come?"

Ser Ryman had dismounted to help Petyr Pimple back to his feet. The lad was muddy, but unhurt.

"I've come to make my apology for the wrong I did your House, and to see my uncle wed." Robb swung down from the saddle. "Petyr, take my horse. Yours is almost back to the stable."

Petyr looked to his father and said, "I can ride behind one of my brothers."

The Freys made no sign of obeisance. "You come late," Ser Ryman declared.

"The rains delayed us," said Robb. "I sent a bird."

"I do not see the woman."

By *the woman* Ser Ryman meant Jeyne Westerling, all knew. Lady Catelyn smiled apologetically. "Queen Jeyne was weary after so much travel, sers. No doubt she will be pleased to visit when times are more settled."

"My grandfather will be displeased." Though Black Walder had sheathed his sword, his tone was no friendlier.

"I've told him much of the lady, and he wished to behold her with his own eyes."

Edwyn cleared his throat. "We have chambers prepared for you in the Water Tower, Your Grace," he told Robb with careful courtesy, "as well as for Lord Tully and Lady Stark. Your lords bannermen are also welcome to shelter under our roof and partake of the wedding feast."

"And my men?" asked Robb.

"My lord grandfather regrets that he cannot feed nor house so large a host. We have been sore pressed to find fodder and provender for our own levies. Nonetheless, your men shall not be neglected. If they will cross and set up their camp beside our own, we will bring out enough casks of wine and ale for all to drink the health of Lord Edmure and his bride. We have thrown up three great feast tents on the far bank, to provide them with some shelter from the rains."

"Your lord father is most kind. My men will thank him. They have had a long wet ride."

Edmure Tully edged his horse forward. "When shall I meet my betrothed?"

"She waits for you within," promised Edwyn Frey. "You will forgive her if she seems shy, I know. She has been awaiting this day most anxiously, poor maid. But perhaps we might continue this out of the rain?"

"Truly." Ser Ryman mounted up again, pulling Petyr Pimple up behind him. "If you would follow me, my father awaits." He turned the palfrey's head back towrd the Twins.

Edmure fell in beside Catelyn. "The Late Lord Frey might have seen fit to welcome us in person," he complained. "I am his liege lord as well as his son-to-be, and Robb's his king."

"When you are one-and-ninety, Brother, see how eager *you* are to go riding in the rain." Yet she wondered if that was the whole truth of it. Lord Walder normally went about in a covered litter, which would have kept the worst of the rain off him. *A deliberate slight*? If so, it might be the first of many yet to come.

There was more trouble at the gatehouse. Grey Wind balked in the middle of the drawbridge, shook the rain off, and howled at the portcullis. Robb whistled impatiently.

"Grey Wind. What is it? Grey Wind, with me." But the direwolf only bared his teeth. *He does not like this place,* Catelyn thought. Robb had to squat and speak softly to the wolf before he would consent to pass beneath the portcullis. By then Lame Lothar and Walder Rivers had come up. "It's the sound of the water he fears," Rivers said. "Beasts know to avoid the river in flood."

"A dry kennel and a leg of mutton will see him right again," said Lothar cheerfully. "Shall I summon our master of hounds?"

"He's a direwolf, not a dog," said Robb, "and dangerous to men he does not trust. Ser Raynald, stay with him. I won't take him into Lord Walder's hall like this."

Deftly done, Catelyn decided. *Robb keeps the Westerling out of Lord Walder's sight as well.*

Gout and brittle bones had taken their toll of old Walder Frey. They found him propped up in his high seat with a cushion beneath him and an ermine robe across his lap. His chair was black oak, its back carved into the semblance of two stout towers joined by an arched bridge, so massive that its embrace turned the old man into a grotesque child. There was something of the vulture about Lord Walder, and rather more of the weasel. His bald head, spotted with age, thrust out from his scrawny shoulders on a long pink neck. Loose skin dangled beneath his receding chin, his eyes were runny and clouded, and his toothless mouth moved constantly, sucking at the empty air as a babe sucks at his mother's breast.

The eighth Lady Frey stood beside Lord Walder's high seat. At his feet sat a somewhat younger version of himself, a stooped thin man of fifty whose costly garb of blue wool and grey satin was strangely accented by a crown and collar ornamented with tiny brass bells. The likeness between him and his lord was striking, save for their eyes; Lord Frey's small, dim, and suspicious, the other's large, amiable, and vacant. Catelyn recalled that one of Lord Walder's brood had fathered a halfwit long years ago. During past visits, the Lord of the Crossing had always taken care to hide this one away. *Did he always wear a fool's crown, or is that meant as mockery of Robb?* It was a question she dare not ask.

Frey sons, daughters, children, grandchildren, husbands,

wives and servants crowded the rest of the hall. But it was the old man who spoke. "You will forgive me if I do not kneel, I know. My legs no longer work as they did, though that which hangs between 'em serves well enough, *heh*." His mouth split in a toothless smile as he eyed Robb's crown. "Some would say it's a poor king who crowns himself with bronze, Your Grace."

"Bronze and iron are stronger than gold and silver," Robb answered. "The old Kings of Winter wore such a sword-crown."

"Small good it did them when the dragons came. *Heh*." That *heh* seemed to please the lackwit, who bobbed his head from side to side, jingling crown and collar. "Sire," Lord Walder said, "forgive my Aegon the noise. He has less wits than a crannogman, and he's never met a king before. One of Stevron's boys. We call him Jinglebell."

"Ser Stevron mentioned him, my lord." Robb smiled at the lackwit. "Well met, Aegon. Your father was a brave man."

Jinglebell jingled his bells. A thin line of spit ran from one corner of his mouth when he smiled.

"Save your royal breath. You'd do as well talking to a chamberpot." Lord Walder shifted his gaze to the others. "Well, Lady Catelyn, I see you have returned to us. And young Ser Edmure, the victor of the Stone Mill. Lord Tully now, I'll need to remember that. You're the fifth Lord Tully I've known. I outlived the other four, *heh*. Your bride's about here somewhere. I suppose you want a look at her."

"I would, my lord."

"Then you'll have it. But clothed. She's a modest girl, and a maid. You won't see her naked till the bedding." Lord Walder cackled. "*Heh*. Soon enough, soon enough." He craned his head about. "Benfrey, go fetch your sister. Be quick about it, Lord Tully's come all the way from Riverrun." A young knight in a quartered surcoat bowed and took his leave, and the old man turned back to Robb. "And where's *your* bride, Your Grace? The fair Queen Jeyne. A Westerling of the Crag, I'm told, *heh*."

"I left her at Riverrun, my lord. She was too weary for more travel, as we told Ser Ryman."

"That makes me grievous sad. I wanted to behold her

with mine own weak eyes. We all did, *heh*. Isn't that so, my lady?"

Pale wispy Lady Frey seemed startled that she would be called upon to speak. "Y-yes, my lord. We all so wanted to pay homage to Queen Jeyne. She must be fair to look on."

"She is most fair, my lady." There was an icy stillness in Robb's voice that reminded Catelyn of his father.

The old man either did not hear it or refused to pay it any heed. "Fairer than my own get, *heh?* Elsewise how could her face and form have made the King's Grace forget his solemn promise."

Robb suffered the rebuke with dignity. "No words can set that right, I know, but I have come to make my apologies for the wrong I did your House, and to beg for your forgiveness, my lord."

"Apologies, *heh*. Yes, you vowed to make one, I recall. I'm old, but I don't forget such things. Not like some kings, it seems. The young remember nothing when they see a pretty face and a nice firm pair of teats, isn't that so? I was the same. Some might say I still am, *heh heh*. They'd be wrong, though, wrong as you were. But now you're here to make amends. It was my girls you spurned, though. Mayhaps it's them should hear you beg for pardon, Your Grace. My maiden girls. Here, have a look at them." When he waggled his fingers, a flurry of femininity left their places by the walls to line up beneath the dais. Jinglebell started to rise as well, his bells ringing merrily, but Lady Frey grabbed the lackwit's sleeve and tugged him back down.

Lord Walder named the names. "My daughter Arwyn," he said of a girl of fourteen. "Shirei, my youngest trueborn daughter. Ami and Marianne are granddaughters. I married Ami to Ser Pate of Sevenstreams, but the Mountain killed the oaf so I got her back. That's a Cersei, but we call her Little Bee, her mother's a Beesbury. More granddaughters. One's a Walda, and the others . . . well, they have names, whatever they are . . ."

"I'm Merry, Lord Grandfather," one girl said.

"You're noisy, that's for certain. Next to Noisy is my daughter Tyta. Then another Walda. Alyx, Marissa . . . are you Marissa? I thought you were. She's not always bald. The maester shaved her hair off, but he swears it will soon grow back. The twins are Serra and Sarra." He squinted down at one of the younger girls. "*Heh*, are you another Walda?"

The girl could not have been more than four. "I'm Ser Aemon Rivers's Walda, lord great grandfather." She curtsied.

"How long have you been talking? Not that you're like to have anything sensible to say, your father never did. He's a bastard's son besides, *heh*. Go away, I wanted only Freys up here. The King in the North has no interest in base stock." Lord Walder glanced to Robb, as Jinglebell bobbed his head and chimed. "There they are, all maidens. Well, and one widow, but there's some who like a woman broken in. You might have had any one of them."

"It would have been an impossible choice, my lord," said Robb with careful courtesy. "They're all too lovely."

Lord Walder snorted. "And they say *my* eyes are bad. Some will do well enough, I suppose. Others . . . well, it makes no matter. They weren't good enough for the King in the North, *heh*. Now what is it you have to say?"

"My ladies." Robb looked desperately uncomfortable, but he had known this moment must come, and he faced it without flinching. "All men should keep their word, kings most of all. I was pledged to marry one of you and I broke that vow. The fault is not in you. What I did was not done to slight you, but because I loved another. No words can set it right, I know, yet I come before you to ask forgiveness, that the Freys of the Crossing and the Starks of Winterfell may once again be friends."

The smaller girls fidgeted anxiously. Their older sisters waited for Lord Walder on his black oak throne. Jinglebell rocked back and forth, bells chiming on collar and crown.

"Good," the Lord of the Crossing said. "That was very good, Your Grace. 'No words can set it right,' *heh*. Well said, well said. At the wedding feast I hope you will not refuse to dance with my daughters. It would please an old man's heart, *heh*." He bobbed his wrinkled pink head up and down, in much the same way his lackwit grandson did, though Lord Walder wore no bells. "And here she is, Lord Edmure. My daughter Roslin, my most precious little blossom, *heh*."

Ser Benfrey led her into the hall. They looked enough

alike to be full siblings. Judging from their age, both were children of the sixth Lady Frey; a Rosby, Catelyn seemed to recall.

Roslin was small for her years, her skin as white as if she had just risen from a milk bath. Her face was comely, with a small chin, delicate nose, and big brown eyes. Thick chestnut hair fell in loose waves to a waist so tiny that Edmure would be able to put his hands around it. Beneath the lacy bodice of her pale blue gown, her breasts looked small but shapely.

"Your Grace." The girl went to her knees. "Lord Edmure, I hope I am not a disappointment to you."

Far from it, thought Catelyn. Her brother's face had lit up at the sight of her. "You are a delight to me, my lady," Edmure said. "And ever will be, I know."

Roslin had a small gap between two of her front teeth that made her shy with her smiles, but the flaw was almost endearing. *Pretty enough*, Catelyn thought, *but so small, and she comes of Rosby stock*. The Rosbys had never been robust. She much preferred the frames of some of the older girls in the hall; daughters or granddaughters, she could not be sure. They had a Crakehall look about them, and Lord Walder's third wife had been of that House. *Wide hips to bear children, big breasts to nurse them, strong arms to carry them. The Crakehalls have always been a big-boned family, and strong.*

"My lord is kind," the Lady Roslin said to Edmure.

"My lady is beautiful." Edmure took her hand and drew her to her feet. "But why are you crying?"

"For joy," Roslin said. "I weep for joy, my lord."

"*Enough*," Lord Walder broke in. "You may weep and whisper after you're wed, *heh*. Benfrey, see your sister back to her chambers, she has a wedding to prepare for. And a bedding, *heh*, the sweetest part. For all, for all." His mouth moved in and out. "We'll have music, such sweet music, and wine, *heh*, the red will run, and we'll put some wrongs aright. But now you're weary, and wet as well, dripping on my floor. There's fires waiting for you, and hot mulled wine, and baths if you want 'em. Lothar, show our guests to their quarters."

"I need to see my men across the river, my lord," Robb said.

"They shan't get lost," Lord Walder complained. "They're crossed before, haven't they? When you came down from the north. You wanted crossing and I gave it to you, and you never said mayhaps, *heh*. But suit yourself. Lead each man across by the hand if you like, it's naught to me."

"*My lord!*" Catelyn had almost forgotten. "Some food would be most welcome. We have ridden many leagues in the rain."

Walder Frey's mouth moved in and out. "Food, *heh*. A loaf of bread, a bite of cheese, mayhaps a sausage."

"Some wine to wash it down," Robb said. "And salt."

"Bread and salt. *Heh*. Of course, of course." The old man clapped his hands together, and servants came into the hall, bearing flagons of wine and trays of bread, cheese, and butter. Lord Walder took a cup of red himself, and raised it high with a spotted hand. "My guests," he said. "My honored guests. Be welcome beneath my roof, and at my table."

"We thank you for your hospitality, my lord," Robb replied. Edmure echoed him, along with the Greatjon, Ser Marq Piper, and the others. They drank his wine and ate his bread and butter. Catelyn tasted the wine and nibbled at some bread, and felt much the better for it. *Now we should be safe*, she thought.

Knowing how petty the old man could be, she had expected their rooms to be bleak and cheerless. But the Freys had made more than ample provision for them, it seemed. The bridal chamber was large and richly appointed, dominated by a great featherbed with corner posts carved in the likeness of castle towers. Its draperies were Tully red and blue, a nice courtesy. Sweet-smelling carpets covered a plank floor, and a tall shuttered window opened to the south. Catelyn's own room was smaller, but handsomely furnished and comfortable, with a fire burning in the hearth. Lame Lothar assured them that Robb would have an entire suite, as befit a king. "If there is anything you require, you need only tell one of the guards." He bowed and withdrew, limping heavily as he made his way down the curving steps.

"We should post our own guards," Catelyn told her brother. She would rest easier with Stark and Tully men outside her door. The audience with Lord Walder had not been as painful as she feared, yet all the same she would be glad to be done with this. *A few more days, and Robb will be off to battle, and me to a comfortable captivity at Seagard.* Lord Jason would show her every courtesy, she had no doubt, but the prospect still depressed her.

She could hear the sounds of horses below as the long column of mounted men wound their way across the bridge from castle to castle. The stones rumbled to the passage of heavy-laden wayns. Catelyn went to the window and gazed out, to watch Robb's host emerge from the eastern twin. "The rain seems to be lessening."

"Now that we're inside." Edmure stood before the fire, letting the warmth wash over him. "What did you make of Roslin?"

Too small and delicate. Childbirth will go hard on her. But her brother seemed well pleased with the girl, so all she said was, "Sweet."

"I believe she liked me. Why was she crying?"

"She's a maid on the eve of her wedding. A few tears are to be expected." Lysa had wept lakes the morning of their own wedding, though she had managed to be dry-eyed and radiant when Jon Arryn swept his cream-and-blue cloak about her shoulders.

"She's prettier than I dared hope." Edmure raised a hand before she could speak. "I know there are more important things, spare me the sermon, septa. Even so . . . did you see some of those other maids Frey trotted out? The one with the twitch? Was that the shaking sickness? And those twins had more craters and eruptions on their faces than Petyr Pimple. When I saw that lot, I knew Roslin would be bald and one-eyed, with Jinglebell's wits and Black Walder's temper. But she seems gentle as well as fair." He looked perplexed. "Why would the old weasel refuse to let me choose unless he meant to foist off someone hideous?"

"Your fondness for a pretty face is well known," Catelyn reminded him. "Perhaps Lord Walder actually wants you to be happy with your bride." *Or more like, he did not want you balking over a boil and upsetting all his plans.* "Or it may be that Roslin is the old man's favorite. The Lord of Riverrun is a much better match than most of his daughters can hope for."

"True." Her brother still seemed uncertain, however. "Is it possible the girl is barren?"

"Lord Walder wants his grandson to inherit Riverrun. How would it serve him to give you a barren wife?"

"It rids him of a daughter no one else would take."

"Small good that will do him. Walder Frey is a peevish man, not a stupid one."

"Still . . . it *is* possible?"

"Yes," Catelyn conceded, reluctantly. "There are illnesses a girl can have in childhood that leave her unable to conceive. There's no reason to believe that Lady Roslin was so afflicted, though." She looked round the room. "The Freys have received us more kindly than I had anticipated, if truth be told."

Edmure laughed. "A few barbed words and some unseemly gloating. From him that's courtesy. I expected the old weasel to piss in our wine and make us praise the vintage."

The jest left Catelyn strangely disquieted. "If you will excuse me, I should change from these wet clothes.

"As you wish." Edmure yawned. "I may nap an hour."

She retreated to her own room. The chest of clothes she'd brought from Riverrun had been carried up and laid at the foot of the bed. After she'd undressed and hung her wet clothing by the fire, she donned a warm wool dress of Tully red and blue, washed and brushed her hair and let it dry, and went in search of Freys.

Lord Walder's black oak throne was empty when she entered the hall, but some of his sons were drinking by the fire. Lame Lothar rose clumsily when he saw her. "Lady Catelyn, I thought you would be resting. How may I be of service?"

"Are these your brothers?" she asked.

"Brothers, half-brothers, good brothers, and nephews. Raymund and I shared a mother. Lord Lucias Vypren is my half-sister Lythene's husband, and Ser Damon is their son. My half-brother Ser Hosteen I believe you know. And this is Ser Leslyn Haigh and his sons, Ser Harys and Ser Donnel."

"Well met, sers. Is Ser Perwyn about? He helped escort me to Storm's End and back, when Robb sent me to speak with Lord Renly. I was looking forward to seeing him again."

"Perwyn is away," Lame Lothar said. "I shall give him your regards. I know he will regret having missed you."

"Surely he will return in time for Lady Roslin's wedding?"

"He had hoped to," said Lame Lothar, "but with this rain . . . you saw how the rivers ran, my lady."

"I did indeed," said Catelyn. "I wonder if you would be so good as to direct me to your maester?"

"Are you unwell, my lady?" asked Ser Hosteen, a powerful man with a square strong jaw.

"A woman's complaint. Nothing to concern you, ser."

Lothar, ever gracious, escorted her from the hall, up some steps, and across a covered bridge to another stair. "You should find Maester Brenett in the turret on the top, my lady."

Catelyn half expected that the maester would be yet another son of Walder Frey's, but Brenett did not have the look. He was a great fat man, bald and double-chinned and none too clean, to judge from the raven droppings that stained the sleeves of his robes, yet he seemed amiable enough. When she told him of Edmure's concerns about Lady Roslin's fertility, he chuckled. "Your lord brother need have no fear, Lady Catelyn. She's small, I'll grant you, and narrow in the hips, but her mother was the same, and Lady Bethany gave Lord Walder a child every year."

"How many lived past infancy?" she asked bluntly.

"Five." He ticked them off on fingers plump as sausages. "Ser Perwyn. Ser Benfrey. Maester Willamen, who took his vows last year and now serves Lord Hunter in the Vale. Olyvar, who squired for your son. And Lady Roslin, the youngest. Four boys to one girl. Lord Edmure will have more sons than he knows what to do with."

"I am sure that will please him." So the girl was like to be fertile as well as fair of face. *That should put Edmure's mind at ease.* Lord Walder had left her brother no cause for complaint, so far as she could see.

Catelyn did not return to her own room after leaving the maester; instead she went to Robb. She found Robin Flint and Ser Wendel Manderly with him, along with the Greatjon and his son, who was still called the Smalljon though he threatened to overtop his father. They were all damp. Another man, still wetter, stood before the fire in a pale pink cloak trimmed with white fur. "Lord Bolton," she said.

"Lady Catelyn," he replied, his voice faint, "it is a pleasure to look on you again, even in such trying times."

"You are kind to say so." Catelyn could feel gloom in the room. Even the Greatjon seemed somber and subdued. She looked at their grim faces and said, "What's happened?"

"Lannisters on the Trident," said Ser Wendel unhappily. "My brother is taken again."

"And Lord Bolton has brought us further word of Winterfell," Robb added. "Ser Rodrik was not the only good man to die. Cley Cerwyn and Leobald Tallhart were slain as well."

"Cley Cerwyn was only a boy," she said, saddened. "Is this true, then? All dead, and Winterfell gone?"

Bolton's pale eyes met her own. "The ironmen burned both castle and winter town. Some of your people were taken back to the Dreadfort by my son, Ramsay."

"Your bastard was accused of grievous crimes," Catelyn reminded him sharply. "Of murder, rape, and worse."

"Yes," Roose Bolton said. "His blood is tainted, that cannot be denied. Yet he is a good fighter, as cunning as he is fearless. When the ironmen cut down Ser Rodrik, and Leobald Tallhart soon after, it fell to Ramsay to lead the battle, and he did. He swears that he shall not sheathe his sword so long as a single Greyjoy remains in the north. Perhaps such service might atone in some small measure for whatever crimes his bastard blood has led him to commit." He shrugged. "Or not. When the war is done, His Grace must weigh and judge. By then I hope to have a trueborn son by Lady Walda."

This is a cold man, Catelyn realized, not for the first time.

"Did Ramsay mention Theon Greyjoy?" Robb demanded. "Was he slain as well, or did he flee?"

Roose Bolton removed a ragged strip of leather from the pouch at his belt. "My son sent this with his letter."

Ser Wendel turned his fat face away. Robin Flint and

Smalljon Umber exchanged a look, and the Greatjon snorted like a bull. "Is that . . . skin?" said Robb.

"The skin from the little finger of Theon Greyjoy's left hand. My son is cruel, I confess it. And yet . . . what is a little skin, against the lives of two young princes? You were their mother, my lady. May I offer you this . . . small token of revenge?"

Part of Catelyn wanted to clutch the grisly trophy to her heart, but she made herself resist. "Put it away. Please."

"Flaying Theon will not bring my brothers back," Robb said. "I want his head, not his skin."

"He is Balon Greyjoy's only living son," Lord Bolton said softly, as if they had forgotten, "and now rightful King of the Iron Islands. A captive king has great value as a hostage."

"Hostage?" The word raised Catelyn's hackles. Hostages were oft exchanged. "Lord Bolton, I hope you are not suggesting that we *free* the man who killed my sons."

"Whoever wins the Seastone Chair will want Theon Greyjoy dead," Bolton pointed out. "Even in chains, he has a better claim than any of his uncles. Hold him, I say, and demand concessions from the ironborn as the price of his execution."

Robb considered that reluctantly, but in the end he nodded. "Yes. Very well. Keep him alive, then. For the present. Hold him secure at the Dreadfort till we've retaken the north."

Catelyn turned back to Roose Bolton. "Ser Wendel said something of Lannisters on the Trident?"

"He did, my lady. I blame myself. I delayed too long before leaving Harrenhal. Aenys Frey departed several days before me and crossed the Trident at the ruby ford, though not without difficulty. But by the time we came up the river was a torrent. I had no choice but to ferry my men across in small boats, of which we had too few. Two-thirds of my strength was on the north side when the Lannisters attacked those still waiting to cross. Norrey, Locke, and Burley men chiefly, with Ser Wylis Manderly and his White Harbor knights as rear guard. I was on the wrong side of the Trident, powerless to help them. Ser Wylis rallied our men as best he could, but Gregor Clegane attacked with heavy horse and drove them into the river. As many drowned as were cut down. More fled, and the rest were taken captive."

Gregor Clegane was always ill news, Catelyn reflected. Would Robb need to march south again to deal with him? Or was the Mountain coming here? "Is Clegane across the river, then?"

"No." Bolton's voice was soft, but certain. "I left six hundred men at the ford. Spearmen from the rills, the mountains, and the White Knife, a hundred Hornwood longbows, some freeriders and hedge knights, and a strong force of Stout and Cerwyn men to stiffen them. Ronnel Stout and Ser Kyle Condon have the command. Ser Kyle was the late Lord Cerwyn's right hand, as I'm sure you know, my lady. Lions swim no better than wolves. So long as the river runs high, Ser Gregor will not cross."

"The last thing we need is the Mountain at our backs when we start up the causeway," said Robb. "You did well, my lord."

"Your Grace is too kind. I suffered grievous losses on the Green Fork, and Glover and Tallhart worse at Duskendale."

"*Duskendale.*" Robb made the word a curse. "Robett Glover will answer for that when I see him, I promise you."

"A folly," Lord Bolton agreed, "but Glover was heedless after he learned that Deepwood Motte had fallen. Grief and fear will do that to a man."

Duskendale was done and cold; it was the battles still to come that worried Catelyn. "How many men have you brought my son?" she asked Roose Bolton pointedly.

His queer colorless eyes studied her face a moment before he answered. "Some five hundred horse and three thousand foot, my lady. Dreadfort men, in chief, and some from Karhold. With the loyalty of the Karstarks so doubtful now, I thought it best to keep them close. I regret there are not more."

"It should be enough," said Robb. "You will have command of my rear guard, Lord Bolton. I mean to start for the Neck as soon as my uncle has been wedded and bedded. We're going home."

ARYA

The outriders came on them an hour from the Green Fork, as the wayn was slogging down a muddy road. "Keep your head down and your mouth shut," the Hound warned her as the three spurred toward them; a knight and two squires, lightly armored and mounted on fast palfreys. Clegane cracked his whip at the team, a pair of old drays that had known better days. The wayn was creaking and swaying, its two huge wooden wheels squeezing mud up out of the deep ruts in the road with every turn. Stranger followed, tied to the wagon.

The big bad-tempered courser wore neither armor, barding, nor harness, and the Hound himself was garbed in splotchy green roughspun and a soot-grey mantle with a hood that swallowed his head. So long as he kept his eyes down you could not see his face, only the whites of his eyes peering out. He looked like some down-at-heels farmer. A *big* farmer, though. And under the roughspun was boiled leather and oiled mail, Arya knew. She looked like a farmer's son, or maybe a swineherd. And behind them were four squat casks of salt pork and one of pickled pigs' feet.

The riders split and circled them for a look before they came up close. Clegane drew the wayn to a halt and waited patiently on their pleasure. The knight bore spear and sword while his squires carried longbows. The badges on their jerkins were smaller versions of the sigil sewn on their master's surcoat; a black pitchfork on a golden bar sinister, upon a russet field. Arya had thought of revealing herself to the first outriders they encountered, but she had always pictured grey-cloaked men with the direwolf on their breasts. She might have risked it even if they'd worn the Umber giant or the Glover fist, but she did not know this pitchfork knight or whom he served. The closest thing to a pitchfork she had ever seen at Winterfell was the trident in the hand of Lord Manderly's merman.

"You have business at the Twins?" the knight asked.

"Salt pork for the wedding feast, if it please you, ser." The Hound mumbled his reply, his eyes down, his face hidden.

"Salt pork never pleases me." The pitchfork knight gave Clegane only the most cursory glance, and paid no attention at all to Arya, but he looked long and hard at Stranger. The stallion was no plow horse, that was plain at a glance. One of the squires almost wound up in the mud when the big black courser bit at his own mount. "How did you come by this beast?" the pitchfork knight demanded.

"M'lady told me to bring him, ser," Clegane said humbly. "He's a wedding gift for young Lord Tully."

"What lady? Who is it you serve?"

"Old Lady Whent, ser."

"Does she think she can buy Harrenhal back with a horse?" the knight asked. "Gods, is there any fool like an old fool?" Yet he waved them down the road. "Go on with you, then."

"Aye, m'lord." The Hound snapped his whip again, and the old drays resumed their weary trek. The wheels had settled deep into the mud during the halt, and it took several moments for the team to pull them free again. By then the outriders were riding off. Clegane gave them one last look and snorted. "Ser Donnel Haigh," he said. "I've taken more horses off him than I can count. Armor as well. Once I near killed him in a mêlée."

"How come he didn't know you, then?" Arya asked.

"Because knights are fools, and it would have been be-neath him to look twice at some poxy peasant." He gave the horses a lick with the whip. "Keep your eyes down and your tone respectful and say *ser* a lot, and most knights will never see you. They pay more mind to horses than to smallfolk. He might have known Stranger if he'd ever seen me ride him."

He would have known your face, though. Arya had no doubt of that. Sandor Clegane's burns would not be easy to forget, once you saw them. He couldn't hide the scars be-hind a helm, either; not so long as the helm was made in the shape of a snarling dog.

That was why they'd needed the wayn and the pickled pigs' feet. "I'm not going to be dragged before your brother in chains," the Hound had told her, "and I'd just as soon not have to cut through his men to get to him. So we play a little game."

A farmer chance-met on the kingsroad had provided them with wayn, horses, garb, and casks, though not will-ingly. The Hound had taken them at swordpoint. When the farmer cursed him for a robber, he said, "No, a forager. Be grateful you get to keep your smallclothes. Now take those boots off. Or I'll take your legs off. Your choice." The farmer was as big as Clegane, but all the same he chose to give up his boots and keep his legs.

Evenfall found them still trudging toward the Green Fork and Lord Frey's twin castles. *I am almost there,* Arya thought. She knew she ought to be excited, but her belly was all knotted up tight. Maybe that was just the fever she'd been fighting, but maybe not. Last night she'd had a bad dream, a *terrible* dream. She couldn't remember what she'd dreamed of now, but the feeling had lingered all day. If anything, it had only gotten stronger. *Fear cuts deeper than swords.* She had to be strong now, the way her father told her. There was nothing between her and her mother but a castle gate, a river, and an army . . . but it was *Robb's* army, so there was no real danger there. Was there?

Roose Bolton was one of them, though. The Leech Lord, as the outlaws called him. That made her uneasy. She had fled Harrenhal to get away from Bolton as much as from the Bloody Mummers, and she'd had to cut the throat of one of his guards to escape. Did he know she'd done that?

Or did he blame Gendry or Hot Pie? Would he have told her mother? What would he do if he saw her? *He probably won't even know me.* She looked more like a drowned rat than a lord's cupbearer these days. A drowned *boy* rat. The Hound had hacked handfuls of her hair off only two days past. He was an even worse barber than Yoren, and he'd left her half bald on one side. *Robb won't know me either, I bet. Or even Mother.* She had been a little girl the last time she saw them, the day Lord Eddard Stark left Winterfell.

They heard the music before they saw the castle; the distant rattle of drums, the brazen blare of horns, the thin skirling of pipes faint beneath the growl of the river and the sound of the rain beating on their heads. "We've missed the wedding," the Hound said, "but it sounds as though the feast is still going. I'll be rid of you soon."

No, I'll be rid of you, Arya thought.

The road had been running mostly northwest, but now it turned due west between an apple orchard and a field of drowned corn beaten down by the rain. They passed the last of the apple trees and crested a rise, and the castles, river, and camps all appeared at once. There were hundreds of horses and thousands of men, most of them milling about the three huge feast tents that stood side by side facing the castle gates, like three great canvas longhalls. Robb had made his camp well back from the walls, on higher, drier ground, but the Green Fork had overflown its bank and even claimed a few carelessly placed tents.

The music from the castles was louder here. The sound of the drums and horns rolled across the camp. The musicians in the nearer castle were playing a different song than the ones in the castle on the far bank, though, so it sounded more like a battle than a song. "They're not very good," Arya observed.

The Hound made a sound that might have been a laugh. "There's old deaf women in Lannisport complaining of the din, I'll warrant. I'd heard Walder Frey's eyes were failing, but no one mentioned his bloody ears."

Arya found herself wishing it were day. If the sun was out and the wind was blowing, she would have been able to see the banners better. She would have looked for the direwolf of Stark, or maybe the Cerwyn battleaxe or the Glover fist. But in the gloom of night all the colors looked grey.

The rain had dwindled down to a fine drizzle, almost a mist, but an earlier downpour had left the banners wet as dishrags, sodden and unreadable.

A hedge of wagons and carts had been drawn up along the perimeter to make a crude wooden wall against any attack. That was where the guards stopped them. The lantern their sergeant carried shed enough light for Arya to see that his cloak was a pale pink, spotted with red teardrops. The men under him had the Leech Lord's badge sewn over their hearts, the flayed man of the Dreadfort. Sandor Clegane gave them the same tale he'd used on the outriders, but the Bolton sergeant was a harder sort of nut than Ser Donnel Haigh had been. "Salt pork's no fit meat for a lord's wedding feast," he said scornfully.

"Got pickled pigs' feet too, ser."

"Not for the feast, you don't. The feast's half done. And I'm a northman, not some milksuck southron knight."

"I was told to see the steward, or the cook . . ."

"Castle's closed. The lordlings are not to be disturbed." The sergeant considered a moment. "You can unload by the feast tents, there." He pointed with a mailed hand. "Ale makes a man hungry, and old Frey won't miss a few pigs' feet. He don't have the teeth for such anyhow. Ask for Sedgekins, he'll know what's to be done with you." He barked a command, and his men rolled one of the wagons aside for them to enter.

The Hound's whip spurred the team toward the tents. No one seemed to pay them any mind. They splashed past rows of brightly colored pavilions, their walls of wet silk lit up like magic lanterns by lamps and braziers inside; pink and gold and green they glimmered, striped and fretty and chequy, emblazoned with birds and beasts, chevrons and stars, wheels and weapons. Arya spotted a yellow tent with six acorns on its panels, three over two over one. *Lord Smallwood*, she knew, remembering Acorn Hall so far away, and the lady who'd said she was pretty.

But for every shimmering silk pavilion there were two dozen of felt or canvas, opaque and dark. There were barracks tents too, big enough to shelter two score footsoldiers, though even those were dwarfed by the three great feast tents. The drinking had been going on for hours, it seemed. Arya heard shouted toasts and the clash of cups, mixed in with all the usual camp sounds, horses whinny-ing and dogs barking, wagons rumbling through the dark, laughter and curses, the clank and clatter of steel and wood. The music grew still louder as they approached the castle, but under that was a deeper, darker sound: the river, the swollen Green Fork, growling like a lion in its den.

Arya twisted and turned, trying to look everywhere at once, hoping for a glimpse of a direwolf badge, for a tent done up in grey and white, for a face she knew from Winterfell. All she saw were strangers. She stared at a man relieving himself in the reeds, but he wasn't Alebelly. She saw a half-dressed girl burst from a tent laughing, but the tent was pale blue, not grey like she'd thought at first, and the man who went running after her wore a treecat on his doublet, not a wolf. Beneath a tree, four archers were slip-ping waxed strings over the notches of their longbows, but they were not her father's archers. A maester crossed their path, but he was too young and thin to be Maester Luwin. Arya gazed up at the Twins, their high tower windows glowing softly wherever a light was burning. Through the haze of rain, the castles looked spooky and mysterious, like something from one of Old Nan's tales, but they weren't Winterfell.

The press was thickest at the feast tents. The wide flaps were tied back, and men were pushing in and out with drinking horns and tankards in their hands, some with camp followers. Arya glanced inside as the Hound drove past the first of the three, and saw hundreds of men crowd-ing the benches and jostling around the casks of mead and ale and wine. There was hardly room to move inside, but none of them seemed to mind. At least they were warm and dry. Cold wet Arya envied them. Some were even singing. The fine misty rain was steaming all around the door from the heat escaping from inside. "Here's to Lord Edmure and Lady Roslin," she heard a voice shout. They all drank, and someone yelled, "Here's to the Young Wolf and Queen Jeyne."

Who is Queen Jeyne? Arya wondered briefly. The only queen she knew was Cersei.

Firepits had been dug outside the feast tents, sheltered beneath rude canopies of woven wood and hides that kept the rain out, so long as it fell straight down. The wind was blowing off the river, though, so the drizzle came in anyway, enough to make the fires hiss and swirl. Serving men were turning joints of meat on spits above the flames. The smells made Arya's mouth water. "Shouldn't we stop?" she asked Sandor Clegane. "There's northmen in the tents." She knew them by their beards, by their faces, by their cloaks of bearskin and sealskin, by their half-heard toasts and the songs they sang; Karstarks and Umbers and men of the mountain clans. "I bet there are Winterfell men too." Her father's men, the Young Wolf's men, the direwolves of Stark.

"Your brother will be in the castle," he said. "Your mother too. You want them or not?"

"Yes," she said. "What about Sedgekins?" The sergeant had told them to ask for Sedgekins.

"Sedgekins can bugger himself with a hot poker." Clegane shook out his whip, and sent it hissing through the soft rain to bite at a horse's flank. "It's your bloody brother I want."

CATELYN

The drums were pounding, pounding, pounding, and her head with them. Pipes wailed and flutes trilled from the musicians' gallery at the foot of the hall; fiddles screeched, horns blew, the skins skirled a lively tune, but the drumming drove them all. The sounds echoed off the rafters, whilst the guests ate, drank, and shouted at one another below. *Walder Frey must be deaf as a stone to call this music.* Catelyn sipped a cup of wine and watched Jinglebell prance to the sounds of "Alysanne." At least she thought it was meant to be "Alysanne." With these players, it might as easily have been "The Bear and the Maiden Fair."

Outside the rain still fell, but within the Twins the air was thick and hot. A fire roared in the hearth and rows of torches burned smokily from iron sconces on the walls. Yet most of the heat came off the bodies of the wedding guests, jammed in so thick along the benches that every man who tried to lift his cup poked his neighbor in the ribs.

Even on the dais they were closer than Catelyn would have liked. She had been placed between Ser Ryman Frey and Roose Bolton, and had gotten a good noseful of both. Ser Ryman drank as if Westeros was about to run short of wine, and sweated it all out under his arms. He had bathed in lemonwater, she judged, but no lemon could mask so much sour sweat. Roose Bolton had a sweeter smell to him, yet no more pleasant. He sipped hippocras in preference to wine or mead, and ate but little.

Catelyn could not fault him for his lack of appetite. The wedding feast began with a thin leek soup, followed by a salad of green beans, onions, and beets, river pike poached in almond milk, mounds of mashed turnips that were cold before they reached the table, jellied calves' brains, and a leche of stringy beef. It was poor fare to set before a king, and the calves' brains turned Catelyn's stomach. Yet Robb ate it uncomplaining, and her brother was too caught up with his bride to pay much attention.

You would never guess Edmure complained of Roslin all the way from Riverrun to the Twins. Husband and wife ate from a single plate, drank from a single cup, and exchanged chaste kisses between sips. Most of the dishes Edmure waved away. She could not blame him for that. She remembered little of the food served at her own wedding feast. *Did I even taste it? Or spend the whole time gazing at Ned's face, wondering who he was?*

Poor Roslin's smile had a fixed quality to it, as if someone had sewn it onto her face. *Well, she is a maid wedded, but the bedding's yet to come. No doubt she's as terrified as I was.* Robb was seated between Alyx Frey and Fair Walda, two of the more nubile Frey maidens. "At the wedding feast I hope you will not refuse to dance with my daughters," Walder Frey had said. "It would please an old man's heart." His heart should be well pleased, then; Robb had done his duty like a king. He had danced with each of the girls, with Edmure's bride and the eighth Lady Frey, with the widow Ami and Roose Bolton's wife Fat Walda, with the pimply twins Serra and Sarra, even with Shirei, Lord Walder's youngest, who must have been all of six. Catelyn wondered whether the Lord of the Crossing would be satisfied, or if he would find cause for complaint in all the other daughters and granddaughters who had not had a turn with the king. "Your sisters dance very well," she said to Ser Ryman Frey, trying to be pleasant.

"They're aunts and cousins." Ser Ryman drank a swallow of wine, the sweat trickling down his cheek into his beard.

A sour man, and in his cups, Catelyn thought. The Late Lord Frey might be niggardly when it came to feeding his guests, but he did not stint on the drink. The ale, wine, and mead were flowing as fast as the river outside. The Greatjon was already roaring drunk. Lord Walder's son Merrett was matching him cup for cup, but Ser Whalen Frey had passed out trying to keep up with the two of them. Catelyn would sooner Lord Umber had seen fit to stay sober, but telling the Greatjon not to drink was like telling him not to breathe for a few hours.

Smalljon Umber and Robin Flint sat near Robb, to the other side of Fair Walda and Alyx, respectively. Neither of them was drinking; along with Patrek Mallister and Dacey Mormont, they were her son's guards this evening. A wedding feast was not a battle, but there were always dangers when men were in their cups, and a king should never be unguarded. Catelyn was glad of that, and even more glad of the swordbelts hanging on pegs along the walls. *No man needs a longsword to deal with jellied calves' brains.*

"Everyone thought my lord would choose Fair Walda," Lady Walda Bolton told Ser Wendel, shouting to be heard above the music. Fat Walda was a round pink butterball of a girl with watery blue eyes, limp yellow hair, and a huge bosom, yet her voice was a fluttering squeak. It was hard to picture her in the Dreadfort in her pink lace and cape of vair. "My lord grandfather offered Roose his bride's weight in silver as a dowry, though, so my lord of Bolton picked *me.*" The girl's chins jiggled when she laughed. "I weigh six stone more than Fair Walda, but that was the first time I was glad of it. I'm Lady Bolton now and my cousin's still a maid, and she'll be *nineteen* soon, poor thing."

The Lord of the Dreadfort paid the chatter no mind, Catelyn saw. Sometimes he tasted a bite of this, a spoon of that, tearing bread from the loaf with short strong fingers, but the meal could not distract him. Bolton had made a toast to Lord Walder's grandsons when the wedding feast began, pointedly mentioning that Walder and Walder were in the care of his bastard son. From the way the old man

had squinted at him, his mouth sucking at the air, Catelyn
knew he had heard the unspoken threat.

Was there ever a wedding less joyful? she wondered, until she remembered her poor Sansa and her marriage to the
Imp. *Mother take mercy on her. She has a gentle soul.* The
heat and smoke and noise were making her sick. The musicians in the gallery might be numerous and loud, but
they were not especially gifted. Catelyn took another swallow of wine and allowed a page to refill her cup. *A few
more hours, and the worst will be over.* By this hour tomorrow Robb would be off to another battle, this time
with the ironmen at Moat Cailin. Strange, how that
prospect seemed almost a relief. *He will win his battle. He
wins all his battles, and the ironborn are without a king.
Besides, Ned taught him well.* The drums were pounding.
Jinglebell hopped past her once again, but the music was so
loud she could scarcely hear his bells.

Above the din came a sudden snarling as two dogs fell
upon each other over a scrap of meat. They rolled across
the floor, snapping and biting, as a howl of mirth went up.
Someone doused them with a flagon of ale and they broke
apart. One limped toward the dais. Lord Walder's toothless
mouth opened in a bark of laughter as the dripping wet dog
shook ale and hair all over three of his grandsons.

The sight of the dogs made Catelyn wish once more for
Grey Wind, but Robb's direwolf was nowhere to be seen.
Lord Walder had refused to allow him in the hall. "Your
wild beast has a taste for human flesh, I hear, *heh,*" the old
man had said. "Rips out throats, yes. I'll have no such creature at my Roslin's feast, amongst women and little ones,
all my sweet innocents."

"Grey Wind is no danger to them, my lord," Robb
protested. "Not so long as I am there."

"You were there at my gates, were you not? When the
wolf attacked the grandsons I sent to greet you? I heard all
about that, don't think I didn't, *heh.*"

"No harm was done—"

"No harm, the king says? No harm? Petyr fell from his
horse, *fell.* I lost a wife the same way, falling." His mouth
worked in and out. "Or was she just some strumpet?
Bastard Walder's mother, yes, now I recall. She fell off her
horse and cracked her head. What would Your Grace do if

Petyr had broken his neck, *heh*? Give me another apology in place of a grandson? No, no, no. Might be you're king, I won't say you're not, the King in the North, *heh*, but under my roof, my rule. Have your wolf or have your wedding, sire. You'll not have both."

Catelyn could tell that her son was furious, but he yielded with as much courtesy as he could summon. *If it pleases Lord Walder to serve me stewed crow smothered in maggots*, he'd told her, *I'll eat it and ask for a second bowl*. And so he had.

The Greatjon had drunk another of Lord Walder's brood under the table, Petyr Pimple this time. *The lad has a third his capacity, what did he expect?* Lord Umber wiped his mouth, stood, and began to sing. *"A bear there was, a bear, a BEAR! All black and brown and covered with hair!"* His voice was not at all bad, though somewhat thick from drink. Unfortunately the fiddlers and drummers and flutists up above were playing "Flowers of Spring," which suited the words of "The Bear and the Maiden Fair" as well as snails might suit a bowl of porridge. Even poor Jinglebell covered his ears at the cacophony.

Roose Bolton murmured some words too soft to hear and went off in search of a privy. The cramped hall was in a constant uproar of guests and servants coming and going. A second feast, for knights and lords of somewhat lesser rank, was roaring along in the other castle, she knew. Lord Walder had exiled his baseborn children and their offspring to that side of the river, so that Robb's northmen had taken to referring to it as "the bastard feast." Some guests were no doubt stealing off to see if the bastards were having a better time than they were. Some might even be venturing as far as the camps. The Freys had provided wagons of wine, ale, and mead, so the common soldiers could drink to the wedding of Riverrun and the Twins.

Robb sat down in Bolton's vacant place. "A few more hours and this farce is done, Mother," he said in a low voice, as the Greatjon sang of the maid with honey in her hair. "Black Walder's been mild as a lamb for once. And Uncle Edmure seems well content in his bride." He leaned across her. "Ser Ryman?"

Ser Ryman Frey blinked and said, "Sire. Yes?"

"I'd hoped to ask Olyvar to squire for me when we

march north," said Robb, "but I do not see him here. Would he be at the other feast?"

"Olyvar?" Ser Ryman shook his head. "No. Not Olyvar. Gone . . . gone from the castles. Duty."

"I see." Robb's tone suggested otherwise. When Ser Ryman offered nothing more, the king got to his feet again. "Would you care for a dance, Mother?"

"Thank you, but no." A dance was the last thing she needed, the way her head was throbbing. "No doubt one of Lord Walder's daughters would be pleased to partner you."

"Oh, no doubt." His smile was resigned.

The musicians were playing "Iron Lances" by then, while the Greatjon sang "The Lusty Lad." *Someone should acquaint them with each other, it might improve the harmony.* Catelyn turned back to Ser Ryman. "I had heard that one of your cousins was a singer."

"Alesander. Symond's son. Alyx is his sister." He raised a cup toward where she danced with Robin Flint.

"Will Alesander be playing for us tonight?"

Ser Ryman squinted at her. "Not him. He's away." He wiped sweat from his brow and lurched to his feet. "Pardons, my lady. Pardons." Catelyn watched him stagger toward the door.

Edmure was kissing Roslin and squeezing her hand. Elsewhere in the hall, Ser Marq Piper and Ser Danwell Frey played a drinking game, Lame Lothar said something amusing to Ser Hosteen, one of the younger Freys juggled three daggers for a group of giggly girls, and Jinglebell sat on the floor sucking wine off his fingers. The servers were bringing out huge silver platters piled high with cuts of juicy pink lamb, the most appetizing dish they'd seen all evening. And Robb was leading Dacey Mormont in a dance.

When she wore a dress in place of a hauberk, Lady Maege's eldest daughter was quite pretty; tall and willowy, with a shy smile that made her long face light up. It was pleasant to see that she could be as graceful on the dance floor as in the training yard. Catelyn wondered if Lady Maege had reached the Neck as yet. She had taken her other daughters with her, but as one of Robb's battle companions Dacey had chosen to remain by his side. *He has Ned's gift for inspiring loyalty.* Olyvar Frey had been devoted to her son as well. Hadn't Robb said that Olyvar wanted to remain with him even *after* he'd married Jeyne?

Seated betwixt his black oak towers, the Lord of the Crossing clapped his spotted hands together. The noise they made was so faint that even those on the dais scarce heard it, but Ser Aenys and Ser Hosteen saw and began to pound their cups on the table. Lame Lothar joined them, then Marq Piper and Ser Danwell and Ser Raymund. Half the guests were soon pounding. Finally even the mob of musicians in the gallery took note. The piping, drumming, and fiddling trailed off into quiet.

"Your Grace," Lord Walder called out to Robb, "the septon has prayed his prayers, some words have been said, and Lord Edmure's wrapped my sweetling in a fish cloak, but they are not yet man and wife. A sword needs a sheath, *heh*, and a wedding needs a bedding. What does my sire say? Is it meet that we should bed them?"

A score or more of Walder Frey's sons and grandsons began to bang their cups again, shouting, "To bed! To bed! *To bed with them!*" Roslin had gone white. Catelyn wondered whether it was the prospect of losing her maidenhead that frightened the girl, or the bedding itself. With so many siblings, she was not like to be a stranger to the custom, but it was different when you were the one being bedded. On Catelyn's own wedding night, Jory Cassell had torn her gown in his haste to get her out of it, and drunken Desmond Grell kept apologizing for every bawdy joke, only to make another. When Lord Dustin had beheld her naked, he'd told Ned that her breasts were enough to make him wish he'd never been weaned. *Poor man*, she thought. He had ridden south with Ned, never to return. Catelyn wondered how many of the men here tonight would be dead before the year was done. *Too many, I fear.*

Robb raised a hand. "If you think the time is meet, Lord Walder, by all means let us bed them."

A roar of approval greeted his pronouncement. Up in the gallery the musicians took up their pipes and horns and fiddles again, and began to play "The Queen Took Off Her Sandal, the King Took Off His Crown." Jinglebell hopped from foot to foot, his own crown ringing. "I hear Tully men have trout between their legs instead of cocks," Alyx Frey called out boldly. "Does it take a worm to make them rise?" To which Ser Marq Piper threw back, "*I hear that Frey women have two gates in place of one!*" and Alyx said, "Aye, but both are closed and barred to little things like you!" A gust of laughter followed, until Patrek Mallister climbed up onto a table to propose a toast to Edmure's one-eyed fish. "And a mighty pike it is!" he proclaimed. "Nay, I'll wager it's a minnow," Fat Walda Bolton shouted out from Catelyn's side. Then the general cry of *"Bed them! Bed them!"* went up again.

The guests swarmed the dais, the drunkest in the forefront as ever. The men and boys surrounded Roslin and lifted her into the air whilst the maids and mothers in the hall pulled Edmure to his feet and began tugging at his clothing. He was laughing and shouting bawdy jokes back at them, though the music was too loud for Catelyn to hear. She heard the Greatjon, though. "Give this little bride to me," he bellowed as he shoved through the other men and threw Roslin over one shoulder. "Look at this little thing! No meat on her at all!"

Catelyn felt sorry for the girl. Most brides tried to return the banter, or at least pretended to enjoy it, but Roslin was stiff with terror, clutching the Greatjon as if she feared he might drop her. *She's crying too*, Catelyn realized as she watched Ser Marq Piper pull off one of the bride's shoes. *I hope Edmure is gentle with the poor child.* Jolly, bawdy music still poured down from the gallery; the queen was taking off her kirtle now, and the king his tunic.

She knew she should join the throng of women round her brother, but she would only ruin their fun. The last thing she felt just now was bawdy. Edmure would forgive her absence, she did not doubt; much jollier to be stripped and bedded by a score of lusty, laughing Freys than by a sour, stricken sister.

As man and maid were carried from the hall, a trail of clothing behind them, Catelyn saw that Robb had also remained. Walder Frey was prickly enough to see some insult to his daughter in that. *He should join in Roslin's bedding, but is it my place to tell him so?* She tensed, until she saw that others had stayed as well. Petyr Pimple and Ser Whalen Frey slept on, their heads on the table. Merrett Frey poured himself another cup of wine, while Jinglebell wandered about stealing bites off the plates of those who'd left. Ser Wendel Manderly was lustily attacking a leg of lamb. And of course Lord Walder was far too feeble to leave his seat without help. *He will expect Robb to go, though.* She could almost hear the old man asking why His Grace did not want to see his daughter naked. The drums were pounding again, pounding and pounding and pounding.

Dacey Mormont, who seemed to be the only woman left in the hall besides Catelyn, stepped up behind Edwyn Frey, and touched him lightly on the arm as she said something in his ear. Edwyn wrenched himself away from her with unseemly violence. "No," he said, too loudly. "I'm done with dancing for the nonce." Dacey paled and turned away. Catelyn got slowly to her feet. *What just happened there?* Doubt gripped her heart, where an instant before had been only weariness. *It is nothing,* she tried to tell herself, *you are seeing grumkins in the woodpile, you are become an old silly woman sick with grief and fear.* But something must have shown on her face. Even Ser Wendel Manderly took note. "Is something amiss?" he asked, the leg of lamb in his hands.

She did not answer him. Instead she went after Edwyn Frey. The players in the gallery had finally gotten both king and queen down to their name-day suits. With scarcely a moment's respite, they began to play a very different sort of song. No one sang the words, but Catelyn knew "The Rains of Castamere" when she heard it. Edwyn was hurrying toward a door. She hurried faster, driven by the music. Six quick strides and she caught him. *And who are you, the proud lord said, that I must bow so low?* She grabbed Edwyn by the arm to turn him and went cold all over when she felt the iron rings beneath his silken sleeve.

Catelyn slapped him so hard she broke his lip. *Olyvar,* she thought, *and Perwyn, Alesander, all absent. And Roslin wept . . .*

Edwyn Frey shoved her aside. The music drowned all other sound, echoing off the walls as if the stones themselves were playing. Robb gave Edwyn an angry look and moved to block his way . . . and staggered suddenly as a quarrel sprouted from his side, just beneath the shoulder. If he screamed then, the sound was swallowed by the pipes and horns and fiddles. Catelyn saw a second bolt pierce his leg, saw him fall. Up in the gallery, half the musicians had crossbows in their hands instead of drums or lutes. She ran toward her son, until something punched in the small of the back and the hard stone floor came up to slap her. "*Robb!*" she screamed. She saw Smalljon Umber wrestle a table off its trestles. Crossbow bolts thudded into the wood, one two three, as he flung it down on top of his king. Robin Flint was ringed by Freys, their daggers rising and falling. Ser Wendel Manderly rose ponderously to his feet, holding his leg of lamb. A quarrel went in his open mouth and came out the back of his neck. Ser Wendel crashed forward, knocking the table off its trestles and sending cups, flagons, trenchers, platters, turnips, beets, and wine bouncing, spilling, and sliding across the floor.

Catelyn's back was on fire. *I have to reach him.* The Smalljon bludgeoned Ser Raymund Frey across the face with a leg of mutton. But when he reached for his sword-belt a crossbow bolt drove him to his knees. *In a coat of gold or a coat of red, a lion still has claws.* She saw Lucas Blackwood cut down by Ser Hosteen Frey. One of the Vances was hamstrung by Black Walder as he was wrestling with Ser Harys Haigh. *And mine are long and sharp, my lord, as long and sharp as yours.* The crossbows took Donnel Locke, Owen Norrey, and half a dozen more. Young Ser Benfrey had seized Dacey Mormont by the arm, but Catelyn saw her grab up a flagon of wine with her other hand, smash it full in his face, and run for the door. It flew open before she reached it. Ser Ryman Frey pushed into the hall, clad in steel from helm to heel. A dozen Frey men-at-arms packed the door behind him. They were armed with heavy longaxes.

"*Mercy!*" Catelyn cried, but horns and drums and the clash of steel smothered her plea. Ser Ryman buried the head of his axe in Dacey's stomach. By then men were pouring in the other doors as well, mailed men in shaggy fur cloaks with steel in their hands. *Northmen!* She took them for rescue for half a heartbeat, till one of them struck the Smalljon's head off with two huge blows of his axe. Hope blew out like a candle in a storm.

In the midst of slaughter, the Lord of the Crossing sat on his carved oaken throne, watching greedily.

There was a dagger on the floor a few feet away. Perhaps it had skittered there when the Smalljon knocked the table

off its trestles, or perhaps it had fallen from the hand of
some dying man. Catelyn crawled toward it. Her limbs
were leaden, and the taste of blood was in her mouth. *I will
kill Walder Frey*, she told herself. Jinglebell was closer to
the knife, hiding under a table, but he only cringed away as
she snatched up the blade. *I will kill the old man, I can do
that much at least.*

Then the tabletop that the Smalljon had flung over Robb
shifted, and her son struggled to his knees. He had an arrow
in his side, a second in his leg, a third through his chest.
Lord Walder raised a hand, and the music stopped, all but
one drum. Catelyn heard the crash of distant battle, and
closer the wild howling of a wolf. *Grey Wind*, she remembered too late. "*Heh*," Lord Walder cackled at Robb, "the
King in the North arises. Seems we killed some of your
men, Your Grace. Oh, but I'll make you an *apology*, that
will mend them all again, *heh*."

Catelyn grabbed a handful of Jinglebell Frey's long grey
hair and dragged him out of his hiding place. "Lord
Walder!" she shouted. "*LORD WALDER!*" The drum beat
slow and sonorous, *doom boom doom*. "Enough," said
Catelyn. "*Enough*, I say. You have repaid betrayal with betrayal, let it end." When she pressed her dagger to
Jinglebell's throat, the memory of Bran's sickroom came
back to her, with the feel of steel at her own throat. The
drum went *boom doom boom doom boom doom*.
"Please," she said. "He is my son. My first son, and my
last. Let him go. Let him go and I swear we will forget
this . . . forget all you've done here. I swear it by the old
gods and new, we . . . we will take no vengeance . . ."

Lord Walder peered at her in mistrust. "Only a fool
would believe such blather. D'you take me for a fool, my
lady?"

"I take you for a father. Keep me for a hostage, Edmure
as well if you haven't killed him. But let Robb go."

"No." Robb's voice was whisper faint. "Mother, no . . ."

"Yes. Robb, get up. Get up and walk out, please, *please*.
Save yourself . . . if not for me, for Jeyne."

"Jeyne?" Robb grabbed the edge of the table and forced
himself to stand. "Mother," he said, "Grey Wind . . ."

"Go to him. Now. Robb, *walk out of here.*"

Lord Walder snorted. "And why would I let him do that?"

She pressed the blade deeper into Jinglebell's throat. The lackwit rolled his eyes at her in mute appeal. A foul stench assailed her nose, but she paid it no more mind than she did the sullen ceaseless pounding of that drum, *boom doom boom doom boom doom.* Ser Ryman and Black Walder were circling round her back, but Catelyn did not care. They could do as they wished with her; imprison her, rape her, kill her, it made no matter. She had lived too long, and Ned was waiting. It was Robb she feared for. "On my honor as a Tully," she told Lord Walder, "on my honor as a Stark, I will trade your boy's life for Robb's. A son for a son." Her hand shook so badly she was ringing Jinglebell's head.

Boom, the drum sounded, *boom doom boom doom.* The old man's lips went in and out. The knife trembled in Catelyn's hand, slippery with sweat. "A son for a son, *heh*," he repeated. "But that's a grandson . . . and he never was much use."

A man in dark armor and a pale pink cloak spotted with blood stepped up to Robb. "Jaime Lannister sends his regards." He thrust his longsword through her son's heart, and twisted.

Robb had broken his word, but Catelyn kept hers. She tugged hard on Aegon's hair and sawed at his neck until the blade grated on bone. Blood ran hot over her fingers. His little bells were ringing, ringing, ringing, and the drum went *boom doom boom.*

Finally someone took the knife away from her. The tears burned like vinegar as they ran down her cheeks. Ten fierce ravens were raking her face with sharp talons and tearing off strips of flesh, leaving deep furrows that ran red with blood. She could taste it on her lips.

It hurts so much, she thought. *Our children, Ned, all our sweet babes. Rickon, Bran, Arya, Sansa, Robb . . . Robb . . . please, Ned, please, make it stop, make it stop hurting . . .* The white tears and the red ones ran together until her face was torn and tattered, the face that Ned had loved. Catelyn Stark raised her hands and watched the blood run down her long fingers, over her wrists, beneath the sleeves of her gown. Slow red worms crawled along her arms and under her clothes. *It tickles*. That made her laugh until she screamed. "Mad," someone said, "she's lost her wits," and someone else said, "Make an end," and a hand grabbed her scalp just as she'd done with Jinglebell, and she thought, *No, don't, don't cut my hair, Ned loves my hair*. Then the steel was at her throat, and its bite was red and cold.

ARYA

The feast tents were behind them now. They squished over wet clay and torn grass, out of the light and back into the gloom. Ahead loomed the castle gatehouse. She could see torches moving on the walls, their flames dancing and blowing in the wind. The light shone dully against the wet mail and helms. More torches were moving on the dark stone bridge that joined the Twins, a column of them streaming from the west bank to the east.

"The castle's not closed," Arya said suddenly. The sergeant had said it would be, but he was wrong. The portcullis was being drawn upward even as she watched, and the drawbridge had already been lowered to span the swollen moat. She had been afraid that Lord Frey's guardsmen would refuse to let them in. For half a heartbeat she chewed her lip, too anxious to smile.

The Hound reined up so suddenly that she almost fell off the wayn. "Seven bloody buggering hells," Arya heard him curse, as their left wheel began to sink in soft mud. The wayn tilted slowly. "Get *down*," Clegane roared at her, slamming the heel of his hand into her shoulder to knock her sideways. She landed light, the way Syrio had taught her, and bounced up at once with a face full of mud. *"Why did you do that?"* she screamed. The Hound had leapt down as well. He tore the seat off the front of the wayn and reached in for the swordbelt he'd hidden beneath it.

It was only then that she heard the riders pouring out the castle gate in a river of steel and fire, the thunder of their destriers crossing the drawbridge almost lost beneath the drumming from the castles. Men and mounts wore plate armor, and one in every ten carried a torch. The rest had axes, longaxes with spiked heads and heavy bone-crushing armor-smashing blades.

Somewhere far off she heard a wolf howling. It wasn't very loud compared to the camp noise and the music and the low ominous growl of the river running wild, but she heard it all the same. Only maybe it wasn't her ears that heard it. The sound shivered through Arya like a knife, sharp with rage and grief. More and more riders were emerging from the castle, a column four wide with no end to it, knights and squires and freeriders, torches and long-axes. And there was noise coming from behind as well.

When Arya looked around, she saw that there were only two of the huge feast tents where once there had been three. The one in the middle had collapsed. For a moment she did not understand what she was seeing. Then the flames went licking up from the fallen tent, and now the other two were collapsing, heavy oiled cloth settling down on the men beneath. A flight of fire arrows streaked through the air. The second tent took fire, and then the third. The screams grew so loud she could hear words through the music. Dark shapes moved in front of the flames, the steel of their armor shining orange from afar.

A battle, Arya knew. *It's a battle. And the riders . . .*

She had no more time to watch the tents then. With the river overflowing its banks, the dark swirling waters at the end of the drawbridge reached as high as a horse's belly, but the riders splashed through them all the same, spurred on by the music. For once the same song was coming from both castles. *I know this song*, Arya realized suddenly. Tom o' Sevens had sung it for them, that rainy night the outlaws had sheltered in the brewhouse with the brothers.

And who are you, the proud lord said, that I must bow so low?

The Frey riders were struggling through the mud and reeds, but some of them had seen the wayn. She watched as three riders left the main column, pounding through the shallows. *Only a cat of a different coat, that's all the truth I know.*

Clegane cut Stranger loose with a single slash of his sword and leapt onto his back. The courser knew what was wanted of him. He pricked up his ears and wheeled toward the charging destriers. *In a coat of gold or a coat of red, a lion still has claws. And mine are long and sharp, my lord, as long and sharp as yours.* Arya had prayed a hundred hundred times for the Hound to die, but now . . . there was a rock in her hand, slimy with mud, and she didn't even remember picking it up. *Who do I throw it at?*

She jumped at the clash of metal as Clegane turned aside the first longaxe. While he was engaged with the first man, the second circled behind him and aimed a blow for the small of his back. Stranger was wheeling, so the Hound took only a glancing blow, enough to rip a great gash in his baggy peasant's blouse and expose the mail below. *He is one against three.* Arya still clutched her rock. *They're sure to kill him.* She thought of Mycah, the butcher's boy who had been her friend so briefly.

Then she saw the third rider coming her way. Arya moved behind the wayn. *Fear cuts deeper than swords.* She could hear drums and warhorns and pipes, stallions trumpeting, the shriek of steel on steel, but all the sounds seemed so far away. There was only the oncoming horseman and the longaxe in his hand. He wore a surcoat over his armor and she saw the two towers that marked him for a Frey. She did not understand. Her uncle was marrying Lord Frey's daughter, the Freys were her brother's friends. "*Don't!*" she screamed as he rode around the wayn, but he paid no mind.

When he charged Arya threw the rock, the way she'd once thrown a crabapple at Gendry. She'd gotten Gendry right between the eyes, but this time her aim was off, and the stone caromed sideways off his temple. It was enough to break his charge, but no more. She retreated, darting across the muddy ground on the balls of her feet, putting the wayn between them once more. The knight followed at a trot, only darkness behind his eyeslit. She hadn't even dented his helm. They went round once, twice, a third time. The knight cursed her. *"You can't run for—"*

The axehead caught him square in the back of the head, crashing through his helm and the skull beneath and sending him flying face first from his saddle. Behind him was the Hound, still mounted on Stranger. *How did you get an axe?* she almost asked, before she saw. One of the other Freys was trapped beneath his dying horse, drowning in a foot of water. The third man was sprawled on his back, unmoving. He hadn't worn a gorget, and a foot of broken sword jutted from beneath his chin.

"Get my helm," Clegane growled at her.

It was stuffed at the bottom of a sack of dried apples, in the back of the wayn behind the pickled pigs' feet. Arya upended the sack and tossed it to him. He snatched it one-handed from the air and lowered it over his head, and where the man had sat only a steel dog remained, snarling at the fires.

"My brother . . ."

"Dead," he shouted back at her. "Do you think they'd slaughter his men and leave him alive?" He turned his head back toward the camp. "Look. *Look,* damn you."

The camp had become a battlefield. *No, a butcher's den.* The flames from the feasting tents reached halfway up the sky. Some of the barracks tents were burning too, and half a hundred silk pavilions. Everywhere swords were singing. *And now the rains weep o'er his hall, with not a soul to hear.* She saw two knights ride down a running man. A wooden barrel came crashing onto one of the burning tents and burst apart, and the flames leapt twice as high. *A catapult,* she knew. The castle was flinging oil or pitch or something.

"Come with me." Sandor Clegane reached down a hand. "We have to get away from here, and now." Stranger tossed his head impatiently, his nostrils flaring at the scent of blood. The song was done. There was only one solitary drum, its slow monotonous beats echoing across the river like the pounding of some monstrous heart. The black sky wept, the river grumbled, men cursed and died. Arya had mud in her teeth and her face was wet. *Rain. It's only rain.*

That's all it is. "We're *here*," she shouted. Her voice sounded thin and scared, a little girl's voice. "Robb's just in the castle, and my mother. The gate's even open." There were no more Freys riding out. *I came so far.* "We have to go get my *mother*."

"Stupid little bitch." Fires glinted off the snout of his helm, and made the steel teeth shine. "You go in there, you won't come out. Maybe Frey will let you kiss your mother's corpse."

"Maybe we can *save* her . . ."

"Maybe you can. I'm not done living yet." He rode toward her, crowding her back toward the wayn. "Stay or go, she-wolf. Live or die. Your—"

Arya spun away from him and darted for the gate. The portcullis was coming down, but slowly. *I have to run faster.* The mud slowed her, though, and then the water. *Run fast as a wolf.* The drawbridge had begun to lift, the water running off it in a sheet, the mud falling in heavy clots. *Faster.* She heard loud splashing and looked back to see Stranger pounding after her, sending up gouts of water with every stride. She saw the longaxe too, still wet with blood and brains. And Arya ran. Not for her brother now, not even for her mother, but for herself. She ran faster than she had ever run before, her head down and her feet churning up the river, she ran from him as Mycah must have run.

His axe took her in the back of the head.

TYRION

They supped alone, as they did so often.

"The pease are overcooked," his wife ventured once.

"No matter," he said. "So is the mutton."

It was a jest, but Sansa took it for criticism. "I am sorry, my lord."

"Why? Some cook should be sorry. Not you. The pease are not your province, Sansa."

"I . . . I am sorry that my lord husband is displeased."

"Any displeasure I'm feeling has naught to do with pease. I have Joffrey and my sister to displease me, and my lord father, and three hundred bloody Dornishmen." He had settled Prince Oberyn and his lords in a cornerfort facing the city, as far from the Tyrells as he could put them without evicting them from the Red Keep entirely. It was not nearly far enough. Already there had been a brawl in a Flea Bottom pot-shop that left one Tyrell man-at-arms dead and two of Lord Gargalen's scalded, and an ugly confrontation in the yard when Mace Tyrell's wizened little mother called Ellaria Sand "the serpent's whore." Every time he chanced to see

Oberyn Martell the prince asked when the justice would be served. Overcooked pease were the least of Tyrion's troubles, but he saw no point in burdening his young wife with any of that. Sansa had enough griefs of her own.

"The pease suffice," he told her curtly. "They are green and round, what more can one expect of pease? Here, I'll have another serving, if it please my lady." He beckoned, and Podrick Payne spooned so many pease onto his plate that Tyrion lost sight of his mutton. *That was stupid*, he told himself. *Now I have to eat them all, or she'll be sorry all over again.*

The supper ended in a strained silence, as so many of their suppers did. Afterward, as Pod was removing the cups and platters, Sansa asked Tyrion for leave to visit the godswood.

"As you wish." He had become accustomed to his wife's nightly devotions. She prayed at the royal sept as well, and often lit candles to Mother, Maid, and Crone. Tyrion found all this piety excessive, if truth be told, but in her place he might want the help of the gods as well. "I confess, I know little of the old gods," he said, trying to be pleasant. "Perhaps someday you might enlighten me. I could even accompany you."

"No," Sansa said at once. "You . . . you are kind to offer, but . . . there are no *devotions*, my lord. No priests or songs or candles. Only trees, and silent prayer. You would be bored."

"No doubt you're right." *She knows me better than I thought.* "Though the sound of rustling leaves might be a pleasant change from some septon droning on about the seven aspects of grace." Tyrion waved her off. "I won't intrude. Dress warmly, my lady, the wind is brisk out there." He was tempted to ask what she prayed for, but Sansa was so dutiful she might actually tell him, and he didn't think he wanted to know.

He went back to work after she left, trying to track some golden dragons through the labyrinth of Littlefinger's ledgers. Petyr Baelish had not believed in letting gold sit about and grow dusty, that was for certain, but the more Tyrion tried to make sense of his accounts the more his head hurt. It was all very well to talk of breeding dragons instead of locking them up in the treasury, but some of these ventures smelled worse than week-old fish. *I wouldn't have been so quick to let Joffrey fling the Antler Men over the walls if I'd known how many of the bloody bastards had taken loans from the crown.* He would have to send Bronn to find their heirs, but he feared that would prove as fruitful as trying to squeeze silver from a silverfish.

When the summons from his lord father arrived, it was the first time Tyrion could ever recall being pleased to see Ser Boros Blount. He closed the ledgers gratefully, blew out the oil lamp, tied a cloak around his shoulders, and waddled across the castle to the Tower of the Hand. The wind *was* brisk, just as he'd warned Sansa, and there was a smell of rain in the air. Perhaps when Lord Tywin was done with him he should go to the godswood and fetch her home before she got soaked.

But all that went straight out of his head when he entered the Hand's solar to find Cersei, Ser Kevan, and Grand Maester Pycelle gathered about Lord Tywin and the king. Joffrey was almost bouncing, and Cersei was savoring a smug little smile, though Lord Tywin looked as grim as ever. *I wonder if he could smile even if he wanted to.* "What's happened?" Tyrion asked.

His father offered him a roll of parchment. Someone had flattened it, but it still wanted to curl. *"Roslin caught a fine fat trout,"* the message read. *"Her brothers gave her a pair of wolf pelts for her wedding."* Tyrion turned it over to inspect the broken seal. The wax was silvery-grey, and pressed into it were the twin towers of House Frey. "Does the Lord of the Crossing imagine he's being poetic? Or is this meant to confound us?" Tyrion snorted. "The trout would be Edmure Tully, the pelts . . ."

"He's *dead!*" Joffrey sounded so proud and happy you might have thought he'd skinned Robb Stark himself.

First Greyjoy and now Stark. Tyrion thought of his child wife, praying in the godswood even now. *Praying to her father's gods to bring her brother victory and keep her mother safe, no doubt.* The old gods paid no more heed to prayer than the new ones, it would seem. Perhaps he should take comfort in that. "Kings are falling like leaves this autumn," he said. "It would seem our little war is winning itself."

"Wars do not win themselves, Tyrion," Cersei said with poisonous sweetness. "Our lord father won this war."

"Nothing is won so long as we have enemies in the field," Lord Tywin warned them.

"The river lords are no fools," the queen argued. "Without the northmen they cannot hope to stand against the combined power of Highgarden, Casterly Rock, and Dorne. Surely they will choose submission rather than destruction."

"Most," agreed Lord Tywin. "Riverrun remains, but so long as Walder Frey holds Edmure Tully hostage, the Blackfish dare not mount a threat. Jason Mallister and Tytos Blackwood will fight on for honor's sake, but the Freys can keep the Mallisters penned up at Seagard, and with the right inducement Jonos Bracken can be persuaded to change his allegiance and attack the Blackwoods. In the end they will bend the knee, yes. I mean to offer generous terms. Any castle that yields to us will be spared, save one."

"Harrenhal?" said Tyrion, who knew his sire.

"The realm is best rid of these Brave Companions. I have commanded Ser Gregor to put the castle to the sword."

Gregor Clegane. It appeared as if his lord father meant to mine the Mountain for every last nugget of ore before turning him over to Dornish justice. The Brave Companions would end as heads on spikes, and Littlefinger would stroll into Harrenhal without so much as a spot of blood on those fine clothes of his. He wondered if Petyr Baelish had reached the Vale yet. *If the gods are good, he ran into a storm at sea and sank.* But when had the gods ever been especially good?

"They should all be put to the sword," Joffrey declared suddenly. "The Mallisters and Blackwoods and Brackens . . . all of them. They're traitors. I want them killed, Grandfather. I won't have any *generous terms.*" The king turned to Grand Maester Pycelle. "And I want Robb Stark's head too. Write to Lord Frey and tell him. The king commands. I'm going to have it served to Sansa at my wedding feast."

"Sire," Ser Kevan said, in a shocked voice, "the lady is now your aunt by marriage."

"A jest." Cersei smiled. "Joff did not mean it."

"Yes I did," Joffrey insisted. "He was a traitor, and I want his stupid head. I'm going to make Sansa kiss it."

"*No.*" Tyrion's voice was hoarse. "Sansa is no longer yours to torment. Understand that, monster."

Joffrey sneered. "You're the monster, Uncle."

"Am I?" Tyrion cocked his head. "Perhaps you should speak more softly to me, then. Monsters are dangerous beasts, and just now kings seem to be dying like flies."

"I could have your tongue out for saying that," the boy king said, reddening. "I'm the king."

Cersei put a protective hand on her son's shoulder. "Let the dwarf make all the threats he likes, Joff. I want my lord father and my uncle to see what he is."

Lord Tywin ignored that; it was Joffrey he addressed. "Aerys also felt the need to remind men that he was king. And he was passing fond of ripping tongues out as well. You could ask Ser Ilyn Payne about that, though you'll get no reply."

"Ser Ilyn never dared provoke Aerys the way your Imp provokes Joff," said Cersei. "You heard him. 'Monster,' he said. To the King's Grace. And he threatened him . . ."

"Be quiet, Cersei. Joffrey, when your enemies defy you, you must serve them steel and fire. When they go to their knees, however, you must help them back to their feet. Elsewise no man will ever bend the knee to you. And any man who must say 'I am the king' is no true king at all. Aerys never understood that, but you will. When I've won your war for you, we will restore the king's peace and the king's justice. The only head that need concern you is Margaery Tyrell's maidenhead."

Joffrey had that sullen, sulky look he got. Cersei had him firmly by the shoulder, but perhaps she should have had him by the throat. The boy surprised them all. Instead of scuttling safely back under his rock, Joff drew himself up defiantly and said, "You talk about Aerys, Grandfather, but you were scared of him."

Oh, my, hasn't this gotten interesting? Tyrion thought.

Lord Tywin studied his grandchild in silence, gold flecks shining in his pale green eyes. "Joffrey, apologize to your grandfather," said Cersei.

He wrenched free of her. "Why should I? Everyone

knows it's true. My father won all the battles. He killed Prince Rhaegar and took the crown, while *your* father was hiding under Casterly Rock." The boy gave his grandfather a defiant look. "A *strong* king acts boldly, he doesn't just talk."

"Thank you for that wisdom, Your Grace," Lord Tywin said, with a courtesy so cold it was like to freeze their ears off. "Ser Kevan, I can see the king is tired. Please see him safely back to his bedchamber. Pycelle, perhaps some gentle potion to help His Grace sleep restfully?"

"Dreamwine, my lord?"

"I don't want any dreamwine," Joffrey insisted.

Lord Tywin would have paid more heed to a mouse squeaking in the corner. "Dreamwine will serve. Cersei, Tyrion, remain."

Ser Kevan took Joffrey firmly by the arm and marched him out the door, where two of the Kingsguard were waiting. Grand Maester Pycelle scurried after them as fast as his shaky old legs could take him. Tyrion remained where he was.

"Father, I am sorry," Cersei said, when the door was shut. "Joff has always been willful, I did warn you . . ."

"There is a long league's worth of difference between willful and stupid. 'A strong king acts boldly?' Who told him that?"

"Not me, I promise you," said Cersei. "Most like it was something he heard Robert say . . ."

"The part about you hiding under Casterly Rock does sound like Robert." Tyrion didn't want Lord Tywin forgetting that bit.

"Yes, I recall now," Cersei said, "Robert *often* told Joff that a king must be bold."

"And what were *you* telling him, pray? I did not fight a war to seat Robert the Second on the Iron Throne. You gave me to understand the boy cared nothing for his father."

"Why would he? Robert ignored him. He would have *beat* him if I'd allowed it. That brute you made me marry once hit the boy so hard he knocked out two of his baby teeth, over some mischief with a cat. I told him I'd kill him in his sleep if he ever did it again, and he never did, but sometimes he would say things . . ."

"It appears things needed to be said." Lord Tywin waved two fingers at her, a brusque dismissal. "Go."

She went, seething.

"Not Robert the Second," Tyrion said. "Aerys the Third."

"The boy is thirteen. There is time yet." Lord Tywin paced to the window. That was unlike him; he was more upset than he wished to show. "He requires a sharp lesson."

Tyrion had gotten his own sharp lesson at thirteen. He felt almost sorry for his nephew. On the other hand, no one deserved it more. "Enough of Joffrey," he said. "Wars are won with quills and ravens, wasn't that what you said? I must congratulate you. How long have you and Walder Frey been plotting this?"

"I mislike that word," Lord Tywin said stiffly.

"And I mislike being left in the dark."

"There was no reason to tell you. You had no part in this."

"Was Cersei told?" Tyrion demanded to know.

"No one was told, save those who had a part to play. And they were only told as much as they needed to know. You ought to know that there is no other way to keep a secret—here, especially. My object was to rid us of a dangerous enemy as cheaply as I could, not to indulge your curiosity or make your sister feel important." He closed the shutters, frowning. "You have a certain cunning, Tyrion, but the plain truth is *you talk too much*. That loose tongue of yours will be your undoing."

"You should have let Joff tear it out," suggested Tyrion.

"You would do well not to tempt me," Lord Tywin said. "I'll hear no more of this. I have been considering how best to appease Oberyn Martell and his entourage."

"Oh? Is this something I'm allowed to know, or should I leave so you can discuss it with yourself?"

His father ignored the sally. "Prince Oberyn's presence here is unfortunate. His brother is a cautious man, a *reasoned* man, subtle, deliberate, even indolent to a degree. He is a man who weighs the consequences of every word and every action. But Oberyn has always been half-mad."

"Is it true he tried to raise Dorne for Viserys?"

"No one speaks of it, but yes. Ravens flew and riders

rode, with what secret messages I never knew. Jon Arryn sailed to Sunspear to return Prince Lewyn's bones, sat down with Prince Doran, and ended all the talk of war. But Robert never went to Dorne thereafter, and Prince Oberyn seldom left it."

"Well, he's here now, with half the nobility of Dorne in his tail, and he grows more impatient every day," said Tyrion. "Perhaps I should show him the brothels of King's Landing, that might distract him. A tool for every task, isn't that how it works? My tool is yours, Father. Never let it be said that House Lannister blew its trumpets and I did not respond."

Lord Tywin's mouth tightened. "Very droll. Shall I have them sew you a suit of motley, and a little hat with bells on it?"

"If I wear it, do I have leave to say anything I want about His Grace King Joffrey?"

Lord Tywin seated himself again and said, "I was made to suffer my father's follies. I will not suffer yours. Enough."

"Very well, as you ask so pleasantly. The Red Viper is *not* going to be pleasant, I fear . . . nor will he content himself with Ser Gregor's head alone."

"All the more reason not to give it to him."

"*Not* to . . . ?" Tyrion was shocked. "I thought we were agreed that the woods were full of beasts."

"Lesser beasts." Lord Tywin's fingers laced together under his chin. "Ser Gregor has served us well. No other knight in the realm inspires such terror in our enemies."

"Oberyn *knows* that Gregor was the one who . . ."

"He knows nothing. He has heard tales. Stable gossip and kitchen calumnies. He has no crumb of proof. Ser Gregor is certainly not about to confess to him. I mean to keep him well away for so long as the Dornishmen are in King's Landing."

"And when Oberyn demands the justice he's come for?"

"I will tell him that Ser Amory Lorch killed Elia and her children," Lord Tywin said calmly. "So will you, if he asks."

"Ser Amory Lorch is dead," Tyrion said flatly.

"Precisely. Vargo Hoat had Ser Amory torn apart by a

bear after the fall of Harrenhal. That ought to be sufficiently grisly to appease even Oberyn Martell."

"You may call that justice . . ."

"It *is* justice. It was Ser Amory who brought me the
girl's body, if you must know. He found her hiding under
her father's bed, as if she believed Rhaegar could still protect her. Princess Elia and the babe were in the nursery a
floor below."

"Well, it's a tale, and Ser Amory's not like to deny it.
What will you tell Oberyn when he asks who gave Lorch
his orders?"

"Ser Amory acted on his own in the hope of winning favor from the new king. Robert's hatred for Rhaegar was
scarcely a secret."

It might serve, Tyrion had to concede, *but the snake
will not be happy.* "Far be it from me to question your cunning, Father, but in your place I do believe I'd have let
Robert Baratheon bloody his own hands."

Lord Tywin stared at him as if he had lost his wits. "You
deserve that motley, then. We had come late to Robert's
cause. It was necessary to demonstrate our loyalty. When
I laid those bodies before the throne, no man could doubt
that we had forsaken House Targaryen forever. And
Robert's relief was palpable. As stupid as he was, even he
knew that Rhaegar's children had to die if his throne was
ever to be secure. Yet he saw himself as a hero, and heroes
do not kill children." His father shrugged. "I grant you, it
was done too brutally. Elia need not have been harmed at
all, that was sheer folly. By herself she was nothing."

"Then why did the Mountain kill her?"

"Because I did not tell him to spare her. I doubt I mentioned her at all. I had more pressing concerns. Ned Stark's
van was rushing south from the Trident, and I feared it
might come to swords between us. And it was in Aerys to
murder Jaime, with no more cause than spite. That was the
thing I feared most. That, and what Jaime himself might
do." He closed a fist. "Nor did I yet grasp what I had in
Gregor Clegane, only that he was huge and terrible in battle. The rape . . . even you will not accuse me of giving *that*
command, I would hope. Ser Amory was almost as bestial
with Rhaenys. I asked him afterward why it had required
half a hundred thrusts to kill a girl of . . . two? Three? He

said she'd kicked him and would not stop screaming. If Lorch had half the wits the gods gave a turnip, he would have calmed her with a few sweet words and used a soft silk pillow." His mouth twisted in distaste. "The blood was in him."

But not in you, Father. There is no blood in Tywin Lannister. "Was it a soft silk pillow that slew Robb Stark?"

"It was to be an arrow, at Edmure Tully's wedding feast. The boy was too wary in the field. He kept his men in good order, and surrounded himself with outriders and bodyguards."

"So Lord Walder slew him under his own roof, at his own table?" Tyrion made a fist. "What of Lady Catelyn?"

"Slain as well, I'd say. *A pair of wolfskins.* Frey had intended to keep her captive, but perhaps something went awry."

"So much for guest right."

"The blood is on Walder Frey's hands, not mine."

"Walder Frey is a peevish old man who lives to fondle his young wife and brood over all the slights he's suffered. I have no doubt he hatched this ugly chicken, but he would never have dared such a thing without a promise of protection."

"I suppose you would have spared the boy and told Lord Frey you had no need of his allegiance? That would have driven the old fool right back into Stark's arms and won you another year of war. Explain to me why it is more noble to kill ten thousand men in battle than a dozen at dinner." When Tyrion had no reply to that, his father continued. "The price was cheap by any measure. The crown shall grant Riverrun to Ser Emmon Frey once the Blackfish yields. Lancel and Daven must marry Frey girls, Joy is to wed one of Lord Walder's natural sons when she's old enough, and Roose Bolton becomes Warden of the North and takes home Arya Stark."

"*Arya* Stark?" Tyrion cocked his head. "And Bolton? I might have known Frey would not have the stomach to act alone. But Arya . . . Varys and Ser Jacelyn searched for her for more than half a year. Arya Stark is surely dead."

"So was Renly, until the Blackwater."

"What does that mean?"

"Perhaps Littlefinger succeeded where you and Varys

failed. Lord Bolton will wed the girl to his bastard son. We shall allow the Dreadfort to fight the ironborn for a few years, and see if he can bring Stark's other bannermen to heel. Come spring, all of them should be at the end of their strength and ready to bend the knee. The north will go to your son by Sansa Stark . . . if you ever find enough manhood in you to breed one. Lest you forget, it is not only Joffrey who must needs take a maidenhead."

I had not forgotten, though I'd hoped you had. "And when do you imagine Sansa will be at her most fertile?" Tyrion asked his father in tones that dripped acid. "Before or after I tell her how we murdered her mother and her brother?"

DAVOS

For a moment it seemed as though the king had not heard. Stannis showed no pleasure at the news, no anger, no disbelief, not even relief. He stared at his Painted Table with teeth clenched hard. "You are certain?" he asked.

"I am not seeing the body, no, Your Kingliness," said Salladhor Saan. "Yet in the city, the lions prance and dance. *The Red Wedding*, the smallfolk are calling it. They swear Lord Frey had the boy's head hacked off, sewed the head of his direwolf in its place, and nailed a crown about his ears. His lady mother was slain as well, and thrown naked in the river."

At a wedding, thought Davos. *As he sat at his slayer's board, a guest beneath his roof. These Freys are cursed.* He could smell the burning blood again, and hear the leech hissing and spitting on the brazier's hot coals.

"It was the Lord's wrath that slew him," Ser Axell Florent declared. "It was the hand of R'hllor!"

"*Praise the Lord of Light!*" sang out Queen Selyse, a pinched thin hard woman with large ears and a hairy upper lip.

"Is the hand of R'hllor spotted and palsied?" asked Stannis. "This sounds more Walder Frey's handiwork than any god's."

"R'hllor chooses such instruments as he requires." The ruby at Melisandre's throat shone redly. "His ways are mysterious, but no man may withstand his fiery will."

"No man may withstand him!" the queen cried.

"Be quiet, woman. You are not at a nightfire now." Stannis considered the Painted Table. "The wolf leaves no heirs, the kraken too many. The lions will devour them unless . . . Saan, I will require your fastest ships to carry envoys to the Iron Islands and White Harbor. I shall offer pardons." The way he snapped his teeth showed how little he liked that word. "Full pardons, for all those who repent of treason and swear fealty to their rightful king. They must see . . ."

"They will not." Melisandre's voice was soft. "I am sorry, Your Grace. This is not an end. More false kings will soon rise to take up the crowns of those who've died."

"More?" Stannis looked as though he would gladly have throttled her. "More usurpers? *More* traitors?"

"I have seen it in the flames."

Queen Selyse went to the king's side. "The Lord of Light sent Melisandre to guide you to your glory. Heed her, I beg you. R'hllor's holy flames do not lie."

"There are lies and lies, woman. Even when these flames speak truly, they are full of tricks, it seems to me."

"An ant who hears the words of a king may not comprehend what he is saying," Melisandre said, "and all men are ants before the fiery face of god. If sometimes I have mistaken a warning for a prophecy or a prophecy for a warning, the fault lies in the reader, not the book. But this I know for a certainty—envoys and pardons will not serve you now, no more than leeches. You must show the realm a sign. A sign that proves your power!"

"Power?" The king snorted. "I have thirteen hundred men on Dragonstone, another three hundred at Storm's End." His hand swept over the Painted Table. "The rest of Westeros is in the hands of my foes. I have no fleet but Salladhor Saan's. No coin to hire sellswords. No prospect of plunder or glory to lure freeriders to my cause."

"Lord husband," said Queen Selyse, "you have more

men than Aegon did three hundred years ago. All you lack are dragons."

The look Stannis gave her was dark. "Nine mages crossed the sea to hatch Aegon the Third's cache of eggs. Baelor the Blessed prayed over his for half a year. Aegon the Fourth built dragons of wood and iron. Aerion Brightflame drank wildfire to transform himself. The mages failed, King Baelor's prayers went unanswered, the wooden dragons burned, and Prince Aerion died screaming."

Queen Selyse was adamant. "None of these was the chosen of R'hllor. No red comet blazed across the heavens to herald their coming. None wielded Lightbringer, the red sword of heroes. And none of them paid the price. Lady Melisandre will tell you, my lord. Only death can pay for life."

"The boy?" The king almost spat the words.

"The boy," agreed the queen.

"The boy," Ser Axell echoed.

"I was sick unto death of this wretched boy before he was even born," the king complained. "His very name is a roaring in my ears and a dark cloud upon my soul."

"Give the boy to me and you need never hear his name spoken again," Melisandre promised.

No, but you'll hear him screaming when she burns him. Davos held his tongue. It was wiser not to speak until the king commanded it.

"Give me the boy for R'hllor," the red woman said, "and the ancient prophecy shall be fulfilled. Your dragon shall awaken and spread his stony wings. The kingdom shall be yours."

Ser Axell went to one knee. "On bended knee I beg you, sire. Wake the stone dragon and let the traitors tremble. Like Aegon you begin as Lord of Dragonstone. Like Aegon you shall conquer. Let the false and the fickle feel your flames."

"Your own wife begs as well, lord husband." Queen Selyse went down on both knees before the king, hands clasped as if in prayer. "Robert and Delena defiled our bed and laid a curse upon our union. This boy is the foul fruit of their fornications. Lift his shadow from my womb and I will bear you many trueborn sons, I know it." She threw her arms around his legs. "He is only one boy, born of your brother's lust and my cousin's shame."

"He is mine own blood. Stop clutching me, woman." King Stannis put a hand on her shoulder, awkwardly untangling himself from her grasp. "Perhaps Robert did curse our marriage bed. He swore to me that he never meant to shame me, that he was drunk and never knew which bedchamber he entered that night. But does it matter? The boy was not at fault, whatever the truth."

Melisandre put her hand on the king's arm. "The Lord of Light cherishes the innocent. There is no sacrifice more precious. From his king's blood and his untainted fire, a dragon shall be born."

Stannis did not pull away from Melisandre's touch as he had from his queen's. The red woman was all Selyse was not; young, full-bodied, and strangely beautiful, with her heart-shaped face, coppery hair, and unearthly red eyes. "It would be a wondrous thing to see stone come to life," he admitted, grudging. "And to mount a dragon . . . I remember the first time my father took me to court, Robert had to hold my hand. I could not have been older than four, which would have made him five or six. We agreed afterward that the king had been as noble as the dragons were fearsome." Stannis snorted. "Years later, our father told us that Aerys had cut himself on the throne that morning, so his Hand had taken his place. It was Tywin Lannister who'd so impressed us." His fingers touched the surface of the table, tracing a path lightly across the varnished hills. "Robert took the skulls down when he donned the crown, but he could not bear to have them destroyed. Dragon wings over Westeros . . . there would be such a . . ."

"Your Grace!" Davos edged forward. "Might I speak?"

Stannis closed his mouth so hard his teeth snapped. "My lord of the Rainwood. Why do you think I made you Hand, if not to speak?" The king waved a hand. "Say what you will."

Warrior, make me brave. "I know little of dragons and less of gods . . . but the queen spoke of curses. No man is as cursed as the kinslayer, in the eyes of gods and men."

"There are no gods save R'hllor and the Other, whose name must not be spoken." Melisandre's mouth made a hard red line. "And small men curse what they cannot understand."

"I am a small man," Davos admitted, "so tell me why you need this boy Edric Storm to wake your great stone dragon, my lady." He was determined to say the boy's name as often as he could.

"Only death can pay for life, my lord. A great gift requires a great sacrifice."

"Where is the greatness in a baseborn child?"

"He has kings' blood in his veins. You have seen what even a little of that blood could do—"

"I saw you burn some leeches."

"And two false kings are dead."

"Robb Stark was murdered by Lord Walder of the Crossing, and we have heard that Balon Greyjoy fell from a bridge. Who did your leeches kill?"

"Do you doubt the power of R'hllor?"

No. Davos remembered too well the living shadow that had squirmed from out her womb that night beneath Storm's End, its black hands pressing at her thighs. *I must go carefully here, or some shadow may come seeking me as well.* "Even an onion smuggler knows two onions from three. You are short a king, my lady."

Stannis gave a snort of laughter. "He has you there, my lady. Two is not three."

"To be sure, Your Grace. One king might die by chance, even two . . . but three? If Joffrey should die in the midst of all his power, surrounded by his armies and his Kingsguard, would not that show the power of the Lord at work?"

"It might." The king spoke as if he grudged each word.

"Or not." Davos did his best to hide his fear.

"Joffrey *shall* die," Queen Selyse declared, serene in her confidence.

"It may be that he is dead already," Ser Axell added.

Stannis looked at them with annoyance. "Are you trained crows, to croak at me in turns? Enough."

"Husband, hear me—" the queen entreated.

"Why? Two is not three. Kings can count as well as smugglers. You may go." Stannis turned his back on them.

Melisandre helped the queen to her feet. Selyse swept stiffly from the chamber, the red woman trailing behind.

Ser Axell lingered long enough to give Davos one last look. *An ugly look on an ugly face*, he thought as he met the stare.

After the others had gone, Davos cleared his throat. The king looked up. "Why are you still here?"

"Sire, about Edric Storm . . ."

Stannis made a sharp gesture. "Spare me."

Davos persisted. "Your daughter takes her lessons with him, and plays with him every day in Aegon's Garden."

"I know that."

"Her heart would break if anything ill should—"

"I know that as well."

"If you would only see him—"

"I have seen him. He looks like Robert. Aye, and worships him. Shall I tell him how often his beloved father ever gave him a thought? My brother liked the making of children well enough, but after birth they were a bother."

"He asks after you every day, he—"

"You are making me angry, Davos. I will hear no more of this bastard boy."

"His name is Edric Storm, sire."

"I know his name. Was there ever a name so apt? It proclaims his bastardy, his high birth, and the turmoil he brings with him. Edric Storm. There, I have said it. Are you satisfied, my lord Hand?"

"Edric—" he started.

"—is *one boy!* He may be the best boy who ever drew breath and it would not matter. My duty is to the realm." His hand swept across the Painted Table. "How many boys dwell in Westeros? How many girls? How many men, how many women? The darkness will devour them all, she says. The night that never ends. She talks of prophecies . . . a hero reborn in the sea, living dragons hatched from dead stone . . . she speaks of *signs* and swears they point to me. I never asked for this, no more than I asked to be king. Yet dare I disregard her?" He ground his teeth. "We do not choose our destinies. Yet we must . . . we must do our duty, no? Great or small, *we must do our duty*. Melisandre swears that she has seen me in her flames, facing the dark with Lightbringer raised on high. *Lightbringer!*" Stannis gave a derisive snort. "It glimmers prettily, I'll grant you, but on the Blackwater this magic sword served me no better than any common steel. A dragon would have turned that battle. Aegon once stood here as I do, looking down on this table. Do you think we would name him Aegon the Conqueror today if he had not had *dragons?*"

"Your Grace," said Davos, "the cost . . ."

"*I know the cost!* Last night, gazing into that hearth, I saw things in the flames as well. I saw a king, a crown of fire on his brows, burning . . . *burning,* Davos. His own crown consumed his flesh and turned him into ash. Do you think I need Melisandre to tell me what that means? Or *you?*" The king moved, so his shadow fell upon King's Landing. "If Joffrey should die . . . what is the life of one bastard boy against a kingdom?"

"Everything," said Davos, softly.

Stannis looked at him, jaw clenched. "Go," the king said at last, "before you talk yourself back into the dungeon."

Sometimes the storm winds blow so strong a man has no choice but to furl his sails. "Aye, Your Grace." Davos bowed, but Stannis had seemingly forgotten him already.

It was chilly in the yard when he left the Stone Drum. A wind blew briskly from the east, making the banners snap and flap noisily along the walls. Davos could smell salt in the air. *The sea.* He loved that smell. It made him want to walk a deck again, to raise his canvas and sail off south to Marya and his two small ones. He thought of them most every day now, and even more at night. Part of him wanted nothing so much as to take Devan and go home. *I cannot. Not yet. I am a lord now, and the King's Hand, I must not fail him.*

He raised his eyes to gaze up at the walls. In place of merlons, a thousand grotesques and gargoyles looked down on him, each different from all the others; wyverns, griffins, demons, manticores, minotaurs, basilisks, hellhounds, cockatrices, and a thousand queerer creatures sprouted from the castle's battlements as if they'd grown there. And the dragons were everywhere. The Great Hall was a dragon lying on its belly. Men entered through its open mouth. The kitchens were a dragon curled up in a ball, with the smoke and steam of the ovens vented through its nostrils. The towers were dragons hunched above the walls or poised for flight; the Windwyrm seemed to scream defiance, while Sea Dragon Tower gazed serenely out across the waves. Smaller dragons framed the gates. Dragon claws emerged from walls to grasp at torches, great stone wings enfolded the smith and armory, and tails formed arches, bridges, and exterior stairs.

Davos had often heard it said that the wizards of Valyria did not cut and chisel as common masons did, but worked stone with fire and magic as a potter might work clay. But now he wondered. *What if they were real dragons, somehow turned to stone?*

"If the red woman brings them to life, the castle will come crashing down, I am thinking. What kind of dragons are full of rooms and stairs and furniture? And windows. And chimneys. And privy shafts."

Davos turned to find Salladhor Saan beside him. "Does this mean you have forgiven my treachery, Salla?"

The old pirate wagged a finger at him. "Forgiving, yes. Forgetting, no. All that good gold on Claw Isle that might have been mine, it makes me old and tired to think of it. When I die impoverished, my wives and concubines will curse you, Onion Lord. Lord Celtigar had many fine wines that now I am not tasting, a sea eagle he had trained to fly from the wrist, and a magic horn to summon krakens from the deep. Very useful such a horn would be, to pull down Tyroshi and other vexing creatures. But do I have this horn to blow? No, because the king made my old friend his Hand." He slipped his arm through Davos's and said, "The queen's men love you not, old friend. I am hearing that a certain Hand has been making friends of his own. This is true, yes?"

You hear too much, you old pirate. A smuggler had best know men as well as tides, or he would not live to smuggle long. The queen's men might remain fervent followers of the Lord of Light, but the lesser folk of Dragonstone were drifting back to the gods they'd known all their lives. They said Stannis was ensorceled, that Melisandre had turned him away from the Seven to bow before some demon out of shadow, and . . . worst sin of all . . . that she and her god had failed him. And there were knights and lordlings who felt the same. Davos had sought them out, choosing them with the same care with which he'd once picked his crews. Ser Gerald Gower fought stoutly on the Blackwater, but afterward had been heard to say that R'hllor must be a fee-ble god to let his followers be chased off by a dwarf and a dead man. Ser Andrew Estermont was the king's cousin, and had served as his squire years ago. The Bastard of Nightsong had commanded the rearguard that allowed Stannis to reach the safety of Salladhor Saan's galleys, but he worshiped the Warrior with a faith as fierce as he was. *King's men, not queen's men.* But it would not do to boast of them.

"A certain Lysene pirate once told me that a good smug-gler stays out of sight," Davos replied carefully. "Black sails, muffled oars, and a crew that knows how to hold their tongues."

The Lyseni laughed. "A crew with no tongues is even better. Big strong mutes who cannot read or write." But then he grew more somber. "But I am glad to know that someone watches your back, old friend. Will the king give the boy to the red priestess, do you think? One little dragon could end this great big war."

Old habit made him reach for his luck, but his finger-bones no longer hung about his neck, and he found noth-ing. "He will not do it," said Davos. "He could not harm his own blood."

"Lord Renly will be glad to hear this."

"Renly was a traitor in arms. Edric Storm is innocent of any crime. His Grace is a just man."

Salla shrugged. "We shall be seeing. Or you shall. For myself, I am returning to sea. Even now, rascally smugglers may be sailing across the Blackwater Bay, hoping to avoid paying their lord's lawful duties." He slapped Davos on the back. "Take care. You with your mute friends. You are grown so very great now, yet the higher a man climbs the farther he has to fall."

Davos reflected on those words as he climbed the steps of Sea Dragon Tower to the maester's chambers below the rookery. He did not need Salla to tell him that he had risen too high. *I cannot read, I cannot write, the lords despise me, I know nothing of ruling, how can I be the King's Hand? I belong on the deck of a ship, not in a castle tower.*

He had said as much to Maester Pylos. "You are a no-table captain," the maester replied. "A captain rules his ship, does he not? He must navigate treacherous waters, set his sails to catch the rising wind, know when a storm is coming and how best to weather it. This is much the same."

Pylos meant it kindly, but his assurances rang hollow. "It is not at all the same!" Davos had protested. "A kingdom's not a ship . . . and a good thing, or this kingdom would be sinking. I know wood and rope and water, yes, but how will that serve me now? Where do I find the wind to blow King Stannis to his throne?"

The maester laughed at that. "And there you have it, my lord. Words are wind, you know, and you've blown mine away with your good sense. His Grace knows what he has in you, I think."

"Onions," said Davos glumly. "That is what he has in me. The King's Hand should be a highborn lord, someone wise and learned, a battle commander or a great knight . . ."

"Ser Ryam Redwyne was the greatest knight of his day, and one of the worst Hands ever to serve a king. Septon Murmison's prayers worked miracles, but as Hand he soon had the whole realm praying for his death. Lord Butterwell was renowned for wit, Myles Smallwood for courage, Ser Otto Hightower for learning, yet they failed as Hands, every one. As for birth, the dragonkings oft chose Hands from amongst their own blood, with results as various as Baelor Breakspear and Maegor the Cruel. Against this, you have Septon Barth, the blacksmith's son the Old King plucked from the Red Keep's library, who gave the realm forty years of peace and plenty." Pylos smiled. "Read your history, Lord Davos, and you will see that your doubts are groundless."

"How can I read history, when I cannot read?"

"Any man can read, my lord," said Maester Pylos. "There is no magic needed, nor high birth. I am teaching the art to your son, at the king's command. Let me teach you as well."

It was a kindly offer, and not one that Davos could refuse. And so every day he repaired to the maester's chambers high atop Sea Dragon Tower, to frown over scrolls and parchments and great leather tomes and try to puzzle out a few more words. His efforts often gave him headaches, and made him feel as big a fool as Patchface besides. His son

Devan was not yet twelve, yet he was well ahead of his father, and for Princess Shireen and Edric Storm reading seemed as natural as breathing. When it came to books, Davos was more a child than any of them. Yet he persisted. He was the King's Hand now, and a King's Hand should read.

The narrow twisting steps of Sea Dragon Tower had been a sore trial to Maester Cressen after he broke his hip. Davos still found himself missing the old man. He thought Stannis must as well. Pylos seemed clever and diligent and well-meaning, but he was so young, and the king did not confide in him as he had in Cressen. The old man had been with Stannis so long . . . *Until he ran afoul of Melisandre, and died for it.*

At the top of the steps Davos heard a soft jingle of bells that could only herald Patchface. The princess's fool was waiting outside the maester's door for her like a faithful hound. Dough-soft and slump-shouldered, his broad face tattooed in a motley pattern of red and green squares, Patchface wore a helm made of a rack of deer antlers strapped to a tin bucket. A dozen bells hung from the tines and rang when he moved . . . which meant constantly, since the fool seldom stood still. He jingled and jangled his way everywhere he went; small wonder that Pylos had exiled him from Shireen's lessons. "Under the sea the old fish eat the young fish," the fool muttered at Davos. He bobbed his head, and his bells clanged and chimed and sang. "I know, I know, oh oh oh."

"Up here the young fish teach the old fish," said Davos, who never felt so ancient as when he sat down to try and read. It might have been different if aged Master Cressen had been the one teaching him, but Pylos was young enough to be his son.

He found the maester seated at his long wooden table covered with books and scrolls, across from the three children. Princess Shireen sat between the two boys. Even now Davos could take great pleasure in the sight of his own blood keeping company with a princess and a king's bastard. *Devan will be a lord now, not merely a knight. The Lord of the Rainwood.* Davos took more pride in that than in wearing the title himself. *He reads too. He reads and he writes, as if he had been born to it.* Pylos had naught but praise for his diligence, and the master-at-arms said Devan was showing promise with sword and lance as well. *And he is a godly lad, too.* "My brothers have ascended to the Hall of Light, to sit beside the Lord," Devan had said when his father told him how his four elder brothers had died. "I will pray for them at the nightfires, and for you as well, Father, so you might walk in the Light of the Lord till the end of your days."

"Good morrow to you, Father," the boy greeted him. *He looks so much like Dale did at his age,* Davos thought. His eldest had never dressed so fine as Devan in his squire's raiment, to be sure, but they shared the same square plain face, the same forthright brown eyes, the same thin brown flyaway hair. Devan's cheeks and chin were dusted with blond hair, a fuzz that would have shamed a proper peach, though the boy was fiercely proud of his "beard." *Just as Dale was proud of his, once.* Devan was the oldest of the three children at the table.

Yet Edric Storm was three inches taller and broader in the chest and shoulders. He was his father's son in that; nor did he ever miss a morning's work with sword and shield. Those old enough to have known Robert and Renly as children said that the bastard boy had more of their look than Stannis had ever shared; the coal-black hair, the deep blue eyes, the mouth, the jaw, the cheekbones. Only his ears reminded you that his mother had been a Florent.

"Yes, good morrow, my lord," Edric echoed. The boy could be fierce and proud, but the maesters and castellans and masters-at-arms who'd raised him had schooled him well in courtesy. "Do you come from my uncle? How fares His Grace?"

"Well," Davos lied. If truth be told, the king had a haggard, haunted look about him, but he saw no need to burden the boy with his fears. "I hope I have not disturbed your lesson."

"We had just finished, my lord," Maester Pylos said.

"We were reading about King Daeron the First." Princess Shireen was a sad, sweet, gentle child, far from pretty. Stannis had given her his square jaw and Selyse her Florent ears, and the gods in their cruel wisdom had seen fit to compound her homeliness by afflicting her with greyscale in the cradle. The disease had left one cheek and half her neck grey and cracked and hard, though it had spared both her life and her sight. "He went to war and conquered Dorne. The Young Dragon, they called him."

"He worshiped false gods," said Devan, "but he was a great king otherwise, and very brave in battle."

"He was," agreed Edric Storm, "but my father was braver. The Young Dragon never won three battles in a day."

The princess looked at him wide-eyed. "Did Uncle Robert win three battles in a day?"

The bastard nodded. "It was when he'd first come home to call his banners. Lords Grandison, Cafferen, and Fell planned to join their strength at Summerhall and march on Storm's End, but he learned their plans from an informer and rode at once with all his knights and squires. As the plotters came up on Summerhall one by one, he defeated each of them in turn before they could join up with the others. He slew Lord Fell in single combat and captured his son Silveraxe."

Devan looked to Pylos. "Is that how it happened?"

"I *said* so, didn't I?" Edric Storm said before the maester could reply. "He smashed all three of them, and fought so bravely that Lord Grandison and Lord Cafferen became his men afterward, and Silveraxe too. No one ever beat my father."

"Edric, you ought not boast," Maester Pylos said. "King Robert suffered defeats like any other man. Lord Tyrell bested him at Ashford, and he lost many a tourney tilt as well."

"He won more than he lost, though. And he killed Prince Rhaegar on the Trident."

"That he did," the maester agreed. "But now I must give my attention to Lord Davos, who has waited so patiently. We will read more of King Daeron's *Conquest of Dorne* on the morrow."

Princess Shireen and the boys said their farewells courteously. When they had taken their leaves, Maester Pylos moved closer to Davos. "My lord, perhaps you would like to try a bit of *Conquest of Dorne* as well?" He slid the slender leather-bound book across the table. "King Daeron wrote with an elegant simplicity, and his history is rich with blood, battle, and bravery. Your son is quite engrossed."

"My son is not quite twelve. I am the King's Hand. Give me another letter, if you would."

"As you wish, my lord." Maester Pylos rummaged about his table, unrolling and then discarding various scraps of parchment. "There are no new letters. Perhaps an old one . . ."

Davos enjoyed a good story as well as any man, but Stannis had not named him Hand for his enjoyment, he felt. His first duty was to help his king rule, and for that he must needs understand the words the ravens brought. The best way to learn a thing was to do it, he had found; sails or scrolls, it made no matter.

"This might serve our purpose." Pylos passed him a letter.

Davos flattened down the little square of crinkled parchment and squinted at the tiny crabbed letters. Reading was hard on the eyes, that much he had learned early. Sometimes he wondered if the Citadel offered a champion's purse to the maester who wrote the smallest hand. Pylos had laughed at the notion, but . . .

"To the . . . five kings," read Davos, hesitating briefly over *five*, which he did not often see written out. "The king . . . be . . . the king . . . beware?"

"*Beyond*," the maester corrected.

Davos grimaced. "The King beyond the Wall comes . . . comes *south*. He leads a . . . a . . . fast . . ."

"Vast."

". . . a *vast* host of wil . . . wild . . . wildlings. Lord M . . . Mmmor . . . Mormont sent a . . . raven from the . . . ha . . . ha . . ."

"Haunted. The *haunted forest*." Pylos underlined the words with the point of his finger.

". . . the haunted forest. He is . . . *under* a . . . attack?"

"Yes."

Pleased, he plowed onward. "Oth . . . other birds have come since, with no words. We . . . fear . . . Mormont slain with all . . . with all his . . . stench . . . no, *strength*. We fear Mormont slain with all his strength . . ." Davos suddenly realized just what he was reading. He turned the letter over, and saw that the wax that had sealed it had been black. "This is from the Night's Watch. Maester, has King Stannis seen this letter?"

"I brought it to Lord Alester when it first arrived. He was the Hand then. I believed he discussed it with the queen. When I asked him if he wished to send a reply, he told me not to be a fool. 'His Grace lacks the men to fight his own battles, he has none to waste on wildlings,' he said to me."

That was true enough. And this talk of five kings would certainly have angered Stannis. "Only a starving man begs bread from a beggar," he muttered.

"Pardon, my lord?"

"Something my wife said once." Davos drummed his shortened fingers against the tabletop. The first time he had seen the Wall he had been younger than Devan, serving aboard the *Cobblecat* under Roro Uhoris, a Tyroshi known up and down the narrow sea as the Blind Bastard, though he was neither blind nor baseborn. Roro had sailed past Skagos into the Shivering Sea, visiting a hundred little coves that had never seen a trading ship before. He brought steel; swords, axes, helms, good chainmail hauberks, to trade for furs, ivory, amber, and obsidian. When the *Cobblecat* turned back south her holds were stuffed, but in the Bay of Seals three black galleys came out to herd her into Eastwatch. They lost their cargo and the Bastard lost his head, for the crime of trading weapons to the wildlings.

Davos had traded at Eastwatch in his smuggling days. The black brothers made hard enemies but good customers, for a ship with the right cargo. But while he might have taken their coin, he had never forgotten how the Blind Bastard's head had rolled across the *Cobblecat*'s deck. "I met some wildlings when I was a boy," he told Maester Pylos. "They were fair thieves but bad hagglers. One made off with our cabin girl. All in all, they seemed men like any other men, some fair, some foul."

"Men are men," Maester Pylos agreed. "Shall we return to our reading, my lord Hand?"

I am the Hand of the King, yes. Stannis might be the King of Westeros in name, but in truth he was the King of the Painted Table. He held Dragonstone and Storm's End, and had an ever-more-uneasy alliance with Salladhor Saan, but that was all. How could the Watch have looked to him for help? *They may not know how weak he is, how lost his cause.* "King Stannis never saw this letter, you are quite certain? Nor Melisandre?"

"No. Should I bring it to them? Even now?"

"No," Davos said at once. "You did your duty when you brought it to Lord Alester." *If Melisandre knew of this letter . . .* What was it she had said? *One whose name may not be spoken is marshaling his power, Davos Seaworth. Soon comes the cold, and the night that never ends . . .* And Stannis had seen a vision in the flames, a ring of torches in the snow with terror all around.

"My lord, are you unwell?" asked Pylos.

I am frightened, Maester, he might have said. Davos was remembering a tale Salladhor Saan had told him, of how Azor Ahai tempered Lightbringer by thrusting it through the heart of the wife he loved. *He slew his wife to fight the dark. If Stannis is Azor Ahai come again, does that mean Edric Storm must play the part of Nissa Nissa?* "I was thinking, Maester. My pardons." *What harm if some wildling king conquers the north?* It was not as though Stannis *held* the north. His Grace could scarcely be expected to defend people who refused to acknowledge him as king. "Give me another letter," he said abruptly. "This one is too . . ."

". . . difficult?" suggested Pylos.

Soon comes the cold, whispered Melisandre, *and the night that never ends.* "Troubling," said Davos. "Too . . . troubling. A different letter, please."

JON

They woke to the smoke of Mole's Town burning.
Atop the King's Tower, Jon Snow leaned on the
padded crutch that Maester Aemon had given him
and watched the grey plume rise. Styr had lost all hope of
taking Castle Black unawares when Jon escaped him, yet
even so, he need not have warned of his approach so
bluntly. *You may kill us,* he reflected, *but no one will be
butchered in their beds. That much I did, at least.*

His leg still hurt like blazes when he put his weight on
it. He'd needed Clydas to help him don his fresh-washed
blacks and lace up his boots that morning, and by the time
they were done he'd wanted to drown himself in the milk
of the poppy. Instead he had settled for half a cup of
dreamwine, a chew of willow bark, and the crutch. The
beacon was burning on Weatherback Ridge, and the
Night's Watch had need of every man.

"I can fight," he insisted when they tried to stop him.

"Your leg's healed, is it?" Noye snorted. "You won't
mind me giving it a little kick, then?"

"I'd sooner you didn't. It's stiff, but I can hobble around well enough, and stand and fight if you have need of me."

"I have need of every man who knows which end of the spear to stab into the wildlings."

"The pointy end." Jon had told his little sister something like that once, he remembered.

Noye rubbed the bristle on his chin. "Might be you'll do. We'll put you on a tower with a longbow, but if you bloody well fall off don't come crying to me."

He could see the kingsroad wending its way south through stony brown fields and over windswept hills. The Magnar would be coming up that road before the day was done, his Thenns marching behind him with axes and spears in their hands and their bronze-and-leather shields on their backs. *Grigg the Goat, Quort, Big Boil, and the rest will be coming as well. And Ygritte.* The wildlings had never been his friends, he had not *allowed* them to be his friends, but her . . .

He could feel the throb of pain where her arrow had gone through the meat and muscle of his thigh. He remembered the old man's eyes too, and the black blood rushing from his throat as the storm cracked overhead. But he remembered the grotto best of all, the look of her naked in the torchlight, the taste of her mouth when it opened under his. *Ygritte, stay away. Go south and raid, go hide in one of those roundtowers you liked so well. You'll find nothing here but death.*

Across the yard, one of the bowmen on the roof of the old Flint Barracks had unlaced his breeches and was pissing through a crenel. *Mully,* he knew from the man's greasy orange hair. Men in black cloaks were visible on other roofs and tower tops as well, though nine of every ten happened to be made of straw. "The scarecrow sentinels," Donal Noye called them. *Only we're the crows,* Jon mused, *and most of us were scared enough.*

Whatever you called them, the straw soldiers had been Maester Aemon's notion. They had more breeches and jerkins and tunics in the storerooms than they'd had men to fill them, so why not stuff some with straw, drape a cloak around their shoulders, and set them to standing watches? Noye had placed them on every tower and in half the windows. Some were even clutching spears, or had crossbows cocked under their arms. The hope was that the Thenns would see them from afar and decide that Castle Black was too well defended to attack.

Jon had six scarecrows sharing the roof of the King's Tower with him, along with two actual breathing brothers. Deaf Dick Follard sat in a crenel, methodically cleaning and oiling the mechanism of his crossbow to make sure the wheel turned smoothly, while the Oldtown boy wandered restlessly around the parapets, fussing with the clothes on straw men. *Maybe he thinks they will fight better if they're posed just right. Or maybe this waiting is fraying his nerves the way it's fraying mine.*

The boy claimed to be eighteen, older than Jon, but he was green as summer grass for all that. Satin, they called him, even in the wool and mail and boiled leather of the Night's Watch; the name he'd gotten in the brothel where he'd been born and raised. He was pretty as a girl with his dark eyes, soft skin, and raven's ringlets. Half a year at Castle Black had toughened up his hands, however, and Noye said he was passable with a crossbow. Whether he had the courage to face what was coming, though . . .

Jon used the crutch to limp across the tower top. The King's Tower was not the castle's tallest—the high, slim, crumbling Lance held that honor, though Othell Yarwyck had been heard to say it might topple any day. Nor was the King's Tower strongest—the Tower of Guards beside the kingsroad would be a tougher nut to crack. But it was tall enough, strong enough, and well placed beside the Wall, overlooking the gate and the foot of the wooden stair.

The first time he had seen Castle Black with his own eyes, Jon had wondered why anyone would be so foolish as to build a castle without walls. How could it be defended?

"It can't," his uncle told him. "That is the point. The Night's Watch is pledged to take no part in the quarrels of the realm. Yet over the centuries certain Lords Commander, more proud than wise, forgot their vows and near destroyed us all with their ambitions. Lord Commander Runcel Hightower tried to bequeathe the Watch to his bastard son. Lord Commander Rodrik Flint thought to make himself King-beyond-the-Wall. Tristan Mudd, Mad Marq Rankenfell, Robin Hill . . . did you know that six hundred years ago, the commanders at Snowgate and the Nightfort went to war *against each other*? And when the Lord Commander tried to stop them, they joined forces to murder him? The Stark in Winterfell had to take a hand . . . and both their heads. Which he did easily, because *their strongholds were not defensible*. The Night's Watch had nine hundred and ninety-six Lords Commander before Jeor Mormont, most of them men of courage and honor . . . but we have had cowards and fools as well, our tyrants and our madmen. We survive because the lords and kings of the Seven Kingdoms know that we pose no threat to them, no matter *who* should lead us. Our only foes are to the north, and to the north we have the Wall."

Only now those foes have gotten past the Wall to come up from the south, Jon reflected, *and the lords and kings of the Seven Kingdoms have forgotten us. We are caught between the hammer and the anvil.* Without a wall Castle Black could not be held; Donal Noye knew that as well as any. "The castle does them no good," the armorer told his little garrison. "Kitchens, common hall, stables, even the towers . . . let them take it all. We'll empty the armory and move what stores we can to the top of the Wall, and make our stand around the gate."

So Castle Black had a wall of sorts at last, a crescent-shaped barricade ten feet high made of stores; casks of nails and barrels of salt mutton, crates, bales of black broadcloth, stacked logs, sawn timbers, fire-hardened stakes, and sacks and sacks of grain. The crude rampart enclosed the two things most worth defending; the gate to the north, and the foot of the great wooden switchback stair that clawed and climbed its way up the face of the Wall like a drunken thunderbolt, supported by wooden beams as big as tree trunks driven deep into the ice.

The last few moles were still making the long climb, Jon saw, urged on by his brothers. Grenn was carrying a little boy in his arms, while Pyp, two flights below, let an old man lean upon his shoulder. The oldest villagers still waited below for the cage to make its way back down to them. He saw a mother pulling along two children, one on either hand, as an older boy ran past her up the steps. Two hundred feet above them, Sky Blue Su and Lady Meliana (who was no lady, all her friends agreed) stood on a landing, looking south. They had a better view of the smoke than he did, no doubt. Jon wondered about the villagers who had chosen not to flee. There were always a few, too stubborn or too stupid or too brave to run, a few who preferred to fight or hide or bend the knee. Maybe the Thenns would spare them.

The thing to do would be to take the attack to them, he thought. *With fifty rangers well mounted, we could cut them apart on the road.* They did not have fifty rangers, though, nor half as many horses. The garrison had not returned, and there was no way to know just where they were, or even whether the riders that Noye had sent out had reached them.

We are the garrison, Jon told himself, *and look at us.* The brothers Bowen Marsh had left behind were old men, cripples, and green boys, just as Donal Noye had warned him. He could see some wrestling barrels up the steps, others on the barricade; stout old Kegs, as slow as ever, Spare Boot hopping along briskly on his carved wooden leg, half-mad Easy who fancied himself Florian the Fool reborn, Dornish Dilly, Red Alyn of the Rosewood, Young Henly (well past fifty), Old Henly (well past seventy), Hairy Hal, Spotted Pate of Maidenpool. A couple of them saw Jon looking down from atop the King's Tower and waved up at him. Others turned away. *They still think me a turncloak.* That was a bitter draft to drink, but Jon could not blame them. He was a bastard, after all. Everyone knew that bastards were wanton and treacherous by nature, having been born of lust and deceit. And he had made as many enemies as friends at Castle Black . . . Rast, for one. Jon had once threatened to have Ghost rip his throat out unless he stopped tormenting Samwell Tarly, and Rast did not forget things like that. He was raking dry leaves into piles under the stairs just now, but every so often he stopped long enough to give Jon a nasty look.

"No," Donal Noye roared at three of the Mole's Town men, down below. "The pitch goes to the hoist, the oil up the steps, crossbow bolts to the fourth, fifth, and sixth landings, spears to first and second. Stack the lard under the stair, yes, there, behind the planks. The casks of meat are for the barricade. *Now*, you poxy plow pushers, *NOW!*"

He has a lord's voice, Jon thought. His father had always said that in battle a captain's lungs were as important as his sword arm. "It does not matter how brave or brilliant a man is, if his commands cannot be heard," Lord Eddard told his sons, so Robb and he used to climb the towers of Winterfell to shout at each other across the yard. Donal Noye could have drowned out both of them. The moles all went in terror of him, and rightfully so, since he was always threatening to rip their heads off.

Three-quarters of the village had taken Jon's warning to heart and come to Castle Black for refuge. Noye had decreed that every man still spry enough to hold a spear or swing an axe would help defend the barricade, else they could damn well go home and take their chances with the Thenns. He had emptied the armory to put good steel in their hands; big double-bladed axes, razor-sharp daggers, longswords, maces, spiked morningstars. Clad in studded leather jerkins and mail hauberks, with greaves for their legs and gorgets to keep their heads on their shoulders, a few of them even looked like soldiers. *In a bad light. If you squint.*

Noye had put the women and children to work as well. Those too young to fight would carry water and tend the fires, the Mole's Town midwife would assist Clydas and Maester Aemon with any wounded, and Three-Finger Hobb suddenly had more spit boys, kettle stirrers, and onion choppers than he knew what to do with. Two of the whores had even offered to fight, and had shown enough skill with the crossbow to be given a place on the steps forty feet up.

"It's cold." Satin stood with his hands tucked into his armpits under his cloak. His cheeks were bright red.

Jon made himself smile. "The Frostfangs are cold. This is a brisk autumn day."

"I hope I never see the Frostfangs then. I knew a girl in Oldtown who liked to ice her wine. That's the best place for ice, I think. In wine." Satin glanced south, frowned. "You think the scarecrow sentinels scared them off, my lord?"

"We can hope." It was possible, Jon supposed . . . but more likely the wildlings had simply paused for a bit of rape and plunder in Mole's Town. Or maybe Styr was waiting for nightfall, to move up under cover of darkness.

Midday came and went, with still no sign of Thenns on

the kingsroad. Jon heard footsteps inside the tower, though, and Owen the Oaf popped up out of the trapdoor, red-faced from the climb. He had a basket of buns under one arm, a wheel of cheese under the other, a bag of onions dangling from one hand. "Hobb said to feed you, in case you're stuck up here awhile."

That, or for our last meal. "Thank him for us, Owen."

Dick Follard was deaf as a stone, but his nose worked well enough. The buns were still warm from the oven when he went digging in the basket and plucked one out. He found a crock of butter as well, and spread some with his dagger. "Raisins," he announced happily. "Nuts, too." His speech was thick, but easy enough to understand once you got used to it.

"You can have mine too," said Satin. "I'm not hungry."

"Eat," Jon told him. "There's no knowing when you'll have another chance." He took two buns himself. The nuts were pine nuts, and besides the raisins there were bits of dried apple.

"Will the wildlings come today, Lord Snow?" Owen asked.

"You'll know if they do," said Jon. "Listen for the horns."

"Two. Two is for wildlings." Owen was tall, towheaded, and amiable, a tireless worker and surprisingly deft when it came to working wood and fixing catapults and the like, but as he'd gladly tell you, his mother had dropped him on his head when he was a baby, and half his wits had leaked out through his ear.

"You remember where to go?" Jon asked him.

"I'm to go to the stairs, Donal Noye says. I'm to go up to the third landing and shoot my crossbow down at the wildlings if they try to climb over the barrier. The *third* landing, one two three." His head bobbed up and down. "If the wildlings attack, the king will come and help us, won't he? He's a mighty warrior, King Robert. He's sure to come. Maester Aemon sent him a bird."

There was no use telling him that Robert Baratheon was dead. He would forget it, as he'd forgotten it before. "Maester Aemon sent him a bird," Jon agreed. That seemed to make Owen happy.

Maester Aemon had sent a lot of birds . . . not to one

king, but to four. *Wildlings at the gate*, the message ran. *The realm in danger. Send all the help you can to Castle Black.* Even as far as Oldtown and the Citadel the ravens flew, and to half a hundred mighty lords in their castles. The northern lords offered their best hope, so to them Aemon had sent two birds. To the Umbers and the Boltons, to Castle Cerwyn and Torrhen's Square, Karhold and Deepwood Motte, to Bear Island, Oldcastle, Widow's Watch, White Harbor, Barrowton, and the Rills, to the mountain fastnesses of the Liddles, the Burleys, the Norreys, the Harclays, and the Wulls, the black birds brought their plea. *Wildlings at the gate. The north in danger. Come with all your strength.*

Well, ravens might have wings, but lords and kings do not. If help was coming, it would not come today.

As morning turned to afternoon, the smoke of Mole's Town blew away and the southern sky was clear again. *No clouds*, thought Jon. That was good. Rain or snow could doom them all.

Clydas and Maester Aemon rode the winch cage up to safety at the top of the Wall, and most of the Mole's Town wives as well. Men in black cloaks paced restlessly on the tower tops and shouted back and forth across the courtyards. Septon Cellador led the men on the barricade in a prayer, beseeching the Warrior to give them strength. Deaf Dick Follard curled up beneath his cloak and went to sleep. Satin walked a hundred leagues in circles, round and round the crenellations. The Wall wept and the sun crept across a hard blue sky. Near evenfall, Owen the Oaf returned with a loaf of black bread and a pail of Hobb's best mutton, cooked in a thick broth of ale and onions. Even Dick woke up for that. They ate every bit of it, using chunks of bread to wipe the bottom of the pail. By the time they were done the sun was low in the west, the shadows sharp and black throughout the castle. "Light the fire," Jon told Satin, "and fill the kettle with oil."

He went downstairs himself to bar the door, to try and work some of the stiffness from his leg. That was a mistake, and Jon soon knew it, but he clutched the crutch and saw it through all the same. The door to the King's Tower was oak studded with iron. It might delay the Thenns, but it would not stop them if they wanted to come in. Jon slammed the bar down in its notches, paid a visit to the privy—it might well be his last chance—and hobbled back up to the roof, grimacing at the pain.

The west had gone the color of a blood bruise, but the sky above was cobalt blue, deepening to purple, and the stars were coming out. Jon sat between two merlons with only a scarecrow for company and watched the Stallion gallop up the sky. Or was it the Horned Lord? He wondered where Ghost was now. He wondered about Ygritte as well, and told himself that way lay madness.

They came in the night, of course. *Like thieves*, Jon thought. *Like murderers*.

Satin pissed himself when the horns blew, but Jon pretended not to notice. "Go shake Dick by the shoulder," he told the Oldtown boy, "else he's liable to sleep through the fight."

"I'm frightened." Satin's face was a ghastly white.

"So are they." Jon leaned his crutch up against a merlon and took up his longbow, bending the smooth thick Dornish yew to slip a bowstring through the notches. "Don't waste a quarrel unless you know you have a good clean shot," he said when Satin returned from waking Dick. "We have an ample supply up here, but *ample* doesn't mean inexhaustible. And step behind a merlon to reload, don't try and hide in back of a scarecrow. They're made of straw, an arrow will punch through them." He did not bother telling Dick Follard anything. Dick could read your lips if there was enough light and he gave a damn what you were saying, but he knew it all already.

The three of them took up positions on three sides of the round tower. Jon hung a quiver from his belt and pulled an arrow. The shaft was black, the fletching grey. As he notched it to his string, he remembered something that Theon Greyjoy had once said after a hunt. "The boar can keep his tusks and the bear his claws," he had declared, smiling that way he did. "There's nothing half so mortal as a grey goose feather."

Jon had never been half the hunter that Theon was, but he was no stranger to the longbow either. There were dark shapes slipping around the armory, backs against the stone, but he could not see them well enough to waste an arrow. He heard distant shouts, and saw the archers on the Tower of Guards loosing shafts at the ground. That was too far off to concern Jon. But when he glimpsed three shadows detach themselves from the old stables fifty yards away, he stepped up to the crenel, raised his bow, and drew. They were running, so he led them, waiting, waiting . . .

The arrow made a soft *hiss* as it left his string. A moment later there was a grunt, and suddenly only two shadows were loping across the yard. They ran all the faster, but Jon had already pulled a second arrow from his quiver. This time he hurried the shot too much, and missed. The wildlings were gone by the time he nocked again. He searched for another target, and found four, rushing around the empty shell of the Lord Commander's Keep. The moonlight glimmered off their spears and axes, and the gruesome devices on their round leathern shields; skulls and bones, serpents, bear claws, twisted demonic faces. *Free folk*, he knew. The Thenns carried shields of black boiled leather with bronze rims and bosses, but theirs were plain and unadorned. These were the lighter wicker shields of raiders.

Jon pulled the goose feather back to his ear, aimed, and loosed the arrow, then nocked and drew and loosed again. The first shaft pierced the bearclaw shield, the second one a throat. The wildling screamed as he went down. He heard the deep *thrum* of Deaf Dick's crossbow to his left, and Satin's a moment later. "I got one!" the boy cried hoarsely. "I got one in the chest."

"Get another," Jon called.

He did not have to search for targets now; only choose them. He dropped a wildling archer as he was fitting an arrow to his string, then sent a shaft toward the axeman hacking at the door of Hardin's Tower. That time he missed, but the arrow quivering in the oak made the wildling reconsider. It was only as he was running off that Jon recognized Big Boil. Half a heartbeat later, old Mully put an arrow through his leg from the roof of the Flint Barracks, and he crawled off bleeding. *That will stop him bitching about his boil*, Jon thought.

When his quiver was empty, he went to get another, and moved to a different crenel, side by side with Deaf Dick Follard. Jon got off three arrows for every bolt Deaf Dick discharged, but that was the advantage of the longbow. The crossbow penetrated better, some insisted, but it was slow and cumbersome to reload. He could hear the wildlings shouting to each other, and somewhere to the west a warhorn blew. The world was moonlight and shadow, and time became an endless round of notch and draw and loose. A wildling arrow ripped through the throat of the straw sentinel beside him, but Jon Snow scarcely noticed. *Give me one clean shot at the Magnar of Thenn*, he prayed to his father's gods. The Magnar at least was a foe that he could hate. *Give me Styr*.

His fingers were growing stiff and his thumb was bleeding, but still Jon notched and drew and loosed. A gout of flame caught his eye, and he turned to see the door of the common hall afire. It was only a few moments before the whole great timbered hall was burning. Three-Finger Hobb and his Mole's Town helpers were safe atop the Wall, he knew, but it felt like a punch in the belly all the same. "*JON*," Deaf Dick yelled in his thick voice, "*the armory*." They were on the roof, he saw. One had a torch. Dick hopped up on the crenel for a better shot, jerked his crossbow to his shoulder, and sent a quarrel thrumming toward the torch man. He missed.

The archer down below him didn't.

Follard never made a sound, only toppled forward headlong over the parapet. It was a hundred feet to the yard below. Jon heard the thump as he was peering round a straw soldier, trying to see where the arrow had come from. Not ten feet from Deaf Dick's body, he glimpsed a leather shield, a ragged cloak, a mop of thick red hair. *Kissed by fire*, he thought, *lucky*. He brought his bow up, but his fingers would not part, and she was gone as suddenly as she'd appeared. He swiveled, cursing, and loosed a shaft at the men on the armory roof instead, but he missed them as well.

By then the east stables were afire too, black smoke and wisps of burning hay pouring from the stalls. When the roof collapsed, flames rose up roaring, so loud they almost drowned out the warhorns of the Thenns. Fifty of them were pounding up the kingsroad in tight column, their shields held up above their heads. Others were swarming through the vegetable garden, across the flagstone yard, around the old dry well. Three had hacked their way through the doors of Maester Aemon's apartments in the timber keep below the rookery, and a desperate fight was going on atop the Silent Tower, longswords against bronze axes. None of that mattered. *The dance has moved on,* he thought.

Jon hobbled across to Satin and grabbed him by the shoulder. "With me," he shouted. Together they moved to the north parapet, where the King's Tower looked down on the gate and Donal Noye's makeshift wall of logs and barrels and sacks of corn. The Thenns were there before them. They wore halfhelms, and had thin bronze disks sewn to their long leather shirts. Many wielded bronze axes, though a few were chipped stone. More had short stabbing spears with leaf-shaped heads that gleamed redly in the light from the burning stables. They were screaming in the Old Tongue as they stormed the barricade, jabbing with their spears, swinging their bronze axes, spilling corn and blood with equal abandon while crossbow quarrels and arrows rained down on them from the archers that Donal Noye had posted on the stair.

"What do we *do*?" Satin shouted.

"We kill them," Jon shouted back, a black arrow in his hand.

No archer could have asked for an easier shot. The Thenns had their backs to the King's Tower as they charged the crescent, clambering over bags and barrels to reach the men in black. Both Jon and Satin chanced to choose the same target. He had just reached the top of the barricade when an arrow sprouted from his neck and a quarrel between his shoulder blades. Half a heartbeat later a longsword took him in the belly and he fell back onto the man behind him. Jon reached down to his quiver and found it empty again. Satin was winding back his crossbow. He left him to it and went for more arrows, but he hadn't taken more than three steps before the trap slammed open three feet in front of him. *Bloody hell, I never even heard the door break.*

There was no time to think or plan or shout for help. Jon dropped his bow, reached back over his shoulder, ripped Longclaw from its sheath, and buried the blade in the middle of the first head to pop out of the tower. Bronze was no match for Valyrian steel. The blow sheared right through the Thenn's helm and deep into his skull, and he went crashing back down where he'd come from. There were more behind him, Jon knew from the shouting. He fell back and called to Satin. The next man to make the climb got a quarrel through his cheek. He vanished too. "The oil," Jon said. Satin nodded. Together they snatched up the thick quilted pads they'd left beside the fire, lifted the heavy kettle of boiling oil, and dumped it down the hole on the Thenns below. The shrieks were as bad as anything he had ever heard, and Satin looked as though he was going to be sick. Jon kicked the trapdoor shut, set the heavy iron kettle on top of it, and gave the boy with the pretty face a hard shake. "Retch later," Jon yelled. "*Come.*"

They had only been gone from the parapets for a few moments, but everything below had changed. A dozen black brothers and a few Mole's Town men still stood atop the crates and barrels, but the wildlings were swarming over all along the crescent, pushing them back. Jon saw one shove his spear up through Rast's belly so hard he lifted him into the air. Young Henly was dead and Old Henly was dying, surrounded by foes. He could see Easy spinning and slashing, laughing like a loon, his cloak flapping as he leapt from cask to cask. A bronze axe caught him just below the knee and the laughter turned into a bubbling shriek.

"They're breaking," Satin said.

"No," said Jon, "they're broken."

It happened quickly. One mole fled and then another, and suddenly all the villagers were throwing down their weapons and abandoning the barricade. The brothers were too few to hold alone. Jon watched them try and form a line to fall back in order, but the Thenns washed over them with spear and axe, and then they were fleeing too. Dornish Dilly slipped and went down on his face, and a wildling planted a spear between his shoulder blades. Kegs, slow and short of breath, had almost reached the bottom step when a Thenn caught the end of his cloak and yanked him around . . . but a crossbow quarrel dropped the man before his axe could fall. "*Got* him," Satin crowed, as Kegs staggered to the stair and began to crawl up the steps on hands and knees.

The gate is lost. Donal Noye had closed and chained it, but it was there for the taking, the iron bars glimmering red with reflected firelight, the cold black tunnel behind. No one had fallen back to defend it; the only safety was on top of the Wall, seven hundred feet up the crooked wooden stairs.

"What gods do you pray to?" Jon asked Satin.

"The Seven," the boy from Oldtown said.

"Pray, then," Jon told him. "Pray to your new gods, and I'll pray to my old ones." It all turned here.

With the confusion at the trapdoor, Jon had forgotten to fill his quiver. He limped back across the roof and did that now, and picked up his bow as well. The kettle had not moved from where he'd left it, so it seemed as though they were safe enough for the nonce. *The dance has moved on, and we're watching from the gallery*, he thought as he hobbled back. Satin was loosing quarrels at the wildlings on the steps, then ducking down behind a merlon to cock the crossbow. *He may be pretty, but he's quick*.

The real battle was on the steps. Noye had put spearmen on the two lowest landings, but the headlong flight of the villagers had panicked them and they had joined the flight, racing up toward the third landing with the Thenns killing anyone who fell behind. The archers and crossbowmen on the higher landings were trying to drop shafts over their heads. Jon nocked an arrow, drew, and loosed, and was pleased when one of the wildlings went rolling down the steps. The heat of the fires was making the Wall weep, and the flames danced and shimmered against the ice. The steps shook to the footsteps of men running for their lives.

Again Jon notched and drew and loosed, but there was only one of him and one of Satin, and a good sixty or seventy Thenns pounding up the stairs, killing as they went, drunk on victory. On the fourth landing, three brothers in black cloaks stood shoulder to shoulder with longswords in their hands, and battle was joined again, briefly. But there were only three and soon enough the wildling tide washed over them, and their blood dripped down the steps. "A man is never so vulnerable in battle as when he flees," Lord Eddard had told Jon once. "A running man is like a wounded animal to a soldier. It gets his bloodlust up." The archers on the fifth landing fled before the battle even reached them. It was a rout, a red rout.

"Fetch the torches," Jon told Satin. There were four of

them stacked beside the fire, their heads wrapped in oily rags. There were a dozen fire arrows too. The Oldtown boy thrust one torch into the fire until it was blazing brightly, and brought the rest back under his arm, unlit. He looked frightened again, as well he might. Jon was frightened too.

It was then that he saw Styr. The Magnar was climbing up the barricade, over the gutted corn sacks and smashed barrels and the bodies of friends and foe alike. His bronze scale armor gleamed darkly in the firelight. Styr had taken off his helm to survey the scene of his triumph, and the bald earless whoreson was smiling. In his hand was a long weirwood spear with an ornate bronze head. When he saw the gate, he pointed the spear at it and barked something in the Old Tongue to the half-dozen Thenns around him. *Too late*, Jon thought. *You should have led your men over the barricade, you might have been able to save a few.*

Up above, a warhorn sounded, long and low. Not from the top of the Wall, but from the ninth landing, some two hundred feet up, where Donal Noye was standing.

Jon notched a fire arrow to his bowstring, and Satin lit it from the torch. He stepped to the parapet, drew, aimed, loosed. Ribbons of flame trailed behind as the shaft sped downward and thudded into its target, crackling.

Not Styr. The steps. Or more precisely, the casks and kegs and sacks that Donal Noye had piled up *beneath* the steps, as high as the first landing; the barrels of lard and lamp oil, the bags of leaves and oily rags, the split logs, bark, and wood shavings. "Again," said Jon, and, "Again," and, "Again." Other longbowmen were firing too, from every tower top in range, some sending their arrows up in high arcs to drop before the Wall. When Jon ran out of fire arrows, he and Satin began to light the torches and fling them from the crenels.

Up above another fire was blooming. The old wooden steps had drunk up oil like a sponge, and Donal Noye had drenched them from the ninth landing all the way down to the seventh. Jon could only hope that most of their own people had staggered up to safety before Noye threw the torches. The black brothers at least had known the plan, but the villagers had not.

Wind and fire did the rest. All Jon had to do was watch. With flames below and flames above, the wildlings had nowhere to go. Some continued upward, and died. Some went downward, and died. Some stayed where they were. They died as well. Many leapt from the steps before they burned, and died from the fall. Twenty-odd Thenns were still huddled together between the fires when the ice cracked from the heat, and the whole lower third of the stair broke off, along with several tons of ice. That was the last that Jon Snow saw of Styr, the Magnar of Thenn. *The Wall defends itself*, he thought.

Jon asked Satin to help him down to the yard. His wounded leg hurt so badly that he could hardly walk, even with the crutch. "Bring the torch," he told the boy from Oldtown. "I need to look for someone." It had been mostly Thenns on the steps. Surely some of the free folk had escaped. Mance's people, not the Magnar's. She might have been one. So they climbed down past the bodies of the men who'd tried the trapdoor, and Jon wandered through the dark with his crutch under one arm, and the other around the shoulders of a boy who'd been a whore in Oldtown.

The stables and the common hall had burned down to smoking cinders by then, but the fire still raged along the wall, climbing step by step and landing by landing. From time to time they'd hear a groan and then a *craaaack*, and another chunk would come crashing off the Wall. The air was full of ash and ice crystals.

He found Quort dead, and Stone Thumbs dying. He found some dead and dying Thenns he had never truly known. He found Big Boil, weak from all the blood he'd lost but still alive.

He found Ygritte sprawled across a patch of old snow beneath the Lord Commander's Tower, with an arrow between her breasts. The ice crystals had settled over her face, and in the moonlight it looked as though she wore a glittering silver mask.

The arrow was black, Jon saw, but it was fletched with white duck feathers. *Not mine*, he told himself, *not one of mine*. But he felt as if it were.

When he knelt in the snow beside her, her eyes opened. "Jon Snow," she said, very softly. It sounded as though the arrow had found a lung. "Is *this* a proper castle now? Not just a tower?"

"It is." Jon took her hand.

"Good," she whispered. "I wanted t' see one proper castle, before . . . before I . . ."

"You'll see a hundred castles," he promised her. "The battle's done. Maester Aemon will see to you." He touched her hair. "You're kissed by fire, remember? Lucky. It will take more than an arrow to kill you. Aemon will draw it out and patch you up, and we'll get you some milk of the poppy for the pain."

She just smiled at that. "D'you remember that cave? We should have stayed in that cave. I told you so."

"We'll go back to the cave," he said. "You're not going to die, Ygritte. You're not."

"Oh." Ygritte cupped his cheek with her hand. "You know nothing, Jon Snow," she sighed, dying.

BRAN

"I t is only another empty castle," Meera Reed said as she gazed across the desolation of rubble, ruins, and weeds.

No, thought Bran, *it is the Nightfort, and this is the end of the world.* In the mountains, all he could think of was reaching the Wall and finding the three-eyed crow, but now that they were here he was filled with fears. The dream he'd had . . . the dream *Summer* had had . . . *No, I mustn't think about that dream.* He had not even told the Reeds, though Meera at least seemed to sense that something was wrong. If he never talked of it maybe he could forget he ever dreamed it, and then it wouldn't have happened and Robb and Grey Wind would still be . . .

"Hodor." Hodor shifted his weight, and Bran with it. He was tired. They had been walking for hours. *At least he's not afraid.* Bran was scared of this place, and almost as scared of admitting it to the Reeds. *I'm a prince of the north, a Stark of Winterfell, almost a man grown, I have to be as brave as Robb.*

Jojen gazed up at him with his dark green eyes. "There's nothing here to hurt us, Your Grace."

Bran wasn't so certain. The Nightfort had figured in some of Old Nan's scariest stories. It was here that Night's King had reigned, before his name was wiped from the memory of man. This was where the Rat Cook had served the Andal king his prince-and-bacon pie, where the seventy-nine sentinels stood their watch, where brave young Danny Flint had been raped and murdered. This was the castle where King Sherrit had called down his curse on the Andals of old, where the 'prentice boys had faced the thing that came in the night, where blind Symeon Star-Eyes had seen the hellhounds fighting. Mad Axe had once walked these yards and climbed these towers, butchering his brothers in the dark.

All that had happened hundreds and thousands of years ago, to be sure, and some maybe never happened at all. Maester Luwin always said that Old Nan's stories shouldn't be swallowed whole. But once his uncle came to see Father, and Bran asked about the Nightfort. Benjen Stark never said the tales were true, but he never said they weren't; he only shrugged and said, "We left the Nightfort two hundred years ago," as if that was an answer.

Bran forced himself to look around. The morning was cold but bright, the sun shining down from a hard blue sky, but he did not like the *noises*. The wind made a nervous whistling sound as it shivered through the broken towers, the keeps groaned and settled, and he could hear rats scrabbling under the floor of the great hall. *The Rat Cook's children running from their father.* The yards were small forests where spindly trees rubbed their bare branches together and dead leaves scuttled like roaches across patches of old snow. There were trees growing where the stables had been, and a twisted white weirwood pushing up through the gaping hole in the roof of the domed kitchen. Even Summer was not at ease here. Bran slipped inside his skin, just for an instant, to get the smell of the place. He did not like that either.

And there was no way through.

Bran had told them there wouldn't be. He had told them and *told* them, but Jojen Reed had insisted on seeing for himself. He had had a green dream, he said, and his green dreams did not lie. *They don't open any gates either*, thought Bran.

The gate the Nightfort guarded had been sealed since the day the black brothers had loaded up their mules and garrons and departed for Deep Lake; its iron portcullis lowered, the chains that raised it carried off, the tunnel packed with stone and rubble all frozen together until they were as impenetrable as the Wall itself. "We should have followed Jon," Bran said when he saw it. He thought of his bastard brother often, since the night that Summer had watched him ride off through the storm. "We should have found the kingsroad and gone to Castle Black."

"We dare not, my prince," Jojen said. "I've told you why."

"But there are *wildlings*. They killed some man and they wanted to kill Jon too. Jojen, there were a *hundred* of them."

"So you said. We are four. You helped your brother, if that was him in truth, but it almost cost you Summer."

"I know," said Bran miserably. The direwolf had killed three of them, maybe more, but there had been too many. When they formed a tight ring around the tall earless man, he had tried to slip away through the rain, but one of their arrows had come flashing after him, and the sudden stab of pain had driven Bran out of the wolf's skin and back into his own. After the storm finally died, they had huddled in the dark without a fire, talking in whispers if they talked at all, listening to Hodor's heavy breathing and wondering if the wildlings might try and cross the lake in the morning. Bran had reached out for Summer time and time again, but the pain he found drove him back, the way a red-hot kettle makes you pull your hand back even when you mean to grab it. Only Hodor slept that night, muttering "Hodor, hodor," as he tossed and turned. Bran was terrified that Summer was off dying in the darkness. *Please, you old gods*, he prayed, *you took Winterfell, and my father, and my legs, please don't take Summer too. And watch over Jon Snow too, and make the wildlings go away.*

No weirwoods grew on that stony island in the lake, yet somehow the old gods must have heard. The wildlings took their sweet time about departing the next morning, stripping the bodies of their dead and the old man they'd

killed, even pulling a few fish from the lake, and there was
a scary moment when three of them found the causeway
and started to walk out . . . but the path turned and they
didn't, and two of them nearly drowned before the others
pulled them out. The tall bald man yelled at them, his
words echoing across the water in some tongue that even
Jojen did not know, and a little while later they gathered up
their shields and spears and marched off north by east, the
same way Jon had gone. Bran wanted to leave too, to look
for Summer, but the Reeds said no. "We will stay another
night," said Jojen, "put some leagues between us and the
wildlings. You don't want to meet them again, do you?"
Late that afternoon Summer returned from wherever he'd
been hiding, dragging his back leg. He ate parts of the bodies in the inn, driving off the crows, then swam out to the
island. Meera had drawn the broken arrow from his leg and
rubbed the wound with the juice of some plants she found
growing around the base of the tower. The direwolf was
still limping, but a little less each day, it seemed to Bran.
The gods had heard.

"Maybe we should try another castle," Meera said to
her brother. "Maybe we could get through the gate somewhere else. I could go scout if you wanted, I'd make better
time by myself."

Bran shook his head. "If you go east there's Deep Lake,
then Queensgate. West is Icemark. But they'll be the same,
only smaller. All the gates are sealed except the ones at
Castle Black, Eastwatch, and the Shadow Tower."

Hodor said, "Hodor," to that, and the Reeds exchanged a
look. "At least I should climb to the top of the Wall,"
Meera decided. "Maybe I'll see something up there."

"What could you hope to see?" Jojen asked.

"*Something*," said Meera, and for once she was
adamant.

It should be me. Bran raised his head to look up at the
Wall, and imagined himself climbing inch by inch, squirming his fingers into cracks in the ice and kicking footholds
with his toes. That made him smile in spite of everything,
the dreams and the wildlings and Jon and *everything*. He
had climbed the walls of Winterfell when he was little, and
all the towers too, but none of them had been so high, and
they were only stone. The Wall could *look* like stone, all

grey and pitted, but then the clouds would break and the sun would hit it differently, and all at once it would transform, and stand there white and blue and glittering. It was the end of the world, Old Nan always said. On the other side were monsters and giants and ghouls, but they could not pass so long as the Wall stood strong. *I want to stand on top with Meera*, Bran thought. *I want to stand on top and see.*

But he was a broken boy with useless legs, so all he could do was watch from below as Meera went up in his stead.

She wasn't really *climbing*, the way he used to climb. She was only walking up some steps that the Night's Watch had hewn hundreds and thousands of years ago. He remembered Maester Luwin saying the Nightfort was the only castle where the steps had been cut from the ice of the Wall itself. Or maybe it had been Uncle Benjen. The newer castles had wooden steps, or stone ones, or long ramps of earth and gravel. *Ice is too treacherous.* It was his uncle who'd told him that. He said that the outer surface of the Wall wept icy tears sometimes, though the core inside stayed frozen hard as rock. The steps must have melted and refrozen a thousand times since the last black brothers left the castle, and every time they did they shrunk a little and got smoother and rounder and more treacherous.

And smaller. *It's almost like the Wall was swallowing them back into itself.* Meera Reed was very surefooted, but even so she was going slowly, moving from nub to nub. In two places where the steps were hardly there at all she got down on all fours. *It will be worse when she comes down*, Bran thought, watching. Even so, he wished it was him up there. When she reached the top, crawling up the icy knobs that were all that remained of the highest steps, Meera vanished from his sight.

"When will she come down?" Bran asked Jojen.

"When she is ready. She will want to have a good look . . . at the Wall and what's beyond. We should do the same down here."

"Hodor?" said Hodor, doubtfully.

"We might find something," Jojen insisted.

Or something might find us. Bran couldn't say it, though; he did not want Jojen to think he was craven.

So they went exploring, Jojen Reed leading, Bran in his basket on Hodor's back, Summer padding by their side. Once the direwolf bolted through a dark door and returned a moment later with a grey rat between his teeth. *The Rat Cook*, Bran thought, but it was the wrong color, and only as big as a cat. The Rat Cook was white, and almost as huge as a sow . . .

There were a lot of dark doors in the Nightfort, and a lot of rats. Bran could hear them scurrying through the vaults and cellars, and the maze of pitch-black tunnels that connected them. Jojen wanted to go poking around down there, but Hodor said "*Hodor*" to that, and Bran said "No." There were worse things than rats down in the dark beneath the Nightfort.

"This seems an old place," Jojen said as they walked down a gallery where the sunlight fell in dusty shafts through empty windows.

"Twice as old as Castle Black," Bran said, remembering. "It was the first castle on the Wall, and the largest." But it had also been the first abandoned, all the way back in the time of the Old King. Even then it had been three-quarters empty and too costly to maintain. Good Queen Alysanne had suggested that the Watch replace it with a smaller, newer castle at a spot only seven miles east, where the Wall curved along the shore of a beautiful green lake. Deep Lake had been paid for by the queen's jewels and built by the men the Old King had sent north, and the black brothers had abandoned the Nightfort to the rats.

That was two centuries past, though. Now Deep Lake stood as empty as the castle it had replaced, and the Nightfort . . .

"There are ghosts here," Bran said. Hodor had heard all the stories before, but Jojen might not have. "*Old* ghosts, from before the Old King, even before Aegon the Dragon, seventy-nine deserters who went south to be outlaws. One was Lord Ryswell's youngest son, so when they reached the barrowlands they sought shelter at his castle, but Lord Ryswell took them captive and returned them to the Nightfort. The Lord Commander had holes hewn in the top of the Wall and he put the deserters in them and sealed them up alive in the ice. They have spears and horns and they all face north. The seventy-nine sentinels, they're called. They left their posts in life, so in death their watch goes on forever. Years later, when Lord Ryswell was old and dying, he had himself carried to the Nightfort so he could take the black and stand beside his son. He'd sent him back to the Wall for honor's sake, but he loved him still, so he came to share his watch."

They spent half the day poking through the castle. Some of the towers had fallen down and others looked unsafe, but they climbed the bell tower (the bells were gone) and the rookery (the birds were gone). Beneath the brewhouse they found a vault of huge oaken casks that boomed hollowly when Hodor knocked on them. They found a library (the shelves and bins had collapsed, the books were gone, and rats were everywhere). They found a dank and dim-lit dungeon with cells enough to hold five hundred captives, but when Bran grabbed hold of one of the rusted bars it broke off in his hand. Only one crumbling wall remained of the great hall, the bathhouse seemed to be sinking into the ground, and a huge thornbush had conquered the practice yard outside the armory where black brothers had once labored with spear and shield and sword. The armory and the forge still stood, however, though cobwebs, rats, and dust had taken the places of blades, bellows, and anvil. Sometimes Summer would hear sounds that Bran seemed deaf to, or bare his teeth at nothing, the fur on the back of his neck bristling . . . but the Rat Cook never put in an appearance, nor the seventy-nine sentinels, nor Mad Axe. Bran was much relieved. *Maybe it is only a ruined empty castle.*

By the time Meera returned, the sun was only a sword's breath above the western hills. "What did you see?" her brother Jojen asked her.

"I saw the haunted forest," she said in a wistful tone. "Hills rising wild as far as the eye can see, covered with trees that no axe has ever touched. I saw the sunlight glinting off a lake, and clouds sweeping in from the west. I saw patches of old snow, and icicles long as pikes. I even saw an eagle circling. I think he saw me too. I waved at him."

"Did you see a way down?" asked Jojen.

She shook her head. "No. It's a sheer drop, and the ice is so smooth . . . I might be able to make the descent if I had a good rope and an axe to chop out handholds, but . . ."

". . . but not us," Jojen finished.

"No," his sister agreed. "Are you sure this is the place you saw in your dream? Maybe we have the wrong castle."

"No. This is the castle. There is a gate here."

Yes, thought Bran, *but it's blocked by stone and ice.*

As the sun began to set the shadows of the towers lengthened and the wind blew harder, sending gusts of dry dead leaves rattling through the yards. The gathering gloom put Bran in mind of another of Old Nan's stories, the tale of Night's King. He had been the thirteenth man to lead the Night's Watch, she said; a warrior who knew no fear. "And that was the fault in him," she would add, "for all men must know fear." A woman was his downfall; a woman glimpsed from atop the Wall, with skin as white as the moon and eyes like blue stars. Fearing nothing, he chased her and caught her and loved her, though her skin was cold as ice, and when he gave his seed to her he gave his soul as well.

He brought her back to the Nightfort and proclaimed her a queen and himself her king, and with strange sorceries he bound his Sworn Brothers to his will. For thirteen years they had ruled, Night's King and his corpse queen, till finally the Stark of Winterfell and Joramun of the wildlings had joined to free the Watch from bondage. After his fall, when it was found he had been sacrificing to the Others, all records of Night's King had been destroyed, his very name forbidden.

"Some say he was a Bolton," Old Nan would always end. "Some say a Magnar out of Skagos, some say Umber, Flint, or Norrey. Some would have you think he was a Woodfoot, from them who ruled Bear Island before the ironmen came. He never was. He was a Stark, the brother of the man who brought him down." She always pinched Bran on the nose then, he would never forget it. "He was a Stark of Winterfell, and who can say? Mayhaps his name was *Brandon*. Mayhaps he slept in this very bed in this very room."

No, Bran thought, *but he walked in this castle, where we'll sleep tonight.* He did not like that notion very much at all. Night's King was only a man by light of day, Old Nan would always say, but the night was his to rule. *And it's getting dark.*

The Reeds decided that they would sleep in the kitchens, a stone octagon with a broken dome. It looked to offer better shelter than most of the other buildings, even though a crooked weirwood had burst up through the slate floor beside the huge central well, stretching slantwise toward the hole in the roof, its bone-white branches reaching for the sun. It was a queer kind of tree, skinnier than any other weirwood that Bran had ever seen and faceless as well, but it made him feel as if the old gods were with him here, at least.

That was the only thing he liked about the kitchens, though. The roof was mostly there, so they'd be dry if it rained again, but he didn't think they would ever get *warm* here. You could feel the cold seeping up through the slate floor. Bran did not like the shadows either, or the huge brick ovens that surrounded them like open mouths, or the rusted meat hooks, or the scars and stains he saw in the butcher's block along one wall. *That was where the Rat Cook chopped the prince to pieces,* he knew, *and he baked the pie in one of these ovens.*

The well was the thing he liked the least, though. It was a good twelve feet across, all stone, with *steps* built into its side, circling down and down into darkness. The walls were damp and covered with niter, but none of them could see the water at the bottom, not even Meera with her sharp hunter's eyes. "Maybe it doesn't have a bottom," Bran said uncertainly.

Hodor peered over the knee-high lip of the well and said, "*HODOR!*" The word echoed down the well, "Hodorhodorhodorhodor," fainter and fainter, "hodorhodorhodorhodor," until it was less than a whisper. Hodor looked startled. Then he laughed, and bent to scoop a broken piece of slate off the floor.

"Hodor, *don't!*" said Bran, but too late. Hodor tossed the slate over the edge. "You shouldn't have done that. You don't know what's down there. You might have hurt something, or . . . or woken something up."

Hodor looked at him innocently. "Hodor?"

Far, far, far below, they heard the sound as the stone found water. It wasn't a *splash*, not truly. It was more a *gulp*, as if whatever was below had opened a quivering gelid mouth to swallow Hodor's stone. Faint echoes traveled up the well, and for a moment Bran thought he heard something moving, thrashing about in the water. "Maybe we shouldn't stay here," he said uneasily.

"By the well?" asked Meera. "Or in the Nightfort?"

"Yes," said Bran.

She laughed, and sent Hodor out to gather wood. Summer went too. It was almost dark by then, and the direwolf wanted to hunt.

Hodor returned alone with both arms full of deadwood and broken branches. Jojen Reed took his flint and knife and set about lighting a fire while Meera boned the fish she'd caught at the last stream they'd crossed. Bran wondered how many years had passed since there had last been a supper cooked in the kitchens of the Nightfort. He wondered who had cooked it too, though maybe it was better not to know.

When the flames were blazing nicely Meera put the fish on. *At least it's not a meat pie.* The Rat Cook had cooked the son of the Andal king in a big pie with onions, carrots, mushrooms, lots of pepper and salt, a rasher of bacon, and a dark red Dornish wine. Then he served him to his father, who praised the taste and had a second slice. Afterward the gods transformed the cook into a monstrous white rat who could only eat his own young. He had roamed the Nightfort ever since, devouring his children, but still his hunger was not sated. "It was not for murder that the gods cursed him," Old Nan said, "nor for serving the Andal king his son in a pie. A man has a right to vengeance. But he slew a *guest* beneath his roof, and that the gods cannot forgive."

"We should sleep," Jojen said solemnly, after they were full. The fire was burning low. He stirred it with a stick. "Perhaps I'll have another green dream to show us the way."

Hodor was already curled up and snoring lightly. From time to time he thrashed beneath his cloak, and whimpered something that might have been "Hodor." Bran wriggled closer to the fire. The warmth felt good, and the soft crackling of flames soothed him, but sleep would not come. Outside the wind was sending armies of dead leaves marching across the courtyards to scratch faintly at the doors and windows. The sounds made him think of Old

Nan's stories. He could almost hear the ghostly sentinels calling to each other atop the Wall and winding their ghostly warhorns. Pale moonlight slanted down through the hole in the dome, painting the branches of the weirwood as they strained up toward the roof. It looked as if the tree was trying to catch the moon and drag it down into the well. *Old gods*, Bran prayed, *if you hear me, don't send a dream tonight. Or if you do, make it a good dream*. The gods made no answer.

Bran made himself close his eyes. Maybe he even slept some, or maybe he was just drowsing, floating the way you do when you are half awake and half asleep, trying not to think about Mad Axe or the Rat Cook or the thing that came in the night.

Then he heard the noise.

His eyes opened. *What was that?* He held his breath. *Did I dream it? Was I having a stupid nightmare?* He didn't want to wake Meera and Jojen for a bad dream, but . . . *there . . . a soft scuffling sound, far off . . . Leaves, it's leaves rattling off the walls outside and rustling together . . . or the wind, it could be the wind . . .* The sound wasn't coming from outside, though. Bran felt the hairs on his arm start to rise. *The sound's inside, it's in here with us, and it's getting louder.* He pushed himself up onto an elbow, listening. There *was* wind, and blowing leaves as well, but this was something else. *Footsteps.* Someone was coming this way. Some*thing* was coming this way.

It wasn't the sentinels, he knew. The sentinels never left the Wall. But there might be other ghosts in the Nightfort, ones even more terrible. He remembered what Old Nan had said of Mad Axe, how he took his boots off and prowled the castle halls barefoot in the dark, with never a sound to tell you where he was except for the drops of blood that fell from his axe and his elbows and the end of his wet red beard. Or maybe it wasn't Mad Axe at all, maybe it was the thing that came in the night. The 'prentice boys all saw it, Old Nan said, but afterward when they told their Lord Commander every description had been different. *And three died within the year, and the fourth went mad, and a hundred years later when the thing had come again, the 'prentice boys were seen shambling along behind it, all in chains.*

That was only a story, though. He was just scaring himself. There was no thing that comes in the night, Maester Luwin had said so. If there had ever been such a thing, it was gone from the world now, like giants and dragons. *It's nothing,* Bran thought.

But the sounds were louder now.

It's coming from the well, he realized. That made him even more afraid. Something was coming up from under the ground, coming up out of the dark. *Hodor woke it up. He woke it up with that stupid piece of slate, and now it's coming.* It was hard to hear over Hodor's snores and the thumping of his own heart. Was that the sound blood made dripping from an axe? Or was it the faint, far-off rattling of ghostly chains? Bran listened harder. *Footsteps.* It was definitely footsteps, each one a little louder than the one before. He couldn't tell how many, though. The well made the sounds echo. He didn't hear any dripping, or chains either, but there *was* something else . . . a high thin whimpering sound, like someone in pain, and heavy muffled breathing. But the footsteps were loudest. The footsteps were coming closer.

Bran was too frightened to shout. The fire had burned down to a few faint embers and his friends were all asleep. He almost slipped his skin and reached out for his wolf, but Summer might be miles away. He couldn't leave his friends helpless in the dark to face whatever was coming up out of the well. *I told them not to come here,* he thought miserably. *I told them there were ghosts. I told them that we should go to Castle Black.*

The footfalls sounded heavy to Bran, slow, ponderous, scraping against the stone. *It must be huge.* Mad Axe had been a big man in Old Nan's story, and the thing that came in the night had been monstrous. Back in Winterfell, Sansa had told him that the demons of the dark couldn't touch him if he hid beneath his blanket. He almost did that now, before he remembered that he was a prince, and almost a man grown.

Bran wriggled across the floor, dragging his dead legs behind him until he could reach out and touch Meera on the foot. She woke at once. He had never known anyone to wake as quick as Meera Reed, or to be so alert so fast. Bran pressed a finger to his mouth so she'd know not to speak. She heard the sound at once, he could see that on her face; the echoing footfalls, the faint whimpering, the heavy breathing.

Meera rose to her feet without a word and reclaimed her weapons. With her three-pronged frog spear in her right hand and the folds of her net dangling from her left, she slipped barefoot toward the well. Jojen dozed on, oblivious, while Hodor muttered and thrashed in restless sleep. She kept to the shadows as she moved, stepped around the shaft of moonlight as quiet as a cat. Bran was watching her all the while, and even he could barely see the faint sheen of her spear. *I can't let her fight the thing alone*, he thought. Summer was far away, but . . .

. . . he slipped his skin, and reached for Hodor.

It was not like sliding into Summer. That was so easy now that Bran hardly thought about it. This was harder, like trying to pull a left boot on your right foot. It fit all wrong, and the boot was *scared* too, the boot didn't know what was happening, the boot was pushing the foot away. He tasted vomit in the back of *Hodor's* throat, and that was almost enough to make him flee. Instead he squirmed and shoved, sat up, gathered his legs under him—his huge strong legs—and rose. *I'm standing.* He took a step. *I'm walking.* It was such a strange feeling that he almost fell. He could see himself on the cold stone floor, a little broken thing, but he wasn't broken now. He grabbed Hodor's longsword. The breathing was as loud as a blacksmith's bellows.

From the well came a wail, a piercing *creech* that went through him like a knife. A huge black shape heaved itself up into the darkness and lurched toward the moonlight, and the fear rose up in Bran so thick that before he could even *think* of drawing Hodor's sword the way he'd meant to, he found himself back on the floor again with Hodor roaring "*Hodor hodor HODOR,*" the way he had in the lake tower whenever the lightning flashed. But the thing that came in the night was screaming too, and thrashing wildly in the folds of Meera's net. Bran saw her spear dart out of the darkness to snap at it, and the thing staggered and fell, struggling with the net. The wailing was still coming from the well, even louder now. On the floor the black thing flopped and fought, screeching, *"No, no, don't, please, DON'T . . ."*

Meera stood over him, the moonlight shining silver off the prongs of her frog spear. "Who are you?" she demanded.

"I'm *SAM*," the black thing sobbed. "Sam, Sam, I'm Sam, let me *out*, you *stabbed* me . . ." He rolled through the puddle of moonlight, flailing and flopping in the tangles of Meera's net. Hodor was still shouting, "Hodor hodor hodor."

It was Jojen who fed the sticks to the fire and blew on them until the flames leapt up crackling. Then there was light, and Bran saw the pale thin-faced girl by the lip of the well, all bundled up in furs and skins beneath an enormous black cloak, trying to shush the screaming baby in her arms. The thing on the floor was pushing an arm through the net to reach his knife, but the loops wouldn't let him. He wasn't any monster beast, or even Mad Axe drenched in gore; only a big fat man dressed up in black wool, black fur, black leather, and black mail. "He's a black brother," said Bran. "Meera, he's from the Night's Watch."

"Hodor?" Hodor squatted down on his haunches to peer at the man in the net. "Hodor," he said again, hooting.

"The Night's Watch, yes." The fat man was still breathing like a bellows. "I'm a brother of the Watch." He had one cord under his chins, forcing his head up, and others digging deep into his cheeks. "I'm a crow, please. Let me out of this."

Bran was suddenly uncertain. "Are you the three-eyed crow?" *He can't be the three-eyed crow.*

"I don't think so." The fat man rolled his eyes, but there were only two of them. "I'm only Sam. Samwell Tarly. Let me *out*, it's hurting me." He began to struggle again.

Meera made a disgusted sound. "Stop flopping around. If you tear my net I'll throw you back down the well. Just lie still and I'll untangle you."

"Who are you?" Jojen asked the girl with the baby.

"Gilly," she said. "For the gillyflower. He's Sam. We never meant to scare you." She rocked her baby and murmured at it, and finally it stopped crying.

Meera was untangling the fat brother. Jojen went to the well and peered down. "Where did you come from?"

"From Craster's," the girl said. "Are you the one?"

Jojen turned to look at her. "The one?"

"He said that Sam wasn't the one," she explained. "There was someone else, he said. The one he was sent to find."

"Who said?" Bran demanded.

"Coldhands," Gilly answered softly.

Meera peeled back one end of her net, and the fat man managed to sit up. He was shaking, Bran saw, and still struggling to catch his breath. "He said there would be people," he huffed. "People in the castle. I didn't know you'd be right at the top of the steps, though. I didn't know you'd throw a net on me or stab me in the stomach." He touched his belly with a black-gloved hand. "Am I bleeding? I can't see."

"It was just a poke to get you off your feet," said Meera. "Here, let me have a look." She went to one knee, and felt around his navel. "You're wearing *mail*. I never got near your skin."

"Well, it hurt all the same," Sam complained.

"Are you *really* a brother of the Night's Watch?" Bran asked.

The fat man's chins jiggled when he nodded. His skin looked pale and saggy. "Only a steward. I took care of Lord Mormont's ravens." For a moment he looked like he was going to cry. "I lost them at the Fist, though. It was my fault. I got us lost too. I couldn't even find the Wall. It's a hundred leagues long and seven hundred feet high and *I couldn't find it!*"

"Well, you've found it now," said Meera. "Lift your rump off the ground, I want my net back."

"How did you get through the Wall?" Jojen demanded as Sam struggled to his feet. "Does the well lead to an underground river, is that where you came from? You're not even wet . . ."

"There's a gate," said fat Sam. "A hidden gate, as old as the Wall itself. *The Black Gate*, he called it."

The Reeds exchanged a look. "We'll find this gate at the bottom of the well?" asked Jojen.

Sam shook his head. "*You* won't. I have to take you."

"Why?" Meera demanded. "If there's a gate . . ."

"You won't find it. If you did it wouldn't open. Not for

you. It's the *Black* Gate." Sam plucked at the faded black
wool of his sleeve. "Only a man of the Night's Watch can
open it, he said. A Sworn Brother who has said his words."

"*He* said." Jojen frowned. "This . . . Coldhands?"

"That wasn't his true name," said Gilly, rocking. "We
only called him that, Sam and me. His hands were cold as
ice, but he saved us from the dead men, him and his ravens,
and he brought us here on his elk."

"His elk?" said Bran, wonderstruck.

"His elk?" said Meera, startled.

"His *ravens*?" said Jojen.

"Hodor?" said Hodor.

"Was he green?" Bran wanted to know. "Did he have
antlers?"

The fat man was confused. "The elk?"

"*Coldhands*," said Bran impatiently. "The green men
ride on elks, Old Nan used to say. Sometimes they have
antlers too."

"He wasn't a green man. He wore blacks, like a brother
of the Watch, but he was pale as a wight, with hands so
cold that at first I was afraid. The wights have blue eyes,
though, and they don't have tongues, or they've forgotten
how to use them." The fat man turned to Jojen. "He'll be
waiting. We should go. Do you have anything warmer to
wear? The Black Gate is cold, and the other side of the Wall
is even colder. You—"

"Why didn't he come with you?" Meera gestured toward Gilly and her babe. "*They* came with you, why not
him? Why didn't you bring him through this Black Gate
too?"

"He . . . he can't."

"Why not?"

"The Wall. The Wall is more than just ice and stone, he
said. There are spells woven into it . . . old ones, and
strong. He cannot pass beyond the Wall."

It grew very quiet in the castle kitchen then. Bran could
hear the soft crackle of the flames, the wind stirring the
leaves in the night, the creak of the skinny weirwood
reaching for the moon. *Beyond the gates the monsters live,
and the giants and the ghouls*, he remembered Old Nan
saying, *but they cannot pass so long as the Wall stands*

strong. So go to sleep, my little Brandon, my baby boy. You needn't fear. There are no monsters here.

"I am not the one you were told to bring," Jojen Reed told fat Sam in his stained and baggy blacks. "*He* is."

"Oh." Sam looked down at him uncertainly. It might have been just then that he realized Bran was crippled. "I don't . . . I'm not strong enough to carry you, I . . ."

"Hodor can carry me." Bran pointed at his basket. "I ride in that, up on his back."

Sam was staring at him. "You're Jon Snow's brother. The one who fell . . ."

"No," said Jojen. "That boy is dead."

"Don't tell," Bran warned. "Please."

Sam looked confused for a moment, but finally he said, "I . . . I can keep a secret. Gilly too." When he looked at her, the girl nodded. "Jon . . . Jon was *my* brother too. He was the best friend I ever had, but he went off with Qhorin Halfhand to scout the Frostfangs and never came back. We were waiting for him on the Fist when . . . when . . ."

"Jon's here," Bran said. "Summer saw him. He was with some wildlings, but they killed a man and Jon took his horse and escaped. I bet he went to Castle Black."

Sam turned big eyes on Meera. "You're certain it was Jon? You saw him?"

"I'm Meera," Meera said with a smile. "Summer is . . ."

A shadow detached itself from the broken dome above and leapt down through the moonlight. Even with his injured leg, the wolf landed as light and quiet as a snowfall. The girl Gilly made a frightened sound and clutched her babe so hard against her that it began to cry again.

"He won't hurt you," Bran said. "*That*'s Summer."

"Jon said you all had wolves." Sam pulled off a glove. "I know Ghost." He held out a shaky hand, the fingers white and soft and fat as little sausages. Summer padded closer, sniffed them, and gave the hand a lick.

That was when Bran made up his mind. "We'll go with you."

"All of you?" Sam seemed surprised by that.

Meera ruffled Bran's hair. "He's our prince."

Summer circled the well, sniffing. He paused by the top step and looked back at Bran. *He wants to go.*

"Will Gilly be safe if I leave her here till I come back?" Sam asked them.

"She should be," said Meera. "She's welcome to our fire."

Jojen said, "The castle is empty."

Gilly looked around. "Craster used to tell us tales of castles, but I never knew they'd be so big."

It's only the kitchens. Bran wondered what she'd think when she saw Winterfell, if she ever did.

It took them a few minutes to gather their things and hoist Bran into his wicker seat on Hodor's back. By the time they were ready to go, Gilly sat nursing her babe by the fire. "You'll come back for me," she said to Sam.

"As soon as I can," he promised, "then we'll go somewhere warm." When he heard that, part of Bran wondered what he was doing. *Will I ever go someplace warm again?*

"I'll go first, I know the way." Sam hesitated at the top. "There's just so many *steps*," he sighed, before he started down. Jojen followed, then Summer, then Hodor with Bran riding on his back. Meera took the rear, with her spear and net in hand.

It was a long way down. The top of the well was bathed in moonlight, but it grew smaller and dimmer every time they went around. Their footsteps echoed off the damp stones, and the water sounds grew louder. "Should we have brought torches?" Jojen asked.

"Your eyes will adjust," said Sam. "Keep one hand on the wall and you won't fall."

The well grew darker and colder with every turn. When Bran finally lifted his head around to look back up the shaft, the top of the well was no bigger than a half-moon. "*Hodor*," Hodor whispered, "*Hodorhodorhodorhodorhodorhodor*," the well whispered back. The water sounds were close, but when Bran peered down he saw only blackness.

A turn or two later Sam stopped suddenly. He was a quarter of the way around the well from Bran and Hodor and six feet farther down, yet Bran could barely see him. He could see the door, though. *The Black Gate*, Sam had called it, but it wasn't black at all.

It was white weirwood, and there was a face on it.

A glow came from the wood, like milk and moonlight,

so faint it scarcely seemed to touch anything beyond the door itself, not even Sam standing right before it. The face was old and pale, wrinkled and shrunken. *It looks dead.* Its mouth was closed, and its eyes; its cheeks were sunken, its brow withered, its chin sagging. *If a man could live for a thousand years and never die but just grow older, his face might come to look like that.*

The door opened its eyes.

They were white too, and blind. "Who are you?" the door asked, and the well whispered, *"Who-who-who-who-who-who-who."*

"I am the sword in the darkness," Samwell Tarly said. "I am the watcher on the walls. I am the fire that burns against the cold, the light that brings the dawn, the horn that wakes the sleepers. I am the shield that guards the realms of men."

"Then pass," the door said. Its lips opened, wide and wider and wider still, until nothing at all remained but a great gaping mouth in a ring of wrinkles. Sam stepped aside and waved Jojen through ahead of him. Summer followed, sniffing as he went, and then it was Bran's turn. Hodor ducked, but not low enough. The door's upper lip brushed softly against the top of Bran's head, and a drop of water fell on him and ran slowly down his nose. It was strangely warm, and salty as a tear.

DAENERYS

Meereen was as large as Astapor and Yunkai combined. Like her sister cities she was built of brick, but where Astapor had been red and Yunkai yellow, Meereen was made with bricks of many colors. Her walls were higher than Yunkai's and in better repair, studded with bastions and anchored by great defensive towers at every angle. Behind them, huge against the sky, could be seen the top of the Great Pyramid, a monstrous thing eight hundred feet tall with a towering bronze harpy at its top.

"The harpy is a craven thing," Daario Naharis said when he saw it. "She has a woman's heart and a chicken's legs. Small wonder her sons hide behind their walls."

But the hero did not hide. He rode out the city gates, armored in scales of copper and jet and mounted upon a white charger whose striped pink-and-white barding matched the silk cloak flowing from the hero's shoulders. The lance he bore was fourteen feet long, swirled in pink and white, and his hair was shaped and teased and lacquered into two great curling ram's horns. Back and forth he rode beneath the walls of multicolored bricks, challenging the besiegers to send a champion forth to meet him in single combat.

Her bloodriders were in such a fever to go meet him that they almost came to blows. "Blood of my blood," Dany told them, "your place is here by me. This man is a buzzing fly, no more. Ignore him, he will soon be gone." Aggo, Jhogo, and Rakharo were brave warriors, but they were young, and too valuable to risk. They kept her *khalasar* together, and were her best scouts too.

"That was wisely done," Ser Jorah said as they watched from the front of her pavilion. "Let the fool ride back and forth and shout until his horse goes lame. He does us no harm."

"He does," Arstan Whitebeard insisted. "Wars are not won with swords and spears alone, ser. Two hosts of equal strength may come together, but one will break and run whilst the other stands. This hero builds courage in the hearts of his own men and plants the seeds of doubt in ours."

Ser Jorah snorted. "And if our champion were to lose, what sort of seed would that plant?"

"A man who fears battle wins no victories, ser."

"We're not speaking of battle. Meereen's gates will not open if that fool falls. Why risk a life for naught?"

"For honor, I would say."

"I have heard enough." Dany did not need their squabbling on top of all the other troubles that plagued her. Meereen posed dangers far more serious than one pink-and-white hero shouting insults, and she could not let herself be distracted. Her host numbered more than eighty thousand after Yunkai, but fewer than a quarter of them were soldiers. The rest . . . well, Ser Jorah called them mouths with feet, and soon they would be starving.

The Great Masters of Meereen had withdrawn before Dany's advance, harvesting all they could and burning what they could not harvest. Scorched fields and poisoned wells had greeted her at every hand. Worst of all, they had nailed a slave child up on every milepost along the coast road from Yunkai, nailed them up still living with their entrails hanging out and one arm always outstretched to point the way to Meereen. Leading her van, Daario had given orders for the children to be taken down before Dany had to see them, but she had countermanded him as soon as she was told. "I *will* see them," she said. "I will see every one, and count them, and look upon their faces. And I will remember."

By the time they came to Meereen sitting on the salt coast beside her river, the count stood at one hundred and sixty-three. *I will have this city*, Dany pledged to herself once more.

The pink-and-white hero taunted the besiegers for an hour, mocking their manhood, mothers, wives, and gods. Meereen's defenders cheered him on from the city walls. "His name is Oznak zo Pahl," Brown Ben Plumm told her when he arrived for the war council. He was the new commander of the Second Sons, chosen by a vote of his fellow sellswords. "I was bodyguard to his uncle once, before I joined the Second Sons. The Great Masters, what a ripe lot o' maggots. The women weren't so bad, though it was worth your life to look at the wrong one the wrong way. I knew a man, Scarb, this Oznak cut his liver out. Claimed to be defending a lady's honor, he did, said Scarb had raped her with his eyes. How do you rape a wench with *eyes*, I ask you? But his uncle is the richest man in Meereen and his father commands the city guard, so I had to run like a rat before he killed me too."

They watched Oznak zo Pahl dismount his white charger, undo his robes, pull out his manhood, and direct a stream of urine in the general direction of the olive grove where Dany's gold pavilion stood among the burnt trees. He was still pissing when Daario Naharis rode up, *arakh* in hand. "Shall I cut that off for you and stuff it down his mouth, Your Grace?" His tooth shone gold amidst the blue of his forked beard.

"It's his city I want, not his meager manhood." She was growing angry, however. *If I ignore this any longer, my own people will think me weak.* Yet who could she send? She needed Daario as much as she did her bloodriders. Without the flamboyant Tyroshi, she had no hold on the Stormcrows, many of whom had been followers of Prendahl na Ghezn and Sallor the Bald.

High on the walls of Meereen, the jeers had grown louder, and now hundreds of the defenders were taking their lead from the hero and pissing down through the ramparts to show their contempt for the besiegers. *They are pissing on slaves, to show how little they fear us,* she thought. *They would never dare such a thing if it were a Dothraki khalasar outside their gates.*

"This challenge must be met," Arstan said again.

"It will be." Dany said, as the hero tucked his penis away again. "Tell Strong Belwas I have need of him."

They found the huge brown eunuch sitting in the shade of her pavilion, eating a sausage. He finished it in three bites, wiped his greasy hands clean on his trousers, and sent Arstan Whitebeard to fetch him his steel. The aged squire honed Belwas's *arakh* every evening and rubbed it down with bright red oil.

When Whitebeard brought the sword, Strong Belwas squinted down the edge, grunted, slid the blade back into its leather sheath, and tied the swordbelt about his vast waist. Arstan had brought his shield as well: a round steel disk no larger than a pie plate, which the eunuch grasped with his off hand rather than strapping to his forearm in the manner of Westeros. "Find liver and onions, Whitebeard," Belwas said. "Not for now, for after. Killing makes Strong Belwas hungry." He did not wait for a reply, but lumbered from the olive grove toward Oznak zo Pahl.

"Why that one, *Khaleesi?*" Rakharo demanded of her. "He is fat and stupid."

"Strong Belwas was a slave here in the fighting pits. If this highborn Oznak should fall to such the Great Masters will be shamed, while if he wins . . . well, it is a poor victory for one so noble, one that Meereen can take no pride in." And unlike Ser Jorah, Daario, Brown Ben, and her three bloodriders, the eunuch did not lead troops, plan battles, or give her counsel. *He does nothing but eat and boast and bellow at Arstan.* Belwas was the man she could most easily spare. And it was time she learned what sort of protector Magister Illyrio had sent her.

A thrum of excitement went through the siege lines when Belwas was seen plodding toward the city, and from the walls and towers of Meereen came shouts and jeers. Oznak zo Pahl mounted up again, and waited, his striped lance held upright. The charger tossed his head impatiently and pawed the sandy earth. As massive as he was, the eunuch looked small beside the hero on his horse.

"A chivalrous man would dismount," said Arstan.

Oznak zo Pahl lowered his lance and charged.

Belwas stopped with legs spread wide. In one hand was his small round shield, in the other the curved *arakh* that Arstan tended with such care. His great brown stomach and sagging chest were bare above the yellow silk sash knotted about his waist, and he wore no armor but his studded leather vest, so absurdly small that it did not even cover his nipples. "We should have given him chainmail," Dany said, suddenly anxious.

"Mail would only slow him," said Ser Jorah. "They wear no armor in the fighting pits. It's blood the crowds come to see."

Dust flew from the hooves of the white charger. Oznak thundered toward Strong Belwas, his striped cloak streaming from his shoulders. The whole city of Meereen seemed to be screaming him on. The besiegers' cheers seemed few and thin by comparison; her Unsullied stood in silent ranks, watching with stone faces. Belwas might have been made of stone as well. He stood in the horse's path, his vest stretched tight across his broad back. Oznak's lance was leveled at the center of his chest. Its bright steel point winked in the sunlight. *He's going to be impaled*, she thought . . . as the eunuch spun sideways. And quick as the blink of an eye the horseman was beyond him, wheeling, raising the lance. Belwas made no move to strike at him. The Meereenese on the walls screamed even louder. "What is he doing?" Dany demanded.

"Giving the mob a show," Ser Jorah said.

Oznak brought the horse around Belwas in a wide circle, then dug in with his spurs and charged again. Again Belwas waited, then spun and knocked the point of the lance aside. She could hear the eunuch's booming laughter echoing across the plain as the hero went past him. "The lance is too long," Ser Jorah said. "All Belwas needs do is avoid the point. Instead of trying to spit him so prettily, the fool should ride right over him."

Oznak zo Pahl charged a third time, and now Dany could see plainly that he was riding *past* Belwas, the way a Westerosi knight might ride at an opponent in a tilt, rather than *at* him, like a Dothraki riding down a foe. The flat level ground allowed the charger to get up a good speed, but it also made it easy for the eunuch to dodge the cumbersome fourteen-foot lance.

Meereen's pink-and-white hero tried to anticipate this time, and swung his lance sideways at the last second to catch Strong Belwas when he dodged. But the eunuch had anticipated too, and this time he dropped down instead of spinning sideways. The lance passed harmlessly over his head. And suddenly Belwas was rolling, and bringing the razor-sharp *arakh* around in a silver arc. They heard the charger scream as the blade bit into his legs, and then the horse was falling, the hero tumbling from the saddle.

A sudden silence swept along the brick parapets of Meereen. Now it was Dany's people who were screaming and cheering.

Oznak leapt clear of his horse and managed to draw his sword before Strong Belwas was on him. Steel sang against steel, too fast and furious for Dany to follow the blows. It could not have been a dozen heartbeats before Belwas's chest was awash in blood from a slice below his breasts, and Oznak zo Pahl had an *arakh* planted right between his ram's horns. The eunuch wrenched the blade loose and parted the hero's head from his body with three savage blows to the neck. He held it up high for the Meereenese to see, then flung it toward the city gates and let it bounce and roll across the sand.

"So much for the hero of Meereen," said Daario, laughing.

"A victory without meaning," Ser Jorah cautioned. "We will not win Meereen by killing its defenders one at a time."

"No," Dany agreed, "but I'm pleased we killed this one."

The defenders on the walls began firing their crossbows at Belwas, but the bolts fell short or skittered harmlessly along the ground. The eunuch turned his back on the steel-tipped rain, lowered his trousers, squatted, and shat in the direction of the city. He wiped himself with Oznak's striped cloak, and paused long enough to loot the hero's corpse and put the dying horse out of its agony before trudging back to the olive grove.

The besiegers gave him a raucous welcome as soon as he

reached the camp. Her Dothraki hooted and screamed, and the Unsullied sent up a great clangor by banging their spears against their shields. "Well done," Ser Jorah told him, and Brown Ben tossed the eunuch a ripe plum and said, "A sweet fruit for a sweet fight." Even her Dothraki handmaids had words of praise. "We would braid your hair and hang a bell in it, Strong Belwas," said Jhiqui, "but you have no hair to braid."

"Strong Belwas needs no tinkly bells." The eunuch ate Brown Ben's plum in four big bites and tossed aside the stone. "Strong Belwas needs liver and onions."

"You shall have it," said Dany. "Strong Belwas is hurt." His stomach was red with the blood sheeting down from the meaty gash beneath his breasts.

"It is nothing. I let each man cut me once, before I kill him." He slapped his bloody belly. "Count the cuts and you will know how many Strong Belwas has slain."

But Dany had lost Khal Drogo to a similar wound, and she was not willing to let it go untreated. She sent Missandei to find a certain Yunkish freedman renowned for his skill in the healing arts. Belwas howled and complained, but Dany scolded him and called him a big bald baby until he let the healer stanch the wound with vinegar, sew it shut, and bind his chest with strips of linen soaked in fire wine. Only then did she lead her captains and commanders inside her pavilion for their council.

"I must have this city," she told them, sitting cross-legged on a pile of cushions, her dragons all about her. Irri and Jhiqui poured wine. "Her granaries are full to bursting. There are figs and dates and olives growing on the terraces of her pyramids, and casks of salt fish and smoked meat buried in her cellars."

"And fat chests of gold, silver, and gemstones as well," Daario reminded them. "Let us not forget the gemstones."

"I've had a look at the landward walls, and I see no point of weakness," said Ser Jorah Mormont. "Given time, we might be able to mine beneath a tower and make a breach, but what do we eat while we're digging? Our stores are all but exhausted."

"No weakness in the *landward* walls?" said Dany. Meereen stood on a jut of sand and stone where the slow brown Skahazadhan flowed into Slaver's Bay. The city's north wall ran along the riverbank, its west along the bay shore. "Does that mean we might attack from the river or the sea?"

"With three ships? We'll want to have Captain Groleo take a good look at the wall along the river, but unless it's crumbling that's just a wetter way to die."

"What if we were to build siege towers? My brother Viserys told tales of such, I know they can be made."

"From wood, Your Grace," Ser Jorah said. "The slavers have burnt every tree within twenty leagues of here. Without wood, we have no trebuchets to smash the walls, no ladders to go over them, no siege towers, no turtles, and no rams. We can storm the gates with axes, to be sure, but . . ."

"Did you see them bronze heads above the gates?" asked Brown Ben Plumm. "Rows of harpy heads with open mouths? The Meereenese can squirt boiling oil out them mouths, and cook your axemen where they stand."

Daario Naharis gave Grey Worm a smile. "Perhaps the Unsullied should wield the axes. Boiling oil feels like no more than a warm bath to you, I have heard."

"This is false." Grey Worm did not return the smile. "These ones do not feel burns as men do, yet such oil blinds and kills. The Unsullied do not fear to die, though. Give these ones rams, and we will batter down these gates or die in the attempt."

"You would die," said Brown Ben. At Yunkai, when he took command of the Second Sons, he claimed to be the veteran of a hundred battles. "Though I will not say I fought bravely in all of them. There are old sellswords and bold sellswords, but no old bold sellswords." She saw that it was true.

Dany sighed. "I will not throw away Unsullied lives, Grey Worm. Perhaps we can starve the city out."

Ser Jorah looked unhappy. "We'll starve long before they do, Your Grace. There's no food here, nor fodder for our mules and horses. I do not like this river water either. Meereen shits into the Skahazadhan but draws its drinking water from deep wells. Already we've had reports of sickness in the camps, fever and brownleg and three cases of the bloody flux. There will be more if we remain. The slaves are weak from the march."

"Freedmen," Dany corrected. "They are slaves no longer."

"Slave or free, they are hungry and they'll soon be sick. The city is better provisioned than we are, and can be resupplied by water. Your three ships are not enough to deny them access to both the river and the sea."

"Then what do you advise, Ser Jorah?"

"You will not like it."

"I would hear it all the same."

"As you wish. I say, let this city be. You cannot free every slave in the world, *Khaleesi*. Your war is in Westeros."

"I have not forgotten Westeros." Dany dreamt of it some nights, this fabled land that she had never seen. "If I let Meereen's old brick walls defeat me so easily, though, how will I ever take the great stone castles of Westeros?"

"As Aegon did," Ser Jorah said, "with fire. By the time we reach the Seven Kingdoms, your dragons will be grown. And we will have siege towers and trebuchets as well, all the things we lack here . . . but the way across the Lands of the Long Summer is long and grueling, and there are dangers we cannot know. You stopped at Astapor to buy an army, not to start a war. Save your spears and swords for the Seven Kingdoms, my queen. Leave Meereen to the Meereenese and march west for Pentos."

"Defeated?" said Dany, bristling.

"When cowards hide behind great walls, it is they who are defeated, *Khaleesi*," Ko Jhogo said.

Her other bloodriders concurred. "Blood of my blood," said Rakharo, "when cowards hide and burn the food and fodder, great *khals* must seek for braver foes. This is known."

"It is known," Jhiqui agreed, as she poured.

"Not to me." Dany set great store by Ser Jorah's counsel, but to leave Meereen untouched was more than she could stomach. She could not forget the children on their posts, the birds tearing at their entrails, their skinny arms pointing up the coast road. "Ser Jorah, you say we have no food left. If I march west, how can I feed my freedmen?"

"You can't. I am sorry, *Khaleesi*. They must feed themselves or starve. Many and more will die along the march, yes. That will be hard, but there is no way to save them. We need to put this scorched earth well behind us."

Dany had left a trail of corpses behind her when she crossed the red waste. It was a sight she never meant to see again. "No," she said. "I will not march my people off to die." *My children.* "There must be *some* way into this city."

"I know a way." Brown Ben Plumm stroked his speckled grey-and-white beard. "Sewers."

"Sewers? What do you mean?"

"Great brick sewers empty into the Skahazadhan, carrying the city's wastes. They might be a way in, for a few. That was how I escaped Meereen, after Scarb lost his head." Brown Ben made a face. "The smell has never left me. I dream of it some nights."

Ser Jorah looked dubious. "Easier to go out than in, it would seem to me. These sewers empty into the river, you say? That would mean the mouths are right below the walls."

"And closed with iron grates," Brown Ben admitted, "though some have rusted through, else I would have drowned in shit. Once inside, it is a long foul climb in pitch-dark through a maze of brick where a man could lose himself forever. The filth is never lower than waist high, and can rise over your head from the stains I saw on the walls. There's *things* down there too. Biggest rats you ever saw, and worse things. Nasty."

Daario Naharis laughed. "As nasty as you, when you came crawling out? If any man were fool enough to try this, every slaver in Meereen would smell them the moment they emerged."

Brown Ben shrugged. "Her Grace asked if there was a way in, so I told her . . . but Ben Plumm isn't going down in them sewers again, not for all the gold in the Seven Kingdoms. If there's others want to try it, though, they're welcome."

Aggo, Jhogo, and Grey Worm all tried to speak at once, but Dany raised her hand for silence. "These sewers do not sound promising." Grey Worm would lead his Unsullied down the sewers if she commanded it, she knew; her bloodriders would do no less. But none of them was suited to the task. The Dothraki were horsemen, and the strength of the Unsullied was their discipline on the battlefield. *Can I send men to die in the dark on such a slender hope?* "I must think on this some more. Return to your duties."

Her captains bowed and left her with her handmaids and her dragons. But as Brown Ben was leaving, Viserion spread his pale white wings and flapped lazily at his head. One of the wings buffeted the sellsword in his face. The white dragon landed awkwardly with one foot on the man's head and one on his shoulder, shrieked, and flew off again. "He likes you, Ben," said Dany.

"And well he might." Brown Ben laughed. "I have me a drop of the dragon blood myself, you know."

"You?" Dany was startled. Plumm was a creature of the free companies, an amiable mongrel. He had a broad brown face with a broken nose and a head of nappy grey hair, and his Dothraki mother had bequeathed him large, dark, almond-shaped eyes. He claimed to be part Braavosi, part Summer Islander, part Ibbenese, part Qohorik, part Dothraki, part Dornish, and part Westerosi, but this was the first she had heard of Targaryen blood. She gave him a searching look and said, "How could that be?"

"Well," said Brown Ben, "there was some old Plumm in the Sunset Kingdoms who wed a dragon princess. My grandmama told me the tale. He lived in King Aegon's day."

"Which King Aegon?" Dany asked. "Five Aegons have ruled in Westeros." Her brother's son would have been the sixth, but the Usurper's men had dashed his head against a wall.

"Five, were there? Well, that's a confusion. I could not give you a number, my queen. This old Plumm was a lord, though, must have been a famous fellow in his day, the talk of all the land. The thing was, begging your royal pardon, he had himself a cock six foot long."

The three bells in Dany's braid tinkled when she laughed. "You mean inches, I think."

"Feet," Brown Ben said firmly. "If it was inches, who'd want to talk about it, now? Your Grace."

Dany giggled like a little girl. "Did your grandmother claim she'd actually seen this prodigy?"

"That the old crone never did. She was half-Ibbenese

and half-Qohorik, never been to Westeros, my grandfather must have told her. Some Dothraki killed him before I was born."

"And where did your grandfather's knowledge come from?"

"One of them tales told at the teat, I'd guess." Brown Ben shrugged. "That's all I know about Aegon the Unnumbered or old Lord Plumm's mighty manhood, I fear. I best see to my Sons."

"Go do that," Dany told him.

When Brown Ben left, she lay back on her cushions. "If you were grown," she told Drogon, scratching him between the horns, "I'd fly you over the walls and melt that harpy down to slag." But it would be years before her dragons were large enough to ride. *And when they are, who shall ride them? The dragon has three heads, but I have only one.* She thought of Daario. *If ever there was a man who could rape a woman with his eyes . . .*

To be sure, she was just as guilty. Dany found herself stealing looks at the Tyroshi when her captains came to council, and sometimes at night she remembered the way his gold tooth glittered when he smiled. That, and his eyes. *His bright blue eyes.* On the road from Yunkai, Daario had brought her a flower or a sprig of some plant every evening when he made his report . . . to help her learn the land, he said. Waspwillow, dusky roses, wild mint, lady's lace, daggerleaf, broom, prickly ben, harpy's gold . . . *He tried to spare me the sight of the dead children too.* He should not have done that, but he meant it kindly. And Daario Naharis made her laugh, which Ser Jorah never did.

Dany tried to imagine what it would be like if she allowed Daario to kiss her, the way Jorah had kissed her on the ship. The thought was exciting and disturbing, both at once. *It is too great a risk.* The Tyroshi sellsword was not a good man, no one needed to tell her that. Under the smiles and the jests he was dangerous, even cruel. Sallor and Prendahl had woken one morning as his partners; that very night he'd given her their heads. *Khal Drogo could be cruel as well, and there was never a man more dangerous.* She had come to love him all the same. *Could I love Daario? What would it mean, if I took him into my bed? Would that make him one of the heads of the dragon?* Ser Jorah would be angry, she knew, but he was the one who'd said she had to take two husbands. *Perhaps I should marry them both and be done with it.*

But these were foolish thoughts. She had a city to take, and dreaming of kisses and some sellsword's bright blue eyes would not help her breach the walls of Meereen. *I am the blood of the dragon,* Dany reminded herself. Her thoughts were spinning in circles, like a rat chasing its tail. Suddenly she could not stand the close confines of the pavilion another moment. *I want to feel the wind on my face, and smell the sea.* "Missandei," she called, "have my silver saddled. Your own mount as well."

The little scribe bowed. "As Your Grace commands. Shall I summon your bloodriders to guard you?"

"We'll take Arstan. I do not mean to leave the camps." She had no enemies among her children. And the old squire would not talk too much as Belwas would, or look at her like Daario.

The grove of burnt olive trees in which she'd raised her pavilion stood beside the sea, between the Dothraki camp and that of the Unsullied. When the horses had been saddled, Dany and her companions set out along the shoreline, away from the city. Even so, she could feel Meereen at her back, mocking her. When she looked over one shoulder, there it stood, the afternoon sun blazing off the bronze harpy atop the Great Pyramid. Inside Meereen the slavers would soon be reclining in their fringed *tokars* to feast on lamb and olives, unborn puppies, honeyed dormice and other such delicacies, whilst outside her children went hungry. A sudden wild anger filled her. *I will bring you down,* she swore.

As they rode past the stakes and pits that surrounded the eunuch encampment, Dany could hear Grey Worm and his sergeants running one company through a series of drills with shield, shortsword, and heavy spear. Another company was bathing in the sea, clad only in white linen breechclouts. The eunuchs were very clean, she had noticed. Some of her sellswords smelled as if they had not washed or changed their clothes since her father lost the Iron Throne, but the Unsullied bathed each evening, even if they'd marched all day. When no water was available they cleansed themselves with sand, the Dothraki way.

The eunuchs knelt as she passed, raising clenched fists to their breasts. Dany returned the salute. The tide was coming in, and the surf foamed about the feet of her silver. She could see her ships standing out to sea. *Balerion* floated nearest; the great cog once known as *Saduleon*, her sails furled. Further out were the galleys *Meraxes* and *Vhagar*, formerly *Joso's Prank* and *Summer Sun*. They were Magister Illyrio's ships, in truth, not hers at all, and yet she had given them new names with hardly a thought. Dragon names, and more; in old Valyria before the Doom, Balerion, Meraxes, and Vhagar had been gods.

South of the ordered realm of stakes, pits, drills, and bathing eunuchs lay the encampments of her freedmen, a far noisier and more chaotic place. Dany had armed the former slaves as best she could with weapons from Astapor and Yunkai, and Ser Jorah had organized the fighting men into four strong companies, yet she saw no one drilling here. They passed a driftwood fire where a hundred people had gathered to roast the carcass of a horse. She could smell the meat and hear the fat sizzling as the spit boys turned, but the sight only made her frown.

Children ran behind their horses, skipping and laughing. Instead of salutes, voices called to her on every side in a babble of tongues. Some of the freedmen greeted her as "Mother," while others begged for boons or favors. Some prayed for strange gods to bless her, and some asked her to bless them instead. She smiled at them, turning right and left, touching their hands when they raised them, letting those who knelt reach up to touch her stirrup or her leg. Many of the freedmen believed there was good fortune in her touch. *If it helps give them courage, let them touch me,* she thought. *There are hard trials yet ahead . . .*

Dany had stopped to speak to a pregnant woman who wanted the Mother of Dragons to name her baby when someone reached up and grabbed her left wrist. Turning, she glimpsed a tall ragged man with a shaved head and a sunburnt face. "Not so hard," she started to say, but before she could finish he'd yanked her bodily from the saddle. The ground came up and knocked the breath from her, as her silver whinnied and backed away. Stunned, Dany rolled to her side and pushed herself onto one elbow . . .

. . . and then she saw the sword.

"There's the treacherous sow," he said. "I knew you'd come to get your feet kissed one day." His head was bald as a melon, his nose red and peeling, but she knew that voice and those pale green eyes. "I'm going to start by cutting off your teats." Dany was dimly aware of Missandei shouting for help. A freedman edged forward, but only a step. One quick slash, and he was on his knees, blood running down his face. Mero wiped his sword on his breeches. "Who's next?"

"I am." Arstan Whitebeard leapt from his horse and stood over her, the salt wind riffling through his snowy hair, both hands on his tall hardwood staff.

"Grandfather," Mero said, "run off before I break your stick in two and bugger you with—"

The old man feinted with one end of the staff, pulled it back, and whipped the other end about faster than Dany would have believed. The Titan's Bastard staggered back into the surf, spitting blood and broken teeth from the ruin of his mouth. Whitebeard put Dany behind him. Mero slashed at his face. The old man jerked back, cat-quick. The staff thumped Mero's ribs, sending him reeling. Arstan splashed sideways, parried a looping cut, danced away from a second, checked a third mid-swing. The moves were so fast she could hardly follow. Missandei was pulling Dany to her feet when she heard a *crack*. She thought Arstan's staff had snapped until she saw the jagged bone jutting from Mero's calf. As he fell, the Titan's Bastard twisted and lunged, sending his point straight at the old man's chest. Whitebeard swept the blade aside almost contemptuously and smashed the other end of his staff against the big man's temple. Mero went sprawling, blood bubbling from his mouth as the waves washed over him. A moment later the freedmen washed over him too, knives and stones and angry fists rising and falling in a frenzy.

Dany turned away, sickened. She was more frightened now than when it had been happening. *He would have killed me.*

"Your Grace." Arstan knelt. "I am an old man, and shamed. He should never have gotten close enough to seize you. I was lax. I did not know him without his beard and hair."

"No more than I did." Dany took a deep breath to stop her shaking. *Enemies everywhere.* "Take me back to my tent. Please."

By the time Mormont arrived, she was huddled in her lion pelt, drinking a cup of spice wine. "I had a look at the river wall," Ser Jorah started. "It's a few feet higher than the others, and just as strong. And the Meereenese have a dozen fire hulks tied up beneath the ramparts—"

She cut him off. "You might have warned me that the Titan's Bastard had escaped."

He frowned. "I saw no need to frighten you, Your Grace. I have offered a reward for his head—"

"Pay it to Whitebeard. Mero has been with us all the way from Yunkai. He shaved his beard off and lost himself amongst the freedmen, waiting for a chance for vengeance. Arstan killed him."

Ser Jorah gave the old man a long look. "A squire with a stick slew Mero of Braavos, is that the way of it?"

"A stick," Dany confirmed, "but no longer a squire. Ser Jorah, it's my wish that Arstan be knighted."

"*No.*"

The loud refusal was surprise enough. Stranger still, it came from both men at once.

Ser Jorah drew his sword. "The Titan's Bastard was a nasty piece of work. And good at killing. Who are you, old man?"

"A better knight than you, ser," Arstan said coldly.

Knight? Dany was confused. "You said you were a squire."

"I was, Your Grace." He dropped to one knee. "I squired for Lord Swann in my youth, and at Magister Illyrio's behest I have served Strong Belwas as well. But during the years between, I was a knight in Westeros. I have told you no lies, my queen. Yet there are truths I have withheld, and for that and all my other sins I can only beg your forgiveness."

"What truths have you withheld?" Dany did not like this. "You will tell me. Now."

He bowed his head. "At Qarth, when you asked my name, I said I was called Arstan. That much was true. Many men had called me by that name while Belwas and I were making our way east to find you. But it is not my true name."

She was more confused than angry. *He has played me false, just as Jorah warned me, yet he saved my life just now.*

Ser Jorah flushed red. "Mero shaved his beard, but you grew one, didn't you? No wonder you looked so bloody familiar . . ."

"You know him?" Dany asked the exile knight, lost.

"I saw him perhaps a dozen times . . . from afar most often, standing with his brothers or riding in some tourney. But every man in the Seven Kingdoms knew Barristan the Bold." He laid the point of his sword against the old man's neck. "*Khaleesi*, before you kneels Ser Barristan Selmy, Lord Commander of the Kingsguard, who betrayed your House to serve the Usurper Robert Baratheon."

The old knight did not so much as blink. "The crow calls the raven black, and *you* speak of betrayal."

"Why are you here?" Dany demanded of him. "If Robert sent you to kill me, why did you save my life?" *He served the Usurper. He betrayed Rhaegar's memory, and abandoned Viserys to live and die in exile. Yet if he wanted me dead, he need only have stood aside . . .* "I want the *whole* truth now, on your honor as a knight. Are you the Usurper's man, or mine?"

"Yours, if you will have me." Ser Barristan had tears in his eyes. "I took Robert's pardon, aye. I served him in Kingsguard and council. Served with the Kingslayer and others near as bad, who soiled the white cloak I wore. Nothing will excuse that. I might be serving in King's Landing still if the vile boy upon the Iron Throne had not cast me aside, it shames me to admit. But when he took the cloak that the White Bull had draped about my shoulders, and sent men to kill me that selfsame day, it was as though he'd ripped a caul off my eyes. That was when I knew I must find my true king, and die in his service—"

"I can grant that wish," Ser Jorah said darkly.

"Quiet," said Dany. "I'll hear him out."

"It may be that I must die a traitor's death," Ser Barristan said. "If so, I should not die alone. Before I took Robert's pardon I fought against him on the Trident. You were on the other side of that battle, Mormont, were you not?" He did not wait for an answer. "Your Grace, I am sorry I misled you. It was the only way to keep the Lannisters from learning that I had joined you. You are watched, as your brother was. Lord Varys reported every move Viserys made, for years. Whilst I sat on the small council, I heard a hundred such reports. And since the day you wed Khal Drogo, there has been an informer by your side selling your secrets, trading whispers to the Spider for gold and promises."

He cannot mean . . . "You are mistaken." Dany looked at Jorah Mormont. "Tell him he's mistaken. There's no informer. Ser Jorah, tell him. We crossed the Dothraki sea together, and the red waste . . ." Her heart fluttered like a bird in a trap. "Tell him, Jorah. Tell him how he got it wrong."

"The Others take you, Selmy." Ser Jorah flung his longsword to the carpet. "*Khaleesi*, it was only at the start, before I came to know you . . . before I came to love . . ."

"*Do not say that word!*" She backed away from him. "*How could you?* What did the Usurper promise you? Gold, was it gold?" The Undying had said she would be betrayed twice more, once for gold and once for love. "Tell me what you were promised?"

"Varys said . . . I might go home." He bowed his head.

I was going to take you home! Her dragons sensed her fury. Viserion roared, and smoke rose grey from his snout. Drogon beat the air with black wings, and Rhaegal twisted his head back and belched flame. *I should say the word and burn the two of them.* Was there no one she could trust, no one to keep her safe? "Are all the knights of Westeros so false as you two? Get out, before my dragons roast you both. What does roast liar smell like? As foul as Brown Ben's sewers? *Go!*"

Ser Barristan rose stiff and slow. For the first time, he looked his age. "Where shall we go, Your Grace?"

"To hell, to serve King Robert." Dany felt hot tears on her cheeks. Drogon screamed, lashing his tail back and forth. "The Others can have you both." *Go, go away forever, both of you, the next time I see your faces I'll have your traitors' heads off.* She could not say the words, though. *They betrayed me. But they saved me. But they lied.* "You go . . ." *My bear, my fierce strong bear, what will I do without him? And the old man, my brother's friend.* "You go . . . go . . ." *Where?*

And then she knew.

TYRION

Tyrion dressed himself in darkness, listening to his wife's soft breathing from the bed they shared. *She dreams*, he thought, when Sansa murmured something softly—a name, perhaps, though it was too faint to say—and turned onto her side. As man and wife they shared a marriage bed, but that was all. *Even her tears she hoards to herself.*

He had expected anguish and anger when he told her of her brother's death, but Sansa's face had remained so still that for a moment he feared she had not understood. It was only later, with a heavy oaken door between them, that he heard her sobbing. Tyrion had considered going to her then, to offer what comfort he could. *No*, he had to remind himself, *she will not look for solace from a Lannister.* The most he could do was to shield her from the uglier details of the Red Wedding as they came down from the Twins. Sansa did not need to hear how her brother's body had been hacked and mutilated, he decided; nor how her mother's corpse had been dumped naked into the Green Fork in a savage mockery of House Tully's funeral customs. The last thing the girl needed was more fodder for her nightmares.

It was not enough, though. He had wrapped his cloak around her shoulders and sworn to protect her, but that was as cruel a jape as the crown the Freys had placed atop the head of Robb Stark's direwolf after they'd sewn it onto his headless corpse. Sansa knew that as well. The way she looked at him, her stiffness when she climbed into their bed . . . when he was with her, never for an instant could he forget who he was, or *what* he was. No more than she did. She still went nightly to the godswood to pray, and Tyrion wondered if she were praying for his death. She had lost her home, her place in the world, and everyone she had ever loved or trusted. *Winter is coming*, warned the Stark words, and truly it had come for them with a vengeance. *But it is high summer for House Lannister. So why am I so bloody cold?*

He pulled on his boots, fastened his cloak with a lion's head brooch, and slipped out into the torchlit hall. There was this much to be said for his marriage; it had allowed him to escape Maegor's Holdfast. Now that he had a wife and household, his lord father had agreed that more suitable accommodations were required, and Lord Gyles had found himself abruptly dispossessed of his spacious apartments atop the Kitchen Keep. And splendid apartments they were too, with a large bedchamber and adequate solar, a bath and dressing room for his wife, and small adjoining chambers for Pod and Sansa's maids. Even Bronn's cell by the stair had a window of sorts. *Well, more an arrow slit, but it lets in light.* The castle's main kitchen was just across the courtyard, true, but Tyrion found those sounds and smells infinitely preferable to sharing Maegor's with his sister. The less he had to see of Cersei the happier he was like to be.

Tyrion could hear Brella's snoring as he passed her cell. Shae complained of that, but it seemed a small enough price to pay. Varys had suggested the woman to him; in former days, she had run Lord Renly's household in the city, which had given her a deal of practice at being blind, deaf, and mute.

Lighting a taper, he made his way back to the servants' steps and descended. The floors below his own were still, and he heard no footsteps but his own. Down he went, to the ground floor and beyond, to emerge in a gloomy cellar with a vaulted stone ceiling. Much of the castle was connected underground, and the Kitchen Keep was no exception. Tyrion waddled along a long dark passageway until he found the door he wanted, and pushed through.

Within, the dragon skulls were waiting, and so was Shae. "I thought m'lord had forgotten me." Her dress was draped over a black tooth near as tall as she was, and she stood within the dragon's jaws, nude. *Balerion*, he thought. Or was it Vhagar? One dragon skull looked much like another.

Just the sight of her made him hard. "Come out of there."

"I won't." She smiled her wickedest smile. "M'lord will pluck me from the dragon's jaws, I know." But when he waddled closer she leaned forward and blew out the taper.

"Shae . . ." He reached, but she spun and slipped free.

"You have to catch me." Her voice came from his left. "M'lord must have played monsters and maidens when he was little."

"Are you calling me a monster?"

"No more than I'm a maiden." She was behind him, her steps soft against the floor. "You need to catch me all the same."

He did, finally, but only because she let herself be caught. By the time she slipped into his arms, he was flushed and out of breath from stumbling into dragon skulls. All that was forgotten in an instant when he felt her small breasts pressed against his face in the dark, her stiff little nipples brushing lightly over his lips and the scar where his nose had been. Tyrion pulled her down onto the floor. "My giant," she breathed as he entered her. "My giant's come to save me."

After, as they lay entwined amongst the dragon skulls, he rested his head against her, inhaling the smooth clean smell of her hair. "We should go back," he said reluctantly. "It must be near dawn. Sansa will be waking."

"You should give her dreamwine," Shae said, "like Lady Tanda does with Lollys. A cup before she goes to sleep, and we could fuck in bed beside her without her waking." She giggled. "Maybe we should, some night. Would m'lord like that?" Her hand found his shoulder, and began to knead the muscles there. "Your neck is hard as stone. What troubles you?"

Tyrion could not see his fingers in front of his face, but he ticked his woes off on them all the same. "My wife. My sister. My nephew. My father. The Tyrells." He had to move to his other hand. "Varys. Pycelle. Littlefinger. The Red Viper of Dorne." He had come to his last finger. "The face that stares back out of the water when I wash."

Shae kissed his maimed scarred nose. "A brave face. A kind and good face. I wish I could see it now."

All the sweet innocence of the world was in her voice. *Innocence? Fool, she's a whore, all she knows of men is the bit between their legs. Fool, fool.* "Better you than me!" Tyrion sat. "We have a long day before us, both of us. You shouldn't have blown out that taper. How are we to find our clothing?"

She laughed. "Maybe we'll have to go naked."

And if we're seen, my lord father will hang you. Hiring Shae as one of Sansa's maids had given him an excuse to be seen talking with her, but Tyrion did not delude himself that they were safe. Varys had warned him. "I gave Shae a false history, but it was meant for Lollys and Lady Tanda. Your sister is of a more suspicious mind. If she should ask me what I know . . ."

"You will tell her some clever lie."

"No. I will tell her that the girl is a common camp follower that you acquired before the battle on the Green Fork and brought to King's Landing against your lord father's express command. I will not lie to the queen."

"You have lied to her before. Shall I tell her that?"

The eunuch sighed. "That cuts more deeply than a knife, my lord. I have served you loyally, but I must also serve your sister when I can. How long do you think she would let me live if I were of no further use to her whatsoever? I have no fierce sellsword to protect me, no valiant brother to avenge me, only some little birds who whisper in my ear. With those whisperings I must buy my life anew each day."

"Pardon me if I do not weep for you."

"I shall, but you must pardon me if I do not weep for

Shae. I confess, I do not understand what there is in her to make a clever man like you act such a fool."

"You might, if you were not a eunuch."

"Is that the way of it? A man may have wits, or a bit of meat between his legs, but not both?" Varys tittered. "Perhaps I should be grateful I was cut, then."

The Spider was right. Tyrion groped through the dragon-haunted darkness for his smallclothes, feeling wretched. The risk he was taking left him tight as a drumhead, and there was guilt as well. *The Others can take my guilt,* he thought as he slipped his tunic over his head. *Why should I be guilty? My wife wants no part of me, and most especially not the part that seems to want her.* Perhaps he ought to *tell* her about Shae. It was not as though he was the first man ever to keep a concubine. Sansa's own oh-so-honorable father had given her a bastard brother. For all he knew, his wife might be thrilled to learn that he was fucking Shae, so long as it spared her his unwelcome touch.

No, I dare not. Vows or no, his wife could not be trusted. She might be maiden between the legs, but she was hardly innocent of betrayal; she had once spilled her own father's plans to Cersei. And girls her age were not known for keeping secrets.

The only safe course was to rid himself of Shae. *I might send her to Chataya,* Tyrion reflected, reluctantly. In Chataya's brothel, Shae would have all the silks and gems she could wish for, and the gentlest highborn patrons. It would be a better life by far than the one she had been living when he'd found her.

Or, if she was tired of earning her bread on her back, he might arrange a marriage for her. *Bronn, perhaps?* The sellsword had never balked at eating off his master's plate, and he was a knight now, a better match than she could elsewise hope for. *Or Ser Tallad?* Tyrion had noticed that one gazing wistfully at Shae more than once. *Why not? He's tall, strong, not hard to look upon, every inch the gifted young knight.* Of course, Tallad knew Shae only as a pretty young lady's maid in service at the castle. *If he wed her and then learned she was a whore . . .*

"M'lord, where are you? Did the dragons eat you up?"

"No. Here." He groped at a dragon skull. "I have found a shoe, but I believe it's yours."

"M'lord sounds very solemn. Have I displeased you?"

"No," he said, too curtly. "You always please me." *And therein is our danger.* He might dream of sending her away at times like this, but that never lasted long. Tyrion saw her dimly through the gloom, pulling a woolen sock up a slender leg. *I can see.* A vague light was leaking through the row of long narrow windows set high in the cellar wall. The skulls of the Targaryen dragons were emerging from the darkness around them, black amidst grey. "Day comes too soon." *A new day. A new year. A new century. I survived the Green Fork and the Blackwater, I can bloody well survive King Joffrey's wedding.*

Shae snatched her dress down off the dragon's tooth and slipped it over her head. "I'll go up first. Brella will want help with the bathwater." She bent over to give him one last kiss, upon the brow. "My giant of Lannister. I love you so."

And I love you as well, sweetling. A whore she might well be, but she deserved better than what he had to give her. *I will wed her to Ser Tallad. He seems a decent man. And tall . . .*

SANSA

That was such a sweet dream, Sansa thought drowsily. She had been back in Winterfell, running through the godswood with her Lady. Her father had been there, and her brothers, all of them warm and safe. *If only dreaming could make it so . . .*

She threw back the coverlets. *I must be brave.* Her torments would soon be ended, one way or the other. *If Lady was here, I would not be afraid.* Lady was dead, though; Robb, Bran, Rickon, Arya, her father, her mother, even Septa Mordane. *All of them are dead but me.* She was alone in the world now.

Her lord husband was not beside her, but she was used to that. Tyrion was a bad sleeper and often rose before the dawn. Usually she found him in the solar, hunched beside a candle, lost in some old scroll or leatherbound book. Sometimes the smell of the morning bread from the ovens took him to the kitchens, and sometimes he would climb up to the roof garden or wander all alone down Traitor's Walk.

She threw back the shutters and shivered as gooseprickles

rose along her arms. There were clouds massing in the eastern sky, pierced by shafts of sunlight. *They look like two huge castles afloat in the morning sky*. Sansa could see their walls of tumbled stone, their mighty keeps and barbicans. Wispy banners swirled from atop their towers and reached for the fast-fading stars. The sun was coming up behind them, and she watched them go from black to grey to a thousand shades of rose and gold and crimson. Soon the wind mushed them together, and there was only one castle where there had been two.

She heard the door open as her maids brought the hot water for her bath. They were both new to her service; Tyrion said the women who'd tended to her previously had all been Cersei's spies, just as Sansa had always suspected. "Come see," she told them. "There's a castle in the sky."

They came to have a look. "It's made of gold." Shae had short dark hair and bold eyes. She did all that was asked of her, but sometimes she gave Sansa the most insolent looks. "A castle all of gold, there's a sight I'd like to see."

"A castle, is it?" Brella had to squint. "That tower's tumbling over, looks like. It's all ruins, that is."

Sansa did not want to hear about falling towers and ruined castles. She closed the shutters and said, "We are expected at the queen's breakfast. Is my lord husband in the solar?"

"No, m'lady," said Brella. "I have not seen him."

"Might be he went to see his father," Shae declared. "Might be the King's Hand had need of his counsel."

Brella gave a sniff. "Lady Sansa, you'll be wanting to get into the tub before the water gets too cool."

Sansa let Shae pull her shift up over her head and climbed into the big wooden tub. She was tempted to ask for a cup of wine, to calm her nerves. The wedding was to be at midday in the Great Sept of Baelor across the city. And come evenfall the feast would be held in the throne room; a thousand guests and seventy-seven courses, with singers and jugglers and mummers. But first came breakfast in the Queen's Ballroom, for the Lannisters and the Tyrell men—the Tyrell women would be breaking their fast with Margaery—and a hundred odd knights and lordlings. *They have made me a Lannister*, Sansa thought bitterly.

Brella sent Shae to fetch more hot water while she washed Sansa's back. "You are trembling, m'lady."

"The water is not hot enough," Sansa lied.

Her maids were dressing her when Tyrion appeared, Podrick Payne in tow. "You look lovely, Sansa." He turned to his squire. "Pod, be so good as to pour me a cup of wine."

"There will be wine at the breakfast, my lord," Sansa said.

"There's wine here. You don't expect me to face my sister sober, surely? It's a new century, my lady. The three hundredth year since Aegon's Conquest." The dwarf took a cup of red from Podrick and raised it high. "To Aegon. What a fortunate fellow. Two sisters, two wives, and three big dragons, what more could a man ask for?" He wiped his mouth with the back of his hand.

The Imp's clothing was soiled and unkempt, Sansa noticed; it looked as though he'd slept in it. "Will you be changing into fresh garb, my lord? Your new doublet is very handsome."

"The *doublet* is handsome, yes." Tyrion put the cup aside. "Come, Pod, let us see if we can find some garments to make me look less dwarfish. I would not want to shame my lady wife."

When the Imp returned a short time later, he was presentable enough, and even a little taller. Podrick Payne had changed as well, and looked almost a proper squire for once, although a rather large red pimple in the fold beside his nose spoiled the effect of his splendid purple, white, and gold raiment. *He is such a timid boy.* Sansa had been wary of Tyrion's squire at first; he was a Payne, cousin to Ser Ilyn Payne who had taken her father's head off. However, she'd soon come to realize that Pod was as frightened of her as she was of his cousin. Whenever she spoke to him, he turned the most alarming shade of red.

"Are purple, gold, and white the colors of House Payne, Podrick?" she asked him politely.

"No. I mean, yes." He blushed. "The colors. Our arms are purple and white chequy, my lady. With gold coins. In the checks. Purple and white. Both." He studied her feet.

"There's a tale behind those coins," said Tyrion. "No doubt Pod will confide it to your toes one day. Just now we are expected at the Queen's Ballroom, however. Shall we?"

Sansa was tempted to beg off. *I could tell him that my tummy was upset, or that my moon's blood had come.* She wanted nothing more than to crawl back in bed and pull the drapes. *I must be brave, like Robb,* she told herself, as she took her lord husband stiffly by the arm.

In the Queen's Ballroom they broke their fast on honey-cakes baked with blackberries and nuts, gammon steaks, bacon, fingerfish crisped in breadcrumbs, autumn pears, and a Dornish dish of onions, cheese, and chopped eggs cooked up with fiery peppers. "Nothing like a hearty breakfast to whet one's appetite for the seventy-seven-course feast to follow," Tyrion commented as their plates were filled. There were flagons of milk and flagons of mead and flagons of a light sweet golden wine to wash it down. Musicians strolled among the tables, piping and fluting and fiddling, while Ser Dontos galloped about on his broom-stick horse and Moon Boy made farting sounds with his cheeks and sang rude songs about the guests.

Tyrion scarce touched his food, Sansa noticed, though he drank several cups of the wine. For herself, she tried a little of the Dornish eggs, but the peppers burned her mouth. Otherwise she only nibbled at the fruit and fish and honeycakes. Every time Joffrey looked at her, her tummy got so fluttery that she felt as though she'd swal-lowed a bat.

When the food had been cleared away, the queen solemnly presented Joff with the wife's cloak that he would drape over Margaery's shoulders. "It is the cloak I donned when Robert took me for his queen, the same cloak my mother Lady Joanna wore when wed to my lord father." Sansa thought it looked threadbare, if truth be told, but perhaps because it was so used.

Then it was time for gifts. It was traditional in the Reach to give presents to bride and groom on the morning of their wedding; on the morrow they would receive more presents as a couple, but today's tokens were for their sepa-rate persons.

From Jalabhar Xho, Joffrey received a great bow of golden wood and quiver of long arrows fletched with green and scarlet feathers; from Lady Tanda a pair of supple rid-ing boots; from Ser Kevan a magnificent red leather joust-ing saddle; a red gold brooch wrought in the shape of a scorpion from the Dornishman, Prince Oberyn; silver spurs from Ser Addam Marbrand; a red silk tourney pavilion from Lord Mathis Rowan. Lord Paxter Redwyne brought forth a beautiful wooden model of the war galley of two hundred oars being built even now on the Arbor. "If it please Your Grace, she will be called *King Joffrey's Valor*," he said, and Joff allowed that he was very pleased indeed. "I will make it my flagship when I sail to Dragonstone to kill my traitor uncle Stannis," he said.

He plays the gracious king today. Joffrey could be gallant when it suited him, Sansa knew, but it seemed to suit him less and less. Indeed, all his courtesy vanished at once when Tyrion presented him with their own gift: a huge old book called *Lives of Four Kings*, bound in leather and gorgeously illuminated. The king leafed through it with no interest. "And what is this, Uncle?"

A book. Sansa wondered if Joffrey moved those fat wormy lips of his when he read.

"Grand Maester Kaeth's history of the reigns of Daeron the Young Dragon, Baelor the Blessed, Aegon the Unworthy, and Daeron the Good," her small husband answered.

"A book every king should read, Your Grace," said Ser Kevan.

"My father had no time for books." Joffrey shoved the tome across the table. "If you read less, Uncle Imp, perhaps Lady Sansa would have a baby in her belly by now." He laughed . . . and when the king laughs, the court laughs with him. "Don't be sad, Sansa, once I've gotten Queen Margaery with child I'll visit your bedchamber and show my little uncle how it's done."

Sansa reddened. She glanced nervously at Tyrion, afraid of what he might say. This could turn as nasty as the bedding had at their own feast. But for once the dwarf filled his mouth with wine instead of words.

Lord Mace Tyrell came forward to present his gift: a golden chalice three feet tall, with two ornate curved handles and seven faces glittering with gemstones. "Seven faces for Your Grace's seven kingdoms," the bride's father explained. He showed them how each face bore the sigil of one of the great houses: ruby lion, emerald rose, onyx stag, silver trout, blue jade falcon, opal sun, and pearl direwolf.

"A splendid cup," said Joffrey, "but we'll need to chip the wolf off and put a squid in its place, I think."

Sansa pretended that she had not heard.

"Margaery and I shall drink deep at the feast, good father." Joffrey lifted the chalice above his head, for everyone to admire.

"The damned thing's as tall as I am," Tyrion muttered in a low voice. "Half a chalice and Joff will be falling down drunk."

Good, she thought. *Perhaps he'll break his neck.*

Lord Tywin waited until last to present the king with his own gift: a longsword. Its scabbard was made of cherry-wood, gold, and oiled red leather, studded with golden lions' heads. The lions had ruby eyes, she saw. The ballroom fell silent as Joffrey unsheathed the blade and thrust the sword above his head. Red and black ripples in the steel shimmered in the morning light.

"Magnificent," declared Mathis Rowan.

"A sword to sing of, sire," said Lord Redwyne.

"A *king's* sword," said Ser Kevan Lannister.

King Joffrey looked as if he wanted to kill someone right then and there, he was so excited. He slashed at the air and laughed. "A great sword must have a great name, my lords! What shall I call it?"

Sansa remembered Lion's Tooth, the sword Arya had flung into the Trident, and Hearteater, the one he'd made her kiss before the battle. She wondered if he'd want Margaery to kiss this one.

The guests were shouting out names for the new blade. Joff dismissed a dozen before he heard one he liked. *"Widow's Wail!"* he cried. "Yes! It shall make many a widow, too!" He slashed again. "And when I face my uncle Stannis it will break his magic sword clean in two." Joff tried a downcut, forcing Ser Balon Swann to take a hasty step backward. Laughter rang through the hall at the look on Ser Balon's face.

"Have a care, Your Grace," Ser Addam Marbrand warned the king. "Valyrian steel is perilously sharp."

"I remember." Joffrey brought Widow's Wail down in a savage two-handed slice, onto the book that Tyrion had given him. The heavy leather cover parted at a stroke. "Sharp! I told you, I am no stranger to Valyrian steel." It took him half a dozen further cuts to hack the thick tome apart, and the boy was breathless by the time he was done. Sansa could feel her husband struggling with his fury as Ser Osmund Kettleblack shouted, "I pray you never turn that wicked edge on me, sire."

"See that you never give me cause, ser." Joffrey flicked a chunk of *Lives of Four Kings* off the table at swordpoint, then slid Widow's Wail back into its scabbard.

"Your Grace," Ser Garlan Tyrell said. "Perhaps you did not know. In all of Westeros there were but four copies of that book illuminated in Kaeth's own hand."

"Now there are three." Joffrey undid his old swordbelt to don his new one. "You and Lady Sansa owe me a better present, Uncle Imp. This one is all chopped to pieces."

Tyrion was staring at his nephew with his mismatched eyes. "Perhaps a knife, sire. To match your sword. A dagger of the same fine Valyrian steel . . . with a dragonbone hilt, say?"

Joff gave him a sharp look. "You . . . yes, a dagger to match my sword, good." He nodded. "A . . . a gold hilt with rubies in it. Dragonbone is too plain."

"As you wish, Your Grace." Tyrion drank another cup of wine. He might have been all alone in his solar for all the attention he paid Sansa. But when the time came to leave for the wedding, he took her by the hand.

As they were crossing the yard, Prince Oberyn of Dorne fell in beside them, his black-haired paramour on his arm. Sansa glanced at the woman curiously. She was baseborn and unwed, and had borne two bastard daughters for the prince, but she did not fear to look even the queen in the eye. Shae had told her that this Ellaria worshiped some Lysene love goddess. "She was almost a whore when he found her, m'lady," her maid confided, "and now she's near a princess." Sansa had never been this close to the Dornishwoman before. *She is not truly beautiful*, she thought, *but something about her draws the eye.*

"I once had the great good fortune to see the Citadel's copy of *Lives of Four Kings*," Prince Oberyn was telling her lord husband. "The illuminations were wondrous to behold, but Kaeth was too kind by half to King Viserys."

Tyrion gave him a sharp look. "Too kind? He scants

Viserys shamefully, in my view. It should have been *Lives of Five Kings.*"

The prince laughed. "Viserys hardly reigned a fortnight."

"He reigned more than a year," said Tyrion.

Oberyn gave a shrug. "A year or a fortnight, what does it matter? He poisoned his own nephew to gain the throne and then did nothing once he had it."

"Baelor starved himself to death, fasting," said Tyrion. "His uncle served him loyally as Hand, as he had served the Young Dragon before him. Viserys might only have reigned a year, but he ruled for fifteen, while Daeron warred and Baelor prayed." He made a sour face. "And if he did remove his nephew, can you blame him? Someone had to save the realm from Baelor's follies."

Sansa was shocked. "But Baelor the Blessed was a great king. He walked the Boneway barefoot to make peace with Dorne, and rescued the Dragonknight from a snakepit. The vipers refused to strike him because he was so pure and holy."

Prince Oberyn smiled. "If you were a viper, my lady, would you want to bite a bloodless stick like Baelor the Blessed? I'd sooner save my fangs for someone juicier . . ."

"My prince is playing with you, Lady Sansa," said the woman Ellaria Sand. "The septons and singers like to say that the snakes did not bite Baelor, but the truth is very different. He was bitten half a hundred times, and should have died from it."

"If he had, Viserys would have reigned a dozen years," said Tyrion, "and the Seven Kingdoms might have been better served. Some believe Baelor was deranged by all that venom."

"Yes," said Prince Oberyn, "but I've seen no snakes in this Red Keep of yours. So how do you account for Joffrey?"

"I prefer not to." Tyrion inclined his head stiffly. "If you will excuse us. Our litter awaits." The dwarf helped Sansa up inside and clambered awkwardly after her. "Close the curtains, my lady, if you'd be so good."

"Must we, my lord?" Sansa did not want to be shut behind the curtains. "The day is so lovely."

"The good people of King's Landing are like to throw

dung at the litter if they see me inside it. Do us both a kind-ness, my lady. Close the curtains."

She did as he bid her. They sat for a time, as the air grew warm and stuffy around them. "I was sorry about your book, my lord," she made herself say.

"It was Joffrey's book. He might have learned a thing or two if he'd read it." He sounded distracted. "I should have known better. I should have seen . . . a good many things."

"Perhaps the dagger will please him more."

When the dwarf grimaced, his scar tightened and twisted. "The boy's earned himself a dagger, wouldn't you say?" Thankfully Tyrion did not wait for her reply. "Joff quarreled with your brother Robb at Winterfell. Tell me, was there ill feeling between Bran and His Grace as well?"

"Bran?" The question confused her. "Before he fell, you mean?" She had to try and think back. It was all so long ago. "Bran was a sweet boy. Everyone loved him. He and Tommen fought with wooden swords, I remember, but just for play."

Tyrion lapsed back into moody silence. Sansa heard the distant clank of chains from outside; the portcullis was be-ing drawn up. A moment later there was a shout, and their litter swayed into motion. Deprived of the passing scenery, she chose to stare at her folded hands, uncomfortably aware of her husband's mismatched eyes. *Why is he look-ing at me that way?*

"You loved your brothers, much as I love Jaime."

Is this some Lannister trap to make me speak treason? "My brothers were traitors, and they've gone to traitors' graves. It is treason to love a traitor."

Her little husband snorted. "Robb rose in arms against his rightful king. By law, that made him a traitor. The oth-ers died too young to know what treason was." He rubbed his nose. "Sansa, do you know what happened to Bran at Winterfell?"

"Bran fell. He was always climbing things, and finally he fell. We always feared he would. And Theon Greyjoy killed him, but that was later."

"Theon Greyjoy." Tyrion sighed. "Your lady mother once accused me . . . well, I will not burden you with the ugly details. She accused me falsely. I never harmed your brother Bran. And I mean no harm to you."

What does he want me to say? "That is good to know, my lord." He wanted something from her, but Sansa did not know what it was. *He looks like a starving child, but I have no food to give him. Why won't he leave me be?*

Tyrion rubbed at his scarred, scabby nose yet again, an ugly habit that drew the eye to his ugly face. "You have never asked me how Robb died, or your lady mother."

"I . . . would sooner not know. It would give me bad dreams."

"Then I will say no more."

"That . . . that's kind of you."

"Oh, yes," said Tyrion. "I am the very soul of kindness. And I know about bad dreams."

TYRION

The new crown that his father had given the Faith stood twice as tall as the one the mob had smashed, a glory of crystal and spun gold. Rainbow light flashed and shimmered every time the High Septon moved his head, but Tyrion had to wonder how the man could bear the weight. And even he had to concede that Joffrey and Margaery made a regal couple, as they stood side-by-side between the towering gilded statues of the Father and the Mother.

The bride was lovely in ivory silk and Myrish lace, her skirts decorated with floral patterns picked out in seed pearls. As Renly's widow, she might have worn the Baratheon colors, gold and black, yet she came to them a Tyrell, in a maiden's cloak made of a hundred cloth-of-gold roses sewn to green velvet. He wondered if she really was a maiden. *Not that Joffrey is like to know the difference.*

The king looked near as splendid as his bride, in his doublet of dusky rose, beneath a cloak of deep crimson velvet blazoned with his stag and lion. The crown rested easily on his curls, gold on gold. *I saved that bloody crown for him.*

Tyrion shifted his weight uncomfortably from one foot to the other. He could not stand still. *Too much wine.* He should have thought to relieve himself before they set out from the Red Keep. The sleepless night he'd spent with Shae was making itself felt too, but most of all he wanted to strangle his bloody royal nephew.

I am no stranger to Valyrian steel, the boy had boasted. The septons were always going on about how the Father Above judges us all. *If the Father would be so good as to topple over and crush Joff like a dung beetle, I might even believe it.*

He ought to have seen it long ago. Jaime would never send another man to do his killing, and Cersei was too cunning to use a knife that could be traced back to her, but Joff, arrogant vicious stupid little wretch that he was . . .

He remembered a cold morning when he'd climbed down the steep exterior steps from Winterfell's library to find Prince Joffrey jesting with the Hound about killing wolves. *Send a dog to kill a wolf,* he said. Even Joffrey was not so foolish as to command Sandor Clegane to slay a son of Eddard Stark, however; the Hound would have gone to Cersei. Instead the boy found his catspaw among the unsavory lot of freeriders, merchants, and camp followers who'd attached themselves to the king's party as they made their way north. *Some poxy lackwit willing to risk his life for a prince's favor and a little coin.* Tyrion wondered whose idea it had been to wait until Robert left Winterfell before opening Bran's throat. *Joff's, most like. No doubt he thought it was the height of cunning.*

The prince's own dagger had a jeweled pommel and inlaid goldwork on the blade, Tyrion seemed to recall. At least Joff had not been stupid enough to use that. Instead he went poking among his father's weapons. Robert Baratheon was a man of careless generosity, and would have given his son any dagger he wanted . . . but Tyrion guessed that the boy had just taken it. Robert had come to Winterfell with a long tail of knights and retainers, a huge wheelhouse, and a baggage train. No doubt some diligent servant had made certain that the king's weapons went with him, in case he should desire any of them.

The blade Joff chose was nice and plain. No goldwork, no jewels in the hilt, no silver inlay on the blade. King Robert never wore it, had likely forgotten he owned it. Yet the Valyrian steel was deadly sharp . . . sharp enough to slice through skin, flesh, and muscle in one quick stroke. *I am no stranger to Valyrian steel.* But he had been, hadn't he? Else he would never have been so foolish as to pick Littlefinger's knife.

The *why* of it still eluded him. *Simple cruelty, perhaps?* His nephew had that in abundance. It was all Tyrion could do not to retch up all the wine he'd drunk, piss in his breeches, or both. He squirmed uncomfortably. He ought to have held his tongue at breakfast. *The boy knows I know now. My big mouth will be the death of me, I swear it.*

The seven vows were made, the seven blessings invoked, and the seven promises exchanged. When the wedding song had been sung and the challenge had gone unanswered, it was time for the exchange of cloaks. Tyrion shifted his weight from one stunted leg to the other, trying to see between his father and his uncle Kevan. *If the gods are just, Joff will make a hash of this.* He made certain not to look at Sansa, lest his bitterness show in his eyes. *You might have knelt, damn you. Would it have been so bloody hard to bend those stiff Stark knees of yours and let me keep a little dignity?*

Mace Tyrell removed his daughter's maiden cloak tenderly, while Joffrey accepted the folded bride's cloak from his brother Tommen and shook it out with a flourish. The boy king was as tall at thirteen as his bride was at sixteen; he would not require a fool's back to climb upon. He draped Margaery in the crimson-and-gold and leaned close to fasten it at her throat. And that easily she passed from her father's protection to her husband's. *But who will protect her from Joff?* Tyrion glanced at the Knight of Flowers, standing with the other Kingsguard. *You had best keep your sword well honed, Ser Loras.*

"With this kiss I pledge my love!" Joffrey declared in ringing tones. When Margaery echoed the words he pulled her close and kissed her long and deep. Rainbow lights danced once more about the High Septon's crown as he solemnly declared Joffrey of the Houses Baratheon and Lannister and Margaery of House Tyrell to be one flesh, one heart, one soul.

Good, that's done with. Now let's get back to the bloody castle so I can have a piss.

Ser Loras and Ser Meryn led the procession from the sept in their white scale armor and snowy cloaks. Then came Prince Tommen, scattering rose petals from a basket before the king and queen. After the royal couple followed Queen Cersei and Lord Tyrell, then the bride's mother arm-in-arm with Lord Tywin. The Queen of Thorns tottered after them with one hand on Ser Kevan Lannister's arm and the other on her cane, her twin guardsmen close behind her in case she fell. Next came Ser Garlan Tyrell and his lady wife, and finally it was their turn.

"My lady." Tyrion offered Sansa his arm. She took it dutifully, but he could feel her stiffness as they walked up the aisle together. She never once looked down at him.

He heard them cheering outside even before he reached the doors. The mob loved Margaery so much they were even willing to love Joffrey again. She had belonged to Renly, the handsome young prince who had loved them so well he had come back from beyond the grave to save them. And the bounty of Highgarden had come with her, flowing up the roseroad from the south. The fools didn't seem to remember that it had been Mace Tyrell who *closed* the roseroad to begin with, and made the bloody famine.

They stepped out into the crisp autumn air. "I feared we'd never escape," Tyrion quipped.

Sansa had no choice but to look at him then. "I . . . yes, my lord. As you say." She looked sad. "It was such a beautiful ceremony, though."

As ours was not. "It was long, I'll say that much. I need to return to the castle for a good piss." Tyrion rubbed the stump of his nose. "Would that I'd contrived some mission to take me out of the city. Littlefinger was the clever one."

Joffrey and Margaery stood surrounded by Kingsguard atop the steps that fronted on the broad marble plaza. Ser Addam and his gold cloaks held back the crowd, while the statue of King Baelor the Blessed gazed down on them benevolently. Tyrion had no choice but to queue up with the rest to offer congratulations. He kissed Margaery's fingers and wished her every happiness. Thankfully, there were others behind them waiting their turn, so they did not need to linger long.

Their litter had been sitting in the sun, and it was very warm inside the curtains. As they lurched into motion,

Tyrion reclined on an elbow while Sansa sat staring at her hands. *She is just as comely as the Tyrell girl.* Her hair was a rich autumn auburn, her eyes a deep Tully blue. Grief had given her a haunted, vulnerable look; if anything, it had only made her more beautiful. He wanted to reach her, to break through the armor of her courtesy. Was that what made him speak? Or just the need to distract himself from the fullness in his bladder?

"I had been thinking that when the roads are safe again, we might journey to Casterly Rock." *Far from Joffrey and my sister.* The more he thought about what Joff had done to *Lives of Four Kings,* the more it troubled him. *There was a message there, oh yes.* "It would please me to show you the Golden Gallery and the Lion's Mouth, and the Hall of Heroes where Jaime and I played as boys. You can hear thunder from below where the sea comes in . . ."

She raised her head slowly. He knew what she was seeing; the swollen brutish brow, the raw stump of his nose, his crooked pink scar and mismatched eyes. Her own eyes were big and blue and empty. "I shall go wherever my lord husband wishes."

"I had hoped it might please you, my lady."

"It will please me to please my lord."

His mouth tightened. *What a pathetic little man you are. Did you think babbling about the Lion's Mouth would make her smile? When have you ever made a woman smile but with gold?* "No, it was a foolish notion. Only a Lannister can love the Rock."

"Yes, my lord. As you wish."

Tyrion could hear the commons shouting out King Joffrey's name. *In three years that cruel boy will be a man, ruling in his own right . . . and every dwarf with half his wits will be a long way from King's Landing.* Oldtown, perhaps. Or even the Free Cities. He had always had a yen to see the Titan of Braavos. *Perhaps that would please Sansa.* Gently, he spoke of Braavos, and met a wall of sullen courtesy as icy and unyielding as the Wall he had walked once in the north. It made him weary. Then and now.

They passed the rest of the journey in silence. After a while, Tyrion found himself hoping that Sansa would say something, anything, the merest word, but she never spoke. When the litter halted in the castle yard, he let one of the grooms help her down. "We will be expected at the feast an hour hence, my lady. I will join you shortly." He walked off stiff-legged. Across the yard, he could hear Margaery's breathless laugh as Joffrey swept her from the saddle. *The boy will be as tall and strong as Jaime one day,* he thought, *and I'll still be a dwarf beneath his feet. And one day he's like to make me even shorter . . .*

He found a privy and sighed gratefully as he relieved himself of the morning's wine. There were times when a piss felt near as good as a woman, and this was one. He wished he could relieve himself of his doubts and guilts half as easily.

Podrick Payne was waiting outside his chambers. "I laid out your new doublet. Not here. On your bed. In the bedchamber."

"Yes, that's where we keep the bed." Sansa would be in there, dressing for the feast. *Shae as well.* "Wine, Pod."

Tyrion drank it in his window seat, brooding over the chaos of the kitchens below. The sun had not yet touched the top of the castle wall, but he could smell breads baking and meats roasting. The guests would soon be pouring into the throne room, full of anticipation; this would be an evening of song and splendor, designed not only to unite Highgarden and Casterly Rock but to trumpet their power and wealth as a lesson to any who might still think to oppose Joffrey's rule.

But who would be mad enough to contest Joffrey's rule now, after what had befallen Stannis Baratheon and Robb Stark? There was still fighting in the riverlands, but everywhere the coils were tightening. Ser Gregor Clegane had crossed the Trident and seized the ruby ford, then captured Harrenhal almost effortlessly. Seagard had yielded to Black Walder Frey, Lord Randyll Tarly held Maidenpool, Duskendale, and the kingsroad. In the west, Ser Daven Lannister had linked up with Ser Forley Prester at the Golden Tooth for a march on Riverrun. Ser Ryman Frey was leading two thousand spears down from the Twins to join them. And Paxter Redwyne claimed his fleet would soon set sail from the Arbor, to begin the long voyage around Dorne and through the Stepstones. Stannis's Lyseni pirates would be outnumbered ten to one. The struggle that the maesters were calling the War of the Five Kings was all but at an end.

Mace Tyrell had been heard complaining that Lord Tywin had left no victories for him.

"My lord?" Pod was at his side. "Will you be changing? I laid out the doublet. On your bed. For the feast."

"Feast?" said Tyrion sourly. "What feast?"

"The wedding feast." Pod missed the sarcasm, of course. "King Joffrey and Lady Margaery. Queen Margaery, I mean."

Tyrion resolved to get very, very drunk tonight. "Very well, young Podrick, let us go make me festive."

Shae was helping Sansa with her hair when they entered the bedchamber. *Joy and grief*, he thought when he beheld them there together. *Laughter and tears*. Sansa wore a gown of silvery satin trimmed in vair, with dagged sleeves that almost touched the floor, lined in soft purple felt. Shae had arranged her hair artfully in a delicate silver net winking with dark purple gemstones. Tyrion had never seen her look more lovely, yet she wore sorrow on those long satin sleeves. "Lady Sansa," he told her, "you shall be the most beautiful woman in the hall tonight."

"My lord is too kind."

"My lady," said Shae wistfully. "Couldn't I come serve at table? I so want to see the pigeons fly out of the pie."

Sansa looked at her uncertainly. "The queen has chosen all the servers."

"And the hall will be too crowded." Tyrion had to bite back his annoyance. "There will be musicians strolling all through the castle, though, and tables in the outer ward with food and drink for all." He inspected his new doublet, crimson velvet with padded shoulders and puffed sleeves slashed to show the black satin underlining. *A handsome garment. All it wants is a handsome man to wear it.* "Come, Pod, help me into this."

He had another cup of wine as he dressed, then took his wife by the arm and escorted her from the Kitchen Keep to join the river of silk, satin, and velvet flowing toward the throne room. Some guests had gone inside to find their places on the benches. Others were milling in front of the doors, enjoying the unseasonable warmth of the afternoon. Tyrion led Sansa around the yard, to perform the necessary courtesies.

She is good at this, he thought, as he watched her tell Lord Gyles that his cough was sounding better, compliment Elinor Tyrell on her gown, and question Jalabhar Xho about wedding customs in the Summer Isles. His cousin Ser Lancel had been brought down by Ser Kevan, the first time he'd left his sickbed since the battle. *He looks ghastly.* Lancel's hair had turned white and brittle, and he was thin as a stick. Without his father beside him holding him up, he would surely have collapsed. Yet when Sansa praised his valor and said how good it was to see him getting strong again, both Lancel and Ser Kevan beamed. *She would have made Joffrey a good queen and a better wife if he'd had the sense to love her.* He wondered if his nephew was capable of loving anyone.

"You do look quite exquisite, child," Lady Olenna Tyrell told Sansa when she tottered up to them in a cloth-of-gold gown that must have weighed more than she did. "The wind has been at your hair, though." The little old woman reached up and fussed at the loose strands, tucking them back into place and straightening Sansa's hair net. "I was very sorry to hear about your losses," she said as she tugged and fiddled. "Your brother was a terrible traitor, I know, but if we start killing men at weddings they'll be even more frightened of marriage than they are presently. There, that's better." Lady Olenna smiled. "I am pleased to say I shall be leaving for Highgarden the day after next. I have had quite enough of this smelly city, thank you. Perhaps you would like to accompany me for a little visit, whilst the men are off having their war? I shall miss my Margaery so dreadfully, and all her lovely ladies. Your company would be such sweet solace."

"You are too kind, my lady," said Sansa, "but my place is with my lord husband."

Lady Olenna gave Tyrion a wrinkled, toothless smile. "Oh? Forgive a silly old woman, my lord, I did not mean to steal your lovely wife. I assumed you would be off leading a Lannister host against some wicked foe."

"A host of dragons and stags. The master of coin must remain at court to see that all the armies are paid for."

"To be sure. Dragons and stags, that's very clever. And dwarf's pennies as well. I have heard of these dwarf's pennies. No doubt collecting those is *such* a dreadful chore."

"I leave the collecting to others, my lady."

"Oh, do you? I would have thought you might want to tend to it yourself. We can't have the crown being cheated of its dwarf's pennies, now. Can we?"

"Gods forbid." Tyrion was beginning to wonder whether Lord Luthor Tyrell had ridden off that cliff intentionally. "If you will excuse us, Lady Olenna, it is time we were in our places."

"Myself as well. Seventy-seven courses, I daresay. Don't you find that a bit *excessive*, my lord? I shan't eat more than three or four bites myself, but you and I are very little, aren't we?" She patted Sansa's hair again and said, "Well, off with you, child, and try to be merrier. Now where have my guardsmen gone? Left, Right, where are you? Come help me to the dais."

Although evenfall was still an hour away, the throne room was already a blaze of light, with torches burning in every sconce. The guests stood along the tables as heralds called out the names and titles of the lords and ladies making their entrance. Pages in the royal livery escorted them down the broad central aisle. The gallery above was packed with musicians; drummers and pipers and fiddlers, strings and horns and skins.

Tyrion clutched Sansa's arm and made the walk with a heavy waddling stride. He could feel their eyes on him, picking at the fresh new scar that had left him even uglier than he had been before. *Let them look*, he thought as he hopped up onto his seat. *Let them stare and whisper until they've had their fill, I will not hide myself for their sake.* The Queen of Thorns followed them in, shuffling along with tiny little steps. Tyrion wondered which of them looked more absurd, him with Sansa or the wizened little woman between her seven-foot-tall twin guardsmen.

Joffrey and Margaery rode into the throne room on matched white chargers. Pages ran before them, scattering rose petals under their hooves. The king and queen had changed for the feast as well. Joffrey wore striped black-and-crimson breeches and a cloth-of-gold doublet with black satin sleeves and onyx studs. Margaery had exchanged the demure gown that she had worn in the sept for one much more revealing, a confection in pale green samite with a tight-laced bodice that bared her shoulders and the tops of her small breasts. Unbound, her soft brown hair tumbled over her white shoulders and down her back almost to her waist. Around her brows was a slim golden crown. Her smile was shy and sweet. *A lovely girl,* thought Tyrion, *and a kinder fate than my nephew deserves.*

The Kingsguard escorted them onto the dais, to the seats of honor beneath the shadow of the Iron Throne, draped for the occasion in long silk streamers of Baratheon gold, Lannister crimson, and Tyrell green. Cersei embraced Margaery and kissed her cheeks. Lord Tywin did the same, and then Lancel and Ser Kevan. Joffrey received loving kisses from the bride's father and his two new brothers, Loras and Garlan. No one seemed in any great rush to kiss Tyrion. When the king and queen had taken their seats, the High Septon rose to lead a prayer. *At least he does not drone as badly as the last one,* Tyrion consoled himself.

He and Sansa had been seated far to the king's right, beside Ser Garlan Tyrell and his wife, the Lady Leonette. A dozen others sat closer to Joffrey, which a pricklier man might have taken for a slight, given that he had been the King's Hand only a short time past. Tyrion would have been glad if there had been a hundred.

"Let the cups be filled!" Joffrey proclaimed, when the gods had been given their due. His cupbearer poured a whole flagon of dark Arbor red into the golden wedding chalice that Lord Tyrell had given him that morning. The king had to use both hands to lift it. *"To my wife the queen!"*

"Margaery!" the hall shouted back at him. *"Margaery! Margaery! To the queen!"* A thousand cups rang together, and the wedding feast was well and truly begun. Tyrion Lannister drank with the rest, emptying his cup on that first toast and signaling for it to be refilled as soon as he was seated again.

The first dish was a creamy soup of mushrooms and buttered snails, served in gilded bowls. Tyrion had scarcely touched the breakfast, and the wine had already gone to his head, so the food was welcome. He finished quickly. *One done, seventy-six to come. Seventy-seven dishes, while there are still starving children in this city, and men who would kill for a radish. They might not love the Tyrells half so well if they could see us now.*

Sansa tasted a spoonful of soup and pushed the bowl away. "Not to your liking, my lady?" Tyrion asked.

"There's to be so much, my lord. I have a little tummy." She fiddled nervously with her hair and looked down the table to where Joffrey sat with his Tyrell queen.

Does she wish it were her in Margaery's place? Tyrion frowned. *Even a child should have better sense.* He turned away, wanting distraction, but everywhere he looked were women, fair fine beautiful happy women who belonged to other men. Margaery, of course, smiling sweetly as she and Joffrey shared a drink from the great seven-sided wedding chalice. Her mother Lady Alerie, silver-haired and handsome, still proud beside Mace Tyrell. The queen's three young cousins, bright as birds. Lord Merryweather's dark-haired Myrish wife with her big black sultry eyes. Ellaria Sand among the Dornishmen (Cersei had placed them at their own table, just below the dais in a place of high honor but as far from the Tyrells as the width of the hall would allow), laughing at something the Red Viper had told her.

And there was one woman, sitting almost at the foot of the third table on the left . . . the wife of one of the Fossoways, he thought, and heavy with his child. Her delicate beauty was in no way diminished by her belly, nor was her pleasure in the food and frolics. Tyrion watched as her husband fed her morsels off his plate. They drank from the same cup, and would kiss often and unpredictably. Whenever they did, his hand would gently rest upon her stomach, a tender and protective gesture.

He wondered what Sansa would do if he leaned over and kissed her right now. *Flinch away, most likely.* Or be brave and suffer through it, as was her duty. *She is nothing if not dutiful, this wife of mine.* If he told her that he wished to have her maidenhead tonight, she would suffer that dutifully as well, and weep no more than she had to.

He called for more wine. By the time he got it, the second course was being served, a pastry coffyn filled with pork, pine nuts, and eggs. Sansa ate no more than a bite of hers, as the heralds were summoning the first of the seven singers.

Grey-bearded Hamish the Harper announced that he would perform "for the ears of gods and men, a song ne'er heard before in all the Seven Kingdoms." He called it "Lord Renly's Ride."

His fingers moved across the strings of the high harp, filling the throne room with sweet sound. *"From his throne of bones the Lord of Death looked down on the murdered lord,"* Hamish began, and went on to tell how Renly, repenting his attempt to usurp his nephew's crown, had defied the Lord of Death himself and crossed back to the land of the living to defend the realm against his brother.

And for this poor Symon wound up in a bowl of brown, Tyrion mused. Queen Margaery was teary-eyed by the end, when the shade of brave Lord Renly flew to Highgarden to steal one last look at his true love's face. "Renly Baratheon never repented of anything in his life," the Imp told Sansa, "but if I'm any judge, Hamish just won himself a gilded lute."

The Harper also gave them several more familiar songs. "A Rose of Gold" was for the Tyrells, no doubt, as "The Rains of Castamere" was meant to flatter his father. "Maiden, Mother, and Crone" delighted the High Septon, and "My Lady Wife" pleased all the little girls with romance in their hearts, and no doubt some little boys as well. Tyrion listened with half a ear, as he sampled sweet-corn fritters and hot oatbread baked with bits of date, apple, and orange, and gnawed on the rib of a wild boar.

Thereafter dishes and diversions succeeded one another in a staggering profusion, buoyed along upon a flood of wine and ale. Hamish left them, his place taken by a small-ish elderly bear who danced clumsily to pipe and drum while the wedding guests ate trout cooked in a crust of crushed almonds. Moon Boy mounted his stilts and strode around the tables in pursuit of Lord Tyrell's ludicrously fat fool Butterbumps, and the lords and ladies sampled roast herons and cheese-and-onion pies. A troupe of Pentoshi tumblers performed cartwheels and handstands, balanced platters on their bare feet, and stood upon each other's shoulders to form a pyramid. Their feats were accompanied by crabs boiled in fiery eastern spices, trenchers filled with chunks of chopped mutton stewed in almond milk with carrots, raisins, and onions, and fish tarts fresh from the ovens, served so hot they burned the fingers.

Then the heralds summoned another singer; Collio Quaynis of Tyrosh, who had a vermilion beard and an accent as ludicrous as Symon had promised. Collio began with his version of "The Dance of the Dragons," which was more properly a song for two singers, male and female. Tyrion suffered through it with a double helping of honey-ginger partridge and several cups of wine. A haunting ballad of two dying lovers amidst the Doom of Valyria might have pleased the hall more if Collio had not sung it in High Valyrian, which most of the guests could not speak. But "Bessa the Barmaid" won them back with its ribald lyrics. Peacocks were served in their plumage, roasted whole and stuffed with dates, while Collio summoned a drummer, bowed low before Lord Tywin, and launched into "The Rains of Castamere."

If I have to hear seven versions of that, I may go down to Flea Bottom and apologize to the stew. Tyrion turned to his wife. "So which did you prefer?"

Sansa blinked at him. "My lord?"

"The singers. Which did you prefer?"

"I . . . I'm sorry, my lord. I was not listening."

She was not eating, either. "Sansa, is aught amiss?" He spoke without thinking, and instantly felt the fool. *All her kin are slaughtered and she's wed to me, and I wonder what's amiss.*

"No, my lord." She looked away from him, and feigned an unconvincing interest in Moon Boy pelting Ser Dontos with dates.

Four master pyromancers conjured up beasts of living flame to tear at each other with fiery claws whilst the serving men ladeled out bowls of blandissory, a mixture of beef broth and boiled wine sweetened with honey and dotted with blanched almonds and chunks of capon. Then came some strolling pipers and clever dogs and sword swallowers, with buttered pease, chopped nuts, and slivers of swan poached in a sauce of saffron and peaches. ("Not swan again," Tyrion muttered, remembering his supper with his sister on the eve of battle.) A juggler kept a half-dozen swords and axes whirling through the air as skewers of blood sausage were brought sizzling to the tables, a juxtaposition that Tyrion thought passing clever, though not perhaps in the best of taste.

The heralds blew their trumpets. "To sing for the golden lute," one cried, "we give you Galyeon of Cuy."

Galyeon was a big barrel-chested man with a black beard, a bald head, and a thunderous voice that filled every corner of the throne room. He brought no fewer than six musicians to play for him. "Noble lords and ladies fair, I sing but one song for you this night," he announced. "It is the song of the Blackwater, and how a realm was saved." The drummer began a slow ominous beat.

"The dark lord brooded high in his tower," Galyeon began, *"in a castle as black as the night."*

"Black was his hair and black was his soul," the musicians chanted in unison. A flute came in.

"He feasted on bloodlust and envy, and filled his cup full up with spite," sang Galyeon. *"My brother once ruled seven kingdoms, he said to his harridan wife. I'll take what was his and make it all mine. Let his son feel the point of my knife."*

"A brave young boy with hair of gold," his players chanted, as a woodharp and a fiddle began to play.

"If I am ever Hand again, the first thing I'll do is hang all the singers," said Tyrion, too loudly.

Lady Leonette laughed lightly beside him, and Ser Garlan leaned over to say, "A valiant deed unsung is no less valiant."

"The dark lord assembled his legions, they gathered around him like crows. And thirsty for blood they boarded their ships . . ."

". . . and cut off poor Tyrion's nose," Tyrion finished.

Lady Leonette giggled. "Perhaps you should be a singer, my lord. You rhyme as well as this Galyeon."

"No, my lady," Ser Garlan said. "My lord of Lannister was made to do great deeds, not to sing of them. But for his chain and his wildfire, the foe would have been across the river. And if Tyrion's wildlings had not slain most of Lord Stannis's scouts, we would never have been able to take him unawares."

His words made Tyrion feel absurdly grateful, and helped to mollify him as Galyeon sang endless verses about the valor of the boy king and his mother, the golden queen.

"She never did that," Sansa blurted out suddenly.

"Never believe anything you hear in a song, my lady."
Tyrion summoned a serving man to refill their wine cups.

Soon it was full night outside the tall windows, and still
Galyeon sang on. His song had seventy-seven verses,
though it seemed more like a thousand. *One for every
guest in the hall.* Tyrion drank his way through the last
twenty or so, to help resist the urge to stuff mushrooms in
his ears. By the time the singer had taken his bows, some of
the guests were drunk enough to begin providing uninten-
tional entertainments of their own. Grand Maester Pycelle
fell asleep while dancers from the Summer Isles swirled
and spun in robes made of bright feathers and smoky silk.
Roundels of elk stuffed with ripe blue cheese were being
brought out when one of Lord Rowan's knights stabbed a
Dornishman. The gold cloaks dragged them both away, one
to a cell to rot and the other to get sewn up by Maester
Ballabar.

Tyrion was toying with a leche of brawn, spiced with
cinnamon, cloves, sugar, and almond milk, when King
Joffrey lurched suddenly to his feet. *"Bring on my royal
jousters!"* he shouted in a voice thick with wine, clapping
his hands together.

My nephew is drunker than I am, Tyrion thought as the
gold cloaks opened the great doors at the end of the hall.
From where he sat, he could only see the tops of two
striped lances as a pair of riders entered side by side. A
wave of laughter followed them down the center aisle toward the king. *They must be riding ponies,* he concluded . . . until they came into full view.

The jousters were a pair of dwarfs. One was mounted on
an ugly grey dog, long of leg and heavy of jaw. The other
rode an immense spotted sow. Painted wooden armor clattered and clacked as the little knights bounced up and
down in their saddles. Their shields were bigger than they
were, and they wrestled manfully with their lances as they
clomped along, swaying this way and that and eliciting
gusts of mirth. One knight was all in gold, with a black
stag painted on his shield; the other wore grey and white,
and bore a wolf device. Their mounts were barded likewise.

Tyrion glanced along the dais at all the laughing faces.
Joffrey was red and breathless, Tommen was hooting and
hopping up and down in his seat, Cersei was chuckling

politely, and even Lord Tywin looked mildly amused. Of all those at the high table, only Sansa Stark was not smiling. He could have loved her for that, but if truth be told the Stark girl's eyes were far away, as if she had not even seen the ludicrous riders loping toward her.

The dwarfs are not to blame, Tyrion decided. *When they are done, I shall compliment them and give them a fat purse of silver. And come the morrow, I will find whoever planned this little diversion and arrange for a different sort of thanks.*

When the dwarfs reined up beneath the dais to salute the king, the wolf knight dropped his shield. As he leaned over to grab for it, the stag knight lost control of his heavy lance and slammed him across the back. The wolf knight fell off his pig, and his lance tumbled over and boinked his foe on the head. They both wound up on the floor in a great tangle. When they rose, both tried to mount the dog. Much shouting and shoving followed. Finally they regained their saddles, only mounted on each other's steed, holding the wrong shield and facing backward.

It took some time to sort that out, but in the end they spurred to opposite ends of the hall, and wheeled about for the tilt. As the lords and ladies guffawed and giggled, the little men came together with a crash and a clatter, and the wolf knight's lance struck the helm of the stag knight and knocked his head clean off. It spun through the air spattering blood to land in the lap of Lord Gyles. The headless dwarf careened around the tables, flailing his arms. Dogs barked, women shrieked, and Moon Boy made a great show of swaying perilously back and forth on his stilts, until Lord Gyles pulled a dripping red melon out of the shattered helm, at which point the stag knight poked his face up out of his armor, and another storm of laughter rocked the hall. The knights waited for it to die, circled around each other trading colorful insults, and were about to separate for another joust when the dog threw its rider to the floor and mounted the sow. The huge pig squealed in distress, while the wedding guests squealed with laughter, especially when the stag knight leapt onto the wolf knight, let down his wooden breeches, and started to pump away frantically at the other's nether portions.

"I yield, I yield," the dwarf on the bottom screamed. "Good ser, put up your sword!"

"I would, I would, if you'll stop moving the sheath!" the dwarf on the top replied, to the merriment of all.

Joffrey was snorting wine from both nostrils. Gasping, he lurched to his feet, almost knocking over his tall two-handed chalice. "A champion," he shouted. "We have a champion!" The hall began to quiet when it was seen that the king was speaking. The dwarfs untangled, no doubt anticipating the royal thanks. "Not a *true* champion, though," said Joff. "A true champion defeats *all* challengers." The king climbed up on the table. "Who else will challenge our tiny champion?" With a gleeful smile, he turned toward Tyrion. "*Uncle!* You'll defend the honor of my realm, won't you? You can ride the pig!"

The laughter crashed over him like a wave. Tyrion Lannister did not remember rising, nor climbing on his chair, but he found himself standing on the table. The hall was a torchlit blur of leering faces. He twisted his face into the most hideous mockery of a smile the Seven Kingdoms had ever seen. "Your Grace," he called, "I'll ride the pig . . . but only if you ride the dog!"

Joff scowled, confused. "Me? I'm no dwarf. Why me?"

Stepped right into the cut, Joff. "Why, you're the only man in the hall that I'm certain of defeating!"

He could not have said which was sweeter; the instant of shocked silence, the gale of laughter that followed, or the look of blind rage on his nephew's face. The dwarf hopped back to the floor well satisfied, and by the time he looked back Ser Osmund and Ser Meryn were helping Joff climb down as well. When he noticed Cersei glaring at him, Tyrion blew her a kiss.

It was a relief when the musicians began to play. The tiny jousters led dog and sow from the hall, the guests returned to their trenchers of brawn, and Tyrion called for another cup of wine. But suddenly he felt Ser Garlan's hand on his sleeve. "My lord, beware," the knight warned. "The king."

Tyrion turned in his seat. Joffrey was almost upon him, red-faced and staggering, wine slopping over the rim of the great golden wedding chalice he carried in both hands. "Your Grace," was all he had time to say before the king upended the chalice over his head. The wine washed down over his face in a red torrent. It drenched his hair, stung his eyes, burned in his wound, ran down his cheeks, and soaked the velvet of his new doublet. "How do you like that, Imp?" Joffrey mocked.

Tyrion's eyes were on fire. He dabbed at his face with the back of a sleeve and tried to blink the world back into clarity. "That was ill done, Your Grace," he heard Ser Garlan say quietly.

"Not at all, Ser Garlan." Tyrion dare not let this grow any uglier than it was, not here, with half the realm looking on. "Not every king would think to honor a humble subject by serving him from his own royal chalice. A pity the wine spilled."

"It didn't *spill*," said Joffrey, too graceless to take the retreat Tyrion offered him. "And I wasn't *serving* you, either."

Queen Margaery appeared suddenly at Joffrey's elbow. "My sweet king," the Tyrell girl entreated, "come, return to your place, there's another singer waiting."

"Alaric of Eysen," said Lady Olenna Tyrell, leaning on her cane and taking no more notice of the wine-soaked dwarf than her granddaughter had done. "I do so hope he plays us 'The Rains of Castamere.' It has been an hour, I've forgotten how it goes."

"Ser Addam has a toast he wants to make as well," said Margaery. "Your Grace, please."

"I have no wine," Joffrey declared. "How can I drink a toast if I have no wine? Uncle Imp, you can serve me. Since you won't joust you'll be my cupbearer."

"I would be most honored."

"*It's not meant to be an honor!*" Joffrey screamed. "Bend down and pick up my chalice." Tyrion did as he was bid, but as he reached for the handle Joff kicked the chalice through his legs. "Pick it *up!* Are you as clumsy as you are ugly?" He had to crawl under the table to find the thing. "Good, now fill it with wine." He claimed a flagon from a serving girl and filled the goblet three-quarters full. "No, on your knees, dwarf." Kneeling, Tyrion raised up the heavy cup, wondering if he was about to get a second bath. But Joffrey took the wedding chalice one-handed, drank deep, and set it on the table. "You can get up now, Uncle."

His legs cramped as he tried to rise, and almost spilled him again. Tyrion had to grab hold of a chair to steady himself. Ser Garlan lent him a hand. Joffrey laughed, and Cersei as well. Then others. He could not see who, but he heard them.

"Your Grace." Lord Tywin's voice was impeccably correct. "They are bringing in the pie. Your sword is needed."

"The pie?" Joffrey took his queen by the hand. "Come, my lady, it's the pie."

The guests stood, shouting and applauding and smashing their wine cups together as the great pie made its slow way down the length of the hall, wheeled along by a half-dozen beaming cooks. Two yards across it was, crusty and golden brown, and they could hear squeaks and thumpings coming from inside it.

Tyrion pulled himself back into his chair. All he needed now was for a dove to shit on him and his day would be complete. The wine had soaked through his doublet and smallclothes, and he could feel the wetness against his skin. He ought to change, but no one was permitted to leave the feast until the time came for the bedding ceremony. That was still a good twenty or thirty dishes off, he judged.

King Joffrey and his queen met the pie below the dais. As Joff drew his sword, Margaery laid a hand on his arm to restrain him. "Widow's Wail was not meant for slicing pies."

"True." Joffrey lifted his voice. "Ser Ilyn, your sword!"

From the shadows at the back of the hall, Ser Ilyn Payne appeared. *The specter at the feast*, thought Tyrion as he watched the King's Justice stride forward, gaunt and grim. He had been too young to have known Ser Ilyn before he'd lost his tongue. *He would have been a different man in those days, but now the silence is as much a part of him as those hollow eyes, that rusty chainmail shirt, and the greatsword on his back.*

Ser Ilyn bowed before the king and queen, reached back over his shoulder, and drew forth six feet of ornate silver bright with runes. He knelt to offer the huge blade to Joffrey, hilt first; points of red fire winked from ruby eyes on the pommel, a chunk of dragonglass carved in the shape of a grinning skull.

Sansa stirred in her seat. "What sword is that?"

Tyrion's eyes still stung from the wine. He blinked and looked again. Ser Ilyn's greatsword was as long and wide as Ice, but it was too silvery-bright; Valyrian steel had a darkness to it, a smokiness in its soul. Sansa clutched his arm. "What has Ser Ilyn done with my father's sword?"

I should have sent Ice back to Robb Stark, Tyrion thought. He glanced at his father, but Lord Tywin was watching the king.

Joffrey and Margaery joined hands to lift the greatsword and swung it down together in a silvery arc. When the piecrust broke, the doves burst forth in a swirl of white feathers, scattering in every direction, flapping for the windows and the rafters. A roar of delight went up from the benches, and the fiddlers and pipers in the gallery began to play a sprightly tune. Joff took his bride in his arms, and whirled her around merrily.

A serving man placed a slice of hot pigeon pie in front of Tyrion and covered it with a spoon of lemon cream. The pigeons were well and truly cooked in *this* pie, but he found them no more appetizing than the white ones fluttering about the hall. Sansa was not eating either. "You're deathly pale, my lady," Tyrion said. "You need a breath of cool air, and I need a fresh doublet." He stood and offered her his hand. "Come."

But before they could make their retreat, Joffrey was back. "Uncle, where are you going? You're my cupbearer, remember?"

"I need to change into fresh garb, Your Grace. May I have your leave?"

"No. I like the look of you this way. Serve me my wine."

The king's chalice was on the table where he'd left it. Tyrion had to climb back onto his chair to reach it. Joff yanked it from his hands and drank long and deep, his throat working as the wine ran purple down his chin. "My lord," Margaery said, "we should return to our places. Lord Buckler wants to toast us."

"My uncle hasn't eaten his pigeon pie." Holding the chalice one-handed, Joff jammed his other into Tyrion's pie. "It's ill luck not to eat the pie," he scolded as he filled his mouth with hot spiced pigeon. "See, it's good." Spitting

out flakes of crust, he coughed and helped himself to another fistful. "Dry, though. Needs washing down." Joff
took a swallow of wine and coughed again, more violently.
"I want to see, *kof*, see you ride that, *kof kof*, pig, Uncle. I
want . . ." His words broke up in a fit of coughing.

Margaery looked at him with concern. "Your Grace?"

"It's, *kof*, the pie, noth—*kof*, pie." Joff took another
drink, or tried to, but all the wine came spewing back out
when another spate of coughing doubled him over. His face
was turning red. "I, *kof*, I can't, *kof kof kof kof* . . ." The
chalice slipped from his hand and dark red wine went running across the dais.

"He's choking," Queen Margaery gasped.

Her grandmother moved to her side. "Help the poor
boy!" the Queen of Thorns screeched, in a voice ten times
her size. "*Dolts!* Will you all stand about gaping? *Help* your
king!"

Ser Garlan shoved Tyrion aside and began to pound
Joffrey on the back. Ser Osmund Kettleblack ripped open
the king's collar. A fearful high thin sound emerged from
the boy's throat, the sound of a man trying to suck a river
through a reed; then it stopped, and that was more terrible
still. "Turn him over!" Mace Tyrell bellowed at everyone
and no one. "Turn him over, shake him by his heels!" A
different voice was calling, "Water, give him some *water!*"
The High Septon began to pray loudly. Grand Maester
Pycelle shouted for someone to help him back to his chambers, to fetch his potions. Joffrey began to claw at his
throat, his nails tearing bloody gouges in the flesh. Beneath
the skin, the muscles stood out hard as stone. Prince
Tommen was screaming and crying.

He is going to die, Tyrion realized. He felt curiously
calm, though pandemonium raged all about him. They
were pounding Joff on the back again, but his face was only
growing darker. Dogs were barking, children were wailing,
men were shouting useless advice at each other. Half the
wedding guests were on their feet, some shoving at each
other for a better view, others rushing for the doors in their
haste to get away.

Ser Meryn pried the king's mouth open to jam a spoon
down his throat. As he did, the boy's eyes met Tyrion's. *He
has Jaime's eyes.* Only he had never seen Jaime look so

scared. *The boy's only thirteen.* Joffrey was making a dry clacking noise, trying to speak. His eyes bulged white with terror, and he lifted a hand . . . reaching for his uncle, or pointing . . . *Is he begging my forgiveness, or does he think I can save him?* "Noooo," Cersei wailed, "Father help him, someone help him, my son, my *son* . . ."

Tyrion found himself thinking of Robb Stark. *My own wedding is looking much better in hindsight.* He looked to see how Sansa was taking this, but there was so much confusion in the hall that he could not find her. But his eyes fell on the wedding chalice, forgotten on the floor. He went and scooped it up. There was still a half-inch of deep purple wine in the bottom of it. Tyrion considered it a moment, then poured it on the floor.

Margaery Tyrell was weeping in her grandmother's arms as the old lady said, "Be brave, be brave." Most of the musicians had fled, but one last flutist in the gallery was blowing a dirge. In the rear of the throne room scuffling had broken out around the doors, and the guests were trampling on each other. Ser Addam's gold cloaks moved in to restore order. Guests were rushing headlong out into the night, some weeping, some stumbling and retching, others white with fear. It occurred to Tyrion belatedly that it might be wise to leave himself.

When he heard Cersei's scream, he knew that it was over.

I should leave. Now. Instead he waddled toward her.

His sister sat in a puddle of wine, cradling her son's body. Her gown was torn and stained, her face white as chalk. A thin black dog crept up beside her, sniffing at Joffrey's corpse. "The boy is gone, Cersei," Lord Tywin said. He put his gloved hand on his daughter's shoulder as one of his guardsmen shooed away the dog. "Unhand him now. Let him go." She did not hear. It took two Kingsguard to pry loose her fingers, so the body of King Joffrey Baratheon could slide limp and lifeless to the floor.

The High Septon knelt beside him. "Father Above, judge our good King Joffrey justly," he intoned, beginning the prayer for the dead. Margaery Tyrell began to sob, and Tyrion heard her mother Lady Alerie saying, "He choked, sweetling. He choked on the pie. It was naught to do with you. He choked. We all saw."

"He did not choke." Cersei's voice was sharp as Ser Ilyn's sword. "My son was poisoned." She looked to the white knights standing helplessly around her. "Kingsguard, do your duty."

"My lady?" said Ser Loras Tyrell, uncertain.

"Arrest my brother," she commanded him. "He did this, the dwarf. Him and his little wife. They killed my son. Your king. *Take them!* Take them both!"

SANSA

Far across the city, a bell began to toll.

Sansa felt as though she were in a dream. "Joffrey is dead," she told the trees, to see if that would wake her.

He had not been dead when she left the throne room. He had been on his knees, though, clawing at his throat, tearing at his own skin as he fought to breathe. The sight of it had been too terrible to watch, and she had turned and fled, sobbing. Lady Tanda had been fleeing as well. "You have a good heart, my lady," she said to Sansa. "Not every maid would weep so for a man who set her aside and wed her to a dwarf."

A good heart. I have a good heart. Hysterical laughter rose up her gullet, but Sansa choked it back down. The bells were ringing, slow and mournful. Ringing, ringing, ringing. They had rung for King Robert the same way. Joffrey was dead, he was dead, he was dead, dead, dead. Why was she crying, when she wanted to dance? Were they tears of joy?

She found her clothes where she had hidden them, the

night before last. With no maids to help her, it took her longer than it should have to undo the laces of her gown. Her hands were strangely clumsy, though she was not as frightened as she ought to have been. "The gods are cruel to take him so young and handsome, at his own wedding feast," Lady Tanda had said to her.

The gods are just, thought Sansa. Robb had died at a wedding feast as well. It was Robb she wept for. *Him and Margaery.* Poor Margaery, twice wed and twice widowed. Sansa slid her arm from a sleeve, pushed down the gown, and wriggled out of it. She balled it up and shoved it into the bole of an oak, shook out the clothing she had hidden there. *Dress warmly,* Ser Dontos had told her, *and dress dark.* She had no blacks, so she chose a dress of thick brown wool. The bodice was decorated with freshwater pearls, though. *The cloak will cover them.* The cloak was a deep green, with a large hood. She slipped the dress over her head, and donned the cloak, though she left the hood down for the moment. There were shoes as well, simple and sturdy, with flat heels and square toes. *The gods heard my prayer,* she thought. She felt so numb and dreamy. *My skin has turned to porcelain, to ivory, to steel.* Her hands moved stiffly, awkwardly, as if they had never let down her hair before. For a moment she wished Shae was there, to help her with the net.

When she pulled it free, her long auburn hair cascaded down her back and across her shoulders. The web of spun silver hung from her fingers, the fine metal glimmering softly, the stones black in the moonlight. *Black amethysts from Asshai.* One of them was missing. Sansa lifted the net for a closer look. There was a dark smudge in the silver socket where the stone had fallen out.

A sudden terror filled her. Her heart hammered against her ribs, and for an instant she held her breath. *Why am I so scared, it's only an amethyst, a black amethyst from Asshai, no more than that. It must have been loose in the setting, that's all. It was loose and it fell out, and now it's lying somewhere in the throne room, or in the yard, unless . . .*

Ser Dontos had said the hair net was magic, that it would take her home. He told her she must wear it tonight at Joffrey's wedding feast. The silver wire stretched tight across her knuckles. Her thumb rubbed back and forth against the hole where the stone had been. She tried to stop, but her fingers were not her own. Her thumb was drawn to the hole as the tongue is drawn to a missing tooth. *What kind of magic?* The king was dead, the cruel king who had been her gallant prince a thousand years ago. If Dontos had lied about the hair net, had he lied about the rest as well? *What if he never comes? What if there is no ship, no boat on the river, no escape?* What would happen to her then?

She heard a faint rustle of leaves, and stuffed the silver hair net down deep in the pocket of her cloak. "Who's there?" she cried. "Who is it?" The godswood was dim and dark, and the bells were ringing Joff into his grave.

"Me." He staggered out from under the trees, reeling drunk. He caught her arm to steady himself. "Sweet Jonquil, I've come. Your Florian has come, don't be afraid."

Sansa pulled away from his touch. "You said I must wear the hair net. The silver net with . . . what sort of stones are those?"

"Amethysts. Black amethysts from Asshai, my lady."

"They're no amethysts. Are they? *Are they?* You lied."

"Black amethysts," he swore. "There was magic in them."

"There was *murder* in them!"

"Softly, my lady, softly. No murder. He choked on his pigeon pie." Dontos chortled. "Oh, tasty tasty pie. Silver and stones, that's all it was, silver and stone and magic."

The bells were tolling, and the wind was making a noise like *he* had made as he tried to suck a breath of air. "You poisoned him. You did. You took a stone from my hair . . ."

"Hush, you'll be the death of us. I did nothing. Come, we must away, they'll search for you. Your husband's been arrested."

"Tyrion?" she said, shocked.

"Do you have another husband? The Imp, the dwarf uncle, she thinks he did it." He grabbed her hand and pulled at her. "This way, we must away, quickly now, have no fear."

Sansa followed unresisting. *I could never abide the weeping of women*, Joff once said, but his mother was the only woman weeping now. In Old Nan's stories the grumkins crafted magic things that could make a wish come true. *Did I wish him dead?* she wondered, before she remembered that she was too old to believe in grumkins. "*Tyrion* poisoned him?" Her dwarf husband had hated his nephew, she knew. Could he truly have killed him? *Did he know about my hair net, about the black amethysts? He brought Joff wine.* How could you make someone choke by putting an amethyst in their wine? *If Tyrion did it, they will think I was part of it as well*, she realized with a start of fear. How not? They were man and wife, and Joff had killed her father and mocked her with her brother's death. *One flesh, one heart, one soul.*

"Be quiet now, my sweetling," said Dontos. "Outside the godswood, we must make no sound. Pull up your hood and hide your face." Sansa nodded, and did as he said.

He was so drunk that sometimes Sansa had to lend him her arm to keep him from falling. The bells were ringing out across the city, more and more of them joining in. She kept her head down and stayed in the shadows, close behind Dontos. While descending the serpentine steps he stumbled to his knees and retched. *My poor Florian*, she thought, as he wiped his mouth with a floppy sleeve. *Dress dark*, he'd said, yet under his brown hooded cloak he was wearing his old surcoat; red and pink horizontal stripes beneath a black chief bearing three gold crowns, the arms of House Hollard. "Why are you wearing your surcoat? Joff decreed it was death if you were caught dressed as a knight again, he . . . oh . . ." Nothing Joff had decreed mattered any longer.

"I wanted to be a knight. For this, at least." Dontos lurched back to his feet and took her arm. "Come. Be quiet now, no questions."

They continued down the serpentine and across a small sunken courtyard. Ser Dontos shoved open a heavy door and lit a taper. They were inside a long gallery. Along the walls stood empty suits of armor, dark and dusty, their helms crested with rows of scales that continued down their backs. As they hurried past, the taper's light made the shadows of each scale stretch and twist. *The hollow knights are turning into dragons*, she thought.

One more stair took them to an oaken door banded with iron. "Be strong now, my Jonquil, you are almost there."

When Dontos lifted the bar and pulled open the door, Sansa felt a cold breeze on her face. She passed through twelve feet of wall, and then she was outside the castle, standing at the top of the cliff. Below was the river, above the sky, and one was as black as the other.

"We must climb down," Ser Dontos said. "At the bottom, a man is waiting to row us out to the ship."

"I'll fall." Bran had fallen, and he had loved to climb.

"No you won't. There's a sort of ladder, a secret ladder, carved into the stone. Here, you can feel it, my lady." He got down on his knees with her and made her lean over the edge of the cliff, groping with her fingers until she found the handhold cut into the face of the bluff. "Almost as good as rungs."

Even so, it was a long way down. "I *can't.*"

"You must."

"Isn't there another way?"

"This is the way. It won't be so hard for a strong young girl like you. Hold on tight and never look down and you'll be at the bottom in no time at all." His eyes were shiny. "Your poor Florian is fat and old and drunk, I'm the one should be afraid. I used to fall off my horse, don't you remember? That was how we began. I was drunk and fell off my horse and Joffrey wanted my fool head, but you saved me. You *saved* me, sweetling."

He's weeping, she realized. "And now you have saved me."

"Only if you go. If not, I have killed us both."

It was him, she thought. *He killed Joffrey.* She had to go, for him as much as for herself. "You go first, ser." If he *did* fall, she did not want him falling down on her head and knocking both of them off the cliff.

"As you wish, my lady." He gave her a sloppy kiss and swung his legs clumsily over the precipice, kicking about until he found a foothold. "Let me get down a bit, and come after. You will come now? You must swear it."

"I'll come," she promised.

Ser Dontos disappeared. She could hear him huffing and puffing as he began the descent. Sansa listened to the tolling of the bell, counting each ring. At ten, gingerly, she eased herself over the edge of the cliff, poking with her toes until they found a place to rest. The castle walls loomed large above her, and for a moment she wanted nothing so much as to pull herself up and run back to her warm rooms in the Kitchen Keep. *Be brave*, she told herself. *Be brave, like a lady in a song.*

Sansa dared not look down. She kept her eyes on the face of the cliff, making certain of each step before reaching for the next. The stone was rough and cold. Sometimes she could feel her fingers slipping, and the handholds were not as evenly spaced as she would have liked. The bells would not stop ringing. Before she was halfway down her arms were trembling and she knew that she was going to fall. *One more step*, she told herself, *one more step.* She had to keep moving. If she stopped, she would never start again, and dawn would find her still clinging to the cliff, frozen in fear. *One more step, and one more step.*

The ground took her by surprise. She stumbled and fell, her heart pounding. When she rolled onto her back and stared up at from where she had come, her head swam dizzily and her fingers clawed at the dirt. *I did it. I did it, I didn't fall, I made the climb and now I'm going home.*

Ser Dontos pulled her back onto her feet. "This way. Quiet now, quiet, quiet." He stayed close to the shadows that lay black and thick beneath the cliffs. Thankfully they did not have to go far. Fifty yards downriver, a man sat in a small skiff, half-hidden by the remains of a great galley that had gone aground there and burned. Dontos limped up to him, puffing. "Oswell?"

"No names," the man said. "In the boat." He sat hunched over his oars, an old man, tall and gangling, with long white hair and a great hooked nose, with eyes shaded by a cowl. "Get in, be quick about it," he muttered. "We need to be away."

When both of them were safe aboard, the cowled man slid the blades into the water and put his back into the oars, rowing them out toward the channel. Behind them the bells were still tolling the boy king's death. They had the dark river all to themselves.

With slow, steady, rhythmic strokes, they threaded their way downstream, sliding above the sunken galleys, past broken masts, burned hulls, and torn sails. The oarlocks had been muffled, so they moved almost soundlessly. A mist was rising over the water. Sansa saw the embattled ramparts of one of the Imp's winch towers looming above, but the great chain had been lowered, and they rowed unimpeded past the spot where a thousand men had burned. The shore fell away, the fog grew thicker, the sound of the bells began to fade. Finally even the lights were gone, lost somewhere behind them. They were out in Blackwater Bay, and the world shrank to dark water, blowing mist, and their silent companion stooped over the oars. "How far must we go?" she asked.

"No talk." The oarsman was old, but stronger than he looked, and his voice was fierce. There was something oddly familiar about his face, though Sansa could not say what it was.

"Not far." Ser Dontos took her hand in his own and rubbed it gently. "Your friend is near, waiting for you."

"*No talk!*" the oarsman growled again. "Sound carries over water, Ser Fool."

Abashed, Sansa bit her lip and huddled down in silence. The rest was rowing, rowing, rowing.

The eastern sky was vague with the first hint of dawn when Sansa finally saw a ghostly shape in the darkness ahead; a trading galley, her sails furled, moving slowly on a single bank of oars. As they drew closer, she saw the ship's figurehead, a merman with a golden crown blowing on a great seashell horn. She heard a voice cry out, and the galley swung slowly about.

As they came alongside, the galley dropped a rope ladder over the rail. The rower shipped the oars and helped Sansa to her feet. "Up now. Go on, girl, I got you." Sansa thanked him for his kindness, but received no answer but a grunt. It was much easier going up the rope ladder than it had been coming down the cliff. The oarsman Oswell followed close behind her, while Ser Dontos remained in the boat.

Two sailors were waiting by the rail to help her onto the deck. Sansa was trembling. "She's cold," she heard someone say. He took off his cloak and put it around her shoulders. "There, is that better, my lady? Rest easy, the worst is past and done."

She knew the voice. *But he's in the Vale,* she thought. Ser Lothor Brune stood beside him with a torch.

"Lord Petyr," Dontos called from the boat. "I must needs row back, before they think to look for me."

Petyr Baelish put a hand on the rail. "But first you'll want your payment. Ten thousand dragons, was it?"

"Ten thousand." Dontos rubbed his mouth with the back of his hand. "As you promised, my lord."

"Ser Lothor, the reward."

Lothor Brune dipped his torch. Three men stepped to the gunwale, raised crossbows, fired. One bolt took Dontos in the chest as he looked up, punching through the left crown on his surcoat. The others ripped into throat and belly. It happened so quickly neither Dontos nor Sansa had time to cry out. When it was done, Lothor Brune tossed the torch down on top of the corpse. The little boat was blazing fiercely as the galley moved away.

"You *killed* him." Clutching the rail, Sansa turned away and retched. Had she escaped the Lannisters to tumble into worse?

"My lady," Littlefinger murmured, "your grief is wasted on such a man as that. He was a sot, and no man's friend."

"But he *saved* me."

"He sold you for a promise of ten thousand dragons. Your disappearance will make them suspect you in Joffrey's death. The gold cloaks will hunt, and the eunuch will jingle his purse. Dontos . . . well, you heard him. He sold you for gold, and when he'd drunk it up he would have sold you again. A bag of dragons buys a man's silence for a while, but a well-placed quarrel buys it forever." He smiled sadly. "All he did he did at my behest. I dared not befriend you openly. When I heard how you saved his life at Joff's tourney, I knew he would be the perfect catspaw."

Sansa felt sick. "He said he was my Florian."

"Do you perchance recall what I said to you that day your father sat the Iron Throne?"

The moment came back to her vividly. "You told me that life was not a song. That I would learn that one day, to my sorrow." She felt tears in her eyes, but whether she wept for Ser Dontos Hollard, for Joff, for Tyrion, or for herself, Sansa could not say. "Is it *all* lies, forever and ever, everyone and everything?"

"Almost everyone. Save you and I, of course." He smiled. "*Come to the godswood tonight if you want to go home.*"

"The note . . . it was you?"

"It had to be the godswood. No other place in the Red Keep is safe from the eunuch's little birds . . . or little rats, as I call them. There are trees in the godswood instead of walls. Sky above instead of ceiling. Roots and dirt and rock in place of floor. The rats have no place to scurry. Rats need to hide, lest men skewer them with swords." Lord Petyr took her arm. "Let me show you to your cabin. You have had a long and trying day, I know. You must be weary."

Already the little boat was no more than a swirl of smoke and fire behind them, almost lost in the immensity of the dawn sea. There was no going back; her only road was forward. "Very weary," she admitted.

As he led her below, he said, "Tell me of the feast. The queen took such pains. The singers, the jugglers, the dancing bear . . . did your little lord husband enjoy my jousting dwarfs?"

"Yours?"

"I had to send to Braavos for them and hide them away in a brothel until the wedding. The expense was exceeded only by the bother. It is surprisingly difficult to hide a dwarf, and Joffrey . . . you can lead a king to water, but with Joff one had to splash it about before he realized he could drink it. When I told him about my little surprise, His Grace said, 'Why would I want some ugly dwarfs at my feast? I hate dwarfs.' I had to take him by the shoulder and whisper, 'Not as much as your uncle will.' "

The deck rocked beneath her feet, and Sansa felt as if the world itself had grown unsteady. "They think Tyrion poisoned Joffrey. Ser Dontos said they seized him."

Littlefinger smiled. "Widowhood will become you, Sansa."

The thought made her tummy flutter. She might never need to share a bed with Tyrion again. That *was* what she'd wanted . . . wasn't it?

The cabin was low and cramped, but a featherbed had been laid upon the narrow sleeping shelf to make it more comfortable, and thick furs piled atop it. "It will be snug, I know, but you shouldn't be too uncomfortable." Littlefinger pointed out a cedar chest under the porthole. "You'll find fresh garb within. Dresses, smallclothes, warm stockings, a cloak. Wool and linen only, I fear. Unworthy of a maid so beautiful, but they'll serve to keep you dry and clean until we can find you something finer."

He had this all prepared for me. "My lord, I . . . I do not understand . . . Joffrey gave you Harrenhal, made you Lord Paramount of the Trident . . . why . . ."

"Why should I wish him dead?" Littlefinger shrugged. "I had no motive. Besides, I am a thousand leagues away in the Vale. Always keep your foes confused. If they are never certain who you are or what you want, they cannot know what you are like to do next. Sometimes the best way to baffle them is to make moves that have no purpose, or even seem to work against you. Remember that, Sansa, when you come to play the game."

"What . . . what game?"

"The only game. The game of thrones." He brushed back a strand of her hair. "You are old enough to know that your mother and I were more than friends. There was a time when Cat was all I wanted in this world. I dared to dream of the life we might make and the children she would give me . . . but she was a daughter of Riverrun, and Hoster Tully. *Family, Duty, Honor*, Sansa. *Family, Duty, Honor* meant I could never have her hand. But she gave me something finer, a gift a woman can give but once. How could I turn my back upon her daughter? In a better world, you might have been mine, not Eddard Stark's. My loyal loving daughter . . . Put Joffrey from your mind, sweetling. Dontos, Tyrion, all of them. They will never trouble you again. You are safe now, that's all that matters. You are safe with me, and sailing home."

JAIME

The king is dead, they told him, never knowing that Joffrey was his son as well as his sovereign.

"The Imp opened his throat with a dagger," a costermonger declared at the roadside inn where they spent the night. "He drank his blood from a big gold chalice." The man did not recognize the bearded one-handed knight with the big bat on his shield, no more than any of them, so he said things he might otherwise have swallowed, had he known who was listening.

"It was poison did the deed," the innkeep insisted. "The boy's face turned black as a plum."

"May the Father judge him justly," murmured a septon.

"The dwarf's wife did the murder with him," swore an archer in Lord Rowan's livery. "Afterward, she vanished from the hall in a puff of brimstone, and a ghostly direwolf was seen prowling the Red Keep, blood dripping from his jaws."

Jaime sat silent through it all, letting the words wash over him, a horn of ale forgotten in his one good hand. *Joffrey. My blood. My firstborn. My son.* He tried to bring the boy's face to mind, but his features kept turning into Cersei's. *She will be in mourning, her hair in disarray and her eyes red from crying, her mouth trembling as she tries to speak. She will cry again when she sees me, though she'll fight the tears.* His sister seldom wept but when she was with him. She could not stand for others to think her weak. Only to her twin did she show her wounds. *She will look to me for comfort and revenge.*

They rode hard the next day, at Jaime's insistence. His son was dead, and his sister needed him.

When he saw the city before him, its watchtowers dark against the gathering dusk, Jaime Lannister cantered up to Steelshanks Walton, behind Nage with the peace banner.

"What's that awful stink?" the northman complained.

Death, thought Jaime, but he said, "Smoke, sweat, and shit. King's Landing, in short. If you have a good nose you can smell the treachery too. You've never smelled a city before?"

"I smelled White Harbor. It never stank like this."

"White Harbor is to King's Landing as my brother Tyrion is to Ser Gregor Clegane."

Nage led them up a low hill, the seven-tailed peace banner lifting and turning in the wind, the polished seven-pointed star shining bright upon its staff. He would see Cersei soon, and Tyrion, and their father. *Could my brother truly have killed the boy?* Jaime found that hard to believe.

He was curiously calm. Men were supposed to go mad with grief when their children died, he knew. They were supposed to tear their hair out by the roots, to curse the gods and swear red vengeance. So why was it that he felt so little? *The boy lived and died believing Robert Baratheon his sire.*

Jaime had seen him born, that was true, though more for Cersei than the child. But he had never held him. "How would it look?" his sister warned him when the women finally left them. "Bad enough Joff looks like you without you mooning over him." Jaime yielded with hardly a fight. The boy had been a squalling pink thing who demanded too much of Cersei's time, Cersei's love, and Cersei's breasts. Robert was welcome to him.

And now he's dead. He pictured Joff lying still and cold

with a face black from poison, and still felt nothing. Perhaps he *was* the monster they claimed. If the Father Above came down to offer him back his son or his hand, Jaime knew which he would choose. He had a second son, after all, and seed enough for many more. *If Cersei wants another child I'll give her one . . . and this time I'll hold him, and the Others take those who do not like it.* Robert was rotting in his grave, and Jaime was sick of lies.

He turned abruptly and galloped back to find Brienne. *Gods know why I bother. She is the least companionable creature I've ever had the misfortune to meet.* The wench rode well behind and a few feet off to the side, as if to proclaim that she was no part of them. They had found men's garb for her along the way; a tunic here, a mantle there, a pair of breeches and a cowled cloak, even an old iron breastplate. She looked more comfortable dressed as a man, but nothing would ever make her look handsome. *Nor happy.* Once out of Harrenhal, her usual pighead stubbornness had soon reasserted itself. "I want my arms and armor back," she had insisted. "Oh, by all means, let us have you back in steel," Jaime replied. "A helm, especially. We'll all be happier if you keep your mouth shut and your visor down."

That much Brienne could do, but her sullen silences soon began to fray his good humor almost as much as Qyburn's endless attempts to be ingratiating. *I never thought I would find myself missing the company of Cleos Frey, gods help me.* He was beginning to wish he had left her for the bear after all.

"King's Landing," Jaime announced when he found her. "Our journey's done, my lady. You've kept your vow, and delivered me to King's Landing. All but a few fingers and a hand."

Brienne's eyes were listless. "That was only half my vow. I told Lady Catelyn I would bring her back her daughters. Or Sansa, at the least. And now . . ."

She never met Robb Stark, yet her grief for him runs deeper than mine for Joff. Or perhaps it was Lady Catelyn she mourned. They had been at Brindlewood when they had *that* news, from a red-faced tub of a knight named Ser Bertram Beesbury, whose arms were three beehives on a field striped black and yellow. A troop of Lord Piper's men

had passed through Brindlewood only yesterday, Beesbury
told them, rushing to King's Landing beneath a peace banner of their own. "With the Young Wolf dead Piper saw no
point to fighting on. His son is captive at the Twins."
Brienne gaped like a cow about to choke on her cud, so it
fell to Jaime to draw out the tale of the Red Wedding.

"Every great lord has unruly bannermen who envy him
his place," he told her afterward. "My father had the
Reynes and Tarbecks, the Tyrells have the Florents, Hoster
Tully had Walder Frey. Only strength keeps such men in
their place. The moment they smell weakness . . . during
the Age of Heroes, the Boltons used to flay the Starks and
wear their skins as cloaks." She looked so miserable that
Jaime almost found himself wanting to comfort her.

Since that day Brienne had been like one half-dead. Even
calling her "wench" failed to provoke any response. *The
strength is gone from her.* The woman had dropped a rock
on Robin Ryger, battled a bear with a tourney sword, bitten
off Vargo Hoat's ear, and fought Jaime to exhaustion . . .
but she was broken now, done. "I'll speak to my father
about returning you to Tarth, if it please you," he told her.
"Or if you would rather stay, I could perchance find some
place for you at court."

"As a lady companion to the queen?" she said dully.

Jaime remembered the sight of her in that pink satin
gown, and tried not to imagine what his sister might say of
such a companion. "Perhaps a post with the City
Watch . . ."

"I will not serve with oathbreakers and murderers."

Then why did you ever bother putting on a sword?
he might have said, but he bit back the words. "As you
will, Brienne." One-handed, he wheeled his horse about
and left her.

The Gate of the Gods was open when they reached
it, but two dozen wayns were lined up along the roadside,
loaded with casks of cider, barrels of apples, bales of hay,
and some of the biggest pumpkins Jaime had ever seen.
Almost every wagon had its guards; men-at-arms wearing
the badges of small lordlings, sellswords in mail and boiled
leather, sometimes only a pink-cheeked farmer's son
clutching a homemade spear with a fire-hardened point.
Jaime smiled at them all as he trotted past. At the gate, the

gold cloaks were collecting coin from each driver before waving the wagons through. "What's this?" Steelshanks demanded.

"They got to pay for the right to sell inside the city. By command of the King's Hand and the master of coin."

Jaime looked at the long line of wayns, carts, and laden horses. "Yet they still line up to pay?"

"There's good coin to be made here now that the fighting's done," the miller in the nearest wagon told them cheerfully. "It's the Lannisters hold the city now, old Lord Tywin of the Rock. They say he shits silver."

"Gold," Jaime corrected dryly. "And Littlefinger mints the stuff from goldenrod, I vow."

"The Imp is master of coin now," said the captain of the gate. "Or was, till they arrested him for murdering the king." The man looked the northmen over suspiciously. "Who are you lot?"

"Lord Bolton's men, come to see the King's Hand."

The captain glanced at Nage with his peace banner. "Come to bend the knee, you mean. You're not the first. Go straight up to the castle, and see you make no trouble." He waved them through and turned back to the wagons.

If King's Landing mourned its dead boy king, Jaime would never have known it. On the Street of Seeds a begging brother in threadbare robes was praying loudly for Joffrey's soul, but the passersby paid him no more heed than they would a loose shutter banging in the wind. Elsewhere milled the usual crowds; gold cloaks in their black mail, bakers' boys selling tarts and breads and hot pies, whores leaning out of windows with their bodices half unlaced, gutters redolent of nightsoil. They passed five men trying to drag a dead horse from the mouth of an alley, and elsewhere a juggler spinning knives through the air to delight a throng of drunken Tyrell soldiers and small children.

Riding down familiar streets with two hundred northmen, a chainless maester, and an ugly freak of a woman at his side, Jaime found he scarcely drew a second look. He did not know whether he ought to be amused or annoyed. "They do not know me," he said to Steelshanks as they rode through Cobbler's Square.

"Your face is changed, and your arms as well," the northman said, "and they have a new Kingslayer now."

The gates to the Red Keep were open, but a dozen gold cloaks armed with pikes barred the way. They lowered their points as Steelshanks came trotting up, but Jaime recognized the white knight commanding them. "Ser Meryn."

Ser Meryn Trant's droopy eyes went wide. "Ser Jaime?"

"How nice to be remembered. Move these men aside."

It had been a long time since anyone had leapt to obey him quite so fast. Jaime had forgotten how well he liked it.

They found two more Kingsguard in the outer ward; two who had not worn white cloaks when Jaime last served here. *How like Cersei to name me Lord Commander and then choose my colleagues without consulting me.* "Someone has given me two new brothers, I see," he said as he dismounted.

"We have that honor, ser." The Knight of Flowers shone so fine and pure in his white scales and silk that Jaime felt a tattered and tawdry thing by contrast.

Jaime turned to Meryn Trant. "Ser, you've been remiss in teaching our new brothers their duties."

"What duties?" said Meryn Trant defensively.

"Keeping the king alive. How many monarchs have you lost since I left the city? Two, is it?"

Then Ser Balon saw the stump. *"Your hand . . ."*

Jaime made himself smile. "I fight with my left now. It makes for more of a contest. Where will I find my lord father?"

"In the solar with Lord Tyrell and Prince Oberyn."

Mace Tyrell and the Red Viper breaking bread together? Strange and stranger. "Is the queen with them as well?"

"No, my lord," Ser Balon answered. "You'll find her in the sept, praying over King Joff—"

"*You!*"

The last of the northmen had dismounted, Jaime saw, and now Loras Tyrell had seen Brienne.

"Ser Loras." She stood stupidly, holding her bridle.

Loras Tyrell strode toward her. "Why?" he said. "You will tell me why. He treated you kindly, gave you a rainbow cloak. Why would you kill him?"

"I never did. I would have died for him."

"You will." Ser Loras drew his longsword.

"It was not me."

"Emmon Cuy swore it was, with his dying breath."

"He was outside the tent, he never saw—"

"There was no one *in* the tent but you and Lady Stark.
Do you claim that old woman could cut through hardened
steel?"

"There was a *shadow*. I know how mad it sounds,
but . . . I was helping Renly into his armor, and the candles
blew out and there was blood everywhere. It was Stannis,
Lady Catelyn said. His . . . his shadow. I had no part in it,
on my honor . . ."

"You have no honor. Draw your sword. I won't have it
said that I slew you while your hand was empty."

Jaime stepped between them. "Put the sword away,
ser."

Ser Loras edged around him. "Are you a craven as well
as a killer, Brienne? Is that why you ran, with his blood on
your hands? *Draw your sword, woman!*"

"Best hope she doesn't." Jaime blocked his path again.
"Or it's like to be your corpse we carry out. The wench is
as strong as Gregor Clegane, though not so pretty."

"This is no concern of yours." Ser Loras shoved him
aside.

Jaime grabbed the boy with his good hand and yanked
him around. "I am the *Lord Commander of the Kingsguard*, you arrogant pup. *Your* commander, so long as you
wear that white cloak. Now *sheathe your bloody sword*, or
I'll take it from you and shove it up some place even Renly
never found."

The boy hesitated half a heartbeat, long enough for Ser
Balon Swann to say, "Do as the Lord Commander says,
Loras." Some of the gold cloaks drew their steel then, and
that made some Dreadfort men do the same. *Splendid*,
thought Jaime, *no sooner do I climb down off my horse
than we have a bloodbath in the yard.*

Ser Loras Tyrell slammed his sword back into its sheath.

"That wasn't so difficult, was it?"

"I want her arrested." Ser Loras pointed. "Lady Brienne,
I charge you with the murder of Lord Renly Baratheon."

"For what it's worth," said Jaime, "the wench does have honor. More than I have seen from you. And it may even be she's telling it true. I'll grant you, she's not what you'd call clever, but even my horse could come up with a better lie, if it was a lie she meant to tell. As you insist, however . . . Ser Balon, escort Lady Brienne to a tower cell and hold her there under guard. And find some suitable quarters for Steelshanks and his men, until such time as my father can see them."

"Yes, my lord."

Brienne's big blue eyes were full of hurt as Balon Swann and a dozen gold cloaks led her away. *You ought to be blowing me kisses, wench,* he wanted to tell her. Why must they misunderstand every bloody thing he did? *Aerys. It all grows from Aerys.* Jaime turned his back on the wench and strode across the yard.

Another knight in white armor was guarding the doors of the royal sept; a tall man with a black beard, broad shoulders, and a hooked nose. When he saw Jaime he gave a sour smile and said, "And where do you think you're going?"

"Into the sept." Jaime lifted his stump to point. "That one right there. I mean to see the queen."

"Her Grace is in mourning. And why would she be wanting to see the likes of you?"

Because I'm her lover, and the father of her murdered son, he wanted to say. "Who in seven hells are you?"

"A knight of the Kingsguard, and you'd best learn some respect, cripple, or I'll have that other hand and leave you to suck up your porridge of a morning."

"I am the queen's brother, ser."

The white knight thought that funny. "Escaped, have you? And grown a bit as well, m'lord?"

"Her *other* brother, dolt. And the Lord Commander of the Kingsguard. Now stand aside, or you'll wish you had."

The dolt took a long look this time. "Is it . . . Ser Jaime." He straightened. "My pardons, milord. I did not know you. I have the honor to be Ser Osmund Kettleblack."

Where's the honor in that? "I want some time alone with my sister. See that no one else enters the sept, ser. If we're disturbed, I'll have your bloody head."

"Aye, ser. As you say." Ser Osmund opened the door.

Cersei was kneeling before the altar of the Mother. Joffrey's bier had been laid out beneath the Stranger, who led the newly dead to the other world. The smell of incense hung heavy in the air, and a hundred candles burned, sending up a hundred prayers. *Joff's like to need every one of them, too.*

His sister looked over her shoulder. "Who?" she said, then, "Jaime?" She rose, her eyes brimming with tears. "Is it truly you?" She did not come to him, however. *She has never come to me,* he thought. *She has always waited, letting me come to her. She gives, but I must ask.* "You should have come sooner," she murmured, when he took her in his arms. "Why couldn't you have come sooner, to keep him safe? My boy . . ."

Our boy. "I came as fast I could." He broke from the embrace, and stepped back a pace. "It's war out there, Sister."

"You look so thin. And your hair, your golden hair . . ."

"The hair will grow back." Jaime lifted his stump. *She needs to see.* "This won't."

Her eyes went wide. "The Starks . . ."

"No. This was Vargo Hoat's work."

The name meant nothing to her. "Who?"

"The Goat of Harrenhal. For a little while."

Cersei turned to gaze at Joffrey's bier. They had dressed the dead king in gilded armor, eerily similar to Jaime's own. The visor of the helm was closed, but the candles reflected softly off the gold, so the boy shimmered bright and brave in death. The candlelight woke fires in the rubies that decorated the bodice of Cersei's mourning dress as well. Her hair fell to her shoulders, undressed and unkempt. "He killed him, Jaime. Just as he'd warned me. One day when I thought myself safe and happy he would turn my joy to ashes in my mouth, he said."

"Tyrion said that?" Jaime had not wanted to believe it. Kinslaying was worse than kingslaying, in the eyes of gods and men. *He knew the boy was mine. I loved Tyrion. I was good to him.* Well, but for that one time . . . but the Imp did not know the truth of that. *Or did he?* "Why would he kill Joff?"

"For a whore." She clutched his good hand and held it tight in hers. "He *told* me he was going to do it. Joff knew. As he was dying, he *pointed* at his murderer. At our twisted little monster of a brother." She kissed Jaime's fingers. "You'll kill him for me, won't you? You'll avenge our son."

Jaime pulled away. "He is still my brother." He shoved his stump at her face, in case she failed to see it. "And I am in no fit state to be killing anyone."

"You have another hand, don't you? I am not asking you to best the Hound in battle. Tyrion is a *dwarf*, locked in a cell. The guards would stand aside for *you*."

The thought turned his stomach. "I must know more of this. Of how it happened."

"You shall," Cersei promised. "There's to be a trial. When you hear all he did, you'll want him dead as much as I do." She touched his face. "I was lost without you, Jaime. I was afraid the Starks would send me your head. I could not have borne that." She kissed him. A light kiss, the merest brush of her lips on his, but he could feel her tremble as he slid his arms around her. "I am not whole without you."

There was no tenderness in the kiss he returned to her, only hunger. Her mouth opened for his tongue. "No," she said weakly when his lips moved down her neck, "not here. The septons . . ."

"The Others can take the septons." He kissed her again, kissed her silent, kissed her until she moaned. Then he knocked the candles aside and lifted her up onto the Mother's altar, pushing up her skirts and the silken shift beneath. She pounded on his chest with feeble fists, murmuring about the risk, the danger, about their father, about the septons, about the wrath of gods. He never heard her. He undid his breeches and climbed up and pushed her bare white legs apart. One hand slid up her thigh and underneath her smallclothes. When he tore them away, he saw that her moon's blood was on her, but it made no difference.

"Hurry," she was whispering now, "quickly, *quickly*, now, do it now, do me now. Jaime Jaime Jaime." Her hands helped guide him. "Yes," Cersei said as he thrust, "my brother, sweet brother, yes, like that, yes, I have you, you're home now, you're home now, you're *home*." She kissed his ear and stroked his short bristly hair. Jaime lost himself in her flesh. He could feel Cersei's heart beating in time with his own, and the wetness of blood and seed where they were joined.

But no sooner were they done than the queen said, "Let me up. If we are discovered like this . . ."

Reluctantly he rolled away and helped her off the altar. The pale marble was smeared with blood. Jaime wiped it clean with his sleeve, then bent to pick up the candles he had knocked over. Fortunately they had all gone out when they fell. *If the sept had caught fire I might never have noticed.*

"This was folly." Cersei pulled her gown straight. "With Father in the castle . . . Jaime, we must be careful."

"I am sick of being careful. The Targaryens wed brother to sister, why shouldn't we do the same? Marry me, Cersei. Stand up before the realm and say it's me you want. We'll have our own wedding feast, and make another son in place of Joffrey."

She drew back. "That's not funny."

"Do you hear me chuckling?"

"Did you leave your wits at Riverrun?" Her voice had an edge to it. "Tommen's throne derives from Robert, you know that."

"He'll have Casterly Rock, isn't that enough? Let Father sit the throne. All I want is you." He made to touch her cheek. Old habits die hard, and it was his right arm he lifted.

Cersei recoiled from his stump. "*Don't* . . . don't talk like this. You're scaring me, Jaime. Don't be *stupid*. One wrong word and you'll cost us everything. What did they do to you?"

"They cut off my hand."

"No, it's more, you're *changed*." She backed off a step. "We'll talk later. On the morrow. I have Sansa Stark's maids in a tower cell, I need to question them . . . you should go to Father."

"I crossed a thousand leagues to come to you, and lost the best part of me along the way. Don't tell me to leave."

"*Leave me*," she repeated, turning away.

Jaime laced up his breeches and did as she commanded. Weary as he was, he could not seek a bed. By now his lord father knew that he was back in the city.

The Tower of the Hand was guarded by Lannister household guards, who knew him at once. "The gods are good, to give you back to us, ser," one said, as he held the door.

"The gods had no part in it. Catelyn Stark gave me back. Her, and the Lord of the Dreadfort."

He climbed the stairs and pushed into the solar unannounced, to find his father sitting by the fire. Lord Tywin was alone, for which Jaime was thankful. He had no desire to flaunt his maimed hand for Mace Tyrell or the Red Viper just now, much less the two of them together.

"Jaime," Lord Tywin said, as if they'd last seen each other at breakfast. "Lord Bolton led me to expect you earlier. I had hoped you'd be here for the wedding."

"I was delayed." Jaime closed the door softly. "My sister outdid herself, I'm told. Seventy-seven courses and a regicide, never a wedding like it. How long have you known I was free?"

"The eunuch told me a few days after your escape. I sent men into the riverlands to look for you. Gregor Clegane, Samwell Spicer, the brothers Plumm. Varys put out the word as well, but quietly. We agreed that the fewer people who knew you were free, the fewer would be hunting you."

"Did Varys mention this?" He moved closer to the fire, to let his father see.

Lord Tywin pushed himself out of his chair, breath hissing between his teeth. *"Who did this?* If Lady Catelyn thinks—"

"Lady Catelyn held a sword to my throat and made me swear to return her daughters. This was your goat's work. Vargo Hoat, the Lord of Harrenhal!"

Lord Tywin looked away, disgusted. "No longer. Ser Gregor's taken the castle. The sellswords deserted their erstwhile captain almost to a man, and some of Lady Whent's old people opened a postern gate. Clegane found Hoat sitting alone in the Hall of a Hundred Hearths, half-mad with pain and fever from a wound that festered. His ear, I'm told."

Jaime had to laugh. *Too sweet! His ear!* He could scarcely wait to tell Brienne, though the wench wouldn't find it half so funny as he did. "Is he dead yet?"

"Soon. They have taken off his hands and feet, but Clegane seems amused by the way the Qohorik slobbers."

Jaime's smile curdled. "What about his Brave Companions?"

"The few who stayed at Harrenhal are dead. The others scattered. They'll make for ports, I'll warrant, or try and lose themselves in the woods." His eyes went back to Jaime's stump, and his mouth grew taut with fury. "We'll have their heads. Every one. Can you use a sword with your left hand?"

I can hardly dress myself in the morning. Jaime held up the hand in question for his father's inspection. "Four fingers, a thumb, much like the other. Why shouldn't it work as well?"

"Good." His father sat. "That is good. I have a gift for you. For your return. After Varys told me . . ."

"Unless it's a new hand, let it wait." Jaime took the chair across from him. "How did Joffrey die?"

"Poison. It was meant to appear as though he choked on a morsel of food, but I had his throat slit open and the maesters could find no obstruction."

"Cersei claims that Tyrion did it."

"Your brother served the king the poisoned wine, with a thousand people looking on."

"That was rather foolish of him."

"I have taken Tyrion's squire into custody. His wife's maids as well. We shall see if they have anything to tell us. Ser Addam's gold cloaks are searching for the Stark girl, and Varys has offered a reward. The king's justice will be done."

The king's justice. "You would execute your own son?"

"He stands accused of regicide and kinslaying. If he is innocent, he has nothing to fear. First we must needs consider the evidence for and against him."

Evidence. In this city of liars, Jaime knew what sort of evidence would be found. "Renly died strangely as well, when Stannis needed him to."

"Lord Renly was murdered by one of his own guards, some woman from Tarth."

"That woman from Tarth is the reason I'm here. I tossed her into a cell to appease Ser Loras, but I'll believe in Renly's ghost before I believe she did him any harm. But Stannis—"

"It was poison that killed Joffrey, not sorcery." Lord

Tywin glanced at Jaime's stump again. "You cannot serve in the Kingsguard without a sword hand—"

"I can," he interrupted. "And I will. There's precedent. I'll look in the White Book and find it, if you like. Crippled or whole, a knight of the Kingsguard serves for life."

"Cersei ended that when she replaced Ser Barristan on grounds of age. A suitable gift to the Faith will persuade the High Septon to release you from your vows. Your sister was foolish to dismiss Selmy, admittedly, but now that she has opened the gates—"

"—someone needs to close them again." Jaime stood. "I am tired of having highborn women kicking pails of shit at me, Father. No one ever asked me if I wanted to be Lord Commander of the Kingsguard, but it seems I am. I have a duty—"

"You do." Lord Tywin rose as well. "A duty to House Lannister. You are the heir to Casterly Rock. That is where you should be. Tommen should accompany you, as your ward and squire. The Rock is where he'll learn to be a Lannister, and I want him away from his mother. I mean to find a new husband for Cersei. Oberyn Martell perhaps, once I convince Lord Tyrell that the match does not threaten Highgarden. And it is past time you were wed. The Tyrells are now insisting that Margaery be wed to Tommen, but if I were to offer you instead—"

"NO!" Jaime had heard all that he could stand. No, more than he could stand. He was sick of it, sick of lords and lies, sick of his father, his sister, sick of the whole bloody business. "No. No. No. No. No. How many times must I say no before you'll hear it? Oberyn Martell? The man's infamous, and not just for poisoning his sword. He has more bastards than Robert, and beds with boys as well. And if you think for one misbegotten moment that I would wed Joffrey's widow . . ."

"Lord Tyrell swears the girl's still maiden."

"She can die a maiden as far as I'm concerned. I don't want her, and I don't want your Rock!"

"You are my son—"

"I am a knight of the Kingsguard. The Lord Commander of the Kingsguard! And that's all I mean to be!"

Firelight gleamed golden in the stiff whiskers that

framed Lord Tywin's face. A vein pulsed in his neck, but he did not speak. And did not speak. And did not speak.

The strained silence went on until it was more than Jaime could endure. "Father . . ." he began.

"You are not my son." Lord Tywin turned his face away. "You say you are the Lord Commander of the Kingsguard, and only that. Very well, ser. Go do your duty."

DAVOS

Their voices rose like cinders, swirling up into purple evening sky. "Lead us from the darkness, O my Lord. Fill our hearts with fire, so we may walk your shining path."

The nightfire burned against the gathering dark, a great bright beast whose shifting orange light threw shadows twenty feet tall across the yard. All along the walls of Dragonstone the army of gargoyles and grotesques seemed to stir and shift.

Davos looked down from an arched window in the gallery above. He watched Melisandre lift her arms, as if to embrace the shivering flames. "R'hllor," she sang in a voice loud and clear, "you are the light in our eyes, the fire in our hearts, the heat in our loins. Yours is the sun that warms our days, yours the stars that guard us in the dark of night."

"Lord of Light, defend us. The night is dark and full of terrors." Queen Selyse led the responses, her pinched face full of fervor. King Stannis stood beside her, jaw clenched hard, the points of his red-gold crown shimmering whenever he moved his head. *He is with them, but not of them,* Davos thought. Princess Shireen was between them, the mottled grey patches on her face and neck almost black in the firelight.

"*Lord of Light, protect us,*" the queen sang. The king did not respond with the others. He was staring into the flames. Davos wondered what he saw there. *Another vision of the war to come? Or something closer to home?*

"R'hllor who gave us breath, we thank you," sang Melisandre. "R'hllor who gave us day, we thank you."

"*We thank you for the sun that warms us,*" Queen Selyse and the other worshipers replied. "*We thank you for the stars that watch us. We thank you for our hearths and for our torches, that keep the savage dark at bay.*" There were fewer voices saying the responses than there had been the night before, it seemed to Davos; fewer faces flushed with orange light about the fire. But would there be fewer still on the morrow . . . or more?

The voice of Ser Axell Florent rang loud as a trumpet. He stood barrel-chested and bandy-legged, the firelight washing his face like a monstrous orange tongue. Davos wondered if Ser Axell would thank him, after. The work they did tonight might well make him the King's Hand, as he dreamed.

Melisandre cried, "We thank you for Stannis, by your grace our king. We thank you for the pure white fire of his goodness, for the red sword of justice in his hand, for the love he bears his leal people. Guide him and defend him, R'hllor, and grant him strength to smite his foes."

"*Grant him strength,*" answered Queen Selyse, Ser Axell, Devan, and the rest. "*Grant him courage. Grant him wisdom.*"

When he was a boy, the septons had taught Davos to pray to the Crone for wisdom, to the Warrior for courage, to the Smith for strength. But it was the Mother he prayed to now, to keep his sweet son Devan safe from the red woman's demon god.

"Lord Davos? We'd best be about it." Ser Andrew touched his elbow gently. "My lord?"

The title still rang queer in his ears, yet Davos turned away from the window. "Aye. It's time." Stannis, Melisandre, and the queen's men would be at their prayers an hour or more. The red priests lit their fires every day at sunset, to thank R'hllor for the day just ending, and beg him to send his sun back on the morrow to banish the gathering darkness. *A smuggler must know the tides and when to seize them.* That was all he was at the end of the day; Davos the smuggler. His maimed hand rose to his throat for his luck, and found nothing. He snatched it down and walked a bit more quickly.

His companions kept pace, matching their strides to his own. The Bastard of Nightsong had a pox-ravaged face and an air of tattered chivalry; Ser Gerald Gower was broad, bluff, and blond; Ser Andrew Estermont stood a head taller, with a spade-shaped beard and shaggy brown eye-brows. They were all good men in their own ways, Davos thought. *And they will all be dead men soon, if this night's work goes badly.*

"Fire is a living thing," the red woman told him, when he asked her to teach him how to see the future in the flames. "It is always moving, always changing . . . like a book whose letters dance and shift even as you try to read them. It takes years of training to see the shapes beyond the flames, and more years still to learn to tell the shapes of what will be or what may be or what was. Even then it comes hard, *hard*. You do not understand that, you men of the sunset lands." Davos asked her then how it was that Ser Axell had learned the trick of it so quickly, but to that she only smiled enigmatically and said, "Any cat may stare into a fire and see red mice at play."

He had not lied to his king's men, about that or any of it. "The red woman may see what we intend," he warned them.

"We should start by killing her, then," urged Lewys the Fishwife. "I know a place where we could waylay her, four of us with sharp swords . . ."

"You'd doom us all," said Davos. "Maester Cressen tried to kill her, and she knew at once. From her flames, I'd guess. It seems to me that she is very quick to sense any threat to her own person, but surely she cannot see *everything*. If we ignore her, perhaps we might escape her notice."

"There is no honor in hiding and sneaking," objected

Ser Triston of Tally Hill, who had been a Sunglass man before Lord Guncer went to Melisandre's fires.

"Is it so honorable to burn?" Davos asked him. "You saw Lord Sunglass die. Is that what you want? I don't need men of honor now. I need *smugglers*. Are you with me, or no?"

They were. Gods be good, they were.

Maester Pylos was leading Edric Storm through his sums when Davos pushed open the door. Ser Andrew was close behind him; the others had been left to guard the steps and cellar door. The maester broke off. "That will be enough for now, Edric."

The boy was puzzled by the intrusion. "Lord Davos, Ser Andrew. We were doing sums."

Ser Andrew smiled. "I hated sums when I was your age, coz."

"I don't mind them so much. I like history best, though. It's full of tales."

"Edric," said Maester Pylos, "run and get your cloak now. You're to go with Lord Davos."

"I am?" Edric got to his feet. "Where are we going?" His mouth set stubbornly. "I won't go pray to the Lord of Light. I am a Warrior's man, like my father."

"We know," Davos said. "Come, lad, we must not dawdle."

Edric donned a thick hooded cloak of undyed wool. Maester Pylos helped him fasten it, and pulled the hood up to shadow his face. "Are you coming with us, Maester?" the boy asked.

"No." Pylos touched the chain of many metals he wore about his neck. "My place is here on Dragonstone. Go with Lord Davos now, and do as he says. He is the King's Hand, remember. What did I tell you about the King's Hand?"

"The Hand speaks with the king's voice."

The young maester smiled. "That's so. Go now."

Davos had been uncertain of Pylos. Perhaps he resented him for taking old Cressen's place. But now he could only admire the man's courage. *This could mean his life as well.*

Outside the maester's chambers, Ser Gerald Gower waited by the steps. Edric Storm looked at him curiously. As they made their descent he asked, "Where are we going, Lord Davos?"

"To the water. A ship awaits you."

The boy stopped suddenly. "A ship?"

"One of Salladhor Saan's. Salla is a good friend of mine."

"I shall go with you, Cousin," Ser Andrew assured him. "There's nothing to be frightened of."

"I am not *frightened*," Edric said indignantly. "Only . . . is Shireen coming too?"

"No," said Davos. "The princess must remain here with her father and mother."

"I have to see her then," Edric explained. "To say my farewells. Otherwise she'll be sad."

Not so sad as if she sees you burn. "There is no time," Davos said. "I will tell the princess that you were thinking of her. And you can write her, when you get to where you're going."

The boy frowned. "Are you sure I must go? Why would my uncle send me from Dragonstone? Did I displease him? I never meant to." He got that stubborn look again. "I want to see my uncle. I want to see King Stannis."

Ser Andrew and Ser Gerald exchanged a look. "There's no time for that, Cousin," Ser Andrew said.

"I want to see him!" Edric insisted, louder.

"He does not want to see you." Davos had to say something, to get the boy moving. "I am his Hand, I speak with his voice. Must I go to the king and tell him that you would not do as you were told? Do you know how angry that will make him? Have you ever seen your uncle angry?" He pulled off his glove and showed the boy the four fingers that Stannis had shortened. "I have."

It was all lies; there had been no anger in Stannis Baratheon when he cut the ends off his onion knight's fingers, only an iron sense of justice. But Edric Storm had not been born then, and could not know that. And the threat had the desired effect. "He should not have done that," the boy said, but he let Davos take him by the hand and draw him down the steps.

The Bastard of Nightsong joined them at the cellar door. They walked quickly, across a shadowed yard and down some steps, under the stone tail of a frozen dragon. Lewys the Fishwife and Omer Blackberry waited at the postern gate, two guards bound and trussed at their feet. "The boat?" Davos asked them.

"It's there," Lewys said. "Four oarsmen. The galley is anchored just past the point. *Mad Prendos*."

Davos chuckled. *A ship named after a madman. Yes, that's fitting.* Salla had a streak of the pirate's black humor.

He went to one knee before Edric Storm. "I must leave you now," he said. "There's a boat waiting, to row you out to a galley. Then it's off across the sea. You are Robert's son so I know you will be brave, no matter what happens."

"I will. Only . . ." The boy hesitated.

"Think of this as an adventure, my lord." Davos tried to sound hale and cheerful. "It's the start of your life's great adventure. May the Warrior defend you."

"And may the Father judge you justly, Lord Davos." The boy went with his cousin Ser Andrew out the postern gate. The others followed, all but the Bastard of Nightsong. *May the Father judge me justly*, Davos thought ruefully. But it was the king's judgment that concerned him now.

"These two?" asked Ser Rolland of the guards, when he had closed and barred the gate.

"Drag them into a cellar," said Davos. "You can cut them free when Edric's safely under way."

The Bastard gave a curt nod. There were no more words to say; the easy part was done. Davos pulled his glove on, wishing he had not lost his luck. He had been a better man and a braver one with that bag of bones around his neck. He ran his shortened fingers through thinning brown hair, and wondered if it needed to be cut. He must look presentable when he stood before the king.

Dragonstone had never seemed so dark and fearsome. He walked slowly, his footsteps echoing off black walls and dragons. *Stone dragons who will never wake, I pray.* The Stone Drum loomed huge ahead of him. The guards at the door uncrossed their spears as he approached. *Not for the onion knight, but for the King's Hand.* Davos was the Hand going in, at least. He wondered what he would be coming out. *If I ever do . . .*

The steps seemed longer and steeper than before, or perhaps it was just that he was tired. *The Mother never made me for tasks like this.* He had risen too high and too fast, and up here on the mountain the air was too thin for him to breathe. As a boy he'd dreamed of riches, but that was long ago. Later, grown, all he had wanted was a few acres of good land, a hall to grow old in, a better life for his sons. The Blind Bastard used to tell him that a clever smuggler did not overreach, nor draw too much attention to himself. *A few acres, a timbered roof, a "ser" before my name, I should have been content.* If he survived this night, he would take Devan and sail home to Cape Wrath and his gentle Marya. *We will grieve together for our dead sons, raise the living ones to be good men, and speak no more of kings.*

The Chamber of the Painted Table was dark and empty when Davos entered; the king would still be at the night-fire, with Melisandre and the queen's men. He knelt and made a fire in the hearth, to drive the chill from the round chamber and chase the shadows back into their corners. Then he went around the room to each window in turn, opening the heavy velvet curtains and unlatching the wooden shutters. The wind came in, strong with the smell of salt and sea, and pulled at his plain brown cloak.

At the north window, he leaned against the sill for a breath of the cold night air, hoping to catch a glimpse of *Mad Prendos* raising sail, but the sea seemed black and empty as far as the eye could see. *Is she gone already?* He could only pray that she was, and the boy with her. A half moon was sliding in and out amongst thin high clouds, and Davos could see familiar stars. There was the Galley, sailing west; there the Crone's Lantern, four bright stars that enclosed a golden haze. The clouds hid most of the Ice Dragon, all but the bright blue eye that marked due north. *The sky is full of smugglers' stars.* They were old friends, those stars; Davos hoped that meant good luck.

But when he lowered his gaze from the sky to the castle ramparts, he was not so certain. The wings of the stone dragons cast great black shadows in the light from the nightfire. He tried to tell himself that they were no more than carvings, cold and lifeless. *This was their place, once. A place of dragons and dragonlords, the seat of House Targaryen.* The Targaryens were the blood of old Valyria . . .

The wind sighed through the chamber, and in the hearth the flames gusted and swirled. He listened to the logs crackle and spit. When Davos left the window his shadow went before him, tall and thin, and fell across the Painted

Table like a sword. And there he stood for a long time, waiting. He heard their boots on the stone steps as they ascended. The king's voice went before him. ". . . is not three," he was saying.

"Three is three," came Melisandre's answer. "I swear to you, Your Grace, I saw him die and heard his mother's wail."

"In the nightfire." Stannis and Melisandre came through the door together. "The flames are full of tricks. What is, what will be, what may be. You cannot tell me for a certainty . . ."

"Your Grace." Davos stepped forward. "Lady Melisandre saw it true. Your nephew Joffrey is dead."

If the king was surprised to find him at the Painted Table, he gave no sign. "Lord Davos," he said. "He was not my nephew. Though for years I believed he was."

"He choked on a morsel of food at his wedding feast," Davos said. "It may be that he was poisoned."

"He is the third," said Melisandre.

"I can count, woman." Stannis walked along the table, past Oldtown and the Arbor, up toward the Shield Islands and the mouth of the Mander. "Weddings have become more perilous than battles, it would seem. Who was the poisoner? Is it known?"

"His uncle, it's said. The Imp."

Stannis ground his teeth. "A dangerous man. I learned that on the Blackwater. How do you come by this report?"

"The Lyseni still trade at King's Landing. Salladhor Saan has no reason to lie to me."

"I suppose not." The king ran his fingers across the table. "Joffrey . . . I remember once, this kitchen cat . . . the cooks were wont to feed her scraps and fish heads. One told the boy that she had kittens in her belly, thinking he might want one. Joffrey opened up the poor thing with a dagger to see if it were true. When he found the kittens, he brought them to show to his father. Robert hit the boy so hard I thought he'd killed him." The king took off his crown and placed it on the table. "Dwarf or leech, this killer served the kingdom well. They *must* send for me now."

"They will not," said Melisandre. "Joffrey has a brother."

"Tommen." The king said the name grudgingly.

"They will crown Tommen, and rule in his name."

Stannis made a fist. "Tommen is gentler than Joffrey, but born of the same incest. Another monster in the making. Another leech upon the land. Westeros needs a man's hand, not a child's."

Melisandre moved closer. "Save them, sire. Let me wake the stone dragons. Three is three. Give me the boy."

"Edric Storm," Davos said.

Stannis rounded on him in a cold fury. "*I know his name*. Spare me your reproaches. I like this no more than you do, but my duty is to the realm. My duty . . ." He turned back to Melisandre. "You swear there is no other way? Swear it on your life, for I promise, you shall die by inches if you lie."

"You are he who must stand against the Other. The one whose coming was prophesied five thousand years ago. The red comet was your herald. You are the prince that was promised, and if you fail the world fails with you." Melisandre went to him, her red lips parted, her ruby throbbing. "Give me this boy," she whispered, "and I will give you your kingdom."

"He can't," said Davos. "Edric Storm is gone."

"Gone?" Stannis turned. "What do you mean, *gone?*"

"He is aboard a Lyseni galley, safely out to sea." Davos watched Melisandre's pale, heart-shaped face. He saw the flicker of dismay there, the sudden uncertainty. *She did not see it!*

The king's eyes were dark blue bruises in the hollows of his face. "The bastard was taken from Dragonstone without my leave? A galley, you say? If that Lysene pirate thinks to use the boy to squeeze gold from me—"

"This is your Hand's work, sire." Melisandre gave Davos a knowing look. "You will bring him back, my lord. You will."

"The boy is out of my reach," said Davos. "And out of your reach as well, my lady."

Her red eyes made him squirm. "I should have left you to the dark, ser. Do you know what you have done?"

"My duty."

"Some might call it treason." Stannis went to the window to stare out into the night. *Is he looking for the ship?*

"I raised you up from dirt, Davos." He sounded more tired than angry. "Was loyalty too much to hope for?"

"Four of my sons died for you on the Blackwater. I might have died myself. You have my loyalty, always." Davos Seaworth had thought long and hard about the words he said next; he knew his life depended on them. "Your Grace, you made me swear to give you honest counsel and swift obedience, to defend your realm against your foes, to *protect your people.* Is not Edric Storm one of your people? One of those I swore to protect? I kept my oath. How could that be treason?"

Stannis ground his teeth again. "I never asked for this crown. Gold is cold and heavy on the head, but so long as I *am* the king, I have a duty . . . If I must sacrifice one child to the flames to save a million from the dark . . . *Sacrifice* . . . is never easy, Davos. Or it is no true sacrifice. Tell him, my lady."

Melisandre said, "Azor Ahai tempered Lightbringer with the heart's blood of his own beloved wife. If a man with a thousand cows gives one to god, that is nothing. But a man who offers the only cow he owns . . ."

"She talks of cows," Davos told the king. "I am speaking of a boy, your daughter's friend, your brother's son."

"A king's son, with the power of kingsblood in his veins." Melisandre's ruby glowed like a red star at her throat. "Do you think you've saved this boy, Onion Knight? When the long night falls, Edric Storm shall die with the rest, wherever he is hidden. Your own sons as well. Darkness and cold will cover the earth. You meddle in matters you do not understand."

"There's much I don't understand," Davos admitted. "I have never pretended elsewise. I know the seas and rivers, the shapes of the coasts, where the rocks and shoals lie. I know hidden coves where a boat can land unseen. And I know that a king protects his people, or he is no king at all."

Stannis's face darkened. "Do you mock me to my face? Must I learn a king's duty from an onion smuggler?"

Davos knelt. "If I have offended, take my head. I'll die as I lived, your loyal man. But hear me first. Hear me for the sake of the onions I brought you, and the fingers you took."

Stannis slid Lightbringer from its scabbard. Its glow

filled the chamber. "Say what you will, but say it quickly." The muscles in the king's neck stood out like cords.

Davos fumbled inside his cloak and drew out the crinkled sheet of parchment. It seemed a thin and flimsy thing, yet it was all the shield he had. "A King's Hand should be able to read and write. Maester Pylos has been teaching me." He smoothed the letter flat upon his knee and began to read by the light of the magic sword.

JON

He dreamt he was back in Winterfell, limping past the stone kings on their thrones. Their grey granite eyes turned to follow him as he passed, and their grey granite fingers tightened on the hilts of the rusted swords upon their laps. *You are no Stark*, he could hear them mutter, in heavy granite voices. *There is no place for you here. Go away.* He walked deeper into the darkness. "Father?" he called. "Bran? Rickon?" No one answered. A chill wind was blowing on his neck. "Uncle?" he called. "Uncle Benjen? Father? Please, Father, help me." Up above he heard drums. *They are feasting in the Great Hall, but I am not welcome there. I am no Stark, and this is not my place.* His crutch slipped and he fell to his knees. The crypts were growing darker. *A light has gone out somewhere.* "Ygritte?" he whispered. "Forgive me. Please." But it was only a direwolf, grey and ghastly, spotted with blood, his golden eyes shining sadly through the dark . . .

The cell was dark, the bed hard beneath him. His own bed, he remembered, his own bed in his steward's cell beneath the Old Bear's chambers. By rights it should have brought him sweeter dreams. Even beneath the furs, he was cold. Ghost had shared his cell before the ranging, warming it against the chill of night. And in the wild, Ygritte had slept beside him. *Both gone now*. He had burned Ygritte himself, as he knew she would have wanted, and Ghost . . . *Where are you?* Was *he* dead as well, was that what his dream had meant, the bloody wolf in the crypts? But the wolf in the dream had been grey, not white. *Grey, like Bran's wolf*. Had the Thenns hunted him down and killed him after Queenscrown? If so, Bran was lost to him for good and all.

Jon was trying to make sense of that when the horn blew.

The Horn of Winter, he thought, still confused from sleep. But Mance never found Joramun's horn, so that couldn't be. A second blast followed, as long and deep as the first. Jon had to get up and go to the Wall, he knew, but it was so hard . . .

He shoved aside his furs and sat. The pain in his leg seemed duller, nothing he could not stand. He had slept in his breeches and tunic and smallclothes, for the added warmth, so he had only to pull on his boots and don leather and mail and cloak. The horn blew again, two long blasts, so he slung Longclaw over one shoulder, found his crutch, and hobbled down the steps.

It was the black of night outside, bitter cold and overcast. His brothers were spilling out of towers and keeps, buckling their swordbelts and walking toward the Wall. Jon looked for Pyp and Grenn, but could not find them. Perhaps one of them was the sentry blowing the horn. *It is Mance*, he thought. *He has come at last*. That was good. *We will fight a battle, and then we'll rest. Alive or dead, we'll rest.*

Where the stair had been, only an immense tangle of charred wood and broken ice remained below the Wall. The winch raised them up now, but the cage was only big enough for ten men at a time, and it was already on its way up by the time Jon arrived. He would need to wait for its return. Others waited with him; Satin, Mully, Spare Boot, Kegs, big blond Hareth with his buck teeth. Everyone called him Horse. He had been a stablehand in Mole's Town, one of the few moles who had stayed at Castle Black. The rest had run back to their fields and hovels, or their beds in the underground brothel. Horse wanted to take the black, though, the great buck-toothed fool. Zei remained as well, the whore who'd proved so handy with a crossbow, and Noye had kept three orphan boys whose father had died on the steps. They were young—nine and eight and five—but no one else seemed to want them.

As they waited for the cage to come back, Clydas brought them cups of hot mulled wine, while Three-Finger Hobb passed out chunks of black bread. Jon took a heel from him and gnawed on it.

"Is it Mance Rayder?" Satin asked anxiously.

"We can hope so." There were worse things than wildlings in the dark. Jon remembered the words the wildling king had spoken on the Fist of the First Men, as they stood amidst that pink snow. *When the dead walk, walls and stakes and swords mean nothing. You cannot fight the dead, Jon Snow. No man knows that half so well as me.* Just thinking of it made the wind seem a little colder.

Finally the cage came clanking back down, swaying at the end of the long chain, and they crowded in silently and shut the door.

Mully yanked the bell rope three times. A moment later they began to rise, by fits and starts at first, then more smoothly. No one spoke. At the top the cage swung sideways and they clambered out one by one. Horse gave Jon a hand down onto the ice. The cold hit him in the teeth like a fist.

A line of fires burned along the top of the Wall, contained in iron baskets on poles taller than a man. The cold knife of the wind stirred and swirled the flames, so the lurid orange light was always shifting. Bundles of quarrels, arrows, spears, and scorpion bolts stood ready on every hand. Rocks were piled ten feet high, big wooden barrels of pitch and lamp oil lined up beside them. Bowen Marsh had left Castle Black well supplied in everything save men. The wind was whipping at the black cloaks of the scarecrow sentinels who stood along the ramparts, spears in hand. "I hope it wasn't one of them who blew the horn," Jon said to Donal Noye when he limped up beside him.

"Did you hear that?" Noye asked.

There was the wind, and horses, and something else. "A mammoth," Jon said. "That was a mammoth."

The armorer's breath was frosting as it blew from his broad, flat nose. North of the Wall was a sea of darkness that seemed to stretch forever. Jon could make out the faint red glimmer of distant fires moving through the wood. It was Mance, certain as sunrise. The Others did not light torches.

"How do we fight them if we can't see them?" Horse asked.

Donal Noye turned toward the two great trebuchets that Bowen Marsh had restored to working order. "Give me *light!*" he roared.

Barrels of pitch were loaded hastily into the slings and set afire with a torch. The wind fanned the flames to a brisk red fury. "*NOW!*" Noye bellowed. The counterweights plunged downward, the throwing arms rose to *thud* against the padded crossbars. The burning pitch went tumbling through the darkness, casting an eerie flickering light upon the ground below. Jon caught a glimpse of mammoths moving ponderously through the half-light, and just as quickly lost them again. *A dozen, maybe more.* The barrels struck the earth and burst. They heard a deep bass trumpeting, and a giant roared something in the Old Tongue, his voice an ancient thunder that sent shivers up Jon's spine.

"*Again!*" Noye shouted, and the trebuchets were loaded once more. Two more barrels of burning pitch went crackling through the gloom to come crashing down amongst the foe. This time one of them struck a dead tree, enveloping it in flame. *Not a dozen mammoths,* Jon saw, *a hundred.*

He stepped to the edge of the precipice. *Careful,* he reminded himself, *it is a long way down.* Red Alyn sounded his sentry's horn once more, *Aaaaahooooooooooooooooooooooooooooo, aaaaahoooooooooooooooooooooo.* And now the wildlings answered, not with one horn but with a dozen, and with drums and pipes as well. *We are come,* they seemed to say, *we are come to break your Wall, to take your lands and steal your daughters.* The wind howled, the trebuchets creaked and thumped, the barrels flew. Behind the giants and the mammoths, Jon saw men advancing on the Wall with bows and axes. Were there twenty or twenty thousand? In the dark there was no way to tell. *This is a battle of blind men, but Mance has a few thousand more of them than we do.*

"The gate!" Pyp cried out. "They're at the *GATE!*"

The Wall was too big to be stormed by any conventional means; too high for ladders or siege towers, too thick for battering rams. No catapult could throw a stone large enough to breach it, and if you tried to set it on fire, the icemelt would quench the flames. You could climb over, as the raiders did near Greyguard, but only if you were strong and fit and sure-handed, and even then you might end up like Jarl, impaled on a tree. *They must take the gate, or they cannot pass.*

But the gate was a crooked tunnel through the ice, smaller than any castle gate in the Seven Kingdoms, so narrow that rangers must lead their garrons through single file. Three iron grates closed the inner passage, each locked and chained and protected by a murder hole. The outer door was old oak, nine inches thick and studded with iron, not easy to break through. *But Mance has mammoths,* he reminded himself, *and giants as well.*

"Must be cold down there," said Noye. "What say we warm them up, lads?" A dozen jars of lamp oil had been lined up on the precipice. Pyp ran down the line with a torch, setting them alight. Owen the Oaf followed, shoving them over the edge one by one. Tongues of pale yellow fire swirled around the jars as they plunged downward. When the last was gone, Grenn kicked loose the chocks on a barrel of pitch and sent it rumbling and rolling over the edge as well. The sounds below changed to shouts and screams, sweet music to their ears.

Yet still the drums beat on, the trebuchets shuddered and thumped, and the sound of skinpipes came wafting through the night like the songs of strange fierce birds. Septon Cellador began to sing as well, his voice tremulous and thick with wine.

Gentle Mother, font of mercy,
save our sons from war, we pray,
stay the swords and stay the arrows,
let them know . . .

Donal Noye rounded on him. "Any man here stays his sword, I'll chuck his puckered arse right off this Wall . . . starting with you, Septon. *Archers!* Do we have any bloody archers?"

"Here," said Satin.

"And here," said Mully. "But how can I find a target? It's black as the inside of a pig's belly. Where are they?"

Noye pointed north. "Loose enough arrows, might be you'll find a few. At least you'll make them fretful." He looked around the ring of firelit faces. "I need two bows and two spears to help me hold the tunnel if they break the gate." More than ten stepped forward, and the smith picked his four. "Jon, you have the Wall till I return."

For a moment Jon thought he had misheard. It had sounded as if Noye were leaving him in command. "My lord?"

"*Lord?* I'm a blacksmith. I said, the Wall is yours."

There are older men, Jon wanted to say, *better men. I am still as green as summer grass. I'm wounded, and I stand accused of desertion.* His mouth had gone bone dry. "Aye," he managed.

Afterward it would seem to Jon Snow as if he'd dreamt that night. Side by side with the straw soldiers, with long-bows or crossbows clutched in half-frozen hands, his archers launched a hundred flights of arrows against men they never saw. From time to time a wildling arrow came flying back in answer. He sent men to the smaller catapults and filled the air with jagged rocks the size of a giant's fist, but the darkness swallowed them as a man might swallow a handful of nuts. Mammoths trumpeted in the gloom, strange voices called out in stranger tongues, and Septon Cellador prayed so loudly and drunkenly for the dawn to come that Jon was tempted to chuck him over the edge himself. They heard a mammoth dying at their feet and saw another lurch burning through the woods, trampling down men and trees alike. The wind blew cold and colder. Hobb rode up the chain with cups of onion broth, and

Owen and Clydas served them to the archers where they stood, so they could gulp them down between arrows. Zei took a place among them with her crossbow. Hours of repeated jars and shocks knocked something loose on the right-hand trebuchet, and its counterweight came crashing free, suddenly and catastrophically, wrenching the throwing arm sideways with a splintering crash. The left-hand trebuchet kept throwing, but the wildlings had quickly learned to shun the place where its loads were landing.

We should have twenty trebuchets, not two, and they should be mounted on sledges and turntables so we could move them. It was a futile thought. He might as well wish for another thousand men, and maybe a dragon or three.

Donal Noye did not return, nor any of them who'd gone down with him to hold that black cold tunnel. *The Wall is mine,* Jon reminded himself whenever he felt his strength flagging. He had taken up a longbow himself, and his fingers felt crabbed and stiff, half-frozen. His fever was back as well, and his leg would tremble uncontrollably, sending a white-hot knife of pain right through him. *One more arrow, and I'll rest,* he told himself, half a hundred times. *Just one more.* Whenever his quiver was empty, one of the orphaned moles would bring him another. *One more quiver, and I'm done.* It couldn't be long until the dawn.

When morning came, none of them quite realized it at first. The world was still dark, but the black had turned to grey and shapes were beginning to emerge half-seen from the gloom. Jon lowered his bow to stare at the mass of heavy clouds that covered the eastern sky. He could see a glow behind them, but perhaps he was only dreaming. He notched another arrow.

Then the rising sun broke through to send pale lances of light across the battleground. Jon found himself holding his breath as he looked out over the half-mile swath of cleared land that lay between the Wall and the edge of the forest. In half a night they had turned it into a wasteland of blackened grass, bubbling pitch, shattered stone, and corpses. The carcass of the burned mammoth was already drawing crows. There were giants dead on the ground as well, but behind them . . .

Someone moaned to his left, and he heard Septon

Cellador say, "Mother have mercy, oh. Oh, oh, oh, *Mother have mercy.*"

Beneath the trees were all the wildlings in the world; raiders and giants, wargs and skinchangers, mountain men, salt sea sailors, ice river cannibals, cave dwellers with dyed faces, dog chariots from the Frozen Shore, Hornfoot men with their soles like boiled leather, all the queer wild folk Mance had gathered to break the Wall. *This is not your land*, Jon wanted to shout at them. *There is no place for you here. Go away.* He could hear Tormund Giantsbane laughing at that. "You know nothing, Jon Snow," Ygritte would have said. He flexed his sword hand, opening and closing the fingers, though he knew full well that swords would not come into it up here.

He was chilled and feverish, and suddenly the weight of the longbow was too much. The battle with the Magnar had been nothing, he realized, and the night fight less than nothing, only a probe, a dagger in the dark to try and catch them unprepared. The real battle was only now beginning.

"I never knew there would be so *many*," Satin said.

Jon had. He had seen them before, but not like this, not drawn up in battle array. On the march the wildling column had sprawled over long leagues like some enormous worm, but you never saw all of it at once. But now . . .

"Here they come," someone said in a hoarse voice.

Mammoths centered the wildling line, he saw, a hundred or more with giants on their backs clutching mauls and huge stone axes. More giants loped beside them, pushing along a tree trunk on great wooden wheels, its end sharpened to a point. *A ram*, he thought bleakly. If the gate still stood below, a few kisses from that thing would soon turn it into splinters. On either side of the giants came a wave of horsemen in boiled leather harness with fire-hardened lances, a mass of running archers, hundreds of foot with spears, slings, clubs, and leathern shields. The bone chariots from the Frozen Shore clattered forward on the flanks, bouncing over rocks and roots behind teams of huge white dogs. *The fury of the wild*, Jon thought as he listened to the skirl of skins, to the dogs barking and baying, the mammoths trumpeting, the free folk whistling and screaming, the giants roaring in the Old Tongue. Their drums echoed off the ice like rolling thunder.

He could feel the despair all around him. "There must be a hundred thousand," Satin wailed. "How can we stop so many?"

"The Wall will stop them," Jon heard himself say. He turned and said it again, louder. "The *Wall* will stop them. *The Wall defends itself.*" Hollow words, but he needed to say them, almost as much as his brothers needed to hear them. "Mance wants to unman us with his numbers. Does he think we're *stupid?*" He was shouting now, his leg forgotten, and every man was listening. "The chariots, the horsemen, all those fools on foot . . . what are they going to do to us up here? Any of you ever see a mammoth climb a wall?" He laughed, and Pyp and Owen and half a dozen more laughed with him. "They're *nothing*, they're less use than our straw brothers here, they can't reach us, they can't hurt us, and they don't frighten us, do they?"

"*NO!*" Grenn shouted.

"They're down there and we're up here," Jon said, "and so long as we hold the gate they cannot pass. *They cannot pass!*" They were all shouting then, roaring his own words back at him, waving swords and longbows in the air as their cheeks flushed red. Jon saw Kegs standing there with a warhorn slung beneath his arm. "Brother," he told him, "sound for battle."

Grinning, Kegs lifted the horn to his lips, and blew the two long blasts that meant *wildlings*. Other horns took up the call until the Wall itself seemed to shudder, and the echo of those great deep-throated moans drowned all other sound.

"Archers," Jon said when the horns had died away, "you'll aim for the giants with that ram, every bloody one of you. Loose *at my command*, not before. *THE GIANTS AND THE RAM.* I want arrows raining on them with every step, but we'll wait till they're in range. Any man who wastes an arrow will need to climb down and fetch it back, do you hear me?"

"I do," shouted Owen the Oaf. "I hear you, Lord Snow."

Jon laughed, laughed like a drunk or a madman, and his men laughed with him. The chariots and the racing horsemen on the flanks were well ahead of the center now, he saw. The wildlings had not crossed a third of the half mile, yet their battle line was dissolving. "Load the trebuchet with caltrops," Jon said. "Owen, Kegs, angle the catapults toward the center. Scorpions, load with fire spears and loose at my command." He pointed at the Mole's Town boys. "You, you, and you, stand by with torches."

The wildling archers shot as they advanced; they would dash forward, stop, loose, then run another ten yards. There were so many that the air was constantly full of arrows, all falling woefully short. *A waste*, Jon thought. *Their want of discipline is showing.* The smaller horn-and-wood bows of the free folk were outranged by the great yew longbows of the Night's Watch, and the wildlings were trying to shoot at men seven hundred feet above them. "*Let them shoot*," Jon said. "Wait. Hold." Their cloaks were flapping behind them. "The wind is in our faces, it will cost us range. Wait." *Closer, closer*. The skins wailed, the drums thundered, the wildling arrows fluttered and fell.

"*DRAW*." Jon lifted his own bow and pulled the arrow to his ear. Satin did the same, and Grenn, Owen the Oaf, Spare Boot, Black Jack Bulwer, Arron and Emrick. Zei hoisted her crossbow to her shoulder. Jon was watching the ram come on and on, the mammoths and giants lumbering forward on either side. They were so small he could have crushed them all in one hand, it seemed. *If only my hand was big enough*. Through the killing ground they came. A hundred crows rose from the carcass of the dead mammoth as the wildlings thundered past to either side of them. Closer and closer, until . . .

"*LOOSE!*"

The black arrows hissed downward, like snakes on feathered wings. Jon did not wait to see where they struck. He reached for a second arrow as soon as the first left his bow. "*NOTCH. DRAW. LOOSE.*" As soon as the arrow flew he found another. "*NOTCH. DRAW. LOOSE.*" Again, and then again. Jon shouted for the trebuchet, and heard the creak and heavy *thud* as a hundred spiked steel caltrops went spinning through the air. "*Catapults*," he called, "*scorpions. Bowmen, loose at will.*" Wildling arrows were striking the Wall now, a hundred feet below them. A second giant spun and staggered. *Notch, draw, loose.* A mammoth veered into another beside it, spilling giants on the ground. *Notch, draw, loose.* The ram was down and done, he saw, the giants who'd pushed it dead or dying. "*Fire arrows*," he shouted. "I want that ram burning." The screams of wounded mammoths and the booming cries of giants mingled with the drums and pipes to make an awful music, yet still his archers drew and loosed, as if they'd all gone as deaf as dead Dick Follard. They might be the dregs of the order, but they were men of the Night's Watch, or near enough as made no matter. *That's why they shall not pass*.

One of the mammoths was running berserk, smashing wildlings with his trunk and crushing archers underfoot. Jon pulled back his bow once more, and launched another arrow at the beast's shaggy back to urge him on. To east and west, the flanks of the wildling host had reached the Wall unopposed. The chariots drew in or turned while the horsemen milled aimlessly beneath the looming cliff of ice. "*At the gate!*" a shout came. Spare Boot, maybe. "*Mammoth at the gate!*"

"Fire," Jon barked. "Grenn, Pyp."

Grenn thrust his bow aside, wrestled a barrel of oil onto its side, and rolled it to the edge of the Wall, where Pyp hammered out the plug that sealed it, stuffed in a twist of cloth, and set it alight with a torch. They shoved it over together. A hundred feet below it struck the Wall and burst, filling the air with shattered staves and burning oil. Grenn was rolling a second barrel to the precipice by then, and Kegs had one as well. Pyp lit them both. "*Got him!*" Satin shouted, his head sticking out so far that Jon was certain he was about to fall. "*Got him, got him, GOT him!*" He could hear the roar of fire. A flaming giant lurched into view, stumbling and rolling on the ground.

Then suddenly the mammoths were fleeing, running from the smoke and flames and smashing into those behind them in their terror. Those went backward too, the giants and wildlings behind them scrambling to get out of their way. In half a heartbeat the whole center was collapsing. The horsemen on the flanks saw themselves being abandoned and decided to fall back as well, not one so much as blooded. Even the chariots rumbled off, having done nothing but look fearsome and make a lot of noise. *When they break, they break hard*, Jon Snow thought as he watched them reel away. The drums had all gone silent.

How do you like that music, Mance? How do you like the taste of the Dornishman's wife? "Do we have anyone hurt?" he asked.

"The bloody buggers got my leg." Spare Boot plucked the arrow out and waved it above his head. "The wooden one!"

A ragged cheer went up. Zei grabbed Owen by the hands, spun him around in a circle, and gave him a long wet kiss right there for all to see. She tried to kiss Jon too, but he held her by the shoulder and pushed her gently but firmly away. "No," he said. *I am done with kissing.* Suddenly he was too weary to stand, and his leg was agony from knee to groin. He fumbled for his crutch. "Pyp, help me to the cage. Grenn, you have the Wall."

"*Me?*" said Grenn. "*Him?*" said Pyp. It was hard to tell which of them was more horrified. "But," Grenn stammered, "b-but what do I do if the wildlings attack again?"

"Stop them," Jon told him.

As they rode down in the cage, Pyp took off his helm and wiped his brow. "Frozen sweat. Is there anything as disgusting as frozen sweat?" He laughed. "Gods, I don't think I have ever been so hungry. I could eat an aurochs whole, I swear it. Do you think Hobb will cook up Grenn for us?" When he saw Jon's face, his smile died. "What's wrong? Is it your leg?"

"My leg," Jon agreed. Even the words were an effort.

"Not the battle, though? We won the battle."

"Ask me when I've seen the gate," Jon said grimly. *I want a fire, a hot meal, a warm bed, and something to make my leg stop hurting,* he told himself. But first he had to check the tunnel and find what had become of Donal Noye.

After the battle with the Thenns it had taken them almost a day to clear the ice and broken beams away from the inner gate. Spotted Pate and Kegs and some of the other builders had argued heatedly that they ought just leave the debris there, another obstacle for Mance. That would have meant abandoning the defense of the tunnel, though, and Noye was having none of it. With men in the murder holes and archers and spears behind each inner grate, a few determined brothers could hold off a hundred times as many wildlings and clog the way with corpses. He did not mean to give Mance Rayder free passage through the ice. So with pick and spade and ropes, they had moved the broken steps aside and dug back down to the gate.

Jon waited by the cold iron bars while Pyp went to Maester Aemon for the spare key. Surprisingly, the maester himself returned with him, and Clydas with a lantern. "Come see me when we are done," the old man told Jon while Pyp was fumbling with the chains. "I need to change your dressing and apply a fresh poultice, and you will want some more dreamwine for the pain."

Jon nodded weakly. The door swung open. Pyp led them in, followed by Clydas and the lantern. It was all Jon could do to keep up with Maester Aemon. The ice pressed close around them, and he could feel the cold seeping into his bones, the weight of the Wall above his head. It felt like walking down the gullet of an ice dragon. The tunnel took a twist, and then another. Pyp unlocked a second iron gate. They walked farther, turned again, and saw light ahead, faint and pale through the ice. *That's bad*, Jon knew at once. *That's very bad*.

Then Pyp said, "There's blood on the floor."

The last twenty feet of the tunnel was where they'd fought and died. The outer door of studded oak had been hacked and broken and finally torn off its hinges, and one of the giants had crawled in through the splinters. The lantern bathed the grisly scene in a sullen reddish light. Pyp turned aside to retch, and Jon found himself envying Maester Aemon his blindness.

Noye and his men had been waiting within, behind a gate of heavy iron bars like the two Pyp had just unlocked. The two crossbows had gotten off a dozen quarrels as the giant struggled toward them. Then the spearmen must have come to the fore, stabbing through the bars. Still the giant found the strength to reach through, twist the head off Spotted Pate, seize the iron gate, and wrench the bars apart. Links of broken chain lay strewn across the floor. *One giant. All this was the work of one giant.*

"Are they all dead?" Maester Aemon asked softly.

"Yes. Donal was the last." Noye's sword was sunk deep in the giant's throat, halfway to the hilt. The armorer had always seemed such a big man to Jon, but locked in the giant's massive arms he looked almost like a child. "The giant crushed his spine. I don't know who died first." He took the lantern and moved forward for a better look. "Mag." *I am the last of the giants.* He could feel the sadness there, but he had no time for sadness. "It was Mag the Mighty. The king of the giants."

He needed sun then. It was too cold and dark inside the tunnel, and the stench of blood and death was suffocating. Jon gave the lantern back to Clydas, squeezed around the bodies and through the twisted bars, and walked toward the daylight to see what lay beyond the splintered door.

The huge carcass of a dead mammoth partially blocked the way. One of the beast's tusks snagged his cloak and tore it as he edged past. Three more giants lay outside, half buried beneath stone and slush and hardened pitch. He could see where the fire had melted the Wall, where great sheets of ice had come sloughing off in the heat to shatter on the blackened ground. He looked up at where they'd come from. *When you stand here it seems immense, as if it were about to crush you.*

Jon went back inside to where the others waited. "We need to repair the outer gate as best we can and then block up this section of the tunnel. Rubble, chunks of ice, anything. All the way to the second gate, if we can. Ser Wynton will need to take command, he's the last knight left, but he needs to move *now*, the giants will be back before we know it. We have to tell him—"

"Tell him what you will," said Maester Aemon, gently. "He will smile, nod, and forget. Thirty years ago Ser Wynton Stout came within a dozen votes of being Lord Commander. He would have made a fine one. Ten years ago he would still have been capable. No longer. You know that as well as Donal did, Jon."

It was true. "You give the order, then," Jon told the maester. "You have been on the Wall your whole life, the men will follow you. We have to close the gate."

"I am a maester chained and sworn. My order serves, Jon. We give counsel, not commands."

"Someone must—"

"You. You must lead."

"No."

"Yes, Jon. It need not be for long. Only until such time as the garrison returns. Donal chose you, and Qhorin Halfhand before him. Lord Commander Mormont made you his steward. You are a son of Winterfell, a nephew of Benjen Stark. It must be you or no one. The Wall is yours, Jon Snow."

ARYA

She could feel the hole inside her every morning when she woke. It wasn't hunger, though sometimes there was that too. It was a hollow place, an emptiness where her heart had been, where her brothers had lived, and her parents. Her head hurt too. Not as bad as it had at first, but still pretty bad. Arya was used to that, though, and at least the lump was going down. But the hole inside her stayed the same. *The hole will never feel any better,* she told herself when she went to sleep.

Some mornings Arya did not want to wake at all. She would huddle beneath her cloak with her eyes squeezed shut and try to will herself back to sleep. If the Hound would only have left her alone, she would have slept all day and all night.

And dreamed. That was the best part, the dreaming. She dreamed of wolves most every night. A great pack of wolves, with her at the head. She was bigger than any of them, stronger, swifter, faster. She could outrun horses and out-fight lions. When she bared her teeth even men would run from her, her belly was never empty long, and her fur kept her warm even when the wind was blowing cold. And her brothers and sisters were with her, many and more of them, fierce and terrible and *hers*. They would never leave her.

But if her nights were full of wolves, her days belonged to the dog. Sandor Clegane made her get up every morning, whether she wanted to or not. He would curse at her in his raspy voice, or yank her to her feet and shake her. Once he dumped a helm full of cold water all over her head. She bounced up sputtering and shivering and tried to kick him, but he only laughed. "Dry off and feed the bloody horses," he told her, and she did.

They had two now, Stranger and a sorrel palfrey mare Arya had named Craven, because Sandor said she'd likely run off from the Twins the same as them. They'd found her wandering riderless through a field the morning after the slaughter. She was a good enough horse, but Arya could not love a coward. *Stranger would have fought.* Still, she tended the mare as best she knew. It was better than riding double with the Hound. And Craven might have been a coward, but she was young and strong as well. Arya thought that she might be able to outrun Stranger, if it came to it.

The Hound no longer watched her as closely as he had. Sometimes he did not seem to care whether she stayed or went, and he no longer bound her up in a cloak at night. *One night I'll kill him in his sleep*, she told herself, but she never did. *One day I'll ride away on Craven, and he won't be able to catch me*, she thought, but she never did that either. Where would she go? Winterfell was gone. Her grandfather's brother was at Riverrun, but he didn't know her, no more than she knew him. Maybe Lady Smallwood would take her in at Acorn Hall, but maybe she wouldn't. Besides, Arya wasn't even sure she could *find* Acorn Hall again. Sometimes she thought she might go back to Sharna's inn, if the floods hadn't washed it away. She could stay with Hot Pie, or maybe Lord Beric would find her there. Anguy would teach her to use a bow, and she could ride with Gendry and be an outlaw, like Wenda the White Fawn in the songs.

But that was just stupid, like something Sansa might dream. Hot Pie and Gendry had left her just as soon as they could, and Lord Beric and the outlaws only wanted to ransom her, just like the Hound. None of them wanted her around. *They were never my pack, not even Hot Pie and Gendry. I was stupid to think so, just a stupid little girl, and no wolf at all.*

So she stayed with the Hound. They rode every day, never sleeping twice in the same place, avoiding towns and villages and castles as best they could. Once she asked Sandor Clegane where they were going. "Away," he said. "That's all you need to know. You're not worth spit to me now, and I don't want to hear your whining. I should have let you run into that bloody castle."

"You should have," she agreed, thinking of her mother.

"You'd be dead if I had. You ought to thank me. You ought to sing me a pretty little song, the way your sister did."

"Did you hit her with an axe too?"

"I hit you with the *flat* of the axe, you stupid little bitch. If I'd hit you with the blade there'd still be chunks of your head floating down the Green Fork. Now shut your bloody mouth. If I had any sense I'd give you to the silent sisters. They cut the tongues out of girls who talk too much."

That wasn't fair of him to say. Aside from that one time, Arya hardly talked at all. Whole days passed when neither of them said anything. She was too empty to talk, and the Hound was too angry. She could feel the fury in him; she could see it on his face, the way his mouth would tighten and twist, the looks he gave her. Whenever he took his axe to chop some wood for a fire, he would slide into a cold rage, hacking savagely at the tree or the deadfall or the broken limb, until they had twenty times as much kindling and firewood as they'd needed. Sometimes he would be so sore and tired afterward that he would lie down and go right to sleep without even lighting a fire. Arya hated it when that happened, and hated him too. Those were the nights when she stared the longest at the axe. *It looks awfully heavy, but I bet I could swing it.* She wouldn't hit him with the flat, either.

Sometimes in their wanderings they glimpsed other people; farmers in their fields, swineherds with their pigs, a milkmaid leading a cow, a squire carrying a message down a rutted road. She never wanted to speak to them either. It was as if they lived in some distant land and spoke a queer alien tongue; they had nothing to do with her, or her with them.

Besides, it wasn't safe to be seen. From time to time columns of horsemen passed down the winding farm roads, the twin towers of Frey flying before them. "Hunting for stray northmen," the Hound said when they had passed. "Any time you hear hooves, get your head down fast, it's not like to be a friend."

One day, in an earthen hollow made by the roots of a fallen oak, they came face to face with another survivor of the Twins. The badge on his breast showed a pink maiden dancing in a swirl of silk, and he told them he was Ser Marq Piper's man; a bowman, though he'd lost his bow. His left shoulder was all twisted and swollen where it met his arm; a blow from a mace, he said, it had broken his shoulder and smashed his chainmail deep into his flesh. "A northman, it was," he wept. "His badge was a bloody man, and he saw mine and made a jape, red man and pink maiden, maybe they should get together. I drank to his Lord Bolton, he drank to Ser Marq, and we drank together to Lord Edmure and Lady Roslin and the King in the North. And then he killed me." His eyes were fever bright when he said that, and Arya could tell that it was true. His shoulder was swollen grotesquely, and pus and blood had stained his whole left side. There was a stink to him too. *He smells like a corpse.* The man begged them for a drink of wine.

"If I'd had any wine, I'd have drunk it myself," the Hound told him. "I can give you water, and the gift of mercy."

The archer looked at him a long while before he said, "You're Joffrey's dog."

"My own dog now. Do you want the water?"

"Aye." The man swallowed. "And the mercy. Please."

They had passed a small pond a short ways back. Sandor gave Arya his helm and told her to fill it, so she trudged back to the water's edge. Mud squished over the toe of her boots. She used the dog's head as a pail. Water ran out through the eyeholes, but the bottom of the helm still held a lot.

When she came back, the archer turned his face up and she poured the water into his mouth. He gulped it down as fast as she could pour, and what he couldn't gulp ran down his cheeks into the brown blood that crusted his whiskers, until pale pink tears dangled from his beard. When the water was gone he clutched the helm and licked the steel. "Good," he said. "I wish it was wine, though. I wanted wine."

"Me too." The Hound eased his dagger into the man's chest almost tenderly, the weight of his body driving the point through his surcoat, ringmail, and the quilting beneath. As he slid the blade back out and wiped it on the dead man, he looked at Arya. "That's where the heart is, girl. That's how you kill a man."

That's one way. "Will we bury him?"

"Why?" Sandor said. "He don't care, and we've got no spade. Leave him for the wolves and wild dogs. Your brothers and mine." He gave her a hard look. "First we rob him, though."

There were two silver stags in the archer's purse, and almost thirty coppers. His dagger had a pretty pink stone in the hilt. The Hound hefted the knife in his hand, then flipped it toward Arya. She caught it by the hilt, slid it through her belt, and felt a little better. It wasn't Needle, but it was steel. The dead man had a quiver of arrows too, but arrows weren't much good without a bow. His boots were too big for Arya and too small for the Hound, so those they left. She took his kettle helm as well, even though it came down almost past her nose, so she had to tilt it back to see. "He must have had a horse as well, or he wouldn't have got away," Clegane said, peering about, "but it's bloody well gone, I'd say. No telling how long he's been here."

By the time they found themselves in the foothills of the Mountains of the Moon, the rains had mostly stopped. Arya could see the sun and moon and stars, and it seemed to her that they were heading eastward. "Where are we going?" she asked again.

This time the Hound answered her. "You have an aunt in the Eyrie. Might be she'll want to ransom your scrawny arse, though the gods know why. Once we find the high road, we can follow it all the way to the Bloody Gate."

Aunt Lysa. The thought left Arya feeling empty. It was her mother she wanted, not her mother's sister. She didn't know her mother's sister any more than she knew her great uncle Blackfish. *We should have gone into the castle.* They didn't really *know* that her mother was dead, or Robb either. It wasn't like they'd seen them die or anything. Maybe Lord Frey had just taken them captive. Maybe they were chained up in his dungeon, or maybe the Freys were taking them to King's Landing so Joffrey could chop their heads off. They didn't *know.* "We should go back," she suddenly decided. "We should go back to the Twins and get my mother. She can't be dead. We have to help her."

"I thought your sister was the one with a head full of songs," the Hound growled. "Frey might have kept your mother alive to ransom, that's true. But there's no way in seven hells I'm going to pluck her out of his castle all by my bloody self."

"Not by yourself. I'd come too."

He made a sound that was almost a laugh. "*That* will scare the piss out of the old man."

"You're just afraid to die!" she said scornfully.

Now Clegane *did* laugh. "Death don't scare me. Only fire. Now be quiet, or I'll cut your tongue out myself and save the silent sisters the bother. It's the Vale for us."

Arya didn't think he'd *really* cut her tongue out; he was just saying that the way Pinkeye used to say he'd beat her bloody. All the same, she wasn't going to try him. Sandor Clegane was no Pinkeye. Pinkeye didn't cut people in half or hit them with axes. Not even with the flat of axes.

That night she went to sleep thinking of her mother, and wondering if she should kill the Hound in his sleep and rescue Lady Catelyn herself. When she closed her eyes she saw her mother's face against the back of her eyelids. *She's so close I could almost smell her . . .*

. . . and then she *could* smell her. The scent was faint beneath the other smells, beneath moss and mud and water, and the stench of rotting reeds and rotting men. She padded slowly through the soft ground to the river's edge, lapped up a drink, then lifted her head to sniff. The sky was grey and thick with cloud, the river green and full of floating things. Dead men clogged the shallows, some still moving as the water pushed them, others washed up on the banks. Her brothers and sisters swarmed around them, tearing at the rich ripe flesh.

The crows were there too, screaming at the wolves and

filling the air with feathers. Their blood was hotter, and one of her sisters had snapped at one as it took flight and caught it by the wing. It made her want a crow herself. She wanted to taste the blood, to hear the bones crunch between her teeth, to fill her belly with warm flesh instead of cold. She was hungry and the meat was all around, but she knew she could not eat.

The scent was stronger now. She pricked her ears up and listened to the grumbles of her pack, the shriek of angry crows, the whirr of wings and sound of running water. Somewhere far off she could hear horses and the calls of living men, but they were not what mattered. Only the scent mattered. She sniffed the air again. There it was, and now she saw it too, something pale and white drifting down the river, turning where it brushed against a snag. The reeds bowed down before it.

She splashed noisily through the shallows and threw herself into the deeper water, her legs churning. The current was strong but she was stronger. She swam, following her nose. The river smells were rich and wet, but those were not the smells that pulled her. She paddled after the sharp red whisper of cold blood, the sweet cloying stench of death. She chased them as she had often chased a red deer through the trees, and in the end she ran them down, and her jaw closed around a pale white arm. She shook it to make it move, but there was only death and blood in her mouth. By now she was tiring, and it was all she could do to pull the body back to shore. As she dragged it up the muddy bank, one of her little brothers came prowling, his tongue lolling from his mouth. She had to snarl to drive him off, or else he would have fed. Only then did she stop to shake the water from her fur. The white thing lay facedown in the mud, her dead flesh wrinkled and pale, cold blood trickling from her throat. *Rise*, she thought. *Rise and eat and run with us.*

The sound of horses turned her head. *Men.* They were coming from downwind, so she had not smelled them, but now they were almost here. Men on horses, with flapping black and yellow and pink wings and long shiny claws in hand. Some of her younger brothers bared their teeth to defend the food they'd found, but she snapped at them until they scattered. That was the way of the wild. Deer and hares and crows fled before wolves, and wolves fled from men. She abandoned the cold white prize in the mud where she had dragged it, and ran, and felt no shame.

When morning came, the Hound did not need to shout at Arya or shake her awake. She had woken before him for a change, and even watered the horses. They broke their fast in silence, until Sandor said, "This thing about your mother . . ."

"It doesn't matter," Arya said in a dull voice. "I know she's dead. I saw her in a dream."

The Hound looked at her a long time, then nodded. No more was said of it. They rode on toward the mountains.

In the higher hills, they came upon a tiny isolated village surrounded by grey-green sentinels and tall blue soldier pines, and Clegane decided to risk going in. "We need food," he said, "and a roof over our heads. They're not like to know what happened at the Twins, and with any luck they won't know me."

The villagers were building a wooden palisade around their homes, and when they saw the breadth of the Hound's shoulders they offered them food and shelter and even coin for work. "If there's wine as well, I'll do it," he growled at them. In the end, he settled for ale, and drank himself to sleep each night.

His dream of selling Arya to Lady Arryn died there in the hills, though. "There's frost above us and snow in the high passes," the village elder said. "If you don't freeze or starve, the shadowcats will get you, or the cave bears. There's the clans as well. The Burned Men are fearless since Timett One-Eye came back from the war. And half a year ago, Gunthor son of Gurn led the Stone Crows down on a village not eight miles from here. They took every woman and every scrap of grain, and killed half the men. They have *steel* now, good swords and mail hauberks, and they watch the high road—the Stone Crows, the Milk Snakes, the Sons of the Mist, all of them. Might be you'd take a few with you, but in the end they'd kill you and make off with your daughter."

I'm not his daughter, Arya might have shouted, if she hadn't felt so tired. She was no one's daughter now. She was no one. Not Arya, not Weasel, not Nan nor Arry nor

Squab, not even Lumpyhead. She was only some girl who ran with a dog by day, and dreamed of wolves by night.

It was quiet in the village. They had beds stuffed with straw and not too many lice, the food was plain but filling, and the air smelled of pines. All the same, Arya soon decided that she hated it. The villagers were cowards. None of them would even look at the Hound's face, at least not for long. Some of the women tried to put her in a dress and make her do needlework, but they weren't Lady Smallwood and she was having none of it. And there was one girl who took to following her, the village elder's daughter. She was of an age with Arya, but just a *child*; she cried if she skinned a knee, and carried a stupid cloth doll with her everywhere she went. The doll was made up to look like a man-at-arms, sort of, so the girl called him Ser Soldier and bragged how he kept her safe. "Go away," Arya told her half a hundred times. "Just leave me be." She wouldn't, though, so finally Arya took the doll away from her, ripped it open, and pulled the rag stuffing out of its belly with a finger. "Now he *really* looks like a soldier!" she said, before she threw the doll in a brook. After that the girl stopped pestering her, and Arya spent her days grooming Craven and Stranger or walking in the woods. Sometimes she would find a stick and practice her needlework, but then she would remember what had happened at the Twins and smash it against a tree until it broke.

"Might be we should stay here awhile," the Hound told her, after a fortnight. He was drunk on ale, but more brooding than sleepy. "We'd never reach the Eyrie, and the Freys will still be hunting survivors in the riverlands. Sounds like they need swords here, with these clansmen raiding. We can rest up, maybe find a way to get a letter to your aunt." Arya's face darkened when she heard that. She didn't want to stay, but there was nowhere to go, either. The next morning, when the Hound went off to chop down trees and haul logs, she crawled back into bed.

But when the work was done and the tall wooden palisade was finished, the village elder made it plain that there was no place for them. "Come winter, we will be hard pressed to feed our own," he explained. "And you . . . a man like you brings blood with him."

Sandor's mouth tightened. "So you do know who I am."

"Aye. We don't get travelers here, that's so, but we go to market, and to fairs. We know about King Joffrey's dog."

"When these Stone Crows come calling, you might be glad to have a dog."

"Might be." The man hesitated, then gathered up his courage. "But they say you lost your belly for fighting at the Blackwater. They say—"

"I know what they say." Sandor's voice sounded like two woodsaws grinding together. "Pay me, and we'll be gone."

When they left, the Hound had a pouch full of coppers, a skin of sour ale, and a new sword. It was a very old sword, if truth be told, though new to him. He swapped its owner the longaxe he'd taken at the Twins, the one he'd used to raise the lump on Arya's head. The ale was gone in less than a day, but Clegane sharpened the sword every night, cursing the man he'd swapped with for every nick and spot of rust. *If he lost his belly for fighting, why does he care if his sword is sharp?* It was not a question Arya dared ask him, but she thought on it a lot. Was that why he'd run from the Twins and carried her off?

Back in the riverlands, they found that the rains had ebbed away, and the flood waters had begun to recede. The Hound turned south, back toward the Trident. "We'll make for Riverrun," he told Arya as they roasted a hare he'd killed. "Maybe the Blackfish wants to buy himself a she-wolf."

"He doesn't know me. He won't even know I'm really me." Arya was tired of making for Riverrun. She had been making for Riverrun for years, it seemed, without ever getting there. Every time she made for Riverrun, she ended up someplace worse. "He won't give you any ransom. He'll probably just hang you."

"He's free to try." He turned the spit.

He doesn't talk like he's lost his belly for fighting. "I know where we could go," Arya said. She still had one brother left. *Jon will want me, even if no one else does. He'll call me "little sister" and muss my hair.* It was a long way, though, and she didn't think she could get there by herself. She hadn't even been able to reach Riverrun. "We could go to the Wall."

Sandor's laugh was half a growl. "The little wolf bitch wants to join the Night's Watch, does she?"

"My brother's on the Wall," she said stubbornly.

His mouth gave a twitch. "The Wall's a thousand leagues from here. We'd need to fight through the bloody Freys just to reach the Neck. There's lizard lions in those swamps that eat wolves every day for breakfast. And if we did reach the north with our skins intact, there's ironborn in half the castles, and thousands of bloody buggering northmen as well."

"Are you scared of them?" she asked. "Have you lost your belly for fighting?"

For a moment she thought he was going to hit her. By then the hare was brown, though, skin crackling and grease popping as it dripped down into the cookfire. Sandor took it off the stick, ripped it apart with his big hands, and tossed half of it into Arya's lap. "There's nothing wrong with my belly," he said as he pulled off a leg, "but I don't give a rat's arse for you *or* your brother. I have a brother too."

TYRION

"Tyrion," Ser Kevan Lannister said wearily, "if you are indeed innocent of Joffrey's death, you should have no difficulty proving it at trial."

Tyrion turned from the window. "Who is to judge me?"

"Justice belongs to the throne. The king is dead, but your father remains Hand. Since it is his own son who stands accused and his grandson who was the victim, he has asked Lord Tyrell and Prince Oberyn to sit in judgment with him."

Tyrion was scarcely reassured. Mace Tyrell had been Joffrey's good-father, however briefly, and the Red Viper was . . . well, a snake. "Will I be allowed to demand trial by battle?"

"I would not advise that."

"Why not?" It had saved him in the Vale, why not here? "Answer me, Uncle. Will I be allowed a trial by battle, and a champion to prove my innocence?"

"Certainly, if such is your wish. However, you had best know that your sister means to name Ser Gregor Clegane as *her* champion, in the event of such a trial."

The bitch checks my moves before I make them. A pity she didn't choose a Kettleblack. Bronn would make short work of any of the three brothers, but the Mountain That Rides was a kettle of a different color. "I shall need to sleep on this." *I need to speak with Bronn, and soon.* He didn't want to think about what this was like to cost him. Bronn had a lofty notion of what his skin was worth. "Does Cersei have witnesses against me?"

"More every day."

"Then I must have witnesses of my own."

"Tell me who you would have, and Ser Addam will send the Watch to bring them to the trial."

"I would sooner find them myself."

"You stand accused of regicide and kinslaying. Do you truly imagine you will be allowed to come and go as you please?" Ser Kevan waved at the table. "You have quill, ink, and parchment. Write the names of such witnesses as you require, and I shall do all in my power to produce them, you have my word as a Lannister. But you shall not leave this tower, except to go to trial."

Tyrion would not demean himself by begging. "Will you permit my squire to come and go? The boy Podrick Payne?"

"Certainly, if that is your wish. I shall send him to you."

"Do so. Sooner would be better than later, and now would be better than sooner." He waddled to the writing table. But when he heard the door open, he turned back and said, "Uncle?"

Ser Kevan paused. "Yes?"

"I did not do this."

"I wish I could believe that, Tyrion."

When the door closed, Tyrion Lannister pulled himself up into the chair, sharpened a quill, and pulled a blank parchment. *Who will speak for me?* He dipped his quill in the inkpot.

The sheet was still maiden when Podrick Payne appeared, sometime later. "My lord," the boy said.

Tyrion put down the quill. "Find Bronn and bring him at once. Tell him there's gold in it, more gold than he's ever dreamt of, and see that you don't return without him."

"Yes, my lord. I mean, no. I won't. Return." He went.

He had not returned by sunset, nor by moonrise. Tyrion

fell asleep in the window seat to wake stiff and sore at dawn. A serving man brought porridge and apples to break his fast, with a horn of ale. He ate at the table, the blank parchment before him. An hour later, the serving man returned for the bowl. "Have you seen my squire?" Tyrion asked him. The man shook his head.

Sighing, he turned back to the table, and dipped the quill again. *Sansa*, he wrote upon the parchment. He sat staring at the name, his teeth clenched so hard they hurt.

Assuming Joffrey had not simply choked to death on a bit of food, which even Tyrion found hard to swallow, Sansa must have poisoned him. *Joff practically put his cup down in her lap, and he'd given her ample reason.* Any doubts Tyrion might have had vanished when his wife did. *One flesh, one heart, one soul.* His mouth twisted. *She wasted no time proving how much those vows meant to her, did she? Well, what did you expect, dwarf?*

And yet . . . where would Sansa have gotten poison? He could not believe the girl had acted alone in this. *Do I really want to find her?* Would the judges believe that Tyrion's child bride had poisoned a king without her husband's knowledge? *I wouldn't.* Cersei would insist that they had done the deed together.

Even so, he gave the parchment to his uncle the next day. Ser Kevan frowned at it. "Lady Sansa is your only witness?"

"I will think of others in time."

"Best think of them now. The judges mean to begin the trial three days hence."

"That's too soon. You have me shut up here under guard, how am I to find witnesses to my innocence?"

"Your sister's had no difficulty finding witnesses to your guilt." Ser Kevan rolled up the parchment. "Ser Addam has men hunting for your wife. Varys has offered a hundred stags for word of her whereabouts, and a hundred dragons for the girl herself. If the girl can be found she will be found, and I shall bring her to you. I see no harm in husband and wife sharing the same cell and giving comfort to one another."

"You are too kind. Have you seen my squire?"

"I sent him to you yesterday. Did he not come?"

"He came," Tyrion admitted, "and then he went."

"I shall send him to you again."

But it was the next morning before Podrick Payne returned. He stepped inside the room hesitantly, with fear written all over his face. Bronn came in behind him. The sellsword knight wore a jerkin studded with silver and a heavy riding cloak, with a pair of fine-tooled leather gloves thrust through his swordbelt.

One look at Bronn's face gave Tyrion a queasy feeling in the pit of his stomach. "It took you long enough."

"The boy begged, or I wouldn't have come at all. I am expected at Castle Stokeworth for supper."

"Stokeworth?" Tyrion hopped from the bed. "And pray, what is there for you in Stokeworth?"

"A bride." Bronn smiled like a wolf contemplating a lost lamb. "I'm to wed Lollys the day after next."

"Lollys." *Perfect, bloody perfect.* Lady Tanda's lackwit daughter gets a knightly husband and a father of sorts for the bastard in her belly, and Ser Bronn of the Blackwater climbs another rung. It had Cersei's stinking fingers all over it. "My bitch sister has sold you a lame horse. The girl's dim-witted."

"If I wanted wits, I'd marry you."

"Lollys is big with another man's child."

"And when she pops him out, I'll get her big with mine."

"She's not even heir to Stokeworth," Tyrion pointed out. "She has an elder sister. Falyse. A *married* sister."

"Married ten years, and still barren," said Bronn. "Her lord husband shuns her bed. It's said he prefers virgins."

"He could prefer goats and it wouldn't matter. The lands will still pass to his wife when Lady Tanda dies."

"Unless Falyse should die before her mother."

Tyrion wondered whether Cersei had any notion of the sort of serpent she'd given Lady Tanda to suckle. *And if she does, would she care?* "Why are you here, then?"

Bronn shrugged. "You once told me that if anyone ever asked me to sell you out, you'd double the price."

Yes. "Is it two wives you want, or two castles?"

"One of each would serve. But if you want me to kill Gregor Clegane for you, it had best be a damned *big* castle."

The Seven Kingdoms were full of highborn maidens, but even the oldest, poorest, and ugliest spinster in the realm would balk at wedding such lowborn scum as Bronn. *Unless she was soft of body and soft of head, with a fatherless child in her belly from having been raped half a hundred times.* Lady Tanda had been so desperate to find a husband for Lollys that she had even pursued Tyrion for a time, and that had been *before* half of King's Landing enjoyed her. No doubt Cersei had sweetened the offer somehow, and Bronn *was* a knight now, which made him a suitable match for a younger daughter of a minor house.

"I find myself woefully short of both castles and highborn maidens at the moment," Tyrion admitted. "But I can offer you gold and gratitude, as before."

"I have gold. What can I buy with gratitude?"

"You might be surprised. A Lannister pays his debts."

"Your sister is a Lannister too."

"My lady wife is heir to Winterfell. Should I emerge from this with my head still on my shoulders, I may one day rule the north in her name. I could carve you out a big piece of it."

"If and when and might be," said Bronn. "And it's bloody cold up there. Lollys is soft, warm, and close. I could be poking her two nights hence."

"Not a prospect I would relish."

"Is that so?" Bronn grinned. "Admit it, Imp. Given a choice between fucking Lollys and fighting the Mountain, you'd have your breeches down and cock up before a man could blink."

He knows me too bloody well. Tyrion tried a different tack. "I'd heard that Ser Gregor was wounded on the Red Fork, and again at Duskendale. The wounds are bound to slow him."

Bronn looked annoyed. "He was never fast. Only freakish big and freakish strong. I'll grant you, he's quicker than you'd expect for a man that size. He has a monstrous long reach, and doesn't seem to feel blows the way a normal man would."

"Does he frighten you so much?" asked Tyrion, hoping to provoke him.

"If he didn't frighten me, I'd be a bloody fool." Bronn gave a shrug. "Might be I could take him. Dance around him until he was so tired of hacking at me that he couldn't lift his sword. Get him off his feet somehow. When they're flat on their backs it don't matter how tall they are. Even so, it's chancy. One misstep and I'm dead. Why should I risk it? I like you well enough, ugly little whoreson that you are . . . but if I fight your battle, I lose either way. Either the Mountain spills my guts, or I kill him and lose Stokeworth. I sell my sword, I don't give it away. I'm not your bloody brother."

"No," said Tyrion sadly. "You're not." He waved a hand. "Begone, then. Run to Stokeworth and Lady Lollys. May you find more joy in your marriage bed than I ever found in mine."

Bronn hesitated at the door. "What will you do, Imp?"

"Kill Gregor myself. Won't *that* make for a jolly song?"

"I hope I hear them sing it." Bronn grinned one last time, and walked out of the door, the castle, and his life.

Pod shuffled his feet. "I'm sorry."

"Why? Is it your fault that Bronn's an insolent black-hearted rogue? He's always been an insolent black-hearted rogue. That's what I liked about him." Tyrion poured himself a cup of wine and took it to the window seat. Outside the day was grey and rainy, but the prospect was still more cheerful than his. He could send Podrick Payne questing after Shagga, he supposed, but there were so many hiding places in the deep of the kingswood that outlaws often evaded capture for decades. *And Pod sometimes has difficulty finding the kitchens when I sent him down for cheese.* Timett son of Timett would likely be back in the Mountains of the Moon by now. And despite what he'd told Bronn, going up against Ser Gregor Clegane in his own person would be a bigger farce than Joffrey's jousting dwarfs. He did not intend to die with gales of laughter ringing in his ears. *So much for trial by combat.*

Ser Kevan paid him another call later that day, and again the day after. Sansa had not been found, his uncle informed him politely. Nor the fool Ser Dontos, who'd vanished the same night. Did Tyrion have any more witnesses he wished to summon? He did not. *How do I bloody well prove I didn't poison the wine, when a thousand people saw me fill Joff's cup?*

He did not sleep at all that night.

Instead he lay in the dark, staring up at the canopy and counting his ghosts. He saw Tysha smiling as she kissed him, saw Sansa naked and shivering in fear. He saw Joffrey clawing his throat, the blood running down his neck as his face turned black. He saw Cersei's eyes, Bronn's wolfish smile, Shae's wicked grin. Even thought of Shae could not arouse him. He fondled himself, thinking that perhaps if he woke his cock and satisfied it, he might rest more easily afterward, but it was no good.

And then it was dawn, and time for his trial to begin.

It was not Ser Kevan who came for him that morning, but Ser Addam Marbrand with a dozen gold cloaks. Tyrion had broken his fast on boiled eggs, burned bacon, and fried bread, and dressed in his finest. "Ser Addam," he said. "I had thought my father might send the Kingsguard to escort me to trial. I am still a member of the royal family, am I not?"

"You are, my lord, but I fear that most of the Kingsguard stand witness against you. Lord Tywin felt it would not be proper for them to serve as your guards."

"Gods forbid we do anything *improper*. Please, lead on."

He was to be tried in the throne room, where Joffrey had died. As Ser Addam marched him through the towering bronze doors and down the long carpet, he felt the eyes upon him. Hundreds had crowded in to see him judged. At least he hoped that was why they had come. *For all I know, they're all witnesses against me.* He spied Queen Margaery up in the gallery, pale and beautiful in her mourning. *Twice wed and twice widowed, and only sixteen.* Her mother stood tall to one side of her, her grandmother small on the other, with her ladies in waiting and her father's household knights packing the rest of the gallery.

The dais still stood beneath the empty Iron Throne, though all but one table had been removed. Behind it sat stout Lord Mace Tyrell in a gold mantle over green, and slender Prince Oberyn Martell in flowing robes of striped orange, yellow, and scarlet. Lord Tywin Lannister sat between them. *Perhaps there's hope for me yet.* The Dornishman and the Highgardener despised each other. *If I can find a way to use that . . .*

The High Septon began with a prayer, asking the Father Above to guide them to justice. When he was done the father below leaned forward to say, "Tyrion, did you kill King Joffrey?"

He would not waste a heartbeat. "No."

"Well, that's a relief," said Oberyn Martell dryly.

"Did Sansa Stark do it, then?" Lord Tyrell demanded.

I would have, if I'd been her. Yet wherever Sansa was and whatever her part in this might have been, she remained his wife. He had wrapped the cloak of his protection about her shoulders, though he'd had to stand on a fool's back to do it. "The gods killed Joffrey. He choked on his pigeon pie."

Lord Tyrell reddened. "You would blame the bakers?"

"Them, or the pigeons. Just leave me out of it." Tyrion heard nervous laughter, and knew he'd made a mistake. *Guard your tongue, you little fool, before it digs your grave.*

"There are witnesses against you," Lord Tywin said. "We shall hear them first. Then you may present your own witnesses. You are to speak only with our leave."

There was naught that Tyrion could do but nod.

Ser Addam had told it true; the first man ushered in was Ser Balon Swann of the Kingsguard. "Lord Hand," he began, after the High Septon had sworn him to speak only truth, "I had the honor to fight beside your son on the bridge of ships. He is a brave man for all his size, and I will not believe he did this thing."

A murmur went through the hall, and Tyrion wondered what mad game Cersei was playing. *Why offer a witness that believes me innocent?* He soon learned. Ser Balon spoke reluctantly of how he had pulled Tyrion away from Joffrey on the day of the riot. "He did strike His Grace, that's so. It was a fit of wroth, no more. A summer storm. The mob near killed us all."

"In the days of the Targaryens, a man who struck one of the blood royal would lose the hand he struck him with," observed the Red Viper of Dorne. "Did the dwarf regrow his little hand, or did you White Swords forget your duty?"

"He was of the blood royal himself," Ser Balon answered. "And the King's Hand beside."

"No," Lord Tywin said. "He was *acting* Hand, in my stead."

Ser Meryn Trant was pleased to expand on Ser Balon's account, when he took his place as witness. "He knocked the king to the ground and began kicking him. He shouted that it was unjust that His Grace had escaped unharmed from the mobs."

Tyrion began to grasp his sister's plan. *She began with a man known to be honest, and milked him for all he would give. Every witness to follow will tell a worse tale, until I seem as bad as Maegor the Cruel and Aerys the Mad together, with a pinch of Aegon the Unworthy for spice.*

Ser Meryn went on to relate how Tyrion had stopped Joffrey's chastisement of Sansa Stark. "The dwarf asked His Grace if he knew what had happened to Aerys Targaryen. When Ser Boros spoke up in defense of the king, the Imp threatened to have him killed."

Blount himself came next, to echo *that* sorry tale. Whatever mislike Ser Boros might harbor toward Cersei for dismissing him from the Kingsguard, he said the words she wanted all the same.

Tyrion could no longer hold his tongue. "Tell the judges what Joffrey was *doing*, why don't you?"

The big jowly man glared at him. "You told your savages to kill me if I opened my mouth, that's what I'll tell them."

"Tyrion," Lord Tywin said. "You are to speak only when we call upon you. Take this for a warning."

Tyrion subsided, seething.

The Kettleblacks came next, all three of them in turn. Osney and Osfryd told the tale of his supper with Cersei before the Battle of the Blackwater, and of the threats he'd made.

"He told Her Grace that he meant to do her harm," said Ser Osfryd. "To hurt her." His brother Osney elaborated. "He said he would wait for a day when she was happy, and make her joy turn to ashes in her mouth." Neither mentioned Alayaya.

Ser Osmund Kettleblack, a vision of chivalry in immaculate scale armor and white wool cloak, swore that King Joffrey had long known that his uncle Tyrion meant to murder him. "It was the day they gave me the white cloak, my lords," he told the judges. "That brave boy said to me, 'Good Ser Osmund, guard me well, for my uncle loves me not. He means to be king in my place.' "

That was more than Tyrion could stomach. "*Liar!*" He took two steps forward before the gold cloaks dragged him back.

Lord Tywin frowned. "Must we have you chained hand and foot like a common brigand?"

Tyrion gnashed his teeth. *A second mistake, fool, fool, fool of a dwarf. Keep your calm or you're doomed.* "No. I beg your pardons, my lords. His lies angered me."

"His truths, you mean," said Cersei. "Father, I beg you to put him in fetters, for your own protection. You see how he is."

"I see he's a dwarf," said Prince Oberyn. "The day I fear a dwarf's wrath is the day I drown myself in a cask of red."

"We need no fetters." Lord Tywin glanced at the windows, and rose. "The hour grows late. We shall resume on the morrow."

That night, alone in his tower cell with a blank parchment and a cup of wine, Tyrion found himself thinking of his wife. Not Sansa; his *first* wife, Tysha. *The whore wife, not the wolf wife.* Her love for him had been pretense, and yet he had believed, and found joy in that belief. *Give me sweet lies, and keep your bitter truths.* He drank his wine and thought of Shae. Later, when Ser Kevan paid his nightly visit, Tyrion asked for Varys.

"You believe the eunuch will speak in your defense?"

"I won't know until I have talked with him. Send him here, Uncle, if you would be so good."

"As you wish."

Maesters Ballabar and Frenken opened the second day of trial. They had opened King Joffrey's noble corpse as well, they swore, and found no morsel of pigeon pie nor any other food lodged in the royal throat. "It was poison that killed him, my lords," said Ballabar, as Frenken nodded gravely.

Then they brought forth Grand Maester Pycelle, leaning heavily on a twisted cane and shaking as he walked, a few white hairs sprouting from his long chicken's neck. He had grown too frail to stand, so the judges permitted a chair to be brought in for him, and a table as well. On the table were laid a number of small jars. Pycelle was pleased to put a name to each.

"Greycap," he said in a quavery voice, "from the toadstool. Nightshade, sweetsleep, demon's dance. This is blindeye. Widow's blood, this one is called, for the color. A cruel potion. It shuts down a man's bladder and bowels, until he drowns in his own poisons. This wolfsbane, here basilisk venom, and this one the tears of Lys. Yes. I know them all. The Imp Tyrion Lannister stole them from my chambers, when he had me falsely imprisoned."

"*Pycelle,*" Tyrion called out, risking his father's wrath, "could any of these poisons choke off a man's breath?"

"No. For that, you must turn to a rarer poison. When I was a boy at the Citadel, my teachers named it simply *the strangler.*"

"But this rare poison was not found, was it?"

"No, my lord." Pycelle blinked at him. "You used it all to kill the noblest child the gods ever put on this good earth."

Tyrion's anger overwhelmed his sense. "Joffrey was cruel and stupid, but I did not kill him. Have my head off if you like, I had no hand in my nephew's death."

"*Silence!*" Lord Tywin said. "I have told you thrice. The next time, you shall be gagged and chained."

After Pycelle came the procession, endless and wearisome. Lords and ladies and noble knights, highborn and humble alike, they had all been present at the wedding feast, had all seen Joffrey choke, his face turning as black as a Dornish plum. Lord Redwyne, Lord Celtigar, and Ser Flement Brax had heard Tyrion threaten the king; two serving men, a juggler, Lord Gyles, Ser Hobber Redwyne, and Ser Philip Foote had observed him fill the wedding chalice; Lady Merryweather swore that she had seen the dwarf drop something into the king's wine while Joff and Margaery were cutting the pie; old Estermont, young Peckledon, the singer Galyeon of Cuy, and the squires Morros and Jothos Slynt told how Tyrion had picked up the chalice as Joff was dying and poured out the last of the poisoned wine onto the floor.

When did I make so many enemies? Lady Merryweather was all but a stranger. Tyrion wondered if she was blind or bought. At least Galyeon of Cuy had not set his account to music, or else there might have been seventy-seven bloody verses to it.

When his uncle called that night after supper, his manner was cold and distant. *He thinks I did it too.* "Do you have witnesses for us?" Ser Kevan asked him.

"Not as such, no. Unless you've found my wife."

His uncle shook his head. "It would seem the trial is going very badly for you."

"Oh, do you think so? I hadn't noticed." Tyrion fingered his scar. "Varys has not come."

"Nor will he. On the morrow he testifies against you."

Lovely. "I see." He shifted in his seat. "I am curious. You were always a fair man, Uncle. What convinced you?"

"Why steal Pycelle's poisons, if not to use them?" Ser Kevan said bluntly. "And Lady Merryweather saw—"

"—*nothing!* There was nothing to see. But how do I prove that? How do I prove *anything*, penned up here?"

"Perhaps the time has come for you to confess."

Even through the thick stone walls of the Red Keep, Tyrion could hear the steady wash of rain. "Say that again, Uncle? I could swear you urged me to confess."

"If you were to admit your guilt before the throne and repent of your crime, your father would withhold the sword. You would be permitted to take the black."

Tyrion laughed in his face. "Those were the same terms Cersei offered Eddard Stark. We all know how *that* ended."

"Your father had no part in that."

That much was true, at least. "Castle Black teems with murderers, thieves and rapists," Tyrion said, "but I don't recall meeting many regicides while I was there. You expect me to believe that if I admit to being a kinslayer and kingslayer, my father will simply nod, forgive me, and pack me off to the Wall with some warm woolen smallclothes." He hooted rudely.

"Naught was said of forgiveness," Ser Kevan said sternly. "A confession would put this matter to rest. It is for that reason your father sends me with this offer."

"Thank him kindly for me, Uncle," said Tyrion, "but tell him I am not presently in a confessing mood."

"Were I you, I'd change my mood. Your sister wants your head, and Lord Tyrell at least is inclined to give it to her."

"So one of my judges has already condemned me, without hearing a word in my defense?" It was no more than he expected. "Will I still be allowed to speak and present witnesses?"

"You *have* no witnesses," his uncle reminded him. "Tyrion, if you are guilty of this enormity, the Wall is a kinder fate than you deserve. And if you are blameless . . . there is fighting in the north, I know, but even so it will be a safer place for you than King's Landing, whatever the outcome of this trial. The mob is convinced of your guilt. Were you so foolish as to venture out into the streets, they would tear you limb from limb."

"I can see how much that prospect upsets you."

"You are my brother's son."

"You might remind *him* of that."

"Do you think he would allow you to take the black if you were not his own blood, and Joanna's? Tywin seems a hard man to you, I know, but he is no harder than he's had to be. Our own father was gentle and amiable, but so weak his bannermen mocked him in their cups. Some saw fit to defy him openly. Other lords borrowed our gold and never troubled to repay it. At court they japed of toothless lions. Even his mistress stole from him. A woman scarcely one step above a whore, and she helped herself to my mother's jewels! It fell to Tywin to restore House Lannister to its proper place. Just as it fell to him to rule this realm, when he was no more than twenty. He bore that heavy burden for *twenty years*, and all it earned him was a mad king's envy. Instead of the honor he deserved, he was made to suffer slights beyond count, yet he gave the Seven Kingdoms peace, plenty, and justice. He is a just man. You would be wise to trust him."

Tyrion blinked in astonishment. Ser Kevan had always been solid, stolid, pragmatic; he had never heard him speak with such fervor before. "You love him."

"He is my brother."

"I . . . I will think on what you've said."

"Think carefully, then. And quickly."

He thought of little else that night, but come morning was no closer to deciding if his father could be trusted. A servant brought him porridge and honey to break his fast, but all he could taste was bile at the thought of confession. *They will call me kinslayer till the end of my days. For a thousand years or more, if I am remembered at all, it will be as the monstrous dwarf who poisoned his young nephew at his wedding feast.* The thought made him so bloody angry that he flung the bowl and spoon across the room and left a smear of porridge on the wall. Ser Addam

Marbrand looked at it curiously when he came to escort Tyrion to trial, but had the good grace not to inquire.

"Lord Varys," the herald said, "master of whisperers."

Powdered, primped, and smelling of rosewater, the Spider rubbed his hands one over the other all the time he spoke. *Washing my life away*, Tyrion thought, as he listened to the eunuch's mournful account of how the Imp had schemed to part Joffrey from the Hound's protection and spoken with Bronn of the benefits of having Tommen as king. *Half-truths are worth more than outright lies*. And unlike the others, Varys had documents; parchments painstakingly filled with notes, details, dates, whole conversations. So much material that its recitation took all day, and so much of it damning. Varys confirmed Tyrion's midnight visit to Grand Maester Pycelle's chambers and the theft of his poisons and potions, confirmed the threat he'd made to Cersei the night of their supper, confirmed every bloody thing but the poisoning itself. When Prince Oberyn asked him how he could possibly know all this, not having been present at any of these events, the eunuch only giggled and said, "My little birds told me. Knowing is their purpose, and mine."

How do I question a little bird? thought Tyrion. *I should have had the eunuch's head off my first day in King's Landing. Damn him. And damn me for whatever trust I put in him.*

"Have we heard it all?" Lord Tywin asked his daughter as Varys left the hall.

"Almost," said Cersei. "I beg your leave to bring one final witness before you, on the morrow."

"As you wish," Lord Tywin said.

Oh, good, thought Tyrion savagely. *After this farce of a trial, execution will almost come as a relief.*

That night, as he sat by his window drinking, he heard voices outside his door. *Ser Kevan, come for my answer*, he thought at once, but it was not his uncle who entered.

Tyrion rose to give Prince Oberyn a mocking bow. "Are judges permitted to visit the accused?"

"Princes are permitted to go where they will. Or so I told your guards." The Red Viper took a seat.

"My father will be displeased with you."

"The happiness of Tywin Lannister has never been high

on my list of concerns. Is it Dornish wine you're drinking?"

"From the Arbor."

Oberyn made a face. "Red water. Did you poison him?"

"No. Did you?"

The prince smiled. "Do all dwarfs have tongues like yours? Someone is going to cut it out one of these days."

"You are not the first to tell me that. Perhaps I should cut it out myself, it seems to make no end of trouble."

"So I've seen. I think I may drink some of Lord Redwyne's grape juice after all."

"As you like." Tyrion served him a cup.

The man took a sip, sloshed it about in his mouth, and swallowed. "It will serve, for the moment. I will send you up some strong Dornish wine on the morrow." He took another sip. "I have turned up that golden-haired whore I was hoping for."

"So you found Chataya's?"

"At Chataya's I bedded the black-skinned girl. Alayaya, I believe she is called. Exquisite, despite the stripes on her back. But the whore I referred to is your sister."

"Has she seduced you yet?" Tyrion asked, unsurprised.

Oberyn laughed aloud. "No, but she will if I meet her price. The queen has even hinted at marriage. Her Grace needs another husband, and who better than a prince of Dorne? Ellaria believes I should accept. Just the thought of Cersei in our bed makes her wet, the randy wench. And we should not even need to pay the dwarf's penny. All your sister requires from me is one head, somewhat overlarge and missing a nose."

"And?" said Tyrion, waiting.

By way of answer Prince Oberyn swirled his wine, and said, "When the Young Dragon conquered Dorne so long ago, he left the Lord of Highgarden to rule us after the Submission of Sunspear. This Tyrell moved with his tail from keep to keep, chasing rebels and making certain that our knees stayed bent. He would arrive in force, take a castle for his own, stay a moon's turn, and ride on to the next castle. It was his custom to turn the lords out of their own chambers and take their beds for himself. One night he found himself beneath a heavy velvet canopy. A sash hung down near the pillows, should he wish to summon a wench. He had a taste for Dornish women, this Lord Tyrell, and who can blame him? So he pulled upon the sash, and when he did the canopy above him split open, and a hundred red scorpions fell down upon his head. His death lit a fire that soon swept across Dorne, undoing all the Young Dragon's victories in a fortnight. The kneeling men stood up, and we were free again."

"I know the tale," said Tyrion. "What of it?"

"Just this. If I should ever find a sash beside my own bed, and pull on it, I would sooner have the scorpions fall upon me than the queen in all her naked beauty."

Tyrion grinned. "We have that much in common, then."

"To be sure, I have much to thank your sister for. If not for her accusation at the feast, it might well be you judging me instead of me judging you." The prince's eyes were dark with amusement. "Who knows more of poison than the Red Viper of Dorne, after all? Who has better reason to want to keep the Tyrells far from the crown? And with Joffrey in his grave, by *Dornish* law the Iron Throne should pass next to his sister Myrcella, who as it happens is betrothed to mine own nephew, thanks to you."

"Dornish law does not apply." Tyrion had been so ensnared in his own troubles that he'd never stopped to consider the succession. "My father will crown Tommen, count on that."

"He may indeed crown Tommen, here in King's Landing. Which is not to say that my brother may not crown Myrcella, down in Sunspear. Will your father make war on your niece on behalf of your nephew? Will your sister?" He gave a shrug. "Perhaps I should marry Queen Cersei after all, on the condition that she support her daughter over her son. Do you think she would?"

Never, Tyrion wanted to say, but the word caught in his throat. Cersei always resented being excluded from power on account of her sex. *If Dornish law applied in the west, she would be the heir to Casterly Rock in her own right.* She and Jaime were twins, but Cersei had come first into the world, and that was all it took. By championing Myrcella's cause she would be championing her own. "I do not know how my sister would choose, between Tommen and Myrcella," he admitted. "It makes no matter. My father will never give her that choice."

"Your father," said Prince Oberyn, "may not live forever."

Something about the way he said it made the hairs on the back of Tyrion's neck bristle. Suddenly he was mindful of Elia again, and all that Oberyn had said as they crossed the field of ashes. *He wants the head that spoke the words, not just the hand that swung the sword.* "It is not wise to speak such treasons in the Red Keep, my prince. The little birds are listening."

"Let them. Is it treason to say a man is mortal? *Valar morghulis* was how they said it in Valyria of old. *All men must die.* And the Doom came and proved it true." The Dornishman went to the window to gaze out into the night. "It is being said that you have no witnesses for us."

"I was hoping one look at this sweet face of mine would be enough to persuade you all of my innocence."

"You are mistaken, my lord. The Fat Flower of Highgarden is quite convinced of your guilt, and determined to see you die. His precious Margaery was drinking from that chalice too, as he has reminded us half a hundred times."

"And you?" said Tyrion.

"Men are seldom as they appear. You look so very guilty that I am convinced of your innocence. Still, you will likely be condemned. Justice is in short supply this side of the mountains. There has been none for Elia, Aegon, or Rhaenys. Why should there be any for you? Perhaps Joffrey's real killer was eaten by a bear. That seems to happen quite often in King's Landing. Oh, wait, the bear was at Harrenhal, now I remember."

"Is that the game we are playing?" Tyrion rubbed at his scarred nose. He had nothing to lose by telling Oberyn the truth. "There *was* a bear at Harrenhal, and it did kill Ser Amory Lorch."

"How sad for him," said the Red Viper. "And for you. Do all noseless men lie so badly, I wonder?"

"I am not lying. Ser Amory dragged Princess Rhaenys out from under her father's bed and stabbed her to death. He had some men-at-arms with him, but I do not know their names." He leaned forward. "It was Ser Gregor Clegane who smashed Prince Aegon's head against a wall and raped your sister Elia with his blood and brains still on his hands."

"What is this, now? Truth, from a Lannister?" Oberyn smiled coldly. "Your father gave the commands, yes?"

"No." He spoke the lie without hesitation, and never stopped to ask himself why he should.

The Dornishman raised one thin black eyebrow. "Such a dutiful son. And such a very feeble lie. It was Lord Tywin who presented my sister's children to King Robert all wrapped up in crimson Lannister cloaks."

"Perhaps you ought to have this discussion with my father. He was there. I was at the Rock, and still so young that I thought the thing between my legs was only good for pissing."

"Yes, but you are here now, and in some difficulty, I would say. Your innocence may be as plain as the scar on your face, but it will not save you. No more than your father will." The Dornish prince smiled. "But I might."

"You?" Tyrion studied him. "You are one judge in three. How could you save me?"

"Not as your judge. As your champion."

JAIME

A white book sat on a white table in a white room. The room was round, its walls of whitewashed stone hung with white woolen tapestries. It formed the first floor of White Sword Tower, a slender structure of four stories built into an angle of the castle wall overlooking the bay. The undercroft held arms and armor, the second and third floors the small spare sleeping cells of the six brothers of the Kingsguard.

One of those cells had been his for eighteen years, but this morning he had moved his things to the topmost floor, which was given over entirely to the Lord Commander's apartments. Those rooms were spare as well, though spacious; and they were above the outer walls, which meant he would have a view of the sea. *I will like that*, he thought. *The view, and all the rest.*

As pale as the room, Jaime sat by the book in his Kingsguard whites, waiting for his Sworn Brothers. A longsword hung from his hip. *From the wrong hip.* Before he had always worn his sword on his left, and drawn it across his body when he unsheathed. He had shifted it to his right hip this morning, so as to be able to draw it with his left hand in the same manner, but the weight of it felt strange there, and when he had tried to pull the blade from the scabbard the whole motion seemed clumsy and unnatural. His clothing fit badly as well. He had donned the winter raiment of the Kingsguard, a tunic and breeches of bleached white wool and a heavy white cloak, but it all seemed to hang loose on him.

Jaime had spent his days at his brother's trial, standing well to the back of the hall. Either Tyrion never saw him there or he did not know him, but that was no surprise. Half the court no longer seemed to know him. *I am a stranger in my own House.* His son was dead, his father had disowned him, and his sister . . . she had not allowed him to be alone with her once, after that first day in the royal sept where Joffrey lay amongst the candles. Even when they bore him across the city to his tomb in the Great Sept of Baelor, Cersei kept a careful distance.

He looked about the Round Room once more. White wool hangings covered the walls, and there was a white shield and two crossed longswords mounted above the hearth. The chair behind the table was old black oak, with cushions of blanched cowhide, the leather worn thin. *Worn by the bony arse of Barristan the Bold and Ser Gerold Hightower before him, by Prince Aemon the Dragon-knight, Ser Ryam Redwyne, and the Demon of Darry, by Ser Duncan the Tall and the Pale Griffin Alyn Connington.* How could the Kingslayer belong in such exalted company?

Yet here he was.

The table itself was old weirwood, pale as bone, carved in the shape of a huge shield supported by three white stallions. By tradition the Lord Commander sat at the top of the shield, and the brothers three to a side, on the rare occasions when all seven were assembled. The book that rested by his elbow was massive; two feet tall and a foot and a half wide, a thousand pages thick, fine white vellum bound between covers of bleached white leather with gold hinges and fastenings. *The Book of the Brothers* was its formal name, but more often it was simply called the White Book.

Within the White Book was the history of the Kingsguard.

Every knight who'd ever served had a page, to record his name and deeds for all time. On the top left-hand corner of each page was drawn the shield the man had carried at the time he was chosen, inked in rich colors. Down in the bottom right corner was the shield of the Kingsguard; snow-white, empty, pure. The upper shields were all different; the lower shields were all the same. In the space between were written the facts of each man's life and service. The heraldic drawings and illuminations were done by septons sent from the Great Sept of Baelor three times a year, but it was the duty of the Lord Commander to keep the entries up to date.

My duty, now. Once he learned to write with his left hand, that is. The White Book was well behind. The deaths of Ser Mandon Moore and Ser Preston Greenfield needed to be entered, and the brief bloody Kingsguard service of Sandor Clegane as well. New pages must be started for Ser Balon Swann, Ser Osmund Kettleblack, and the Knight of Flowers. *I will need to summon a septon to draw their shields.*

Ser Barristan Selmy had preceded Jaime as Lord Commander. The shield atop his page showed the arms of House Selmy: three stalks of wheat, yellow, on a brown field. Jaime was amused, though unsurprised, to find that Ser Barristan had taken the time to record his own dismissal before leaving the castle.

Ser Barristan of House Selmy. Firstborn son of Ser Lyonel Selmy of Harvest Hall. Served as squire to Ser Manfred Swann. Named "the Bold" in his 10th year, when he donned borrowed armor to appear as a mystery knight in the tourney at Blackhaven, where he was defeated and unmasked by Duncan, Prince of Dragonflies. Knighted in his 16th year by King Aegon V Targaryen, after performing great feats of prowess as a mystery knight in the winter tourney at King's Landing, defeating Prince Duncan the Small and Ser Duncan the Tall, Lord Commander of the Kingsguard. Slew Maelys the Monstrous, last of the Blackfyre Pretenders, in single combat during the War of the Ninepenny Kings. Defeated Lormelle Long Lance and Cedrik Storm, the Bastard of Bronzegate. Named to the Kingsguard in his 23rd year, by Lord Commander Ser Gerold Hightower. Defended the passage against all chal-

lengers in the tourney of the Silver Bridge. Victor in the mêlée at Maidenpool. Brought King Aerys II to safety during the Defiance of Duskendale, despite an arrow wound in the chest. Avenged the murder of his Sworn Brother, Ser Gwayne Gaunt. Rescued Lady Jeyne Swann and her septa from the Kingswood Brotherhood, defeating Simon Toyne and the Smiling Knight, and slaying the former. In the Oldtown tourney, defeated and unmasked the mystery knight Blackshield, revealing him as the Bastard of Uplands. Sole champion of Lord Steffon's tourney at Storm's End, whereat he unhorsed Lord Robert Baratheon, Prince Oberyn Martell, Lord Leyton Hightower, Lord Jon Connington, Lord Jason Mallister, and Prince Rhaegar Targaryen. Wounded by arrow, spear, and sword at the Battle of the Trident whilst fighting beside his Sworn Brothers and Rhaegar Prince of Dragonstone. Pardoned, and named Lord Commander of the Kingsguard, by King Robert I Baratheon. Served in the honor guard that brought Lady Cersei of House Lannister to King's Landing to wed King Robert. Led the attack on Old Wyk during Balon Greyjoy's Rebellion. Champion of the tourney at King's Landing, in his 57th year. Dismissed from service by King Joffrey I baratheon in his 61st year, for reasons of advanced age.

The earlier part of Ser Barristan's storied career had been entered by Ser Gerold Hightower in a big forceful hand. Selmy's own smaller and more elegant writing took over with the account of his wounding on the Trident.

Jaime's own page was scant by comparison.

Ser Jaime of House Lannister. Firstborn son of Lord Tywin and Lady Joanna of Casterly Rock. Served against the Kingswood Brotherhood as squire to Lord Summer Crakehall. Knighted in his 15th year by Ser Arthur Dayne of the Kingsguard, for valor in the field. Chosen for the Kingsguard in his 15th year by King Aerys II Targaryen. During the Sack of King's Landing, slew King Aerys II at the foot of the Iron Throne. Thereafter known as the "Kingslayer." Pardoned for his crime by King Robert I Baratheon. Served in the honor guard that brought his sister the Lady Cersei Lannister to King's Landing to wed

King Robert. Champion in the tourney held at King's Landing on the occasion of their wedding.

Summed up like that, his life seemed a rather scant and mingy thing. Ser Barristan could have recorded a few of his other tourney victories, at least. And Ser Gerold might have written a few more words about the deeds he'd performed when Ser Arthur Dayne broke the Kingswood Brotherhood. He *had* saved Lord Sumner's life as Big Belly Ben was about to smash his head in, though the outlaw had escaped him. And he'd held his own against the Smiling Knight, though it was Ser Arthur who slew him. *What a fight that was, and what a foe.* The Smiling Knight was a madman, cruelty and chivalry all jumbled up together, but he did not know the meaning of fear. *And Dayne, with Dawn in hand . . .* The outlaw's longsword had so many notches by the end that Ser Arthur had stopped to let him fetch a new one. "It's that white sword of yours I want," the robber knight told him as they resumed, though he was bleeding from a dozen wounds by then. "Then you shall have it, ser," the Sword of the Morning replied, and made an end of it.

The world was simpler in those days, Jaime thought, *and men as well as swords were made of finer steel.* Or was it only that he had been fifteen? They were all in their graves now, the Sword of the Morning and the Smiling Knight, the White Bull and Prince Lewyn, Ser Oswell Whent with his black humor, earnest Jon Darry, Simon Toyne and his Kingswood Brotherhood, bluff old Sumner Crakehall. *And me, that boy I was . . . when did he die, I wonder? When I donned the white cloak? When I opened Aerys's throat?* That boy had wanted to be Ser Arthur Dayne, but someplace along the way he had become the Smiling Knight instead.

When he heard the door open, he closed the White Book and stood to receive his Sworn Brothers. Ser Osmund Kettleblack was the first to arrive. He gave Jaime a grin, as if they were old brothers-in-arms. "Ser Jaime," he said, "had you looked like this t'other night, I'd have known you at once."

"Would you indeed?" Jaime doubted that. The servants had bathed him, shaved him, and washed and brushed his hair. When he looked in a glass, he no longer saw the man who had crossed the riverlands with Brienne . . . but he did not see himself either. His face was thin and hollow, and he had lines under his eyes. *I look like some old man.* "Stand by your seat, ser."

Kettleblack complied. The other Sworn Brothers filed in one by one. "Sers," Jaime said in a formal tone when all five had assembled, "who guards the king?"

"My brothers Ser Osney and Ser Osfryd," Ser Osmund replied.

"And my brother Ser Garlan," said the Knight of Flowers.

"Will they keep him safe?"

"They will, my lord."

"Be seated, then." The words were ritual. Before the seven could meet in session, the king's safety must be assured.

Ser Boros and Ser Meryn sat to his right, leaving an empty chair between them for Ser Arys Oakheart, off in Dorne. Ser Osmund, Ser Balon, and Ser Loras took the seats to his left. *The old and the new.* Jaime wondered if that meant anything. There had been times during its history where the Kingsguard had been divided against itself, most notably and bitterly during the Dance of the Dragons. Was that something he needed to fear as well?

It seemed queer to him to sit in the Lord Commander's seat where Barristan the Bold had sat for so many years. *And even queerer to sit here crippled.* Nonetheless, it was his seat, and this was his Kingsguard now. *Tommen's seven.*

Jaime had served with Meryn Trant and Boros Blount for years; adequate fighters, but Trant was sly and cruel, and Blount a bag of growly air. Ser Balon Swann was better suited to his cloak, and of course the Knight of Flowers was supposedly all a knight should be. The fifth man was a stranger to him, this Osmund Kettleblack.

He wondered what Ser Arthur Dayne would have to say of this lot. *"How is it that the Kingsguard has fallen so low,"* most like. *"It was my doing,"* I would have to answer. *"I opened the door, and did nothing when the vermin began to crawl inside."*

"The king is dead," Jaime began. "My sister's son, a boy

of thirteen, murdered at his own wedding feast in his own hall. All five of you were present. All five of you were *protecting* him. And yet he's dead." He waited to see what they would say to that, but none of them so much as cleared a throat. *The Tyrell boy is angry, and Balon Swann's ashamed*, he judged. From the other three Jaime sensed only indifference. "Did my brother do this thing?" he asked them bluntly. "Did Tyrion poison my nephew?"

Ser Balon shifted uncomfortably in his seat. Ser Boros made a fist. Ser Osmund gave a lazy shrug. It was Meryn Trant who finally answered. "He filled Joffrey's cup with wine. That must have been when he slipped the poison in."

"You are certain it was the *wine* that was poisoned?"

"What else?" said Ser Boros Blount. "The Imp emptied the dregs on the floor. Why, but to spill the wine that might have proved him guilty?"

"He knew the wine was poisoned," said Ser Meryn.

Ser Balon Swann frowned. "The Imp was not alone on the dais. Far from it. That late in the feast, we had people standing and moving about, changing places, slipping off to the privy, servants were coming and going . . . the king and queen had just opened the wedding pie, every eye was on them or those thrice-damned doves. No one was watching the wine cup."

"Who else was on the dais?" asked Jaime.

Ser Meryn answered. "The king's family, the bride's family, Grand Maester Pycelle, the High Septon . . ."

"There's your poisoner," suggested Ser Oswald Kettleblack with a sly grin. "Too holy by half, that old man. Never liked the look o' him, myself." He laughed.

"No," the Knight of Flowers said, unamused. "Sansa Stark was the poisoner. You all forget, my sister was drinking from that chalice as well. Sansa Stark was the only person in the hall who had reason to want Margaery dead, as well as the king. By poisoning the wedding cup, she could hope to kill both of them. And why did she run afterward, unless she was guilty?"

The boy makes sense. Tyrion might yet be innocent. No one was any closer to finding the girl, however. Perhaps Jaime should look into that himself. For a start, it would be good to know how she had gotten out of the castle. *Varys may have a notion or two about that.* No one knew the Red Keep better than the eunuch.

That could wait, however. Just now Jaime had more immediate concerns. *You say you are the Lord Commander of the Kingsguard,* his father had said. *Go do your duty.* These five were not the brothers he would have chosen, but they were the brothers he had; the time had come to take them in hand.

"Whoever did it," he told them, "Joffrey is dead, and the Iron Throne belongs to Tommen now. I mean for him to sit on it until his hair turns white and his teeth fall out. And not from poison." Jaime turned to Ser Boros Blount. The man had grown stout in recent years, though he was big-boned enough to carry it. "Ser Boros, you look like a man who enjoys his food. Henceforth you'll taste everything Tommen eats or drinks."

Ser Osmund Kettleblack laughed aloud and the Knight of Flowers smiled, but Ser Boros turned a deep beet red. "I am no food taster! I am a knight of the Kingsguard!"

"Sad to say, you are." Cersei should never have stripped the man of his white cloak. But their father had only compounded the shame by restoring it. "My sister has told me how readily you yielded my nephew to Tyrion's sellswords. You will find carrots and pease less threatening, I hope. When your Sworn Brothers are training in the yard with sword and shield, you may train with spoon and trencher. Tommen loves applecakes. Try not to let any sellswords make off with them."

"You speak to me thus? *You?*"

"You should have died before you let Tommen be taken."

"As you died protecting Aerys, ser?" Ser Boros lurched to his feet, and clasped the hilt of his sword. "I *won't* . . . I won't suffer this. You should be the food taster, it seems to me. What else is a cripple good for?"

Jaime smiled. "I agree. I am as unfit to guard the king as you are. So draw that sword you're fondling, and we shall see how your two hands fare against my one. At the end one of us will be dead, and the Kingsguard will be improved." He rose. "Or, if you prefer, you may return to your duties."

"*Bah!*" Ser Boros hawked up a glob of green phlegm,

spat it at Jaime's feet, and walked out, his sword still in its sheath.

The man is craven, and a good thing. Though fat, aging, and never more than ordinary, Ser Boros could still have hacked him into bloody pieces. *But Boros does not know that, and neither must the rest. They feared the man I was; the man I am they'd pity.*

Jaime seated himself again and turned to Kettleblack. "Ser Osmund. I do not know you. I find that curious. I've fought in tourneys, mêlées, and battles throughout the Seven Kingdoms. I know of every hedge knight, freerider, and upjumped squire of any skill who has ever presumed to break a lance in the lists. So how is it that I have never heard of you, Ser Osmund?"

"That I couldn't say, my lord." He had a great wide smile on his face, did Ser Osmund, as if he and Jaime were old comrades in arms playing some jolly little game. "I'm a soldier, though, not no tourney knight."

"Where had you served, before my sister found you?"

"Here and there, my lord."

"I have been to Oldtown in the south and Winterfell in the north. I have been to Lannisport in the west, and King's Landing in the east. But I have never been to Here. Nor There." For want of a finger, Jaime pointed his stump at Ser Osmund's beak of a nose. "I will ask once more. *Where have you served?*"

"In the Stepstones. Some in the Disputed Lands. There's always fighting there. I rode with the Gallant Men. We fought for Lys, and some for Tyrosh."

You fought for anyone who would pay you. "How did you come by your knighthood?"

"On a battlefield."

"Who knighted you?"

"Ser Robert . . . Stone. He's dead now, my lord."

"To be sure." Ser Robert Stone might have been some bastard from the Vale, he supposed, selling his sword in the Disputed Lands. On the other hand, he might be no more than a name Ser Osmund cobbled together from a dead king and a castle wall. *What was Cersei thinking when she gave this one a white cloak?*

At least Kettleblack would likely know how to use a sword and shield. Sellswords were seldom the most honorable of men, but they had to have a certain skill at arms to stay alive. "Very well, ser," Jaime said. "You may go."

The man's grin returned. He left swaggering.

"Ser Meryn." Jaime smiled at the sour knight with the rust-red hair and the pouches under his eyes. "I have heard it said that Joffrey made use of you to chastise Sansa Stark." He turned the White Book around one-handed. "Here, show me where it is in our vows that we swear to beat women and children."

"I did as His Grace commanded me. We are sworn to obey."

"Henceforth you will temper that obedience. My sister is Queen Regent. My father is the King's Hand. I am Lord Commander of the Kingsguard. Obey us. None other."

Ser Meryn got a stubborn look on his face. "Are you telling us not to obey the king?"

"The king is eight. Our first duty is to *protect* him, which includes protecting him from himself. Use that ugly thing you keep inside your helm. If Tommen wants you to saddle his horse, obey him. If he tells you to kill his horse, come to me."

"Aye. As you command, my lord."

"Dismissed." As he left, Jaime turned to Ser Balon Swann. "Ser Balon, I have watched you tilt many a time, and fought with and against you in mêlées. I'm told you proved your valor a hundred times over during the Battle of the Blackwater. The Kingsguard is honored by your presence."

"The honor's mine, my lord." Ser Balon sounded wary.

"There is only one question I would put to you. You served us loyally, it's true . . . but Varys tells me that your brother rode with Renly and then Stannis, whilst your lord father chose not to call his banners at all and remained behind the walls of Stonehelm all through the fighting."

"My father is an old man, my lord. Well past forty. His fighting days are done."

"And your brother?"

"Donnel was wounded in the battle and yielded to Ser Elwood Harte. He was ransomed afterward and pledged his fealty to King Joffrey, as did many other captives."

"So he did," said Jaime. "Even so . . . Renly, Stannis, Joffrey, Tommen . . . how did he come to omit Balon

Greyjoy and Robb Stark? He might have been the first knight in the realm to swear fealty to all six kings."

Ser Balon's unease was plain. "Donnel erred, but he is Tommen's man now. You have my word."

"It's not Ser Donnel the Constant who concerns me. It's you." Jaime leaned forward. "What will you do if brave Ser Donnel gives his sword to yet another usurper, and one day comes storming into the throne room? And there you stand all in white, between your king and your blood. What will you do?"

"I . . . my lord, that will never happen."

"It happened to me," Jaime said.

Swann wiped his brow with the sleeve of his white tunic.

"You have no answer?"

"My lord." Ser Balon drew himself up. "On my sword, on my honor, on my father's name, I swear . . . I shall not do as you did."

Jaime laughed. "Good. Return to your duties . . . and tell Ser Donnel to add a weathervane to his shield."

And then he was alone with the Knight of Flowers.

Slim as a sword, lithe and fit, Ser Loras Tyrell wore a snowy linen tunic and white wool breeches, with a gold belt around his waist and a gold rose clasping his fine silk cloak. His hair was a soft brown tumble, and his eyes were brown as well, and bright with insolence. *He thinks this is a tourney, and his tilt has just been called.* "Seventeen and a knight of the Kingsguard," said Jaime. "You must be proud. Prince Aemon the Dragonknight was seventeen when he was named. Did you know that?"

"Yes, my lord."

"And did you know that I was *fifteen*?"

"That as well, my lord." He smiled.

Jaime hated that smile. "I was better than you, Ser Loras. I was bigger, I was stronger, and I was quicker."

"And now you're older," the boy said. "My lord."

He had to laugh. *This is too absurd. Tyrion would mock me unmercifully if he could hear me now, comparing cocks with this green boy.* "Older and wiser, ser. You should learn from me."

"As you learned from Ser Boros and Ser Meryn?"

That arrow hit too close to the mark. "I learned from

the White Bull and Barristan the Bold," Jaime snapped. "I learned from Ser Arthur Dayne, the Sword of the Morning, who could have slain all five of you with his left hand while he was taking a piss with the right. I learned from Prince Lewyn of Dorne and Ser Oswell Whent and Ser Jonothor Darry, good men every one."

"Dead men, every one."

He's me, Jaime realized suddenly. *I am speaking to myself, as I was, all cocksure arrogance and empty chivalry. This is what it does to you, to be too good too young.*

As in a swordfight, sometimes it is best to try a different stroke. "It's said you fought magnificently in the battle . . . almost as well as Lord Renly's ghost beside you. A Sworn Brother has no secrets from his Lord Commander. Tell me, ser. Who was wearing Renly's armor?"

For a moment Loras Tyrell looked as though he might refuse, but in the end he remembered his vows. "My brother," he said sullenly. "Renly was taller than me, and broader in the chest. His armor was too loose on me, but it suited Garlan well."

"Was the masquerade your notion, or his?"

"Lord Littlefinger suggested it. He said it would frighten Stannis's ignorant men-at-arms."

"And so it did." *And some knights and lordlings too.* "Well, you gave the singers something to make rhymes about, I suppose that's not to be despised. What did you do with Renly?"

"I buried him with mine own hands, in a place he showed me once when I was a squire at Storm's End. No one shall ever find him there to disturb his rest." He looked at Jaime defiantly. "I will defend King Tommen with all my strength, I swear it. I will give my life for his if need be. But I will never betray Renly, by word or deed. He was the king that should have been. He was the best of them."

The best dressed perhaps, Jaime thought, but for once he did not say it. The arrogance had gone out of Ser Loras the moment he began to speak of Renly. *He answered truly. He is proud and reckless and full of piss, but he is not false. Not yet.* "As you say. One more thing, and you may return to your duties."

"Yes, my lord?"

"I still have Brienne of Tarth in a tower cell."

The boy's mouth hardened. "A black cell would be better."

"You are certain that's what she deserves?"

"She deserves death. I told Renly that a woman had no place in the Rainbow Guard. She won the mêlée with a trick."

"I seem to recall another knight who was fond of tricks. He once rode a mare in heat against a foe mounted on a bad-tempered stallion. What sort of trickery did Brienne use?"

Ser Loras flushed. "She leapt . . . it makes no matter. She won, I grant her that. His Grace put a rainbow cloak around her shoulders. And she killed him. Or let him die."

"A large difference there." *The difference between my crime and the shame of Boros Blount.*

"She had sworn to protect him. Ser Emmon Cuy, Ser Robar Royce, Ser Parmen Crane, they'd sworn as well. How could anyone have hurt him, with her inside his tent and the others just outside? Unless they were part of it."

"There were five of you at the wedding feast," Jaime pointed out. "How could Joffrey die? Unless you were part of it?"

Ser Loras drew himself up stiffly. "There was nothing we could have done."

"The wench says the same. She grieves for Renly as you do. I promise you, I never grieve for Aerys. Brienne's ugly, and pighead stubborn. But she lacks the wits to be a liar, and she is loyal past the point of sense. She swore an oath to bring me to King's Landing, and here I sit. This hand I lost . . . well, that was my doing as much as hers. Considering all she did to protect me, I have no doubt that she would have fought for Renly, had there been a foe to fight. But a shadow?" Jaime shook his head. "Draw your sword, Ser Loras. Show me how *you'd* fight a shadow. I should like to see that."

Ser Loras made no move to rise. "She fled," he said. "She and Catelyn Stark, they left him in his blood and ran. Why would they, if it was not their work?" He stared at the table. "Renly gave me the van. Otherwise it would have been me helping him don his armor. He often entrusted that task to me. We had . . . we had prayed together that night. I left him with her. Ser Parmen and Ser Emmon were guarding the tent, and Ser Robar Royce was there as well. Ser Emmon swore Brienne had . . . although . . ."

"Yes?" Jaime prompted, sensing a doubt.

"The gorget was cut through. One clean stroke, through a steel gorget. Renly's armor was the best, the finest steel. How could she do that? I tried myself, and it was not possible. She's freakish strong for a woman, but even the Mountain would have needed a heavy axe. And why armor him and *then* cut his throat?" He gave Jaime a confused look. "If not her, though . . . how could it be a *shadow?*"

"Ask her." Jaime came to a decision. "Go to her cell. Ask your questions and hear her answers. If you are still convinced that she murdered Lord Renly, I will see that she answers for it. The choice will be yours. Accuse her, or release her. All I ask is that you judge her fairly, on your honor as a knight."

Ser Loras stood. "I shall. On my honor."

"We are done, then."

The younger man started for the door. But there he turned back. "Renly thought she was absurd. A woman dressed in man's mail, pretending to be a knight."

"If he'd ever seen her in pink satin and Myrish lace, he would not have complained."

"I asked him why he kept her close, if he thought her so grotesque. He said that all his other knights wanted things of him, castles or honors or riches, but all that Brienne wanted was to die for him. When I saw him all bloody, with her fled and the three of them unharmed . . . if she's innocent, then Robar and Emmon . . ." He could not seem to say the words.

Jaime had not stopped to consider that aspect of it. "I would have done the same, ser." The lie came easy, but Ser Loras seemed grateful for it.

When he was gone, the Lord Commander sat alone in the white room, wondering. The Knight of Flowers had been so mad with grief for Renly that he had cut down two of his own Sworn Brothers, but it had never occurred to Jaime to do the same with the five who had failed Joffrey. *He was my son, my secret son . . . What am I, if I do not lift the hand I have left to avenge mine own blood and seed?* He ought to kill Ser Boros at least, just to be rid of him.

He looked at his stump and grimaced. *I must do something about that.* If the late Ser Jacelyn Bywater could wear an iron hand, he should have a gold one. *Cersei might like that. A golden hand to stroke her golden hair, and hold her hard against me.*

His hand could wait, though. There were other things to tend to first. There were other debts to pay.

SANSA

The ladder to the forecastle was steep and splintery, so Sansa accepted a hand up from Lothor Brune. *Ser Lothor,* she had to remind herself; the man had been knighted for his valor in the Battle of the Blackwater. Though no proper knight would wear those patched brown breeches and scuffed boots, nor that cracked and water-stained leather jerkin. A square-faced stocky man with a squashed nose and a mat of nappy grey hair, Brune spoke seldom. *He is stronger than he looks, though.* She could tell by the ease with which he lifted her, as if she weighed nothing at all.

Off the bow of the *Merling King* stretched a bare and stony strand, windswept, treeless, and uninviting. Even so, it made a welcome sight. They had been a long while clawing their way back on course. The last storm had swept them out of sight of land, and sent such waves crashing over the sides of the galley that Sansa had been certain they were all going to drown. Two men had been swept overboard, she had heard old Oswell saying, and another had fallen from the mast and broken his neck.

She had seldom ventured out on deck herself. Her little cabin was dank and cold, but Sansa had been sick for most of the voyage . . . sick with terror, sick with fever, or sea-sick . . . she could keep nothing down, and even sleep came hard. Whenever she closed her eyes she saw Joffrey tearing at his collar, clawing at the soft skin of his throat, dying with flakes of pie crust on his lips and wine stains on his doublet. And the wind keening in the lines reminded her of the terrible thin sucking sound he'd made as he fought to draw in air. Sometimes she dreamed of Tyrion as well. "He did nothing," she told Littlefinger once, when he paid a visit to her cabin to see if she were feeling any better.

"He did not kill Joffrey, true, but the dwarf's hands are far from clean. He had a wife before you, did you know that?"

"He told me."

"And did he tell you that when he grew bored with her, he made a gift of her to his father's guardsmen? He might have done the same to you, in time. Shed no tears for the Imp, my lady."

The wind ran salty fingers through her hair, and Sansa shivered. Even this close to shore, the rolling of the ship made her tummy queasy. She desperately needed a bath and a change of clothes. *I must look as haggard as a corpse, and smell of vomit.*

Lord Petyr came up beside her, cheerful as ever. "Good morrow. The salt air is bracing, don't you think? It always sharpens my appetite." He put a sympathetic arm about her shoulders. "Are you quite well? You look so pale."

"It's only my tummy. The seasickness."

"A little wine will be good for that. We'll get you a cup, as soon as we're ashore." Petyr pointed to where an old flint tower stood outlined against a bleak grey sky, the breakers crashing on the rocks beneath it. "Cheerful, is it not? I fear there's no safe anchorage here. We'll put ashore in a boat."

"Here?" She did not want to go ashore here. The Fingers were a dismal place, she'd heard, and there was something forlorn and desolate about the little tower. "Couldn't I stay on the ship until we make sail for White Harbor?"

"From here the *King* turns east for Braavos. Without us."

"But . . . my lord, you said . . . you said we were sailing home."

"And there it stands, miserable as it is. My ancestral home. It has no name, I fear. A great lord's seat ought to have a name, wouldn't you agree? Winterfell, the Eyrie, Riverrun, those are *castles*. Lord of Harrenhal now, that has a sweet ring to it, but what was I before? Lord of Sheepshit and Master of the Drearfort? It lacks a certain something." His grey-green eyes regarded her innocently. "You look distraught. Did you think we were making for Winterfell, sweetling? Winterfell has been taken, burned, and sacked. All those you knew and loved are dead. What northmen who have not fallen to the ironmen are warring amongst themselves. Even the Wall is under attack. Winterfell was the home of your childhood, Sansa, but you are no longer a child. You're a woman grown, and you need to make your own home."

"But not here," she said, dismayed. "It looks so . . ."

". . . small and bleak and mean? It's all that, and less. The Fingers are a lovely place, if you happen to be a stone. But have no fear, we shan't stay more than a fortnight. I expect your aunt is already riding to meet us." He smiled. "The Lady Lysa and I are to be wed."

"Wed?" Sansa was stunned. "You and my aunt?"

"The Lord of Harrenhal and the Lady of the Eyrie."

You said it was my mother you loved. But of course Lady Catelyn was dead, so even if she had loved Petyr secretly and given him her maidenhood, it made no matter now.

"So silent, my lady?" said Petyr. "I was certain you would wish to give me your blessing. It is a rare thing for a boy born heir to stones and sheep pellets to wed the daughter of Hoster Tully and the widow of Jon Arryn."

"I . . . I pray you will have long years together, and many children, and be very happy in one another." It had been years since Sansa last saw her mother's sister. *She will be kind to me for my mother's sake, surely. She's my own blood.* And the Vale of Arryn was beautiful, all the songs said so. Perhaps it would not be so terrible to stay here for a time.

Lothor and old Oswell rowed them ashore. Sansa huddled in the bow under her cloak with the hood drawn up against the wind, wondering what awaited her. Servants emerged from the tower to meet them; a thin old woman and a fat middle-aged one, two ancient white-haired men, and a girl of two or three with a sty on one eye. When they recognized Lord Petyr they knelt on the rocks. "My household," he said. "I don't know the child. Another of Kella's bastards, I suppose. She pops one out every few years."

The two old men waded out up to their thighs to lift Sansa from the boat so she would not get her skirts wet. Oswell and Lothor splashed their way ashore, as did Littlefinger himself. He gave the old woman a kiss on the cheek and grinned at the younger one. "Who fathered this one, Kella?"

The fat woman laughed. "I can't rightly say, m'lord. I'm not one for telling them no."

"And all the local lads are grateful, I am quite sure."

"It is good to have you home, my lord," said one old man. He looked to be at least eighty, but he wore a studded brigantine and a longsword at his side. "How long will you be in residence?"

"As short a time as possible, Bryen, have no fear. Is the place habitable just now, would you say?"

"If we knew you was coming we would have laid down fresh rushes, m'lord," said the crone. "There's a dung fire burning."

"Nothing says *home* like the smell of burning dung." Petyr turned to Sansa. "Grisel was my wet nurse, but she keeps my castle now. Umfred's my steward, and Bryen—didn't I name you captain of the guard the last time I was here?"

"You did, my lord. You said you'd be getting some more men too, but you never did. Me and the dogs stand all the watches."

"And very well, I'm sure. No one has made off with any of my rocks or sheep pellets, I see that plainly." Petyr gestured toward the fat woman. "Kella minds my vast herds. How many sheep do I have at present, Kella?"

She had to think a moment. "Three and twenty, m'lord. There was nine and twenty, but Bryen's dogs killed one and we butchered some others and salted down the meat."

"Ah, cold salt mutton. I *must* be home. When I break my fast on gulls' eggs and seaweed soup, I'll be certain of it."

"If you like, m'lord," said the old woman Grisel.

Lord Petyr made a face. "Come, let's see if my hall is as dreary as I recall." He led them up the strand over rocks slick with rotting seaweed. A handful of sheep were wandering about the base of the flint tower, grazing on the thin grass that grew between the sheepfold and thatched stable. Sansa had to step carefully; there were pellets everywhere.

Within, the tower seemed even smaller. An open stone stair wound round the inside wall, from undercroft to roof. Each floor was but a single room. The servants lived and slept in the kitchen at ground level, sharing the space with a huge brindled mastiff and a half-dozen sheep-dogs. Above that was a modest hall, and higher still the bedchamber. There were no windows, but arrowslits were embedded in the outer wall at intervals along the curve of the stair. Above the hearth hung a broken longsword and a battered oaken shield, its paint cracked and flaking.

The device painted on the shield was one Sansa did not know; a grey stone head with fiery eyes, upon a light green field. "My grandfather's shield," Petyr explained when he saw her gazing at it. "His own father was born in Braavos and came to the Vale as a sellsword in the hire of Lord Corbray, so my grandfather took the head of the Titan as his sigil when he was knighted."

"It's very fierce," said Sansa.

"Rather too fierce, for an amiable fellow like me," said Petyr. "I much prefer my mockingbird."

Oswell made two more trips out to the *Merling King* to offload provisions. Among the loads he brought ashore were several casks of wine. Petyr poured Sansa a cup, as promised. "Here, my lady, that should help your tummy, I would hope."

Having solid ground beneath her feet had helped already, but Sansa dutifully lifted the goblet with both hands and took a sip. The wine was very fine; an Arbor vintage, she thought. It tasted of oak and fruit and hot summer nights, the flavors blossoming in her mouth like flowers opening to the sun. She only prayed that she could keep it down. Lord Petyr was being so kind, she did not want to spoil it all by retching on him.

He was studying her over his own goblet, his bright grey-green eyes full of . . . was it amusement? Or something

GEORGE R. R. MARTIN

else? Sansa was not certain. "Grisel," he called to the old woman, "bring some food up. Nothing too heavy, my lady has a tender tummy. Some fruit might serve, perhaps. Oswell's brought some oranges and pomegranates from the *King*."

"Yes, m'lord."

"Might I have a hot bath as well?" asked Sansa.

"I'll have Kella draw some water, m'lady."

Sansa took another sip of wine and tried to think of some polite conversation, but Lord Petyr saved her the effort. When Grisel and the other servants had gone, he said, "Lysa will not come alone. Before she arrives, we must be clear on who you are."

"Who I . . . I don't understand."

"Varys has informers everywhere. If Sansa Stark should be seen in the Vale, the eunuch will know within a moon's turn, and that would create unfortunate . . . complications. It is not safe to be a Stark just now. So we shall tell Lysa's people that you are my natural daughter."

"Natural?" Sansa was aghast. "You mean, a bastard?"

"Well, you can scarcely be my trueborn daughter. I've never taken a wife, that's well known. What should you be called?"

"I . . . I could call myself after my mother . . ."

"Catelyn? A bit too obvious . . . but after *my* mother, that would serve. Alayne. Do you like it?"

"Alayne is pretty." Sansa hoped she would remember. "But couldn't I be the trueborn daughter of some knight in your service? Perhaps he died gallantly in the battle, and . . ."

"I have no gallant knights in my service, Alayne. Such a tale would draw unwanted questions as a corpse draws crows. It is rude to pry into the origins of a man's natural children, however." He cocked his head. "So, who are you?"

"Alayne . . . Stone, would it be?" When he nodded, she said, "But who is my mother?"

"Kella?"

"Please no," she said, mortified.

"I was teasing. Your mother was a gentlewoman of Braavos, daughter of a merchant prince. We met in Gulltown when I had charge of the port. She died giving you birth, and entrusted you to the Faith. I have some devotional books you can look over. Learn to quote from them. Nothing discourages unwanted questions as much as a flow of pious bleating. In any case, at your flowering you decided you did not wish to be a septa and wrote to me. That was the first I knew of your existence." He fingered his beard. "Do you think you can remember all that?"

"I hope. It will be like playing a game, won't it?"

"Are you fond of games, Alayne?"

The new name would take some getting used to. "Games? I . . . I suppose it would depend . . ."

Grisel reappeared before he could say more, balancing a large platter. She set it down between them. There were apples and pears and pomegranates, some sad-looking grapes, a huge blood orange. The old woman had brought a round of bread as well, and a crock of butter. Petyr cut a pomegranate in two with his dagger, offering half to Sansa. "You should try and eat, my lady."

"Thank you, my lord." Pomegranate seeds were so messy; Sansa chose a pear instead, and took a small delicate bite. It was very ripe. The juice ran down her chin.

Lord Petyr loosened a seed with the point of his dagger. "You must miss your father terribly, I know. Lord Eddard was a brave man, honest and loyal . . . but quite a hopeless player." He brought the seed to his mouth with the knife. "In King's Landing, there are two sorts of people. The players and the pieces."

"And I was a piece?" She dreaded the answer.

"Yes, but don't let that trouble you. You're still half a child. Every man's a piece to start with, and every maid as well. Even some who think they are players." He ate another seed. "Cersei, for one. She thinks herself sly, but in truth she is utterly predictable. Her strength rests on her beauty, birth, and riches. Only the first of those is truly her own, and it will soon desert her. I pity her then. She wants power, but has no notion what to do with it when she gets it. Everyone wants something, Alayne. And when you know what a man wants you know who he is, and how to move him."

"As you moved Ser Dontos to poison Joffrey?" It *had* to have been Dontos, she had concluded.

Littlefinger laughed. "Ser Dontos the Red was a skin of

wine with legs. He could never have been trusted with a task of such enormity. He would have bungled it or betrayed me. No, all Dontos had to do was lead you from the castle . . . and make certain you wore your silver hair net."

The black amethysts. "But . . . if not Dontos, who? Do you have other . . . pieces?"

"You could turn King's Landing upside down and not find a single man with a mockingbird sewn over his heart, but that does not mean I am friendless." Petyr went to the steps. "Oswell, come up here and let the Lady Sansa have a look at you."

The old man appeared a few moments later, grinning and bowing. Sansa eyed him uncertainly. "What am I supposed to see?"

"Do you know him?" asked Petyr.

"No."

"Look closer."

She studied the old man's lined windburnt face, hook nose, white hair, and huge knuckly hands. There *was* something familiar about him, yet Sansa had to shake her head. "I don't. I never saw Oswell before I got into his boat, I'm certain."

Oswell grinned, showing a mouth of crooked teeth. "No, but m'lady might of met my three sons."

It was the "three sons," and that smile too. *"Kettleblack!"* Sansa's eyes went wide. "You're a Kettleblack!"

"Aye, m'lady, as it please you."

"She's beside herself with joy." Lord Petyr dismissed him with a wave, and returned to the pomegranate again as Oswell shuffled down the steps. "Tell me, Alayne—which is more dangerous, the dagger brandished by an enemy, or the hidden one pressed to your back by someone you never even see?"

"The hidden dagger."

"There's a clever girl." He smiled, his thin lips bright red from the pomegranate seeds. "When the Imp sent off her guards, the queen had Ser Lancel hire sellswords for her. Lancel found her the Kettleblacks, which delighted your little lord husband, since the lads were in his pay through his man Bronn." He chuckled. "But it was me who told Oswell to get his sons to King's Landing when I learned that Bronn was looking for swords. Three hidden daggers, Alayne, now perfectly placed."

"So one of the Kettleblacks put the poison in Joff's cup?" Ser Osmund had been near the king all night, she remembered.

"Did I say that?" Lord Petyr cut the blood orange in two with his dagger and offered half to Sansa. "The lads are far too treacherous to be part of any such scheme . . . and Osmund has become especially unreliable since he joined the Kingsguard. That white cloak does things to a man, I find. Even a man like him." He tilted his chin back and squeezed the blood orange, so the juice ran down into his mouth. "I love the juice but I loathe the sticky fingers," he complained, wiping his hands. "Clean hands, Sansa. Whatever you do, make certain your hands are clean."

Sansa spooned up some juice from her own orange. "But if it wasn't the Kettleblacks and it wasn't Ser Dontos . . . you weren't even in the city, and it couldn't have been Tyrion . . ."

"No more guesses, sweetling?"

She shook her head. "I don't . . ."

Petyr smiled. "I will wager you that at some point during the evening someone told you that your hair net was crooked and straightened it for you."

Sansa raised a hand to her mouth. "You cannot mean . . . she wanted to take me to Highgarden, to marry me to her grandson . . ."

"Gentle, pious, good-hearted Willas Tyrell. Be grateful you were spared, he would have bored you spitless. The old woman is not boring, though, I'll grant her that. A fearsome old harridan, and not near as frail as she pretends. When I came to Highgarden to dicker for Margaery's hand, she let her lord son bluster while she asked pointed questions about Joffrey's nature. I praised him to the skies, to be sure . . . whilst my men spread disturbing tales amongst Lord Tyrell's servants. That is how the game is played.

"I also planted the notion of Ser Loras taking the white. Not that I *suggested* it, that would have been too crude. But men in my party supplied grisly tales about how the mob had killed Ser Preston Greenfield and raped the Lady Lollys, and slipped a few silvers to Lord Tyrell's army of singers to sing of Ryam Redwyne, Serwyn of the Mirror

Shield, and Prince Aemon the Dragonknight. A harp can be as dangerous as a sword, in the right hands.

"Mace Tyrell actually thought it was his own idea to make Ser Loras's inclusion in the Kingsguard part of the marriage contract. Who better to protect his daughter than her splendid knightly brother? And it relieved him of the difficult task of trying to find lands and a bride for a third son, never easy, and doubly difficult in Ser Loras's case.

"Be that as it may. Lady Olenna was not about to let Joff harm her precious darling granddaughter, but unlike her son she also realized that under all his flowers and finery, Ser Loras is as hot-tempered as Jaime Lannister. Toss Joffrey, Margaery, and Loras in a pot, and you've got the makings for kingslayer stew. The old woman understood something else as well. Her son was determined to make Margaery a queen, and for that he needed a king . . . but he did not need *Joffrey*. We shall have another wedding soon, wait and see. Margaery will marry Tommen. She'll keep her queenly crown and her maidenhead, neither of which she especially wants, but what does that matter? The great western alliance will be preserved . . . for a time, at least."

Margaery and Tommen. Sansa did not know what to say. She had liked Margaery Tyrell, and her small sharp grandmother as well. She thought wistfully of Highgarden with its courtyards and musicians, and the pleasure barges on the Mander; a far cry from this bleak shore. *At least I am safe here. Joffrey is dead, he cannot hurt me anymore, and I am only a bastard girl now. Alayne Stone has no husband and no claim.* And her aunt would soon be here as well. The long nightmare of King's Landing was behind her, and her mockery of a marriage as well. She could make herself a new home here, just as Petyr said.

It was eight long days until Lysa Arryn arrived. On five of them it rained, while Sansa sat bored and restless by the fire, beside the old blind dog. He was too sick and toothless to walk guard with Bryen anymore, and mostly all he did was sleep, but when she patted him he whined and licked her hand, and after that they were fast friends. When the rains let up, Petyr walked with her around his holdings, which took less than half a day. He owned a lot of rocks, just as he had said. There was one place where the tide came jetting up out of a blowhole to shoot thirty feet into the air, and another where someone had chiseled the seven-pointed star of the new gods upon a boulder. Petyr said that marked one of the places the Andals had landed, when they came across the sea to wrest the Vale from the First Men.

Farther inland a dozen families lived in huts of piled stone beside a peat bog. "Mine own smallfolk," Petyr said, though only the oldest seemed to know him. There was a hermit's cave on his land as well, but no hermit. "He's dead now, but when I was a boy my father took me to see him. The man had not washed in forty years, so you can imagine how he smelled, but supposedly he had the gift of prophecy. He groped me a bit and said I would be a great man, and for that my father gave him a skin of wine." Petyr snorted. "I would have told him the same thing for half a cup."

Finally, on a grey windy afternoon, Bryen came running back to the tower with his dogs barking at his heels, to announce that riders were approaching from the southwest. "Lysa," Lord Petyr said. "Come, Alayne, let us greet her."

They put on their cloaks and waited outside. The riders numbered no more than a score; a very modest escort, for the Lady of the Eyrie. Three maids rode with her, and a dozen household knights in mail and plate. She brought a septon as well, and a handsome singer with a wisp of a mustache and long sandy curls.

Could that be my aunt? Lady Lysa was two years younger than Mother, but this woman looked ten years older. Thick auburn tresses fell down past her waist, but beneath the costly velvet gown and jeweled bodice her body sagged and bulged. Her face was pink and painted, her breasts heavy, her limbs thick. She was taller than Littlefinger, and heavier; nor did she show any grace in the clumsy way she climbed down off her horse.

Petyr knelt to kiss her fingers. "The king's small council commanded me to woo and win you, my lady. Do you think you might have me for your lord and husband?"

Lady Lysa pooched her lips and pulled him up to plant a kiss upon his cheek. "Oh, mayhaps I could be persuaded." She giggled. "Have you brought gifts to melt my heart?"

"The king's peace."

"Oh, poo to the peace, what else have you brought me?"

"My daughter." Littlefinger beckoned Sansa forward with a hand. "My lady, allow me to present you Alayne Stone."

Lysa Arryn did not seem greatly pleased to see her. Sansa did a deep curtsy, her head bowed. "A bastard?" she heard her aunt say. "Petyr, have you been wicked? Who was her mother?"

"The wench is dead. I'd hoped to take Alayne to the Eyrie."

"What am I to do with her there?"

"I have a few notions," said Lord Petyr. "But just now I am more interested in what I might do with you, my lady."

All the sternness melted off her aunt's round pink face, and for a moment Sansa thought Lysa Arryn was about to cry. "Sweet Petyr, I've missed you so, you don't know, you can't know. Yohn Royce has been stirring up all sorts of trouble, demanding that I call my banners and go to war. And the others all swarm around me, Hunter and Corbray and that *dreadful* Nestor Royce, all wanting to wed me and take my son to ward, but none of them truly love me. Only you, Petyr. I've dreamed of you so long."

"And I of you, my lady." He slid an arm around behind her and kissed her on the neck. "How soon can we be wed?"

"Now," said Lady Lysa, sighing. "I've brought my own septon, and a singer, and mead for the wedding feast."

"Here?" That did not please him. "I'd sooner wed you at the Eyrie, with your whole court in attendance."

"Poo to my court. I have waited so long, I could not bear to wait another moment." She put her arms around him. "I want to share your bed tonight, my sweet. I want us to make another child, a brother for Robert or a sweet little daughter."

"I dream of that as well, sweetling. Yet there is much to be gained from a great public wedding, with all the Vale—"

"No." She stamped a foot. "I want you now, this very night. And I must warn you, after all these years of silence and whisperings, I mean to *scream* when you love me. I am going to scream so loud they'll hear me in the Eyrie!"

"Perhaps I could bed you now, and wed you later?"

The Lady Lysa giggled like a girl. "Oh, Petyr Baelish,

you are so *wicked*. No, I say no, I am the Lady of the Eyrie, and I command you to wed me this very moment!"

Petyr gave a shrug. "As my lady commands, then. I am helpless before you, as ever."

They said their vows within the hour, standing beneath a sky-blue canopy as the sun sank in the west. Afterward trestle tables were set up beneath the small flint tower, and they feasted on quail, venison, and roast boar, washing it down with a fine light mead. Torches were lit as dusk crept in. Lysa's singer played "The Vow Unspoken" and "Seasons of My Love" and "Two Hearts That Beat as One." Several younger knights even asked Sansa to dance. Her aunt danced as well, her skirts whirling when Petyr spun her in his arms. Mead and marriage had taken years off Lady Lysa. She laughed at everything so long as she held her husband's hand, and her eyes seemed to glow whenever she looked at him.

When it was time for the bedding, her knights carried her up to the tower, stripping her as they went and shouting bawdy jests. *Tyrion spared me that*, Sansa remembered. It would not have been so bad being undressed for a man she loved, by friends who loved them both. *By Joffrey, though* . . . She shuddered.

Her aunt had brought only three ladies with her, so they pressed Sansa to help them undress Lord Petyr and march him up to his marriage bed. He submitted with good grace and a wicked tongue, giving as good as he got. By the time they had gotten him into the tower and out of his clothes, the other women were flushed, with laces unlaced, kirtles crooked, and skirts in disarray. But Littlefinger only smiled at Sansa as they marched him up to the bedchamber where his lady wife was waiting.

Lady Lysa and Lord Petyr had the third-story bedchamber to themselves, but the tower was small . . . and true to her word, her aunt screamed. It had begun to rain outside, driving the feasters into the hall one floor below, so they heard most every word. "Petyr," her aunt moaned. "Oh, Petyr, Petyr, sweet *Petyr*, oh oh oh. There, Petyr, there. That's where you belong." Lady Lysa's singer launched into a bawdy version of "Milady's Supper," but even his singing and playing could not drown out Lysa's cries. "Make me a baby, Petyr," she screamed, "make me another sweet little

baby. Oh, Petyr, my precious, my precious, *PEEEEEETYR!*"
Her last shriek was so loud that it set the dogs to barking,
and two of her aunt's ladies could scarce contain their
mirth.

Sansa went down the steps and out into the night. A
light rain was falling on the remains of the feast, but the air
smelled fresh and clean. The memory of her own wedding
night with Tyrion was much with her. *In the dark, I am
the Knight of Flowers*, he had said. *I could be good to you.*
But that was only another Lannister lie. *A dog can smell a
lie, you know*, the Hound had told her once. She could almost hear the rough rasp of his voice. *Look around you,
and take a good whiff. They're all liars here, and every one
better than you.* She wondered what had become of Sandor
Clegane. Did he know that they'd killed Joffrey? Would he
care? He had been the prince's sworn shield for years.

She stayed outside for a long time. When at last she
sought her own bed, wet and chilled, only the dim glow of
a peat fire lit the darkened hall. There was no sound from
above. The young singer sat in a corner, playing a slow
song to himself. One of her aunt's maids was kissing a
knight in Lord Petyr's chair, their hands busy beneath each
other's clothing. Several men had drunk themselves to
sleep, and one was in the privy, being noisily sick. Sansa
found Bryen's old blind dog in her little alcove beneath the
steps, and lay down next to him. He woke and licked her
face. "You sad old hound," she said, ruffling his fur.

"Alayne." Her aunt's singer stood over her. "Sweet
Alayne. I am Marillion. I saw you come in from the rain.
The night is chill and wet. Let me warm you."

The old dog raised his head and growled, but the singer
gave him a cuff and sent him slinking off, whimpering.

"Marillion?" she said, uncertain. "You are . . . kind to
think of me, but . . . pray forgive me. I am very tired."

"And very beautiful. All night I have been making songs
for you in my head. A lay for your eyes, a ballad for your
lips, a duet to your breasts. I will not sing them, though.
They were poor things, unworthy of such beauty." He sat
on her bed and put his hand on her leg. "Let me sing to you
with my body instead."

She caught a whiff of his breath. "You're drunk."

"I never get drunk. Mead only makes me merry. I am on fire." His hand slipped up to her thigh. "And you as well."

"Unhand me. You forget yourself."

"Mercy. I have been singing love songs for hours. My blood is stirred. And yours, I know . . . there's no wench half so lusty as one bastard born. Are you wet for me?"

"I'm a *maiden*," she protested.

"Truly? Oh, Alayne, Alayne, my fair maid, give me the gift of your innocence. You will thank the gods you did. I'll have you singing louder than the Lady Lysa."

Sansa jerked away from him, frightened. "If you don't leave me, my au—my *father* will hang you. Lord Petyr."

"Littlefinger?" He chuckled. "Lady Lysa loves me well, and I am Lord Robert's favorite. If your father offends me, I will destroy him with a verse." He put a hand on her breast, and squeezed. "Let's get you out of these wet clothes. You wouldn't want them ripped, I know. Come, sweet lady, heed your heart—"

Sansa heard the soft sound of steel on leather. "Singer," a rough voice said, "best go, if you want to sing again." The light was dim, but she saw a faint glimmer of a blade.

The singer saw it too. "Find your own wench—" The knife flashed, and he cried out. "You *cut* me!"

"I'll do worse, if you don't go."

And quick as that, Marillion was gone. The other remained, looming over Sansa in the darkness. "Lord Petyr said watch out for you." It was Lothor Brune's voice, she realized. *Not the Hound's, no, how could it be? Of course it had to be Lothor . . .*

That night Sansa scarcely slept at all, but tossed and turned just as she had aboard the *Merling King*. She dreamt of Joffrey dying, but as he clawed at his throat and the blood ran down across his fingers she saw with horror that it was her brother Robb. And she dreamed of her wedding night too, of Tyrion's eyes devouring her as she undressed. Only then he was bigger than Tyrion had any right to be, and when he climbed into the bed his face was scarred only on one side. "*I'll have a song from you*," he rasped, and Sansa woke and found the old blind dog beside her once again. "I wish that you were Lady," she said.

Come the morning, Grisel climbed up to the bedchamber to serve the lord and lady a tray of morning bread, with butter, honey, fruit, and cream. She returned to say that Alayne was wanted. Sansa was still drowsy from sleep. It took her a moment to remember that *she* was Alayne.

Lady Lysa was still abed, but Lord Petyr was up and dressed. "Your aunt wishes to speak with you," he told Sansa, as he pulled on a boot. "I've told her who you are."

Gods be good. "I . . . I thank you, my lord."

Petyr yanked on the other boot. "I've had about as much home as I can stomach. We'll leave for the Eyrie this afternoon." He kissed his lady wife and licked a smear of honey off her lips, then headed down the steps.

Sansa stood by the foot of the bed while her aunt ate a pear and studied her. "I see it now," the Lady Lysa said, as she set the core aside. "You look so much like Catelyn."

"It's kind of you to say so."

"It was not meant as flattery. If truth be told, you look too much like Catelyn. Something must be done. We shall darken your hair before we bring you back to the Eyrie, I think."

Darken my hair? "If it please you, Aunt Lysa."

"You must not call me that. No word of your presence here must be allowed to reach King's Landing. I do not mean to have my son endangered." She nibbled the corner of a honeycomb. "I have kept the Vale out of this war. Our harvest has been plentiful, the mountains protect us, and the Eyrie is impregnable. Even so, it would not do to draw Lord Tywin's wroth down upon us." Lysa set the comb down and licked honey from her fingers. "You were wed to Tyrion Lannister, Petyr says. That vile *dwarf*."

"They made me marry him. I never wanted it."

"No more than I did," her aunt said. "Jon Arryn was no dwarf, but he was *old*. You may not think so to see me now, but on the day we wed I was so lovely I put your mother to shame. But all Jon desired was my father's swords, to aid his darling boys. I should have refused him, but he was such an old man, how long could he live? Half his teeth were gone, and his breath smelled like bad cheese. I cannot abide a man with foul breath. Petyr's breath is always fresh . . . he was the first man I ever kissed, you know. My father said he was too lowborn, but *I* knew how high he'd rise. Jon gave him the customs for Gulltown to please me, but when he increased the incomes tenfold my lord husband saw how clever he was and gave him other appointments, even brought him to King's Landing to be master of coin. That was hard, to see him every day and still be wed to that old cold man. Jon did his *duty* in the bedchamber, but he could no more give me pleasure than he could give me children. His seed was old and weak. All my babies died but Robert, three girls and two boys. All my sweet little babies dead, and that old man just went on and on with his stinking breath. So you see, I have suffered too." Lady Lysa sniffed. "You do know that your poor mother is dead?"

"Tyrion told me," said Sansa. "He said the Freys murdered her at The Twins, with Robb."

Tears welled suddenly in Lady Lysa's eyes. "We are women alone now, you and I. Are you afraid, child? Be brave. I would never turn away Cat's daughter. We are bound by blood." She beckoned Sansa closer. "You may come kiss my cheek, Alayne."

Dutifully she approached and knelt beside the bed. Her aunt was drenched in sweet scent, though under that was a sour milky smell. Her cheek tasted of paint and powder.

As Sansa stepped back, Lady Lysa caught her wrist. "Now tell me," she said sharply. "Are you with child? The truth now, I will know if you lie."

"No," she said, startled by the question.

"You *are* a woman flowered, are you not?"

"Yes." Sansa knew the truth of her flowering could not be long hidden in the Eyrie. "Tyrion didn't . . . he never . . ." She could feel the blush creeping up her cheeks. "I am still a maid."

"Was the dwarf incapable?"

"No. He was only . . . he was . . ." *Kind?* She could not say that, not here, not to this aunt who hated him so. "He . . . he had whores, my lady. He told me so."

"Whores." Lysa released her wrist. "Of course he did. What woman would bed such a creature, but for gold? I should have killed the Imp when he was in my power, but he tricked me. He is full of low cunning, that one. His sellsword slew my good Ser Vardis Egen. Catelyn should not have brought him here, I told her that. She made off with our uncle too. That was wrong of her. The Blackfish was my Knight of the Gate, and since he left us the mountain clans are growing very bold. Petyr will soon set all that to rights, though. I shall make him Lord Protector of the Vale." Her aunt smiled for the first time, almost warmly. "He may not look as tall or strong as some, but he is worth more than all of them. Trust in him and do as he says."

"I shall, Aunt . . . my lady."

Lady Lysa seemed pleased by that. "I knew that boy Joffrey. He used to call my Robert cruel names, and once he slapped him with a wooden sword. A man will tell you poison is dishonorable, but a woman's honor is different. The Mother shaped us to protect our children, and our only dishonor is in failure. You'll know that, when you have a child."

"A child?" said Sansa, uncertainly.

Lysa waved a hand negligently. "Not for many years. You are too young to be a mother. One day you shall want children, though. Just as you will want to marry."

"I . . . I *am* married, my lady."

"Yes, but soon a widow. Be glad the Imp preferred his whores. It would not be fitting for my son to take that *dwarf*'s leavings, but as he never touched you . . . How would you like to marry your cousin, the Lord Robert?"

The thought made Sansa weary. All she knew of Robert Arryn was that he was a little boy, and sickly. *It is not me she wants her son to marry, it is my claim. No one will ever marry me for love.* But lying came easy to her now. "I . . . can scarcely wait to meet him, my lady. But he is still a child, is he not?"

"He is eight. And not robust. But such a good boy, so bright and clever. He will be a great man, Alayne. *The seed is strong*, my lord husband said before he died. His last words. The gods sometimes let us glimpse the future as we lay dying. I see no reason why you should not be wed as soon as we know that your Lannister husband is dead. A secret wedding, to be sure. The Lord of the Eyrie could scarcely be thought to have married a bastard, that would not be fitting. The ravens should bring us the word from King's Landing once the Imp's head rolls. You and Robert can be wed the next day, won't that be joyous? It will be good for him to have a little companion. He played with Vardis Egen's boy when we first returned to the Eyrie, and my steward's sons as well, but they were much too rough and I had no choice but to send them away. Do you read well, Alayne?"

"Septa Mordane was good enough to say so."

"Robert has weak eyes, but he loves to be read to," Lady Lysa confided. "He likes stories about animals the best. Do you know the little song about the chicken who dressed as a fox? I sing him that all the time, he never grows tired of it. And he likes to play hopfrog and spin-the-sword and come-into-my-castle, but you must always let him win. That's only proper, don't you think? He is the Lord of the Eyrie, after all, you must never forget that. You are well born, and the Starks of Winterfell were always proud, but Winterfell has fallen and you are really just a beggar now, so put that pride aside. Gratitude will better become you, in your present circumstances. Yes, and obedience. My son will have a grateful and obedient wife."

JON

Day and night the axes rang.

Jon could not remember the last time he had slept. When he closed his eyes he dreamed of fighting; when he woke he fought. Even in the King's Tower he could hear the ceaseless *thunk* of bronze and flint and stolen steel biting into wood, and it was louder when he tried to rest in the warming shed atop the Wall. Mance had sledgehammers at work as well, and long saws with teeth of bone and flint. Once, as he was drifting off into an exhausted sleep, there came a great cracking from the haunted forest, and a sentinel tree came crashing down in a cloud of dirt and needles.

He was awake when Owen came to him, lying restless under a pile of furs on the floor of the warming shed. "Lord Snow," said Owen, shaking his shoulder, "the dawn." He gave Jon a hand to help pull him back onto his feet. Others were waking as well, jostling one another as they pulled on their boots and buckled their swordbelts in the close confines of the shed. No one spoke. They were all too tired for talk. Few of them ever left the Wall these days. It took too long to ride up and down in the cage. Castle Black had been abandoned to Maester Aemon, Ser Wynton Stout, and a few others too old or ill to fight.

"I had a dream that the king had come," Owen said happily. "Maester Aemon sent a raven, and King Robert came with all his strength. I dreamed I saw his golden banners."

Jon made himself smile. "That would be a welcome sight to see, Owen." Ignoring the twinge of pain in his leg, he swept a black fur cloak about his shoulders, gathered up his crutch, and went out onto the Wall to face another day.

A gust of wind sent icy tendrils wending through his long brown hair. Half a mile north, the wildling encampments were stirring, their campfires sending up smoky fingers to scratch against the pale dawn sky. Along the edge of the forest they had raised their tents of hide and fur, even a crude longhall of logs and woven branches; there were horselines to the east, mammoths to the west, and men everywhere, sharpening their swords, putting points on crude spears, donning makeshift armor of hide and horn and bone. For every man that he could see, Jon knew there were a score unseen in the wood. The brush gave them some shelter from the elements and hid them from the eyes of the hated crows.

Already their archers were stealing forward, pushing their rolling mantlets. "Here come our breakfast arrows," Pyp announced cheerfully, as he did every morning. *It's good that he can make a jape of it*, Jon thought. *Someone has to.* Three days ago, one of those breakfast arrows had caught Red Alyn of the Rosewood in the leg. You could still see his body at the foot of the Wall, if you cared to lean out far enough. Jon had to think that it was better for them to smile at Pyp's jest than to brood over Alyn's corpse.

The mantlets were slanting wooden shields, wide enough for five of the free folk to hide behind. The archers pushed them close, then knelt behind them to loose their arrows through slits in the wood. The first time the wildlings rolled them out, Jon had called for fire arrows and set a half-dozen ablaze, but after that Mance started covering them with raw hides. All the fire arrows in the world couldn't make them catch now. The brothers had even started wagering as to which of the straw sentinels would collect the most arrows before they were done. Dolorous

Edd was leading with four, but Othell Yarwyck, Tumberjon, and Watt of Long Lake had three apiece. It was Pyp who'd started naming the scarecrows after their missing brothers, too. "It makes it seem as if there's more of us," he said.

"More of us with arrows in our bellies," Grenn complained, but the custom did seem to give his brothers heart, so Jon let the names stand and the wagering continue.

On the edge of the Wall an ornate brass Myrish eye stood on three spindly legs. Maester Aemon had once used it to peer at the stars, before his own eyes had failed him. Jon swung the tube down to have a look at the foe. Even at this distance there was no mistaking Mance Rayder's huge white tent, sewn together from the pelts of snow bears. The Myrish lenses brought the wildlings close enough for him to make out faces. Of Mance himself he saw no sign this morning, but his woman Dalla was outside tending the fire, while her sister Val milked a she-goat beside the tent. Dalla looked so big it was a wonder she could move. *The child must be coming very soon*, Jon thought. He swiveled the eye east and searched amongst the tents and trees till he found the turtle. *That will be coming very soon as well.* The wildlings had skinned one of the dead mammoths during the night, and they were lashing the raw bloody hide over the turtle's roof, one more layer on top of the sheepskins and pelts. The turtle had a rounded top and eight huge wheels, and under the hides was a stout wooden frame. When the wildlings had begun knocking it together, Satin thought they were building a ship. *Not far wrong.* The turtle was a hull turned upside down and opened fore and aft; a longhall on wheels.

"It's done, isn't it?" asked Grenn.

"Near enough." Jon shoved away the eye. "It will come today, most like. Did you fill the barrels?"

"Every one. They froze hard during the night, Pyp checked."

Grenn had changed a great deal from the big, clumsy, red-necked boy Jon had first befriended. He had grown half a foot, his chest and shoulders had thickened, and he had not cut his hair nor trimmed his beard since the Fist of the First Men. It made him look as huge and shaggy as an aurochs, the mocking name that Ser Alliser Thorne had hung on him during training. He looked weary now, though. When Jon said as much, he nodded. "I heard their axes all night. Couldn't sleep for all the chopping."

"Then go sleep now."

"I don't need—"

"You do. I want you rested. Go on, I'm not going to let you sleep through the fight." He made himself smile. "You're the only one who can move those bloody barrels."

Grenn went off muttering, and Jon returned to the far eye, searching the wildling camp. From time to time an arrow would sail past overhead, but he had learned to ignore those. The range was long and the angle was bad, the chances of being hit were small. He still saw no sign of Mance Rayder in the camp, but he spied Tormund Giantsbane and two of his sons around the turtle. The sons were struggling with the mammoth hide while Tormund gnawed on the roast leg of a goat and bellowed orders. Elsewhere he found the wildling skinchanger, Varamyr Sixskins, walking through the trees with his shadowcat dogging his heels.

When he heard the rattle of the winch chains and the iron groan of the cage door opening, he knew it would be Hobb bringing their breakfast as he did every morning. The sight of Mance's turtle had robbed Jon of his appetite. Their oil was all but gone, and the last barrel of pitch had been rolled off the Wall two nights ago. They would soon run short of arrows as well, and there were no fletchers making more. And the night before last, a raven had come from the west, from Ser Denys Mallister. Bowen Marsh had chased the wildlings all the way to the Shadow Tower, it seemed, and then farther, down into the gloom of the Gorge. At the Bridge of Skulls he had met the Weeper and three hundred wildlings and won a bloody battle. But the victory had been a costly one. More than a hundred brothers slain, among them Ser Endrew Tarth and Ser Aladale Wynch. The Old Pomegranate himself had been carried back to the Shadow Tower sorely wounded. Maester Mullin was tending him, but it would be some time before he was fit to return to Castle Black.

When he had read that, Jon had dispatched Zei to Mole's Town on their best horse to plead with the villagers to help man the Wall. She never returned. When he sent Mully after her, he came back to report the whole village deserted, even the brothel. Most likely Zei had followed them, straight down the kingsroad. *Maybe we should all do the same,* Jon reflected glumly.

He made himself eat, hungry or no. Bad enough he could not sleep, he could not go on without food as well. *Besides, this might be my last meal. It might be the last meal for all of us.* So it was that Jon had a belly full of bread, bacon, onions, and cheese when he heard Horse shout, *"IT'S COMING!"*

No one needed to ask what "it" was. Nor did Jon need the maester's Myrish eye to see it creeping out from amongst the tents and trees. "It doesn't really look much like a turtle," Satin commented. "Turtles don't have fur."

"Most of them don't have wheels either," said Pyp.

"Sound the warhorn," Jon commanded, and Kegs blew two long blasts, to wake Grenn and the other sleepers who'd had the watch during the night. If the wildlings were coming, the Wall would need every man. *Gods know, we have few enough.* Jon looked at Pyp and Kegs and Satin, Horse and Owen the Oaf, Tim Tangletongue, Mully, Spare Boot, and the rest, and tried to imagine them going belly to belly and blade to blade against a hundred screaming wildlings in the freezing darkness of that tunnel, with only a few iron bars between them. That was what it would come down to, unless they could stop the turtle before the gate was breached.

"It's big," Horse said.

Pyp smacked his lips. "Think of all the soup it will make." The jape was stillborn. Even Pyp sounded tired. *He looks half dead,* thought Jon, *but so do we all.* The King-beyond-the-Wall had so many men that he could throw fresh attackers at them every time, but the same handful of black brothers had to meet every assault, and it had worn them ragged.

The men beneath the wood and hides would be pulling hard, Jon knew, putting their shoulders into it, straining to keep the wheels turning, but once the turtle was flush against the gate they would exchange their ropes for axes. At least Mance was not sending his mammoths today. Jon was glad of that. Their awesome strength was wasted on the Wall, and their size only made them easy targets. The last had been a day and a half in the dying, its mournful trumpetings terrible to hear.

The turtle crept slowly through stones and stumps and brush. The earlier attacks had cost the free folk a hundred lives or more. Most still lay where they had fallen. In the lulls the crows would come and pay them court, but now the birds fled screeching. They liked the look of that turtle no more than he did.

Satin, Horse, and the others were looking to him, Jon knew, waiting for his orders. He was so tired, he hardly knew any more. *The Wall is mine*, he reminded himself. "Owen, Horse, to the catapults. Kegs, you and Spare Boot on the scorpions. The rest of you string your bows. Fire arrows. Let's see if we can burn it." It was likely to be a futile gesture, Jon knew, but it had to be better than standing helpless.

Cumbersome and slow-moving, the turtle made for an easy shot, and his archers and crossbowmen soon turned it into a lumbering wooden hedgehog . . . but the wet hides protected it, just as they had the mantlets, and the flaming arrows guttered out almost as soon as they struck. Jon cursed under his breath. "Scorpions," he commanded. "Catapults."

The scorpions bolts punched deep into the pelts, but did no more damage than the fire arrows. The rocks went bouncing off the turtle's roof, leaving dimples in the thick layers of hides. A stone from one of the trebuchets might have crushed it, but the one machine was still broken, and the wildlings had gone wide around the area where the other dropped its loads.

"Jon, it's still coming," said Owen the Oaf.

He could see that for himself. Inch by inch, yard by yard, the turtle crept closer, rolling, rumbling and rocking as it crossed the killing ground. Once the wildlings got it flush against the Wall, it would give them all the shelter they needed while their axes crashed through the hastily-repaired outer gates. Inside, under the ice, they would clear the loose rubble from the tunnel in a matter of hours, and then there would be nothing to stop them but two iron gates, a few half-frozen corpses, and whatever brothers Jon

cared to throw in their path, to fight and die down in the
dark.

To his left, the catapult made a *thunk* and filled the air
with spinning stones. They plonked down on the turtle
like hail, and caromed harmlessly aside. The wildling
archers were still loosing arrows from behind their
mantlets. One thudded into the face of a straw man, and
Pyp said, "Four for Watt of Long Lake! We have a tie!" The
next shaft whistled past his own ear, however. "*Fie!*" he
shouted down. "I'm not in the tourney!"

"The hides won't burn," Jon said, as much to himself as
to the others. Their only hope was to try and crush the turtle when it reached the Wall. For that, they needed boulders. No matter how stoutly built the turtle was, a huge
chunk of rock crashing straight down on top of it from
seven hundred feet was bound to do some damage. "Grenn,
Owen, Kegs, it's time."

Alongside the warming shed a dozen stout oaken barrels
were lined up in a row. They were full of crushed rock; the
gravel that the black brothers customarily spread on the
footpaths to give themselves better footing atop the Wall.
Yesterday, after he'd seen the free folk covering the turtle
with sheepskins, Jon told Grenn to pour water into the barrels, as much as they would take. The water would seep
down through the crushed stone, and overnight the whole
thing would freeze solid. It was the nearest thing to a boulder they were going to get.

"Why do we need to freeze it?" Grenn had asked him.
"Why don't we just roll the barrels off the way they are?"

Jon answered, "If they crash against the Wall on the way
down they'll burst, and loose gravel will spray everywhere.
We don't want to rain pebbles on the whoresons."

He put his shoulder to the one barrel with Grenn, while
Kegs and Owen were wrestling with another. Together
they rocked it back and forth to break the grip of the ice
that had formed around its bottom. "The bugger weighs a
ton," said Grenn.

"Tip it over and roll it," Jon said. "Careful, if it rolls
over your foot you'll end up like Spare Boot."

Once the barrel was on its side, Jon grabbed a torch and
waved it above the surface of the Wall, back and forth, just
enough to melt the ice a little. The thin film of water

helped the barrel roll more easily. Too easily, in fact; they almost lost it. But finally, with four of them pooling their efforts, they rolled their boulder to the edge and stood it up again.

They had four of the big oak barrels lined up above the gate by the time Pyp shouted, "There's a turtle at our door!" Jon braced his injured leg and leaned out for a look. *Hoardings, Marsh should have built hoardings.* So many things they should have done. The wildlings were dragging the dead giants away from the gate. Horse and Mully were dropping rocks down on them, and Jon thought he saw one man go down, but the stones were too small to have any effect on the turtle itself. He wondered what the free folk would do about the dead mammoth in the path, but then he saw. The turtle was almost as wide as a longhall, so they simply pushed it *over* the carcass. His leg twitched, but Horse caught his arm and drew him back to safety. "You shouldn't lean out like that," the boy said.

"We should have built hoardings." Jon thought he could hear the crash of axes on wood, but that was probably just fear ringing in his ears. He looked to Grenn. "Do it."

Grenn got behind a barrel, put his shoulder against it, grunted, and began to push. Owen and Mully moved to help him. They shoved the barrel out a foot, and then another. And suddenly it was gone.

They heard the *thump* as it struck the Wall on the way down, and then, much louder, the crash and *crack* of splintering wood, followed by shouts and screams. Satin whooped and Owen the Oaf danced in circles, while Pyp leaned out and called, "The turtle was stuffed full of rabbits! Look at them hop away!"

"*Again*," Jon barked, and Grenn and Kegs slammed their shoulders against the next barrel, and sent it tottering out into empty air.

By the time they were done, the front of Mance's turtle was a crushed and splintered ruin, and wildlings were spilling out the other end and scrambling for their camp. Satin scooped up his crossbow and sent a few quarrels after them as they ran, to see them off the faster. Grenn was grinning through his beard, Pyp was making japes, and none of them would die today.

On the morrow, though . . . Jon glanced toward the

shed. Eight barrels of gravel remained where twelve had stood a few moments before. He realized how tired he was then, and how much his wound was hurting. *I need to sleep. A few hours, at least.* He could go to Maester Aemon for some dreamwine, that would help. "I am going down to the King's Tower," he told them. "Call me if Mance gets up to anything. Pyp, you have the Wall."

"Me?" said Pyp.

"Him?" said Grenn.

Smiling, he left them to it and rode down in the cage.

A cup of dreamwine *did* help, as it happened. No sooner had he stretched out on the narrow bed in his cell than sleep took him. His dreams were strange and formless, full of strange voices, shouts and cries, and the sound of a warhorn, blowing low and loud, a single deep booming note that lingered in the air.

When he awoke the sky was black outside the arrow slit that served him for a window, and four men he did not know were standing over him. One held a lantern. "Jon Snow," the tallest of them said brusquely, "pull on your boots and come with us."

His first groggy thought was that somehow the Wall had fallen whilst he slept, that Mance Rayder had sent more giants or another turtle and broken through the gate. But when he rubbed his eyes he saw that the strangers were all in black. *They're men of the Night's Watch,* Jon realized. "Come where? Who are you?"

The tall man gestured, and two of the others pulled Jon from the bed. With the lantern leading the way they marched him from his cell and up a half turn of stair, to the Old Bear's solar. He saw Maester Aemon standing by the fire, his hands folded around the head of a blackthorn cane. Septon Cellador was half drunk as usual, and Ser Wynton Stout was asleep in a window seat. The other brothers were strangers to him. All but one.

Immaculate in his fur-trimmed cloak and polished boots, Ser Alliser Thorne turned to say, "Here's the turn-cloak now, my lord. Ned Stark's bastard, of Winterfell."

"I'm no turncloak, Thorne," Jon said coldly.

"We shall see." In the leather chair behind the table where the Old Bear wrote his letters sat a big, broad, jowly man Jon did not know. "Yes, we shall see," he said again.

"You will not deny that you are Jon Snow, I hope? Stark's bastard?"

"*Lord* Snow, he likes to call himself." Ser Alliser was a spare, slim man, compact and sinewy, and just now his flinty eyes were dark with amusement.

"You're the one who named me Lord Snow," said Jon. Ser Alliser had been fond of naming the boys he trained, during his time as Castle Black's master-at-arms. The Old Bear had sent Thorne to Eastwatch-by-the-Sea. *These others must be Eastwatch men. The bird reached Cotter Pyke and he's sent us help.* "How many men have you brought?" he asked the man behind the table.

"It's me who'll ask the questions," the jowly man replied. "You've been charged with oathbreaking, cowardice, and desertion, Jon Snow. Do you deny that you abandoned your brothers to die on the Fist of the First Men and joined the wildling Mance Rayder, this self-styled King-beyond-the-Wall?"

"*Abandoned* . . . ?" Jon almost choked on the word.

Maester Aemon spoke up then. "My lord, Donal Noye and I discussed these issues when Jon Snow first returned to us, and were satisfied by Jon's explanations."

"Well, *I* am not satisfied, Maester," said the jowly man. "I will hear these *explanations* for myself. Yes I will!"

Jon swallowed his anger. "I abandoned no one. I left the Fist with Qhorin Halfhand to scout the Skirling Pass. I joined the wildlings under orders. The Halfhand feared that Mance might have found the Horn of Winter . . ."

"The Horn of Winter?" Ser Alliser chuckled. "Were you commanded to count their snarks as well, Lord Snow?"

"No, but I counted their *giants* as best I could."

"*Ser*," snapped the jowly man. "You will address Ser Alliser as *ser*, and myself as *m'lord*. I am Janos Slynt, Lord of Harrenhal, and commander here at Castle Black until such time as Bowen Marsh returns with his garrison. You will grant us our courtesies, yes. I will not suffer to hear an anointed knight like the good Ser Alliser mocked by a traitor's bastard." He raised a hand and pointed a meaty finger at Jon's face. "Do you deny that you took a wildling woman into your bed?"

"No." Jon's grief over Ygritte was too fresh for him to deny her now. "No, my lord."

"I suppose it was also the Halfhand who commanded you to fuck this unwashed whore?" Ser Alliser asked with a smirk.

"*Ser*. She was no whore, *ser*. The Halfhand told me not to balk, whatever the wildlings asked of me, but . . . I will not deny that I went beyond what I had to do, that I . . . cared for her."

"You admit to being an oathbreaker, then," said Janos Slynt.

Half the men at Castle Black visited Mole's Town from time to time to dig for buried treasures in the brothel, Jon knew, but he would not dishonor Ygritte by equating her with the Mole's Town whores. "I broke my vows with a woman. I admit that. Yes."

"Yes, *m'lord!*" When Slynt scowled, his jowls quivered. He was as broad as the Old Bear had been, and no doubt would be as bald if he lived to Mormont's age. Half his hair was gone already, though he could not have been more than forty.

"Yes, my lord," Jon said. "I rode with the wildlings and ate with them, as the Halfhand commanded me, and I shared my furs with Ygritte. But I swear to you, I never turned my cloak. I escaped the Magnar as soon as I could, and never took up arms against my brothers or the realm."

Lord Slynt's small eyes studied him. "Ser Glendon," he commanded, "bring in the other prisoner."

Ser Glendon was the tall man who had dragged Jon from his bed. Four other men went with him when he left the room, but they were back soon enough with a captive, a small, sallow, battered man fettered hand and foot. He had a single eyebrow, a widow's peak, and a mustache that looked like a smear of dirt on his upper lip, but his face was swollen and mottled with bruises, and most of his front teeth had been knocked out.

The Eastwatch men threw the captive roughly to the floor. Lord Slynt frowned down at him. "Is this the one you spoke of?"

The captive blinked yellow eyes. "Aye." Not until that instant did Jon recognize Rattleshirt. *He is a different man without his armor*, he thought. "Aye," the wildling repeated, "he's the craven killed the Halfhand. Up in the Frostfangs, it were, after we hunted down t'other crows and killed them, every one. We would have done for this one too, only he begged f' his worthless life, offered t' join us if we'd have him. The Halfhand swore he'd see the craven dead first, but the wolf ripped Qhorin half t' pieces and this one opened his throat." He gave Jon a cracktooth smile then, and spat blood on his foot.

"Well?" Janos Slynt demanded of Jon harshly. "Do you deny it? Or will you claim Qhorin commanded you to kill him?"

"He told me . . ." The words came hard. "He told me to do *whatever* they asked of me."

Slynt looked about the solar, at the other Eastwatch men. "Does this boy think I fell off a turnip wagon onto my head?"

"Your lies won't save you now, Lord Snow," warned Ser Alliser Thorne. "We'll have the truth from you, bastard."

"I've told you the truth. Our garrons were failing, and Rattleshirt was close behind us. Qhorin told me to pretend to join the wildlings. '*You must not balk, whatever is asked of you*,' he said. He knew they would make me kill him. Rattleshirt was going to kill him anyway, he knew that too."

"So now you claim the great Qhorin Halfhand feared *this* creature?" Slynt looked at Rattleshirt, and snorted.

"All men fear the Lord o' Bones," the wildling grumbled. Ser Glendon kicked him, and he lapsed back into silence.

"I never said that," Jon insisted.

Slynt slammed a fist on the table. "I heard you! Ser Alliser had your measure true enough, it seems. You lie through your bastard's teeth. Well, I will not suffer it. I will not! You might have fooled this crippled *blacksmith*, but not Janos Slynt! Oh, no. Janos Slynt does not swallow lies so easily. Did you think my skull was stuffed with cabbage?"

"I don't know what your skull is stuffed with. My lord."

"Lord Snow is nothing if not arrogant," said Ser Alliser. "He murdered Qhorin just as his fellow turncloaks did Lord Mormont. It would not surprise me to learn that it was all part of the same fell plot. Benjen Stark may well have a hand in all this as well. For all we know, he is sitting in Mance Rayder's tent even now. You know these Starks, my lord."

"I do," said Janos Slynt. "I know them too well."

Jon peeled off his glove and showed them his burned hand. "I burned my hand defending Lord Mormont from a wight. And my uncle was a man of honor. He would never have betrayed his vows."

"No more than you?" mocked Ser Alliser.

Septon Cellador cleared his throat. "Lord Slynt," he said, "this boy refused to swear his vows properly in the sept, but went beyond the Wall to say his words before a heart tree. His father's gods, he said, but they are wildling gods as well."

"They are the gods of the north, Septon." Maester Aemon was courteous, but firm. "My lords, when Donal Noye was slain, it was this young man Jon Snow who took the Wall and held it, against all the fury of the north. He has proved himself valiant, loyal, and resourceful. Were it not for him, you would have found Mance Rayder sitting here when you arrived, Lord Slynt. You are doing him a great wrong. Jon Snow was Lord Mormont's own steward and squire. He was chosen for that duty because the Lord Commander saw much promise in him. As do I."

"Promise?" said Slynt. "Well, promise may turn false. Qhorin Halfhand's blood is on his hands. Mormont trusted him, you say, but what of that? I know what it is to be betrayed by men you trusted. Oh, yes. And I know the ways of wolves as well." He pointed at Jon's face. "Your father died a traitor."

"My father was murdered." Jon was past caring what they did to him, but he would not suffer any more lies about his father.

Slynt purpled. "Murder? You insolent pup. King Robert was not even cold when Lord Eddard moved against his son." He rose to his feet; a shorter man than Mormont, but thick about the chest and arms, with a gut to match. A small gold spear tipped with red enamel pinned his cloak at the shoulder. "Your father died by the sword, but he was highborn, a King's Hand. For you, a noose will serve. Ser Alliser, take this turncloak to an ice cell."

"My lord is wise." Ser Alliser seized Jon by the arm.

Jon yanked away and grabbed the knight by the throat

with such ferocity that he lifted him off the floor. He would have throttled him if the Eastwatch men had not pulled him off. Thorne staggered back, rubbing the marks Jon's fingers had left on his neck. "You see for yourselves, brothers. The boy is a wildling."

TYRION

When dawn broke, he found he could not face the thought of food. *By evenfall I may stand condemned.* His belly was acid with bile, and his nose itched. Tyrion scratched at it with the point of his knife. *One last witness to endure, then my turn.* But what to do? Deny everything? Accuse Sansa and Ser Dontos? Confess, in the hope of spending the rest of his days on the Wall? Let the dice fly and pray the Red Viper could defeat Ser Gregor Clegane?

Tyrion stabbed listlessly at a greasy grey sausage, wishing it were his sister. *It is bloody cold on the Wall, but at least I would be shut of Cersei.* He did not think he would make much of a ranger, but the Night's Watch needed clever men as well as strong ones. Lord Commander Mormont had said as much, when Tyrion had visited Castle Black. *There are those inconvenient vows, though.* It would mean the end of his marriage and whatever claim he might ever have made for Casterly Rock, but he did not seem destined to enjoy either in any case. And he seemed to recall that there was a brothel in a nearby village.

It was not a life he'd ever dreamed of, but it was life. And all he had to do to earn it was trust in his father, stand up on his little stunted legs, and say, "Yes, I did it, I confess." That was the part that tied his bowels in knots. He almost wished he *had* done it, since it seemed he must suffer for it anyway.

"My lord?" said Podrick Payne. "They're here, my lord. Ser Addam. And the gold cloaks. They wait without."

"Pod, tell me true . . . do you think I did it?"

The boy hesitated. When he tried to speak, all he managed to produce was a weak sputter.

I am doomed. Tyrion sighed. "No need to answer. You've been a good squire to me. Better than I deserved. Whatever happens, I thank you for your leal service."

Ser Addam Marbrand waited at the door with six gold cloaks. He had nothing to say this morning, it seemed. *Another good man who thinks me a kinslayer.* Tyrion summoned all the dignity he could find and waddled down the steps. He could feel them all watching him as he crossed the yard; the guards on the walls, the grooms by the stables, the scullions and washerwomen and serving girls. Inside the throne room, knights and lordlings moved aside to let them through, and whispered to their ladies.

No sooner had Tyrion taken his place before the judges than another group of gold cloaks led in Shae.

A cold hand tightened round his heart. *Varys betrayed her,* he thought. Then he remembered. *No. I betrayed her myself. I should have left her with Lollys. Of course they'd question Sansa's maids, I'd do the same.* Tyrion rubbed at the slick scar where his nose had been, wondering why Cersei had bothered. *Shae knows nothing that can hurt me.*

"They plotted it together," she said, this girl he'd loved. "The Imp and Lady Sansa plotted it after the Young Wolf died. Sansa wanted revenge for her brother and Tyrion meant to have the throne. He was going to kill his sister next, and then his own lord father, so he could be Hand for Prince Tommen. But after a year or so, before Tommen got too old, he would have killed him too, so as to take the crown for his own head."

"How could you know all this?" demanded Prince Oberyn. "Why would the Imp divulge such plans to his wife's maid?"

"I overheard some, m'lord," said Shae, "and m'lady let things slip too. But most I had from his own lips. I wasn't only Lady Sansa's maid. I was his whore, all the time he was here in King's Landing. On the morning of the wedding, he dragged me down where they keep the dragon skulls and fucked me there with the monsters all around. And when I cried, he said I ought to be more grateful, that it wasn't every girl who got to be the king's whore. That was when he told me how he meant to be king. He said that poor boy Joffrey would never know his bride the way he was knowing me." She started sobbing then. "I never meant to be a whore, m'lords. I was to be married. A squire, he was, and a good brave boy, gentle born. But the Imp saw me at the Green Fork and put the boy I meant to marry in the front rank of the van, and after he was killed he sent his wildlings to bring me to his tent. Shagga, the big one, and Timett with the burned eye. He said if I didn't pleasure him, he'd give me to them, so I did. Then he brought me to the city, so I'd be close when he wanted me. He made me do such shameful things . . ."

Prince Oberyn looked curious. "What sorts of things?"

"*Unspeakable* things." As the tears rolled slowly down that pretty face, no doubt every man in the hall wanted to take Shae in his arms and comfort her. "With my mouth and . . . other parts, m'lord. All my parts. He used me every way there was, and . . . he used to make me tell him how big he was. *My giant*, I had to call him, *my giant of Lannister*."

Oswald Kettleblack was the first to laugh. Boros and Meryn joined in, then Cersei, Ser Loras, and more lords and ladies than he could count. The sudden gale of mirth made the rafters ring and shook the Iron Throne. "It's true," Shae protested. "My giant of Lannister." The laughter swelled twice as loud. Their mouths were twisted in merriment, their bellies shook. Some laughed so hard that snot flew from their nostrils.

I saved you all, Tyrion thought. *I saved this vile city and all your worthless lives.* There were hundreds in the throne room, every one of them laughing but his father. Or so it seemed. Even the Red Viper chortled, and Mace Tyrell looked like to bust a gut, but Lord Tywin Lannister sat between them as if made of stone, his fingers steepled beneath his chin.

Tyrion pushed forward. "*MY LORDS!*" he shouted. He had to shout, to have any hope of being heard.

His father raised a hand. Bit by bit, the hall grew silent.

"Get this lying whore out of my sight," said Tyrion, "and I will give you your confession."

Lord Tywin nodded, gestured. Shae looked half in terror as the gold cloaks formed up around her. Her eyes met Tyrion's as they marched her from the wall. Was it shame he saw there, or fear? He wondered what Cersei had promised her. *You will get the gold or jewels, whatever it was you asked for*, he thought as he watched her back recede, *but before the moon has turned she'll have you entertaining the gold cloaks in their barracks.*

Tyrion stared up at his father's hard green eyes with their flecks of cold bright gold. "Guilty," he said, "so guilty. Is that what you wanted to hear?"

Lord Tywin said nothing. Mace Tyrell nodded. Prince Oberyn looked mildly disappointed. "You admit you poisoned the king?"

"Nothing of the sort," said Tyrion. "Of Joffrey's death I am innocent. I am guilty of a more monstrous crime." He took a step toward his father. "I was born. I lived. I am guilty of being a dwarf, I confess it. And no matter how many times my good father forgave me, I have persisted in my infamy."

"This is folly, Tyrion," declared Lord Tywin. "Speak to the matter at hand. You are not on trial for being a dwarf."

"That is where you err, my lord. I have been on trial for being a dwarf my entire life."

"Have you nothing to say in your defense?"

"Nothing but this: I did not do it. Yet now I wish I had." He turned to face the hall, that sea of pale faces. "I wish I had enough poison for you all. You make me sorry that I am not the monster you would have me be, yet there it is. I am innocent, but I will get no justice here. You leave me no choice but to appeal to the gods. I demand trial by battle."

"Have you taken leave of your wits?" his father said.

"No, I've found them. *I demand trial by battle!*"

His sweet sister could not have been more pleased. "He has that right, my lords," she reminded the judges. "Let the gods judge. Ser Gregor Clegane will stand for Joffrey. He returned to the city the night before last, to put his sword at my service."

Lord Tywin's face was so dark that for half a heartbeat Tyrion wondered if he'd drunk some poisoned wine as well. He slammed his fist down on the table, too angry to speak. It was Mace Tyrell who turned to Tyrion and asked the question. "Do you have a champion to defend your innocence?"

"He does, my lord." Prince Oberyn of Dorne rose to his feet. "The dwarf has quite convinced me."

The uproar was deafening. Tyrion took especial pleasure in the sudden doubt he glimpsed in Cersei's eyes. It took a hundred gold cloaks pounding the butts of their spears against the floor to quiet the throne room again. By then Lord Tywin Lannister had recovered himself. "Let the issue be decided on the morrow," he declared in iron tones. "I wash my hands of it." He gave his dwarf son a cold angry look, then strode from the hall, out the king's door behind the Iron Throne, his brother Kevan at his side.

Later, back in his tower cell, Tyrion poured himself a cup of wine and sent Podrick Payne off for cheese, bread, and olives. He doubted whether he could keep down anything heavier just now. *Did you think I would go meekly, Father?* he asked the shadow his candles etched upon the wall. *I have too much of you in me for that.* He felt strangely at peace, now that he had snatched the power of life and death from his father's hands and placed it in the hands of the gods. *Assuming there are gods, and they give a mummer's fart. If not, then I'm in Dornish hands.* No matter what happened, Tyrion had the satisfaction of knowing that he'd kicked Lord Tywin's plans to splinters. If Prince Oberyn won, it would further inflame Highgarden against the Dornish; Mace Tyrell would see the man who crippled his son helping the dwarf who almost poisoned his daughter to escape his rightful punishment. And if the Mountain triumphed, Doran Martell might well demand to know why his brother had been served with death instead of the justice Tyrion had promised him. Dorne might crown Myrcella after all.

It was almost worth dying to know all the trouble he'd made. *Will you come to see the end, Shae? Will you stand there with the rest, watching as Ser Ilyn lops my ugly head off? Will you miss your giant of Lannister when he's dead?* He drained his wine, flung the cup aside, and sang lustily.

> *He rode through the streets of the city,*
> *down from his hill on high,*
> *O'er the wynds and the steps and the cobbles,*
> *he rode to a woman's sigh.*
> *For she was his secret treasure,*
> *she was his shame and his bliss.*
> *And a chain and a keep are nothing,*
> *compared to a woman's kiss.*

Ser Kevan did not visit him that night. He was probably with Lord Tywin, trying to placate the Tyrells. *I have seen the last of that uncle, I fear.* He poured another cup of wine. A pity he'd had Symon Silver Tongue killed before learning all the words of that song. It wasn't a bad song, if truth be told. Especially compared to the ones that would be written about him henceforth. *"For hands of gold are always cold, but a woman's hands are warm,"* he sang. Perhaps he should write the other verses himself. If he lived so long.

That night, surprisingly, Tyrion Lannister slept long and deep. He rose at first light, well rested and with a hearty appetite, and broke his fast on fried bread, blood sausage, applecakes, and a double helping of eggs cooked with onions and fiery Dornish peppers. Then he begged leave of his guards to attend his champion. Ser Addam gave his consent.

Tyrion found Prince Oberyn drinking a cup of red wine as he donned his armor. He was attended by four of his younger Dornish lordlings. "Good morrow to you, my lord," the prince said. "Will you take a cup of wine?"

"Should you be drinking before battle?"

"I always drink before battle."

"That could get you killed. Worse, it could get *me* killed."

Prince Oberyn laughed. "The gods defend the innocent. You *are* innocent, I trust?"

"Only of killing Joffrey," Tyrion admitted. "I do hope you know what you are about to face. Gregor Clegane is—"

"—large? So I have heard."

"He is almost eight feet tall and must weigh thirty stone, all of it muscle. He fights with a two-handed greatsword, but needs only one hand to wield it. He has been known to cut men in half with a single blow. His armor is so heavy that no lesser man could bear the weight, let alone move in it."

Prince Oberyn was unimpressed. "I have killed large men before. The trick is to get them off their feet. Once they go down, they're dead." The Dornishman sounded so blithely confident that Tyrion felt almost reassured, until he turned and said, "Daemon, my spear!" Ser Daemon tossed it to him, and the Red Viper snatched it from the air.

"You mean to face the Mountain with a *spear?*" That made Tyrion uneasy all over again. In battle, ranks of massed spears made for a formidable front, but single combat against a skilled swordsman was a very different matter.

"We are fond of spears in Dorne. Besides, it is the only way to counter his reach. Have a look, Lord Imp, but see you do not touch." The spear was turned ash eight feet long, the shaft smooth, thick, and heavy. The last two feet of that was steel: a slender leaf-shaped spearhead narrowing to a wicked spike. The edges looked sharp enough to shave with. When Oberyn spun the haft between the palms of his hand, they glistened black. *Oil? Or poison?* Tyrion decided that he would sooner not know. "I hope you are good with that," he said doubtfully.

"You will have no cause for complaint. Though Ser Gregor may. However thick his plate, there will be gaps at the joints. Inside the elbow and knee, beneath the arms . . . I will find a place to tickle him, I promise you." He set the spear aside. "It is said that a Lannister always pays his debts. Perhaps you will return to Sunspear with me when the day's bloodletting is done. My brother Doran would be most pleased to meet the rightful heir to Casterly Rock . . . especially if he brought his lovely wife, the Lady of Winterfell."

Does the snake think I have Sansa squirreled away somewhere, like a nut I'm hoarding for winter? If so, Tyrion was not about to disabuse him. "A trip to Dorne might be very pleasant, now that I reflect on it."

"Plan on a lengthy visit." Prince Oberyn sipped his wine. "You and Doran have many matters of mutual interest to discuss. Music, trade, history, wine, the dwarf's penny . . . the laws of inheritance and succession. No doubt an uncle's counsel would be of benefit to Queen Myrcella in the trying times ahead."

If Varys had his little birds listening, Oberyn was giving them a ripe earful. "I believe I will have that cup of wine," said Tyrion. *Queen Myrcella?* It would have been more tempting if only he did have Sansa tucked beneath his cloak. *If she declared for Myrcella over Tommen, would the north follow?* What the Red Viper was hinting at was treason. Could Tyrion truly take up arms against Tommen, against his own father? *Cersei would spit blood.* It might be worth it for that alone.

"Do you recall the tale I told you of our first meeting, Imp?" Prince Oberyn asked, as the Bastard of Godsgrace knelt before him to fasten his greaves. "It was not for your tail alone that my sister and I came to Casterly Rock. We were on a quest of sorts. A quest that took us to Starfall, the Arbor, Oldtown, the Shield Islands, Crakehall, and finally Casterly Rock . . . but our true destination was marriage. Doran was betrothed to Lady Mellario of Norvos, so he had been left behind as castellan of Sunspear. My sister and I were yet unpromised.

"Elia found it all exciting. She was of that age, and her delicate health had never permitted her much travel. I preferred to amuse myself by mocking my sister's suitors. There was Little Lord Lazyeye, Squire Squishlips, one I named the Whale That Walks, that sort of thing. The only one who was even halfway presentable was young Baelor Hightower. A pretty lad, and my sister was half in love with him until he had the misfortune to fart once in our presence. I promptly named him Baelor Breakwind, and after that Elia couldn't look at him without laughing. I was a monstrous young fellow, someone should have sliced out my vile tongue."

Yes, Tyrion agreed silently. Baelor Hightower was no longer young, but he remained Lord Leyton's heir; wealthy, handsome, and a knight of splendid repute. *Baelor Brightsmile*, they called him now. Had Elia wed him in place of Rhaegar Targaryen, she might be in Oldtown with her children growing tall around her. He wondered how many lives had been snuffed out by that fart.

"Lannisport was the end of our voyage," Prince Oberyn went on, as Ser Arron Qorgyle helped him into a padded leather tunic and began lacing it up the back. "Were you aware that our mothers knew each other of old?"

"They had been at court together as girls, I seem to recall. Companions to Princess Rhaella?"

"Just so. It was my belief that the mothers had cooked up this plot between them. Squire Squishlips and his ilk and the various pimply young maidens who'd been paraded before me were the almonds before the feast, meant only to whet our appetites. The main course was to be served at Casterly Rock."

"Cersei and Jaime."

"Such a clever dwarf. Elia and I were older, to be sure. Your brother and sister could not have been more than eight or nine. Still, a difference of five or six years is little enough. And there was an empty cabin on our ship, a very nice cabin, such as might be kept for a person of high birth. As if it were intended that we take someone back to Sunspear. A young page, perhaps. Or a companion for Elia. Your lady mother meant to betroth Jaime to my sister, or Cersei to me. Perhaps both."

"Perhaps," said Tyrion, "but my father—"

"—ruled the Seven Kingdoms, but was ruled at home by his lady wife, or so *my* mother always said." Prince Oberyn raised his arms, so Lord Dagos Manwoody and the Bastard of Godsgrace could slip a chainmail byrnie down over his head. "At Oldtown we learned of your mother's death, and the monstrous child she had borne. We might have turned back there, but my mother chose to sail on. I told you of the welcome we found at Casterly Rock.

"What I did not tell you was that my mother waited as long as was decent, and then broached your father about our purpose. Years later, on her deathbed, she told me that Lord Tywin had refused us brusquely. His daughter was meant for Prince Rhaegar, he informed her. And when she asked for Jaime, to espouse Elia, he offered her you instead."

"Which offer she took for an outrage."

"It *was*. Even you can see that, surely?"

"Oh, surely." *It all goes back and back,* Tyrion thought, *to our mothers and fathers and theirs before them. We are puppets dancing on the strings of those who came before us, and one day our own children will take up our strings and dance on in our steads.* "Well, Prince Rhaegar married Elia of Dorne, not Cersei Lannister of Casterly Rock. So it would seem your mother won that tilt."

"She thought so," Prince Oberyn agreed, "but your father is not a man to forget such slights. He taught that lesson to Lord and Lady Tarbeck once, and to the Reynes of Castamere. And at King's Landing, he taught it to my sister. My helm, Dagos." Manwoody handed it to him; a high golden helm with a copper disk mounted on the brow, the sun of Dorne. The visor had been removed, Tyrion saw. "Elia and her children have waited long for justice." Prince Oberyn pulled on soft red leather gloves, and took up his spear again. "But this day they shall have it."

The outer ward had been chosen for the combat. Tyrion had to skip and run to keep up with Prince Oberyn's long strides. *The snake is eager,* he thought. *Let us hope he is venomous as well.* The day was grey and windy. The sun was struggling to break through the clouds, but Tyrion could no more have said who was going to win that fight than the one on which his life depended.

It looked as though a thousand people had come to see if he would live or die. They lined the castle wallwalks and elbowed one another on the steps of keeps and towers. They watched from the stable doors, from windows and bridges, from balconies and roofs. And the yard was packed with them, so many that the gold cloaks and the knights of the Kingsguard had to shove them back to make enough room for the fight. Some had dragged out chairs to watch more comfortably, while others perched on barrels. *We should have done this in the Dragonpit,* Tyrion thought sourly. *We could have charged a penny a head and paid for Joffrey's wedding and funeral both.* Some of the onlookers even had small children sitting on their shoulders, to get a better view. They shouted and pointed at the sight of Tyrion.

Cersei seemed half a child herself beside Ser Gregor. In his armor, the Mountain looked bigger than any man had any right to be. Beneath a long yellow surcoat bearing the three black dogs of Clegane, he wore heavy plate over chainmail, dull grey steel dinted and scarred in battle. Beneath that would be boiled leather and a layer of quilting. A flat-topped greathelm was bolted to his gorget, with breaths around the mouth and nose and a narrow slit for vision. The crest atop it was a stone fist.

If Ser Gregor was suffering from wounds, Tyrion could see no sign of it from across the yard. *He looks as though he was chiseled out of rock, standing there.* His greatsword was planted in the ground before him, six feet of scarred metal. Ser Gregor's huge hands, clad in gauntlets of lobstered steel, clasped the crosshilt to either side of the grip. Even Prince Oberyn's paramour paled at the sight of him. "You are going to fight *that?*" Ellaria Sand said in a hushed voice.

"I am going to kill that," her lover replied carelessly.

Tyrion had his own doubts, now that they stood on the brink. When he looked at Prince Oberyn, he found himself wishing he had Bronn defending him . . . or even better, Jaime. The Red Viper was lightly armored; greaves, vambraces, gorget, spaulder, steel codpiece. Elsewise Oberyn was clad in supple leather and flowing silks. Over his byrnie he wore his scales of gleaming copper, but mail and scale together would not give him a quarter the protection of Gregor's heavy plate. With its visor removed, the prince's helm was effectively no better than a half-helm, lacking even a nasal. His round steel shield was brightly polished, and showed the sun-and-spear in red gold, yellow gold, white gold, and copper.

Dance around him until he's so tired he can hardly lift his arm, then put him on his back. The Red Viper seemed to have the same notion as Bronn. But the sellsword had been blunt about the risks of such tactics. *I hope to seven hells that you know what you are doing, snake.*

A platform had been erected beside the Tower of the Hand, halfway between the two champions. That was where Lord Tywin sat with his brother Ser Kevan. King Tommen was not in evidence; for that, at least, Tyrion was grateful.

Lord Tywin glanced briefly at his dwarf son, then lifted his hand. A dozen trumpeters blew a fanfare to quiet the crowd. The High Septon shuffled forward in his tall crystal crown, and prayed that the Father Above would help them in this judgment, and that the Warrior would lend his strength to the arm of the man whose cause was just. *That would be me*, Tyrion almost shouted, but they would only laugh, and he was sick unto death of laughter.

Ser Osmund Kettleblack brought Clegane his shield, a massive thing of heavy oak rimmed in black iron. As the Mountain slid his left arm through the straps, Tyrion saw that the hounds of Clegane had been painted over. This morning Ser Gregor bore the seven-pointed star the Andals had brought to Westeros when they crossed the narrow sea to overwhelm the First Men and their gods. *Very pious of you, Cersei, but I doubt the gods will be impressed.*

There were fifty yards between them. Prince Oberyn advanced quickly, Ser Gregor more ominously. *The ground does not shake when he walks*, Tyrion told himself. *That is only my heart fluttering*. When the two men were ten yards apart, the Red Viper stopped and called out, "Have they told you who I am?"

Ser Gregor grunted through his breaths. "Some dead man." He came on, inexorable.

The Dornishman slid sideways. "I am Oberyn Martell, a prince of Dorne," he said, as the Mountain turned to keep him in sight. "Princess Elia was my sister."

"Who?" asked Gregor Clegane.

Oberyn's long spear jabbed, but Ser Gregor took the point on his shield, shoved it aside, and bulled back at the prince, his great sword flashing. The Dornishman spun away untouched. The spear darted forward. Clegane slashed at it, Martell snapped it back, then thrust again. Metal screamed on metal as the spearhead slid off the Mountain's chest, slicing through the surcoat and leaving a long bright scratch on the steel beneath. "Elia Martell, Princess of Dorne," the Red Viper hissed. "You raped her. You murdered her. You killed her children."

Ser Gregor grunted. He made a ponderous charge to hack at the Dornishman's head. Prince Oberyn avoided him easily. "You raped her. You murdered her. You killed her children."

"Did you come to talk or to fight?"

"I came to hear you confess." The Red Viper landed a quick thrust on the Mountain's belly, to no effect. Gregor cut at him, and missed. The long spear lanced in above his sword. Like a serpent's tongue it flickered in and out, feinting low and landing high, jabbing at groin, shield, eyes. *The Mountain makes for a big target, at the least,* Tyrion thought. Prince Oberyn could scarcely miss, though none of his blows was penetrating Ser Gregor's heavy plate. The Dornishman kept circling, jabbing, then darting back again, forcing the bigger man to turn and turn again. *Clegane is losing sight of him.* The Mountain's helm had a narrow eyeslit, severely limiting his vision. Oberyn was making good use of that, and the length of his spear, and his quickness.

It went on that way for what seemed a long time. Back and forth they moved across the yard, and round and round in spirals, Ser Gregor slashing at the air while Oberyn's spear struck at arm, and leg, twice at his temple. Gregor's big wooden shield took its share of hits as well, until a dog's head peeped out from under the star, and elsewhere the raw oak showed through. Clegane would grunt from time to time, and once Tyrion heard him mutter a curse, but otherwise he fought in a sullen silence.

Not Oberyn Martell. "You raped her," he called, feinting. "You murdered her," he said, dodging a looping cut from Gregor's greatsword. "You killed her children," he shouted, slamming the spearpoint into the giant's throat, only to have it glance off the thick steel gorget with a screech.

"Oberyn is toying with him," said Ellaria Sand.

That is fool's play, thought Tyrion. "The Mountain is too bloody big to be any man's toy."

All around the yard, the throng of spectators was creeping in toward the two combatants, edging forward inch by inch to get a better view. The Kingsguard tried to keep them back, shoving at the gawkers forcefully with their big white shields, but there were hundreds of gawkers and only six of the men in white armor.

"You raped her." Prince Oberyn parried a savage cut with his spearhead. "You murdered her." He sent the spearpoint at Clegane's eyes, so fast the huge man flinched back. "You killed her children." The spear flickered sideways and down, scraping against the Mountain's breastplate. "You raped her. You murdered her. You killed her children." The spear was two feet longer than Ser Gregor's sword, more than enough to keep him at an awkward distance. He hacked at the shaft whenever Oberyn lunged at him, trying to lop off the spearhead, but he might as well have been trying to hack the wings off a fly. "You raped her. You murdered her. You killed her children." Gregor tried to bull rush, but Oberyn skipped aside and circled round his back. "You raped her. You murdered her. You killed her children."

"Be quiet." Ser Gregor seemed to be moving a little slower, and his greatsword no longer rose quite so high as it had when the contest began. "Shut your bloody mouth."

"You raped her," the prince said, moving to the right.

"*Enough!*" Ser Gregor took two long strides and brought his sword down at Oberyn's head, but the Dornishman backstepped once more. "You murdered her," he said.

"*SHUT UP!*" Gregor charged headlong, right at the point of the spear, which slammed into his right breast then slid aside with a hideous steel shriek. Suddenly the Mountain was close enough to strike, his huge sword flashing in a steel blur. The crowd was screaming as well. Oberyn slipped the first blow and let go of the spear, useless now that Ser Gregor was inside it. The second cut the Dornishman caught on his shield. Metal met metal with an ear-splitting clang, sending the Red Viper reeling. Ser Gregor followed, bellowing. *He doesn't use words, he just roars like an animal,* Tyrion thought. Oberyn's retreat became a headlong backward flight mere inches ahead of the greatsword as it slashed at his chest, his arms, his head.

The stable was behind him. Spectators screamed and shoved at each other to get out of the way. One stumbled into Oberyn's back. Ser Gregor hacked down with all his savage strength. The Red Viper threw himself sideways, rolling. The luckless stableboy behind him was not so quick. As his arm rose to protect his face, Gregor's sword took it off between elbow and shoulder. "*Shut UP!*" the Mountain howled at the stableboy's scream, and this time he swung the blade sideways, sending the top half of the lad's head across the yard in a spray of blood and brains. Hundreds of spectators suddenly seemed to lose all interest in the guilt or innocence of Tyrion Lannister, judging by the way they pushed and shoved at each other to escape the yard.

But the Red Viper of Dorne was back on his feet, his long spear in hand. "Elia," he called at Ser Gregor. "You raped her. You murdered her. You killed her children. Now say her name."

The Mountain whirled. Helm, shield, sword, surcoat; he was spattered with gore from head to heels. "You talk too much," he grumbled. "You make my head hurt."

"I will hear you say it. She was Elia of Dorne."

The Mountain snorted contemptuously, and came on . . . and in that moment, the sun broke through the low clouds that had hidden the sky since dawn.

The sun of Dorne, Tyrion told himself, but it was Gregor Clegane who moved first to put the sun at his back. *This is a dim and brutal man, but he has a warrior's instincts.*

The Red Viper crouched, squinting, and sent his spear darting forward again. Ser Gregor hacked at it, but the thrust had only been a feint. Off balance, he stumbled forward a step.

Prince Oberyn tilted his dinted metal shield. A shaft of sunlight blazed blindingly off polished gold and copper, into the narrow slit of his foe's helm. Clegane lifted his own shield against the glare. Prince Oberyn's spear flashed like lightning and found the gap in the heavy plate, the joint under the arm. The point punched through mail and boiled leather. Gregor gave a choked grunt as the Dornishman twisted his spear and yanked it free."Elia. Say it! Elia of Dorne!" He was circling, spear poised for another thrust. "*Say it!*"

Tyrion had his own prayer. *Fall down and die*, was how it went. *Damn you, fall down and die!* The blood trickling from the Mountain's armpit was his own now, and he must be bleeding even more heavily inside the breastplate. When he tried to take a step, one knee buckled. Tyrion thought he was going down.

Prince Oberyn had circled behind him. "*ELIA OF DORNE!*" he shouted. Ser Gregor started to turn, but too slow and too late. The spearhead went through the back of the knee this time, through the layers of chain and leather between the plates on thigh and calf. The Mountain reeled, swayed, then collapsed face first on the ground. His huge sword went flying from his hand. Slowly, ponderously, he rolled onto his back.

The Dornishman flung away his ruined shield, grasped the spear in both hands, and sauntered away. Behind him the Mountain let out a groan, and pushed himself onto an elbow. Oberyn whirled cat-quick, and *ran* at his fallen foe. "*EEEEELLLLLLLIIIIIAAAAA!*" he screamed, as he drove the spear down with the whole weight of his body behind it. The *crack* of the ashwood shaft snapping was almost as sweet a sound as Cersei's wail of fury, and for an instant Prince Oberyn had wings. *The snake has vaulted over the Mountain.* Four feet of broken spear jutted from Clegane's belly as Prince Oberyn rolled, rose, and dusted himself off. He tossed aside the splintered spear and claimed his foe's greatsword. "If you die before you say her name, ser, I will hunt you through all seven hells," he promised.

Ser Gregor tried to rise. The broken spear had gone through him, and was pinning him to the ground. He wrapped both hands about the shaft, grunting, but could not pull it out. Beneath him was a spreading pool of red. "I am feeling more innocent by the instant," Tyrion told Ellaria Sand beside him.

Prince Oberyn moved closer. "*Say the name!*" He put a foot on the Mountain's chest and raised the greatsword with both hands. Whether he intended to hack off Gregor's head or shove the point through his eyeslit was something Tyrion would never know.

Clegane's hand shot up and grabbed the Dornishman behind the knee. The Red Viper brought down the greatsword in a wild slash, but he was off-balance, and the edge did no more than put another dent in the Mountain's vambrace. Then the sword was forgotten as Gregor's hand tightened and twisted, yanking the Dornishman down on top of him. They wrestled in the dust and blood, the broken spear wobbling back and forth. Tyrion saw with horror that the Mountain had wrapped one huge arm around the prince, drawing him tight against his chest, like a lover.

"Elia of Dorne," they all heard Ser Gregor say, when they were close enough to kiss. His deep voice boomed within the helm. "I killed her screaming whelp." He thrust his free hand into Oberyn's unprotected face, pushing steel fingers into his eyes. "*Then* I raped her." Clegane slammed his fist into the Dornishman's mouth, making splinters of his teeth. "Then I smashed her fucking head in. Like this." As he drew back his huge fist, the blood on his gauntlet seemed to smoke in the cold dawn air. There was a sickening *crunch*. Ellaria Sand wailed in terror, and Tyrion's breakfast came boiling back up. He found himself on his knees retching bacon and sausage and applecakes, and that double helping of fried eggs cooked up with onions and fiery Dornish peppers.

He never heard his father speak the words that condemned him. Perhaps no words were necessary. *I put my life in the Red Viper's hands, and he dropped it.* When he remembered, too late, that snakes had no hands, Tyrion began to laugh hysterically.

He was halfway down the serpentine steps before he realized that the gold cloaks were not taking him back to his tower room. "I've been consigned to the black cells," he said. They did not bother to answer. *Why waste your breath on the dead?*

DAENERYS

Dany broke her fast under the persimmon tree that grew in the terrace garden, watching her dragons chase each other about the apex of the Great Pyramid where the huge bronze harpy once stood. Meereen had a score of lesser pyramids, but none stood even half as tall. From here she could see the whole city: the narrow twisty alleys and wide brick streets, the temples and granaries, hovels and palaces, brothels and baths, gardens and fountains, the great red circles of the fighting pits. And beyond the walls was the pewter sea, the winding Skahazadhan, the dry brown hills, burnt orchards, and blackened fields. Up here in her garden Dany sometimes felt like a god, living atop the highest mountain in the world.

Do all gods feel so lonely? Some must, surely. Missandei had told her of the Lord of Harmony, worshiped by the Peaceful People of Naath; he was the only true god, her little scribe said, the god who always was and always would be, who made the moon and stars and earth, and all the creatures that dwelt upon them. *Poor Lord of Harmony.*

Dany pitied him. It must be terrible to be alone for all time, attended by hordes of butterfly women you could make or unmake at a word. Westeros had seven gods at least, though Viserys had told her that some septons said the seven were only aspects of a single god, seven facets of a single crystal. That was just confusing. The red priests believed in two gods, she had heard, but two who were eternally at war. Dany liked that even less. She would not want to be eternally at war.

Missandei served her duck eggs and dog sausage, and half a cup of sweetened wine mixed with the juice of a lime. The honey drew flies, but a scented candle drove them off. The flies were not so troublesome up here as they were in the rest of her city, she had found, something else she liked about the pyramid. "I must remember to do something about the flies," Dany said. "Are there many flies on Naath, Missandei?"

"On Naath there are butterflies," the scribe responded in the Common Tongue. "More wine?"

"No. I must hold court soon." Dany had grown very fond of Missandei. The little scribe with the big golden eyes was wise beyond her years. *She is brave as well. She had to be, to survive the life she's lived.* One day she hoped to see this fabled isle of Naath. Missandei said the Peaceful People made music instead of war. They did not kill, not even animals; they ate only fruit and never flesh. The butterfly spirits sacred to their Lord of Harmony protected their isle against those who would do them harm. Many conquerors had sailed on Naath to blood their swords, only to sicken and die. *The butterflies do not help them when the slave ships come raiding, though.* "I am going to take you home one day, Missandei," Dany promised. *If I had made the same promise to Jorah, would he still have sold me?* "I swear it."

"This one is content to stay with you, Your Grace. Naath will be there, always. You are good to this—to me."

"And you to me." Dany took the girl by the hand. "Come help me dress."

Jhiqui helped Missandei bathe her while Irri was laying out her clothes. Today she wore a robe of purple samite and a silver sash, and on her head the three-headed dragon crown the Tourmaline Brotherhood had given her in Qarth.

Her slippers were silver as well, with heels so high that she was always half afraid she was about to topple over. When she was dressed, Missandei brought her a polished silver glass so she could see how she looked. Dany stared at herself in silence. *Is this the face of a conqueror?* So far as she could tell, she still looked like a little girl.

No one was calling her Daenerys the Conqueror yet, but perhaps they would. Aegon the Conqueror had won Westeros with three dragons, but she had taken Meereen with sewer rats and a wooden cock, in less than a day. *Poor Groleo.* He still grieved for his ship, she knew. If a war galley could ram another ship, why not a gate? That had been her thought when she commanded the captains to drive their ships ashore. Their masts had become her battering rams, and swarms of freedmen had torn their hulls apart to build mantlets, turtles, catapults, and ladders. The sellswords had given each ram a bawdy name, and it had been the mainmast of *Meraxes*—formerly *Joso's Prank*—that had broken the eastern gate. Joso's Cock, they called it. The fighting had raged bitter and bloody for most of a day and well into the night before the wood began to splinter and *Meraxes'* iron figurehead, a laughing jester's face, came crashing through.

Dany had wanted to lead the attack herself, but to a man her captains said that would be madness, and her captains never agreed on anything. Instead she remained in the rear, sitting atop her silver in a long shirt of mail. She *heard* the city fall from half a league away, though, when the defenders' shouts of defiance changed to cries of fear. Her dragons had roared as one in that moment, filling the night with flame. *The slaves are rising*, she knew at once. *My sewer rats have gnawed off their chains.*

When the last resistance had been crushed by the Unsullied and the sack had run its course, Dany entered her city. The dead were heaped so high before the broken gate that it took her freedmen near an hour to make a path for her silver. Joso's Cock and the great wooden turtle that had protected it, covered with horsehides, lay abandoned within. She rode past burned buildings and broken windows, through brick streets where the gutters were choked with the stiff and swollen dead. Cheering slaves lifted bloodstained hands to her as she went by, and called her "Mother."

In the plaza before the Great Pyramid, the Meereenese huddled forlorn. The Great Masters had looked anything but great in the morning light. Stripped of their jewels and their fringed *tokars*, they were contemptible; a herd of old men with shriveled balls and spotted skin and young men with ridiculous hair. Their women were either soft and fleshy or as dry as old sticks, their face paint streaked by tears. "I want your leaders," Dany told them. "Give them up, and the rest of you shall be spared."

"How many?" one old woman had asked, sobbing. "How many must you have to spare us?"

"One hundred and sixty-three," she answered.

She had them nailed to wooden posts around the plaza, each man pointing at the next. The anger was fierce and hot inside her when she gave the command; it made her feel like an avenging dragon. But later, when she passed the men dying on the posts, when she heard their moans and smelled their bowels and blood . . .

Dany put the glass aside, frowning. *It was just. It was. I did it for the children.*

Her audience chamber was on the level below, an echoing high-ceilinged room with walls of purple marble. It was a chilly place for all its grandeur. There had been a throne there, a fantastic thing of carved and gilded wood in the shape of a savage harpy. She had taken one long look and commanded it be broken up for firewood. "I will not sit in the harpy's lap," she told them. Instead she sat upon a simple ebony bench. It served, though she had heard the Meereenese muttering that it did not befit a queen.

Her bloodriders were waiting for her. Silver bells tinkled in their oiled braids, and they wore the gold and jewels of dead men. Meereen had been rich beyond imagining. Even her sellswords seemed sated, at least for now. Across the room, Grey Worm wore the plain uniform of the Unsullied, his spiked bronze cap beneath one arm. These at least she could rely on, or so she hoped . . . and Brown Ben Plumm as well, solid Ben with his grey-white hair and weathered face, so beloved of her dragons. And Daario beside him, glittering in gold. Daario and Ben Plumm, Grey Worm, Irri, Jhiqui, Missandei . . . as she looked at them

Dany found herself wondering which of them would betray her next.

The dragon has three heads. There are two men in the world who I can trust, if I can find them. I will not be alone then. We will be three against the world, like Aegon and his sisters.

"Was the night as quiet as it seemed?" Dany asked.

"It seems it was, Your Grace," said Brown Ben Plumm.

She was pleased. Meereen had been sacked savagely, as new-fallen cities always were, but Dany was determined that should end now that the city was hers. She had decreed that murderers were to be hanged, that looters were to lose a hand, and rapists their manhood. Eight killers swung from the walls, and the Unsullied had filled a bushel basket with bloody hands and soft red worms, but Meereen was calm again. *But for how long?*

A fly buzzed her head. Dany waved it off, irritated, but it returned almost at once. "There are too many flies in this city."

Ben Plumm gave a bark of laughter. "There were flies in my ale this morning. I swallowed one of them."

"Flies are the dead man's revenge." Daario smiled, and stroked the center prong of his beard. "Corpses breed maggots, and maggots breed flies."

"We will rid ourselves of the corpses, then. Starting with those in the plaza below. Grey Worm, will you see to it?"

"The queen commands, these ones obey."

"Best bring sacks as well as shovels, Worm," Brown Ben counseled. "Well past ripe, those ones. Falling off those poles in bits and pieces, and crawling with . . ."

"He knows. So do I." Dany remembered the horror she had felt when she had seen the Plaza of Punishment in Astapor. *I made a horror just as great, but surely they deserved it. Harsh justice is still justice.*

"Your Grace," said Missandei, "Ghiscari inter their honored dead in crypts below their manses. If you would boil the bones clean and return them to their kin, it would be a kindness."

The widows will curse me all the same. "Let it be done." Dany beckoned to Daario. "How many seek audience this morning?"

"Two have presented themselves to bask in your radiance."

Daario had plundered himself a whole new wardrobe in Meereen, and to match it he had redyed his trident beard and curly hair a deep rich purple. It made his eyes look almost purple too, as if he were some lost Valyrian. "They arrived in the night on the *Indigo Star*, a trading galley out of Qarth."

A slaver, you mean. Dany frowned. "Who are they?"

"The *Star*'s master and one who claims to speak for Astapor."

"I will see the envoy first."

He proved to be a pale ferret-faced man with ropes of pearls and spun gold hanging heavy about his neck. "Your Worship!" he cried. "My name is Ghael. I bring greetings to the Mother of Dragons from King Cleon of Astapor, Cleon the Great."

Dany stiffened. "I left a council to rule Astapor. A healer, a scholar, and a priest."

"Your Worship, those sly rogues betrayed your trust. It was revealed that they were scheming to restore the Good Masters to power and the people to chains. Great Cleon exposed their plots and hacked their heads off with a cleaver, and the grateful folk of Astapor have crowned him for his valor."

"Noble Ghael," said Missandei, in the dialect of Astapor, "is this the same Cleon once owned by Grazdan mo Ullhor?"

Her voice was guileless, yet the question plainly made the envoy anxious. "The same," he admitted. "A great man."

Missandei leaned close to Dany. "He was a butcher in Grazdan's kitchen," the girl whispered in her ear. "It was said he could slaughter a pig faster than any man in Astapor."

I have given Astapor a butcher king. Dany felt ill, but she knew she must not let the envoy see it. "I will pray that King Cleon rules well and wisely. What would he have of me?"

Ghael rubbed his mouth. "Perhaps we should speak more privily, Your Grace?"

"I have no secrets from my captains and commanders."

"As you wish. Great Cleon bids me declare his devotion to the Mother of Dragons. Your enemies are his enemies, he says, and chief among them are the Wise Masters of Yunkai. He proposes a pact between Astapor and Meereen, against the Yunkai'i."

"I swore no harm would come to Yunkai if they released their slaves," said Dany.

"These Yunkish dogs cannot be trusted, Your Worship. Even now they plot against you. New levies have been raised and can be seen drilling outside the city walls, warships are being built, envoys have been sent to New Ghis and Volantis in the west, to make alliances and hire sellswords. They have even dispatched riders to Vaes Dothrak to bring a *khalasar* down upon you. Great Cleon bid me tell you not to be afraid. Astapor remembers. Astapor will not forsake you. To prove his faith, Great Cleon offers to seal your alliance with a marriage."

"A marriage? To me?"

Ghael smiled. His teeth were brown and rotten. "Great Cleon will give you many strong sons."

Dany found herself bereft of words, but little Missandei came to her rescue. "Did his first wife give him sons?"

The envoy looked at her unhappily. "Great Cleon has three daughters by his first wife. Two of his newer wives are with child. But he means to put all of them aside if the Mother of Dragons will consent to wed him."

"How noble of him," said Dany. "I will consider all you've said, my lord." She gave orders that Ghael be given chambers for the night, somewhere lower in the pyramid.

All my victories turn to dross in my hands, she thought. *Whatever I do, all I make is death and horror.* When word of what had befallen Astapor reached the streets, as it surely would, tens of thousands of newly freed Meereenese slaves would doubtless decide to follow her when she went west, for fear of what awaited them if they stayed . . . yet it might well be that worse would await them on the march. Even if she emptied every granary in the city and left Meereen to starve, how could she feed so many? The way before her was fraught with hardship, bloodshed, and danger. Ser Jorah had warned her of that. He'd warned her of so many things . . . he'd . . . *No, I will not think of Jorah Mormont. Let him keep a little longer.* "I shall see this trader captain," she announced. Perhaps he would have some better tidings.

That proved to be a forlorn hope. The master of the *Indigo Star* was Qartheen, so he wept copiously when asked about Astapor. "The city bleeds. Dead men rot unburied in the streets, each pyramid is an armed camp, and the markets have neither food nor slaves for sale. And the poor children! King Cleaver's thugs have seized every highborn boy in Astapor to make new Unsullied for the trade, though it will be years before they are trained."

The thing that surprised Dany most was how unsurprised she was. She found herself remembering Eroeh, the Lhazarene girl she had once tried to protect, and what had happened to her. *It will be the same in Meereen once I march*, she thought. The slaves from the fighting pits, bred and trained to slaughter, were already proving themselves unruly and quarrelsome. They seemed to think they owned the city now, and every man and woman in it. Two of them had been among the eight she'd hanged. *There is no more I can do*, she told herself. "What do you want of me, Captain?"

"Slaves," he said. "My holds are full to bursting with ivory, ambergris, zorse hides, and other fine goods. I would trade them here for slaves, to sell in Lys and Volantis."

"We have no slaves for sale," said Dany.

"My queen?" Daario stepped forward. "The riverside is full of Meereenese, begging leave to be allowed to sell themselves to this Qartheen. They are thicker than the flies."

Dany was shocked. "They *want* to be slaves?"

"The ones who come are well spoken and gently born, sweet queen. Such slaves are prized. In the Free Cities they will be tutors, scribes, bed slaves, even healers and priests. They will sleep in soft beds, eat rich foods, and dwell in manses. Here they have lost all, and live in fear and squalor."

"I see." Perhaps it was not so shocking, if these tales of Astapor were true. Dany thought a moment. "Any man who wishes to sell *himself* into slavery may do so. Or woman." She raised a hand. "But they may not sell their children, nor a man his wife."

"In Astapor the city took a tenth part of the price, each time a slave changed hands," Missandei told her.

"We'll do the same," Dany decided. Wars were won with gold as much as swords. "A tenth part. In gold or silver coin, or ivory. Meereen has no need of saffron, cloves, or zorse hides."

"It shall be done as you command, glorious queen," said Daario. "My Stormcrows will collect your tenth."

If the Stormcrows saw to the collections at least half the gold would somehow go astray, Dany knew. But the Second Sons were just as bad, and the Unsullied were as unlettered as they were incorruptible. "Records must be kept," she said. "Seek among the freedmen for men who can read, write, and do sums."

His business done, the captain of the *Indigo Star* bowed and took his leave. Dany shifted uncomfortably on the ebony bench. She dreaded what must come next, yet she knew she had put it off too long already. Yunkai and Astapor, threats of war, marriage proposals, the march west looming over all . . . *I need my knights. I need their swords, and I need their counsel.* Yet the thought of seeing Jorah Mormont again made her feel as if she'd swallowed a spoonful of flies; angry, agitated, sick. She could almost feel them buzzing round her belly. *I am the blood of the dragon. I must be strong. I must have fire in my eyes when I face them, not tears.* "Tell Belwas to bring my knights," Dany commanded, before she could change her mind. "My good knights."

Strong Belwas was puffing from the climb when he marched them through the doors, one meaty hand wrapped tight around each man's arm. Ser Barristan walked with his head held high, but Ser Jorah stared at the marble floor as he approached. *The one is proud, the other guilty.* The old man had shaved off his white beard. He looked ten years younger without it. But her balding bear looked older than he had. They halted before the bench. Strong Belwas stepped back and stood with his arms crossed across his scarred chest. Ser Jorah cleared his throat. "*Khaleesi* . . ."

She had missed his voice so much, but she had to be stern. "Be quiet. I will tell you when to speak." She stood. "When I sent you down into the sewers, part of me hoped I'd seen the last of you. It seemed a fitting end for liars, to drown in slavers' filth. I thought the gods would deal with you, but instead you returned to me. My gallant knights of Westeros, an informer and a turncloak. My brother would have hanged you both." Viserys would have, anyway. She did not know what Rhaegar would have done. "I will admit you helped win me this city . . ."

Ser Jorah's mouth tightened. "We won you this city. We sewer rats."

"Be quiet," she said again . . . though there *was* truth to what he said. While Joso's Cock and the other rams were battering the city gates and her archers were firing flights of flaming arrows over the walls, Dany had sent two hundred men along the river under cover of darkness to fire the hulks in the harbor. But that was only to hide their true purpose. As the flaming ships drew the eyes of the defenders on the walls, a few half-mad swimmers found the sewer mouths and pried loose a rusted iron grating. Ser Jorah, Ser Barristan, Strong Belwas, and twenty brave fools slipped beneath the brown water and up the brick tunnel, a mixed force of sellswords, Unsullied, and freedmen. Dany had told them to choose only men who had no families . . . and preferably no sense of smell.

They had been lucky as well as brave. It had been a moon's turn since the last good rain, and the sewers were only thigh-high. The oilcloth they'd wrapped around their torches kept them dry, so they had light. A few of the freedmen were frightened of the huge rats until Strong Belwas caught one and bit it in two. One man was killed by a great pale lizard that reared up out of the dark water to drag him off by the leg, but when next ripples were spied Ser Jorah butchered the beast with his blade. They took some wrong turnings, but once they found the surface Strong Belwas led them to the nearest fighting pit, where they surprised a few guards and struck the chains off the slaves. Within an hour, half the fighting slaves in Meereen had risen.

"You *helped* win this city," she repeated stubbornly. "And you have served me well in the past. Ser Barristan saved me from the Titan's Bastard, and from the Sorrowful Man in Qarth. Ser Jorah saved me from the poisoner in Vaes Dothrak, and again from Drogo's bloodriders after my sun-and-stars had died." So many people wanted her dead, sometimes she lost count. "And yet you lied, deceived me, betrayed me." She turned to Ser Barristan. "You protected my father for many years, fought beside my brother on the Trident, but you abandoned Viserys in his exile and bent your knee to the Usurper instead. Why? And tell it *true*."

"Some truths are hard to hear. Robert was a . . . a good knight . . . chivalrous, brave . . . he spared my life, and the lives of many others . . . Prince Viserys was only a boy, it would have been years before he was fit to rule, and . . . forgive me, my queen, but you asked for truth . . . even as a child, your brother Viserys oft seemed to be his father's son, in ways that Rhaegar never did."

"His father's son?" Dany frowned. "What does that mean?"

The old knight did not blink. "Your father is called 'the Mad King' in Westeros. Has no one ever told you?"

"Viserys did." *The Mad King.* "The *Usurper* called him that, the Usurper and his dogs." *The Mad King.* "It was a lie."

"Why ask for truth," Ser Barristan said softly, "if you close your ears to it?" He hesitated, then continued. "I told you before that I used a false name so the Lannisters would not know that I'd joined you. That was less than half of it, Your Grace. The truth is, I wanted to watch you for a time before pledging you my sword. To make certain that you were not . . ."

". . . my father's daughter?" If she was not her father's daughter, who was she?

". . . mad," he finished. "But I see no taint in you."

"*Taint?*" Dany bristled.

"I am no maester to quote history at you, Your Grace. Swords have been my life, not books. But every child knows that the Targaryens have always danced too close to madness. Your father was not the first. King Jaehaerys once told me that madness and greatness are two sides of the same coin. Every time a new Targaryen is born, he said, the gods toss the coin in the air and the world holds its breath to see how it will land."

Jaehaerys. This old man knew my grandfather. The thought gave her pause. Most of what she knew of Westeros had come from her brother, and the rest from Ser Jorah. Ser Barristan would have forgotten more than the two of them had ever known. *This man can tell me what I came from.* "So I am a coin in the hands of some god, is that what you are saying, ser?"

"No," Ser Barristan replied. "You are the trueborn heir of Westeros. To the end of my days I shall remain your faithful knight, should you find me worthy to bear a sword again. If not, I am content to serve Strong Belwas as his squire."

"What if I decide you're only worthy to be my fool?" Dany asked scornfully. "Or perhaps my cook?"

"I would be honored, Your Grace," Selmy said with quiet dignity. "I can bake apples and boil beef as well as any man, and I've roasted many a duck over a campfire. I hope you like them greasy, with charred skin and bloody bones."

That made her smile. "I'd have to be mad to eat such fare. Ben Plumm, come give Ser Barristan your longsword."

But Whitebeard would not take it. "I flung my sword at Joffrey's feet and have not touched one since. Only from the hand of my queen will I accept a sword again."

"As you wish." Dany took the sword from Brown Ben and offered it hilt first. The old man took it reverently. "Now kneel," she told him, "and swear it to my service."

He went to one knee and lay the blade before her as he said the words. Dany scarcely heard them. *He was the easy one,* she thought. *The other will be harder.* When Ser Barristan was done, she turned to Jorah Mormont. "And now you, ser. Tell me true."

The big man's neck was red; whether from anger or shame she did not know. "I have tried to tell you true, half a hundred times. I told you Arstan was more than he seemed. I warned you that Xaro and Pyat Pree were not to be trusted. I warned you—"

"You warned me against everyone except yourself." His insolence angered her. *He should be humbler. He should beg for my forgiveness.* "Trust no one but Jorah Mormont, you said . . . and all the time you were the Spider's creature!"

"I am no man's *creature.* I took the eunuch's gold, yes. I learned some ciphers and wrote some letters, but that was all—"

"*All?* You spied on me and sold me to my enemies!"

"For a time." He said it grudgingly. "I stopped."

"When? When did you stop?"

"I made one report from Qarth, but—"

"From *Qarth?*" Dany had been hoping it had ended much earlier. "What did you write from Quarth? That you were my man now, that you wanted no more of their schemes?" Ser Jorah could not meet her eyes. "When Khal Drogo died, you asked me to go with you to Yi Ti and the Jade Sea. Was that your wish or Robert's?"

"That was to protect you," he insisted. "To keep you away from them. I knew what snakes they were . . ."

"*Snakes?* And what are you, ser?" Something unspeakable occurred to her. "You told them I was carrying Drogo's child . . ."

"*Khaleesi* . . ."

"Do not think to deny it, ser," Ser Barristan said sharply. "I was there when the eunuch told the council, and Robert decreed that Her Grace and her child must die. You were the source, ser. There was even talk that you might do the deed, for a pardon."

"A lie." Ser Jorah's face darkened. "I would never . . . Daenerys, it was me who *stopped* you from drinking the wine."

"Yes. And how was it you knew the wine was poisoned?"

"I . . . I but suspected . . . the caravan brought a letter from Varys, he warned me there would be attempts. He wanted you watched, yes, but not harmed." He went to his knees. "If I had not told them someone else would have. You *know* that."

"I know you betrayed me." She touched her belly, where her son Rhaego had perished. "I know a poisoner tried to kill my son, because of you. That's what I *know*."

"No . . . no." He shook his head. "I never meant . . . forgive me. You have to forgive me."

"*Have* to?" It was too late. *He should have begun by begging forgiveness.* She could not pardon him as she'd intended. She had dragged the wineseller behind her horse until there was nothing left of him. Didn't the man who brought him deserve the same? *This is Jorah, my fierce bear, the right arm that never failed me. I would be dead without him, but . . .* "I can't forgive you," she said. "I can't."

"You forgave the old man . . ."

"He lied to me about his name. You sold my secrets to the men who killed my father and stole my brother's throne."

"I protected you. I fought for you. Killed for you."

Kissed me, she thought, *betrayed me.*

"I went down into the sewers like a rat. For you."

It might have been kinder if you'd died there. Dany said nothing. There was nothing to say.

"Daenerys," he said, "I have loved you."

And there it was. *Three treasons will you know. Once for blood and once for gold and once for love.* "The gods do nothing without a purpose, they say. You did not die in battle, so it must be they still have some use for you. But I don't. I will not have you near me. You are banished, ser. Go back to your masters in King's Landing and collect your pardon, if you can. Or to Astapor. No doubt the butcher king needs knights."

"No." He reached for her. "Daenerys, please, hear me . . ."

She slapped his hand away. "Do not ever presume to touch me again, or to speak my name. You have until dawn to collect your things and leave this city. If you're found in Meereen past break of day, I will have Strong Belwas twist your head off. I will. Believe that." She turned her back on him, her skirts swirling. *I cannot bear to see his face.* "Remove this liar from my sight," she commanded. *I must not weep. I must not. If I weep I will forgive him.* Strong Belwas seized Ser Jorah by the arm and dragged him out. When Dany glanced back, the knight was walking as if drunk, stumbling and slow. She looked away until she heard the doors open and close. Then she sank back onto the ebony bench. *He's gone, then. My father and my mother, my brothers, Ser Willem Darry, Drogo who was my sun-and-stars, his son who died inside me, and now Ser Jorah . . .*

"The queen has a good heart," Daario purred through his deep purple whiskers, "but that one is more dangerous than all the Oznaks and Meros rolled up in one." His strong hands caressed the hilts of his matched blades, those wanton golden women. "You need not even say the word, my radiance. Only give the tiniest nod, and your Daario shall fetch you back his ugly head."

"Leave him be. The scales are balanced now. Let him go home." Dany pictured Jorah moving amongst old gnarled oaks and tall pines, past flowering thornbushes, grey stones bearded with moss, and little creeks running icy down steep hillsides. She saw him entering a hall built of huge logs, where dogs slept by the hearth and the smell of meat and mead hung thick in the smoky air. "We are done for now," she told her captains.

It was all she could do not to run back up the wide marble stairs. Irri helped her slip from her court clothes and into more comfortable garb; baggy woolen breeches, a loose felted tunic, a painted Dothraki vest. "You are trembling, *Khaleesi*," the girl said as she knelt to lace up Dany's sandals.

"I'm cold," Dany lied. "Bring me the book I was reading last night." She wanted to lose herself in the words, in other times and other places. The fat leather-bound volume was full of songs and stories from the Seven Kingdoms. Children's stories, if truth be told; too simple and fanciful to be true history. All the heroes were tall and handsome, and you could tell the traitors by their shifty eyes. Yet she loved them all the same. Last night she had been reading of the three princesses in the red tower, locked away by the king for the crime of being beautiful.

When her handmaid brought the book, Dany had no trouble finding the page where she had left off, but it was no good. She found herself reading the same passage half a dozen times. *Ser Jorah gave me this book as a bride's gift, the day I wed Khal Drogo. But Daario is right, I shouldn't have banished him. I should have kept him, or I should have killed him.* She played at being a queen, yet sometimes she still felt like a scared little girl. *Viserys always said what a dolt I was. Was he truly mad?* She closed the book. She could still recall Ser Jorah, if she wished. Or send Daario to kill him.

Dany fled from the choice, out onto the terrace. She found Rhaegal asleep beside the pool, a green and bronze coil basking in the sun. Drogon was perched up atop the pyramid, in the place where the huge bronze harpy had stood before she had commanded it to be pulled down. He spread his wings and roared when he spied her. There was no sign of Viserion, but when she went to the parapet and scanned the horizon she saw pale wings in the far distance, sweeping above the river. *He is hunting. They grow bolder every day.* Yet it still made her anxious when they flew too far away. *One day one of them may not return,* she thought.

"Your Grace?"

She turned to find Ser Barristan behind her. "What more would you have of me, ser? I spared you, I took you into my service, now give me some peace."

"Forgive me, Your Grace. It was only . . . now that you know who I am . . ." The old man hesitated. "A knight of the Kingsguard is in the king's presence day and night. For that reason, our vows require us to protect his secrets as we would his life. But your father's secrets by rights belong to you now, along with his throne, and . . . I thought perhaps you might have questions for me."

Questions? She had a hundred questions, a thousand, ten thousand. Why couldn't she think of one? "Was my father truly mad?" she blurted out. *Why do I ask that?* "Viserys said this talk of madness was a ploy of the Usurper's . . ."

"Viserys was a child, and the queen sheltered him as much as she could. Your father always had a little madness in him, I now believe. Yet he was charming and generous as well, so his lapses were forgiven. His reign began with such promise . . . but as the years passed, the lapses grew more frequent, until . . ."

Dany stopped him. "Do I want to hear this now?"

Ser Barristan considered a moment. "Perhaps not. Not now."

"Not now," she agreed. "One day. One day you must tell me all. The good and the bad. There is *some* good to be said of my father, surely?"

"There is, Your Grace. Of him, and those who came before him. Your grandfather Jaehaerys and his brother, their father Aegon, your mother . . . and Rhaegar. Him most of all."

"I wish I could have known him." Her voice was wistful.

"I wish he could have known you," the old knight said. "When you are ready, I will tell you all."

Dany kissed him on the cheek and sent him on his way. That night her handmaids brought her lamb, with a salad of raisins and carrots soaked in wine, and a hot flaky bread dripping with honey. She could eat none of it. *Did Rhaegar ever grow so weary?* she wondered. *Did Aegon, after his conquest?*

Later, when the time came for sleep, Dany took Irri into bed with her, for the first time since the ship. But even as she shuddered in release and wound her fingers through her handmaid's thick black hair, she pretended it was Drogo holding her . . . only somehow his face kept turning into Daario's. *If I want Daario I need only say so.* She lay with Irri's legs entangled in her own. *His eyes looked almost purple today . . .*

Dany's dreams were dark that night, and she woke three times from half-remembered nightmares. After the third time she was too restless to return to sleep. Moonlight streamed through the slanting windows, silvering the marble floors. A cool breeze was blowing through the open terrace doors. Irri slept soundly beside her, her lips slightly parted, one dark brown nipple peeping out above the sleeping silks. For a moment Dany was tempted, but it was Drogo she wanted, or perhaps Daario. Not Irri. The maid was sweet and skillful, but all her kisses tasted of duty.

She rose, leaving Irri asleep in the moonlight. Jhiqui and Missandei slept in their own beds. Dany slipped on a robe and padded barefoot across the marble floor, out onto the terrace. The air was chilly, but she liked the feel of grass between her toes and the sound of the leaves whispering to one another. Wind ripples chased each other across the surface of the little bathing pool and made the moon's reflection dance and shimmer.

She leaned against a low brick parapet to look down upon the city. Meereen was sleeping too. *Lost in dreams of kinder days, perhaps.* Night covered the streets like a black blanket, hiding the corpses and the grey rats that came up from the sewers to feast on them, the swarms of stinging flies. Distant torches glimmered red and yellow where her sentries walked their rounds, and here and there she saw the faint glow of lanterns bobbing down an alley. Perhaps one was Ser Jorah, leading his horse slowly toward the gate. *Farewell, old bear. Farewell, betrayer.*

She was Daenerys Stormborn, the Unburnt, *khaleesi* and queen, Mother of Dragons, slayer of warlocks, breaker of chains, and there was no one in the world that she could trust.

"Your Grace?" Missandei stood at her elbow wrapped in a bedrobe, wooden sandals on her feet. "I woke, and saw that you were gone. Did you sleep well? What are you looking at?"

"My city," said Dany. "I was looking for a house with a red door, but by night all the doors are black."

"A red door?" Missandei was puzzled. "What house is this?"

"No house. It does not matter." Dany took the younger girl by the hand. "Never lie to me, Missandei. Never betray me."

"I never would," Missandei promised. "Look, dawn comes."

The sky had turned a cobalt blue from the horizon to the zenith, and behind the line of low hills to the east a glow could be seen, pale gold and oyster pink. Dany held Missandei's hand as they watched the sun come up. All the grey bricks became red and yellow and blue and green and orange. The scarlet sands of the fighting pits transformed them into bleeding sores before her eyes. Elsewhere the golden dome of the Temple of the Graces blazed bright, and bronze stars winked along the walls where the light of the rising sun touched the spikes on the helms of the Unsullied. On the terrace, a few flies stirred sluggishly. A bird began to chirp in the persimmon tree, and then two more. Dany cocked her head to hear their song, but it was not long before the sounds of the waking city drowned them out.

The sounds of my city.

That morning she summoned her captains and commanders to the garden, rather than descending to the audience chamber. "Aegon the Conqueror brought fire and blood to Westeros, but afterward he gave them peace, prosperity, and justice. But all I have brought to Slaver's Bay is death and ruin. I have been more *khal* than queen, smashing and plundering, then moving on."

"There is nothing to stay for," said Brown Ben Plumm.

"Your Grace, the slavers brought their doom on themselves," said Daario Naharis.

"You have brought freedom as well," Missandei pointed out.

"Freedom to starve?" asked Dany sharply. "Freedom to die? Am I a dragon, or a harpy?" *Am I mad? Do I have the taint?*

"A dragon," Ser Barristan said with certainty. "Meereen is not Westeros, Your Grace."

"But how can I rule seven kingdoms if I cannot rule a single city?" He had no answer to that. Dany turned away from them, to gaze out over the city once again. "My children need time to heal and learn. My dragons need time to grow and test their wings. And I need the same. I will not let this city go the way of Astapor. I will not let the harpy of Yunkai chain up those I've freed all over again." She turned back to look at their faces. "I will not march."

"What will you do then, *Khaleesi?*" asked Rakharo.

"Stay," she said. "Rule. And be a queen."

JAIME

The king sat at the head of the table, a stack of cushions under his arse, signing each document as it was presented to him.

"Only a few more, Your Grace," Ser Kevan Lannister assured him. "This is a bill of attainder against Lord Edmure Tully, stripping him of Riverrun and all its lands and incomes, for rebelling against his lawful king. This is a similar attainder, against his uncle Ser Brynden Tully, the Blackfish." Tommen signed them one after the other, dipping the quill carefully and writing his name in a broad childish hand.

Jaime watched from the foot of the table, thinking of all those lords who aspired to a seat on the king's small council. *They can bloody well have mine.* If this was power, why did it taste like tedium? He did not feel especially powerful, watching Tommen dip his quill in the inkpot again. He felt bored.

And sore. Every muscle in his body ached, and his ribs and shoulders were bruised from the battering they'd gotten, courtesy of Ser Addam Marbrand. Just thinking of it made him wince. He could only hope the man would keep his mouth shut. Jaime had known Marbrand since he was a boy, serving as a page at Casterly Rock; he trusted him as much as he trusted anyone. Enough to ask him to take up shields and tourney swords. He had wanted to know if he could fight with his left hand.

And now I do. The knowledge was more painful than the beating that Ser Addam had given him, and the beating was so bad he could hardly dress himself this morning. If they had been fighting in earnest, Jaime would have died two dozen deaths. It seemed so simple, changing hands. It wasn't. Every instinct he had was wrong. He had to *think* about everything, where once he'd just moved. And while he was thinking, Marbrand was thumping him. His left hand couldn't even seem to *hold* a longsword properly; Ser Addam had disarmed him thrice, sending his blade spinning.

"This grants said lands, incomes, and castle to Ser Emmon Frey and his lady wife, Lady Genna." Ser Kevan presented another sheaf of parchments to the king. Tommen dipped and signed. "This is a decree of legitimacy for a natural son of Lord Roose Bolton of the Dreadfort. And this names Lord Bolton your Warden of the North." Tommen dipped, signed, dipped, signed. "This grants Ser Rolph Spicer title to the castle Castamere and raises him to the rank of lord." Tommen scrawled his name.

I should have gone to Ser Ilyn Payne, Jaime reflected. The King's Justice was not a friend as Marbrand was, and might well have beat him bloody . . . but without a tongue, he was not like to boast of it afterward. All it would take would be one chance remark by Ser Addam in his cups, and the whole world would soon know how useless he'd become. *Lord Commander of the Kingsguard.* It was a cruel jape, that . . . though not quite so cruel as the gift his father had sent him.

"This is your royal pardon for Lord Gawen Westerling, his lady wife, and his daughter Jeyne, welcoming them back into the king's peace," Ser Kevan said. "This is a pardon for Lord Jonos Bracken of Stone Hedge. This is a pardon for Lord Vance. This for Lord Goodbrook. This for Lord Mooton of Maidenpool."

Jaime pushed himself to his feet. "You seem to have

these matters well in hand, Uncle. I shall leave His Grace to you."

"As you wish." Ser Kevan rose as well. "Jaime, you should go to your father. This breach between you—"

"—is his doing. Nor will he mend it by sending me mocking gifts. Tell him that, if you can pry him away from the Tyrells long enough."

His uncle looked distressed. "The gift was heartfelt. We thought that it might encourage you—"

"—to grow a new hand?" Jaime turned to Tommen. Though he had Joffrey's golden curls and green eyes, the new king shared little else with his late brother. He inclined to plumpness, his face was pink and round, and he even liked to read. *He is still shy of nine, this son of mine. The boy is not the man*. It would be seven years before Tommen was ruling in his own right. Until then the realm would remain firmly in the hands of his lord grandfather. "Sire," he asked, "do I have your leave to go?"

"As you like, Ser Uncle." Tommen looked back to Ser Kevan. "Can I seal them now, Great-Uncle?" Pressing his royal seal into the hot wax was his favorite part of being king, so far.

Jaime strode from the council chamber. Outside the door he found Ser Meryn Trant standing stiff at guard in white scale armor and snowy cloak. *If this one should learn how feeble I am, or Kettleblack or Blount should hear of it . . .* "Remain here until His Grace is done," he said, "then escort him back to Maegor's."

Trant inclined his head. "As you say, my lord."

The outer ward was crowded and noisy that morning. Jaime made for the stables, where a large group of men were saddling their horses. "Steelshanks!" he called. "Are you off, then?"

"As soon as m'lady is mounted," said Steelshanks Walton. "My lord of Bolton expects us. Here she is now."

A groom led a fine grey mare out the stable door. On her back was mounted a skinny hollow-eyed girl wrapped in a heavy cloak. Grey, it was, like the dress beneath it, and trimmed with white satin. The clasp that pinned it to her breast was wrought in the shape of a wolf's head with slitted opal eyes. The girl's long brown hair blew wild in the wind. She had a pretty face, he thought, but her eyes were sad and wary.

When she saw him, she inclined her head. "Ser Jaime," she said in a thin anxious voice. "You are kind to see me off."

Jaime studied her closely. "You know me, then?"

She bit her lip. "You may not recall, my lord, as I was littler then . . . but I had the honor to meet you at Winterfell when King Robert came to visit my father Lord Eddard." She lowered her big brown eyes and mumbled, "I'm Arya Stark."

Jaime had never paid much attention to Arya Stark, but it seemed to him that this girl was older. "I understand you're to be married."

"I am to wed Lord Bolton's son, Ramsay. He used to be a Snow, but His Grace has made him a Bolton. They say he's very brave. I am so happy."

Then why do you sound so frightened? "I wish you joy, my lady." Jaime turned back to Steelshanks. "You have the coin you were promised?"

"Aye, and we've shared it out. You have my thanks." The northman grinned. "A Lannister always pays his debts."

"Always," said Jaime, with a last glance at the girl. He wondered if there was much resemblance. Not that it mattered. The real Arya Stark was buried in some unmarked grave in Flea Bottom in all likelihood. With her brothers dead, and both parents, who would dare name this one a fraud? "Good speed," he told Steelshanks. Nage raised his peace banner, and the northmen formed a column as ragged as their fur cloaks and trotted out the castle gate. The thin girl on the grey mare looked small and forlorn in their midst.

A few of the horses still shied away from the dark splotch on the hard-packed ground where the earth had drunk the life's blood of the stableboy Gregor Clegane had killed so clumsily. The sight of it made Jaime angry all over again. He had told his Kingsguard to keep the crowd out of the way, but that oaf Ser Boros had let himself be distracted by the duel. The fool boy himself shared some of the blame, to be sure; the dead Dornishman as well. And

Clegane most of all. The blow that took the boy's arm off had been mischance, but that second cut . . .

Well, Gregor is paying for it now. Grand Maester Pycelle was tending to the man's wounds, but the howls heard ringing from the maester's chambers suggested that the healing was not going as well as it might. "The flesh mortifies and the wounds ooze pus," Pycelle told the council. "Even maggots will not touch such foulness. His convulsions are so violent that I have had to gag him to prevent him from biting off his tongue. I have cut away as much tissue as I dare, and treated the rot with boiling wine and bread mold, to no avail. The veins in his arm are turning black. When I leeched him, all the leeches died. My lords, I must know what malignant substance Prince Oberyn used on his spear. Let us detain these other Dornishmen until they are more forthcoming."

Lord Tywin had refused him. "There will be trouble enough with Sunspear over Prince Oberyn's death. I do not mean to make matters worse by holding his companions captive."

"Then I fear Ser Gregor may die."

"Undoubtedly. I swore as much in the letter I sent to Prince Doran with his brother's body. But it must be seen to be the sword of the King's Justice that slays him, not a poisoned spear. Heal him."

Grand Maester Pycelle blinked in dismay. "My lord—"

"*Heal him,*" Lord Tywin said again, vexed. "You are aware that Lord Varys has sent fishermen into the waters around Dragonstone. They report that only a token force remains to defend the island. The Lyseni are gone from the bay, and the great part of Lord Stannis's strength with them."

"Well and good," announced Pycelle. "Let Stannis rot in Lys, I say. We are well rid of the man and his ambitions."

"Did you turn into an utter fool when Tyrion shaved your beard? This is *Stannis Baratheon.* The man will fight to the bitter end and then some. If he is gone, it can only mean he intends to resume the war. Most likely he will land at Storm's End and try and rouse the storm lords. If so, he's finished. But a bolder man might roll the dice for Dorne. If he should win Sunspear to his cause, he might prolong this war for years. So we will *not* offend the

Martells any further, for *any* reason. The Dornishmen are free to go, and you *will* heal Ser Gregor."

And so the Mountain screamed, day and night. Lord Tywin Lannister could cow even the Stranger, it would seem.

As Jaime climbed the winding steps of White Sword Tower, he could hear Ser Boros snoring in his cell. Ser Balon's door was shut as well; he had the king tonight, and would sleep all day. Aside from Blount's snores, the tower was very quiet. That suited Jaime well enough. *I ought to rest myself.* Last night, after his dance with Ser Addam, he'd been too sore to sleep.

But when he stepped into his bedchamber, he found his sister waiting for him.

She stood beside the open window, looking over the curtain walls and out to sea. The bay wind swirled around her, flattening her gown against her body in a way that quickened Jaime's pulse. It was white, that gown, like the hangings on the wall and the draperies on his bed. Swirls of tiny emeralds brightened the ends of her wide sleeves and spiraled down her bodice. Larger emeralds were set in the golden spiderweb that bound her golden hair. The gown was cut low, to bare her shoulders and the tops of her breasts. *She is so beautiful.* He wanted nothing more than to take her in his arms.

"Cersei." He closed the door softly. "Why are you here?"

"Where else could I go?" When she turned to him there were tears in her eyes. "Father's made it clear that I am no longer wanted on the council. Jaime, won't you talk to him?"

Jaime took off his cloak and hung it from a peg on the wall. "I talk to Lord Tywin every day."

"*Must* you be so stubborn? All he wants . . ."

". . . is to force me from the Kingsguard and send me back to Casterly Rock."

"That need not be so terrible. He is sending me back to Casterly Rock as well. He wants me far away, so he'll have a free hand with Tommen. Tommen is *my* son, not his!"

"Tommen is the king."

"He is a boy! A frightened little boy who saw his brother *murdered* at his own wedding. And now they are telling him that *he* must marry. The girl is twice his age and twice a widow!"

He eased himself into a chair, trying to ignore the ache of bruised muscles. "The Tyrells are insisting. I see no harm in it. Tommen's been lonely since Myrcella went to Dorne. He likes having Margaery and her ladies about. Let them wed."

"He is your son . . ."

"He is my seed. He's never called me Father. No more than Joffrey ever did. You warned me a thousand times never to show any undue interest in them."

"To keep them safe! You as well. How would it have looked if my brother had played the father to the king's children? Even Robert might have grown suspicious."

"Well, he's beyond suspicion now." Robert's death still left a bitter taste in Jaime's mouth. *It should have been me who killed him, not Cersei.* "I only wished he'd died at my hands." *When I still had two of them.* "If I'd let kingslaying become a habit, as he liked to say, I could have taken you as my wife for all the world to see. I'm not ashamed of loving you, only of the things I've done to hide it. That boy at Winterfell . . ."

"Did I tell you to throw him out the window? If you'd gone hunting as I begged you, nothing would have happened. But no, you had to have me, you could not wait until we returned to the city."

"I'd waited long enough. I hated watching Robert stumble to your bed every night, always wondering if maybe this night he'd decide to claim his rights as husband." Jaime suddenly remembered something else that troubled him about Winterfell. "At Riverrun, Catelyn Stark seemed convinced I'd sent some footpad to slit her son's throat. That I'd given him a dagger."

"That," she said scornfully. "Tyrion asked me about that."

"There *was* a dagger. The scars on Lady Catelyn's hands were real enough, she showed them to me. Did you . . . ?"

"Oh, don't be absurd." Cersei closed the window. "Yes, I hoped the boy would die. So did you. Even *Robert* thought that would have been for the best. 'We kill our horses when they break a leg, and our dogs when they go blind, but we

are too weak to give the same mercy to crippled children,'
he told me. He was blind himself at the time, from drink."

Robert? Jaime had guarded the king long enough to
know that Robert Baratheon said things in his cups that he
would have denied angrily the next day. "Were you alone
when Robert said this?"

"You don't think he said it to Ned Stark, I hope? Of
course we were alone. Us and the children." Cersei removed her hairnet and draped it over a bedpost, then shook
out her golden curls. "Perhaps Myrcella sent this man with
the dagger, do you think so?"

It was meant as mockery, but she'd cut right to the heart
of it, Jaime saw at once. "Not Myrcella. Joffrey."

Cersei frowned. "Joffrey had no love for Robb Stark, but
the younger boy was nothing to him. He was only a child
himself."

"A child hungry for a pat on the head from that sot you
let him believe was his father." He had an uncomfortable
thought. "Tyrion almost died because of this bloody dagger. If he knew the whole thing was Joffrey's work, that
might be why . . ."

"I don't care *why*," Cersei said. "He can take his reasons
down to hell with him. If you had seen how Joff died . . . he
fought, Jaime, he fought for every breath, but it was as if
some malign spirit had its hands about his throat. He had
such terror in his eyes . . . When he was little, he'd run to
me when he was scared or hurt and I would protect him.
But that night there was nothing I could do. Tyrion murdered him in front of me, and *there was nothing I could
do*." Cersei sank to her knees before his chair and took
Jaime's good hand between both of hers. "Joff is dead and
Myrcella's in Dorne. Tommen's all I have left. You mustn't
let Father take him from me. Jaime, please."

"Lord Tywin has not asked for my approval. I can talk to
him, but he will not listen . . ."

"He will if you agree to leave the Kingsguard."

"I'm not leaving the Kingsguard."

His sister fought back tears. "Jaime, you're my shining
knight. You cannot abandon me when I need you most! He
is stealing my son, sending me away . . . and unless you
stop him, Father is going to force me to wed again!"

Jaime should not have been surprised, but he was. The

words were a blow to his gut harder than any that Ser Addam Marbrand had dealt him. "Who?"

"Does it matter? Some lord or other. Someone Father thinks he needs. I don't care. I will not have another husband. You are the only man I want in my bed, ever again."

"Then *tell* him that!"

She pulled her hands away. "You are talking madness again. Would you have us ripped apart, as Mother did that time she caught us playing? Tommen would lose the throne, Myrcella her marriage . . . I *want* to be your wife, we belong to each other, but it can never be, Jaime. We are brother and sister."

"The Targaryens . . ."

"We are not Targaryens!"

"Quiet," he said, scornfully. "So loud, you'll wake my Sworn Brothers. We can't have that, now, can we? People might learn that you had come to see me."

"Jaime," she sobbed, "don't you think *I* want it as much as you do? It makes no matter who they wed me to, I want you at my side, I want you in my bed, I want you inside me. Nothing has changed between us. Let me prove it to you." She pushed up his tunic and began to fumble with the laces of his breeches.

Jaime felt himself responding. "No," he said, "not here." They had never done it in White Sword Tower, much less in the Lord Commander's chambers. "Cersei, this is not the place."

"You took me in the sept. This is no different." She drew out his cock and bent her head over it.

Jaime pushed her away with the stump of his right hand. *"No.* Not here, I said." He forced himself to stand.

For an instant he could see confusion in her bright green eyes, and fear as well. Then rage replaced it. Cersei gathered herself together, got to her feet, straightened her skirts. "Was it your hand they hacked off in Harrenhal, or your manhood?" As she shook her head, her hair tumbled around her bare white shoulders. "I was a fool to come. You lacked the courage to avenge Joffrey, why would I think that you'd protect Tommen? Tell me, if the Imp had killed all three of your children, would *that* have made you wroth?"

"Tyrion is not going to harm Tommen or Myrcella. I am still not certain he killed Joffrey."

Her mouth twisted in anger. "How can you *say* that? After all his threats—"

"Threats mean nothing. He swears he did not do it."

"Oh, he *swears*, is that it? And dwarfs don't lie, is that what you think?"

"Not to me. No more than you would."

"You great golden fool. He's lied to you a thousand times, and so have I." She bound up her hair again, and scooped up the hairnet from the bedpost where she'd hung it. "Think what you will. The little monster is in a black cell, and soon Ser Ilyn will have his head off. Perhaps you'd like it for a keepsake." She glanced at the pillow. "He can watch over you as you sleep alone in that cold white bed. Until his eyes rot out, that is."

"You had best go, Cersei. You're making me angry."

"Oh, an angry cripple. How terrifying." She laughed. "A pity Lord Tywin Lannister never had a son. I could have been the heir he wanted, but I lacked the cock. And speaking of such, best tuck yours away, brother. It looks rather sad and small, hanging from your breeches like that."

When she was gone Jaime took her advice, fumbling one-handed at his laces. He felt a bone-deep ache in his phantom fingers. *I've lost a hand, a father, a son, a sister, and a lover, and soon enough I will lose a brother. And yet they keep telling me House Lannister won this war.*

Jaime donned his cloak and went downstairs, where he found Ser Boros Blount having a cup of wine in the common room. "When you're done with your drink, tell Ser Loras I'm ready to see her."

Ser Boros was too much of a coward to do much more than glower. "You are ready to see who?"

"Just tell Loras."

"Aye." Ser Boros drained his cup. "Aye, Lord Commander."

He took his own good time about it, though, or else the Knight of Flowers proved hard to find. Several hours had passed by the time they arrived, the slim handsome youth and the big ugly maid. Jaime was sitting alone in the round room, leafing idly through the White Book. "Lord

Commander," Ser Loras said, "you wished to see the Maid of Tarth?"

"I did." Jaime waved them closer with his left hand. "You have talked with her, I take it?"

"As you commanded, my lord."

"And?"

The lad tensed. "I . . . it may be it happened as she says, ser. That it was Stannis. I cannot be certain."

"Varys tells me that the castellan of Storm's End perished strangely as well," said Jaime.

"Ser Cortnay Penrose," said Brienne sadly. "A good man."

"A stubborn man. One day he stood square in the way of the King of Dragonstone. The next he leapt from a tower." Jaime stood. "Ser Loras, we will talk more of this later. You may leave Brienne with me."

The wench looked as ugly and awkward as ever, he decided when Tyrell left them. Someone had dressed her in woman's clothes again, but this dress fit much better than that hideous pink rag the goat had made her wear. "Blue is a good color on you, my lady," Jaime observed. "It goes well with your eyes." *She does have astonishing eyes.*

Brienne glanced down at herself, flustered. "Septa Donyse padded out the bodice, to give it that shape. She said you sent her to me." She lingered by the door, as if she meant to flee at any second. "You look . . ."

"Different?" He managed a half-smile. "More meat on the ribs and fewer lice in my hair, that's all. The stump's the same. Close the door and come here."

She did as he bid her. "The white cloak . . ."

". . . is new, but I'm sure I'll soil it soon enough."

"That wasn't . . . I was about to say that it becomes you."

She came closer, hesitant. "Jaime, did you mean what you told Ser Loras? About . . . about King Renly, and the shadow?"

Jaime shrugged. "I would have killed Renly myself if we'd met in battle, what do I care who cut his throat?"

"You said I had honor . . ."

"I'm the bloody Kingslayer, remember? When I say you have honor, that's like a whore vouchsafing your maidenhood." He leaned back and looked up at her. "Steelshanks is on his way back north, to deliver Arya Stark to Roose Bolton."

"You gave her to *him?*" she cried, dismayed. "You swore an oath to Lady Catelyn . . ."

"With a sword at my throat, but never mind. Lady Catelyn's dead. I could not give her back her daughters even if I had them. And the girl my father sent with Steelshanks was not Arya Stark."

"*Not* Arya Stark?"

"You heard me. My lord father found some skinny northern girl more or less the same age with more or less the same coloring. He dressed her up in white and grey, gave her a silver wolf to pin her cloak, and sent her off to wed Bolton's bastard." He lifted his stump to point at her. "I wanted to tell you that before you went galloping off to rescue her and got yourself killed for no good purpose. You're not half bad with a sword, but you're not good enough to take on two hundred men by yourself."

Brienne shook her head. "When Lord Bolton learns that your father paid him with false coin . . ."

"Oh, he knows. *Lannisters lie*, remember? It makes no matter, this girl serves his purpose just as well. Who is going to say that she *isn't* Arya Stark? Everyone the girl was close to is dead except for her sister, who has disappeared."

"Why would you tell me all this, if it's true? You are betraying your father's secrets."

The Hand's secrets, he thought. *I no longer have a father.* "I pay my debts like every good little lion. I did promise Lady Stark her daughters . . . and one of them is still alive. My brother may know where she is, but if so he isn't saying. Cersei is convinced that Sansa helped him murder Joffrey."

The wench's mouth got stubborn. "I will not believe that gentle girl a poisoner. Lady Catelyn said that she had a loving heart. It was your brother. There was a trial, Ser Loras said."

"Two trials, actually. Words and swords both failed him. A bloody mess. Did you watch from your window?"

"My cell faces the sea. I heard the shouting, though."

"Prince Oberyn of Dorne is dead, Ser Gregor Clegane lies dying, and Tyrion stands condemned before the eyes of gods and men. They're keeping him in a black cell till they kill him."

Brienne looked at him. "You do not believe he did it."

Jaime gave her a hard smile. "See, wench? We know each other too well. Tyrion's wanted to be me since he took his first step, but he'd never follow me in kingslaying. Sansa Stark killed Joffrey. My brother's kept silent to protect her. He gets these fits of gallantry from time to time. The last one cost him a nose. This time it will mean his head."

"No," Brienne said. "It was not my lady's daughter. It could not have been her."

"There's the stubborn stupid wench that I remember."

She reddened. "My name is . . ."

"Brienne of Tarth." Jaime sighed. "I have a gift for you." He reached down under the Lord Commander's chair and brought it out, wrapped in folds of crimson velvet.

Brienne approached as if the bundle was like to bite her, reached out a huge freckled hand, and flipped back a fold of cloth. Rubies glimmered in the light. She picked the treasure up gingerly, curled her fingers around the leather grip, and slowly slid the sword free of its scabbard. Blood and black the ripples shone. A finger of reflected light ran red along the edge. "Is this Valyrian steel? I have never seen such colors."

"Nor I. There was a time that I would have given my right hand to wield a sword like that. Now it appears I have, so the blade is wasted on me. Take it." Before she could think to refuse, he went on. "A sword so fine must bear a name. It would please me if you would call this one Oathkeeper. One more thing. The blade comes with a price."

Her face darkened. "I told you, I will never serve . . ."

". . . such foul creatures as us. Yes, I recall. Hear me out, Brienne. Both of us swore oaths concerning Sansa Stark. Cersei means to see that the girl is found and killed, wherever she has gone to ground . . ."

Brienne's homely face twisted in fury. "If you believe that I would harm my lady's daughter for a *sword*, you—"

"*Just listen*," he snapped, angered by her assumption. "I want you to find Sansa first, and get her somewhere safe.

How else are the two of us going to make good our stupid vows to your precious dead Lady Catelyn?"

The wench blinked. "I . . . I thought . . ."

"I know what you *thought.*" Suddenly Jaime was sick of the sight of her. *She bleats like a bloody sheep.* "When Ned Stark died, his greatsword was given to the King's Justice," he told her. "But my father felt that such a fine blade was wasted on a mere headsman. He gave Ser Ilyn a new sword, and had Ice melted down and reforged. There was enough metal for two new blades. You're holding one. So you'll be defending Ned Stark's daughter with Ned Stark's own steel, if that makes any difference to you."

"Ser, I . . . I owe you an apolo . . ."

He cut her off. "Take the bloody sword and go, before I change my mind. There's a bay mare in the stables, as homely as you are but somewhat better trained. Chase after Steelshanks, search for Sansa, or ride home to your isle of sapphires, it's naught to me. I don't want to look at you anymore."

"Jaime . . ."

"*Kingslayer,*" he reminded her. "Best use that sword to clean the wax out of your ears, wench. We're done."

Stubbornly, she persisted. "Joffrey was your . . ."

"My king. Leave it at that."

"You say Sansa killed him. Why protect her?"

Because Joff was no more to me than a squirt of seed in Cersei's cunt. And because he deserved to die. "I have made kings and unmade them. Sansa Stark is my last chance for honor." Jaime smiled thinly. "Besides, kingslayers should band together. Are you ever going to go?"

Her big hand wrapped tight around Oathkeeper. "I will. And I will find the girl and keep her safe. For her lady mother's sake. And for yours." She bowed stiffly, whirled, and went.

Jaime sat alone at the table while the shadows crept across the room. As dusk began to settle, he lit a candle and opened the White Book to his own page. Quill and ink he found in a drawer. Beneath the last line Ser Barristan had entered, he wrote in an awkward hand that might have done credit to a six-year-old being taught his first letters by a maester:

Defeated in the Whispering Wood by the Young Wolf

Robb Stark during the War of the Five Kings. Held captive at Riverrun and ransomed for a promise unfulfilled. Captured again by the Brave Companions, and maimed at the word of Vargo Hoat their captain, losing his sword hand to the blade of Zollo the Fat. Returned safely to King's Landing by Brienne, the Maid of Tarth.

When he was done, more than three-quarters of his page still remained to be filled between the gold lion on the crimson shield on top and the blank white shield at the bottom. Ser Gerold Hightower had begun his history, and Ser Barristan Selmy had continued it, but the rest Jaime Lannister would need to write for himself. He could write whatever he chose, henceforth.

Whatever he chose . . .

JON

The wind was blowing wild from the east, so strong the heavy cage would rock whenever a gust got it in its teeth. It skirled along the Wall, shivering off the ice, making Jon's cloak flap against the bars. The sky was slate grey, the sun no more than a faint patch of brightness behind the clouds. Across the killing ground, he could see the glimmer of a thousand campfires burning, but their lights seemed small and powerless against such gloom and cold.

A grim day. Jon Snow wrapped gloved hands around the bars and held tight as the wind hammered at the cage once more. When he looked straight down past his feet, the ground was lost in shadow, as if he were being lowered into some bottomless pit. *Well, death is a bottomless pit of sorts,* he reflected, *and when this day's work is done my name will be shadowed forever.*

Bastard children were born from lust and lies, men said; their nature was wanton and treacherous. Once Jon had meant to prove them wrong, to show his lord father that he could be as good and true a son as Robb. *I made a botch of that*. Robb had become a hero king; if Jon was remembered at all, it would be as a turncloak, an oathbreaker, and a murderer. He was glad that Lord Eddard was not alive to see his shame.

I should have stayed in that cave with Ygritte. If there was a life beyond this one, he hoped to tell her that. *She will claw my face the way the eagle did, and curse me for a coward, but I'll tell her all the same.* He flexed his sword hand, as Maester Aemon had taught him. The habit had become part of him, and he would need his fingers to be limber to have even half a chance of murdering Mance Rayder.

They had pulled him out this morning, after four days in the ice, locked up in a cell five by five by five, too low for him to stand, too tight for him to stretch out on his back. The stewards had long ago discovered that food and meat kept longer in the icy storerooms carved from the base of the Wall . . . but prisoners did not. "You will die in here, Lord Snow," Ser Alliser had said just before he closed the heavy wooden door, and Jon had believed it. But this morning they had come and pulled him out again, and marched him cramped and shivering back to the King's Tower, to stand before jowly Janos Slynt once more

"That old maester says I cannot hang you," Slynt declared. "He has written Cotter Pyke, and even had the bloody gall to show me the letter. He says you are no turncloak."

"Aemon's lived too long, my lord," Ser Alliser assured him. "His wits have gone dark as his eyes."

"Aye," Slynt said. "A blind man with a chain about his neck, who does he think he is?"

Aemon Targaryen, Jon thought, *a king's son and a king's brother and a king who might have been.* But he said nothing.

"Still," Slynt said, "I will not have it said that Janos Slynt hanged a man unjustly. I will not. I have decided to give you one last chance to prove you are as loyal as you claim, Lord Snow. One last chance to do your duty, yes!" He stood. "Mance Rayder wants to parley with us. He knows he has no chance now that Janos Slynt has come, so he wants to talk, this King-beyond-the-Wall. But the man is craven, and will not come to us. No doubt he knows I'd hang him. Hang him by his feet from the top of the Wall, on a rope two hundred feet long! But he will not come. He asks that we send an envoy to him."

"We're sending you, Lord Snow." Ser Alliser smiled.

"Me." Jon's voice was flat. "Why me?"

"You rode with these wildlings," said Thorne. "Mance Rayder knows you. He will be more inclined to trust you."

That was so wrong Jon might have laughed. "You've got it backward. Mance suspected me from the first. If I show up in his camp wearing a black cloak again and speaking for the Night's Watch, he'll know that I betrayed him."

"He asked for an envoy, we are sending one," said Slynt. "If you are too craven to face this turncloak king, we can return you to your ice cell. This time without the furs, I think. Yes."

"No need for that, my lord," said Ser Alliser. "Lord Snow will do as we ask. He wants to show us that he is no turncloak. He wants to prove himself a loyal man of the Night's Watch."

Thorne was much the more clever of the two, Jon realized; this had his stink all over it. He was trapped. "I'll go," he said in a clipped, curt voice.

"*M'lord*," Janos Slynt reminded him. "You'll address me—"

"I'll go, *my lord*. But you are making a mistake, *my lord*. You are sending the wrong man, *my lord*. Just the sight of me is going to anger Mance. *My lord* would have a better chance of reaching terms if he sent—"

"Terms?" Ser Alliser chuckled.

"Janos Slynt does not make terms with lawless savages, Lord Snow. No, he does not."

"We're not sending you to *talk* with Mance Rayder," Ser Alliser said. "We're sending you to kill him."

The wind whistled through the bars, and Jon Snow shivered. His leg was throbbing, and his head. He was not fit to kill a kitten, yet here he was. *The trap had teeth.* With Maester Aemon insisting on Jon's innocence, Lord Janos had not dared to leave him in the ice to die. This was better. "Our honor means no more than our lives, so long as the realm is safe," Qhorin Halfhand had said in the Frostfangs. He must remember that. Whether he slew Mance or only tried and failed, the free folk would kill him.

Even desertion was impossible, if he'd been so inclined; to Mance he was a proven liar and betrayer.

When the cage jerked to a halt, Jon swung down onto the ground and rattled Longclaw's hilt to loosen the bastard blade in its scabbard. The gate was a few yards to his left, still blocked by the splintered ruins of the turtle, the carcass of a mammoth ripening within. There were other corpses too, strewn amidst broken barrels, hardened pitch, and patches of burnt grass, all shadowed by the Wall. Jon had no wish to linger here. He started walking toward the wildling camp, past the body of a dead giant whose head had been crushed by a stone. A raven was pulling out bits of brain from the giant's shattered skull. It looked up as he walked by. "*Snow*," it screamed at him. "*Snow, snow.*" Then it opened its wings and flew away.

No sooner had he started out than a lone rider emerged from the wildling camp and came toward him. He wondered if Mance was coming out to parley in no-man's-land. *That might make it easier, though nothing will make it easy.* But as the distance between them diminished Jon saw that the horseman was short and broad, with gold rings glinting on thick arms and a white beard spreading out across his massive chest.

"*Har!*" Tormund boomed when they came together. "Jon Snow the crow. I feared we'd seen the last o' you."

"I never knew you feared anything, Tormund."

That made the wildling grin. "Well said, lad. I see your cloak is black. Mance won't like that. If you've come to change sides again, best climb back on that Wall o' yours."

"They've sent me to treat with the King-beyond-the-Wall."

"Treat?" Tormund laughed. "Now there's a word. Har! Mance wants to talk, that's true enough. Can't say he'd want to talk with *you*, though."

"I'm the one they've sent."

"I see that. Best come along, then. You want to ride?"

"I can walk."

"You fought us hard here." Tormund turned his garron back toward the wildling camp. "You and your brothers. I give you that. Two hundred dead, and a dozen giants. Mag himself went in that gate o' yours and never did come out."

"He died on the sword of a brave man named Donal Noye."

"Aye? Some great lord was he, this Donal Noye? One of your shiny knights in their steel smallclothes?"

"A blacksmith. He only had one arm."

"A one-armed smith slew Mag the Mighty? Har! That must o' been a fight to see. Mance will make a song of it, see if he don't." Tormund took a waterskin off his saddle and pulled the cork. "This will warm us some. To Donal Noye, and Mag the Mighty." He took a swing, and handed it down to Jon.

"To Donal Noye, and Mag the Mighty." The skin was full of mead, but a mead so potent that it made Jon's eyes water and sent tendrils of fire snaking through his chest. After the ice cell and the cold ride down in the cage, the warmth was welcome.

Tormund took the skin back and downed another swig, then wiped his mouth. "The Magnar of Thenn swore t'us that he'd have the gate wide open, so all we'd need to do was stroll through singing. He was going to bring the whole Wall down."

"He brought down part," Jon said. "On his head."

"Har!" said Tormund. "Well, I never had much use for Styr. When a man's got no beard nor hair nor ears, you can't get a good grip on him when you fight." He kept his horse at a slow walk so Jon could limp beside him. "What happened to that leg?"

"An arrow. One of Ygritte's, I think."

"That's a woman for you. One day she's kissing you, the next she's filling you with arrows."

"She's dead."

"Aye?" Tormund gave a sad shake of the head. "A waste. If I'd been ten years younger, I'd have stolen her meself. That hair she had. Well, the hottest fires burn out quickest." He lifted the skin of mead. "To Ygritte, kissed by fire!" He drank deep.

"To Ygritte, kissed by fire," Jon repeated when Tormund handed him back the skin. He drank even deeper.

"Was it you killed her?"

"My brother." Jon had never learned which one, and hoped he never would.

"You bloody crows." Tormund's tone was gruff, yet

strangely gentle. "That Longspear stole me daughter. Munda, me little autumn apple. Took her right out o' my tent with all four o' her brothers about. Toregg slept through it, the great lout, and Torwynd . . . well, Torwynd the Tame, that says all that needs saying, don't it? The young ones gave the lad a fight, though."

"And Munda?" asked Jon.

"She's my own blood," said Tormund proudly. "She broke his lip for him and bit one ear half off, and I hear he's got so many scratches on his back he can't wear a cloak. She likes him well enough, though. And why not? He don't fight with no spear, you know. Never has. So where do you think he got that name? *Har!*"

Jon had to laugh. Even now, even here. Ygritte had been fond of Longspear Ryk. He hoped he found some joy with Tormund's Munda. Someone needed to find some joy somewhere.

"You know nothing, Jon Snow," Ygritte would have told him. *I know that I am going to die*, he thought. *I know that much, at least.* "All men die," he could almost hear her say, "and women too, and every beast that flies or swims or runs. It's not the *when* o' dying that matters, it's the *how* of it, Jon Snow." *Easy for you to say*, he thought back. *You died brave in battle, storming the castle of a foe. I'm going to die a turncloak and a killer.* Nor would his death be quick, unless it came on the end of Mance's sword.

Soon they were among the tents. It was the usual wildling camp; a sprawling jumble of cookfires and piss pits, children and goats wandering freely, sheep bleating among the trees, horse hides pegged up to dry. There was no plan to it, no order, no defenses. But there were men and women and animals everywhere.

Many ignored him, but for every one who went about his business there were ten who stopped to stare; children squatting by the fires, old women in dog carts, cave dwellers with painted faces, raiders with claws and snakes and severed heads painted on their shields, all turned to have a look. Jon saw spearwives too, their long hair streaming in the piney wind that sighed between the trees.

There were no true hills here, but Mance Rayder's white fur tent had been raised on a spot of high stony ground right on the edge of the trees. The King-beyond-the-Wall was waiting outside, his ragged red-and-black cloak blowing in the wind. Harma Dogshead was with him, Jon saw, back from her raids and feints along the Wall, and Varamyr Sixskins as well, attended by his shadowcat and two lean grey wolves.

When they saw who the Watch had sent, Harma turned her head and spat, and one of Varamyr's wolves bared its teeth and growled. "You must be very brave or very stupid, Jon Snow," Mance Rayder said, "to come back to us wearing a black cloak."

"What else would a man of the Night's Watch wear?"

"Kill him," urged Harma. "Send his body back up in that cage o' theirs and tell them to send us someone else. I'll keep his head for my standard. A turncloak's worse than a dog."

"I warned you he was false." Varamyr's tone was mild, but his shadow-cat was staring at Jon hungrily through slitted grey eyes. "I never did like the smell o' him."

"Pull in your claws, beastling." Tormund Giantsbane swung down off his horse. "The lad's here to hear. You lay a paw on him, might be I'll take me that shadowskin cloak I been wanting."

"Tormund Crowlover," Harma sneered. "You are a great sack o' wind, old man."

The skinchanger was grey-faced, round-shouldered, and bald, a mouse of a man with a wolfling's eyes. "Once a horse is broken to the saddle, any man can mount him," he said in a soft voice. "Once a beast's been joined to a man, any skinchanger can slip inside and ride him. Orell was withering inside his feathers, so I took the eagle for my own. But the joining works both ways, warg. Orell lives inside me now, whispering how much he hates you. And I can soar above the Wall, and see with eagle eyes."

"So we know," said Mance. "We know how few you were, when you stopped the turtle. We know how many came from Eastwatch. We know how your supplies have dwindled. Pitch, oil, arrows, spears. Even your stair is gone, and that cage can only lift so many. We know. And now you know we know." He opened the flap of the tent. "Come inside. The rest of you, wait here."

"What, even me?" said Tormund.

"Particularly you. Always."

It was warm within. A small fire burned beneath the smoke holes, and a brazier smouldered near the pile of furs where Dalla lay, pale and sweating. Her sister was holding her hand. *Val,* Jon remembered. "I was sorry when Jarl fell," he told her.

Val looked at him with pale grey eyes. "He always climbed too fast." She was as fair as he'd remembered, slender, full-breasted, graceful even at rest, with high sharp cheekbones and a thick braid of honey-colored hair that fell to her waist.

"Dalla's time is near," Mance explained. "She and Val will stay. They know what I mean to say."

Jon kept his face as still as ice. *Foul enough to slay a man in his own tent under truce. Must I murder him in front of his wife as their child is being born?* He closed the fingers of his sword hand. Mance was not wearing armor, but his own sword was sheathed on his left hip. And there were other weapons in the tent, daggers and dirks, a bow and a quiver of arrows, a bronze-headed spear lying beside that big black . . .

. . . horn.

Jon sucked in his breath.

A warhorn, a bloody great warhorn.

"Yes," Mance said. "The Horn of Winter, that Joramun once blew to wake giants from the earth."

The horn was huge, eight feet along the curve and so wide at the mouth that he could have put his arm inside up to the elbow. *If this came from an aurochs, it was the biggest that ever lived.* At first he thought the bands around it were bronze, but when he moved closer he realized they were gold. *Old gold, more brown than yellow, and graven with runes.*

"Ygritte said you never found the horn."

"Did you think only crows could lie? I liked you well enough, for a bastard . . . but I never trusted you. A man needs to earn my trust."

Jon faced him. "If you've had the Horn of Joramun all along, why haven't you used it? Why bother building turtles and sending Thenns to kill us in our beds? If this horn is all the songs say, why not just sound it and be done?"

It was Dalla who answered him, Dalla great with child,

lying on her pile of furs beside the brazier. "We free folk know things you kneelers have forgotten. Sometimes the short road is not the safest, Jon Snow. The Horned Lord once said that sorcery is a sword without a hilt. There is no safe way to grasp it."

Mance ran a hand along the curve of the great horn. "No man goes hunting with only one arrow in his quiver," he said. "I had hoped that Styr and Jarl would take your brothers unawares, and open the gate for us. I drew your garrison away with feints and raids and secondary attacks. Bowen Marsh swallowed that lure as I knew he would, but your band of cripples and orphans proved to be more stubborn than anticipated. Don't think you've stopped us, though. The truth is, you are too few and we are too many. I could continue the attack here and still send ten thousand men to cross the Bay of Seals on rafts and take Eastwatch from the rear. I could storm the Shadow Tower too, I know the approaches as well as any man alive. I could send men and mammoths to dig out the gates at the castles you've abandoned, all of them at once."

"Why don't you, then?" Jon could have drawn Longclaw then, but he wanted to hear what the wildling had to say.

"Blood," said Mance Rayder. "I'd win in the end, yes, but you'd bleed me, and my people have bled enough."

"Your losses haven't been that heavy."

"Not at your hands." Mance studied Jon's face. "You saw the Fist of the First Men. You know what happened there. You know what we are facing."

"The Others . . ."

"They grow stronger as the days grow shorter and the nights colder. First they kill you, then they send your dead against you. The giants have not been able to stand against them, nor the Thenns, the ice river clans, the Hornfoots."

"Nor you?"

"Nor me." There was anger in that admission, and bitterness too deep for words. "Raymun Redbeard, Bael the Bard, Gendel and Gorne, the Horned Lord, they all came south to conquer, but I've come with my tail between my legs to hide behind your Wall." He touched the horn again. "If I sound the Horn of Winter, the Wall will fall. Or so the songs would have me believe. There are those among my people who want nothing more . . ."

"But once the Wall is fallen," Dalla said, "*what will stop the Others?*"

Mance gave her a fond smile. "It's a wise woman I've found. A true queen." He turned back to Jon. "Go back and tell them to open their gate and let us pass. If they do, I will give them the horn, and the Wall will stand until the end of days."

Open the gate and let them pass. Easy to say, but what must follow? Giants camping in the ruins of Winterfell? Cannibals in the wolfswood, chariots sweeping across the barrowlands, free folk stealing the daughters of shipwrights and silversmiths from White Harbor and fishwives off the Stony Shore? "Are you a true king?" Jon asked suddenly.

"I've never had a crown on my head or sat my arse on a bloody throne, if that's what you're asking," Mance replied. "My birth is as low as a man's can get, no septon's ever smeared my head with oils, I don't own any castles, and my queen wears furs and amber, not silk and sapphires. I am my own champion, my own fool, and my own harpist. You don't become King-beyond-the-Wall because your father was. The free folk won't follow a name, and they don't care which brother was born first. They follow fighters. When I left the Shadow Tower there were five men making noises about how they might be the stuff of kings. Tormund was one, the Magnar another. The other three I slew, when they made it plain they'd sooner fight than follow."

"You can kill your enemies," Jon said bluntly, "but can you rule your friends? If we let your people pass, are you strong enough to make them keep the king's peace and obey the laws?"

"Whose laws? The laws of Winterfell and King's Landing?" Mance laughed. "When we want laws we'll make our own. You can keep your king's justice too, and your king's taxes. I'm offering you the horn, not our freedom. We will not kneel to you."

"What if we refuse the offer?" Jon had no doubt that they would. The Old Bear might at least have listened, though he would have balked at the notion of letting thirty or forty thousand wildlings loose on the Seven Kingdoms.

But Alliser Thorne and Janos Slynt would dismiss the notion out of hand.

"If you refuse," Mance Rayder said, "Tormund Giantsbane will sound the Horn of Winter three days hence, at dawn."

He could carry the message back to Castle Black and tell them of the horn, but if he left Mance still alive Lord Janos and Ser Alliser would seize on that as proof that he was a turncloak. A thousand thoughts flickered through Jon's head. *If I can destroy the horn, smash it here and now . . .* but before he could begin to think that through, he heard the low moan of some other horn, made faint by the tent's hide walls. Mance heard it too. Frowning, he went to the door. Jon followed.

The warhorn was louder outside. Its call had stirred the wildling camp. Three Hornfoot men jogged past, carrying long spears. Horses were whinnying and snorting, giants roaring in the Old Tongue, and even the mammoths were restless.

"Outrider's horn," Tormund told Mance.

"Something's coming." Varamyr sat crosslegged on the half-frozen ground, his wolves circled restlessly around him. A shadow swept over him, and Jon looked up to see the eagle's blue-grey wings. "Coming, from the east."

When the dead walk, walls and stakes and swords mean nothing, he remembered. *You cannot fight the dead, Jon Snow. No man knows that half so well as me.*

Harma scowled. "East? The wights should be behind us."

"East," the skinchanger repeated. "*Something's coming.*"

"The Others?" Jon asked.

Mance shook his head. "The Others never come when the sun is up." Chariots were rattling across the killing ground, jammed with riders waving spears of sharpened bone. The king groaned. "Where the bloody hell do they think they're going? Quenn, get those fools back where they belong. Someone bring my horse. The mare, not the stallion. I'll want my armor too." Mance glanced suspiciously at the Wall. Atop the icy parapets, the straw soldiers stood collecting arrows, but there was no sign of any other activity. "Harma, mount up your raiders. Tormund, find your sons and give me a triple line of spears."

"Aye," said Tormund, striding off.

The mousy little skinchanger closed his eyes and said, "I see them. They're coming along the streams and game trails . . ."

"Who?"

"Men. Men on horses. Men in steel and men in black."

"Crows." Mance made the word a curse. He turned on Jon. "Did my old brothers think they'd catch me with my breeches down if they attacked while we were talking?"

"If they planned an attack they never told me about it." Jon did not believe it. Lord Janos lacked the men to attack the wildling camp. Besides, he was on the wrong side of the Wall, and the gate was sealed with rubble. *He had a different sort of treachery in mind, this can't be his work.*

"If you're lying to me again, you won't be leaving here alive," Mance warned. His guards brought him his horse and armor. Elsewhere around the camp, Jon saw people running at cross purposes, some men forming up as if to storm the Wall while others slipped into the woods, women driving dog carts east, mammoths wandering west. He reached back over his shoulder and drew Longclaw just as a thin line of rangers emerged from the fringes of the wood three hundred yards away. They wore black mail, black halfhelms, and black cloaks. Half-armored, Mance drew his sword. "You knew nothing of this, did you?" he said to Jon, coldly.

Slow as honey on a cold morning, the rangers swept down on the wildling camp, picking their way through clumps of gorse and stands of trees, over roots and rocks. Wildlings flew to meet them, shouting war cries and waving clubs and bronze swords and axes made of flint, galloping headlong at their ancient enemies. *A shout, a slash, and a fine brave death*, Jon had heard brothers say of the free folk's way of fighting.

"Believe what you will," Jon told the King-beyond-the-Wall, "but I knew nothing of any attack."

Harma thundered past before Mance could reply, riding at the head of thirty raiders. Her standard went before her; a dead dog impaled on a spear, raining blood at every stride. Mance watched as she smashed into the rangers. "Might be you're telling it true," he said. "Those look like Eastwatch men. Sailors on horses. Cotter Pyke always had more guts than sense. He took the Lord of Bones at Long Barrow, he might have thought to do the same with me. If so, he's a fool. He doesn't have the men, he—"

"*Mance!*" the shout came. It was a scout, bursting from the trees on a lathered horse. "*Mance*, there's more, they're all around us, iron men, *iron*, a *host* of iron men."

Cursing, Mance swung up into the saddle. "Varamyr, stay and see that no harm comes to Dalla." The King-beyond-the-Wall pointed his sword at Jon. "And keep a few extra eyes on this crow. If he runs, rip out his throat."

"Aye, I'll do that." The skinchanger was a head shorter than Jon, slumped and soft, but that shadowcat could disembowel him with one paw. "They're coming from the north too," Varamyr told Mance. "You best go."

Mance donned his helm with its raven wings. His men were mounted up as well. "Arrowhead," Mance snapped, "to me, form wedge." Yet when he slammed his heels into the mare and flew across the field at the rangers, the men who raced to catch him lost all semblance of formation.

Jon took a step toward the tent, thinking of the Horn of Winter, but the shadowcat blocked him, tail lashing. The beast's nostrils flared, and slaver ran from his curved front teeth. *He smells my fear.* He missed Ghost more than ever then. The two wolves were behind him, growling.

"Banners," he heard Varamyr murmur, "I see golden banners, oh . . ." A mammoth lumbered by, trumpeting, a half-dozen bowmen in the wooden tower on its back. "The king . . . no . . ."

Then the skinchanger threw back his head and *screamed*.

The sound was shocking, ear-piercing, thick with agony. Varamyr fell, writhing, and the 'cat was screaming too . . . and high, high in the eastern sky, against the wall of cloud, Jon saw the eagle *burning*. For a heartbeat it flamed brighter than a star, wreathed in red and gold and orange, its wings beating wildly at the air as if it could fly from the pain. Higher it flew, and higher, and higher still.

The scream brought Val out of the tent, white-faced. "What is it, what's happened?" Varamyr's wolves were fighting each other, and the shadowcat had raced off into the trees, but the man was still twisting on the ground. "What's wrong with him?" Val demanded, horrified. "Where's Mance?"

"There." Jon pointed. "Gone to fight." The king led his ragged wedge into a knot of rangers, his sword flashing.

"Gone? He can't be gone, not now. It's started."

"The battle?" He watched the rangers scatter before Harma's bloody dog's head. The raiders screamed and hacked and chased the men in black back into the trees. But there were more men coming from the wood, a column of horse. *Knights on heavy horse,* Jon saw. Harma had to regroup and wheel to meet them, but half of her men had raced too far ahead.

"The *birth!*" Val was shouting at him.

Trumpets were blowing all around, loud and brazen. *The wildlings have no trumpets, only warhorns.* They knew that as well as he did; the sound sent free folk running in confusion, some toward the fighting, others away. A mammoth was stomping through a flock of sheep that three men were trying to herd off west. The drums were beating as the wildlings ran to form squares and lines, but they were too late, too disorganized, too slow. The enemy was emerging from the forest, from the east, the northeast, the north; three great columns of heavy horse, all dark glinting steel and bright wool surcoats. Not the men of Eastwatch, those had been no more than a line of scouts. An army. *The king!* Jon was as confused as the wildlings. Could Robb have returned? Had the boy on the Iron Throne finally bestirred himself? "You best get back inside the tent," he told Val.

Across the field one column had washed over Harma Dogshead. Another smashed into the flank of Tormund's spearmen as he and his sons desperately tried to turn them. The giants were climbing onto their mammoths, though, and the knights on their barded horses did not like that at all; he could see how the coursers and destriers screamed and scattered at the sight of those lumbering mountains. But there was fear on the wildling side as well, hundreds of women and children rushing away from the battle, some of them blundering right under the hooves of garrons. He saw an old woman's dog cart veer into the path of three chariots, to send them crashing into each other.

"Gods," Val whispered, "gods, why are they doing this?"

"Go inside the tent and stay with Dalla. It's not safe out

here." It wouldn't be a great deal safer inside, but she didn't need to hear that.

"I need to find the midwife," Val said.

"You're the midwife. I'll stay here until Mance comes back." He had lost sight of Mance but now he found him again, cutting his way through a knot of mounted men. The mammoths had shattered the center column, but the other two were closing like pincers. On the eastern edge of the camps, some archers were loosing fire arrows at the tents. He saw a mammoth pluck a knight from his saddle and fling him forty feet with a flick of its trunk. Wildlings streamed past, women and children running from the battle, some with men hurrying them along. A few of them gave Jon dark looks but Longclaw was in his hand, and no one troubled him. Even Varamyr fled, crawling off on his hands and knees.

More and more men were pouring from the trees, not only knights now but freeriders and mounted bowmen and men-at-arms in jacks and kettle helms, dozens of men, hundreds of men. A blaze of banners flew above them. The wind was whipping them too wildly for Jon to see the sigils, but he glimpsed a seahorse, a field of birds, a ring of flowers. And yellow, so much yellow, yellow banners with a red device, whose arms were those?

East and north and northeast, he saw bands of wildlings trying to stand and fight, but the attackers rode right over them. The free folk still had the numbers, but the attackers had steel armor and heavy horses. In the thickest part of the fray, Jon saw Mance standing tall in his stirrups. His red-and-black cloak and raven-winged helm made him easy to pick out. He had his sword raised and men were rallying to him when a wedge of knights smashed into them with lance and sword and longaxe. Mance's mare went up on her hind legs, kicking, and a spear took her through the breast. Then the steel tide washed over him.

It's done, Jon thought, *they're breaking*. The wildlings were running, throwing down their weapons, Hornfoot men and cave dwellers and Thenns in bronze scales, they were running. Mance was gone, someone was waving Harma's head on a pole, Tormund's lines had broken. Only the giants on their mammoths were holding, hairy islands in a red steel sea. The fires were leaping from tent to tent and some of the tall pines were going up as well. And through the smoke another wedge of armored riders came, on barded horses. Floating above them were the largest banners yet, royal standards as big as sheets; a yellow one with long pointed tongues that showed a flaming heart, and another like a sheet of beaten gold, with a black stag prancing and rippling in the wind.

Robert, Jon thought for one mad moment, remembering poor Owen, but when the trumpets blew again and the knights charged, the name they cried was *"Stannis! Stannis! STANNIS!"*

Jon turned away, and went inside the tent.

ARYA

Outside the inn on a weathered gibbet, a woman's bones were twisting and rattling at every gust of wind.

I know this inn. There hadn't been a gibbet outside the door when she had slept here with her sister Sansa under the watchful eye of Septa Mordane, though. "We don't want to go in," Arya decided suddenly, "there might be ghosts."

"You know how long it's been since I had a cup of wine?" Sandor swung down from the saddle. "Besides, we need to learn who holds the ruby ford. Stay with the horses if you want, it's no hair off my arse."

"What if they know you?" Sandor no longer troubled to hide his face. He no longer seemed to care who knew him. "They might want to take you captive."

"Let them try." He loosened his longsword in its scabbard, and pushed through the door.

Arya would never have a better chance to escape. She could ride off on Craven and take Stranger too. She chewed her lip. Then she led the horses to the stables, and went in after him.

They know him. The silence told her that. But that wasn't the worst thing. She knew them too. Not the skinny innkeep, nor the women, nor the fieldhands by the hearth. But the others. The soldiers. She knew the soldiers.

"Looking for your brother, Sandor?" Polliver's hand was down the bodice of the girl on his lap, but now he slid it out.

"Looking for a cup of wine. Innkeep, a flagon of red." Clegane threw a handful of coppers on the floor.

"I don't want no trouble, ser," the innkeep said.

"Then don't call me *ser.*" His mouth twitched. "Are you deaf, fool? I ordered wine." As the man ran off, Clegane shouted after him, "*Two cups!* The girl's thirsty too!"

There are only three, Arya thought. Polliver gave her a fleeting glance and the boy beside him never looked at her at all, but the third one gazed long and hard. He was a man of middling height and build, with a face so ordinary that it was hard to say how old he was. *The Tickler. The Tickler and Polliver both.* The boy was a squire, judging by his age and dress. He had a big white pimple on one side of his nose, and some red ones on his forehead. "Is this the lost puppy Ser Gregor spoke of?" he asked the Tickler. "The one who piddled in the rushes and ran off?"

The Tickler put a warning hand on the boy's arm, and gave a short sharp shake of his head. Arya read that plain enough.

The squire didn't, or else he didn't care. "Ser said his puppy brother tucked his tail between his legs when the battle got too warm at King's Landing. He said he ran off whimpering." He gave the Hound a stupid mocking grin.

Clegane studied the boy and never said a word. Polliver shoved the girl off his lap and got to his feet. "The lad's drunk," he said. The man-at-arms was almost as tall as the Hound, though not so heavily muscled. A spade-shaped beard covered his jaws and jowls, thick and black and neatly trimmed, but his head was more bald than not. "He can't hold his wine, is all."

"Then he shouldn't drink."

"The puppy doesn't scare . . ." the boy began, till the

Tickler casually twisted his ear between thumb and fore-finger. The words became a squeal of pain.

The innkeep came scurrying back with two stone cups and a flagon on a pewter platter. Sandor lifted the flagon to his mouth. Arya could see the muscles in his neck work-ing as he gulped. When he slammed it back down on the table, half the wine was gone. "Now you can pour. Best pick up those coppers too, it's the only coin you're like to see today."

"We'll pay when we're done drinking," said Polliver.

"When you're done drinking you'll tickle the innkeep to see where he keeps his gold. The way you always do."

The innkeep suddenly remembered something in the kitchen. The locals were leaving too, and the girls were gone. The only sound in the common room was the faint crackling of the fire in the hearth. *We should go too*, Arya knew.

"If you're looking for Ser, you come too late," Polliver said. "He was at Harrenhal, but now he's not. The queen sent for him." He wore three blades on his belt, Arya saw; a longsword on his left hip, and on his right a dagger and a slimmer blade, too long to be a dirk and too short to be a sword. "King Joffrey's dead, you know," he added. "Poisoned at his own wedding feast."

Arya edged farther into the room. *Joffrey's dead.* She could almost see him, with his blond curls and his mean smile and his fat soft lips. *Joffrey's dead!* She knew it ought to make her happy, but somehow she still felt empty in-side. Joffrey was dead, but if Robb was dead too, what did it matter?

"So much for my brave brothers of the Kingsguard." The Hound gave a snort of contempt. "Who killed him?"

"The Imp, it's thought. Him and his little wife."

"What wife?"

"I forgot, you've been hiding under a rock. The northern girl. Winterfell's daughter. We heard she killed the king with a spell, and afterward changed into a wolf with big leather wings like a bat, and flew out a tower window. But she left the dwarf behind and Cersei means to have his head."

That's stupid, Arya thought. *Sansa only knows songs, not spells, and she'd never marry the Imp.*

The Hound sat on the bench closest to the door. His mouth twitched, but only the burned side. "She ought to dip him in wildfire and cook him. Or tickle him till the moon turns black." He raised his wine cup and drained it straightaway.

He's one of them, Arya thought when she saw that. She bit her lip so hard she tasted blood. *He's just like they are. I should kill him when he sleeps.*

"So Gregor took Harrenhal?" Sandor said.

"Didn't require much taking," said Polliver. "The sell-swords fled as soon as they knew we were coming, all but a few. One of the cooks opened a postern gate for us, to get back at Hoat for cutting off his foot." He chuckled. "We kept him to cook for us, a couple wenches to warm our beds, and put all the rest to the sword."

"*All* the rest?" Arya blurted out.

"Well, Ser kept Hoat to pass the time."

Sandor said, "The Blackfish is still in Riverrun?"

"Not for long," said Polliver. "He's under siege. Old Frey's going to hang Edmure Tully unless he yields the castle. The only real fighting's around Raventree. Blackwoods and Brackens. The Brackens are ours now."

The Hound poured a cup of wine for Arya and another for himself, and drank it down while staring at the hearth-fire. "The little bird flew away, did she? Well, bloody good for her. She shit on the Imp's head and flew off."

"They'll find her," said Polliver. "If it takes half the gold in Casterly Rock."

"A pretty girl, I hear," said the Tickler. "Honey sweet." He smacked his lips and smiled.

"And courteous," the Hound agreed. "A proper little lady. Not like her bloody sister."

"They found her too," said Polliver. "The sister. She's for Bolton's bastard, I hear."

Arya sipped her wine so they could not see her mouth. She didn't understand what Polliver was talking about. *Sansa has no other sister.* Sandor Clegane laughed aloud.

"What's so bloody funny?" asked Polliver.

The Hound never flicked an eye at Arya. "If I'd wanted you to know, I'd have told you. Are there ships at Saltpans?"

"Saltpans? How should I know? The traders are back at

Maidenpool, I heard. Randyll Tarly took the castle and locked Mooton in a tower cell. I haven't heard shit about Saltpans."

The Tickler leaned forward. "Would you put to sea without bidding farewell to your brother?" It gave Arya chills to hear him ask a question. "Ser would sooner you returned to Harrenhal with us, Sandor. I bet he would. Or King's Landing . . ."

"Bugger that. Bugger him. Bugger you."

The Tickler shrugged, straightened, and reached a hand behind his head to rub the back of his neck. Everything seemed to happen at once then; Sandor lurched to his feet, Polliver drew his longsword, and the Tickler's hand whipped around in a blur to send something silver flashing across the common room. If the Hound had not been moving, the knife might have cored the apple of his throat; instead it only grazed his ribs, and wound up quivering in the wall near the door. He laughed then, a laugh as cold and hollow as if it had come from the bottom of a deep well. "I was hoping you'd do something stupid." His sword slid from its scabbard just in time to knock aside Polliver's first cut.

Arya took a step backward as the long steel song began. The Tickler came off the bench with a shortsword in one hand and a dagger in the other. Even the chunky brown-haired squire was up, fumbling for his swordhilt. She snatched her wine cup off the table and threw it at his face. Her aim was better than it had been at the Twins. The cup hit him right on his big white pimple and he went down hard on his tail.

Polliver was a grim, methodical fighter, and he pressed Sandor steadily backward, his heavy longsword moving with brutal precision. The Hound's own cuts were sloppier, his parries rushed, his feet slow and clumsy. *He's drunk*, Arya realized with dismay. *He drank too much too fast, with no food in his belly.* And the Tickler was sliding around the wall to get behind him. She grabbed the second wine cup and flung it at him, but he was quicker than the squire had been and ducked his head in time. The look he gave her then was cold with promise. *Is there gold hidden in the village?* she could hear him ask. The stupid squire was clutching the edge of a table and pulling himself to his knees. Arya could taste the beginnings of panic in the back of her throat. *Fear cuts deeper than swords. Fears cuts deeper . . .*

Sandor gave a grunt of pain. The burned side of his face ran red from temple to cheek, and the stub of his ear was gone. That seemed to make him angry. He drove back Polliver with a furious attack, hammering at him with the old nicked longsword he had swapped for in the hills. The bearded man gave way, but none of the cuts so much as touched him. And then the Tickler leapt over a bench quick as a snake, and slashed at the back of the Hound's neck with the edge of his short sword.

They're killing him. Arya had no more cups, but there was something better to throw. She drew the dagger they'd robbed off the dying archer and tried to fling it at the Tickler the way he'd done. It wasn't the same as throwing a rock or a crabapple, though. The knife wobbled, and hit him in the arm hilt first. *He never even felt it.* He was too intent on Clegane.

As he stabbed, Clegane twisted violently aside, winning himself half a heartbeat's respite. Blood ran down his face and from the gash in his neck. Both of the Mountain's men came after him hard, Polliver hacking at his head and shoulders while the Tickler darted in to stab at back and belly. The heavy stone flagon was still on the table. Arya grabbed it with two hands, but as she lifted it someone grabbed her arm. The flagon slipped from her fingers and crashed to the floor. Wrenched around, she found herself nose to nose with the squire. *You stupid, you forgot all about him.* His big white pimple had burst, she saw.

"Are you the puppy's puppy?" He had his sword in his right hand and her arm in his left, but her own hands were free, so she jerked his knife from its sheath and sheathed it again in his belly, twisting. He wasn't wearing mail or even boiled leather, so it went right in, the same way Needle had when she killed the stableboy at King's Landing. The squire's eyes got big and he let go of her arm. Arya spun to the door and wrenched the Tickler's knife from the wall.

Polliver and the Tickler had driven the Hound into a corner behind a bench, and one of them had given him an ugly red gash on his upper thigh to go with his other wounds. Sandor was leaning against the wall, bleeding and breathing noisily. He looked as though he could barely stand, let alone fight. "Throw down the sword, and we'll take you back to Harrenhal," Polliver told him.

"So Gregor can finish me himself?"

The Tickler said, "Maybe he'll give you to me."

"If you want me, come get me." Sandor pushed away from the wall and stood in a half-crouch behind the bench, his sword held across his body.

"You think we won't?" said Polliver. "You're drunk."

"Might be," said the Hound, "but you're dead." His foot lashed out and caught the bench, driving it hard into Polliver's shins. Somehow the bearded man kept his feet, but the Hound ducked under his wild slash and brought his own sword up in a vicious backhand cut. Blood spattered on the ceiling and walls. The blade caught in the middle of Polliver's face, and when the Hound wrenched it loose half his head came with it.

The Tickler backed away. Arya could smell his fear. The shortsword in his hand suddenly seemed almost a toy against the long blade the Hound was holding, and he wasn't armored either. He moved swiftly, light on his feet, never taking his eyes off Sandor Clegane. It was the easiest thing in the world for Arya to step up behind him and stab him.

"Is there gold hidden in the village?" she shouted as she drove the blade up through his back. "Is there silver? Gems?" She stabbed twice more. "Is there food? Where is Lord Beric?" She was on top of him by then, still stabbing. "Where did he go? How many men were with him? How many knights? How many bowmen? How many, how many, how many, how many, how many, how many? Is there *gold* in the village?"

Her hands were red and sticky when Sandor dragged her off him. "Enough," was all he said. He was bleeding like a butchered pig himself, and dragging one leg when he walked.

"There's one more," Arya reminded him.

The squire had pulled the knife out of his belly and was trying to stop the blood with his hands. When the Hound yanked him upright, he screamed and started to blubber like a baby. "Mercy," he wept, "please. Don't kill me. Mother have mercy."

"Do I look like your bloody mother?" The Hound looked like nothing human. "You killed this one too," he told Arya. "Pricked him in his bowels, that's the end of him. He'll be a long time dying, though."

The boy didn't seemed to hear him. "I came for the girls," he whimpered. ". . . make me a man, Polly said . . . oh, gods, please, take me to a castle . . . a maester, take me to a maester, my father's got gold . . . it was only for the girls . . . mercy, ser."

The Hound gave him a crack across the face that made him scream again. "Don't call me ser." He turned back to Arya. "This one is yours, she-wolf. You do it."

She knew what he meant. Arya went to Polliver and knelt in his blood long enough to undo his swordbelt. Hanging beside his dagger was a slimmer blade, too long to be a dirk, too short to be a man's sword . . . but it felt just right in her hand.

"You remember where the heart is?" the Hound asked.

She nodded. The squire rolled his eyes. "Mercy."

Needle slipped between his ribs and gave it to him.

"Good." Sandor's voice was thick with pain. "If these three were whoring here, Gregor must hold the ford as well as Harrenhal. More of his pets could ride up any moment, and we've killed enough of the bloody buggers for one day."

"Where will we go?" she asked.

"Saltpans." He put a big hand on her shoulder to keep from falling. "Get some wine, she-wolf. And take whatever coin they have as well, we'll need it. If there's ships at Saltpans, we can reach the Vale by sea." His mouth twitched at her, as more blood ran down from where his ear had been. "Maybe Lady Lysa will marry you to her little Robert. *There's* a match I'd like to see." He started to laugh, then groaned instead.

When the time came to leave, he needed Arya's help to get back up on Stranger. He had tied a strip of cloth about his neck and another around his thigh, and taken the squire's cloak off its peg by the door. The cloak was green, with a green arrow on a white bend, but when the Hound wadded it up and pressed it to his ear it soon turned red. Arya was afraid he would collapse the moment they set out, but somehow he stayed in the saddle.

They could not risk meeting whoever held the ruby

ford, so instead of following the kingsroad they angled south by east, through weedy fields, woods, and marshes. It was hours before they reached the banks of the Trident. The river had returned meekly to its accustomed channel, Arya saw, all its wet brown rage vanished with the rains. *It's tired too*, she thought.

Close by the water's edge, they found some willows rising from a jumble of weathered rocks. Together the rocks and trees formed a sort of natural fort where they could hide from both river and trail. "Here will do," the Hound said. "Water the horses and gather some deadwood for a fire." When he dismounted, he had to catch himself on a tree limb to keep from falling.

"Won't the smoke be seen?"

"Anyone wants to find us, all they need to do is follow my blood. Water and wood. But bring me that wineskin first."

When he got the fire going, Sandor propped up his helm in the flames, emptied half the wineskin into it, and collapsed back against a jut of moss-covered stone as if he never meant to rise again. He made Arya wash out the squire's cloak and cut it into strips. Those went into his helm as well. "If I had more wine, I'd drink till I was dead to the world. Maybe I ought to send you back to that bloody inn for another skin or three."

"No," Arya said. *He wouldn't, would he? If he does, I'll just leave him and ride off.*

Sandor laughed at the fear on her face. "A jest, wolf girl. A bloody jest. Find me a stick, about so long and not too big around. And wash the mud off it. I hate the taste of mud."

He didn't like the first two sticks she brought him. By the time she found one that suited him, the flames had scorched his dog's snout black all the way to the eyes. Inside the wine was boiling madly. "Get the cup from my bedroll and dip it half full," he told her. "Be careful. You knock the damn thing over, I *will* send you back for more. Take the wine and pour it on my wounds. Think you can do that?" Arya nodded. "Then what are you waiting for?" he growled.

Her knuckles brushed the steel the first time she filled the cup, burning her so badly she got blisters. Arya had to bite her lip to keep from screaming. The Hound used the stick for the same purpose, clamping it between his teeth as she poured. She did the gash in his thigh first, then the shallower cut on the back of his neck. Sandor coiled his right hand into a fist and beat against the ground when she did his leg. When it came to his neck, he bit the stick so hard it broke, and she had to find him a new one. She could see the terror in his eyes. "Turn your head." She trickled the wine down over the raw red flesh where his ear had been, and fingers of brown blood and red wine crept over his jaw. He *did* scream then, despite the stick. Then he passed out from the pain.

Arya figured the rest out by herself. She fished the strips they'd made of the squire's cloak out of the bottom of the helm and used them to bind the cuts. When she came to his ear, she had to wrap up half his head to stop the bleeding. By then dusk was settling over the Trident. She let the horses graze, then hobbled them for the night and made herself as comfortable as she could in a niche between two rocks. The fire burned a while and died. Arya watched the moon through the branches overhead.

"Ser Gregor the Mountain," she said softly. "Dunsen, Raff the Sweetling, Ser Ilyn, Ser Meryn, Queen Cersei." It made her feel queer to leave out Polliver and the Tickler. And Joffrey too. She was glad he was dead, but she wished she could have been there to see him die, or maybe kill him herself. *Polliver said that Sansa killed him, and the Imp.* Could that be true? The Imp was a Lannister, and Sansa . . . *I wish I could change into a wolf and grow wings and fly away.*

If Sansa was gone too, there were no more Starks but her. Jon was on the Wall a thousand leagues away, but he was a Snow, and these different aunts and uncles the Hound wanted to sell her to, they weren't Starks either. They weren't *wolves.*

Sandor moaned, and she rolled onto her side to look at him. She had left his name out too, she realized. Why had she done that? She tried to think of Mycah, but it was hard to remember what he'd looked like. She hadn't known him long. *All he ever did was play at swords with me.* "The Hound," she whispered, and, "*Valar morghulis.*" Maybe he'd be dead by morning . . .

But when the pale dawn light came filtering through the

trees, it was him who woke her with the toe of his boot. She had dreamed she was a wolf again, chasing a riderless horse up a hill with a pack behind her, but his foot brought her back just as they were closing for the kill.

The Hound was still weak, every movement slow and clumsy. He slumped in the saddle, and sweated, and his ear began to bleed through the bandage. He needed all his strength just to keep from falling off Stranger. Had the Mountain's men come hunting them, she doubted if he would even be able to lift a sword. Arya glanced over her shoulder, but there was nothing behind them but a crow flitting from tree to tree. The only sound was the river.

Long before noon, Sandor Clegane was reeling. There were hours of daylight still remaining when he called a halt. "I need to rest," was all he said. This time when he dismounted he *did* fall. Instead of trying to get back up he crawled weakly under a tree, and leaned up against the trunk. "Bloody hell," he cursed. "Bloody hell." When he saw Arya staring at him, he said, "I'd skin you alive for a cup of wine, girl."

She brought him water instead. He drank a little of it, complained that it tasted of mud, and slid into a noisy fevered sleep. When she touched him, his skin was burning up. Arya sniffed at his bandages the way Maester Luwin had done sometimes when treating her cut or scrape. His face had bled the worst, but it was the wound on his thigh that smelled funny to her.

She wondered how far this Saltpans was, and whether she could find it by herself. *I wouldn't have to kill him. If I just rode off and left him, he'd die all by himself. He'll die of fever, and lie there beneath that tree until the end of days.* But maybe it would be better if she killed him herself. She had killed the squire at the inn and he hadn't done anything except grab her arm. The Hound had killed Mycah. *Mycah and more. I bet he's killed a hundred Mycahs.* He probably would have killed her too, if not for the ransom.

Needle glinted as she drew it. Polliver had kept it nice and sharp, at least. She turned her body sideways in a water dancer's stance without even thinking about it. Dead leaves crunched beneath her feet. *Quick as a snake*, she thought. *Smooth as summer silk.*

His eyes opened. "You remember where the heart is?" he asked in a hoarse whisper.

As still as stone she stood. "I . . . I was only . . ."

"Don't lie," he growled. "I hate liars. I hate gutless frauds even worse. Go on, do it." When Arya did not move, he said, "I killed your butcher's boy. I cut him near in half, and laughed about it after." He made a queer sound, and it took her a moment to realize he was sobbing. "And the little bird, your pretty sister, I stood there in my white cloak and let them beat her. I *took* the bloody song, she never gave it. I meant to take her too. I should have. I should have fucked her bloody and ripped her heart out before leaving her for that dwarf." A spasm of pain twisted his face. "Do you mean to make me beg, bitch? *Do it!* The gift of mercy . . . avenge your little Michael . . ."

"Mycah." Arya stepped away from him. "You don't deserve the gift of mercy."

The Hound watched her saddle Craven through eyes bright with fever. Not once did he attempt to rise and stop her. But when she mounted, he said, "A real wolf would finish a wounded animal."

Maybe some real wolves will find you, Arya thought. *Maybe they'll smell you when the sun goes down.* Then he would learn what wolves did to dogs. "You shouldn't have hit me with an axe," she said. "You should have saved my mother." She turned her horse and rode away from him, and never looked back once.

On a bright morning six days later, she came to a place where the Trident began to widen out and the air smelled more of salt than trees. She stayed close to the water, passing fields and farms, and a little after midday a town appeared before her. *Saltpans*, she hoped. A small castle dominated the town; no more than a holdfast, really, a single tall square keep with a bailey and a curtain wall. Most of the shops and inns and alehouses around the harbor had been plundered or burned, though some looked still inhabited. But the port was there, and eastward spread the Bay of Crabs, its waters shimmering blue and green in the sun.

And there were ships.

Three, thought Arya, *there are three.* Two were only river galleys, shallow draft boats made to ply the waters of the Trident. The third was bigger, a salt sea trader with two banks of oars, a gilded prow, and three tall masts with furled purple sails. Her hull was painted purple too. Arya rode Craven down to the docks to get a better look. Strangers are not so strange in a port as they are in little villages, and no one seemed to care who she was or why she was here.

I need silver. The realization made her bite her lip. They had found a stag and a dozen coppers on Polliver, eight silvers on the pimply squire she'd killed, and only a couple of pennies in the Tickler's purse. But the Hound had told her to pull off his boots and slice open his blood-drenched clothes, and she'd turned up a stag in each toe, and three golden dragons sewn in the lining of his jerkin. Sandor had kept it all, though. *That wasn't fair. It was mine as much as his.* If she had given him the gift of mercy . . . she hadn't, though. She couldn't go back, no more than she could beg for help. *Begging for help never gets you any.* She would have to sell Craven, and hope she brought enough.

The stable had been burnt, she learned from a boy by the docks, but the woman who'd owned it was still trading behind the sept. Arya found her easily; a big, robust woman with a good horsey smell to her. She liked Craven at first look, asked Arya how she'd come by her, and grinned at her answer. "She's a well-bred horse, that's plain enough, and I don't doubt she belonged to a knight, sweetling," she said. "But the knight wasn't no dead brother o' yours. I been dealing with the castle there many a year, so I know what gentleborn folk is like. This mare is well-bred, but you're not." She poked a finger at Arya's chest. "Found her or stole her, never mind which, that's how it was. Only way a scruffy little thing like you comes to ride a palfrey."

Arya bit her lip. "Does that mean you won't buy her?"

The woman chuckled. "It means you'll take what I give you, sweetling. Else we go down to the castle, and maybe you get nothing. Or even hanged, for stealing some good knight's horse."

A half-dozen other Saltpans folks were around, going about their business, so Arya knew she couldn't kill the woman. Instead she had to bite her lip and let herself be cheated. The purse she got was pitifully flat, and when she asked for more for the saddle and bridle and blanket, the woman just laughed at her.

She would never have cheated the Hound, she thought during the long walk back to the docks. The distance seemed to have grown by miles since she'd ridden it.

The purple galley was still there. If the ship had sailed while she was being robbed, that would have been too much to bear. A cask of mead was being rolled up the plank when she arrived. When she tried to follow, a sailor up on deck shouted down at her in a tongue she did not know. "I want to see the captain," Arya told him. He only shouted louder. But the commotion drew the attention of a stout grey-haired man in a coat of purple wool, and he spoke the Common Tongue. "I am captain here," he said. "What is your wish? Be quick, child, we have a tide to catch."

"I want to go north, to the Wall. Here, I can pay." She gave him the purse. "The Night's Watch has a castle on the sea."

"Eastwatch." The captain spilled out the silver onto his palm and frowned. "Is this all you have?"

It is not enough, Arya knew without being told. She could see it on his face. "I wouldn't need a cabin or anything," she said. "I could sleep down in the hold, or . . ."

"Take her on as cabin girl," said a passing oarsman, a bolt of wool over one shoulder. "She can sleep with me."

"Mind your tongue," the captain snapped.

"I could work," said Arya. "I could scrub the decks. I scrubbed a castle steps once. Or I could row . . ."

"No," he said, "you couldn't." He gave her back her coins. "It would make no difference if you could, child. The north has nothing for us. Ice and war and pirates. We saw a dozen pirate ships making north as we rounded Crackclaw Point, and I have no wish to meet them again. From here we bend our oars for home, and I suggest you do the same."

I have no home, Arya thought. *I have no pack. And now I don't even have a horse.*

The captain was turning away when she said, "What ship is this, my lord?"

He paused long enough to give her a weary smile. "This is the galleas *Titan's Daughter*, of the Free City of Braavos."

"Wait," Arya said suddenly. "I have something else." She had stuffed it down inside her smallclothes to keep it safe, so she had to dig deep to find it, while the oarsmen laughed and the captain lingered with obvious impatience. "One more silver will make no difference, child," he finally said.

"It's not silver." Her fingers closed on it. "It's iron. Here." She pressed it into his hand, the small black iron coin that Jaqen H'ghar had given her, so worn the man whose head it bore had no features. *It's probably worthless, but . . .*

The captain turned it over and blinked at it, then looked at her again. "This . . . how . . . ?"

Jaqen said to say the words too. Arya crossed her arms against her chest. "*Valar morghulis*," she said, as loud as if she'd known what it meant.

"*Valar dohaeris*," he replied, touching his brow with two fingers. "Of *course* you shall have a cabin."

SAMWELL

He sucks harder than mine." Gilly stroked the babe's head as she held him to her nipple.

"He's hungry," said the blonde woman Val, the one the black brothers called the wildling princess. "He's lived on goats' milk up to now, and potions from that blind maester."

The boy did not have a name yet, no more than Gilly's did. That was the wildling way. Not even Mance Rayder's son would get a name till his third year, it would seem, though Sam had heard the brothers calling him "the little prince" and "born-in-battle."

He watched the child nurse at Gilly's breast, and then he watched Jon watch. *Jon is smiling*. A sad smile, still, but definitely a smile of sorts. Sam was glad to see it. *It is the first time I've seen him smile since I got back*.

They had walked from the Nightfort to Deep Lake, and from Deep Lake to Queensgate, following a narrow track from one castle to the next, never out of sight of the Wall. A day and a half from Castle Black, as they trudged along on callused feet, Gilly heard horses behind them, and turned to see a column of black riders coming from the west. "My brothers," Sam assured her. "No one uses this road but the Night's Watch." It had turned out to be Ser Denys Mallister from the Shadow Tower, along with the wounded Bowen Marsh and the survivors from the fight at the Bridge of Skulls. When Sam saw Dywen, Giant, and Dolorous Edd Tollett, he broke down and wept.

It was from them that he learned about the battle beneath the Wall. "Stannis landed his knights at Eastwatch, and Cotter Pyke led him along the ranger's roads, to take the wildlings unawares," Giant told him. "He smashed them. Mance Rayder was taken captive, a thousand of his best slain, including Harma Dogshead. The rest scattered like leaves before a storm, we heard." *The gods are good*, Sam thought. If he had not gotten lost as he made his way south from Craster's Keep, he and Gilly might have walked right into the battle . . . or into Mance Rayder's camp, at the very least. That might have been well enough for Gilly and the boy, but not for him. Sam had heard all the stories about what wildlings did with captured crows. He shuddered.

Nothing that his brothers told him prepared him for what he found at Castle Black, however. The common hall had burned to the ground and the great wooden stair was a mound of broken ice and scorched timbers. Donal Noye was dead, along with Rast, Deaf Dick, Red Alyn, and so many more, yet the castle was more crowded than Sam had ever seen, not with black brothers, but with the king's soldiers, more than a thousand of them. There was a king in the King's Tower for the first time in living memory, and banners flew from the Lance, Hardin's Tower, the Grey Keep, the Shieldhall, and other buildings that had stood empty and abandoned for long years. "The big one, the gold with the black stag, that's the royal standard of House Baratheon," he told Gilly, who had never seen banners before. "The fox-and-flowers is House Florent. The turtle is Estermont, the swordfish is Bar Emmon, and the crossed trumpets are for Wensington."

"They're all bright as flowers." Gilly pointed. "I like those yellow ones, with the fire. Look, and some of the fighters have the same thing on their blouses."

"A fiery heart. I don't know whose sigil that is."

He found out soon enough. *"Queen's men,"* Pyp told him—after he let out a whoop, and shouted, "Run and bar the doors, lads, it's Sam the Slayer come back from the grave," while Grenn was hugging Sam so hard he thought his ribs might break—"but best you don't go asking where the queen is. Stannis left her at Eastwatch, with their daughter and his fleet. He brought no woman but the red one."

"The red one?" said Sam uncertainly.

"Melisandre of Asshai," said Grenn. "The king's sorceress. They say she burned a man alive at Dragonstone so Stannis would have favorable winds for his voyage north. She rode beside him in the battle too, and gave him his magic sword. Lightbringer, they call it. Wait till you see it. It glows like it had a piece of sun inside it." He looked at Sam again and grinned a big helpless stupid grin. "I still can't believe you're here."

Jon Snow had smiled to see him too, but it was a tired smile, like the one he wore now. "You made it back after all," he said. "And brought Gilly out as well. You've done well, Sam."

Jon had done more than well himself, to hear Grenn tell it. Yet even capturing the Horn of Winter and a wildling prince had not been enough for Ser Alliser Thorne and his friends, who still named him turncloak. Though Maester Aemon said his wound was healing well, Jon bore other scars, deeper than the ones around his eye. *He grieves for his wildling girl, and for his brothers.*

"It's strange," he said to Sam. "Craster had no love for Mance, nor Mance for Craster, but now Craster's daughter is feeding Mance's son."

"I have the milk," Gilly said, her voice soft and shy. "Mine takes only a little. He's not so greedy as this one."

The wildling woman Val turned to face them. "I've heard the queen's men saying that the red woman means to give Mance to the fire, as soon as he is strong enough."

Jon gave her a weary look. "Mance is a deserter from the Night's Watch. The penalty for that is death. If the Watch had taken him, he would have been hanged by now, but he's the king's captive, and no one knows the king's mind but the red woman."

"I want to see him," Val said. "I want to show him his son. He deserves that much, before you kill him."

Sam tried to explain. "No one is permitted to see him but Maester Aemon, my lady."

"If it were in my power, Mance could hold his son." Jon's smile was gone. "I'm sorry, Val." He turned away. "Sam and I have duties to return to. Well, Sam does, anyway. We'll ask about your seeing Mance. That's all I can promise."

Sam lingered long enough to give Gilly's hand a squeeze and promise to return again after supper. Then he hurried after. There were guards outside the door, queen's men with spears. Jon was halfway down the steps, but he waited when he heard Sam puffing after him. "You're more than fond of Gilly, aren't you?"

Sam reddened. "Gilly's good. She's good and kind." He was glad that his long nightmare was done, glad to be back with his brothers at Castle Black . . . but some nights, alone in his cell, he thought of how warm Gilly had been when they'd curled up beneath the furs with the babe between them. "She . . . she made me braver, Jon. Not *brave*, but . . . braver."

"You know you cannot keep her," Jon said gently, "no more than I could stay with Ygritte. You said the words, Sam, the same as I did. The same as all of us."

"I know. Gilly said she'd be a wife to me, but . . . I told her about the words, and what they meant. I don't know if that made her sad or glad, but I told her." He swallowed nervously and said, "Jon, could there be honor in a lie, if it were told for a . . . a good purpose?"

"It would depend on the lie and the purpose, I suppose." Jon looked at Sam. "I wouldn't advise it. You're not made to lie, Sam. You blush and squeak and stammer."

"I do," said Sam, "but I could lie in a letter. I'm better with a quill in hand. I had a . . . a thought. When things are more settled here, I thought maybe the best thing for Gilly . . . I thought I might send her to Horn Hill. To my mother and sisters and my . . . my f-f-father. If Gilly were to say the babe was m-mine . . ." He was blushing again. "My mother would want him, I know. She would find some place for Gilly, some kind of service, it wouldn't be as hard as serving Craster. And Lord R-Randyll, he . . . he would never *say* so, but he might be pleased to believe I got a bastard on some wildling girl. At least it would prove I was man enough to lie with a woman and father a child. He told me once that I was sure to die a maiden, that no woman would ever . . . you know . . . Jon, if I did this, wrote this lie . . . would that be a good thing? The life the boy would have . . ."

"Growing up a bastard in his grandfather's castle?" Jon shrugged. "That depends in great part on your father, and what sort of boy this is. If he takes after you . . ."

"He won't. Craster's his real father. You saw him, he was hard as an old tree stump, and Gilly is stronger than she looks."

"If the boy shows any skill with sword or lance, he should have a place with your father's household guard at the least," Jon said. "It's not unknown for bastards to be trained as squires and raised to knighthood. But you'd best be sure Gilly can play this game convincingly. From what you've told me of Lord Randyll, I doubt he would take kindly to being deceived."

More guards were posted on the steps outside the tower. These were king's men, though; Sam had quickly learned the difference. The king's men were as earthy and impious as any other soldiers, but the queen's men were fervid in their devotion to Melisandre of Asshai and her Lord of Light. "Are you going to the practice yard again?" Sam asked as they crossed the yard. "Is it wise to train so hard before your leg's done healing?"

Jon shrugged. "What else is there for me to do? Marsh has removed me from duty, for fear that I'm still a turn-cloak."

"It's only a few who believe that," Sam assured him. "Ser Alliser and his friends. Most of the brothers know better. King Stannis knows as well, I'll wager. You brought him the Horn of Winter and captured Mance Rayder's son."

"All I did was protect Val and the babe against looters when the wildlings fled, and keep them there until the rangers found us. I never *captured* anyone. King Stannis keeps his men well in hand, that's plain. He lets them plunder some, but I've only heard of three wildling women being raped, and the men who did it have all been gelded. I suppose I should have been killing the free folk as they ran. Ser Alliser has been putting it about that the only time I bared my sword was to defend our foes. I failed to kill Mance Rayder because I was in league with him, he says."

"That's only Ser Alliser," said Sam. "Everyone knows the sort of man he is." With his noble birth, his knighthood, and his long years in the Watch, Ser Alliser Thorne might have been a strong challenger for the Lord Commander's title, but almost all the men he'd trained during his years as master-at-arms despised him. His name had been offered, of course, but after running a weak sixth on the first day and actually *losing* votes on the second, Thorne had withdrawn to support Lord Janos Slynt.

"What everyone knows is that Ser Alliser is a knight from a noble line, and trueborn, while I'm the bastard who killed Qhorin Halfhand and bedded with a spearwife. The *warg*, I've heard them call me. How can I be a warg without a wolf, I ask you?" His mouth twisted. "I don't even dream of Ghost anymore. All my dreams are of the crypts, of the stone kings on their thrones. Sometimes I hear Robb's voice, and my father's, as if they were at a feast. But there's a wall between us, and I know that no place has been set for me."

The living have no place at the feasts of the dead. It tore the heart from Sam to hold his silence then. *Bran's not dead, Jon,* he wanted to stay. *He's with friends, and they're going north on a giant elk to find a three-eyed crow in the depths of the haunted forest.* It sounded so mad that there were times Sam Tarly thought he must have dreamt it all, conjured it whole from fever and fear and hunger . . . but he would have blurted it out anyway, if he had not given his word.

Three times he had sworn to keep the secret; once to Bran himself, once to that strange boy Jojen Reed, and last of all to Coldhands. "The world believes the boy is dead," his rescuer had said as they parted. "Let his bones lie undisturbed. We want no seekers coming after us. Swear it, Samwell of the Night's Watch. Swear it for the life you owe me."

Miserable, Sam shifted his weight and said, "Lord Janos will never be chosen Lord Commander." It was the best comfort he had to offer Jon, the only comfort. "That won't happen."

"Sam, you're a sweet fool. Open your eyes. It's been happening for days." Jon pushed his hair back out of his eyes and said, "I may know nothing, but I know that. Now pray excuse me, I need to hit someone very hard with a sword."

There was naught that Sam could do but watch him stride off toward the armory and the practice yard. That was where Jon Snow spent most of his waking hours. With Ser Endrew dead and Ser Alliser disinterested, Castle Black had no master-at-arms, so Jon had taken it on himself to work with some of the rawer recruits; Satin, Horse, Hop-Robin with his clubfoot, Arron and Emrick. And when they had duties, he would train alone for hours with sword and shield and spear, or match himself against anyone who cared to take him on.

Sam, you're a sweet fool, he could hear Jon saying, all the way back to the maester's keep. *Open your eyes. It's been happening for days.* Could he be right? A man needed the votes of two-thirds of the Sworn Brothers to become the Lord Commander of the Night's Watch, and after nine days and nine votes no one was even close to that. Lord Janos *had* been gaining, true, creeping up past first Bowen Marsh and then Othell Yarwyck, but he was still well behind Ser Denys Mallister of the Shadow Tower and Cotter Pyke of Eastwatch-by-the-Sea. *One of them will be the new Lord Commander, surely*, Sam told himself.

Stannis had posted guards outside the maester's door too. Within, the rooms were hot and crowded with the wounded from the battle; black brothers, king's men, and queen's men, all three. Clydas was shuffling amongst them with flagons of goats' milk and dreamwine, but Maester Aemon had not yet returned from his morning call on Mance Rayder. Sam hung his cloak upon a peg and went to lend a hand. But even as he fetched and poured and changed dressings, Jon's words nagged at him. *Sam, you're a sweet fool. Open your eyes. It's been happening for days.*

It was a good hour before he could excuse himself to feed the ravens. On the way up to the rookery, he stopped to check the tally he had made of last night's count. At the start of the choosing, more than thirty names had been offered, but most had withdrawn once it became clear they could not win. Seven remained as of last night. Ser Denys Mallister had collected two hundred and thirteen tokens,

Cotter Pyke one hundred and eighty-seven, Lord Slynt seventy-four, Othell Yarwyck sixty, Bowen Marsh forty-nine, Three-Finger Hobb five, and Dolorous Edd Tollett one. *Pyp and his stupid japes.* Sam shuffled through the earlier counts. Ser Denys, Cotter Pyke, and Bowen Marsh had all been falling since the third day, Othell Yarwyck since the sixth. Only Lord Janos Slynt was climbing, day after day after day.

He could hear the birds *quorking* in the rookery, so he put the papers away and climbed the steps to feed them. Three more ravens had come in, he saw with pleasure. "*Snow,*" they cried at him. "*Snow, snow, snow.*" He had taught them that. Even with the newcomers, the ravenry seemed dismally empty. Few of the birds that Aemon had sent off had returned as yet. *One reached Stannis, though. One found Dragonstone, and a king who still cared.* A thousand leagues south, Sam knew, his father had joined House Tarly to the cause of the boy on the Iron Throne, but neither King Joffrey nor little King Tommen had bestirred himself when the Watch cried out for help. *What good is a king who will not defend his realm?* he thought angrily, remembering the night on the Fist of the First Men and the terrible trek to Craster's Keep through darkness, fear, and falling snow. The queen's men made him uneasy, it was true, but at least they had *come.*

That night at supper Sam looked for Jon Snow, but did not see him anywhere in the cavernous stone vault where the brothers now took their meals. He finally took a place on the bench near his other friends. Pyp was telling Dolorous Edd about the contest they'd had to see which of the straw soldiers could collect the most wildling arrows. "You were leading most of the way, but Watt of Long Lake got three in the last day and passed you."

"I never win anything," Dolorous Edd complained. "The gods always smiled on Watt, though. When the wildlings knocked him off the Bridge of Skulls, somehow he landed in a nice deep pool of water. How lucky was that, missing all those rocks?"

"Was it a long fall?" Grenn wanted to know. "Did landing in the pool of water save his life?"

"No," said Dolorous Edd. "He was dead already, from

that axe in his head. Still, it was pretty lucky, missing the rocks."

Three-Finger Hobb had promised the brothers roast haunch of mammoth that night, maybe in hopes of cadging a few more votes. *If that was his notion, he should have found a younger mammoth*, Sam thought, as he pulled a string of gristle out from between his teeth. Sighing, he pushed the food away.

There would be another vote shortly, and the tensions in the air were thicker than the smoke. Cotter Pyke sat by the fire, surrounded by rangers from Eastwatch. Ser Denys Mallister was near the door with a smaller group of Shadow Tower men. *Janos Slynt has the best place*, Sam realized, *halfway between the flames and the drafts*. He was alarmed to see Bowen Marsh beside him, wan-faced and haggard, his head still wrapped in linen, but listening to all that Lord Janos had to say. When he pointed that out to his friends, Pyp said, "And look down there, that's Ser Alliser whispering with Othell Yarwyck."

After the meal Maester Aemon rose to ask if any of the brothers wished to speak before they cast their tokens. Dolorous Edd got up, stone-faced and glum as ever. "I just want to say to whoever is voting for me that I would certainly make an awful Lord Commander. But so would all these others." He was followed by Bowen Marsh, who stood with one hand on Lord Slynt's shoulder. "Brothers and friends, I am asking that my name be withdrawn from this choosing. My wound still troubles me, and the task is too large for me, I fear . . . but not for Lord Janos here, who commanded the gold cloaks of King's Landing for many years. Let us all give him our support."

Sam heard angry mutters from Cotter Pyke's end of the room, and Ser Denys looked at one of his companions and shook his head. *It is too late, the damage is done.* He wondered where Jon was, and why he had stayed away.

Most of the brothers were unlettered, so by tradition the choosing was done by dropping tokens into a big potbellied iron kettle that Three-Finger Hobb and Owen the Oaf had dragged over from the kitchens. The barrels of tokens were off in a corner behind a heavy drape, so the voters could make their choice unseen. You were allowed to have a friend cast your token if you had duty, so some men took two tokens, three, or four, and Ser Denys and Cotter Pyke voted for the garrisons they had left behind.

When the hall was finally empty, save for them, Sam and Clydas upended the kettle in front of Maester Aemon. A cascade of seashells, stones, and copper pennies covered the table. Aemon's wrinkled hands sorted with surprising speed, moving the shells here, the stones there, the pennies to one side, the occasional arrowhead, nail, and acorn off to themselves. Sam and Clydas counted the piles, each of them keeping his own tally.

Tonight it was Sam's turn to give his results first. "Two hundred and three for Ser Denys Mallister," he said. "One hundred and sixty-nine for Cotter Pyke." One hundred and thirty-seven for Lord Janos Slynt, seventy-two for Othell Yarwyck, five for Three-Finger Hobb, and two for Dolorous Edd."

"I had one hundred and sixty-eight for Pyke," Clydas said. "We are two votes short by my count, and one by Sam's."

"Sam's count is correct," said Maester Aemon. "Jon Snow did not cast a token. It makes no matter. No one is close."

Sam was more relieved than disappointed. Even with Bowen Marsh's support, Lord Janos was still only third. "Who are these five who keep voting for Three-Finger Hobb?" he wondered.

"Brothers who want him out of the kitchens?" said Clydas.

"Ser Denys is down ten votes since yesterday," Sam pointed out. "And Cotter Pyke is down almost twenty. That's not good."

"Not good for their hopes of becoming Lord Commander, certainly," said Maester Aemon. "Yet it may be good for the Night's Watch, in the end. That is not for us to say. Ten days is not unduly long. There was once a choosing that lasted near two years, some seven hundred votes. The brothers will come to a decision in their own time."

Yes, Sam thought, *but what decision?*

Later, over cups of watered wine in the privacy of Pyp's cell, Sam's tongue loosened and he found himself thinking aloud. "Cotter Pyke and Ser Denys Mallister have been losing ground, but between them they still have almost two-thirds," he told Pyp and Grenn. "Either one would be fine as Lord Commander. Someone needs to convince one of them to withdraw and support the other."

"Someone?" said Grenn, doubtfully. "What someone?"

"Grenn is so dumb he thinks *someone* might be him," said Pyp. "Maybe when someone is done with Pyke and Mallister, he should convince King Stannis to marry Queen Cersei too."

"King Stannis is married," Grenn objected.

"What am I going to do with him, Sam?" sighed Pyp.

"Cotter Pyke and Ser Denys don't like each other much," Grenn argued stubbornly. "They fight about *everything*."

"Yes, but only because they have different ideas about what's best for the Watch," said Sam. "If we explained—"

"*We!*" said Pyp. "How did *someone* change to *we?* I'm the mummer's monkey, remember? And Grenn is, well, *Grenn*." He smiled at Sam, and wiggled his ears. "You, now . . . you're a lord's son, and the maester's steward . . ."

"And Sam the Slayer," said Grenn. "You slew an Other."

"It was the *dragonglass* that killed it," Sam told him for the hundredth time.

"A lord's son, the maester's steward, and Sam the Slayer," Pyp mused. "*You* could talk to them, might be . . ."

"I could," said Sam, sounding as gloomy as Dolorous Edd, "if I wasn't too craven to face them."

JON

Jon prowled around Satin in a slow circle, sword in hand, forcing him to turn. "Get your shield up," he said.

"It's too heavy," the Oldtown boy complained.

"It's as heavy as it needs to be to stop a sword," Jon said. "Now get it up." He stepped forward, slashing. Satin jerked the shield up in time to catch the sword on its rim, and swung his own blade at Jon's ribs. "Good," Jon said, when he felt the impact on his own shield. "That was good. But you need to put your body into it. Get your weight behind the steel and you'll do more damage than with arm strength alone. Come, try it again, drive at me, but keep the shield up or I'll ring your head like a bell . . ."

Instead Satin took a step backward and raised his visor. "Jon," he said, in an anxious voice.

When he turned, she was standing behind him, with half a dozen queen's men around her. *Small wonder the yard grew so quiet.* He had glimpsed Melisandre at her nightfires, and coming and going about the castle, but never so close. *She's beautiful*, he thought . . . but there was something more than a little unsettling about red eyes. "My lady."

"The king would speak with you, Jon Snow."

Jon thrust the practice sword into the earth. "Might I be allowed to change? I am in no fit state to stand before a king."

"We shall await you atop the Wall," said Melisandre. *We*, Jon heard, *not he. It's as they say. This is his true queen, not the one he left at Eastwatch.*

He hung his mail and plate inside the armory, returned to his own cell, discarded his sweat-stained clothes, and donned a fresh set of blacks. It would be cold and windy in the cage, he knew, and colder and windier still on top of the ice, so he chose a heavy hooded cloak. Last of all he collected Longclaw, and slung the bastard sword across his back.

Melisandre was waiting for him at the base of the Wall. She had sent her queen's men away. "What does His Grace want of me?" Jon asked her as they entered the cage.

"All you have to give, Jon Snow. He is a king."

He shut the door and pulled the bell cord. The winch began to turn. They rose. The day was bright and the Wall was weeping, long fingers of water trickling down its face and glinting in the sun. In the close confines of the iron cage, he was acutely aware of the red woman's presence. *She even smells red.* The scent reminded him of Mikken's forge, of the way iron smelled when red-hot; the scent was smoke and blood. *Kissed by fire*, he thought, remembering Ygritte. The wind got in amongst Melisandre's long red robes and sent them flapping against Jon's legs as he stood beside her. "You are not cold, my lady?" he asked her.

She laughed. "Never." The ruby at her throat seemed to pulse, in time with the beating of her heart. "The Lord's fire lives within me, Jon Snow. Feel." She put her hand on his cheek, and held it there while he felt how warm she was. "That is how life should feel," she told him. "Only death is cold."

They found Stannis Baratheon standing alone at the edge of the Wall, brooding over the field where he had won his battle, and the great green forest beyond. He was dressed in the same black breeches, tunic, and boots that a brother of the Night's Watch might wear. Only his cloak set him apart; a heavy golden cloak trimmed in black fur, and pinned with a brooch in the shape of a flaming heart. "I have brought you the Bastard of Winterfell, Your Grace," said Melisandre.

Stannis turned to study him. Beneath his heavy brow were eyes like bottomless blue pools. His hollow cheeks and strong jaw were covered with a short-cropped blue-black beard that did little to conceal the gauntness of his face, and his teeth were clenched. His neck and shoulders were clenched as well, and his right hand. Jon found himself remembering something Donal Noye once said about the Baratheon brothers. *Robert was the true steel. Stannis is pure iron, black and hard and strong, but brittle, the way iron gets. He'll break before he bends.* Uneasily, he knelt, wondering why this brittle king had need of him.

"Rise. I have heard much and more of you, Lord Snow."

"I am no lord, sire." Jon rose. "I know what you have heard. That I am a turncloak, and craven. That I slew my brother Qhorin Halfhand so the wildlings would spare my life. That I rode with Mance Rayder, and took a wildling wife."

"Aye. All that, and more. You are a warg too, they say, a skinchanger who walks at night as a wolf." King Stannis had a hard smile. "How much of it is true?"

"I had a direwolf, Ghost. I left him when I climbed the Wall near Greyguard, and have not seen him since. Qhorin Halfhand commanded me to join the wildlings. He knew they would make me kill him to prove myself, and told me to do whatever they asked of me. The woman was named Ygritte. I broke my vows with her, but I swear to you on my father's name that I never turned my cloak."

"I believe you," the king said.

That startled him. "Why?"

Stannis snorted. "I know Janos Slynt. And I knew Ned Stark as well. Your father was no friend of mine, but only a fool would doubt his honor or his honesty. You have his look." A big man, Stannis Baratheon towered over Jon, but he was so gaunt that he looked ten years older than he was. "I know more than you might think, Jon Snow. I know it was you who found the dragonglass dagger that Randyll Tarly's son used to slay the Other."

"Ghost found it. The blade was wrapped in a ranger's

cloak and buried beneath the Fist of the First Men. There were other blades as well . . . spearheads, arrowheads, all dragonglass."

"I know you held the gate here," King Stannis said. "If not, I would have come too late."

"Donal Noye held the gate. He died below in the tunnel, fighting the king of the giants."

Stannis grimaced. "Noye made my first sword for me, and Robert's warhammer as well. Had the god seen fit to spare him, he would have made a better Lord Commander for your order than any of these fools who are squabbling over it now."

"Cotter Pyke and Ser Denys Mallister are no fools, sire," Jon said. "They're good men, and capable. Othell Yarwyck as well, in his own way. Lord Mormont trusted each of them."

"Your Lord Mormont trusted too easily. Else he would not have died as he did. But we were speaking of you. I have not forgotten that it was you who brought us this magic horn, and captured Mance Rayder's wife and son."

"Dalla died." Jon was saddened by that still. "Val is her sister. She and the babe did not require much capturing, Your Grace. You had put the wildlings to flight, and the skinchanger Mance had left to guard his queen went mad when the eagle burned." Jon looked at Melisandre. "Some say that was your doing."

She smiled, her long copper hair tumbling across her face. "The Lord of Light has fiery talons, Jon Snow."

Jon nodded, and turned back to the king. "Your Grace, you spoke of Val. She has asked to see Mance Rayder, to bring his son to him. It would be a . . . a kindness."

"The man is a deserter from your order. Your brothers are all insisting on his death. Why should I do him a kindness?"

Jon had no answer for that. "If not for him, for Val. For her sister's sake, the child's mother."

"You are fond of this Val?"

"I scarcely know her."

"They tell me she is comely."

"Very," Jon admitted.

"Beauty can be treacherous. My brother learned that lesson from Cersei Lannister. She murdered him, do not doubt it. Your father and Jon Arryn as well." He scowled. "You rode with these wildlings. Is there any honor in them, do you think?"

"Yes," Jon said, "but their own sort of honor, sire."

"In Mance Rayder?"

"Yes. I think so."

"In the Lord of Bones?"

Jon hesitated. "Rattleshirt, we called him. Treacherous and blood-thirsty. If there's honor in him, he hides it down beneath his suit of bones."

"And this other man, this Tormund of the many names who eluded us after the battle? Answer me truly."

"Tormund Giantsbane seemed to me the sort of man who would make a good friend and a bad enemy, Your Grace."

Stannis gave a curt nod. "Your father was a man of honor. He was no friend to me, but I saw his worth. Your brother was a rebel and a traitor who meant to steal half my kingdom, but no man can question his courage. What of you?"

Does he want me to say I love him? Jon's voice was stiff and formal as he said, "I am a man of the Night's Watch."

"Words. Words are wind. Why do you think I abandoned Dragonstone and sailed to the Wall, Lord Snow?"

"I am no lord, sire. You came because we sent for you, I hope. Though I could not say why you took so long about it."

Surprisingly, Stannis smiled at that. "You're bold enough to be a Stark. Yes, I should have come sooner. If not for my Hand, I might not have come at all. Lord Seaworth is a man of humble birth, but he reminded me of my duty, when all I could think of was my rights. I had the cart before the horse, Davos said. I was trying to win the throne to save the kingdom, when I should have been trying to save the kingdom to win the throne." Stannis pointed north. "There is where I'll find the foe that I was born to fight."

"His name may not be spoken," Melisandre added softly. "He is the God of Night and Terror, Jon Snow, and these shapes in the snow are his creatures."

"They tell me that you slew one of these walking corpses to save Lord Mormont's life," Stannis said. "It may be that this is your war as well, Lord Snow. If you will give me your help."

"My sword is pledged to the Night's Watch, Your Grace," Jon Snow answered carefully.

That did not please the king. Stannis ground his teeth and said, "I need more than a sword from you."

Jon was lost. "My lord?"

"I need the north."

The north. "I . . . my brother Robb was King in the North . . ."

"Your brother was the rightful Lord of Winterfell. If he had stayed home and done his duty, instead of crowning himself and riding off to conquer the riverlands, he might be alive today. Be that as it may. You are not Robb, no more than I am Robert."

The harsh words had blown away whatever sympathy Jon might have had for Stannis. "I loved my brother," he said.

"And I mine. Yet they were what they were, and so are we. I am the only true king in Westeros, north or south. And you are Ned Stark's bastard." Stannis studied him with those dark blue eyes. "Tywin Lannister has named Roose Bolton his Warden of the North, to reward him for betraying your brother. The ironmen are fighting amongst themselves since Balon Greyjoy's death, yet they still hold Moat Cailin, Deepwood Motte, Torrhen's Square, and most of the Stony Shore. Your father's lands are bleeding, and I have neither the strength nor the time to stanch the wounds. What is needed is a Lord of Winterfell. A *loyal* Lord of Winterfell."

He is looking at me, Jon thought, stunned. "Winterfell is no more. Theon Greyjoy put it to the torch."

"Granite does not burn easily," Stannis said. "The castle can be rebuilt, in time. It's not the walls that make a lord, it's the man. Your northmen do not know me, have no reason to love me, yet I will need their strength in the battles yet to come. I need a son of Eddard Stark to win them to my banner."

He would make me Lord of Winterfell. The wind was gusting, and Jon felt so light-headed he was half afraid it would blow him off the Wall. "Your Grace," he said, "you forget. I am a Snow, not a Stark."

"It's you who are forgetting," King Stannis replied.

Melisandre put a warm hand on Jon's arm. "A king can remove the taint of bastardy with a stroke, Lord Snow."

Lord Snow. Ser Alliser Thorne had named him that, to mock his bastard birth. Many of his brothers had taken to using it as well, some with affection, others to wound. But suddenly it had a different sound to it in Jon's ears. It sounded . . . real. "Yes," he said, hesitantly, "kings have legitimized bastards before, but . . . I am still a brother of the Night's Watch. I knelt before a heart tree and swore to hold no lands and father no children."

"Jon." Melisandre was so close he could feel the warmth of her breath. "R'hllor is the only true god. A vow sworn to a tree has no more power than one sworn to your shoes. Open your heart and let the light of the Lord come in. Burn these weirwoods, and accept Winterfell as a gift of the Lord of Light."

When Jon had been very young, too young to understand what it meant to be a bastard, he used to dream that one day Winterfell might be his. Later, when he was older, he had been ashamed of those dreams. Winterfell would go to Robb and then his sons, or to Bran or Rickon should Robb die childless. And after them came Sansa and Arya. Even to dream otherwise seemed disloyal, as if he were betraying them in his heart, wishing for their deaths. *I never wanted this*, he thought as he stood before the blue-eyed king and the red woman. *I loved Robb, loved all of them . . . I never wanted any harm to come to any of them, but it did. And now there's only me.* All he had to do was say the word, and he would be Jon Stark, and nevermore a Snow. All he had to do was pledge this king his fealty, and Winterfell was his. All he had to do . . .

. . . was forswear his vows again.

And this time it would not be a ruse. To claim his father's castle, he must turn against his father's gods.

King Stannis gazed off north again, his gold cloak streaming from his shoulders. "It may be that I am mistaken in you, Jon Snow. We both know the things that are said of bastards. You may lack your father's honor, or your brother's skill in arms. But you are the weapon the Lord has given me. I have found you here, as you found the cache of dragonglass beneath the Fist, and I mean to make use of you. Even Azor

Ahai did not win his war alone. I killed a thousand wildlings, took another thousand captive, and scattered the rest, but we both know they will return. Melisandre has seen that in her fires. This Tormund Thunderfist is likely re-forming them even now, and planning some new assault. And the more we bleed each other, the weaker we shall all be when the real enemy falls upon us."

Jon had come to that same realization. "As you say, Your Grace." He wondered where this king was going.

"Whilst your brothers have been struggling to decide who shall lead them, I have been speaking with this Mance Rayder." He ground his teeth. "A stubborn man, that one, and prideful. He will leave me no choice but to give him to the flames. But we took other captives as well, other leaders. The one who calls himself the Lord of Bones, some of their clan chiefs, the new Magnar of Thenn. Your brothers will not like it, no more than your father's lords, but I mean to allow the wildlings through the Wall . . . those who will swear me their fealty, pledge to keep the king's peace and the king's laws, and take the Lord of Light as their god. Even the giants, if those great knees of theirs can bend. I will settle them on the Gift, once I have wrested it away from your new Lord Commander. When the cold winds rise, we shall live or die together. It is time we made alliance against our common foe." He looked at Jon. "Would you agree?"

"My father dreamed of resettling the Gift," Jon admitted. "He and my uncle Benjen used to talk of it." *He never thought of settling it with wildlings, though . . . but he never rode with wildlings, either.* He did not fool himself; the free folk would make for unruly subjects and dangerous neighbors. Yet when he weighed Ygritte's red hair against the cold blue eyes of the wights, the choice was easy. "I agree."

"Good," King Stannis said, "for the surest way to seal a new alliance is with a marriage. I mean to wed my Lord of Winterfell to this wildling princess."

Perhaps Jon had ridden with the free folk too long; he could not help but laugh. "Your Grace," he said, "captive or no, if you think you can just *give* Val to me, I fear you have a deal to learn about wildling women. Whoever weds her had best be prepared to climb in her tower window and carry her off at swordpoint . . ."

"*Whoever?*" Stannis gave him a measuring look. "Does this mean you will not wed the girl? I warn you, she is part of the price you must pay, if you want your father's name and your father's castle. This match is necessary, to help assure the loyalty of our new subjects. Are you refusing me, Jon Snow?"

"No," Jon said, too quickly. It was Winterfell the king was speaking of, and Winterfell was not to be lightly refused. "I mean . . . this has all come very suddenly, Your Grace. Might I beg you for some time to consider?"

"As you wish. But consider quickly. I am not a patient man, as your black brothers are about to discover." Stannis put a thin, fleshless hand on Jon's shoulder. "Say nothing of what we've discussed here today. To anyone. But when you return, you need only bend your knee, lay your sword at my feet, and pledge yourself to my service, and you shall rise again as Jon Stark, the Lord of Winterfell."

TYRION

When he heard noises through the thick wooden door of his cell, Tyrion Lannister prepared to die.

Past time, he thought. *Come on, come on, make an end to it*. He pushed himself to his feet. His legs were asleep from being folded under him. He bent down and rubbed the knives from them. *I will not go stumbling and waddling to the headsman's block*.

He wondered whether they would kill him down here in the dark or drag him through the city so Ser Ilyn Payne could lop his head off. After his mummer's farce of a trial, his sweet sister and loving father might prefer to dispose of him quietly, rather than risk a public execution. *I could tell the mob a few choice things, if they let me speak*. But would they be that foolish?

As the keys rattled and the door to his cell pushed inward, creaking, Tyrion pressed back against the dampness of the wall, wishing for a weapon. *I can still bite and kick. I'll die with the taste of blood in my mouth, that's something*. He wished he'd been able to think of some rousing last words. "Bugger you all" was not like to earn him much of a place in the histories.

Torchlight fell across his face. He shielded his eyes with a hand. "*Come on*, are you frightened of a dwarf? Do it, you son of a poxy whore." His voice had grown hoarse from disuse.

"Is that any way to speak about our lady mother?" The man moved forward, a torch in his left hand. "This is even more ghastly than my cell at Riverrun, though not quite so dank."

For a moment Tyrion could not breathe. "You?"

"Well, most of me." Jaime was gaunt, his hair hacked short. "I left a hand at Harrenhal. Bringing the Brave Companions across the narrow sea was not one of Father's better notions." He lifted his arm, and Tyrion saw the stump.

A bark of hysterical laughter burst from his lips. "Oh, gods," he said. "Jaime, I am so sorry, but . . . gods be good, look at the two of us. Handless and Noseless, the Lannister boys."

"There were days when my hand smelled so bad I wished I was noseless." Jaime lowered the torch, so the light bathed his brother's face. "An impressive scar."

Tyrion turned away from the glare. "They made me fight a battle without my big brother to protect me."

"I heard tell you almost burned the city down."

"A filthy lie. I only burned the river." Abruptly, Tyrion remembered where he was, and why. "Are you here to kill me?"

"Now that's ungrateful. Perhaps I should leave you here to rot if you're going to be so discourteous."

"Rotting is not the fate Cersei has in mind for me."

"Well no, if truth be told. You're to be beheaded on the morrow, out on the old tourney grounds."

Tyrion laughed again. "Will there be food? You'll have to help me with my last words, my wits have been running about like a rat in a root cellar."

"You won't need last words. I'm rescuing you." Jaime's voice was strangely solemn.

"Who said I required rescue?"

"You know, I'd almost forgotten what an annoying little

man you are. Now that you've reminded me, I do believe I'll let Cersei cut your head off after all."

"Oh no you won't." He waddled out of the cell. "Is it day or night up above? I've lost all sense of time."

"Three hours past midnight. The city sleeps." Jaime slid the torch back into its sconce, on the wall between the cells.

The corridor was so poorly lit that Tyrion almost stumbled on the turnkey, sprawled across the cold stone floor. He prodded him with a toe. "Is he dead?"

"Asleep. The other three as well. The eunuch dosed their wine with sweetsleep, but not enough to kill them. Or so he swears. He is waiting back at the stair, dressed up in a septon's robe. You're going down into the sewers, and from there to the river. A galley is waiting in the bay. Varys has agents in the Free Cities who will see that you do not lack for funds . . . but try not to be conspicuous. Cersei will send men after you, I have no doubt. You might do well to take another name."

"Another name? Oh, certainly. And when the Faceless Men come to kill me, I'll say, 'No, you have the wrong man, I'm a *different* dwarf with a hideous facial scar.'" Both Lannisters laughed at the absurdity of it all. Then Jaime went to one knee and kissed him quickly once on each cheek, his lips brushing against the puckered ribbon of scar tissue.

"Thank you, Brother," Tyrion said. "For my life."

"It was . . . a debt I owed you." Jaime's voice was strange.

"A debt?" He cocked his head. "I do not understand."

"Good. Some doors are best left closed."

"Oh, dear," said Tyrion. "Is there something grim and ugly behind it? Could it be that someone said something *cruel* about me once? I'll try not to weep. Tell me."

"Tyrion . . ."

Jaime is afraid. "Tell me," Tyrion said again.

His brother looked away. "Tysha," he said softly.

"Tysha?" His stomach tightened. "What of her?"

"She was no whore. I never bought her for you. That was a lie that Father commanded me to tell. Tysha was . . . she was what she seemed to be. A crofter's daughter, chance met on the road."

Tyrion could hear the faint sound of his own breath whistling hollowly through the scar of his nose. Jaime could not meet his eyes. *Tysha.* He tried to remember what she had looked like. *A girl, she was only a girl, no older than Sansa.* "My wife," he croaked. "She wed me."

"For your gold, Father said. She was lowborn, you were a Lannister of Casterly Rock. All she wanted was the gold, which made her no different from a whore, so . . . so it would not be a lie, not truly, and . . . he said that you required a sharp lesson. That you would learn from it, and thank me later . . ."

"*Thank* you?" Tyrion's voice was choked. "He gave her to his guards. A barracks full of guards. He made me . . . watch." *Aye, and more than watch. I took her too . . . my wife . . .*

"I never knew he would do that. You must believe me."

"Oh, *must* I?" Tyrion snarled. "Why should I believe you about anything, ever? She was my *wife!*"

"Tyrion—"

He hit him. It was a slap, backhanded, but he put all his strength into it, all his fear, all his rage, all his pain. Jaime was squatting, unbalanced. The blow sent him tumbling backward to the floor. "I . . . I suppose I earned that."

"Oh, you've earned more than that, Jaime. You and my sweet sister and our loving father, yes, I can't begin to tell you what you've earned. But you'll have it, that I swear to you. A Lannister always pays his debts." Tyrion waddled away, almost stumbling over the turnkey again in his haste. Before he had gone a dozen yards, he bumped up against an iron gate that closed the passage. *Oh, gods.* It was all he could do not to scream.

Jaime came up behind him. "I have the gaoler's keys."

"Then use them." Tyrion stepped aside.

Jaime unlocked the gate, pushed it open, and stepped through. He looked back over his shoulder. "Are you coming?"

"Not with you." Tyrion stepped through. "Give me the keys and go. I will find Varys on my own." He cocked his head and stared up at his brother with his mismatched eyes. "Jaime, can you fight left-handed?"

"Rather less well than you," Jaime said bitterly.

"Good. Then we will be well matched if we should ever meet again. The cripple and the dwarf."

Jaime handed him the ring of keys. "I gave you the truth. You owe me the same. Did you do it? Did you kill him?"

The question was another knife, twisting in his guts. "Are you sure you want to know?" asked Tyrion. "Joffrey would have been a worse king than Aerys ever was. He stole his father's dagger and gave it to a footpad to slit the throat of Brandon Stark, did you know that?"

"I . . . I thought he might have."

"Well, a son takes after his father. Joff would have killed me as well, once he came into his power. For the crime of being short and ugly, of which I am so conspicuously guilty."

"You have not answered my question."

"You poor stupid blind crippled fool. Must I spell every little thing out for you? Very well. Cersei is a lying whore, she's been fucking Lancel and Osmund Kettleblack and probably Moon Boy for all I know. And I am the monster they all say I am. Yes, I killed your vile son." He made himself grin. It must have been a hideous sight to see, there in the torchlit gloom.

Jaime turned without a word and walked away.

Tyrion watched him go, striding on his long strong legs, and part of him wanted to call out, to tell him that it wasn't true, to beg for his forgiveness. But then he thought of Tysha, and he held his silence. He listened to the receding footsteps until he could hear them no longer, then waddled off to look for Varys.

The eunuch was lurking in the dark of a twisting turnpike stair, garbed in a moth-eaten brown robe with a hood that hid the paleness of his face. "You were so long, I feared that something had gone amiss," he said when he saw Tyrion.

"Oh, no," Tyrion assured him, in poisonous tones. "What could *possibly* have gone amiss?" He twisted his head back to stare up. "I sent for you during my trial."

"I could not come. The queen had me watched, night and day. I dared not help you."

"You're helping me now."

"Am I? Ah." Varys giggled. It seemed strangely out of

place in this place of cold stone and echoing darkness. "Your brother can be most persuasive."

"Varys, you are as cold and slimy as a slug, has anyone ever told you? You did your best to kill me. Perhaps I ought to return the favor."

The eunuch sighed. "The faithful dog is kicked, and no matter how the spider weaves, he is never loved. But if you slay me here, I fear for you, my lord. You may never find your way back to daylight." His eyes glittered in the shifting torchlight, dark and wet. "These tunnels are full of traps for the unwary."

Tyrion snorted. "Unwary? I'm the wariest man who ever lived, you helped see to that." He rubbed at his nose. "So tell me, wizard, where is my innocent maiden wife?"

"I have found no trace of Lady Sansa in King's Landing, sad to say. Nor of Ser Dontos Hollard, who by rights should have turned up somewhere drunk by now. They were seen together on the serpentine steps the night she vanished. After that, nothing. There was much confusion that night. My little birds are silent." Varys gave a gentle tug at the dwarf's sleeve and pulled him into the stair. "My lord, we must away. Your path is down."

That's no lie, at least. Tyrion waddled along in the eunuch's wake, his heels scraping against the rough stone as they descended. It was very cold within the stairwell, a damp bone-chilling cold that set him to shivering at once. "What part of the dungeons are these?" he asked.

"Maegor the Cruel decreed four levels of dungeons for his castle," Varys replied. "On the upper level, there are large cells where common criminals may be confined together. They have narrow windows set high in the walls. The second level has the smaller cells where highborn captives are held. They have no windows, but torches in the halls cast light through the bars. On the third level the cells are smaller and the doors are wood. The black cells, men call them. That was where you were kept, and Eddard Stark before you. But there is a level lower still. Once a man is taken down to the fourth level, he never sees the sun again, nor hears a human voice, nor breathes a breath free of agonizing pain. Maegor had the cells on the fourth level built for torment." They had reached the bottom of the steps. An unlighted door opened before them. "This is the fourth level. Give me your hand, my lord. It is safer to walk in darkness here. There are things you would not wish to see."

Tyrion hung back a moment. Varys had already betrayed him once. Who knew what game the eunuch was playing? And what better place to murder a man than down in the darkness, in a place that no one knew existed? His body might never be found.

On the other hand, what choice did he have? To go back up the steps and walk out the main gate? No, that would not serve.

Jaime would not be afraid, he thought, before he remembered what Jaime had done to him. He took the eunuch by the hand and let himself be led through the black, following the soft scrape of leather on stone. Varys walked quickly, from time to time whispering, "Careful, there are three steps ahead," or, "The tunnel slopes downward here, my lord." *I arrived here a King's Hand, riding through the gates at the head of my own sworn men*, Tyrion reflected, *and I leave like a rat scuttling through the dark, holding hands with a spider.*

A light appeared ahead of them, too dim to be daylight, and grew as they hurried toward it. After a while he could see it was an arched doorway, closed off by another iron gate. Varys produced a key. They stepped through into a small round chamber. Five other doors opened off the room, each barred in iron. There was an opening in the ceiling as well, and a series of rungs set in the wall below, leading upward. An ornate brazier stood to one side, fashioned in the shape of a dragon's head. The coals in the beast's yawning mouth had burnt down to embers, but they still glowed with a sullen orange light. Dim as it was, the light was welcome after the blackness of the tunnel.

The juncture was otherwise empty, but on the floor was a mosaic of a three-headed dragon wrought in red and black tiles. Something niggled at Tyrion for a moment. Then it came to him. *This is the place Shae told me of, when Varys first led her to my bed.* "We are below the Tower of the Hand."

"Yes." Frozen hinges screamed in protest as Varys pulled open a long-closed door. Flakes of rust drifted to the floor. "This will take us out to the river."

Tyrion walked slowly to the ladder, ran his hand across the lowest rung. "This will take me up to my bedchamber."

"Your lord father's bedchamber now."

He looked up the shaft. "How far must I climb?"

"My lord, you are too weak for such follies, and there is besides no time. We must go."

"I have business above. How far?"

"Two hundred and thirty rungs, but whatever you intend—"

"Two hundred and thirty rungs, and then?"

"The tunnel to the left, but hear me—"

"How far along to the bedchamber?" Tyrion lifted a foot to the lowest rung of the ladder.

"No more than sixty feet. Keep one hand on the wall as you go. You will feel the doors. The bedchamber is the third." He sighed. "This is folly, my lord. Your brother has given you your life back. Would you cast it away, and mine with it?"

"Varys, the only thing I value less than my life just now is yours. Wait for me here." He turned his back on the eunuch and began to climb, counting silently as he went.

Rung by rung, he ascended into darkness. At first he could see the dim outline of each rung as he grasped it, and the rough grey texture of the stone behind, but as he climbed the black grew thicker. *Thirteen fourteen fifteen sixteen.* By thirty, his arms trembled with the strain of pulling. He paused a moment to catch his breath and glanced down. A circle of faint light shone far below, half obscured by his own feet. Tyrion resumed his ascent. *Thirty-nine forty forty-one.* By fifty, his legs burned. The ladder was endless, numbing. *Sixty-eight sixty-nine seventy.* By eighty, his back was a dull agony. Yet still he climbed. He could not have said why. *One thirteen one fourteen one fifteen.*

At two hundred and thirty, the shaft was black as pitch, but he could *feel* the warm air flowing from the tunnel to his left, like the breath of some great beast. He poked about awkwardly with a foot and edged off the ladder. The tunnel was even more cramped than the shaft. Any man of normal size would have had to crawl on hands and knees, but Tyrion was short enough to walk upright. *At last, a place made for dwarfs.* His boots scuffed softly against the stone. He walked slowly, counting steps, feeling for gaps in the walls. Soon he began to hear voices, muffled and indistinct at first, then clearer. He listened more closely. Two of his father's guardsmen were joking about the Imp's whore, saying how sweet it would be to fuck her, and how bad she must want a real cock in place of the dwarf's stunted little thing. "Most like it's got a crook in it," said Lum. That led him into a discussion of how Tyrion would die on the morrow. "He'll weep like a woman and beg for mercy, you'll see," Lum insisted. Lester figured he'd face the axe brave as a lion, being a Lannister, and he was willing to bet his new boots on it. "Ah, shit in your boots," said Lum, "you know they'd never fit these feet o'mine. Tell you what, if I win you can scour my bloody mail for a fortnight."

For the space of a few feet, Tyrion could hear every word of their haggling, but when he moved on, the voices faded quickly. *Small wonder Varys did not want me to climb the bloody ladder*, Tyrion thought, smiling in the dark. *Little birds indeed.*

He came to the third door and fumbled about for a long time before his fingers brushed a small iron hook set between two stones. When he pulled down on it, there was a soft rumble that sounded loud as an avalanche in the stillness, and a square of dull orange light opened a foot to his left.

The hearth! He almost laughed. The fireplace was full of hot ash, and a black log with a hot orange heart burning within. He edged past gingerly, taking quick steps so as not to burn his boots, the warm cinders crunching softly under his heels. When he found himself in what had once been his bedchamber, he stood a long moment, breathing the silence. Had his father heard? Would he reach for his sword, raise the hue and cry?

"M'lord?" a woman's voice called.

That might have hurt me once, when I still felt pain. The first step was the hardest. When he reached the bed Tyrion pulled the draperies aside and there she was, turning toward him with a sleepy smile on her lips. It died when she saw him. She pulled the blankets up to her chin, as if that would protect her.

"Were you expecting someone taller, sweetling?"

Big wet tears filled her eyes. "I never meant those things I said, the queen made me. *Please*. Your father frightens me so." She sat up, letting the blanket slide down to her lap. Beneath it she was naked, but for the chain about her throat. A chain of linked golden hands, each holding the next.

"My lady Shae," Tyrion said softly. "All the time I sat in the black cell waiting to die, I kept remembering how beautiful you were. In silk or roughspun or nothing at all . . ."

"M'lord will be back soon. You should go, or . . . did you come to take me away?"

"Did you ever like it?" He cupped her cheek, remembering all the times he had done this before. All the times he'd slid his hands around her waist, squeezed her small firm breasts, stroked her short dark hair, touched her lips, her cheeks, her ears. All the times he had opened her with a finger to probe her secret sweetness and make her moan. "Did you ever like my touch?"

"More than anything," she said, "my giant of Lannister."

That was the worst thing you could have said, sweetling.

Tyrion slid a hand under his father's chain, and twisted. The links tightened, digging into her neck. "For hands of gold are always cold, but a woman's hands are warm," he said. He gave cold hands another twist as the warm ones beat away his tears.

Afterward he found Lord Tywin's dagger on the bedside table and shoved it through his belt. A lion-headed mace, a poleaxe, and a crossbow had been hung on the walls. The poleaxe would be clumsy to wield inside a castle, and the mace was too high to reach, but a large wood-and-iron chest had been placed against the wall directly under the crossbow. He climbed up, pulled down the bow and a leather quiver packed with quarrels, jammed a foot into the stirrup, and pushed down until the bowstring cocked. Then he slipped a bolt into the notch.

Jaime had lectured him more than once on the drawbacks of crossbows. If Lum and Lester emerged from wherever they were talking, he'd never have time to reload, but at least he'd take one down to hell with him. Lum, if he had a choice. *You'll have to clean your own mail, Lum. You lose.*

Waddling to the door, he listened a moment, then eased it open slowly. A lamp burned in a stone niche, casting wan yellow light over the empty hallway. Only the flame was moving. Tyrion slid out, holding the crossbow down against his leg.

He found his father where he knew he'd find him, seated in the dimness of the privy tower, bedrobe hiked up around his hips. At the sound of steps, Lord Tywin raised his eyes.

Tyrion gave him a mocking half bow. "My lord."

"Tyrion." If he was afraid, Tywin Lannister gave no hint of it. "Who released you from your cell?"

"I'd love to tell you, but I swore a holy oath."

"The eunuch," his father decided. "I'll have his head for this. Is that my crossbow? Put it down."

"Will you punish me if I refuse, Father?"

"This escape is folly. You are not to be killed, if that is what you fear. It's still my intent to send you to the Wall, but I could not do it without Lord Tyrell's consent. Put down the crossbow and we will go back to my chambers and talk of it."

"We can talk here just as well. Perhaps I don't choose to go to the Wall, Father. It's bloody cold up there, and I believe I've had enough coldness from you. So just tell me something, and I'll be on my way. One simple question, you owe me that much."

"I owe you nothing."

"You've given me less than that, all my life, but you'll give me this. What did you do with Tysha?"

"Tysha?"

He does not even remember her name. "The girl I married."

"Oh, yes. Your first whore."

Tyrion took aim at his father's chest. "The next time you say that word, I'll kill you."

"You do not have the courage."

"Shall we find out? It's a short word, and it seems to come so easily to your lips." Tyrion gestured impatiently with the bow. "Tysha. What did you do with her, after my little lesson?"

"I don't recall."

"Try harder. Did you have her killed?"

His father pursed his lips. "There was no reason for that, she'd learned her place . . . and had been well paid for her day's work, I seem to recall. I suppose the steward sent her on her way. I never thought to inquire."

"On her way *where?*"

"Wherever whores go."

Tyrion's finger clenched. The crossbow *whanged* just as Lord Tywin started to rise. The bolt slammed into him above the groin and he sat back down with a grunt. The quarrel had sunk deep, right to the fletching. Blood seeped out around the shaft, dripping down into his pubic hair and over his bare thighs. "You shot me," he said incredulously, his eyes glassy with shock.

"You always were quick to grasp a situation, my lord," Tyrion said. "That must be why you're the Hand of the King."

"You . . . you are no . . . no son of mine."

"Now that's where you're wrong, Father. Why, I believe I'm you writ small. Do me a kindness now, and die quickly. I have a ship to catch."

For once, his father did what Tyrion asked him. The proof was the sudden stench, as his bowels loosened in the moment of death. *Well, he was in the right place for it,* Tyrion thought. But the stink that filled the privy gave ample evidence that the oft-repeated jape about his father was just another lie.

Lord Tywin Lannister did not, in the end, shit gold.

SAMWELL

The king was angry. Sam saw that at once.

As the black brothers entered one by one and knelt before him, Stannis shoved away his breakfast of hardbread, salt beef, and boiled eggs, and eyed them coldly. Beside him, the red woman Melisandre looked as if she found the scene amusing.

I have no place here, Sam thought anxiously, when her red eyes fell upon him. *Someone had to help Maester Aemon up the steps. Don't look at me, I'm just the maester's steward.* The others were contenders for the Old Bear's command, all but Bowen Marsh, who had withdrawn from the contest but remained castellan and Lord Steward. Sam did not understand why Melisandre should seem so interested in *him.*

King Stannis kept the black brothers on their knees for an extraordinarily long time. "Rise," he said at last. Sam gave Maester Aemon his shoulder to help him back up.

The sound of Lord Janos Slynt clearing his throat broke the strained silence. "Your Grace, let me say how pleased we are to be summoned here. When I saw your banners from the Wall, I knew the realm was saved. 'There comes a man who ne'er forgets his duty,' I said to good Ser Alliser. 'A *strong* man, and a true king.' May I congratulate you on your victory over the savages? The singers will make much of it, I know—"

"The singers may do as they like," Stannis snapped. "Spare me your fawning, Janos, it will not serve you." He rose to his feet and frowned at them all. "Lady Melisandre tells me that you have not yet chosen a Lord Commander. I am displeased. How much longer must this folly last?"

"Sire," said Bowen Marsh in a defensive tone, "no one has achieved two-thirds of the vote yet. It has only been ten days."

"Nine days too long. I have captives to dispose of, a realm to order, a war to fight. Choices must be made, decisions that involve the Wall and the Night's Watch. By rights your Lord Commander should have a voice in those decisions."

"He should, yes," said Janos Slynt. "But it must be said. We brothers are only simple soldiers. Soldiers, yes! And Your Grace will know that soldiers are most comfortable taking orders. They would benefit from your royal guidance, it seems to me. For the good of the realm. To help them choose wisely."

The suggestion outraged some of the others. "Do you want the king to wipe our arses for us too?" said Cotter Pyke angrily. "The choice of a Lord Commander belongs to the Sworn Brothers, and to them alone," insisted Ser Denys Mallister. "If they choose wisely they won't be choosing me," moaned Dolorous Edd. Maester Aemon, calm as always, said, "Your Grace, the Night's Watch has been choosing its own leader since Brandon the Builder raised the Wall. Through Jeor Mormont we have had nine hundred and ninety-seven Lords Commander in unbroken succession, each chosen by the men he would lead, a tradition many thousands of years old."

Stannis ground his teeth. "It is not my wish to tamper with your rights and traditions. As to *royal guidance*, Janos, if you mean that I ought to tell your brothers to choose you, have the courage to say so."

That took Lord Janos aback. He smiled uncertainly and began to sweat, but Bowen Marsh beside him said, "Who better to command the black cloaks than a man who once commanded the gold, sire?"

"Any of you, I would think. Even the cook." The look the king gave Slynt was cold. "Janos was hardly the first gold cloak ever to take a bribe, I grant you, but he may have been the first commander to fatten his purse by selling places and promotions. By the end he must have had half the officers in the City Watch paying him part of their wages. Isn't that so, Janos?"

Slynt's neck was purpling. "Lies, all lies! A strong man makes enemies, Your Grace knows that, they whisper lies behind your back. Naught was ever proven, not a man came forward . . ."

"Two men who were prepared to come forward died suddenly on their rounds." Stannis narrowed his eyes. "Do not trifle with me, my lord. I saw the proof Jon Arryn laid before the small council. If I had been king you would have lost more than your office, I promise you, but Robert shrugged away your little lapses. 'They all steal,' I recall him saying. 'Better a thief we know than one we don't, the next man might be worse.' Lord Petyr's words in my brother's mouth, I'll warrant. Littlefinger had a nose for gold, and I'm certain he arranged matters so the crown profited as much from your corruption as you did yourself."

Lord Slynt's jowls were quivering, but before he could frame a further protest Maester Aemon said, "Your Grace, by law a man's past crimes and transgressions are wiped clean when he says his words and becomes a Sworn Brother of the Night's Watch."

"I am aware of that. If it happens that Lord Janos here is the best the Night's Watch can offer, I shall grit my teeth and choke him down. It is naught to me which man of you is chosen, so long as you *make a choice*. We have a war to fight."

"Your Grace," said Ser Denys Mallister, in tones of wary courtesy. "If you are speaking of the wildlings . . ."

"I am not. And you know that, ser."

"And you must know that whilst we are thankful for the aid you rendered us against Mance Rayder, we can offer you no help in your contest for the throne. The Night's

Watch takes no part in the wars of the Seven Kingdoms. For eight thousand years—"

"I know your history, Ser Denys," the king said brusquely. "I give you my word, I shall not ask you to lift your swords against any of the rebels and usurpers who plague me. I do expect that you will continue to defend the Wall as you always have."

"We'll defend the Wall to the last man," said Cotter Pyke.

"Probably me," said Dolorous Edd, in a resigned tone.

Stannis crossed his arms. "I shall require a few other things from you as well. Things that you may not be so quick to give. I want your castles. And I want the Gift."

Those blunt words burst among the black brothers like a pot of wildfire tossed onto a brazier. Marsh, Mallister, and Pyke all tried to speak at once. King Stannis let them talk. When they were done, he said, "I have three times the men you do. I can take the lands if I wish, but I would prefer to do this legally, with your consent."

"The Gift was given to the Night's Watch in perpetuity, Your Grace," Bowen Marsh insisted.

"Which means it cannot be lawfully seized, attained, or taken from you. But what was given once can be given again."

"What will you do with the Gift?" demanded Cotter Pyke.

"Make better use of it than you have. As to the castles, Eastwatch, Castle Black, and the Shadow Tower shall remain yours. Garrison them as you always have, but I must take the others for *my* garrisons if we are to hold the Wall."

"You do not have the men," objected Bowen Marsh.

"Some of the abandoned castles are scarce more than ruins," said Othell Yarwyck, the First Builder.

"Ruins can be rebuilt."

"Rebuilt?" Yarwyck said. "But who will do the work?"

"That is my concern. I shall require a list from you, detailing the present state of every castle and what might be required to restore it. I mean to have them all garrisoned again within the year, and nightfires burning before their gates."

"Nightfires?" Bowen Marsh gave Melisandre an uncertain look. "We're to light nightfires now?"

"You are." The woman rose in a swirl of scarlet silk, her long copper-bright hair tumbling about her shoulders. "Swords alone cannot hold this darkness back. Only the light of the Lord can do that. Make no mistake, good sers and valiant brothers, the war we've come to fight is no petty squabble over lands and honors. Ours is a war for life itself, and should we fail the world dies with us."

The officers did not know how to take that, Sam could see. Bowen Marsh and Othell Yarwyck exchanged a doubtful look, Janos Slynt was fuming, and Three-Finger Hobb looked as though he would sooner be back chopping carrots. But all of them seemed surprised to hear Maester Aemon murmur, "It is the war for the dawn you speak of, my lady. But where is the prince that was promised?"

"He stands before you," Melisandre declared, "though you do not have the eyes to see. Stannis Baratheon is Azor Ahai come again, the warrior of fire. In him the prophecies are fulfilled. The red comet blazed across the sky to herald his coming, and he bears Lightbringer, the red sword of heroes."

Her words seemed to make the king desperately uncomfortable, Sam saw. Stannis ground his teeth, and said, "You called and I came, my lords. Now you must live with me, or die with me. Best get used to that." He made a brusque gesture. "That's all. Maester, stay a moment. And you, Tarly. The rest of you may go."

Me? Sam thought, stricken, as his brothers were bowing and making their way out. *What does he want with me?*

"You are the one that killed the creature in the snow," King Stannis said, when only the four of them remained.

"Sam the Slayer." Melisandre smiled.

Sam felt his face turning red. "No, my lady. Your Grace. I mean, I am, yes. I'm Samwell Tarly, yes."

"Your father is an able soldier," King Stannis said. "He defeated my brother once, at Ashford. Mace Tyrell has been pleased to claim the honors for that victory, but Lord Randyll had decided matters before Tyrell ever found the battlefield. He slew Lord Cafferen with that great Valyrian sword of his and sent his head to Aerys." The king rubbed his jaw with a finger. "You are not the sort of son I would expect such a man to have."

"I . . . I am not the sort of son he wanted, sire."

"If you had not taken the black, you would make a useful hostage," Stannis mused.

"He has taken the black, sire," Maester Aemon pointed out.

"I am well aware of that," the king said. "I am aware of more than you know, Aemon Targaryen."

The old man inclined his head. "I am only Aemon, sire. We give up our House names when we forge our maester's chains."

The king gave that a curt nod, as if to say he knew and did not care. "You slew this creature with an obsidian dagger, I am told," he said to Sam.

"Y-yes, Your Grace. Jon Snow gave it to me."

"Dragonglass." The red woman's laugh was music. "*Frozen fire*, in the tongue of old Valyria. Small wonder it is anathema to these cold children of the Other."

"On Dragonstone, where I had my seat, there is much of this obsidian to be seen in the old tunnels beneath the mountain," the king told Sam. "Chunks of it, boulders, ledges. The great part of it was black, as I recall, but there was some green as well, some red, even purple. I have sent word to Ser Rolland my castellan to begin mining it. I will not hold Dragonstone for very much longer, I fear, but perhaps the Lord of Light shall grant us enough *frozen fire* to arm ourselves against these creatures, before the castle falls."

Sam cleared his throat. "S-sire. The dagger . . . the dragonglass only shattered when I tried to stab a wight."

Melisandre smiled. "Necromancy animates these wights, yet they are still only dead flesh. Steel and fire will serve for them. The ones you call the Others are something more."

"Demons made of snow and ice and cold," said Stannis Baratheon. "The ancient enemy. The only enemy that matters." He considered Sam again. "I am told that you and this wildling girl passed beneath the Wall, through some magic gate."

"The B-black Gate," Sam stammered. "Below the Nightfort."

"The Nightfort is the largest and oldest of the castles on the Wall," the king said. "That is where I intend to make my seat, whilst I fight this war. You will show me this gate."

"I," said Sam, "I w-will, if . . ." *If it is still there. If it will open for a man not of the black. If . . .*

"You will," snapped Stannis. "I shall tell you when."

Maester Aemon smiled. "Your Grace," he said, "before we go, I wonder if you would do us the great honor of showing us this wondrous blade we have all heard so very much of."

"You want to see Lightbringer? A *blind* man?"

"Sam shall be my eyes."

The king frowned. "Everyone else has seen the thing, why not a blind man?" His swordbelt and scabbard hung from a peg near the hearth. He took the belt down and drew the longsword out. Steel scraped against wood and leather, and radiance filled the solar; shimmering, shifting, a dance of gold and orange and red light, all the bright colors of fire.

"Tell me, Samwell." Maester Aemon touched his arm.

"It *glows*," said Sam, in a hushed voice. "As if it were on fire. There are no flames, but the steel is yellow and red and orange, all flashing and glimmering, like sunshine on water, but prettier. I wish you could see it, Maester."

"I see it now, Sam. A sword full of sunlight. So lovely to behold." The old man bowed stiffly. "Your Grace. My lady. This was most kind of you."

When King Stannis sheathed the shining sword, the room seemed to grow very dark, despite the sunlight streaming through the window. "Very well, you've seen it. You may return to your duties now. And remember what I said. Your brothers will choose a Lord Commander tonight, or I shall make them wish they had."

Maester Aemon was lost in thought as Sam helped him down the narrow turnpike stair. But as they were crossing the yard, he said, "I felt no heat. Did you, Sam?"

"Heat? From the sword?" He thought back. "The air around it was shimmering, the way it does above a hot brazier."

"Yet you *felt* no heat, did you? And the scabbard that held this sword, it is wood and leather, yes? I heard the sound when His Grace drew out the blade. Was the leather scorched, Sam? Did the wood seem burnt or blackened?"

"No," Sam admitted. "Not that I could see."

Maester Aemon nodded. Back in his own chambers, he asked Sam to set a fire and help him to his chair beside the hearth. "It is hard to be so old," he sighed as he settled onto the cushion. "And harder still to be so blind. I miss the sun. And books. I miss books most of all." Aemon waved a hand. "I shall have no more need of you till the choosing."

"The choosing . . . Maester, isn't there something you could do? What the king said of Lord Janos . . ."

"I recall," Maester Aemon said, "but Sam, I am a maester, chained and sworn. My duty is to counsel the Lord Commander, whoever he might be. It would not be proper for me to be seen to favor one contender over another."

"I'm not a maester," said Sam. "Could *I* do something?"

Aemon turned his blind white eyes toward Sam's face, and smiled softly. "Why, I don't know, Samwell. Could you?"

I could, Sam thought. *I have to.* He had to do it right away, too. If he hesitated he was certain to lose his courage. *I am a man of the Night's Watch*, he reminded himself as he hurried across the yard. *I am. I can do this.* There had been a time when he had quaked and squeaked if Lord Mormont so much as looked at him, but that was the old Sam, before the Fist of the First Men and Craster's Keep, before the wights and Coldhands and the Other on his dead horse. He was braver now. *Gilly made me braver*, he'd told Jon. It was true. It had to be true.

Cotter Pyke was the scarier of the two commanders, so Sam went to him first, while his courage was still hot. He found him in the old Shieldhall, dicing with three of his Eastwatch men and a red-headed sergeant who had come from Dragonstone with Stannis.

When Sam begged leave to speak with him, though, Pyke barked an order, and the others took the dice and coins and left them.

No man would ever call Cotter Pyke handsome, though the body under his studded brigantine and roughspun breeches was lean and hard and wiry strong. His eyes were small and close-set, his nose broken, his widow's peak as sharply pointed as the head of a spear. The pox had ravaged his face badly, and the beard he'd grown to hide the scars was thin and scraggly.

"Sam the Slayer!" he said, by way of greeting. "Are you sure you stabbed an Other, and not some child's snow knight?"

This isn't starting well. "It was the dragonglass that killed it, my lord," Sam explained feebly.

"Aye, no doubt. Well, out with it, Slayer. Did the maester send you to me?"

"The maester?" Sam swallowed. "I . . . I just left him, my lord." That wasn't truly a lie, but if Pyke chose to read it wrong, it might make him more inclined to listen. Sam took a deep breath and launched into his plea.

Pyke cut him off before he'd said twenty words. "You want me to kneel down and kiss the hem of Mallister's pretty cloak, is that it? I might have known. You lordlings all flock like sheep. Well, tell Aemon that he's wasted your breath and my time. If anyone withdraws it should be Mallister. The man's too bloody *old* for the job, maybe you ought to go tell him that. We choose him, and we're like to be back here in a year, choosing someone else."

"He's old," Sam agreed, "but he's well ex-experienced."

"At sitting in his tower and fussing over maps, maybe. What does he plan to do, write letters to the wights? He's a knight, well and good, but he's not a *fighter*, and I don't give a kettle of piss who he unhorsed in some fool tourney fifty years ago. The Halfhand fought all his battles, even an old blind man should see that. And we need a fighter more than ever with this bloody king on top of us. Today it's ruins and empty fields, well and good, but what will *His Grace* want come the morrow? You think *Mallister* has the belly to stand up to Stannis Baratheon and that red bitch?" He laughed. "I don't."

"You won't support him, then?" said Sam, dismayed.

"Are you Sam the Slayer or Deaf Dick? No, I won't support him." Pyke jabbed a finger at his face. "Understand this, boy. I don't *want* the bloody job, and never did. I fight best with a deck beneath me, not a horse, and Castle Black is too far from the sea. But I'll be buggered with a red-hot sword before I turn the Night's Watch over to that preening eagle from the Shadow Tower. And you can run back to the old man and tell him I said so, if he asks." He stood. "Get out of my sight."

It took all the courage Sam had left in him to say,

"W-what if there was someone else? Could you s-support someone else?"

"Who? Bowen Marsh? The man counts spoons. Othell's a follower, does what he's told and does it well, but no more'n that. Slynt . . . well, his men like him, I'll grant you, and it would almost be worth it to stick him down the royal craw and see if Stannis gagged, but no. There's too much of King's Landing in that one. A toad grows wings and thinks he's a bloody dragon." Pyke laughed. "Who does that leave, Hobb? We could pick him, I suppose, only then who's going to boil your mutton, Slayer? You look like a man who likes his bloody mutton."

There was nothing more to say. Defeated, Sam could only stammer out his thanks and take his leave. *I will do better with Ser Denys*, he tried to tell himself as he walked through the castle. Ser Denys was a knight, highborn and well-spoken, and he had treated Sam most courteously when he'd found him and Gilly on the road. *Ser Denys will listen to me, he has to.*

The commander of the Shadow Tower had been born beneath the Booming Tower of Seagard, and looked every inch a Mallister. Sable trimmed his collar and accented the sleeves of his black velvet doublet. A silver eagle fastened its claws in the gathered folds of his cloak. His beard was white as snow, his hair was largely gone, and his face was deeply lined, it was true. Yet he still had grace in his movements and teeth in his mouth, and the years had dimmed neither his blue-grey eyes nor his courtesy.

"My lord of Tarly," he said, when his steward brought Sam to him in the Lance, where the Shadow Tower men were staying. "I am pleased to see that you've recovered from your ordeal. Might I offer you a cup of wine? Your lady mother is a Florent, I recall. One day I must tell you about the time I unhorsed both of your grandfathers in the same tourney. Not today, though, I know we have more pressing concerns. You come from Maester Aemon, to be sure. Does he have counsel to offer me?"

Sam took a sip of wine, and chose his words with care. "A maester chained and sworn . . . it would not be proper for him to be seen as having influenced the choice of Lord Commander . . ."

The old knight smiled. "Which is why he has not come

to me himself. Yes, I quite understand, Samwell. Aemon and I are both old men, and wise in such matters. Say what you came to say."

The wine was sweet, and Ser Denys listened to Sam's plea with grave courtesy, unlike Cotter Pyke. But when he was done, the old knight shook his head. "I agree that it would be a dark day in our history if a king were to name our Lord Commander. This king especially. He is not like to keep his crown for long. But truly, Samwell, it ought to be Pyke who withdraws. I have more support than he does, and I am better suited to the office."

"You are," Sam agreed, "but Cotter Pyke might serve. It's said he has oft proved himself in battle." He did not mean to offend Ser Denys by praising his rival, but how else could he convince him to withdraw?

"Many of my brothers have proved themselves in battle. It is not enough. Some matters cannot be settled with a battleaxe. Maester Aemon will understand that, though Cotter Pyke does not. The Lord Commander of the Night's Watch is a *lord*, first and foremost. He must be able to treat with other lords . . . and with kings as well. He must be a man worthy of respect." Ser Denys leaned forward. "We are the sons of great lords, you and I. We know the importance of birth, blood, and that early training that can ne'er be replaced. I was a squire at twelve, a knight at eighteen, a champion at two-and-twenty. I have been the commander at the Shadow Tower for thirty-three years. Blood, birth, and training have fitted me to deal with kings. Pyke . . . well, did you hear him this morning, asking if His Grace would wipe his bottom? Samwell, it is not my habit to speak unkindly of my brothers, but let us be frank . . . the ironborn are a race of pirates and thieves, and Cotter Pyke was raping and murdering when he was still half a boy. Maester Harmune reads and writes his letters, and has for years. No, loath as I am to disappoint Maester Aemon, I could not in honor stand aside for Pyke of Eastwatch."

This time Sam was ready. "Might you for someone else? If it was someone more suitable?"

Ser Denys considered a moment. "I have never desired the honor for its own sake. At the last choosing, I stepped aside gratefully when Lord Mormont's name was offered, just as I had for Lord Qorgyle at the choosing before that. So long as the Night's Watch remains in good hands, I am content. But Bowen Marsh is not equal to the task, no more than Othell Yarwyck. And this so-called Lord of Harrenhal is a butcher's whelp unjumped by the Lannisters. Small wonder he is venal and corrupt."

"There's another man," Sam blurted out. "Lord Commander Mormont trusted him. So did Donal Noye and Qhorin Halfhand. Though he's not as highly born as you, he comes from old blood. He was castle-born and castle-raised, and he learned sword and lance from a knight and letters from a maester of the Citadel. His father was a lord, and his brother a king."

Ser Denys stroked his long white beard. "Mayhaps," he said, after a long moment. "He is very young, but . . . mayhaps. He might serve, I grant you, though I would be more suitable. I have no doubt of that. I would be the wiser choice."

Jon said there could be honor in a lie, if it were told for the right reason. Sam said, "If we do not choose a Lord Commander tonight, King Stannis means to name Cotter Pyke. He said as much to Maester Aemon this morning, after all of you had left."

"I see." Ser Denys rose. "I must think on this. Thank you, Samwell. And give my thanks to Maester Aemon as well."

Sam was trembling by the time he left the Lance. *What have I done?* he thought. *What have I said?* If they caught him in his lie, they would . . . *what? Send me to the Wall? Rip my entrails out? Turn me into a wight?* Suddenly it all seemed absurd. How could he be so frightened of Cotter Pyke and Ser Denys Mallister, when he had seen a raven eating Small Paul's face?

Pyke was not pleased by his return. "You again? Make it quick, you are starting to annoy me."

"I only need a moment more," Sam promised. "You won't withdraw for Ser Denys, you said, but you might for someone else."

"Who is it this time, Slayer? You?"

"No. A fighter. Donal Noye gave him the Wall when the wildlings came, and he was the Old Bear's squire. The only thing is, he's bastard-born."

Cotter Pyke laughed. "Bloody hell. That would shove a

1086   GEORGE R. R. MARTIN

spear up Mallister's arse, wouldn't it? Might be worth it just for that. How bad could the boy be?" He snorted. "I'd be better, though. I'm what's needed, any fool can see that."

"Any fool," Sam agreed, "even me. But . . . well, I shouldn't be telling you, but . . . King Stannis means to force Ser Denys on us, if we do not choose a man tonight. I heard him tell Maester Aemon that, after the rest of you were sent away."

JON

Iron Emmett was a long, lanky young ranger whose endurance, strength, and swordsmanship were the pride of Eastwatch. Jon always came away from their sessions stiff and sore, and woke the next day covered with bruises, which was just the way he wanted it. He would never get any better going up against the likes of Satin and Horse, or even Grenn.

Most days he gave as good as he got, Jon liked to think, but not today. He had hardly slept last night, and after an hour of restless tossing he had given up even the attempt, dressed, and walked the top of the Wall till the sun came up, wrestling with Stannis Baratheon's offer. The lack of sleep was catching up with him now, and Emmett was hammering him mercilessly across the yard, driving him back on his heels with one long looping cut after another, and slamming him with his shield from time to time for good measure. Jon's arm had gone numb from the shock of impact, and the edgeless practice sword seemed to be growing heavier with every passing moment.

He was almost ready to lower his blade and call a halt

when Emmett feinted low and came in over his shield with a savage forehand slash that caught Jon on the temple. He staggered, his helm and head both ringing from the force of the blow. For half a heartbeat the world beyond his eyeslit was a blur.

And then the years were gone, and he was back at Winterfell once more, wearing a quilted leather coat in place of mail and plate. His sword was made of wood, and it was Robb who stood facing him, not Iron Emmett.

Every morning they had trained together, since they were big enough to walk; Snow and Stark, spinning and slashing about the wards of Winterfell, shouting and laughing, sometimes crying when there was no one else to see. They were not little boys when they fought, but knights and mighty heroes. "I'm Prince Aemon the Dragonknight," Jon would call out, and Robb would shout back, "Well, I'm Florian the Fool." Or Robb would say, "I'm the Young Dragon," and Jon would reply, "I'm Ser Ryam Redwyne."

That morning he called it first. "I'm Lord of Winterfell!" he cried, as he had a hundred times before. Only this time, *this* time, Robb had answered, "You can't be Lord of Winterfell, you're bastard-born. My lady mother says you can't ever be the Lord of Winterfell."

I thought I had forgotten that. Jon could taste blood in his mouth, from the blow he'd taken.

In the end Halder and Horse had to pull him away from Iron Emmett, one man on either arm. The ranger sat on the ground dazed, his shield half in splinters, the visor of his helm knocked askew, and his sword six yards away. "Jon, enough," Halder was shouting, "he's down, you disarmed him. *Enough!*"

No. Not enough. Never enough. Jon let his sword drop. "I'm sorry," he muttered. "Emmett, are you hurt?"

Iron Emmett pulled his battered helm off. "Was there some part of *yield* you could not comprehend, Lord Snow?" It was said amiably, though. Emmett was an amiable man, and he loved the song of swords. "Warrior defend me," he groaned, "now I know how Qhorin Halfhand must have felt."

That was too much. Jon wrenched free of his friends and retreated to the armory, alone. His ears were still ringing from the blow Emmett had dealt him. He sat on the bench and buried his head in his hands. *Why am I so angry?* he asked himself, but it was a stupid question. *Lord of Winterfell. I could be the Lord of Winterfell. My father's heir.*

It was not Lord Eddard's face he saw floating before him, though; it was Lady Catelyn's. With her deep blue eyes and hard cold mouth, she looked a bit like Stannis. *Iron,* he thought, *but brittle.* She was looking at him the way she used to look at him at Winterfell, whenever he had bested Robb at swords or sums or most anything. *Who are you?* that look had always seemed to say. *This is not your place. Why are you here?*

His friends were still out in the practice yard, but Jon was in no fit state to face them. He left the armory by the back, descending a steep flight of stone steps to the wormways, the tunnels that linked the castle's keeps and towers below the earth. It was short walk to the bathhouse, where he took a cold plunge to wash the sweat off and soaked in a hot stone tub. The warmth took some of the ache from his muscles and made him think of Winterfell's muddy pools, steaming and bubbling in the godswood. *Winterfell,* he thought. *Theon left it burned and broken, but I could restore it.* Surely his father would have wanted that, and Robb as well. They would never have wanted the castle left in ruins.

You can't be the Lord of Winterfell, you're bastard-born, he heard Robb say again. And the stone kings were growling at him with granite tongues. *You do not belong here. This is not your place.* When Jon closed his eyes he saw the heart tree, with its pale limbs, red leaves, and solemn face. The weirwood was the heart of Winterfell, Lord Eddard always said . . . but to save the castle Jon would have to tear that heart up by its ancient roots, and feed it to the red woman's hungry fire god. *I have no right,* he thought. *Winterfell belongs to the old gods.*

The sound of voices echoing off the vaulted ceiling brought him back to Castle Black. "I don't know," a man was saying, in a voice thick with doubts. "Maybe if I knew the man better . . . Lord Stannis didn't have much good to say of him, I'll tell you that."

"When has Stannis Baratheon ever had much good to

say of anyone?" Ser Alliser's flinty voice was unmistakable. "If we let Stannis choose our Lord Commander, we become his bannermen in all but name. Tywin Lannister is not like to forget that, and you know it will be Lord Tywin who wins in the end. He's already beaten Stannis once, on the Blackwater."

"Lord Tywin favors Slynt," said Bowen Marsh, in a fretful, anxious voice. "I can show you his letter, Othell. 'Our faithful friend and servant,' he called him."

Jon Snow sat up suddenly, and the three men froze at the sound of the slosh. "My lords," he said with cold courtesy.

"What are you doing here, bastard?" Thorne asked.

"Bathing. But don't let me spoil your plotting." Jon climbed from the water, dried, dressed, and left them to conspire.

Outside, he found he had no idea where he was going. He walked past the shell of the Lord Commander's Tower, where once he'd saved the Old Bear from a dead man; past the spot where Ygritte had died with that sad smile on her face; past the King's Tower where he and Satin and Deaf Dick Follard had waited for the Magnar and his Thenns; past the heaped and charred remains of the great wooden stair. The inner gate was open, so Jon went down the tunnel, through the Wall. He could feel the cold around him, the weight of all the ice above his head. He walked past the place where Donal Noye and Mag the Mighty had fought and died together, through the new outer gate, and back into the pale cold sunlight.

Only then did he permit himself to stop, to take a breath, to think. Othell Yarwyck was not a man of strong convictions, except when it came to wood and stone and mortar. The Old Bear had known that. *Thorne and Marsh will sway him, Yarwyck will support Lord Janos, and Lord Janos will be chosen Lord Commander. And what does that leave me, if not Winterfell?*

A wind swirled against the Wall, tugging at his cloak. He could feel the cold coming off the ice the way heat comes off a fire. Jon pulled up his hood and began to walk again. The afternoon was growing old, and the sun was low in the west. A hundred yards away was the camp where King Stannis had confined his wildling captives within a ring of ditches, sharpened stakes, and high wooden fences.

To his left were three great firepits, where the victors had burned the bodies of all the free folk to die beneath the Wall, huge pelted giants and little Hornfoot men alike. The killing ground was still a desolation of scorched weeds and hardened pitch, but Mance's people had left traces of themselves everywhere; a torn hide that might have been part of a tent, a giant's maul, the wheel of a chariot, a broken spear, a pile of mammoth dung. On the edge of the haunted forest, where the tents had been, Jon found an oakwood stump and sat.

Ygritte wanted me to be a wildling. Stannis wants me to be the Lord of Winterfell. But what do I want? The sun crept down the sky to dip behind the Wall where it curved through the western hills. Jon watched as that towering expanse of ice took on the reds and pinks of sunset. *Would I sooner be hanged for a turncloak by Lord Janos, or forswear my vows, marry Val, and become the Lord of Winterfell?* It seemed an easy choice when he thought of it in those terms . . . though if Ygritte had still been alive, it might have been even easier. Val was a stranger to him. She was not hard on the eyes, certainly, and she had been sister to Mance Rayder's queen, but still . . .

I would need to steal her if I wanted her love, but she might give me children. I might someday hold a son of my own blood in my arms. A son was something Jon Snow had never dared dream of, since he decided to live his life on the Wall. *I could name him Robb. Val would want to keep her sister's son, but we could foster him at Winterfell, and Gilly's boy as well. Sam would never need to tell his lie. We'd find a place for Gilly too, and Sam could come visit her once a year or so. Mance's son and Craster's would grow up brothers, as I once did with Robb.*

He wanted it, Jon knew then. He wanted it as much as he had ever wanted anything. *I have always wanted it,* he thought, guiltily. *May the gods forgive me.* It was a hunger inside him, sharp as a dragonglass blade. A hunger . . . he could feel it. It was food he needed, prey, a red deer that stank of fear or a great elk proud and defiant. He needed to kill and fill his belly with fresh meat and hot dark blood. His mouth began to water with the thought.

It was a long moment before he understood what was happening. When he did, he bolted to his feet. "*Ghost?*" He turned toward the wood, and there he came, padding silently out of the green dusk, the breath coming warm and white from his open jaws. *"Ghost!"* he shouted, and the direwolf broke into a run. He was leaner than he had been, but bigger as well, and the only sound he made was the soft crunch of dead leaves beneath his paws. When he reached Jon he leapt, and they wrestled amidst brown grass and long shadows as the stars came out above them. "Gods, wolf, where have you *been?*" Jon said when Ghost stopped worrying at his forearm. "I thought you'd died on me, like Robb and Ygritte and all the rest. I've had no sense of you, not since I climbed the Wall, not even in dreams." The direwolf had no answer, but he licked Jon's face with a tongue like a wet rasp, and his eyes caught the last light and shone like two great red suns.

Red eyes, Jon realized, *but not like Melisandre's.* He had a weirwood's eyes. *Red eyes, red mouth, white fur. Blood and bone, like a heart tree. He belongs to the old gods, this one.* And he alone of all the direwolves was white. Six pups they'd found in the late summer snows, him and Robb; five that were grey and black and brown, for the five Starks, and one white, as white as Snow.

He had his answer then.

Beneath the Wall, the queen's men were kindling their nightfire. He saw Melisandre emerge from the tunnel with the king beside her, to lead the prayers she believed would keep the dark away. "Come, Ghost," Jon told the wolf. "With me. You're hungry, I know. I could feel it." They ran together for the gate, circling wide around the nightfire, where reaching flames clawed at the black belly of the night.

The king's men were much in evidence in the yards of Castle Black. They stopped as Jon went by, and gaped at him. None of them had ever seen a direwolf before, he realized, and Ghost was twice as large as the common wolves that prowled their southron greenwoods. As he walked toward the armory, Jon chanced to look up and saw Val standing in her tower window. *I'm sorry*, he thought. *I'm not the man to steal you out of there.*

In the practice yard he came upon a dozen king's men with torches and long spears in their hands. Their sergeant looked at Ghost and scowled, and a couple of his men lowered their spears until the knight who led them said, "Move aside and let them pass." To Jon he said, "You're late for your supper."

"Then get out of my way, ser," Jon replied, and he did.

He could hear the noise even before he reached the bottom of the steps; raised voices, curses, someone pounding on a table. Jon stepped into the vault all but unnoticed. His brothers crowded the benches and the tables, but more were standing and shouting than were sitting, and no one was eating. There was no food. *What's happening here?* Lord Janos Slynt was bellowing about turncloaks and treason, Iron Emmett stood on a table with a naked sword in his fist, Three-Finger Hobb was cursing a ranger from the Shadow Tower . . . some Eastwatch man slammed his fist onto the table again and again, demanding quiet, but all that did was add to the din echoing off the vaulted ceiling.

Pyp was the first to see Jon. He grinned at the sight of Ghost, put two fingers in his mouth, and whistled as only a mummer's boy could whistle. The shrill sound cut through the clamor like a sword. As Jon walked toward the tables, more of the brothers took note, and fell quiet. A hush spread across the cellar, until the only sounds were Jon's heels clicking on the stone floor, and the soft crackle of the logs in the hearth.

Ser Alliser Thorne shattered the silence. "The turncloak graces us with his presence at last."

Lord Janos was red-faced and quivering. "The *beast*," he gasped. "Look! The beast that tore the life from Halfhand. A warg walks among us, brothers. A *WARG!* This . . . this *creature* is not fit to lead us! This *beastling* is not fit to live!"

Ghost bared his teeth, but Jon put a hand on his head. "My lord," he said, "will you tell me what's happened here?"

Maester Aemon answered, from the far end of the hall. "Your name has been put forth as Lord Commander, Jon."

That was so absurd Jon had to smile. "By who?" he said, looking for his friends. This had to be one of Pyp's japes, surely. But Pyp shrugged at him, and Grenn shook his head. It was Dolorous Edd Tollett who stood. "By me. Aye, it's a terrible cruel thing to do to a friend, but better you than me."

Lord Janos started sputtering again. "This, this is an outrage. We ought to hang this *boy*. Yes! Hang him, I say, hang him for a turncloak and a warg, along with his friend Mance Rayder. Lord *Commander*? I will not have it, I will not suffer it!"

Cotter Pyke stood up. "*You* won't suffer it? Might be you had those gold cloaks trained to lick your bloody arse, but you're wearing a black cloak now."

"Any brother may offer any name for our consideration, so long as the man has said his vows," Ser Denys Mallister said. "Tollett is well within his rights, my lord."

A dozen men started to talk at once, each trying to drown out the others, and before long half the hall was shouting once more. This time it was Ser Alliser Thorne who leapt up on the table, and raised his hands for quiet. "*Brothers!*" he cried, "this gains us naught. I say we vote. This *king* who has taken the King's Tower has posted men at all the doors to see that we do not eat nor leave till we have made a choice. So be it! We will choose, and choose again, all night if need be, until we have our lord . . . but before we cast our tokens, I believe our First Builder has something to say to us."

Othell Yarwyck stood up slowly, frowning. The big builder rubbed his long lantern jaw and said, "Well, I'm pulling my name out. If you wanted me, you had ten chances to choose me, and you didn't. Not enough of you, anyway. I was going to say that those who were casting a token for me ought to choose Lord Janos . . ."

Ser Alliser nodded. "Lord Slynt is the best possible—"

"I wasn't *done*, Alliser," Yarwyck complained. "Lord Slynt commanded the City Watch in King's Landing, we all know, and he was Lord of Harrenhal . . ."

"He's never *seen* Harrenhal," Cotter Pyke shouted out.

"Well, that's so," said Yarwyck. "Anyway, now that I'm standing here, I don't recall why I thought Slynt would be such a good choice. That would be sort of kicking King Stannis in the mouth, and I don't see how that serves us. Might be Snow would be better. He's been longer on the Wall, he's Ben Stark's nephew, and he served the Old Bear as squire." Yarwyck shrugged. "Pick who you want, just so it's not me." He sat down.

Janos Slynt had turned from red to purple, Jon saw, but

Ser Alliser Thorne had gone pale. The Eastwatch man was pounding his fist on the table again, but now he was shouting for the kettle. Some of his friends took up the cry. "*Kettle!*" they roared, as one. "*Kettle, kettle, KETTLE!*"

The kettle was in the corner by the hearth, a big black potbellied thing with two huge handles and a heavy lid. Maester Aemon said a word to Sam and Clydas and they went and grabbed the handles and dragged the kettle over to the table. A few of the brothers were already queueing up by the token barrels as Clydas took the lid off and almost dropped it on his foot. With a raucous scream and a clap of wings, a huge raven burst out of the kettle. It flapped upward, seeking the rafters perhaps, or a window to make its escape, but there were no rafters in the vault, nor windows either. The raven was trapped. Cawing loudly, it circled the hall, once, twice, three times. And Jon heard Samwell Tarly shout, "I know that bird! That's Lord Mormont's raven!"

The raven landed on the table nearest Jon. "*Snow*," it cawed. It was an old bird, dirty and bedraggled. "*Snow*," it said again, "*Snow, snow, snow*." It walked to the end of the table, spread its wings again, and flew to Jon's shoulder.

Lord Janos Slynt sat down so heavily he made a *thump*, but Ser Alliser filled the vault with mocking laughter. "Ser Piggy thinks we're all fools, brothers," he said. "He's taught the bird this little trick. They all say *snow*, go up to the rookery and hear for yourselves. Mormont's bird had more words than that."

The raven cocked its head and looked at Jon. "*Corn?*" it said hopefully. When it got neither corn nor answer, it *quorked* and muttered, "*Kettle? Kettle? Kettle?*"

The rest was arrowheads, a torrent of arrowheads, a flood of arrowheads, arrowheads enough to drown the last few stones and shells, and all the copper pennies too.

When the count was done, Jon found himself surrounded. Some clapped him on the back, whilst others bent the knee to him as if he were a lord in truth. Satin, Owen the Oaf, Halder, Toad, Spare Boot, Giant, Mully, Ulmer of the Kingswood, Sweet Donnel Hill, and half a hundred more pressed around him. Dywen clacked his wooden teeth and said, "Gods be good, our Lord Commander's still in swaddling clothes." Iron Emmett said, "I hope this don't mean I can't beat the bloody piss out of you next time we train, my lord." Three-Finger Hobb wanted to know if he'd still be eating with the men, or if he'd want his meals sent up to his solar. Even Bowen Marsh came up to say he would be glad to continue as Lord Steward if that was Lord Snow's wish.

"Lord Snow," said Cotter Pyke, "if you muck this up, I'm going to rip your liver out and eat it raw with onions."

Ser Denys Mallister was more courteous. "It was a hard thing young Samwell asked of me," the old knight confessed. "When Lord Qorgyle was chosen, I told myself, 'No matter, he has been longer on the Wall than you have, your time will come.' When it was Lord Mormont, I thought, 'He is strong and fierce, but he is old, your time may yet come.' But you are half a boy, Lord Snow, and now I must return to the Shadow Tower knowing that my time will never come." He smiled a tired smile. "Do not make me die regretful. Your uncle was a great man. Your lord father and his father as well. I shall expect full as much of you."

"Aye," said Cotter Pyke. "And you can start by telling those king's men that it's done, and we want our bloody supper."

"*Supper*," screamed the raven. "*Supper, supper.*"

The king's men cleared the door when they told them of the choosing, and Three-Finger Hobb and half a dozen helpers went trotting off to the kitchen to fetch the food. Jon did not wait to eat. He walked across the castle, wondering if he were dreaming, with the raven on his shoulder and Ghost at his heels. Pyp, Grenn, and Sam trailed after him, chattering, but he hardly heard a word until Grenn whispered, "*Sam* did it," and Pyp said, "Sam *did* it!" Pyp had brought a wineskin with him, and he took a long drink and chanted, "Sam, Sam, Sam the wizard, Sam the wonder, Sam Sam the marvel man, he did it. But when did you hide the raven in the kettle, Sam, and how in seven hells could you be certain it would fly to Jon? It would have mucked up everything if the bird had decided to perch on Janos Slynt's fat head."

"I had nothing to do with the bird," Sam insisted. "When it flew out of the kettle I almost wet myself."

Jon laughed, half amazed that he still remembered how. "You're all a bunch of mad fools, do you know that?"

"Us?" said Pyp. "You call *us* fools? We're not the ones who got chosen as the nine-hundredth-and-ninety-eighth Lord Commander of the Night's Watch. You best have some wine, Lord Jon. I think you're going to need a *lot* of wine."

So Jon Snow took the wineskin from his hand and had a swallow. But only one. The Wall was his, the night was dark, and he had a king to face.

SANSA

She awoke all at once, every nerve atingle. For a moment she did not remember where she was. She had dreamt that she was little, still sharing a bedchamber with her sister Arya. But it was her maid she heard tossing in sleep, not her sister, and this was not Winterfell, but the Eyrie. *And I am Alayne Stone, a bastard girl.* The room was cold and black, though she was warm beneath the blankets. Dawn had not yet come. Sometimes she dreamed of Ser Ilyn Payne and woke with her heart thumping, but this dream had not been like that. *Home. It was a dream of home.*

The Eyrie was no home. It was no bigger than Maegor's Holdfast, and outside its sheer white walls was only the mountain and the long treacherous descent past Sky and Snow and Stone to the Gates of the Moon on the valley floor. There was no place to go and little to do. The older servants said these halls rang with laughter when her father and Robert Baratheon had been Jon Arryn's wards, but those days were many years gone. Her aunt kept a small household, and seldom permitted any guests to ascend past the Gates of the Moon. Aside from her aged maid, Sansa's only companion was the Lord Robert, eight going on three.

And Marillion. There is always Marillion. When he played for them at supper, the young singer often seemed to be singing directly at her. Her aunt was far from pleased. Lady Lysa doted on Marillion, and had banished two serving girls and even a page for telling lies about him.

Lysa was as lonely as she was. Her new husband seemed to spend more time at the foot of the mountain than he did atop it. He was gone now, had been gone the past four days, meeting with the Corbrays. From bits and pieces of overheard conversations Sansa knew that Jon Arryn's bannermen resented Lysa's marriage and begrudged Petyr his authority as Lord Protector of the Vale. The senior branch of House Royce was close to open revolt over her aunt's failure to aid Robb in his war, and the Waynwoods, Redforts, Belmores, and Templetons were giving them every support. The mountain clans were being troublesome as well, and old Lord Hunter had died so suddenly that his two younger sons were accusing their elder brother of having murdered him. The Vale of Arryn might have been spared the worst of the war, but it was hardly the idyllic place that Lady Lysa had made it out to be.

I am not going back to sleep, Sansa realized. *My head is all a tumult.* She pushed her pillow away reluctantly, threw back the blankets, went to her window, and opened the shutters.

Snow was falling on the Eyrie.

Outside the flakes drifted down as soft and silent as memory. *Was this what woke me?* Already the snowfall lay thick upon the garden below, blanketing the grass, dusting the shrubs and statues with white and weighing down the branches of the trees. The sight took Sansa back to cold nights long ago, in the long summer of her childhood.

She had last seen snow the day she'd left Winterfell. *That was a lighter fall than this*, she remembered. *Robb had melting flakes in his hair when he hugged me, and the snowball Arya tried to make kept coming apart in her hands.* It hurt to remember how happy she had been that morning. Hullen had helped her mount, and she'd ridden out with the snowflakes swirling around her, off to see the great wide world. *I thought my song was beginning that day, but it was almost done.*

Sansa left the shutters open as she dressed. It would be cold, she knew, though the Eyrie's towers encircled the garden and protected it from the worst of the mountain winds. She donned silken smallclothes and a linen shift, and over that a warm dress of blue lambswool. Two pairs of hose for her legs, boots that laced up to her knees, heavy leather gloves, and finally a hooded cloak of soft white fox fur.

Her maid rolled herself more tightly in her blanket as the snow began to drift in the window. Sansa eased open the door, and made her way down the winding stair. When she opened the door to the garden, it was so lovely that she held her breath, unwilling to disturb such perfect beauty. The snow drifted down and down, all in ghostly silence, and lay thick and unbroken on the ground. All color had fled the world outside. It was a place of whites and blacks and greys. White towers and white snow and white statues, black shadows and black trees, the dark grey sky above. *A pure world*, Sansa thought. *I do not belong here.*

Yet she stepped out all the same. Her boots tore ankle-deep holes into the smooth white surface of the snow, yet made no sound. Sansa drifted past frosted shrubs and thin dark trees, and wondered if she were still dreaming. Drifting snowflakes brushed her face as light as lover's kisses, and melted on her cheeks. At the center of the garden, beside the statue of the weeping woman that lay broken and half-buried on the ground, she turned her face up to the sky and closed her eyes. She could feel the snow on her lashes, taste it on her lips. It was the taste of Winterfell. The taste of innocence. The taste of dreams.

When Sansa opened her eyes again, she was on her knees. She did not remember falling. It seemed to her that the sky was a lighter shade of grey. *Dawn*, she thought. *Another day. Another new day.* It was the old days she hungered for. Prayed for. But who could she pray to? The garden had been meant for a godswood once, she knew, but the soil was too thin and stony for a weirwood to take root. *A godswood without gods, as empty as me.*

She scooped up a handful of snow and squeezed it between her fingers. Heavy and wet, the snow packed easily. Sansa began to make snowballs, shaping and smoothing them until they were round and white and perfect. She remembered a summer's snow in Winterfell when Arya and Bran had ambushed her as she emerged from the keep one morning. They'd each had a dozen snowballs to hand, and she'd had none. Bran had been perched on the roof of the covered bridge, out of reach, but Sansa had chased Arya through the stables and around the kitchen until both of them were breathless. She might even have caught her, but she'd slipped on some ice. Her sister came back to see if she was hurt. When she said she wasn't, Arya hit her in the face with another snowball, but Sansa grabbed her leg and pulled her down and was rubbing snow in her hair when Jory came along and pulled them apart, laughing.

What do I want with snowballs? She looked at her sad little arsenal. *There's no one to throw them at.* She let the one she was making drop from her hand. *I could build a snow knight instead,* she thought. *Or even . . .*

She pushed two of her snowballs together, added a third, packed more snow in around them, and patted the whole thing into the shape of a cylinder. When it was done, she stood it on end and used the tip of her little finger to poke holes in it for windows. The crenellations around the top took a little more care, but when they were done she had a tower. *I need some walls now,* Sansa thought, *and then a keep.* She set to work.

The snow fell and the castle rose. Two walls ankle-high, the inner taller than the outer. Towers and turrets, keeps and stairs, a round kitchen, a square armory, the stables along the inside of the west wall. It was only a castle when she began, but before very long Sansa knew it was Winterfell. She found twigs and fallen branches beneath the snow and broke off the ends to make the trees for the godswood. For the gravestones in the lichyard she used bits of bark. Soon her gloves and her boots were crusty white, her hands were tingling, and her feet were soaked and cold, but she did not care. The castle was all that mattered. Some things were hard to remember, but most came back to her easily, as if she had been there only yesterday. The Library Tower, with the steep stonework stair twisting about its exterior. The gatehouse, two huge bulwarks, the arched gate between them, crenellations all along the top . . .

And all the while the snow kept falling, piling up in drifts around her buildings as fast as she raised them. She was patting down the pitched roof of the Great Hall when she heard a voice, and looked up to see her maid calling from her window. Was my lady well? Did she wish to break her fast? Sansa shook her head, and went back to shaping snow, adding a chimney to one end of the Great Hall, where the hearth would stand inside.

Dawn stole into her garden like a thief. The grey of the sky grew lighter still, and the trees and shrubs turned a dark green beneath their stoles of snow. A few servants came out and watched her for a time, but she paid them no mind and they soon went back inside where it was warmer. Sansa saw Lady Lysa gazing down from her balcony, wrapped up in a blue velvet robe trimmed with fox fur, but when she looked again her aunt was gone. Maester Colemon popped out of the rookery and peered down for a while, skinny and shivering but curious.

Her bridges kept falling down. There was a covered bridge between the armory and the main keep, and another that went from the fourth floor of the bell tower to the second floor of the rookery, but no matter how carefully she shaped them, they would not hold together. The third time one collapsed on her, she cursed aloud and sat back in helpless frustration.

"Pack the snow around a stick, Sansa."

She did not know how long he had been watching her, or when he had returned from the Vale. "A stick?" she asked.

"That will give it strength enough to stand, I'd think," Petyr said. "May I come into your castle, my lady?"

Sansa was wary. "Don't break it. Be . . ."

". . . gentle?" He smiled. "Winterfell has withstood fiercer enemies than me. It *is* Winterfell, is it not?"

"Yes," Sansa admitted.

He walked along outside the walls. "I used to dream of it, in those years after Cat went north with Eddard Stark. In my dreams it was ever a dark place, and cold."

"No. It was always warm, even when it snowed. Water from the hot springs is piped through the walls to warm them, and inside the glass gardens it was always like the hottest day of summer." She stood, towering over the great white castle. "I can't think how to do the glass roof over the gardens."

Littlefinger stroked his chin, where his beard had been before Lysa had asked him to shave it off. "The glass was locked in frames, no? Twigs are your answer. Peel them and cross them and use bark to tie them together into frames. I'll show you." He moved through the garden, gathering up twigs and sticks and shaking the snow from them. When he had enough, he stepped over both walls with a single long stride and squatted on his heels in the middle of the yard. Sansa came closer to watch what he was doing. His hands were deft and sure, and before long he had a crisscrossing latticework of twigs, very like the one that roofed the glass gardens of Winterfell. "We will need to imagine the glass, to be sure," he said when he gave it to her.

"This is just right," she said.

He touched her face. "And so is that."

Sansa did not understand. "And so is what?"

"Your smile, my lady. Shall I make another for you?"

"If you would."

"Nothing could please me more."

She raised the walls of the glass gardens while Littlefinger roofed them over, and when they were done with that he helped her extend the walls and build the guardshall. When she used sticks for the covered bridges, they stood, just as he had said they would. The First Keep was simple enough, an old round drum tower, but Sansa was stymied again when it came to putting the gargoyles around the top. Again he had the answer. "It's been snowing on your castle, my lady," he pointed out. "What do the gargoyles look like when they're covered with snow?"

Sansa closed her eyes to see them in memory. "They're just white lumps."

"Well, then. Gargoyles are hard, but white lumps should be easy." And they were.

The Broken Tower was easier still. They made a tall tower together, kneeling side by side to roll it smooth, and when they'd raised it Sansa stuck her fingers through the top, grabbed a handful of snow, and flung it full in his face. Petyr yelped, as the snow slid down under his collar. "That was unchivalrously done, my lady."

"As was bringing me here, when you swore to take me home."

She wondered where this courage had come from, to speak to him so frankly. *From Winterfell*, she thought. *I am stronger within the walls of Winterfell.*

His face grew serious. "Yes, I played you false in that . . . and in one other thing as well."

Sansa's stomach was aflutter. "What other thing?"

"I told you that nothing could please me more than to help you with your castle. I fear that was a lie as well. Something else would please me more." He stepped closer. "This."

Sansa tried to step back, but he pulled her into his arms and suddenly he was kissing her. Feebly, she tried to squirm, but only succeeded in pressing herself more tightly against him. His mouth was on hers, swallowing her words. He tasted of mint. For half a heartbeat she yielded to his kiss . . . before she turned her face away and wrenched free. "What are you *doing?*"

Petyr straightened his cloak. "Kissing a snow maid."

"You're supposed to kiss *her.*" Sansa glanced up at Lysa's balcony, but it was empty now. "Your lady wife."

"I do. Lysa has no cause for complaint." He smiled. "I wish you could see yourself, my lady. You are so beautiful. You're crusted over with snow like some little bear cub, but your face is flushed and you can scarcely breathe. How long have you been out here? You must be very cold. Let me warm you, Sansa. Take off those gloves, give me your hands."

"I won't." He sounded almost like Marillion, the night he'd gotten so drunk at the wedding. Only this time Lothor Brune would not appear to save her; Ser Lothor was Petyr's man. "You shouldn't kiss me. I might have been your own daughter . . ."

"Might have been," he admitted, with a rueful smile. "But you're not, are you? You are Eddard Stark's daughter, and Cat's. But I think you might be even more beautiful than your mother was, when she was your age."

"Petyr, please." Her voice sounded so weak. "Please . . ."

"A *castle!*"

The voice was loud, shrill, and childish. Littlefinger

turned away from her. "Lord Robert." He sketched a bow. "Should you be out in the snow without your gloves?"

"Did you make the snow castle, Lord Littlefinger?"

"Alayne did most of it, my lord."

Sansa said, "It's meant to be Winterfell."

"Winterfell?" Robert was small for eight, a stick of a boy with splotchy skin and eyes that were always runny. Under one arm he clutched the threadbare cloth doll he carried everywhere.

"Winterfell is the seat of House Stark," Sansa told her husband-to-be. "The great castle of the north."

"It's not so great." The boy knelt before the gatehouse. "Look, here comes a giant to knock it down." He stood his doll in the snow and moved it jerkily. "*Tromp tromp I'm a giant, I'm a giant,*" he chanted. "*Ho ho ho, open your gates or I'll mash them and smash them.*" Swinging the doll by the legs, he knocked the top off one gatehouse tower and then the other.

It was more than Sansa could stand. "Robert, *stop that.*" Instead he swung the doll again, and a foot of wall exploded. She grabbed for his hand but she caught the doll instead. There was a loud ripping sound as the thin cloth tore. Suddenly she had the doll's head, Robert had the legs and body, and the rag-and-sawdust stuffing was spilling in the snow.

Lord Robert's mouth trembled. "You *killlllllllled* him," he wailed. Then he began to shake. It started with no more than a little shivering, but within a few short heartbeats he had collapsed across the castle, his limbs flailing about violently. White towers and snowy bridges shattered and fell on all sides. Sansa stood horrified, but Petyr Baelish seized her cousin's wrists and shouted for the maester.

Guards and serving girls arrived within instants to help restrain the boy, Maester Colemon a short time later. Robert Arryn's shaking sickness was nothing new to the people of the Eyrie, and Lady Lysa had trained them all to come rushing at the boy's first cry. The maester held the little lord's head and gave him half a cup of dreamwine, murmuring soothing words. Slowly the violence of the fit seemed to ebb away, till nothing remained but a small shaking of the hands. "Help him to my chambers," Colemon told the guards. "A leeching will help calm him."

"It was my fault." Sansa showed them the doll's head. "I ripped his doll in two. I never meant to, but . . ."

"His lordship was destroying the castle," said Petyr.

"A giant," the boy whispered, weeping. "It wasn't me, it was a giant hurt the castle. She *killed* him! I hate her! She's a bastard and I *hate* her! I don't *want* to be leeched!"

"My lord, your blood needs thinning," said Maester Colemon. "It is the bad blood that makes you angry, and the rage that brings on the shaking. Come now."

They led the boy away. *My lord husband*, Sansa thought, as she contemplated the ruins of Winterfell. The snow had stopped, and it was colder than before. She wondered if Lord Robert would shake all through their wedding. *At least Joffrey was sound of body.* A mad rage seized hold of her. She picked up a broken branch and smashed the torn doll's head down on top of it, then pushed it down atop the shattered gatehouse of her snow castle. The servants looked aghast, but when Littlefinger saw what she'd done he laughed. "If the tales be true, that's not the first giant to end up with his head on Winterfell's walls."

"Those are only stories," she said, and left him there.

Back in her bedchamber, Sansa took off her cloak and her wet boots and sat beside the fire. She had no doubt that she would be made to answer for Lord Robert's fit. *Perhaps Lady Lysa will send me away.* Her aunt was quick to banish anyone who displeased her, and nothing displeased her quite so much as people she suspected of mistreating her son.

Sansa would have welcomed banishment. The Gates of the Moon was much larger than the Eyrie, and livelier as well. Lord Nestor Royce seemed gruff and stern, but his daughter Myranda kept his castle for him, and everyone said how frolicsome she was. Even Sansa's supposed bastardy might not count too much against her below. One of King Robert's baseborn daughters was in service to Lord Nestor, and she and the Lady Myranda were said to be fast friends, as close as sisters.

I will tell my aunt that I don't want to marry Robert. Not even the High Septon himself could declare a woman married if she refused to say the vows. She wasn't a beggar, no matter what her aunt said. She was thirteen, a woman flowered and wed, the heir to Winterfell. Sansa felt sorry for her little cousin sometimes, but she could not imagine ever wanting to be his wife. *I would sooner be married to Tyrion again*. If Lady Lysa knew that, surely she'd send her away . . . away from Robert's pouts and shakes and runny eyes, away from Marillion's lingering looks, away from Petyr's kisses. *I will tell her. I will!*

It was late that afternoon when Lady Lysa summoned her. Sansa had been marshaling her courage all day, but no sooner did Marillion appear at her door than all her doubts returned. "Lady Lysa requires your presence in the High Hall." The singer's eyes undressed her as he spoke, but she was used to that.

Marillion was comely, there was no denying it; boyish and slender, with smooth skin, sandy hair, a charming smile. But he had made himself well hated in the Vale, by everyone but her aunt and little Lord Robert. To hear the servants talk, Sansa was not the first maid to suffer his advances, and the others had not had Lothor Brune to defend them. But Lady Lysa would hear no complaints against him. Since coming to the Eyrie, the singer had become her favorite. He sang Lord Robert to sleep every night, and tweaked the noses of Lady Lysa's suitors with verses that made mock of their foibles. Her aunt had showered him with gold and gifts; costly clothes, a gold arm ring, a belt studded with moonstones, a fine horse. She had even given him her late husband's favorite falcon. It all served to make Marillion unfailingly courteous in Lady Lysa's presence, and unfailingly arrogant outside it.

"Thank you," Sansa told him stiffly. "I know the way."

He would not leave. "My lady said to bring you."

Bring me? She did not like the sound of that. "Are you a guardsman now?" Littlefinger had dismissed the Eyrie's captain of guards and put Ser Lothor Brune in his place.

"Do you require guarding?" Marillion said lightly. "I am composing a new song, you should know. A song so sweet and sad it will melt even your frozen heart. 'The Roadside Rose,' I mean to call it. About a baseborn girl so beautiful she bewitched every man who laid eyes upon her."

I am a Stark of Winterfell, she longed to tell him. Instead she nodded, and let him escort her down the tower steps and along a bridge. The High Hall had been closed as long as she'd been at the Eyrie. Sansa wondered why her aunt had opened it. Normally she preferred the comfort of her solar, or the cozy warmth of Lord Arryn's audience chamber with its view of the waterfall.

Two guards in sky-blue cloaks flanked the carved wooden doors of the High Hall, spears in hand. "No one is to enter so long as Alayne is with Lady Lysa," Marillion told them.

"Aye." The men let them pass, then crossed their spears. Marillion swung the doors shut and barred them with a third spear, longer and thicker than those the guards had borne.

Sansa felt a prickle of unease. "Why did you do that?"

"My lady awaits you."

She looked about uncertainly. Lady Lysa sat on the dais in a high-backed chair of carved weirwood, alone. To her right was a second chair, taller than her own, with a stack of blue cushions piled on the seat, but Lord Robert was not in it. Sansa hoped he'd recovered. Marillion was not like to tell her, though.

Sansa walked down the blue silk carpet between rows of fluted pillars slim as lances. The floors and walls of the High Hall were made of milk-white marble veined with blue. Shafts of pale daylight slanted down through narrow arched windows along the eastern wall. Between the windows were torches, mounted in high iron sconces, but none of them was lit. Her footsteps fell softly on the carpet. Outside the wind blew cold and lonely.

Amidst so much white marble even the sunlight looked chilly, somehow . . . though not half so chilly as her aunt. Lady Lysa had dressed in a gown of cream-colored velvet and a necklace of sapphires and moon-stones. Her auburn hair had been done up in a thick braid, and fell across one shoulder. She sat in the high seat watching her niece approach, her face red and puffy beneath the paint and powder. On the wall behind her hung a huge banner, the moon-and-falcon of House Arryn in cream and blue.

Sansa stopped before the dais, and curtsied. "My lady. You sent for me." She could still hear the sound of the wind, and the soft chords Marillion was playing at the foot of the hall.

"I saw what you did," the Lady Lysa said.

Sansa smoothed down the folds of her skirt. "I trust

Lord Robert is better? I never meant to rip his doll. He was smashing my snow castle, I only . . ."

"Will you play the coy deceiver with me?" her aunt said. "I was not speaking of Robert's doll. I *saw* you kissing him."

The High Hall seemed to grow a little colder. The walls and floor and columns might have turned to ice. "He kissed me."

Lysa's nostrils flared. "And why would he do that? He has a wife who loves him. A woman grown, not a little girl. He has no need for the likes of you. Confess, child. You threw yourself at him. That was the way of it."

Sansa took a step backward. "That's not true."

"Where are you going? Are you afraid? Such wanton behavior must be punished, but I will not be hard on you. We keep a whipping boy for Robert, as is the custom in the Free Cities. His health is too delicate for him to bear the rod himself. I shall find some common girl to take your whipping, but first you must own up to what you've done. I cannot abide a liar, Alayne."

"I was building a snow castle," Sansa said. "Lord Petyr was helping me, and then he kissed me. That's what you saw."

"Have you no honor?" her aunt said sharply. "Or do you take me for a fool? You do, don't you? You take me for a fool. Yes, I see that now. I am not a fool. You think you can have any man you want because you're young and beautiful. Don't think I haven't seen the looks you give Marillion. I know everything that happens in the Eyrie, little lady. And I have known your like before, too. But you are mistaken if you think big eyes and strumpet's smiles will win you Petyr. He is mine." She rose to her feet. "They all tried to take him from me. My lord father, my husband, your mother . . . Catelyn most of all. She liked to kiss my Petyr too, oh yes she did."

Sansa retreated another step. "My mother?"

"Yes, your mother, your precious mother, my own sweet sister Catelyn. Don't you think to play the innocent with me, you vile little liar. All those years in Riverrun, she played with Petyr as if he were her little toy. She teased him with smiles and soft words and wanton looks, and made his nights a torment."

"No." *My mother is dead*, she wanted to shriek. *She was your own sister, and she's dead*. "She didn't. She wouldn't."

"How would you know? Were you there?" Lysa descended from the high seat, her skirts swirling. "Did you come with Lord Bracken and Lord Blackwood, the time they visited to lay their feud before my father? Lord Bracken's singer played for us, and Catelyn danced six dances with Petyr that night, *six*, I counted. When the lords began to argue my father took them up to his audience chamber, so there was no one to stop us drinking. Edmure got drunk, young as he was . . . and Petyr tried to kiss your mother, only she pushed him away. She *laughed* at him. He looked so wounded I thought my heart would burst, and afterward he drank until he passed out at the table. Uncle Brynden carried him up to bed before my father could find him like that. But you remember none of it, do you?" She looked down angrily. "*Do you?*"

Is she drunk, or mad? "I was not born, my lady."

"You were not born. But I was, so do not presume to tell what is true. I *know* what is true. You kissed him!"

"He kissed me," Sansa insisted again. "I never wanted—"

"Be quiet, I haven't given you leave to speak. You enticed him, just as your mother did that night in Riverrun, with her smiles and her dancing. You think I could forget? That was the night I stole up to his bed to give him comfort. I bled, but it was the sweetest hurt. He told me he loved me then, but he called me *Cat*, just before he fell back to sleep. Even so, I stayed with him until the sky began to lighten. Your mother did not deserve him. She would not even give him her favor to wear when he fought Brandon Stark. *I* would have given him my favor. I gave him everything. He is mine now. Not Catelyn's and not yours."

All of Sansa's resolve had withered in the face of her aunt's onslaught. Lysa Arryn was frightening her as much as Queen Cersei ever had. "He's yours, my lady," she said, trying to sound meek and contrite. "May I have your leave to go?"

"You may not." Her aunt's breath smelled of wine. "If you were anyone else, I would banish you. Send you down to Lord Nestor at the Gates of the Moon, or back to the Fingers. How would you like to spend your life on that bleak shore, surrounded by slatterns and sheep pellets? That was what my father meant for Petyr. Everyone thought it was because of that stupid duel with Brandon Stark, but that wasn't so. Father said I ought to thank the gods that so great a lord as Jon Arryn was willing to take me soiled, but I knew it was only for the swords. I had to marry Jon, or my father would have turned me out as he did his brother, but it was Petyr I was meant for. I am telling you all this so you will understand how much we love each other, how long we have suffered and dreamed of one another. We made a baby together, a precious little baby." Lysa put her hands flat against her belly, as if the child was still there. "When they stole him from me, I made a promise to myself that I would never let it happen again. Jon wished to send my sweet Robert to Dragonstone, and that sot of a king would have given him to Cersei Lannister, but I never let them . . . no more than I'll let you steal my Petyr Littlefinger. Do you hear me, Alayne or Sansa or whatever you call yourself? Do you hear what I am telling you?"

"Yes. I swear, I won't ever kiss him again, or . . . or entice him." Sansa thought that was what her aunt wanted to hear.

"So you admit it now? It was you, just as I thought. You are as wanton as your mother." Lysa grabbed her by the wrist. "Come with me now. There is something I want to show you."

"You're hurting me." Sansa squirmed. "Please, Aunt Lysa, I haven't done anything. I swear it."

Her aunt ignored her protests. "*Marillion!*" she shouted. "I need you, Marillion! I *need* you!"

The singer had remained discreetly in the rear of the hall, but at Lady Arryn's shout he came at once. "My lady?"

"Play us a song. Play 'The False and the Fair.'"

Marillion's fingers brushed the strings. "*The lord he came a-riding upon a rainy day, hey-nonny, hey-nonny, hey-nonny-hey . . .*"

Lady Lysa pulled at Sansa's arm. It was either walk or be dragged, so she chose to walk, halfway down the hall and between a pair of pillars, to a white weirwood door set in the marble wall. The door was firmly closed, with three heavy bronze bars to hold it in place, but Sansa could hear the wind outside worrying at its edges. When she saw the crescent moon carved in the wood, she planted her feet. "The Moon Door." She tried to yank free. "Why are you showing me the Moon Door?"

"You squeak like a mouse now, but you were bold enough in the garden, weren't you? You were bold enough in the snow."

"*The lady sat a-sewing upon a rainy day,*" Marillion sang. "*Hey-nonny, hey-nonny, hey-nonny-hey.*"

"Open the door," Lysa commanded. "*Open* it, I say. You will do it, or I'll send for my guards." She shoved Sansa forward. "Your mother was brave, at least. Lift off the bars."

If I do as she says, she will let me go. Sansa grabbed one of the bronze bars, yanked it loose, and tossed it down. The second bar clattered to the marble, then the third. She had barely touched the latch when the heavy wooden door *flew* inward and slammed back against the wall with a bang. Snow had piled up around the frame, and it all came blowing in at them, borne on a blast of cold air that left Sansa shivering. She tried to step backward, but her aunt was behind her. Lysa seized her by the wrist and put her other hand between her shoulder blades, propelling her forcefully toward the open door.

Beyond was white sky, falling snow, and nothing else.

"Look down," said Lady Lysa. "Look *down.*"

She tried to wrench free, but her aunt's fingers were digging into her arm like claws. Lysa gave her another shove, and Sansa shrieked. Her left foot broke through a crust of snow and knocked it loose. There was nothing in front of her but empty air, and a waycastle six hundred feet below clinging to the side of the mountain. "Don't!" Sansa screamed. "You're scaring me!" Behind her, Marillion was still playing his woodharp and singing, "*Hey-nonny, hey-nonny, hey-nonny-hey.*"

"Do you still want my leave to go? Do you?"

"No." Sansa planted her feet and tried to squirm backward, but her aunt did not budge. "Not this way. Please . . ." She put a hand up, her fingers scrabbling at the doorframe, but she could not get a grip, and her feet were sliding on the wet marble floor. Lady Lysa pressed her forward inexorably. Her aunt outweighed her by three stone. "*The lady lay a-kissing, upon a mound of hay,*" Marillion was singing. Sansa twisted sideways, hysterical with fear, and one foot slipped out over the void. She screamed. "*Hey-nonny, hey-nonny, hey-nonny-hey.*" The wind flapped her skirts up and bit at her bare legs with cold teeth. She could feel snowflakes melting on her cheeks. Sansa flailed, found Lysa's thick auburn braid, and clutched it tight. "My hair!" her aunt shrieked. "*Let go of my hair!*" She was shaking, sobbing. They teetered on the edge. Far off, she heard the guards pounding on the door with their spears, demanding to be let in. Marillion broke off his song.

"*Lysa!* What's the meaning of this?" The shout cut through the sobs and heavy breathing. Footsteps echoed down the High Hall. "Get *back* from there! Lysa, what are you doing?" The guards were still beating at the door; Littlefinger had come in the back way, through the lords' entrance behind the dais.

As Lysa turned, her grip loosened enough for Sansa to rip free. She stumbled to her knees, where Petyr Baelish saw her. He stopped suddenly. "Alayne. What is the trouble here?"

"*Her.*" Lady Lysa grabbed a handful of Sansa's hair. "*She's* the trouble. She *kissed* you."

"Tell her," Sansa begged. "Tell her we were just building a castle . . ."

"*Be quiet!*" her aunt screamed. "I never gave you leave to speak. No one cares about your castle."

"She's a child, Lysa. Cat's daughter. What did you think you were doing?"

"I was going to marry her to *Robert!* She has no gratitude. No . . . no *decency*. You are not hers to kiss. *Not hers!* I was teaching her a lesson, that was all."

"I see." He stroked his chin. "I think she understands now. Isn't that so, Alayne?"

"Yes," sobbed Sansa. "I understand."

"I don't want her here." Her aunt's eyes were shiny with tears. "Why did you bring her to the Vale, Petyr? This isn't her place. She doesn't belong here."

"We'll send her away, then. Back to King's Landing, if

you like." He took a step toward them. "Let her up, now. Let her away from the door."

"*NO!*" Lysa gave Sansa's head another wrench. Snow eddied around them, making their skirts snap noisily. "You can't want her. You *can't.* She's a stupid empty-headed little girl. She doesn't love you the way I have. I've always loved you. I've proved it, haven't I?" Tears ran down her aunt's puffy red face. "I gave you my maiden's gift. I would have given you a son too, but they murdered him with moon tea, with tansy and mint and wormwood, a spoon of honey and a drop of pennyroyal. It wasn't me, I never *knew,* I only drank what Father gave me . . ."

"That's past and done, Lysa. Lord Hoster's dead, and his old maester as well." Littlefinger moved closer. "Have you been at the wine again? You ought not to talk so much. We don't want Alayne to know more than she should, do we? Or Marillion?"

Lady Lysa ignored that. "Cat never gave you anything. It was me who got you your first post, who made Jon bring you to court so we could be close to one another. You promised me you would never forget that."

"Nor have I. We're together, just as you always wanted, just as we always planned. Just let go of Sansa's hair . . ."

"I won't! I saw you kissing in the snow. She's just like her mother. Catelyn kissed you in the godswood, but she never *meant* it, she never wanted you. Why did you love her best? It was me, it was always *meeee!*"

"I know, love." He took another step. "And I am here. All you need to do is take my hand, come on." He held it out to her. "There's no cause for all these tears."

"Tears, tears, *tears,*" she sobbed hysterically. "No need for tears . . . but that's not what you said in King's Landing. You told me to put the tears in Jon's wine, and I did. For Robert, and for *us!* And I wrote Catelyn and told her the Lannisters had killed my lord husband, just as you said. That was so clever . . . you were always clever, I told Father that, I said Petyr's so clever, he'll rise high, he will, he *will,* and he's sweet and gentle and I have his little baby in my belly . . . Why did you kiss her? *Why?* We're together now, we're together after so long, so very long, why would you want to kiss *herrrrrr?*"

"Lysa," Petyr sighed, "after all the storms we've suffered, you should trust me better. I swear, I shall never leave your side again, for as long as we both shall live."

"Truly?" she asked, weeping. "Oh, *truly?*"

"Truly. Now unhand the girl and come give me a kiss."

Lysa threw herself into Littlefinger's arms, sobbing. As they hugged, Sansa crawled from the Moon Door on hands and knees and wrapped her arms around the nearest pillar. She could feel her heart pounding. There was snow in her hair and her right shoe was missing. *It must have fallen.* She shuddered, and hugged the pillar tighter.

Littlefinger let Lysa sob against his chest for a moment, then put his hands on her arms and kissed her lightly. "My sweet silly jealous wife," he said, chuckling. "I've only loved one woman, I promise you."

Lysa Arryn smiled tremulously. "Only one? Oh, Petyr, do you swear it? Only one?"

"Only Cat." He gave her a short, sharp shove.

Lysa stumbled backward, her feet slipping on the wet marble. And then she was gone. She never screamed. For the longest time there was no sound but the wind.

Marillion gasped, "You . . . you . . ."

The guards were shouting outside the door, pounding with the butts of their heavy spears. Lord Petyr pulled Sansa to her feet. "You're not hurt?" When she shook her head, he said, "Run let my guards in, then. Quick now, there's no time to lose. This singer's killed my lady wife."

EPILOGUE

The road up to Oldstones went twice around the hill before reaching the summit. Overgrown and stony, it would have been slow going even in the best of times, and last night's snow had left it muddy as well. *Snow in autumn in the riverlands, it's unnatural,* Merrett thought gloomily. It had not been much of a snow, true; just enough to blanket the ground for a night. Most of it had started melting away as soon as the sun came up. Still, Merrett took it for a bad omen. Between rains, floods, fire, and war, they had lost two harvests and a good part of a third. An early winter would mean famine all across the riverlands. A great many people would go hungry, and some of them would starve. Merrett only hoped he wouldn't be one of them. *I may, though. With my luck, I just may. I never did have any luck.*

Beneath the castle ruins, the lower slopes of the hill were so thickly forested that half a hundred outlaws could well have been lurking there. *They could be watching me even now.* Merrett glanced about, and saw nothing but gorse, bracken, thistle, sedge, and blackberry bushes between the pines and grey-green sentinels. Elsewhere skeletal elm and ash and scrub oaks choked the ground like weeds. He saw no outlaws, but that meant little. Outlaws were better at hiding than honest men.

Merrett hated the woods, if truth be told, and he hated outlaws even more. "Outlaws stole my life," he had been known to complain when in his cups. He was too often in his cups, his father said, often and loudly. *Too true*, he thought ruefully. *You needed some sort of distinction in the Twins, else they were liable to forget you were alive, but a reputation as the biggest drinker in the castle had done little to enhance his prospects, he'd found. I once hoped to be the greatest knight who ever couched a lance. The gods took that away from me. Why shouldn't I have a cup of wine from time to time? It helps my headaches. Besides, my wife is a shrew, my father despises me, my children are worthless. What do I have to stay sober for?*

He was sober now, though. Well, he'd had two horns of ale when he broke his fast, and a small cup of red when he set out, but that was just to keep his head from pounding. Merrett could feel the headache building behind his eyes, and he knew that if he gave it half a chance he would soon feel as if he had a thunderstorm raging between his ears. Sometimes his headaches got so bad that it even hurt too much to weep. Then all he could do was rest on his bed in a dark room with a damp cloth over his eyes, and curse his luck and the nameless outlaw who had done this to him.

Just thinking about it made him anxious. He could no wise afford a headache now. *If I bring Petyr back home safely, all my luck will change.* He had the gold, all he needed to do was climb to the top of Oldstones, meet the bloody outlaws in the ruined castle, and make the exchange. A simple ransom. Even he could not muck it up . . . unless he got a headache, one so bad that it left him unable to ride. He was supposed to be at the ruins by sunset, not weeping in a huddle at the side of the road. Merrett rubbed two fingers against his temple. *Once more around the hill, and there I am.* When the message had come in and he had stepped forward to offer to carry the ransom, his father had squinted down and said, "*You*, Merrett?" and started laughing through his nose, that hideous *heh heh*

heh laugh of his. Merrett practically had to beg before they'd give him the bloody bag of gold.

Something moved in the underbrush along the side of the road. Merrett reined up hard and reached for his sword, but it was only a squirrel. "Stupid," he told himself, shoving the sword back in its scabbard without ever having gotten it out. "Outlaws don't have tails. Bloody hell, Merrett, get hold of yourself." His heart was thumping in his chest as if he were some green boy on his first campaign. *As if this were the kingswood and it was the old Brotherhood I was going to face, not the lightning lord's sorry lot of brigands.* For a moment he was tempted to trot right back down the hill and find the nearest alehouse. That bag of gold would buy a lot of ale, enough for him to forget all about Petyr Pimple. *Let them hang him, he brought this on himself. It's no more than he deserves, wandering off with some bloody camp follower like a stag in rut.*

His head had begun to pound; soft now, but he knew it would get worse. Merrett rubbed the bridge of his nose. He really had no right to think so ill of Petyr. *I did the same myself when I was his age.* In his case all it got him was a pox, but still, he shouldn't condemn. Whores did have charms, especially if you had a face like Petyr's. The poor lad had a wife, to be sure, but she was half the problem. Not only was she twice his age, but she was bedding his brother Walder too, if the talk was true. There was always lots of talk around the Twins, and only a little was ever true, but in this case Merrett believed it. Black Walder was a man who took what he wanted, even his brother's wife. He'd had Edwyn's wife too, that was common knowledge, Fair Walda had been known to slip into his bed from time to time, and some even said he'd known the seventh Lady Frey a deal better than he should have. Small wonder he refused to marry. Why buy a cow when there were udders all around begging to be milked?

Cursing under his breath, Merrett jammed his heels into his horse's flanks and rode on up the hill. As tempting as it was to drink the gold away, he knew that if he didn't come back with Petyr Pimple, he had as well not come back at all.

Lord Walder would soon turn two-and-ninety. His ears had started to go, his eyes were almost gone, and his gout was so bad that he had to be carried everywhere. He could not possibly last much longer, all his sons agreed. *And when he goes, everything will change, and not for the better.* His father was querulous and stubborn, with an iron will and a wasp's tongue, but he did believe in taking care of his own. *All* of his own, even the ones who had displeased and disappointed him. *Even the ones whose names he can't remember.* Once he was gone, though . . .

When Ser Stevron had been heir, that was one thing. The old man had been grooming Stevron for sixty years, and had pounded it into his head that blood was blood. But Stevron had died whilst campaigning with the Young Wolf in the west—"of waiting, no doubt," Lame Lothar had quipped when the raven brought them the news—and his sons and grandsons were a different sort of Frey. Stevron's son Ser Ryman stood to inherit now; a thick-witted, stubborn, greedy man. And after Ryman came his own sons, Edwyn and Black Walder, who were even worse. "Fortunately," Lame Lothar once said, "they hate each other even more than they hate us."

Merrett wasn't certain that was fortunate at all, and for that matter Lothar himself might be more dangerous than either of them. Lord Walder had ordered the slaughter of the Starks at Roslin's wedding, but it had been Lame Lothar who had plotted it out with Roose Bolton, all the way down to which songs would be played. Lothar was a very amusing fellow to get drunk with, but Merrett would never be so foolish as to turn his back on him. In the Twins, you learned early that only full blood siblings could be trusted, and them not very far.

It was like to be every son for himself when the old man died, and every daughter as well. The new Lord of the Crossing would doubtless keep on *some* of his uncles, nephews, and cousins at the Twins, the ones he happened to like or trust, or more likely the ones he thought would prove useful to him. *The rest of us he'll shove out to fend for ourselves.*

The prospect worried Merrett more than words could say. He would be forty in less than three years, too old to take up the life of a hedge knight . . . even if he'd *been* a knight, which as it happened he wasn't. He had no land, no wealth of his own. He owned the clothes on his back but not much else, not even the horse he was riding. He wasn't clever enough to be a maester, pious enough to be a septon, or savage enough to be a sellsword. *The gods gave me no gift but birth, and they stinted me there.* What good was it to be the son of a rich and powerful House if you were the *ninth* son? When you took grandsons and great-grandsons into account, Merrett stood a better chance of being chosen High Septon than he did of inheriting the Twins.

I have no luck, he thought bitterly. *I have never had any bloody luck.* He was a big man, broad around the chest and shoulders if only of middling height. In the last ten years he had grown soft and fleshy, he knew, but when he'd been younger Merrett had been almost as robust as Ser Hosteen, his eldest full brother, who was commonly regarded as the strongest of Lord Walder Frey's brood. As a boy he'd been packed off to Crakehall to serve his mother's family as a page. When old Lord Sumner had made him a squire, everyone had assumed he would be Ser Merrett in no more than a few years, but the outlaws of the Kingswood Brotherhood had pissed on those plans. While his fellow squire Jaime Lannister was covering himself in glory, Merrett had first caught the pox from a camp follower, then managed to get captured by a *woman*, the one called the White Fawn. Lord Sumner had ransomed him back from the outlaws, but in the very next fight he'd been felled by a blow from a mace that had broken his helm and left him insensible for a fortnight. Everyone gave him up for dead, they told him later.

Merrett hadn't died, but his fighting days were done. Even the lightest blow to his head brought on blinding pain and reduced him to tears. Under these circumstances knighthood was out of the question, Lord Sumner told him, not unkindly. He was sent back to the Twins to face Lord Walder's poisonous disdain.

After that, Merrett's luck had only grown worse. His father had managed to make a good marriage for him, somehow; he wed one of Lord Darry's daughters, back when the Darrys stood high in King Aerys's favor. But it seemed as if he no sooner had deflowered his bride than Aerys lost his throne. Unlike the Freys, the Darrys had been prominent Targaryen loyalists, which cost them half their lands, most of their wealth, and almost all their power. As for his lady wife, she found him a great disappointment from the first, and insisted on popping out nothing but girls for years; three live ones, a stillbirth, and one that died in infancy before she finally produced a son. His eldest daughter had turned out to be a slut, his second a glutton. When Ami was caught in the stables with no fewer than *three* grooms, he'd been forced to marry her off to a bloody *hedge knight*. That situation could not possibly get any worse, he'd thought . . . until Ser Pate decided he could win renown by defeating Ser Gregor Clegane. Ami had come running back a widow, to Merrett's dismay and the undoubted delight of every stablehand in the Twins.

Merrett had dared to hope that his luck was finally changing when Roose Bolton chose to wed *his* Walda instead of one of her slimmer, comelier cousins. The Bolton alliance was important for House Frey and his daughter had helped secure it; he thought that must surely count for something. The old man had soon disabused him. "He picked her because she's *fat*," Lord Walder said. "You think Bolton gave a mummer's fart that she was your whelp? Think he sat about thinking, '*Heh*, Merrett Muttonhead, that's the very man I need for a good-father'? Your Walda's a sow in silk, that's why he picked her, and I'm not like to thank you for it. We'd have had the same alliance at half the price if your little porkling put down her spoon from time to time."

The final humiliation had been delivered with a smile, when Lame Lothar had summoned him to discuss his role in Roslin's wedding. "We must each play our part, according to our gifts," his half-brother told him. "You shall have one task and one task only, Merrett, but I believe you are well suited to it. I want you to see to it that Greatjon Umber is so bloody drunk that he can hardly stand, let alone fight."

And even that I failed at. He'd cozened the huge northman into drinking enough wine to kill any three normal men, yet after Roslin had been bedded the Greatjon still managed to snatch the sword of the first man to accost him and break his arm in the snatching. It had taken eight of them to get him into chains, and the effort had left two men wounded, one dead, and poor old Ser Leslyn Haigh short half an ear. When he couldn't fight with his hands any longer, Umber had fought with his teeth.

Merrett paused a moment and closed his eyes. His head was throbbing like that bloody drum they'd played at the wedding, and for a moment it was all he could do to stay in the saddle. *I have to go on*, he told himself. If he could bring back Petyr Pimple, surely it would put him in Ser Ryman's good graces. Petyr might be a whisker on the hapless side, but he wasn't as cold as Edwyn, nor as hot as Black Walder. *The boy will be grateful for my part, and his father will see that I'm loyal, a man worth having about.*

But only if he was there by sunset with the gold. Merrett glanced at the sky. *Right on time.* He needed something to steady his hands. He pulled up the waterskin hung from his saddle, uncorked it, and took a long swallow. The wine was thick and sweet, so dark it was almost black, but gods it tasted good.

The curtain wall of Oldstones had once encircled the brow of the hill like the crown on a king's head. Only the foundation remained, and a few waist-high piles of crumbling stone spotted with lichen. Merrett rode along the line of the wall until he came to the place where the gatehouse would have stood. The ruins were more extensive here, and he had to dismount to lead his palfrey through them. In the west, the sun had vanished behind a bank of low clouds. Gorse and bracken covered the slopes, and once inside the vanished walls the weeds were chest high. Merrett loosened his sword in its scabbard and looked about warily, but saw no outlaws. *Could I have come on the wrong day?* He stopped and rubbed his temples with his thumbs, but that did nothing to ease the pressure behind his eyes. *Seven bloody hells . . .*

From somewhere deep within the castle, faint music came drifting through the trees.

Merrett found himself shivering, despite his cloak. He pulled open his waterskin and had another drink of wine. *I could just get back on my horse, ride to Oldtown, and drink the gold away. No good ever came from dealing with outlaws.* That vile little bitch Wenda had burned a fawn into the cheek of his arse while she had him captive. No wonder his wife despised him. *I have to go through with this. Petyr Pimple might be Lord of the Crossing one day,*

Edwyn has no sons and Black Walder's only got bastards. Petyr will remember who came to get him. He took another swallow, corked the skin up, and led his palfrey through broken stones, gorse, and thin wind-whipped trees, following the sounds to what had been the castle ward.

Fallen leaves lay thick upon the ground, like soldiers after some great slaughter. A man in patched, faded greens was sitting crosslegged atop a weathered stone sepulcher, fingering the strings of a woodharp. The music was soft and sad. Merrett knew the song. *High in the halls of the kings who are gone, Jenny would dance with her ghosts . . .*

"Get off there," Merrett said. "You're sitting on a king."

"Old Tristifer don't mind my bony arse. The Hammer of Justice, they called him. Been a long while since he heard any new songs." The outlaw hopped down. Trim and slim, he had a narrow face and foxy features, but his mouth was so wide that his smile seemed to touch his ears. A few strands of thin brown hair were blowing across his brow. He pushed them back with his free hand and said, "Do you remember me, my lord?"

"No." Merrett frowned. "Why would I?"

"I sang at your daughter's wedding. And passing well, I thought. That Pate she married was a cousin. We're all cousins in Sevenstreams. Didn't stop him from turning niggard when it was time to pay me." He shrugged. "Why is it your lord father never has me play at the Twins? Don't I make enough noise for his lordship? He likes it loud, I have been hearing."

"You bring the gold?" asked a harsher voice, behind him.

Merrett's throat was dry. *Bloody outlaws, always hiding in the bushes.* It had been the same in the kingswood. you'd think you'd caught five of them, and ten more would spring from nowhere.

When he turned, they were all around him; an ill-favored gaggle of leathery old men and smooth-cheeked lads younger than Petyr Pimple, the lot of them clad in roughspun rags, boiled leather, and bits of dead men's armor. There was one woman with them, bundled up in a hooded cloak three times too big for her. Merrett was too flustered to count them, but there seemed to be a dozen at the least, maybe a score.

"I asked a question." The speaker was a big bearded man with crooked green teeth and a broken nose; taller than Merrett, though not so heavy in the belly. A halfhelm covered his head, a patched yellow cloak his broad shoulders. "Where's our gold?"

"In my saddlebag. A hundred golden dragons." Merrett cleared his throat. "You'll get it when I see that Petyr—"

A squat one-eyed outlaw strode forward before he could finish, reached into the saddlebag bold as you please, and found the sack. Merrett started to grab him, then thought better of it. The outlaw opened the drawstring, removed a coin, and bit it. "Tastes right." He hefted the sack. "Feels right too."

They're going to take the gold and keep Petyr too, Merrett thought in sudden panic. "That's the whole ransom. All you asked for." His palms were sweating. He wiped them on his breeches. "Which one of you is Beric Dondarrion?" Dondarrion had been a lord before he turned outlaw, he might still be a man of honor.

"Why, that would be me," said the one-eyed man.

"You're a bloody liar, Jack," said the big bearded man in the yellow cloak. "It's my turn to be Lord Beric."

"Does that mean I have to be Thoros?" The singer laughed. "My lord, sad to say, Lord Beric was needed elsewhere. The times are troubled, and there are many battles to fight. But we'll sort you out just as he would, have no fear."

Merrett had plenty of fear. His head was pounding too. Much more of this and he'd be sobbing. "You have your gold," he said. "Give me my nephew, and I'll be gone." Petyr was actually more a great half-nephew, but there was no need to go into that.

"He's in the godswood," said the man in the yellow cloak. "We'll take you to him. Notch, you hold his horse."

Merrett handed over the bridle reluctantly. He did not see what other choice he had. "My water skin," he heard himself say. "A swallow of wine, to settle my—"

"We don't drink with your sort," yellow cloak said curtly. "It's this way. Follow me."

Leaves crunched beneath their heels, and every step

sent a spike of pain through Merrett's temple. They walked in silence, the wind gusting around them. The last light of the setting sun was in his eyes as he clambered over the mossy hummocks that were all that remained of the keep. Behind was the godswood.

Petyr Pimple was hanging from the limb of an oak, a noose tight around his long thin neck. His eyes bulged from a black face, staring down at Merrett accusingly. *You came too late*, they seemed to say. But he hadn't. He *hadn't!* He had come when they told him. "You killed him," he croaked.

"Sharp as a blade, this one," said the one-eyed man.

An aurochs was thundering through Merrett's head. *Mother have mercy*, he thought. "I brought the gold."

"That was good of you," said the singer amiably. "We'll see that it's put to good use."

Merrett turned away from Petyr. He could taste the bile in the back of his throat. "You . . . you had no right."

"We had a rope," said yellow cloak. "That's right enough."

Two of the outlaws seized Merrett's arms and bound them tight behind his back. He was too deep in shock to struggle. "No," was all he could manage. "I only came to ransom Petyr. You said if you had the gold by sunset he wouldn't be harmed . . ."

"Well," said the singer, "you've got us there, my lord. That was a lie of sorts, as it happens."

The one-eyed outlaw came forward with a long coil of hempen rope. He looped one end around Merrett's neck, pulled it tight, and tied a hard knot under his ear. The other end he threw over the limb of the oak. The big man in the yellow cloak caught it.

"What are you doing?" Merrett knew how stupid that sounded, but he could not believe what was happening, even then. "You'd never dare hang a Frey."

Yellow cloak laughed. "That other one, the pimply boy, he said the same thing."

He doesn't mean it. He cannot mean it. "My father will pay you. I'm worth a good ransom, more than Petyr, twice as much."

The singer sighed. "Lord Walder might be half-blind and gouty, but he's not so stupid as to snap at the same bait twice. Next time he'll send a hundred swords instead of a hundred dragons, I fear."

"He will!" Merrett tried to sound stern, but his voice betrayed him. "He'll send a thousand swords, and kill you all."

"He has to catch us first." The singer glanced up at poor Petyr. "And he can't hang us twice, now can he?" He drew a melancholy air from the strings of his woodharp. "Here now, don't soil yourself. All you need to do is answer me a question, and I'll tell them to let you go."

Merrett would tell them anything if it meant his life. "What do you want to know? I'll tell you true, I swear it."

The outlaw gave him an encouraging smile. "Well, as it happens, we're looking for a dog that ran away."

"A dog?" Merrett was lost. "What kind of dog?"

"He answers to the name Sandor Clegane. Thoros says he was making for the Twins. We found the ferrymen who took him across the Trident, and the poor sod he robbed on the kingsroad. Did you see him at the wedding, perchance?"

"The Red Wedding?" Merrett's skull felt as if it were about to split, but he did his best to recall. There had been so much confusion, but surely someone would have mentioned Joffrey's dog sniffing round the Twins. "He wasn't in the castle. Not at the main feast . . . he might have been at the bastard feast, or in the camps, but . . . no, someone would have said . . ."

"He would have had a child with him," said the singer. "A skinny girl, about ten. Or perhaps a boy the same age."

"I don't think so," said Merrett. "Not that I knew."

"No? Ah, that's a pity. Well, up you go."

"*No*," Merrett squealed loudly. "No, *don't*, I gave you your answer, you said you'd let me go."

"Seems to me that what I said was I'd *tell* them to let you go." The singer looked at yellow cloak. "Lem, let him go."

"Go bugger yourself," the big outlaw replied brusquely.

The singer gave Merrett a helpless shrug and began to play, "The Day They Hanged Black Robin."

"*Please.*" The last of Merrett's courage was running down his leg. "I've done you no harm. I brought the gold, the way you said. I answered your question. I have *children*."

"That Young Wolf never will," said the one-eyed outlaw.

Merrett could hardly think for the pounding in his head. "He shamed us, the whole realm was laughing, we had to cleanse the stain on our honor." His father had said all that and more.

"Maybe so. What do a bunch o' bloody peasants know about a lord's honor?" Yellow cloak wrapped the end of the rope around his hand three times. "We know some about murder, though."

"Not murder." His voice was shrill. "It was vengeance, we had a right to our vengeance. It was *war*. Aegon, we called him Jinglebell, a poor lackwit never hurt anyone, Lady Stark cut his throat. We lost half a hundred men in the camps. Ser Garse Goodbrook, Kyra's husband, and Ser Tytos, Jared's son . . . someone smashed his head in with an axe . . . Stark's direwolf killed four of our wolfhounds and tore the kennelmaster's arm off his shoulder, even after we'd filled him full of quarrels . . ."

"So you sewed his head on Robb Stark's neck after both o' them were dead," said yellow cloak.

"My father did that. All I did was drink. You wouldn't kill a man for drinking." Merrett remembered something then, something that might be the saving of him. "They say Lord Beric always gives a man a trial, that he won't kill a man unless something's proved against him. You can't prove anything against me. The Red Wedding was my father's work, and Ryman's and Lord Bolton's. Lothar rigged the tents to collapse and put the crossbowmen in the gallery with the musicians, Bastard Walder led the attack on the camps . . . they're the ones you want, not me, I only drank some wine . . . *you have no witness*."

"As it happens, you're wrong there." The singer turned to the hooded woman. "Milady?"

The outlaws parted as she came forward, saying no word. When she lowered her hood, something tightened inside Merrett's chest, and for a moment he could not breathe. *No. No, I saw her die. She was dead for a day and night before they stripped her naked and threw her body in the river. Raymund opened her throat from ear to ear. She was dead.*

Her cloak and collar hid the gash his brother's blade had made, but her face was even worse than he remembered. The flesh had gone pudding soft in the water and turned the color of curdled milk. Half her hair was gone and the rest had turned as white and brittle as a crone's. Beneath her ravaged scalp, her face was shredded skin and black blood where she had raked herself with her nails. But her eyes were the most terrible thing. Her eyes saw him, and they hated.

"She don't speak," said the big man in the yellow cloak. "You bloody bastards cut her throat too deep for that. But she remembers." He turned to the dead woman and said, "What do you say, m'lady? Was he part of it?"

Lady Catelyn's eyes never left him. She nodded.

Merrett Frey opened his mouth to plead, but the noose choked off his words. His feet left the ground, the rope cutting deep into the soft flesh beneath his chin. Up into the air he jerked, kicking and twisting, up and up and up.

APPENDIX

THE KINGS AND THEIR COURTS

THE KING ON THE IRON THRONE

JOFFREY BARATHEON, the First of His Name, a boy of thirteen years, the eldest son of King Robert I Baratheon and Queen Cersei of House Lannister,
—his mother, QUEEN CERSEI, of House Lannister, Queen Regent and Protector of the Realm,
  —Cersei's sworn swords:
    —SER OSFRYD KETTLEBLACK, younger brother to Ser Osmund Kettleblack of the Kingsguard,
    —SER OSNEY KETTLEBLACK, youngest brother of Ser Osmund and Ser Osfryd,
—his sister, PRINCESS MYRCELLA, a girl of nine, a ward of Prince Doran Martell at Sunspear,
—his brother, PRINCE TOMMEN, a boy of eight, next heir to the Iron Throne,
—his grandfather, TYWIN LANNISTER, Lord of Casterly Rock, Warden of the West, and Hand of the King,
—his uncles and cousins, paternal,
  —his father's brother, STANNIS BARATHEON, rebel Lord of Dragonstone, styling himself King Stannis the First,
    —Stannis's daughter, SHIREEN, a girl of eleven,
  —his father's brother, {RENLY BARATHEON}, rebel Lord of Storm's End, murdered in the midst of his army,
  —his grandmother's brother, SER ELDON ESTERMONT,
    —Ser Eldon's son, SER AEMON ESTERMONT,
      —Ser Aemon's son, SER ALYN ESTERMONT,
—his uncles and cousins, maternal,
  —his mother's brother, SER JAIME LANNISTER, called THE KINGSLAYER, a captive at Riverrun,
  —his mother's brother, TYRION LANNISTER, called

THE IMP, a dwarf, wounded in the Battle of the Blackwater,
  —Tyrion's squire, PODRICK PAYNE,
  —Tyrion's captain of guards, SER BRONN OF THE BLACKWATER, a former sellsword,
  —Tyrion's concubine, SHAE, a camp follower now serving as bedmaid to Lollys Stokeworth,
  —his grandfather's brother, SER KEVAN LANNISTER,
  —Ser Kevan's son, SER LANCEL LANNISTER, formerly squire to King Robert, wounded in the Battle of the Blackwater, near death,
  —his grandfather's brother, {TYGETT LANNISTER}, died of a pox,
  —Tygett's son, TYREK LANNISTER, a squire, missing since the great riot,
  —Tyrek's infant wife, LADY ERMESANDE HAYFORD,
—his baseborn siblings, King Robert's bastards:
  —MYA STONE, a maid of nineteen, in the service of Lord Nestor Royce, of the Gates of the Moon,
  —GENDRY, an apprentice smith, a fugitive in the riverlands and ignorant of his heritage,
  —EDRIC STORM, King Robert's only acknowledged bastard son, a ward of his uncle Stannis on Dragonstone,

—his Kingsguard:
  —SER JAIME LANNISTER, Lord Commander,
  —SER MERYN TRANT,
  —SER BALON SWANN,
  —SER OSMUND KETTLEBLACK,
  —SER LORAS TYRELL, the Knight of Flowers,
  —SER ARYS OAKHEART,

—his small council:
  —LORD TYWIN LANNISTER, Hand of the King,
  —SER KEVAN LANNISTER, master of laws,
  —LORD PETYR BAELISH, called LITTLEFINGER, master of coin,
  —VARYS, a eunuch, called THE SPIDER, master of whisperers,
  —LORD MACE TYRELL, master of ships,
  —GRAND MAESTER PYCELLE,

—his court and retainers:

  —SER ILYN PAYNE, the King's Justice, a headsman,
  —LORD HALLYNE THE PYROMANCER, a Wisdom of the Guild of Alchemists,
  —MOON BOY, a jester and fool,
  —ORMOND OF OLDTOWN, the royal harper and bard,
  —DONTOS HOLLARD, a fool and a drunkard, formerly a knight called SER DONTOS THE RED,
  —JALABHAR XHO, Prince of the Red Flower Vale, an exile from the Summer Isles,
  —LADY TANDA STOKEWORTH,
    —her daughter, FALYSE, wed to Ser Balman Byrch,
    —her daughter, LOLLYS, thirty-four, unwed, and soft of wits, with child after being raped,
    —her healer and counselor, MAESTER FRENKEN,
  —LORD GYLES ROSBY, a sickly old man,
  —SER TALLAD, a promising young knight,
  —LORD MORROS SLYNT, a squire, eldest son of the former Commander of the City Watch,
    —JOTHOS SLYNT, his younger brother, a squire,
    —DANOS SLYNT, younger still, a page,
  —SER BOROS BLOUNT, a former knight of the Kingsguard, dismissed for cowardice by Queen Cersei,
  —JOSMYN PECKLEDON, a squire, and a hero of the Battle of the Blackwater,
  —SER PHILIP FOOTE, made Lord of the Marches for his valor during the Battle of the Blackwater,
  —SER LOTHOR BRUNE, named LOTHOR APPLE-EATER for his deeds during the Battle of the Blackwater, a former free-rider in service to Lord Baelish,
—other lords and knights at King's Landing:
  —MATHIS ROWAN, Lord of Goldengrove,
  —PAXTER REDWYNE, Lord of the Arbor,
    —Lord Paxter's twin sons, SER HORAS and SER HOBBER, mocked as HORROR and SLOBBER,
    —Lord Redwyne's healer, MAESTER BALLABAR,
  —ARDRIAN CELTIGAR, the Lord of Claw Isle,
  —LORD ALESANDER STAEDMON, called PENNYLOVER,
  —SER BONIFER HASTY, called THE GOOD, a famed knight,
  —SER DONNEL SWANN, heir to Stonehelm,

—SER RONNET CONNINGTON, called RED RONNET, the Knight of Griffin's Roost,
—AURANE WATERS, the Bastard of Driftmark,
—SER DERMOT OF THE RAINWOOD, a famed knight,
—SER TIMON SCRAPESWORD, a famed knight,

—the people of King's Landing:
—the City Watch (the "gold cloaks"),
—{SER JACELYN BYWATER, called IRONHAND}, Commander of the City Watch, slain by his own men during the Battle of the Blackwater,
—SER ADDAM MARBRAND, Commander of the City Watch, Ser Jacelyn's successor,
—CHATAYA, owner of an expensive brothel,
—ALAYAYA, her daughter,
—DANCY, MAREI, JAYDE, Chataya's girls,
—TOBHO MOTT, a master armorer,
—IRONBELLY, a blacksmith,
—HAMISH THE HARPER, a famed singer,
—COLLIO QUAYNIS, a Tyroshi singer,
—BETHANY FAIR-FINGERS, a woman singer,
—ALARIC OF EYSEN, a singer, far-traveled,
—GALYEON OF CUY, a singer notorious for the length of his songs,
—SYMON SILVER TONGUE, a singer.

King Joffrey's banner shows the crowned stag of Baratheon, black on gold, and the lion of Lannister, gold on crimson, combatant.

THE KING IN THE NORTH
THE KING OF THE TRIDENT

ROBB STARK, Lord of Winterfell, King in the North, and King of the Trident, the eldest son of Eddark Stark, Lord of Winterfell, and Lady Catelyn of House Tully,
  —his direwolf, GREY WIND,
—his mother, LADY CATELYN, of House Tully, widow of Lord Eddard Stark,
—his siblings:
  —his sister, PRINCESS SANSA, a maid of twelve, a captive in King's Landing,
    —Sansa's direwolf, {LADY}, killed at Castle Darry,
  —his sister, PRINCESS ARYA, a girl of ten, missing and presumed dead,
    —Arya's direwolf, NYMERIA, lost near the Trident,
  —his brother, PRINCE BRANDON, called BRAN, heir to the north, a boy of nine, believed dead,
    —Bran's direwolf, SUMMER,
    —Bran companions and protectors:
      —MEERA REED, a maid of sixteen, daughter of Lord Howland Reed of Greywater Watch,
      —JOJEN REED, her brother, thirteen,
      —HODOR, a simpleminded stableboy, seven feet tall,
  —his brother, PRINCE RICKON, a boy of four, believed dead,
    —Rickon's direwolf, SHAGGYDOG,
    —Rickon's companion and protector:
      —OSHA, a wildling captive who served as a scullion at Winterfell,

—his half-brother, JON SNOW, a Sworn Brother of
the Night's Watch,
  —Jon's direwolf, GHOST,

—his uncles and aunts, paternal:
  —his father's elder brother, {BRANDON STARK}, slain
  at the command of King Aerys II Targaryen,
  —his father's sister, {LYANNA STARK}, died in the
  Mountains of Dorne during Robert's Rebellion,
  —his father's younger brother, BENJEN STARK, a man
  of the Night's Watch, lost beyond the Wall,
—his uncles, aunts, and cousins, maternal:
  —his mother's younger sister, LYSA ARRYN, Lady of
  the Eyrie and widow of Lord Jon Arryn,
  —their son, ROBERT ARRYN, Lord of the Eyrie,
  —his mother's younger brother, SER EDMURE TULLY,
  heir to Riverrun,
  —his grandfather's brother, SER BRYNDEN TULLY,
  called THE BLACKFISH,
—his sworn swords and companions:
  —his squire, OLYVAR FREY,
  —SER WENDEL MANDERLY, second son to the Lord of
  White Harbor,
  —PATREK MALLISTER, heir to Seagard,
  —DACEY MORMONT, eldest daughter of Lady Maege
  Mormont and heir to Bear Island,
  —JON UMBER, called THE SMALLJON, heir to Last
  Hearth,
  —DONNEL LOCKE, OWEN NORREY, ROBIN FLINT,
  northmen,

—his lords bannermen, captains and commanders:
—{with Robb's army in the Westerlands}
  —SER BRYNDEN TULLY, the BLACKFISH, commanding
  the scouts and outriders,
  —JON UMBER, called THE GREATJON, commanding
  the van,
  —RICKARD KARSTARK, Lord of Karhold,
  —GALBART GLOVER, Master of Deepwood Motte,
  —MAEGE MORMONT, Lady of Bear Island,
  —{SER STEVRON FREY}, eldest son of Lord Walder
  Frey and heir to the Twins, died at Oxcross,

—Ser Stevron's eldest son, SER RYMAN FREY,
—Ser Ryman's son, BLACK WALDER FREY,
—MARTYN RIVERS, a bastard son of Lord Walder Frey,

—(with Roose Bolton's host at Harrengal),
—ROOSE BOLTON, Lord of the Dreadfort,
—SER AENYS FREY, SER JARED FREY, SER HOSTEEN FREY, SER DANWELL FREY
   —their bastard half-brother, RONEL RIVERS,
—SER WYLIS MANDERLY, heir to White Harbor,
   —SER KYLE CONDON, a knight in his service,
—RONNEL STOUT,
—VARGO HOAT of the Free City of Qohor, captain of a sellsword company, the Brave Companions,
   —his lieutenant, URSWYCK called THE FAITHFUL,
   —his lieutenant, SEPTON UTT,
   —TIMEON OF DORNE, RORGE, IGGO, FAT ZOLLO, BITER, TOGG JOTH of Ibben, PYG, THREE TOES, his men,
   —QYBURN, a chainless maester and sometime necromancer, his healer,

—(with the northern army attacking Duskendale)
—ROBETT GLOVER, of Deepwood Motte,
—SER HELMAN TALLHART, of Torrhen's Square,
—HARRION KARSTARK, sole surviving son of Lord Rickard Karstark, and heir to Karhold,

—(traveling north with Lord Eddard's bones)
—HALLIS MOLLEN, captain of guards for Winterfell,
   —JACKS, QUENT, SHADD, guardsmen,

—his lord bannermen and castellans, in the north:
—WYMAN MANDERLY, Lord of White Harbor,
—HOWLAND REED, Lord of Greywater Watch, a crannogman,
—MORS UMBER, called CROWFOOD, and HOTHER UMBER, called WHORESBANE, uncles to Greatjon Umber, joint castellans at the Last Hearth,
—LYESSA FLINT, Lady of Widow's Watch,
—ONDREW LOCKE, Lord of Oldcastle, an old man,
—(CLEY CERWYN), Lord of Cerwyn, a boy of fourteen, killed in battle at Winterfell,

—his sister, JONELLE CERWYN, a maid of two-and-thirty, now the Lady of Cerwyn,

—{LEOBALD TALLHART}, younger brother to Ser Helman, castellan at Torrhen's Square, killed in battle at Winterfell,

—Leobald's wife, BERENA of House Hornwood,
—Leobald's son, BRANDON, a boy of fourteen,
—Leobald's son, BEREN, a boy of ten,
—Ser Helman's son, {BENFRED}, killed by ironmen on the Stony Shore,
—Ser Helman's daughter, EDDARA, a girl of nine, heir to Torrhen's Square,

—LADY SYBELLE, wife to Robett Glover, a captive of Asha Greyjoy at Deepwood Motte,

—Robett's son, GAWEN, three, rightful heir to Deepwood Motte, a captive of Asha Greyjoy,
—Robett's daughter, ERENA, a babe of one, a captive of Asha Greyjoy at Deepwood Motte,
—LARENCE SNOW, a bastard son of Lord Hornwood, and ward of Galbart Glover, thirteen, a captive of Asha Greyjoy at Deepwood Motte.

The banner of the King in the North remains as it has for thousands of years: the grey direwolf of the Starks of Winterfell, running across an ice-white field.

THE KING IN THE NARROW SEA

STANNIS BARATHEON, the First of His Name, second son of Lord Steffon Baratheon and Lady Cassana of House Estermont, formerly Lord of Dragonstone,
—his wife, QUEEN SELYSE of House Florent,
  —PRINCESS SHIREEN, their daughter, a girl of eleven,
    —PATCHFACE, her lackwit fool,
—his baseborn nephew, EDRIC STORM, a boy of twelve, bastard son of King Robert by Delena Florent,
—his squires, DEVAN SEAWORTH and BRYEN FARRING,
—his court and retainers:
  —LORD ALESTER FLORENT, Lord of Brightwater Keep and Hand of the King, the queen's uncle,
  —SER AXELL FLORENT, castellan of Dragonstone and leader of the queen's men, the queen's uncle,
  —LADY MELISANDRE OF ASSHAI, called THE RED WOMAN, priestess of R'hllor, the Lord of Light and God of Flame and Shadow,
  —MAESTER PYLOS, healer, tutor, counselor,
  —SER DAVOS SEAWORTH, called THE ONION KNIGHT and sometimes SHORTHAND, once a smuggler,
    —Davos's wife, LADY MARYA, a carpenter's daughter,
      —their seven sons:
        —{DALE}, lost on the Blackwater,
        —{ALLARD}, lost on the Blackwater,
        —{MATTHOS}, lost on the Blackwater,
        —{MARIC}, lost on the Blackwater,
        —DEVAN, squire to King Stannis,
        —STANNIS, a boy of nine years,
        —STEFFON, a boy of six years,
—SALLADHOR SAAN, of the Free City of Lys, styling

himself Prince of the Narrow Sea and Lord of Blackwater Bay, master of the *Valyrian* and a fleet of sister galleys,

    —MEIZO MAHR, a eunuch in his hire,

    —KHORANE SATHMANTES, captain of his galley *Shayala's Dance*,

—"PORRIDGE" and "LAMPREY," two gaolers,

—his lords bannermen,

    —MONTERYS VELARYON, Lord of the Tides and Master of Driftmark, a boy of six,

    —DURAM BAR EMMON, Lord of Sharp Point, a boy of fifteen years,

    —SER GILBERT FARRING, castellan of Storm's End,

      —LORD ELWOOD MEADOWS, Ser Gilbert's second,

      —MAESTER JURNE, Ser Gilbert's counselor and healer,

    —LORD LUCOS CHYTTERING, called LITTLE LUCOS, a youth of sixteen,

    —LESTER MORRIGEN, Lord of Crows Nest,

—his knights and sworn swords,

    —SER LOMAS ESTERMONT, the king's maternal uncle,

      —his son, SER ANDREW ESTERMONT,

    —SER ROLLAND STORM, called THE BASTARD OF NIGHT-SONG, a baseborn son of the late Lord Bryen Caron,

    —SER PARMEN CRANE, called PARMEN THE PURPLE, held captive at Highgarden,

    —SER ERREN FLORENT, younger brother to Queen Selyse, held captive at Highgarden,

    —SER GERALD GOWER,

    —SER TRISTON OF TALLY HILL, formerly in service to Lord Guncer Sunglass,

    —LEWYS, called THE FISHWIFE,

    —OMER BLACKBERRY.

King Stannis has taken for his banner the fiery heart of the Lord of Light: a red heart surrounded by orange flames upon a yellow field. Within the heart is the crowned stag of House Baratheon, in black.

THE QUEEN ACROSS THE WATER

DAENERYS TARGARYEN, the First of Her Name, *Khaleesi* of the Dothraki, called DAENERYS STORMBORN, the UNBURNT, MOTHER OF DRAGONS, sole surviving heir of Aerys II Targaryen widow of Khal Drogo of the Dothraki,
—her growing dragons, DROGON, VISERION, RHAEGAL,
—her Queensguard:
  —SER JORAH MORMONT, formerly Lord of Bear Island, exiled for slaving,
  —JHOGO, *ko* and bloodrider, the whip,
  —AGGO, *ko* and bloodrider, the bow,
  —RAKHARO, *ko* and bloodrider, the *arakh*,
  —STRONG BELWAS, a former eunuch slave from the fighting pits of Meereen,
    —his aged squire, ARSTAN called WHITEBEARD; a man of Westeros,
—her handmaids:
  —IRRI, a Dothraki girl, fifteen,
  —JHIQUI, a Dothraki girl, fourteen,
—GROLEO, captain of the great cog *Balerion*, a Pentoshi seafarer in the hire of Illyrio Mopatis,

—her late kin:
  —{RHAEGAR}, her brother, Prince of Dragonstone and heir to the Iron Throne, slain by Robert Baratheon on the Trident,
    —{RHAENYS}, Rhaegar's daughter by Elia of Dorne, murdered during the Sack of King's Landing,
    —{AEGON}, Rhaegar's son by Elia of Dorne, murdered during the Sack of King's Landing,
  —{VISERYS}, her brother, styling himself King Viserys,

the Third of His Name, called THE BEGGAR KING, slain in Vaes Dothrak by Khal Drogo,
—{DROGO}, her husband, a great *khal* of the Dothraki, never defeated in battle, died of a wound,
    —{RHAEGO}, her stillborn son by Khal Drogo, slain in the womb by Mirri Maz Duur,

—her known enemies:
    —KHAL PONO, once *ko* to Drogo,
    —KHAL JHAQO, once *ko* to Drogo,
        —MAGGO, his bloodrider,
    —THE UNDYING OF QARTH, a band of warlocks,
        —PYAT PREE, a Qartheen warlock,
    —THE SORROWFUL MEN, a guild of Qartheen assassins,

—her uncertain allies, past and present:
    —XARO XHOAN DAXOS, a merchant prince of Qarth,
    —QUAITHE, a masked shadowbinder from Asshai,
    —ILLYRIO MOPATIS, a magister of the Free City of Pentos, who brokered her marriage to Khal Drogo,

—in Astapor:
    —KRAZNYS MO NAKLOZ, a wealthy slave trader,
        —his slave, MISSANDEI, a girl of ten, of the Peaceful People of Naath,
    —GRAZDAN MO ULLHOR, an old slave trader, very rich,
        —his slave, CLEON, a butcher and cook,
    —GREY WORM, an eunuch of the Unsullied,

—in Yunkai:
    —GRAZDAN MO ERAZ, envoy and nobleman,
    —MERO OF BRAAVOS, called THE TITAN'S BASTARD, captain of the Second Sons, a free company,
        —BROWN BEN PLUMM, a sergeant in the Second Sons, a sellsword of dubious descent,
    —PRENDAHL NA GHEZN, a Ghiscari sellsword, captain of the Stormcrows, a free company,

—SALLOR THE BALD, a Qartheen sellsword, captain
  of the Stormcrows,
—DAARIO NAHARIS, a flamboyant Tyroshi
  sellsword, captain of the Stormcrows,

—in Meereen:
  —OZNAK ZO PAHL, a hero of the city.

The banner of Daenerys Targaryen is the banner of Aegon
the Conqueror and the dynasty he established: a three-
headed dragon, red on black.

KING OF THE ISLES
AND THE NORTH

BALON GREYJOY, the Ninth of His Name Since the Grey King, styling himself King of the Iron Islands and the North, King of Salt and Rock, Son of the Sea Wind, and Lord Reaper of Pyke,
—his wife, QUEEN ALANNYS, of House Harlaw,
—their children:
——{RODRIK}, their eldest son, slain at Seagard during Greyjoy's Rebellion,
——{MARON}, their second son, slain at Pyke during Greyjoy's Rebellion,
——ASHA, their daughter, captain of the *Black Wind* and conqueror of Deepwood Motte,
——THEON, their youngest son, captain of the *Sea Bitch* and briefly Prince of Winterfell,
———Theon's squire, WEX PYKE, bastard son of Lord Botley's half-brother, a mute lad of twelve,
———Theon's crew, the men of the *Sea Bitch*:
————URZEN, MARON BOTLEY called FISHWHISKERS, STYGG, GEVIN HARLAW, CADWYLE,

—his brothers:
——EURON, called Crow's Eye, captain of the *Silence*, a notorious outlaw, pirate, and raider,
——VICTARION, Lord Captain of the Iron Fleet, master of the *Iron Victory*,
——AERON, called DAMPHAIR, a priest of the Drowned God,
—his household on Pyke:
——MAESTER WENDAMYR, healer and counselor,

    —HELYA, keeper of the castle,
—his warriors and sworn swords:
    —DAGMER called CLEFTJAW, captain of
      Foamdrinker,
    —BLUETOOTH, a longship captain,
    —ULLER, SKYTE, oarsmen and warriors,
    —ANDRIK THE UNSMILING, a giant of a man,
    —QARL, called QARL THE MAID, beardless but
      deadly,

—people of Lordsport:
    —OTTER GIMPKNEE, innkeeper and whoremonger,
    —SIGRIN, a shipwright,

—his lords bannermen:
    —SAWANE BOTLEY, Lord of Lordsport, on Pyke,
    —LORD WYNCH, of Iron Holt, on Pyke,
    —STONEHOUSE, DRUMM, and GOODBROTHER of Old
      Wyk,
    —LORD GOODBROTHER, SPARR, LORD MERLYN, and
      LORD FARWYND of Great Wyk,
    —LORD HARLAW, of Harlaw,
    —VOLMARK, MYRE, STONETREE, and KENNING, of
      Harlaw,
    —ORKWOOD and TAWNEY of Orkmont,
    —LORD BLACKTYDE of Blacktyde,
    —LORD SALTCLIFFE and LORD SUNDERLY of Saltcliffe.

OTHER HOUSES GREAT
AND SMALL

HOUSE ARRYN

The Arryns are descended from the Kings of Mountain and Vale, one of the oldest and purest lines of Andal nobility. House Arryn has taken no part in the War of the Five Kings, holding back its strength to protect the Vale of Arryn. The Arryn sigil is the moon-and-falcon, white, upon a sky-blue field. The Arryn words are *As High As Honor*.

ROBERT ARRYN, Lord of the Eyrie, Defender of the Vale, Warden of the East, a sickly boy of eight years,
—his mother, LADY LYSA, of House Tully, third wife and widow of Lord Jon Arryn, and sister to Catelyn Stark,
—their household:
  —MARILLION, a handsome young singer, much favored by Lady Lysa,
  —MAESTER COLEMON, counselor, healer, and tutor,
  —SER MARWYN BELMORE, captain of guards,
  —MORD, a brutal gaoler,

—his lords bannermen, knights, and retainers:
  —LORD NESTOR ROYCE, High Steward of the Vale and castellan of the Gates of the Moon, of the junior branch of House Royce,
    —Lord Nestor's son, SER ALBAR,
    —Lord Nestor's daughter, MYRANDA,
    —MYA STONE, a bastard girl in his service, natural daughter of King Robert I Baratheon,
  —LORD YOHN ROYCE, called BRONZE YOHN, Lord of Runestone, of the senior branch of House Royce, cousin to Lord Nestor,
    —Lord Yohn's eldest son, SER ANDAR,

—Lord Yohn's second son, {SER ROBAR}, a knight of Renly Baratheon's Rainbow Guard, slain at Storm's End by Ser Loras Tyrell,

—Lord Yohn's youngest son, {SER WAYMAR}, a man of the Night's Watch, lost beyond the Wall,

—SER LYN CORBRAY, a suitor to Lady Lysa,

—MYCHEL REDFORT, his squire,

—LADY ANYA WAYNWOOD,

—Lady Anya's eldest son and heir, SER MORTON, a suitor to Lady Lysa,

—Lady Anya's second son, SER DONNEL, the Knight of the Gate,

—EON HUNTER, Lord of Longbow Hall, an old man, and a suitor to Lady Lysa,

—HORTON REDFORT, Lord of Redfort.

HOUSE FLORENT

The Florents of Brightwater Keep are Tyrell bannermen, despite a superior claim to Highgarden by virtue of a blood tie to House Gardener, the old Kings of the Reach. At the outbreak of the War of the Five Kings, Lord Alester Florent followed the Tyrells in declaring for King Renly, but his brother Ser Axell chose King Stannis, whom he had served for years as castellan of Dragonstone. Their niece Selyse was and is King Stannis's queen. When Renly died at Storm's End, the Florents went over to Stannis with all their strength, the first of Renly's bannermen to do so. The sigil of House Florent shows a fox head in a circle of flowers.

ALESTER FLORENT, Lord of Brightwater,
—his wife, LADY MELARA, of House Crane,
—their children:
——ALEKYNE, heir to Brightwater,
——MELESSA, wed to Lord Randyll Tarly,
——RHEA, wed to Lord Leyton Hightower,
—his siblings:
——SER AXELL, castellan of Dragonstone,
——{SER RYAM}, died in a fall from a horse,
———Ser Ryam's daughter, QUEEN SELYSE, wed to King Stannis Baratheon,
———Ser Ryam's son, {SER IMRY}, commanding Stannis Baratheon's fleet on the Blackwater, lost with the *Fury*,
———Ser Ryam's second son, SER ERREN, held captive at Highgarden,
——SER COLIN,
———Ser Colin's daughter, DELENA, wed to SER HOSMAN NORCROSS,

—Delena's son, EDRIC STORM, a bastard of King Robert I Baratheon, twelve years of age,

—Delena's son, ALESTER NORCROSS, eight,

—Delena's son, RENLY NORCROSS, a boy of two,

—Ser Colin's son, MAESTER OMER, in service at Old Oak,

—Ser Colin's son, MERRELL, a squire on the Arbor,

—his sister, RYLENE, wed to Ser Rycherd Crane.

HOUSE FREY

Powerful, wealthy, and numerous, the Freys are banner-men to House Tully, but they have not always been diligent in their duty. When Robert Baratheon met Rhaegar Targaryen on the Trident, the Freys did not arrive until the battle was done, and thereafter Lord Hoster Tully always called Lord Walder "the Late Lord Frey." It is also said of Walder Frey that he is the only lord in the Seven Kingdoms who could field an army out of his breeches.

At the onset of the War of the Five Kings, Robb Stark won Lord Walder's allegiance by pledging to wed one of his daughters or granddaughters. Two of Lord Walder's grandsons were sent to Winterfell to be fostered.

WALDER FREY, Lord of the Crossing,
—by his first wife, {LADY PERRA, of House Royce}:
  —{SER STEVRON}, their eldest son, died after the
    Battle of Oxcross,
      —m. {Corenna Swann, died of a wasting illness},
      —Stevron's eldest son, SER RYMAN, heir to the
        Twins,
          —Ryman's son, EDWYN, wed to Janyce Hunter,
            —Edwyn's daughter, WALDA, a girl of eight,
          —Ryman's son, WALDER, called BLACK WALDER,
          —Ryman's son, PETYR, called PETYR PIMPLE,
            —m. Mylenda Caron,
            —Petyr's daughter, PERRA, a girl of five,
      —m. {Jeyne Lydden, died in a fall from a horse},
      —Stevron's son, AEGON, a halfwit called
        JINGLEBELL,
      —Stevron's daughter, {MAEGELLE, died in
        childbed}, m. Ser Dafyn Vance,
          —Maegelle's daughter, MARIANNE, a maiden,

　　　—Maegelle's son, WALDER VANCE, a squire,
　　　—Maegelle's son, PATREK VANCE,
　　—m. {Marsella Waynwood, died in childbed},
　　—Stevron's son, WALTON, m. Deana Hardyng,
　　　—Walton's son, STEFFON, called THE SWEET,
　　　—Walton's daughter, WALDA, called FAIR
　　　　WALDA,
　　　—Walton's son, BRYAN, a squire,
　—SER EMMON, m. Genna of House Lannister,
　　—Emmon's son, SER CLEOS, m. Jeyne Darry,
　　　—Cleos's son, TYWIN, a squire of eleven,
　　　—Cleos's son, WILLEM, a page at Ashemark,
　　　　nine,
　　—Emmon's son, SER LYONEL, m. Melesa
　　　Crakehall,
　　—Emmon's son, TION, a captive at Riverrun,
　　—Emmon's son, WALDER, called RED WALDER,
　　　fourteen, a squire at Casterly Rock,
　—SER AENYS, m. {Tyana Wylde, died in childbed},
　　—Aenys's son, AEGON BLOODBORN, an outlaw,
　　—Aenys's son, RHAEGAR, m. Jeyne Beesbury,
　　　—Rhaegar's son, ROBERT, a boy of thirteen,
　　　—Rhaegar's daughter, WALDA, a girl of ten,
　　　　called WHITE WALDA,
　　　—Rhaegar's son, JONOS, a boy of eight,
　—PERRIANE, m. Ser Leslyn Haigh,
　　—Perriane's son, SER HARYS HAIGH,
　　　—Harys's son, WALDER HAIGH, a boy of
　　　　four,
　　—Perriane's son, SER DONNEL HAIGH,
　　—Perriane's son, ALYN HAIGH, a squire,

　—by his second wife, {LADY CYRENNA, of House
　　Swann}:
　　—SER JARED, their eldest son, m. {Alys Frey},
　　　—Jared's son, SER TYTOS, m. Zhoe Blanetree,
　　　　—Tytos's daughter, ZIA, a maid of fourteen,
　　　　—Tytos's son, ZACHERY, a boy of twelve,
　　　　　training at the Sept of Oldtown,
　　　—Jared's daughter, KYRA, m. Ser Garse
　　　　Goodbrook,

—Kyra's son, WALDER GOODBROOK, a boy of nine,

—Kyra's daughter, JEYNE GOODBROOK, six,

—SEPTON LUCEON, in service at the Great Sept of Baelor in King's Landing,

—by his third wife, {LADY AMAREI of House Crakehall}:

—SER HOSTEEN, their eldest son, m. Bellena Hawick,

—Hosteen's son, SER ARWOOD, m. Ryella Royce,

—Arwood's daughter, RYELLA, a girl of five,

—Arwood's twin sons, ANDROW and ALYN, three,

—LADY LYTHENE, m. Lord Lucias Vypren,

—Lythene's daughter, ELYANA, m. Ser Jon Wylde,

—Elyana's son, RICKARD WYLDE, four,

—Lythene's son, SER DAMON VYPREN,

—SYMOND, m. Betharios of Braavos,

—Symond's son, ALESANDER, a singer,

—Symond's daughter, ALYX, a maid of seventeen,

—Symond's son, BRADAMAR, a boy of ten, fostered on Braavos as a ward of Oro Tendyris, a merchant of that city,

—SER DANWELL, m. Wynafrei Whent,

—{many stillbirths and miscarriages},

—MERRETT, m. Mariya Darry,

—Merrett's daughter, AMEREI, called AMI, a widow of sixteen, m. {Ser Pate of the Blue Fork},

—Merrett's daughter, WALDA, called FAT WALDA, a wife of fifteen years, m. Lord Roose Bolton,

—Merrett's daughter, MARISSA, a maid of thirteen,

—Merrett's son, WALDER, called LITTLE WALDER, a boy of seven, taken captive at Winterfell while a ward of Lady Catelyn Stark,

—{SER GEREMY, drowned}, m. Carolei Waynwood,

—Geremy's son, SANDOR, a boy of twelve, a squire to Ser Donnel Waynwood,

—Geremy's daughter, CYNTHEA, a girl of nine, a ward of Lady Anya Waynwood,

—SER RAYMUND, m. Beony Beesbury,

    —Raymund's son, ROBERT, sixteen, in training at the Citadel in Oldtown,

    —Raymund's son, MALWYN, fifteen, apprenticed to an alchemist in Lys,

    —Raymund's twin daughters, SERRA and SARRA, maiden girls of fourteen,

    —Raymund's daughter, CERSEI, six, called LITTLE BEE,

—by his fourth wife, {LADY ALYSSA, of House Blackwood}:

    —LOTHAR, their eldest son, called LAME LOTHAR, m. Leonella Lefford,

        —Lothar's daughter, TYSANE, a girl of seven,

        —Lothar's daughter, WALDA, a girl of four,

        —Lothar's daughter, EMBERLEI, a girl of two,

    —SER JAMMOS, m. Sallei Paege,

        —Jammos's son, WALDER, called BIG WALDER, a boy of eight, taken captive at Winterfell while a ward of Lady Catelyn Stark,

        —Jammos's twin sons, DICKON and MATHIS, five,

    —SER WHALEN, m. Sylwa Paege,

        —Whalen's son, HOSTER, a boy of twelve, squire to Ser Damon Paege,

        —Whalen's daughter, MERIANNE, called MERRY, a girl of eleven,

    —LADY MORYA, m. Ser Flement Brax,

        —Morya's son, ROBERT BRAX, nine, fostered at Casterly Rock as a page,

        —Morya's son, WALDER BRAX, a boy of six,

        —Morya's son, JON BRAX, a babe of three,

    —TYTA, called TYTA THE MAID, a maid of twenty-nine,

—by his fifth wife, {LADY SARYA of House Whent}:

    —no progeny,

—by his sixth wife, {LADY BETHANY of House Rosby}:

    —SER PERWYN, their eldest son,

—SER BENFREY, m. Jyanna Frey, a cousin,
  —Benfrey's daughter, DELLA, called DEAF DELLA,
    a girl of three,
  —Benfrey's son, OSMUND, a boy of two,
—MAESTER WILLAMEN, in service at Longbow Hall,
—OLYVAR, squire to Robb Stark,
—ROSLIN, a maid of sixteen,

—by his seventh wife, {LADY ANNARA of House
  Farring}:
  —ARWYN, a maid of fourteen,
  —WENDEL, their eldest son, a boy of thirteen,
    fostered at Seagard as a page,
  —COLMAR, promised to the Faith, eleven,
  —WALTYR, called TYR, a boy of ten,
  —ELMAR, formerly betrothed to Arya Stark, a boy of
    nine,
  —SHIREI, a girl of six,

—his eighth wife, LADY JOYEUSE of House Erenford,
—no progeny as yet,

—Lord Walder's natural children, by sundry mothers,
  —WALDER RIVERS, called BASTARD WALDER,
      —Bastard Walder's son, SER AEMON RIVERS,
      —Bastard Walder's daughter, WALDA RIVERS,
  —MAESTER MELWYS, in service at Rosby,
  —JEYNE RIVERS, MARTYN RIVERS, RYGER RIVERS,
    RONEL RIVERS, MELLARA RIVERS, others.

HOUSE LANNISTER

The Lannisters of Casterly Rock remain the principal support of King Joffrey's claim to the Iron Throne. They boast of descent from Lann the Clever, the legendary trickster of the Age of Heroes. The gold of Casterly Rock and the Golden Tooth has made them the wealthiest of the Great Houses. The Lannister sigil is a golden lion upon a crimson field. Their words are *Hear Me Roar!*

TYWIN LANNISTER, Lord of Casterly Rock, Warden of the West, Shield of Lannisport, and Hand of the King,
—his son, SER JAIME, called THE KINGSLAYER, a twin to Queen Cersei, Lord Commander of the Kingsguard, and Warden of the East, a captive at Riverrun,
—his daughter, QUEEN CERSEI, twin to Jaime, widow of King Robert I Baratheon, Queen Regent for her son Joffrey,
——her son, KING JOFFREY BARATHEON, a boy of thirteen,
——her daughter, PRINCESS MYRCELLA BARATHEON, a girl of nine, a ward of Prince Doran Martell in Dorne,
——her son, PRINCE TOMMEN BARATHEON, a boy of eight, heir to the Iron Throne,
—his dwarf son, TYRION, called THE IMP, called HALFMAN, wounded and scarred on the Blackwater,

—his siblings:
——SER KEVAN, Lord Tywin's eldest brother,
———Ser Kevan's wife, DORNA, of House Swyft,
———their son, SER LANCEL, formerly a squire to King Robert, wounded and near death,
———their son, WILLEM, twin to Martyn, a squire, captive at Riverrun,

—their son, MARTYN, twin to Willem, a squire, a captive with Robb Stark,
     —their daughter, JANEI, a girl of two,
—GENNA, his sister, wed to Ser Emmon Frey,
     —their son, SER CLEOS FREY, a captive at Riverrun,
     —their son, SER LYONEL,
     —their son, TION FREY, a squire, captive at Riverrun,
     —their son, WALDER, called RED WALDER, a squire at Casterly Rock,
—{SER TYGETT}, his second brother, died of a pox,
     —Tygett's widow, DARLESSA, of House Marbrand,
     —their son, TYREK, squire to the king, missing,
—{GERION}, his youngest brother, lost at sea,
     —Gerion's bastard daughter, JOY, eleven,

—his cousin, {SER STAFFORD LANNISTER}, brother to the late Lady Joanna, slain at Oxcross,
     —Ser Stafford's daughters, CERENNA and MYRIELLE,
     —Ser Stafford's son, SER DAVEN,
—his cousins:
     —SER DAMION LANNISTER, m. Lady Shiera Crakehall,
        —his son, SER LUCION,
        —his daughter, LANNA, m. Lord Antario Jast,
     —MARGOT, m. Lord Titus Peake,

—his household:
     —MAESTER CREYLEN, healer, tutor, and counselor,
     —VYLARR, captain-of-guards,
        —LUM and RED LESTER, guardsmen,
     —WHITESMILE WAT, a singer,
     —SER BENEDICT BROOM, master-at-arms,

—his lords bannermen:
     —DAMON MARBRAND, Lord of Ashemark,
        —SER ADDAM MARBRAND, his son and heir,
     —ROLAND CRAKEHALL, Lord of Crakehall,
        —his brother, {SER BURTON CRAKEHALL}, killed by Lord Beric Dondarrion and his outlaws,
        —his son and heir, SER TYBOLT CRAKEHALL,
        —his second son, SER LYLE CRAKEHALL, called STRONGBOAR, a captive at Pinkmaiden Castle,

—his youngest son, SER MERLON CRAKEHALL,
—{ANDROS BRAX}, Lord of Hornvale, drowned during
the Battle of the Camps,
   —his brother, {SER RUPERT BRAX}, slain at Oxcross,
   —his eldest son, SER TYTOS BRAX, now Lord of
   Hornvale, a captive at the Twins,
   —his second son, {SER ROBERT BRAX}, slain at the
   Battle of the Fords,
   —his third son, SER FLEMENT BRAX, now heir,
—{LORD LEO LEFFORD}, drowned at the Stone Mill,
—REGENARD ESTREN, Lord of Wyndhall, a captive at
the Twins,
—GAWEN WESTERLING, Lord of the Crag, a captive at
Seagard,
   —his wife, LADY SYBELL, of House Spicer,
      —her brother, SER ROLPH SPICER,
      —her cousin, SER SAMWELL SPICER,
   —their children:
      —SER RAYNALD WESTERLING,
      —JEYNE, a maid of sixteen years,
      —ELEYNA, a girl of twelve,
      —ROLLAM, a boy of nine,
—LEWYS LYDDEN, Lord of the Deep Den,
—LORD ANTARIO JAST, a captive at Pinkmaiden
Castle,
—LORD PHILIP PLUMM,
   —his sons, SER DENNIS PLUMM, SER PETER PLUMM,
   and SER HARWYN PLUMM, called HARDSTONE,
—QUENTEN BANEFORT, Lord of Banefort, a captive
of Lord Jonos Bracken,
—his knights and captains:
   —SER HARYS SWYFT, good-father to Ser Kevan
   Lannister,
      —Ser Harys's son, SER STEFFON SWYFT,
         —Ser Steffon's daughter, JOANNA,
      —Ser Harys's daughter, SHIERLE, m. Ser Melwyn
      Sarsfield,
   —SER FORLEY PRESTER,
   —SER GARTH GREENFIELD, a captive at Raventree
   Hall,
   —SER LYMOND VIKARY, a captive at Wayfarer's Rest,
   —LORD SELMOND STACKSPEAR,

—his son, SER STEFFON STACKSPEAR,

—his younger son, SER ALYN STACKSPEAR,

—TERRENCE KENNING, Lord of Kayce,

—SER KENNOS OF KAYCE, a knight in his service,

—SER GREGOR CLEGANE, the Mountain That Rides,

—POLLIVER, CHISWYCK, RAFF THE SWEETLING, DUNSEN, and THE TICKLER, soldiers in his service,

—{SER AMORY LORCH}, fed to a bear by Vargo Hoat after the fall of Harrenhal.

HOUSE MARTELL

Dorne was the last of the Seven Kingdoms to swear fealty to the Iron Throne. Blood, custom, and history all set the Dornishmen apart from the other kingdoms. At the outbreak of the War of the Five Kings, Dorne took no part. With the betrothal of Myrcella Baratheon to Prince Trystane, Sunspear declared its support for King Joffrey and called its banners. The Martell banner is a red sun pierced by a golden spear. Their words are *Unbowed, Unbent, Unbroken*.

DORAN NYMEROS MARTELL, Lord of Sunspear, Prince of Dorne,
—his wife, MELLARIO, of the Free City of Norvos,
—their children:
    —PRINCESS ARIANNE, their eldest daughter, heir to Sunspear,
    —PRINCE QUENTYN, their elder son,
    —PRINCE TRYSTANE, their younger son, betrothed to Myrcella Baratheon,
—his siblings:
    —his sister, {PRINCESS ELIA}, wife of Prince Rhaegar Targaryen, slain during the Sack of King's Landing,
    —their children:
        —{PRINCESS RHAENYS}, a young girl, slain during the Sack of King's Landing,
        —{PRINCE AEGON}, a babe, slain during the Sack of King's Landing,
    —his brother, PRINCE OBERYN, called THE RED VIPER,
        —Prince Oberyn's paramour, ELLARIA SAND,
        —Prince Oberyn's bastard daughters, OBARA,

NYMERIA, TYENE, SARELLA, ELIA, OBELLA,
DOREA, LOREZA, called THE SAND SNAKES,
—Prince Oberyn's companions:
  —HARMEN ULLER, Lord of Hellholt,
    —Harmen's brother, SER ULWYCK ULLER,
  —SER RYON ALLYRION,
    —Ser Ryon's natural son, SER DAEMON
    SAND, the Bastard of Godsgrace,
  —DAGOS MANWOODY, Lord of Kingsgrave,
    —Dagos's sons, MORS and DICKON,
    —Dagos's brother, SER MYLES MANWOODY,
  —SER ARRON QORGYLE,
  —SER DEZIEL DALT, the Knight of Lemonwood,
  —MYRIA JORDAYNE, heir to the Tor,
  —LARRA BLACKMONT, Lady of Blackmont,
    —her daughter, JYNESSA BLACKMONT,
    —her son, PERROS BLACKMONT, a squire,
—his household:
  —AREO HOTAH, a Norvoshi sellsword, captain of
  guards,
  —MAESTER CALEOTTE, counselor, healer, and tutor,
—his lords bannermen:
  —HARMEN ULLER, Lord of Hellholt,
  —EDRIC DAYNE, Lord of Starfall,
  —DELONNE ALLYRION, Lady of Godsgrace,
  —DAGOS MANWOODY, Lord of Kingsgrave,
  —LARRA BLACKMONT, Lady of Blackmont,
  —TREMOND GARGALEN, Lord of Salt Shore,
  —ANDERS YRONWOOD, Lord of Yronwood,
  —NYMELLA TOLAND.

HOUSE TULLY

Lord Edmyn Tully of Riverrun was one of the first of the river lords to swear fealty to Aegon the Conqueror. The victorious Aegon rewarded him by raising House Tully to dominion over all the lands of the Trident. The Tully sigil is a leaping trout, silver, on a field of rippling blue and red. The Tully words are *Family, Duty, Honor*.

HOSTER TULLY, Lord of Riverrun,
—his wife, {LADY MINISA, of House Whent}, died in childbed,
—their children:
—CATELYN, widow of Lord Eddard Stark of Winterfell,
—her eldest son, ROBB STARK, Lord of Winterfell, King in the North, and King of the Trident,
—her daughter, SANSA STARK, a maid of twelve, captive at King's Landing,
—her daughter, ARYA STARK, ten, missing for a year,
—her son, BRANDON STARK, eight, believed dead,
—her son, RICKON STARK, four, believed dead,
—LYSA, widow of Lord Jon Arryn of the Eyrie,
—her son, ROBERT, Lord of the Eyrie and Defender of the Vale, a sickly boy of seven years,
—SER EDMURE, his only son, heir to Riverrun,
—Ser Edmure's friends and companions:
—SER MARQ PIPER, heir to Pinkmaiden,
—LORD LYMOND GOODBROOK,
—SER RONALD VANCE, called THE BAD, and his brothers, SER HUGO, SER ELLERY, and KIRTH,
—PATREK MALLISTER, LUCAS BLACKWOOD, SER

PERWYN FREY, TRISTAN RYGER, SER ROBERT PAEGE,

—his brother, SER BRYNDEN, called THE BLACKFISH,

—his household:

- —MAESTER VYMAN, counselor, healer, and tutor,
- —SER DESMOND GRELL, master-at-arms,
- —SER ROBIN RYGER, captain of the guard,
  - —LONG LEW, ELWOOD, DELP, guardsmen,
- —UTHERYDES WAYN, steward of Riverrun,
- —RYMUND THE RHYMER, a singer,

—his lords bannermen:

- —JONOS BRACKEN, Lord of the Stone Hedge,
- —JASON MALLISTER, Lord of Seagard,
- —WALDER FREY, Lord of the Crossing,
- —CLEMENT PIPER, Lord of Pinkmaiden Castle,
- —KARYL VANCE, Lord of Wayfarer's Rest,
- —NORBERT VANCE, Lord of Atranta,
- —THEOMAR SMALLWOOD, Lord of Acorn Hall,
  - —his wife, LADY RAVELLA, of House Swann,
  - —their daughter, CARELLEN,
- —WILLIAM MOOTON, Lord of Maidenpool,
- —SHELLA WHENT, dispossessed Lady of Harrenhal,
- —SER HALMON PAEGE.
- —TYTOS BLACKWOOD, Lord of Raventree

HOUSE TYRELL

The Tyrells rose to power as stewards to the Kings of the Reach, whose domain included the fertile plains of the southwest from the Dornish marches and Blackwater Rush to the shores of the Sunset Sea. Through the female line, they claim descent from Garth Greenhand, gardener king of the First Men, who wore a crown of vines and flowers and made the land bloom. When Mern IX, last king of House Gardener, was slain on the Field of Fire, his steward Harlen Tyrell surrendered Highgarden to Aegon the Conqueror. Aegon granted him the castle and dominion over the Reach. The Tyrell sigil is a golden rose on a grass-green field. Their words are *Growing Strong*.

Lord Mace Tyrell declared his support for Renly Baratheon at the onset of the War of the Five Kings, and gave him the hand of his daughter Margaery. Upon Renly's death, Highgarden made alliance with House Lannister, and Margaery was betrothed to King Joffrey.

MACE TYRELL, Lord of Highgarden, Warden of the South, Defender of the Marches, and High Marshall of the Reach,
  —his wife, LADY ALERIE, of House Hightower of Oldtown,
  —their children:
    —WILLAS, their eldest son, heir to Highgarden,
    —SER GARLAN, called THE GALLANT, their second son,
      —his wife, LADY LEONETTE of House Fossoway,
    —SER LORAS, the Knight of Flowers, their youngest son, a Sworn Brother of the Kingsguard,
    —MARGAERY, their daughter, a widow of fifteen years, betrothed to King Joffrey I Baratheon,
      —Margaery's companions and ladies-in-waiting:

—her cousins, MEGGA, ALLA, and ELINOR
TYRELL,
—Elinor's betrothed, ALYN AMBROSE, squire,
—LADY ALYSANNE BULWER, a girl of eight,
—MEREDYTH CRANE, called MERRY,
—TAENA OF MYR, wife to LORD ORTON MERRY-
WEATHER,
—LADY ALYCE GRACEFORD,
—SEPTA NYSTERICA, a sister of the Faith,
—his widowed mother, LADY OLENNA of House
Redwyne, called the QUEEN OF THORNS,
—Lady Olenna's guardsmen, ARRYK and ERRYK,
called LEFT and RIGHT,
—his sisters:
—LADY MINA, wed to Paxter Redwyne, Lord of the
Arbor,
—their children:
—SER HORAS REDWYNE, twin to Hobber, mocked
as HORROR,
—SER HOBBER REDWYNE, twin to Horas, mocked
as SLOBBER,
—DESMERA REDWYNE, a maid of sixteen,
—LADY JANNA, wed to Ser Jon Fossoway,
—his uncles and cousins:
—his father's brother, GARTH, called THE GROSS,
Lord Seneschal of Highgarden,
—Garth's bastard sons, GARSE and GARRETT
FLOWERS,
—his father's brother, SER MORYN, Lord
Commander of the City Watch of Oldtown,
—Moryn's son, [SER LUTHOR], m. Lady Elyn
Norridge,
—Luthor's son, SER THEODORE, m. Lady Lia
Serry,
—Theodore's daughter, ELINOR,
—Theodore's son, LUTHOR, a squire,
—Luthor's son, MAESTER MEDWICK,
—Luthor's daughter, OLENE, m. Ser Leo
Blackbar,
—Moryn's son, LEO, called LEO THE LAZY,
—his father's brother, MAESTER GORMON, a scholar
of the Citadel,

—his cousin, {SER QUENTIN}, died at Ashford,
  —Quentin's son, SER OLYMER, m. Lady Lysa
    Meadows,
      —Olymer's sons, RAYMUND and RICKARD,
      —Olymer's daughter, MEGGA,
—his cousin, MAESTER NORMUND, in service at
  Blackcrown,
—his cousin, {SER VICTOR}, slain by the Smiling
  Knight of the Kingswood Brotherhood,
—Victor's daughter, VICTARIA, m. {Lord Jon Bulwer},
  died of a summer fever,
  —their daughter, LADY ALYSANNE BULWER, eight,
—Victor's son, SER LEO, m. Lady Alys Beesbury,
  —Leo's daughters, ALLA and LEONA,
  —Leo's sons, LYONEL, LUCAS, and LORENT,

—his household at Highgarden:
  —MAESTER LOMYS, counselor, healer, and tutor,
  —IGON VYRWEL, captain of the guard,
  —SER VORTIMER CRANE, master-at-arms,
  —BUTTERBUMPS, fool and jester, hugely fat,

—his lords bannermen:
  —RANDYLL TARLY, Lord of Horn Hill,
  —PAXTER REDWYNE, Lord of the Arbor,
  —ARWYN OAKHEART, Lady of Old Oak,
  —MATHIS ROWAN, Lord of Goldengrove,
  —ALESTER FLORENT, Lord of Brightwater Keep, a
    rebel in support of Stannis Baratheon,
  —LEYTON HIGHTOWER, Voice of Oldtown, Lord of
    the Port,
  —ORTON MERRYWEATHER, Lord of Longtable,
  —LORD ARTHUR AMBROSE,
—his knights and sworn swords:
  —SER MARK MULLENDORE, crippled during the
    Battle of the Blackwater,
  —SER JON FOSSOWAY, of the green-apple Fossoways,
  —SER TANTON FOSSOWAY, of the red-apple
    Fossoways.

REBELS, ROGUES, AND SWORN BROTHERS

THE SWORN BROTHERS OF THE NIGHT'S WATCH

(ranging Beyond the Wall)

JEOR MORMONT, called THE OLD BEAR, Lord Commander of the Night's Watch,
- —JON SNOW, the Bastard of Winterfell, his steward and squire, lost while scouting the Skirling Pass,
    - —GHOST, his direwolf, white and silent,
    - —EDDISON TOLLETT, called DOLOROUS EDD, his squire,
- —THOREN SMALLWOOD, commanding the rangers,
    - —DYWEN, DIRK, SOFTFOOT, GRENN, BEDWYCK called GIANT, OLLO LOPHAND, GRUBBS, BERNARR called BROWN BERNARR, another BERNARR called BLACK BERNARR, TIM STONE, ULMER OF KINGSWOOD, GARTH called GREYFEATHER, GARTH OF GREENAWAY, GARTH OF OLDTOWN, ALAN OF ROSBY, RONNEL HARCLAY, AETHAN, RYLES, MAWNEY, rangers,
- —JARMEN BUCKWELL, commanding the scouts,
    - —BANNEN, KEDGE WHITEYE, TUMBERJON, FORNIO, GOADY, rangers and scouts,
- —SER OTTYN WYTHERS, commanding the rearguard,
- —SER MALADOR LOCKE, commanding the baggage,
    - —DONNEL HILL, called SWEET DONNEL, his squire and steward,
    - —HAKE, a steward and cook,
    - —CHETT, an ugly steward, keeper of hounds,
    - —SAMWELL TARLY, a fat steward, keeper of ravens, mocked as SER PIGGY,
    - —LARK called THE SISTERMAN, his cousin ROLLEY OF SISTERTON, CLUBFOOT KARL, MASLYN, SMALL PAUL,

SAWWOOD, LEFT HAND LEW, ORPHAN OSS, MUTTERING BILL, stewards,
—{QHORIN HALFHAND}, commanding the rangers from the Shadow Tower, slain in the Skirling Pass,
—{SQUIRE DALBRIDGE, EGGEN}, rangers, slain in the Skirling Pass,
—STONESNAKE, a ranger and mountaineer, lost afoot in Skirling Pass,
—BLANE, Qhorin Halfhand's second, commanding the Shadow Tower men on the Fist of the First Men,
—SER BYAM FLINT,

(at Castle Black)
BOWEN MARSH, Lord Steward and castellan,
—MAESTER AEMON (TARGARYEN), healer and counselor, a blind man, one hundred years old,
—his steward, CLYDAS,
—BENJEN STARK, First Ranger, missing, feared dead,
—SER WYNTON STOUT, eighty years a ranger,
—SER ALADALE WYNCH, PYPAR, DEAF DICK FOLLARD, HAIRY HAL, BLACK JACK BULWER, ELRON, MATTHAR, rangers,
—OTHELL YARWYCK, First Builder,
—SPARE BOOT, YOUNG HENLY, HALDER, ALBETT, KEGS, SPOTTED PATE OF MAIDENPOOL, builders,
—DONAL NOYE, armorer, smith, and steward, one-armed,
—THREE-FINGER HOBB, steward and chief cook,
—TIM TANGLETONGUE, EASY, MULLY, OLD HENLY, CUGEN, RED ALYN OF THE ROSEWOOD, JEREN, stewards,
—SEPTON CELLADOR, a drunken devout,
—SER ENDREW TARTH, master-at-arms,
—RAST, ARRON, EMRICK, SATIN, HOP-ROBIN, recruits in training,
—CONWY, GUEREN, recruiters and collectors,

(at Eastwatch-by-the-Sea)
—COTTER PYKE, Commander Eastwatch,
—MAESTER HARMUNE, healer and counselor,
—SER ALLISER THORNE, master-at-arms,

—JANOS SLYNT, former commander of the City Watch of King's Landing, briefly Lord of Harrenhal,

—SER GLENDON HEWETT,

—DAREON, steward and singer,

—IRON EMMETT, a ranger famed for his strength,

(at Shadow Tower)

SER DENYS MALLISTER, Commander, Shadow Tower

—his steward and squire, WALLACE MASSEY,

—MAESTER MULLIN, healer and counselor.

THE BROTHERHOOD WITHOUT BANNERS
AN OUTLAW FELLOWSHIP

BERIC DONDARRION, Lord of Blackhaven, called THE
LIGHTNING LORD, oft reported dead,
—his right hand, THOROS OF MYR, a red priest,
—his squire, EDRIC DAYNE, Lord of Starfall, twelve,
—his followers:
    —LEM, called LEM LEMONCLOAK, a one-time soldier,
    —HARWIN, son of Hullen, formerly in service to
      Lord Eddard Stark at Winterfell,
    —GREENBEARD, a Tyroshi sellsword,
    —TOM OF SEVENSTREAMS, a singer of dubious report,
      called TOM SEVENSTRINGS and TOM O' SEVENS,
    —ANGUY THE ARCHER, a bowman from the Dornish
      Marches,
    —JACK-BE-LUCKY, a wanted man, short an eye,
    —THE MAD HUNTSMAN, of Stoney Sept,
    —KYLE, NOTCH, DENNETT, longbowmen,
    —MERRIT O' MOONTOWN, WATTY THE MILLER, LIKELY
      LUKE, MUDGE, BEARDLESS DICK, outlaws in his band,

—at the Inn of the Kneeling Man:
    —SHARNA, the innkeep, a cook and midwife,
      —her husband, called HUSBAND,
      —BOY, an orphan of the war,

—at the Peach, a brothel in Stoney Sept:
    —TANSY, the red-haired proprietor,
      —ALYCE, CASS, LANNA, JYZENE, HELLY, BELLA,
      some of her peaches,

—at Acorn Hall, the seat of House Smallwood:
  —LADY RAVELLA, formerly of House Swann, wife to
  Lord Theomar Smallwood,

—here and there and elsewhere:
  —LORD LYMOND LYCHESTER, an old man of
  wandering wit, who once held Ser Maynard at the
  bridge,
    —his young caretaker, MAESTER ROONE,
  —the ghost of High Heart,
  —the Lady of the Leaves,
  —the septon at Sallydance.

the WILDLINGS, or
the FREE FOLK

MANCE RAYDER, King-beyond-the-Wall,
—DALLA, his pregnant wife,
—VAL, her younger sister,

—his chiefs and captains:
—HARMA, called DOGSHEAD, commanding his van,
—THE LORD OF BONES, mocked as RATTLESHIRT,
leader of a war band,
—YGRITTE, a young spearwife, a member of his
band,
—RYK, called LONGSPEAR, a member of his band,
—RAGWYLE, LENYL, members of his band,
—his captive, JON SNOW, the crow-come-over,
—GHOST, Jon's direwolf, white and silent,
—STYR, Magnar of Thenn,
—JARL, a young raider, Val's lover,
—GRIGG THE GOAT, ERROK, QUORT, BODGER, DEL,
BIG BOIL, HEMPEN DAN, HENK THE HELM, LENN,
TOEFINGER, STONE THUMBS, raiders,
—TORMUND, Mead-King of Ruddy Hall, called
GIANTS-BANE, TALL-TALKER, HORN-BLOWER, and
BREAKER OF ICE, also THUNDERFIST, HUSBAND TO
BEARS, SPEAKER TO GODS, and FATHER OF HOSTS,
leader of a war band,
—his sons, TOREGG THE TALL, TORWYRD THE
TAME, DORMUND, and DRYN, his daughter
MUNDA,
—{ORELL, called ORELL THE EAGLE}, a skinchanger
slain by Jon Snow in the Skirling Pass,

—MAG MAR TUN DOH WEG, called MAG THE MIGHTY, of the giants,

—VARMYR called SIXSKINS, a skinchanger, master of three wolves, a shadowcat, and a snow bear,

—THE WEEPER, a raider and leader of a war band,

—{ALFYN CROWKILLER}, a raider, slain by Qhorin Halfhand of the Night's Watch,

CRASTER, of Craster's Keep, who kneels to none,

—GILLY, his daughter and wife, great with child,

—DYAH, FERNY, NELLA, three of his nineteen wives.

ACKNOWLEDGMENTS

If bricks aren't well made, the wall falls down.

This is an awfully big wall I'm building here, so I need a lot of bricks. Fortunately, I know a lot of brickmakers, and all sorts of other useful folk as well.

Thanks and appreciation, once more, to those good friends who so kindly lent me their expertise (and in some cases, even their *books*) so my bricks would be nice and solid—to my Archmaester Sage Walker, to First Builder Carl Keim, to Melinda Snodgrass my master of horse.

And as ever, to Parris.

ABOUT THE AUTHOR

GEORGE R. R. MARTIN sold his first story in 1971 and hasn't stopped. As a writer/producer, he worked on *The Twilight Zone, Beauty and the Beast,* and various feature films and pilots that were never made. In the mid '90s he returned to prose and began work on A Song of Ice and Fire. He has been in the Seven Kingdoms ever since. He lives in Santa Fe, New Mexico, with the lovely Parris.

George R. R. Martin's
epic fantasy saga
A Song of Ice and Fire

begins with
A GAME OF THRONES

and continues in
A CLASH OF KINGS

A STORM OF SWORDS

A FEAST FOR CROWS

The long-awaited next volume
in the series!

Now, here's a special preview of
the next book in

George R. R. Martin's

landmark series

A FEAST FOR CROWS

the riveting sequel to

A GAME OF THRONES
A CLASH OF KINGS
and
A STORM OF SWORDS

Available now

CERSEI

A cold rain fell from a slate grey sky, turning the walls and ramparts of the Red Keep dark as blood. The queen held the king's hand and led him firmly across the muddy yard to where her litter waited with its escort. "Uncle Jaime said I could ride my horse and throw pennies to the smallfolk," the boy objected.

"Do you want to catch a chill?" Tommen had never been as robust as Joffrey. "Your lord grandfather would want you to look a proper king at his wake. We cannot appear at the Great Sept wet and bedraggled." *Bad enough I must wear mourning again.* Black had never been a happy color on her. With her fair skin, it made her look half a corpse herself. Cersei had risen an hour before dawn to bathe and fix her hair, and she did not intend to let the rain destroy her efforts.

Inside the litter, Tommen settled back against his pillows and peered out at the falling rain. "The gods are weeping for grandfather. Lady Jocelyn says the raindrops are their tears."

"Jocelyn Swyft is a fool. If the gods could weep, they would have wept for your brother. Rain is rain. Close the curtain before you let any more in. That mantle is sable, would you have it soaked?"

Tommen did as he was bid. She was glad of that, yet his

meekness troubled her as well. A king had to be strong. *Joffrey would have argued with me. He was never easy to cow.* "You should not slump so," she told Tommen, just to see. "Sit like a king. Put your shoulders back, and straighten your crown. Would you have it falling off of your head in front of all your lords?"

"No, Mother." The boy sat straight and reached up to fix the crown. Joff's crown was too big for him. Tommen had always been inclined to plumpness, but his face seemed thinner now. *Is he eating well?* She must remember to ask the steward. She could not risk Tommen growing ill, not with Myrcella in the hands of the Dornishmen. *He will grow into Joff's crown in time.* But until he did, a smaller one might be needed, one that did not threaten to swallow his head. She would take it up with the goldsmiths.

The litter made its slow way down Aegon's High Hill. Two Kingsguard went before them, white knights on white horses with their cloaks hanging sodden from their shoulders. Behind came fifty Lannister guardsmen in gold and crimson.

Tommen peered through the drapes at the empty streets. "I thought there would be more people. When Father died all the people came out and watched us go by."

"This rain has driven them inside." The Kingslanders had never loved Lord Tywin, not even before the Sack. *He never wanted love, though. Only respect, and all the honors due him. 'You cannot eat love, nor buy a horse with it, nor warm your halls on a cold night,' she heard him tell Jaime once, when her brother had been as young as Tommen.*

At the Great Sept of Baelor, that magnificence in marble atop Visenya's Hill, the little knot of mourners were outnumbered by the gold cloaks that Ser Addam Marbrand had drawn up across the plaza. *More will turn out later*, the queen told herself as Ser Meryn Trant helped her from the litter. Only the highborn and their retinues were to be admitted to the morning service; there would be another in the afternoon for the commons, and the evening prayers were open to all. Cersei would need to return for that, so that the smallfolk might see her mourn. Certain things were expected of her. *The mob must have its show.* It was a nuisance, though. She had offices to fill, letters to write, a war to win, a realm to rule.

The High Septon met them at the top of the steps. A bent old man with a wispy grey beard, he was so stooped by the weight of his ornate embroidered robes that his eyes were on a level with the queen's breasts . . . though his crown, an airy confection of cut crystal and spun gold, added a good foot and a half to his height. Lord Tywin had given him that crown to replace the one that was lost when the mob killed the previous High Septon. They had pulled the fat fool from his litter and torn him apart, the day Myrcella sailed for Dorne. *That one was a great glutton, and biddable. This one . . .* This High Septon was of Tyrion's making, Cersei recalled suddenly. It was a disquieting thought.

The old man's spotted hand looked like a chicken claw as it poked from a sleeve encrusted with golden scrollwork and small crystals. Cersei knelt on the wet marble and kissed his fingers, and bid Tommen to do the same. *What does he know of me? How much did the dwarf tell him?* The High Septon smiled as he helped her back to her feet and escorted her inside, but was it a threatening smile full of unspoken knowledge, or just some vacuous twitch of an old man's wrinkled lips? She found it impossible to tell.

She held Tommen's hand as they made their way through the Hall of Lamps beneath globes of leaded glass. Trant and Kettleblack flanked them, water dripping from their wet cloaks to puddle on the floor. The High Septon walked slowly, leaning on a weirwood staff topped by an crystal orb. Seven of the Most Devout attended him, shimmering in cloth-of-silver. Tommen followed, dressed in cloth-of-gold beneath his sable mantle. The queen wore an old gown of black velvet lined with ermine. There'd been no time to have a new one made, and she could not wear the same dress she had worn for Joffrey, nor the one she'd buried Robert in.

At least I will not be expected to don mourning for Tyrion. I shall dress in crimson silk and cloth-of-gold for that, and wear rubies in my hair. The man who brought her the dwarf's head would be raised to lordship, no matter how mean and low his birth or station. Pycelle's ravens were carrying her promise to every part of the Seven Kingdoms even now, and soon enough word would cross the narrow sea to the Nine Free Cities and the lands beyond. *Let the Imp run to the ends of the earth, he will not escape me.*

They stepped through the inner doors together, into the cavernous heart of the Great Sept, and began their slow progress down a wide aisle, one of seven that met beneath the dome. To right and left, highborn mourners sank at their passing. Many of her father's bannermen were here, and knights who had fought beside Lord Tywin in half a hundred battles. The sight of them made her feel more confident. *I am not without friends.*

Under the lofty dome of glass and gold and crystal, Lord Tywin Lannister's body rested upon a stepped marble bier. At its head Jaime stood at vigil, his one good hand curled about the hilt of a tall golden greatsword whose point rested on the floor. The hooded cloak he wore was as white as freshly fallen snow, and the scales of his long hauberk were mother-of-pearl chased with gold. *Lord Tywin would have wanted him in Lannister gold and crimson,* she thought when she saw his garb. *It always angered him to see Jaime all in white.* Her brother was growing his beard again as well. The stubble covered his jaw and cheeks, and gave him a rough, uncouth look. *He might at least have waited till Father's bones were interred beneath the Rock.*

Cersei led the king up three short steps to kneel beside the body. Tommen's eyes were filled with tears. "Weep quietly," she told him, leaning close. "You are a king, not a squalling child. Your lords are watching you." The boy swiped the tears away with the back of his hand. He had her eyes, emerald green, as large and bright as Jaime's eyes had been when he was Tommen's age. Her brother had been such a *pretty* boy . . . but fierce as Joffrey, a lion cub in truth. The queen put her arm around Tommen and kissed his golden curls. *He will need me to teach him how to rule, and keep him safe from his enemies.* Some of them stood around them even now, pretending to be friends.

The silent sisters had armored Lord Tywin as if to fight some final battle. He wore his finest plate, heavy steel enameled a deep, dark crimson, with gold inlay on his gauntlets, greaves, and breastplate. His rondels were golden sunbursts; a golden lioness crouched upon each shoulder; a maned lion crested the greathelm beside his head. Upon his chest lay a longsword in a gilded scabbard studded with rubies, his hands folded about its hilt in gloves of gilded mail. *Even in death his face is noble,* she thought, *although the mouth . . .* The corners of her father's lips curved upward ever so slightly, giving him a look of vague bemusement. *That should not be.* She blamed Pycelle; she should have told the silent sisters that Lord Tywin Lannister never smiled. *The man is as useless as nipples on a breastplate.* Cersei resolved once more to demand a replacement of the Citadel.

That odd half-smile made Lord Tywin seem less fearful, somehow. That, and the fact that his eyes were closed. Her father's eyes had always been unsettling; pale green, almost luminous, and flecked with gold. His eyes could see inside you, could see how weak and worthless and ugly you were down deep. *When he looked at you, you knew.*

Unbidden, a memory came back to her, of the feast King Aerys had thrown to welcome her when first she'd come to court, a girl as green as summer grass. When old Merryweather the master of coin said something about raising the duty on wine, Lord Rykker boomed out, "If the crown wants for gold, His Grace can keep Lord Tywin on his chamberpot." The king and his lickspittles laughed loudly, whilst Father stared at Rykker over his wine cup. Long after the merriment had died that gaze lingered. Rykker turned away, turned back, met Father's eyes and then ignored them, drank a tankard of ale, and finally bolted to his feet and stalked off red-faced, defeated by a pair of unflinching eyes.

His eyes are closed forever now, she thought, *but my eyes are green as well. It is my look they will flinch from now, my frown that they must fear. I am a lion too.*

It was gloomy within the sept, with the sky so grey outside. If the rain ever stopped, the sun would slant down through the hanging crystals to drape the corpse from head to heel in rainbows. The Lord of Casterly Rock deserved rainbows, Cersei thought. He had been a great man. *I shall be greater, though. A thousand years from now, when the maesters write about this time, you shall be remembered only as Queen Cersei's sire.*

"Mother." Tommen tugged her sleeve. "What smells so bad?"

My lord father. "Death." She could smell it too; a faint whisper of decay that made her want to wrinkle her nose. Cersei paid it no mind. The seven septons in the silver robes stood behind the bier, beseeching the Father Above to judge Lord Tywin justly. When they were done, seventy-seven septas gathered beneath the statue of the Mother and began to sing to her for mercy. Tommen was fidgeting by then, and even the queen's knees had begun to ache. She glanced up at Jaime. Her twin stood there as if he had been carved from stone, and would not meet her eyes.

On the benches behind him her uncle Kevan knelt with his thick shoulders slumped, his son beside him. *Lancel looks worse than Father.* Only seventeen, her cousin might have passed for seventy: grey-faced, gaunt, with hollow cheeks, sunken eyes, and hair as white and brittle as chalk.

How can Lancel be among the living when Tywin Lannister is dead? Have the gods taken leave of their wits?

Lord Gyles was coughing more than usual, and covering his nose with a square of red silk. *He can smell it too.* Grand Maester Pycelle had his eyes closed. *Asleep again,* she decided.

To the right of the bier were the Tyrells, the Lord of Highgarden foremost amongst them, flanked by his hideous mother and vacuous wife, his son Garlan and his daughter Margaery. *Queen Margaery,* she reminded herself; Joff's widow and Tommen's future wife. Twice wedded and never bedded, they said, but Cersei had her own suspicions. Margaery looked very much like her brother, the Knight of Flowers. The queen wondered if they had other things as common as well. *Our little rose has a good many ladies waiting attendance on her, night and day.* They stood behind her now, almost a dozen of them. Cersei studied their faces, wondering which of them might have the loosest tongue. *Who is the most fearful, the most wanton, the hungriest for favor?* She really must find out.

It was a relief when the singing ended. The smell coming off her father's corpse seemed to have grown stronger. Most of the mourners had the decency to pretend that nothing was amiss, but Cersei saw some of Margaery's ladies wrinkling their little Tyrell noses. As she and Tommen were walking back down the aisle the queen thought she heard someone mutter "privy" and chortle, but when she turned her head to see who had spoken a sea of solemn faces gazed at her blankly. *They would never have dared make japes about him when he was still alive. He would have turned their bowels to water with a look.*

Back out in the Hall of Lamps, the mourners were buzzing thick as flies. The Redwyne twins kissed her hand, and their father her cheek. Hallyne the Pyromancer promised that a flaming hand would burn in the sky above the city on the day her father's bones went west. Lord Gyles announced that he had hired a master stonecarver to make a mighty statue of Lord Tywin, to stand eternal vigil beside the Lion Gate. Ser Lyman Turnberry appeared with a patch over his right eye, swearing that he would wear it until he could bring her the head of her dwarf brother.

"You are too kind." Cersei kissed his cheek and moved away quickly, looking for Tommen. He was easy enough to find, with two Kingsguard beside him in white armor, but to her annoyance she saw that he had fallen into the clutches of Margaery Tyrell and her grandmother. The Queen of Thorns was almost of a height with Tommen, and for an instant Cersei took her for another child.

Before she could rescue him, the press brought her face-to-face with her uncle. When the queen reminded him of their meeting later, Ser Kevan gave a weary nod, and begged leave to withdraw. But Lancel lingered behind, the very picture of a man with one foot in the grave. *But is he climbing in or climbing out?*

Cersei forced herself to smile. "Lancel, I am happy to see you looking so much stronger. Maester Ballabar brought us such dire reports, we feared for your life. But I would have thought you on your way to Darry by now, to take up your lordship." Her father had made Lancel a lord after the Battle of the Blackwater, as a sop to his brother Kevan.

"My father will ride with me to Darry when he escorts Lord Tywin's bones back to Casterly Rock." Her cousin's voice was as wispy as the mustache on his upper lip. Though his hair had gone white, his mustache fuzz remained a sandy color. Cersei had often gazed up at it while the boy was inside her, pumping dutifully away. *It looks like a smudge of dirt on his lip.* She used to threaten to scrub it off with a little spit. "The riverlands have need of a strong hand," Lancel added.

A pity that they're getting such a feeble one, she wanted to say. Instead she smiled. "And you are to be wed as well."

A gloomy look passed across the young knight's ravaged face. "A Frey girl, and not of my choosing. She is not even maiden. A widow, of Darry blood. My father says that will help me with the peasants, but the peasants are all dead." He reached for her hand, looking as if he might burst into tears. "It is cruel, Cersei. Your Grace knows that I love—"

"—House Lannister," she finished for him. "No one can doubt that, Lancel. May your wife give you strong sons." *Best not let her father host the wedding, though.* "I know you will do many noble deeds in Darry."

Lancel nodded, plainly miserable. "When it seemed that I might die, my father brought the High Septon to pray for me. He is a good man, Cersei. He says the Mother spared me for some holy purpose, so I might atone for my sins." His eyes were wet and shiny, a child's eyes in an old man's face.

Cersei wondered how he intended to atone for her. *Mine own blood,* she thought, disgusted. Was she the only lion left alive? *Knighting him was a mistake, and bedding him a bigger one.* Lancel was a weak reed, and she liked this newfound piety of his not at all; he had been much more amusing when he was trying to be Jaime. *What has this mewling fool told the High Septon? And what will he tell his little Frey when they lay together in the dark?* If he wished to boast of bedding a queen, well, men were always lying about women. She would put it down as the braggadocio of a callow boy smitten by unrequited love. *But if he sings of Robert and the strongwine . . .* "Atonement is best achieved through prayer," Cersei told her cousin pointedly. "*Silent* prayer." She left him to think about that, and girded herself to face the Tyrell host.

Margaery embraced her like a sister, which the queen found presumptuous, but this was not the place to reproach her. Lady Alerie and the cousins contended themselves with kissing fingers. Lady Graceford, who was large with child, asked the queen's leave to name it Tywin if it were a boy, or Lanna if it were a girl. *Lickspittles like you will drown the realm in Tywins,* she reflected, but she graciously gave consent, feigning delight.

Lady Merryweather was the only one who truly pleased her. "Your Grace," she said, in her sultry Myrish tones, "I have sent word to my friends across the narrow sea, asking them to seize the Imp at once should he show his ugly face in the Free Cities."

"Do you have many friends across the water?"

"In Myr, many. In Lys as well, and Tyrosh. Men of power."

Cersei could well believe it. The Myrish woman was too beautiful by half; long-legged and full-breasted, with smooth olive skin, ripe lips, huge dark eyes, and thick black hair that always looked as if she'd just come from bed. *She even smells like sin, like some exotic lotus.* "Lord Merryweather and I wish only to serve Your Grace and the little king," the woman said, with a look that was as pregnant as Lady Graceford.

This one is ambitious, and her lord is proud but poor. "We must speak again, my lady. Taena, is it? You are most kind. I know that we shall be great friends."

And then the Lord of Highgarden himself fell upon her.

Mace Tyrell was no more than ten years older than Cersei, yet she thought of him as her father's age, not her own. He was not quite so tall as Lord Tywin had been, but elsewise he was bigger, with a thick chest and a gut that had grown even thicker. His hair was chestnut colored and his eyes looked a bit like chestnuts too, but there were specks of white and grey in his beard. His face was often red. "Lord

Tywin was a great man, and will be greatly missed," he declared ponderously after he had kissed both her cheeks. "No man alive is fit to don his armor, that is plain. We all grieve for him."

"My lord is good to say so."

"If there is aught that I might do to serve in this dark hour, Your Grace need only ask."

If you want to be Hand, my lord, at least have the courage to say it plainly. The queen smiled at him warmly. *Let him read into that as much as he likes.* "His Grace will be heartened to hear it . . . though surely you are needed in the Reach."

"My son Willas is an able lad," the man replied, refusing to take her pefectly good hint. "His leg may be twisted but he has no want of wits. And Garlan will soon take Brightwater. Between them the Reach will be in good hands, if it happens that I am needed elsewhere. The governance of the realm must come first, Lord Tywin often said. And I am pleased to bring Your Grace good tidings in that regard. My uncle Garth has agreed to serve as master of coin, as your lord father wished. He is making his way to Oldtown to take ship. His sons will accompany him. Lord Tywin mentioned something about finding places for the two of them as well. Perhaps in the City Watch."

The queen's smile had frozen so hard she feared her teeth might crack. *Garth the Gross on the small council and his two bastards in the gold cloaks. Do the Tyrells think I will just serve the realm up to them on a gilded platter?* The arrogance of it took her breath away.

"Garth has served me well as Lord Seneschal, as he served my father before me," Tyrell was going on. "Littlefinger had a nose for gold, I grant you, but Garth—"

"My lord," Cersei broke in, "I fear there has been some misunderstanding. I have asked Lord Gyles Rosby to serve as our new master of coin, and he has done me the honor of accepting."

Mace gaped at her. "Rosby? That . . . *cougher?* But . . . the matter was agreed, Your Grace. Garth is on his way to Oldtown."

"Best send a raven to Lord Hightower and ask him to make certain your uncle does not take ship. We would hate for Garth to brave an autumn sea for nought." She smiled pleasantly.

A flush crept up Lord Tyrell's thick neck and spread across his cheeks. "This . . . your lord father assured me . . ."

His mother appeared beside him, and slid her arm through his own. "It would seem that Lord Tywin did not share his plans with our regent, I can't *imagine* why. Still, there 'tis, no use hectoring Her Grace. She is quite right, you must write Lord Leyton before Garth boards a ship. You know the sea will sicken him, and make his farting worse." She gave Cersei a toothless smile. "Your council chambers will smell sweeter with Lord Gyles, though I daresay that coughing would drive me to distraction. We all adore dear old Uncle Garth, but the man is flatulent, that cannot be gainsaid. I do abhor foul smells." Her wrinkled face wrinkled up even more. "I caught a whiff of something unpleasant in the holy sept, in truth. Mayhaps you smelled it too?"

"No," Cersei said coldly. "A scent, you say?"

"More like a stink."

"Perhaps you miss your autumn roses. We have kept you here too long." The sooner she rid the court of Lady Olenna the better. Lord Tyrell would doubtless send off a goodly number of his soldiers to see his mother safely home.

"I do long for the fragrances of Highgarden, I confess it," said the old lady, "but of course I can not leave until I have seen my sweet Margaery wed to your precious little Tommen."

"I await that day eagerly as well," Lord Tyrell put in, too loudly. "Lord Tywin and I were on the very point of setting a date, as it happens. Perhaps you and I might take up that discussion, Your Grace."

"Soon."

"Soon will serve," said Lady Olenna, with a sniff. "Now come along, Mace, let Her Grace get on with her . . . grief."

I will see you dead, old woman, Cersei promised herself as the Queen of Thorns tottered off to her towering guardsmen, a pair of seven footers she called Left and Right. *We'll see how sweet a corpse you make.*

She went in search of Tommen again, rescued him from Margaery and her cousins, and made for the doors. Outside, the rain had finally stopped. The autumn air smelled sweet and fresh. Tommen started to take his crown off.

"Put that back on," Cersei commanded him.

"It makes my neck hurt," he said, but he did as he was bid. "Will I be married soon? Margaery says that as soon we're wed we can go to Highgarden."

"You are not going to Highgarden, but you can ride back to

the castle." Cersei beckoned to Ser Meryn Trant. "Bring His Grace a mount, and ask Lord Gyles if he would do me the honor of sharing my litter." Things were moving more quickly than she had anticipated; there was no time to be squandered.

Tommen was happy at the prospect of a ride, and of course Lord Gyles was honored by her invitation . . . though when she asked him to be her master of coin, he began coughing so violently that she feared he might die right then and there. But the Mother was merciful, and Gyles eventually recover sufficiently to accept, and even began coughing out the names of men he wanted to replace, customs officers and wool factors appointed by Littlefinger, even one of the keepers of the keys.

"Name the cow what you will, so long as the milk flows. And should the question arise, you joined the council yesterday."

"Yester—" A fit of coughing bent him over. "Yesterday. To be sure." Lord Gyles coughed into a square of red silk, as if to hide the blood in his spittle. Cersei pretended not to notice. She did not think that he would be her master of coin for very long. *When he dies I will find someone else.* Perhaps she would recall Littlefinger. The queen could not imagine that Petyr Baelish would be allowed to remain Lord Protector of the Vale for very long, with Lysa Arryn dead. The Vale lords were already stirring, if what Pycelle said was true. *They will take that wretched boy away from him, and he will come crawling back.*

"Your, *kaf*, Grace?" Lord Gyles dabbed his mouth. "Might I, *kaf*, ask, *kaf kaf*, who will be, *kaf*, the King's Hand?"

"My uncle," she replied absently.

It was a relief to see the gates of the Red Keep looming large before her. She gave Tommen over to the charge of his squires, and retired gratefully to her own chambers to rest.

No sooner had she eased off her shoes than Jocelyn entered timidly to say that Qyburn was without and craved audience. "Send him in," the queen commanded. *A ruler gets no rest.*

Qyburn was old, but his hair still had more ash than snow in it, and the laugh lines around his mouth made him look like some little girl's favorite grandfather. *A rather shabby grandfather, though.* The collar of his robe was frayed, and one sleeve had been torn and badly sewn. "Your Grace," he began, "I have examined Ser Gregor Clegane, as you commanded. The poison on the Viper's spear was manticore venom from the east, I would stake my life on that."

"Pycelle says no. He told my lord father that manticore venom kills the instant it reaches the heart."

"And so it does. But this venom has been *thickened* somehow so as to draw out the Mountain's dying."

"Thickened? Thickened *how*? With some other substance?"

"It may be as Your Grace suggests, though in most cases adulterating a poison only lessens its potency. It may be that the cause is . . . less natural, let us say. A spell, I think."

Is this one as big a fool as Pycelle? "So are you telling me that the Mountain is dying of some black *sorcery*?"

Qyburn ignored the mockery in her voice. "He is dying of the venom, but slowly, and in exquisite agony. My efforts to ease his pain have proved as fruitless as Pycelle's. Ser Gregor is overly accustomed to the poppy, I fear. His squire tells me that he is plagued by blinding headaches and oft quaffs the milk of the poppy as lesser men quaff ale. Be that as it may, his veins have turned black from head to heel, his water is clouded with pus, and the venom has eaten a hole in his side as large as my fist. It is a wonder that the man is still alive, if truth be told."

"His size," the queen suggested, frowning. "Gregor is a very large man. Also a very stupid one. Too stupid to know when he should die, it seems." She held out her cup, and Senelle filled it once again. "The Dornishmen want his head, and his screaming frightens Tommen. It has even been known to wake me of a night. I would say it is past time we summoned Ilyn Payn."

"Your Grace," said Qyburn, "mayhaps I might move Ser Gregor to the dungeons? His screams will not disturb you there, and I will be able to tend to him more freely."

"Tend to him?" She laughed. "Let Ser Ilyn tend to him."

"If that is Your Grace's wish," Qyburn said, "but this poison . . . it would be useful to know more about it, would it not? Send a knight to slay a knight and an archer to kill an archer, the smallfolk often say. To combat the black arts . . ." He did not finish the thought, but only smiled at her.

He is not Pycelle, that much is plain. The queen weighed him, wondering. "Why did the Citadel take your chain? Tell me true, I warn you. I will have your tongue if you lie to me."

"The archmaesters are cravens at heart. The grey sheep, Marwyn calls them. I was as skilled a healer as Ebrose, but aspired to surpass him. For hundreds of years the men of the Citadel have opened the bodies of the dead, to study the nature of life. I wished to understand the nature of death, so I opened the bodies of the living. For that crime the grey sheep shamed me and forced me into exile . . . but even now I know more of life and death than any man in Oldtown."

"Do you?" She smiled. "Very well. The Mountain is yours. Do what you will with him, but confine your studies to the black cells. When he dies, bring me his head. My father promised it to Dorne. Prince Doran would no doubt prefer to kill Gregor himself, but we all must suffer disappointments in this life."

"Very good, Your Grace." Qyburn cleared his throat. "I am am not so well provided as Pycelle, however. I must needs equip myself with certain . . ."

"I shall instruct Lord Gyles to provide you with gold sufficient for your needs. Buy yourself some new robes as well. You look as though you've wandered up from Flea Bottom. Now go."

He bowed, and went.

Her uncle arrived promptly at sunset, wearing a quilted doublet of charcoal-colored wool as somber as his face. Like all the Lannisters, Ser Kevan was fair-skinned and blond, though at five-and-fifty he had lost most of his hair. No one would ever call him comely. Thick of waist, round of shoulder, with a square jutting chin that his close-cropped yellow beard did little to conceal, he reminded her of some old mastiff . . . but a faithful old mastiff was the very thing that she required.

They ate a simple supper of beets and bread and bloody beef with a flagon of Dornish red to wash it all down. Ser Kevan ate slowly and said little, and scarcely touched his wine cup. *He broods too much on Father,* the queen decided. *He needs to be put to work to get beyond his grief.*

She said as much, when the last of the food had been cleared away and the servants had departed. "I know how much my father relied on you, Uncle. Now I must do the same."

"You need a Hand," he said, "and Jaime has refused you."

He is blunt. Very well. She glanced away. "Jaime . . . I felt so lost with Father dead, I scarce knew what I was saying. Jaime is gallant, but a bit of a fool, let us be frank. Tommen needs a more seasoned man. Someone older . . ."

"Mace Tyrell is older."

Her nostrils flared. "Never." Cersei pushed a lock of hair off her brow. "The Tyrells overreach themselves."

"You would be a fool to make Mace Tyrell your Hand," Ser Kevan warned, "but a bigger fool to make him your foe.

I've heard what happened in the Hall of Lamps. Mace should have known better than to broach such matters in public, but even so, you were unwise to shame him in front of half the Reach."

"It was that, or kiss his hand and welcome another Tyrell to the small council." His reproach annoyed her. "Rosby will be more than adequate as master of coin. You've seen his horses, and that litter of his. A man that rich should have no problem finding gold. As for the Hand . . . who better to finish my father's work than the brother who shared his counsels?"

"Every man needs someone he can trust. Tywin had me, and once your mother."

"He loved her very much." Cersei refused to think about the dead whore in his bed. "I know they are together now."

"So I pray." Ser Kevan studied her face for a long moment before he replied. "You ask much of me, Cersei."

"No more than my father did."

"I am tired." Her uncle reached for his wine cup and took a swallow. "I have a wife I have not seen in two years, a dead son whose tomb I have yet to visit, another son who might have died as well. And Lancel must needs establish himself in Darry. There are outlaws stabling their horses in his great hall. Castle Darry must be made strong again, its lands protected, its burned fields ploughed and planted anew. He needs my help."

"As does Tommen." Cersei had not expected Kevan to require coaxing. *He never played coy with Father.* "The realm needs you."

"The realm. Aye. And House Lannister." He sipped his wine again. "Very well. I will remain and serve His Grace . . ."

"Very good," she started to say, but Ser Kevan raised his voice and bulled right over her.

". . . so long as you name me regent as well as Hand, and take yourself back to Casterly Rock."

For half a heartbeat Cersei could only stare at him. *What did he say?* "I am the regent," she reminded him.

"You were. Your father did not intend that you continue in that role. He told me of his plans to send you back to the Rock and find a new husband for you."

Cersei could feel her anger rising. "He spoke of such, yes. And I told him it was not my wish to wed again."

Her uncle was unmoved. "There are good reasons why you should, but if you are resolved against another marriage I will not force it on you. As to the other, though . . . you are the Lady of Casterly Rock now. Your place is there."

How dare you? she wanted to scream. Instead she said, "I am also the Queen Regent. My place is with my son."

"Your father thought not."

"My father is dead."

"To my grief, and the woe of all the realm. Open your eyes and look about you, Cersei. The kingdom is in ruins. Tywin might have been able to set matters aright, but . . ."

"*I* shall set matters aright!" That sounded shrill. Cersei softened her tone. "With your help, Uncle. If you will serve me as faithfully as you served my father—"

"You are not your father." His voice was hard. "Tywin regarded Jaime as his rightful heir."

"*Jaime* . . . Jaime has taken vows. The Kingsguard serve for life. Jaime never thinks, he laughs at everything and everyone and says whatever comes into his head. Jaime is a handsome fool."

"And yet he was your first choice to be the King's Hand. What does that make you, Cersei?"

"I told you, I was sick with grief, I did not think—"

"No," Ser Kevan agreed, "which is why you should return to Casterly Rock, and leave the king with those who do."

"*The king is my son!*" Cersei rose to her feet.

"Aye," her uncle said, "and from what I saw of Joffrey, you are as unfit as a mother as you are as a ruler."

She threw the contents of her wine cup full in his face.

Ser Kevan rose with a ponderous dignity. "Your Grace." Wine trickled down his cheeks and dripped from his close-cropped beard. "With your leave, might I withdraw?"

"By what right do you presume to give *me* terms? You are no more than one of my father's household knights."

"I hold no lands, that is true. But I have certain incomes, and chests of coin set aside. My own father forgot none of his children when he died, and Tywin knew how to reward good service. I feed two hundred knights and can double that number if need be. There are freeriders who will follow my banner, and I have the gold to hire sellswords. You would be wise not to take me lightly, Your Grace . . . and wiser still not to make of me a foe."

"Are you *threatening* me?"

"Say rather than I am counseling you."

"I should throw you in a black cell."

"No. You should yield the regency to me. As you will

not, however, then name me your castellan for Casterly Rock, and make either Mathis Rowan or Randyll Tarly the Hand of the King."

Tyrell bannermen, both of them. The suggestion left her speechless. *Is he bought?* she wondered. *Has he taken Tyrell gold to betray House Lannister?*

"Mathis Rowan is sensible, prudent, well-liked," her uncle went on, oblivious. "Randyll Tarly is the finest soldier in the realm. A poor Hand for peacetime, but with Tywin dead there's no better man to finish this war. Lord Tyrell cannot openly take offense if you choose one of his own bannermen as Hand. Both Tarly and Towan are able men . . . and *loyal.* Name either one, and you make him yours. You will strengthen yourself and weaken Highgarden at the same time, yet Mace will likely thank you for it." He gave a shrug. "That is my counsel, take it or no. You may make Moon Boy your Hand for all I care. My brother is dead, woman. I am going to take him home."

Traitor, she thought. *Turncloak.* She wondered how much Mace Tyrell had given him. "You would abandon your king when he needs you most," she told him. "You would abandon Tommen."

"Tommen has his mother." Ser Kevan's green eyes met her own, unblinking. A last drop of wine trembled wet and red beneath his chin, and finally fell. "Aye," he added softly, after a pause, "and his father too, I think."

GAME OF THRONES

THE COMPLETE FIRST SEASON

INCLUDES HOURS OF BONUS CONTENT INCLUDING INTERACTIVE GUIDES, SEVEN AUDIO COMMENTARIES, AND NEVER-BEFORE-SEEN FOOTAGE FROM THE SET.

NOW AVAILABLE
ON BLU-RAY™, DVD
AND DIGITAL DOWNLOAD

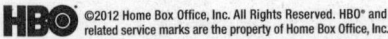

Also by
GEORGE R. R. MARTIN

─── Novels ───

Fevre Dream

Windhaven

The
Armageddon Rag

Dying of the Light

─── Short Stories ───

Dreamsongs:
Volume I

Dreamsongs:
Volume II

Also available in Audio and eBook

THE RANDOM HOUSE PUBLISHING GROUP

www.GeorgeRRMartin.com